THE VERNACULAR TRADITION
O'Meally

THE LITERATURE OF SLAVERY AND FREEDOM
Andrews

LITERATURE OF THE RECONSTRUCTION TO THE NEW NEGRO RENAISSANCE
Foster / Yarborough

HARLEM RENAISSANCE
Rampersad

REALISM, NATURALISM, MODERNISM
McDowell / Spillers

THE BLACK ARTS MOVEMENT
Baker

LITERATURE SINCE 1970
Christian

The Norton Anthology
of African American
Literature

The Norton Anthology of African American Literature

Henry Louis Gates Jr., *General Editor*

W. E. B. Du Bois Professor of Humanities

Harvard University

Nellie Y. McKay, *General Editor*

Professor of American and Afro-American Literature

University of Wisconsin, Madison

W · W · NORTON & COMPANY · *New York* · *London*

The text of this book is composed in Electra, with display set in Bernhard Modern.
Composition by ComCom. Manufacturing by R. R. Donnelley. Book design by
Antonina Krass.

Cover and jacket illustration: *Family* (1955) by Charles H. Alston. Reproduced courtesy of
the Whitney Museum of American Art.

The design element was inspired by Aaron Douglas's "Flight," from the *Emperor Jones*
series, c. 1926. Collection of Stephanie E. Pogue, Hyattsville, Maryland.

ISBN 0-393-04001-1
ISBN 0-393-95908-2 (pbk.)

W. W. Norton & Company, Inc., 500 Fifth Avenue, New York, N.Y. 10110
http://www.wwnorton.com
W. W. Norton & Company Ltd., 10 Coptic Street, London WC1A 1PU

1 2 3 4 5 6 7 8 9 0

Contents

THE LITERATURE OF SLAVERY AND FREEDOM: 1746–1865

HARLEM RENAISSANCE: 1919–1940   929

REALISM, NATURALISM, MODERNISM: 1940–1960   1319

Preface

Talking Books

The lesson to be drawn from this cursory glance at what I may call the past, present and future of our Race Literature apart from its value as first beginnings, not only to us as a people but literature in general, is that unless earnest and systematic effort be made to procure and preserve for transmission to our successors, the records, books and various publications already produced by us, not only will the sturdy pioneers who paved the way and laid the foundation for our Race literature be robbed of their just due, but an irretrievable wrong will be inflicted upon the generations that shall come after us.

—VICTORIA EARLE MATTHEWS, 1895

In the history of the world's great literatures, few traditions have origins as curious as that created by African slaves and ex-slaves writing in the English language in the third quarter of the eighteenth century. In the stubbornly durable history of human slavery, it was only the black slaves in England and the United States who created a genre of literature that, at once, testified against their captors and bore witness to the urge to be free and literate, to embrace the European Enlightenment's dream of reason and the American Enlightenment's dream of civil liberty, wedded together gloriously in a great republic of letters.

For what could be more peculiar to the institution of human slavery than liberal learning, than "the arts and sciences," as the French philosophes put it? Slavery, as Lucius C. Matlock argued in 1845 in a review of Frederick Douglass's now classic *Narrative of the Life*, "naturally and necessarily" is "the enemy of literature." Despite that antagonistic relation, Matlock continued, slavery had by the middle of the nineteenth century "become the prolific theme of much that is profound in argument, sublime in poetry, and thrilling in narrative." What's more, he concluded with as much astonishment as satisfaction, "the soil of slavery itself"—and the demands for its abolition—had turned out to be an ironically fertile ground for the creation of a new literature, a literature indicting oppression, a literature created by the oppressed: "From the soil of slavery itself have sprung forth some of the most brilliant productions, whose logical levers will ultimately upheave and overthrow the system." It will be from "the pen of self-emancipated slaves," Matlock predicted, that "startling incidents authenticated, far excelling fiction in their touching pathos," will "secure the execrations of all good men and become a monument more enduring than marble, in testimony strong as sacred wit. . . ."

African American slaves, remarkably, sought to write themselves out of

slavery by mastering the Anglo-American bellettristic tradition. To say that
they did so against the greatest odds does not begin to suggest the heroic
proportions that the task of registering a black voice in printed letters entailed. James Albert Ukawsaw Gronniosaw, the author of the first full-
length black autobiography, A narrative of the most remarkable particulars
in the life of James Albert Ukawsaw Gronniosaw, an African Prince (1770),
and the source of the genre of the slave narrative, accounted for this animosity, as well as the slave's anxiety before it, in the trope of the talking
book:

> [My Master] used to read prayers in public to the ship's crew every
> Sabbath day; and then I saw him read. I was never so surprised in my
> life, as when I saw the book talk to my master, for I thought it did as I
> observed him to look upon it, and move his lips. I wished it would do
> so with me. As soon as my master had done reading, I followed him to
> the place where he put the book, being mightily delighted with it, and
> when nobody saw me, I opened it, and put my ear down close upon it,
> in great hopes that it would say something to me; but I was sorry, and
> greatly disappointed, when I found that it would not speak. This
> thought immediately presented itself to me, that every body and every
> thing despised me because I was black.

The text of Western letters refused to speak to the person of African descent; paradoxically, we read about that refusal in a text created by that very
person of African descent. In a very real sense, the Anglo-African literary
tradition was created two centuries ago in order to demonstrate that persons
of African descent possessed the requisite degrees of reason and wit to create literature, that they were, indeed, full and equal members of the community of rational, sentient beings, that they could, indeed, write. With
Gronniosaw's An African Prince, a distinctively "African" voice registered
its presence in the republic of letters; it was a text that both talked "black,"
and, through its unrelenting indictment of the institution of slavery, talked
back.

Making the text "speak" in the full range of timbres that the African enslaved in England and America brought to the process of writing became
the dominant urge of the ex-slave authors. So compelling did Gronniosaw's trope of the talking book prove to be that, between 1770 and 1815,
no fewer than five authors of slave narratives used the same metaphor as a
crucial scene of instruction to dramatize the author's own road to literacy,
initially, and to authorship, ultimately. John Marrant in 1785, Cugoano in
1787, Equiano in 1789, and John Jea in 1815—all modified Gronniosaw's
figure of the talking book as the signal structural element of their autobiographical narratives, thereby providing the formal links of repetition and
revision that, in part, define any literary tradition. So related, in theme and
structure, were these texts that by 1790 Gronniosaw's Dublin publisher
also included John Marrant's Narrative on his list and advertised its sale on
Gronniosaw's endpapers.

Still, the resistance even to the idea that an African could create literature was surprisingly resilient. As early as 1680, Morgan Godwyn, the self-described "Negro and Indian's Advocate," had accounted for the resistance in this way:

[a] disingenuous and unmanly *Position* had been formed; and privately *(as it were in the dark)* handed to and again, which is this, That the Negro's though in their Figure they carry some resemblances of manhood, yet are indeed no men . . . the consideration of the shape and figure of our Negro's Bodies, their Limbs and members; their Voice and Countenance, in all things according with other mens; together with their *Risibility* and *Discourse* (man's *peculiar* Faculties) should be sufficient Conviction. How should they otherwise be capable of Trades, and other no less manly imployments; as also of *Reading* and *Writing*, or show so much Discretion in management of Business; . . . but wherein (we know) that many of our People are *deficient*, were they not truly Men?

Godwyn's account of the claims that Africans were not human beings and his use of the possession of reason and its manifestations through "Reading and Writing" to refute these claims were widely debated during the Enlightenment, generally at the African's expense.

The putative relation between literacy and the quest for freedom provided the subtext for this larger debate over the African's "place in nature," his or her place in the great chain of being. Following the Stono Rebellion of 1739 in South Carolina, the largest uprising of slaves in the colonies before the American Revolution, legislators there enacted a draconian body of public laws, making two forms of literacy punishable by law: the mastery of letters, and the mastery of the drum. The law against literacy read as follows:

And *whereas* the having of slaves taught to write, or suffering them to be employed in writing, may be attending with great inconveniences; *Be it enacted*, that all and every person and persons whatsoever, who shall hereafter teach, or cause any slave or slaves to be taught to write, or shall use or employ any slave as a scribe in any manner of writing whatsoever, hereafter taught to write; every such person or persons shall, for every offense, forfeit the sum of one hundred pounds current money.

The law against the use of the talking drum was just as strong:

And for that as it is absolutely necessary to the safety of this Province, that all due care be taken to restrain the wanderings and meetings of negroes and other slaves, at all times, and more especially on Saturday nights, Sundays and other holidays, and their using and carrying wooden swords, and other mischievous and dangerous weapons, or using or keeping of drums, horns, or other loud instruments, which may call together or give sign or notice to one another of their wicked designs and purposes. . . . And whatsoever master, owner or overseer shall permit or suffer his or their negro or other slave or slaves, at any time hereafter, or beat drums, blow horns, or use any other loud instruments, or whosoever shall suffer and countenance any public meetings or seatings or strange negroes or slaves in their plantations, shall forfeit 10 current money, for every such offence.

In the Stono Rebellion, both forms of literacy—of English letters and of the black vernacular—had been pivotal to the slave's capacity to rebel.

Writing, many philosophers argued in the Enlightenment, stood alone among the fine arts as the most salient repository of "genius," the visible sign of reason itself. In this subordinate role, however, writing, although secondary to reason, was nevertheless the *medium* of reason's expression. We *know* reason by its representations. Such representations could assume spoken or written form. Eighteenth-century European writers privileged *writing*—in their writings about Africans, at least—as the principal measure of the Africans' humanity, their capacity for progress, their very place in the great chain of being. As the Scottish philosopher David Hume put it in a footnote to the second edition of his widely read essay "Of National Characters":

I am apt to suspect the negroes, and in general all the other species of men (for there are four or five different kinds) to be naturally inferior to the whites. There never was a civilized nation of any other complexion than white, nor even any individual eminent either in action or speculation. No ingenious manufacturers amongst them, no arts, no sciences. On the other hand, the most rude and barbarous of the whites, such as the ancient *Germans*, the present *Tartars*, have still something eminent about them, in their valour, form of government, or some other particular.

Such a uniform and constant difference could not happen, in so many countries and ages, if nature had not made an original distinction betwixt these breeds of men. Not to mention our colonies, there are *negro* slaves dispersed all over *Europe*, of which none ever discovered any symptoms of ingenuity; tho' low people, without education, will start up amongst us, and distinguish themselves in every profession. In *Jamaica* indeed they talk of one negro as a man of parts and learning [Francis Williams]; but 'tis likely he is admired for every slender accomplishment, like a parrot, who speaks a few words plainly.

Immanuel Kant, the German philosopher, responding to Hume's essay a decade later, had this to say:

The negroes of Africa have by nature no feeling that rises above the trifling. Mr. Hume challenges anyone to cite a single example in which a Negro has shown talents, and asserts that among the hundreds of thousands of blacks who are transported elsewhere from the countries, although many of them have been set free, still not a single one was ever found who presented anything great in art or science or any other praise-worthy quality, even though among the whites some continually rise aloft from the lowest rabble, and through superior gifts earn respect in the world. So fundamental is the difference between these two races of man, and it appears to be as great in regard to mental capacities as in color. The religion of fetishes so wide-spread among them is perhaps a sort of idolatry that sinks as deeply into the trifling as appears to be possible to human nature. A bird feather, a cow horn, a conch shell, or any other common object, as soon as it becomes consecrated by a few words, is an object of veneration and of invocation in swearing oaths. The blacks are very vain but in the Negro's way, and so talkative that they must be driven apart from each other with thrashings.

Thomas Jefferson, in his *Notes on the State of Virginia* (1787), echoed this discourse in his disparaging remarks about Phillis Wheatley's book of poems:

Misery is often the parent of the most affecting touches in poetry. Among the blacks is misery enough, God knows, but not poetry. Love is the peculiar oestrum of the poet. Their love is ardent, but it kindles the senses only, not the imagination. Religion, indeed, has produced a Phillis Wheatley; but it could not produce a poet. The compositions published under her name are below the dignity of criticism.

To test assertions such as these, various Europeans and Americans educated young black slaves along with their own children. "El negro Juan Latino," who published three books of poetry in Latin between 1573 and 1585, was one of the earliest examples of such an experiment, followed by Wilhelm Amo, Jacobus Capitein, and Francis Williams, in the first quarter of the eighteenth century. The first black person to publish a book of poetry in English, Phillis Wheatley, was also the subject of such an experiment. But whether Wheatley had the capacity to write, *herself*, poems of such accomplishment, was a matter of considerable controversy in Boston in 1773.

Let us imagine a scene. One bright morning in the spring of 1773, a young African girl walked demurely into the courthouse at Boston to undergo an oral examination, the results of which would determine the direction of her life and work. Perhaps she was shocked upon entering the appointed room. For there, gathered in a semicircle, sat eighteen of Boston's most notable citizens. Among them was John Erving, a prominent Boston merchant; the Reverend Charles Chauncey, pastor of the Tenth Congregational Church; and John Hancock, who would later gain fame for his signature on the Declaration of Independence. At the center of this group would have sat His Excellency, Thomas Hutchinson, governor of the colony, with Andrew Oliver, his lieutenant governor, close by his side.

Why had this august group been assembled? Why had it seen fit to summon this adolescent African woman, scarcely eighteen years old, before it? This group of "the most respectable characters in Boston," as it would later define itself, had assembled to question closely the African adolescent on the slender sheaf of poems that she claimed to have written by herself.

We can only speculate on the nature of the questions posed to the fledgling poet. Perhaps they asked her to identify and explain—for all to hear—exactly who were the Greek and Latin gods and poets alluded to so frequently in her work. Perhaps they asked her to conjugate a verb in Latin, or even to translate randomly selected passages from the Latin, which she and her master, John Wheatley, claimed that she "had made some progress in." Or perhaps they asked her to recite from memory key passages from the texts of John Milton and Alexander Pope, the two poets by whom the African seems to have been most directly influenced. We do not know.

We do know, however, that the African poet's responses were more than sufficient to prompt these eighteen august gentlemen to compose, sign, and publish a two-paragraph "Attestation," an open letter "To the Publick" that prefaces Phillis Wheatley's book, and which reads in part:

> We whose Names are under-written, do assure the World, that the POEMS specified in the following Page, were (as we verily believe) written by PHILLIS, a young Negro Girl, who was but a few Years since, brought an uncultivated Barbarian from *Africa*, and has ever since been, and now is under the Disadvantage of serving as a Slave in a Family in this Town. She has been examined by some of the best Judges, and is thought qualified to write them.

So important was this document in securing a publisher for Phillis Wheatley's poems that it forms the signal element in the prefatory matter printed in the opening pages of her *Poems on Various Subjects, Religious and Moral*, which was issued in London in the fall of 1773 because Boston printers remained skeptical about her authorship and refused to publish the book. Without the printed "Attestation," Phillis Wheatley's publisher claimed, few would have believed that an African could possibly have written poetry all by herself. As the eighteen put the matter clearly in their letter, "Numbers would be ready to suspect they were not really the Writings of PHILLIS."

This curious anecdote, surely one of the oddest oral examinations on record, is only a tiny part of a larger, and even more curious, episode in the Enlightenment. At least since the end of the seventeenth century, Europeans had wondered aloud whether or not the African "species of men," as they most commonly put it, could ever create formal literature, could ever master "the arts and sciences." If they could, the argument ran, then the African variety of humanity and the European variety were fundamentally related. If not, then it seemed clear that the African was destined by nature to be a slave, rightly relegated to a low place in the great chain of being, an ancient construct that arranged all of creation on a vertical scale ascending from plants, insects, and animals through human beings to the angels and God himself.

By 1750, the chain had become minutely calibrated; the human scale rose from "the lowliest Hottentot" (black South African) to "glorious Milton and Newton." If blacks could write and publish imaginative literature, then they could, in effect, take a few "giant steps" up the chain of being, in a pernicious metaphysical game of "Mother, May I?" For example, reviewers of Wheatley's book argued that the publication of her poems meant that the African was indeed a human being and should not be enslaved. Indeed, Wheatley herself was manumitted soon after her poems were published.

That which was only implicit in Wheatley's case would become explicit fifty years later. George Moses Horton had, by the mid 1820s, gained a considerable reputation at Chapel Hill as the "slave-poet." His master printed full-page advertisements in northern newspapers soliciting subscriptions for a book of Horton's poems and promising to exchange the slave's freedom for a sufficient return on sales of the book. Writing, for these slaves, was not only an activity of mind; it was also a commodity that gained them access to their full humanity—Horton literally bought freedom with his poems.

Two centuries separate the publication of Phillis Wheatley's curious book of poems and Toni Morrison's reception of the Nobel Prize for literature in 1993. Morrison's success is part of a larger phenomenon. African American literature has been enjoying a renaissance in quality and quantity for the past decade or so, even vaster than the New Negro, or Harlem, Renaissance of the 1920s, spurred on to a significant extent since 1970 by the writings of African American women such as Morrison, Alice Walker, Maya Angelou, Rita Dove, Gloria Naylor, Jamaica Kincaid, and Terry McMillan, among a host of others. The number of literary prizes won by black authors in the past decade, including Pulitzer Prizes, National and American Book Awards, far exceeds the total number of such honors won by African Americans during the rest of the century. And several times since 1990, as many as three or four black authors have appeared simultaneously on the best-seller list of the *New York Times*. While the audience for this magnificent flowering of black literature crosses all racial boundaries, black readers have never been more numerous: in June 1996 the *Times* reported that African Americans purchase 160 million books a year.

This prominence in the marketplace has had its counterpart in the curriculum. Black literature courses have in the past two decades become a central part of the offerings in English departments and in departments of American studies, African American studies, and Women's studies. Maya Angelou's appearance at President Bill Clinton's inauguration in 1993, the first poet to read at an inauguration since Robert Frost did so for John F. Kennedy in 1961, and Rita Dove's unprecedented two-term appointment as Poet Laureate of the United States are further signs of the pervasive presence of African American literature in American society, just as the sustained popularity of rap poetry has revitalized a "Spoken Word" movement in cafés, the postmodern end-of-the-century heir to poetry readings by Beats in the coffeehouses of the 1950s.

This broad acceptance of the authority of African American writing was, of course, not always the case. Leonard Deutsch, a professor of English at Marshall University, recalls the harsh resistance that greeted his request to write a Ph.D. dissertation on Ralph Ellison at Kent State University in 1970. When his prospectus was approved, a member of his thesis committee—a well-known Melville scholar—resigned in protest, arguing that

> To write this dissertation is bad on two counts: for Len Deutsch himself, and subsequently for the university. A doctoral dissertation implies substance, weight (stuffiness often accompanying this), and spread, and not concentration upon the wings of a gnat. If it be con-

centration, the dissertation must by concentration bring together and sum-up worlds of thought and material—the dissertation as metonymy or synecdoche, which it generally is. One could, for instance, write about Hemingway, Faulkner, or Bellow (recently living or still kicking) because men like them have established a respectable and accepted corpus of work ranging sufficiently to call for comment.

Ellison's work, he concluded, was not of the stature to warrant being studied for a Ph.D. in English. Other stories of white professors and predominantly white institutions of higher education discouraging scholarly interests and careers in African American literature abound in contemporary academic folklore.

The resistance to the literary merits of black literature, as we have seen, has its origins in the Enlightenment and in the peculiar institution of slavery. The social and political uses to which this literature has been put have placed a tremendous burden on these writers, casting an author and her or his works in the role of synecdoche, a part standing for the ethnic whole, signifying who "the Negro" was, what his or her "inherent" intellectual potential might be, and whether or not the larger group was entitled to the full range of rights and responsibilities of American citizenship. Because of the perilous stature of African Americans in American society, their literature has suffered under tremendous extraliterary burdens.

Writing in the "Preface" to *An Anthology of American Negro Literature* (1929), V. F. Calverton, a Marxist critic, argued that black literature was primarily a reflection of the Negro's historical economic exploitation:

> In a subtle way, Negro art and literature in America have had an *economic origin*. All that is original in Negro folk-lore, or singular in Negro spirituals and Blues, can be traced to the economic institution of slavery and its influence upon the Negro soul.

Richard Wright would echo these sentiments in his "Blueprint for Negro Writing," published in 1937. Calverton went on to argue that the Negro's music and folk art were never "purely imitative," and that black vernacular cultural forms were "definitely and unequivocally American," the only "original" American culture yet created. Wright, too, would repeat this claim. If black writers turned to their own vernacular traditions, he concluded, black literature could be as original and as compelling as black music and folklore. The literary movement of the 1920s, he maintained, was more important for what it implied about what historian Carter G. Woodson called "the public Negro mind" than for what it had contributed to the canon of the world's great literatures:

> If this new literature of the Negro in America does not constitute a renaissance, it does signify rapid growth in racial art and culture. It is a growth that is as yet unfinished. Indeed we may say it illustrates a growth that in a dynamic sense has just begun. It indicates more than the rise of a literature. It marks the rise of an entire people.

Calverton's argument about the production of literary arts and "the rise of an entire people" echoed the eloquent argument that the poet James

Weldon Johnson had made in his important anthology, *The Book of American Negro Poetry*, published in 1922, at the very beginning of the Harlem Renaissance. Johnson's preface remains one of the major critical essays on the nature and function of black literature. In it Johnson states explicitly what had been implicit in the critical reception of black literary production since Phillis Wheatley: blacks must create literature because it is, inevitably, a fundamental aspect of their larger struggle for civil rights, and it can never escape this role because it serves as *prima facie* evidence of the Negro's intellectual potential:

> A people may become great through many means, but there is only one measure by which its greatness is recognized and acknowledged. The final measure of the greatness of all peoples is the amount and standard of the literature and art they have produced. The world does not know that a people is great until that people produces great literature and art. No people that has produced great literature and art has ever been looked upon by the world as distinctly inferior.

Johnson here was drawing upon Ralph Waldo Emerson's claim (made in 1844 in his speech "On the Emancipation of the West Indies") about the necessity for blacks to contribute "an indispensable element" to the American nation's cultural mix before they would be granted full citizenship:

> If the black man carries in his bosom an indispensable element of a new and coming civilization, for the sake of that element, no money, nor strength, nor circumstance can hurt him; he will survive and play his part. . . . The intellect—that is miraculous! Who has it, has the talisman. His skin and bones, though they were the color of night, are transparent, and the everlasting stars shine through with attractive beams.

In large part because of these extraliterary expectations—and because of the pernicious withholding of literary and formal education from blacks— African American literature did not come of age until well into this century. As Sylvestre C. Watkins put it in his *Anthology of American Negro Literature* (1944),

> Negro history and Negro literature have maintained a very close relationship through the years. In his struggle for a better way of life, the Negro has, through necessity, made his literature a purposeful thing born of his great desire to become a full-fledged citizen of the United States. His late start did not allow him the pleasure of creating a new phrase, or a more beautiful expression. The struggle against ignorance, indifference and racial bigotry had first claim upon his time and energy.

Indeed, the tension inherent in the African American tradition between even the most private utterances of a poet such as Phillis Wheatley—whose mastery of the English language and whose grace under pressure as *the* synecdoche for the African in Western culture would merit for her a place in the canon, even if her work were not as layered as it is—and the political uses to which those utterances are put obtains to this day. What is the "black voice" that Gronniosaw sought to place in his text? What, exactly, accounts for the "African" element in African American literature? What is the relation between vernacular literature, the blues, gospel, the sermon, and jazz and the formal African American literary tradition? And what relation does the canon of African American literature bear to that of the American tradition? To begin to address these questions, we and our nine colleagues decided to produce this anthology.

Principles of Selection

The Norton Anthology of African American Literature is a celebration of two centuries of imaginative writing in English by persons of African descent in the United States. It is most certainly not the first anthology seeking to define the canon of African American literature. But it is the most comprehensive; its sheer scope and inclusiveness enable readers to trace the repetitions, tropes, and signifying that define the tradition.

Just as the eighteenth-century slave narrators revised the trope of the talking book, writers in the black tradition have repeated and revised figures, tropes, and themes in prior works, leading to formal links in a chain of tradition that connects the slave narratives to autobiographical strategies employed a full century later in works such as Richard Wright's Black Boy, Claude Brown's Manchild in the Promised Land, Ralph Ellison's Invisible Man, and Toni Morrison's Beloved. Precisely because "blackness" is a socially constructed category, it must be learned through imitation, and its literary representations must also be learned in the same way—like jazz—through repetition and revision. The African American literary tradition exists as a formal entity because of this historical practice, which the editors of the monumental anthology The Negro Caravan (1944) called "a sort of literary inbreeding which causes Negro writers to be influenced by other Negroes more than should ordinarily be expected." If Virginia Woolf was correct when she claimed that "books speak to other books," it is also true that works of literature created by African Americans often extend, or signify upon, other works in the black tradition, structurally and thematically. Tracing these formal connections is the task of the teacher, and is most certainly a central function of this anthology.

If African American literature is flourishing dramatically at the end of the century, so too is the academic study of this field. Critical studies, anthologies, encyclopedias, companions, chronological histories, reprints, and reference works of all sorts are enabling us to reassemble the fragmented history of African American writing, buried so often in what one commentator in 1854 called "the ephemeral caskets" of periodical literature, pamphlets, occasional publications, and limited, even vanity, editions. This scholarly work of recovery will most likely end the cycle of each generation of scholars being forced to reinvent the proverbial wheel. Such duplication of effort has been the great curse confronting scholars of African American culture throughout this century. These tools—the collective scholarship of the last few decades—will enable future scholarship and creative learning.

The Norton Anthology of African American Literature builds upon a distinguished tradition of anthology editing that began at least as early as the mid-nineteenth century, with the publication of Les cenelles, Coix de Poesies Indigenes in New Orleans in 1845. These forays into canon formation—for every anthology defines a canon—were also acts of love, arduously grafted together under the most difficult circumstances. Often, a black writer's work exists today only because of his or her presence in a scarce or rare anthology. Robert Thomas Kerlin's superbly edited Negro Poets and Their Poems (1923), for example, includes works by poets such as J. Monrad Allen, Joshua Henry Jones Jr., Eva A. Jessye, Irvin W. Underhill, and Andre Razafkeriefo, whose works are seldom, if ever, taught or anthologized today. Today's canonical figures can often be another generation's amusing footnote to literary history.

The editors of this anthology have followed two dicta in making selections in their respective periods. The first dictum is a caution advised by the writer and social critic Victoria Earle Matthews in 1895 in her important speech "The Value of Race Literature":

> Race literature does not mean things uttered in praise, thoughtless praise of ourselves, wherein each goose thinks her gosling a swan. We have had too much of this. . . . Race literature does mean though the preserving of all records of a Race, and thus cherishing the material saving from destruction and obliteration what is good, helpful and stimulating. But for our Race Literature, how will future generations know of the pioneers in Literature, our statesmen, soldiers, divines, musicians, artists, lawyers, critics, and scholars?

We have endeavored to choose for the Norton Anthology works of such a quality that they merit preservation and sustain classroom interest.

The second dictum, inspired by our friend and advisor M. H. Abrams, is to create an anthology that serves the classroom in a number of specific ways: (1) that the selections allow in-depth study of the major writers in the tradition; (2) that works be so far as feasible complete, and abundant enough to give instructors choices; (3) that introductions and annotation free the student from the need for reference books, so that the anthology can be read anywhere; (4) that each editor, while subject to agreed-upon guidelines, be allowed to keep his or her own distinctive voice; (5) that the anthology be comfortably portable, so students can carry it to class.

Our task, again as defined by M. H. Abrams, has been to bring together into one comprehensive anthology texts we believe to be indispensable for "the indispensable courses that introduce students to the unparalleled excellence and variety" of African American literature. Insofar as possible, we have included those texts necessary to teach, ideally, a survey course in African American literature. With the exceptions of the poetry of Jay Wright, Zora Neale Hurston's novel Their Eyes Were Watching God, and the short fiction of Gayl Jones, which could not be included here for reasons of copyright, our anthology contains the texts that, in the judgment of the editors, define the canon of African American literature at the present time.

Like several historically important anthologies—Kerlin's Negro Poets *and Their Poetry*, Calverton's *Anthology of American Negro Literature*, Sterling Brown, Arthur P. Davis, and Ulysses Lee's *Negro Caravan*, among others—we have given a prominent place to the black vernacular tradition. We have placed this section at the beginning of our text because, historically, anonymous vernacular literature certainly preceded the tradition of written letters among African Americans, and because *all* of the world's literatures have developed from an oral base. In the instance of our literary tradition, the oral, or the vernacular, is never far from the written. Oral expression—the dozens, signifying, rap poetry—surrounds the written tradition rather as a Möbius strip intertwines above and below a plane, in the traditional antiphonal "call/response" structures peculiar to African and African American expressive cultural forms. Not only has the vernacular tradition served as the foundation of the written tradition, but it continues to nurture it, comment upon it, and criticize it in a dialectical, reciprocal relation that surely obtained historically in every major literary tradition. (A visit today to a black beauty parlor, or barbershop, in a black neighborhood, verifies this claim.) The vernacular tradition, however, does not live on the page, but in community and in performance. The Norton Anthology, with its accompanying audio CD, is the first anthology to offer side by side the written and oral traditions, thus illuminating the connections between them. With this technological innovation, we have come full circle from James Gronniosaw's imaginary trope of 1770: this unique feature of our anthology is a literal response to his compelling metaphor, an electronic talking book that makes concrete the black tradition's first structuring metaphor.

The *Norton Anthology of African American Literature* is divided into seven periods, beginning with "The Vernacular Tradition," edited by Robert G. O'Meally, which ranges from eighteenth-century, anonymous black sacred music to twentieth-century blues, jazz, and rap. We have divided the formal tradition into six chronological periods: "The Literature of Slavery and Freedom," edited by William L. Andrews, encompasses the century between 1746 and 1865; "Literature of the Reconstruction to the New Negro Renaissance," edited by Frances Smith Foster and Richard Yarborough, encompasses the half century between 1865 and 1919; "The Harlem Renaissance," edited by Arnold Rampersad, we define as commencing in 1919 and ending in the late 1930s, just before the landmark publication of *Native Son* in 1940; "Realism, Modernism, and Naturalism," edited by Deborah E. McDowell and Hortense Spillers, covers the years from 1940 to 1960, when black authors sought to adapt the conventions of these literary movements to new formal modes that would be adequate to the complex interplay of race and class and gender in modernity; "The Black Arts Movement," edited by Houston A. Baker Jr., covers the 1960s by representing an aesthetic that was no less political than literary—an aesthetic born out of the great movement for civil rights and catalyzed by the demand for Black Power. Our anthology concludes with "Literature since 1970," edited by Barbara T. Christian, the period that has witnessed a renaissance in writings by African American women, a prodigious production of superb work by more African American authors than had been published in the preceding seven decades, and the receipt by black authors of every major award for literary excellence, culminating in Morrison's receipt of the Nobel Prize.

Editorial Procedures

Convinced that this generation of scholars could play a pivotal role in opening the canon and the classroom to African American authors, in 1986 Henry Louis Gates Jr. approached M. H. Abrams, then a colleague in the English department at Cornell, seeking support for a Norton anthology of African American literature. M. H. Abrams responded enthusiastically, as did John Benedict, the stellar in-house editor of various Norton anthologies.

Producing this anthology in the intervening decade has been a truly collaborative effort. The project has moved forward with the help of hundreds of colleagues in the field, who evaluated its general merits, made early recommendations for individual selections, and later proposed refinements and expansions. We have learned from the past, gathering tables of contents from earlier collections as a record of changing definitions of the canon between 1849 and the present. Most importantly, we have collaborated with the nine colleagues who have served as period editors, and whose individual expertise constitutes the foundation of an anthology of central importance in the teaching of African American literature.

The anthology, comprising the work of 120 writers, 52 of whom are women, richly represents African American vernacular literature, poetry, drama, short fiction, the novel, slave narratives, and autobiography. Given the limitations of space, a major question was whether or not to include entire texts of longer works, despite their availability in other editions. After considerable debate, we decided to make available, where possible, texts that we believe represent the origins of a genre: among these "firsts" are Lucy Terry's only poem, *Bars Fight* (1746), the earliest known poem by an African American; Victor Séjour's *The Mulatto*, the earliest short story by an African American (published in Paris in 1837), here published for the first time in English; and the first African American novel, Harriet E. Wilson's *Our Nig* (1859). We have also tried to select texts that best reflect the technical and rhetorical development of the various genres over time.

We have included the following longer texts in their entirety: Frederick Douglass, *Narrative of the Life of Frederick Douglass, an American Slave*; W. E. B. Du Bois, *The Souls of Black Folk*; James Weldon Johnson, *Autobiography of an Ex-Colored Man*; Jean Toomer, *Cane*; Melvin B. Tolson, *Libretto for the Republic of Liberia*; Richard Wright, *The Man Who Lived Underground*; Gwendolyn Brooks, *Maud Martha*; Lorraine Hansberry, *A Raisin in the Sun*; Amiri Baraka, *Dutchman*; Ed Bullins, *Goin'a Buffalo: A Tragifantasy*; Toni Morrison, *Sula*; Adrienne Kennedy, *A Movie Star Has to Star in Black and White*; and August Wilson, *Fences*.

In each literary period, the anthology presents the writers in the order of their birth dates, and the works of each writer in the order of their publication. Thus, the anthology's organization facilitates a chronological approach to African American authors as well as generic or thematic approaches.

Each editor has been responsible for defining the canonical writings of his or her period, and for writing introductory essays, headnotes, and footnotes reflecting the best available scholarship. As in other Norton anthologies, period introductions and author headnotes are meant to be self-sufficient, thereby minimizing the student's need for supplementary biographical, political, or cultural material. After each work, we cite (when known) the date of composition on the left, and the date of first publication on the right. Annotations gloss words that have special meanings in the black vernacular. When a work has been excerpted, the word "From" appears before the title, the omissions are indicated in the text by three asterisks, and summaries of deleted material are provided. The Selected Bibliographies at the end of the volume provide guides to further readings and research and complete the self-sufficiency of the anthology. For instructors, the course guide to *The Norton Anthology of African American Literature*, by Frances Smith Foster, H. R. Houston, and Jewel Parham, offers a wealth of suggestions for teaching with the anthology, including several sample syllabi. A copy can be obtained on request to the publisher.

The editors are deeply indebted to the hundred of teachers who helped us to arrive at the contents of this anthology. A list of "Acknowledgments" names advisors who prepared detailed critiques of the selections both for discrete periods and for the anthology as a whole.

The editors would like to thank M. H. Abrams and the late John Benedict for believing in this project and supporting it from its inception, as did Donald Lamm, chairman of W. W. Norton and Company. The late Barry Wade eagerly accepted editorship upon the untimely death of John Benedict. Julia Reidhead, our third in-house editor, not only has been a tireless advocate of this project but also has displayed a dazzling attention to detail. With her assistant, Tara Parmiter, she helped us to systematically address the dilemmas of anthology making. Without her support, this project would not have been realized. We also give special thanks to Marian Johnson, whose skillful and tactful development work has greatly enhanced this book. We thank too Candace Levy, manuscript editor; Diane O'Connor, production manager; Anna Karvellas, coordinator of the audio CD; and Fred Courtright, permissions manager.

We have attempted to reconstruct the African American literary heritage, at the turn of the century, without pretending to completeness. Limitations of space and prohibitions on copyright have prevented us from including several authors whose texts are important to the canon and whose level of excellence warrants inclusion here. Despite these limitations, we believe that we have represented justly the African American literary tradition by reprinting many of its most historically important and aesthetically sophisticated works. The authors of these works (whose births range from 1730 to 1957) have made the text of Western letters speak in voices and timbres resonant, resplendent, and variously "black." Taken together, they form a literary tradition in which African American authors collectively affirm that the will to power is the will to write, and to testify eloquently in aesthetic forms never far removed from the language of music and the rhythmic resonance of the spoken word.

Henry Louis Gates Jr.
Cambridge, Massachusetts

Nellie Y. McKay
Madison, Wisconsin

July 16, 1996

Acknowledgments

More than ten years in the making, this First Edition of *The Norton Anthology of African American Literature* benefited immeasurably from the advice, assistance, and encouragement of colleagues. Among our many critics, advisors, and friends, the following were of especial help in the preparation of the book. Jennifer Burton (Harvard University) prepared the detailed contextual timeline of African American literature and provided essential research and administrative help. For other research assistance we wish to thank Vermonja Alston (University of Pennsylvania), Cynthia Bond (Cornell University), Keisha Bowman (University of Wisconsin, Madison), Charity Burton (Harvard University), Mike Davis (Princeton University), Geoffrey Ferguson (Harvard University), Michael Furlough (University of Virginia), Lisa Gates (Harvard University), Karin Halil (Harvard University), Candy Heineman (Duke University), Cheryl Higashida (Cornell University), Adam Hotek (University of Pennsylvania), Helena Kaminski (Harvard University), Joanne Kendall (Harvard University), Kathryne Lindberg (Wayne State University), Ruth Lindeborg (University of Pennsylvania), Claudia May (University of California, Berkeley), Richard Newman (W. E. B. Du Bois Research Center, Harvard), Terri Oliver (Harvard University), James Peterson (University of Pennsylvania), Patricia Redmond (University of Pennsylvania), Leslie Reynard (University of Kansas), Michael Roy (Harvard University), María Sánchez (Harvard University), Bruce N. Simon (Princeton University), Kimberly Slaughter-White (University of California, Los Angeles), Mary Ann Stewart-Boelcskevy (Harvard University), Mason Stokes (University of Virginia), Mike Vasquez (Harvard University), Natalie Weathers (University of Pennsylvania), and Lisa Woolfork (University of Wisconsin). For bringing to light new scholarship, we thank Randall K. Burkett, who called attention to an edition in his private library of Gronniosaw's *Narrative*, which contains an advertisement for John Marrant's *Narrative*, and Philip Barnard (University of Kansas), whose new translation of Victor Séjour's *The Mulatto* enables us to introduce to the classroom this previously unavailable work.

From its inception, our Board of Editorial Advisors played a central role in shaping the project. We are indebted to Gerald Barrax (North Carolina State University), Bernard Bell (Penn State University), Kimberly Benston (Haverford College), C. W. E. Bigsby, Sterling A. Brown (late of Howard University), Dickson D. Bruce, John Callahan, Hazel Carby (Yale University), Arthur P. Davis (late of Howard University), Thadious Davis (Vanderbilt University), Melvin Dixson (late of Queens College of CUNY), Genevieve Fabre (University of Paris), Michel Fabre (Universite de la Sorbonne Nouvelle), Addison Gayle Jr. (late of Baruch College of CUNY), Donald

Gibson (Rutgers University), Hugh Gloster (Morehouse College), Mary-emma Graham (Northeastern University), Yoshinobu Hakutani (Kent State University), James V. Hatch (New York University), Trudier Harris (University of North Carolina, Chapel Hill), William J. Harris (Pennsylvania State University), Robert E. Hemenway (University of Kansas, Lawrence), Mae Henderson (University of North Carolina, Chapel Hill), Stephen Henderson (Howard University), Cason L. Hill (Morehouse College), Sue Houchins, Gloria Hull (University of California, Santa Cruz), Blyden Jackson (University of North Carolina, Chapel Hill), Lemuell Johnson (University of Michigan), Bernice Johnson-Reagan (Smithsonian Institute), Laurence W. Levine (George Mason University), R. Baxter Miller (University of Tennessee), James A. Miller (Trinity College), Claudia Mitchell-Kernan (University of California, Los Angeles), Charles Nichols (late of Brown University), Charles Nilon (University of Colorado), James Olney (Louisiana State University), Dorothy Porter (late of Howard University), J. Saunders Redding (late of Cornell University), John Reilly (State University of New York, Albany), Marilyn Richardson, William Robinson (Rhode Island College), Charles Rowell (University of Virginia), Joan Rita Sherman, Amiritjit Singh (Rhode Island College), Barbara Smith, Valerie Smith (University of California, Los Angeles), Werner Sollors (Harvard University), Robert Stepto (Yale University), Dorothy Sterling, Claudia Tate (George Washington University), Clyde Taylor (Tufts University), Darwin T. Turner (late of the University of Iowa), Gloria Wade-Gayles (Spellman College), Cheryl A. Wall (Rutgers University), Mary Helen Washington (University of Maryland), Jerry Ward (Tougaloo College), Joseph N. Weixlmann Jr. (Indiana State University), Craig Werner (University of Wisconsin, Madison), Margaret Wilkerson (University of California, Berkeley), Kenny J. Williams (Duke University), Sherley Anne Williams (University of California, San Diego), and Jean Fagan Yellin (Pace University).

Over the long road to publication, during which time African American literature broke new ground at a breathtaking pace, our table of contents required several rounds of reshaping. For their clear-eyed advice, we wish to thank our many reviewers: Lionel Arnold (Oklahoma State University), Fahamisha Patricia Brown (Boston College), Lois Brown (Cornell University), Kenneth Byerman (Indiana State University), Rudolph P. Byrd (Emory University), Maura L. Conron, Selwyn R. Cudjoe (Wellesley College), Jeffrey Louis Decker (University of California, Los Angeles), Manthia Diawara (New York University), Gerald Early (Washington University), Shelley Fisher Fishkin (University of Texas at Austin), Robert Jones (Rice University), Kenneth Kinnamon (University of Arkansas), John E. Kirby (San Diego Mesa College), Thomas Knipp (St. Louis University), Missy Kubischek (University of Nebraska, Omaha), Mary Hope Lee (San Diego Mesa College), Colleen McElroy (University of Washington), Cornelius Page (San Diego Mesa College), Erskine Peters (University of California, Berkeley), Carla Peterson (University of Maryland), Horace Porter (Stanford University), Tricia Rose (New York University), Donald Schweda (Quincy College), J. T. Skerrett (University of Massachusetts, Amherst), Tracey L. Stewart, Priscilla Wald (Columbia University), and Kenneth Warren (University of Chicago).

The Norton Anthology
of African American
Literature

The Vernacular Tradition*

In African American literature, *the vernacular* refers to the church songs, blues, ballads, sermons, stories, and, in our own era, rap songs that are part of the oral, not primarily the literate (or written-down) tradition of black expression. What distinguishes this body of work is its in-group and, at times, secretive, defensive, and aggressive character: it is not, generally speaking, produced for circulation beyond the black group itself (though it sometimes is bought and sold as exotic material by those outside its circle). This highly charged material has been extraordinarily influential for writers of poetry, fiction, drama, and so on. What would the work of Langston Hughes, Sterling A. Brown, Zora Neale Hurston, and Ralph Ellison be like without its black vernacular ingredients? What, for that matter, would the writing of Mark Twain or William Faulkner be without these same elements? Still, this vernacular material also has its own shapes, its own integrity, its own place in the black literary canon: *the literature of the vernacular.*

Defining the vernacular and delineating it as a category of African American literary studies have been difficult and controversial projects. Some critics note the vernacular's typical demarcation as a category of things that are male, attached only to lower-class groups, and otherwise simplistically expressive of a vast and complexly layered and dispersed group of people. Others warn both against the sentimentalization of a stereotyped "folk" and their "lore" and against the impulse to define black people and their literature solely in terms of the production of unconscious but somehow definitive work from the bottom of the social hierarchy. With these critiques often come warnings against forming too easy an idea about the shape and direction of African American literary history. Most emphatic is the argument against a "modernist" view that would posit an almost sacred set of foundational vernacular texts by "black and unknown bards" (to borrow James Weldon Johnson's ringing phrase) leading to ever more complex works by higher and higher artists marching into the future. Is contemporary music really more "progressive" or "complex" than the work of Bessie Smith or Louis Armstrong?

And yet even after these questions and criticisms have been raised, somehow such distinctive forms as church songs, blues, tall tales, work songs, games, jokes, dozens, and rap songs—along with myriad other such forms, past and present—persist among African Americans, as they have for decades. They are, as a Langston Hughes poem announces, *still here.* Indeed, the vernacular is not a body of quaint, folksy items. It is not a male province. Nor is it associated with a particular level of society or with a particular historical era. It is neither long ago, far away, nor fading. Instead the vernacular encompasses vigorous, dynamic processes of expression, past and present. It makes up a rich storehouse of materials wherein the values, styles, and character types of black American life are reflected in language that is highly energized and often marvelously eloquent.

*Throughout this section, titles followed by • are included on the Audio Companion.

1

Ralph Ellison argued that vernacular art accounts, to a large degree, for the black American's legacy of self-awareness and endurance. For black performers and listeners (as well as readers) it has often served the classic function of teaching as it delights. Refusing to subscribe wholly to the white Americans' ethos and world-view, African Americans expressed in these vernacular forms their own ways of seeing the world, its history, and its meanings. The vernacular comprises, Ellison said, nothing less than another instance of humanity's "triumph over chaos." In it experiences of the past are remembered and evaluated; through it African Americans attempt to humanize an often harsh world, and to do so with honesty, with toughness, and often with humor.

THE VERNACULAR: A BRIEF HISTORY

Eighteenth- and nineteenth-century observers, black and white, recorded their fascination with these black oral forms. Thomas Jefferson, for example, observed that musically the slaves "are more generally gifted than the whites with accurate ears for tune and time." Nearly fifty years later, a Mississippi planter used conventionally racialized language to inform Frederick Law Olmstead that "niggers is allers good singers nat'rally. I reckon they got better lungs than white folks, they hev such powerful voices." Frederick Douglass took pains in each of his autobiographies to define the meaning of the songs of slaves. He points out, for instance, that those who hear the music as evidence that the slaves are happy with their station in life miss the slave song's deeper, troubled meanings. By the end of the nineteenth century, some black writers were declaring these forms evidence of special "Negro genius," a keystone proof of black contribution to world culture and of black readiness for full U.S. citizenship.

Early landmark anthologies of black literature, *The New Negro* (1925), *The Book of American Negro Poetry* (1931), and *The Negro Caravan* (1941), included careful discussions of black songs and stories; *Caravan* presented vernacular texts as forms to be enjoyed and studied both as art and as part of the usually unseen historical record. These books opened the way to the realization that black writers, most obviously poets, were sometimes strongly influenced by vernacular forms. Certain Negro writers of the 1920s and 1930s (and their literary offspring of later decades) consciously sought to draw artistic power from the vernacular into their writing. In some cases—one thinks of works by Langston Hughes, Sterling Brown, and Zora Neale Hurston as examples—writers celebrated such forms as blues and sermons and tried to capture them on the page with as little intrusion as possible.

By the late 1930s, however, Richard Wright, Ralph Ellison, and other African American writers who were close students of the black vernacular warned against the sentimentalization of "the folk" and declared the writer's responsibility to do what they saw Eliot, Stein, and Joyce (along with Louis Armstrong, Jelly Roll Morton, and Duke Ellington) doing in their art: to capture the note and trick of the vernacular at the same time that he or she transformed it into something drawing on artistic sources and traditions beyond the vernacular. These writers warned, too, against the danger of winning audiences for black writing with the "easy tears" of a simplified black folklore at the expense of political engagement. What Ellison in particular advocated was a literature as conscious of the best new thinking in political science and modern writing as it was of the ways of Brer Rabbit and the down-home blues. Sounding a similar note in the late 1970s, Albert Murray pronounced what he termed (with a reference to literary critic Kenneth Burke) the "vernacular imperative" for writers: all writers, said Murray, must be thoroughly knowledgeable of the local materials surrounding them (what else could they write about with true authority?) as well as of the artistic traditions for transforming those materials—the vernacular—into the silver and gold of personalized modern artistic expression.

The Black Arts movement of the 1960s and 1970s reflected many of these controversies and convictions about the vernacular. It was a period of the rediscovery of Hurston, who was widely celebrated by the rising new group of feminist writers as well as by various factions of the male-centered black aesthetic group. At the same time, it was a period of rediscovery of Wright and Hughes, whose radical politics and celebration of the potential within black working-class communities were widely heralded and imitated. More than ever there was a general sense of black vernacular expression as something of current value not just among working classes but throughout the African American "nation." Such students of black speech and story as Roger Abrahams, John Szwed, and Geneva Smitherman helped define the peculiarities of black vernacular expression and noted its relation to black oral forms throughout the Americas and in Africa. By the 1980s and 1990s, many scholars and writers recognized the black vernacular as an enormously rich and various source. Key analytical books by Lawrence Levine, Sterling Stuckey, Albert Murray, Ralph Ellison, Houston A. Baker Jr., Henry Louis Gates Jr., and others paved the way for the ongoing contemporary analysis of the forms as sources for historical and critical insight as well as wellsprings for the writer.

DEFINING THE VERNACULAR

What is the vernacular? According to Webster's second edition, the term comes from the Latin—"vernaculus: Born in one's house, native, from verna, a slave born in his master's house, a native"—and counts among its meanings the following: (1) "belonging to, developed in, and spoken or used by the people of a particular place, region, or country; native; indigenous. . . . (2) characteristic of a locality; local." In the context of American art, the vernacular may be defined as expression that springs from the creative interaction between the received or learned traditions and that which is locally invented, "made in America." This definition, derived from American cultural historian John A. Kouwenhoven and Ralph Ellison, sees Manhattan's skyscrapers as well as Appalachian quilts as vernacular because they use modern techniques and forms (machines, factory-made materials, etc.) along with what Ellison calls the play-it-by-ear methods and local products that give American forms their distinctive resonances and power. What, then, is the African American vernacular? It consists of forms sacred—songs, prayers, and sermons—as well as secular—work songs, secular rhymes and songs, blues, jazz, and stories of many kinds. It also consists of dances, wordless musical performances, stage shows, and visual art forms of many sorts.

As Houston A. Baker Jr. has noted, the word vernacular has been used to describe developments in the world of architecture. In contrast to the exalted, refined, or learned styles of making buildings, the vernacular in architecture refers both to local styles by builders unaware of or unconcerned with developments beyond their particular province and to works by inspired, cosmopolitan architects such as Frank Lloyd Wright, a careful student of architecture as a worldwide enterprise and of the latest technologies, but also one who wanted his buildings custom-made for their surroundings.

This example from architecture is relevant insofar as the makers of black vernacular art used the American language and everything at their disposal to make art that paid a minimum of attention to the Thou-shalt-nots of the academy or the arbiters of high style. Coming from the bottom of the American social ladder, blacks have been relatively free from scrutiny by the official cultural monitors. As a group they tended to care little about such opinions; what the black social dance called the Black Bottom looked like to the proctors at the local ballet class (be they white or black) was of no interest to them. Thus it is no surprise that the black inventors of this rich array of definitively American forms have had such a potent impact on America's cultural life and history.

The forms included here are varied and resist aesthetic generalizations. One is drawn nonetheless to parts of Zora Neale Hurston's wonderful catalog of the *Characteristics of Negro Expression*: "angularity," "assymmetry," a tendency toward "mimicry" and the "will to adorn." In addition, the forms share traits that reflect their African background: call/response patterns of many kinds; group creation; and a percussive, often dance-beat orientation not only in musical forms but in the rhythm of a tale or rhyme. Not surprisingly, improvisation is a highly prized aspect of vernacular performance. Then too one finds European, Euro-American, and American Indian forms reshaped to African American purposes and sensibilities. For example, like black folktales, tales from Europe often lack clear delineations of sacred and profane, good and evil, righteous punishers and righteously punished. Similarly, the blues offer few such consolations, solutions, or even scapegoats. At times what seems revealed is the starkness of a life that is real, that is tough, and that must be confronted without the convenience of formulaic dodges or wishful escapes. Even the spirituals admit that "I've been 'buked and I've been scorned, I've been talked about, / Sure as you're born." And the church songs involve—along with the yearning for heaven's peace—confrontation with real troubles of the world and the will to do something about them.

One of the most compelling efforts at generalization about African American aesthetics is drawn by Henry Louis Gates Jr. from the vernacular itself. Drawing on linguistic research by Geneva Smitherman and others, Gates has defined *signifying*—the often competitively figurative, subversively parodying speech of tales and of less formalized talk as well as of various forms of music—as an impulse that operates not only between contesting tale tellers but between writers (and painters, and dancers, etc.) as well. According to this view, Toni Morrison signifies on writers who precede her by revising their conceptions of character and scene, for example, or perhaps she even signifies on aspects of the novelistic tradition itself. In Gates's complex formulations about how African Americans create, the vernacular meets not only formal art, it meets the world of scholarly criticism as well.

How were this section's entries selected? Whence came these particular texts? Pouring over dozens of anthologies and collections, hymnals, songbooks, recordings, and literary works per se yielded texts that are not only historically representative but also distinctive and resonant with meaning. One abiding problem with capturing such works is that they were not originally constructed for the printed page but for performance within complicated social and often highly ritualized settings. Nonstandard pronunciations in texts transcribed from records are generally represented with a minimum of invented spellings—the "eye dialect" so often used by American writers to designate déclassé or politically disempowered groups. This effort was informed by those of writers who captured black speech by getting the rhythms right, the pauses, the special emphases and colors. But contractions and new spellings were allowed when they seemed called for.

What determines the order of the vernacular selections, genre by genre? Whenever possible, works are presented in the chronological order and are clustered according to authorship. But since when it comes to the vernacular, both authorship and chronology are often unknown or ambiguous (for example: who first told the tale of the rabbit and the tar-baby?), we simply have done our best to ascertain credits and dates when they are available. In the folktales section, works are credited and dated in footnotes but—recognizing that in this instance the "authors" are the recorders (brilliantly artistic ones though they may be) of works created incrementally by many, many voices over many, many years—they are listed not by date or writer but by subject: the animal tales precede the ones with human characters and follow a general chronological arc. Such broad thematic and timeline concerns govern all of the vernacular section's orderings—even when specific dates and authors are given. For even in the case of a Duke Ellington song or a Martin Luther King sermon/speech, where date and "author" seem so specific, what we reproduce here is one particular text or version of a performance given over and over, according to changing settings and moments. And both Ellington and King draw on rich vernacular traditions (on black and unknown bards) to fashion and project their works. (In Ellington's case, the best text may be the recorded "text," with its performance by sixteen members of his band, each of whom adds much more to the creative process than is the case with European "classical" music.) More than any other form of black literature, the vernacular resists being captured on a page or in a historical frame: by definition, it is about gradual, group creation; it is about *change*.

Clearly, the selections here and on the Audio Companion to *The Norton Anthology of African American Literature* are not meant to be definitive but to invite further explorations and findings. Black vernacular forms are works-in-progress, experiments in a still new country. They have not survived because they are perfect, polished jewels that are sonnetlike in their finish but because they are vigorous fountains of expression. Not only are they influential for writers, they are wonderful creations on their own. In the black tradition, no forms are more quick or overflowing with black power and black meaning.

SPIRITUALS

Negro spirituals are the religious songs sung by African Americans since the earliest days of slavery and first gathered in a book in 1801 by the black church leader Richard Allen. As scholars have observed, this term, whether abbreviated to *spirituals* or not, is somewhat misleading: for many black slaves, and for their offspring, the divisions between secular and sacred were not as definite as the designation *spirituals* would suggest. Certainly these religious songs were not sung only in churches or in religious ritual settings. Travelers in the Old South and slaves themselves reported that music about God and the Bible was sung during work time, play time, and rest time as well as on Sundays at praise meetings. As historian Lawrence Levine observes, for slaves the concept of the sacred signified a strong will to incorporate "within this world all the elements of the divine."

That the songs were sung not just in ritual worship but throughout the day meant that they served as powerful shields against the values of the slaveholders and their killing definitions of black humanity. For one thing, along with a sense of the slaves' personal self-worth as children of a mighty God, the spirituals offered them much-needed psychic escape from the workaday world of slavery's restrictions and cruelties. Certainly, "this world is not my home" was a steady theme in the spirituals, one that offered its singer/hearers visions of a peaceful, loving realm beyond the one in which they labored. Some of the songs bespoke the dream of flying away, leaving the world of care behind:

> I've got two wings for to veil my face
> I've got two wings for to fly away . . .

Along with such visions of displacement and escape, many of the spirituals offered images of a steady and just King Jesus who had a comfortable space around his altar where those in Heaven could rest a while (significant for people forced to work all day), a place where they would be reunited with "friends and kindreds" who had gone before. One song makes clear the vision of familiarity and ease:

> A-settin' down with Jesus
> Eatin' hone and drinkin' wine
> Marchin' round de throne
> Wid Peter, James, and John.

And:

> I'm gonna tell God all my troubles,
> When I get home . . .
> I'm gonna tell him the road was rocky
> When I get home.

In such visions of justice and peace resided both a healthful impulse to escape the sorrowful world and an implied criticism of life's earthly overwork, injustice, and violence.

Most of the spirituals were not about easeful King Jesus at all, however, but about the Old Testament God and His heroes and prophets. Moses, Job, Daniel, Samson, and Ezekiel are celebrated in scores of spirituals along with the Chosen People, protected by their furiously watchful God. According to poet and critic Sterling A. Brown, "Fairly easy allegories identified Egypt-land with the South, Pharaoh with the masters, the Israelites with themselves and Moses with their leader." Not surprisingly, some of the songs offered not just psychic escapes and veiled criticisms but calls for this-worldly attentiveness and direct action:

> Didn't my Lord deliver Daniel,
> And why not every man?

Frederick Douglass and others spoke of references in the spirituals to escapes not to Heaven but to freedomland, whether in the non-slave-holding states or all the way to Canada. "Swing low sweet chariot, Coming for to carry me home" was evidently one of those songs that referred to the urge, and perhaps the specific plan, to make a run out of the jaws of slavery into the land of freedom. Many songs, doubtless sung well out of the master's earshot, celebrated the coming of freedom:

> O Freedom;
> O Freedom!
> And before I'll be a slave,
> I'll be buried in my grave!
> And go home to my Lord and be free.

Other secret songs were equally direct and stark:

> No more driver's lash for me;
> No more, no more . . .
> No more peck of corn for me;
> Many thousands go.

In terms of form, these songs employ the call/response patterns of West and Central Africa, patterns that were encouraged by the lining-out (i.e., the calling out of the song lyrics in anticipation of the group's singing of the lyrics) of hymns that the New World Africans encountered in the Protestant services of America. The single voice of the chorus would be answered by a group of singers, usually the entire group gathered together. The songs varied in rhythm. Dirgelike sorrow songs, rightly named by W. E. B. Du Bois in his marvelous chapter on the music in The Souls of Black Folk, were quite appropriate for such plaintive lyrics as

> Don't know what my mother wants to stay here fuh,
> Dis ole world ain't been no friend to huh.

Only slightly less dark was the meditative poetry that clergyman, writer, and army officer Thomas Wentworth Higginson, one of the first to pay respectful attention to the spiritual, heard among black Civil War soldiers:

> I'll lie in de grave
> And stretch out my arms,
> When I lay dis body down.

Elsewhere, the spirituals presented a drivingly percussive vision of Judgment Day. *That Great Gittin' Up Morning!*, a song of Gabriel, trumpet song, and jubilation, might have been used in a ring shout where the possessed worshipers were inspired to raise their voices and move their bodies in praise of the Lord.

Further study of spirituals would investigate their African and European sources; the debates over the originality of their forms and verses; their presentation in minstrel shows and other commercial venues; their fund-raising importance for nineteenth- and twentieth-century black schools; their uses by classically trained black composers and arrangers as a concert "art music"; their uses by Dvořák, William Grant Still, and other composers in search of an indigenous American music that used large forms; their importance for "race men and women" of the nineteenth and twentieth centuries, who often pointed to the songs as evidence of "Negro genius"; and their relation to gospel and to other African American musics. Suffice it to say that even when read they are both moving and inspiring in their complex expression of sorrow and a possible far-off joy.

Were You There When They Crucified My Lord?

Were you there, when they crucified my Lord?
Were you there, when they crucified my Lord?
Oh, sometimes, it causes me to tremble, tremble, tremble.
Were you there, when they crucified my Lord?

Were you there, when they nailed him to the tree?   5
Were you there, when they nailed him to the tree?
Oh, sometimes, it causes me to tremble, tremble, tremble.
Were you there, when they nailed him to the tree?

Were you there, when they pierced him in the side?
Were you there, when they pierced him in the side?   10
Oh, sometimes, it causes me to tremble, tremble, tremble.
Were you there, when they pierced him in the side?

Were you there, when the sun refused to shine?
Were you there, when the sun refused to shine?
Oh, sometimes, it causes me to tremble, tremble, tremble.   15
Were you there, when the sun refused to shine?

Were you there, when they laid him in the tomb?
Were you there, when they laid him in the tomb?
Oh, sometimes, it causes me to tremble, tremble, tremble.
Were you there, when they laid him in the tomb?   20

City Called Heaven

I am a poor pilgrim of sorrow.
I'm in this wide world alone.
No hope in this world for tomorrow.
I'm tryin' to make heaven my home.

Sometimes I am tossed and driven.   5
Sometimes I don't know where to roam.
I've heard of a city called heaven.
I've started to make it my home.

My mother's gone on to pure glory.
My father's still walkin' in sin.   10
My sisters and brothers won't own me
Because I'm tryin' to get in.

Sometimes I am tossed and driven.
Sometimes I don't know where to roam,
But I've heard of a city called heaven   15
And I've started to make it my home.

God's A-Gonna Trouble the Water

Wade in the water, children,
Wade in the water, children,
Wade in the water, children,
God's a-gonna trouble the water.

See that host all dressed in white,   5
God's a-gonna trouble the water;
The leader looks like the Israelite, [1]
God's a-gonna trouble the water.

Wade in the water, children,
Wade in the water, children,   10
Wade in the water, children,
God's a-gonna trouble the water.

See that host all dressed in red,
God's a-gonna trouble the water;
Looks like the band that Moses led,   15
God's a-gonna trouble the water.

Wade in the water, children,
Wade in the water, children,
Wade in the water, children,
God's a-gonna trouble the water.   20

1. Moses.

8

Walk Together Children

Walk together children,
Don't you get weary,
Walk together children,
Don't you get weary.
Oh, talk together children,   5
Don't you get weary,
There's a great camp meeting[2] in the Promised Land.

Sing together children,
Don't you get weary,
Sing together children,   10
Don't you get weary.
Oh, shout together children,
Don't you get weary,
There's a great camp meeting in the Promised Land.

Gwineter mourn and never tire,   15
Mourn and never tire,
Mourn and never tire.
There's a great camp meeting in the Promised Land.

Oh, get you ready children,
Don't you get weary,   20
Get you ready children,
Don't you get weary.
We'll enter there, oh, children,
Don't you get weary,
There's a great camp meeting in the Promised Land.   25

I Know Moon-Rise[3]

"I know moon-rise, I know star-rise,
    Lay dis body down.
I walk in de moonlight, I walk in de starlight,
    To lay dis body down.
I'll walk in de graveyard, I'll walk through de graveyard,   5
    To lay dis body down.
I'll lie in de grave and stretch out my arms;
    Lay dis body down.
I go to de judgment in de evenin' of de day,
    When I lay dis body down;   10
And my soul and your soul will meet in de day
    When I lay dis body down."

2. A religious gathering.
3. This particular spiritual was singled out by nineteenth-century scholar, abolitionist, and army officer Thomas Wentworth Higginson for special
praise. Of the words "I'll lie in de grave and stretch
out my arms," he wrote in 1867: "Never, it seems to
me, since man first lived and suffered, was his infinite longing for peace uttered more plaintively
than in that line."

I'm A-Rollin'

I'm a-rollin', I'm a-rollin', I'm a-rollin' through an unfriendly world,
I'm a-rollin', I'm a-rollin', I'm a-rollin' through an unfriendly world,
I'm a-rollin', I'm a-rollin', I'm a-rollin' through an unfriendly world,
I'm a-rollin', I'm a-rollin', I'm a-rollin' through an unfriendly world,

O, brothers, won't you help me,   5
O, brothers, won't you help me to pray;
O, brothers, won't you help me,
Won't you help me in de service of de Lord.

I'm a-rollin', I'm a-rollin', I'm a-rollin' through an unfriendly world,
I'm a-rollin', I'm a-rollin', I'm a-rollin' through an unfriendly world,   10
I'm a-rollin', I'm a-rollin', I'm a-rollin' through an unfriendly world,
I'm a-rollin', I'm a-rollin', I'm a-rollin' through an unfriendly world,

O, sisters, won't you help me,
O, sisters, won't you help me to pray;
O, sisters, won't you help me,   15
Won't you help me in de service of de Lord.

I'm a-rollin', I'm a-rollin', I'm a-rollin' through an unfriendly world,
I'm a-rollin', I'm a-rollin', I'm a-rollin' through an unfriendly world.

I Been Rebuked and I Been Scorned[4]

I been rebuked and I been scorned,
I been rebuked and I been scorned,
Chillun, I been rebuked and I been scorned,
I'se had a hard time, sho's you born.

Talk about me much as you please,   5
Talk about me much as you please,
Chillun, talk about me much as you please,
Gonna talk about you when I get on my knees.

Didn't My Lord Deliver Daniel?•

Didn't my Lord deliver Daniel,[5]
Deliver Daniel, deliver Daniel?
Didn't my Lord deliver Daniel?
An' why not everyman?

He delivered Daniel from de lion's den,   5
Jonah[6] from de belly of de whale.

4. Note the direct sense in which this song expresses the slave's dissatisfaction not just with personal spiritual shortcomings but with being
"rebuked" and "scorned" in *this* world.
5. When the Babylonians threw Daniel into a
lions' den, God sent an angel to shut the lions'
mouths, thus delivering him from harm (Daniel
6:22).
6. After he had been swallowed by a great fish,
Jonah was saved when God heard his prayers
(Jonah 2:7–10).

And de Hebrew children from de fiery furnace,
An' why not everyman?

Didn't my Lord deliver Daniel,
Deliver Daniel, deliver Daniel?
Didn't my Lord deliver Daniel?   10
An' why not everyman?

De moon run down in a purple stream,
De sun forbear to shine,
And every star disappear,   15
King Jesus shall be mine.

Didn't my Lord deliver Daniel,
Deliver Daniel, deliver Daniel?
Didn't my Lord deliver Daniel?
An' why not everyman?   20

De wind blows east and de wind blows west,
It blows like de judgment day,
And every poor soul dat never did pray'll
Be glad to pray dat day.

Didn't my Lord deliver Daniel,   25
Deliver Daniel, deliver Daniel?
Didn't my Lord deliver Daniel?
An' why not everyman?

I set my foot on de Gospel ship,
An' de ship begin to sail.   30
It landed me over on Canaan's[7] shore
And I'll never come back no more.

Didn't my Lord deliver Daniel,
Deliver Daniel, deliver Daniel?
Didn't my Lord deliver Daniel?   35
An' why not every man?

Soon I Will Be Done•

Soon I will be done with the troubles of the world,
Troubles of the world, the troubles of the world,
Soon I will be done with the troubles of the world.
Goin' home to live with God.

No more weepin' and a-wailing,   5
No more weepin' and a-wailing,
No more weepin' and a-wailing,
I'm goin' to live with God.

7. The Promised Land, encompassing present-day Israel and parts of Syria; here a symbol of Heaven.

Soon I will be done with the troubles of the world,
Troubles of the world, the troubles of the world,   10
Soon I will be done with the troubles of the world.
Goin' home to live with God.

I want t' meet my mother,
I want t' meet my mother,
I want t' meet my mother,   15
I'm goin' to live with God.

Soon I will be done with the troubles of the world,
Troubles of the world, the troubles of the world,
Soon I will be done with the troubles of the world.
Goin' home to live with God.   20

I want t' meet my Jesus,
I want t' meet my Jesus,
I want t' meet my Jesus,
I'm goin' to live with God.

Soon I will be done with the troubles of the world,   25
Troubles of the world, the troubles of the world,
Soon I will be done with the troubles of the world.
Goin' home to live with God.

No More Auction Block[8]

No more auction block for me,
No more, no more,
No more auction block for me,
Many thousand gone.

No more peck of corn for me,[9]   5
No more, no more,
No more peck of corn for me,
Many thousand gone.

No more pint of salt for me,
No more, no more,   10
No more pint of salt for me,
Many thousand gone.

No more driver's lash for me,
No more, no more,
No more driver's lash for me,   15
Many thousand gone.

---

8. No spiritual's lyrics speak more explicitly about
the hardness of the slave's life—and of the "many
thousand" gone to the unknown fate of the auction
block, gone to death.
9. A reference to the limited rations — corn, and in
the next stanza, salt — granted the slave.

Swing Low, Sweet Chariot [1]

Swing low, sweet chariot,
Coming for to carry me home,
Swing low, sweet chariot,
Coming for to carry me home.

I looked over Jordan [2] and what did I see   5
Coming for to carry me home,
A band of angels, coming after me,
Coming for to carry me home.

If you get there before I do,
Coming for to carry me home,   10
Tell all my friends I'm coming too,
Coming for to carry me home.

Swing low, sweet chariot,
Coming for to carry me home,
Swing low, sweet chariot,   15
Coming for to carry me home.

Steal Away to Jesus [3]•

Steal away, steal away, steal away to Jesus,
Steal away, steal away home,
I ain't got long to stay here.

My Lord, He calls me,
He calls me by the thunder,
The trumpet sounds within-a my soul,   5
I ain't got long to stay here.

Steal away, steal away, steal away to Jesus,
Steal away, steal away home,
I ain't got long to stay here.   10

Green trees a-bending,
Po' sinner stands a-trembling,
The trumpet sounds within-a my soul,
I ain't got long to stay here.

Steal away, steal away, steal away to Jesus,   15
Steal away, steal away home,
I ain't got long to stay here.

---

1. This is often cited as a song not just celebrating the hope of release into Heaven but signaling the plan or the moment—or the general aspiration—to be carried "home" to freedom by the underground railroad system.
2. A river in the Mideast. "Crossing over Jordan" is a metaphor for going to Heaven.
3. Often cited as a signal song for runaway slaves. If so, its lyrics—especially using the dangerous word *steal*—must have been kept secret from white supporters of slavery.

Go Down, Moses [4]•

Go down, Moses,
Way down in Egyptland
Tell old Pharaoh
To let my people go.

When Israel was in Egyptland   5
Let my people go
Oppressed so hard they could not stand
Let my people go.

Go down, Moses,
Way down in Egyptland   10
Tell old Pharaoh
"Let my people go."

"Thus saith the Lord," bold Moses said,
"Let my people go;
If not I'll smite your first-born dead   15
Let my people go.

"No more shall they in bondage toil,
    Let my people go;
Let them come out with Egypt's spoil,
    Let my people go."   20

The Lord told Moses what to do
    Let my people go;
To lead the children of Israel through,
    Let my people go.

Go down, Moses,   25
    Way down in Egyptland,
Tell old Pharaoh,
    "Let my people go!"

Been in the Storm So Long [5]•

I've been in the storm so long,
You know I've been in the storm so long,
Oh Lord, give me more time to pray,
I've been in the storm so long.

I am a motherless child,   5
Singin' I am a motherless child,
Singin' Oh Lord, give me more time to pray,
I've been in the storm so long.

4. The scholar and poet Sterling A. Brown observed in 1953 that this song was so direct in its protest that it was banned on many slave plantations.
5. That this version differs quite a bit from the one
on the Audio Companion illustrates the dynamism
of the oral form. Here and throughout this vernacular section, no single, final authoritative text ever
exists.

14

This is a needy time,
This is a needy time,   10
Singin' Oh Lord, give me more time to pray,
I've been in the storm so long.

Lord, I need you now,
Lord, I need you now,
Singin' Oh Lord, give me more time to pray,   15
I've been in the storm so long.

My neighbors need you now,
My neighbors need you now,
Singin' Oh Lord, give me more time to pray,
I've been in the storm so long.   20

My children need you now,
My children need you now,
Singin' Oh Lord, give me more time to pray,
I've been in the storm so long.

Just look what a shape I'm in,   25
Just look what a shape I'm in,
Cryin' Oh Lord, give me more time to pray,
I've been in the storm so long.

Oh, Freedom!

Oh, freedom,
Oh, freedom,
Oh, freedom over me!
An' befo' I'd be a slave,
I'll be buried in my grave,   5
An' go home to my Lord an' be free.

No mo' moanin',
No mo' moanin',
No mo' moanin' over me!
An' befo' I'd be a slave,   10
I'll be buried in my grave,
An' go home to my Lord an' be free.

No mo' weepin',
No mo' weepin',
No mo' weepin' over me!   15
An' befo' I'd be a slave,
I'll be buried in my grave,
An' go home to my Lord an' be free.

There'll be singin',
There'll be singin',
There'll be singin' over me!   20
An' befo' I'd be a slave,

I'll be buried in my grave,
An' go home to my Lord an' be free.

There'll be shoutin',   25
There'll be shoutin',
There'll be shoutin' over me!
An' befo' I'd be a slave,
I'll be buried in my grave,
An' go home to my Lord an' be free.   30

There'll be prayin',
There'll be prayin',
There'll be prayin' over me!
An' befo' I'd be a slave,
I'll be buried in my grave,   35
An' go home to my Lord an' be free.

GOSPEL

In a sense, the distinction between spirituals and gospel is so slight that it seems contrived. Both are black sacred songs, church songs that are constructed in a variety of forms within the African American musical tradition. Both are born and nurtured in the context of ritualized Christian worship, and yet both comment widely on the circumstances of black life in white America. To complicate the picture even more, it is possible to render a traditional Negro spiritual in a *gospel manner*. Sometimes, indeed, songs from eighteenth- and nineteenth-century English hymnals—most notably the songs of Isaac Watts—may be rendered in so convincing a gospel version that observers have thought them generated as the spirituals were generated: within the richly dramatic space of the black church service itself.

What is the gospel manner? And what is its history? Briefly, gospel music emerged in the first decades of the twentieth century as blues and early jazz styles of singing and playing instruments began to exert a powerful impact on the way church musicians conceived their task. Especially in holiness churches, Churches of God in Christ—those farthest from the genteel European models of churchly decorum—a highly percussive, polyrhythmically syncopated and bluesy music began to appear. These singers, says poet and critic Sterling A. Brown,

> fight the devil by using what have been considered the devil's weapons. Tambourines, cymbals, trumpets and even trombones and bass fiddles are now accepted in some churches. The devil has no right to all that fine rhythm, so a joyful noise is made unto the Lord with bounce and swing.

Eventually, not only gospelized versions of familiar church songs but also songs composed in this particular idiom—a body of gospel songs per se—began to be heard in certain churches, notably in Chicago, where the music first claimed a citywide and then a national audience.

According to historian Anthony Heilbut, it is important to note the presence of gospel quartets such as the Dinwiddie Colored Quartet (recorded in 1902, arguably the first gospel music to be commercially waxed) and singing preachers such as the Reverends J. M. Gates and J. C. Burnett along with street singers and singing evangelists such as Blind Willie Johnson and Blind Arizona Dranes (all first recorded in the 1920s) as early performers of the music that became more stylized and codified as gospel.

The 1930s were the key years in the music's development. During those years, Thomas A. Dorsey, known during his blues playing and composing days as "Georgia Tom," became active in Chicago's black Protestant churches; and his experience as a blues player gave the music a truly great composer. Among his compositions are *Take My Hand, Precious Lord, I'm Going to Live the Life I Sing about in My Song, Old Ship of Zion*, and many others. Born the son of a Baptist minister and nephew of church organists in Villa Rica, Georgia, in 1899, Dorsey was a child prodigy who absorbed the musical styles and techniques surrounding him, including circus songs, vaudeville tunes, hillbilly ballads, and revival hymns. His single major influence was C. A. Tindley, the black religious songwriter who, like certain other late-nineteenth-century musicians, distinguished himself by combining the themes and melodies of the white religious revivals with the blues tonalities and other features of black music. Among Tindley's major hymns are the universally acclaimed *We'll Understand It Better By and By, Stand by Me*, and *Take Your Burdens to the Lord*. Dorsey's wide range of musical experience permitted him to take Tindley's example and combine it with what he knew from the secular world to create the bedrock compositions in this new musical form.

Using vehicles by Dorsey, Tindley, and others were such "gospel warriors" and "gospel pioneers" as Mitchell's Christian Singers, the Golden Gate Jubilee Quartet, the Dixie Hummingbirds, Alex Bradford, Sallie Martin, Clara Hudman (the Georgia Peach), Willie Mae Ford Smith, Marion Williams, Sister Rosetta Tharpe, Edna Gallmon Cooke, and Mahalia Jackson. Jackson's spectacular art has been best described in an essay by Ralph Ellison, whose "The World's Greatest Gospel Singer" stands as a statement about gospel's range of influences and special powers. He writes:

> It is an art which depends upon the employment of the full expressive resources of the human voice—from the rough growl employed by blues singers, the intermediate sounds, half-cry, half-recitative, which are common to Eastern music; the shouts and hollers of American Negro folk cries; the rough-edged tones and broad vibratos, the high, shrill and grating tones which rasp one's ears like the agonized flourishes of flamenco, to the gut tones, which remind us of where the jazz trombone found its human source. . . . In Mahalia's own "Move On Up a Little Higher" there is a riff straight out of early Ellington. Most of all it is an art which swings, and in the South there are many crudely trained groups who use it naturally for the expression of religious feeling who could teach the jazz modernists quite a bit about polyrhythmics and polytonality.

Gospel's ongoing practice of absorbing new music has continued into the present day, with current gospel groups dipping into the treasure trove of works by Dorsey and Tindley and of Negro spirituals at the same time that they invent new works influenced by the forms and instrumental mixes of rhythm and blues music, Broadway, opera, and rap. Like jazz, gospel has managed to absorb these various influences while maintaining a distinctiveness and power all its own.

This Little Light of Mine

Oh, this little light of mine,
I'm gonna let it shine.
This little light of mine,
I'm gonna let it shine.

This little light of mine,   5
I'm gonna let it shine.
Let it shine, shine, shine,
Let it shine.

All in my home,
I'm gonna let it shine.   10
All in my home,
I'm gonna let it shine.
All in my home,
I'm gonna let it shine.
Let it shine, shine, shine,   15
Let it shine.

God give it to me,
I'm gonna let it shine.
God give it to me,
I'm gonna let it shine.   20
God give it to me,
I'm gonna let it shine.
Let it shine, shine, shine,
Let it shine.

This little light of mine,   25
I'm gonna let it shine.
This little light of mine,
I'm gonna let it shine.
This little light of mine,
I'm gonna let it shine.   30
Let it shine, shine, shine,
Let it shine.

Everywhere I go,
I'm gonna let it shine
Everywhere I go,   35
I'm gonna let it shine
Everywhere I go, I'm gonna let it shine
Let it shine, shine, shine,
Let it shine.

Down by the Riverside

I'm gonna lay down my sword and shield
Down by the riverside
Down by the riverside
Down by the riverside
I'm gonna lay down my sword and shield   5
Down by the riverside
Study war no more

I ain't gonna study war no more
Ain't gonna study war no more

I ain't gonna study war no more   10
I ain't gonna study war no more
Ain't gonna study war no more
Ain't gonna study war no more

I'm gonna put on my long white robes
Down by the riverside   15
Down by the riverside
Down by the riverside
I'm gonna put on my long white robes
Down by the riverside
Study war no more   20

I ain't gonna study war no more
Ain't gon' study war no more
Study war no more
Ain't gon' study war no more
Study war no more   25
I ain't gonna study war no more

I'm gonna meet all my friends who're gone
Down by the riverside
Down by the riverside
Down by the riverside   30
Gonna meet all my friends who're gone
Down by the riverside
Study war no more

I ain't gonna study war no more
Study war no more   35
Ain't gon' study war no more
I ain't gonna study war no more
Study war no more
Ain't gonna study war no more

I'm gonna put on my golden shoes   40
Down by the riverside
Down by the riverside
Down by the riverside
Gonna put on my golden shoes
Down by the riverside   45
Study war no more

Well, I ain't gon' study war no more
Study war no more
I ain't gonna study war no more
I ain't gonna study war no more   50
Study war no more
Study war no more

I'm gonna meet my dear old mother
Down by the riverside
Down by the riverside   55

Down by the riverside
Gonna meet my dear old mother
Down by the riverside
Study war no more

Well, I ain' gon' study war no more   60
Lawd, study war no more
Ain't gonna study war no more
Halleluljah
Ain't gonna study war no more
No, study war no more   65
Ain't gonna study war no more

Freedom in the Air

Over my head
I see freedom in the air
Over my head, Oh Lord
I see freedom in the air
Over my head   5
I see freedom in the air
There must be a God somewhere

Take My Hand, Precious Lord [1]•

Precious Lord, take my hand,
Lead me on, let me stand,
I am tired, I am weak, I am worn.
Through the storm, through the night
Lead me on to the light,   5
Take my hand, precious Lord,
Lead me home.

When my way grows drear,
Precious Lord, linger near.
When my life is almost gone,   10
Hear my cry, hear my call,
Hold my hand lest I fall.
Take my hand, precious Lord,
Lead me home.

When the darkness appears   15
And the night draws near,
And the day is past and gone,
At the river I stand,
Guide my feet, hold my hand.
Take my hand, precious Lord,   20
Lead me home.

1. By Thomas A. Dorsey.

Peace Be Still

Master, the tempest is raging
The billows are tossing high
The sky is overshadowed with blackness
No shelter or hope is nigh
Carest thou not that we perish?   5
How can thou lie asleep?
When it seems each moment is threatening
A grave in the angry deep

Get up Jesus because:
The winds and the waves shall obey thy will   10
Peace be still, Peace be still
Whether the wrath of the storm-tossed sea
Or demons or man or whatever it be
No water can swallow the ship where lies
The master of ocean and earth and skies   15
They shall sweetly obey thy will
Peace, peace be still

Stand by Me [2]

When the storms of life are raging,
Stand by me, stand by me.
When the storms of life are raging,
Stand by me, stand by me.

When the world is tossing me,   5
Like a ship out on the sea:
Thou who knowest all about it,
Stand by your child, stand by me.

In the midst of persecution,
Stand by me, stand by me.   10
In the midst of persecution,
Stand by me, stand by me.

When my foes in battle array
Undertake to stop my way,
Thou who rescued Paul and Silas, [3]   15
Stand by me, stand by me.

When I'm growing old and feeble,
Stand by me, stand by me.
When I'm growing old and feeble,
Stand by me, stand by me.   20

2. By C. A. Tindley. The title and tune of this gospel song were appropriated for a rhythm and blues song in the early 1960s.

3. In the New Testament, he was a missionary for the Apostles. Paul was one of the twelve Apostles chosen by Jesus.

When my life becomes a burden,
And I'm nearing chilly Jordan[4]
O thou Lily of the Valley,[5]
Stand by me, stand by me.

4. A river in the Mideast. "Crossing over Jordan" is   "I am the rose of Sharon, and the lily of the val-
a metaphor for going to Heaven.   leys."
5. See Song of Solomon 2:1, where the bride says,

THE BLUES

At the beginning of the twentieth century, observers in New Orleans and elsewhere in the South began to notice a new kind of music. This music borrowed harmonic and structural devices and vocal techniques from work songs and spirituals. But unlike these other forms, this music was usually sung not by a chorus but by a single voice accompanied by one or more instruments. Like the earlier forms, blues, as this music came to be known, involved a compellingly rhythmical sound that relied on patterns of call/response between singer and audience, and at times between singer and instrument too. In spite of all the affinities with church songs, blues music was decidedly secular; it promised no heavenly grace or home but offered instead a stylized complaint about earthly trials and troubles, a complaint countered, if at all, by the flickering promise of an occasional good time or loving companion. Its dances were not the holy possession dances of church ritual but the courtship dances of Saturday night revelry and after-hours fun that held at bay, albeit temporarily, the melancholia often described in blues lyrics.

Songwriter and bandleader W. C. Handy (1873–1958) is called "the father of the blues" because he took careful note of this form of expression and transcribed its songs. But Handy was more than just a copyist. Having mastered the idiomatic forms, he combined and extended them to produce the first storehouse of blues compositions that were both true to their beginnings and inventive. Like the earlier blues of uncertain authorship—so widely circulated and so often reinvented that they may somewhat justly be termed group creations—Handy's blues were most often twelve-bar forms: three lines of four beats each, the first line repeated twice and followed by a third end-rhymed line:

I hate to see the evening sun go down.
I hate to see that evening sun go down.
'Cause my baby, he done left this town.*

Other blues songs vary from this particular pattern but still are defined as blues because of their use of "blue notes" and other characteristic blues patterns and sounds. All blues songs involve improvisation, sometimes just in terms of timing and emphasis, sometimes more elaborate reinvention of melodies and even meanings. They also involve particular sounds—train bells and whistles, sexual groans, conversational whispers, rhapsodies, shouts, stories, and especially in their first rural incarnations, barnyard noises as well.

A full discussion of the blues would take into account the early southern farms where black singing flourished; the background in African and European forms; the impact of minstrelsy, medicine shows, and carnivals on the music; early blues centers such as New Orleans, Memphis, and the Mississippi delta; the movement of the blues to the Southwest, the Midwest, and up the eastern seaboard; and the

*From Handy's St. Louis Blues.

persistence of the blues in jazz and other American musics. Worth noting here is how this powerful form has inspired writers and artists throughout the twentieth century. In 1953, as a headnote to his first published fiction, Albert Murray wrote: "We all learn from Mann, Joyce, Hemingway, Eliot, and the rest, but I'm also trying to write in terms of the tradition I grew up in, the Negro tradition of blues, stomps, ragtimes, jumps, and swing. After all, very few writers have done as much with American experience as Jelly Roll Morton, Count Basie, and Duke Ellington." Ralph Ellison said that Richard Wright's *Black Boy* was like the blues in "its refusal to offer solutions"; he also penned the following compelling definition of the form:

> The blues is an impulse to keep the painful detail and episodes of a brutal existence alive in one's aching consciousness, to finger its jazzed grain, and to transcend it, not by the consolation of philosophy but by squeezing from it a near-tragic, near-comic lyricism. As a form, the blues is an autobiographical chronicle of personal catastrophe expressed lyrically.

As Murray's and Ellison's words show, to term a poem or work of fiction a "blues piece" or to note blues influence within it is to associate it with modern black American vernacular expression at its finest.

Yellow Dog Blues [1]

Ever since Miss Susan Johnson lost her jockey, Lee,
There has been much excitement, more to be;
You can hear her moaning night and morn.
Wonder where my easyrider's gone?

Cablegrams come of sympathy,   5
Telegrams go of inquiry,
Letters come from down in "Bam." [2]
And ev'rywhere that Uncle Sam
Has even a rural delivery.
All day the phone rings but it's not for me.   10
At last good tidings fill our hearts with glee;
This message comes from Tennessee:

Dear Sue, your easyrider struck this burg today,
On a southbound rattler, sidedoor Pullman car.
See him here, and he was on the hog. [3]   15

Easy Rider's gotta stay away
He has to vamp it but the hike ain't far.
He's gone somewhere the Southern 'cross the Yellow Dog. [4]

Dear Sue, your easyrider struck this burg today,
On a southbound rattler, sidedoor Pullman car.   20
See him here, and he was on the hog.

---

1. By W. C. Handy (1873–1958); published in 1914.
2. Alabama.
3. I.e., living promiscuously.
4. Railroad line; official name = Yazoo Delta Railroad.

Easy Rider's gotta stay away
He has to vamp it but the hike ain't far.
He's gone somewhere the Southern 'cross the Yellow Dog.

St. Louis Blues[5]

I hate to see de evenin' sun go down
I hate to see de evenin' sun go down
Cause mah baby, he done lef' dis town

Feelin' tomorrow lak I feel today
Feelin' tomorrow lak I feel today   5
I'll pack mah trunk, an' make mah getaway

St. Louis woman wid her diamon' rings
Pulls dat man aroun' by her apron strings
'Twant for powder an' for store-bought hair
De man I love would not gone nowhere   10

Got de St. Louis blues, jes as blue as I can be
Dat man got a heart lak a rock cast in de sea
Or else he wouldn't have gone so far from me

Been to de gypsy to get mah fortune tol'
To de gypsy, done got mah fortune tol'   15
Cause I'm most wild 'bout mah jelly roll

Gypsy done tol' me, "Don't you wear no black"
Yes, she done tol' me, "Don't you wear no black.
Go to St. Louis, you can win him back"

Help me to Cairo;[6] make St. Louis by mahself   20
Git to Cairo, find mah ol' frien', Jeff
Gwine to pin mahself close to his side
If I flag his train, I sho can ride

I loves dat man lak a schoolboy loves his pie
Lak a Kentucky Colonel loves his mint an' rye   25
I'll love mah baby till de day I die

You ought to see dat stovepipe brown o' mine
Lak he owns de Dimon' Joseph line
He'd make a cross-eyed 'oman go stone blind

Blacker than midnight, teeth lak flags of truce   30
Blackest man in de whole St. Louis
Blacker de berry, sweeter is de juice. . . .

.   .   .   .   .

5. By W. C. Handy (1873–1958); published in   6. Town in Illinois.
1914.

A black headed gal make a freight train jump de track
Said, a black headed gal make a freight train jump de track
But a long tall gal makes a preacher "Ball de Jack"[7]   35

Lawd, a blond headed woman makes a good man leave the town
I said, blond headed woman makes a good man leave the town
But a red headed woman make a boy slap his papa down. . . .

Beale Street Blues[8]

I've seen the lights of gay Broadway,
Old Market Street, down by the Frisco Bay,
I've strolled the Prado,[9]
I've gambled on the Bourse,[1]
The seven wonders of the world I've seen,   5
And many are the places I have been.

Take my advice folks
And see Beale Street[2] first.

You'll see pretty browns in beautiful gowns,
You'll see tailor-mades and hand-me-downs,   10
You'll meet honest men and pick-pockets skilled,
You'll find that business never closes till somebody gets killed.

I'd rather be here than any place I know,
I'd rather be here than any place I know.
It's goin' to take the Sergeant   15
For to make me go.

Goin' to the river
Maybe, by and by,
Goin' to the river,
And there's a reason why: 20
Because the river's wet,
and Beale Street's gone dry.

You'll see Hog Nose rest'rants and Chitlin'[3] Cafes,
You'll see jugs that tell of by-gone days,
And places, once places, now just a sham,   25
You'll see Golden Balls enough to pave the New Jerusalem.[4]

Goin' to the river
Maybe, by and by,
Goin' to the river,
And there's a reason why: 30

7. Social dance step of the 1920s.
8. By W. C. Handy (1873–1958); published in 1917.
9. Spanish national museum in Madrid.
1. Paris money market; equivalent of the New York Stock Exchange.

2. The main black street of Memphis, Tennessee, lined with commercial buildings, churches, theaters, parks, and houses.
3. Pork dish—the small intestines of hogs.
4. Heaven. "Golden Balls": the sign of the pawnshop.

Because the river's wet,
and Beale Street's gone dry.

I'd rather be here than any place I know,
I'd rather be here than any place I know.
It's goin' to take the Sergeant   35
For to make me go

Goin' to the river
Maybe, by and by,
Goin' to the river,
And there's a reason why: 40
Because the river's wet,
and Beale Street's gone dry.

If Beale Street could talk,[5] if Beale Street could talk
Married men would have to take their beds and walk,
Except one or two, who never drink booze,   45
And the blind man on the corner who sings the Beale Street Blues.

I'd rather be here than any place I know,
I'd rather be here than any place I know.
It's goin' to take the Sergeant
For to make me go   50

Down-Hearted Blues[6]

Gee, but it's hard to love someone, when that someone don't love you,
I'm so disgusted, heartbroken too,
I've got those down-hearted blues.
Once I was crazy about a man, he mistreated me all the time,
The next man I see, he's got to promise to be mine, all mine.   5

Trouble, trouble, I've had it all my days,
Trouble, trouble, I've had it all my days,
It seems that trouble's going to follow me to my grave.

If I could only find the man, oh, how happy I would be,
To the Good Lord ev'rynight I pray, please send my man back to me   10
I've almost worried myself to death wond'ring why he went away,
But just wait and see, he's gonna want me back some sweet day.

World in a jug, the stopper's in my hand,
Got the world in a jug, the stopper's in my hand,
Going to hold it baby till you come under my command.   15

Say, I ain't never loved but three men in my life,
No, I ain't never loved but three men in my life,
T'was my father, my brother, and the man who wrecked my life.

5. James Baldwin's novel *If Beale Street Could*   tin (1897–1972); this song of 1922 was a big hit for
Talk (1974) derives its title from this line.   Bessie Smith in 1923.
6. By Albert Hunter (1897–1984) and Louie Aus-

'Cause he mistreated me and he drove me from his door,
Yes, he mistreated me and he drove me from his door   20
But the Good Book says you'll reap just what you sow.

Oh, it may be a week and it may be a month or two,
Yes, it may be a week and it may be a month or two,
But the day you quit me honey, it's coming home to you.
Oh, I walked the floor and I wrung my hands and cried,   25
Yes, I walked the floor and I wrung my hands and cried,
Had the down-hearted blues and couldn't be satisfied

See, See Rider[7] •

See See Rider, see what you done done!
    Lord, Lord, Lord!
You made me love you, now your gal done come.
You made me love you, now your gal done come.

I'm goin' away, baby, I won't be back till fall.   5
    Lord, Lord, Lord!
Goin' away, baby, won't be back till fall.
If I find me a good man, I won't be back at all.

I'm gonna buy me a pistol just as long as I am tall.
    Lord, Lord, Lord!   10
Kill my man and catch the Cannon Ball.[8]
If he won't have me, he won't have no gal at all.

See See Rider, where did you stay last night?
    Lord, Lord, Lord!
Your shoes ain't buttoned, clothes don't fit you right.   15
You didn't come home till the sun was shinin' bright.

Prove It on Me Blues[9]

Went out last night, had a great big fight,
Everything seemed to go on wrong;
I looked up, to my surprise,
The gal I was with was gone.

Where she went, I don't know,   5
I mean to follow everywhere she goes;
Folks said I'm crooked, I didn't know where she took it,
I want the whole world to know:

7. By Ma Rainey (1886–1939); first recorded in 1924.
8. A train—either the Wabash Cannonball or the express line from Cincinnati to New Orleans.
9. This song by Ma Rainey (1886–1939) is cited as an example of lesbian themes in blues music. It was first recorded in 1928.

They say I do it, ain't nobody caught me,
Sure got to prove it on me;   10
Went out last night with a crowd of my friends,
They must've been women, 'cause I don't like no men.

It's true I wear a collar and a tie,
Make the wind blow all the while;
They say I do it, ain't nobody caught me,   15
They sure got to prove it on me.

Say I do it, ain't nobody caught me,
Sure got to prove it on me;
I went out last night with a crowd of my friends,
They must've been women, 'cause I don't like no men.   20

Wear my clothes just like a fan,
Talk to the gals just like any old man;
'Cause they say I do it, ain't nobody caught me,
Sure got to prove it on me.

Gulf Coast Blues [1]

I've been blue all day, my gal's gone away;
She left her daddy cold, for another man I'm told.
I tried to treat her kind, I thought she would be mine;
That gal I hate to lose, that's why daddy's got the blues.

Gal that I love, she has left me in this town,   5
The gal I love has left me in this town.
And if it keep on snowing, I will be Gulf Coast bound.

I've done packed my clothes, gonna leave my woes,
Goin' to a better place, with a smile on my face,
Say, when the steamboat blows, and when that Gulf train goes, 10
You'll hear me say "Goodbye," because here's the reason why:

Mailman passed by, but he didn't leave no news,
The mailman passed by he didn't leave no news,
I'll tell the world he left me crying the Gulf Coast blues.

These women up North, honey, sure do make me tired,   15
These women up North, honey, sure do make me tired,
They've got a mouthful of "gimme,"
Handful of "much obliged."

Broadway's all right and the lights shine nice and bright,
Broadway's all right and the lights shine nice and bright,   20
I'd rather walk down home,
By my little lantern light.

1. By musician/composer/impresario Clarence Williams (1898–1965); recorded by Bessie Smith in 1923.

The Gulf of Mexico flows into Mobile Bay,
The Gulf of Mexico flows into Mobile Bay,
I'm gonna let that cold water   25
Flow over me someday.

Trouble in Mind[2]

Trouble in mind, I'm blue,
But I won't be blue always,
For the sun will shine in my backdoor someday.

Trouble in mind, that's true,
I have almost lost my mind;   5
Life ain't worth livin', feel like I could die,

I'm gonna lay my head on some lonesome railroad line:
Let the two nineteen train ease my troubled mind.

Trouble in mind, I'm blue,
My poor heart is beatin' slow;   10
Never had no trouble in my life before.

I'm all alone at midnight,
And my lamp is burning low,
Never had so much trouble in my life before.

I'm gonna lay my head   15
On that lonesome railroad track,
But when I hear the whistle,
Lord, I'm gonna pull it back.

I'm goin' down to the river
Take along my rocking chair,   20
And if the blues don't leave me,
I'll rock on away from there.

Well, trouble, oh, trouble,
Trouble on my worried mind,
When you see me laughin',   25
I'm laughin' just to keep from cryin'.

Backwater Blues[3]•

When it rain five days an' de skies turned dark as night
When it rain five days an' de skies turned dark as night
Then trouble taken place in the lowland that night

---

2. By Richard M. Jones (c. 1889–1945); published   3. By Bessie Smith (1895–1937); first recorded in
in 1926.   1927.

I woke up this mornin', can't even get outa mah do'
I woke up this mornin', can't even get outa mah do'   5
That's enough trouble to make a po' girl wonder where she wanta go

Then they rowed a little boat about five miles 'cross the pond
They rowed a little boat about five miles 'cross the pond
I packed all mah clothes, th'owed 'em in, an' they rowed me along

When it thunder an' a-lightnin', an' the wind begin to blow   10
When it thunder an' a-lightnin', an' the wind begin to blow
An' thousan' people ain' got no place to go

Then I went an' stood up on some high ol' lonesome hill
I went an' stood up on some high ol' lonesome hill
An' looked down on the house where I used to live   15

Backwater blues done cause me to pack mah things an' go
Backwater blues done cause me to pack mah things an' go
Cause mah house fell down an' I cain' live there no mo'

O-o-o-oom, I cain' move no mo'
O-o-o-oom, I cain' move no mo'   20
There ain' no place fo' a po' ol' girl to go

In the House Blues[4]

Setting in the house with everything on my mind,
Setting in the house with everything on my mind.
Looking at the clock and can't even tell the time.

Walk into my window and looking out of my door,
Walk into my window and looking out of my door.   5
Wishing that my man would come home once more.

Can't eat, can't sleep, so weak I can't walk my floor,
Can't eat, can't sleep, so weak I can't walk my floor.
Feel like hollering murder, let the police squad get me once more.

They woke me up before day with trouble on my mind,   10
They woke me up before day with trouble on my mind.
Wringing my hands and screaming, walking the floor hollering and
     crying.

Catch 'em, don't let them blues in here,
Catch 'em, don't let them blues in here.
They shakes me in my bed, can't set down in my chair.   15

Ooooooh, the blues has got me on the go.
Ooooooh, they've got me on the go.
They runs around my house in and out of my front door.

4. By Bessie Smith (1895–1937), who first recorded it in 1927.

How Long Blues [5]•

How long, how long, has that evenin' train been gone?
How long, how long, baby, how long?
Heard the whistle blowin', couldn't see no train,
'Way down in my heart I had an achin' pain,
How long, how long, baby, how long?   5

I'm sad and lonely the whole day through,
Why don't you write me and give me the news?
You have left me singin' those how long blues.

If I could holler like a Mountain Jack,
I'd go up on the mountain and call my baby back,   10
How long, how long, baby, how long?

I went up on the mountain looked as far as I could see,
The man had my woman and the blues had poor me,
How long, how long, how long?

I can see the green grass growing on the hill,   15
But I ain't seen the green grass on a dollar bill,
For so long, so long, baby, so long.

If you don't believe I'm sinkin' see what a hole I'm in,
If you don't believe I love you, baby, look what a fool I've been,
Well, I'm gone how long, baby, how long?   20

I'm goin' down to Georgia, been up in Tennessee,
So look me over, baby, the last you'll see of me,
For so long, so long, baby, so long.

The brook runs into the river, the river runs into the sea,
If I don't run into my baby, a train is goin' to run into me,   25
How long, how long, how long?

Hellhound on My Trail [6]

I've got to keep moving
          I've got to keep moving
                              blues falling down like hail
                                   blues falling down like hail
Ummmmmmmmmmmmmmmmmmmmm
                                   blues falling down like hail
                                        blues falling down
                                                  like hail

---

5. By Leroy Carr (1905–1935); recorded in 1928.
6. This song was written by Robert Johnson (c. 1912–1938), who recorded it in 1937. Eric Sackheim arranged this song on the page as a modern poet might have done; his arrangement emphasizes the idea that blues are part of contemporary poetic expression.

And the days keeps on 'minding me
                    there's a hellhound on my trail
                              hellhound on
                                    my trail
                    hellhound on my trail

If today was Christmas Eve
        If today was Christmas Eve
                        and tomorrow was Christmas Day
If today was Christmas Eve
                and tomorrow was Christmas Day
                        (aw wouldn't we have a
                                time baby)
All I would need my little sweet rider just
                        to pass the time away
                            uh huh
                                to pass the
                                time away

You sprinkled hot foot powder[7]
                umm around my door
                        all around my door
You sprinkled hot foot powder
                all around your daddy's door
                        hmmm hmmm hmmm
It keeps me with a rambling mind, rider,
                        every old place I go
                            every old place I go

I can tell the wind is rising
                the leaves trembling on the trees
                        trembling on the trees
I can tell the wind is rising
                leaves trembling on the trees
                        umm hmm hmm hmm
All I need my little sweet woman
                    and to keep my company
                        hmmm hmmm hmmm
                                hmmm
        my company

It's a Low Down Dirty Shame[8]

It's a low down dirty, low down dirty shame,
It's a low down dirty, low down dirty shame.
I'm in love with a married woman,
I'm afraid to call her name.

7. Magic, goopher, or hoodoo powder, presumed to have special powers when prescribed by a conjure doctor.

8. By Ollie Shepard (1897–1984), who first recorded it in 1937. The first widely popular version was recorded in 1940 by Joe Turner (1911–1985).

She's a no good woman, don't mean no one man no good,   5
She's a no good woman, don't mean no one man no good.
I don't blame that woman, I'd be the same way if I could.

It's a low down dirty, low down dirty shame,
It's a low down dirty, low down dirty shame.
I'm in love with a married woman,   10
I'm afraid to call her name.

Baby, that's all right, that's all right for you,
Baby, that's all right, that's all right for you,
Baby, that's all right, any old thing you do.

It's a low down dirty, low down dirty shame,   15
It's a low down dirty, low down dirty shame.
I'm in love with a married woman,
I'm afraid to call her name.

Good Morning, Blues[9]•

Good mornin', blues,
Blues, how do you do?
Good mornin', blues,
Blues, how do you do?
Good morning, how are you?   5

I laid down last night,
Turning from side to side;
Yes, I was turning from side to side,
I was not sick,
I was just dissatisfied.   10

When I got up this mornin',
Blues walking round my bed;
Yes, the blues walkin' round my bed,
I went to eat my breakfast,
The blues was all in my bread.   15

I sent for you yesterday baby,
Here you come a walking today;
Yes, here you come a walking today,
Got your mouth wide open,
You don't know what to say.   20

Good mornin', blues,
Blues, how do you do?
Yes, blues, how do you do?
I'm doing all right,
Good morning, how are you?   25

9. By Jimmy Rushing (1903–1972), who recorded it in 1937. As with many works in the vernacular tradition, this classic blues has been sung in many different versions. Compare this one with the version on the Audio Companion, by Huddie ("Leadbelly") Ledbetter.

Sent for You Yesterday[1]

Don't the moon look lonesome shining through the trees?
Don't the moon look lonesome shining through the trees?
Don't your house look lonesome when your baby's packed up to
    leave?

Yeah, she's little and low and built up from the ground,
She's little and low and built up from the ground.   5
Just a while before day she'll make your love come down.

Sent for you yesterday, and here you come today,
Sent for you yesterday, and here you come today
Baby, you can't love me and treat me thataway.

Goin' to Chicago Blues[2]

Going to Chicago, sorry that I can't take you,
Going to Chicago, sorry that I can't take you.
There's nothing in Chicago that a monkey woman[3] can do.

When you see me coming, baby, raise your window high,
When you see me coming, baby, raise your window high,   5
When you see me passing, baby, hang your head and cry.

Hurry down sunshine, see what tomorrow brings,
Hurry down sunshine, see what tomorrow brings.
And the sun went down, tomorrow brought us rain.

You so mean and evil, you do things you ought not do,   10
You so mean and evil, you do things you ought not do.
You got my brand new money, guess I'll have to put up with you.

Anybody ask you who was it sang this song,
Anybody ask you who was it sang this song,
Tell 'em Little Jimmy Rushing,[4] he's been here and gone.   15

Fine and Mellow[5]

My man don't love me
Treats me oh so mean
My man he don't love me
Treats me awful mean

---

1. By Jimmy Rushing (1903–1972), who recorded
it in 1938.
2. This song of the thirties celebrates an expected
move to the urban North: Chicago — city of promise. The composer is unknown; first recorded, by
Jimmy Rushing, in 1939.
3. Derogatory (and then sometimes flattering)
term for an African American woman.

4. Blues and ballad singer; for many years the principal vocalist with the Count Basie Orchestra.
5. This is one of the few twelve-bar blues songs associated with Billie Holiday. Though the song uses
traditional blues progressions and lyrics, Holiday
(1915–1959) is credited as its composer and lyricist
(1939).

He's the lowest man   5
That I've ever seen

He wears high draped pants
Stripes are really yellow
He wears high draped pants
Stripes are really yellow   10
But when he starts in to love me
He is so fine and mellow

Love will make you drink and gamble
Make you stay out all night long
Love will make you drink and gamble   15
Make you stay out all night long
Love will make you do things
That you know is wrong

But if you treat me right baby
I'll stay home everyday   20
Just treat me right baby
I'll stay home night and day
But you're so mean to me baby
I know you're gonna drive me away

Love is just like a faucet   25
It turns off and on
Love is just like a faucet
It turns off and on
Sometimes when you think it's on baby
It has turned off and gone   30

Hoochie Coochie[6]

The gypsy woman told my mother
Before I was born
I got a boy child's coming
Gonna be a son of a gun
He gonna make pretty womens   5
Jump and shout
Then the world wanna know
What this all about

'Cause you know I'm here
Everybody knows I'm here   10
Yeah, you know I'm a hoochie coochie man
Everybody knows I'm here

I got a black cat bone
I got a mojo[7] too

6. This song is associated with Muddy Waters   corded it in 1954.
(McKinley Morganfield) (1915–1983). He first re-   7. Conjurer's potion.

I got the John the Conqueroo[8]   15
I'm gonna mess with you
I'm gonna make you girls
Lead me by the hand
Then the world'll know
The hoochie coochie man   20

But you know I'm here
Everybody knows I'm here
Yeah, you know I'm a hoochie coochie man
Everybody knows I'm here

On a seven hours   25
On the seventh day
On the seventh month
The seven doctors said
He was born for good luck
And that you'll see   30
I got seven hundred dollars
Don't you mess with me

But you know I'm here
Everybody knows I'm here
Well you know I'm a hoochie coochie man   35
Everybody knows I'm here

Sunnyland[9]•

Seems like I heard
That lonesome Sunnyland blow.
Seems like I heard
That lonesome Sunnyland blow.
She blows just like   5
She won't be back no more.

I feel bad this morning,
Feel just like I wanna cry.
Feel bad this morning,
Feel just like I wanna cry.   10
My baby caught the train this morning,
And she didn't even say goodbye.

I had a letter from my baby,
She said she was coming home.
Had a letter from my baby,   15
And she said she was coming home.
Well, I'm just sitting here waiting,
And I hope it won't be long.

8. A root prepared by a conjurer to grant extraordinary powers.

9. By Elmore James (1918–1963); recorded in
1961. "Sunnyland": train.

Secular Rhymes and Songs, Ballads, and Work Songs

As pervasive as were the sacred forms of expression among African Americans, secular forms were nearly as important for the slaves. Perhaps over time such forms have become more important than sacred ones; certainly, this seems to be the case for many blacks of the second half of the twentieth century.

Slave narrators reported mock-prayers, mock-sermons, and other parodies of the forms celebrated in church. Doubtless these provided a kind of outlet for the deeply faithful: the black laughter may have humanized an awesome God and His earthly saints (along with a powerful preacher, the subject of many a joke in this category) and thereby sustained belief. Elsewhere, aside from religion and its purposes, such secular parodies of sacred texts contained their own stinging elements of truth:

> "Our Fadder, Which are in Heaben!"—
> White man owe me leben and pay me seben
> "D'y Kingdom come! D'y Will be done!"—
> An' if I hadn't tuck dat, I wouldn' git none.

In addition, they expressed with humor the bitter disappointments of slave existence:

> My ole Mistiss promise me,
> W'en she died, she'd set me free.
> She lived so long dat 'er head got bal',
> An' she give out 'n de notion a dyin' at all.

Superb narrative rhymes, sometimes framed as songs, also enliven this group. Here one finds praise songs to such fast-moving heroes as Travelin' Man; Long Gone Lost John; Railroad Bill; Po' Lazarus; and John Henry, the hard-muscled steel driver who died trying to outhammer the steam-driven hammer machine. Their more contemporary (i.e., current and dating back to the beginning of the twentieth century) cousins are Shine and Stackolee, who, like certain earlier heroic ballad figures, are fast-talking figures of action and, if necessary, violence. Badman figures who "don't mind dying" have become more numerous in the twentieth-century lore. At times what makes sense in the tales is a figure with an oversized gun who not only can outsmart The Man (or however the square white authority figure is designated) but (and almost invariably these characters are male) can blow him to hell, too. These hero and badman forms have had a strong impact on the blues, that other stronghold of secular expression, and, in current times, on rap music, where modern wish-fulfillment avengers roam, bragging, daring trouble, ready for war.

In this broad category of the secular, one finds children's game songs, rhyming snatches of advice ("a still tongue makes a wise head"), and other miscellaneous pieces. All are materials of play that is sometimes fun and frivolous, sometimes instructive, sometimes frighteningly reflective of the violence of American society.

Work songs of slavery and (relatively) freedom also fall within this space of secular black vernacular expression. These often ruggedly eloquent songs functioned to pass the time, to synchronize the work pace, and to reflect on the scene the workers witnessed.

It should be added that these story songs and rhymes were often expressed by virtuoso singers and wordsmiths whose underground talents, unseen by the broader society, are celebrated in the worlds in which they reign as "men of words," power figures. Doubtless their energy and unofficial artistry are part of the story of how Africans in America have managed to survive and even to prevail.

SECULAR RHYMES AND SONGS

[We raise de wheat]

We raise de wheat,
Dey gib us de corn:
We bake de bread,
Dey gib us de crust;
We sif de meal,   5
Dey gib us de huss;
We peel de meat,
Dey gib us de skin;
And dat's de way
Dey take us in;   10
We skim de pot,
Dey gib us de liquor,
And say dat's good enough for nigger.

Me and My Captain

Me an my captain don't agree,
But he don't know, 'cause he don't ask me;
He don't know, he don't know my mind,
When he see me laughing
Just laughing to keep from crying.   5

Oh what's the matter now,
Me and my captain can't get along nohow;
He don't know, he don't know my mind,
When he see me laughing
Just laughing to keep from crying.   10

He call me low down I just laugh,
Kick seat of my pants and that ain't half;
He don't know, he don't know my mind,
When he see me laughing
Just laughing to keep from crying.   15

Got one mind for white folks to see,
'Nother for what I know is me;
He don't know, he don't know my mind,
When he see me laughing
Just laughing to keep from crying.   20

Promises of Freedom

My ole Mistiss promise me,
W'en she died, she'd set me free.
She lived so long dat 'er head got bal',
An' she give out'n de notion a dyin' at all.

My ole Mistiss say to me: 5
"Sambo, I'se gwine ter set you free."
But w'en dat head git slick an' bal',
De Lawd couldn' a' killed 'er wid a big green maul. [1]

My ole Mistiss never die,
Wid 'er nose all hooked an' skin all dry.   10
But my ole Miss, she's somehow gone,
An' she lef' "Uncle Sambo" a-hillin' up co'n.

Ole Mosser lakwise promise me,
W'en he died, he'd set me free.
But ole Mosser go an' make his Will   15
Fer to leave me a-plowin' ole Beck still.

Yes, my ole Mosser promise me;
But "his papers" didn't leave me free.
A dose of pizen he'ped 'im along.
May de Devil preach 'is funer'l song.   20

Jack and Dinah Want Freedom

Ole Aunt Dinah, she's jes lak me.
She wuk so hard dat she want to be free.
But, you know, Aunt Dinah's gittin' sorter ole;
An' she's feared to go to Canada, caze it's so col'.

Dar wus ole Uncle Jack, he want to git free.   5
He find de way Norf by de moss on de tree.
He cross dat river a-floatin' in a tub.
Dem Patterollers [2] give 'im a mighty close rub.

Dar is ole Uncle Billy, he's a mighty good Nigger.
He tote all de news to Mosser a little bigger.   10
When you tells Uncle Billy, you wants free fer a fac';
De nex' day de hide drap off'n yo' back.

---

1. A heavy club, mallet, or staff.
2. Formally and informally appointed police agents charged with intercepting fugitive slaves.

Run, Nigger, Run

Run, nigger run; de patter-roller[3] catch you;
Run, nigger, run, it's almost day.
Run, nigger, run; de patter-roller catch you;
Run, nigger, run, and try to get away.

Dis nigger run, he run his best,   5
Stuck his head in a hornet's nest,
Jumped de fence and run fru de paster;
White man run, but nigger run faster.

Dat nigger run, dat nigger flew,
Dat nigger tore his shirt in two.   10

Learn to Count

Naught's a naught,
Five's a figger.
All fer de white man,
None fer de Nigger.

Ten's a ten,   5
But it's mighty funny;
When you cain't count good,
You hain't got no money.

Another Man Done Gone•

Another man done gone,
Another man done gone,
Uh—from the county farm,
Another man done gone.

I didn't know his name,   5
I didn't know his name,
I didn't know his name,
I didn't know his name.

He had a long chain on,
He had a long chain on,   10
He had a long chain on,
He had a long chain on.

He killed another man,
He killed another man,
He killed another man,   15
He killed another man.

3. See n. 2, above.

I don' know where he's gone,
I don' know where he's gone,
I don' know where he's gone,
I don' know where he's gone.   20

I'm going to walk your log,
I'm going to walk your log,
I'm going to walk your log,
I'm going to walk your log.

You May Go But This Will Bring You Back [4]•

You may leave and go to Hali-ma-fack, [5]
But my slow-drag will-a bring you back,
A-well-a you may go but this will bring you back.

Ahhh, I been in the country but I moved to town,
I'm a toe-low shaker [6] from a-head on down,   5
Well-a you may go but this will bring you back.

Ahh, some folks call me a toe-low shaker,
It's a doggone lie, I'm a backbone breaker,
Well-a you may go but this will bring you back.

Aw, you like my peaches but you don't like me,   10
Don't you like my peaches, don't you shake my tree,
Well-a you may go but this will bring you back.

A-hoodoo, a-hoodoo, a-hoodoo working,
My heels are popping and my toenails cracking,
Well-a you may go but this will bring you back.   15

4. This song was sung by Zora Neale Hurston in 1935 during an interview conducted by the Library of Congress.
5. I.e., a long distance. Hali-ma-fack is a facetious reference to the Halifax River in Florida and/or to Halifax in Nova Scotia. Moreover, it refers to a faraway mythic realm, like the "Philamayork" of many tales.
6. Toe-low shaker and backbone breaker (line 8) refer to juke-house dances and dancers.

BALLADS

Poor Lazarus

High sheriff tol' de deputy, "Go out an' bring me Laz'us."
High sheriff tol' de deputy, "Go out an' bring me Laz'us.
Bring him dead or alive, Lawd, Lawd, bring him dead or alive."

Oh, bad man Laz'us done broke in de commissary winder,
Oh, bad man Laz'us done broke in de commissary winder,   5
He been paid off, Lawd, Lawd, he been paid off.

Oh, de deputy 'gin to wonder, where in de worl' he could fin' him;
Oh, de deputy 'gin to wonder, where in de worl' he could fin' him;
Well, I don' know, Lawd, Lawd, I jes' don' know.

Oh, dey found po' Laz'us way out between two mountains,   10
Oh, dey found po' Laz'us way out between two mountains,
An' dey blowed him down, Lawd, Lawd, an' dey blowed him down.

Ol' Laz'us tol' de deputy he had never been arrested,
Ol' Laz'us tol' de deputy he had never been arrested,
By no one man, Lawd, Lawd, by no one man.   15

So dey shot po' Laz'us, shot him wid a great big number,
Dey shot po' Laz'us, shot him wid a great big number,
Number 45, Lawd, Lawd, number 45.

An' dey taken po' Laz'us an' dey laid him on de commissary county,
Dey taken po' Laz'us an' dey laid him on de commissary county,   20
An' dey walked away, Lawd, Lawd, an' dey walked away.

Laz'us' sister run an' tol' her mother,
Laz'us' sister run an' tol' her mother,
Dat po' Laz'us dead, Lawd, Lawd, po' Laz'us dead.

Laz'us' mother, she laid down her sewin',   25
Laz'us' mother, she laid down her sewin',
'Bout de trouble, Lawd, Lawd, she had wid Laz'us.

Laz'us' mother she come a-screamin' an' a-cryin',
Laz'us' mother she come a-screamin' an' a-cryin',
"Dat's my only son, Lawd, Lawd, dat's my only son."   30

The Signifying Monkey[1]

The Monkey and the Lion
Got to talking one day.
Monkey looked down and said, Lion,
I hear you's king in every way.
But I know somebody   5
Who do not think that is true—
He told me he could whip
The living daylights out of you.
Lion said, Who?
Monkey said, Lion,   10
He talked about your mama
And talked about your grandma, too,
And I'm too polite to tell you
What he said about you.

1. This somewhat sanitized version of this ballad was presented by Langston Hughes and Arna Bontemps in *The Book of American Negro Folklore* (1958). "Signifying" refers to a wide variety of African American verbal games involving ritual insult, competition, innuendo, parody, and other forms of loaded expression.

Lion said, Who said what? Who?   15
Monkey in the tree,
Lion on the ground.
Monkey kept on signifying
But he didn't come down.
Monkey said, His name is Elephant—   20
He stone sure is not your friend.
Lion said, He don't need to be
Because today will be his end.
Lion took off through the jungle
Lickity-split,   25
Meaning to grab Elephant
And tear him bit to bit. Period!
He come across Elephant copping a righteous nod
Under a fine cool shady tree.
Lion said, You big old no-good so-and-so,   30
It's either you or me.
Lion let out a solid roar
And bopped Elephant with his paw.
Elephant just took his trunk
And busted old Lion's jaw.   35
Lion let out another roar,
Reared up six feet tall.
Elephant just kicked him in the belly
And laughed to see him drop and fall.
Lion rolled over,   40
Copped Elephant by the throat.
Elephant just shook him loose
And butted him like a goat,
Then he tromped him and he stomped him
Till the Lion yelled, Oh, no!   45
And it was near-nigh sunset
When Elephant let Lion go.
The signifying Monkey
Was still setting in his tree
When he looked down and saw the Lion   50
Said, Why, Lion, who can that there be?
Lion said, It's me.
Monkey rapped, Why, Lion,
You look more dead than alive!
Lion said, Monkey, I don't want   55
To hear your jive-end jive.
Monkey just kept on signifying,
Lion, you for sure caught hell—
Mister Elephant's done whipped you
To a fare-thee-well!   60
Why, Lion, you look like to me
You been in the precinct station
And had the third-degree,
Else you look like
You been high on gage [2]   65

2. Marijuana.

And done got caught
In a monkey cage!
You ain't no king to me.
Facts, I don't think that you
Can even as much as roar—   70
And if you try I'm liable
To come down out of this tree and
Whip your tail some more.
The Monkey started laughing
And jumping up and down.   75
But he jumped so hard the limb broke
And he landed—*bam!*—on the ground.
When he went to run, his foot slipped
And he fell flat down.
Grrr-rrr-rr-r! The Lion was on him   80
With his front feet and his hind.
Monkey hollered, Ow!
I didn't mean it, Mister Lion!
Lion said, You little flea-bag you!
Why, I'll eat you up alive.   85
I wouldn't a-been in this fix a-tall
Wasn't for your signifying jive.
Please, said Monkey, Mister Lion,
If you'll just let me go,
I got something to tell you, *please*,   90
I think you ought to know.
Lion let the Monkey loose
To see what his tale could be—
And Monkey jumped right back on up
Into his tree.   95
What I was gonna tell you, said Monkey,
Is you square old so-and-so,
If you fool with me I'll get
Elephant to whip your head some more.
Monkey, said the Lion,   100
Beat to his unbooted knees,
You and all your signifying children
Better stay up in them trees.
Which is why today
Monkey does his signifying   105
A-*way-up* out of the way.

Wild Negro Bill

I'se wild Nigger Bill
Frum Redpepper Hill.
I never did wo'k, an' I never will.

I'se done killed de Boss.
I'se knocked down de hoss.   5
I eats up raw goose widout apple sauce!

I'se Run-a-way Bill,
I knows dey mought kill;
But ole Mosser hain't cotch me, an' he never will!

John Henry[3]•

When John Henry was a little fellow,
 You could hold him in the palm of your hand,
He said to his pa, "When I grow up
 I'm gonna be a steel-driving man.
  Gonna be a steel-driving man."   5

When John Henry was a little baby,
 Setting on his mammy's knee,
He said "The Big Bend Tunnel on the C. & O. Road
 Is gonna be the death of me,
  Gonna be the death of me."   10

One day his captain told him,
 How he had bet a man
That John Henry would beat his steam-drill down,
 Cause John Henry was the best in the land,
  John Henry was the best in the land.   15

John Henry kissed his hammer,
 White man turned on steam,
Shaker held John Henry's trusty steel,
 Was the biggest race the world had ever seen,
  Lord, biggest race the world ever seen.   20

John Henry on the right side
 The steam drill on the left,
"Before I'll let your steam drill beat me down,
 I'll hammer my fool self to death,
  Hammer my fool self to death."   25

John Henry walked in the tunnel,
 His captain by his side,
The mountain so tall, John Henry so small,
 He laid down his hammer and he cried,
  Laid down his hammer and he cried.   30

Captain heard a mighty rumbling,
 Said "The mountain must be caving in,"
John Henry said to the captain,
 "It's my hammer swinging in de wind,
  "My hammer swinging in de wind."   35

3. The Audio Companion features a different version of the ballad of John Henry. "C. & O. Road" (line 8): Chesapeake and Ohio Railroad line.

John Henry said to his shaker,[4]
    "Shaker, you'd better pray;
For if ever I miss this piece of steel,
    Tomorrow'll be your burial day,
        Tomorrow'll be your burial day."   40

John Henry said to his shaker,
    "Lordy, shake it while I sing,
I'm pulling my hammer from my shoulders down,
    Great Gawdamighty, how she ring,
        Great Gawdamighty, how she ring!"   45

John Henry said to his captain,
    "Before I ever leave town,
Gimme one mo' drink of dat tom-cat gin,
    And I'll hammer dat steam driver down,
        I'll hammer dat steam driver down."   50

John Henry said to his captain,
    "Before I ever leave town,
Gimme a twelve-pound hammer wid a whale-bone handle,
    And I'll hammer dat steam driver down,
        I'll hammer dat steam drill on down."   55

John Henry said to his captain,
    "A man ain't nothin' but a man,
But before I'll let dat steam drill beat me down,
    I'll die wid my hammer in my hand,
        Die wid my hammer in my hand."   60

The man that invented the steam drill
    He thought he was mighty fine,
John Henry drove down fourteen feet,
    While the steam drill only made nine,
        Steam drill only made nine.   65

"Oh, lookaway over yonder, captain,
    You can't see like me,"
He gave a long and loud and lonesome cry,
    "Lawd, a hammer be the death of me,
        A hammer be the death of me!"   70

John Henry had a little woman,
    Her name was Polly Ann,
John Henry took sick, she took his hammer,
    She hammered like a natural man,
        Lawd, she hammered like a natural man.   75

John Henry hammering on the mountain
    As the whistle blew for half-past two,
The last words his captain heard him say,

---

4. The railroad worker who holds the drill upright and rotates it between the blows of the hammer.

"I've done hammered my insides in two,
    Lawd, I've hammered my insides in two."   80

The hammer that John Henry swung
    It weighed over twelve pound,
He broke, a rib in his left hand side
    And his intrels fell on the ground,
        And his intrels fell on the ground.   85

John Henry, O, John Henry,
    His blood is running red,
Fell right down with his hammer to the ground,
    Said, "I beat him to the bottom but I'm dead,
        Lawd, beat him to the bottom but I'm dead."   90

When John Henry was laying there dying,
    The people all by his side,
The very last words they heard him say,
    "Give me a cool drink of water 'fore I die,
        Cool drink of water 'fore I die."   95

John Henry had a little woman,
    The dress she wore was red,
She went down the track, and she never looked back,
    Going where her man fell dead,
        Going where her man fell dead.   100

John Henry had a little woman,
    The dress she wore was blue,
De very last words she said to him,
    "John Henry, I'll be true to you,
        John Henry, I'll be true to you."   105

"Who's gonna shoes yo' little feet,
    Who's gonna glove yo' hand,
Who's gonna kiss yo' pretty, pretty cheek,
    Now you done lost yo' man?
        Now you done lost yo' man?"   110

"My mammy's gonna shoes my little feet,
    Pappy gonna glove my hand,
My sister's gonna kiss my pretty, pretty cheek,
    Now I done lost my man,
        Now I done lost my man."   115

They carried him down by the river,
    And buried him in the sand,
And everybody that passed that way,
    Said, "There lies that steel-driving man,
        There lies a steel-driving man."   120

They took John Henry to the river,
    And buried him in the sand,
And every locomotive come a-roaring by,

Says "There lies that steel-drivin' man,
    Lawd, there lies a *steel*-drivin' man."   125

Some say he came from Georgia,
    And some from Alabam,
But its wrote on the rock at the Big Bend Tunnel,
    That he was an East Virginia man,
        Lord, Lord, an East Virginia man.   130

Frankie and Johnny

Frankie and Johnny were lovers,
    Lordy, how they could love,
Swore to be true to each other,
    True as the stars up above,
        He was her man, but he done her wrong.   5

Frankie went down to the corner,
    To buy her a bucket of beer,
Frankie says "Mister Bartender,
    Has my lovin' Johnnie been here?
        He is my man, but he's doing me wrong."   10

"I don't want to cause you no trouble
    Don't want to tell you no lie,
I saw your Johnnie half-an-hour ago
    Making love to Nelly Bly.
        He is your man, but he's doing you wrong."   15

Frankie went down to the hotel
    Looked over the transom so high,
There she saw her lovin' Johnnie
    Making love to Nelly Bly
        He was her man; he was doing her wrong.   20

Frankie threw back her kimono,
    Pulled out her big forty-four;
Rooty-toot-toot: three times she shot
    Right through that hotel door,
        She shot her man, who was doing her wrong.   25

"Roll me over gently,
    Roll me over slow,
Roll me over on my right side,
    Cause these bullets hurt me so,
        I was your man, but I done you wrong."   30

Bring all your rubber-tired hearses
    Bring all your rubber-tired hacks,
They're carrying poor Johnny to the burying ground
    And they ain't gonna bring him back,
        He was her man, but he done her wrong.   35

Frankie says to the sheriff,
   "What are they going to do?"
The sheriff he said to Frankie,
   "It's the 'lectric chair for you.
      He was your man, and he done you wrong."   40

"Put me in that dungeon,
   Put me in that cell,
Put me where the northeast wind
   Blows from the southeast corner of hell,
      I shot my man, 'cause he done me wrong."   45

Railroad Bill

CHORUS:

Railroad Bill, Railroad Bill,
He never worked and he never will
I'm gonna ride old Railroad Bill.

VERSES:

Railroad Bill he was a mighty mean man
He shot the midnight lantern out the brakeman's hand   5
I'm going to ride old Railroad Bill.

Railroad Bill took my wife,
Said if I didn't like it, he would take my life,
I'm going to ride old Railroad Bill.

Going up on a mountain, going out west,   10
Thirty-eight special sticking out of my vest,
I'm going to ride old Railroad Bill.

Buy me a pistol just as long as my arm,
Kill everybody ever done me harm,
I'm going to ride old Railroad Bill.   15

I've got a thirty-eight special on a forty-five frame,
How in the world can I miss him when I got dead aim,
I'm going to ride old Railroad Bill.

Buy me a pistol just as long as my arm,
Kill everybody ever done me harm,   20
I'm going to ride old Railroad Bill.

Honey, honey, think I'm a fool,
Think I would quit you while the weather is cool,
I'm going to ride old Railroad Bill.

Stackolee

One dark and dusty day
I was strolling down the street.
I thought I heard some old dog bark,
But it warn't nothing but Stackolee gambling in the dark.
Stackolee threw seven.   5
Billy said, It ain't that way.
You better go home and come back another day.
Stackolee shot Billy four times in the head
And left that fool on the floor damn near dead.
Stackolee decided he'd go up to Sister Lou's.   10
Said, Sister Lou! Sister Lou, guess what I done done?
I just shot and killed Billy, your big-head son.
Sister Lou said, Stackolee, that can't be true!
You and Billy been friends for a year or two.
Stackolee said, Woman, if you don't believe what I said,   15
Go count the bullet holes in that son-of-a-gun's head.
Sister Lou got frantic and all in a rage,
Like a tea hound dame on some frantic gage.
She got on the phone, Sheriff, Sheriff, I want you to help poor me.
I want you to catch that bad son-of-a-gun they call Stackolee.   20
Sheriff said, My name might begin with an s and end with an f
But if you want that bad Stackolee you got to get him yourself.
So Stackolee left, he went walking down the New Haven track.
A train come along and flattened him on his back.
He went up in the air and when he fell   25
Stackolee landed right down in hell.
He said, Devil, devil, put your fork up on the shelf
Cause I'm gonna run this devilish place myself.
There came a rumbling on the earth and a tumbling on the ground,
That bad son-of-a-gun, Stackolee, was turning hell around.   30
He ran across one of his ex-girl friends down there.
She was Chock-full-o'-nuts and had pony-tail hair.
She said, Stackolee, Stackolee, wait for me.
I'm trying to please you, can't you see?
She said, I'm going around the corner but I'll be right back.   35
I'm gonna see if I can't stack my sack.
Stackolee said, Susie Belle, go on and stack your sack.
But I just might not be here when you get back.
Meanwhile, Stackolee went with the devil's wife and with his girl
        friend, too.
Winked at the devil and said, I'll go with you.   40
The devil turned around to hit him a lick.
Stackolee knocked the devil down with a big black stick.
Now, to end this story, so I heard tell,
Stackolee, all by his self, is running hell.

Sinking of the *Titanic* [5]

It was 1912 when the awful news got around
That the great *Titanic* was sinking down.
Shine came running up on deck, told the Captain, "Please,
The water in the boiler room is up to my knees."

Captain said, "Take your black self on back down there!   5
I got a hundred-fifty pumps to keep the boiler room clear."
Shine went back in the hole, started shovelling coal,
Singing, "Lord, have mercy, Lord, on my soul!"

Just then half the ocean jumped across the boiler room deck.
Shine yelled to the Captain,"The water's 'round my neck!"   10
Captain said, "Go back! Neither fear nor doubt!
I got a hundred more pumps to keep the water out."

"Your words sound happy and your words sound true,
But this is one time, Cap, your words won't do
I don't like chicken and I don't like ham—   15
And I don't believe your pumps is worth a damn!"

The old *Titanic* was beginning to sink.
Shine pulled off his clothes and jumped in the brink.
He said, "Little fish, big fish, and shark fishes, too,
Get out of my way because I'm coming through."   20

Captain on bridge hollered, "Shine, Shine, save poor me,
And I'm make you as rich as any man can be."
Shine said, "There's more gold on land than there is on sea."
And he swimmed on.

Big fat banker begging, "Shine, Shine, save poor me!   25
I'll give you a thousand shares of T and T."
Shine said, "More stocks on land than there is on sea."
And he swimmed on.

When all them white folks went to heaven,
Shine was in Sugar Ray's Bar drinking Seagrams Seven.   30

Shine and the *Titanic* [6]

One day when the great *Titanic* was sinking away,
Captain was in his quarters one lonely night,
This old man came up the port side.
He said, "Captain, Captain, the water's over the first fireroom
     door."
He said, "Shine, Shine, have no doubt.   5

5. This sanitized version of the *Titanic* ballad was presented by Langston Hughes and Arna Bontemps in *The Book of American Negro Folklore* (1958). 6. This typically bawdy version of the *Titanic* bal-lad was recorded as spoken in Philadelphia and published in Roger Abraham's *Deep Down in the Jungle* (1964).

We got forty-nine pumps to pump the water out."
Shine went down and he came up again.
He said, "Captain, look! That damn water's still coming in."
Captain said, "Shine, Shine, have no doubt,
Now we have ninety-nine pumps to pump the water out."   10
He said, "Captain, there was a time when your word might be true,
But this is one damn time your word won't do."
So Shine he jumped overboard. He took two kicks, one stroke,
He was off like a PT boat.[7]
Captain came up on the deck. He said, "Shine, Shine, save poor me.   15
I'll give you more money than any black man want to see."
Shine said, "You know my color and you guessed my race."
Come in here and give these sharks a chase."
Captain's daughter came up on deck,
Drawers in her hand, brassiere around her neck.   20
She said, "Shine, Shine, save poor me.
Give you more pregnant pussy than a black man want to see."
Shine said, "I know you're pregnant, 'bout to have a kid,
But if that boat sink two more inches, you'll swim this coast just like
      Shine did."
The Captain's wife came up on deck. She said, "Shine, Shine, save
      poor me.   25
I'll let you eat pussy like a rat eats cheese."
Shine said, "I like pussy, I ain't no rat.
I like cock, but not like that."
Shine kept a-swimming.
Shine came past the whale's den.   30
The whale invited old Shine in.
Shine said, "I know you're king of the ocean, king of the sea,
But you gotta be a water-splashing motherfucker to outswim me."
So Shine kept on stroking.
Now Shine met up with the shark.   35
Shark said, "Shine, Shine, can't you see.
When you jump in these waters you belongs to me."
Shine said, "I know you outswim the barracuda, outsmart every fish
      in the sea,
But you gotta be a stroking motherfucker to outswim me."
Shine kept a-swimming.   40
When the word got to Washington that the great *Titanic* had sunk,
Shine was on Broadway, one-third drunk.

7. A fast, maneuverable U.S. fighting vessel that specialized in torpedoing enemy ships.

WORK SONGS

Pick a Bale of Cotton

Jump down, turn around to pick a bale of cotton.
Jump down, turn around, pick a bale a day.

Jump down, turn around to pick a bale of cotton.
Jump down, turn around, pick a bale a day.

Oh, Lordy, pick a bale of cotton!   5
Oh, Lordy, pick a bale a day!

Me and my gal can pick a bale of cotton,
Me and my gal can pick a bale a day
Me and my wife can pick a bale of cotton,
Me and my wife can pick a bale a day. . . .   10

Me and my friend can pick a bale of cotton,
Me and my friend can pick a bale a day. . . .

Me and my poppa can pick a bale of cotton,
Me and my poppa can pick a bale a day.
Oh, Lordy, pick a bale of cotton!   15
Oh, Lordy, pick a bale a day!

Go Down, Old Hannah [1]

Go down, old Hannah,
    Won't you rise no more?
Go down, old Hannah,
    Won't you rise no more?

Lawd, if you rise,   5
    Bring judgment on.
Lawd, if you rise,
    Bring judgment on.

Oh, did you hear
    What the captain said?   10
Oh, did you hear
    What the captain said?

That if you work
    He'll treat you well,
And if you don't   15
    He'll give you hell.

Oh, go down, old Hannah,
    Won't you rise no more?
Won't you go down, old Hannah,
    Won't you rise no more?   20

Oh, long-time man,
    Hold up your head.
Well, you may get a pardon
    And you may drop dead.

1. The sun.

Lawdy, nobody feels sorry   25
For the life-time man.
Nobody feels sorry
For the life-time man.

Can't You Line It? [2]

1   When I get in Illinois
    I'm going to spread the news about the Florida boys.

CHORUS:

(All men straining at rail in concert.)
Shove it over! Hey, hey, can't you line it?
(Shaking rail.) Ah, shack-a-lack-a-lack-a-lack-a-lack-a-lack-a-lack.
(Grunt as they move rail.) Can't you move it? Hey, hey, can't you try.   5

2   Tell what the hobo told the bum,
    If you get any corn-bread save me some.

CHORUS

3   A nickle's worth of bacon, and a dime's worth of lard,
    I would buy more but the time's too hard.

CHORUS

4   Wonder what's the matter with the walking boss,   10
    It's done five-thirty and he won't knock off.

CHORUS

5   I ast my Cap'n what's the time of day,
    He got mad and throwed his watch away.

CHORUS

6   Cap'n got a pistol and he try to play bad,
    But I'm going to take it if he make me mad.   15

CHORUS

7   Cap'n got a burner [3] I'd like to have,
    A 32:20 with a shiny barrel.

CHORUS

8   De Cap'n can't read, de Cap'n can't write,
    How do he know that the time is right?

2. This song is common to the railroad camps. It is   placed in position to be spiked down [Zora Neale
suited to the "lining" rhythm. That is, it fits the   Hurston's note].
straining of the men at the lining bars as the rail is 3. Gun [Hurston's note].

CHORUS

9 Me and my buddy and two three more,   20
   Going to ramshack Georgy everywhere we go.

CHORUS

10 Here come a woman walking 'cross the field,
    Her mouth exhausting like an automobile.

JAZZ

The music that came to be called jazz emerged in the first decades of the twentieth century from the artistic meeting of elements including ragtime, marching band music, opera and other European classical musics, Native American musics, spirituals, work songs, and especially the blues. No seedbed for the new music was richer than that of New Orleans, where, in spite of separatist racial policies, musicians could tap into the city's spectacularly broad range of musical influences and where the opportunities to hear, play, and practice music—and to do so under expert musician-tutors—were extraordinarily abundant.

By the teens and twenties, the good news of early jazz was beginning to spread to a wide variety of places across the nation, including Mobile, Alabama; Washington, D.C.; Chicago; St. Louis and Kansas City, Missouri; Minneapolis; New York; Boston; and beyond. Jazz crystallized from disparate elements: rural and urban, portside and inland, long settled and frontier. Still, it developed primarily as a city phenomenon, one that attempted to capture in music the cadences, voices, and even the rising skylines, of new urban America. Particularly was it influenced by the tremendousness and the music-in-motion of the modern train, the beautiful machine that seems to have represented both the power and the promise of moving away from the land where one's parents and grandparents had been slaves (which occurred in a mighty wave during this period's Great Migration) and the remembrance of such earlier train images in the spirituals (with their trains bound for glory) and in the underground railroad (with its stations, conductors, and hard-riding runners for freedom). From the beginning, jazz was a music of train-whistle guitars, bell-ringing pianos and horns, "conductors" calling and squalling. *Honky-Tonk Train, Daybreak Express, 9:20 Special,* and *Take the A Train* are just a tiny sampling of jazz compositions with titles bearing this locomotive influence. Both Thelonious Monk's *Little Rootie Tootie* and Elmore James's *Sunnyland,* the latter on the Audio Companion, involve significant railroad onomatopoeia.

From the beginning, too, jazz was primarily an instrumental music strongly impacted by the sound of the African American voice. What this music can sound like more than anything else is the jam-session-like talk and song from the Harlems of America and from its southern roads. In a real sense, the sound of jazz is that of the African American voice scored as band music, with all of black talk's flair for storytelling as well as the dirty dozens, understatement as well as braggadocio, whispery romance as well as loud-talk menace, the exalted eloquence of a Martin Luther King and the spare dry poetry of a pool-hall boast or a jump-rope rhyme. All of that "talking and testifying" and "speaking and speechifying" boldly make their way into this music, giving it great force and flavor. Once singers got into the jazz act, they tended to follow Louis Armstrong in using their voices as if they were jazz instruments—which meant, ironically, that they were voices imitating instruments that were imitating voices!

Jazz is not, generally speaking, an art of unaccompanied solo making. In this collaborative music, one hears the instruments and the singers in conversation with each other in patterns often called call and response or call and recall. Jazz instrumentalists often sing the blues through their horns and boxes. Even when singing a nonblues number, they may improvise on it as if it were a blues, and they may inject it with the spirit of blue demons and devils. Like the blues singer's art, the jazz musicians' is defined by blue notes, blue timbres, and improvisations. And jazz has a blueslike tragic dimension, too: it knows that life is a low-down dirty shame or that, as the bluesman Elmore James puts it, "the sky is crying." As opposed to pop music, which comes and goes with every era, jazz music fingers the jagged grain of experience and knows that, despite all hopes and efforts, things might not work out for the best.

And yet with the deep sea blue tragic sense of life that underlies the music comes an overwhelming impulse to celebrate human experience. For jazz is a music with a strong sense of possibility and humor. It is a music of rejuvenation. What makes it so is that again, like all blues-idiom music, jazz proclaims the human will to keep on keeping on in spite of the troubles traditionally sung about in blues lyrics. Jazz swings and stomps and laughs and finger snaps these blues troubles out of town for a while. It is a music that, as Jelly Roll Morton (and many others) has said, "opens up the window and lets the bad air out."

In its early forms and in forms that persist into our own times, jazz was music that wanted to get up and dance. Duke Ellington once said that you had to be able to dance to play his music properly. Whatever its key and time signatures, whatever its paces, it has remained a dance music, one defined by the urge to make the body rock in rhythm, to swing: to exult in physical movement and in music's dance-beat orientation, its groove that moves singers, instrumentalists, and dancers in dynamically syncopated coordination. No wonder Ralph Ellison said that jazz makers function in society as bringers of great joy.

In other words, jazz heralds the human capacity to do more than merely survive, to create an individual self or voice that can maintain itself, under pressure, with style and equipoise, that can confront trouble and improvise ways of coping no matter what changes or disjunctures may get in the way. Whether labeled "hot" or "cool," jazz is a music of black American endurance under the fast-changing circumstances of a new century. Wrung from the rock of U.S. black life, it has become a (some would say it has become the) quintessential modern music, the soundtrack adopted by the world as it realizes, intellectually, what this music symbolizes and also as it finds the music's beat, now heartbeat steady, now fast-train syncopated, too swinging for body or soul to resist.

In many cases, writers have written about jazz music as such, or they have made detailed references to it in their work. Ellison, Albert Murray, James Baldwin, Toni Morrison, Gloria Naylor, Al Young, and Amiri Baraka are among those in this large group. Others have performed to jazz music or have written works meant to be performed to jazz accompaniment. What is just as interesting is to trace the influences of jazz, as a set of artistic forms and body of techniques, on African American writing's shapes and purposes. There is very good new criticism in this direction, suggesting that in the years to come, students of African American culture will find more ways to talk about the elements of jazz—its vamps (or introductory statements), breaks (or solos), riffs (repeated structural phrases), choruses (main themes), bridges (secondary, connecting themes), call/response patterns, improvisations, syncopated cadences, and other definitive structures—and the ways in which they operate in the pages of a book. Perhaps above all the key point to make here is that jazz (and much jazz-inflected black literature) expresses what Ellison has termed "the American joke" as well as the "real secret of life," which is, he says, "to make life swing"; and the bittersweet bluesy knowledge that though we be dismembered every day, somehow still another day we rise.

(What Did I Do to Be So) Black and Blue? [1]•

Out in the street,
Shufflin' feet,
Couples passin' two by two.
While here am I,
Left high and dry,   5
Black, and 'cause I'm black I'm blue.

Browns and yellers,
All have fellers,
Gentlemen prefer them light.
Wish I could fade,   10
Can't make the grade,
Nothin' but dark days in sight.

Cold empty bed,
Springs hard as lead,
Pains in my head,   15
Feel like old Ned.
What did I do to be so black and blue?

No joys for me,
No company,
Even the mouse   20
Ran from my house.
All my life through, I've been so black and blue.

I'm white inside,
It don't help my case,
'Cause I can't hide what is on my face.   25

I'm so forlorn,
Life's like a thorn,
My heart is torn.
Why was I born?
What did I do to be so black and blue?   30

Just 'cause you're black,
Folks think you lack,
They laugh at you and scorn you too.
What did I do to be so black and blue?

---

1. Written by Thomas "Fats" Waller, Andy Razaf, and Harry Brooks for the 1929 Broadway review called *Hot Chocolates*, this song gained new, powerful meaning in Louis Armstrong's recorded ver- sion of that same year. This song also plays an important role in Ralph Ellison's novel *Invisible Man* (1952).

When you are near,   35
They laugh and sneer,
Set you aside
And you're denied.
What did I do to be so black and blue?

How sad I am, each day I feel worse.   40
My mark of Ham [2] seems to be a curse.

How will it end?
Ain't got a friend,
My only sin is in my skin.
What did I do to be so black and blue?   45

It Don't Mean a Thing (If It Ain't Got That Swing) [3]•

Wah-dah do, wah-dah do,
Wah-dah do, dah-dah do, dah-dah do.

It don't mean a thing
If it ain't got that swing!

It don't mean a thing,   5
All you've got to do is sing!

It makes no difference if it's sweet or hot,
Just keep that rhythm,
Give it everything you've got!

It don't mean a thing   10
If it ain't got that swing!

Wah-dah-dah doo!
Yah-yah-yah-yah-dah doo!

Bup be-duh be-duh be-dut,
Dat-dat-dat   15

Ohhh, it don't mean a thing
If it ain't got that swing!

2. In the Old Testament, Ham was Noah's second, cursed son—marked for the sin of seeing his father naked and neglecting to cover him and designated by racial lore (and sometimes by "science" and "history") as the "original Ethiopian," the first black person on earth. Thus "the mark of Ham" refers, often with irony when blacks make the reference, to evidence of African ancestry.
3. Transcribed from a performance by Ivie Anderson with Duke Ellington (1899–1974). Recorded in 1932, this song gave a motto to the Swing Era of the 1930s, and to jazz music in general.

Parker's Mood [4]•

Come with me,
If you want to go to Kansas City.

I'm feeling lowdown and blue,
My heart's full of sorrow.
Don't hardly know what to do.   5
Where will I be tomorrow?

Going to Kansas City.
Want to go too?
No, you can't make it with me.
Going to Kansas City,   10
Sorry that I can't take you.

When you see me coming,
Raise your window high.
When you see me leaving, baby,
Hang your head and cry.   15

I'm afraid there's nothing in this cream, this dreamy town
A honky-tonky monkey-woman can do.
She'd only bring herself down.

So long everybody!
The time has come   20
And I must leave you
So if I don't ever see your smiling face again:
Make a promise you'll remember
Like a Christmas Day in December
That I told you   25
All through thick and thin
On up until the end
Parker's been your friend.

Don't hang your head
When you see, when you see those six pretty horses pulling
   me.   30
Put a twenty dollar silver-piece on my watchchain,
Look at the smile on my face,
And sing a little song
To let the world know I'm really free.
Don't cry for me,   35
'Cause I'm going to Kansas City.

---

4. Parker is Charlie Parker, alto saxophonist and key contributor to the modern (post World War II) movement in jazz called "bebop." The lyrics of this song were written by the singer King Pleasure (Clarence Beeks) in 1953 to fit the Parker sax solo on his recorded slow blues, also called *Parker's Mood.*

Rap

Emerging from U.S. black urban centers of the 1970s and 1980s, rap draws from such varied sources as jump-rope rhymes and other game chants and songs; competitive trickster toasts and badman boasts such as those of Stackolee and Shine; chanted sermons of black churches (including those of the Nation of Islam); the scat singing of jazz musicians such as Louis Armstrong and Cab Calloway; "vocalese" jazz singing (fitting words and scat phrases to recorded jazz solos); favorite radio disc-jockeys' patter; and the widely popular Black Arts movement poetry of such writers as Nikki Giovanni, Amiri Baraka, Jayne Cortez, Gil Scott-Heron, and the Last Poets—these latter, in turn, influenced by the poetry of Langston Hughes, Sterling Brown, and other black poets working (in the circling pattern of influence so typical of the arts in America) in a black vernacular idiom.

Rappers themselves often cite African musical forms and their underlying sensibilities (along with ongoing political struggles on that continent) as keystone influences on their music, based, they say, on the idea of spoken or chanted words as the beats of a modern-but-ancient, spirit-driven drum. Musically speaking, rappers also draw strength from the dancing rhythm-and-blues and reggae drum- and basslines and the highly charged and irreverently sexualized and politicized talk-sing styles of such musicians as James Brown, Sly Stone, and George Clinton.

Rap music is characterized by sometimes extremely deft rhymes and highly percussive stylized verse—one observer calls it "verbal fire and ice"—performed against a background of sounds "sampled" from snatches of previously recorded music. This sampling has given the music a self-consciously created, postmodern mix. It is a patchwork music vigorously quilted together from fragments granting it a sparklingly pastichelike effect and a parodist's attitude both toward the songs that are quoted and toward their traditions. Like much art associated with postmodernism, rap is often whimsically comical and self-mockingly reflexive.

It is important to remember that like its parents, rhythm and blues and jazz, rap is at once an in-group ritual music, a performance music, and a *dance music*, designed to make dancers move together to its boom-box-busting drumlines and machine-gun-like firings of chanted sound. It is animated music that celebrates black verbal and musical style; but it is also music that rejoices in the poetry of the human body in soulful, dance-hall-rocking motion.

Many rap performances, drawing directly from vernacular sources, describe (sometimes in the bawdiest of terms) sexual quests and imagined conquests along with fantasies of power, mobility, and access to money and its trinkets. One strain of this music, sometimes called "gangsta rap," offers raw and raucous testimony—in language often intentionally offensive in its blunt vulgarity, brutal sexist diction, and occasional anti-Semitism—from those who laugh at the idea that rappers should be role models. What the group N.W.A. (Niggahs Wid Attitude) says it wants is simply put: it wants sex and money. Like badman boasts and trickster narratives dating back at least to the 1940s, N.W.A.'s lyrics broadcast the will to meet a violent world with alluring, shocking fast talk and, if necessary, with hard fists and bullets. Despite disclaimers, gangsta rappers and others do teach their listeners (in something like the way that realist fiction writers teach their readers) by detailing in rivetingly raw terms the severe, violent nature of life in the no-exit realm of the black urban underclass. Some even tap into the black prophetic tradition by urging listeners to awaken to new levels of political and spiritual consciousness, to read and to prepare to take forthright action in a far-downfallen world.

Profoundly, rap is a music that makes room for young black performers to address black audiences (and anyone else who may be listening) in virtuoso-rhyming language, about serious matters of disempowerment and spiritual drift and the urgent, booming need for fundamental change.

The Revolution Will Not Be Televised [1]

You will not be able to stay home, brother.
You will not be able to plug in, turn on and cop out.
You will not be able to lose yourself on scag and
skip out for beer during commercials because
The revolution will not be televised.   5

The revolution will not be televised.
The revolution will not be brought to you by Xerox in four parts
    without commercial interruption.
The revolution will not show you pictures of Nixon blowing a bugle
    and leading a charge by John Mitchell, General Abramson and
    Spiro Agnew to eat hog maws confiscated from a Harlem
    sanctuary.
The revolution will not be televised.

The revolution will not be brought to you by   10
The Schaeffer Award Theatre and will not star
Natalie Wood and Steve McQueen or Bullwinkle and Julia.
The revolution will not give your mouth sex appeal.
The revolution will not get rid of the nubs.
The revolution will not make you look five pounds thinner.   15
The revolution will not be televised, brother.

There will be no pictures of you and Willie Mae
pushing that shopping cart down the block on the dead run
or trying to slide that color t.v. in a stolen ambulance.
NBC will not be able to predict the winner at 8:32 on reports from
    twenty-nine districts.   20
The revolution will not be televised.

There will be no pictures of pigs shooting down brothers
on the instant replay.
There will be no pictures of pigs shooting down brothers
on the instant replay.   25
The will be no slow motion or still lifes of Roy Wilkins strolling
    through Watts in a red, black and green liberation jumpsuit
    that he has been saving for just the proper occasion.

Green Acres, Beverly Hillbillies and Hooterville Junction
will no longer be so damned relevant
and women will not care if Dick finally got down with Jane
on Search for Tomorrow   30
because black people will be in the streets looking for

1. This recorded poem of 1970 by Gil Scott-Heron is not rap music *per se* but it had a vital influence on rap music's forms and themes.

A Brighter Day.
The revolution will not be televised.

There will be no highlights on the Eleven O'Clock News
and no pictures of hairy armed women liberationists   35
and Jackie Onassis blowing her nose.
The theme song will not be written by Jim Webb or Francis Scott
    Key
nor sung by Glen Campbell, Tom Jones, Johnny Cash,
Englebert Humperdink or Rare Earth.
The revolution will not be televised.   40

The revolution will not be right back after a
message about a white tornado, white lightning or white people.
You will not have to worry about a dove in your bedroom,
the tiger in your tank or the giant in your toilet bowl.
The revolution will not go better with coke.   45
The revolution will not fight germs that may cause bad breath.
The revolution *will* put you in the driver's seat.
The revolution will not be televised
            will not be televised
                not be televised   50
                    be televised
The revolution will be no re-run, brothers.
The revolution will be LIVE.

The Message[1]•

It's like a jungle sometimes, it makes me wonder
How I keep from going under
It's like a jungle sometimes, it makes me wonder
How I keep from going under

Broken glass everywhere   5
People pissing on the stairs
You know they just don't care
I can't take the smell, can't take the noise
Got no money to move out, I guess I got no choice
Rats in the front room, roaches in the back   10
Junkies in the alley with a baseball bat
I tried to get away but I couldn't get far
'Cause the man with the tow truck repossessed my car

Don't push me 'cause I'm close to the edge
I'm trying not to lose my head   15
Ah huh huh huh huh
It's like a jungle sometimes, it makes me wonder
How I keep from going under

1. Recorded by Grandmaster Flash & the Furious Five in 1982.

Standing on the front stoop, hanging out the window
Watching all the cars go by, roaring as the breezes blow   20
Crazy lady, living in a bag
Eating outta garbage pails, used to be a fag hag
Says she danced the tango, skip the light fandango
Was zircon princess seemed to lost her senses
Down at the peep show, watching all the creeps so   25
She could tell the story to the girls back home
She went to the city and got social security
She had to get a pension, she couldn't make it on her own

Don't push me 'cause I'm close to the edge
I'm trying not to lose my head   30
Ah huh huh huh huh
It's like a jungle sometimes, it makes me wonder
How I keep from going under
Huh ah huh huh huh
It's like a jungle sometimes, it makes me wonder   35
How I keep from going under

My brother's doing bad, stole my mother's TV
Says she watches too much, it's just not healthy
"All My Children" in the daytime, "Dallas" at night
Can't even see the game or the Sugar Ray fight   40
The bill collectors, they ring my phone
And scare my wife when I'm not home
Got a bum education, double-digit inflation
Can't train to the job, there's a strike at the station
Neon King Kong, standing on my back   45
Can't stop to turn around, broke my sacroiliac
A mid-range migraine, cancered membrane
Sometimes I think I'm going insane
I swear, I might hijack a plane

Don't push me 'cause I'm close to the edge   50
I'm trying not to lose my head
It's like a jungle sometimes, it makes me wonder
How I keep from going under

My son said, "Daddy, I don't want to go to school
'Cause the teacher's a jerk, he must think I'm a fool   55
And all the kids smoke reefer, I think it'd be cheaper
If I just got a job, learned to be a street sweeper
Dance to the beat, shuffle my feet
Wear a shirt and tie and run with the creeps
'Cause it's all about money, ain't a damn thing funny   60
You got to have a con in this land of milk and honey"

They pushed that girl in front of the train
Took her to the doctor, sewed her arm on again
Stabbed that man right in his heart
Gave him a transplant for a brand new start   65
I can't walk through the park 'cause it's crazy after dark

Keep my hand on my gun
'Cause they got me on the run
I feel like a outlaw
Broke my last glass jaw   70
Hear them say, "You want some more?"
Livin' on a seesaw

Don't push me 'cause I'm close to the edge
I'm trying not to lose my head
Say what?   75
It's like a jungle sometimes, it makes me wonder
How I keep from going under

A child is born with no state of mind
Blind to the ways of mankind
God is smiling on you but he's frowning too   80
Because only God knows what you go through
You grow in the ghetto, living second rate
And your eyes will sing a song of deep hate
The place that you play and where you stay
Looks like one great big alleyway   85
You'll admire all the number book-takers
Thugs, pimps, and pushers and the big money makers
Driving big cars, spending twenties and tens
And you wanna grow up to be just like them, huh
Smugglers, scramblers, burglars, gamblers   90
Pickpockets, peddlers, even panhandlers
You say, "I'm cool, huh, I'm no fool"
But then you wind up dropping out of high school
Now you're unemployed, all nonvoid
Walking 'round like you're Pretty Boy Floyd   95
Turned stick-up kid but look what you done did
Got sent up for a eight-year bid
Now your manhood is took and you're a Maytag
Spend the next two years as a undercover fag

Being used and abused to serve like hell   100
'Til one day you was found hung dead in the cell
It was plain to see that your life was lost
You was cold and your body swung back and forth
But now your eyes sing the sad sad song
Of how ya lived so fast and died so young   105

So don't push me 'cause I'm close to the edge
I'm trying not to lose my head
Ah huh huh huh huh
It's like a jungle sometimes, it makes me wonder
How I keep from going under   110

(Dialogue)
Yo, Mel, you see that girl man?
Yeah, man
Cowboy

Yo! That sound like Cowboy, man
That's cool   115
Yo! What's up money?
Yo!
Hey, where's Creole and Rahiem at, man?
They upstairs cooling out
So, what's up for tonight y'all?   120
Yo! We could go down to Fever, man
Let's go check out June Bug, man
Hey yo! You know that girl Betty?
Yeah, man
Her moms got robbed, man   125
What?
Not again?
She got hurt real bad
When this happen? When this happen?
(Tires squeal)
Everybody freeze! Don't nobody move nothing, y'all know what
    this is   130
Get 'em up!
What?
Get 'em up!
Man, we down with Grandmaster Flash and the Furious Five
What's that? A gang?   135
No!
Look, shut up! I don't want to hear your mouth
'Scuse me, Officer, Officer, what's the problem?
You the problem, you the problem
You ain't got to push me, man   140
Get in the car! Get in the car! Get in the godda—
Get in the car!

Don't Believe the Hype [1]

Don't believe the hype

Back—caught you lookin' for the same thing
It's a new thing—check out this I bring
Uh-oh, the roll below the level
'Cause I'm livin' low   5
Next to the bass (c'mon)
Turn up the radio
They claim that I'm a criminal
By now I wonder how
Some people never know   10
The enemy could be their friend, guardian
I'm not a hooligan
I rock the party and
Clear all the madness, I'm not a racist
Preach to teach to all   15

1. Recorded by Public Enemy in 1988.

'Cause some, they never had this
Number one, not born to run
About the gun
I wasn't licensed to have one
The minute they see me, fear me   20
I'm the epitome—a public enemy
Used, abused, without clues
I refused to blow a fuse
They even had it on the news
Don't believe the hype   25

Don't believe the hype

Yes—was the start of my last jam
So here it is again, another def jam
But since I gave you all a little something
That we knew you lacked   30
They still consider me a new jack
All the critics, you can hang 'em
I'll hold the rope
But they hope to the pope
And pray it ain't dope   35
The follower of Farrakhan
Don't tell me that you understand
Until you hear the man
The book of the new school rap game
Writers treat me like Coltrane, insane   40
Yes to them, but to me I'm a different kind
We're brothers of the same mind, unblind
Caught in the middle and
Not surrenderin'
I don't rhyme for the sake of riddlin'   45
Some claim that I'm a smuggler
Some say I never heard of ya
A rap burglar, false media
We don't need it, do we?
It's fake, that's what it be to ya, dig me?   50
Yo, Terminator X, step up on the stand and show the people what
        time it is, boyyyyy!

Don't believe the hype

Don't believe the hype—it's a sequel
As an equal, can I get this through to you
My 98's boomin' with a trunk of funk   55
All the jealous punks can't stop the dunk
Comin' from the school of hard knocks
Some perpetrate, they drink Clorox
Attack the Black, because I know they lack exact
The cold facts, and still they try to xerox   60
The leader of the new school, uncool
Never played the fool, just made the rules
Remember there's a need to get alarmed

Again I said I was a timebomb
In the daytime, radio's scared of me   65
'Cause I'm mad, 'cause I'm the enemy
They can't come on and play me in prime time
'Cause I know the time, plus I'm gettin' mine
I get on the mix late in the night
They know I'm livin' right, so here go the mike, psych   70
Before I let it go, don't rush my show
You try to reach and grab and get elbowed
Word to Herb, yo if you can't swing this
Learn the words, you might sing this
Just a little bit of the taste of the bass for you   75
As you get up and dance at the LQ
When some deny it, defy it, I swing bolos
And then they clear the lane, I go solo
The meaning of all of that
Some media is the wack   80
As you believe it's true
It blows me through the roof
Suckers, liars, get me a shovel
Some writers I know are damn devils
For them I say, "Don't believe the hype"   85
Yo Chuck, they must be on the pipe, right?
Their pens and pads I'll snatch
'Cause I've had it
I'm not an addict, fiendin' for static
I'll see their tape recorder and grab it   90
No, you can't have it back, silly rabbit
I'm goin' to my media assassin
Harry Allen, I gotta ask him
Yo Harry, you're a writer, are we that type?

Don't believe the hype   95
Don't believe the hype

I got Flavor and all those things you know
Yeah boy, part two bum rush the show
Yo Griff, get the green, black, red, and
Gold down, countdown to Armageddon   100
'88 you wait the S-One's will
Put the left in effect and I still will
Rock the hard jams, treat it like a seminar
Reach the bourgeois, and rock the boulevard
Some say I'm negative   105
But they're not positive
But what I got to give
The media says this
Red black and green
Know what I mean   110
Yo, don't believe the hype

The Evil That Men Do [1]

You asked, I came
So behold the Queen
Let's add a little sense to the scene
I'm livin' positive
Not out here knocked up   5
But the lines are so dangerous
I oughta be locked up
This rhyme doesn't require prime time
I'm just sharin' thoughts in mind
Back again because I knew you wanted it   10
From the Latifah with the Queen in front of it
Droppin' bombs, you're up in arms and puzzled
The lines will flow like fluid while you guzzle
You slip, I'll drop you on a BDP-produced track
From KRS to be exact   15
It's a Flavor Unit quest that today has me speakin'
'Cause it's knowledge I'm seekin'
Enough about myself, I think it's time that I tell you
About the Evil That Men Do

Situations, reality, what a concept   20
Nothin' ever seems to stay in step
So today here is a message for my sisters and brothers
Here are some things I want to cover
A woman strives for a better life
But who the hell cares   25
Because she's livin' on welfare
The government can't come up with a decent housin' plan
So she's in no man's land
It's a sucker who tells you you're equal
(You don't need 'em   30
Johannesburg cries for freedom)
We the people hold these truths to be self-evident
(But there's no response from the president)
Someone's livin' the good life tax-free
'Cause some poor girl can't find   35
A way to be crack-free
And that's just part of the message
I thought I had to send you
About the Evil That Men Do

Tell me, don't you think it's a shame   40
When someone can put a quarter in a video game
But when a homeless person approaches you on the street
You can't treat him the same
It's time to teach the deaf, the dumb, the blind
That black on black crime only shackles and binds   45
You to a doom, a fate worse than death
But there's still time left

1. Recorded by Queen Latifah in 1989.

To stop puttin' your conscience on cease
And bring about some type of peace
Not only in your heart but also in your mind 50
It will benefit all mankind
Then there will be one thing
That will never stop you
And it's the Evil That Men Do

SERMONS

The African American sermon is a complex oratorical form with significant differences from religion to religion, denomination to denomination, region to region, and era to era. Sermons heard in a northern Nation of Islam mosque differ significantly from those heard in a down-home Southern Baptist church. Those flattening out all of these differences to expound on *the* black sermon deny this pulchritudinous variety and do a serious injustice to history and its unfurling. Still, there is a sense of continuity in black homiletics (or sermon making), especially observable within those black churches that are independent (or relatively independent) from non–African American leadership hierarchies and cultural values.

The folklorist Gerald L. Davis has outlined several features that define the black sermon as a distinctive form. According to Davis, the African American sermon typically has these parts: (1) the disclaimer, in which the preacher makes clear that the morning's message comes not from him or her alone but from God; (2) the statement of theme as drawn from specific biblical readings; (3) the literal and then the broad interpretation of the biblical Word; (4) the formulaic body of the sermon, the morning's main message; and (5) the closing statement, rarely a summary as such but rather an open-ended conclusion leading to the next part of the church service.

Within this frame, black preachers are storytellers, actors, and singers who use their voices and bodies to lend dynamism to the performed word. Sometimes, as in Rev. C. L. Franklin's "The Eagle Stirreth Her Nest," a sermon will take the form of the preacher's own personal witnessing of God's ways in the world. There is also an important body of black folk sermons, and of fragments of sermons, that have become part of the black sermonic canon. *The Valley of Dry Bones* and *The Eagle Stirreth Her Nest* are examples of canonized sermons. Like other vernacular forms, black sermons have developed by incremental repetition—from Africa through slavery (that cultural cauldron in which not only Christianity but Christian forms of worship were learned and then refashioned to meet black values) to freedom—and have become part of a nationwide black creative process.

Despite the relative rigidity of the black sermon's architecture, it is jazzlike in its insistence that the preacher find his or her own "voice" and imprint on each sermon his or her own particular style. Jazzlike too is black preaching's emphasis on the improvisational mode. For like the jazz player the preacher participates in a dynamic collaborative process in which he or she listens with the greatest care while playing, as it were, *with and against* the congregation. The result is that often the best sermons are not just individual productions in the usual Western sense of the artist's product but spring from a creative process involving all those in a given congregation who participate with a full spirit. The most successful preacher can listen through handclaps and countercalls for a *"Well"* from the Amen Corner (that section of a congregation, positioned near the pulpit, where older members sit and lead the church in responses to the service), a word voiced in a tone or timbre that says "Slow down" or "Explain that" or "Keep building, sister, we hear you!" And of course the preacher also plays with and against the conventions of black preaching itself, plays with the *tradition* of the form. He or she knows what formal elements the congregation expects, and, like the artist, delays them, pretends to ignore or undermine them, then hammers them home or slips them in, to the congregation's aesthetic satisfaction and delight.

Again like other artists in the black vernacular tradition, the black preacher is involved not just in call-and-response patterns but in patterns of call-and-*recall*: inspiration and memory. The black preacher presents a rhythmically sophisticated statement in which repetitions, dramatic pauses, shifts in tone and pitch, and a variety of other devices associated with black music (and the other arts) are used. At times, too, the man or woman of the Word drops words altogether and moans, chants, sings, grunts, hums, and/or hollers the morning message in a way that transcends what one of Ralph Ellison's characters calls "the straight meaning of the words." In these most musical portions of the "sermonic narrative," as Davis says, perhaps the deepest African American take-home lessons resound. Inspiration and memory.

Still, it is crucial also to note the black sermon's steadfast linking of spiritual lessons to those of the here and the now. Sometimes the here and now references—to the foibles of the congregation, to current events, or to contemporary media forms, for example—take a comical turn. But then again the references to current affairs can be deadly serious. For the black sermon typically is a vehicle not only for conversion and worship but for sociopolitical exposition and analysis. It is in this sense, as Cornel West has observed, that preachers are vital intellectual presences—and, in the cases of those such as Martin Luther King and Malcolm X, prophetic seers—in our communities. For even as the unmistakably black forms of their presentations implicitly celebrate black Americans as a group, the sermons aim too to help congregations comprehend the mysterious and often unfriendly world through which they are rolling. Little wonder that so many preachers have been political movers and shakers: organizers, analysts, spokespersons, office seekers, and community leaders on a very large scale.

Many black writers—including James Weldon Johnson, Zora Neale Hurston, James Baldwin, and Ralph Ellison—have written brilliantly about the Church and have movingly rendered sermons in their work. In Baldwin's play *Amen Corner* you can hear the fans fanning and smell the after-service food cooking through the church's thumping floorboards. Doubtless the best way to experience the sermon is to attend a black church, to hear and see the Word performed in context; second best is to experience the sermon in literature, where the sense of context also can be very full. But reading transcripts of actual sermons and listening to recordings of them—especially for those who have the original cultural settings in mind—also makes the case that they comprise a wonderfully rich site of African American vernacular expression, an art form in its own right.

The styles of the black preacher have become part of American oratorical style. Martin Luther King and Malcolm X—both masters of the drama of the sermon, though of different faiths—gave the mid-twentieth century its greatest examples of black church rhetoric and of the black sermon's possibilities for persuasive force. Recent collections of prayers and testimonials—notably James Washington's masterful *Conversations with God*—have made clear the depth and range of church forms other than songs and sermons. These collections also make the point that here again is a vernacular form that is very much alive and well within the congregations of black America.

God[1]

I vision God standing
On the heights of heaven,
Throwing the devil like
A burning torch
Over the gulf   5
Into the valleys of hell.
His eye the lightning's flash,
His voice the thunder's roll.
Wid one hand He snatched
The sun from its socket,   10
And the other He clapped across the moon.

I vision God wringing
A storm from the heavens;
Rocking the world
Like an earthquake;   15
Blazing the sea
Wid a trail er fire.
His eye the lightning's flash,
His voice the thunder's roll.
Wid one hand He snatched   20
The sun from its socket,
And the other He clapped across the moon.

I vision God standing
On a mountain
Of burnished gold,   25
Blowing His breath
Of silver clouds
Over the world.
His eye the lightning's flash,
His voice the thunder's roll.   30

Wid one hand He snatched
The sun from its socket,
And the other He clapped across the moon.

1. Collected in the Congaree River area of South Carolina by E. C. L. Adams (1876–1946) and published in 1928.

C. L. FRANKLIN

The Eagle Stirreth Her Nest[1]

"As an eagle stirreth up her nest, fluttereth over her young, spreadeth abroad on her wings, taketh them, beareth them on her wings: So the Lord

1. Franklin (1915–1984) uses Deuteronomy 32:11–12 as his opening text.

alone did lead him, and there was no strange god with him." The eagle stirreth her nest.

The eagle here is used to symbolize God's care and God's concern for his people. Many things have been used as symbolic expressions to give us a picture of God or some characteristic of one of his attributes: the ocean, with her turbulent majesty; the mountains, the lions. Many things have been employed as pictures of either God's strength or God's power or God's love or God's mercy. And the psalmist has said that The heavens declare the glory of God and the firmament shows forth his handiworks.

So the eagle here is used as a symbol of God. Now in picturing God as an eagle stirring her nest, I believe history has been one big nest that God has been eternally stirring to make man better and to help us achieve world brotherhood. Some of the things that have gone on in your own experiences have merely been God stirring the nest of your circumstances. Now the Civil War, for example, and the struggle in connection with it, was merely the promptings of Providence to lash man to a point of being brotherly to all men. In fact, all of the wars that we have gone through, we have come out with new outlooks and new views and better people. So that throughout history, God has been stirring the various nests of circumstances surrounding us, so that he could discipline us, help us to know ourselves, and help us to love another, and to help us hasten on the realization of the kingdom of God.

The eagle symbolizes God because there is something about an eagle that is a fit symbol of things about God. In the first place, the eagle is the king of fowls. And if he is a regal or kingly bird, in that majesty he represents the kingship of God or symbolizes the kingship of God. (Listen if you please.) For God is not merely a king, he is *the* king. Somebody has said that he is the king of kings. For you see, these little kings that we know, they've got to have a king over them. They've got to account to somebody for the deeds done in their bodies. For God is *the* king. And if the eagle is a kingly bird, in that way he symbolizes the regalness and kingliness of our God.

In the second place, the eagle is strong. Somebody has said that as the eagle goes winging his way through the air he can look down on a young lamb grazing by a mountainside, and can fly down and just with the strength of his claws, pick up this young lamb and fly away to yonder's cleft and devour it—because he's strong. If the eagle is strong, then, in that he is a symbol of God, for our God is strong. Our God is strong. Somebody has called him a fortress. So that when the enemy is pursuing me I can run behind him. Somebody has called him a citadel of protection and redemption. Somebody else has said that he's so strong until they call him a leaning-post that thousands can lean on him, and he'll never get away. (I don't believe you're praying with me.) People have been leaning on him ever since time immemorial. Abraham leaned on him. Isaac and Jacob leaned on him. Moses[2] and the prophets leaned on him. All the Christians leaned

---

2. All great leaders of the Old Testament. Abraham was the father of Isaac who was the father of Jacob. Moses delivered the Israelites from slavery under the Pharaoh.

on him. People are leaning on him all over the world today. He's never given way. He's strong. That's strong. Isn't it so?

In the second place, he's swift. The eagle is swift. And it is said that he could fly with such terrific speed that his wings can be heard rowing in the air. He's swift. And if he's swift in that way, he's a symbol of our God. For our God is swift. I said he's swift. Sometimes, sometimes he'll answer you while you're calling him. He's swift. Daniel was thrown in a lions' den. And Daniel rung him on the way to the lions' den. And having rung him, why, God had dispatched the angel from heaven. And by the time that Daniel got to the lions' den, the angel had changed the nature of lions and made them lay down and act like lambs. [3] He's swift. Swift. One night Peter [4] was put in jail and the church went down on its knees to pray for him. And while the church was praying, Peter knocked on the door. God was so swift in answering prayer. So that if the eagle is a swift bird, in that way he represents or symbolizes the fact that God is swift. He's swift. If you get in earnest tonight and tell him about your troubles, he's swift to hear you. All you do is need a little faith, and ask him in grace.

Another thing about the eagle is that he has extraordinary sight. Extraordinary sight. Somewhere it is said that he can rise to a lofty height in the air and look in the distance and see a storm hours away. That's extraordinary sight. And sometimes he can stand and gaze right in the sun because he has extraordinary sight. I want to tell you my God has extraordinary sight. He can see every ditch that you have dug for me and guide me around them. God has extraordinary sight. He can look behind that smile on your face and see that frown in your heart. God has extraordinary sight.

Then it is said that an eagle builds a nest unusual. It is said that the eagle selects rough material, basically, for the construction of his nest. And then as the nest graduates toward a close or a finish, the material becomes finer and softer right down at the end. And then he goes about to set up residence in that nest. And when the little eaglets are born, she goes out and brings in food to feed them. But when they get to the point where they're old enough to be out on their own, why, the eagle will begin to pull out some of that down and let some of those thorns come through so that the nest won't be, you know, so comfortable. So when they get to lounging around and rolling around, the thorns prick 'em here and there. (Pray with me if you please.)

I believe that God has to do that for us sometimes. Things are going so well and we are so satisfied that we just lounge around and forget to pray. You'll walk around all day and enjoy God's life, God's health and God's strength, and go climb into bed without saying, "Thank you, Lord, for another day's journey." We'll do that. God has to pull out a little of the plush around us, a little of the comfort around us, and let a few thorns of trial and tribulation stick through the nest to make us pray sometime. Isn't it so? For most of us forget God when things are going well with us. Most of us forget him.

It is said that there was a man who had a poultry farm. And that he raised chickens for the market. And one day in one of his broods he discovered a

<hr>

3. See Daniel 6:16–22.   4. One of the apostles chosen by Jesus.

strange looking bird that was very much unlike the other chickens on the
yard. [*Whooping:*]

And[5]
    the man
        didn't pay too much attention.
    But he noticed
        as time went on
that
    this strange looking bird
        was unusual.
    He outgrew
        the other little chickens,
    his habits were stranger
        and different.
O Lord.
    But he let him grow on,
    and let him mingle
        with the other chickens.
O Lord.
    And then one day a man
    who knew eagles
        when he saw them,
    came along
        and saw that little eagle
        walking in the yard.
And
    he said to his friend,
    "Do you know
        that you have an eagle here?"
    The man said, "Well,
        I didn't really know it.
    But I knew he was different
        from the other chickens.
And
    I knew that his ways
        were different.
And
    I knew that his habits
        were different.
And
    he didn't act like
        the other chickens.
    But I didn't know
        that he was an eagle."
    But the man said, "Yes,
        you have an eagle here on your yard.
    And what you ought to do
        is build a cage.
    After a while
        when he's a little older

---

5. Note that from here on the preached words are presented in a form that approximates the rhythmic chanting quality of their presentation.

        he's going to get tired
            of the ground.
Yes he will.
        He's going to rise up
            on the pinion of his wings.
Yes,
and
        as he grows,
why,
        you can change the cage,
and
        make it a little larger
            as he grows older
            and grows larger."
        The man went out
            and built a cage.
And
        every day he'd go in
            and feed the eagle.
But
        he grew
            a little older
            and a little older.
Yes he did.
        His wings
            began
        to scrape on the sides
            of the cage.
And
        he had to build
            another cage
        and open the door of the old cage
            and let him into
        a larger cage.
Yes he did.
O Lord.
And
        after a while
            he outgrew that one day
            and then he had to build
            another cage.
        So one day
            when the eagle had gotten grown,
Lord God,
        and his wings
            were twelve feet
            from tip to tip,
O Lord,
        he began to get restless
        in the cage.
Yes he did.
        He began to walk around
            and be uneasy.

Why,
    he heard
        noises
        in the air.
    A flock of eagles flew over
        and he heard
        their voices.
And

    though he'd never been around eagles,
    there was something about that voice
        that he heard
    that moved
        down in him,
    and made him
        dissatisfied.
O Lord.
And

    the man watched him
        as he walked around
        uneasy.
O Lord.

    He said, "Lord,
        my heart goes out to him.
    I believe I'll go
        and open the door
        and set the eagle free."
O Lord.

    He went there
        and opened the door.
Yes.

    The eagle walked out,
        yes,
    spreaded his wings,
        then took 'em down.
Yes.

    The eagle walked around
        a little longer,
and

    he flew up a little higher
        and went to the barnyard.
And,
yes,

    he set there for a while.
    He wiggled up a little higher
    and flew in yonder's tree.
Yes.

    And then he wiggled up a little higher
    and flew to yonder's mountain.
Yes.
Yes!
Yes.

    One of these days,
        one of these days.

My soul
    is an eagle
in the cage that the Lord
    has made for me.
My soul,
    my soul,
my soul
    is caged in,
    in this old body,
    yes it is,
and one of these days
the man who made the cage
will open the door
and let my soul
    go.
Yes he will.
You ought to
    be able to see me
    take the wings of my soul.
Yes, yes,
yes,
yes!
Yes, one of these days.
One of these old days.
One of these old days.
Did you hear me say it?
I'll fly away
    and be at rest.
Yes.
Yes!
Yes!
Yes!
Yes!
Yes.
One of these old days.
One of these old days.
And
    when troubles
    and trials are over,
    when toil
    and tears are ended,
    when burdens
    are through burdening,
ohh!
Ohh.
Ohh!
Ohh one of these days.
Ohh one of these days.
One of these days.
One of these days,
my soul will take wings,
my soul will take wings.
Ohh!

Ohh, a few more days.
Ohh, a few more days.
A few more days.
O Lord.

[Faith hasn't got no eyes][1]

Faith hasn't got no eyes, but she long-legged
But take de spy-glass of Faith
And look into dat upper room
When you are alone to yourself
When yo' heart is burnt with fire, ha!   5
When de blood is lopin' thru yo' veins
Like de iron monasters (monsters) on de rail
Look into dat upper chamber, ha!
We notice at de supper table
As He gazed upon His friends, ha!   10
His eyes flowin' wid tears, ha! He said
"My soul is exceedingly sorrowful unto death, ha!
For this night, ha!
One of you shall betray me, ha!
It were not a Roman officer, ha!   15
It were not a centurion
But one of you
Who I have chosen my bosom friend
That sops in the dish with me shall betray me."
I want to draw a parable.   20
I see Jesus
Leaving heben with all of His grandeur
Dis-robin' Hisself of His matchless honor
Yielding up de scepter of revolvin' worlds
Clothing Hisself in de garment of humanity   25
Coming into de world to rescue His friends.
Two thousand years have went by on their rusty ankles
But with the eye of faith, I can see Him
Look down from his high tower of elevation
I can hear Him when He walks about the golden streets   30
I can hear 'em ring under His footsteps
Sol me-e-e, Sol do
Sol me-e-e, Sol do
I can hear Him step out upon the rim bones of nothing
Crying I am de way   35
De truth and de light
Ah!
God A'mighty!
I see Him grab de throttle
Of de well ordered train of mercy   40

1. This is part of John Pearson's final sermon in the climactic chapter of Zora Neale Hurston's first novel, *Jonah's Gourd Vine* (1934). After finishing the sermon, Pearson literally walks out of the church and declares that the community cannot accept an imperfect pastor—or, in his words, "dey's ready fuh uh preacher tuh be uh man uhmongst men, but dey ain't ready yet fuh 'im to be uh man uhmongst women."

I see kingdoms crush and crumble
Whilst de archangels held de winds in de corner chambers
I see Him arrive on dis earth
And walk de streets thirty and three years
Oh-h-hhh!   45
I see Him walking beside de sea of Galilee wid His disciples
This declaration gendered on His lips
"Let us go on to the other side."
God A'mighty!
Dey entered de boat   50
Wid their oarus (oars) stuck in de back
Sails unfurled to de evenin' breeze
And de ship was now sailin'
As she reached de center of de lake
Jesus was sleep on a pillow in de rear of de boat   55
And de dynamic powers of nature became disturbed
And de mad winds broke de heads of de Western drums
And fell down on de lake of Galilee
And buried themselves behind de gallopin' waves
And de white-caps marbilized themselves like an army   60

And walked out like soldiers goin' to battle
And de zig-zag lightning
Licked out her fiery tongue
And de flying clouds
Threw their wings in the channels of the deep   65
And bedded de waters like a road-plow
And faced de current of de chargin' billows
And de terrific bolts of thunder—they bust in de clouds
And de ship begin to reel and rock
God A'mighty!   70
And one of de disciples called Jesus
"Master!! Carest Thou not that we perish?"
And He arose
And de storm was in its pitch
And de lightnin' played on His raiments as He stood on de prow of
    the boat   75
And placed His foot upon de neck of the storm
And spoke to the howlin' winds
And de sea fell at His feet like a marble floor
And de thunders went back in their vault
Then He set down on de rim of de ship   80
And took de hooks of His power
And lifted de billows in His lap
And rocked de winds to sleep on His arm
And said, "Peace, be still."
And de Bible says there was a calm.   85

MARTIN LUTHER KING JR.

I Have a Dream [1]

I am happy to join with you today in what will go down in history as the greatest demonstration for freedom in the history of our nation.

Fivescore years ago, a great American, in whose symbolic shadow we stand today, signed the Emancipation Proclamation. This momentous decree came as a great beacon light of hope to millions of Negro slaves who had been seared in the flames of withering injustice. It came as a joyous daybreak to end the long night of their captivity.

But one hundred years later, the Negro still is not free; one hundred years later, the life of the Negro is still sadly crippled by the manacles of segregation and the chains of discrimination; one hundred years later, the Negro lives on a lonely island of poverty in the midst of a vast ocean of material prosperity; one hundred years later, the Negro is still languished in the corners of American society and finds himself in exile in his own land.

So we've come here today to dramatize a shameful condition. In a sense we've come to our nation's capital to cash a check. When the architects of our republic wrote the magnificent words of the Constitution and the Declaration of Independence, they were signing a promissory note to which every American was to fall heir. This note was the promise that all men, yes, black men as well as white men, would be guaranteed the unalienable rights of life, liberty, and the pursuit of happiness.

It is obvious today that America has defaulted on this promissory note in so far as her citizens of color are concerned. Instead of honoring this sacred obligation, America has given the Negro people a bad check; a check which has come back marked "insufficient funds." We refuse to believe that there are insufficient funds in the great vaults of opportunity of this nation. And so we've come to cash this check, a check that will give us upon demand the riches of freedom and the security of justice.

We have also come to this hallowed spot to remind America of the fierce urgency of now. This is no time to engage in the luxury of cooling off or to take the tranquilizing drug of gradualism. Now is the time to make real the promises of democracy; now is the time to rise from the dark and desolate valley of segregation to the sunlit path of racial justice; now is the time to lift our nation from the quicksands of racial injustice to the solid rock of brotherhood; now is the time to make justice a reality for all of God's children. It would be fatal for the nation to overlook the urgency of the moment. This sweltering summer of the Negro's legitimate discontent will not pass until there is an invigorating autumn of freedom and equality.

1. King (1929–1968) delivered this speech in front of the Lincoln Memorial on August 28, 1963, at the March on Washington, D.C., for Civil Rights.

Nineteen sixty-three is not an end, but a beginning. And those who hope that the Negro needed to blow off steam and will now be content, will have a rude awakening if the nation returns to business as usual.

There will be neither rest nor tranquility in America until the Negro is granted his citizenship rights. The whirlwinds of revolt will continue to shake the foundations of our nation until the bright day of justice emerges.

But there is something that I must say to my people who stand on the warm threshold which leads into the palace of justice. In the process of gaining our rightful place we must not be guilty of wrongful deeds.

Let us not seek to satisfy our thirst for freedom by drinking from the cup of bitterness and hatred. We must forever conduct our struggle on the high plane of dignity and discipline. We must not allow our creative protest to degenerate into physical violence. Again and again we must rise to the majestic heights of meeting physical force with soul force.

The marvelous new militancy which has engulfed the Negro community must not lead us to a distrust of all white people, for many of our white brothers, as evidenced by their presence here today, have come to realize that their destiny is tied up with our destiny and they have come to realize that their freedom is inextricably bound to our freedom. This offense we share mounted to storm the battlements of injustice must be carried forth by a biracial army. We cannot walk alone.

And as we walk, we must make the pledge that we shall always march ahead. We cannot turn back. There are those who are asking the devotees of civil rights, "When will you be satisfied?" We can never be satisfied as long as the Negro is the victim of the unspeakable horrors of police brutality.

We can never be satisfied as long as our bodies, heavy with fatigue of travel, cannot gain lodging in the motels of the highways and the hotels of the cities. We cannot be satisfied as long as the Negro's basic mobility is from a smaller ghetto to a larger one.

We can never be satisfied as long as our children are stripped of their selfhood and robbed of their dignity by signs stating "for whites only." We cannot be satisfied as long as a Negro in Mississippi cannot vote and a Negro in New York believes he has nothing for which to vote. No, we are not satisfied, and we will not be satisfied until justice rolls down like waters and righteousness like a mighty stream.

I am not unmindful that some of you have come here out of excessive trials and tribulation. Some of you have come fresh from narrow jail cells. Some of you have come from areas where your quest for freedom left you battered by the storms of persecution and staggered by the winds of police brutality. You have been the veterans of creative suffering. Continue to work with the faith that unearned suffering is redemptive.

Go back to Mississippi; go back to Alabama; go back to South Carolina; go back to Georgia; go back to Louisiana; go back to the slums and ghettos of the northern cities, knowing that somehow this situation can, and will be changed. Let us not wallow in the valley of despair.

So I say to you, my friends that even though we must face the difficulties of today and tomorrow, I still have a dream. It is a dream deeply rooted in the American dream that one day this nation will rise up and live out the true meaning of its creed—we hold these truths to be self-evident, that all men are created equal.

I have a dream that one day on the red hills of Georgia, sons of former slaves and sons of former slave-owners will be able to sit down together at the table of brotherhood.

I have a dream that one day, even the state of Mississippi, a state sweltering with the heat of injustice, sweltering with the heat of oppression, will be transformed into an oasis of freedom and justice.

I have a dream my four little children will one day live in a nation where they will not be judged by the color of their skin but by content of their character. I have a dream today!

I have a dream that one day, down in Alabama, with its vicious racists, with its governor having his lips dripping with the words of interposition and nullification, that one day, right there in Alabama, little black boys and black girls will be able to join hands with little white boys and white girls as sisters and brothers. I have a dream today!

I have a dream that one day every valley shall be exalted, every hill and mountain shall be made low, the rough places shall be made plain, and the crooked places shall be made straight and the glory of the Lord will be revealed and all flesh shall see it together.[2]

This is our hope. This is the faith that I go back to the South with.

With this faith we will be able to hear out of the mountain of despair a stone of hope. With this faith we will be able to transform the jangling discords of our nation into a beautiful symphony of brotherhood.

With this faith we will be able to work together, to pray together, to struggle together, to go to jail together, to stand up for freedom together, knowing that we will be free one day. This will be the day when all of God's children will be able to sing with new meaning—"my country 'tis of thee; sweet land of liberty; of thee I sing; land where my fathers died, land of the pilgrim's pride; from every mountain side, let freedom ring"—and if America is to be a great nation, this must become true.

So let freedom ring from the prodigious hilltops of New Hampshire.

Let freedom ring from the mighty mountains of New York.

Let freedom ring from the heightening Alleghenies of Pennsylvania.

Let freedom ring from the snow-capped Rockies of Colorado.

Let freedom ring from the curvaceous slopes of California.

But not only that.

Let freedom ring from Stone Mountain of Georgia.

Let freedom ring from Lookout Mountain of Tennessee.

Let freedom ring from every hill and molehill of Mississippi, from every mountainside, let freedom ring.

And when we allow freedom to ring, when we let it ring from every village and hamlet, from every state and city, we will be able to speed up that day when all of God's children—black men and white men, Jews and Gentiles, Catholics and Protestants—will be able to join hands and to sing in

---

2. Isaiah 40:4–5: "Every valley shall be exalted, and every mountain and hill shall be made low: and the crooked shall be made straight, and the rough places plain: and the glory of the Lord shall be revealed, and all flesh shall see it together."

the words of the old Negro spiritual, "Free at last, free at last; thank God Almighty, we are free at last."

I've Been to the Mountaintop [1]

Thank you very kindly, my friends. As I listened to Ralph Abernathy [2] in his eloquent and generous introduction and then thought about myself, I wondered who he was talking about. It's always good to have your closest friend and associate say something good about you. And Ralph is the best friend that I have in the world.

I'm delighted to see each of you here tonight in spite of a storm warning. You reveal that you are determined to go on anyhow. Something is happening in Memphis, something is happening in our world.

You know, if I were standing at the beginning of time, with the possibility of general and panoramic view of the whole human history up to now, and the Almighty said to me, "Martin Luther King, which age would you like to live in?"—I would take my mental flight by Egypt through, or rather across the Red Sea, through the wilderness on toward the promised land. And in spite of its magnificence, I wouldn't stop there. I would move on by Greece, and take my mind to Mount Olympus. And I would see Plato, Aristotle, Socrates, Euripides and Aristophanes assembled around the Parthenon as they discussed the great and eternal issues of reality.

But I wouldn't stop there. I would go on, even to the great heyday of the Roman Empire. And I would see developments around there, through various emperors and leaders. But I wouldn't stop there. I would even come up to the day of the Renaissance, and get a quick picture of all that the Renaissance did for the cultural and esthetic life of man. But I wouldn't stop there. I would even go by the way that the man for whom I'm named had his habitat. And I would watch Martin Luther as he tacked his ninety-five theses on the door at the church in Wittenberg.

But I wouldn't stop there. I would come on up even to 1863, and watch a vacillating president by the name of Abraham Lincoln finally come to the conclusion that he had to sign the Emancipation Proclamation. But I wouldn't stop there. I would even come up to the early thirties, and see a man grappling with the problems of the bankruptcy of his nation. And come with an eloquent cry that we have nothing to fear but fear itself.

But I wouldn't stop there. Strangely enough, I would turn to the Almighty, and say, "If you allow me to live just a few years in the second half of the twentieth century, I will be happy." Now that's a strange statement to make, because the world is all messed up. The nation is sick. Trouble is in the land. Confusion all around. That's a strange statement. But I know, somehow, that only when it is dark enough, can you see the stars. And I see God working in this period of the twentieth century in a way that men, in some strange way, are responding—something is happening in our world.

1. King delivered this sermon, his last, on April 3, 1968, at the Bishop Charles Mason Temple in Memphis, Tennessee, on behalf of the city's largely black body of sanitation workers, who were pressing for higher wages and an end to maltreatment by white supervisors. King was assassinated on the following day.
2. Civil rights leader (1926–1990).

The masses of people are rising up. And wherever they are assembled today, whether they are in Johannesburg, South Africa: Nairobi, Kenya; Accra, Ghana; New York City; Atlanta, Georgia; Jackson, Mississippi; or Memphis, Tennessee—the cry is always the same—"We want to be free."

And another reason that I'm happy to live in this period is that we have been forced to a point where we're going to have to grapple with the problems that men have been trying to grapple with through history, but the demands didn't force them to do it. Survival demands that we grapple with them. Men, for years now, have been talking about war and peace. But now, no longer can they just talk about it. It is no longer a choice between violence and nonviolence in this world; it's nonviolence or nonexistence.

That is where we are today. And also in the human rights revolution, if something isn't done, and in a hurry, to bring the colored peoples of the world out of their long years of poverty, their long years of hurt and neglect, the whole world is doomed. Now, I'm just happy that God has allowed me to live in this period, to see what is unfolding. And I'm happy that he's allowed me to be in Memphis.

I can remember, I can remember when Negroes were just going around as Ralph has said, so often, scratching where they didn't itch, and laughing when they were not tickled. But that day is all over. We mean business now, and we are determined to gain our rightful place in God's world.

And that's all this whole thing is about. We aren't engaged in any negative protest and in any negative arguments with anybody. We are saying that we are determined to be men. We are determined to be people. We are saying that we are God's children. And that we don't have to live like we are forced to live.

Now, what does all of this mean in this great period of history? It means that we've got to stay together. We've got to stay together and maintain unity. You know, whenever Pharaoh wanted to prolong the period of slavery in Egypt, he had a favorite, favorite formula for doing it. What was that? He kept the slaves fighting among themselves. But whenever the slaves get together, something happens in Pharaoh's court, and he cannot hold the slaves in slavery. When the slaves get together, that's the beginning of getting out of slavery. Now let us maintain unity.

Secondly, let us keep the issues where they are. The issue is injustice. The issue is the refusal of Memphis to be fair and honest in its dealings with its public servants, who happen to be sanitation workers. Now, we've got to keep attention on that. That's always the problem with a little violence. You know what happened the other day, and the press dealt only with the window-breaking. I read the articles. They very seldom got around to mentioning the fact that one thousand, three hundred sanitation workers were on strike, and that Memphis is not being fair to them, and that Mayor Loeb[3] is in dire need of a doctor. They didn't get around to that.

Now we're going to march again, and we've got to march again, in order to put the issue where it is supposed to be. And force everybody to see that there are thirteen hundred of God's children here suffering, sometimes going hungry, going through dark and dreary nights wondering how this

3. Henry Loeb, mayor of Memphis (1960–63, 1968–71).

thing is going to come out. That's the issue. And we've got to say to the nation: we know it's coming out. For when people get caught up with that which is right and they are willing to sacrifice for it, there is no stopping point short of victory.

We aren't going to let any mace stop us. We are masters in our nonviolent movement in disarming police forces; they don't know what to do. I've seen them so often. I remember in Birmingham, Alabama, when we were in that majestic struggle there we would move out of the 16th Street Baptist Church day after day; by the hundreds we would move out. And Bull Connor [1] would tell them to send the dogs forth and they did come; but we just went before the dogs singing, "Ain't gonna let nobody turn me round." Bull Connor next would say, "Turn the fire hoses on." And as I said to you the other night, Bull Connor didn't know history. He knew a kind of physics that somehow didn't relate to the transphysics that we knew about. And that was the fact that there was a certain kind of fire that no water could put out. And we went before the fire hoses; we had known water. If we were Baptist or some other denomination, we had been immersed. If we were Methodist, and some others, we had been sprinkled, but we knew water.

That couldn't stop us. And we just went on before the dogs and we would look at them; and we'd go on before the water hoses and we would look at it, and we'd just go on singing "Over my head I see freedom in the air." And then we would be thrown in the paddy wagons, and sometimes we were stacked in there like sardines in a can. And they would throw us in, and old Bull would say, "Take them off," and they did; and we would just go in the paddy wagon singing, "We Shall Overcome." And every now and then we'd get in the jail, and we'd see the jailers looking through the windows being moved by our prayers, and being moved by our words and our songs. And there was a power there which Bull Connor couldn't adjust to: and so we ended up transforming Bull into a steer, and we won our struggle in Birmingham.

Now we've got to go on in Memphis just like that. I call upon you to be with us Monday. Now about injunctions: We have an injunction and we're going into court tomorrow morning to fight this illegal, unconstitutional injunction. All we say to America is, "Be true to what you said on paper." If I lived in China or even Russia, or any totalitarian country, maybe I could understand the denial of certain basic First Amendment privileges, because they hadn't committed themselves to that over there. But somewhere I read of the freedom of assembly. Somewhere I read of the freedom of speech. Somewhere I read of the freedom of the press. Somewhere I read that the greatness of America is the right to protest for right. And so just as I say, we aren't going to let any injunction turn us around. We are going on. We need all of you. And you know what's beautiful to me, is to see all of these ministers of the Gospel. It's a marvelous picture. Who is it that is supposed to articulate the longings and aspirations of the people more than the preacher? Somehow the preacher must be an Amos, and say, "Let justice roll down like waters and righteousness like a mighty stream." Some-

---

4. Eugene "Bull" Connor, Birmingham's Commissioner of Public Safety, who repeatedly tangled with civil rights workers during demonstrations and marches.

how, the preacher must say with Jesus, "The spirit of the Lord is upon me, because he hath anointed me to deal with the problems of the poor."

And I want to commend the preachers, under the leadership of these noble men: James Lawson, one who has been in this struggle for many years; he's been to jail for struggling, but he's still going on, fighting for the rights of his people. Rev. Ralph Jackson, Billy Kiles; I could just go right on down the list, but time will not permit. But I want to thank them all. And I want you to thank them, because so often, preachers aren't concerned about anything but themselves. And I'm always happy to see a relevant ministry.

It's alright to talk about "long white robes over yonder," in all of its symbolism. But ultimately people want some suits and dresses and shoes to wear down here. It's alright to talk about "streets flowing with milk and honey," but God has commanded us to be concerned about the slums down here, and his children who can't eat three square meals a day. It's alright to talk about the new Jerusalem, but one day, God's preacher must talk about the New York, the new Atlanta, the new Philadelphia, the new Los Angeles, the new Memphis, Tennessee. This is what we have to do.

Now the other thing we'll have to do is this: Always anchor our external direct action with the power of economic withdrawal. Now, we are poor people, individually, we are poor when you compare us with white society in America. We are poor. Never stop and forget that collectively, that means all of us together, collectively we are richer than all the nations in the world, with the exception of nine. Did you ever think about that? After you leave the United States, Soviet Russia, Great Britain, West Germany, France, and I could name the others, the Negro collectively is richer than most nations of the world. We have an annual income of more than thirty billion dollars a year, which is more than all of the exports of the United States, and more than the national budget of Canada. Did you know that? That's power right there, if we know how to pool it.

We don't have to argue with anybody. We don't have to curse and go around acting bad with our words. We don't need any bricks and bottles, we don't need any Molotov cocktails, we just need to go around to these stores, and to these massive industries in our country, and say, "God sent us by here, to say to you that you're not treating his children right. And we've come by here to ask you to make the first item on your agenda—fair treatment, where God's children are concerned. Now, if you are not prepared to do that, we do have an agenda that we must follow. And our agenda calls for withdrawing economic support from you."

And so, as a result of this, we are asking you tonight, to go out and tell your neighbors not to buy Coca-Cola in Memphis. Go by and tell them not to buy Sealtest milk. Tell them not to buy—what is the other bread?—Wonder Bread. And what is the other bread company, Jesse? Tell them not to buy Hart's bread. As Jesse Jackson has said, up to now, only the garbage men have been feeling pain; now we must kind of redistribute the pain. We are choosing these companies because they haven't been fair in their hiring policies; and we are choosing them because they can begin the process of saying, they are going to support the needs and the rights of these men who are on strike. And then they can move on downtown and tell Mayor Loeb to do what is right.

But not only that, we've got to strengthen black institutions. I call upon you to take your money out of the banks downtown and deposit your money in Tri-State Bank—we want a "bank-in" movement in Memphis. So go by the savings and loan association. I'm not asking you something that we don't do ourselves at SCLC. Judge Hooks and others will tell you that we have an account here in the savings and loan association from the Southern Christian Leadership Conference. We're just telling you to follow what we're doing. Put your money there. You have six or seven black insurance companies in Memphis. Take out your insurance there. We want to have an "insurance-in."

Now these are some practical things we can do. We begin the process of building a greater economic base. And at the same time, we are putting pressure where it really hurts. I ask you to follow through here.

Now, let me say as I move to my conclusion that we've got to give ourselves to this struggle until the end. Nothing would be more tragic than to stop at this point, in Memphis. We've got to see it through. And when we have our march, you need to be there. Be concerned about your brother. You may not be on strike. But either we go up together, or we go down together.

Let us develop a kind of dangerous unselfishness. One day a man came to Jesus; and he wanted to raise some questions about some vital matters in life. At points, he wanted to trick Jesus, and show him that he knew a little more than Jesus knew and through this, throw him off base. Now that question could have easily ended up in a philosophical and theological debate. But Jesus immediately pulled that question from mid-air, and placed it on a dangerous curve between Jerusalem and Jericho. And he talked about a certain man, who fell among thieves. You remember that a Levite and a priest passed by on the other side. They didn't stop to help him. And finally a man of another race came by. He got down from his beast, decided not to be compassionate by proxy. But with him, administered first aid, and helped the man in need. Jesus ended up saying, this was the good man, this was the great man, because he had the capacity to project the "I" into the "thou," and to be concerned about his brother. Now you know, we use our imagination a great deal to try to determine why the priest and the Levite didn't stop. At times we say they were busy going to a church meeting—an ecclesiastical gathering—and they had to get on down to Jerusalem so they wouldn't be late for their meeting. At other times we would speculate that there was a religious law that "One who was engaged in religious ceremonials was not to touch a human body twenty-four hours before the ceremony." And every now and then we begin to wonder whether maybe they were not going down to Jerusalem, or down to Jericho, rather to organize a "Jericho Road Improvement Association." That's a possibility. Maybe they felt that it was better to deal with the problem from the causal root, rather than to get bogged down with an individual effort.

But I'm going to tell you what my imagination tells me. It's possible that these men were afraid. You see, the Jericho road is a dangerous road. I remember when Mrs. King and I were first in Jerusalem. We rented a car and drove from Jerusalem down to Jericho. And as soon as we got on that road, I said to my wife, "I can see why Jesus used this as a setting for his parable." It's a winding, meandering road. It's really conducive for ambushing. You start out in Jerusalem, which is about 1200 miles, or rather 1200 feet above sea level. And by the time you get down to Jericho, fifteen or twenty minutes later, you're about 2200 feet below sea level. That's a dangerous road. In the days of Jesus it came to be known as the "Bloody Pass." And you know, it's possible that the priest and the Levite looked over that man on the ground and wondered if the robbers were still around. Or it's possible that they felt that the man on the ground was merely faking. And he was acting like he had been robbed and hurt, in order to seize them over there, lure them there for quick and easy seizure. And so the first question that the Levite asked was, "If I stop to help this man, what will happen to me?" But then the Good Samaritan came by. And he reversed the question: "If I do not stop to help this man, what will happen to him?"

That's the question before you tonight. Not, "If I stop to help the sanitation workers, what will happen to all of the hours that I usually spend in my office every day and every week as a pastor?" The question is not, "If I stop to help this man in need, what will happen to me?" "If I do not stop to help the sanitation workers, what will happen to them?" That's the question.

Let us rise up tonight with a greater readiness. Let us stand with a greater determination. And let us move on in these powerful days, these days of challenge to make America what it ought to be. We have an opportunity to make America a better nation. And I want to thank God, once more, for allowing me to be here with you.

You know, several years ago, I was in New York City autographing the first book that I had written. And while sitting there autographing books, a demented black woman came up. The only question I heard from her was, "Are you Martin Luther King?"

And I was looking down writing, and I said yes. And the next minute I felt something beating on my chest. Before I knew it I had been stabbed by this demented woman. I was rushed to Harlem Hospital. It was a dark Saturday afternoon. And that blade had gone through, and the X-rays revealed that the tip of the blade was on the edge of my aorta, the main artery. And once that's punctured, you drown in your own blood—that's the end of you.

It came out in the New York Times the next morning, that if I had sneezed, I would have died. Well, about four days later, they allowed me, after the operation, after my chest had been opened, and the blade had been taken out, to move around in the wheel chair in the hospital. They allowed me to read some of the mail that came in, and from all over the states, and the world, kind letters came in. I read a few, but one of them I will never forget. I had received one from the President and the Vice-President. I've forgotten what those telegrams said. I'd received a visit and a letter from the Governor of New York, but I've forgotten what the letter said. But there was another letter that came from a little girl, a young girl who was a student at the White Plains High School. And I looked at that letter, and I'll never forget it. It said simply, "Dear Dr. King: I am a ninth-grade student at the White Plains High School." She said, "While it should not matter, I would like to mention that I am a white girl. I read in the paper of your misfortune, and of your suffering. And I read that if you had sneezed, you would have died. And I'm simply writing you to say that I'm so happy that you didn't sneeze."

And I want to say tonight, I want to say that I am happy that I didn't sneeze. Because if I had sneezed, I wouldn't have been around here in 1960, when students all over the South started sitting-in at lunch counters. And I knew that as they were sitting in, they were really standing up for the best in the American dream. And taking the whole nation back to those great walls of democracy which were dug deep by the Founding Fathers in the Declaration of Independence and the Constitution. If I had sneezed, I wouldn't have been around in 1962, when Negroes in Albany, Georgia, decided to straighten their backs up. And whenever men and women straighten their backs up, they are going somewhere, because a man can't ride your back unless it is bent. If I had sneezed, I wouldn't have been here in 1963, when the black people of Birmingham, Alabama, aroused the conscience of this nation, and brought into being the Civil Rights Bill. If I had sneezed, I wouldn't have had a chance later that year, in August, to try to tell America about a dream that I had had. If I had sneezed, I wouldn't have been down in Selma, Alabama, to see the great movement there. If I had sneezed, I wouldn't have been in Memphis to see a community rally around those brothers and sisters who are suffering. I'm so happy that I didn't sneeze.

And they were telling me, now it doesn't matter now. It really doesn't matter what happens now. I left Atlanta this morning, and as we got started on the plane, there were six of us, the pilot said over the public address system, "We are sorry for the delay, but we have Dr. Martin Luther King on the plane. And to be sure that all of the bags were checked, and to be sure that nothing would be wrong with the plane, we had to check out everything carefully. And we've had the plane protected and guarded all night."

And then I got into Memphis. And some began to say the threats, or talk about the threats that were out. What would happen to me from some of our sick white brothers?

Well, I don't know what will happen now. We've got some difficult days ahead. But it doesn't matter with me now. Because I've been to the mountaintop. And I don't mind. Like anybody, I would like to live a long life. Longevity has its place. But I'm not concerned about that now. I just want to do God's will. And He's allowed me to go up to the mountain. And I've looked over. And I've seen the promised land. I may not get there with you. But I want you to know tonight, that we, as a people, will get to the promised land. And I'm happy, tonight. I'm not worried about anything. I'm not fearing any man. Mine eyes have seen the glory of the coming of the Lord.

MALCOLM X

The Ballot or the Bullet[1]•

Brothers and sisters and friends, and I see some enemies.

In fact I think we'd be fooling ourselves if we had an audience this large and didn't realize that there were some enemies present.

This afternoon, we want to talk about *The Ballot or the Bullet. The Ballot or the Bullet* explains itself. But before we get into it, since this is the year of the ballot or the bullet, I would like to clarify some things that refer to me, personally, concerning my own personal position. I'm still a Muslim, that is my religion is still Islam.

My religion is still Islam. I still credit Mr. Muhammad for what I know and what I am. He's the one who opened my eyes. At present I am the minister of the newly founded Muslim Mosque Incorporated, which has its offices in the Theresa Hotel, right in that heart of Harlem—that's the black belt in New York City. And when we realize that Adam Clayton Powell[2] is a Christian minister, he heads the Abyssinian Baptist Church, but at the same time, he's more famous for his political struggling. And Dr. King[3] is a Christian minister from Atlanta, Georgia—or in Atlanta, Georgia—but he's become more famous for being involved in the Civil Rights struggle. The same as they are Christian ministers, I'm a Muslim minister. And I don't believe in fighting today in any one front, but on all fronts.

In fact I'm a black nationalist freedom fighter.

Islam is my religion, but I believe my religion is my personal business. It governs my personal life and my personal morals. And my religious philosophy is personal between me and the God in whom I believe—just as the religious philosophy of these others is between them and the God in whom they believe. And this is best this way. Were we to come out here discussing religion, we'd have too many differences from the out-start, and we could never get together. So today, though Islam is my religious philosophy, my political, economic, and social philosophy is black nationalism. As I say, if we bring up religion, we'll have differences, we'll have arguments, we'll never be able to get together. But if we keep our religion at home, keep our religion in the closet, keep our religion between ourselves and our God, but when we come out here, we have a fight that is common to all of us against a enemy who is common to all of us.

The political philosophy of black nationalism only means that the black man should control the politics and the politicians in his own community. The time when white people can come in our community, and get us to vote for them so that they can be our political leaders and tell us what to do

1. After his break with Black Muslim leader Elijah Muhammad in 1964, Malcolm X (1925–1965) spoke with more forthrightness about politics in the United States. That year, he delivered versions of this speech many times, in New York, Cleveland, and Detroit. He gave this particular version in De- troit on April 14, 1964, at a rally sponsored by the Group on Advanced Leadership (GOAL).
2. Congressional representative from New York (1945–70).
3. Martin Luther King.

and what not to do is long gone. Those days are gone. By the same token, the time when that same white man, knowing that your eyes are too far open, can send another Negro into the community and get you and me to support him, so he can use him to lead us astray, those days are long gone, too.

The political philosophy of black nationalism only means that if you and I are going to live in a black community—and that's where we're going to live, 'cause soon as you move out of the black community into their community it's mixed for a period of time, but they're gone and you're right there by yourself again.

We must, we must understand the politics of our community. And we must know what politics is supposed to produce. We must know what part politics play in our lives. And until we become politically mature, we will always be misled, led astray, or deceived, or maneuvered into supporting someone politically who doesn't have the good of our community at heart.

So the political philosophy of black nationalism only means that we will have to carry on a program, a political program, of re-education, to open our people's eyes, make us become more politically conscious, politically mature. And then whenever we get ready to cast our ballot, that ballot will be cast for a man of the community who has the good of the community at heart.

The economic philosophy of black nationalism only means that we should own and operate and control the economy of our community. You can't open up a black store in a white community; the white man won't even patronize you. And he's not wrong, he's got sense enough to look out for himself. It's you, it's you who don't have sense enough to look out for yourself.

The white man is too intelligent to let someone else come and gain control of the economy of his community. But you will let anybody come in and control the economy of your community—control the housing, control the education, control the jobs, control the businesses—under the pretext that you want to integrate. Naw, you're out of your mind.

The economic philosophy of black nationalism only means that we have to become involved in a program of re-education, to educate our people into the importance of knowing that when you spend your dollar out of the community in which you live, the community in which you spend your money becomes richer and richer. The community out of which you take your money becomes poorer and poorer. And because these Negroes who have been misled and misguided are breaking their necks to take their money and spend it with the man, the man is becoming richer and richer and you're becoming poorer and poorer. And then what happens? The community in which you live becomes a slum. It becomes a ghetto. The conditions become run down. And then you have the audacity to complain about poor housing in a run-down community. Why, you run it down yourself, when you take your dollar out.

And you and I are in a double trap because, not only do we lose by taking our money someplace else and spending it, when we try and spend it in *our own* community, we're trapped because we haven't had sense enough to set up stores and control the businesses of our community. The man who's controlling the stores in our community is a man who doesn't look like we do. He's a man who doesn't even live in the community. So you and I, even when we try and spend our money in the block where we live, or the area where we live, we're spending it with a man who when the sun goes down takes that basket full of money in another part of the town.

So we're trapped. Trapped. Double trapped. Triple trapped. Any way we go, we find that we're trapped. And any kind of solution that someone comes up with is just another trap. But the economic philosophy of black nationalism shows our people the importance of setting up these little stores, and developing them and expanding them into larger operations. Woolworth didn't start out big like they are today. They started out with a dime store and expanded and expanded and then expanded until today, they're all over the country and all over the world and they're getting some of everybody's money. Now, this is what you and I—General Motors, the same way, didn't start out like it is. It started out like a little rat-race type operation, and it expanded and it expanded until today it is where it is right now. And you and I have to make a start. And the best place to start is right in the community where we live.

So our people not only have to be re-educated to the importance of supporting black business, but the black man himself has to be made aware of the importance of going into business. And once you and I go into business, we own and operate *at least* the businesses in our community, what we will be doing is developing a situation wherein we will actually be able to create employment for the people in the community. And once you can create some employment in the community where you live, it will eliminate the necessity of you and me having to act ignorantly and disgracefully, boycotting and picketing some cracker someplace else, trying to beg him for a job.

Anytime you have to rely upon your enemy for a job, you're in bad shape.

He is your enemy. You wouldn't be in this country if some enemy hadn't kidnapped you and brought you here.

On the other hand, some of you think you came here on the *Mayflower*.

So, as you can see, brothers and sisters, today, this afternoon, it's not our intention to discuss religion. We're going to forget religion. If we bring up religion, we'll be in an argument. And the best way to keep away from arguments and differences, as I said earlier . . . put your religion at home, in the closet. Keep it between you and your God. Because if it hasn't done anything more for you than it has, you need to forget it anyway.

Whether you are a Christian or a Muslim or a Nationalist, we all have the same problem. They don't hang you because you're a Baptist, they hang you 'cause you're black. They don't attack me because I'm a Muslim, they attack me 'cause I'm black. They attack all of us for the same reason. All of us catch hell from the same enemy. We're all in the same bag. In the same boat. We suffer political oppression. Economic exploitation. And social degradation. All of 'em from the same enemy. The government has failed us. You can't deny that. Anytime you're living in the twentieth century, and you're walking around here singing "We Shall Overcome," the government has failed us.

This is part of what's wrong with you. You do too much singing. Today, it's time to stop singing and start swinging.

You can't sing up on freedom. But you can *swing* up on some freedom. Cassius Clay[4] can sing. But singing didn't help him to become the heavyweight champion of the world. *Swinging* helped him become the heavyweight champion of the world.

So this government has failed us. The government itself has failed us. And the white liberals, who have been posing as our friends, have failed us. And once we see that all these other sources to which we've turned have failed, we stop turning to them and turn to ourselves. We need a self-help program. A do-it-yourself philosophy. A do-it-right-now philosophy. A it's-already-too-late philosophy. This is what you and I need to get with. And the only way we're going to solve our problem is with a self-help program. Before we can get a self-help program started, we have to have a self-help philosophy. Black nationalism is a self-help philosophy. What's so good about it, you can stay right in the church where you are and still take black nationalism as your philosophy. You can stay in any kind of civic organization that you belong to and still take black nationalism as your philosophy. You can be an atheist and still take black nationalism as your philosophy. This is a philosophy that eliminates the necessity for division and argument. Because if you are black, you should be thinking black. And if you're a black, and you're not thinking black at this late date, why, I'm sorry for you.

Once you change your philosophy, you change your thought pattern. Once you change your thought pattern, you change your attitude. Once you change your attitude, it changes your behavior pattern. And then you go on into some action. As long as you got a sit-down philosophy, you'll have a sit-down thought pattern. And as long as you think that old sit-down thought, you'll be in some kind of sit-down action. They'll have you sitting-in everywhere.

It's not so good to refer to what you're going to do as a sit-in. Then right there it castrates you. Right there it brings you down. What goes with it? Think of the image of someone sitting. An old woman can sit. An old man can sit. A chump can sit. A coward can sit. Anything can sit. For you and I have been *sitting* long enough and it's time today for you and I to be doing some *standing*. And some *fighting* to back that up.

When we look at other parts of this earth in which we live, we find that black, brown, red and yellow people in Africa and Asia are getting their independence. They're not getting it by singing "We Shall Overcome." No, they're getting it through *nationalism*. It is nationalism that brought about the independence of the people in Asia. Every nation in Asia gained its independence through the philosophy of nationalism. Every nation on the African continent that has gotten its independence brought it about through the philosophy of nationalism. And it will take *black* nationalism to bring about the freedom of twenty-two million Afro-Americans here in this country where we have suffered *colonialism* for the past four hundred years.

4. Prizefighter who, in 1964, took the name Muhammad Ali.

America is just as much a colonial power as England ever was. America is just as much a colonial power as France ever was. In fact, America is more so a colonial power than they. Because she's a hypocritical colonial power behind it. What do you call second class citizenship? Why, that's colonization. Second-class citizenship is nothing but twentieth-century slavery. How are you going to tell me you're a second-class citizen? They don't have second class citizenship in any other government on this earth. They just have slaves and people who are free. Well, this country is a hypocrite. They try and make you think they set you free by calling you a second class citizen. Naw, you're nothing but a twentieth-century slave.

Just as it took nationalism to remove colonialism from Asia and Africa, it'll take black nationalism today to remove colonialism from the backs and the minds of twenty-two million Afro-Americans here in this country. Looks like it might be the year of the ballot or the bullet.

Why does it look like it might be the year of the ballot or the bullet? Because Negroes have listened to the trickery and the lies and the false promises of the white man now for too long. And they're fed up. They've become disenchanted. They've become disillusioned. They've become dissatisfied. And all of this has built up frustrations in the black community that makes the black community throughout America today more explosive than all of the atomic bombs the Russians can ever invent. Whenever you got a racial powder keg sitting in your lap, you're in more trouble than if you had an atomic power keg sitting in your lap. When a racial powder keg goes off, it doesn't care who it knocks out the way. Understand this: it's dangerous. Because what can the white man use, now, to fool us? After he put down that march on Washington, and you see all through that now. He tricked you, had you marching down to Washington. Yes, had you marching back and forth between the feet of a dead man named Lincoln and another dead man named George Washington, singing "We Shall Overcome."

He made a chump out of you. He made a fool out of you. He made you think you were going somewhere and you end up going nowhere but between Lincoln and Washington.

So today our people are disillusioned. They've become disenchanted. They've become dissatisfied. And in their frustrations they want action. You can see this young black man, this new generation, asking for the ballot or the bullet. That old Uncle Tom action is outdated. The young generation don't want to hear anything about "The odds are against us." What do we care about odds?

When this country here was first being founded, there were thirteen colonies. The whites were colonized. They were fed up with this taxation without representation. So some of them stood up and said "liberty or death." Well, I went to a white school over here in Mason, Michigan. The white man made the mistake of letting me read his history books. He made the mistake of teaching me that Patrick Henry[5] was a patriot. And George Washington—wasn't nothing non-violent about old Pat. Or George Wash-

5. American Revolutionary leader and orator (1736–1799), famous for his pronouncement "Give me liberty or give me death."

ington. "Liberty or death" was what brought about the freedom of whites in this country from the English.

They didn't care about the odds. Why, they faced the wrath of the entire British Empire. And in those days, they used to say that the British Empire was so vast and so powerful that the sun would never set on it. This is how big it was. Yet these thirteen little scrawny states, tired of taxation without representation, tired of being exploited and oppressed and degraded, told that big British Empire, "liberty or death." And here you have twenty-two million Afro-Americans, black people today, catching more hell than Patrick Henry ever saw.

And I'm here to tell you, in case you don't know it, that you got a new, you got a new generation of black people in this country who don't care anything whatsoever about odds. They don't want to hear you old Uncle Tom handkerchief-heads talking about the odds. No.

This is a new generation. If they're going to draft these young black men and send them over to Korea or South Vietnam to face eight hundred million Chinese . . . if you're not afraid of those odds, you shouldn't be afraid of these odds.

Why does this loom to be such an explosive *political* year? Because this is the year of politics. This is the year when all of the white politicians are going to come into the Negro community. You've never seen them until election time. You can't find them until election time. They're going to come in with false promises. And as they make these false promises, they're going to feed our frustrations. And this will only serve to make matters worse. I'm no politician. I'm not even a student of politics. I'm not a Republican nor a Democrat, nor an American. And got sense enough to know it.

I'm one of the twenty-two million black *victims* of the Democrats. One of the twenty-two million black *victims* of the Republicans. And one of the twenty-two million black *victims* of Americanism.

And when I speak, I don't speak as a Democrat, or a Republican, nor an American. I speak as a *victim* of America's so-called democracy. You and I have never seen democracy; all we've seen is hypocrisy. When we open our eyes today and look around America, we see America not through the eyes of someone who has enjoyed the fruits of Americanism, we see America through the eyes of someone who has been the victim of Americanism. We don't see any American dream. We've experienced only the American nightmare.

We haven't benefited from America's democracy. We've only suffered from America's hypocrisy. And the generation that is coming up now can see it, and are not afraid to say it. If you go to jail, so what? If you're black, you were born in jail. In the North as well as the South. Stop talking about the South. Long as you're south of the Canadian border, you're South.

Don't call Governor Wallace a Dixie governor; *Romney*[6] is a Dixie governor.

Twenty-two million black victims of Americanism are waking up. And

6. George Romney, governor of Michigan (1963–69). George Wallace, segregationist governor of Alabama (1963–66, 1971–79).

they're gaining a new political consciousness, becoming politically mature. And as they develop this political maturity, they are able to see the recent trends in these political elections. They see that the whites are so evenly divided that every time they vote, the race is so close, they have to go back and count the votes all over again. Which means that any block, any minority that has a block of votes that stick together is in a strategic position. Either way you go, that's who gets it. You're in a position to determine who'll go to the White House and who'll stay in the dog house.

You're the one who has that power. You can keep Johnson in Washington, D.C. or you can send him back to his Texas cotton patch.

You're the one who sent Kennedy to Washington. You're the one who put the present Democratic administration in Washington, D.C. The whites were evenly divided. It was the fact that you threw 80 percent of your votes behind the Democrats that put the Democrats in the White House. When you see this, you can see that the Negro vote is the key factor. And despite the fact that you are in a position to be the determining factor, what do you get out of it? The Democrats have been in Washington, D.C., only because of the Negro vote. They've been down there four years. And there, all other legislation they wanted to bring up, they've brought it up and gotten it out of the way, and now they bring up you. And *now* they bring up you. You put them first and they put you last . . . 'cause you're a chump . . . a political chump.

In Washington, D.C., in the House of Representatives, there are 257 who are Democrats. Only 177 are Republican. In the Senate there are 67 Democrats. Only 33 are Republicans. The party that *you* backed controls two-thirds of the House of Representatives and the Senate. And *still* they can't keep their promise to you. 'Cause you're a chump.

Anytime you throw your weight behind a political party that controls two-thirds of the government, and that party can't keep the promise that it made to you during election time, and you're dumb enough to walk around continuing to identify yourself with that party, you're not only a chump but you're a traitor to your race.

And what kind of alibi do they come up with? They try and pass the buck to the Dixiecrats. Now, back during the days when you were blind, deaf, and dumb, ignorant, politically immature, naturally you went along with that. But today, as your eyes come open, and you develop political maturity, you're able to see and think for yourself. And you can see that a Dixiecrat is nothing but a Democrat . . . in disguise.

You look at the structure of the government that controls this country. It's controlled by sixteen senatorial committees and twenty congressional committees. Of the sixteen senatorial committees that run the government, ten of them are in the hands of southern segregationists. Of the twenty congressional committees that run the government, twelve of them are in the hands of southern segregationists. And they going to tell you and me that the South lost the war.

You today are in the hands of a government of segregationists: Racists, white supremacists . . . who belong to the Democratic Party but disguise themselves as Dixiecrats. A Dixiecrat is nothing but a Democrat. Whoever runs the Democrats is also the follower of the Dixiecrats. And the follower of all of them is sitting in the White House.

I say and I say it again: You got a president who's nothing but a southern segregationist. From the state of Texas. They'll lynch you in Texas as quick as they'll lynch you in Mississippi. Only, in Texas, they lynch you with a Texas accent; in Mississippi, they lynch you with a Mississippi accent.

And the first thing the cracker does when he comes in power, he takes all the Negro leaders and invites them for coffee. To show that he's all right. And those Uncle Toms can't pass up the coffee.

They come away from the coffee table, telling you and me that this man is all right. 'Cause he's from the South. And since he's from the South, he can deal with the South. Look at the logic that they're using. What about Eastland? He's from the South. Make him the president. If Johnson[7] is a good man 'cause he's from Texas, and being from Texas will enable him to deal with the South, Eastland can deal with the South better than Johnson.

Naw, I say, you've been misled. You've been had. You been took.

I was in Washington a couple weeks ago—while the senators were filibustering. And I noticed at the back of the Senate a huge map. And on this map, it showed the distribution of Negroes in America. And surprisingly, the same senators that were involved in the filibuster were from the states where there were the most Negroes. Why were they filibustering the civil rights legislation? Because the civil rights legislation is supposed to guarantee voting rights to Negroes in those states. And those senators from those states know that if the Negroes in those states can vote, those senators are down the drain.

The representatives of those states go down the drain. And in the Constitution of this country, it has a stipulation wherein whenever the rights, the voting rights of people in a certain district are violated, then the representative who's from a particular district, according to the Constitution is supposed to be expelled from the Congress. Now, if this particular aspect of the Constitution was enforced, why you wouldn't have a cracker in Washington, D.C.

But what would happen? When you expel the Dixiecrat, you're expelling the Democrat. When you destroy the power of the Dixiecrat, you're destroying the power of the Democratic Party. So how in the world can the Democratic Party in the South actually side with you, in sincerity, when all of this power is based in the South? These northern Democrats are in cahoots with the southern Democrats.

They're playing a giant con game. A political con game. You know how it goes. Whenever one of them comes to you, and make believe he's for you. And he's in cahoots with the other one that's not for you. Why? Because neither one of them is for you. But they got to make you go with one of them or the other. So this is a con game. And this is what they been doing with you and me all these years. First thing Johnson got off the plane, when he became president, he asked, "Where's Dicky?" You know who "Dicky" is? Dicky is old southern cracker Richard Russell.[8] Look a-here! Yes! Lyndon B. Johnson's best friend is the one who is the head, who's heading the forces that are filibustering civil rights legislation. You tell me how in the hell is he going to be Johnson's best friend?

7. Lyndon Johnson, U.S. president (1963–69). James Eastland, U.S. senator from Mississippi (1943–78). 8. Governor of Georgia (1931–33), U.S. Senator from Georgia (1932–71).

How can Johnson be his friend and your friend too? Naw, that man is too tricky. Especially if his friend is still old Dicky.

Whenever the Negroes keep the Democrats in power, they're keeping the Dixiecrats in power. Is this true? A vote for a Democrat is nothing but a vote for a Dixiecrat. I know you don't like me saying that. But I'm not the kind of person who'll come here to say what you like. I'm going to tell you the truth whether you like it or not.

Up here in the North, you have the same thing. The Democratic Party . . . they don't do it that way. They got a thing that they call gerrymandering. They maneuver you out of power. Even though you can vote, they fix it so you're voting for nobody.

They got you going and coming. In the South, they're outright political wolves. In the North they're political foxes. A fox and a wolf are both canine—both belong to the dog family. Now, you take your choice. You going to choose a northern dog or a southern dog? Because either dog you choose, I guarantee you, you'll still be in the doghouse.

This is why I say it's the ballot or the bullet. It's liberty or it's death. It's freedom for everybody or freedom for nobody.

America today finds herself in a unique situation. Historically, revolutions are bloody, oh yes they are. They haven't ever had a blood*less* revolution. Or a non-violent revolution. That don't happen even in Hollywood. You don't have a revolution in which you love your enemy. And you don't have a revolution in which you're begging the system of exploitation to integrate you into it. Revolutions overturn systems. Revolutions destroy systems. A revolution is bloody.

But America is in a unique position. She's the only country in history in a position actually to become involved in a bloodless revolution. The Russian revolution was bloody. The Chinese revolution was bloody. The French revolution was bloody. The Cuban revolution was bloody. And there was nothing more bloody than the American revolution. But today, this country can become involved in a revolution that won't take bloodshed. All she's got to do is give the black man in this country everything that's due him. Everything.

I hope that the white man can see this. 'Cause if you don't see it, you're finished. If you don't see it, you're going to become involved in some action in which you don't have a chance. And we don't care about your atomic bomb, it's useless. Because other countries have atomic bombs. When two or three different countries have atomic bombs, nobody can use it. So it means that the white man today is without a weapon. And if you want some action, you got to come on down to earth. And there's more black people on earth than there are white people on earth.

I only got a couple more minutes. The white man can never win another war on the ground. His days of war victory, his days of ground victory are over. Can I prove it? Yes. Take all the action that's going on on this earth, right now, that he's involved in. Tell me where he's winning. Nowhere. Why some rice farmers, some rice farmers, some rice eaters, ran him out of Korea. Yes, they ran him out of Korea. Rice eaters, with nothing but gym shoes and a rifle and a bowl of rice. Took him and his tanks and his napalm and all that other action he's supposed to have, and ran him 'cross the Yalu.

Why? 'Cause the day that he can win on the ground is past. Up in French Indochina, those little peasants, rice growers, took on the might of the French army. And ran all the Frenchmen—you don't remember Dien Bien Phu???[9] Naw!!! The same thing happened in Algeria, in Africa. They didn't have anything but a rifle. The French had all these highly mechanized instruments of warfare. But they put some guerrilla action on 'em. And a white man can't fight a guerrilla war. Guerrilla action takes heart, takes nerve, and he doesn't have that.

He's brave when he's got tanks. He's brave when he's got planes. He's brave when he's got bombs. He's brave when he's got a whole lot of company along with him. But you take that little man from Africa and Asia, turn him loose in the woods with a blade, with a blade. That's all he needs, all he needs is a blade. And when the sun goes down, and it's dark, it's even-steven.

So it's the ballot or the bullet. Today our people can see that we're faced with a government conspiracy. This government has failed us. The senators who are filibustering concerning your and my rights—that's the government. Don't say it's southern senators. This is the *government*. I his is the *government* filibuster. It's not a segregationist filibuster. It's the *government* filibuster. Any kind of activity that takes place on the floor of the Congress or the Senate, that's the government. Any kind of dilly-dallying, that's the government. Any kind of pussyfooting, that's the government. Any kind of act that's designed to delay or deprive you and me, right now, of getting full rights, that's the government that's responsible. And anytime you find the government involved in a conspiracy, to violate the citizenship, or the civil rights of a people, then you are wasting your time going to that government expecting redress. Instead you have to take that government to the World Court and accuse it of genocide and all of the other crimes that it is guilty of today.

So those of us whose political and economic and social philosophy is black nationalism have become involved in the civil rights struggle, we have injected ourselves into the civil rights struggle, and we intend to expand it from the level of civil rights to the level of human rights. As long as you fight it on the level of civil rights, you're under Uncle Sam's jurisdiction. You're going to his court expecting him to correct the problem. He *created* the problem. He's the criminal. You don't take your case to the criminal. You take your criminal to court.

When the government of South Africa began to trample upon the human rights of the people of South Africa, they were taken to the U.N. When the government of Portugal began to trample upon the rights of our brothers and sisters in Angola, it was taken before the U.N. Why even the white man took the Hungarian question to the U.N. and just this week, Chief Justice Goldberg[1] was crying over three million Jews in Russia about their human rights, charging Russia with violating the U.N. charter, because of its mistreatment of the human rights of Jews in Russia. Now you

---

9. The Vietnamese victory in the battle of Dien Bien Phu (1954) inspired the permanent withdrawal of the French from Indochina and the Geneva Accords of 1954.

1. Arthur Joseph Goldberg, lawyer, associate Supreme Court Justice (1962–65), U.S. representative to the United Nations (1965–68).

tell me, how can the plight of everybody on this earth reach the halls of the United Nations, and you have twenty-two million Afro-Americans whose churches are being bombed? Whose little girls are being murdered. Whose leaders are being shot down in broad daylight. Now you tell me why the leaders of this struggle have never taken it before the United Nations.

So, our next move, is to take the entire civil rights struggle, problem, into the United Nations.

And let the world see that Uncle Sam is guilty of violating the human rights of twenty-two million Afro-Americans and still has the audacity or the nerve to stand up and to represent himself as the leader of the free world.

Not only is he a crook, he's a hypocrite. Here he is, standing up in front of other people, Uncle Sam, with the blood of your and my mothers and fathers on his hands. With the blood dripping down his jaws like a bloody-jawed wolf. And still got the nerve to point his finger at other countries. You can't even get civil rights legislation. And this man has got the nerve to stand up and talk about South Africa. Or talk about Nazi Germany. Or talk about Portugal. Naw, no more days like those.

So I say in my conclusion, the only way we're going to solve it, we got to unite, we got to work together in unity and harmony. And black nationalism is the key. How we going to overcome the tendency to be at each other's throats that always exists in our neighborhood? And the reason this tendency exists—the strategy of the white man has always been divide and conquer. He keeps us divided in order to conquer us. He tells you I'm for separation and you're for integration and keep us fighting with each other. No, I'm not for separation and you're not for integration. What you and I are for is freedom.

Only you think that integration will get you freedom, I think that separation will get me freedom. We both got the same objective. We just both got different ways of getting at it.

So, I studied this man Billy Graham,[2] who preaches white nationalism. That's what he preaches. I say, that's what he preaches. The whole church structure in this country is white nationalism. You go inside a white church, that's what they preaching, white nationalism. They got Jesus white, Mary white, God white, everybody white, that's white nationalism.

So, what he does, the way he circumvents the jealousy and envy that he ordinarily would incur among the heads of the church, whenever you go into an area where the church already is, you going to run into trouble. Because they got that thing, what you call it, syndicated, they got a syndicate, just like the racketeers have. I'm going to say what's on my mind, cause the church, the preachers have already proved to you that they got a syndicate.

And when you're out in the rackets, whenever you're getting in another man's territory, you know, they gang up on you. And that's the same way with you—you run into the same thing. So how Billy Graham gets around that, instead of going into somebody else's territory, like he going to start a new church, he doesn't try to start a church, he just goes in preaching

2. American evangelist (b. 1918).

Christ. And he says, everybody who believes in Him, you go wherever you find Him. So this helps all the churches, and so since it helps all the churches, they don't fight him. Well, we're going to do the same thing, only our gospel is black nationalism. His gospel is white nationalism, our gospel is black nationalism. And the gospel of black nationalism, as I told you, means you should control your own—the politics of your community, the economy of your community, and all of the society in which you live should be under your control. And once you feel that this philosophy will solve your problem, go join any church where that's preached. Don't join a church where white nationalism is preached. Now, you can go to a Negro church and be exposed to white nationalism. 'Cause when you walk in a Negro church and you see a white Jesus and a white Mary and some white angels, that Negro church is preaching white nationalism.

But when you go to a church and you see the pastor of that church with a philosophy and a program that's designed to bring black people together and elevate black people, join that church. Join that church. If you see where the NAACP is preaching and practicing that which is designed to make black nationalism materialize, join the NAACP. Join any kind of organization, civic, religious, fraternal, political, or otherwise, that's based on lifting the black man up and making him master of his own community.

It'll be the ballot or it'll be the bullet. It'll be liberty or it'll be death. And if you're not ready to pay that price, don't use the word freedom in your vocabulary.

One more thing: I was on the program in Illinois recently with Senator Paul Douglas[3] the so-called liberal, the so-called Democrat, the so-called white man. At which time he told me that our African brothers were not interested in us in Africa. He says the Africans are not interested in the American Negro. I knew he was lying. But, during the next two or three weeks, it's my intention and plan to make a tour of our African homeland. And I hope that when I come back I'll be able to come back and let you know how our African brothers and sisters feel toward us.

And I know before I go there, that they love us. We're one. We're the same. It's the same man that colonized them all these years that colonized you and me too, all these years. And all we have to do now is wake up and work in unity and harmony and the battle will be over.

I want to thank the Freedom Now Party in the gold; I want to thank Milton and Richard Henry for inviting me here this afternoon, and also a Reverend Cley. And I want them to know that anything that I can ever do at anytime to work with anybody in any kind of program that is sincerely designed to eliminate the political, the economic, and the social evils that confront all of our people in Detroit and elsewhere, all you've got to do is give me a telephone call, and I'll be on the next jet right on into the city.

Thank you.

3. U.S. senator from Massachusetts (1948–66).

Folktales

In his novel *Train-Whistle Guitar* (1974), Albert Murray introduces a character named Scooter who revels in the rare chances he gets to sit at the front room fireside within earshot of family and neighborhood elders when the mood and moonlight are right for the telling of tales. The novel's setting is black semirural Alabama of the 1920s, but the ritual moment of telling and retelling lifts it into an almost timeless zone. The group's jewels of wisdom (along with some highfalutin talk and sheer nonsense) will be handed around with an attitude that combines high solemnity and playfulness. Elders entertain elders with traditional tales (with topical twists and variations), but no one is unaware of the presence of the eleven-year-old youngster who needs to hear these stories—their styles of telling and their substantive values along with their mysteries and incongruities. Since their arrival in the New World from Africa, the tales have been a key part of the African American's equipment for survival and sustenance.

Many new black arrivals, whether coming in the seventeenth century, the eighteenth, or the nineteenth century, could immediately communicate together using a common creole language that had facilitated commerce back home in Africa. What is clearer than ever now is that the Africans also brought with them a vast storehouse of stories—along with other such expressive forms as songs, dances, styles of worship, games, patterns of adornment, and the like that helped them to maintain on the new continent at least the broad outlines of their original worldview. (These forms were what the blacks had instead of freedom. They had *rites* and not *rights*, as Ralph Ellison once put it; rhythmic freedom if not political freedom, said Cornel West.) Despite the ravages of the Middle Passage and the violence of slavery as an institution, one finds among African Americans story types, characters, motifs, and styles of telling that bear the distinctive traits of south Saharan Africa's ways of making stories. One finds, for example, many kinds of trickster tales (forerunners of the Brer Rabbit cycle) along with tales of metamorphoses and wonder which have distinctive counterparts in the New World.

Before long, African Americans had taken hold of American Indian and Euro-American tales and passed them around the fireside. But whatever the sources—Old or New World; black, white, red—African Americans hammered these myriad tales into unmistakably black American shapes and themes. The voices of the stories (sometimes one story could involve several voices—of Bear, perhaps, or Sis Cat, or Brer Fox—operating in different octaves and vocal timbres) marked them as African American. So did the particular turns of the plot as well as the particular heroes, dupes, and villains, and their values.

This section contains several kinds of tales: animal trickster tales, tales of slave tricksters, tales explaining how things came to be as they are, tales with other lessons about life in the tough briar patch of the United States, and tales where there's simply one darned thing happening after another. All of them invite us along for the narrative ride.

One warning: do not accept any simplistic explanation for the stories' meanings. Watch for the easy interpretation of trickster tales as Weak-but-Cunning Black versus Strong-but-Duller White. This formula often will hold. But then again it will not. Frequently, the "weak" rabbits of these tales are (like tricksters the world over) greedy monsters of selfish pride, dangerously out of sync with their surroundings and fellow creatures. Or the rabbits can be just plain pretentious. In a sense, that is what gets Brer Rabbit into trouble in the famous Tar-Baby Tale: he insists on being addressed with genteel etiquette, and to say the least, the effort fails. Often the rabbits' foes are infinitely more community minded and responsible than the rabbits are. At times, as in tales of Rabbit and Fox, both antagonists are tricksters; in such cases, both may embody characteristics closer to those of the slave holder, as usually imagined, than to those of the slave; certainly, both Rabbit and Fox can serve more as warnings than as exemplars of how to live.

Be aware too that like other oral forms these tales were originally invented not for the printed page but for spoken performance. Something vital is lost when we are not at the fireside with Scooter, hearing the sounds, watching the tellers and their tellings, full of whispery asides, silences, dramatic clicks, calls, and other story sounds. Without being there we miss the sense of the tale as part of a process of verbal exchange that involves audience responses and sometimes a competitive round of tale set against tale. Some of these actual performances would surely have consisted not of complete and finished products but of fragments and loose bits of a familiar yarn handed around in brief before the next talk takes over. Some tales might have been introduced by one teller and finished off by one or more others. Some might have been hooted down before they got off the ground.

Keeping in mind this sense of the tales as part of a performance process, note in particular the entries reported by Zora Neale Hurston, who did her best to let her readers see and hear the work in its complex social and ritual contexts. But even while reading Hurston, remember that she was a literary intellectual who came to the party with pen (and/or tape recorder) in hand; even her best efforts to catch the dancing spirit of the thrice-told tale on paper betray her own sense of life and inevitable identity as something of an outsider.

Because of the unavoidable difficulties of translation from oral to written forms, purity cannot be a central concern in choosing selections. Joel Chandler Harris, the late-nineteenth-century collector, is here with all his bags and baggages as a white southerner of his era. Harris invents his own frame to encase the tales—in his case as stories told by a somewhat stereotyped Uncle Remus to a curious white youngster in his charge. Other literary renderings of the tales, including ones by black writers Zora Neale Hurston and Julius Lester, also are here along with more unvarnished (and in this sense scientific) reports by such scholars as Roger Abrahams. Sometimes the literary renderings of the tales involve phonetical spellings which at first obscure meaning but which—once the reader breaks the code— can help bring the work to life. Sometimes, on the other hand, faithful scientific renderings of the material can lie stillborn on the page. (They may also delight, or offend.) All these efforts are now part of a tradition in which modern readers, like Murray's Scooter, can pull up as close as we can to the flesh and blood and spirit of the tales and their tellers.

All God's Chillen Had Wings [1]

Once all Africans could fly like birds; but owing to their many transgressions, their wings were taken away. There remained, here and there, in the sea islands and out-of-the-way places in the low country, some who had been overlooked, and had retained the power of flight, though they looked like other men.

There was a cruel master on one of the sea islands who worked his people till they died. When they died he bought others to take their places.

---

1. As told by Caesar Grant, of John's Island, carter and laborer. Published in John Bennet's *Doctor to the Dead* (1943, 1946) and in Langston Hughes and Arna Bontemps's *Book of Negro Folklore* (1958). Tales of black flight inspired Toni Morrison's *Song of Solomon* and several other works by African American writers.

These also he killed with overwork in the burning summer sun, through the middle hours of the day, although this was against the law.

One day, when all the worn-out Negroes were dead of overwork, he bought, of a broker in the town, a company of native Africans just brought into the country, and put them at once to work in the cottonfield.

He drove them hard. They went to work at sunrise and did not stop until dark. They were driven with unsparing harshness all day long, men, women and children. There was no pause for rest during the unendurable heat of the midsummer noon, though trees were plenty and near. But through the hardest hours, when fair plantations gave their Negroes rest, this man's driver pushed the work along without a moment's stop for breath, until all grew weak with heat and thirst.

There was among them one young woman who had lately borne a child. It was her first; she had not fully recovered from bearing, and should not have been sent to the field until her strength had come back. She had her child with her, as the other women had, astraddle on her hip, or piggyback.

The baby cried. She spoke to quiet it. The driver could not understand her words. She took her breast with her hand and threw it over her shoulder that the child might suck and be content. Then she went back to chopping knot-grass; but being very weak, and sick with the great heat, she stumbled, slipped and fell.

The driver struck her with his lash until she rose and staggered on.

She spoke to an old man near her, the oldest man of them all, tall and strong, with a forked beard. He replied; but the driver could not understand what they said; their talk was strange to him.

She returned to work; but in a little while she fell again. Again the driver lashed her until she got to her feet. Again she spoke to the old man. But he said: "Not yet, daughter; not yet." So she went on working, though she was very ill.

Soon she stumbled and fell again. But when the driver came running with his lash to drive her on with her work, she turned to the old man and asked: "Is it time yet, daddy?" He answered: "Yes, daughter; the time has come. Go; and peace be with you!" . . . and stretched out his arms toward her . . . so.

With that she leaped straight up into the air and was gone like a bird, flying over field and wood.

The driver and overseer ran after her as far as the edge of the field; but she was gone, high over their heads, over the fence, and over the top of the woods, gone, with her baby astraddle of her hip, sucking at her breast.

Then the driver hurried the rest to make up for her loss; and the sun was very hot indeed. So hot that soon a man fell down. The overseer himself lashed him to his feet. As he got up from where he had fallen the old man called to him in an unknown tongue. My grandfather told me the words that he said; but it was a long time ago, and I have forgotten them. But when he had spoken, the man turned and laughed at the overseer, and leaped up into the air, and was gone, like a gull, flying over field and wood.

Soon another man fell. The driver lashed him. He turned to the old man. The old man cried out to him, and stretched out his arms as he had done for the other two; and he, like them, leaped up, and was gone through the air, flying like a bird over field and wood.

Then the overseer cried to the driver, and the master cried to them both: "Beat the old devil! He is the doer!"

The overseer and the driver ran at the old man with lashes ready; and the master ran too, with a picket pulled from the fence, to beat the life out of the old man who had made those Negroes fly.

But the old man laughed in their faces, and said something loudly to all the Negroes in the field, the new Negroes and the old Negroes.

And as he spoke to them they all remembered what they had forgotten, and recalled the power which once had been theirs. Then all the Negroes, old and new, stood up together; the old man raised his hands; and they all leaped up into the air with a great shout; and in a moment were gone, flying, like a flock of crows, over the field, over the fence, and over the top of the wood; and behind them flew the old man.

The men went clapping their hands; and the women went singing; and those who had children gave them their breasts; and the children laughed and sucked as their mothers flew, and were not afraid.

The master, the overseer, and the driver looked after them as they flew, beyond the wood, beyond the river, miles on miles, until they passed beyond the last rim of the world and disappeared in the sky like a handful of leaves. They were never seen again.

Where they went I do not know; I never was told. Nor what it was that the old man said . . . that I have forgotten. But as he went over the last fence he made a sign in the master's face, and cried "Kuli-ba! Kuli-ba!" I don't know what that means.

But if I could only find the old wood sawyer, he could tell you more; for he was there at the time, and saw the Africans fly away with their women and children. He is an old, old man, over ninety years of age, and remembers a great many strange things.

Big Talk[1]

During slavery time two ole niggers wuz talkin' an' one said tuh de other one, "Ole Massa made me so mad yistiddy till Ah give 'im uh good cussin' out. Man, Ah called 'im everything wid uh handle on it."

De other one says, "You didn't cuss Ole Massa, didja? Good God! Whut did he do tuh you?"

"He didn't do nothin', an' man, Ah laid one cussin' on 'im! Ah'm uh man lak dis, Ah won't stan' no hunchin'. Ah betcha he won't bother me no mo'."

"Well, if you cussed 'im an' he didn't do nothin' tuh you, de nex' time he make me mad Ah'm goin' tuh lay uh hearin' on him."

Nex' day de nigger did somethin'. Ole Massa got in behind 'im and he turnt 'round an' give Ole Massa one good cussin' an Ole Massa had 'im took down and whipped nearly tuh death. Nex' time he saw dat other nigger he says tuh 'im. "Thought you tole me, you cussed Ole Massa out and he never opened his mouf."

"Ah did."

1. From Zora Neale Hurston's *Mules and Men* (1935).

"Well, how come he never did nothin' tuh yuh? Ah did it an' he come nigh uh killin' *me*."

"Man, you didn't go cuss 'im tuh his face, didja?"

"Sho Ah did. Ain't dat whut you tole me you done?"

"Naw, Ah didn't say Ah cussed 'im tuh his face. You sho is crazy. Ah thought you had mo' sense than dat. When Ah cussed Ole Massa he wuz settin' on de front porch an' Ah wuz down at de big gate."

De other nigger wuz mad but he didn't let on. Way after while he 'proached de nigger dat got 'im de beatin' an' tole 'im, "Know whut Ah done tuhday?"

"Naw, whut you done? Give Ole Massa 'nother cussin'?"

"Naw, Ah ain't never goin' do dat no mo'. Ah peeped up under Ole Miss's drawers."

"Man, hush yo' mouf! You knows you ain't looked up under Ole Miss's clothes!"

"Yes, Ah did too. Ah looked right up her very drawers."

"You better hush dat talk! Somebody goin' hear you and Ole Massa'll have you kilt."

"Well, Ah sho done it an' she never done nothin' neither."

"Well, whut did she say?"

"Not uh mumblin' word, an' Ah stopped and looked jus' as long as Ah wanted tuh an' went on 'bout mah business."

"Well, de nex' time Ah see her settin' out on de porch Ah'm goin' tuh look too."

"Help yo'self."

Dat very day Ole Miss wuz settin' out on de porch in de cool uh de evenin' all dressed up in her starchy white clothes. She had her legs all crossed up and de nigger walked up tuh de edge uh de porch and peeped up under Ole Miss's clothes. She took and hollored an' Ole Massa come out an' had dat nigger almost kilt alive.

When he wuz able tuh be 'bout again he said tuh de other nigger; "Thought you tole me you peeped up under Ole Miss's drawers?"

"Ah sho did."

"Well, how come she never done nothin' tuh *you*? She got me nearly kilt."

"Man, when Ah looked under Ole Miss's drawers they wuz hangin' out on de clothes line. You didn't go look up in 'em while she had 'em on, didja? You sho is uh fool! Ah thought you had mo' sense than dat, Ah claire Ah did. It's uh wonder he didn't kill yuh dead. Umph, umph, umph. You sho ain't got no sense atall."

Deer Hunting Story [1]

You know Ole Massa took a nigger deer huntin' and posted him in his place and told him, says: "Now you wait right here and keep yo' gun reformed and ready. Ah'm goin' 'round de hill and skeer up de deer and head him dis way. When he come past, you shoot."

1. From Zora Neale Hurston's *Mules and Men* (1935). Note the deliberate spoofing of the white "Massa" by the ostensibly respectful "nigger."

De nigger says: "Yessuh, Ah sho' will, Massa."

He set there and waited wid de gun all cocked and after a while de deer come tearin' past him. He didn't make a move to shoot de deer so he went on 'bout his business. After while de white man come on 'round de hill and ast de nigger: "Did you kill de deer?"

De nigger says: "Ah ain't seen no deer pass here yet."

Massa says: "Yes, you did. You couldn't help but see him. He come right dis way."

Nigger says: "Well Ah sho' ain't seen none. All Ah seen was a white man come along here wid a pack of chairs on his head and Ah tipped my hat to him and waited for de deer."

How to Write a Letter[1]

Ah know another man wid a daughter.

The man sent his daughter off to school for seben years, den she come home all finished up. So he said to her, "Daughter, git yo' things and write me a letter to my brother!" So she did.

He says, "Head it up," and she done so.

"Now tell 'im, 'Dear Brother, our chile is done come home from school and all finished up and we is very proud of her.' "

Then he ast de girl "Is you got dat?"

She tole 'im "yeah."

"Now tell him some mo'. 'Our mule is dead but Ah got another mule and when Ah say (clucking sound of tongue and teeth) he moved from de word.' "

"Is you got dat?" he ast de girl.

"Naw suh," she tole 'im.

He waited a while and he ast her again, "You got dat down yet?"

"Naw suh, Ah ain't got it yet."

"How come you ain't got it yet?"

"Cause Ah can't spell (clucking sound)."

"You mean to tell me you been off to school seben years and can't spell (clucking sound)? Why Ah could spell dat myself and Ah ain't been to school a day in mah life. Well jes' say (clucking sound) he'll know what yo' mean and go on wid de letter."

" 'Member Youse a Nigger"[1]

Ole John was a slave, you know. Ole Massa and Ole Missy and de two li' children—a girl and a boy.

Well, John was workin' in de field and he seen de children out on de lake in a boat, just a hollerin'. They had done lost they oars and was 'bout to turn over. So then he went and tole Ole Massa and Ole Missy.

Well, Ole Missy, she hollered and said: "It's so sad to lose these 'cause

1. From Zora Neale Hurston's *Mules and Men* (1935). This tale illustrates, among other things, the unwritable dimension of oral materials.

1. From Zora Neale Hurston's *Mules and Men* (1935).

Ah ain't never goin' to have no more children." Ole Massa made her hush and they went down to de water and follered de shore on 'round till they found 'em. John pulled off his shoes and hopped in and swum out and got in de boat wid de children and brought 'em to shore.

Well, Massa and John take 'em to de house. So they was all so glad 'cause de children got saved. So Massa told 'im to make a good crop dat year and fill up de barn, and den when he lay by de crops nex' year, he was going to set him free.

So John raised so much crop dat year he filled de barn and had to put some of it in de house.

So Friday come, and Massa said, "Well, de day done come that I said I'd set you free. I hate to do it, but I don't like to make myself out a lie. I hate to git rid of a good nigger lak you."

So he went in de house and give John one of his old suits of clothes to put on. So John put it on and come in to shake hands and tell 'em goodbye. De children they cry, and Ole Missy she cry. Didn't want to see John go. So John took his bundle and put it on his stick and hung it crost his shoulder.

Well, Ole John started on down de road. Well, Ole Massa said, "John, de children love yuh."

"Yassuh."

"John, I love yuh."

"Yassuh."

"And Missy *like* yuh!"

"Yassuh."

"But 'member, John, youse a nigger."

"Yassuh."

Fur as John could hear 'im down de road he wuz hollerin', "John, Oh John! De children loves you. And I love you. De Missy *like* you."

John would holler back, "Yassuh."

"But 'member youse a nigger, tho!"

Ole Massa kept callin' 'im and his voice was pitiful. But John kept right on steppin' to Canada. He answered Old Massa every time he called 'im, but he consumed on wid his bag.

"Ah'll Beatcher Makin' Money" [1]

De rooster chew t'backer, de hen dip snuff.
De biddy can't do it, but he struts his stuff.

Ole John, he was workin' for Massa and Massa had two hawses and he lakted John, so he give John one of his hawses.

When John git to workin' 'em he'd haul off and bet Massa's hawse, but he never would hit his'n. So then some white folks tole ole Massa 'bout John beatin' his hawse and never beatin' his own. So Massa tole John if he ever heard tell of him layin' a whip on his hawse again he was gointer take and kill John's hawse dead as a nit.

1. From Zora Neale Hurston's *Mules and Men* (1935).

John tole 'im, "Massa, if you kill my hawse, Ah'll beatcher makin' money."

One day John hit ole Massa's hawse agin. Dey went and tole Massa' 'bout it. He come down dere where John was haulin' trash, wid a great big ole knife and cut John's hawse's th'oat and he fell dead.

John jumped down off de wagon and skint his hawse, and tied de hide up on a stick and throwed it cross his shoulder, and went on down town.

Ole John was a fortune teller hisself but nobody 'round dere didn't know it. He met a man and de man ast John, "Whut's dat you got over yo' shoulder dere, John?"

"It's a fortune teller, boss."

"Make it talk some, John, and I'll give you a sack of money and a hawse and saddle, and five head of cattle."

John put de hide on de ground and pulled out de stick and hit 'cross de hawse hide and hold his head down dere to lissen.

"Dere's a man in yo' bed-room behind de bed talkin' to yo' wife."

De man went inside his house to see. When he come back out he said, "Yeah, John, you oho tellin' de truth. Make him talk some mo'."

John went to puttin' de stick back in de hide. "Naw, Massa, he's tired now."

De white man says, "Ah'll give you six head of sheeps and fo' hawses and fo' sacks of money."

John pulled out de stick and hit down on de hide and hold down his head to lissen.

"It's a man in yo' kitchen openin' yo' stove." De man went back into his house and come out again and tole John, "Yo, fortune-teller sho is right. Here's de things Ah promised you."

John rode on past Ole Massa's house wid all his sacks of money and drivin' his sheeps and cattle, whoopin' and crackin' his whip. "Yee, whoo-pee, yee!" Crack!

Massa said, "John, where did you git all dat?"

John said, "Ah tole you if you kilt mah hawse Ah'd beatcher makin' money."

Massa said to 'im, "Reckon if Ah kilt mah hawse Ah'd make dat much money?"

"Yeah, Massa, Ah reckon so."

So ole Massa went out and kilt his hawse and went to town hollerin', "Hawse hide for sale! Hawse hide for sale!"

One man said, "Hold on dere. Ah'll give you two-bits for it to bottom some chears."[2]

Ole Massa tole 'im, "Youse crazy!" and went on hollerin' "Hawse hide for sale!"

"Ah'll gi' you twenty cents for it to cover some chears," another man said.

"You must be stone crazy! Why, dis hide is worth five thousand dollars."

De people all laughed at 'im so he took his hawse hide and throwed it away and went and bought hisself another hawse.

---

2. I.e., to use to repair the seats of some chairs.

Ole John, he already rich, he didn't have to work but he jus' love to fool 'round hawses so he went to drivin' hawse and buggy for Massa. And when nobody wasn't wid him, John would let his grandma ride in Massa's buggy. Dey tole ole Massa 'bout it and he said, "John, Ah hear you been had yo' grandma ridin' in mah buggy. De first time Ah ketch her in it, Ah'm gointer kill 'er."

John tole 'im, "If you kill my grandma, Ah'll beatcher makin' money."

Pretty soon some white folks tole Massa dat John was takin' his gran'ma to town in his buggy and was hittin' his hawse and showin' off. So ole Massa come out dere and cut John's gran'ma's th'oat.

So John buried his gran'ma in secret and went and got his same ole hawse hide and keered it up town agin and went 'round talkin' 'bout, "Fortune-teller, fortune-teller!"

One man tole 'im, "Why, John, make it talk some for me. Ah'll give you six head of goats, six sheeps, and a hawse and a saddle to ride 'im wid."

So John made it talk and de man was pleased so he give John more'n he promised 'im, and John went on back past Massa's house wid his stuff so ole Massa could see 'im.

Ole Massa run out and ast, "Oh, John, where did you git all dat?"

John said, "Ah tole you if you kill mah gran'ma Ah'd beatcher makin' money."

Massa said, "You reckon if Ah kill mine, Ah'll make all dat?"

"Yeah, Ah reckon so."

So Massa runned and cut his gran'ma's th'oat and went up town hollerin' "gran'ma for sale! gran'ma for sale!"

Wouldn't nobody break a breath wid him. Dey thought he was crazy. He went on back home and grabbed John and tole 'im, "You made me kill my gran'ma and my good hawse and Ah'm gointer throw you in de river."

John tole 'im, "If you throw me in de river, Ah'll beatcher makin' money."

"Naw you won't neither," Massa tole 'im. "You done made yo' last money and done yo' las' do."

He got ole John in de sack and keered 'im down to de river, but he done forgot his weights, so he went back home to git some.

While he was gone after de weights a toad frog come by dere and John seen 'im. So he hollered and said, "Mr. Hoptoad, if you open dis sack and let me out Ah'll give you a dollar."

Toad frog let 'im out, so he got a soft-shell turtle and put it in de sack wid two big ole bricks. Then ole Massa got his weights and come tied 'em on de sack and throwed it in de river.

Whilst Massa was down to de water foolin' wid dat sack, John had done got out his hawse hide and went on up town agin hollerin', "Fortune-teller! fortune-teller!"

One rich man said "Make it talk for me, John."

John pulled out de stick and hit on de hide, and put his ear down. "Uh man is in yo' smoke-house stealin' meat and another one is in yo' money-safe."

De man went inside to see and when he come back he said, "You sho kin tell de truth."

So John went by Massa's house on a new hawse, wid a sack of money tied on each side of de saddle. Ole Massa seen 'im and ast, "Oh, John, where'd you git all dat?"

"Ah tole you if you throw me in de river Ah'd beatcher makin' money."

Massa ast, "Reckon if Ah let you throw me in de river, Ah'd make all dat?"

"Yeah, Massa, Ah *know* so."

John got ole Massa in de sack and keered 'im down to de river. John didn't forgit *his* weights. He put de weights on ole Massa and jus' befo' he throwed 'im out he said, "Goodbye, Massa, Ah hope you find all you lookin' for."

And dat wuz de las' of ole Massa.

Why the Sister in Black Works Hardest[1]

Know how it happened? After God got thru makin' de world and de varmints and de folks, he made up a great big bundle and let it down in de middle of de road. It laid dere for thousands of years, then Ole Missus said to Ole Massa: "Go pick up dat box, Ah want to see whut's in it." Ole Massa look at de box and it look so heavy dat he says to de nigger, "Go fetch me dat big ole box out dere in de road." De nigger been stumblin' over de box a long time so he tell his wife:

" 'Oman, go git dat box." So de nigger 'oman she runned to git de box. She says:

"Ah always lak to open up a big box 'cause there's nearly always something good in great big boxes." So she run and grabbed a-hold of de box and opened it up and it was full of hard work.

Dat's de reason de sister in black works harder than anybody else in de world. De white man tells de nigger to work and he takes and tells his wife.

Why Women Always Take Advantage of Men[1]

You see in de very first days, God made a man and a woman and put 'em in a house together to live. 'Way back in them days de woman was just as strong as de man and both of 'em did de same things. They useter get to fussin' 'bout who gointer do this and that and sometime they'd fight, but they was even balanced and neither one could whip de other one.

One day de man said to hisself, "B'lieve Ah'm gointer go see God and ast Him for a li'l mo' strength so Ah kin whip dis 'oman and make her mind. Ah'm tired of de way things is." So he went on up to God.

"Good mawnin', Ole Father."

"Howdy man. Whut you doin' 'round my throne so soon dis mawnin'?"

"Ah'm troubled in mind, and nobody can't ease mah spirit 'ceptin' you."

God said: "Put yo' plea in de right form and Ah'll hear and answer."

"Ole Maker, wid de mawnin' stars glitterin' in yo' shinin' crown, wid de

1. From Zora Neale Hurston's *Mules and Men* (1935).

1. From Zora Neale Hurston's *Mules and Men* (1935).

dust from yo' footsteps makin' worlds upon worlds, wid de blazin' bird we call de sun flyin' out of yo' right hand in de mawnin' and consumin' all de flesh and blood of stump-black darkness, and comes flyin' home every evenin' to rest on yo' left hand, and never once in all yo' eternal years, mistood de left hand for de right, Ah ast you *please* to give me mo' strength than dat woman you give me, so Ah kin make her mind. Ah know you don't want to be always comin' down way past de moon and stars to be straightenin' her out and its got to be done. So give me a li'l mo' strength, Ole Maker and Ah'll do it."

"All right, Man, you got mo' strength than woman."

So de man run all de way down de stairs from Heben till he got home. He was so anxious to try his strength on de woman dat he couldn't take his time. Soon's he got in de house he hollered "Woman! Here's yo' boss. God done tole me to handle you in which ever way Ah please. Ah'm yo' boss."

De woman flew to fightin' 'im right off. She fought 'im frightenin' but he beat her. She got her wind and tried 'im agin but he whipped her agin. She got herself together and made de third try on him vigorous but he beat her every time. He was so proud he could whip 'er at last, dat he just crowed over her and made her do a lot of things she didn't like. He told her, "Long as you obey me, Ah'll be good to yuh, but every time yuh rear up Ah'm gointer put plenty wood on yo' back and plenty water in yo' eyes."

De woman was so mad she went straight up to Heben and stood befo' de Lawd. She didn't waste no words. She said, "Lawd, Ah come befo' you mighty mad t'day. Ah want back my strength and power Ah useter have."

"Woman, you got de same power you had since de beginnin'."

"Why is it then, dat de man kin beat me now and he useter couldn't do it?"

"He got mo' strength than he useter have. He come and ast me for it and Ah give it to 'im. Ah gives to them that ast, and you ain't never ast me for no mo' power."

"Please suh, God, Ah'm astin' you for it now. Jus' gimme de same as you give him."

God shook his head. "It's too late now, woman. Whut Ah give, Ah never take back. Ah give him mo' strength than you and no matter how much Ah give you, he'll have mo'."

De woman was so mad she wheeled around and went on off. She went straight to de devil and told him what had happened.

He said, "Don't be dis-incouraged, woman. You listen to me and you'll come out mo' than conqueror. Take dem frowns out yo' face and turn round and go right on back to Heben and ast God to give you dat bunch of keys hangin' by de mantel-piece. Then you bring 'em to me and Ah'll show you what to do wid 'em."

So de woman climbed back up to Heben agin. She was mighty tired but she was more out-done that she was tired so she climbed all night long and got back up to Heben agin. When she got befo' de throne, butter wouldn't melt in her mouf.

"O Lawd and Master of de rainbow, Ah know yo' power. You never make two mountains without you put a valley in between. Ah know you kin hit a straight lick wid a crooked stick."

"Ast for whut you want, woman."

"God, gimme dat bunch of keys hangin' by yo' mantel-piece."

"Take 'em."

So de woman took de keys and hurried on back to de devil wid 'em. There was three keys on de bunch. Devil say, "See dese three keys? They got mo' power in 'em than all de strength de man kin ever git if you handle 'em right. Now dis first big key is to de do' of de kitchen, and you know a man always favors his stomach. Dis second one is de key to de bedroom and he don't like to be shut out from dat neither and dis last key is de key to de cradle and he don't want to be cut off from his generations at all. So now you take dese keys and go lock up everything and wait till he come to you. Then don't you unlock nothin' until he use his strength for yo' benefit and yo' desires."

De woman thanked 'im and tole 'im, "If it wasn't for you, Lawd knows whut us po' women folks would do."

She started off but de devil halted her. "Jus' one mo' thing: don't go home braggin' 'bout yo' keys. Jus' lock up everything and say nothin' until you git asked. And then don't talk too much."

De woman went on home and did like de devil tole her. When de man come home from work she was settin' on de porch singin' some song 'bout "Peck on de wood make de bed go good."

When de man found de three doors fastened what useter stand wide open he swelled up like pine lumber after a rain. First thing he tried to break in cause he figgered his strength would overcome all obstacles. When he saw he couldn't do it, he ast de woman, "Who locked dis do'?"

She tole 'im, "Me."

"Where did you git de key from?"

"God give it to me."

He run up to God and said, "God, woman got me locked 'way from my vittles, my bed and my generations, and she say you give her the keys."

God said, "I did, Man, Ah give her de keys, but de devil showed her how to use 'em!"

"Well, Ole Maker, please gimme some keys jus' lak 'em so she can't git de full control."

"No, Man, what Ah give Ah give. Woman got de key."

"How kin Ah know 'bout my generations?"

"Ast de woman."

So de man come on back and submitted hisself to de woman and she opened de doors.

He wasn't satisfied but he had to give in. 'Way after while he said to de woman, "Le's us divide up. Ah'll give you half of my strength if you lemme hold de keys in my hands."

De woman thought dat over so de devil popped and tol her, "Tell 'im, naw. Let 'im keep his strength and you keep yo' keys."

So de woman wouldn't trade wid 'im and de man had to mortgage his strength to her to live. And dat's why de man makes and de woman takes. You men is still braggin' 'bout yo' strength and de women is sittin' on de keys and lettin' you blow off till she git ready to put de bridle on you.

"De Reason Niggers Is Working So Hard"[1]

Dis is de way *dat* was.

God let down two bundles 'bout five miles down de road. So de white man and de nigger raced to see who would git there first. Well, de nigger out-run de white man and grabbed de biggest bundle. He was so skeered de white man would git it away from him he fell on top of de bundle and hollered back: "Oh, Ah got here first and dis biggest bundle is mine." De white man says: "All right, Ah'll take yo' leavings," and picked up de li'l tee-ninchy bundle layin' in de road. When de nigger opened up his bundle he found a pick and shovel and a hoe and a plow and chop-axe and then de white man opened up his bundle and found a writin'-pen and ink. So ever since then de nigger been out in de hot sun, usin' his tools and de white man been sittin' up figgerin', ought's a ought, figger's a figger; all for de white man, none for de nigger.

The Ventriloquist[1]

TAD. Is you hear de tale 'bout de white man an' de nigger an' de mule?

VOICE. I hear a heap er tales 'bout white folks an' niggers an' mules. Wuh you have in mind?

TAD. One time dere was a white man an' he runned a big farm, an' he notice one er he mule was gitten mighty poor, so he got to watchin'. He s'picion dat de nigger wuh was workin' de mule was stealin' he feed. Dis white man was one er dem people wha' kin pitch dey voice any wey dey wants. He could throw he voice into a cow or dog or any kind er animal an' have 'em talkin'—make 'em carry on reg'lar compersation.

VOICE. I has heared dem kind er people.

TAD. Well, he git to de crack er de stable an' he seed de nigger wid a bag reach in de mule' trough an' take out some corn an' put it in de bag. When de nigger do dat, de white man pitched he voice right into de mule' mout' an' make de mule say:

"Nigger, don't take my little bit er feed."

When he say dat, de nigger walk off an' look at de mule for awhile an' de mule ain' say nothin' more. Den he walk back an' dip in de trough again an' start takin' de mule' corn, an' de white folks make de mule say again:

"Nigger, please don't take my feed."

An' again de nigger walk off an' look at de mule.

VOICE. Ain' no mule ever would er spoke but one time to me.

TAD. Dis here nigger ain' have good sense, an' he went back de third time an' dive into dat corn. An' dis time de mule turn he head an' look at him, an' de white folks th'owed he voice into de mule' mout' one more time an' make de mule say:

1. From Zora Neale Hurston's *Mules and Men* (1935).

1. Collected by E. C. L. Adams and published in 1928.

"Nigger, ain' I axe you please for God' sake quit takin' my feed. You mighty nigh done perish me to de't'."

When he say dat, de nigger drap he bag an' bu's' out er dat stable, an' de next mornin' he went to the boss an' say:

"Boss, I guh quit."

An' he boss say:

"John, I ain' want you to quit me. I satisfy wid you."

An' de nigger say:

"Well, Boss, I ain' zackly satisfy. You mought as well gee me my time, kaze I done quit."

SCIP. Dere ain' no nigger ever would er been zackly satisfy after he heared a mule talkin'.

VOICE. It was quittin' time.

TAD. Dat ain' all. De white folks paid de nigger he wages an' de nigger walk off a piece down de road an' turn 'round an' walk back to de white folks an' say:

"Boss, I done quit. Dere ain' no nuse for nobody to say nothin' to me. I done quit an' I is guine, but 'fore I goes I got one thing to say to you."

An' de white folks look at him jes as kind an' say:

"Wha' it is, John?"

An' de nigger say:

"Boss, I done quit sho' 'nough, but 'fore I goes I wants to tell you one thing. Anything dat mule say to you is a damn lie."

An' den he leff.

SCIP. I knowed in de first place dat de white folks done loss a nigger.

You Talk Too Much, Anyhow[1]

Once, during the time of slavery, the pond was somewhat low. A negro happened to walk down there and found this turtle down there about the size of the bottom of a big tin tub, lying on the bank. So the negro said to the turtle, "Good morning, Mr. Turtle." The turtle at first didn't say anything, but finally said, "Good morning, Mr. Man." The negro said, "My, Mr. Turtle, I didn't know you could talk." Turtle said, "What I say about you niggers is you talk too much." So the negro goes back to his house and tells Old Massa about the turtle. He said, "Massa, don't you know, I was down at the creek this morning, and there was a great big turtle on the bank, and he could talk." Massa said, "Get away from here, you're just lying." The negro said he was telling the truth, but Master told him he lied like a dog. But the negro said, "No sir, he can really talk."

So the master said he would go down to see this turtle, but if he didn't talk he was going to beat the slave half to death. Both of them went back down to the creek and they found the turtle lying on the bank. The negro walked right up to the turtle and said, "Good morning, Mr. Turtle." Turtle didn't say anything, so the negro repeated, "I say, good morning, Mr. Tur-

1. As published in Roger D. Abrahams, ed., *Afro-American Folktales* (1985).

tle." Turtle still didn't say anything. This time the negro got scared. He said, "Please sir, Mr. Turtle, please say good morning," but Turtle wouldn't talk.

The Master took the negro back to the house and beat him half to death. After he got his beating, he went on back to the creek. He saw the turtle again and said to him, "Why didn't you say good morning? You knew I was going to get a beating if you didn't talk." Turtle said, "Well, that's what I say about you negroes, you talk too much anyhow."

The King Buzzard [1]

(A group around the camp-fire.)

TOM.   I wonder wey Tad.

CRICKET.   I ain' know. Look like he wants to git out er draggin' dis here seine. He leff here ever since 'fore day. Say he guh see kin he kill a turkey.

VOICE.   Who wid him?

CRICKET.   Ain' nobody wid him. He leff here by his self.

TOM.   I sho' ain't loves to wander 'round dese here swamps by my lonesome.

CRICKET.   Tad is a ole swamper. I reckon he know wuh he doin'.

VOICE.   He ain' tooken nothin' to eat wid him, an' it atter midnight. I reckon he must er had some kind er trouble.

CRICKET.   Looks to me like I hear sump'n comin'.

[*Tad approaches, his clothes badly torn. He is wet and covered with yellow mud.*]

TOM.   Tad, wey you been? You sho' looks like you loves to wander 'round dese here swamps by you'self.

TAD.   Look at me. Is I look like I been enjoyin' myself?

TOM.   You sho' is tored up. A bear must er had you.

TAD.   I seen sump'n wuss 'an a bear.

VOICE.   Wuh it been?

TAD.   I been walkin' 'long on de edge er Big Alligator Hole, an' de air been stink, an' I walk on an' I see sump'n riz up in front er me bigger 'an a man. An' he spread he whing out an' say, "Uuh!" He eye been red an' he de nastiest lookin' thing I ever see. He stink in my nostrils. He so stink, he stink to my eye an' my year. An' I look at him an' see he been eat a dead hog right dere in de night time. I ain' never see buzzard settin' on a carcass in de night 'fore dis. An' he look so vigus, he look like he ain' care ef he stay dere an' fight or no.

An' I been so oneasy an' frighten, till I ain' kin do nothin an' 'fore I knowed it, I jump at him. An' he riz up—makin' dat same dreadful sound—an' start flyin' all 'round me. Look like he tryin' to vomick on me. An' I dodge, an' dere in de moonlight dat ole thing circle 'round— look like he guh tackle me. An' he spewed he vomick every which er

---

1. Collected by E. C. L. Adams and published in 1928.

way, an' I see de leaf an' de grass wuh it fall on dry up. All de air seem like it were pizen.

An' I turned to leff, an' it keep on gittin' nigher an' nigher to me. An' I ain' know wuh would er happen, ef I ain' git in a canebrake wey he ain' kin fly. An' I crawl 'round for God knows how long, an' when I find myself, I been lost. Jesus know I ain' never wan' see no more buzzard like dat.

CRICKET. My God!

VOICE Wuh kind er buzzard dat?

TAD. God knows.

TOM. Dat ain' no buzzard. I hear 'bout dat ole thing 'fore dis.

My pa tell me dat 'way back in slavery time—'way back in Af'ica—dere been a nigger, an' he been a big nigger. He been de chief er he tribe, an' when dem white folks was ketchin' niggers for slavery, dat ole nigger nuse to entice 'em into trap. He'd git 'em on boat wey dem white folks could ketch 'em an' chain 'em. White folks nused to gee him money an' all kind er little thing, an' he'd betray 'em. An' one time atter he betray thousands into bondage, an' de white folks say dey ain' guh come to dat coast no more—dat was dey last trip—so dey knocked dat nigger down an' put chain on him an' brung him to dis country.

An' when he dead, dere were no place in heaven for him an' he were not desired in hell. An' de Great Master decide dat he were lower dan all other mens or beasts; he punishment were to wander for eternal time over de face er de earth. Dat as he had kilt de sperrits of mens an' womens as well as dere bodies, he must wander on an' on. Dat his sperrit should always travel in de form of a great buzzard, an' dat carrion must be he food.

An' sometimes he appears to mens, but he doom is settled, an' he ain' would er hurt Tad, kaze one er he punishment is dat he evil beak an' claw shall never tech no livin' thing. An' dey say he are known to all de sperrit world as de King Buzzard, an' dat forever he must travel alone.

A Flying Fool [1]

This colored man died and went up there to meet his Maker. But when he got to the gates, St. Peter said that God wasn't home or having any visitors—by which he meant no negroes allowed. Well, this old boy, he had been a good man all his life and his preacher had told him that Heaven would be his place, so he didn't exactly know what to do. So he just kind of hung around the gates, until one time St. Peter just had to go and take a pee. So while Pete was gone, this old boy slipped through, stole himself a pair of wings, and he really took off. Sailed around the trees, in and out of those golden houses and all, swooped down and buzzed some of those heavenly singers and all, and had himself a good old time. Meanwhile, of course, St. Pete came back and found out what had happened and called

1. This tale, published in Roger D. Abrahams, ed., *Afro-American Folktales* (1985), is often referred to in novels, poems, and short stories. See Richard Wright's *Lawd Today*, Ralph Ellison's *Flying Home*, and Sterling Brown's *Slim in Hell*.

out the heavenly police force to go get him. Well, this guy was just getting the feel of wearing wings, and he really took off, zoomed off. They had some little time bringing him down, him flying all over Heaven fast as he could go. Finally, they got him cornered and he racked up on one of those trees, and I tell you, he looked like a mess with broken wings and all. So they took him and threw him out the gates. Now here comes one of his friends, who asked him, "What happened, man?" He said, "Oh, man, when I got here they wouldn't let me in to the white man's Heaven, but I grabbed me some wings and I had me a fly." He said, "Oh yeah?" Man said, "Yeah, they may not let any colored folks in, but while I was there I was a flying fool."

Bur Rabbit in Red Hill Churchyard [1]

I pass 'long one night by Red Hill churchyard an' I hear all kind er chune.[2] I stop an' look an' my eye like to jump out er my head at wha' I see. De ground was kiver all over wid snow, an' de palin's on de graveyard fence was cracklin', it been so cold. De moon was shinin' bright—mighty nigh like day. De only diff'ence been it ain' look as natu'al. An' I look an' listen— an' ain' nothin' been de matter wid my eye an' ain' nothin' been wrong wid my hearin'—an' I seen a rabbit settin' on top of a grave playin' a fiddle, for God's sake. All kind er little beasts been runnin' 'round, dancin' an' callin' numbers. An' dere was wood rats an' squirrels cuttin' capers wid dey fancy self, an' diff'ent kind er birds an' owl. Even dem ole owl was sachayin' 'round—look like dey was enjoyin' dey self. An' dat ole rabbit was puttin' on more airs dan a poor buckra wid a jug er liquor an' a new suit er clothes on.

Well, sir, I jes stood der wid my heart in my mout' an' my eyes bu'stin' out my head. I been natu'ally paralyze, I been so scared. An' while I were lookin', Bur Rabbit stop playin', put he fiddle under he arm an' step off de grave. He walk off a little piece an' guin some sort er sign to de little birds an' beasts, an' dey form dey self into a circle 'round de grave. An' dat was when I knowed sump'n strange was guh happen.

You know a rabbit is cunnin'. He got more sense dan people. He sharp. My brother, he ain't trust no mistake.

Well, I watch an' I see Bur Rabbit take he fiddle from under he arm an' start to fiddlin' some more, an' he were doin' some fiddlin' out dere in dat snow. An' Bur Mockin' Bird jine him an' whistle a chune dat would er made de angels weep. Even dem ole owl had tear drappin' from dey eye. Dat mockin' bird an dat rabbit—Lord, dey had chunes floatin' all 'round on de night air. Dey could stand a chune on end, grab it up an' throw it away an' ketch it an' bring it back an' hold it; an' make dem chunes sound like dey was strugglin' to git away one minute, an' de next dey sound like sump'n gittin' up close an' whisperin'.

An' as I watch, I see Bur Rabbit lower he fiddle, wipe he face an' stick he han'k'ch'ef in he pocket, an' take off he hat an' bow mighty nigh to de

1. Collected by E. C. L. Adams and published in 1928. Note that this tale presents an image of the Rabbit as musician with supernatural powers.
2. Tune.

ground. Bur Mockin' Bird stop he chune an' all de little beasts an' birds an' dem ole owl bow down.

An' wuh you reckon? While I been watch all dese strange guines on, I see de snow on de grave crack an' rise up, an' de grave open an' I see Simon[3] rise up out er dat grave. I see him an' he look jest as natu'al as he done 'fore dey bury him. An' he look satisfy, an' he look like he taken a great interest in Bur Rabbit an' de little beasts an' birds. An' he set down on de top er he own grave, an' carry on a long compersation wid all dem animals. An' dem owl look like dey never was guh git through. You know dem ole owl—de ole folks always is say dey is dead folks.

But dat ain' all. Atter dey done wored dey self out wid compersation, I see Bur Rabbit take he fiddle an' put it under he chin an' start to playin'. An' while I watch, I see Bur Rabbit step back on de grave an' Simon were gone.

Brer Rabbit Tricks Brer Fox Again[1]

When all the animals saw how well Brer Rabbit and Brer Fox were getting along, they decided to patch up their quarrels.

One hot day Brer Rabbit, Brer Fox, Brer Coon, Brer Bear, and a whole lot of the other animals were clearing new ground so they could plant corn and have some roasting ears when autumn came.

Brer Rabbit got tired about three minutes after he started, but he couldn't say anything if he didn't want the other animals calling him lazy. So he kept carrying off the weeds and brambles the others were pulling out of the ground. After a while he screamed real loud and said a briar was stuck in his hand. He wandered off, picking at his hand. As soon as he was out of sight, he started looking for a shady place where he could take a nap.

He saw a well with a bucket in it. That was the very thing he'd been looking for. He climbed, jumped in, and whoops! The bucket went down, down, down until—SPLASH!—it hit the water.

Now, I know you don't know nothing about no well. You probably think that when God made water, He made the faucet too. Well, God don't know nothing about no faucet, and I don't care too much for them myself. When I was coming up, everybody had their own well. Over the well was a pulley with a rope on it. Tied to each end of the rope was a bucket, and when you pulled one bucket up, the other one went down. Brer Rabbit found out about them kind of wells as he looked up at the other bucket.

He didn't know what he was going to do. He couldn't even move around very much or else he'd tip over and land in the water.

Brer Fox and Brer Rabbit might've made up and become friends, but that didn't mean Brer Fox trusted Brer Rabbit. Brer Fox had seen him sneaking off, so he followed. He watched Brer Rabbit get in the bucket and

---

3. Simon is described in the New Testament variously as the son of Jonah or John; Jesus gave him the name Peter.

1. From *The Tales of Uncle Remus: The Adventures of Brer Rabbit*, as told by Julius Lester (1987).

go to the bottom of the well. That was the most astonishing thing he had ever seen. Brer Rabbit had to be up to something.

"I bet you anything that's where Brer Rabbit hides all his money. Or he's probably discovered a gold mine down there!"

Brer Fox peeked down into the well. "Hey, Brer Rabbit! What you doing down there?"

"Who? Me? Fishing. I thought I'd surprise everybody and catch a mess of fish for dinner."

"Many of 'em down there?"

"Is there stars in the sky? I'm glad you come, 'cause there's more fish down here than I can haul up. Why don't you come on down and give me a hand?"

"How do I get down there?"

"Jump in the bucket."

Brer Fox did that and started going down. The bucket Brer Rabbit was in started up. As Brer Rabbit passed Brer Fox, he sang out:

> Goodbye, Brer Fox, take care of your clothes,
> For this is the way the world goes;
> Some goes up and some goes down,
> You'll get to the bottom all safe and sound.

Just as Brer Fox hit the water—SPLASH!—Brer Rabbit jumped out at the top. He ran and told the other animals that Brer Fox was muddying up the drinking water.

They ran to the well and hauled Brer Fox out, chastising him for muddying up some good water. Wasn't nothing he could say.

Everybody went back to work, and every now and then Brer Rabbit looked at Brer Fox and laughed. Brer Fox had to give a little dry grin himself.

The Wonderful Tar-Baby Story [1]

"Didn't the fox *never* catch the rabbit, Uncle Remus?" asked the little boy the next evening.

"He come mighty nigh it, honey, sho's you bawn—Brer Fox did. One day atter Brer Rabbit fool 'im wid dat calamus root,[2] Brer Fox went ter wuk en got 'im some tar, en mix it wid some turbentime, en fix up a contrapshun wat he call a Tar-Baby, en he tuck dish yer Tar-Baby en he sot 'er in de big road, en den he lay off in de bushes fer ter see wat de news wuz gwineter be. En he didn't hatter wait long, nudder, kaze bimeby here come Brer Rabbit pacin' down de road—lippity-clippity, clippity-lippity—dez ez sassy ez a jay-bird. Brer Fox, he lay low. Brer Rabbit come prancin' 'long twel he spy de Tar-Baby, en den he fotch up on his behime legs like he wuz 'stonished. De Tar-Baby, she sot dar, she did, en Brer Fox, he lay low.

" 'Mawnin'!' sez Brer Rabbit, sezee—'nice wedder dis mawnin',' sezee.

---

1. From Joel Chandler Harris, *Uncle Remus: His Songs and Sayings* (1880).

2. The aromatic root of the tropical plant also called "sweet flag."

"Tar-Baby ain't sayin' nuthin', en Brer Fox, he lay low.

" 'How duz yo' sym'tums seem ter segashuate?' sez Brer Rabbit, sezee.

"Brer Fox, he wink his eye slow, en lay low, en de Tar-Baby, she ain't sayin' nuthin'.

" 'How you come on, den? Is you deaf?' sez Brer Rabbit, sezee. 'Kaze if you is, I kin holler louder,' sezee.

"Tar-Baby stay still, en Brer Fox, he lay low.

" 'Youer stuck up, dat's w'at you is,' says Brer Rabbit, sezee, 'en I'm gwineter kyore you, dat's w'at I'm a gwineter do,' sezee.

"Brer Fox, he sorter chuckle in his stummuck, he did, but Tar-Baby ain't sayin' nuthin'.

" 'I'm gwineter larn you howter talk ter 'specttubble fokes ef hit's de las' ack,' sez Brer Rabbit, sezee. 'Ef you don't take off dat hat en tell me howdy, I'm gwineter bus' you wide open,' sezee.

"Tar-Baby stay still, en Brer Fox, he lay low.

"Brer Rabbit keep on axin' 'im, en de Tar-Baby, she keep on sayin' nuthin', twel present'y Brer Rabbit draw back wid his fis', he did, en blip he tuck 'er side er de head. Right dar's whar he broke his merlasses jug. His fis' stuck, en he can't pull loose. De tar hilt 'im. But Tar-Baby, she stay still, en Brer Fox, he lay low.

" 'Ef you don't lemme loose, I'll knock you agin,' sez Brer Rabbit, sezee, en wid dat he fotch 'er a wipe wid de udder han', en dat stuck. Tar-Baby, she ain't sayin' nuthin', en Brer Fox, he lay low.

" 'Tu'n me loose, fo' I kick de natal stuffin' outen you,' sez Brer Rabbit, sezee, but de Tar-Baby, she ain't sayin' nuthin'. She des hilt on, en den Brer Rabbit lose de use er his feet in de same way. Brer Fox, he lay low. Den Brer Rabbit squall out dat ef de Tar-Baby don't tu'n 'im loose he butt 'er cranksided. En den he butted, en his head got stuck. Den Brer Fox, he sa'ntered fort', lookin' des ez innercent ez wunner yo' mammy's mockin'-birds.

" 'Howdy, Brer Rabbit,' sez Brer Fox, sezee. 'You look sorter stuck up dis mawnin',' sezee, en den he rolled on de groun', en laft en laft twel he couldn't laff no mo'. 'I speck you'll take dinner wid me dis time, Brer Rabbit. I done laid in some calamus root, en I ain't gwineter take no skuse,' sez Brer Fox, sezee."

Here Uncle Remus paused, and drew a two-pound yam out of the ashes.

"Did the fox eat the rabbit?" asked the little boy to whom the story had been told.

"Dat's all de fur de tale goes," replied the old man. "He mout, en den agin he mountent. Some say Jedge B'ar come 'long en loosed 'im—some say he didn't. I hear Miss Sally callin'. You better run 'long."

How Mr. Rabbit Was Too Sharp for Mr. Fox[1]

"Uncle Remus," said the little boy one evening, when he had found the old man with little or nothing to do, "did the fox kill and eat the rabbit when he caught him with the Tar-Baby?"

---

1. From Joel Chandler Harris, *Uncle Remus: His Songs and Sayings* (1880).

"Law, honey, ain't I tell you 'bout dat?" replied the old darkey, chuckling slyly. "I 'clar ter grashus I ought er tole you dat, but ole man Nod wuz ridin' on my eyeleds 'twel a leetle mo'n I'd a dis'member'd my own name, en den on to dat here come yo' mammy hollerin' atter you.

"W'at I tell you w'en I fus' begin? I tole you Brer Rabbit wuz a monstus soon beas'; leas'ways dat's w'at I laid out fer ter tell you. Well, den, honey, don't you go en make no udder kalkalashuns, kaze in dem days Brer Rabbit en his fambly wuz at de head er de gang w'en enny racket wuz on han', en dar dey stayed. 'Fo' you begins fer ter wipe yo' eyes 'bout Brer Rabbit, you wait en see whar'bouts Brer Rabbit gwineter fetch up at. But dat's needer yer ner dar.

"W'en Brer Fox fine Brer Rabbit mixt up wid de Tar-Baby, he feel mighty good, en he roll on de groun' en laff. Bimeby he up'n say, sezee:

"'Well, I speck I got you dis time, Brer Rabbit,' sezee; 'maybe I ain't, but I speck I is. You been runnin' roun' here sassin' atter me a mighty long time, but I speck you done come ter de een' er de row. You bin cuttin' up yo' capers en bouncin' 'roun' in dis naberhood ontwel you come ter b'leeve yo'se'f de boss er de whole gang. En den youer allers some'rs whar you got no bizness,' sez Brer Fox, sezee. 'Who ax you fer ter come en strike up a 'quaintence wid dish yer Tar-Baby? En who stuck you up dar whar you iz? Nobody in de roun' worril. You des tuck en jam yo'se'f on dat Tar-Baby widout waitin' fer enny invite,' sez Brer Fox, sezee, 'en dar you is, en dar you'll stay twel I fixes up a bresh-pile and fires her up, kaze I'm gwineter bobbycue you dis day, sho,' sez Brer Fox, sezee.

"Den Brer Rabbit talk mighty 'umble.

"'I don't keer w'at you do wid me, Brer Fox,' sezee, 'so you don't fling me in dat brier-patch. Roas' me, Brer Fox,' sezee, 'but don't fling me in dat brier-patch,' sezee.

"'Hit's so much trouble fer ter kindle a fire,' sez Brer Fox, sezee, 'dat I speck I'll hatter hang you,' sezee.

"'Hang me des ez high ez you please, Brer Fox,' sez Brer Rabbit, sezee, 'but do fer de Lord's sake don't fling me in that brier-patch,' sezee.

"'I ain't got no string,' sez Brer Fox, sezee, 'en now I speck I'll hatter drown you,' sezee.

"'Drown me des ez deep ez you please, Brer Fox,' sez Brer Rabbit, sezee, 'but do don't fling me in dat brier-patch,' sezee.

"'Dey ain't no water nigh,' sez Brer Fox, sezee, 'en now I speck I'll hatter skin you,' sezee.

"'Skin me, Brer Fox,' sez Brer Rabbit, sezee, 'snatch out my eyeballs, t'ar out my years by de roots, en cut off my legs,' sezee, 'but do please, Brer Fox, don't fling me in dat brier-patch,' sezee.

"Co'se Brer Fox wanter hurt Brer Rabbit bad ez he kin, so he cotch 'im by de behime legs en slung 'im right in de middle er de brier-patch. Dar was a considerbul flutter whar Brer Rabbit struck de bushes, en Brer Fox sorter hang 'roun' fer ter see w'at wuz gwineter happen. Bimeby he hear somebody call 'im, en way up de hill he see Brer Rabbit settin' cross-legged a chinkapin log koamin' de pitch outen his har wid a chip. Den Brer know dat he bin swop off mighty bad. Brer Rabbit wuz bleedzed fer ter ack some er his sass, en he holler out:

" 'Bred en bawn in a brier-patch, Brer Fox—bred en bawn in a brier-patch!' en wid dat he skip out des ez lively ez a cricket in de embers."

The Awful Fate of Mr. Wolf.[1]

Uncle Remus was half-soling[2] one of his shoes, and his Miss Sally's little boy had been handling his awls, his hammers, and his knives to such an extent that the old man was compelled to assume a threatening attitude; but peace reigned again, and the little boy perched himself on a chair, watching Uncle Remus driving in pegs.

"Folks w'at's allers pesterin' people, en bodderin' 'longer dat w'at ain't dern, don't never come ter no good eend. Dar wuz Brer Wolf; stidder mindin' un his own bizness, he hatter take en go in pardnerships wid Brer Fox, en dey want skacely a minnit in de day dat he want atter Brer Rabbit, en he kep' on en kep' on twel fus' news you knowed he got kotch up wid—en he got kotch up wid monstus bad."

"Goodness, Uncle Remus! I thought the Wolf let the Rabbit alone, atter he tried to fool him about the Fox being dead."

"Better lemme tell dish yer my way. Bimeby hit'll be yo' bed time, en Miss Sally'll be a hollerin' atter you, en you'll be a whimplin' roun', en den Mars John'll fetch up de re'r wid dat ar strop w'at I made fer 'im."

The child laughed, and playfully shook his fist in the simple, serious face of the venerable old darkey, but said no more. Uncle Remus waited awhile to be sure there was to be no other demonstration, and then proceeded:

"Brer Rabbit ain't see no peace w'atsumever. He can't leave home 'cep' Brer Wolf 'ud make a raid en tote off some er de fambly. Brer Rabbit b'ilt 'im a straw house, en hit wuz tored down; den he made a house outen pine-tops, en dat went de same way; den he made 'im a bark house, en dat wuz raided on, en eve'y time he los' a house he los' wunner his chilluns. Las' Brer Rabbit got mad, he did, en cust, en den he went off, he did, en got some kyarpinters, en dey b'ilt 'im a plank house wid rock foundashuns. Atter dat he could have some peace en quietness. He could go out en pass de time er day wid his nabers, en come back en set by de fier, en smoke his pipe, en read de newspapers same like enny man w'at got a fambly. He made a hole, he did, in de cellar whar de little Rabbits could hide out w'en dar wuz much uv a racket in de naberhood, en de latch er de front do' kotch on de inside. Brer Wolf, he see how de lan' lay, he did, en he lay low. De little Rabbits wuz mighty skittish, but hit got so dat cole chills ain't run up Brer Rabbit's back no mo' w'en he heerd Brer Wolf go gallopin' by.

"Bimeby, one day w'en Brer Rabbit wuz fixin' fer ter call on Miss Coon, he heerd a monstus fuss en clatter up de big road, en 'mos' 'fo' he could fix his years fer ter lissen, Brer Wolf run in de do'. De little Rabbits dey went inter dere hole in de cellar, dey did, like blowin' out a cannle. Brer Wolf wuz far'ly kivver'd wid mud, en mighty nigh outer win'.

" 'Oh, do pray save me, Brer Rabbit!' sez Brer Wolf, sezee. 'Do please,

---

1. From Joel Chandler Harris, *Uncle Remus: His Songs and Sayings* (1880). Note the contrast between the outer tale's ostensible peace and the inner tale's extraordinary violence.
2. Performing a shoe repair.

Brer Rabbit! de dogs is atter me, en dey'll t'ar me up. Don't you year um comin'? Oh, do please save me, Brer Rabbit! Hide me some'rs whar de dogs won't git me.'

"No quicker sed dan done.

" 'Jump in dat big chist dar, Brer Wolf,' sez Brer Rabbit, sezee; 'jump in dar en make yo'se'f at home.'

"In jump Brer Wolf, down come de led, en inter de hasp went de hook, en dar Mr. Wolf wuz. Den Brer Rabbit went ter de lookin' glass, he did, en wink at hisse'f, en den he drawd de rockin'-cheer in front er de fier, he did, en tuck a big chaw terbarker."

"Tobacco, Uncle Remus?" asked the little boy, incredulously.

"Rabbit terbarker, honey. You know dis yer life ev'lastin' w'at Miss Sally puts 'mong de cloze in de trunk; well, dat's rabbit terbarker. Den Brer Rabbit sot dar long time, he did, turnin' his mine over en wukken his thinkin' masheen. Bimeby he got up, en sorter stir 'roun'. Den Brer Wolf open up.

" 'Is de dogs all gone, Brer Rabbit?'

" 'Seem like I hear one un um smellin' roun' de chimbly-cornder des now.'

"Den Brer Rabbit git de kittle en fill it full er water, en put it on de fier.

" 'W'at you doin' now, Brer Rabbit?'

" 'I'm fixin' fer ter make you a nice cup er tea, Brer Wolf.'

"Den Brer Rabbit went ter de cubberd en git de gimlet,[3] en commence fer ter bo' little holes in de chist-led.

" 'W'at you doin' now, Brer Rabbit?'

" 'I'm a bo'in' little holes so you kin get bref, Brer Wolf.'

"Den Brer Rabbit went out en git some mo' wood, en fling it on de fier.

" 'W'at you doin' now, Brer Rabbit?'

" 'I'm a chunkin' up de fier so you won't git cole, Brer Wolf.'

"Den Brer Rabbit went down inter de cellar en fotch out all his chilluns.

" 'W'at you doin' now, Brer Rabbit?'

" 'I'm a tellin' my chilluns w'at a nice man you is, Brer Wolf.'

"En de chilluns, dey had ter put der han's on der moufs fer ter keep fum laffin'. Den Brer Rabbit he got de kittle en commenced fer ter po' de hot water on de chist-lid.

" 'W'at dat I hear, Brer Rabbit?'

" 'You hear de win' a blowin', Brer Wolf.'

"Den de water begin fer ter sif thoo.

" 'W'at dat I feel, Brer Rabbit?'

" 'You feels de fleas a bitin', Brer Wolf.'

" 'Dey er bitin' mighty hard, Brer Rabbit.'

" 'Tu'n over on de udder side, Brer Wolf.'

" 'W'at dat I feel now, Brer Rabbit?'

" 'Still you feels de fleas, Brer Wolf.'

" 'Dey er eatin' me up, Brer Rabbit,' en dem wuz de las' words er Brer Wolf, kase de scaldin' water done de bizness.

"Den Brer Rabbit call in his nabers, he did, en dey hilt a reg'lar juberlee; en ef you go ter Brer Rabbit's house right now, I dunno but w'at you'll fine

---

3. A small hand tool for boring holes.

Brer Wolf's hide hangin' in de back-po'ch, en all bekaze he wuz so bizzy wid udder fo'kses doin's."

What the Rabbit Learned [1]

So they had a convention. De rabbit took de floor and said they was tired of runnin', and dodgin' all de time, and they asted de dogs to please leave rabbits alone and run somethin' else. So de dogs put it to a vote and 'greed to leave off runnin' rabbits.

So after de big meetin' Brer Dog invites de rabbit over to his house to have dinner wid him.

He started on thru de woods wid Brer Dog but every now and then he'd stop and scratch his ear and listen. He stop right in his tracks. Dog say:

"Aw, come on Brer Rabbit, you too suscautious. Come on."

Kept dat up till they come to de branch just 'fore they got to Brer Dog's house. Just as Brer Rabbit started to step out on de foot-log, he heard some dogs barkin' way down de creek. He heard de old hound say, "How o-l-d is he?" and the young dogs answer him: "Twenty-one or two, twenty-one or two!" So Brer Rabbit say, "Excuse me, but Ah don't reckon Ah better go home wid you today, Brer Dog."

"Aw, come on, Brer Rabbit, you always gitten scared for nothin'. Come on."

"Ah hear dogs barkin', Brer Dog."

"Naw, you don't, Brer Rabbit."

"Yes, Ah do. Ah know, dat's dogs barkin'."

"S'posin' it is, it don't make no difference. Ain't we done held a convention and passed a law dogs run no mo' rabbits? Don't pay no 'tention to every li'l bit of barkin' you hear."

Rabbit scratch his ear and say,

"Yeah, but all de dogs ain't been to no convention, and anyhow some of dese fool dogs ain't got no better sense than to run all over dat law and break it up. De rabbits didn't go to school much and he didn't learn but three letter, and that's trust no mistake. Run every time de bush shake."

So he raced on home without breakin' another breath wid de dog.

1. From Zora Neale Hurston's *Mules and Men* (1935).

The Literature of Slavery and Freedom

1746–1865

THE RELIGIOUS AND POLITICAL MISSION OF AFRICAN AMERICAN LITERATURE

The engendering impulse of African American literature is resistance to human tyranny. The sustaining spirit of African American literature is dedication to human dignity. As resistance to tyranny and dedication to human dignity became increasingly synonymous with the idea of America itself in the latter half of the eighteenth century, early African American writers identified themselves as Americans with a special mission. They would articulate the spiritual and political ideals of America to inspire and justify the struggle of blacks for their birthright as American citizens. They would also demand fidelity to those same ideals from whites whose moral complacency and racial prejudices had blinded them to the obligations of their own heritage.

Although the ideals of equality and liberty celebrated by the founders of the United States drew their legitimacy from intertwined religious and political traditions, the racial chauvinism of most white Americans in the early republic forced a separation of their religious and political responsibilities to blacks. In the realm of the spirit, most whites were content with African American claims to an equal right to God's grace, as long as African American salvation did not entail a radical redemption of the white-dominated social order. In the political sphere, however, whites presumed themselves alone to be the arbiters of rights and privileges.

Recognizing this contradiction in white America's attitude toward black advancement, the first African American writers in the United States appealed to the traditional Christian gospel of the universal brotherhood of humanity as a way of initiating a discussion with whites that did not directly confront their prejudices and anxieties. Readers of Phillis Wheatley's *Poems on Various Subjects, Religious and Moral* (1773), which won international attention as the first African American work of literature, found much more evidence of the Boston slave poet's piety than her politics. Even in one of her rare poems about her personal experience as an African American, *On Being Brought from Africa to America*, Wheatley spoke of black equality to whites in terms that appeared limited to matters of the spirit:

> Some view our sable race with scornful eye,
> "Their colour is a diabolic die."
> Remember, *Christians*, *Negros*, black as *Cain*,
> May be refin'd, and join th' angelic train.

Despite the self-deprecating treatment of color in this poem, by insisting that color is no barrier to black ascension to spiritual heights, Wheatley may have been inviting her white reader to consider whether color should bar African Americans from rising in the social and political scale either.

Wheatley and her fellow pioneers in African American poetry, Massachusetts balladeer Lucy Terry and Jupiter Hammon, a New York slave, as well as Briton Hammon, who produced the first work of African American prose, *A Narrative of the Uncommon Sufferings and Surprising Deliverance of Briton Hammon, a Negro Man* (1760), all seem to have been motivated primarily by a desire to win a popular Christian readership. Nevertheless, their appearance on the American literary scene, however safely conventional their piety and its expression may seem today, had social significance. As slaves or former slaves, all placed white readers on notice that even the least advantaged of black Americans had feelings to voice and stories to tell to the public at large. Moreover, as *writers* who employed the arts of literacy with independent purpose—which the white-authored preface to Wheatley's *Poems* was at pains to attest—poets such as Wheatley and Jupiter Hammon contradicted a widespread European prejudice that black people were incapable of literary expression. Mastery of language, the essential sign of a civilized mind to the European, implicitly qualified a black writer, and by analogy those whom he or she represented, for self-mastery and a place of respect within white civilization.

From the outset, African American literature challenged the dominant culture's attempt to segregate the religious from the political, the spirit from the flesh, insofar as racial affairs were concerned. Within two years of the publication of her landmark book of poems, Wheatley was articulating without equivocation the holistic view of spiritual and political issues on which later generations of African American writing would be founded. In 1774 she commented that she could discern "more and more clearly, the glorious Dispensation of civil and religious Liberty, which are so inseparably united, that there is little or no Enjoyment of one without the other." By the early nineteenth century, civil rights agitators like Maria W. Stewart felt no compunction in affirming God's investment in both the eternal and the earthly redemption of black people. Echoing, perhaps even alluding to, Wheatley's famous quatrain in *On Being Brought from Africa to America*, Stewart announced to African Americans in 1831: "Many think, because your skins are tinged with a sable hue, that you are an inferior race of beings; but God does not consider you as such." By invoking divine sanction for African American social strivings, writers like Stewart brought to fruition the earliest black writers' efforts to dignify black experience with spiritual significance and divinely ordained importance.

In the eyes of the standard-bearers of early African American literature, all of God's laws were indivisible because all of God's people were one. Jesus, the suffering servant, bore powerful witness to God's love of mercy; Moses, the deliverer of the Israelites from bondage in Egypt, testified just as compellingly to God's devotion to justice. Spurred by a conviction of their own special calling to witness against America's spiritual and political degeneration, early black writers such as Olaudah Equiano, David Walker, Maria Stewart, and ultimately Frederick Douglass exhorted their white readers like preachers imploring a backsliding congregation to live up to the standards of their reputed religion and their professed political principles. "O, ye nominal Christians!" Equiano thundered to the white readers of his *Interesting Narrative of the Life of Olaudah Equiano, or Gustavus Vassa, the African* (1789) after surveying the horrors of the notorious Middle Passage endured by millions of Africans before they were sold into slavery in the Americas: "might not an African ask you—Learned you this from your God, who says unto you, Do unto all men as you would men should do unto you?" In a similar vein, Benjamin Banneker, a black mathematician and almanac maker, wrote Secretary of State Thomas Jefferson in 1791 to ask how the author of the Declaration of Independence could denounce Britain's tyranny over its American colonies in 1776 without also opposing "that state of tyrannical thraldom and inhuman captivity to which too many of my brethren are doomed" in the newly formed United States. Are you not also "guilty of that most criminal act which you professedly detested in others?" Banneker inquired with unassailable logic.

Representing themselves as faithful adherents to the humanitarian ideals of Christianity and the American Revolution, early African American writers explored through various forms of irony the chasm between white America's words and its deeds, between its propaganda about freedom and its widespread practice of slavery. David Walker's Appeal, in Four Articles; Together with a Preamble, to the Coloured Citizens of the World (1829) is predicated on a structural irony anticipated in its very title. Like the U.S. Constitution, Walker's Appeal begins with a preamble followed by four articles. Unlike the Constitution, which legalized slavery in the United States, Walker's text demands slavery's abolition and warns of the deconstitution of the United States by God's avenging power if slavery is not ended. One of the most famous instances of irony in early African American literature appears in James M. Whitfield's America (1853), a bitter parody of the popular patriotic hymn America the Beautiful. The opening lines of Whitfield's poem announce:

> America, it is to thee,
> Thou boasted land of liberty,—
> It is to thee I raise my song,
> Thou land of blood, and crime, and wrong.

Whitfield's cry of betrayal at the hands of America summarized decades of increasingly vocal black outrage over the fundamental hypocrisy of the United States' self-congratulatory image as the "land of the free."

The grotesque inconsistency between the United States' championing of "life, liberty, and the pursuit of happiness" in its own Declaration of Independence and its sanctioning of the crime of chattel slavery furnished early African American literature with its most enduring theme. Initially, African American writers like Benjamin Banneker used the egalitarian language of the Declaration of Independence to try to shame white America into abolishing slavery. But as early as the expatriate Victor Séjour's pioneering short story The Mulatto (1837), and with increasing vehemence in the speeches of mid-century black America's most eloquent platform orators, such as Henry Highland Garnet and Frederick Douglass, the right of African Americans to armed resistance to slavery was proclaimed. The Founding Fathers' justification of revolution—particularly Patrick Henry's "Give me liberty or give me death" speech in 1775 to the Virginia assembly—gave ample precedent for violent action in the name of freedom. Regardless of the means of rhetorical attack, African American literature throughout the pre–Civil War era maintained as its central priorities the abolition of slavery and the promotion of the black man and woman to a status in the civil and cultural order equal to that of whites.

SLAVERY IN THE AMERICAS

To prosecute their war of words against slavery, early black advocates of freedom became students of the long and sordid history of human bondage, which dated back to ancient Egypt, Greece, and Rome. One such self-educated historian, David Walker, acknowledged that slavery had long been practiced in Africa, but he charged white Christian slaveholders with greater crimes against humanity and greater hypocrisy in justifying those crimes than any prior slave system had been guilty of. Twentieth-century scholarship has lent much support to the contentions of Walker and others in the African American antislavery vanguard that slavery as perpetrated by the European colonizers of Africa and the Americas brought man's inhumanity to man to a level of technological efficiency unimagined by previous generations.

When Portuguese mariners began trading gold, ivory, and spices with the chieftains of the coast of West Africa in the mid-fifteenth century, they discovered that African prisoners of war and their children could be readily supplied for sale as slaves. The slave trade among North and West Africans was an established institution, though the status of slave in these parts of Africa did not carry with it the stigma with which European and American slave traders and slaveholders branded the African. After the discovery of the so-called New World, its Spanish conquerors instituted particularly brutal forms of slavery as soon as enough power could be consolidated to turn the native population into a compulsory work force. Ironically, the horrific effects of the Spanish enslavement of the indigenous peoples of Central America triggered the first importation of African slaves into the Western Hemisphere. In 1517 Bartolomé de las Casas, a Spanish missionary to the Caribbean island of Hispaniola, recommended to his political superiors that Africans be imported to the Spanish colonies to relieve the appalling mistreatment of the indigenous peoples of New Spain. Before the slave trade to the Americas was abolished in the late nineteenth century, at least ten million human beings had been brought to North and South America against their will, to be subjected to one of the most inhuman systems of social and economic oppression the world has ever seen.

The first black people who came to North America were not slaves, however, but explorers. Among the most famous were Estevanico (d. 1539), who opened up what is now New Mexico and Arizona for Spanish settlement, and Jean Baptiste Point du Sable (1745?–1818), who founded a trading post on the southern shore of Lake Michigan from which the city of Chicago grew. The first Africans in British North America were brought to work as laborers. They arrived at Jamestown, Virginia, in 1619 aboard a Dutch slave ship. Only twenty in number, including at least three women, these people had survived the desperate Middle Passage from their homeland to America, a voyage so harsh that it is estimated that one in eight Africans died in transit without ever reaching the slave markets of the New World. Initially, the black people brought to the Virginia colony were not considered slaves. They were classed as indentured servants who could become free if they worked satisfactorily for their masters for a stipulated number of years. But by 1700, the growing plantation economy of Virginia demanded a work force that was cheaper than free labor and more easily controlled. By establishing the institution of chattel slavery, in which a black person became not just a temporary servant but the lifetime property of his or her white master, the tobacco, cotton, and rice planters of British North America ensured their rise to economic and political preeminence over the southern half of what would become the United States.

Under chattel slavery, the African imported to North America was divested as much as possible of his or her culture. The newly minted slave was relegated to a condition that the historian Orlando Patterson has termed "social death." Although much evidence demonstrates that some African religious beliefs, cultural practices, and linguistic forms survived the Middle Passage, the system of chattel slavery was designed to prevent Africans and their descendants from building a new identity except in accordance with the dictates of their oppressors. Instead of an individual, slavery devised what Patterson calls "a social nonperson," a being that by legal definition could have no family, no personal honor, no community, no past, and no future. The intention of slavery was to create in the slave a sense of complete alienation from all human ties except those that bound him or her in absolute dependence to the master's will. Self-reliance, a cardinal tenet of the popular American doctrine of rugged individualism, was forbidden the slave, since the very notion of selfhood had no meaning or application to those who could not even possess themselves.

SLAVERY AND AMERICAN RACISM

What gave American chattel slavery its uniquely oppressive character and power was its insistence that enslavement was the natural and proper condition for partic- ular *races* of people. Reinforced by theories of racial difference promoted by such prestigious philosophers as Friedrich Hegel, Immanuel Kant, and David Hume, most Europeans and Americans assumed that differences in externals—complex- ion, hair, and other physical features—between blacks and whites signified differ- ences in the inherent character—intelligence, morality, and spirituality—of the two groups. When Thomas Jefferson reviewed what he considered to be the major dif- ferences between whites and blacks, he concluded that these differences were so deep and ineradicable that only complete separation of the races, with whites in control until such time as blacks could be removed from the country, could avert race war in the United States.

Jefferson's *Notes on the State of Virginia* (1787) contained a powerful condemna- tion of slavery, but the book also became an influential statement of early American racism because of Jefferson's persistent association of blackness with absence. After celebrating "the fine mixtures of red and white" that endow the complexions of whites with their "superior beauty," Jefferson contemplated with an almost palpa- ble shudder "that eternal monotony, which reigns in the countenances [of black people], that immoveable veil of black which covers all the emotions of the other race." Thus darkness of skin symbolized for Jefferson an absence of light within the African American, a void that made blackness the sign not merely of skin difference but also of an unknowable alien, a threatening other. Providing intellectual and moral cover for slavery's naked politics of exploitation, a sizable school of racist writers in the first half of the nineteenth century in the United States followed Jef- ferson in arguing that the African American's physical and cultural difference amounted to an intellectual, spiritual, and moral otherness that only slavery could manage and turn to some productive account.

RESISTANCE TO SLAVERY AND RACISM

After the United States won its war for independence from Britain in 1783, the cause of African American freedom earned a number of notable regional victories despite being stymied in the national political arena. To win the endorsement of the southern states, the framers of the U.S. Constitution wrote into law several mea- sures that protected slavery, in particular the infamous "three-fifths compromise," which stipulated that a slave could be counted as three-fifths of a person for the purpose of apportioning representation for a given district in the Congress. Since slaves could not vote, the three-fifths compromise did nothing but augment the size and power of the southern bloc in the U.S. House of Representatives. Undaunted, antislavery advocates in Pennsylvania and New York, supported by the Society of Friends (Quakers), the most vocal religious group to oppose slavery in the North American colonies, issued a call for the gradual abolition of slavery in the new re- public. The gradualism of those known as "moral suasionists" enjoyed genuine suc- cess when Vermont banned slavery in 1777 and emancipationists pushed through abolition laws in Pennsylvania (1780), Rhode Island (1784), Connecticut (1784), New York (1799), and New Jersey (1804). By the end of the first decade of the nineteenth century, slavery was effectively a dead letter in all the states of the North and in the burgeoning Northwest Territory. Bowing to antislavery pressure in 1807, the U.S. Congress went so far as to outlaw the African slave trade, though it left the internal slave trade alone.

In the early decades of the nineteenth century, African Americans in the North joined with fair-minded whites to bring about additional social and political advances. African American newspapers, inaugurated by *Freedom's Journal* in 1827, urged through essays, poetry, and fiction as well as more conventional journalism the achievements of black people in the North and the need for an end to slavery in the South. Committed to improved educational opportunity, African Americans pushed for the admission of their children to the early public schools of the North and vigorously protested against laws that excluded them. Independent black Methodist and Baptist churches, led by thoughtful and respected black leaders, bore witness to the solidarity and progressive outlook of northern black communities, as did the rise of various mutual-aid, fraternal, and debating societies in cities such as New York, Philadelphia, and Boston. Racial prejudice, discrimination, and segregation remained endemic in the states of North, however, indifferent to the evidence of the self-improvement and good citizenship of many African Americans.

In the South, where racism provided the cornerstone of the social, economic, and political order, African Americans could do little to alter their circumstances. The living conditions of slaves remained almost totally dependent on the disposition of individual masters. The legal status of free persons of color deteriorated as their numbers shrank in the South after 1800. Antislavery proponents in the upper South were able to liberalize laws that made it easier to emancipate slaves. But the expansion of the British textile industry, together with changes in the farming and processing of cotton in the United States during the 1790s, wedded the South more and more tightly to slavery. The invention of the cotton gin, a labor-saving device that provided a cheap means of separating cotton fiber from its seed, turned Southern agriculture at the turn of the century into "the cotton kingdom." Cotton plantations, on which a hundred or more slaves labored from dawn to dusk six days a week, sprang up over the lower South and in the opening territories of the trans-Mississippi Valley. Slaveholding seemed the key to unlocking vast new wealth from the land. As a consequence the slave population in the South grew rapidly, from seven hundred thousand in 1790 to two million in 1830.

In the late summer of 1831 in Southampton County, Virginia, an insurrection of slaves fomented by a black preacher named Nat Turner crystallized the impending crisis into which slavery was taking the South. Convinced that he had been called by God to usher in the biblically prophesied Day of Judgment, Turner led his followers, who numbered between sixty and eighty, in a bloody march toward Jerusalem, the county seat, where he intended to seize its arsenal and munitions supply. Before they were scattered and apprehended by state and federal troops, Turner's loosely disciplined army executed sixty whites, including Prophet Nat's master and family. Turner remained at large until his capture in late October. After dictating a narrative hurried into publication under the title *The Confessions of Nat Turner*, the leader of the most successful slave revolt in U.S. history was hanged on November 11, 1831. It is estimated that fifty thousand copies of Turner's decidedly unrepentant "confessions" were printed, making this the most widely read African American personal narrative since Equiano's in 1789.

The slaveholding South was permanently traumatized by Turner's insurrection. The Virginia state legislature debated whether to abolish slavery or make it more repressive, deciding in the end to follow the latter course. Throughout the South tighter restrictions were placed on free blacks; on black opportunities to assemble, especially in church; on black ministers; and on the access of slaves to books (even the Bible) as well as to literacy. Those who held the reins of power in the South became increasingly belligerent in their defense of slavery and their determination to see it extended into the new territories beyond the Mississippi River that were lobbying for statehood. Regarding each other with heightening suspicion, representatives of the slave and the free states in the U.S. Congress seemed powerless to prevent the polarization of the two regions of the country. Various compromises were enacted—the most controversial of which was the Compromise of 1850, which among other things instituted the Fugitive Slave Law—so that a balance of power might be maintained between the North and South. Nevertheless, compromise only intensified the feeling in each section that the opposition was gaining an unfair share of power.

RADICAL ABOLITIONISM AND THE FUGITIVE SLAVE NARRATIVE

In the aftermath of the Turner revolt and the South's iron-fisted response to it, a new generation of reformers in the North proclaimed their absolute and uncompromising opposition to slavery. Led by the crusading white journalist William Lloyd Garrison, these abolitionists demanded the immediate end of slavery throughout the United States. Free blacks in the North lent their support to Garrison's American Anti-Slavery Society, editing newspapers, holding conventions, circulating petitions, and investing their money and their energies in protest actions. Searching for a means of galvanizing public concern for the slave as "a man and a brother," this generation of black and white radical abolitionists sponsored a new departure in African American literature, the fugitive slave narrative. From 1830 to the end of the slavery era, the fugitive slave narrative dominated the literary landscape of antebellum black America, far outnumbering the autobiographies of free people of color, not to mention the handful of novels published by African Americans. Most of the major authors of African American literature before 1865, including Olaudah Equiano, Frederick Douglass, William Wells Brown, and Harriet Jacobs, launched their writing careers via narratives of their experience as slaves.

Typically the antebellum slave narrative carried a black message inside a white envelope. Prefatory (and sometimes appended) matter by whites attested to the reliability and good character of the narrator and called attention to what the narrative would reveal about the moral abominations of slavery. The former slave's contribution to the text centered on his or her rite of passage from slavery in the South to freedom in the North. Usually the antebellum slave narrator portrayed slavery as a condition of extreme physical, intellectual, emotional, and spiritual deprivation, a kind of hell on earth. Precipitating the narrator's decision to escape was some sort of personal crisis, such as the sale of a loved one or a dark night of the soul in which hope contends with despair for the spirit of the slave. Impelled by faith in God and a commitment to liberty and human dignity comparable (the slave narrative often stressed) to that of America's Founding Fathers, the slave undertook an arduous quest for freedom that climaxed in his or her arrival in the North. In many antebellum narratives, the attainment of freedom was signaled not simply by reaching the free states but by renaming oneself and dedicating one's future to antislavery activism.

Advertised in the abolitionist press and sold at antislavery meetings throughout the English-speaking world, a significant number of antebellum slave narratives went through multiple editions and sold in the tens of thousands. This popularity was not solely attributable to the publicity the narratives received from the antislavery movement. Readers could see that, as one reviewer put it, "the slave who endeavours to recover his freedom is associating with himself no small part of the romance of the time." To the noted transcendentalist clergyman Theodore Parker, slave narratives qualified as America's only indigenous literary form, for "all the original romance of Americans is in them, not in the white man's novel." The most widely read and hotly debated American novel of the nineteenth century, Harriet Beecher Stowe's *Uncle Tom's Cabin* (1852), was profoundly influenced by its author's reading of a number of slave narratives, to which she owed many graphic incidents and the models for some of her most memorable characters.

In 1845 the slave narrative reached its epitome with the publication of the *Narrative of the Life of Frederick Douglass, an American Slave, Written by Himself.* A fugitive from Maryland slavery, Douglass spent four years honing his skills as an abolitionist lecturer before setting about the task of writing his autobiography. In deciding to author his own story rather than enlist a white editor to transcribe his oral testimony and fashion that into a book, Douglass made a crucial break with established procedure in the publishing of slave narratives. At the risk of public censure for egotism and incompetence (he had never had a day's schooling in his life), Douglass resolved to write his own story in his own way. He was determined to bear witness to the self-awareness, intellectual independence, and literary authority of the slave. After Douglass's immensely successful *Narrative,* the presence of the subtitle, *Written by Himself,* on a slave narrative bore increasing significance as an indicator of a narrator's political and literary self-reliance. In the late 1840s well-known fugitive slaves such as William Wells Brown, Henry Bibb, and James W. C. Pennington reinforced the rhetorical self-consciousness of the slave narrative by incorporating into their stories trickster motifs from African American folk culture, extensive literary and biblical allusion, and a picaresque perspective on the meaning of the slave's flight from bondage to freedom.

As social and political conflict in the United States at mid-century centered more and more on the presence and fate of African Americans, the slave narrative took on an unprecedented urgency and candor, unmasking as never before the moral and social complexities of the American caste and class system in the North as well as the South. *My Bondage and My Freedom* (1855), Douglass's second autobiography, conducted a fresh inquiry into the meaning of slavery and freedom, adopting the standpoint of one who had spent enough time in the so-called free states to understand how pervasive racism and paternalism was, even among the most liberal whites, the Garrisonians themselves. Harriet Jacobs, the earliest known African American female slave to author her own narrative, also challenged conventional ideas about slavery and freedom in her strikingly original *Incidents in the Life of a Slave Girl* (1861). Jacobs's autobiography shows how sexual exploitation made slavery especially oppressive for black women. But in demonstrating how she fought back and ultimately gained both her own freedom and that of her two children, Jacobs proved the inadequacy of the image of victim that had been pervasively applied to female slaves in the male-authored slave narrative. The writing of Jacobs; the feminist oratory of the "Libyan sybil," Sojourner Truth; and the renowned example of Harriet Tubman, the fearless conductor of runaways on the Underground Railroad enriched African American literature with new models of female self-expression and heroism.

THE FIRST AFRICAN AMERICAN LITERARY RENAISSANCE

These developments in the slave narrative, along with the publication of several pioneering experiments in fiction, justify calling the 1850s and early 1860s the first renaissance in African American letters. In these years black writers began to expand their horizons, both in terms of the forms they developed and the themes they adopted. In 1853 Frederick Douglass published a historical novella, *The Heroic Slave,* in his own newspaper, *Frederick Douglass' Paper.* The protagonist of Douglass's story, Madison Washington, who actually led a successful slave mutiny in 1841, gave American readers a model of black manhood that carefully balanced the violent desire for justice of Nat Turner and the Christian pacifism of Stowe's Uncle Tom. Soon after *The Heroic Slave* the first full-length African American novel was published in England under the title *Clotel; or, The President's Daughter*. Authored by William Wells Brown, who had already distinguished himself as the writer of an internationally celebrated slave narrative as well as the first travel book by an African American, *Clotel* blurred the line between fact and fiction by recounting the tragic career of a beautiful and idealistic light-skinned woman reputed to be the daughter of Thomas Jefferson and his slave mistress. *Clotel* helped popularize the sentimental image of the "tragic mulatta" in American fiction and drama. But the ultimate outcome of her story, in which Clotel transforms herself into a combative trickster figure to rescue her daughter from slavery, shows Brown testing the limits of gender conventions in fiction. Five years later, Brown contributed again to the outpouring of literary creativity among blacks at mid-century by fashioning the first African American play, *The Escape; or, A Leap for Freedom*, based on scenes and themes familiar to readers of fugitive slave narratives.

In 1859 Martin R. Delany, a black journalist and physician who would later serve as a major in the Federal Army during the Civil War, produced *Blake; or, The Huts of America*, a novel whose hero plots a slave revolt in the South. Delany's Blake represents the first black nationalist culture hero in African American literature. In the same year the first African American women's fiction also appeared. *The Two Offers*, a short story by Frances Ellen Watkins Harper, and *Our Nig; or, Sketches from the Life of a Free Black*, an autobiographical novel by Harriet E. Wilson. Among the poetic voices of black America Harper's was preeminent at mid-century. The African American reading community embraced her as a writer who spoke to the needs and aspirations of slaves and free people alike in verse that was direct, impassioned, and morally inspiring. In contrast, the literary work of Harriet Wilson received little or no notice, despite (or perhaps because of) her unprecedented, tough-minded investigation of the socioeconomic realities of life for a black working-class woman in the North.

FOLK TRADITIONS

Behind the achievements of individual African American writers during the antislavery period lies the communal consciousness of millions of slaves, whose oral tradition in song and story has given form and substance to literature by black people since they first began writing in English. In his *Narrative*, Frederick Douglass recalled having received his first glimmering sense of the awful evil of slavery by listening to the work songs of his fellow slaves in Maryland. Later in his life he revealed that the familiar plantation spiritual "Run to Jesus" had first suggested to him the thought of making his escape from slavery. The genius of the spirituals rested in their double meaning, their blending of the spiritual and the political. When slaves sang "I thank God I'm free at las' " only they knew whether they were referring to freedom from sin or from slavery. Even in those spirituals that express a poignant yearning for deliverance in heaven from earthly burdens, one can hear a powerful complaint against the institutions that forced black people to believe that only in the next world would they find justice.

A second great fund of southern black folklore, the animal tales, testified to the slaves' commonsense understanding of human psychology and everyday justice in this world. Although many of these tales explained in comic fashion how the world came to be as it is, many more concentrated on the exploits of trickster figures, most notably Brer Rabbit, who used their wits to overcome stronger animal antagonists. Tales that celebrate the trickster, whether in animal or human form, are universal in human folklore. Still the popularity of Brer Rabbit in the folklore of the slaves attests to the enduring faith of black Americans in the power of mind over matter. The spirit of Brer Rabbit lived in every slave who deceived his master with a smile of loyalty while stealing from his storehouse and making plans for escape.

THE CIVIL WAR AND EMANCIPATION

In 1860 the first avowedly antislavery candidate for president, Abraham Lincoln of the Republican Party, was elected in one of the bitterest campaigns ever waged in the United States. Southern extremists began to beat the drum for secession. Lincoln promised the South that he would not demand the abolition of slavery, but he warned the secessionists that he would not allow them to split the Union apart. When South Carolina bombarded federal troops at Fort Sumter in Charleston on April 12, 1861, Lincoln issued a call for seventy-five thousand volunteers to help put down what northern politicians called the southern rebellion. During the next four years, while the American Civil War raged on, African Americans played an increasingly important role in the Union cause. Initially forbidden to serve in the Union army, black men waited until the summer of 1862, when Lincoln finally heeded the counsel of advisers like Frederick Douglass and permitted free blacks in liberated portions of Louisiana and South Carolina to form regiments. When two South Carolina regiments, combining both free blacks and former slaves, captured and occupied Jacksonville, Florida, in March 1863, Lincoln decided to engage in the full-scale recruitment of black soldiers for the army. By the war's end, more than 186,000 blacks had served in the artillery, cavalry, engineers, and infantry as well as in the U.S. Navy. Black troops left a notable record of valor in major battles throughout the South in the last two years of the war even though they were routinely paid less than the wages white soldiers received. More than 38,000 African Americans gave their lives for the Union cause.

Although northern whites joined the Union army for many reasons, blacks fought for one overriding purpose—to bring an end to slavery. For more than two years after the outbreak of hostilities, African Americans waited for their president to link the Union cause with the extinction of slavery. When Lincoln issued the Emancipation Proclamation in the summer of 1862, which declared all slaves in the rebellious states to be free as of January 1, 1863, blacks in the North felt that, at long last, their country had committed itself to an ideal worth dying for. Few African Americans criticized Lincoln for failing to declare freedom for the slaves in the border states, such as Kentucky and Maryland, that had not joined the southern confederacy. Charlotte Forten, daughter of an influential Philadelphia civil rights activist and author of the most widely read African American diary of the nineteenth century, probably spoke for most in the black American leadership class when she entered in her diary on January 1, 1863: "Ah, what a grand, glorious day this has been. The dawn of freedom which it heralds may not break upon us at once; but it will surely come, and sooner, I believe, than we have ever dared hope before." When the final surrender came at Appomatox, Virginia, on April 9, 1865, African Americans pressed for the enactment of laws ensuring a new era of freedom and opportunity for every black American. On December 6, 1865, the Thirteenth Amendment to the U.S. Constitution, which abolished "slavery and involuntary servitude" throughout the country, was ratified by the newly united states of America, including eight from the former Confederacy. But the long-anticipated era of freedom, equality, and opportunity for all would prove much more difficult to bring into reality.

LUCY TERRY

c. 1730–1821

Lucy Terry's only poem, *Bars Fight*, is the earliest known work of literature by an African American. Composed in rhymed tetrameter couplets and probably designed to be sung, Terry's ballad records an Indian ambush of two white families on August 25, 1746, in a section of Deerfield, Massachusetts, known as "the Bars," a colonial term for the meadows. Although Terry had grown up a slave in Deerfield, her poem conveys genuine sympathy for the white men and women who died in the fight. The poem was preserved orally in local memory until it was published in Springfield, Massachusetts, in 1855.

Terry was born in Africa, kidnapped as an infant, and sold into slavery in Rhode Island. In 1735, when she was about five years old, she became the property of Ensign Ebenezer Wells of Deerfield, Massachusetts. She was converted to Christianity and became a member of her master's church in 1744. She remained a slave until Obijah Prince, a wealthy free black, bought her freedom and married her in 1756. In 1760 the Princes moved to Guilford, Vermont, where her reputation as a raconteur and a strong defender of black civil rights grew. Committed to an education for each of her six children, Lucy Terry Prince encouraged her oldest son to apply for admission to Williams College. When he was refused, she traveled to Williamstown, Massachusetts, and delivered a three-hour argument to the college's trustees against Williams's policy of racial discrimination. Though unsuccessful, this effort augmented Terry's regional reputation as a skilled orator. After her husband's death in 1794, Terry moved to Sunderland, Vermont, where she died in 1821.

Bars[1] Fight

> August, 'twas the twenty-fifth,
> Seventeen hundred forty-six,
> The Indians did in ambush lay,
> Some very valient men to slay,
> The names of whom I'll not leave out: 5
> Samuel Allen like a hero fout,[2]
> And though he was so brave and bold,
> His face no more shall we behold.
>
> Eleazer Hawks was killed outright,
> Before he had time to fight,—   10
> Before he did the Indians see,
> Was shot and killed immediately.
>
> Oliver Amsden he was slain,
> Which caused his friends much grief and pain.
> Simeon Amsden they found dead   15
> Not many rods distant from his head.

1. Meadows.   2. Fought.

137

Adonijah Gillett, we do hear,
Did lose his life which was so dear.
John Sadler fled across the water,
And thus escaped the dreadful slaughter.   20

Eunice Allen see the Indians coming,
And hopes to save herself by running;
And had not her petticoats stopped her,
The awful creatures had not catched her,
Nor tommy hawked her on the head,   25
And left her on the ground for dead.
Young Samuel Allen, Oh, lack-a-day!
Was taken and carried to Canada.

1746   1855

OLAUDAH EQUIANO
c. 1745–1797

The Interesting Narrative of the Life of Olaudah Equiano, or Gustavus Vassa, the African, Written by Himself (1789) is widely regarded as the prototype of the slave narrative, a form of autobiography that in the early nineteenth century gained a wide international readership because of its compelling firsthand testimony against slavery. In its bulky two volumes, Olaudah Equiano's Life tells a richly detailed story of seagoing adventure, spiritual enlightenment, and economic success in England and the Americas. Equiano's ability to espouse the highest ideals of his era in the language of the everyday man and woman had much to do with the impressive publication record of the Life, which went through thirty-six editions between 1789 and 1857 and was translated into Dutch and German. Equiano's autobiography was the most influential work of English prose by an African American in the eighteenth century. With Phillis Wheatley's Poems on Various Subjects, Religious and Moral (1773), the Life of Olaudah Equiano verified the claim, much disputed during the Enlightenment, that blacks could represent themselves effectively through writing. Equiano's seriousness of purpose, sophisticated self-analysis, and sustained attention to the craft of storytelling have identified his autobiography as an inaugural text of African American letters.

Equiano was not the first African-born former slave to recount his experiences in bondage and freedom. But he was the first to write the story of his life himself, without the aid or direction of white ghostwriters or editors, such as his predecessors in the slave narrative relied on. Equiano's independence in this regard may be one reason why his story places much more emphasis on the atrocities of slavery and pleads more insistently for its total and immediate abolition than any previous slave narrative. Most slave narrators of Equiano's era impressed their white sponsors with their piety and their willingness to forgive those who had once oppressed and exploited them. Although Equiano made much of his conversion to Christianity, he made clear his dedication to social change by venting his moral outrage toward slavery and by structuring his story so that freedom, not the consolations of religion, emerges as the top priority of his life in slavery. Equiano's twin desires at the end of the Life—to become a Christian missionary to Africa and to lobby for an end to the African slave trade—suggest that Christianity and abolitionism, the pursuit of individual and social perfection, go hand in hand. This mating of the spiritual and the secular in the *Life* was prophetic of the ideological orientation of most nineteenth-century African American protest literature.

One of Equiano's more remarkable rhetorical strategies is his use of his African origins to establish his credibility as a critic of European rapacity. Born around 1745 in the village of Essaka in the interior of modern-day eastern Nigeria, Olaudah Equiano grew up among the Ibo people before he was kidnapped at the age of eleven and sold as a slave to other Africans. His memories of Ibo life are almost unreservedly positive, stressing the simplicity of his people's manners, the justice of their moral values, and the harmony of their society. Even his months with his first master, a black chieftain, are portrayed as benign when compared to his grisly initiation into the savagery of European slavery. Recreating the terror and awe he felt on seeing "those white men with horrible looks, red faces, and long hair" engaged in packing the slave ships with their human cargo, Equiano thrusts his white reader into the mind and heart of a black youth innocent of the monstrous injustice that was about to befall him. In this way Equiano attempted to liberate his white reader from a culturally enforced sense of superiority that prevented many whites from feeling a common bond of humanity with black people.

The *Life of Olaudah Equiano* reveals in unforgettable ways the atrocity that was the Middle Passage. Yet Equiano survived his early years in slavery by tempering his fear of whites with a self-interested desire to master their technology and thus carve out a place for himself in their world. The major part of Equiano's autobiography describes his successful assimilation in practically every sphere of economic activity to which he applies himself. As the personal servant to a lieutenant in the English navy (who renamed him Gustavus Vassa after a sixteenth-century Swedish king) and later as a ship's steward during campaigns in the Mediterranean and off the coast of France, the slave youth makes the most of his maritime opportunities. Expecting from his master's assurances to be freed after six years of good service, Equiano was instead sold to a West Indian trader in 1762, who soon sold him to Robert King, a Philadelphia Quaker and merchant. Working for King taught Equiano, by that time a well-trained seaman, a good deal about seagoing commercial practices, so that by 1766, at the age of twenty-one, the aspiring black man was able not only to buy his freedom but also to launch his own business career. In 1767 the self-emancipated Equiano returned to England to work as a hairdresser for affluent Londoners, during which time he learned the French horn, expanded his study of mathematics, and underwent a profound religious conversion and became a Methodist. In 1773 he returned to the sea to participate in an expedition in search of the North Pole. After voyages to ports as far off as Central America and Turkey, Equiano settled down in England in 1777. During the next few years he became increasingly interested in returning to Africa; in 1787 he was rewarded with an appointment as a "comissary of provisions and stores" for a colonization venture in Sierra Leone on the west coast of Africa. Political infighting occasioned by his public criticism of the management of this venture prevented Equiano from fulfilling his dream of returning to his native land.

After the publication of his autobiography in 1789, Equiano traveled extensively in England and Ireland promoting his book. He married an Englishwoman, Susanna Cullen, in 1792 and died in London on March 31, 1797. Equiano's *Life* bequeaths to modern African American literature a prescient and provocative example of what W. E. B. Du Bois would call "double-consciousness"—the African American's fateful sense of "twoness" born of a bicultural identification with both an African heritage and a European education.

From The Interesting Narrative of the Life of Olaudah Equiano, or Gustavus Vassa, the African, Written by Himself

Volume I

> Behold, God is my salvation; I will trust and not be afraid, for the Lord Jehovah is my strength and my song; he also is become my salvation. And in that day shall ye say, Praise the Lord, call upon his name, declare his doings among the people.
>
> —ISAIAH 12:2, 4

To the Lords Spiritual and Temporal, and the Commons of the Parliament of Great Britain.

My Lords and Gentlemen,

Permit me, with the greatest deference and respect, to lay at your feet the following genuine Narrative; the chief design of which is to excite in your august assemblies a sense of compassion for the miseries which the Slave-Trade has entailed on my unfortunate countrymen. By the horrors of that trade was I first torn away from all the tender connexions that were naturally dear to my heart; but these, through the mysterious ways of Providence, I ought to regard as infinitely more than compensated by the introduction I have thence obtained to the knowledge of the Christian religion, and of a nation which, by its liberal sentiments, its humanity, the glorious freedom of its government, and its proficiency in arts and sciences, has exalted the dignity of human nature.

I am sensible I ought to entreat your pardon for addressing to you a work so wholly devoid of literary merit; but, as the production of an unlettered African, who is actuated by the hope of becoming an instrument towards the relief of his suffering countrymen, I trust that *such a man*, pleading in *such a cause*, will be acquitted of boldness and presumption.

May the God of heaven inspire your hearts with peculiar benevolence on that important day when the question of Abolition is to be discussed, when thousands, in consequence of your Determination, are to look for Happiness or Misery!

I am,

MY LORDS AND GENTLEMEN,

Your most obedient,

And devoted humble Servant,

OLAUDAH EQUIANO,

OR

GUSTAVUS VASSA.

Union-Street, Mary-le-bone,
March 24, 1789.

CHAPTER I

I believe it is difficult for those who publish their own memoirs to escape the imputation of vanity; nor is this the only disadvantage under which they labour: it is also their misfortune, that what is uncommon is rarely, if ever, believed, and what is obvious we are apt to turn from with disgust, and to charge the writer with impertinence. People generally think those memoirs only worthy to be read or remembered which abound in great or striking events, those, in short, which in a high degree excite either admiration or pity. all others they consign to contempt and oblivion. It is therefore, I confess, not a little hazardous in a private and obscure individual, and a stranger too, thus to solicit the indulgent attention of the public; especially when I own I offer here the history of neither a saint, a hero, nor a tyrant. I believe there are few events in my life, which have not happened to many: it is true the incidents of it are numerous; and, did I consider myself an European, I might say my sufferings were great: but when I compare my lot with that of most of my countrymen, I regard myself as a *particular favourite of Heaven*, and acknowledge the mercies of Providence in every occurrence of my life. If then the following narrative does not appear sufficiently interesting to engage general attention, let my motive be some excuse for its publication. I am not so foolishly vain as to expect from it either immortality or literary reputation. If it affords any satisfaction to my numerous friends, at whose request it has been written, or in the smallest degree promotes the interests of humanity, the ends for which it was undertaken will be fully attained, and every wish of my heart gratified. Let it therefore be remembered, that, in wishing to avoid censure, I do not aspire to praise.

That part of Africa, known by the name of Guinea, to which the trade for slaves is carried on, extends along the coast above 3400 miles, from the Senegal to Angola, and includes a variety of kingdoms. Of these the most considerable is the kingdom of Benen,[1] both as to extent and wealth, the richness and cultivation of the soil, the power of its king, and the number and warlike disposition of the inhabitants. It is situated nearly under the line,[2] and extends along the coast about 170 miles, but runs back into the interior part of Africa to a distance hitherto I believe unexplored by any traveller; and seems only terminated at length by the empire of Abyssinia,[3] near 1500 miles from its beginning. This kingdom is divided into many provinces or districts: in one of the most remote and fertile of which, called Eboe,[4] I was born, in the year 1745, in a charming fruitful vale, named Essaka. The distance of this province from the capital of Benin and the sea coast must be very considerable; for I had never heard of white men or Europeans, nor of the sea: and our subjection to the king of Benin was little more than nominal; for every transaction of the government, as far as my slender observation extended, was conducted by the chiefs or elders of the place. The manners and government of a people who have little commerce with other countries are generally very simple; and the history of what

1. Or Benin, a West African country, home of the kingdom of Dahomey.
2. South of the equator.
3. An African kingdom comprising modern-day Ethiopia and parts of the Sudan.
4. The Ibo people live in what is now southern Nigeria.

passes in one family or village may serve as a specimen of a nation. My father was one of those elders or chiefs I have spoken of, and was styled Embrenche; a term, as I remember, importing the highest distinction, and signifying in our language a *mark* of grandeur. This mark is conferred on the person entitled to it, by cutting the skin across at the top of the forehead, and drawing it down to the eye-brows; and while it is in this situation applying a warm hand, and rubbing it until it shrinks up into a thick *weal* across the lower part of the forehead. Most of the judges and senators were thus marked; my father had long born it: I had seen it conferred on one of my brothers, and I was also *destined* to receive it by my parents. Those Embrence, or chief men, decided disputes and punished crimes; for which purpose they always assembled together. The proceedings were generally short; and in most cases the law of retaliation prevailed. I remember a man was brought before my father, and the other judges, for kidnapping a boy; and, although he was the son of a chief or senator, he was condemned to make recompense by a man or woman slave. Adultery, however, was sometimes punished with slavery or death; a punishment which I believe is inflicted on it throughout most of the nations of Africa:[5] so sacred among them is the honour of the marriage bed, and so jealous are they of the fidelity of their wives. Of this I recollect an instance:—a woman was convicted before the judges of adultery, and delivered over, as the custom was, to her husband to be punished. Accordingly he determined to put her to death: but it being found, just before her execution, that she had an infant at her breast; and no woman being prevailed on to perform the part of a nurse, she was spared on account of the child. The men, however, do not preserve the same constancy to their wives, which they expect from them; for they indulge in a plurality, though seldom in more than two. Their mode of marriage is thus:—both parties are usually betrothed when young by their parents, (though I have known the males to betroth themselves). On this occasion a feast is prepared, and the bride and bridegroom stand up in the midst of all their friends, who are assembled for the purpose, while he declares she is thenceforth to be looked upon as his wife, and that no other person is to pay any addresses to her. This is also immediately proclaimed in the vicinity, on which the bride retires from the assembly. Some time after she is brought home to her husband, and then another feast is made, to which the relations of both parties are invited: her parents then deliver her to the bridegroom, accompanied with a number of blessings, and at the same time they tie round her waist a cotton string of the thickness of a goose-quill, which none but married women are permitted to wear: she is now considered as completely his wife; and at this time the dowry is given to the new married pair, which generally consists of portions of land, slaves, and cattle, household goods, and implements of husbandry. These are offered by the friends of both parties; besides which the parents of the bridegroom present gifts to those of the bride, whose property she is looked upon before marriage; but after it she is esteemed the sole property of her husband. The ceremony being now ended the festival begins, which

---

5. "See Benezet's 'Account of Guinea' through-   *Some Historical Account of Guinea, with an Inquiry*
out" [Equiano's note]. Anthony Benezet (1713–   *into the Rise and Progress of the Slave Trade* (1772).
1784), American antislavery activist and author of

is celebrated with bonefires, and loud acclamations of joy, accompanied with music and dancing.

We are almost a nation of dancers, musicians, and poets. Thus every great event, such as a triumphant return from battle, or other cause of public rejoicing is celebrated in public dances, which are accompanied with songs and music suited to the occasion. The assembly is separated into four divisions, which dance either apart or in succession, and each with a character peculiar to itself. The first division contains the married men, who in their dances frequently exhibit feats of arms, and the representation of a battle. To these succeed the married women, who dance in the second division. The young men occupy the third; and the maidens the fourth. Each represents some interesting scene of real life, such as a great achievement, domestic employment, a pathetic story, or some rural sport; and as the subject is generally founded on some recent event, it is therefore ever new. This gives our dances a spirit and variety which I have scarcely seen elsewhere.[6] We have many musical instruments, particularly drums of different kinds, a piece of music which resembles a guitar, and another much like a stickado.[7] These last are chiefly used by betrothed virgins, who play on them on all grand festivals.

As our manners are simple, our luxuries are few. The dress of both sexes is nearly the same. It generally consists of a long piece of callico, or muslin, wrapped loosely round the body, somewhat in the form of a highland plaid. This is usually dyed blue, which is our favourite colour. It is extracted from a berry, and is brighter and richer than any I have seen in Europe. Besides this, our women of distinction wear golden ornaments; which they dispose with some profusion on their arms and legs. When our women are not employed with the men in tillage, their usual occupation is spinning and weaving cotton, which they afterwards dye, and make it into garments. They also manufacture earthen vessels, of which we have many kinds. Among the rest tobacco pipes, made after the same fashion, and used in the same manner, as those in Turkey.[8]

Our manner of living is entirely plain; for as yet the natives are unacquainted with those refinements in cookery which debauch the taste: bullocks, goats, and poultry, supply the greatest part of their food. These constitute likewise the principal wealth of the country, and the chief articles of its commerce. The flesh is usually stewed in a pan; to make it savoury we sometimes use also pepper, and other spices, and we have salt made of wood ashes. Our vegetables are mostly plantains, eadas, yams, beans, and Indian corn.[9] The head of the family usually eats alone; his wives and slaves have also their separate tables. Before we taste food we always wash our hands: indeed our cleanliness on all occasions is extreme; but on this it is an indispensable ceremony. After washing, libation is made, by pouring out a small portion of the food, in a certain place, for the

6. "When I was in Smyrna I have frequently seen the Greeks dance after this manner" [Equiano's note]. Smyrna is a city in western Turkey founded by the Greeks.
7. The sticcado pastorale, an Italian musical instrument resembling a xylophone.
8. The bowl is earthen, curiously figured, to which a long reed is fixed as a tube. This tube is sometimes so long as to be borne by one, and frequently out of grandeur by two boys [Equiano's note].
9. Also known as maize, a New World plant cultivated by Native American peoples and brought to Africa in the 16th century by the Portuguese, where it quickly became a staple. "Eadas": types of yams.

spirits of departed relations, which the natives suppose to preside over their conduct, and guard them from evil. They are totally unacquainted with strong or spirituous liquors; and their principal beverage is palm wine. This is gotten from a tree of that name by tapping it at the top, and fastening a large gourd to it; and sometimes one tree will yield three or four gallons in a night. When just drawn it is of a most delicious sweetness; but in a few days it acquires a tartish and more spirituous flavour: though I never saw any one intoxicated by it. The same tree also produces nuts and oil. Our principal luxury is in perfumes; one sort of these is an odoriferous wood of delicious fragrance: the other a kind of earth; a small portion of which thrown into the fire diffuses a most powerful odour.[1] We beat this wood into powder, and mix it with palm oil; with which both men and women perfume themselves.

In our buildings we study convenience rather than ornament. Each master of a family has a large square piece of ground, surrounded with a moat or fence, or enclosed with a wall made of red earth tempered; which, when dry, is as hard as brick. Within this are his houses to accommodate his family and slaves; which, if numerous, frequently present the appearance of a village. In the middle stands the principal building, appropriated to the sole use of the master, and consisting of two apartments; in one of which he sits in the day with his family, the other is left apart for the reception of his friends. He has besides these a distinct apartment in which he sleeps, together with his male children. On each side are the apartments of his wives, who have also their separate day and night houses. The habitations of the slaves and their families are distributed throughout the rest of the enclosure. These houses never exceed one story in height: they are always built of wood, or stakes driven into the ground, crossed with wattles,[2] and neatly plastered within, and without. The roof is thatched with reeds. Our day-houses are left open at the sides; but those in which we sleep are always covered, and plastered in the inside, with a composition mixed with cowdung, to keep off the different insects, which annoy us during the night. The walls and floors also of these are generally covered with mats. Our beds consist of a platform, raised three or four feet from the ground, on which are laid skins, and different parts of a spungy tree called plaintain. Our covering is calico or muslin, the same as our dress. The usual seats are a few logs of wood; but we have benches, which are generally perfumed, to accommodate strangers: these compose the greater part of our household furniture. Houses so constructed and furnished require but little skill to erect them. Every man is a sufficient architect for the purpose. The whole neighbourhood afford their unanimous assistance in building them and in return receive, and expect no other recompense than a feast.

As we live in a country where nature is prodigal of her favours, our wants are few and easily supplied; of course we have few manufactures. They consist for the most part of calicoes, earthern ware, ornaments, and instruments of war and husbandry. But these make no part of our commerce, the principal articles of which, as I have observed, are provisions. In such a state money is of little use; however we have some small pieces of coin, if I may

---

1. When I was in Smyrna I saw the same kind of earth, and brought some of it with me to England; it resembles musk in strength, but is more delicious in scent, and is not unlike the smell of a rose [Equiano's note].

2. Slender branches or reeds.

call them such. They are made something like an anchor; but I do not remember either their value or denomination. We have also markets, at which I have been frequently with my mother. These are sometimes visited by stout mahogany-coloured men from the south west of us: we call them Oye-Eboe, which term signifies red men living at a distance. They generally bring us fire-arms, gunpowder, hats, beads, and dried fish. The last we esteemed a great rarity, as our waters were only brooks and springs. These articles they barter with us for odoriferous woods and earth, and our salt of wood ashes. They always carry slaves through our land; but the strictest account is exacted of their manner of procuring them before they are suffered to pass. Sometimes indeed we sold slaves to them, but they were only prisoners of war, or such among us as had been convicted of kidnapping, or adultery, and some other crimes, which we esteemed heinous. This practice of kidnapping induces me to think, that, notwithstanding all our strictness, their principal business among us was to trepan[3] our people. I remember too they carried great sacks along with them, which not long after I had an opportunity of fatally seeing applied to that infamous purpose.

Our land is uncommonly rich and fruitful, and produces all kinds of vegetables in great abundance. We have plenty of Indian corn, and vast quantities of cotton and tobacco. Our pine apples grow without culture; they are about the size of the largest sugar-loaf,[4] and finely flavoured. We have also spices of different kinds, particularly pepper; and a variety of delicious fruits which I have never seen in Europe; together with gums of various kinds, and honey in abundance. All our industry is exerted to improve those blessings of nature. Agriculture is our chief employment; and every one, even the children and women, are engaged in it. Thus we are all habituated to labour from our earliest years. Every one contributes something to the common stock; and as we are unacquainted with idleness, we have no beggars. The benefits of such a mode of living are obvious. The West India planters prefer the slaves of Benin or Eboe to those of any other part of Guinea, for their hardiness, intelligence, integrity, and zeal. Those benefits are felt by us in the general healthiness of the people, and in their vigour and activity; I might have added too in their comeliness. Deformity is indeed unknown amongst us, I mean that of shape. Numbers of the natives of Eboe now in London might be brought in support of this assertion: for, in regard to complexion, ideas of beauty are wholly relative. I remember while in Africa to have seen three negro children, who were tawny, and another quite white, who were universally regarded by myself, and the natives in general, as far as related to their complexions, as deformed. Our women too were in my eyes at least uncommonly graceful, alert, and modest to a degree of bashfulness; nor do I remember to have ever heard of an instance of incontinence amongst them before marriage. They are also remarkably cheerful. Indeed cheerfulness and affability are two of the leading characteristics of our nation.

Our tillage is exercised in a large plain or common, some hours walk from our dwellings, and all the neighbours resort thither in a body. They use no beasts of husbandry; and their only instruments are hoes, axes, shovels, and beaks, or pointed iron to dig with. Sometimes we are visited by

---

3. To trap by trickery.   4. Refined sugar molded into a cone.

locusts, which come in large clouds, so as to darken the air, and destroy our harvest. This however happens rarely, but when it does, a famine is produced by it. I remember an instance or two wherein this happened. This common is often the theatre of war; and therefore when our people go out to till their land, they not only go in a body, but generally take their arms with them for fear of a surprise; and when they apprehend an invasion they guard the avenues to their dwellings, by driving sticks into the ground, which are so sharp at one end as to pierce the foot, and are generally dipped in poison. From what I can recollect of these battles, they appear to have been irruptions of one little state or district on the other, to obtain prisoners or booty. Perhaps they were incited to this by those traders who brought the European goods I mentioned amongst us. Such a mode of obtaining slaves in Africa is common; and I believe more are procured this way and by kidnapping, than any other.[5] When a trader wants slaves, he applies to a chief for them, and tempts him with his wares. It is not extraordinary, if on this occasion he yields to the temptation with as little firmness, and accepts the price of his fellow creatures liberty with as little reluctance as the enlightened merchant. Accordingly he falls on his neighbours, and a desperate battle ensues. If he prevails and takes prisoners, he gratifies his avarice by selling them; but, if his party be vanquished, and he falls into the hands of the enemy, he is put to death: for, as he has been known to foment their quarrels, it is thought dangerous to let him survive, and no ransom can save him, though all other prisoners may be redeemed. We have firearms, bows and arrows, broad two-edged swords and javelins: we have shields also which cover a man from head to foot. All are taught the use of these weapons; even our women are warriors, and march boldly out to fight along with the men. Our whole district is a kind of militia: on a certain signal given, such as the firing of a gun at night, they all rise in arms and rush upon their enemy. It is perhaps something remarkable, that when our people march to the field a red flag or banner is borne before them. I was once a witness to a battle in our common. We had been all at work in it one day as usual, when our people were suddenly attacked. I climbed a tree at some distance, from which I beheld the fight. There were many women as well as men on both sides; among others my mother was there, and armed with a broad sword. After fighting for a considerable time with great fury, and after many had been killed our people obtained the victory, and took their enemy's Chief prisoner. He was carried off in great triumph, and, though he offered a large ransom for his life, he was put to death. A virgin of note among our enemies had been slain in the battle, and her arm was exposed in our market-place, where our trophies were always exhibited. The spoils were divided according to the merit of the warriors. Those prisoners which were not sold or redeemed we kept as slaves: but how different was their condition from that of the slaves in the West Indies! With us they do no more work than other members of the community, even their masters; their food, clothing and lodging were nearly the same as theirs, (except that they were not permitted to eat with those who were free-born); and there was scarce any other difference between them, than a superior degree

5. See Benezet's "Account of Africa" throughout [Equiano's note].

of importance which the head of a family possesses in our state, and that authority which, as such, he exercises over every part of his household. Some of these slaves have even slaves under them as their own property, and for their own use.

As to religion, the natives believe that there is one Creator of all things, and that he lives in the sun, and is girted round with a belt that he may never eat or drink; but, according to some, he smokes a pipe, which is our own favourite luxury. They believe he governs events, especially our deaths or captivity; but, as for the doctrine of eternity, I do not remember to have ever heard of it: some however believe in the transmigration of souls[6] in a certain degree. Those spirits, which are not transmigrated, such as our dear friends or relations, they believe always attend them, and guard them from the bad spirits or their foes. For this reason they always before eating, as I have observed, put some small portion of the meat, and pour some of their drink, on the ground for them; and they often make oblations of the blood of beasts or fowls at their graves. I was very fond of my mother, and almost constantly with her. When she went to make these oblations at her mother's tomb, which was a kind of small solitary thatched house, I some-times attended her. There she made her libations, and spent most of the night in cries and lamentations. I have been often extremely terrified on these occasions. The loneliness of the place, the darkness of the night, and the ceremony of libation, naturally awful and gloomy, were heightened by my mother's lamentations; and these, concurring with the cries of doleful birds, by which these places were frequented, gave an inexpressible terror to the scene.

We compute the year from the day on which the sun crosses the line, and on its setting that evening there is a general shout throughout the land; at least I can speak from my own knowledge throughout our vicinity. The people at the same time make a great noise with rattles, not unlike the bas-ket rattles used by children here, though much larger, and hold up their hands to heaven for a blessing. It is then the greatest offerings are made; and those children whom our wise men foretell will be fortunate are then presented to different people. I remember many used to come to see me, and I was carried about to others for that purpose. They have many offer-ings, particularly at full moons; generally two at harvest before the fruits are taken out of the ground: and when any young animals are killed, some-times they offer up part of them as a sacrifice. These offerings, when made by one of the heads of a family, serve for the whole. I remember we often had them at my father's and my uncle's, and their families have been pre-sent. Some of our offerings are eaten with bitter herbs. We had a saying among us to any one of a cross temper, "That if they were to be eaten, they should be eaten with bitter herbs."

We practised circumcision like the Jews, and made offerings and feasts on that occasion in the same manner as they did. Like them also, our chil-dren were named from some event, some circumstance, or fancied fore-boding at the time of their birth. I was named *Olaudah*, which, in our

---

6. A concept of reincarnation in which the soul is reborn into successive existences that may be human, animal, or vegetable.

language, signifies vicissitude or fortune also, one favoured, and having a loud voice and well spoken. I remember we never polluted the name of the object of our adoration; on the contrary, it was always mentioned with the greatest reverence; and we were totally unacquainted with swearing, and all those terms of abuse and reproach which find their way so readily and copiously into the languages of more civilized people. The only expressions of that kind I remember were "May you rot, or may you swell, or may a beast take you."

I have before remarked that the natives of this part of Africa are extremely cleanly. This necessary habit of decency was with us a part of religion, and therefore we had many purifications and washings; indeed almost as many, and used on the same occasions, if my recollection does not fail me, as the Jews. Those that touched the dead at any time were obliged to wash and purify themselves before they could enter a dwelling-house. Every woman too, at certain times, was forbidden to come into a dwelling-house, or touch any person, or any thing we ate. I was so fond of my mother I could not keep from her, or avoid touching her at some of those periods, in consequence of which I was obliged to be kept out with her, in a little house made for that purpose, till offering was made, and then we were purified.

Though we had no places of public worship, we had priests and magicians, or wise men. I do not remember whether they had different offices, or whether they were united in the same persons, but they were held in great reverence by the people. They calculated our time, and foretold events, as their name imported, for we called them Ah-affoe-way-cah, which signifies calculators or yearly men, our year being called Ah-affoe. They wore their beards, and when they died they were succeeded by their sons. Most of their implements and things of value were interred along with them. Pipes and tobacco were also put into the grave with the corpse, which was always perfumed and ornamented, and animals were offered in sacrifice to them. None accompanied their funerals but those of the same profession or tribe. These buried them after sunset, and always returned from the grave by a different way from that which they went.

These magicians were also our doctors or physicians. They practised bleeding by cupping;[7] and were very successful in healing wounds and expelling poisons. They had likewise some extraordinary method of discovering jealousy, theft, and poisoning; the success of which no doubt they derived from their unbounded influence over the credulity and superstition of the people. I do not remember what those methods were, except that as to poisoning: I recollect an instance or two, which I hope it will not be deemed impertinent here to insert, as it may serve as a kind of specimen of the rest, and is still used by the negroes in the West Indies. A virgin had been poisoned, but it was not known by whom: the doctors ordered the corpse to be taken up by some persons, and carried to the grave. As soon as the bearers had raised it on their shoulders, they seemed seized with some[8] sudden impulse, and ran to and fro unable to stop themselves. At last, after having passed through a number of thorns and prickly bushes unhurt, the

7. Drawing blood with a heated glass vessel.
8. "See also Leut. Matthew's Voyage, p. 123"   [Equiano's note]. John Matthews's A *Voyage to the River Sierra Leone* (1788).

corpse fell from them close to a house, and defaced it in the fall; and, the owner being taken up, he immediately confessed the poisoning.[9]

The natives are extremely cautious about poison. When they buy any eatable the seller kisses it all round before the buyer, to shew him it is not poisoned; and the same is done when any meat or drink is presented, particularly to a stranger. We have serpents of different kinds, some of which are esteemed ominous when they appear in our houses, and these we never molest. I remember two of those ominous snakes, each of which was as thick as the calf of a man's leg, and in colour resembling a dolphin in the water, crept at different times into my mother's night-house, where I always lay with her, and coiled themselves into folds, and each time they crowed like a cock. I was desired by some of our wise men to touch these, that I might be interested in the good omens, which I did, for they were quite harmless, and would tamely suffer themselves to be handled; and then they were put into a large open earthen pan, and set on one side of the highway. Some of our snakes, however, were poisonous: one of them crossed the road one day when I was standing on it, and passed between my feet without offering to touch me, to the great surprise of many who saw it; and these incidents were accounted by the wise men, and therefore by my mother and the rest of the people, as remarkable omens in my favour.

Such is the imperfect sketch my memory has furnished me with of the manners and customs of a people among whom I first drew my breath. And here I cannot forbear suggesting what has long struck me very forcibly, namely, the strong analogy which even by this sketch, imperfect as it is, appears to prevail in the manners and customs of my countrymen and those of the Jews, before they reached the Land of Promise, and particularly the patriarchs[1] while they were yet in that pastoral state which is described in Genesis—an analogy, which alone would induce me to think that the one people had sprung from the other. Indeed this is the opinion of Dr. Gill,[2] who, in his commentary on Genesis, very ably deduces the pedigree of the Africans from Aster and Asra, the descendants of Abraham by Keturah his wife and concubine (for both these titles are applied to her). It is also comformable to the sentiments of Dr. John Clarke, formerly Dean of Sarum,[3] in his Truth of the Christian Religion: both these authors concur in ascribing to us this original. The reasonings of these gentlemen are still further confirmed by the scripture chronology; and if any further corroboration were required, this resemblance in so many respects is a strong

9. An instance of this kind happened at Montserrat in the West Indies in the year 1763. I then belonged to the Charming Sally, Capt. Doran.—The chief mate, Mr. Mansfield, and some of the crew being one day on shore, were present at the burying of a poisoned negro girl. Though they had often heard of the circumstance of the running in such cases, and had even seen it, they imagined it to be a trick of the corpse-bearers. The mate therefore desired two of the sailors to take up the coffin, and carry it to the grave. The sailors, who were all of the same opinion, readily obeyed; but they had scarcely raised it to their shoulders, before they began to run furiously about, quite unable to direct themselves, till, at last, without intention, they came to the hut of him who had poisoned the girl. The coffin then immediately fell from their shoulders against the hut, and damaged part of the wall. The owner of the hut was taken into custody on this, and confessed the poisoning.—I give this story as it was related by the mate and crew on their return to the ship. The credit which is due to it I leave with the reader [Equiano's note].
1. The forefathers of the Israelites, including Abraham, Isaac, Jacob, and Jacob's twelve sons. "Land of Promise": Canaan, which God promised to the ancient Israelites after their exodus from Egypt.
2. John Gill (1697–1771), English Baptist theologian.
3. The ecclesiastical name for Salisbury, England. John Clarke (1682–1757), mathematician and theologian, author of The Truth of the Christian Religion (1711).

evidence in support of the opinion. Like the Israelites in their primitive state, our government was conducted by our chiefs or judges, our wise men and elders; and the head of a family with us enjoyed a similar authority over his household with that which is ascribed to Abraham and the other patriarchs. The law of retaliation obtained almost universally with us as with them: and even their religion appeared to have shed upon us a ray of its glory, though broken and spent in its passage, or eclipsed by the cloud with which time, tradition, and ignorance might have enveloped it; for we had our circumcision (a rule I believe peculiar to that people:) we had also our sacrifices and burnt-offerings, our washings and purifications, on the same occasions as they had.

As to the difference of colour between the Eboan Africans and the modern Jews, I shall not presume to account for it. It is a subject which has engaged the pens of men of both genius and learning, and is far above my strength. The most able and Reverend Mr. T. Clarkson, however, in his much admired Essay on the Slavery and Commerce of the Human Species,[4] has ascertained the cause, in a manner that at once solves every objection on that account, and, on my mind at least, has produced the fullest conviction. I shall therefore refer to that performance for the theory,[5] contenting myself with extracting a fact as related by Dr. Mitchel.[6] "The Spaniards, who have inhabited America, under the torrid zone, for any time, are become as dark coloured as our native Indians of Virginia; of which I *myself have been a witness.*" There is also another instance[7] of a Portuguese settlement at Mitomba, a river in Sierra Leona;[8] where the inhabitants are bred from a mixture of the first Portuguese discoverers with the natives, and are now become in their complexion, and in the woolly quality of their hair, *perfect negroes,* retaining however a smattering of the Portuguese language.

These instances, and a great many more which might be adduced, while they shew how the complexions of the same persons vary in different climates, it is hoped may tend also to remove the prejudice that some conceive against the natives of Africa on account of their colour. Surely the minds of the Spaniards did not change with their complexions! Are there not causes enough to which the apparent inferiority of an African may be ascribed, without limiting the goodness of God, and supposing he forbore to stamp understanding on certainly his own image, because "carved in ebony." Might it not naturally be ascribed to their situation? When they come among Europeans, they are ignorant of their language, religion, manners, and customs. Are any pains taken to teach them these? Are they treated as men? Does not slavery itself depress the mind, and extinguish all its fire and every noble sentiment? But, above all, what advantages do not a refined people possess over those who are rude and uncultivated. Let the polished and haughty European recollect that his ancestors were once, like the Africans, uncivilized, and even barbarous. Did Nature make *them* in-

---

4. Thomas Clarkson (1760–1846), antislavery agitator, wrote his essay in 1785.
5. Page 178 to 216 [Equiano's note].
6. Philos. Trans. No. 476, Set. 4, cited by Mr. Clarkson, p. 205 [Equiano's note].

7. Same page [Equiano's note].
8. A West African port for the Portuguese ivory and slave trade, later a colony established by British abolitionists for the resettlement of freed slaves.

ferior to their sons? and should *they too* have been made slaves? Every rational mind answers, No. Let such reflections as these melt the pride of their superiority into sympathy for the wants and miseries of their sable[9] brethren, and compel them to acknowledge, that understanding is not confined to feature or colour. If, when they look round the world, they feel exultation, let it be tempered with benevolence to others, and gratitude to God, "who hath made of one blood all nations of men for to dwell on all the face of the earth;[1] and whose wisdom is not our wisdom, neither are our ways his ways."[2]

CHAPTER II

I hope the reader will not think I have trespassed on his patience in introducing myself to him with some account of the manners and customs of my country. They had been implanted in me with great care, and made an impression on my mind, which time could not erase, and which all the adversity and variety of fortune I have since experienced served only to rivet and record, for, whether the love of one's country be real or imaginary, or a lesson of reason, or an instinct of nature, I still look back with pleasure on the first scenes of my life, though that pleasure has been for the most part mingled with sorrow.

I have already acquainted the reader with the time and place of my birth. My father, besides many slaves, had a numerous family, of which seven lived to grow up, including myself and a sister, who was the only daughter. As I was the youngest of the sons, I became, of course, the greatest favourite with my mother, and was always with her; and she used to take particular pains to form my mind. I was trained up from my earliest years in the art of war; my daily exercise was shooting and throwing javelins; and my mother adorned me with emblems, after the manner of our greatest warriors. In this way I grew up till I was turned the age of eleven, when an end was put to my happiness in the following manner:—Generally when the grown people in the neighbourhood were gone far in the fields to labour, the children assembled together in some of the neighbours' premises to play; and commonly some of us used to get up a tree to look out for any assailant, or kidnapper, that might come upon us; for they sometimes took those opportunities of our parents' absence to attack and carry off as many as they could seize. One day, as I was watching at the top of a tree in our yard, I saw one of those people come into the yard of our next neighbour but one, to kidnap, there being many stout young people in it. Immediately on this I gave the alarm of the rogue, and he was surrounded by the stoutest of them, who entangled him with cords, so that he could not escape till some of the grown people came and secured him. But alas! ere long it was my fate to be thus attacked, and to be carried off, when none of the grown people were nigh. One day, when all our people were gone out to their works as usual, and only I and my dear sister were left to mind the house, two men and a woman got over our walls, and in a moment seized us both, and, without

9. Black.
1. Acts 17:26.
2. Compare Isaiah 55:8: "For my thoughts are not your thoughts, neither are your ways my ways, saith the Lord."

giving us time to cry out, or make resistance, they stopped our mouths, and ran off with us into the nearest wood. Here they tied our hands, and continued to carry us as far as they could, till night came on, when we reached a small house, where the robbers halted for refreshment, and spent the night. We were then unbound, but were unable to take any food; and, being quite overpowered by fatigue and grief, our only relief was some sleep, which allayed our misfortune for a short time. The next morning we left the house, and continued travelling all the day. For a long time we had kept the woods, but at last we came into a road which I believed I knew. I had now some hopes of being delivered; for we had advanced but a little way before I discovered some people at a distance, on which I began to cry out for their assistance: but my cries had no other effect than to make them tie me faster and stop my mouth, and then they put me into a large sack. They also stopped my sister's mouth, and tied her hands; and in this manner we proceeded till we were out of the sight of these people. When we went to rest the following night they offered us some victuals;[3] but we refused it; and the only comfort we had was in being in one another's arms all that night, and bathing each other with our tears. But alas! we were soon deprived of even the small comfort of weeping together. The next day proved a day of greater sorrow than I had yet experienced; for my sister and I were then separated, while we lay clasped in each other's arms. It was in vain that we besought them not to part us; she was torn from me, and immediately carried away, while I was left in a state of distraction not to be described. I cried and grieved continually; and for several days I did not eat any thing but what they forced into my mouth. At length, after many days travelling, during which I had often changed masters, I got into the hands of a chieftain, in a very pleasant country. This man had two wives and some children, and they all used me extremely well, and did all they could to comfort me; particularly the first wife, who was something like my mother. Although I was a great many days journey from my father's house, yet these people spoke exactly the same language with us. This first master of mine, as I may call him, was a smith, and my principal employment was working his bellows, which were the same kind as I had seen in my vicinity. They were in some respects not unlike the stoves here in gentlemen's kitchens; and were covered over with leather, and in the middle of that leather a stick was fixed, and a person stood up, and worked it, in the same manner as is done to pump water out of a cask with a hand pump. I believe it was gold he worked, for it was of a lovely bright yellow colour, and was worn by the women on their wrists and ankles. I was there I suppose about a month, and they at last used to trust me some little distance from the house. This liberty I used in embracing every opportunity to inquire the way to my own home: and I also sometimes, for the same purpose, went with the maidens, in the cool of the evenings, to bring pitchers of water from the springs for the use of the house. I had also remarked where the sun rose in the morning, and set in the evening, as I had travelled along; and I had observed that my father's house was towards the rising of the sun. I therefore determined to

3. Food.

seize the first opportunity of making my escape, and to shape my course for
that quarter; for I was quite oppressed and weighed down by grief after my
mother and friends; and my love of liberty, ever great, was strengthened by
the mortifying circumstance of not daring to eat with the free-born children, although I was mostly their companion. While I was projecting my
escape, one day an unlucky event happened, which quite disconcerted my
plan, and put an end to my hopes. I used to be sometimes employed in
assisting an elderly woman slave to cook and take care of the poultry; and
one morning, while I was feeding some chickens, I happened to toss a
small pebble at one of them, which hit it on the middle and directly killed
it. The old slave, having soon after missed the chicken, inquired after it;
and on my relating the accident (for I told her the truth, because my
mother would never suffer me to tell a lie) she flew into a violent passion,
threatened that I should suffer for it; and, my master being out, she immediately went and told her mistress what I had done. This alarmed me very
much, and I expected an instant flogging, which to me was uncommonly
dreadful; for I had seldom been beaten at home. I therefore resolved to fly;
and accordingly I ran into a thicket that was hard by, and hid myself in the
bushes. Soon afterwards my mistress and the slave returned, and, not seeing me, they searched all the house, but not finding me, and I not making
answer when they called to me, they thought I had run away, and the
whole neighbourhood was raised in the pursuit of me. In that part of the
country (as in ours) the houses and villages were skirted with woods, or
shrubberies, and the bushes were so thick that a man could readily conceal
himself in them, so as to elude the strictest search. The neighbours continued the whole day looking for me, and several times many of them came
within a few yards of the place where I lay hid. I then gave myself up for lost
entirely, and expected every moment, when I heard a rustling among the
trees, to be found out, and punished by my master: but they never discovered me, though they were often so near that I even heard their conjectures
as they were looking about for me; and I now learned from them, that any
attempt to return home would be hopeless. Most of them supposed I had
fled towards home, but the distance was so great, and the way so intricate,
that they thought I could never reach it, and that I should be lost in the
woods. When I heard this I was seized with a violent panic, and abandoned
myself to despair. Night too began to approach, and aggravated all my fears.
I had before entertained hopes of getting home, and I had determined
when it should be dark to make the attempt; but I was now convinced it was
fruitless, and I began to consider that, if possibly I could escape all other
animals, I could not those of the human kind; and that, not knowing the
way, I must perish in the woods. Thus was I like the hunted deer:

—Ev'ry leaf and ev'ry whisp'ring breath
Convey'd a foe, and ev'ry foe a death.[4]

4. From John Denham's *Cooper Hill* (1642), lines 286–88.

I heard frequent rustlings among the leaves; and being pretty sure they were snakes I expected every instant to be stung by them. This increased my anguish, and the horror of my situation became now quite insupportable. I at length quitted the thicket, very faint and hungry, for I had not eaten or drank any thing all the day; and crept to my master's kitchen, from whence I set out at first, and which was an open shed, and laid myself down in the ashes with an anxious wish for death to relieve me from all my pains. I was scarcely awake in the morning when the old woman slave, who was the first up, came to light the fire, and saw me in the fire place. She was very much surprised to see me, and could scarcely believe her own eyes. She now promised to intercede for me, and went for her master, who soon after came, and, having slightly reprimanded me, ordered me to be taken care of, and not to be ill-treated.

Soon after this my master's only daughter, and child by his first wife, sickened and died, which affected him so much that for some time he was almost frantic, and really would have killed himself, had he not been watched and prevented. However, in a small time afterwards he recovered, and I was again sold. I was now carried to the left of the sun's rising, through many different countries, and a number of large woods. The people I was sold to used to carry me very often, when I was tired, either on their shoulders or on their backs. I saw many convenient well-built sheds along the roads, at proper distances, to accommodate the merchants and travellers, who lay in those buildings along with their wives, who often accompany them; and they always go well armed.

From the time I left my own nation I always found somebody that understood me till I came to the sea coast. The languages of different nations did not totally differ, nor were they so copious as those of the Europeans, particularly the English. They were therefore easily learned; and, while I was journeying thus through Africa, I acquired two or three different tongues. In this manner I had been travelling for a considerable time, when one evening, to my great surprise, whom should I see brought to the house where I was but my dear sister! As soon as she saw me she gave a loud shriek, and ran into my arms—I was quite overpowered: neither of us could speak; but, for a considerable time, clung to each other in mutual embraces, unable to do any thing but weep. Our meeting affected all who saw us; and indeed I must acknowledge, in honour of those sable destroyers of human rights, that I never met with any ill treatment, or saw any offered to their slaves, except tying them, when necessary, to keep them from running away. When these people knew we were brother and sister they indulged us together; and the man, to whom I supposed we belonged, lay with us, he in the middle, while she and I held one another by the hands across his breast all night; and thus for a while we forgot our misfortunes in the joy of being together: but even this small comfort was soon to have an end; for scarcely had the fatal morning appeared, when she was again torn from me for ever! I was now more miserable, if possible, than before. The small relief which her presence gave me from pain was gone, and the wretchedness of my situation was redoubled by my anxiety after her fate, and my apprehensions lest her sufferings should be greater than mine, when I could not be with her to alleviate them. Yes, thou dear partner of all my childish sports! thou sharer of my joys and sorrows! happy should I have ever esteemed myself to encounter every misery for you, and to procure your freedom by the sacrifice of my own. Though you were early forced from my arms, your image has been always rivetted in my heart, from which neither *time nor fortune* have been able to remove it; so that, while the thoughts of your sufferings have damped my prosperity, they have mingled with adversity and increased its bitterness. To that Heaven which protects the weak from the strong, I commit the care of your innocence and virtues, if they have not already received their full reward, and if your youth and delicacy have not long since fallen victims to the violence of the African trader, the pestilential stench of a Guinea ship, the seasoning[5] in the European colonies, or the lash and lust of a brutal and unrelenting overseer.

I did not long remain after my sister. I was again sold, and carried through a number of places, till, after travelling a considerable time, I came to a town called Tinmah, in the most beautiful country I had yet seen in Africa. It was extremely rich, and there were many rivulets which flowed through it, and supplied a large pond in the centre of the town, where the people washed. Here I first saw and tasted cocoa nuts, which I thought superior to any nuts I had ever tasted before; and the trees, which were loaded, were also interspersed amongst the houses, which had commodious shades adjoining, and were in the same manner as ours, the insides being neatly plastered and whitewashed. Here I also saw and tasted for the first time sugar-cane. Their money consisted of little white shells, the size of the finger nail. I was sold here for one hundred and seventy-two of them by a merchant who lived and brought me there. I had been about two or three days at his house, when a wealthy widow, a neighbour of his, came there one evening, and brought with her an only son, a young gentleman about my own age and size. Here they saw me; and, having taken a fancy to me, I was bought of the merchant, and went home with them. Her house and premises were situated close to one of those rivulets I have mentioned, and were the finest I ever saw in Africa: they were very extensive, and she had a number of slaves to attend her. The next day I was washed and perfumed, and when meal-time came I was led into the presence of my mistress, and ate and drank before her with her son. This filled me with astonishment; and I could scarce help expressing my surprise that the young gentleman should suffer me, who was bound, to eat with him who was free; and not only so, but that he would not at any time either eat or drink till I had taken first, because I was the eldest, which was agreeable to our custom. Indeed every thing here, and all their treatment of me, made me forget that I was a slave. The language of these people resembled ours so nearly, that we understood each other perfectly. They had also the very same customs as we. There were likewise slaves daily to attend us, while my young master and I with other boys sported with our darts and bows and arrows, as I had been used to do at home. In this resemblance to my former happy state I passed about two months; and I now began to think I was to be adopted into the family, and was beginning to be reconciled to my situation, and to forget by degrees my misfortunes, when all at once the delu-

5. Rigorous preparation for use. "Guinea": west coast of Africa (archaic).

sion vanished; for, without the least previous knowledge, one morning early, while my dear master and companion was still asleep, I was wakened out of my reverie to fresh sorrow, and hurried away even amongst the uncircumcised.

Thus, at the very moment I dreamed of the greatest happiness, I found myself most miserable; and it seemed as if fortune wished to give me this taste of joy, only to render the reverie more poignant. The change I now experienced was as painful as it was sudden and unexpected. It was a change indeed from a state of bliss to a scene which is inexpressible by me, as it discovered to me an element I had never before beheld, and till then had no idea of, and wherein such instances of hardship and cruelty continually occurred as I can never reflect on but with horror.

All the nations and people I had hitherto passed through resembled our own in their manners, customs, and language: but I came at length to a country, the inhabitants of which differed from us in all those particulars. I was very much struck with this difference, especially when I came among a people who did not circumcise, and are without washing their hands. They cooked also in iron pots, and had European cutlasses and cross bows, which were unknown to us, and fought with their fists amongst themselves. Their women were not so modest as ours, for they ate, and drank, and slept, with their men. But, above all, I was amazed to see no sacrifices or offerings among them. In some of those places the people ornamented themselves with scars, and likewise filed their teeth very sharp. They wanted sometimes to ornament me in the same manner, but I would not suffer them; hoping that I might some time be among a people who did not thus disfigure themselves, as I thought they did. At last I came to the banks of a large river, which was covered with canoes, in which the people appeared to live with their household utensils and provisions of all kinds. I was beyond measure astonished at this, as I had never before seen any water larger than a pond or a rivulet: and my surprise was mingled with no small fear when I was put into one of these canoes, and we began to paddle and move along the river. We continued going on thus till night; and when we came to land, and made fires on the banks, each family by themselves, some dragged their canoes on shore, others stayed and cooked in theirs, and laid in them all night. Those on the land had mats, of which they made tents, some in the shape of little houses: in these we slept; and after the morning meal we embarked again and proceeded as before. I was often very much astonished to see some of the women, as well as the men, jump into the water, dive to the bottom, come up again, and swim about. Thus I continued to travel, sometimes by land, sometimes by water, through different countries and various nations, till, at the end of six or seven months after I had been kidnapped, I arrived at the sea coast. It would be tedious and uninteresting to relate all the incidents which befell me during this journey, and which I have not yet forgotten; of the various hands I passed through, and the manners and customs of all the different people among whom I lived: I shall therefore only observe, that in all the places where I was the soil was exceedingly rich; the pomkins, eadas, plantains, yams, etc., etc. were in great abundance, and of incredible size. There were also vast quantities of different gums, though not used for any purpose; and every where a great deal of tobacco. The cotton even grew quite wild; and there was plenty of red-wood.[6] I saw no mechanics whatever in all the way, except such as I have mentioned. The chief employment in all these countries was agriculture, and both the males and females, as with us, were brought up to it, and trained in the arts of war.

The first object which saluted my eyes when I arrived on the coast was the sea, and a slave ship, which was then riding at anchor, and waiting for its cargo. These filled me with astonishment, which was soon converted into terror when I was carried on board. I was immediately handled and tossed up to see if I were found by some of the crew; and I was now persuaded that I had gotten into a world of bad spirits, and that they were going to kill me. Their complexions too differing so much from ours, their long hair, and the language they spoke, (which was very different from any I had ever heard) united to confirm me in this belief. Indeed such were the horrors of my views and fears at the moment, that, if ten thousand worlds had been my own, I would have freely parted with them all to have exchanged my condition with that of the meanest slave in my own country. When I looked round the ship too and saw a large furnace of copper boiling, and a multitude of black people of every description chained together, every one of their countenances expressing dejection and sorrow, I no longer doubted of my fate; and, quite overpowered with horror and anguish, I fell motionless on the deck and fainted. When I recovered a little I found some black people about me, who I believed were some of those who brought me on board, and had been receiving their pay; they talked to me in order to cheer me, but all in vain. I asked them if we were not to be eaten by those white men with horrible looks, red faces, and loose hair. They told me I was not; and one of the crew brought me a small portion of spirituous liquor in a wine glass; but, being afraid of him, I would not take it out of his hand. One of the blacks therefore took it from him and gave it to me, and I took a little down my palate, which, instead of reviving me, as they thought it would, threw me into the greatest consternation at the strange feeling it produced, having never tasted any such liquor before. Soon after this the blacks who brought me on board went off, and left me abandoned to despair. I now saw myself deprived of all chance of returning to my native country, or even the least glimpse of hope of gaining the shore, which I now considered as friendly; and I even wished for my former slavery in preference to my present situation, which was filled with horrors of every kind, still heightened by my ignorance of what I was to undergo. I was not long suffered to indulge my grief; I was soon put down under the decks, and there I received such a salutation in my nostrils as I had never experienced in my life: so that, with the loathsomeness of the stench, and crying together, I became so sick and low that I was not able to eat, nor had I the least desire to taste any thing. I now wished for the last friend, death, to relieve me; but soon, to my grief, two of the white men offered me eatables; and, on my refusing to eat, one of them held me fast by the hands, and laid me across I think the windlass, and tied my feet, while the other flogged me severely. I had never experienced any thing of this kind before; and al-

6. Probably mahogany.

though, not being used to the water, I naturally feared that element the first time I saw it, yet nevertheless, could I have got over the nettings, I would have jumped over the side, but I could not; and, besides, the crew used to watch us very closely who were not chained down to the decks, lest we should leap into the water: and I have seen some of these poor African prisoners most severely cut for attempting to do so, and hourly whipped for not eating. This indeed was often the case with myself. In a little time after, amongst the poor chained men, I found some of my own nation, which in a small degree gave ease to my mind. I inquired of these what was to be done with us; they gave me to understand we were to be carried to these white people's country to work for them. I then was a little revived, and thought, if it were no worse than working, my situation was not so desperate: but still I feared I should be put to death, the white people looked and acted, as I thought, in so savage a manner; for I had never seen among any people such instances of brutal cruelty; and this not only shewn towards us blacks, but also to some of the whites themselves. One white man in particular I saw, when we were permitted to be on deck, flogged so unmercifully with a large rope near the foremast, that he died in consequence of it; and they tossed him over the side as they would have done a brute. This made me fear these people the more; and I expected nothing less than to be treated in the same manner. I could not help expressing my fears and apprehensions to some of my countrymen: I asked them if these people had no country, but lived in this hollow place (the ship): they told me they did not, but came from a distant one. "Then," said I, "how comes it in all our country we never heard of them?" They told me because they lived so very far off. I then asked where were their women? had they any like themselves? I was told they had: "and why," said I, "do we not see them?" they answered, because they were left behind. I asked how the vessel could go? they told me they could not tell; but that there were cloths put upon the masts by the help of the ropes I saw, and then the vessel went on; and the white men had some spell or magic they put in the water when they liked in order to stop the vessel. I was exceedingly amazed at this account, and really thought they were spirits. I therefore wished much to be from amongst them, for I expected they would sacrifice me: but my wishes were vain; for we were so quartered that it was impossible for any of us to make our escape. While we stayed on the coast I was mostly on deck; and one day, to my great astonishment, I saw one of these vessels coming in with the sails up. As soon as the whites saw it, they gave a great shout, at which we were amazed; and the more so as the vessel appeared larger by approaching nearer. At last she came to an anchor in my sight, and when the anchor was let go I and my countrymen who saw it were lost in astonishment to observe the vessel stop; and were now convinced it was done by magic. Soon after this the other ship got her boats out, and they came on board of us, and the people of both ships seemed very glad to see each other. Several of the strangers also shook hands with us black people, and made motions with their hands, signifying I suppose we were to go to their country; but we did not understand them. At last, when the ship we were in had got in all her cargo, they made ready with many fearful noises, and we were all put under deck, so that we could not see how they managed the vessel. But this disappointment was the least of my sorrow. The stench of the hold while we were on the coast was so intolerably loathsome, that it was dangerous to remain there for any time, and some of us had been permitted to stay on the deck for the fresh air; but now that the whole ship's cargo were confined together, it became absolutely pestilential. The closeness of the place, and the heat of the climate, added to the number in the ship, which was so crowded that each had scarcely room to turn himself, almost suffocated us. This produced copious perspirations, so that the air soon became unfit for respiration, from a variety of loathsome smells, and brought on a sickness among the slaves, of which many died, thus falling victims to the improvident avarice, as I may call it, of their purchasers. This wretched situation was again aggravated by the galling of the chains, now become insupportable; and the filth of the necessary tubs,[7] into which the children often fell, and were almost suffocated. The shrieks of the women, and the groans of the dying, rendered the whole a scene of horror almost inconceivable. Happily perhaps for myself I was soon reduced so low here that it was thought necessary to keep me almost always on deck; and from my extreme youth I was not put in fetters. In this situation I expected every hour to share the fate of my companions, some of whom were almost daily brought upon deck at the point of death, which I began to hope would soon put an end to my miseries. Often did I think many of the inhabitants of the deep much more happy than myself. I envied them the freedom they enjoyed, and as often wished I could change my condition for theirs. Every circumstance I met with served only to render my state more painful, and heighten my apprehensions, and my opinion of the cruelty of the whites. One day they had taken a number of fishes; and when they had killed and satisfied themselves with as many as they thought fit, to our astonishment who were on the deck, rather than give any of them to us to eat as we expected, they tossed the remaining fish into the sea again, although we begged and prayed for some as well as we could, but in vain; and some of my countrymen, being pressed by hunger, took an opportunity, when they thought no one saw them, of trying to get a little privately; but they were discovered, and the attempt procured them some very severe floggings. One day, when we had a smooth sea and moderate wind, two of my wearied countrymen who were chained together (I was near them at the time), preferring death to such a life of misery, somehow made through the nettings and jumped into the sea: immediately another quite dejected fellow, who, on account of his illness, was suffered to be out of irons, also followed their example; and I believe many more would very soon have done the same if they had not been prevented by the ship's crew, who were instantly alarmed. Those of us that were the most active were in a moment put down under the deck, and there was such a noise and confusion amongst the people of the ship as I never heard before, to stop her, and get the boat out to go after the slaves. However two of the wretches were drowned, but they got the other, and afterwards flogged him unmercifully for thus attempting to prefer death to slavery. In this manner we continued to undergo more hardships than I can now relate, hardships which are inseparable from this

7. I.e., human waste.

accursed trade. Many a time we were near suffocation from the want of fresh air, which we were often without for whole days together. This, and the stench of the necessary tubs, carried off many. During our passage I first saw flying fishes, which surprised me very much: they used frequently to fly across the ship, and many of them fell on the deck. I also now first saw the use of the quadrant;[8] I had often with astonishment seen the mariners make observations with it, and I could not think what it meant. They at last took notice of my surprise; and one of them, willing to increase it, as well as to gratify my curiosity, made me one day look through it. The clouds appeared to me to be land, which disappeared as they passed along. This heightened my wonder; and I was now more persuaded than ever that I was in another world, and that every thing about me was magic. At last we came in sight of the island of Barbadoes,[9] at which the whites on board gave a great shout, and made many signs of joy to us. We did not know what to think of this; but as the vessel drew nearer we plainly saw the harbour, and other ships of different kinds and sizes; and we soon anchored amongst them off Bridge Town.[1] Many merchants and planters now came on board, though it was in the evening. They put us in separate parcels, and examined us attentively. They also made us jump, and pointed to the land, signifying we were to go there. We thought by this we should be eaten by these ugly men, as they appeared to us; and, when soon after we were all put down under the deck again, there was much dread and trembling among us, and nothing but bitter cries to be heard all the night from these apprehensions, insomuch that at last the white people got some old slaves from the land to pacify us. They told us we were not to be eaten, but to work, and were soon to go on land, where we should see many of our country people. This report eased us much; and sure enough, soon after we were landed, there came to us Africans of all languages. We were conducted immediately to the merchant's yard, where we were all pent up together like so many sheep in a fold, without regard to sex or age. As every object was new to me every thing I saw filled me with surprise. What struck me first was that the houses were built with stories, and in every other respect different from those in Africa: but I was still more astonished on seeing people on horseback. I did not know what this could mean; and indeed I thought these people were full of nothing but magical arts. While I was in this astonishment one of my fellow prisoners spoke to a countryman of his about the horses, who said they were the same kind they had in their country. I understood them, though they were from a distant part of Africa, and I thought it odd I had not seen any horses there; but afterwards, when I came to converse with different Africans, I found they had many horses amongst them, and much larger than those I then saw. We were not many days in the merchant's custody before we were sold after their usual manner, which is this:—On a signal given, (as the beat of a drum) the buyers rush at once into the yard where the slaves are confined, and make choice of that parcel they like best. The noise and clamour with which this is attended, and the eagerness visible in the countenances of the buyers, serve not a

8. A navigation instrument used for measuring altitudes.
9. Or Barbados, the most easterly of the Caribbean islands.
1. The capital of Barbados.

little to increase the apprehensions of the terrified Africans, who may well be supposed to consider them as the ministers of that destruction to which they think themselves devoted. In this manner, without scruple, are relations and friends separated, most of them never to see each other again. I remember in the vessel in which I was brought over, in the men's apartment, there were several brothers, who, in the sale, were sold in different lots; and it was very moving on this occasion to see and hear their cries at parting. O, ye nominal Christians! might not an African ask you, learned you this from your God, who says unto you, Do unto all men as you would men should do unto you?[2] Is it not enough that we are torn from our country and friends to toil for your luxury and lust of gain? Must every tender feeling be likewise sacrificed to your avarice? Are the dearest friends and relations, now rendered more dear by their separation from their kindred, still to be parted from each other, and thus prevented from cheering the gloom of slavery with the small comfort of being together and mingling their sufferings and sorrows? Why are parents to lose their children, brothers their sisters, or husbands their wives? Surely this is a new refinement in cruelty, which, while it has no advantage to atone for it, thus aggravates distress, and adds fresh horrors even to the wretchedness of slavery.

FROM CHAPTER III

I now totally lost the small remains of comfort I had enjoyed in conversing with my countrymen; the women too, who used to wash and take care of me, were all gone different ways, and I never saw one of them afterwards.

I stayed in this island for a few days; I believe it could not be above a fortnight; when I, and some few more slaves, that were not saleable amongst the rest, from very much fretting, were shipped off in a sloop for North America. On the passage we were better treated than when we were coming from Africa, and we had plenty of rice and fat pork. We were landed up a river a good way from the sea, about Virginia county, where we saw few or none of our native Africans, and not one soul who could talk to me. I was a few weeks weeding grass, and gathering stones in a plantation; and at last all my companions were distributed different ways, and only myself was left. I was now exceedingly miserable, and thought myself worse off than any of the rest of my companions, for they could talk to each other, but I had no person to speak to that I could understand. In this state, I was constantly grieving and pining, and wishing for death rather than anything else. While I was in this plantation the gentleman, to whom I suppose the estate belonged, being unwell, I was one day sent for to his dwelling-house to fan him; when I came into the room where he was I was very much affrighted at some things I saw, and the more so as I had seen a black woman slave as I came through the house, who was cooking the dinner, and the poor creature was cruelly loaded with various kinds of iron machines; she had one particularly on

2. Compare Matthew 7:12: "Therefore all things whatsoever ye would that men should do to you, do ye even so to them."

her head, which locked her mouth so fast that she could scarcely speak;
and could not eat nor drink. I was much astonished and shocked at this
contrivance, which I afterwards learned was called the iron muzzle. Soon
after I had a fan put in my hand, to fan the gentleman while he slept;
and so I did indeed with great fear. While he was fast asleep I indulged
myself a great deal in looking about the room, which to me appeared
very fine and curious. The first object that engaged my attention was a
watch which hung on the chimney, and was going. I was quite surprised
at the noise it made, and was afraid it would tell the gentleman anything
I might do amiss; and when I immediately after observed a picture hanging in the room, which appeared constantly to look at me, I was still
more affrighted, having never seen such things as these before. At one
time I thought it was something relative to magic; and not seeing it move
I thought it might be some way the whites had to keep their great men
when they died, and offer them libations as we used to do to our friendly
spirits. In this state of anxiety I remained till my master awoke, when I
was dismissed out of the room, to my no small satisfaction and relief; for I
thought that these people were all made up of wonders. In this place I
was called Jacob; but on board the *African Snow*, I was called Michael. I
had been some time in this miserable, forlorn, and much dejected state,
without having anyone to talk to, which made my life a burden, when
the kind and unknown hand of the Creator (who in very deed leads the
blind in a way they know not) now began to appear, to my comfort; for
one day the captain of a merchant ship, called the *Industrious Bee*, came
on some business to my master's house. This gentleman, whose name
was Michael Henry Pascal, was a lieutenant in the royal navy, but now
commanded this trading ship, which was somewhere in the confines of
the county many miles off. While he was at my master's house it happened that he saw me, and liked me so well that he made a purchase of
me. I think I have often heard him say he gave thirty or forty pounds sterling for me; but I do not now remember which. However, he meant me
for a present to some of his friends in England: and as I was sent accordingly from the house of my then master (one Mr. Campbell) to the place
where the ship lay; I was conducted on horseback by an elderly black
man (a mode of travelling which appeared very odd to me). When I arrived I was carried on board a fine large ship, loaded with tobacco, etc.,
and just ready to sail for England. I now thought my condition much
mended; I had sails to lie on, and plenty of good victuals to eat; and everybody on board used me very kindly, quite contrary to what I had seen
of any white people before; I therefore began to think that they were not
all of the same disposition. A few days after I was on board we sailed for
England. I was still at a loss to conjecture my destiny. By this time, however, I could smatter a little imperfect English; and I wanted to know as
well as I could where we were going. Some of the people of the ship
used to tell me they were going to carry me back to my own country, and
this made me very happy. I was quite rejoiced at the sound of going back;
and thought if I should get home what wonders I should have to tell. But
I was reserved for another fate, and was soon undeceived when we came
within sight of the English coast. While I was on board this ship, my cap-

tain and master named me *Gustavus Vassa*. [3] I at that time began to understand him a little, and refused to be called so, and told him as well as I could that I would be called Jacob; but he said I should not, and still called me Gustavus: and when I refused to answer to my new name, which at first I did, it gained me many a cuff; so at length I submitted, and was obliged to bear the present name, by which I have been known ever since.

                    *   *   *

    It was about the beginning of the spring 1757, when I arrived in England and I was near twelve years of age at that time. I was very much struck with the buildings and the pavement of the streets in Falmouth; and, indeed, every object I saw, filled me with new surprise. One morning, when I got upon deck, I saw it covered all over with the snow that fell over-night. As I had never seen anything of the kind before, I thought it was salt; so I immediately ran down to the mate and desired him, as well as I could, to come and see how somebody in the night had thrown salt all over the deck. He, knowing what it was, desired me to bring some of it down to him. Accordingly I took up a handful of it, which I found very cold indeed; and when I brought it to him he desired me to taste it. I did so, and I was surprised beyond measure. I then asked him what it was; he told me it was snow, but I could not in anywise understand him. He asked me if we had no such thing in my country; I told him, No. I then asked him the use of it, and who made it; he told me a great man in the heavens, called God. But here again I was to all intents and purposes at a loss to understand him; and the more so, when a little after I saw the air filled with it, in a heavy shower, which fell down on the same day. After this I went to church; and having never been at such a place before, I was again amazed at seeing and hearing the service. I asked all I could about it; and they gave me to understand it was worshipping God, who made us and all things. I was still at a great loss, and soon got into an endless field of inquiries, as well as I was able to speak and ask about things. However, my little friend Dick [4] used to be my best interpreter; for I could make free with him, and he always instructed me with pleasure. And from what I could understand by him of this God, and in seeing these white people did not sell one another as we did, I was much pleased; and in this I thought they were much happier than we Africans. I was astonished at the wisdom of the white people in all things I saw; but was amazed at their not sacrificing, or making any offerings, and eating with unwashed hands, and touching the dead. I likewise could not help remarking the particular slenderness of their women, which I did not at first like; and I thought they were not so modest and shame faced as the African women.

    I had often seen my master and Dick employed in reading; and I had a great curiosity to talk to the books, as I thought they did; and so to learn how all things had a beginning: for that purpose I have often taken up a book, and have talked to it, and then put my ears to it, when alone, in hopes it would answer me; and I have been very much concerned when I found it remained silent.

---

3. Gustavus Vassa became king of Sweden in 1523.

4. Richard Baxter, a white American youth whom Equiano met on his first voyage to England.

FROM CHAPTER IV

It was now between two and three years since I first came to England, a great part of which I had spent at sea; so that I became inured to that service, and began to consider myself as happily situated; for my master treated me always extremely well; and my attachment and gratitude to him were very great. From the various scenes I had beheld on ship-board, I soon grew a stranger to terror of every kind, and was, in that respect at least, almost an Englishman. I have often reflected with surprise that I never felt half the alarm at any of the numerous dangers I have been in, that I was filled with at the first sight of the Europeans, and at every act of theirs, even the most trifling, when I first came among them, and for some time afterwards. That fear, however, which was the effect of my ignorance, wore away as I began to know them. I could now speak English tolerably well, and I perfectly understood every thing that was said. I now not only felt myself quite easy with these new countrymen, but relished their society and manners. I no longer looked upon them as spirits, but as men superior to us; and therefore I had the stronger desire to resemble them; to imbibe their spirit, and imitate their manners; I therefore embraced every occasion of improvement; and every new thing that I observed I treasured up in my memory. I had long wished to be able to read and write; and for this purpose I took every opportunity to gain instruction, but had made as yet very little progress. However, when I went to London with my master, I had soon an opportunity of improving myself, which I gladly embraced. Shortly after my arrival, he sent me to wait upon the Miss Guerins, who had treated me with much kindness when I was there before; and they sent me to school.

While I was attending these ladies their servants told me I could not go to Heaven unless I was baptized. This made me very uneasy; for I had now some faint idea of a future state: accordingly I communicated my anxiety to the eldest Miss Guerin, with whom I was become a favourite, and pressed her to have me baptized; when to my great joy she told me I should. She had formerly asked my master to let me be baptized, but he had refused; however she now insisted on it; and he being under some obligation to her brother complied with her request; so I was baptized in St. Margaret's church, Westminster, in February 1759, by my present name.

* * *

1789

PHILLIS WHEATLEY
1753?–1784

Phillis Wheatley, the first African American to publish a book and the first to achieve an international reputation as a writer, has been one of the most controversial and enigmatic figures in the history of African American literature. She seems to have had little taste for controversy herself, but with a pen in her hand and a book in her name, Wheatley became, inevitably, a point of contention for others. Born in

West Africa and enslaved in America, Phillis Wheatley grew up in a fixed and pre-judged position in the white social order; she was the alien, the dependent, the talking chattel. But sometime in her teens Wheatley decided, on her own, to add to the list of her predetermined social identities—the Negro, the woman, the slave—a new name, that of poet. Ever since that decision, the question of how to interpret and evaluate Wheatley the poet in light of her status as a black female slave in eighteenth-century New England has been the critical crux, the first order of busi-ness, for students of Wheatley and the beginnings of African American literature.

The mere fact of an African born slave woman's writing poetry in English, her adopted language, was stunning news to whites who encountered *Poems on Various Subjects, Religious and Moral by Phillis Wheatley, Negro Servant to Mr. John Wheatley, of Boston, in New England* when it first appeared in London in Septem-ber 1773. Since the revolution in European thought and expression known as the Enlightenment, the assumption among even the educated white elite was that black Africans were incapable of the highest forms of civilization, such as poetic expression and mathematical calculation, and were, therefore, fit only for enslave-ment by their supposed superiors in Europe. To the whites of Europe and the Americas, writing provided demonstrable evidence of reason. Creative writing, of which poetry was considered the highest expression, constituted indisputable proof of genius. Because Europeans knew of no blacks in Africa who had distinguished themselves in written literature (Europeans ignored the fact that African literatures tended to be oral rather than written), slavery's defenders claimed that blacks lacked the imagination, originality, and vision to qualify as fully human, the equals of whites. Wheatley's landmark volume of poetry challenged these prejudices on its title page alone. How could poems, especially serious verse on profound matters of the spirit, be written by a "Negro" and a "servant"? "It was not natural," contempo-rary African American poet June Jordan has ironically observed in a tribute to the literary foremother she calls "Phillis Miracle." But because Wheatley wrote her poems, exploitative assumptions about the African's "nature" would never again be so easy to maintain in European and American letters.

The white sponsors of *Poems on Various Subjects*, chiefly the poet's master, John Wheatley, realized that publishing Phillis's book represented an act of potentially disturbing intervention into an established literary and cultural tradition. Readers discovering the virtually unprecedented example of a black woman slave poet would not be satisfied merely to read and ponder her verse. They would have to be convinced that it was truly hers; they would want an explanation as to how and why she had taken to writing in the first place. Thus *Poems on Various Subjects* offers its reader several introductory documents designed to authenticate Phillis Wheatley and her poetry and to legitimate her literary motives. These prefatory materials helped establish a convention, a kind of interracial literary etiquette, that white readers soon came to expect when encountering an African American author. The authenticating documents that preface Wheatley's poems attest to the extent of the challenge facing the emerging African American writer, when even her friends and sponsors could not see how a black writer's work could speak for itself without first being spoken for by whites.

Among the documents that introduce *Poems on Various Subjects* is a short bio-graphical sketch of the poet written by her master, John Wheatley, a respected and well-to-do Boston merchant. John Wheatley knew nothing of the personal history of the frail girl whom he purchased in July 1761 from the human cargo transported from West Africa aboard the slave ship *Phillis*. Judging the child "between seven and eight years of age," John Wheatley turned the new slave over to his wife, Susanna, to serve as a personal maid. Responding to early indications of intellectual precociousness in Phillis, the Wheatley family encouraged her to study the Bible and to read English and Latin literature, history, and geography. After only four years' exposure to the English language, Phillis began to write poetry; her first published poem appeared in a Rhode Island newspaper in 1767. Impressed by their slave's literary dedication and anxious about her delicate health, the Wheatleys reduced Phillis's work obligations to relatively light duties around the house.

In the fall of 1770 Phillis Wheatley earned her first extensive fame as a poet with an elegy on the death of the Reverend George Whitefield, an internationally popular Methodist evangelist. After publishing several more well-received elegies in broadsides and newspapers in North America and England, Phillis Wheatley sailed to England in the spring of 1773 to see through to publication a volume of her poetry. In London the poet received a warm welcome from such highly placed persons as Benjamin Franklin and Brooke Watson, the future mayor of London, who gave her a copy of John Milton's *Paradise Lost* as a token of his admiration. But Susanna Wheatley's serious illness required Phillis's return to Boston a little more than a month before *Poems on Various Subjects* came out. Soon after her arrival in Boston in September 1773, John Wheatley emancipated his twenty-year-old slave.

After securing her freedom, Phillis remained in the Wheatley household, where she tended to her former mistress and master in their last years. The poet's letters from this time acknowledge her continuing regard for the Wheatley family and her keen interest in the business side of publishing poetry. An unusually forthright statement of her opposition to slavery, originally included in a 1774 personal letter, was reprinted in at least eleven New England newspapers. As popular agitation against British rule mounted into cries for revolution, Wheatley undertook patriotic poetry as a way to affirm her allegiance to the cause of liberty. In October 1775, while living in Providence, Rhode Island, where John Wheatley had moved his household after the British occupation of Boston, Phillis wrote to George Washington, commander in chief of the American Revolutionary Army, enclosing a poem of praise and encouragement. General Washington acknowledged receipt of the poem and invited the poet to visit him at his headquarters in Cambridge. Wheatley did so the following year.

In March 1778 John Wheatley died. On April 1, Phillis Wheatley married a free black man, John Peters, about whom little is known other than he was talented but financially unsuccessful in the occupations he pursued. The Peters family gradually descended into poverty. During the first five years of the marriage, Phillis Wheatley Peters published nothing. In the eleven months before her death on December 5, 1784, however, she published three elegies and *Liberty and Peace*, a tribute to the triumphant American Revolution. Wheatley also advertised for subscribers to a second volume of her poetry, but the volume was never completed.

The literary reputation of Phillis Wheatley rests primarily on the thirty-eight poems in *Poems on Various Subjects*. Composed largely of neoclassical occasional and elegiac verse in the heroic couplet form popularized by Alexander Pope, *Poems* testifies to Wheatley's devout Christianity, her knowledge of the classic Greek, Latin, and English poets, and her desire to write a poetry that addressed current events and prominent people of the day as well as weighty life-and-death matters. In general, reviewers of *Poems* complimented Wheatley on an achievement that promised much from a poet barely out of her teens. As the abolitionist movement progressed in the first half of the nineteenth century, Wheatley became almost an icon, a model of native "African genius," proof positive of "the capacity of the African's intellect for improvement." But Wheatley the sociological symbol gradually eclipsed Wheatley the individual poet in the nineteenth century.

Since the twentieth-century revival of scholarly interest in her work, Wheatley's poems have sometimes been criticized for failing to live up to standards of self-expressiveness and political engagement that seem appropriate expectations of poetry today but were not nearly so aesthetically acceptable in her own time. To some readers Wheatley's poetry seems conventional and conformist; to others it has a detached correctness that lacks feeling. Her harshest critics have attacked Wheatley for failing to use her gifts in the service of antislavery or to identify herself plainly enough with African American people and their social and cultural, as well as political, needs. Wheatley's defenders maintain that her poetry is a good deal more politically subversive and individually expressive than it appears at first glance.

Wherever these debates lead us, it is important to remember the task that Wheatley had before her when she undertook a career as a black woman poet in a white man's country. Wheatley had first to write her way *into* American literature before she or any other black writer could claim a special mission and purpose for an *African* American literature. She had no models other than European American ones for her poetry, and she could not assume that her white readers would want to know what a slave woman thought or felt unless she could demonstrate her capacity to express her ideas and feelings in a manner sanctioned by the dominant culture. In response to these conditions, Wheatley adopted a literary persona and style that affirmed her seriousness as an African American artist and created a precedent on which subsequent black poets could build with confidence. No single writer has contributed more to the founding of African American literature.

FROM POEMS ON VARIOUS SUBJECTS, RELIGIOUS AND MORAL

Preface

The following Poems were written originally for the Amusement of the Author, as they were the products of her leisure Moments. She had no Intention ever to have published them; nor would they now have made their Appearance, but at the Importunity of many of her best, and most generous Friends; to whom she considers herself, as under the greatest Obligations.

As her Attempts in Poetry are now sent into the World, it is hoped the Critic will not severely censure their Defects; and we presume they have too much Merit to be cast aside with Contempt, as worthless and trifling Effusions.

As to the Disadvantages she has laboured under, with Regard to Learning, nothing needs to be offered, as her Master's Letter in the following Page will sufficiently shew the Difficulties in this Respect she had to encounter.

With all their Imperfections, the Poems are now humbly submitted to the Perusal of the Public.

[Letter Sent by the Author's Master to the Publisher]

Phillis was brought from *Africa* to *America* in the Year 1761, between Seven and Eight Years of Age. Without any Assistance from School Education, and by only what she was taught in the Family, she, in sixteen Months Time from her Arrival, attained the English Language, to which she was an utter Stranger before, to such a Degree, as to read any, the most difficult Parts of the Sacred Writings, to the great Astonishment of all who heard her.

As to her Writing, her own Curiosity led her to it; and this she learnt in so short a Time, that in the Year 1765, she wrote a Letter to the Rev. Mr. Occom,[1] the *Indian* Minister, while in *England*.

She has a great Inclination to learn the Latin Tongue, and has made some Progress in it. This Relation is given by her Master who bought her, and with whom she now lives.

JOHN WHEATLEY

Boston, Nov. 14, 1772.

[To the Publick]

As it has been repeatedly suggested to the Publisher, by Persons, who have seen the Manuscript, that Numbers would be ready to suspect they were not really the Writings of PHILLIS, he has procured the following attestation, from the most respectable Characters in *Boston*, that none might have the least Ground for Disputing their *Original*.

We whose Names are under-written, do assure the World, that the POEMS specified in the following Page, were (as we verily believe) written by PHILLIS, a young Negro Girl, who was but a few Years since, brought an uncultivated Barbarian from *Africa*, and has ever since been, and now is, under the Disadvantage of serving as a Slave in a Family in this Town. She has been examined by some of the best Judges, and is thought qualified to write them.

His Excellency Thomas Hutchinson,[2] *Governor*

The Hon. Andrew Oliver, *Lieu-
tenant-Governor.*
The Hon. Thomas Hubbard,
The Hon. John Erving,
The Hon. James Pitts,
The Hon. Harrison Gray,
The Hon. James Bowdoin,
John Hancock, *Esq;*
Joseph Green, *Esq;*

Richard Carey, *Esq;*
The Rev. Charles Chauncy, D.D.
The Rev. Mather Byles, D.D.
The Rev. Ed. Pemberton, D.D.
The Rev. Andrew Elliot, D.D.
The Rev. Samuel Cooper, D.D.
The Rev. Mr. Samuel Mather,
The Rev. Mr. John Moorhead,
Mr. John Wheatley, *her Master.*

N.B. The original Attestations, signed by the above Gentlemen, may be seen by applying to *Archibald Bell*, Bookseller, No. 8, *Aldgate-Street.*

1773

---

1. Samson Occom (1723–1792), a Mohegan Indian ordained a Presbyterian minister.
2. Hutchinson (1711–1780) was governor of Massachusetts from 1771 to 1774. The following list includes the names of some of the most prominent political and religious leaders in Boston.

To Mæcenas[1]

Mæcenas, you, beneath the myrtle[2] shade,
Read o'er what poets sung, and shepherds play'd.
What felt those poets but you feel the same?
Does not your soul possess the sacred flame?
Their noble strains your equal genius shares   5
In softer language, and diviner airs.

    While *Homer*[3] paints lo! circumfus'd in air,
Celestial Gods in mortal forms appear;
Swift as they move hear each recess rebound,
Heav'n quakes, earth trembles, and the shores resound.   10
Great Sire of verse, before my mortal eyes,
The lightnings blaze across the vaulted skies,
And, as the thunder shakes the heav'nly plains,
A deep-felt horror thrills through all my veins.
When gentler strains demand thy graceful song,   15
The length'ning line moves languishing along.
When great *Patroclus* courts *Achilles'*[4] aid,
The grateful tribute of my tears is paid;
Prone on the shore he feels the pangs of love,
And stern *Pelides*[5] tend'rest passions move.   20

    Great *Maro's*[6] strain in heav'nly numbers flows,
The *Nine*[7] inspire, and all the bosom glows.
O could I rival thine and *Virgil's* page,
Or claim the *Muses* with the *Mantuan*[8] Sage;
Soon the same beauties should my mind adorn,   25
And the same ardors in my soul should burn:
Then should my song in bolder notes arise,
And all my numbers pleasingly surprize;
But here I sit, and mourn a grov'ling mind,
That fain would mount, and ride upon the wind.   30

    Not you, my friend, these plaintive strains become,
Not you, whose bosom is the *Muses* home;
When they from tow'ring *Helicon*[9] retire,
They fan in you the bright immortal fire,
But I less happy, cannot raise the song,   35
The fault'ring music dies upon my tongue.

    The happier *Terence*[1] all the choir inspir'd,
His soul replenish'd, and his bosom fir'd;
But say, ye *Muses*, why this partial grace,

1. A Roman aristocrat (74–8 b.c.) who befriended and supported the poets Horace and Virgil.
2. An evergreen held sacred to the worship of Venus, the Roman goddess of love.
3. The epic poet of ancient Greece.
4. The hero of the Greeks in Homer's *Iliad*. Patroclus was his favorite companion.
5. I.e., Achilles, son of Peleus.
6. The family name of the Roman epic poet Virgil.
7. I.e., the nine Muses, Greek goddesses of literature and the arts.
8. Mantua was thought to be the birthplace of Virgil.
9. Mount Helicon in Greece, the legendary home of the Muses.
1. "He was an *African* by birth" [Wheatley's note]. Terence was a celebrated Roman comic dramatist of the 2nd century b.c.

To one alone of *Afric's* sable[2] race;   40
From age to age transmitting thus his name
With the first glory in the rolls of fame?

Thy virtues, great *Mæcenas!* shall be sung
In praise of him, from whom those virtues sprung;
While blooming wreaths around thy temples spread,   45
I'll snatch a laurel[3] from thine honour'd head,
While you indulgent smile upon the deed.

As long as *Thames* in streams majestic flows,
Or *Naiads*[4] in their oozy beds repose,
While Phœbus reigns above the starry train,   50
While bright *Aurora*[5] purples o'er the main,
So long, great Sir, the muse thy praise shall sing,
So long thy praise shall make *Parnassus*[6] ring:
Then grant, *Mæcenas,* thy paternal rays,
Hear me propitious, and defend my lays.   55

1773

To the University of Cambridge,[1] in New-England

While an intrinsic ardor prompts to write,
The muses promise to assist my pen;
'Twas not long since I left my native shore
The land of errors, and *Egyptian* gloom:
Father of mercy, 'twas thy gracious hand   5
Brought me in safety from those dark abodes.

Students, to you 'tis giv'n to scan the heights
Above, to traverse the ethereal[2] space,
And mark the systems of revolving worlds.
Still more, ye sons of science ye receive   10
The blissful news by messengers from heav'n,
How *Jesus'* blood for your redemption flows.
See him with hands out-stretcht upon the cross;
Immense compassion in his bosom glows;
He hears revilers, nor resents their scorn: 15
What matchless mercy in the Son of God!
When the whole human race by sin had fall'n,
He deign'd to die that they might rise again,
And share with him in the sublimest skies,
Life without death, and glory without end.   20

Improve your privileges while they stay,
Ye pupils, and each hour redeem, that bears

2. Black.
3. Emblem of honor and distinction.
4. In Greek folklore, nymphs (i.e., fairylike women) of springs, rivers, and lakes. The Thames is a river that runs through London.
5. The Roman goddess of the dawn. "Phoebus":

i.e., Apollo, Greek god of the sun.
6. A mountain in Greece associated with the worship of Apollo and the Muses.
1. I.e., Harvard College.
2. Heavenly.

Or good or bad report of you to heav'n.
Let sin, that baneful evil to the soul,
By you be shunn'd, nor once remit your guard;   25
Suppress the deadly serpent in its egg.
Ye blooming plants of human race devine,
An *Ethiop*[3] tells you 'tis your greatest foe;
Its transient sweetness turns to endless pain,
And in immense perdition[4] sinks the soul.   30

1773

On Being Brought from Africa to America

'Twas mercy brought me from my *Pagan* land,
Taught my benighted soul to understand
That there's a God, that there's a *Saviour* too:
Once I redemption neither sought nor knew.
Some view our sable[1] race with scornful eye,   5
"Their colour is a diabolic die."
Remember, *Christians*, *Negros*, black as *Cain*,[2]
May be refin'd, and join th' angelic train.

1773

On the Death of the Rev. Mr. George Whitefield.[1] 1770

Hail, happy saint, on thine immortal throne,
Possest of glory, life, and bliss unknown;
We hear no more the music of thy tongue,
Thy wonted[2] auditories cease to throng.
Thy sermons in unequall'd accents flow'd,   5
And ev'ry bosom with devotion glow'd;
Thou didst in strains of eloquence refin'd
Inflame the heart, and captivate the mind.
Unhappy we the setting sun deplore,
So glorious once, but ah! it shines no more.   10

Behold the prophet in his tow'ring flight!
He leaves the earth for heav'n's unmeasur'd height,
And worlds unknown receive him from our sight.
There *Whitefield* wings with rapid course his way,
And sails to *Zion*[3] through vast seas of day.   15
Thy pray'rs, great saint, and thine incessant cries
Have pierc'd the bosom of thy native skies.
Thou moon hast seen, and all the stars of light,
How he has wrestled with his God by night.

---

3. Black African.
4. Eternal damnation.
1. Black.
2. Because he murdered his brother Abel (Genesis 4:1–15), Cain is said to have been "marked" by God. Some readers of the Bible thought that Cain thereby became the first black man.

1. An English Methodist evangelist (1714–1770), one of the most famous revivalists in America and Great Britain during the 18th century. This was Wheatley's first published poem, and it gave her considerable notoriety.
2. Accustomed.
3. Here, the heavenly city of God.

He pray'd that grace in ev'ry heart might dwell,   20
He long'd to see *America* excel;
He charg'd[4] its youth that ev'ry grace divine
Should with full lustre in their conduct shine;
That Saviour,[5] which his soul did first receive,
The greatest gift that ev'n a God can give,   25
He freely offer'd to the num'rous throng,
That on his lips with list'ning pleasure hung.

   "Take him, ye wretched, for your only good,
"Take him ye starving sinners, for your food;
"Ye thirsty, come to this life-giving stream,   30
"Ye preachers, take him for your joyful theme;
"Take him my dear *Americans,* he said,
"Be your complaints on his kind bosom laid:
"Take him, ye *Africans,* he longs for you,
"*Impartial Saviour* is his title due: 35
"Wash'd in the fountain of redeeming blood,
"You shall be sons, and kings, and priests to God."[6]

   Great *Countess,*[7] we *Americans* revere
Thy name, and mingle in thy grief sincere;
New England deeply feels, the *Orphans* mourn,   40
Their more than father will no more return.

   But, though arrested by the hand of death,
Whitefield no more exerts his lab'ring breath,
Yet let us view him in th' eternal skies,
Let ev'ry heart to this bright vision rise;   45
While the tomb safe retains its sacred trust,
Till life divine re-animates his dust.

                                                              1773

To the Right Honourable William,[1] Earl of Dartmouth, His Majesty's Principal Secretary of State for North-America, Etc.

Hail, happy day, when, smiling like the morn,
Fair *Freedom* rose *New-England* to adorn:
The northern clime[2] beneath her genial ray,
Dartmouth, congratulates thy blissful sway:
Elate with hope her race no longer mourns,   5
Each soul expands, each grateful bosom burns,
While in thine hand with pleasure we behold
The silken reins, and *Freedom's* charms unfold.

---

4. Exhorted.
5. I.e., Christ.
6. In a version of this poem published in London in 1771, this line reads "He'll make you free, and Kings, and Priests to God."
7. "The Countess of *Huntingdon,* to whom Mr. *Whitefield* was Chaplain" [Wheatley's note]. Selina Shirley Hastings (1707–1791), countess of Huntingdon, was a strong supporter of Whitefield. Wheatley visited her in England in 1773.
1. William Legge, Lord Dartmouth, was appointed secretary in charge of the American colonies in August 1772. Wheatley hoped that Dartmouth would prove more amenable to the grievances of the colonists.
2. Region.

Long lost to realms beneath the northern skies
She shines supreme, while hated *faction* dies: 10
Soon as appear'd the *Goddess* long desir'd,
Sick at the view, she [3] lanquish'd and expir'd;
Thus from the splendors of the morning light
The owl in sadness seeks the caves of night.

No more, *America*, in mournful strain   15
Of wrongs, and grievance unredress'd complain,
No longer shalt thou dread the iron chain,
Which wanton *Tyranny* with lawless hand
Had made, and with it meant t' enslave the land.

Should you, my lord, while you peruse my song,   20
Wonder from whence my love of *Freedom* sprung,
Whence flow these wishes for the common good,
By feeling hearts alone best understood,
I, young in life, by seeming cruel fate
Was snatch'd from *Afric's* fancy'd happy seat: [1]   25
What pangs excruciating must molest,
What sorrows labour in my parent's breast?
Steel'd was that soul and by no misery mov'd
That from a father seiz'd his babe belov'd:
Such, such my case. And can I then but pray   30
Others may never feel tyrannic sway?

For favours past, great Sir, our thanks are due,
And thee we ask thy favours to renew,
Since in thy pow'r, as in thy will before,
To sooth the griefs, which thou did'st once deplore.   35
May heav'nly grace the sacred sanction give
To all thy works, and thou for ever live
Not only on the wings of fleeting *Fame*,
Though praise immortal crowns the patriot's name,
But to conduct to heav'ns refulgent fane,   40
May fiery coursers [5] sweep th' ethereal plain,
And bear thee upwards to that blest abode,
Where, like the prophet, [6] thou shalt find thy God.

                                                                  1773

On Imagination

Thy various works, imperial queen, we see,
How bright their forms! how deck'd with pomp by thee!
Thy wond'rous acts in beauteous order stand,
And all attest how potent is thine hand.

3. I.e., faction (internal conflict). "The Goddess":   5. Horses. "Refulgent fane": shining temple.
freedom.   6. Elijah, who was carried to heaven in a chariot of
4. Abode or home. "Fancy'd": imagined.   fire (2 Kings 2:11).

From *Helicon's* refulgent heights attend,   5
Ye sacred choir,[1] and my attempts befriend:
To tell her glories with a faithful tongue,
Ye blooming graces, triumph in my song.

Now here, now there, the roving *Fancy* flies,
Till some lov'd object strikes her wand'ring eyes,   10
Whose silken fetters all the senses bind,
And soft captivity involves the mind.

Imagination! who can sing thy force?
Or who describe the swiftness of thy course?
Soaring through air to find the bright abode,   15
Th' empyreal[2] palace of the thund'ring God,
We on thy pinions can surpass the wind,
And leave the rolling universe behind:
From star to star the mental optics rove,
Measure the skies, and range the realms above.   20
There in one view we grasp the mighty whole,
Or with new worlds amaze th' unbounded soul.

Though *Winter* frowns to *Fancy's* raptur'd eyes
The fields may flourish, and gay scenes arise;
The frozen deeps may break their iron bands,   25
And bid their waters murmur o'er the sands.
Fair *Flora*[3] may resume her fragrant reign,
And with her flow'ry riches deck the plain;
Sylvanus[4] may diffuse his honours round,
And all the forest may with leaves be crown'd: 30
Show'rs may descend, and dews their gems disclose,
And nectar sparkle on the blooming rose.

Such is thy pow'r, nor are thine orders vain,
O thou the leader of the mental train:
In full perfection all thy works are wrought,   35
And thine the sceptre o'er the realms of thought.
Before thy throne the subject-passions bow,
Of subject-passions sov'reign ruler Thou,
At thy command joy rushes on the heart,
And through the glowing veins the spirits dart.   40

Fancy might now her silken pinions try
To rise from earth, and sweep th' expanse on high;
From *Tithon's* bed now might *Aurora*[5] rise,
Her cheeks all glowing with celestial dies,[6]
While a pure stream of light o'erflows the skies.   45
The monarch of the day I might behold,
And all the mountains tipt with radiant gold,

1. I.e., the nine Muses, goddesses of literature and
art. Mount Helicon, in Greece, was the legendary
home of the Muses.
2. Celestial.
3. Roman goddess of fertility and flowers.

4. Roman goddess of the forest.
5. Roman goddess of dawn, who, according to
Greek myth, loved Tithonus, a Trojan.
6. Colors.

But I reluctant leave the pleasing views,
Which *Fancy* dresses to delight the *Muse;*
Winter austere forbids me to aspire,   50
And northern tempests damp the rising fire;
They chill the tides of *Fancy's* flowing sea,
Cease then, my song, cease the unequal lay.[7]

1773

To S. M.,[1] a Young *African* Painter, on Seeing His Works

To show the lab'ring bosom's deep intent,
And thought in living characters to paint,
When first thy pencil did those beauties give,
And breathing figures learnt from thee to live,
How did those prospects give my soul delight,   5
A new creation rushing on my sight?
Still, wond'rous youth! each noble path pursue,
On deathless glories fix thine ardent view:
Still may the painter's and the poet's fire
To aid thy pencil, and thy verse conspire!   10
And may the charms of each seraphic[2] theme
Conduct thy footsteps to immortal fame!
High to the blissful wonders of the skies
Elate thy soul, and raise thy wishful eyes.
Thrice happy, when exalted to survey   15
That splendid city, crown'd with endless day,
Whose twice six gates on radiant hinges ring:
Celestial *Salem*[3] blooms in endless spring.

Calm and serene thy moments glide along,
And may the muse inspire each future song!   20
Still, with the sweets of contemplation bless'd,
May peace with balmy wings your soul invest!
But when these shades of time are chas'd away,
And darkness ends in everlasting day,
On what seraphic pinions shall we move,   25
And view the landscapes in the realms above?
There shall thy tongue in heav'nly murmurs flow,
And there my muse with heav'nly transport glow:
No more to tell of *Damon's* tender sighs,
Or rising radiance of *Aurora's*[4] eyes,   30
For nobler themes demand a nobler strain,
And purer language on th' ethereal plain.
Cease, gentle muse! the solemn gloom of night
Now seals the fair creation from my sight.

1773

7. Ballad.
1. Scipio Moorhead, slave of the Reverend John Moorhead of Boston.
2. Angelic.
3. Heavenly Jerusalem, which Revelation 21:12

describes as having twelve gates ("twice six gates").
4. The Roman goddess of the dawn. In classical mythology Damon pledged his life for his friend Pythias.

To Samson Occom [1]

Rev'd and honor'd Sir,

I have this Day received your obliging kind Epistle, and am greatly satisfied with your Reasons respecting the Negroes, and think highly reasonable what you offer in Vindication of their natural Rights: Those that invade them cannot be insensible that the divine Light is chasing away the thick Darkness which broods over the Land of Africa; and the Chaos which has reign'd so long, is converting into beautiful Order, and [r]eveals more and more clearly, the glorious Dispensation of civil and religious Liberty, which are so inseparably united, that there is little or no Enjoyment of one without the other: Otherwise, perhaps, the Israelites [2] had been less solicitous for their Freedom from Egyptian slavery; I do not say they would have been contented without it, by no means, for in every human Breast, God has implanted a Principle, which we call Love of Freedom; it is impatient of Oppression, and pants for Deliverance; and by the Leave of our modern Egyptians I will assert, that the same Principle lives in us. God grant Deliverance in his own Way and Time, and get him honour upon all those whose Avarice impels them to countenance and help forward the Calamities of their fellow Creatures. This I desire not for their Hurt, but to convince them of the strange Absurdity of their Conduct whose Words and Actions are so diametrically opposite. How well the Cry for Liberty, and the reverse Disposition for the exercise of oppressive Power over others agree,— I humbly think it does not require the Penetration of a Philosopher to determine.—

1774

To His Excellency General Washington [1]

Sir,

I have taken the freedom to address your Excellency in the enclosed poem, and entreat your acceptance, though I am not insensible of its inaccuracies. Your being appointed by the Grand Continental Congress to be Generalissimo of the armies of North America, together with the fame of your virtues, excite sensations not easy to suppress. Your generosity, therefore, I presume, will pardon the attempt. Wishing your Excellency all possible success in the great cause you are so generously engaged in. I am,

Your Excellency's most obedient humble servant,

Phillis Wheatley

1776

---

1. A Mohegan Indian (1723–1792) ordained a Presbyterian minister, who had written an indictment of slave-holding Christian ministers with which Wheatley, who was his friend, strongly concurred.
2. The Hebrews held in bondage to the ancient Egyptians.

1. As a demonstration of her patriotism, Wheatley sent this introductory letter and the following poem to Washington four months after he had been named commander in chief of the American Revolutionary Army. On February 28, 1776, Washington replied, thanking Wheatley for the poem and inviting her to visit him.

Celestial choir! enthron'd in realms of light,
  Columbia's² scenes of glorious toils I write.
While freedom's cause her anxious breast alarms,
She flashes dreadful in refulgent arms.
See mother earth her offspring's fate bemoan,   5
And nations gaze at scenes before unknown!
See the bright beams of heaven's revolving light
Involved in sorrows and veil of night!

  The goddess comes, she moves divinely fair,
Olive and laurel³ bind her golden hair: 10
Wherever shines this native of the skies,
Unnumber'd charms and recent graces rise.

  Muse! bow propitious while my pen relates
How pour her armies through a thousand gates,
As when Eolus⁴ heaven's fair face deforms,   15
Enwrapp'd in tempest and a night of storms;
Astonish'd ocean feels the wild uproar,
The refluent surges beat the sounding shore;
Or thick as leaves in Autumn's golden reign,
Such, and so many, moves the warrior's train.   20
In bright array they seek the work of war,
Where high unfurl'd the ensign⁵ waves in air.
Shall I to Washington their praise recite?
Enough thou know'st them in the fields of fight.
Thee, first in peace and honours,—we demand   25
The grace and glory of thy martial band.
Fam'd for thy valour, for thy virtues more,
Hear every tongue thy guardian aid implore!

  One century scarce perform'd its destined round,
When Gallic⁶ powers Columbia's fury found;   30
And so may you, whoever dares disgrace
The land of freedom's heaven-defended race!
Fix'd are the eyes of nations on the scales,
For in their hopes Columbia's arm prevails.
Anon Britannia droops the pensive head,   35
While round increase the rising hills of dead.
Ah! cruel blindness to Columbia's state!
Lament thy thirst of boundless power too late.

  Proceed, great chief, with virtue on thy side,
Thy ev'ry action let the goddess guide.   40
A crown, a mansion, and a throne that shine,
With gold unfading, WASHINGTON! be thine.

                  1776

---

2. This reference to America as the land of Columbus is thought to be the first in print. "Celestial
choir": the nine Muses, goddesses of literature and
art.
3. Emblems of victory.

4. In classical mythology, the keeper of the winds.
5. Flag or banner.
6. French; a reference to the French and Indian
War (1689–1763) in North America.

DAVID WALKER

1785–1830

The most militant voice among the early African American protest writers belonged to David Walker, whose call to violent resistance against slavery so alarmed authorities in the South that they were reputed to have put a price on his head. *David Walker's Appeal*, published by its author in 1829, shocked and alarmed many white readers in the North as well as the South because of Walker's insistence on white racism as a national problem, of which slavery was only its most egregious manifestation. Most black readers found the *Appeal* an inspiring articulation of African American pride and a fearless call to radical action in the name of those principles of justice to which Americans, white as well as black, were supposed to be dedicated.

In an ironically patriotic spirit, Walker, a self-avowed "restless disturber of the peace," took pains to pattern the title and structure of his *Appeal* on the U.S. Constitution. Hence the formal and stately character of the full title of the text: *David Walker's Appeal in Four Articles; Together with a Preamble, to the Coloured Citizens of the World, but in Particular and Very Expressly, to Those of the United States of America.* In addition to drawing on American political precedent for his argument for black nationalism, Walker also allied himself with the biblical tradition of the prophet crying in the wilderness, denouncing the hypocrisy of the prevailing religious practice and calling for divine punishment "in behalf of the oppressed." Walker's devastating historical analysis of slavery and racism in Europe and the Americas, promulgated in the *Preamble* and *Article I* of the *Appeal*, is probably the most memorable feature of his writing. But subsequent articles of the *Appeal* urge a program of African American educational, spiritual, and political renewal that proves Walker's dedication to constructive social change, not just retribution. By demonstrating that biblical as well as American history amply justified forcible resistance against tyranny, Walker tried to galvanize into unity of purpose both the religious and the worldly communities of black America. No wonder, therefore, that white southerners demanded the *Appeal* be suppressed and took stringent measures to keep it out of the hands of slaves.

Born in Wilmington, North Carolina, to a slave father and a free mother, David Walker, though never actually a slave, learned from his father's example and from extensive travel in the slave states all he needed to know about the South's "peculiar institution." Boston became his home in 1827; there he married a fugitive slave in 1828. He supported his family well as a secondhand clothes dealer, but he spent much of his available time studying the history of slavery in classical and recent times. In Boston's black community Walker became a leader, gaining local recognition for his antislavery speeches, one of which was printed in 1828 in *Freedom's Journal*, the first African American newspaper published in the United States. Growing in militancy and outspokenness during the last two years of his life, Walker published three editions of his *Appeal* in 1829 and 1830, each one increasingly urgent and frank in its denunciation of racial injustice. Southern hysteria in response to the appearance of the *Appeal* made Walker a marked man. He died mysteriously on June 28, 1830, purportedly the victim of poison.

Walker did not live to see Nat Turner's insurrection in Southampton County, Virginia, in August 1831, only fourteen months after the publication of the last edition of the *Appeal*. But slaveholders were convinced that Turner had put into action what Walker had proposed in words. Efforts in Virginia to bar black ministers from preaching to their own people—on the supposition that some would use the *Appeal* as their text—were only some of many repressive measures taken in that state to keep the ideas of Walker and the example of Turner from inciting the enslaved to revolt. Nevertheless, Walker's admirers in the North, such as the fiery antislavery minister Henry Highland Garnet, kept the *Appeal* and Walker's compelling story in print well into the middle of the nineteenth century. In the twentieth century, particularly during times of crisis and heightened black consciousness, *David Walker's Appeal* reclaims our attention as an enabling text and a touchstone by which its successors, from Garnet's own "Call to Rebellion" speech in 1843 to Eldridge Cleaver's *Soul on Ice* (1967), can be measured, valued, and preserved in a tradition.

From David Walker's Appeal in Four Articles; Together with a Preamble, to the Coloured Citizens of the World

Preamble

My dearly beloved Brethren and Fellow Citizens.

Having travelled over a considerable portion of these United States, and having, in the course of my travels, taken the most accurate observations of things as they exist—the result of my observations has warranted the full and unshaken conviction, that we, (coloured people of these United States,) are the most degraded, wretched, and abject set of beings that ever lived since the world began; and I pray God that none like us ever may live again until time shall be no more. They tell us of the Israelites in Egypt, the Helots[1] in Sparta, and of the Roman Slaves, which last were made up from almost every nation under heaven, whose sufferings under those ancient and heathen nations, were, in comparison with ours, under this enlightened and Christian nation, no more than a cypher—or, in other words, those heathen nations of antiquity, had but little more among them than the name and form of slavery; while wretchedness and endless miseries were reserved, apparently in a phial, to be poured out upon our fathers, ourselves and our children, by *Christian* Americans!

These positions I shall endeavour, by the help of the Lord, to demonstrate in the course of this *Appeal*, to the satisfaction of the most incredulous mind—and may God Almighty, who is the Father of our Lord Jesus Christ, open your hearts to understand and believe the truth.

The *causes*, my brethren, which produce our wretchedness and miseries, are so very numerous and aggravating, that I believe the pen only of a Josephus or a Plutarch,[2] can well enumerate and explain them. Upon subjects, then, of such incomprehensible magnitude, so impenetrable, and so notorious, I shall be obliged to omit a large class of, and content myself with giving you an exposition of a few of those, which do indeed rage to such an alarming pitch, that they cannot but be a perpetual source of terror and dismay to every reflecting mind.

1. A state-owned serf in the ancient Greek city-state of Sparta.
2. Greek biographer and moral philosopher (A.D. 46–120?). Josephus (A.D. 37–100?), Jewish statesman and historian.

I am fully aware, in making this appeal to my much afflicted and suffering brethren, that I shall not only be assailed by those whose greatest earthly desires are, to keep us in abject ignorance and wretchedness, and who are of the firm conviction that Heaven has designed us and our children to be slaves and *beasts of burden* to them and their children. I say, I do not only expect to be held up to the public as an ignorant, impudent and restless disturber of the public peace, by such avaricious creatures, as well as a mover of insubordination—and perhaps put in prison or to death, for giving a superficial exposition of our miseries, and exposing tyrants. But I am persuaded, that many of my brethren, particularly those who are ignorantly in league with slave-holders or tyrants, who acquire their daily bread by the blood and sweat of their more ignorant brethren—and not a few of those too, who are too ignorant to see an inch beyond their noses, will rise up and call me cursed—Yea, the jealous ones among us will perhaps use more abject subtlety, by affirming that this work is not worth perusing, that we are well situated, and there is no use in trying to better our condition, for we cannot. I will ask one question here.—Can our condition be any worse?—Can it be more mean and abject? If there are any changes, will they not be for the better, though they may appear for the worst at first? Can they get us any lower? Where can they get us? They are afraid to treat us worse, for they know well, the day they do it they are gone. But against all accusations which may or can be preferred against me, I appeal to Heaven for my motive in writing—who knows that my object is, if possible, to awaken in the breasts of my afflicted, degraded and slumbering brethren, a spirit of inquiry and investigation respecting our miseries and wretchedness in this *Republican Land of Liberty!!!!!!*

The sources from which our miseries are derived, and on which I shall comment, I shall not combine in one, but shall put them under distinct heads and expose them in their turn; in doing which, keeping truth on my side, and not departing from the strictest rules of morality, I shall endeavour to penetrate, search out, and lay them open for your inspection. If you cannot or will not profit by them, I shall have done *my* duty to you, my country and my God.

And as the inhuman system of *slavery,* is the *source* from which most of our miseries proceed, I shall begin with that *curse to nations,* which has spread terror and devastation through so many nations of antiquity, and which is raging to such a pitch at the present day in Spain and in Portugal. It had one tug in England, in France, and in the United States of America; yet the inhabitants thereof, do not learn wisdom, and erase it entirely from their dwellings and from all with whom they have to do. The fact is, the labour of slaves comes so cheap to the avaricious usurpers, and is (as they think) of such great utility to the country where it exists, that those who are actuated by sordid avarice only, overlook the evils, which will as sure as the Lord lives, follow after the good. In fact, they are so happy to keep in ignorance and degradation, and to receive the homage and the labour of the slaves, they forget that God rules in the armies of heaven and among the inhabitants of the earth, having his ears continually open to the cries, tears and groans of his oppressed people; and being a just and holy Being will at one day appear fully in behalf of the oppressed, and arrest the progress of the avaricious oppressors; for although the destruction of the oppressors God may not effect by the oppressed, yet the Lord our God will bring other destructions upon them—for not unfrequently will he cause them to rise up one against another, to be split and divided, and to oppress each other, and sometimes to open hostilities with sword in hand. Some may ask, what is the matter with this united and happy people?—Some say it is the cause of political usurpers, tyrants, oppressors, etc. But has not the Lord an oppressed and suffering people among them? Does the Lord condescend to hear their cries and see their tears in consequence of oppression? Will he let the oppressors rest comfortably and happy always? Will he not cause the very children of the oppressors to rise up against them, and oftimes put them to death? "God works in many ways his wonders to perform."[3]

I will not here speak of the destructions which the Lord brought upon Egypt, in consequence of the oppression and consequent groans of the oppressed—of the hundreds and thousands of Egyptians whom God hurled into the Red Sea for afflicting his people in their land—of the Lord's suffering people in Sparta or Lacedaemon, the land of the truly famous Lycurgus[4]—nor have I time to comment upon the cause which produced the fierceness with which Sylla usurped the title, and absolutely acted as dictator of the Roman people—the conspiracy of Cataline—the conspiracy against, and murder of Cæsar in the Senate house—the spirit with which Marc Antony made himself master of the commonwealth—his associating Octavius and Lipidus with himself in power—their dividing the provinces of Rome among themselves—their attack and defeat, on the plains of Phillippi, of the last defenders of their liberty, (Brutus and Cassius)—the tyranny of Tiberius,[5] and from him to the final overthrow of Constantinople by the Turkish Sultan, Mahomed II.[6] A.D. 1453. I say, I shall not take up time to speak of the *causes* which produced so much wretchedness and massacre among those heathen nations, for I am aware that you know too well, that God is just, as well as merciful!—I shall call your attention a few moments to that *Christian* nation, the Spaniards—while I shall leave almost unnoticed, that avaricious and cruel people, the Portuguese, among whom all true hearted Christians and lovers of Jesus Christ, must evidently see the judgments of God displayed. To show the judgments of God upon the Spaniards, I shall occupy but a little time, leaving a plenty of room for the candid and unprejudiced to reflect.

All persons who are acquainted with history, and particularly the Bible, who are not blinded by the God of this world, and are not actuated solely by avarice—who are able to lay aside prejudice long enough to view candidly and impartially, things as they were, are, and probably will be—who are willing to admit that God made man to serve Him *alone*, and that man should have no other Lord or Lords but Himself—that God Almighty is the *sole proprietor* or *master* of the WHOLE human family, and will not on any consideration admit of a colleague, being unwilling to divide his glory with

---

3. Slightly adapted from William Cowper's hymn "Walking with God" (1779).
4. A legendary reformer and legislator of Sparta.
5. Walker is tracing the major events and leaders of the civil wars that, during the last century before

Christ, transformed Rome from a republic into a dictatorship under the emperor Augustus and his successor Tiberius (d. A.D. 37).
6. Muhammad II (1429–1481) conquered the Byzantine Empire in 1453.

another—and who can dispense with prejudice long enough to admit that we are *men*, notwithstanding our *improminent noses* and *woolly heads*, and believe that we feel for our fathers, mothers, wives and children, as well as the whites do for theirs.—I say, all who are permitted to see and believe these things, can easily recognize the judgments of God among the Spaniards. Though others may lay the cause of the fierceness with which they cut each other's throats, to some other circumstance, yet they who believe that God is a God of justice, will believe that SLAVERY *is the principal cause.*

While the Spaniards are running about upon the field of battle cutting each other's throats, has not the Lord an afflicted and suffering people in the midst of them, whose cries and groans in consequence of oppression are continually pouring into the ears of the God of justice? Would they not cease to cut each other's throats, if they could? But how can they? The very support which they draw from government to aid them in perpetrating such enormities, does it not arise in a great degree from the wretched victims of oppression among them? And yet they are calling for *Peace!— Peace!!* Will any peace be given unto them? Their destruction may indeed be procrastinated awhile, but can it continue long, while they are oppressing the Lord's people? Has He not the hearts of all men in His hand? Will he suffer one part of his creatures to go on oppressing another like brutes always, with impunity? And yet, those avaricious wretches are calling for *Peace!!!!* I declare, it does appear to me, as though some nations think God is asleep, or that he made the Africans for nothing else but to dig their mines and work their farms, or they cannot believe history, sacred or profane. I ask every man who has a heart, and is blessed with the privilege of believing—Is not God a God of justice to *all* his creatures? Do you say he is? Then if he gives peace and tranquillity to tyrants, and permits them to keep our fathers, our mothers, ourselves and our children in eternal ignorance and wretchedness, to support them and their families, would he be to us a God of *justice?* I ask, O ye *Christians!!!* who hold us and our children in the most abject ignorance and degradation, that ever a people were afflicted with since the world began—I say, if God gives you peace and tranquillity, and suffers you thus to go on afflicting us, and our children, who have never given you the least provocation—would he be to us *a God of justice?* If you will allow that we are MEN, who feel for each other, does not the blood of our fathers and of us their children, cry aloud to the Lord of Sabaoth against you, for the cruelties and murders with which you have, and do continue to afflict us. But it is time for me to close my remarks on the suburbs, just to enter more fully into the interior of this system of cruelty and oppression.

Article I

OUR WRETCHEDNESS IN CONSEQUENCE OF SLAVERY

My beloved brethren:—The Indians of North and of South America— the Greeks—the Irish, subjected under the king of Great Britain—the Jews, that ancient people of the Lord—the inhabitants of the islands of the sea— in fine, all the inhabitants of the earth, (except however, the sons of Africa) are called *men,* and of course are, and ought to be free. But we, (coloured people) and our children are *brutes!!* and of course are, and *ought to be* SLAVES to the American people and their children forever!! to dig their mines and work their farms; and thus go on enriching them, from one generation to another with our *blood* and our *tears!!!!*

I promised in a preceding page to demonstrate to the satisfaction of the most incredulous, that we, (coloured people of these United States of America) are the *most wretched, degraded* and *abject* set of beings that *ever lived* since the world began, and that the white Americans having reduced us to the wretched state of *slavery,* treat us in that condition *more cruel* (they being an enlightened and Christian people,) than any heathen nation did any people whom it had reduced to our condition. These affirmations are so well confirmed in the minds of all unprejudiced men, who have taken the trouble to read histories, that they need no elucidation from me. But to put them beyond all doubt, I refer you in the first place to the children of Jacob, or of Israel in Egypt, under Pharaoh and his people. Some of my brethren do not know who Pharaoh and the Egyptians were—I know it to be a fact, that some of them take the Egyptians to have been a gang of *devils,* not knowing any better, and that they (Egyptians) having got possession of the Lord's people, treated them *nearly* as cruel as *Christian Americans* do us, at the present day. For the information of such, I would only mention that the Egyptians, were Africans or coloured people, such as we are—some of them yellow and others dark—a mixture of Ethiopians and the natives of Egypt—about the same as you see the coloured people of the United States at the present day.—I say, I call your attention then, to the children of Jacob, while I point out particularly to you his son Joseph, among the rest, in Egypt.

"And Pharaoh, said unto Joseph, . . . thou shalt be over my house, and according unto thy word shall all my people be ruled: only in the throne will I be greater than thou."[7]

"And Pharaoh said unto Joseph, see, I have set thee over all the land of Egypt."[8]

"And Pharaoh said unto Joseph, I am Pharaoh, and without thee shall no man lift up his hand or foot in all the land of Egypt."[9]

Now I appeal to heaven and to earth, and particularly to the American people themselves, who cease not to declare that our condition is not *hard,* and that we are comparatively satisfied to rest in wretchedness and misery, under them and their children. Not, indeed, to show me a coloured President, a Governor, a Legislator, a Senator, a Mayor, or an Attorney at the Bar.—But to show me a man of colour, who holds the low office of a Constable, or one who sits in a Juror Box, even on a case of one of his wretched brethren, throughout this great Republic! !—But let us pass Joseph the son of Israel a little farther in review, as he existed with that heathen nation.

"And Pharaoh called Joseph's name Zaphnathpaaneah; and he gave him to wife Asenath the daughter of Potipherah priest of On. And Joseph went out over all the land of Egypt."[1]

7. "See Genesis, chap. xli" [Walker's note]. The verses are 39–40.
8. Genesis 44:41.
9. Genesis 41:44.
1. Genesis 41:45 [Walker's note].

Compare the above, with the American institutions. Do they not institute laws to prohibit us from marrying among the whites? I would wish, candidly, however, before the Lord, to be understood, that I would not give a *pinch of snuff* to be married to any white person I ever saw in all the days of my life. And I do say it, that the black man, or man of colour, who will leave his own colour (provided he can get one, who is good for any thing) and marry a white woman, to be a double slave to her, just because she is *white*, ought to be treated by her as he surely will be, viz: as a NIGGER!!!! It is not, indeed, what I care about inter-marriages with the whites, which induced me to pass this subject in review; for the Lord knows, that there is a day coming when they will be glad enough to get into the company of the blacks, notwithstanding, we are, in this generation, levelled by them, almost on a level with the brute creation: and some of us they treat even worse than they do the brutes that perish. I only made this extract to show how much lower we are held, and how much more cruel we are treated by the Americans, than were the children of Jacob, by the Egyptians.—We will notice the sufferings of Israel some further, under *heathen Pharaoh*, compared with ours under the *enlightened Christians of America*.

"And Pharaoh spoke unto Joseph, saying, thy father and thy brethren are come unto thee:

"The land of Egypt is before thee: in the best of the land make thy father and brethren to dwell; in the land of Goshen let them dwell: and if thou knowest any men of activity among them, then make them rulers over my cattle."[2]

I ask those people who treat us so *well*, Oh! I ask them, where is the most barren spot of land which they have given unto us? Israel had the most fertile land in all Egypt. Need I mention the very notorious fact, that I have known a poor man of colour, who laboured night and day, to acquire a little money, and having acquired it, he vested it in a small piece of land, and got him a house erected thereon, and having paid for the whole, he moved his family into it, where he was suffered to remain but nine months, when he was cheated out of his property by a white man, and driven out of door! And is not this the case generally? Can a man of colour buy a piece of land and keep it peaceably? Will not some white man try to get it from him, even if it is in a *mud hole?* I need not comment any farther on a subject, which all, both black and white, will readily admit. But I must, really, observe that in this very city, when a man of colour dies, if he owned any real estate it most generally falls into the hands of some white person. The wife and children of the deceased may weep and lament if they please, but the estate will be kept snug enough by its white possessor.

But to prove farther that the condition of the Israelites was better under the Egyptians than ours is under the whites. I call upon the professing Christians, I call upon the philanthropist, I call upon the very tyrant himself, to show me a page of history, either sacred or profane, on which a verse can be found, which maintains, that the Egyptians heaped the *insupportable insult* upon the children of Israel, by telling them that they were not of the *human family*. Can the whites deny this charge? Have they not, after having reduced us to the deplorable condition of slaves under their feet,

2. Genesis, chap. xlvii. 5, 6 [Walker's note].

held us up as descending originally from the tribes of *Monkeys* or *Orang-Outangs?* O! my God! I appeal to every man of feeling—is not this insupportable? Is it not heaping the most gross insult upon our miseries, because they have got us under their feet and we cannot help ourselves? Oh! pity us we pray thee, Lord Jesus, Master.—Has Mr. Jefferson declared to the world, that we are inferior to the whites, both in the endowments of our bodies and our minds?[3] It is indeed surprising, that a man of such great learning, combined with such excellent natural parts, should speak so of a set of men in chains. I do not know what to compare it to, unless, like putting one wild deer in an iron cage, where it will be secured, and hold another by the side of the same, then let it go, and expect the one in the cage to run as fast as the one at liberty. So far, my brethren, were the Egyptians from heaping these insults upon their slaves, that Pharaoh's daughter took Moses, a son of Israel for her own, as will appear by the following.

"And Pharaoh's daughter said unto her, [Moses' mother] take this child away, and nurse it for me, and I will pay thee thy wages. And the woman took the child [Moses] and nursed it.

"And the child grew, and she brought him unto Pharaoh's daughter and he became her son. And she called his name Moses: and she said because I drew him out of the water."[4]

In all probability, Moses would have become Prince Regent to the throne, and no doubt, in process of time but he would have been seated on the throne of Egypt. But he had rather suffer shame, with the people of God, than to enjoy pleasures with that wicked people for a season. O! that the coloured people were long since of Moses' excellent disposition, instead of courting favour with, and telling news and lies to our *natural enemies*, against each other—aiding them to keep their hellish chains of slavery upon us. Would we not long before this time, have been respectable men, instead of such wretched victims of oppression as we are? Would they be able to drag our mothers, our fathers, our wives, our children and ourselves, around the world in chains and hand-cuffs as they do, to dig up gold and silver for them and theirs? This question, my brethren, I leave for you to digest; and may God Almighty force it home to your hearts. Remember that unless you are united, keeping your tongues within your teeth, you will be afraid to trust your secrets to each other, and thus perpetuate our miseries under the *Christians!!!!* ☞ ADDITION.—Remember, also to lay humble at the feet of our Lord and Master Jesus Christ, with prayers and fastings. Let our enemies go on with their butcheries, and at once fill up their cup. Never make an attempt to gain our freedom or *natural right*, from under our cruel oppressors and murderers, until you see your way clear[5]—when that hour arrives and you move, be not afraid or dismayed; for be you as-

<hr />

3. In his *Notes on the State of Virginia* (1787), Thomas Jefferson judged black people less beautiful than whites and intellectually inferior to them as well.

4. See Exodus, chap. ii. 9, 10 [Walker's note].

5. It is not to be understood here, that I mean for us to wait until God shall take us by the hair of our heads and drag us out of abject wretchedness and slavery, nor do I mean to convey the idea for us to wait until our enemies shall make preparations, and call us to seize those preparations, take it away from them, and put every thing before us to death, in order to gain our freedom which God has given us. For you must remember that we are men as well as they. God has been pleased to give us two eyes, two hands, two feet, and some sense in our heads as well as they. They have no more right to hold us in slavery than we have to hold them, we have just as much right, in the sight of God, to hold them and their children in slavery and wretchedness, as they have to hold us, and no more [Walker's note].

ured that Jesus Christ the King of heaven and of earth who is the God of justice and of armies, will surely go before you. And those enemies who have for hundreds of years stolen our *rights*, and kept us ignorant of Him and His divine worship, he will remove. Millions of whom, are this day, so ignorant and avaricious, that they cannot conceive how God can have an attribute of justice, and show mercy to us because it pleased Him to make us black—which colour, Mr. Jefferson calls unfortunate!!!!!! As though we are not as thankful to our God, for having made us as it pleased himself, as they, (the whites,) are for having made them white. They think because they hold us in their infernal chains of slavery, that we wish to be white, or of their color—but they are dreadfully deceived—we wish to be just as it pleased our Creator to have made us, and no avaricious and unmerciful wretches, have any business to make slaves of, or hold us in slavery. How would they like for us to make slaves of, and hold them in cruel slavery, and murder them as they do us?—But is Mr. Jefferson's assertions true? viz. "that it is unfortunate for us that our Creator has been pleased to make us *black*." We will not take his say so, for the fact. The world will have an opportunity to see whether it is unfortunate for us, that our Creator *has made us* darker than the *whites*.

Fear not the number and education of our *enemies*, against whom we shall have to contend for our lawful right; guaranteed to us by our Maker; for why should we be afraid, when God is, and will continue, (if we continue humble) to be on our side?

The man who would not fight under our Lord and Master Jesus Christ, in the glorious and heavenly cause of freedom and of God—to be delivered from the most wretched, abject and servile slavery, that ever a people was afflicted with since the foundation of the world, to the present day—ought to be kept with all of his children or family, in slavery, or in chains, to be butchered by his *cruel enemies.*

I saw a paragraph, a few years since, in a South Carolina paper, which, speaking of the barbarity of the Turks, it said: "The Turks are the most barbarous people in the world—they treat the Greeks more like *brutes* than human beings." And in the same paper was an advertisement, which said: "Eight well built Virginia and Maryland *Negro fellows* and four *wenches* will positively be *sold* this day, *to the highest bidder!*" And what astonished me still more was, to see in this same *humane* paper!! the cuts of three men, with clubs and budgets[6] on their backs, and an advertisement offering a considerable sum of money for their apprehension and delivery. I declare, it is really so amusing to hear the Southerners and Westerners of this country talk about *barbarity*, that it is positively, enough to make a man *smile*.

The sufferings of the Helots among the Spartans, were somewhat severe, it is true, but to say that theirs, were as severe as ours among the Americans, I do most strenuously deny—for instance, can any man show me an article on a page of ancient history which specifies, that, the Spartans chained, and handcuffed the Helots, and dragged them from their wives and children, children from their parents, mothers from their suckling babes, wives from their husbands, driving them from one end of the country to the

6. Leather bags. "Cuts": images from woodcuts.

other? Notice the Spartans were heathens, who lived long before our Divine Master made his appearance in the flesh. Can Christian Americans deny these barbarous cruelties? Have you not, Americans, having subjected us under you, added to these miseries, by insulting us in telling us to our face, because we are helpless, that we are not of the human family? I ask you, O! Americans, I ask you, in the name of the Lord, can you deny these charges? Some perhaps may deny, by saying, that they never thought or said that we were not men. But do not actions speak louder than words?—have they not made provisions for the Greeks, and Irish? Nations who have never done the least thing for them, while *we*, who have enriched their country with our blood and tears—have dug up gold and silver for them and their children, from generation to generation, and are in more miseries than any other people under heaven, are not seen, but by comparatively, a handful of the American people? There are indeed, more ways to kill a dog, besides choking it to death with butter. Further—The Spartans or Lacedaemonians, had some frivolous pretext, for enslaving the Helots, for they (Helots) while being free inhabitants of Sparta, stirred up an intestine commotion, and were, by the Spartans subdued, and made prisoners of war. Consequently they and their children were condemned to perpetual slavery.[7]

I have been for years troubling the pages of historians, to find out what our fathers have done to the *white Christians of America*, to merit such condign punishment as they have inflicted on them, and do continue to inflict on us their children. But I must aver, that my researches have hitherto been to no effect. I have therefore, come to the immoveable conclusion, that they (Americans) have, and do continue to punish us for nothing else, but for enriching them and their country. For I cannot conceive of anything else. Nor will I ever believe otherwise, until the Lord shall convince me.

The world knows, that slavery as it existed among the Romans, (which was the primary cause of their destruction) was, comparatively speaking, no more than a *cypher*,[8] when compared with ours under the Americans. Indeed I should not have noticed the Roman slaves, had not the very learned and penetrating Mr. Jefferson said, "when a master was murdered, all his slaves in the same house, or within hearing, were condemned to death."[9]— Here let me ask Mr. Jefferson, (but he is gone to answer at the bar of God, for the deeds done in his body while living,) I therefore ask the whole American people, had I not rather die, or be put to death, than to be a slave to any tyrant, who takes not only my own, but my wife and children's lives by the inches? Yea, would I meet death with avidity far! far!! in preference to such *servile submission* to the murderous hands of tyrants. Mr. Jefferson's very severe remarks on us have been so extensively argued upon by men whose attainments in literature, I shall never be able to reach, that I would not have meddled with it, were it not to solicit each of my brethren, who has the spirit of a man, to buy a copy of Mr. Jefferson's "Notes on Virginia,"

---

7. "See Dr. Goldsmith's History of Greece— page 9. See also, Plutarch's Lives. The Helot's subdued by Agis, king of Sparta" [Walker's note]. Walker's citation is to Oliver Goldsmith's *A History* of *Greece* (1774).

8. Something of no consequence.

9. See his Notes on Virginia, page 210 [Walker's note].

and put it in the hand of his son. For let no one of us suppose that the refutations which have been written by our white friends are enough—they are *whites*—we are *blacks*. We, and the world wish to see the charges of Mr. Jefferson refuted by the blacks *themselves*, according to their chance; for we must remember that what the whites have written respecting this subject, is other men's labours, and did not emanate from the blacks. I know well, that there are some talents and learning among the coloured people of this country, which we have not a chance to develope, in consequence of oppression; but our oppression ought not to hinder us from acquiring all we can. For we will have a chance to develope them by and by. God will not suffer us, always to be oppressed. Our sufferings will come to an *end*, in spite of all the Americans this side of *eternity*. Then we will want all the learning and talents among ourselves, and perhaps more, to govern ourselves.—"Every dog must have its day," the American's is coming to an end.

But let us review Mr. Jefferson's remarks respecting us some further. Comparing our miserable fathers, with the learned philosophers of Greece, he says: "Yet notwithstanding these and other discouraging circumstances among the Romans, their slaves were often their rarest artists. They excelled too, in science, insomuch as to be usually employed as tutors to their master's children; Epictetus, Terence and Phædrus,[1] were slaves,—but they were of the race of whites. It is not their *condition* then, but *nature*, which has produced the distinction."[2] See this, my brethren!! Do you believe that this assertion is swallowed by millions of the whites? Do you know that Mr. Jefferson was one of as great characters as ever lived among the whites? See his writings for the world, and public labours for the United States of America. Do you believe that the assertions of such a man, will pass away into oblivion unobserved by this people and the world? If you do you are much mistaken—See how the American people treat us— have we souls in our bodies? Are we men who have any spirits at all? I know that there are many *swell-bellied* fellows among us, whose greatest object is to fill their stomachs. Such I do not mean—I am after those who know and feel, that we are MEN, as well as other people; to them, I say, that unless we try to refute Mr. Jefferson's arguments respecting us, we will only establish them.

But the slaves among the Romans. Every body who has read history, knows, that as soon as a slave among the Romans obtained his freedom, he could rise to the greatest eminence in the State, and there was no law instituted to hinder a slave from buying his freedom. Have not the Americans instituted laws to hinder us from obtaining our freedom? Do any deny this charge? Read the laws of Virginia, North Carolina, etc. Further: have not the Americans instituted laws to prohibit a man of colour from obtaining and holding any office whatever, under the government of the United States of America? Now, Mr. Jefferson tells us, that our condition is not so hard, as the slaves were under the Romans!!!!!!

It is time for me to bring this article to a close. But before I close it, I must observe to my brethren that at the close of the first Revolution in this

---

1. A classical Roman philosopher, dramatist, and author of fables, respectively, each one born in slavery.

2. See his Notes on Virginia, page 211 [Walker's note].

country, with Great Britain, there were but thirteen States in the Union, now there are twenty-four, most of which are slave-holding States, and the whites are dragging us around in chains and in handcuffs, to their new States and Territories to work their mines and farms, to enrich them and their children—and millions of them believing firmly that we being a little darker than they, were made by our Creator to be an inheritance to them and their children for ever—the same as a parcel of *brutes*.

Are we MEN!!—I ask you, O my brethren! are we MEN? Did our Creator make us to be slaves to dust and ashes like ourselves? Are they not dying worms as well as we? Have they not to make their appearance before the tribunal of Heaven, to answer for the deeds done in the body, as well as we? Have we any other Master but Jesus Christ alone? Is he not their Master as well as ours?—What right then, have we to obey and call any other Master, but Himself? How we could be so *submissive* to a gang of men, whom we cannot tell whether they are *as good* as ourselves or not, I never could conceive. However, this is shut up with the Lord, and we cannot precisely tell—but I declare, we judge men by their works.

The whites have always been an unjust, jealous, unmerciful, avaricious and blood-thirsty set of beings, always seeking after power and authority.— We view them all over the confederacy of Greece, where they were first known to be any thing, (in consequence of education) we see them there, cutting each other's throats—trying to subject each other to wretchedness and misery—to effect which, they used all kinds of deceitful, unfair, and unmerciful means. We view them next in Rome, where the spirit of tyranny and deceit raged still higher. We view them in Gaul,[3] Spain, and in Britain.—In fine, we view them all over Europe, together with what were scattered about in Asia and Africa, as heathens, and we see them acting more like devils than accountable men. But some may ask, did not the blacks of Africa, and the mulattoes of Asia, go on in the same way as did the whites of Europe. I answer, no—they never were half so avaricious, deceitful and unmerciful as the whites, according to their knowledge.

But we will leave the whites or Europeans as heathens, and take a view of them as Christians, in which capacity we see them as cruel, if not more so than ever. In fact, take them as a body, they are ten times more cruel, avaricious and unmerciful than ever they were; for while they were heathens, they were bad enough it is true, but it is positively a fact that they were not quite so audacious as to go and take vessel loads of men, women and children, and in cold blood, and through devilishness, throw them into the sea, and murder them in all kinds of ways. While they were heathens, they were too ignorant for such barbarity. But being Christians, enlightened and sensible, they are completely prepared for such hellish cruelties. Now suppose God were to give them more sense, what would they do? If it were possible, would they not *dethrone* Jehovah[4] and seat themselves upon his throne? I therefore, in the name and fear of the Lord God of Heaven and of earth, divested of prejudice either on the side of my colour or that of the whites, advance my suspicion of them, whether they are *as good by nature* as we are or not. Their actions, since they were known as a people, have been the

3. France.   4. God.

reverse, I do indeed suspect them, but this, as I before observed, is shut up with the Lord, we cannot exactly tell, it will be proved in succeeding generations.—The whites have had the essence of the gospel as it was preached by my master and his apostles—the Ethiopians have not, who are to have it in its meridian splendor—the Lord will give it to them to their satisfaction. I hope and pray my God, that they will make good use of it, that it may be well with them.[5]

5. It is my solemn belief, that if ever the world becomes Christianized, (which must certainly take place before long) it will be through the means, under God of the *Blacks*, who are now held in wretchedness, and degradation, by the white *Christians* of the world, who before they learn to do justice to us before our Maker—and be reconciled to us, and reconcile us to them, and by that means have clear consciences before God and man.— Send out Missionaries to convert the Heathens, many of whom after they cease to worship gods, which neither see nor hear, become ten times more the children of Hell, than ever they were, why what is the reason? Why the reason is obvious, they must learn to do justice at home, before they go into distant lands, to display their charity, Christianity, and benevolence; when they learn to do justice, God will accept their offering, (no man may think that I am against Missionaries for I am not, my object is to see justice done at home, before we go to convert the Heathens) [Walker's note].

GEORGE MOSES HORTON
1797?–1883?

For most of his persistent, often frustrated life, George Moses Horton was both a slave and a poet. Unlike Phillis Wheatley, his only significant predecessor in the history of African American poetry, Horton made the conflict between the condition of his birth and the aspiration of his life a salient and individualizing theme of his writing. In 1925 Countee Cullen became Harlem's most famous poet by composing the poignant and plainly self-referential couplet: "Yet do I marvel at this curious thing: / To make a poet black, and bid him sing." It was Horton, however, who introduced to American verse the agonizing contradiction epitomized in Cullen's lines. Not only black but also a slave, not just a versifier but a poet intent on a professional literary career in a society that denied him the right to write, Horton's experience and articulation of the contradictory status of the black poet were paradigmatic, a crucial reference point in the history of African American literature.

Born a slave in Northampton County, North Carolina, George Moses Horton endured bondage to three generations of the William Horton family until emancipation finally came in 1865 with the end of the Civil War. George grew up working on his masters' farms but discovered by the age of ten a strong affinity toward music and verse. After teaching himself to read, the teenager began composing hymns in his head. By the time he was twenty years old he had begun to make a reputation at the state university at Chapel Hill, a ten-mile walk from his home, because of his ability to create made-to-order love poems for students willing to pay twenty-five to seventy-five cents per lyric, depending on the length and complexity. Some students compensated Horton for his work by giving him collections of poetry by Homer, Virgil, Shakespeare, John Milton, Lord Byron, and other classic English authors, all of whom became models for Horton's own verse. Caroline Lee Hentz, a Chapel Hill professor's wife and antislavery author, helped Horton learn to write; in 1828 she helped him break into print by sending two poems critical of slavery to the Lancaster, Massachusetts, *Gazette*, Hentz's hometown newspaper.

In 1828 an unlikely biracial coalition of southerners and northerners tried to raise money for Horton's freedom by sponsoring his first volume of poetry, *The*

Hope of Liberty, which was published in Raleigh in 1829. *The Hope of Liberty* was the first book of African American poetry in more than half a century and the first book authored by a black southerner. Only three of the twenty-one poems in *The Hope of Liberty* shed light on Horton's feelings about his enslavement; the rest are concerned with romantic love, religion, and death. But the poem titled *On Hearing of the Intention of a Gentleman to Purchase the Poet's Freedom* proved that the facile creator of sentimental complaints like *The Lover's Farewell* had also been through depths of "deep despair" in his pursuit of a "dismal path" toward freedom.

Although *The Hope of Liberty* did not accomplish its purpose, Horton's master did allow him to settle in Chapel Hill and hire his time by working as a professional poet, waiter, and handyman and by publishing his verse in various abolitionist periodicals, such as the *Liberator*, the *North Star*, and the *National Anti-Slavery Standard*. In 1845 Horton saw his second book into print, *The Poetical Works of George M. Horton, The Colored Bard of North Carolina*. Published in Hillsborough, North Carolina, *The Poetical Works* did not risk the goodwill Horton enjoyed among local southern whites by opposing slavery overtly. But the most remarkable poem in the volume, *Division of an Estate*, has impressed a number of modern critics with its subtle rhetoric of protest and its pathetic rendition of the slave's plight at the moment of auction.

During the last months of the Civil War, Horton managed to interest Captain Will Banks, a Michigan cavalry officer in the occupying Union Army, in his plans for the publication of a third book of poems. Shortly after the fall of the Confederacy, *Naked Genius*, a compendium of 133 poems, most of them previously unpublished, appeared from a Raleigh, North Carolina, printer. Horton's final book of poetry does not stray far from the subjects and manner that pervade his earlier collections, but the poems on slavery attack the injustices, rather than simply complain of the constraints, of slavery and racism. Perhaps the poet felt finally at liberty to speak his mind not only about slavery but also about the trammels that had bound him and his poetic talents. If so, *George Moses Horton, Myself*, one of the relatively few remarkable poems in *Naked Genius*, stands as a fitting autobiographical summary to the life and work of the poet. Although freedom brought him the opportunity to move to Philadelphia, where he is thought to have resided until his death sometime in 1883, Horton's silence as a poet after 1865 suggests that he had been identified for so long as "the slave poet" and "the colored bard of North Carolina" that he could not see clearly how to remake himself in a new place for a new time.

The Lover's Farewell

And wilt thou, love, my soul display,
And all my secret thoughts betray?
I strove but could not hold thee fast,
My heart flies off with thee at last.

The favorite daughter of the dawn,   5
On love's mild breeze will soon be gone
I strove but could not cease to love,
Nor from my heart the weight remove.

And wilt thou, love, my soul beguile,
And gull[1] thy fav'rite with a smile?   10

1. Trick or cheat.

Nay, soft affection answers, nay,
And beauty wings my heart away.

I steal on tiptoe from these bowers,
All spangled with a thousand flowers;
I sigh, yet leave them all behind,   15
To gain the object of my mind.

And wilt thou, love, command my soul,
And waft me with a light controul?—
Adieu to all the blooms of May,
Farewell—I fly with love away!   20

I leave my parents here behind,
And all my friends—to love resigned—
'Tis grief to go, but death to stay:
Farewell—I'm gone with love away!

1829

On Hearing of the Intention of a Gentleman to Purchase the Poet's Freedom

When on life's ocean first I spread my sail,
I then implored a mild auspicious gale;
And from the slippery strand I took my flight,
And sought the peaceful haven of delight.

Tyrannic storms arose upon my soul,   5
And dreadful did their mad'ning thunders roll;
The pensive muse[1] was shaken from her sphere,
And hope, it vanish'd in the clouds of fear.

At length a golden sun broke thro' the gloom,
And from his smiles arose a sweet perfume—   10
A calm ensued, and birds began to sing,
And lo! the sacred muse resumed her wing.

With frantic joy she chaunted as she flew,
And kiss'd the clement[2] hand that bore her thro'
Her envious foes did from her sight retreat,   15
Or prostrate fall beneath her burning feet.

'Twas like a proselyte,[3] allied to Heaven—
Or rising spirits' boast of sins forgiven,
Whose shout dissolves the adamant away
Whose melting voice the stubborn rocks obey.   20

'Twas like the salutation of the dove,
Borne on the zephyr[4] thro' some lonesome grove,

1. Greek goddess of literature.
2. Kind, tender. "Chaunted": chanted.
3. A new convert to a religion.
4. Breeze or wind.

When Spring returns, and Winter's chill is past,
And vegetation smiles above the blast.

'Twas like the evening of a nuptial pair,   25
When love pervades the hour of sad despair—
'Twas like fair Helen's sweet return to Troy, [5]
When every Grecian bosom swell'd with joy.

The silent harp which on the osiers hung,
Was then attuned, and manumission [6] sung: 30
Away by hope the clouds of fear were driven,
And music breathed my gratitude to heaven.

Hard was the race to reach the distant goal,
The needle oft was shaken from the pole;
In such distress, who could forbear to weep?   35
Toss'd by the headlong billows of the deep!

The tantalizing beams which shone so plain,
Which turn'd my former pleasures into pain—
Which falsely promised all the joys of fame,
Gave way, and to a more substantial flame.   40

Some philanthropic souls as from afar,
With pity strove to break the slavish bar;
To whom my floods of gratitude shall roll,
And yield with pleasure to their soft control.

And sure of Providence this work begun—.   45
He shod my feet this rugged race to run;
And in despite of all the swelling tide,
Along the dismal path will prove my guide.

Thus on the dusky verge of deep despair,
Eternal Providence was with me there;   50
When pleasure seemed to fade on life's gay dawn,
And the last beam of hope was almost gone.

                                                                    1829

Division of an Estate

It well bespeaks a man beheaded, quite
Divested of the laurel [1] robe of life,
When every member struggles for its base,
The head; the power of order now recedes,
Unheeded efforts rise on every side,   5
With dull emotion rolling through the brain
Of apprehending slaves. The flocks and herds,

5. In Homer's *Iliad*, the Greeks went to war with   of a willow tree.
Troy to return the beautiful Helen.   1. An emblem of respect and honor.
6. Emancipation, freedom. "Osiers": branches

In sad confusion, now run to and fro,
And seem to ask, distressed, the reason why
That they are thus prostrated. Howl, ye dogs!   10
Ye cattle, low! ye sheep, astonish'd, bleat!
Ye bristling swine, trudge squealing through the glades,
Void of an owner to impart your food!
Sad horses, lift your heads and neigh aloud,
And caper frantic from the dismal scene: 15
Mow the last food upon your grass-clad lea.[2]
And leave a solitary home behind,
In hopeless widowhood no longer gay!
The trav'ling sun of gain his journey ends
In unavailing pain; he sets with tears;   20
A king sequester'd sinking from his throne,
Succeeded by a train of busy friends.
Like stars which rise with smiles, to mark the flight
Of awful Phoebus[3] to another world;
Stars after stars in fleet succession rise   25
Into the wide empire of fortune clear,
Regardless of the donor of their lamps;
Like heirs forgetful of parental care,
Without a grateful smile or filial tear,
Redound in rev'rence to expiring age.   30
But soon parental benediction flies
Like vivid meteors; in a moment gone,
As though they ne'er had been. But O! the state,
The dark suspense in which poor vassals[4] stand
Each mind upon the spire of chance hangs fluctuant;   35
The day of separation is at hand;
Imagination lifts her gloomy curtains,
Like ev'ning's mantle at the flight of day,
Thro' which the trembling pinnacle we spy,
On which we soon must stand with hopeful smiles,   40
Or apprehending frowns; to tumble on
The right or left forever.

                                                              1845

The Creditor to His Proud Debtor

Ha! tott'ring Johnny strut and boast,
But think of what your feathers cost;
Your crowing days are short at most,
    You bloom but soon to fade.
Surely you could not stand so wide,   5
If strictly to the bottom tried;
The wind would blow your plume aside,
    If half your debts were paid.
        Then boast and bear the crack,
        With the Sheriff at your back,   10

2. Meadow.   Apollo, god of the sun.
3. The bright; a Greek epithet associated with   4. Here, the slaves.

Huzza for dandy Jack,
My jolly fop,[1] my Jo—

The blue smoke from your segar[2] flies,
Offensive to my nose and eyes,
The most of people would be wise,   15
    Your presence to evade.
Your pockets jingle loud with cash,
And thus you cut a foppish dash,
But alas! dear boy, you would be trash,
    If your accounts were paid.   20
      Then boast and bear the crack, etc.

My duck bill[3] boots would look as bright,
Had you in justice served me right,
Like you, I then could step as light,
    Before a flaunting maid.   25
As nicely could I clear my throat,
And to my tights, my eyes devote,
But I'd leave you bear,[4] without coat,
    For which you have not paid.
      Then boast and bear the crack, etc.   30

I'd toss myself with a scornful air,
And to a poor man pay no care,
I could rock cross-legged in my chair,
    Within the cloister[5] shade.
I'd gird my neck with a light cravat,   35
And creaming wear my bell-crown hat;
But away my down would fly at that,
    If once my debts were paid.
      Then boast and bear the crack,
      With the Sheriff at your back,   40
      Huzza for dandy Jack,
      My jolly fop, my Jo—

          1845

George Moses Horton, Myself

I feel myself in need
    Of the inspiring strains of ancient lore,
My heart to lift, my empty mind to feed,
    And all the world explore.

I know that I am old   5
    And never can recover what is past,
But for the future may some light unfold
    And soar from ages blast.

1. A vain, affected man; a dude.   4. I.e., bare.
2. Cigar.   5. A place where one can live a secluded life.
3. Broad-toed.

I feel resolved to try,
My wish to prove, my calling to pursue,   10
Or mount up from the earth into the sky,
To show what Heaven can do.

My genius from a boy,
Has fluttered like a bird within my heart,
But could not thus confined her powers employ,   15
Impatient to depart.

She like a restless bird,
Would spread her wing, her power to be unfurl'd,
And let her songs be loudly heard,
And dart from world to world.   20

1865

SOJOURNER TRUTH

1797–1883

More than any other African American of her era, Sojourner Truth was the stuff of antislavery legend. She is said to have been accosted once by a white policeman in Rochester, New York, as she walked alone, cane in hand, from Corinthian Hall after delivering an antislavery lecture earlier that evening. The policeman demanded that she identify herself. Truth paused, planted her cane firmly, drew herself up to her full six-foot height, and in her deep, resonant voice, replied, "*I am that I am.*" The unnerved officer vanished. Sojourner Truth went on to her destination undisturbed.

A leading exponent of liberty in both the abolitionist and feminist movements in the mid-nineteenth century, Sojourner Truth was an extraordinarily self-possessed person. The singularity of her identity and the impossibility of labeling her are epitomized in her appropriation of "I am that I am," the words God speaks in the Bible in answer to Moses' attempt to give the Lord a name. Sojourner Truth was the name triumphantly adopted by Isabella, a one-time slave, after forty years of struggle first to become free and then to settle on the mission she felt God intended for her.

Isabella's experience in slavery was harsh. Born in Ulster County, New York, to a wealthy Dutch master, she was separated from her parents as a child and sold to a succession of owners who exploited her unusual strength and did not hesitate to enforce their discipline with beatings. She bore at least five children in slavery and took one of them with her when she left her final master in 1826, seizing her freedom a year before she was emancipated by New York law in 1827. Two years later she sued successfully for the return of her son Peter from enslavement in Alabama. Attracted to New York City, Isabella worked there as a domestic. She pursued both unorthodox and conventional religious paths toward the spiritual fulfillment she longed for. In 1843 Isabella became convinced that God had called her to leave the city and go out into the countryside "testifying of the hope that was in her," the hope that others, regardless of color or condition, could experience the spiritual conversion and empowerment that she now felt. The new name she assumed, Sojourner Truth, was to signify the new person she had become in the spirit, a traveler dedicated to speaking the Truth as God revealed it.

Early in her career as an itinerant preacher, Sojourner Truth met William Lloyd Garrison, Frederick Douglass, and other prominent antislavery activists in Massachusetts. She enthusiastically joined their ranks, earning fame for her ability to deliver folksy as well as fiery speeches that denounced slavery as a moral abomination tempting the wrath of God on America. This commitment to human rights impelled Truth into the budding feminist movement of the 1850s as well. By the onset of the Civil War, Sojourner Truth had come to represent a brand of female, communitarian, vernacular African American leadership that rivaled the masculine, individualist, self-consciously literary model of black spokesman espoused by Douglass himself.

In 1863 Harriet Beecher Stowe gave Truth lasting celebrity in an *Atlantic Monthly* tribute titled *Sojourner Truth, the Libyan Sibyl*, in which Stowe declared, "I do not recollect ever to have been conversant with any one who had more of that silent and subtle power which we call personal presence than this woman." During the Civil War, despite advancing age and infirmities brought on by the rigors of slavery and the antislavery struggle, Truth worked tirelessly on several civil rights fronts. She recruited black troops in Michigan; helped with relief efforts for the freedmen and women escaping from the South; led a successful effort to desegregate the streetcars of Washington, D.C.; and counseled President Abraham Lincoln. After the war she crusaded for improvements in the lot of African Americans in the South and the Midwest. She died at her home in Battle Creek, Michigan, in 1883, an icon of American progressivism and reform.

Sojourner Truth never learned to read or write. "I cannot read a book, but I can read the people," she asserted. Two efforts were made during her lifetime to preserve her biography and the flavor of her remarkable manner of self-expression. In 1850 Truth worked with Olive Gilbert, a sympathetic white woman, to write and publish the *Narrative of Sojourner Truth*, a contribution to both the slave narrative and female spiritual autobiography traditions of African American literature. In 1875 with the aid of a white friend, Frances Titus, Truth reprinted her *Narrative*, supplementing it with her *Book of Life*, which included personal correspondence, newspaper accounts of her activities, and tributes from her friends. This expanded edition of Truth's biography was reprinted in 1878, 1881, and 1884 under the title *Narrative of Sojourner Truth; A Bondswoman of Olden Time, with a History of Her Labors and Correspondence Drawn from Her "Book of Life."* Yet it is not her lengthy life story but rather a single speech that has preserved Sojourner Truth in cultural memory.

In the early summer of 1851 during a women's rights convention in Akron, Ohio, Truth took the podium to defend the dignity of women against theological attacks from a group of ministers. The president of the convention, Frances Gage, recalled some years later the pressure applied by white women to keep Truth from speaking lest she antagonize the ministers' racial as well as gender prejudices. But Truth spoke nonetheless. Her extemporaneous oration, scarcely more than three hundred words punctuated by homely metaphors and a deceptively simple argument for women's unique role in the liberation struggles of the day, was admiringly reported in the *Anti-Slavery Bugle* on June 21, 1851. In 1878 a second and more elaborate version of the speech as Gage recollected it was incorporated into the *Book of Life* section of the *Narrative of Sojourner Truth*. The rhetorical question that Gage records Truth asking repeatedly in her speech—"and ar'n't I a woman?"—became not only the de facto title of Truth's most famous oration but also the crux of her challenge as a black woman to racial and sexual stereotypes that few had had the foresight to address so courageously. As the importance of Sojourner Truth's ideas and example has mounted in recent years, the reliability of the Gage account of the famed *Ar'n't I a Woman?* speech has been questioned. The more direct and less dialectal Sojourner Truth of the *Anti-Slavery Bugle*'s report now sounds more authentic to many analysts. Yet by comparing both versions of this classic oral text of African American literature, we can usefully reconsider Sojourner Truth's message from two perspectives and thereby appreciate its complex impact on those in her own time who tried, with varying success, to convey the power of her verbal artistry.

Ar'n't I a Woman?
Speech to the Women's Rights Convention in Akron, Ohio, 1851

From *The* Anti-Slavery Bugle, *June 21, 1851*

One of the most unique and interesting speeches of the Convention was made by Sojourner Truth, an emancipated slave. It is impossible to transfer it to paper, or convey any adequate idea of the effect it produced upon the audience. Those only can appreciate it who saw her powerful form, her whole-souled, earnest gesture, and listened to her strong and truthful tones. She came forward to the platform and addressing the President said with great simplicity: "May I say a few words?" Receiving an affirmative answer, she proceeded:

I want to say a few words about this matter. I am a woman's rights. I have as much muscle as any man, and can do as much work as any man. I have plowed and reaped and husked and chopped and mowed, and can any man do more than that? I have heard much about the sexes being equal. I can carry as much as any man, and can eat as much too, if I can get it. I am as strong as any man that is now. As for intellect, all I can say is, if woman have a pint, and man a quart—why can't she have her little pint full? You need not be afraid to give us our rights for fear we will take too much,—for we can't take more than our pint'll hold. The poor men seem to be all in confusion, and don't know what to do. Why children, if you have woman's rights, give it to her and you will feel better. You will have your own rights, and they won't be so much trouble. I can't read, but I can hear. I have heard the bible and have learned that Eve caused man to sin. Well, if woman upset the world, do give her a chance to set it right side up again. The Lady has spoken about Jesus, how he never spurned woman from him, and she was right. When Lazarus died, Mary and Martha came to him with faith and love and besought him to raise their brother.[1] And Jesus wept and Lazarus came forth. And how came Jesus into the world? Through God who created him and a woman who bore him. Man, where is your part? But the women are coming up blessed be God and a few of the men are coming up with them. But man is in a tight place, the poor slave is on him, woman is coming on him, he is surely between a hawk and a buzzard.

---

1. John 11:1–44 records the story of Jesus' raising of Lazarus, the brother of the disciples Mary and Martha, from the dead.

From *The Narrative of Sojourner Truth*, 1878

In the year 1851 she left her home in Northampton, Mass., for a lecturing tour in Western New York, accompanied by the Hon. George Thompson of England, and other distinguished abolitionists. To advocate the cause of the enslaved at this period was both unpopular and unsafe. Their meetings were frequently disturbed or broken up by the pro-slavery mob, and their lives imperiled. At such times, Sojourner fearlessly maintained her ground, and by her dignified manner and opportune remarks would disperse the rabble and restore order.

She spent several months in Western New York, making Rochester her head-quarters. Leaving this State, she traveled westward, and the next glimpse we get of her is in a Woman's Rights Convention at Akron, Ohio. Mrs. Frances D. Gage, who presided at that meeting, relates the following:—

"The cause was unpopular then. The leaders of the movement trembled on seeing a tall, gaunt black woman, in a gray dress and white turban, surmounted by an uncouth sun-bonnet, march deliberately into the church, walk with the air of a queen up the aisle, and take her seat upon the pulpit steps. A buzz of disapprobation was heard all over the house, and such words as these fell upon listening ears:—

" 'An abolition affair!' 'Woman's rights and niggers!' 'We told you so!' 'Go it, old darkey!'

"I chanced upon that occasion to wear my first laurels in public life as president of the meeting. At my request, order was restored and the business of the hour went on. The morning session was held; the evening exercises came and went. Old Sojourner, quiet and reticent as the 'Libyan Statue,'[2] sat crouched against the wall on the corner of the pulpit stairs, her sun-bonnet shading her eyes, her elbows on her knees, and her chin resting upon her broad, hard palm. At intermission she was busy, selling 'The Life of Sojourner Truth,'[3] a narrative of her own strange and adventurous life. Again and again timorous and trembling ones came to me and said with earnestness, 'Don't let her speak, Mrs. Gage, it will ruin us. Every newspaper in the land will have our cause mixed with abolition and niggers, and we shall be utterly denounced.' My only answer was, 'We shall see when the time comes.'

"The second day the work waxed warm. Methodist, Baptist, Episcopal, Presbyterian, and Universalist ministers came in to hear and discuss the resolutions presented. One claimed superior rights and privileges for man on the ground of superior intellect; another, because of the manhood of Christ. 'If God had desired the equality of woman, he would have given some token of his will through the birth, life, and death of the Saviour.' Another gave us a theological view of the sin of our first mother. There were few women in those days that dared to 'speak in meeting,' and the august teachers of the people were seeming to get the better of us, while the boys in the galleries and the sneerers among the pews were hugely enjoying

2. A reference to the title of Harriet Beecher Stowe's *Sojourner Truth, the Libyan Sibyl,* which was published in the *Atlantic Monthly* (April 1863).

3. *Narrative of Sojourner Truth* (1850).

the discomfiture, as they supposed, of the 'strong minded.' Some of the tender-skinned friends were on the point of losing dignity, and the atmosphere of the convention betokened a storm.

"Slowly from her seat in the corner rose Sojourner Truth, who, till now, had scarcely lifted her head. 'Don't let her speak!' gasped half a dozen in my ear. She moved slowly and solemnly to the front, laid her old bonnet at her feet, and turned her great, speaking eyes to me. There was a hissing sound of disapprobation above and below. I rose and announced 'Sojourner Truth,' and begged the audience to keep silence for a few moments. The tumult subsided at once, and every eye was fixed on this almost Amazon form, which stood nearly six feet high, head erect, and eye piercing the upper air, like one in a dream. At her first word, there was a profound hush. She spoke in deep tones, which, though not loud, reached every ear in the house, and away through the throng at the doors and windows:—

"'Well, chilern, whar dar is so much racket dar must be something out o' kilter. I tink dat 'twixt de niggers of de Souf and de women at de Norf all a talkin' 'bout rights, de white men will be in a fix pretty soon. But what's all dis here talkin' 'bout? Dat man ober dar say dat women needs to be helped into carriages, and lifted ober ditches, and to have de best place every whar. Nobody eber help me into carriages, or ober mud puddles, or gives me any best place [and raising herself to her full height and her voice to a pitch like rolling thunder, she asked], and ar'n't I a woman? Look at me! Look at my arm! [And she bared her right arm to the shoulder, showing her tremendous muscular power.] I have plowed, and planted, and gathered into barns, and no man could head me—and ar'n't I a woman? I could work as much and eat as much as a man (when I could get it), and bear de lash as well—and ar'n't I a woman? I have borne thirteen chilern and seen 'em mos' all sold off into slavery, and when I cried out with a mother's grief, none but Jesus heard—and ar'n't I a woman? Den dey talks 'bout dis ting in de head—what dis dey call it?' 'Intellect,' whispered some one near. 'Dat's it honey. What's dat got to do with women's rights or niggers' rights? If my cup won't hold but a pint and yourn holds a quart, would n't ye be mean not to let me have my little half-measure full?' And she pointed her significant finger and sent a keen glance at the minister who had made the argument. The cheering was long and loud.

"'Den dat little man in black dar, he say women can't have as much rights as man, cause Christ want a woman. Whar did your Christ come from?' Rolling thunder could not have stilled that crowd as did those deep, wonderful tones, as she stood there with outstretched arms and eye of fire. Raising her voice still louder, she repeated, 'Whar did your Christ come from? From God and a woman. Man had nothing to do with him.' Oh! what a rebuke she gave the little man.

"'Turning again to another objector, she took up the defense of mother Eve. I cannot follow her through it all. It was pointed, and witty, and solemn, eliciting at almost every sentence deafening applause; and she ended by asserting that 'if de fust woman God ever made was strong enough to turn the world upside down, all 'lone, dese togedder [and she glanced her eye over us], ought to be able to turn it back and get it right side up again, and now dey is asking to do it, de men better let em.' Long-continued cheering. 'Bleeged to ye for hearin' on me, and now ole Sojourner ha'n't got nothing more to say.'

"Amid roars of applause, she turned to her corner, leaving more than one of us with streaming eyes and hearts beating with gratitude. She had taken us up in her strong arms and carried us safely over the slough of difficulty, turning the whole tide in our favor. I have never in my life seen anything like the magical influence that subdued the mobbish spirit of the day and turned the jibes and sneers of an excited crowd into notes of respect and admiration. Hundreds rushed up to shake hands, and congratulate the glorious old mother and bid her God speed on her mission of 'testifying again concerning the wickedness of this 'ere people.' "

MARIA W. STEWART
1803–1879

Maria Stewart has been called America's first black woman political writer. Her *Productions of Mrs. Maria W. Stewart* (1835), a collection of speeches and essays on such topics as slavery, women's rights, and African American uplift, opened the door through which subsequent black women activists of the pen—Frances Ellen Watkins Harper and Mary Ann Shadd, to name just two—marched. Stewart is also thought to have been the first American woman of any color to step onto a lecture platform and speak her political mind to what was then called "a promiscuous audience," that is, an audience of men as well as women. The date of this bold foray into new territory for women, especially black women, was September 21, 1832; the place was Franklin Hall in Boston, the site of the regular monthly meeting of the New England Anti-Slavery Society. Stewart knew that this audience, composed of some of the most liberal-minded people in the northern states, would be attentive rather than appalled by her appearance in direct defiance of accepted nineteenth-century ideas about "woman's place." Rather than congratulating them on their progressive views, however, Stewart challenged her audience, both its white and black members, to greater efforts on behalf of educational and economic opportunity for young black women as well as men in the city of Boston. When it was published in her *Productions*, Stewart called her remarks at Franklin Hall a lecture. But it might just as well have been received as a political sermon, for it is certainly a vintage decanter of piety, political exhortation, and social prophesy poured out in a distinctively nineteenth-century African American rhetorical vein.

Maria Miller was born in Hartford, Connecticut, and orphaned at the age of five. With no other means of support, she went to work as a servant girl in a minister's family, where she received religious instruction but little else in the way of an education. In her teens she was able to make up somewhat for this deficit through her own efforts. In 1826 she married James W. Stewart, a shipping agent in the Boston fishing industry, who left her a widow three years later. The publication of David Walker's *Appeal* in Boston in 1829 seems to have given real impetus to Maria Stewart's desire to address the issues facing African American men and women on the eve of the most militant phase of the antislavery struggle in America. A conversion experience in 1830 galvanized Stewart into action, confident that she possessed "that spirit of independence that, were I called upon, I would willingly sacrifice my life for the cause of God and my brethren." In the early 1830s, Stewart introduced herself as a writer of religious tracts designed to edify and inspire black people. In 1832 and 1833 she moved into the world of secular controversy, undertaking a series of lectures and essays advertised and sometimes published in William Lloyd Garrison's new antislavery periodical, *The Liberator*, which were collected in 1835 as her *Productions*.

Stewart's social criticism in the *Productions* is usually couched in traditional appeals to Christian charity and individual moral reform. Her feminist agenda is at times predicated on pleas to women to rededicate themselves to their conventional duties as mothers and wives. Nevertheless, Stewart's conviction that "religion and the pure principles of morality" were "the sure foundation" on which African Americans had to build for the future did not keep her from recommending a blueprint for a new social order that was radically opposed to the hierarchies of class and caste that dominated the world in which she lived. For Stewart, the egalitarianism of the Christian gospel demanded a fundamental rethinking of the roles that men and women as well as blacks and whites assumed were natural, God-given, and inevitable. At the end of the *Productions*, Stewart proclaimed "a mighty work of reformation" in the minds of her people, particularly among women of color, even as she admitted that public opposition to her work had grown to such proportions as to compel her to move from Boston to New York. If she was dispirited by the response to her speaking and writing in Boston, Stewart's career in New York does not show permanent evidence of it. She joined women's organizations, attended antislavery conventions, and did some lecturing. She worked as a schoolteacher in Brooklyn and Long Island and, after 1852, in Baltimore and Washington, D.C. In 1879, just months before her death, Stewart brought out a reprinted edition of her essays, speeches, and meditations of the 1830s, adding to this material a memoir, which she titled *Sufferings during the War*. The message of the new book, *Meditations from the Pen of Mrs. Maria W. Stewart*, is epitomized in an observation that brought the memoir, and Stewart's career, to a fitting conclusion: "by grace I overcame."

From Religion and the Pure Principles of Morality, the Sure Foundation on Which We Must Build

Introduction

Feeling a deep solemnity of soul, in view of our wretched and degraded situation, and sensible of the gross ignorance that prevails among us, I have thought proper thus publicly to express my sentiments before you. I hope my friends will not scrutinize these pages with too severe an eye, as I have not calculated to display either elegance or taste in their composition, but have merely written the meditations of my heart as far as my imagination led; and have presented them before you in order to arouse you to exertion, and to enforce upon your minds the great necessity of turning your attention to knowledge and improvement.

I was born in Hartford, Connecticut, in 1803; was left an orphan at five years of age; was bound out in a clergyman's family; had the seeds of piety and virtue early sown in my mind, but was deprived of the advantages of education, though my soul thirsted for knowledge. Left them at fifteen years of age; attended Sabbath schools[1] until I was twenty; in 1826 was

---

1. Sunday schools.

married to James W. Stewart; was left a widow in 1829; was, as I humbly hope and trust, brought to the knowledge of the truth, as it is in Jesus, in 1830; in 1831 made a public profession of my faith in Christ.

From the moment I experienced the change, I felt a strong desire, with the help and assistance of God, to devote the remainder of my days to piety and virtue, and now possess that spirit of independence that, were I called upon, I would willingly sacrifice my life for the cause of God and my brethren.

All the nations of the earth are crying out for liberty and equality. Away, away with tyranny and oppression! And shall Afric's sons be silent any longer? Far be it from me to recommend to you either to kill, burn, or destroy. But I would strongly recommend to you to improve your talents; let not one lie buried in the earth. Show forth your powers of mind. Prove to the world that

> Though black your skins as shades of night,
> your hearts are pure, your souls are white.

This is the land of freedom. The press is at liberty. Every man has a right to express his opinion. Many think, because your skins are tinged with a sable hue, that you are an inferior race of beings; but God does not consider you as such. He hath formed and fashioned you in his own glorious image, and hath bestowed upon you reason and strong powers of intellect. He hath made you to have dominion over the beasts of the field, the fowls of the air, and the fish of the sea.[2] He hath crowned you with glory and honor; hath made you but a little lower than the angels.[3] and according to the Constitution of these United States, he hath made all men free and equal. Then why should one worm say to another, "Keep you down there, while I sit up yonder; for I am better than thou?"[4] It is not the color of the skin that makes the man, but it is the principles formed within the soul.

Many will suffer for pleading the cause of oppressed Africa, and I shall glory in being one of her martyrs; for I am firmly persuaded, that the God in whom I trust is able to protect me from the rage and malice of mine enemies, and from them that will rise up against me; and if there is no other way for me to escape, he is able to take me to himself, as he did the most noble, fearless, and undaunted David Walker.[5]

1831

2. Genesis 1:26.
3. Psalm 8:5.
4. An ironic allusion to Isaiah 65:5: "Stand by thyself, come not near to me; for I am holier than thou."

5. African American polemicist (1785–1830), author of David Walker's Appeal (1829).

Lecture Delivered at the Franklin Hall

Boston, September 21, 1832

Why sit ye here and die? If we say we will go to a foreign land, the famine and the pestilence are there, and there we shall die. If we sit here, we shall die. Come let us plead our cause before the whites: if they save us alive, we shall live—and if they kill us, we shall but die. [1]

Methinks I heard a spiritual interrogation—"Who shall go forward, and take off the reproach that is cast upon the people of color? Shall it be a woman?" And my heart made this reply—"If it is thy will, be it even so, Lord Jesus!"

I have heard much respecting the horrors of slavery; but may Heaven forbid that the generality of my color throughout these United States should experience any more of its horrors than to be a servant of servants, or hewers of wood and drawers of water! [2] Tell us no more of southern slavery; for with few exceptions, although I may be very erroneous in my opinion, yet I consider our condition but little better than that. Yet, after all, methinks there are no chains so galling as those that bind the soul, and exclude it from the vast field of useful and scientific knowledge. O, had I received the advantages of an early education, my ideas would, ere now, have expanded far and wide; but, alas! I possess nothing but moral capability—no teachings but the teachings of the Holy Spirit.

I have asked several individuals of my sex, who transact business for themselves, if providing our girls were to give them the most satisfactory references, they would not be willing to grant them an equal opportunity with others? Their reply has been—for their own part, they had no objection; but as it was not the custom, were they to take them into their employ, they would be in danger of losing the public patronage.

And such is the powerful force of prejudice. Let our girls possess whatever amiable qualities of soul they may; let their characters be fair and spotless as innocence itself; let their natural taste and ingenuity be what they may; it is impossible for scarce an individual of them to rise above the condition of servants. Ah! why is this cruel and unfeeling distinction? Is it merely because God has made our complexion to vary? If it be, O shame to soft, relenting humanity! "Tell it not in Gath! publish it not in the streets of Askelon!" [3] Yet, after all, methinks were the American free people of color to turn their attention more assiduously to moral worth and intellectual improvement, this would be the result: prejudice would gradually diminish, and the whites would be compelled to say, unloose those fetters!

> Though black their skins as shades of night
> Their hearts are pure, their souls are white.

Few white persons of either sex, who are calculated for anything else, are willing to spend their lives and bury their talents in performing mean, ser-

---

1. A paraphrase of 2 Kings 7:4.
2. Joshua 9:23: "Now therefore ye are cursed, and there shall none of you be freed from being bond-men, and hewers of wood and drawers of water for the house of my God."
3. 2 Samuel 1:20.

vile labor. And such is the horrible idea that I entertain respecting a life of servitude, that if I conceived of their [sic] being no possibility of my rising above the condition of servant, I would gladly hail death as a welcome messenger. O, horrible idea, indeed! to possess noble souls aspiring after high and honorable acquirements, yet confined by the chains of ignorance and poverty to lives of continual drudgery and toil. Neither do I know of any who have enriched themselves by spending their lives as house-domestics, washing windows, shaking carpets, brushing boots, or tending upon gentlemen's tables. I can but die for expressing my sentiments: and I am as willing to die by the sword as the pestilence; for I am a true born American; your blood flows in my veins, and your spirit fires my breast.

I observed a piece in the Liberator a few months since, stating that the colonizationists[4] had published a work respecting us, asserting that we were lazy and idle. I confute them on that point. Take us generally as a people, we are neither lazy nor idle; and considering how little we have to excite or stimulate us, I am almost astonished that there are so many industrious and ambitious ones to be found; although I acknowledge, with extreme sorrow, that there are some who never were and never will be serviceable to society. And have you not a similar class among yourselves?

Again. It was asserted that we were "a ragged set, crying for liberty." I reply to it, the whites have so long and so loudly proclaimed the theme of equal rights and privileges, that our souls have caught the flame also, ragged as we are. As far as our merit deserves, we feel a common desire to rise above the condition of servants and drudges. I have learnt, by bitter experience, that continual hard labor deadens the energies of the soul, and benumbs the faculties of the mind; the ideas become confined, the mind barren, and, like the scorching sands of Arabia, produces nothing; or like the uncultivated soil, brings forth thorns and thistles.

Again, continual and hard labor irritates our tempers and sours our dispositions; the whole system becomes worn out with toil and fatigue; nature herself becomes almost exhausted, and we care but little whether we live or die. It is true, that the free people of color throughout these United States are neither bought nor sold, nor under the lash of the cruel driver; many obtain a comfortable support; but few, if any, have an opportunity of becoming rich and independent; and the enjoyments we most pursue are as unprofitable to us as the spider's web or the floating bubbles that vanish into air. As servants, we are respected; but let us presume to aspire any higher, our employer regards us no longer. And were it not that the King eternal has declared that Ethiopia shall stretch forth her hands unto God,[5] I should indeed despair.

I do not consider it derogatory, my friends, for persons to live out to service. There are many whose inclination leads them to aspire no higher; and I would highly commend the performance of almost anything for an honest livelihood; but where constitutional strength is wanting, labor of this kind, in its mildest form, is painful. And doubtless many are the prayers that have ascended to Heaven from Afric's daughters for strength to per-

4. Persons who believed that blacks should be freed on the condition that they return to Africa. "The Liberator": the official journal of the Ameri-can Anti-Slavery Society, edited by William Lloyd Garrison.
5. Psalm 68:31.

form their work. Oh, many are the tears that have been shed for the want of that strength! Most of our color have dragged out a miserable existence of servitude from the cradle to the grave. And what literary acquirement can be made, or useful knowledge derived, from either maps, books, or charts, by those who continually drudge from Monday morning until Sunday noon? O, ye fairer sisters, whose hands are never soiled, whose nerves and muscles are never strained, go learn by experience! Had we had the opportunity that you have had, to improve our moral and mental faculties, what would have hindered our intellects from being as bright, and our manners from being as dignified as yours? Had it been our lot to have been nursed in the lap of affluence and ease, and to have basked beneath the smiles and sunshine of fortune, should we not have naturally supposed that we were never made to toil? And why are not our forms as delicate, and our constitutions as slender, as yours? Is not the workmanship as curious and complete? Have pity upon us, have pity upon us, O ye who have hearts to feel for other's woes; for the hand of God has touched us. Owing to the disadvantages under which we labor, there are many flowers among us that are

>   ... born to bloom unseen
>   And waste their fragrance on the desert air.[6]

My beloved brethren, as Christ has died in vain for those who will not accept his offered mercy, so will it be vain for the advocates of freedom to spend their breath in our behalf, unless with united hearts and souls you make some mighty efforts to raise your sons and daughters from the horrible state of servitude and degradation in which they are placed. It is upon you that woman depends; she can do but little besides using her influence; and it is for her sake and yours that I have come forward and made myself a hissing and a reproach among the people;[7] for I am also one of the wretched and miserable daughters of the descendants of fallen Africa. Do you ask, why are you wretched and miserable? I reply, look at many of the most worthy and most interesting of us doomed to spend our lives in gentlemen's kitchens. Look at our young men, smart, active and energetic, with souls filled with ambitious fire; if they look forward, alas! What are their prospects? They can be nothing but the humblest laborers, on account of their dark complexions; hence many of them lose their ambition, and become worthless. Look at our middle-aged men, clad in their rusty plaids and coats; in winter, every cent they earn goes to buy their wood and pay their rents; the poor wives also toil beyond their strength, to help support their families. Look at our aged sires, whose heads are whitened with the frosts of seventy winters, with their old wood-saws on their backs. Alas, what keeps us so? Prejudice, ignorance and poverty. But ah! methinks our oppression is soon to come to an end; yea, before the Majesty of heaven, our groans and cries have reached the ears of the Lord of Sabaoth.[8] As the pray-

---

6. Compare Thomas Gray's famous *Elegy Written in a Country Churchyard* (1751), lines 55–56: "born to blush unseen, / And waste its sweetness on the desert air."
7. Jeremiah 29:18: "And I will . . . deliver them to be removed to all the kingdoms of the earth, to be a curse, and an astonishment, and an hissing, and a reproach, among all the nations whither I have driven them."
8. James 5:4.

ers and tears of Christians will avail the finally impenitent nothing; neither will the prayers and tears of the friends of humanity avail us anything, unless we possess a spirit of virtuous emulation within our breasts. Did the pilgrims, when they first landed on these shores, quietly compose themselves and say, "The Britons have all the money and all the power, and we must continue their servants forever?" Did they sluggishly sigh and say, "Our lot is hard, the Indians own the soil, and we cannot cultivate it?" No; they first made powerful efforts to raise themselves, and then God raised up those illustrious patriots, WASHINGTON and LAFAYETTE,[9] to assist and defend them. And, my brethren, have you made a powerful effort? Have you prayed the legislature for mercy's sake to grant you all the rights and privileges of free citizens, that your daughters may rise to that degree of respectability which true merit deserves, and your sons above the servile situations which most of them fill?

1832   1835

9. Marquis de Lafayette (1757–1834), Frenchman who served as an aide to General George Washington, commander in chief of the American Revolutionary Army.

HARRIET JACOBS

c. 1813–1897

Harriet Jacobs was the first woman to author a slave narrative in the United States. Before the publication of *Incidents in the Life of a Slave Girl* (1861), several freeborn African American women, such as Jarena Lee and Zilpha Elaw, had proudly portrayed their spiritual journeys and social struggles in autobiographies that featured the trials and triumphs of true Christian womanhood. Jacobs's successful struggle for freedom, not only for herself but for her two children, represented no less profoundly a black woman's indomitable spirit. Yet nowhere in her autobiography, not even on its title page, did Jacobs disclose her own identity as the subject and author of her story. Instead, she called herself "Linda Brent" and masked the important places and persons in her story in the manner of a novelist. "I had no motive for secrecy on my own account," Jacobs insisted in the preface to her autobiography, but given the harrowing and sensational story she had to tell, the one-time fugitive slave felt she had little alternative but to shield herself from a readership whose understanding and empathy she could not take for granted.

Jacobs's task in writing her narrative was considerably more complicated than that of Lee or Elaw because Jacobs felt obliged to disclose through her firsthand example the special injustices that women suffered under what sentimental defenders of slavery often referred to as the "patriarchal institution." Famous male fugitive slave narrators like Frederick Douglass and William Wells Brown had called attention to the sexual victimization of slave women by white men. But these men had said little about how slave women resisted such exploitation and tried to exercise a measure of freedom within the restrictions of their oppression. Though she knew that she risked losing her reader's respect by speaking out, Jacobs refused to suppress the truth about her sexual exploitation in slavery or her use of her own sexuality as a weapon against such exploitation. Writing an unprecedented mixture of confession, self-justification, and societal exposé, Jacobs turned her autobiography into a unique analysis of the myths and the realities that defined the situation of the

African American woman and her relationship to the nineteenth century's "cult of true womanhood." As a result, *Incidents in the Life of a Slave Girl* occupies a crucial place in the history of both African American and American women's literature.

Harriet Jacobs was born a slave in Edenton, North Carolina, around 1813. Orphaned as a child, she grew up under the tutelage of her grandmother and her white mistress, who taught her to read and sew. The death of her mistress when Jacobs was eleven conveyed her into the hands of Dr. James Norcom, the licentious and abusive master called Dr. Flint in *Incidents*. During her early teenage years, Jacobs was subjected to relentless sexual harassment from Norcom. In desperation she formed a clandestine liaison with Samuel Tredwell Sawyer, a white attorney (Mr. Sands in *Incidents*), by whom Jacobs had two children by the time she was twenty years old. Hoping that by seeming to run away she could induce Norcom to sell her children to their father, Jacobs hid herself in a crawl space above a storeroom in her grandmother's house in the summer of 1835. In that "little dismal hole" she remained for the next seven years, sewing, reading the Bible, keeping watch over her children as best she could, and writing occasional letters to Flint designed to confuse him as to her actual whereabouts. In 1842 Jacobs escaped to the North, determined to reclaim her daughter from Sawyer, who had purchased the child and sent her to Brooklyn, New York, without emancipating her. In New York, Jacobs was reunited with her daughter, secured a place for her son to live in Boston, and went to work as a nursemaid to the baby daughter of Mary Stace Willis, wife of the popular editor, poet, and magazine writer Nathaniel Parker Willis.

For ten years after her escape from North Carolina, Harriet Jacobs lived the tense and uncertain life of a fugitive slave. Norcom made several attempts to locate her in New York, which forced Jacobs to keep on the move and enlist the aid of antislavery activists in Rochester, New York, where she took up an eighteen-month residence in 1849. Working in an antislavery reading room and bookstore above the offices of Frederick Douglass's newspaper, *The North Star*, Jacobs met and began to confide in Amy Post, an abolitionist and pioneering feminist who gently urged her to consider making her story public. After the tremendous response to *Uncle Tom's Cabin* (1852), Jacobs thought of enlisting the aid of the novel's author, Harriet Beecher Stowe, in getting Jacobs's story published. But Stowe had little interest in any sort of creative partnership with Jacobs. After receiving, early in 1852, the gift of her freedom from Cornelia Grinnell Willis, the second wife of her employer, Jacobs decided to write her autobiography herself.

Incidents in the Life of a Slave Girl is the only nineteenth-century slave narrative whose genesis can be traced, through a series of letters from Jacobs to various friends and advisors, including Post and the eventual editor of *Incidents*, Lydia Maria Child. Discovered and published by Jean Fagan Yellin in her admirable edition of *Incidents in the Life of a Slave Girl* (1987), Jacobs's correspondence with Child helps lay to rest the long-standing charge against *Incidents* that it is at worst a fiction and at best the product of Child's pen, not Jacobs's. Child's letters to Jacobs and others make clear that her role as editor was no more than she acknowledged in her introduction to *Incidents*: to ensure the orderly arrangement and directness of the narrative, without adding anything to the text or altering in any significant way Jacobs's manner of recounting her story.

Incidents in the Life of a Slave Girl appeared inauspiciously in early 1861, its publication underwritten by its author. The narrative was favorably reviewed in the abolitionist press, but with the onset of the Civil War in April of that year, Jacobs's book claimed little attention beyond antislavery circles. From 1862 to 1866 Jacobs devoted herself to relief efforts in and around Washington, D.C., among former slaves who had become refugees of the war. In the war's immediate aftermath she went to Savannah, Georgia, to engage in further relief work among the freedmen and freedwomen. By the mid-1880s Jacobs had returned to Washington, D.C., and was helping to organize the National Association of Colored Women. She died in that city on March 7, 1897.

From Incidents in the Life of a Slave Girl

Preface

BY THE AUTHOR

Reader, be assured this narrative is no fiction. I am aware that some of my adventures may seem incredible; but they are, nevertheless, strictly true. I have not exaggerated the wrongs inflicted by Slavery; on the contrary, my descriptions fall far short of the facts. I have concealed the names of places, and given persons fictitious names. I had no motive for secrecy on my own account, but I deemed it kind and considerate towards others to pursue this course.

I wish I were more competent to the task I have undertaken. But I trust my readers will excuse deficiencies in consideration of circumstances. I was born and reared in Slavery; and I remained in a Slave State twenty-seven years. Since I have been at the North, it has been necessary for me to work diligently for my own support, and the education of my children. This has not left me much leisure to make up for the loss of early opportunities to improve myself; and it has compelled me to write these pages at irregular intervals, whenever I could snatch an hour from household duties.

When I first arrived in Philadelphia, Bishop Paine [1] advised me to publish a sketch of my life, but I told him I was altogether incompetent to such an undertaking. Though I have improved my mind somewhat since that time, I still remain of the same opinion; but I trust my motives will excuse what might otherwise seem presumptuous. I have not written my experiences in order to attract attention to myself; on the contrary, it would have been more pleasant to me to have been silent about my own history. Neither do I care to excite sympathy for my own sufferings. But I do earnestly desire to arouse the women of the North to a realizing sense of the condition of two millions of women at the South, still in bondage, suffering what I suffered, and most of them far worse. I want to add my testimony to that of abler pens to convince the people of the Free States what Slavery really is. Only by experience can any one realize how deep, and dark, and foul is that pit of abominations. May the blessing of God rest on this imperfect effort in behalf of my persecuted people!

LINDA BRENT.

---

1. Daniel A. Payne (1811–1893), bishop of the African Methodist Episcopal Church. Jacobs met him in Philadelphia in 1842.

I. Childhood

I was born a slave; but I never knew it till six years of happy childhood had passed away. My father was a carpenter, and considered so intelligent and skillful in his trade, that, when buildings out of the common line were to be erected, he was sent for from long distances, to be head workman. On condition of paying his mistress two hundred dollars a year, and supporting himself, he was allowed to work at his trade, and manage his own affairs. His strongest wish was to purchase his children; but, though he several times offered his hard earnings for that purpose, he never succeeded. In complexion my parents were a light shade of brownish yellow, and were termed mulattoes. They lived together in a comfortable home; and, though we were all slaves, I was so fondly shielded that I never dreamed I was a piece of merchandise, trusted to them for safe keeping, and liable to be demanded of them at any moment. I had one brother, William, who was two years younger than myself—a bright, affectionate child. I had also a great treasure in my maternal grandmother, who was a remarkable woman in many respects. She was the daughter of a planter in South Carolina, who, at his death, left her mother and his three children free, with money to go to St. Augustine, where they had relatives. It was during the Revolutionary War; and they were captured on their passage, carried back, and sold to different purchasers. Such was the story my grandmother used to tell me; but I do not remember all the particulars. She was a little girl when she was captured and sold to the keeper of a large hotel. I have often heard her tell how hard she fared during childhood. But as she grew older she evinced so much intelligence, and was so faithful, that her master and mistress could not help seeing it was for their interest to take care of such a valuable piece of property. She became an indispensable personage in the household, officiating in all capacities, from cook and wet nurse to seamstress. She was much praised for her cooking; and her nice crackers became so famous in the neighborhood that many people were desirous of obtaining them. In consequence of numerous requests of this kind, she asked permission of her mistress to bake crackers at night, after all the household work was done; and she obtained leave to do it, provided she would clothe herself and her children from the profits. Upon these terms, after working hard all day for her mistress, she began her midnight bakings, assisted by her two oldest children. The business proved profitable; and each year she laid by a little, which was saved for a fund to purchase her children. Her master died, and the property was divided among his heirs. The widow had her dower in the hotel, which she continued to keep open. My grandmother remained in her service as a slave; but her children were divided among her master's children. As she had five, Benjamin, the youngest one, was sold, in order that each heir might have an equal portion of dollars and cents. There was so little difference in our ages that he seemed more like my brother than my uncle. He was a bright, handsome lad, nearly white; for he inherited the complexion my grandmother had derived from Anglo-Saxon ancestors. Though only ten years old, seven hundred and twenty dollars were paid for him. His sale was a terrible blow to my grandmother; but she was naturally hopeful, and she went to work with renewed energy, trusting in time to be able to purchase some of her children. She had laid up three hundred dollars, which her mistress one day begged as a loan, promising to pay her soon. The reader probably knows that no promise or writing given to a slave is legally binding; for, according to Southern laws, a slave, *being* property, can *hold* no property. When my grandmother lent her hard earnings to her mistress, she trusted solely to her honor. The honor of a slaveholder to a slave!

To this good grandmother I was indebted for many comforts. My brother Willie and I often received portions of the crackers, cakes, and preserves, she made to sell, and after we ceased to be children we were indebted to her for many more important services.

Such were the unusually fortunate circumstances of my early childhood. When I was six years old, my mother died; and then, for the first time, I learned, by the talk around me, that I was a slave. My mother's mistress was the daughter of my grandmother's mistress. She was the foster sister of my mother; they were both nourished at my grandmother's breast. In fact, my mother had been weaned at three months old, that the babe of the mistress might obtain sufficient food. They played together as children; and, when they became women, my mother was a most faithful servant to her whiter foster sister. On her death-bed her mistress promised that her children should never suffer for any thing; and during her lifetime she kept her word. They all spoke kindly of my dead mother, who had been a slave merely in name, but in nature was noble and womanly. I grieved for her, and my young mind was troubled with the thought who would now take care of me and my little brother. I was told that my home was now to be with her mistress; and I found it a happy one. No toilsome or disagreeable duties were imposed upon me. My mistress was so kind to me that I was always glad to do her bidding, and proud to labor for her as much as my young years would permit. I would sit by her side for hours, sewing diligently, with a heart as free from care as that of any free-born white child. When she thought I was tired, she would send me out to run and jump; and away I bounded, to gather berries or flowers to decorate her room. Those were happy days—too happy to last. The slave child had no thought for the morrow; but there came that blight, which too surely waits on every human being born to be a chattel.

When I was nearly twelve years old, my kind mistress sickened and died. As I saw the cheek grow paler, and the eye more glassy, how earnestly I prayed in my heart that she might live! I loved her; for she had been almost like a mother to me. My prayers were not answered. She died, and they buried her in the little churchyard, where, day after day, my tears fell upon her grave.

I was sent to spend a week with my grandmother. I was now old enough to begin to think of the future; and again and again I asked myself what they would do with me. I felt sure I should never find another mistress so kind as the one who was gone. She had promised my dying mother that her children should never suffer for any thing; and when I remembered that, and recalled her many proofs of attachment to me, I could not help having some hopes that she had left me free. My friends were almost certain it would be so. They thought she would be sure to do it, on account of my mother's love and faithful service. But, alas! we all know that the memory of a faithful slave does not avail much to save her children from the auction block.

After a brief period of suspense, the will of my mistress was read, and we learned that she had bequeathed me to her sister's daughter, a child of five years old. So vanished our hopes. My mistress had taught me the precepts of God's Word: "Thou shalt love thy neighbor as thyself."[2] "Whatsoever ye would that men should do unto you, do ye even so unto them."[3] But I was her slave, and I suppose she did not recognize me as her neighbor. I would give much to blot out from my memory that one great wrong. As a child, I loved my mistress; and, looking back on the happy days I spent with her, I try to think with less bitterness of this act of injustice. While I was with her, she taught me to read and spell; and for this privilege, which so rarely falls to the lot of a slave, I bless her memory.

She possessed but few slaves; and at her death those were all distributed among her relatives. Five of them were my grandmother's children, and had shared the same milk that nourished her mother's children. Notwithstanding my grandmother's long and faithful service to her owners, not one of her children escaped the auction block. These God-breathing machines are no more, in the sight of their masters, than the cotton they plant, or the horses they tend.

II. The New Master and Mistress

Dr. Flint, a physician in the neighborhood, had married the sister of my mistress, and I was now the property of their little daughter. It was not without murmuring that I prepared for my new home; and what added to my unhappiness, was the fact that my brother William was purchased by the same family. My father, by his nature, as well as by the habit of transacting business as a skillful mechanic, had more of the feelings of a freeman than is common among slaves. My brother was a spirited boy; and being brought up under such influences, he early detested the name of master and mistress. One day, when his father and his mistress had happened to call him at the same time, he hesitated between the two; being perplexed to know which had the strongest claim upon his obedience. He finally concluded to go to his mistress. When my father reproved him for it, he said, "You both called me, and I didn't know which I ought to go to first."

"You are *my* child," replied our father, "and when I call you, you should come immediately, if you have to pass through fire and water."

Poor Willie! He was now to learn his first lesson of obedience to a master. Grandmother tried to cheer us with hopeful words, and they found an echo in the credulous hearts of youth.

When we entered our new home we encountered cold looks, cold words, and cold treatment. We were glad when the night came. On my narrow bed I moaned and wept, I felt so desolate and alone.

I had been there nearly a year, when a dear little friend of mine was buried. I heard her mother sob, as the clods fell on the coffin of her only

2. Mark 12:31.   3. Matthew 7:12.

child, and I turned away from the grave, feeling thankful that I still had something left to love. I met my grandmother, who said, "Come with me, Linda;" and from her tone I knew that something sad had happened. She led me apart from the people, and then said, "My child, your father is dead." Dead! How could I believe it? He had died so suddenly I had not even heard that he was sick. I went home with my grandmother. My heart rebelled against God, who had taken from me mother, father, mistress, and friend. The good grandmother tried to comfort me. "Who knows the ways of God?" said she. "Perhaps they have been kindly taken from the evil days to come." Years afterwards I often thought of this. She promised to be a mother to her grandchildren, so far as she might be permitted to do so; and strengthened by her love, I returned to my master's. I thought I should be allowed to go to my father's house the next morning; but I was ordered to go for flowers, that my mistress's house might be decorated for an evening party. I spent the day gathering flowers and weaving them into festoons, while the dead body of my father was lying within a mile of me. What cared my owners for that? he was merely a piece of property. Moreover, they thought he had spoiled his children, by teaching them to feel that they were human beings. This was blasphemous doctrine for a slave to teach; presumptuous in him, and dangerous to the masters.

The next day I followed his remains to a humble grave beside that of my dear mother. There were those who knew my father's worth, and respected his memory.

My home now seemed more dreary than ever. The laugh of the little slave-children sounded harsh and cruel. It was selfish to feel so about the joy of others. My brother moved about with a very grave face. I tried to comfort him, by saying, "Take courage, Willie; brighter days will come by and by."

"You don't know any thing about it, Linda," he replied. "We shall have to stay here all our days; we shall never be free."

I argued that we were growing older and stronger, and that perhaps we might, before long, be allowed to hire our own time, and then we could earn money to buy our freedom. William declared this was much easier to say than to do; moreover, he did not intend to *buy* his freedom. We held daily controversies upon this subject.

Little attention was paid to the slaves' meals in Dr. Flint's house. If they could catch a bit of food while it was going, well and good. I gave myself no trouble on that score, for on my various errands I passed my grandmother's house, where there was always something to spare for me. I was frequently threatened with punishment if I stopped there; and my grandmother, to avoid detaining me, often stood at the gate with something for my breakfast or dinner. I was indebted to *her* for all my comforts, spiritual or temporal. It was *her* labor that supplied my scanty wardrobe. I have a vivid recollection of the linsey-woolsey[4] dress given me every winter by Mrs. Flint. How I hated it! It was one of the badges of slavery.

While my grandmother was thus helping to support me from her hard earnings, the three hundred dollars she had lent her mistress were never

4. A cheap fabric made of linen and wool.

repaid. When her mistress died, her son-in-law, Dr. Flint, was appointed executor. When grandmother applied to him for payment, he said the estate was insolvent, and the law prohibited payment. It did not, however, prohibit him from retaining the silver candelabra, which had been purchased with that money. I presume they will be handed down in the family, from generation to generation.

My grandmother's mistress had always promised her that, at her death, she should be free; and it was said that in her will she made good the promise. But when the estate was settled, Dr. Flint told the faithful old servant that, under existing circumstances, it was necessary she should be sold.

On the appointed day, the customary advertisement was posted up, proclaiming that there would be a "public sale of negroes, horses, etc." Dr. Flint called to tell my grandmother that he was unwilling to wound her feelings by putting her up at auction, and that he would prefer to dispose of her at private sale. My grandmother saw through his hypocrisy; she understood very well that he was ashamed of the job. She was a very spirited woman, and if he was base enough to sell her, when her mistress intended she should be free, she was determined the public should know it. She had for a long time supplied many families with crackers and preserves; consequently, "Aunt Marthy," as she was called, was generally known, and every body who knew her respected her intelligence and good character. Her long and faithful service in the family was also well known, and the intention of her mistress to leave her free. When the day of sale came, she took her place among the chattels, and at the first call she sprang upon the auction-block. Many voices called out, "Shame! Shame! Who is going to sell *you*, aunt Marthy? Don't stand there! That is no place for *you*." Without saying a word, she quietly awaited her fate. No one bid for her. At last, a feeble voice said, "Fifty dollars." It came from a maiden lady, seventy years old, the sister of my grandmother's deceased mistress. She had lived forty years under the same roof with my grandmother; she knew how faithfully she had served her owners, and how cruelly she had been defrauded of her rights; and she resolved to protect her. The auctioneer waited for a higher bid; but her wishes were respected; no one bid above her. She could neither read nor write; and when the bill of sale was made out, she signed it with a cross. But what consequence was that, when she had a big heart overflowing with human kindness? She gave the old servant her freedom.

At that time, my grandmother was just fifty years old. Laborious years had passed since then; and now my brother and I were slaves to the man who had defrauded her of her money, and tried to defraud her of her freedom. One of my mother's sisters, called Aunt Nancy, was also a slave in his family. She was a kind, good aunt to me; and supplied the place of both housekeeper and waiting maid to her mistress. She was, in fact, at the beginning and end of every thing.

Mrs. Flint, like many southern women, was totally deficient in energy. She had not strength to superintend her household affairs; but her nerves were so strong, that she could sit in her easy chair and see a woman whipped, till the blood trickled from every stroke of the lash. She was a member of the church; but partaking of the Lord's supper did not seem to put her in a Christian frame of mind. If dinner was not served at the exact time on that particular Sunday, she would station herself in the kitchen, and wait till it was dished, and then spit in all the kettles and pans that had been used for cooking. She did this to prevent the cook and her children from eking out their meagre fare with the remains of the gravy and other scrapings. The slaves could get nothing to eat except what she chose to give them. Provisions were weighed out by the pound and ounce, three times a day. I can assure you she gave them no chance to eat wheat bread from her flour barrel. She knew how many biscuits a quart of flour would make, and exactly what size they ought to be.

Dr. Flint was an epicure.[5] The cook never sent a dinner to his table without fear and trembling; for if there happened to be a dish not to his liking, he would either order her to be whipped, or compel her to eat every mouthful of it in his presence. The poor, hungry creature might not have objected to eating it; but she did object to having her master cram it down her throat till she choked.

They had a pet dog, that was a nuisance in the house. The cook was ordered to make some Indian mush[6] for him. He refused to eat, and when his head was held over it, the froth flowed from his mouth into the basin. He died a few minutes after. When Dr. Flint came in, he said the mush had not been well cooked, and that was the reason the animal would not eat it. He sent for the cook, and compelled her to eat it. He thought that the woman's stomach was stronger than the dog's; but her sufferings afterwards proved that he was mistaken. This poor woman endured many cruelties from her master and mistress; sometimes she was locked up, away from her nursing baby, for a whole day and night.

When I had been in the family a few weeks, one of the plantation slaves was brought to town, by order of his master. It was near night when he arrived, and Dr. Flint ordered him to be taken to the work house, and tied up to the joist, so that his feet would just escape the ground. In that situation he was to wait till the doctor had taken his tea. I shall never forget that night. Never before, in my life, had I heard hundreds of blows fall, in succession, on a human being. His piteous groans, and his "O, pray don't, massa," rang in my ear for months afterwards. There were many conjectures as to the cause of this terrible punishment. Some said master accused him of stealing corn; others said the slave had quarrelled with his wife, in presence of the overseer, and had accused his master of being the father of her child. They were both black, and the child was very fair.

I went into the work house next morning, and saw the cowhide still wet with blood, and the boards all covered with gore. The poor man lived, and continued to quarrel with his wife. A few months afterwards Dr. Flint handed them both over to a slavetrader. The guilty man put their value into his pocket, and had the satisfaction of knowing that they were out of sight and hearing. When the mother was delivered into the trader's hands, she said, "You *promised* to treat me well." To which he replied, "You have let your tongue run too far; damn you!" She had forgotten that it was a crime for a slave to tell who was the father of her child.

5. One who has discriminating taste in food and   6. A mush made of corn, or maize.
drink.

From others than the master persecution also comes in such cases. I once saw a young slave girl dying soon after the birth of a child nearly white. In her agony she cried out, "O Lord, come and take me!" Her mistress stood by, and mocked at her like an incarnate fiend. "You suffer, do you?" she exclaimed. "I am glad of it. You deserve it all, and more too."

The girl's mother said, "The baby is dead, thank God; and I hope my poor child will soon be in heaven, too."

"Heaven!" retorted the mistress. "There is no such place for the like of her and her bastard."

The poor mother turned away, sobbing. Her dying daughter called her, feebly, and as she bent over her, I heard her say, "Don't grieve so, mother; God knows all about it; and HE will have mercy upon me."

Her sufferings, afterwards, became so intense, that her mistress felt unable to stay; but when she left the room, the scornful smile was still on her lips. Seven children called her mother. The poor black woman had but the one child, whose eyes she saw closing in death, while she thanked God for taking her away from the greater bitterness of life.

* * *

V. The Trials of Girlhood

During the first years of my service in Dr. Flint's family, I was accustomed to share some indulgences with the children of my mistress. Though this seemed to me no more than right, I was grateful for it, and tried to merit the kindness by the faithful discharge of my duties. But I now entered on my fifteenth year—a sad epoch in the life of a slave girl. My master began to whisper foul words in my ear. Young as I was, I could not remain ignorant of their import. I tried to treat them with indifference or contempt. The master's age, my extreme youth, and the fear that his conduct would be reported to my grandmother, made him bear this treatment for many months. He was a crafty man, and resorted to many means to accomplish his purposes. Sometimes he had stormy, terrific ways, that made his victims tremble; sometimes he assumed a gentleness that he thought must surely subdue. Of the two, I preferred his stormy moods, although they left me trembling. He tried his utmost to corrupt the pure principles my grandmother had instilled. He peopled my young mind with unclean images, such as only a vile monster could think of. I turned from him with disgust and hatred. But he was my master. I was compelled to live under the same roof with him—where I saw a man forty years my senior daily violating the most sacred commandments of nature. He told me I was his property; that I must be subject to his will in all things. My soul revolted against the mean tyranny. But where could I turn for protection? No matter whether the slave girl be as black as ebony or as fair as her mistress. In either case, there is no shadow of law to protect her from insult, from violence, or even from death; all these are inflicted by fiends who bear the shape of men. The mistress, who ought to protect the helpless victim, has no other feelings towards her but those of jealousy and rage. The degradation, the wrongs, the vices, that grow out of slavery, are more than I can describe. They are greater than you would willingly believe. Surely, if you

credited one half the truths that are told you concerning the helpless millions suffering in this cruel bondage, you at the north would not help to
tighten the yoke. You surely would refuse to do for the master, on your own
soil, the mean and cruel work which trained bloodhounds and the lowest
class of whites do for him at the south.

Every where the years bring to all enough of sin and sorrow; but in slavery the very dawn of life is darkened by these shadows. Even the little child,
who is accustomed to wait on her mistress and her children, will learn,
before she is twelve years old, why it is that her mistress hates such and such
a one among the slaves. Perhaps the child's own mother is among those
hated ones. She listens to violent outbreaks of jealous passion, and cannot
help understanding what is the cause. She will become prematurely knowing in evil things. Soon she will learn to tremble when she hears her master's footfall. She will be compelled to realize that she is no longer a child.
If God has bestowed beauty upon her, it will prove her greatest curse. That
which commands admiration in the white woman only hastens the degradation of the female slave. I know that some are too much brutalized by
slavery to feel the humiliation of their position; but many slaves feel it most
acutely, and shrink from the memory of it. I cannot tell how much I suffered in the presence of these wrongs, nor how I am still pained by the
retrospect. My master met me at every turn, reminding me that I belonged
to him, and swearing by heaven and earth that he would compel me to
submit to him. If I went out for a breath of fresh air, after a day of unwearied toil, his footsteps dogged me. If I knelt by my mother's grave, his
dark shadow fell on me even there. The light heart which nature had given
me became heavy with sad forebodings. The other slaves in my master's
house noticed the change. Many of them pitied me; but none dared to ask
the cause. They had no need to inquire. They knew too well the guilty
practices under that roof; and they were aware that to speak of them was an
offence that never went unpunished.

I longed for some one to confide in. I would have given the world to have
laid my head on my grandmother's faithful bosom, and told her all my
troubles. But Dr. Flint swore he would kill me, if I was not as silent as the
grave. Then, although my grandmother was all in all to me, I feared her as
well as loved her. I had been accustomed to look up to her with a respect
bordering upon awe. I was very young, and felt shamefaced about telling
her such impure things, especially as I knew her to be very strict on such
subjects. Moreover, she was a woman of a high spirit. She was usually very
quiet in her demeanor; but if her indignation was once roused, it was not
very easily quelled. I had been told that she once chased a white gentleman
with a loaded pistol, because he insulted one of her daughters. I dreaded
the consequences of a violent outbreak; and both pride and fear kept me
silent. But though I did not confide in my grandmother, and even evaded
her vigilant watchfulness and inquiry, her presence in the neighborhood
was some protection to me. Though she had been a slave, Dr. Flint was
afraid of her. He dreaded her scorching rebukes. Moreover, she was known
and patronized by many people; and he did not wish to have his villainy
made public. It was lucky for me that I did not live on a distant plantation,
but in a town not so large that the inhabitants were ignorant of each other's

affairs. Bad as are the laws and customs in a slaveholding community, the doctor, as a professional man, deemed it prudent to keep up some outward show of decency.

O, what days and nights of fear and sorrow that man caused me! Reader, it is not to awaken sympathy for myself that I am telling you truthfully what I suffered in slavery. I do it to kindle a flame of compassion in your hearts for my sisters who are still in bondage, suffering as I once suffered.

I once saw two beautiful children playing together. One was a fair white child; the other was her slave, and also her sister. When I saw them embracing each other, and heard their joyous laughter, I turned sadly away from the lovely sight. I foresaw the inevitable blight that would fall on the little slave's heart. I knew how soon her laughter would be changed to sighs. The fair child grew up to be a still fairer woman. From childhood to womanhood her pathway was blooming with flowers, and overarched by a sunny sky. Scarcely one day of her life had been clouded when the sun rose on her happy bridal morning.

How had those years dealt with her slave sister, the little playmate of her childhood? She, also, was very beautiful; but the flowers and sunshine of love were not for her. She drank the cup of sin, and shame, and misery, whereof her persecuted race are compelled to drink.

In view of these things, why are ye silent, ye free men and women of the north? Why do your tongues falter in maintenance of the right? Would that I had more ability! But my heart is so full, and my pen is so weak! There are noble men and women who plead for us, striving to help those who cannot help themselves. God bless them! God give them strength and courage to go on! God bless those, every where, who are laboring to advance the cause of humanity!

[After appealing futilely to Dr. Flint's jealous wife for protection, Brent receives a marriage proposal from a free black carpenter, but Dr. Flint refuses to let her purchase her freedom.]

X. A Perilous Passage in the Slave Girl's Life

After my lover went away, Dr. Flint contrived a new plan. He seemed to have an idea that my fear of my mistress was his greatest obstacle. In the blandest tones, he told me that he was going to build a small house for me, in a secluded place, four miles away from the town. I shuddered; but I was constrained to listen, while he talked of his intention to give me a home of my own, and to make a lady of me. Hitherto, I had escaped my dreaded fate, by being in the midst of people. My grandmother had already had high words with my master about me. She had told him pretty plainly what she thought of his character, and there was considerable gossip in the neighborhood about our affairs, to which the open-mouthed jealousy of Mrs. Flint contributed not a little. When my master said he was going to build a house for me, and that he could do it with little trouble and expense, I was in hopes something would happen to frustrate his scheme; but I soon heard that the house was actually begun. I vowed before my Maker that I would never enter it. I had rather toil on the plantation from dawn till dark; I had rather live and die in jail, than drag on, from day to day, through such a living death. I was determined that the master, whom I so hated and loathed, who had blighted the prospects of my youth, and made my life a desert, should not, after my long struggle with him, succeed at last in trampling his victim under his feet. I would do any thing, every thing, for the sake of defeating him. What *could* I do? I thought and thought, till I became desperate, and made a plunge into the abyss.

And now, reader, I come to a period in my unhappy life, which I would gladly forget if I could. The remembrance fills me with sorrow and shame It pains me to tell you of it; but I have promised to tell you the truth, and I will do it honestly, let it cost me what it may. I will not try to screen myself behind the plea of compulsion from a master; for it was not so. Neither can I plead ignorance or thoughtlessness. For years, my master had done his utmost to pollute my mind with foul images, and to destroy the pure principles inculcated by my grandmother, and the good mistress of my childhood. The influences of slavery had had the same effect on me that they had on other young girls; they had made me prematurely knowing, concerning the evil ways of the world. I knew what I did, and I did it with deliberate calculation.

But, O, ye happy women, whose purity has been sheltered from childhood, who have been free to choose the objects of your affection, whose homes are protected by law, do not judge the poor desolate slave girl too severely! If slavery had been abolished, I, also, could have married the man of my choice; I could have had a home shielded by the laws; and I should have been spared the painful task of confessing what I am now about to relate; but all my prospects had been blighted by slavery. I wanted to keep myself pure; and, under the most adverse circumstances, I tried hard to preserve my self-respect; but I was struggling alone in the powerful grasp of the demon Slavery; and the monster proved too strong for me. I felt as if I was forsaken by God and man; as if all my efforts must be frustrated; and I became reckless in my despair.

I have told you that Dr. Flint's persecutions and his wife's jealousy had given rise to some gossip in the neighborhood. Among others, it chanced that a white unmarried gentleman had obtained some knowledge of the circumstances in which I was placed. He knew my grandmother, and often spoke to me in the street. He became interested for me, and asked questions about my master, which I answered in part. He expressed a great deal of sympathy, and a wish to aid me. He constantly sought opportunities to see me, and wrote to me frequently. I was a poor slave girl, only fifteen years old.

So much attention from a superior person was, of course, flattering; for human nature is the same in all. I also felt grateful for his sympathy, and encouraged by his kind words. It seemed to me a great thing to have such a friend. By degrees, a more tender feeling crept into my heart. He was an educated and eloquent gentleman; too eloquent, alas, for the poor slave girl who trusted in him. Of course I saw whither all this was tending. I knew the impassable gulf between us; but to be an object of interest to a man who is not married, and who is not her master, is agreeable to the pride and feelings of a slave, if her miserable situation has left her any pride or sentiment. It seems less degrading to give one's self, than to submit to compulsion. There is something akin to freedom in having a lover who has no control over you, except that which he gains by kindness and attachment. A master may treat you as rudely as he pleases, and you dare not speak; moreover, the wrong does not seem so great with an unmarried man, as with one who has a wife to be made unhappy. There may be sophistry in all this; but the condition of a slave confuses all principles of morality, and, in fact, renders the practice of them impossible.

When I found that my master had actually begun to build the lonely cottage, other feelings mixed with those I have described. Revenge, and calculations of interest, were added to flattered vanity and sincere gratitude for kindness. I knew nothing would enrage Dr. Flint so much as to know that I favored another; and it was something to triumph over my tyrant even in that small way. I thought he would revenge himself by selling me, and I was sure my friend, Mr. Sands, would buy me. He was a man of more generosity and feeling than my master, and I thought my freedom could be easily obtained from him. The crisis of my fate now came so near that I was desperate. I shuddered to think of being the mother of children that should be owned by my old tyrant. I knew that as soon as a new fancy took him, his victims were sold far off to get rid of them; especially if they had children. I had seen several women sold, with his babies at the breast. He never allowed his offspring by slaves to remain long in sight of himself and his wife. Of a man who was not my master I could ask to have my children well supported; and in this case, I felt confident I should obtain the boon.[7] I also felt quite sure that they would be made free. With all these thoughts revolving in my mind, and seeing no other way of escaping the doom I so much dreaded, I made a headlong plunge. Pity me, and pardon me, O virtuous reader! You never knew what it is to be a slave; to be entirely unprotected by law or custom; to have the laws reduce you to the condition of a chattel, entirely subject to the will of another. You never exhausted your ingenuity in avoiding the snares, and eluding the power of a hated tyrant; you never shuddered at the sound of his footsteps, and trembled within hearing of his voice. I know I did wrong. No one can feel it more sensibly than I do. The painful and humiliating memory will haunt me to my dying day. Still, in looking back, calmly, on the events of my life, I feel that the slave woman ought not to be judged by the same standard as others.

The months passed on. I had many unhappy hours. I secretly mourned over the sorrow I was bringing on my grandmother, who had so tried to shield me from harm. I knew that I was the greatest comfort of her old age, and that it was a source of pride to her that I had not degraded myself, like most of the slaves. I wanted to confess to her that I was no longer worthy of her love; but I could not utter the dreaded words.

As for Dr. Flint, I had a feeling of satisfaction and triumph in the thought of telling *him*. From time to time he told me of his intended arrangements, and I was silent. At last, he came and told me the cottage was completed, and ordered me to go to it. I told him I would never enter it. He said, "I

7. Favor.

have heard enough of such talk as that. You shall go, if you are carried by force; and you shall remain there."

I replied, "I will never go there. In a few months I shall be a mother."

He stood and looked at me in dumb amazement, and left the house without a word. I thought I should be happy in my triumph over him. But now that the truth was out, and my relatives would hear of it, I felt wretched. Humble as were their circumstances, they had pride in my good character. Now, how could I look them in the face? My self-respect was gone! I had resolved that I would be virtuous, though I was a slave. I had said, "Let the storm beat! I will brave it till I die." And now, how humiliated I felt!

I went to my grandmother. My lips moved to make confession, but the words stuck in my throat. I sat down in the shade of a tree at her door and began to sew. I think she saw something unusual was the matter with me. The mother of slaves is very watchful. She knows there is no security for her children. After they have entered their teens she lives in daily expectation of trouble. This leads to many questions. If the girl is of a sensitive nature, timidity keeps her from answering truthfully, and this well-meant course has a tendency to drive her from maternal counsels. Presently, in came my mistress, like a mad woman, and accused me concerning her husband. My grandmother, whose suspicions had been previously awakened, believed what she said. She exclaimed, "O Linda! has it come to this? I had rather see you dead than to see you as you now are. You are a disgrace to your dead mother." She tore from my fingers my mother's wedding ring and her silver thimble. "Go away!" she exclaimed, "and never come to my house, again." Her reproaches fell so hot and heavy, that they left me no chance to answer. Bitter tears, such as the eyes never shed but once, were my only answer. I rose from my seat, but fell back again, sobbing. She did not speak to me; but the tears were running down her furrowed cheeks, and they scorched me like fire. She had always been so kind to me! So kind! How I longed to throw myself at her feet, and tell her all the truth! But she had ordered me to go, and never to come there again. After a few minutes, I mustered strength, and started to obey her. With what feelings did I now close that little gate, which I used to open with such an eager hand in my childhood! It closed upon me with a sound I never heard before.

Where could I go? I was afraid to return to my master's. I walked on recklessly, not caring where I went, or what would become of me. When I had gone four or five miles, fatigue compelled me to stop. I sat down on the stump of an old tree. The stars were shining through the boughs above me. How they mocked me, with their bright, calm light! The hours passed by, and as I sat there alone a chilliness and deadly sickness came over me. I sank on the ground. My mind was full of horrid thoughts. I prayed to die; but the prayer was not answered. At last, with great effort I roused myself, and walked some distance further, to the house of a woman who had been a friend of my mother. When I told her why I was there, she spoke soothingly to me; but I could not be comforted. I thought I could bear my shame if I could only be reconciled to my grandmother. I longed to open my heart to her. I thought if she could know the real state of the case, and all I had been bearing for years, she would perhaps judge me less harshly. My friend advised me to send for her. I did so; but days of agonizing suspense passed before she came. Had she utterly forsaken me? No. She came at last. I knelt before her, and told her the things that had poisoned my life; how long I had been persecuted; that I saw no way of escape; and in an hour of extremity I had become desperate. She listened in silence. I told her I would bear any thing and do any thing, if in time I had hopes of obtaining her forgiveness. I begged of her to pity me, for my dead mother's sake. And she did pity me. She did not say, "I forgive you;" but she looked at me lovingly, with her eyes full of tears. She laid her old hand gently on my head, and murmured, "Poor child! Poor child!"

[Outraged when he learns that Brent is pregnant, Dr. Flint threatens her but fails to coerce Brent into revealing the identity of her lover. Brent gives birth to a son, Benjamin, and goes to live with Aunt Martha.]

XIV. *Another Link to Life*

I had not returned to my master's house since the birth of my child. The old man raved to have me thus removed from his immediate power; but his wife vowed, by all that was good and great, she would kill me if I came back; and he did not doubt her word. Sometimes he would stay away for a season. Then he would come and renew the old threadbare discourse about his forbearance and my ingratitude. He labored, most unnecessarily, to convince me that I had lowered myself. The venomous old reprobate[8] had no need of descanting on that theme. I felt humiliated enough. My unconscious babe was the ever-present witness of my shame. I listened with silent contempt when he talked about my having forfeited *his* good opinion; but I shed bitter tears that I was no longer worthy of being respected by the good and pure. Alas! slavery still held me in its poisonous grasp. There was no chance for me to be respectable. There was no prospect of being able to lead a better life.

Sometimes, when my master found that I still refused to accept what he called his kind offers, he would threaten to sell my child. "Perhaps that will humble you," said he.

Humble *me!* Was I not already in the dust? But his threat lacerated my heart. I knew the law gave him power to fulfill it; for slaveholders have been cunning enough to enact that "the child shall follow the condition of the *mother*," not of the *father*; thus taking care that licentiousness shall not interfere with avarice. This reflection made me clasp my innocent babe all the more firmly to my heart. Horrid visions passed through my mind when I thought of his liability to fall into the slave trader's hands. I wept over him, and said, "O my child! perhaps they will leave you in some cold cabin to die, and then throw you into a hole, as if you were a dog."

When Dr. Flint learned that I was again to be a mother, he was exasperated beyond measure. He rushed from the house, and returned with a pair of shears. I had a fine head of hair; and he often railed about my pride of arranging it nicely. He cut every hair close to my head, storming and swearing all the time. I replied to some of his abuse, and he struck me.

8. A depraved, vicious person.

Some months before, he had pitched me down stairs in a fit of passion; and the injury I received was so serious that I was unable to turn myself in bed for many days. He then said, "Linda, I swear by God I will never raise my hand against you again;" but I knew that he would forget his promise.

After he discovered my situation, he was like a restless spirit from the pit. He came every day; and I was subjected to such insults as no pen can describe. I would not describe them if I could; they were too low, too revolting. I tried to keep them from my grandmother's knowledge as much as I could. I knew she had enough to sadden her life, without having my troubles to bear. When she saw the doctor treat me with violence, and heard him utter oaths terrible enough to palsy a man's tongue, she could not always hold her peace. It was natural and motherlike that she should try to defend me; but it only made matters worse.

When they told me my new-born babe was a girl, my heart was heavier than it had ever been before. Slavery is terrible for men; but it is far more terrible for women. Superadded to the burden common to all, *they* have wrongs, and sufferings, and mortifications peculiarly their own.

Dr. Flint had sworn that he would make me suffer, to my last day, for this new crime against *him*, as he called it; and as long as he had me in his power he kept his word. On the fourth day after the birth of my babe, he entered my room suddenly, and commanded me to rise and bring my baby to him. The nurse who took care of me had gone out of the room to prepare some nourishment, and I was alone. There was no alternative. I rose, took up my babe, and crossed the room to where he sat. "Now stand there," said he, "till I tell you to go back!" My child bore a strong resemblance to her father, and to the deceased Mrs. Sands, her grandmother. He noticed this; and while I stood before him, trembling with weakness, he heaped upon me and my little one every vile epithet he could think of. Even the grandmother in her grave did not escape his curses. In the midst of his vituperations[9] I fainted at his feet. This recalled him to his senses. He took the baby from my arms, laid it on the bed, dashed cold water in my face, took me up, and shook me violently, to restore my consciousness before any one entered the room. Just then my grandmother came in, and he hurried out of the house. I suffered in consequence of this treatment; but I begged my friends to let me die, rather than send for the doctor. There was nothing I dreaded so much as his presence. My life was spared; and I was glad for the sake of my little ones. Had it not been for these ties to life, I should have been glad to be released by death, though I had lived only nineteen years.

Always it gave me a pang that my children had no lawful claim to a name. Their father offered his; but, if I had wished to accept the offer, I dared not while my master lived. Moreover, I knew it would not be accepted at their baptism. A Christian name they were at least entitled to; and we resolved to call my boy for our dear good Benjamin, who had gone far away from us.

My grandmother belonged to the church; and she was very desirous of having the children christened. I knew Dr. Flint would forbid it, and I did not venture to attempt it. But chance favored me. He was called to visit a

9. Bitter, abusive language.

patient out of town, and was obliged to be absent during Sunday. "Now is the time," said my grandmother; "we will take the children to church, and have them christened."

When I entered the church, recollections of my mother came over me, and I felt subdued in spirit. There she had presented me for baptism, without any reason to feel ashamed. She had been married, and had such legal rights as slavery allows to a slave. The vows had at least been sacred to her, and she had never violated them. I was glad she was not alive, to know under what different circumstances her grandchildren were presented for baptism. Why had my lot been so different from my mother's? *Her* master had died when she was a child; and she remained with her mistress till she married. She was never in the power of any master; and thus she escaped one class of the evils that generally fall upon slaves.

When my baby was about to be christened, the former mistress of my father stepped up to me, and proposed to give it her Christian name. To this I added the surname of my father, who had himself no legal right to it; for my grandfather on the paternal side was a white gentleman. What tangled skeins are the genealogies of slavery! I loved my father; but it mortified me to be obliged to bestow his name on my children.

When we left the church, my father's old mistress invited me to go home with her. She clasped a gold chain around my baby's neck. I thanked her for this kindness; but I did not like the emblem. I wanted no chain to be fastened on my daughter, not even if its links were of gold. How earnestly I prayed that she might never feel the weight of slavery's chain, whose iron entereth into the soul!

[To remind her of his power over her, Dr. Flint compels Brent to work at his son's nearby plantation. She forms a plan to get her freedom by hiding in the house of a local friend until such time as Flint will give up hope of finding her. Brent hopes that Flint will eventually sell her along with her children to their father, Mr. Sands.]

XVII. *The Flight*

Mr. Flint[1] was hard pushed for house servants, and rather than lose me he had restrained his malice. I did my work faithfully, though not, of course, with a willing mind. They were evidently afraid I should leave them. Mr. Flint wished that I should sleep in the great house instead of the servants' quarters. His wife agreed to the proposition, but said I mustn't bring my bed into the house, because it would scatter feathers on her carpet. I knew when I went there that they would never think of such a thing as furnishing a bed of any kind for me and my little one. I therefore carried my own bed, and now I was forbidden to use it. I did as I was ordered. But now that I was certain my children were to be put in their power, in order to give them a stronger hold on me, I resolved to leave them that night. I remembered the grief this step would bring upon my dear old grandmother; and nothing less than the freedom of my children would have induced me to disregard her advice. I went about my evening work with trembling steps. Mr. Flint twice

1. Dr. Flint's son.

called from his chamber door to inquire why the house was not locked up. I replied that I had not done my work. "You have had time enough to do it," said he. "Take care how you answer me!"

I shut all the windows, locked all the doors, and went up to the third story, to wait till midnight. How long those hours seemed, and how fervently I prayed that God would not forsake me in this hour of utmost need! I was about to risk every thing on the throw of a die; and if I failed, O what would become of me and my poor children? They would be made to suffer for my fault.

At half past twelve I stole softly down stairs. I stopped on the second floor, thinking I heard a noise. I felt my way down into the parlor, and looked out of the window. The night was so intensely dark that I could see nothing. I raised the window very softly and jumped out. Large drops of rain were falling, and the darkness bewildered me. I dropped on my knees, and breathed a short prayer to God for guidance and protection. I groped my way to the road, and rushed towards the town with almost lightning speed. I arrived at my grandmother's house, but dared not see her. She would say, "Linda, you are killing me;" and I knew that would unnerve me. I tapped softly at the window of a room, occupied by a woman, who had lived in the house several years. I knew she was a faithful friend, and could be trusted with my secret. I tapped several times before she heard me. At last she raised the window, and I whispered, "Sally, I have run away. Let me in, quick." She opened the door softly, and said in low tones, "For God's sake, don't. Your grandmother is trying to buy you and de chillern. Mr. Sands was here last week. He tole her he was going away on business, but he wanted her to go ahead about buying you and de chillern, and he would help her all he could. Don't run away, Linda. Your grandmother is all bowed down wid trouble now."

I replied, "Sally, they are going to carry my children to the plantation to-morrow; and they will never sell them to any body so long as they have me in their power. Now, would you advise me to go back?"

"No, chile, no," answered she. "When dey finds you is gone, dey won't want de plague ob de chillern; but where is you going to hide? Dey knows ebery inch ob dis house."

I told her I had a hiding-place, and that was all it was best for her to know. I asked her to go into my room as soon as it was light, and take all my clothes out of my trunk, and pack them in hers; for I knew Mr. Flint and the constable would be there early to search my room. I feared the sight of my children would be too much for my full heart; but I could not go out into the uncertain future without one last look. I bent over the bed where lay my little Benny and baby Ellen. Poor little ones! fatherless and motherless! Memories of their father came over me. He wanted to be kind to them; but they were not all to him, as they were to my womanly heart. I knelt and prayed for the innocent little sleepers. I kissed them lightly, and turned away.

As I was about to open the street door, Sally laid her hand on my shoulder, and said, "Linda, is you gwine all alone? Let me call your uncle."

"No, Sally," I replied, "I want no one to be brought into trouble on my account."

I went forth into the darkness and rain. I ran on till I came to the house of the friend who was to conceal me.

Early the next morning Mr. Flint was at my grandmother's inquiring for me. She told him she had not seen me, and supposed I was at the plantation. He watched her face narrowly, and said, "Don't you know any thing about her running off?" She assured him that she did not. He went on to say, "Last night she ran off without the least provocation. We had treated her very kindly. My wife liked her. She will soon be found and brought back. Are her children with you?" When told that they were, he said, "I am very glad to hear that. If they are here, she cannot be far off. If I find out that any of my niggers have had any thing to do with this damned business, I'll give 'em five hundred lashes." As he started to go to his father's, he turned round and added, persuasively, "Let her be brought back, and she shall have her children to live with her."

The tidings made the old doctor rave and storm at a furious rate. It was a busy day for them. My grandmother's house was searched from top to bottom. As my trunk was empty, they concluded I had taken my clothes with me. Before ten o'clock every vessel northward bound was thoroughly examined, and the law against harboring fugitives was read to all on board. At night a watch was set over the town. Knowing how distressed my grandmother would be, I wanted to send her a message; but it could not be done. Every one who went in or out of her house was closely watched. The doctor said he would take my children, unless she became responsible for them; which of course she willingly did. The next day was spent in searching. Before night, the following advertisement was posted at every corner, and in every public place for miles round:—

"$300 REWARD! Ran away from the subscriber, an intelligent, bright, mulatto girl, named Linda, 21 years of age. Five feet four inches high. Dark eyes, and black hair inclined to curl; but it can be made straight. Has a decayed spot on a front tooth. She can read and write, and in all probability will try to get to the Free States. All persons are forbidden, under penalty of the law, to harbor or employ said slave. $150 will be given to whoever takes her in the state, and $300 if taken out of the state and delivered to me, or lodged in jail.

DR. FLINT."

[A handful of sympathetic black and white women keep Brent in safe hiding. Dr. Flint retaliates by selling Brent's children and her brother, William, to a slave trader, unaware that the trader represents Mr. Sands. A permanent hiding place is secured in Brent's grandmother's house.]

XXI. The Loophole of Retreat

A small shed had been added to my grandmother's house years ago. Some boards were laid across the joists at the top, and between these boards and the roof was a very small garret, never occupied by any thing but rats and mice. It was a pent roof, covered with nothing but shingles, according to the southern custom for such buildings. The garret was only nine feet long and seven wide. The highest part was three feet high, and sloped down abruptly to the loose board floor. There was no admission for either light or air. My uncle Phillip, who was a carpenter, had very skillfully made a concealed trap-door, which communicated with the storeroom. He had been doing this while I was waiting in the swamp. The storeroom opened upon a piazza.[2] To this hole I was conveyed as soon as I entered the house. The air was stifling; the darkness total. A bed had been spread on the floor. I could sleep quite comfortably on one side; but the slope was so sudden that I could not turn on the other without hitting the roof. The rats and mice ran over my bed; but I was weary, and I slept such sleep as the wretched may, when a tempest has passed over them. Morning came. I knew it only by the noises I heard; for in my small den day and night were all the same. I suffered for air even more than for light. But I was not comfortless. I heard the voices of my children. There was joy and there was sadness in the sound. It made my tears flow. How I longed to speak to them! I was eager to look on their faces; but there was no hole, no crack, through which I could peep. This continued darkness was oppressive. It seemed horrible to sit or lie in a cramped position day after day, without one gleam of light. Yet I would have chosen this, rather than my lot as a slave, though white people considered it an easy one; and it was so compared with the fate of others. I was never cruelly over-worked; I was never lacerated with the whip from head to foot; I was never so beaten and bruised that I could not turn from one side to the other; I never had my heel-strings cut to prevent my running away; I was never chained to a log and forced to drag it about, while I toiled in the fields from morning till night; I was never branded with hot iron, or torn by bloodhounds. On the contrary, I had always been kindly treated, and tenderly cared for, until I came into the hands of Dr. Flint. I had never wished for freedom till then. But though my life in slavery was comparatively devoid of hardships, God pity the woman who is compelled to lead such a life!

My food was passed up to me through the trap-door my uncle had contrived; and my grandmother, my uncle Phillip, and aunt Nancy would seize such opportunities as they could, to mount up there and chat with me at the opening. But of course this was not safe in the daytime. It must all be done in darkness. It was impossible for me to move in an erect position, but I crawled about my den for exercise. One day I hit my head against something, and found it was a gimlet. My uncle had left it sticking there when he made the trap-door. I was as rejoiced as Robinson Crusoe could have been at finding such a treasure. It put a lucky thought into my head. I said to myself, "Now I will have some light. Now I will see my children." I did not dare to begin my work during the daytime, for fear of attracting attention. But I groped round; and having found the side next the street, where I could frequently see my children, I stuck the gimlet in and waited for evening. I bored three rows of holes, one above another; then I bored out the interstices between. I thus succeeded in making one hole about an inch long and an inch broad. I sat by it till late into the night, to enjoy the little whiff of air that floated in. In the morning I watched for my children. The

2. A large covered porch.

first person I saw in the street was Dr. Flint. I had a shuddering, superstitious feeling that it was a bad omen. Several familiar faces passed by. At last I heard the merry laugh of children, and presently two sweet little faces were looking up at me, as though they knew I was there, and were conscious of the joy they imparted. How I longed to *tell* them I was there!

My condition was now a little improved. But for weeks I was tormented by hundreds of little red insects, fine as a needle's point, that pierced through my skin, and produced an intolerable burning. The good grandmother gave me herb teas and cooling medicines, and finally I got rid of them. The heat of my den was intense, for nothing but thin shingles protected me from the scorching summer's sun. But I had my consolations. Through my peeping-hole I could watch the children, and when they were near enough, I could hear their talk. Aunt Nancy brought me all the news she could hear at Dr. Flint's. From her I learned that the doctor had written to New York to a colored woman, who had been born and raised in our neighborhood, and had breathed his contaminating atmosphere. He offered her a reward if she could find out any thing about me. I know not what was the nature of her reply; but he soon after started for New York in haste, saying to his family that he had business of importance to transact. I peeped at him as he passed on his way to the steamboat. It was a satisfaction to have miles of land and water between us, even for a little while; and it was a still greater satisfaction to know that he believed me to be in the Free States. My little den seemed less dreary than it had done. He returned, as he did from his former journey to New York, without obtaining any satisfactory information. When he passed our house next morning, Benny was standing at the gate. He had heard them say that he had gone to find me, and he called out, "Dr. Flint, did you bring my mother home? I want to see her." The doctor stamped his foot at him in a rage, and exclaimed, "Get out of the way, you little damned rascal! If you don't, I'll cut off your head."

Benny ran terrified into the house, saying, "You can't put me in jail again. I don't belong to you now." It was well that the wind carried the words away from the doctor's ear. I told my grandmother of it, when we had our next conference at the trap-door; and begged of her not to allow the children to be impertinent to the irascible old man.

Autumn came, with a pleasant abatement of heat. My eyes had become accustomed to the dim light, and by holding my book or work in a certain position near the aperture I contrived to read and sew. That was a great relief to the tedious monotony of my life. But when winter came, the cold penetrated through the thin shingle roof, and I was dreadfully chilled. The winters there are not so long, or so severe, as in northern latitudes; but the houses are not built to shelter from cold, and my little den was peculiarly comfortless. The kind grandmother brought me bed-clothes and warm drinks. Often I was obliged to lie in bed all day to keep comfortable; but with all my precautions, my shoulders and feet were frostbitten. O, those long, gloomy days, with no object for my eye to rest upon, and no thoughts to occupy my mind, except the dreary past and the uncertain future! I was thankful when there came a day sufficiently mild for me to wrap myself up and sit at the loophole to watch the passers by. Southerners have the habit of stopping and talking in the streets, and I heard many conversations not

intended to meet my ears. I heard slave-hunters planning how to catch
some poor fugitive. Several times I heard allusions to Dr. Flint, myself, and
the history of my children, who, perhaps, were playing near the gate. One
would say, "I wouldn't move my little finger to catch her, as old Flint's
property." Another would say, "I'll catch *any* nigger for the reward. A man
ought to have what belongs to him, if he *is* a damned brute." The opinion
was often expressed that I was in the Free States. Very rarely did any one
suggest that I might be in the vicinity. Had the least suspicion rested on my
grandmother's house, it would have been burned to the ground. But it was
the last place they thought of. Yet there was no place, where slavery existed,
that could have afforded me so good a place of concealment.

Dr. Flint and his family repeatedly tried to coax and bribe my children to
tell something they had heard said about me. One day the doctor took
them into a shop, and offered them some bright little silver pieces and gay
handkerchiefs if they would tell where their mother was. Ellen shrank away
from him, and would not speak; but Benny spoke up, and said, "Dr. Flint, I
don't know where my mother is. I guess she's in New York; and when you
go there again, I wish you'd ask her to come home, for I want to see her;
but if you put her in jail, or tell her you'll cut her head off, I'll tell her to go
right back."

[Brent passes the years hidden in her garret, suffering from exposure, lack of exercise, poor ventilation, and illness. Mr. Sands is elected to Congress. Risking discovery, Brent pleads with him to free their children. He does not live up to his promises
to do so but instead conveys their daughter, Ellen, to some of his relatives in Brooklyn, New York. Meanwhile Dr. Flint continues to search for Brent both locally and
in New York.]

XXIX. Preparations for Escape

I hardly expect that the reader will credit me, when I affirm that I lived in
that little dismal hole, almost deprived of light and air, and with no space to
move my limbs, for nearly seven years. But it is a fact; and to me a sad one,
even now; for my body still suffers from the effects of that long imprisonment, to say nothing of my soul. Members of my family, now living in New
York and Boston, can testify to the truth of what I say.

Countless were the nights that I sat late at the little loophole scarcely
large enough to give me a glimpse of one twinkling star. There, I heard the
patrols and slave-hunters conferring together about the capture of runaways, well knowing how rejoiced they would be to catch me.

Season after season, year after year, I peeped at my children's faces, and
heard their sweet voices, with a heart yearning all the while to say, "Your
mother is here." Sometimes it appeared to me as if ages had rolled away
since I entered upon that gloomy, monotonous existence. At times, I was
stupefied and listless; at other times I became very impatient to know when
these dark years would end, and I should again be allowed to feel the sunshine, and breathe the pure air.

After Ellen left us, this feeling increased. Mr. Sands had agreed that
Benny might go to the north whenever his uncle Phillip could go with

him; and I was anxious to be there also, to watch over my children, and protect them so far as I was able. Moreover, I was likely to be drowned out of my den, if I remained much longer; for the slight roof was getting badly out of repair, and uncle Phillip was afraid to remove the shingles, lest some one should get a glimpse of me. When storms occurred in the night, they spread mats and bits of carpet, which in the morning appeared to have been laid out to dry; but to cover the roof in the daytime might have attracted attention. Consequently, my clothes and bedding were often drenched; a process by which the pains and aches in my cramped and stiffened limbs were greatly increased. I revolved various plans of escape in my mind, which I sometimes imparted to my grandmother, when she came to whisper with me at the trap-door. The kind-hearted old woman had an intense sympathy for runaways. She had known too much of the cruelties inflicted on those who were captured. Her memory always flew back at once to the sufferings of her bright and handsome son, Benjamin, the youngest and dearest of her flock. So, whenever I alluded to the subject, she would groan out, "Oh, don't think of it, child. You'll break my heart." I had no good old aunt Nancy now to encourage me; but my brother William and my children were continually beckoning me to the north.

And now I must go back a few months in my story. I have stated that the first of January was the time for selling slaves, or leasing them out to new masters. If time were counted by heart-throbs, the poor slaves might reckon years of suffering during that festival so joyous to the free. On the New Year's day preceding my aunt's death, one of my friends, named Fanny, was to be sold at auction, to pay her master's debts. My thoughts were with her during all the day, and at night I anxiously inquired what had been her fate. I was told that she had been sold to one master, and her four little girls to another master, far distant; that she had escaped from her purchaser, and was not to be found. Her mother was the old Aggie I have spoken of. She lived in a small tenement belonging to my grandmother, and built on the same lot with her own house. Her dwelling was searched and watched, and that brought the patrols so near me that I was obliged to keep very close in my den. The hunters were somehow eluded; and not long afterwards Benny accidentally caught sight of Fanny in her mother's hut. He told his grandmother, who charged him never to speak of it, explaining to him the frightful consequences; and he never betrayed the trust. Aggie little dreamed that my grandmother knew where her daughter was concealed, and that the stooping form of her old neighbor was bending under a similar burden of anxiety and fear; but these dangerous secrets deepened the sympathy between the two old persecuted mothers.

My friend Fanny and I remained many weeks hidden within call of each other; but she was unconscious of the fact. I longed to have her share my den, which seemed a more secure retreat than her own; but I had brought so much trouble on my grandmother, that it seemed wrong to ask her to incur greater risks. My restlessness increased. I had lived too long in bodily pain and anguish of spirit. Always I was in dread that by some accident, or some contrivance, slavery would succeed in snatching my children from me. This thought drove me nearly frantic, and I determined to steer for the

North Star at all hazards. At this crisis, Providence opened an unexpected way for me to escape. My friend Peter came one evening, and asked to speak with me. "Your day has come, Linda," said he. "I have found a chance for you to go to the Free States. You have a fortnight to decide." The news seemed too good to be true; but Peter explained his arrangements, and told me all that was necessary was for me to say I would go. I was going to answer him with a joyful yes, when the thought of Benny came to my mind. I told him the temptation was exceedingly strong, but I was terribly afraid of Dr. Flint's alleged power over my child, and that I could not go and leave him behind. Peter remonstrated earnestly. He said such a good chance might never occur again; that Benny was free, and could be sent to me; and that for the sake of my children's welfare I ought not to hesitate a moment. I told him I would consult with uncle Phillip. My uncle rejoiced in the plan, and bade me go by all means. He promised, if his life was spared, that he would either bring or send my son to me as soon as I reached a place of safety. I resolved to go, but thought nothing had better be said to my grandmother till very near the time of departure. But my uncle thought she would feel it more keenly if I left her so suddenly. "I will reason with her," said he, "and convince her how necessary it is, not only for your sake, but for hers also. You cannot be blind to the fact that she is sinking under her burdens." I was not blind to it. I knew that my concealment was an ever-present source of anxiety, and that the older she grew the more nervously fearful she was of discovery. My uncle talked with her, and finally succeeded in persuading her that it was absolutely necessary for me to seize the chance so unexpectedly offered.

The anticipation of being a free woman proved almost too much for my weak frame. The excitement stimulated me, and at the same time bewildered me. I made busy preparations for my journey, and for my son to follow me. I resolved to have an interview with him before I went, that I might give him cautions and advice, and tell him how anxiously I should be waiting for him at the north. Grandmother stole up to me as often as possible to whisper words of counsel. She insisted upon my writing to Dr. Flint, as soon as I arrived in the Free States, and asking him to sell me to her. She said she would sacrifice her house, and all she had in the world, for the sake of having me safe with my children in any part of the world. If she could only live to know *that* she could die in peace. I promised the dear old faithful friend that I would write to her as soon as I arrived, and put the letter in a safe way to reach her; but in my own mind I resolved that not another cent of her hard earnings should be spent to pay rapacious slaveholders for what they called their property. And even if I had not been unwilling to buy what I had already a right to possess, common humanity would have prevented me from accepting the generous offer, at the expense of turning my aged relative out of house and home, when she was trembling on the brink of the grave.

I was to escape in a vessel; but I forbear to mention any further particulars. I was in readiness, but the vessel was unexpectedly detained several days. Meantime, news came to town of a most horrible murder committed on a fugitive slave, named James. Charity, the mother of this unfortunate young man, had been an old acquaintance of ours. I have told the shocking

particulars of his death,[3] in my description of some of the neighboring
slaveholders. My grandmother, always nervously sensitive about runaways,
was terribly frightened. She felt sure that a similar fate awaited me, if I did
not desist from my enterprise. She sobbed, and groaned, and entreated
me not to go. Her excessive fear was somewhat contagious, and my heart
was not proof against her extreme agony. I was grievously disappointed, but
I promised to relinquish my project.

When my friend Peter was apprised of this, he was both disappointed
and vexed. He said, that judging from our past experience, it would be a
long time before I had such another chance to throw away. I told him it
need not be thrown away; that I had a friend concealed near by, who would
be glad enough to take the place that had been provided for me. I told him
about poor Fanny, and the kind-hearted, noble fellow, who never turned
his back upon any body in distress, white or black, expressed his readiness
to help her. Aggie was much surprised when she found that we knew her
secret. She was rejoiced to hear of such a chance for Fanny, and arrangements were made for her to go on board the vessel the next night. They
both supposed that I had long been at the north, therefore my name was
not mentioned in the transaction. Fanny was carried on board at the appointed time, and stowed away in a very small cabin. This accommodation
had been purchased at a price that would pay for a voyage to England. But
when one proposes to go to fine old England, they stop to calculate
whether they can afford the cost of the pleasure; while in making a bargain
to escape from slavery, the trembling victim is ready to say, "Take all I have,
only don't betray me!"

The next morning I peeped through my loophole, and saw that it was
dark and cloudy. At night I received news that the wind as ahead, and the
vessel had not sailed. I was exceedingly anxious about Fanny, and Peter
too, who was running a tremendous risk at my instigation. Next day the
wind and weather remained the same. Poor Fanny had been half dead with
fright when they carried her on board, and I could readily imagine how she
must be suffering now. Grandmother came often to my den, to say how
thankful she was I did not go. On the third morning she rapped for me to
come down to the storeroom. The poor old sufferer was breaking down
under her weight of trouble. She was easily flurried now. I found her in a
nervous, excited state, but I was not aware that she had forgotten to lock the
door behind her, as usual. She was exceedingly worried about the detention of the vessel. She was afraid all would be discovered, and then Fanny,
and Peter, and I, would all be tortured to death, and Phillip would be utterly ruined, and her house would be torn down. Poor Peter! If he should
die such a horrible death as the poor slave James had lately done, and all
for his kindness in trying to help me, how dreadful it would be for us all!
Alas, the thought was familiar to me, and had sent many a sharp pang
through my heart. I tried to suppress my own anxiety, and speak soothingly
to her. She brought in some allusion to aunt Nancy, the dear daughter she
had recently buried, and then she lost all control of herself. As she stood

---

3. To illustrate the cruelty of slaveholders, Jacobs recalled, earlier in her narrative, the sadistic tortures
suffered by a local slave named James.

there, trembling and sobbing, a voice from the piazza called out, "Whar is you, aunt Marthy?" Grandmother was startled, and in her agitation opened the door, without thinking of me. In stepped Jenny, the mischievous housemaid, who had tried to enter my room, when I was concealed in the house of my white benefactress. "I's bin huntin ebery what for you, aunt Marthy," said she. "My missis wants you to send her some crackers." I had slunk down behind a barrel, which entirely screened me, but I imagined that Jenny was looking directly at the spot, and my heart beat violently. My grandmother immediately thought what she had done, and went out quickly with Jenny to count the crackers locking the door after her. She returned to me, in a few minutes, the perfect picture of despair. "Poor child!" she exclaimed, "my carelessness has ruined you. The boat ain't gone yet. Get ready immediately, and go with Fanny. I ain't got another word to say against it now; for there's no telling what may happen this day."

Uncle Phillip was sent for, and he agreed with his mother in thinking that Jenny would inform Dr. Flint in less than twenty-four hours. He advised getting me on board the boat, if possible; if not, I had better keep very still in my den, where they could not find me without tearing the house down. He said it would not do for him to move in the matter, because suspicion would be immediately excited; but he promised to communicate with Peter. I felt reluctant to apply to him again, having implicated him too much already; but there seemed to be no alternative. Vexed as Peter had been by my indecision, he was true to his generous nature, and said at once that he would do his best to help me, trusting I should show myself a stronger woman this time.

He immediately proceeded to the wharf, and found that the wind had shifted, and the vessel was slowly beating down stream. On some pretext of urgent necessity, he offered two boatmen a dollar apiece to catch up with her. He was of lighter complexion than the boatmen he hired, and when the captain saw them coming so rapidly, he thought officers were pursuing his vessel in search of the runaway slave he had on board. They hoisted sails, but the boat gained upon them, and the indefatigable Peter sprang on board.

The captain at once recognized him. Peter asked him to go below, to speak about a bad bill he had given him. When he told his errand, the captain replied, "Why, the woman's here already; and I've put her where you or the devil would have a tough job to find her."

"But it is another woman I want to bring," said Peter. "*She* is in great distress, too, and you shall be paid any thing within reason, if you'll stop and take her."

"What's her name?" inquired the captain.

"Linda," he replied.

"That's the name of the woman already here," rejoined the captain. "By George! I believe you mean to betray me."

"O!" exclaimed Peter, "God knows I wouldn't harm a hair of your head. I am too grateful to you. But there really *is* another woman in great danger. Do have the humanity to stop and take her!"

After a while they came to an understanding. Fanny, not dreaming I was any where about in that region, had assumed my name, though she had called herself Johnson. "Linda is a common name," said Peter, "and the woman I want to bring is Linda Brent."

The captain agreed to wait at a certain place till evening, being handsomely paid for his detention.

Of course, the day was an anxious one for us all. But we concluded that if Jenny had seen me, she would be too wise to let her mistress know of it; and that she probably would not get a chance to see Dr. Flint's family till evening, for I knew very well what were the rules in that household. I afterwards believed that she did not see me; for nothing ever came of it, and she was one of those base characters that would have jumped to betray a suffering fellow being for the sake of thirty pieces of silver.

I made all my arrangements to go on board as soon as it was dusk. The intervening time I resolved to spend with my son. I had not spoken to him for seven years, though I had been under the same roof, and seen him every day, when I was well enough to sit at the loophole. I did not dare to venture beyond the storeroom; so they brought him there, and locked us up together, in a place concealed from the piazza door. It was an agitating interview for both of us. After we had talked and wept together for a little while, he said, "Mother, I'm glad you're going away. I wish I could go with you. I knew you was here; and I have been so afraid they would come and catch you!"

I was greatly surprised, and asked him how he had found it out.

He replied, "I was standing under the eaves, one day, before Ellen went away, and I heard somebody cough up over the wood shed. I don't know what made me think it was you, but I did think so. I missed Ellen, the night before she went away; and grandmother brought her back into the room in the night; and I thought maybe she'd been to see you, before she went, for I heard grandmother whisper to her, 'Now go to sleep; and remember never to tell.'"

I asked him if he ever mentioned his suspicions to his sister. He said he never did; but after he heard the cough, if he saw her playing with other children on that side of the house, he always tried to coax her round to the other side, for fear they would hear me cough, too. He said he had kept a close lookout for Dr. Flint, and if he saw him speak to a constable, or a patrol, he always told grandmother. I now recollected that I had seen him manifest uneasiness, when people were on that side of the house, and I had at the time been puzzled to conjecture a motive for his actions. Such prudence may seem extraordinary in a boy of twelve years, but slaves, being surrounded by mysteries, deceptions, and dangers, early learn to be suspicious and watchful, and prematurely cautious and cunning. He had never asked a question of grandmother, or uncle Phillip, and I had often heard him chime in with other children, when they spoke of my being at the north.

I told him I was now really going to the Free States, and if he was a good, honest boy, and a loving child to his dear old grandmother, the Lord would bless him, and bring him to me, and we and Ellen would live together. He began to tell me that grandmother had not eaten any thing all day. While he was speaking, the door was unlocked, and she came in with a small bag of money, which she wanted me to take. I begged her to keep a part of it, at least, to pay for Benny's being sent to the north; but she insisted, while her tears were falling fast, that I should take the whole. "You may be sick among strangers," she said, "and they would send you to the poorhouse to die." Ah, that good grandmother!

For the last time I went up to my nook. Its desolate appearance no longer chilled me, for the light of hope had risen in my soul. Yet, even with the blessed prospect of freedom before me, I felt very sad at leaving forever that old homestead, where I had been sheltered so long by the dear old grandmother; where I had dreamed my first young dream of love; and where, after that had faded away, my children came to twine themselves so closely round my desolate heart. As the hour approached for me to leave, I again descended to the storeroom. My grandmother and Benny were there. She took me by the hand, and said, "Linda, let us pray." We knelt down together, with my child pressed to my heart, and my other arm round the faithful, loving old friend I was about to leave forever. On no other occasion has it ever been my lot to listen to so fervent a supplication for mercy and protection. It thrilled through my heart, and inspired me with trust in God.

Peter was waiting for me in the street. I was soon by his side, faint in body, but strong of purpose. I did not look back upon the old place, though I felt that I should never see it again.

[Brent escapes to Philadelphia by boat. She goes to New York and visits her daughter, who is being trained to become a lady's personal servant instead of receiving schooling and her freedom. Brent finds employment in New York providing child care for Mary, the infant daughter of Mrs. Bruce, "a true and sympathizing friend." Mrs. Bruce's death increases Brent's insecurity. Fearful of slave catchers, she is forced to flee to Boston, where she is able to support her children by working as a seamstress.]

XXXIX. The Confession

For two years my daughter and I supported ourselves comfortably in Boston. At the end of that time, my brother William offered to send Ellen to a boarding school. It required a great effort for me to consent to part with her, for I had few near ties, and it was her presence that made my two little rooms seem home-like. But my judgment prevailed over my selfish feelings. I made preparations for her departure. During the two years we had lived together I had often resolved to tell her something about her father; but I had never been able to muster sufficient courage. I had a shrinking dread of diminishing my child's love. I knew she must have curiosity on the subject, but she had never asked a question. She was always very careful not to say any thing to remind me of my troubles. Now that she was going from me, I thought if I should die before she returned, she might hear my story from some one who did not understand the palliating circumstances; and that if she were entirely ignorant on the subject, her sensitive nature might receive a rude shock.

When we retired for the night, she said, "Mother, it is very hard to leave you alone. I am almost sorry I am going, though I do want to improve myself. But you will write to me often; won't you, mother?"

I did not throw my arms round her. I did not answer her. But in a calm, solemn way, for it cost me great effort, I said, "Listen to me, Ellen; I have something to tell you!" I recounted my early sufferings in slavery, and told her how nearly they had crushed me. I began to tell her how they had driven me into a great sin, when she clasped me in her arms, and exclaimed, "Oh, don't, mother! Please don't tell me any more."

I said, "But, my child, I want you to know about your father."

"I know all about it, mother," she replied; "I am nothing to my father, and he is nothing to me. All my love is for you. I was with him five months in Washington, and he never cared for me. He never spoke to me as he did to his little Fanny. I knew all the time he was my father, for Fanny's nurse told me so; but she said I must never tell any body, and I never did. I used to wish he would take me in his arms and kiss me, as he did Fanny; or that he would sometimes smile at me, as he did at her. I thought if he was my own father, he ought to love me. I was a little girl then, and didn't know any better. But now I never think any thing about my father. All my love is for you." She hugged me closer as she spoke, and I thanked God that the knowledge I had so much dreaded to impart had not diminished the affection of my child. I had not the slightest idea she knew that portion of my history. If I had, I should have spoken to her long before; for my pent-up feelings had often longed to pour themselves out to some one I could trust. But I loved the dear girl better for the delicacy she had manifested towards her unfortunate mother.

The next morning, she and her uncle started on their journey to the village in New York, where she was to be placed at school. It seemed as if all the sunshine had gone away. My little room was dreadfully lonely. I was thankful when a message came from a lady, accustomed to employ me, requesting me to come and sew in her family for several weeks. On my return, I found a letter from brother William. He thought of opening an anti-slavery reading room in Rochester, and combining with it the sale of some books and stationery; and he wanted me to unite with him. We tried it, but it was not successful. We found warm anti-slavery friends there, but the feeling was not general enough to support such an establishment. I passed nearly a year in the family of Isaac and Amy Post,[4] practical believers in the Christian doctrine of human brotherhood. They measured a man's worth by his character, not by his complexion. The memory of those beloved and honored friends will remain with me to my latest hour.

XL. The Fugitive Slave Law[5]

My brother, being disappointed in his project, concluded to go to California; and it was agreed that Benjamin should go with him. Ellen liked her school, and was a great favorite there. They did not know her history, and she did not tell it, because she had no desire to make capital out of their sympathy. But when it was accidentally discovered that her mother

---

4. Quaker abolitionists living in Rochester, New York. Amy Post was a participant in the first Woman's Rights Convention held at Seneca Falls, New York, in 1848.

5. The most controversial feature of the Compromise of 1850, the Fugitive Slave Law made any action that aided a runaway slave a federal crime.

was a fugitive slave, every method was used to increase her advantages and diminish her expenses.

I was alone again. It was necessary for me to be earning money, and I preferred that it should be among those who knew me. On my return from Rochester, I called at the house of Mr. Bruce, to see Mary, the darling little babe that had thawed my heart, when it was freezing into a cheerless distrust of all my fellow-beings. She was growing a tall girl now, but I loved her always. Mr. Bruce had married again, and it was proposed that I should become nurse to a new infant. I had but one hesitation, and that was my feeling of insecurity in New York, now greatly increased by the passage of the Fugitive Slave Law. However, I resolved to try the experiment. I was again fortunate in my employer. The new Mrs. Bruce was an American, brought up under aristocratic influences, and still living in the midst of them; but if she had any prejudice against color, I was never made aware of it; and as for the system of slavery, she had a most hearty dislike of it. No sophistry of Southerners could blind her to its enormity. She was a person of excellent principles and a noble heart. To me, from that hour to the present, she has been a true and sympathizing friend. Blessings be with her and hers!

About the time that I reentered the Bruce family, an event occurred of disastrous import to the colored people. The slave Hamlin, the first fugitive that came under the new law, was given up by the bloodhounds of the north to the bloodhounds of the south. It was the beginning of a reign of terror to the colored population. The great city rushed on in its whirl of excitement, taking no note of the "short and simple annals of the poor."[6] But while fashionables were listening to the thrilling voice of Jenny Lind[7] in Metropolitan Hall, the thrilling voices of poor hunted colored people went up, in an agony of supplication, to the Lord, from Zion's church. Many families, who had lived in the city for twenty years, fled from it now. Many a poor washerwoman, who, by hard labor, had made herself a comfortable home, was obliged to sacrifice her furniture, bid a hurried farewell to friends, and seek her fortune among strangers in Canada. Many a wife discovered a secret she had never known before—that her husband was a fugitive, and must leave her to insure his own safety. Worse still, many a husband discovered that his wife had fled from slavery years ago, and as "the child follows the condition of its mother," the children of his love were liable to be seized and carried into slavery. Every where, in those humble homes, there was consternation and anguish. But what cared the legislators of the "dominant race" for the blood they were crushing out of trampled hearts?

When my brother William spent his last evening with me, before he went to California, we talked nearly all the time of the distress brought on our oppressed people by the passage of this iniquitous law; and never had I seen him manifest such bitterness of spirit, such stern hostility to our oppressors. He was himself free from the operation of the law; for he did not run from any Slaveholding State, being brought into the Free States by his

6. From Thomas Grey's famous *Elegy in a Country Churchyard*, line 32.   7. Internationally popular Swedish singer.

master.[8] But I was subject to it; and so were hundreds of intelligent and industrious people all around us. I seldom ventured into the streets; and when it was necessary to do an errand for Mrs. Bruce, or any of the family, I went as much as possible through back streets and by-ways. What a disgrace to a city calling itself free, that inhabitants, guiltless of offence, and seeking to perform their duties conscientiously, should be condemned to live in such incessant fear, and have nowhere to turn for protection! This state of things, of course, gave rise to many impromptu vigilance committees. Every colored person, and every friend of their persecuted race, kept their eyes wide open. Every evening I examined the newspapers carefully, to see what Southerners had put up at the hotels. I did this for my own sake, thinking my young mistress and her husband might be among the list; I wished also to give information to others, if necessary; for if many were "running to and fro," I resolved that "knowledge should be increased."[9]

This brings up one of my Southern reminiscences, which I will here briefly relate. I was somewhat acquainted with a slave named Luke, who belonged to a wealthy man in our vicinity. His master died, leaving a son and daughter heirs to his large fortune. In the division of the slaves, Luke was included in the son's portion. This young man became a prey to the vices growing out of the "patriarchal institution," and when he went to the north, to complete his education, he carried his vices with him. He was brought home, deprived of the use of his limbs, by excessive dissipation. Luke was appointed to wait upon his bed-ridden master, whose despotic habits were greatly increased by exasperation at his own helplessness. He kept a cowhide beside him, and, for the most trivial occurrence, he would order his attendant to bare his back, and kneel beside the couch, while he whipped him till his strength was exhausted. Some days he was not allowed to wear any thing but his shirt, in order to be in readiness to be flogged. A day seldom passed without his receiving more or less blows. If the slightest resistance was offered, the town constable was sent for to execute the punishment, and Luke learned from experience how much more the constable's strong arm was to be dreaded than the comparatively feeble one of his master. The arm of his tyrant grew weaker, and was finally palsied; and then the constable's services were in constant requisition. The fact that he was entirely dependent on Luke's care, and was obliged to be tended like an infant, instead of inspiring any gratitude or compassion towards his poor slave, seemed only to increase his irritability and cruelty. As he lay there on his bed, a mere degraded wreck of manhood, he took into his head the strangest freaks of despotism; and if Luke hesitated to submit to his orders, the constable was immediately sent for. Some of these freaks were of a nature too filthy to be repeated. When I fled from the house of bondage, I left poor Luke still chained to the bedside of this cruel and disgusting wretch.

One day, when I had been requested to do an errand for Mrs. Bruce, I was hurrying through back streets, as usual, when I saw a young man approaching, whose face was familiar to me. As he came nearer, I recognized Luke. I always rejoiced to see or hear of any one who had escaped from the

---

8. William escaped from his master, Mr. Sands,   9. Daniel 12:4.
when Sands moved to Washington, D.C.

black pit; but, remembering this poor fellow's extreme hardships, I was peculiarly glad to see him on Northern soil, though I no longer called it *free* soil. I well remembered what a desolate feeling it was to be alone among strangers, and I went up to him and greeted him cordially. At first, he did not know me; but when I mentioned my name, he remembered all about me. I told him of the Fugitive Slave Law, and asked him if he did not know that New York was a city of kidnappers.

He replied, "De risk ain't so bad for me, as 'tis fur you. 'Cause I runned away from de speculator, and you runned away from de massa. Dem speculators vont spen dar money to come here fur a runaway, if dey ain't sartin sure to put dar hans right on him. An I tell you I's tuk good car 'bout dat. I had too hard times down dar, to let 'em ketch dis nigger."

He then told me of the advice he had received, and the plans he had laid. I asked if he had money enough to take him to Canada. "'Pend upon it, I hab," he replied. "I tuk car fur dat. I'd bin workin all my days fur dem cussed whites, an got no pay but kicks and cuffs. So I tought dis nigger had a right to money nuff to bring him to de Free States. Massa Henry he lib till ebery body vish him dead; an ven he did die, I knowed de debbil would hab him, an vouldn't vant him to bring his money 'long too. So I tuk some of his bills, and put 'em in de pocket of his old trousers. An ven he was buried, dis nigger ask fur dem ole trousers, an dey gub 'em to me." With a low, chuckling laugh, he added, "You see I didn't *steal* it; dey *gub* it to me. I tell you, I had mighty hard time to keep de speculator from findin it; but he didn't git it."

This is a fair specimen of how the moral sense is educated by slavery. When a man has his wages stolen from him, year after year, and the laws sanction and enforce the theft, how can he be expected to have more regard to honesty than has the man who robs him? I have become somewhat enlightened, but I confess that I agree with poor, ignorant, much-abused Luke, in thinking he had a *right* to that money, as a portion of his unpaid wages. He went to Canada forthwith, and I have not since heard from him.

All that winter I lived in a state of anxiety. When I took the children out to breathe the air, I closely observed the countenances of all I met. I dreaded the approach of summer, when snakes and slaveholders make their appearance. I was, in fact, a slave in New York, as subject to slave laws as I had been in a Slave State. Strange incongruity in a State called free!

Spring returned, and I received warning from the south that Dr. Flint knew of my return to my old place, and was making preparations to have me caught. I learned afterwards that my dress, and that of Mrs. Bruce's children, had been described to him by some of the Northern tools, which slaveholders employ for their base purposes, and then indulge in sneers at their cupidity and mean servility.

I immediately informed Mrs. Bruce of my danger, and she took prompt measures for my safety. My place as nurse could not be supplied immediately, and this generous, sympathizing lady proposed that I should carry her baby away. It was a comfort to me to have the child with me; for the heart is reluctant to be torn away from every object it loves. But how few mothers would have consented to have one of their own babes become a fugitive, for the sake of a poor, hunted nurse, on whom the legislators of the country had let loose the bloodhounds! When I spoke of the sacrifice she was making, in depriving herself of her dear baby, she replied, "It is better for you to have baby with you, Linda; for if they get on your track, they will be obliged to bring the child to me; and then, if there is a possibility of saving you, you shall be saved."

This lady had a very wealthy relative, a benevolent gentleman in many respects, but aristocratic and pro-slavery. He remonstrated with her for harboring a fugitive slave; told her she was violating the laws of her country; and asked her if she was aware of the penalty. She replied, "I am very well aware of it. It is imprisonment and one thousand dollars fine. Shame on my country that it *is* so! I am ready to incur the penalty. I will go to the state's prison, rather than have any poor victim torn from *my* house, to be carried back to slavery."

The noble heart! The brave heart! The tears are in my eyes while I write of her. May the God of the helpless reward her for her sympathy with my persecuted people!

I was sent into New England, where I was sheltered by the wife of a senator, whom I shall always hold in grateful remembrance. This honorable gentleman would not have voted for the Fugitive Slave Law, as did the senator in "Uncle Tom's Cabin"; [1] on the contrary, he was strongly opposed to it; but he was enough under its influence to be afraid of having me remain in his house many hours. So I was sent into the country, where I remained a month with the baby. When it was supposed that Dr. Flint's emissaries had lost track of me, and given up the pursuit for the present, I returned to New York.

XLI. *Free at Last*

Mrs. Bruce, and every member of her family, were exceedingly kind to me. I was thankful for the blessings of my lot, yet I could not always wear a cheerful countenance. I was doing harm to no one; on the contrary, I was doing all the good I could in my small way; yet I could never go out to breathe God's free air without trepidation at my heart. This seemed hard; and I could not think it was a right state of things in any civilized country.

From time to time I received news from my good old grandmother. She could not write; but she employed others to write for her. The following is an extract from one of her last letters:—

"Dear Daughter: I cannot hope to see you again on earth; but I pray to God to unite us above, where pain will no more rack this feeble body of mine; where sorrow and parting from my children will be no more. God has promised these things if we are faithful unto the end. My age and feeble health deprive me of going to church now; but God is with me here at home. Thank your brother for his kindness. Give much love to him, and tell him to remember the Creator in the days of his youth, and strive to meet me in the Father's kingdom. Love to Ellen and Benjamin. Don't neglect him. Tell him for me, to be a good

1. An allusion to Senator Bird of Ohio in Harriet Beecher Stowe's novel *Uncle Tom's Cabin* (1852).

boy. Strive, my child, to train them for God's children. May he protect and provide for you, is the prayer of your loving old mother."

These letters both cheered and saddened me. I was always glad to have tidings from the kind, faithful old friend of my unhappy youth; but her messages of love made my heart yearn to see her before she died, and I mourned over the fact that it was impossible. Some months after I returned from my flight to New England, I received a letter from her, in which she wrote, "Dr. Flint is dead. He has left a distressed family. Poor old man! I hope he made his peace with God."

I remembered how he had defrauded my grandmother of the hard earnings she had loaned; how he had tried to cheat her out of the freedom her mistress had promised her, and how he had persecuted her children; and I thought to myself that she was a better Christian than I was, if she could entirely forgive him. I cannot say, with truth, that the news of my old master's death softened my feelings towards him. There are wrongs which even the grave does not bury. The man was odious to me while he lived, and his memory is odious now.

His departure from this world did not diminish my danger. He had threatened my grandmother that his heirs should hold me in slavery after he was gone; that I never should be free so long as a child of his survived. As for Mrs. Flint, I had seen her in deeper afflictions than I supposed the loss of her husband would be, for she had buried several children; yet I never saw any signs of softening in her heart. The doctor had died in embarrassed circumstances, and had little to will to his heirs, except such property as he was unable to grasp. I was well aware what I had to expect from the family of Flints; and my fears were confirmed by a letter from the south, warning me to be on my guard, because Mrs. Flint openly declared that her daughter could not afford to lose so valuable a slave as I was.

I kept close watch of the newspapers for arrivals; but one Saturday night, being much occupied, I forgot to examine the Evening Express as usual. I went down into the parlor for it, early in the morning, and found the boy about to kindle a fire with it. I took it from him and examined the list of arrivals. Reader, if you have never been a slave, you cannot imagine the acute sensation of suffering at my heart, when I read the names of Mr. and Mrs. Dodge, at a hotel in Courtland Street. It was a third-rate hotel, and that circumstance convinced me of the truth of what I had heard, that they were short of funds and had need of my value, as *they* valued me; and that was by dollars and cents. I hastened with the paper to Mrs. Bruce. Her heart and hand were always open to every one in distress, and she always warmly sympathized with mine. It was impossible to tell how near the enemy was. He might have passed and repassed the house while we were sleeping. He might at that moment be waiting to pounce upon me if I ventured out of doors. I had never seen the husband of my young mistress, and therefore I could not distinguish him from any other stranger. A carriage was hastily ordered; and, closely veiled, I followed Mrs. Bruce, taking the baby again with me into exile. After various turnings and crossings, and returnings, the carriage stopped at the house of one of Mrs. Bruce's friends, where I was kindly received. Mrs. Bruce returned immediately, to instruct the domestics what to say if any one came to inquire for me.

It was lucky for me that the evening paper was not burned up before I had a chance to examine the list of arrivals. It was not long after Mrs. Bruce's return to her house, before several people came to inquire for me. One inquired for me, another asked for my daughter Ellen, and another said he had a letter from my grandmother, which he was requested to deliver in person.

They were told, "She *has* lived here, but she has left."

"How long ago?"

"I don't know, sir."

"Do you know where she went?"

"I do not, sir." And the door was closed.

This Mr. Dodge, who claimed me as his property, was originally a Yankee pedler in the south; then he became a merchant, and finally a slaveholder. He managed to get introduced into what was called the first society, and married Miss Emily Flint. A quarrel arose between him and her brother, and the brother cowhided him. This led to a family feud, and he proposed to remove to Virginia. Dr. Flint left him no property, and his own means had become circumscribed, while a wife and children depended upon him for support. Under these circumstances, it was very natural that he should make an effort to put me into his pocket.

I had a colored friend, a man from my native place, in whom I had the most implicit confidence. I sent for him, and told him that Mr. and Mrs. Dodge had arrived in New York. I proposed that he should call upon them to make inquiries about his friends at the south, with whom Dr. Flint's family were well acquainted. He thought there was no impropriety in his doing so, and he consented. He went to the hotel, and knocked at the door of Mr. Dodge's room, which was opened by the gentleman himself, who gruffly inquired, "What brought you here? How came you to know I was in the city?"

"Your arrival was published in the evening papers, sir; and I called to ask Mrs. Dodge about my friends at home. I didn't suppose it would give any offence."

"Where's that negro girl, that belongs to my wife?"

"What girl, sir?"

"You know well enough. I mean Linda, that ran away from Dr. Flint's plantation, some years ago. I dare say you've seen her, and know where she is."

"Yes, sir, I've seen her, and know where she is. She is out of your reach, sir."

"Tell me where she is, or bring her to me, and I will give her a chance to buy her freedom."

"I don't think it would be of any use, sir. I have heard her say she would go to the ends of the earth, rather than pay any man or woman for her freedom, because she thinks she has a right to it. Besides, she couldn't do it, if she would, for she has spent her earnings to educate her children."

This made Mr. Dodge very angry, and some high words passed between them. My friend was afraid to come where I was; but in the course of the day I received a note from him. I supposed they had not come from the south, in the winter, for a pleasure excursion; and now the nature of their business was very plain.

Mrs. Bruce came to me and entreated me to leave the city the next morning. She said her house was watched, and it was possible that some clew to me might be obtained. I refused to take her advice. She pleaded with an earnest tenderness, that ought to have moved me; but I was in a bitter, disheartened mood. I was weary of flying from pillar to post. I had been chased during half my life, and it seemed as if the chase was never to end. There I sat, in that great city, guiltless of crime, yet not daring to worship God in any of the churches. I heard the bells ringing for afternoon service, and, with contemptuous sarcasm, I said, "Will the preachers take for their text, 'Proclaim liberty to the captive, and the opening of prison doors to them that are bound'?[2] or will they preach from the text, 'Do unto others as ye would they should do unto you'?"[3] Oppressed Poles and Hungarians could find a safe refuge in that city; John Mitchell[4] was free to proclaim in the City Hall his desire for "a plantation well stocked with slaves"; but there I sat, an oppressed American, not daring to show my face. God forgive the black and bitter thoughts I indulged on that Sabbath day! The Scripture says, "Oppression makes even a wise man mad";[5] and I was not wise.

I had been told that Mr. Dodge said his wife had never signed away her right to my children, and if he could not get me, he would take them. This it was, more than any thing else, that roused such a tempest in my soul. Benjamin was with his uncle William in California, but my innocent young daughter had come to spend a vacation with me. I thought of what I had suffered in slavery at her age, and my heart was like a tiger's when a hunter tries to seize her young.

Dear Mrs. Bruce! I seem to see the expression of her face, as she turned away discouraged by my obstinate mood. Finding her expostulations[6] unavailing, she sent Ellen to entreat me. When ten o'clock in the evening arrived and Ellen had not returned, this watchful and unwearied friend became anxious. She came to us in a carriage, bringing a well-filled trunk for my journey—trusting that by this time I would listen to reason. I yielded to her, as I ought to have done before.

The next day, baby and I set out in a heavy snow storm, bound for New England again. I received letters from the City of Iniquity, addressed to me under an assumed name. In a few days one came from Mrs. Bruce, informing me that my new master was still searching for me, and that she intended to put an end to this persecution by buying my freedom. I felt grateful for the kindness that prompted this offer, but the idea was not so pleasant to me as might have been expected. The more my mind had become enlightened, the more difficult it was for me to consider myself an article of property; and to pay money to those who had so grievously oppressed me seemed like taking from my sufferings the glory of triumph. I

2. Isaiah 61:1.
3. Compare Matthew 7:12: "Therefore all things whatsoever ye would that men should do to you, do ye even so to them."

4. Irish nationalist and advocate of slavery.
5. Ecclesiastes 7:7.
6. Earnest reasoning designed to change someone's conduct.

wrote to Mrs. Bruce, thanking her, but saying that being sold from one owner to another seemed too much like slavery; that such a great obligation could not be easily cancelled; and that I preferred to go to my brother in California.

Without my knowledge, Mrs. Bruce employed a gentleman in New York to enter into negotiations with Mr. Dodge. He proposed to pay three hundred dollars down, if Mr. Dodge would sell me, and enter into obligations to relinquish all claim to me or my children forever after. He who called himself my master said he scorned so small an offer for such a valuable servant. The gentleman replied, "You can do as you choose, sir. If you reject this offer you will never get any thing; for the woman has friends who will convey her and her children out of the country."

Mr. Dodge concluded that "half a loaf was better than no bread," and he agreed to the proffered terms. By the next mail I received this brief letter from Mrs. Bruce: "I am rejoiced to tell you that the money for your freedom has been paid to Mr. Dodge. Come home to-morrow. I long to see you and my sweet babe."

My brain reeled as I read these lines. A gentleman near me said, "It's true; I have seen the bill of sale." "The bill of sale!" Those words struck me like a blow. So I was *sold* at last! A human being *sold* in the free city of New York! The bill of sale is on record, and future generations will learn from it that women were articles of traffic in New York, late in the nineteenth century of the Christian religion. It may hereafter prove a useful document to antiquaries, [7] who are seeking to measure the progress of civilization in the United States. I well know the value of that bit of paper; but much as I love freedom, I do not like to look upon it. I am deeply grateful to the generous friend who procured it, but I despise the miscreant who demanded payment for what never rightfully belonged to him or his.

I had objected to having my freedom bought, yet I must confess that when it was done I felt as if a heavy load had been lifted from my weary shoulders. When I rode home in the cars I was no longer afraid to unveil my face and look at people as they passed. I should have been glad to have met Daniel Dodge himself; to have had him seen me and known me, that he might have mourned over the untoward circumstances which compelled him to sell me for three hundred dollars.

When I reached home, the arms of my benefactress were thrown round me, and our tears mingled. As soon as she could speak, she said, "O Linda, I'm so glad it's all over! You wrote to me as if you thought you were going to be transferred from one owner to another. But I did not buy you for your services. I should have done just the same, if you had been going to sail for California tomorrow. I should, at least, have the satisfaction of knowing that you left me a free woman."

My heart was exceedingly full. I remembered how my poor father had tried to buy me, when I was a small child, and how he had been disappointed. I hoped his spirit was rejoicing over me now. I remembered how my good old grandmother had laid up her earnings to purchase me in later years, and how often her plans had been frustrated. How that faithful, lov-

7. Those who study rare, old things.

ing old heart would leap for joy, if she could look on me and my children now that we were free! My relatives had been foiled in all their efforts, but God had raised me up a friend among strangers, who had bestowed on me the precious, long-desired boon. Friend! It is a common word, often lightly used. Like other good and beautiful things, it may be tarnished by careless handling; but when I speak of Mrs. Bruce as my friend, the word is sacred.

My grandmother lived to rejoice in my freedom; but not long after, a letter came with a black seal. She had gone "where the wicked cease from troubling, and the weary are at rest." [8]

Time passed on, and a paper came to me from the south, containing an obituary notice of my uncle Phillip. It was the only case I ever knew of such an honor conferred upon a colored person. It was written by one of his friends, and contained these words: "Now that death has laid him low, they call him a good man and a useful citizen; but what are eulogies to the black man, when the world has faded from his vision? It does not require man's praise to obtain rest in God's kingdom." So they called a colored man a *citizen!* Strange words to be uttered in that region!

Reader, my story ends with freedom; not in the usual way, with marriage. I and my children are now free! We are as free from the power of slaveholders as are the white people of the north; and though that, according to my ideas, is not saying a great deal, it is a vast improvement in *my* condition. The dream of my life is not yet realized. I do not sit with my children in a home of my own. I still long for a hearthstone of my own, however humble. I wish it for my children's sake far more than for my own. But God so orders circumstances as to keep me with my friend Mrs. Bruce. Love, duty, gratitude, also bind me to her side. It is a privilege to serve her who pities my oppressed people, and who has bestowed the inestimable boon of freedom on me and my children.

It has been painful to me, in many ways, to recall the dreary years I passed in bondage. I would gladly forget them if I could. Yet the retrospection is not altogether without solace; for with those gloomy recollections come tender memories of my good old grandmother, like light, fleecy clouds floating over a dark and troubled sea.

1861

8. Job 3:17.

WILLIAM WELLS BROWN
1814?–1884

William Wells Brown is generally regarded as the first African American to achieve distinction in what the nineteenth century called *belles lettres*, or "fine letters." A number of black Americans contemporary with Brown, most notably Frederick Douglass, enjoyed popular success as journalists and orators. In addition to these forms of expression, however, Brown tried his hand at genres considered more prestigiously "literary," authoring the first novel, *Clotel; or, The President's Daughter* (1853) and the first drama, *The Escape; or, A Leap for Freedom* (1858), in African

American literature. Less well known but still remarkable works from Brown's pen include *Three Years in Europe* (1852), the first travel book by a black American, and two volumes of history, *The Black Man: His Antecedents, His Genius, and His Achievements* (1863) and *The Negro in the American Rebellion* (1867), the latter of which is the first military history of the African American in the United States. Brown was an antislavery lecturer and an activist long before he became a literary man. He saw *belles lettres* as a fresh and potent way to dramatize his case against slavery while promoting a sympathetic image of African Americans in both the United States and England. Brown's critics have sometimes judged his fiction and poetry overburdened by abolitionist propaganda and sentimentality, but few deny that he originated some of the most persistent and provocative character types and motifs in the African American narrative tradition.

William Wells Brown was born on a plantation near Lexington, Kentucky, the son of a white man who never acknowledged his fatherhood and a slave woman whose only name was Elizabeth. Light complexioned and quick witted, William spent his boyhood and teenage years mainly in St. Louis, Missouri, and its vicinity, working as a house servant, a field hand, a tavernkeeper's assistant, a printer's helper, an assistant in a medical office, and finally a handyman for James Walker— a Missouri slave trader with whom William made three trips up and down the Mississippi River between St. Louis and the New Orleans slave market. After a year's service to Walker, William returned to his master in the spring of 1832, only to learn that he was to be put up for sale. This news precipitated the slave's first escape attempt, which failed in part because he was determined to take his mother with him. William suffered the usual punishment for trying to run away—beatings, hard labor as a field hand, and sale. In the fall of 1833 he fell into the hands of owners who were so unwary as to take him on a family excursion to Cincinnati in the last weeks of the year. On New Year's Day, 1834, William made his escape from slavery, traveling by night alone in the cold from Cincinnati across Ohio to Cleveland. On his way, the fugitive was befriended by Mr. and Mrs. Wells Brown, a Quaker couple whose kindness the slave acknowledged by adding the names of his benefactor to his own.

After seizing his freedom, William Wells Brown worked for nine years as a steamboatman on Lake Erie and conductor for the Underground Railroad in Buffalo, New York. In 1843 Brown became a lecturing agent for the Western New York Anti-Slavery Society. Moving to Boston in 1847, Brown wrote his autobiography, *Narrative of William W. Brown, a Fugitive Slave*, which went through four American and five British editions before 1850, earning its author international fame. Brown's *Narrative* was exceeded in popularity and sales only by the *Narrative of the Life of Frederick Douglass, an American Slave*, which had appeared in 1845. The contrasts between Brown's self-portrait and that of Douglass are mirrored in the differences between the styles of the two men's narratives. Douglass's storytelling incorporates the rhetorical conventions of nineteenth-century platform oratory and the structure of Protestant conversion narratives to emphasize how Douglass had fashioned himself into an exemplary figure. Brown's modest, understated plain style, displaying few flourishes and little self-reflection, refuses to make great claims for the man himself. Instead, it is often the ordinary, the representative, and the nonheroic—even the antiheroic—that come to the fore in Brown's narrative of his life. Yet in Brown's willingness to focus on himself as a slave trickster and to explore the contradictions between a slave's survival ethic and the dominant morality of his time, we discover a striking brand of realism.

In the summer of 1849 Brown went abroad to attend the International Peace Congress in Paris and to encourage British support for the antislavery movement in the United States. Brown remained in England until 1854, delivering more than one thousand antislavery lectures and publishing *Three Years in Europe* and *Clotel* in London. *Clotel*, Brown's panoramic story of the fate of a mixed-race daughter of Thomas Jefferson, draws substantially on its author's personal experience in bondage as well as on the slave narrative and antislavery novel traditions. But in the development of the character of Clotel, Brown's book moves beyond the stereotypes and conventions of its time. While Clotel, like many a "tragic mulatta" in nineteenth-century American fiction, is distinguished by her beauty, her idealism, her barely traceable African ancestry, and her disappointments in love, she also proves herself an active and combative figure by the end of her story. Like many of his black literary contemporaries during the 1850s, Brown felt obliged to create characters that epitomized the ideals of aspiring African American men and women in order to educate an American readership that saw mostly the defamation of African American character in newspapers, magazines, and books. The real and the ideal maintain at best an uncertain balance in Brown's writing. But the tension between them and the problematic ways Brown tried to resolve them tell us much about the conflicting aesthetic and ideological agendas underlying early African American writing.

When Brown's friends purchased his freedom in 1854, he returned to the United States and continued agitating for abolitionism until the end of the Civil War. After the war, he practiced medicine in Boston and promoted temperance while researching and writing several significant books, among them *Clotelle; or, The Colored Heroine* (1867), a revision of *Clotel* that left Brown's heroine in charge of a school for the education of the freedmen and freedwomen at the end of the Civil War. In 1874 Brown produced his most comprehensive work of African American history, *The Rising Son; or, The Antecedents and Advancement of the Colored Race*, which contained biographical sketches of 110 prominent black Americans. In 1880 the last of Brown's books, a reminiscence of his life in slavery and a tough-minded report on conditions in the Reconstruction South, appeared with the curiously nostalgic title (for a one-time fugitive slave) of *My Southern Home*. Brown died at his home in Chelsea, a suburb of Boston, on November 6, 1884.

From Narrative of William W. Brown, a Fugitive Slave

Chapter V

My master[1] had family worship, night and morning. At night, the slaves were called in to attend; but in the mornings, they had to be at their work, and master did all the praying. My master and mistress were great lovers of mint julep, and every morning, a pitcherfull was made, of which they all partook freely, not excepting little master William. After drinking freely all round, they would have family worship, and then breakfast. I cannot say but I loved the julep as well as any of them, and during prayer was always careful to seat myself close to the table where it stood, so as to help myself when they were all busily engaged in their devotions. By the time prayer was over, I was about as happy as any of them. A sad accident happened one morning. In helping myself, and at the same time keeping an eye on

1. Dr. John Young, a St. Louis physician and plantation owner, owned Brown from his birth until 1834.

my old mistress, I accidentally let the pitcher fall upon the floor, breaking it in pieces, and spilling the contents. This was a bad affair for me; for as soon as prayer was over, I was taken and severely chastised.

My master's family consisted of himself, his wife, and their nephew, William Moore. He was taken into the family, when only a few weeks of age. His name being that of my own, mine was changed,[2] for the purpose of giving precedence to his, though I was his senior by ten or twelve years. The plantation being four miles from the city, I had to drive the family to church. I always dreaded the approach of the Sabbath; for, during service, I was obliged to stand by the horses in the hot broiling sun, or in the rain, just as it happened.

One Sabbath, as we were driving past the house of D. D. Page, a gentleman who owned a large baking establishment, as I was sitting upon the box of the carriage, which was very much elevated, I saw Mr. Page pursuing a slave around the yard, with a long whip, cutting him at every jump. The man soon escaped from the yard, and was followed by Mr. Page. They came running past us, and the slave perceiving that he would be overtaken, stopped suddenly, and Page stumbled over him, and falling on the stone pavement, fractured one of his legs, which crippled him for life. The same gentleman, but a short time previous, tied up a woman of his, by the name of Delphia, and whipped her nearly to death; yet he was a deacon in the Baptist church, in good and regular standing. Poor Delphia! I was well acquainted with her, and called to see her while upon her sick bed; and I shall never forget her appearance. She was a member of the same church with her master.

Soon after this, I was hired out to Mr. Walker; the same man whom I have mentioned as having carried a gang of slaves down the river, on the steamboat Enterprize. Seeing me in the capacity of steward on the boat, and thinking that I would make a good hand to take care of slaves, he determined to have me for that purpose; and finding that my master would not sell me, he hired me for the term of one year.

When I learned the fact of my having been hired to a negro speculator, or a "soul-driver" as they are generally called among slaves, no one can tell my emotions. Mr. Walker had offered a high price for me, as I afterwards learned, but I suppose my master was restrained from selling me by the fact that I was a near relative of his. On entering the service of Mr. Walker, I found that my opportunity of getting to a land of liberty was gone, at least for the time being. He had a gang of slaves in readiness to start for New Orleans, and in a few days we were on our journey. I am at a loss for language to express my feelings on that occasion. Although my master had told me that he had not sold me, and Mr. Walker had told me that he had not purchased me, I did not believe them; and not until I had been to New Orleans, and was on my return, did I believe that I was not sold.

There was on the boat a large room on the lower deck, in which the slaves were kept, men and women, promiscuously—all chained two and two, and a strict watch kept that they did not get loose; for cases have

2. To Sanford.

occurred in which slaves have got off their chains, and made their escape at landing-places, while the boats were taking in wood;—and with all our care, we lost one woman who had been taken from her husband and children, and having no desire to live without them, in the agony of her soul jumped overboard, and drowned herself. She was not chained.

It was almost impossible to keep that part of the boat clean.

On landing at Natchez,[3] the slaves were all carried to the slavepen, and there kept one week, during which time, several of them were sold. Mr. Walker fed his slaves well. We took on board, at St. Louis, several hundred pounds of bacon (smoked meat) and cornmeal, and his slaves were better fed than slaves generally were in Natchez, so far as my observation extended.

At the end of a week, we left for New Orleans, the place of our final destination, which we reached in two days. Here the slaves were placed in a negro-pen, where those who wished to purchase could call and examine them. The negro-pen is a small yard, surrounded by buildings, from fifteen to twenty feet wide, with the exception of a large gate with iron bars. The slaves are kept in the buildings during the night, and turned out into the yard during the day. After the best of the stock was sold at private sale at the pen, the balance were taken to the Exchange Coffee House Auction Rooms, kept by Isaac L. McCoy, and sold at public auction. After the sale of this lot of slaves, we left New Orleans for St. Louis.

From *Chapter VI*

On our arrival at St. Louis, I went to Dr. Young, and told him that I did not wish to live with Mr. Walker any longer. I was heart-sick at seeing my fellow-creatures bought and sold. But the Dr. had hired me for the year, and stay I must. Mr. Walker again commenced purchasing another gang of slaves. He bought a man of Colonel John O'Fallon, who resided in the suburbs of the city. This man had a wife and three children. As soon as the purchase was made, he was put in jail for safe keeping, until we should be ready to start for New Orleans. His wife visited him while there, several times, and several times when she went for that purpose was refused admittance.

In the course of eight or nine weeks Mr. Walker had his cargo of human flesh made up. There was in this lot a number of old men and women, some of them with gray locks. We left St. Louis in the steamboat Carlton, Captain Swan, bound for New Orleans. On our way down, and before we reached Rodney,[4] the place where we made our first stop, I had to prepare the old slaves for market. I was ordered to have the old men's whiskers shaved off, and the gray hairs plucked out where they were not too numerous, in which case he had a preparation of blacking to color it, and with a blacking-brush we would put it on. This was new business to me, and was performed in a room where the passengers could not see us. These slaves were also taught how old they were by Mr. Walker, and after going through

---

3. In Mississippi.   4. Also in Mississippi.

the blacking process, they looked ten or fifteen years younger; and I am sure that some of those who purchased slaves of Mr. Walker, were dreadfully cheated, especially in the ages of the slaves which they bought.

We landed at Rodney, and the slaves were driven to the pen in the back part of the village. Several were sold at this place, during our stay of four or five days, when we proceeded to Natchez. There we landed at night, and the gang were put in the warehouse until morning, when they were driven to the pen. As soon as the slaves are put in these pens, swarms of planters may be seen in and about them. They knew when Walker was expected, as he always had the time advertised beforehand when he would be in Rodney, Natchez, and New Orleans. These were the principal places where he offered his slaves for sale.

When at Natchez the second time, I saw a slave very cruelly whipped. He belonged to a Mr. Broadwell, a merchant who kept a store on the wharf. The slave's name was Lewis. I had known him several years, as he was formerly from St. Louis. We were expecting a steamboat down the river, in which we were to take passage for New Orleans. Mr. Walker sent me to the landing to watch for the boat, ordering me to inform him on its arrival. While there, I went into the store to see Lewis. I saw a slave in the store, and asked him where Lewis was. Said he, "They have got Lewis hanging between the heavens and the earth." I asked him what he meant by that. He told me to go into the warehouse and see. I went in, and found Lewis there. He was tied up to a beam, with his toes just touching the floor. As there was no one in the warehouse but himself, I inquired the reason of his being in that situation. He said Mr. Broadwell had sold his wife to a planter six miles from the city, and that he had been to visit her,—that he went in the night, expecting to return before daylight, and went without his master's permission. The patrol had taken him up before he reached his wife. He was put in jail, and his master had to pay for his catching and keeping, and that was what he was tied up for.

Just as he finished his story, Mr. Broadwell came in, and inquired what I was doing there. I knew not what to say, and while I was thinking what reply to make, he struck me over the head with the cowhide, the end of which struck me over my right eye, sinking deep into the flesh, leaving a scar which I carry to this day. Before I visited Lewis, he had received fifty lashes. Mr. Broadwell gave him fifty more after I came out, as I was afterwards informed by Lewis himself.

The next day we proceeded to New Orleans, and put the gang in the same negro-pen which we occupied before. In a short time, the planters came flocking to the pen to purchase slaves. Before the slaves were exhibited for sale, they were dressed and driven out into the yard. Some were set to dancing, some to jumping, some to singing, and some to playing cards. This was done to make them appear cheerful and happy. My business was to see that they were placed in those situations before the arrival of the purchasers, and I have often set them to dancing when their cheeks were wet with tears. As slaves were in good demand at that time, they were all soon disposed of, and we again set out for St. Louis.

On our arrival, Mr. Walker purchased a farm five or six miles from the city. He had no family, but made a housekeeper of one of his female slaves.

Poor Cynthia! I knew her well. She was a quadroon,[5] and one of the most beautiful women I ever saw. She was a native of St. Louis, and bore an irreproachable character for virtue and propriety of conduct. Mr. Walker bought her for the New Orleans market, and took her down with him on one of the trips that I made with him. Never shall I forget the circumstances of that voyage! On the first night that we were on board the steamboat, he directed me to put her into a state-room he had provided for her, apart from the other slaves. I had seen too much of the workings of slavery, not to know what this meant. I accordingly watched him into the stateroom, and listened to hear what passed between them. I heard him make his base offers, and her reject them. He told her that if she would accept his vile proposals, he would take her back with him to St. Louis, and establish her as his housekeeper at his farm. But if she persisted in rejecting them, he would sell her as a field hand on the worst plantation on the river. Neither threats nor bribes prevailed, however, and he retired, disappointed of his prey.

The next morning, poor Cynthia told me what had past, and bewailed her sad fate with floods of tears. I comforted and encouraged her all I could; but I foresaw but too well what the result must be. Without entering into any farther particulars, suffice it to say that Walker performed his part of the contract, at that time. He took her back to St. Louis, established her as his mistress and housekeeper at his farm, and before I left, he had two children by her. But, mark the end! Since I have been at the North, I have been credibly informed that Walker has been married, and, as a previous measure, sold poor Cynthia and her four children (she having had two more since I came away) into hopeless bondage!

He soon commenced purchasing to make up the third gang. We took steamboat, and went to Jefferson City, a town on the Missouri river. Here we landed, and took stage for the interior of the State. He bought a number of slaves as he passed the different farms and villages. After getting twenty-two or twenty-three men and women, we arrived at St. Charles, a village on the banks of the Missouri. Here he purchased a woman who had a child in her arms, appearing to be four or five weeks old.

We had been travelling by land for some days, and were in hopes to have found a boat at this place for St. Louis, but were disappointed. As no boat was expected for some days, we started for St. Louis by land. Mr. Walker had purchased two horses. He rode one, and I the other. The slaves were chained together, and we took up our line of march, Mr. Walker taking the lead, and I bringing up the rear. Though the distance was not more than twenty miles, we did not reach it the first day. The road was worse than any that I have ever travelled.

Soon after we left St. Charles, the young child grew very cross, and kept up a noise during the greater part of the day. Mr. Walker complained of its crying several times, and told the mother to stop the child's d——d noise, or he would. The woman tried to keep the child from crying, but could not. We put up at night with an acquaintance of Mr. Walker, and in the morning, just as we were about to start, the child again commenced crying.

5. A person who has one-quarter black ancestry.

Walker stepped up to her, and told her to give the child to him. The mother tremblingly obeyed. He took the child by one arm, as you would a cat by the leg, walked into the house, and said to the lady,

"Madam, I will make you a present of this little nigger; it keeps such a noise that I can't bear it."

"Thank you, sir," said the lady.

The mother, as soon as she saw that her child was to be left, ran up to Mr. Walker, and falling upon her knees begged him to let her have her child; she clung around his legs, and cried, "Oh, my child! my child! master, do let me have my child! oh, do, do, do. I will stop its crying, if you will only let me have it again." When I saw this woman crying for her child so piteously, a shudder,—a feeling akin to horror, shot through my frame. I have often since in imagination heard her crying for her child:—

O, master, let me stay to catch
 My baby's sobbing breath,
His little glassy eye to watch,
 And smooth his limbs in death,

And cover him with grass and leaf,
 Beneath the large oak tree:
It is not sullenness, but grief,—
 O, master, pity me!

The morn was chill—I spoke no word,
 But feared my babe might die,
And heard all day, or thought I heard,
 My little baby cry.

At noon, oh, how I ran and took
 My baby to my breast!
I lingered—and the long lash broke
 My sleeping infant's rest.

I worked till night—till darkest night,
 In torture and disgrace;
Went home and watched till morning light,
 To see my baby's face.

Then give me but one little hour—
 O! do not lash me so!
One little hour—one little hour—
 And gratefully I'll go.

Mr. Walker commanded her to return into the ranks with the other slaves. Women who had children were not chained, but those that had none were. As soon as her child was disposed of, she was chained in the gang.

The following song I have often heard the slaves sing, when about to be carried to the far south. It is said to have been composed by a slave.

See these poor souls from Africa
Transported to America;
We are stolen, and sold to Georgia,
Will you go along with me?
We are stolen, and sold to Georgia,
Come sound the jubilee!

See wives and husbands sold apart,
Their children's screams will break my heart;—
There's a better day a coming,
Will you go along with me?
There's a better day a coming,
Go sound the jubilee!

O, gracious Lord! when shall it be,
That we poor souls shall all be free;
Lord, break them slavery powers—
Will you go along with me?
Lord break them slavery powers,
Go sound the jubilee!

Dear Lord, dear Lord, when slavery'll cease,
Then we poor souls will have our peace;—
There's a better day a coming,
Will you go along with me?
There's a better day a coming,
Go sound the jubilee!"

We finally arrived at Mr. Walker's farm. He had a house built during our absence to put slaves in. It was a kind of domestic jail. The slaves were put in the jail at night, and worked on the farm during the day. They were kept here until the gang was completed, when we again started for New Orleans, on board the steamboat North America, Capt. Alexander Scott. We had a large number of slaves in this gang. One, by the name of Joe, Mr. Walker was training up to take my place, as my time was nearly out, and glad was I. We made our first stop at Vicksburg,[6] where we remained one week and sold several slaves.

Mr. Walker, though not a good master, had not flogged a slave since I had been with him, though he had threatened me. The slaves were kept in the pen, and he always put up at the best hotel, and kept his wines in his room, for the accommodation of those who called to negotiate with him for the purchase of slaves. One day while we were at Vicksburg, several gentlemen came to see him for this purpose, and as usual the wine was called for. I took the tray and started around with it, and having accidentally filled some of the glasses too full, the gentlemen spilled the wine on their clothes as they went to drink. Mr. Walker apologized to them for my carelessness, but looked at me as though he would see me again on this subject.

After the gentlemen had left the room, he asked me what I meant by my carelessness, and said that he would attend to me. The next morning, he

6. In Mississippi.

gave me a note to carry to the jailer, and a dollar in money to give to him. I suspected that all was not right, so I went down near the landing where I met with a sailor, and walking up to him, asked him if he would be so kind as to read the note for me. He read it over, and then looked at me. I asked him to tell me what was in it. Said he,

"They are going to give you hell."

"Why?" said I.

He said, "This is a note to have you whipped, and says that you have a dollar to pay for it."

He handed me back the note, and off I started. I knew not what to do, but was determined not to be whipped. I went up to the jail—took a look at it, and walked off again. As Mr. Walker was acquainted with the jailer, I feared that I should be found out if I did not go, and be treated in consequence of it still worse.

While I was meditating on the subject, I saw a colored man about my size walk up, and the thought struck me in a moment to send him with my note. I walked up to him, and asked him who he belonged to. He said he was a free man, and had been in the city but a short time. I told him I had a note to go into the jail, and get a trunk to carry to one of the steamboats; but was so busily engaged that I could not do it, although I had a dollar to pay for it. He asked me if I would not give him the job. I handed him the note and the dollar, and off he started for the jail.

I watched to see that he went in, and as soon as I saw the door close behind him, I walked around the corner, and took my station, intending to see how my friend looked when he came out. I had been there but a short time, when a colored man came around the corner, and said to another colored man with whom he was acquainted—

"They are giving a nigger scissors[7] in the jail."

"What for?" said the other. The man continued,

"A nigger came into the jail, and asked for the jailer. The jailer came out, and he handed him a note, and said he wanted to get a trunk. The jailer told him to go with him, and he would give him the trunk. So he took him into the room, and told the nigger to give up the dollar. He said a man had given him the dollar to pay for getting the trunk. But that lie would not answer. So they made him strip himself, and then they tied him down, and are now whipping him."

I stood by all the while listening to their talk, and soon found out that the person alluded to was my customer. I went into the street opposite the jail, and concealed myself in such a manner that I could not be seen by any one coming out. I had been there but a short time, when the young man made his appearance, and looked around for me. I, unobserved, came forth from my hiding-place, behind a pile of brick, and he pretty soon saw me and came up to me complaining bitterly, saying that I had played a trick upon him. I denied any knowledge of what the note contained, and asked him what they had done to him. He told me in substance what I heard the man tell who had come out of the jail.

"Yes," said he, "they whipped me and took my dollar, and gave me this note."

---

7. I.e., giving him a lashing.

He showed me the note which the jailer had given him, telling him to give it to his master. I told him I would give him fifty cents for it,—that being all the money I had. He gave it to me, and took his money. He had received twenty lashes on his bare back, with the negro-whip.

I took the note and started for the hotel where I had left Mr. Walker. Upon reaching the hotel, I handed it to a stranger whom I had not seen before, and requested him to read it to me. As near as I can recollect, it was as follows:—

> Dear Sir:—By your direction, I have given your boy twenty lashes. He is a very saucy boy, and tried to make me believe that he did not belong to you, and I put it on to him well for lying to me.
>
> > I remain,
> > Your obedient servant.

It is true that in most of the slave-holding cities, when a gentleman wishes his servants whipped, he can send him to the jail and have it done. Before I went in where Mr. Walker was, I wet my cheeks a little, as though I had been crying. He looked at me, and inquired what was the matter. I told him that I had never had such a whipping in my life, and handed him the note. He looked at it and laughed;—"and so you told him that you did not belong to me." "Yes, sir," said I. "I did not know that there was any harm in that." He told me I must behave myself, if I did not want to be whipped again.

This incident shows how it is that slavery makes its victims lying and mean; for which vices it afterwards reproaches them, and uses them as arguments to prove that they deserve no better fate. I have often, since my escape, deeply regretted the deception I practised upon this poor fellow; and I heartily desire that it may be, at some time or other, in my power to make him amends for his vicarious sufferings in my behalf.

* * *

1847

From Clotel; or, The President's Daughter

Chapter I. The Negro Sale

> Why stands she near the auction stand,
> That girl so young and fair?
> What brings her to this dismal place,
> Why stands she weeping there? [1]

With the growing population of slaves in the Southern States of America, there is a fearful increase of half whites, most of whose fathers are slave-owners, and their mothers slaves. Society does not frown upon the man who sits with his mulatto child upon his knee, whilst its mother stands a

---

1. Most of the verses that serve as epigraphs and conclusions to chapters in *Clotel* were taken from popular American antislavery poetry published, often anonymously, in the periodical press and in collections such as Brown's own *The Anti-Slavery Harp* (1848).

slave behind his chair. The late Henry Clay,[2] some years since, predicted that the abolition of negro slavery would be brought about by the amalgamation of the races. John Randolph,[3] a distinguished slaveholder of Virginia, and a prominent statesman, said in a speech in the legislature of his native state, that "the blood of the first American statesmen coursed through the veins of the slave of the South." In all the cities and towns of the slave states, the real negro, or clear black, does not amount to more than one in every four of the slave population. This fact is, of itself, the best evidence of the degraded and immoral condition of the relation of master and slave in the United States of America.

In all the slave states, the law says:—"Slaves shall be deemed, sold, taken, reputed, and adjudged in law to be chattels personal in the hands of their owners and possessors, and their executors, administrators and assigns, to all intents, constructions, and purposes whatsoever." A slave is one who is in the power of a master to whom he belongs. The master may sell him, dispose of his person, his industry, and his labour. He can do nothing, possess nothing, nor acquire anything, but what must belong to his master. The slave is entirely subject to the will of his master, who may correct and chastise him, though not with unusual rigour, or so as to maim and mutilate him, or expose him to the danger of loss of life, or to cause his death. The slave, to remain a slave, must be sensible that there is no appeal from his master. Where the slave is placed by law entirely under the control of the man who claims him, body and soul, as property, what else could be expected than the most depraved social condition? The marriage relation, the oldest and most sacred institution given to man by his Creator, is unknown and unrecognised in the slave laws of the United States. Would that we could say, that the moral and religious teaching in the slave states were better than the laws; but, alas! we cannot. A few years since, some slaveholders became a little uneasy in their minds about the rightfulness of permitting slaves to take to themselves husbands and wives, while they still had others living, and applied to their religious teachers for advice; and the following will show how this grave and important subject was treated:—

Is a servant, whose husband or wife has been sold by his or her master into a distant country, to be permitted to marry again?

The query was referred to a committee, who made the following report; which, after discussion, was adopted:—

That, in view of the circumstances in which servants in this country are placed, the committee are unanimous in the opinion, that it is better to permit servants thus circumstanced to take another husband or wife.

Such was the answer from a committee of the "Shiloh Baptist Association;" and instead of receiving light, those who asked the question were plunged into deeper darkness!

A similar question was put to the "Savannah River Association," and the

---

2. U.S. senator from Kentucky and leader of the Whig Party (1777–1852).

3. U.S. congressman and defender of states' rights (1773–1833).

answer, as the following will show, did not materially differ from the one we have already given:—

> Whether, in a case of involuntary separation, of such a character as to preclude all prospect of future intercourse, the parties ought to be allowed to marry again.

Answer—

> That such separation among persons situated as our slaves are, is civilly a separation by death; and they believe that, in the sight of God, it would be so viewed. To forbid second marriages in such cases would be to expose the parties, not only to stronger hardships and strong temptation, but to church-censure for acting in obedience to their masters, who cannot be expected to acquiesce in a regulation at variance with justice to the slaves, and to the spirit of that command which regulates marriage among Christians. The slaves are not free agents; and a dissolution by death is not more entirely without their consent, and beyond their control, than by such separation.

Although marriage, as the above indicates, is a matter which the slaveholders do not think is of any importance, or of any binding force with their slaves; yet it would be doing that degraded class an injustice, not to acknowledge that many of them do regard it as a sacred obligation, and show a willingness to obey the commands of God on this subject. Marriage is, indeed, the first and most important institution of human existence—the foundation of all civilisation and culture—the root of church and state. It is the most intimate covenant of heart formed among mankind; and for many persons the only relation in which they feel the true sentiments of humanity. It gives scope for every human virtue, since each of these is developed from the love and confidence which here predominate. It unites all which enobles and beautifies life,—sympathy, kindness of will and deed, gratitude, devotion, and every delicate, intimate feeling. As the only asylum for true education, it is the first and last sanctuary of human culture. As husband and wife through each other become conscious of complete humanity, and every human feeling, and every human virtue; so children, at their first awakening in the fond covenant of love between parents, both of whom are tenderly concerned for the same object, find an image of complete humanity leagued in free love. The spirit of love which prevails between them acts with creative power upon the young mind, and awakens every germ of goodness within it. This invisible and incalculable influence of parental life acts more upon the child than all the efforts of education, whether by means of instruction, precept, or exhortation. If this be a true picture of the vast influence for good of the institution of marriage, what must be the moral degradation of that people to whom marriage is denied? Not content with depriving them of all the higher and holier enjoyments of this relation, by degrading and darkening their souls, the slaveholder denies to his victim even that slight alleviation of his misery, which would result from the marriage relation being protected by law and public opinion. Such is the influence of slavery in the United States, that the ministers of religion, even in the so-called free states, are the mere echoes, instead of the correctors, of public sentiment.

We have thought it advisable to show that the present system of chattel slavery in America undermines the entire social condition of man, so as to prepare the reader for the following narrative of slave life, in that otherwise happy and prosperous country.

In all the large towns in the Southern States, there is a class of slaves who are permitted to hire their time of their owners, and for which they pay a high price. These are mulatto women, or quadroons, [4] as they are familiarly known, and are distinguished for their fascinating beauty. The handsomest usually pays the highest price for her time. Many of these women are the favourites of persons who furnish them with the means of paying their owners, and not a few are dressed in the most extravagant manner. Reader, when you take into consideration the fact, that amongst the slave population no safeguard is thrown around virtue, and no inducement held out to slave women to be chaste, you will not be surprised when we tell you that immorality and vice pervade the cities of the Southern States in a manner unknown in the cities and towns of the Northern States. Indeed most of the slave women have no higher aspiration than that of becoming the finely-dressed mistress of some white man. And at negro balls and parties, this class of women usually cut the greatest figure.

At the close of the year—the following advertisement appeared in a newspaper published in Richmond, the capital of the state of Virginia:—"Notice: Thirty-eight negroes will be offered for sale on Monday, November 10th, at twelve o'clock, being the entire stock of the late John Graves Esq. The negroes are in good condition, some of them very prime; among them are several mechanics, able-bodied field hands, plough-boys, and women with children at the breast, and some of them very prolific in their generating qualities, affording a rare opportunity to any one who wishes to raise a strong and healthy lot of servants for their own use. Also several mulatto girls of rare personal qualities: two of them very superior. Any gentleman or lady wishing to purchase, can take any of the above slaves on trial for a week, for which no charge will be made." Amongst the above slaves to be sold were Currer and her two daughters, Clotel and Althesa; the latter were the girls spoken of in the advertisement as "very superior." Currer was a bright mulatto, and of prepossessing appearance, though then nearly forty years of age. She had hired her time for more than twenty years, during which time she had lived in Richmond. In her younger days Currer had been the housekeeper of a young slaveholder; but of later years had been a laundress or washerwoman, and was considered to be a woman of great taste in getting up linen. The gentleman for whom she had kept house was Thomas Jefferson, [5] by whom she had two daughters. Jefferson being called to Washington to fill a government appointment, Currer was left behind, and thus she took herself to the business of washing, by which means she paid her master, Mr. Graves, and supported herself and two children. At the time of the decease of her master, Currer's daughters, Clotel and Althesa, were aged respectively sixteen and fourteen years, and both, like most of their own sex in America, were well grown. Currer early resolved to bring her daughters up as ladies, as she termed it, and therefore imposed little or no work upon them. As her daughters grew older, Currer had to pay a stipulated price for them; yet her notoriety as a laundress of the first class enabled her to put an extra price upon her charges, and thus she and her daughters lived in comparative luxury. To bring up Clotel and Althesa to attract attention, and especially at balls and parties, was the great aim of Currer. Although the term "negro ball" is applied to most of these gatherings, yet a majority of the attendants are often whites. Nearly all the negro parties in the cities and towns of the Southern States are made up of quadroon and mulatto girls, and white men. These are democratic gatherings, where gentlemen, shopkeepers, and their clerks, all appear upon terms of perfect equality. And there is a degree of gentility and decorum in these companies that is not surpassed by similar gatherings of white people in the Slave States. It was at one of these parties that Horatio Green, the son of a wealthy gentleman of Richmond, was first introduced to Clotel. The young man had just returned from college, and was in his twenty-second year. Clotel was sixteen, and was admitted by all to be the most beautiful girl, coloured or white, in the city. So attentive was the young man to the quadroon during the evening that it was noticed by all, and became a matter of general conversation; while Currer appeared delighted beyond measure at her daughter's conquest. From that evening, young Green became the favourite visitor at Currer's house. He soon promised to purchase Clotel, as speedily as it could be effected, and make her mistress of her own dwelling; and Currer looked forward with pride to the time when she should see her daughter emancipated and free. It was a beautiful moonlight night in August, when all who reside in tropical climes are eagerly gasping for a breath of fresh air, that Horatio Green was seated in the small garden behind Currer's cottage, with the object of his affections by his side. And it was here that Horatio drew from his pocket the newspaper, wet from the press, and read the advertisement for the sale of the slaves to which we have alluded; Currer and her two daughters being of the number. At the close of the evening's visit, and as the young man was leaving, he said to the girl, "You shall soon be free and your own mistress."

As might have been expected, the day of sale brought an unusual large number together to compete for the property to be sold. Farmers who make a business of raising slaves for the market were there; slave-traders and speculators were also numerously represented; and in the midst of this throng was one who felt a deeper interest in the result of the sale than any other of the bystanders; this was young Green. True to his promise, he was there with a blank bank check in his pocket, awaiting with impatience to enter the list as a bidder for the beautiful slave. The less valuable slaves were first placed upon the auction block, one after another, and sold to the highest bidder. Husbands and wives were separated with a degree of indifference that is unknown in any other relation of life, except that of slavery. Brothers and sisters were torn from each other; and mothers saw their children leave them for the last time on this earth.

It was late in the day, when the greatest number of persons were thought to be present, that Currer and her daughters were brought forward to the place of sale. Currer was first ordered to ascend the auction stand, which she did with a trembling step. The slave mother was sold to a trader. Althesa, the youngest, and who was scarcely less beautiful than her sister, was sold to the same trader for one thousand dollars. Clotel was the last, and, as was expected, commanded a higher price than any that had been offered for sale that day. The appearance of Clotel on the auction block created a deep sensation amongst the crowd. There she stood, with a complexion as white as most of those who were waiting with a wish to become her purchasers; her features as finely defined as any of her sex of pure Anglo-Saxon; her long black wavy hair done up in the neatest manner; her form tall and graceful, and her whole appearance indicating one superior to her position. The auctioneer commenced by saying, that "Miss Clotel had been reserved for the last, because she was the most valuable. How much, gentlemen? Real Albino, fit for a fancy girl for any one. She enjoys good health, and has a sweet temper. How much do you say?" "Five hundred dollars." "Only five hundred for such a girl as this? Gentlemen, she is worth a deal more than that sum; you certainly don't know the value of the article you are bidding upon. Here, gentlemen, I hold in my hand a paper certifying that she has a good moral character." "Seven hundred." "Ah, gentlemen, that is something like. This paper also states that she is very intelligent." "Eight hundred." "She is a devoted Christian, and perfectly trustworthy." "Nine hundred." "Nine fifty." "Ten." "Eleven." "Twelve hundred." Here the sale came to a dead stand. The auctioneer stopped, looked around, and began in a rough manner to relate some anecdotes relative to the sale of slaves, which, he said, had come under his own observation. At this juncture the scene was indeed strange. Laughing, joking, swearing, smoking, spitting, and talking kept up a continual hum and noise amongst the crowd; while the slave-girl stood with tears in her eyes, at one time looking towards her mother and sister, and at another towards the young man whom she hoped would become her purchaser. "The chastity of this girl is pure; she has never been from under her mother's care; she is a virtuous creature." "Thirteen." "Fourteen." "Fifteen." "Fifteen hundred dollars," cried the auctioneer, and the maiden was struck for that sum. This was a Southern auction, at which the bones, muscles, sinews, blood, and nerves of a young lady of sixteen were sold for five hundred dollars; her moral character for two hundred; her improved intellect for one hundred; her Christianity for three hundred; and her chastity and virtue for four hundred dollars more. And this, too, in a city thronged with churches, whose tall spires look like so many signals pointing to heaven, and whose ministers preach that slavery is a God-ordained institution!

What words can tell the inhumanity, the atrocity, and the immorality of that doctrine which, from exalted office, commends such a crime to the favour of enlightened and Christian people? What indignation from all the world is not due to the government and people who put forth all their strength and power to keep in existence such an institution? Nature abhors it; the age repels it; and Christianity needs all her meekness to forgive it.

Clotel was sold for fifteen hundred dollars, but her purchaser was Horatio Green. Thus closed a negro sale, at which two daughters of

Thomas Jefferson, the writer of the Declaration of American Independence, and one of the presidents of the great republic, were disposed of to the highest bidder!

> O God! my every heart-string cries,
> Dost thou these scenes behold
> In this our boasted Christian land,
> And must the truth be told?
>
> Blush, Christian, blush! for e'en the dark,
> Untutored heathen see
> Thy inconsistency; and, lo!
> They scorn thy God, and thee!

Chapter II. Going to the South

> My country, shall thy honoured name,
> Be as a bye-word through the world?
> Rouse! for, as if to blast thy fame,
> This keen reproach is at thee hurled;
> The banner that above thee waves,
> Is floating o'er three million slaves.

Dick Walker, the slave speculator, who had purchased Currer and Althesa, put them in prison until his gang was made up, and then, with his forty slaves, started for the New Orleans market. As many of the slaves had been brought up in Richmond, and had relations residing there, the slave trader determined to leave the city early in the morning, so as not to witness any of those scenes so common where slaves are separated from their relatives and friends, when about departing for the Southern market. This plan was successful, for not even Clotel, who had been every day at the prison to see her mother and sister, knew of their departure. A march of eight days through the interior of the state, and they arrived on the banks of the Ohio river, where they were all put on board a steamer, and then speedily sailed for the place of their destination.

Walker had already advertised in the New Orleans papers, that he would be there at a stated time with "a prime lot of able-bodied slaves ready for field service; together with a few extra ones, between the ages of fifteen and twenty-five." But, like most who make a business of buying and selling slaves for gain, he often bought some who were far advanced in years, and would always try to sell them for five or ten years younger than they actually were. Few persons can arrive at anything like the age of a negro, by mere observation, unless they are well acquainted with the race. Therefore the slavetrader very frequently carried out this deception with perfect impunity. After the steamer had left the wharf, and was fairly on the bosom of the Father of Waters,[6] Walker called his servant Pompey to him, and instructed him as to "getting the negroes ready for market." Amongst the forty negroes were several whose appearance indicated that they had seen some years, and had gone through some services. Their grey hair and whiskers at

6. The Mississippi River.

once pronounced them to be above the ages set down in the trader's advertisement. Pompey had long been with the trader, and knew his business; and if he did not take delight in discharging his duty, he did it with a degree of alacrity, so that he might receive the approbation of his master. "Pomp," as Walker usually called him, was of real negro blood, and would often say, when alluding to himself, "Dis nigger is no countefit; he is de genewine artekil." Pompey was of low stature, round face, and, like most of his race, had a set of teeth, which for whiteness and beauty could not be surpassed; his eyes large, lips thick, and hair short and woolly. Pompey had been with Walker so long, and had seen so much of the buying and selling of slaves, that he appeared perfectly indifferent to the heartrending scenes which daily occurred in his presence. It was on the second day of the steamer's voyage that Pompey selected five of the old slaves, took them into a room by themselves, and commenced preparing them for the market. "Well," said Pompey, addressing himself to the company, "I is de gentman dat is to get you ready, so dat you will bring marser a good price in de Orleans market. How old is you?" addressing himself to a man who, from appearance, was not less than forty. "If I live to see next corn-planting time I will either be forty-five or fifty-five, I don't know which." "Dat may be," replied Pompey; "But now you is only thirty years old; dat is what marser says you is to be." "I know I is more den dat," responded the man. "I knows nothing about dat," said Pompey; "but when you get in de market, an anybody axe you how old you is, an you tell 'em forty-five, marser will tie you up an gib you de whip like smoke. But if you tell 'em dat you is only thirty, den he wont." "Well den, I guess I will only be thirty when dey axe me," replied the chattel.

"What your name?" inquired Pompey. "Geemes," answered the man. "Oh, Uncle Jim, is it?" "Yes." "Den you must have off dem dare whiskers of yours, and when you get to Orleans you must grease dat face an make it look shiney." This was all said by Pompey in a manner which clearly showed that he knew what he was about. "How old is you?" asked Pompey of a tall, strong-looking man. "I was twenty-nine last potato-digging time," said the man. "What's your name?" "My name is Tobias, but dey call me 'Toby.'" "Well, Toby, or Mr. Tobias, if dat will suit you better, you is now twenty-three years old, an no more. Dus you hear dat?" "Yes," responded Toby. Pompey gave each to understand how old he was to be when asked by persons who wished to purchase, and then reported to his master that the "old boys" were all right. At eight o'clock on the evening of the third day, the lights of another steamer were seen in the distance, and apparently coming up very fast. This was a signal for a general commotion on the Patriot, and everything indicated that a steamboat race was at hand. Nothing can exceed the excitement attendant upon a steamboat on the Mississippi river. By the time the boats had reached Memphis, they were side by side, and each exerting itself to keep the ascendancy in point of speed. The night was clear, the moon shining brightly, and the boats so near to each other that the passengers were calling out from one boat to the other. On board the Patriot, the firemen were using oil, lard, butter, and even bacon, with the wood, for the purpose of raising the steam to its highest pitch. The blaze, mingled with the black smoke, showed plainly that the other boat was burning more than wood. The two boats soon locked, so that the hands of the boats were passing from vessel to vessel, and the wildest excitement prevailed throughout amongst both passengers and crew. At this moment the engineer of the Patriot was seen to fasten down the safety-valve, so that no steam should escape. This was, indeed, a dangerous resort. A few of the boat hands who saw what had taken place, left that end of the boat for more secure quarters.

The Patriot stopped to take in passengers, and still no steam was permitted to escape. At the starting of the boat cold water was forced into the boilers by the machinery, and, as might have been expected, one of the boilers immediately exploded. One dense fog of steam filled every part of the vessel, while shrieks, groans, and cries were heard on every hand. The saloons and cabins soon had the appearance of a hospital. By this time the boat had landed, and the Columbia, the other boat, had come alongside to render assistance to the disabled steamer. The killed and scalded (nineteen in number) were put on shore, and the Patriot, taken in tow by the Columbia, was soon again on its way.

It was now twelve o'clock at night, and instead of the passengers being asleep the majority were gambling in the saloons. Thousands of dollars change hands during a passage from Louisville or St. Louis to New Orleans on a Mississippi steamer, and many men, and even ladies, are completely ruined. "Go call my boy, steward," said Mr. Smith, as he took his cards one by one from the table. In a few moments a fine looking, bright-eyed mulatto boy, apparently about fifteen years of age, was standing by his master's side at the table. "I will see you, and five hundred dollars better," said Smith, as his servant Jerry approached the table. "What price do you set on that boy?" asked Johnson, as he took a roll of bills from his pocket. "He will bring a thousand dollars, any day, in the New Orleans market," replied Smith. "Then you bet the whole of the boy, do you?" "Yes." "I call you, then," said Johnson, at the same time spreading his cards out upon the table. "You have beat me," said Smith, as soon as he saw the cards. Jerry, who was standing on top of the table, with the bank notes and silver dollars round his feet, was now ordered to descend from the table. "You will not forget that you belong to me," said Johnson, as the young slave was stepping from the table to a chair. "No, sir," replied the chattel. "Now go back to your bed, and be up in time to-morrow morning to brush my clothes and clean my boots, do you hear?" "Yes, sir," responded Jerry, as he wiped the tears from his eyes.

Smith took from his pocket the bill of sale and handed it to Johnson; at the same time saying, "I claim the right of redeeming that boy, Mr. Johnson. My father gave him to me when I came of age, and I promised not to part with him." "Most certainly, sir, the boy shall be yours, whenever you hand me over a cool thousand," replied Johnson. The next morning, as the passengers were assembling in the breakfast saloons and upon the guards of the vessel, and the servants were seen running about waiting upon or looking for their masters, poor Jerry was entering his new master's state-room with his boots. "Who do you belong to?" said a gentleman to an old black man, who came along leading a fine dog that he had been feeding. "When I went to sleep last night, I belonged to Governor

Lucas; but I understand dat he is bin gambling all night, so I don't know who owns me dis morning." Such is the uncertainty of a slave's position. He goes to bed at night the property of the man with whom he has lived for years, and gets up in the morning the slave of some one whom he has never seen before! To behold five or six tables in a steamboat's cabin, with half-a-dozen men playing at cards, and money, pistols, bowie-knives, etc. all in confusion on the tables, is what may be seen at almost any time on the Mississippi river.

On the fourth day, while at Natchez,[7] taking in freight and passengers, Walker, who had been on shore to see some of his old customers, returned, accompanied by a tall, thin-faced man, dressed in black, with a white neck-cloth, which immediately proclaimed him to be a clergyman. "I vant a good, trusty woman for house service," said the stranger, as they entered the cabin where Walker's slaves were kept. "Here she is, and no mistake," replied the trader. "Stand up, Currer, my gal; here's a gentleman who wishes to see if you will suit him." Althesa clung to her mother's side, as the latter rose from her seat. "She is a rare cook, a good washer, and will suit you to a T, I am sure." "If you buy me, I hope you will buy my daughter too," said the woman, in rather an excited manner. "I only want one for my own use and would not need another," said the man in black, as he and the trader left the room. Walker and the parson went into the saloon, talked over the matter, the bill of sale was made out, the money paid over, and the clergyman left, with the understanding that the woman should be delivered to him at his house. It seemed as if poor Althesa would have wept herself to death, for the first two days after her mother had been torn from her side by the hand of the ruthless trafficker in human flesh. On the arrival of the boat at Baton Rouge, an additional number of passengers were taken on board; and, amongst them, several persons who had been attending the races. Gambling and drinking were now the order of the day. Just as the ladies and gentlemen were assembling at the suppertable, the report of a pistol was heard in the direction of the Social Hall, which caused great uneasiness to the ladies, and took the gentlemen to that part of the cabin. However, nothing serious had occurred. A man at one of the tables where they were gambling had been seen attempting to conceal a card in his sleeve, and one of the party seized his pistol and fired; but fortunately the barrel of the pistol was knocked up, just as it was about to be discharged, and the ball passed through the upper deck, instead of the man's head, as intended. Order was soon restored; all went on well the remainder of the night, and the next day, at ten o'clock, the boat arrived at New Orleans, and the passengers went to the hotels and the slaves to the market!

> Our eyes are yet on Afric's shores,
> Her thousand wrongs we still deplore;
> We see the grim slave trader there;
> We hear his fettered victim's prayer;
> And hasten to the sufferer's aid,
> Forgetful of *our own "slave trade."*

7. In Mississippi.

The Ocean "Pirate's" fiend-like form
Shall sink beneath the vengeance-storm;
His heart of steel shall quake before
The battle-din and havoc roar:
The knave shall die, the Law hath said,
While it protects *our own "slave trade."*

What earthly eye presumes to scan
The wily Proteus[8]-heart of man?—
What potent hand will e'er unroll
The mantled treachery of his soul!—
O where is he who hath surveyed
The horrors of *our own "slave trade?"*

There is an eye that wakes in light,
There is a hand of peerless might;
Which, soon or late, shall yet assail
And rend dissimulation's veil:
Which *will* unfold the masquerade
Which justifies *our own "slave trade."*

*   *   *

Chapter IV. The Quadroon's Home

How sweetly on the hill-side sleeps
    The sunlight with its quickening rays!
The verdant trees that crown the steeps,
    Grow greener in its quivering blaze.

About three miles from Richmond is a pleasant plain, with here and there a beautiful cottage surrounded by trees so as scarcely to be seen. Among them was one far retired from the public roads, and almost hidden among the trees. It was a perfect model of rural beauty. The piazzas[9] that surrounded it were covered with clematis and passion flower. The pride of China mixed its oriental looking foliage with the majestic magnolia, and the air was redolent with the fragrance of flowers, peeping out of every nook and nodding upon you with a most unexpected welcome. The tasteful hand of art had not learned to imitate the lavish beauty and harmonious disorder of nature, but they lived together in loving amity, and spoke in accordant tones. The gateway rose in a gothic arch, with graceful tracery in iron work, surmounted by a cross, round which fluttered and played the mountain fringe, that lightest and most fragile of vines. This cottage was hired by Horatio Green for Clotel, and the quadroon girl soon found herself in her new home.

The tenderness of Clotel's conscience, together with the care her mother had with her and the high value she placed upon virtue, required an outward marriage; though she well knew that a union with her proscribed race was unrecognised by law, and therefore the ceremony would give her no legal hold on Horatio's constancy. But her high poetic nature

8. A Greek god of the sea who has the power to as-   9. Large covered porches.
sume different shapes.

regarded reality rather than the semblance of things; and when he playfully
asked how she could keep him if he wished to run away, she replied, "If the
mutual love we have for each other, and the dictates of your own conscience do not cause you to remain my husband, and your affections fall
from me, I would not, if I could, hold you by a single fetter." It was indeed
a marriage sanctioned by heaven, although unrecognised on earth. There
the young couple lived secluded from the world, and passed their time as
happily as circumstances would permit. It was Clotel's wish that Horatio
should purchase her mother and sister, but the young man pleaded that he
was unable, owing to the fact that he had not come into possession of his
share of property, yet he promised that when he did, he would seek them
out and purchase them. Their first-born was named Mary, and her complexion was still lighter than her mother. Indeed she was not darker than
other white children. As the child grew older, it more and more resembled
its mother. The iris of her large dark eye had the melting mezzotinto,[1]
which remains the last vestige of African ancestry, and gives that plaintive
expression, so often observed, and so appropriate to that docile and injured
race. Clotel was still happier after the birth of her dear child; for Horatio, as
might have been expected, was often absent day and night with his friends
in the city, and the edicts of society had built up a wall of separation between the quadroon and them. Happy as Clotel was in Horatio's love, and
surrounded by an outward environment of beauty, so well adapted to her
poetic spirit, she felt these incidents with inexpressible pain. For herself
she cared but little; for she had found a sheltered home in Horatio's heart,
which the world might ridicule, but had no power to profane. But when
she looked at her beloved Mary, and reflected upon the unavoidable and
dangerous position which the tyranny of society had awarded her, her soul
was filled with anguish. The rare loveliness of the child increased daily,
and was evidently ripening into most marvellous beauty. The father
seemed to rejoice in it with unmingled pride; but in the deep tenderness of
the mother's eye, there was an indwelling sadness that spoke of anxious
thoughts and fearful foreboding. Clotel now urged Horatio to remove to
France or England, where both her and her child would be free, and where
colour was not a crime. This request excited but little opposition, and was
so attractive to his imagination, that he might have overcome all intervening obstacles, had not "a change come over the spirit of his dreams."[2] He
still loved Clotel; but he was now becoming engaged in political and other
affairs which kept him oftener and longer from the young mother; and ambition to become a statesman was slowly gaining the ascendancy over him.

Among those on whom Horatio's political success most depended was a
very popular and wealthy man, who had an only daughter. His visits to the
house were at first purely of a political nature; but the young lady was pleasing, and he fancied he discovered in her a sort of timid preference for himself. This excited his vanity, and awakened thoughts of the great worldly
advantages connected with a union. Reminiscences of his first love kept

---

1. A delicate half-tint.
2. Compare Lord Byron's *The Dream* (stanza 3,
line 75): "A change came o'er the spirit of my
dream."

these vague ideas in check for several months; for with it was associated the idea of restraint. Moreover, Gertrude, though inferior in beauty, was yet a pretty contrast to her rival. Her light hair fell in silken ringlets down her shoulders, her blue eyes were gentle though inexpressive, and her healthy cheeks were like opening rosebuds. He had already become accustomed to the dangerous experiment of resisting his own inward convictions; and this new impulse to ambition, combined with the strong temptation of variety in love, met the ardent young man weakened in moral principle, and un-fettered by laws of the land. The change wrought upon him was soon no-ticed by Clotel.

[Currer becomes a cook in the home of John Peck, a transplanted Connecticut clergyman turned slaveholder. The courtship of Peck's antislavery daughter, Geor-giana, by Mr. Carlton, a freethinker, arouses much debate about abolition among the principal white characters. Meanwhile Horatio discards Clotel and Mary for marriage to a white woman. Although initially purchased by a New Orleans bank teller, Althesa wins the love of a white man, Henry Morton, who buys, frees, and marries her.]

Chapter XV. To-Day a Mistress, To-Morrow a Slave

> I promised thee a sister tale
> Of man's perfidious cruelty;
> Come, then, and hear what cruel wrong
> Befel the dark ladie.
> —COLERIDGE[3]

Let us return for a moment to the home of Clotel. While she was passing lonely and dreary hours with none but her darling child, Horatio Green was trying to find relief in that insidious enemy of man, the intoxicating cup. Defeated in politics, forsaken in love by his wife, he seemed to have lost all principle of honour, and was ready to nerve himself up to any deed, no matter how unprincipled. Clotel's existence was now well known to Horatio's wife, and both her and her father demanded that the beautiful quadroon and her child should be sold and sent out of the state. To this proposition he at first turned a deaf ear; but when he saw that his wife was about to return to her father's roof, he consented to leave the matter in the hands of his father-in-law. The result was, that Clotel was immediately sold to the slavetrader, Walker, who, a few years previous, had taken her mother and sister to the far South. But, as if to make her husband drink of the cup of humiliation to its very dregs, Mrs. Green resolved to take his child under her own roof for a servant. Mary was, therefore, put to the meanest work that could be found, and although only ten years of age, she was often com-pelled to perform labour, which, under ordinary circumstances, would have been thought too hard for one much older. One condition of the sale of Clotel to Walker was, that she should be taken out of the state, which was accordingly done. Most quadroon women who are taken to the lower countries to be sold are either purchased by gentlemen for their own use,

3. Samuel Taylor Coleridge's *Introduction to the Tale of the Dark Ladie* (1799).

or sold for waiting-maids; and Clotel, like her sister, was fortunate enough to be bought for the latter purpose. The town of Vicksburgh stands on the left bank of the Mississippi, and is noted for the severity with which slaves are treated. It was here that Clotel was sold to Mr. James French, a merchant.

Mrs. French was severe in the extreme to her servants. Well dressed, but scantily fed, and overworked were all who found a home with her. The quadroon had been in her new home but a short time ere she found that her situation was far different from what it was in Virginia. What social virtues are possible in a society of which injustice is the primary characteristic? in a society which is divided into two classes, masters and slaves? Every married woman in the far South looks upon her husband as unfaithful, and regards every quadroon servant as a rival. Clotel had been with her new mistress but a few days, when she was ordered to cut off her long hair. The negro, constitutionally, is fond of dress and outward appearance. He that has short, woolly hair, combs it and oils it to death. He that has long hair, would sooner have his teeth drawn than lose it. However painful it was to the quadroon, she was soon seen with her hair cut as short as any of the full-blooded negroes in the dwelling.

Even with her short hair, Clotel was handsome. Her life had been a secluded one, and though now nearly thirty years of age, she was still beautiful. At her short hair, the other servants laughed, "Miss Clo needn't strut round so big, she got short nappy har well as I," said Nell, with a broad grin that showed her teeth. "She tinks she white, when she come here wid dat long har of hers," replied Mill. "Yes," continued Nell; "missus make her take down her wool so she no put it up to-day."

The fairness of Clotel's complexion was regarded with envy as well by the other servants as by the mistress herself. This is one of the hard features of slavery. To-day the woman is mistress of her own cottage; to-morrow she is sold to one who aims to make her life as intolerable as possible. And be it remembered, that the house servant has the best situation which a slave can occupy. Some American writers have tried to make the world believe that the condition of the labouring classes of England is as bad as the slaves of the United States.

The English labourer may be oppressed, he may be cheated, defrauded, swindled, and even starved; but it is not slavery under which he groans. He cannot be sold; in point of law he is equal to the prime minister. "It is easy to captivate the unthinking and the prejudiced, by eloquent declamation about the oppression of English operatives being worse than that of American slaves, and by exaggerating the wrongs on one side and hiding them on the other. But all informed and reflecting minds, knowing that bad as are the social evils of England, those of Slavery are immeasurably worse." But the degradation and harsh treatment that Clotel experienced in her new home was nothing compared with the grief she underwent at being separated from her dear child. Taken from her without scarcely a moment's warning, she knew not what had become of her. The deep and heartfelt grief of Clotel was soon perceived by her owners, and fearing that her refusal to take food would cause her death, they resolved to sell her. Mr. French found no difficulty in getting a purchaser for the quadroon woman, for such are usually the most marketable kind of property. Clotel was sold at private sale to a young man for a housekeeper; but even he had missed his aim.

[On the death of Rev. Peck, Georgiana marries Carlton and establishes on their plantation "a system of gradual emancipation" that includes cash bonuses for superior work. Currer dies from yellow fever.]

Chapter XIX. Escape of Clotel

The fetters galled my weary soul—
A soul that seemed but thrown away:
I spurned the tyrant's base control,
Resolved at least the man to play.

No country has produced so much heroism in so short a time, connected with escapes from peril and oppression, as has occurred in the United States among fugitive slaves, many of whom show great shrewdness in their endeavours to escape from this land of bondage. A slave was one day seen passing on the high road from a border town in the interior of the state of Virginia to the Ohio river. The man had neither hat upon his head or coat upon his back. He was driving before him a very nice fat pig, and appeared to all who saw him to be a labourer employed on an adjoining farm. "No negro is permitted to go at large in the Slave States without a written pass from his or her master, except on business in the neighbourhood." "Where do you live, my boy?" asked a white man of the slave, as he passed a white house with green blinds. "Jist up de road, sir," was the answer. "That's a fine pig." "Yes, sir, marser like dis choat[4] berry much." And the negro drove on as if he was in great haste. In this way he and the pig travelled more than fifty miles before they reached the Ohio river. Once at the river they crossed over; the pig was sold; and nine days after the runaway slave passed over the Niagara river, and, for the first time in his life, breathed the air of freedom. A few weeks later, and, on the same road, two slaves were seen passing; one was on horseback, the other was walking before him with his arms tightly bound, and a long rope leading from the man on foot to the one on horseback. "Oh, ho, that's a runaway rascal, I suppose," said a farmer, who met them on the road. "Yes, sir, he bin runaway, and I got him fast. Marser will tan his jacket for him nicely when he gets him." "You are a trustworthy fellow, I imagine," continued the farmer. "Oh yes, sir; marser puts a heap of confidence in dis nigger." And the slaves travelled on. When the one on foot was fatigued they would change positions, the other being tied and driven on foot. This they called "ride and tie." After a journey of more than two hundred miles they reached the Ohio river, turned the horse loose, told him to go home, and proceeded on their way to Canada. However they were not to have it all their own way. There are men in the Free States, and especially in the states adjacent to the Slave States, who make their living by catching the runaway slave, and returning him for the reward that may be offered. As the two slaves above

4. Or shoat, a young hog.

mentioned were travelling on towards the land of freedom, led by the North Star, they were set upon by four of these slave-catchers, and one of them unfortunately captured. The other escaped. The captured fugitive was put under the torture, and compelled to reveal the name of his owner and his place of residence. Filled with delight, the kidnappers started back with their victim. Overjoyed with the prospect of receiving a large reward, they gave themselves up on the third night to pleasure. They put up at an inn. The negro was chained to the bed-post, in the same room with his captors. At dead of night, when all was still, the slave arose from the floor upon which he had been lying, looked around, and saw that the white men were fast asleep. The brandy punch had done its work. With palpitating heart and trembling limbs he viewed his position. The door was fast, but the warm weather had compelled them to leave the window open. If he could but get his chains off, he might escape through the window to the piazza, and reach the ground by one of the posts that supported the piazza. The sleeper's clothes hung upon chairs by the bedside; the slave thought of the padlock key, examined the pockets and found it. The chains were soon off, and the negro stealthily making his way to the window: he stopped and said to himself, "These men are villains, they are enemies to all who like me are trying to be free. Then why not I teach them a lesson?" He then undressed himself, took the clothes of one of the men, dressed himself in them, and escaped through the window, and, a moment more, he was on the high road to Canada. Fifteen days later, and the writer of this gave him a passage across Lake Erie, and saw him safe in her Britannic Majesty's dominions.

We have seen Clotel sold to Mr. French in Vicksburgh, her hair cut short, and everything done to make her realise her position as a servant. Then we have seen her re-sold, because her owners feared she would die through grief. As yet her new purchaser treated her with respectful gentleness, and sought to win her favour by flattery and presents, knowing that whatever he gave her he could take back again. But she dreaded every moment lest the scene should change, and trembled at the sound of every footfall. At every interview with her new master Clotel stoutly maintained that she had left a husband in Virginia, and would never think of taking another. The gold watch and chain, and other glittering presents which he purchased for her, were all laid aside by the quadroon, as if they were of no value to her. In the same house with her was another servant, a man, who had from time to time hired himself from his master. William was his name. He could feel for Clotel, for he, like her, had been separated from near and dear relatives, and often tried to console the poor woman. One day the quadroon observed to him that her hair was growing out again. "Yes," replied William, "you look a good deal like a man with your short hair." "Oh," rejoined she, "I have often been told that I would make a better looking man than a woman. If I had the money," continued she, "I would bid farewell to this place." In a moment more she feared that she had said too much, and smilingly remarked, "I am always talking nonsense." William was a tall, full-bodied negro, whose very countenance beamed with intelligence. Being a mechanic, he had, by his own industry, made more than what he paid his owner; this he laid aside, with the hope that some day he might get enough to purchase his freedom. He had in his chest one hundred and fifty dollars. His was a heart that felt for others, and he had again and again wiped the tears from his eyes as he heard the story of Clotel as related by herself. "If she can get free with a little money, why not give her what I have?" thought he, and then he resolved to do it. An hour after, he came into the quadroon's room, and laid the money in her lap, and said, "There, Miss Clotel, you said if you had the means you would leave this place; there is money enough to take you to England, where you will be free. You are much fairer than many of the white women of the South, and can easily pass for a free white lady." At first Clotel feared that it was a plan by which the negro wished to try her fidelity to her owner; but she was soon convinced by his earnest manner, and the deep feeling with which he spoke, that he was honest. "I will take the money only on one condition," said she; "and that is, that I effect your escape as well as my own." "How can that be done?" he inquired. "I will assume the disguise of a gentleman and you that of a servant, and we will take passage on a steamboat and go to Cincinnati, and thence to Canada."[5] Here William put in several objections to the plan. He feared detection, and he well knew that, when a slave is once caught when attempting to escape, if returned is sure to be worse treated than before. However, Clotel satisfied him that the plan could be carried out if he would only play his part.

The resolution was taken, the clothes for her disguise procured, and before night everything was in readiness for their departure. That night Mr. Cooper, their master, was to attend a party, and this was their opportunity. William went to the wharf to look out for a boat, and had scarcely reached the landing ere he heard the puffing of a steamer. He returned and reported the fact. Clotel had already packed her trunk, and had only to dress and all was ready. In less than an hour they were on board the boat. Under the assumed name of "Mr. Johnson," Clotel went to the clerk's office and took a private state room for herself, and paid her own and servant's fare. Besides being attired in a neat suit of black, she had a white silk handkerchief tied round her chin, as if she was an invalid. A pair of green glasses covered her eyes; and fearing that she would be talked to too much and thus render her liable to be detected, she assumed to be very ill. On the other hand, William was playing his part well in the servants' hall; he was talking loudly of his master's wealth. Nothing appeared as good on the boat as in his master's fine mansion. "I don't like dees steamboats no how," said William; "I hope when marser goes on a journey agin he will take de carriage and de hosses." Mr. Johnson (for such was the name by which Clotel now went) remained in his room, to avoid, as far as possible, conversation with others. After a passage of seven days they arrived at Louisville, and put up at Gough's Hotel. Here they had to await the departure of another boat for the North. They were now in their most critical position. They were still in a slave state, and John C. Calhoun,[6] a distinguished slave-owner, was a guest at this hotel. They feared, also, that trouble would attend their attempt to leave this place for the North, as all persons taking negroes with

---

5. The escape of Clotel and William is based on the actual escape of Ellen and William Craft from Georgia in 1848.

6. U.S. senator from South Carolina and a leading proponent of states' rights (1782–1850).

them have to give bail that such negroes are not runaway slaves. The law upon this point is very stringent: all steamboats and other public convey-ances are liable to a fine for every slave that escapes by them, besides pay-ing the full value for the slave. After a delay of four hours, Mr. Johnson and servant took passage on the steamer Rodolph, for Pittsburgh. It is usual, before the departure of the boats, for an officer to examine every part of the vessel to see that no slave secretes himself on board. "Where are you going?" asked the officer of William, as he was doing his duty on this occa-sion. "I am going with marser," was the quick reply. "Who is your master?" "Mr. Johnson, sir, a gentleman in the cabin." "You must take him to the office and satisfy that captain that all is right, or you can't go on this boat." William informed his master what the officer had said. The boat was on the eve of going, and no time could be lost, yet they knew not what to do. At last they went to the office, and Mr. Johnson, addressing the captain, said, "I am informed that my boy can't go with me unless I give security that he belongs to me." "Yes," replied the captain, "that is the law." "A very strange law indeed," rejoined Mr. Johnson, "that one can't take his property with him." After a conversation of some minutes, and a plea on the part of John-son that he did not wish to be delayed owing to his illness, they were per-mitted to take their passage without farther trouble, and the boat was soon on its way up the river. The fugitives had now passed the Rubicon,[7] and the next place at which they would land would be in a Free State. Clotel called William to her room, and said to him, "We are now free, you can go on your way to Canada, and I shall go to Virginia in search of my daugh-ter." The announcement that she was going to risk her liberty in a Slave State was unwelcome news to William. With all the eloquence he could command, he tried to persuade Clotel that she could not escape detection, and was only throwing her freedom away. But she had counted the cost, and made up her mind for the worst. In return for the money he had fur-nished, she had secured for him his liberty, and their engagement was at an end.

After a quick passage the fugitives arrived at Cincinnati, and there sepa-rated. William proceeded on his way to Canada, and Clotel again resumed her own apparel, and prepared to start in search of her child. As might have been expected, the escape of those two valuable slaves created no little sen-sation in Vicksburgh. Advertisements and messages were sent in every di-rection in which the fugitives were thought to have gone. It was soon, however, known that they had left the town as master and servant; and many were the communications which appeared in the newspapers, in which the writers thought, or pretended, that they had seen the slaves in their disguise. One was to the effect that they had gone off in a chaise; one as master, and the other as servant. But the most probable was an account given by a correspondent of one of the Southern newspapers, who hap-pened to be a passenger in the same steamer in which the slaves escaped, and which we here give:—

　　One bright starlight night, in the month of December last, I found myself in the cabin of the steamer Rodolph, then lying in the port of

7. Figuratively, the point of no turning back.

Vicksburgh, and bound to Louisville. I had gone early on board, in order to select a good berth, and having got tired of reading the papers, amused myself with watching the appearance of the passengers as they dropped in, one after another, and I being a believer in physiognomy,[8] formed my own opinion of their characters.

The second bell rang, and as I yawningly returned my watch to my pocket, my attention was attracted by the appearance of a young man who entered the cabin supported by his servant, a strapping negro.

The man was bundled up in a capacious overcoat; his face was bandaged with a white handkerchief, and its expression entirely hid by a pair of enormous spectacles.

There was something so mysterious and unusual about the young man as he sat restless in the corner, that curiosity led me to observe him more closely.

He appeared anxious to avoid notice, and before the steamer had fairly left the wharf, requested, in a low, womanly voice, to be shown his berth, as he was an invalid, and must retire early: his name he gave as Mr. Johnson. His servant was called, and he was put quietly to bed. I paced the deck until Tybee light grew dim in the distance, and then went to my berth.

I awoke in the morning with the sun shining in my face; we were then just passing St. Helena. It was a mild beautiful morning, and most of the passengers were on deck, enjoying the freshness of the air, and stimulating their appetites for breakfast. Mr. Johnson soon made his appearance, arrayed as on the night before, and took his seat quietly upon the guard of the boat.

From the better opportunity afforded by daylight, I found that he was a slight built, apparently handsome young man, with black hair and eyes, and of a darkness of complexion that betokened Spanish extraction. Any notice from others seemed painful to him; so to satisfy my curiosity, I questioned his servant, who was standing near, and gained the following information.

His master was an invalid—he had suffered for a long time under a complication of diseases, that had baffled the skill of the best physicians in Mississippi, he was now suffering principally with the "rheumatism," and he was scarcely able to walk or help himself in any way. He came from Vicksburgh, and was now on his way to Philadelphia, at which place resided his uncle, a celebrated physician, and through whose means he hoped to be restored to perfect health.

This information, communicated in a bold, off-hand manner, enlisted my sympathies for the sufferer, although it occurred to me that he walked rather too gingerly for a person afflicted with so many ailments.

After thanking Clotel for the great service she had done him in bringing him out of slavery, William bade her farewell. The prejudice that exists in the Free States against coloured persons, on account of their colour, is attributable solely to the influence of slavery, and is but another form of slav-

---

8. The practice of judging personality and mental ability by observing facial characteristics.

ery itself. And even the slave who escapes from the Southern plantations, is surprised when he reaches the North, at the amount and withering influence of this prejudice. William applied at the railway station for a ticket for the train going to Sandusky, and was told that if he went by that train he would have to ride in the luggage-van. "Why?" asked the astonished negro. "We don't send a Jim Crow carriage but once a day, and that went this morning." The "Jim Crow" carriage is the one in which the blacks have to ride. Slavery is a school in which its victims learn much shrewdness, and William had been an apt scholar. Without asking any more questions, the negro took his seat in one of the first-class carriages. He was soon seen and ordered out. Afraid to remain in the town longer, he resolved to go by that train; and consequently seated himself on a goods' box in the luggage-van. The train started at its proper time, and all went on well. Just before arriving at the end of the journey, the conductor called on William for his ticket. "I have none," was the reply. "Well, then, you can pay your fare to me," said the officer. "How much is it?" asked the black man. "Two dollars." "What do you charge those in the passenger-carriage?" "Two dollars." "And do you charge me the same as you do those who ride in the best carriages?" asked the negro. "Yes," was the answer. "I shan't pay it," returned the man. "You black scamp, do you think you can ride on this road without paying your fare?" "No, I don't want to ride for nothing; I only want to pay what's right." "Well, launch out two dollars, and that's right." "No, I shan't; I will pay what I ought, and won't pay any more." "Come, come, nigger, your fare and be done with it," said the conductor, in a manner that is never used except by Americans to blacks. "I won't pay you two dollars, and that enough," said William. "Well, as you have come all the way in the luggage-van, pay me a dollar and a half and you may go." "I shan't do any such thing." "Don't you mean to pay for riding?" "Yes, but I won't pay a dollar and a half for riding up here in the freight-van. If you had let me come in the carriage where others ride, I would have paid you two dollars." "Where were you raised? You seem to think yourself as good as white folks." "I want nothing more than my rights." "Well, give me a dollar, and I will let you off." "No, sir, I shan't do it." "What do you mean to do then—don't you wish to pay anything?" "Yes, sir, I want to pay you the full price." "What do you mean by full price?" "What do you charge per hundred-weight for goods?" inquired the negro with a degree of gravity that would have astonished Diogenes[9] himself. "A quarter of a dollar per hundred," answered the conductor. "I weigh just one hundred and fifty pounds," returned William, "and will pay you three eighths of a dollar." "Do you expect that you will pay only thirty-seven cents for your ride?" "This, sir, is your own price. I came in a luggage-van, and I'll pay for luggage." After a vain effort to get the negro to pay more, the conductor took the thirty-seven cents, and noted in his cash-book, "Received for one hundred and fifty pounds of luggage, thirty-seven cents." This, reader, is no fiction; it actually occurred in the railway above described.

Thomas Corwin,[1] a member of the American Congress, is one of the blackest white men in the United States. He was once on his way to Con-

---

9. Greek philosopher (d. c. 320 B.C.).
1. U.S. congressman and senator from Ohio (1794–1865).

gress, and took passage in one of the Ohio river steamers. As he came just at the dinner hour, he immediately went into the dining saloon, and took his seat at the table. A gentleman with his whole party of five ladies at once left the table. "Where is the captain," cried the man in an angry tone. The captain soon appeared, and it was sometime before he could satisfy the old gent. that Governor Corwin was not a nigger. The newspapers often have notices of mistakes made by innkeepers and others who undertake to accommodate the public, one of which we give below.

On the 6th inst., the Hon. Daniel Webster and family entered Edgartown,[2] on a visit for health and recreation. Arriving at the hotel, without alighting from the coach, the landlord was sent for to see if suitable accommodation could be had. That dignitary appearing, and surveying Mr. Webster, while the hon. senator addressed him, seemed woefully to mistake the dark features of the traveller as he sat back in the corner of the carriage, and to suppose him a *coloured man*, particularly as there were two coloured servants of Mr. W. outside. So he promptly declared that there was no room for him and his family, and he could not be accommodated there—at the same time suggesting that he might perhaps find accommodation at some of the huts "up back," to which he pointed. So deeply did the prejudice of looks possess him, that he appeared not to notice that the stranger introduced himself to him as Daniel Webster, or to be so ignorant as not to have heard of such a personage; and turning away, he expressed to the driver his astonishment that he should bring *black* people there for *him* to take in. It was not till he had been repeatedly assured and made to understand that the said Daniel Webster was a real live senator of the United States, that he perceived his awkward mistake and the distinguished honour which he and his house were so near missing.

In most of the Free States, the coloured people are disfranchised on account of their colour. The following scene, which we take from a newspaper in the state of Ohio, will give some idea of the extent to which this prejudice is carried.

The whole of Thursday last was occupied by the Court of Common Pleas for this county in trying to find out whether one Thomas West was of the VOTING COLOUR, as some had very *constitutional doubts* as to whether his colour was orthodox, and whether his hair was of the official crisp! Was it not a dignified business? Four profound judges, four acute lawyers, twelve grave jurors, and I don't know how many venerable witnesses, making in all about thirty men, perhaps, all engaged in the profound, laborious, and illustrious business, of finding out whether a man who pays tax, works on the road, and is an industrious farmer, has been born according to the republican, Christian constitution of Ohio—so that he can vote! And they wisely, gravely, and "JUDGMATICALLY" decided that he should not vote! What wisdom—what research it must have required to evolve this truth! It was left for the Court of Common Pleas for Columbian county, Ohio, in the United States of North America, to find out what Solomon[3] never dreamed

2. On the island of Martha's Vineyard, Massachusetts. Daniel Webster (1782–1852), U.S. senator from Massachusetts and leader of the Whig Party.

3. King of Israel, celebrated in the Bible for his wisdom (d. 922 B.C.).

of—the courts of all civilised, heathen, or Jewish countries, never contemplated. Lest the wisdom of our courts should be circumvented by
some such men as might be named, who are so near being born constitutionally that they might be taken for white by sight, I would suggest
that our court be invested with SMELLING powers, and that if a man
don't exhale the constitutional smell, he shall not vote! This would be
an additional security to our liberties.

William found, after all, that liberty in the so-called Free States was
more a name than a reality; that prejudice followed the coloured man into
every place that he might enter. The temples erected for the worship of the
living God are no exception. The finest Baptist church in the city of Boston
has the following paragraph in the deed that conveys its seats to pew-
holders:

> And it is a further condition of these presents, that if the owner or
> owners of said pew shall determine hereafter to sell the same, it shall
> first be offered, in writing, to the standing committee of said society for
> the time being, at such price as might otherwise be obtained for it; and
> the said committee shall have the right, for ten days after such offer, to
> purchase said pew for said society, at that price, first deducting there-
> from all taxes and assessments on said pew then remaining unpaid.
> And if the said committee shall not so complete such purchase within
> said ten days, then the pew may be sold by the owner or owners thereof
> (after payment of all such arrears) to any one respectable *white person*,
> but upon the same conditions as are contained in this instrument; and
> immediate notice of such sale shall be given in writing, by the vendor,
> to the treasurer of said society.

Such are the conditions upon which the Rowe Street Baptist Church, Boston, disposes of its seats. The writer of this is able to put that whole congregation, minister and all, to flight, by merely putting his coloured face in
that church. We once visited a church in New York that had a place set
apart for the sons of Ham.[4] It was a dark, dismal looking place in one corner of the gallery, grated in front like a hen-coop, with a black border
around it. It had two doors; over one was B. M.—black men; over the other
B. W.—black women.

* * *

[Dying young of consumption, Georgiana Carlton frees her slaves. Disguised as a
"Spanish or Italian gentleman," Clotel goes to Richmond to find her daughter.
Althesa and her husband die in a yellow fever epidemic in New Orleans. Their two
daughters are sold into slavery and soon die tragically. Clotel is apprehended in
Richmond and conveyed to Washington, D.C., to be sold back into slavery. When
her dramatic escape attempt is thwarted, she chooses to drown herself in the Potomac River, within sight of the White House. Clotel's daughter, Mary, ultimately
marries the light-skinned George Green, a fugitive slave with whom she is provi-
dentially reunited in France after a ten-year separation.]

1853

4. Son of the biblical patriarch Noah, who was thought to be the progenitor of African peoples.

ADA [SARAH L. FORTEN]

1814–1898?

"Ada" was the pen name that Sarah L. Forten adopted when she contributed poems and essays to antislavery journals such as *The Liberator* and *The Abolitionist* in the 1830s. A member of one of the most highly respected free black families in the antebellum North, Sarah Forten was the third daughter of James and Charlotte Forten of Philadelphia. James Forten's business acumen made him one of the more affluent men of Philadelphia in the early nineteenth century. His early dedication to abolitionism and civil rights for blacks and women made his home a regular meeting place for some of the most famous reformers and intellectuals of the era, such as William Lloyd Garrison, the fiery editor of *The Liberator*, and John Greenleaf Whittier, the most revered antislavery poet of his time. Sarah Forten grew up in an atmosphere charged with discussion of social, intellectual, and literary issues. Her writing, which she started publishing as a teenager, showed a high-minded devotion to antislavery and women's rights. She supported these causes in action as well as words by helping to found the Philadelphia Female Anti-Slavery Society in 1833 and serving on its board of managers. In 1838 Forten married Joseph Purvis, brother of Robert Purvis, a prominent northern African American civil rights leader. The couple moved to a country home in Bucks County, Pennsylvania, where Sarah devoted herself to raising a large family.

A year before her marriage in 1837, Forten read Angelina E. Grimké's *Appeal to the Christian Women of the South*, an unprecedented call to southern women, by a daughter of slaveholders, to acknowledge the evil of slavery and to refuse to comply further with it. In *Lines Suggested on Reading "An Appeal to Christian Women of the South,"* Forten wholeheartedly welcomes Grimké as a newcomer to "the sacred cause." Despite popular opposition to women's speaking their minds in public, Forten seizes on Grimké's example to show women that "the pen is ours to wield" in defense of justice. *Lines* does more than celebrate Forten's sense of literary sisterhood with Grimké, however. The poem also charges white feminist writers to follow Grimké's lead by channeling their revolutionary form of "woman's work" into literary agitation on behalf of black women in chains.

Lines Suggested on Reading "An Appeal to Christian Women of the South," by A. E. Grimke [1]

My spirit leaps in joyousness tow'rd thine,
My gifted sister, as with gladdened heart
My vision flies along thy "speaking pages."
Well hast thou toiled in Mercy's sacred cause;
And thus another strong and lasting thread   5
Is added to the woof [2] our sex is weaving,
With skill and industry, for Freedom's garb.
Precious the privilege to labor here,—
Worthy the lofty mind and handy-work

---

1. Angelina Emily Grimké (1805–1879), southern-born feminist and abolitionist author.

2. The threads that cross the warp of a woven fabric.

Of Chapman, Chandler, Child,[3] and Grimke too.   10
There's much in woman's influence, ay much,
To swell the rolling tide of sympathy,
And aid those champions of a fettered race,
Now laboring arduous in the moral field.
We may not "cry aloud," as they are bid,   15
And lift our voices in the *public* ear;
Nor yet be mute. The pen is ours to wield;
The heart to will, and hands to execute.
And more the gracious promise gives to all—
Ask, says the Saviour, and ye shall receive.   20
In concert then, Father of love, we join,
To wrestle with thy presence, as of old
Did Israel, and will not let thee go
Until thou bless.[4] The cause is thine—for 'tis
Thy guiltless poor who are oppressed, on whom   25
The sun of Freedom may not cast his beams,
Nor dew of heavenly knowledge e'er descend.
And for their fearless advocates we ask
The wisdom of the serpent—above all,
Our heavenly Father, clothe, oh clothe them with   30
The dove-like spirit of thine own dear Son:
Then are they safe, tho' Persecution's waves
Dash o'er their bark, and furious winds assail—
Still they are safe.

      ——Yes, this *is* woman's work,   35
Her own appropriate sphere; and nought should drive
Her from the mercy seat, till Mercy's work
Be finished.

       Whose is that wail, piercing the ear
Of night, with agony too deep for words   40
To give it birth? 'Tis woman's—she of Ramah—
Another Rachel, weeping for her babes,
And will not be consoled, for they are not.[5]
Oh! slavery, with all its withering power,
Can never wholly quench the flame of love,   45
Nor dry the stream of tenderness that flows
In breasts maternal. A *mother's love!* deep grows
That plant of Heaven, fast by the well of life,
And nought can pluck it thence till woman cease
To be.——Then, long as mothers' hearts are breaking   50
Beneath the hammer of the auctioneer,
And ruthless Avarice tears asunder bonds,
That the fat of the Almighty joined,
So long should woman's melting voice be heard,

3. Maria Weston Chapman (1806–1885), Elizabeth Margaret Chandler (1807–1834), and Lydia Maria Child (1802–1880), American antislavery authors and editors.
4. An allusion to Genesis 32:24–29, in which the patriarch Jacob wrestles with an angel who blesses him with the name Israel.
5. See Matthew 2:18: "In Rama was there a voice heard, lamentation and weeping, and great mourning, Rachel weeping for her children, and would not be comforted, because they are not."

In intercession strong and deep, that this   55
Accursed thing, this Achan[6] in our camp,
May be removed.

Pawtucket, 1836.   ADA

1836

6. A traitor to his people, the Israelites (Joshua 7).

HENRY HIGHLAND GARNET

1815–1882

Growing up as a slave in Maryland, Henry Highland Garnet was inspired by a family tradition that identified his grandfather as a tribal ruler in the legendary Mandingo Empire of West Africa. The example of that grandfather, as well as that of Garnet's father George, who successfully engineered the escape of his entire family from slavery in 1825, gave young Henry a model of black manhood based in African as well as African American styles of leadership; to this model he remained dedicated throughout his life. In New York City, where his family lived after leaving Maryland, Garnet received an unusually thorough preparation for the role he would play in the antislavery struggle. He was befriended by such influential African American activists as the Reverend Theodore S. Wright and the teachers of the New York African Free School; his classmates at the school included Alexander Crummell, who would become perhaps the leading black intellectual of the mid-nineteenth century, and Ira Aldridge, later to achieve international acclaim as a Shakespearean actor. Garnet studied at the Noyes Academy in Canaan, New Hampshire, before being driven out by bigoted whites, and at the Oneida Institute in Whitesboro, New York, where he decided on a career as a Presbyterian minister. Licensed to preach in 1842, the Reverend Mr. Garnet assumed the pastorate of the predominately white Presbyterian church of Troy, New York. Soon he became famous as one of black America's most eloquent and controversial platform orators.

In 1843 at the National Negro Convention in Buffalo, New York, Garnet delivered the speech that defined him as an unabashed radical revolutionary in regard to the black struggle for liberation in the United States. Garnet's *Address to the Slaves of the United States of America* vigorously argued the justifiability of noncompliance and violent resistance if necessary in the slaves' dealings with their masters. The "Call to Rebellion" speech, as the address has come to be known, sparked a strong denunciation from Frederick Douglass, at that time an adherent of the nonviolent "moral suasion" school of abolitionism. The speech fell only a single vote short of being approved as an official resolution of the 1843 convention. But in 1847, the National Negro Convention endorsed Garnet's militance, as would Douglass by the mid-1850s. With the financial aid of abolitionist John Brown, Garnet in 1848 combined his hitherto unpublished "Call to Rebellion" speech with *David Walker's Appeal* to form a pamphlet uniquely prophetic of the armed conflict over slavery to which the United States was fatefully committed.

During the Civil War, Garnet was among the first to urge President Lincoln to authorize the enlistment of African American troops. After accepting a call in 1864 to lead the fashionable Fifteenth Street Presbyterian Church of Washington, D.C., the black minister became the first man of color to deliver a sermon to the U.S. House of Representatives. Despite his advocacy since the late 1850s of black emigration to Africa and the Caribbean, Garnet never ceased to agitate for reform at home, both on the social and on the political front, as in the case of slavery, but in the economic arena as well, particularly in regard to post–Civil War land monopolies held by southern whites, which Garnet felt would perpetuate free African Americans in second-class citizenship. In 1882 Garnet's long devotion to pan-Africanism reached its culmination in his appointment as U.S. minister to Liberia. Hoping to help build a black nation, Garnet died the next year. He was buried in a Liberian cemetery overlooking the Atlantic Ocean.

An Address to the Slaves of the United States of America

Brethren and Fellow Citizens: Your brethren of the North, East, and West have been accustomed to meet together in National Conventions, [1] to sympathize with each other, and to weep over your unhappy condition. In these meetings we have addressed all classes of the free, but we have never, until this time, sent a word of consolation and advice to you. We have been contented in sitting still and mourning over your sorrows, earnestly hoping that before this day your sacred liberties would have been restored. But, we have hoped in vain. Years have rolled on, and tens of thousands have been borne on streams of blood and tears to the shores of eternity. While you have been oppressed, we have also been partakers with you; nor can we be free while you are enslaved. We, therefore, write to you as being bound with you.

Many of you are bound to us, not only by the ties of a common humanity, but we are connected by the more tender relations of parents, wives, husbands, and sisters, and friends. As such we most affectionately address you.

Slavery has fixed a deep gulf between you and us, and while it shuts out from you the relief and consolation which your friends would willingly render, it afflicts and persecutes you with a fierceness which we might not expect to see in the fiends of hell. But still the Almighty Father of mercies has left to us a glimmering ray of hope, which shines out like a lone star in a cloudy sky. Mankind are becoming wiser, and better—the oppressor's power is fading, and you, every day, are becoming better informed, and more numerous. Your grievances, brethren, are many. We shall not attempt, in this short address, to present to the world all the dark catalogue of the nation's sins, which have been committed upon an innocent people. Nor is it indeed necessary, for you feel them from day to day, and all the civilized world looks upon them with amazement.

Two hundred and twenty-seven years ago the first of our injured race were brought to the shores of America. They came not with glad spirits to select their homes in the New World. They came not with their own consent, to find an unmolested enjoyment of the blessings of this fruitful soil. The first dealings they had with men calling themselves Christians exhibited to them the worst features of corrupt and sordid hearts: and convinced them that no cruelty is too great, no villainy and no robbery too abhorrent

---

1. In 1830 African Americans began to hold national conventions to consider social, economic, and political issues.

for even enlightened men to perform, when influenced by avarice and lust. Neither did they come flying upon the wings of liberty to a land of freedom. But they came with broken hearts, from their beloved native land, and were doomed to unrequited toil and deep degradation. Nor did the evil of their bondage end at their emancipation by death. Succeeding generations inherited their chains, and millions have come from eternity into time, and have returned again to the world of spirits, cursed and ruined by American slavery.

The propagators of the system, or their immediate successors, very soon discovered its growing evil, and its tremendous wickedness, and secret promises were made to destroy it. The gross inconsistency of a people holding slaves, who had themselves "ferried o'er the wave" for freedom's sake, was too apparent to be entirely overlooked. The voice of Freedom cried, "Emancipate your slaves." Humanity supplicated with tears for the deliverance of the children of Africa. Wisdom urged her solemn plea. The bleeding captive plead his innocence, and pointed to Christianity who stood weeping at the cross. Jehovah frowned upon the nefarious institution, and thunderbolts, red with vengeance, struggled to leap forth to blast the guilty wretches who maintained it. But all was vain. Slavery had stretched its dark wings of death over the land, the Church stood silently by—the priests prophesied falsely, and the people loved to have it so. Its throne is established, and now it reigns triumphant.

Nearly three millions of your fellow-citizens are prohibited by law and public opinion (which in this country is stronger than law) from reading the Book of Life. [2] Your intellect has been destroyed as much as possible, and every ray of light they have attempted to shut out from your minds. The oppressors themselves have become involved in the ruin. They have become weak, sensual, and rapacious—they have cursed you—they have cursed themselves—they have cursed the earth which they have trod.

The colonies threw the blame upon England. They said that the mother country entailed the evil upon them, and they would rid themselves of it if they could. The world thought they were sincere, and the philanthropic pitied them. But time soon tested their sincerity. In a few years the colonists grew strong, and severed themselves from the British Government. Their independence was declared, and they took their station among the sovereign powers of the earth. The declaration was a glorious document. Sages admired it, and the patriotic of every nation reverenced the God-like sentiments which it contained. When the power of Government returned to their hands, did they emancipate the slaves? No; they rather added new links to our chains. Were they ignorant of the principles of Liberty? Certainly they were not. The sentiments of their revolutionary orators fell in burning eloquence upon their hearts, and with one voice they cried, LIBERTY OR DEATH. Oh, what a sentence was that! It ran from soul to soul like electric fire, and nerved the arms of thousands to fight in the holy cause of Freedom. Among the diversity of opinions that are entertained in regard to physical resistance, there are but a few found to gainsay the stern declaration. We are among those who do not.

2. The Bible.

SLAVERY! How much misery is comprehended in that single word. What mind is there that does not shrink from its direful effects? Unless the image of God be obliterated from the soul, all men cherish the love of liberty. The nice discerning political economist does not regard the sacred right more than the untutored African who roams in the wilds of Congo. Nor has the one more right to the full enjoyment of his freedom than the other. In every man's mind the good seeds of liberty are planted, and he who brings his fellow down so low, as to make him contented with a condition of slavery, commits the highest crime against God and man. Brethren, your oppressors aim to do this. They endeavor to make you as much like brutes as possible. When they have blinded the eyes of your mind—when they have embittered the sweet waters of life—when they have shut out the light which shines from the word of God—then, and not till then, has American slavery done its perfect work.

TO SUCH DEGRADATION IT IS SINFUL IN THE EXTREME FOR YOU TO MAKE VOLUNTARY SUBMISSION. The divine commandments you are in duty bound to reverence and obey. If you do not obey them, you will surely meet with the displeasure of the Almighty. He requires you to love Him supremely, and your neighbor as yourself—to keep the Sabbath day holy— to search the Scriptures—and bring up your children with respect for His laws, and to worship no other God but Him. But slavery sets all these at nought, and hurls defiance in the face of Jehovah. The forlorn condition in which you are placed does not destroy your obligation to God. You are not certain of heaven, because you allow yourselves to remain in a state of slavery, where you cannot obey the commandments of the Sovereign of the universe. If the ignorance of slavery is a passport to heaven, then it is a blessing, and no curse, and you should rather desire its perpetuity than its abolition. God will not receive slavery, nor ignorance, nor any other state of mind, for love and obedience to Him. Your condition does not absolve you from your moral obligation. The diabolical injustice by which your liberties are cloven down, NEITHER GOD NOR ANGELS, OR JUST MEN, COMMAND YOU TO SUFFER FOR A SINGLE MOMENT. THEREFORE IT IS YOUR SOLEMN AND IMPERATIVE DUTY TO USE EVERY MEANS, BOTH MORAL, INTELLECTUAL, AND PHYSICAL, THAT PROMISES SUCCESS. If a band of heathen men should attempt to enslave a race of Christians, and to place their children under the influence of some false religion, surely Heaven would frown upon the men who would not resist such aggression, even to death. If, on the other hand, a band of Christians should attempt to enslave a race of heathen men, and to entail slavery upon them, and to keep them in heathenism in the midst of Christianity, the God of heaven would smile upon every effort which the injured might make to disenthral themselves.

Brethren, it is as wrong for your lordly oppressors to keep you in slavery as it was for the man thief to steal our ancestors from the coast of Africa. You should therefore now use the same manner of resistance as would have been just in our ancestors when the bloody foot-prints of the first remorseless soul-thief was placed upon the shores of our fatherland. The humblest peasant is as free in the sight of God as the proudest monarch that ever swayed a sceptre. Liberty is a spirit sent out from God, and like its great Author, is no respecter of persons.

Brethren, the time has come when you must act for yourselves. It is an old and true saying that, "if hereditary bondmen would be free, they must themselves strike the blow."[3] You can plead your own cause, and do the work of emancipation better than any others. The nations of the Old World are moving in the great cause of universal freedom, and some of them at least will, ere long, do you justice. The combined powers of Europe have placed their broad seal of disapprobation upon the African slave-trade. But in the slaveholding parts of the United States the trade is as brisk as ever. They buy and sell you as though you were brute beasts. The North has done much—her opinion of slavery in the abstract is known. But in regard to the South, we adopt the opinion of the *New York Evangelist*—"We have advanced so far, that the cause apparently waits for a more effectual door to be thrown open than has been yet." We are about to point you to that more effectual door. Look around you, and behold the bosoms of your loving wives heaving with untold agonies! Here the cries of your poor children! Remember the stripes your fathers bore. Think of the torture and disgrace of your noble mothers. Think of your wretched sisters, loving virtue and purity, as they are driven into concubinage and are exposed to the unbridled lusts of incarnate devils. Think of the undying glory that hangs around the ancient name of Africa—and forget not that you are native-born American citizens, and as such you are justly entitled to all the rights that are granted to the freest. Think how many tears you have poured out upon the soil which you have cultivated with unrequited toil and enriched with your blood; and then go to your lordly enslavers and tell them plainly, that you *are determined to be free*. Appeal to their sense of justice, and tell them that they have no more right to oppress you than you have to enslave them. Entreat them to remove the grievous burdens which they have imposed upon you, and to remunerate you for your labor. Promise them renewed diligence in the cultivation of the soil, if they will render to you an equivalent for your services. Point them to the increase of happiness and prosperity in the British West Indies since the Act of Emancipation.[4] Tell them in language which they cannot misunderstand of the exceeding sinfulness of slavery, and of a future judgment, and of the righteous retributions of an indignant God. Inform them that all you desire is FREEDOM, and that nothing else will suffice. Do this, and forever after cease to toil for the heartless tyrants, who give you no other reward but stripes and abuse. If they then commence work of death, they, and not you, will be responsible for the consequences. You had far better all die—*die immediately*, than live slaves, and entail your wretchedness upon your posterity. If you would be free in this generation, here is your only hope. However much you and all of us may desire it, there is not much hope of redemption without the shedding of blood. If you must bleed, let it all come at once—rather *die freemen than live to be the slaves*. It is impossible, like the children of Israel, to make a grand exodus from the land of bondage. The Pharaohs are on both sides of the blood-red waters! You cannot move *en masse* to the dominions of the British Queen—nor can you pass through Florida and overrun Texas, and

3. Compare Lord Byron's *Childe Harold's Pilgrim-age* 2.76: "Hereditary bondsmen! Know ye not / Who would be free themselves must strike the blow?"

4. Slavery was abolished in the British Empire in 1833.

at last find peace in Mexico. The propagators of American slavery are spending their blood and treasure that they may plant the black flag in the heart of Mexico and riot in the halls of the Montezumas.[5] In language of the Reverend Robert Hall,[6] when addressing the volunteers of Bristol, who were rushing forth to repel the invasion of Napoleon, who threatened to lay waste the fair homes of England, "Religion is too much interested in your behalf not to shed over you her most gracious influences."

You will not be compelled to spend much time in order to become inured to hardships. From the first movement that you breathed the air of heaven, you have been accustomed to nothing else but hardships. The heroes of the American Revolution were never put upon harder fare than a peck of corn and few herrings per week. You have not become enervated by the luxuries of life. Your sternest energies have been beaten out upon the anvil of severe trial. Slavery has done this to make you subservient to its own purposes; but it has done more than this, it has prepared you for any emergency. If you receive good treatment, it is what you can hardly expect; if you meet with pain, sorrow, and even death, these are the common lot of the slaves.

Fellowmen! patient sufferers! behold your dearest rights crushed to the earth! See your sons murdered, and your wives, mothers and sisters doomed to prostitution. In the name of the merciful God, and by all that life is worth, let it no longer be a debatable question, whether it is better to choose *liberty* or *death*.

In 1822, Denmark Veazie,[7] of South Carolina, formed a plan for the liberation of his fellowmen. In the whole history of human efforts to overthrow slavery, a more complicated and tremendous plan was never formed. He was betrayed by the treachery of his own people, and died a martyr to freedom. Many a brave hero fell, but history, faithful to her high trust, will transcribe his name on the same monument with Moses, Hampden, Tell, Bruce and Wallace, Toussaint L'Ouverture, Lafayette, and Washington.[8] That tremendous movement shook the whole empire of slavery. The guilty soul-thieves were overwhelmed with fear. It is a matter of fact that at this time, and in consequence of the threatened revolution, the slave States talked strongly of emancipation. But they blew but one blast of the trumpet of freedom, and then laid it aside. As these men became quiet, the slaveholders ceased to talk about emancipation: and now behold your condition to-day! Angels sigh over it, and humanity has long since exhausted her tears in weeping on your account!

The patriotic Nathaniel Turner[9] followed Denmark Veazie. He was

5. Montezuma (1408?–1520), Aztec emperor at the time of the Spanish conquest. A reference to proslavery imperialists anxious to seize Mexican territory for slavery.
6. English Baptist clergyman (1764–1831).
7. Or Veazey.
8. George Washington (1732–1799), commander in chief of the army that won the North American colonies' revolution against Great Britain in 1781. Moses led the Hebrews out of Egyptian bondage in the 13th century B.C. John Hampden (1594–1643) fought against Charles I in the English Civil War. William Tell, legendary Swiss patriot in Switzer-

land's struggle against Austrian domination. Robert the Bruce, king of Scotland (1274–1329), and Sir William Wallace (1270–1305) led their country in wars of independence against England. Toussaint L'Ouverture (c. 1744–1803) led the revolution that freed the black population of Haiti from French rule in 1803. Marquis de Lafayette (1757–1834) volunteered his services to the American revolutionaries and became a major general in the Revolutionary Army.
9. Leader of a Southampton, Virginia, slave insurrection in 1831 (1800–1831).

goaded to desperation by wrong and injustice. By despotism, his name has been recorded on the list of infamy, and future generations will remember him among the noble and brave.

Next arose the immortal Joseph Cinque,[1] the hero of the Amistad. He was a native African, and by the help of God he emancipated a whole ship-load of his fellowmen on the high seas. And he now sings of liberty on the sunny hills of Africa and beneath his native palm-trees, where he hears the lion roar and feels himself as free as the king of the forest.

Next arose Madison Washington,[2] that bright star of freedom, and took his station in the constellation of true heroism. He was a slave on board the brig *Creole*, of Richmond, bound to New Orleans, that great slave mart, with a hundred and four others. Nineteen struck for liberty or death. But one life was taken, and the whole were emancipated, and the vessel was carried into Nassau, New Providence.

Noble men! Those who have fallen in freedom's conflict, their memories will be cherished by the true-hearted and the God-fearing in all future generations; those who are living, their names are surrounded by a halo of glory.

Brethren, arise, arise! Strike for your lives and liberties. Now is the day and the hour. Let every slave throughout the land do this, and the days of slavery are numbered. You cannot be more oppressed than you have been—you cannot suffer greater cruelties than you have already. *Rather die freemen than live to be slaves.* Remember that you are FOUR MILLIONS!

It is in your power so to torment the God-cursed slaveholders that they will be glad to let you go free. If the scale was turned, and black men were the masters and white men the slaves, every destructive agent and element would be employed to lay the oppressor low. Danger and death would hang over their heads day and night. Yes, the tyrants would meet with plagues more terrible than those of Pharaoh. But you are a patient people. You act as though you were made for the special use of these devils. You act as though your daughters were born to pamper the lusts of your masters and overseers. And worse than all, you tamely submit while your lords tear your wives from your embraces and defile them before your eyes. In the name of God, we ask, are you men? Where is the blood of your fathers? Has it all run out of your veins? Awake, awake; millions of voices are calling you! Your dead fathers speak to you from their graves. Heaven, as with a voice of thunder, calls on you to arise from the dust.

Let your motto be resistance! *resistance!* RESISTANCE! No oppressed people have ever secured their liberty without resistance. What kind of resistance you had better make you must decide by the circumstances that surround you, and according to the suggestion of expediency. Brethren, adieu! Trust in the living God. Labor for the peace of the human race, and remember that you are FOUR MILLIONS!

1843   1848

---

1. Leader of successful slave mutiny aboard the Spanish schooner *Amistad* in 1839.

2. Leader of a successful slave mutiny aboard the *Creole* in 1841.

VICTOR SÉJOUR

1817–1874

Victor Séjour's chilling short story *Le Mulâtre* ("The Mulatto") is the earliest known work of African American fiction. It first appeared in 1837 in a journal published in Paris, *La Revue des Colonies*, sponsored by a society of men of color. This is the first English translation of Séjour's pioneering story of racial exploitation and violent revenge.

Juan Victor Séjour Marcou et Ferrand was born in New Orleans, Louisiana, the son of a free man of color from Santo Domingo and a free mixed-race woman of New Orleans. Séjour's parents were sufficiently prosperous to send their son to a private school, where he came under the influence of a respected black journalist who wrote for French newspapers in New Orleans. Following a custom of New Orleans's free black class, Séjour went to Paris when he was nineteen to further his education. He stayed on to launch a literary career unhampered by the racial proscriptions of the antebellum South.

Soon after his arrival in Paris, Séjour made the acquaintance of influential literary men of color, such as Alexandre Dumas *père*, the popular French novelist, and abolitionist Cyrille Bisette, who edited *La Revue des Colonies*. Turning away from fiction after *Le Mulâtre*, Séjour wrote an intensely nationalistic ode, *Le Retour de Napoléon*, which expressed his admiration for Napoléon and his identification with France. After its initial publication in Paris in 1841, *Le Retour de Napoléon* was reprinted in *Les Cenelles* (1845), the first anthology of African American poetry, edited by the black New Orleans writer Armand Lanusse. Like all the contributors to *Les Cenelles*, Séjour wrote in French, undoubtedly the language he grew up speaking in New Orleans.

In 1844 Séjour's first play, a verse drama set in fifteenth-century Spain, was accepted for production by the French national theater. During the next twenty-five years, Séjour's plays were regularly staged in Paris and, until 1865, enjoyed considerable popular success. After initial success as a historical dramatist, he specialized in the 1850s in lavishly staged melodramas, heroic adventure plays, and romantic comedies, at least three of which were performed in New Orleans. Shakespeare, whose works were often featured in the New Orleans theater of Séjour's youth, was a major influence on Séjour's most acclaimed drama, *Richard III* (1852). During the late 1860s, however, Séjour's brand of costume drama fell out of fashion in France; ill health and a changing social and cultural climate contributed to a major decline in Séjour's fortunes in the last years of his life.

Victor Séjour was the first in a series of distinguished African American literary expatriates who settled and wrote in Paris. Unlike Chester Himes, Richard Wright, and James Baldwin in the twentieth century, Séjour seems to have gone to France not only to find a social refuge but also to create himself anew as a Continental man of letters unburdened by the responsibilities his black literary contemporaries in America felt to speak directly to racial issues. After *Le Mulâtre* Séjour published little directly concerned with color or caste and evidently nothing concerned with slavery in the United States. Nevertheless, *Le Mulâtre* provided a remarkable precedent for the tradition of African American antislavery protest fiction that, a decade and a half later, made an auspicious start in English with Frederick Douglass's *The Heroic Slave* (1853) and William Wells Brown's *Clotel* (1853). Publishing *Le Mulâtre* in French probably cost the author an American readership outside the city of his birth; even the most cosmopolitan of African American writers, such as

Douglass and Brown, seem to have known nothing about Séjour's early foray into antislavery fiction.

Yet who is to say that Séjour's decision to publish in a black-owned journal in France was not the right—indeed, the only—way to ensure that his explicit and grisly tale of racial exploitation, rape, murder, and suicide would ever see print? Even William Faulkner and Richard Wright, whose probing fictional accounts of perverse desire and sadistic retribution look back to Séjour's evocation of the psychological and social tragedy of black-white relationships under slavery, were attacked in the twentieth century for writing in veins first probed by *Le Mulâtre*. Edgar Allan Poe had some success in the mid-nineteenth century United States writing about violent death, sexual obsession, and the human psyche under extreme mental or emotional strain. But in *Le Mulâtre* Séjour took a literary risk his white American contemporary never attempted. Séjour grounded his study of similarly extreme manifestations of individual pathology in a *social* reality, the system of slavery, which the African American writer treats as the source of the depravity and misery that infects the minds and hearts of all, black and white alike, in his story.

The Mulatto [1]

I

The first rays of dawn were just beginning to light the black mountaintops when I left the Cape for Saint-Marc, a small town in St. Domingue, now known as Haiti. [2] I had seen so many exquisite landscapes and thick, tall forests that, truth to tell, I had begun to believe myself indifferent to these virile beauties of creation. But at the sight of this town, with its picturesque vegetation, its bizarre and novel nature, I was stunned; I stood dumbstruck before the sublime diversity of God's works. The moment I arrived, I was accosted by an old negro, at least seventy years of age; his step was firm, his head held high, his form imposing and vigorous; save the remarkable whiteness of his curly hair, nothing betrayed his age. As is common in that country, he wore a large straw hat and was dressed in trousers of coarse gray linen, with a kind of jacket made from plain batiste. [3]

"Good day, Master," he said, tipping his hat when he saw me.

"Ah! There you are . . . ," and I offered him my hand, which he shook in return.

"Master," he said, "that's quite noble-hearted of you. . . . But you know, do you not, that a negro's as vile as a dog; society rejects him; men detest him; the laws curse him. . . . Yes, he's a most unhappy being, who hasn't even the consolation of always being virtuous. . . . He may be born good, noble, and generous; God may grant him a great and loyal soul; but despite all that, he often goes to his grave with bloodstained hands, and a heart hungering after yet more vengeance. For how many times has he seen the dreams of his youth destroyed? How many times has experience taught him that his good deeds count for nothing, and that he should love neither his wife nor his son; for one day the former will be seduced by the master, and

---

1. First published in French in *La Revue des Colonies* in 1837. This translation is by Philip Barnard.
2. A republic occupying the western third of the is-

land of Hispaniola in the Caribbean Sea.
3. A fine plain-woven fabric.

his own flesh and blood will be sold and transported away despite his despair. What, then, can you expect him to become? Shall he smash his skull
against the paving stones? Shall he kill his torturer? Or do you believe the
human heart can find a way to bear such misfortune?"

The old negro fell silent a moment, as if awaiting my response.

"You'd have to be mad to believe that," he continued, heatedly. "If he
continues to live, it can only be for vengeance; for soon he shall rise . . .
and, from the day he shakes off his servility, the master would do better to
have a starving tiger raging beside him than to meet that man face to face."
While the old man spoke, his face lit up, his eyes sparkled, and his heart
pounded forcefully. I would not have believed one could discover that
much life and power beneath such an aged exterior. Taking advantage of
this moment of excitement, I said to him: "Antoine, you promised you'd
tell me the story of your friend Georges."

"Do you want to hear it now?"

"Certainly . . ." We sat down, he on my trunk, myself on my valise. Here
is what he told me:

"Do you see this edifice that rises so graciously toward the sky and whose
reflection seems to rise from the sea; this edifice that in its peculiarity
resembles a temple and in its pretense a palace? This is the house of
Saint-M***. Each day, in one of this building's rooms, one finds an assemblage of hangers-on, men of independent means, and the great plantation
owners. The first two groups play billiards or smoke the delicious cigars of
Havana, while the third purchases negroes; that is, free men who have
been torn from their country by ruse or by force, and who have become, by
violence, the goods, the property of their fellow men. . . . Over here we
have the husband without the wife; there, the sister without the brother;
farther on, the mother without the children. This makes you shudder? Yet
this loathsome commerce goes on continuously. Soon, in any case, the offering is a young Senegalese[4] woman, so beautiful that from every mouth
leaps the exclamation: 'How pretty!' Everyone there wants her for his mistress, but not one of them dares dispute the prize with the young Alfred,
now twenty-one years old and one of the richest planters in the country.

" 'How much do you want for this woman?'

" 'Fifteen hundred piasters,' replied the auctioneer.

" 'Fifteen hundred piasters,' Alfred rejoined dryly.

" 'Yes indeed, Sir.'

" 'That's your price?'

" 'That's my price.'

" 'That's awfully expensive.'

" 'Expensive?' replied the auctioneer, with an air of surprise. 'But surely
you see how pretty she is; how clear her skin is, how firm her flesh is. She's
eighteen years old at the most. . . .' Even as he spoke, he ran his shameless
hands all over the ample and half-naked form of the beautiful African.

" 'Is she guaranteed?' asked Alfred, after a moment of reflection.

" 'As pure as the morning dew,' the auctioneer responded. But, for that
matter, you yourself can. . . .'

---

4. From Senegal, a country in West Africa.

" 'No no, there's no need,' said Alfred, interrupting him. 'I trust you.'

" 'I've never sold a single piece of bad merchandise,' replied the vendor, twirling his whiskers with a triumphant air. When the bill of sale had been signed and all formalities resolved, the auctioneer approached the young slave.

" 'This man is now your master,' he said, pointing toward Alfred.

" 'I know it,' the negress answered coldly.

" 'Are you content?'

" 'What does it matter to me . . . him or some other. . . .'

" 'But surely. . . .' stammered the auctioneer, searching for some answer.

" 'But surely what?' said the African, with some humor. 'And if he doesn't suit me?'

" 'My word, that would be unfortunate, for everything is finished. . . .'

" 'Well then, I'll keep my thoughts to myself.'

"Ten minutes later, Alfred's new slave stepped into a carriage that set off along the *chemin des quepes*, a well-made road that leads out into those delicious fields that surround Saint-Marc like young virgins at the foot of the altar. A somber melancholy enveloped her soul, and she began to weep. The driver understood only too well what was going on inside her, and thus made no attempt to distract her. But when he saw Alfred's white house appear in the distance, he involuntarily leaned down toward the unfortunate girl and, with a voice full of tears, said to her: 'Sister, what's your name?'

" 'Laïsa,' she answered, without raising her head.

"At the sound of this name, the driver shivered. Then, gaining control of his emotions, he asked: 'Your mother?'

" 'She's dead. . . .'

" 'Your father?'

" 'He's dead. . . .'

" 'Poor child,' he murmured. 'What country are you from, Laïsa?'

" 'From Senegal. . . .'

"Tears rose in his eyes; she was a fellow countrywoman.

" 'Sister,' he said, wiping his eyes, 'perhaps you know old Chambo and his daughter. . . .'

" 'Why?' answered the girl, raising her head quickly.

" 'Why?' continued the driver, in obvious discomfort, 'well, old Chambo is my father, and . . .'

" 'My God,' cried out the orphan, cutting off the driver before he could finish. 'You are?'

" 'Jacques Chambo.'

" 'You're my brother!'

" 'Laïsa!'

"They threw themselves into each other's arms. They were still embracing when the carriage passed through the main entrance to Alfred's property. The overseer was waiting. . . . 'What's this I see,' he shouted, uncoiling an immense whip that he always carried on his belt; 'Jacques kissing the new arrival before my very eyes. . . . What impertinence!' With this, lashes began to fall on the unhappy man, and spurts of blood leaped from his face."

II

"Alfred may have been a decent man, humane and loyal with his equals; but you can be certain he was a hard, cruel man toward his slaves. I won't tell you everything he did in order to possess Laïsa; for in the end she was virtually raped. For almost a year, she shared her master's bed. But Alfred was already beginning to tire of her; he found her ugly, cold, and insolent. About this time the poor woman gave birth to a boy and gave him the name Georges. Alfred refused to recognize him, drove the mother from his presence, and relegated her to the most miserable hut on his lands, despite the fact that he knew very well, as well as one can, that he was the child's father.

"Georges grew up without ever hearing the name of his father; and when, at times, he attempted to penetrate the mystery surrounding his birth, his mother remained inflexible, never yielding to his entreaties. On one occasion only, she said to him: 'My son, you shall learn your name only when you reach twenty-five, for then you will be a man; you will be better able to guard its secret. You don't realize that he has forbidden me to speak to you about him and threatens you if I do. . . . And Georges, don't you see, this man's hatred would be your death.'

" 'What does that matter,' Georges shouted impetuously. 'At least I could reproach him for his unspeakable conduct.'

" 'Hush. . . . Hush, Georges. The walls have ears and someone will talk,' moaned the poor mother as she trembled.

"A few years later this unhappy woman died, leaving to Georges, her only son, as his entire inheritance, a small leather pouch containing a portrait of the boy's father. But she exacted a promise that the pouch not be opened until his twenty-fifth year; then she kissed him, and her head fell back onto the pillow. . . . She was dead. The painful cries that escaped the orphan drew the other slaves around him. . . . They all set to crying, they beat their chests, they tore their hair in agony. Following these gestures of suffering, they bathed the dead woman's body and laid it out on a kind of long table, raised on wooden supports. The dead woman is placed on her back, her face turned to the East, dressed in her finest clothing, with her hands folded on her chest. At her feet is a bowl filled with holy water, in which a sprig of jasmine is floating; and, finally, at the four corners of this funereal bed, the flames of torches rise up. . . . Each of them, having blessed the remains of the deceased, kneels and prays; for most of the negro races, despite their fetishism, [5] have profound faith in the existence of God. When this first ceremony is finished, another one, no less singular, commences. . . . There are shouts, tears, songs, and then funeral dances!"

III

"Georges had all the talents necessary for becoming a well-regarded gentleman; yet he was possessed of a haughty, tenacious, willful nature; he had one of those oriental sorts of dispositions, the kind that, once pushed far enough from the path of virtue, will stride boldly down the path of crime.

---

5. Worship or belief in objects thought to have magical powers.

He would have given ten years of his life to know the name of his father,
but he dared not violate the solemn oath he had made to his dying mother.
It was as if nature pushed him toward Alfred; he liked him, as much as one
can like a man; and Alfred esteemed him, but with that esteem that the
horseman bears for the most handsome and vigorous of his chargers. In
those days, a band of thieves was spreading desolation through the region;
already several of the settlers had fallen victim to them. One night, by what
chance I know not, Georges learned of their plans. They had sworn to murder Alfred. The slave ran immediately to his master's side.

" 'Master, master,' he shouted. . . . 'In heaven's name, follow me.'

"Alfred raised his eyebrows.

" 'Please! come, come, master,' the mulatto insisted passionately.

" 'Good God,' Alfred replied, 'I believe you're commanding me.'

" 'Forgive me, master . . . forgive me . . . I'm beside myself . . . I
don't know what I'm saying . . . but in heaven's name, come, follow me, because. . . .'

" 'Explain yourself,' said Alfred, in an angry tone. . . .

"The mulatto hesitated.

" 'At once; I order you,' continued Alfred, as he rose menacingly.

" 'Master, you're to be murdered tonight.'

" 'By the Virgin, you're lying. . . .'

" 'Master, they mean to take your life.'

" 'Who?'

" 'The bandits.'

" 'Who told you this?'

" 'Master, that's my secret. . . .' said the mulatto in a submissive voice.

" 'Do you have weapons?' rejoined Alfred, after a moment of silence.

" 'The mulatto pulled back a few of the rags that covered him, revealing
an axe and a pair of pistols.

" 'Good,' said Alfred, hastily arming himself.

" 'Master, are you ready?'

" 'Let's go. . . .'

" 'Let's go,' repeated the mulatto as he stepped toward the door.

"Alfred held him back by the arm.

" 'But where to?'

" 'To your closest friend, Monsieur Arthur.'

"As they were about to leave the room, there was a ferocious pounding at
the door.

" 'The devil,' exclaimed the mulatto, 'it's too late. . . .'

" 'What say you?'

" 'They're here,' replied Georges, pointing at the door. . . .

" 'Ah!'

" 'Master, what's wrong?'

" 'Nothing . . . a sudden pain. . . .'

" 'Don't worry, master, they'll have to walk over my body before they get
to you,' said the slave with a calm and resigned air.

"This calm, this noble devotion, were calculated to reassure the most
cowardly of men. Yet at these last words, Alfred trembled even more, overwhelmed by a horrible thought. He reckoned that Georges, despite his gen-

erosity, was an accomplice of the murderers. Such is the tyrant: he believes all other men incapable of elevated sentiments or selfless dedication, for they must be small-minded, perfidious souls. . . . Their souls are but uncultivated ground, where nothing grows but thorns and weeds. The door shook violently. At this point, Alfred could no longer control his fears; he had just seen the mulatto smiling, whether from joy or anger he knew not.

" 'Scoundrel!' he shouted, dashing into the next room; 'you're trying to have me murdered, but your plot will fail'—upon which he disappeared. Georges bit his lips in rage, but had no time to think, for the door flew open and four men stood in the threshold. Like a flash of lightning, the mulatto drew his pistols and pressed his back to the wall, crying out in a deep voice:

" 'Wretches! What do you want?'

" 'We want to have a talk with you,' rejoined one of them, firing a bullet at Georges from point-blank range.

" 'A fine shot,' muttered Georges, shaking.

"The bullet had broken his left arm. Georges let off a shot. The brigand whirled three times about and fell stone dead. A second followed instantly. At this point, like a furious lion tormented by hunters, Georges, with his axe in his fist and his dagger in his teeth, threw himself upon his adversaries. . . . A hideous struggle ensues. . . . The combatants grapple . . . collide again . . . they seem bound together. . . . The axe blade glistens. . . . The dagger, faithful to the hand that guides it, works its way into the enemy's breast. . . . But never a shout, not a word . . . not a whisper escapes the mouths of these three men, wallowing among the cadavers as if at the heart of some intoxicating orgy. . . . To see them thus, pale and blood-spattered, silent and full of desperation, one must imagine three phantoms throwing themselves against each other, tearing themselves to pieces, in the depths of a grave. . . . Meanwhile, Georges is covered with wounds; he can barely hold himself up. . . . Oh! the intrepid mulatto has reached his end; the severing axe is lifted above his head. . . . Suddenly two explosions are heard, and the two brigands slump to the floor, blaspheming God as they drop. At the same moment, Alfred returns, followed by a young negro. He has the wounded man carried to his hut, and instructs his doctor to attend to him. Now, how is it that Georges was saved by the same man who had just accused him of treachery? As he ran off, Alfred heard the sound of a gun, and the clash of steel; blushing at his own cowardice, he awoke his valet de chambre and flew to the aid of his liberator. Ah, I've forgotten to tell you that Georges had a wife, by the name Zelia, whom he loved with every fiber of his being; she was a mulatto about eighteen or twenty years old, standing very straight and tall, with black hair and a gaze full of tenderness and love. Georges lay for twelve days somewhere between life and death. Alfred visited him often; and, driven on by some fateful chance, he became enamored of Zelia. But, unfortunately for him, she was not one of these women who sell their favors or use them to pay tribute to their master. She repelled Alfred's propositions with humble dignity; for she never forgot that this was a master speaking to a slave. Instead of being moved by this display of a virtue that is so rare among women, above all among those who, like Zelia, are slaves, and who, every day, see their shameless companions pros-

titute themselves to the colonists, thereby only feeding more licentiousness; instead of being moved, as I said, Alfred flew into a rage. . . . What!—
him, the despot, the Bey, the Sultan of the Antilles,[6] being spurned by a
slave . . . how ironic! Thus he swore he would possess
her. . . . A few days before Georges was recovered, Alfred summoned Zelia
to his chamber. Then, attending to nothing but his criminal desires, he
threw his arms around her and planted a burning kiss on her face. The
young slave begged, pleaded, resisted; but all in vain. . . . Already he draws
her toward the adulterous bed; already. . . . Then, the young slave, filled
with a noble indignation, repulses him with one final effort, but one so
sudden, so powerful, that Alfred lost his balance and struck his head as he
fell. . . . At this sight, Zelia began to tear her hair in despair, crying tears of
rage; for she understood perfectly, the unhappy girl, that death was her fate
for having drawn the blood of a being so vile. After crying for some time,
she left to be at her husband's side. He must have been dreaming about
her, for there was a smile on his lips.

"'Georges . . . Georges. . . .' she cried out in agony.

"The mulatto opened his eyes; and his first impulse was to smile at the
sight of his beloved. Zelia recounted for him everything that had happened. He didn't want to believe it, but soon he was convinced of his misfortune; for some men entered his hut and tied up his wife while she stood
sobbing. . . . Georges made an effort to rise up; but, still weakened, he fell
back onto his bed, his eyes haggard, his hands clenched, his mouth gasping
for air."

IV

"Ten days later, two white creole[7] children were playing in the street.

"'Charles,' one said to the other: 'is it true that the mulatto woman who
wanted to kill her master is to be hung tomorrow?'

"'At eight o'clock,' answered the other.

"'Will you go?'

"'Oh yes, certainly.'

"'Won't that be fine, to see her pirouetting between the earth and the
sky,' rejoined the first, laughing as they walked off.

"Does it surprise you to hear two children, at ten years of age, conversing
so gayly on the death of another? This is, perhaps, an inevitable consequence of their education. From their earliest days, they have heard it
ceaselessly repeated, that we were born to serve them, that we were created
to attend to their whims, and that they need have no more or less consideration for us than for a dog. . . . Indeed, what is our agony and suffering to
them? Have they not, just as often, seen their best horses die? They don't
weep for them, for they're rich, and tomorrow they'll buy others. . . . While
these two children were speaking, Georges was at the feet of his master.

"'Master, have mercy . . . mercy. . . .' he cried out, weeping. . . . 'Have

6. The main island group of the West Indies.   7. Someone of European descent born in the West
"Bey": Turkish title for a lord or a prince. "Sultan":   Indies.
ruler of a Muslim country.

pity on her . . . Master, pardon her. . . . Oh! yes, pardon her, it is in your power . . . oh! speak . . . you have only to say the word . . . just one word . . . and she will live.'

"Alfred made no answer.

" 'Oh! for pity's sake . . . master . . . for pity's sake, tell me you pardon her . . . oh! speak . . . answer me, master . . . won't you pardon her. . . .' The unhappy man was bent double with pain. . . .

"Alfred remained impassive, turning his head aside. . . .

" 'Oh!' continued Georges, begging, 'please answer . . . just one word . . . please say something; you see how your silence is tearing my heart in two . . . it's killing me. . . .'

" 'There's nothing I can do,' Alfred finally answered, in an icy tone.

"The mulatto dried his tears, and raised himself to his full height.

" 'Master,' he continued in a hollow voice, 'do you remember what you said to me, as I lay twisting in agony on my bed?'

" 'No. . . .'

" 'Well! I can remember . . . the master said to the slave: you saved my life; what can I grant you in return? Do you want your freedom? 'Master,' answered the slave, 'I can never be free, while my son and my wife are slaves.' To which the master replied: 'If ever you ask me, I swear that your wishes shall be granted'; and the slave did not ask, for he was content that he had saved his master's life . . . but today, today when he knows that, in eighteen hours, his wife will no longer be among the living, he flies to throw himself at your feet, and to call out to you: master, in God's name, save my wife.' And the mulatto, his hands clasped, with a supplicating gaze, fell to his knees and began to cry, his tears falling like rain. . . .

"Alfred turned his head away. . . .

" 'Master . . . master . . . for pity, give me an answer. . . . Oh! say that you want her to live . . . in God's name . . . in your mother's name . . . mercy . . . have mercy upon us. . . .' and the mulatto kissed the dust at his feet.

"Alfred stood silent.

" 'But speak, at least, to this poor man who begs you,' he said, sobbing.

"Alfred said nothing.

" 'My God . . . my God! how miserable I am . . .' and he rolled on the floor, pulling at his hair in torment.

"Finally, Alfred decided to speak: 'I have already told you that it is no longer up to me to pardon her.'

" 'Master,' murmured Georges, still crying, 'she will probably be condemned; for only you and I know that she is innocent.'

"At these words from the mulatto, the blood rose to Alfred's face, and fury to his heart. . . .

"Georges understood that it was no longer time to beg, for he had raised the veil that covered his master's crime; thus he stood up resolutely.

" 'Leave . . . get out,' Alfred shouted at him.

"Instead of leaving, the mulatto crossed his arms on his chest and, with a fierce look, eyed his master scornfully from head to foot.

" 'Get out! get out, I say,' continued Alfred, more and more angrily.

" 'I'm not leaving,' answered Georges.

" 'This is defiance, you wretch.' He made a motion to strike him, but his hand remained at his side, so full of pride and hatred was George's gaze.

" 'What! you can leave her to be killed, to have her throat cut, to be murdered,' said the mulatto, 'when you know her to be innocent . . . when, like a coward, you wanted to seduce her?'

" 'Insolent! What are you saying?'

" 'I'm saying that it would be an infamous deed to let her die. . . .'

" 'Georges . . . Georges. . . .'

" 'I am saying that you're a scoundrel,' screamed Georges, giving full rein to his anger, and seizing Alfred by the arm . . . 'ah! she'll die . . . she will die because she didn't prostitute herself to you . . . because you're white . . . because you're her master . . . you lying coward.'

" 'Careful, Georges,' replied Alfred, trying to take a tone of assurance. 'Be careful that instead of one victim tomorrow, the executioner does not find two.'

" 'You talk of victim and executioner, wretch,' shouted Georges. . . . 'So that means she dies . . . her . . . my Zelia . . . but you should know that her life is linked to your own.'

" 'Georges!'

" 'You should know that your head will remain on your shoulders only so long as she lives.'

" 'Georges . . . Georges!'

" 'You should know that I will kill you, that I'll drink your blood, if even a hair on her head is harmed.'

"During all this time, the mulatto was shaking Alfred with all his strength.

" 'Let me go,' cried Alfred.

" 'Ah! she's dying . . . she's dying' . . . the mulatto screamed deliriously.

" 'Georges, let me go!'

" 'Shut your mouth . . . shut it, you scoundrel . . . ah! she's dying . . . well then, should the executioner put an end to my wife . . .' he continued with a hideous smile.

"Alfred was so agitated he didn't even know that Georges had left. He went directly to his hut, where his child of two years was sleeping in a light cradle made from lianas;[8] taking up the child, he slipped away. In order to understand what follows, you must know that there was only a small river to cross from Alfred's home before one arrives in the midst of those thick forests that seem to hold the new world in their arms.

"For six long hours, Georges walked without a rest; at last he stopped, a few steps from a hut built in the deepest heart of the forest; you'll understand the joy that shone in his eyes when you realize that this tiny hut, isolated as it is, is the camp of the Maroons; that is, of slaves who have fled the tyranny of their masters. At this moment the hut was filled with murmurs; for a rustling had been heard in the forest, and the leader, swearing that the noise was not that of any animal, had taken his rifle and gone

---

8. A woody vine common in the tropics.

out. . . . Suddenly the underbrush parted before him and he found himself face to face with a stranger.

" 'By my freedom,' he cried, looking over the newcomer, 'you found our recess all too easily.'

" 'Africa and freedom,' Georges replied calmly, as he pushed aside the barrel of the rifle. . . . 'I'm one of you.'

" 'Your name.'

" 'Georges, slave of Alfred.'

"They shook hands and embraced.

"The next day the crowd clamored round a scaffold, from which hung the body of a young mulatto woman. . . . When she had expired, the executioner let her corpse down into a pine coffin and, ten minutes later, body and coffin were thrown into a ditch that was opened at the edge of the forest.

"Thus this woman, for having been too virtuous, died the kind of death meted out to the vilest criminal. Would this alone not suffice to render the gentlest of men dangerous and bloodthirsty?"

V

"Three years had passed since the death of the virtuous Zelia. For a time, Alfred was in extreme torment; by day, he seemed to see a vengeful hand descending toward his head; he trembled at night because the darkness brought him hideous, frightful dreams. Soon, however, he banished from his thoughts both the painful memory of the martyr and the terrible threat Georges had made; he married and became a father. . . . Oh! how gratified he felt, when he was told that his prayers were answered, he who had humbly kissed the church floor each evening, beseeching the Virgin of Sorrows to grant him a son.

"For Georges also, there was happiness in this child's arrival. For if he had hoped for three years without attempting to strike back at his wife's executioner; if he had lain sleepless so many nights, with fury in his heart and a hand on his dagger, it was because he was waiting for Alfred to find himself, like Georges, with a wife and a son. It was because he wished to kill him only when dear and precious bonds linked him to this world. . . . Georges had always maintained close ties with one of Alfred's slaves; indeed, he visited him each week; and that slave had never given Georges any news more important than that of the newborn's arrival. . . . He immediately set out for the house of his enemy. On his way he met a negress who was bringing a cup of broth to Madame Alfred; he stopped her, exchanged a few insignificant words, and went on. . . . After many difficulties, he managed to slip his way, like a snake, into Alfred's rooms; once there, hidden in the space between the bed and the wall, he awaited his master. . . . A moment later, Alfred entered the room, humming a tune; he opened his secretary and took out a superb jewel box, set with diamonds, that he had promised his wife, should she give him a son; but, filled with joy and happiness, he sat down and put his head between his hands, like a man who can't believe his unexpected good fortune. Then, on raising his head, he saw before him a kind of motionless shadow, with arms crossed on its breast and two burning eyes that possessed all the ferocity of a tiger preparing to tear its prey to pieces. Alfred made a motion to stand, but a powerful arm held him down in his chair.

"'What do you want with me,' Alfred whispered, in a trembling voice.

"'To compliment you on the birth of your child,' answered a voice that seemed to emerge from the tomb.

"Alfred shook from head to toe, his hair stood on end, and a cold sweat poured over his limbs.

"'I don't know you,' Alfred muttered weakly. . . .

"'Georges is the name.'

"'You. . . .'

"'You thought I was dead, I suppose,' said the mulatto with a convulsive laugh.

"'Help . . . help,' cried Alfred.

"'Who will help you,' rejoined the mulatto . . . haven't you dismissed your servants, haven't you closed your doors, to be alone with your wife . . . so you see, your cries are useless . . . you should commend your soul to God.'

"Alfred had begun to rise from his chair, but at these last words he fell back, pale and trembling.

"'Oh! have pity, Georges . . . don't kill me, not today.'

"Georges shrugged his shoulders. 'Master, isn't it horrible to die when you're happy; to lie down in the grave at the moment you see your fondest dreams coming true . . . oh! it's horrible, isn't it,' said the mulatto with an infernal laugh. . . .

"'Mercy, Georges. . . .'

"'And yet,' he continued, 'such is your destiny . . . you shall die today, this hour, this minute, without giving your wife your last farewell. . . .'

"'Have pity . . . pity. . . .'

"'Without kissing your newborn son a second time. . . .'

"'Oh! mercy . . . mercy.'

"'I think my vengeance is worthy of your own . . . I would have sold my soul to the Devil, had he promised me this moment.'

"'Oh! mercy . . . please take pity on me,' said Alfred, throwing himself at the feet of the mulatto.

"Georges shrugged his shoulders and raised his axe.

"'Oh! one more hour of life!'

"'To embrace your wife, is that it?'

"'One minute. . . .'

"'To see your son again, right?'

"'Oh! have pity. . . .'

"'You might as well plead with the starving tiger to let go his prey.'

"'In God's name, Georges.'

"'I don't believe in that any longer.'

"'In the name of your father. . . .'

"At this, Georges's fury subsided.

"'My father . . . my father,' repeated the mulatto, tears in his eyes. 'Do you know him . . . oh! tell me his name. . . . What's his name . . . oh! tell me, tell me his name . . . I'll pardon you . . . I'll bless you.'

"And the mulatto nearly fell on his knees before his master. But suddenly, sharp cries were heard. . . .

" 'Good heavens . . . that's my wife's voice,' cried Alfred, dashing toward the sounds. . . .

"As if he were coming back to his senses, the mulatto remembered that he had come to the house of his master, not to learn the name of his father, but to settle accounts with him for his wife's blood. Holding Alfred back, he told him with a hideous grin: 'Hold on, master; it's nothing.'

" 'Jesus and Mary . . . don't you hear her calling for help.'

" 'It's nothing, I tell you.'

" 'Let me go . . . let me go . . . it's my wife's voice.'

" 'No, it's the gasps of a dying woman.'

" 'Wretch, you're lying. . . .'

" 'I poisoned her. . . .'

" 'Oh!'

" 'Do you hear those cries . . . they're hers.'

" 'The Devil. . . .'

" 'Do you hear those screams . . . they're hers.'

" 'A curse. . . .'

"During all this time, Alfred had been trying to shake free of the mulatto's grip; but he held him fast, tighter and tighter. As he did, his head rose higher, his heart beat fiercely, he steadied himself for his awful task.

" 'Alfred . . . help . . . water . . . I'm suffocating,' shouted a woman, as she threw herself into the middle of the room. She was pale and disheveled, her eyes were starting out of her head, her hair was in wild disarray.

" 'Alfred, Alfred . . . for heaven's sake, help me . . . some water . . . I need water . . . my blood is boiling . . . my heart is twitching . . . oh! water, water. . . .'

"Alfred struggled mightily to help her, but Georges held him fast with an iron hand. Laughing like one of the damned, he cried out: 'No, master . . . I'm afraid not . . . I want your wife to die . . . right there . . . before your eyes . . . right in front of you . . . do you understand, master; right in front of you, asking you for water, for air, while you can do nothing to help her.'

" 'Damnation . . . may you be damned,' howled Alfred, as he struggled like a madman.

" 'You can curse and blaspheme all you want,' answered the mulatto . . . 'this is the way it's going to be. . . .'

" 'Alfred,' the dying woman moaned again, 'good-bye . . . good-bye . . . I'm dying. . . .'

" 'Look well,' responded the mulatto, still laughing. . . . 'Look . . . she's gasping . . . goodness! a single drop of this water would restore her to life.' He showed him a small vial.

" 'My entire fortune for that drop of water. . . .' cried Alfred.

" 'Have you gone mad, master. . . .'

" 'Ah! that water . . . that water . . . don't you see she's dying . . . give it to me . . . please give it to me. . . .'

" 'Here . . .' and the mulatto flung the vial against the wall.

" 'Accursed,' screamed Alfred, seizing Georges by the neck. 'Oh! my entire life, my soul, for a dagger. . . .'

"Georges released Alfred's hands.

" 'Now that she's dead, it's your turn, master,' he said as he lifted his axe.

" 'Strike, executioner . . . strike . . . after poisoning her, you might as well kill your own fa—.' The ax fell, and Alfred's head rolled across the floor, but, as it rolled, the head distinctly pronounced the final syllable, '—ther . . .' Georges at first believed he had misheard, but the word *father*, like a funeral knell, rang in his ears. To be certain, he opened the fateful pouch. . . . 'Ah!' he cried out, 'I'm cursed. . . .' An explosion was heard; and the next day, near the corpse of Alfred, was discovered the corpse of the unhappy Georges. . . ."

1837

FREDERICK DOUGLASS
1818–1895

In his introduction to Frederick Douglass's second autobiography, *My Bondage and My Freedom* (1855), James McCune Smith, a black physician and abolitionist, hailed Douglass as "a Representative American man—a type of his countrymen." To Smith Douglass's record of "self-elevation" from the lowest to the highest condition in society marked him as a "noble example" for all Americans to emulate. Rising through the ranks of the antislavery movement in the 1840s and 1850s to become black America's most electrifying speaker and commanding writer, Douglass by the outbreak of the Civil War was generally recognized as the premier African American leader and spokesman for his people. Through the latter half of the nineteenth century Douglass dedicated his leadership to the ideal of building a racially integrated America in which skin color would cease to determine an individual's social value and economic options. As the most highly regarded African American man of letters in the nineteenth century, Douglass devoted his literary efforts primarily to the creation of a heroic image of himself that would inspire in blacks the belief that color need not be a permanent bar to their achievement of the American Dream, while reminding whites of their obligation as Americans to support free and equal access to that dream for Americans of all races.

The man who became internationally famous as Frederick Douglass was born in the backcountry of Maryland's Eastern Shore, the son of Harriet Bailey, a slave, and an unknown white man. Throughout his adult life, Douglass tried futilely to obtain reliable information about the date of his birth, which as far as he knew was never recorded. Recent biographical scholarship, however, has uncovered the property book of Douglass's first master, Aaron Anthony, in which Frederick Augustus Bailey's birth is listed as February 1818. In his first autobiography, *Narrative of the Life of Frederick Douglass* (1845), Douglass cites the resentment he felt over not knowing his birthday as early evidence of "a restless spirit" within that would goad him into increasing defiance of the institution into which he had been born. But in many respects Douglass's childhood in slavery was not as miserable as it might have been, despite the fact that his mother died when he was about seven years old. In his *Narrative* Douglass recalls having suffered much more from hunger and cold as a child than from beatings or other forms of overt abuse.

Before he was old enough to do fieldwork Frederick was selected to go to Baltimore in 1826 to become a servant in the home of Sophia and Hugh Auld. Like her sister-in-law Lucretia Anthony Auld, who had befriended Frederick on the Eastern Shore plantation where he spent his early childhood, Sophia Auld treated her obviously talented new servant with unusual kindness. She went so far as to begin reading lessons for Frederick, until her husband angrily closed the books on further efforts to brighten the mental outlook of their slave. Refusing to accept Hugh Auld's dictates, Frederick took his first covertly rebellious steps by teaching himself to read and write.

In 1833 a quarrel between Hugh Auld and his brother Thomas, Frederick's legal owner, resulted in Frederick's return to his boyhood home in St. Michaels, Maryland. Tensions between the recalcitrant black youth and his owner convinced Auld to hire Frederick out as a farm worker under the supervision of Edward Covey, a local slave breaker. After six months of unstinting labor, merciless whippings, and repeated humiliations, the desperate sixteen-year-old slave fought back, resisting one of Covey's attempted beatings and intimidating his tormentor sufficiently to prevent future attacks. Douglass's dramatic account of his struggle with Covey would become the heroic turning point of his future autobiographies and one of the most celebrated scenes in all of antebellum African American literature.

In the spring of 1836 Frederick went back to Baltimore to learn the calking trade in the city's shipyards. What Hugh Auld did not take from his earnings Frederick invested in a scheme to seize his freedom. With the aid of his future spouse, Anna Murray, and masquerading as a free black merchant sailor, Frederick Bailey took a northbound train out of Baltimore on September 3, 1838, and arrived in New York City the next day. Before a month had passed he and Anna were reunited, married, and living in New Bedford, Connecticut, as Mr. and Mrs. Frederick Douglass, the new last name recommended by a friend in New Bedford's thriving black community. Less than three years later Douglass joined the abolitionist movement as a full-time lecturer. His natural brilliance, imposing physique, and rhetorical skill soon brought him national notoriety.

Although he was best known in his own time as a speaker, Douglass worked hard to deserve the recognition he enjoys today as a writer. Rumors that a man of such accomplished address could never have been a slave drove Douglass to the decision to put his life's story into print in 1845. He was far from the first fugitive slave to put into print an account of his experiences in bondage. But the *Narrative of the Life of Frederick Douglass, an American Slave, Written by Himself* was unquestionably the epitome of the antebellum fugitive slave narrative. Selling more than thirty thousand copies in the first five years of its existence, Douglass's *Narrative* became an international best-seller, its contemporary readership far outstripping that of such classic white autobiographies as Henry David Thoreau's *Walden* (1854). The abolitionist leader William Lloyd Garrison introduced Douglass's *Narrative* by stressing how representative Douglass's experience of slavery had been. But Garrison could not help but note the extraordinary individuality of the black author's manner of rendering that experience. It is Douglass's style of self-presentation, through which he recreated the slave as an evolving self bound for mental as well as physical freedom, that makes his autobiography so memorable. After Douglass's *Narrative*, the presence of the subtitle, *Written by Himself*, on a slave narrative bore increasing political and literary significance as an indicator of a narrator's self-determination independent of external expectations and conventions.

Fearing that the added attention that his *Narrative* would attract would make him an easy target for slave catchers, Douglass went on a lecture tour in England immediately after the publication of his *Narrative*. When he came back to the United States in the spring of 1847, he had resolved, against the advice of many of his associates in Garrison's American Anti-Slavery Society, to launch his own news-paper, *The North Star*. In part Douglass wanted to prove that a black-run newspaper could succeed; in part he needed a forum from which to express himself freely, without consulting his former mentors and sponsors in the abolitionist movement. Douglass kept his newspaper going from 1847 to 1863, authoring most of the arti-cles and editorials himself. One of the literary highlights of his newspaper was a novella he wrote and published in March 1853, under the title *The Heroic Slave*. Based on an actual slave mutiny, *The Heroic Slave* brought Douglass, and with him black America, into the war of words that Harriet Beecher Stowe's *Uncle Tom's Cabin* (1852) precipitated in American literary fiction.

During the early 1850s the once close relationship between Douglass and Wil-liam Lloyd Garrison ruptured in a split that forced the black man to reassess his philosophy and goals as a reformer. Out of this time of soul searching came Dou-glass's second autobiography, *My Bondage and My Freedom* (1855). In this remark-able reevaluation of his life from the standpoint of almost fifteen years of freedom, Douglass addressed the problems of slavery and racism with unprecedented can-dor, unmasking as never before the moral and social complexities of the American caste and class system in the North as well as the South. He admitted that his search for freedom had not reached its fulfillment among the Garrisonian abolitionists, despite the implication of his *Narrative*'s conclusion. "Progress is yet possible," he asserted at the end of *My Bondage and My Freedom*, but he had come to realize his need for an anchor in the northern black community if he was ever to achieve a fully liberated sense of self.

After the outbreak of the Civil War, Douglass lobbied President Lincoln to let black troops join the fighting. When mass recruitment of African Americans for the Union Army finally began in the spring of 1863, Douglass's speeches rallied north-ern black men to the cause. When the war ended, Douglass pleaded with President Andrew Johnson for a national voting rights act that would allow African Americans to vote in all the states. His loyalty to the Republican Party, whose candidates he supported throughout his later years, won Douglass appointment to the highest po-litical offices that any black man from the North had ever won: federal marshall and recorder of deeds for the District of Columbia, president of the Freedman's Bureau Bank, consul to Haiti, and charge d'affaires for the Dominican Republic. The income he earned from these political jobs, when coupled with the fees he received for his popular lectures, most notably the one titled *Self-Made Men*, al-lowed Douglass and his family to live in comfort in Washington, D.C., during the last two decades of his life. His final memoir, *Life and Times of Frederick Douglass*, first published in 1881 and expanded in 1892, did not excite the admiration of re-viewers or sell widely, as his first two autobiographies had. But it was enough for Douglass to express through the *Life and Times* his confidence that his had been a "life of victory, if not complete, at least assured." Douglass died of a heart attack on February 20, 1895, a few hours after he had delivered a rousing speech to a women's rights rally.

Although the early twentieth century heard an occasional plea for the recogni-tion of Frederick Douglass as a major contributor to the tradition of American auto-biographical literature, not until the civil rights movement of the 1950s and the agitation for black studies in the 1960s did the *Narrative of the Life of Frederick Douglass* begin its ascent into the higher echelons of the canon of nineteenth-century American prose. After years of obscurity, *My Bondage and My Freedom* is now being advanced as one of the crucial "I-narratives" of the American 1850s, comparable in significance to the first-person writings of such renowned figures as Thoreau and Walt Whitman. In the history of African American literature, Dou-glass's importance and influence are virtually immeasurable. His *Narrative* gave the English-speaking world the most compelling and sophisticated rendition of an African American selfhood ever fashioned by a black writer up to that time. Douglass's literary artistry invested this model of selfhood with a moral and political authority that subsequent aspirants to the role of African American culture hero—from the conservative Booker T. Washington to the radical W. E. B. Du Bois—would seek to appropriate for their own autobiographical self-portraits. In twentieth-century African American literature, from Paul Laurence Dunbar's brooding poetic tribute *Douglass* (1903) to the idealistic characterization of Ned Douglass in Ernest J. Gaines's novel *The Autobiography of Miss Jane Pittman* (1971), the criterion for a black heroism that uses words as a weapon in the struggle for self and communal liberation remains the example set by Frederick Douglass.

Narrative of the Life of Frederick Douglass, an American Slave, Written by Himself[1]

Preface[2]

In the month of August, 1841, I attended an anti-slavery convention in Nantucket, at which it was my happiness to become acquainted with FREDERICK DOUGLASS, the writer of the following Narrative. He was a stranger to nearly every member of that body; but, having recently made his escape from the southern prison-house of bondage, and feeling his curiosity excited to ascertain the principles and measures of the abolitionists,—of whom he had heard a somewhat vague description while he was a slave,—he was induced to give his attendance, on the occasion alluded to, though at that time a resident in New Bedford.[3]

Fortunate, most fortunate occurrence!—fortunate for the millions of his manacled brethren, yet panting for deliverance from their awful thraldom!—fortunate for the cause of negro emancipation, and of universal liberty!—fortunate for the land of his birth, which he has already done so much to save and bless!—fortunate for a large circle of friends and acquaintances, whose sympathy and affection he has strongly secured by the many sufferings he has endured, by his virtuous traits of character, by his ever-abiding remembrance of those who are in bonds, as being bound with them!—fortunate for the multitudes, in various parts of our republic, whose minds he has enlightened on the subject of slavery, and who have been melted to tears by his pathos, or roused to virtuous indignation by his stirring eloquence against the enslavers of men!—fortunate for himself, as it at once brought him into the field of public usefulness, "gave the world assurance of a MAN,"[4] quickened the slumbering energies of his soul, and consecrated him to the great work of breaking the rod of the oppressor, and letting the oppressed go free!

I shall never forget his first speech at the convention—the extraordinary emotion it excited in my own mind—the powerful impression it created

1. First printed in May 1845 by the Anti-Slavery Office in Boston, the source of the present text.
2. The preface is by William Lloyd Garrison (1805–1879), American journalist and social reformer, and one of the most radical spokesmen for militant abolition in the United States.

3. Douglass escaped from Baltimore on September 3, 1838, and settled in New Bedford, Massachusetts, where he became active in the antislavery movement.
4. Shakespeare's *Hamlet* 3.4.62.

upon a crowded auditory, completely taken by surprise—the applause which followed from the beginning to the end of his felicitous remarks. I think I never hated slavery so intensely as at that moment; certainly, my perception of the enormous outrage which is inflicted by it, on the godlike nature of its victims, was rendered far more clear than ever. There stood one, in physical proportion and stature commanding and exact—in intellect richly endowed—in natural eloquence a prodigy—in soul manifestly "created but a little lower than the angels"[5]—yet a slave, ay, a fugitive slave,—trembling for his safety, hardly daring to believe that on the American soil, a single white person could be found who would befriend him at all hazards, for the love of God and humanity! Capable of high attainments as an intellectual and moral being—needing nothing but a comparatively small amount of cultivation to make him an ornament to society and a blessing to his race—by the law of the land, by the voice of the people, by the terms of the slave code, he was only a piece of property, a beast of burden, a chattel personal, nevertheless!

A beloved friend[6] from New Bedford prevailed on Mr. DOUGLASS to address the convention: He came forward to the platform with a hesitancy and embarrassment, necessarily the attendants of a sensitive mind in such a novel position. After apologizing for his ignorance, and reminding the audience that slavery was a poor school for the human intellect and heart, he proceeded to narrate some of the facts in his own history as a slave, and in the course of his speech gave utterance to many noble thoughts and thrilling reflections. As soon as he had taken his seat, filled with hope and admiration, I rose, and declared that PATRICK HENRY,[7] of revolutionary fame, never made a speech more eloquent in the cause of liberty, than the one we had just listened to from the lips of that hunted fugitive. So I believed at that time—such is my belief now. I reminded the audience of the peril which surrounded this self-emancipated young man at the North,—even in Massachusetts, on the soil of the Pilgrim Fathers, among the descendants of revolutionary sires; and I appealed to them, whether they would ever allow him to be carried back into slavery,—law or no law, constitution or no constitution. The response was unanimous and in thunder-tones—"NO!" "Will you succor and protect him as a brother-man—a resident of the old Bay State."[8] "YES!" shouted the whole mass, with an energy so startling, that the ruthless tyrants south of Mason and Dixon's line might almost have heard the mighty burst of feeling, and recognized it as the pledge of an invincible determination, on the part of those who gave it, never to betray him that wanders, but to hide the outcast, and firmly to abide the consequences.

It was at once deeply impressed upon my mind, that, if Mr. DOUGLASS could be persuaded to consecrate his time and talents to the promotion of the anti-slavery enterprise, a powerful impetus would be given to it, and a stunning blow at the same time inflicted on northern prejudice against a

5. God created humans "a little lower than the angels" to have authority over all other living creatures (Psalm 8:5). Paul calls the Hebrews to look at Christ, who was made "a little lower than the angels" (Hebrews 2:7, 9).
6. William C. Coffin, New Bedford's leading abolitionist at the time.
7. American patriot (1736–1799), famous for the words: "I know not what course others may take, but as for me, give me liberty or give me death."
8. I.e., Massachusetts.

colored complexion. I therefore endeavored to instill hope and courage into his mind, in order that he might dare to engage in a vocation so anomalous and responsible for a person in his situation; and I was seconded in this effort by warm-hearted friends, especially by the late General Agent of the Massachusetts Anti-Slavery Society, Mr. JOHN A. COLLINS, whose judgment in this instance entirely coincided with my own. At first, he could give no encouragement; with unfeigned diffidence, he expressed his conviction that he was not adequate to the performance of so great a task; the path marked out was wholly an untrodden one; he was sincerely apprehensive that he should do more harm than good. After much deliberation, however, he consented to make a trial; and ever since that period, he has acted as a lecturing agent, under the auspices either of the American or the Massachusetts Anti-Slavery Society. In labors he has been most abundant; and his success in combating prejudice, in gaining proselytes, in agitating the public mind, has far surpassed the most sanguine expectations that were raised at the commencement of his brilliant career. He has borne himself with gentleness and meekness, yet with true manliness of character. As a public speaker, he excels in pathos, wit, comparison, imitation, strength of reasoning, and fluency of language. There is in him that union of head and heart, which is indispensable to an enlightenment of the heads and a winning of the hearts of others. May his strength continue to be equal to his day! May he continue to "grow in grace, and in the knowledge of God," that he may be increasingly serviceable in the cause of bleeding humanity, whether at home or abroad!

It is certainly a very remarkable fact, that one of the most efficient advocates of the slave population, now before the public, is a fugitive slave, in the person of FREDERICK DOUGLASS; and that the free colored population of the United States are as ably represented by one of their own number, in the person of CHARLES LENOX REMOND, [9] whose eloquent appeals have extorted the highest applause of multitudes on both sides of the Atlantic. Let the calumniators of the colored race despise themselves for their baseness and illiberality of spirit, and henceforth cease to talk of the natural inferiority of those who require nothing but time and opportunity to attain to the highest point of human excellence.

It may, perhaps, be fairly questioned, whether any other portion of the population of the earth could have endured the privations, sufferings and horrors of slavery, without having become more degraded in the scale of humanity than the slaves of African descent. Nothing has been left undone to cripple their intellects, darken their minds, debase their moral nature, obliterate all traces of their relationship to mankind; and yet how wonderfully they have sustained the mighty load of a most frightful bondage, under which they have been groaning for centuries! To illustrate the effect of slavery on the white man,—to show that he has no powers of endurance, in such a condition, superior to those of his black brother,—DANIEL O'CONNELL, [1] the distinguished advocate of universal emancipation, and

---

9. A free-born black man (1810–1873), the first African American employed by the Massachusetts Anti-Slavery Society as a lecturer. He toured with Douglass in 1842.

1. Irish statesman (1775–1847), fighter for Catholic emancipation and Irish independence, called "the Liberator."

the mightiest champion of prostrate but not conquered Ireland, relates the following anecdote in a speech delivered by him in the Conciliation Hall, Dublin, before the Loyal National Repeal Association, March 31, 1845. "No matter," said Mr. O'CONNELL, "under what specious term it may disguise itself, slavery is still hideous. *It has a natural, an inevitable tendency to brutalize every noble faculty of man.* An American sailor, who was cast away on the shore of Africa, where he was kept in slavery for three years, was at the expiration of that period, found to be imbruted and stultified—he had lost all reasoning power; and having forgotten his native language, could only utter some savage gibberish between Arabic and English, which nobody could understand, and which even he himself found difficulty in pronouncing. So much for the humanizing influence of THE DOMESTIC INSTITUTION!" Admitting this to have been an extraordinary case of mental deterioration, it proves at least that the white slave can sink as low in the scale of humanity as the black one.

Mr. DOUGLASS has very properly chosen to write his own Narrative, in his own style, and according to the best of his ability, rather than to employ some one else. It is, therefore, entirely his own production; and, considering how long and dark was the career he had to run as a slave,—how few have been his opportunities to improve his mind since he broke his iron fetters,—it is, in my judgment, highly creditable to his head and heart. He who can peruse it without a tearful eye, a heaving breast, an afflicted spirit,—without being filled with an unutterable abhorrence of slavery and all its abettors, and animated with a determination to seek the immediate overthrow of that execrable system,—without trembling for the fate of this country in the hands of a righteous God, who is ever on the side of the oppressed, and whose arm is not shortened that it cannot save,—must have a flinty heart, and be qualified to act the part of a trafficker "in slaves and the souls of men."[2] I am confident that it is essentially true in all its statements; that nothing has been set down in malice, nothing exaggerated, nothing drawn from the imagination; that it comes short of the reality, rather than overstates a single fact in regard to SLAVERY AS IT IS. The experience of FREDERICK DOUGLASS, as a slave, was not a peculiar one; his lot was not especially a hard one; his case may be regarded as a very fair specimen of the treatment of slaves in Maryland, in which State it is conceded that they are better fed and less cruelly treated than in Georgia, Alabama, or Louisiana. Many have suffered incomparably more, while very few on the plantations have suffered less, than himself. Yet how deplorable was his situation! what terrible chastisements were inflicted upon his person! what still more shocking outrages were perpetrated upon his mind! with all his noble powers and sublime aspirations, how like a brute was he treated, even by those professing to have the same mind in them that was in Christ Jesus! to what dreadful liabilities was he continually subjected! how destitute of friendly counsel and aid, even in his greatest extremities! how heavy was the midnight of woe which shrouded in blackness the last ray of hope, and filled the future with terror and gloom! what longings after freedom took possession of his breast, and how his misery augmented, in proportion

2. Compare Revelation 18:13.

as he grew reflective and intelligent,—thus demonstrating that a happy slave is an extinct man! how he thought, reasoned, felt, under the lash of the driver, with the chains upon his limbs! what perils he encountered in his endeavors to escape from his horrible doom! and how signal have been his deliverance and preservation in the midst of a nation of pitiless enemies!

This Narrative contains many affecting incidents, many passages of great eloquence and power; but I think the most thrilling one of them all is the description DOUGLASS gives of his feelings, as he stood soliloquizing respecting his fate, and the chances of his one day being a freeman, on the banks of the Chesapeake Bay—view in the receding vessels as they flew with their white wings before the breeze, and apostrophizing them as animated by the living spirit of freedom. Who can read that passage, and be insensible to its pathos and sublimity? Compressed into it is a whole Alexandrian library[3] of thought, feeling, and sentiment—all that can, all that need be urged, in the form of expostulation, entreaty, rebuke, against that crime of crimes,—making man the property of his fellow-man! O, how accursed is that system, which entombs the godlike mind of man, defaces the divine image, reduces those who by creation were crowned with glory and honor to a level with four-footed beasts, and exalts the dealer in human flesh above all that is called God! Why should its existence be prolonged one hour? Is it not evil, only evil, and that continually? What does its presence imply but the absence of all fear of God, all regard for man, on the part of the people of the United States? Heaven speed its eternal overthrow!

So profoundly ignorant of the nature of slavery are many persons, that they are stubbornly incredulous whenever they read or listen to any recital of the cruelties which are daily inflicted on its victims. They do not deny that the slaves are held as property; but that terrible fact seems to convey to their minds no idea of injustice, exposure to outrage, or savage barbarity. Tell them of cruel scourgings, of mutilations and brandings, of scenes of pollution and blood, of the banishment of all light and knowledge, and they affect to be greatly indignant at such enormous exaggerations, such wholesale misstatements, such abominable libels on the character of the southern planters! As if all these direful outrages were not the natural results of slavery! As if it were less cruel to reduce a human being to the condition of a thing, than to give him a severe flagellation, or to deprive him of necessary food and clothing! As if whips, chains, thumb-screws, paddles, bloodhounds, overseers, drivers, patrols, were not all indispensable to keep the slaves down, and to give protection to their ruthless oppressors! As if, when the marriage institution is abolished, concubinage, adultery, and incest, must not necessarily abound; when all the rights of humanity are annihilated, any barrier remains to protect the victim from the fury of the spoiler; when absolute power is assumed over life and liberty, it will not be wielded with destructive sway! Skeptics of this character abound in society. In some few instances, their incredulity arises from a want of reflection;

3. Alexandria, in Egypt, housed the great library center of the Greco-Roman world.

but, generally, it indicates a hatred of the light, a desire to shield slavery from the assaults of its foes, a contempt of the colored race, whether bond or free. Such will try to discredit the shocking tales of slaveholding cruelty which are recorded in this truthful Narrative; but they will labor in vain. Mr. DOUGLASS has frankly disclosed the place of his birth, the names of those who claimed ownership in his body and soul, and the names also of those who committed the crimes which he has alleged against them. His statements, therefore, may easily be disproved, if they are untrue.

In the course of his Narrative, he relates two instances of murderous cruelty,—in one of which a planter deliberately shot a slave belonging to a neighboring plantation, who had unintentionally gotten within his lordly domain in quest of fish; and in the other, an overseer blew out the brains of a slave who had fled to a stream of water to escape a bloody scourging. Mr. DOUGLASS states that in neither of these instances was any thing done by way of legal arrest or judicial investigation. The Baltimore American, of March 17, 1845, relates a similar case of atrocity, perpetrated with similar impunity—as follows:—"*Shooting a Slave.*—We learn, upon the authority of a letter from Charles county, Maryland, received by a gentleman of this city, that a young man, named Matthews, a nephew of General Matthews, and whose father, it is believed, holds an office at Washington, killed one of the slaves upon his father's farm by shooting him. The letter states that young Matthews had been left in charge of the farm; that he gave an order to the servant, which was disobeyed, when he proceeded to the house, *obtained a gun, and, returning, shot the servant.* He immediately, the letter continues, fled to his father's residence, where he still remains unmolested."—Let it never be forgotten, that no slaveholder or overseer can be convicted of any outrage perpetrated on the person of a slave, however diabolical it may be, on the testimony of colored witnesses, whether bond or free. By the slave code, they are adjudged to be as incompetent to testify against a white man, as though they were indeed a part of the brute creation. Hence, there is no legal protection in fact, whatever there may be in form, for the slave population; and any amount of cruelty may be inflicted on them with impunity. Is it possible for the human mind to conceive of a more horrible state of society?

The effect of a religious profession on the conduct of southern masters is vividly described in the following Narrative, and shown to be any thing but salutary. In the nature of the case, it must be in the highest degree pernicious. The testimony of Mr. DOUGLASS, on this point, is sustained by a cloud of witnesses, whose veracity is unimpeachable. "A slaveholder's profession of Christianity is a palpable imposture. He is a felon of the highest grade. He is a manstealer. It is of no importance what you put in the other scale."

Reader! are you with the man-stealers in sympathy and purpose, or on the side of their down-trodden victims? If with the former, then are you the foe of God and man. If with the latter, what are you prepared to do and dare in their behalf? Be faithful, be vigilant, be untiring in your efforts to break every yoke, and let the oppressed go free. Come what may—cost what it may—inscribe on the banner which you unfurl to the breeze, as your religious and political motto—"No Compromise with Slavery! No Union with Slaveholders!"

WM. LLOYD GARRISON

Boston, May 1, 1845.

Letter from Wendell Phillips, Esq. [4]

Boston, April 22, 1845.

My Dear Friend:

You remember the old fable of "The Man and the Lion" where the lion complained that he should not be so misrepresented "when the lions wrote history."

I am glad the time has come when the "lions write history." We have been left long enough to gather the character of slavery from the involuntary evidence of the masters. One might, indeed, rest sufficiently satisfied with what, it is evident, must be, in general, the results of such a relation, without seeking farther to find whether they have followed in every instance. Indeed, those who stare at the half-peck of corn a week, and love to count the lashes on the slave's back, are seldom the "stuff" out of which reformers and abolitionists are to be made. I remember that, in 1838, many were waiting for the results of the West India experiment, [5] before they could come into our ranks. Those "results" have come long ago; but, alas! few of that number have come with them, as converts. A man must be disposed to judge of emancipation by other tests than whether it has increased the produce of sugar,—and to hate slavery for other reasons than because it starves men and whips womens,—before he is ready to lay the first stone of his anti-slavery life.

I was glad to learn, in your story, how early the most neglected of God's children waken to a sense of their rights, and of the injustice done them. Experience is a keen teacher; and long before you had mastered your A B C, or knew where the "white sails" of the Chesapeake were bound, you began, I see, to gauge the wretchedness of the slave, not by his hunger and want, not by his lashes and toil, but by the cruel and blighting death which gathers over his soul.

In connection with this, there is one circumstance which makes your recollections peculiarly valuable, and renders your early insight the more remarkable. You come from that part of the country where we are told slavery appears with its fairest features. Let us hear, then, what it is at its best estate—gaze on its bright side, if it has one; and then imagination may task her powers to add dark lines to the picture, as she travels southward to that (for the colored man) Valley of the Shadow of Death, where the Mississippi sweeps along.

---

4. A leading abolitionist (1811–1884).
5. Slavery was officially abolished in the West Indies and throughout the British Empire in 1833.

The process of emancipation was completed in 1838.

Again, we have known you long, and can put the most entire confidence in your truth, candor, and sincerity. Every one who has heard you speak has felt, and, I am confident, every one who reads your book will feel, persuaded that you give them a fair specimen of the whole truth. No one-sided portrait,—no wholesale complaints,—but strict justice done, whenever individual kindliness has neutralized, for a moment, the deadly system with which it was strangely allied. You have been with us, too, some years, and can fairly compare the twilight of rights, which your race enjoy at the North, with that "noon of night" under which they labor south of Mason and Dixon's line. Tell us whether, after all, the half-free colored man of Massachusetts is worse off than the pampered slave of the rice swamps!

In reading your life, no one can say that we have unfairly picked out some rare specimens of cruelty. We know that the bitter drops, which even you have drained from the cup, are no incidental aggravations, no individual ills, but such as must mingle always and necessarily in the lot of every slave. They are the essential ingredients, not the occasional results, of the system.

After all, I shall read your book with trembling for you. Some years ago, when you were beginning to tell me your real name and birthplace, you may remember I stopped you, and preferred to remain ignorant of all. With the exception of a vague description, so I continued, till the other day, when you read me your memoirs. I hardly knew, at the time, whether to thank you or not for the sight of them, when I reflected that it was still dangerous, in Massachusetts, for honest men to tell their names! They say the fathers, in 1776, signed the Declaration of Independence with the halter about their necks. You, too, publish your declaration of freedom with danger compassing you around. In all the broad lands which the Constitution of the United States overshadows, there is no single spot,—however narrow or desolate,—where a fugitive slave can plant himself and say, "I am safe." The whole armory of Northern Law has no shield for you. I am free to say that, in your place, I should throw the MS. into the fire.

You, perhaps, may tell your story in safety, endeared as you are to so many warm hearts by rare gifts, and a still rarer devotion of them to the service of others. But it will be owing only to your labors, and the fearless efforts of those who, trampling the laws and Constitution of the country under their feet, are determined that they will "hide the outcast," and that their hearths shall be, spite of the law, an asylum for the oppressed, if, some time or other, the humblest may stand in our streets, and bear witness in safety against the cruelties which he has been the victim.

Yet it is sad to think, that these very throbbing hearts which welcome your story, and form your best safeguard in telling it, are all beating contrary to the "statute in such case made and provided." Go on, my dear friend, till you, and those who, like you, have been saved, so as by fire, from the dark prison-house, shall stereotype these free, illegal pulses into statutes; and New England, cutting loose from a blood-stained Union, shall glory in being the house of refuge for the oppressed;—till we no longer merely "*hide* the outcast," or make a merit of standing idly by while he is hunted in our midst; but, consecrating anew the soil of the Pilgrims as an asylum for the oppressed, proclaim our *welcome* to the slave so loudly, that the tones shall reach every hut in the Carolinas, and make the broken-hearted bondman leap up at the thought of old Massachusetts.

God speed the day!

Till then, and ever,
Yours truly,
WENDELL PHILLIPS

Chapter I

I was born in Tuckahoe, near Hillsborough, and about twelve miles from Easton, in Talbot county, Maryland. I have no accurate knowledge of my age, never having seen any authentic record containing it. By far the larger part of the slaves know as little of their ages as horses know of theirs, and it is the wish of most masters within my knowledge to keep their slaves thus ignorant. I do not remember to have ever met a slave who could tell of his birthday. They seldom come nearer to it than planting-time, harvest-time, cherry-time, spring-time, or fall-time. A want of information concerning my own was a source of unhappiness to me even during childhood. The white children could tell their ages. I could not tell why I ought to be deprived of the same privilege. I was not allowed to make any inquiries of my master concerning it. He deemed all such inquiries on the part of a slave improper and impertinent, and evidence of a restless spirit. The nearest estimate I can give makes me now between twenty-seven and twenty-eight years of age. I come to this, from hearing my master say, some time during 1835, I was about seventeen years old.

My mother was named Harriet Bailey. She was the daughter of Isaac and Betsey Bailey, both colored, and quite dark. My mother was of a darker complexion than either my grandmother or grandfather.

My father was a white man. He was admitted to be such by all I ever heard speak of my parentage. The opinion was also whispered that my master was my father; but of the correctness of this opinion, I know nothing; the means of knowing was withheld from me. My mother and I were separated when I was but an infant—before I knew her as my mother. It is a common custom, in the part of Maryland from which I ran away, to part children from their mothers at a very early age. Frequently, before the child has reached its twelfth month, its mother is taken from it, and hired out on some farm a considerable distance off, and the child is placed under the care of an old woman, too old for field labor. For what this separation is done, I do not know, unless it be to hinder the development of the child's affection toward its mother, and to blunt and destroy the natural affection of the mother for the child. This is the inevitable result.

I never saw my mother, to know her as such, more than four or five times in my life; and each of these times was very short in duration, and at night. She was hired by a Mr. Stewart, who lived about twelve miles from my home. She made her journeys to see me in the night, travelling the whole distance on foot, after the performance of her day's work. She was a field hand, and a whipping is the penalty of not being in the field at sunrise, unless a slave has special permission from his or her master to the contrary—a permission which they seldom get, and one that gives to him that gives it the proud name of being a kind master. I do not recollect of ever seeing my mother by the light of day. She was with me in the night. She would lie down with me, and get me to sleep, but long before I waked she was gone. Very little communication ever took place between us. Death soon ended what little we could have while she lived, and with it her hardships and suffering. She died when I was about seven years old, on one of my master's farms, near Lee's Mill. I was not allowed to be present during her illness, at her death, or burial. She was gone long before I knew anything about it. Never having enjoyed, to any considerable extent, her soothing presence, her tender and watchful care, I received the tidings of her death with much the same emotions I should have probably felt at the death of a stranger.

Called thus suddenly away, she left me without the slightest intimation of who my father was. The whisper that my master was my father, may or may not be true; and, true or false, it is of but little consequence to my purpose whilst the fact remains, in all its glaring odiousness, that slaveholders have ordained, and by law established, that the children of slave women shall in all cases follow the condition of their mothers; and this is done too obviously to administer to their own lusts, and make a gratification of their wicked desires profitable as well as pleasureable; for by this cunning arrangement, the slaveholder, in cases not a few, sustains to his slaves the double relation of master and father.

I know of such cases; and it is worthy of remark that such slaves invariably suffer greater hardships, and have more to contend with, than others. They are, in the first place, a constant offence to their mistress. She is ever disposed to find fault with them; they can seldom do any thing to please her; she is never better pleased than when she sees them under the lash, especially when she suspects her husband of showing to his mulatto children favors which he withholds from his black slaves. The master is frequently compelled to sell this class of his slaves, out of deference to the feelings of his white wife; and, cruel as the deed may strike any one to be, for a man to sell his own children to human flesh-mongers, it is often the dictate of humanity for him to do so; for, unless he does this, he must not only whip them himself, but must stand by and see one white son tie up his brother, of but few shades darker complexion than himself, and ply the gory lash to his naked back; and if he lisp one word of disapproval, it is set down to his parental partiality, and only makes a bad matter worse, both for himself and the slave whom he would protect and defend.

Every year brings with it multitudes of this class of slaves. It was doubtless in consequence of a knowledge of this fact, that one great statesman of the south predicted the downfall of slavery by the inevitable laws of population. Whether this prophecy is ever fulfilled or not, it is nevertheless plain that a very different-looking class of people are springing up at the south, and are now held in slavery, from those originally brought to this country from Africa; and if their increase will do no other good, it will do away the force of the argument, that God cursed Ham,[6] and therefore American slavery is right. If the lineal descendants of Ham are alone to be scripturally enslaved, it is certain that slavery at the south must soon become unscriptural; for thousands are ushered into the world, annually, who, like myself, owe their existence to white fathers, and those fathers most frequently their own masters.

I have had two masters. My first master's name was Anthony. I do not remember his first name. He was generally called Captain Anthony—a title which, I presume, he acquired by sailing a craft on the Chesapeake Bay. He was not considered a rich slaveholder. He owned two or three farms, and about thirty slaves. His farms and slaves were under the care of an overseer. The overseer's name was Plummer. Mr. Plummer was a miserable drunkard, a profane swearer, and a savage monster. He always went armed with a cowskin and a heavy cudgel.[7] I have known him to cut and slash the women's heads so horribly, that even master would be enraged at his cruelty, and would threaten to whip him if he did not mind himself. Master, however, was not a humane slaveholder. It required extraordinary barbarity on the part of an overseer to affect him. He was a cruel man, hardened by a long life of slaveholding. He would at times seem to take great pleasure in whipping a slave. I have often been awakened at the dawn of day by the most heartrending shrieks of an own aunt of mine, whom he used to tie up to a joist, and whip upon her naked back till she was literally covered with blood. No words, no tears, no prayers, from his gory victim, seemed to move his iron heart from its bloody purpose. The louder she screamed, the harder he whipped; and where the blood ran fastest, there he whipped longest. He would whip her to make her scream, and whip her to make her hush; and not until overcome by fatigue, would he cease to swing the blood-clotted cowskin. I remember the first time I ever witnessed this horrible exhibition. I was quite a child, but I will remember it. I never shall forget it whilst I remember any thing. It was the first of a long series of such outrages, of which I was doomed to be a witness and a participant. It struck me with awful force. It was the blood-stained gate, the entrance to the hell of slavery, through which I was about to pass. It was a most terrible spectacle. I wish I could commit to paper the feelings with which I beheld it.

This occurrence took place very soon after I went to live with my old master, and under the following circumstances. Aunt Hester went out one night,—where or for what I do not know,—and happened to be absent when my master desired her presence. He had ordered her not to go out evenings, and warned her that she must never let him catch her in company with a young man, who was paying attention to her, belonging to Colonel Lloyd. The young man's name was Ned Roberts, generally called Lloyd's Ned. Why master was so careful of her, may be safely left to conjecture. She was a woman of noble form, and of graceful proportions, having very few equals, and fewer superiors, in personal appearance, among the colored or white women of our neighborhood.

6. The specious argument referred to is based on an interpretation of Genesis 9:20–27, in which Noah curses his son Ham and condemns him to bondage to his brothers.

7. A short, thick stick of wood. "Cowskin": a whip made of raw cowhide.

Aunt Hester had not only disobeyed his orders in going out, but had been found in company with Lloyd's Ned; which circumstance, I found, from what he said while whipping her, was the chief offence. Had he been a man of pure morals himself, he might have been thought interested in protecting the innocence of my aunt; but those who knew him will not suspect him of any such virtue. Before he commenced whipping Aunt Hester, he took her into the kitchen, and stripped her from neck to waist, leaving her neck, shoulders, and back, entirely naked. He then told her to cross her hands, calling her at the same time a d——d b——h. After crossing her hands, he tied them with a strong rope, and led her to a stool under a large hook in the joist, put in for the purpose. He made her get upon the stool, and tied her hands to the hook. She now stood fair for his infernal purpose. Her arms were stretched up at their full length, so that she stood upon the ends of her toes. He then said to her, "Now, you d——d b——h, I'll learn you how to disobey my orders!" and after rolling up his sleeves, he commenced to lay on the heavy cowskin, and soon the warm, red blood (amid heart-rending shrieks from her, and horrid oaths from him) came dripping to the floor. I was so terrified and horror-stricken at the sight, that I hid myself in a closet, and dared not venture out till long after the bloody transaction was over. I expected it would be my turn next. It was all new to me. I had never seen any thing like it before. I had always lived with my grandmother on the outskirts of the plantation, where she was put to raise the children of the younger women. I had therefore been, until now, out of the way of the bloody scenes that often occurred on the plantation.

Chapter II

My master's family consisted of two sons, Andrew and Richard; one daughter, Lucretia, and her husband, Captain Thomas Auld. They lived in one house, upon the home plantation of Colonel Edward Lloyd. My master was Colonel Lloyd's clerk and superintendent. He was what might be called the overseer of the overseers. I spent two years of childhood on this plantation in my old master's family. It was here that I witnessed the bloody transaction recorded in the first chapter; and as I received my first impressions of slavery on this plantation, I will give some description of it, and of slavery as it there existed. The plantation is about twelve miles north of Easton, in Talbot county, and is situated on the border of Miles River. The principal products raised upon it were tobacco, corn, and wheat. These were raised in great abundance; so that, with the products of this and the other farms belonging to him, he was able to keep in almost constant employment a large sloop, in carrying them to market at Baltimore. This sloop was named Sally Lloyd, in honor of one of the colonel's daughters. My master's son-in-law, Captain Auld, was master of the vessel; she was otherwise manned by the colonel's own slaves. Their names were Peter, Isaac, Rich, and Jake. These were esteemed very highly by the other slaves, and looked upon as the privileged ones of the plantation; for it was no small affair, in the eyes of the slaves, to be allowed to see Baltimore.

Colonel Lloyd kept from three to four hundred slaves on his home plantation, and owned a large number more on the neighboring farms belonging to him. The names of the farms nearest to the home plantation were Wye Town and New Design. "Wye Town" was under the overseership of a man named Noah Willis. New Design was under the overseership of a Mr. Townsend. The overseers of these, and all the rest of the farms, numbering over twenty, received advice and direction from the managers of the home plantation. This was the great business place. It was the seat of government for the whole twenty farms. All disputes among the overseers were settled here. If a slave was convicted of any high misdemeanor, became unmanageable, or evinced a determination to run away, he was brought immediately here, severely whipped, put on board the sloop, carried to Baltimore, and sold to Austin Woolfolk, or some other slave-trader, as a warning to the slaves remaining.

Here, too, the slaves of all the other farms received their monthly allowance of food, and their yearly clothing. The men and women slaves received, as their monthly allowance of food, eight pounds of pork, or its equivalent in fish, and one bushel of corn meal. Their yearly clothing consisted of two coarse linen shirts, one pair of linen trousers, like the shirts, one jacket, one pair of trousers for winter, made of coarse negro cloth, one pair of stockings, and one pair of shoes; the whole of which could not have cost more than seven dollars. The allowance of the slave children was given to their mothers, or the old women having the care of them. The children unable to work in the field had neither shoes, stockings, jackets, nor trousers, given to them; their clothing consisted of two coarse linen shirts per year. When these failed them, they went naked until the next allowance-day. Children from seven to ten years old, of both sexes, almost naked, might be seen at all seasons of the year.

There were no beds given the slaves, unless one coarse blanket be considered such, and none but the men and women had these. This, however, is not considered a very great privation. They find less difficulty from the want of beds, than from the want of time to sleep; for when their day's work in the field is done, the most of them having their washing, mending, and cooking to do, and having few or none of the ordinary facilities for doing either of these, very many of their sleeping hours are consumed in preparing for the field the coming day; and when this is done, old and young, male and female, married and single, drop down side by side; on one common bed,—the cold, damp floor,—each covering himself or herself with their miserable blankets; and here they sleep till they are summoned to the field by the driver's horn. At the sound of this, all must rise, and be off to the field. There must be no halting; every one must be at his or her post; and woe betides them who hear not this morning summons to the field; for if they are not awakened by the sense of hearing, they are by the sense of feeling: no age nor sex finds any favor. Mr. Severe, the overseer, used to stand by the door of the quarter, armed with a large hickory stick and heavy cowskin, ready to whip any one who was so unfortunate as not to hear, or, from any other cause, was prevented from being ready to start for the field at the sound of the horn.

Mr. Severe was rightly named: he was a cruel man. I have seen him whip a woman, causing the blood to run half an hour at the time; and this, too, in the midst of her crying children, pleading for their mother's release. He seemed to take pleasure in manifesting his fiendish barbarity. Added to his cruelty, he was a profane swearer. It was enough to chill the blood and stiffen the hair of an ordinary man to hear him talk. Scarce a sentence escaped him but that was commenced or concluded by some horrid oath. The field was the place to witness his cruelty and profanity. His presence made it both the field of blood and of blasphemy. From the rising till the going down of the sun, he was cursing, raving, cutting, and slashing among the slaves of the field, in the most frightful manner. His career was short. He died very soon after I went to Colonel Lloyd's; and he died as he lived, uttering, with his dying groans, bitter curses and horrid oaths. His death was regarded by the slaves as the result of a merciful providence.

Mr. Severe's place was filled by a Mr. Hopkins. He was a very different man. He was less cruel, less profane, and made less noise, than Mr. Severe. His course was characterized by no extraordinary demonstrations of cruelty. He whipped, but seemed to take no pleasure in it. He was called by the slaves a good overseer.

The home plantation of Colonel Lloyd wore the appearance of a country village. All the mechanical operations for all the farms were performed here. The shoemaking and mending, the blacksmithing, cartwrighting, coopering, weaving, and grain-grinding, were all performed by the slaves on the home plantation. The whole place wore a business-like aspect very unlike the neighboring farms. The number of houses, too, conspired to give it advantage over the neighboring farms. It was called by the slaves the *Great House Farm*. Few privileges were esteemed higher, by the slaves of the out-farms, than that of being selected to do errands at the Great House Farm. It was associated in their minds with greatness. A representative could not be prouder of his election to a seat in the American Congress, than a slave on one of the out-farms would be of his election to do errands at the Great House Farm. They regarded it as evidence of great confidence reposed in them by their overseers; and it was on this account, as well as a constant desire to be out of the field from under the driver's lash, that they esteemed it a high privilege, one worth careful living for. He was called the smartest and most trusty fellow, who had this honor conferred upon him the most frequently. The competitors for this office sought as diligently to please their overseers, as the office-seekers in the political parties seek to please and deceive the people. The same traits of character might be seen in Colonel Lloyd's slaves, as are seen in the slaves of the political parties.

The slaves selected to go to the Great House Farm, for the monthly allowance for themselves and their fellow-slaves, were peculiarly enthusiastic. While on their way, they would make the dense old woods, for miles around, reverberate with their wild songs, revealing at once the highest joy and the deepest sadness. They would compose and sing as they went along, consulting neither time nor tune. The thought that came up, came out—if not in the word, in the sound;—and as frequently in the one as in the other. They would sometimes sing the most pathetic sentiment in the most rapturous tone, and the most rapturous sentiment in the most pathetic tone. Into all of their songs they would manage to weave something of the Great House Farm. Especially would they do this, when leaving home. They would then sing most exultingly the following words:—

"I am going away to the Great House Farm!
O, yea! O, yea! O!"

This they would sing, as a chorus, to words which to many would seem unmeaning jargon, but which, nevertheless, were full of meaning to themselves. I have sometimes thought that the mere hearing of those songs would do more to impress some minds with the horrible character of slavery, than the reading of whole volumes of philosophy on the subject could do.

I did not, when a slave, understand the deep meaning of those rude and apparently incoherent songs. I was myself within the circle; so that I neither saw nor heard as those without might see and hear. They told a tale of woe which was then altogether beyond my feeble comprehension; they were tones loud, long, and deep; they breathed the prayer and complaint of souls boiling over with the bitterest anguish. Every tone was a testimony against slavery, and a prayer to God for deliverance from chains. The hearing of those wild notes always depressed my spirit, and filled me with ineffable sadness. I have frequently found myself in tears while hearing them. The mere recurrence to those songs, even now, afflicts me; and while I am writing these lines, an expression of feeling has already found its way down my cheek. To those songs I trace my first glimmering conception of the dehumanizing character of slavery. I can never get rid of that conception. Those songs still follow me, to deepen my hatred of slavery, and quicken my sympathies for my brethren in bonds. If any one wishes to be impressed with the soul-killing effects of slavery, let him go to Colonel Lloyd's plantation, and, on allowance-day, place himself in the deep pine woods, and there let him, in silence, analyze the sounds that shall pass through the chambers of his soul,—and if he is not thus impressed, it will only be because "there is no flesh in his obdurate heart." [8]

I have often been utterly astonished, since I came to the north, to find persons who could speak of the singing, among slaves, as evidence of their contentment and happiness. It is impossible to conceive of a greater mistake. Slaves sing most when they are most unhappy. The songs of the slave represent the sorrows of his heart; and he is relieved by them, only as an aching heart is relieved by its tears. At least, such is my experience. I have often sung to drown my sorrow, but seldom to express my happiness. Crying for joy, and singing for joy, were alike uncommon to me while in the jaws of slavery. The singing of a man cast away upon a desolate island might be as appropriately considered as evidence of contentment and happiness, as the singing of a slave; the songs of the one and of the other are prompted by the same emotion.

Chapter III

Colonel Lloyd kept a large and finely cultivated garden, which afforded almost constant employment for four men, besides the chief gardener, (Mr. M'Durmond.) This garden was probably the greatest attraction of the

8. From William Cowper's popular poem *The Task* (1785): *The Time-Piece* 2.8.

place. During the summer months, people came from far and near—from Baltimore, Easton, and Annapolis—to see it. It abounded in fruits of almost every description, from the hardy apple of the north to the delicate orange of the south. This garden was not the least source of trouble on the plantation. Its excellent fruit was quite a temptation to the hungry swarms of boys, as well as the older slaves, belonging to the colonel, few of whom had the virtue or the vice to resist it. Scarcely a day passed, during the summer, but that some slave had to take the lash for stealing fruit. The colonel had to resort to all kinds of stratagems to keep his slaves out of the garden. The last and most successful one was that of tarring his fence all around, after which, if a slave was caught with any tar upon his person, it was deemed sufficient proof that he had either been into the garden, or had tried to get in. In either case, he was severely whipped by the chief gardener. This plan worked well; the slaves became as fearful of tar as of the lash. They seemed to realize the impossibility of touching *tar* without being defiled.

The colonel also kept a splendid riding equipage. His stable and carriage-house presented the appearance of some of our large city livery establishments. His horses were of the finest form and noblest blood. His carriage-house contained three splendid coaches, three or four gigs, besides dearborns and barouches[9] of the most fashionable style.

This establishment was under the care of two slaves—old Barney and young Barney—father and son. To attend to this establishment was their sole work. But it was by no means an easy employment; for in nothing was Colonel Lloyd more particular than in the management of his horses. The slightest inattention to these was unpardonable, and was visited upon those, under whose care they were placed, with the severest punishment; no excuse could shield them, if the colonel only suspected any want of attention to his horses—a supposition which he frequently indulged, and one which, of course, made the office of old and young Barney a very trying one. They never knew when they were safe from punishment. They were frequently whipped when least deserving, and escaped whipping when most deserving it. Every thing depended upon the looks of the horses, and the state of Colonel Lloyd's own mind when his horses were brought to him for use. If a horse did not move fast enough, or hold his head high enough, it was owing to some fault of his keepers. It was painful to stand near the stable door, and hear the various complaints against the keepers when a horse was taken out for use. "This horse has not had proper attention. He has not been sufficiently rubbed and curried, or he has not been properly fed; his food was too wet or too dry; he got it too soon or too late; he was too hot or too cold; he had too much hay, and not enough of grain; or he had too much grain, and not enough of hay; instead of old Barney's attending to the horse, he had very improperly left it to his son." To all these complaints, no matter how unjust, the slave must answer never a word. Colonel Lloyd could not brook any contradiction from a slave. When he spoke, a slave must stand, listen, and tremble; and such was literally the case. I have seen Colonel Lloyd make old Barney, a man between fifty and sixty years of age, uncover his bald head, kneel down upon the

9. Different kinds of carriages.

cold, damp ground, and receive upon his naked and toil-worn shoulders more than thirty lashes at the time. Colonel Lloyd had three sons— Edward, Murray, and Daniel,—and three sons-in-law, Mr. Winder, Mr. Nicholson, and Mr. Lowndes. All of these lived at the Great House Farm, and enjoyed the luxury of whipping the servants when they pleased, from old Barney down to William Wilkes, the coach-driver. I have seen Winder make one of the house-servants stand off from him a suitable distance to be touched with the end of his whip, and at every stroke raise great ridges upon his back.

To describe the wealth of Colonel Lloyd would be almost equal to describing the riches of Job. He kept from ten to fifteen house-servants. He was said to own a thousand slaves, and I think this estimate quite within the truth. Colonel Lloyd owned so many that he did not know them when he saw them; nor did all the slaves of the out-farms know him. It is reported of him, that, while riding along the road one day, he met a colored man, and addressed him in the usual manner of speaking to colored people on the public highways of the south: "Well, boy, whom do you belong to?" "To Colonel Lloyd," replied the slave. "Well, does the colonel treat you well?" "No, sir," was the ready reply. "What, does he work you too hard?" "Yes, sir." "Well, don't he give you enough to eat?" "Yes, sir, he gives me enough, such as it is."

The colonel, after ascertaining where the slave belonged, rode on; the man also went on about his business, not dreaming that he had been conversing with his master. He thought, said, and heard nothing more of the matter, until two or three weeks afterwards. The poor man was then informed by his overseer that, for having found fault with his master, he was now to be sold to a Georgia trader. He was immediately chained and handcuffed; and thus, without a moment's warning, he was snatched away, and forever sundered, from his family and friends, by a hand more unrelenting than death. This is the penalty of telling the truth, of telling the simple truth, in answer to a series of plain questions.

It is partly in consequence of such facts, that slaves, when inquired of as to their condition and the character of their masters, almost universally say they are contented, and that their masters are kind. The slaveholders have been known to send in spies among their slaves, to ascertain their views and feelings in regard to their condition. The frequency of this has had the effect to establish among the slaves the maxim, that a still tongue makes a wise head. They suppress the truth rather than take the consequences of telling it, and in so doing prove themselves a part of the human family. If they have any thing to say of their masters, it is generally in their master's favor, especially when speaking to an untried man. I have been frequently asked, when a slave, if I had a kind master, and do not remember ever to have given a negative answer; nor did I, in pursuing this course, consider myself as uttering what was absolutely false; for I always measured the kindness of my master by the standard of kindness set up among slaveholders around us. Moreover, slaves are like other people, and imbibe prejudices quite common to others. They think their own better than that of others. Many, under the influence of this prejudice, think their own masters are better than the masters of other slaves; and this, too, in some cases, when the very reverse is true. Indeed, it is not uncommon for slaves even to fall out and quarrel among themselves about the relative goodness of their masters, each contending for the superior goodness of his own over that of the others. At the very same time, they mutually execrate their masters when viewed separately. It was so on our plantation. When Colonel Lloyd's slaves met the slaves of Jacob Jepson, they seldom parted without a quarrel about their masters; Colonel Lloyd's slaves contending that he was the richest, and Mr. Jepson's slaves that he was the smartest, and most of a man. Colonel Lloyd's slaves would boast his ability to buy and sell Jacob Jepson. Mr. Jepson's slaves would boast his ability to whip Colonel Lloyd. These quarrels would almost always end in a fight between the parties, and those that whipped were supposed to have gained the point at issue. They seemed to think that the greatness of their masters was transferable to themselves. It was considered as being bad enough to be a slave; but to be a poor man's slave was deemed a disgrace indeed!

Chapter IV

Mr. Hopkins remained but a short time in the office of overseer. Why his career was so short, I do not know, but suppose he lacked the necessary severity to suit Colonel Lloyd. Mr. Hopkins was succeeded by Mr. Austin Gore, a man possessing, in an eminent degree, all those traits of character indispensable to what is called a first-rate overseer. Mr. Gore had served Colonel Lloyd, in the capacity of overseer, upon one of the out-farms, and had shown himself worthy of the high station of overseer upon the home or Great House Farm.

Mr. Gore was proud, ambitious, and persevering. He was artful, cruel, and obdurate. He was just the man for such a place, and it was just the place for such a man. It afforded scope for the full exercise of all his powers, and he seemed to be perfectly at home in it. He was one of those who could torture the slightest look, word, or gesture, on the part of the slave, into impudence, and would treat it accordingly. There must be no answering back to him; no explanation was allowed a slave, showing himself to have been wrongfully accused. Mr. Gore acted fully up to the maxim laid down by slaveholders,— "It is better that a dozen slaves suffer under the lash, than that the overseer should be convicted, in the presence of the slaves, of having been at fault." No matter how innocent a slave might be—it availed him nothing, when accused by Mr. Gore of any misdemeanor. To be accused was to be convicted, and to be convicted was to be punished; the one always following the other with immutable certainty. To escape punishment was to escape accusation; and few slaves had the fortune to do either, under the overseership of Mr. Gore. He was just proud enough to demand the most debasing homage of the slave, and quite servile enough to crouch, himself, at the feet of the master. He was ambitious enough to be contented with nothing short of the highest rank of overseers, and persevering enough to reach the height of his ambition. He was cruel enough to inflict the severest punishment, artful enough to descend to the lowest trickery, and obdurate enough to be insensible to the voice of a reproving conscience. He was, of all the overseers, the most dreaded by the slaves. His presence was painful; his eye flashed confusion; and seldom was his sharp, shrill voice heard, without producing horror and trembling in their ranks.

Mr. Gore was a grave man, and, though a young man, he indulged in no jokes, said no funny words, seldom smiled. His words were in perfect keeping with his looks, and his looks were in perfect keeping with his words. Overseers will sometimes indulge in a witty word, even with the slaves; not so with Mr. Gore. He spoke but to command, and commanded but to be obeyed; he dealt sparingly with his words, and bountifully with his whip, never using the former where the latter would answer as well. When he whipped, he seemed to do so from a sense of duty, and feared no consequences. He did nothing reluctantly, no matter how disagreeable; always at his post, never inconsistent. He never promised but to fulfil. He was, in a word, a man of the most inflexible firmness and stone-like coolness.

His savage barbarity was equalled only by the consummate coolness with which he committed the grossest and most savage deeds upon the slaves under his charge. Mr. Gore once undertook to whip one of Colonel Lloyd's slaves, by the name of Demby. He had given Demby but a few stripes, when, to get rid of the scourging, he ran and plunged himself into a creek, and stood there at the depth of his shoulders, refusing to come out. Mr. Gore told him that he would give him three calls, and that, if he did not come out at the third call, he would shoot him. The first call was given. Demby made no response, but stood his ground. The second and third calls were given with the same result. Mr. Gore then, without consultation or deliberation with any one, not even giving Demby an additional call, raised his musket to his face, taking deadly aim at his standing victim, and in an instant poor Demby was no more. His mangled body sank out of sight, and blood and brains marked the water where he had stood.

A thrill of horror flashed through every soul upon the plantation, excepting Mr. Gore. He alone seemed cool and collected. He was asked by Colonel Lloyd and my old master, why he resorted to this extraordinary expedient. His reply was, (as well as I can remember,) that Demby had become unmanageable. He was setting a dangerous example to the other slaves,—one which, if suffered to pass without some such demonstration on his part, would finally lead to the total subversion of all rule and order upon the plantation. He argued that if one slave refused to be corrected, and escaped with his life, the other slaves would soon copy the example; the result of which would be, the freedom of the slaves, and the enslavement of the whites. Mr. Gore's defence was satisfactory. He was continued in his station as overseer upon the home plantation. His fame as an overseer went abroad. His horrid crime was not even submitted to judicial investigation. It was committed in the presence of slaves, and they of course could neither institute a suit, nor testify against him; and thus the guilty perpetrator of one of the bloodiest and most foul murders goes unwhipped of justice, and uncensured by the community in which he lives. Mr. Gore lived in St. Michael's, Talbot county, Maryland, when I left there; and if he is still alive, he very probably lives there now; and if so, he is now as he was then, as highly esteemed and as much respected as though his guilty soul had not been stained with his brother's blood.

I speak advisedly when I say this,—that killing a slave, or any colored person, in Talbot county, Maryland, is not treated as a crime, either by the courts or the community. Mr. Thomas Lanman, of St. Michael's, killed two slaves, one of whom he killed with a hatchet, by knocking his brains out. He used to boast of the commission of the awful and bloody deed. I have heard him do so laughingly, saying, among other things, that he was the only benefactor of his country in the company, and that when others would do as much as he had done, we should be relieved of "the d—d niggers."

The wife of Mr. Giles Hicks, living but a short distance from where I used to live, murdered my wife's cousin, a young girl between fifteen and sixteen years of age, mangling her person in the most horrible manner, breaking her nose and breastbone with a stick, so that the poor girl expired in a few hours afterward. She was immediately buried, but had not been in her untimely grave but a few hours before she was taken up and examined by the coroner, who decided that she had come to her death by severe beating. The offence for which this girl was thus murdered was this:—She had been set that night to mind Mrs. Hicks's baby, and during the night she fell asleep, and the baby cried. She, having lost her rest for several nights previous, did not hear the crying. They were both in the room with Mrs. Hicks. Mrs. Hicks, finding the girl slow to move, jumped from her bed, seized an oak stick of wood by the fireplace, and with it broke the girl's nose and breastbone, and thus ended her life. I will not say that this most horrid murder produced no sensation in the community. It did produce sensation, but not enough to bring the murderess to punishment. There was a warrant issued for her arrest, but it was never served. Thus she escaped not only punishment, but even the pain of being arraigned before a court for her horrid crime.

Whilst I am detailing bloody deeds which took place during my stay on Colonel Lloyd's plantation, I will briefly narrate another, which occurred about the same time as the murder of Demby by Mr. Gore.

Colonel Lloyd's slaves were in the habit of spending a part of their nights and Sundays in fishing for oysters, and in this way made up the deficiency of their scanty allowance. An old man belonging to Colonel Lloyd, while thus engaged, happened to get beyond the limits of Colonel Lloyd's, and on the premises of Mr. Beal Bondly. At this trespass, Mr. Bondly took offence, and with his musket came down to the shore, and blew its deadly contents into the poor old man.

Mr. Bondly came over to see Colonel Lloyd the next day, whether to pay him for his property, or to justify himself in what he had done, I know not. At any rate, this whole fiendish transaction was soon hushed up. There was very little said about it at all, and nothing done. It was a common saying, even among little white boys, that it was worth a half-cent to kill a "nigger," and a half-cent to bury one.

Chapter V

As to my own treatment while I lived on Colonel Lloyd's plantation, it was very similar to that of the other slave children. I was not old enough to work in the field, and there being little else than field work to do, I had a great deal of leisure time. The most I had to do was to drive up the cows at evening, keep the fowls out of the garden, keep the front yard clean, and run of errands for my old master's daughter, Mrs. Lucretia Auld. The most of my leisure time I spent in helping Master Daniel Lloyd in finding his birds, after he had shot them. My connection with Master Daniel was of some advantage to me. He became quite attached to me, and was a sort of protector of me. He would not allow the older boys to impose upon me, and would divide his cakes with me.

I was seldom whipped by my old master, and suffered little from any thing else than hunger and cold. I suffered much from hunger, but much more from cold. In hottest summer and coldest winter, I was kept almost naked—no shoes, no stockings, no jacket, no trousers, nothing on but a coarse tow linen shirt, reaching only to my knees. I had no bed. I must have perished with cold, but that, the coldest nights, I used to steal a bag which was used for carrying corn to the mill. I would crawl into this bag, and there sleep on the cold, damp, clay floor, with my head in and feet out. My feet have been so cracked with the frost, that the pen with which I am writing might be laid in the gashes.

We were not regularly allowanced. Our food was coarse corn meal boiled. This was called *mush*. It was put into a large wooden tray or trough, and set down upon the ground. The children were then called, like so many pigs, and like so many pigs they would come and devour the mush; some with oystershells, others with pieces of shingle, some with naked hands, and none with spoons. He that ate fastest got most; he that was strongest secured the best place; and few left the trough satisfied.

I was probably between seven and eight years old when I left Colonel Lloyd's plantation. I left it with joy. I shall never forget the ecstasy with which I received the intelligence that my old master (Anthony) had determined to let me go to Baltimore, to live with Mr. Hugh Auld, brother to my old master's son-in-law, Captain Thomas Auld. I received this information about three days before my departure. They were three of the happiest days I ever enjoyed. I spent the most part of all these three days in the creek, washing off the plantation scurf, and preparing myself for my departure.

The pride of appearance which this would indicate was not my own. I spent the time in washing, not so much because I wished to, but because Mrs. Lucretia had told me I must get all the dead skin off my feet and knees before I could go to Baltimore; for the people of Baltimore were very cleanly, and would laugh at me if I looked dirty. Besides, she was going to give me a pair of trousers, which I should not put on unless I got all the dirt off me. The thought of owning a pair of trousers was great indeed! It was almost a sufficient motive, not only to make me take off what would be called by pigdrovers the mange, but the skin itself. I went at it in good earnest, working for the first time with the hope of reward.

The ties that ordinarily bind children to their homes were all suspended in my case. I found no severe trial in my departure. My home was charmless; it was not home to me; on parting from it, I could not feel that I was leaving any thing which I could have enjoyed by staying. My mother was dead, my grandmother lived far off, so that I seldom saw her. I had two sisters and one brother, that lived in the same house with me; but the early separation of us from our mother had well nigh blotted the fact of our relationship from our memories. I looked for home elsewhere, and was confident of finding none which I should relish less than the one which I was leaving. If, however, I found in my new home hardship, hunger, whipping, and nakedness, I had the consolation that I should not have escaped any one of them by staying. Having already had more than a taste of them in the house of my old master, and having endured them there, I very naturally inferred my ability to endure them elsewhere, and especially at Baltimore; for I had something of the feeling about Baltimore that is expressed in the proverb, that "being hanged in England is preferable to dying a natural death in Ireland." I had the strongest desire to see Baltimore. Cousin Tom, though not fluent in speech, had inspired me with that desire by his eloquent description of the place. I could never point out any thing at the Great House, no matter how beautiful or powerful, but that he had seen something at Baltimore far exceeding, both in beauty and strength, the object which I pointed out to him. Even the Great House itself, with all its pictures, was far inferior to many buildings in Baltimore. So strong was my desire, that I thought a gratification of it would fully compensate for whatever loss of comforts I should sustain by the exchange. I left without a regret, and with the highest hopes of future happiness.

We sailed out of Miles River for Baltimore on a Saturday morning. I remember only the day of the week, for at that time I had no knowledge of the days of the month, nor the months of the year. On setting sail, I walked aft, and gave to Colonel Lloyd's plantation what I hoped would be the last look. I then placed myself in the bows of the sloop, and there spent the remainder of the day in looking ahead, interesting myself in what was in the distance rather than in things near or behind.

In the afternoon of that day, we reached Annapolis, the capital of the State. We stopped but a few moments, so that I had no time to go on shore. It was the first large town that I had ever seen, and though it would look small compared with some of our New England factory villages, I thought it a wonderful place for its size—more imposing even than the Great House Farm!

We arrived at Baltimore early on Sunday morning, landing at Smith's Wharf, not far from Bowley's Wharf. We had on board the sloop a large flock of sheep; and after aiding in driving them to the slaughterhouse of Mr. Curtis on Louden Slater's Hill, I was conducted by Rich, one of the hands belonging on board of the sloop to my new home in Alliciana Street near Mr. Gardner's ship-yard, on Fells Point.

Mr. and Mrs. Auld were both at home, and met me at the door with their little son Thomas, to take care of whom I had been given. And here I saw what I had never seen before; it was a white face beaming with the most kindly emotions; it was the face of my new mistress, Sophia Auld. I wish I could describe the rapture that flashed through my soul as I beheld it. It was a new and strange sight to me, brightening up my pathway with the light of happiness. Little Thomas was told, there was his Freddy,—and I was told to take care of little Thomas; and thus I entered upon the duties of my new home with the most cheering prospect ahead.

I look upon my departure from Colonel Lloyd's plantation as one of the most interesting events of my life. It is possible, and even quite probable, that but for the mere circumstance of being removed from that plantation to Baltimore, I should have to-day, instead of being here seated by my own table, in the enjoyment of freedom and the happiness of home, writing this Narrative, been confined in the galling chains of slavery. Going to live at Baltimore laid the foundation, and opened the gateway, to all my subsequent prosperity. I have ever regarded it as the first plain manifestation of that kind providence which has ever since attended me, and marked my life with so many favors. I regarded the selection of myself as being somewhat remarkable. There were a number of slave children that might have been sent from the plantation to Baltimore. There were those younger, those older, and those of the same age. I was chosen from among them all, and was the first, last, and only choice.

I may be deemed superstitious, and even egotistical, in regarding this event as a special interposition of divine Providence in my favor. But I should be false to the earliest sentiments of my soul, if I suppressed the opinion. I prefer to be true to myself, even at the hazard of incurring the ridicule of others, rather than to be false, and incur my own abhorrence. From my earliest recollection, I date the entertainment of a deep conviction that slavery would not always be able to hold me within its foul embrace; and in the darkest hours of my career in slavery, this living word of faith and spirit of hope departed from me, but remained like ministering angels to cheer me through the gloom. This good spirit was from God, and to him I offer thanksgiving and praise.

Chapter VI

My new mistress proved to be all she appeared when I first met her at the door,—a woman of the kindest heart and finest feelings. She had never had a slave under her control previously to myself, and prior to her marriage she had been dependent upon her own industry for a living. She was by trade a weaver; and by constant application to her business, she had been in a good degree preserved from the blighting and dehumanizing effects of slavery. I was utterly astonished at her goodness. I scarcely knew how to behave towards her. She was entirely unlike any other white woman I had ever seen. I could not approach her as I was accustomed to approach other white ladies. My early instruction was all out of place. The crouching servility, usually so acceptable a quality in a slave, did not answer when manifested toward her. Her favor was not gained by it; she seemed to be disturbed by it. She did not deem it impudent or unmannerly for a slave to look her in the face. The meanest slave was put fully at ease in her presence, and none left without feeling better for having seen her. Her face was made of heavenly smiles, and her voice of tranquil music.

But, alas! this kind heart had but a short time to remain such. The fatal poison of irresponsible power was already in her hands; and soon commenced its infernal work. That cheerful eye, under the influence of slavery, soon became red with rage; that voice, made all of sweet accord, changed to one of harsh and horrid discord; and that angelic face gave place to that of a demon.

Very soon after I went to live with Mr. and Mrs. Auld, she very kindly commenced to teach me the A, B, C. After I had learned this, she assisted me in learning to spell words of three or four letters. Just at this point of my progress, Mr. Auld found out what was going on, and at once forbade Mrs. Auld to instruct me further, telling her, among other things, that it was unlawful, as well as unsafe, to teach a slave to read. To use his own words, further, he said, "If you give a nigger an inch, he will take an ell. A nigger should know nothing but to obey his master—to do as he is told to do. Learning would *spoil* the best nigger in the world. Now," said he, "if you teach that nigger (speaking of myself) how to read, there would be no keeping him. It would forever unfit him to be a slave. He would at once become unmanageable, and of no value to his master. As to himself, it could do him no good, but a great deal of harm. It would make him discontented and unhappy." These words sank deep into my heart, stirred up sentiments within that lay slumbering, and called into existence an entirely new train of thought. It was a new and special revelation, explaining dark and mysterious things, with which my youthful understanding had struggled, but struggled in vain. I now understood what had been to me a most perplexing difficulty—to wit, the white man's power to enslave the black man. It was a grand achievement, and I prized it highly. From that moment, I understood the pathway from slavery to freedom. It was just what I wanted, and I got it at a time when I the least expected it. Whilst I was saddened by the thought of losing the aid of my kind mistress, I was gladdened by the invaluable instruction which, by the merest accident, I had gained from my master. Though conscious of the difficulty of learning without a teacher, I set out with high hope, and a fixed purpose, at whatever cost of trouble, to learn how to read. The very decided manner with which he spoke, and strove to impress his wife with the evil consequences of giving me instruction, served to convince me that he was deeply sensible of the truths he was uttering. It gave me the best assurance that I might rely with the utmost confidence on the results which, he said, would flow from teaching me to read. What he most dreaded, that I most desired. What he most loved, that I most hated. That which to him was a great evil, to be carefully shunned, was to me a great good, to be diligently sought; and the argument which he so warmly urged, against my learning to read, only served to inspire me with a desire and determination to learn. In learning to read, I owe almost as much to the bitter opposition of my master, as to the kindly aid of my mistress. I acknowledge the benefit of both.

I had resided but a short time in Baltimore before I observed a marked difference, in the treatment of slaves, from that which I had witnessed in the country. A city slave is almost a freeman, compared with a slave on the plantation. He is much better fed and clothed, and enjoys privileges altogether unknown to the slave on the plantation. There is a vestige of decency, a sense of shame, that does much to curb and check those outbreaks of atrocious cruelty so commonly enacted upon the plantation. He is a desperate slaveholder, who will shock the humanity of his non-slaveholding neighbors with the cries of his lacerated slave. Few are willing to incur the odium attaching to the reputation of being a cruel master; and above all things, they would not be known as not giving a slave enough to eat. Every city slaveholder is anxious to have it known of him, that he feeds his slaves well; and it is due to them to say, that most of them do give their slaves enough to eat. There are, however, some painful exceptions to this rule. Directly opposite to us, on Philpot Street, lived Mr. Thomas Hamilton. He owned two slaves. Their names were Henrietta and Mary. Henrietta was about twenty-two years of age, Mary was about fourteen; and of all the mangled and emaciated creatures I ever looked upon, these two were the most so. His heart must be harder than stone, that could look upon these unmoved. The head, neck, and shoulders of Mary were literally cut to pieces. I have frequently felt her head, and found it nearly covered with festering sores, caused by the lash of her cruel mistress. I do not know that her master ever whipped her, but I have been an eye-witness to the cruelty of Mrs. Hamilton. I used to be in Mr. Hamilton's house nearly every day. Mrs. Hamilton used to sit in a large chair in the middle of the room, with a heavy cowskin always by her side, and scarce an hour passed during the day but was marked by the blood of one of these slaves. The girls seldom passed her without her saying, "Move faster, you *black gip!*" at the same time giving them a blow with the cowskin over the head or shoulders, often drawing the blood. She would then say, "Take that, you *black gip!*"— continuing, "If you don't move faster, I'll move you!" Added to the cruel lashings to which these slaves were subjected, they were kept nearly halfstarved. They seldom knew what it was to eat a full meal. I have seen Mary contending with the pigs for the offal thrown into the street. So much was Mary kicked and cut to pieces, that she was oftener called "*pecked*" than by her name.

Chapter VII

I lived in Master Hugh's family about seven years. During this time, I succeeded in learning to read and write. In accomplishing this, I was compelled to resort to various stratagems. I had no regular teacher. My mistress, who had kindly commenced to instruct me, had, in compliance with the advice and direction of her husband, not only ceased to instruct, but had set her face against my being instructed by any one else. It is due, however, to my mistress to say of her, that she did not adopt this course of treatment immediately. She at first lacked the depravity indispensable to shutting me up in mental darkness. It was at least necessary for her to have some training in the exercise of irresponsible power, to make her equal to the task of treating me as though I were a brute.

My mistress was, as I have said, a kind and tender-hearted woman; and in the simplicity of her soul she commenced, when I first went to live with her, to treat me as she supposed one human being ought to treat another. In entering upon the duties of a slaveholder, she did not seem to perceive that I sustained to her the relation of a mere chattel, and that for her to treat me as a human being was not only wrong, but dangerously so. Slavery proved as injurious to her as it did to me. When I went there, she was a pious, warm, and tender-hearted woman. There was no sorrow or suffering for which she had not a tear. She had bread for the hungry, clothes for the naked, and comfort for every mourner that came within her reach. Slavery soon proved its ability to divest her of these heavenly qualities. Under its influence, the tender heart became stone, and the lamblike disposition gave way to one of tigerlike fierceness. The first step in her downward course was in her ceasing to instruct me. She now commenced to practise her husband's precepts. She finally became even more violent in her opposition than her husband himself. She was not satisfied with simply doing as well as he had commanded; she seemed anxious to do better. Nothing seemed to make her more angry than to see me with a newspaper. She seemed to think that here lay the danger. I have had her rush at me with a face made all up of fury, and snatch from me a newspaper, in a manner that fully revealed her apprehension. She was an apt woman; and a little experience soon demonstrated, to her satisfaction, that education and slavery were incompatible with each other.

From this time I was most narrowly watched. If I was in a separate room any considerable length of time, I was sure to be suspected of having a book and was at once called to give an account of myself. All this, however, was too late. The first step had been taken. Mistress, in teaching me the alphabet, had given me the *inch*, and no precaution could prevent me from taking the *ell*.

The plan which I adopted, and the one by which I was most successful, was that of making friends of all the little white boys whom I met in the street. As many of these as I could, I converted into teachers. With their kindly aid obtained at different times and in different places, I finally succeeded in learning to read. When I was sent of errands, I always took my book with me, and by going one part of my errand quickly, I found time to get a lesson before my return. I used also to carry bread with me, enough of which was always in the house, and to which I was always welcome; for I was much better off in this regard than many of the poor white children in our neighborhood. This bread I used to bestow upon the hungry little urchins, who, in return, would give me that more valuable bread of knowledge. I am strongly tempted to give the names of two or three of those little boys, as a testimonial of the gratitude and affection I bear them; but prudence forbids;—not that it would injure me, but it might embarrass them; for it is almost an unpardonable offence to teach slaves to read in this Christian country. It is enough to say of the dear little fellows, that they lived on Philpot Street, very near Durgin and Bailey's ship-yard. I used to talk this matter of slavery over with them. I would sometimes say to them, I wished I could be as free as they would be when they got to be men. "You will be free as soon as you are twenty-one, *but I am a slave for life!* Have not I as good a right to be free as you have?" These words used to trouble them; they would express for me the liveliest sympathy, and console me with the hope that something would occur by which I might be free.

I was now about twelve years old, and the thought of being *a slave for life* began to bear heavily upon my heart. Just about this time, I got hold of a book entitled "The Columbian Orator." [1] Every opportunity I got, I used to read this book. Among much of other interesting matter, I found in it a

1. A popular collection of classic poems, dialogues, plays, and speeches that Douglass used as a model for his own speeches. "Columbian": American.

dialogue between a master and his slave. The slave was represented as having run away from his master three times. The dialogue represented the conversation which took place between them, when the slave was retaken the third time. In this dialogue, the whole argument in behalf of slavery was brought forward by the master, all of which was disposed of by the slave. The slave was made to say some very smart as well as impressive things in reply to his master—things which had the desired though unexpected effect; for the conversation resulted in the voluntary emancipation of the slave on the part of the master.

In the same book, I met with one of Sheridan's mighty speeches on and in behalf of Catholic emancipation.[2] These were choice documents to me. I read them over and over again with unabated interest. They gave tongue to interesting thoughts of my own soul, which had frequently flashed through my mind, and died away for want of utterance. The moral which I gained from the dialogue was the power of truth over the conscience of even a slaveholder. What I got from Sheridan was a bold denunciation of slavery, and a powerful vindication of human rights. The reading of these documents enabled me to utter my thoughts, and to meet the arguments brought forward to sustain slavery; but while they relieved me of one difficulty, they brought on another even more painful than the one of which I was relieved. The more I read, the more I was led to abhor and detest my enslavers. I could regard them in no other light than a band of successful robbers, who had left their homes, and gone to Africa, and stolen us from our homes, and in a strange land reduced us to slavery. I loathed them as being the meanest as well as the most wicked of men. As I read and contemplated the subject, behold! that very discontentment which Master Hugh had predicted would follow my learning to read had already come, to torment and sting my soul to unutterable anguish. As I writhed under it, I would at times feel that learning to read had been a curse rather than a blessing. It had given me a view of my wretched condition, without the remedy. It opened my eyes to the horrible pit, but to no ladder upon which to get out. In moments of agony, I envied my fellow-slaves for their stupidity. I have often wished myself a beast. I preferred the condition of the meanest reptile to my own. Any thing, no matter what, to get rid of thinking! It was this everlasting thinking of my condition that tormented me. There was no getting rid of it. It was pressed upon me by every object within sight or hearing, animate or inanimate. The silver trump of freedom had roused my soul to eternal wakefulness. Freedom now appeared, to disappear no more forever. It was heard in every sound, and seen in every thing. It was ever present to torment me with a sense of my wretched condition. I saw nothing without seeing it, I heard nothing without hearing it, and felt nothing without feeling it. It looked from every star, it smiled in every calm, breathed in every wind, and moved in every storm.

I often found myself regretting my own existence, and wishing myself dead; and but for the hope of being free, I have no doubt but that I should have killed myself, or done something for which I should have been killed.

---

2. The speech in the *Columbian Orator* to which Douglass refers was actually made by the Irish patriot Arthur O'Connor. Richard Brinsley Sheridan (1751–1816), Irish dramatist and political leader.

While in this state of mind, I was eager to hear any one speak of slavery. I was a ready listener. Every little while, I could hear something about the abolitionists. It was some time before I found what the word meant. It was always used in such connections as to make it an interesting word to me. If a slave ran away and succeeded in getting clear, or if a slave killed his master, set fire to a barn, or did any thing very wrong in the mind of a slave-holder, it was spoken of as the fruit of *abolition*. Hearing the word in this connection very often, I set about learning what it meant. The dictionary afforded me little or no help. I found it was "the act of abolishing;" but then I did not know what was to be abolished. Here I was perplexed. I did not dare to ask any one about its meaning, for I was satisfied that it was something they wanted me to know very little about. After a patient waiting, I got one of our city papers, containing an account of the number of petitions from the north, praying for the abolition of slavery in the District of Columbia, and of the slave trade between the States. From this time I understood the words *abolition* and *abolitionist,* and always drew near when that word was spoken, expecting to hear something of importance to myself and fellow-slaves. The light broke in upon me by degrees. I went one day down on the wharf of Mr. Waters; and seeing two Irishmen unloading a scow of stone, I went, unasked and helped them. When we had finished, one of them came to me and asked me if I were a slave. I told him I was. He asked, "Are ye a slave for life?" I told him that I was. The good Irishman seemed to be deeply affected by the statement. He said to the other that it was a pity so fine a little fellow as myself should be a slave for life. He said it was a shame to hold me. They both advised me to run away to the north; that I should find friends there, and that I should be free. I pretended not to be interested in what they said, and treated them as if I did not understand them; for I feared they might be treacherous. White men have been known to encourage slaves to escape, and then, to get the reward, catch them and return them to their masters. I was afraid that these seemingly good men might use me so; but I nevertheless remembered their advice, and from that time I resolved to run away. I looked forward to a time at which it would be safe for me to escape. I was too young to think of doing so immediately; besides, I wished to learn how to write, as I might have occasion to write my own pass. I consoled myself with the hope that I should one day find a good chance. Meanwhile, I would learn to write.

The idea as to how I might learn to write was suggested to me by being in Durgin and Bailey's ship-yard, and frequently seeing the ship carpenters, after hewing, and getting a piece of timber ready for use, write on the timber the name of that part of the ship for which it was intended. When a piece of timber was intended for the larboard side, it would be marked thus—"L." When a piece was for the starboard side, it would be marked thus—"S." A piece for the larboard side forward, would marked thus—"L. F." When a piece was for starboard side forward, it would be marked thus—"S. F." For larboard aft, it would be marked thus—"L. A." For starboard aft, it would be marked thus—"S. A." I soon learned the names of these letters, and for what they were intended when placed upon a piece of timber in the ship-yard. I immediately commenced copying them, and in a short time was able to make the four letters named. After that, when I met with any boy who I knew could write, I would tell him I could write as well as he. The next word would be, "I don't believe you. Let me see you try it." I would then make the letters which I had been so fortunate as to learn, and ask him to beat that. In this way I got a good many lessons in writing, which it is quite possible I should never have gotten in any other way. During this time, my copy-book was the board fence, brick wall, and pavement; my pen and ink was a lump of chalk. With these, I learned mainly how to write. I then commenced and continued copying the Italics in Webster's Spelling Book,[3] until I could make them all without looking on the book. By this time, my little Master Thomas had gone to school, and learned how to write, and had written over a number of copy-books. These had been brought home, and shown to some of our near neighbors, and then laid aside. My mistress used to go to class meeting at the Wilk Street meeting-house every Monday afternoon, and leave me to take care of the house. When left thus, I used to spend the time in writing in the spaces left in Master Thomas's copy-book, copying what he had written. I continued to do this until I could write a hand very similar to that of Master Thomas. Thus, after a long, tedious effort for years, I finally succeeded in learning how to write.

Chapter VIII

In a very short time after I went to live at Baltimore, my old master's youngest son Richard died; and in about three years and six months after his death, my old master, Captain Anthony died, leaving only his son, Andrew, and daughter, Lucretia, to share his estate. He died while on a visit to see his daughter at Hillsborough. Cut off thus unexpectedly, he left no will as to the disposal of his property. It was therefore necessary to have a valuation of the property, that it might be equally divided between Mrs. Lucretia and Master Andrew. I was immediately sent for, to be valued with the other property. Here again my feelings rose up in detestation of slavery. I had now a new conception of my degraded condition. Prior to this, I had become, if not insensible to my lot, at least partly so. I left Baltimore with a young heart overborne with sadness, and a soul full of apprehension. I took passage with Captain Rowe, in the schooner Wild Cat and, after a sail of about twenty-four hours, I found myself near the place of my birth. I had now been absent from it almost, if not quite, five years. I, however, remembered the place very well. I was only about five years old when I left it, to go and live with my old master on Colonel Lloyd's plantation; so that I was now between ten and eleven years old.

We were all ranked together at the valuation. Men and women, old and young, married and single, were ranked with horses, sheep, and swine. There were horses and men, cattle and women, pigs and children, all holding the same rank in the scale of being, and were all subjected to the same narrow examination. Silvery-headed age and sprightly youth, maids and matrons, had to undergo the same indelicate inspection. At this moment, I saw more clearly than ever the brutalizing effects of slavery upon both slave and slaveholder.

---

3. The *American Spelling Book* (1783) by Noah Webster (1758–1843), the leading American lexicographer of the time.

After the valuation, then came the division. I have no language to express the high excitement and deep anxiety which were felt among us poor slaves during this time. Our fate for life was now to be decided. We had no more voice in that decision than the brutes among whom we were ranked. A single word from the white men was enough—against all our wishes, prayers, and entreaties—to sunder forever the dearest friends, dearest kindred, and strongest ties known to human beings. In addition to the pain of separation, there was the horrid dread of falling into the hands of Master Andrew. He was known to us all as being a most cruel wretch,—a common drunkard, who had, by his reckless mismanagement and profligate dissipation, already wasted a large portion of his father's property. We all felt that we might as well be sold at once to the Georgia traders, as to pass into his hands; for we knew that that would be our inevitable condition,—a condition held by us all in the utmost horror and dread.

I suffered more anxiety than most of my fellowslaves. I had known what it was to be kindly treated; they had known nothing of the kind. They had seen little or nothing of the world. They were in very deed men and women of sorrow, and acquainted with grief. Their back had been made familiar with the bloody lash, so that they had become callous; mine was yet tender; for while at Baltimore I got few whippings, and few slaves could boast of a kinder master and mistress than myself; and the thought of passing out of their hands into those of Master Andrew—a man who, but a few day before, to give me a sample of his bloody disposition, took my little brother by the throat, threw him on the ground, and with the heel of his boot stamped upon his head till the blood gushed from his nose and ears—was well calculated to make me anxious as to my fate. After he had committed this savage outrage upon my brother, he turned to me, and said that was the way he meant to serve me one of these days,—meaning, I suppose, when I came into his possession.

Thanks to a kind Providence, I fell to the portion of Mrs. Lucretia, and was sent immediately back to Baltimore, to live again in the family of Master Hugh. Their joy at my return equalled their sorrow at my departure. It was a glad day to me. I had escaped a [fate] worse than lion's jaws. I was absent from Baltimore, for the purpose of valuation and division, just about one month, and it seemed to have been six.

Very soon after my return to Baltimore, my mistress, Lucretia, died, leaving her husband and one child, Amanda; and in a very short time after her death, Master Andrew died. Now all the property of my old master, slaves included, was in the hands of strangers,—strangers who had had nothing to do with accumulating it. Not a slave was left free. All remained slaves, from the youngest to the oldest. If any one thing in my experience, more than another, served to deepen my conviction of the infernal character of slavery, and to fill me with unutterable loathing of slaveholders, it was their base ingratitude to my poor old grandmother. She had served my old master faithfully from youth to old age. She had been the source of all his wealth; she had peopled his plantation with slaves; she had become a great grandmother in his service. She had rocked him in infancy, attended him in childhood, served him through life, and at his death wiped from his icy brow the cold death-sweat, and closed his eyes forever. She was nevertheless left a slave—a slave for life—a slave in the hands of strangers; and in their hands she saw her children, her grandchildren, and her great-grand-children, divided, like so many sheep, without being gratified with the small privilege of a single word, as to their or her own destiny. And, to cap the climax of their base ingratitude and fiendish barbarity, my grand-mother, who was now very old, having outlived my old master and all his children, having seen the beginning and end of all of them, and her pre-sent owners finding she was of but little value, her frame already racked with the pains of old age, and complete helplessness fast stealing over her once active limbs, they took her to the woods, built her a little hut, put up a little mud-chimney, and then made her welcome to the privilege of sup-porting herself there in perfect loneliness; thus virtually turning her out to die! If my poor old grandmother now lives, she lives to suffer in utter loneli-ness; she lives to remember and mourn over the loss of children, the loss of grandchildren, and the loss of great-grandchildren. They are, in the lan-guage of the slave's poet, Whittier,[4]—

> "Gone, gone, sold and gone
> To the rice swamp dank and lone,
> Where the slave-whip ceaseless swings,
> Where the noisome insect stings,
> Where the fever-demon strews
> Poison with the falling dews,
> Where the sickly sunbeams glare
> Through the hot and misty air:—
> Gone, gone, sold and gone
> To the rice swamp dank and lone,
> From Virginia hills and waters—
> Woe is me, my stolen daughters!"

The hearth is desolate. The children, the unconscious children, who once sang and danced in her presence, are gone. She gropes her way, in the darkness of age, for a drink of water. Instead of the voices of her chil-dren, she hears by day the moans of the dove, and by night the screams of the hideous owl. All is gloom. The grave is at the door. And now, when weighed down by the pains and aches of old age, when the head inclines to the feet, when the beginning and ending of human existence meet, and helpless infancy and painful old age combine together—at this time, this most needful time, the time for the exercise of that tenderness and affec-tion which children only can exercise toward a declining parent—my poor old grandmother, the devoted mother of twelve children, is left all alone, in yonder little hut, before a few dim embers. She stands—she sits—she stag-gers—she falls—she groans—she dies—and there are none of her children or grandchildren present, to wipe from her wrinkled brow the cold sweat of death, or to place beneath the sod her fallen remains. Will not a righteous God visit for these things?

In about two years after the death of Mrs. Lucretia, Master Thomas mar-ried his second wife. Her name was Rowena Hamilton. She was the eldest

4. John Greenleaf Whittier (1807–1892), Ameri-can poet and abolitionist. The lines Douglass quotes below are from Whittier's antislavery poem *The Farewell of a Virginia Slave Mother to Her Daughters, Sold into Southern Bondage* (1838).

daughter of Mr. William Hamilton. Master now lived in St. Michael's. Not long after his marriage, a misunderstanding took place between himself and Master Hugh; and as a means of punishing his brother, he took me from him to live with himself at St. Michael's. Here I underwent another most painful separation. It, however, was not so severe as the one I dreaded at the division of property; for, during this interval, a great change had taken place in Master Hugh and his once kind and affectionate wife. The influence of brandy upon him, and of slavery upon her, had effected a disastrous change in the characters of both; so that, as far as they were concerned, I thought I had little to lose by the change. But it was not to them that I was attached. It was to those little Baltimore boys that I felt the strongest attachment. I had received many good lessons from them, and was still receiving them, and the thought of leaving them was painful indeed. I was leaving, too, without the hope of ever being allowed to return. Master Thomas had said he would never let me return again. The barrier betwixt himself and brother he considered impassable.

I then had to regret that I did not at least make the attempt to carry out my resolution to run away; for the chances of success are tenfold greater from the city than from the country.

I sailed from Baltimore for St. Michael's in the sloop Amanda, Captain Edward Dodson. On my passage, I paid particular attention to the direction which the steamboats took to go to Philadelphia. I found, instead of going down, on reaching North Point they went up the bay, in a northeasterly direction. I deemed this knowledge of the utmost importance. My determination to run away was again revived. I resolved to wait only so long as the offering of a favorable opportunity. When that came, I was determined to be off.

Chapter IX

I have now reached a period of my life when I can give dates. I left Baltimore, and went to live with Master Thomas Auld, at St. Michael's in March, 1832. It was now more than seven years since I lived with him in the family of my old master, on Colonel Lloyd's plantation. We of course were now almost entire strangers to each other. He was to me a new master, and I to him a new slave. I was ignorant of his temper and disposition; he was equally so of mine. A very short time, however brought us into full acquaintance with each other. I was made acquainted with his wife not less than with himself. They were well matched, being equally mean and cruel. I was now, for the first time during a space of more than seven years, made to feel the painful gnawings of hunger—a something which I had not experienced before since I left Colonel Lloyd's plantation. It went hard enough with me then, when I could look back to no period at which I had enjoyed a sufficiency. It was tenfold harder after living in Master Hugh's family, where I had always had enough to eat, and of that which was good. I have said Master Thomas was a mean man. He was so. Not to give a slave enough to eat, is regarded as the most aggravated development of meanness even among slaveholders. The rule is, no matter how coarse the food, only let there be enough of it. This is the theory; and in the part of Maryland from which I came, it is the general practice,—though there are many exceptions. Master Thomas gave us enough of neither coarse nor fine food. There were four slaves of us in the kitchen—my sister Eliza, my aunt Priscilla, Henny, and myself; and we were allowed less than half of a bushel of cornmeal per week, and very little else, either in the shape of meat or vegetables. It was not enough for us to subsist upon. We were therefore reduced to the wretched necessity of living at the expense of our neighbors. This we did by begging and stealing, whichever came handy in the time of need, the one being considered as legitimate as the other. A great many times have we poor creatures been nearly perishing with hunger, when food in abundance lay mouldering in the safe and smoke-house,[5] and our pious mistress was aware of the fact; and yet that mistress and her husband would kneel every morning, and pray that God would bless them in basket and store!

Bad as all slaveholders are, we seldom meet one destitute of every element of character commanding respect. My master was one of this rare sort. I do not know of one single noble act ever performed by him. The leading trait in his character was meanness; and if there were any other element in his nature, it was made subject to this. He was mean; and, like most other mean men, he lacked the ability to conceal his meanness. Captain Auld was not born a slaveholder. He had been a poor man, master only of a Bay craft. He came into possession of all his slaves by marriage; and of all men, adopted slaveholders are the worst. He was cruel, but cowardly. He commanded without firmness. In the enforcement of his rules he was at times rigid, and at times lax. At times, he spoke to his slaves with the firmness of Napoleon and the fury of a demon; at other times, he might well be mistaken for an inquirer who had lost his way. He did nothing of himself. He might have passed for a lion, but for his ears. In all things noble which he attempted, his own meanness shone most conspicuous. His airs, words, and actions, were the airs, words, and actions of born slaveholders, and, being assumed, were awkward enough. He was not even a good imitator. He possessed all the disposition to deceive, but wanted the power. Having no resources within himself, he was compelled to be the copyist of many, and being such, he was forever the victim of inconsistency; and of consequence he was an object of contempt, and was held as such even by his slaves. The luxury of having slaves of his own to wait upon him was something new and unprepared for. He was a slaveholder without the ability to hold slaves. He found himself incapable of managing his slaves either by force, fear, or fraud. We seldom called him "master;" we generally called him "Captain Auld," and were hardly disposed to title him at all. I doubt not that our conduct had much to do with making him appear awkward, and of consequence fretful. Our want of reverence for him must have perplexed him greatly. He wished to have us call him master, but lacked the firmness necessary to command us to do so. His wife used to insist upon our calling him so, but to no purpose. In August, 1832, my master attended a Methodist camp-meeting[6] held in the Bay-side, Talbot county, and there

5. Used both to cure and to store meat and fish. "Safe": i.e., a meat safe, a structure for preserving food.

6. A popular form of 19th-century evangelical religious gathering held in rural areas.

experienced religion. I indulged a faint hope that his conversion would lead him to emancipate his slaves, and that, if he did not do this, it would at any rate, make him more kind and humane. I was disappointed in both these respects. It neither made him to be humane to his slaves, nor to emancipate them. If it had any effect on his character, it made him more cruel and hateful in all his ways; for I believe him to have been a much worse man after his conversion than before. Prior to his conversion, he relied upon his own depravity to shield and sustain him in his savage barbarity; but after his conversion, he found religious sanction and support for his slaveholding cruelty. He made the greatest pretensions to piety. His house was the house of prayer. He prayed morning, noon, and night. He very soon distinguished himself among his brethren, and was soon made a class-leader and exhorter. His activity in revivals was great, and he proved himself an instrument in the hands of the church in converting many souls. His house was the preachers' home. They used to take great pleasure in coming there to put up; for while he starved us, he stuffed them. We have had three or four preachers there at a time. The names of those who used to come most frequently while I lived there, were Mr. Storks, Mr. Ewery, Mr. Humphry, and Mr. Hickey. I have also seen Mr. George Cookman at our house. We slaves loved Mr. Cookman. We believed him to be a good man. We thought him instrumental in getting Mr. Samuel Harrison, a very rich slaveholder, to emancipate his slaves; and by some means got the impression that he was laboring to effect the emancipation of all the slaves. When he was at our house, we were sure to be called in to prayers. When the others were there, we were sometimes called in and sometimes not. Mr. Cookman took more notice of us than either of the other ministers. He could not come among us with betraying his sympathy for us, and, stupid as we were, we had the sagacity to see it.

While I lived with my master in St. Michael's, there was a white young man, a Mr. Wilson, who proposed to keep a Sabbath school for the instruction of such slaves as might be disposed to learn to read the New Testament. We met but three times, when Mr. West and Mr. Fairbanks, both class-leaders, with many others, came upon with us with sticks and other missiles, drove us off, and forbade us to meet again. Thus ended our little Sabbath school in the pious town of St. Michael's.

I have said my master found religious sanction for his cruelty. As an example, I will state one of many facts going to prove the charge. I have seen him tie up a lame young woman, and whip her with a heavy cowskin upon her naked shoulders, causing the warm red blood to drip; and, in justification of the bloody deed, he would quote this passage of Scripture—"He that knoweth his master's will, and doeth it not, shall be beaten with many stripes."[7]

Master would keep this lacerated young woman tied up in this horrid situation four or five hours at a time. I have known him to tie her up early in the morning, and whip her before breakfast; leave her, go to his store, return at dinner, and whip her again, cutting her in the places already made raw with his cruel lash. The secret of master's cruelty toward

7. Luke 12:47.

"Henny" is found in the fact of her being almost helpless. When quite a child, she fell into the fire, and burned herself horribly. Her hands were so burnt that she never got the use of them. She could do very little but bear heavy burdens. She was to master a bill of expense; and as he was a mean man, she was a constant offence to him. He seemed desirous of getting the poor girl out of existence. He gave her away once to his sister; but, being a poor gift, she was not disposed to keep her. Finally, my benevolent master, to use his own words, "set her adrift to take care of herself." Here was a recently-converted man, holding on upon the mother, and at the same time turning out her helpless child, to starve and die! Master Thomas was one of the many pious slaveholders who hold slaves for the very charitable purpose of taking care of them.

My master and myself had quite a number of differences. He found me unsuitable to his purpose. My city life, he said, had had a very pernicious effect upon me. It had almost ruined me for every good purpose, and fitted me for every thing which was bad. One of my greatest faults was that of letting his horse run away, and go down to his father-in-law's farm, which was about five miles from St. Michael's. I would then have to go after it. My reason for this kind of carelessness, or carefulness, was, that I could always get something to eat when I went there. Master William Hamilton, my master's father-in-law, always gave his slaves enough to eat. I never left there hungry, no matter how great the need of my speedy return. Master Thomas at length said he would stand it no longer. I had lived with him nine months, during which time he had given me a number of severe whippings, all to no good purpose. He resolved to put me out, as he said, to be broken; and, for this purpose, he let me for one year to a man named Edward Covey. Mr. Covey was a poor man, a farm-renter. He rented the place upon which he lived, as also the hands with which he tilled it. Mr. Covey had acquired a very high reputation for breaking young slaves, and this reputation was of immense value to him. It enabled him to get his farm tilled with much less expense to himself than he could have had it done without such a reputation. Some slaveholders thought it not much loss to allow Mr. Covey to have their slaves one year, for the sake of training to which they were subjected, without any other compensation. He could hire young help with great ease, in consequence of this reputation. Added to the natural good qualities of Mr. Covey, he was a professor of religion—a pious soul—a member and a class-leader in the Methodist church. All of this added weight to his reputation as a "nigger-breaker." I was aware of all the facts, having been made acquainted with them by a young man who had lived there. I nevertheless made the change gladly; for I was sure of getting enough to eat, which is not the smallest consideration to a hungry man.

Chapter X

I left Master Thomas's house, and went to live with Mr. Covey, on the 1st of January, 1833. I was now, for the first time in my life, a field hand. In my new employment, I found myself even more awkward than a country boy appeared to be in a large city. I had been at my new home but one week before Mr. Covey gave me a very severe whipping, cutting my back, causing the blood to run, and raising ridges on my flesh as large as my little finger. The details of this affair are as follows: Mr. Covey sent me, very early in the morning of one of our coldest days in the month of January, to the woods, to get a load of wood. He gave me a team of unbroken oxen. He told me which was the in-hand ox, and which the off-hand one.[8] He then tied the end of a large rope around the horns of the in-hand-ox, and gave me the other end of it, and told me, if the oxen started to run, that I must hold on upon the rope. I had never driven oxen before, and of course I was very awkward. I, however, succeeded in getting to the edge of the woods with little difficulty; but I had got a very few rods into the woods, when the oxen took fright, and started full tilt, carrying the cart against trees, and over stumps, in the most frightful manner. I expected every moment that my brains would be dashed out against the trees. After running thus for a considerable distance, they finally upset the cart, dashing it with great force against a tree, and threw themselves into a dense thicket. How I escaped death, I do not know. There I was, entirely alone, in a thick wood, in a place new to me. My cart was upset and shattered, my oxen were entangled among the young trees, and there was none to help me. After a long spell of effort, I succeeded in getting my cart righted, my oxen disentangled, and again yoked to the cart. I now proceeded with my team to the place where I had, the day before, been chopping wood, and loaded my cart pretty heavily, thinking in this way to tame my oxen. I then proceeded on my way home. I had now consumed one half of the day. I got out of the woods safely, and now felt out of danger. I stopped my oxen to open the woods gate; and just as I did so, before I could get hold of my ox-rope, the oxen again started, rushed through the gate, catching it between the wheel and the body of the cart, tearing it to pieces, and coming within a few inches of crushing me against the gate-post. Thus twice, in one short day, I escaped death by the merest chance. On my return, I told Mr. Covey what had happened, and how it happened. He ordered me to return to the woods again immediately. I did so, and he followed on after me. Just as I got into the woods, he came up and told me to stop my cart, and that he would teach me how to trifle away my time, and break gates. He then went to a large gum-tree, and with his axe cut three large switches, and, after trimming them up neatly with his pocketknife, he ordered me to take off my clothes. I made him no answer, but stood with my clothes on. He repeated his order. I still made him no answer, nor did I move to strip myself. Upon this he rushed at me with the fierceness of a tiger, tore off my clothes, and lashed me till he had worn out his switches, cutting me so savagely as to leave the marks visible for a long time after. This whipping was the first of a number just like it, and for similar offences.

I lived with Mr. Covey one year. During the first six months, of that year, scarce a week passed without his whipping me. I was seldom free from a sore back. My awkwardness was almost always his excuse for whipping me. We were worked fully up to the point of endurance. Long before day we were up, our horses fed, and by the first approach of day we were off to the

8. I.e., the ox to the right of a pair hitched to a wagon. "The in-hand ox": the one to the left.

field with our hoes and ploughing teams. Mr. Covey gave us enough to eat, but scarce time to eat it. We were often less than five minutes taking our meals. We were often in the field from the first approach of day till its last lingering ray had left us; and at saving-fodder time, midnight often caught us in the field binding blades.[9]

Covey would be out with us. The way he used to stand it, was this. He would spend the most of his afternoons in bed. He would then come out fresh in the evening, ready to urge us on with his words, example, and frequently with the whip. Mr. Covey was one of the few slaveholders who could and did work with his hands. He was a hard-working man. He knew by himself just what a man or a boy could do. There was no deceiving him. His work went on in his absence almost as well as in his presence; and he had the faculty of making us feel that he was ever present with us. This he did by surprising us. He seldom approached the spot where we were at work openly, if he could do it secretly. He always aimed at taking us by surprise. Such was his cunning, that we used to call him, among ourselves, "the snake." When we were at work in the cornfield, he would sometimes crawl on his hands and knees to avoid detection, and all at once he would rise nearly in our midst, and scream out, "Ha, ha! Come, come! Dash on, dash on!" This being his mode of attack, it was never safe to stop a single minute. His comings were like a thief in the night. He appeared to us as being ever at hand. He was under every tree, behind every stump, in every bush, and at every window, on the plantation. He would sometimes mount his horse, as if bound to St. Michael's, a distance of seven miles, and in half an hour afterwards you would see him coiled up in the corner of the wood-fence, watching every motion of the slaves. He would, for this purpose, leave his horse tied up in the woods. Again, he would sometimes walk up to us, and give us orders as though he was upon the point of starting on a long journey, turn his back upon us, and make as though he was going to the house to get ready; and, before he would get half way thither, he would turn short and crawl into a fence-corner, or behind some tree, and there watch us till the going down of the sun.

Mr. Covey's *forte* consisted in his power to deceive. His life was devoted to planning and perpetrating the grossest deceptions. Every thing he possessed in the shape of learning or religion, he made conform to his disposition to deceive. He seemed to think himself equal to deceiving the Almighty. He would make a short prayer in the morning, and a long prayer at night; and, strange as it may seem, few men would at times appear more devotional than he. The exercises of his family devotions were always commenced with singing; and, as he was a very poor singer himself, the duty of raising the hymn generally came upon me. He would read his hymn, and nod at me to commence. I would at times do so; at others, I would not. My non-compliance would almost always produce much confusion. To show himself independent of me, he would start and stagger through with his hymn in the most discordant manner. In this state of mind, he prayed with more than ordinary spirit. Poor man! such was his disposition, and success at deceiving, I do verily believe that he sometimes deceived himself into

9. I.e., of wheat or other crops. "Saving-fodder time": a reference to the harvest of the crops.

the solemn belief, that he was a sincere worshiper of the most high God; and this, too, at a time when he may be said to have been guilty of compelling his woman slave to commit the sin of adultery. The facts in the case are these: Mr. Covey was a poor man; he was just commencing in life; he was only able to buy one slave; and, shocking as is the fact, he bought her, as he said, for a *breeder*. This woman was named Caroline. Mr. Covey bought her from Mr. Thomas Lowe, about six miles from St. Michael's. She was a large, able-bodied woman, about twenty years old. She had already given birth to one child, which proved her to be just what he wanted. After buying her, he hired a married man of Mr. Samuel Harrison, to live with him one year; and him he used to fasten up with her every night! The result was, that, at the end of the year, the miserable woman gave birth to twins. At this result Mr. Covey seemed to be highly pleased, both with the man and the wretched woman. Such was his joy, and that of his wife, that nothing they could do for Caroline during her confinement was too good, or too hard to be done. The children were regarded as being quite an addition to his wealth.

If at any one time of my life more than another, I was made to drink the bitterest dregs of slavery, that time was during the first six months of my stay with Mr. Covey. We were worked in all weathers. It was never too hot or too cold; it could never rain, blow, hail, or snow, too hard for us to work in the field. Work, work, work, was scarcely more the order of the day than of the night. The longest days were too short for him, and the shortest nights too long for him. I was somewhat unmanageable when I first went there, but a few months of this discipline tamed me. Mr. Covey succeed in breaking me. I was broken in body, soul, and spirit. My natural elasticity was crushed, my intellect languished, the disposition to read departed, the cheerful spark that lingered about my eye died; the dark night of slavery closed in upon me, and behold a man transformed into a brute!

Sunday was my only leisure time. I spent this in a sort of beastlike stupor, between sleep and wake, under some large tree. At times I would rise up, a flash of energetic freedom would dart through my soul, accompanied with a faint beam of hope, that flickered for a moment, and then vanished. I sank down again, mourning over my wretched condition. I was sometimes prompted to take my life, and that of Covey, but was prevented by a combination of hope and fear. My sufferings on this plantation seem now like a dream rather than a stern reality.

Our house stood within a few rods of the Chesapeake Bay, whose broad bosom was ever white with sails from every quarter of the habitable globe. These beautiful vessels, robed in purest white, so delightful to the eye of freemen, were to me so many shrouded ghosts, to terrify and torment me with thoughts of my wretched condition. I have often, in the deep stillness of a summer's Sabbath, stood all alone upon the lofty banks of that noble bay, and traced, with saddened heart and tearful eye, the countless number of sails moving off to the mighty ocean. The sight of these always affected me powerfully. My thoughts would compel utterance; and there, with no audience but the Almighty, I would pour out my soul's complaint, in my rude way, with an apostrophe to the moving multitude of ships:—

"You are loosed from your moorings, and are free; I am fast in my chains, and am a slave! You move merrily before the gentle gale, and I sadly before the bloody whip! You are freedom's swift-winged angels, that fly round the world; I am confined in bands of iron! O that I were free! Oh, that I were on one of your gallant decks, and under your protecting wing! Alas! betwixt me and you, the turbid waters roll. Go on, go on. O that I could also go! Could I but swim! If I could fly! Oh, why was I born a man, of whom to make a brute! The glad ship is gone; she hides in the dim distance. I am left in the hottest hell of unending slavery. O God, save me! God, deliver me! Let me be free! Is there any God? Why am I a slave? I will run away. I will not stand it. Get caught, or get clear, I'll try it. I had as well die with ague as the fever. I have only one life to lose. I had as well be killed running as die standing. Only think of it; one hundred miles straight north, and I am free! Try it? Yes! God helping me, I will. It cannot be that I shall live and die a slave. I will take to the water. This very bay shall yet bear me into freedom. The steamboats steered in a north-east course from North Point. I will do the same; and when I get to the head of the bay, I will turn my canoe adrift, and walk straight through Delaware into Pennsylvania. When I get there, I shall not be required to have a pass; I can travel without being disturbed. Let but the first opportunity offer, and, come what will, I am off. Meanwhile, I will try to bear up under the yoke. I am not the only slave in the world. Why should I fret? I can bear as much as any one of them. Besides, I am but a boy, and all boys are bound to some one. It may be that my misery in slavery will only increase my happiness when I get free. There is a better day coming."

Thus I used to think, and thus I used to speak to myself; goaded almost to madness at one moment, and at the next reconciling myself to my wretched lot.

I have already intimated that my condition was much worse, during the first six months of my stay at Mr. Covey's, than in the last six. The circumstances leading to the change in Mr. Covey's course toward me form an epoch in my humble history. You have seen how a man was made a slave; you shall see how a slave was made a man. On one of the hottest days of the month of August, 1833, Bill Smith, William Hughes, a slave named Eli, and myself, were engaged in fanning wheat.[1] Hughes was clearing the fanned wheat from before the fan. Eli was turning, Smith was feeding, and I was carrying wheat to the fan. The work was simple, requiring strength rather than intellect; yet, to one entirely unused to such work, it came very hard. About three o'clock of that day, I broke down; my strength failed me; I was seized with a violent aching of the head, attended with extreme dizziness; I trembled in every limb. Finding what was coming, I nerved myself up, feeling it would never do to stop work. I stood as long as I could stagger to the hopper with grain. When I could stand no longer, I fell, and felt as if held down by an immense weight. The fan of course stopped; every one had his own work to do; and no one could do the work of the other, and have his own go on at the same time.

Mr. Covey was at the house, about one hundred yards from the treading-yard where we were fanning. On hearing the fan stop, he left immediately,

---

1. I.e., separating the wheat from the chaff.

and came to the spot where we were. He hastily inquired what the matter was. Bill answered that I was sick, and there was no one to bring wheat to the fan. I had by this time crawled away under the side of the post and rail-fence by which the yard was enclosed, hoping to find relief by getting out of the sun. He then asked where I was. He was told by one of the hands. He came to the spot, and, after looking at me awhile, asked me what was the matter. I told him as well as I could, for I scarce had strength to speak. He then gave me a savage kick in the side, and told me to get up. I tried to do so, but fell back in the attempt. He gave me another kick, and again told me to rise. I again tried, and succeeded in gaining my feet; but, stooping to get the tub with which I was feeding the fan, I again staggered and fell. While down in this situation, Mr. Covey took up the hickory slat with which Hughes had been striking off the half-bushel measure, and with it gave me a heavy blow upon the head, making a large wound, and the blood ran freely; and with this again told me to get up. I made no effort to comply, having now made up my mind to let him do his worst. In a short time after receiving this blow, my head grew better. Mr. Covey had now left me to my fate. At this moment I resolved, for the first time, to go to my master, enter a complaint, and ask his protection. In order to do this, I must that afternoon walk seven miles; and this, under the circumstances, was truly a severe undertaking. I was exceedingly feeble; made so as much by the kicks and blows which I received, as by the severe fit of sickness to which I had been subjected. I, however, watched my chance, while Covey was looking in an opposite direction, and started for St. Michael's. I succeeded in getting a considerable distance on my way to the woods, when Covey discovered me, and called after me to come back, threatening what he would do if I did not come. I disregarded both his calls and his threats, and made my way to the woods as fast as my feeble state would allow; and thinking I might be overhauled by him if I kept the road, I walked through the woods, keeping far enough from the road to avoid detection, and near enough to prevent losing my way. I had not gone far before my little strength again failed me. I could go no farther. I fell down, and lay for a considerable time. The blood was yet oozing from the wound on my head. For a time I thought I should bleed to death; and think now that I should have done so, but that the blood so matted my hair as to stop the wound. After lying there about three quarters of an hour, I nerved myself up again, and started on my way, through bogs and briers, barefooted and bareheaded, tearing my feet sometimes at nearly every step; and after a journey of about seven miles, occupying some five hours to perform it, I arrived at master's store. I then presented an appearance enough to affect any but a heart of iron. From the crown of my head to my feet, I was covered with blood. My hair was all clotted with dust and blood; my shirt was stiff with blood. My legs and feet were torn in sundry places with briers and thorns, and were also covered with blood. I suppose I looked like a man who had escaped a den of wild beasts, and barely escaped them. In this state I appeared before my master, humbly entreating him to interpose his authority for my protection. I told him all the circumstances as well as I could, and it seemed, as I spoke, at times to affect him. He would then walk the floor, and seek to justify Covey by saying he expected I deserved it. He asked me what I wanted. I told him, to let me get a new home; that as sure as I lived with Mr. Covey again, I should live with but to die with him; that Covey would surely kill me; he was in a fair way for it. Master Thomas ridiculed the idea that there was any danger of Mr. Covey's killing me, and said that he knew Mr. Covey; that he was a good man, and that he could not think of taking me from him; that, should he do so, he would lose the whole year's wages; that I belonged to Mr. Covey for one year, and that I must go back to him, come what might; and that I must not trouble him with any more stories, or that he would himself *get hold of me*. After threatening me thus, he gave me a very large dose of salts, telling me that I might remain in St. Michael's that night, (it being quite late,) but that I must be off back to Mr. Covey's early in the morning; and that if I did not, he would *get hold of me*, which meant that he would whip me. I remained all night, and, according to his orders I started off to Covey's in the morning, (Saturday morning), wearied in body and broken in spirit. I got no supper that night, or breakfast that morning. I reached Covey's about nine o'clock; and just as I was getting over the fence that divided Mrs. Kemp's fields from ours, out ran Covey with his cowskin, to give me another whipping. Before he could reach me, I succeeded in getting to the cornfield; and as the corn was very high, it afforded me the means of hiding. He seemed very angry, and searched for me a long time. My behavior was altogether unaccountable. He finally gave up the chase, thinking, I suppose, that I must come home for something to eat; he would give himself no further trouble in looking for me. I spent that day mostly in the woods, having the alternative before me,—to go home and be whipped to death, or stay in the woods and be starved to death. That night, I fell in with Sandy Jenkins, a slave with whom I was somewhat acquainted. Sandy had a free wife [2] who lived about four miles from Mr. Covey's; and it being Saturday, he was on his way to see her. I told him my circumstances, and he very kindly invited me to go home with him. I went home with him, and talked this whole matter over, and got his advice as to what course it was best for me to pursue. I found Sandy an old adviser. He told me, with great solemnity, I must go back to Covey; but that before I went, I must go with him into another part of the woods, where there was a certain *root*, which, if I would take some of it with me, carrying it *always on my right side*, would render it impossible for Mr. Covey, or any other white man, to whip me. He said he had carried it for years; and since he had done so, he had never received a blow, and never expected to while he carried it. I at first rejected the idea, that the simple carrying of a root in my pocket would have any such effect as he had said, and was not disposed to take it; but Sandy impressed the necessity with much earnestness, telling me it could do no harm, if it did no good. To please him, I at length took the root, and, according to his direction, carried it upon my right side. This was Sunday morning. I immediately started for home; and upon entering the yard gate, out came Mr. Covey on his way to meeting. He spoke to me very kindly, bade me drive the pigs from a lot near by, and passed on towards the church. Now, this singular conduct of Mr. Covey really made me begin to think that there was something in the *root* which Sandy had given me; and

2. I.e., she was not legally a slave.

had it been on any other day than Sunday, I could have attributed the conduct to no other cause than the influence of that root; and as it was, I was half inclined to think the *root* to be something more than I at first had taken it to be. All went well till Monday morning. On this morning, the virtue of the *root* was fully tested. Long before daylight, I was called to go and rub, curry, and feed, the horses. I obeyed, and was glad to obey. But whilst thus engaged, whilst in the act of throwing down some blades from the loft, Mr. Covey entered the stable with a long rope; and just as I was half out of the loft, he caught hold of my legs, and was about tying me. As soon as I found what he was up to, I gave a sudden spring, and as I did so, he holding to my legs, I was brought sprawling on the stable floor. Mr. Covey seemed now to think he had me, and could do what he pleased; but at this moment—from whence came the spirit I don't know—I resolved to fight; and, suiting my action to the resolution, I seized Covey hard by the throat; and as I did so, I rose. He held on to me, and I to him. My resistance was so entirely unexpected, that Covey seemed taken all aback. He trembled like a leaf. This gave me assurance, and I held him uneasy, causing the blood to run where I touched him with the ends of my fingers. Mr. Covey soon called out to Hughes for help. Hughes came, and while Covey held me, attempted to tie my right hand. While he was in the act of doing so, I watched my chance, and gave him a heavy kick close under the ribs. This kick fairly sickened Hughes, so that he left me in the hands of Mr. Covey. This kick had the effect of not only weakening Hughes, but Covey also. When he saw Hughes bending over with pain, his courage quailed. He asked me if I meant to persist in my resistance. I told him I did, come what might; that he had used me like a brute for six months, and that I was determined to be used so no longer. With that, he strove to drag me to a stick that was lying just out of the stable door. He meant to knock me down. But just as he was leaning over to get the stick, I seized him with both hands by his collar, and brought him by a sudden snatch to the ground. By this time, Bill came. Covey called upon him for assistance. Bill wanted to know what he could do. Covey said, "Take hold of him, take hold of him!" Bill said his master hired him out to work, and not to help to whip me; so he left Covey and myself to fight our own battle out. We were at it for nearly two hours. Covey at length let me go, puffing and blowing at a great rate, saying that if I had not resisted, he would not have whipped me half so much. The truth was, that he had not whipped me at all. I considered him as getting entirely the worst end of the bargain; for he had drawn no blood from me, but I had from him. The whole six months afterwards, that I spent with Mr. Covey, he never laid the weight of his finger upon me in anger. He would occasionally say, he didn't want to get hold of me again. "No," thought I, "you need not; for you will come off worse than you did before."

This battle with Mr. Covey was the turning-point in my career as a slave. It rekindled the few expiring embers of freedom, and revived within me a sense of my own manhood. It recalled the departed self-confidence, and inspired me again with a determination to be free. The gratification afforded by the triumph was a full compensation for whatever else might follow, even death itself. He only can understand the deep satisfaction which I experienced, who has himself repelled by force the bloody arm of slavery. I felt as I never felt before. It was a glorious resurrection, from the tomb of slavery, to the heaven of freedom. My long-crushed spirit rose, cowardice departed, bold defiance took its place; and I now, resolved that, however long I might remain a slave in form, the day had passed forever when I could be a slave in fact. I did not hesitate to let it be known of me, that the white man who expected to succeed in whipping, must also succeed in killing me.

From this time I was never again what might be called fairly whipped, though I remained a slave four years afterwards. I had several fights, but was never whipped.

It was for a long time a matter of surprise to me why Mr. Covey did not immediately have me taken by the constable to the whipping-post, and there regularly whipped for the crime of raising my hand against a white man in defence of myself. And the only explanation I can now think of does not entirely satisfy me; but such as it is, I will give it. Mr. Covey enjoyed the most unbounded reputation for being a first-rate overseer and negro-breaker. It was of considerable importance to him. That reputation was at stake; and had he sent me—a boy about sixteen years old—to the public whipping post, his reputation would have been lost; so, to save his reputation, he suffered me to go unpunished.

My term of actual service to Mr. Edward Covey ended on Christmas day, 1833. The days between Christmas and New Year's day are allowed as holidays; and, accordingly, we were not required to perform any labor, more than to feed and take care of the stock. This time we regarded as our own, by the grace of our masters; and we therefore used or abused it nearly as we pleased. Those of us who had families at a distance, were generally allowed to spend the whole six days in their society. This time, however, was spent in various ways. The staid, sober, thinking and industrious ones of our number would employ themselves in making corn-brooms, mats, horse-collars, and baskets; and another class of us would spend the time hunting opossums, hares, and coons. But by far the larger part engaged in such sports and merriments as playing ball, wrestling, running foot-races, fiddling, dancing, and drinking whisky; and this latter mode of spending the time was by far the most agreeable to the feelings of our master. A slave who would work during the holidays was considered by our masters as scarcely deserving them. He was regarded as one who rejected the favor of his master. It was deemed a disgrace not to get drunk at Christmas; and he was regarded as lazy indeed, who had not provided himself with the necessary means, during the year, to get whisky enough to last him through Christmas.

From what I know of the effect of these holidays upon the slave, I believe them to be among the most effective means in the hands of the slaveholder in keeping down the spirit of insurrection. Were the slaveholders at once to abandon this practice, I have not the slightest doubt it would lead to an immediate insurrection among the slaves. These holidays serve as conductors, or safety-valves, to carry off the rebellious spirit of enslaved humanity. But for these, the slave would be forced up to the wildest desperation; and woe betide the slaveholder, the day he ventures to remove or hinder the operation of those conductors! I warn him that, in such an event, a spirit will go forth in their midst, more to be dreaded than the most appalling earthquake.

The holidays are part and parcel of the gross fraud, wrong, and inhumanity of slavery. They are professedly a custom established by the benevolence of the slaveholders; but I undertake to say, it is the result of selfishness, and one of the grossest fraud committed upon the down-trodden slave. They do not give the slaves this time because they would not like to have their work during its continuance, but because they know it would be unsafe to deprive them of it. This will be seen by the fact, that the slaveholders like to have their slaves spend those days just in such a manner as to make them as glad of their ending as of their beginning. Their object seems to be, to disgust their slaves with freedom, by plunging them into the lowest depths of dissipation. For instance, the slaveholders not only like to see the slave drink of his own accord, but will adopt various plans to make him drunk. One plan is, to make bets on their slaves, as to who can drink the most whisky without getting drunk; and in this way they succeed in getting whole multitudes to drink to excess. Thus, when the slave asks for virtuous freedom, the cunning slaveholder, knowing his ignorance, cheats him with a dose of vicious dissipation, artfully labelled with the name of liberty. The most of us used to drink it down, and the result was just what might be supposed: many of us were led to think that there was little to choose between liberty and slavery. We felt, and very properly too, that we had almost as well be slaves to man as to rum. So, when the holidays ended, we staggered up from the filth of our wallowing, took a long breath, and marched to the field,—feeling, upon the whole, rather glad to go, from what our master had deceived us into a belief was freedom, back to the arms of slavery.

I have said that this mode of treatment is a part of the whole system of fraud and inhumanity of slavery. It is so. The mode here adopted to disgust the slave with freedom, by allowing him to see only the abuse of it, is carried out in other things. For instance, a slave loves molasses; he steals some. His master, in many cases, goes off to town, and buys a large quantity; he returns, takes his whip, and commands the slave to eat the molasses, until the poor fellow is made sick at the very mention of it. The same mode is sometimes adopted to make the slaves refrain from asking for more food than their regular allowance. A slave runs through his allowance, and applies for more. His master is enraged at him; but, not willing to send him off without food, gives more than is necessary, and compels him to eat it within a given time. Then, if he complains that he cannot eat it, he is said to be satisfied neither full nor fasting, and is whipped for being hard to please! I have an abundance of such illustrations of the same principle, drawn from my own observation, but think the cases I have cited sufficient. The practice is a very common one.

On the first of January, 1834, I left Mr. Covey, and went to live with Mr. William Freeland, who lived about three miles from St. Michael's. I soon found Mr. Freeland a very different man from Mr. Covey. Though not rich, he was what would be called an educated southern gentleman. Mr. Covey, as I have shown, was a well-trained negro-breaker and slave-driver. The former (slaveholder though he was) seemed to possess some regard for

honor, some reverence for justice, and some respect for humanity. The
latter seemed totally insensible to all such sentiments. Mr. Freeland had
many of the faults peculiar to slaveholders, such as being very passionate
and fretful; but I must do him the justice to say, that he was exceedingly
free from those degrading vices to which Mr. Covey was constantly addicted. The one was open and frank, and we always knew where to find
him. The other was a most artful deceiver, and could be understood only
by such as were skilful enough to detect his cunningly-devised frauds. Another advantage I gained in my new master was, he made no pretensions to,
or profession of, religion; and this, in my opinion, was truly a great advantage. I assert most unhesitatingly, that the religion of the south is a mere
covering for the most horrid crimes,—a justifier of the most appalling barbarity,—a sanctifier of the most hateful frauds,—and a dark shelter under,
which the darkest, foulest, grossest, and most infernal deeds of slaveholders
find the strongest protection. Were I to be again reduced to the chains of
slavery, next to that enslavement, I should regard being the slave of a religious master the greatest calamity that could befall me. For of all slaveholders with whom I have ever met, religious slaveholders are the worst. I have
ever found them the meanest and basest, the most cruel and cowardly, of
all others. It was my unhappy lot not only to belong to a religious slaveholder, but to live in a community of such religionists. Very near Mr. Freeland lived the Rev. Daniel Weeden, and in the same neighborhood lived
the Rev. Rigby Hopkins. These were members and ministers in the Reformed Methodist Church. Mr. Weeden owned, among others, a woman
slave, whose name I have forgotten. This woman's back, for weeks, was kept
literally raw, made so by the lash of this merciless, *religious* wretch. He
used to hire hands. His maxim was, Behave well or behave ill, it is the duty
of a master occasionally to whip a slave, to remind him of his master's authority. Such was his theory, and such his practice.

Mr. Hopkins was even worse than Mr. Weeden. His chief boast was his
ability to manage slaves. The peculiar feature of his government was that of
whipping slaves in advance of deserving it. He always managed to have one
or more of his slaves to whip every Monday morning. He did this to alarm
their fears, and strike terror into those who escaped. His plan was to whip
for the smallest offences, to prevent the commission of large ones. Mr.
Hopkins could always find some excuse for whipping a slave. It would astonish one, unaccustomed to a slave-holding life, to see with what wonderful ease a slave-holder can find things, of which to make occasion to whip a
slave. A mere look, word, or motion,—a mistake, accident, or want of
power,—are all matters for which a slave may be whipped at any time. Does
a slave look dissatisfied? It is said, he has the devil in him, and it must be
whipped out. Does he speak loudly when spoken to by his master? Then he
is wanting in reverence, and should be whipped for it. Does he ever venture to vindicate his conduct, when censured for it? Then he is guilty of
impudence,—one of the greatest crimes of which a slave can be guilty.
Does he ever venture to suggest a different mode of doing things from that
pointed out by his master? He is indeed presumptuous, and getting above
himself; and nothing less than a flogging will do for him. Does he, while
ploughing, break a plough,—or, while hoeing, break a hoe? It is owing to

his carelessness, and for it a slave must always be whipped. Mr. Hopkins could always find something of this sort to justify the use of the lash, and he seldom failed to embrace such opportunities. There was not a man in the whole county, with whom the slaves who had the getting their own home, would not prefer to live, rather than with this Rev. Mr. Hopkins. And yet there was not a man any where round, who made higher professions of religion, or was more active in revivals—more attentive to the class, love-feast, prayer and preaching meetings, or more devotional in his family,—that prayed earlier, later, louder, and longer,—than this same reverend slave-driver, Rigby Hopkins.

But to return to Mr. Freeland, and to my experience while in his employment. He, like Mr. Covey, gave us enough to eat; but unlike Mr. Covey, he also gave us sufficient time to take our meals. He worked us hard, but always between sunrise and sunset. He required a good deal of work to be done, but gave us good tools with which to work. His farm was large, but he employed hands enough to work it, and with ease, compared with many of his neighbors. My treatment, while in his employment, was heavenly, compared with what I experienced at the hands of Mr. Edward Covey.

Mr. Freeland was himself the owner of but two slaves. Their names were Henry Harris and John Harris. The rest of his hands he hired. These consisted of myself, Sandy Jenkins[3] and Handy Caldwell. Henry and John were quite intelligent, and in a very little while after I went there, I succeeded in creating in them a strong desire to learn how to read. This desire soon sprang up in the others also. They very soon mustered up some old spelling-books, and nothing would do but that I must keep a Sabbath school. I agreed to do so, and accordingly devoted my Sundays to teaching these my loved fellow-slaves how to read. Neither of them knew his letters when I went there. Some of the slaves of the neighboring farms found what was going on, and also availed themselves of this little opportunity to learn to read. It was understood, among all who came, that there must be as little display about it as possible. It was necessary to keep our religious masters at St. Michael's unacquainted with the fact, that, instead of spending the Sabbath in wrestling, boxing, and drinking whisky, we were trying to learn how to read the will of God; for they had much rather see us engaged in those degrading sports, than to see us behaving like intellectual, moral, and accountable beings. My blood boils as I think of the bloody manner in which Messrs. Wright Fairbanks and Garrison West, both class-leaders, in connection with many others, rushed in upon us with sticks and stones, and broke up our virtuous little Sabbath school, at St. Michael's—all calling themselves Christians! humble followers of the Lord Jesus Christ! But I am again digressing.

I held my Sabbath school at the house of a free colored man, whose name I deem it imprudent to mention; for should it be known, it might

3. This is the same man who gave me the roots to prevent my being whipped by Mr. Covey. He was "a clever soul." We used frequently to talk about the fight with Covey, and as often as we did so, he would claim my success as the result of the roots he gave me. This superstition is very common among the more ignorant slaves. A slave seldom dies but that his death is attributed to trickery [Douglass's note].

embarrass him greatly, though the crime of holding the school was committed ten years ago. I had at one time over forty scholars, and those of the right sort, ardently desiring to learn. They were of all ages, though mostly men and women. I look back to those Sundays with an amount of pleasure not to be expressed. They were great days to my soul. The work of instructing my dear fellow-slaves was the sweetest engagement with which I was ever blessed. We loved each other, and to leave them at the close of the Sabbath was a severe cross indeed. When I think that those precious souls are to-day shut up in the prison-house of slavery, my feelings overcome me, and I am almost ready to ask, "Does a righteous God govern the universe? and for what does he hold the thunders in his right hand, if not to smite the oppressor, and deliver the spoiled out of the hand of the spoiler?" These dear souls came not to Sabbath school because it was popular to do so, nor did I teach them because it was reputable to be thus engaged. Every moment they spent in that school, they were liable to be taken up, and given thirty-nine lashes. They came because they wished to learn. Their minds had been starved by their cruel masters. They had been shut up in mental darkness. I taught them, because it was the delight of my soul to be doing something that looked like bettering the condition of my race. I kept up my school nearly the whole year I lived with Mr. Freeland; and, beside my Sabbath school, I devoted three evenings in the week, during the winter, to teaching the slaves at home. And I have the happiness to know, that several of those who came to Sabbath school learned how to read; and that one, at least, is now free through my agency.

The year passed off smoothly. It seemed only about half as long as the year which preceded it. I went through it without receiving a single blow. I will give Mr. Freeland the credit of being the best master I ever had, *till I became my own master.* For the ease with which I passed the year, I was, however, somewhat indebted to the society of my fellow-slaves. They were noble souls; they not only possessed loving hearts, but brave ones. We were linked and interlinked with each other. I loved them with a love stronger than any thing I have experienced since. It is sometimes said that we slaves do not love and confide in each other. In answer to this assertion, I can say, I never loved any or confided in any people more than my fellow-slaves, and especially those with whom I lived at Mr. Freeland's. I believe we would have died for each other. We never undertook to do any thing, of any importance, without a mutual consultation. We never moved separately. We were one; and as much so by our tempers and dispositions, as by the mutual hardships to which we were necessarily subjected by our condition as slaves.

At the close of the year 1834, Mr. Freeland again hired me of my master, for the year 1835. But, by this time, I began to want to live *upon free land* as well as *with Freeland;* and I was no longer content, therefore, to live with him or any slaveholder. I began, with the commencement of the year, to prepare myself for a final struggle, which should decide my fate one way or the other. My tendency was upward. I was fast approaching manhood, and year after year had passed, and I was still a slave. These thoughts roused me—I must do something. I therefore resolved that 1835 should not pass without witnessing an attempt, on my part, to secure my liberty. But I was not willing to cherish this determination alone. My fellow-slaves were dear to me. I was anxious to have them participate with me in this, my life-giving determination. I therefore, though with great prudence, commenced early to ascertain their views and feelings in regard to their condition, and to imbue their minds with thoughts of freedom. I bent myself to devising ways and means for our escape, and meanwhile strove, on all fitting occasions, to impress them with the gross fraud and inhumanity of slavery. I went first to Henry, next to John, then to the others. I found, in them all, warm hearts and noble spirits. They were ready to hear, and ready to act when a feasible plan should be proposed. This was what I wanted. I talked to them of our want of manhood, if we submitted to our enslavement without at least one noble effort to be free. We met often, and consulted frequently, and told our hopes and fears, recounted the difficulties, real and imagined, which we should be called on to meet. At times we were almost disposed to give up and try to content ourselves with our wretched lot; at others, we were firm and unbending in our determination to go. Whenever we suggested any plan, there was shrinking—the odds were fearful. Our path was beset with the greatest obstacles; and if we succeeded in gaining the end of it, our right to be free was yet questionable—we were yet liable to be returned to bondage. We could see no spot, this side of the ocean, where we could be free. We knew nothing about Canada. Our knowledge of the north did not extend farther than New York; and to go there, and be forever harassed with the frightful liability of being returned to slavery—with the certainty of being treated tenfold worse than before—the thought was truly a horrible one, and one which it was not easy to overcome. The case sometimes stood thus: At every gate through which we were to pass, we saw a watchman—at every ferry a guard—on every bridge a sentinel—and in every wood a patrol. We were hemmed in upon every side. Here were the difficulties, real or imagined—the good to be sought, and the evil to be shunned. On the one hand, there stood slavery, a stern reality, glaring frightfully upon us,—its robes already crimsoned with the blood of millions, and even now feasting itself greedily upon our own flesh. On the other hand, away back in the dim distance, under the flickering light of the north star, behind some craggy hill or snow-covered mountain, stood a doubtful freedom—half frozen—beckoning us to come and share its hospitality. This in itself was sometimes enough to stagger us; but when we permitted ourselves to survey the road, we were frequently appalled. Upon either side we saw grim death, assuming the most horrid shapes. Now it was starvation, causing us to eat our own flesh;—now we were contending with the waves, and were drowned;—now we were overtaken, and torn to pieces by the fangs of the terrible bloodhound. We were stung by scorpions, chased by wild beasts, bitten by snakes, and finally, after having nearly reached the desired spot,—after swimming rivers, encountering wild beasts, sleeping in the woods, suffering hunger and nakedness,—we were overtaken by our pursuers, and in our resistance, we were shot dead upon the spot! I say, this picture sometimes appalled us, and made us

"rather bear those ills we had,
Than fly to others, that we knew not of."[4]

In coming to a fixed determination to run away, we did more than Patrick Henry, when he resolved upon liberty or death. With us it was a doubtful liberty at most, and almost certain death if we failed. For my part, I should prefer death to hopeless bondage.

Sandy, one of our number, gave up the notion, but still encouraged us. Our company then consisted of Henry Harris, John Harris, Henry Bailey, Charles Roberts, and myself. Henry Bailey was my uncle, and belonged to my master. Charles married my aunt: he belonged to my master's father-in-law, Mr. William Hamilton.

The plan we finally concluded upon was, to get a large canoe belonging to Mr. Hamilton, and upon the Saturday night previous to Easter holidays, paddle directly up the Chesapeake Bay. On our arrival at the head of the bay, a distance of seventy or eighty miles from where we lived, it was our purpose to turn our canoe adrift, and follow the guidance of the north star till we got beyond the limits of Maryland. Our reason for taking the water route was, that we were less liable to be suspected as runaways; we hoped to be regarded as fishermen; whereas, if we should take the land route, we should be subjected to interruptions of almost every kind. Any one having a white face, and being so disposed, could stop us, and subject us to examination.

The week before our intended start, I wrote several protections, one for each of us. As well as I can remember they were in the following words, to wit:—

"This is to certify that I, the undersigned, have given the bearer, my servant, full liberty to go to Baltimore, and spend the Easter holidays. Written with mine own hand, etc., 1835

"WILLIAM HAMILTON,
"Near St. Michael's, in Talbot county, Maryland."

We were not going to Baltimore; but, in going up the bay, we went toward Baltimore, and these protections were only intended to protect us while on the bay.

As the time drew near for our departure, our anxiety became more and more intense. It was truly a matter of life and death with us. The strength of our determination was about to be fully tested. At this time, I was very active in explaining every difficulty, removing every doubt, dispelling every fear, and inspiring all with the firmness indispensable to success in our undertaking; assuring them that half was gained the instant we made the move; we had talked long enough; we were now ready to move; if not now, we never should be; and if we did not intend to move now, we had as well fold our arms, sit down, and acknowledge ourselves fit only to be slaves. This, none of us were prepared to acknowledge. Every man stood firm; and at our last meeting, we pledged ourselves afresh, in the most solemn man-

4. Shakespeare's *Hamlet* 3.1.81–82.

ner, that at the time appointed, we would certainly start in pursuit of freedom. This was in the middle of the week, at the end of which we were to be
off. We went, as usual, to our several fields of labor, but with bosoms highly
agitated with thoughts of our truly hazardous undertaking. We tried to conceal our feelings as much as possible; and I think we succeeded very well.

After a painful waiting, the Saturday morning, whose night was to witness our departure, came. I hailed it with joy, bring what of sadness it
might. Friday night was a sleepless one for me. I probably felt more anxious
than the rest, because I was, by common consent, at the head of the whole
affair. The responsibility of success or failure lay heavily upon me. The
glory of the one, and the confusion of the other, were alike mine. The first
two hours of that morning were such as I never experienced before, and
hope never to again. Early in the morning, we went, as usual, to the field.
We were spreading manure; and all at once, while thus engaged, I was
overwhelmed with an indescribable feeling, in the fulness of which I
turned to Sandy, who was near by, and said, "We are betrayed!" "Well,"
said he, "that thought has this moment struck me." We said no more. I was
never more certain of any thing.

The horn was blown as usual, and we went up from the field to the
house for breakfast. I went for the form, more than for want of any thing to
eat that morning. Just as I got to the house, in looking out at the lane gate, I
saw four white men, with two colored men. The white men were on horseback, and the colored ones were walking behind, as if tied. I watched them
a few moments till they got up to our lane gate. Here they halted, and tied
the colored men to the gate-post. I was not yet certain as to what the matter
was. In a few moments, in rode Mr. Hamilton, with a speed betokening
great excitement. He came to the door, and inquired if Master William was
in. He was told he was at the barn. Mr. Hamilton, without dismounting,
rode up to the barn with extraordinary speed. In a few moments, he and
Mr. Freeland returned to the house. By this time, the three constables rode
up, and in great haste dismounted, tied their horses, and met Master William and Mr. Hamilton returning from the barn; and after talking awhile,
they all walked up to the kitchen door. There was no one in the kitchen but
myself and John. Henry and Sandy were up at the barn. Mr. Freeland put
his head in at the door, and called me by name, saying, there were some
gentlemen at the door who wished to see me. I stepped to the door, and
inquired what they wanted. They at once seized me, and, without giving
me any satisfaction, tied me—lashing my hands closely together. I insisted
upon knowing what the matter was. They at length said, that they had
learned I had been in a "scrape," and that I was to be examined before my
master; and if their information proved false, I should not be hurt.

In a few moments, they succeeded in tying John. They then turned to
Henry, who had by this time returned, and commanded him to cross his
hands. "I won't!" said Henry, in a firm tone, indicating his readiness to
meet the consequences of his refusal. "Won't you?" said Tom Graham, the
constable. "No, I won't!" said Henry, in a still stronger tone. With this, two
of the constables pulled out their shining pistols, and swore, by their Creator, that they would make him cross his hands or kill him. Each cocked
his pistol, and, with fingers on the trigger, walked up to Henry, saying, at

the same time, if he did not cross his hands, they would blow his damned heart out. "Shoot me, shoot me!" said Henry; "you can't kill me but once. Shoot, shoot,—and be damned! *I won't be tied!*" This he said in a tone of loud defiance; and at the same time, with a motion as quick as lightning, he with one single stroke dashed the pistols from the hand of each constable. As he did this, all hands fell upon him, and, after beating him some time, they finally overpowered him, and got him tied.

During the scuffle, I managed, I know not how, to get my pass out, and, without being discovered, put it into the fire. We were all now tied; and just as we were to leave for Easton jail, Betsy Freeland, mother of William Freeland, came to the door with her hands full of biscuits, and divided them between Henry and John. She then delivered herself of a speech, to the following effect:—addressing herself to me, she said, *"You devil! You yellow devil!* it was you that put it into the heads of Henry and John to run away. But for you, you long-legged mulatto devil! Henry nor John would never have thought of such a thing." I made no reply, and was immediately hurried off towards St. Michael's. Just a moment previous to the scuffle with Henry, Mr. Hamilton suggested the propriety of making a search for the protections which he had understood Frederick had written for himself and the rest. But, just at the moment he was about carrying his proposal into effect, his aid was needed in helping to tie Henry; and the excitement attending the scuffle caused them either to forget, or to deem it unsafe, under the circumstances, to search. So we were not yet convicted of the intention to run away.

When we got about half way to St. Michael's, while the constables having us in charge were looking ahead, Henry inquired of me what he should do with his pass. I told him to eat it with his biscuit, and own nothing; and we passed the word around, *"Own nothing;"* and *"Own nothing!"* said we all. Our confidence in each other was unshaken. We were resolved to succeed or fail together, after the calamity had befallen us as much as before. We were now prepared for any thing. We were to be dragged that morning fifteen miles behind horses, and then to be placed in the Easton jail. When we reached St. Michael's, we underwent a sort of examination. We all denied that we ever intended to run away. We did this more to bring out the evidence against us, than from any hope of getting clear of being sold; for, as I have said, we were ready for that. The fact was, we cared but little where we went, so we went together. Our greatest concern was about separation. We dreaded that more than any thing this side of death. We found the evidence against us to be the testimony of one person; our master would not tell who it was; but we came to a unanimous decision among ourselves as to who their informant was. We were sent off to the jail at Easton. When we got there, we were delivered up to the sheriff, Mr. Joseph Graham, and by him placed in jail. Henry, John, and myself, were placed in one room together—Charles, and Henry Bailey, in another. Their object in separating us was to hinder concert.

We had been in jail scarcely twenty minutes, when a swarm of slave traders, and agents for slave traders, flocked into jail to look at us, and to ascertain if we were for sale. Such a set of beings I never saw before! I felt myself surrounded by so many fiends from perdition. A band of pirates never looked more like their father, the devil. They laughed and grinned over us, saying, "Ah, my boys! we have got you, haven't we?" And after taunting us in various ways, they one by one went into an examination of us, with intent to ascertain our value. They would impudently ask us if we would not like to have them for our masters. We would make them no answer, and leave them to find out as best they could. Then they would curse and swear at us, telling us that they could take the devil out of us in a very little while, if we were only in their hands.

While in jail, we found ourselves in much more comfortable quarters than we expected when we went there. We did not get much to eat, nor that which was very good; but we had a good clean room, from the windows of which we could see what was going on in the street, which was very much better than though we had been placed in one of the dark, damp cells. Upon the whole, we got along very well, so far as the jail and its keeper were concerned. Immediately after the holidays were over, contrary to all our expectations, Mr. Hamilton and Mr. Freeland came up to Easton, and took Charles, the two Henrys, and John, out of jail, and carried them home, leaving me alone. I regarded this separation as a final one. It caused me more pain than any thing else in the whole transaction. I was ready for any thing rather than separation. I supposed that they had consulted together, and had decided that, as I was the whole cause of the intention of the others to run away, it was hard to make the innocent suffer with the guilty; and that they had, therefore, concluded to take the others home, and sell me, as a warning to the others that remained. It is due to the noble Henry to say, he seemed almost as reluctant at leaving the prison as at leaving home to come to the prison. But we knew we should, in all probability, be separated, if we were sold; and since he was in their hands, he concluded to go peaceably home.

I was now left to my fate. I was all alone, and within the walls of a stone prison. But a few days before, and I was full of hope. I expected to have been safe in a land of freedom; but now I was covered with gloom, sunk down to the utmost despair. I thought the possibility of freedom was gone. I was kept in this way about one week, at the end of which, Captain Auld, my master, to my surprise and utter astonishment, came up, and took me out, with the intention of sending me, with a gentleman of his acquaintance, into Alabama. But, from some cause or other, he did not send me to Alabama, but concluded to send me back to Baltimore, to live again with his brother Hugh, and to learn a trade.

Thus, after an absence of three years and one month, I was once more permitted to return to my old home at Baltimore. My master sent me away, because there existed against me a very great prejudice in the community, and he feared I might be killed.

In a few weeks after I went to Baltimore, Master Hugh hired me to Mr. William Gardner, an extensive ship-builder, on Fell's Point. I was put there to learn how to calk. It, however, proved a very unfavorable place for the accomplishment of this object. Mr. Gardner was engaged that spring in building two large man-of-war brigs, professedly for the Mexican government. The vessels were to be launched in the July of that year, and in failure thereof, Mr. Gardner was to lose a considerable sum; so that when I

entered, all was hurry. There was no time to learn any thing. Every man
had to do that which he knew how to do. In entering the shipyard, my
orders from Mr. Gardner were, to do whatever the carpenters commanded
me to do. This was placing me at the beck and call of about seventy-five
men. I was to regard all these as masters. Their word was to be my law. My
situation was a most trying one. At times I needed a dozen pair of hands. I
was called a dozen ways in the space of a single minute. Three or four
voices would strike my ear at the same moment. It was—"Fred., come help
me to cant this timber here."—"Fred., come carry this timber yonder."—
"Fred., bring that roller here."—"Fred., go get a fresh can of water."—
"Fred., come help saw off the end of this timber."—"Fred., go quick, and
get the crowbar."—"Fred., hold on the end of this fall."[5]—"Fred., go to the
blacksmith's shop, and get a new punch."—"Hurra, Fred.! run and bring
me a cold chisel."—"I say, Fred., bear a hand, and get up a fire as quick as
lightning under that steam-box."—"Halloo, nigger! come, turn this grind-
stone."—"Come, come! move, move! and *bowse*[6] this timber forward."—"I
say, darky, blast your eyes, why don't you heat up some pitch?"—"Halloo!
halloo! halloo!" (Three voices at the same time.) "Come here!—Go
there!—Hold on where you are! Damn you, if you move, I'll knock your
brains out!"

   This was my school for eight months; and I might have remained there
longer, but for a most horrid fight I had with four of the white apprentices,
in which my left eye was nearly knocked out, and I was horribly mangled in
other respects. The facts in the case were these: Until a very little while
after I went there, white and black ship-carpenters worked side by side, and
no one seemed to see any impropriety in it. All hands seemed to be very
well satisfied. Many of the black carpenters were freemen. Things seemed
to be going on very well. All at once, the white carpenters knocked off, and
said they would not work with free colored workmen. Their reason for this,
as alleged, was, that if free colored carpenters were encouraged, they would
soon take the trade into their own hands, and poor white men would be
thrown out of employment. They therefore felt called upon at once to put a
stop to it. And, taking advantage of Mr. Gardner's necessities, they broke
off, swearing they would work no longer, unless he would discharge his
black carpenters. Now, though this did not extend to me in form, it did
reach me in fact. My fellow-apprentices very soon began to feel it degrading to them to work with me. They began to put on airs, and talk about the
"niggers" taking the country, saying we all ought to be killed; and, being
encouraged by the journeymen, they commenced making my condition as
hard as they could, by hectoring me around, and sometimes striking me. I,
of course, kept the vow I made after the fight with Mr. Covey, and struck
back again, regardless of consequences; and while I kept them from combining, I succeeded very well; for I could whip the whole of them, taking
them separately. They, however, at length combined, and came upon me,
armed with sticks, stones, and heavy handspikes. One came in front with a
half brick. There was one at each side of me, and one behind me. While I

---

5. Nautical term for the free end of a rope of a   6. To haul the timber by pulling on the rope.
tackle or hoisting device.

was attending to those in front, and on either side, the one behind ran up with the handspike, and struck me a heavy blow upon the head. It stunned me. I fell, and with this they all ran upon me, and fell to beating me with their fists. I let them lay on for a while, gathering strength. In an instant, I gave a sudden surge, and rose to my hands and knees. Just as I did that, one of their number gave me, with his heavy boot, a powerful kick in the left eye. My eyeball seemed to have burst. When they saw my eye closed, and badly swollen, they left me. With this I seized the handspike, and for a time pursued them. But here the carpenters interfered, and I thought I might as well give it up. It was impossible to stand my hand against so many. All this took place in sight of not less than fifty white ship-carpenters, and not one interposed a friendly word; but some cried, "Kill the damned nigger! Kill him! kill him! He struck a white person." I found my only chance for life was in flight. I succeeded in getting away without an additional blow, and barely so, for to strike a white man is death by Lynch law,[7]—and that was the law in Mr. Gardner's ship-yard; nor is there much of any other out of Mr. Gardner's ship-yard.

I went directly home, and told the story of my wrongs to Master Hugh; and I am happy to say of him, irreligious as he was, his conduct was heavenly, compared with that of his brother Thomas under similar circumstances. He listened attentively to my narration of the circumstances leading to the savage outrage, and gave many proofs of his strong indignation at it. The heart of my once overkind mistress was again melted into pity. My puffed-out eye and blood-covered face moved her to tears. She took a chair by me, washed the blood from my face, and, with a mother's tenderness, bound up my head, covering the wounded eye with a lean piece of fresh beef. It was almost compensation for my suffering to witness, once more, a manifestation of kindness from this, my once affectionate old mistress. Master Hugh was very much enraged. He gave expression to his feelings by pouring out curses upon the heads of those who did the deed. As soon as I got a little the better of my bruises, he took me with him to Esquire Watson's, on Bond Street, to see what could be done about the matter. Mr. Watson inquired who saw the assault committed. Master Hugh told him it was done in Mr. Gardner's ship-yard, at midday, where there were a large company of men at work. "As to that," he said, "the deed was done, and there was no question as to who did it." His answer was, he could do nothing in the case, unless some white man would come forward and testify. He could issue no warrant on my word. If I had been killed in the presence of a thousand colored people, their testimony combined would have been insufficient to have arrested one of the murderers. Master Hugh, for once, was compelled to say this state of things was too bad. Of course, it was impossible to get any white man to volunteer his testimony in my behalf, and against the white young men. Even those who may have sympathized with me were not prepared to do this. It required a degree of courage unknown to them to do so; for just at that time, the slightest manifestation of humanity toward a colored person was denounced as abolitionism, and that name subjected its bearer to frightful liabilities. The watchwords of the

7. I.e., to be subject to lynching, without benefit of legal procedures.

bloody-minded in that region, and in those days, were, "Damn the aboli-tionists!" and "Damn the niggers!" There was nothing done, and probably nothing would have been done if I had been killed. Such was, and such remains, the state of things in the Christian city of Baltimore.

Master Hugh, finding he could get no redress, refused to let me go back again to Mr. Gardner. He kept me himself, and his wife dressed my wound till I was again restored to health. He then took me into the ship-yard of which he was foreman, in the employment of Mr. Walter Price. There I was immediately set to calking, and very soon learned the art of using my mallet and irons. In the course of one year from the time I left Mr. Gard-ner's, I was able to command the highest wages given to the most experi-enced calkers. I was now of some importance to my master. I was bringing him from six to seven dollars per week. I sometimes brought him nine dol-lars per week: my wages were a dollar and a half a day. After learning how to calk, I sought my own employment, made my own contracts, and collected the money which I earned. My pathway became much more smooth than before; my condition was now much more comfortable. When I could get no calking to do, I did nothing. During these leisure times, those old no-tions about freedom would steal over me again. When in Mr. Gardner's employment, I was kept in such a perpetual whirl of excitement, I could think of nothing, scarcely, but my life; and in thinking of my life, I almost forgot my liberty. I have observed this in my experience of slavery,—that whenever my condition was improved, instead of its increasing my content-ment, it only increased my desire to be free, and set me to thinking of plans to gain my freedom. I have found that, to make a contented slave, it is nec-essary to make a thoughtless one. It is necessary to darken his moral and mental vision, and, as far as possible, to annihilate the power of reason. He must be able to detect no inconsistencies in slavery; he must be made to feel that slavery is right; and he can be brought to that only when he ceases to be a man.

I was now getting, as I have said, one dollar and fifty cents per day. I contracted for it; I earned it; it was paid to me; it was rightfully my own; yet, upon each returning Saturday night, I was compelled to deliver every cent of that money to Master Hugh. And why? Not because he earned it,—not because he had any hand in earning it,—not because I owed it to him,—nor because he possessed the slightest shadow of a right to it; but solely because he had the power to compel me to give it up. The right of the grim-visaged pirate upon the high seas is exactly the same.

Chapter XI

I now come to that part of my life during which I planned, and finally succeeded in making, my escape from slavery. But before narrating any of the peculiar circumstances, I deem it proper to make known my intention not to state all the facts connected with the transaction. My reasons for pur-suing this course may be understood from the following: First, were I to give a minute statement of all the facts, it is not only possible but quite probable, that others would thereby be involved in the most embarrassing difficulties. Secondly, such a statement would most undoubtedly induce greater vigilance on the part of slaveholders than has existed heretofore among them; which would, of course, be the means of guarding a door whereby some dear brother bondman might escape his galling chains. I deeply regret the necessity that impels me to suppress any thing of importance connected with my experience in slavery. It would afford me great pleasure indeed, as well as materially add to the interest of my narrative, were I at liberty to gratify a curiosity, which I know exists in the minds of many, by an accurate statement of all the facts pertaining to my most fortunate escape. But I must deprive myself of this pleasure, and the curious of the gratification which such a statement would afford. I would allow myself to suffer under the greatest imputations which evil-minded men might suggest, rather than exculpate myself, and thereby run the hazard of closing the slightest avenue by which a brother slave might clear himself of the chains and fetters of slavery.

I have never approved of the very public manner in which some of our western friends have conducted what they call the *underground railroad*, but which I think, by their own declarations, had been made most emphatically the *upperground railroad*. I honor those good men and women for their noble daring; and applaud them for willingly subjecting themselves to bloody persecution, by openly avowing their participation in the escape of slaves. I, however, can see very little good resulting from such a course, either to themselves or the slaves escaping; while, upon the other hand, I see and feel assured that those open declarations are a positive evil to the slaves remaining, who are seeking to escape. They do nothing towards enlightening the slave, whilst they do much towards enlightening the master. They stimulate him to greater watchfulness, and enhance his power to capture his slave. We owe something to the slave south of the line as well as to those north of it; and in aiding the latter on their way to freedom, we should be careful to do nothing which would be likely to hinder the former from escaping from slavery. I would keep the merciless slaveholder profoundly ignorant of the means of flight adopted by the slave. I would leave him to imagine himself surrounded by myriads of invisible tormentors, ever ready to snatch from his infernal grasp his trembling prey. Let him be left to feel his way in the dark; let darkness commensurate with his crime hover over him; and let him feel that at every step he takes, in pursuit of the flying bondman, he is running the frightful risk of having his hot brains dashed out by an invisible agency. Let us render the tyrant no aid; let us not hold the light by which he can trace the footprints of our flying brother. But enough of this. I will now proceed to the statement of those facts, connected with my escape, for which I am alone responsible, and for which no one can be made to suffer but myself.

In the early part of the year 1838, I became quite restless. I could see no reason why I should, at the end of each week, pour the reward of my toil into the purse of my master. When I carried to him my weekly wages, he would, after counting the money, look me in the face with a robber-like fierceness, and say, "Is this all?" He was satisfied with nothing less than the last cent. He would, however, when I made him six dollars, sometimes give me six cents, to encourage me. It had the opposite effect. I regarded it as a sort of admission of my right to the whole. The fact that he gave me any part of my wages was proof, to my mind, that he believed me entitled to the whole of them. I always felt worse for having received any thing; for I feared that the giving me a few cents would ease his conscience, and make him feel himself to be a pretty honorable sort of robber. My discontent grew upon me. I was ever on the lookout for means of escape; and, finding no direct means, I determined to try to hire my time, with a view of getting money with which to make my escape. In the spring of 1838, when Master Thomas came to Baltimore to purchase his spring goods, I got an opportunity, and applied to him to allow me to hire my time. He unhesitatingly refused my request, and told me this was another stratagem by which to escape. He told me I could go nowhere but that he could get me; and that, in the event of my running away, he should spare no pains in his efforts to catch me. He exhorted me to content myself, and be obedient. He told me, if I would be happy, I must lay out no plans for the future. He said, if I behaved myself properly, he would take care of me. Indeed, he advised me to complete thoughtlessness of the future, and taught me to depend solely upon him for happiness. He seemed to see fully the pressing necessity of setting aside my intellectual nature, in order to [insure] contentment in slavery. But in spite of him, and even in spite of myself, I continued to think, and to think about the injustice of my enslavement, and the means of escape.

About two months after this, I applied to Master Hugh for the privilege of hiring my time. He was not acquainted with the fact that I had applied to Master Thomas, and had been refused. He too, at first, seemed disposed to refuse; but, after some reflection, he granted me the privilege, and proposed the following terms: I was to be allowed all my time, make all contracts with those for whom I worked, and find my own employment; and, in return for this liberty, I was to pay him three dollars at the end of each week; find myself in calking tools, and in board and clothing. My board was two dollars and a half per week. This, with the wear and tear of clothing and calking tools, made my regular expenses about six dollars per week. This amount I was compelled to make up, or relinquish the privilege of hiring my time. Rain or shine, work or no work, at the end of each week the money must be forthcoming, or I must give up my privilege. This arrangement, it will be perceived, was decidedly in my master's favor. It relieved him of all needs of looking after me. His money was sure. He received all the benefits of slaveholding without its evils; while I endured all the evils of a slave, and suffered all the care and anxiety of a freeman. I found it a hard bargain. But, hard as it was I thought it better than the old mode of getting along. It was a step towards freedom to be allowed to bear the responsibilities of a freeman, and I was determined to hold on upon it. I bent myself to the work of making money. I was ready to work at night as well as day, and by the most untiring perseverance and industry, I made enough to meet my expenses, and lay up a little money each week. I went on thus from May till August. Master Hugh then refused to allow me to hire my time longer. The ground for his refusal was a failure on my part, one Saturday night, to pay him for my week's time. This failure was occasioned by my attending a camp meeting about ten miles from Baltimore. During the week, I had entered into an engagement with a number of young friends to start from

Baltimore to the camp ground early Saturday evening; and being detained by my employer, I was unable to get down to Master Hugh's without disappointing the company. I knew that Master Hugh was in no special need of the money that night. I therefore decided to go to camp meeting, and upon my return pay him the three dollars. I staid at the camp meeting one day longer than I intended when I left. But as soon as I returned, I called upon him to pay him what he considered his due. I found him very angry; he could scarce restrain his wrath. He said he had a great mind to give me a severe whipping. He wished to know how I dared go out of the city without asking his permission. I told him I hired my time, and while I paid him the price which he asked for it, I did not know that I was bound to ask him when and where I should go. This reply troubled him; and, after reflecting a few moments, he turned to me, and said I should hire my time no longer; that the next thing he should know if, I would be running away. Upon the same plea, he told me to bring my tools and clothing home forthwith. I did so; but instead of seeking work, as I had been accustomed to do previously to hiring my time, I spent the whole week without the performance of a single stroke of work. I did this in retaliation. Saturday night, he called upon me as usual for my week's wages. I told him I had no wages; I had done no work that week. Here we were upon the point of coming to blows. He raved, and swore his determination to get hold of me. I did not allow myself a single word; but was resolved, if he laid the weight of his hand upon me, it should be blow for blow. He did not strike me, but told me that he would find me in constant employment in future. I thought the matter over during the next day, Sunday, and finally resolved upon the third day of September, as the day upon which I would make a second attempt to secure my freedom. I now had three weeks during which to prepare for my journey. Early on Monday morning, before Master Hugh had time to make any engagement for me, I went out and got employment of Mr. Butler, at his ship-yard near the drawbridge, upon what is called the City Block, thus making it unnecessary for him to seek employment for me. At the end of the week, I brought him between eight and nine dollars. He seemed very well pleased, and asked why I did not do the same the week before. He little knew what my plans were. My object in working steadily was to remove any suspicion he might entertain of my intent to run away; and in this I succeeded admirably. I suppose he thought I was never better satisfied with my condition than at the very time during which I was planning my escape. The second week passed, and again I carried him my full wages; and so well pleased was he, that he gave me twenty-five cents, (quite a large sum for a slaveholder to give a slave), and bade me to make a good use of it. I told him I would.

Things went on without very smoothly indeed, but within there was trouble. It is impossible for me to describe my feelings as the time of my contemplated start drew near. I had a number of warm-hearted friends in Baltimore,—friends that I loved almost as I did my life,—and the thought of being separated from them forever was painful beyond expression. It is my opinion that thousands would escape from slavery, who now remain, but for the strong cords of affection that bind them to their friends. The thought of leaving my friends was decidedly the most painful thought with which I had to contend. The love of them was my tender point, and shook my decision more than all things else. Besides the pain of separation, the dread and apprehension of a failure exceeded what I had experienced at my first attempt. The appalling defeat I then sustained returned to torment me. I felt assured that, if I failed in this attempt, my case would be a hopeless one—it would seal my fate as a slave forever. I could not hope to get off with any thing less than the several punishment, and being placed beyond the means of escape. It required no very vivid imagination to depict the most frightful scenes through which I should have to pass, in case I failed. The wretchedness of slavery, and the blessedness of freedom, were perpetually before me. It was life and death with me. But I remained firm, and, according to my resolution, on the third day of September, 1838, I left my chains, and succeeded in reaching New York without the slightest interruption of any kind. How I did so,—what means I adopted,—what direction I travelled, and by what mode of conveyance,—I must leave unexplained, for the reasons before mentioned.

I have been frequently asked how I felt when I found myself in a free State. I have never been able to answer the question with any satisfaction to myself. It was a moment of the highest excitement I ever experienced. I suppose I felt as one may imagine the unarmed mariner to feel when he is rescued by a friendly man-of-war from the pursuit of a pirate. In writing to a dear friend, immediately after my arrival at New York, I said I felt like one who had escaped a den of hungry lions. This state of mind, however, very soon subsided; and I was again seized with a feeling of great insecurity and loneliness. I was yet liable to be taken back, and subjected to all the tortures of slavery. This in itself was enough to damp the ardor of my enthusiasm. But the loneliness overcame me. There I was in the midst of thousands, and yet a perfect stranger; without home and without friends, in the midst of thousands of my own brethren—children of a common Father, and yet I dared not to unfold to any one of them my sad condition. I was afraid to speak to any one for fear of speaking to the wrong one, and thereby falling into the hands of money-loving kidnappers, whose business it was to lie in wait for the panting fugitive, as the ferocious beasts of the forest lie in wait for their prey. The motto which I adopted when I started from slavery was this—"Trust no man!" I saw in every white man an enemy, and in almost every colored man cause for distrust. It was a most painful situation; and, to understand it, one must needs experience it, or imagine himself in similar circumstances. Let him be a fugitive slave in a strange land—a land given up to be the hunting-ground for slaveholders—whose inhabitants are legalized kidnappers—where he is every moment subjected to the terrible liability of being seized upon by his fellowmen, as the hideous crocodile seizes upon his prey!—I say, let him place himself in my situation—without home or friends—without money or credit—wanting shelter, and no one to give it—wanting bread, and no money to buy it,—and at the same time let him feel that he is pursued by merciless men-hunters, and in total darkness as to what to do, where to go, or where to stay,—perfectly helpless both as to the means of defence and means of escape,—in the midst of plenty, yet suffering the terrible gnawings of hunger,—in the midst of houses, yet having no home,—among fellow-men, yet feeling as if in the midst of wild beasts, whose greediness to swallow up the trembling and half-famished fugitive is only equalled by that with which the monsters of the deep swallow up the helpless fish upon which they subsist,—I say, let him be placed in this most trying situation,—the situation in which I was placed,—then, and not till then, will he fully appreciate the hardships of, and know how to sympathize with, the toil-worn and whip-scarred fugitive slave.

Thank Heaven, I remained but a short time in this distressed situation. I was relieved from it by the humane hand of MR. DAVID RUGGLES, [8] whose vigilance, kindness, and perseverance, I shall never forget. I am glad of an opportunity to express, as far as words can, the love and gratitude I bear him. Mr. Ruggles is now afflicted with blindness, and is himself in need of the same kind offices which he was once so forward in the performance of toward others. I had been in New York but a few days, when Mr. Ruggles sought me out, and very kindly took me to his boarding-house at the corner of Church and Lespenard Streets. Mr. Ruggles was then very deeply engaged in the memorable *Darg* case, [9] as well as attending to a number of other fugitive slaves; devising ways and means for their successful escape; and, though watched and hemmed in on almost every side, he seemed to be more than a match for his enemies.

Very soon after I went to Mr. Ruggles, he wished to know of me where I wanted to go; as he deemed it unsafe for me to remain in New York. I told him I was a calker, and should like to go where I could get work. I thought of going to Canada; but he decided against it, and in favor of my going to New Bedford, thinking I should be able to get work there at my trade. At this time, Anna, [1] my intended wife, came on; for I wrote to her immediately after my arrival at New York, (notwithstanding my homeless, houseless, and helpless condition,) informing her of my successful flight, and wishing her to come on forthwith. In a few days after her arrival, Mr. Ruggles called in the Rev. J. W. C. Pennington, who, in the presence of Mr. Ruggles, Mrs. Michaels, and two or three others, performed the marriage ceremony, and gave us a certificate, of which the following is an exact copy:—

"This may certify, that I joined together in holy matrimony Frederick Johnson [2] and Anna Murray, as man and wife, in the presence of Mr. David Ruggles and Mrs. Michaels.

"JAMES W. C. PENNINGTON [3]

"*New York, Sept.* 15, 1838."

Upon receiving this certificate, and a five-dollar bill from Mr. Ruggles, I shouldered one part of our baggage, and Anna took up the other, and we set out forthwith to take passage on board of the steamboat John W. Richmond for Newport, on our way to New Bedford. Mr. Ruggles gave me a letter to a

---

8. A journalist and abolitionist (1810–1849), who aided Douglass in his escape from Maryland and in whose house Douglass stayed on his way to New Bedford in 1838.
9. Ruggles had been arrested in 1839 and charged with harboring a fugitive slave who had escaped from John P. Darg of Arkansas.

1. "She was free" [Douglass's note]. Anna Murray (d. 1882) had been a self-supporting domestic worker before moving to New York to marry.
2. I had changed my name from Frederick *Bailey* to that of *Johnson* [Douglass's note].
3. Fugitive slave, abolitionist orator, and Congregationalist pastor (1807–1870).

Mr. Shaw in Newport, and told me, in case my money did not serve me to New Bedford, to stop in Newport and obtain further assistance; but upon our arrival at Newport, we were so anxious to get to a place of safety, that, notwithstanding we lacked the necessary money to pay our fare, we decided to take seats in the stage, and promise to pay when we got to New Bedford. We were encouraged to do this by two excellent gentlemen, residents of New Bedford, whose names I afterward ascertained to be Joseph Ricketson and William C. Taber. They seemed at once to understand our circumstances, and gave us such assurance of their friendliness as put us fully at ease in their presence. It was good indeed to meet with such friends, at such a time. Upon reaching New Bedford, we were directed to the house of Mr. Nathan Johnson, by whom we were kindly received, and hospitably provided for. Both Mr. and Mrs. Johnson took a deep and lively interest in our welfare. They proved themselves quite worthy of the name of abolitionists. When the stage-driver found us unable to pay our fare, he held on upon our baggage as security for the debt. I had but to mention the fact to Mr. Johnson, and he forthwith advanced the money.

We now began to feel a degree of safety, and to prepare ourselves for the duties and responsibilities of a life of freedom. On the morning after our arrival at New Bedford, while at the breakfast-table, the question arose as to what name I should be called by. The name given me by my mother was, "Frederick Augustus Washington Bailey." I, however, had dispensed with the two middle names long before I left Maryland so that I was generally known by the name of "Frederick Bailey." I started from Baltimore bearing the name of "Stanley." When I got to New York, I again changed my name to "Frederick Johnson," and thought that would be the last change. But when I got to New Bedford, I found it necessary again to change my name. The reason of this necessity was, that there were so many Johnsons in New Bedford, it was already quite difficult to distinguish between them. I gave Mr. Johnson the privilege of choosing me a name, but told him he must not take from me the name of "Frederick." I must hold on to that, to preserve a sense of my identity. Mr. Johnson had just been reading the "Lady of the Lake," and at once suggested that my name be "Douglass."[4] From that time until now I have been called "Frederick Douglass;" and as I am more widely known by that name than by either of the others, I shall continue to use it as my own.

I was quite disappointed at the general appearance of things in New Bedford. The impression which I had received respecting the character and condition of the people of the north, I found to be singularly erroneous. I had very strangely supposed, while in slavery, that few of the comforts, and scarcely any of the luxuries, of life were enjoyed at the north; compared with what were enjoyed by the slaveholders of the south. I probably came to this conclusion from the fact that northern people owned no slaves. I supposed that they were about upon a level with the non-slaveholding population of the south. I knew *they* were exceedingly poor, and I had been accustomed to regard their poverty as the necessary consequence of their

4. Sir Walter Scott's (1771–1832) poem *Lady of the Lake* (1810) is a historical romance set in the Scottish highlands in the 16th century. Douglass is named after the wrongfully exiled Lord James of Douglas, a Scottish chieftain revered for his bravery and virtue.

being non-slaveholders. I had somehow imbibed the opinion that, in the absence of slaves, there could be no wealth, and very little refinement. And upon coming to the north, I expected to meet with a rough, hard-handed, and uncultivated population, living in the most Spartanlike simplicity, knowing nothing of the ease, luxury, pomp, and grandeur of southern slaveholders. Such being my conjectures, any one acquainted with the appearance of New Bedford may very readily infer how palpably I must have seen my mistake.

In the afternoon of the day when I reached New Bedford, I visited the wharves, to take a view of the shipping. Here I found myself surrounded with the strongest proofs of wealth. Lying at the wharves, and riding in the stream, I saw many ships of the finest model, in the best order, and of the largest size. Upon the right and left, I was walled in by granite warehouses of the widest dimensions, stowed to their utmost capacity with the necessaries and comforts of life. Added to this, almost every body seemed to be at work, but noiselessly so, compared with what I had been accustomed to in Baltimore. There were no loud songs heard from those engaged in loading and unloading ships. I heard no deep oaths or horrid curses on the laborer. I saw no whipping of men; but all seemed to go smoothly on. Every man appeared to understand his work, and went at it with a sober, yet cheerful earnestness, which betokened the deep interest which he felt in what he was doing, as well as a sense of his own dignity as man. To me this looked exceedingly strange. From the wharves I strolled around and over the town, gazing with wonder and admiration at the splendid churches, beautiful dwellings, and finely-cultivated gardens; evincing an amount of wealth, comfort, taste, and refinement, such as I had never seen in any part of slaveholding Maryland.

Every thing looked clean, new, and beautiful. I saw few or no dilapidated houses, with poverty-stricken inmates; no half-naked children and barefooted women, such as I had been accustomed to see in Hillsborough, Easton, St. Michael's, and Baltimore. The people looked more able, stronger, healthier, and happier, than those of Maryland. I was for once made glad by a view of extreme wealth, without being saddened by seeing extreme poverty. But the most astonishing as well as the most interesting thing to me was the condition of the colored people, a great many of whom, like myself, had escaped thither as a refuge from the hunters of men. I found many, who had not been seven years out of their chains, living in finer houses, and evidently enjoying more of the comforts of life, than the average of slaveholders in Maryland. I will venture to assert, that my friend Mr. Nathan Johnson (of whom I can say with a grateful heart, "I was hungry, and he gave me meat; I was thirsty, and he gave me drink; I was a stranger, and he took me in")[5] lived in a neater house, dined at a better table; took, paid for, and read, more newspapers; better understood the moral, religious, and political character of the nation,—than nine tenths of the slaveholders in Talbot county Maryland. Yet Mr. Johnson was a working man. His hands were hardened by toil, and not his alone, but those also of Mrs. Johnson. I found the colored people much more spirited than I had sup-

5. Matthew 25:35.

posed they would be. I found among them a determination to protect each other from the blood-thirsty kidnapper, at all hazards. Soon after my arrival, I was told a circumstance which illustrated their spirit. A colored man and a fugitive slave were on unfriendly terms. The former was heard to threaten the latter with informing his master of his whereabouts. Straightway a meeting was called among the colored people, under the stereotyped notice, "Business of importance!" The betrayer was invited to attend. The people came at the appointed hour, and organized the meeting by appointing a very religious old gentleman as president, who, I believe, made a prayer, after which he addressed the meeting as follows: *"Friends, we have got him here, and I would recommend that you young men just take him outside the door, and kill him!"* With this, a number of them bolted at him; but they were intercepted by some more timid than themselves, and the betrayer escaped their vengeance, and has not been seen in New Bedford since. I believe there have been no more such threats, and should there be hereafter, I doubt not that death would be the consequence.

I found employment, the third day after my arrival, in stowing a sloop with a load of oil. It was new, dirty, and hard work for me; but I went at it with a glad heart and a willing hand. I was now my own master. It was a happy moment, the rapture of which can be understood only by those who have been slaves. It was the first work, the reward of which was to be entirely my own. There was no Master Hugh standing ready, the moment I earned the money, to rob me of it. I worked that day with a pleasure I had never before experienced. I was at work for myself and newly-married wife. It was to me the starting-point of a new existence. When I got through with that job, I went in pursuit of a job of calking; but such was the strength of prejudice against color, among the white calkers, that they refused to work with me, and of course I could get no employment.[6] Finding my trade of no immediate benefit, I threw off my calking habiliments, and prepared myself to do any kind of work I could get to do. Mr. Johnson kindly let me have his wood-horse and saw, and I very soon found myself, a plenty of work. There was no work too hard—none too dirty. I was ready to saw wood, shovel coal, carry the hod, sweep the chimney, or roll oil casks,—all of which I did for nearly three years in New Bedford, before I became known to the anti-slavery world.

In about four months after I went to New Bedford, there came a young man to me, and inquired if I did not wish to take the "Liberator."[7] I told him I did; but, just having made my escape from slavery, I remarked that I was unable to pay for it then. I, however, finally became a subscriber to it. The paper came, and I read it from week to week with such feelings as it would be quite idle for me to attempt to describe. The paper became my meat and my drink. My soul was set all on fire. Its sympathy for my brethren in bonds—its scathing denunciations of slaveholders—its faithful exposures of slavery—and its powerful attacks upon the upholders of the institution—sent a thrill of joy through my soul, such as I had never felt before!

6. I am told that colored persons can now get employment at calking in New Bedford—a result of anti-slavery effort [Douglass's note].

7. Edited by William Lloyd Garrison, the *Liberator* was a widely read abolitionist newspaper.

I had not long been a reader of the "Liberator," before I got a pretty correct idea of the principles, measures and spirit of the anti-slavery reform. I took right hold of the cause. I could do but little; but what I could, I did with a joyful heart, and never felt happier than when in an anti-slavery meeting. I seldom had much to say at the meetings, because what I wanted to say was said so much better by others. But, while attending an anti-slavery convention at Nantucket, on the 11th of August, 1841, I felt strongly moved to speak, and was at the same time much urged to do so by Mr. William C. Coffin, a gentleman who had heard me speak in the colored people's meeting at New Bedford. It was a severe cross, and I took it up reluctantly. The truth was, I felt myself a slave, and the idea of speaking to white people weighed me down. I spoke but a few moments, when I felt a degree of freedom, and said what I desired with considerable ease. From that time until now, I have been engaged in pleading the cause of my brethren—with what success, and with what devotion, I leave those acquainted with my labors to decide.

Appendix

I find, since reading over the foregoing Narrative, that I have, in several instances, spoken in such a tone and manner, respecting religion, as may possibly lead those unacquainted with my religious views to suppose me an opponent of all religion. To remove the liability of such misapprehension, I deem it proper to append the following brief explanation. What I have said respecting and against religion, I mean strictly to apply to the *slave-holding religion* of this land, and with no possible reference to Christianity proper; for, between the Christianity of this land, and the Christianity of Christ, I recognize the widest possible difference—so wide, that to receive the one as good, pure, and holy, is of necessity to reject the other as bad, corrupt, and wicked. To be the friend of the one, is of necessity to be the enemy of the other. I love the pure, peaceable, and impartial Christianity of Christ: I therefore hate the corrupt, slaveholding, women-whipping, cradle-plundering, partial and hypocritical Christianity of this land. Indeed, I can see no reason, but the most deceitful one, for calling the religion of this land Christianity. I look upon it as the climax of all misnomers, the boldest of all frauds, and the grossest of all libels. Never was there a clearer case of "stealing the livery of the court of heaven to serve the devil in." [8] I am filled with unutterable loathing when I contemplate the religious pomp and show, together with the horrible inconsistencies, which every where surround me. We have menstealers for ministers, women-whippers for missionaries, and cradle-plunderers for church members. The man who wields the blood-clotted cowskin during the week fills the pulpit on Sunday, and claims to be a minister of the meek and lowly Jesus. The man who robs me of my earnings at the end of each week meets me as a class-leader on Sunday morning, to show me the way of life, and the path of salvation. He who sells my sister, for purposes of prostitution, stands forth as the pious advocate of purity. He who proclaims it a religious duty to read

8. Compare Robert Pollok's *The Course of Time* (1827) 8.616–18: "He was a man / Who stole the livery of the court of Heaven / To serve the Devil in."

the Bible denies me the right of learning to read the name of the God who
made me. He who is the religious advocate of marriage robs whole millions
of its sacred influence, and leaves them to the ravages of wholesale pollution. The warm defender of the sacredness of the family relation is the
same that scatters whole families,—sundering husbands and wives, parents
and children, sisters and brothers,—leaving the hut vacant, and the hearth
desolate. We see the thief preaching against theft, and the adulterer against
adultery. We have men sold to build churches, women sold to support the
gospel, and babies sold to purchase Bibles for the *poor heathen! all for the
glory of God and the good of souls!* The slave auctioneer's bell and the
church-going bell chime in with each other, and the bitter cries of the
heartbroken slave are drowned in the religious shouts of his pious master.
Revivals of religion and revivals in the slave-trade go hand in hand together. The slave prison and the church stand near each other. The clanking of fetters and the rattling of chains in the prison, and the pious psalm
and solemn prayer in the church, may be heard at the same time. The
dealers in the bodies and souls of men erect their stand in the presence of
the pulpit, and they mutually help each other. The dealer gives his blood-
stained gold to support the pulpit, and the pulpit, in return, covers his infernal business with the garb of Christianity. Here we have religion and
robbery the allies of each other—devils dressed in angels' robes, and hell
presenting the semblance of paradise.

> "Just God! and these are they,
>   Who minister at thine alter, God of right!
> Men who their hands, with prayer and blessing, lay
>   On Israel's ark of light.[9]

> "What! preach, and kidnap men?
>   Give thanks, and rob thy own afflicted poor?
> Talk of thy glorious liberty, and then
>   Bolt hard the captive's door?

> "What! servants of thy own
>   Merciful Son, who came to seek and save
> The homeless and the outcast, fettering down
>   The tasked and plundered slave!

> "Pilate and Herod[1] friends!
>   Chief priests and rulers, as of old, combine!
> Just God and holy! is that church which lends
>   Strength to the spoiler thine?"[2]

The Christianity of America is a Christianity, of whose votaries it may be
as truly said, as it was of the ancient scribes and Pharisees, "They bind
heavy burdens, and grievous to be borne, and lay them on men's shoulders,

---

9. I.e., the Holy Ark containing the Torah; by extension, the entire body of law as contained in the
Old Testament of the Bible and Talmud.
1. Herod Antipas, ruler of Galilee, ordered the execution of John the Baptist and participated in the
trial of Christ. Pontius Pilate was the Roman authority who condemned Christ to death.
2. From Whittier's antislavery poem *Clerical Oppressors* (1836).

but they themselves will not move them with one of their fingers. All their works they do for to be seen of men.——They love the uppermost rooms at feasts, and the chief seats in the synagogues, ... and to be called of men, Rabbi, Rabbi.——But woe unto you, scribes and Pharisees, hypocrites! for ye shut up the kingdom of heaven against men; for ye neither go in yourselves, neither suffer ye them that are entering to go in. Ye devour widows' houses, and for a pretence make long prayers; therefore ye shall receive the greater damnation. Ye compass sea and land to make one proselyte, and when he is made, ye make him twofold more the child of hell than yourselves.——Woe unto you, scribes and Pharisees, hypocrites! for ye pay tithe of mint, and anise, and cumin, and have omitted the weightier matters of the law, judgment, mercy, and faith; these ought ye to have done, and not to leave the other undone. Ye blind guides! which strain at a gnat, and swallow a camel. Woe unto you, scribes and Pharisees, hypocrites! for ye make clean the outside of the cup and of the platter; but within, they are full of extortion and excess.——Woe unto you, scribes and Pharisees, hypocrites! for ye are like unto whited sepulchres, which indeed appear beautiful outward, but are within full of dead men's bones, and of all uncleanness. Even so ye also outwardly appear righteous unto men, but within ye are full of hypocrisy and iniquity."[3]

Dark and terrible as is this picture, I hold it to be strictly true of the overwhelming mass of professed Christians in America. They strain at a gnat, and swallow a camel. Could any thing be more true of our churches? They would be shocked at the proposition of fellowshipping a *sheep*-stealer; and at the same time they hug to their communion a *man*-stealer, and brand me with being an infidel, if I find fault with them for it. They attend with Pharisaical strictness to the outward forms of religion, and at the same time neglect the weightier matters of the law, judgment, mercy, and faith. They are always ready to sacrifice, but seldom to show mercy. They are they who are represented as professing to love God whom they have not seen, whilst they hate their brother whom they have seen. They love the heathen on the other side of the globe. They can pray for him, pay money to have the Bible put into his hand, and missionaries to instruct him; while they despise and totally neglect the heathen at their own doors.

Such is, very briefly, my view of the religion of this land; and to avoid any misunderstanding, growing out of the use of general terms, I mean, by the religion of this land, that which is revealed in the words, deeds, and actions, of those bodies, north and south, calling themselves Christian churches, and yet in union with slaveholders. It is against religion, as presented by these bodies, that I have felt it my duty to testify.

I conclude these remarks by copying the following portrait of the religion of the south, (which is, by communion and fellowship, the religion of the north,) which I soberly affirm is "true to the life," and without caricature or the slightest exaggeration. It is said to have been drawn, several years before the present anti-slavery agitation began, by a northern Methodist preacher, who, while residing at the south, had an opportunity to see slave-

---

3. Christ's denunciation of the Scribes and Pharisees in Matthew 23:4–28. The scribes were the Jewish scholars who taught Jewish law and edited and interpreted the Bible; the Pharisees were members of a powerful Jewish sect that insisted on strict observance of written and oral religious laws.

holding morals, manners, and piety, with his own eyes. "Shall I not visit for these things? saith the Lord. Shall not my soul be avenged on such a nation as this?"[4]

A PARODY

"Come, saints and sinners, hear me tell
How pious priests whip Jack and Nell,
And women buy and children sell,
And preach all sinners down to hell,
    And sing of heavenly union.

"They'll bleat and baa, dona like goats,
Gorge down black sheep, and strain at motes,
Array their backs in fine black coats,
Then seize their negroes by their throats,
    And choke, for heavenly union.

"They'll church you if you sip a dram,
And damn you if you steal a lamb;
Yet rob old Tony, Doll, and Sam,
Of human rights, and bread and ham;
    Kidnapper's heavenly union.

"They'll loudly talk of Christ's reward,
And bind his image with a cord,
And scold, and swing the lash abhorred,
And sell their brother in the Lord
    To handcuffed heavenly union.

"They'll read and sing a sacred song,
And make a prayer both loud and long,
And teach the right and do the wrong,
Hailing the brother, sister throng,
    With words of heavenly union.

"We wonder how such saints can sing,
Or praise the Lord upon the wing,
Who roar, and scold, and whip, and sting,
And to their slaves and mammon cling,
    In guilty conscience union.

"They'll raise tobacco, corn, and rye,
And drive, and thieve, and cheat, and lie,
And lay up treasures in the sky,
By making switch and cowskin fly,
    In hope of heavenly union.

"They'll crack old Tony on the skull,
And preach and roar like Bashan[5] bull,
Or braying ass, of mischief full,

4. Jeremiah speaks God's charges against the sins   5. Strong bulls mentioned in the Bible.
of the House of Israel (Jeremiah 5:9).

Then seize old Jacob by the wool,
    And pull for heavenly union.

"A roaring, ranting, sleek man-thief,
Who lived on mutton, veal, and beef,
Yet never would afford relief
To needy, sable sons of grief,
    Was big with heavenly union.

" 'Love not the world,' the preacher said,
And winked his eye, and shook his head;
He seized on Tom, and Dick, and Ned,
Cut short their meat, and clothes, and bread,
    Yet still loved heavenly union.

"Another preacher whining spoke
Of One whose heart for sinners broke:
He tied old Nanny to an oak,
And drew the blood at every stroke,
    And prayed for heavenly union.

"Two others oped their iron jaws,
And waved their children-stealing paws;
There sat their children in gewgaws;
By stinting negroes' backs and maws,
    They kept up heavenly union.

"All good from Jack another takes,
And entertains their flirts and rakes,
Who dress as sleek as glossy snakes,
And cram their mouths with sweetened cakes;
    And this goes down for union."[6]

    Sincerely and earnestly hoping that this little book may do something toward throwing light on the American slave system, and hastening the glad day of deliverance to the millions of my brethren in bonds—faithfully relying upon the power of truth, love, and justice, for success in my humble efforts—and solemnly pledging my self anew to the sacred cause,—I subscribe myself,

                         FREDERICK DOUGLASS

Lynn, Mass., April 28, 1845.

                                    1845

From My Bondage and My Freedom

Chapter XXIII. Introduced to the Abolitionists

    In the summer of 1841, a grand anti-slavery convention was held in Nantucket, under the auspices of Mr. Garrison[1] and his friends. Until now, I

---

6. Douglass is parodying "Heavenly Union," a popular hymn in the South.
1. William Lloyd Garrison (1805–1879), Ameri-

can journalist, reformer, and one of the most radical spokesmen for militant abolition in the United States.

had taken no holiday since my escape from slavery.[2] Having worked very hard that spring and summer, in Richmond's brass foundery—sometimes working all night as well as all day—and needing a day or two of rest, I attended this convention, never supposing that I should take part in the proceedings. Indeed, I was not aware that any one connected with the convention even so much as knew my name. I was, however, quite mistaken. Mr. William C. Coffin, a prominent abolitionist in those days of trial, had heard me speaking to my colored friends, in the little schoolhouse on Second street, New Bedford, where we worshiped. He sought me out in the crowd, and invited me to say a few words to the convention. Thus sought out, and thus invited, I was induced to speak out the feelings inspired by the occasion, and the fresh recollection of the scenes through which I had passed as a slave. My speech on this occasion is about the only one I ever made, of which I do not remember a single connected sentence. It was with the utmost difficulty that I could stand erect, or that I could command and articulate two words without hesitation and stammering. I trembled in every limb. I am not sure that my embarrassment was not the most effective part of my speech, if speech it could be called. At any rate, this is about the only part of my performance that I now distinctly remember. But excited and convulsed as I was, the audience, though remarkably quiet before, became as much excited as myself. Mr. Garrison followed me, taking me as his text; and now, whether I had made an eloquent speech in behalf of freedom or not, his was one never to be forgotten by those who heard it. Those who had heard Mr. Garrison oftenest, and had known him longest, were astonished. It was an effort of unequaled power, sweeping down, like a very tornado, every opposing barrier, whether of sentiment or opinion. For a moment, he possessed that almost fabulous inspiration, often referred to but seldom attained, in which a public meeting is transformed, as it were, into a single individuality—the orator wielding a thousand heads and hearts at once, and by the simple majesty of his all controlling thought, converting his hearers into the express image of his own soul. That night there were at least one thousand Garrisonians in Nantucket! At the close of this great meeting, I was duly waited on by Mr. John A. Collins—then the general agent of the Massachusetts anti-slavery society—and urgently solicited by him to become an agent of that society, and to publicly advocate its anti-slavery principles. I was reluctant to take the proffered position. I had not been quite three years from slavery—was honestly distrustful of my ability—wished to be excused; publicity exposed me to discovery and arrest by my master; and other objections came up, but Mr. Collins was not to be put off, and I finally consented to go out for three months, for I supposed that I should have got to the end of my story and my usefulness, in that length of time.

Here, opened upon me a new life—a life for which I had had no preparation. I was a "graduate from the peculiar institution," Mr. Collins used to say, when introducing me, *with my diploma written on my back!* The three years of my freedom had been spent in the hard school of adversity.

2. Douglass escaped from Baltimore on September 3, 1838, and settled in New Bedford, Massachusetts.

My hands had been furnished by nature with something like a solid leather coating, and I had bravely marked out for myself a life of rough labor, suited to the hardness of my hands, as a means of supporting myself and rearing my children.

Now what shall I say of this fourteen years' experience as a public advocate of the cause of my enslaved brothers and sisters? The time is but as a speck, yet large enough to justify a pause for retrospection—and a pause it must only be.

Young, ardent, and hopeful, I entered upon this new life in the full gush of unsuspecting enthusiasm. The cause was good; the men engaged in it were good; the means to attain its triumph, good; Heaven's blessing must attend all, and freedom must soon be given to the pining millions under a ruthless bondage. My whole heart went with the holy cause, and my most fervent prayer to the Almighty Disposer of the hearts of men, were continually offered for its early triumph. "Who or what," thought I, "can withstand a cause so good, so holy, so indescribably glorious. The God of Israel is with us. The might of the Eternal is on our side. Now let but the truth be spoken, and a nation will start forth at the sound!" In this enthusiastic spirit, I dropped into the ranks of freedom's friends, and went forth to the battle. For a time I was made to forget that my skin was dark and my hair crisped. For a time I regretted that I could not have shared the hardships and dangers endured by the earlier workers for the slave's release. I soon, however, found that my enthusiasm had been extravagant; that hardships and dangers were not yet passed; and that the life now before me, had shadows as well as sunbeams.

Among the first duties assigned me, on entering the ranks, was to travel, in company with Mr. George Foster, to secure subscribers to the "Antislavery Standard" and the "Liberator."[3] With him I traveled and lectured through the eastern counties of Massachusetts. Much interest was awakened—large meetings assembled. Many came, no doubt, from curiosity to hear what a negro could say in his own cause. I was generally introduced as a *"chattel"*—a *"thing"*—a piece of southern *"property"*—the chairman assuring the audience that *it* could speak. Fugitive slaves, at that time, were not so plentiful as now; and as a fugitive slave lecturer, I had the advantage of being a *"brand new fact"*—the first one out. Up to that time, a colored man was deemed a fool who confessed himself a runaway slave, not only because of the danger to which he exposed himself of being retaken, but because it was a confession of a very *low* origin! Some of my colored friends in New Bedford thought very badly of my wisdom for thus exposing and degrading myself. The only precaution I took, at the beginning, to prevent Master Thomas[4] from knowing where I was, and what I was about, was the withholding my former name, my master's name, and the name of the state and county from which I came. During the first three or four months, my speeches were almost exclusively made up of narrations of my own personal experience as a slave. "Let us have the facts," said the people. So also said Friend George Foster, who always wished to pin me down to my sim-

3. Newspapers that espoused immediate abolition-   4. Douglass's former master, Thomas Auld.
ism.

ple narrative. "Give us the facts," said Collins, "we will take care of the philosophy." Just here arose some embarrassment. It was impossible for me to repeat the same old story month after month, and to keep up my interest in it. It was new to the people, it is true, but it was an old story to me; and to go through with it night after night, was a task altogether too mechanical for my nature. "Tell your story, Frederick," would whisper my then revered friend, William Lloyd Garrison, as I stepped upon the platform. I could not always obey, for I was now reading and thinking. New views of the subject were presented to my mind. It did not entirely satisfy me to *narrate* wrongs; I felt like *denouncing* them. I could not always curb my moral indignation for the perpetrators of slaveholding villainy, long enough for a circumstantial statement of the facts which I felt almost everybody must know. Besides, I was growing, and needed room. "People won't believe you ever was a slave, Frederick, if you keep on this way," said Friend Foster. "Be yourself," said Collins, "and tell your story." It was said to me, "Better have a *little* of the plantation manner of speech than not; 'tis not best that you seem too learned." These excellent friends were actuated by the best of motives, and were not altogether wrong in their advice; and still I must speak just the word that seemed to *me* the word to be spoken *by* me.

At last the apprehended trouble came. People doubted if I had ever been a slave. They said I did not talk like a slave, look like a slave, nor act like a slave, and that they believed I had never been south of Mason and Dixon's line. "He don't tell us where he came from—what his master's name was—how he got away—nor the story of his experience. Besides, he is educated, and is, in this, a contradiction of all the facts we have concerning the ignorance of the slaves." Thus, I was in a pretty fair way to be denounced as an impostor. The committee of the Massachusetts anti-slavery society knew all the facts in my case, and agreed with me in the prudence of keeping them private. They, therefore, never doubted my being a genuine fugitive; but going down the aisles of the churches in which I spoke, and hearing the free spoken Yankees saying, repeatedly, *"He's never been a slave, I'll warrent ye,"* I resolved to dispel all doubt, at no distant day, by such a revelation of facts as could not be made by any other than a genuine fugitive.

In a little less than four years, therefore, after becoming a public lecturer, I was induced to write out the leading facts connected with my experience in slavery, giving names of persons, places, and dates [5]—thus putting it in the power of any who doubted, to ascertain the truth or falsehood of my story of being a fugitive slave. This statement soon became known in Maryland, and I had reason to believe that an effort would be made to recapture me.

It is not probable that any open attempt to secure me as a slave could have succeeded, further than the obtainment, by my master, of the money value of my bones and sinews. Fortunately for me, in the four years of my labors in the abolition cause, I had gained many friends, who would have suffered themselves to be taxed to almost any extent to save me from slavery. It was felt that I had committed the double offense of running away, and exposing the secrets and crimes of slavery and slaveholders. There was

5. I.e., the *Narrative of the Life of Frederick Douglass* (1845).

a double motive for seeking my reenslavement—avarice and vengeance; and while, as I have said, there was little probability of successful recapture, if attempted openly, I was constantly in danger of being spirited away, at a moment when my friends could render me no assistance. In traveling about from place to place—often alone—I was much exposed to this sort of attack. Any one cherishing the design to betray me, could easily do so, by simply tracing my whereabouts through the anti-slavery journals, for my meetings and movements were promptly made known in advance. My true friends, Mr. Garrison and Mr. Phillips,[6] had no faith in the power of Massachusetts to protect me in my right to liberty. Public sentiment and the law, in their opinion, would hand me over to the tormentors. Mr. Phillips, especially, considered me in danger, and said, when I showed him the manuscript of my story, if in my place, he would throw it into the fire. Thus, the reader will observe, the settling of one difficulty only opened the way for another; and that though I had reached a free state, and had attained a position for public usefulness, I was still tormented with the liability of losing my liberty. How this liability was dispelled, will be related, with other incidents, in the next chapter.

Chapter XXIV. Twenty-One Months in Great Britain

The allotments of Providence, when coupled with trouble and anxiety, often conceal from finite vision the wisdom and goodness in which they are sent; and, frequently, what seemed a harsh and invidious dispensation, is converted by after experience into a happy and beneficial arrangement. Thus, the painful liability to be returned again to slavery, which haunted me by day, and troubled my dreams by night, proved to be a necessary step in the path of knowledge and usefulness. The writing of my pamphlet, in the spring of 1845, endangered my liberty, and led me to seek a refuge from republican slavery in monarchical England. A rude, uncultivated fugitive slave was driven, by stern necessity, to that country to which young American gentlemen go to increase their stock of knowledge, to seek pleasure, to have their rough, democratic manners softened by contact with English aristocratic refinement. On applying for a passage to England, on board the Cambria, of the Cunard line, my friend, James N. Buffum,[7] of Lynn, Massachusetts, was informed that I could not be received on board as a cabin passenger. American prejudice against color triumphed over British liberality and civilization, and erected a color test and condition for crossing the sea in the cabin of a British vessel. The insult was keenly felt by my white friends, but to me, it was common, expected, and therefore, a thing of no great consequence, whether I went in the cabin or in the steerage. Moreover, I felt that if I could not go into the first cabin, first-cabin passengers could come into the second cabin, and the result justified my anticipations to the fullest extent. Indeed, I soon found myself an object of more general interest than I wished to be; and so far from being degraded by being placed in the second cabin, that part of the ship became the scene of as much pleasure and refinement, during the voyage, as the cabin itself. The

6. Massachusetts reformer, antislavery agitator, and orator (1811–1884).

7. Businessman, Massachusetts politician, and civil rights activist (1807–1887).

Hutchinson Family, celebrated vocalists—fellow-passengers—often came to my rude forecastle deck, and sung their sweetest songs, enlivening the place with eloquent music, as well as spirited conversation, during the voyage. In two days after leaving Boston, one part of the ship was about as free to me as another. My fellow-passengers not only visited me, but invited me to visit them, on the saloon deck. My visits there, however, were but seldom. I preferred to live within my privileges, and keep upon my own premises. I found this quite as much in accordance with good policy, as with my own feelings. The effect was, that with the majority of the passengers, all color distinctions were flung to the winds, and I found myself treated with every mark of respect, from the beginning to the end of the voyage, except in a single instance; and in that, I came near being mobbed, for complying with an invitation given me by the passengers, and the captain of the "Cambria," to deliver a lecture on slavery. Our New Orleans and Georgia passengers were pleased to regard my lecture as an insult offered to them, and swore I should not speak. They went so far as to threaten to throw me overboard, and but for the firmness of Captain Judkins, probably would have (under the inspiration of *slavery* and *brandy*) attempted to put their threats into execution. I have no space to describe this scene, although its tragic and comic peculiarities are well worth describing. An end was put to the *melee*, by the captain's calling the ship's company to put the salt water mobocrats in irons. At this determined order, the gentlemen of the lash scampered, and for the rest of the voyage conducted themselves very decorously.

This incident of the voyage, in two days after landing at Liverpool, brought me at once before the British public, and that by no act of my own. The gentlemen so promptly snubbed in their meditated violence, flew to the press to justify their conduct, and to denounce me as a worthless and insolent negro. This course was even less wise than the conduct it was intended to sustain; for, besides awakening something like a national interest in me, and securing me an audience, it brought out counter statements, and threw the blame upon themselves, which they had sought to fasten upon me and the gallant captain of the ship.

Some notion may be formed of the difference in my feelings and circumstances, while abroad, from the following extract from one of a series of letters addressed by me to Mr. Garrison, and published in the Liberator. It was written on the first day of January, 1846:

> "MY DEAR FRIEND GARRISON: Up to this time, I have given no direct expression of the views, feelings, and opinions which I have formed, respecting the character and condition of the people of this land. I have refrained thus, purposely. I wish to speak advisedly, and in order to do this, I have waited till, I trust, experience has brought my opinions to an intelligent maturity. I have been thus careful, not because I think what I say will have much effect in shaping the opinions of the world, but because whatever of influence I may possess, whether little or much, I wish it to go in the right direction, and according to truth. I hardly need say that, in speaking of Ireland, I shall be influenced by no prejudices in favor of America. I think my circum-

stances all forbid that. I have no end to serve, no creed to uphold, no government to defend; and as to nation, I belong to none. I have no protection at home, or resting-place abroad. The land of my birth welcomes me to her shores only as a slave, and spurns with contempt the idea of treating me differently; so that I am an outcast from the society of my childhood, and an outlaw in the land of my birth. 'I am a stranger with thee, and a sojourner, as all my fathers were.'[8] That men should be patriotic, is to me perfectly natural; and as a philosophical fact, I am able to give it an *intellectual* recognition. But no further can I go. If ever I had any patriotism, or any capacity for the feeling, it was whipped out of me long since, by the lash of the American soul-drivers.

"In thinking of America, I sometimes find myself admiring her bright blue sky, her grand old woods, her fertile fields, her beautiful rivers, her mighty lakes, and star-crowned mountains. But my rapture is soon checked, my joy is soon turned to mourning. When I remember that all is cursed with the infernal spirit of slaveholding, robbery, and wrong; when I remember that with the waters of her noblest rivers, the tears of my brethren are borne to the ocean, disregarded and forgotten, and that her most fertile fields drink daily of the warm blood of my outraged sisters; I am filled with unutterable loathing, and led to reproach myself that anything could fall from my lips in praise of such a land. America will not allow her children to love her. She seems bent on compelling those who would be her warmest friends, to be her worst enemies. May God give her repentance, before it is too late, is the ardent prayer of my heart. I will continue to pray, labor, and wait, believing that she cannot always be insensible to the dictates of justice, or deaf to the voice of humanity.

"My opportunities for learning the character and condition of the people of this land have been very great. I have traveled almost from the Hill of Howth to the Giant's Causeway, and from the Giant's Causeway to Cape Clear. During these travels, I have met with much in the character and condition of the people to approve, and much to condemn; much that has thrilled me with pleasure, and very much that has filled me with pain. I will not, in this letter, attempt to give any description of those scenes which have given me pain. This I will do hereafter. I have enough, and more than your subscribers will be disposed to read at one time, of the bright side of the picture. I can truly say, I have spent some of the happiest moments of my life since landing in this country. I seem to have undergone a transformation. I live a new life. The warm and generous cooperation extended to me by the friends of my despised race; the prompt and liberal manner with which the press has rendered me its aid; the glorious enthusiasm with which thousands have flocked to hear the cruel wrongs of my downtrodden and long-enslaved fellow-countrymen portrayed; the deep sympathy for the slave, and the strong abhorrence of the slaveholder, everywhere evinced; the cordiality with which members and ministers

8. Psalm 39:12.

of various religious bodies, and of various shades of religious opinion, have embraced me, and lent me their aid; the kind hospitality constantly proffered to me by persons of the highest rank in society; the spirit of freedom that seems to animate all with whom I come in contact, and the entire absence of everything that looked like prejudice against me, on account of the color of my skin—contrasted so strongly with my long and bitter experience in the United States, that I look with wonder and amazement on the transition. In the southern part of the United States, I was a slave, thought of and spoken of as property; in the language of the Law, *'held, taken, reputed, ajudged to be a chattel in the hands of my owners and possessors, and their executors, administrators, and assigns, to all intents, constructions, and purposes whatsoever.'* (Brev. Digest, 224.) In the northern states, a fugitive slave, liable to be hunted at any moment, like a felon, and to be hurled into the terrible jaws of slavery—doomed by an inveterate prejudice against color to insult and outrage on every hand, (Massachusetts out of the question)—denied the privileges and courtesies common to others in the use of the most humble means of conveyance—shut out from the cabins on steamboats—refused admission to respectable hotels—caricatured, scorned, scoffed, mocked, and maltreated with impunity by any one, (no matter how black his heart,) so he has a white skin. But now behold the change! Eleven days and a half gone, and I have crossed three thousand miles of the perilous deep. Instead of a democratic government, I am under a monarchical government. Instead of the bright, blue sky of America, I am covered with the soft, grey fog of the Emerald Isle.[9] I breathe, and lo! the chattel becomes a man. I gaze around in vain for one who will question my equal humanity, claim me as his slave, or offer me an insult. I employ a cab—I am seated beside white people—I reach the hotel—I enter the same door—I am shown into the same parlor—I dine at the same table—and no one is offended. No delicate nose grows deformed in my presence. I find no difficulty here in obtaining admission into any place of worship, instruction, or amusement, on equal terms with people as white as any I ever saw in the United States. I meet nothing to remind me of my complexion. I find myself regarded and treated at every turn with the kindness and deference paid to white people. When I go to church, I am met by no upturned nose and scornful lip to tell me, *'We don't allow niggers in here!'*

"I remember, about two years ago, there was in Boston, near the southwest corner of Boston Common, a menagerie. I had long desired to see such a collection as I understood was being exhibited there. Never having had an opportunity while a slave, I resolved to seize this, my first, since my escape. I went, and as I approached the entrance to gain admission, I was met and told by the door-keeper, in a harsh and contemptuous tone, *'We don't allow niggers in here.'* I also remember attending a revival meeting in the Rev. Henry Jackson's meeting-

9. I.e., Ireland.

house, at New Bedford, and going up the broad aisle to find a seat, I was met by a good deacon, who told me, in a pious tone, 'We don't allow niggers in here!' Soon after my arrival in New Bedford, from the south, I had a strong desire to attend the Lyceum, [1] but was told, 'They don't allow niggers in here!' While passing from New York to Boston, on the steamer Massachusetts, on the night of the 9th of December, 1843, when chilled almost through with the cold, I went to the cabin to get a little warm. I was soon touched upon the shoulder, and told, 'We don't allow niggers in here!' On arriving in Boston, from an anti-slavery tour, hungry and tired, I went into an eating-house, near my friend, Mr. Campbell's, to get some refreshments. I was met by a lad in a white apron, 'We don't allow niggers in here!' A week or two before leaving the United States, I had a meeting appointed at Weymouth, the home of that glorious band of true abolitionists, the Weston family, and others. On attempting to take a seat in the omnibus to that place, I was told by the driver, (and I never shall forget his fiendish hate,) 'I don't allow niggers in here!' Thank heaven for the respite I now enjoy! I had been in Dublin but a few days, when a gentleman of great respectability kindly offered to conduct me through all the public buildings of that beautiful city; and a little afterward, I found myself dining with the lord mayor of Dublin. What a pity there was not some American democratic christian at the door of his splendid mansion, to bark out at my approach, 'They don't allow niggers in here!' The truth is, the people here know nothing of the republican negro hate prevalent in our glorious land. They measure and esteem men according to their moral and intellectual worth, and not according to the color of their skin. Whatever may be said of the aristocracies here, there is none based on the color of a man's skin. This species of aristocracy belongs preeminently to 'the land of the free, and the home of the brave.' I have never found it abroad, in any but Americans. It sticks to them wherever they go. They find it almost as hard to get rid of, as to get rid of their skins.

"The second day after my arrival at Liverpool, in company with my friend, Buffum, and several other friends, I went to Eaton Hall, the residence of the Marquis of Westminster, one of the most splendid buildings in England. On approaching the door, I found several of our American passengers, who came out with us in the Cambria, waiting for admission, as but one party was allowed in the house at a time. We all had to wait till the company within came out. And of all the faces, expressive of chagrin, those of the Americans were preeminent. They looked as sour as vinegar, and as bitter as gall when they found I was to be admitted on equal terms with themselves. When the door was opened, I walked in, on an equal footing with my white fellow-citizens, and from all I could see, I had as much attention paid me by the servants that showed us through the house, as any with a paler skin. As I walked through the building, the statuary did not fall down, the pic-

---

1. The lyceum movement brought popular education to the American masses through lectures, debates, concerts, and scientific demonstrations.

tures did not leap from their places, the doors did not refuse to open, and the servants did not say, 'We don't allow niggers in here!'
"A happy new-year to you, and all the friends of freedom."

My time and labors, while abroad, were divided between England, Ireland, Scotland, and Wales. Upon this experience alone, I might write a book twice the size of this, "My Bondage and my Freedom." I visited and lectured in nearly all the large towns and cities in the United Kingdom, and enjoyed many favorable opportunities for observation and information. But books on England are abundant, and the public may, therefore, dismiss any fear that I am meditating another infliction in that line; though, in truth, I should like much to write a book on those countries, if for nothing else, to make grateful mention of the many dear friends, whose benevolent actions toward me are ineffaceably stamped upon my memory, and warmly treasured in my heart. To these friends I owe my freedom in the United States. On their own motion, without any solicitation from me (Mrs. Henry Richardson, a clever lady, remarkable for her devotion to every good work, taking the lead,) they raised a fund sufficient to purchase my freedom, and actually paid it over, and placed the papers[2] of my manumission in my hands, before they would tolerate the idea of my returning to this, my native country. To this commercial transaction I owe my exemption from the democratic operation of the fugitive slave bill of 1850.[3] But for this, I might at any time become a victim of this most cruel and scandalous enactment, and be doomed to end my life, as I began it, a slave. The sum paid for my freedom was one hundred and fifty pounds sterling.[4]
Some of my uncompromising anti-slavery friends in this country failed

2. The following is a copy of these curious papers, both of my transfer from Thomas to Hugh Auld, and from Hugh to myself:
"Know all men by these Presents, That I, Thomas Auld, of Talbot county, and state of Maryland, for and in consideration of the sum of one hundred dollars, current money, to me paid by Hugh Auld, of the city of Baltimore, in the said state, at and before the sealing and delivery of these presents, the receipt whereof, I, the said Thomas Auld, do hereby acknowledge, have granted, bargained, and sold, and by these presents do grant, bargain, and sell unto the said Hugh Auld, his executors, administrators, and assigns, ONE NEGRO MAN, by the name of FREDERICK BAILY, or DOUGLASS, as he calls himself—he is now about twenty-eight years of age—to have and to hold the said negro man for life. And I, the said Thomas Auld, for myself, my heirs, executors, and administrators, all and singular, the said FREDERICK BAILY, alias DOUGLASS, unto the said Hugh Auld, his executors, administrators, and assigns, against me, the said Thomas Auld, my executors, and administrators, and against all and every other person or persons whatsoever, shall and will warrant and forever defend by these presents. In witness whereof, I set my hand and seal, this thirteenth day of November, eighteen hundred and forty-six. THOMAS AULD.
"Signed, sealed, and delivered in presence of Wrightson Jones.
"JOHN C. LEAS."
The authenticity of this bill of sale is attested by N. Harrington, a justice of the peace of the state of

Maryland, and for the county of Talbot, dated same day as above.

"To all whom it may concern: Be it known, that I, Hugh Auld, of the city of Baltimore, in Baltimore county, in the state of Maryland, for divers good causes and considerations, me thereunto moving, have released from slavery, liberated, manumitted, and set free, and by these presents do hereby release from slavery, liberate, manumit, and set free, MY NEGRO MAN, named FREDERICK BAILY, otherwise called DOUGLASS, being of the age of twenty-eight years, or thereabouts, and able to work and gain a sufficient livelihood and maintenance; and him the said negro man, named FREDERICK BAILY, otherwise called FREDERICK DOUGLASS, I do declare to be henceforth free, manumitted, and discharged from all manner of servitude to me, my executors, and administrators forever.
"In witness whereof, I, the said Hugh Auld, have hereunto set my hand and seal, the fifth of December, in the year one thousand eight hundred and forty-six. HUGH AULD
"Sealed and delivered in the presence of T. Hanson Belt.
"JAMES N. S. T. WRIGHT" [Douglass's note].
3. A provision of the Compromise of 1850, the Fugitive Slave Act criminalized any interference with a slaveowner's attempt to recapture an escaped slave anywhere in the United States.
4. The equivalent of $711.66 in U.S. currency at that time.

to see the wisdom of this arrangement, and were not pleased that I consented to it, even by my silence. They thought it a violation of anti-slavery principles—conceding a right of property in man—and a wasteful expenditure of money. On the other hand, viewing it simply in the light of a ransom, or as money extorted by a robber, and my liberty of more value than one hundred and fifty pounds sterling, I could not see either a violation of the laws of morality, or those of economy, in the transaction.

It is true, I was not in the possession of my claimants, and could have easily remained in England, for the same friends who had so generously purchased my freedom, would have assisted me in establishing myself in that country. To this, however, I could not consent. I felt that I had a duty to perform—and that was, to labor and suffer with the oppressed in my native land. Considering, therefore, all the circumstances—the fugitive slave bill included—I think the very best thing was done in letting Master Hugh have the hundred and fifty pounds sterling and leaving me free to return to my appropriate field of labor. Had I been a private person, having no other relations or duties than those of a personal and family nature, I should never have consented to the payment of so large a sum for the privilege of living securely under our glorious republican form of government. I could have remained in England, or have gone to some other country; and perhaps I could even have lived unobserved in this. But to this I could not consent. I had already become somewhat notorious; and withal quite as unpopular as notorious; and I was, therefore, much exposed to arrest and recapture.

1855

From What to the Slave Is the Fourth of July?: An Address Delivered in Rochester, New York, on 5 July 1852

Mr. President, Friends and Fellow Citizens: He who could address this audience without a quailing sensation, has stronger nerves than I have. I do not remember ever to have appeared as a speaker before any assembly more shrinkingly, nor with greater distrust of my ability, than I do this day. A feeling has crept over me, quite unfavorable to the exercise of my limited powers of speech. The task before me is one which requires much previous thought and study for its proper performance. I know that apologies of this sort are generally considered flat and unmeaning. I trust, however, that mine will not be so considered. Should I seem at ease, my appearance would much misrepresent me. The little experience I have had in addressing public meetings, in country school houses, avails me nothing on the present occasion.

The papers and placards say, that I am to deliver a 4th [of] July oration. This certainly sounds large, and out of the common way, for me. It is true that I have often had the privilege to speak in this beautiful Hall, and to address many who now honor me with their presence. But neither their familiar faces, nor the perfect gage I think I have of Corinthian Hall, seems to free me from embarrassment.

The fact is, ladies and gentlemen, the distance between this platform and the slave plantation, from which I escaped, is considerable—and the difficulties to be overcome in getting from the latter to the former, are by no means slight. That I am here to-day is, to me, a matter of astonishment as well as of gratitude. You will not, therefore, be surprised, if in what I have to say, I evince no elaborate preparation, nor grace my speech with any high sounding exordium. With little experience and with less learning, I have been able to throw my thoughts hastily and imperfectly together; and trusting to your patient and generous indulgence, I will proceed to lay them before you.

This, for the purpose of this celebration, is the 4th of July. It is the birthday of your National Independence, and of your political freedom. This, to you, is what the Passover[1] was to the emancipated people of God. It carries your minds back to the day, and to the act of your great deliverance; and to the signs, and to the wonders, associated with that act, and that day. This celebration also marks the beginning of another year of your national life; and reminds you that the Republic of America is now 76 years old. I am glad, fellow-citizens, that your nation is so young. Seventy-six years, though a good old age for a man, is but a mere speck in the life of a nation. Three score years and ten is the allotted time for individual men; but nations number their years by thousands. According to this fact, you are, even now, only in the beginning of your national career, still lingering in the period of childhood. I repeat, I am glad this is so. There is hope in the thought, and hope is much needed, under the dark clouds which lower above the horizon. The eye of the reformer is met with angry flashes, portending disastrous times; but his heart may well beat lighter at the thought that America is young, and that she is still in the impressible stage of her existence. May he not hope that high lessons of wisdom, of justice and of truth, will yet give direction to her destiny? Were the nation older, the patriot's heart might be sadder, and the reformer's brow heavier. Its future might be shrouded in gloom, and the hope of its prophets go out in sorrow. There is consolation in the thought that America is young. Great streams are not easily turned from channels, worn deep in the course of ages. They may sometimes rise in quiet and stately majesty, and inundate the land, refreshing and fertilizing the earth with their mysterious properties. They may also rise in wrath and fury, and bear away, on their angry waves, the accumulated wealth of years of toil and hardship. They, however, gradually flow back to the same old channel, and flow on as serenely as ever. But, while the river may not be turned aside, it may dry up, and leave nothing behind but the withered branch, and the unsightly rock, to howl in the abyss-sweeping wind, the sad tale of departed glory. As with rivers so with nations.

Fellow-citizens, I shall not presume to dwell at length on the associations that cluster about this day. The simple story of it is that, 76 years ago, the people of this country were British subjects. The style and title of your "sovereign people" (in which you now glory) was not then born. You were under the British Crown. Your fathers esteemed the English Government as the home government; and England as the fatherland. This home gov-

---

1. A Jewish festival celebrating the Jews' deliverance from bondage in Egypt.

ernment, you know, although a considerable distance from your home, did, in the exercise of its parental prerogatives, impose upon its colonial children, such restraints, burdens and limitations, as, in its mature judgement, it deemed wise, right and proper.

But, your fathers, who had not adopted the fashionable idea of this day, of the infallibility of government, and the absolute character of its acts, presumed to differ from the home government in respect to the wisdom and the justice of some of those burdens and restraints. They went so far in their excitement as to pronounce the measures of government unjust, unreasonable, and oppressive, and altogether such as ought not to be quietly submitted to. I scarcely need say, fellow-citizens, that my opinion of those measures fully accords with that of your fathers. Such a declaration of agreement on my part would not be worth much to anybody. It would, certainly, prove nothing, as to what part I might have taken, had I lived during the great controversy of 1776. To say *now* that America was right, and England wrong, is exceedingly easy. Everybody can say it; the dastard, not less than the noble brave, can flippantly discant on the tyranny of England towards the American Colonies. It is fashionable to do so; but there was a time when to pronounce against England, and in favor of the cause of the colonies, tried men's souls. [2] They who did so were accounted in their day, plotters of mischief, agitators and rebels, dangerous men. To side with the right, against the wrong, with the weak against the strong, and with the oppressed against the oppressor! *here* lies the merit, and the one which, of all others, seems unfashionable in our day. The cause of liberty may be stabbed by the men who glory in the deeds of your fathers. But, to proceed.

Feeling themselves harshly and unjustly treated by the home government, your fathers, like men of honesty, and men of spirit, earnestly sought redress. They petitioned and remonstrated; they did so in a decorous, respectful, and loyal manner. Their conduct was wholly unexceptionable. This, however, did not answer the purpose. They saw themselves treated with sovereign indifference, coldness and scorn. Yet they persevered. They were not the men to look back.

As the sheet anchor takes a firmer hold, when the ship is tossed by the storm, so did the cause of your fathers grow stronger, as it breasted the chilling blasts of kingly displeasure. The greatest and best of British statesmen admitted its justice, and the loftiest eloquence of the British Senate came to its support. But, with that blindness which seems to be the unvarying characteristic of tyrants, since Pharoah and his hosts were drowned in the Red Sea, the British Government persisted in the exactions complained of.

The madness of this course, we believe, is admitted now, even by England; but we fear the lesson is wholly lost on our present rulers.

Oppression makes a wise man mad. Your fathers were wise men, and if they did not go mad, they became restive under this treatment. They felt themselves the victims of grievous wrongs, wholly incurable in their colonial capacity. With brave men there is always a remedy for oppression. Just here, the idea of a total separation of the colonies from the crown was born!

---

2. An allusion to the famous opening of Thomas Paine's revolutionary pamphlet *The American Crisis* (1776): "These are the times that try men's souls."

It was a startling idea, much more so, than we, at this distance of time, regard it. The timid and the prudent (as has been intimated) of that day, were, of course, shocked and alarmed by it.

Such people lived then, had lived before, and will, probably, ever have a place on this planet; and their course, in respect to any great change, (no matter how great the good to be attained, or the wrong to be redressed by it), may be calculated with as much precision as can be the course of the stars. They hate all changes, but silver, gold and copper change! Of this sort of change they are always strongly in favor.

These people were called tories in the days of your fathers; and the appellation, probably, conveyed the same idea that is meant by a more modern, though a somewhat less euphonious term, [3] which we often find in our papers, applied to some of our old politicians.

Their opposition to the then dangerous thought was earnest and powerful; but, amid all their terror and affrighted vociferations against it, the alarming and revolutionary idea moved on, and the country with it.

On the 2d of July, 1776, the old Continental Congress, to the dismay of the lovers of ease, and the worshippers of property, clothed that dreadful idea with all the authority of national sanction. They did so in the form of a resolution; and as we seldom hit upon resolutions, drawn up in our day, whose transparency is at all equal to this, it may refresh your minds and help my story if I read it.

"Resolved, That these united colonies *are*, and of right, ought to be free and Independent States; that they are absolved from all allegiance to the British Crown; and that all political connection between them and the State of Great Britain *is*, and ought to be, dissolved."

Citizens, your fathers made good that resolution. They succeeded; and to-day you reap the fruits of their success. The freedom gained is yours; and you, therefore, may properly celebrate this anniversary. The 4th of July is the first great fact in your nation's history—the very ring-bolt in the chain of your yet undeveloped destiny.

Pride and patriotism, not less than gratitude, prompt you to celebrate and to hold it in perpetual remembrance. I have said that the Declaration of Independence is the RING-BOLT to the chain of your nation's destiny; so, indeed, I regard it. The principles contained in that instrument are saving principles. Stand by those principles, be true to them on all occasions, in all places, against all foes, and at whatever cost.

From the round top of your ship of state, dark and threatening clouds may be seen. Heavy billows, like mountains in the distance, disclose to the leeward huge forms of flinty rocks! That *bolt* drawn, that *chain* broken, and all is lost. *Cling to this day—cling to it*, and to its principles, with the grasp of a storm-tossed mariner to a spar at midnight.

The coming into being of a nation, in any circumstances, is an interesting event. But, besides general considerations, there were peculiar circum-

---

3. Douglass is probably referring to the term *Hunker*, which was applied to conservative Democrats. "Euphonious": having a pleasant sound.

stances which make the advent of this republic an event of special attractiveness.

The whole scene, as I look back to it, was simple, dignified and sublime.

The population of the country, at the time, stood at the insignificant number of three millions. The country was poor in the munitions of war. The population was weak and scattered, and the country a wilderness unsubdued. There were then no means of concert and combination, such as exist now. Neither steam nor lightning had then been reduced to order and discipline. From the Potomac to the Delaware was a journey of many days. Under these, and innumerable other disadvantages, your fathers declared for liberty and independence and triumphed.

Fellow Citizens, I am not wanting in respect for the fathers of this republic. The signers of the Declaration of Independence were brave men. They were great men too—great enough to give fame to a great age. It does not often happen to a nation to raise, at one time, such a number of truly great men. The point from which I am compelled to view them is not, certainly, the most favorable; and yet I cannot contemplate their great deeds with less than admiration. They were statesmen, patriots and heroes, and for the good they did, and the principles they contended for, I will unite with you to honor their memory.

They loved their country better than their own private interests; and, though this is not the highest form of human excellence, all will concede that it is a rare virtue, and that when it is exhibited, it ought to command respect. He who will, intelligently, lay down his life for his country, is a man whom it is not in human nature to despise. Your fathers staked their lives, their fortunes, and their sacred honor, on the cause of their country. In their admiration of liberty, they lost sight of all other interests.

They were peace men; but they preferred revolution to peaceful submission to bondage. They were quiet men; but they did not shrink from agitating against oppression. They showed forbearance; but that they knew its limits. They believed in order; but not in the order of tyranny. With them, nothing was "settled" that was not right. With them, justice, liberty and humanity were "final"; not slavery and oppression. You may well cherish the memory of such men. They were great in their day and generation. Their solid manhood stands out the more as we contrast it with these degenerate times.

How circumspect, exact and proportionate were all their movements! How unlike the politicians of an hour! Their statesmanship looked beyond the passing moment, and stretched away in strength into the distant future. They seized upon eternal principles, and set a glorious example in their defence. Mark them!

Fully appreciating the hardship to be encountered, firmly believing in the right of their cause, honorably inviting the scrutiny of an on-looking world, reverently appealing to heaven to attest their sincerity, soundly comprehending the solemn responsibility they were about to assume, wisely measuring the terrible odds against them, your fathers, the fathers of this republic, did, most deliberately, under the inspiration of a glorious patriotism, and with a sublime faith in the great principles of justice and freedom, lay deep the corner-stone of the national superstructure, which has risen and still rises in grandeur around you.

Of this fundamental work, this day is the anniversary. Our eyes are met with demonstrations of joyous enthusiasm. Banners and pennants wave exultingly on the breeze. The din of business, too, is hushed. Even Mammon [4] seems to have quitted his grasp on this day. The ear-piercing fife and the stirring drum unite their accents with the ascending peal of a thousand church bells. Prayers are made, hymns are sung, and sermons are preached in honor of this day; while the quick martial tramp of a great and multitudinous nation, echoed back by all the hills, valleys and mountains of a vast continent, bespeak the occasion one of thrilling and universal interest—a nation's jubilee.

Friends and citizens, I need not enter further into the causes which led to this anniversary. Many of you understand them better than I do. You could instruct me in regard to them. That is a branch of knowledge in which you feel, perhaps, a much deeper interest than your speaker. The causes which led to the separation of the colonies from the British crown have never lacked for a tongue. They have all been taught in your common schools, narrated at your firesides, unfolded from your pulpits, and thundered from your legislative halls, and are as familiar to you as household words. They form the staple of your national poetry and eloquence.

I remember, also, that, as a people, Americans are remarkably familiar with all facts which make in their own favor. This is esteemed by some as a national trait—perhaps a national weakness. It is a fact, that whatever makes for the wealth or for the reputation of Americans, and can be had *cheap!* will be found by Americans. I shall not be charged with slandering Americans, if I say I think the American side of any question may be safely left in American hands.

I leave, therefore, the great deeds of your fathers to other gentlemen whose claim to have been regularly descended will be less likely to be disputed than mine!

The Present

My business, if I have any here to-day, is with the present. The accepted time with God and his cause is the ever-living now.

> "Trust no future, however pleasant,
>   Let the dead past bury its dead;
> Act, act in the living present,
>   Heart within, and God overhead." [5]

We have to do with the past only as we can make it useful to the present and to the future. To all inspiring motives, to noble deeds which can be gained from the past, we are welcome. But now is the time, the important time. Your fathers have lived, died, and have done their work, and have done much of it well. You live and must die, and you must do your work.

4. The false god of riches and greed.
5. From Henry Wadsworth Longfellow's popular poem A *Psalm of Life* (1838).

You have no right to enjoy a child's share in the labor of your fathers, unless your children are to be blest by your labors. You have no right to wear out and waste the hard-earned fame of your fathers to cover your indolence. Sydney Smith[6] tells us that men seldom eulogize the wisdom and virtues of their fathers, but to excuse some folly or wickedness of their own. This truth is not a doubtful one. There are illustrations of it near and remote, ancient and modern. It was fashionable, hundreds of years ago, for the children of Jacob to boast, we have "Abraham to our father,"[7] when they had long lost Abraham's faith and spirit. That people contented themselves under the shadow of Abraham's great name, while they repudiated the deeds which made his name great. Need I remind you that a similar thing is being done all over this country to-day? Need I tell you that the Jews are not the only people who built the tombs of the prophets, and garnished the sepulchres of the righteous? Washington could not die till he had broken the chains of his slaves.[8] Yet his monument is built up by the price of human blood, and the traders in the bodies and souls of men, shout—"We have Washington to *our father.*" Alas! that it should be so; yet so it is.

> "The evil that men do, lives after them,
> The good is oft' interred with their bones."[9]

Fellow-citizens, pardon me, allow me to ask, why am I called upon to speak here to-day? What have I, or those I represent, to do with your national independence? Are the great principles of political freedom and of natural justice, embodied in that Declaration of Independence, extended to us? and am I, therefore, called upon to bring our humble offering to the national altar, and to confess the benefits and express devout gratitude for the blessings resulting from your independence to us?

Would to God, both for your sakes and ours, that an affirmative answer could be truthfully returned to these questions! Then would my task be light, and my burden easy and delightful. For *who* is there so cold, that a nation's sympathy could not warm him? Who so obdurate and dead to the claims of gratitude, that would not thankfully acknowledge such priceless benefits? Who so stolid and selfish, that would not give his voice to swell the hallelujahs of a nation's jubilee, when the chains of servitude had been torn from his limbs? I am not that man. In a case like that, the dumb might eloquently speak, and the "lame man leap as an hart."[1]

But, such is not the state of the case. I say it with a sad sense of the disparity between us. I am not included within the pale of this glorious anniversary! Your high independence only reveals the immeasurable distance between us. The blessings in which you, this day, rejoice, are not enjoyed in common. The rich inheritance of justice, liberty, prosperity and independence, bequeathed by your fathers, is shared by you, not by me. The sunlight that brought life and healing to you, has brought stripes and death

6. English minister and satirical essayist (1771–1845).
7. Luke 3:8. Abraham was the first patriarch of the Hebrews. Jacob, whose sons were the ancestors of the twelve tribes of Israel, was Abraham's grandson.
8. In his will George Washington authorized the emancipation of his three hundred slaves upon the death of his wife.
9. Shakespeare's *Julius Caesar* 3.2.76.
1. Isaiah 35:6.

to me. This Fourth [of] July is *yours*, not *mine*. *You* may rejoice, *I* must mourn. To drag a man in fetters into the grand illuminated temple of liberty, and call upon him to join you in joyous anthems, were inhuman mockery and sacrilegious irony. Do you mean, citizens, to mock me, by asking me to speak to-day? If so, there is a parallel to your conduct. And let me warn you that it is dangerous to copy the example of a nation whose crimes, towering up to heaven, were thrown down by the breath of the Almighty, burying that nation in irrecoverable ruin! I can to-day take up the plaintive lament of a peeled and woe-smitten people!

"By the rivers of Babylon, there we sat down. Yea! we wept when we remembered Zion. We hanged our harps upon the willows in the midst thereof. For there, they that carried us away captive, required of us a song; and they who wasted us required of us mirth, saying, Sing us one of the songs of Zion. How can we sing the Lord's song in a strange land? If I forget thee, O Jerusalem, let my right hand forget her cunning. If I do not remember thee, let my tongue cleave to the roof of my mouth."[2]

Fellow-citizens; above your national, tumultuous joy, I hear the mournful wail of millions! whose chains, heavy and grievous yesterday, are, to-day, rendered more intolerable by the jubilee shouts that reach them. If I do forget, if I do not faithfully remember those bleeding children of sorrow this day, "may my right hand forget her cunning, and may my tongue cleave to the roof of my mouth!" To forget them, to pass lightly over their wrongs, and to chime in with the popular theme, would be treason most scandalous and shocking, and would make me a reproach before God and the world. My subject, then fellow-citizens, is AMERICAN SLAVERY. I shall see, this day, and its popular characteristics, from the slave's point of view. Standing, there, identified with the American bondman, making his wrongs mine, I do not hesitate to declare, with all my soul, that the character and conduct of this nation never looked blacker to me than on this 4th of July! Whether we turn to the declarations of the past, or to the professions of the present, the conduct of the nation seems equally hideous and revolting. America is false to the past, false to the present, and solemnly binds herself to be false to the future. Standing with God and the crushed and bleeding slave on this occasion, I will, in the name of humanity which is outraged, in the name of liberty which is fettered, in the name of the constitution and the Bible, which are disregarded and trampled upon, dare to call in question and to denounce, with all the emphasis I can command, everything that serves to perpetuate slavery—the great sin and shame of America! "I will not equivocate; I will not excuse";[3] I will use the severest language I can command; and yet not one word shall escape me that any man, whose judgement is not blinded by prejudice, or who is not at heart a slaveholder, shall not confess to be right and just.

But I fancy I hear some one of my audience say, it is just in this circumstance that you and your brother abolitionists fail to make a favorable impression on the public mind. Would you argue more, and denounce less, would you persuade more, and rebuke less, your cause would be much

---

2. Psalm 137:1–6.
3. From the first issue of William Lloyd Garrison's pioneering antislavery newspaper, the *Liberator*.

more likely to succeed. But, I submit, where all is plain there is nothing to be argued. What point in the anti-slavery creed would you have me argue? On what branch of the subject do the people of this country need light? Must I undertake to prove that the slave is a man? That point is conceded already. Nobody doubts it. The slaveholders themselves acknowledge it in the enactment of laws for their government. They acknowledge it when they punish disobedience on the part of the slave. There are seventy-two crimes in the State of Virginia, which, if committed by a black man, (no matter how ignorant he be), subject him to the punishment of death; while only two of the same crimes will subject a white man to the like punishment. What is this but the acknowledgement that the slave is a moral, intellectual and responsible being? The manhood of the slave is conceded. It is admitted in the fact that Southern statute books are covered with enactments forbidding, under severe fines and penalties, the teaching of the slave to read or to write. When you can point to any such laws, in reference to the beasts of the field, then I may consent to argue the manhood of the slave. When the dogs in your streets, when the fowls of the air, when the cattle on your hills, when the fish of the sea, and the reptiles that crawl, shall be unable to distinguish the slave from a brute, *then* will I argue with you that the slave is a man!

For the present, it is enough to affirm the equal manhood of the negro race. Is it not astonishing that, while we are ploughing, planting and reaping, using all kinds of mechanical tools, erecting houses, constructing bridges, building ships, working in metals of brass, iron, copper, silver and gold; that, while we are reading, writing and cyphering, acting as clerks, merchants and secretaries, having among us lawyers, doctors, ministers, poets, authors, editors, orators and teachers; that, while we are engaged in all manner of enterprises common to other men, digging gold in California, capturing the whale in the Pacific, feeding sheep and cattle on the hill-side, living, moving, acting, thinking, planning, living in families as husbands, wives and children, and, above all, confessing and worshipping the Christian's God, and looking hopefully for life and immortality beyond the grave, we are called upon to prove that we are men!

Would you have me argue that man is entitled to liberty? that he is the rightful owner of his own body? You have already declared it. Must I argue the wrongfulness of slavery? Is that a question for Republicans? Is it to be settled by the rules of logic and argumentation, as a matter beset with great difficulty, involving a doubtful application of the principle of justice, hard to be understood? How should I look to-day, in the presence of Americans, dividing, and subdividing a discourse, to show that men have a natural right to freedom? speaking of it relatively, and positively, negatively, and affirmatively. To do so, would be to make myself ridiculous, and to offer an insult to your understanding. There is not a man beneath the canopy of heaven, that does not know that slavery is wrong *for him.*

What, am I to argue that it is wrong to make men brutes, to rob them of their liberty, to work them without wages, to keep them ignorant of their relations to their fellow men, to beat them with sticks, to flay their flesh with the lash, to load their limbs with irons, to hunt them with dogs, to sell them at auction, to sunder their families, to knock out their teeth, to burn their flesh, to starve them into obedience and submission to their masters? Must I argue that a system thus marked with blood, and stained with pollution, is *wrong*? No! I will not. I have better employments for my time and strength, than such arguments would imply.

What, then, remains to be argued? Is it that slavery is not divine; that God did not establish it; that our doctors of divinity are mistaken? There is blasphemy in the thought. That which is inhuman, cannot be divine! *Who* can reason on such a proposition? They that can, may; I cannot. The time for such argument is past.

At a time like this, scorching irony, not convincing argument, is needed. O! had I the ability, and could I reach the nation's ear, I would, to-day, pour out a fiery stream of biting ridicule, blasting reproach, withering sarcasm, and stern rebuke. For it is not light that is needed, but fire; it is not the gentle shower, but thunder. We need the storm, the whirlwind, and the earthquake. The feeling of the nation must be quickened; the conscience of the nation must be roused; the propriety of the nation must be startled; the hypocrisy of the nation must be exposed; and its crimes against God and man must be proclaimed and denounced.

What, to the American slave, is your 4th of July? I answer: a day that reveals to him, more than all other days in the year, the gross injustice and cruelty to which he is the constant victim. To him, your celebration is a sham; your boasted liberty, an unholy license; your national greatness, swelling vanity; your sounds of rejoicing are empty and heartless; your denunciations of tyrants, brass fronted impudence; your shouts of liberty and equality, hollow mockery; your prayers and hymns, your sermons and thanksgivings, with all your religious parade, and solemnity, are, to him, mere bombast, fraud, deception, impiety, and hypocrisy—a thin veil to cover up crimes which would disgrace a nation of savages. There is not a nation on the earth guilty of practices, more shocking and bloody, than are the people of these United States, at this very hour.

Go where you may, search where you will, roam through all the monarchies and despotisms of the old world, travel through South America, search out every abuse, and when you have found the last, lay your facts by the side of the everyday practices of this nation, and you will say with me, that, for revolting barbarity and shameless hypocrisy, America reigns without a rival.

The Internal Slave Trade

*   *   *

Americans! your republican politics, not less than your republican religion, are flagrantly inconsistent. You boast of your love of liberty, your superior civilization, and your pure Christianity, while the whole political power of the nation (as embodied in the two great political parties), is solemnly pledged to support and perpetuate the enslavement of three millions of your countrymen. You hurl your anathemas[4] at the crowned headed tyrants of Russia and Austria, and pride yourselves on your Demo-

4. Denunciations or curses.

cratic institutions, while you yourselves consent to be the mere *tools* and *body-guards* of the tyrants of Virginia and Carolina. You invite to your shores fugitives of oppression from abroad, honor them with banquets, greet them with ovations, cheer them, toast them, salute them, protect them, and pour out your money to them like water; but the fugitives from your own land you advertise, hunt, arrest, shoot and kill. You glory in your refinement and your universal education; yet you maintain a system as barbarous and dreadful as ever stained the character of a nation—a system begun in avarice, supported in pride, and perpetuated in cruelty. You shed tears over fallen Hungary,[5] and make the sad story of her wrongs the theme of your poets, statesmen and orators, till your gallant sons are ready to fly to arms to vindicate her cause against her oppressors; but, in regard to the ten thousand wrongs of the American slave, you would enforce the strictest silence, and would hail him as an enemy of the nation who dares to make those wrongs the subject of public discourse! You are all on fire at the mention of liberty for France or for Ireland; but are as cold as an iceberg at the thought of liberty for the enslaved of America. You discourse eloquently on the dignity of labor; yet, you sustain a system which, in its very essence, casts a stigma upon labor. You can bare your bosom to the storm of British artillery to throw off a threepenny tax on tea; and yet wring the last hard-earned farthing from the grasp of the black laborers of your country. You profess to believe "that, of one blood, God made all nations of men to dwell on the face of all the earth,"[6] and hath commanded all men, everywhere to love one another; yet you notoriously hate, (and glory in your hatred), all men whose skins are not colored like your own. You declare, before the world, and are understood by the world to declare, that you *"hold these truths to be self evident, that all men are created equal; and are endowed by their Creator with certain inalienable rights; and that, among these are, life, liberty, and the pursuit of happiness";*[7] and yet, you hold securely, in a bondage which, according to your own Thomas Jefferson, *"is worse than ages of that which your fathers rose in rebellion to oppose,"*[8] a seventh part of the inhabitants of your country.

Fellow-citizens! I will not enlarge further on your national inconsistencies. The existence of slavery in this country brands your republicanism as a sham, your humanity as a base pretence, and your Christianity as a lie. It destroys your moral power abroad; it corrupts your politicians at home. It saps the foundation of religion; it makes your name a hissing, and a byword to a mocking earth. It is the antagonistic force in your government, the only thing that seriously disturbs and endangers your *Union*. It fetters your progress; it is the enemy of improvement, the deadly foe of education; it fosters pride; it breeds insolence; it promotes vice; it shelters crime; it is a curse to the earth that supports it; and yet, you cling to it, as if it were the sheet anchor of all your hopes. Oh! be warned! be warned! a horrible reptile is coiled up in your nation's bosom; the venomous creature is nursing

---

5. In August 1849 the republic of Hungary was overthrown by invading Russian and Austrian troops.
6. Acts 17:26.
7. From the U.S. Declaration of Independence.
8. Compare Jefferson's June 26, 1786, letter to Nicholas Demeunier: "Who can endure toil, famine, stripes, imprisonment or death itself in vindication of his own liberty . . . and inflict upon his fellow men a bondage, one hour of which is fraught with more misery than ages of that which he rose in rebellion to oppose."

at the tender breast of your youthful republic; *for the love of God, tear away,* and fling from you the hideous monster, and *let the weight of twenty millions crush and destroy it forever!*

The Constitution

* * *

Allow me to say, in conclusion, notwithstanding the dark picture I have this day presented of the state of the nation, I do not despair of this country. There are forces in operation, which must inevitably work the downfall of slavery. *"The arm of the Lord is not shortened,"*[9] and the doom of slavery is certain. I, therefore, leave off where I began, with *hope.* While drawing encouragement from the Declaration of Independence, the great principles it contains, and the genius of American Institutions, my spirit is also cheered by the obvious tendencies of the age. Nations do not now stand in the same relation to each other that they did ages ago. No nation can now shut itself up from the surrounding world, and trot round in the same old path of its fathers without interference. The time *was* when such could be done. Long established customs of hurtful character could formerly fence themselves in, and do their evil work with social impunity. Knowledge was then confined and enjoyed by the privileged few, and the multitude walked on in mental darkness. But a change has now come over the affairs of mankind. Walled cities and empires have become unfashionable. The arm of commerce has borne away the gates of the strong city. Intelligence is penetrating the darkest corners of the globe. It makes its pathway over and under the sea, as well as on the earth. Wind, steam, and lightning are its chartered agents. Oceans no longer divide, but link nations together. From Boston to London is now a holiday excursion. Space is comparatively annihilated. Thoughts expressed on one side of the Atlantic are distinctly heard on the other.

The far off and almost fabulous Pacific rolls in grandeur at our feet. The Celestial Empire, the mystery of ages, is being solved. The fiat of the Almighty, *"Let there be Light,"*[1] has not yet spent its force. No abuse, no outrage whether in taste, sport or avarice, can now hide itself from the all-pervading light. The iron shoe, and crippled foot of China must be seen, in contrast with nature. *Africa must rise and put on her yet unwoven garment.* *"Ethiopia shall stretch out her hand unto God."*[2] In the fervent aspirations of William Lloyd Garrison, I say, and let every heart join in saying it:

> God speed the year of jubilee
>> The wide world o'er!
> When from their galling chains set free,
> Th' oppress'd shall vilely bend the knee,
> And wear the yoke of tyranny
>> Like brutes no more.
> That year will come, and freedom's reign,

9. Compare Isaiah 59:1: "Behold the Lord's hand is not shortened, that it cannot save; neither his ear heavy, that it cannot hear."
1. Genesis 1:3.

2. Compare Psalm 68:31: "Princes shall come out of Egypt; Ethiopia shall soon stretch out her hands unto God."

To man his plundered rights again
   Restore.

God speed the day when human blood
   Shall cease to flow!
In every clime be understood,
The claims of human brotherhood,
And each return for evil, good,
   Not blow for blow;
That day will come all feuds to end,
And change into a faithful friend
   Each foe.

God speed the hour, the glorious hour,
   When none on earth
Shall exercise a lordly power,
Nor in a tyrant's presence cower;
But all to manhood's stature tower,
   By equal birth!
THAT HOUR WILL COME, to each, to all,
And from his prison-house, the thrall
   Go forth.

Until that year, day, hour, arrive,
With head, and heart, and hand I'll strive,
To break the rod, and rend the gyve,
The spoiler of his prey deprive—
   So witness Heaven!
And never from my chosen post,
Whate'er the peril or the cost,
   Be driven.[3]

1852

From Life and Times of Frederick Douglass

From Second Part

FROM CHAPTER XV. WEIGHED IN THE BALANCE

The most of my story is now before the reader. Whatever of good or ill the future may have in store for me, the past at least is secure. As I review the last decade up to the present writing, I am impressed with a sense of completeness; a sort of rounding up of the arch to the point where the keystone may be inserted, the scaffolding removed, and the work, with all its perfections or faults, left to speak for itself. This decade, from 1871 to 1881, has been crowded, if time is capable of being thus described, with incidents and events which may well enough be accounted remarkable. To me they certainly appear strange, if not wonderful. My early life not only gave no visible promise, but no hint of such experience. On the contrary, that

3. William Lloyd Garrison's *The Triumph of Freedom* (1845).

life seemed to render it, in part at least, impossible. In addition to what is narrated in the foregoing chapter, I have, as belonging to this decade, to speak of my mission to Santo Domingo;[1] of my appointment as a member of the council for the government of the District of Columbia; of my election as elector at large for the State of New York; of my invitation to speak at the monument of the unknown loyal dead, at Arlington, on Decoration day;[2] of my address on the unveiling of Lincoln monument, at Lincoln Park, Washington; of my appointment to bring the electoral vote from New York to the national capital; of my invitation to speak near the statue of Abraham Lincoln, Madison Square, New York; of my accompanying the body of Vice-President Wilson from Washington to Boston; of my conversations with Senator Sumner and President Grant; of my welcome to the receptions of Secretary Hamilton Fish; of my appointment by President R. B. Hayes to the office of Marshal of the District of Columbia; of my visit to Thomas Auld, the man who claimed me as his slave, and from whom I was purchased by my English friends; of my visit, after an absence of fifty-six years, to Lloyd's plantation, the home of my childhood; and of my appointment by President James A. Garfield[3] to the office of Recorder of Deeds of the District of Columbia.

Those who knew of my more than friendly relations with Hon. Charles Sumner, and of his determined opposition to the annexation of Santo Domingo to the United States, were surprised to find me earnestly taking sides with General Grant upon that question. Some of my white friends, and a few of those of my own color—who, unfortunately, allow themselves to look at public questions more through the medium of feeling than of reason, and who follow the line of what is grateful to their friends rather than what is consistent with their own convictions—thought my course was an ungrateful return for the eminent services of the Massachusetts senator. I am free to say that, had I been guided only by the promptings of my heart, I should in this controversy have followed the lead of Charles Sumner. He was not only the most clearsighted, brave, and uncompromising friend of my race who had ever stood upon the floor of the Senate, but was to me a loved, honored, and precious personal friend; a man possessing the exalted and matured intellect of a statesman, with the pure and artless heart of a child. Upon any issue, as between him and others, when the right seemed in anywise doubtful, I should have followed his counsel and advice. But the annexation of Santo Domingo, to my understanding, did not seem to be any such question. The reasons in its favor were many and obvious; and those against it, as I thought, were easily answered. To Mr. Sumner, annexation was a measure to extinguish a colored nation, and to do so by dishonorable means and for selfish motives. To me it meant the alliance of a weak and defenseless people, having few or none of the attributes of a nation, torn and rent by internal feuds and unable to maintain order at home or

1. Capital of the Dominican Republic on the island of Hispaniola in the Caribbean Sea.
2. Now called Memorial Day. Douglass spoke on May 30, 1871.
3. Served in 1881 as twentieth president of the United States (1831–1881). Charles Sumner (1811–1874), Republican Party leader and U.S.

Senator (1851–74). Ulysses S. Grant (1822–1885), eighteenth president of the United States (1869–77). Hamilton Fish (1808–1893), U.S. secretary of state (1869–77). Rutherford B. Hayes (1822–1893), nineteenth president of the United States (1877–81).

command respect abroad, to a government which would give it peace, stability, prosperity, and civilization, and make it helpful to both countries. To favor annexation at the time when Santo Domingo asked for a place in our union, was a very different thing from what it was when Cuba and Central America were sought by fillibustering expeditions. When the slave power bore rule, and a spirit of injustice and oppression animated and controlled every part of our government, I was for limiting our dominion to the smallest possible margin; but since liberty and equality have become the law of our land, I am for extending our dominion whenever and wherever such extension can peaceably and honorably, and with the approval and desire of all the parties concerned, be accomplished. Santo Domingo wanted to come under our government upon the terms thus described; and for more reasons than I can stop here to give, I then believed, and do now believe, it would have been wise to have received her into our sisterhood of States.

The idea that annexation meant degradation to a colored nation was altogether fanciful; there was no more dishonor to Santo Domingo in making her a State of the American Union, than in making Kansas, Nebraska, or any other territory such a State. It was giving to a part the strength of the whole, and lifting what must be despised for its isolation into an organization and relationship which would compel consideration and respect.

*　*　*

An appointment to any important and lucrative office under the United States government usually brings its recipient a large measure of praise and congratulation on the one hand, and much abuse and disparagement on the other; and he may think himself singularly fortunate if the censure does not exceed the praise. I need not dwell upon the causes of this extravagance, but I may say that there is no office of any value in the country which is not desired and sought by many persons equally meritorious and equally deserving. But as only one person can be appointed to any one office, only one can be pleased, while many are offended. Unhappily, resentment follows disappointment, and this resentment often finds expression in disparagement and abuse of the successful man. As in most else that I have said, I borrow this reflection from my own experience.

My appointment as United States Marshal of the District of Columbia,[4] was in keeping with the rest of my life, as a free-man. It was an innovation upon long established usage, and opposed to the general current of sentiment in the community. It came upon the people of the District as a gross surprise, and almost a punishment; and provoked something like a scream—I will not say a *yell*—of popular displeasure. As soon as I was named by President Hayes for the place, efforts were made by members of the bar to defeat my confirmation before the Senate. All sorts of reasons against my appointment, but the true one, were given, and that was withheld more from a sense of shame, than from a sense of justice. The apprehension doubtless was, that if appointed marshal, I would surround myself with colored deputies, colored bailiffs and colored messengers and pack the jury-box with colored jurors; in a word, Africanize the courts. But the

4. From 1877 to 1881.

most dreadful thing threatened, was a colored man at the *Executive Mansion* in white kid gloves, sparrow-tailed coat, patent-leather boots, and alabaster cravat, performing the ceremony—a very empty one—of introducing the aristocratic citizens of the republic to the President of the United States. This was something entirely too much to be borne; and men asked themselves in view of it, To what is the world coming? and where will these things stop? Dreadful! Dreadful!

It is creditable to the manliness of the American Senate, that it was moved by none of these things, and that it lost no time in the matter of my confirmation. I learn, and believe my information correct, that foremost among those who supported my confirmation against the objections made to it, was Hon. Roscoe Conkling of New York. His speech in executive session is said by the senators who heard it, to have been one of the most masterly and eloquent ever delivered on the floor of the Senate; and this too I readily believe, for Mr. Conkling possesses the ardor and fire of Henry Clay, the subtlety of Calhoun, and the massive grandeur of Daniel Webster.[5]

* * *

In all my forty years of thought and labor to promote the freedom and welfare of my race, I never found myself more widely and painfully at variance with leading colored men of the country than when I opposed the effort to set in motion a wholesale exodus of colored people of the South to the Northern States;[6] and yet I never took a position in which I felt myself better fortified by reason and necessity. It was said of me, that I had deserted to the old master class, and that I was a traitor to my race; that I had run away from slavery myself, and yet I was opposing others in doing the same. When my opponents condescended to argue, they took the ground that the colored people of the South needed to be brought into contact with the freedom and civilization of the North; that no emancipated and persecuted people ever had or ever could rise in the presence of the people by whom they had been enslaved, and that the true remedy for the ills which the freedmen were suffering, was to initiate the Israelitish departure from our modern Egypt to a land abounding, if not in "milk and honey,"[7] certainly in pork and hominy.

Influenced, no doubt, by the dazzling prospects held out to them by the advocates of the exodus movement, thousands of poor, hungry, naked and destitute colored people were induced to quit the South amid the frosts and snows of a dreadful winter in search of a better country. I regret to say that there was something sinister in this so-called exodus, for it transpired that some of the agents most active in promoting it had an understanding with certain railroad companies, by which they were to receive one dollar per head upon all such passengers. Thousands of these poor people, traveling only so far as they had money to bear their expenses, were dropped in the extremest destitution on the levees of St. Louis, and their tales of woe were such as to move a heart much less sensitive to human suffering than mine. But while I felt for these poor deluded people, and did what I could

5. Henry Clay, John C. Calhoun, and Daniel Webster were pre–Civil War national political leaders renowned for their oratory.
6. The migration of African Americans from the South to the Midwest, especially Kansas, in search of economic opportunity and legal protection, gained national attention in 1879.
7. Numbers 13:27.

to put a stop to their ill-advised and ill-arranged stampede, I also did what I could to assist such of them as were within my reach, who were on their way to this land of promise. Hundreds of these people came to Washington, and at one time there were from two to three hundred lodgers here unable to get further for the want of money. I lost no time in appealing to my friends for the means of assisting them.

* * *

How little justice was done me by those who accused me of indifference to the welfare of the colored people of the South on account of my opposition to the so-called exodus will be seen by the following extracts from a paper [8] on that subject laid before the Social Science Congress at Saratoga, when the question was before the country:

> "Important as manual labor everywhere is, it is nowhere more important and absolutely indispensable to the existence of society than in the more southern of the United States. Machinery may continue to do, as it has done, much of the work of the North, but the work of the South requires for its performance bone, sinew and muscle of the strongest and most enduring kind. Labor in that section must know no pause. Her soil is pregnant and prolific with life and energy. All the forces of nature within her borders are wonderfully vigorous, persistent, and active. Aided by an almost perpetual summer, abundantly supplied with heat and moisture, her soil readily and rapidly covers itself with noxious weeds, dense forests, and impenetrable jungles. Only a few years of non-tillage would be needed to give the sunny and fruitful South to the bats and owls of a desolate wilderness. From this condition, shocking for a southern man to contemplate, it is now seen that nothing less powerful than the naked iron arm of the negro can save her. For him, as a Southern laborer there is no competitor or substitute.

* * *

> "Hence it is seen that the dependence upon the negro of the planters, land-owners, and the old master-class of the South, however galling and humiliating to Southern pride and power, is nearly complete and perfect. There is only one mode of escape for them, and that mode they will certainly not adopt. It is to take off their own coats, cease to whittle sticks and talk politics at cross-roads, and go themselves to work in their broad and sunny fields of cotton and sugar. An invitation to do this is about as harsh and distasteful to all their inclinations as would be an invitation to step down into their graves. With the negro all this is different. Neither natural, artificial nor traditional causes stand in the way of the freedman's laboring in the South. Neither the heat nor the fever-demon which lurks in her tangled and oozy swamps affrights him, and he stands to-day the admitted author of whatever prosperity, beauty, and civilization are now possessed by the South, and the admitted arbiter of her destiny.

8. Douglass's paper The Negro Exodus from the Gulf States was read to the American Social Sciences Association at Saratoga, New York, on September 12, 1879.

"This, then, is the high vantage ground of the negro; he has labor; the South wants it, and must have it or perish. Since he is free he can now give it or withhold it; use it where he is, or take it elsewhere as he pleases. His labor made him a slave, and his labor can, if he will, make him free, comfortable, and independent. It is more to him than fire, swords, ballot-boxes, or bayonets. It touches the heart of the South through its pocket. This power served him well years ago, when in the bitterest extremity of destitution. But for it he would have perished when he dropped out of slavery. It saved him then, and it will save him again.

* * *

"Bad as is the condition of the negro to-day at the South, there was a time when it was flagrantly and incomparably worse. A few years ago he had nothing—he had not even himself. He belonged to somebody else, who could dispose of his person and his labor as he pleased. Now he has himself, his labor, and his right to dispose of one and the other as shall best suit his own happiness. He has more. He has a standing in the supreme law of the land—in the Constitution of the United States—not to be changed or affected by any conjunction of circumstances likely to occur in the immediate or remote future. The Fourteenth Amendment makes him a citizen, and the Fifteenth [9] makes him a voter. With power behind him, at work for him, and which cannot be taken from him, the negro of the South may wisely bide his time. The situation at the moment is exceptional and transient. The permanent powers of the government are all on his side. What though for the moment the hand of violence strikes down the negro's rights in the South, those rights will revive, survive, and flourish again. They are not the only people who have been, in a moment of popular passion, maltreated and driven from the polls. The Irish and Dutch have frequently been so treated. Boston, Baltimore, and New York have been the scenes of lawless violence; but those scenes have now disappeared. . . . . Without abating one jot of our horror and indignation at the outrages committed in some parts of the Southern States against the negro, we cannot but regard the present agitation of an African exodus from the South as ill-timed and, in some respects, hurtful. We stand to-day at the beginning of a grand and beneficent reaction. There is a growing recognition of the duty and obligation of the American people to guard, protect, and defend the personal and political rights of all the people of all the States, and to uphold the principles upon which rebellion was suppressed, slavery abolished, and the country saved from dismemberment and ruin.

* * *

"Besides the objection thus stated, it is manifest that the public and noisy advocacy of a general stampede of the colored people from the South to the North is necessarily an abandonment of the great and paramount principle of protection to person and property in every

---

9. The Fourteenth Amendment to the U.S. Constitution extended citizenship rights to the former slaves. The Fifteenth guaranteed the right to vote to all male citizens regardless of race or color.

State in the Union. It is an evasion of a solemn obligation and duty. The business of this nation is to protect its citizens *where they are*, not to transport them where they will not need protection. The best that can be said of this exodus in this respect is, that it is an attempt to climb up some other way—it is an expedient, a half-way measure, and tends to weaken in the public mind a sense of the absolute right, power and duty of the government, inasmuch as it concedes, by implication at least, that on the soil of the South the law of the land cannot command obedience, the ballot-box cannot be kept pure, peaceable elections cannot be held, the Constitution cannot be enforced, and the lives and liberties of loyal and peaceable citizens cannot be protected. It is a surrender, a premature disheartening surrender, since it would secure freedom and free institutions by migration rather than by protection, by flight rather than by right, by going into a strange land rather than by staying in one's own. It leaves the whole question of equal rights on the soil of the South open and still to be settled, with the moral influence of the exodus against us, since it is a confession of the utter impracticability of equal rights and equal protection in any State where those rights may be struck down by violence.

"It does not appear that the friends of freedom should spend either time or talent in furtherance of this exodus as a desirable measure, either for the North or the South. If the people of this country cannot be protected in every State of the Union, the government of the United States is shorn of its rightful dignity and power, the late rebellion has triumphed, the sovereignty of the nation is an empty name, and the power and authority in individual States is greater than the power and authority of the United States. . . . . .

From *Third Part*

CHAPTER I. LATER LIFE

Ten years ago when the preceding chapters of this book were written,[1] having then reached in the journey of life the middle of the decade beginning at sixty and ending at seventy, and naturally reminded that I was no longer young, I laid aside my pen with some such sense of relief as might be felt by a weary and over-burdened traveler when arrived at the desired end of a long journey, or as an honest debtor wishing to be square with all the world might feel when the last dollar of an old debt was paid off. Not that I wished to be discharged from labor and service in the cause to which I have devoted my life, but from this peculiar kind of labor and service. I hardly need say to those who know me, that writing for the public eye never came quite as easily to me as speaking to the public ear. It is a marvel to me that under the circumstances I learned to write at all. It has been a still greater marvel that in the brief working period in which they lived and wrought, such men as Dickens, Dumas, Carlyle and Sir Walter Scott[2]

1. The first edition of *Life and Times of Frederick Douglass* was published in 1881. In 1892 Douglass revised and updated the *Life and Times*.

2. Charles Dickens, Alexandre Dumas, Thomas Carlyle, and Sir Walter Scott were all renowned 19th-century European literary figures.

could have produced the works ascribed to them. But many have been the impediments with which I have had to struggle. I have, too, been embarrassed by the thought of writing so much about myself when there was so much else of which to write. It is far easier to write about others than about one's self. I write freely of myself, not from choice, but because I have, by my cause, been morally forced into thus writing. Time and events have summoned me to stand forth both as a witness and an advocate for a people long dumb, not allowed to speak for themselves, yet much misunderstood and deeply wronged. In the earlier days of my freedom, I was called upon to expose the direful nature of the slave system, by telling my own experience while a slave, and to do what I could thereby to make slavery odious and thus to hasten the day of emancipation. It was no time to mince matters or to stand upon a delicate sense of propriety, in the presence of a crime so gigantic as our slavery was, and the duty to oppose it so imperative. I was called upon to expose even my stripes, and with many misgivings obeyed the summons and tried thus to do my whole duty in this my first public work and what I may say proved to be the best work of my life.

Fifty years have passed since I entered upon that work, and now that it is ended, I find myself summoned again by the popular voice and by what is called the negro problem, to come a second time upon the witness stand and give evidence upon disputed points concerning myself and my emancipated brothers and sisters who, though free, are yet oppressed and are in as much need of an advocate as before they were set free. Though this is not altogether as agreeable to me as was my first mission, it is one that comes with such commanding authority as to compel me to accept it as a present duty. In it I am pelted with all sorts of knotty questions, some of which might be difficult even for Humboldt, Cuvier or Darwin, [3] were they alive, to answer. They are questions which range over the whole field of science, learning and philosophy, and some descend to the depths of impertinent, unmannerly and vulgar curiosity. To be able to answer the higher range of these questions I should be profoundly versed in psychology, anthropology, ethnology, sociology, theology, biology, and all the other ologies, philosophies and sciences. There is no disguising the fact that the American people are much interested and mystified about the mere matter of color as connected with manhood. It seems to them that color has some moral or immoral qualities and especially the latter. They do not feel quite reconciled to the idea that a man of different color from themselves should have all the human rights claimed by themselves. When an unknown man is spoken of in their presence, the first question that arises in the average American mind concerning him and which must be answered is, Of what color is he? and he rises or falls in estimation by the answer given. It is not whether he is a good man or a bad man. That does not seem of primary importance. Hence I have often been bluntly and sometimes very rudely asked, of what color my mother was, and of what color was my father? In what proportion does the blood of the various races mingle in my veins, especially how much white blood and how much

3. Alexander von Humboldt, German naturalist; George Cuvier, French zoologist; and Charles Darwin, English naturalist and evolutionist, preeminent 19th-century scientists.

black blood entered into my composition? Whether I was not part Indian
as well as African and Caucasian? Whether I considered myself more African than Caucasian, or the reverse? Whether I derived my intelligence
from my father, or from my mother, from my white, or from my black
blood? Whether persons of mixed blood are as strong and healthy as persons of either of the races whose blood they inherit? Whether persons of
mixed blood do permanently remain of the mixed complexion or finally
take on the complexion of one or the other of the two or more races of
which they may be composed? Whether they live as long and raise as large
families as other people? Whether they inherit only evil from both parents
and good from neither? Whether evil dispositions are more transmissible
than good? Why did I marry a person of my father's complexion instead of
marrying one of my mother's complexion? How is the race problem to be
solved in this country? Will the negro go back to Africa or remain here?
Under this shower of purely American questions, more or less personal, I
have endeavored to possess my soul in patience and get as much good out
of life as was possible with so much to occupy my time; and, though often
perplexed, seldom losing my temper, or abating heart or hope for the future
of my people. Though I cannot say I have satisfied the curiosity of my countrymen on all the questions raised by them, I have, like all honest men on
the witness stand, answered to the best of my knowledge and belief, and I
hope I have never answered in such wise as to increase the hardships of any
human being of whatever race or color.

When the first part of this book was written, I was, as before intimated,
already looking toward the sunset of human life and thinking that my children would probably finish the recital of my life, or that possibly some
other persons outside of family ties to whom I am known might think it
worth while to tell what he or she might know of the remainder of my story.
I considered, as I have said, that my work was done. But friends and publishers concur in the opinion that the unity and completeness of the work
require that it shall be finished by the hand by which it was begun.

Many things touched me and employed my thoughts and activities between the years 1881 and 1891. I am willing to speak of them. Like most
men who give the world their autobiographies I wish my story to be told as
favorably towards myself as it can be with a due regard to truth. I do not
wish it to be imagined by any that I am insensible to the singularity of my
career, or to the peculiar relation I sustain to the history of my time and
country. I know and feel that it is something to have lived at all in this
Republic during the latter part of this eventful century, but I know it is
more to have had some small share in the great events which have distinguished it from the experience of all other centuries. No man liveth unto
himself, or ought to live unto himself. My life has conformed to this Bible
saying, for, more than most men, I have been the thin edge of the wedge to
open for my people a way in many directions and places never before occupied by them. It has been mine, in some degree, to stand as their defense in
moral battle against the shafts of detraction, calumny and persecution, and
to labor in removing and overcoming those obstacles which, in the shape
of erroneous ideas and customs, have blocked the way to their progress. I
have found this to be no hardship, but the natural and congenial vocation

of my life. I had hardly become a thinking being when I first learned to hate slavery, and hence I was no sooner free than I joined the noble band of Abolitionists in Massachusetts, headed by William Lloyd Garrison and Wendell Phillips. Afterward, by voice and pen, in season and out of season, it was mine to stand for the freedom of people of all colors, until in our land the last yoke was broken and the last bondsman was set free. In the war for the Union I persuaded the colored man to become a soldier. In the peace that followed, I asked the Government to make him a citizen. In the construction of the rebellious States I urged his enfranchisement.

Much has been written and published during the last ten years purporting to be a history of the anti-slavery movement and of the part taken by the men and women engaged in it, myself among the number. In some of these narrations I have received more consideration and higher estimation than I perhaps deserved. In others I have not escaped undeserved disparagement, which I may leave to the reader and to the judgment of those who shall come after me to reply to and to set right.

The anti-slavery movement, that truly great moral conflict which rocked the land during thirty years, and the part taken by the men and women engaged in it, are not quite far enough removed from us in point of time to admit at present of an impartial history. Some of the sects and parties that took part in it still linger with us and are zealous for distinction, for priority and superiority. There is also the disposition to unduly magnify the importance of some men and to diminish the importance of others. While over all this I spread the mantle of charity, it may in a measure explain whatever may seem like prejudice, bigotry and partiality in some attempts already made at the history of the anti-slavery movement. As in a great war, amid the roar of cannon, the smoke of powder, the rising dust and the blinding blaze of fire and counterfire of battle, no one participant may be blamed for not being able to see and correctly to measure and report the efficiency of the different forces engaged, and to render honor where honor is due; so we may say of the late historians who have essayed to write the history of the anti-slavery movement. It is not strange that those who write in New England from the stand occupied by William Lloyd Garrison and his friends, should fail to appreciate the services of the political abolitionists and of the Free Soil and Republican parties. Perhaps a political abolitionist would equally misjudge and underrate the value of the non-voting and moral-suasion party, of which Mr. Garrison was the admitted leader; while in fact the two were the halves necessary to make the whole. Without Adams, Giddings, Hale, Chase, Wade, Seward, Wilson and Sumner[4] to plead our cause in the councils of the nation, the taskmasters would have remained the contented and undisturbed rulers of the Union, and no condition of things would have been brought about authorizing the Federal Government to abolish slavery in the country's defense. As one of those whose bonds have been broken, I cannot see without pain any attempt to disparage and undervalue any man's work in this cause.

Hereafter, when we get a little farther away from the conflict, some brave

---

4. John Quincy Adams, Joshua R. Giddings, John Parker Hale, Salmon P. Chase, Benjamin F. Wade, William H. Seward, Henry Wilson, and Charles Sumner were leading figures in the American anti-slavery movement.

and truth-loving man, with all the facts before him, uninfluenced by filial love and veneration for men, or party associations, or pride of name, will gather from here and there the scattered fragments, my small contribution perhaps among the number, and give to those who shall come after us an impartial history of this the grandest moral conflict of the century. Truth is patient and time is just. With these and like reflections, which have often brought consolation to better men than myself, when upon them has fallen the keen edge of censure, and with the scrupulous justice done me in the biography of myself lately written by Mr. Frederick May Holland[5] of Concord, Massachusetts, I can easily rest contented.

1892

5. *Frederick Douglass, the Colored Orator* (1891).

JAMES M. WHITFIELD
1822–1871

Admired and endorsed by both Frederick Douglass and William Wells Brown, James M. Whitfield's talent and commitment to his people earned him lasting recognition as the standard bearer of black America's antislavery poets. Yet even in his own time Whitfield's achievement was often measured more by what he and others felt he could have attained than by what he actually did accomplish as a poet. Douglass was perhaps the first to declare Whitfield a disheartening example of genius shackled to an uninspiring job—that of barbering—that sapped the poet's energies and consumed his time while returning to him and his family only minimal support. Some of Whitfield's contemporaries thought the barber-poet had the potential to become another Edgar Allan Poe, the epitome of blighted genius among antebellum white American poets, or John Greenleaf Whittier, the leading white antislavery poet of the time. One might approach Whitfield as simply another candidate for the kind of romanticizing that Americans have often indulged in when considering their supposedly frustrated geniuses. But Whitfield deserves an introduction more in line with Langston Hughes's poetic self-characterization in *Me and the Mule*, which Hughes concludes by affirming, unapologetically, that like his mule he's "Black—and don't give a damn! / You got to take me / Like I am."

James M. Whitfield was born free in Exeter, New Hampshire, in 1822. He was working in a basement barber shop in Buffalo, New York, when Douglass first met him in 1850. From 1849 to 1852, readers of Douglass's newspapers, the *North Star* and *Frederick Douglass' Paper*, found Whitfield's impassioned antislavery poetry published on a regular basis. In 1853 Whitfield assembled the collection for which he is remembered, *America and Other Poems*, and saw it through to publication in Buffalo. The anonymous writer of the introduction to the volume, perhaps Whitfield himself, appealed to the buying public for support so that the poet might "fully develop the talent which God hath given him." Although *America and Other Poems* was well received, it did not compensate Whitfield sufficiently to enable him to leave his trade and devote himself full time to writing. But the collection did demonstrate the poet's craftsmanship, especially in his use of classical imagery, his high seriousness, and his distinctive powers of socially conscious invective. The title poem of the collection, the 160-line *America*, begins as a sardonic parody of a nationalistic hymn familiar to all Whitfield's countrymen and evolves into a systematic and trenchant analysis of the hypocrisies and lies that undergirded "slavery's accursed plan." Despite the moral outrage and bitterness of Whitfield's attack on slavery, however, *America* closes in the spirit of a prayer of supplication to a just God, the poet refusing to give in to the despair that tempts him to cynicism. Ironically, however, Whitfield has often been characterized as a cynical and pessimistic poet imitative of Byron in both the form and philosophy of his verse. Yet although Whitfield understood and could convincingly represent "this soul, long crushed and sad," his poem *Yes! Strike Again That Sounding String* articulates a counter-desire to find in poetry a way out of bleak self-absorption. The love poems and religious verse included in *America and Other Poems*, while fairly conventional, testify to Whitfield's determination to explore the full range of his art.

In 1854 Whitfield affiliated himself with Martin R. Delany, one of the foremost champions of black emigration, and helped to organize that year's National Emigration Convention. Later in the decade he is thought to have traveled in Central America as an emigration agent commissioned to search for likely settlement locales for African Americans disenchanted with the United States. The outbreak of the Civil War found Whitfield in San Francisco, where he worked at his trade and wrote occasional poems for the *San Francisco Elevator*, an African American newspaper, until 1870. Although his last poems notably softened the anger and bitterness that made his early verse so compelling, Whitfield remains nineteenth-century black America's best example of the poet as culture-hero, "wielding, with unfaltering arm, / The utmost power which God has given."

America

America, it is to thee,
Thou boasted land of liberty,—
It is to thee I raise my song,
Thou land of blood, and crime, and wrong.
It is to thee, my native land,   5
From whence has issued many a band
To tear the black man from his soil,
And force him here to delve and toil;
Chained on your blood-bemoistened sod,
Cringing beneath a tyrant's rod,   10
Stripped of those rights which Nature's God
    Bequeathed to all the human race,
Bound to a petty tyrant's nod,
    Because he wears a paler face.
Was it for this, that freedom's fires   15
Were kindled by your patriot sires?
Was it for this, they shed their blood,
On hill and plain, on field and flood?
Was it for this, that wealth and life
Were staked upon that desperate strife,   20
Which drenched this land for seven long years
With blood of men, and women's tears?
When black and white fought side by side,
    Upon the well-contested field,—
Turned back the fierce opposing tide,   25
    And made the proud invader yield—

When, wounded, side by side they lay,
   And heard with joy the proud hurrah
From their victorious comrades say
   That they had waged successful war,   30
The thought ne'er entered in their brains
That they endured those toils and pains,
To forge fresh fetters, heavier chains
For their own children, in whose veins
Should flow that patriotic blood,   35
So freely shed on field and flood.
Oh no; they fought, as they believed,
   For the inherent rights of man;
But mark, how they have been deceived
   By slavery's accursed plan.   40
They never thought, when thus they shed
   Their heart's best blood, in freedom's cause.
That their own sons would live in dread,
   Under unjust, oppressive laws:
That those who quietly enjoyed   45
   The rights for which they fought and fell,
Could be the framers of a code,
   That would disgrace the fiends of hell!
Could they have looked, with prophet's ken, [1]
   Down to the present evil time,   50
   Seen free-born men, uncharged with crime,
Consigned unto a slaver's pen,—
Or thrust into a prison cell,
With thieves and murderers to dwell—
While that same flag whose stripes and stars   55
Had been their guide through freedom's wars
As proudly waved above the pen
Of dealers in the souls of men!
Or could the shades [2] of all the dead,
   Who fell beneath that starry flag,   60
Visit the scenes where they once bled,
   On hill and plain, on vale and crag,
By peaceful brook, or ocean's strand,
   By inland lake, or dark green wood,
Where'er the soil of this wide land   65
   Was moistened by their patriot blood,—
And then survey the country o'er,
   From north to south, from east to west,
And hear the agonizing cry
Ascending up to God on high,   70
From western wilds to ocean's shore,
   The fervent prayer of the oppressed;
The cry of helpless infancy
   Torn from the parent's fond caress
By some base tool of tyranny,   75
   And doomed to woe and wretchedness;

1. Knowledge.   2. Spirits.

The indignant wail of fiery youth,
　　Its noble aspirations crushed,
Its generous zeal, its love of truth,
　　Trampled by tyrants in the dust;   80
The aerial piles which fancy reared,
　　And hopes too bright to be enjoyed,
Have passed and left his young heart scared,
　　And all its dreams of bliss destroyed.
The shriek of virgin purity,   85
　　Doomed to some libertine's embrace,
Should rouse the strongest sympathy
　　Of each one of the human race;
And weak old age, oppressed with care,
　　As he reviews the scene of strife,   90
Puts up to God a fervent prayer,
　　To close his dark and troubled life.
The cry of fathers, mothers, wives,
　　Severed from all their hearts hold dear,
And doomed to spend their wretched lives   95
　　In gloom, and doubt, and hate, and fear;
And manhood, too, with soul of fire,
And arm of strength, and smothered ire,
Stands pondering with brow of gloom,
Upon his dark unhappy doom,   100
Whether to plunge in battle's strife,
And buy his freedom with his life,
And with stout heart and weapon strong,
Pay back the tyrant wrong for wrong,
Or wait the promised time of God,   105
　　When his Almighty ire shall wake,
And smite the oppressor in his wrath,
And hurl red ruin in his path,
And with the terrors of his rod,
　　Cause adamantine [3] hearts to quake.   110
Here Christian writhes in bondage still,
　　Beneath his brother Christian's rod,
And pastors trample down at will,
　　The image of the living God.
While prayers go up in lofty strains,   115
　　And pealing hymns ascend to heaven,
The captive, toiling in his chains,
　　With tortured limbs and bosom riven,
Raises his fettered hand on high,
　　And in the accents of despair,   120
To him who rules both earth and sky,
　　Puts up a sad, a fervent prayer,
To free him from the awful blast
　　Of slavery's bitter galling shame—
Although his portion should be cast   125
　　With demons in eternal flame!

3. Unyielding.

Almighty God! 'tis this they call
   The land of liberty and law;
Part of its sons in baser thrall
   Than Babylon [4] or Egypt saw—   130
Worse scenes of rapine, lust and shame,
   Than Babylonian ever knew,
Are perpetrated in the name
   Of God, the holy, just, and true;
And darker doom than Egypt felt, [5]   135
May yet repay this nation's guilt.
Almighty God! thy aid impart,
And fire anew each faltering heart,
And strengthen every patriot's hand,
Who aims to save our native land.   140
We do not come before thy throne,
   With carnal weapons drenched in gore,
Although our blood has freely flown,
   In adding to the tyrant's store.
Father! before thy throne we come,   145
   Not in the panoply of war,
With pealing trump, and rolling drum,
   And cannon booming loud and far;
Striving in blood to wash out blood,
   Through wrong to seek redress for wrong;   150
For while thou'rt holy, just and good,
   The battle is not to the strong;
But in the sacred name of peace,
   Of justice, virtue, love and truth,
We pray, and never mean to cease,   155
   Till weak old age and fiery youth
In freedom's cause their voices raise,
And burst the bonds of every slave;
Till, north and south, and east and west,
The wrongs we bear shall be redressed.   160

                             1853

Yes! Strike Again That Sounding String

Yes! strike again that sounding string,
   And let the wildest numbers roll;
Thy song of fiercest passion sing—
   It breathes responsive to my soul!

A soul, whose gentlest hours were nursed,   5
   In stern adversity's dark way,
And o'er whose pathway never burst
   One gleam of hope's enlivening ray.

4. Ancient city of Mesopotamia and center of an empire that flourished in the 6th century B.C.
5. A reference to the plagues described in Exodus 7–12 suffered by Egypt because of its resistance to the liberation of the Jews.

If thou wouldst soothe my burning brain,
   Sing not to me of joy and gladness;   10
'Twill but increase the raging pain,
   And turn the fever into madness.

Sing not to me of landscapes bright,
   Of fragrant flowers and fruitful trees—
Of azure skies and mellow light,   15
   Or whisperings of the gentle breeze;

But tell me of the tempest roaring
   Across the angry foaming deep,
Or torrents from the mountains pouring
   Down precipices dark and steep.   20

Sing of the lightning's lurid flash,
   The ocean's roar, the howling storm,
The earthquake's shock, the thunder's crash,
   Where ghastly terrors teeming swarm.

Sing of the battle's deadly strife,   25
   The ruthless march of war and pillage,
The awful waste of human life,
   The plundered town, the burning village!

Of streets with human gore made red,
   Of priests upon the altar slain;   30
The scenes of rapine, woe and dread,
   That fill the warrior's horrid train.

Thy song may then an echo wake,
   Deep in this soul, long crushed and sad,
The direful impressions shake   35
   Which threaten now to drive it mad.

                                 1853

Self-Reliance

I love the man whose lofty mind
   On God and its own strength relies;
Who seeks the welfare of his kind,
   And dare be honest though he dies;
Who cares not for the world's applause,   5
   But, to his own fixed purpose true,
The path which God and nature's laws
   Point out, doth earnestly pursue.
When adverse clouds around him lower,
   And stern oppression bars his way,   10
When friends desert in trial's hour,
   And hope sheds but a feeble ray;

When all the powers of earth and hell
   Combine to break his spirit down,
And strive, with their terrific yell,   15
   To crush his soul beneath their frown—
When numerous friends, whose cheerful tone
   In happier hours once cheered him on,
With visions that full brightly shone,
   But now, alas! are dimmed and gone!   20
When love, which in his bosom burned
   With all the fire of ardent youth,
And which he fondly thought returned
   With equal purity and truth,
Mocking his hopes, falls to the ground,   25
   Like some false vision of the night,
Its vows a hollow, empty sound,
   Scathing his heart with deadly blight,
Choking that welling spring of love,
Which lifts the soul to God above,   30
In bonds mysterious to unite
The finite with the infinite;
And draw a blessing from above,
Of infinite on finite love.
When hopes of better, fear of worse,   35
   Alike are fled, and naught remains
To stimulate him on his course:
   No hope of bliss, no fear of pains
Fiercer than what already rend,
   With tortures keen, his inmost heart,   40
Without a hope, without a friend,
   With nothing to allay the smart
From blighted love, affections broken,
   From blasted hopes and cankering care,
When every thought, each word that's spoken   45
   Urges him onward to despair.
When through the opening vista round,
   Shines on him no pellucid[1] ray,
Like beam of early morning found,
   The harbinger of perfect day;   50
But like the midnight's darkening frown,
   When stormy tempests rear on high,
When pealing thunder shakes the ground,
   And lurid lightning rends the sky!
When clothed in more than midnight gloom,   55
Like some foul specter from the tomb,
Despair, with stern and fell control,
Sits brooding o'er his inmost soul—
'Tis then the faithful mind is proved,
   That, true alike to man and God,   60
By all the ills of life unmoved,
   Pursues its straight and narrow road.

---

1. Transparent.

For such a man the siren song
   Of pleasure hath no lasting charm;
Nor can the mighty and the strong   65
   His spirit tame with powerful arm.
His pleasure is to wipe the tear
   Of sorrow from the mourner's cheek,
The languid, fainting heart to cheer,
   To succor and protect the weak.   70
When the bright face of fortune smiles
   Upon his path with cheering ray,
And pleasure, with alluring wiles,
   Flatters, to lead his heart astray,
His soul in conscious virtue strong,   75
   And armed with innate rectitude,
Loving the right, detesting wrong,
   And seeking the eternal good
Of all alike, the high or low,
His dearest friend, or direst foe,   80
Seeks out the brave and faithful few,
Who, to themselves and Maker true,
Dare, in the name and fear of God,
To spread the living truth abroad!
Armed with the same sustaining power,   85
Against adversity's dark hour,
And from the deep deceitful guile
Which lurks in pleasure's hollow smile,
Or from the false and fitful beam
   That marks ambition's meteor fire,   90
Or from the dark and lurid gleam
   Revealing passion's deadly ire.
His steadfast soul fearing no harm,
   But trusting in the aid of Heaven,
And wielding, with unfaltering arm,   95
   The utmost power which God has given—
Conscious that the Almighty power
   Will nerve the faithful soul with might,
Whatever storms may round him lower,
   Strikes boldly for the true and right.   100

1853

FRANCES E. W. HARPER

1825–1911

Author of four novels, several volumes of poetry, and numerous stories, poems, essays and letters, Frances Ellen Watkins Harper was one of the most prolific and popular African American writers prior to the twentieth century. Like that of her contemporaries William Wells Brown, Frederick Douglass, John Greenleaf Whittier, Harriet Beecher Stowe, and Harriet Jacobs, Harper's life and literature were inseparably entwined. Local and national newspapers regularly noted her activities and advertised her lecture tours. Histories such as Brown's *The Rising Son; or, The*

Antecedents and Advances of the Colored Race (1873) and Phebe A. Hanaford's *Daughters of America; or, Women of the Century* (1883) routinely referred to her accomplishments. Many African American women's service clubs named themselves in her honor, and across the nation, in cities such as St. Louis, St. Paul, and Pittsburgh, F. E. W. Harper Leagues and Frances E. Harper Women's Christian Temperance Unions thrived well into the twentieth century.

Harper was born Frances Ellen Watkins to free parents on September 24, 1825, in Baltimore, Maryland, then a slave state. By the age of three, she was orphaned and living with relatives, most likely her uncle, William Watkins, and his large, close-knit family. A deeply religious and politically active man, Watkins was a writer, educator, and minister. Harper received an uncommonly thorough education at her uncle's school, where she showed promise in writing and elocution, a strong interest in radical politics and religion, and a special sense of responsibility and devotion to lofty ideals.

As with all but the most privileged students, Harper left school at an early age to work in domestic service. Even so, around 1845 Harper reportedly published a small collection of poems called *Forest Leaves* (no copy is known to have survived). About five years later, she was hired as the first female teacher at the Union Seminary, a school newly established by the African Methodist Episcopal Church near Columbus, Ohio. The next year she took another teaching position, this time in Little York, Pennsylvania. Her frequent encounters with fugitive slaves and her own refugee status (the result of a Maryland law that made it a crime, punishable by enslavement, for a free black person to enter the state) moved her toward more direct political involvement. Around 1853 she quit teaching and moved to Philadelphia to devote herself to the antislavery movement.

The 1853 publication of *Eliza Harris*, one of many responses to Harriet Beecher Stowe's vastly popular *Uncle Tom's Cabin*, brought Harper national attention. Frederick Douglass often prefaced Harper's poems with flattering remarks about her lectures and recommendations of her books. William Lloyd Garrison also regularly allocated space in the *Liberator* for her writings and notices of her activities.

After Harper was hired by the Maine Anti-Slavery Society, her schedule was grueling. In the first six weeks of fall 1854, Harper traveled to twenty cities and gave at least thirty-one lectures. Yet she managed to find time to write and publish poems, essays, and letters. In 1854 her book *Poems on Miscellaneous Subjects*, a collection of poems and essays prefaced by William Lloyd Garrison, was published both in Boston and in Philadelphia. *Poems* was an immediate success, selling more than ten thousand copies and meriting reprinting in an enlarged version within three years. During Harper's lifetime the collection was reprinted at least twenty times.

Poems on Miscellaneous Subjects includes several of the works for which Harper is most famous today, poems that are generally agreed to have ushered in the tradition of African American protest poetry. A classic example is *The Slave Mother*, which focuses on the separation of families and the devastating pain that women, in particular, suffered in bondage. The works in *Poems* address the need to end slavery and the importance of Christian living, civil rights, and racial pride, ideals that Harper advocated throughout her long career.

Although Harper was often characterized as "a noble Christian woman" and "one of the most scholarly and well-read women of her day," she did not shy away from difficult daily work. Her position with the Maine Anti-Slavery Society took her to parts of Canada and most of New England. The ordinary difficulties of prerailroad travel were compounded by the danger posed to abolitionists by slavery advocates and by those opposed to both women and African Americans speaking publicly. Despite these circumstances, Harper next signed on as an agent and lecturer for the Pennsylvania Society for Promoting the Abolition of Slavery and proceeded on a series of tours across the old Northwest.

As the repressive measures against blacks, especially slaves, increased, Harper's writings became increasingly militant. When a group of armed men led by John Brown stormed the arsenal at Harpers Ferry, West Virginia, in October 1859, Harper gathered support for the captured men and their families. She wrote letters, one of which is anthologized here, and joined efforts to raise money for the families of the jailed men. "It is not enough to express our sympathy by words," she wrote; "we should be ready to crystallize it into actions." It is also likely that she violated the Fugitive Slave Law herself by accompanying runaway slaves along the Underground Railroad.

In 1859 Harper published in the newly created *Anglo-American Magazine* several pieces, including *The Two Offers* and *Our Greatest Want*. *The Two Offers* argues against social complacency and asserts that marriage is but one option for a woman of intelligence and social conscience. *Our Greatest Want* argues that acquisition of material wealth was necessary for African Americans but that their development as "true men and true women" was a higher priority. As in several earlier poems, Harper emphasizes the importance of personal faith and self-discipline.

In November 1860, Frances Watkins married Fenton Harper, a widower with three children, and moved to a farm near Columbus, Ohio. The Harpers had one child, Mary. Despite the demands of family life, Frances Harper still found time for occasional lectures and publications. When Fenton Harper died in 1864, creditors claimed their property and most of their belongings. To support her family, the widowed mother returned to the lecture circuit, where she soon met large and receptive audiences. Shortly thereafter, Harper joined Frederick Douglass, Robert and Harriet Purvis, Sojourner Truth, Susan B. Anthony, Lucretia Mott, and Elizabeth Cady Stanton in the newly founded American Equal Rights Association. But Harper's equal rights advocacy was complicated by the racism of her feminist colleagues and the sexism of some of her black brothers. During the debate over the Fifteenth Amendment to the Constitution, this group divided over support for black men's suffrage or votes for white women. Harper, then and later, often assumed the role of mediator between sometimes naive, often competitive, and frequently hostile sectors. "We are all bound up together in one great bundle of humanity," she repeatedly admonished.

After the Civil War, educated northern women from many racial backgrounds traveled into the South to teach and to provide other social services for the newly freed slaves. From 1866 to 1871, Harper crossed and recrossed the South, teaching and lecturing to southern audiences and recording her impressions for northern readers. In her lectures, Harper argued that the future of the nation depended upon the ability of its citizens to unite behind a common goal. "Between the white people and the colored there is a community of interests," she asserted, "and the sooner they find it out, the better it will be for both parties." Her other theme, and the one that increasingly dominated her published writings, was that Emancipation had opened a new era, a time for blacks, particularly black women, to "consecrate their lives to the work of upbuilding the race." Her first serialized novel, *Minnie's Sacrifice* (1869), advocated this type of personal commitment and devotion to higher ideals.

Harper published three collections of poetry during the decade following Emancipation. *Moses: A Story of the Nile* (1869), approximately seven hundred lines of free verse, is a remarkable departure from Harper's typical four-line, rhymed stanzas. Here Harper uses an especially common African American trope for the slave experience, the enslavement of the Hebrews in Egypt, to create an example of personal sacrifice. Two years later Harper published *Poems* (1871), which explores themes similar to those of *Poems on Miscellaneous Subjects* now updated for a new era. From the horrific and unnatural experiences of slavery, her poems turn to the redemptive suffering of divinely ordained separations and establish a Reconstruction ideal of heroic effort, sacrifice, and courage rewarded, striking a more hopeful tone than in the earlier collection.

The following year Harper published *Sketches of Southern Life,* a significant marker in African American literature as well as in Harper's career. Unlike the slave narratives and much of Harper's antebellum writings, *Sketches* treats slavery as a literary construct. The heart of this volume is a series of six poems, narrated by Aunt Chloe, that form at once the autobiography of a former slave and an oral history of slavery and Reconstruction. Aunt Chloe may well prove to be Harper's most important contribution to American letters. Although she is sixty years old, Aunt Chloe learns to read, takes an active interest in politics (though she cannot vote), and does what she can to ensure that the men "voted clean." She helps build schools and churches for the community, and she works to buy herself a cabin, which she enlarges to accommodate her children after they are reunited.

Sometime around 1871 Harper settled in Philadelphia, where she continued to interweave her literary production with her political commitment. In 1873 Harper began a newspaper column (first named *Fancy Etchings,* then *Fancy Sketches*) that discussed contemporary issues, moral dilemmas, and aesthetics through the conversations and activities of Jenny, a recent college graduate who wants to be a poet; her Aunt Jane, who encourages her to use her talent to improve society; and a variety of other fictitious characters. Later, other African American writers including Olivia Ward Bush-Banks and Langston Hughes created similar series. Two of her next three novels, *Sowing and Reaping: A Temperance Story* (1876) and *Trial and Triumph* (1888–89), as well as numerous essays and poems, deal with temperance, now one of her top priorities. *Trial* is also one of Harper's most obvious attempts to combat the mythology of the chivalrous South, the happy slave, and the treacherous free black then being created by plantation school literature. *Iola Leroy* (1892), Harper's best-known novel, builds on both her own corrective work in *Trial* and the methods, characters, and plots of earlier African American novels. Although Iola is superficially similar to the figure of the tragic mulatta, she is not a suffering victim. In addition, Harper pairs her mulatto characters with "pure African" counterparts who are generally superior to their noble and accomplished lighter-skinned friends. Further extending the conventions of earlier African American fiction, Harper includes several folk characters whose intelligence, dedication, and resourcefulness are models for the emerging black middle class.

After *Iola Leroy,* Harper published at least five collections of poetry. Even in her seventies, Harper continued to be active, working with the National Council of Women, the Universal Peace Union, the Women's Christian Temperance Union, and other organizations, and writing essays and poems for their journals. In 1892 she addressed the Women's Congress at the Columbian Exposition, one of a handful of black women to do so. In 1896, she took part in founding the National Association of Colored Women, for which she served as vice president and as consultant for several years.

Harper died on February 20, 1911. During her career, Harper worked in virtually every literary genre available to her. Although she appreciated beauty and enjoyed the honors she received, she believed that literature which could not be used to represent, to reprimand, and to revise was useless. Born during slavery, Harper was buried during the period that historians now refer to as the nadir of American race relations. Through it all she combined pragmatic idealism, courageous action, and lyrical words to dispel the shadows and usher in what she knew would be brighter coming days.

Ethiopia [1]

Yes! Ethiopia yet shall stretch
   Her bleeding hands abroad;
Her cry of agony shall reach
   The burning throne of God. [2]

The tyrant's yoke from off her neck,   5
   His fetters from her soul,
The mighty hand of God shall break,
   And spurn the base control.

Redeemed from dust and freed from chains,
   Her sons shall lift their eyes;   10
From cloud-capt hills and verdant plains
   Shall shouts of triumph rise.

Upon her dark, despairing brow,
   Shall play a smile of peace;
For God shall bend unto her wo,   15
   And bid her sorrows cease.

'Neath sheltering vines and stately palms
   Shall laughing children play,
And aged sires with joyous psalms
   Shall gladden every day.   20

Secure by night, and blest by day,
   Shall pass her happy hours;
Nor human tigers hunt for prey
   Within her peaceful bowers.

Then, Ethiopia! stretch, oh! stretch   25
   Thy bleeding hands abroad;
Thy cry of agony shall reach
   And find redress from God.

1853?

Eliza Harris [1]

Like a fawn from the arrow, startled and wild,
A woman swept by us, bearing a child;

---

1. If Kletzing and Crogman (*Progress of a Race; or, The Remarkable Advancement of the Afro-American*, 1897) are correct, this poem was published before 1853 and is Harper's earliest extant poem. The poem also appears in *Frederick Douglass' Paper*, March 31, 1854, and in *Poems on Miscellaneous Subjects* (1854). In the 19th century, the term *Ethiopia* was often considered to be synonymous with "black Africa."
2. An allusion to Psalm 68:31–35. Psalm 68 was often quoted and revised in 19th-century African American literature.

1. Versions of this poem appeared in the *Liberator* on December 16, 1853, and in *Frederick Douglass' Paper* on December 23, 1853. There are references that cite an even earlier publication in the *Alienated American*. Stanzas 11 and 12, reprinted here from the *Liberator*, were included in the early versions but not in *Poems on Miscellaneous Subjects*. Both the *Liberator* and *Frederick Douglass' Paper* reprinted *Eliza Harris* in 1860. Like Harriet Beecher Stowe in *Uncle Tom's Cabin* and other writers of that time, Harper based her poem on a recent incident that occurred in Cincinnati, Ohio.

In her eye was the night of a settled despair,
And her brow was o'ershaded with anguish and care.

She was nearing the river—in reaching the brink,   5
She heeded no danger, she paused not to think!
For she is a mother—her child is a slave—
And she'll give him his freedom, or find him a grave!

It was a vision to haunt us, that innocent face—
So pale in its aspect, so fair in its grace;   10
As the tramp of the horse and the bay of the hound,
With the fetters that gall, were trailing the ground!

She was nerv'd by despair, and strengthened by woe,
As she leap'd o'er the chasms that yawn'd from below;
Death howl'd in the tempest, and rav'd in the blast,   15
But she heard not the sound till the danger was past.

Oh! how shall I speak of my proud country's shame?
Of the stains on her glory, how give them their name?
How say that her banner in mockery waves—
Her "star spangled banner"—o'er millions of slaves?   20

How say that the lawless may torture and chase
A woman whose crime is the hue of her face?
How the depths of the forest may echo around
With the shrieks of despair, and the bay of the hound?

With her step on the ice, and her arm on her child,   25
The danger was fearful, the pathway was wild;
But, aided by Heaven, she gained a free shore,
Where the friends of humanity open'd their door.

So fragile and lovely, so fearfully pale,
Like a lily that bends to the breath of the gale,   30
Save the heave of her breast, and the sway of her hair,
You'd have thought her a statue of fear and despair.

In agony close to her bosom she press'd
The life of her heart, the child of her breast:—
Oh! love from its tenderness gathering might,   35
Had strengthen'd her soul for the dangers of flight.

But she's free—yes, free from the land where the slave
From the hand of oppression must rest in the grave;
Where bondage and torture, where scourges and chains,
Have plac'd on our banner indelible stains.   40

Did a fever e'er burning through bosom and brain,
Send a lava-like flood through every vein,
Till it suddenly cooled 'neath a healing spell,
And you knew, oh! the joy! you knew you were well?

So felt this young mother, as a sense of the rest   45
Stole gently and sweetly o'er *her* weary breast,
As her boy looked up, and, wondering, smiled
On the mother whose love had freed her child.

The bloodhounds have miss'd the scent of her way;
The hunter is rifled and foil'd of his prey;   50
Fierce jargon and cursing, with clanking of chains,
Make sounds of strange discord on Liberty's plains.

With the rapture love and fulness of bliss,
She plac'd on his brow a mother's fond kiss:—
Oh! poverty, danger and death she can brave,   55
For the child of her love is no longer a slave!

                                            1853

The Slave Mother

Heard you that shriek? It rose
     So wildly on the air,
It seemed as if a burden'd heart
     Was breaking in despair.

Saw you those hands so sadly clasped—   5
     The bowed and feeble head—
The shuddering of that fragile form—
     That look of grief and dread?

Saw you the sad, imploring eye?
     Its every glance was pain,   10
As if a storm of agony
     Were sweeping through the brain.

She is a mother, pale with fear,
     Her boy clings to her side,
And in her kirtle[1] vainly tries   15
     His trembling form to hide.

He is not hers, although she bore
     For him a mother's pains;
He is not hers, although her blood
     Is coursing through his veins!   20

He is not hers, for cruel hands
     May rudely tear apart
The only wreath of household love
     That binds her breaking heart.

His love has been a joyous light   25
     That o'er her pathway smiled,

1. Loose gown.

A fountain gushing ever new,
   Amid life's desert wild.

His lightest word has been a tone
   Of music round her heart,   30
Their lives a streamlet blent in one—
   Oh, Father! must they part?

They tear him from her circling arms,
   Her last and fond embrace.
Oh! never more may her sad eyes   35
   Gaze on his mournful face.

No marvel, then, these bitter shrieks
   Disturb the listening air:
She is a mother, and her heart
   Is breaking in despair.   40

             1854

Vashti [1]

She leaned her head upon her hand
   And heard the king's decree—
"My lords are feasting in my halls,
   Bid Vashti come to me.

"I've shown the treasures of my house,   5
   My costly jewels rare,
But with the glory of her eyes
   No rubies can compare.

"Adorn'd and crown'd I'd have her come,
   With all her queenly grace,   10
And, 'mid my lords and mighty men,
   Unveil her lovely face.

"Each gem that sparkles in my crown,
   Or glitters on my throne,
Grows poor and pale when she appears,   15
   My beautiful, my own!"

All waiting stood the chamberlains
   To hear the Queen's reply,
They saw her cheek grow deathly pale,
   But light flash'd to her eye: 20

"Go, tell the King," she proudly said,
   "That I am Persia's [2] Queen,

1. This poem was published in *Poems* (1857) and
in the *New National Era* on September 22, 1870. It
is based on an incident described in Esther 1:13–

22.
2. Now Iran.

And by his crowds of merry men
   I never will be seen.

"I'll take the crown from off my head   25
   And tread it 'neath my feet
Before their rude and careless gaze
   My shrinking eyes shall meet.

"A queen unveil'd before the crowd!—
   Upon each lip my name!—   30
Why, Persia's women all would blush
   And weep for Vashti's shame!

"Go back!" she cried, and waived her hand,
   And grief was in her eye:
"Go, tell the King," she sadly said,   35
   "That I would rather die."

They brought her message to the King,
   Dark flash'd his angry eye;
'Twas as the lightning ere the storm
   Hath swept in fury by.   40

Then bitterly outspoke the King,
   Through purple lips of wrath—
"What shall be done to her who dares
   To cross your monarch's path?"

Then spake his wily counsellors—   45
   "O King of this fair land!
From distant Ind[3] to Ethiop,
   All bow to thy command.

"But if, before thy servants' eyes,
   This thing they plainly see,   50
That Vashti doth not heed thy will
   Nor yield herself to thee,

"The women, restive 'neath our rule,
   Would learn to scorn our name,
And from her deed to us would come   55
   Reproach and burning shame.

"Then, gracious King, sign with thy hand
   This stern but just decree,
That Vashti lay aside her crown,
   Thy Queen no more to be."   60

She heard again the King's command,
   And left her high estate,

3. I.e., India.

Strong in her earnest womanhood,
She calmly met her fate,

And left the palace of the King,   65
Proud of her spotless name—
A woman who could bend to grief,
But would not bow to shame.

1857

Bury Me in a Free Land [1]

Make me a grave where'er you will,
In a lowly plain or a lofty hill;
Make it among earth's humblest graves,
But not in a land where men are slaves.

I could not rest, if around my grave   5
I heard the steps of a trembling slave;
His shadow above my silent tomb
Would make it a place of fearful gloom.

I could not sleep, if I heard the tread
Of a coffle-gang to the shambles [2] led,   10
And the mother's shriek of wild despair
Rise, like a curse, on the trembling air.

I could not rest, if I saw the lash
Drinking her blood at each fearful gash;
And I saw her babes torn from her breast,   15
Like trembling doves from their parent nest.

I'd shudder and start, if I heard the bay
Of a bloodhound seizing his human prey;
And I heard the captive plead in vain,
As they bound, afresh, his galling [3] chain.   20

If I saw young girls from their mother's arms
Bartered and sold for their youthful charms,
My eye would flash with a mournful flame,
My death-pale cheek grow red with shame.

I would sleep, dear friends, where bloated Might   25
Can rob no man of his dearest right;
My rest shall be calm in any grave
Where none can call his brother a slave.

I ask no monument, proud and high,
To arrest the gaze of the passers by;   30

1. This poem was published in the *Liberator* on
January 14, 1864. Harper included a copy of this
poem in a letter she wrote to one of John Brown's
men who was awaiting execution for his part in the
raid on Harpers Ferry.
2. Slaughterhouse. "Coffle-gang": chained slaves.
3. Chafing, irritating.

All that my yearning spirit craves
Is—*Bury me not in a land of slaves!*

1864

Aunt Chloe's Politics

Of course, I don't know very much
  About these politics,
But I think that some who run 'em
  Do mighty ugly tricks.

I've seen 'em honey-fugle[1] round,   5
  And talk so awful sweet,
That you'd think them full of kindness,
  As an egg is full of meat.

Now I don't believe in looking
  Honest people in the face,   10
And saying when you're doing wrong,
  That "I haven't sold my race."[2]

When we want to school our children,
  If the money isn't there,
Whether black or white have took it,   15
  The loss we all must share.

And this buying up each other[3]
  Is something worse than mean,
Though I thinks a heap of voting,
  I go for voting clean.   20

1872

Learning to Read

Very soon the Yankee teachers
  Came down and set up school;
But, oh! how the Rebs[1] did hate it,—
  It was agin' their rule.

Our masters always tried to hide   5
  Book learning from our eyes;
Knowledge did'nt agree with slavery—
  'Twould make us all too wise.

But some of us would try to steal
  A little from the book,   10

1. Or honey fogle; act in an ingratiating manner so
as to deceive or cheat.
2. Betrayed one's own group or culture.

3. Paying someone to vote a certain way.
1. Rebel, or Confederate, forces during the Civil
War.

And put the words together,
    And learn by hook or crook.

I remember Uncle Caldwell,
    Who took pot-liquor[2] fat
And greased the pages of his book,   15
    And hid it in his hat.

And had his master ever seen
    The leaves upon his head,
He'd have thought them greasy papers,
    But nothing to be read.   20

And there was Mr. Turner's Ben,
    Who heard the children spell,
And picked the words right up by heart,
    And learned to read 'em well.

Well, the Northern folks kept sending   25
    The Yankee teachers down;
And they stood right up and helped us,
    Though Rebs did sneer and frown.

And, I longed to read my Bible,
    For precious words it said;   30
But when I begun to learn it,
    Folks just shook their heads,

And said there is no use trying,
    Oh! Chloe, you're too late;
But as I was rising sixty,   35
    I had no time to wait.

So I got a pair of glasses,
    And straight to work I went,
And never stopped till I could read
    The hymns and Testament.[3]   40

Then I got a little cabin—
    A place to call my own—
And I felt as independent
    As the queen upon her throne.

1872

A Double Standard

Do you blame me that I loved him?
    If when standing all alone
I cried for bread a careless world
    Pressed to my lips a stone.

2. Fatty broth from cooking meat and vegetables.   3. I.e., the Bible.

Do you blame me that I loved him,   5
    That my heart beat glad and free,
When he told me in the sweetest tones
    He loved but only me?

Can you blame me that I did not see
    Beneath his burning kiss   10
The serpent's wiles, nor even hear
    The deadly adder hiss?

Can you blame me that my heart grew cold
    That the tempted, tempter turned;
When he was feted and caressed   15
    And I was coldly spurned?

Would you blame him, when you draw from me
    Your dainty robes aside,
If he with gilded baits should claim
    Your fairest as his bride?   20

Would you blame the world if it should press
    On him a civic crown;
And see me struggling in the depth
    Then harshly press me down?

Crime has no sex and yet to-day   25
    I wear the brand of shame;
Whilst he amid the gay and proud
    Still bears an honored name.

Can you blame me if I've learned to think
    Your hate of vice a sham,　 30
When you so coldly crushed me down
    And then excused the man?

Would you blame me if to-morrow
    The coroner should say,
A wretched girl, outcast, forlorn,   35
    Has thrown her life away?

Yes, blame me for my downward course,
    But oh! remember well,
Within your homes you press the hand
    That led me down to hell.   40

I'm glad God's ways are not our ways,
    He does not see as man;
Within His love I know there's room
    For those whom others ban.

I think before His great white throne,   45
    His throne of spotless light,

That whited sepulchres[1] shall wear
  The hue of endless night.

That I who fell, and he who sinned,
  Shall reap as we have sown;   50
That each the burden of his loss
  Must bear and bear alone.

No golden weights can turn the scale
  Of justice in His sight;
And what is wrong in woman's life   55
  In man's cannot be right.

                              1895

Songs for the People

Let me make the songs for the people,
  Songs for the old and young;
Songs to stir like a battle-cry
  Wherever they are sung.

Not for the clashing of sabres,   5
  For carnage nor for strife;
But songs to thrill the hearts of men
  With more abundant life.

Let me make the songs for the weary,
  Amid life's fever and fret,   10
Till hearts shall relax their tension,
  And careworn brows forget.

Let me sing for little children,
  Before their footsteps stray,
Sweet anthems of love and duty,   15
  To float o'er life's highway.

I would sing for the poor and aged,
  When shadows dim their sight;
Of the bright and restful mansions,
  Where there shall be no night.   20

Our world, so worn and weary,
  Needs music, pure and strong,
To hush the jangle and discords
  Of sorrow, pain, and wrong.

Music to soothe all its sorrow,   25
  Till war and crime shall cease;

1. Crypts or tombs.

And the hearts of men grown tender
    Girdle the world with peace.

1895

An Appeal to My Country Women

You can sigh o'er the sad-eyed Armenian
    Who weeps in her desolate home.
You can mourn o'er the exile of Russia
    From kindred and friends doomed to roam.

You can pity the men who have woven   5
    From passion and appetite chains
To coil with a terrible tension
    Around their heartstrings and brains.

You can sorrow o'er little children
    Disinherited from their birth,   10
The wee waifs and toddlers neglected,
    Robbed of sunshine, music and mirth.

For beasts you have gentle compassion;
    Your mercy and pity they share.
For the wretched, outcast and fallen   15
    You have tenderness, love and care.

But hark! from our Southland are floating
    Sobs of anguish, murmurs of pain,
And women heart-stricken are weeping
    Over their tortured and their slain.   20

On their brows the sun has left traces;
    Shrink not from their sorrow in scorn.
When they entered the threshold of being
    The children of a King were born.

Each comes as a guest to the table   25
    The hands of our God has outspread,
To fountains that ever leap upward,
    To share in the soil we all tread.

When we plead for the wrecked and fallen,
    The exile from far-distant shores,   30
Remember that men are still wasting
    Life's crimson around our own doors.

Have ye not, oh, my favored sisters,
    Just a plea, a prayer or a tear,
For mothers who dwell 'neath the shadows   35
    Of agony, hatred and fear?

Men may tread down the poor and lowly,
    May crush them in anger and hate,
But surely the mills of God's justice
    Will grind out the grist of their fate.   40

Oh, people sin-laden and guilty,
    So lusty and proud in your prime,
The sharp sickles of God's retribution
    Will gather your harvest of crime.

Weep not, oh my well-sheltered sisters,   45
    Weep not for the Negro alone,
But weep for your sons who must gather
    The crops which their fathers have sown.

Go read on the tombstones of nations
    Of chieftains who masterful trod,   50
The sentence which time has engraven,
    That they had forgotten their God.

'Tis the judgment of God that men reap
    The tares[1] which in madness they sow,
Sorrow follows the footsteps of crime,   55
    And Sin is the consort of Woe.

            1900

The Two Offers

"What is the matter with you, Laura, this morning? I have been watching you this hour, and in that time you have commenced a half dozen letters and torn them all up. What matter of such grave moment is puzzling your dear little head, that you do not know how to decide?"

"Well, it is an important matter: I have two offers for marriage, and I do not know which to choose."

"I should accept neither, or to say the least, not at present."

"Why not?"

"Because I think a woman who is undecided between two offers, has not love enough for either to make a choice; and in that very hesitation, indecision, she has a reason to pause and seriously reflect, lest her marriage, instead of being an affinity of souls or a union of hearts, should only be a mere matter of bargain and sale, or an affair of convenience and selfish interest."

"But I consider them both very good offers, just such as many a girl would gladly receive. But to tell you the truth, I do not think that I regard either as a woman should the man she chooses for her husband. But then if I refuse, there is the risk of being an old maid, and that is not to be thought of."

"Well, suppose there is, is that the most dreadful fate that can befall a

---

1. Plants, especially noxious weeds.

woman? Is there not more intense wretchedness in an ill-assorted marriage—more utter loneliness in a loveless home, than in the lot of the old maid who accepts her earthly mission as a gift from God, and strives to walk the path of life with earnest and unfaltering steps?"

"Oh! what a little preacher you are. I really believe that you were cut out for an old maid; that when nature formed you, she put in a double portion of intellect to make up for a deficiency of love; and yet you are kind and affectionate. But I do not think that you know anything of the grand, overmastering passion, or the deep necessity of woman's heart for loving."

"Do you think so?" resumed the first speaker; and bending over her work she quietly applied herself to the knitting that had lain neglected by her side, during this brief conversation; but as she did so, a shadow flitted over her pale and intellectual brow, a mist gathered in her eyes, and a slight quivering of the lips, revealed a depth of feeling to which her companion was a stranger.

But before I proceed with my story, let me give you a slight history of the speakers. They were cousins, who had met life under different auspices. Laura Lagrange, was the only daughter of rich and indulgent parents, who had spared no pains to make her an accomplished lady. Her cousin, Janette Alston, was the child of parents, rich only in goodness and affection. Her father had been unfortunate in business, and dying before he could retrieve his fortunes, left his business in an embarrassed state. His widow was unacquainted with his business affairs, and when the estate was settled, hungry creditors had brought their claims and the lawyers had received their fees, she found herself homeless and almost penniless, and she who had been sheltered in the warm clasp of loving arms, found them too powerless to shield her from the pitiless pelting storms of adversity. Year after year she struggled with poverty and wrestled with want, till her toil-worn hands became too feeble to hold the shattered chords of existence, and her tear-dimmed eyes grew heavy with the slumber of death. Her daughter had watched over her with untiring devotion, had closed her eyes in death, and gone out into the busy, restless world, missing a precious tone from the voices of earth, a beloved step from the paths of life. Too self reliant to depend on the charity of relations, she endeavored to support herself by her own exertions, and she had succeeded. Her path for a while was marked with struggle and trial, but instead of uselessly repining, she met them bravely, and her life became not a thing of ease and indulgence, but of conquest, victory, and accomplishments. At the time when this conversation took place, the deep trials of her life had passed away. The achievements of her genius had won her a position in the literary world, where she shone as one of its bright particular stars. And with her fame came a competence of worldly means, which gave her leisure for improvement, and the riper development of her rare talents. And she, that pale intellectual woman, whose genius gave life and vivacity to the social circle, and whose presence threw a halo of beauty and grace around the charmed atmosphere in which she moved, had at one period of her life, known the mystic and solemn strength of an all-absorbing love. Years faded into the misty past, had seen the kindling of her eye, the quick flushing of her cheek, and the wild throbbing of her heart, at tones of a voice long since hushed to the stillness of death. Deeply, wildly, passionately, she had loved. Her whole life seemed like the pouring out of rich, warm and gushing affections. This love quickened her talents, inspired her genius, and threw over her life a tender and spiritual earnestness. And then came a fearful shock, a mournful waking from that "dream of beauty and delight." A shadow fell around her path; it came between her and the object of her heart's worship; first a few cold words, estrangement, and then a painful separation; the old story of woman's pride—digging the sepulchre of her happiness, and then a new-made grave, and her path over it to the spirit world; and thus faded out from that young heart her bright, brief and saddened dream of life. Faint and spirit-broken, she turned from the scenes associated with the memory of the loved and lost. She tried to break the chain of sad associations that bound her to the mournful past; and so, pressing back the bitter sobs from her almost breaking heart, like the dying dolphin, whose beauty is born of its death anguish, her genius gathered strength from suffering and wonderous power and brilliancy from the agony she hid within the desolate chambers of her soul. Men hailed her as one of earth's strangely gifted children, and wreathed the garlands of fame for her brow, when it was throbbing with a wild and fearful unrest. They breathed her name with applause, when through the lonely halls of her stricken spirit, was an earnest cry for peace, a deep yearning for sympathy and heart-support.

But life, with its stern realities, met her; its solemn responsibilities confronted her, and turning, with an earnest and shattered spirit, to life's duties and trials, she found a calmness and strength that she had only imagined in her dreams of poetry and song. We will now pass over a period of ten years, and the cousins have met again. In that calm and lovely woman, in whose eyes is a depth of tenderness, tempering the flashes of her genius, whose looks and tones are full of sympathy and love, we recognize the once smitten and stricken Janette Alston. The bloom of her girlhood had given way to a higher type of spiritual beauty, as if some unseen hand had been polishing and refining the temple in which her lovely spirit found its habitation; and this had been the fact. Her inner life had grown beautiful, and it was this that was constantly developing the outer. Never, in the early flush of womanhood, when an absorbing love had lit up her eyes and glowed in her life, had she appeared so interesting as when, with a countenance which seemed overshadowed with a spiritual light, she bent over the deathbed of a young woman, just lingering at the shadowy gates of the unseen land.

"Has he come?" faintly but eagerly exclaimed the dying woman. "Oh! how I have longed for his coming, and even in death he forgets me."

"Oh, do not say so, dear Laura, some accident may have detained him," said Janette to her cousin; for on that bed, from whence she will never rise, lies the once-beautiful and light-hearted Laura Lagrange, the brightness of whose eyes has long since been dimmed with tears, and whose voice had become like a harp whose every chord is tuned to sadness—whose faintest thrill and loudest vibrations are but the variations of agony. A heavy hand was laid upon her once warm and bounding heart, and a voice came whispering through her soul, that she must die. But, to her, the tidings was a message of deliverance—a voice, hushing her wild sorrows to the calmness of resignation and hope. Life had grown so weary upon her head—the future looked so hopeless—she had no wish to tread again the track where thorns had pierced her feet, and clouds overcast her sky; and she hailed the coming of death's angel as the footsteps of a welcome friend. And yet, earth had one object so very dear to her weary heart. It was her absent and recreant husband; for, since that conversation, she had accepted one of her offers, and become a wife. But, before she married, she learned that great lesson of human experience and woman's life, to love the man who bowed at her shrine, a willing worshipper. He had a pleasing address, raven hair, flashing eyes, a voice of thrilling sweetness, and lips of persuasive eloquence; and being well versed in the ways of the world, he won his way to her heart, and she became his bride, and he was proud of his prize. Vain and superficial in his character, he looked upon marriage not as a divine sacrament for the soul's development and human progression, but as the title-deed that gave him possession of the woman he thought he loved. But alas for her, the laxity of his principles had rendered him unworthy of the deep and undying devotion of a pure-hearted woman; but, for awhile, he hid from her his true character, and she blindly loved him, and for a short period was happy in the consciousness of being beloved; though sometimes a vague unrest would fill her soul, when, overflowing with a sense of the good, the beautiful, and the true, she would turn to him, but find no response to the deep yearnings of her soul—no appreciation of life's highest realities—its solemn grandeur and significant importance. Their souls never met, and soon she found a void in her bosom, that his earth-born love could not fill. He did not satisfy the wants of her mental and moral nature—between him and her there was no affinity of minds, no intercommunion of souls.

Talk as you will of woman's deep capacity for loving, of the strength of her affectional nature. I do not deny it; but will the mere possession of any human love, fully satisfy all the demands of her whole being? You may paint her in poetry or fiction, as a frail vine, clinging to her brother man for support, and dying when deprived of it; and all this may sound well enough to please the imaginations of school-girls, or love-lorn maidens. But woman—the true woman—if you would render her happy, it needs more than the mere development of her affectional nature. Her conscience should be enlightened, her faith in the true and right established, and scope given to her Heaven-endowed and God-given faculties. The true aim of female education should be, not a development of one or two, but all the faculties of the human soul, because no perfect womanhood is developed by imperfect culture. Intense love is often akin to intense suffering, and to trust the whole wealth of a woman's nature on the frail bark of human love, may often be like trusting a cargo of gold and precious gems, to a bark that has never battled with the storm, or buffetted the waves. Is it any wonder, then, that so many life-barks go down, paving the ocean of time with precious hearts and wasted hopes? that so many float around us, shattered and dismasted wrecks? that so many are stranded on the shoals of existence, mournful beacons and solemn warnings for the thoughtless, to whom marriage is a careless and hasty rushing together of the affections? Alas that an institution so fraught with good for humanity should be so perverted, and that state of life, which should be filled with happiness, become so replete with misery. And this was the fate of Laura Lagrange. For a brief period after her marriage her life seemed like a bright and beautiful dream, full of hope and radiant with joy. And then there came a change—he found other attractions that lay beyond the pale of home influences. The gambling saloon had power to win him from her side, he had lived in an element of unhealthy and unhallowed excitements, and the society of a loving wife, the pleasures of a well-regulated home, were enjoyments too tame for one who had vitiated his tastes by the pleasures of sin. There were charmed houses of vice, built upon dead men's loves, where, amid a flow of song, laughter, wine, and careless mirth, he would spend hour after hour, forgetting the cheek that was paling through his neglect, heedless of the tear-dimmed eyes, peering anxiously into the darkness, waiting, or watching his return.

The influence of old associations was upon him. In early life, home had been to him a place of ceilings and walls, not a true home, built upon goodness, love and truth. It was a place where velvet carpets hushed his tread, where images of loveliness and beauty invoked into being by painter's art and sculptor's skill, pleased the eye and gratified the taste, where magnificence surrounded his way and costly clothing adorned his person; but it was not the place for the true culture and right development of his soul. His father had been too much engrossed in making money, and his mother in spending it, in striving to maintain a fashionable position in society, and shining in the eyes of the world, to give the proper direction to the character of their wayward and impulsive son. His mother put beautiful robes upon his body, but left ugly scars upon his soul; she pampered his appetite, but starved his spirit. Every mother should be a true artist, who knows how to weave into her child's life images of grace and beauty, the true poet capable of writing on the soul of childhood the harmony of love and truth, and teaching it how to produce the grandest of all poems—the poetry of a true and noble life. But in his home, a love for the good, the true and right, had been sacrificed at the shrine of frivolity and fashion. That parental authority which should have been preserved as a string of precious pearls, unbroken and unscattered, was simply the administration of chance. At one time obedience was enforced by authority, at another time by flattery and promises, and just as often it was not enforced at all. His early associations were formed as chance directed, and from his want of home-training, his character received a bias, his life a shade, which ran through every avenue of his existence, and darkened all his future hours. Oh, if we would trace the history of all the crimes that have o'ershadowed this sin-shrouded and sorrow-darkened world of ours, how many might be seen arising from the wrong home influences, or the weakening of the home ties. Home should always be the best school for the affections, the birthplace of high resolves, and the altar upon which lofty aspirations are kindled, from whence the soul may go forth strengthened, to act its part aright in the great drama of life, with conscience enlightened, affections cultivated, and reason and judgment dominant. But alas for the young wife. Her husband had not been blessed with such a home. When he entered the arena of life, the voices from home did not linger around his path as angels of guidance about his steps; they were not like so many messages to invite him to deeds of high and holy worth. The memory of no sainted mother arose between him and deeds of darkness; the earnest prayers of no father arrested him in his downward course; and before a year of his married life had waned, his young wife had learned to wait and mourn his frequent and uncalled-for absence. More than once had she seen him come home from his midnight haunts, the bright intelligence of his eye displaced by the drunkard's stare, and his manly gait changed to the inebriate's stagger; and she was beginning to know the bitter agony that is compressed in the mournful words, a drunkard's wife. And then there came a bright but brief episode in her experience; the angel of life gave to her existence a deeper meaning and loftier significance: she sheltered in the warm clasp of her loving arms, a dear babe, a precious child, whose love filled every chamber of her heart, and felt the fount of maternal love gushing so new within her soul. That child was hers. How overshadowing was the love with which she bent over its helplessness, how much it helped to fill the void and chasms in her soul. How many lonely hours were beguiled by its winsome ways, its answering smiles and fond caresses. How exquisite and solemn was the feeling that thrilled her heart when she clasped the tiny hands together and taught her dear child to call God "Our Father."

What a blessing was that child. The father paused in his headlong career, awed by the strange beauty and precocious intellect of his child; and the mother's life had a better expression through her ministrations of love. And then there came hours of bitter anguish, shading the sunlight of her home and hushing the music of her heart. The angel of death bent over the couch of her child and beaconed it away. Closer and closer the mother strained her child to her wildly heaving breast, and struggled with the heavy hand that lay upon its heart. Love and agony contended with death, and the language of the mother's heart was,

> "Oh, Death, away! that innocent is mine;
>   I cannot spare him from my arms
> To lay him, Death, in thine.
>   I am a mother, Death; I gave that darling birth
> I could not bear his lifeless limbs
>   Should moulder in the earth."

But death was stronger than love and mightier than agony and won the child for the land of crystal founts and deathless flowers, and the poor, stricken mother sat down beneath the shadow of her mighty grief, feeling as if a great light had gone out from her soul, and that the sunshine had suddenly faded around her path. She turned in her deep anguish to the father of her child, the loved and cherished dead. For awhile his words were kind and tender, his heart seemed subdued, and his tenderness fell upon her worn and weary heart like rain on perishing flowers, or cooling waters to lips all parched with thirst and scorched with fever; but the change was evanescent, the influence of unhallowed associations and evil habits had vitiated and poisoned the springs of his existence. They had bound him in their meshes, and he lacked the moral strength to break his fetters, and stand erect in all the strength and dignity of a true manhood, making life's highest excellence his ideal, and striving to gain it.

And yet moments of deep contrition would sweep over him, when he would resolve to abandon the wine-cup forever, when he was ready to forswear the handling of another card, and he would try to break away from the associations that he felt were working his ruin; but when the hour of temptation came his strength was weakness, his earnest purposes were cobwebs, his well-meant resolutions ropes of sand, and thus passed year after year of the married life of Laura Lagrange. She tried to hide her agony from the public gaze, to smile when her heart was almost breaking. But year after year her voice grew fainter and sadder, her once light and bounding step grew slower and faltering. Year after year she wrestled with agony, and strove with despair, till the quick eyes of her brother read, in the paling of her cheek and the dimming eye, the secret anguish of her worn and weary spirit. On that wan, sad face, he saw the death-tokens, and he knew the dark wing of the mystic angel swept coldly around her path. "Laura," said her brother to her one day, "you are not well, and I think you need our mother's tender care and nursing. You are daily losing strength, and if you will go I will accompany you." At first, she hesitated, she shrank almost instinctively from presenting that pale sad face to the loved ones at home. That face was such a tell-tale; it told of heart-sickness, of hope deferred, and the mournful story of unrequited love. But then a deep yearning for home sympathy woke within her a passionate longing for love's kind words, for tenderness and heart-support, and she resolved to seek the home of her childhood, and lay her weary head upon her mother's bosom, to be folded again in her loving arms, to lay that poor, bruised and aching heart where it might beat and throb closely to the loved ones at home. A kind welcome awaited her. All that love and tenderness could devise was done to bring the bloom to her cheek and the light to her eye; but it was all in vain; her's was a disease that no medicine could cure, no earthly balm would heal. It was a slow wasting of the vital forces, the sickness of the soul. The unkindness and neglect of her husband, lay like a leaden weight upon her heart, and slowly oozed away its life-drops. And where was he that had won her love, and then cast it aside as a useless thing, who rifled her heart of its wealth and spread bitter ashes upon its broken altars? He was lingering away from her when the death-damps were gathering on her brow, when his name was trembling on her lips! lingering away! when she was watching his coming, though the death films were gathering before her eyes, and earthly things were fading from her vision. "I think I hear him now," said the dying woman, "surely that is his step;" but the sound died away in the distance. Again she started from an uneasy slumber, "That is his voice! I am so glad he has come." Tears gathered in the eyes of the sad watchers by that dying bed, for they knew that she was deceived. He had not returned. For her sake they wished his coming. Slowly the hours waned away, and then came the sad, soul-sickening thought that she was forgotten, forgotten in the last hour of human need, forgotten when the spirit, about to be dissolved, paused for the last time on the threshold of existence, a weary watcher at the gates of death. "He has forgotten me," again she faintly murmured, and the last tears she would ever shed on earth sprung to her mournful eyes, and clasping her hands together in silent anguish, a few broken sentences issued from her pale and quivering lips. They were prayers for strength and earnest pleading for him who had desolated her young life, by turning its sunshine to shadows, its smiles to tears. "He has forgotten me," she murmured again, "but I can bear it, the bitterness of death is passed, and soon I hope to exchange the shadows of death for the brightness of eternity, the rugged paths of life for the golden streets of glory, and the care and turmoils of earth for the peace and rest of heaven." Her voice grew fainter and fainter, they saw the shadows that never deceive flit over her pale and faded face, and knew that the death angel waited to soothe their weary one to rest, to calm the throbbing of her bosom and cool the fever of her brain. And amid the silent hush of their grief the freed spirit, refined through suffering, and brought into divine harmony through the spirit of the living Christ, passed over the dark waters of death as on a bridge of light, over whose radiant arches hovering angels bent. They parted the dark locks from her marble brow, closed the waxen lids over the once bright and laughing eye, and left her to the dreamless slumber of the grave. Her cousin turned from that deathbed a sadder and wiser woman. She resolved more earnestly than ever to make the world better by her example, gladder by her presence, and to kindle the fires of her genius on the altars of universal love and truth. She had a higher and better object in all her writings than the mere acquisition of gold, or acquirement of fame. She felt that she had a high and holy mission on the battle-field of existence, that life was not given her to be frittered away in nonsense, or wasted away in trifling pursuits. She would willingly espouse an unpopular cause but not an unrighteous one. In her the down-trodden slave found an earnest advocate; the flying fugitive remembered her kindness as he stepped cautiously through our Republic, to gain his freedom in a monarchial land, having broken the chains on which the rust of centuries had gathered. Little children learned to name her with affection, the poor called her blessed, as she broke her bread to the pale lips of hunger. Her life was like a beautiful story, only it was clothed with the dignity of reality and invested with the sublimity of truth. True, she was an old maid, no husband brightened her life with his love, or shaded it with his neglect. No children nestling lovingly in her arms called her mother. No one appended Mrs. to her name; she was indeed an old maid, not vainly striving to keep up an appearance of girlishness, when departed was written on her youth. Not vainly pining at her loneliness and isolation: the world was full of warm, loving hearts, and her own beat in unison with them. Neither was she always sentimentally sighing for something to love, objects of affection were all around her, and the world was not so wealthy in love that it had no use for her's; in blessing others she made a life and benediction, and as old age descended peacefully and gently upon her, she had learned one of life's most precious lessons, that true happiness consists not so much in the fruition of our wishes as in the regulation of desires and the full development and right culture of our whole natures.

1859

Our Greatest Want

Leading ideas impress themselves upon communities and countries. A thought is evolved and thrown out among the masses, they receive it and it becomes interwoven with their mental and moral life—if the thought be good the receivers are benefited, and helped onward to the truer life; if it is not, the reception of the idea is a detriment. A few earnest thinkers, and workers infuse into the mind of Great Britain, a sentiment of human brotherhood. The hue and cry of opposition is raised against it. Avarice and cupidity oppose it, but the great heart of the people throbs for it. A healthy public opinion dashes and surges against the British throne, the idea gains ground and progresses till hundreds of thousands of men, women and children arise, redeemed from bondage, and freed from chains, and the nation gains moral power by the act.[1] Visions of dominion, proud dreams of conquest fill the soul of Napoleon Bonaparte, and he infuses them into the mind of France, and the peace of Europe is invaded. His bloodstained armies dazzled and misled, follow him through carnage and blood, to shake earth's proudest kingdoms to their base, and the march of a true progression is stayed by a river of blood. In America, where public opinion exerts such a sway, a leading is success. The politician who chooses for his candidate not the best man but the most available one.—The money getter, who virtually says let me make money, though I coin it from blood and extract it from tears—The minister, who stoops from his high position to the slave power, and in a word all who barter principle for expediency, the true and right for the available and convenient, are worshipers at the shrine of success. And we, or at least some of us, upon whose faculties the rust of centuries has lain, are beginning to awake and worship at the same altar, and bow to the idols. The idea if I understand it aright, that is interweaving itself with our thoughts, is that the greatest need of our people at present is money, and that as money is a symbol of power, the possession of it will gain for us the rights which power and prejudice now deny us.—And it may be true that the richer we are the nearer we are to social and political equality; but somehow, (and I may not fully comprehend the idea,) it does not seem to me that money, as little as we possess of it, is our greatest want. Neither do I think that the possession of intelligence and talent is our greatest want. If I understand our greatest wants aright they strike deeper than any want that gold or knowledge can supply. We want more soul, a higher cultivation of all our spiritual faculties. We need more unselfishness, earnestness and integrity. Our greatest need is not gold or silver, talent or genius, but true men and true women. We have millions of our race in the prison house of slavery, but have we yet a single Moses in freedom. And if we had who among us would be led by him?

I like the character of Moses. He is the first disunionist[2] we read of in the Jewish Scriptures. The magnificence of Pharaoh's throne loomed up before his vision, its oriental splendors glittered before his eyes; but he turned from them all and chose rather to suffer with the enslaved, than

---

1. Great Britain had abolished slavery in the British Empire in 1833.
2. In the antebellum period, this word meant any-
one who advocated secession from or dissolution of the United States.

rejoice with the free. He would have no union with the slave power of Egypt. When we have a race of men whom this blood stained government cannot tempt or flatter, who would sternly refuse every office in the nation's gift, from a president down to a tide-waiter, until she shook her hands from complicity in the guilt of cradle plundering and man stealing, then for us the foundations of an historic character will have been laid. We need men and women whose hearts are the homes of a high and lofty enthusiasm, and a noble devotion to the cause of emancipation, who are ready and willing to lay time, talent and money on the altar of universal freedom. We have money among us, but how much of it is spent to bring deliverance to our captive brethren? Are our wealthiest men the most liberal sustainers of the Anti-slavery enterprise? Or does the bare fact of their having money, really help mould public opinion and reverse its sentiments? We need what money cannot buy and what affluence is too beggarly to purchase. Earnest, self sacrificing souls that will stamp themselves not only on the present but the future. Let us not then defer all our noble opportunities till we get rich. And here I am not aiming to enlist a fanatical crusade against the desire for riches, but I do protest against chaining down the soul, with its Heaven endowed faculties and God given attributes to the one idea of getting money as stepping into power or even gaining our rights in common with others. The respect that is only bought by gold is not worth much. It is no honor to shake hands politically with men who whip women and steal babies. If this government has no call for our services, no aim for your children, we have the greater need of them to build up a true manhood and womanhood for ourselves. The important lesson we should learn and be able to teach, is how to make every gift, whether gold or talent, fortune or genius, subserve the cause of crushed humanity and carry out the greatest idea of the present age, the glorious idea of human brotherhood.

1859

From Fancy Etchings

[Enthusiasm and Lofty Aspirations]

2/20/73

"Aunt Jane? Aunt Jane?"

I lifted up my eyes as a fresh young voice sang out my name in tones of pleasurable excitement, and before me stood my niece; her face aglow with one of those beautiful enthusiasms which ever lend a charm to the plainest face.

"What is it, darling?"

"Why Aunty, I want you to immortalize yourself. I want you to write a book, a good book, full of hard, earnest thoughts. A book that will make people better and happier because they read it. I wish I had your power of utterance, and I would write such a book. I am just from College and I mean to do something for my race."

I said, "What do you mean to do?" for her words had awakened my interest.

"I hardly know what I shall succeed in doing, but I want to be a living loving force, not a mere intellectual force, eager about and excited only for my own welfare; but a moral and spiritual force. A woman who can and will do something for women, especially for our own women because they will need me most."

"I am glad, very glad, Jenny, that you have concluded to make something out of your young life. I am always delighted when I see young people full of enthusiasm and lofty aspirations. Our women have been treated as the 'fag' end [1] women of the country; but now that advantages are thrown open to you, which were denied to us older women, I hope that you will prove that your minds are widening with the cycles of the sun. Jenny, darling, permit me to say to you, set your mark high; aim at perfection, and if you would succeed yourself, always be ready to acknowledge the success of others, and do not place the culture of your intellect before the development of your soul. The culture of the intellect may bring you money and applause, but the right training of your soul will give you character and influence; but really Jenny you did not ask me for a sermon and I will stop moralizing."

"Oh! no dear Aunty, I love to hear you talk. You often regret your limited knowledge of books; but you are a book yourself, and I am passionately fond of reading you."

"Thank you, darling, you are quite complimentary to me this morning, but I suppose you like to say pleasant things to Aunty."

"But Aunty if they are pleasant, they are true. If some of us younger women have more learning, you have more knowledge; and if we know more of books, you know more of life; and one knowledge should supplement the other. I felt rather provoked, when Thomas Pemroy, who was discussing with you on some disputed point, asked you in such a tone of conceited superiority, 'Don't you know any better than that?' and, I thought that you felt a little sensitive when Mary Talbot took the liberty to correct a mispronounced word of yours in the presence of several persons."

"Of course I did not feel as if she were treating me very politely; but I attributed it to her lack of social training. Of course I don't suppose that any of us like to be treated as if our words were mice, and that a critic sat beside us like a watchful cat, ever ready to pounce upon a mishap or slipshod word. I think an undue cultivation of the spirit of criticism becomes a kill joy to genial conversation, and a repressive force in society."

"I think Aunty, that conversation ought to be made one of the finest and most excellent of all arts. Have you not met with some people with whom you feel it easy to converse? They seem to unlock your heart and loosen your lips. Then there are others who do not talk to you; they make speeches at you; they step through their sentences as if their words were eggs and they were afraid of hatching them, and they convey to your mind an idea of a self-consciousness that annoys you."

"Yes, I have met with just such people; but how I do enjoy those genial

1. The last part or the very end of something.

souls, whose fine social tact, and generous appreciation, unloosen your lips and make you feel at home with them. I often desire these people with tact, more than I do the people of mere talent; but when both are combined, I think it creates a delightful companionship. But Jenny we have wandered from our original subject, what do you intend doing in the future."

"Well Aunty I will tell you when I come again. It is a pleasant little secret, but it will keep; and I must go now for I have an engagement at eleven o'clock, and it is now half past ten, so good-bye Aunty."

"Good-bye, Jenny, come again soon, and unfold to Aunty's willing ear, all the wise schemes and loving plans you have for the good of our people, and in the meantime rest assured of my hearty sympathy for the cause in which you are interested."

[Dangerous Economies]

5/23/73

"Well! sister," said Jenny to Annie, "what shall be the order of the day?"

"I have some shopping to do, and as I am going to New Paradose, I suppose that I must furbish up a little. I hear that it is a dressy place, and of course I don't want to appear odd. In Rome it is said, you must do as the Romans do,"

"Provided," said Aunt Jane, "that Rome is right. Whether I went to New Paradose or remained in Moontown, I should want my dress to be an expression of my own individuality. If the manners and customs of New Paradose were better than mine, I should try and adopt them, but if I thought that mine were better, I should endeavor to stamp myself on New Paradose; and not let New Paradose stamp itself on me."

"But Aunty," said Anna, "you must remember that we all have not your self reliance and independence of character. We are not all fully emancipated from gaudiness."

"Well, if you are not, the sooner you break your fetters the better, and yet I was not always as self-reliant as I am now. Self reliance is a lesson that I learned in the fire."

"How so, Aunty?"

"Well girls, when I was young, I had just as much longing for sympathy, and hunger for appreciation, I suppose as any other person, but I had too much individuality of character to mould myself after other people's patterns, too much reverence for truth to be the mere echo of their opinions. I could not help thinking for myself, and that style of thinking gave a tone and color to my character which made me seem peculiar; and mankind are more ready to forgive aberrations of conduct than they are aberrations of opinion. Nonconformity is a social heresy that people are slow to tolerate, and so I learned to stand alone. But girls do not let me detain you any longer. Go and do your shopping and let me see your purchases."

"Well Aunty, we'll do our shopping this morning, and then have, I hope, a pleasant reunion this evening. Jenny, had we not better call on a dressmaker today? Do you know of a good dressmaker we can get?"

"Yes I know a first rate dressmaker, and she works very cheaply. She is quite poor, and very anxious for work. She worked for me, and I don't think that I could have gotten the same work done so well and so cheaply anywhere else in town."

"Let us call on her."

"Very well."

"Jenny," said Aunt Jane, suddenly raising her head from her knitting, and laying it on her lap, "don't be too careful of your silks and rags."

"Why, what is the matter Aunt Jane? is my dress torn, or some of my forbelows, [1] as you call them, out of place?"

"Not at all, you look as neat and nice as a new pin."

"Well, I don't know what you mean, your words are a riddle to me."

"Now, Jenny, let me tell you what I mean. I heard you say just now, that Mrs. Anderson worked for you more cheaply, than other women in town, do you know why she does it?"

"I suppose," said Jenny, slightly embarassed, "it is because she is very poor and wants work."

"And is it right for my niece to take advantage of her necessity?"

"But, Aunty, doesn't everybody try to have their work done as cheaply as possible?"

"No, Jenny, not everyone. I have given a number of times, a larger sum for work than was demanded, because I thought the work was worth more."

"Well, Aunty, I guess that you are an exception."

"I hope not, Jenny. I am not conceited enough to think that I am better than my neighbors."

"But Aunty, are not such people the best judges of their own business? I should think that Mrs. Anderson knows better than I do on what terms she can afford to make dresses."

"I suppose she does, but Mrs. Anderson has too many hungry mouths to feed to run the risk of losing her work by chaffering about prices. Now Jenny, you and I, in dealing with poor dependent women should act on the principle of doing as we would be done by. We both belong to societies for the relief of poverty and the salvation of fellow women, but would we not better serve humanity by trying to prevent pauperism and striving to save women from falling?"

"But, Aunty, how can we do it?"

"Jenny, I think one of the great lessons we women have to learn is to know how to treat each other better. We fail, I think, in fully comprehending our relations to society, and the reflex influence of that ignorance upon its purity and progress, and evil may be wrought by want of thought as well as want of heart. Now, Jenny, let me tell you plainly wherein I think you failed in your duty to Mrs. Anderson. In getting your summer outfit you spared no expense, every tradesman with whom you dealt received his full pay for what you received, they were in a situation to dictate their terms; but this poor, careworn, struggling woman was the most poorly paid of all. Jenny, I would have curtailed my expenses in the price of every article I purchased, rather than have given Mrs. Anderson one 25 cents less than her work was worth. I think if you had said 'Mrs. Anderson, your work is

---

1. Ruffles or flounces on a skirt or petticoat.

worth more, and I cannot consent for you to take less,' that you would have
lifted a load from her heart and that your own would have been lighter."

"Well Aunty, I am glad that you have called my attention to this subject.
I think that she would feel more courage to face life when she knew that
she was sustained by sympathy and kindness."

"The Bible says, 'blessed is he who considereth the poor,' and how many
unavailing regrets this consideration might save us. A kind word, a pleasant
smile, a sympathizing look, a generous recognition, may seem very little
things to give, but they are so pleasant to receive, and I fear that poor,
lonely, struggling women are often more wounded by the little slights and
neglects of society, than they are by the keen arrows of poverty and privation, and this is just where we save our silks and rags. We help to keep up
their poverty by our exactions, and their depression by our social pride, and
we save for ourselves by taking advantage of their wants."

"Well, Aunty, I mean to be more careful in the future. I should scorn to
feel that I held my position in society by keeping my foot on the neck of
someone else."

"Jenny dear, you will succeed if you will follow the injunction which
says 'honor all men.' The Bible has not only the highest code of morals, but
also the best rule of manners."

1873

Woman's Political Future [1]

If before sin had cast its deepest shadows or sorrow had distilled its bitterest tears, it was true that it was not good for man to be alone, it is no less
true, since the shadows have deepened and life's sorrows have increased,
that the world has need of all the spiritual aid that woman can give for the
social advancement and moral development of the human race. The tendency of the present age, with its restlessness, religious upheavals, failures,
blunders, and crimes, is toward broader freedom, an increase of knowledge, the emancipation of thought, and a recognition of the brotherhood
of man; in this movement woman, as the companion of man, must be a
sharer. So close is the bond between man and woman that you can not
raise one without lifting the other. The world can not move without
woman's sharing in the movement, and to help give a right impetus to that
movement is woman's highest privilege.

If the fifteenth century discovered America to the Old World, the nineteenth is discovering woman to herself. Little did Columbus imagine,
when the New World broke upon his vision like a lovely gem in the coronet of the universe, the glorious possibilities of a land where the sun should
be our engraver, the winged lightning our messenger, and steam our beast
of burden. But as mind is more than matter, and the highest ideal always
the true real, so to woman comes the opportunity to strive for richer and
grander discoveries than ever gladdened the eye of the Genoese mariner.

1. Speech given at the World's Congress of Repre-   covery" of the Americas. Harper was one of four
sentative Women at the Columbian Exposition,   African American women to address this audience.
the 1893 World's Fair commemorating the "dis-

Not the opportunity of discovering new worlds, but that of filling this old world with fairer and higher aims than the greed of gold and the lust of power, is hers. Through weary, wasting years men have destroyed, dashed in pieces, and overthrown, but to-day we stand on the threshold of woman's era, and woman's work is grandly constructive. In her hand are possibilities whose use or abuse must tell upon the political life of the nation, and send their influence for good or evil across the track of unborn ages.

As the saffron tints and crimson flushes of morn herald the coming day, so the social and political advancement which woman has already gained bears the promise of the rising of the full-orbed sun of emancipation. The result will be not to make home less happy, but society more holy; yet I do not think the mere extension of the ballot a panacea for all the ills of our national life. What we need to-day is not simply more voters, but better voters. To-day there are red-handed men[2] in our republic, who walk unwhipped of justice, who richly deserve to exchange the ballot of the freeman for the wristlets of the felon; brutal and cowardly men, who torture, burn, and lynch their fellow-men, men whose defenselessness should be their best defense and their weakness an ensign of protection. More than the changing of institutions we need the development of a national conscience, and the upbuilding of national character. Men may boast of the aristocracy of blood, may glory in the aristocracy of talent, and be proud of the aristocracy of wealth, but there is one aristocracy which must ever outrank them all, and that is the aristocracy of character; and it is the women of a country who help to mold its character, and to influence if not determine its destiny; and in the political future of our nation woman will not have done what she could if she does not endeavor to have our republic stand foremost among the nations of the earth, wearing sobriety as a crown and righteousness as a garment and a girdle. In coming into her political estate woman will find a mass of illiteracy to be dispelled. If knowledge is power, ignorance is also power. The power that educates wickedness may manipulate and dash against the pillars of any state when they are undermined and honeycombed by injustice.

I envy neither the heart nor the head of any legislator who has been born to an inheritance of privileges, who has behind him ages of education, dominion, civilization, and Christianity, if he stands opposed to the passage of a national education bill, whose purpose is to secure education to the children of those who were born under the shadow of institutions which made it a crime to read.

To-day women hold in their hands influence and opportunity, and with these they have already opened doors which have been closed to others. By opening doors of labor woman has become a rival claimant for at least some of the wealth monopolized by her stronger brother. In the home she is the priestess, in society the queen, in literature she is a power, in legislative halls law-makers have responded to her appeals, and for her sake have humanized and liberalized their laws. The press has felt the impress of her hand. In the pews of the church she constitutes the majority; the pulpit has welcomed her, and in the school she has the blessed privilege of teaching

2. I.e., those in the act of committing a crime or wrongdoing.

children and youth. To her is apparently coming the added responsibility of political power; and what she now possesses should only be the means of preparing her to use the coming power for the glory of God and the good of mankind; for power without righteousness is one of the most dangerous forces in the world.

Political life in our country has plowed in muddy channels, and needs the infusion of clearer and cleaner waters. I am not sure that women are naturally so much better than men that they will clear the stream by the virtue of their womanhood; it is not through sex but through character that the best influence of women upon the life of the nation must be exerted.

I do not believe in unrestricted and universal suffrage for either men or women. I believe in moral and educational tests. I do not believe that the most ignorant and brutal man is better prepared to add value to the strength and durability of the government than the most cultured, upright, and intelligent woman. I do not think that willful ignorance should swamp earnest intelligence at the ballot-box, nor that educated wickedness, violence, and fraud should cancel the votes of honest men. The unsteady hands of a drunkard can not cast the ballot of a freeman. The hands of lynchers are too red with blood to determine the political character of the government for even four short years. The ballot in the hands of woman means power added to influence. How well she will use that power I can not foretell. Great evils stare us in the face that need to be throttled by the combined power of an upright manhood and an enlightened womanhood; and I know that no nation can gain its full measure of enlightenment and happiness if one-half of it is free and the other half is fettered. China compressed the feet of her women and thereby retarded the steps of her men. The elements of a nation's weakness must ever be found at the hearthstone.

More than the increase of wealth, the power of armies, and the strength of fleets is the need of good homes, of good fathers, and good mothers.

The life of a Roman citizen was in danger in ancient Palestine, and men had bound themselves with a vow that they would eat nothing until they had killed the Apostle Paul. Pagan Rome threw around that imperiled life a bulwark of living clay consisting of four hundred and seventy human hearts, and Paul was saved.[3] Surely the life of the humblest American citizen should be as well protected in America as that of a Roman citizen was in heathen Rome. A wrong done to the weak should be an insult to the strong. Woman coming into her kingdom will find enthroned three great evils, for whose overthrow she should be as strong in a love of justice and humanity as the warrior is in his might. She will find intemperance sending its flood of shame, and death, and sorrow to the homes of men, a fretting leprosy in our politics, and a blighting curse in our social life; the social evil sending to our streets women whose laughter is sadder than their tears, who slide from the paths of sin and shame to the friendly shelter of the grave; and lawlessness enacting in our republic deeds over which angels might weep, if heaven knows sympathy.

---

3. Because he was a Roman citizen, the government went to great lengths to protect Paul from physical assault by those who disagreed with his teachings. See Acts 23–26.

How can any woman send petitions to Russia against the horrors of Siberian prisons if, ages after the Inquisition has ceased to devise its tortures, she has not done all she could by influence, tongue, and pen to keep men from making bonfires of the bodies of real or supposed criminals?

O women of America! into your hands God has pressed one of the sublimest opportunities that ever came into the hands of the women of any race or people. It is yours to create a healthy public sentiment; to demand justice, simple justice, as the right of every race; to brand with everlasting infamy the lawless and brutal cowardice that lynches, burns, and tortures your own countrymen.

To grapple with the evils which threaten to undermine the strength of the nation and to lay magazines of powder under the cribs of future generations is no child's play.

Let the hearts of the women of the world respond to the song of the herald angels of peace on earth and good will to men. Let them throb as one heart unified by the grand and holy purpose of uplifting the human race, and humanity will breathe freer, and the world grow brighter. With such a purpose Eden would spring up in our path, and Paradise be around our way.

1893

HARRIET E. WILSON
1828?–1863?

The first novel by an African American woman, Harriet E. Wilson's *Our Nig; or, Sketches from the Life of a Free Black, in a Two-Story White House, North* (1859), is also the first novel in black American literature to examine the life of an ordinary black person in realistic detail. The central figure in *Our Nig* is undoubtedly based on Wilson herself, a working-class woman who set out to reveal from her actual experience in the North that "slavery's shadows fall even there." The mockery of freedom that northern black people had to endure during the antebellum era first received serious attention in fiction in Frank J. Webb's *The Garies and Their Friends* (1857), the third novel, after Douglass's *The Heroic Slave* (1853) and Brown's *Clotel* (1853), authored by an African American. But Wilson's experimental text—a hybrid of autobiography, fiction, and exposé—makes a more cogent case than Webb's novel for the connection between racism and the economic domination of whites over blacks in the antebellum North. Moreover, Wilson's sensitivity to gender factors in her representation of a black servant girl as a sympathetic and admirable figure makes *Our Nig* a noteworthy intervention in the history of American fiction's treatment of women of color.

Little was known about the identity or the biography of Harriet E. Wilson until Henry Louis Gates Jr. undertook research on her and her novel in the early 1980s. As a consequence of his findings, we now know that Wilson's maiden name was Harriet Adams; that she was born in Milford, New Hampshire, around 1828, and was married in her hometown to Thomas Wilson in 1851; that she bore a son in the late spring of 1852, who died seven and a half years later; and that she had moved to Boston or its vicinity by the time her novel was published, at her own expense by an obscure job printer of that city, in 1859. Of Wilson's death nothing is known for certain.

The correspondences between *Our Nig*, the letters of recommendation that append it, and the few facts that have been uncovered about its author, suggest that Wilson suffered in an employment situation (probably in Milford) similar to that of Alfrado, the much-mistreated protagonist of *Our Nig*. That Wilson married a reputed fugitive slave, as Alfrado does in the novel, and was abandoned in pregnancy by her husband, as Alfrado notes in her story, is also attested to by one of the writers of a recommendation letter for *Our Nig*. Wilson's and Alfrado's struggles for dignity and self-sufficiency finally dovetail in the literary venture that was *Our Nig*. After years of emotional and physical abuse at the hands of her female employer, which left her so weakened that she had to depend on public assistance for herself and her son, Harriet Wilson turned to novel writing as a means of earning a living and supporting her family. Thus African American women's fiction originated in necessity, if not virtual desperation, but took form and meaning in Wilson's eloquent testimony to the economics of class as well as race and gender in her life.

Our Nig is a woman's growing-up story. More than one critic has noted its similarities to white American women's fiction of the mid-nineteenth century, particularly in its focus on the struggles of a young single woman to achieve economic independence and self-respect. Alfrado's fundamental motivation throughout her story is to defend herself against the assaults on her psyche perpetrated by her mistress, Mrs. Bellmont, and to find some means by which she might "succeed in providing for her own wants." A want of money and social connections handicaps Alfrado profoundly, but, unlike white working-class girls, she must also negotiate racial prejudice against her, which manifests itself in Mrs. Bellmont's conviction that Alfrado has neither the right nor the need to aspire to anything beyond a subordinate relationship to whites. Although Mrs. Bellmont and her daughter Mary dedicate themselves to breaking Alfrado's spirit, they never succeed in doing so.

Our Nig joins forces with antebellum black women's spiritual autobiographies by Jarena Lee and Zilpha Elaw and Harriet Jacobs's pioneering slave narrative to pay special tribute to the strength of character and moral resolution of the African American woman. Alfrado's out-of-wedlock birth to a white woman and a black man, which Wilson records with rare candor and understanding, would have disqualified her from serious attention at the hands of almost any conventional novelist of the era. By focusing on Alfrado's struggle to attain a sense of dignity and self-assurance founded in religious faith, Wilson asserted her determination to depart from literary norms and invest in her black female protagonist the qualities of genuine heroism. Consistent with a view of Christianity put forward in much nineteenth-century African American writing, Alfrado's faith transforms her self-estimate, endows her with a genuine sense of power and hope, and spurs her toward direct confrontation with her oppressor. Like Douglass's famous battle with Covey the slave breaker, Alfrado's climactic defiance of Mrs. Bellmont is represented as an act of self-reclamation and spiritual regeneration. Wilson signals Alfrado's victory in classic slave narrative fashion: escaping the "two-story white house, North," Alfrado sets out in quest of economic, intellectual, and spiritual "self-improvement." Marriage, ironically, does not bring her the security that it usually symbolizes for women in sentimental fiction of the time. But Alfrado does not give in to hopeless dependency; instead she concludes her story with the promise to her reader that "nothing turns her from her steadfast purpose of elevating herself." Whatever actually happened to Harriet Wilson, in the voice of the narrator of *Our Nig* she articulated a self-confidence and a dauntless dedication to a better future that remain a hallmark of black women's fiction in the United States.

From Our Nig; or, Sketches from the Life of a Free Black, in a Two-Story White House, North

Preface

In offering to the public the following pages, the writer confesses her inability to minister to the refined and cultivated, the pleasure supplied by abler pens. It is not for such these crude narrations appear. Deserted by kindred, disabled by failing health, I am forced to some experiment which shall aid me in maintaining myself and child without extinguishing this feeble life. I would not from these motives even palliate slavery at the South, by disclosures of its appurtenances North. My mistress was wholly imbued with *southern* principles. I do not pretend to divulge every transaction in my own life, which the unprejudiced would declare unfavorable in comparison with treatment of legal bondmen; I have purposely omitted what would most provoke shame in our good anti-slavery friends at home.

My humble position and frank confession of errors will, I hope, shield me from severe criticism. Indeed, defects are so apparent it requires no skilful hand to expose them.

I sincerely appeal to my colored brethren universally for patronage, hoping they will not condemn this attempt of their sister to be erudite, but rally around me a faithful band of supporters and defenders.

H. E. W.

Chapter I. Mag Smith, My Mother

> Oh, Grief beyond all other griefs, when fate
> First leaves the young heart lone and desolate
> In the wide world, without that only tie
> For which it loved to live or feared to die;
> Lorn as the hung-up lute, that ne'er hath spoken
> Since the sad day its master-chord was broken!
> MOORE.[1]

Lonely Mag Smith! See her as she walks with downcast eyes and heavy heart. It was not always thus. She *had* a loving, trusting heart. Early deprived of parental guardianship, far removed from relatives, she was left to guide her tiny boat over life's surges alone and inexperienced. As she merged into womanhood, unprotected, uncherished, uncared for, there fell on her ear the music of love, awakening an intensity of emotion long dormant. It whispered of an elevation before unaspired to; of ease and plenty her simple heart had never dreamed of as hers. She knew the voice of her charmer, so ravishing, sounded far above her. It seemed like an angel's, alluring her upward and onward. She thought she could ascend to him and become an equal. She surrendered to him a priceless gem, which he proudly garnered as a trophy, with those of other victims, and left her to her fate. The world seemed full of hateful deceivers and crushing arro-

---

1. From Thomas Moore's immensely popular *Lalla Rookh* (1817), a series of Oriental tales in verse.

gance. Conscious that the great bond of union to her former companions was severed, that the disdain of others would be insupportable, she determined to leave the few friends she possessed, and seek an asylum among strangers. Her offspring came unwelcomed, and before its nativity numbered weeks, it passed from earth, ascending to a purer and better life.

"God be thanked," ejaculated Mag, as she saw its breathing cease; "no one can taunt *her* with my ruin."

Blessed release! may we all respond. How many pure, innocent children not only inherit a wicked heart of their own, claiming life-long scrutiny and restraint, but are heirs also of parental disgrace and calumny, from which only long years of patient endurance in paths of rectitude can disencumber them.

Mag's new home was soon contaminated by the publicity of her fall; she had a feeling of degradation oppressing her; but she resolved to be circumspect, and try to regain in a measure what she had lost. Then some foul tongue would jest of her shame, and averted looks and cold greetings disheartened her. She saw she could not bury in forgetfulness her misdeed, so she resolved to leave her home and seek another in the place she at first fled from.

Alas, how fearful are we to be first in extending a helping hand to those who stagger in the mires of infamy; to speak the first words of hope and warning to those emerging into the sunlight of morality! Who can tell what numbers, advancing just far enough to hear a cold welcome and join in the reserved converse of professed reformers, disappointed, disheartened, have chosen to dwell in unclean places, rather than encounter these "holier-than-thou" of the great brotherhood of man!

Such was Mag's experience; and disdaining to ask favor or friendship from a sneering world, she resolved to shut herself up in a hovel she had often passed in better days, and which she knew to be untenanted. She vowed to ask no favors of familiar faces; to die neglected and forgotten before she would be dependent on any. Removed from the village, she was seldom seen except as upon your introduction, gentle reader, with downcast visage, returning her work to her employer, and thus providing herself with the means of subsistence. In two years many hands craved the same avocation; foreigners who cheapened toil and clamored for a livelihood, competed with her, and she could not thus sustain herself. She was now above no drudgery. Occasionally old acquaintances called to be favored with help of some kind, which she was glad to bestow for the sake of the money it would bring her; but the association with them was such a painful reminder of by-gones, she returned to her hut morose and revengeful, refusing all offers of a better home than she possessed. Thus she lived for years, hugging her wrongs, but making no effort to escape. She had never known plenty, scarcely competency; but the present was beyond comparison with those innocent years when the coronet of virtue was hers.

Every year her melancholy increased, her means diminished. At last no one seemed to notice her, save a kind-hearted African, who often called to inquire after her health and to see if she needed any fuel, he having the responsibility of furnishing that article, and she in return mending or making garments.

"How much you earn dis week, Mag?" asked he one Saturday evening.

"Little enough, Jim. Two or three days without any dinner. I washed for the Reeds, and did a small job for Mrs. Bellmont; that's all. I shall starve soon, unless I can get more to do. Folks seem as afraid to come here as if they expected to get some awful disease. I don't believe there is a person in the world but would be glad to have me dead and out of the way."

"No, no, Mag! don't talk so. You shan't starve so long as I have barrels to hoop. Peter Greene boards me cheap. I'll help you, if nobody else will."

A tear stood in Mag's faded eye. "I'm glad," she said, with a softer tone than before, "if there is *one* who isn't glad to see me suffer. I b'lieve all Singleton wants to see me punished, and feel as if they could tell when I've been punished long enough. It's a long day ahead they'll set it, I reckon."

After the usual supply of fuel was prepared, Jim returned home. Full of pity for Mag, he set about devising measures for her relief. "By golly!" said he to himself one day—for he had become so absorbed in Mag's interest that he had fallen into a habit of musing aloud—"By golly! I wish she'd *marry* me."

"Who?" shouted Pete Greene, suddenly starting from an unobserved corner of the rude shop.

"Where you come from, you sly nigger!" exclaimed Jim.

"Come, tell me, who is 't?" said Pete; "Mag Smith, you want to marry?"

"Git out, Pete! and when you come in dis shop again, let a nigger know it. Don't steal in like a thief."

Pity and love know little severance. One attends the other. Jim acknowledged the presence of the former, and his efforts in Mag's behalf told also of a finer principle.

This sudden expedient which he had unintentionally disclosed, roused his thinking and inventive powers to study upon the best method of introducing the subject to Mag.

He belted his barrels, with many a scheme revolving in his mind, none of which quite satisfied him, or seemed, on the whole, expedient. He thought of the pleasing contrast between her fair face and his own dark skin; the smooth, straight hair, which he had once, in expression of pity, kindly stroked on her now wrinkled but once fair brow. There was a tempest gathering in his heart, and at last, to ease his pent-up passion, he exclaimed aloud, "By golly!" Recollecting his former exposure, he glanced around to see if Pete was in hearing again. Satisfied on this point, he continued: "She'd be as much of a prize to me as she'd fall short of coming up to the mark with white folks. I don't care for past things. I've done things 'fore now I's 'shamed of. She's good enough for me, any how."

One more glance about the premises to be sure Pete was away.

The next Saturday night brought Jim to the hovel again. The cold was fast coming to tarry its apportioned time. Mag was nearly despairing of meeting its rigor.

"How's the wood, Mag?" asked Jim.

"All gone; and no more to cut, any how," was the reply.

"Too bad!" Jim said. His truthful reply would have been, I'm glad.

"Anything to eat in the house?" continued he.

"No," replied Mag.

"Too bad!" again, orally, with the same *inward* gratulation as before.

"Well, Mag," said Jim, after a short pause, "you's down low enough. I don't see but I've got to take care of ye. 'Sposin' we marry!"

Mag raised her eyes, full of amazement, and uttered a sonorous "What?" Jim felt abashed for a moment. He knew well what were her objections.

"You's had trial of white folks, any how. They run off and left ye, and now none of 'em come near ye to see if you's dead or alive. I's black outside, I know, but I's got a white heart inside. Which you rather have, a black heart in a white skin, or a white heart in a black one?"

"Oh, dear!" sighed Mag; "Nobody on earth cares for *me*—"

"I do," interrupted Jim.

"I can do but two things," said she, "beg my living, or get it from you."

"Take me, Mag. I can give you a better home than this, and not let you suffer so."

He prevailed; they married. You can philosophize, gentle reader, upon the impropriety of such unions, and preach dozens of sermons on the evils of amalgamation. Want is a more powerful philosopher and preacher. Poor Mag. She has sundered another bond which held her to her fellows. She has descended another step down the ladder of infamy.

Chapter II. My Father's Death

> Misery! we have known each other,
> Like a sister and a brother,
> Living in the same lone home
> Many years—we must live some
> Hours or ages yet to come.
>   SHELLEY.[2]

Jim, proud of his treasure,—a white wife,—tried hard to fulfil his promises; and furnished her with a more comfortable dwelling, diet, and apparel. It was comparatively a comfortable winter she passed after her marriage. When Jim could work, all went on well. Industrious, and fond of Mag, he was determined she should not regret her union to him. Time levied an additional charge upon him, in the form of two pretty mulattos, whose infantile pranks amply repaid the additional toil. A few years, and a severe cough and pain in his side compelled him to be an idler for weeks together, and Mag had thus a reminder of by-gones. She cared for him only as a means to subserve her own comfort; yet she nursed him faithfully and true to marriage vows till death released her. He became the victim of consumption.[3] He loved Mag to the last. So long as life continued, he stifled his sensibility to pain, and toiled for her sustenance long after he was able to do so.

A few expressive wishes for her welfare; a hope of better days for her; an anxiety lest they should not all go to the "good place"; brief advice about their children; a hope expressed that Mag would not be neglected as she used to be; the manifestation of Christian patience; these were *all* the legacy of miserable Mag. A feeling of cold desolation came over her, as she turned from the grave of one who had been truly faithful to her.

---

2. From *Invocation to Misery* (1818) by the English Romantic poet Percy Bysshe Shelley.　　3. Tuberculosis.

She was now expelled from companionship with white people; this last step—her union with a black—was the climax of repulsion.

Seth Shipley, a partner in Jim's business, wished her to remain in her present home; but she declined, and returned to her hovel again, with obstacles threefold more insurmountable than before. Seth accompanied her, giving her a weekly allowance which furnished most of the food necessary for the four inmates. After a time, work failed; their means were reduced.

How Mag toiled and suffered, yielding to fits of desperation, bursts of anger, and uttering curses too fearful to repeat. When both were supplied with work, they prospered; if idle, they were hungry together. In this way their interests became united; they planned for the future together. Mag had lived an outcast for years. She had ceased to feel the gushings of penitence; she had crushed the sharp agonies of an awakened conscience. She had no longings for a purer heart, a better life. Far easier to descend lower. She entered the darkness of perpetual infamy. She asked not the rite of civilization or Christianity. Her will made her the wife of Seth. Soon followed scenes familiar and trying.

"It's no use," said Seth one day; "we must give the children away, and try to get work in some other place."

"Who'll take the black devils?" snarled Mag.

"They're none of mine," said Seth; "what you growling about?"

"Nobody will want any thing of mine, or yours either," she replied.

"We'll make 'em, p'r'aps," he said. "There's Frado's six years old, and pretty, if she is yours, and white folks'll say so. She'd be a prize somewhere," he continued, tipping his chair back against the wall, and placing his feet upon the rounds, as if he had much more to say when in the right position.

Frado, as they called one of Mag's children, was a beautiful mulatto, with long, curly black hair, and handsome, roguish eyes, sparkling with an exuberance of spirit almost beyond restraint.

Hearing her name mentioned, she looked up from her play, to see what Seth had to say of her.

"Wouldn't the Bellmonts take her?" asked Seth.

"Bellmonts?" shouted Mag. "His wife is a right she-devil! and if—"

"Hadn't they better be all together?" interrupted Seth, reminding her of a like epithet used in reference to her little ones.

Without seeming to notice him, she continued, "She can't keep a girl in the house over a week; and Mr. Bellmont wants to hire a boy to work for him, but he can't find one that will live in the house with her; she's so ugly, they can't."

"Well, we've got to make a move soon," answered Seth; "if you go with me, we shall go right off. Had you rather spare the other one?" asked Seth, after a short pause.

"One's as bad as t' other," replied Mag. "Frado is such a wild, frolicky thing, and means to do jest as she's a mind to; she won't go if she don't want to. I don't want to tell her she is to be given away."

"I will," said Seth. "Come here, Frado?"

The child seemed to have some dim foreshadowing of evil, and declined.

"Come here," he continued; "I want to tell you something."

She came reluctantly. He took her hand and said: "We're going to move, by-'m-bye; will you go?"

"No!" screamed she; and giving a sudden jerk which destroyed Seth's equilibrium, left him sprawling on the floor, while she escaped through the open door.

"She's a hard one," said Seth, brushing his patched coat sleeve. "I'd risk her at Bellmont's."

They discussed the expediency of a speedy departure. Seth would first seek employment, and then return for Mag. They would take with them what they could carry, and leave the rest with Pete Greene, and come for them when they were wanted. They were long in arranging affairs satisfactorily, and were not a little startled at the close of their conference to find Frado missing. They thought approaching night would bring her. Twilight passed into darkness, and she did not come. They thought she had understood their plans, and had, perhaps, permanently withdrawn. They could not rest without making some effort to ascertain her retreat. Seth went in pursuit, and returned without her. They rallied others when they discovered that another little colored girl was missing, a favorite playmate of Frado's. All effort proved unavailing. Mag felt sure her fears were realized, and that she might never see her again. Before her anxieties became realities, both were safely returned, and from them and their attendant they learned that they went to walk, and not minding the direction soon found themselves lost. They had climbed fences and walls, passed through thickets and marshes, and when night approached selected a thick cluster of shrubbery as a covert for the night. They were discovered by the person who now restored them, chatting of their prospects, Frado attempting to banish the childish fears of her companion. As they were some miles from home, they were kindly cared for until morning. Mag was relieved to know her child was not driven to desperation by their intentions to relieve themselves of her, and she was inclined to think severe restraint would be healthful.

The removal was all arranged; the few days necessary for such migrations passed quickly, and one bright summer morning they bade farewell to their Singleton hovel, and with budgets and bundles commenced their weary march. As they neared the village, they heard the merry shouts of children gathered around the schoolroom, awaiting the coming of their teacher.

"Halloo!" screamed one, "Black, white and yeller!" "Black, white and yeller," echoed a dozen voices.

It did not grate so harshly on poor Mag as once it would. She did not even turn her head to look at them. She had passed into an insensibility no childish taunt could penetrate, else she would have reproached herself as she passed familiar scenes, for extending the separation once so easily annihilated by steadfast integrity. Two miles beyond lived the Bellmonts, in a large, old fashioned, two-story white house, environed by fruitful acres, and embellished by shrubbery and shade trees. Years ago a youthful couple consecrated it as home; and after many little feet had worn paths to favorite fruit trees, and over its green hills, and mingled at last with brother man in the race which belongs neither to the swift or strong, the sire became grey-haired and decrepid, and went to his last repose. His aged consort soon followed him. The old homestead thus passed into the hands of a son, to whose wife Mag had applied the epithet "she-devil," as may be remembered. John, the son, had not in his family arrangements departed from the example of the father. The pastimes of his boyhood were ever freshly revived by witnessing the games of his own sons as they rallied about the same goal his youthful feet had often won; as well as by the amusements of his daughters in their imitations of maternal duties.

At the time we introduce them, however, John is wearing the badge of age. Most of his children were from home; some seeking employment; some were already settled in homes of their own. A maiden sister shared with him the estate on which he resided, and occupied a portion of the house.

Within sight of the house, Seth seated himself with his bundles and the child he had been leading, while Mag walked onward to the house leading Frado. A knock at the door brought Mrs. Bellmont, and Mag asked if she would be willing to let that child stop there while she went to the Reed's house to wash, and when she came back she would call and get her. It seemed a novel request, but she consented.Why the impetuous child entered the house, we cannot tell; the door closed, and Mag hastily departed. Frado waited for the close of day, which was to bring back her mother. Alas! it never came. It was the last time she ever saw or heard of her mother.

Chapter III. A New Home for Me

> Oh! did we but know of the shadows so nigh,
>   The world would indeed be a prison of gloom;
> All light would be quenched in youth's eloquent eye,
>   And the prayer-lisping infant would ask for the tomb.
>
> For if Hope be a star that may lead us astray,
>   And "deceiveth the heart," as the aged ones preach;
> Yet 'twas Mercy that gave it, to beacon our way,
>   Though its halo illumes where it never can reach.
>   ELIZA COOK. [4]

As the day closed and Mag did not appear, surmises were expressed by the family that she never intended to return. Mr. Bellmont was a kind, humane man, who would not grudge hospitality to the poorest wanderer, nor fail to sympathize with any sufferer, however humble. The child's desertion by her mother appealed to his sympathy, and he felt inclined to succor her. To do this in opposition to Mrs. Bellmont's wishes, would be like encountering a whirlwind charged with fire, daggers and spikes. She was not as susceptible of fine emotions as her spouse. Mag's opinion of her was not without foundation. She was self-willed, haughty, undisciplined, arbitrary and severe. In common parlance, she was a *scold*, a thorough one. Mr. B. remained silent during the consultation which follows, engaged in by mother, Mary and John, or Jack, as he was familiarly called.

"Send her to the County House," said Mary, in reply to the query what should be done with her, in a tone which indicated self-importance in the

---

4. A popular 19th-century English periodical poet.

speaker. She was indeed the idol of her mother, and more nearly resembled her in disposition and manners than the others.

Jane, an invalid daughter, the eldest of those at home, was reclining on a sofa apparently uninterested.

"Keep her," said Jack. "She's real handsome and bright, and not very black, either."

"Yes," rejoined Mary; "that's just like you, Jack. She'll be of no use at all these three years, right under foot all the time."

"Poh! Miss Mary; if she should stay, it wouldn't be two days before you would be telling the girls about *our* nig, *our* nig!" retorted Jack.

"I don't want a nigger 'round *me*, do you, mother?" asked Mary.

"I don't mind the nigger in the child. I should like a dozen better than one," replied her mother. "If I could make her do my work in a few years, I would keep her. I have so much trouble with girls I hire, I am almost persuaded if I have one to train up in my way from a child, I shall be able to keep them awhile. I am tired of changing every few months."

"Where could she sleep?" asked Mary. "I don't want her near me."

"In the L chamber," answered the mother.

"How'll she get there?" asked Jack. "She'll be afraid to go through that dark passage, and she can't climb the ladder safely."

"She'll have to go there; it's good enough for a nigger," was the reply.

Jack was sent on horseback to ascertain if Mag was at her home. He returned with the testimony of Pete Greene that they were fairly departed, and that the child was intentionally thrust upon their family.

The imposition was not at all relished by Mrs. B., or the pert, haughty Mary, who had just glided into her teens.

"Show the child to bed, Jack," said his mother. "You seem most pleased with the little nigger, so you may introduce her to her room."

He went to the kitchen, and, taking Frado gently by the hand, told her he would put her in bed now; perhaps her mother would come the next night after her.

It was not yet quite dark, so they ascended the stairs without any light, passing through nicely furnished rooms, which were a source of great amazement to the child. He opened the door which connected with her room by a dark, unfinished passage-way. "Don't bump your head," said Jack, and stepped before to open the door leading into her apartment,—an unfinished chamber over the kitchen, the roof slanting nearly to the floor, so that the bed could stand only in the middle of the room. A small half window furnished light and air. Jack returned to the sitting room with the remark that the child would soon outgrow those quarters.

"When she *does*, she'll outgrow the house," remarked the mother.

"What can she do to help you?" asked Mary. "She came just in the right time, didn't she? Just the very day after Bridget left," continued she.

"I'll see what she can do in the morning," was the answer.

While this conversation was passing below, Frado lay, revolving in her little mind whether she would remain or not until her mother's return. She was of wilful, determined nature, a stranger to fear, and would not hesitate to wander away should she decide to. She remembered the conversation of her mother with Seth, the words "given away" which she heard used in reference to herself; and though she did not know their full import, she thought she should, by remaining, be in some relation to white people she was never favored with before. So she resolved to tarry, with the hope that mother would come and get her some time. The hot sun had penetrated her room, and it was long before a cooling breeze reduced the temperature so that she could sleep.

Frado was called early in the morning by her new mistress. Her first work was to feed the hens. She was shown how it was *always* to be done, and in no other way; any departure from this rule to be punished by a whipping. She was then accompanied by Jack to drive the cows to pasture, so she might learn the way. Upon her return she was allowed to eat her breakfast, consisting of a bowl of skimmed milk, with brown bread crusts, which she was told to eat, standing, by the kitchen table, and must not be over ten minutes about it. Meanwhile the family were taking their morning meal in the dining-room. This over, she was placed on a cricket[5] to wash the common dishes; she was to be in waiting always to bring wood and chips, to run hither and thither from room to room.

A large amount of dish-washing for small hands followed dinner. Then the same after tea and going after the cows finished her first day's work. It was a new discipline to the child. She found some attractions about the place, and she retired to rest at night more willing to remain. The same routine followed day after day, with slight variation; adding a little more work, and spicing the toil with "words that burn," and frequent blows on her head. These were great annoyances to Frado, and had she known where her mother was, she would have gone at once to her. She was often greatly wearied, and silently wept over her sad fate. At first she wept aloud, which Mrs. Bellmont noticed by applying a rawhide, always at hand in the kitchen. It was a symptom of discontent and complaining which must be "nipped in the bud," she said.

Thus passed a year. No intelligence of Mag. It was now certain Frado was to become a permanent member of the family. Her labors were multiplied; she was quite indispensable, although but seven years old. She had never learned to read, never heard of a school until her residence in the family.

Mrs. Bellmont was in doubt about the utility of attempting to educate people of color, who were incapable of elevation. This subject occasioned a lengthy discussion in the family. Mr. Bellmont, Jane and Jack arguing for Frado's education; Mary and her mother objecting. At last Mr. Bellmont declared decisively that she *should* go to school. He was a man who seldom decided controversies at home. The word once spoken admitted of no appeal; so, notwithstanding Mary's objection that she would have to attend the same school she did, the word became law.

It was to be a new scene to Frado, and Jack had many queries and conjectures to answer. He was himself too far advanced to attend the summer school, which Frado regretted, having had too many opportunities of witnessing Miss Mary's temper to feel safe in her company alone.

The opening day of school came. Frado sauntered on far in the rear of

5. A footstool.

Mary, who was ashamed to be seen "walking with a nigger." As soon as she appeared, with scanty clothing and bared feet, the children assembled, noisily published her approach: "See that nigger," shouted one. "Look! look!" cried another. "I won't play with her," said one little girl. "Nor I neither," replied another.

Mary evidently relished these sharp attacks, and saw a fair prospect of lowering Nig where, according to her views, she belonged. Poor Frado, chagrined and grieved, felt that her anticipations of pleasure at such a place were far from being realized. She was just deciding to return home, and never come there again, when the teacher appeared, and observing the downcast looks of the child, took her by the hand, and led her into the school-room. All followed, and, after the bustle of securing seats was over, Miss Marsh inquired if the children knew "any cause for the sorrow of that little girl?" pointing to Frado. It was soon all told. She then reminded them of their duties to the poor and friendless; their cowardice in attacking a young innocent child; referred them to one who looks not on outward appearances, but on the heart. "She looks like a good girl; I think I shall love her, so lay aside all prejudice, and vie with each other in shewing kindness and good-will to one who seems different from you," were the closing remarks of the kind lady. Those kind words! The most agreeable sound which ever meets the ear of sorrowing, grieving childhood.

Example rendered her words efficacious. Day by day there was a manifest change of deportment towards "Nig." Her speeches often drew merriment from the children; no one could do more to enliven their favorite pastimes than Frado. Mary could not endure to see her thus noticed, yet knew not how to prevent it. She could not influence her schoolmates as she wished. She had not gained their affections by winning ways and yielding points of controversy. On the contrary, she was self-willed, domineering; every day reported "mad" by some of her companions. She availed herself of the only alternative, abuse and taunts, as they returned from school. This was not satisfactory; she wanted to use physical force "to subdue her," to "keep her down."

There was, on their way home, a field intersected by a stream over which a single plank was placed for a crossing. It occurred to Mary that it would be a punishment to Nig to compel her to cross over; so she dragged her to the edge, and told her authoritatively to go over. Nig hesitated, resisted. Mary placed herself behind the child, and, in the struggle to force her over, lost her footing and plunged into the stream. Some of the larger scholars being in sight, ran, and thus prevented Mary from drowning and Frado from falling. Nig scampered home fast as possible, and Mary went to the nearest house, dripping, to procure a change of garments. She came loitering home, half crying, exclaiming, "Nig pushed me into the stream!" She then related the particulars. Nig was called from the kitchen. Mary stood with anger flashing in her eyes. Mr. Bellmont sat quietly reading his paper. He had witnessed too many of Miss Mary's outbreaks to be startled. Mrs. Bellmont interrogated Nig.

"I didn't do it! I didn't do it!" answered Nig, passionately, and then related the occurrence truthfully.

The discrepancy greatly enraged Mrs. Bellmont. With loud accusations and angry gestures she approached the child. Turning to her husband, she asked,

"Will you sit still, there, and hear that black nigger call Mary a liar?"

"How do we know but she has told the truth? I shall not punish her," he replied, and left the house, as he usually did when a tempest threatened to envelop him. No sooner was he out of sight than Mrs. B. and Mary commenced beating her inhumanly; then propping her mouth open with a piece of wood, shut her up in a dark room, without any supper. For employment, while the tempest raged within, Mr. Bellmont went for the cows, a task belonging to Frado, and thus unintentionally prolonged her pain. At dark Jack came in, and seeing Mary, accosted her with, "So you thought you'd vent your spite on Nig, did you? Why can't you let her alone? It was good enough for you to get a ducking, only you did not stay in half long enough."

"Stop!" said his mother. "You shall never talk so before me. You would have that little nigger trample on Mary, would you? She came home with a lie; it made Mary's story false."

"What was Mary's story?" asked Jack.

It was related.

"Now," said Jack, sallying into a chair, "the school-children happened to see it all, and they tell the same story Nig does. Which is most likely to be true, what a dozen agree they saw, or the contrary?"

"It is very strange you will believe what others say against your sister," retorted his mother, with flashing eye. "I think it is time your father subdued you."

"Father is a sensible man," argued Jack. "He would not wrong a dog. Where is Frado?" he continued.

"Mother gave her a good whipping and shut her up," replied Mary.

Just then Mr. Bellmont entered, and asked if Frado was "shut up yet."

The knowledge of her innocence, the perfidy of his sister, worked fearfully on Jack. He bounded from his chair, searched every room till he found the child; her mouth wedged apart, her face swollen, and full of pain.

How Jack pitied her! He relieved her jaws, brought her some supper, took her to her room, comforted her as well as he knew how, sat by her till she fell asleep, and then left for the sitting room. As he passed his mother, he remarked, "If that was the way Frado was to be treated, he hoped she would never wake again!" He then imparted her situation to his father, who seemed untouched, till a glance at Jack exposed a tearful eye. Jack went early to her next morning. She awoke sad, but refreshed. After breakfast Jack took her with him to the field, and kept her through the day. But it could not be so generally. She must return to school, to her household duties. He resolved to do what he could to protect her from Mary and his mother. He bought her a dog, which became a great favorite with both. The invalid, Jane, would gladly befriend her; but she had not the strength to brave the iron will of her mother. Kind words and affectionate glances were the only expressions of sympathy she could safely indulge in. The men employed on the farm were always glad to hear her prattle; she was a great favorite with them. Mrs. Bellmont allowed them the privilege of talking with her in the kitchen. She did not fear but she should have ample opportunity of subduing her when they were away. Three months of schooling, summer and winter, she enjoyed for three years. Her winter over-dress was a cast-off overcoat, once worn by Jack, and a sun-bonnet. It was a source of great merriment to the scholars, but Nig's retorts were so mirthful, and their satisfaction so evident in attributing the selection to "Old Granny Bellmont," that it was not painful to Nig or pleasurable to Mary. Her jollity was not to be quenched by whipping or scolding. In Mrs. Bellmont's presence she was under restraint; but in the kitchen, and among her schoolmates, the pent up fires burst forth. She was ever at some sly prank when unseen by her teacher, in school hours; not unfrequently some outburst of merriment, of which she was the original, was charged upon some innocent mate, and punishment inflicted which she merited. They enjoyed her antics so fully that any of them would suffer wrongfully to keep open the avenues of mirth. She would venture far beyond propriety, thus shielded and countenanced.

The teacher's desk was supplied with drawers, in which were stored his books and other *et ceteras*[6] of the profession. The children observed Nig very busy there one morning before school, as they flitted in occasionally from their play outside. The master came; called the children to order; opened a drawer to take the book the occasion required; when out poured a volume of smoke. "Fire! fire!" screamed he, at the top of his voice. By this time he had become sufficiently acquainted with the peculiar odor, to know he was imposed upon. The scholars shouted with laughter to see the terror of the dupe, who, feeling abashed at the needless fright, made no very strict investigation, and Nig once more escaped punishment. She had provided herself with cigars, and puffing, puffing away at the crack of the drawer, had filled it with smoke, and then closed it tightly to deceive the teacher, and amuse the scholars. The interim of terms was filled up with a variety of duties new and peculiar. At home, no matter how powerful the heat when sent to rake hay or guard the grazing herd, she was never permitted to shield her skin from the sun. She was not many shades darker than Mary now; what a calamity it would be ever to hear the contrast spoken of. Mrs. Bellmont was determined the sun should have full power to darken the shade which nature had first bestowed upon her as best befitting.

[Mrs. Bellmont halts Frado's schooling when she reaches the age of nine. Mr. Bellmont's unmarried sister, Abby, and James Bellmont, a grown son home for a recuperative visit, befriend Frado in the face of Mrs. Bellmont's violent persecution of the black girl. In defiance of her mother, Jane Bellmont marries modest George Means instead of Henry Reed, a wealthy suitor, and moves away. Not long after Jack Bellmont heads west to seek his fortune.]

From *Chapter VIII. Visitor and Departure*

* * *

Frado, under the instructions of Aunt Abby and the minister, became a believer in a future existence—one of happiness or misery. Her doubt was, *is* there a heaven for the black? She knew there was one for James, and

6. Additional things.

Aunt Abby, and all good white people; but was there any for blacks? She had listened attentively to all the minister said, and all Aunt Abby had told her; but then it was all for white people.

As James approached that blessed world, she felt a strong desire to follow, and be with one who was such a dear, kind friend to her.

While she was exercised with these desires and aspirations, she attended an evening meeting with Aunt Abby, and the good man urged all, young or old, to accept the offers of mercy, to receive a compassionate Jesus as their Saviour. "Come to Christ," he urged, "all, young or old, white or black, bond or free, come all to Christ for pardon; repent, believe."

This was the message she longed to hear; it seemed to be spoken for her. But he had told them to repent; "what was that?" she asked. She knew she was unfit for any heaven, made for whites or blacks. She would gladly repent, or do anything which would admit her to share the abode of James.

Her anxiety increased; her countenance bore marks of solicitude unseen before; and though she said nothing of her inward contest, they all observed a change.

James and Aunt Abby hoped it was the springing of good seed sown by the Spirit of God. Her tearful attention at the last meeting encouraged his aunt to hope that her mind was awakened, her conscience aroused. Aunt Abby noticed that she was particularly engaged in reading the Bible; and this strengthened her conviction that a heavenly Messenger was striving with her. The neighbors dropped in to inquire after the sick, and also if Frado was "serious?" They noticed she seemed very thoughtful and tearful at the meetings. Mrs. Reed was very inquisitive; but Mrs. Belmont saw no appearance of change for the better. She did not feel responsible for her spiritual culture, and hardly believed she had a soul.

Nig was in truth suffering much; her feelings were very intense on any subject, when once aroused. She read her Bible carefully, and as often as an opportunity presented, which was when entirely secluded in her own apartment, or by Aunt Abby's side, who kindly directed her to Christ, and instructed her in the way of salvation.

Mrs. Bellmont found her one day quietly reading her Bible. Amazed and half crediting the reports of officious neighbors, she felt it was time to interfere. Here she was, reading and shedding tears over the Bible. She ordered her to put up the book, and go to work, and not be snivelling about the house, or stop to read again.

But there was one little spot seldom penetrated by her mistress' watchful eye: this was her room, uninviting and comfortless; but to herself a safe retreat. Here she would listen to the pleadings of a Saviour, and try to penetrate the veil of doubt and sin which clouded her soul, and long to cast off the fetters of sin, and rise to the communion of saints.

Mrs. Bellmont, as we before said, did not trouble herself about the future destiny of her servant. If she did what she desired for *her* benefit, it was all the responsibility she acknowledged. But she seemed to have great aversion to the notice Nig would attract should she become pious. How could she meet this case? She resolved to make her complaint to John. Strange, when she was always foiled in this direction, she should resort to him. It was time something was done; she had begun to read the Bible openly.

The night of this discovery, as they were retiring, Mrs. Bellmont introduced the conversation, by saying:

"I want your attention to what I am going to say. I have let Nig go out to evening meetings a few times, and, if you will believe it, I found her reading the Bible to-day, just as though she expected to turn pious nigger, and preach to white folks. So now you see what good comes of sending her to school. If she should get converted she would have to go to meeting: at least, as long as James lives. I wish he had not such queer notions about her. It seems to trouble him to know he must die and leave her. He says if he should get well he would take her home with him, or educate her here. Oh, how awful! What can the child mean? So careful, too, of her! He says we shall ruin her health making her work so hard, and sleep in such a place. O, John! do you think he is in his right mind?"

"Yes, yes; she is slender."

"Yes, yes!" she repeated sarcastically, "you know these niggers are just like black snakes; you *can't* kill them. If she wasn't tough she would have been killed long ago. There was never one of my girls could do half the work."

"Did they ever try?" interposed her husband. "I think she can do more than all of them together."

"What a man!" said she, peevishly. "But I want to know what is going to be done with her about getting pious?"

"Let her do just as she has a mind to. If it is a comfort to her, let her enjoy the privilege of being good. I see no objection."

"I should think *you* were crazy, sure. Don't you know that every night she will want to go toting off to meeting? and Sundays, too? and you know we have a great deal of company Sundays, and she can't be spared."

"I thought you Christians held to going to church," remarked Mr. B.

"Yes, but who ever thought of having a nigger go, except to drive others there? Why, according to you and James, we should very soon have her in the parlor, as smart as our own girls. It's of no use talking to you or James. If you should go on as you would like, it would not be six months before she would be leaving me; and that won't do. Just think how much profit she was to us last summer. We had no work hired out; she did the work of two girls—"

"And got the whippings for two with it!" remarked Mr. Bellmont.

"I'll beat the money out of her, if I can't get her worth any other way," retorted Mrs. B. sharply. While this scene was passing, Frado was trying to utter the prayer of the publican, "God be merciful to me a sinner."[7]

[Frado is disconsolate on the death of James Bellmont, but clings to the religious hope he encourages in her.]

---

7. Luke 18:13.

Chapter X. Perplexities.—Another Death

Neath the billows of the ocean,
Hidden treasures wait the hand,
That again to light shall raise them
With the diver's magic wand.
G. W. COOK.

The family, gathered by James' decease, returned to their homes. Susan and Charles [8] returned to Baltimore. Letters were received from the absent, expressing their sympathy and grief. The father bowed like a "bruised reed," under the loss of his beloved son. He felt desirous to die the death of the righteous; also, conscious that he was unprepared, he resolved to start on the narrow way, and some time solicit entrance through the gate which leads to the celestial city. He acknowledged his too ready acquiescence with Mrs. B., in permitting Frado to be deprived of her only religious privileges for weeks together. He accordingly asked his sister to take her to meeting once more, which she was ready at once to do.

The first opportunity they once more attended meeting together. The minister conversed faithfully with every person present. He was surprised to find the little colored girl so solicitous, and kindly directed her to the flowing fountain [9] where she might wash and be clean. He inquired of the origin of her anxiety, of her progress up to this time, and endeavored to make Christ, instead of James, the attraction of Heaven. He invited her to come to his house, to speak freely her mind to him, to pray much, to read her Bible often.

The neighbors, who were at meeting,—among them Mrs. Reed,—discussed the opinions Mrs. Bellmont would express on the subject. Mrs. Reed called and informed Mrs. B. that her colored girl "related her experience the other night at the meeting."

"What experience?" asked she, quickly, as if she expected to hear the number of times she had whipped Frado, and the number of lashes set forth in plain Arabic numbers.

"Why, you know she is serious, don't you? She told the minister about it."

Mrs. B. made no reply, but changed the subject adroitly. Next morning she told Frado she "should not go out of the house for one while, except on errands; and if she did not stop trying to be religious, she would whip her to death."

Frado pondered; her mistress was a professor of religion; was *she* going to heaven? then she did not wish to go. If she should be near James, even, she could not be happy with those fiery eyes watching her ascending path. She resolved to give over all thought of the future world, and strove daily to put her anxiety far from her.

Mr. Bellmont found himself unable to do what James or Jack could accomplish for her. He talked with her seriously, told her he had seen her many times punished undeservedly; he did not wish to have her saucy or disrespectful, but when she was *sure* she did not deserve a whipping, to

8. Wife and son of James Bellmont.   9. I.e., Christ.

avoid it if she could. "You are looking sick," he added, "you cannot endure beating as you once could."

It was not long before an opportunity offered of profiting by his advice. She was sent for wood, and not returning as soon as Mrs. B. calculated, she followed her, and, snatching from the pile a stick, raised it over her.

"Stop!" shouted Frado, "strike me, and I'll never work a mite more for you;" and throwing down what she had gathered, stood like one who feels the stirring of free and independent thoughts.

By this unexpected demonstration, her mistress, in amazement, dropped her weapon, desisting from her purpose of chastisement. Frado walked towards the house, her mistress following with the wood she herself was sent after. She did not know, before, that she had a power to ward off assaults. Her triumph in seeing her enter the door with *her* burden, repaid her for much of her former suffering.

It was characteristic of Mrs. B. never to rise in her majesty, unless she was sure she should be victorious.

This affair never met with an "after clap," like many others.

Thus passed a year. The usual amount of scolding, but fewer whippings. Mrs. B. longed once more for Mary's return, who had been absent over a year; and she wrote imperatively for her to come quickly to her. A letter came in reply, announcing that she would comply as soon as she was sufficiently recovered from an illness which detained her.

No serious apprehensions were cherished by either parent, who constantly looked for notice of her arrival, by mail. Another letter brought tidings that Mary was seriously ill; her mother's presence was solicited.

She started without delay. Before she reached her destination, a letter came to the parents announcing her death.

No sooner was the astounding news received, than Frado rushed into Aunt Abby's, exclaiming:—

"She's dead, Aunt Abby!"

"Who?" she asked, terrified by the unprefaced announcement.

"Mary; they've just had a letter."

As Mrs. B. was away, the brother and sister could freely sympathize, and she sought him in this fresh sorrow, to communicate such solace as she could, and to learn particulars of Mary's untimely death, and assist him in his journey thither.

It seemed a thanksgiving to Frado. Every hour or two she would pop in into Aunt Abby's room with some strange query:

"She got into the *river* again, Aunt Abby, didn't she; the Jordan[1] is a big one to tumble into, any how. S'posen she goes to hell, she'll be as black as I am. Wouldn't mistress be mad to see her a nigger!" and others of a similar stamp, not at all acceptable to the pious, sympathetic dame; but she could not evade them.

The family returned from their sorrowful journey, leaving the dead behind. Nig looked for a change in her tyrant; what could subdue her, if the loss of her idol could not?

---

1. The Jordan River of the Mideast, used here figuratively to represent the transition from death to the afterlife.

Never was Mrs. B. known to shed tears so profusely, as when she reiterated to one and another the sad particulars of her darling's sickness and death. There was, indeed, a season of quiet grief; it was the lull of the fiery elements. A few weeks revived the former tempests, and so at variance did they seem with chastisement sanctified, that Frado felt them to be unbearable. She determined to flee. But where? Who would take her? Mrs. B. had always represented her ugly. Perhaps every one thought her so. Then no one would take her. She was black, no one would love her. She might have to return, and then she would be more in her mistress' power than ever.

She remembered her victory at the wood-pile. She decided to remain to do as well as she could; to assert her rights when they were trampled on; to return once more to her meeting in the evening, which had been prohibited. She had learned how to conquer; she would not abuse the power while Mr. Bellmont was at home.

But had she not better run away? Where? She had never been from the place far enough to decide what course to take. She resolved to speak to Aunt Abby. *She* mapped the dangers of her course, her liability to fail in finding so good friends as John and herself. Frado's mind was busy for days and nights. She contemplated administering poison to her mistress, to rid herself and the house of so detestable a plague.

But she was restrained by an overruling Providence; and finally decided to stay contentedly through her period of service,[2] which would expire when she was eighteen years of age.

In a few months Jane returned home with her family, to relieve her parents, upon whom years and affliction had left the marks of age. The years intervening since she had left her home, had, in some degree, softened the opposition to her unsanctioned marriage with George. The more Mrs. B. had about her, the more energetic seemed her directing capabilities, and her fault-finding propensities. Her own, she had full power over; and Jane after vain endeavors, became disgusted, weary, and perplexed, and decided that, though her mother might suffer, she could not endure her home. They followed Jack to the West. Thus vanished all hopes of sympathy or relief from this source to Frado. There seemed no one capable of enduring the oppressions of the house but her. She turned to the darkness of the future with the determination previously formed, to remain until she should be eighteen. Jane begged her to follow her so soon as she should be released; but so wearied out was she by her mistress, she felt disposed to flee from any and every one having her similitude of name or feature.

[Frado completes her long term of service to the Bellmonts and departs with one dress and a Bible. She finds work as a seamstress but illness compounded by years of mistreatment compels her to return to the Bellmont house, where Abby nurses her back to a fragile health. Frado takes a job as a domestic, but soon suffers a physical breakdown. Aided by charity, she is able to continue her efforts at self-support by sewing and bonnet making.]

---

2. Frado is an indentured servant, obliged to remain with the Bellmonts until she reaches adulthood.

Chapter XII. The Winding Up of the Matter

Nothing new under the sun.
SOLOMON.[3]

A few years ago, within the compass of my narrative, there appeared often in some of our New England villages, professed fugitives from slavery, who recounted their personal experience in homely phrase, and awakened the indignation of non-slaveholders against brother Pro.[4] Such a one appeared in the new home of Frado; and as people of color were rare there, was it strange she should attract her dark brother; that he should inquire her out; succeed in seeing her; feel a strange sensation in his heart towards her; that he should toy with her shining curls, feel proud to provoke her to smile and expose the ivory concealed by thin, ruby lips; that her sparkling eyes should fascinate; that he should propose; that they should marry? A short acquaintance was indeed an objection, but she saw him often, and thought she knew him. He never spoke of his enslavement to her when alone, but she felt that, like her own oppression, it was painful to disturb oftener than was needful.

He was a fine, straight negro, whose back showed no marks of the lash, erect as if it never crouched beneath a burden. There was a silent sympathy which Frado felt attracted her, and she opened her heart to the presence of love—that arbitrary and inexorable tyrant.

She removed to Singleton, her former residence, and there was married. Here were Frado's first feelings of trust and repose on human arm. She realized, for the first time, the relief of looking to another for comfortable support. Occasionally he would leave her to "lecture."

Those tours were prolonged often to weeks. Of course he had little spare money. Frado was again feeling her self-dependence, and was at last compelled to resort alone to that. Samuel was kind to her when at home, but made no provision for his absence, which was at last unprecedented.

He left her to her fate—embarked at sea, with the disclosure that he had never seen the South, and that his illiterate harangues were humbugs for hungry abolitionists. Once more alone! Yet not alone. A still newer companionship would soon force itself upon her. No one wanted her with such prospects. Herself was burden enough; who would have an additional one?

The horrors of her condition nearly prostrated her, and she was again thrown upon the public for sustenance. Then followed the birth of her child. The long absent Samuel unexpectedly returned, and rescued her from charity. Recovering from her expected illness, she once more commenced toil for herself and child, in a room obtained of a poor woman, but with better fortune. One so well known would not be wholly neglected. Kind friends watched her when Samuel was from home, prevented her from suffering, and when the cold weather pinched the warmly clad, a kind friend took them in, and thus preserved them. At last Samuel's business

3. King of Israel during the 10th century B.C. and traditionally credited with authorship of the Book of Ecclesiastes. The epigraph is after Ecclesiastes 1:9: "There is no new thing under the sun.
4. Proslavery.

became very engrossing, and after long desertion, news reached his family that he had become a victim of yellow fever, in New Orleans.

So much toil as was necessary to sustain Frado, was more than she could endure. As soon as her babe could be nourished without his mother, she left him in charge of a Mrs. Capon, and procured an agency,[5] hoping to recruit her health, and gain an easier livelihood for herself and child. This afforded her better maintenance than she had yet found. She passed into the various towns of the State she lived in, then into Massachusetts. Strange were some of her adventures. Watched by kidnappers, maltreated by professed abolitionists, who didn't want slaves at the South, nor niggers in their own houses, North. Faugh! to lodge one; to eat with one; to admit one through the front door; to sit next one; awful!

Traps slyly laid by the vicious to ensnare her, she resolutely avoided. In one of her tours, Providence favored her with a friend who, pitying her cheerless lot, kindly provided her with a valuable recipe, from which she might herself manufacture a useful article for her maintenance. This proved a more agreeable, and an easier way of sustenance.

And thus, to the present time, may you see her busily employed in preparing her merchandise; then sallying forth to encounter many frowns, but some kind friends and purchasers. Nothing turns her from her steadfast purpose of elevating herself. Reposing on God, she has thus far journeyed securely. Still an invalid, she asks your sympathy, gentle reader. Refuse not, because some part of her history is unknown, save by the Omniscient God. Enough has been unrolled to demand your sympathy and aid.

Do you ask the destiny of those connected with her *early* history? A few years only have elapsed since Mr. and Mrs. B. passed into another world. As age increased, Mrs. B. became more irritable, so that no one, even her own children, could remain with her; and she was accompanied by her husband to the home of Lewis,[6] where, after an agony in death unspeakable, she passed away. Only a few months since, Aunt Abby entered heaven. Jack and his wife rest in heaven, disturbed by no intruders; and Susan and her child are yet with the living. Jane has silver locks in place of auburn tresses, but she has the early love of Henry still, and has never regretted her exchange of lovers. Frado has passed from their memories, as Joseph from the butler's,[7] but she will never cease to track them till beyond mortal vision.

1859

Literature of the
Reconstruction to the
New Negro Renaissance
1865–1919

The Civil War was, President Lincoln proclaimed, a test of whether this nation or any nation "conceived in liberty and dedicated to the proposition that all men are created equal" could long endure. While Lincoln was not as candid about the fact that from its conception, a substantial portion of this nation's inhabitants were neither free nor treated equally, African Americans and others knew that the institution of slavery was one of the primary practices being tested. They recognized that the war was also to determine the power relationship between the federal and state governments and the nature and control of the economy, that it was affected by the changes in demographics caused by immigration and emigration, and that the role of free northern blacks was also at issue. Everyone in the United States was experiencing the tensions generated by the increasing number of religious denominations and by the rise of scientific inquiry that challenged traditional explanations and introduced new social theories and practices. African Americans, both former slaves and longtime free citizens; Euro-Americans, whether newly immigrated or descendants of the founding families; and the indigenous peoples of the territories now claimed as Mexico, Canada, and the United States were all affected by changes that were transforming or obliterating their way of life.

The great postbellum task was one of reaffirming the blueprint for a new and better version of the Pilgrims' City upon a Hill and of rebuilding its institutions and reconciling its populations. Those who had survived the Civil War sought to salvage from their various pasts their best and truest ideals and—using the spirit, experience, and technology of the present—to fashion a new and greater *United* States of America. The majority was in favor of removing debris and shoring up weight-bearing beams, but some groups insisted this could not be accomplished without replacing or redesigning certain structural problems left intact during the war and others that the war had actually created. For example, slavery had been abolished, in word if not in deed, but the societal role of the freed slaves was yet to be determined. Nor was the negotiation of roles a question only for those who had once been slaves. Many who had never been legally enslaved—African Americans, women, indigenous Americans, and recent immigrants—were convinced that their rights must be incorporated into the fundamental architecture of the reconstructed country. Although they considered abolition a giant step toward a truly United

States of America and acknowledged the thousands of lives lost and millions of acres devastated in the Civil War, most agreed that the United States had in fact passed its test. The challenge now was to produce a society more faithful to the language and intent of the Constitution than the antebellum one, a nation more under God than ever before.

This desire to remake, not merely repair, the country was especially apparent in discussions of gender roles and rights. Women had been the backbone of the anti-slavery movement. Through their involvement in it, they had developed administrative skills and political savvy. They had become accomplished speakers and writers. They had recognized and articulated the comparisons between their own status and the conditions of enslaved blacks. The demands of war had given them greater experience and further independence. During the years between 1861 and 1865, women expanded their roles, establishing hospitals, schools, recreation centers, and other institutions to care for the newly freed slaves and the fighting men and the families they'd left behind. Most were entirely unwilling to return silently to the patriarchal definitions that reserved liberty and equality for the fraternity. In addition, many wanted to continue to work with people regardless of differences in gender, religion, national origin, and class. Thus at the Eleventh National Woman's Rights Convention in May 1866, Frances Ellen Watkins Harper proclaimed:

> We are all bound up together in one great bundle of humanity, and society cannot trample on the weakest and feeblest of its members without receiving the curse in its own soul. . . . The grand and glorious revolution which has commenced, will fail to reach its climax of success, until throughout the length and breadth of the American Republic, the nation shall be so color-blind, as to know no man by the color of his skin or the curl of his hair. It will then have not privileged class, trampling upon and outraging the under-privileged classes, but will be then one great privileged nation, whose privilege will be to produce the loftiest manhood and womanhood that humanity can attain.

While some poets and activists agreed with Harper, hers was not a majority position. Knowing that the nation was at a historical watershed, that the war had settled the question of whether the agricultural South, supported by slave labor, would dominate the economy or whether the mercantile North, aided by European immigrants, would determine the national future, some people envisioned a reconstructed economy that integrated the produce of the South with the manufacturing of the North and exploited the potential treasures of the western frontier. They recognized the possibilities of applying scientific knowledge to a burgeoning technology and thereby establishing the United States as a world power. The argument for a shared community of interests and a classless society represented by Harper's "we are all bound up together" speech directly conflicted with the rugged and rapacious individualism that imperialistic expansion required.

The conflict in vision for the future of the United States was not a regional one, nor was it entirely along racial lines. While the Civil War had wrecked some individual fortunes, it had not dismantled the plantation system. Postwar industrial expansion enabled it to be refigured as sharecropping and tenant farming. And, for those not satisfied with staying at home, the changes wrought by war and mobility had opened many areas to virtually anyone with the desire and design to exploit them. One of the deciding factors in this contest for new territory was the completion of the first transcontinental railroad in 1869. Built by exploited Asians and blacks and serviced by the poor, the railroad opened up the frontier and made the distribution of minerals and raw materials, meat, produce, and finished goods quicker and easier than before. Soon the nation boasted four transcontinental rail-roads as well as an impressive array of canals. Both forms of transportation encour-aged its transformation from a land of small towns and rural communities to one of urban metropolises. Gradually, as the western territories beckoned, coastal New England lost its position as cultural and commercial center. At the same time, im-migration was doubling, tripling, and quadrupling the size of some cities. Between 1860 and 1900 estimates are that fourteen million immigrants, primarily from Europe, settled in the Northeast and Midwest. In 1850 New York counted five hun-dred thousand residents. By 1900 it was home to three and a half million. In a similar time period, Chicago went from a small outpost of twenty thousand to the center of the meat packing and other industries with two million inhabitants.

Never before had so many different cultures lived so closely to one another. Though westward expansion allowed greater than usual class and culture interac-tion and assimilation, that same expansion practically destroyed other cultures, par-ticularly Native American, and the environments that had sustained them. Moreover, the physical space of the United States was limited, and as the pioneers and social misfits reached the Pacific, they had to settle down and live with one another. Increased cultural diversity in decreased physical territory multiplied the normal pressures to conform. Many saw the answer in a melting pot concept, but their tastes favored a stew characterized by meat and potatoes, mildly flavored with a little salt and almost no pepper. Rice, yams, and maize were excluded from the recipe, and the rice, yam, or maize eaters were allowed at the table only to serve.

A DECADE OF RECONSTRUCTION

Reconstruction is generally identified as the years between 1865 and 1877. Actu-ally, it began even before the end of the Civil War when numerous volunteers fol-lowed the armies south and established refugee centers, hospitals, schools, and other social services. It ended in the late 1870s, with the withdrawal from the South of federal forces and the passing by the reunited states of laws designed to limit African Americans socially, politically, and economically. With slavery officially outlawed, the white South moved quickly to protect its interests by codifying the very white supremacist ideology that had undergirded the chattel slave system. Some legislation even took away freedoms and outlawed practices that had been relatively common before the war; divorce and other domestic issues were particu-larly hard pressed. In March 1867 the Republican-dominated Congress passed the Reconstruction Act, which struck down many of those restrictive codes that tar-geted African Americans. In addition, it established the Freedmen's Bureau to pro-tect the rights and the lives of black people in the South. Through the Freedmen's Bureau, thousands of northerners—men and women, black and white—traveled to the South to set up schools, establish cooperatives, and train the newly freed slaves in the rituals of citizenship. During its brief history, from 1865 to about 1870, the bureau established four thousand schools staffed by educated northerners. Some of these schools, along with those founded by churches and by philanthropic vision-aries, became independent colleges. Between 1866 and 1868, for example, Fisk, Morehouse, Howard, Atlanta, Talladega, and Hampton were established.

The most significant pieces of Reconstruction legislation were three Constitu-tional amendments. The Thirteenth Amendment (1865) outlawed slavery, the Fourteenth (1868) provided equal protection to African Americans under the law, and the Fifteenth (1870) granted suffrage to black men. These provided limited but dramatic results. The passage of the Fifteenth Amendment gave African American men some political clout. In Louisiana, they had enough voting strength to elect a governor. Newly enfranchised African Americans sent sixteen of their number to

Congress and significantly influenced several state legislatures. However, in many places African Americans never actually obtained the vote. And the Constitutional amendments, like other reform legislation, were neither uniformly enforced nor even recognized in all parts of the country. Consequently, the daily lives of far too many African Americans were not substantially different in freedom than they had been under slavery. For example, most continued to work on farms and in forests for the same people who had once owned them. Their bosses still exercised considerable authority over their actions and their activities. Those who could not adjust or who lost favor were evicted or imprisoned. And the establishment of the convict-lease system, by which prisoners were rented to private individuals or companies, proved to be another version of slavery.

The limited social and economic gains that African Americans experienced immediately after the war were quickly reversed when, in 1877, withdrawal of federal troops, reversal by state and federal courts of protective legislation for African Americans, and the return to power of the Democrats signaled the end of Reconstruction. Along with other vigilante groups, the Ku Klux Klan, established in 1866, embarked on a wave of suppression so brutal that the federal government could not pursue its rebuilding program without intervening.

SEPARATE AND UNEQUAL

It took only two or three years to deconstruct the institutions and to repeal or replace the legislation of the Reconstruction decade. Random violence and systematic oppression were supported by Jim Crow laws, which legalized racial segregation in virtually every area of life. The last part of the nineteenth century and the first few years of the twentieth became known in African American history as the "Decades of Disappointment" or, as black scholar Rayford Logan termed it, "the Nadir of Black Experience."

The reasons for this downfall were many. For example, while some abolitionists believed in equal rights for blacks, many did not. The antislavery societies, by and large, had been segregated. The mass of northern whites whose support was crucial for the war effort and the abolition of slavery wanted to put sectional divisions behind them and had turned in the meantime to issues such as suffrage, temperance, and pacifism. In addition, issues of equal rights were diverse and often conflicting. For example, when it appeared that Congress would grant the vote to black men but not to any women, white suffragist Elizabeth Cady Stanton declared, "I will cut off this right arm of mine before I will ever work for or demand the ballot for the Negro and not the woman." Racism split the Equal Rights Association into two separate organizations when Stanton, Susan B. Anthony, and others withdrew to form the National Woman Suffrage Association. As the century progressed, abolitionist leaders such as Charles Sumner, Frederick Douglass, and William Lloyd Garrison died. Other activists such as Harriet Tubman and Frances Harper became old and infirm. More important, their prestige and influence, founded as it had been on conditions that no longer existed, had seriously eroded. Their successors had come of age during Reconstruction. They had been firmly enchanted by the American Dream of economic prosperity and social mobility. Fewer and fewer African American leaders had actually experienced slavery. Although they fought against repressive legislation, they shared much of the optimism engendered by the postbellum economic reconstruction still under way. Giant leaps in manufacturing and transportation and provocative expansion of physical territory and scientific know-how fueled visions far more extravagant than that of being a model democracy. European immigrants provided much of the labor for northern factories. In both the North and the South, they were given priority over African Americans in skilled trades and personal services. Soon the carpenters, blacksmiths, coopers, shipbuilders, and of course, factory workers had formed all-white unions. Nannies replaced mammies, and black butlers became corner bootblacks. Waiters were demoted to dishwashers, and cooks were replaced by European chefs. Barbers could not use their scissors on the hair of blacks if they wished to keep a white clientele, and even bootblacks could not use the same rag on shoes worn by African Americans and on those that shod the feet of Anglo-Americans.

When Booker T. Washington founded the Tuskegee Institute in 1881, it was one of the rare and rapidly disappearing examples of interracial cooperation. Tuskegee was one of the first schools for African Americans financially sponsored by both blacks and whites but headed by a black president. Yet with its emphasis on vocational training and manual labor, Washington's school did not challenge segregation. Tuskegee was founded on a philosophy of thrift, hard work, self-reliance, and patience, which Washington later articulated in his famous Atlanta Exposition speech (1895). "Cast down your bucket where you are," he counseled, both blacks and whites, and while he did include "commerce" and "the professions" in the fountains from which southern blacks might nourish their ambitions, agriculture, mechanics, and domestic service dominated Tuskegee's curriculum and the minds of the white power brokers who supported his cause. While Washington acknowledged that it was "important and right" that African Americans share the "privileges of the law," his caveat that it "is vastly more important" that African Americans "be *prepared* for the exercise of those privileges" (emphasis added) implied that they were not then ready for equal protection under the law, for suffrage or other manifestations of citizenship.

Two years after the opening of Tuskegee, in 1883, the Supreme Court outlawed the Civil Rights Act of 1875 by upholding the Jim Crow laws of Tennessee. In rapid succession, state and federal courts supported laws and changes in state constitutions that segregated public transportation and buildings, that made integrated schools and many gatherings illegal, and that disenfranchised black men. By 1896, with the Supreme Court in *Plessy v. Ferguson* declaring the legality of the "separate but equal" ideology, a hold had been placed on real progress for African Americans, a hold that was to withstand serious legal challenge until the middle of the twentieth century.

RACIAL CONFLICT INTO THE TWENTIETH CENTURY

The decades just before and after the start of the twentieth century are characterized in many U.S. history books as the Progressive Period. For African Americans they are more accurately called the Decades of Disappointment, years marked by a "great migration" from South to North, from farmlands to cities in search of succor and sufferance if not success. Still, the turn of the century did see the establishment of nationwide reform movements. Laws were passed governing working conditions and hours, providing worker's compensation, and improving the health, education, and welfare of the poor and the working classes. Settlement houses such as Hull House in Chicago, child care for working mothers, and other crucial institutions came into being. And a small but significant number of individuals preached a social gospel that advocated change according to the ethics of Christianity, emphasized morality over blind theology, and social over individual redemption.

All this is not to say that African Americans took no part in the public life of the nation. Some played important roles in the national expansion efforts. In 1898, four "special" black units joined the four regular black units in the U.S. military. The regular units had already displayed their loyalty and valor in the frontier wars. During the Spanish-American War, two of these units, the Ninth and Tenth Cavalries, were said to have saved Teddy Roosevelt's Rough Riders from "complete annihilation." Inventors such as Jan E. Matzeliger, Elijah McCoy, and Granville T. Woods received patents for important mechanical and electrical devices. And African Americans participated effectively in groups such as the Populist Party and the Knights of Labor.

As the nation moved into the twentieth century, its mood was cautiously optimistic. Big business was providing an improved standard of living for most Americans. Still, the wealth and power were clearly not evenly distributed. To investigate and address this inequity, philanthropists funded an increasing number of reform movements. Writers such as Upton Sinclair stirred the public to protest the most blatant abuses. That most of these efforts were segregated did not concern white Americans. African Americans, having endured decades of disappointment, were generally less interested in integration than in their physical safety and economic security. They were convinced that their progress was their own problem. Questions of African American destiny would be answered, they believed, by African Americans themselves if their fellow citizens would stop the violence and live up to their Constitutional promises.

In 1895 Frederick Douglass died and Booker T. Washington gave his Atlanta Exposition speech. These events nicely symbolize the changes in philosophy and options that faced the race. In the ensuing years the debate arose among African Americans over the merits of Washington's privileging industrial education and economic advancement against W. E. B. Du Bois's advocacy of political agitation and leadership from the "talented tenth." Washington stated time and again that he would "set no limits to the attainments of the Negro in arts, in letters or statesmanship," but he argued that "knowledge must be harnessed to the things of real life," and he "pleaded for industrial education and development" because that was the foundation on which the race could prosper. Du Bois asserted that "the Negro race, like all races, is going to be saved by its exceptional men." Less discussed are the numerous statements by other leaders, including many African American women, who advocated a blend of these two extremes.

Despite the violence and blatant inequalities in the separate but equal United States, literacy among African Americans increased in the late nineteenth century, and the black middle class and even a small but wealthy social elite grew in number and influence. Throughout the country, a diverse set of African American institutions prospered. Many churches, for example, became active in providing academic education and expanded their ministries to include the establishment of day care centers, employment bureaus, housing projects, and orphanages. Organizations such as the Afro-American League, the Negro Business League, and the National Council of Negro Women worked both with the churches and independently to create educational, economic, social, and recreational opportunities. Still, though African Americans paid market rates and were taxed as if they had equal access to the wealth and privileges of the nation, they did not. Discrimination in education and in job opportunities increased as the twentieth century neared. And to make matters worse, not only were African Americans unwelcome outside their neighborhoods but they were often not safe even in their own communities. According to historian John Hope Franklin, during the last sixteen years of the nineteenth century there were more than twenty-five hundred lynchings, mostly of blacks in the South. When one recalls that lynchings often entailed not just death by hanging but also torture and burning alive and that such horrible events were sometimes advertised in advance and attracted large crowds of white men, women, and children, the pre–World War I years almost make the antebellum South seem a dress rehearsal.

The southern depression of 1914 was exacerbated by several natural disasters, including a plague of boll weevils that destroyed the cotton crops in 1915. Black tenant farmers were plunged further into debt, and laborers saw their daily wages decrease to seventy-five cents a day and below. Despite Washington's admonition to "cast down your buckets where you are," large numbers of African Americans left the South, fleeing violence, segregation, and poverty and seeking work in the industrial cities of Chicago, Detroit, New York, and Pittsburgh. Though these refugees found more freedom in the urban North, even there they were subject to intimidation and exploitation. With the advent of World War I, the steady stream of emigrants became a flood as the military accepted more African Americans and factories, railroads, and major employers found themselves desperate for workers to fill the positions left vacant by enlisted men. In 1916, for example, the Pennsylvania Railroad hired twelve thousand blacks, the majority of whom they had recruited in the South and brought up by the trainload.

WRITING THINGS RIGHT

The years between the Civil War and World War I were characterized by mountaintop experiences and valley travails. Reconstruction promised renewal. Post-Reconstruction not only destroyed those dreams but imposed harsh new realities. If the end of the nineteenth century was marked by contradictions and compromises, deaths and rebirths, African American writers recorded it all in ways parallel to, intersecting with, and diverging from the methods of other American writers. From its colonial beginnings, American literature has been inextricably connected with its perceived political and religious usefulness. From the Puritan sermons and hymnals that were the first products of the American printing presses to the captivity and conversion narratives that proved Divine Providence's intervention in individual lives to the novels, poems, and sketches that demonstrated the efficacy of moral and mannered living, the most popular literature in the United States was that which taught and confirmed social mores. Yet increasingly the artist's obligation to instruct was accompanied by mutual desires that it be done pleasingly and in a manner that showed off the writer's familiarity with the literary canon. Thus nineteenth-century American literature tried not merely to delight and instruct but also to highlight intellectual achievement and aesthetic sophistication.

African Americans generally understood these expectations and strove to produce literary works that both pleased and taught. For them, as for their Anglo-American contemporaries, writing was primarily a means of instructing themselves and others and of correcting the historical record. However, for African American writers, the challenge of producing literature both *utile* and *dulce* was exacerbated by the disparagement of their intellectual and creative capacities and by the exoticization and marginalization of African American culture and aspirations at the very time that the nation was working toward unification. Such were the circumstances when William Wells Brown wrote, in his introduction to *The Black Man, His Genius and His Achievements* (1863), "If this work shall aid in vindicating the Negro's character, and show that he is endowed with those intellectual and amiable qualities which adorn and dignify human nature, it will meet the most sanguine hopes of the writer." And such were the catalysts for Victoria Earle Matthews's declaration in *The Value of Race Literature* (1895) that there was

> indubitable evidence of the need of thoughtful, well-defined and intelligently placed efforts on our part, to serve as counterirritants against all such writing that shall stand, having as an aim the supplying of influential and accurate information, on all subjects relating to the Negro and his environments, to inform the American mind at least, for literary purposes. We cannot afford any more than any other people to be indifferent to the fact, that the surest road to real fame is through literature.

Thus African American literature in the mid-nineteenth and early twentieth centuries was used to confirm and to manifest creativity and genius while also documenting and shaping social, political, and spiritual aspirations and conditions.

PERSONAL TESTIMONIES

Before the Civil War, literature had played a vital role in influencing public attitudes. Songs and poems, essays and sermons, autobiographies and novels had stirred both hearts and minds. Slave narratives had been critical to the abolitionist effort. Small wonder then that in the Reconstruction period, African Americans relied heavily on personal testimony. In the fifty years after the Civil War, the number of extant published autobiographies by former slaves was double that of the one hundred years before it. Generally using their slave past as prelude, warning, and resource, postbellum narrators recast the sin and suffering of slavery as trials and tribulations from which they and former slaves, like other survivors of the Civil War or another trauma past, emerged wiser and stronger. Slavery was, in Elizabeth Keckley's words, "a cruel custom" and a "plant of evil" that had been allowed to grow until it had choked, and nearly destroyed, the nation.

Postbellum slave narratives championed the rugged individualism and successful transcendence that characterized both the American Dream, as exemplified by Benjamin Franklin and Abraham Lincoln, and the Horatio Alger myth put forth in popular literature. But the postbellum narrators combined these capitalist possibilities with the strong spirit of community and mutual effort that typified the social, political, and religious sentiments of postwar America. During Reconstruction, especially, narrators concentrated on the lessons learned from slavery and the progress made after emancipation that would entitle African Americans to full participation in the building and maintaining of the new and improved versions of the "City upon the Hill."

The postbellum slave narrative's focus is clearly shown in the titles of works such as Elizabeth Keckley's *Behind the Scenes: Thirty Years a Slave and Four Years in the White House* (1868); *The Experience and Personal Narrative of Uncle Tom Jones: What Was a Slave for Forty-Three Years* (1871); *Life and Adventures of James Williams, a Fugitive Slave, with a Full Description of the Underground Railroad* (1874); *From Slave Cabin to Pulpit, the Autobiography of Peter Randolph* (1893); *From the Virginia Plantation to the National Capitol; or The First and Only Negro Representative in Congress from the Old Dominion* by John Mercer Langston (1894); Henry Clay Bruce's *The New Man: Twenty-Nine Years a Slave, Twenty-Nine Years a Free Man* (1895); *Thirty Years a Slave, From Bondage to Freedom* by Louis Hughes (1896); and Booker T. Washington's *Up From Slavery* (1901).

As social and economic conditions changed and as legal segregation and racial persecution increased, so too did the number of African Americans who presented their experiences in overcoming past adversity as models for the present and blueprints for a better future. Joining the postbellum slave narratives was a series of "progress report autobiographies"—that is, personal accounts by individuals who could not claim unmitigated success but whose achievements thus far were deemed sufficient to instruct and to inspire others. These included works such as *Early Recollections and Life of Dr. James Still* (1877), *The Colored Cadet at West Point* by Henry Ossian Flipper (1878), *Meditations from the Pen of Mrs. Maria W. Stewart* (1879), Susie King Taylor's *Reminiscences of My Life with the 33rd United States Colored Troops* (1902), William Pickens's *The Heir of Slaves* (1910), and James David Corrothers's *In Spite of the Handicap* (1916). Individual studies of those who had endured trials but experienced triumph assuaged the fears of whites and others who worried about revenge against or dependency on them. These autobiographical texts served also to instruct other blacks that they could and should buy into the American Dream.

LITERACY FOR LIBERATION

African American literature and African American literacy had always gone hand in hand, and many works were written expressly for use in schools. As public education developed across the country, and with the advent of the freedman's schools particularly, so did the need for relevant and accurate texts grow. A few schools had curricula that stressed Greek, rhetoric, elocution and higher mathematics. African American scholars, such as William Sanders Scarboroggh and Anna J. Cooper, published textbooks of Greek grammar and translations of literature originally in French, German, and other languages. The majority of the schools that African Americans attended, however, offered reading, writing, arithmetic, and vocational skills. Yet, even for these institutions, writers saw a need for books that adequately expressed the history, position, and aspirations of African Americans. As such, they published an ever increasing number of individual biographies and compendiums of African American contributions. Among the biographies by African Americans about African Americans are *Life and Public Services of Martin R. Delany* (1868) by Frances Anne Rollin, *Frederick Douglass* (1899) by Charles Chesnutt, and *Norris Wright Cuney: A Tribune of the Black People* (1913) by Maud Cuney Hare. Generally, these texts were designed for at least two purposes: to show white readers that blacks were capable of contributing to the rebuilding of the nation and to inform, inspire, and instruct other African Americans of the way to a more satisfying future. This dual purpose is clearly stated in Martin Robison Delany's "Preface" to his *Condition, Elevation, Emigration and Destiny of the Colored People of the United States* (1868). Delany's "sole purpose," he wrote, was "to place before the public in general, and the colored people of the United States in particular, great truths concerning this class of citizens, which appears [sic] to have been heretofore avoided, as well by friends as enemies to their elevation."

During Reconstruction, Delany's efforts were joined by those such as William Wells Brown's *The Negro in the American Rebellion* (1867) and *The Rising Son; or, The Antecedents and Advancement of the Colored Race* (1874), and William Still's *The Underground Rail Road: A Record of Facts, Authentic Narratives, Letters* (1872). As the century advanced, the projects became more grand and more diverse. Alexander Crummell compiled *The Greatness of Christ, and Other Sermons* and Albery A. Whitman versified on *Twasinat's Seminoles; or, The Rape of Florida* (1884). Daniel Payne accepted the challenge of writing *The History of the African American Episcopal Church* (1891) and George Washington Williams needed two volumes for his *History of the Negro Race in America from 1619 to 1880* (1893). W. E. B. Du Bois offered a sociological study, *The Philadelphia Negro* (1899); Booker T. Washington was one of several contributors to the massive "History and Reminiscence of the Afro-American" titled *A New Negro for a New Century* (1900); and Charles Fred White offered *Who's Who in Philadelphia* (1912). Pauline Hopkins's *Primer of Facts Pertaining to the Early Greatness of the African Race* (1905), Alice Dunbar Nelson's *Masterpieces of Negro Eloquence* (1914), and Delilah L. Beasley's *Negro Trail Blazers of California* (1919) were all attempts to enlighten and inspire.

POPULAR LITERATURE AND PUBLISHING

The intended readership for these works was not limited by race, class, or cultural aspiration. African American writers in general wrote what Roy Harvey Pearce calls "popular literature," that is, a literature accessible to all, composed and produced for mass production while not unduly compromising itself or its mission. African

American writers participated in the major literary trends that appeared between the two wars. They tried virtually every genre and every style. They wrote realistic, naturalistic, sentimental fiction. They created epics and lyrics in dialect and in highly romanticized or formalized diction. Often, they subtly revised the themes and techniques of white writers. For example, although the folk tales told by Charles Chesnutt and by Joel Chandler Harris have obvious similarities, Chesnutt's Uncle Junius more clearly recognizes the power of his words and uses them to his own ends. Often, African American writers revised character types and situations to fit the changes in society. One such case is that of the mulatto protagonist, the depictions of which moved from the pitiful victimization of William Wells Brown's Clotel (1867) to the proud claiming of heritage in Frances E. W. Harper's Iola Leroy (1892) and presented possibilities of racial and personal identity that ranged from the militant nationalism of Bernard Belgrave in Sutton Griggs's Imperium in Imperio (1899) to the pathetic self-betrayal of the protagonist in James Weldon Johnson's Autobiography of an Ex-Colored Man (1912).

Finding a publisher is a major problem for any writer. For African American writers this obstacle was often insurmountable. Sometimes special-interest presses such as those dedicated to temperance, peace, and other social reform movements published writers whose work accorded with their goals and did not overtly challenge their assumptions about African Americans. For example, her affiliations with the Women's Christian Temperance Union, the Unitarian Church, and the YMCA often allowed Frances Ellen Watkins Harper to publish in such journals as the Englishwoman's Review, the Woman's Journal and the Peacemaker and Board of Arbitration. Others, such as Frederick Douglass and Booker T. Washington, enjoyed extensive political ties and national stature so high that their essays were sometimes commissioned or reprinted by newspapers and magazines that catered almost exclusively to white readers. During the period when realism and local color were in vogue, stories and poems in dialect or about folk figures enjoyed enthusiastic acceptance. Writers such as Paul Laurence Dunbar and Charles Chesnutt were welcomed in the pages of the Atlantic Monthly, favorably reviewed in the North American Quarterly, and published by established presses such as Dodd, Mead and Houghton Mifflin. Occasionally, a book or two was printed and marketed not as the production of an African American writer but in a series also containing texts by Anglo-Americans. This was the case with William Wells Brown, whose third revision of Clotel was included in James Redpath's Campfire Series, and with Amelia Johnson, whose Clarence and Corrine; or, God's Way (1890) and The Hazeley Family (1894) were part of the Sunday School material produced by the American Baptist Publication Society. William Stanley Braithwaite's success within the white publishing industry was such that he subordinated his own writing to his editing of the Anthology of Magazine Verse (1913–29), The Book of Elizabethan Verse, The Book of Restoration Verse, and other such collections. The majority of African American writers, however, were published first and most frequently in an outlet largely ignored by most literary scholars, the African American Press.

THE AFRICAN AMERICAN PRESS

The African American Press was not a single company but a diverse group of African American individuals and institutions unified by two basic attributes. First, their goal was to promulgate the writings of African Americans to a readership that was primarily African American. And, second, their publications were, as Frankie Hutton characterizes them, "uplifting, positive, and forward thinking both in the messages conveyed and in spirit." African American Press publications encouraged black Americans to write stories and poems, essays and letters by sponsoring contests, advertising, and often distributing the resulting volumes. From *Freedom's Journal* in 1837 and *The Anglo African Magazine* (1859) to *The Mystery* (1843) and *The North Star* (1847), which was reincarnated as *Frederick Douglass's Paper* (1851), African American writers had gained their own audiences for their artistic and philosophical utterances as well as their theological and political declarations. With the end of slavery, African American publications flourished. By 1896 more than 150 newspapers and magazines had been founded. Boston, New York, and Pennsylvania were the most favored headquarters, but Ohio, Minnesota, and California also entered into the publishing stream, and its tributaries flowed through Alabama, Louisiana, Kansas, Iowa, and Oklahoma territories with much passion and purpose. Like the ventures of Anglo-Americans and others, most of the presses were undercapitalized, short lived, and local; but many formed coalitions with other papers and had a significant impact on national and international perspectives.

It was with the African American Press that journalists such as Ida B. Wells, T. Thomas Fortune, Phillip A. Bell, and Victoria Earle Matthews gained their audiences. Some, such as Thomas Detter, author of *Nellie Brown; or, The Jealous Wife* (1871) and Pauline Hopkins, author of *Contending Forces* (1900), were not only reporters but also novelists. And it was as serializations in the pages of the African American Press that Frances Ellen Watkins Harper published three of her four novels and that Clarissa Minnie Thompson presented *Treading the Winepress*.

In *The Afro American Press and Its Editors* (1891), I. Garland Penn makes it clear that art was also politics and that quantity was not to be confused with quality:

> That the measure of a people's literary qualifications is its press facilities has been accepted, we think, as a fact; yet a people's literary worth is not to be estimated solely by the number of its newspapers, magazines and periodicals. . . . Press facilities may be a measure of a people's literary worth only insomuch as the press is able, practical, and efficient; and so far as it expresses itself clearly and produces sentiment in accordance with the principles of right, truth and justice.

The African American Press included publications by special-interest groups such as churches, labor unions, sororities, and fraternities. An unusual number of these groups did not limit their aspirations to providing mere in-house organs. In the spirit of its motto, "Lifting as We Climb," the National Association of Colored Women began publishing *Women's Era* in 1894. The NAACP founded the *Crisis* in 1910 and published a magazine for children called *The Brownie's Book*. The Urban League created *Opportunity*, which, along with *Crisis*, provided the foundation of the Harlem Renaissance. Sutton Griggs, using the expertise gained by privately publishing his own five novels, founded in 1914 the Public Welfare League as a means of encouraging African American talent and influencing public opinion. Among other influential members of the African American Press in the second half of the nineteenth century were McGirt's Publishing Company, which published *McGirt's Magazine* as well as individual books, and the Colored Co-Operative Publishing Company, which presented individual titles and serialized novels in its periodical the *Colored American*.

Of particular interest is the period between 1890 and 1910, a time known to many as "the women's era." In 1892, for example, appeared *Iola Leroy; or, Shadows Uplifted* by Frances E. W. Harper, *A Voice from the South by a Black Woman of the South* by Anna Julia Cooper, *From Darkness Cometh the Light; or, Struggles for Freedom* by Lucy A. Delaney, and *Southern Horrors: Lynch Law in All Its Phases* by Ida B. Wells. In fiction, in essays, in autobiographies, and in investigative reporting, African American women were voicing their perspectives and recording their activities. Nor were their voices alone, for during this time volumes testifying to the women now claiming the era for themselves and their race appeared. Their tenor is evident in their titles, such as Monroe Majors's *Noted Negro Women: Their Triumphs and Activities* (1893), Lawson Andrews Scruggs's *Women of Distinction: Remarkable in Works and Invincible in Character* (1893), and Gertrude Mossell's *The Work of the Afro-American Woman* (1894).

The lines between secular and special interest presses were not so clearly drawn as they are today, and it is true that the African American Press was, to a great extent, created by and strongly dependent on African American church leaders. The AME Book Concern, for example, was established in 1817 not only to provide the disciplines, hymns, and records of the newly organized African Methodist Episcopal Church but also to publish educational materials for church literacy programs. From that enterprise developed bookstores, national distribution systems, and a variety of texts of literary and social importance. The Book Concern created the *Repository of Religion and Literature and of Science and Art* (1858); the *Christian Recorder*, whose masthead proclaimed that it was published "for the dissemination of Religion, Morality, Literature and Science"; and the *A.M.E. Church Review*, which was founded as "a literary magazine" in 1884. While no copies are known to have survived, the AME Book Concern is also stated to have published *The Ladies' Magazine* and *The Children's Recorder*.

Similar influence was offered by other denominations. Beginning in 1896 the National Baptist Publishing Company soon became a major conduit for songs, poems, autobiographies, histories, and fiction composed by African American writers. It was from the offices of the *South Western Christian Advocate* that Victoria Rogers Albert's *House of Bondage* (1900) was presented. Generally, the newspapers and magazines of the Afro-Protestant Press championed abolition, temperance, suffrage, education, and economic development and encouraged the editorials, essays, and letters as well as the poems, plays, short stories, and serialized novels of African Americans. They held literary contests, published book reviews, argued points of aesthetics, and advertised books by and for African Americans.

As World War I began, African Americans were reading and writing, publishing and pontificating in virtually every genre and in every literary style. African American writers had become skilled at correcting misinformation and challenging literary movements such as the Plantation School and other revisionist, and sometimes repulsive, literary trends. Some, such as Alice Moore Dunbar Nelson, Daniel Webster Davis, and Charles Chesnutt, had contributed to the local color movement. Others had written biographies, histories, autobiographies, sermons, meditations, and patriotic poems. Many had achieved both national and international prominence. Others were known and celebrated primarily within their communities or through the national African American press. All had set the stage and established the stories from (and against) which the next generations could create their own renaissance.

CHARLOTTE FORTEN GRIMKÉ

1837–1914

For four generations, the Fortens of Philadelphia had been free, wealthy, educated, and politically active. Because the Philadelphia schools were racially segregated, the Forten children were tutored at home. But when sixteen-year-old Charlotte decided she wanted to become a teacher, she was sent to live in Salem, Massachusetts. Two years later she had graduated from Higginson Grammar School, and her

Parting Hymn had been selected over thirty-nine other entries as the class song. While studying at Salem Normal School, Forten followed the example of her aunts and grandmother by joining the local antislavery committee and by publishing occasional poems and essays. She became the first African American to teach in the Salem schools. During the Civil War, she spent two years in Port Royal, South Carolina, participating in an experimental program for educating former slaves. Forten provided several northern periodicals with firsthand accounts of the project's success. One of her best known essays, *Life in the Sea Islands,* appeared in the *Atlantic Monthly.* Forten taught in Philadelphia and Washington, D.C., before ill health forced her to accept the less demanding but prestigious position as clerk in the Treasury Department. In 1876, she married the Reverend Francis James Grimké, a former fugitive slave and a graduate of the Princeton Theological Seminary. For the next thirty-six years, the Grimké home was a center for those who loved literature, art, and music and hated racism and oppression.

During her life Forten enjoyed a modest reputation as a poet and essayist and as translator of Emil Erckmann and Alexander Chatrain's novel *Madame Therese; or, The Volunteers of '92.* Today, however, she is best known for works she never intended for publication, the journals that she kept between 1854 and 1864 and between 1885 and 1889. Beginning with her arrival in Salem and chronicling her experiences during the Civil War and Reconstruction, these works provide rare insight into the coming of age of a nineteenth-century free black woman; the culture and traditions of middle-class African Americans; and the lesser known activities of individuals such as Frederick Douglass, John Greenleaf Whittier, Wendell Phillips, Mary Shepard, and Laura Towne.

A Parting Hymn

When Winter's royal robes of white
    From hill and vale are gone,
And the glad voices of the spring
    Upon the air are borne,
Friends, who have met with us before,   5
Within these walls shall meet no more.

Forth to a noble work they go:
    O, may their hearts keep pure,
And hopeful zeal and strength be theirs
    To labor and endure,   10
That they an earnest faith may prove
By words of truth and deeds of love.

May those, whose holy task it is
    To guide impulsive youth,
Fail not to cherish in their souls   15
    A reverence for truth;
For teachings which the lips impart
Must have their source within the heart.

May all who suffer share their love—
    The poor and the oppressed;   20
So shall the blessing of our God
    Upon their labors rest.

And may we meet again where all
Are blest and freed from every thrall.

1856

JOURNALS

A wish to record the passing events of my life, which, even if quite unimportant to others, naturally possess great interest to myself, and of which it will be pleasant to have some remembrance, has induced me to commence this journal. I feel that keeping a diary will be a pleasant and profitable employment of my leisure hours, and will afford me much pleasure in other years, by recalling to my mind the memories of other days, thoughts of much-loved friends from whom I may then be separated, with whom I now pass many happy hours, in taking delightful walks, and holding "sweet converse"; the interesting books that I read; and the different people, places and things that I am permitted to see.

Besides this, it will doubtless enable me to judge correctly of the growth and improvement of my mind from year to year.

—C. L. F., *Salem, May 1854.*

From Journal One

Wednesday, May 24, 1854

Rose at five. The sun was shining brightly through my window, and I felt vexed with myself that he should have risen before me; I shall not let him have that advantage again very soon. How bright and beautiful are these May mornings! The air is so pure and balmy, the trees are in full blossom, and the little birds sing sweetly. I stand by the window listening to their music, but suddenly remember that I have an Arithmetic lesson which employes me until breakfast; then to school, recited my lessons, and commenced my journal. After dinner practised a music lesson, did some sewing, and then took a pleasant walk by the water. I stood for some time admiring the waves as they rose and fell, sparkling in the sun, and could not help envying a party of boys who were enjoying themselves in a sailing boat. On my way home, I stopped at Mrs. [Caroline] Putnam's and commenced reading "Hard Times," a new story by Dickens. The scene opens in a very matter-of-fact school, where teacher and committee deal in stern facts, and allow no flights of fancy in the youthful minds committed to their charge. One interesting little girl is severely reprimanded for wishing a carpet of flowers (not natural ones); while a repulsive looking boy receives much praise for a very long definition of the word "horse," which seems quite unintelligible to every one else. I anticipate to much pleasure in reading this story.—Saw some agreeable friends, [Jonathan] McBuffum and his family from Lynn, prepared tea, and spent the evening in writing.

Thursday, May 25

Did not intend to write this evening, but have just heard of something that is worth recording;—something which must ever rouse in the mind of every true friend of liberty and humanity, feelings of the deepest indignation and sorrow. Another fugitive [Anthony Burns] from bondage has been arrested; a poor man, who for two short months has trod the soil and breathed the air of the "Old Bay State," was arrested like a criminal in the streets of her capital, and is now kept strictly guarded,—a double police force is required, the military are in readiness; and all this is done to prevent a man, whom God has created in his own image, from regaining that freedom with which, he, in common with every other human being, is endowed. I can only hope and pray most earnestly that Boston will not again disgrace herself by sending him back to a bondage worse than death; or rather that she will redeem herself from the disgrace which his arrest alone has brought upon her. [1] The weather is gloomy and my feelings correspond with it, how applicable now are the words of the immortal Cowper, [2]

> "My ear is pained,
> My soul is sick with every day's report
> Of wrong and outrage, with which earth is filled;
> There is no flesh in man's obdurate heart,
> It does not feel for man; the nat'ral bond
> Of brotherhood, is severed as the flax.
> He finds his fellow guilty of a skin
> Not coloured like his own; and having power
> T'enforce the wrong, for such a worthy cause
> Dooms and devotes him as his lawful prey."

Friday, May 26, 1854

Had a conversation with Miss Mary Shepard about slavery; she is, as I thought, thoroughly opposed to it, but does not agree with me in thinking that the churches and ministers are generally supporters of the infamous system; I believe it firmly. Mr. [Albert] Barnes, one of the most prominent of the Philadelphia clergy, who does not profess to be an abolitionist, has declared his belief that 'the American church is the bulwark of slavery.' Words cannot express all that I feel; all that is felt by the friends of Freedom, when thinking of this great obstacle to the removal of slavery from our land. Alas! that it should be so. I was much disappointed in not seeing the eclipse, which, it [sic] was expected to be the most entire that has taken place for years, but the weather was rainy and the sky obscured by clouds, so after spending half the afternoon on the roof of the house in eager expectation, I saw nothing; heard since that the sun made his appearance for a minute or two, but I was not fortunate enough to catch even the momentary glimpse of him. Father left yesterday for Providence and N.[orth] Bed-

1. The federal court decided that Anthony Burns was the property of Charles F. Suttle and should be immediately returned to him. So intense was the opposition to the decision that the Marines had to provide security for the transfer.
2. William Cowper (1731–1800), English poet. The quotation is from *The Task: A Poem in Six Books*, book 2, *The Time-Piece* 5–15.

ford; thinks he will return tomorrow evening. I write to the sound of music sweet; Sarah [Cassey Smith] is playing the "Bords Du Rhin," and I imagine myself standing on the banks of that beautiful river which flows so placidly past the happy homes of Germany. All around is lovely and calm; the sun is shedding his last rays upon the distant hills, and the gentle warbling of the shepherd's flute is heard as he returns home with his flock. I wish that this delightful day-dream could last, but it cannot, and I must rouse myself from it and return to sober reality. It is already time that I should be indulging in nightly dreams.—

> "Ah—visions less beguiling far,
> Than waking dreams by daylight are."

Saturday, May 27

Have been very busy all morning, sweeping, dusting, sewing, and doing sundry other little things which are always to be done on Saturday.—Spent a delightful hour in the afternoon at Miss [Mary] Shepard's, looking with her and Miss [Elizabeth] Church, over some beautiful engravings, representing those parts of France, Italy and Switzerland in which the persecuted Waldenses[3] lived. Some of the scenery was very lovely, with smooth lakes and quiet valleys; sparkling streams on the banks of which cattle and sheep were very demurely grazing, and near them small groups of peasants in their pretty and fanciful costume; the spirit of repose seems breathed around.—And then we turn to another scene where the lofty mountains rise in grandeur to the very clouds; how sublime, how very grand they appear! The views were all beautiful, and looking at them has increased my desire to visit these countries. Miss Shepard showed us some of her beautiful books, and read one or two exquisite pieces of poetry. I enjoyed myself very much.—Returned home, read the Anti-Slavery papers, and then went down to the depot to meet father; he had arrived in Boston early in the morning, regretted very much that he had not reached there in the evening before to attend the great meeting at Faneuil Hall. He says that the excitement in Boston is very great; the trial of the poor man takes place on Monday. We scarcely dare to think of what may be the result; there seems to be nothing too bad for those Northern tools of slavery to do.

Sunday, May 28

A lovely day; in the morning I read in the Bible and wrote letters; in the afternoon took a quiet walk in Harmony Grove, and as I passed by many 'an unknown grave,' the question 'who sleeps below?' rose often to my mind, and led to a long train of thoughts, of who those departed ones might have been, how much beloved, how deeply regretted and how worthy of such love and such regret. I love to walk on the Sabbath, for all is so peaceful; the noise and labor of every-day life has ceased; and in perfect silence we can commune with Nature and with Nature's God. Spent the evening very pleasantly at Mrs. [Cecelia] Babcock's.

---

3. Protestant religious sect of medieval origin.

Tuesday, May 30

Rose very early and was busy until nine o'clock; then, at Mrs. Putnam's urgent request, went to keep store for her while she went to Boston to attend the Anti-Slavery Convention. I was very anxious to go, and will certainly do so to-morrow; the arrest of the alleged fugitive will give additional interest to the meetings, I should think. His trial is still going on and I can scarcely think of anything else; read again to-day as most suitable to my feelings and to the times, "The Runaway Slave at Pilgrim's Point," by Elizabeth B. Browning;[4] how powerfully it is written! how earnestly and touchingly does the writer portray the bitter anguish of the poor fugitive as she thinks over all the wrongs and sufferings that she has endured, and of the sin to which tyrants have driven her but which they alone must answer for! It seems as if no one could read this poem without having his sympathies roused to the utmost on behalf of the oppressed. After a long conversation with my friends on their return, on this all-absorbing subject, we separated for the night, and I went to bed, weary and sad.

Wednesday, May 31

The last day of spring. She has not been very pleasant this year, until within a few weeks, during which her smiles have been so bountiful and bright, her character so very lovable, that we part from her with regret. Sarah [Cassey Smith] and I went to Boston in the morning. Everything was much quieter—outwardly than we expected, but still much real indignation and excitement prevail. We walked past the Court-House, which is now lawlessly converted into a prison, and filled with soldiers, some of whom were looking from the windows, with an air of insolent authority, which made my blood boil, while I felt the strongest contempt for their cowardice and servility. We went to the meeting, but the best speakers were absent, engaged in the most arduous and untiring efforts in behalf of the poor fugitive; but though we missed the glowing eloquence of [Wendell] Phillips, [William Lloyd] Garrison, and [Theodore] Parker,[5] still there were excellent speeches made, and our hearts responded to the exalted sentiments of Truth and Liberty which were uttered. The exciting intelligence which occasionally came in relation to the trial, added fresh zeal to the speakers, of whom Stephen Foster and his wife [Abigail Kelley][6] were the principal. The latter addressed, in the most eloquent language, the women present, entreating them to urge their husbands and brothers to action, and also to give their aid on all occasions in our just and holy cause.—I did not see father the whole day; he, of course, was deeply interested in the trial.— Dined at Mr. Garrison's; his wife is one of the loveliest persons I have ever seen, worthy of such a husband. At the table, I watched earnestly the expression of that noble face, as he spoke beautifully in support of the non-resistant principles to which he has kept firm; his is indeed the very highest Christian spirit, to which I cannot hope to reach, however, for I believe in

---

4. British poet (1806–1861).
5. All prominent abolitionists.
6. Equal rights activist (1810–1887) whose election to the executive board of the American Anti-

Slavery Society led to a split in the organization and the formation of the American and Foreign Anti-Slavery Society. Stephen Seymonds Foster (1809–1881), New England equal rights activist.

resistance to tyrants, and would fight for liberty until death. We came home in the evening, and felt sick at heart as we passed through the streets of Boston on our way to the depot, seeing the military as they rode along, ready at any time to prove themselves the minions of the South.

Thursday, June 1

I am keeping store for Mrs. Putnam again. Miss [Sarah Parker] Remond is still in Boston, and Mrs. [Nancy] R.[emond] has gone also; father and Aunt Harriet [Purvis] are there. The trial is over at last; the commissioner's decision will be given to-morrow. We are all in the greatest suspense; what will that decision be? Alas! that any one should have the power to decide the right of a fellow being to himself! It is thought by many that he will be acquitted of the *great crime* of leaving a life of bondage, as the legal evidence is not thought sufficient to convict him. But it is only too probable that they will sacrifice him to propitiate the South, since so many at the North dared oppose the passage of the infamous Nebraska Bill.[7] Miss [Helen] Putnam was married this evening. Mr. [Octavius B.] Frothingham performed the ceremony, and in his prayer alluded touchingly to the events of this week; he afterwards in conversation with the bridegroom, (Mr. [Jacob] Gilliard), spoke in the most feeling manner about this case,— his sympathies are on the right side. The wedding was a pleasant one; the bride looked very lovely; and we enjoyed ourselves as much as is possible in these exciting times. It is impossible to be happy now.

Friday, June 2

Our worst fears are realized; the decision was against poor [Anthony] Burns, and he has been sent back to a bondage worse, a thousand times worse than death. Even an attempt at rescue was utterly impossible; the prisoner was completely surrounded by soldiers with bayonets fixed, a canon loaded, ready to be fired at the slightest sign. To-day Massachusetts has again been disgraced; again has she showed her submissions to the Slave Power; and Oh! with what deep sorrow do we think of what will doubtless be the fate of that poor man, when he is again consigned to the horrors of slavery. With what scorn must that government be regarded which cowardly assembles thousands of soldiers to satisfy the demands of slaveholders; to deprive of his freedom a man, created in God's own image, whose sole offense is the color of his skin! And if resistance is offered to this outrage, these soldiers are to shoot down American citizens without mercy; and this by express orders of a government which proudly boasts of being the freest in the world; this on the very soil where the Revolution of 1776 began; in sight of the battlefield, where thousands of brave men fought and died in opposing British tyranny, which was nothing compared with the American oppression of today. In looking over my diary, I perceive that I did not mention that there was on the Friday night after the man's arrest,

7. I.e., the Kansas-Nebraska Act of 1854, which provided for the organization of Kansas and Nebraska into territories but led to great controversy over the presence or nonpresence of slavery within them.

an attempt made to rescue him, but although it failed, on account of there not being men enough engaged in it, all honor should be given to those who bravely made the attempt. I can write no more. A cloud seems hanging over me, over all our persecuted race, which nothing can dispel.

Sunday, June 4

A beautiful day. The sky is cloudless, the sun shines warm and bright, and a delicious breeze fans my cheeks as I sit by the window writing. How strange it is that in a world so beautiful, there can be so much wickedness, on this delightful day, while many are enjoying themselves in their happy homes, not poor Burns only, but millions beside are suffering in chains; and how many Christian ministers to-day will mention him, or those who suffer with him? How many will speak from the pulpit against the cruel outrage on humanity which has just been committed, or against the many, even worse ones, which are committed in this country every day? Too well do we know that there are but very few, and these few alone deserve to be called the ministers of Christ, whose doctrine was 'Break every yoke, and let the oppressed go free.'—During the past week, we have had a vacation, which I had expected to enjoy very much, but it was, of course, impossible for me to do so. To-morrow school commences, and although the pleasure I shall feel in again seeing my beloved teacher, and in resuming my studies will be much saddened by recent events, yet they shall be a fresh incentive to more earnest study, to aid me in fitting myself for laboring in a holy cause, for enabling me to do much towards changing the condition of my oppressed and suffering people. Would that those with whom I shall recite to-morrow could sympathize with me in this; would that they could look upon all God's creatures without respect to color, feeling that it is character alone which makes the true man or woman! I earnestly hope that the time will come when they will feel thus.—I have several letters to write to-day to send by Aunt Harriet [Purvis] who leaves for Philadelphia tomorrow. Father left yesterday, he has not yet decided to come here to live; he will write and tell me what he has determined to do, as soon as he has consulted mother. I fear he has not now a very favorable opinion of Massachusetts; still I hope they will come; I long to see the children again.

*   *   *

Tuesday, June 6

Studied my lesson, then went to school. How pleasant it is after a few days separation, to see our kind teacher and the happy faces around her again, and to resume our studies with renewed energy and perseverance! The day has been so beautiful and bright that it seems as if not a single moment should be wasted. After school Henry [Cassey] and I went to Mr. [Charles] Hoffman's garden and walked through the hot houses. We saw some very splendid cactuses, some of a bright scarlet color, others of the deepest crimson. Their gorgeous hues seemed fitter for "the clime of the East, the land of the sun," than for our colder climate. Then we stopped to admire the graceful and beautiful fuchsias, and saw some superb emblem of "devotion." I love flowers; they beautify our homes, and seem to diffuse cheerfulness as well as fragrance around us; and there are no purer or more beautiful ornaments than these natural ones.—Began to read "A Peep at Number Five." I like it very much; Miss Shepard gave me a slight sketch of the author who was a very lovely person. To know something of the author always adds greatly to the interest of a book.—In the evening, wrote until bed-time.

* * *

From Journal Three

Tuesday Night [October 28, 1862]

T'was a strange sight as our boat approached the landing at Hilton Head.[1] On the wharf was a motley assemblage,—soldiers, officers, and "contrabands"[2] of every hue and size. They were mostly black, however, and certainly the most dismal specimens I ever saw. H.[ilton] H.[ead] looks like a very desolate place; just a long low, sandy point running out into the sea with no visible dwellings upon it but the soldiers' white roofed tents.

Thence, after an hour's delay, during which we signed a paper, which was virtually taking the oath of allegiance, we left the "United States," most rocking of rockety propellers,—and took a steamboat for Beaufort.[3] On board the boat was General [Rufus] Saxton to whom we were introduced. I like his face exceedingly. And his manners were very courteous and affable. He looks like a thoroughly *good* man.—From H.[ilton] H.[ead] to B.[eaufort] the same low line of sandy shore bordered by trees[,] almost the only object of interest to me were the remains of an old Huguenot Fort,[4] built many, many years ago.

Arrived at B.[eaufort;] we found that we had yet not reached our home. Went to Mr. [Mansfield] French's, and saw there Reuben T.[omlinson] whom I was very glad to meet, and Mrs. [Francis] Gage, who seemed to be in rather a dismal state of mind. B.[eaufort] looks like a pleasant place. The houses are large and quite handsome, built in the usual Southern style with verandahs around them, and beautiful trees. One magnolia tree in Mr. F.[rench]'s yard is splendid,—quite as large as some of our large shade trees, and with the most beautiful foliage, a dark rich glossy green.

Went into the Commissary's Office to wait for the boat which was to take us to St. Helena's Island which is about six miles from B.[eaufort]. Tis here that Miss [Laura] Towne has her school, in which I am to teach and that Mr. Hunn will have his store. While waiting in the office we saw several military gentleman [sic], *not* very creditable specimens, I sh'ld say. The little Commissary himself, Capt. T. is a perfect little popinjay, and he and a Colonel somebody who didn't look any too sensible, talked in a very smart

1. South Carolina port.
2. When slaves were abandoned or escaped during the war, the U.S. government declared them "con-

traband of war" and under its supervision.
3. In South Carolina.
4. A fort built by early French Protestant settlers.

manner, evidently for our especial benefit. The word "nigger" was plentifully used, whereupon I set them down at once as *not* gentleman [*sic*]. Then they talked a great deal about rebel attacks and yellow fever, and other alarming things, with significant nods and looks at each other. We saw through them at once, and were not at all alarmed by any of their representations. But if they are a fair example of army officers, I sh'ld pray to see as little of them as possible.

To my great joy found that we were to be rowed by a crew of negro boatmen. Young Mr. F.[rench—] whom I like—accompanied us, while Mr. H.[unn] went with a flat to get our baggage. The row was delightful. It was just at sunset—a grand Southern sunset; and the gorgeous clouds of crimson and gold were reflected in the waters below, which were smooth and calm as a mirror. Then, as we glided along, the rich sonorous tones of the boatmen broke upon the evening stillness. Their singing impressed me much. It was so sweet and strange and solemn. "Roll, Jordan, Roll" was grand, and another

> "Jesus make de blind to see
> Jesus make de deaf to hear
> Jesus make de cripple walk
> Walk in, dear Jesus,"

and the refrain

> "No man can hender me."

It was very, very impressive. I want to hear these men sing [John Greenleaf] Whittier's[5] "Song of the Negro Boatmen." I am going to see if it can't be brought about in some way.

It was nearly dark when we reached St. Helena's, where we found Miss T.[owne]'s carriage awaiting us, and then we three and our driver, had a long drive along the lonely roads in the dark night. How easy it sh'ld have been for a band of guerillas—had any chanced that way—to seize and hang us. But we found nothing of the kind. We were in a jubilant state of mind and sang "John Brown" with a will as we drove through the pines and palmettos. Arrived at the Superintendent's house[;] we were kindly greeted by him and the ladies and shown into a lofty *ceilinged* parlor where a cheerful wood fire glowed in the grate, and we soon began to feel quite at home in the very heart of Rebeldom; only that I do not at all realize yet that we are in S.[outh] C.[arolina]. It is all a strange wild dream, from which I am constantly expecting to awake. But I can write no more now. I am tired, and still feel the motion of the ship in my poor head. Good night, dear A!

Wednesday, October 29

A lovely day, but rather cool, I sh'ld think, for the "sunny South." The ship still reals [*sic*] in my head, and everything is most unreal, yet I went to

---

5. American poet and abolitionist (1807–1892).

drive . . . We drove to Oaklands, our future home. It is very pleasantly situated, but the house is in rather a dilapidated condition, as are most of the houses here, and the and the [sic] yard and garden have a neglected look, when it is cleaned up, and the house made habitable I think it will be quite a pleasant place. There are some lovely roses growing there and quantities of ivy creeping along the ground, even under the house, in wild luxuriance—The negroes on the place are very kind and polite. I think I shall get on amicably with them[.]

After walking about and talking with them, and plucking some roses and ivy to send home, we left Oaklands and drove to the school. It is kept by Miss [Ellen] Murray and Miss Towne in the little Baptist Church, which is beautifully situated in a grove of live oaks. Never saw anything more beautiful than these trees. It is strange that we do not hear of them at the North. They are the first objects that attract one's attention here. They are large, noble trees with small glossy green leaves. Their beauty consists in the long bearded moss with which every branch is heavily draped. This moss is singularly beautiful, and gives a solemn almost funeral aspect to the trees.

We went into the school, and heard the children read and spell. The teachers tell us that they have made great improvement in a very short time, and I noticed with pleasure how bright, how eager to learn many of them seem. The singing delighted me most. They sang beautifully in their rich, sweet clear tones, and with that peculiar swaying motion which I had noticed before in the older people, and which seems to make their singing all the more effective. Besides several other tunes they sang "Marching Along" with much spirit, and then one of their own hymns "Down in the Lonesome Valley," which is sweetly solemn and most beautiful. Dear children! born in slavery, but free at last? May God preserve to you all the blessings of freedom, and may you be in every possible way fitted to enjoy them. My heart goes out to you. I shall be glad to do all that I can to help you.—

As we drove homeward I noticed that the trees are just beginning to turn; some beautiful scarlet berries were growing along the roadside, and everywhere the beautiful live oak with its moss drapery. The palmettos disappoint me much. Most of them have a very jagged appearance, and are yet stiff and ungraceful. The country is very level—as flat as that in eastern Penn.[sylvania]. There are plenty of woods, but I think they have not the grandeur of our Northern woods. The cotton fields disappoint me too. They have a very straggling look, and the pods are small, not at all the great snowballs that I had imagined. Altogether the country w'ld be rather desolate looking were it not for my beautiful and evergreen live oaks.

Friday, October 31

Miss T.[owne] went to B.[eaufort] to-day, and I taught for her. I enjoyed it much. The children are well-behaved and eager to learn. It will be a happiness to teach here. I like Miss [Ellen] Murray so much. She is of English parentage, born in the Provinces. She is one of the most whole-souled warm-hearted women I ever met. I felt drawn to her from the first (before I knew she was English) and of course I like her none the less for that. Miss Towne also is a delightful person. "A charming lady" Gen. Saxton calls her and my heart echoes the words. She is housekeeper, physician, everything, here. The most indispensable person on the place, and the people are devoted to her. And indeed she is quite a remarkable young lady. She is one of the earliest comers, and has done much good in teaching and superintending the negroes. She is quite young; not more than twenty-two or three I sh'ld think, and is superintendent of two plantations. I like her energy and decision of character. Her appearance too is very interesting. Mr. [Richard] S.[oule] the superintendent, is a very kind, agreeable person. I like him.

Sunday, November 2

Drove to church to-day—to the same little Baptist Church that the school is held in. The people came in slowly. They have no way of telling the time. About eleven they had all assembled; the church was full. Old and young were there assembled in their Sunday dresses. Clean gowns on, clean head handkerchiefs, bright colored, of course, I noticed that some had even reached the dignity of straw hats, with bright feathers. The services were very interesting. The minister, Mr. P.[hillips?] is an earnest N.[ew] E.[ngland] man. The singing was very beautiful, sat there in a kind of trance and listened to it, and while I listened looked through the open windows into the beautiful grove of oaks with their moss drapery. "Ah w'ld that my tongue c'ld utter the thoughts that arise in me." But it cannot. The sermon was quite good. But I enjoyed nothing so much as the singing—the wonderful, beautiful singing. There can be no doubt that these people have a great deal of musical talent. It was a beautiful sight,—their enthusiasm. After the service two couples were married. Then the meeting was out. The various groups under the trees forming a very pretty picture. We drove to the Episcopal Church afterward where the aristocracy of Rebeldom was to worship. The building is much smaller than the others, but there is a fine organ there on which Miss W.[ay?] played while some of the young superintendents sang very finely, and then we came home. It is all like a dream still, and will be for a long time, I suppose; a strange wild dream. When we get settled in our own house and I have fairly entered into teaching, perhaps I shall begin to realize it all. What we are to do for furniture I know not. Our sole possessions now consist of two bureaus and a bedstead. Mr. H.[unn] had not time to get the mattresses in N.[ew] York. So I suppose we must use blanket substitutes till we can do better. I am determined not to be discouraged at anything. I have never felt more hopeful, more cheerful than I do now.

Oaklands. Tuesday, November 4

Came to our new home to-day. Felt sorry to leave the friends who have been so kind to us, but as they are only three miles distant[,] hope to see them occasionally. But nobody here has much time for visiting. Our home looks rather desolate; the only furniture consisting of two bureaus, three small pine tables and two chairs, one of which has a broken back. L.[izzie] and I have manufactured a tolerable drugget out of some woollen stuff, red and black plaid which will give our "parlor" a somewhat more comfortable look. I have already hung up my lovely Evangeline, and two or three other prints and gathered some beautiful roses. This has been a busy day. A few more such and we hope that our home will begin to look homelike. I am tired, dear A. Good night, and God be with you.

Wednesday, November 5

Had my first regular teaching experience, and to you and you only friend beloved, will acknowledge that it was *not* a very pleasant one. Part of my scholars are very tiny,—babies, I call them—and it is hard to keep them quiet and interested while I am hearing the larger ones. They are too young even for the alphabet, it seems to me. I think I must write home and ask somebody to send me picture-books and toys to amuse them with. I fancied Miss T.[owne] looked annoyed when, at one time the little ones were usually restless. Perhaps it was only my fancy. Dear Miss M.[urray] was kind and considerate as usual. She is very lovable. Well I *must* not be discouraged. Perhaps things will go on better to-morrow. I am sure I enjoyed the walk to school. Through those lovely woods, just brightening to scarlet now. Met the ladies about halfway, and they gave me a drive to the church. Lizzie H.[unn] tells me that the store has been crowded all day. Her father hasn't had time to arrange his goods. I foresee that his store, to which people from all the neighboring plantations come,—will be a source of considerable interest and amusement. We've established our household on—as we hope—a firm basis. We have *Rose* for our little maid-of-all-work, *Amoretta* for cook, washer, and ironer, and *Cupid*, yes, Cupid himself, for clerk, oysterman and future coachman. I must also inform you dear A., that we have made ourselves a bed, whereon we hope to rest to-night, for rest *I* certainly did not last night, despite innumerable blankets designed to conceal and render inactive the bones of the bed. But said bones did so protrude that sleep was almost an impossibility to our poor little body. Everything is still very, very strange. I am not at all homesick, but it does seem *so* long since I saw some who are very dear, and I believe *I* am quite sick for want of a letter. But patience! patience! *That* is a luxury which cannot possibly be enjoyed before the last of next week.

Thursday, November 6

Rained all day so that I c'ldn't go to school. Attended store part of the day. T'was crowded nearly all the time. It was quite amusing to see how eager the people are to buy. The bright handkerchiefs—imitation Madras—are an especial attraction. I think they were very quiet and orderly considering how crowded the place was. This afternoon made another bed; and this eve. finished a very long letter to father, the first part of which was begun last month. I wish I c'ld see them all. It w'ld be such a happiness. My dear, dear Quincy [Forten]—I wonder if he w'ld know me now, God bless him! God be with him! Cut out a dress to-day for an old woman—Venus,—who thanked and blessed me enough poor old soul. It was a pleasure to hear her say what a happy year this has been for her[:] "Nobody to whip me nor dribe me, and plenty to eat. Nebber had such a happy year in my life before." Promised to make a little dress for her great-grandchild—only a few weeks old. It shall be a bright pink calico, such as will delight the little free baby's eyes, when it shall be old enough to appreciate it.

Friday, November 7

Had a lovely walk to school. The trees,—a few of them are thinning beautifully now, but they have not the general brilliant hues of the northern woods. The mocking birds were singing sweetly this morn. I think my "babies" were rather more manageable to-day, but they were certainly troublesome enough. This afternoon L.[izzie] and I went round to the "quarters." Some of the people are really quite interesting, and all were pleasant and seemed glad to see us. One poor woman has a very sick child. The poor little thing is only a few months old, and is suffering dreadfully with whooping cough. It is pitiful to hear it moan. If our good doctor Miss T.[owne] were only here. But she does not come to-day.

Saturday

This eve. after sewing, read part of "Alexandre"[6] aloud. I must practice my French every day, or I shall entirely forget it. I wish I had my chessmen.

Saturday, November 8

Spent part of the morn. in the store which was more crowded than ever. So much gold and silver I've not seen for many months. These people must have been hoarding it up for a long time. They are rather unreasonable, and expect one to wait on a dozen at once. But it is not strange. Miss T.[owne] came this afternoon, and gave medicine to Tilla's baby, which seems, I think, a little better; and all the other children. Everyone of them has the whooping cough. I've put my books and a vase of lovely roses and oleanders on our little table. The fire burns brightly, and the little room looks quite cheerful and homelike. Have done some sewing and reading.

Monday, November 10

We taught—or rather commenced teaching the children "John Brown" which they entered into eagerly. I felt to the full the significance of *that* song being sung here in S.[outh] C.[arolina] by little negro children, by those whom he—the glorious old man—died to save. Miss [Laura] T.[owne] told them about him. A poor mulatto man is in one of our people's houses, a man from the North, who assisted Mr. [Samuel D.] Phillips (a nephew of Wendell P.[hillips]) when he was here, in teaching school; he seems to be quite an intelligent man. He is suffering from fever. I shall

6. Probably Jean Racine's *Alexandre le Grand* (1665).

be glad to take as good care of him as I can. It is so sad to be ill, helpless and poor, and so far away from home. This eve. though I felt wretchedly, had a long exercise in irregular French verbs. The work of reviewing did me good. Forgot bodily ills—even so great an ill as a bad cold in the head for a while.

Thursday, November 13

Was there ever a lovelier road than that through part of my way to school lies? Oh, I wish you were here to go with me, *cher ami*. It is lined with woods on both sides. On the one tall stately pines, on the other the noble live oaks with their graceful moss drapery. And the road is captured with those brown odorous pine leaves that I love so well. It is perfectly lovely. I forgot that I was almost ill to-day, while sauntering along, listening to the birds and breathing the soft delicious air. Of the last part of the walk, through sun and sand, the less said the better. Talked to the children a little while to-day about the noble Toussaint. [7] They listened very attentively. It is well that they sh'ld know what one of their own color c'ld do for his race. I long to inspire them with courage and ambition (of a noble sort), and high purposes. It is noticeable how very few mulattoes there are here. Indeed in our school, with one or two exceptions, the children are all black. A little mulatto child strayed into the school house yesterday—a pretty little thing with large beautiful black eyes and lovely long lashes. But so dirty! I longed to seize and thoroughly cleanse her. The mother is a good-looking woman, but quite black. "Thereby," I doubt not, "hangs a tale." This eve. Harry, one of the men on the place, came in for a lesson. He is most eager to learn, and is really a scholar to be proud of. He learns rapidly. I gave him his first lesson in writing to-night, and his progress was wonderful. He held his pen almost perfectly right the first time. He will very soon learn to write, I think. I must inquire who w'ld like to take lessons at night. Whenever I am well enough it will be a real pleasure to teach them. Finished translating into French Adelaide Proctor's [8] poem "A Woman's Question," which I like so much. It was an experiment, and I assure you, *mon ami*, tis a queer translation. But it was good practice in French. Shall finish this eve. by copying some of my Journal for my dear Mary [Shepard].

Sunday, November 16

Felt too tired to go to church to-day. Some of the grown people came in this morn. I read them the Sermon on the Mount. And then they sang some of their own beautiful hymns; among them "Down in the Lonesome Valley" which I like best of all. I want to hear it every day. This afternoon some of the children came in and sang a long time. Then I commenced teaching them the 23d Psalm, which Miss M.[urray] is teaching the children in school. Ours here are too ill with whooping cough to attend school.

7. Toussaint L'Ouverture (1750?–1803), slave leader who not only freed his people but helped establish Haiti as an independent nation.

8. British writer and activist (1825–1864). A *Woman's Question* was in her *Legends and Lyrics* (1858).

I have enjoyed this day very much. For my own especial benefit, have read
and re-read my dear Mrs. Browning. Can anything be more exquisite than
those "Sonnets from the Portuguese." Is *any* man, even Browning himself,
worthy of such homage from such a soul? yes, yes, *he* is, I do believe. But
few others are. This eve. finished my Journal for Mary S.[hepard]. Tis so
voluminous, so badly written, and so stupid that I am ashamed to send it.
But I suppose almost anything from this region w'ld be interesting to people at the N.[orth] so it might as well go.

Monday, November 17

Had a dreadfully wearying day in school, of which the less said the better. Afterward drove the ladies to "The Corner," a collection of negro
houses, whither Miss T.[owne] went on a doctoring expedition. The people there are very pleasant. Saw a little baby, just borne [sic] today—and
another—old Venus' great grandchild for whom I made the little pink
frock. These people are very grateful. The least kindness that you do them
they insist on repaying in some way. We have had a quantity of eggs and
potatoes brought us despite our remonstrances. Today one of the women
gave me some Tanias. Tania is a queer looking root. After it is boiled it
looks a little like potato, but is much larger. I don't like the taste.

Tuesday, November 18

After school went to the Corner again. Stopped at old Susy's house to see
some sick children. Old Susy is a character. Miss T.[owne] asked her if she
wanted her old master to come back again. Most emphatically she answered. "No *indeed*, missus, no indeed dey treat we too bad. Dey tuk ebery
one of my chilen away from me. When we sick and c'ldnt work dey tuk
away all our food from us; gib us nutten to eat. Dey's orful hard Missis."
When Miss T.[owne] told her that some of the people wanted their old
masters to come back, a look of supreme contempt came to old Susy's withered face. "That's cause dey's got no sense den, missus," she said indignantly. Susy has any quantity of children and grandchildren, and she
thanks God that she can now have some of them with her in her old age.
To-night gave Cupid a lesson in the alphabet. He is not a brilliant scholar,
but he tries hard to learn, and so I am sure will succeed in time. A man
from another plantation came in for a lesson. L.[izzie Hunn] attended to
him while I had Cupid. He knows his letters, and seems very bright.

Wednesday, November 19

A steamer is in! Miss T.[owne] had letters from Phila.[delphia] to-day.
The mail is not yet all distributed. If I don't get any I shall be *perfectly*
desperate. But I surely will get some to-morrow. To-night had another
pupil—Robert—brighter than Cupid—not so bright as Harry. He will do
well I think.

Thursday, November 20

Had letters from Aunt M.[argaretta], Annie [Woods Webb], and Sarah P.[itman?]. Was delighted to hear from them, but so disappointed at not hearing from my dear brother Henry [Cassey]. Aunt M.[argaretta] writes me that he did not receive any letter from me. Strange! When I wrote to him the same time that I wrote to her. Am very sorry. Wrote to-night to Aunt M.[argaretta], Lizzie C.[hurch?], Charlotte, E.[llen Shearman?], Sarah P.[itman?] and to Whittier asking him to write a little Christmas hymn for our children to sing. I hope he will do it. Asked Aunt M.[argaretta] to see Mrs. Rachel Moore about sending some thick clothing for the people, and some blocks, etc. for our "babies." I hope they can get here by Christmas. It w'ld be so nice to distribute them for Christmas presents.

*　*　*

BOOKER T. WASHINGTON
1856–1915

After witnessing the systematic legalization of racial segregation throughout the South in the 1890s, many African Americans concluded that self-reliance and racial solidarity were their last best hopes for a decent life in the United States. These people embraced Booker T. Washington as their champion and adopted his autobiography, *Up From Slavery* (1901), as their guide to a better future. In 1895, the year of the death of Frederick Douglass, Washington had been catapulted to national leadership of black America on the strength of an address he had given at the Cotton States Exposition in Atlanta, Georgia. In that speech the slave-born school principal from Tuskegee, Alabama, suggested that the best way to ensure progress and peace in the South was for whites to respect the blacks' desire for improved economic opportunities and for blacks to respect the whites' desire for social separation of the races. Washington advised his fellow African Americans that they could regain their rights in the South only by accepting the political status quo and working gradually to change it by proving themselves valuable, productive members of society who deserved fair treatment before the law. Washington's supporters welcomed *Up From Slavery* as a demonstration of the good that a black man could do for himself and his people if given a chance to obtain an education and engage in useful, productive work.

Washington was born in Franklin County, Virginia (now West Virginia), in what he described in *Up From Slavery* as "the most miserable, desolate, and discouraging surroundings." Ignored by the white father he never knew, Booker was raised by his mother, Jane, who worked as a cook for a small planter until emancipation came at the end of the Civil War. Soon thereafter Booker moved with his mother and three siblings to Malden, West Virginia, where he went to work at a salt furnace and later in the coal mines. Determined to get an education, he attended night school and fit classes into his daily work schedule until the fall of 1872, when he embarked on an arduous, five-hundred-mile journey to Hampton, Virginia, to seek admission to the Hampton Institute, an industrial school for blacks and American Indians. After graduating with honors in 1875, Washington served on the faculty of

Hampton until 1881, when the Alabama legislature authorized him to found a school for black teachers in the heart of Alabama's "black belt."

From July 4, 1881, the official opening date of the Tuskegee Normal and Industrial Institute, until his death in 1915, Washington concentrated on maintaining Tuskegee as a major black-run educational institution and on promoting and defending his philosophy of African American education and socioeconomic progress. The keynotes of Washington's philosophy of progress—industrial education; accommodation of southern white supremacy; and an emphasis on racial pride, solidarity, and self-help—were hardly new or original with Washington. But the Tuskegeean was a master publicist who knew how to use his connections among the white business, philanthropic, and political elite to advance his enterprises on a national front. A commanding speaker and tireless traveler, Washington made a name for himself as an author, hiring ghostwriters to help him churn out a great quantity of magazine articles and essays, a two-volume history of black America, and a biography of Frederick Douglass. But his greatest literary asset was his own life story, which he invested in repeatedly in a perpetual effort to maintain his power and prestige in early-twentieth-century America.

Washington's first foray into autobiography was *The Story of My Life and Work* (1900), a ghostwritten account published by an African American firm and marketed primarily to a black audience. Seeking a wider readership, Washington serialized in 1900–01 a new version of his life, *Up From Slavery*, in *Outlook*, a popular national family magazine. Over the writing of this narrative and its subsequent publication as a book Washington exercised careful editorial control. This book, Washington confided to the publisher of his first autobiography, was designed to appeal to "a class of people who have money and to whom I must look for money for endowment and other purposes."

What virtually guaranteed *Up From Slavery*'s popularity among whites was Washington's deftness in masking his personal and social agenda behind an apparently simple, almost folksy, brand of unassuming storytelling. His style in the most popular portions of *Up From Slavery* is almost drained of personal emotion or self-reference. The overall impression that Washington's style left on his white readers—that of an almost saintly self-forgetfulness balanced by a businesslike worldliness in the art of getting things done—went a long way toward creating the myth of the Tuskegeean as the Moses of his people.

Up From Slavery won praise from prestigious literary magazines for its inspirational tone, its lucidity of style, and its constructive contribution to racial problems in the South. More than one reviewer likened *Up From Slavery* to the archetypal American success story, the *Autobiography of Benjamin Franklin*. Translations of *Up From Slavery* into French, Spanish, German, Russian, and a half-dozen other European languages testified to the interest that Washington's story aroused worldwide. For the most part African American readers responded favorably to *Up From Slavery*, although a handful of those Washington scornfully labeled "the intellectuals" doubted the effectiveness of the author's conciliatory approach to race relations in the South.

As a contribution to the African American slave narrative tradition headed by Frederick Douglass's *Narrative* (1845) and Harriet Jacobs's *Incidents in the Life of a Slave Girl* (1861), *Up From Slavery* quickly eclipsed all that had gone before it. Instead of the hell on earth that antebellum slave narrators claimed slavery was like, Washington termed slavery a "school" from which his fellow blacks had graduated with honors, so to speak, and with the will and the skill to keep rising. In part, Washington incorporated this revisionist estimate of slavery into his autobiography because he wanted white Americans to see the freedmen and freedwomen of the

South as a resource, not a liability, for the United States as it entered the twentieth century. Washington also played the revisionist card because he wanted to be recognized as a forward-looking, progressive leader who would not allow past disadvantages to dismay him.

This revisionist estimate of the impact of slavery and the significance of race on the prospects of African Americans epitomizes the double-edged interpretative possibilities that Washington's rhetoric presents for his readers. On the one hand, in portraying enslavement and all the injustices attendant to it as more of a help than a hindrance to the tempering of his rugged individualism, Washington came close to implying that slavery and racism had not really been so bad for African Americans after all. On the other hand, the same revisionist treatment of slavery and race could be welcomed as a rejoinder to the long-standing assumption among whites that under slavery black people suffered a disabling demoralization that left them unfit for any role in freedom except that of ward of the state.

The problem of how to interpret such a perspective on African American history and the post–Civil War struggle for dignity and opportunity has divided readers of Up From Slavery practically since it first appeared. To some, Washington's autobiography seems to paper over centuries of accumulated white responsibility for the evils of slavery, and instead of demanding the reform of white American institutions, it calls for African American conformity to the dominant myth of individualism in the United States. To other readers, however, Washington's message in Up From Slavery puts its priorities exactly where they had to be—on the necessity of self-help within the African American community—because of the refusal of whites to accept responsibility for the evils of their institutions or to tolerate any form of black leadership that did not seem to subscribe to the ideology of the dominant order. No small part of the genius of Up From Slavery lies in the fact that neither those who condemn Washington as a cynical sell-out nor those who praise him as a shrewd power broker have ever fully convinced readers of the autobiography of the true identity of the man known contradictorily as both "the Sage of Tuskegee" and "the Wizard of the Tuskegee Machine."

From Up From Slavery

Chapter I. A Slave among Slaves

I was born a slave on a plantation in Franklin County, Virginia. I am not quite sure of the exact place or exact date of my birth, but at any rate I suspect I must have been born somewhere and at some time. As nearly as I have been able to learn, I was born near a cross-roads post-office called Hale's Ford, and the year was 1858 or 1859.[1] I do not know the month or the day. The earliest impressions I can now recall are of the plantation and the slave quarters—the latter being the part of the plantation where the slaves had their cabins.

My life had its beginning in the midst of the most miserable, desolate, and discouraging surroundings. This was so, however, not because my owners were especially cruel, for they were not, as compared with many others. I was born in a typical log cabin, about fourteen by sixteen feet square. In this cabin I lived with my mother and a brother and sister till after the Civil War, when we were all declared free.

---

1. According to biographer Louis H. Harlan, Washington was born in 1856.

Of my ancestry I know almost nothing. In the slave quarters, and even later, I heard whispered conversations among the coloured people of the tortures which the slaves, including, no doubt, my ancestors on my mother's side, suffered in the middle passage of the slave ship while being conveyed from Africa to America. I have been unsuccessful in securing any information that would throw any accurate light upon the history of my family beyond my mother. She, I remember, had a half-brother and a half-sister. In the days of slavery not very much attention was given to family history and family records—that is, black family records. My mother, I suppose, attracted the attention of a purchaser who was afterward my owner and hers. Her addition to the slave family attracted about as much attention as the purchase of a new horse or cow. Of my father I know even less than of my mother. I do not even know his name. I have heard reports to the effect that he was a white man who lived on one of the near-by plantations. Whoever he was, I never heard of his taking the least interest in me or providing in any way for my rearing. But I do not find especial fault with him. He was simply another unfortunate victim of the institution which the Nation unhappily had engrafted upon it at that time.

The cabin was not only our living-place, but was also used as the kitchen for the plantation. My mother was the plantation cook. The cabin was without glass windows; it had only openings in the side which let in the light, and also the cold, chilly air of winter. There was a door to the cabin—that is, something that was called a door—but the uncertain hinges by which it was hung, and the large cracks in it, to say nothing of the fact that it was too small, made the room a very uncomfortable one. In addition to these openings there was, in the lower right-hand corner of the room, the "cat-hole,"—a contrivance which almost every mansion or cabin in Virginia possessed during the ante-bellum period.[2] The "cat-hole" was a square opening, about seven by eight inches, provided for the purpose of letting the cat pass in and out of the house at will during the night. In the case of our particular cabin I could never understand the necessity for this convenience, since there were at least a half-dozen other places in the cabin that would have accommodated the cats. There was no wooden floor in our cabin, the naked earth being used as a floor. In the centre of the earthen floor there was a large, deep opening covered with boards, which was used as a place in which to store sweet potatoes during the winter. An impression of this potato-hole is very distinctly engraved upon my memory, because I recall that during the process of putting the potatoes in or taking them out I would often come into possession of one or two, which I roasted and thoroughly enjoyed. There was no cooking-stove on our plantation, and all the cooking for the whites and slaves my mother had to do over an open fireplace, mostly in pots and "skillets." While the poorly built cabin caused us to suffer with cold in the winter, the heat from the open fireplace in summer was equally trying.

The early years of my life, which were spent in the little cabin, were not very different from those of thousands of other slaves. My mother, of course, had little time in which to give attention to the training of her chil-

2. The era before the Civil War began in 1861.

dren during the day. She snatched a few moments for our care in the early morning before her work began, and at night after the day's work was done. One of my earliest recollections is that of my mother cooking a chicken late at night, and awakening her children for the purpose of feeding them. How or where she got it I do not know. I presume, however, it was procured from our owner's farm. Some people may call this theft. If such a thing were to happen now, I should condemn it as theft myself. But taking place at the time it did, and for the reason that it did, no one could ever make me believe that my mother was guilty of thieving. She was simply a victim of the system of slavery. I cannot remember having slept in a bed until after our family was declared free by the Emancipation Proclamation. Three children—John, my older brother, Amanda, my sister, and myself—had a pallet on the dirt floor, or, to be more correct, we slept in and on a bundle of filthy rags laid upon the dirt floor.

I was asked not long ago to tell something about the sports and pastimes that I engaged in during my youth. Until that question was asked it had never occurred to me that there was no period of my life that was devoted to play. From the time that I can remember anything, almost every day of my life has been occupied in some kind of labour; though I think I would now be a more useful man if I had had time for sports. During the period that I spent in slavery I was not large enough to be of much service, still I was occupied most of the time in cleaning the yards, carrying water to the men in the fields, or going to the mill, to which I used to take the corn, once a week, to be ground. The mill was about three miles from the plantation. This work I always dreaded. The heavy bag of corn would be thrown across the back of the horse, and the corn divided about evenly on each side; but in some way, almost without exception, on these trips, the corn would so shift as to become unbalanced and would fall off the horse, and often I would fall with it. As I was not strong enough to reload the corn upon the horse, I would have to wait, sometimes for many hours, till a chance passer-by came along who would help me out of my trouble. The hours while waiting for some one were usually spent in crying. The time consumed in this way made me late in reaching the mill, and by the time I got my corn ground and reached home it would be far into the night. The road was a lonely one, and often led through dense forests. I was always frightened. The woods were said to be full of soldiers who had deserted from the army, and I had been told that the first thing a deserter did to a Negro boy when he found him alone was to cut off his ears. Besides, when I was late in getting home I knew I would always get a severe scolding or a flogging.

I had no schooling whatever while I was a slave, though I remember on several occasions I went as far as the schoolhouse door with one of my young mistresses to carry her books. The picture of several dozen boys and girls in a schoolroom engaged in study made a deep impression upon me, and I had the feeling that to get into a schoolhouse and study in this way would be about the same as getting into paradise.

So far as I can now recall, the first knowledge that I got of the fact that we were slaves, and that freedom of the slaves was being discussed, was early one morning before day, when I was awakened by my mother kneeling over her children and fervently praying that Lincoln and his armies might be successful, and that one day she and her children might be free. In this connection I have never been able to understand how the slaves throughout the South, completely ignorant as were the masses so far as books or newspapers were concerned, were able to keep themselves so accurately and completely informed about the great National questions that were agitating the country. From the time that Garrison, Lovejoy,[3] and others began to agitate for freedom, the slaves throughout the South kept in close touch with the progress of the movement. Though I was a mere child during the preparation for the Civil War and during the war itself, I now recall the many late-at-night whispered discussions that I heard my mother and the other slaves on the plantation indulge in. These discussions showed that they understood the situation, and that they kept themselves informed of events by what was termed the "grape-vine" telegraph.

During the campaign when Lincoln was first a candidate for the Presidency, the slaves on our far-off plantation, miles from any railroad or large city or daily newspaper, knew what the issues involved were. When war was begun between the North and the South, every slave on our plantation felt and knew that, though other issues were discussed, the primal one was that of slavery. Even the most ignorant members of my race on the remote plantations felt in their hearts, with a certainty that admitted of no doubt, that the freedom of the slaves would be the one great result of the war, if the Northern armies conquered. Every success of the Federal armies and every defeat of the Confederate forces was watched with the keenest and most intense interest. Often the slaves got knowledge of the results of great battles before the white people received it. This news was usually gotten from the coloured man who was sent to the post-office for the mail. In our case the post-office was about three miles from the plantation, and the mail came once or twice a week. The man who was sent to the office would linger about the place long enough to get the drift of the conversation from the group of white people who naturally congregated there, after receiving their mail, to discuss the latest news. The mail-carrier on his way back to our master's house would as naturally retail the news that he had secured among the slaves, and in this way they often heard of important events before the white people at the "big house," as the master's house was called.

I cannot remember a single instance during my childhood or early boyhood when our entire family sat down to the table together, and God's blessing was asked, and the family ate a meal in a civilized manner. On the plantation in Virginia, and even later, meals were gotten by the children very much as dumb animals get theirs. It was a piece of bread here and a scrap of meat there. It was a cup of milk at one time and some potatoes at another. Sometimes a portion of our family would eat out of the skillet or pot, while some one else would eat from a tin plate held on the knees, and often using nothing but the hands with which to hold the food. When I had grown to sufficient size, I was required to go to the "big house" at meal-times to fan the flies from the table by means of a large set of paper fans

3. Elijah P. Lovejoy (1802–1837), antislavery editor, who was murdered while defending his press from a mob in Alton, Illinois. William Lloyd Garri- son (1805–1879), uncompromising editor of *The Liberator* and leader of the American Anti-Slavery Society.

operated by a pulley. Naturally much of the conversation of the white people turned upon the subject of freedom and the war, and I absorbed a good deal of it. I remember that at one time I saw two of my young mistresses and some lady visitors eating ginger-cakes, in the yard. At that time those cakes seemed to me to be absolutely the most tempting and desirable things that I had ever seen; and I then and there resolved that, if I ever got free, the height of my ambition would be reached if I could get to the point where I could secure and eat ginger-cakes in the way that I saw those ladies doing.

Of course as the war was prolonged the white people, in many cases, often found it difficult to secure food for themselves. I think the slaves felt the deprivation less than the whites, because the usual diet for the slaves was corn bread and pork, and these could be raised on the plantation; but coffee, tea, sugar, and other articles which the whites had been accustomed to use could not be raised on the plantation, and the conditions brought about by the war frequently made it impossible to secure these things. The whites were often in great straits. Parched corn was used for coffee, and a kind of black molasses was used instead of sugar. Many times nothing was used to sweeten the so-called tea and coffee.

The first pair of shoes that I recall wearing were wooden ones. They had rough leather on the top, but the bottoms, which were about an inch thick, were of wood. When I walked they made a fearful noise, and besides this they were very inconvenient, since there was no yielding to the natural pressure of the foot. In wearing them one presented an exceedingly awkward appearance. The most trying ordeal that I was forced to endure as a slave boy, however, was the wearing of a flax[4] shirt. In the portion of Virginia where I lived it was common to use flax as part of the clothing for the slaves. That part of the flax from which our clothing was made was largely the refuse, which of course was the cheapest and roughest part. I can scarcely imagine any torture, except, perhaps, the pulling of a tooth, that is equal to that caused by putting on a new flax shirt for the first time. It is almost equal to the feeling that one would experience if he had a dozen or more chestnut burrs, or a hundred small pin-points, in contact with his flesh. Even to this day I can recall accurately the tortures that I underwent when putting on one of these garments. The fact that my flesh was soft and tender added to the pain. But I had no choice. I had to wear the flax shirt or none; and had it been left to me to choose, I should have chosen to wear no covering. In connection with the flax shirt, my brother John, who is several years older than I am, performed one of the most generous acts that I ever heard of one slave relative doing for another. On several occasions when I was being forced to wear a new flax shirt, he generously agreed to put it on in my stead and wear it for several days, till it was "broken in." Until I had grown to be quite a youth this single garment was all that I wore.

One may get the idea, from what I have said, that there was bitter feeling toward the white people on the part of my race, because of the fact that most of the white population was away fighting in a war which would result in keeping the Negro in slavery if the South was successful. In the case of the slaves on our place this was not true, and it was not true of any large

---

4. A coarse fiber used for rope and clothes until replaced by softer textiles made of cotton.

portion of the slave population in the South where the Negro was treated
with anything like decency. During the Civil War one of my young masters
was killed, and two were severely wounded. I recall the feeling of sorrow
which existed among the slaves when they heard of the death of "Mars'
Billy." It was no sham sorrow, but real. Some of the slaves had nursed
"Mars' Billy"; others had played with him when he was a child. "Mars'
Billy" had begged for mercy in the case of others when the overseer or master was thrashing them. The sorrow in the slave quarter was only second to
that in the "big house." When the two young masters were brought home
wounded, the sympathy of the slaves was shown in many ways. They were
just as anxious to assist in the nursing as the family relatives of the
wounded. Some of the slaves would even beg for the privilege of sitting up
at night to nurse their wounded masters. This tenderness and sympathy on
the part of those held in bondage was a result of their kindly and generous
nature. In order to defend and protect the women and children who were
left on the plantations when the white males went to war, the slaves would
have laid down their lives. The slave who was selected to sleep in the "big
house" during the absence of the males was considered to have the place of
honour. Any one attempting to harm "young Mistress" or "old Mistress"
during the night would have had to cross the dead body of the slave to do
so. I do not know how many have noticed it, but I think that it will be found
to be true that there are few instances, either in slavery or freedom, in
which a member of my race has been known to betray a specific trust.

As a rule, not only did the members of my race entertain no feelings of
bitterness against the whites before and during the war, but there are many
instances of Negroes tenderly caring for their former masters and mistresses
who for some reason have become poor and dependent since the war. I
know of instances where the former masters of slaves have for years been
supplied with money by their former slaves to keep them from suffering. I
have known of still other cases in which the former slaves have assisted in
the education of the descendants of their former owners. I know of a case
on a large plantation in the South in which a young white man, the son of
the former owner of the estate, has become so reduced in purse and self-
control by reason of drink that he is a pitiable creature; and yet, notwithstanding the poverty of the coloured people themselves on this plantation,
they have for years supplied this young white man with the necessities of
life. One sends him a little coffee or sugar, another a little meat, and so on.
Nothing that the coloured people possess is too good for the son of "old
Mars' Tom," who will perhaps never be permitted to suffer while any remain on the place who knew directly or indirectly of "old Mars' Tom."

I have said that there are few instances of a member of my race betraying
a specific trust. One of the best illustrations of this which I know of is in the
case of an ex-slave from Virginia whom I met not long ago in a little town in
the state of Ohio. I found that this man had made a contract with his master, two or three years previous to the Emancipation Proclamation, to the
effect that the slave was to be permitted to buy himself, by paying so much
per year for his body; and while he was paying for himself, he was to be
permitted to labour where and for whom he pleased. Finding that he could
secure better wages in Ohio, he went there. When freedom came, he was

still in debt to his master some three hundred dollars. Notwithstanding that the Emancipation Proclamation freed him from any obligation to his master, this black man walked the greater portion of the distance back to where his old master lived in Virginia, and placed the last dollar, with interest, in his hands. In talking to me about this, the man told me that he knew that he did not have to pay the debt, but that he had given his word to his master, and his word he had never broken. He felt that he could not enjoy his freedom till he had fulfilled his promise.

From some things that I have said one may get the idea that some of the slaves did not want freedom. This is not true. I have never seen one who did not want to be free, or one who would return to slavery.

I pity from the bottom of my heart any nation or body of people that is so unfortunate as to get entangled in the net of slavery. I have long since ceased to cherish any spirit of bitterness against the Southern white people on account of the enslavement of my race. No one section of our country was wholly responsible for its introduction, and, besides, it was recognized and protected for years by the General Government. Having once got its tentacles fastened on to the economic and social life of the Republic, it was no easy matter for the country to relieve itself of the institution. Then, when we rid ourselves of prejudice, or racial feeling, and look facts in the face, we must acknowledge that, notwithstanding the cruelty and moral wrong of slavery, the ten million Negroes inhabiting this country, who themselves or whose ancestors went through the school of American slavery, are in a stronger and more hopeful condition, materially, intellectually, morally, and religiously, than is true of an equal number of black people in any other portion of the globe. This is so to such an extent that Negroes in this country, who themselves or whose forefathers went through the school of slavery, are constantly returning to Africa as missionaries to enlighten those who remained in the fatherland. This I say, not to justify slavery—on the other hand, I condemn it as an institution, as we all know that in America it was established for selfish and financial reasons, and not from a missionary motive—but to call attention to a fact, and to show how Providence so often uses men and institutions to accomplish a purpose. When persons ask me in these days how, in the midst of what sometimes seem hopelessly discouraging conditions, I can have such faith in the future of my race in this country, I remind them of the wilderness through which and out of which, a good Providence has already led us.

Ever since I have been old enough to think for myself, I have entertained the idea that, notwithstanding the cruel wrongs inflicted upon us, the black man got nearly as much out of slavery as the white man did. The hurtful influences of the institution were not by any means confined to the Negro. This was fully illustrated by the life upon our own plantation. The whole machinery of slavery was so constructed as to cause labour, as a rule, to be looked upon as a badge of degradation, of inferiority. Hence labour was something that both races on the slave plantation sought to escape. The slave system on our place, in a large measure, took the spirit of self-reliance and self-help out of the white people. My old master had many boys and girls, but not one, so far as I know, ever mastered a single trade or special line of productive industry. The girls were not taught to cook, sew, or to take care of the house. All of this was left to the slaves. The slaves, of course, had little personal interest in the life of the plantation, and their ignorance prevented them from learning how to do things in the most improved and thorough manner. As a result of the system, fences were out of repair, gates were hanging half off the hinges, doors creaked, window-panes were out, plastering had fallen but was not replaced, weeds grew in the yard. As a rule, there was food for whites and blacks, but inside the house, and on the dining-room table, there was wanting that delicacy and refinement of touch and finish which can make a home the most convenient, comfortable, and attractive place in the world. Withal there was a waste of food and other materials which was sad. When freedom came, the slaves were almost as well fitted to begin life anew as the master, except in the matter of book-learning and ownership of property. The slave owner and his sons had mastered no special industry. They unconsciously had imbibed the feeling that manual labour was not the proper thing for them. On the other hand, the slaves, in many cases, had mastered some handicraft, and none were ashamed, and few unwilling, to labour.

Finally the war closed, and the day of freedom came. It was a momentous and eventful day to all upon our plantation. We had been expecting it. Freedom was in the air, and had been for months. Deserting soldiers returning to their homes were to be seen every day. Others who had been discharged, or whose regiments had been paroled, were constantly passing near our place. The "grape-vine telegraph" was kept busy night and day. The news and mutterings of great events were swiftly carried from one plantation to another. In the fear of "Yankee" invasions, the silverware and other valuables were taken from the "big house," buried in the woods, and guarded by trusted slaves. Woe be to any one who would have attempted to disturb the buried treasure. The slaves would give the Yankee soldiers food, drink, clothing—anything but that which had been specifically intrusted to their care and honour. As the great day drew nearer, there was more singing in the slave quarters than usual. It was bolder, had more ring, and lasted later into the night. Most of the verses of the plantation songs had some reference to freedom. True, they had sung those same verses before, but they had been careful to explain that the "freedom" in these songs referred to the next world, and had no connection with life in this world. Now they gradually threw off the mask, and were not afraid to let it be known that the "freedom" in their songs meant freedom of the body in this world. The night before the eventful day, word was sent to the slave quarters to the effect that something unusual was going to take place at the "big house" the next morning. There was little, if any, sleep that night. All was excitement and expectancy. Early the next morning word was sent to all the slaves, old and young, to gather at the house. In company with my mother, brother, and sister, and a large number of other slaves, I went to the master's house. All of our master's family were either standing or seated on the veranda of the house, where they could see what was to take place and hear what was said. There was a feeling of deep interest, or perhaps sadness, on their faces, but not bitterness. As I now recall the impression they made upon me, they did not at the moment seem to be sad because of the loss of property, but rather because of parting with those whom they had reared and who were in many ways very close to them. The most distinct thing that I now recall in connection with the scene was that some man who seemed to be a stranger (a United States officer, I presume) made a little speech and then read a rather long paper—the Emancipation Proclamation, I think. After the reading we were told that we were all free, and could go when and where we pleased. My mother, who was standing by my side, leaned over and kissed her children, while tears of joy ran down her cheeks. She explained to us what it all meant, that this was the day for which she had been so long praying, but fearing that she would never live to see.

For some minutes there was great rejoicing, and thanksgiving, and wild scenes of ecstasy. But there was no feeling of bitterness. In fact, there was pity among the slaves for our former owners. The wild rejoicing on the part of the emancipated coloured people lasted but for a brief period, for I noticed that by the time they returned to their cabins there was a change in their feelings. The great responsibility of being free, of having charge of themselves, of having to think and plan for themselves and their children, seemed to take possession of them. It was very much like suddenly turning a youth of ten or twelve years out into the world to provide for himself. In a few hours the great questions with which the Anglo-Saxon race had been grappling for centuries had been thrown upon these people to be solved. These were the questions of a home, a living, the rearing of children, education, citizenship, and the establishment and support of churches. Was it any wonder that within a few hours the wild rejoicing ceased and a feeling of deep gloom seemed to pervade the slave quarters? To some it seemed that, now that they were in actual possession of it, freedom was a more serious thing than they had expected to find it. Some of the slaves were seventy or eighty years old; their best days were gone. They had no strength with which to earn a living in a strange place and among strange people, even if they had been sure where to find a new place of abode. To this class the problem seemed especially hard. Besides, deep down in their hearts there was a strange and peculiar attachment to "old Marster" and "old Missus," and to their children, which they found it hard to think of breaking off. With these they had spent in some cases nearly a half-century, and it was no light thing to think of parting. Gradually, one by one, stealthily at first, the older slaves began to wander from the slave quarters back to the "big house" to have a whispered conversation with their former owners as to the future.

Chapter II. Boyhood Days

After the coming of freedom there were two points upon which practically all the people on our place were agreed, and I find that this was generally true throughout the South: that they must change their names, and that they must leave the old plantation for at least a few days or weeks in order that they might really feel sure that they were free.

In some way a feeling got among the coloured people that it was far from proper for them to bear the surname of their former owners, and a great many of them took other surnames. This was one of the first signs of freedom. When they were slaves, a coloured person was simply called "John" or

"Susan." There was seldom occasion for more than the use of the one name. If "John" or "Susan" belonged to a white man by the name of "Hatcher," sometimes he was called "John Hatcher," or as often "Hatcher's John." But there was a feeling that "John Hatcher" or "Hatcher's John" was not the proper title by which to denote a freeman; and so in many cases "John Hatcher" was changed to "John S. Lincoln" or "John S. Sherman," the initial "S" standing for no name, it being simply a part of what the coloured man proudly called his "entitles."

As I have stated, most of the coloured people left the old plantation for a short while at least, so as to be sure, it seemed, that they could leave and try their freedom on to see how it felt. After they had remained away for a time, many of the older slaves, especially, returned to their old homes and made some kind of contract with their former owners by which they remained on the estate.

My mother's husband, who was the stepfather of my brother John and myself, did not belong to the same owners as did my mother. In fact, he seldom came to our plantation. I remember seeing him there perhaps once a year, that being about Christmas time. In some way, during the war, by running away and following the Federal soldiers, it seems, he found his way into the new state of West Virginia. As soon as freedom was declared, he sent for my mother to come to the Kanawha Valley, in West Virginia. At that time a journey from Virginia over the mountains to West Virginia was rather a tedious and in some cases a painful undertaking. What little clothing and few household goods we had were placed in a cart, but the children walked the greater portion of the distance, which was several hundred miles.

I do not think any of us ever had been very far from the plantation, and the taking of a long journey into another state was quite an event. The parting from our former owners and the members of our own race on the plantation was a serious occasion. From the time of our parting till their death we kept up a correspondence with the older members of the family, and in later years we have kept in touch with those who were the younger members. We were several weeks making the trip, and most of the time we slept in the open air and did our cooking over a log fire out-of-doors. One night I recall that we camped near an abandoned log cabin, and my mother decided to build a fire in that for cooking, and afterward to make a "pallet" on the floor for our sleeping. Just as the fire had gotten well started a large black snake fully a yard and a half long dropped down the chimney and ran out on the floor. Of course we at once abandoned that cabin. Finally we reached our destination—a little town called Malden, which is about five miles from Charleston, the present capital of the state.

At that time salt-mining was the great industry in that part of West Virginia, and the little town of Malden was right in the midst of the salt-furnaces. My stepfather had already secured a job at a salt-furnace, and he had also secured a little cabin for us to live in. Our new house was no better than the one we had left on the old plantation in Virginia. In fact, in one respect it was worse. Notwithstanding the poor condition of our plantation cabin, we were at all times sure of pure air. Our new home was in the midst of a cluster of cabins crowded closely together, and as there were no sanitary regulations, the filth about the cabins was often intolerable. Some of our neighbours were coloured people, and some were the poorest and most ignorant and degraded white people. It was a motley mixture. Drinking, gambling, quarrels, fights, and shockingly immoral practices were frequent. All who lived in the little town were in one way or another connected with the salt business. Though I was a mere child, my stepfather put me and my brother at work in one of the furnaces. Often I began work as early as four o'clock in the morning.

The first thing I ever learned in the way of book knowledge was while working in this salt-furnace. Each salt-packer had his barrels marked with a certain number. The number allotted to my stepfather was "18." At the close of the day's work the boss of the packers would come around and put "18" on each of our barrels, and I soon learned to recognize that figure wherever I saw it, and after a while got to the point where I could make that figure, though I knew nothing about any other figures or letters.

From the time that I can remember having any thoughts about anything, I recall that I had an intense longing to learn to read. I determined, when quite a small child, that, if I accomplished nothing else in life, I would in some way get enough education to enable me to read common books and newspapers. Soon after we got settled in some manner in our new cabin in West Virginia, I induced my mother to get hold of a book for me. How or where she got it I do not know, but in some way she procured an old copy of Webster's[5] "blue-black" spelling-book, which contained the alphabet, followed by such meaningless words as "ab," "ba," "ca," "da." I began at once to devour this book, and I think that it was the first one I ever had in my hands. I had learned from somebody that the way to begin to read was to learn the alphabet, so I tried in all the ways I could think of to learn it,— all of course without a teacher, for I could find no one to teach me. At that time there was not a single member of my race anywhere near us who could read, and I was too timid to approach any of the white people. In some way, within a few weeks, I mastered the greater portion of the alphabet. In all my efforts to learn to read my mother shared fully my ambition, and sympathized with me and aided me in every way that she could. Though she was totally ignorant, so far as mere book knowledge was concerned, she had high ambitions for her children, and a large fund of good, hard, common sense which seemed to enable her to meet and master every situation. If I have done anything in life worth attention, I feel sure that I inherited the disposition from my mother.

In the midst of my struggles and longing for an education, a young coloured boy who had learned to read in the state of Ohio came to Malden. As soon as the coloured people found out that he could read, a newspaper was secured, and at the close of nearly every day's work this young man would be surrounded by a group of men and women who were anxious to hear him read the news contained in the papers. How I used to envy this man! He seemed to me to be the one young man in all the world who ought to be satisfied with his attainments.

5. Noah Webster (1758–1843), author of the most widely used spelling books in the 19th-century United States.

About this time the question of having some kind of a school opened for the coloured children in the village began to be discussed by members of the race. As it would be the first school for Negro children that had ever been opened in that part of Virginia, it was, of course, to be a great event, and the discussion excited the widest interest. The most perplexing question was where to find a teacher. The young man from Ohio who had learned to read the papers was considered, but his age was against him. In the midst of the discussion about a teacher, another young coloured man from Ohio, who had been a soldier, in some way found his way into town. It was soon learned that he possessed considerable education, and he was engaged by the coloured people to teach their first school. As yet no free schools had been started for coloured people in that section, hence each family agreed to pay a certain amount per month, with the understanding that the teacher was to "board 'round"—that is, spend a day with each family. This was not bad for the teacher, for each family tried to provide the very best on the day the teacher was to be its guest. I recall that I looked forward with an anxious appetite to the "teacher's day" at our little cabin.

This experience of a whole race beginning to go to school for the first time, presents one of the most interesting studies that has ever occurred in connection with the development of any race. Few people who were not right in the midst of the scenes can form any exact idea of the intense desire which the people of my race showed for an education. As I have stated, it was a whole race trying to go to school. Few were too young, and none too old, to make the attempt to learn. As fast as any kind of teachers could be secured, not only were day-schools filled, but night-schools as well. The great ambition of the older people was to try to learn to read the Bible before they died. With this end in view, men and women who were fifty or seventy-five years old would often be found in the night-school. Sunday-schools were formed soon after freedom, but the principal book studied in the Sunday-school was the spelling-book. Day-school, night-school, Sunday-school, were always crowded, and often many had to be turned away for want of room.

The opening of the school in the Kanawha Valley, however, brought to me one of the keenest disappointments that I ever experienced. I had been working in a salt-furnace for several months, and my stepfather had discovered that I had a financial value, and so, when the school opened, he decided that he could not spare me from my work. This decision seemed to cloud my every ambition. The disappointment was made all the more severe by reason of the fact that my place of work was where I could see the happy children passing to and from school, mornings and afternoons. Despite this disappointment, however, I determined that I would learn something, anyway. I applied myself with greater earnestness than ever to the mastering of what was in the "blue-back" speller.

My mother sympathized with me in my disappointment, and sought to comfort me in all the ways she could, and to help me find a way to learn. After a while I succeeded in making arrangements with the teacher to give me some lessons at night, after the day's work was done. These night lessons were so welcome that I think I learned more at night than the other children did during the day. My own experiences in the night-school gave me faith in the night-school idea, with which, in after years, I had to do both at Hampton and Tuskegee. But my boyish heart was still set upon going to the day-school, and I let no opportunity slip to push my case. Finally I won, and was permitted to go to the school in the day for a few months, with the understanding that I was to rise early in the morning and work in the furnace till nine o'clock, and return immediately after school closed in the afternoon for at least two more hours of work.

The schoolhouse was some distance from the furnace, and as I had to work till nine o'clock, and the school opened at nine, I found myself in a difficulty. School would always be begun before I reached it, and sometimes my class had recited. To get around this difficulty I yielded to a temptation for which most people, I suppose, will condemn me; but since it is a fact, I might as well state it. I have great faith in the power and influence of facts. It is seldom that anything is permanently gained by holding back a fact. There was a large clock in a little office in the furnace. This clock, of course, all the hundred or more workmen depended upon to regulate their hours of beginning and ending the day's work. I got the idea that the way for me to reach school on time was to move the clock hands from half-past eight up to the nine o'clock mark. This I found myself doing morning after morning, till the furnace "boss" discovered that something was wrong, and locked the clock in a case. I did not mean to inconvenience anybody. I simply meant to reach that schoolhouse in time.

When, however, I found myself at the school for the first time, I also found myself confronted with two other difficulties. In the first place, I found that all of the other children wore hats or caps on their heads, and I had neither hat nor cap. In fact, I do not remember that up to the time of going to school I had ever worn any kind of covering upon my head, nor do I recall that either I or anybody else had even thought anything about the need of covering for my head. But, of course, when I saw how all the other boys were dressed, I began to feel quite uncomfortable. As usual, I put the case before my mother, and she explained to me that she had no money with which to buy a "store hat," which was a rather new institution at that time among the members of my race and was considered quite the thing for young and old to own, but that she would find a way to help me out of the difficulty. She accordingly got two pieces of "homespun" (jeans) and sewed them together, and I was soon the proud possessor of my first cap.

The lesson that my mother taught me in this has always remained with me, and I have tried as best I could to teach it to others. I have always felt proud, whenever I think of the incident, that my mother had strength of character enough not to be led into the temptation of seeming to be that which she was not—of trying to impress my schoolmates and others with the fact that she was able to buy me a "store hat" when she was not. I have always felt proud that she refused to go into debt for that which she did not have the money to pay for. Since that time I have owned many kinds of caps and hats, but never one of which I have felt so proud as of the cap made of the two pieces of cloth sewed together by my mother. I have noted the fact, but without satisfaction, I need not add, that several of the boys who began their careers with "store hats" and who were my schoolmates and used to join in the sport that was made of me because I had only a "homespun" cap, have ended their careers in the penitentiary, while others are not able now to buy any kind of hat.

My second difficulty was with regard to my name, or rather *a* name. From the time when I could remember anything, I had been called simply "Booker." Before going to school it had never occurred to me that it was needful or appropriate to have an additional name. When I heard the school-roll called, I noticed that all of the children had at least two names, and some of them indulged in what seemed to me the extravagance of having three. I was in deep perplexity, because I knew that the teacher would demand of me at least two names, and I had only one. By the time the occasion came for the enrolling of my name, an idea occurred to me which I thought would make me equal to the situation; and so, when the teacher asked me what my full name was, I calmly told him "Booker Washington," as if I had been called by that name all my life; and by that name I have since been known. Later in my life I found that my mother had given me the name of "Booker Taliaferro" soon after I was born, but in some way that part of my name seemed to disappear and for a long while was forgotten, but as soon as I found out about it I revived it, and made my full name "Booker Taliaferro Washington." I think there are not many men in our country who have had the privilege of naming themselves in the way that I have.

More than once I have tried to picture myself in the position of a boy or man with an honoured and distinguished ancestry which I could trace back through a period of hundreds of years, and who had not only inherited a name, but fortune and a proud family homestead; and yet I have sometimes had the feeling that if I had inherited these, and had been a member of a more popular race, I should have been inclined to yield to the temptation of depending upon my ancestry and my colour to do that for me which I should do for myself. Years ago I resolved that because I had no ancestry myself I would leave a record of which my children would be proud, and which might encourage them to still higher effort.

The world should not pass judgment upon the Negro, and especially the Negro youth, too quickly or too harshly. The Negro boy has obstacles, discouragements, and temptations to battle with that are little known to those not situated as he is. When a white boy undertakes a task, it is taken for granted that he will succeed. On the other hand, people are usually surprised if the Negro boy does not fail. In a word, the Negro youth starts out with the presumption against him.

The influence of ancestry, however, is important in helping forward any individual or race, if too much reliance is not placed upon it. Those who constantly direct attention to the Negro youth's moral weaknesses, and compare his advancement with that of white youths, do not consider the influence of the memories which cling about the old family homesteads. I have no idea, as I have stated elsewhere, who my grandmother was. I have, or have had, uncles and aunts and cousins, but I have no knowledge as to where most of them are. My case will illustrate that of hundreds of thousands of black people in every part of our country. The very fact that the white boy is conscious that, if he fails in life, he will disgrace the whole family record, extending back through many generations, is of tremendous value in helping him to resist temptations. The fact that the individual has behind and surrounding him proud family history and connection serves as a stimulus to help him to overcome obstacles when striving for success.

The time that I was permitted to attend school during the day was short, and my attendance was irregular. It was not long before I had to stop attending day-school altogether, and devote all of my time again to work. I resorted to the night-school again. In fact, the greater part of the education I secured in my boyhood was gathered through the night-school after my day's work was done. I had difficulty often in securing a satisfactory teacher. Sometimes, after I had secured some one to teach me at night, I would find, much to my disappointment, that the teacher knew but little more than I did. Often I would have to walk several miles at night in order to recite my night-school lessons. There was never a time in my youth, no matter how dark and discouraging the days might be, when one resolve did not continually remain with me, and that was a determination to secure an education at any cost.

Soon after we moved to West Virginia, my mother adopted into our family, notwithstanding our poverty, an orphan boy, to whom afterward we gave the name of James B. Washington. He has ever since remained a member of the family.

After I had worked in the salt-furnace for some time, work was secured for me in a coal-mine which was operated mainly for the purpose of securing fuel for the salt-furnace. Work in the coal-mine I always dreaded. One reason for this was that any one who worked in a coal-mine was always unclean, at least while at work, and it was a very hard job to get one's skin clean after the day's work was over. Then it was fully a mile from the opening of the coal-mine to the face of the coal, and all, of course, was in the blackest darkness. I do not believe that one ever experiences anywhere else such darkness as he does in a coal-mine. The mine was divided into a large number of different "rooms" or departments, and, as I never was able to learn the location of all these "rooms," I many times found myself lost in the mine. To add to the horror of being lost, sometimes my light would go out, and then, if I did not happen to have a match, I would wander about in the darkness until by chance I found some one to give me a light. The work was not only hard, but it was dangerous. There was always the danger of being blown to pieces by a premature explosion of powder, or of being crushed by falling slate. Accidents from one or the other of these causes were frequently occurring, and this kept me in constant fear. Many children of the tenderest years were compelled then, as is now true I fear, in most coal-mining districts, to spend a large part of their lives in these coal-mines, with little opportunity to get an education; and, what is worse, I have often noted that, as a rule, young boys who begin life in a coal-mine are often physically and mentally dwarfed. They soon lose ambition to do anything else than to continue as a coal-miner.

In those days, and later as a young man, I used to try to picture in my imagination the feelings and ambitions of a white boy with absolutely no limit placed upon his aspirations and activities. I used to envy the white boy who had no obstacles placed in the way of his becoming a Congressman, Governor, Bishop, or President by reason of the accident of his birth or race. I used to picture the way that I would act under such circumstances; how I would begin at the bottom and keep rising until I reached the highest round of success.

In later years, I confess that I do not envy the white boy as I once did. I have learned that success is to be measured not so much by the position that one has reached in life as by the obstacles which he has overcome while trying to succeed. Looked at from this standpoint, I almost reach the conclusion that often the Negro boy's birth and connection with an unpopular race is an advantage, so far as real life is concerned. With few exceptions, the Negro youth must work harder and must perform his tasks even better than a white youth in order to secure recognition. But out of the hard and unusual struggle through which he is compelled to pass, he gets a strength, a confidence, that one misses whose pathway is comparatively smooth by reason of birth and race.

From any point of view, I had rather be what I am, a member of the Negro race, than be able to claim membership with the most favoured of any other race. I have always been made sad when I have heard members of any race claiming rights and privileges, or certain badges of distinction, on the ground simply that they were members of this or that race, regardless of their own individual worth or attainments. I have been made to feel sad for such persons because I am conscious of the fact that mere connection with what is known as a superior race will not permanently carry an individual forward unless he has individual worth, and mere connection with what is regarded as an inferior race will not finally hold an individual back if he possesses intrinsic, individual merit. Every persecuted individual and race should get much consolation out of the great human law, which is universal and eternal, that merit, no matter under what skin found, is, in the long run, recognized and rewarded. This I have said here, not to call attention to myself as an individual, but to the race to which I am proud to belong.

Chapter III. The Struggle for an Education

One day, while at work in the coal-mine, I happened to overhear two miners talking about a great school for coloured people somewhere in Virginia. This was the first time that I had ever heard anything about any kind of school or college that was more pretentious than the little coloured school in our town.

In the darkness of the mine I noiselessly crept as close as I could to the two men who were talking. I heard one tell the other that not only was the school established for the members of my race, but that opportunities were provided by which poor but worthy students could work out all or a part of the cost of board, and at the same time be taught some trade or industry.

As they went on describing the school, it seemed to me that it must be the greatest place on earth, and not even Heaven presented more attractions for me at that time than did the Hampton Normal and Agricultural Institute[6] in Virginia, about which these men were talking. I resolved at

6. Founded in 1868, a school that offered industrial, agricultural, and teacher training for African Americans and American Indians.

once to go to that school, although I had no idea where it was, or how many miles away, or how I was going to reach it; I remembered only that I was on fire constantly with one ambition, and that was to go to Hampton. This thought was with me day and night.

After hearing of the Hampton Institute, I continued to work for a few months longer in the coal-mine. While at work there, I heard of a vacant position in the household of General Lewis Ruffner, the owner of the salt-furnace and coal-mine. Mrs. Viola Ruffner, the wife of General Ruffner, was a "Yankee" woman from Vermont. Mrs. Ruffner had a reputation all through the vicinity for being very strict with her servants, and especially with the boys who tried to serve her. Few of them had remained with her more than two or three weeks. They all left with the same excuse: she was too strict. I decided, however, that I would rather try Mrs. Ruffner's house than remain in the coal-mine, and so my mother applied to her for the vacant position. I was hired at a salary of $5 per month.

I had heard so much about Mrs. Ruffner's severity that I was almost afraid to see her, and trembled when I went into her presence. I had not lived with her many weeks, however, before I began to understand her. I soon began to learn that, first of all, she wanted everything kept clean about her, that she wanted things done promptly and systematically, and that at the bottom of everything she wanted absolute honesty and frankness. Nothing must be sloven or slipshod; every door, every fence, must be kept in repair.

I cannot now recall how long I lived with Mrs. Ruffner before going to Hampton, but I think it must have been a year and a half. At any rate, I here repeat what I have said more than once before, that the lessons that I learned in the home of Mrs. Ruffner were as valuable to me as any education I have ever gotten anywhere since. Even to this day I never see bits of paper scattered around a house or in the street that I do not want to pick them up at once. I never see a filthy yard that I do not want to clean it, a paling off of a fence that I do not want to put it on, an unpainted or unwhitewashed house that I do not want to paint or whitewash it, or a button off one's clothes, or a grease-spot on them or on a floor, that I do not want to call attention to it.

From fearing Mrs. Ruffner I soon learned to look upon her as one of my best friends. When she found that she could trust me she did so implicitly. During the one or two winters that I was with her she gave me an opportunity to go to school for an hour in the day during a portion of the winter months, but most of my studying was done at night, sometimes alone, sometimes under some one whom I could hire to teach me. Mrs. Ruffner always encouraged and sympathized with me in all my efforts to get an education. It was while living with her that I began to get together my first library. I secured a dry-goods box, knocked out one side of it, put some shelves in it, and began putting into it every kind of book that I could get my hands upon, and called it my "library."

Notwithstanding my success at Mrs. Ruffner's I did not give up the idea of going to the Hampton Institute. In the fall of 1872 I determined to make an effort to get there, although, as I have stated, I had no definite idea of the direction in which Hampton was, or of what it would cost to go there. I do not think that any one thoroughly sympathized with me in my ambition to go to Hampton unless it was my mother, and she was troubled with a grave fear that I was starting out on a "wild-goose chase." At any rate, I got only a half-hearted consent from her that I might start. The small amount of money that I had earned had been consumed by my stepfather and the remainder of the family, with the exception of a very few dollars, and so I had very little with which to buy clothes and pay my travelling expenses. My brother John helped me all that he could, but of course that was not a great deal, for his work was in the coal-mine, where he did not earn much, and most of what he did earn went in the direction of paying the household expenses.

Perhaps the thing that touched and pleased me most in connection with my starting for Hampton was the interest that many of the older coloured people took in the matter. They had spent the best days of their lives in slavery, and hardly expected to live to see the time when they would see a member of their race leave home to attend a boarding-school. Some of these older people would give me a nickel, others a quarter, or a handkerchief.

Finally the great day came, and I started for Hampton. I had only a small, cheap satchel that contained what few articles of clothing I could get. My mother at the time was rather weak and broken in health. I hardly expected to see her again, and thus our parting was all the more sad. She, however, was very brave through it all. At that time there were no through trains connecting that part of West Virginia with eastern Virginia. Trains ran only a portion of the way, and the remainder of the distance was travelled by stage-coaches.

The distance from Malden to Hampton is about five hundred miles. I had not been away from home many hours before it began to grow painfully evident that I did not have enough money to pay my fare to Hampton. One experience I shall long remember. I had been travelling over the mountains most of the afternoon in an old-fashioned stagecoach, when, late in the evening, the coach stopped for the night at a common, unpainted house called a hotel. All the other passengers except myself were whites. In my ignorance I supposed that the little hotel existed for the purpose of accommodating the passengers who travelled on the stage-coach. The difference that the colour of one's skin would make I had not thought anything about. After all the other passengers had been shown rooms and were getting ready for supper, I shyly presented myself before the man at the desk. It is true I had practically no money in my pocket with which to pay for bed or food, but I had hoped in some way to beg my way into the good graces of the landlord, for at that season in the mountains of Virginia the weather was cold, and I wanted to get indoors for the night. Without asking as to whether I had any money, the man at the desk firmly refused to even consider the matter of providing me with food or lodging. This was my first experience in finding out what the colour of my skin meant. In some way I managed to keep warm by walking about, and so got through the night. My whole soul was so bent upon reaching Hampton that I did not have time to cherish any bitterness toward the hotel-keeper.

By walking, begging rides both in wagons and in the cars, in some way, after a number of days, I reached the city of Richmond, Virginia, about eighty-two miles from Hampton. When I reached there, tired, hungry, and dirty, it was late in the night. I had never been in a large city, and this rather added to my misery. When I reached Richmond, I was completely out of money. I had not a single acquaintance in the place, and, being unused to city ways, I did not know where to go. I applied at several places for lodging, but they all wanted money, and that was what I did not have. Knowing nothing else better to do, I walked the streets. In doing this I passed by many foodstands where fried chicken and half-moon apple pies were piled high and made to present a most tempting appearance. At that time it seemed to me that I would have promised all that I expected to possess in the future to have gotten hold of one of those chicken legs or one of those pies. But I could not get either of these, nor anything else to eat.

I must have walked the streets till after midnight. At last I became so exhausted that I could walk no longer. I was tired, I was hungry, I was every-thing but discouraged. Just about the time when I reached extreme physi-cal exhaustion, I came upon a portion of a street where the board sidewalk was considerably elevated. I waited for a few minutes, till I was sure that no passers-by could see me, and then crept under the sidewalk and lay for the night upon the ground, with my satchel of clothing for a pillow. Nearly all night I could hear the tramp of feet over my head. The next morning I found myself somewhat refreshed, but I was extremely hungry, because it had been a long time since I had had sufficient food. As soon as it became light enough for me to see my surroundings I noticed that I was near a large ship, and that this ship seemed to be unloading a cargo of pig iron. I went at once to the vessel and asked the captain to permit me to help unload the vessel in order to get money for food. The captain, a white man, who seemed to be kind-hearted, consented. I worked long enough to earn money for my breakfast, and it seems to me, as I remember it now, to have been about the best breakfast that I have ever eaten.

My work pleased the captain so well that he told me if I desired I could continue working for a small amount per day. This I was very glad to do. I continued working on this vessel for a number of days. After buying food with the small wages I received there was not much left to add to the amount I must get to pay my way to Hampton. In order to economize in every way possible, so as to be sure to reach Hampton in a reasonable time, I continued to sleep under the same sidewalk that gave me shelter the first night I was in Richmond. Many years after that the coloured citizens of Richmond very kindly tendered me a reception at which there must have been two thousand people present. This reception was held not far from the spot where I slept the first night I spent in that city, and I must confess that my mind was more upon the sidewalk that first gave me shelter than upon the reception, agreeable and cordial as it was.

When I had saved what I considered enough money with which to reach Hampton, I thanked the captain of the vessel for his kindness, and started again. Without any unusual occurrence I reached Hampton, with a sur-plus of exactly fifty cents with which to begin my education. To me it had been a long, eventful journey; but the first sight of the large, three-story, brick school building seemed to have rewarded me for all that I had under-gone in order to reach the place. If the people who gave the money to pro-vide that building could appreciate the influence the sight of it had upon me, as well as upon thousands of other youths, they would feel all the more encouraged to make such gifts. It seemed to me to be the largest and most beautiful building I had ever seen. The sight of it seemed to give me new life. I felt that a new kind of existence had now begun—that life would now have a new meaning. I felt that I had reached the promised land, and I resolved to let no obstacle prevent me from putting forth the highest effort to fit myself to accomplish the most good in the world.

As soon as possible after reaching the grounds of the Hampton Institute, I presented myself before the head teacher for assignment to a class. Hav-ing been so long without proper food, a bath, and change of clothing, I did not, of course, make a very favourable impression upon her, and I could see at once that there were doubts in her mind about the wisdom of admitting me as a student. I felt that I could hardly blame her if she got the idea that I was a worthless loafer or tramp. For some time she did not refuse to admit me, neither did she decide in my favour, and I continued to linger about her, and to impress her in all the ways I could with my worthiness. In the meantime I saw her admitting other students, and that added greatly to my discomfort, for I felt, deep down in my heart, that I could do as well as they, if I could only get a chance to show what was in me.

After some hours had passed, the head teacher said to me: "The adjoin-ing recitation-room needs sweeping. Take the broom and sweep it."

It occurred to me at once that here was my chance. Never did I receive an order with more delight. I knew that I could sweep, for Mrs. Ruffner had thoroughly taught me how to do that when I lived with her.

I swept the recitation-room three times. Then I got a dusting-cloth and I dusted it four times. All the woodwork around the walls, every bench, table, and desk, I went over four times with my dusting-cloth. Besides, every piece of furniture had been moved and every closet and corner in the room had been thoroughly cleaned. I had the feeling that in a large measure my fu-ture depended upon the impression I made upon the teacher in the clean-ing of that room. When I was through, I reported to the head teacher. She was a "Yankee" woman who knew just where to look for dirt. She went into the room and inspected the floor and closets; then she took her handker-chief and rubbed it on the woodwork about the walls, and over the table and benches. When she was unable to find one bit of dirt on the floor, or a particle of dust on any of the furniture, she quietly remarked, "I guess you will do to enter this institution."

I was one of the happiest souls on earth. The sweeping of that room was my college examination, and never did any youth pass an examination for entrance into Harvard or Yale that gave him more genuine satisfaction. I have passed several examinations since then, but I have always felt that this was the best one I ever passed.

I have spoken of my own experience in entering the Hampton Institute. Perhaps few, if any, had anything like the same experience that I had, but about that same period there were hundreds who found their way to Hamp-

ton and other institutions after experiencing something of the same difficulties that I went through. The young men and women were determined
to secure an education at any cost.

The sweeping of the recitation-room in the manner that I did it seems to
have paved the way for me to get through Hampton. Miss Mary F. Mackie,
the head teacher, offered me a position as janitor. This, of course, I gladly
accepted, because it was a place where I could work out nearly all the cost
of my board. The work was hard and taxing, but I stuck to it. I had a large
number of rooms to care for, and had to work late into the night, while at
the same time I had to rise by four o'clock in the morning, in order to build
the fires and have a little time in which to prepare my lessons. In all my
career at Hampton, and ever since I have been out in the world, Miss Mary
F. Mackie, the head teacher to whom I have referred, proved one of my
strongest and most helpful friends. Her advice and encouragement were
always helpful and strengthening to me in the darkest hour.

I have spoken of the impression that was made upon me by the buildings
and general appearance of the Hampton Institute, but I have not spoken of
that which made the greatest and most lasting impression upon me, and
that was a great man—the noblest, rarest human being that it has ever been
my privilege to meet. I refer to the late General Samuel C. Armstrong.[7]

It has been my fortune to meet personally many of what are called great
characters, both in Europe and America, but I do not hesitate to say that I
never met any man who, in my estimation, was the equal of General Armstrong. Fresh from the degrading influences of the slave plantation and the
coal-mines, it was a rare privilege for me to be permitted to come into direct contact with such a character as General Armstrong. I shall always remember that the first time I went into his presence he made the impression
upon me of being a perfect man; I was made to feel that there was something about him that was superhuman. It was my privilege to know the
General personally from the time I entered Hampton till he died, and the
more I saw of him the greater he grew in my estimation. One might have
removed from Hampton all the buildings, class-rooms, teachers, and industries, and given the men and women there the opportunity of coming into
daily contact with General Armstrong, and that alone would have been a
liberal education. The older I grow, the more I am convinced that there is
no education which one can get from books and costly apparatus that is
equal to that which can be gotten from contact with great men and
women. Instead of studying books so constantly, how I wish that our
schools and colleges might learn to study men and things!

General Armstrong spent two of the last six months of his life in my
home at Tuskegee. At that time he was paralyzed to the extent that he had
lost control of his body and voice in a very large degree. Notwithstanding
his affliction, he worked almost constantly night and day for the cause to
which he had given his life. I never saw a man who so completely lost sight
of himself. I do not believe he ever had a selfish thought. He was just as
happy in trying to assist some other institution in the South as he was when

7. Former officer in the Union Army, educational reformer, and founder of Hampton Institute (1839–
1893).

working for Hampton. Although he fought the Southern white man in the Civil War, I never heard him utter a bitter word against him afterward. On the other hand, he was constantly seeking to find ways by which he could be of service to the Southern whites.

It would be difficult to describe the hold that he had upon the students at Hampton, or the faith they had in him. In fact, he was worshipped by his students. It never occurred to me that General Armstrong could fail in anything that he undertook. There is almost no request that he could have made that would not have been complied with. When he was a guest at my home in Alabama, and was so badly paralyzed that he had to be wheeled about in an invalid's chair, I recall that one of the General's former students had occasion to push his chair up a long, steep hill that taxed his strength to the utmost. When the top of the hill was reached, the former pupil, with a glow of happiness on his face, exclaimed, "I am so glad that I have been permitted to do something that was real hard for the General before he dies!" While I was a student at Hampton, the dormitories became so crowded that it was impossible to find room for all who wanted to be admitted. In order to help remedy the difficulty, the General conceived the plan of putting up tents to be used as rooms. As soon as it became known that General Armstrong would be pleased if some of the older students would live in the tents during the winter, nearly every student in school volunteered to go.

I was one of the volunteers. The winter that we spent in those tents was an intensely cold one, and we suffered severely—how much I am sure General Armstrong never knew, because we made no complaints. It was enough for us to know that we were pleasing General Armstrong, and that we were making it possible for an additional number of students to secure an education. More than once, during a cold night, when a stiff gale would be blowing, our tent was lifted bodily, and we would find ourselves in the open air. The General would usually pay a visit to the tents early in the morning, and his earnest, cheerful, encouraging voice would dispel any feeling of despondency.

I have spoken of my admiration for General Armstrong, and yet he was but a type of that Christlike body of men and women who went into the Negro schools at the close of the war by the hundreds to assist in lifting up my race. The history of the world fails to show a higher, purer, and more unselfish class of men and women than those who found their way into those Negro schools.

Life at Hampton was a constant revelation to me; was constantly taking me into a new world. The matter of having meals at regular hours, of eating on a tablecloth, using a napkin, the use of the bathtub and of the toothbrush, as well as the use of sheets upon the bed, were all new to me.

I sometimes feel that almost the most valuable lesson I got at the Hampton Institute was in the use and value of the bath. I learned there for the first time some of its value, not only in keeping the body healthy, but in inspiring self-respect and promoting virtue. In all my travels in the South and elsewhere since leaving Hampton I have always in some way sought my daily bath. To get it sometimes when I have been the guest of my own people in a single-roomed cabin has not always been easy to do, except by slipping away to some stream in the woods. I have always tried to teach my people that some provision for bathing should be a part of every house.

For some time, while a student at Hampton, I possessed but a single pair of socks, but when I had worn these till they became soiled, I would wash them at night and hang them by the fire to dry, so that I might wear them again the next morning.

The charge for my board at Hampton was ten dollars per month. I was expected to pay a part of this in cash and to work out the remainder. To meet this cash payment, as I have stated, I had just fifty cents when I reached the institution. Aside from a very few dollars that my brother John was able to send me once in a while, I had no money with which to pay my board. I was determined from the first to make my work as janitor so valuable that my services would be indispensable. This I succeeded in doing to such an extent that I was soon informed that I would be allowed the full cost of my board in return for my work. The cost of tuition was seventy dollars a year. This, of course, was wholly beyond my ability to provide. If I had been compelled to pay the seventy dollars for tuition, in addition to providing for my board, I would have been compelled to leave the Hampton school. General Armstrong, however, very kindly got Mr. S. Griffitts Morgan,[8] of New Bedford, Mass., to defray the cost of my tuition during the whole time that I was at Hampton. After I finished the course at Hampton and had entered upon my lifework at Tuskegee, I had the pleasure of visiting Mr. Morgan several times.

After having been for a while at Hampton, I found myself in difficulty because I did not have books and clothing. Usually, however, I got around the trouble about books by borrowing from those who were more fortunate than myself. As to clothes, when I reached Hampton I had practically nothing. Everything that I possessed was in a small hand satchel. My anxiety about clothing was increased because of the fact that General Armstrong made a personal inspection of the young men in ranks, to see that their clothes were clean. Shoes had to be polished, there must be no buttons off the clothing, and no grease-spots. To wear one suit of clothes continually, while at work and in the schoolroom, and at the same time keep it clean, was rather a hard problem for me to solve. In some way I managed to get on till the teachers learned that I was in earnest and meant to succeed, and then some of them were kind enough to see that I was partly supplied with second-hand clothing that had been sent in barrels from the North. These barrels proved a blessing to hundreds of poor but deserving students. Without them I question whether I should ever have gotten through Hampton.

When I first went to Hampton I do not recall that I had ever slept in a bed that had two sheets on it. In those days there were not many buildings there, and room was very precious. There were seven other boys in the same room with me; most of them, however, students who had been there for some time. The sheets were quite a puzzle to me. The first night I slept under both of them, and the second night I slept on top of both of them; but by watching the other boys I learned my lesson in this, and have been trying to follow it ever since and to teach it to others.

8. A merchant.

I was among the youngest of the students who were in Hampton at that time. Most of the students were men and women—some as old as forty years of age. As I now recall the scene of my first year, I do not believe that one often has the opportunity of coming into contact with three or four hundred men and women who were so tremendously in earnest as these men and women were. Every hour was occupied in study or work. Nearly all had had enough actual contact with the world to teach them the need of education. Many of the older ones were, of course, too old to master the text-books very thoroughly, and it was often sad to watch their struggles; but they made up in earnestness much of what they lacked in books. Many of them were as poor as I was, and, besides having to wrestle with their books, they had to struggle with a poverty which prevented their having the necessities of life. Many of them had aged parents who were dependent upon them, and some of them were men who had wives whose support in some way they had to provide for.

The great and prevailing idea that seemed to take possession of every one was to prepare himself to lift up the people at his home. No one seemed to think of himself. And the officers and teachers, what a rare set of human beings they were! They worked for the students night and day, in season and out of season. They seemed happy only when they were helping the students in some manner. Whenever it is written—and I hope it will be— the part that the Yankee teachers played in the education of the Negroes immediately after the war will make one of the most thrilling parts of the history of this country. The time is not far distant when the whole South will appreciate this service in a way that it has not yet been able to do.

* * *

Chapter XIV. The Atlanta Exposition [9] Address

The Atlanta Exposition, at which I had been asked to make an address as a representative of the Negro race, as stated in the last chapter, was opened with a short address from Governor Bullock. [1] After other interesting exercises, including an invocation from Bishop Nelson, of Georgia, a dedicatory ode by Albert Howell, Jr., and addresses by the President of the Exposition and Mrs. Joseph Thompson, [2] the President of the Woman's Board, Governor Bullock introduced me with the words, "We have with us to-day a representative of Negro enterprise and Negro civilization."

When I arose to speak, there was considerable cheering, especially from the coloured people. As I remember it now, the thing that was uppermost in my mind was the desire to say something that would cement the friendship of the races and bring about hearty coöperation between them. So far as my outward surroundings were concerned, the only thing that I recall distinctly now is that when I got up, I saw thousands of eyes looking intently into my face. The following is the address which I delivered:—

9. The Cotton States and International Exposition, which officially opened on September 18, 1895, was a trade fair for the promotion of the New South.

1. Rufus B. Bullock (1834–1907), governor of Georgia from 1868 to 1871 and president of the exposition.

2. An active clubwoman and president of the Woman's Board of the Atlanta Exposition.

MR. PRESIDENT AND GENTLEMEN OF THE BOARD OF DIRECTORS
AND CITIZENS.

One-third of the population of the South is of the Negro race. No enterprise seeking the material, civil, or moral welfare of this section can disregard this element of our population and reach the highest success. I but convey to you, Mr. President and Directors, the sentiment of the masses of my race when I say that in no way have the value and manhood of the American Negro been more fittingly and generously recognized than by the managers of this magnificent Exposition at every stage of its progress. It is a recognition that will do more to cement the friendship of the two races than any occurrence since the dawn of our freedom.

Not only this, but the opportunity here afforded will awaken among us a new era of industrial progress. Ignorant and inexperienced, it is not strange that in the first years of our new life we began at the top instead of at the bottom; that a seat in Congress or the state legislature was more sought than real estate or industrial skill; that the political convention or stump speaking had more attractions than starting a dairy farm or truck garden.

A ship lost at sea for many days suddenly sighted a friendly vessel. From the mast of the unfortunate vessel was seen a signal, "Water, water; we die of thirst!" The answer from the friendly vessel at once came back, "Cast down your bucket where you are." A second time the signal, "Water, water; send us water!" ran up from the distressed vessel, and was answered, "Cast down your bucket where you are." And a third and fourth signal for water was answered, "Cast down your bucket where you are." The captain of the distressed vessel, at last heeding the injunction, cast down his bucket, and it came up full of fresh, sparkling water from the mouth of the Amazon River. To those of my race who depend on bettering their condition in a foreign land or who underestimate the importance of cultivating friendly relations with the Southern white man, who is their next-door neighbour, I would say: "Cast down your bucket where you are"—cast it down in making friends in every manly way of the people of all races by whom we are surrounded.

Cast it down in agriculture, mechanics, in commerce, in domestic service, and in the professions. And in this connection it is well to bear in mind that whatever other sins the South may be called to bear, when it comes to business, pure and simple, it is in the South that the Negro is given a man's chance in the commercial world, and in nothing is this Exposition more eloquent than in emphasizing this chance. Our greatest danger is that in the great leap from slavery to freedom we may overlook the fact that the masses of us are to live by the productions of our hands, and fail to keep in mind that we shall prosper in proportion as we learn to dignify and glorify common labour and put brains and skill into the common occupations of life; shall prosper in proportion as we learn to draw the line between the superficial and the substantial, the ornamental gewgaws of life and the useful. No race can prosper till it learns that there is as much dignity in tilling a field as in writing a poem. It is at the bottom of life we must begin, and not at the top. Nor should we permit our grievances to overshadow our opportunities.

To those of the white race who look to the incoming of those of foreign birth and strange tongue and habits for the prosperity of the South, were I permitted I would repeat what I say to my own race, "Cast down your bucket where you are." Cast it down among the eight millions of Negroes whose habits you know, whose fidelity and love you have tested in days when to have proved treacherous meant the ruin of your firesides. Cast down your bucket among these people who have, without strikes and labour wars, tilled your fields, cleared your forests, builded your railroads and cities, and brought forth treasures from the bowels of the earth, and helped make possible this magnificent representation of the progress of the South. Casting down your bucket among my people, helping and encouraging them as you are doing on these grounds, and to education of head, hand, and heart, you will find that they will buy your surplus land, make blossom the waste places in your fields, and run your factories. While doing this, you can be sure in the future, as in the past, that you and your families will be surrounded by the most patient, faithful, law-abiding, and unresentful people that the world has seen. As we have proved our loyalty to you in the past, in nursing your children, watching by the sick-bed of your mothers and fathers, and often following them with tear-dimmed eyes to their graves, so in the future, in our humble way, we shall stand by you with a devotion that no foreigner can approach, ready to lay down our lives, if need be, in defence of yours, interlacing our industrial, commercial, civil, and religious life with yours in a way that shall make the interests of both races one. In all things that are purely social we can be as separate as the fingers, yet one as the hand in all things essential to mutual progress.

There is no defence or security for any of us except in the highest intelligence and development of all. If anywhere there are efforts tending to curtail the fullest growth of the Negro, let these efforts be turned into stimulating, encouraging, and making him the most useful and intelligent citizen. Effort or means so invested will pay a thousand per cent interest. These efforts will be twice blessed—"blessing him that gives and him that takes."[3]

There is no escape through law of man or God from the inevitable:—

> The laws of changeless justice bind
>   Oppressor with oppressed;
> And close as sin and suffering joined
>   We march to fate abreast.[4]

Nearly sixteen millions of hands will aid you in pulling the load upward, or they will pull against you the load downward. We shall constitute one-third and more of the ignorance and crime of the South, or one-third its intelligence and progress; we shall contribute one-third to the business and industrial prosperity of the South, or we shall prove a veritable body of death, stagnating, depressing, retarding every effort to advance the body politic.

Gentlemen of the Exposition, as we present to you our humble effort at

3. Shakespeare's *The Merchant of Venice* 4.1.187.   *Royal* (1862) by the American antislavery poet
4. From *The Song of the Negro Boatmen* in *At Port*   John Greenleaf Whittier.

an exhibition of our progress, you must not expect overmuch. Starting thirty years ago with ownership here and there in a few quilts and pumpkins and chickens (gathered from miscellaneous sources), remember the path that has led from these to the inventions and production of agricultural implements, buggies, steam-engines, newspapers, books, statuary, carving, paintings, the management of drug-stores and banks, has not been trodden without contact with thorns and thistles. While we take pride in what we exhibit as a result of our independent efforts, we do not for a moment forget that our part in this exhibition would fall far short of your expectations but for the constant help that has come to our educational life, not only from the Southern states, but especially from Northern philanthropists, who have made their gifts a constant stream of blessing and encouragement.

The wisest among my race understand that the agitation of questions of social equality is the extremest folly, and that progress in the enjoyment of all the privileges that will come to us must be the result of severe and constant struggle rather than of artificial forcing. No race that has anything to contribute to the markets of the world is long in any degree ostracized. It is important and right that all privileges of the law be ours, but it is vastly more important that we be prepared for the exercises of these privileges. The opportunity to earn a dollar in a factory just now is worth infinitely more than the opportunity to spend a dollar in an opera-house.

In conclusion, may I repeat that nothing in thirty years has given us more hope and encouragement, and drawn us so near to you of the white race, as this opportunity offered by the Exposition; and here bending, as it were, over the altar that represents the results of the struggles of your race and mine, both starting practically empty-handed three decades ago, I pledge that in your effort to work out the great and intricate problem which God has laid at the doors of the South, you shall have at all times the patient, sympathetic help of my race; only let this be constantly in mind, that, while from representations in these buildings of the product of field, of forest, of mine, of factory, letters, and art, much good will come, yet far above and beyond material benefits will be that higher good, that, let us pray God, will come, in a blotting out of sectional differences and racial animosities and suspicions, in a determination to administer absolute justice, in a willing obedience among all classes to the mandates of law. This, this, coupled with our material prosperity, will bring into our beloved South a new heaven and a new earth.

The first thing that I remember, after I had finished speaking, was that Governor Bullock rushed across the platform and took me by the hand, and that others did the same. I received so many and such hearty congratulations that I found it difficult to get out of the building. I did not appreciate to any degree, however, the impression which my address seemed to have made, until the next morning, when I went into the business part of the city. As soon as I was recognized, I was surprised to find myself pointed out and surrounded by a crowd of men who wished to shake hands with me. This was kept up on every street on to which I went, to an extent which embarrassed me so much that I went back to my boarding-place. The next morning I returned to Tuskegee. At the station in Atlanta, and at almost all of the stations at which the train stopped between that city and Tuskegee, I found a crowd of people anxious to shake hands with me.

The papers in all parts of the United States published the address in full, and for months afterward there were complimentary editorial references to it. Mr. Clark Howell, the editor of the Atlanta *Constitution*, telegraphed to a New York paper, among other words, the following, "I do not exaggerate when I say that Professor Booker T. Washington's address yesterday was one of the most notable speeches, both as to character and as to the warmth of its reception, ever delivered to a Southern audience. The address was a revelation. The whole speech is a platform upon which blacks and whites can stand with full justice to each other."

The Boston *Transcript* said editorially: "The speech of Booker T. Washington at the Atlanta Exposition, this week, seems to have dwarfed all the other proceedings and the Exposition itself. The sensation that it has caused in the press has never been equalled."

I very soon began receiving all kinds of propositions from lecture bureaus, and editors of magazines and papers, to take the lecture platform, and to write articles. One lecture bureau offered me fifty thousand dollars, or two hundred dollars a night and expenses, if I would place my services at its disposal for a given period. To all these communications I replied that my life-work was at Tuskegee; and that whenever I spoke it must be in the interests of the Tuskegee school and my race, and that I would enter into no arrangements that seemed to place a mere commercial value upon my services.

Some days after its delivery I sent a copy of my address to the President of the United States, the Hon. Grover Cleveland. I received from him the following autograph reply:—

Gray Gables, Buzzard's Bay, Mass.,
October 6, 1895.

BOOKER T. WASHINGTON, ESQ.:

MY DEAR SIR: I thank you for sending me a copy of your address delivered at the Atlanta Exposition.

I thank you with much enthusiasm for making the address. I have read it with intense interest, and I think the Exposition would be fully justified if it did not do more than furnish the opportunity for its delivery. Your words cannot fail to delight and encourage all who wish well for your race; and if our coloured fellow-citizens do not from your utterances gather new hope and form new determinations to gain every valuable advantage offered them by their citizenship, it will be strange indeed.

Yours very truly,
GROVER CLEVELAND.

Later I met Mr. Cleveland, for the first time, when, as President, he visited the Atlanta Exposition. At the request of myself and others he consented to spend an hour in the Negro Building, for the purpose of

inspecting the Negro exhibit and of giving the coloured people in attendance an opportunity to shake hands with him. As soon as I met Mr. Cleveland I became impressed with his simplicity, greatness, and rugged
honesty. I have met him many times since then, both at public functions
and at his private residence in Princeton, and the more I see of him the
more I admire him. When he visited the Negro Building in Atlanta he
seemed to give himself up wholly, for that hour, to the coloured people. He
seemed to be as careful to shake hands with some old coloured "auntie"
clad partially in rags, and to take as much pleasure in doing so, as if he were
greeting some millionnaire. Many of the coloured people took advantage
of the occasion to get him to write his name in a book or on a slip of paper.
He was as careful and patient in doing this as if he were putting his signature to some great state document.

Mr. Cleveland has not only shown his friendship for me in many personal ways, but has always consented to do anything I have asked of him for
our school. This he has done, whether it was to make a personal donation
or to use his influence in securing the donations of others. Judging from
my personal acquaintance with Mr. Cleveland, I do not believe that he is
conscious of possessing any colour prejudice. He is too great for that. In my
contact with people I find that, as a rule, it is only the little, narrow people
who live for themselves, who never read good books, who do not travel,
who never open up their souls in a way to permit them to come into contact with other souls—with the great outside world. No man whose vision is
bounded by colour can come into contact with what is highest and best in
the world. In meeting men, in many places, I have found that the happiest
people are those who do the most for others; the most miserable are those
who do the least. I have also found that few things, if any, are capable of
making one so blind and narrow as race prejudice. I often say to our students, in the course of my talks to them on Sunday evenings in the chapel,
that the longer I live and the more experience I have of the world, the more
I am convinced that, after all, the one thing that is most worth living for—
and dying for, if need be—is the opportunity of making some one else more
happy and more useful.

The coloured people and the coloured newspapers at first seemed to be
greatly pleased with the character of my Atlanta address, as well as with its
reception. But after the first burst of enthusiasm began to die away, and the
coloured people began reading the speech in cold type, some of them
seemed to feel that they had been hypnotized. They seemed to feel that I
had been too liberal in my remarks toward the Southern whites, and that I
had not spoken out strongly enough for what they termed the "rights" of
the race. For a while there was a reaction, so far as a certain element of my
own race was concerned, but later these reactionary ones seemed to have
been won over to my way of believing and acting.

While speaking of changes in public sentiment, I recall that about ten
years after the school at Tuskegee was established, I had an experience that
I shall never forget. Dr. Lyman Abbott,[5] then the pastor of Plymouth

---

5. American editor and writer (1835–1922) who was the minister of the Plymouth Congregational Church
in Brooklyn, New York.

Church, and also editor of the *Outlook* (then the *Christian Union*), asked me to write a letter for his paper giving my opinion of the exact condition, mental and moral, of the coloured ministers in the South, as based upon my observations. I wrote the letter, giving the exact facts as I conceived them to be. The picture painted was a rather black one—or, since I am black, shall I say "white"? It could not be otherwise with a race but a few years out of slavery, a race which had not had time or opportunity to produce a competent ministry.

What I said soon reached every Negro minister in the country, I think, and the letters of condemnation which I received from them were not few. I think that for a year after the publication of this article every association and every conference or religious body of any kind, of my race, that met, did not fail before adjourning to pass a resolution condemning me, or calling upon me to retract or modify what I had said. Many of these organizations went so far in their resolutions as to advise parents to cease sending their children to Tuskegee. One association even appointed a "missionary" whose duty it was to warn the people against sending their children to Tuskegee. This missionary had a son in the school, and I noticed that, whatever the "missionary" might have said or done with regard to others, he was careful not to take his son away from the institution. Many of the coloured papers, especially those that were the organs of religious bodies, joined in the general chorus of condemnation or demands for retraction.

During the whole time of the excitement, and through all the criticism, I did not utter a word of explanation or retraction. I knew that I was right, and that time and the sober second thought of the people would vindicate me. It was not long before the bishops and other church leaders began to make a careful investigation of the conditions of the ministry, and they found out that I was right. In fact, the oldest and most influential bishop in one branch of the Methodist Church said that my words were far too mild. Very soon public sentiment began making itself felt, in demanding a purifying of the ministry. While this is not yet complete by any means, I think I may say, without egotism, and I have been told by many of our most influential ministers, that my words had much to do with starting a demand for the placing of a higher type of men in the pulpit. I have had the satisfaction of having many who once condemned me thank me heartily for my frank words.

The change of the attitude of the Negro ministry, so far as regards myself, is so complete that at the present time I have no warmer friends among any class than I have among the clergymen. The improvement in the character and life of the Negro ministers is one of the most gratifying evidences of the progress of the race. My experience with them, as well as other events in my life, convince me that the thing to do, when one feels sure that he has said or done the right thing, and is condemned, is to stand still and keep quiet. If he is right, time will show it.

In the midst of the discussion which was going on concerning my Atlanta speech, I received the letter which I give below, from Dr. Gilman, the President of Johns Hopkins University, who had been made chairman of the judges of award in connection with the Atlanta Exposition:—

Johns Hopkins University, Baltimore,
President's Office, September 30, 1895.

DEAR MR. WASHINGTON:

Would it be agreeable to you to be one of the Judges of Award in the Department of Education at Atlanta? If so, I shall be glad to place your name upon the list. A line by telegraph will be welcomed.

Yours very truly,
D. C. GILMAN.

I think I was even more surprised to receive this invitation than I had been to receive the invitation to speak at the opening of the Exposition. It was to be a part of my duty, as one of the jurors, to pass not only upon the exhibits of the coloured schools, but also upon those of the white schools. I accepted the position, and spent a month in Atlanta in performance of the duties which it entailed. The board of jurors was a large one, consisting in all of sixty members. It was about equally divided between Southern white people and Northern white people. Among them were college presidents, leading scientists and men of letters, and specialists in many subjects. When the group of jurors to which I was assigned met for organization, Mr. Thomas Nelson Page,[6] who was one of the number, moved that I be made secretary of that division, and the motion was unanimously adopted. Nearly half of our division were Southern people. In performing my duties in the inspection of the exhibits of white schools I was in every case treated with respect, and at the close of our labours I parted from my associates with regret.

I am often asked to express myself more freely than I do upon the political condition and the political future of my race. These recollections of my experience in Atlanta give me the opportunity to do so briefly. My own belief is, although I have never before said so in so many words, that the time will come when the Negro in the South will be accorded all the political rights which his ability, character, and material possessions entitle him to. I think, though, that the opportunity to freely exercise such political rights will not come in any large degree through outside or artificial forcing, but will be accorded to the Negro by the Southern white people themselves, and that they will protect him in the exercise of those rights. Just as soon as the South gets over the old feeling that it is being forced by "foreigners," or "aliens," to do something which it does not want to do, I believe that the change in the direction that I have indicated is going to begin. In fact, there are indications that it is already beginning in a slight degree.

Let me illustrate my meaning. Suppose that some months before the opening of the Atlanta Exposition there had been a general demand from the press and public platform outside the South that a Negro be given a

6. Popular Virginia author (1853–1922) who wrote *In Ole Virginia* (1887) and other southern romances.

place on the opening programme, and that a Negro be placed upon the board of jurors of award. Would any such recognition of the race have taken place? I do not think so. The Atlanta officials went as far as they did because they felt it to be a pleasure, as well as a duty, to reward what they considered merit in the Negro race. Say what we will, there is something in human nature which we cannot blot out, which makes one man, in the end, recognize and reward merit in another, regardless of colour or race.

I believe it is the duty of the Negro—as the greater part of the race is already doing—to deport himself modestly in regard to political claims, depending upon the slow but sure influences that proceed from the possession of property, intelligence, and high character for the full recognition of his political rights. I think that the according of the full exercise of political rights is going to be a matter of natural, slow growth, not an over-night, gourd-vine affair. I do not believe that the Negro should cease voting, for a man cannot learn the exercise of self-government by ceasing to vote, any more than a boy can learn to swim by keeping out of the water, but I do believe that in his voting he should more and more be influenced by those of intelligence and character who are his next-door neighbours.

I know coloured men who, through the encouragement, help, and advice of Southern white people, have accumulated thousands of dollars' worth of property, but who, at the same time, would never think of going to those same persons for advice concerning the casting of their ballots. This, it seems to me, is unwise and unreasonable, and should cease. In saying this I do not mean that the Negro should truckle, or not vote from principle, for the instant he ceases to vote from principle he loses the confidence and respect of the Southern white man even.

I do not believe that any state should make a law that permits an ignorant and poverty-stricken white man to vote, and prevents a black man in the same condition from voting. Such a law is not only unjust, but it will react, as all unjust laws do, in time; for the effect of such a law is to encourage the Negro to secure education and property, and at the same time it encourages the white man to remain in ignorance and poverty. I believe that in time, through the operation of intelligence and friendly race relations, all cheating at the ballot-box in the South will cease. It will become apparent that the white man who begins by cheating a Negro out of his ballot soon learns to cheat a white man out of his, and that the man who does this ends his career of dishonesty by the theft of property or by some equally serious crime. In my opinion, the time will come when the South will encourage all of its citizens to vote. It will see that it pays better, from every standpoint, to have healthy, vigorous life than to have that political stagnation which always results when one-half of the population has no share and no interest in the Government.

As a rule, I believe in universal, free suffrage, but I believe that in the South we are confronted with peculiar conditions that justify the protection of the ballot in many of the states, for a while at least, either by an educational test, a property test, or by both combined; but whatever tests are required, they should be made to apply with equal and exact justice to both races.

1901

CHARLES W. CHESNUTT
1858–1932

Charles W. Chesnutt was the first African American writer of fiction to enlist the white-controlled publishing industry in the service of his social message. From 1899 to 1905, during which time he published two collections of short stories and three novels, Chesnutt was the most influential and widely respected African American fiction writer in the United States, reaching a significant portion of the national reading audience with his analyses and indictments of racism.

Born in Cleveland, Ohio, in 1858, the son of free black émigrés from the South, Chesnutt grew up in Fayetteville, North Carolina, during the turbulent Reconstruction era. A quiet, bookish boy, he attended school regularly at an institution founded by the Freedmen's Bureau. In his late teens he was appointed assistant principal of the normal school established for blacks in Fayetteville by the North Carolina State Legislature. But his marriage in 1878 and his impatience with the restrictions of his life in the South fueled his ambitions to find better opportunities elsewhere. Before his twenty-first birthday he had confided to his journal a plan to move to the North to "get employment in some literary avocation, or something leading in that direction." Confident that he could succeed, Chesnutt moved to New York City in 1883 and to Cleveland in 1884, where he settled his family, passed the Ohio State bar, and launched a business career as a legal stenographer.

In August 1887, the *Atlantic Monthly* printed Chesnutt's *The Goophered Grapevine*, his first important work of fiction. Set in North Carolina and featuring an ex-slave raconteur who could spin wonderful tales about antebellum southern life, *The Goophered Grapevine* appeared to be part of the "plantation tradition" of contemporary southern literature, typified in the work of white writers such as Joel Chandler Harris and Thomas Nelson Page, who had made their fame writing nostalgic tales of the Old South in Negro dialect. But Chesnutt's story was singular in two respects. It presented the lore of "conjuration," African American hoodoo beliefs and practices, to a white reading public largely ignorant of black folk culture. It also introduced a new kind of black storytelling protagonist, Uncle Julius McAdoo, who shrewdly adapted his recollections of the past to secure his economic advantage in the present, sometimes at the expense of his white employer.

In March 1899, *The Conjure Woman*, a collection of "conjure stories" based on the model established in *The Goophered Grapevine*, made its debut, delighting its reviewers with its peculiar blend of realism and fantasy. The most memorable stories in the collection, such as *The Goophered Grapevine*, portrayed slavery as a crucible that placed black people under almost unbearable psychological pressures and demanded of them tenacity of purpose, firmness of character, and imaginative ingenuity to preserve themselves, their families, and their community. Appearing during an era when most whites questioned the African American's capacity for full and equal civil rights, the stories of *The Conjure Woman* implicitly argued that, having confirmed their human dignity and heroic fortitude in the face of the worst that slavery could do, the free black man and woman were amply qualified for the rights and responsibilities of American citizenship.

In the fall of 1899 a second Chesnutt short fiction collection, *The Wife of His Youth and Other Stories of the Color Line*, was published. The majority of the stories in *The Wife of His Youth* explore the moral conflicts and psychological strains experienced by those who lived closest to the color line in Chesnutt's day, namely mixed-race persons like himself. The title story of the volume typifies its creator's sensitive portrayal of the manners and mores of the African American urban elite in the post–Civil War North. *The Passing of Grandison*, a clever burlesque of senti-mental southern portrayals of master-slave relationships, returns to the antebellum South with a comic exuberance rare in Chesnutt's fiction. After reading *The Wife of His Youth*, some critics, like the noted white novelist William Dean Howells, called Chesnutt a literary realist of the first order. But other reviewers were put off by his unapologetic inquiries into topics considered too delicate or volatile for short fic-tion, such as southern segregation and interracial marriage.

In the fall of 1899, Chesnutt closed his prosperous court-reporting business in Cleveland to pursue his lifelong dream—a career as a full-time author. In the next six years he published three novels of purpose, *The House behind the Cedars* (1900), *The Marrow of Tradition* (1901), and *The Colonel's Dream* (1905), which surveyed racial problems in the postwar South and tested a number of possible so-cial, economic, and political solutions. *The House behind the Cedars* was generally well received, and *The Marrow of Tradition* was reviewed extensively throughout the country as a disturbing but timely study of the contemporary South in the throes of the white supremacist revolution. Yet by the time Chesnutt began writing *The Colonel's Dream*, he knew that his brand of fiction would not sell well enough to sustain his experimental literary career. Rather than subject himself and his fam-ily to a permanently diminished standard of living, Chesnutt reopened his court-reporting business. Although he continued writing and speaking on various social and political issues after *The Colonel's Dream* was published, Chesnutt produced only a handful of short stories in the last twenty-five years of his life. Among African American readers, however, admiration for his achievement never waned. In 1928 the National Association for the Advancement of Colored People awarded him its Spingarn Medal for his "pioneer work as a literary artist depicting the life and strug-gles of Americans of Negro descent, and for his long and useful career as scholar, worker, and freeman of one of America's greatest cities."

In 1931, in *Post-Bellum—Pre-Harlem*, an essay in literary autobiography, Ches-nutt accepted the fact that writing fashions had passed him by, but he took pride in pointing out how far African American literature and the attitude of the white liter-ary world toward it had come since the days when he first broke into print. Al-though he was too modest to do so, Chesnutt might have claimed an important role in preparing the American public for the advent of the New Negro author of the 1920s, for in a basic sense, the new movement followed his precedent in unmask-ing the false poses and images of their era to refocus attention on the real racial issues facing their America. Today, historians of African American writing point out that Charles Chesnutt almost singlehandedly inaugurated a truly African American literary tradition in the short story. He was the first writer to make the broad range of African American experience his artistic province and to consider practically every issue and problem endemic to the American color line worthy of literary attention. Because he developed literary modes appropriate to his materials, Chesnutt also left to his successors a rich formal legacy that underlies major trends in twentieth-century black fiction, from the ironies of James Weldon Johnson's classic African American fiction of manners to the magical realism of Charles Johnson's contem-porary neo-slave narratives.

The Goophered Grapevine

Some years ago my wife was in poor health, and our family doctor, in whose skill and honesty I had implicit confidence, advised a change of cli-mate. I shared, from an unprofessional standpoint, his opinion that the raw winds, the chill rains, and the violent changes of temperature that characterized the winters in the region of the Great Lakes tended to aggravate my wife's difficulty, and would undoubtedly shorten her life if she remained exposed to them. The doctor's advice was that we seek, not a temporary place of sojourn, but a permanent residence, in a warmer and more equable climate. I was engaged at the time in grape-culture in northern Ohio, and, as I liked the business and had given it much study, I decided to look for some other locality suitable for carrying it on. I thought of sunny France, of sleepy Spain, of Southern California, but there were objections to them all. It occurred to me that I might find what I wanted in some one of our own Southern States. It was a sufficient time after the war for conditions in the South to have become somewhat settled; and I was enough of a pioneer to start a new industry, if I could not find a place where grape-culture had been tried. I wrote to a cousin who had gone into the turpentine business in central North Carolina. He assured me, in response to my inquiries, that no better place could be found in the South than the State and neighborhood where he lived; the climate was perfect for health, and, in conjunction with the soil, ideal for grape-culture; labor was cheap, and land could be bought for a mere song. He gave us a cordial invitation to come and visit him while we looked into the matter. We accepted the invitation, and after several days of leisurely travel, the last hundred miles of which were up a river on a sidewheel steamer, we reached our destination, a quaint old town, which I shall call Patesville, because, for one reason, that is not its name. There was a red brick market-house in the public square, with a tall tower, which held a four-faced clock that struck the hours, and from which there pealed out a curfew at nine o'clock. There were two or three hotels, a court-house, a jail, stores, offices, and all the appurtenances of a county seat and a commercial emporium; for while Patesville numbered only four or five thousand inhabitants, of all shades of complexion, it was one of the principal towns in North Carolina, and had a considerable trade in cotton and naval stores. This business activity was not immediately apparent to my unaccustomed eyes. Indeed, when I first saw the town, there brooded over it a calm that seemed almost sabbatic in its restfulness, though I learned later on that underneath its somnolent exterior the deeper currents of life—love and hatred, joy and despair, ambition and avarice, faith and friendship—flowed not less steadily than in livelier latitudes.

We found the weather delightful at that season, the end of summer, and were hospitably entertained. Our host was a man of means and evidently regarded our visit as a pleasure, and we were therefore correspondingly at our case, and in a position to act with the coolness of judgment desirable in making so radical a change in our lives. My cousin placed a horse and buggy at our disposal, and himself acted as our guide until I became somewhat familiar with the country.

I found that grape-culture, while it had never been carried on to any great extent, was not entirely unknown in the neighborhood. Several planters thereabouts had attempted it on a commercial scale, in former years, with greater or less success; but like most Southern industries, it had felt the blight of war and had fallen into desuetude.

I went several times to look at a place that I thought might suit me. It was

a plantation of considerable extent, that had formerly belonged to a
wealthy man by the name of McAdoo. The estate had been for years involved in litigation between disputing heirs, during which period shiftless
cultivation had well-nigh exhausted the soil. There had been a vineyard of
some extent on the place, but it had not been attended to since the war,
and had lapsed into utter neglect. The vines—here partly supported by
decayed and broken-down trellises, there twining themselves among the
branches of the slender saplings which had sprung up among them—grew
in wild and unpruned luxuriance, and the few scattered grapes they bore
were the undisputed prey of the first comer. The site was admirably
adapted to grape-raising; the soil, with a little attention, could not have
been better; and with the native grape, the luscious scuppernong, as my
main reliance in the beginning, I felt sure that I could introduce and cultivate successfully a number of other varieties.

One day I went over with my wife to show her the place. We drove out of
the town over a long wooden bridge that spanned a spreading mill-pond,
passed the long whitewashed fence surrounding the county fair-ground,
and struck into a road so sandy that the horse's feet sank to the fetlocks. Our
route lay partly up hill and partly down, for we were in the sand-hill county;
we drove past cultivated farms, and then by abandoned fields grown up in
scrub-oak and short-leaved pine, and once or twice through the solemn
aisles of the virgin forest, where the tall pines, well-nigh meeting over the
narrow road, shut out the sun, and wrapped us in cloistral solitude. Once,
at a cross-roads, I was in doubt as to the turn to take, and we sat there waiting ten minutes—we had already caught some of the native infection of
restfulness—for some human being to come along, who could direct us on
our way. At length a little negro girl appeared, walking straight as an arrow,
with a piggin full of water on her head. After a little patient investigation,
necessary to overcome the child's shyness, we learned what we wished to
know, and at the end of about five miles from the town reached our destination.

We drove between a pair of decayed gateposts—the gate itself had long
since disappeared—and up a straight sandy lane, between two lines of rotting rail fence, partly concealed by jimsonweeds and briers, to the open
space where a dwelling-house had once stood, evidently a spacious mansion, if we might judge from the ruined chimneys that were still standing,
and the brick pillars on which the sills rested. The house itself, we had
been informed, had fallen a victim to the fortunes of war.

We alighted from the buggy, walked about the yard for a while, and then
wandered off into the adjoining vineyard. Upon Annie's complaining of
weariness I led the way back to the yard, where a pine log, lying under a
spreading elm, afforded a shady though somewhat hard seat. One end of
the log was already occupied by a venerable-looking colored man. He held
on his knees a hat full of grapes, over which he was smacking his lips with
great gusto, and a pile of grapeskins near him indicated that the performance was no new thing. We approached him at an angle from the rear, and
were close to him before he perceived us. He respectfully rose as we drew
near, and was moving away, when I begged him to keep his seat.

"Don't let us disturb you," I said. "There is plenty of room for us all."

He resumed his seat with somewhat of embarrassment. While he had been standing, I had observed that he was a tall man, and, though slightly bowed by the weight of years, apparently quite vigorous. He was not entirely black, and this fact, together with the quality of his hair, which was about six inches long and very bushy, except on the top of his head, where he was quite bald, suggested a slight strain of other than negro blood. There was a shrewdness in his eyes, too, which was not altogether African, and which, as we afterwards learned from experience, was indicative of a corresponding shrewdness in his character. He went on eating the grapes, but did not seem to enjoy himself quite so well as he had apparently done before he became aware of our presence.

"Do you live around here?" I asked, anxious to put him at his ease.

"Yas, suh. I lives des ober yander, behine de nex' san'-hill, on de Lumberton plank-road."

"Do you know anything about the time when this vineyard was cultivated?"

"Lawd bless you, suh, I knows all about it. Dey ain' na'er a man in dis settlement w'at won' tell you ole Julius McAdoo 'uz bawn en raise' on dis yer same plantation. Is you de Norv'n gemman w'at's gwine ter buy de ole vimya'd?"

"I am looking at it," I replied; "but I don't know that I shall care to buy unless I can be reasonably sure of making something out of it."

"Well, suh, you is a stranger ter me, en I is a stranger ter you, en we is bofe strangers ter one anudder, but 'f I 'uz in yo' place, I would n' buy dis vimya'd."

"Why not?" I asked.

"Well, I dunno whe'r you b'lieves in cunj'in' er not,—some er de w'ite folks don't, er says dey don't,—but de truf er de matter is dat dis yer ole vimya'd is goophered."

"Is what?" I asked, not grasping the meaning of this unfamiliar word.

"Is goophered,—cunju'd, bewitch'."

He imparted this information with such solemn earnestness, and with such an air of confidential mystery, that I felt somewhat interested, while Annie was evidently much impressed, and drew closer to me.

"How do you know it is bewitched?" I asked.

"I would n' spec' fer you ter b'lieve me 'less you know all 'bout de fac's. But ef you en young miss dere doan' min' lis'nin' ter a ole nigger run on a minute er two w'ile you er restin', I kin 'splain to you how it all happen'."

We assured him that we would be glad to hear how it all happened, and he began to tell us. At first the current of his memory—or imagination—seemed somewhat sluggish; but as his embarrassment wore off, his language flowed more freely, and the story acquired perspective and coherence. As he became more and more absorbed in the narrative, his eyes assumed a dreamy expression, and he seemed to lose sight of his auditors, and to be living over again in monologue his life on the old plantation.

"Ole Mars Dugal' McAdoo," he began, "bought dis place long many years befo' de wah, en I 'member well w'en he sot out all dis yer part er de plantation in scuppernon's. De vimes growed monst'us fas', en Mars Dugal' made a thousan' gallon er scuppernon' wine eve'y year.

"Now, ef dey's an'thing a nigger lub, nex' ter 'possum, en chick'n, en watermillyums, it's scuppernon's. Dey ain' nuffin dat kin stan' up side'n de scuppernon' fer sweetness; sugar ain't a suckumstance ter scuppernon'. W'en de season is nigh 'bout ober, en de grapes begin ter swivel up des a little wid de wrinkles er ole age,—w'en de skin git sof' en brown,—den de scuppernon' make you smack yo' lip en roll yo' eye en wush fer mo'; so I reckon it ain' very 'stonishin' dat niggers lub scuppernon'.

"Dey wuz a sight er niggers in de naberhood er de vimya'd. Dere wuz ole Mars Henry Brayboy's niggers, en ole Mars Jeems McLean's niggers, en Mars Dugal's own niggers; den dey wuz a settlement er free niggers en po' buckrahs[1] down by de Wim'l'ton Road, en Mars Dugal' had de only vimya'd in de naberhood. I reckon it ain' so much so nowadays, but befo' de wah, in slab'ry times, a nigger did n' mine goin' fi' er ten mile in a night, w'en dey wuz sump'n good ter eat at de yuther een'.

"So atter a w'ile Mars Dugal' begin ter miss his scuppernon's. Co'se he 'cuse' de niggers er it, but dey all 'nied it ter de las'. Mars Dugal' sot spring guns en steel traps, en he en de oberseah sot up nights once't er twice't, tel one night Mars Dugal'—he 'uz a monst'us keerless man—got his leg shot full er cow-peas. But somehow er nudder dey could n' nebber ketch none er de niggers. I dunner how it happen, but it happen des like I tell you, en de grapes kep' on a-goin' des de same.

"But bimeby ole Mars Dugal' fix' up a plan ter stop it. Dey wuz a cunjuh 'oman livin' down 'mongs' de free niggers on de Wim'l'ton Road, en all de darkies fum Rockfish ter Beaver Crick wuz feared er her. She could wuk de mos' powerfulles' kin' er goopher,—could make people hab fits, er rheuma- tiz, er make 'em des dwinel away en die; en dey say she went out ridin' de niggers at night, fer she wuz a witch 'sides bein' a cunjuh 'oman. Mars Dugal' hearn 'bout Aun' Peggy's doin's, en begun ter 'flect whe'r er no he could n' git her ter he'p him keep de niggers off'n de grapevimes. One day in de spring er de year, ole miss pack' up a basket er chick'n en poun'-cake, en a bottle er scuppernon' wine, en Mars Dugal' tuk it in his buggy en driv ober ter Aun' Peggy's cabin. He tuk de basket in, en had a long talk wid Aun' Peggy.

"De nex' day Aun' Peggy come up ter de vimya'd. De niggers seed her slippin' 'roun', en dey soon foun' out what she 'uz doin' dere. Mars Dugal' had hi'ed her ter goopher de grapevimes. She sa'ntered 'roun' 'mongs' de vimes, en tuk a leaf fum dis one, en a grape-hull fum dat one, en a grape- seed fum anudder one; en den a little twig fum here, en a little pinch er dirt fum dere,—en put it all in a big black bottle, wid a snake's toof en a speckle' hen's gall en some ha'rs fum a black cat's tail, en den fill' de bottle wid scuppernon' wine. W'en she got de goopher all ready en fix', she tuk 'n went out in de woods en buried it under de root uv a red oak tree, en den come back en tole one er de niggers she done goopher de grapevines, en a'er a nigger w'at eat dem grapes 'ud be sho ter die inside'n twel' mont's.

"Atter dat de niggers let de scuppernon's 'lone, en Mars Dugal' did n' hab no 'casion ter fine no mo' fault; en de season wuz mos' gone, w'en a strange gemman stop at de plantation one night ter see Mars Dugal' on some business; en his coachman, seein' de scuppernon's growin' so nice en

---

1. White men (regionalism).

sweet, slip 'roun' behine de smoke-house, en et all de scuppernon's he could hole. Nobody did n' notice it at de time, but dat night, on de way home, de gemman's hoss runned away en kill' de coachman. W'en we hearn de noos, Aun' Lucy, de cook, she up 'n say she seed de strange nigger eat'n' er de scuppernon's behine de smokehouse; en den we knowed de goopher had b'en er wukkin'. Den one er de nigger chilluns runned away fum de quarters one day, en got in de scuppernon's, en died de nex' week. W'ite folks say he die' er de fevuh, but de niggers knowed it wuz de goopher. So you k'n be sho de darkies did n' hab much ter do wid dem scuppernon' vimes.

"W'en de scuppernon' season 'uz ober fer dat year, Mars Dugal' foun' he had made fifteen hund'ed gallon er wine; en one er de niggers hearn him laffin' wid de oberseah fit ter kill, en sayin' dem fifteen hund'ed gallon er wine wuz monst'us good intrus' on de ten dollars he laid out on de vimya'd. So I 'low ez he paid Aun' Peggy ten dollars fer to goopher de grapevimes.

"De goopher did n' wuk no mo' tel de nex' summer, w'en 'long to'ds de middle er de season one er de fiel' han's died; en ez dat lef' Mars Dugal' sho't er han's, he went off ter town fer ter buy anudder. He fotch de noo nigger home wid 'im. He wuz er ole nigger, er de color er a gingy-cake, en ball ez a hoss-apple on de top er his head. He wuz a peart ole nigger, do', en could do a big day's wuk.

"Now it happen dat one er de niggers on de nex' plantation, one er ole Mars Henry Brayboy's niggers, had runned away de day befo', en tuk ter de swamp, en ole Mars Dugal' en some er de yuther nabor w'ite folks had gone out wid dere guns en dere dogs fer ter he'p 'em hunt fer de nigger; en de han's on our own plantation wuz all so flusterated dat we fuhgot ter tell de noo han' 'bout de goopher on de scuppernon' vimes. Co'se he smell de grapes en see de vimes, an atter dahk de fus' thing he done wuz ter slip off ter de grapevimes 'dout sayin' nuffin ter nobody. Nex' mawnin' he tole some er de niggers 'bout de fine bait er scuppernon' he et de night befo'.

"W'en dey tole 'im 'bout de goopher on de grapevimes, he 'uz dat tarrified dat he turn pale, en look des like he gwine ter die right in his tracks. De oberseah come up en axed w'at 'uz de matter; en w'en dey tole 'im Henry be'n eatin' er de scuppernon's, en got de goopher on 'im, he gin Henry a big drink er w'iskey, en 'low dat de nex' rainy day he take 'im ober ter Aun' Peggy's, en see ef she would n' take de goopher off'n him, seein' ez he did n' know nuffin erbout it tel he done et de grapes.

"Sho nuff, it rain de nex' day, en de oberseah went ober ter Aun' Peggy's wid Henry. En Aun' Peggy say dat bein' ez Henry did n' know 'bout de goopher, en et de grapes in ign'ance er de conseq'ences, she reckon she mought be able fer ter take de goopher off'n him. So she fotch out er bottle wid some cunjuh medicine in it, en po'd some out in a go'd fer Henry ter drink. He manage ter git it down; he say it tas'e like whiskey wid sump'n bitter in it. She 'lowed dat 'ud keep de goopher off'n him tel de spring; but w'en de sap begin ter rise in de grapevimes he ha' ter come en see her ag'in, en she tell him w'at e's ter do.

"Nex' spring, w'en de sap commence' ter rise in de scuppernon' vime, Henry tuk a ham one night. Whar'd he git de ham? *I* doan know; dey wa'n't no hams on de plantation 'cep'n' w'at 'uz in de smoke-house, but *I* never

see Henry 'bout de smoke-house. But ez I wuz a-sayin', he tuk de ham ober
ter Aun' Peggy's; en Aun' Peggy tole 'im dat w'en Mars Dugal' begin ter
prune de grapevimes, he mus' go en take 'n scrape off de sap whar it ooze
out'n de cut een's er de vimes, en 'n'int his ball head wid it; en ef he do dat
once't a year de goopher would n' wuk agin 'im long ez he done it. En bein'
ez he fotch her de ham, she fix' it so he kin eat all de scuppernon' he want.

"So Henry 'n'int his head wid de sap out'n de big grapevime des ha'f way
'twix' de quarters en de big house, en de goopher nebber wuk agin him dat
summer. But de beatenes' thing you eber see happen ter Henry. Up ter dat
time he wuz ez ball ez a sweeten' 'tater, but des ez soon ez de young leaves
begun ter come out on de grapevimes, de ha'r begun ter grow out on
Henry's head, en by de middle er de summer he had de bigges' head er ha'r
on de plantation. Befo' dat, Henry had tol'able good ha'r 'roun' de aidges,
but soon ez de young grapes begun ter come, Henry's ha'r begun to quirl
all up in little balls, des like dis yer reg'lar grapy ha'r, en by de time de
grapes got ripe his head look des like a bunch er grapes. Combin' it did n'
do no good; he wuk at it ha'f de night wid er Jim Crow,[2] en think he git it
straighten' out, but in de mawnin' de grapes 'ud be dere des de same. So he
gin it up, en tried ter keep de grapes down by havin' his ha'r cut sho't.

"But dat wa'n't de quares' thing 'bout de goopher. When Henry come ter
de plantation, he wuz gittin' a little ole an stiff in de j'ints. But dat summer
he got des ez spry en libely ez any young nigger on de plantation; fac', he
got so biggity dat Mars Jackson, de oberseah, ha' ter th'eaten ter whip 'im,
ef he did n' stop cuttin' up his didos en behave hisse'f. But de mos'
cur'ouses' thing happen' in de fall, when de sap begin ter go down in de
grapevimes. Fus', when de grapes 'uz gethered, de knots begun ter
straighten out'n Henry's ha'r; en w'en de leaves begin ter fall, Henry's ha'r
'mence' ter drap out; en when de vimes 'uz bar', Henry's head wuz baller'n
it wuz in de spring, en he begin ter git ole en stiff in de j'ints ag'in, en paid
no mo' 'tention ter de gals dyoin' er de whole winter. En nex' spring, w'en
he rub de sap on ag'in, he got young ag'in, en so soopl en libely dat none er
de young niggers on de plantation could n' jump, ner dance, ner hoe ez
much cotton ez Henry. But in de fall er de year his grapes 'mence' ter
straighten out, en his j'ints ter git stiff, en his ha'r drap off, en de rheumatiz
begin ter wrastle wid 'im.

"Now, ef you'd 'a' knowed ole Mars Dugal' McAdoo, you'd 'a' knowed
dat it ha' ter be a mighty rainy day when he could n' fine sump'n fer his
niggers ter do, en it ha' ter be a mighty little hole he could n' crawl thoo, en
ha' ter be a monst'us cloudy night when a dollar git by him in de dahkness;
en w'en he see how Henry git young in de spring en ole in de fall, he 'lowed
ter hisse'f ez how he could make mo' money out'n Henry dan by wukkin'
him in de cotton-fiel'. 'Long de nex' spring, atter de sap 'mence' ter rise, en
Henry 'n'int 'is head en sta'ted fer ter git young en soopl, Mars Dugal' up 'n
tuk Henry ter town, en sole 'im fer fifteen hunder' dollars. Co'se de man
w'at bought Henry did n' know nuffin 'bout de goopher, en Mars Dugal'
did n' see no 'casion fer ter tell 'im. Long to'ds de fall, w'en de sap went

2. A small card, resembling a currycomb in construction, and used by negroes in the rural districts instead
of a comb [Chesnutt's note].

down, Henry begin ter git ole ag'in same ez yuzhal, en his noo marster begin ter git skeered les'n he gwine ter lose his fifteen-hunder'-dollar nigger. He sent fer a mighty fine doctor, but de med'cine did n' 'pear ter do no good; de goopher had a good holt. Henry tole de doctor 'bout de goopher, but de doctor des laff at 'im.

"One day in de winter Mars Dugal' went ter town, en wuz santerin' 'long de Main Street, when who should he meet but Henry's noo marster. Dey said 'Hoddy,' en Mars Dugal' ax 'im ter hab a seegyar; en atter dey run on awhile 'bout de craps en de weather, Mars Dugal' ax 'im, sorter keerless, like ez ef he des thought of it,—

"'How you like de nigger I sole you las' spring?'

"Henry's marster shuck his head en knock de ashes off'n his seegyar.

"'Spec' I made a bad bahgin when I bought dat nigger. Henry done good wuk all de summer, but sence de fall set in he 'pears ter be sorter pinin' away. Dey ain' nuffin pertickler de matter wid 'im—leastways de doctor say so—'cep'n' a tech er de rheumatiz; but his ha'r is all fell out, en ef he don't pick up his strenk mighty soon, I spec' I'm gwine ter lose 'im.'

"Dey smoked on awhile, en bimeby ole mars say, 'Well, a bahgin's a bahgin, but you en me is good fren's, en I doan wan' ter see you lose all de money you paid fer dat nigger; en ef w'at you say is so, en I ain't 'sputin' it, he ain't wuf much now. I 'spec's you wukked him too ha'd dis summer, er e'se de swamps down here don't agree wid de san'-hill nigger. So you des lemme know, en ef he gits any wusser I'll be willin' ter gib yer five hund'ed dollars fer 'im, en take my chances on his livin'.'

"Sho 'nuff, when Henry begun ter draw up wid de rheumatiz en it look like he gwine ter die fer sho, his noo marster sen' fer Mars Dugal', en Mars Dugal' gin him what he promus, en brung Henry home ag'in. He tuk good keer uv 'im dyoin' er de winter,—give 'im w'iskey ter rub his rheumatiz, en terbacker ter smoke, en all he want ter eat,—'caze a nigger w'at he could make a thousan' dollars a year off'n did n' grow on eve'y huckleberry bush.

"Nex' spring, w'en de sap ris en Henry's ha'r commence' ter sprout, Mars Dugal' sole 'im ag'in, down in Robeson County dis time; en he kep' dat sellin' business up fer five year er mo'. Henry nebber say nuffin 'bout de goopher ter his noo marsters, 'caze he know he gwine ter be tuk good keer uv de nex' winter, w'en Mars Dugal' buy him back. En Mars Dugal' made 'nuff money off'n Henry ter buy anudder plantation ober on Beaver Crick.

"But 'long 'bout de een' er dat five year dey come a stranger ter stop at de plantation. De fus' day he 'uz dere he went out wid Mars Dugal' en spent all de mawnin' lookin' ober de vimya'd, en atter dinner dey spent all de evenin' playin' kya'ds. De niggers soon 'skiver' dat he wuz a Yankee, en dat he come down ter Norf C'lina fer ter l'arn de w'ite folks how to raise grapes en make wine. He promus Mars Dugal' he c'd make de grapevimes b'ar twice't ez many grapes, en dat de noo winepress he wuz a-sellin' would make mo' d'n twice't ez many gallons er wine. En ole Mars Dugal' des drunk it all in, des 'peared ter be bewitch' wid dat Yankee. W'en de darkies see dat Yankee runnin' 'roun' de vimya'd en diggin' under de grapevimes, dey shuk dere heads, en 'lowed dat dey feared Mars Dugal' losin' his min'. Mars Dugal' had all de dirt dug away fum under de roots er all de scuppernon' vimes, an' let 'em stan' dat away fer a week er mo'. Den dat Yankee

made de niggers fix up a mixtry er lime en ashes en manyo,[3] en po' it 'roun'
de roots er de grapevimes. Den he 'vise Mars Dugal' fer ter trim de vimes
close't, en Mars Dugal' tuck 'n done eve'ything de Yankee tole him ter do.
Dyoin' all er dis time, mind yer, dis yer Yankee wuz libbin' off'n de fat er de
lan', at de big house, en playin' kya'ds wid Mars Dugal' eve'y night; en dey
say Mars Dugal' los' mo'n a thousan' dollars dyoin' er de week dat Yankee
wuz a-ruinin' de grapevimes.

"W'en de sap ris nex' spring, ole Henry 'n'inted his head ez yuzhal, en
his ha'r 'mence' ter grow des de same ez it done eve'y year. De scuppernon'
vimes growed monst's fas', en de leaves wuz greener en thicker dan dey
eber be'n dyoin' my rememb'ance; en Henry's ha'r growed out thicker dan
eber, en he 'peared ter git younger 'n younger, en sooper 'n sooper; en
seein' ez he wuz sho't er han's dat spring, havin' tuk in consid'able noo
groun', Mars Dugal' 'cluded he would n' sell Henry 'tel he git de crap in en
de cotton chop'. So he kep' Henry on de plantation.

"But 'long 'bout time fer de grapes ter come on de scuppernon' vimes,
dey 'peared ter come a change ober 'em; de leaves withered en swivel' up,
en de young grapes turn' yaller, en bimeby eve'ybody on de plantation
could see dat de whole vimya'd wuz dyin'. Mars Dugal' tuk'n water de
vimes en done all he could, but 't wa'n' no use: dat Yankee had done bus'
de watermillyum. One time de vimes picked up a bit, en Mars Dugal'
'lowed dey wuz gwine ter come out ag'in; but dat Yankee done dug too
close under de roots, en prune de branches too close ter de vime, en all dat
lime en ashes done burn' de life out'n de vimes, en dey des kep' a-with'in'
en a-swivelin'.

"All dis time de goopher wuz a-wukkin'. When de vimes sta'ted ter
wither, Henry 'mence' ter complain er his rheumatiz; en when de leaves
begin ter dry up, his ha'r 'mence' ter drap out. When de vimes fresh' up a
bit, Henry 'd git peart ag'in, en when de vimes wither' ag'in, Henry 'd git
ole ag'in, en des kep' gittin' mo' en mo' fitten fer nuffin; he des pined away,
en pined away, en fine'ly tuk ter his cabin; en when de big vime whar he
got de sap ter 'n'int his head withered en turned yaller en died, Henry died
too,—des went out sorter like a cannel. Dey did n't 'pear ter be nuffin de
matter wid 'im, 'cep'n' de rheumatiz, but his strenk des dwinel' away 'tel he
did n' hab ernuff lef' ter draw his bref. De goopher had got de under holt,
en th'owed Henry dat time fer good en all.

"Mars Dugal' tuk on might'ly 'bout losin' his vimes en his nigger in de
same year; en he swo' dat ef he could git holt er dat Yankee he'd wear 'im
ter a frazzle, en den chaw up de frazzle; en he'd done it, too, for Mars
Dugal' 'uz a monst'us brash man w'en he once git started. He sot de
vimya'd out ober ag'in, but it wuz th'ee er fo' year befo' de vimes got ter
b'arin' any scuppernon's.

"W'en de wah broke out, Mars Dugal' raise' a comp'ny, en went off ter
fight de Yankees. He say he wuz mighty glad dat wah come, en he des want
ter kill a Yankee fer eve'y dollar he los' 'long er dat grape-raisin' Yankee. En
I 'spec' he would 'a' done it, too, ef de Yankees had n' s'picioned sump'n,
en killed him fus'. Atter de s'render ole miss move' ter town, de niggers all

---

3. Manure.

scattered 'way fum de plantation, en de vimya'd ain' be'n cultervated sence."

"Is that story true?" asked Annie doubtfully, but seriously, as the old man concluded his narrative.

"It 's des ez true ez I 'm a-settin' here, miss. Dey's a easy way ter prove it: I kin lead de way right ter Henry's grave ober yander in de plantation buryin'-groun'. En I tell yer w'at, marster, I would n' 'vise you to buy dis yer ole vimya'd, 'caze de goopher's on it yit, en dey ain' no tellin' w'en it's gwine ter crap out."

"But I thought you said all the old vines died."

"Dey did 'pear ter die, but a few un 'em come out ag'in, en is mixed in 'mongs' de yuthers. I ain' skeered ter eat de grapes, 'caze I knows de old vimes fum de noo ones; but wid strangers dey ain' no tellin' w'at mought happen. I would n' 'vise yer ter buy dis vimya'd."

I bought the vineyard, nevertheless, and it has been for a long time in a thriving condition, and is often referred to by the local press as a striking illustration of the opportunities open to Northern capital in the development of Southern industries. The luscious scuppernong holds first rank among our grapes, though we cultivate a great many other varieties, and our income from grapes packed and shipped to the Northern markets is quite considerable. I have not noticed any developments of the goopher in the vineyard, although I have a mild suspicion that our colored assistants do not suffer from want of grapes during the season.

I found, when I bought the vineyard, that Uncle Julius had occupied a cabin on the place for many years, and derived a respectable revenue from the product of the neglected grapevines. This, doubtless, accounted for his advice to me not to buy the vineyard, though whether it inspired the goopher story I am unable to state. I believe, however, that the wages I paid him for his services as coachman, for I gave him employment in that capacity, were more than an equivalent for anything he lost by the sale of the vineyard.

1899

The Passing of Grandison

I

When it is said that it was done to please a woman, there ought perhaps to be enough said to explain anything; for what a man will not do to please a woman is yet to be discovered. Nevertheless, it might be well to state a few preliminary facts to make it clear why young Dick Owens tried to run one of his father's negro men off to Canada.

In the early fifties, when the growth of anti-slavery sentiment and the constant drain of fugitive slaves into the North had so alarmed the slaveholders of the border States as to lead to the passage of the Fugitive Slave

Law,[1] a young white man from Ohio, moved by compassion for the sufferings of a certain bondman who happened to have a "hard master," essayed to help the slave to freedom. The attempt was discovered and frustrated; the abductor was tried and convicted for slave-stealing, and sentenced to a term of imprisonment in the penitentiary. His death, after the expiration of only a small part of the sentence, from cholera contracted while nursing stricken fellow prisoners, lent to the case a melancholy interest that made it famous in anti-slavery annals.

Dick Owens had attended the trial. He was a youth of about twenty-two, intelligent, handsome, and amiable, but extremely indolent, in a graceful and gentlemanly way; or, as old Judge Fenderson put it more than once, he was lazy as the Devil,—a mere figure of speech, of course, and not one that did justice to the Enemy of Mankind. When asked why he never did anything serious, Dick would good-naturedly reply, with a well-modulated drawl, that he did n't have to. His father was rich; there was but one other child, an unmarried daughter, who because of poor health would probably never marry, and Dick was therefore heir presumptive to a large estate. Wealth or social position he did not need to seek, for he was born to both. Charity Lomax had shamed him into studying law, but notwithstanding an hour or so a day spent at old Judge Fenderson's office, he did not make remarkable headway in his legal studies.

"What Dick needs," said the judge, who was fond of tropes,[2] as became a scholar, and of horses, as was befitting a Kentuckian, "is the whip of necessity, or the spur of ambition. If he had either, he would soon need the snaffle[3] to hold him back."

But all Dick required, in fact, to prompt him to the most remarkable thing he accomplished before he was twenty-five, was a mere suggestion from Charity Lomax. The story was never really known to but two persons until after the war, when it came out because it was a good story and there was no particular reason for its concealment.

Young Owens had attended the trial of this slave-stealer, or martyr,—either or both,—and, when it was over, had gone to call on Charity Lomax, and, while they sat on the veranda after sundown, had told her all about the trial. He was a good talker, as his career in later years disclosed, and described the proceedings very graphically.

"I confess," he admitted, "that while my principles were against the prisoner, my sympathies were on his side. It appeared that he was of good family, and that he had an old father and mother, respectable people, dependent upon him for support and comfort in their declining years. He had been led into the matter by pity for a negro whose master ought to have been run out of the county long ago for abusing his slaves. If it had been merely a question of old Sam Briggs's negro, nobody would have cared anything about it. But father and the rest of them stood on the principle of the thing, and told the judge so, and the fellow was sentenced to three years in the penitentiary."

1. It made a federal crime any action that aided a runaway slave and was the most controversial feature of the Compromise of 1850.

2. Figures of speech.
3. The bit of a bridle.

Miss Lomax had listened with lively interest.

"I've always hated old Sam Briggs," she said emphatically, "ever since the time he broke a negro's leg with a piece of cordwood. When I hear of a cruel deed it makes the Quaker blood that came from my grandmother assert itself. Personally I wish that all Sam Briggs's negroes would run away. As for the young man, I regard him as a hero. He dared something for humanity. I could love a man who would take such chances for the sake of others."

"Could you love me, Charity, if I did something heroic?"

"You never will, Dick. You're too lazy for any use. You'll never do anything harder than playing cards or fox-hunting."

"Oh, come now, sweetheart! I've been courting you for a year, and it's the hardest work imaginable. Are you never going to love me?" he pleaded.

His hand sought hers, but she drew it back beyond his reach.

"I'll never love you, Dick Owens, until you have done something. When that time comes, I'll think about it."

"But it takes so long to do anything worth mentioning, and I don't want to wait. One must read two years to become a lawyer, and work five more to make a reputation. We shall both be gray by then."

"Oh, I don't know," she rejoined. "It doesn't require a lifetime for a man to prove that he is a man. This one did something, or at least tried to."

"Well, I'm willing to attempt as much as any other man. What do you want me to do, sweetheart? Give me a test."

"Oh, dear me!" said Charity, "I don't care what you *do*, so you do *something*. Really, come to think of it, why should I care whether you do anything or not?"

"I'm sure I don't know why you should, Charity," rejoined Dick humbly, "for I'm aware that I'm not worthy of it."

"Except that I do hate," she added, relenting slightly, "to see a really clever man so utterly lazy and good for nothing."

"Thank you, my dear; a word of praise from you has sharpened my wits already. I have an idea! Will you love me if *I* run a negro off to Canada?"

"What nonsense!" said Charity scornfully. "You must be losing your wits. Steal another man's slave, indeed, while your father owns a hundred!"

"Oh, there'll be no trouble about that," responded Dick lightly; "I'll run off one of the old man's; we've got too many anyway. It may not be quite as difficult as the other man found it, but it will be just as unlawful, and will demonstrate what I am capable of."

"Seeing's believing," replied Charity. "Of course, what you are talking about now is merely absurd. I'm going away for three weeks, to visit my aunt in Tennessee. If you're able to tell me, when I return, that you've done something to prove your quality, I'll—well, you may come and tell me about it."

II

Young Owens got up about nine o'clock next morning, and while making his toilet put some questions to his personal attendant, a rather bright looking young mulatto of about his own age.

"Tom," said Dick.

"Yas, Mars Dick," responded the servant.

"I'm going on a trip North. Would you like to go with me?"

Now, if there was anything that Tom would have liked to make, it was a trip North. It was something he had long contemplated in the abstract, but had never been able to muster up sufficient courage to attempt in the concrete. He was prudent enough, however, to dissemble his feelings.

"I wouldn't min' it, Mars Dick, ez long ez you'd take keer er me an' fetch me home all right."

Tom's eyes belied his words, however, and his young master felt well assured that Tom needed only a good opportunity to make him run away. Having a comfortable home, and a dismal prospect in case of failure, Tom was not likely to take any desperate chances; but young Owens was satisfied that in a free State but little persuasion would be required to lead Tom astray. With a very logical and characteristic desire to gain his end with the least necessary expenditure of effort, he decided to take Tom with him, if his father did not object.

Colonel Owens had left the house when Dick went to breakfast, so Dick did not see his father till luncheon.

"Father," he remarked casually to the colonel, over the fried chicken, "I'm feeling a trifle run down. I imagine my health would be improved somewhat by a little travel and change of scene."

"Why don't you take a trip North?" suggested his father. The colonel added to paternal affection a considerable respect for his son as the heir of a large estate. He himself had been "raised" in comparative poverty, and had laid the foundations of his fortune by hard work; and while he despised the ladder by which he had climbed, he could not entirely forget it, and unconsciously manifested, in his intercourse with his son, some of the poor man's deference toward the wealthy and well-born.

"I think I'll adopt your suggestion, sir," replied the son, "and run up to New York; and after I've been there awhile I may go on to Boston for a week or so. I've never been there, you know."

"There are some matters you can talk over with my factor in New York," rejoined the colonel, "and while you are up there among the Yankees, I hope you'll keep your eyes and ears open to find out what the rascally abolitionists are saying and doing. They're becoming altogether too active for our comfort, and entirely too many ungrateful niggers are running away. I hope the conviction of that fellow yesterday may discourage the rest of the breed. I'd just like to catch any one trying to run off one of my darkeys. He'd get short shrift; I don't think any Court would have a chance to try him."

"They are a pestiferous lot," assented Dick, "and dangerous to our institutions. But say, father, if I go North I shall want to take Tom with me."

Now, the colonel, while a very indulgent father, had pronounced views on the subject of negroes, having studied them, as he often said, for a great many years, and, as he asserted oftener still, understanding them perfectly. It is scarcely worth while to say, either, that he valued more highly than if he had inherited them the slaves he had toiled and schemed for.

"I don't think it safe to take Tom up North," he declared, with prompt-ness and decision. "He's a good enough boy, but too smart to trust among those low-down abolitionists. I strongly suspect him of having learned to read, though I can't imagine how. I saw him with a newspaper the other day, and while he pretended to be looking at a woodcut, I'm almost sure he was reading the paper. I think it by no means safe to take him."

Dick did not insist, because he knew it was useless. The colonel would have obliged his son in any other matter, but his negroes were the outward and visible sign of his wealth and station, and therefore sacred to him.

"Whom do you think it safe to take?" asked Dick. "I suppose I'll have to have a body-servant."

"What's the matter with Grandison?" suggested the colonel. "He's handy enough, and I reckon we can trust him. He's too fond of good eating, to risk losing his regular meals; besides, he's sweet on your mother's maid, Betty, and I've promised to let 'em get married before long. I'll have Gran-dison up, and we'll talk to him. Here, you boy Jack," called the colonel to a yellow youth in the next room who was catching flies and pulling their wings off to pass the time, "go down to the barn and tell Grandison to come here."

"Grandison," said the colonel, when the negro stood before him, hat in hand.

"Yas, marster."

"Haven't I always treated you right?"

"Yas, marster."

"Haven't you always got all you wanted to eat?"

"Yas, marster."

"And as much whiskey and tobacco as was good for you, Grandison?"

"Y-a-s, marster."

"I should just like to know, Grandison, whether you don't think yourself a great deal better off than those poor free negroes down by the plank road, with no kind master to look after them and no mistress to give them medi-cine when they're sick and—and"—

"Well, I sh'd jes' reckon I is better off, suh, dan dem low-down free nig-gers, suh! Ef anybody ax 'em who dey b'long ter, dey has ter say nobody, er e'se lie erbout it. Anybody ax me who I b'longs ter, I ain' got no 'casion ter be shame' ter tell 'em, no, suh, 'deed I ain', suh!"

The colonel was beaming. This was true gratitude, and his feudal heart thrilled at such appreciative homage. What cold-blooded, heartless mon-sters they were who would break up this blissful relationship of kindly pro-tection on the one hand, of wise subordination and loyal dependence on the other! The colonel always became indignant at the mere thought of such wickedness.

"Grandison," the colonel continued, "your young master Dick is going North for a few weeks, and I am thinking of letting him take you along. I shall send you on this trip, Grandison, in order that you may take care of your young master. He will need some one to wait on him, and no one can ever do it so well as one of the boys brought up with him on the old plantation. I am going to trust him in your hands, and I'm sure you'll do your duty faithfully, and bring him back home safe and sound—to old Kentucky."

Grandison grinned. "Oh yas, marster, I'll take keer er young Mars Dick."

"I want to warn you, though, Grandison," continued the colonel impressively, "against these cussed abolitionists, who try to entice servants from their comfortable homes and their indulgent masters, from the blue skies, the green fields, and the warm sunlight of their southern home, and send them away off yonder to Canada, a dreary country, where the woods are full of wildcats and wolves and bears, where the snow lies up to the eaves of the houses for six months of the year, and the cold is so severe that it freezes your breath and curdles your blood; and where, when runaway niggers get sick and can't work, they are turned out to starve and die, unloved and uncared for. I reckon, Grandison, that you have too much sense to permit yourself to be led astray by any such foolish and wicked people."

" 'Deed, suh, I would n' low none er dem cussed, low-down abolitioners ter come nigh me, suh. I'd—I'd—would I be 'lowed ter hit 'em, suh?"

"Certainly, Grandison," replied the colonel, chuckling, "hit 'em as hard as you can. I reckon they'd rather like it. Begad, I believe they would! It would serve 'em right to be hit by a nigger!"

"Er ef I didn't hit 'em, suh," continued Grandison reflectively, "I'd tell Mars Dick, en *he'd* fix 'em. He'd smash de face off'n 'em, suh, I jes' knows he would."

"Oh yes, Grandison, your young master will protect you. You need fear no harm while he is near."

"Dey won't try ter steal me, will dey, marster?" asked the negro, with sudden alarm.

"I don't know, Grandison," replied the colonel, lighting a fresh cigar. "They're a desperate set of lunatics, and there's no telling what they may resort to. But if you stick close to your young master, and remember always that he is your best friend, and understands your real needs, and has your true interests at heart, and if you will be careful to avoid strangers who try to talk to you, you'll stand a fair chance of getting back to your home and your friends. And if you please your master Dick, he'll buy you a present, and a string of beads for Betty to wear when you and she get married in the fall."

"Thanky, marster, thanky, suh," replied Grandison, oozing gratitude at every pore; "you is a good marster, to be sho', suh; yas, 'deed you is. You kin jes' bet me and Mars Dick gwine git 'long jes' lack I wuz own boy ter Mars Dick. En it won't be my fault ef he don' want me fer his boy all de time, w'en we come back home ag'in."

"All right, Grandison, you may go now. You needn't work any more today, and here's a piece of tobacco for you off my own plug."

"Thanky, marster, thanky, marster! You is de bes' marster any nigger ever had in dis worl'." And Grandison bowed and scraped and disappeared round the corner, his jaws closing around a large section of the colonel's best tobacco.

"You may take Grandison," said the colonel to his son. "I allow he's abolitionist-proof."

III

Richard Owens, Esq., and servant, from Kentucky, registered at the fashionable New York hostelry for Southerners in those days, a hotel where an atmosphere congenial to Southern institutions was sedulously maintained. But there were negro waiters in the dining-room, and mulatto bell-boys, and Dick had no doubt that Grandison, with the native gregariousness and garrulousness of his race, would foregather and palaver with them sooner or later, and Dick hoped that they would speedily inoculate him with the virus of freedom. For it was not Dick's intention to say anything to his servant about his plan to free him, for obvious reasons. To mention one of them, if Grandison should go away, and by legal process be recaptured, his young master's part in the matter would doubtless become known, which would be embarrassing to Dick, to say the least. If, on the other hand, he should merely give Grandison sufficient latitude, he had no doubt he would eventually lose him. For while not exactly skeptical about Grandison's perfervid loyalty, Dick had been a somewhat keen observer of human nature, in his own indolent way, and based his expectations upon the force of the example and argument that his servant could scarcely fail to encounter. Grandison should have a fair chance to become free by his own initiative; if it should become necessary to adopt other measures to get rid of him, it would be time enough to act when the necessity arose; and Dick Owens was not the youth to take needless trouble.

The young master renewed some acquaintances and made others, and spent a week or two very pleasantly in the best society of the metropolis, easily accessible to a wealthy, well-bred young Southerner, with proper introductions. Young women smiled on him, and young men of convivial habits pressed their hospitalities; but the memory of Charity's sweet, strong face and clear blue eyes made him proof against the blandishments of the one sex and the persuasions of the other. Meanwhile he kept Grandison supplied with pocket-money, and left him mainly to his own devices. Every night when Dick came in he hoped he might have to wait upon himself, and every morning he looked forward with pleasure to the prospect of making his toilet unaided. His hopes, however, were doomed to disappointment, for every night when he came in Grandison was on hand with a bootjack, and a nightcap mixed for his young master as the colonel had taught him to mix it, and every morning Grandison appeared with his master's boots blacked and his clothes brushed, and laid his linen out for the day.

"Grandison," said Dick one morning, after finishing his toilet, "this is the chance of your life to go around among your own people and see how they live. Have you met any of them?"

"Yas, suh, I's seen some of 'em. But I don' keer nuffin fer 'em, suh. Dey 're diffe'nt f'm de niggers down ou' way. Dey 'lows dey 're free, but dey ain' got sense 'nuff ter know dey ain' half as well off as dey would be down Souf, whar dey'd be 'preciated."

When two weeks had passed without any apparent effect of evil example upon Grandison, Dick resolved to go on to Boston, where he thought the atmosphere might prove more favorable to his ends. After he had been at the Revere House for a day or two without losing Grandison, he decided upon slightly different tactics.

Having ascertained from a city directory the addresses of several well-known abolitionists, he wrote them each a letter something like this:—

Dear Friend and Brother:—

A wicked slaveholder from Kentucky, stopping at the Revere House, has dared to insult the liberty-loving people of Boston by bringing his slave into their midst. Shall this be tolerated? Or shall steps be taken in the name of liberty to rescue a fellow-man from bondage? For obvious reasons I can only sign myself,

A Friend of Humanity.

That his letter might have an opportunity to prove effective, Dick made it a point to send Grandison away from the hotel on various errands. On one of these occasions Dick watched him for quite a distance down the street. Grandison had scarcely left the hotel when a long-haired, sharp-featured man came out behind him, followed him, soon overtook him, and kept along beside him until they turned the next corner. Dick's hopes were roused by this spectacle, but sank correspondingly when Grandison returned to the hotel. As Grandison said nothing about the encounter, Dick hoped there might be some self-consciousness behind this unexpected reticence, the results of which might develop later on.

But Grandison was on hand again when his master came back to the hotel at night, and was in attendance again in the morning, with hot water, to assist at his master's toilet. Dick sent him on further errands from day to day, and upon one occasion came squarely up to him—inadvertently of course—while Grandison was engaged in conversation with a young white man in clerical garb. When Grandison saw Dick approaching, he edged away from the preacher and hastened toward his master, with a very evident expression of relief upon his countenance.

"Mars Dick," he said, "dese yer abolitioners is jes' pesterin' de life out er me tryin' ter git me ter run away. I don' pay no 'tention ter 'em, but dey riles me so sometimes dat I'm feared I'll hit some of 'em some er dese days, an' dat mought git me inter trouble. I ain' said nuffin' ter you 'bout it, Mars Dick, fer I did n' wanter 'sturb yo' min'; but I don' like it, suh; no, suh, I don'! Is we gwine back home 'fo' long, Mars Dick?"

"We'll be going back soon enough," replied Dick somewhat shortly, while he inwardly cursed the stupidity of a slave who could be free and would not, and registered a secret vow that if he were unable to get rid of Grandison without assassinating him, and were therefore compelled to take him back to Kentucky, he would see that Grandison got a taste of an article of slavery that would make him regret his wasted opportunities. Meanwhile he determined to tempt his servant yet more strongly.

"Grandison," he said next morning, "I'm going away for a day or two, but I shall leave you here. I shall lock up a hundred dollars in this drawer and give you the key. If you need any of it, use it and enjoy yourself,—spend it all if you like,—for this is probably the last chance you'll have for some time to be in a free State, and you'd better enjoy your liberty while you may."

When he came back a couple of days later and found the faithful Grandison at his post, and the hundred dollars intact, Dick felt seriously annoyed. His vexation was increased by the fact that he could not express his feelings adequately. He did not even scold Grandison; how could he, indeed, find fault with one who so sensibly recognized his true place in the economy of civilization, and kept it with such touching fidelity?

"I can't say a thing to him," groaned Dick. "He deserves a leather medal, made out of his own hide tanned. I reckon I'll write to father and let him know what a model servant he has given me."

He wrote his father a letter which made the colonel swell with pride and pleasure. "I really think," the colonel observed to one of his friends, "that Dick ought to have the nigger interviewed by the Boston papers, so that they may see how contented and happy our darkeys really are."

Dick also wrote a long letter to Charity Lomax, in which he said, among many other things, that if she knew how hard he was working, and under what difficulties, to accomplish something serious for her sake, she would no longer keep him in suspense, but overwhelm him with love and admiration.

Having thus exhausted without result the more obvious methods of getting rid of Grandison, and diplomacy having also proved a failure, Dick was forced to consider more radical measures. Of course he might run away himself, and abandon Grandison, but this would be merely to leave him in the United States, where he was still a slave, and where, with his notions of loyalty, he would speedily be reclaimed. It was necessary, in order to accomplish the purpose of his trip to the North, to leave Grandison permanently in Canada, where he would be legally free.

"I might extend my trip to Canada," he reflected, "but that would be too palpable. I have it! I'll visit Niagara Falls on the way home, and lose him on the Canada side. When he once realizes that he is actually free, I'll warrant that he'll stay."

So the next day saw them westward bound, and in due course of time, by the somewhat slow conveyances of the period, they found themselves at Niagara. Dick walked and drove about the Falls for several days, taking Grandison along with him on most occasions. One morning they stood on the Canadian side, watching the wild whirl of the waters below them.

"Grandison," said Dick, raising his voice above the roar of the cataract, "do you know where you are now?"

"I's wid you, Mars Dick; dat's all I keers."

"You are now in Canada, Grandison, where your people go when they run away from their masters. If you wished, Grandison, you might walk away from me this very minute, and I could not lay my hand upon you to take you back."

Grandison looked around uneasily.

"Let's go back ober de ribber, Mars Dick. I's feared I'll lose you ovuh heah, an' den I won' hab no marster, an' won't nebber be able to git back home no mo'.''

Discouraged, but not yet hopeless, Dick said, a few minutes later,—

"Grandison, I'm going up the road a bit, to the inn over yonder. You stay here until I return. I'll not be gone a great while."

Grandison's eyes opened wide and he looked somewhat fearful.

"Is dey any er dem dadblasted abolitioners roun' heah, Mars Dick?"

"I don't imagine that there are," replied his master, hoping there might be. "But I'm not afraid of *your* running away, Grandison. I only wish I were," he added to himself.

Dick walked leisurely down the road to where the whitewashed inn, built of stone, with true British solidity, loomed up through the trees by the roadside. Arrived there he ordered a glass of ale and a sandwich, and took a seat at a table by a window, from which he could see Grandison in the distance. For a while he hoped that the seed he had sown might have fallen on fertile ground, and that Grandison, relieved from the restraining power of a master's eye, and finding himself in a free country, might get up and walk away; but the hope was vain, for Grandison remained faithfully at his post, awaiting his master's return. He had seated himself on a broad flat stone, and, turning his eyes away from the grand and awe-inspiring spectacle that lay close at hand, was looking anxiously toward the inn where his master sat cursing his ill-timed fidelity.

By and by a girl came into the room to serve his order, and Dick very naturally glanced at her; and as she was young and pretty and remained in attendance, it was some minutes before he looked for Grandison. When he did so his faithful servant had disappeared.

To pay his reckoning and go away without the change was a matter quickly accomplished. Retracing his footsteps toward the Falls, he saw, to his great disgust, as he approached the spot where he had left Grandison, the familiar form of his servant stretched out on the ground, his face to the sun, his mouth open, sleeping the time away, oblivious alike to the grandeur of the scenery, the thunderous roar of the cataract, or the insidious voice of sentiment.

"Grandison," soliloquized his master, as he stood gazing down at his ebony encumbrance, "I do not deserve to be an American citizen; I ought not to have the advantages I possess over you; and I certainly am not worthy of Charity Lomax, if I am not smart enough to get rid of you. I have an idea! You shall yet be free, and I will be the instrument of your deliverance. Sleep on, faithful and affectionate servitor, and dream of the blue grass and the bright skies of old Kentucky, for it is only in your dreams that you will ever see them again!"

Dick retraced his footsteps towards the inn. The young woman chanced to look out of the window and saw the handsome young gentleman she had waited on a few minutes before, standing in the road a short distance away, apparently engaged in earnest conversation with a colored man employed as hostler[4] for the inn. She thought she saw something pass from the white man to the other, but at that moment her duties called her away from the

4. A person who takes care of horses.

window, and when she looked out again the young gentleman had disappeared, and the hostler, with two other young men of the neighborhood, one white and one colored, were walking rapidly towards the Falls.

IV

Dick made the journey homeward alone, and as rapidly as the conveyances of the day would permit. As he drew near home his conduct in going back without Grandison took on a more serious aspect than it had borne at any previous time, and although he had prepared the colonel by a letter sent several days ahead, there was still the prospect of a bad quarter of an hour with him; not, indeed, that his father would upbraid him, but he was likely to make searching inquiries. And notwithstanding the vein of quiet recklessness that had carried Dick through his preposterous scheme, he was a very poor liar, having rarely had occasion or inclination to tell anything but the truth. Any reluctance to meet his father was more than offset, however, by a stronger force drawing him homeward, for Charity Lomax must long since have returned from her visit to her aunt in Tennessee.

Dick got off easier than he had expected. He told a straight story, and a truthful one, so far as it went.

The colonel raged at first, but rage soon subsided into anger, and anger moderated into annoyance, and annoyance into a sort of garrulous sense of injury. The colonel thought he had been hardly used; he had trusted this negro, and he had broken faith. Yet, after all, he did not blame Grandison so much as he did the abolitionists, who were undoubtedly at the bottom of it.

As for Charity Lomax, Dick told her, privately of course, that he had run his father's man, Grandison, off to Canada, and left him there.

"Oh, Dick," she had said with shuddering alarm, "what have you done? If they knew it they'd send you to the penitentiary, like they did that Yankee."

"But they don't know it," he had replied seriously; adding, with an injured tone, "you don't seem to appreciate my heroism like you did that of the Yankee; perhaps it 's because I wasn't caught and sent to the penitentiary. I thought you wanted me to do it."

"Why, Dick Owens!" she exclaimed. "You know I never dreamed of any such outrageous proceeding.

"But I presume I'll have to marry you," she concluded, after some insistence on Dick's part, "if only to take care of you. You are too reckless for anything; and a man who goes chasing all over the North, being entertained by New York and Boston society and having negroes to throw away, needs some one to look after him."

"It's a most remarkable thing," replied Dick fervently, "that your views correspond exactly with my profoundest convictions. It proves beyond question that we were made for one another."

They were married three weeks later. As each of them had just returned from a journey, they spent their honeymoon at home.

A week after the wedding they were seated, one afternoon, on the piazza of the colonel's house, where Dick had taken his bride, when a negro from the yard ran down the lane and threw open the big gate for the colonel's buggy to enter. The colonel was not alone. Beside him, ragged and travel-stained, bowed with weariness, and upon his face a haggard look that told of hardship and privation, sat the lost Grandison.

The colonel alighted at the steps.

"Take the lines, Tom," he said to the man who had opened the gate, "and drive round to the barn. Help Grandison down,—poor devil, he's so stiff he can hardly move!—and get a tub of water and wash him and rub him down, and feed him, and give him a big drink of whiskey, and then let him come round and see his young master and his new mistress."

The colonel's face wore an expression compounded of joy and indignation,—joy at the restoration of a valuable piece of property; indignation for reasons he proceeded to state.

"It 's astounding, the depths of depravity the human heart is capable of! I was coming along the road three miles away, when I heard some one call me from the roadside. I pulled up the mare, and who should come out of the woods but Grandison. The poor nigger could hardly crawl along, with the help of a broken limb. I was never more astonished in my life. You could have knocked me down with a feather. He seemed pretty far gone,—he could hardly talk above a whisper,—and I had to give him a mouthful of whiskey to brace him up so he could tell his story. It's just as I thought from the beginning, Dick; Grandison had no notion of running away; he knew when he was well off, and where his friends were. All the persuasions of abolition liars and runaway niggers did not move him. But the desperation of those fanatics knew no bounds; their guilty consciences gave them no rest. They got the notion somehow that Grandison belonged to a nigger-catcher, and had been brought North as a spy to help capture ungrateful runaway servants. They actually kid-naped him—just think of it!—and gagged him and bound him and threw him rudely into a wagon, and carried him into the gloomy depths of a Canadian forest, and locked him in a lonely hut, and fed him on bread and water for three weeks. One of the scoundrels wanted to kill him, and persuaded the others that it ought to be done; but they got to quarreling about how they should do it, and before they had their minds made up Grandison escaped, and, keeping his back steadily to the North Star, made his way, after suffering incredible hardships, back to the old plan-tation, back to his master, his friends, and his home. Why, it's as good as one of Scott's novels! Mr. Simms[5] or some other one of our Southern authors ought to write it up."

"Don't you think, sir," suggested Dick, who had calmly smoked his cigar throughout the colonel's animated recital, "that that kidnaping yarn sounds a little improbable? Isn't there some more likely explanation?"

"Nonsense, Dick; it's the gospel truth! Those infernal abolitionists are

5. William Gilmore Simms (1806–1870), the most widely read novelist of the antebellum South. Sir Wal-ter Scott (1771–1832), popular British historical novelist.

capable of anything—everything! Just think of their locking the poor, faithful nigger up, beating him, kicking him, depriving him of his liberty, keeping him on bread and water for three long, lonesome weeks, and he all the time pining for the old plantation!"

There were almost tears in the colonel's eyes at the picture of Grandison's sufferings that he conjured up. Dick still professed to be slightly skeptical, and met Charity's severely questioning eye with bland unconsciousness.

The colonel killed the fatted calf for Grandison, and for two or three weeks the returned wanderer's life was a slave's dream of pleasure. His fame spread throughout the county, and the colonel gave him a permanent place among the house servants, where he could always have him conveniently at hand to relate his adventures to admiring visitors.

About three weeks after Grandison's return the colonel's faith in sable humanity was rudely shaken, and its foundations almost broken up. He came near losing his belief in the fidelity of the negro to his master,—the servile virtue most highly prized and most sedulously cultivated by the colonel and his kind. One Monday morning Grandison was missing. And not only Grandison, but his wife, Betty the maid; his mother, aunt Eunice; his father, uncle Ike; his brothers, Tom and John, and his little sister Elsie, were likewise absent from the plantation; and a hurried search and inquiry in the neighborhood resulted in no information as to their whereabouts. So much valuable property could not be lost without an effort to recover it, and the wholesale nature of the transaction carried consternation to the hearts of those whose ledgers were chiefly bound in black. Extremely energetic measures were taken by the colonel and his friends. The fugitives were traced, and followed from point to point, on their northward run through Ohio. Several times the hunters were close upon their heels, but the magnitude of the escaping party begot unusual vigilance on the part of those who sympathized with the fugitives, and strangely enough, the underground railroad seemed to have had its tracks cleared and signals set for this particular train. Once, twice, the colonel thought he had them, but they slipped through his fingers.

One last glimpse he caught of his vanishing property, as he stood, accompanied by a United States marshal, on a wharf at a port on the south shore of Lake Erie. On the stern of a small steamboat which was receding rapidly from the wharf, with her nose pointing toward Canada, there stood a group of familiar dark faces, and the look they cast backward was not one of longing for the fleshpots of Egypt.[6] The colonel saw Grandison point him out to one of the crew of the vessel, who waved his hand derisively toward the colonel. The latter shook his fist impotently—and the incident was closed.

1899

6. An allusion to Exodus 16:2–3.

The Wife of His Youth

I

Mr. Ryder was going to give a ball. There were several reasons why this was an opportune time for such an event.

Mr. Ryder might aptly be called the dean of the Blue Veins. The original Blue Veins were a little society of colored persons organized in a certain Northern city shortly after the war. Its purpose was to establish and maintain correct social standards among a people whose social standards among a people whose social condition presented almost unlimited room for improvement. By accident, combined perhaps with some natural affinity, the society consisted of individuals who were, generally speaking, more white than black. Some envious outsider made the suggestion that no one was eligible for membership who was not white enough to show blue veins. The suggestion was readily adopted by those who were not of the favored few, and since that time the society, though possessing a longer and more pretentious name, had been known far and wide as the "Blue Vein Society," and its members as the "Blue Veins."

The Blue Veins did not allow that any such requirement existed for admission to their circle, but, on the contrary, declared that character and culture were the only things considered; and that if most of their members were light-colored, it was because such persons, as a rule, had had better opportunities to qualify themselves for membership. Opinions differed, too, as to the usefulness of the society. There were those who had been known to assail it violently as a glaring example of the very prejudice from which the colored race had suffered most; and later, when such critics had succeeded in getting on the inside, they had been heard to maintain with zeal and earnestness that the society was a lifeboat, an anchor, a bulwark and a shield,—a pillar of cloud by day and of fire by night, to guide their people through the social wilderness. Another alleged prerequisite for Blue Vein membership was that of free birth; and while there was really no such requirement, it is doubtless true that very few of the members would have been unable to meet it if there had been. If there were one or two of the older members who had come up from the South and from slavery, their history presented enough romantic circumstances to rob their servile origin of its grosser aspects.

While there were no such tests of eligibility, it is true that the Blue Veins had their notions on these subjects, and that not all of them were equally liberal in regard to the things they collectively disclaimed. Mr. Ryder was one of the most conservative. Though he had not been among the founders of the society, but had come in some years later, his genius for social leadership was such that he had speedily become its recognized adviser and head, the custodian of its standards, and the preserver of its traditions. He shaped its social policy, was active in providing for its entertainment, and when the interest fell off, as it sometimes did, he fanned the embers until they burst again into a cheerful flame.

There were still other reasons for his popularity. While he was not as white as some of the Blue Veins, his appearance was such as to confer distinction upon them. His features were of a refined type, his hair was almost straight; he was always neatly dressed; his manners were irreproachable, and his morals above suspicion. He had come to Groveland a young man, and obtaining employment in the office of a railroad company as messenger had in time worked himself up to the position of stationery clerk, having charge of the distribution of the office supplies for the whole company. Although the lack of early training had hindered the orderly development of a naturally fine mind, it had not prevented him from doing a great deal of reading or from forming decidedly literary tastes. Poetry was his passion. He could repeat whole pages of the great English poets; and if his pronunciation was sometimes faulty, his eye, his voice, his gestures, would respond to the changing sentiment with a precision that revealed a poetic soul and disarmed criticism. He was economical, and had saved money; he owned and occupied a very comfortable house on a respectable street. His residence was handsomely furnished, containing among other things a good library, especially rich in poetry, a piano, and some choice engravings. He generally shared his house with some young couple, who looked after his wants and were company for him; for Mr. Ryder was a single man. In the early days of his connection with the Blue Veins he had been regarded as quite a catch, and young ladies and their mothers had manœuvred with much ingenuity to capture him. Not, however, until Mrs. Molly Dixon visited Groveland had any woman ever made him wish to change his condition to that of a married man.

Mrs. Dixon had come to Groveland from Washington in the spring, and before the summer was over she had won Mr. Ryder's heart. She possessed many attractive qualities. She was much younger than he; in fact, he was old enough to have been her father, though no one knew exactly how old he was. She was whiter than he, and better educated. She had moved in the best colored society of the country, at Washington, and had taught in the schools of that city. Such a superior person had been eagerly welcomed to the Blue Vein Society, and had taken a leading part in its activities. Mr. Ryder had at first been attracted by her charms of person, for she was very good looking and not over twenty-five; then by her refined manners and the vivacity of her wit. Her husband had been a government clerk, and at his death had left a considerable life insurance. She was visiting friends in Groveland, and, finding the town and the people to her liking, had prolonged her stay indefinitely. She had not seemed displeased at Mr. Ryder's attentions, but on the contrary had given him every proper encouragement; indeed, a younger and less cautious man would long since have spoken. But he had made up his mind, and had only to determine the time when he would ask her to be his wife. He decided to give a ball in her honor, and at some time during the evening of the ball to offer her his heart and hand. He had no special fears about the outcome, but, with a little touch of romance, he wanted the surroundings to be in harmony with his own feelings when he should have received the answer he expected.

Mr. Ryder resolved that this ball should mark an epoch in the social history of Groveland. He knew, of course,—no one could know better,—the entertainments that had taken place in past years, and what must be done to surpass them. His ball must be worthy of the lady in whose honor it was to be given, and must, by the quality of its guests, set an example for the future. He had observed of late a growing liberality, almost a laxity, in social matters, even among members of his own set, and had several times been forced to meet in a social way persons whose complexions and callings in life were hardly up to the standard which he considered proper for the society to maintain. He had a theory of his own.

"I have no race prejudice," he would say, "but we people of mixed blood are ground between the upper and the nether millstone. Our fate lies between absorption by the white race and extinction in the black. The one doesn't want us yet, but may take us in time. The other would welcome us, but it would be for us a backward step. 'With malice towards none, with charity for all,'[1] we must do the best we can for ourselves and those who are to follow us. Self-preservation is the first law of nature."

His ball would serve by its exclusiveness to counteract leveling tendencies, and his marriage with Mrs. Dixon would help to further the upward process of absorption he had been wishing and waiting for.

II

The ball was to take place on Friday night. The house had been put in order, the carpets covered with canvas, the halls and stairs decorated with palms and potted plants; and in the afternoon Mr. Ryder sat on his front porch, which the shade of a vine running up over a wire netting made a cool and pleasant lounging place. He expected to respond to the toast "The Ladies" at the supper, and from a volume of Tennyson[2]—his favorite poet—was fortifying himself with apt quotations. The volume was open at "A Dream of Fair Women." His eyes fell on these lines, and he read them aloud to judge better of their effect:—

> "At length I saw a lady within call,
>   Stiller than chisell'd marble, standing there;
> A daughter of the gods, divinely tall,
>   And most divinely fair."

He marked the verse, and turning the page read the stanza beginning,—

> "O sweet pale Margaret,
>   O rare pale Margaret."[3]

He weighed the passage a moment, and decided that it would not do. Mrs. Dixon was the palest lady he expected at the ball, and she was of a rather ruddy complexion, and of lively disposition and buxom build. So he ran over the leaves until his eye rested on the description of Queen Guinevere:[4]—

1. From Abraham Lincoln's second inaugural address (1865).
2. Alfred, Lord Tennyson (1809–1892), poet laureate of England. He published A Dream of Fair Women in 1832.
3. Tennyson's Margaret (1832).
4. Wife of the legendary King Arthur.

"She seem'd a part of joyous Spring:
A gown of grass-green silk she wore,
Buckled with golden clasps before;
A light-green tuft of plumes she bore
Closed in a golden ring.

"She look'd so lovely, as she sway'd
The rein with dainty finger-tips,
A man had given all other bliss,
And all his worldly worth for this,
To waste his whole heart in one kiss
Upon her perfect lips." [5]

As Mr. Ryder murmured these words audibly, with an appreciative thrill, he heard the latch of his gate click, and a light footfall sounding on the steps. He turned his head, and saw a woman standing before his door.

She was a little woman, not five feet tall, and proportioned to her height. Although she stood erect, and looked around her with very bright and restless eyes, she seemed quite old; for her face was crossed and recrossed with a hundred wrinkles, and around the edges of her bonnet could be seen protruding here and there a tuft of short gray wool. She wore a blue calico gown of ancient cut, a little red shawl fastened around her shoulders with an old-fashioned brass brooch, and a large bonnet profusely ornamented with faded red and yellow artificial flowers. And she was very black,—so black that her toothless gums, revealed when she opened her mouth to speak, were not red, but blue. She looked like a bit of the old plantation life, summoned up from the past by the wave of a magician's wand, as the poet's fancy had called into being the gracious shapes of which Mr. Ryder had just been reading.

He rose from his chair and came over to where she stood.

"Good-afternoon, madam," he said.

"Good-evenin', suh," she answered, ducking suddenly with a quaint curtsy. Her voice was shrill and piping, but softened somewhat by age. "Is dis yere whar Mistuh Ryduh lib, suh?" she asked, looking around her doubtfully, and glancing into the open windows, through which some of the preparations for the evening were visible.

"Yes," he replied, with an air of kindly patronage, unconsciously flattered by her manner, "I am Mr. Ryder. Did you want to see me?"

"Yas, suh, ef I ain't 'sturbin' of you too much."

"Not at all. Have a seat over here behind the vine, where it is cool. What can I do for you?"

" 'Scuse me, suh," she continued, when she had sat down on the edge of a chair, " 'scuse me, suh, I's lookin' for my husban'. I heerd you wuz a big man an' had libbed heah a long time, an' I 'lowed you would n't min' ef I'd come roun' an' ax you ef you 'd ever heerd of a merlatter [6] man by de name er Sam Taylor 'quirin' roun' in de chu'ches ermongs' de people fer his wife 'Liza Jane?"

---

5. Tennyson's *Sir Launcelot and Queen Guinevere* (1842).   6. Mulatto.

Mr. Ryder seemed to think for a moment.

"There used to be many such cases right after the war," he said, "but it has been so long that I have forgotten them. There are very few now. But tell me your story, and it may refresh my memory."

She sat back farther in her chair so as to be more comfortable, and folded her withered hands in her lap.

"My name 's 'Liza," she began, " 'Liza Jane. W'en I wuz young I us'ter b'long ter Marse Bob Smif, down in ole Missoura. I wuz bawn down dere. W'en I wuz a gal I wuz married ter a man named Jim. But Jim died, an' after dat I married a merlatter man named Sam Taylor. Sam wuz freebawn, but his mammy and daddy died, an' de w'ite folks 'prenticed him ter my marster fer ter work fer 'im 'tel he wuz growed up. Sam worked in de fiel', an' I wuz de cook. One day Ma'y Ann, ole miss's maid, came rushin' out ter de kitchen, an' says she, ' 'Liza Jane, ole marse gwine sell yo' Sam down de ribber.'

" 'Go way f'm yere,' says I; 'my husban' 's free!'

" 'Don' make no diff'ence. I heerd ole marse tell ole miss he wuz gwine take yo' Sam 'way wid 'im ter-morrow, fer he needed money, an' he knowed whar he could git a t'ousan' dollars fer Sam an' no questions axed.'

"W'en Sam come home f'm de fiel' dat night, I tole him 'bout ole marse gwine steal 'im, an' Sam run erway. His time wuz mos' up, an' he swo' dat w'en he wuz twenty-one he would come back an' he'p me run erway, er else save up de money ter buy my freedom. An' I know he'd 'a' done it, fer he thought a heap er me, Sam did. But w'en he come back he did n' fin' me, fer I wuz n' dere. Ole marse had heerd dat I warned Sam, so he had me whip' an' sol' down de ribber.

"Den de wah broke out, an' w'en it wuz ober de cullud folks wuz scattered. I went back ter de ole home; but Sam wuz n' dere, an' I could n' l'arn nuffin' 'bout 'im. But I knowed he 'd be'n dere to look fer me an' had n' foun' me, an' had gone erway ter hunt fer me.

" I's be'n lookin' fer 'im eber sence," she added simply, as though twenty-five years were but a couple of weeks, "an' I knows he 's be'n lookin' fer me. Fer he sot a heap er sto' by me, Sam did, an' I know he 's be'n huntin' fer me all dese years,—'less'n he 's be'n sick er sump'n, so he could n' work, er out'n his head, so he could n' 'member his promise. I went back down de ribber, fer I 'lowed he'd gone down dere lookin' fer me. I's be'n ter Noo Orleans, an' Atlanty, an' Charleston, an' Richmon'; an' w'en I'd be'n all ober de Souf I come ter de Norf. Fer I knows I'll fin' 'im some er dese days," she added softly, "er he 'll fin' me, an' den we 'll bofe be as happy in freedom as we wuz in de ole days befo' de wah." A smile stole over her withered countenance as she paused a moment, and her bright eyes softened into a faraway look.

This was the substance of the old woman's story. She had wandered a little here and there. Mr. Ryder was looking at her curiously when she finished.

"How have you lived all these years?" he asked.

"Cookin', suh. I's a good cook. Does you know anybody w'at needs a good cook, suh? I's stoppin' wid a cullud fam'ly roun' de corner yonder 'tel I kin git a place."

"Do you really expect to find your husband? He may be dead long ago."

She shook her head emphatically. "Oh no, he ain' dead. De signs an' de tokens tells me. I dremp three nights runnin' on'y dis las' week dat I foun' him."

"He may have married another woman. Your slave marriage would not have prevented him, for you never lived with him after the war, and without that your marriage doesn't count."[7]

"Would n' make no diff'ence wid Sam. He would n' marry no yuther 'ooman 'tel he foun' out 'bout me. I knows it," she added. "Sump'n 's be'n tellin' me all dese years dat I's gwine fin' Sam 'fo' I dies."

"Perhaps he's outgrown you, and climbed up in the world where he would n't care to have you find him."

"No, indeed, suh," she replied, "Sam ain' dat kin' er man. He wuz good ter me, Sam wuz, but he wuz n' much good ter nobody e'se, fer he wuz one er de triflin'es' han's on de plantation. I 'spec's ter haf ter suppo't 'im w'en I fin' 'im, fer he nebber would work 'less'n he had ter. But den he wuz free, an' he did n' git no pay fer his work, an' I don' blame 'im much. Mebbe he 's done better sence he run erway, but I ain' 'spectin' much."

"You may have passed him on the street a hundred times during the twenty-five years, and not have known him; time works great changes."

She smiled incredulously. "I'd know 'im 'mongs' a hund'ed men. Fer dey wuz n' no yuther merlatter man like my man Sam, an' I could n' be mistook. I's toted his picture roun' wid me twenty-five years."

"May I see it?" asked Mr. Ryder. "It might help me to remember whether I have seen the original."

As she drew a small parcel from her bosom he saw that it was fastened to a string that went around her neck. Removing several wrappers, she brought to light an old-fashioned daguerreotype in a black case. He looked long and intently at the portrait. It was faded with time, but the features were still distinct, and it was easy to see what manner of man it had represented.

He closed the case, and with a slow movement handed it back to her.

"I don't know of any man in town who goes by that name," he said, "nor have I heard of any one making such inquiries. But if you will leave me your address, I will give the matter some attention, and if I find out anything I will let you know."

She gave him the number of a house in the neighborhood, and went away, after thanking him warmly.

He wrote the address on the fly-leaf of the volume of Tennyson, and, when she had gone, rose to his feet and stood looking after her curiously. As she walked down the street with mincing step, he saw several persons whom she passed turn and look back at her with a smile of kindly amusement. When she had turned the corner, he went upstairs to his bedroom, and stood for a long time before the mirror of his dressing-case, gazing thoughtfully at the reflection of his own face.

---

7. Although slave marriages had no legal standing before 1865, after the fall of the Confederacy many ex-slave couples—previously separated by sale or war—made serious efforts to reunite and register themselves formally as husband and wife.

III

At eight o'clock the ballroom was a blaze of light and the guests had begun to assemble; for there was a literary programme and some routine business of the society to be gone through with before the dancing. A black servant in evening dress waited at the door and directed the guests to the dressing-rooms.

The occasion was long memorable among the colored people of the city; not alone for the dress and display, but for the high average of intelligence and culture that distinguished the gathering as a whole. There were a number of school-teachers, several young doctors, three or four lawyers, some professional singers, an editor, a lieutenant in the United States army spending his furlough in the city, and others in various polite callings; these were colored, though most of them would not have attracted even a casual glance because of any marked difference from white people. Most of the ladies were in evening costume, and dress coats and dancing pumps were the rule among the men. A band of string music, stationed in an alcove behind a row of palms, played popular airs while the guests were gathering.

The dancing began at half past nine. At eleven o'clock supper was served. Mr. Ryder had left the ballroom some little time before the intermission, but reappeared at the supper-table. The spread was worthy of the occasion, and the guests did full justice to it. When the coffee had been served, the toastmaster, Mr. Solomon Sadler, rapped for order. He made a brief introductory speech, complimenting host and guests, and then presented in their order the toasts of the evening. They were responded to with a very fair display of after-dinner wit.

"The last toast," said the toast-master, when he reached the end of the list, "is one which must appeal to us all. There is no one of us of the sterner sex who is not at some time dependent upon woman,—in infancy for protection, in manhood for companionship, in old age for care and comforting. Our good host has been trying to live alone, but the fair faces I see around me to-night prove that he too is largely dependent upon the gentler sex for most that makes life worth living,—the society and love of friends,—and rumor is at fault if he does not soon yield entire subjection to one of them. Mr. Ryder will now respond to the toast,—The Ladies."

There was a pensive look in Mr. Ryder's eyes as he took the floor and adjusted his eyeglasses. He began by speaking of woman as the gift of Heaven to man, and after some general observations on the relations of the sexes he said: "But perhaps the quality which most distinguishes woman is her fidelity and devotion to those she loves. History is full of examples, but has recorded none more striking than one which only to-day came under my notice."

He then related, simply but effectively, the story told by his visitor of the afternoon. He gave it in the same soft dialect, which came readily to his lips, while the company listened attentively and sympathetically. For the story had awakened a responsive thrill in many hearts. There were some present who had seen, and others who had heard their fathers and grandfathers tell, the wrongs and sufferings of this past generation, and all of them still felt, in their darker moments, the shadow hanging over them. Mr. Ryder went on:—

"Such devotion and confidence are rare even among women. There are many who would have searched a year, some who would have waited five years, a few who might have hoped ten years; but for twenty-five years this woman has retained her affection for and her faith in a man she has not seen or heard of in all that time.

"She came to me to-day in the hope that I might be able to help her find this long-lost husband. And when she was gone I gave my fancy rein, and imagined a case I will put to you.

"Suppose that this husband, soon after his escape, had learned that his wife had been sold away, and that such inquiries as he could make brought no information of her whereabouts. Suppose that he was young, and she much older than he; that he was light, and she was black; that their marriage was a slave marriage, and legally binding only if they chose to make it so after the war. Suppose, too, that he made his way to the North, as some of us have done, and there, where he had larger opportunities, had improved them, and had in the course of all these years grown to be as different from the ignorant boy who ran away from fear of slavery as the day is from the night. Suppose, even, that he had qualified himself, by industry, by thrift, and by study, to win the friendship and be considered worthy the society of such people as these I see around me to-night, gracing my board and filling my heart with gladness; for I am old enough to remember the day when such a gathering would not have been possible in this land. Suppose, too, that, as the years went by, this man's memory of the past grew more and more indistinct, until at last it was rarely, except in his dreams, that any image of this bygone period rose before his mind. And then suppose that accident should bring to his knowledge the fact that the wife of his youth, the wife he had left behind him,—not one who had walked by his side and kept pace with him in his upward struggle, but one upon whom advancing years and a laborious life had set their mark,—was alive and seeking him, but that he was absolutely safe from recognition or discovery, unless he chose to reveal himself. My friends, what would the man do? I will presume that he was one who loved honor, and tried to deal justly with all men. I will even carry the case further, and suppose that perhaps he had set his heart upon another, whom he had hoped to call his own. What would he do, or rather what ought he to do, in such a crisis of a lifetime?

"It seemed to me that he might hesitate, and I imagined that I was an old friend, a near friend, and that he had come to me for advice; and I argued the case with him. I tried to discuss it impartially. After we had looked upon the matter from every point of view, I said to him, in words that we all know:—

> 'This above all: to thine own self be true,
> And it must follow, as the night the day,
> Thou canst not then be false to any man.'[8]

Then, finally, I put the question to him, 'Shall you acknowledge her?'

8. Shakespeare's *Hamlet* 1.3.

"And now, ladies and gentlemen, friends and companions, I ask you, what should he have done?"

There was something in Mr. Ryder's voice that stirred the hearts of those who sat around him. It suggested more than mere sympathy with an imaginary situation; it seemed rather in the nature of a personal appeal. It was observed, too, that his look rested more especially upon Mrs. Dixon, with a mingled expression of renunciation and inquiry.

She had listened, with parted lips and streaming eyes. She was the first to speak: "He should have acknowledged her."

"Yes," they all echoed, "he should have acknowledged her."

"My friends and companions," responded Mr. Ryder, "I thank you, one and all. It is the answer I expected, for I knew your hearts."

He turned and walked toward the closed door of an adjoining room, while every eye followed him in wondering curiosity. He came back in a moment, leading by the hand his visitor of the afternoon, who stood startled and trembling at the sudden plunge into this scene of brilliant gayety. She was neatly dressed in gray, and wore the white cap of an elderly woman.

"Ladies and gentlemen," he said, "this is the woman, and I am the man, whose story I have told you. Permit me to introduce to you the wife of my youth."

1899

ANNA JULIA COOPER
1858?–1964

Born enslaved in North Carolina, Anna Julia Cooper eventually became one of the most well respected black scholars and teachers of her time. Today she is remembered not only for her personal accomplishments—she was one of the first African Americans to receive a Ph.D.—but for her lifelong commitment to education for black people, women in particular.

Cooper's remarkable career in education began at the age of nine, when she received a scholarship to St. Augustine's Normal School, a North Carolina institution developed to train teachers for service among formerly enslaved people. She stayed there fourteen years, eventually joining the faculty. In 1881, she entered Oberlin College, graduating three years later. She taught briefly at Wilberforce, then returned to St. Augustine's in 1885. Within two years, she was awarded a master's degree in mathematics from Oberlin based largely on her teaching experience. In 1887, as a teacher of science and mathematics, she began a long and sometimes difficult tenure at Washington Colored High School, also known as M Street School, in Washington, D.C., academic producer of many well-known African American professionals, artists, and politicians. In 1902 Cooper became principal of M Street. Some years later she attended Columbia University, and in 1925 she earned her Ph.D. in French from the University of Paris. Her commitment to both education and black people led her in 1930 to the presidency of Frelinghuysen University, a school dedicated to serving working black residents of Washington, D.C.

A *Voice from the South by a Black Woman of the South* (1892) emerged out of

Cooper's most productive and politically active period. In the year of *Voice*'s publication, Cooper helped to organize the Colored Woman's League of Washington, D.C.; in 1893 she, Fannie Jackson Coppin, Frances E. W. Harper, and Fannie Barrier Williams were the only African American women to address the Women's Congress, convened during the Columbian Exposition in Chicago. Two years later she took part in the first meeting of the National Conference of Colored Women, and in 1900 she participated in the Pan-African Conference in London. During the 1890s Cooper also helped to edit *The Southland* magazine.

Womanhood a Vital Element in the Regeneration and Progress of a Race, included in *Voice*, argues that the education and elevation of black women is crucial to racial uplift, for societies may be evaluated best by the status of their female members. In Cooper's words, "the fundamental agency under God in the regeneration, the retraining of the race, as well as the ground work and starting point of its progress upward, must be the *black woman*." Cooper shared with many contemporaries the belief that the 1890s was a "woman's era," a time when women would usher in a moral and just society more congruent with the founding ideals of the United States. Black women were especially well situated to analyze and offer solutions to society's injustices because of their position as women in a sexist society and as black people in a racist society. Cooper thus considered the development of black women's faculties through higher education crucial not only to the "regeneration of a race" but to the progress of the nation and the world. Replete with references to important figures from Western culture and spiced by Cooper's insightful sarcasm and good humor, *Womanhood a Vital Element* is not only an argument for black women's centrality to human progress but an illustration of what one black woman can do if given access to the halls of academe.

Womanhood a Vital Element in the Regeneration and Progress of a Race[1]

The two sources from which, perhaps, modern civilization has derived its noble and ennobling ideal of woman are Christianity and the Feudal System.

In Oriental[2] countries woman has been uniformly devoted to a life of ignorance, infamy, and complete stagnation. The Chinese shoe of to-day does not more entirely dwarf, cramp, and destroy her physical powers, than have the customs, laws, and social instincts, which from remotest ages have governed our Sister of the East, enervated and blighted her mental and moral life.

Mahomet[3] makes no account of woman whatever in his polity. The Koran, which, unlike our Bible, was a product and not a growth, tried to address itself to the needs of Arabian civilization as Mahomet with his circumscribed powers saw them. The Arab was a nomad. Home to him meant his present camping place. That deity who, according to our western ideals, makes and sanctifies the home, was to him a transient bauble to be toyed with so long as it gave pleasure and then to be thrown aside for a new one. As a personality, an individual soul, capable of eternal growth and unlimited development, and destined to mould and shape the civilization of the future to an incalculable extent, Mahomet did not know woman.

1. Read before the convocation of colored clergy of the Protestant Episcopal Church at Washington, D.C., 1886 [Cooper's note].

2. Includes the Mideast and North Africa as well as East Asia.

3. Muhammad.

There was no hereafter, no paradise for her. The heaven of the Mussulman[4] is peopled and made gladsome not by the departed wife, or sister, or mother, but by *houri*[5]—a figment of Mahomet's brain, partaking of the ethereal qualities of angels, yet imbued with all the vices and inanity of Oriental women. The harem here, and—"dust to dust" hereafter, this was the hope, the inspiration, the *summum bonum*[6] of the Eastern woman's life! With what result on the life of the nation, the "Unspeakable Turk," the "sick man" of modern Europe can to-day exemplify.

Says a certain writer: "The private life of the Turk is vilest of the vile, unprogressive, unambitious, and inconceivably low." And yet Turkey is not without her great men. She has produced most brilliant minds; men skilled in all the intricacies of diplomacy and statesmanship; men whose intellects could grapple with the deep problems of empire and manipulate the subtle agencies which check-mate kings. But these minds were not the normal outgrowth of a healthy trunk. They seemed rather ephemeral excrescencies[7] which shoot far out with all the vigor and promise, apparently, of strong branches; but soon alas fall into decay and ugliness because there is no soundness in the root, no life-giving sap, permeating, strengthening and perpetuating the whole. There is a worm at the core! The home-life is impure! and when we look for fruit, like apples of Sodom,[8] it crumbles within our grasp into dust and ashes.

It is pleasing to turn from this effete and immobile civilization to a society still fresh and vigorous, whose seed is in itself, and whose very name is synonymous with all that is progressive, elevating and inspiring, viz., the European bud and the American flower of modern civilization.

And here let me say parenthetically that our satisfaction in American institutions rests not on the fruition we now enjoy, but springs rather from the possibilities and promise that are inherent in the system, though as yet, perhaps, far in the future.

"Happiness," says Madame de Stael,[9] "consists not in perfections attained, but in a sense of progress, the result of our own endeavor under conspiring circumstances *toward* a goal which continually advances and broadens and deepens till it is swallowed up in the Infinite." Such conditions in embryo are all that we claim for the land of the West. We have not yet reached our ideal in American civilization. The pessimists even declare that we are not marching in that direction. But there can be no doubt that here in America is the arena in which the next triumph of civilization is to be won; and here too we find promise abundant and possibilities infinite.

Now let us see on what basis this hope for our country primarily and fundamentally rests. Can any one doubt that it is chiefly on the homelife and on the influence of good women in those homes? Says Macaulay:[1] "You may judge a nation's rank in the scale of civilization from the way they treat their women." And Emerson,[2] "I have thought that a sufficient measure of civilization is the influence of good women." Now this high

---

4. Muslim.
5. One of the beautiful virgins promised to faithful Muslim men in Paradise.
6. Highest good.
7. Short-lived abnormalities.
8. Biblical city known for the unnatural wickedness of its citizens.
9. French-Swiss woman of letters (1766–1817).
1. Thomas Babington Macaulay (1800–1859), British writer and statesman.
2. Ralph Waldo Emerson (1803–1882), American poet and essayist.

regard for woman, this germ of a prolific idea which in our own day is bearing such rich and varied fruit, was ingrafted into European civilization, we have said, from two sources, the Christian Church and the Feudal System. For although the Feudal System can in no sense be said to have originated the idea, yet there can be no doubt that the habits of life and modes of thought to which Feudalism gave rise, materially fostered and developed it; for they gave us chivalry, than which no institution has more sensibly magnified and elevated woman's position in society.

Tacitus[3] dwells on the tender regard for woman entertained by these rugged barbarians before they left their northern homes to overrun Europe. Old Norse legends too, and primitive poems, all breathe the same spirit of love of home and veneration for the pure and noble influence there presiding—the wife, the sister, the mother.

And when later on we see the settled life of the Middle Ages "oozing out," as M. Guizot[4] expresses it, from the plundering and pillaging life of barbarism and crystallizing into the Feudal System, the tiger of the field is brought once more within the charmed circle of the goddesses of his castle, and his imagination weaves around them a halo whose reflection possibly has not yet altogether vanished.

It is true the spirit of Christianity had not yet put the seal of catholicity on this sentiment. Chivalry, according to Bascom,[5] was but the toning down and softening of a rough and lawless period. It gave a roseate glow to a bitter winter's day. Those who looked out from castle windows revelled in its "amethyst tints." But God's poor, the weak, the unlovely, the commonplace were still freezing and starving none the less in unpitied, unrelieved loneliness.

Respect for woman, the much lauded chivalry of the Middle Ages, meant what I fear it still means to some men in our own day—respect for the elect few among whom they expect to consort.

The idea of the radical amelioration of womankind, reverence for woman as woman regardless of rank, wealth, or culture, was to come from that rich and bounteous fountain from which flow all our liberal and universal ideas—the Gospel of Jesus Christ.

And yet the Christian Church at the time of which we have been speaking would seem to have been doing even less to protect and elevate woman than the little done by secular society. The Church as an organization committed a double offense against woman in the Middle Ages. Making of marriage a sacrament and at the same time insisting on the celibacy of the clergy and other religious orders, she gave an inferior if not an impure character to the marriage relation, especially fitted to reflect discredit on woman. Would this were all or the worst! but the Church by the licentiousness of its chosen servants invaded the household and established too often as vicious connections those relations which it forbade to assume openly and in good faith. "Thus," to use the words of our authority, "the religious corps became as numerous, as searching, and as unclean as the frogs of

3. Publius Cornelius Tacitus (c. 55–c. 120), Roman historian.
4. Francois Pierre Guillaume Guizot (1787–1874), French historian and statesman.

5. John Bascom (1827–1911), author of *Philosophy of English Literature: A Course of Lectures Delivered in the Lowel Institute* (1874).

Egypt, which penetrated into all quarters, into the ovens and kneading troughs, leaving their filthy trail wherever they went." Says Chaucer[6] with characteristic satire, speaking of the Friars:

'Women may now go safely up and doun,
In every bush, and under every tree,
Ther is non other incubus but he,
And he ne will don hem no dishonour.'

Henry, Bishop of Liege, could unblushingly boast the birth of twenty-two children in fourteen years.[7]

It may help us under some of the perplexities which beset our way in "the one Catholic and Apostolic Church" to-day, to recall some of the corruptions and incongruities against which the Bride of Christ has had to struggle in her past history and in spite of which she has kept, through many vicissitudes, the faith once delivered to the saints. Individuals, organizations, whole sections of the Church militant may outrage the Christ whom they profess, may ruthlessly trample under foot both the spirit and the letter of his precepts, yet not till we hear the voices audibly saying "Come let us depart hence," shall we cease to believe and cling to the promise, "*I am with you to the end of the world.*"

"Yet saints their watch are keeping,
The cry goes up 'How long!'
And soon the night of weeping
Shall be the morn of song."

However much then the facts of any particular period of history may seem to deny it, I for one do not doubt that the source of the vitalizing principle of woman's development and amelioration is the Christian Church, so far as that church is coincident with Christianity.

Christ gave ideals not formulæ. The Gospel is a germ requiring millennia for its growth and ripening. It needs and at the same time helps to form around itself a soil enriched in civilization, and perfected in culture and insight without which the embryo can neither be unfolded or comprehended. With all the strides our civilization has made from the first to the nineteenth century, we can boast not an idea, not a principle of action, not a progressive social force but was already mutely foreshadowed, or directly enjoined in that simple tale of a meek and lowly life. The quiet face of the Nazarene[8] is ever seen a little way ahead, never too far to come down to and touch the life of the lowest in days the darkest, yet ever leading onward, still onward, the tottering childish feet of our strangely boastful civilization.

By laying down for woman the same code of morality, the same standard of purity, as for man; by refusing to countenance the shameless and equally guilty monsters who were gloating over her fall,—graciously stooping in all the majesty of his own spotlessness to wipe away the filth and grime of her

6. Geoffrey Chaucer (c. 1340–1400), English poet. The quotation is from his *Canterbury Tales*.
7. Bascom [Cooper's note].
8. Jesus Christ.

guilty past and bid her go in peace and sin no more; and again in the moments of his own careworn and footsore dejection, turning trustfully and lovingly, away from the heartless snubbing and sneers, away from the cruel malignity of mobs and prelates in the dusty marts of Jerusalem to the ready sympathy, loving appreciation and unfaltering friendship of that quiet home at Bethany;[9] and even at the last, by his dying bequest to the disciple whom he loved, signifying the protection and tender regard to be extended to that sorrowing mother and ever afterward to the sex she represented;— throughout his life and in his death he has given to men a rule and guide for the estimation of woman as an equal, as a helper, as a friend, and as a sacred charge to be sheltered and cared for with a brother's love and sympathy, lessons which nineteen centuries' gigantic strides in knowledge, arts, and sciences, in social and ethical principles have not been able to probe to their depth or to exhaust in practice.

It seems not too much to say then of the vitalizing, regenerating, and progressive influence of womanhood on the civilization of today, that, while it was foreshadowed among Germanic nations in the far away dawn of their history as a narrow, sickly and stunted growth, it yet owes its catholicity and power, the deepening of its roots and broadening of its branches to Christianity.

The union of these two forces, the Barbaric and the Christian, was not long delayed after the Fall of the Empire. The Church, which fell with Rome, finding herself in danger of being swallowed up by barbarism, with characteristic vigor and fertility of resources, addressed herself immediately to the task of conquering her conquerers. The means chosen does credit to her power of penetration and adaptability, as well as to her profound, unerring, all-compassing diplomacy; and makes us even now wonder if aught human can successfully and ultimately withstand her far-seeing designs and brilliant policy, or gainsay her well-earned claim to the word *Catholic*.

She saw the barbarian, little more developed than a wild beast. She forbore to antagonize and mystify his warlike nature by a full blaze of the heartsearching and humanizing tenets of her great Head. She said little of the rule "If thy brother smite thee on one cheek, turn to him the other also;" but thought it sufficient for the needs of those times, to establish the so-called "Truce of God" under which men were bound to abstain from butchering one another for three days of each week and on Church festivals. In other words, she respected their individuality: non-resistance pure and simple being for them an utter impossibility, she contented herself with less radical measures calculated to lead up finally to the full measure of the benevolence of Christ.

Next she took advantage of the barbarian's sensuous love of gaudy display and put all her magnificent garments on. She could not capture him by physical force, she would dazzle him by gorgeous spectacles. It is said that Romanism gained more in pomp and ritual during this trying period of the Dark Ages than throughout all her former history.

The result was she carried her point. Once more Rome laid her ambi-

---

9. Village associated with the final scenes of Jesus' life.

tious hand on the temporal power, and allied with Charlemagne,[1] aspired to rule the world through a civilization dominated by Christianity and permeated by the traditions and instincts of those sturdy barbarians.

Here was the confluence of the two streams we have been tracing, which, united now, stretch before us as a broad majestic river. In regard to woman it was the meeting of two noble and ennobling forces, two kindred ideas the resultant of which, we doubt not, is destined to be a potent force in the betterment of the world.

Now after our appeal to history comparing nations destitute of this force and so destitute also of the principle of progress, with other nations among whom the influence of woman is prominent coupled with a brisk, progressive, satisfying civilization,—if in addition we find this strong presumptive evidence corroborated by reason and experience, we may conclude that these two equally varying concomitants are linked as cause and effect; in other words, that the position of woman in society determines the vital elements of its regeneration and progress.

Now that this is so on *a priori* grounds all must admit. And this not because woman is better or stronger or wiser than man, but from the nature of the case, because it is she who must first form the man by directing the earliest impulses of his character.

Byron and Wordsworth[2] were both geniuses and would have stamped themselves on the thought of their age under any circumstances; and yet we find the one a savor of life unto life, the other of death unto death. "Byron, like a rocket, shot his way upward with scorn and repulsion, flamed out in wild, explosive, brilliant excesses and disappeared in darkness made all the more palpable."[3]

Wordsworth lent of his gifts to reinforce that "power in the Universe which makes for righteousness" by taking the harp handed him from Heaven and using it to swell the strains of angelic choirs. Two locomotives equally mighty stand facing opposite tracks; the one to rush headlong to destruction with all its precious freight, the other to toil grandly and gloriously up the steep embattlements to Heaven and to God. Who—who can say what a world of consequences hung on the first placing and starting of these enormous forces!

Woman, Mother,—your responsibility is one that might make angels tremble and fear to take hold! To trifle with it, to ignore or misuse it, is to treat lightly the most sacred and solemn trust ever confided by God to human kind. The training of children is a task on which an infinity of weal[4] or woe depends. Who does not covet it? Yet who does not stand awestruck before its momentous issues! It is a matter of small moment, it seems to me, whether that lovely girl in whose accomplishments you take such pride and delight, can enter the gay and crowded salon with the ease and elegance of this or that French or English gentlewoman, compared with the decision as to whether her individuality is going to reinforce the good or the evil elements of the world. The lace and the diamonds, the dance

---

1. King of the Franks (742–814) and emperor of the Holy Roman Empire.
2. George Gordon, Lord Byron (1788–1824), and William Wordsworth (1770–1850), both English poets.
3. Bascom's Eng. Lit. p. 253 [Cooper's note].
4. Happiness.

and the theater, gain a new significance when scanned in their bearings on such issues. Their influence on the individual personality, and through her on the society and civilization which she vitalizes and inspires—all this and more must be weighed in the balance before the jury can return a just and intelligent verdict as to the innocence or banefulness of these apparently simple amusements.

Now the fact of woman's influence on society being granted, what are its practical bearings on the work which brought together this conference of colored clergy and laymen in Washington? "We come not here to talk." Life is too busy, too pregnant with meaning and far reaching consequences to allow you to come this far for mere intellectual entertainment.

The vital agency of womanhood in the regeneration and progress of a race, as a general question, is conceded almost before it is fairly stated. I confess one of the difficulties for me in the subject assigned lay in its obviousness. The plea is taken away by the opposite attorney's granting the whole question.

"Woman's influence on social progress"—who in Christendom doubts or questions it? One may as well be called on to prove that the sun is the source of light and heat and energy to this many-sided little world.

Nor, on the other hand, could it have been intended that I should apply the position when taken and proven, to the needs and responsibilities of the women of our race in the South. For is it not written, "Cursed is he that cometh after the king?" and has not the King already preceded me in "The Black Woman of the South"?[5]

They have had both Moses and the Prophets in Dr. Crummell and if they hear not him, neither would they be persuaded though one came up from the South.

I would beg, however, with the Doctor's permission, to add my plea for the *Colored Girls* of the South:—that large, bright, promising fatally beautiful class that stand shivering like a delicate plantlet before the fury of tempestuous elements, so full of promise and possibilities, yet so sure of destruction; often without a father to whom they dare apply the loving term, often without a stronger brother to espouse their cause and defend their honor with his life's blood; in the midst of pitfalls and snares, waylaid by the lower classes of white men, with no shelter, no protection nearer than the great blue vault above, which half conceals and half reveals the one Care-Taker they know so little of. Oh, save them, help them, shield, train, develop, teach, inspire them! Snatch them, in God's name, as brands[6] from the burning! There is material in them well worth your while, the hope in germ of a staunch, helpful, regenerating womanhood on which, primarily, rests the foundation stones of our future as a race.

It is absurd to quote statistics showing the Negro's bank account and rent rolls, to point to the hundreds of newspapers edited by colored men and lists of lawyers, doctors, professors, D. D's, LL D's, etc., etc., etc., while the source from which the life-blood of the race is to flow is subject to taint and corruption in the enemy's camp.

<hr />

5. "Pamphlet published by Dr. Alex. Crummell" [Cooper's note]. Alexander Crummell (1819–1898), U.S. essayist, theologian, and political spokesperson who was "proud of his unmixed African blood."

6. Partly burned pieces of wood.

True progress is never made by spasms. Real progress is growth. It must begin in the seed. Then, "first the blade, then the ear, after that the full corn in the ear." There is something to encourage and inspire us in the advancement of individuals since their emancipation from slavery. It at least proves that there is nothing irretrievably wrong in the shape of the black man's skull, and that under given circumstances his development, downward or upward, will be similar to that of other average human beings.

But there is no time to be wasted in mere felicitation. That the Negro has his niche in the infinite purposes of the Eternal, no one who has studied the history of the last fifty years in America will deny. That much depends on his own right comprehension of his responsibility and rising to the demands of the hour, it will be good for him to see; and how best to use his present so that the structure of the future shall be stronger and higher and brighter and nobler and holier than that of the past, is a question to be decided each day by every one of us.

The race is just twenty-one years removed from the conception and experience of a chattel, just at the age of ruddy manhood. It is well enough to pause a moment for retrospection, introspection, and prospection. We look back, not to become inflated with conceit because of the depths from which we have arisen, but that we may learn wisdom from experience. We look within that we may gather together once more our forces, and, by improved and more practical methods, address ourselves to the tasks before us. We look forward with hope and trust that the same God whose guiding hand led our fathers through and out of the gall and bitterness of oppression, will still lead and direct their children, to the honor of His name, and for their ultimate salvation.

But this survey of the failures or achievements of the past, the difficulties and embarrassments of the present, and the mingled hopes and fears for the future, must not degenerate into mere dreaming nor consume the time which belongs to the practical and effective handling of the crucial questions of the hour; and there can be no issue more vital and momentous than this of the womanhood of the race.

Here is the vulnerable point, not in the heel, but at the heart of the young Achilles;[7] and here must the defenses be strengthened and the watch redoubled.

We are the heirs of a past which was not our fathers' moulding. "Every man the arbiter of his own destiny" was not true for the American Negro of the past: and it is no fault of his that he finds himself to-day the inheritor of a manhood and womanhood impoverished and debased by two centuries and more of compression and degradation.

But weaknesses and malformations, which to-day are attributable to a vicious schoolmaster and a pernicious system, will a century hence be rightly regarded as proofs of innate corruptness and radical incurability.

Now the fundamental agency under God in the regeneration, the retraining of the race, as well as the ground work and starting point of its progress upward, must be the *black woman*.

---

7. In Greek mythology, the foremost hero of the Trojan War. His vulnerable spot was the heel by which his mother held him when she dipped him in the river Styx to make him immortal.

With all the wrongs and neglects of her past, with all the weakness, the debasement, the moral thralldom of her present, the black woman of to-day stands mute and wondering at the Herculean task devolving upon her. But the cycles wait for her. No other hand can move the lever. She must be loosed from her bands and set to work.

Our meager and superficial results from past efforts prove their futility; and every attempt to elevate the Negro, whether undertaken by himself or through the philanthropy of others, cannot but prove abortive unless so directed as to utilize the indispensable agency of an elevated and trained womanhood.

A race cannot be purified from without. Preachers and teachers are helps, and stimulants and conditions as necessary as the gracious rain and sunshine are to plant growth. But what are rain and dew and sunshine and cloud if there be no life in the plant germ? We must go to the root and see that that is sound and healthy and vigorous; and not deceive ourselves with waxen flowers and painted leaves of mock chlorophyll.

We too often mistake individuals' honor for race development and so are ready to substitute pretty accomplishments for sound sense and earnest purpose.

A stream cannot rise higher than its source. The atmosphere of homes is no rarer and purer and sweeter than are the mothers in those homes. A race is but a total of families. The nation is the aggregate of its homes. As the whole is sum of all its parts, so the character of the parts will determine the characteristics of the whole. These are all axioms and so evident that it seems gratuitous to remark it; and yet, unless I am greatly mistaken, most of the unsatisfaction from our past results arises from just such a radical and palpable error, as much almost on our own part as on that of our benevolent white friends.

The Negro is constitutionally hopeful and proverbially irrepressible; and naturally stands in danger of being dazzled by the shimmer and tinsel of superficials. We often mistake foliage for fruit and overestimate or wrongly estimate brilliant results.

The late Martin R. Delany,[8] who was an unadulterated black man, used to say when honors of state fell upon him, that when he entered the council of kings the black race entered with him; meaning, I suppose, that there was no discounting his race identity and attributing his achievements to some admixture of Saxon blood. But our present record of eminent men, when placed beside the actual status of the race in America to-day, proves that no man can represent the race. Whatever the attainments of the individual may be, unless his home has moved on *pari passu*,[9] he can never be regarded as identical with or representative of the whole.

Not by pointing to sun-bathed mountain tops do we prove that Phœbus[1] warms the valleys. We must point to homes, average homes, homes of the rank and file of horny handed toiling men and women of the South (where the masses are) lighted and cheered by the good, the beautiful, and the

---

8. African American medical doctor, abolitionist, and writer (1812–1885).   9. At the same pace (Latin).   1. Apollo, god of the sun.

true,—then and not till then will the whole plateau be lifted into the sunlight.

Only the BLACK WOMAN can say "when and where I enter, in the quiet, undisputed dignity of my womanhood, without violence and without suing or special patronage, then and there the whole *Negro race enters with me.*" Is it not evident then that as individual workers for this race we must address ourselves with no half-hearted zeal to this feature of our mission. The need is felt and must be recognized by all. There is a call for workers, for missionaries, for men and women with the double consecration of a fundamental love of humanity and a desire for its melioration through the Gospel; but superadded to this we demand an intelligent and sympathetic comprehension of the interests and special needs of the Negro.

I see not why there should not be an organized effort for the protection and elevation of our girls such as the White Cross League [2] in England. English women are strengthened and protected by more than twelve centuries of Christian influences, freedom and civilization; English girls are dispirited and crushed down by no such all-levelling prejudice as that supercilious caste spirit in America which cynically assumes "A Negro woman cannot be a lady." English womanhood is beset by no such snares and traps as betray the unprotected, untrained colored girl of the South, whose only crime and dire destruction often is her unconscious and marvelous beauty. Surely then if English indignation is aroused and English manhood thrilled under the leadership of a Bishop of the English church to build up bulwarks around their wronged sisters, Negro sentiment cannot remain callous and Negro effort nerveless in view of the imminent peril of the mothers of the next generation. "*I am my Sister's keeper!*" should be the hearty response of every man and woman of the race, and this conviction should purify and exalt the narrow, selfish and petty personal aims of life into a noble and sacred purpose.

We need men who can let their interest and gallantry extend outside the circle of their æsthetic appreciation; men who can be a father, a brother, a friend to every weak, struggling unshielded girl. We need women who are so sure of their own social footing that they need not fear leaning to lend a hand to a fallen or falling sister. We need men and women who do not exhaust their genius splitting hairs on aristocratic distinctions and thanking God they are not as others; but earnest, unselfish souls, who can go into the highways and byways, lifting up and leading, advising and encouraging with the truly catholic benevolence of the Gospel of Christ.

As Church workers we must confess our path of duty is less obvious; or rather our ability to adapt our machinery to our conception of the peculiar exigencies of this work as taught by experience and our own consciousness of the needs of the Negro, is as yet not demonstrable. Flexibility and aggressiveness are not such strong characteristics of the Church to-day as in the Dark Ages.

As a Mission field for the Church the Southern Negro is in some aspects most promising; in others, perplexing. Aliens neither in language and cus-

---

2. Founded in the early 1800s in England, it was also known as the White Cross Army or Bishop of Durham's Movement; an organization of men who vowed to uphold chastity and purity.

toms, nor in associations and sympathies, naturally of deeply rooted religious instincts and taking most readily and kindly to the worship and teachings of the Church, surely the task of proselytizing the American Negro is infinitely less formidable than that which confronted the Church in the Barbarians of Europe. Besides, this people already look to the Church as the hope of their race. Thinking colored men almost uniformly admit that the Protestant Episcopal Church with its quiet, chaste dignity and decorous solemnity, its instructive and elevating ritual, its bright chanting and joyous hymning, is eminently fitted to correct the peculiar faults of worship—the rank exuberance and often ludicrous demonstrativeness of their people. Yet, strange to say, the Church, claiming to be missionary and Catholic, urging that schism is sin and denominationalism inexcusable, has made in all these years almost no inroads upon this semi-civilized religionism.

Harvests from this over ripe field of home missions have been gathered in by Methodists, Baptists, and not least by Congregationalists, who were unknown to the Freedmen before their emancipation.

Our clergy numbers less than two dozen[3] priests of Negro blood and we have hardly more than one self-supporting colored congregation in the entire Southland. While the organization known as the A. M. E. Church[4] has 14,063 ministers, itinerant and local, 4,069 self-supporting churches, 4,275 Sunday-schools, with property valued at $7,772,284, raising yearly for church purposes $1,427,000.

Stranger and more significant than all, the leading men of this race (I do not mean demagogues and politicians, but men of intellect, heart, and race devotion, men to whom the elevation of their people means more than personal ambition and sordid gain—and the men of that stamp have not all died yet) the Christian workers for the race, of younger and more cultured growth, are noticeably drifting into sectarian churches, many of them declaring all the time that they acknowledge the historic claims of the Church, believe her apostolicity, and would experience greater personal comfort, spiritual and intellectual, in her revered communion. It is a fact which any one may verify for himself, that representative colored men, professing that in their heart of hearts they are Episcopalians, are actually working in Methodist and Baptist pulpits, while the ranks of the Episcopal clergy are left to be filled largely by men who certainly suggest the propriety of a *"perpetual* Diaconate"[5] if they cannot be said to have created the necessity for it.

Now where is the trouble? Something must be wrong. What is it?

A certain Southern Bishop of our Church reviewing the situation, whether in Godly anxiety or in "Gothic antipathy" I know not, deprecates the fact that the colored people do not seem *drawn* to the Episcopal Church, and comes to the sage conclusion that the Church is not adapted to the rude untutored minds of the Freedmen, and that they may be left to

---

3. The published report of '91 shows 26 priests for the entire country, including one not engaged in work and one a professor in a non-sectarian school, since made Dean of an episcopal Annex to Howard University known as King Hall [Cooper's note].

4. African Methodist Episcopal Church, oldest independent black church in the United States.
5. The subordinate officers of a church, usually in charge of running it.

go to the Methodists and Baptists whither their racial proclivities undeniably tend. How the good Bishop can agree that all-foreseeing Wisdom, and Catholic Love would have framed his Church as typified in his seamless garment and unbroken body, and yet not leave it broad enough and deep enough and loving enough to seek and save and hold seven millions of God's poor, I cannot see.

But the doctors while discussing their scientifically conclusive diagnosis of the disease, will perhaps not think it presumptuous in the patient if he dares to suggest where at least the pain is. If this be allowed, a *Black woman of the South* would beg to point out two possible oversights in this southern work which may indicate in part both a cause and a remedy for some failure. The first is *not calculating for the Black man's personality*; not having respect, if I may so express it, to his manhood or deferring at all to his conceptions of the needs of his people. When colored persons have been employed it was too often as machines or as manikins. There has been no disposition, generally, to get the black man's ideal or to let his individuality work by its own gravity, as it were. A conference of earnest Christian men have met at regular intervals for some years past to discuss the best methods of promoting the welfare and development of colored people in this country. Yet, strange as it may seem, they have never invited a colored man or even intimated that one would be welcome to take part in their deliberations. Their remedial contrivances are purely theoretical or empirical, therefore, and the whole machinery devoid of soul.

The second important oversight in my judgment is closely allied to this and probably grows out of it, and that is not developing Negro womanhood as an essential fundamental for the elevation of the race, and utilizing this agency in extending the work of the Church.

Of the first I have possibly already presumed to say too much since it does not strictly come within the province of my subject. However, Macaulay somewhere criticises the Church of England as not knowing how to use fanatics, and declares that had Ignatius Loyola[6] been in the Anglican instead of the Roman communion, the Jesuits would have been schismatics instead of Catholics; and if the religious awakenings of the Wesleys[7] had been in Rome, she would have shaven their heads, tied ropes around their waists, and sent them out under her own banner and blessing. Whether this be true or not, there is certainly a vast amount of force potential for Negro evangelization rendered latent, or worse, antagonistic by the halting, uncertain, I had almost said, *trimming* policy of the Church in the South. This may sound both presumptuous and ungrateful. It is mortifying, I know, to benevolent wisdom, after having spent itself in the execution of well conned theories for the ideal development of a particular work, to hear perhaps the weakest and humblest element of that work asking "what doest thou?"

Yet so it will be in life. The "thus far and no farther" pattern cannot be fitted to any growth in God's kingdom. The universal law of development is "onward and upward." It is God-given and inviolable. From the unfolding

6. Spanish priest (1491–1556), founder of the Jesuit order.
7. English preacher (1703–1791), founder of Methodism.

of the germ in the acorn to reach the sturdy oak, to the growth of a human soul into the full knowledge and likeness of its Creator, the breadth and scope of the movement in each and all are too grand, too mysterious, too like God himself, to be encompassed and locked down in human molds.

After all the Southern slave owners were right: either the very alphabet of intellectual growth must be forbidden and the Negro dealt with absolutely as a chattel having neither rights nor sensibilities; or else the clamps and irons of mental and moral, as well as civil compression must be riven asunder and the truly enfranchised soul led to the entrance of that boundless vista through which it is to toil upwards to its beckoning God as the buried seed germ to meet the sun.

A perpetual colored diaconate, carefully and kindly superintended by the white clergy; congregations of shiny faced peasants with their clean white aprons and sunbonnets catechised at regular intervals and taught to recite the creed, the Lord's prayer and the ten commandments—duty towards God and duty towards neighbor, surely such well tended sheep ought to be grateful to their shepherds and content in that station of life to which it pleased God to call them. True, like the old professor lecturing to his solitary student, we make no provision here for irregularities. "Questions must be kept till after class," or dispensed with altogether. That some do ask questions and insist on answers, in class too, must be both impertinent and annoying. Let not our spiritual pastors and masters however be grieved at such self-assertion as merely signifies we have a destiny to fulfill and as men and women we must *be about our Father's business.*

It is a mistake to suppose that the Negro is prejudiced against a white ministry. Naturally there is not a more kindly and implicit follower of a white man's guidance than the average colored peasant. What would to others be an ordinary act of friendly or pastoral interest he would be more inclined to regard gratefully as a condescension. And he never forgets such kindness. Could the Negro be brought near to his white priest or bishop, he is not suspicious. He is not only willing but often longs to unburden his soul to this intelligent guide. There are no reservations when he is convinced that you are his friend. It is a saddening satire on American history and manners that it takes something to convince him.

That our people are not "drawn" to a church whose chief dignitaries they see only in the chancel, and whom they reverence as they would a painting or an angel, whose life never comes down to and touches theirs with the inspiration of an objective reality, may be "perplexing" truly (American caste and American Christianity both being facts) but it need not be surprising. There must be something of human nature in it, the same as that which brought about that "the Word was made flesh and dwelt among us" that He might "draw" us towards God.

Men are not "drawn" by abstractions. Only sympathy and love can draw, and until our Church in America realizes this and provides a clergy that can come in touch with our life and have a fellow feeling for our woes, without being imbedded and frozen up in their "Gothic antipathies," the good bishops are likely to continue "perplexed" by the sparsity of colored Episcopalians.

A colored priest of my acquaintance recently related to me, with tears in his eyes, how his reverend Father in God, the Bishop who had ordained him, had met him on the cars on his way to the diocesan convention and warned him, not unkindly, not to take a seat in the body of the convention with the white clergy. To avoid disturbance of their godly placidity he would of cource please sit back and somewhat apart. I do not imagine that that clergyman had very much heart for the Christly (!) deliberations of that convention.

To return, however, it is not on this broader view of Church work, which I mentioned as a primary cause of its halting progress with the colored people, that I am to speak. My proper theme is the second oversight of which in my judgment our Christian propagandists have been guilty: or, the necessity of church training, protecting and uplifting our colored womanhood as indispensable to the evangelization of the race.

Apelles[8] did not disdain even that criticism of his lofty art which came from an uncouth cobbler; and may I not hope that the writer's oneness with her subject both in feeling and in being may palliate undue obtrusiveness of opinions here. That the race cannot be effectually lifted up till its women are truly elevated we take as proven. It is not for us to dwell on the needs, the neglects, and the ways of succor, pertaining to the black woman of the South. The ground has been ably discussed and an admirable and practical plan proposed by the oldest Negro priest in America, advising and urging that special organizations such as Church Sisterhoods and industrial schools be devised to meet her pressing needs in the Southland. That some such movements are vital to the life of this people and the extension of the Church among them, is not hard to see. Yet the pamphlet fell stillborn from the press. So far as I am informed the Church has made no motion towards carrying out Dr. Crummell's suggestion.

The denomination which comes next our own in opposing the proverbial emotionalism of Negro worship in the South, and which in consequence like ours receives the cold shoulder from the old heads, resting as we do under the charge of not "having religion" and not believing in conversion—the Congregationalists—have quietly gone to work on the young, have established industrial and training schools, and now almost every community in the South is yearly enriched by a fresh infusion of vigorous young hearts, cultivated heads, and helpful hands that have been trained at Fisk, at Hampton, in Atlanta University, and in Tuskegee, Alabama.

These young people are missionaries actual or virtual both here and in Africa. They have learned to love the methods and doctrines of the Church which trained and educated them; and so Congregationalism surely and steadily progresses.

Need I compare these well known facts with results shown by the Church in the same field and during the same or even a longer time.

The institution of the Church in the South to which she mainly looks for the training of her colored clergy and for the help of the "Black Woman" and "Colored Girl" of the South, has graduated since the year 1868, when the school was founded, *five young women;*[9] and while yearly numerous young men have been kept and trained for the ministry by the charities of

8. Greek painter (360?–315? B.C.).
9. Five have been graduated since '86, two in '91, two in '92 [Cooper's note].

the Church, the number of indigent females who have here been supported, sheltered and trained, is phenomenally small. Indeed, to my mind, the attitude of the Church toward this feature of her work is as if the solution of the problem of Negro missions depended solely on sending a quota of deacons and priests into the field, girls being a sort of *tertium quid* [1] whose development may be promoted if they can pay their way and fall in with the plans mapped out for the training of the other sex. Now I would ask in all earnestness, does not this force potential deserve by education and stimulus to be made dynamic? Is it not a solemn duty incumbent on all colored churchmen to make it so? Will not the aid of the Church be given to prepare our girls in head, heart, and hand for the duties and responsibilities that await the intelligent wife, the Christian mother, the earnest, virtuous, helpful woman, at once both the lever and the fulcrum for uplifting the race.

As Negroes and churchmen we cannot be indifferent to these questions. They touch us most vitally on both sides. We believe in the Holy Catholic Church. We believe that however gigantic and apparently remote the consummation, the Church will go on conquering and to conquer till the kingdoms of this world, not excepting the black man and the black woman of the South, shall have become the kingdoms of the Lord and of his Christ.

That past work in this direction has been unsatisfactory we must admit. That without a change of policy results in the future will be as meagre, we greatly fear. Our life as a race is at stake. The dearest interests of our hearts are in the scales. We must either break away from dear old landmarks and plunge out in any line and every line that enables us to meet the pressing need of our people, or we must ask the Church to allow and help us, untrammelled by the prejudices and theories of individuals, to work agressively under her direction as we alone can, with God's help, for the salvation of our people.

The time is ripe for action. Self-seeking and ambition must be laid on the altar. The battle is one of sacrifice and hardship, but our duty is plain. We have been recipients of missionary bounty in some sort for twenty-one years. Not even the senseless vegetable is content to be a mere reservoir. Receiving without giving is an anomaly in nature. Nature's cells are all little workshops for manufacturing sunbeams, the product to be *given out* to earth's inhabitants in warmth, energy, thought, action. Inanimate creation always pays back an equivalent.

Now, *How much owest thou my Lord?* Will his account be overdrawn if he call for singleness of purpose and self-sacrificing labor for your brethren? Having passed through your drill school, will you refuse a general's commission even if it entail responsibility, risk and anxiety, with possibly some adverse criticism? Is it too much to ask you to step forward and direct the work for your race along those lines which you know to be of first and vital importance?

Will you allow these words of Ralph Waldo Emerson? "In ordinary,"

1. Related to two things but distinctly different from both (Latin).

says he, "we have a snappish criticism which watches and contradicts the opposite party. We want the will which advances and dictates [acts]. Nature has made up her mind that what cannot defend itself, shall not be defended. Complaining never so loud and with never so much reason, is of no use. What cannot stand must fall; *and the measure of our sincerity and therefore of the respect of men is the amount of health and wealth we will hazard in the defense of our right.*"

1892

PAULINE E. HOPKINS

1859–1930

Born in 1859 in Portland, Maine, Pauline Elizabeth Hopkins was raised in Boston in an environment in which she was encouraged to develop her considerable literary gifts. At fifteen, she won a writing contest for her essay *The Evils of Intemperance and Their Remedy*, and her ten-dollar prize was presented to her by the pioneering African American author William Wells Brown. In her youth she also performed with and wrote for the Hopkins Colored Troubadours, a family theatrical group. Such experiences provided the foundation for her lifelong commitment to art and racial uplift, and Hopkins went on to become the single most productive black literary woman of her generation.

Hopkins's entry into the writing profession came as a result of her involvement with the *Colored American Magazine*, a journal founded in Boston in 1900. One of a number of important black periodicals at the turn of the century, the *Colored American* was a crucial forum for creative writing, reportage, scholarship, and progressive political commentary. Shaping it both as its literary editor and as a major contributor, Hopkins soon became one of the magazine's dominant voices. From 1900 through 1904, she published in the *Colored American* an astounding body of diverse prose, including short fiction, historical articles, and biographical sketches. What establishes her preeminent position in the African American literary canon, however, are the four novels that she produced during this period, three of which were serialized in the *Colored American* (one under the pseudonym Sarah A. Allen, derived from her mother's maiden name). Published in 1900 by the press that issued the *Colored American*, *Contending Forces: A Romance of Negro Life North and South* is the best known of these novels and the only one to appear initially in book form.

As does much black fiction around the turn of the century, *Contending Forces* attempts to work within the general confines of mainstream literary genres (here, domestic and historical romances), while at the same time addressing some of the pressing social issues confronting blacks at the time. *Contending Forces*, however, is especially noteworthy because of its complexity and unusual scope. Not only does the setting range from Bermuda in the 1790s to late-nineteenth-century Boston, but Hopkins displays a mature grasp of the diverse political positions that marked contemporary black thought. If, on the one hand, she treats these different perspectives with a characteristic evenhandedness, on the other hand, she makes clear her ultimate endorsement of what Du Bois termed "agitation" in contrast to the less aggressive strategy identified with Booker T. Washington. Hopkins also gives us in *Contending Forces* possibly our most vivid fictional look at the experiences of African American bourgeois women. In doing so, she alerts us to the fact that the do-

mestic sphere, broadly defined, was as important a site of resistance for blacks as the
public arena, which was generally dominated by males. While not unblemished by
some stereotypical characterizations (especially of its lower-class figures), overly
melodramatic scenes, and incredible coincidences, *Contending Forces* is, nonetheless, an extremely compelling look at the long-term effects of the violation of the
black family during slavery, the necessary political activism of the black middle
class in the North, and the power of romantic love and domestic bonds to enable a
transcending of even the most deleterious results of racist victimization, particularly the sexual exploitation of black women. Although less polished than *Contending Forces*, Hopkins's other novels show many of the same themes and motifs that
inform her first book. What is perhaps most striking about her three serialized novels is the free rein the format evidently allowed her imagination. In *Of One Blood;
or, The Hidden Self*, for instance, she produced an early example of what can quite
appropriately be termed black science fiction.

In 1904 Hopkins left the *Colored American*, supposedly for medical reasons.
However, one suspects that her departure had something to do with the magazine's
falling under the control of Booker T. Washington, who was displeased with its
political stance. Regardless, Hopkins's productivity continued. In 1905 she published A *Primer of Facts Pertaining to the Early Greatness of the African Race and
the Possibility of Restoration by its Descendants—with Epilogue*, and in 1916 she
established *New Era*, a periodical to which she also contributed both fiction and
nonfiction. As she was compelled for much of her career, however, she had to work
as a stenographer in order to support herself during these years. Little is known of
Hopkins's later life; in August 1930, a relatively forgotten figure, she died from injuries suffered in a fire.

From Contending Forces

[The bulk of the action takes place in late-nineteenth-century Boston, with attention centering primarily on the black Smith family. The matriarch, Ma Smith, runs
a boarding house; residents include her two children, Will and Dora, and Sappho
Clark, a mysterious and beautiful woman who becomes romantically involved with
Will.]

Chapter VIII

THE SEWING-CIRCLE

Where village statesmen talked with looks profound,
Imagination fondly stoops to trace
The parlor splendors of that festive place.
. . . .
Yes! let the rich deride, the proud disdain,
These simple blessings of the lowly train;
To me more dear,
One native charm than all the gloss of art.
                                        —GOLDSMITH[1]

Ma Smith was a member of the church referred to in the last chapter,
the most prominent one of color in New England. It was situated in the
heart of the West End, and was a very valuable piece of property. Every
winter this church gave many entertainments to aid in paying off the mort-

---

1. Oliver Goldsmith (1730?–1774), British author. The quotation is from his *The Deserted Village*.

gage, which at this time amounted to about eight thousand dollars. Mrs. Smith, as the chairman of the board of stewardesses, was inaugurating a fair—one that should eclipse anything of a similar nature ever attempted by the colored people, and numerous sewing-circles were being held among the members all over the city. Parlor entertainments where an admission fee of ten cents was collected from every patron, were also greatly in vogue, and the money thus obtained was put into a fund to defray the expense of purchasing eatables and decorations, and paying for the printing of tickets, circulars, etc., for the fair. The strongest forces of the colored people in the vicinity were to combine and lend their aid in making a supreme effort to clear this magnificent property.

Boston contains a number of well-to-do families of color whose tax-bills show a most comfortable return each year to the city treasury. Strange as it may seem, these well-to-do people, in goodly numbers, distribute themselves and their children among the various Episcopal churches with which the city abounds, the government of which holds out the welcome hand to the brother in black, who is drawn to unite his fortunes with the members of this particular denomination. It may be true that the beautiful ritual of the church is responsible in some measure for this. Colored people are nothing if not beauty-lovers, and for such a people the grandeur of the service has great attractions. But in justice to this church one must acknowledge that it has been instrumental in doing much toward helping this race to help itself, along the lines of brotherly interest.

These people were well represented within the precincts of Mrs. Smith's pretty parlor one afternoon, all desirous of lending their aid to help along the great project.

As we have said, Mrs. Smith occupied the back parlor of the house as her chamber, and within this room the matrons had assembled to take charge of the cutting out of different garments; and here, too, the sewing machine was placed ready for use. In the parlor proper all the young ladies were seated ready to perform any service which might be required of them in the way of putting garments together.

By two o'clock all the members of the sewing-circle were in their places. The parlor was crowded. Mrs. Willis, the brilliant widow of a bright Negro politician, had charge of the girls, and after the sewing had been given out the first business of the meeting was to go over events of interest to the Negro race which had transpired during the week throughout the country. These facts had been previously tabulated upon a blackboard which was placed upon an easel, and occupied a conspicuous position in the room. Each one was supposed to contribute anything of interest that she had read or heard in that time for the benefit of all. After these points had been gone over, Mrs. Willis gave a talk upon some topic of interest. At six o'clock tea was to be served in the kitchen, the company taking refreshment in squads of five. At eight o'clock all unfinished work would be folded and packed away in the convenient little Boston bag,[2] to be finished at home, and the male friends of the various ladies were expected to put in an appearance.

2. A two-handled satchel.

Music and recitations were to be enjoyed for two hours, ice cream and cake being sold for the benefit of the cause.

Mrs. Willis was a good example of a class of women of color that came into existence at the close of the Civil War. She was not a *rara avis*,[3] but one of many possibilities which the future will develop from among the colored women of New England. Every city or town from Maine to New York has its Mrs. Willis. Keen in her analysis of human nature, most people realized, after a short acquaintance, in which they ran the gamut of emotions from strong attraction to repulsion, that she had sifted them thoroughly, while they had gained nothing in return. Shrewd in business matters, many a subtle business man had been worsted by her apparent womanly weakness and charming simplicity. With little money, she yet contrived to live in quiet elegance, even including the little journeys from place to place, so adroitly managed as to increase her influence at home and her fame abroad. Well-read and thoroughly conversant with all current topics, she impressed one as having been liberally educated and polished by travel, whereas a high-school course more than covered all her opportunities.

Even today it is erroneously believed that all racial development among colored people has taken place since emancipation. It is impossible of belief for some, that little circles of educated men and women of color have existed since the Revolutionary War. Some of these people were born free, some have lost the memory of servitude in the dim past; a greater number by far were recruited from the energetic slaves of the South, who toiled when they should have slept, for the money that purchased their freedom, or else they boldly took the rights which man denied. Mrs. Willis was one from among these classes. The history of her descent could not be traced, but somewhere, somehow, a strain of white blood had filtered through the African stream. At sixty odd she was vigorous, well-preserved, broad and comfortable in appearance, with an aureole of white hair crowning a pleasant face.

She had loved her husband with a love ambitious for his advancement. His foot on the stairs mounting to the two-room tenement which constituted their home in the early years of married life, had sent a thrill to her very heart as she sat sewing baby clothes for the always expected addition to the family. But twenty years make a difference in all our lives. It brought many changes to the colored people of New England— social and business changes. Politics had become the open sesame for the ambitious Negro. A seat in the Legislature then was not a dream to this man, urged by the loving woman behind him. Other offices of trust were quickly offered him when his worth became known. He grasped his opportunity; grew richer, more polished, less social, and the family broadened out and overflowed from old familiar "West End" environments across the River Charles into the aristocratic suburbs of Cambridge.[4] Death comes to us all.

Money, the sinews of living and social standing, she did not possess upon

3. A rare bird (Latin, literal trans.); here, an unusual person.   4. A community in the Boston area.

her husband's death. Therefore she was forced to begin a weary pilgrimage—a hunt for the means to help her breast the social tide. The best opening, she decided after looking carefully about her, was in the great cause of the evolution of true womanhood in the work of the "Woman Question" as embodied in marriage and suffrage. She could talk dashingly on many themes, for which she had received much applause in by-gone days, when in private life she had held forth in the drawing-room of some Back Bay[5] philanthropist who sought to use her talents as an attraction for a worthy charitable object, the discovery of a rare species of versatility in the Negro character being a sure drawing-card. It was her boast that she had made the fortunes of her family and settled her children well in life. The advancement of the colored woman should be the new problem in the woman question that should float her upon its tide into the prosperity she desired. And she succeeded well in her plans: conceived in selfishness, they yet bore glorious fruit in the formation of clubs of colored women banded together for charity, for study, for every reason under God's glorious heavens that can better the condition of mankind.

Trivialities are not to be despised. Inborn love implanted in a woman's heart for a luxurious, esthetic home life, running on well-oiled wheels amid flowers, sunshine, books and priceless pamphlets, easy chairs and French gowns, may be the means of developing a Paderewski[6] or freeing a race from servitude. It was amusing to watch the way in which she governed societies and held her position. In her hands committees were as wax, and loud murmurings against the tyranny of her rule died down to judicious whispers. If a vote went contrary to her desires, it was in her absence. Thus she became the pivot about which all the social and intellectual life of the colored people of her section revolved. No one had yet been found with the temerity to contest her position, which, like a title of nobility, bade fair to descend to her children. It was thought that she might be eclipsed by the younger and more brilliant women students on the strength of their alma mater, but she still held her own by sheer force of will-power and indomitable pluck.

The subject of the talk at this meeting was: "The place which the virtuous woman occupies in upbuilding a race." After a few explanatory remarks, Mrs. Willis said:

"I am particularly anxious that you should think upon this matter seriously, because of its intrinsic value to all of us as race women. I am not less anxious because you represent the coming factors of our race. Shortly, you must fill the positions now occupied by your mothers, and it will rest with you and your children to refute the charges brought against us as to our moral irresponsibility, and the low moral standard maintained by us in comparison with other races."

"Did I understand you to say that the Negro woman in her native state is truly a virtuous woman?" asked Sappho, who had been very silent during the bustle attending the opening of the meeting.

5. An upper-class community in Boston.
6. Ignace J. Paderewski (1860–1941), a Polish pianist and statesman.

"Travelers tell us that the native African woman is impregnable in her virtue," replied Mrs. Willis.

"So we have sacrificed that attribute in order to acquire civilization," chimed in Dora.

"No, not 'sacrificed,' but pushed one side by the force of circumstances. Let us thank God that it *is* an essential attribute peculiar to us—a racial characteristic which is slumbering but not lost," replied Mrs. Willis. "But let us not forget the definition of virtue—'Strength to do the right thing under all temptations.' Our ideas of virtue are too narrow. We confine them to that conduct which is ruled by our animal passions alone. It goes deeper than that—general excellence in every duty of life is what we may call virtue."

"Do you think, then, that Negro women will be held responsible for all the lack of virtue that is being laid to their charge today? I mean, do you think that God will hold us responsible for the *illegitimacy* with which our race has been obliged, as it were, to flood the world?" asked Sappho.

"I believe that we shall not be held responsible for wrongs which we have *unconsciously* committed, or which we have committed under *compulsion*. We are virtuous or non-virtuous only when we have a *choice* under temptation. We cannot by any means apply the word to a little child who has never been exposed to temptation, nor to the Supreme Being 'who cannot be tempted with evil.' So with the African brought to these shores against his will—the state of morality which implies willpower on his part does not exist, therefore he is not a responsible being. The sin and its punishment lies with the person *consciously* false to his *knowledge* of right. From this we deduce the truism that 'the civility of no race is perfect whilst another race is degraded.' "

"I shall never forget my feelings," chimed in Anna Stevens, a school teacher of a very studious temperament, "at certain remarks made by the Rev. John Thomas at one of his noonday lectures in the Temple. He was speaking on 'Different Races,' and had in his vigorous style been sweeping his audience with him at a high elevation of thought which was dazzling to the faculties, and almost impossible to follow in some points. Suddenly he touched upon the Negro, and with impressive gesture and lowered voice thanked God that the mulatto race was dying out, because it was a mongrel mixture which combined the worst elements of two races. Lo, the poor mulatto![7] despised by the blacks of his own race, scorned by the whites! Let him go out and hang himself!" In her indignation Anna forgot the scissors, and bit her thread off viciously with her little white teeth.

Mrs. Willis smiled as she said calmly: "My dear Anna, I would not worry about the fate of the mulatto, for the fate of the mulatto will be the fate of the entire race. Did you never think that today the black race on this continent has developed into a race of mulattoes?"

"Why, Mrs. Willis!" came in a chorus of voices.

"Yes," continued Mrs. Willis, still smiling. "It is an incontrovertible truth that there is no such thing as an unmixed black on the American continent. Just bear in mind that we cannot tell by a person's complexion

---

7. A person of mixed Negro and Caucasian ancestry.

whether he be dark or light in blood, for by the working of the natural laws the white father and black mother produce the mulatto offspring; the black father and white mother the mulatto offspring also, while the *black father* and *quadroon*[8] mother produce the black child, which to the eye alone is a child of unmixed black blood. I will venture to say that out of a hundred apparently pure black men not one will be able to trace an unmixed flow of African blood since landing upon these shores! What an unhappy example of the frailty of all human intellects, when such a man and scholar as Doctor Thomas could so far allow his prejudices to dominate his better judgment as to add one straw to the burden which is popularly supposed to rest upon the unhappy mulattoes of a despised race," finished the lady, with a dangerous flash of her large dark eyes.

"Mrs. Willis," said Dora, with a scornful little laugh, "I am not unhappy, and I am a mulatto. I just enjoy my life, and I don't want to die before my time comes, either. There are lots of good things left on earth to be enjoyed even by mulattoes, and I want my share."

"Yes, my dear; and I hope you may all live and take comfort in the proper joys of your lives. While we are all content to accept life, and enjoy it along the lines which God has laid down for us as individuals as well as a race, we shall be happy and get the best out of life. Now, let me close this talk by asking you to remember one maxim written of your race by a good man: 'Happiness and social position are not to be gained by pushing.' Let the world, by its need of us along certain lines, and our intrinsic fitness for these lines, push us into the niche which God has prepared for us. So shall our lives be beautified and our race raised in the civilization of the future as we grow away from all these prejudices which have been the instruments of our advancement according to the intention of an All-seeing Omnipotence, from the beginning. Never mind our poverty, ignorance, and the slights and injuries which we bear at the hands of a higher race. With the thought ever before us of what the Master suffered to raise all humanity to its present degree of prosperity and intelligence, let us cultivate, while we go about our daily tasks, no matter how inferior they may seem to us, beauty of the soul and mind, which being transmitted to our children by the law of heredity, shall improve the race by eliminating *immorality* from our midst and raising *morality* and virtue to their true place. Thirty-five years of liberty have made us a new people. The marks of servitude and oppression are dropping slowly from us; let us hasten the transformation of the body by the nobility of the soul."

> For of the soul the body form doth take,
> For soul is form and doth the body make,[9]

quoted Dora.

"Yes," said Mrs. Willis with a smile, "that is the idea exactly, and well expressed. Now I hope that through the coming week you will think of what we have talked about this afternoon, for it is of the very first importance to all people, but particularly so to young folks."

---

8. A person with one-quarter Negro and three-quarters Caucasian blood.

9. From Edmund Spenser's (1552–1599) *An Hymne in Honour of Beautie.*

Sappho, who had been thoughtfully embroidering pansies on white linen, now leaned back in her chair for a moment and said: "Mrs. Willis, there is one thing which puzzles me—how are we to overcome the nature which is given us? I mean how can we eliminate passion from our lives, and emerge into the purity which marked the life of Christ? So many of us desire purity and think to have found it, but in a moment of passion, or under the pressure of circumstances which we cannot control, we commit some horrid sin, and the taint of it sticks and will not leave us, and we grow to loathe ourselves."

"Passion, my dear Miss Clark, is a state in which the will lies dormant, and all other desires become subservient to one. Enthusiasm for any one object or duty may become a passion. I believe that in some degree passion may be beneficial, but we must guard ourselves against a sinful growth of any appetite. All work of whatever character, as I look at it, needs a certain amount of absorbing interest to become successful, and it is here that the Christian life gains its greatest glory in teaching us how to keep ourselves from abusing any of our human attributes. We are not held responsible for compulsory sin, only for the sin that is pleasant to our thoughts and palatable to our appetites. All desires and hopes with which we are endowed are good in the sight of God, only it is left for us to discover their right uses. Do I cover your ground?"

"Yes and no," replied Sappho; "but perhaps at some future time you will be good enough to talk with me personally upon this subject."

"Dear child, sit here by me. It is a blessing to look at you. Beauty like yours is inspiring. You seem to be troubled; what is it? If I can comfort or strengthen, it is all I ask." She pressed the girl's hand in hers and drew her into a secluded corner. For a moment the flood-gates of suppressed feeling flew open in the girl's heart, and she longed to lean her head on that motherly breast and unburden her sorrows there.

"Mrs. Willis, I am troubled greatly," she said at length.

"I am so sorry; tell me, my love, what it is all about."

Just as the barriers of Sappho's reserve seemed about to be swept away, there followed, almost instantly, a wave of repulsion toward this woman and her effusiveness, so forced and insincere. Sappho was very impressionable, and yielded readily to the influence which fell like a cold shadow between them. She drew back as from an abyss suddenly beheld stretching before her.

"On second thoughts, I think I ought to correct my remarks. It is not really *trouble*, but more a desire to confirm me in my own ideas."

"Well, if you feel you are right, dear girl, stand for the uplifting of the race and womanhood. Do not shrink from duty."

"It was simply a thought raised by your remarks on morality. I once knew a woman who had sinned. No one in the community in which she lived knew it but herself. She married a man who would have despised her had he known her story; but as it is, she is looked upon as a pattern of virtue for all women."

"And then what?" asked Mrs. Willis, with a searching glance at the fair face beside her.

"Ought she not to have told her husband before marriage? Was it not her duty to have thrown herself upon his clemency?"

"I think not," replied Mrs. Willis dryly. "See here, my dear, I am a practical woman of the world, and I think your young woman builded wiser than she knew. I am of the opinion that most men are like the lower animals in many things—they don't always know what is for their best good. If the husband had been left to himself, he probably would not have married the one woman in the world best fitted to be his wife. I think in her case she did her duty."

"Ah, that word 'duty.' What is our duty?" queried the girl, with a sad droop to the sensitive mouth. "It is so hard to know our duty. We are told that all hidden things shall be revealed. Must repented and atoned-for sin rise at last to be our curse?"

"Here is a point, dear girl. God does not look upon the constitution of sin as we do. His judgment is not ours; ours is finite, his infinite. Your duty is not to be morbid, thinking these thoughts that have puzzled older heads than yours. Your duty is, also, to be happy and bright for the good of those about you. Just blossom like the flowers, have faith and *trust*." At this point the entrance of the men made an interruption, and Mrs. Willis disappeared in a crowd of other matrons. Sappho was impressed in spite of herself, by the woman's words. She sat buried in deep thought.

There was evidently more in this woman than appeared upon the surface. With all the centuries of civilization and culture that have come to this grand old world, no man has yet been found able to trace the windings of God's inscrutable ways. There are men and women whose seeming uselessness fit perfectly into the warp and woof of Destiny's web. All things work together for good.

Chapter XV

WILL SMITH'S DEFENSE OF HIS RACE

> Thank God for the token!
> Thank God that one man as a free
> Man has spoken!
> —Whittier [1]

Someone at this moment began to sing that grand old hymn, ever new and consoling:

> "Jesus, Lover of my soul,
> Let me to thy bosom fly,
> While the nearer waters roll,
> While the tempest still is nigh."

When quiet once more reigned, amid intense silence the chairman arose and introduced Mr. William Smith as the last speaker of the evening. Tremendous applause greeted him, for he was known to be an able and eloquent debater.

"Friends," he said, "I shall not attempt a lengthy and discursive argument; I shall simply try to answer some of the arguments which have been

---

1. John Greenleaf Whittier (1807–1892), U.S. writer. The quotation is from his poem *Ritner*.

advanced by other speakers. I have no doubt that they have spoken their honest convictions. Now let us look at the other side of the question.

"We know that the Negro question is the most important issue in the affairs of the American Republic today. We are told that there are but two ways of solving the vexed question of the equality of the two races: miscegenation by law, which can *never* take place, or complete domination by the white race—meaning by that *comparative servitude.*

"Miscegenation, either *lawful* or *unlawful,* we *do not want.* The Negro dwells less on such a social cataclysm than any other race among us. Social equality does not exist; no man is forced to receive another within the environments of intimate social life. 'Social position is not to be gained by pushing.' That much for miscegenation. The question now stands: Which race shall dominate within certain parallels of latitude south of Mason and Dixon's line? The Negro, if given his full political rights, would carry the balance of power every time. This power the South has sworn that he shall never exercise. All sorts of arguments are brought forward to prove the inferiority of intellect, hopeless depravity, and God knows what not, to uphold the white man in his wanton cruelty toward the American Ishmael. [2]

"We are told that we can receive education only along certain elementary lines, and in the next breath we are taunted with not producing a genius in science or art. A Southern white man will tell you that of all politicians the Negro is the vilest, ignoring the fact that for corrupt politics no race ever can or ever will excel the venality of a certain class of whites. Let us, for the sake of illustration, glance at the position of the Irish element in politics. They come to this country poor, unlettered, despised. Fifty years ago Pat [3] was as little welcome at the North as the Negro at the South. What has changed the status of his citizenship? *Politics.* The Irishman dominates politics at the North, and there is no gift within the power of the government that does not feel his influence. I remember a story I heard once of an Irishman just landed at Castle Garden. [4] A friend met him, and as they walked up the street said to him: 'Well, Pat, you are just in time to vote for the city government election.' 'Begorra,' [5] replied Pat, 'an' is it a guvimint they have here? Sure, thin, I'll vote agin it.'

"The Irish vote, then, is massed at certain strategic points in the North, and its power is feared and respected. The result has been a rapid and dazzling advance all along the avenues of education and wealth in this country for that incisive race. To the Negro alone politics shall bring no fruit.

"To the defense of slavery in the past, and the inhuman treatment of the Negro in the present, the South has consecrated her best energies. Literature, politics, theology, history have been ransacked and perverted to prove the hopeless inferiority of the Negro and the design of God that he should serve by right of color and physique. She has convinced no one but herself. Bitterer than double-distilled gall was the Federal success which brought Negro emancipation, domination and supremacy.

"Disfranchisement is what is wanted by the South. Disfranchise the

2. In Genesis (16–17) the son of Abraham and Hagar, who was the Egyptian servant of Sarah, Abraham's wife.
3. Used as a slang term for someone of Irish descent.
4. An entry station in New York City for immigrants to the United States.
5. By God (Irish oath).

Negro and the South will be content. He, as the weaker race, can soon be crowded out.

"Many solutions of the question of Negro domination have been advanced; among them the deportation of the Negro to Africa has been most warmly advocated by public men all over the country. They argue that in this way the prophecy of the Bible will soonest be fulfilled; that 'Ethiopia shall stretch forth her hand and princes shall come out of Egypt.'[6]

"The late Henry Grady[7] told us 'that in the wise and humane administration, in the lifting the slave to heights of which he had not dreamed in his savage home, and giving him a happiness he has not yet found in freedom—our fathers (Southern men) left their sons a saving and excellent heritage (slavery).' Another man, also a Southerner, has told us: 'In education and industrial progress this race has accomplished more than it could have achieved in centuries in different environment, without the aid of the whites. The Negro has needed the example as well as the aid of the white man. In sections where the colored population is massed and removed from contact with the whites, the Negro has retrograded. Segregate the colored population and you take away the object-lesson.' Here, then, is the testimony of two intellectual white men as to the dependence of the Negro upon his proximity to the whites for a continuance of what advancement he has made since the abolishment of slavery. Is such a race as this fit at the present time to carry enlightenment into a savage and barbarous country? Can the blind lead the blind? Would not the Negro gradually fall into the same habits of ignorance and savagery from which the white slave-trader so humanely rescued him when he transported him into the blissful lap of American slavery? The Negro cannot be deported.

"It is being argued that the Negro is receiving education beyond his needs or his capacity. In short, that a Negro highly educated is a Negro spoiled. I agree with the gentleman on the other side that education alone will not produce a good citizen. But, of those who would curtail his endeavors to reach the highest that may be opened to him, I would ask: Of what use has education been to you in the upbuilding of the social and political structure which you designate the United States of America? What are the uses of education anyhow?

"To those who know the constitution of the brain as the organ of the moral and intellectual powers of man, education is of the highest importance in the formation of the character of the individual, the race, the government, the social life of any community under heaven. The objects presented to the mind by education stimulate in the same manner that the physical elements of nature do the nerves and muscles—they afford the faculties scope for action. Education is knowledge of nature in all its departments. The moment the mind discovers its own constitution and discerns the importance of the natural laws, the great advantage of moral and intellectual cultivation as a means of invigorating the brain and mental faculties, and of directing the conduct in obedience to the laws of God and man, is apparent. It is important that the Negro should not be hampered in

6. See Psalms 68:31 (King James Version).
7. White political leader (1850–1889), who was an influential editor of the *Atlanta Constitution*.

his search after knowledge if we would eliminate from his nature any tendency toward vice that he may be thought to possess, and *which has been largely increased by what he has imbibed from the example and the close,* IMMORAL ASSOCIATION *which often existed between the master and the slave.* From my own observation I should say that in this country today the science of man's whole nature—animal, moral and intellectual—was never more required to guide him than at present, when he seems to wield a giant's power, and in the application of it to display the selfish ignorance of an overgrown child.

"We come now to the crime of rape, with which the Negro is accused. For the sake of argument, we will allow that in one case out of a hundred the Negro is guilty of the crime with which he is charged; in the other ninety-nine cases the white man gratifies his lust, either of passion or vengeance. None of us will ever forget the tales told us tonight by Luke Sawyer; the wanton passions he revealed and which it has taken centuries of white civilization to develop, disclosing a dire hell to which the common crime of the untutored Negro is as white as alabaster. And it is from such men as these that the appeal comes for protection for woman's virtue! Do such examples as these render the Negro gentle and pacific? No; he sees himself traveling for years the barren Sahara of poverty, imprisonment, broken hopes and violated home ties; the ignorant, half-savage, irresponsible human animal who forms the rank and file of a race so recently emancipated from servitude, sees only revenge before his short-sighted vision.

"Rape is the outgrowth of a fiendish animus of the whites toward the blacks and of the blacks toward the whites. The Southern white is unable to view the feared domination of the blacks with the dispassionate reasoning of the unprejudiced mind. He exaggerates the nearness of that possibility, which is not desired by the blacks, and, like the physician sick of a mortal disease, is unable to prescribe for himself, and cannot realize that the simple remedy, gently applied, will lift him from his couch of pain. Lynch law prevails as the only sure cure for the ills of the South.

" 'Lynchings are justifiable on two grounds,' says a thoughtful writer: 'First, if they are consonant with the moral dignity and well-being of the people; and secondly, if they stop, and are the only sure means of stopping, the crime they avenge.' Lynching does not stop crime; it is but a subterfuge for killing men. It is a good excuse, to use a rough expression, to 'go a-gunning for niggers.'

"Lynching was instituted to crush the manhood of the enfranchised black. Rape is the crime which appeals most strongly to the heart of the home life. Merciful God! Irony of ironies! *The men who created the mulatto race, who recruit its ranks year after year by the very means which they invoked lynch law to suppress,* bewailing the sorrows of violated womanhood!

"No; it is not rape. If the Negro votes, he is shot; if he marries a white woman, he is shot; if he accumulates property, he is shot or lynched—he is a pariah whom the National Government cannot defend. But if he defends himself and his home, then is heard the tread of marching feet as the Federal troops move southward to quell a 'race riot.'

"The South declares that she is no worse than the North, and that the North would do the same under like provocation. Perhaps so, if the offender were a Negro. Take the case of Christie Warden and Frank Almy, which occurred in New Hampshire only a few years ago. Where could a more atrocious crime be perpetrated? The refinement of intellectual pursuits, the elegancies of social intercourse, were the attributes which went to make up the personnel of the most brutal murderer that ever disgraced the history of crime. Centuries of culture and civilization were combined in his make-up. The community where the girl lived and was respected and beloved did not lynch the brute. The white heat of passion led men to lay aside all pursuits for days in order to hunt the criminal from his hiding-place. New Hampshire justice gave him counsel and every means to defend himself from the penalty of his horrid crime. *That was in the North!*

"Human nature is the same in everything. The characteristic traits of the master will be found in his dog. Black, devilish, brutal as they may picture the Negro to be, he but reflects the nature of his environments. *He is the Hyde who torments the Dr. Jekyll* [8] *of the white man's refined civilization!*

"My friends, it is going to take time to straighten out this problem; it will only be done by the formation of public opinion. Brute force will not accomplish anything. We must *agitate*. As the anti-slavery apostles went everywhere, preaching the word fifty years before emancipation, *so must we do to-day*. Appeal for the justice of our cause to every civilized nation under the heavens. Lift ourselves upward and forward in this great march of life until 'Ethiopia shall indeed stretch forth her hand, and princes shall come out of Egypt.' "

When he had finished there was not a dry eye in that vast audience. Every heart followed the words of the pastor as with broken utterance he invoked the divine blessing upon the meeting just ended. Slowly they dispersed to their homes, filled with thoughts that burn but cannot be spoken.

The papers said next day that a very interesting meeting occurred the night before at the church on X Street.

1900

Famous Men of the Negro Race

Booker T. Washington

The subject of this sketch is probably the most talked of Afro-American in the civilized world today, and the influence of his words and acts on the future history of the Negro race will be carefully scrutinized by future generations.

Dr. Washington's life-story has been rehearsed so frequently by writers of both races, that it has become familiar in the households of the land.

We all know that he was born a slave on a plantation in Franklin County, Virginia, in 1858 or 1859. He describes Hale's Ford, near his birthplace, as a town with one house and a post-office. His master's name was John Burroughs, for whose family his mother cooked.

---

8. A reference to Robert Louis Stevenson's (1850–1894) novel *Dr. Jekyll and Mr. Hyde* (1886) in which a scientist's experiments lead to his splitting into two conflicting personalities, the rational, cultured Dr. Jekyll and the monstrous, brutal Hyde.

Dr. Washington's early life and struggles are stories common to thousands of Negroes,—freedom, poverty, a desire for education, the hardships encountered to compass the coveted end, his admission to Hampton and his final graduation from that college, a year at Wayland Seminary, Washington, D. C., and his "slumbering ambition" to become a lawyer. We read with pleasure the account of his life as a teacher at Malden, West Virginia, where he had received his first training in the three r's "reading, 'riting and 'rithmetic." His own description of his work there is highly entertaining:

"I not only taught school in the day, but for a great portion of the time taught night school. In addition to this I had two Sunday schools: the average attendance in my day school was, I think, between 80 and 90. As I had no assistant it was a very difficult task to keep all the pupils interested and to see that they made progress in their work.

"One thing that gave me great satisfaction and pleasure in teaching this school was the conducting of a debating society, which met weekly and was largely attended by the young and older people."

After an interval of successful work in this field, Dr. Washington tells of his work as a teacher at Hampton. He says: "I was surprised by being asked by Gen. Armstrong[1] to return to Hampton Institute and take a position, partly as a teacher and partly as a post-graduate student. This, I gladly consented to do. Gen. Armstrong had decided to start a night class at Hampton for students who wanted to work all day and study for two hours at night. He asked me to organize and teach this class. At first there were only about a half dozen students, but the number soon grew to about thirty. The night class at Hampton has since grown to the point where it numbers six or seven hundred.

"At the end of my second year at Hampton as a teacher, in 1881, there came a call from the little town of Tuskegee, Alabama, to Gen. Armstrong for some one to organize and become the Principal of a Normal School, which the people wanted to start in that town. Gen. Armstrong asked me to give up my work at Hampton and go to Tuskegee in answer to this call. I decided to undertake the work, and after spending a few days at my old home in Malden, West Virginia, I proceeded to the town of Tuskegee."

No one will question the assertion that Dr. Washington and Tuskegee are one.

Tuskegee Institute is the soul of the man outlined in wood, in brick and stone, pulsating with the life of the human hive within on whom he has stamped his individuality.

As the absorbing topic of two continents, wherever the Negro is discussed, is the "Washington Industrial Propaganda," which has gained proselytes in every section of our country among influential and wealthy citizens, we shall trace the growth of the Institute from its inception, quoting from the founder's story as given in his book, "The Story of My Life and Work."

"When I reached Tuskegee, the only thing that had been done toward starting the school was the securing of $2,000. There was no land, building,

---

1. General Samuel Chapman Armstrong (1839–1893), founder in 1868 of the Hampton Institute, a school for former slaves, in Virginia.

or apparatus. I opened the school on July 4, 1881, in an old church and a shanty that was almost ready to fall down from decay. On the first day there was an attendance of thirty students, mainly those engaged in teaching in the public schools of the vicinity. I remember that, during the first months I taught in this little shanty, it was in such a dilapidated condition that, when it rained, one of the larger pupils would cease his lessons and hold the umbrella over me while I heard the recitation. After the school had been in session for several months, I began to see the necessity of having a permanent location for the institution, where we could have the students not only in their class rooms, but get hold of them in their home life, and teach them how to take care of their bodies in the matter of general cleanliness. It was rather noticeable that, notwithstanding the poverty of most of the students who came to us in the earlier months of the institution, most of them had the idea of getting an education in order that they might find some method of living without manual labor; that is, they had the feeling that to work with the hands was not conducive to being of the highest type of lady or gentleman."

We can well believe this prejudice against labor was true of the Negro, and we ought to expect nothing different from a class so long accustomed to see nought but excellence in the behavior of the white race. "Massa Charles" lolled in his hammock while the slave worked. All the training of the Negro was in the direction that despised labor and made it a crime for a gentleman to labor.

Irony of fate! that sees the Southern gentleman adopting today, for the salvation of his section, the despised tactics of the "greasy Northern mechanic."

Feeling that it was necessary to make a great effort to improve the school, Dr. Washington secured a loan of $500 from Gen. J. F. B. Marshall, treasurer of Hampton Institute, and with this money bought an abandoned farm of 100 acres. Purchases of adjacent land and gifts of the same have increased the site to 2,460 acres.

Speaking of the great amount of assistance given him by the white inhabitants of the town, Dr. Washington says:

"I have been in a good many Southern towns, but I think I have never seen one where the general average of culture and intelligence is so high as that of the people of Tuskegee. We have in this town and its surroundings a good example of the friendly relations that exist between the two races when both races are enlightened and educated."

Through the efforts of Miss Davidson, Dr. Washington's first assistant teacher at Tuskegee in the North, money enough was secured to repay Gen. Marshall's loan and build Porter Hall, the first building on the grounds, which was dedicated on Thanksgiving Day, 1882. From this time on the school's reputation grew, and it soon became a problem what to do with the increasing number of applicants, anxious to secure an education.

In May, 1882, Dr. Washington had married Miss Fannie N. Smith of Malden, W. Virginia; she died in 1884, leaving one child, Miss Portia Washington, recently graduated from the Normal School at Framingham, Mass. In 1885, Miss Olivia Davidson became Mrs. Washington; this esti-

mable woman died in 1889. Two sons survive her—Baker Taliaferro and
Ernest Davidson.

In 1893, Dr. Washington married Miss Maggie James Murray, a graduate of Fisk University,[2] who is well known to the public in all sections of
the country.

In February, 1883, the State Legislature of Alabama was so impressed
with the excellent character of the school that they voted to increase the
annual appropriation from two to three thousand dollars. That summer a
four-room cottage was put up to hold sixteen young men, and three board
shanties were rented which would accommodate thirty-six additional students.

In September, 1885, $1,100 was secured through Rev. R. C. Bedford
from the Trustees of the States of the Slater Fund. "I might add right here
that the interest of the Trustees of the Slater Fund, now under the control
of Dr. J. L. M. Curry, special agent, has continued from that time until this,
so that now the institution receives $11,000 from the Fund," says Dr.
Washington; also: "With this impetus a carpenter shop was built, a windmill set up to pump water into the school building, a sewing machine
bought for girls' industrial room, mules and wagons for the farm, and work
on the new buildings, Alabama Hall, was vigorously pushed."

In March, 1884, through influence of Gen. Armstrong, meetings were
held in Baltimore, Philadelphia, New York and Boston, having for their
object the completion of Alabama Hall, and by much hard work funds
were secured, $10,000 in all.

In the spring of same year Dr. Washington was invited by Hon. Thomas
W. Bicknall, of Boston, President of the National Educational Association,
to address that body at its session during the summer at Madison, Wisconsin. At that assembly there were at least five thousand teachers present,
representing every State in the Union. This was the first great meeting, national in character, at which the doctor had had an opportunity of presenting his work.

Between 1884 and 1894, the hardest work was done in securing money
for Tuskegee. This was the period of growth. In 1884, the enrollment was
169. In 1894 the enrollment had increased to 712, and 54 officers and
teachers employed, and 30 buildings practically all built by the labor of the
students.

In 1883, they received their first donation of $500 from the Peabody
Fund through Dr. J. L. M. Curry, general agent. This amount has been
increased to twelve or fifteen hundred dollars each year.

In 1895, Dr. Washington lectured on "Industrial Education," under the
auspices of the Students' Lecture Bureau of Fisk University. We give two
extracts from the speech: "Despite all our disadvantages and hardships ever
since our forefathers set foot upon the American soil as slaves, our pathway
has been marked by progress. Think of it: We went into slavery pagans; we
came out Christians. We went into slavery pieces of property; we came out
American citizens. We went into slavery without a language; we came out

2. Founded for freed slaves in 1866 in Nashville, Tennessee.

speaking the proud Anglo-Saxon tongue. We went into slavery with slave chains clanking about our wrists; we came out with the American ballot in our hands." Continuing his speech, he said: "As a race there are two things we must learn to do—one is to put brains into the common occupations of life, and the other is to dignify common labor. Twenty years ago every large and paying barber shop was in the hands of black men; today in all the large cities you cannot find a single large or first-class barber shop operated by colored men. The black man had had a monopoly of that industry, but had gone on from day to day in the same old monotonous way without improving anything about the industry. As a result, the white man has taken it up, put brains into it, watched all the fine points, improved and progressed, until his shop today is not known as a barber shop, but as a tonsorial parlor, and he is no longer called a barber, but a tonsorial artist."

In the spring of 1895 he accompanied a committee of Atlanta, Ga., people to Washington to appear before the Committee on Appropriation for the purpose of inducing Congress to help forward the Exposition which the citizens of Atlanta were planning to have. The bill passed with little opposition.

Dr. Washington was proposed for chief commissioner, but declined to serve, accepting instead the position of commissioner for the State of Alabama, and was also made one of the judges of award in the Department of Education. Tuskegee Normal and Industrial Institute prepared a large and creditable exhibit, having with one exception (Hampton Institute) the largest exhibit in the Negro building. Three gold medals were awarded to institutions of learning, and Tuskegee got one of them.

On September 18, Dr. Washington made his great speech,[3] tendering the Negro exhibit of which the New York World said that it was one of the most notable speeches, both as to character and the warmth of its reception, ever delivered to a Southern audience. For this address Dr. Washington received many flattering encomiums from leading men all over the country.

In 1896, Harvard College conferred the honorary degree of Master of Arts upon him. Mr. Washington is the first of his race to receive an honorary degree from a New England University.

In 1897 occurred the dedication of the Robert Gould Shaw[4] monument in Boston. The dedicatory exercises were held in Music Hall, Boston, which was packed from top to bottom with a distinguished audience. Many old anti-slavery men were there. Hon. Roger Wolcott, Governor of Massachusetts, presided. Again Mr. Washington's address was the feature of the occasion, and he scored another great hit.

By dint of hard work and much persuasive eloquence, Dr. Washington secured the honor of a visit from President McKinley[5] to Tuskegee, at the time of the Atlanta Peace Jubilee, December 14 and 15, 1898. On the morning of December 16, at eight o'clock, the President, Mrs. McKinley,

3. I.e., Washington's 1895 Atlanta Exposition address.
4. White commander of the black Fifty-Fourth Massachusetts Volunteer Infantry unit in the Civil War (1837–1863).
5. William McKinley (1843–1901), the twenty-fifth president of the United States.

with his cabinet, their families and distinguished generals, including Generals Shafter, Joseph Wheeler, Lawton, etc., were met by Governor Joseph F. Johnston of Alabama, and his staff and the Alabama Legislature, at Tuskegee. The morning was spent in a parade and inspection of the grounds, all of which were witnessed by more than six thousand visitors. After this they retired to the large chapel, where the President and others made addresses.

Dr. Washington's public career as a speaker is full of interest: we can, of course, in an article like this, give but a bare outline of many brilliant occasions in which he has participated as the central figure. His speeches on the Negro problem, and in behalf of the Institute, are able and teem with humor, and they possess also the essential property of attracting the attention of the monied element, for Dr. Washington is without a peer in this particular line, and as a result Tuskegee is the richest Negro educational plant in the world.

Immediately after the public meeting held at the Hollis Street Theatre in 1899, friends quietly started a movement to raise a certain sum of money, to be used in sending Dr. and Mrs. Washington to Europe. They remained abroad from May 10 until August 5, gaining much needed rest. While abroad lynching was especially frequent in the South, and Mr. Washington addressed a letter to the Southern people through the medium of the press. We give an excerpt:

"With all the earnestness of my heart I want to appeal, not to the President of the United States, Mr. McKinley, not to the people of New York nor of the New England States, but to the citizens of our Southern States, to assist in creating a public sentiment such as will make human life here just as safe and sacred as it is anywhere else in the world.

"For a number of years the South has appealed to the North and to Federal authorities, through the public press, from the public platform and most eloquently through the late Henry W. Grady, to leave the whole matter of the rights and protection of the Negro to the South, declaring that it would see to it that the Negro would be made secure in his citizenship. During the last half dozen years the whole country, from the President down, has been inclined more than ever to pursue this policy, leaving the whole matter of the destiny of the Negro to the Negro himself and to the Southern white people among whom the great bulk of the Negroes live.

"By the present policy of non-interference on the part of the North and the Federal Government, the South is given a sacred trust. How will she execute this trust?" It is all very well to talk of the Negro's immorality and illiteracy, and that raising him out of the Slough of Despond will benefit the South and remove unpleasantness between the races, but until the same course is pursued with the immoral and illiterate *white* Southerner that is pursued with the Negro, there will be no peace in that section. Ignorance is as harmful in one race as in another. The South keeps on in her mad carnage of blood: she refuses to be conciliated. The influence and wealth which have flowed into Hampton and Tuskegee have awakened jealous spite. She doesn't care a rap for the "sacred trust" of Grady or any other man. We hear a lot of talk against the methods of the anti-slavery leaders, but no abolitionist ever used stronger language than the Rev.

Quincy Ewing of Mississippi, in his recent great speech against lynching. We wonder how they like it down that way? Will they hang him or burn him?

The effect of that speech has been as electrical as was the first gun from Sumter. We could shout for joy over the words: "I have always been and am now a States-right Democrat; but I say with no sort of hesitation that if Mississippi cannot put a stop to the lynching of Negroes within her borders—Negroes, let us remember, who are citizens of the United States as well as of Mississippi—then the Federal Government ought to take a hand in this business!" The reverend gentleman does not believe in treating a cancer with rose water.

Through the generosity of wealthy friends, Tuskegee has now an endowment fund of $150,000, from which the school is receiving interest.

The site of the Institute is now 835 acres. The other large tract is about four miles southeast of the Institute and is composed of 800 acres and known as "Marshall farm." Upon the home farm is located forty-two buildings. Of these, Alabama, Davidson, Huntington, Cassidy and Science Halls, the Agricultural Trades and Laundry Buildings, and the chapel are built of brick. There are also two large frame halls—Porter and Phelps Halls, small frame buildings and cottages used for commissary storerooms, recitation rooms, dormitories and teachers' residences. There are also the shop and saw-mill, with engine rooms and dynamo in conjunction. The brickyard, where the bricks needed in the construction of all brick buildings are made by pupils, turned out 1,500,000 bricks in 1899.

The Agricultural Department, Prof. G. W. Carver,[6] of the Iowa State University, in charge, attracts much attention on account of changes wrought in old methods by scientific agriculture. The building is well-equipped at a cost of $10,000, and contains a fine chemical laboratory. Agriculture is an important feature in the life of the school. 135 acres of the home farm are devoted to raising vegetables, strawberries, grapes and other fruits. The Marshall farm is worked by student labor, keeping from thirty to forty-five boys on it constantly. It produces a large amount of the farm products used by the school and 800 head of live stock.

The Mechanical Department is in the Slater-Armstrong Memorial Trades' Building, dedicated in 1900. It is built entirely of brick, and contains twenty-seven rooms. The bricks were made by student labor. The building contains directors' office, reading room, exhibit room, wheelwright shop, blacksmith shop, tin shop, printing office, carpenter shop, repair shop, wood-working machine room, iron-working machine room, foundry, brick-making and plastering rooms, general stock and supply room, and a boiler and engine room. The second floor contains the mechanical drawing room, harness shop, paint shop, tailor shop, shoe shop, and electrical laboratory, and a room for carriage trimming and upholstering.

The Department of Domestic Science is directed by Mrs. Booker T. Washington, and embraces laundering, cooking, dressmaking, plain sew-

6. George Washington Carver (1864–1943), African American scientist who joined the faculty at Tuskegee Institute in 1896.

ing, millinery and mattress making. A training school for nurses has for instructors the resident physician and a competent trained nurse.

There is also a division of music, a Bible training department and an academic department, all of which are carried on extensively with elaborate equipments.

From this brief review of the life of the founder of Tuskegee Institute and the prodigious growth of the work there we can but conclude that this is a phenomenal age in which we are living, and one of the most remarkable features of this age is Booker T. Washington,—his humble birth and rise to eminence and wealth.

View his career in whatever light we may, be we for or against his theories, his personality is striking, his life uncommon, and the magnetic influence which radiates from him in all direction, bending and swaying great minds and pointing the ultimate conclusion of colossal schemes as the wind the leaves of the trees, is stupendous. When the happenings of the Twentieth Century have become matters of history, Dr. Washington's motives will be open to as many constructions and discussions as are those of Napoleon today, or of other men of extraordinary ability, whether for good or evil, who have had like phenomenal careers.

1901

From Famous Women of the Negro Race

Literary Workers

FRANCES E. W. HARPER

In presenting to our readers a short sketch of the labors of Frances Ellen Watkins Harper[1] we feel more than glad of an opportunity to add our mead of praise to the just encomiums of many other writers for the noble deeds of an eminent Christian woman. We need give but the simple facts of the many acts that composed her life work, but these speak in trumpet tones, louder than extravagant praise or fulsome compliment.

Mrs. Harper was born in Baltimore, Maryland, in 1825; freeborn she yet partook of the cup of woe under the oppressive influence which was the heritage of bond and free alike under slave laws. She was an only child and was left an orphan at the tender age of three years. Happily an aunt took charge of her, and until she was thirteen she was sent to a private school for free colored children in Baltimore kept by an uncle, the Rev. William Watkins. At the conclusion of this period the little girl was deemed fit for labor and was put out to work in order that she might earn her own living. She endured many trials, but in the midst of the most trying ordeals preserved her desire for knowledge. She possessed a remarkable talent for composition, and when but fourteen wrote an article which attracted the attention of the lady for whom she was working. To the honor of this woman be it said that she appreciated the girl's extraordinary talent, and while she was

---

1. African American author and reformer (1825–1911).

zealously taught sewing, housework and the care of children, books were furnished her and many leisure hours were permitted her in which she was able to indulge her longing for intellectual food.

At eighteen the young girl published her first volume, called "Forest Leaves." Some of her productions were also published in the newspapers, attracting much attention.

In 1851 she left Baltimore and resided a short time in Ohio, where she was engaged in teaching. Becoming dissatisfied with her surroundings, she removed to Little York, Penn., and engaged in teaching again. While there she saw much of the underground railroad and her mind became imbued with the desire to help her people in some way. About this time Maryland enacted a law forbidding free people of color from the North from coming into the State on pain of being imprisoned and sold into slavery. A free man violated this law and was sold to Georgia; he escaped, was discovered and remanded to slavery. He died soon after from the effects of exposure and suffering. In a letter to a friend, referring to this outrage, Mrs. Harper wrote: "Upon that grave I pledged myself to the Anti-Slavery cause." In another letter she wrote: "It may be that God himself has written upon both my heart and brain a commission to use time, talent and energy in the cause of freedom." In this faith she began the study of Anti-Slavery methods and documents, finally visiting Boston, where she was received with great kindness by the Anti-Slavery people. From there she proceeded to New Bedford, where she addressed a public meeting on the "Education and Elevation of the Colored Race." The following month she was engaged by the State Anti-Slavery Society of Maine, with what success is shown from one of her letters:

"Bucksport Centre,
"Sept. 28, 1854.

"The agent of the State Anti-Slavery Society travels with me, and she is a pleasant, sweet lady. I do like her so. We eat together, sleep together. (She is a white woman.) In fact, I have not been in one colored person's house since I left Massachusetts; but I have a pleasant time. My life reminds me of a beautiful dream. What a difference between this and York! I have lectured three times this week. I have met with some of the kindest treatment I have ever received."

Her ability and labors were everywhere appreciated, and her meetings largely attended. She breakfasted with the Governor of Maine.

For a year and a half she continued speaking in the Eastern States with marked success; the papers commending her efforts highly. The following extract is from the Portland Daily Press respecting a lecture delivered after the war:

"She spoke for nearly an hour and a half, her subject being 'The Mission of the War, and the Demands of the Colored Race in the Work of Reconstruction.' Mrs. Harper has a splendid articulation, uses chaste, pure language, has a pleasant voice, and allows no one to tire of hearing her. We shall attempt no abstract of her address; none that we could make would do her justice. It was one of which any lecturer might feel proud, and her reception by a Portland audience was all that could be desired. We have seen no praises of her that were overdrawn. We have heard Miss Dickinson,[2] and do not hesitate to award the palm to her darker colored sister."

In 1856, desiring to see the fugitives in Canada, she visited the Upper Province. While in Toronto she lectured, where she was well received and listened to with great interest. We give an extract from a letter unfolding her mind and showing her impressions of the land where her race found a refuge:

"Well, I have gazed for the first time upon Free Land, and, would you believe it, tears sprang to my eyes, and I wept. Oh, it was a glorious sight to gaze for the first time on a land where a poor slave flying from our glorious land of liberty would in a moment find his fetters broken, his shackles loosed, and whatever he was in the land of Washington, beneath the shadow of Bunker Hill Monument or even Plymouth Rock, 'here he becomes a man and a brother.' I have gazed on Harper's Ferry, or rather the rock at the Ferry; I have seen it towering up in simple grandeur, with the gentle Potomac gliding peacefully at its feet, and felt that it was God's masonry, and my soul had expanded in gazing on its sublimity. I have seen the ocean singing its wild chorus of sounding waves, and ecstacy has thrilled upon the living chords of my heart. I have since then seen the rainbow crowned Niagara chanting the choral hymn of Omnipotence, girdled with grandeur and robed with glory; but none of these things have melted me as the first sight of Free Land. Towering mountains lifting their hoary summits to catch the first faint flush of day when the sunbeams kiss the shadows from morning's drowsy face may expand and exalt your soul. The first view of the ocean may fill you with strange delight. Niagara—the great, the glorious Niagara—may hush your spirit with its ceaseless thunder; it may charm you with its robe of crested spray and rainbow crown; but the Land of Freedom was a lesson of deeper significance than foaming waves or towering mounts."

Mrs. Harper was not contented to make speeches and receive plaudits, but was ready to do the rough work, and gave freely of all the moneys that her literary labors brought her. Indeed, it was often found necessary to restrain her open hand and to counsel her to be more careful of her hard-earned income.

When the John Brown[3] episode was agitating the nation, no one was more deeply affected than Mrs. Harper. To John Brown's wife she sent a letter saying: "May God, our God, sustain you in the hour of trial. If there is one thing on earth I can do for you or yours, let me be apprized. I am at your service."

Not forgetting Brown's comrades, then in prison under sentence of death, true to the impulses of her generous heart, she wrote to their relations offering financial aid—sending clothing and money. "Spare no expense," she says, "to make their last hours as bright as possible. Now, my friend, fulfil this to the letter. Oh, is it not a privilege, if you are sisterless

2. Probably Anna E. Dickinson (1842–1932), advocate for women's suffrage and civil rights for blacks.

3. White militant abolitionist (1800–1859), who was hanged as a result of his attack in 1859 on a federal arsenal at Harpers Ferry, Virginia.

and lonely, to be a sister to the human race and to place your heart where it may throb close to down-trodden humanity?" In the fall of 1860, in Cincinnati, O., Mrs. Harper married Fenton Harper, a widower. She then retired to a small farm bought from the accumulated sales of her books, etc., and for a time was absorbed by the cares of married life. Mr. Harper died May 23, 1864.

After this event Mrs. Harper again appeared as an advocate for her race. She had battled for freedom under slavery and through the war. She now began laboring as earnestly for equality before the law—education, and a higher manhood, especially in the South.

She traveled for several years, extensively through Southern cities, visiting the plantations and lowly cabin homes, addressing schools, churches, meetings in Court Houses and Legislative Halls, under most trying conditions.

Her private lectures to freedwomen are particularly worthy of notice. Desiring to speak to women, along the objects of wrong and abuse under slavery, and whom emancipation found in deepest ignorance, Mrs. Harper made it her business to talk to them of their morals and general improvement, giving them the wisest counsel in her possession. For all this work she made no charge, working and preaching as did the Master—for the love of humanity.

After her labors in the South ceased, Mrs. Harper returned to Philadelphia and began active work in the Sabbath schools. Her work in the temperance field must also be noticed.

Mrs. Harper has always read the best magazines and ablest weeklies published; she is familiar with the best authors, including De Socqueville, Mill, Ruskin, Buckle, Guizot, etc.[4]

Before the learned and unlearned Mrs. Harper has spoken in behalf of her race; during seventeen years of public speaking she has never once been other than successful in delivering thousands of speeches. By personal effort alone she has removed mountains of prejudice. At least we may be allowed to hope that the rising generation will be encouraged by her example to renewed courage in surmounting prejudice and racial difficulties. Fifty thousand copies of her four books have been sold. They have been used to entertain and delight hundreds of audiences.

Grace Greenwood,[5] in noticing a course of lectures in which Mrs. Harper spoke, pays her this tribute:

"Next on the course was Mrs. Harper, a colored woman; about as colored as some of the Cuban belles I have met at Saratoga. She has a noble head, this bronze muse; a strong face, with a shadowed glow upon it, indicative of thoughtful fervor, and of a nature most femininely sensitive, but not in the least morbid. Her form is delicate, her hands daintily small. She stands quietly beside her desk, and speaks without notes, with gestures few and fitting. Her manner is marked by dignity and composure. She is never assuming, never theatrical. Every glance of her sad eyes was a mournful

4. "De Socqueville": probably Alexis de Tocqueville (1805–1859), French author. John Stuart Mill (1806–1873), British philosopher. John Ruskin (1819–1900), British philosopher and reformer. Henry Thomas Buckle (1821–1862), British historian. François Pierre Guillaume Guizot (1787–1874), French politician and historian. 5. Writer (1823–1904).

remonstrance against injustice and wrong. Feeling in her soul, as she must have felt it, the chilling weight of caste, she seemed to say:

> 'I lift my heart up solemnly,
> As once Electra her sepulchral urn.'

As I listened to her there swept over me a chill wave of horror, the realization that this noble woman, had she not been rescued from her mother's condition, might have been sold on the auction block to the highest bidder—her intellect, fancy, eloquence, the flashing wit that might make the delight of a Parisian salon, and her pure, Christian character all thrown in—the recollection that women like her could be dragged out of public conveyances in our own city, so frowned out of fashionable churches by Anglo-Saxon saints."

Mrs. Harper is still living in Philadelphia; she is eighty odd years old, and is lovingly spoken of and known to her friends and acquaintances as "Mother Harper."

We append her poem published in 1871, "Words for the Hour," because it fits the times and our present needs:

> Men of the North! it is no time
> To quit the battle-field;
> When danger fronts your rear and van
> It is no time to yield.
>
> No time to bend the battle's crest
> Before the wily foe,
> And, ostrich-like, to hide your heads
> From the impending blow.
>
> The minions of a baffled wrong
> Are marshalling their clan;
> Rise up! rise up enchanted North!
> And strike for God and man.
>
> This is no time for careless ease;
> No time for idle sleep;
> Go light the fires in every camp,
> And solemn sentries keep.
>
> The foe you foiled upon the field
> Has only changed his base;
> New dangers crowd around you
> And stare you in the face.
>
> O Northern men! within your hands
> Is held no common trust;
> Secure the victories won by blood
> When treason bit the dust.

'Tis yours to banish from the land
  Oppression's iron rule;
And o'er the ruined auction block
  Erect the common school.

To wipe from labor's branded brow
  The curse that shamed the land,
And teach the Freedman how to wield
  The ballot in his hand.

This is the nation's golden hour,
  Nerve every heart and hand,
To build on Justice as a rock,
  The future of the land.

True to your trust, oh, never yield
  One citadel of right!
With Truth and Justice clasping hands
  Ye yet shall win the fight!

1902

Letter from Cordelia A. Condict and Pauline Hopkins's Reply (March 1903)

We are constantly in receipt of letters from our readers in all sections of the country, in fact of the world, and it gives us a great deal of pleasure to note how warm a reception is given our publication among all classes and races. Some friends offer kindly suggestions as to how we can improve and make more helpful "The Colored American Magazine," while others tell of the grand work already accomplished by our periodical. The following letter, recently received from one of our *white* readers, is of more than passing interest to us all:

Dear Sirs:—

With Miss Floto I have been taking and reading with interest the COLORED AMERICAN MAGAZINE.

If I found it more helpful to Christian work among your people I would continue to take it.

May I make a comment on the stories, especially those that have been serial. Without exception they have been of love between the colored and whites. Does that mean that your novelists can imagine no love beautiful and sublime within the range of the colored race, for each other? I have seen beautiful home life and love in families altogether of Negro blood.

The stories of these tragic mixed loves will not commend themselves to your white readers and will not elevate the colored readers. I believe your novelists could do with a consecrated imagination and pen, more for the elevation of home life and love, than perhaps any other one class of writers.

What Dickens[1] did for the neglected working class of England, some writer could do for the neglected colored people of America.

For several years I worked (superintended a Sunday school) among a greatly mixed people, Indian, Negro, Spanish and Anglo-Saxon.

My sympathies are with the earnest and spiritual work that is being done for your people, by yourselves or others.

We have kindred who are cultured Christian ladies, who for years have borne the ostracism of the white women of the South for the sake of the colored girls and women of the great South land.

> Very respectfully,
> CORNELIA A. CONDICT.

Following is Miss Hopkins' reply, which we feel will be of general interest:—

With regard to your enclosure (letter from Mrs. Condict) will say, it is the same old story. One religion for the whites and another for the blacks. The story of Jesus for us, that carries with it submission to the abuses of our people and blindness to the degrading of our youth. I think Mrs. Condict has a great work to do—greater than she can accomplish, I fear—to carry religion to the Southern whites.

My stories are definitely planned to show the obstacles persistently placed in our paths by a dominant race to subjugate us spiritually. Marriage is made illegal between the races and yet the mulattoes increase. Thus the shadow of corruption falls on the blacks and on the whites, without whose aid the mulattoes would not exist. And then the hue and cry goes abroad of the immorality of the Negro and the disgrace that the mulattoes are to this nation. Amalgamation is an institution designed by God for some wise purpose, and mixed bloods have always exercised a great influence on the progress of human affairs. I sing of the *wrongs* of a race that ignorance of their pitiful condition may be changed to intelligence and must awaken compassion in the hearts of the just.

The home life of Negroes is beautiful in many instances; warm affection is there between husband and wife, and filial and paternal tenderness in them is not surpassed by any other race of the human family. But Dickens wrote not of the joys and beauties of English society; I believe he was the author of "Bleak House" and "David Copperfield."[2] If he had been an American, and with his trenchant pen had exposed the abuses practiced by the Southern whites upon the blacks—had told the true story of how wealth, intelligence and femininity has stooped to choose for a partner in sin, the degraded (?) Negro whom they affect to despise, Dickens would have been advised to shut up or get out. I believe Jesus Christ when on earth rebuked the Pharisees in this wise: "Ye hypocrites, ye expect to be heard for your much speaking"; "O wicked and adulterous (?) nation, how can ye escape the damnation of hell?" He didn't go about patting those old

1. Charles Dickens (1812–1870), British novelist.
2. Dickens's novels, published in 1852–53 and 1849–50, respectively.

sinners on the back and saying, "All right, boys, fix me up and the Jews will get there all right. Money talks. Divy on the money you take in the exchange business of the synagogue, and it'll be all right with God." Jesus told the thing as it was and the Jews crucified him! I am glad to receive this criticism for it shows more clearly than ever that white people don't understand *what pleases Negroes*. You are between Scylla and Charybdis:[3] If you please the author of this letter and your white clientele, you will lose your Negro patronage. If you cater to the *demands* of the Negro trade, away goes Mrs. ——. I have sold to many whites and have received great praise for the work I am doing in exposing the social life of the Southerners and the wickedness of their caste prejudice.

Let the good work go on. Opposition is the life of an enterprise; criticism tells you that you are doing something.

Respect.,
PAULINE E. HOPKINS.

3. Two monsters in Greek mythology. Scylla is usually depicted as a ravenous six-headed sea creature and Charybdis as a whirlpool.

IDA B. WELLS-BARNETT
1862–1931

Ida B. Wells-Barnett is best known as an investigative journalist who delivered factual reporting and scholarly analyses on lynching in a courageous, tenacious, consciousness-raising style. However, it is more accurate to consider her a literary activist who wrote stirring essays to inform and to persuade people to demand and to give equal rights.

Born to slave parents six months before Emancipation, she was the oldest of seven children. When the Freedman's Aid association opened a school in Holly Springs, Mississippi, Wells-Barnett's father became a member of the trustee board and Ida B. Wells became one of its first students. Her parents died in the yellow fever epidemic of 1878, and sixteen-year-old Ida had to drop out of school. She obtained a teaching position, and with its twenty-five-dollar-a-month salary, she supported the entire family. Later, she moved to Memphis where the salaries were higher, and during the summer breaks, she attended Fisk University. There Wells-Barnett began her journalism career by writing for the student newspaper. She became editor of a small church related paper, *The Evening Star*, and then was hired to edit *The Living Way*, a weekly black Baptist newspaper. Wells-Barnett later wrote, "I had an instinctive feeling that the people who had little or no school training should have something coming into their homes weekly which dealt with their problems in a simple, helpful way. So in weekly letters to the *Living Way*, I wrote in a plain, common-sense way on the things which concerned our people." One subject was her own lawsuit against the Chesapeake, Ohio, and Southwestern Railroad. Wells-Barnett had sued the railroad company for attempting to expel her from the ladies' car. Though she won her case in a lower court, the Tennessee Supreme Court later overturned the ruling. Her columns written under the pen name Iola were reprinted in newspapers throughout the country. When she was twenty-seven, Wells-Barnett became editor and part owner of the *Memphis Free Speech*. Two years later when she wrote an article denouncing inadequate schools for black children, she was fired from her teaching position. Not long afterward another article almost cost her her life. In March 1892 three black businessmen opened a grocery store that competed with a white merchant. They were lynched. Outraged, Wells-Barnett wrote a scathing report that challenged the purported cause of the lynching with this statement: "Nobody in this section believes the old thread-bare lie that Negro men assault white women. If southern white men are not careful they will over-reach themselves and a conclusion will be reached which will be very damaging to the moral reputation of their women." Fortunately, Wells-Barnett had left Memphis to visit Frances E. W. Harper when the white mob destroyed the office of the *Free Speech*. Her partner, J. C. Fleming, was run out of town and Wells-Barnett was advised not to return.

Making the best of her exile, Wells-Barnett soon became writer, editor, and part owner of the *New York Age*. She continued to develop her critiques of lynch law and to publicize events in the South, believing that northerners would be moved to action if they were made aware of what was happening. *A Red Record* was one of several publications written to inspire her readers to positive action. Among her other well-publicized crusades was that against the decision to bar blacks from participating in the Chicago World's Fair. Along with Frederick Douglass, Ferdinand Lee Barnett, and I. Garland Penn, Wells-Barnett wrote and distributed a pamphlet titled *The Reason Why the Colored American Is Not in the World's Columbian Exposition*.

Though she later married Ferdinand Lee Barnett and had four children, Wells-Barnett continued her activism. She was nationally prominent in the women's club movement and part of the founding group of the National Association for the Advancement of Colored People. She continued to investigate violence against blacks. In 1898, at a rally in Chicago, she presented President William McKinley with a series of resolutions against lynching. In 1913 she organized one of the first suffrage groups made up of black women, and in 1930, she ran as an independent candidate for state senator.

Ida B. Wells-Barnett is remembered as an outspoken and articulate advocate of equal protection under the law and civil rights for black people. Rightly placed among the best muckraking journalists, she put herself at risk to call attention to the inequities and injustices of her day.

From A Red Record

Chapter I

THE CASE STATED

The student of American sociology will find the year 1894 marked by a pronounced awakening of the public conscience to a system of anarchy and outlawry which had grown during a series of ten years to be so common, that scenes of unusual brutality failed to have any visible effect upon the humane sentiments of the people of our land.

Beginning with the emancipation of the Negro, the inevitable result of unbridled power exercised for two and a half centuries, by the white man over the Negro, began to show itself in acts of conscienceless outlawry. During the slave regime, the Southern white man owned the Negro body and soul. It was to his interest to dwarf the soul and preserve the body.

Vested with unlimited power over his slave, to subject him to any and all kinds of physical punishment, the white man was still restrained from such punishment as tended to injure the slave by abating his physical powers and thereby reducing his financial worth. While slaves were scourged mercilessly, and in countless cases inhumanly treated in other respects, still the white owner rarely permitted his anger to go so far as to take a life, which would entail upon him a loss of several hundred dollars. The slave was rarely killed, he was too valuable; it was easier and quite as effective, for discipline or revenge, to sell him "Down South."

But Emancipation came and the vested interests of the white man in the Negro's body were lost. The white man had no right to scourge the emancipated Negro, still less has he a right to kill him. But the Southern white people had been educated so long in that school of practice, in which might makes right, that they disdained to draw strict lines of action in dealing with the Negro. In slave times the Negro was kept subservient and submissive by the frequency and severity of the scourging, but, with freedom, a new system of intimidation came into vogue; the Negro was not only whipped and scourged; he was killed.

Not all nor nearly all of the murders done by white men, during the past thirty years in the South, have come to light, but the statistics as gathered and preserved by white men, and which have not been questioned, show that during these years more than ten thousand Negroes have been killed in cold blood, without the formality of judicial trial and legal execution. And yet, as evidence of the absolute impunity with which the white man dares to kill a Negro, the same record shows that during all these years, and for all these murders only three white men have been tried, convicted, and executed. As no white man has been lynched for the murder of colored people, these three executions are the only instances of the death penalty being visited upon white men for murdering Negroes.

Naturally enough the commission of these crimes began to tell upon the public conscience, and the Southern white man, as a tribute to the nineteenth century civilization, was in a manner compelled to give excuses for his barbarism. His excuses have adapted themselves to the emergency, and are aptly outlined by that greatest of all Negroes, Frederick Douglass, in an article of recent date, in which he shows that there have been three distinct eras of Southern barbarism, to account for which three distinct excuses have been made.

The first excuse given to the civilized world for the murder of unoffending Negroes was the necessity of the white man to repress and stamp out alleged "race riots." For years immediately succeeding the war there was an appalling slaughter of colored people, and the wires usually conveyed to northern people and the world the intelligence, first, that an insurrection was being planned by Negroes, which, a few hours later, would prove to have been vigorously resisted by white men, and controlled with a resulting loss of several killed and wounded. It was always a remarkable feature in these insurrections and riots that only Negroes were killed during the rioting, and that all the white men escaped unharmed.

From 1865 to 1872, hundreds of colored men and women were mercilessly murdered and the almost invariable reason assigned was that they met their death by being alleged participants in an insurrection or riot. But this story at last wore itself out. No insurrection ever materialized; no Negro rioter was ever apprehended and proven guilty, and no dynamite ever recorded the black man's protest against oppression and wrong. It was too much to ask thoughtful people to believe this transparent story, and the southern white people at last made up their minds that some other excuse must be had.

Then came the second excuse, which had its birth during the turbulent times of reconstruction. By an amendment to the Constitution the Negro was given the right of franchise, and, theoretically at least, his ballot became his invaluable emblem of citizenship. In a government "of the people, for the people, and by the people," the Negro's vote became an important factor in all matters of state and national politics. But this did not last long. The southern white man would not consider that the Negro had any right which a white man was bound to respect, and the idea of a republican form of government in the southern states grew into general contempt. It was maintained that "This is a white man's government," and regardless of numbers the white man should rule. "No Negro domination" became the new legend on the sanguinary banner of the sunny South, and under it rode the Ku Klux Klan, the Regulators, and the lawless mobs, which for any cause chose to murder one man or a dozen as suited their purpose best. It was a long, gory campaign; the blood chills and the heart almost loses faith in Christianity when one thinks of Yazoo, Hamburg, Edgefield, Copiah, and the countless massacres of defenseless Negroes, whose only crime was the attempt to exercise their right to vote.

But it was a bootless strife for colored people. The government which had made the Negro a citizen found itself unable to protect him. It gave him the right to vote, but denied him the protection which should have maintained that right. Scourged from his home; hunted through the swamps; hung by midnight raiders, and openly murdered in the light of day, the Negro clung to his right of franchise with a heroism which would have wrung admiration from the hearts of savages. He believed that in that small white ballot there was a subtle something which stood for manhood as well as citizenship, and thousands of brave black men went to their graves, exemplifying the one by dying for the other.

The white man's victory soon became complete by fraud, violence, intimidation and murder. The franchise vouchsafed[1] to the Negro grew to be a "barren ideality," and regardless of numbers, the colored people found themselves voiceless in the councils of those whose duty it was to rule. With no longer the fear of "Negro Domination" before their eyes, the white man's second excuse became valueless. With the Southern governments all subverted and the Negro actually eliminated from all participation in state and national elections, there could be no longer an excuse for killing Negroes to prevent "Negro Domination."

Brutality still continued; Negroes were whipped, scourged, exiled, shot and hung whenever and wherever it pleased the white man so to treat them, and as the civilized world with increasing persistency held the white

----

1. Granted.

people of the South to account for its outlawry, the murderers invented the third excuse—that Negroes had to be killed to avenge their assaults upon women. There could be framed no possible excuse more harmful to the Negro and more unanswerable if true in its sufficiency for the white man.

Humanity abhors the assailant of womanhood, and this charge upon the Negro at once placed him beyond the pale of human sympathy. With such unanimity, earnestness and apparent candor was this charge made and reiterated that the world has accepted the story that the Negro is a monster which the Southern white man has painted him. And to-day, the Christian world feels, that while lynching is a crime, and lawlessness and anarchy the certain precursors of a nation's fall, it can not by word or deed, extend sympathy or help to a race of outlaws, who might mistake their plea for justice and deem it an excuse for their continued wrongs.

The Negro has suffered much and is willing to suffer more. He recognizes that the wrongs of two centuries can not be righted in a day, and he tries to bear his burden with patience for to-day and be hopeful for to-morrow. But there comes a time when the veriest worm will turn, and the Negro feels to-day that after all the work he has done, all the sacrifices he has made, and all the suffering he has endured, if he did not, now, defend his name and manhood from this vile accusation, he would be unworthy even of the contempt of mankind. It is to this charge he now feels he must make answer.

If the Southern people in defense of their lawlessness, would tell the truth and admit that colored men and women are lynched for almost any offense, from murder to a misdemeanor, there would not now be the necessity for this defense. But when they intentionally, maliciously and constantly belie the record and bolster up these falsehoods by the words of legislators, preachers, governors and bishops, then the Negro must give to the world his side of the awful story.

A word as to the charge itself. In considering the third reason assigned by the Southern white people for the butchery of blacks, the question must be asked, what the white man means when he charges the black man with rape. Does he mean the crime which the statutes of the civilized states describe as such? Not by any means. With the Southern white man, any mesalliance existing between a white woman and a colored man is a sufficient foundation for the charge of rape. The Southern white man says that it is impossible for a voluntary alliance to exist between a white woman and a colored man, and therefore, the fact of an alliance is a proof of force. In numerous instances where colored men have been lynched on the charge of rape, it was positively known at the time of lynching, and indisputably proven after the victim's death, that the relationship sustained between the man and woman was voluntary and clandestine, and that in no court of law could even the charge of assault have been successfully maintained.

It was for the assertion of this fact, in the defense of her own race, that the writer hereof became an exile; her property destroyed and her return to her home forbidden under penalty of death, for writing the following editorial which was printed in her paper, the Free Speech, in Memphis, Tenn., May 21, 1892:

"Eight Negroes lynched since last issue of the 'Free Speech' one at Little

Rock, Ark., last Saturday morning where the citizens broke (?) into the penitentiary and got their man; three near Anniston, Ala., one near New Orleans; and three at Clarksville, Ga., the last three for killing a white man, and five on the same old racket—the new alarm about raping white women. The same programme of hanging, then shooting bullets into the lifeless bodies was carried out to the letter. Nobody in this section of the country believes the old threadbare lie that Negro men rape white women. If Southern white men are not careful, they will over-reach themselves and public sentiment will have a reaction; a conclusion will then be reached which will be very damaging to the moral reputation of their women."

But threats cannot suppress the truth, and while the Negro suffers the soul deformity, resultant from two and a half centuries of slavery, he is no more guilty of this vilest of all vile charges than the white man who would blacken his name.

During all the years of slavery, no such charge was ever made, not even during the dark days of the rebellion, when the white man, following the fortunes of war went to do battle for the maintenance of slavery. While the master was away fighting to forge the fetters upon the slave, he left his wife and children with no protectors save the Negroes themselves. And yet during those years of trust and peril, no Negro proved recreant to his trust and no white man returned to a home that had been dispoiled.

Likewise during the period of alleged "insurrection," and alarming "race riots," it never occurred to the white man, that his wife and children were in danger of assault. Nor in the Reconstruction era, when the hue and cry was against "Negro Domination," was there ever a thought that the domination would ever contaminate a fireside or strike to death the virtue of womanhood. It must appear strange indeed, to every thoughtful and candid man, that more than a quarter of a century elapsed before the Negro began to show signs of such infamous degeneration.

In his remarkable apology for lynching, Bishop Haygood, of Georgia, says: "No race, not the most savage, tolerates the rape of woman, but it may be said without reflection upon any other people that the Southern people are now and always have been most sensitive concerning the honor of their women—their mothers, wives, sisters and daughters." It is not the purpose of this defense to say one word against the white women of the South. Such need not be said, but it is their misfortune that the chivalrous white men of that section, in order to escape the deserved execration[2] of the civilized world, should shield themselves by their cowardly and infamously false excuse, and call into question that very honor about which their distinguished priestly apologist claims they are most sensitive. To justify their own barbarism they assume a chivalry which they do not possess. True chivalry respects all womanhood, and no one who reads the record, as it is written in the faces of the million mulattoes in the South, will for a minute conceive that the southern white man had a very chivalrous regard for the honor due the women of his own race or respect for the womanhood which circumstances placed in his power. That chivalry which is "most sensitive concerning the honor of women" can hope for but little respect from the

_____

2. Curse.

civilized world, when it confines itself entirely to the women who happen to be white. Virtue knows no color line, and the chivalry which depends upon complexion of skin and texture of hair can command no honest respect.

When emancipation came to the Negroes, there arose in the northern part of the United States an almost divine sentiment among the noblest, purest and best white women of the North, who felt called to a mission to educate and Christianize the millions of southern ex-slaves. From every nook and corner of the North, brave young white women answered that call and left their cultured homes, their happy associations and their lives of ease, and with heroic determination went to the South to carry light and truth to the benighted blacks. It was a heroism no less than that which calls for volunteers for India, Africa and the Isles of the sea. To educate their unfortunate charges; to teach them the Christian virtues and to inspire in them the moral sentiments manifest in their own lives, these young women braved dangers whose record reads more like fiction than fact. They became social outlaws in the South. The peculiar sensitiveness of the southern white men for women, never shed its protecting influence about them. No friendly word from their own race cheered them in their work; no hospitable doors gave them the companionship like that from which they had come. No chivalrous white man doffed his hat in honor or respect. They were "Nigger teachers"—unpardonable offenders in the social ethics of the South, and were insulted, persecuted and ostracised, not by Negroes, but by the white manhood which boasts of its chivalry toward women.

And yet these northern women worked on, year after year, unselfishly, with a heroism which amounted almost to martyrdom. Threading their way through dense forests, working in schoolhouse, in the cabin and in the church, thrown at all times and in all places among the unfortunate and lowly Negroes, whom they had come to find and to serve, these northern women, thousands and thousands of them, have spent more than a quarter of a century in giving to the colored people their splendid lessons for home and heart and soul. Without protection, save that which innocence gives to every good woman, they went about their work, fearing no assault and suffering none. Their chivalrous protectors were hundreds of miles away in their northern homes, and yet they never feared any "great dark faced mobs," they dared night or day to "go beyond their own roof trees." They never complained of assaults, and no mob was ever called into existence to avenge crimes against them. Before the world adjudges the Negro a moral monster, a vicious assailant of womanhood and a menace to the sacred precincts of home, the colored people ask the consideration of the silent record of gratitude, respect, protection and devotion of the millions of the race in the South, to the thousands of northern white women who have served as teachers and missionaries since the war.

The Negro may not have known what chivalry was, but he knew enough to preserve inviolate the womanhood of the South which was entrusted to his hands during the war. The finer sensibilities of his soul may have been crushed out by years of slavery, but his heart was full of gratitude to the white women of the North, who blessed his home and inspired his soul in all these years of freedom. Faithful to his trust in both of these instances, he should now have the impartial ear of the civilized world, when he dares to speak for himself as against the infamy wherewith he stands charged.

It is his regret, that, in his own defense, he must disclose to the world that degree of dehumanizing brutality which fixes upon America the blot of a national crime. Whatever faults and failings other nations may have in their dealings with their own subjects or with other people, no other civilized nation stands condemned before the world with a series of crimes so peculiarly national. It becomes a painful duty of the Negro to reproduce a record which shows that a large portion of the American people avow anarchy, condone murder and defy the contempt of civilization.

These pages are written in no spirit of vindictiveness, for all who give the subject consideration must concede that far too serious is the condition of that civilized government in which the spirit of unrestrained outlawry constantly increases in violence, and casts its blight over a continually growing area of territory. We plead not for the colored people alone, but for all victims of the terrible injustice which puts men and women to death without form of law. During the year 1894, there were 132 persons executed in the United States by due form of law, while in the same year, 197 persons were put to death by mobs who gave the victims no opportunity to make a lawful defense. No comment need be made upon a condition of public sentiment responsible for such alarming results.

The purpose of the pages which follow shall be to give the record which has been made, not by colored men, but that which is the result of compilations made by white men, of reports sent over the civilized world by white men in the South. Out of their own mouths shall the murderers be condemned. For a number of years the Chicago Tribune, admittedly one of the leading journals of America, has made a specialty of the compilation of statistics touching upon lynching. The data compiled by that journal and published to the world January 1st, 1894, up to the present time has not been disputed. In order to be safe from the charge of exaggeration, the incidents hereinafter reported have been confined to those vouched for by the Tribune.

Chapter X

THE REMEDY

It is a well established principle of law that every wrong has a remedy. Herein rests our respect for law. The Negro does not claim that all of the one thousand black men, women and children, who have been hanged, shot and burned alive during the past ten years, were innocent of the charges made against them. We have associated too long with the white man not to have copied his vices as well as his virtues. But we do insist that the punishment is not the same for both classes of criminals. In lynching, opportunity is not given the Negro to defend himself against the unsupported accusations of white men and women. The word of the accuser is held to be true and the excited bloodthirsty mob demands that the rule of law be reversed and instead of proving the accused to be guilty, the victim of their hate and revenge must prove himself innocent. No evidence he can offer will satisfy the mob; he is bound hand and foot and swung into eternity. Then to excuse its infamy, the mob almost invariably reports the monstrous falsehood that its victim made a full confession before he was hanged.

With all military, legal and political power in their hands, only two of the lynching States have attempted a check by exercising the power which is theirs. Mayor Trout, of Roanoke, Virginia, called out the militia in 1893, to protect a Negro prisoner, and in so doing nine men were killed and a number wounded. Then the mayor and militia withdrew, left the Negro to his fate and he was promptly lynched. The business men realized the blow to the town's financial interests, called the mayor home, the grand jury indicted and prosecuted the ringleaders of the mob. They were given light sentences, the highest being one of twelve months in State prison. The day he arrived at the penitentiary, he was pardoned by the governor of the State.

The only other real attempt made by the authorities to protect a prisoner of the law, and which was more successful, was that of Gov. McKinley, of Ohio, who sent the militia to Washington Courthouse, O., in October, 1894, and five men were killed and twenty wounded in maintaining the principle that the law must be upheld.

In South Carolina, in April, 1893, Gov. Tillman aided the mob by yielding up to be killed, a prisoner of the law, who had voluntarily placed himself under the Governor's protection. Public sentiment by its representatives has encouraged Lynch Law, and upon the revolution of this sentiment we must depend for its abolition.

Therefore, we demand a fair trial by law for those accused of crime, and punishment by law after honest conviction. No maudlin sympathy for criminals is solicited, but we do ask that the law shall punish all alike. We earnestly desire those that control the forces which make public sentiment to join with us in the demand. Surely the humanitarian spirit of this country which reaches out to denounce the treatment of the Russian Jews, the Armenian Christians, the laboring poor of Europe, the Siberian exiles and the native women of India—will not longer refuse to lift its voice on this subject. If it were known that the cannibals or the savage Indians had burned three human beings alive in the past two years, the whole of Christendom would be roused, to devise ways and means to put a stop to it. Can you remain silent and inactive when such things are done in our own community and country? Is your duty to humanity in the United States less binding?

What can you do, reader, to prevent lynching, to thwart anarchy and promote law and order throughout our land?

1st. You can help disseminate the facts contained in this book by bringing them to the knowledge of every one with whom you come in contact, to the end that public sentiment may be revolutionized. Let the facts speak for themselves, with you as a medium.

2d. You can be instrumental in having churches, missionary societies, Y. M. C. A.'s, W. C. T. U.'s and all Christian and moral forces in connection with your religious and social life, pass resolutions of condemnation and protest every time a lynching takes place; and see that they are sent to the place where these outrages occur.

3d. Bring to the intelligent consideration of Southern people the refusal of capital to invest where lawlessness and mob violence hold sway. Many labor organizations have declared by resolution that they would avoid lynch infested localities as they would the pestilence when seeking new homes. If the South wishes to build up its waste places quickly, there is no better way than to uphold the majesty of the law by enforcing obedience to the same, and meting out the same punishment to all classes of criminals, white as well as black. "Equality before the law," must become a fact as well as a theory before America is truly the "land of the free and the home of the brave."

4th. Think and act on independent lines in this behalf, remembering that after all, it is the white man's civilization and the white man's government which are on trial. This crusade will determine whether that civilization can maintain itself by itself, or whether anarchy shall prevail; whether this Nation shall write itself down a success at self government, or in deepest humiliation admit its failure complete; whether the precepts and theories of Christianity are professed and practiced by American white people as Golden Rules of thought and action, or adopted as a system of morals to be preached to heathen until they attain to the intelligence which needs the system of Lynch Law.

5th. Congressman Blair offered a resolution in the House of Representatives, August, 1894. The organized life of the country can speedily make this a law by sending resolutions to Congress indorsing Mr. Blair's bill and asking Congress to create the commission. In no better way can the question be settled, and the Negro does not fear the issue. The following is the resolution:

"Resolved, By the House of Representatives and Senate in congress assembled, That the committee on labor be instructed to investigate and report the number, location and date of all alleged assaults by males upon females throughout the country during the ten years last preceding the passing of this joint resolution, for or on account of which organized but unlawful violence has been inflicted or attempted to be inflicted. Also to ascertain and report all facts of organized but unlawful violence to the person, with the attendant facts and circumstances, which have been inflicted upon accused persons alleged to have been guilty of crimes punishable by due process of law which have taken place in any part of the country within the ten years last preceding the passage of this resolution. Such investigation shall be made by the usual methods and agencies of the Department of Labor, and report made to Congress as soon as the work can be satisfactorily done, and the sum of $25,000, or so much thereof as may be necessary, is hereby appropriated to pay the expenses out of any money in the treasury not otherwise appropriated."

The belief has been constantly expressed in England that in the United States, which has produced Wm. Lloyd Garrison, Henry Ward Beecher, James Russell Lowell, John G. Whittier and Abraham Lincoln there must be those of their descendants who would take hold of the work of inaugurating an era of law and order. The colored people of this country who have been loyal to the flag believe the same, and strong in that belief have begun this crusade. To those who still feel they have no obligation in the matter, we commend the following lines of Lowell on "Freedom."

Men! whose boast it is that ye
Come of fathers brave and free,
If there breathe on earth a slave
Are ye truly free and brave?
If ye do not feel the chain,
When it works a brother's pain,
Are ye not base slaves indeed,
Slaves unworthy to be freed?

Women! who shall one day bear
Sons to breathe New England air,
If ye hear without a blush,
Deeds to make the roused blood rush
Like red lava through your veins,
For your sisters now in chains,—
Answer! are ye fit to be
Mothers of the brave and free?

Is true freedom but to break
Fetters for our own dear sake,
And, with leathern hearts, forget
That we owe mankind a debt?
No! true freedom is to share
All the chains our brothers wear,
And, with heart and hand, to be
Earnest to make others free!

There are slaves who fear to speak
For the fallen and the weak;
They are slaves who will not choose
Hatred, scoffing, and abuse,
Rather than in silence shrink
From the truth they needs must think;
They are slaves who dare not be
In the right with two or three.

A FIELD FOR PRACTICAL WORK

The very frequent inquiry made after my lectures by interested friends is, "What can I do to help the cause?" The answer always is, "Tell the world the facts." When the Christian world knows the alarming growth and extent of outlawry in our land, some means will be found to stop it.

The object of this publication is to tell the facts, and friends of the cause can lend a helping hand by aiding in the distribution of these books. When I present our cause to a minister, editor, lecturer, or representative of any moral agency, the first demand is for facts and figures. Plainly, I can not then hand out a book with a twenty-five cent tariff on the information contained. This would be only a new method in the book agents' art. In all such cases it is a pleasure to submit this book for investigation, with the certain assurance of gaining a friend to the cause.

There are many agencies which may be enlisted in our cause by the general circulation of the facts herein contained. The preachers, teachers, editors and humanitarians of the white race, at home and abroad, must have facts laid before them, and it is our duty to supply these facts. The Central Anti-Lynching League, Room 9, 128 Clark st., Chicago, has established a Free Distribution Fund, the work of which can be promoted by all who are interested in this work.

Anti-lynching leagues, societies and individuals can order books from this fund at agents' rates. The books will be sent to their order, or, if desired, will be distributed by the League among those whose co-operative aid we so greatly need. The writer hereof assures prompt distribution of books according to order, and public acknowledgment of all orders through the public press.

1895

W. E. B. DU BOIS

1868–1963

William Edward Burghardt Du Bois was the Renaissance man of African American letters during the first fifty years of the twentieth century. He was the most multifaceted, prolific, and influential writer that black America has ever produced, with one of the widest-ranging intellects of any of his American contemporaries. Through his extensive publications in the sociology and history of African Americans and in tribute to his pioneering editing of numerous journals of opinion devoted to racial issues, Du Bois has been called, with justification, the founder of black studies in American academic life. His work and his example inspired a twentieth-century African American intelligentsia proud of its heritage and committed to a social as well as an intellectual mission.

Du Bois believed that ideas not slogans, principles not personalities were essential to the eradication of the many forms of bigotry and inequality that had perverted what he called "the ideal of human brotherhood" in America. While engaged in full-time university teaching, scholarly research, and lecturing, he played a pivotal role in the organization of the Niagara movement, which in 1910 became the National Association for the Advancement of Colored People (NAACP). A radical democrat, Du Bois was not afraid to espouse unpopular notions of socialism and communism in the name of full socioeconomic equality. Yet his unflagging critique of the material injustices of America arose from his commitment to spiritual ideals, to "the striving in the souls of black folk" to become "co-worker[s] in the kingdom of culture," creators of an America in which the "best powers" and "latent genius" that Du Bois believed were inherent in all races could find expression and fulfillment. Thus, although Du Bois was educated as a scholar and his manner of writing was often professorial, he repeatedly turned to traditional literary forms, such as poetry, fiction, and an introspective, impressionistic prose when impelled by the need to express his most deeply felt emotions.

On his twenty-fifth birthday, while studying for his Ph.D. at the University of Berlin, Du Bois confided to his journal the following goals: "to make a name in science, to make a name in art and thus to raise my race." From his childhood in Great Barrington, Massachusetts, he had cherished a fondness for books and a desire for intellectual distinction. His mother, Mary Burghardt Du Bois, and her extended family (which could trace its ancestry back to the earliest settlers of the valley where Du Bois grew up), protected and encouraged William after his father,

Alfred Du Bois, deserted his family when his son was still an infant. Attending predominantly white schools and churches, Du Bois graduated with honors from the local high school in 1884 with "no thought of discrimination on the part of my [white] fellows," as he recalled in his autobiography, *Dusk of Dawn*, in 1940.

In 1885 the "quite thoroughly New England" youth went to Fisk University in Nashville, Tennessee, his first foray into the South and southern racism and, more important, his first deep immersion in the lives of African Americans. Earning his bachelor's degree in 1888, Du Bois applied to Harvard University for a scholarship, which he won; he graduated from Harvard with another bachelor's degree in 1890 and a master's degree the next year. Between 1892 and 1894, he pursued his education at the University of Berlin. In 1895 Du Bois earned his doctorate in history from Harvard; his dissertation, *The Suppression of the African Slave-Trade to the United States*, was published in 1896, the first volume in the Harvard Historical Studies series.

By the time his first book saw print, Du Bois was busy at his first teaching post, at Wilberforce University, a black institution established by the African Methodist Episcopal church in central Ohio. In 1896 he married Nina Gomer, a Wilberforce student, and soon thereafter accepted an offer from the University of Pennsylvania to do research on the black people of Philadelphia. Despite a paltry salary, no assistance, and lack of even an office, Du Bois did his work in exemplary fashion, producing *The Philadelphia Negro* (1899), the first sociological text on an African American community published in the United States. In 1897 Du Bois joined the faculty of Atlanta University, where for the next thirteen years through his teaching and research he laid the foundation for twentieth-century African American sociology with a series of academic conferences and empirically based annual reports on such topics as black landowners, the black church, the black family, black urbanization, and black mortality.

Increasingly alarmed by the incidence of white violence against blacks in the South and chafing against the restraints of segregation, the college professor sought out forums beyond academe from which he could address fundamental problems of race and justice in the United States. In articles for such magazines as the *Atlantic Monthly*, *The Dial*, and *World's Work*, Du Bois wrote not as a detached social scientist but as a cultural interpreter, a historian, advocate, and oracle of his people. By the turn of the century, he had become convinced that the distinctive artistic traditions, expressive culture, and communal values of African Americans—what he called the "soul" of the black folk in the United States—had to be recognized, respected, and conserved by white and black Americans alike. In 1903 Du Bois voiced this conviction and this plea in the eloquent and experimental book for which he is now best known, *The Souls of Black Folk*.

Ostensibly a collection of essays on African American history, sociology, religion, politics, and music, *The Souls of Black Folk* reads in important respects like a personal exposition of a collective experience, "life within the Veil," as Du Bois termed it. The metaphor of the veil denotes throughout *The Souls of Black Folk* the shadowy yet substantial line that separated whites from persons of African descent in the turn-of-the-century United States. "The problem of the Twentieth Century is the problem of the color-line," Du Bois announced prophetically in the "forethought" to *The Souls of Black Folk*. But it was Du Bois's genius to realize that to protest the color line most effectively and originally in a new century, he had to find ways to personalize it, to make its reality not merely a social and legal fact but a profound psychological factor in the African American's sense of self and relationship to society. Thus, from the beginning of his book, Du Bois introduces his white reader to peculiar dualities and conflicts in African American self-perception—known ever since by Du Bois's term *double-consciousness*—which for Du Bois de-

fined both the crux of black Americans' struggle to identify themselves and the crucible in which their African and American identities could be merged into a unity
of which they and the nation could be proud. *Of Mr. Booker T. Washington and
Others*—the most influential essay in *The Souls of Black Folk*—attacked the political
program of the acknowledged leader of black America in a way that gave Du Bois a
national following as an uncompromising civil rights champion. But the volume
begins and ends in a prose more evocative than provocative, as Du Bois celebrates
the spiritual aspirations of black America through its folklore, its music, and its
"simple faith and reverence" in "the ultimate justice of things," when "America
shall rend the Veil and the prisoned shall go free."

Between 1903 and 1910, Du Bois wrote some of his memorable work in poetry and
narrative prose. He published his prose poem *A Litany of Atlanta* in the wake of a
brutal outbreak of violence against blacks in Atlanta in September 1906. A year later
The Song of the Smoke testified to Du Bois's desire for an alternative to the traditional
deity he prayed to in the *Litany*, while also pioneering an aesthetic of unabashed
blackness. In 1909 came a biography of John Brown based mainly on
its author's attempt to plumb the mysteries of the mind of the radical abolitionist
martyr. A year later Du Bois launched the *Crisis*, the official organ of the NAACP,
which as editor he fashioned into the most widely read African American magazine
of its time. In 1911 Du Bois tried his hand at long fiction. His novel *The Quest of the
Silver Fleece* (1911), partly an exposé of the southern cotton industry, partly a romantic love story, and partly a brief for socialism, did not receive much notice, but its
unhackneyed depiction of black women and its barely disguised political radicalism
were remarkable in African American fiction. Du Bois's feminism, though imperfect
by today's standards, came to the fore again in his essay *The Damnation of Women*,
one of the most notable essays in *Darkwater: Voices within the Veil* (1920).

Although the *Crisis* served Du Bois well as a forum for his ideas on American
racial issues, he devoted considerable energy during the 1910s and 1920s to international questions. In 1915 he published *The Negro*, a study that embraced peoples
of African descent worldwide. Attempting to combat colonialism, Du Bois organized several Pan-African congresses in Europe and New York. His second novel,
Dark Princess (1928), imagined an international "Great Council of Darker Peoples" poised to overthrow European imperialism and American racism. The blend
of socialist propaganda and romantic fantasy at the heart of *Dark Princess* was designed to illustrate Du Bois's contention in *Criteria of Negro Art* (1926) that art and
propaganda were one. Du Bois felt obliged to insist on this because many writers of
the New Negro Renaissance in the 1920s were unsympathetic to the explicitly political agenda of his fiction and to what they saw as his outmoded Victorian values
in writing about love and sex. Despite the friction between Du Bois and some of the
firebrands of the New Negro Renaissance, the editor of the *Crisis* published several
of the best of the new writers, in particular Langston Hughes and Countee Cullen.
Hughes and other notable writers such as Jessie Fauset also made important contributions to *The Brownie's Book*, a magazine for African American children that Du
Bois initiated in 1920.

The Depression of the 1930s confirmed in Du Bois's mind the need for fundamental socioeconomic change in America according to Marxist principles. He resigned from the NAACP in 1934 and returned to Atlanta University. His massive
history, *Black Reconstruction* (1935), revised conventional accounts of Reconstruction in the South as a debacle and emphasized the efforts of the freed people to
transform the South into a society free of social and economic exploitation. In 1940
Du Bois published his first full-length autobiography, *Dusk of Dawn: An Autobiography of a Concept of Race*, in which he focused on the evolution of his ideas about
race, "human difference," and social justice, concluding with an argument for

black "voluntary segregation" as the most effective means of organizing and advancing African Americans socially and economically. Although *Dusk of Dawn* firmly stated that its author was not a communist, Du Bois's writing later in the 1940s affirmed his growing affinities to Marxism, his admiration of the Soviet Union, his vigorous anticolonialism, and his heightened militancy in the struggle for African American civil rights in the United States.

Du Bois's left-wing politics had more than a little to do with his forced retirement from Atlanta University in 1944 and his firing in 1948 by the NAACP from his position as director of special research. In 1951 the U.S. government indicted Du Bois and his colleagues in the New York–based Peace Information Center, an organization that promoted the banning of atomic weapons, as subversive agents of a foreign power. Acquitted in November 1951, Du Bois found himself ostracized by many African American leaders and civil rights organizations. But he went on writing (although most of his outlets were limited to the leftwing press): *In Battle for Peace* (1952), an autobiography; a trilogy of novels, *The Black Flame* (1957), *Mansart Builds a School* (1959), and *Worlds of Color* (1961); and *The Autobiography of W. E. B. Du Bois* (1968), posthumously published. In 1963 Du Bois renounced his American citizenship and became a citizen of Ghana, where he had moved in 1961. When he died he was planning the multivolume *Encyclopaedia Africana*.

A Litany of Atlanta [1]

O Silent God, Thou whose voice afar in mist and mystery hath left our ears an-hungered in these fearful days—
    Hear us, good Lord!

Listen to us, Thy children: our faces dark with doubt, are made a mockery in Thy sanctuary. With uplifted hands we front Thy heaven, O God, crying:
    We beseech Thee to hear us, good Lord!

We are not better than our fellows, Lord, we are but weak and human men. When our devils do deviltry, curse Thou the doer and the deed: curse them as we curse them, do to them all and more than ever they have done to innocence and weakness, to womanhood and home.
    Have mercy upon us, miserable sinners!

And yet whose is the deeper guilt? Who made these devils? Who nursed them in crime and fed them on injustice? Who ravished and debauched their mothers and their grandmothers? Who bought and sold their crime, and waxed fat and rich on public iniquity?
    Thou knowest, good God!

Is this Thy justice, O Father, that guile be easier than innocence, and the innocent crucified for the guilt of the untouched guilty?
    Justice, O Judge of men!

---

1. In September 1906 a three-day race riot instigated by whites raged through Atlanta, Georgia. Du Bois wrote this poem on a train as he returned to the city unsure of the fate of his family there. "Litany": a prayer of entreaty in which a minister and a congregation alternately speak.

Wherefore do we pray? Is not the God of the fathers dead? Have not seers seen in Heaven's halls Thine hearsed and lifeless form stark amidst the black and rolling smoke of sin, where all along bow bitter forms of endless dead?

Awake, Thou that sleepest!

Thou art not dead, but flown afar, up hills of endless light, thru blazing corridors of suns, where worlds do swing of good and gentle men, of women strong and free—far from the cozenage,[2] black hypocrisy and chaste prostitution of this shameful speck of dust!

Turn again, O Lord, leave us not to perish in our sin!

From lust of body and lust of blood
  Great God deliver us!

From lust of power and lust of gold,
  Great God deliver us!

From the leagued lying of despot and of brute,
  Great God deliver us!

A city lay in travail, God our Lord, and from her loins sprang twin Murder and Black Hate. Red was the midnight; clang, crack and cry of death and fury filled the air and trembled underneath the stars when church spires pointed silently to Thee. And all this was to sate the greed of greedy men who hide behind the veil of vengeance!

Bend us Thine ear, O Lord!

In the pale, still morning we looked upon the deed. We stopped our ears and held our leaping hands, but they—did they not wag their heads and leer and cry with bloody jaws: *Cease from Crime!* The word was mockery, for thus they train a hundred crimes while we do cure one.

Turn again our captivity, O Lord!

Behold this maimed and broken thing; dear God it was an humble black man who toiled and sweat to save a bit from the pittance paid him. They told him: *Work and Rise.* He worked. Did this man sin? Nay, but some one told how some one said another did—one whom he had never seen nor known. Yet for that man's crime this man lieth maimed and murdered, his wife naked to shame, his children, to poverty and evil.

Hear us, O heavenly Father!

Doth not this justice of hell stink in Thy nostrils, O God? How long shall the mounting flood of innocent blood roar in Thine ears and pound in our hearts for vengeance? Pile the pale frenzy of blood-crazed brutes who do such deeds high on Thine altar, Jehovah Jireh,[3] and burn it in hell forever and forever!

Forgive us, good Lord; we know not what we say!

---

2. Fraud, trickery.   3. God.

Bewildered we are, and passion-tost, mad with the madness of a mobbed and mocked and murdered people; straining at the armposts of Thy Throne, we raise our shackled hands and charge Thee, God, by the bones of our stolen fathers, by the tears of our dead mothers, by the very blood of Thy crucified Christ: *What meaneth this?* Tell us the Plan; give us the Sign!

 Keep not thou silence, O God!

Sit no longer blind, Lord God, deaf to our prayer and dumb to our dumb suffering. Surely Thou too art not white, O Lord, a pale, bloodless, heartless thing?

 Ah! Christ of all the Pities!

Forgive the thought! Forgive these wild, blasphemous words. Thou art still the God of our black fathers, and in Thy soul's soul sit some soft darkenings of the evening, some shadowings of the velvet night.

But whisper—speak—call, great God, for Thy silence is white terror to our hearts! The way, O God, show us the way and point us the path.

Whither? North is greed and South is blood; within, the coward, and without, the liar. Whither? To death?

 Amen! Welcome dark sleep!

Whither? To life? But not this life, dear God, not this. Let the cup pass from us, tempt us not beyond our strength, for there is that clamoring and clawing within, to whose voice we would not listen, yet shudder lest we must, and it is red, Ah! God! It is a red and awful shape.

 Selah! [4]

In yonder East trembles a star.

 Vengeance is mine; I will repay, saith the Lord!

Thy will, O Lord, be done!

 Kyrie Eleison! [5]

Lord, we have done these pleading, wavering words.

 We beseech Thee to hear us, good Lord!

We bow our heads and hearken soft to the sobbing of women and little children.

 We beseech Thee to hear us, good Lord!

Our voices sink in silence and in night.

 Hear us, good Lord!

In night, O God of a godless land!

 Amen!

4. Forever (Hebrew).   5. Lord, have mercy on us (Greek).

In silence, O Silent God.
   Selah!

1906

The Song of the Smoke

     I am the Smoke King
     I am black!
I am swinging in the sky,
I am wringing worlds awry;
  I am the thought of the throbbing mills,   5
  I am the soul of the soul-toil kills,
  Wraith of the ripple of trading rills;
Up I'm curling from the sod,
I am whirling home to God;
     I am the Smoke King   10
     I am black.

     I am the Smoke King,
     I am black!
I am wreathing broken hearts,
I am sheathing love's light darts;   15
  Inspiration of iron times
  Wedding the toil of toiling climes,
  Shedding the blood of bloodless crimes—
Lurid lowering 'mid the blue,
Torrid towering toward the true,   20
     I am the Smoke King,
     I am black.

     I am the Smoke King,
     I am black!
I am darkening with song,   25
I am hearkening to wrong!
  I will be black as blackness can—
  The blacker the mantle, the mightier the man!
  For blackness was ancient ere whiteness began.
I am daubing God in night,   30
I am swabbing Hell in white:
     I am the Smoke King
     I am black.

     I am the Smoke King,
     I am black!   35
I am cursing ruddy morn,
I am hearsing hearts unborn:
  Souls unto me are as stars in a night,
  I whiten my black men—I blacken my white!
  What's the hue of a hide to a man in his might?   40
Hail! great, gritty, grimy hands—
Sweet Christ, pity toiling lands!

I am the Smoke King
I am black.

1907

The Souls of Black Folk

The Forethought

Herein lie buried many things which if read with patience may show the strange meaning of being black here in the dawning of the Twentieth Century. This meaning is not without interest to you, Gentle Reader; for the problem of the Twentieth Century is the problem of the color-line.

I pray you, then, receive my little book in all charity, studying my words with me, forgiving mistake and foible for sake of the faith and passion that is in me, and seeking the grain of truth hidden there.

I have sought here to sketch, in vague, uncertain outline, the spiritual world in which ten thousand thousand Americans live and strive. First, in two chapters I have tried to show what Emancipation meant to them, and what was its aftermath. In a third chapter I have pointed out the slow rise of personal leadership, and criticised candidly the leader who bears the chief burden of his race to-day. Then, in two other chapters I have sketched in swift outline the two worlds within and without the Veil, and thus have come to the central problem of training men for life. Venturing now into deeper detail, I have in two chapters studied the struggles of the massed millions of the black peasantry, and in another have sought to make clear the present relations of the sons of master and man.

Leaving, then, the world of the white man, I have stepped within the Veil, raising it that you may view faintly its deeper recesses,—the meaning of its religion, the passion of its human sorrow, and the struggle of its greater souls. All this I have ended with a tale twice told but seldom written.

Some of these thoughts of mine have seen the light before in other guise. For kindly consenting to their republication here, in altered and extended form, I must thank the publishers of *The Atlantic Monthly, The World's Work, The Dial, The New World,* and the *Annals of the American Academy of Political and Social Science.*

Before each chapter, as now printed, stands a bar of the Sorrow Songs,[1] —some echo of haunting melody from the only American music which welled up from black souls in the dark past. And, finally, need I add that I who speak here am bone of the bone and flesh of the flesh of them that live within the Veil?

W. E. B. Du B.

ATLANTA, GA., Feb. 1, 1903.

---

1. Du Bois's term for African American spirituals communally composed by southern slaves.

I. Of Our Spiritual Strivings

O water, voice of my heart, crying in the sand,
  All night long crying with a mournful cry,
As I lie and listen, and cannot understand
    The voice of my heart in my side or the voice of the sea,
  O water, crying for rest, is it I, is it I?
    All night long the water is crying to me.

Unresting water, there shall never be rest
  Till the last moon droop and the last tide fail,
And the fire of the end begin to burn in the west;
    And the heart shall be weary and wonder and cry like the sea,
  All life long crying without avail,
    As the water all night long is crying to me.

                                         ARTHUR SYMONS[2]

Between me and the other world there is ever an unasked question: unasked by some through feelings of delicacy; by others through the difficulty of rightly framing it. All, nevertheless, flutter round it. They approach me in a half-hesitant sort of way, eye me curiously or compassionately, and then, instead of saying directly, How does it feel to be a problem? they say, I know an excellent colored man in my town; or, I fought at Mechanicsville;[3] or, Do not these Southern outrages make your blood boil? At these I smile, or am interested, or reduce the boiling to a simmer, as the occasion may require. To the real question, How does it feel to be a problem? I answer seldom a word.

And yet, being a problem is a strange experience,—peculiar even for one who has never been anything else, save perhaps in babyhood and in Europe. It is in the early days of rollicking boyhood that the revelation first bursts upon one, all in a day, as it were. I remember well when the shadow swept across me. I was a little thing, away up in the hills of New England, where the dark Housatonic[4] winds between Hoosac and Taghkanic to the sea. In a wee wooden schoolhouse, something put it into the boys' and girls' heads to buy gorgeous visiting-cards—ten cents a package—and exchange. The exchange was merry, till one girl, a tall newcomer, refused my card,—refused it peremptorily, with a glance. Then it dawned upon me with a certain suddenness that I was different from the others; or like, mayhap, in heart and life and longing, but shut out from their world by a vast veil. I had thereafter no desire to tear down that veil, to creep through; I held all beyond it in common contempt, and lived above it in a region of blue sky and great wandering shadows. That sky was bluest when I could beat my mates at examination-time, or beat them at a foot-race, or even beat their stringy heads. Alas, with the years all this fine contempt began to fade; for the worlds I longed for, and all their dazzling opportunities, were

2. English poet (1865–1945). The quotation is
from *The Crying of Water* (1903).
    3. A Civil War battle in Virginia.
    4. A river in western Massachusetts.

theirs, not mine. But they should not keep these prizes, I said; some, all, I would wrest from them. Just how I would do it I could never decide: by reading law, by healing the sick, by telling the wonderful tales that swam in my head,—some way. With other black boys the strife was not so fiercely sunny: their youth shrunk into tasteless sycophancy, or into silent hatred of the pale world about them and mocking distrust of everything white; or wasted itself in a bitter cry, Why did God make me an outcast and a stranger in mine own house? The shades of the prison-house closed round about us all: walls strait and stubborn to the whitest, but relentlessly narrow, tall, and unscalable to sons of night who must plod darkly on in resignation, or beat unavailing palms against the stone, or steadily, half hopelessly, watch the streak of blue above.

After the Egyptian and Indian, the Greek and Roman, the Teuton and Mongolian, the Negro is a sort of seventh son, born with a veil, and gifted with second-sight in this American world,—a world which yields him no true self-consciousness, but only lets him see himself through the revelation of the other world. It is a peculiar sensation, this double-consciousness, this sense of always looking at one's self through the eyes of others, of measuring one's soul by the tape of a world that looks on in amused contempt and pity. One ever feels his two-ness,—an American, a Negro; two souls, two thoughts, two unreconciled strivings; two warring ideals in one dark body, whose dogged strength alone keeps it from being torn asunder.

The history of the American Negro is the history of this strife,—this longing to attain self-conscious manhood, to merge his double self into a better and truer self. In this merging he wishes neither of the older selves to be lost. He would not Africanize America, for America has too much to teach the world and Africa. He would not bleach his Negro soul in a flood of white Americanism, for he knows that Negro blood has a message for the world. He simply wishes to make it possible for a man to be both a Negro and an American, without being cursed and spit upon by his fellows, without having the doors of Opportunity closed roughly in his face.

This, then, is the end of his striving: to be a co-worker in the kingdom of culture, to escape both death and isolation, to husband and use his best powers and his latent genius. These powers of body and mind have in the past been strangely wasted, dispersed, or forgotten. The shadow of a mighty Negro past flits through the tale of Ethiopia the Shadowy and of Egypt the Sphinx. Throughout history, the powers of single black men flash here and there like falling stars, and die sometimes before the world has rightly gauged their brightness. Here in America, in the few days since Emancipation, the black man's turning hither and thither in hesitant and doubtful striving has often made his very strength to lose effectiveness, to seem like absence of power, like weakness. And yet it is not weakness,—it is the contradiction of double aims. The double-aimed struggle of the black artisan—on the one hand to escape white contempt for a nation of mere hewers of wood and drawers of water, and on the other hand to plough and nail and dig for a poverty-stricken horde—could only result in making him a poor craftsman, for he had but half a heart in either cause. By the poverty and ignorance of his people, the Negro minister or doctor was tempted toward quackery and demagogy; and by the criticism of the other world, toward ideals that made him ashamed of his lowly tasks. The would-be black *savant*[5] was confronted by the paradox that the knowledge his people needed was a twice-told tale to his white neighbors, while the knowledge which would teach the white world was Greek to his own flesh and blood. The innate love of harmony and beauty that set the ruder souls of his people a-dancing and a-singing raised but confusion and doubt in the soul of the black artist; for the beauty revealed to him was the soul-beauty of a race which his larger audience despised, and he could not articulate the message of another people. This waste of double aims, this seeking to satisfy two unreconciled ideals, has wrought sad havoc with the courage and faith and deeds of ten thousand thousand people,—has sent them often wooing false gods and invoking false means of salvation, and at times has even seemed about to make them ashamed of themselves.

Away back in the days of bondage they thought to see in one divine event the end of all doubt and disappointment; few men ever worshipped Freedom with half such unquestioning faith as did the American Negro for two centuries. To him, so far as he thought and dreamed, slavery was indeed the sum of all villainies, the cause of all sorrow, the root of all prejudice; Emancipation was the key to a promised land of sweeter beauty than ever stretched before the eyes of wearied Israelites. In song and exhortation swelled one refrain—Liberty; in his tears and curses the God he implored had Freedom in his right hand. At last it came,—suddenly, fearfully, like a dream. With one wild carnival of blood and passion came the message in his own plaintive cadences:—

> "Shout, O children!
> Shout, you're free!
> For God has bought your liberty!"[6]

Years have passed away since then,—ten, twenty, forty; forty years of national life, forty years of renewal and development, and yet the swarthy spectre sits in its accustomed seat at the Nation's feast. In vain do we cry to this our vastest social problem:—

> "Take any shape but that, and my firm nerves
> Shall never tremble!"[7]

The Nation has not yet found peace from its sins; the freedman has not yet found in freedom his promised land. Whatever of good may have come in these years of change, the shadow of a deep disappointment rests upon the Negro people,—a disappointment all the more bitter because the unattained ideal was unbounded save by the simple ignorance of a lowly people.

The first decade was merely a prolongation of the vain search for freedom, the boon that seemed ever barely to elude their grasp,—like a tantalizing will-o'-the-wisp,[8] maddening and misleading the headless host. The

---

5. A learned person. "Demagogy" (previous page): exploitation through appeals to emotion or prejudice.

6. Source unknown.

7. Shakespeare's *Macbeth* 3.2.99.

8. A delusive hope or goal. "Boon": a favor.

holocaust of war, the terrors of the Ku-Klux Klan, the lies of carpet-baggers,[9] the disorganization of industry, and the contradictory advice of friends and foes, left the bewildered serf with no new watchword beyond the old cry for freedom. As the time flew, however, he began to grasp a new idea. The ideal of liberty demanded for its attainment powerful means, and these the Fifteenth Amendment[1] gave him. The ballot, which before he had looked upon as a visible sign of freedom, he now regarded as the chief means of gaining and perfecting the liberty with which war had partially endowed him. And why not? Had not votes made war and emancipated millions? Had not votes enfranchised the freedmen? Was anything impossible to a power that had done all this? A million black men started with renewed zeal to vote themselves into the kingdom. So the decade flew away, the revolution of 1876[2] came, and left the half-free serf weary, wondering, but still inspired. Slowly but steadily, in the following years, a new vision began gradually to replace the dream of political power,—a powerful movement, the rise of another ideal to guide the unguided, another pillar of fire by night after a clouded day. It was the ideal of "book-learning"; the curiosity, born of compulsory ignorance, to know and test the power of the cabalistic letters of the white man, the longing to know. Here at last seemed to have been discovered the mountain path to Canaan;[3] longer than the highway of Emancipation and law, steep and rugged, but straight, leading to heights high enough to overlook life.

Up the new path the advance guard toiled, slowly, heavily, doggedly; only those who have watched and guided the faltering feet, the misty minds, the dull understandings, of the dark pupils of these schools know how faithfully, how piteously, this people strove to learn. It was weary work. The cold statistician wrote down the inches of progress here and there, noted also where here and there a foot had slipped or some one had fallen. To the tired climbers, the horizon was ever dark, the mists were often cold, the Canaan was always dim and far away. If, however, the vistas disclosed as yet no goal, no resting-place, little but flattery and criticism, the journey at least gave leisure for reflection and self-examination; it changed the child of Emancipation to the youth with dawning self-consciousness, self-realization, self-respect. In those sombre forests of his striving his own soul rose before him, and he saw himself,—darkly as through a veil; and yet he saw in himself some faint revelation of his power, of his mission. He began to have a dim feeling that, to attain his place in the world, he must be himself, and not another. For the first time he sought to analyze the burden he bore upon his back, that dead-weight of social degradation partially masked behind a half-named Negro problem. He felt his poverty; without a cent, without a home, without land, tools, or savings, he had entered into competition with rich, landed, skilled neighbors. To be a poor man is hard, but to be a poor race in a land of dollars is the very bottom of hardships. He felt the weight of his ignorance,—not simply of letters, but of life, of business, of

9. Northerners, often viewed as opportunists, who moved to the South to participate in Reconstruction. "Ku-Klux Klan": a secret society founded in the post–Civil War South to reestablish white supremacy.
1. Ratified in 1870, this amendment to the U.S. Constitution guaranteed voting rights to African American men.
2. Opposition to continuing the Reconstruction policy after the 1876 national elections.
3. In the Bible, the Promised Land of the Israelites. "Cabalistic": mystical.

the humanities; the accumulated sloth and shirking and awkwardness of decades and centuries shackled his hands and feet. Nor was his burden all poverty and ignorance. The red stain of bastardy, which two centuries of systematic legal defilement of Negro women had stamped upon his race, meant not only the loss of ancient African chastity, but also the hereditary weight of a mass of corruption from white adulterers, threatening almost the obliteration of the Negro home.

A people thus handicapped ought not to be asked to race with the world, but rather allowed to give all its time and thought to its own social problems. But alas! while sociologists gleefully count his bastards and his prostitutes, the very soul of the toiling, sweating black man is darkened by the shadow of a vast despair. Men call the shadow prejudice, and learnedly explain it as the natural defence of culture against barbarism, learning against ignorance, purity against crime, the "higher" against the "lower" races. To which the Negro cries Amen! and swears that to so much of this strange prejudice as is founded on just homage to civilization, culture, righteousness, and progress, he humbly bows and meekly does obeisance.[4] But before that nameless prejudice that leaps beyond all this he stands helpless, dismayed, and well-nigh speechless; before that personal disrespect and mockery, the ridicule and systematic humiliation, the distortion of fact and wanton license of fancy, the cynical ignoring of the better and the boisterous welcoming of the worse, the all-pervading desire to inculcate disdain for everything black, from Toussaint[5] to the devil,—before this there rises a sickening despair that would disarm and discourage any nation save that black host to whom "discouragement" is an unwritten word.

But the facing of so vast a prejudice could not but bring the inevitable self-questioning, self-disparagement, and lowering of ideals which ever accompany repression and breed in an atmosphere of contempt and hate. Whisperings and portents came borne upon the four winds: Lo! we are diseased and dying, cried the dark hosts; we cannot write, our voting is vain; what need of education, since we must always cook and serve? And the Nation echoed and enforced this self-criticism, saying: Be content to be servants, and nothing more; what need of higher culture for half-men? Away with the black man's ballot, by force or fraud,—and behold the suicide of a race! Nevertheless, out of the evil came something of good,—the more careful adjustment of education to real life, the clearer perception of the Negroes' social responsibilities, and the sobering realization of the meaning of progress.

So dawned the time of *Sturm und Drang*:[6] storm and stress to-day rocks our little boat on the mad waters of the world-sea; there is within and without the sound of conflict, the burning of body and rending of soul; inspiration strives with doubt, and faith with vain questionings. The bright ideals of the past,—physical freedom, political power, the training of brains and the training of hands,—all these in turn have waxed and waned, until even the last grows dim and overcast. Are they all wrong,—all false? No, not that, but each alone was over-simple and incomplete,—the dreams of a credu-

---

4. A gesture of respect.
5. Toussaint L'Ouverture (1743–1803), leader of a

successful slave revolution in Haiti.
6. Storm and stress (German).

lous race-childhood, or the fond imaginings of the other world which does not know and does not want to know our power. To be really true, all these ideals must be melted and welded into one. The training of the schools we need to-day more than ever,—the training of deft hands, quick eyes and ears, and above all the broader, deeper, higher culture of gifted minds and pure hearts. The power of the ballot we need in sheer self-defence,—else what shall save us from a second slavery? Freedom, too, the long-sought, we still seek,—the freedom of life and limb, the freedom to work and think, the freedom to love and aspire. Work, culture, liberty,—all these we need, not singly but together, not successively but together, each growing and aiding each, and all striving toward that vaster ideal that swims before the Negro people, the ideal of human brotherhood, gained through the unifying ideal of Race; the ideal of fostering and developing the traits and talents of the Negro, not in opposition to or contempt for other races, but rather in large conformity to the greater ideals of the American Republic, in order that some day on American soil two world-races may give each to each those characteristics both so sadly lack. We the darker ones come even now not altogether empty-handed: there are to-day no truer exponents of the pure human spirit of the Declaration of Independence than the American Negroes; there is no true American music but the wild sweet melodies of the Negro slave; the American fairy tales and folk-lore are Indian and African; and, all in all, we black men seem the sole oasis of simple faith and reverence in a dusty desert of dollars and smartness. Will America be poorer if she replace her brutal dyspeptic[7] blundering with light-hearted but determined Negro humility? or her coarse and cruel wit with loving jovial good-humor? or her vulgar music with the soul of the Sorrow Songs?

Merely a concrete test of the underlying principles of the great republic is the Negro Problem, and the spiritual striving of the freedmen's sons is the travail of souls whose burden is almost beyond the measure of their strength, but who bear it in the name of an historic race, in the name of this the land of their fathers' fathers, and in the name of human opportunity.

And now what I have briefly sketched in large outline let me on coming pages tell again in many ways, with loving emphasis and deeper detail, that men may listen to the striving in the souls of black folk.

7. Grouchy.

II. Of the Dawn of Freedom

> Careless seems the great Avenger;
> History's lessons but record
> One death-grapple in the darkness
> 'Twixt old systems and the Word;
> Truth forever on the scaffold,
> Wrong forever on the throne;
> Yet that scaffold sways the future,
> And behind the dim unknown
> Standeth God within the shadow
> Keeping watch above His own.
> LOWELL [8]

The problem of the twentieth century is the problem of the color-line,—the relation of the darker to the lighter races of men in Asia and Africa, in America and the islands of the sea. It was a phase of this problem that caused the Civil War; and however much they who marched South and North in 1861 may have fixed on the technical points of union and local autonomy as a shibboleth, [9] all nevertheless knew, as we know, that the question of Negro slavery was the real cause of the conflict. Curious it was, too, how this deeper question ever forced itself to the surface despite effort and disclaimer. No sooner had Northern armies touched Southern soil than this old question, newly guised, sprang from the earth,—What shall be done with Negroes? Peremptory military commands, this way and that, could not answer the query; the Emancipation Proclamation seemed but to broaden and intensify the difficulties; and the War Amendments made the Negro problems of to-day.

It is the aim of this essay to study the period of history from 1861 to 1872 so far as it relates to the American Negro. In effect, this tale of the dawn of Freedom is an account of that government of men called the Freedmen's Bureau, [1]—one of the most singular and interesting of the attempts made by a great nation to grapple with vast problems of race and social condition.

The war has naught to do with slaves, cried Congress, the President, and the Nation; and yet no sooner had the armies, East and West, penetrated Virginia and Tennessee than fugitive slaves appeared within their lines. They came at night, when the flickering camp-fires shone like vast unsteady stars along the black horizon: old men and thin, with gray and tufted hair; women, with frightened eyes, dragging whimpering hungry children; men and girls, stalwart and gaunt,—a horde of starving vagabonds, homeless, helpless, and pitiable, in their dark distress. Two methods of treating these newcomers seemed equally logical to opposite sorts of minds. Ben

---

8. James Russell Lowell (1819–1891), popular American poet. The quotation is from *The Present Crisis* (1844).

9. A test or password.
1. Agency established in 1865 by Congress to aid freed slaves and destitute whites.

Butler, in Virginia, quickly declared slave property contraband of war, and put the fugitives to work; while Fremont, in Missouri, declared the slaves free under martial law. Butler's action was approved, but Fremont's was hastily countermanded, and his successor, Halleck,[2] saw things differently. "Hereafter," he commanded, "no slaves should be allowed to come into your lines at all; if any come without your knowledge, when owners call for them deliver them." Such a policy was difficult to enforce; some of the black refugees declared themselves freemen, others showed that their masters had deserted them, and still others were captured with forts and plantations. Evidently, too, slaves were a source of strength to the Confederacy, and were being used as laborers and producers. "They constitute a military resource," wrote Secretary Cameron,[3] late in 1861; "and being such, that they should not be turned over to the enemy is too plain to discuss." So gradually the tone of the army chiefs changed; Congress forbade the rendition[4] of fugitives, and Butler's "contrabands" were welcomed as military laborers. This complicated rather than solved the problem, for now the scattering fugitives became a steady stream, which flowed faster as the armies marched.

Then the long-headed man with care-chiselled face who sat in the White House saw the inevitable, and emancipated the slaves of rebels on New Year's, 1863. A month later Congress called earnestly for the Negro soldiers whom the act of July, 1862, had half grudgingly allowed to enlist. Thus the barriers were levelled and the deed was done. The stream of fugitives swelled to a flood, and anxious army officers kept inquiring: "What must be done with slaves, arriving almost daily? Are we to find food and shelter for women and children?"

It was a Pierce of Boston who pointed out the way, and thus became in a sense the founder of the Freedmen's Bureau. He was a firm friend of Secretary Chase; and when, in 1861, the care of slaves and abandoned lands devolved upon the Treasury officials, Pierce was specially detailed from the ranks to study the conditions. First, he cared for the refugees at Fortress Monroe; and then, after Sherman[5] had captured Hilton Head, Pierce was sent there to found his Port Royal experiment[6] of making free workingmen out of slaves. Before his experiment was barely started, however, the problem of the fugitives had assumed such proportions that it was taken from the hands of the over-burdened Treasury Department and given to the army officials. Already centres of massed freedmen were forming at Fortress Monroe, Washington, New Orleans, Vicksburg and Corinth, Columbus, Ky., and Cairo, Ill., as well as at Port Royal. Army chaplains found here new and fruitful fields; "superintendents of contrabands" multiplied, and some attempt at systematic work was made by enlisting the able-bodied men and giving work to the others.

Then came the Freedmen's Aid societies, born of the touching appeals from Pierce and from these other centres of distress. There was the Ameri-

2. Henry Wager Halleck (1815–1872), general in chief of the Union army (1862–64). Benjamin Franklin Butler (1818–1893) and John Charles Fremont (1813–1890) were Union army generals.
3. Simon Cameron (1799–1889), U.S. secretary of war (1861–62).
4. Surrender.

5. William Tecumseh Sherman (1820–1891), Union army general. Edward Lillie Pierce (1829–1897), antislavery activist. Salmon Portland Chase (1808–1873), secretary of the treasury (1861–64).
6. An effort by northern reformers and the U.S. Army to train former slaves for freedom on the Sea Islands, South Carolina, from 1862 to 1865.

can Missionary Association, sprung from the *Amistad*, [7] and now full-grown for work; the various church organizations, the National Freedmen's Relief Association, the American Freedmen's Union, the Western Freedmen's Aid Commission,—in all fifty or more active organizations, which sent clothes, money, school-books, and teachers southward. All they did was needed, for the destitution of the freedmen was often reported as "too appalling for belief," and the situation was daily growing worse rather than better.

And daily, too, it seemed more plain that this was no ordinary matter of temporary relief, but a national crisis; for here loomed a labor problem of vast dimensions. Masses of Negroes stood idle, or, if they worked spasmodically, were never sure of pay; and if perchance they received pay, squandered the new thing thoughtlessly. In these and other ways were camp-life and the new liberty demoralizing the freedmen. The broader economic organization thus clearly demanded sprang up here and there as accident and local conditions determined. Here it was that Pierce's Port Royal plan of leased plantations and guided workmen pointed out the rough way. In Washington the military governor, at the urgent appeal of the superintendent, opened confiscated estates to the cultivation of the fugitives, and there in the shadow of the dome gathered black farm villages. General Dix gave over estates to the freedmen of Fortress Monroe, and so on, South and West. The government and benevolent societies furnished the means of cultivation, and the Negro turned again slowly to work. The systems of control, thus started, rapidly grew, here and there, into strange little governments, like that of General Banks in Louisiana, with its ninety thousand black subjects, its fifty thousand guided laborers, and its annual budget of one hundred thousand dollars and more. It made out four thousand payrolls a year, registered all freedmen, inquired into grievances and redressed them, laid and collected taxes, and established a system of public schools. So, too, Colonel Eaton, the superintendent of Tennessee and Arkansas, ruled over one hundred thousand freedmen, leased and cultivated seven thousand acres of cotton land, and fed ten thousand paupers a year. In South Carolina was General Saxton, with his deep interest in black folk. He succeeded Pierce and the Treasury officials, and sold forfeited estates, leased abandoned plantations, encouraged schools, and received from Sherman, after that terribly picturesque march to the sea, thousands of the wretched camp followers.

Three characteristic things one might have seen in Sherman's raid through Georgia, which threw the new situation in shadowy relief: the Conqueror, the Conquered, and the Negro. Some see all significance in the grim front of the destroyer, and some in the bitter sufferers of the Lost Cause. But to me neither soldier nor fugitive speaks with so deep a meaning as that dark human cloud that clung like remorse on the rear of those swift columns, swelling at times to half their size, almost engulfing and choking them. In vain were they ordered back, in vain were bridges hewn from beneath their feet; on they trudged and writhed and surged, until they rolled into Savannah, a starved and naked horde of tens of thousands.

---

7. A Spanish slave ship on which fifty-four slaves mutinied in 1839; they were declared free by a U.S. Supreme Court decision in 1841.

There too came the characteristic military remedy: "The islands from Charleston south, the abandoned rice-fields along the rivers for thirty miles back from the sea, and the country bordering the St. John's River, Florida, are reserved and set apart for the settlement of Negroes now made free by act of war." So read the celebrated "Field-order Number Fifteen."[8]

All these experiments, orders, and systems were bound to attract and perplex the government and the nation. Directly after the Emancipation Proclamation, Representative Eliot[9] had introduced a bill creating a Bureau of Emancipation; but it was never reported. The following June a committee of inquiry, appointed by the Secretary of War, reported in favor of a temporary bureau for the "improvement, protection, and employment of refugee freedmen," on much the same lines as were afterwards followed. Petitions came in to President Lincoln from distinguished citizens and organizations, strongly urging a comprehensive and unified plan of dealing with the freedmen, under a bureau which should be "charged with the study of plans and execution of measures for easily guiding, and in every way judiciously and humanely aiding, the passage of our emancipated and yet to be emancipated blacks from the old condition of forced labor to their new state of voluntary industry."

Some half-hearted steps were taken to accomplish this, in part, by putting the whole matter again in charge of the special Treasury agents. Laws of 1863 and 1864 directed them to take charge of and lease abandoned lands for periods not exceeding twelve months, and to "provide in such leases, or otherwise, for the employment and general welfare" of the freedmen. Most of the army officers greeted this as a welcome relief from perplexing "Negro affairs," and Secretary Fessenden, July 29, 1864, issued an excellent system of regulations, which were afterward closely followed by General Howard.[1] Under Treasury agents, large quantities of land were leased in the Mississippi Valley, and many Negroes were employed; but in August, 1864, the new regulations were suspended for reasons of "public policy," and the army was again in control.

Meanwhile Congress had turned its attention to the subject; and in March the House passed a bill by a majority of two establishing a Bureau for Freedmen in the War Department. Charles Sumner,[2] who had charge of the bill in the Senate, argued that freedmen and abandoned lands ought to be under the same department, and reported a substitute for the House bill attaching the Bureau to the Treasury Department. This bill passed, but too late for action by the House. The debates wandered over the whole policy of the administration and the general question of slavery, without touching very closely the specific merits of the measure in hand. Then the national election took place; and the administration, with a vote of renewed confidence from the country, addressed itself to the matter more seriously. A conference between the two branches of Congress agreed upon a carefully drawn measure which contained the chief provisions of Sumner's bill, but made the proposed organization a department independent of both the War and the Treasury officials. The bill was conservative, giving the new depart-

8. Given in January 1865 by General Sherman.
9. Thomas Dawes Eliot (1808–1870) of Massachusetts.
1. Oliver Otis Howard (1830–1909), Union army general and chief commissioner of the Freedmen's

Bureau in 1865. William Pitt Fessenden (1806–1869), secretary of the treasury (1864–65).
2. U.S. Senator (1811–1874) from Massachusetts from 1851 to 1874.

ment "general superintendence of all freedmen." Its purpose was to "establish regulations" for them, protect them, lease them lands, adjust their wages, and appear in civil and military courts as their "next friend." There were many limitations attached to the powers thus granted, and the organization was made permanent. Nevertheless, the Senate defeated the bill, and a new conference committee was appointed. This committee reported a new bill, February 28, which was whirled through just as the session closed, and became the act of 1865 establishing in the War Department a "Bureau of Refugees, Freedmen, and Abandoned Lands."

This last compromise was a hasty bit of legislation, vague and uncertain in outline. A Bureau was created, "to continue during the present War of Rebellion, and for one year thereafter," to which was given "the supervision and management of all abandoned lands and the control of all subjects relating to refugees and freedmen," under "such rules and regulations as may be presented by the head of the Bureau and approved by the President." A Commissioner, appointed by the President and Senate, was to control the Bureau, with an office force not exceeding ten clerks. The President might also appoint assistant commissioners in the seceded States, and to all these offices military officials might be detailed at regular pay. The Secretary of War could issue rations, clothing, and fuel to the destitute, and all abandoned property was placed in the hands of the Bureau for eventual lease and sale to ex-slaves in forty-acre parcels.

Thus did the United States government definitely assume charge of the emancipated Negro as the ward of the nation. It was a tremendous undertaking. Here at a stroke of the pen was erected a government of millions of men,—and not ordinary men either, but black men emasculated by a peculiarly complete system of slavery, centuries old; and now, suddenly, violently, they come into a new birthright, at a time of war and passion, in the midst of the stricken and embittered population of their former masters. Any man might well have hesitated to assume charge of such a work, with vast responsibilities, indefinite powers, and limited resources. Probably no one but a soldier would have answered such a call promptly; and, indeed, no one but a soldier could be called, for Congress had appropriated no money for salaries and expenses.

Less than a month after the weary Emancipator passed to his rest, his successor[3] assigned Major-Gen. Oliver O. Howard to duty as Commissioner of the new Bureau. He was a Maine man, then only thirty-five years of age. He had marched with Sherman to the sea, had fought well at Gettysburg, and but the year before had been assigned to the command of the Department of Tennessee. An honest man, with too much faith in human nature, little aptitude for business and intricate detail, he had had large opportunity of becoming acquainted at first hand with much of the work before him. And of that work it has been truly said that "no approximately correct history of civilization can ever be written which does not throw out in bold relief, as one of the great landmarks of political and social progress, the organization and administration of the Freedmen's Bureau."

On May 12, 1865, Howard was appointed; and he assumed the duties of his office promptly on the 15th, and began examining the field of work. A

3. Andrew Johnson (1808–1875), U.S. president (1865–69).

curious mess he looked upon: little despotisms, communistic experiments, slavery, peonage,[4] business speculations, organized charity, unorganized almsgiving,—all reeling on under the guise of helping the freedmen, and all enshrined in the smoke and blood of war and the cursing and silence of angry men. On May 19 the new government—for a government it really was—issued its constitution; commissioners were to be appointed in each of the seceded States, who were to take charge of "all subjects relating to refugees and freedmen," and all relief and rations were to be given by their consent alone. The Bureau invited continued coöperation with benevolent societies, and declared: "It will be the object of all commissioners to introduce practicable systems of compensated labor," and to establish schools. Forthwith nine assistant commissioners were appointed. They were to hasten to their fields of work; seek gradually to close relief establishments, and make the destitute self-supporting; act as courts of law where there were no courts, or where Negroes were not recognized in them as free; establish the institution of marriage among ex-slaves, and keep records; see that freedmen were free to choose their employers, and help in making fair contracts for them; and finally, the circular said: "Simple good faith, for which we hope on all hands for those concerned in the passing away of slavery, will especially relieve the assistant commissioners in the discharge of their duties toward the freedmen, as well as promote the general welfare."

No sooner was the work thus started, and the general system and local organization in some measure begun, than two grave difficulties appeared which changed largely the theory and outcome of Bureau work. First, there were the abandoned lands of the South. It had long been the more or less definitely expressed theory of the North that all the chief problems of Emancipation might be settled by establishing the slaves on the forfeited lands of their masters,—a sort of poetic justice, said some. But this poetry done into solemn prose meant either wholesale confiscation of private property in the South, or vast appropriations. Now Congress had not appropriated a cent, and no sooner did the proclamations of general amnesty appear than the eight hundred thousand acres of abandoned lands in the hands of the Freedmen's Bureau melted quickly away. The second difficulty lay in perfecting the local organization of the Bureau throughout the wide field of work. Making a new machine and sending out officials of duly ascertained fitness for a great work of social reform is no child's task; but this task was even harder, for a new central organization had to be fitted on a heterogeneous and confused but already existing system of relief and control of ex-slaves; and the agents available for this work must be sought for in an army still busy with war operations,—men in the very nature of the case ill fitted for delicate social work,—or among the questionable camp followers of an invading host. Thus, after a year's work, vigorously as it was pushed, the problem looked even more difficult to grasp and solve than at the beginning. Nevertheless, three things that year's work did, well worth the doing: it relieved a vast amount of physical suffering; it transported seven thousand fugitives from congested centres back to the farm; and, best of all, it inaugurated the crusade of the New England school-ma'am.

The annals of this Ninth Crusade are yet to be written,—the tale of a

4. A form of debt servitude imposed on former slaves.

mission that seemed to our age far more quixotic than the quest of St. Louis[5] seemed to his. Behind the mists of ruin and rapine waved the calico dresses of women who dared, and after the hoarse mouthings of the field guns rang the rhythm of the alphabet. Rich and poor they were, serious and curious. Bereaved now of a father, now of a brother, now of more than these, they came seeking a life work in planting New England school-houses among the white and black of the South. They did their work well. In that first year they taught one hundred thousand souls, and more.

Evidently, Congress must soon legislate again on the hastily organized Bureau, which had so quickly grown into wide significance and vast possibilities. An institution such as that was well-nigh as difficult to end as to begin. Early in 1866 Congress took up the matter, when Senator Trumbull, of Illinois, introduced a bill to extend the Bureau and enlarge its powers. This measure received, at the hands of Congress, far more thorough discussion and attention than its predecessor. The war cloud had thinned enough to allow a clearer conception of the work of Emancipation. The champions of the bill argued that the strengthening of the Freedmen's Bureau was still a military necessity; that it was needed for the proper carrying out of the Thirteenth Amendment,[6] and was a work of sheer justice to the ex-slave, at a trifling cost to the government. The opponents of the measure declared that the war was over, and the necessity for war measures past; that the Bureau, by reason of its extraordinary powers, was clearly unconstitutional in time of peace, and was destined to irritate the South and pauperize the freedmen, at a final cost of possibly hundreds of millions. These two arguments were unanswered, and indeed unanswerable: the one that the extraordinary powers of the Bureau threatened the civil rights of all citizens; and the other that the government must have power to do what manifestly must be done, and that present abandonment of the freedmen meant their practical re-enslavement. The bill which finally passed enlarged and made permanent the Freedmen's Bureau. It was promptly vetoed by President Johnson as "unconstitutional," "unnecessary," and "extrajudicial," and failed of passage over the veto. Meantime, however, the breach between Congress and the President began to broaden, and a modified form of the lost bill was finally passed over the President's second veto, July 16.

The act of 1866 gave the Freedmen's Bureau its final form,—the form by which it will be known to posterity and judged of men. It extended the existence of the Bureau to July, 1868; it authorized additional assistant commissioners, the retention of army officers mustered out of regular service, the sale of certain forfeited lands to freedmen on nominal terms, the sale of Confederate public property for Negro schools, and a wider field of judicial interpretation and cognizance. The government of the unreconstructed South was thus put very largely in the hands of the Freedmen's Bureau, especially as in many cases the departmental military commander was now made also assistant commissioner. It was thus that the Freedmen's Bureau became a full-fledged government of men. It made laws, executed

---

5. Louis IX, king of France (1214–1270), who was the leader of the Seventh Crusade in 1248. During the Middle Ages, nine crusades were undertaken by European Christians to recover the Holy Land from the Muslims. "Quixotic": impracticably idealistic.
6. A constitutional amendment that abolished slavery in 1865.

them and interpreted them; it laid and collected taxes, defined and punished crime, maintained and used military force, and dictated such measures as it thought necessary and proper for the accomplishment of its varied ends. Naturally, all these powers were not exercised continuously nor to their fullest extent; and yet, as General Howard has said, "scarcely any subject that has to be legislated upon in civil society failed, at one time or another, to demand the action of this singular Bureau."

To understand and criticise intelligently so vast a work, one must not forget an instant the drift of things in the later sixties. Lee had surrendered, Lincoln was dead, and Johnson and Congress were at loggerheads; the Thirteenth Amendment was adopted, the Fourteenth pending, and the Fifteenth declared in force in 1870. Guerrilla raiding, the ever-present flickering after-flame of war, was spending its force against the Negroes, and all the Southern land was awakening as from some wild dream to poverty and social revolution. In a time of perfect calm, amid willing neighbors and streaming wealth, the social uplifting of four million slaves to an assured and self-sustaining place in the body politic and economic would have been a herculean task; but when to the inherent difficulties of so delicate and nice a social operation were added the spite and hate of conflict, the hell of war; when suspicion and cruelty were rife, and gaunt Hunger wept beside Bereavement,—in such a case, the work of any instrument of social regeneration was in large part foredoomed to failure. The very name of the Bureau stood for a thing in the South which for two centuries and better men had refused even to argue,—that life amid free Negroes was simply unthinkable, the maddest of experiments.

The agents that the Bureau could command varied all the way from unselfish philanthropists to narrow-minded busy-bodies and thieves; and even though it be true that the average was far better than the worst, it was the occasional fly that helped spoil the ointment.

Then amid all crouched the freed slave, bewildered between friend and foe. He had emerged from slavery,—not the worst slavery in the world, not a slavery that made all life unbearable, rather a slavery that had here and there something of kindliness, fidelity, and happiness,—but withal slavery, which, so far as human aspiration and desert were concerned, classed the black man and the ox together. And the Negro knew full well that, whatever their deeper convictions may have been, Southern men had fought with desperate energy to perpetuate this slavery under which the black masses, with half-articulate thought, had writhed and shivered. They welcomed freedom with a cry. They shrank from the master who still strove for their chains; they fled to the friends that had freed them, even though those friends stood ready to use them as a club for driving the recalcitrant South back into loyalty. So the cleft between the white and black South grew. Idle to say it never should have been; it was as inevitable as its results were pitiable. Curiously incongruous elements were left arrayed against each other,—the North, the government, the carpet-bagger, and the slave, here; and there, all the South that was white, whether gentleman or vagabond, honest man or rascal, lawless murderer or martyr to duty.

Thus it is doubly difficult to write of this period calmly, so intense was the feeling, so mighty the human passions that swayed and blinded men.

Amid it all, two figures ever stand to typify that day to coming ages,—the one, a gray-haired gentleman, whose fathers had quit themselves like men, whose sons lay in nameless graves; who bowed to the evil of slavery because its abolition threatened untold ill to all; who stood at last, in the evening of life, a blighted, ruined form, with hate in his eyes;—and the other, a form hovering dark and mother-like, her awful face black with the mists of centuries, had aforetime quailed at that white master's command, had bent in love over the cradles of his sons and daughters, and closed in death the sunken eyes of his wife,—aye, too, at his behest had laid herself low to his lust, and borne a tawny man-child to the world, only to see her dark boy's limbs scattered to the winds by midnight marauders riding after "cursed Niggers." These were the saddest sights of that woful day; and no man clasped the hands of these two passing figures of the present-past; but, hating, they went to their long home, and, hating, their children's children live to-day.

Here, then, was the field of work for the Freedmen's Bureau; and since, with some hesitation, it was continued by the act of 1868 until 1869, let us look upon four years of its work as a whole. There were, in 1868, nine hundred Bureau officials scattered from Washington to Texas, ruling, directly and indirectly, many millions of men. The deeds of these rulers fall mainly under seven heads: the relief of physical suffering, the overseeing of the beginnings of free labor, the buying and selling of land, the establishment of schools, the paying of bounties, the administration of justice, and the financiering of all these activities.

Up to June, 1869, over half a million patients had been treated by Bureau physicians and surgeons, and sixty hospitals and asylums had been in operation. In fifty months twenty-one million free rations were distributed at a cost of over four million dollars. Next came the difficult question of labor. First, thirty thousand black men were transported from the refuges and relief stations back to the farms, back to the critical trial of a new way of working. Plain instructions went out from Washington: the laborers must be free to choose their employers, no fixed rate of wages was prescribed, and there was to be no peonage or forced labor. So far, so good; but where local agents differed *toto cœlo* in capacity and character, where the *personnel* [7] was continually changing, the outcome was necessarily varied. The largest element of success lay in the fact that the majority of the freedmen were willing, even eager, to work. So labor contracts were written,—fifty thousand in a single State,—laborers advised, wages guaranteed, and employers supplied. In truth, the organization became a vast labor bureau,—not perfect, indeed, notably defective here and there, but on the whole successful beyond the dreams of thoughtful men. The two great obstacles which confronted the officials were the tyrant and the idler,—the slaveholder who was determined to perpetuate slavery under another name; and the freedman who regarded freedom as perpetual rest,—the Devil and the Deep Sea.

In the work of establishing the Negroes as peasant proprietors, the Bureau was from the first handicapped and at last absolutely checked. Something was done, and larger things were planned; abandoned lands were leased so long as they remained in the hands of the Bureau, and a total

---

7. Persons employed in any work. "*Toto cœlo*": utterly (Latin).

revenue of nearly half a million dollars derived from black tenants. Some other lands to which the nation had gained title were sold on easy terms, and public lands were opened for settlement to the very few freedmen who had tools and capital. But the vision of "forty acres and a mule"—the righteous and reasonable ambition to become a landholder, which the nation had all but categorically promised the freedmen—was destined in most cases to bitter disappointment. And those men of marvellous hindsight who are to-day seeking to preach the Negro back to the present peonage of the soil know well, or ought to know, that the opportunity of binding the Negro peasant willingly to the soil was lost on that day when the Commissioner of the Freedmen's Bureau had to go to South Carolina and tell the weeping freedmen, after their years of toil, that their land was not theirs, that there was a mistake—somewhere. If by 1874 the Georgia Negro alone owned three hundred and fifty thousand acres of land, it was by grace of his thrift rather than by bounty of the government.

The greatest success of the Freedmen's Bureau lay in the planting of the free school among Negroes, and the idea of free elementary education among all classes in the South. It not only called the schoolmistresses through the benevolent agencies and built them schoolhouses, but it helped discover and support such apostles of human culture as Edmund Ware, Samuel Armstrong, and Erastus Cravath. [8] The opposition to Negro education in the South was at first bitter, and showed itself in ashes, insult, and blood; for the South believed an educated Negro to be a dangerous Negro. And the South was not wholly wrong; for education among all kinds of men always has had, and always will have, an element of danger and revolution, of dissatisfaction and discontent. Nevertheless, men strive to know. Perhaps some inkling of this paradox, even in the unquiet days of the Bureau, helped the bayonets allay an opposition to human training which still to-day lies smouldering in the South, but not flaming. Fisk, Atlanta, Howard, and Hampton [9] were founded in these days, and six million dollars were expended for educational work, seven hundred and fifty thousand dollars of which the freedmen themselves gave of their poverty.

Such contributions, together with the buying of land and various other enterprises, showed that the ex-slave was handling some free capital already. The chief initial source of this was labor in the army, and his pay and bounty as a soldier. Payments to Negro soldiers were at first complicated by the ignorance of the recipients, and the fact that the quotas of colored regiments from Northern States were largely filled by recruits from the South, unknown to their fellow soldiers. Consequently, payments were accompanied by such frauds that Congress, by joint resolution in 1867, put the whole matter in the hands of the Freedmen's Bureau. In two years six million dollars was thus distributed to five thousand claimants, and in the end the sum exceeded eight million dollars. Even in this system fraud was frequent; but still the work put needed capital in the hands of practical paupers, and some, at least, was well spent.

The most perplexing and least successful part of the Bureau's work lay in

8. First president of Fisk University (1833–1900). Edmund Asa Ware (1837–1885), founder of Atlanta University. Samuel Chapman Armstrong (1839–1893), founder of Hampton Institute.

9. Colleges for African Americans founded after the Civil War in Nashville, Tennessee; Atlanta, Georgia; Washington, D.C.; and Hampton, Virginia, respectively.

the exercise of its judicial functions. The regular Bureau court consisted of
one representative of the employer, one of the Negro, and one of the Bureau. If the Bureau could have maintained a perfectly judicial attitude, this
arrangement would have been ideal, and must in time have gained confidence; but the nature of its other activities and the character of its *personnel*
prejudiced the Bureau in favor of the black litigants, and led without doubt
to much injustice and annoyance. On the other hand, to leave the Negro
in the hands of Southern courts was impossible. In a distracted land where
slavery had hardly fallen, to keep the strong from wanton abuse of the weak,
and the weak from gloating insolently over the half-shorn strength of the
strong, was a thankless, hopeless task. The former masters of the land were
peremptorily ordered about, seized, and imprisoned, and punished over
and again, with scant courtesy from army officers. The former slaves were
intimidated, beaten, raped, and butchered by angry and revengeful men.
Bureau courts tended to become centres simply for punishing whites,
while the regular civil courts tended to become solely institutions for perpetuating the slavery of blacks. Almost every law and method ingenuity
could devise was employed by the legislatures to reduce the Negroes to
serfdom,—to make them the slaves of the State, if not of individual owners;
while the Bureau officials too often were found striving to put the "bottom
rail on top," and give the freedmen a power and independence which they
could not yet use. It is all well enough for us of another generation to wax
wise with advice to those who bore the burden in the heat of the day. It is
full easy now to see that the man who lost home, fortune, and family at a
stroke, and saw his land ruled by "mules and niggers," was really benefited
by the passing of slavery. It is not difficult now to say to the young freedman, cheated and cuffed about, who has seen his father's head beaten to a
jelly and his own mother namelessly assaulted, that the meek shall inherit
the earth. Above all, nothing is more convenient than to heap on the
Freedmen's Bureau all the evils of that evil day, and damn it utterly for
every mistake and blunder that was made.

All this is easy, but it is neither sensible nor just. Some one had blundered, but that was long before Oliver Howard was born; there was criminal aggression and heedless neglect, but without some system of control
there would have been far more than there was. Had that control been
from within, the Negro would have been re-enslaved, to all intents and purposes. Coming as the control did from without, perfect men and methods
would have bettered all things; and even with imperfect agents and questionable methods, the work accomplished was not undeserving of commendation.

Such was the dawn of Freedom; such was the work of the Freedmen's
Bureau, which, summed up in brief, may be epitomized thus: For some
fifteen million dollars, beside the sums spent before 1865, and the dole of
benevolent societies, this Bureau set going a system of free labor, established a beginning of peasant proprietorship, secured the recognition of
black freedmen before courts of law, and founded the free common school
in the South. On the other hand, it failed to begin the establishment of
good-will between ex-masters and freedmen, to guard its work wholly from
paternalistic methods which discouraged self-reliance, and to carry out to
any considerable extent its implied promises to furnish the freedmen with

land. Its successes were the result of hard work, supplemented by the aid of philanthropists and the eager striving of black men. Its failures were the result of bad local agents, the inherent difficulties of the work, and national neglect.

Such an institution, from its wide powers, great responsibilities, large control of moneys, and generally conspicuous position, was naturally open to repeated and bitter attack. It sustained a searching Congressional investigation at the instance of Fernando Wood[1] in 1870. Its archives and few remaining functions were with blunt discourtesy transferred from Howard's control, in his absence, to the supervision of Secretary of War Belknap in 1872, on the Secretary's recommendation. Finally, in consequence of grave intimations of wrong-doing made by the Secretary and his subordinates, General Howard was court-martialed in 1874. In both of these trials the Commissioner of the Freedmen's Bureau was officially exonerated from any wilful misdoing, and his work commended. Nevertheless, many unpleasant things were brought to light,—the methods of transacting the business of the Bureau were faulty; several cases of defalcation[2] were proved, and other frauds strongly suspected; there were some business transactions which savored of dangerous speculation, if not dishonesty; and around it all lay the smirch of the Freedmen's Bank.

Morally and practically, the Freedmen's Bank was part of the Freedmen's Bureau, although it had no legal connection with it. With the prestige of the government back of it, and a directing board of unusual respectability and national reputation, this banking institution had made a remarkable start in the development of that thrift among black folk which slavery had kept them from knowing. Then in one sad day came the crash,—all the hard-earned dollars of the freedmen disappeared; but that was the least of the loss,—all the faith in saving went too, and much of the faith in men; and that was a loss that a Nation which to-day sneers at Negro shiftlessness has never yet made good. Not even ten additional years of slavery could have done so much to throttle the thrift of the freedmen as the mismanagement and bankruptcy of the series of savings banks chartered by the Nation for their especial aid. Where all the blame should rest, it is hard to say; whether the Bureau and the Bank died chiefly by reason of the blows of its selfish friends or the dark machinations of its foes, perhaps even time will never reveal, for here lies unwritten history.

Of the foes without the Bureau, the bitterest were those who attacked not so much its conduct or policy under the law as the necessity for any such institution at all. Such attacks came primarily from the Border States and the South; and they were summed up by Senator Davis, of Kentucky, when he moved to entitle the act of 1866 a bill "to promote strife and conflict between the white and black races . . . by a grant of unconstitutional power." The argument gathered tremendous strength South and North; but its very strength was its weakness. For, argued the plain common-sense of the nation, if it is unconstitutional, unpractical, and futile for the nation to stand guardian over its helpless wards, then there is left but one alternative,—to make those wards their own guardians by arming them with the

---

1. Twice a congressman from New York City, 1863–65 and 1867–81.
2. Embezzlement of money.

ballot. Moreover, the path of the practical politician pointed the same way;
for, argued this opportunist, if we cannot peacefully reconstruct the South
with white votes, we certainly can with black votes. So justice and force
joined hands.

The alternative thus offered the nation was not between full and restricted Negro suffrage; else every sensible man, black and white, would
easily have chosen the latter. It was rather a choice between suffrage and
slavery, after endless blood and gold had flowed to sweep human bondage
away. Not a single Southern legislature stood ready to admit a Negro,
under any conditions, to the polls; not a single Southern legislature believed free Negro labor was possible without a system of restrictions that
took all its freedom away; there was scarcely a white man in the South who
did not honestly regard Emancipation as a crime, and its practical nullification as a duty. In such a situation, the granting of the ballot to the black
man was a necessity, the very least a guilty nation could grant a wronged
race, and the only method of compelling the South to accept the results of
the war. Thus Negro suffrage ended a civil war by beginning a race feud.
And some felt gratitude toward the race thus sacrificed in its swaddling
clothes on the altar of national integrity; and some felt and feel only indifference and contempt.

Had political exigencies been less pressing, the opposition to government guardianship of Negroes less bitter, and the attachment to the slave
system less strong, the social seer can well imagine a far better policy,—a
permanent Freedmen's Bureau, with a national system of Negro schools; a
carefully supervised employment and labor office; a system of impartial
protection before the regular courts; and such institutions for social betterment as savings-banks, land and building associations, and social settlements. All this vast expenditure of money and brains might have formed a
great school of prospective citizenship, and solved in a way we have not yet
solved the most perplexing and persistent of the Negro problems.

That such an institution was unthinkable in 1870 was due in part to certain acts of the Freedmen's Bureau itself. It came to regard its work as
merely temporary, and Negro suffrage as a final answer to all present perplexities. The political ambition of many of its agents and *protégés* led it far
afield into questionable activities, until the South, nursing its own deep
prejudices, came easily to ignore all the good deeds of the Bureau and hate
its very name with perfect hatred. So the Freedmen's Bureau died, and its
child was the Fifteenth Amendment.

The passing of a great human institution before its work is done, like the
untimely passing of a single soul, but leaves a legacy of striving for other
men. The legacy of the Freedmen's Bureau is the heavy heritage of this
generation. To-day, when new and vaster problems are destined to strain
every fibre of the national mind and soul, would it not be well to count this
legacy honestly and carefully? For this much all men know: despite compromise, war, and struggle, the Negro is not free. In the backwoods of the
Gulf States, for miles and miles, he may not leave the plantation of his
birth; in well-nigh the whole rural South the black farmers are peons,
bound by law and custom to an economic slavery, from which the only
escape is death or the penitentiary. In the most cultured sections and cities
of the South the Negroes are a segregated servile caste, with restricted

rights and privileges. Before the courts, both in law and custom, they stand on a different and peculiar basis. Taxation without representation is the rule of their political life. And the result of all this is, and in nature must have been, lawlessness and crime. That is the large legacy of the Freedmen's Bureau, the work it did not do because it could not.

I have seen a land right merry with the sun, where children sing, and rolling hills lie like passioned women wanton with harvest. And there in the King's Highway sat and sits a figure veiled and bowed, by which the traveller's footsteps hasten as they go. On the tainted air broods fear. Three centuries' thought has been the raising and unveiling of that bowed human heart, and now behold a century new for the duty and the deed. The problem of the Twentieth Century is the problem of the color-line.

III. Of Mr. Booker T. Washington and Others

From birth till death enslaved; in word, in deed, unmanned!
. . . .
Hereditary bondsmen! Know ye not
Who would be free themselves must strike the blow?

BYRON[3]

Easily the most striking thing in the history of the American Negro since 1876 is the ascendancy of Mr. Booker T. Washington. It began at the time when war memories and ideals were rapidly passing; a day of astonishing commercial development was dawning; a sense of doubt and hesitation overtook the freedmen's sons,—then it was that his leading began. Mr. Washington came, with a simple definite programme, at the psychological moment when the nation was a little ashamed of having bestowed so much sentiment on Negroes, and was concentrating its energies on Dollars. His programme of industrial education, conciliation of the South, and submission and silence as to civil and political rights, was not wholly original; the Free Negroes from 1830 up to wartime had striven to build industrial schools, and the American Missionary Association had from the first taught various trades; and Price[4] and others had sought a way of honorable alliance with the best of the Southerners. But Mr. Washington first indissolubly linked these things; he put enthusiasm, unlimited energy, and perfect faith into this programme, and changed it from a by-path into a veritable Way of Life. And the tale of the methods by which he did this is a fascinating study of human life.

It startled the nation to hear a Negro advocating such a programme after

3. George Gordon, Lord Byron (1788–1824), British poet. The quotation is from *Childe Harold's Pilgrimage* (1812).

4. Joseph Charles Price (1854–1893), southern orator, educator, and moderate civil rights spokesman.

many decades of bitter complaint; it startled and won the applause of the South, it interested and won the admiration of the North; and after a confused murmur of protest, it silenced if it did not convert the Negroes themselves.

To gain the sympathy and coöperation of the various elements comprising the white South was Mr. Washington's first task; and this, at the time Tuskegee[5] was founded, seemed, for a black man, well-nigh impossible. And yet ten years later it was done in the word spoken at Atlanta: "In all things purely social we can be as separate as the five fingers, and yet one as the hand in all things essential to mutual progress." This "Atlanta Compromise" is by all odds the most notable thing in Mr. Washington's career. The South interpreted it in different ways: the radicals received it as a complete surrender of the demand for civil and political equality; the conservatives, as a generously conceived working basis for mutual understanding. So both approved it, and to-day its author is certainly the most distinguished Southerner since Jefferson Davis, and the one with the largest personal following.

Next to this achievement comes Mr. Washington's work in gaining place and consideration in the North. Others less shrewd and tactful had formerly essayed to sit on these two stools and had fallen between them; but as Mr. Washington knew the heart of the South from birth and training, so by singular insight he intuitively grasped the spirit of the age which was dominating the North. And so thoroughly did he learn the speech and thought of triumphant commercialism, and the ideals of material prosperity, that the picture of a lone black boy poring over a French grammar amid the weeds and dirt of a neglected home soon seemed to him the acme of absurdities. One wonders what Socrates and St. Francis of Assisi[6] would say to this.

And yet this very singleness of vision and thorough oneness with his age is a mark of the successful man. It is as though Nature must needs make men narrow in order to give them force. So Mr. Washington's cult has gained unquestioning followers, his work has wonderfully prospered, his friends are legion, and his enemies are confounded. To-day he stands as the one recognized spokesman of his ten million fellows, and one of the most notable figures in a nation of seventy millions. One hesitates, therefore, to criticise a life which, beginning with so little, has done so much. And yet the time is come when one may speak in all sincerity and utter courtesy of the mistakes and shortcomings of Mr. Washington's career, as well as of his triumphs, without being thought captious or envious, and without forgetting that it is easier to do ill than well in the world.

The criticism that has hitherto met Mr. Washington has not always been of this broad character. In the South especially has he had to walk warily to avoid the harshest judgments,—and naturally so, for he is dealing with the one subject of deepest sensitiveness to that section. Twice—once when at the Chicago celebration of the Spanish-American War he alluded to the color-prejudice that is "eating away the vitals of the South," and once when

5. Tuskegee Normal and Industrial Institute, a school for African Americans founded by Booker T. Washington in Tuskegee, Alabama, in 1881.

6. Italian preacher (1181?–1226), founder of the Franciscan religious order. Socrates (470?–399 B.C.), Athenian philosopher and teacher.

he dined with President Roosevelt[7]—has the resulting Southern criticism
been violent enough to threaten seriously his popularity. In the North the
feeling has several times forced itself into words, that Mr. Washington's
counsels of submission overlooked certain elements of true manhood, and
that his educational programme was unnecessarily narrow. Usually, however, such criticism has not found open expression, although, too, the spiritual sons of the Abolitionists have not been prepared to acknowledge that
the schools founded before Tuskegee, by men of broad ideals and self-
sacrificing spirit, were wholly failures or worthy of ridicule. While, then,
criticism has not failed to follow Mr. Washington, yet the prevailing public
opinion of the land has been but too willing to deliver the solution of a
wearisome problem into his hands, and say, "If that is all you and your race
ask, take it."

Among his own people, however, Mr. Washington has encountered the
strongest and most lasting opposition, amounting at times to bitterness, and
even to-day continuing strong and insistent even though largely silenced in
outward expression by the public opinion of the nation. Some of this opposition is, of course, mere envy; the disappointment of displaced dema-
gogues and the spite of narrow minds. But aside from this, there is among
educated and thoughtful colored men in all parts of the land a feeling of
deep regret, sorrow, and apprehension at the wide currency and ascendancy which some of Mr. Washington's theories have gained. These same
men admire his sincerity of purpose, and are willing to forgive much to
honest endeavor which is doing something worth the doing. They coöperate with Mr. Washington as far as they conscientiously can; and, indeed, it
is no ordinary tribute to this man's tact and power that, steering as he must
between so many diverse interests and opinions, he so largely retains the
respect of all.

But the hushing of the criticism of honest opponents is a dangerous
thing. It leads some of the best of the critics to unfortunate silence and
paralysis of effort, and others to burst into speech so passionately and in-
temperately as to lose listeners. Honest and earnest criticism from those
whose interests are most nearly touched,—criticism of writers by readers, of
government by those governed, of leaders by those led,—this is the soul of
democracy and the safeguard of modern society. If the best of the American Negroes receive by outer pressure a leader whom they had not recognized before, manifestly there is here a certain palpable gain. Yet there is
also irreparable loss,—a loss of that peculiarly valuable education which a
group receives when by search and criticism it finds and commissions its
own leaders. The way in which this is done is at once the most elementary
and the nicest problem of social growth. History is but the record of such
group-leadership; and yet how infinitely changeful is its type and character!
And of all types and kinds, what can be more instructive than the leadership of a group within a group?—that curious double movement where real
progress may be negative and actual advance be relative retrogression. All
this is the social student's inspiration and despair.

Now in the past the American Negro has had instructive experience in

7. Theodore Roosevelt (1858–1919), U.S. president from 1901 to 1909.

the choosing of group leaders, founding thus a peculiar dynasty which in the light of present conditions is worth while studying. When sticks and stones and beasts form the sole environment of a people, their attitude is largely one of determined opposition to and conquest of natural forces. But when to earth and brute is added an environment of men and ideas, then the attitude of the imprisoned group may take three main forms,—a feeling of revolt and revenge; an attempt to adjust all thought and action to the will of the greater group; or, finally, a determined effort at self-realization and self-development despite environing opinion. The influence of all of these attitudes at various times can be traced in the history of the American Negro, and in the evolution of his successive leaders.

Before 1750, while the fire of African freedom still burned in the veins of the slaves, there was in all leadership or attempted leadership but the one motive of revolt and revenge,—typified in the terrible Maroons, the Danish blacks, and Cato of Stono,[8] and veiling all the Americas in fear of insurrection. The liberalizing tendencies of the latter half of the eighteenth century brought, along with kindlier relations between black and white, thoughts of ultimate adjustment and assimilation. Such aspiration was especially voiced in the earnest songs of Phyllis, in the martyrdom of Attucks, the fighting of Salem and Poor, the intellectual accomplishments of Banneker and Derham, and the political demands of the Cuffes.[9]

Stern financial and social stress after the war cooled much of the previous humanitarian ardor. The disappointment and impatience of the Negroes at the persistence of slavery and serfdom voiced itself in two movements. The slaves in the South, aroused undoubtedly by vague rumors of the Haytian revolt, made three fierce attempts at insurrection,—in 1800 under Gabriel in Virginia, in 1822 under Vesey in Carolina, and in 1831 again in Virginia under the terrible Nat Turner.[1] In the Free States, on the other hand, a new and curious attempt at self-development was made. In Philadelphia and New York color-prescription led to a withdrawal of Negro communicants from white churches and the formation of a peculiar socio-religious institution among the Negroes known as the African Church,—an organization still living and controlling in its various branches over a million of men.

Walker's wild appeal[2] against the trend of the times showed how the world was changing after the coming of the cotton-gin. By 1830 slavery seemed hopelessly fastened on the South, and the slaves thoroughly cowed

8. Leader of an insurrection of slaves in Stono, South Carolina, in 1739. "Maroons": fugitive slave communities in the South that often raided nearby farms and plantations. "Danish blacks": insurrectionary slaves who took control of the island of St. John in the Danish West Indies (now the Virgin Islands) in 1723.
9. Paul Cuffe (1759–1817), merchant-mariner and author who in 1780 with his brother John protested Massachusetts laws that withheld the vote from African Americans and American Indians. Phillis Wheatley (c. 1753–1784), internationally acclaimed African-born poet who grew up a slave in Boston. Crispus Attucks (1723?–1770), believed to have been an escaped slave, was the first man to die in the Boston Massacre, a prelude to the Ameri-

can Revolution. Peter Salem (1750–1816), distinguished slave-born American Revolutionary War soldier. Salem Poor (b. 1758), distinguished free-born American Revolutionary War soldier. Benjamin Banneker (1731–1806), surveyor, astronomer, and almanac maker. James Durham or Derham (b. 1762), earliest known African American physician.
1. Gabriel Prosser (1775–1800), Denmark Vesey (c. 1767–1822), and Nat Turner (1800–1831) were leaders of insurrections inspired to some extent by the successful slave revolt that established an independent nation in Haiti in 1804.
2. David Walker (1785–1830), author of David Walker's Appeal (1829), a revolutionary antislavery tract.

into submission. The free Negroes of the North, inspired by the mulatto immigrants from the West Indies, began to change the basis of their demands; they recognized the slavery of slaves, but insisted that they themselves were freemen, and sought assimilation and amalgamation with the nation on the same terms with other men. Thus, Forten and Purvis of Philadelphia, Shad of Wilmington, Du Bois of New Haven, Barbadoes[3] of Boston, and others, strove singly and together as men, they said, not as slaves; as "people of color," not as "Negroes." The trend of the times, however, refused them recognition save in individual and exceptional cases, considered them as one with all the despised blacks, and they soon found themselves striving to keep even the rights they formerly had of voting and working and moving as freemen. Schemes of migration and colonization arose among them; but these they refused to entertain, and they eventually turned to the Abolition movement as a final refuge.

Here, led by Remond, Nell, Wells-Brown,[4] and Douglass, a new period of self-assertion and self-development dawned. To be sure, ultimate freedom and assimilation was the ideal before the leaders, but the assertion of the manhood rights of the Negro by himself was the main reliance, and John Brown's raid was the extreme of its logic. After the war and emancipation, the great form of Frederick Douglass, the greatest of American Negro leaders, still led the host. Self-assertion, especially in political lines, was the main programme, and behind Douglass came Elliot, Bruce, and Langston, and the Reconstruction politicians, and, less conspicuous but of greater social significance Alexander Crummell and Bishop Daniel Payne.[5]

Then came the Revolution of 1876, the suppression of the Negro votes, the changing and shifting of ideals, and the seeking of new lights in the great night. Douglass, in his old age, still bravely stood for the ideals of his early manhood,—ultimate assimilation *through* self-assertion, and on no other terms. For a time Price arose as a new leader, destined, it seemed, not to give up, but to re-state the old ideals in a form less repugnant to the white South. But he passed away in his prime. Then came the new leader. Nearly all the former ones had become leaders by the silent suffrage of their fellows, had sought to lead their own people alone, and were usually, save Douglass, little known outside their race. But Booker T. Washington arose as essentially the leader not of one race but of two,—a compromiser between the South, the North, and the Negro. Naturally the Negroes resented, at first bitterly, signs of compromise which surrendered their civil and political rights, even though this was to be exchanged for larger chances of economic development. The rich and dominating North, however, was not only weary of the race problem, but was investing largely in Southern enterprises, and welcomed any method of peaceful cooperation.

3. James G. Barbadoes (c. 1796–1841), abolitionist and leader among the free African Americans of Boston. James Forten Sr. (1766–1842), wealthy Philadelphia businessman and civil rights activist. Robert Purvis Sr. (1810–1898), wealthy Philadelphia reformer and abolitionist. Mary Ann Shad or Shadd (1823–1893), newspaper editor and antislavery lecturer. Alexander Du Bois, W. E. B. Du Bois's grandfather.
4. William Wells Brown (c. 1814–1884), internationally famous fugitive slave, lecturer, and author.

Charles Lenox Remond (1810–1874), journalist and antislavery lecturer. William C. Nell (1816–1874), abolitionist journalist and active participant in the Underground Railroad.
5. Daniel A. Payne (1811–1893), African Methodist Episcopal church leader and educator. Robert Brown Elliott (1842–1884), congressman from South Carolina (1870–74). Blanche Kelso Bruce (1841–1898), U.S. senator from Mississippi (1875–81). John Mercer Langston (1829–1897), congressman from Virginia (1890–91).

Thus, by national opinion, the Negroes began to recognize Mr. Washington's leadership; and the voice of criticism was hushed.

Mr. Washington represents in Negro thought the old attitude of adjustment and submission; but adjustment at such a peculiar time as to make his programme unique. This is an age of unusual economic development, and Mr. Washington's programme naturally takes an economic cast, becoming a gospel of Work and Money to such an extent as apparently almost completely to overshadow the higher aims of life. Moreover, this is an age when the more advanced races are coming in closer contact with the less developed races, and the race-feeling is therefore intensified; and Mr. Washington's programme practically accepts the alleged inferiority of the Negro races. Again, in our own land, the reaction from the sentiment of war time has given impetus to race-prejudice against Negroes, and Mr. Washington withdraws many of the high demands of Negroes as men and American citizens. In other periods of intensified prejudice all the Negro's tendency to self-assertion has been called forth; at this period a policy of submission is advocated. In the history of nearly all other races and peoples the doctrine preached at such crises has been that manly self-respect is worth more than lands and houses, and that a people who voluntarily surrender such respect, or cease striving for it, are not worth civilizing.

In answer to this, it has been claimed that the Negro can survive only through submission. Mr. Washington distinctly asks that black people give up, at least for the present, three things,—

First, political power,

Second, insistence on civil rights,

Third, higher education of Negro youth,—and concentrate all their energies on industrial education, the accumulation of wealth, and the conciliation of the South. This policy has been courageously and insistently advocated for over fifteen years, and has been triumphant for perhaps ten years. As a result of this tender of the palm-branch,[6] what has been the return? In these years there have occurred:

1. The disfranchisement of the Negro.

2. The legal creation of a distinct status of civil inferiority for the Negro.

3. The steady withdrawal of aid from institutions for the higher training of the Negro.

These movements are not, to be sure, direct results of Mr. Washington's teachings; but his propaganda has, without a shadow of doubt, helped their speedier accomplishment. The question then comes: Is it possible, and probable, that nine millions of men can make effective progress in economic lines if they are deprived of political rights, made a servile caste, and allowed only the most meagre chance for developing their exceptional men? If history and reason give any distinct answer to these questions, it is an emphatic No. And Mr. Washington thus faces the triple paradox of his career:

1. He is striving nobly to make Negro artisans business men and property-owners; but it is utterly impossible, under modern competitive methods, for workingmen and property-owners to defend their rights and exist without the right of suffrage.

6. A gesture acknowledging victory.

2. He insists on thrift and self-respect, but at the same time counsels a silent submission to civic inferiority such as is bound to sap the manhood of any race in the long run.

3. He advocates common-school[7] and industrial training, and depreciates institutions of higher learning; but neither the Negro common-schools, nor Tuskegee itself, could remain open a day were it not for teachers trained in Negro colleges, or trained by their graduates.

This triple paradox in Mr. Washington's position is the object of criticism by two classes of colored Americans. One class is spiritually descended from Toussaint the Savior, through Gabriel, Vesey, and Turner, and they represent the attitude of revolt and revenge; they hate the white South blindly and distrust the white race generally, and so far as they agree on definite action, think that the Negro's only hope lies in emigration beyond the borders of the United States. And yet, by the irony of fate, nothing has more effectually made this programme seem hopeless than the recent course of the United States toward weaker and darker peoples in the West Indies, Hawaii, and the Philippines,—for where in the world may we go and be safe from lying and brute force?

The other class of Negroes who cannot agree with Mr. Washington has hitherto said little aloud. They deprecate the sight of scattered counsels, of internal disagreement; and especially they dislike making their just criticism of a useful and earnest man an excuse for a general discharge of venom from small-minded opponents. Nevertheless, the questions involved are so fundamental and serious that it is difficult to see how men like the Grimkes, Kelly Miller, J. W. E. Bowen,[8] and other representatives of this group, can much longer be silent. Such men feel in conscience bound to ask of this nation three things:

1. The right to vote.
2. Civic equality.
3. The education of youth according to ability.

They acknowledge Mr. Washington's invaluable service in counselling patience and courtesy in such demands; they do not ask that ignorant black men vote when ignorant whites are debarred, or that any reasonable restrictions in the suffrage should not be applied; they know that the low social level of the mass of the race is responsible for much discrimination against it, but they also know, and the nation knows, that relentless color-prejudice is more often a cause than a result of the Negro's degradation; they seek the abatement of this relic of barbarism, and not its systematic encouragement and pampering by all agencies of social power from the Associated Press to the Church of Christ. They advocate, with Mr. Washington, a broad system of Negro common schools supplemented by thorough industrial training; but they are surprised that a man of Mr. Washington's insight cannot see that no such educational system ever has rested or can rest on any other basis than that of the well-equipped college and university, and they insist that there is a demand

7. Public elementary school.
8. John Wesley Edward Bowen (1855–1933), Methodist church leader and popular lecturer. Archibald H. Grimké (1849–1930), attorney and journalist, and Francis J. Grimké (1850–1937), clergyman and educator, both civil rights activists in the North. Kelly Miller (1863–1939), professor at Howard University and a mediator between conservatives and militants among African Americans.

for a few such institutions throughout the South to train the best of the Negro youth as teachers, professional men, and leaders.

This group of men honor Mr. Washington for his attitude of conciliation toward the white South; they accept the "Atlanta Compromise" in its broadest interpretation; they recognize, with him, many signs of promise, many men of high purpose and fair judgment, in this section; they know that no easy task has been laid upon a region already tottering under heavy burdens. But, nevertheless, they insist that the way to truth and right lies in straightforward honesty, not in indiscriminate flattery; in praising those of the South who do well and criticising uncompromisingly those who do ill; in taking advantage of the opportunities at hand and urging their fellows to do the same, but at the same time in remembering that only a firm adherence to their higher ideals and aspirations will ever keep those ideals within the realm of possibility. They do not expect that the free right to vote, to enjoy civic rights, and to be educated, will come in a moment; they do not expect to see the bias and prejudices of years disappear at the blast of a trumpet; but they are absolutely certain that the way for a people to gain their reasonable rights is not by voluntarily throwing them away and insisting that they do not want them; that the way for a people to gain respect is not by continually belittling and ridiculing themselves; that, on the contrary, Negroes must insist continually, in season and out of season, that voting is necessary to modern manhood, that color discrimination is barbarism, and that black boys need education as well as white boys.

In failing thus to state plainly and unequivocally the legitimate demands of their people, even at the cost of opposing an honored leader, the thinking classes of American Negroes would shirk a heavy responsibility,—a responsibility to themselves, a responsibility to the struggling masses, a responsibility to the darker races of men whose future depends so largely on this American experiment, but especially a responsibility to this nation,—this common Fatherland. It is wrong to encourage a man or a people in evil-doing; it is wrong to aid and abet a national crime simply because it is unpopular not to do so. The growing spirit of kindliness and reconciliation between the North and South after the frightful differences of a generation ago ought to be a source of deep congratulation to all, and especially to those whose mistreatment caused the war; but if that reconciliation is to be marked by the industrial slavery and civic death of those same black men, with permanent legislation into a position of inferiority, then those black men, if they are really men, are called upon by every consideration of patriotism and loyalty to oppose such a course by all civilized methods, even though such opposition involves disagreement with Mr. Booker T. Washington. We have no right to sit silently by while the inevitable seeds are sown for a harvest of disaster to our children, black and white.

First, it is the duty of black men to judge the South discriminatingly. The present generation of Southerners are not responsible for the past, and they should not be blindly hated or blamed for it. Furthermore, to no class is the indiscriminate endorsement of the recent course of the South toward Negroes more nauseating than to the best thought of the South. The South is not "solid"; it is a land in the ferment of social change, wherein forces of all kinds are fighting for supremacy; and to praise the ill the South is to-day perpetrating is just as wrong as to condemn the good. Discriminating and broad-minded criticism is what the South needs,—needs it for the sake of her own white sons and daughters, and for the insurance of robust, healthy mental and moral development.

To-day even the attitude of the Southern whites toward the blacks is not, as so many assume, in all cases the same; the ignorant Southerner hates the Negro, the workingmen fear his competition, the money-makers wish to use him as a laborer, some of the educated see a menace in his upward development, while others—usually the sons of the masters—wish to help him to rise. National opinion has enabled this last class to maintain the Negro common schools, and to protect the Negro partially in property, life, and limb. Through the pressure of the money-makers, the Negro is in danger of being reduced to semi-slavery, especially in the country districts; the workingmen, and those of the educated who fear the Negro, have united to disfranchise him, and some have urged his deportation; while the passions of the ignorant are easily aroused to lynch and abuse any black man. To praise this intricate whirl of thought and prejudice is nonsense; to inveigh indiscriminately against "the South" is unjust; but to use the same breath in praising Governor Aycock, exposing Senator Morgan, arguing with Mr. Thomas Nelson Page, and denouncing Senator Ben Tillman,[9] is not only sane, but the imperative duty of thinking black men.

It would be unjust to Mr. Washington not to acknowledge that in several instances he has opposed movements in the South which were unjust to the Negro; he sent memorials to the Louisiana and Alabama constitutional conventions, he has spoken against lynching, and in other ways has openly or silently set his influence against sinister schemes and unfortunate happenings. Notwithstanding this, it is equally true to assert that on the whole the distinct impression left by Mr. Washington's propaganda is, first, that the South is justified in its present attitude toward the Negro because of the Negro's degradation; secondly, that the prime cause of the Negro's failure to rise more quickly is his wrong education in the past; and, thirdly, that his future rise depends primarily on his own efforts. Each of these propositions is a dangerous half-truth. The supplementary truths must never be lost sight of: first, slavery and race-prejudice are potent if not sufficient causes of the Negro's position; second, industrial and common-school training were necessarily slow in planting because they had to await the black teachers trained by higher institutions,—it being extremely doubtful if any essentially different development was possible, and certainly a Tuskegee was unthinkable before 1880; and, third, while it is a great truth to say that the Negro must strive and strive mightily to help himself, it is equally true that unless his striving be not simply seconded, but rather aroused and encouraged, by the initiative of the richer and wiser environing group, he cannot hope for great success.

In his failure to realize and impress this last point, Mr. Washington is especially to be criticised. His doctrine has tended to make the whites, North and South, shift the burden of the Negro problem to the Negro's

9. Benjamin Ryan Tillman (1847–1918), white supremacist governor of South Carolina (1890–94) and U.S. senator (1895–1918). Charles Brantley Aycock (1859–1912), reformist governor of North Carolina (1901–05). John Tyler Morgan (1824– 1907), white supremacist senator from Alabama (1876–1907). Thomas Nelson Page (1853–1922), author of sentimental fiction about slavery in the pre–Civil War South.

oulders and stand aside as critical and rather pessimistic spectators; when
n fact the burden belongs to the nation, and the hands of none of us are
clean if we bend not our energies to righting these great wrongs.

The South ought to be led, by candid and honest criticism, to assert her
better self and do her full duty to the race she has cruelly wronged and is
still wronging. The North—her co-partner in guilt—cannot salve her conscience by plastering it with gold. We cannot settle this problem by diplomacy and suaveness, by "policy" alone. If worse come to worst, can the
moral fibre of this country survive the slow throttling and murder of nine
millions of men?

The black men of America have a duty to perform, a duty stern and delicate,—a forward movement to oppose a part of the work of their greatest
leader. So far as Mr. Washington preaches Thrift, Patience, and Industrial
Training for the masses, we must hold up his hands and strive with him,
rejoicing in his honors and glorying in the strength of this Joshua[1] called of
God and of man to lead the headless host. But so far as Mr. Washington
apologizes for injustice, North or South, does not rightly value the privilege
and duty of voting, belittles the emasculating effects of caste distinctions,
and opposes the higher training and ambition of our brighter minds,—so
far as he, the South, or the Nation, does this,—we must unceasingly and
firmly oppose them. By every civilized and peaceful method we must strive
for the rights which the world accords to men, clinging unwaveringly to
those great words which the sons of the Fathers would fain[2] forget: "We
hold these truths to be self-evident: That all men are created equal; that
they are endowed by their Creator with certain unalienable rights; that
among these are life, liberty, and the pursuit of happiness."

IV. Of the Meaning of Progress

> Willst Du Deine Macht verkünden,
> Wähle sie die frei von Sünden,
> Steh'n in Deinem ew'gen Haus!
> Deine Geister sende aus!
> Die Unsterblichen, die Reinen,
> Die nicht fühlen, die nicht weinen!
> Nicht die zarte Jungfrau wähle,
> Nicht der Hirtin weiche Seele!
>
> SCHILLER[3]

Once upon a time I taught school in the hills of Tennessee, where the
broad dark vale of the Mississippi begins to roll and crumple to greet the

1. Biblical leader who brought the Israelites into
the Promised Land.
2. Readily.

3. Friedrich von Schiller (1759–1805), German
poet and dramatist. The quotation is from *The
Maid of Orleans* (1801).

Alleghanies. I was a Fisk student then, and all Fisk men thought that Tennessee—beyond the Veil—was theirs alone, and in vacation time they sallied forth in lusty bands to meet the county school-commissioners. Young and happy, I too went, and I shall not soon forget that summer, seventeen years ago.

First, there was a Teachers' Institute at the county-seat; and there distinguished guests of the superintendent taught the teachers fractions and spelling and other mysteries,—white teachers in the morning, Negroes at night. A picnic now and then, and a supper, and the rough world was softened by laughter and song. I remember how— But I wander.

There came a day when all the teachers left the Institute and began the hunt for schools. I learn from hearsay (for my mother was mortally afraid of fire-arms) that the hunting of ducks and bears and men is wonderfully interesting, but I am sure that the man who has never hunted a country school has something to learn of the pleasures of the chase. I see now the white, hot roads lazily rise and fall and wind before me under the burning July sun; I feel the deep weariness of heart and limb as ten, eight, six miles stretch relentlessly ahead; I feel my heart sink heavily as I hear again and again, "Got a teacher? Yes." So I walked on and on—horses were too expensive—until I had wandered beyond railways, beyond stage lines, to a land of "varmints" and rattlesnakes, where the coming of a stranger was an event, and men lived and died in the shadow of one blue hill.

Sprinkled over hill and dale lay cabins and farmhouses, shut out from the world by the forests and the rolling hills toward the east. There I found at last a little school. Josie told me of it; she was a thin, homely girl of twenty, with a dark-brown face and thick, hard hair. I had crossed the stream at Watertown,[4] and rested under the great willows; then I had gone to the little cabin in the lot where Josie was resting on her way to town. The gaunt farmer made me welcome, and Josie, hearing my errand, told me anxiously that they wanted a school over the hill; that but once since the war had a teacher been there; that she herself longed to learn,—and thus she ran on, talking fast and loud, with much earnestness and energy.

Next morning I crossed the tall round hill, lingered to look at the blue and yellow mountains stretching toward the Carolinas, then plunged into the wood, and came out at Josie's home. It was a dull frame cottage with four rooms, perched just below the brow of the hill, amid peach-trees. The father was a quiet, simple soul, calmly ignorant, with no touch of vulgarity. The mother was different,—strong, bustling, and energetic, with a quick, restless tongue, and an ambition to live "like folks." There was a crowd of children. Two boys had gone away. There remained two growing girls; a shy midget of eight; John, tall, awkward, and eighteen; Jim, younger, quicker, and better looking; and two babies of indefinite age. Then there was Josie herself. She seemed to be the centre of the family: always busy at service, or at home, or berry-picking; a little nervous and inclined to scold, like her mother, yet faithful, too, like her father. She had about her a certain fineness, the shadow of an unconscious moral heroism that would willingly give all of life to make life broader, deeper, and fuller for her and hers.

4. A village in eastern Tennessee.

I saw much of this family afterwards, and grew to love them for their honest efforts to be decent and comfortable, and for their knowledge of their own ignorance. There was with them no affectation. The mother would scold the father for being so "easy"; Josie would roundly berate the boys for carelessness; and all knew that it was a hard thing to dig a living out of a rocky sidehill.

I secured the school. I remember the day I rode horseback out to the commissioner's house with a pleasant young white fellow who wanted the white school. The road ran down the bed of a stream; the sun laughed and the water jingled, and we rode on. "Come in," said the commissioner,— "come in. Have a seat. Yes, that certificate will do. Stay to dinner. What do you want a month?" "Oh," thought I, "this is lucky"; but even then fell the awful shadow of the Veil, for they ate first, then I—alone.

The schoolhouse was a log hut, where Colonel Wheeler used to shelter his corn. It sat in a lot behind a rail fence and thorn bushes, near the sweetest of springs. There was an entrance where a door once was, and within, a massive rickety fireplace; great chinks between the logs served as windows. Furniture was scarce. A pale blackboard crouched in the corner. My desk was made of three boards, reinforced at critical points, and my chair, borrowed from the landlady, had to be returned every night. Seats for the children—these puzzled me much. I was haunted by a New England vision of neat little desks and chairs, but, alas! the reality was rough plank benches without backs, and at times without legs. They had the one virtue of making naps dangerous,—possibly fatal, for the floor was not to be trusted.

It was a hot morning late in July when the school opened. I trembled when I heard the patter of little feet down the dusty road, and saw the growing row of dark solemn faces and bright eager eyes facing me. First came Josie and her brothers and sisters. The longing to know, to be a student in the great school at Nashville, hovered like a star above this child-woman amid her work and worry, and she studied doggedly. There were the Dowells from their farm over toward Alexandria,—Fanny, with her smooth black face and wondering eyes; Martha, brown and dull; the pretty girl-wife of a brother, and the younger brood.

There were the Burkes,—two brown and yellow lads, and a tiny haughty-eyed girl. Fat Reuben's little chubby girl came, with golden face and old-gold hair, faithful and solemn. 'Thenie was on hand early,—a jolly, ugly, good-hearted girl, who slyly dipped snuff[5] and looked after her little bow-legged brother. When her mother could spare her, 'Tildy came,—a midnight beauty, with starry eyes and tapering limbs; and her brother, correspondingly homely. And then the big boys,—the hulking Lawrences; the lazy Neills, unfathered sons of mother and daughter; Hickman, with a stoop in his shoulders; and the rest.

There they sat, nearly thirty of them, on the rough benches, their faces shading from a pale cream to a deep brown, the little feet bare and swinging, the eyes full of expectation, with here and there a twinkle of mischief, and the hands grasping Webster's blue-back spelling-book.[6] I

5. Use of a stick to apply powdered tobacco to the gums.

6. The most popular spelling book of the 19th century, authored by Noah Webster (1758–1843).

loved my school, and the fine faith the children had in the wisdom of their teacher was truly marvellous. We read and spelled together, wrote a little, picked flowers, sang, and listened to stories of the world beyond the hill. At times the school would dwindle away, and I would start out. I would visit Mun Eddings, who lived in two very dirty rooms, and ask why little Lugene, whose flaming face seemed ever ablaze with the dark-red hair uncombed, was absent all last week, or why I missed so often the inimitable rags of Mack and Ed. Then the father, who worked Colonel Wheeler's farm on shares, would tell me how the crops needed the boys; and the thin, slovenly mother, whose face was pretty when washed, assured me that Lugene must mind the baby. "But we'll start them again next week." When the Lawrences stopped, I knew that the doubts of the old folks about book-learning had conquered again, and so, toiling up the hill, and getting as far into the cabin as possible, I put Cicero "pro Archia Poeta"[7] into the simplest English with local applications, and usually convinced them—for a week or so.

On Friday nights I often went home with some of the children,—sometimes to Doc Burke's farm. He was a great, loud, thin Black, ever working, and trying to buy the seventy-five acres of hill and dale where he lived; but people said that he would surely fail, and the "white folks would get it all." His wife was a magnificent Amazon,[8] with saffron face and shining hair, uncorseted and barefooted, and the children were strong and beautiful. They lived in a one-and-a-half-room cabin in the hollow of the farm, near the spring. The front room was full of great fat white beds, scrupulously neat; and there were bad chromos[9] on the walls, and a tired centretable. In the tiny back kitchen I was often invited to "take out and help" myself to fried chicken and wheat biscuit, "meat" and corn pone,[1] string-beans and berries. At first I used to be a little alarmed at the approach of bedtime in the one lone bedroom, but embarrassment was very deftly avoided. First, all the children nodded and slept, and were stowed away in one great pile of goose feathers; next, the mother and the father discreetly slipped away to the kitchen while I went to bed; then, blowing out the dim light, they retired in the dark. In the morning all were up and away before I thought of awaking. Across the road, where fat Reuben lived, they all went outdoors while the teacher retired, because they did not boast the luxury of a kitchen.

I liked to stay with the Dowells, for they had four rooms and plenty of good country fare. Uncle Bird had a small, rough farm, all woods and hills, miles from the big road; but he was full of tales,—he preached now and then,—and with his children, berries, horses, and wheat he was happy and prosperous. Often, to keep the peace, I must go where life was less lovely; for instance, 'Tildy's mother was incorrigibly dirty, Reuben's larder was limited seriously, and herds of untamed insects wandered over the Eddingses' beds. Best of all I loved to go to Josie's, and sit on the porch, eating peaches, while the mother bustled and talked: how Josie had bought the sewing-machine; how Josie worked at service in winter, but that four dol-

---

7. Defense of the poet Archias by Marcus Tullius Cicero (106–43 B.C.), Roman statesman and orator.
8. A large, strong woman.

9. Colored pictures printed by a lithographic process.
1. A type of corn bread.

lars a month was "mighty little" wages; how Josie longed to go away to school, but that it "looked like" they never could get far enough ahead to let her; how the crops failed and the well was yet unfinished; and, finally, how "mean" some of the white folks were.

For two summers I lived in this little world; it was dull and humdrum. The girls looked at the hill in wistful longing, and the boys fretted and haunted Alexandria. Alexandria was "town,"—a straggling, lazy village of houses, churches, and shops, and an aristocracy of Toms, Dicks, and Captains. Cuddled on the hill to the north was the village of the colored folks, who lived in three- or four-room unpainted cottages, some neat and homelike, and some dirty. The dwellings were scattered rather aimlessly, but they centred about the twin temples of the hamlet, the Methodist, and the Hard-Shell[2] Baptist churches. These, in turn, leaned gingerly on a sad-colored schoolhouse. Hither my little world wended its crooked way on Sunday to meet other worlds, and gossip, and wonder, and make the weekly sacrifice with frenzied priest at the altar of the "old-time religion." Then the soft melody and mighty cadences of Negro song fluttered and thundered.

I have called my tiny community a world, and so its isolation made it; and yet there was among us but a half-awakened common consciousness, sprung from common joy and grief, at burial, birth, or wedding; from a common hardship in poverty, poor land, and low wages; and, above all, from the sight of the Veil that hung between us and Opportunity. All this caused us to think some thoughts together; but these, when ripe for speech, were spoken in various languages. Those whose eyes twenty-five and more years before had seen "the glory of the coming of the Lord,"[3] saw in every present hindrance or help a dark fatalism bound to bring all things right in His own good time. The mass of those to whom slavery was a dim recollection of childhood found the world a puzzling thing: it asked little of them, and they answered with little, and yet it ridiculed their offering. Such a paradox they could not understand, and therefore sank into listless indifference, or shiftlessness, or reckless bravado. There were, however, some—such as Josie, Jim, and Ben—to whom War, Hell, and Slavery were but childhood tales, whose young appetites had been whetted to an edge by school and story and half-awakened thought. Ill could they be content, born without and beyond the World. And their weak wings beat against their barriers,—barriers of caste, of youth, of life; at last, in dangerous moments, against everything that opposed even a whim.

The ten years that follow youth, the years when first the realization comes that life is leading somewhere,—these were the years that passed after I left my little school. When they were past, I came by chance once more to the walls of Fisk University, to the halls of the chapel of melody. As I lingered there in the joy and pain of meeting old school-friends, there swept over me a sudden longing to pass again beyond the blue hill, and to see the homes and the school of other days, and to learn how life had gone with my school-children; and I went.

2. Uncompromising.
3. From the opening line of Julia Ward Howe's *Battle Hymn of the Republic* (1861).

Josie was dead, and the gray-haired mother said simply, "We've had a heap of trouble since you've been away." I had feared for Jim. With a cultured parentage and a social caste to uphold him, he might have made a venturesome merchant or a West Point cadet. But here he was, angry with life and reckless; and when Farmer Durham charged him with stealing wheat, the old man had to ride fast to escape the stones which the furious fool hurled after him. They told Jim to run away; but he would not run, and the constable came that afternoon. It grieved Josie, and great awkward John walked nine miles every day to see his little brother through the bars of Lebanon jail. At last the two came back together in the dark night. The mother cooked supper, and Josie emptied her purse, and the boys stole away. Josie grew thin and silent, yet worked the more. The hill became steep for the quiet old father, and with the boys away there was little to do in the valley. Josie helped them to sell the old farm, and they moved nearer town. Brother Dennis, the carpenter, built a new house with six rooms; Josie toiled a year in Nashville, and brought back ninety dollars to furnish the house and change it to a home.

When the spring came, and the birds twittered, and the stream ran proud and full, little sister Lizzie, bold and thoughtless, flushed with the passion of youth, bestowed herself on the tempter, and brought home a nameless child. Josie shivered and worked on, with the vision of schooldays all fled, with a face wan and tired,—worked until, on a summer's day, some one married another; then Josie crept to her mother like a hurt child, and slept—and sleeps.

I paused to scent the breeze as I entered the valley. The Lawrences have gone,—father and son forever,—and the other son lazily digs in the earth to live. A new young widow rents out their cabin to fat Reuben. Reuben is a Baptist preacher now, but I fear as lazy as ever, though his cabin has three rooms; and little Ella has grown into a bouncing woman, and is ploughing corn on the hot hillside. There are babies a-plenty, and one half-witted girl. Across the valley is a house I did not know before, and there I found, rocking one baby and expecting another, one of my schoolgirls, a daughter of Uncle Bird Dowell. She looked somewhat worried with her new duties, but soon bristled into pride over her neat cabin and the tale of her thrifty husband, the horse and cow, and the farm they were planning to buy.

My log schoolhouse was gone. In its place stood Progress; and Progress, I understand, is necessarily ugly. The crazy foundation stones still marked the former site of my poor little cabin, and not far away, on six weary boulders, perched a jaunty board house, perhaps twenty by thirty feet, with three windows and a door that locked. Some of the window-glass was broken, and part of an old iron stove lay mournfully under the house. I peeped through the window half reverently, and found things that were more familiar. The blackboard had grown by about two feet, and the seats were still without backs. The county owns the lot now, I hear, and every year there is a session of school. As I sat by the spring and looked on the Old and the New I felt glad, very glad, and yet—

After two long drinks I started on. There was the great double log-house on the corner. I remembered the broken, blighted family that used to live there. The strong, hard face of the mother, with its wilderness of hair, rose before me. She had driven her husband away, and while I taught school a strange man lived there, big and jovial, and people talked. I felt sure that Ben and 'Tildy would come to naught from such a home. But this is an odd world; for Ben is a busy farmer in Smith County, "doing well, too," they say, and he had cared for little 'Tildy until last spring, when a lover married her. A hard life the lad had led, toiling for meat, and laughed at because he was homely and crooked. There was Sam Carlon, an impudent old skin-flint, who had definite notions about "niggers," and hired Ben a summer and would not pay him. Then the hungry boy gathered his sacks together, and in broad daylight went into Carlon's corn; and when the hard-fisted farmer set upon him, the angry boy flew at him like a beast. Doc Burke saved a murder and a lynching that day.

The story reminded me again of the Burkes, and an impatience seized me to know who won in the battle, Doc or the seventy-five acres. For it is a hard thing to make a farm out of nothing, even in fifteen years. So I hurried on, thinking of the Burkes. They used to have a certain magnificent barba-rism about them that I liked. They were never vulgar, never immoral, but rather rough and primitive, with an unconventionality that spent itself in loud guffaws, slaps on the back, and naps in the corner. I hurried by the cottage of the misborn Neill boys. It was empty, and they were grown into fat, lazy farm-hands. I saw the home of the Hickmans, but Albert, with his stooping shoulders, had passed from the world. Then I came to the Burkes' gate and peered through; the inclosure looked rough and untrimmed, and yet there were the same fences around the old farm save to the left, where lay twenty-five other acres. And lo! the cabin in the hollow had climbed the hill and swollen to a half-finished six-room cottage.

The Burkes held a hundred acres, but they were still in debt. Indeed, the gaunt father who toiled night and day would scarcely be happy out of debt, being so used to it. Some day he must stop, for his massive frame is showing decline. The mother wore shoes, but the lion-like physique of other days was broken. The children had grown up. Rob, the image of his father, was loud and rough with laughter. Birdie, my school baby of six, had grown to a picture of maiden beauty, tall and tawny. "Edgar is gone," said the mother, with head half bowed,—"gone to work in Nashville; he and his father couldn't agree."

Little Doc, the boy born since the time of my school, took me horseback down the creek next morning toward Farmer Dowell's. The road and the stream were battling for mastery, and the stream had the better of it. We splashed and waded, and the merry boy, perched behind me, chattered and laughed. He showed me where Simon Thompson had bought a bit of ground and a home; but his daughter Lana, a plump, brown, slow girl, was not there. She had married a man and a farm twenty miles away. We wound on down the stream till we came to a gate that I did not recognize, but the boy insisted that it was "Uncle Bird's." The farm was fat with the growing crop. In that little valley was a strange stillness as I rode up; for death and marriage had stolen youth and left age and childhood there. We sat and talked that night after the chores were done. Uncle Bird was grayer, and his eyes did not see so well, but he was still jovial. We talked of the acres bought,—one hundred and twenty-five,—of the new guest-chamber added, of Martha's marrying. Then we talked of death: Fanny and Fred were gone; a shadow hung over the other daughter, and when it lifted she was to go to Nashville to school. At last we spoke of the neighbors, and as night fell, Uncle Bird told me how, on a night like that, 'Thenie came wandering back to her home over yonder, to escape the blows of her husband. And next morning she died in the home that her little bow-legged brother, working and saving, had bought for their widowed mother.

My journey was done, and behind me lay hill and dale, and Life and Death. How shall man measure Progress there where the dark-faced Josie lies? How many heartfuls of sorrow shall balance a bushel of wheat? How hard a thing is life to the lowly, and yet how human and real! And all this life and love and strife and failure,—is it the twilight of nightfall or the flush of some faint-dawning day?

Thus sadly musing, I rode to Nashville in the Jim Crow car.[4]

V. Of the Wings of Atalanta

> O black boy of Atlanta!
>   But half was spoken;
> The slave's chains and the master's
>   Alike are broken;
> The one curse of the races
>   Held both in tether;
> They are rising—all are rising—
>   The black and white together.
>   WHITTIER[5]

South of the North, yet north of the South, lies the City of a Hundred Hills, peering out from the shadows of the past into the promise of the future. I have seen her in the morning, when the first flush of day had half-roused her; she lay gray and still on the crimson soil of Georgia; then the blue smoke began to curl from her chimneys, the tinkle of bell and scream of whistle broke the silence, the rattle and roar of busy life slowly gathered and swelled, until the seething whirl of the city seemed a strange thing in a sleepy land.

Once, they say, even Atlanta slept dull and drowsy at the foot-hills of the Alleghanies, until the iron baptism of war awakened her with its sullen waters, aroused and maddened her, and left her listening to the sea. And the sea cried to the hills and the hills answered the sea, till the city rose like a widow and cast away her weeds, and toiled for her daily bread; toiled steadily, toiled cunningly,—perhaps with some bitterness, with a touch of *réclame*,[6]—and yet with real earnestness, and real sweat.

It is a hard thing to live haunted by the ghost of an untrue dream; to see

---

4. A railroad car on which African Americans were compelled to ride because of segregation laws.
5. John Greenleaf Whittier (1807–1892), antislav-

ery poet. The quotation is from *Howard at Atlanta* (1869).
6. Publicity.

the wide vision of empire fade into real ashes and dirt; to feel the pang of the conquered, and yet know that with all the Bad that fell on one black day, something was vanquished that deserved to live, something killed that in justice had not dared to die; to know that with the Right that triumphed, triumphed something of Wrong, something sordid and mean, something less than the broadest and best. All this is bitter hard; and many a man and city and people have found in it excuse for sulking, and brooding, and listless waiting.

Such are not men of the sturdier make; they of Atlanta turned resolutely toward the future; and that future held aloft vistas of purple and gold:— Atlanta, Queen of the cotton kingdom; Atlanta, Gateway to the Land of the Sun; Atlanta, the new Lachesis,[7] spinner of web and woof for the world. So the city crowned her hundred hills with factories, and stored her shops with cunning handiwork, and stretched long iron ways to greet the busy Mercury[8] in his coming. And the Nation talked of her striving.

Perhaps Atlanta was not christened for the winged maiden of dull Bœotia; you know the tale,—how swarthy Atalanta, tall and wild, would marry only him who out-raced her; and how the wily Hippomenes laid three apples of gold in the way. She fled like a shadow, paused, startled over the first apple, but even as he stretched his hand, fled again; hovered over the second, then, slipping from his hot grasp, flew over river, vale, and hill; but as she lingered over the third, his arms fell round her, and looking on each other, the blazing passion of their love profaned the sanctuary of Love, and they were cursed. If Atlanta be not named for Atalanta, she ought to have been.

Atlanta is not the first or the last maiden whom greed of gold has led to defile the temple of Love; and not maids alone, but men in the race of life, sink from the high and generous ideals of youth to the gambler's code of the Bourse;[9] and in all our Nation's striving is not the Gospel of Work befouled by the Gospel of Pay? So common is this that one-half think it normal; so unquestioned, that we almost fear to question if the end of racing is not gold, if the aim of man is not rightly to be rich. And if this is the fault of America, how dire a danger lies before a new land and a new city, lest Atlanta, stooping for mere gold, shall find that gold accursed!

It was no maiden's idle whim that started this hard racing; a fearful wilderness lay about the feet of that city after the War,—feudalism, poverty, the rise of the Third Estate,[1] serfdom, the re-birth of Law and Order, and above and between all, the Veil of Race. How heavy a journey for weary feet! what wings must Atalanta have to flit over all this hollow and hill, through sour wood and sullen water, and by the red waste of sun-baked clay! How fleet must Atalanta be if she will not be tempted by gold to profane the Sanctuary!

The Sanctuary of our fathers has, to be sure, few Gods,—some sneer, "all too few." There is the thrifty Mercury of New England, Pluto of the North, and Ceres of the West; and there, too, is the half-forgotten Apollo of the

---

7. In Greek mythology, one of the three Fates who preside over the birth, life, and death of humankind.

8. Roman god of trade.

9. The stock exchange.

1. The middle class.

South, under whose ægis the maiden ran,—and as she ran she forgot him, even as there in Bœotia Venus[2] was forgot. She forgot the old ideal of the Southern gentleman,—that new-world heir of the grace and courtliness of patrician,[3] knight, and noble; forgot his honor with his foibles, his kindliness with his carelessness, and stooped to apples of gold,—to men busier and sharper, thriftier and more unscrupulous. Golden apples are beautiful—I remember the lawless days of boyhood, when orchards in crimson and gold tempted me over fence and field—and, too, the merchant who has dethroned the planter is no despicable *parvenu*.[4] Work and wealth are the mighty levers to lift this old new land; thrift and toil and saving are the highways to new hopes and new possibilities; and yet the warning is needed lest the wily Hippomenes tempt Atalanta to thinking that golden apples are the goal of racing, and not mere incidents by the way.

Atlanta must not lead the South to dream of material prosperity as the touchstone of all success; already the fatal might of this idea is beginning to spread; it is replacing the finer type of Southerner with vulgar money–getters; it is burying the sweeter beauties of Southern life beneath pretence and ostentation. For every social ill the panacea of Wealth has been urged,—wealth to overthrow the remains of the slave feudalism; wealth to raise the "cracker"[5] Third Estate; wealth to employ the black serfs, and the prospect of wealth to keep them working; wealth as the end and aim of politics, and as the legal tender for law and order; and, finally, instead of Truth, Beauty, and Goodness, wealth as the ideal of the Public School.

Not only is this true in the world which Atlanta typifies, but it is threatening to be true of a world beneath and beyond that world,—the Black World beyond the Veil. To-day it makes little difference to Atlanta, to the South, what the Negro thinks or dreams or wills. In the soul-life of the land he is to-day, and naturally will long remain, unthought of, half forgotten; and yet when he does come to think and will and do for himself,—and let no man dream that day will never come,—then the part he plays will not be one of sudden learning, but words and thoughts he has been taught to lisp in his race-childhood. To-day the ferment of his striving toward self-realization is to the strife of the white world like a wheel within a wheel: beyond the Veil are smaller but like problems of ideals, of leaders and the led, of serfdom, of poverty, of order and subordination, and, through all, the Veil of Race. Few know of these problems, few who know notice them; and yet there they are, awaiting student, artist, and seer,—a field for somebody sometime to discover. Hither has the temptation of Hippomenes penetrated; already in this smaller world, which now indirectly and anon directly must influence the larger for good or ill, the habit is forming of interpreting the world in dollars. The old leaders of Negro opinion, in the little groups where there is a Negro social consciousness, are being replaced by new; neither the black preacher nor the black teacher leads as he did two decades ago. Into their places are pushing the farmers and gardeners, the well-paid porters and artisans, the businessmen,—all those with property and money. And with

2. Roman goddess of love. Pluto is the Roman god of the underworld. Ceres is the Roman goddess of agriculture. Apollo is the Greek god of music and poetry.

3. An aristocrat.
4. A wealthy upstart.
5. A poor white person.

all this change, so curiously parallel to that of the Other-world, goes too the same inevitable change in ideals. The South laments to-day the slow, steady disappearance of a certain type of Negro,—the faithful, courteous slave of other days, with his incorruptible honesty and dignified humility. He is passing away just as surely as the old type of Southern gentleman is passing, and from not dissimilar causes,—the sudden transformation of a fair far-off ideal of Freedom into the hard reality of bread-winning and the consequent deification of Bread.

In the Black World, the Preacher and Teacher embodied once the ideals of this people,—the strife for another and a juster world, the vague dream of righteousness, the mystery of knowing; but to-day the danger is that these ideals, with their simple beauty and weird inspiration, will suddenly sink to a question of cash and a lust for gold. Here stands this black young Atalanta, girding herself for the race that must be run; and if her eyes be still toward the hills and sky as in the days of old, then we may look for noble running; but what if some ruthless or wily or even thoughtless Hippomenes lay golden apples before her? What if the Negro people be wooed from a strife for righteousness, from a love of knowing, to regard dollars as the be-all and end-all of life? What if to the Mammonism[6] of America be added the rising Mammonism of the re-born South, and the Mammonism of this South be reinforced by the budding Mammonism of its half-awakened black millions? Whither, then, is the new-world quest of Goodness and Beauty and Truth gone glimmering? Must this, and that fair flower of Freedom which, despite the jeers of latter-day striplings, sprung from our fathers' blood, must that too degenerate into a dusty quest of gold,—into lawless lust with Hippomenes?

The hundred hills of Atlanta are not all crowned with factories. On one, toward the west, the setting sun throws three buildings in bold relief against the sky. The beauty of the group lies in its simple unity:—a broad lawn of green rising from the red street with mingled roses and peaches; north and south, two plain and stately halls; and in the midst, half hidden in ivy, a larger building, boldly graceful, sparingly decorated, and with one low spire. It is a restful group,—one never looks for more; it is all here, all intelligible. There I live, and there I hear from day to day the low hum of restful life. In winter's twilight, when the red sun glows, I can see the dark figures pass between the halls to the music of the nightbell. In the morning, when the sun is golden, the clang of the day-bell brings the hurry and laughter of three hundred young hearts from hall and street, and from the busy city below,—children all dark and heavy-haired,—to join their clear young voices in the music of the morning sacrifice. In a half-dozen class-rooms they gather then,—here to follow the love-song of Dido, here to listen to the tale of Troy divine;[7] there to wander among the stars, there to wander among men and nations,—and elsewhere other well-worn ways of knowing this queer world. Nothing new, no time-saving devices,—simply old time-glorified methods of delving for Truth, and searching out the hidden beau-

6. The worship of riches.
7. I.e., Homer's epic *The Iliad.* In Virgil's epic *The Aeneid,* Dido was the queen of Carthage who loved Aeneas and committed suicide when he left her.

ties of life, and learning the good of living. The riddle of existence is the college curriculum that was laid before the Pharaohs, that was taught in the groves by Plato, that formed the *trivium* and *quadrivium*, [8] and is to-day laid before the freedmen's sons by Atlanta University. And this course of study will not change; its methods will grow more deft and effectual, its content richer by toil of scholar and sight of seer; but the true college will ever have one goal,—not to earn meat, but to know the end and aim of that life which meat nourishes.

The vision of life that rises before these dark eyes has in it nothing mean or selfish. Not at Oxford or at Leipsic, not at Yale or Columbia, [9] is there an air of higher resolve or more unfettered striving; the determination to realize for men, both black and white, the broadest possibilities of life, to seek the better and the best, to spread with their own hands the Gospel of Sacrifice,—all this is the burden of their talk and dream. Here, amid a wide desert of caste and proscription, amid the heart-hurting slights and jars and vagaries of a deep race-dislike, lies this green oasis, where hot anger cools, and the bitterness of disappointment is sweetened by the springs and breezes of Parnassus; [1] and here men may lie and listen, and learn of a future fuller than the past, and hear the voice of Time:

"Entbehren sollst du, sollst entbehren." [2]

They made their mistakes, those who planted Fisk and Howard and Atlanta before the smoke of battle had lifted; they made their mistakes, but those mistakes were not the things at which we lately laughed somewhat uproariously. They were right when they sought to found a new educational system upon the University: where, forsooth, shall we ground knowledge save on the broadest and deepest knowledge? The roots of the tree, rather than the leaves, are the sources of its life; and from the dawn of history, from Academus to Cambridge, [3] the culture of the University has been the broad foundation-stone on which is built the kindergarten's A B C.

But these builders did make a mistake in minimizing the gravity of the problem before them; in thinking it a matter of years and decades; in therefore building quickly and laying their foundation carelessly, and lowering the standard of knowing, until they had scattered haphazard through the South some dozen poorly equipped high schools and miscalled them universities. They forgot, too, just as their successors are forgetting, the rule of inequality:—that of the million black youth, some were fitted to know and some to dig; that some had the talent and capacity of university men, and some the talent and capacity of blacksmiths; and that true training meant neither that all should be college men nor all artisans, but that the one should be made a missionary of culture to an untaught people, and the other a free workman among serfs. And to seek to make the blacksmith a

8. The seven liberal arts of the Middle Ages (Latin). Plato (c. 427–348 B.C.), Greek philosopher.
9. All world-renowned universities, in England, Germany, Connecticut, and New York, respectively.
1. A mountain in Greece considered the well-

spring of poetry and music.
2. Deny yourself, you must deny yourself (German); from Johann Wolfgang von Goethe's *Faust* (1808) I.
3. The site of Cambridge University in England and Harvard University in the United States. Academus is the site of Plato's ancient academy.

scholar is almost as silly as the more modern scheme of making the scholar a blacksmith; almost, but not quite.

The function of the university is not simply to teach bread-winning, or to furnish teachers for the public schools, or to be a centre of polite society; it is, above all, to be the organ of that fine adjustment between real life, and the growing knowledge of life, an adjustment which forms the secret of civilization. Such an institution the South of to-day sorely needs. She has religion, earnest, bigoted:—religion that on both sides the Veil often omits the sixth, seventh, and eighth commandments,[4] but substitutes a dozen supplementary ones. She has, as Atlanta shows, growing thrift and love of toil; but she lacks that broad knowledge of what the world knows and knew of human living and doing, which she may apply to the thousand problems of real life to-day confronting her. The need of the South is knowledge and culture,—not in dainty limited quantity, as before the war, but in broad busy abundance in the world of work; and until she has this, not all the Apples of Hesperides, be they golden and bejewelled, can save her from the curse of the Bœotian lovers.

The Wings of Atalanta are the coming universities of the South. They alone can bear the maiden past the temptation of golden fruit. They will not guide her flying feet away from the cotton and gold; for—ah, thoughtful Hippomenes!—do not the apples lie in the very Way of Life? But they will guide her over and beyond them, and leave her kneeling in the Sanctuary of Truth and Freedom and broad Humanity, virgin and undefiled. Sadly did the Old South err in human education, despising the education of the masses, and niggardly in the support of colleges. Her ancient university foundations dwindled and withered under the foul breath of slavery; and even since the war they have fought a failing fight for life in the tainted air of social unrest and commercial selfishness, stunted by the death of criticism, and starving for lack of broadly cultured men. And if this is the white South's need and danger, how much heavier the danger and need of the freedmen's sons! how pressing here the need of broad ideals and true culture, the conservation of soul from sordid aims and petty passions! Let us build the Southern university—William and Mary, Trinity, Georgia, Texas, Tulane, Vanderbilt, and the others—fit to live; let us build, too, the Negro universities:—Fisk, whose foundation was ever broad; Howard, at the heart of the Nation; Atlanta at Atlanta, whose ideal of scholarship has been held above the temptation of numbers. Why not here, and perhaps elsewhere, plant deeply and for all time centres of learning and living, colleges that yearly would send into the life of the South a few white men and a few black men of broad culture, catholic tolerance, and trained ability, joining their hands to other hands, and giving to this squabble of the Races a decent and dignified peace?

Patience, Humility, Manners, and Taste, common schools and kindergartens, industrial and technical schools, literature and tolerance,—all these spring from knowledge and culture, the children of the university. So must men and nations build, not otherwise, not upside down.

4. The prohibitions against killing, adultery, and theft from the Ten Commandments.

Teach workers to work,—a wise saying; wise when applied to German boys and American girls; wiser when said of Negro boys, for they have less knowledge of working and none to teach them. Teach thinkers to think,—a needed knowledge in a day of loose and careless logic; and they whose lot is gravest must have the carefulest training to think aright. If these things are so, how foolish to ask what is the best education for one or seven or sixty million souls! shall we teach them trades, or train them in liberal arts? Neither and both: teach the workers to work and the thinkers to think; make carpenters of carpenters, and philosophers of philosophers, and fops of fools. Nor can we pause here. We are training not isolated men but a living group of men,—nay, a group within a group. And the final product of our training must be neither a psychologist nor a brickmason, but a man. And to make men, we must have ideals, broad, pure, and inspiring ends of living,—not sordid money-getting, not apples of gold. The worker must work for the glory of his handiwork, not simply for pay; the thinker must think for truth, not for fame. And all this is gained only by human strife and longing; by ceaseless training and education; by founding Right on righteousness and Truth on the unhampered search for Truth; by founding the common school on the university, and the industrial school on the common school; and weaving thus a system, not a distortion, and bringing a birth, not an abortion.

When night falls on the City of a Hundred Hills, a wind gathers itself from the seas and comes murmuring westward. And at its bidding, the smoke of the drowsy factories sweeps down upon the mighty city and covers it like a pall, while yonder at the University the stars twinkle above Stone Hall. And they say that yon gray mist is the tunic of Atalanta pausing over her golden apples. Fly, my maiden, fly, for yonder comes Hippomenes!

VI. Of the Training of Black Men

> Why, if the Soul can fling the Dust aside,
> And naked on the Air of Heaven ride,
>   Were 't not a Shame—were 't not a Shame for him
> In this clay carcase crippled to abide?
>   OMAR KHAYYÁM (FITZGERALD) [5]

From the shimmering swirl of waters where many, many thoughts ago the slave-ship first saw the square tower of Jamestown, [6] have flowed down to our day three streams of thinking: one swollen from the larger world here and overseas, saying, the multiplying of human wants in culture-lands calls

5. Khayyam (fl. A.D. 1000), Persian poet. The quotation is from Edward FitzGerald's translation of *The Rubaiyat of Omar Khayyam* (1859).

6. Virginia, where African slaves were first brought to North America in 1619.

for the world-wide coöperation of men in satisfying them. Hence arises a new human unity, pulling the ends of earth nearer, and all men, black, yellow, and white. The larger humanity strives to feel in this contact of living Nations and sleeping hordes a thrill of new life in the world, crying, "If the contact of Life and Sleep be Death, shame on such Life." To be sure, behind this thought lurks the afterthought of force and dominion,—the making of brown men to delve when the temptation of beads and red calico cloys.

The second thought streaming from the death-ship and the curving river is the thought of the older South,—the sincere and passionate belief that somewhere between men and cattle, God created a *tertium quid*,[7] and called it a Negro,—a clownish, simple creature, at times even lovable within its limitations, but straitly foreordained to walk within the Veil. To be sure, behind the thought lurks the afterthought,—some of them with favoring chance might become men, but in sheer self-defence we dare not let them, and we build about them walls so high, and hang between them and the light a veil so thick, that they shall not even think of breaking through.

And last of all there trickles down that third and darker thought,—the thought of the things themselves, the confused, half-conscious mutter of men who are black and whitened, crying "Liberty, Freedom, Opportunity—vouchsafe[8] to us, O boastful World, the chance of living men!" To be sure, behind the thought lurks the afterthought,—suppose, after all, the World is right and we are less than men? Suppose this mad impulse within is all wrong, some mock mirage from the untrue?

So here we stand among thoughts of human unity, even through conquest and slavery; the inferiority of black men, even if forced by fraud; a shriek in the night for the freedom of men who themselves are not yet sure of their right to demand it. This is the tangle of thought and afterthought wherein we are called to solve the problem of training men for life.

Behind all its curiousness, so attractive alike to sage and *dilettante*,[9] lie its dim dangers, throwing across us shadows at once grotesque and awful. Plain it is to us that what the world seeks through desert and wild we have within our threshold,—a stalwart laboring force, suited to the semi-tropics; if, deaf to the voice of the Zeitgeist,[1] we refuse to use and develop these men, we risk poverty and loss. If, on the other hand, seized by the brutal afterthought, we debauch the race thus caught in our talons, selfishly sucking their blood and brains in the future as in the past, what shall save us from national decadence? Only that saner selfishness, which Education teaches men, can find the rights of all in the whirl of work.

Again, we may decry the color-prejudice of the South, yet it remains a heavy fact. Such curious kinks of the human mind exist and must be reckoned with soberly. They cannot be laughed away, nor always successfully stormed at, nor easily abolished by act of legislature. And yet they must not be encouraged by being let alone. They must be recognized as facts, but unpleasant facts; things that stand in the way of civilization and religion

---

7. A third something (Latin).
8. Grant.

9. A dabbler in arts or science.
1. The spirit of the age (German).

and common decency. They can be met in but one way,—by the breadth and broadening of human reason, by catholicity of taste and culture. And so, too, the native ambition and aspiration of men, even though they be black, backward, and ungraceful, must not lightly be dealt with. To stimulate wildly weak and untrained minds is to play with mighty fires; to flout their striving idly is to welcome a harvest of brutish crime and shameless lethargy in our very laps. The guiding of thought and the deft coördination of deed is at once the path of honor and humanity.

And so, in this great question of reconciling three vast and partially contradictory streams of thought, the one panacea of Education leaps to the lips of all:—such human training as will best use the labor of all men without enslaving or brutalizing; such training as will give us poise to encourage the prejudices that bulwark society, and to stamp out those that in sheer barbarity deafen us to the wail of prisoned souls within the Veil, and the mounting fury of shackled men.

But when we have vaguely said that Education will set this tangle straight, what have we uttered but a truism? Training for life teaches living; but what training for the profitable living together of black men and white? A hundred and fifty years ago our task would have seemed easier. Then Dr. Johnson[2] blandly assured us that education was needful solely for the embellishments of life, and was useless for ordinary vermin. To-day we have climbed to heights where we would open at least the outer courts of knowledge to all, display its treasures to many, and select the few to whom its mystery of Truth is revealed, not wholly by birth or the accidents of the stock market, but at least in part according to deftness and aim, talent and character. This programme, however, we are sorely puzzled in carrying out through that part of the land where the blight of slavery fell hardest, and where we are dealing with two backward peoples. To make here in human education that ever necessary combination of the permanent and the contingent—of the ideal and the practical in workable equilibrium—has been there, as it ever must be in every age and place, a matter of infinite experiment and frequent mistakes.

In rough approximation we may point out four varying decades of work in Southern education since the Civil War. From the close of the war until 1876, was the period of uncertain groping and temporary relief. There were army schools, mission schools, and schools of the Freedman's Bureau in chaotic disarrangement seeking system and coöperation. Then followed ten years of constructive definite effort toward the building of complete school systems in the South. Normal schools and colleges[3] were founded for the freedmen, and teachers trained there to man the public schools. There was the inevitable tendency of war to underestimate the prejudices of the master and the ignorance of the slave, and all seemed clear sailing out of the wreckage of the storm. Meantime, starting in this decade yet especially developing from 1885 to 1895, began the industrial revolution of the South. The land saw glimpses of a new destiny and the stirring of new ideals. The educational system striving to complete itself saw new obstacles

2. Samuel Johnson (1709–1784), English writer and critic.   3. Schools for the training of teachers.

and a field of work ever broader and deeper. The Negro colleges, hurriedly founded, were inadequately equipped, illogically distributed, and of varying efficiency and grade; the normal and high schools were doing little more than common-school work, and the common schools were training but a third of the children who ought to be in them, and training these too often poorly. At the same time the white South, by reason of its sudden conversion from the slavery ideal, by so much the more became set and strengthened in its racial prejudice, and crystallized it into harsh law and harsher custom; while the marvellous pushing forward of the poor white daily threatened to take even bread and butter from the mouths of the heavily handicapped sons of the freedmen. In the midst, then, of the larger problem of Negro education sprang up the more practical question of work, the inevitable economic quandary that faces a people in the transition from slavery to freedom, and especially those who make that change amid hate and prejudice, lawlessness and ruthless competition.

The industrial school springing to notice in this decade, but coming to full recognition in the decade beginning with 1895, was the proffered answer to this combined educational and economic crisis, and an answer of singular wisdom and timeliness. From the very first in nearly all the schools some attention had been given to training in handiwork, but now was this training first raised to a dignity that brought it in direct touch with the South's magnificent industrial development, and given an emphasis which reminded black folk that before the Temple of Knowledge swing the Gates of Toil.

Yet after all they are but gates, and when turning our eyes from the temporary and the contingent in the Negro problem to the broader question of the permanent uplifting and civilization of black men in America, we have a right to inquire, as this enthusiasm for material advancement mounts to its height, if after all the industrial school is the final and sufficient answer in the training of the Negro race; and to ask gently, but in all sincerity, the ever-recurring query of the ages, Is not life more than meat, and the body more than raiment?[4] And men ask this to-day all the more eagerly because of sinister signs in recent educational movements. The tendency is here, born of slavery and quickened to renewed life by the crazy imperialism of the day, to regard human beings as among the material resources of a land to be trained with an eye single to future dividends. Race-prejudices, which keep brown and black men in their "places," we are coming to regard as useful allies with such a theory, no matter how much they may dull the ambition and sicken the hearts of struggling human beings. And above all, we daily hear that an education that encourages aspiration, that sets the loftiest of ideals and seeks as an end culture and character rather than breadwinning, is the privilege of white men and the danger and delusion of black.

Especially has criticism been directed against the former educational efforts to aid the Negro. In the four periods I have mentioned, we find first, boundless, planless enthusiasm and sacrifice; then the preparation of teachers for a vast public-school system; then the launching and expansion

---

4. Matthew 6:25.

of that school system amid increasing difficulties; and finally the training of workmen for the new and growing industries. This development has been sharply ridiculed as a logical anomaly and flat reversal of nature. Soothly[5] we have been told that first industrial and manual training should have taught the Negro to work, then simple schools should have taught him to read and write, and finally, after years, high and normal schools could have completed the system, as intelligence and wealth demanded.

That a system logically so complete was historically impossible, it needs but a little thought to prove. Progress in human affairs is more often a pull than a push, surging forward of the exceptional man, and the lifting of his duller brethren slowly and painfully to his vantage-ground. Thus it was no accident that gave birth to universities centuries before the common schools, that made fair Harvard the first flower of our wilderness. So in the South: the mass of the freedmen at the end of the war lacked the intelligence so necessary to modern workingmen. They must first have the common school to teach them to read, write, and cipher; and they must have higher schools to teach teachers for the common schools. The white teachers who flocked South went to establish such a common-school system. Few held the idea of founding colleges; most of them at first would have laughed at the idea. But they faced, as all men since them have faced, that central paradox of the South,—the social separation of the races. At that time it was the sudden volcanic rupture of nearly all relations between black and white, in work and government and family life. Since then a new adjustment of relations in economic and political affairs has grown up,—an adjustment subtle and difficult to grasp, yet singularly ingenious, which leaves still that frightful chasm at the color-line across which men pass at their peril. Thus, then and now, there stand in the South two separate worlds; and separate not simply in the higher realms of social intercourse, but also in church and school, on railway and street-car, in hotels and theatres, in streets and city sections, in books and newspapers, in asylums and jails, in hospitals and graveyards. There is still enough of contact for large economic and group coöperation, but the separation is so thorough and deep that it absolutely precludes for the present between the races anything like that sympathetic and effective group-training and leadership of the one by the other, such as the American Negro and all backward peoples must have for effectual progress.

This the missionaries of '68 soon saw; and if effective industrial and trade schools were impracticable before the establishment of a common-school system, just as certainly no adequate common schools could be founded until there were teachers to teach them. Southern whites would not teach them; Northern whites in sufficient numbers could not be had. If the Negro was to learn, he must teach himself, and the most effective help that could be given him was the establishment of schools to train Negro teachers. This conclusion was slowly but surely reached by every student of the situation until simultaneously, in widely separated regions, without consultation or systematic plan, there arose a series of institutions designed to furnish teachers for the untaught. Above the sneers of critics at the obvious

5. In truth.

defects of this procedure must ever stand its one crushing rejoinder: in a single generation they put thirty thousand black teachers in the South; they wiped out the illiteracy of the majority of the black people of the land, and they made Tuskegee possible.

Such higher training-schools tended naturally to deepen broader development: at first they were common and grammar schools, then some became high schools. And finally, by 1900, some thirty-four had one year or more of studies of college grade. This development was reached with different degrees of speed in different institutions: Hampton is still a high school, while Fisk University started her college in 1871, and Spelman Seminary[6] about 1896. In all cases the aim was identical,—to maintain the standards of the lower training by giving teachers and leaders the best practicable training; and above all, to furnish the black world with adequate standards of human culture and lofty ideals of life. It was not enough that the teachers of teachers should be trained in technical normal methods; they must also, so far as possible, be broad-minded, cultured men and women, to scatter civilization among a people whose ignorance was not simply of letters, but of life itself.

It can thus be seen that the work of education in the South began with higher institutions of training, which threw off as their foliage common schools, and later industrial schools, and at the same time strove to shoot their roots ever deeper toward college and university training. That this was an inevitable and necessary development, sooner or later, goes without saying; but there has been, and still is, a question in many minds if the natural growth was not forced, and if the higher training was not either overdone or done with cheap and unsound methods. Among white Southerners this feeling is widespread and positive. A prominent Southern journal voiced this in a recent editorial.

"The experiment that has been made to give the colored students classical training has not been satisfactory. Even though many were able to pursue the course, most of them did so in a parrot-like way, learning what was taught, but not seeming to appropriate the truth and import of their instruction, and graduating without sensible aim or valuable occupation for their future. The whole scheme has proved a waste of time, efforts, and the money of the state."

While most fair-minded men would recognize this as extreme and overdrawn, still without doubt many are asking, Are there a sufficient number of Negroes ready for college training to warrant the undertaking? Are not too many students prematurely forced into this work? Does it not have the effect of dissatisfying the young Negro with his environment? And do these graduates succeed in real life? Such natural questions cannot be evaded, nor on the other hand must a Nation naturally skeptical as to Negro ability assume an unfavorable answer without careful inquiry and patient openness to conviction. We must not forget that most Americans answer all queries regarding the Negro *a priori*, and that the least that human courtesy can do is to listen to evidence.

The advocates of the higher education of the Negro would be the last to

6. A school for black women founded in 1881 in Atlanta.

deny the incompleteness and glaring defects of the present system: too many institutions have attempted to do college work, the work in some cases has not been thoroughly done, and quantity rather than quality has sometimes been sought. But all this can be said of higher education throughout the land; it is the almost inevitable incident of educational growth, and leaves the deeper question of the legitimate demand for the higher training of Negroes untouched. And this latter question can be settled in but one way,—by a first-hand study of the facts. If we leave out of view all institutions which have not actually graduated students from a course higher than that of a New England high school, even though they be called colleges; if then we take the thirty-four remaining institutions, we may clear up many misapprehensions by asking searchingly, What kind of institutions are they? what do they teach? and what sort of men do they graduate?

And first we may say that this type of college, including Atlanta, Fisk, and Howard, Wilberforce and Lincoln, Biddle, Shaw,[7] and the rest, is peculiar, almost unique. Through the shining trees that whisper before me as I write, I catch glimpses of a boulder of New England granite, covering a grave, which graduates of Atlanta University have placed there, with this inscription:

"IN GRATEFUL MEMORY OF THEIR
FORMER TEACHER AND FRIEND
AND OF THE UNSELFISH LIFE HE
LIVED, AND THE NOBLE WORK HE
WROUGHT; THAT THEY, THEIR
CHILDREN, AND THEIR CHIL-
DREN'S CHILDREN MIGHT BE
BLESSED."[8]

This was the gift of New England to the freed Negro: not alms, but a friend; not cash, but character. It was not and is not money these seething millions want, but love and sympathy, the pulse of hearts beating with red blood;—a gift which to-day only their own kindred and race can bring to the masses, but which once saintly souls brought to their favored children in the crusade of the sixties, that finest thing in American history, and one of the few things untainted by sordid greed and cheap vainglory. The teachers in these institutions came not to keep the Negroes in their place, but to raise them out of the defilement of the places where slavery had wallowed them. The colleges they founded were social settlements; homes where the best of the sons of the freedmen came in close and sympathetic touch with the best traditions of New England. They lived and ate together, studied and worked, hoped and harkened in the dawning light. In actual formal content their curriculum was doubtless old-fashioned, but in educational power it was supreme, for it was the contact of living souls.

From such schools about two thousand Negroes have gone forth with the bachelor's degree. The number in itself is enough to put at rest the argument that too large a proportion of Negroes are receiving higher train-

7. Colleges for African Americans in Ohio, South Carolina, and North Carolina.

8. A memorial to Edmund Asa Ware, founder of Atlanta University.

ing. If the ratio to population of all Negro students throughout the land, in both college and secondary training, be counted, Commissioner Harris assures us "it must be increased to five times its present average" to equal the average of the land.

Fifty years ago the ability of Negro students in any appreciable numbers to master a modern college course would have been difficult to prove. To-day it is proved by the fact that four hundred Negroes, many of whom have been reported as brilliant students, have received the bachelor's degree from Harvard, Yale, Oberlin, and seventy other leading colleges. Here we have, then, nearly twenty-five hundred Negro graduates, of whom the crucial query must be made, How far did their training fit them for life? It is of course extremely difficult to collect satisfactory data on such a point,— difficult to reach the men, to get trustworthy testimony, and to gauge that testimony by any generally acceptable criterion of success. In 1900, the Conference at Atlanta University undertook to study these graduates, and published the results. First they sought to know what these graduates were doing, and succeeded in getting answers from nearly two-thirds of the living. The direct testimony was in almost all cases corroborated by the reports of the colleges where they graduated, so that in the main the reports were worthy of credence. Fifty-three per cent of these graduates were teachers,—presidents of institutions, heads of normal schools, principals of city school-systems, and the like. Seventeen per cent were clergymen; another seventeen per cent were in the professions, chiefly as physicians. Over six per cent were merchants, farmers, and artisans, and four per cent were in the government civil-service. Granting even that a considerable proportion of the third unheard from are unsuccessful, this is a record of usefulness. Personally I know many hundreds of these graduates, and have corresponded with more than a thousand; through others I have followed carefully the life-work of scores; I have taught some of them and some of the pupils whom they have taught, lived in homes which they have builded, and looked at life through their eyes. Comparing them as a class with my fellow students in New England and in Europe, I cannot hesitate in saying that nowhere have I met men and women with a broader spirit of helpfulness, with deeper devotion to their life-work, or with more consecrated determination to succeed in the face of bitter difficulties than among Negro college-bred men. They have, to be sure, their proportion of ne'er-do-wells, their pedants and lettered fools, but they have a surprisingly small proportion of them; they have not that culture of manner which we instinctively associate with university men, forgetting that in reality it is the heritage from cultured homes, and that no people a generation removed from slavery can escape a certain unpleasant rawness and *gaucherie*,[9] despite the best of training.

With all their larger vision and deeper sensibility, these men have usually been conservative, careful leaders. They have seldom been agitators, have withstood the temptation to head the mob, and have worked steadily and faithfully in a thousand communities in the South. As teachers, they have given the South a commendable system of city schools and large

9. Uncouthness.

numbers of private normal-schools and academies. Colored college-bred men have worked side by side with white college graduates at Hampton; almost from the beginning the backbone of Tuskegee's teaching force has been formed of graduates from Fisk and Atlanta. And to-day the institute is filled with college graduates, from the energetic wife of the principal down to the teacher of agriculture, including nearly half of the executive council and a majority of the heads of departments. In the professions, college men are slowly but surely leavening the Negro church, are healing and prevent-ing the devastations of disease, and beginning to furnish legal protection for the liberty and property of the toiling masses. All this is needful work. Who would do it if Negroes did not? How could Negroes do it if they were not trained carefully for it? If white people need colleges to furnish teach-ers, ministers, lawyers, and doctors, do black people need nothing of the sort?

If it is true that there are an appreciable number of Negro youth in the land capable by character and talent to receive that higher training, the end of which is culture, and if the two and a half thousand who have had something of this training in the past have in the main proved them-selves useful to their race and generation, the question then comes, What place in the future development of the South ought the Negro college and college-bred man to occupy? That the present social separation and acute race-sensitiveness must eventually yield to the influences of culture, as the South grows civilized, is clear. But such transformation calls for singular wisdom and patience. If, while the healing of this vast sore is progressing, the races are to live for many years side by side, united in economic effort, obeying a common government, sensitive to mutual thought and feeling, yet subtly and silently separate in many matters of deeper human inti-macy,—if this unusual and dangerous development is to progress amid peace and order, mutual respect and growing intelligence, it will call for social surgery at once the delicatest and nicest in modern history. It will demand broad-minded, upright men, both white and black, and in its final accomplishment American civilization will triumph. So far as white men are concerned, this fact is to-day being recognized in the South, and a happy renaissance of university education seems imminent. But the very voices that cry hail to this good work are, strange to relate, largely silent or antagonistic to the higher education of the Negro.

Strange to relate! for this is certain, no secure civilization can be built in the South with the Negro as an ignorant, turbulent proletariat. Suppose we seek to remedy this by making them laborers and nothing more: they are not fools, they have tasted of the Tree of Life, and they will not cease to think, will not cease attempting to read the riddle of the world. By taking away their best equipped teachers and leaders, by slamming the door of opportunity in the faces of their bolder and brighter minds, will you make them satisfied with their lot? or will you not rather transfer their leading from the hands of men taught to think to the hands of untrained dema-gogues? We ought not to forget that despite the pressure of poverty, and despite the active discouragement and even ridicule of friends, the demand for higher training steadily increases among Negro youth: there were, in the years from 1875 to 1880, 22 Negro graduates from Northern colleges;

from 1885 to 1890 there were 43, and from 1895 to 1900, nearly 100 graduates. From Southern Negro colleges there were, in the same three periods,
143, 413, and over 500 graduates. Here, then, is the plain thirst for training;
by refusing to give this Talented Tenth the key to knowledge, can any sane
man imagine that they will lightly lay aside their yearning and contentedly
become hewers of wood and drawers of water?

No. The dangerously clear logic of the Negro's position will more and
more loudly assert itself in that day when increasing wealth and more intricate social organization preclude the South from being, as it so largely is,
simply an armed camp for intimidating black folk. Such waste of energy
cannot be spared if the South is to catch up with civilization. And as the
black third of the land grows in thrift and skill, unless skilfully guided in its
larger philosophy, it must more and more brood over the red past and the
creeping, crooked present, until it grasps a gospel of revolt and revenge and
throws its new-found energies athwart the current of advance. Even to-day
the masses of the Negroes see all too clearly the anomalies of their position
and the moral crookedness of yours. You may marshal strong indictments
against them, but their counter-cries, lacking though they be in formal
logic, have burning truths within them which you may not wholly ignore,
O Southern Gentlemen! If you deplore their presence here, they ask, Who
brought us? When you cry, Deliver us from the vision of intermarriage,
they answer that legal marriage is infinitely better than systematic concubinage [1] and prostitution. And if in just fury you accuse their vagabonds
of violating women, they also in fury quite as just may reply: The wrong
which your gentlemen have done against helpless black women in defiance of your own laws is written on the foreheads of two millions of mulattoes, and written in ineffaceable blood. And finally, when you fasten
crime upon this race as its peculiar trait, they answer that slavery was the
arch-crime, and lynching and lawlessness its twin abortion; that color and
race are not crimes, and yet they it is which in this land receives most un-
ceasing condemnation, North, East, South, and West.

I will not say such arguments are wholly justified,—I will not insist that
there is no other side to the shield; but I do say that of the nine millions of
Negroes in this nation, there is scarcely one out of the cradle to whom
these arguments do not daily present themselves in the guise of terrible
truth. I insist that the question of the future is how best to keep these millions from brooding over the wrongs of the past and the difficulties of the
present, so that all their energies may be bent toward a cheerful striving and
co-operation with their white neighbors toward a larger, juster, and fuller
future. That one wise method of doing this lies in the closer knitting of the
Negro to the great industrial possibilities of the South is a great truth. And
this the common schools and the manual training and trade schools are
working to accomplish. But these alone are not enough. The foundations
of knowledge in this race, as in others, must be sunk deep in the college
and university if we would build a solid, permanent structure. Internal
problems of social advance must inevitably come,—problems of work and

1. Cohabitation without legal marriage.

wages, of families and homes, of morals and the true valuing of the things of life; and all these and other inevitable problems of civilization the Negro must meet and solve largely for himself, by reason of his isolation; and can there be any possible solution other than by study and thought and an appeal to the rich experience of the past? Is there not, with such a group and in such a crisis, infinitely more danger to be apprehended from half-trained minds and shallow thinking than from over-education and over-refinement? Surely we have wit enough to found a Negro college so manned and equipped as to steer successfully between the *dilettante* and the fool. We shall hardly induce black men to believe that if their stomachs be full, it matters little about their brains. They already dimly perceive that the paths of peace winding between honest toil and dignified manhood call for the guidance of skilled thinkers, the loving, reverent comradeship between the black lowly and the black men emancipated by training and culture.

The function of the Negro college, then, is clear: it must maintain the standards of popular education, it must seek the social regeneration of the Negro, and it must help in the solution of problems of race contact and co-operation. And finally, beyond all this, it must develop men. Above our modern socialism, and out of the worship of the mass, must persist and evolve that higher individualism which the centres of culture protect; there must come a loftier respect for the sovereign human soul that seeks to know itself and the world about it; that seeks a freedom for expansion and self-development; that will love and hate and labor in its own way, untrammeled alike by old and new. Such souls aforetime have inspired and guided worlds, and if we be not wholly bewitched by our Rhine-gold,[2] they shall again. Herein the longing of black men must have respect: the rich and bitter depth of their experience, the unknown treasures of their inner life, the strange rendings of nature they have seen, may give the world new points of view and make their loving, living, and doing precious to all human hearts. And to themselves in these the days that try their souls, the chance to soar in the dim blue air above the smoke is to their finer spirits boon and guerdon[3] for what they lose on earth by being black.

I sit with Shakespeare and he winces not. Across the color line I move arm in arm with Balzac and Dumas, where smiling men and welcoming women glide in gilded halls. From out the caves of evening that swing between the strong-limbed earth and the tracery of the stars, I summon Aristotle and Aurelius[4] and what soul I will, and they come all graciously with no scorn nor condescension. So, wed with Truth, I dwell above the Veil. Is this the life you grudge us, O knightly America? Is this the life you long to change into the dull red hideousness of Georgia? Are you so afraid lest peering from this high Pisgah, between Philistine and Amalekite,[5] we sight the Promised Land?

2. A reference to Richard Wagner's opera *The Reingold* (1853–54); a mass of pure gold hidden in the Rhine River.
3. A reward.
4. Marcus Aurelius Antoninus (A.D. 121–180), Roman emperor and philosopher. Aristotle (384–

322 B.C.), Greek philosopher.
5. Peoples who repeatedly warred with the Israelites for control of Canaan, the Promised Land. Pisgah is a mountain from which Moses could see the Promised Land.

VII. Of the Black Belt

I am black but comely, O ye daughters of Jerusalem,
As the tents of Kedar, as the curtains of Solomon.
Look not upon me, because I am black,
Because the sun hath looked upon me:
My mother's children were angry with me;
They made me the keeper of the vineyards;
But mine own vineyard have I not kept.

THE SONG OF SOLOMON[6]

Out of the North the train thundered, and we woke to see the crimson soil of Georgia stretching away bare and monotonous right and left. Here and there lay straggling, unlovely villages, and lean men loafed leisurely at the depots; then again came the stretch of pines and clay. Yet we did not nod, nor weary of the scene; for this is historic ground. Right across our track, three hundred and sixty years ago, wandered the cavalcade of Hernando de Soto,[7] looking for gold and the Great Sea; and he and his footsore captives disappeared yonder in the grim forests to the west. Here sits Atlanta, the city of a hundred hills, with something Western, something Southern, and something quite its own, in its busy life. And a little past Atlanta, to the southwest, is the land of the Cherokees, and there, not far from where Sam Hose[8] was crucified, you may stand on a spot which is to-day the centre of the Negro problem,—the centre of those nine million men who are America's dark heritage from slavery and the slave-trade.

Not only is Georgia thus the geographical focus of our Negro population, but in many other respects, both now and yesterday, the Negro problems have seemed to be centered in this State. No other State in the Union can count a million Negroes among its citizens,—a population as large as the slave population of the whole Union in 1800; no other State fought so long and strenuously to gather this host of Africans. Oglethorpe[9] thought slavery against law and gospel; but the circumstances which gave Georgia its first inhabitants were not calculated to furnish citizens over-nice in their ideas about rum and slaves. Despite the prohibitions of the trustees, these Georgians, like some of their descendants, proceeded to take the law into their own hands; and so pliant were the judges, and so flagrant the smuggling, and so earnest were the prayers of Whitefield,[1] that by the middle of

---

6. Song of Solomon 1:5–6.
7. Spanish explorer of southeastern North America (c. 1500–1542).
8. A black farm worker lynched in Palmetto, Georgia, in 1899.

9. James Edward Oglethorpe (1696–1785), founder of the colony of Georgia in 1733.
1. George Whitefield (1714–1770), English evangelist.

the eighteenth century all restrictions were swept away, and the slave-trade
went merrily on for fifty years and more.

Down in Darien, where the Delegal riots took place some summers ago,
there used to come a strong protest against slavery from the Scotch Highlanders; and the Moravians of Ebenezea[2] did not like the system. But not
till the Haytian Terror of Toussaint was the trade in men even checked;
while the national statute of 1808[3] did not suffice to stop it. How the Africans poured in!—fifty thousand between 1790 and 1810, and then, from
Virginia and from smugglers, two thousand a year for many years more. So
the thirty thousand Negroes of Georgia in 1790 were doubled in a decade,—were over a hundred thousand in 1810, had reached two hundred
thousand in 1820, and half a million at the time of the war. Thus like a
snake the black population writhed upward.

But we must hasten on our journey. This that we pass as we leave Atlanta
is the ancient land of the Cherokees,—that brave Indian nation which
strove so long for its fatherland, until Fate and the United States Government drove them beyond the Mississippi. If you wish to ride with me you
must come into the "Jim Crow Car." There will be no objection,—already
four other white men, and a little white girl with her nurse, are in there.
Usually the races are mixed in there; but the white coach is all white. Of
course this car is not so good as the other, but it is fairly clean and comfortable. The discomfort lies chiefly in the hearts of those four black men yonder—and in mine.

We rumble south in quite a business-like way. The bare red clay and
pines of Northern Georgia begin to disappear, and in their place appears a
rich rolling land, luxuriant, and here and there well tilled. This is the land
of the Creek Indians; and a hard time the Georgians had to seize it. The
towns grow more frequent and more interesting, and brand-new cotton
mills rise on every side. Below Macon the world grows darker; for now we
approach the Black Belt,—that strange land of shadows, at which even
slaves paled in the past, and whence come now only faint and half-intelligi-
ble murmurs to the world beyond. The "Jim Crow Car" grows larger and a
shade better; three rough field-hands and two or three white loafers accompany us, and the newsboy still spreads his wares at one end. The sun is
setting, but we can see the great cotton country as we enter it,—the soil now.
dark and fertile, now thin and gray, with fruit-trees and dilapidated buildings,—all the way to Albany.

At Albany, in the heart of the Black Belt, we stop. Two hundred miles
south of Atlanta, two hundred miles west of the Atlantic, and one hundred
miles north of the Great Gulf lies Dougherty County, with ten thousand
Negroes and two thousand whites. The Flint River winds down from And-
ersonville, and, turning suddenly at Albany, the county-seat, hurries on to
join the Chattahoochee and the sea. Andrew Jackson knew the Flint well,
and marched across it once to avenge the Indian Massacre at Fort Mims.

2. A pacifist Protestant Christian sect that founded
a settlement in Ebenezer, Georgia. Darien was a
site of black communal resistance to a threatened
lynching in McIntosh County, Georgia, in 1899.
3. A law passed by U.S. Congress to prohibit the
African slave trade.

That was in 1814, not long before the battle of New Orleans;[4] and by the Creek treaty that followed this campaign, all Dougherty County, and much other rich land, was ceded to Georgia. Still, settlers fought shy of this land, for the Indians were all about, and they were unpleasant neighbors in those days. The panic of 1837, which Jackson bequeathed to Van Buren,[5] turned the planters from the impoverished lands of Virginia, the Carolinas, and east Georgia, toward the West. The Indians were removed to Indian Territory,[6] and settlers poured into these coveted lands to retrieve their broken fortunes. For a radius of a hundred miles about Albany, stretched a great fertile land, luxuriant with forests of pine, oak, ash, hickory, and poplar; hot with the sun and damp with the rich black swamp-land; and here the corner-stone of the Cotton Kingdom was laid.

Albany is to-day a wide-streeted, placid, Southern town, with a broad sweep of stores and saloons, and flanking rows of homes,—whites usually to the north, and blacks to the south. Six days in the week the town looks decidedly too small for itself, and takes frequent and prolonged naps. But on Saturday suddenly the whole county disgorges itself upon the place, and a perfect flood of black peasantry pours through the streets, fills the stores, blocks the sidewalks, chokes the thoroughfares, and takes full possession of the town. They are black, sturdy, uncouth country folk, good-natured and simple, talkative to a degree, and yet far more silent and brooding than the crowds of the Rhine-pfalz, or Naples, or Cracow.[7] They drink considerable quantities of whiskey, but do not get very drunk; they talk and laugh loudly at times, but seldom quarrel or fight. They walk up and down the streets, meet and gossip with friends, stare at the shop windows, buy coffee, cheap candy, and clothes, and at dusk drive home—happy? well no, not exactly happy, but much happier than as though they had not come.

Thus Albany is a real capital,—a typical Southern county town, the centre of the life of ten thousand souls; their point of contact with the outer world, their centre of news and gossip, their market for buying and selling, borrowing and lending, their fountain of justice and law. Once upon a time we knew country life so well and city life so little, that we illustrated city life as that of a closely crowded country district. Now the world has well-nigh forgotten what the country is, and we must imagine a little city of black people scattered far and wide over three hundred lonesome square miles of land, without train or trolley, in the midst of cotton and corn, and wide patches of sand and gloomy soil.

It gets pretty hot in Southern Georgia in July,—a sort of dull, determined heat that seems quite independent of the sun; so it took us some days to muster courage enough to leave the porch and venture out on the long country roads, that we might see this unknown world. Finally we started. It was about ten in the morning, bright with a faint breeze, and we jogged leisurely southward in the valley of the Flint. We passed the scattered box-

---

4. The site of an American victory at the end of the War of 1812. Andrew Jackson (1767–1845), U.S. president (1829–37). Fort Mims was the site of an 1813 massacre of whites and blacks by the Creek Indians in Alabama.
5. Martin Van Buren (1782–1862), U.S. president (1837–41). "Panic of 1837": an economic crisis brought on by land speculation and overextended credit.
6. I.e., Oklahoma.
7. Cities in Germany, Italy, and Poland, respectively.

like cabins of the brick-yard hands, and the long tenement-row facetiously called "The Ark," and were soon in the open country, and on the confines of the great plantations of other days. There is the "Joe Fields place"; a rough old fellow was he, and had killed many a "nigger" in his day. Twelve miles his plantation used to run,—a regular barony. It is nearly all gone now; only straggling bits belong to the family, and the rest has passed to Jews and Negroes. Even the bits which are left are heavily mortgaged, and, like the rest of the land, tilled by tenants. Here is one of them now,—a tall brown man, a hard worker and a hard drinker, illiterate, but versed in farm-lore, as his nodding crops declare. This distressingly new board house is his, and he has just moved out of yonder moss-grown cabin with its one square room.

From the curtains in Benton's house, down the road, a dark comely face is staring at the strangers; for passing carriages are not every-day occurrences here. Benton is an intelligent yellow man with a good-sized family, and manages a plantation blasted by the war and now the broken staff of the widow. He might be well-to-do, they say; but he carouses too much in Albany. And the half-desolate spirit of neglect born of the very soil seems to have settled on these acres. In times past there were cotton-gins and machinery here; but they have rotted away.

The whole land seems forlorn and forsaken. Here are the remnants of the vast plantations of the Sheldons, the Pellots, and the Rensons; but the souls of them are passed. The houses lie in half ruin, or have wholly disappeared; the fences have flown, and the families are wandering in the world. Strange vicissitudes have met these whilom[8] masters. Yonder stretch the wide acres of Bildad Reasor; he died in war-time, but the upstart overseer hastened to wed the widow. Then he went, and his neighbors too, and now only the black tenant remains; but the shadow-hand of the master's grand-nephew or cousin or creditor stretches out of the gray distance to collect the rack-rent[9] remorselessly, and so the land is uncared-for and poor. Only black tenants can stand such a system, and they only because they must. Ten miles we have ridden to-day and have seen no white face.

A resistless feeling of depression falls slowly upon us, despite the gaudy sunshine and the green cotton-fields. This, then, is the Cotton Kingdom,—the shadow of a marvellous dream. And where is the King? Perhaps this is he,—the sweating ploughman, tilling his eighty acres with two lean mules, and fighting a hard battle with debt. So we sit musing, until, as we turn a corner on the sandy road, there comes a fairer scene suddenly in view,—a neat cottage snugly ensconced by the road, and near it a little store. A tall bronzed man rises from the porch as we hail him, and comes out to our carriage. He is six feet in height, with a sober face that smiles gravely. He walks too straight to be a tenant,—yes, he owns two hundred and forty acres. "The land is run down since the boom-days of eighteen hundred and fifty," he explains, and cotton is low. Three black tenants live on his place, and in his little store he keeps a small stock of tobacco, snuff, soap, and soda, for the neighborhood. Here is his ginhouse with new machinery just installed.

8. Former.   9. Excessively high rent.

Three hundred bales of cotton went through it last year. Two children he has sent away to school. Yes, he says sadly, he is getting on, but cotton is down to four cents; I know how Debt sits staring at him.

Wherever the King may be, the parks and palaces of the Cotton Kingdom have not wholly disappeared. We plunge even now into great groves of oak and towering pine, with an undergrowth of myrtle and shrubbery. This was the "home-house" of the Thompsons,—slave-barons who drove their coach and four in the merry past. All is silence now, and ashes, and tangled weeds. The owner put his whole fortune into the rising cotton industry of the fifties, and with the falling prices of the eighties he packed up and stole away. Yonder is another grove, with unkempt lawn, great magnolias, and grass-grown paths. The Big House stands in half-ruin, its great front door staring blankly at the street, and the back part grotesquely restored for its black tenant. A shabby, well-built Negro he is, unlucky and irresolute. He digs hard to pay rent to the white girl who owns the remnant of the place. She married a policeman, and lives in Savannah.

Now and again we come to churches. Here is one now,—Shepherd's, they call it,—a great whitewashed barn of a thing, perched on stilts of stone, and looking for all the world as though it were just resting here a moment and might be expected to waddle off down the road at almost any time. And yet it is the centre of a hundred cabin homes; and sometimes, of a Sunday, five hundred persons from far and near gather here and talk and eat and sing. There is a school-house near,—a very airy, empty shed; but even this is an improvement, for usually the school is held in the church. The churches vary from log-huts to those like Shepherd's, and the schools from nothing to this little house that sits demurely on the county line. It is a tiny plank-house, perhaps ten by twenty, and has within a double row of rough unplaned benches, resting mostly on legs, sometimes on boxes. Opposite the door is a square home-made desk. In one corner are the ruins of a stove, and in the other a dim blackboard. It is the cheerfulest schoolhouse I have seen in Dougherty, save in town. Back of the schoolhouse is a lodge-house two stories high and not quite finished. Societies meet there,—societies "to care for the sick and bury the dead"; and these societies grow and flourish.

We had come to the boundaries of Dougherty, and were about to turn west along the county-line, when all these sights were pointed out to us by a kindly old man, black, white-haired, and seventy. Forty-five years he had lived here, and now supports himself and his old wife by the help of the steer tethered yonder and the charity of his black neighbors. He shows us the farm of the Hills just across the county line in Baker,—a widow and two strapping sons, who raised ten bales (one need not add "cotton" down here) last year. There are fences and pigs and cows, and the soft-voiced, velvet-skinned young Memnon,[1] who sauntered half-bashfully over to greet the strangers, is proud of his home. We turn now to the west along the county line. Great dismantled trunks of pines tower above the green cotton-fields, cracking their naked gnarled fingers toward the border of living forest beyond. There is little beauty in this region, only a sort of crude abandon that suggests power,—a naked grandeur, as it were. The houses are

1. Legendary leader of the Ethiopian allies of Troy in the Trojan War.

bare and straight; there are no hammocks or easy-chairs, and few flowers. So when, as here at Rawdon's, one sees a vine clinging to a little porch, and home-like windows peeping over the fences, one takes a long breath. I think I never before quite realized the place of the Fence in civilization. This is the Land of the Unfenced, where crouch on either hand scores of ugly one-room cabins, cheerless and dirty. Here lies the Negro problem in its naked dirt and penury. And here are no fences. But now and then the criss-cross rails or straight palings break into view, and then we know a touch of culture is near. Of course Harrison Gohagen,—a quiet yellow man, young, smooth-faced, and diligent,—of course he is lord of some hundred acres, and we expect to see a vision of well-kept rooms and fat beds and laughing children. For has he not fine fences? And those over yonder, why should they build fences on the rack-rented land? It will only increase their rent.

On we wind, through sand and pines and glimpses of old plantations, till there creeps into sight a cluster of buildings,—wood and brick, mills and houses, and scattered cabins. It seemed quite a village. As it came nearer and nearer, however, the aspect changed: the buildings were rotten, the bricks were falling out, the mills were silent, and the store was closed. Only in the cabins appeared now and then a bit of lazy life. I could imagine the place under some weird spell, and was half-minded to search out the princess. An old ragged black man, honest, simple, and improvident, told us the tale. The Wizard of the North—the Capitalist—had rushed down in the seventies to woo this coy dark soil. He bought a square mile or more, and for a time the field-hands sang, the gins groaned, and the mills buzzed. Then came a change. The agent's son embezzled the funds and ran off with them. Then the agent himself disappeared. Finally the new agent stole even the books, and the company in wrath closed its business and its houses, refused to sell, and let houses and furniture and machinery rust and rot. So the Waters-Loring plantation was stilled by the spell of dishonesty, and stands like some gaunt rebuke to a scarred land.

Somehow that plantation ended our day's journey; for I could not shake off the influence of that silent scene. Back toward town we glided, past the straight and thread-like pines, past a dark tree-dotted pond where the air was heavy with a dead sweet perfume. White slender-legged curlews[2] flitted by us, and the garnet blooms of the cotton looked gay against the green and purple stalks. A peasant girl was hoeing in the field, white-turbaned and black-limbed. All this we saw, but the spell still lay upon us.

How curious a land is this,—how full of untold story, of tragedy and laughter, and the rich legacy of human life; shadowed with a tragic past, and big with future promise! This is the Black Belt of Georgia. Dougherty County is the west end of the Black Belt, and men once called it the Egypt of the Confederacy. It is full of historic interest. First there is the Swamp, to the west, where the Chickasawhatchee flows sullenly southward. The shadow of an old plantation lies at its edge, forlorn and dark. Then comes the pool; pendent gray moss and brackish waters appear, and forests filled with wild-fowl. In one place the wood is on fire, smouldering in dull red

2. Large wading birds.

anger; but nobody minds. Then the swamp grows beautiful; a raised road, built by chained Negro convicts, dips down into it, and forms a way walled and almost covered in living green. Spreading trees spring from a prodigal luxuriance of undergrowth; great dark green shadows fade into the black background, until all is one mass of tangled semi-tropical foliage, marvellous in its weird savage splendor. Once we crossed a black silent stream, where the sad trees and writhing creepers, all glinting fiery yellow and green, seemed like some vast cathedral,—some green Milan[3] builded of wildwood. And as I crossed, I seemed to see again that fierce tragedy of seventy years ago. Osceola,[4] the Indian-Negro chieftain, had risen in the swamps of Florida, vowing vengeance. His war-cry reached the red Creeks of Dougherty, and their war-cry rang from the Chattahoochee to the sea. Men and women and children fled and fell before them as they swept into Dougherty. In yonder shadows a dark and hideously painted warrior glided stealthily on,—another and another, until three hundred had crept into the treacherous swamp. Then the false slime closing about them called the white men from the east. Waist-deep, they fought beneath the tall trees, until the war-cry was hushed and the Indians glided back into the west. Small wonder the wood is red.

Then came the black slaves. Day after day the clank of chained feet marching from Virginia and Carolina to Georgia was heard in these rich swamp lands. Day after day the songs of the callous, the wail of the motherless, and the muttered curses of the wretched echoed from the Flint to the Chickasawhatchee, until by 1860 there had risen in West Dougherty perhaps the richest slave kingdom the modern world ever knew. A hundred and fifty barons commanded the labor of nearly six thousand Negroes, held sway over farms with ninety thousand acres of tilled land, valued even in times of cheap soil at three millions of dollars. Twenty thousand bales of ginned cotton went yearly to England, New and Old; and men that came there bankrupt made money and grew rich. In a single decade the cotton output increased four-fold and the value of lands was tripled. It was the heyday of the *nouveau riche*,[5] and a life of careless extravagance reigned among the masters. Four and six bob-tailed thoroughbreds rolled their coaches to town; open hospitality and gay entertainment were the rule. Parks and groves were laid out, rich with flower and vine, and in the midst stood the low wide-halled "big house," with its porch and columns and great fire-places.

And yet with all this there was something sordid, something forced,—a certain feverish unrest and recklessness; for was not all this show and tinsel built upon a groan? "This land was a little Hell," said a ragged, brown, and grave-faced man to me. We were seated near a roadside blacksmith-shop, and behind was the bare ruin of some master's home. "I 've seen niggers drop dead in the furrow, but they were kicked aside, and the plough never stopped. And down in the guardhouse, there's where the blood ran."

With such foundations a kingdom must in time sway and fall. The masters moved to Macon and Augusta, and left only the irresponsible overseers

---

3. I.e., the famous cathedral in Milan, Italy.
4. Seminole Indian (1804?–1838) who led his people in their second war against the United States.
5. Newly rich (French).

on the land. And the result is such ruin as this, the Lloyd "home-place":—great waving oaks, a spread of lawn, myrtles and chestnuts, all ragged and wild; a solitary gate-post standing where once was a castle entrance; an old rusty anvil lying amid rotting bellows and wood in the ruins of a blacksmith shop; a wide rambling old mansion, brown and dingy, filled now with the grandchildren of the slaves who once waited on its tables; while the family of the master has dwindled to two lone women, who live in Macon and feed hungrily off the remnants of an earldom. So we ride on, past phantom gates and falling homes,—past the once flourishing farms of the Smiths, the Gandys, and the Lagores,—and find all dilapidated and half ruined, even there where a solitary white woman, a relic of other days, sits alone in state among miles of Negroes and rides to town in her ancient coach each day.

This was indeed the Egypt of the Confederacy,—the rich granary whence potatoes and corn and cotton poured out to the famished and ragged Confederate troops as they battled for a cause lost long before 1861. Sheltered and secure, it became the place of refuge for families, wealth, and slaves. Yet even then the hard ruthless rape of the land began to tell. The red-clay sub-soil already had begun to peer above the loam. The harder the slaves were driven the more careless and fatal was their farming. Then came the revolution of war and Emancipation, the bewilderment of Reconstruction,—and now, what is the Egypt of the Confederacy, and what meaning has it for the nation's weal or woe?

It is a land of rapid contrasts and of curiously mingled hope and pain. Here sits a pretty blue-eyed quadroon[6] hiding her bare feet; she was married only last week, and yonder in the field is her dark young husband, hoeing to support her, at thirty cents a day without board. Across the way is Gatesby, brown and tall, lord of two thousand acres shrewdly won and held. There is a store conducted by his black son, a blacksmith shop, and a ginnery.[7] Five miles below here is a town owned and controlled by one white New Englander. He owns almost a Rhode Island county, with thousands of acres and hundreds of black laborers. Their cabins look better than most, and the farm, with machinery and fertilizers, is much more business-like than any in the county, although the manager drives hard bargains in wages. When now we turn and look five miles above, there on the edge of town are five houses of prostitutes,—two of blacks and three of whites; and in one of the houses of the whites a worthless black boy was harbored too openly two years ago; so he was hanged for rape. And here, too, is the high whitewashed fence of the "stockade," as the county prison is called; the white folks say it is ever full of black criminals,—the black folks say that only colored boys are sent to jail, and they not because they are guilty, but because the State needs criminals to eke out its income by their forced labor.

The Jew is the heir of the slave-baron in Dougherty; and as we ride westward, by wide stretching cornfields and stubby orchards of peach and pear, we see on all sides within the circle of dark forest a Land of Canaan. Here and there are tales of projects for money-getting, born in the swift days of Reconstruction,—"improvement" companies, wine companies, mills and factories; nearly all failed, and the Jew fell heir. It is a beautiful land, this

6. A person who is one-quarter African American.   7. Where cotton seeds are separated from the fiber.

Dougherty, west of the Flint. The forests are wonderful, the solemn pines have disappeared, and this is the "Oakey Woods," with its wealth of hickories, beeches, oaks, and palmettos. But a pall of debt hangs over the beautiful land; the merchants are in debt to the wholesalers, the planters are in debt to the merchants, the tenants owe the planters, and laborers bow and bend beneath the burden of it all. Here and there a man has raised his head above these murky waters. We passed one fenced stock-farm, with grass and grazing cattle, that looked very homelike after endless corn and cotton. Here and there are black freeholders:[8] there is the gaunt dull-black Jackson, with his hundred acres. "I says, 'Look up! If you don't look up you can't get up,' " remarks Jackson, philosophically. And he's gotten up. Dark Carter's neat barns would do credit to New England. His master helped him to get a start, but when the black man died last fall the master's sons immediately laid claim to the estate. "And them white folks will get it, too," said my yellow gossip.

I turn from these well-tended acres with a comfortable feeling that the Negro is rising. Even then, however, the fields, as we proceed, begin to redden and the trees disappear. Rows of old cabins appear filled with renters and laborers,—cheerless, bare, and dirty, for the most part, although here and there the very age and decay makes the scene picturesque. A young black fellow greets us. He is twenty-two, and just married. Until last year he had good luck renting; then cotton fell, and the sheriff seized and sold all he had. So he moved here, where the rent is higher, the land poorer, and the owner inflexible; he rents a forty-dollar mule for twenty dollars a year. Poor lad!—a slave at twenty-two. This plantation, owned now by a Russian Jew, was a part of the famous Bolton estate. After the war it was for many years worked by gangs of Negro convicts,—and black convicts then were even more plentiful than now; it was a way of making Negroes work, and the question of guilt was a minor one. Hard tales of cruelty and mistreatment of the chained freemen are told, but the county authorities were deaf until the free-labor market was nearly ruined by wholesale migration. Then they took the convicts from the plantations, but not until one of the fairest regions of the "Oakey Woods" had been ruined and ravished into a red waste, out of which only a Yankee or a Jew could squeeze more blood from debt-cursed tenants.

No wonder that Luke Black, slow, dull, and discouraged, shuffles to our carriage and talks hopelessly. Why should he strive? Every year finds him deeper in debt. How strange that Georgia, the world-heralded refuge of poor debtors, should bind her own to sloth and misfortune as ruthlessly as ever England did! The poor land groans with its birth-pains, and brings forth scarcely a hundred pounds of cotton to the acre, where fifty years ago it yielded eight times as much. Of this meagre yield the tenant pays from a quarter to a third in rent, and most of the rest in interest on food and supplies bought on credit. Twenty years yonder sunken-cheeked, old black man has labored under that system, and now, turned day-laborer, is supporting his wife and boarding himself on his wages of a dollar and a half a week, received only part of the year.

---

8. People who hold full and free title to their land.

The Bolton convict farm formerly included the neighboring plantation. Here it was that the convicts were lodged in the great log prison still standing. A dismal place it still remains, with rows of ugly huts filled with surly ignorant tenants. "What rent do you pay here?" I inquired. "I don't know,— what is it, Sam?" "All we make," answered Sam. It is a depressing place,— bare, unshaded, with no charm of past association, only a memory of forced human toil,—now, then, and before the war. They are not happy, these black men whom we meet throughout this region. There is little of the joyous abandon and playfulness which we are wont to associate with the plantation Negro. At best, the natural good-nature is edged with complaint or has changed into sullenness and gloom. And now and then it blazes forth in veiled but hot anger. I remember one big red-eyed black whom we met by the roadside. Forty-five years he had labored on this farm, beginning with nothing, and still having nothing. To be sure, he had given four children a common-school training, and perhaps if the new fence-law had not allowed unfenced crops in West Dougherty he might have raised a little stock and kept ahead. As it is, he is hopelessly in debt, disappointed, and embittered. He stopped us to inquire after the black boy in Albany, whom it was said a policeman had shot and killed for loud talking on the sidewalk. And then he said slowly: "Let a white man touch me, and he dies; I don't boast this,—I don't say it around loud, or before the children,—but I mean it. I 've seen them whip my father and my old mother in them cotton-rows till the blood ran; by—" and we passed on.

Now Sears, whom we met next lolling under the chubby oak-trees, was of quite different fibre. Happy?—Well, yes; he laughed and flipped pebbles, and thought the world was as it was. He had worked here twelve years and has nothing but a mortgaged mule. Children? Yes, seven; but they hadn't been to school this year,—couldn't afford books and clothes, and couldn't spare their work. There go part of them to the fields now,—three big boys astride mules, and a strapping girl with bare brown legs. Careless ignorance and laziness here, fierce hate and vindictiveness there;—these are the extremes of the Negro problem which we met that day, and we scarce knew which we preferred.

Here and there we meet distinct characters quite out of the ordinary. One came out of a piece of newly cleared ground, making a wide detour to avoid the snakes. He was an old, hollow-cheeked man, with a drawn and characterful brown face. He had a sort of self-contained quaintness and rough humor impossible to describe; a certain cynical earnestness that puzzled one. "The niggers were jealous of me over on the other place," he said, "and so me and the old woman begged this piece of woods, and I cleared it up myself. Made nothing for two years, but I reckon I 've got a crop now." The cotton looked tall and rich, and we praised it. He curtsied low, and then bowed almost to the ground, with an imperturbable gravity that seemed almost suspicious. Then he continued, "My mule died last week,"—a calamity in this land equal to a devastating fire in town,—"but a white man loaned me another." Then he added, eyeing us, "Oh, I gets along with white folks." We turned the conversation. "Bears? deer?" he answered, "well, I should say there were," and he let fly a string of brave oaths, as he told hunting-tales of the swamp. We left him standing still in the middle of the road looking after us, and yet apparently not noticing us.

The Whistle place, which includes his bit of land, was bought soon after the war by an English syndicate,[9] the "Dixie Cotton and Corn Company." A marvellous deal of style their factor put on, with his servants and coach-and-six; so much so that the concern soon landed in inextricable bankruptcy. Nobody lives in the old house now, but a man comes each winter out of the North and collects his high rents. I know not which are the more touching,—such old empty houses, or the homes of the masters' sons. Sad and bitter tales lie hidden back of those white doors,—tales of poverty, of struggle, of disappointment. A revolution such as that of '63 is a terrible thing; they that rose rich in the morning often slept in paupers' beds. Beggars and vulgar speculators rose to rule over them, and their children went astray. See yonder sad-colored house, with its cabins and fences and glad crops? It is not glad within; last month the prodigal son of the struggling father wrote home from the city for money. Money! Where was it to come from? And so the son rose in the night and killed his baby, and killed his wife, and shot himself dead. And the world passed on.

I remember wheeling around a bend in the road beside a graceful bit of forest and a singing brook. A long low house faced us, with porch and flying pillars, great oaken door, and a broad lawn shining in the evening sun. But the window-panes were gone, the pillars were worm-eaten, and the moss-grown roof was falling in. Half curiously I peered through the unhinged door, and saw where, on the wall across the hall, was written in once gay letters a faded "Welcome."

Quite a contrast to the southwestern part of Dougherty County is the northwest. Soberly timbered in oak and pine, it has none of that half-tropical luxuriance of the southwest. Then, too, there are fewer signs of a romantic past, and more of systematic modern land-grabbing and money-getting. White people are more in evidence here, and farmer and hired labor replace to some extent the absentee landlord and rack-rented tenant. The crops have neither the luxuriance of the richer land nor the signs of neglect so often seen, and there were fences and meadows here and there. Most of this land was poor, and beneath the notice of the slave-baron, before the war. Since then his nephews and the poor whites and the Jews have seized it. The returns of the farmer are too small to allow much for wages, and yet he will not sell off small farms. There is the Negro Sanford; he has worked fourteen years as overseer on the Ladson place, and "paid out enough for fertilizers to have bought a farm," but the owner will not sell off a few acres.

Two children—a boy and a girl—are hoeing sturdily in the fields on the farm where Corliss works. He is smooth-faced and brown, and is fencing up his pigs. He used to run a successful cotton-gin, but the Cotton Seed Oil Trust has forced the price of ginning so low that he says it hardly pays him. He points out a stately old house over the way as the home of "Pa Willis." We eagerly ride over, for "Pa Willis" was the tall and powerful black Moses who led the Negroes for a generation, and led them well. He was a Baptist preacher, and when he died two thousand black people followed him to

9. A group business venture backed by large capital funds.

the grave; and now they preach his funeral sermon each year. His widow lives here,—a weazened,[1] sharp-featured little woman, who curtsied quaintly as we greeted her. Further on lives Jack Delson, the most prosperous Negro farmer in the county. It is a joy to meet him,—a great broad-shouldered, handsome black man, intelligent and jovial. Six hundred and fifty acres he owns, and has eleven black tenants. A neat and tidy home nestled in a flower-garden, and a little store stands beside it.

We pass the Munson place, where a plucky white widow is renting and struggling; and the eleven hundred acres of the Sennet plantation, with its Negro overseer. Then the character of the farms begins to change. Nearly all the lands belong to Russian Jews; the overseers are white, and the cabins are bare board-houses scattered here and there. The rents are high, and day-laborers and "contract" hands abound. It is a keen, hard struggle for living here, and few have time to talk. Tired with the long ride, we gladly drive into Gillonsville. It is a silent cluster of farm-houses standing on the cross-roads, with one of its stores closed and the other kept by a Negro preacher. They tell great tales of busy times at Gillonsville before all the railroads came to Albany; now it is chiefly a memory. Riding down the street, we stop at the preacher's and seat ourselves before the door. It was one of those scenes one cannot soon forget:—a wide, low, little house, whose motherly roof reached over and sheltered a snug little porch. There we sat, after the long hot drive, drinking cool water,—the talkative little storekeeper who is my daily companion; the silent old black woman patching pantaloons and saying never a word; the ragged picture of helpless misfortune who called in just to see the preacher; and finally the neat matronly preacher's wife, plump, yellow, and intelligent. "Own land?" said the wife; "well, only this house." Then she added quietly, "We did buy seven hundred acres up yonder, and paid for it; but they cheated us out of it. Sells was the owner." "Sells!" echoed the ragged misfortune, who was leaning against the balustrade and listening, "he's a regular cheat. I worked for him thirty-seven days this spring, and he paid me in cardboard checks[2] which were to be cashed at the end of the month. But he never cashed them,— kept putting me off. Then the sheriff came and took my mule and corn and furniture—" "Furniture?" I asked; "but furniture is exempt from seizure by law." "Well, he took it just the same," said the hard-faced man.

---

1. Shriveled.   2. Substitute money made of cardboard.

VIII. Of the Quest of the Golden Fleece

But the Brute said in his breast, "Till the mills I grind have ceased,
The riches shall be dust of dust, dry ashes be the feast!

"On the strong and cunning few
    Cynic favors I will strew;
I will stuff their maw with overplus until their spirit dies;
    From the patient and the low
    I will take the joys they know;
    They shall hunger after vanities and still an-hungered go.
Madness shall be on the people, ghastly jealousies arise;
Brother's blood shall cry on brother up the dead and empty skies."
                                        WILLIAM VAUGHN MOODY [3]

Have you ever seen a cotton-field white with the harvest,—its golden fleece hovering above the black earth like a silvery cloud edged with dark green, its bold white signals waving like the foam of billows from Carolina to Texas across the Black and human Sea? I have sometimes half suspected that here the winged ram Chrysomallus left that Fleece after which Jason and his Argonauts [4] went vaguely wandering into the shadowy East three thousand years ago; and certainly one might frame a pretty and not far-fetched analogy of witchery and dragon's teeth, [5] and blood and armed men, between the ancient and the modern Quest of the Golden Fleece in the Black Sea.

And now the golden fleece is found; not only found, but, in its birth-place, woven. For the hum of the cotton-mills is the newest and most significant thing in the New South today. All through the Carolinas and Georgia, away down to Mexico, rise these gaunt red buildings, bare and homely, and yet so busy and noisy withal [6] that they scarce seem to belong to the slow and sleepy land. Perhaps they sprang from dragons' teeth. So the Cotton Kingdom still lives; the world still bows beneath her sceptre. Even the markets that once defied the *parvenu* have crept one by one across the seas, and then slowly and reluctantly, but surely, have started toward the Black Belt.

To be sure, there are those who wag their heads knowingly and tell us that the capital of the Cotton Kingdom has moved from the Black to the White Belt,—that the Negro of to-day raises not more than half of the cotton crop. Such men forget that the cotton crop has doubled, and more than doubled, since the era of slavery, and that, even granting their contention,

3. William Vaughn Moody (1869–1920), American poet and playwright. The quotation is from *The Brute* (1901).
4. In Greek myth, Jason, an adventurer, and his fellow sailors, the Argonauts, sought Chrysomallus's Golden Fleece.
5. Jason sowed dragon's teeth, from which sprang armed men who fought against Jason.
6. Besides.

the Negro is still supreme in a Cotton Kingdom larger than that on which the Confederacy builded its hopes. So the Negro forms to-day one of the chief figures in a great world-industry; and this, for its own sake, and in the light of historic interest, makes the field-hands of the cotton country worth studying.

We seldom study the condition of the Negro to-day honestly and carefully. It is so much easier to assume that we know it all. Or perhaps, having already reached conclusions in our own minds, we are loth to have them disturbed by facts. And yet how little we really know of these millions,—of their daily lives and longings, of their homely joys and sorrows, of their real shortcomings and the meaning of their crimes! All this we can only learn by intimate contact with the masses, and not by wholesale arguments covering millions separate in time and space, and differing widely in training and culture. To-day, then, my reader, let us turn our faces to the Black Belt of Georgia and seek simply to know the condition of the black farm-laborers of one county there.

Here in 1890 lived ten thousand Negroes and two thousand whites. The country is rich, yet the people are poor. The keynote of the Black Belt is debt; not commercial credit, but debt in the sense of continued inability on the part of the mass of the population to make income cover expense. This is the direct heritage of the South from the wasteful economies of the slave *régime*; but it was emphasized and brought to a crisis by the Emancipation of the slaves. In 1860, Dougherty County had six thousand slaves, worth at least two and a half millions of dollars; its farms were estimated at three millions,—making five and a half millions of property, the value of which depended largely on the slave system, and on the speculative demand for land once marvellously rich but already partially devitalized by careless and exhaustive culture. The war then meant a financial crash; in place of the five and a half millions of 1860, there remained in 1870 only farms valued at less than two millions. With this came increased competition in cotton culture from the rich lands of Texas; a steady fall in the normal price of cotton followed, from about fourteen cents a pound in 1860 until it reached four cents in 1898. Such a financial revolution was it that involved the owners of the cotton-belt in debt. And if things went ill with the master, how fared it with the man?

The plantations of Dougherty County in slavery days were not as imposing and aristocratic as those of Virginia. The Big House was smaller and usually one-storied, and sat very near the slave cabins. Sometimes these cabins stretched off on either side like wings; sometimes only on one side, forming a double row, or edging the road that turned into the plantation from the main thoroughfare. The form and disposition of the laborers' cabins throughout the Black Belt is to-day the same as in slavery days. Some live in the self-same cabins, others in cabins rebuilt on the sites of the old. All are sprinkled in little groups over the face of the land, centering about some dilapidated Big House where the head-tenant or agent lives. The general character and arrangement of these dwellings remains on the whole unaltered. There were in the county, outside the corporate town of Albany, about fifteen hundred Negro families in 1898. Out of all these, only a single family occupied a house with seven rooms; only fourteen have five rooms or more. The mass live in one- and two-room homes.

The size and arrangements of a people's homes are no unfair index of their condition. If, then, we inquire more carefully into these Negro homes, we find much that is unsatisfactory. All over the face of the land is the one-room cabin,—now standing in the shadow of the Big House, now staring at the dusty road, now rising dark and sombre amid the green of the cotton-fields. It is nearly always old and bare, built of rough boards, and neither plastered nor ceiled. Light and ventilation are supplied by the single door and by the square hole in the wall with its wooden shutter. There is no glass, porch, or ornamentation without. Within is a fireplace, black and smoky, and usually unsteady with age. A bed or two, a table, a wooden chest, and a few chairs compose the furniture; while a stray show-bill[7] or a newspaper makes up the decorations for the walls. Now and then one may find such a cabin kept scrupulously neat, with merry steaming fireplace and hospitable door; but the majority are dirty and dilapidated, smelling of eating and sleeping, poorly ventilated, and anything but homes.

Above all, the cabins are crowded. We have come to associate crowding with homes in cities almost exclusively. This is primarily because we have so little accurate knowledge of country life. Here in Dougherty County one may find families of eight and ten occupying one or two rooms, and for every ten rooms of house accommodation for the Negroes there are twenty-five persons. The worst tenement abominations of New York do not have above twenty-two persons for every ten rooms. Of course, one small, close room in a city, without a yard, is in many respects worse than the larger single country room. In other respects it is better; it has glass windows, a decent chimney, and a trustworthy floor. The single great advantage of the Negro peasant is that he may spend most of his life outside his hovel, in the open fields.

There are four chief causes of these wretched homes: First, long custom born of slavery has assigned such homes to Negroes; white laborers would be offered better accommodations, and might, for that and similar reasons, give better work. Secondly, the Negroes, used to such accommodations, do not as a rule demand better; they do not know what better houses mean. Thirdly, the landlords as a class have not yet come to realize that it is a good business investment to raise the standard of living among labor by slow and judicious methods; that a Negro laborer who demands three rooms and fifty cents a day would give more efficient work and leave a larger profit than a discouraged toiler herding his family in one room and working for thirty cents. Lastly, among such conditions of life there are few incentives to make the laborer become a better farmer. If he is ambitious, he moves to town or tries other labor; as a tenant-farmer his outlook is almost hopeless, and following it as a makeshift, he takes the house that is given him without protest.

In such homes, then, these Negro peasants live. The families are both small and large; there are many single tenants,—widows and bachelors, and remnants of broken groups. The system of labor and the size of the houses

---

7. A poster announcing a performance.

both tend to the breaking up of family groups: the grown children go away as contract hands or migrate to town, the sister goes into service; and so one finds many families with hosts of babies, and many newly married couples, but comparatively few families with half-grown and grown sons and daughters. The average size of Negro families has undoubtedly decreased since the war, primarily from economic stress. In Russia over a third of the bridegrooms and over half the brides are under twenty; the same was true of the ante-bellum Negroes. To-day, however, very few of the boys and less than a fifth of the Negro girls under twenty are married. The young men marry between the ages of twenty-five and thirty-five; the young women between twenty and thirty. Such postponement is due to the difficulty of earning sufficient to rear and support a family; and it undoubtedly leads, in the country districts, to sexual immorality. The form of this immorality, however, is very seldom that of prostitution, and less frequently that of illegitimacy than one would imagine. Rather, it takes the form of separation and desertion after a family group has been formed. The number of separated persons is thirty-five to the thousand,—a very large number. It would of course be unfair to compare this number with divorce statistics, for many of these separated women are in reality widowed, were the truth known, and in other cases the separation is not permanent. Nevertheless, here lies the seat of greatest moral danger. There is little or no prostitution among these Negroes, and over three-fourths of the families, as found by house-to-house investigation, deserve to be classed as decent people with considerable regard for female chastity. To be sure, the ideas of the mass would not suit New England, and there are many loose habits and notions. Yet the rate of illegitimacy is undoubtedly lower than in Austria or Italy, and the women as a class are modest. The plague-spot in sexual relations is easy marriage and easy separation. This is no sudden development, nor the fruit of Emancipation. It is the plain heritage from slavery. In those days Sam, with his master's consent, "took up" with Mary. No ceremony was necessary, and in the busy life of the great plantations of the Black Belt it was usually dispensed with. If now the master needed Sam's work in another plantation or in another part of the same plantation, or if he took a notion to sell the slave, Sam's married life with Mary was usually unceremoniously broken, and then it was clearly to the master's interest to have both of them take new mates. This widespread custom of two centuries has not been eradicated in thirty years. To-day Sam's grandson "takes up" with a woman without license or ceremony; they live together decently and honestly, and are, to all intents and purposes, man and wife. Sometimes these unions are never broken until death; but in too many cases family quarrels, a roving spirit, a rival suitor, or perhaps more frequently the hopeless battle to support a family, lead to separation, and a broken household is the result. The Negro church has done much to stop this practice, and now most marriage ceremonies are performed by the pastors. Nevertheless, the evil is still deep seated, and only a general raising of the standard of living will finally cure it.

Looking now at the county black population as a whole, it is fair to characterize it as poor and ignorant. Perhaps ten per cent compose the well-to-do and the best of the laborers, while at least nine per cent are thoroughly lewd and vicious. The rest, over eighty per cent, are poor and ignorant, fairly honest and well meaning, plodding, and to a degree shiftless, with some but not great sexual looseness. Such class lines are by no means fixed; they vary, one might almost say, with the price of cotton. The degree of ignorance cannot easily be expressed. We may say, for instance, that nearly two-thirds of them cannot read or write. This but partially expresses the fact. They are ignorant of the world about them, of modern economic organization, of the function of government, of individual worth and possibilities,—of nearly all those things which slavery in self-defence had to keep them from learning. Much that the white boy imbibes from his earliest social atmosphere forms the puzzling problems of the black boy's mature years. America is not another word for Opportunity to *all* her sons.

It is easy for us to lose ourselves in details in endeavoring to grasp and comprehend the real condition of a mass of human beings. We often forget that each unit in the mass is a throbbing human soul. Ignorant it may be, and poverty stricken, black and curious in limb and ways and thought; and yet it loves and hates, it toils and tires, it laughs and weeps its bitter tears, and looks in vague and awful longing at the grim horizon of its life,—all this, even as you and I. These black thousands are not in reality lazy; they are improvident and careless; they insist on breaking the monotony of toil with a glimpse at the great town-world on Saturday; they have their loafers and their rascals; but the great mass of them work continuously and faithfully for a return, and under circumstances that would call forth equal voluntary effort from few if any other modern laboring class. Over eighty-eight per cent of them—men, women, and children—are farmers. Indeed, this is almost the only industry. Most of the children get their schooling after the "crops are laid by," and very few there are that stay in school after the spring work has begun. Child-labor is to be found here in some of its worst phases, as fostering ignorance and stunting physical development. With the grown men of the county there is little variety in work: thirteen hundred are farmers, and two hundred are laborers, teamsters, etc., including twenty-four artisans, ten merchants, twenty-one preachers, and four teachers. This narrowness of life reaches its maximum among the women: thirteen hundred and fifty of these are farm laborers, one hundred are servants and washerwomen, leaving sixty-five housewives, eight teachers, and six seamstresses.

Among this people there is no leisure class. We often forget that in the United States over half the youth and adults are not in the world earning incomes, but are making homes, learning of the world, or resting after the heat of the strife. But here ninety-six per cent are toiling; no one with leisure to turn the bare and cheerless cabin into a home, no old folks to sit beside the fire and hand down traditions of the past; little of careless happy childhood and dreaming youth. The dull monotony of daily toil is broken only by the gayety of the thoughtless and the Saturday trip to town. The toil, like all farm toil, is monotonous, and here there are little machinery and few tools to relieve its burdensome drudgery. But with all this, it is work in the pure open air, and this is something in a day when fresh air is scarce.

The land on the whole is still fertile, despite long abuse. For nine or ten months in succession the crops will come if asked: garden vegetables in April, grain in May, melons in June and July, hay in August, sweet potatoes in September, and cotton from then to Christmas. And yet on two-thirds of the land there is but one crop, and that leaves the toilers in debt. Why is this?

Away down the Baysan road, where the broad flat fields are flanked by great oak forests, is a plantation; many thousands of acres it used to run, here and there, and beyond the great wood. Thirteen hundred human beings here obeyed the call of one,—were his in body, and largely in soul. One of them lives there yet,—a short, stocky man, his dull-brown face seamed and drawn, and his tightly curled hair gray-white. The crops? Just tolerable, he said; just tolerable. Getting on? No—he wasn't getting on at all. Smith of Albany "furnishes" him, and his rent is eight hundred pounds of cotton. Can't make anything at that. Why didn't he buy land? *Humph!* Takes money to buy land. And he turns away. Free! The most piteous thing amid all the black ruin of war-time, amid the broken fortunes of the masters, the blighted hopes of mothers and maidens, and the fall of an empire,—the most piteous thing amid all this was the black freedman who threw down his hoe because the world called him free. What did such a mockery of freedom mean? Not a cent of money, not an inch of land, not a mouthful of victuals,—not even ownership of the rags on his back. Free! On Saturday, once or twice a month, the old master, before the war, used to dole out bacon and meal to his Negroes. And after the first flush of freedom wore off, and his true helplessness dawned on the freedman, he came back and picked up his hoe, and old master still doled out his bacon and meal. The legal form of service was theoretically far different; in practice, task-work or "cropping" was substituted for daily toil in gangs; and the slave gradually became a metayer, or tenant on shares, in name, but a laborer with indeterminate wages in fact.

Still the price of cotton fell, and gradually the landlords deserted their plantations, and the reign of the merchant began. The merchant of the Black Belt is a curious institution,—part banker, part landlord, part contractor, and part despot. His store, which used most frequently to stand at the cross-roads and become the center of a weekly village, has now moved to town; and thither the Negro tenant follows him. The merchant keeps everything,—clothes and shoes, coffee and sugar, pork and meal, canned and dried goods, wagons and ploughs, seed and fertilizer,—and what he has not in stock he can give you an order for at the store across the way. Here, then, comes the tenant, Sam Scott, after he has contracted with some absent landlord's agent for hiring forty acres of land; he fingers his hat nervously until the merchant finishes his morning chat with Colonel Sanders, and calls out, "Well, Sam, what do you want?" Sam wants him to "furnish" him,—*i. e.*, to advance him food and clothing for the year, and perhaps seed and tools, until his crop is raised and sold. If Sam seems a favorable subject, he and the merchant go to a lawyer, and Sam executes a chattel mortgage on his mule and wagon in return for seed and a week's rations. As soon as the green cotton-leaves appear above the ground, another mortgage is given on the "crop." Every Saturday, or at longer intervals, Sam calls upon the merchant for his "rations"; a family of five usually gets about thirty pounds of fat side-pork and a couple of bushels of corn-meal a month. Besides this, clothing and shoes must be furnished; if Sam or his family is sick, there are orders on the druggist and doctor; if the mule wants shoeing, an order on the blacksmith, etc. If Sam is a hard worker and crops promise well, he is often encouraged to buy more,—sugar, extra clothes, perhaps a buggy. But he is seldom encouraged to save. When cotton rose to ten cents last fall, the shrewd merchants of Dougherty County sold a thousand buggies in one season, mostly to black men.

The security offered for such transactions—a crop and chattel mortgage[8]—may at first seem slight. And, indeed, the merchants tell many a true tale of shiftlessness and cheating; of cotton picked at night, mules disappearing, and tenants absconding. But on the whole the merchant of the Black Belt is the most prosperous man in the section. So skilfully and so closely has he drawn the bonds of the law about the tenant, that the black man has often simply to choose between pauperism and crime; he "waives" all homestead exemptions in his contract; he cannot touch his own mortgaged crop, which the laws put almost in the full control of the land-owner and of the merchant. When the crop is growing the merchant watches it like a hawk; as soon as it is ready for market he takes possession of it, sells it, pays the land-owner his rent, subtracts his bill for supplies, and if, as sometimes happens, there is anything left, he hands it over to the black serf for his Christmas celebration.

The direct result of this system is an all-cotton scheme of agriculture and the continued bankruptcy of the tenant. The currency of the Black Belt is cotton. It is a crop always salable for ready money, not usually subject to great yearly fluctuations in price, and one which the Negroes know how to raise. The landlord therefore demands his rent in cotton, and the merchant will accept mortgages on no other crop. There is no use asking the black tenant, then, to diversify his crops,—he cannot under this system. Moreover, the system is bound to bankrupt the tenant. I remember once meeting a little one-mule wagon on the River road. A young black fellow sat in it driving listlessly, his elbows on his knees. His dark-faced wife sat beside him, stolid, silent.

"Hello!" cried my driver,—he has a most impudent way of addressing these people, though they seem used to it,—"what have you got there?"

"Meat and meal," answered the man, stopping. The meat lay uncovered in the bottom of the wagon,—a great thin side of fat pork covered with salt; the meal was in a white bushel bag.

"What did you pay for that meat?"

"Ten cents a pound." It could have been bought for six or seven cents cash.

"And the meal?"

"Two dollars." One dollar and ten cents is the cash price in town. Here was a man paying five dollars for goods which he could have bought for three dollars cash, and raised for one dollar or one dollar and a half.

Yet it is not wholly his fault. The Negro farmer started behind,—started in debt. This was not his choosing, but the crime of this happy-go-lucky nation which goes blundering along with its Reconstruction tragedies, its Spanish war interludes and Philippine matinees,[9] just as though God re-

---

8. A mortgage on personal property.
9. The Spanish-American War (1898) enabled the United States to annex the Philippines.

ally were dead. Once in debt, it is no easy matter for a whole race to
emerge.

In the year of low-priced cotton, 1898, out of three hundred tenant families one hundred and seventy-five ended their year's work in debt to the
extent of fourteen thousand dollars; fifty cleared nothing, and the remaining seventy-five made a total profit of sixteen hundred dollars. The net indebtedness of the black tenant families of the whole county must have
been at least sixty thousand dollars. In a more prosperous year the situation
is far better; but on the average the majority of tenants end the year even, or
in debt, which means that they work for board and clothes. Such an economic organization is radically wrong. Whose is the blame?

The underlying causes of this situation are complicated but discernible.
And one of the chief, outside the carelessness of the nation in letting the
slave start with nothing, is the wide-spread opinion among the merchants
and employers of the Black Belt that only by the slavery of debt can the
Negro be kept at work. Without doubt, some pressure was necessary at the
beginning of the free-labor system to keep the listless and lazy at work; and
even to-day the mass of the Negro laborers need stricter guardianship than
most Northern laborers. Behind this honest and widespread opinion dishonesty and cheating of the ignorant laborers have a good chance to take
refuge. And to all this must be added the obvious fact that a slave ancestry
and a system of unrequited toil has not improved the efficiency or temper
of the mass of black laborers. Nor is this peculiar to Sambo; it has in history
been just as true of John and Hans, of Jacques and Pat, of all ground-down
peasantries. Such is the situation of the mass of the Negroes in the Black
Belt to-day; and they are thinking about it. Crime, and a cheap and dangerous socialism, are the inevitable results of this pondering. I see now that
ragged black man sitting on a log, aimlessly whittling a stick. He muttered
to me with the murmur of many ages, when he said: "White man sit down
whole year; Nigger work day and night and make crop; Nigger hardly gits
bread and meat; white man sittin' down gits all. *It's wrong.*" And what do
the better classes of Negroes do to improve their situation? One of two
things: if any way possible, they buy land; if not, they migrate to town. Just
as centuries ago it was no easy thing for the serf to escape into the freedom
of town-life, even so to-day there are hindrances laid in the way of county
laborers. In considerable parts of all the Gulf States, and especially in Mississippi, Louisiana, and Arkansas, the Negroes on the plantations in the
back-country districts are still held at forced labor practically without
wages. Especially is this true in districts where the farmers are composed of
the more ignorant class of poor whites, and the Negroes are beyond the
reach of schools and intercourse with their advancing fellows. If such a
peon should run away, the sheriff, elected by white suffrage, can usually be
depended on to catch the fugitive, return him, and ask no questions. If he
escape to another county, a charge of petty thieving, easily true, can be
depended upon to secure his return. Even if some unduly officious person
insist upon a trial, neighborly comity [1] will probably make his conviction
sure, and then the labor due the county can easily be bought by the master.

1. Civility.

Such a system is impossible in the more civilized parts of the South, or near the large towns and cities; but in those vast stretches of land beyond the telegraph and the newspaper the spirit of the Thirteenth Amendment is sadly broken. This represents the lowest economic depths of the black American peasant; and in a study of the rise and condition of the Negro freeholder we must trace his economic progress from this modern serfdom.

Even in the better-ordered country districts of the South the free movement of agricultural laborers is hindered by the migration-agent laws. The "Associated Press" recently informed the world of the arrest of a young white man in Southern Georgia who represented the "Atlantic Naval Supplies Company," and who "was caught in the act of enticing hands from the turpentine farm of Mr. John Greer." The crime for which this young man was arrested is taxed five hundred dollars for each county in which the employment agent proposes to gather laborers for work outside the State. Thus the Negroes' ignorance of the labor-market outside his own vicinity is increased rather than diminished by the laws of nearly every Southern State.

Similar to such measures is the unwritten law of the back districts and small towns of the South, that the character of all Negroes unknown to the mass of the community must be vouched for by some white man. This is really a revival of the old Roman idea of the patron under whose protection the new-made freedman was put. In many instances this system has been of great good to the Negro, and very often under the protection and guidance of the former master's family, or other white friends, the freedman progressed in wealth and morality. But the same system has in other cases resulted in the refusal of whole communities to recognize the right of a Negro to change his habitation and to be master of his own fortunes. A black stranger in Baker County, Georgia, for instance, is liable to be stopped anywhere on the public highway and made to state his business to the satisfaction of any white interrogator. If he fails to give a suitable answer, or seems too independent or "sassy," he may be arrested or summarily driven away.

Thus it is that in the country districts of the South, by written or unwritten law, peonage, hindrances to the migration of labor, and a system of white patronage exists over large areas. Besides this, the chance for lawless oppression and illegal exactions is vastly greater in the country than in the city, and nearly all the more serious race disturbances of the last decade have arisen from disputes in the county between master and man,—as, for instance, the Sam Hose affair. As a result of such a situation, there arose, first, the Black Belt; and, second, the Migration to Town. The Black Belt was not, as many assumed, a movement toward fields of labor under more genial climatic conditions; it was primarily a huddling for self-protection,— a massing of the black population for mutual defence in order to secure the peace and tranquillity necessary to economic advance. This movement took place between Emancipation and 1880, and only partially accomplished the desired results. The rush to town since 1880 is the countermovement of men disappointed in the economic opportunities of the Black Belt.

In Dougherty County, Georgia, one can see easily the results of this experiment in huddling for protection. Only ten per cent of the adult population was born in the county, and yet the blacks outnumber the whites four or five to one. There is undoubtedly a security to the blacks in their very numbers,—a personal freedom from arbitrary treatment, which makes hundreds of laborers cling to Dougherty in spite of low wages and economic distress. But a change is coming, and slowly but surely even here the agricultural laborers are drifting to town and leaving the broad acres behind. Why is this? Why do not the Negroes become land-owners, and build up the black landed peasantry, which has for a generation and more been the dream of philanthropist and statesman?

To the car-window sociologist, to the man who seeks to understand and know the South by devoting the few leisure hours of a holiday trip to unravelling the snarl of centuries,—to such men very often the whole trouble with the black field-hand may be summed up by Aunt Ophelia's[2] word, "Shiftless!" They have noted repeatedly scenes like one I saw last summer. We were riding along the highroad to town at the close of a long hot day. A couple of young black fellows passed us in a mule-team, with several bushels of loose corn in the ear. One was driving, listlessly bent forward, his elbows on his knees,—a happy-go-lucky, careless picture of irresponsibility. The other was fast asleep in the bottom of the wagon. As we passed we noticed an ear of corn fall from the wagon. They never saw it,—not they. A rod farther on we noted another ear on the ground; and between that creeping mule and town we counted twenty-six ears of corn. Shiftless? Yes, the personification of shiftlessness. And yet follow those boys: they are not lazy; to-morrow morning they'll be up with the sun; they work hard when they do work, and they work willingly. They have no sordid, selfish, money-getting ways, but rather a fine disdain for mere cash. They'll loaf before your face and work behind your back with good-natured honesty. They'll steal a watermelon, and hand you back your lost purse intact. Their great defect as laborers lies in their lack of incentive to work beyond the mere pleasure of physical exertion. They are careless because they have not found that it pays to be careful; they are improvident because the improvident ones of their acquaintance get on about as well as the provident. Above all, they cannot see why they should take unusual pains to make the white man's land better, or to fatten his mule, or save his corn. On the other hand, the white land-owner argues that any attempt to improve these laborers by increased responsibility, or higher wages, or better homes, or land of their own, would be sure to result in failure. He shows his Northern visitor the scarred and wretched land; the ruined mansions, the worn-out soil and mortgaged acres, and says, This is Negro freedom!

Now it happens that both master and man have just enough argument on their respective sides to make it difficult for them to understand each other. The Negro dimly personifies in the white man all his ills and misfortunes; if he is poor, it is because the white man seizes the fruit of his toil; if he is ignorant, it is because the white man gives him neither time nor facilities to learn; and, indeed, if any misfortune happens to him, it is because of some hidden machinations of "white folks." On the other hand, the masters and the masters' sons have never been able to see why the Negro, in-

---

2. Ophelia St. Clare is a character in Harriet Beecher Stowe's *Uncle Tom's Cabin* (1852).

stead of settling down to be day-laborers for bread and clothes, are infected
with a silly desire to rise in the world, and why they are sulky, dissatisfied,
and careless, where their fathers were happy and dumb and faithful. "Why,
you niggers have an easier time than I do," said a puzzled Albany merchant
to his black customer. "Yes," he replied, "and so does yo' hogs."

Taking, then, the dissatisfied and shiftless field-hand as a starting-point,
let us inquire how the black thousands of Dougherty have struggled from
him up toward their ideal, and what that ideal is. All social struggle is evidenced by the rise, first of economic, then of social classes, among a homogeneous population. To-day the following economic classes are plainly
differentiated among these Negroes.

A "submerged tenth" of croppers, with a few paupers; forty per cent who
are metayers and thirty-nine per cent of semi-metayers and wage-laborers.
There are left five per cent of money-renters and six per cent of freeholders,—
the "Upper Ten" of the land. The croppers are entirely without capital, even
in the limited sense of food or money to keep them from seed-time to harvest.
All they furnish is their labor; the landowner furnishes land, stock, tools,
seed, and house; and at the end of the year the laborer gets from a third to a
half of the crop. Out of his share, however, comes pay and interest for food
and clothing advanced him during the year. Thus we have a laborer without
capital and without wages, and an employer whose capital is largely his employees' wages. It is an unsatisfactory arrangement, both for hirer and hired,
and is usually in vogue on poor land with hard-pressed owners.

Above the croppers come the great mass of the black population who
work the land on their own responsibility, paying rent in cotton and supported by the crop-mortgage system. After the war this system was attractive
to the freedmen on account of its larger freedom and its possibilities for
making a surplus. But with the carrying out of the crop-lien system, the
deterioration of the land, and the slavery of debt, the position of the metayers has sunk to a dead level of practically unrewarded toil. Formerly all
tenants had some capital, and often considerable; but absentee landlor-
dism, rising rack-rent, and falling cotton have stripped them well-nigh of
all, and probably not over half of them to-day own their mules. The change
from cropper to tenant was accomplished by fixing the rent. If, now, the
rent fixed was reasonable, this was an incentive to the tenant to strive. On
the other hand, if the rent was too high, or if the land deteriorated, the
result was to discourage and check the efforts of the black peasantry. There
is no doubt that the latter case is true; that in Dougherty County every economic advantage of the price of cotton in market and of the strivings of the
tenant has been taken advantage of by the landlords and merchants, and
swallowed up in rent and interest. If cotton rose in price, the rent rose even
higher; if cotton fell, the rent remained or followed reluctantly. If a tenant
worked hard and raised a large crop, his rent was raised the next year; if that
year the crop failed, his corn was confiscated and his mule sold for debt.
There were, of course, exceptions to this,—cases of personal kindness and
forbearance; but in the vast majority of cases the rule was to extract the
uttermost farthing from the mass of the black farm laborers.

The average metayer[3] pays from twenty to thirty per cent of his crop in

---

3. A tenant farmer.

rent. The result of such rack-rent can only be evil,—abuse and neglect of the soil, deterioration in the character of the laborers, and a widespread sense of injustice. "Wherever the country is poor," cried Arthur Young,[4] "it is in the hands of metayers," and "their condition is more wretched than that of day-laborers." He was talking of Italy a century ago; but he might have been talking of Dougherty County to-day. And especially is that true to-day which he declares was true in France before the Revolution: "The metayers are considered as little better than menial servants, removable at pleasure, and obliged to conform in all things to the will of the landlords." On this low plane half the black population of Dougherty County— perhaps more than half the black millions of this land—are to-day struggling.

A degree above these we may place those laborers who receive money wages for their work. Some receive a house with perhaps a garden-spot; then supplies of food and clothing are advanced, and certain fixed wages are given at the end of the year, varying from thirty to sixty dollars, out of which the supplies must be paid for, with interest. About eighteen per cent of the population belong to this class of semi-metayers, while twenty-two per cent are laborers paid by the month or year, and are either "furnished" by their own savings or perhaps more usually by some merchant who takes his chances of payment. Such laborers receive from thirty-five to fifty cents a day during the working season. They are usually young unmarried persons, some being women; and when they marry they sink to the class of metayers, or, more seldom, become renters.

The renters for fixed money rentals are the first of the emerging classes, and form five per cent of the families. The sole advantage of this small class is their freedom to choose their crops, and the increased responsibility which comes through having money transactions. While some of the renters differ little in condition from the metayers, yet on the whole they are more intelligent and responsible persons, and are the ones who eventually become land-owners. Their better character and greater shrewdness enable them to gain, perhaps to demand, better terms in rents; rented farms, varying from forty to a hundred acres, bear an average rental of about fifty-four dollars a year. The men who conduct such farms do not long remain renters; either they sink to metayers, or with a successful series of harvests rise to be land-owners.

In 1870 the tax-books of Dougherty report no Negroes as landholders. If there were any such at that time,—and there may have been a few,—their land was probably held in the name of some white patron,—a method not uncommon during slavery. In 1875 ownership of land had begun with seven hundred and fifty acres; ten years later this had increased to over sixty-five hundred acres, to nine thousand acres in 1890 and ten thousand in 1900. The total assessed property has in this same period risen from eighty thousand dollars in 1875 to two hundred and forty thousand dollars in 1900.

Two circumstances complicate this development and make it in some respects difficult to be sure of the real tendencies; they are the panic of 1893,[5] and the low price of cotton in 1898. Besides this, the system of as-

---

4. English agricultural writer (1741–1820).
5. A financial crisis that led to a four-year eco-   nomic depression in the United States.

sessing property in the country districts of Georgia is somewhat antiquated and of uncertain statistical value; there are no assessors, and each man makes a sworn return to a tax-receiver. Thus public opinion plays a large part, and the returns vary strangely from year to year. Certainly these figures show the small amount of accumulated capital among the Negroes, and the consequent large dependence of their property on temporary prosperity. They have little to tide over a few years of economic depression, and are at the mercy of the cotton-market far more than the whites. And thus the land-owners, despite their marvellous efforts, are really a transient class, continually being depleted by those who fall back into the class of renters or metayers, and augmented by newcomers from the masses. Of the one hundred land-owners in 1898, half had bought their land since 1893, a fourth between 1890 and 1893, a fifth between 1884 and 1890, and the rest between 1870 and 1884. In all, one hundred and eighty-five Negroes have owned land in this county since 1875.

If all the black land-owners who had ever held land here had kept it or left it in the hands of black men, the Negroes would have owned nearer thirty thousand acres than the fifteen thousand they now hold. And yet these fifteen thousand acres are a creditable showing,—a proof of no little weight of the worth and ability of the Negro people. If they had been given an economic start at Emancipation, if they had been in an enlightened and rich community which really desired their best good, then we might perhaps call such a result small or even insignificant. But for a few thousand poor ignorant field-hands, in the face of poverty, a falling market, and social stress, to save and capitalize two hundred thousand dollars in a generation has meant a tremendous effort. The rise of a nation, the pressing forward of a social class, means a bitter struggle, a hard and soul-sickening battle with the world such as few of the more favored classes know or appreciate.

Out of the hard economic conditions of this portion of the Black Belt, only six per cent of the population have succeeded in emerging into peasant proprietorship; and these are not all firmly fixed, but grow and shrink in number with the wavering of the cotton-market. Fully ninety-four per cent have struggled for land and failed, and half of them sit in hopeless serfdom. For these there is one other avenue of escape toward which they have turned in increasing numbers, namely, migration to town. A glance at the distribution of land among the black owners curiously reveals this fact. In 1898 the holdings were as follows: Under forty acres, forty-nine families; forty to two hundred and fifty acres, seventeen families; two hundred and fifty to one thousand acres, thirteen families; one thousand or more acres, two families. Now in 1890 there were forty-four holdings, but only nine of these were under forty acres. The great increase of holdings, then, has come in the buying of small homesteads near town, where their owners really share in the town life; this is a part of the rush to town. And for every land-owner who has thus hurried away from the narrow and hard conditions of country life, how many field-hands, how many tenants, how many ruined renters, have joined that long procession? Is it not strange compensation? The sin of the country districts is visited on the town, and the social sores of city life to-day may, here in Dougherty County, and perhaps in many places near and far, look for their final healing without the city walls.

IX. Of the Sons of Master and Man

Life treads on life, and heart on heart;
We press too close in church and mart
To keep a dream or grave apart.
MRS. BROWNING[6]

The world-old phenomenon of the contact of diverse races of men is to
have new exemplification during the new century. Indeed, the characteristic of our age is the contact of European civilization with the world's undeveloped peoples. Whatever we may say of the results of such contact in
the past, it certainly forms a chapter in human action not pleasant to look
back upon. War, murder, slavery, extermination, and debauchery,—this
has again and again been the result of carrying civilization and the blessed
gospel to the isles of the sea and the heathen without the law. Nor does it
altogether satisfy the conscience of the modern world to be told complacently that all this has been right and proper, the fated triumph of strength
over weakness, of righteousness over evil, of superiors over inferiors. It
would certainly be soothing if one could readily believe all this; and yet
there are too many ugly facts for everything to be thus easily explained
away. We feel and know that there are many delicate differences in race
psychology, numberless changes that our crude social measurements are
not yet able to follow minutely, which explain much of history and social
development. At the same time, too, we know that these considerations
have never adequately explained or excused the triumph of brute force and
cunning over weakness and innocence.

It is, then, the strife of all honorable men of the twentieth century to see
that in the future competition of races the survival of the fittest shall mean
the triumph of the good, the beautiful, and the true; that we may be able to
preserve for future civilization all that is really fine and noble and strong,
and not continue to put a premium on greed and impudence and cruelty.
To bring this hope to fruition, we are compelled daily to turn more and
more to a conscientious study of the phenomena of race-contact,—to a
study frank and fair, and not falsified and colored by our wishes or our fears.
And we have in the South as fine a field for such a study as the world affords,—a field, to be sure, which the average American scientist deems
somewhat beneath his dignity, and which the average man who is not a
scientist knows all about, but nevertheless a line of study which by reason
of the enormous race complications with which God seems about to punish this nation must increasingly claim our sober attention, study, and

6. Elizabeth Barrett Browning (1806–1861), British poet. The quotation is from *A Vision of Poets* (1844).

thought, we must ask, what are the actual relations of whites and blacks in the South? and we must be answered, not by apology or fault-finding, but by a plain, unvarnished tale.

In the civilized life of to-day the contact of men and their relations to each other fall in a few main lines of action and communication: there is, first, the physical proximity of homes and dwelling-places, the way in which neighborhoods group themselves, and the contiguity of neighborhoods. Secondly, and in our age chiefest, there are the economic relations,—the methods by which individuals coöperate for earning a living, for the mutual satisfaction of wants, for the production of wealth. Next, there are the political relations, the coöperation in social control, in group government, in laying and paying the burden of taxation. In the fourth place there are the less tangible but highly important forms of intellectual contact and commerce, the interchange of ideas through conversation and conference, through periodicals and libraries; and, above all, the gradual formation for each community of that curious *tertium quid* which we call public opinion. Closely allied with this come the various forms of social contact in everyday life, in travel, in theatres, in house gatherings, in marrying and giving in marriage. Finally, there are the varying forms of religious enterprise, of moral teaching and benevolent endeavor. These are the principal ways in which men living in the same communities are brought into contact with each other. It is my present task, therefore, to indicate, from my point of view, how the black race in the South meet and mingle with the whites in these matters of everyday life.

First, as to physical dwelling. It is usually possible to draw in nearly every Southern community a physical color-line on the map, on the one side of which whites dwell and on the other Negroes. The winding and intricacy of the geographical color line varies, of course, in different communities. I know some towns where a straight line drawn through the middle of the main street separates nine-tenths of the whites from nine-tenths of the blacks. In other towns the older settlement of whites has been encircled by a broad band of blacks; in still other cases little settlements or nuclei of blacks have sprung up amid surrounding whites. Usually in cities each street has its distinctive color, and only now and then do the colors meet in close proximity. Even in the country something of this segregation is manifest in the smaller areas, and of course in the larger phenomena of the Black Belt.

All this segregation by color is largely independent of that natural clustering by social grades common to all communities. A Negro slum may be in dangerous proximity to a white residence quarter, while it is quite common to find a white slum planted in the heart of a respectable Negro district. One thing, however, seldom occurs: the best of the whites and the best of the Negroes almost never live in anything like close proximity. It thus happens that in nearly every Southern town and city, both whites and blacks see commonly the worst of each other. This is a vast change from the situation in the past, when, through the close contact of master and house-servant in the patriarchal big house, one found the best of both races in close contact and sympathy, while at the same time the squalor and dull round of toil among the field-hands was removed from the sight and hear-

ing of the family. One can easily see how a person who saw slavery thus
from his father's parlors, and sees freedom on the streets of a great city, fails
to grasp or comprehend the whole of the new picture. On the other hand,
the settled belief of the mass of the Negroes that the Southern white people
do not have the black man's best interests at heart has been intensified in
later years by this continual daily contact of the better class of blacks with
the worst representatives of the white race.

Coming now to the economic relations of the races, we are on ground
made familiar by study, much discussion, and no little philanthropic effort.
And yet with all this there are many essential elements in the coöperation
of Negroes and whites for work and wealth that are too readily overlooked
or not thoroughly understood. The average American can easily conceive
of a rich land awaiting development and filled with black laborers. To him
the Southern problem is simply that of making efficient workingmen out of
this material, by giving them the requisite technical skill and the help of
invested capital. The problem, however, is by no means as simple as this,
from the obvious fact that these workingmen have been trained for centuries as slaves. They exhibit, therefore, all the advantages and defects of such
training; they are willing and good-natured, but not self-reliant, provident,
or careful. If now the economic development of the South is to be pushed
to the verge of exploitation, as seems probable, then we have a mass of
workingmen thrown into relentless competition with the workingmen of
the world, but handicapped by a training the very opposite to that of the
modern self-reliant democratic laborer. What the black laborer needs is
careful personal guidance, group leadership of men with hearts in their
bosoms, to train them to foresight, carefulness, and honesty. Nor does it
require any fine-spun theories of racial differences to prove the necessity of
such group training after the brains of the race have been knocked out by
two hundred and fifty years of assiduous education in submission, carelessness, and stealing. After Emancipation, it was the plain duty of some one to
assume this group leadership and training of the Negro laborer. I will not
stop here to inquire whose duty it was,—whether that of the white ex-master
who had profited by unpaid toil, or the Northern philanthropist whose persistence brought on the crisis, or the National Government whose edict
freed the bondmen; I will not stop to ask whose duty it was, but I insist it
was the duty of some one to see that these workingmen were not left alone
and unguided, without capital, without land, without skill, without economic organization, without even the bald protection of law, order, and
decency,—left in a great land, not to settle down to slow and careful internal development, but destined to be thrown almost immediately into relentless and sharp competition with the best of modern workingmen under
an economic system where every participant is fighting for himself, and too
often utterly regardless of the rights or welfare of his neighbor.

For we must never forget that the economic system of the South to-day
which has succeeded the old *régime* is not the same system as that of the
old industrial North, of England, or of France, with their trades-unions,
their restrictive laws, their written and unwritten commercial customs, and
their long experience. It is, rather, a copy of that England of the early nineteenth century, before the factory acts,—the England that wrung pity from

thinkers and fired the wrath of Carlyle.[7] The rod of empire that passed
from the hands of Southern gentlemen in 1865, partly by force, partly by
their own petulance, has never returned to them. Rather it has passed to
those men who have come to take charge of the industrial exploitation of
the New South,—the sons of poor whites fired with a new thirst for wealth
and power, thrifty and avaricious Yankees, shrewd and unscrupulous Jews.
Into the hands of these men the Southern laborers, white and black, have
fallen; and this to their sorrow. For the laborers as such there is in these
new captains of industry neither love nor hate, neither sympathy nor romance; it is a cold question of dollars and dividends. Under such a system
all labor is bound to suffer. Even the white laborers are not yet intelligent,
thrifty, and well trained enough to maintain themselves against the powerful inroads of organized capital. The results among them, even, are long
hours of toil, low wages, child labor, and lack of protection against usury
and cheating. But among the black laborers all this is aggravated, first, by a
race prejudice which varies from a doubt and distrust among the best element of whites to a frenzied hatred among the worst; and, secondly, it is
aggravated, as I have said before, by the wretched economic heritage of the
freedmen from slavery. With this training it is difficult for the freedman to
learn to grasp the opportunities already opened to him, and the new opportunities are seldom given him, but go by favor to the whites.

Left by the best elements of the South with little protection or oversight,
he has been made in law and custom the victim of the worst and most
unscrupulous men in each community. The crop-lien system[8] which is
depopulating the fields of the South is not simply the result of shiftlessness
on the part of Negroes, but is also the result of cunningly devised laws as to
mortgages, liens, and misdemeanors, which can be made by conscienceless men to entrap and snare the unwary until escape is impossible, further
toil a farce, and protest a crime. I have seen, in the Black Belt of Georgia,
an ignorant, honest Negro buy and pay for a farm in installments three
separate times, and then in the face of law and decency the enterprising
Russian Jew who sold it to him pocketed money and deed and left the black
man landless, to labor on his own land at thirty cents a day. I have seen a
black farmer fall in debt to a white storekeeper, and that storekeeper go to
his farm and strip it of every single marketable article,—mules, ploughs,
stored crops, tools, furniture, bedding, clocks, looking-glass,—and all this
without a warrant, without process of law, without a sheriff or officer, in the
face of the law for homestead exemptions, and without rendering to a single responsible person any account or reckoning. And such proceedings
can happen, and will happen, in any community where a class of ignorant
toilers are placed by custom and race-prejudice beyond the pale of sympathy and race-brotherhood. So long as the best elements of a community do
not feel in duty bound to protect and train and care for the weaker members of their group, they leave them to be preyed upon by these swindlers
and rascals.

This unfortunate economic situation does not mean the hindrance of all

---

7. Thomas Carlyle (1795–1881), British social
commentator and critic.
8. A means of farming in which a landowner

places a legal claim on the crop of the tenant as security against payment of debt.

advance in the black South, or the absence of a class of black landlords and mechanics who, in spite of disadvantages, are accumulating property and making good citizens. But it does mean that this class is not nearly so large as a fairer economic system might easily make it, that those who survive in the competition are handicapped so as to accomplish much less than they deserve to, and that, above all, the *personnel* of the successful class is left to chance and accident, and not to any intelligent culling or reasonable methods of selection. As a remedy for this, there is but one possible procedure. We must accept some of the race prejudice in the South as a fact,—deplorable in its intensity, unfortunate in results, and dangerous for the future, but nevertheless a hard fact which only time can efface. We cannot hope, then, in this generation, or for several generations, that the mass of the whites can be brought to assume that close sympathetic and self-sacrificing leadership of the blacks which their present situation so eloquently demands. Such leadership, such social teaching and example, must come from the blacks themselves. For some time men doubted as to whether the Negro could develop such leaders; but to-day no one seriously disputes the capability of individual Negroes to assimilate the culture and common sense of modern civilization, and to pass it on, to some extent at least, to their fellows. If this is true, then here is the path out of the economic situation, and here is the imperative demand for trained Negro leaders of character and intelligence,—men of skill, men of light and leading, college-bred men, black captains of industry, and missionaries of culture; men who thoroughly comprehend and know modern civilization, and can take hold of Negro communities and raise and train them by force of precept and example, deep sympathy, and the inspiration of common blood and ideals. But if such men are to be effective they must have some power,—they must be backed by the best public opinion of these communities, and able to wield for their objects and aims such weapons as the experience of the world has taught are indispensable to human progress.

Of such weapons the greatest, perhaps, in the modern world is the power of the ballot; and this brings me to a consideration of the third form of contact between whites and blacks in the South,—political activity.

In the attitude of the American mind toward Negro suffrage can be traced with unusual accuracy the prevalent conceptions of government. In the fifties we were near enough the echoes of the French Revolution to believe pretty thoroughly in universal suffrage. We argued, as we thought then rather logically, that no social class was so good, so true, and so disinterested as to be trusted wholly with the political destiny of its neighbors; that in every state the best arbiters of their own welfare are the persons directly affected; consequently that it is only by arming every hand with a ballot,—with the right to have a voice in the policy of the state,—that the greatest good to the greatest number could be attained. To be sure, there were objections to these arguments, but we thought we had answered them tersely and convincingly; if some one complained of the ignorance of voters, we answered, "Educate them." If another complained of their venality, we replied, "Disfranchise them or put them in jail." And, finally, to the men who feared demagogues and the natural perversity of some human beings we insisted that time and bitter experience would teach the most hardheaded. It was at this time that the question of Negro suffrage in the South was raised. Here was a defenceless people suddenly made free. How were they to be protected from those who did not believe in their freedom and were determined to thwart it? Not by force, said the North; not by government guardianship, said the South; then by the ballot, the sole and legitimate defence of a free people, said the Common Sense of the Nation. No one thought, at the time, that the ex-slaves could use the ballot intelligently or very effectively; but they did think that the possession of so great power by a great class in the nation would compel their fellows to educate this class to its intelligent use.

Meantime, new thoughts came to the nation: the inevitable period of moral retrogression and political trickery that ever follows in the wake of war overtook us. So flagrant became the political scandals that reputable men began to leave politics alone, and politics consequently became disreputable. Men began to pride themselves on having nothing to do with their own government, and to agree tacitly with those who regarded public office as a private perquisite. In this state of mind it became easy to wink at the suppression of the Negro vote in the South, and to advise self-respecting Negroes to leave politics entirely alone. The decent and reputable citizens of the North who neglected their own civic duties grew hilarious over the exaggerated importance with which the Negro regarded the franchise. Thus it easily happened that more and more the better class of Negroes followed the advice from abroad and the pressure from home, and took no further interest in politics, leaving to the careless and the venal of their race the exercise of their rights as voters. The black vote that still remained was not trained and educated, but further debauched by open and unblushing bribery, or force and fraud; until the Negro voter was thoroughly inoculated with the idea that politics was a method of private gain by disreputable means.

And finally, now, to-day, when we are awakening to the fact that the perpetuity of republican institutions on this continent depends on the purification of the ballot, the civic training of voters, and the raising of voting to the plane of a solemn duty which a patriotic citizen neglects to his peril and to the peril of his children's children,—in this day, when we are striving for a renaissance of civic virtue, what are we going to say to the black voter of the South? Are we going to tell him still that politics is a disreputable and useless form of human activity? Are we going to induce the best class of Negroes to take less and less interest in government, and to give up their right to take such an interest, without a protest? I am not saying a word against all legitimate efforts to purge the ballot of ignorance, pauperism, and crime. But few have pretended that the present movement for disfranchisement in the South is for such a purpose; it has been plainly and frankly declared in nearly every case that the object of the disfranchising laws is the elimination of the black man from politics.

Now, is this a minor matter which has no influence on the main question of the industrial and intellectual development of the Negro? Can we establish a mass of black laborers and artisans and landholders in the South who, by law and public opinion, have absolutely no voice in shaping the laws under which they live and work? Can the modern organization of industry, assuming as it does free democratic government and the power and ability of the laboring classes to compel respect for their welfare,—can this system be carried out in the South when half its laboring force is voiceless in the public councils and powerless in its own defence? To-day the black man of the South has almost nothing to say as to how much he shall be taxed, or how those taxes shall be expended; as to who shall execute the laws, and how they shall do it; as to who shall make the laws, and how they shall be made. It is pitiable that frantic efforts must be made at critical times to get lawmakers in some States even to listen to the respectful presentation of the black man's side of a current controversy. Daily the Negro is coming more and more to look upon law and justice, not as protecting safeguards, but as sources of humiliation and oppression. The laws are made by men who have little interest in him; they are executed by men who have absolutely no motive for treating the black people with courtesy or consideration; and, finally, the accused law-breaker is tried, not by his peers, but too often by men who would rather punish ten innocent Negroes than let one guilty one escape.

I should be the last one to deny the patent weaknesses and shortcomings of the Negro people; I should be the last to withhold sympathy from the white South in its efforts to solve its intricate social problems. I freely acknowledge that it is possible, and sometimes best, that a partially undeveloped people should be ruled by the best of their stronger and better neighbors for their own good, until such time as they can start and fight the world's battles alone. I have already pointed out how sorely in need of such economic and spiritual guidance the emancipated Negro was, and I am quite willing to admit that if the representatives of the best white Southern public opinion were the ruling and guiding powers in the South to-day the conditions indicated would be fairly well fulfilled. But the point I have insisted upon, and now emphasize again, is that the best opinion of the South to-day is not the ruling opinion. That to leave the Negro helpless and without a ballot to-day is to leave him, not to the guidance of the best, but rather to the exploitation and debauchment of the worst; that this is no truer of the South than of the North,—of the North than of Europe: in any land, in any country under modern free competition, to lay any class of weak and despised people, be they white, black, or blue, at the political mercy of their stronger, richer, and more resourceful fellows, is a temptation which human nature seldom has withstood and seldom will withstand.

Moreover, the political status of the Negro in the South is closely connected with the question of Negro crime. There can be no doubt that crime among Negroes has sensibly increased in the last thirty years, and that there has appeared in the slums of great cities a distinct criminal class among the blacks. In explaining this unfortunate development, we must note two things: (1) that the inevitable result of Emancipation was to increase crime and criminals, and (2) that the police system of the South was primarily designed to control slaves. As to the first point, we must not forget that under a strict slave system there can scarcely be such a thing as crime. But when these variously constituted human particles are suddenly thrown broadcast on the sea of life, some swim, some sink, and some hang suspended, to be forced up or down by the chance currents of a busy hurrying world. So great an economic and social revolution as swept the South in '63 meant a weeding out among the Negroes of the incompetents and vicious, the beginning of a differentiation of social grades. Now a rising group of people are not lifted bodily from the ground like an inert solid mass, but rather stretch upward like a living plant with its roots still clinging in the mould. The appearance, therefore, of the Negro criminal was a phenomenon to be awaited; and while it causes anxiety, it should not occasion surprise.

Here again the hope for the future depended peculiarly on careful and delicate dealing with these criminals. Their offences at first were those of laziness, carelessness, and impulse, rather than of malignity or ungoverned viciousness. Such misdemeanors needed discriminating treatment, firm but reformatory, with no hint of injustice, and full proof of guilt. For such dealing with criminals, white or black, the South had no machinery, no adequate jails or reformatories; its police system was arranged to deal with blacks alone, and tacitly assumed that every white man was *ipso facto* a member of that police. Thus grew up a double system of justice, which erred on the white side by undue leniency and the practical immunity of red-handed criminals, and erred on the black side by undue severity, injustice, and lack of discrimination. For, as I have said, the police system of the South was originally designed to keep track of all Negroes, not simply of criminals; and when the Negroes were freed and the whole South was convinced of the impossibility of free Negro labor, the first and almost universal device was to use the courts as a means of reënslaving the blacks. It was not then a question of crime, but rather one of color, that settled a man's conviction on almost any charge. Thus Negroes came to look upon courts as instruments of injustice and oppression, and upon those convicted in them as martyrs and victims.

When, now, the real Negro criminal appeared, and instead of petty stealing and vagrancy we began to have highway robbery, burglary, murder, and rape, there was a curious effect on both sides the color-line: the Negroes refused to believe the evidence of white witnesses or the fairness of white juries, so that the greatest deterrent to crime, the public opinion of one's own social caste, was lost, and the criminal was looked upon as crucified rather than hanged. On the other hand, the whites, used to being careless as to the guilt or innocence of accused Negroes, were swept in moments of passion beyond law, reason, and decency. Such a situation is bound to increase crime, and has increased it. To natural viciousness and vagrancy are being daily added motives of revolt and revenge which stir up all the latent savagery of both races and make peaceful attention to economic development often impossible.

But the chief problem in any community cursed with crime is not the punishment of the criminals, but the preventing of the young from being trained to crime. And here again the peculiar conditions of the South have prevented proper precautions. I have seen twelve-year-old boys working in chains on the public streets of Atlanta, directly in front of the schools, in company with old and hardened criminals; and this indiscriminate mingling of men and women and children makes the chain-gangs perfect schools of crime and debauchery. The struggle for reformatories, which has gone on in Virginia, Georgia, and other States, is the one encouraging sign of the awakening of some communities to the suicidal results of this policy.

It is the public schools, however, which can be made, outside the homes, the greatest means of training decent self-respecting citizens. We have been so hotly engaged recently in discussing trade-schools and the higher education that the pitiable plight of the public-school system in the South has almost dropped from view. Of every five dollars spent for public education in the State of Georgia, the white schools get four dollars and the Negro one dollar; and even then the white public-school system, save in the cities, is bad and cries for reform. If this is true of the whites, what of the blacks? I am becoming more and more convinced, as I look upon the system of common-school training in the South, that the national government must soon step in and aid popular education in some way. To-day it has been only by the most strenuous efforts on the part of the thinking men of the South that the Negro's share of the school fund has not been cut down to a pittance in some half-dozen States; and that movement not only is not dead, but in many communities is gaining strength. What in the name of reason does this nation expect of a people, poorly trained and hard pressed in severe economic competition, without political rights, and with ludicrously inadequate common-school facilities? What can it expect but crime and listlessness, offset here and there by the dogged struggles of the fortunate and more determined who are themselves buoyed by the hope that in due time the country will come to its senses?

I have thus far sought to make clear the physical, economic, and political relations of the Negroes and whites in the South, as I have conceived them, including, for the reasons set forth, crime and education. But after all that has been said on these more tangible matters of human contact, there still remains a part essential to a proper description of the South which it is difficult to describe or fix in terms easily understood by strangers. It is, in fine, the atmosphere of the land, the thought and feeling, the thousand and one little actions which go to make up life. In any community or nation it is these little things which are most elusive to the grasp and yet most essential to any clear conception of the group life taken as a whole. What is thus true of all communities is peculiarly true of the South, where, outside of written history and outside of printed law, there has been going on for a generation as deep a storm and stress of human souls, as intense a ferment of feeling, as intricate a writhing of spirit, as ever a people experienced. Within and without the sombre veil of color vast social forces have been at work,—efforts for human betterment, movements toward disintegration and despair, tragedies and comedies in social and economic life, and a swaying and lifting and sinking of human hearts which have made this land a land of mingled sorrow and joy, of change and excitement and unrest.

The centre of this spiritual turmoil has ever been the millions of black freedmen and their sons, whose destiny is so fatefully bound up with that of the nation. And yet the casual observer visiting the South sees at first little of this. He notes the growing frequency of dark faces as he rides along,—but otherwise the days slip lazily on, the sun shines, and this little world seems as happy and contented as other worlds he has visited. Indeed, on the question of questions—the Negro problem—he hears so little that there almost seems to be a conspiracy of silence; the morning papers seldom mention it, and then usually in a far-fetched academic way, and indeed almost everyone seems to forget and ignore the darker half of the land, until the astonished visitor is inclined to ask if after all there *is* any problem here. But if he lingers long enough there comes the awakening: perhaps in a sudden whirl of passion which leaves him gasping at its bitter intensity; more likely in a gradually dawning sense of things he had not at first noticed. Slowly but surely his eyes begin to catch the shadows of the color-line: here he meets crowds of Negroes and whites; then he is suddenly aware that he cannot discover a single dark face; or again at the close of a day's wandering he may find himself in some strange assembly, where all faces are tinged brown or black, and where he has the vague, uncomfortable feeling of the stranger. He realizes at last that silently, resistlessly, the world about flows by him in two great streams: they ripple on in the same sunshine, they approach and mingle their waters in seeming carelessness,—then they divide and flow wide apart. It is done quietly; no mistakes are made, or if one occurs, the swift arm of the law and of public opinion swings down for a moment, as when the other day a black man and a white woman were arrested for talking together on Whitehall Street in Atlanta.

Now if one notices carefully one will see that between these two worlds, despite much physical contact and daily intermingling, there is almost no community of intellectual life or point of transference where the thoughts and feelings of one race can come into direct contact and sympathy with the thoughts and feelings of the other. Before and directly after the war, when all the best of the Negroes were domestic servants in the best of the white families, there were bonds of intimacy, affection, and sometimes blood relationship, between the races. They lived in the same home, shared in the family life, often attended the same church, and talked and conversed with each other. But the increasing civilization of the Negro since then has naturally meant the development of higher classes: there are increasing numbers of ministers, teachers, physicians, merchants, mechanics, and independent farmers, who by nature and training are the aristocracy and leaders of the blacks. Between them, however, and the best element of the whites, there is little or no intellectual commerce. They go to separate churches, they live in separate sections, they are strictly separated in all public gatherings, they travel separately, and they are beginning to read different papers and books. To most libraries, lectures, concerts, and museums, Negroes are either not admitted at all, or on terms peculiarly galling to the pride of the very classes who might otherwise be attracted. The daily paper chronicles the doings of the black world from afar with no great regard for accuracy; and so on, throughout the category of means for intellectual communication,—schools, conferences, efforts for social betterment, and the like,—it is usually true that the very representatives of the two races, who for mutual benefit and the welfare of the land ought to be in complete understanding and sympathy, are so far strangers that one side thinks all whites are narrow and prejudiced, and the other thinks educated Negroes dangerous and insolent. Moreover, in a land where the tyranny of public opinion and the intolerance of criticism is for obvious historical reasons so strong as in the South, such a situation is extremely difficult to correct. The white man, as well as the Negro, is bound and barred by the color-line, and many a scheme of friendliness and philanthropy, of broad-minded sympathy and generous fellowship between the two has dropped still-born because some busybody has forced the color-question to the front and brought the tremendous force of unwritten law against the innovators.

It is hardly necessary for me to add very much in regard to the social contact between the races. Nothing has come to replace that finer sympathy and love between some masters and house servants which the radical and more uncompromising drawing of the color-line in recent years has caused almost completely to disappear. In a world where it means so much to take a man by the hand and sit beside him, to look frankly into his eyes and feel his heart beating with red blood; in a world where a social cigar or a cup of tea together means more than legislative halls and magazine articles and speeches,—one can imagine the consequences of the almost utter absence of such social amenities between estranged races, whose separation extends even to parks and street-cars.

Here there can be none of that social going down to the people,—the opening of heart and hand of the best to the worst, in generous acknowledgment of a common humanity and a common destiny. On the other hand, in matters of simple almsgiving, where there can be no question of social contact, and in the succor of the aged and sick, the South, as if stirred by a feeling of its unfortunate limitations, is generous to a fault. The black beggar is never turned away without a good deal more than a crust, and a call for help for the unfortunate meets quick response. I remember, one cold winter, in Atlanta, when I refrained from contributing to a public relief fund lest Negroes should be discriminated against, I afterward inquired of a friend: "Were any black people receiving aid?" "Why," said he, "they were *all* black."

And yet this does not touch the kernel of the problem. Human advancement is not a mere question of almsgiving, but rather of sympathy and coöperation among classes who would scorn charity. And here is a land where, in the higher walks of life, in all the higher striving for the good and noble and true, the color-line comes to separate natural friends and co-workers; while at the bottom of the social group, in the saloon, the gambling-hell, and the brothel, that same line wavers and disappears.

I have sought to paint an average picture of real relations between the sons of master and man in the South. I have not glossed over matters for policy's sake, for I fear we have already gone too far in that sort of thing. On the other hand, I have sincerely sought to let no unfair exaggerations creep in. I do not doubt that in some Southern communities conditions are better than those I have indicated; while I am no less certain that in other communities they are far worse.

Nor does the paradox and danger of this situation fail to interest and perplex the best conscience of the South. Deeply religious and intensely democratic as are the mass of the whites, they feel acutely the false position in which the Negro problems place them. Such an essentially honest-hearted and generous people cannot cite the caste-levelling precepts of Christianity, or believe in equality of opportunity for all men, without coming to feel more and more with each generation that the present drawing of the color-line is a flat contradiction to their beliefs and professions. But just as often as they come to this point, the present social condition of the Negro stands as a menace and a portent before even the most open-minded: if there were nothing to charge against the Negro but his blackness or other physical peculiarities, they argue, the problem would be comparatively simple; but what can we say to his ignorance, shiftlessness, poverty, and crime? can a self-respecting group hold anything but the least possible fellowship with such persons and survive? and shall we let a mawkish sentiment sweep away the culture of our fathers or the hope of our children? The argument so put is of great strength, but it is not a whit stronger than the argument of thinking Negroes: granted, they reply, that the condition of our masses is bad; there is certainly on the one hand adequate historical cause for this, and unmistakable evidence that no small number have, in spite of tremendous disadvantages, risen to the level of American civilization. And when, by proscription and prejudice, these same Negroes are classed with and treated like the lowest of their people, simply *because* they are Negroes, such a policy not only discourages thrift and intelligence among black men, but puts a direct premium on the very things you complain of,—inefficiency and crime. Draw lines of crime, of incompetency, of vice, as tightly and uncompromisingly as you will, for these things must be proscribed; but a color-line not only does not accomplish this purpose, but thwarts it.

In the face of two such arguments, the future of the South depends on the ability of the representatives of these opposing views to see and appreciate and sympathize with each other's position,—for the Negro to realize more deeply than he does at present the need of uplifting the masses of his people, for the white people to realize more vividly than they have yet done the deadening and disastrous effect of a color-prejudice that classes Phillis Wheatley and Sam Hose in the same despised class.

It is not enough for the Negroes to declare that color-prejudice is the sole cause of their social condition, nor for the white South to reply that their social condition is the main cause of prejudice. They both act as reciprocal cause and effect, and a change in neither alone will bring the desired effect. Both must change, or neither can improve to any great extent. The Negro cannot stand the present reactionary tendencies and unreasoning drawing of the color-line indefinitely without discouragement and retrogression. And the condition of the Negro is ever the excuse for further discrimination. Only by a union of intelligence and sympathy across the color-line in this critical period of the Republic shall justice and right triumph,—

> "That mind and soul according well,
> May make one music as before,
> But vaster."[9]

9. From the prologue of *In Memoriam* (1850), by Alfred, Lord Tennyson (1809–1892).

X. *Of the Faith of the Fathers*

Dim face of Beauty haunting all the world,
　Fair face of Beauty all too fair to see,
Where the lost stars adown the heavens are hurled,—
　　There, there alone for thee
　　May white peace be.

Beauty, sad face of Beauty, Mystery, Wonder,
　What are these dreams to foolish babbling men
Who cry with little noises 'neath the thunder
　　Of Ages ground to sand,
　　To a little sand.
　　　　　　　　　　　　FIONA MACLEOD[1]

It was out in the country, far from home, far from my foster home, on a dark Sunday night. The road wandered from our rambling log-house up the stony bed of a creek, past wheat and corn, until we could hear dimly across the fields a rhythmic cadence of song,—soft, thrilling, powerful, that swelled and died sorrowfully in our ears. I was a country school-teacher then, fresh from the East, and had never seen a Southern Negro revival. To be sure, we in Berkshire were not perhaps as stiff and formal as they in Suffolk of olden time; yet we were very quiet and subdued, and I know not what would have happened those clear Sabbath mornings had some one punctuated the sermon with a wild scream, or interrupted the long prayer with a loud Amen! And so most striking to me, as I approached the village and the little plain church perched aloft, was the air of intense excitement that possessed that mass of black folk. A sort of suppressed terror hung in the air and seemed to seize us,—a pythian madness,[2] a demoniac possession, that lent terrible reality to song and word. The black and massive form of the preacher swayed and quivered as the words crowded to his lips and flew at us in singular eloquence. The people moaned and fluttered, and then the gaunt-cheeked brown woman beside me suddenly leaped straight into the air and shrieked like a lost soul, while round about came wail and groan and outcry, and a scene of human passion such as I had never conceived before.

Those who have not thus witnessed the frenzy of a Negro revival in the untouched backwoods of the South can but dimly realize the religious feeling of the slave; as described, such scenes appear grotesque and funny, but as seen they are awful. Three things characterized this religion of the slave,—the Preacher, the Music, and the Frenzy. The Preacher is the most unique personality developed by the Negro on American soil. A leader, a politician, an orator, a "boss," an intriguer, an idealist,—all these he is, and ever, too, the centre of a group of men, now twenty, now a thousand in

1. Pseudonym of William Sharp (1855–1905),　　2. A trance in which the priestess Pythia uttered
English poet and novelist.　　　　　　　　　　　the oracles at Delphi in Greece.

number. The combination of a certain adroitness with deep-seated earnestness, of tact with consummate ability, gave him his preëminence, and helps him maintain it. The type, of course, varies according to time and place, from the West Indies in the sixteenth century to New England in the nineteenth, and from the Mississippi bottoms to cities like New Orleans or New York.

The Music of Negro religion is that plaintive rhythmic melody, with its touching minor cadences, which, despite caricature and defilement, still remains the most original and beautiful expression of human life and longing yet born on American soil. Sprung from the African forests, where its counterpart can still be heard, it was adapted, changed, and intensified by the tragic soul-life of the slave, until, under the stress of law and whip, it became the one true expression of a people's sorrow, despair, and hope.

Finally the Frenzy or "Shouting," when the Spirit of the Lord passed by, and, seizing the devotee, made him mad with supernatural joy, was the last essential of Negro religion and the one more devoutly believed in than all the rest. It varied in expression from the silent rapt countenance or the low murmur and moan to the mad abandon of physical fervor,—the stamping, shrieking, and shouting, the rushing to and fro and wild waving of arms, the weeping and laughing, the vision and the trance. All this is nothing new in the world, but old as religion, as Delphi and Endor.[3] And so firm a hold did it have on the Negro, that many generations firmly believed that without this visible manifestation of the God there could be no true communion with the Invisible.

These were the characteristics of Negro religious life as developed up to the time of Emancipation. Since under the peculiar circumstances of the black man's environment they were the one expression of his higher life, they are of deep interest to the student of his development, both socially and psychologically. Numerous are the attractive lines of inquiry that here group themselves. What did slavery mean to the African savage? What was his attitude toward the World and Life? What seemed to him good and evil,—God and Devil? Whither went his longings and strivings, and wherefore were his heart-burnings and disappointments? Answers to such questions can come only from a study of Negro religion as a development, through its gradual changes from the heathenism of the Gold Coast to the institutional Negro church of Chicago.

Moreover, the religious growth of millions of men, even though they be slaves, cannot be without potent influence upon their contemporaries. The Methodists and Baptists of America owe much of their condition to the silent but potent influence of their millions of Negro converts. Especially is this noticeable in the South, where theology and religious philosophy are on this account a long way behind the North, and where the religion of the poor whites is a plain copy of Negro thought and methods. The mass of "gospel" hymns which has swept through American churches and wellnigh ruined our sense of song consists largely of debased imitations of Negro melodies made by ears that caught the jingle but not the music, the

---

3. In Palestine where King Saul spoke to the dead prophet Samuel via a sorceress's power (I Samuel 28). Delphi was the site of a shrine to Apollo, the Greek god of prophecy.

body but not the soul, of the Jubilee songs.[4] It is thus clear that the study of Negro religion is not only a vital part of the history of the Negro in America, but no uninteresting part of American history.

The Negro church of to-day is the social centre of Negro life in the United States, and the most characteristic expression of African character. Take a typical church in a small Virginian town: it is the "First Baptist"—a roomy brick edifice seating five hundred or more persons, tastefully finished in Georgia pine, with a carpet, a small organ, and stained-glass windows. Underneath is a large assembly room with benches. This building is the central club-house of a community of a thousand or more Negroes. Various organizations meet here,—the church proper, the Sunday-school, two or three insurance societies, women's societies, secret societies, and mass meetings of various kinds. Entertainments, suppers, and lectures are held beside the five or six regular weekly religious services. Considerable sums of money are collected and expended here, employment is found for the idle, strangers are introduced, news is disseminated and charity distributed. At the same time this social, intellectual, and economic centre is a religious centre of great power. Depravity, Sin, Redemption, Heaven, Hell, and Damnation are preached twice a Sunday with much fervor, and revivals take place every year after the crops are laid by; and few indeed of the community have the hardihood to withstand conversion. Back of this more formal religion, the Church often stands as a real conserver of morals, a strengthener of family life, and the final authority on what is Good and Right.

Thus one can see in the Negro church to-day, reproduced in microcosm, all that great world from which the Negro is cut off by color-prejudice and social condition. In the great city churches the same tendency is noticeable and in many respects emphasized. A great church like the Bethel of Philadelphia[5] has over eleven hundred members, an edifice seating fifteen hundred persons and valued at one hundred thousand dollars, an annual budget of five thousand dollars, and a government consisting of a pastor with several assisting local preachers, an executive and legislative board, financial boards and tax collectors; general church meetings for making laws; subdivided groups led by class leaders, a company of militia, and twenty-four auxiliary societies. The activity of a church like this is immense and far-reaching, and the bishops who preside over these organizations throughout the land are among the most powerful Negro rulers in the world.

Such churches are really governments of men, and consequently a little investigation reveals the curious fact that, in the South, at least, practically every American Negro is a church member. Some, to be sure, are not regularly enrolled, and a few do not habitually attend services; but, practically, a proscribed people must have a social centre, and that centre for this people is the Negro church. The census of 1890 showed nearly twenty-four thousand Negro churches in the country, with a total enrolled membership of over two and a half millions, or ten actual church members to every twenty-

4. Southern African American religious folk songs.
5. "Mother" Bethel was the founding church of the African Methodist Episcopal denomination in the United States.

:ight persons, and in some Southern States one in every two persons. Besides these there is the large number who, while not enrolled as members, attend and take part in many of the activities of the church. There is an organized Negro church for every sixty black families in the nation, and in some States for every forty families, owning, on an average, a thousand dollars' worth of property each, or nearly twenty-six million dollars in all.

Such, then, is the large development of the Negro church since Emancipation. The question now is, What have been the successive steps of this social history and what are the present tendencies? First, we must realize that no such institution as the Negro church could rear itself without definite historical foundations. These foundations we can find if we remember that the social history of the Negro did not start in America. He was brought from a definite social environment,—the polygamous clan life[6] under the headship of the chief and the potent influence of the priest. His religion was nature-worship, with profound belief in invisible surrounding influences, good and bad, and his worship was through incantation and sacrifice. The first rude change in this life was the slave ship and the West Indian sugar-fields. The plantation organization replaced the clan and tribe, and the white master replaced the chief with far greater and more despotic powers. Forced and long-continued toil became the rule of life, the old ties of blood relationship and kinship disappeared, and instead of the family appeared a new polygamy and polyandry,[7] which, in some cases, almost reached promiscuity. It was a terrific social revolution, and yet some traces were retained of the former group life, and the chief remaining institution was the Priest or Medicine-man. He early appeared on the plantation and found his function as the healer of the sick, the interpreter of the Unknown, the comforter of the sorrowing, the supernatural avenger of wrong, and the one who rudely but picturesquely expressed the longing, disappointment, and resentment of a stolen and oppressed people. Thus, as bard, physician, judge, and priest, within the narrow limits allowed by the slave system, rose the Negro preacher, and under him the first Afro-American institution, the Negro church. This church was not at first by any means Christian nor definitely organized; rather it was an adaptation and mingling of heathen rites among the members of each plantation, and roughly designated as Voodooism.[8] Association with the masters, missionary effort and motives of expediency gave these rites an early veneer of Christianity, and after the lapse of many generations the Negro church became Christian.

Two characteristic things must be noticed in regard to this church. First, it became almost entirely Baptist and Methodist in faith; secondly, as a social institution it antedated by many decades the monogamic[9] Negro home. From the very circumstances of its beginning, the church was confined to the plantation, and consisted primarily of a series of disconnected units; although, later on, some freedom of movement was allowed, still this

---

6. A society made up of extended family groups that allows men to have more than one wife at the same time.
7. Having more than one husband at the same time.

8. An underground religion featuring borrowed Christian symbols and the casting of spells and charms.
9. Having only one wife at a time.

geographical limitation was always important and was one cause of the spread of the decentralized and democratic Baptist faith among the slaves. At the same time, the visible rite of baptism appealed strongly to their mystic temperament. To-day the Baptist Church is still largest in membership among Negroes, and has a million and a half communicants. Next in popularity came the churches organized in connection with the white neighboring churches, chiefly Baptist and Methodist, with a few Episcopalian and others. The Methodists still form the second greatest denomination, with nearly a million members. The faith of these two leading denominations was more suited to the slave church from the prominence they gave to religious feeling and fervor. The Negro membership in other denominations has always been small and relatively unimportant, although the Episcopalians and Presbyterians are gaining among the more intelligent classes to-day, and the Catholic Church is making headway in certain sections. After Emancipation, and still earlier in the North, the Negro churches largely severed such affiliations as they had had with the white churches, either by choice or by compulsion. The Baptist churches became independent, but the Methodists were compelled early to unite for purposes of episcopal government. This gave rise to the great African Methodist Church, the greatest Negro organization in the world, to the Zion Church and the Colored Methodist, and to the black conferences and churches in this and other denominations.

The second fact noted, namely, that the Negro church antedates the Negro home, leads to an explanation of much that is paradoxical in this communistic institution and in the morals of its members. But especially it leads us to regard this institution as peculiarly the expression of the inner ethical life of a people in a sense seldom true elsewhere. Let us turn, then, from the outer physical development of the church to the more important inner ethical life of the people who compose it. The Negro has already been pointed out many times as a religious animal,—a being of that deep emotional nature which turns instinctively toward the supernatural. Endowed with a rich tropical imagination and a keen, delicate appreciation of Nature, the transplanted African lived in a world animate with gods and devils, elves and witches; full of strange influences,—of Good to be implored, of Evil to be propitiated. Slavery, then, was to him the dark triumph of Evil over him. All the hateful powers of the Under-world were striving against him, and a spirit of revolt and revenge filled his heart. He called up all the resources of heathenism to aid,—exorcism and witchcraft, the mysterious Obi worship with its barbarous rites, spells, and blood-sacrifice even, now and then, of human victims. Weird midnight orgies and mystic conjurations were invoked, the witch-woman and the voodoo-priest became the centre of Negro group life, and that vein of vague superstition which characterizes the unlettered Negro even to-day was deepened and strengthened.

In spite, however, of such success as that of the fierce Maroons, the Danish blacks, and others, the spirit of revolt gradually died away under the untiring energy and superior strength of the slave masters. By the middle of the eighteenth century the black slave had sunk, with hushed murmurs, to his place at the bottom of a new economic system, and was unconsciously ripe for a new philosophy of life. Nothing suited his condition then better than the doctrines of passive submission embodied in the newly learned Christianity. Slave masters early realized this, and cheerfully aided religious propaganda within certain bounds. The long system of repression and degradation of the Negro tended to emphasize the elements in his character which made him a valuable chattel: courtesy became humility, moral strength degenerated into submission, and the exquisite native appreciation of the beautiful became an infinite capacity for dumb suffering. The Negro, losing the joy of this world, eagerly seized upon the offered conceptions of the next; the avenging Spirit of the Lord enjoining patience in this world, under sorrow and tribulation until the Great Day when He should lead His dark children home,—this became his comforting dream. His preacher repeated the prophecy, and his bards sang,—

> "Children, we all shall be free
> When the Lord shall appear!" [1]

This deep religious fatalism, painted so beautifully in "Uncle Tom," [2] came soon to breed, as all fatalistic faiths will, the sensualist side by side with the martyr. Under the lax moral life of the plantation, where marriage was a farce, laziness a virtue, and property a theft, a religion of resignation and submission degenerated easily, in less strenuous minds, into a philosophy of indulgence and crime. Many of the worst characteristics of the Negro masses of to-day had their seed in this period of the slave's ethical growth. Here it was that the Home was ruined under the very shadow of the Church, white and black; here habits of shiftlessness took root, and sullen hopelessness replaced hopeful strife.

With the beginning of the abolition movement and the gradual growth of a class of free Negroes came a change. We often neglect the influence of the freedman before the war, because of the paucity of his numbers and the small weight he had in the history of the nation. But we must not forget that his chief influence was internal,—was exerted on the black world; and that there he was the ethical and social leader. Huddled as he was in a few centres like Philadelphia, New York, and New Orleans, the masses of the freedmen sank into poverty and listlessness; but not all of them. The free Negro leader early arose and his chief characteristic was intense earnestness and deep feeling on the slavery question. Freedom became to him a real thing and not a dream. His religion became darker and more intense, and into his ethics crept a note of revenge, into his songs a day of reckoning close at hand. The "Coming of the Lord" swept this side of Death, and came to be a thing to be hoped for in this day. Through fugitive slaves and irrepressible discussion this desire for freedom seized the black millions still in bondage, and became their one ideal of life. The black bards caught new notes, and sometimes even dared to sing,—

> "O Freedom, O Freedom, O Freedom over me!
> Before I'll be a slave

---

1. From "Children, We Shall All Be Free," a Negro spiritual.
2. The pious, long-suffering slave hero of *Uncle Tom's Cabin.*

I'll be buried in my grave,
And go home to my Lord
And be free."[3]

For fifty years Negro religion thus transformed itself and identified itself
with the dream of Abolition, until that which was a radical fad in the white
North and an anarchistic plot in the white South had become a religion to
the black world. Thus, when Emancipation finally came, it seemed to the
freedman a literal Coming of the Lord. His fervid imagination was stirred
as never before, by the tramp of armies, the blood and dust of battle, and
the wail and whirl of social upheaval. He stood dumb and motionless
before the whirlwind: what had he to do with it? Was it not the Lord's
doing, and marvellous in his eyes? Joyed and bewildered with what came,
he stood awaiting new wonders till the inevitable Age of Reaction swept
over the nation and brought the crisis of to-day.

It is difficult to explain clearly the present critical stage of Negro religion. First, we must remember that living as the blacks do in close contact
with a great modern nation, and sharing, although imperfectly, the soul-
life of that nation, they must necessarily be affected more or less directly by
all the religious and ethical forces that are to-day moving the United States.
These questions and movements are, however, overshadowed and dwarfed
by the (to them) all-important question of their civil, political, and economic status. They must perpetually discuss the "Negro Problem,"—must
live, move, and have their being in it, and interpret all else in its light or
darkness. With this come, too, peculiar problems of their inner life,—of the
status of women, the maintenance of Home, the training of children, the
accumulation of wealth, and the prevention of crime. All this must mean a
time of intense ethical ferment, of religious heart-searching and intellectual unrest. From the double life every American Negro must live, as a
Negro and as an American, as swept on by the current of the nineteenth
while yet struggling in the eddies of the fifteenth century,—from this must
arise a painful self-consciousness, an almost morbid sense of personality
and a moral hesitancy which is fatal to self-confidence. The worlds within
and without the Veil of Color are changing, and changing rapidly, but not
at the same rate, not in the same way; and this must produce a peculiar
wrenching of the soul, a peculiar sense of doubt and bewilderment. Such a
double life, with double thoughts, double duties, and double social classes,
must give rise to double words and double ideals, and tempt the mind to
pretence or to revolt, to hypocrisy or to radicalism.

In some such doubtful words and phrases can one perhaps most clearly
picture the peculiar ethical paradox that faces the Negro of to-day and is
tingeing and changing his religious life. Feeling that his rights and his dearest ideals are being trampled upon, that the public conscience is ever more
deaf to his righteous appeal, and that all the reactionary forces of prejudice,
greed, and revenge are daily gaining new strength and fresh allies, the Negro
faces no enviable dilemma. Conscious of his impotence, and pessimistic,
he often becomes bitter and vindictive; and his religion, instead of a wor-

3. From "O Freedom!," a Negro spiritual.

ship, is a complaint and a curse, a wail rather than a hope, a sneer rather than a faith. On the other hand, another type of mind, shrewder and keener and more tortuous too, sees in the very strength of the anti-Negro movement its patent weaknesses, and with Jesuitic casuistry[4] is deterred by no ethical considerations in the endeavor to turn this weakness to the black man's strength. Thus we have two great and hardly reconcilable streams of thought and ethical strivings; the danger of the one lies in anarchy, that of the other in hypocrisy. The one type of Negro stands almost ready to curse God and die, and the other is too often found a traitor to right and a coward before force; the one is wedded to ideals remote, whimsical, perhaps impossible of realization; the other forgets that life is more than meat and the body more than raiment. But, after all, is not this simply the writhing of the age translated into black,—the triumph of the Lie which to-day, with its false culture, faces the hideousness of the anarchist assassin?

To-day the two groups of Negroes, the one in the North, the other in the South, represent these divergent ethical tendencies, the first tending toward radicalism, the other toward hypocritical compromise. It is no idle regret with which the white South mourns the loss of the old-time Negro,— the frank, honest, simple old servant who stood for the earlier religious age of submission and humility. With all his laziness and lack of many elements of true manhood, he was at least open-hearted, faithful, and sincere. To-day he is gone, but who is to blame for his going? Is it not those very persons who mourn for him? Is it not the tendency, born of Reconstruction and Reaction, to found a society on lawlessness and deception, to tamper with the moral fibre of a naturally honest and straightforward people until the whites threaten to become ungovernable tyrants and the blacks criminals and hypocrites? Deception is the natural defence of the weak against the strong, and the South used it for many years against its conquerors; to-day it must be prepared to see its black proletariat turn that same two-edged weapon against itself. And how natural this is! The death of Denmark Vesey and Nat Turner proved long since to the Negro the present hopelessness of physical defence. Political defence is becoming less and less available, and economic defence is still only partially effective. But there is a patent defence at hand,—the defence of deception and flattery, of cajoling and lying. It is the same defence which the Jews of the Middle Age used and which left its stamp on their character for centuries. To-day the young Negro of the South who would succeed cannot be frank and outspoken, honest and self-assertive, but rather he is daily tempted to be silent and wary, politic and sly; he must flatter and be pleasant, endure petty insults with a smile, shut his eyes to wrong; in too many cases he sees positive personal advantage in deception and lying. His real thoughts, his real aspirations, must be guarded in whispers; he must not criticise, he must not complain. Patience, humility, and adroitness must, in these growing black youth, replace impulse, manliness, and courage. With this sacrifice there is an economic opening, and perhaps peace and some prosperity. Without this there is riot, migration, or crime. Nor is this situation peculiar to the Southern United States,—is it not rather the only method by which un-

4. Subtle but misleading or false reasoning.

developed races have gained the right to share modern culture? The price of culture is a Lie.

On the other hand, in the North the tendency is to emphasize the radicalism of the Negro. Driven from his birthright in the South by a situation at which every fibre of his more outspoken and assertive nature revolts, he finds himself in a land where he can scarcely earn a decent living amid the harsh competition and the color discrimination. At the same time, through schools and periodicals, discussions and lectures, he is intellectually quickened and awakened. The soul, long pent up and dwarfed, suddenly expands in new-found freedom. What wonder that every tendency is to excess,—radical complaint, radical remedies, bitter denunciation or angry silence. Some sink, some rise. The criminal and the sensualist leave the church for the gambling-hell and the brothel, and fill the slums of Chicago and Baltimore; the better classes segregate themselves from the group-life of both white and black, and form an aristocracy, cultured but pessimistic, whose bitter criticism stings while it points out no way of escape. They despise the submission and subserviency of the Southern Negroes, but offer no other means by which a poor and oppressed minority can exist side by side with its masters. Feeling deeply and keenly the tendencies and opportunities of the age in which they live, their souls are bitter at the fate which drops the Veil between; and the very fact that this bitterness is natural and justifiable only serves to intensify it and make it more maddening.

Between the two extreme types of ethical attitude which I have thus sought to make clear wavers the mass of the millions of Negroes, North and South; and their religious life and activity partake of this social conflict within their ranks. Their churches are differentiating,—now into groups of cold, fashionable devotees, in no way distinguishable from similar white groups save in color of skin; now into large social and business institutions catering to the desire for information and amusement of their members, warily avoiding unpleasant questions both within and without the black world, and preaching in effect if not in word: *Dum vivimus, vivamus.* [5]

But back of this still broods silently the deep religious feeling of the real Negro heart, the stirring, unguided might of powerful human souls who have lost the guiding star of the past and are seeking in the great night a new religious ideal. Some day the Awakening will come, when the pent-up vigor of ten million souls shall sweep irresistibly toward the Goal, out of the Valley of the Shadow of Death, where all that makes life worth living—Liberty, Justice, and Right—is marked "For White People Only."

5. While we live, let us live (Latin).

XI. Of the Passing of the First-Born

> O sister, sister, thy first-begotten,
> The hands that cling and the feet that follow,
> The voice of the child's blood crying yet,
> *Who hath remembered me? who hath forgotten?*
> Thou hast forgotten, O summer swallow,
> But the world shall end when I forget.
>   SWINBURNE [6]

Unto you a child is born," sang the bit of yellow paper that fluttered into my room one brown October morning. Then the fear of fatherhood mingled wildly with the joy of creation; I wondered how it looked and how it felt,—what were its eyes, and how its hair curled and crumpled itself. And I thought in awe of her,—she who had slept with Death to tear a man-child from underneath her heart, while I was unconsciously wandering. I fled to my wife and child, repeating the while to myself half wonderingly, "Wife and child? Wife and child?"—fled fast and faster than boat and steamcar, and yet must ever impatiently await them; away from the hard-voiced city, away from the flickering sea into my own Berkshire Hills that sit all sadly guarding the gates of Massachusetts.

Up the stairs I ran to the wan mother and whimpering babe, to the sanctuary on whose altar a life at my bidding had offered itself to win a life, and won. What is this tiny formless thing, this new-born wail from an unknown world,—all head and voice? I handle it curiously, and watch perplexed its winking, breathing, and sneezing. I did not love it then; it seemed a ludicrous thing to love; but her I loved, my girl-mother, she whom now I saw unfolding like the glory of the morning—the transfigured woman.

Through her I came to love the wee thing, as it grew and waxed strong; as its little soul unfolded itself in twitter and cry and half-formed word, and as its eyes caught the gleam and flash of life. How beautiful he was, with his olive-tinted flesh and dark gold ringlets, his eyes of mingled blue and brown, his perfect little limbs, and the soft voluptuous roll which the blood of Africa had moulded into his features! I held him in my arms, after we had sped far away to our Southern home,—held him, and glanced at the hot red soil of Georgia and the breathless city of a hundred hills, and felt a vague unrest. Why was his hair tinted with gold? An evil omen was golden hair in my life. Why had not the brown of his eyes crushed out and killed the blue?—for brown were his father's eyes, and his father's father's. And thus in the Land of the Color-line I saw, as it fell across my baby, the shadow of the Veil.

Within the Veil was he born, said I; and there within shall he live,—a

6. Charles Algernon Swinburne (1837–1909), British poet. The quotation is from *Itylus* (1866).

Negro and a Negro's son. Holding in that little head—ah, bitterly!—the un-
bowed pride of a hunted race, clinging with that tiny dimpled hand—ah,
wearily!—to a hope not hopeless but unhopeful, and seeing with those
bright wondering eyes that peer into my soul a land whose freedom is to us
a mockery and whose liberty a lie. I saw the shadow of the Veil as it passed
over my baby, I saw the cold city towering above the blood-red land. I held
my face beside his little cheek, showed him the star-children and the twinkling lights as they began to flash, and stilled with an even-song the unvoiced terror of my life.

So sturdy and masterful he grew, so filled with bubbling life so tremulous with the unspoken wisdom of a life but eighteen months distant from
the All-life,—we were not far from worshipping this revelation of the divine,
my wife and I. Her own life builded and moulded itself upon the child; he
tinged her every dream and idealized her every effort. No hands but hers
must touch and garnish those little limbs; no dress or frill must touch them
that had not wearied her fingers; no voice but hers could coax him off to
Dreamland, and she and he together spoke some soft and unknown tongue
and in it held communion. I too mused above his little white bed; saw the
strength of my own arm stretched onward through the ages through the
newer strength of his; saw the dream of my black fathers stagger a step onward in the wild phantasm of the world; heard in his baby voice the voice of
the Prophet that was to rise within the Veil.

And so we dreamed and loved and planned by fall and winter, and the
full flush of the long Southern spring, till the hot winds rolled from the
fetid Gulf, till the roses shivered and the still stern sun quivered its awful
light over the hills of Atlanta. And then one night the little feet pattered
wearily to the wee white bed, and the tiny hands trembled; and a warm
flushed face tossed on the pillow, and we knew baby was sick. Ten days he
lay there,—a swift week and three endless days, wasting, wasting away.
Cheerily the mother nursed him the first days, and laughed into the little
eyes that smiled again. Tenderly then she hovered round him, till the smile
fled away and Fear crouched beside the little bed.

Then the day ended not, and night was a dreamless terror, and joy and
sleep slipped away. I hear now that Voice at midnight calling me from dull
and dreamless trance,—crying, "The Shadow of Death! The Shadow of
Death!" Out into the starlight I crept, to rouse the gray physician,—the
Shadow of Death, the Shadow of Death. The hours trembled on; the night
listened; the ghastly dawn glided like a tired thing across the lamplight.
Then we two alone looked upon the child as he turned toward us with great
eyes, and stretched his string-like hands,—the Shadow of Death! And we
spoke no word, and turned away.

He died at eventide, when the sun lay like a brooding sorrow above the
western hills, veiling its face; when the winds spoke not, and the trees, the
great green trees he loved, stood motionless. I saw his breath beat quicker
and quicker, pause, and then his little soul leapt like a star that travels in
the night and left a world of darkness in its train. The day changed not; the
same tall trees peeped in at the windows, the same green grass glinted in
the setting sun. Only in the chamber of death writhed the world's most
piteous thing—a childless mother.

I shirk not. I long for work. I pant for a life full of striving. I am no coward, to shrink before the rugged rush of the storm, nor even quail before the
awful shadow of the Veil. But hearken, O Death! Is not this my life hard
enough,—is not that dull land that stretches its sneering web about me cold
enough,—is not all the world beyond these four little walls pitiless enough,
but that thou must needs enter here,—thou, O Death? About my head the
thundering storm beat like a heartless voice, and the crazy forest pulsed
with the curses of the weak; but what cared I, within my home beside my
wife and baby boy? Wast thou so jealous of one little coign of happiness
that thou must needs enter there,—thou, O Death?

A perfect life was his, all joy and love, with tears to make it brighter,—
sweet as a summer's day beside the Housatonic. The world loved him; the
women kissed his curls, the men looked gravely into his wonderful eyes,
and the children hovered and fluttered about him. I can see him now,
changing like the sky from sparkling laughter to darkening frowns, and
then to wondering thoughtfulness as he watched the world. He knew no
color-line, poor dear,—and the Veil, though it shadowed him, had not yet
darkened half his sun. He loved the white matron, he loved his black nurse;
and in his little world walked souls alone, uncolored and unclothed. I—
yea, all men—are larger and purer by the infinite breadth of that one little
life. She who in simple clearness of vision sees beyond the stars said when
he had flown, "He will be happy There; he ever loved beautiful things."
And I, far more ignorant, and blind by the web of mine own weaving, sit
alone winding words and muttering, "If still he be, and he be There, and
there be a There, let him be happy, O Fate!"

Blithe was the morning of his burial, with bird and song and sweet-smelling flowers. The trees whispered to the grass, but the children sat with
hushed faces. And yet it seemed a ghostly unreal day,—the wraith of Life.
We seemed to rumble down an unknown street behind a little white bundle of posies, with the shadow of a song in our ears. The busy city dinned
about us; they did not say much, those pale-faced hurrying men and
women; they did not say much,—they only glanced and said, "Niggers!"

We could not lay him in the ground there in Georgia, for the earth there
is strangely red; so we bore him away to the northward, with his flowers and
his little folded hands. In vain, in vain!—for where, O God! beneath thy
broad blue sky shall my dark baby rest in peace,—where Reverence dwells,
and Goodness, and a Freedom that is free?

All that day and all that night there sat an awful gladness in my heart,—
nay, blame me not if I see the world thus darkly through the Veil,—and my
soul whispers ever to me, saying, "Not dead, not dead, but escaped; not
bond, but free." No bitter meanness now shall sicken his baby heart till it
die a living death, no taunt shall madden his happy boyhood. Fool that I
was to think or wish that this little soul should grow choked and deformed
within the Veil! I might have known that yonder deep unworldly look that
ever and anon floated past his eyes was peering far beyond this narrow
Now. In the poise of his little curl-crowned head did there not sit all that
wild pride of being which his father had hardly crushed in his own heart?
For what, forsooth, shall a Negro want with pride amid the studied
humiliations of fifty million fellows? Well sped, my boy, before the world

had dubbed your ambition insolence, had held your ideals unattainable, and taught you to cringe and bow. Better far this nameless void that stops my life than a sea of sorrow for you.

Idle words; he might have borne his burden more bravely than we,—aye, and found it lighter too, some day; for surely, surely this is not the end. Surely there shall yet dawn some mighty morning to lift the Veil and set the prisoned free. Not for me,—I shall die in my bonds,—but for fresh young souls who have not known the night and waken to the morning; a morning when men ask of the workman, not "Is he white?" but "Can he work?" When men ask artists, not "Are they black?" but "Do they know?" Some morning this may be, long, long years to come. But now there wails, on that dark shore within the Veil, the same deep voice, *Thou shalt forego!* And all have I foregone at that command, and with small complaint,—all save that fair young form that lies so coldly wed with death in the nest I had builded.

If one must have gone, why not I? Why may I not rest me from this restlessness and sleep from this wide waking? Was not the world's alembic,[7] Time, in his young hands, and is not my time waning? Are there so many workers in the vineyard that the fair promise of this little body could lightly be tossed away? The wretched of my race that line the alleys of the nation sit fatherless and unmothered; but Love sat beside his cradle, and in his ear Wisdom waited to speak. Perhaps now he knows the All-love, and needs not to be wise. Sleep, then, child,—sleep till I sleep and waken to a baby voice and the ceaseless patter of little feet—above the Veil.

XII. Of Alexander Crummell[8]

Then from the Dawn it seemed there came, but faint
As from beyond the limit of the world,
Like the last echo born of a great cry,
Sounds, as if some fair city were one voice
Around a king returning from his wars.[9]

TENNYSON

This is the history of a human heart,—the tale of a black boy who many long years ago began to struggle with life that he might know the world and know himself. Three temptations he met on those dark dunes that lay gray and dismal before the wonder-eyes of the child: the temptation of Hate, that stood out against the red dawn; the temptation of Despair, that dark-

7. A purifying still.
8. Clergyman, antislavery activist, and African missionary (1819–1898).

9. From Tennyson's *The Passing of Arthur* in *Idylls of the King* (1869).

ened noonday; and the temptation of Doubt, that ever steals along with twilight. Above all, you must hear of the vales he crossed,—the Valley of Humiliation and the Valley of the Shadow of Death.

I saw Alexander Crummell first at a Wilberforce commencement season, amid its bustle and crush. Tall, frail, and black he stood, with simple dignity and an unmistakable air of good breeding. I talked with him apart, where the storming of the lusty young orators could not harm us. I spoke to him politely, then curiously, then eagerly, as I began to feel the fineness of his character,—his calm courtesy, the sweetness of his strength, and his fair blending of the hope and truth of life. Instinctively I bowed before this man, as one bows before the prophets of the world. Some seer he seemed, that came not from the crimson Past or the gray To-come, but from the pulsing Now,—that mocking world which seemed to me at once so light and dark, so splendid and sordid. Four-score years had he wandered in this same world of mine, within the Veil.

He was born with the Missouri Compromise and lay adying amid the echoes of Manila and El Caney:[1] stirring times for living, times dark to look back upon, darker to look forward to. The black-faced lad that paused over his mud and marbles seventy years ago saw puzzling vistas as he looked down the world. The slave-ship still groaned across the Atlantic, faint cries burdened the Southern breeze, and the great black father whispered mad tales of cruelty into those young ears. From the low doorway the mother silently watched her boy at play, and at nightfall sought him eagerly lest the shadows bear him away to the land of slaves.

So his young mind worked and winced and shaped curiously a vision of Life; and in the midst of that vision ever stood one dark figure alone,—ever with the hard, thick countenance of that bitter father, and a form that fell in vast and shapeless folds. Thus the temptation of Hate grew and shadowed the growing child,—gliding stealthily into his laughter, fading into his play, and seizing his dreams by day and night with rough, rude turbulence. So the black boy asked of sky and sun and flower the never-answered Why? and loved, as he grew, neither the world nor the world's rough ways.

Strange temptation for a child, you may think; and yet in this wide land to-day a thousand thousand dark children brood before this same temptation, and feel its cold and shuddering arms. For them, perhaps, some one will some day lift the Veil,—will come tenderly and cheerily into those sad little lives and brush the brooding hate away, just as Beriah Green strode in upon the life of Alexander Crummell. And before the bluff, kind-hearted man the shadow seemed less dark. Beriah Green had a school in Oneida County, New York, with a score of mischievous boys. "I'm going to bring a black boy here to educate," said Beriah Green, as only a crank and an abolitionist would have dared to say. "Oho!" laughed the boys. "Ye-es," said his wife; and Alexander came. Once before, the black boy had sought a school, had travelled, cold and hungry, four hundred miles up into free New Hampshire, to Canaan. But the godly farmers hitched ninety yoke of oxen

---

1. Sites of U.S. victories in the Philippines and Cuba, respectively, during the Spanish-American War in 1898. "Missouri Compromise": passed by the U.S. Congress in 1820 to keep a balance of free and slave states by allowing Missouri to enter the Union as a slave state.

to the abolition schoolhouse and dragged it into the middle of the swamp. The black boy trudged away.

The nineteenth was the first century of human sympathy,—the age when half wonderingly we began to descry in others that transfigured spark of divinity which we call Myself; when clodhoppers and peasants, and tramps and thieves, and millionaires and—sometimes—Negroes, became throbbing souls whose warm pulsing life touched us so nearly that we half gasped with surprise, crying, "Thou too! Hast Thou seen Sorrow and the dull waters of Hopelessness? Hast Thou known Life?" And then all helplessly we peered into those Other-worlds, and wailed, "O World of Worlds, how shall man make you one?"

So in that little Oneida school there came to those schoolboys a revelation of thought and longing beneath one black skin, of which they had not dreamed before. And to the lonely boy came a new dawn of sympathy and inspiration. The shadowy, formless thing—the temptation of Hate, that hovered between him and the world—grew fainter and less sinister. It did not wholly fade away, but diffused itself and lingered thick at the edges. Through it the child now first saw the blue and gold of life,—the sun-swept road that ran 'twixt heaven and earth until in one far-off wan wavering line they met and kissed. A vision of life came to the growing boy,—mystic, wonderful. He raised his head, stretched himself, breathed deep of the fresh new air. Yonder, behind the forests, he heard strange sounds; then glinting through the trees he saw, far, far away, the bronzed hosts of a nation calling,—calling faintly, calling loudly. He heard the hateful clank of their chains, he felt them cringe and grovel, and there rose within him a protest and a prophecy. And he girded himself to walk down the world.

A voice and vision called him to be a priest,—a seer to lead the uncalled out of the house of bondage. He saw the headless host turn toward him like the whirling of mad waters,—he stretched forth his hands eagerly, and then, even as he stretched them, suddenly there swept across the vision the temptation of Despair.

They were not wicked men,—the problem of life is not the problem of the wicked,—they were calm, good men, Bishops of the Apostolic Church of God, and strove toward righteousness. They said slowly, "It is all very natural—it is even commendable; but the General Theological Seminary of the Episcopal Church cannot admit a Negro." And when that thin, half-grotesque figure still haunted their doors, they put their hands kindly, half sorrowfully, on his shoulders, and said, "Now,—of course, we—we know how you feel about it; but you see it is impossible,—that is—well—it is premature. Sometime, we trust—sincerely trust—all such distinctions will fade away; but now the world is as it is."

This was the temptation of Despair; and the young man fought it doggedly. Like some grave shadow he flitted by those halls, pleading, arguing, half angrily demanding admittance, until there came the final No; until men hustled the disturber away, marked him as foolish, unreasonable, and injudicious, a vain rebel against God's law. And then from that Vision Splendid all the glory faded slowly away, and left an earth gray and stern rolling on beneath a dark despair. Even the kind hands that stretched themselves toward him from out the depths of that dull morning seemed but parts of the purple shadows. He saw them coldly, and asked, "Why should I strive by special grace when the way of the world is closed to me?" All gently yet, the hands urged him on,—the hands of young John Jay, [2] that daring father's daring son; the hands of the good folk of Boston, that free city. And yet, with a way to the priesthood of the Church open at last before him, the cloud lingered there; and even when in old St. Paul's the venerable Bishop raised his white arms above the Negro deacon—even then the burden had not lifted from that heart, for there had passed a glory from the earth.

And yet the fire through which Alexander Crummell went did not burn in vain. Slowly and more soberly he took up again his plan of life. More critically he studied the situation. Deep down below the slavery and servitude of the Negro people he saw their fatal weaknesses, which long years of mistreatment had emphasized. The dearth of strong moral character, of unbending righteousness, he felt, was their great shortcoming, and here he would begin. He would gather the best of his people into some little Episcopal chapel and there lead, teach, and inspire them, till the leaven spread, till the children grew, till the world hearkened, till—till—and then across his dream gleamed some faint after-glow of that first fair vision of youth—only an after-glow, for there had passed a glory from the earth.

One day—it was in 1842, and the springtide was struggling merrily with the May winds of New England—he stood at last in his own chapel in Providence, a priest of the Church. The days sped by, and the dark young clergyman labored; he wrote his sermons carefully; he intoned his prayers with a soft, earnest voice; he haunted the streets and accosted the wayfarers; he visited the sick, and knelt beside the dying. He worked and toiled, week by week, day by day, month by month. And yet month by month the congregation dwindled, week by week the hollow walls echoed more sharply, day by day the calls came fewer and fewer, and day by day the third temptation sat clearer and still more clearly within the Veil; a temptation, as it were, bland and smiling, with just a shade of mockery in its smooth tones. First it came casually, in the cadence of a voice: "Oh, colored folks? Yes." Or perhaps more definitely: "What do you *expect?*" In voice and gesture lay the doubt—the temptation of Doubt. How he hated it, and stormed at it furiously! "Of course they are capable," he cried; "of course they can learn and strive and achieve—" and "Of course," added the temptation softly, "they do nothing of the sort." Of all the three temptations, this one struck the deepest. Hate? He had outgrown so childish a thing. Despair? He had steeled his right arm against it, and fought it with the vigor of determination. But to doubt the worth of his lifework,—to doubt the destiny and capability of the race his soul loved because it was his; to find listless squalor instead of eager endeavor; to hear his own lips whispering, "They do not care; they cannot know; they are dumb driven cattle,—why cast your pearls before swine?"—this, this seemed more than man could bear; and he closed the door, and sank upon the steps of the chancel, and cast his robe upon the floor and writhed.

2. Antislavery activist and politician (1817–1894).

The evening sunbeams had set the dust to dancing in the gloomy chapel when he arose. He folded his vestments, put away the hymn-books, and closed the great Bible. He stepped out into the twilight, looked back upon the narrow little pulpit with a weary smile, and locked the door. Then he walked briskly to the Bishop, and told the Bishop what the Bishop already knew. "I have failed," he said simply. And gaining courage by the confession, he added: "What I need is a larger constituency. There are comparatively few Negroes here, and perhaps they are not of the best. I must go where the field is wider, and try again." So the Bishop sent him to Philadelphia, with a letter to Bishop Onderdonk.

Bishop Onderdonk lived at the head of six white steps,—corpulent, red-faced, and the author of several thrilling tracts on Apostolic Succession.[3] It was after dinner, and the Bishop had settled himself for a pleasant season of contemplation, when the bell must needs ring, and there must burst in upon the Bishop a letter and a thin, ungainly Negro. Bishop Onderdonk read the letter hastily and frowned. Fortunately, his mind was already clear on this point; and he cleared his brow and looked at Crummell. Then he said, slowly and impressively: "I will receive you into this diocese on one condition: no Negro priest can sit in my church convention, and no Negro church must ask for representation there."

I sometimes fancy I can see that tableau: the frail black figure, nervously twitching his hat before the massive abdomen of Bishop Onderdonk; his threadbare coat thrown against the dark woodwork of the book-cases, where Fox's "Lives of the Martyrs" nestled happily beside "The Whole Duty of Man."[4] I seem to see the wide eyes of the Negro wander past the Bishop's broadcloth to where the swinging glass doors of the cabinet glow in the sunlight. A little blue fly is trying to cross the yawning keyhole. He marches briskly up to it, peers into the chasm in a surprised sort of way, and rubs his feelers reflectively; then he essays its depths, and, finding it bottomless, draws back again. The dark-faced priest finds himself wondering if the fly too has faced its Valley of Humiliation, and if it will plunge into it,— when lo! it spreads its tiny wings and buzzes merrily across, leaving the watcher wingless and alone.

Then the full weight of his burden fell upon him. The rich walls wheeled away, and before him lay the cold rough moor winding on through life, cut in twain by one thick granite ridge,—here, the Valley of Humiliation; yonder, the Valley of the Shadow of Death. And I know not which be darker,—no, not I. But this I know: in yonder Vale of the Humble stand to-day a million swarthy men, who willingly would

> "... bear the whips and scorns of time,
> The oppressor's wrong, the proud man's contumely,
> The pangs of despised love, the law's delay,
> The insolence of office, and the spurns
> That patient merit of the unworthy takes,"[5]

3. The Christian doctrine that the religious authority conferred by Jesus on St. Peter extends through an unbroken succession of Apostles, bishops, and popes.
4. A Christian devotional book (1658) by an anonymous English author. John Foxe (1516–1578), English clergyman, who wrote *Acts and Monuments of These Latter and Perilous Days* (popularly known as *The Book of Martyrs*).
5. Shakespeare's *Hamlet* 3.1.69–73.

all this and more would they bear did they but know that this were sacrifice and not a meaner thing. So surged the thought within that lone black breast. The Bishop cleared his throat suggestively; then, recollecting that there was really nothing to say, considerately said nothing, only sat tapping his foot impatiently. But Alexander Crummell said, slowly and heavily: "I will never enter your diocese on such terms." And saying this, he turned and passed into the Valley of the Shadow of Death. You might have noted only the physical dying, the shattered frame and hacking cough; but in that soul lay deeper death than that. He found a chapel in New York,—the church of his father; he labored for it in poverty and starvation, scorned by his fellow priests. Half in despair, he wandered across the sea, a beggar with outstretched hands. Englishmen clasped them,—Wilberforce and Stanley, Thirwell and Ingles, and even Froude and Macaulay; Sir Benjamin Brodie[6] bade him rest awhile at Queen's College in Cambridge, and there he lingered, struggling for health of body and mind, until he took his degree in '53. Restless still and unsatisfied, he turned toward Africa, and for long years, amid the spawn of the slave-smugglers, sought a new heaven and a new earth.

So the man groped for light; all this was not Life,—it was the world-wandering of a soul in search of itself, the striving of one who vainly sought his place in the world, ever haunted by the shadow of a death that is more than death,—the passing of a soul that has missed its duty. Twenty years he wandered,—twenty years and more; and yet the hard rasping question kept gnawing within him, "What, in God's name, am I on earth for?" In the narrow New York parish his soul seemed cramped and smothered. In the fine old air of the English University he heard the millions wailing over the sea. In the wild fever-cursed swamps of West Africa he stood helpless and alone.

You will not wonder at his weird pilgrimage,—you who in the swift whirl of living, amid its cold paradox and marvellous vision, have fronted life and asked its riddle face to face. And if you find that riddle hard to read, remember that yonder black boy finds it just a little harder; if it is difficult for you to find and face your duty, it is a shade more difficult for him; if your heart sickens in the blood and dust of battle, remember that to him the dust is thicker and the battle fiercer. No wonder the wanderers fall! No wonder we point to thief and murderer, and haunting prostitute, and the never-ending throng of unhearsed dead! The Valley of the Shadow of Death gives few of its pilgrims back to the world.

But Alexander Crummell it gave back. Out of the temptation of Hate, and burned by the fire of Despair, triumphant over Doubt, and steeled by Sacrifice against Humiliation, he turned at last home across the waters, humble and strong, gentle and determined. He bent to all the gibes and prejudices, to all hatred and discrimination, with that rare courtesy which is the armor of pure souls. He fought among his own, the low, the grasping, and the wicked, with that unbending righteousness which is the sword of

6. Sir Benjamin Collins Brodie (1783–1862), English surgeon. William Wilberforce (1759–1833), English politician and antislavery leader. Arthur Penrhyn Stanley (1815–1881), English Episcopal leader. Connop Thirwall (1797–1875), English Episcopal bishop. James Anthony Froude (1818–1894), English historian. Thomas Babington Macaulay (1800–1859), English historian.

the just. He never faltered, he seldom complained; he simply worked, inspiring the young, rebuking the old, helping the weak, guiding the strong.

So he grew, and brought within his wide influence all that was best of those who walk within the Veil. They who live without knew not nor dreamed of that full power within, that mighty inspiration which the dull gauze of caste decreed that most men should not know. And now that he is gone, I sweep the Veil away and cry, Lo! the soul to whose dear memory I bring this little tribute. I can see his face still, dark and heavy-lined beneath his snowy hair; lighting and shading, now with inspiration for the future, now in innocent pain at some human wickedness, now with sorrow at some hard memory from the past. The more I met Alexander Crummell, the more I felt how much that world was losing which knew so little of him. In another age he might have sat among the elders of the land in purple-bordered toga;[7] in another country mothers might have sung him to the cradles.

He did his work,—he did it nobly and well; and yet I sorrow that here he worked alone, with so little human sympathy. His name to-day, in this broad land, means little, and comes to fifty million ears laden with no incense of memory or emulation. And herein lies the tragedy of the age: not that men are poor,—all men know something of poverty; not that men are wicked,—who is good? not that men are ignorant,—what is Truth? Nay, but that men know so little of men.

He sat one morning gazing toward the sea. He smiled and said, "The gate is rusty on the hinges." That night at star-rise a wind came moaning out of the west to blow the gate ajar, and then the soul I loved fled like a flame across the Seas, and in its seat sat Death.

I wonder where he is to-day? I wonder if in that dim world beyond, as he came gliding in, there rose on some wan throne a King,—a dark and pierced Jew, who knows the writhings of the earthly damned, saying, as he laid those heart-wrung talents down, "Well done!" while round about the morning stars sat singing.

7. A robe denoting high office in ancient Rome.

XIII. Of the Coming of John

What bring they 'neath the midnight,
Beside the River-sea?
They bring the human heart wherein
No nightly calm can be;
That droppeth never with the wind,
Nor drieth with the dew;
O calm it, God; thy calm is broad
To cover spirits too.
The river floweth on. [8]

MRS. BROWNING

Carlisle street runs westward from the centre of Johnstown, across a great black bridge, down a hill and up again, by little shops and meat-markets, past single-storied homes, until suddenly it stops against a wide green lawn. It is a broad, restful place, with two large buildings outlined against the west. When at evening the winds come swelling from the east, and the great pall of the city's smoke hangs wearily above the valley, then the red west glows like a dreamland down Carlisle Street, and, at the tolling of the supper-bell, throws the passing forms of students in dark silhouette against the sky. Tall and black, they move slowly by, and seem in the sinister light to flit before the city like dim warning ghosts. Perhaps they are; for this is Wells Institute, and these black students have few dealings with the white city below.

And if you will notice, night after night, there is one dark form that ever hurries last and late toward the twinkling lights of Swain Hall,—for Jones is never on time. A long, straggling fellow he is, brown and hard-haired, who seems to be growing straight out of his clothes, and walks with a half-apologetic roll. He used perpetually to set the quiet dining-room into waves of merriment, as he stole to his place after the bell had tapped for prayers; he seemed so perfectly awkward. And yet one glance at his face made one forgive him much,—that broad, good-natured smile in which lay no bit of art or artifice, but seemed just bubbling good-nature and genuine satisfaction with the world.

He came to us from Altamaha, away down there beneath the gnarled oaks of Southeastern Georgia, where the sea croons to the sands and the sands listen till they sink half drowned beneath the waters, rising only here and there in long, low islands. The white folk of Altamaha voted John a

8. From Browning's *A Romance of the Ganges* (1838).

good boy,—fine plough-hand, good in the rice-fields, handy everywhere, and always good-natured and respectful. But they shook their heads when his mother wanted to send him off to school. "It'll spoil him,—ruin him," they said; and they talked as though they knew. But full half the black folk followed him proudly to the station, and carried his queer little trunk and many bundles. And there they shook and shook hands, and the girls kissed him shyly and the boys clapped him on the back. So the train came, and he pinched his little sister lovingly, and put his great arms about his mother's neck, and then was away with a puff and a roar into the great yellow world that flamed and flared about the doubtful pilgrim. Up the coast they hurried, past the squares and palmettos of Savannah, through the cotton-fields and through the weary night, to Millville, and came with the morning to the noise and bustle of Johnstown.

And they that stood behind, that morning in Altamaha, and watched the train as it noisily bore playmate and brother and son away to the world, had thereafter one ever-recurring word,—"When John comes." Then what parties were to be, and what speakings in the churches; what new furniture in the front room,—perhaps even a new front room; and there would be a new schoolhouse, with John as teacher; and then perhaps a big wedding; all this and more—when John comes. But the white people shook their heads.

At first he was coming at Christmas-time,—but the vacation proved too short; and then, the next summer,—but times were hard and schooling costly, and so, instead, he worked in Johnstown. And so it drifted to the next summer, and the next,—till playmates scattered, and mother grew gray, and sister went up to the Judge's kitchen to work. And still the legend lingered,—"When John comes."

Up at the Judge's they rather liked this refrain; for they too had a John—a fair-haired, smooth-faced boy, who had played many a long summer's day to its close with his darker name-sake. "Yes, sir! John is at Princeton, sir," said the broad-shouldered gray-haired Judge every morning as he marched down to the post-office. "Showing the Yankees what a Southern gentleman can do," he added; and strode home again with his letters and papers. Up at the great pillared house they lingered long over the Princeton letter,—the Judge and his frail wife, his sister and growing daughters. "It'll make a man of him," said the Judge, "college is the place." And then he asked the shy little waitress, "Well, Jennie, how's your John?" and added reflectively, "Too bad, too bad your mother sent him off,—it will spoil him." And the waitress wondered.

Thus in the far-away Southern village the world lay waiting, half consciously, the coming of two young men, and dreamed in an inarticulate way of new things that would be done and new thoughts that all would think. And yet it was singular that few thought of two Johns,—for the black folk thought of one John, and he was black; and the white folk thought of another John, and he was white. And neither world thought the other world's thought, save with a vague unrest.

Up in Johnstown, at the Institute, we were long puzzled at the case of John Jones. For a long time the clay seemed unfit for any sort of moulding. He was loud and boisterous, always laughing and singing, and never able to work consecutively at anything. He did not know how to study; he had no idea of thoroughness; and with his tardiness, carelessness, and appalling good-humor, we were sore perplexed. One night we sat in faculty-meeting, worried and serious; for Jones was in trouble again. This last escapade was too much, and so we solemnly voted "that Jones, on account of repeated disorder and inattention to work, be suspended for the rest of the term."

It seemed to us that the first time life ever struck Jones as a really serious thing was when the Dean told him he must leave school. He stared at the gray-haired man blankly, with great eyes. "Why,—why," he faltered, "but— I haven't graduated!" Then the Dean slowly and clearly explained, reminding him of the tardiness and the carelessness, of the poor lessons and neglected work, of the noise and disorder, until the fellow hung his head in confusion. Then he said quickly, "But you won't tell mammy and sister,— you won't write mammy, now will you? For if you won't I'll go out into the city and work, and come back next term and show you something." So the Dean promised faithfully, and John shouldered his little trunk, giving neither word nor look to the giggling boys, and walked down Carlisle Street to the great city, with sober eyes and a set and serious face.

Perhaps we imagined it, but someway it seemed to us that the serious look that crept over his boyish face that afternoon never left it again. When he came back to us he went to work with all his rugged strength. It was a hard struggle, for things did not come easily to him,—few crowding memories of early life and teaching came to help him on his new way; but all the world toward which he strove was of his own building, and he builded slow and hard. As the light dawned lingeringly on his new creations, he sat rapt and silent before the vision, or wandered alone over the green campus peering through and beyond the world of men into a world of thought. And the thoughts at times puzzled him sorely; he could not see just why the circle was not square, and carried it out fifty-six decimal places one midnight,—would have gone further, indeed, had not the matron rapped for lights out. He caught terrible colds lying on his back in the meadows of nights, trying to think out the solar system; he had grave doubts as to the ethics of the Fall of Rome, and strongly suspected the Germans of being thieves and rascals, despite his text-books; he pondered long over every new Greek word, and wondered why this meant that and why it couldn't mean something else, and how it must have felt to think all things in Greek. So he thought and puzzled along for himself,—pausing perplexed where others skipped merrily, and walking steadily through the difficulties where the rest stopped and surrendered.

Thus he grew in body and soul, and with him his clothes seemed to grow and arrange themselves; coat sleeves got longer, cuffs appeared, and collars got less soiled. Now and then his boots shone, and a new dignity crept into his walk. And we who saw daily a new thoughtfulness growing in his eyes began to expect something of this plodding boy. Thus he passed out of the preparatory school into college, and we who watched him felt four more years of change, which almost transformed the tall, grave man who bowed to us commencement morning. He had left his queer thought-world and come back to a world of motion and of men. He looked now for the first time sharply about him, and wondered he had seen so little before. He grew slowly to feel almost for the first time the Veil that lay between him and the white world; he first noticed now the oppression that had not seemed oppression before, differences that erstwhile seemed natural, restraints and slights that in his boyhood days had gone unnoticed or been greeted with a laugh. He felt angry now when men did not call him "Mister," he clenched his hands at the "Jim Crow" cars, and chafed at the colorline that hemmed in him and his. A tinge of sarcasm crept into his speech, and a vague bitterness into his life; and he sat long hours wondering and planning a way around these crooked things. Daily he found himself shrinking from the choked and narrow life of his native town. And yet he always planned to go back to Altamaha,—always planned to work there. Still, more and more as the day approached he hesitated with a nameless dread; and even the day after graduation he seized with eagerness the offer of the Dean to send him North with the quartette during the summer vacation, to sing for the Institute. A breath of air before the plunge, he said to himself in half apology.

It was a bright September afternoon, and the streets of New York were brilliant with moving men. They reminded John of the sea, as he sat in the square and watched them, so changelessly changing, so bright and dark, so grave and gay. He scanned their rich and faultless clothes, the way they carried their hands, the shape of their hats; he peered into the hurrying carriages. Then, leaning back with a sigh, he said, "This is the World." The notion suddenly seized him to see where the world was going; since many of the richer and brighter seemed hurrying all one way. So when a tall, light-haired young man and a little talkative lady came by, he rose half hesitatingly and followed them. Up the street they went, past stores and gay shops, across a broad square, until with a hundred others they entered the high portal of a great building.

He was pushed toward the ticket-office with the others, and felt in his pocket for the new five-dollar bill he had hoarded. There seemed really no time for hesitation, so he drew it bravely out, passed it to the busy clerk, and received simply a ticket but no change. When at last he realized that he had paid five dollars to enter he knew not what, he stood stock-still amazed. "Be careful," said a low voice behind him; "you must not lynch the colored gentleman simply because he's in your way," and a girl looked up roguishly into the eyes of her fair-haired escort. A shade of annoyance passed over the escort's face. "You *will* not understand us at the South," he said half impatiently, as if continuing an argument. "With all your professions, one never sees in the North so cordial and intimate relations between white and black as are everyday occurrences with us. Why, I remember my closest playfellow in boyhood was a little Negro named after me, and surely no two,— *well!*" The man stopped short and flushed to the roots of his hair, for there directly beside his reserved orchestra chairs sat the Negro he had stumbled over in the hallway. He hesitated and grew pale with anger, called the usher and gave him his card, with a few peremptory words, and slowly sat down. The lady deftly changed the subject.

All this John did not see, for he sat in a half-maze minding the scene about him; the delicate beauty of the hall, the faint perfume, the moving myriad of men, the rich clothing and low hum of talking seemed all a part of a world so different from his, so strangely more beautiful than anything he had known, that he sat in dreamland, and started when, after a hush, rose high and clear the music of Lohengrin's swan. [9] The infinite beauty of the wail lingered and swept through every muscle of his frame, and put it all a-tune. He closed his eyes and grasped the elbows of the chair, touching unwittingly the lady's arm. And the lady drew away. A deep longing swelled in all his heart to rise with that clear music out of the dirt and dust of that low life that held him prisoned and befouled. If he could only live up in the free air where birds sang and setting suns had no touch of blood! Who had called him to be the slave and butt of all? And if he had called, what right had he to call when a world like this lay open before men?

Then the movement changed, and fuller, mightier harmony swelled away. He looked thoughtfully across the hall, and wondered why the beautiful gray-haired woman looked so listless, and what the little man could be whispering about. He would not like to be listless and idle, he thought, for he felt with the music the movement of power within him. If he but had some master-work, some life-service, hard,—aye, bitter hard, but without the cringing and sickening servility, without the cruel hurt that hardened his heart and soul. When at last a soft sorrow crept across the violins, there came to him the vision of a far-off home,—the great eyes of his sister, and the dark drawn face of his mother. And his heart sank below the waters, even as the sea-sand sinks by the shores of Altamaha, only to be lifted aloft again with that last ethereal wail of the swan that quivered and faded away into the sky.

It left John sitting so silent and rapt that he did not for some time notice the usher tapping him lightly on the shoulder and saying politely, "Will you step this way, please, sir?" A little surprised, he arose quickly at the last tap, and, turning to leave his seat, looked full into the face of the fair-haired young man. For the first time the young man recognized his dark boyhood playmate, and John knew that it was the Judge's son. The white John started, lifted his hand, and then froze into his chair; the black John smiled lightly, then grimly, and followed the usher down the aisle. The manager was sorry, very, very sorry,—but he explained that some mistake had been made in selling the gentleman a seat already disposed of; he would refund the money, of course,—and indeed felt the matter keenly, and so forth, and—before he had finished John was gone, walking hurriedly across the square and down the broad streets, and as he passed the park he buttoned his coat and said, "John Jones, you're a natural-born fool." Then he went to his lodgings and wrote a letter, and tore it up; he wrote another, and threw it in the fire. Then he seized a scrap of paper and wrote: "Dear Mother and Sister—I am coming—John."

"Perhaps," said John, as he settled himself on the train, "perhaps I am to blame myself in struggling against my manifest destiny simply because it looks hard and unpleasant. Here is my duty to Altamaha plain before me; perhaps they'll let me help settle the Negro problems there,—perhaps they won't. 'I will go in to the King, which is not according to the law; and if I perish, I perish.' " [1] And then he mused and dreamed, and planned a life-work; and the train flew south.

9. The guide for the hero of Wagner's opera Lo-hengrin (1850).   1. Esther 4:16.

Down in Altamaha, after seven long years, all the world knew John was coming. The homes were scrubbed and scoured,—above all, one; the gardens and yards had an unwonted trimness, and Jennie bought a new gingham. With some finesse and negotiation, all the dark Methodists and Presbyterians were induced to join in a monster welcome at the Baptist Church; and as the day drew near, warm discussions arose on every corner as to the exact extent and nature of John's accomplishments. It was noontide on a gray and cloudy day when he came. The black town flocked to the depot, with a little of the white at the edges,—a happy throng, with "Goodmawnings" and "Howdys" and laughing and joking and jostling. Mother sat yonder in the window watching; but sister Jennie stood on the platform, nervously fingering her dress,—tall and lithe, with soft brown skin and loving eyes peering from out a tangled wilderness of hair. John rose gloomily as the train stopped, for he was thinking of the "Jim Crow" car; he stepped to the platform, and paused: a little dingy station, a black crowd gaudy and dirty, a half-mile of dilapidated shanties along a straggling ditch of mud. An overwhelming sense of the sordidness and narrowness of it all seized him; he looked in vain for his mother, kissed coldly the tall, strange girl who called him brother, spoke a short, dry word here and there; then, lingering neither for hand-shaking nor gossip, started silently up the street, raising his hat merely to the last eager old aunty, to her open-mouthed astonishment. The people were distinctly bewildered. This silent, cold man,—was this John? Where was his smile and hearty handgrasp? " 'Peared kind o' down in the mouf," said the Methodist preacher thoughtfully. "Seemed monstus stuck up," complained a Baptist sister. But the white postmaster from the edge of the crowd expressed the opinion of his folks plainly. "That damn Nigger," said he, as he shouldered the mail and arranged his tobacco, "has gone North and got plum full o' fool notions; but they won't work in Altamaha." And the crowd melted away.

The meeting of welcome at the Baptist Church was a failure. Rain spoiled the barbecue, and thunder turned the milk in the ice-cream. When the speaking came at night, the house was crowded to overflowing. The three preachers had especially prepared themselves, but somehow John's manner seemed to throw a blanket over everything,—he seemed so cold and preoccupied, and had so strange an air of restraint that the Methodist brother could not warm up to his theme and elicited not a single "Amen"; the Presbyterian prayer was but feebly responded to, and even the Baptist preacher, though he wakened faint enthusiasm, got so mixed up in his favorite sentence that he had to close it by stopping fully fifteen minutes sooner than he meant. The people moved uneasily in their seats as John rose to reply. He spoke slowly and methodically. The age, he said, demanded new ideas; we were far different from those men of the seventeenth and eighteenth centuries,—with broader ideas of human brotherhood and destiny. Then he spoke of the rise of charity and popular education, and particularly of the spread of wealth and work. The question was, then, he added reflectively, looking at the low discolored ceiling, what part the Negroes of this land would take in the striving of the new century. He sketched in vague outline the new Industrial School that might rise among these pines, he spoke in detail of the charitable and philanthropic work that might be organized, of money that might be saved for banks and business. Finally he urged unity, and deprecated especially religious and denominational bickering. "To-day," he said, with a smile, "the world cares little whether a man be Baptist or Methodist, or indeed a churchman at all, so long as he is good and true. What difference does it make whether a man be baptized in river or wash-bowl, or not at all? Let's leave all that littleness, and look higher." Then, thinking of nothing else, he slowly sat down. A painful hush seized that crowded mass. Little had they understood of what he said, for he spoke an unknown tongue, save the last word about baptism; that they knew, and they sat very still while the clock ticked. Then at last a low suppressed snarl came from the Amen corner, and an old bent man arose, walked over the seats, and climbed straight up into the pulpit. He was wrinkled and black, with scant gray and tufted hair; his voice and hands shook as with palsy; but on his face lay the intense rapt look of the religious fanatic. He seized the Bible with his rough, huge hands; twice he raised it inarticulate, and then fairly burst into the words, with rude and awful eloquence. He quivered, swayed, and bent; then rose aloft in perfect majesty, till the people moaned and wept, wailed and shouted, and a wild shrieking arose from the corners where all the pent-up feeling of the hour gathered itself and rushed into the air. John never knew clearly what the old man said; he only felt himself held up to scorn and scathing denunciation for trampling on the true Religion, and he realized with amazement that all unknowingly he had put rough, rude hands on something this little world held sacred. He arose silently, and passed out into the night. Down toward the sea he went, in the fitful starlight, half conscious of the girl who followed timidly after him. When at last he stood upon the bluff, he turned to his little sister and looked upon her sorrowfully, remembering with sudden pain how little thought he had given her. He put his arm about her and let her passion of tears spend itself on his shoulder.

Long they stood together, peering over the gray unresting water.

"John," she said, "does it make every one—unhappy when they study and learn lots of things?"

He paused and smiled. "I am afraid it does," he said.

"And, John, are you glad you studied?"

"Yes," came the answer, slowly but positively.

She watched the flickering lights upon the sea, and said thoughtfully, "I wish I was unhappy,—and—and," putting both arms about his neck, "I think I am, a little, John."

It was several days later that John walked up to the Judge's house to ask for the privilege of teaching the Negro school. The Judge himself met him at the front door, stared a little hard at him, and said brusquely, "Go 'round to the kitchen door, John, and wait." Sitting on the kitchen steps, John stared at the corn, thoroughly perplexed. What on earth had come over him? Every step he made offended some one. He had come to save his people, and before he left the depot he had hurt them. He sought to teach them at the church, and had outraged their deepest feelings. He had schooled himself to be respectful to the Judge, and then blundered into his front door. And all the time he had meant right,—and yet, and yet, somehow he found it so hard and strange to fit his old surroundings again, to find his place in the world about him. He could not remember that he used to have any difficulty in the past, when life was glad and gay. The world seemed smooth and easy then. Perhaps,—but his sister came to the kitchen door just then and said the Judge awaited him.

The Judge sat in the dining-room amid his morning's mail, and he did not ask John to sit down. He plunged squarely into the business. "You've come for the school, I suppose. Well, John, I want to speak to you plainly. You know I'm a friend to your people. I've helped you and your family, and would have done more if you hadn't got the notion of going off. Now I like the colored people, and sympathize with all their reasonable aspirations; but you and I both know, John, that in this country the Negro must remain subordinate, and can never expect to be the equal of white men. In their place, your people can be honest and respectful; and God knows, I'll do what I can to help them. But when they want to reverse nature, and rule white men, and marry white women, and sit in my parlor, then, by God! we'll hold them under if we have to lynch every Nigger in the land. Now, John, the question is, are you, with your education and Northern notions, going to accept the situation and teach the darkies to be faithful servants and laborers as your fathers were,—I knew your father, John, he belonged to my brother, and he was a good Nigger. Well—well, are you going to be like him, or are you going to try to put fool ideas of rising and equality into these folks' heads, and make them discontented and unhappy?"

"I am going to accept the situation, Judge Henderson," answered John, with a brevity that did not escape the keen old man. He hesitated a moment, and then said shortly, "Very well,—we'll try you awhile. Good-morning."

It was a full month after the opening of the Negro school that the other John came home, tall, gay, and headstrong. The mother wept, the sisters sang. The whole white town was glad. A proud man was the Judge, and it was a goodly sight to see the two swinging down Main Street together. And yet all did not go smoothly between them, for the younger man could not and did not veil his contempt for the little town, and plainly had his heart set on New York. Now the one cherished ambition of the Judge was to see his son mayor of Altamaha, representative to the legislature, and—who could say?—governor of Georgia. So the argument often waxed hot between them. "Good heavens, father," the younger man would say after dinner, as he lighted a cigar and stood by the fireplace, "you surely don't expect a young fellow like me to settle down permanently in this—this God-forgotten town with nothing but mud and Negroes?" "I did," the Judge would answer laconically; and on this particular day it seemed from the gathering scowl that he was about to add something more emphatic, but neighbors had already begun to drop in to admire his son, and the conversation drifted.

"Heah that John is livenin' things up at the darky school," volunteered the postmaster, after a pause.

"What now?" asked the Judge, sharply.

"Oh, nothin' in particulah,—just his almighty air and uppish ways. B'lieve I did heah somethin' about his givin' talks on the French Revolution, equality, and such like. He's what I call a dangerous Nigger."

"Have you heard him say anything out of the way?"

"Why, no,—but Sally, our girl, told my wife a lot of rot. Then, too, I don't need to heah: a Nigger what won't say 'sir' to a white man, or—"

"Who is this John?" interrupted the son.

"Why, it's little black John, Peggy's son,—your old playfellow."

The young man's face flushed angrily, and then he laughed.

"Oh," said he, "it's the darky that tried to force himself into a seat beside the lady I was escorting—"

But Judge Henderson waited to hear no more. He had been nettled all day, and now at this he rose with a half-smothered oath, took his hat and cane, and walked straight to the schoolhouse.

For John, it had been a long, hard pull to get things started in the rickety old shanty that sheltered his school. The Negroes were rent into factions for and against him, the parents were careless, the children irregular and dirty, and books, pencils, and slates largely missing. Nevertheless, he struggled hopefully on, and seemed to see at last some glimmering of dawn. The attendance was larger and the children were a shade cleaner this week. Even the booby class in reading showed a little comforting progress. So John settled himself with renewed patience this afternoon.

"Now, Mandy," he said cheerfully, "that's better; but you mustn't chop your words up so: 'If—the—man—goes.' Why, your little brother even wouldn't tell a story that way, now would he?"

"Naw, suh, he cain't talk."

"All right; now let's try again: 'If the man—' "

"John!"

The whole school started in surprise, and the teacher half arose, as the red, angry face of the Judge appeared in the open doorway.

"John, this school is closed. You children can go home and get to work. The white people of Altamaha are not spending their money on black folks to have their heads crammed with impudence and lies. Clear out! I 'll lock the door myself."

Up at the great pillared house the tall young son wandered aimlessly about after his father's abrupt departure. In the house there was little to interest him; the books were old and stale, the local newspaper flat, and the women had retired with headaches and sewing. He tried a nap, but it was too warm. So he sauntered out into the fields, complaining disconsolately, "Good Lord! how long will this imprisonment last!" He was not a bad fellow,—just a little spoiled and self-indulgent, and as headstrong as his proud father. He seemed a young man pleasant to look upon, as he sat on the great black stump at the edge of the pines idly swinging his legs and smoking. "Why, there isn't even a girl worth getting up a respectable flirtation with," he growled. Just then his eye caught a tall, willowy figure hurrying toward him on the narrow path. He looked with interest at first, and then burst into a laugh as he said, "Well, I declare, if it isn't Jennie, the little brown kitchen-maid! Why, I never noticed before what a trim little body she is. Hello, Jennie! Why, you haven't kissed me since I came home," he said gaily. The young girl stared at him in surprise and confusion,—faltered something inarticulate, and attempted to pass. But a wilful mood had seized the young idler, and he caught at her arm. Frightened, she slipped by; and half mischievously he turned and ran after her through the tall pines.

Yonder, toward the sea, at the end of the path, came John slowly, with his head down. He had turned wearily homeward from the schoolhouse; then, thinking to shield his mother from the blow, started to meet his sister as she came from work and break the news of his dismissal to her. "I'll go away," he said slowly; "I'll go away and find work, and send for them. I cannot live here longer." And then the fierce, buried anger surged up into his throat. He waved his arms and hurried wildly up the path.

The great brown sea lay silent. The air scarce breathed. The dying day bathed the twisted oaks and mighty pines in black and gold. There came from the wind no warning, not a whisper from the cloudless sky. There was only a black man hurrying on with an ache in his heart, seeing neither sun nor sea, but starting as from a dream at the frightened cry that woke the pines, to see his dark sister struggling in the arms of a tall and fair-haired man.

He said not a word, but, seizing a fallen limb, struck him with all the pent-up hatred of his great black arm; and the body lay white and still beneath the pines, all bathed in sunshine and in blood. John looked at it dreamily, then walked back to the house briskly, and said in a soft voice, "Mammy, I'm going away,—I'm going to be free."

She gazed at him dimly and faltered, "No'th, honey, is yo' gwine No'th agin?"

He looked out where the North Star glistened pale above the waters, and said, "Yes, mammy, I'm going—North."

Then, without another word, he went out into the narrow lane, up by the straight pines, to the same winding path, and seated himself on the great black stump, looking at the blood where the body had lain. Yonder in the gray past he had played with that dead boy, romping together under the solemn trees. The night deepened; he thought of the boys at Johnstown. He wondered how Brown had turned out, and Carey? And Jones,—Jones? Why, *he* was Jones, and he wondered what they would all say when they knew, when they knew, in that great long dining-room with its hundreds of merry eyes. Then as the sheen of the starlight stole over him, he thought of the gilded ceiling of that vast concert hall, and heard stealing toward him the faint sweet music of the swan. Hark! was it music, or the hurry and shouting of men? Yes, surely! Clear and high the faint sweet melody rose and fluttered like a living thing, so that the very earth trembled as with the tramp of horses and murmur of angry men.

He leaned back and smiled toward the sea, whence rose the strange melody, away from the dark shadows where lay the noise of horses galloping, galloping on. With an effort he roused himself, bent forward, and looked steadily down the pathway, softly humming the "Song of the Bride,"—

"Freudig geführt, ziehet dahin."[2]

Amid the trees in the dim morning twilight he watched their shadows dancing and heard their horses thundering toward him, until at last they came sweeping like a storm, and he saw in front that haggard white-haired

2. Joyfully led, enter within (German); an adaptation of the opening line of the "Wedding March" in Wagner's *Lohengrin*.

man, whose eyes flashed red with fury. Oh, how he pitied him,—pitied him,—and wondered if he had the coiling twisted rope. Then, as the storm burst round him, he rose slowly to his feet and turned his closed eyes toward the Sea.

And the world whistled in his ears.

XIV. *The Sorrow Songs*

> I walk through the churchyard
>   To lay this body down;
> I know moon-rise, I know star-rise;
> I walk in the moonlight, I walk in the starlight;
> I 'll lie in the grave and stretch out my arms,
> I 'll go to judgment in the evening of the day,
> And my soul and thy soul shall meet that day,
>   When I lay this body down. [3]

NEGRO SONG

They that walked in darkness sang songs in the olden days—Sorrow Songs—for they were weary at heart. And so before each thought that I have written in this book I have set a phrase, a haunting echo of these weird old songs in which the soul of the black slave spoke to men. Ever since I was a child these songs have stirred me strangely. They came out of the South unknown to me, one by one, and yet at once I knew them as of me and of mine. Then in after years when I came to Nashville I saw the great temple builded of these songs towering over the pale city. To me Jubilee Hall [4] seemed ever made of the songs themselves, and its bricks were red with the blood and dust of toil. Out of them rose for me morning, noon, and night, bursts of wonderful melody, full of the voices of my brothers and sisters, full of the voices of the past.

Little of beauty has America given the world save the rude grandeur God himself stamped on her bosom; the human spirit in this new world has expressed itself in vigor and ingenuity rather than in beauty. And so by fateful chance the Negro folk-song—the rhythmic cry of the slave—stands today not simply as the sole American music, but as the most beautiful expression of human experience born this side the seas. It has been neglected, it has been, and is, half despised, and above all it has been persistently mistaken and misunderstood; but notwithstanding, it still remains as the singular spiritual heritage of the nation and the greatest gift of the Negro people.

Away back in the thirties the melody of these slave songs stirred the nation, but the songs were soon half forgotten. Some, like "Near the lake

---

3. From "Lay This Body Down," a Negro spiritual.
4. The central building on the Fisk University campus.

where drooped the willow," passed into current airs and their source was forgotten; others were caricatured on the "minstrel" stage and their memory died away. Then in war-time came the singular Port Royal experiment after the capture of Hilton Head, and perhaps for the first time the North met the Southern slave face to face and heart to heart with no third witness. The Sea Islands of the Carolinas, where they met, were filled with a black folk of primitive type, touched and moulded less by the world about them than any others outside the Black Belt. Their appearance was uncouth, their language funny, but their hearts were human and their singing stirred men with a mighty power. Thomas Wentworth Higginson hastened to tell of these songs, and Miss McKim[5] and others urged upon the world their rare beauty. But the world listened only half credulously until the Fisk Jubilee Singers[6] sang the slave songs so deeply into the world's heart that it can never wholly forget them again.

There was once a blacksmith's son born at Cadiz, New York, who in the changes of time taught school in Ohio and helped defend Cincinnati from Kirby Smith.[7] Then he fought at Chancellorsville and Gettysburg and finally served in the Freedman's Bureau at Nashville. Here he formed a Sunday-school class of black children in 1866, and sang with them and taught them to sing. And then they taught him to sing, and when once the glory of the Jubilee songs passed into the soul of George L. White,[8] he knew his life-work was to let those Negroes sing to the world as they had sung to him. So in 1871 the pilgrimage of the Fisk Jubilee Singers began. North to Cincinnati they rode,—four half-clothed black boys and five girl-women,—led by a man with a cause and a purpose. They stopped at Wilberforce, the oldest of Negro schools, where a black bishop blessed them. Then they went, fighting cold and starvation, shut out of hotels, and cheerfully sneered at, ever northward; and ever the magic of their song kept thrilling hearts, until a burst of applause in the Congregational Council at Oberlin revealed them to the world. They came to New York and Henry Ward Beecher[9] dared to welcome them, even though the metropolitan dailies sneered at his "Nigger Minstrels." So their songs conquered till they sang across the land and across the sea, before Queen and Kaiser, in Scotland and Ireland, Holland and Switzerland. Seven years they sang, and brought back a hundred and fifty thousand dollars to found Fisk University.

Since their day they have been imitated—sometimes well, by the singers of Hampton and Atlanta, sometimes ill, by straggling quartettes. Caricature has sought again to spoil the quaint beauty of the music, and has filled the air with many debased melodies which vulgar ears scarce know from the real. But the true Negro folk-song still lives in the hearts of those who have heard them truly sung and in the hearts of the Negro people.

What are these songs, and what do they mean? I know little of music and can say nothing in technical phrase, but I know something of men, and knowing them, I know that these songs are the articulate message of the

---

5. Lucy McKim Garrison, co-editor of *Slave Songs of the United States* (1867). Higginson (1823–1911), commander of the first black regiment in the Civil War and early commentator on spirituals.
6. A traveling singing troupe founded in 1871 to raise funds for Fisk University.

7. Confederate general who laid siege to Cincinnati in 1862.
8. Creator and leader of the Fisk Jubilee Singers (1838–1895).
9. Clergyman and antislavery crusader (1813–1887).

slave to the world. They tell us in these eager days that life was joyous to the black slave, careless and happy. I can easily believe this of some, of many. But not all the past South, though it rose from the dead, can gainsay the heart-touching witness of these songs. They are the music of an unhappy people, of the children of disappointment; they tell of death and suffering and unvoiced longing toward a truer world, of misty wanderings and hidden ways.

The songs are indeed the siftings of centuries; the music is far more ancient than the words, and in it we can trace here and there signs of development. My grandfather's grandmother was seized by an evil Dutch trader two centuries ago; and coming to the valleys of the Hudson and Housatonic, black, little, and lithe, she shivered and shrank in the harsh north winds, looked longingly at the hills, and often crooned a heathen melody to the child between her knees, thus:

The child sang it to his children and they to their children's children, and so two hundred years it has travelled down to us and we sing it to our children, knowing as little as our fathers what its words may mean, but knowing well the meaning of its music.

This was primitive African music; it may be seen in larger form in the strange chant which heralds "The Coming of John":

> "You may bury me in the East,
> You may bury me in the West,
> But I'll hear the trumpet sound in that morning,"

—the voice of exile.

Ten master songs, more or less, one may pluck from this forest of melody—songs of undoubted Negro origin and wide popular currency, and songs peculiarly characteristic of the slave. One of these I have just mentioned. Another whose strains begin this book is "Nobody knows the trouble I've seen." When, struck with a sudden poverty, the United States refused to fulfil its promises of land to the freedmen, a brigadier-general went down to the Sea Islands to carry the news. An old woman on the outskirts of the throng began singing this song; all the mass joined with her, swaying. And the soldier wept.

The third song is the cradle-song of death which all men know,—"Swing low, sweet chariot,"—whose bars begin the life story of "Alexander Crummell." Then there is the song of many waters, "Roll, Jordan, roll," a mighty chorus with minor cadences. There were many songs of the fugitive like that which opens "The Wings of Atalanta," and the more familiar "Been a-listening." The seventh is the song of the End and the Beginning—"My Lord, what a mourning! when the stars begin to fall"; a strain of this is placed before "The Dawn of Freedom." The song of groping—"My way's cloudy"—begins "The Meaning of Progress"; the ninth is the song of this chapter—"Wrestlin' Jacob, the day is a-breaking,"—a pæan of hopeful strife. The last master song is the song of songs—"Steal away,"—sprung from "The Faith of the Fathers."

There are many others of the Negro folk-songs as striking and character-istic as these, as, for instance, the three strains in the third, eighth, and ninth chapters; and others I am sure could easily make a selection on more scientific principles. There are, too, songs that seem to me a step removed from the more primitive types: there is the maze-like medley, "Bright spar-kles," one phrase of which heads "The Black Belt"; the Easter carol, "Dust, dust and ashes"; the dirge, "My mother's took her flight and gone home"; and that burst of melody hovering over "The Passing of the First-Born"—"I hope my mother will be there in that beautiful world on high."

These represent a third step in the development of the slave song, of which "You may bury me in the East" is the first, and songs like "March on" (chapter six) and "Steal away" are the second. The first is African music, the second Afro-American, while the third is a blending of Negro music with the music heard in the foster land. The result is still distinc-tively Negro and the method of blending original, but the elements are both Negro and Caucasian. One might go further and find a fourth step in this development, where the songs of white America have been distinc-tively influenced by the slave songs or have incorporated whole phrases of Negro melody, as "Swanee River" and "Old Black Joe."[1] Side by side, too, with the growth has gone the debasements and imitations—the Negro "minstrel" songs, many of the "gospel" hymns, and some of the contempo-rary "coon" songs,—a mass of music in which the novice may easily lose himself and never find the real Negro melodies.

In these songs, I have said, the slave spoke to the world. Such a message is naturally veiled and half articulate. Words and music have lost each other and new and cant phrases of a dimly understood theology have dis-placed the older sentiment. Once in a while we catch a strange word of an unknown tongue, as the "Mighty Myo," which figures as a river of death; more often slight words or mere doggerel are joined to music of singular sweetness. Purely secular songs are few in number, partly because many of them were turned into hymns by a change of words, partly because the frolics were seldom heard by the stranger, and the music less often caught. Of nearly all the songs, however, the music is distinctly sorrowful. The ten master songs I have mentioned tell in word and music of trouble and exile, of strife and hiding; they grope toward some unseen power and sigh for rest in the End.

---

1. "Old Folks at Home" (1851), also known as "Swanee River," and "Old Black Joe" (1860) were popular songs by Stephen Foster (1826–1864).

The words that are left to us are not without interest, and, cleared of evident dross, they conceal much of real poetry and meaning beneath conventional theology and unmeaning rhapsody. Like all primitive folk, the slave stood near to Nature's heart. Life was a "rough and rolling sea" like the brown Atlantic of the Sea Islands; the "Wilderness" was the home of God, and the "lonesome valley" led to the way of life. "Winter'll soon be over," was the picture of life and death to a tropical imagination. The sudden wild thunderstorms of the South awed and impressed the Negroes,—at times the rumbling seemed to them "mournful," at times imperious:

> "My Lord calls me,
> He calls me by the thunder,
> The trumpet sounds it in my soul."

The monotonous toil and exposure is painted in many words. One sees the ploughmen in the hot, moist furrow, singing:

> "Dere's no rain to wet you,
> Dere's no sun to burn you,
> Oh, push along, believer,
> I want to go home."

The bowed and bent old man cries, with thrice-repeated wail:

> "O Lord, keep me from sinking down,"

and he rebukes the devil of doubt who can whisper:

> "Jesus is dead and God's gone away."

Yet the soul-hunger is there, the restlessness of the savage, the wail of the wanderer, and the plaint is put in one little phrase:

My soul   wants some thing that's new,   that's new

Over the inner thoughts of the slaves and their relations one with another the shadow of fear ever hung, so that we get but glimpses here and there, and also with them, eloquent omissions and silences. Mother and child are sung, but seldom father; fugitive and weary wanderer call for pity and affection, but there is little of wooing and wedding; the rocks and the mountains are well known, but home is unknown. Strange blending of love and helplessness sings through the refrain:

> "Yonder's my ole mudder,
> Been waggin' at de hill so long;
> 'Bout time she cross over,
> Git home bime-by."

Elsewhere comes the cry of the "motherless" and the "Farewell, farewell, my only child."

Love-songs are scarce and fall into two categories—the frivolous and light, and the sad. Of deep successful love there is ominous silence, and in one of the oldest of these songs there is a depth of history and meaning:

A black woman said of the song, "It can't be sung without a full heart and a troubled sperrit." The same voice sings here that sings in the German folk-song:

"Jetz Geh i' an's brunele, trink' aber net."[2]

Of death the Negro showed little fear, but talked of it familiarly and even fondly as simply a crossing of the waters, perhaps—who knows?—back to his ancient forests again. Later days transfigured his fatalism, and amid the dust and dirt the toiler sang:

"Dust, dust and ashes, fly over my grave,
But the Lord shall bear my spirit home."

The things evidently borrowed from the surrounding world undergo characteristic change when they enter the mouth of the slave. Especially is this true of Bible phrases. "Weep, O captive daughter of Zion," is quaintly turned into "Zion, weep-a-low," and the wheels of Ezekiel are turned every way in the mystic dreaming of the slave, till he says:

"There's a little wheel a-turnin' in-a-my heart."

As in olden time, the words of these hymns were improvised by some leading minstrel of the religious band. The circumstances of the gathering, however, the rhythm of the songs, and the limitations of allowable thought, confined the poetry for the most part to single or double lines, and they seldom were expanded to quatrains or longer tales, although there are some few examples of sustained efforts, chiefly paraphrases of the Bible. Three short series of verses have always attracted me,—the one that heads this chapter, of one line of which Thomas Wentworth Higginson has fit-

2. Now I'm going to the well, but I'm not going to drink (German).

tingly said, "Never, it seems to me, since man first lived and suffered was
his infinite longing for peace uttered more plaintively." The second and
third are descriptions of the Last Judgment,—the one a late improvisation,
with some traces of outside influence:

> "Oh, the stars in the elements are falling,
> And the moon drips away into blood,
> And the ransomed of the Lord are returning unto God,
> Blessed be the name of the Lord."

And the other earlier and homelier picture from the low coast lands:

> "Michael, haul the boat ashore,
> Then you'll hear the horn they blow,
> Then you'll hear the trumpet sound,
> Trumpet sound the world around,
> Trumpet sound for rich and poor,
> Trumpet sound the Jubilee,
> Trumpet sound for you and me."

Through all the sorrow of the Sorrow Songs there breathes a hope—a
faith in the ultimate justice of things. The minor cadences of despair
change often to triumph and calm confidence. Sometimes it is faith in
life, sometimes a faith in death, sometimes assurance of boundless justice in some fair world beyond. But whichever it is, the meaning is always clear: that sometime, somewhere, men will judge men by their
souls and not by their skins. Is such a hope justified? Do the Sorrow
Songs sing true?

The silently growing assumption of this age is that the probation of
races is past, and that the backward races of to-day are of proven inefficiency and not worth the saving. Such an assumption is the arrogance of
peoples irreverent toward Time and ignorant of the deeds of men. A
thousand years ago such an assumption, easily possible, would have
made it difficult for the Teuton to prove his right to life. Two thousand
years ago such dogmatism, readily welcome, would have scouted the
idea of blond races ever leading civilization. So wofully unorganized is
sociological knowledge that the meaning of progress, the meaning of
"swift" and "slow" in human doing, and the limits of human perfectabil-
ity, are veiled, unanswered sphinxes on the shores of science. Why
should Æschylus[3] have sung two thousand years before Shakespeare was
born? Why has civilization flourished in Europe, and flickered, flamed,
and died in Africa? So long as the world stands meekly dumb before
such questions, shall this nation proclaim its ignorance and unhallowed
prejudices by denying freedom of opportunity to those who brought the
Sorrow Songs to the Seats of the Mighty?

Your country? How came it yours? Before the Pilgrims landed we were
here. Here we have brought our three gifts and mingled them with yours: a
gift of story and song—soft, stirring melody in an ill-harmonized and un-

---

3. Greek tragic dramatist (525–456 B.C.).

melodious land; the gift of sweat and brawn to beat back the wilderness, conquer the soil, and lay the foundations of this vast economic empire two hundred years earlier than your weak hands could have done it; the third, a gift of the Spirit. Around us the history of the land has centred for thrice a hundred years; out of the nation's heart we have called all that was best to throttle and subdue all that was worst; fire and blood, prayer and sacrifice, have billowed over this people, and they have found peace only in the altars of the God of Right. Nor has our gift of the Spirit been merely passive. Actively we have woven ourselves with the very warp and woof of this nation,—we fought their battles, shared their sorrow, mingled our blood with theirs, and generation after generation have pleaded with a headstrong, careless people to despise not Justice, Mercy, and Truth, lest the nation be smitten with a curse. Our song, our toil, our cheer, and warning have been given to this nation in blood-brotherhood. Are not these gifts worth the giving? Is not this work and striving? Would America have been America without her Negro people?

Even so is the hope that sang in the songs of my fathers well sung. If somewhere in this whirl and chaos of things there dwells Eternal Good, pitiful yet masterful, then anon in His good time America shall rend the Veil and the prisoned shall go free. Free, free as the sunshine trickling down the morning into these high windows of mine, free as yonder fresh young voices welling up to me from the caverns of brick and mortar below—swelling with song, instinct with life, tremulous treble and darkening bass. My children, my little children, are singing to the sunshine, and thus they sing:

- long   the   heav-   en - ly   way,

And the traveller girds himself, and sets his face toward the Morning, and goes his way.

THE AFTER-THOUGHT

Hear my cry, O God the Reader; vouchsafe that this my book fall not still-born into the world-wilderness. Let there spring, Gentle One, from out its leaves vigor of thought and thoughtful deed to reap the harvest wonderful. (Let the ears of a guilty people tingle with truth, and seventy millions sigh for the righteousness which exalteth nations, in this drear day when human brotherhood is mockery and a snare.) Thus in Thy good time may infinite reason turn the tangle straight, and these crooked marks on a fragile leaf be not indeed

THE END

1903

The Damnation of Women

I remember four women of my boyhood: my mother, cousin Inez, Emma, and Ide Fuller. They represented the problem of the widow, the wife, the maiden, and the outcast. They were, in color, brown and light-brown, yellow with brown freckles, and white. They existed not for themselves, but for men; they were named after the men to whom they were related and not after the fashion of their own souls.

They were not beings, they were relations and these relations were en-filmed with mystery and secrecy. We did not know the truth or believe it when we heard it. Motherhood! What was it? We did not know or greatly care. My mother and I were good chums. I liked her. After she was dead I loved her with a fierce sense of personal loss.

Inez was a pretty, brown cousin who married. What was marriage? We did not know, neither did she, poor thing! It came to mean for her a litter of children, poverty, a drunken, cruel companion, sickness, and death. Why?

There was no sweeter sight than Emma,—slim, straight, and dainty, darkly flushed with the passion of youth; but her life was a wild, awful struggle to crush her natural, fierce joy of love. She crushed it and became a cold, calculating mockery.

Last there was that awful outcast of the town, the white woman, Ide Fuller. What she was, we did not know. She stood to us as embodied filth and wrong,—but whose filth, whose wrong?

Grown up I see the problem of these women transfused; I hear all about me the unanswered call of youthful love, none the less glorious because of its clean, honest, physical passion. Why unanswered? Because the youth are too poor to marry or if they marry, too poor to have children. They turn aside, then, in three directions: to marry for support, to what men call shame, or to that which is more evil than nothing. It is an unendurable paradox; it must be changed or the bases of culture will totter and fall.

The world wants healthy babies and intelligent workers. Today we refuse to allow the combination and force thousands of intelligent workers to go childless at a horrible expenditure of moral force, or we damn them if they break our idiotic conventions. Only at the sacrifice of intelligence and the chance to do their best work can the majority of modern women bear children. This is the damnation of women.

All womanhood is hampered today because the world on which it is emerging is a world that tries to worship both virgins and mothers and in the end despises motherhood and despoils virgins.

The future woman must have a life work and economic independence. She must have knowledge. She must have the right of motherhood at her own discretion. The present mincing horror at free womanhood must pass if we are ever to be rid of the bestiality of free manhood; not by guarding the weak in weakness do we gain strength, but by making weakness free and strong.

The world must choose the free woman or the white wraith of the prostitute. Today it wavers between the prostitute and the nun. Civilization must show two things: the glory and beauty of creating life and the need and duty of power and intelligence. This and this only will make the perfect marriage of love and work.

> God is Love,
> Love is God;
> There is no God but Love
> And Work is His Prophet!

All this of woman,—but what of black women?

The world that wills to worship womankind studiously forgets its darker sisters. They seem in a sense to typify that veiled Melancholy:

> "Whose saintly visage is too bright
> To hit the sense of human sight,
> And, therefore, to our weaker view
> O'er-laid with black." [1]

Yet the world must heed these daughters of sorrow, from the primal black All-Mother of men down through the ghostly throng of mighty wom-

---

1. English poet John Milton's (1608–1674) *Il Penseroso* (c. 1631).

anhood, who walked in the mysterious dawn of Asia and Africa; from Neith,[2] the primal mother of all, whose feet rest on hell, and whose almighty hands uphold the heavens; all religion, from beauty to beast, lies on her eager breasts; her body bears the stars, while her shoulders are necklaced by the dragon; from black Neith down to

> "That starr'd Ethiop queen who strove
> To set her beauty's praise above
> The sea-nymphs,"[3]

through dusky Cleopatras, dark Candaces, and darker, fiercer Zinghas, to our own day and our own land,—in gentle Phillis; Harriet, the crude Moses; the sybil, Sojourner Truth; and the martyr, Louise De Mortie.[4]

The father and his worship is Asia; Europe is the precocious, self-centered, forward-striving child; but the land of the mother is and was Africa. In subtle and mysterious way, despite her curious history, her slavery, polygamy, and toil, the spell of the African mother pervades her land. Isis,[5] the mother, is still titular goddess, in thought if not in name, of the dark continent. Nor does this all seem to be solely a survival of the historic matriarchate[6] through which all nations pass,—it appears to be more than this,—as if the great black race in passing up the steps of human culture gave the world, not only the Iron Age,[7] the cultivation of the soil, and the domestication of animals, but also, in peculiar emphasis, the mother-idea.

"No mother can love more tenderly and none is more tenderly loved than the Negro mother," writes Schneider. Robin tells of the slave who bought his mother's freedom instead of his own. Mungo Park[8] writes: "Everywhere in Africa, I have noticed that no greater affront can be offered a Negro than insulting his mother. 'Strike me,' cries a Mandingo to his enemy, 'but revile not my mother!' " And the Krus and Fantis say the same. The peoples on the Zambezi and the great lakes cry in sudden fear or joy: "O, my mother!" And the Herero swear (endless oath) "By my mother's tears!" "As the mist in the swamps," cries the Angola[9] Negro, "so lives the love of father and mother."

A student of the present Gold Coast[1] life describes the work of the village headman, and adds: "It is a difficult task that he is set to, but in this matter he has all-powerful helpers in the female members of the family, who will be either the aunts or the sisters or the cousins or the nieces of the headman, and as their interests are identical with his in every particular,

2. Or Net, ancient Egyptian creator goddess.
3. Milton's *Il Penseroso*.
4. Teacher, lecturer, and social worker among the freed people in the South (d. 1887). Cleopatra (69–30 B.C.), queen of Egypt. Candace was the title for queens in ancient Ethiopia. Zingha was a legendary ancient African queen. Phillis Wheatley (c. 1735–1784), internationally acclaimed African-born poet who grew up a slave in Boston. Harriet Tubman (c. 1820–1913), slave-born "conductor" on the Underground Railroad, a secret organization that aided fugitive slaves in their escape to the North. Sojourner Truth (1797–1883), slave-born antislavery and women's rights activist.

5. Principal goddess of ancient Egypt.
6. A family or tribe headed by a woman.
7. The period beginning in about 4000 B.C. in Egypt when human beings began making things of iron.
8. British explorer of Africa (1771–1806).
9. A country on the southwest coast of Africa. The Mandingo people inhabit the Niger River region in western Suda. The Zambezi is the largest African river flowing into the Indian Ocean. The Herero people live in Botswana and Namibia.
1. The name of the British colony in West Africa that became Ghana.

the good women spontaneously train up their children to implicit obedience to the headman, whose rule in the family thus becomes a simple and an easy matter. 'The hand that rocks the cradle rules the world.' What a power for good in the native state system would the mothers of the Gold Coast and Ashanti[2] become by judicious training upon native lines!"

Schweinfurth declares of one tribe: "A bond between mother and child which lasts for life is the measure of affection shown among the Dyoor" and Ratzel[3] adds:

"Agreeable to the natural relation the mother stands first among the chief influences affecting the children. From the Zulus to the Waganda, we find the mother the most influential counsellor at the court of ferocious sovereigns, like Chaka or Mtesa;[4] sometimes sisters take her place. Thus even with chiefs who possess wives by hundreds the bonds of blood are the strongest and that the woman, though often heavily burdened, is in herself held in no small esteem among the Negroes is clear from the numerous Negro queens, from the medicine women, from the participation in public meetings permitted to women by many Negro peoples."

As I remember through memories of others, backward among my own family, it is the mother I ever recall,—the little, far-off mother of my grandmothers, who sobbed her life away in song, longing for her lost palm-trees and scented waters; the tall and bronzen grandmother, with beaked nose and shrewish eyes, who loved and scolded her black and laughing husband as he smoked lazily in his high oak chair; above all, my own mother, with all her soft brownness,—the brown velvet of her skin, the sorrowful black-brown of her eyes, and the tiny brown-capped waves of her midnight hair as it lay new parted on her forehead. All the way back in these dim distances it is mothers and mothers of mothers who seem to count, while fathers are shadowy memories.

Upon this African mother-idea, the westward slave trade and American slavery struck like doom. In the cruel exigencies of the traffic in men and in the sudden, unprepared emancipation the great pendulum of social equilibrium swung from a time, in 1800,—when America had but eight or less black women to every ten black men,—all too swiftly to a day, in 1870,—when there were nearly eleven women to ten men in our Negro population. This was but the outward numerical fact of social dislocation; within lay polygamy, polyandry, concubinage,[5] and moral degradation. They fought against all this desperately, did these black slaves in the West Indies, especially among the half-free artisans; they set up their ancient household gods, and when Toussaint and Cristophe[6] founded their kingdom in Haiti, it was based on old African tribal ties and beneath it was the mother-idea.

The crushing weight of slavery fell on black women. Under it there was no legal marriage, no legal family, no legal control over children. To be

2. A people who live in Ghana.
3. Friedrich Ratzel (1844–1904), originator of anthropogeography. Georg August Schweinfurth (1836–1925), African explorer and botanist, collaborator with Ratzel. The Dyoor people lived along the Dyoor River in central Africa.
4. Late-19th-century king of Uganda. The Zulu people live in South Africa. The Waganda are Bantu people from Nigeria. Chaka Zulu (1787?–

1828), leader of southeast African Zulus.
5. Cohabitation without legal marriage. "Polygamy": having more than one wife at the same time. "Polyandry": having more than one husband at the same time.
6. Henri Christophe (1767–1820), dictator of Haiti (1811–20). Toussaint L'Ouverture (1743?–1803), leader of a successful slave revolution in Haiti.

sure, custom and religion replaced here and there what the law denied, yet one has but to read advertisements like the following to see the hell beneath the system:

"One hundred dollars reward will be given for my two fellows, Abram and Frank. Abram has a wife at Colonel Stewart's, in Liberty County, and a mother at Thunderbolt, and a sister in Savannah.

"WILLIAM ROBERTS."

"Fifty dollars reward—Ran away from the subscriber a Negro girl named Maria. She is of a copper color, between thirteen and fourteen years of age—bare headed and barefooted. She is small for her age—very sprightly and very likely. She stated she was going to see her mother at Maysville.

"SANFORD THOMSON."

"Fifty dollars reward—Ran away from the subscriber his Negro man Pauladore, commonly called Paul. I understand General R. Y. Hayne has purchased his wife and children from H. L. Pinckney, Esq., and has them now on his plantation at Goose Creek, where, no doubt, the fellow is frequently lurking.

"T. DAVIS."

The Presbyterian synod of Kentucky said to the churches under its care in 1835: "Brothers and sisters, parents and children, husbands and wives, are torn asunder and permitted to see each other no more. These acts are daily occurring in the midst of us. The shrieks and agony often witnessed on such occasions proclaim, with a trumpet tongue, the iniquity of our system. There is not a neighborhood where these heartrending scenes are not displayed. There is not a village or road that does not behold the sad procession of manacled outcasts whose mournful countenances tell that they are exiled by force from all that their hearts hold dear."

A sister of a president of the United States declared: "We Southern ladies are complimented with the names of wives, but we are only the mistresses of seraglios."[7]

Out of this, what sort of black women could be born into the world of today? There are those who hasten to answer this query in scathing terms and who say lightly and repeatedly that out of black slavery came nothing decent in womanhood; that adultery and uncleanness were their heritage and are their continued portion.

Fortunately so exaggerated a charge is humanly impossible of truth. The half-million women of Negro descent who lived at the beginning of the 19th century had become the mothers of two and one-fourth million daughters at the time of the Civil War and five million granddaughters in 1910. Can all these women be vile and the hunted race continue to grow in wealth and character? Impossible. Yet to save from the past the shreds and vestiges of self-respect has been a terrible task. I most sincerely doubt if any other race of women could have brought its fineness up through so devilish a fire.

7. Harems.

Alexander Crummell[8] once said of his sister in the blood: "In her girl-hood all the delicate tenderness of her sex has been rudely outraged. In the field, in the rude cabin, in the press-room, in the factory she was thrown into the companionship of coarse and ignorant men. No chance was given her for delicate reserve or tender modesty. From her childhood she was the doomed victim of the grossest passion. All the virtues of her sex were utterly ignored. If the instinct of chastity asserted itself, then she had to fight like a tiger for the ownership and possession of her own person and ofttimes had to suffer pain and lacerations for her virtuous self-assertion. When she reached maturity, all the tender instincts of her womanhood were ruth-lessly violated. At the age of marriage,—always prematurely anticipated under slavery—she was mated as the stock of the plantation were mated, not to be the companion of a loved and chosen husband, but to be the breeder of human cattle for the field or the auction block."

Down in such mire has the black motherhood of this race struggled,—starving its own wailing offspring to nurse to the world their swaggering masters; welding for its children chains which affronted even the moral sense of an unmoral world. Many a man and woman in the South have lived in wedlock as holy as Adam and Eve and brought forth their brown and golden children, but because the darker woman was helpless, her chiv-alrous and whiter mate could cast her off at his pleasure and publicly sneer at the body he had privately blasphemed.

I shall forgive the white South much in its final judgment day: I shall forgive its slavery, for slavery is a world-old habit; I shall forgive its fighting for a well-lost cause, and for remembering that struggle with tender tears; I shall forgive its so-called "pride of race," the passion of its hot blood, and even its dear, old, laughable strutting and posing; but one thing I shall never forgive, neither in this world nor the world to come: its wanton and continued and persistent insulting of the black womanhood which it sought and seeks to prostitute to its lust. I cannot forget that it is such South-ern gentlemen into whose hands smug Northern hypocrites of today are seeking to place our women's eternal destiny,—men who insist upon with-holding from my mother and wife and daughter those signs and appella-tions of courtesy and respect which elsewhere he withholds only from bawds and courtesans.

The result of this history of insult and degradation has been both fearful and glorious. It has birthed the haunting prostitute, the brawler, and the beast of burden; but it has also given the world an efficient womanhood, whose strength lies in its freedom and whose chastity was won in the teeth of temptation and not in prison and swaddling clothes.

To no modern race does its women mean so much as to the Negro nor come so near to the fulfilment of its meaning. As one of our women writes: "Only the black woman can say 'when and where I enter, in the quiet, undisputed dignity of my womanhood, without violence and without suing or special patronage, then and there the whole Negro race enters with me.'"[9]

They came first, in earlier days, like foam flashing on dark, silent wa-

---

8. Clergyman, antislavery activist, and African mis-sionary (1819–1898).

9. Anna Julia Cooper's *A Voice from the South* (1892).

ters,—bits of stern, dark womanhood here and there tossed almost carelessly aloft to the world's notice. First and naturally they assumed the panoply[1] of the ancient African mother of men, strong and black, whose very nature beat back the wilderness of oppression and contempt. Such a one was that cousin of my grandmother, whom western Massachusetts remembers as "Mum Bett." Scarred for life by a blow received in defense of a sister, she ran away to Great Barrington and was the first slave, or one of the first, to be declared free under the Bill of Rights of 1780. The son of the judge who freed her, writes:

> "Even in her humble station, she had, when occasion required it, an air of command which conferred a degree of dignity and gave her an ascendancy over those of her rank, which is very unusual in persons of any rank or color. Her determined and resolute character, which enabled her to limit the ravages of Shay's mob, was manifested in her conduct and deportment during her whole life. She claimed no distinction, but it was yielded to her from her superior experience, energy, skill, and sagacity. Having known this woman as familiarly as I knew either of my parents, I cannot believe in the moral or physical inferiority of the race to which she belonged. The degradation of the African must have been otherwise caused than by natural inferiority."

It was such strong women that laid the foundations of the great Negro church of today, with its five million members and ninety millions of dollars in property. One of the early mothers of the church, Mary Still, writes thus quaintly, in the forties:

> "When we were as castouts and spurned from the large churches, driven from our knees, pointed at by the proud, neglected by the careless, without a place of worship, Allen, faithful to the heavenly calling, came forward and laid the foundation of this connection. The women, like the women at the sepulcher, were early to aid in laying the foundation of the temple and in helping to carry up the noble structure and in the name of their God set up their banner; most of our aged mothers are gone from this to a better state of things. Yet some linger still on their staves, watching with intense interest the ark as it moves over the tempestuous waves of opposition and ignorance. . . .
>
> "But the labors of these women stopped not here, for they knew well that they were subject to affliction and death. For the purpose of mutual aid, they banded themselves together in society capacity, that they might be better able to administer to each others' sufferings and to soften their own pillows. So we find the females in the early history of the church abounding in good works and in acts of true benevolence."[2]

From such spiritual ancestry came two striking figures of war-time,—Harriet Tubman and Sojourner Truth.

---

1. A complete set of armor.   2. Mary Still's *An Appeal to the Females of the African Methodist Episcopal Church* (1857).

For eight or ten years previous to the breaking out of the Civil War, Harriet Tubman was a constant attendant at anti-slavery conventions, lectures, and other meetings; she was a black woman of medium size, smiling countenance, with her upper front teeth gone, attired in coarse but neat clothes, and carrying always an old-fashioned reticule[3] at her side. Usually as soon as she sat down she would drop off in sound sleep.

She was born a slave in Maryland, in 1820, bore the marks of the lash on her flesh; and had been made partially deaf, and perhaps to some degree mentally unbalanced by a blow on the head in childhood. Yet she was one of the most important agents of the Underground Railroad and a leader of fugitive slaves. She ran away in 1849 and went to Boston in 1854, where she was welcomed into the homes of the leading abolitionists and where every one listened with tense interest to her strange stories. She was absolutely illiterate, with no knowledge of geography, and yet year after year she penetrated the slave states and personally led North over three hundred fugitives without losing a single one. A standing reward of $10,000 was offered for her, but as she said: "The whites cannot catch us, for I was born with the charm, and the Lord has given me the power." She was one of John Brown's closest advisers and only severe sickness prevented her presence at Harper's Ferry.[4]

When the war cloud broke, she hastened to the front, flitting down along her own mysterious paths, haunting the armies in the field, and serving as guide and nurse and spy. She followed Sherman in his great march to the sea and was with Grant at Petersburg, and always in the camps the Union officers silently saluted her.

The other woman belonged to a different type,—a tall, gaunt, black, unsmiling sybil, weighted with the woe of the world. She ran away from slavery and giving up her own name took the name of Sojourner Truth. She says: "I can remember when I was a little, young girl, how my old mammy would sit out of doors in the evenings and look up at the stars and groan, and I would say, 'Mammy, what makes you groan so?' And she would say, 'I am groaning to think of my poor children; they do not know where I be and I don't know where they be. I look up at the stars and they look up at the stars!'"

Her determination was founded on unwavering faith in ultimate good. Wendell Phillips says that he was once in Faneuil Hall, when Frederick Douglass[5] was one of the chief speakers. Douglass had been describing the wrongs of the Negro race and as he proceeded he grew more and more excited and finally ended by saying that they had no hope of justice from the whites, no possible hope except in their own right arms. It must come to blood! They must fight for themselves. Sojourner Truth was sitting, tall and dark, on the very front seat facing the platform, and in the hush of feeling when Douglass sat down she spoke out in her deep, peculiar voice, heard all over the hall:

"Frederick, is God dead?"

Such strong, primitive types of Negro womanhood in America seem to

3. A woman's small handbag.
4. Site in Virginia of abolitionist John Brown's failed attempt in 1859 to seize the U.S. arsenal.

5. Fugitive slave and abolitionist speaker (1818–1895). Wendell Phillips (1811–1884), American abolitionist speaker.

some to exhaust its capabilities. They know less of a not more worthy, but a finer type of black woman wherein trembles all of that delicate sense of beauty and striving for self-realization, which is as characteristic of the Negro soul as is its quaint strength and sweet laughter. George Washington wrote in grave and gentle courtesy to a Negro woman, in 1776, that he would "be happy to see" at his headquarters at any time, a person "to whom nature has been so liberal and beneficial in her dispensations." This child, Phillis Wheatley, sang her trite and halting strain to a world that wondered and could not produce her like. Measured today her muse was slight and yet, feeling her striving spirit, we call to her still in her own words:

"Through thickest glooms look back, immortal shade."[6]

Perhaps even higher than strength and art loom human sympathy and sacrifice as characteristic of Negro womanhood. Long years ago, before the Declaration of Independence, Kate Ferguson[7] was born in New York. Freed, widowed, and bereaved of her children before she was twenty, she took the children of the streets of New York, white and black, to her empty arms, taught them, found them homes, and with Dr. Mason of Murray Street Church established the first modern Sunday School in Manhattan.

Sixty years later came Mary Shadd[8] up out of Delaware. She was tall and slim, of that ravishing dream-born beauty,—that twilight of the races which we call mulatto. Well-educated, vivacious, with determination shining from her sharp eyes, she threw herself singlehanded into the great Canadian pilgrimage when thousands of hunted black men hurried northward and crept beneath the protection of the lion's paw. She became teacher, editor, and lecturer; tramping afoot through winter snows, pushing without blot or blemish through crowd and turmoil to conventions and meetings, and finally becoming recruiting agent for the United States government in gathering Negro soldiers in the West.

After the war the sacrifice of Negro women for freedom and uplift is one of the finest chapters in their history. Let one life typify all: Louise De Mortie, a free-born Virginia girl, had lived most of her life in Boston. Her high forehead, swelling lips, and dark eyes marked her for a woman of feeling and intellect. She began a successful career as a public reader. Then came the War and the Call. She went to the orphaned colored children of New Orleans,—out of freedom into insult and oppression and into the teeth of the yellow fever. She toiled and dreamed. In 1887 she had raised money and built an orphan home and that same year, in the thirty-fourth of her young life, she died, saying simply: "I belong to God."

As I look about me today in this veiled world of mine, despite the noisier and more spectacular advance of my brothers, I instinctively feel and know that it is the five million women of my race who really count. Black women (and women whose grandmothers were black) are today furnishing our teachers; they are the main pillars of those social settlements which we call churches; and they have with small doubt raised three-fourths of our

6. Wheatley's *On the Death of Dr. Samuel Marshall* (1773).
7. Catherine Ferguson (c. 1774–1854), whose in-

tegrated Sunday school was launched in 1793.
8. Mary Ann Shadd Cary (1823–1893), antislavery activist in Canada.

church property. If we have today, as seems likely, over a billion dollars of accumulated goods, who shall say how much of it has been wrung from the hearts of servant girls and washerwomen and women toilers in the fields? As makers of two million homes these women are today seeking in marvelous ways to show forth our strength and beauty and our conception of the truth.

In the United States in 1910 there were 4,931,882 women of Negro descent; over twelve hundred thousand of these were children, another million were girls and young women under twenty, and two and a half-million were adults. As a mass these women were unlettered,—a fourth of those from fifteen to twenty-five years of age were unable to write. These women are passing through, not only a moral, but an economic revolution. Their grandmothers married at twelve and fifteen, but twenty-seven per cent of these women today who have passed fifteen are still single.

Yet these black women toil and toil hard. There were in 1910 two and a half million Negro homes in the United States. Out of these homes walked daily to work two million women and girls over ten years of age,—over half of the colored female population as against a fifth in the case of white women. These, then, are a group of workers, fighting for their daily bread like men; independent and approaching economic freedom! They furnished a million farm laborers, 80,000 farmers, 22,000 teachers, 600,000 servants and washerwomen, and 50,000 in trades and merchandizing.

The family group, however, which is the ideal of the culture with which these folk have been born, is not based on the idea of an economically independent working mother. Rather its ideal harks back to the sheltered harem with the mother emerging at first as nurse and homemaker, while the man remains the sole breadwinner. What is the inevitable result of the clash of such ideals and such facts in the colored group? Broken families.

Among native white women one in ten is separated from her husband by death, divorce, or desertion. Among Negroes the ratio is one in seven. Is the cause racial? No, it is economic, because there is the same high ratio among the white foreign-born. The breaking up of the present family is the result of modern working and sex conditions and it hits the laborers with terrible force. The Negroes are put in a peculiarly difficult position, because the wage of the male breadwinner is below the standard, while the openings for colored women in certain lines of domestic work, and now in industries, are many. Thus while toil holds the father and brother in country and town at low wages, the sisters and mothers are called to the city. As a result the Negro women outnumber the men nine or ten to eight in many cities, making what Charlotte Gilman[9] bluntly calls "cheap women."

What shall we say to this new economic equality in a great laboring class? Some people within and without the race deplore it. "Back to the homes with the women," they cry, "and higher wage for the men." But how impossible this is has been shown by war conditions. Cessation of foreign migration has raised Negro men's wages, to be sure—but it has not only raised Negro women's wages, it has opened to them a score of new avenues of earning a living. Indeed, here, in microcosm and with differ-

9. Charlotte Perkins Gilman (1860–1935), feminist author and lecturer.

ences emphasizing sex equality, is the industrial history of labor in the 19th and 20th centuries. We cannot abolish the new economic freedom of women. We cannot imprison women again in a home or require them all on pain of death to be nurses and housekeepers.

What is today the message of these black women to America and to the world? The uplift of women is, next to the problem of the color line and the peace movement, our greatest modern cause. When, now, two of these movements—woman and color—combine in one, the combination has deep meaning.

In other years women's way was clear: to be beautiful, to be petted, to bear children. Such has been their theoretic destiny and if perchance they have been ugly, hurt, and barren, that has been forgotten with studied silence. In partial compensation for this narrowed destiny the white world has lavished its politeness on its womankind,—its chivalry and bows, its uncoverings and courtesies—all the accumulated homage disused for courts and kings and craving exercise. The revolt of white women against this preordained destiny has in these latter days reached splendid proportions, but it is the revolt of an aristocracy of brains and ability,—the middle class and rank and file still plod on in the appointed path, paid by the homage, the almost mocking homage, of men.

From black women of America, however, (and from some others, too, but chiefly from black women and their daughters' daughters) this gauze has been withheld and without semblance of such apology they have been frankly trodden under the feet of men. They are and have been objected to, apparently for reasons peculiarly exasperating to reasoning human beings. When in this world a man comes forward with a thought, a deed, a vision, we ask not, how does he look,—but what is his message? It is of but passing interest whether or not the messenger is beautiful or ugly,—the *message* is the thing. This, which is axiomatic among men, has been in past ages but partially true if the messenger was a woman. The world still wants to ask that a woman primarily be pretty and if she is not, the mob pouts and asks querulously, "What else are women for?" Beauty "is its own excuse for being," but there are other excuses, as most men know, and when the white world objects to black women because it does not consider them beautiful, the black world of right asks two questions: "What is beauty?" and, "Suppose you think them ugly, what then? If ugliness and unconventionality and eccentricity of face and deed do not hinder men from doing the world's work and reaping the world's reward, why should it hinder women?"

Other things being equal, all of us, black and white, would prefer to be beautiful in face and form and suitably clothed; but most of us are not so, and one of the mightiest revolts of the century is against the devilish decree that no woman is a woman who is not by present standards a beautiful woman. This decree the black women of America have in large measure escaped from the first. Not being expected to be merely ornamental, they have girded themselves for work, instead of adorning their bodies only for play. Their sturdier minds have concluded that if a woman be clean, healthy, and educated, she is as pleasing as God wills and far more useful than most of her sisters. If in addition to this she is pink and white and straight-haired, and some of her fellow-men prefer this, well and good; but if she is black or brown and crowned in curled mists (and this to us is the most beautiful thing on earth), this is surely the flimsiest excuse for spiritual incarceration or banishment.

The very attempt to do this in the case of Negro Americans has strangely over-reached itself. By so much as the defective eyesight of the white world rejects black women as beauties, by so much the more it needs them as human beings,—an enviable alternative, as many a white woman knows. Consequently, for black women alone, as a group, "handsome is that handsome does" and they are asked to be no more beautiful than God made them, but they are asked to be efficient, to be strong, fertile, muscled, and able to work. If they marry, they must as independent workers be able to help support their children, for their men are paid on a scale which makes sole support of the family often impossible.

On the whole, colored working women are paid as well as white working women for similar work, save in some higher grades, while colored men get from one-fourth to three-fourths less than white men. The result is curious and three-fold: the economic independence of black women is increased, the breaking up of Negro families must be more frequent, and the number of illegitimate children is decreased more slowly among them than other evidences of culture are increased, just as was once true in Scotland and Bavaria.

What does this mean? It forecasts a mighty dilemma which the whole world of civilization, despite its will, must one time frankly face: the unhusbanded mother or the childless wife. God send us a world with woman's freedom and married motherhood inextricably wed, but until He sends it, I see more of future promise in the betrayed girl-mothers of the black belt than in the childless wives of the white North, and I have more respect for the colored servant who yields to her frank longing for motherhood than for her white sister who offers up children for clothes. Out of a sex freedom that today makes us shudder will come in time a day when we will no longer pay men for work they do not do, for the sake of their harem; we will pay women what they earn and insist on their working and earning it; we will allow those persons to vote who know enough to vote, whether they be black or female, white or male; and we will ward race suicide, not by further burdening the over-burdened, but by honoring motherhood, even when the sneaking father shirks his duty.

"Wait till the lady passes," said a Nashville white boy.

"She's no lady; she's a nigger," answered another.

So some few women are born free, and some amid insult and scarlet letters [1] achieve freedom; but our women in black had freedom thrust contemptuously upon them. With that freedom they are buying an untrammeled independence and dear as is the price they pay for it, it will in the end be worth every taunt and groan. Today the dreams of the mothers are coming true. We have still our poverty and degradation, our lewdness and

---

1. In Nathaniel Hawthorne's *The Scarlet Letter* (1851), the protagonist is convicted of adultery and compelled by Puritan authorities to wear a scarlet A.

our cruel toil; but we have, too, a vast group of women of Negro blood who
for strength of character, cleanness of soul, and unselfish devotion of purpose, is today easily the peer of any group of women in the civilized world.
And more than that, in the great rank and file of our five million women we
have the up-working of new revolutionary ideals, which must in time have
vast influence on the thought and action of this land.

For this, their promise, and for their hard past, I honor the women of my
race. Their beauty,—their dark and mysterious beauty of midnight eyes,
crumpled hair, and soft, full-featured faces—is perhaps more to me than to
you, because I was born to its warm and subtle spell; but their worth is
yours as well as mine. No other women on earth could have emerged from
the hell of force and temptation which once engulfed and still surrounds
black women in America with half the modesty and womanliness that they
retain. I have always felt like bowing myself before them in all abasement,
searching to bring some tribute to these long-suffering victims, these burdened sisters of mine, whom the world, the wise, white world, loves to affront and ridicule and wantonly to insult. I have known the women of
many lands and nations,—I have known and seen and lived beside them,
but none have I known more sweetly feminine, more unswervingly loyal,
more desperately earnest, and more instinctively pure in body and in soul
than the daughters of my black mothers. This, then,—a little thing—to their
memory and inspiration.

1920

Criteria of Negro Art

I do not doubt but there are some in this audience who are a little disturbed at the subject of this meeting, and particularly at the subject I have
chosen. Such people are thinking something like this: "How is it that an
organization like this, a group of radicals trying to bring new things into the
world, a fighting organization which has come up out of the blood and dust
of battle, struggling for the right of black men to be ordinary human beings—how is it that an organization of this kind can turn aside to talk about
Art? After all, what have we who are slaves and black to do with Art?"

Or perhaps there are others who feel a certain relief and are saying,
"After all it is rather satisfactory after all this talk about rights and fighting to
sit and dream of something which leaves a nice taste in the mouth."

Let me tell you that neither of these groups is right. The thing we are
talking about tonight is part of the great fight we are carrying on and it
represents a forward and an upward look—a pushing onward. You and I
have been breasting hills; we have been climbing upward; there has been
progress and we can see it day by day looking back along blood-filled paths.
But as you go through the valleys and over the foothills, so long as you are
climbing, the direction,—north, south, east or west,—is of less importance.
But when gradually the vista widens and you begin to see the world at your
feet and the far horizon, then it is time to know more precisely whither you
are going and what you really want.

What do we want? What is the thing we are after? As it was phrased last night it had a certain truth: We want to be Americans, full-fledged Americans, with all the rights of other American citizens. But is that all? Do we want simply to be Americans? Once in a while through all of us there flashes some clairvoyance, some clear idea, of what America really is. We who are dark can see America in a way that white Americans can not. And seeing our country thus, are we satisfied with its present goals and ideals?

In the high school where I studied we learned most of Scott's "Lady of the Lake"[1] by heart. In after life once it was my privilege to see the lake. It was Sunday. It was quiet. You could glimpse the deer wandering in unbroken forests; you could hear the soft ripple of romance on the waters. Around me fell the cadence of that poetry of my youth. I fell asleep full of the enchantment of the Scottish border. A new day broke and with it came a sudden rush of excursionists. They were mostly Americans and they were loud and strident. They poured upon the little pleasure boat,—men with their hats a little on one side and drooping cigars in the wet corners of their mouths; women who shared their conversation with the world. They all tried to get everywhere first. They pushed other people out of the way. They made all sorts of incoherent noises and gestures so that the quiet home folk and the visitors from other lands silently and half-wonderingly gave way before them. They struck a note not evil but wrong. They carried, perhaps, a sense of strength and accomplishment, but their hearts had no conception of the beauty which pervaded this holy place.

If you tonight suddenly should become full-fledged Americans; if your color faded, or the color line here in Chicago was miraculously forgotten; suppose, too, you became at the same time rich and powerful;—what is it that you would want? What would you immediately seek? Would you buy the most powerful of motor cars and outrace Cook County? Would you buy the most elaborate estate on the North Shore? Would you be a Rotarian or a Lion or a What-not of the very last degree? Would you wear the most striking clothes, give the richest dinners and buy the longest press notices?

Even as you visualize such ideals you know in your hearts that these are not the things you really want. You realize this sooner than the average white American because, pushed aside as we have been in America, there has come to us not only a certain distaste for the tawdry and flamboyant but a vision of what the world could be if it were really a beautiful world; if we had the true spirit; if we had the Seeing Eye, the Cunning Hand, the Feeling Heart; if we had, to be sure, not perfect happiness, but plenty of good hard work, the inevitable suffering that always comes with life; sacrifice and waiting, all that—but, nevertheless, lived in a world where men know, where men create, where they realize themselves and where they enjoy life. It is that sort of a world we want to create for ourselves and for all America.

After all, who shall describe Beauty? What is it? I remember tonight four beautiful things: The Cathedral at Cologne,[2] a forest in stone, set in light and changing shadow, echoing with sunlight and solemn song; a village of

---

1. Sir Walter Scott (1771–1832) wrote the poem   2. A Gothic cathedral in Germany.
Lady of the Lake in 1810.

the Veys[3] in West Africa, a little thing of mauve and purple, quiet, lying content and shining in the sun; a black and velvet room where on a throne rests, in old and yellowing marble, the broken curves of the Venus of Milo;[4] a single phrase of music in the Southern South—utter melody, haunting and appealing, suddenly arising out of night and eternity, beneath the moon.

Such is Beauty. Its variety is infinite, its possibility is endless. In normal life all may have it and have it yet again. The world is full of it; and yet today the mass of human beings are choked away from it, and their lives distorted and made ugly. This is not only wrong, it is silly. Who shall right this well-nigh universal failing? Who shall let this world be beautiful? Who shall restore to men the glory of sunsets and the peace of quiet sleep?

We black folk may help for we have within us as a race new stirrings; stirrings of the beginning of a new appreciation of joy, of a new desire to create, of a new will to be; as though in this morning of group life we had awakened from some sleep that at once dimly mourns the past and dreams a splendid future; and there has come the conviction that the Youth that is here today, the Negro Youth, is a different kind of Youth, because in some new way it bears this mighty prophecy on its breast, with a new realization of itself, with new determination for all mankind.

What has this Beauty to do with the world? What has Beauty to do with Truth and Goodness—with the facts of the world and the right actions of men? "Nothing", the artists rush to answer. They may be right. I am but an humble disciple of art and cannot presume to say. I am one who tells the truth and exposes evil and seeks with Beauty and for Beauty to set the world right. That somehow, somewhere eternal and perfect Beauty sits above Truth and Right I can conceive, but here and now and in the world in which I work they are for me unseparated and inseparable.

This is brought to us peculiarly when as artists we face our own past as a people. There has come to us—and it has come especially through the man we are going to honor tonight[5]—a realization of that past, of which for long years we have been ashamed, for which we have apologized. We thought nothing could come out of that past which we wanted to remember; which we wanted to hand down to our children. Suddenly, this same past is taking on form, color and reality, and in a half shamefaced way we are beginning to be proud of it. We are remembering that the romance of the world did not die and lie forgotten in the Middle Age; that if you want romance to deal with you must have it here and now and in your own hands.

I once knew a man and woman. They had two children, a daughter who was white and a daughter who was brown; the daughter who was white married a white man; and when her wedding was preparing the daughter who was brown prepared to go and celebrate. But the mother said, "No!" and the brown daughter went into her room and turned on the gas and died. Do you want Greek tragedy swifter than that?

Or again, here is a little Southern town and you are in the public square. On one side of the square is the office of a colored lawyer and on all the

3. One of the Mandingo peoples of Senegal.
4. A Greek statue of the goddess Venus (c. 100 B.C.).
5. "Carter Godwin Woodson, 12th Spingarn Med-

allist" [Du Bois's note]. Woodson (1875–1950), African American historian and author; he received the NAACP medal in 1926.

other sides are men who do not like colored lawyers. A white woman goes into the black man's office and points to the white-filled square and says, "I want five hundred dollars now and if I do not get it I am going to scream."

Have you heard the story of the conquest of German East Africa? Listen to the untold tale: There were 40,000 black men and 4,000 white men who talked German. There were 20,000 black men and 12,000 white men who talked English. There were 10,000 black men and 400 white men who talked French. In Africa then where the Mountains of the Moon raised their white and snow-capped heads into the mouth of the tropic sun, where Nile and Congo rise and the Great Lakes swim, these men fought; they struggled on mountain, hill and valley, in river, lake and swamp, until in masses they sickened, crawled and died; until the 4,000 white Germans had become mostly bleached bones; until nearly all the 12,000 white Englishmen had returned to South Africa, and the 400 Frenchmen to Belgium and Heaven; all except a mere handful of the white men died; but thousands of black men from East, West and South Africa, from Nigeria and the Valley of the Nile, and from the West Indies still struggled, fought and died. For four years they fought and won and lost German East Africa; and all you hear about it is that England and Belgium conquered German Africa for the allies!

Such is the true and stirring stuff of which Romance is born and from this stuff come the stirrings of men who are beginning to remember that this kind of material is theirs; and this vital life of their own kind is beckoning them on.

The question comes next as to the interpretation of these new stirrings, of this new spirit: Of what is the colored artist capable? We have had on the part of both colored and white people singular unanimity of judgment in the past. Colored people have said: "This work must be inferior because it comes from colored people." White people have said: "It is inferior because it is done by colored people." But today there is coming to both the realization that the work of the black man is not always inferior. Interesting stories come to us. A professor in the University of Chicago read to a class that had studied literature a passage of poetry and asked them to guess the author. They guessed a goodly company from Shelley and Robert Browning down to Tennyson and Masefield. The author was Countée Cullen.[6] Or again the English critic John Drinkwater went down to a Southern seminary, one of the sort which "finishes" young white women of the South. The students sat with their wooden faces while he tried to get some response out of them. Finally he said, "Name me some of your Southern poets". They hesitated. He said finally, "I'll start out with your best: Paul Laurence Dunbar"![7]

With the growing recognition of Negro artists in spite of the severe handicaps, one comforting thing is occurring to both white and black. They are whispering, "Here is a way out. Here is the real solution of the color problem. The recognition accorded Cullen, Hughes, Fauset, White[8] and oth-

---

6. African American poet (1903–1946). Percy Bysshe Shelley (1792–1822); Robert Browning (1812–1889); Alfred, Lord Tennyson (1809–1892); and John Masefield (1878–1967) were all English poets.

7. African American poet (1872–1906).
8. Walter White (1893–1955), author and civil rights leader. Langston Hughes (1902–1967), poet dramatist, and fiction writer. Jessie Redmon Fauset (1882–1961), editor and novelist.

ers shows there is no real color line. Keep quiet! Don't complain! Work! All will be well!"

I will not say that already this chorus amounts to a conspiracy. Perhaps I am naturally too suspicious. But I will say that there are today a surprising number of white people who are getting great satisfaction out of these younger Negro writers because they think it is going to stop agitation of the Negro question. They say, "What is the use of your fighting and complaining; do the great thing and the reward is there". And many colored people are all too eager to follow this advice; especially those who are weary of the eternal struggle along the color line, who are afraid to fight and to whom the money of philanthropists and the alluring publicity are subtle and deadly bribes. They say, "What is the use of fighting? Why not show simply what we deserve and let the reward come to us?"

And it is right here that the National Association for the Advancement of Colored People comes upon the field, comes with its great call to a new battle, a new fight and new things to fight before the old things are wholly won; and to say that the Beauty of Truth and Freedom which shall some day be our heritage and the heritage of all civilized men is not in our hands yet and that we ourselves must not fail to realize.

There is in New York tonight a black woman molding clay by herself in a little bare room, because there is not a single school of sculpture in New York where she is welcome. Surely there are doors she might burst through, but when God makes a sculptor He does not always make the pushing sort of person who beats his way through doors thrust in his face. This girl is working her hands off to get out of this country so that she can get some sort of training.

There was Richard Brown. If he had been white he would have been alive today instead of dead of neglect. Many helped him when he asked but he was not the kind of boy that always asks. He was simply one who made colors sing.

There is a colored woman in Chicago who is a great musician. She thought she would like to study at Fontainebleau this summer where Walter Damrosch [9] and a score of leaders of Art have an American school of music. But the application blank of this school says: "I am a white American and I apply for admission to the school."

We can go on the stage; we can be just as funny as white Americans wish us to be; we can play all the sordid parts that America likes to assign to Negroes; but for any thing else there is still small place for us.

And so I might go on. But let me sum up with this: Suppose the only Negro who survived some centuries hence was the Negro painted by white Americans in the novels and essays they have written. What would people in a hundred years say of black Americans? Now turn it around. Suppose you were to write a story and put in it the kind of people you know and like and imagine. You might get it published and you might not. And the "might not" is still far bigger than the "might". The white publishers catering to white folk would say, "It is not interesting"—to white folk, natu-

---

9. German-American conductor and composer (1862–1950). The Fontainebleau is a French resort.

rally not. They want Uncle Toms, Topsies,[1] good "darkies" and clowns. I have in my office a story with all the earmarks of truth. A young man says that he started out to write and had his stories accepted. Then he began to write about the things he knew best about, that is, about his own people. He submitted a story to a magazine which said, "We are sorry, but we cannot take it". "I sat down and revised my story, changing the color of the characters and the locale and sent it under an assumed name with a change of address and it was accepted by the same magazine that had refused it, the editor promising to take anything else I might send in providing it was good enough."

We have, to be sure, a few recognized and successful Negro artists; but they are not all those fit to survive or even a good minority. They are but the remnants of that ability and genius among us whom the accidents of education and opportunity have raised on the tidal waves of chance. We black folk are not altogether peculiar in this. After all, in the world at large, it is only the accident, the remnant, that gets the chance to make the most of itself; but if this is true of the white world it is infinitely more true of the colored world. It is not simply the great clear tenor of Roland Hayes[2] that opened the ears of America. We have had many voices of all kinds as fine as his and America was and is as deaf as she was for years to him. Then a foreign land heard Hayes and put its imprint on him and immediately America with all its imitative snobbery woke up. We approved Hayes because London, Paris and Berlin approved him and not simply because he was a great singer.

Thus it is the bounden duty of black America to begin this great work of the creation of Beauty, of the preservation of Beauty, of the realization of Beauty, and we must use in this work all the methods that men have used before. And what have been the tools of the artist in times gone by? First of all, he has used the Truth—not for the sake of truth, not as a scientist seeking truth, but as one upon whom Truth eternally thrusts itself as the highest handmaid of imagination, as the one great vehicle of universal understanding. Again artists have used Goodness—goodness in all its aspects of justice, honor and right—not for sake of an ethical sanction but as the one true method of gaining sympathy and human interest.

The apostle of Beauty thus becomes the apostle of Truth and Right not by choice but by inner and outer compulsion. Free he is but his freedom is ever bounded by Truth and Justice; and slavery only dogs him when he is denied the right to tell the Truth or recognize an ideal of Justice.

Thus all Art is propaganda and ever must be, despite the wailing of the purists. I stand in utter shamelessness and say that whatever art I have for writing has been used always for propaganda for gaining the right of black folk to love and enjoy. I do not care a damn for any art that is not used for propaganda. But I do care when propaganda is confined to one side while the other is stripped and silent.

In New York we have two plays: "White Cargo" and "Congo."[3] In

---

1. Uncle Tom and Topsy are characters from Harriet Beecher Stowe's *Uncle Tom's Cabin* (1852).
2. Internationally acclaimed African American singer (1887–1976).

3. Or *Kongo* (1926) by Kilbourn Gordon and Chester DeVonde. *White Cargo: A Play of the Primitive* (1925) by Leon Gordon.

"White Cargo" there is a fallen woman. She is black. In "Congo" the fallen woman is white. In "White Cargo" the black woman goes down further and further and in "Congo" the white woman begins with degradation but in the end is one of the angels of the Lord.

You know the current magazine story: A young white man goes down to Central America and the most beautiful colored woman there falls in love with him. She crawls across the whole isthmus to get to him. The white man says nobly, "No". He goes back to his white sweetheart in New York.

In such cases, it is not the positive propaganda of people who believe white blood divine, infallible and holy to which I object. It is the denial of a similar right of propaganda to those who believe black blood human, lovable and inspired with new ideals for the world. White artists themselves suffer from this narrowing of their field. They cry for freedom in dealing with Negroes because they have so little freedom in dealing with whites. DuBose Heywood writes "Porgy"[4] and writes beautifully of the black Charleston underworld. But why does he do this? Because he cannot do a similar thing for the white people of Charleston, or they would drum him out of town. The only chance he had to tell the truth of pitiful human degradation was to tell it of colored people. I should not be surprised if Octavius Roy Cohen[5] had approached the *Saturday Evening Post* and asked permission to write about a different kind of colored folk than the monstrosities he has created; but if he has, the *Post* has replied, "No. You are getting paid to write about the kind of colored people you are writing about."

In other words, the white public today demands from its artists, literary and pictorial, racial pre-judgment which deliberately distorts Truth and Justice, as far as colored races are concerned, and it will pay for no other.

On the other hand, the young and slowly growing black public still wants its prophets almost equally unfree. We are bound by all sorts of customs that have come down as second-hand soul clothes of white patrons. We are ashamed of sex and we lower our eyes when people will talk of it. Our religion holds us in superstition. Our worst side has been so shamelessly emphasized that we are denying we have or ever had a worst side. In all sorts of ways we are hemmed in and our new young artists have got to fight their way to freedom.

The ultimate judge has got to be you and you have got to build yourselves up into that wide judgment, that catholicity[6] of temper which is going to enable the artist to have his widest chance for freedom. We can afford the Truth. White folk today cannot. As it is now we are handing everything over to a white jury. If a colored man wants to publish a book, he has got to get a white publisher and a white newspaper to say it is great; and then you and I say so. We must come to the place where the work of art when it appears is reviewed and acclaimed by our own free and unfettered judgment. And we are going to have a real and valuable and eternal judgment only as we make ourselves free of mind, proud of body and just of soul to all men.

---

4. A 1925 novel about southern African American life by Dubose Heyward (1885–1940).

5. Carolina humorist (1891–1959).
6. Broad sympathy.

And then do you know what will be said? It is already saying. Just as soon as true Art emerges; just as soon as the black artist appears, someone touches the race on the shoulder and says, "He did that because he was an American, not because he was a Negro; he was born here; he was trained here; he is not a Negro—what is a Negro anyhow? He is just human; it is the kind of thing you ought to expect".

I do not doubt that the ultimate art coming from black folk is going to be just as beautiful, and beautiful largely in the same ways, as the art that comes from white folk, or yellow, or red; but the point today is that until the art of the black folk compells recognition they will not be rated as human. And when through art they compell recognition then let the world discover if it will that their art is as new as it is old and as old as new.

I had a classmate once who did three beautiful things and died. One of them was a story of a folk who found fire and then went wandering in the gloom of night seeking again the stars they had once known and lost; suddenly out of blackness they looked up and there loomed the heavens; and what was it that they said? They raised a mighty cry: "It is the stars, it is the ancient stars, it is the young and everlasting stars!"

                                                                          1926

Two Novels

Nella Larsen "Quicksand" (Knopf)
Claude McKay[1] "Home to Harlem" (Harper and Brothers)

I have just read the last two novels of Negro America. The one I liked; the other I distinctly did not. I think that Mrs. Imes, writing under the pen name of Nella Larsen, has done a fine, thoughtful and courageous piece of work in her novel. It is, on the whole, the best piece of fiction that Negro America has produced since the heyday of Chesnutt, and stands easily with Jessie Fauset's "There is Confusion,"[2] in its subtle comprehension of the curious cross currents that swirl about the black American.

Claude McKay's "Home to Harlem", on the other hand, for the most part nauseates me, and after the dirtier parts of its filth I feel distinctly like taking a bath. This does not mean that the book is wholly bad. McKay is too great a poet to make any complete failure in writing. There are bits of "Home to Harlem" beautiful and fascinating: the continued changes upon the theme of the beauty of colored skins; the portrayal of the fascination of their new yearnings for each other which Negroes are developing. The chief character, Jake, has something appealing, and the glimpses of the Haitian, Ray, have all the materials of a great piece of fiction.

But it looks as though, despite this, McKay has set out to cater for that prurient demand on the part of white folk for a portrayal in Negroes of that utter licentiousness which conventional civilization holds white folk back from enjoying—if enjoyment it can be called. That which a certain decadent section of the white American world, centered particularly in New

---

1. Novelist and poet (1890–1948). Nella Larsen   2. A novel published in 1924.
(1891–1964), novelist.

York, longs for with fierce and unrestrained passions, it wants to see written out in black and white, and saddled on black Harlem. This demand, as voiced by a number of New York publishers, McKay has certainly satisfied, and added much for good measure. He has used every art and emphasis to paint drunkenness, fighting, lascivious sexual promiscuity and utter absence of restraint in as bold and as bright colors as he can.

If this had been done in the course of a well-conceived plot or with any artistic unity, it might have been understood if not excused. But "Home to Harlem" is padded. Whole chapters here and there are inserted with no connection to the main plot, except that they are on the same dirty subject. As a picture of Harlem life or of Negro life anywhere, it is, of course, nonsense. Untrue, not so much as on account of its facts, but on account of its emphasis and glaring colors. I am sorry that the author of "Harlem Shadows" stooped to this. I sincerely hope that he will some day rise above it and give us in fiction the strong, well-knit as well as beautiful theme, that it seems to me he might do.

Nella Larsen on the other hand has seized an interesting character and fitted her into a close yet delicately woven plot. There is no "happy ending" and yet the theme is not defeatist like the work of Peterkin and Green.[3] Helga Crane sinks at last still master of her whimsical, unsatisfied soul. In the end she will be beaten down even to death but she never will utterly surrender to hypocrisy and convention. Helga is typical of the new, honest, young fighting Negro woman—the one on whom "race" sits negligibly and Life is always first and its wandering path is but darkened, not obliterated by the shadow of the Veil. White folk will not like this book. It is not near nasty enough for New York columnists. It is too sincere for the South and middle West. Therefore, buy it and make Mrs. Imes write many more novels.

1928

3. Paul Green (1894–1981), white dramatist who often dealt with interracial subjects. Julia Peterkin (1880–1961), white novelist of southern African American life.

JAMES D. CORROTHERS
1869–1917

A productive and widely published author, James D. Corrothers labored for much of his career in the shadow of his more celebrated and prolific peer Paul Laurence Dunbar. As a result, although several of his poems regularly appear in major anthologies of black literature, most contemporary readers would be surprised to learn that late in life, Corrothers was sufficiently established that *Crisis* magazine could describe him and William Stanley Braithwaite as "the greatest of living Negro American poets."

Born in 1869 in Cass County, Michigan, Corrothers was raised primarily by his grandfather in South Haven, Michigan, a largely white community. A promising student who was forced to defend himself physically against the assaults of his white classmates, Corrothers faced tremendous economic hardships in his youth, and he soon found himself expending most of his energy not in the classroom but aboard ships and in lumber mills, factories, and hotels as he struggled to earn a living. He often spent nights, however, reading Longfellow, Tennyson, Heine, Burns, and particularly James Whitcomb Riley, whose verse in midwestern rural dialect made him perhaps the most popular poet in the late-nineteenth-century United States.

In the mid-1880s, Corrothers settled for a time in Springfield, Ohio, where he became involved in Republican politics and was first exposed to formally educated black peers whose aspirations and tastes matched his own. After moving to Chicago, where he took a job as a bootblack, he received the break that launched his literary career when the well-known writer Henry D. Lloyd befriended him and arranged for the publication of one of his poems in a local paper. Through Lloyd, Corrothers found work with the newspaper as a porter and soon was assigned to write an article on the black Chicago community. With the financial assistance of Lloyd, temperance leader Frances Willard, and a relative, Corrothers was also able to continue his formal education at a preparatory school operated by Northwestern University and at Bennett College in North Carolina.

In the wake of the 1893 Columbian Exhibition in Chicago, where he met celebrities such as Frederick Douglass and other young artists such as Paul Laurence Dunbar, Corrothers initially decided to pursue a career in journalism. Then, after producing a series of comic sketches (later collected and published as *The Black Cat Club*), he was inspired by Dunbar's remarkable literary success to turn to dialect verse. In 1899, *Century Magazine* published 'Way in de Woods, and the first phase of his career as a poet had begun. Like Dunbar, Corrothers used both black dialect and conventional English, with his choice of form often reflecting his response to the expectations and demands of white editors. Appearing generally in white publications, many of his dialect pieces from this period demonstrate his assimilation of plantation tradition styles more than the literary skills that he actually possessed. Other of his dialect work—*Me 'N' Dunbar*, for instance—manifests his ability to transcend the considerable limits of the form by steering it toward both political protest and genuinely touching folk tones and images. Corrothers's nondialect work can be similarly divided into his less inspired and less challenging pieces and those in which his desire to comment on the stifling racist oppression of the time spurred him to take more risks.

Even when they incorporate a critique of American racism, Corrothers's poems generally end on a note of faith, sometimes expressed in explicitly religious terms. Indeed, having entered the ministry in the mid-1890s, Corrothers found himself torn during this period between his literary work and that entailed by his assignment to churches in both the East and the Midwest. Corrothers's family life demanded increasing amounts of his time as well. For these and other reasons, he published little after his success in the early years of the century. Then, in 1912, *Century* accepted two of his nondialect poems; and from that point until his death, Corrothers produced some of his best known verse as well as a handful of prose sketches and his autobiography, *In Spite of the Handicap*. If his writing during these years does not consistently reflect a great advance over his previous publications, much of it does manifest his more sophisticated literary aspirations and his more forthright condemnation of white racism, particularly in his poetry in *Crisis* magazine. Hardly as gifted as his friend Dunbar and generally too willing to meet the demands of the popular magazines and newspapers to whom he sold his work, Corrothers, nevertheless, was a talented and ambitious writer who merits serious critical consideration.

The Snapping of the Bow

> "The toad beneath the harrow knows
> Exactly where each harrow-tooth goes;
> The butterfly upon the road,
> Preaches contentment to that toad."
> —KIPLING [1]

I dreamed a dream, and, in my dream, I heard
One wail at midnight by a convent's walls.
And, as he wailed, he clutched the stars, and shook
The pillars of the firmament of God,
And rolled the thunders of Olympus [2] down   5
On men; and they besought their holy ones
To plead with him—lest he might spoil the world.

        His face was bronze; his limbs were bronze but steel;
His mane was blacker than the Steeds of Night.
And his great eyes flashed warnings from beneath   10
A citadel where daring thoughts abode.—
A comely youth—why needed he to weep?

        Alas! upon his brow he wore the brand
Of degradation, and upon his neck
A circlet galling as a crime!—And from   15
The cursèd thing a chain of hate e'er bound
Him where he stood. His hands were manacled;
His limbs wore thongs that cut the flesh agape,
Until, from the pure pain, he writhed and wept,—
As weeps a conquered god—the prisoner of Despair!   20
He flung himself upon his knees, and burst into a prayer:
        "O God, and hast
Thou made me for these miseries? I feel
Myself a man—I have the spirit and
The hopes of one. O, why, then, must I strive   25
And fail?—No lake is clearer than my soul;
No ship is prouder; none more tempest tost.
'Tis true my brow is dark; but, in the night,
My spirit walks the stars, and lightly spurns
Its kinship to this world!—Lord, I have tried;   30
That burden of the failure rests with thee."
So fell he tranced.

        But, on the plain there rose
A phantom of the silent sphinx—the grim,
Spell-casting thought of some deep master dead.   35
And lo! beside its ancient, crumbling base,
Napoleon, [3] fresh from mighty deeds of war,
Halted his band, and spoke in tones of awe.—
All this I saw, and dreamed that yet—aye, yet!—

---

1. From *Pagett, M. P.* by Rudyard Kipling (1865–1936), British writer.
2. Home of the gods in Greek mythology.

3. Napoleon Bonaparte (1769–1821), French leader.

The race might rise that built the awful thing   40
That holds its secret still in Egypt's sands.

1901

Me 'n' Dunbar[1]

One day when me 'n' Dunbar wuz a-hoein' in de co'n,
Bofe uv us tired an' anxious foh to heah de dinnah—ho'n,—
Him in his fiel', and me in mine, a-wo'kin' on togeddah,
A-sweatin' lak de mischief in de hottes' kine o' weddah,
A debblish notion tuck me 't Paul wuz gittin' on too fas';   5
But, thanks I: "Wait untwel he git 'mongst all dem weeds an' grass,
'N' I'll make him ne'ly kill his se'f, an' den come out de las'."

Tuck off ma coat, rolled up ma slebes, spit on ma han's an' say:
"Ef God'll he'p me—'n' not he'p him—I beats ma man today!"
S'I: "Paul, come on, le's have a race!—I see you achin' foh it"—   10
S'e: "All right, Jeems, ma son; strack out—I sho' admire yo' spurrit."
S'I: "Son er father, I'm yo' match—jes' ketch me, ef you ken!"
S'I "You'd gib up now, ef you'd take advice f'om yo' bes' fr'en"—
An' den de way dem two hoes flew wuz scand'l'us—gen-'l'men!

De sun shone on us br'ilin' hot; but, now an' den de breeze   15
Blowed fresh, f'om 'cross de maddah lot, de fragrance ob de trees
In de ole orchard, jes' beyon'. De birds sung clear an' sweet;
De tree toad wuz a-callin' out his 'pinion ob de heat;
De fahm-house looked invitin', an', erbout a mile away,
De town gleamed white—across de road, de fahmers made dey hay:—   20
But me 'n' Paul was hustlin'; 'ca'se dat wuz ouh "busy day."

By'm-by, I got so tired dat I thought ma soul I'd die—
An' all de time a-watchin' Paul, out one side ob ma eye.—
I walks up to de fence, an, le'nt upon ma hoe a spell,
An' say: "Paul, how you mekin' out?" S'e: "Putty middlin' well."   25
"Dat so?" sez I, "you lookin' weak!" Sez he "Am dat a fack?—
Who wuz it lef' his hoein' fuss? You bettah go on back,—
An' go to wo'k, 'r I'll be so fur dat you cain't fine ma track!"

'N' back I went, an' slashed about, an' to'e up mo' good co'n—
An' missed mo' weeds den airy othah mo'tal evah bo'n.   30
An' all de time a-thinkin' thoughts, untwel I come to see
Dat, dat ah' kine o' foolishness wa'n't he'pin' him ner me.
S'I: "Hole on, Paul, le's stop awhile, an' talk an' git ouh breff—
'Ca'se bofe uv us has got to hoe his own patch foh his se'f."
Sez he: "Dat's right; hey ain't no use to wo'k ouhse'fs to deff."   35

1901

---

1. Paul Laurence Dunbar, American writer (1872–1906).

Paul Laurence Dunbar

He came, a dark youth, singing in the dawn
    Of a new freedom, glowing o'er his lyre,
    Refining, as with great Apollo's[1] fire,
    His people's gift of song. And, thereupon,
This Negro singer, come to Helicon,[2]   5
    Constrained the masters, listening, to admire,
    And roused a race to wonder and aspire,
    Gazing which way their honest voice was gone,
With ebon face uplit of glory's crest.
    Men marveled at the singer, strong and sweet,   10
    Who brought the cabin's mirth, the tuneful night,
But faced the morning, beautiful with light,
    To die while shadows yet fell toward the west,
    And leave his laurels at his people's feet.

Dunbar, no poet wears your laurels now;   15
    None rises, singing, from your race like you.
    Dark melodist, immortal, though the dew
Fell early on the bays[3] upon your brow,
    And tinged with pathos every halcyon vow
    And brave endeavor. Silence o'er you threw   20
Flowerets of love. Or, if an envious few
    Of your own people brought no garlands, how
Could Malice smite him whom the gods had crowned?
    If, like the meadow-lark, your flight was low,
    Your flooded lyrics half the hilltops drowned;   25
A wide world heard you, and it loved you so
    It stilled its heart to list the strains you sang,
    And o'er your happy songs its plaudits rang.

                        1912

At the Closed Gate of Justice

To be a Negro in a day like this
    Demands forgiveness. Bruised with blow on blow,
Betrayed, like him whose woe-dimmed eyes gave bliss,
    Still must one succor those who brought one low,
To be a Negro in a day like this.   5

To be a Negro in a day like this
    Demands rare patience—patience that can wait
In utter darkness. 'Tis the path to miss,
    And knock, unheeded, at an iron gate,
To be a Negro in a day like this.   10

To be a Negro in a day like this
    Demands strange loyalty. We serve a flag

---

1. God of prophecy in Greek and Roman mythology.
2. Home of the Muses in Greek mythology.
3. I.e., bay leaves that were made into a wreath or crown, indicative of high praise and honor.

Which is to us white freedom's emphasis.
   Ah! one must love when truth and justice lag,
To be a Negro in a day like this.   15

To be a Negro in a day like this—
   Alas! Lord God, what evil have we done?
Still shines the gate, all gold and amethyst,
   But I pass by, the glorious goal unwon,
"Merely a Negro"—in a day like *this!*   20

                                   1913

An Indignation Dinner

Dey was hard times jes 'fo' Christmas round our neighborhood one
   year;
So we held a secret meetin', whah de white folks couldn't hear,
To 'scuss de situation, an' to see whut could be done
Towa'd a fust-class Christmas dinneh an' a little Christmas fun.

Rufus Green, who called de meetin', ris' an' said: "In dis here town,   5
An' throughout de land, de white folks is a-tryin' to keep us down."
S' 'e: "Dey's bought us, sold us, beat us; now dey 'buse us 'ca'se we's
   free;
But when dey tetch my *stomach,* dey's done gone too fur foh *me!*

"Is I right?" "You sho is, Rufus!" roared a dozen hungry throats.
"Ef you'd keep a mule a-wo'kin', don't you tamper wid his oats.   10
Dat's sense," continued Rufus. "But dese white folks nowadays
Has done got so close an' stingy you can't live on whut dey pays.

"Here 't is Christmas-time, an', folkses, I's indignant 'nough to
   choke.
Whah's our Christmas dinneh comin' when we's 'mos' completely
   broke?
I can't hahdly 'fo'd a toothpick an' a glass o' water. Mad?   15
Say, I'm desp'ut! Dey jes better treat me nice, dese white folks had!"

Well, dey 'bused de white folks scan'lous, till old Pappy Simmons
   ris',
Leanin' on his cane to spote him, on account his rheumatis',
An' s' 'e: "Chilun, whut's dat wintry wind a-sighin' th'ough de street
'Bout yo' wasted summeh wages? But, no matteh, we mus' *eat.*   20

"Now, I seed a beau'ful tuhkey on a certain gemmun's fahm.
He 's a-growin' fat an' sassy, an' a-struttin' to a chahm.
Chickens, sheeps, hogs, sweet pertaters— all de craps is fine dis year;
All we needs is a *committee* foh to tote de goodies here."

Well, we lit right in an' voted dat it was a gran' idee,   25
An' de dinneh we had Christmas was worth trabblin' miles to see;
An' we eat a full an' plenty, big an' little, great an' small,
Not beca'se we was dishonest, but *indignant,* sah. Dat's all.

                                   1915

JAMES WELDON JOHNSON
1871–1938

In his autobiography, *Along This Way* (1933), written soon after his appointment to the Adam K. Spence Chair of Creative Literature at Fisk University in Nashville, Tennessee, James Weldon Johnson recalled his first foray into teaching forty years earlier. In the summer of 1891 the Atlanta University freshman had gone to a rural district in Georgia to instruct the children of former slaves. "In all of my experience there has been no period so brief that has meant so much in my education for life as the three months I spent in the backwoods of Georgia," Johnson wrote. "I was thrown for the first time on my own resources and abilities. I had my first lesson in dealing with men and conditions in the outside world. . . . It was this period that marked the beginning of my psychological change from boyhood to manhood. It was this period which marked also the beginning of my knowledge of my own people as a 'race.'"

Despite having grown up in much different circumstances—a middle-class black family in the city of Jacksonville, Florida—Johnson learned in Georgia that black countryfolk were not "something apart." "They were me, and I was they . . . a force stronger than blood made us one." Thus Johnson "laid the first stones in the foundation of faith in [the black folk] on which I have stood ever since. . . . I discerned that the forces behind the slow but persistent movement forward of the race lie, ultimately, in them; that when the vanguard of that movement must fall back, it must fall back on them." Had he not recognized early on the importance of this identification with and reliance on the folk of black America, it is unlikely that James Weldon Johnson could have ever exemplified, as he eventually did with such unerring aplomb, the African American vanguard in letters and in social activism during the first third of the twentieth century.

Johnson's parents, James and Helen Louise (Dillet) Johnson, educated their first-born son for success in the white world. His mother, a schoolteacher, imparted to him her considerable love and knowledge of English literature and the European tradition in music. The achievement of his father, headwaiter at the St. James Hotel, a luxury establishment built when Jacksonville was one of Florida's first winter havens, gave young Jimmie the wherewithal and the self-confidence to pursue a professional career. Molded by the classical education for which Atlanta University was best known, Johnson regarded his academic training as a trust given him in the expectation that he would dedicate his resources to black people. Immediately after college Johnson responded to this sense of obligation by becoming principal of Stanton School in his hometown. There in February 1900, he wrote *Lift Ev'ry Voice and Sing* for a school commemoration of Lincoln's birthday. Set to music by his brother, Rosamond, the song resonated throughout black America, achieving within Johnson's lifetime the unofficial title of the "Negro National Anthem." In his poetic career, Johnson proved adept at many styles and forms of poetry, from the unaffected dialect of *Sence You Went Away* (1900) to the urbane sonnet *My City* (1923). But his best poems—the graphic, pulsating free-verse sermons collected in *God's Trombones* (1927)—drew on the spiritual aspirations and folk imagination of black people such as Johnson met in the rural South.

In 1901 Johnson left Jacksonville for New York to collaborate with his brother and a black performer named Bob Cole on the writing of popular songs and librettos. Enjoying unusual success as a songwriter for Broadway shows, Johnson moved easily in the upper echelons of African American society in Brooklyn, New York, where he met his future wife, Grace Nail. In 1906, at the urging of some friends in politics, Johnson decided to abandon songwriting for the diplomatic corps, serving first as U.S. consul at Puerto Cabello, Venezuela, and later (in 1909) as head of the U.S. consulate at Corinto, Nicaragua. During those years Johnson published poems in such national periodicals as the *Century Magazine* and the *Independent* and finished a novel, *The Autobiography of an Ex-Colored Man*, which was published in 1912, anonymously at his request. What little attention *The Autobiography of an Ex-Colored Man* received was generally positive, but sales of the novel were not encouraging.

In the fall of 1913 Johnson resigned from the foreign service. A year later he took over the editorial page of the *New York Age*, an influential African American weekly that had supported Booker T. Washington in his struggle with W. E. B. Du Bois for leadership of black America in the early twentieth century. Johnson's writing for the *Age* displayed the political gift that soon propeled him into national prominence. No ideologue himself, he excelled as a reconciler of differences among those whose ideological agendas seemed to preclude unified, cooperative action. For this reason Johnson was asked in the fall of 1916 to become the national organizer for the National Association for the Advancement of Colored People (NAACP). Opposing race riots in northern cities and the lynchings that pervaded the South during and immediately after the end of World War I, Johnson engaged the NAACP in mass tactics, such as a silent protest parade down New York's Fifth Avenue in which ten thousand African Americans took part on July 28, 1917. In 1920 Johnson was elected to head the NAACP, the first African American to hold this position.

In December 1930, Johnson resigned from the leadership of the NAACP to accept the Spence Chair of Creative Literature at Fisk University, which he held until his death in an automobile accident in 1938. The position had been especially created for him, largely out of recognition of his achievements as a poet, editor, and critic during the heyday of the Harlem Renaissance in the 1920s. As editor of *The Book of American Negro Poetry* (1922, rev. 1931), itself a landmark in the history of African American literature, Johnson stated unequivocally that black people had created "the only things artistic that have yet sprung from American soil and been universally acknowledged as distinctive American products." In characterizing the artistic achievements of African Americans, Johnson paid tribute first to the genius of the folk, to whom he attributed the beast fables associated with Uncle Remus, the spirituals and other slave songs, ragtime music, and the cakewalk. If African American poets, Johnson went on, and by implication almost any other kind of African American artist, aligned themselves with the folk, their work would "express the racial spirit by symbols from within rather than by symbols from without."

In 1927 Johnson demonstrated his theory in his own much-acclaimed *God's Trombones*. That same year, Johnson's novel, republished with the spelling of its title slightly altered to read *The Autobiography of an Ex-Colored Man* and with its authorship plainly acknowledged, gave dramatic form to its creator's theory of the roots of African American creativity in the story of an artist who rejected his gifts and his people in exchange for a masked identity in the white world. Johnson's novel of passing, though its subject was in some ways inimical to the more outspoken celebrants of blackness among the New Negroes of the 1920s, spoke tellingly, nevertheless, to the cultural concerns of the Harlem Renaissance. The protagonist of the *Autobiography* registers profoundly, if also pathetically and even tragically, the problematic exploration of racial identity and the conflicted relationship of "the Negro" to "the American" in the twentieth-century African American's struggle for self-definition in the United States.

In *Along This Way* Johnson states that he was pleased when most of the reviewers of the 1912 edition of the *Autobiography* "accepted it as a human document," as a genuine autobiography, not a consciously crafted piece of fiction. "This was a tribute to the writing," Johnson concluded, "for I had done the book with the intention of its being so taken" as a real account of a real man's interior odyssey toward an uneasy solution of his identity problems. The fact that so much has been argued and so little resolved about what motivates the Ex-Colored Man and what Johnson intended him to signify only confirms the *Autobiography*'s inexhaustible appeal as a narrative that movingly evokes the crises of modernity for the early twentieth-century African American man.

Sence You Went Away

Seems lak to me de stars don't shine so bright,
Seems lak to me de sun done loss his light,
Seems lak to me der's nothin' goin' right,
    Sence you went away.

Seems lak to me de sky ain't half so blue,   5
Seems lak to me dat eve'ything wants you,
Seems lak to me I don't know what to do,
    Sence you went away.

Seems lak to me dat eve'ything is wrong,
Seems lak to me de day's jes twice ez long,   10
Seems lak to me de bird's forgot his song,
    Sence you went away.

Seems lak to me I jes can't he'p but sigh,
Seems lak to me ma th'oat keeps gittin' dry,
Seems lak to me a tear stays in ma eye,   15
    Sence you went away.

                                                       1900

Lift Ev'ry Voice and Sing

Lift ev'ry voice and sing,
Till earth and heaven ring,
Ring with the harmonies of Liberty;
Let our rejoicing rise
High as the list'ning skies,   5
Let it resound loud as the rolling sea.
Sing a song full of the faith that the dark past has taught us,
Sing a song full of the hope that the present has brought us;
Facing the rising sun of our new day begun,
Let us march on till victory is won.   10

Stony the road we trod,
Bitter the chast'ning rod,

Felt in the days when hope unborn had died;
Yet with a steady beat,
Have not our weary feet   15
Come to the place for which our fathers sighed?
We have come over a way that with tears has been watered,
We have come, treading our path through the blood of the
        slaughtered,
Out from the gloomy past,
Till now we stand at last   20
Where the white gleam of our bright star is cast.

God of our weary years,
God of our silent tears,
Thou who hast brought us thus far on the way;
Thou who hast by Thy might,   25
Led us into the light,
Keep us forever in the path, we pray.
Lest our feet stray from the places, our God, where we met Thee,
Lest our hearts, drunk with the wine of the world, we forget Thee;
Shadowed beneath Thy hand,   30
May we forever stand,
True to our God,
True to our native land.

1900   1921

O Black and Unknown Bards

O Black and unknown bards of long ago,
How came your lips to touch the sacred fire?
How, in your darkness, did you come to know
The power and beauty of the minstrel's lyre?
Who first from midst his bonds lifted his eyes?   5
Who first from out the still watch, lone and long,
Feeling the ancient faith of prophets rise
Within his dark-kept soul, burst into song?

Heart of what slave poured out such melody
As "Steal away to Jesus"?[1] On its strains   10
His spirit must have nightly floated free,
Though still about his hands he felt his chains.
Who heard great "Jordan roll"?[2] Whose starward eye
Saw chariot "swing low"?[3] And who was he
That breathed that comforting, melodic sigh,   15
"Nobody knows de trouble I see"?[4]

What merely living clod, what captive thing,
Could up toward God through all its darkness grope,
And find within its deadened heart to sing
These songs of sorrow, love, and faith, and hope?   20

1. A Negro spiritual.
2. "Roll, Jordan, Roll," a Negro spiritual. The Jordan River is in Palestine.
3. "Swing Low, Sweet Chariot," a Negro spiritual.
4. A Negro spiritual.

How did it catch that subtle undertone,
That note in music heard not with the ears?
How sound the elusive reed, so seldom blown,
Which stirs the soul or melts the heart to tears?

Not that great German master[5] in his dream   25
Of harmonies that thundered 'mongst the stars
At the creation, ever heard a theme
Nobler than "Go down, Moses."[6] Mark its bars,
How like a mighty trumpet-call they stir
The blood. Such are the notes that men have sung,   30
Going to valorous deeds; such tones there were
That helped make history when Time was young.

There is a wide, wide wonder in it all,
That from degraded rest and service toil
The fiery spirit of the seer should call   35
These simple children of the sun and soil.
O black slave singers, gone, forgot, unfamed,
You—you alone, of all the long, long line
Of those who've sung untaught, unknown, unnamed,
Have stretched out upward, seeking the divine.   40

You sang not deeds of heroes or of kings;
No chant of bloody war, no exulting pæan[7]
Of arms-won triumphs; but your humble strings
You touched in chord with music empyrean.[8]
You sang far better than you knew; the songs   45
That for your listeners' hungry hearts sufficed
Still live,—but more than this to you belongs:
You sang a race from wood and stone to Christ.

                                        1908

Fifty Years

Today Is the Fiftieth Anniversary of Lincoln's Emancipation Proclamation

O brothers mine, to-day we stand
   Where half a century sweeps our ken,
Since God, through Lincoln's ready hand,
   Struck off our bonds and made us men.

Just fifty years—a Winter's day—   5
   As runs the history of a race;
Yet, as we look back o'er the way,
   How distant seems our starting-place!

Look farther back! Three centuries!
   To where a naked, shivering score,   10

5. Gottfried Wilhelm Leibniz (1646–1716), phi-   7. A song of triumph.
losopher.   8. The highest heaven.
6. A Negro spiritual.

Snatched from their haunts across the seas,
   Stood, wild-eyed, on Virginia's shore.

Far, far the way that we have trod,
   From heathen kraals[1] and jungle dens,
To freedmen, freemen, sons of God,   15
   Americans and Citizens.

A part of His unknown design,
   We've lived within a mighty age;
And we have helped to write a line
   On history's most wondrous page.   20

A few black bondmen strewn along
   The borders of our eastern coast.
Now grown a race, ten million strong,
   An upward, onward, marching host.

Then let us here erect a stone,   25
   To mark the place, to mark the time;
A witness to God's mercies shown,
   A pledge to hold this day sublime.

And let that stone an altar be
   Whereon thanksgivings we may lay—   30
Where we, in deep humility,
   For faith and strength renewed may pray,

With open hearts ask from above
   New zeal, new courage and new pow'rs,
That we may grow more worthy of   35
   This country and this land of ours.

For never let the thought arise
   That we are here on sufferance[2] bare;
Outcasts, asylumed 'neath these skies,
   And aliens without part or share.   40

This land is ours by right of birth,
   This land is ours by right of toil;
We helped to turn its virgin earth,
   Our sweat is in its fruitful soil.

Where once the tangled forest stood,   45
   Where flourished once rank weed and thorn,
Behold the path-traced, peaceful wood,
   The cotton white, the yellow corn.

To gain these fruits that have been earned,
   To hold these fields that have been won,   50

---

1. Villages in South Africa.   2. Permission.

Our arms have strained, our backs have burned,
  Bent bare beneath a ruthless sun.

That Banner, which is now the type
  Of victory on field and flood—
Remember, its first crimson stripe   55
  Was dyed by Attucks'[3] willing blood.

And never yet has come the cry—
  When that fair flag has been assailed—
For men to do, for men to die,
  That have we faltered or have failed.   60

We've helped to bear it, rent and torn,
  Through many a hot-breath'd battle breeze;
Held in our hands, it has been borne
  And planted far across the seas.

And, never yet, O haughty Land—   65
  Let us, at least, for this be praised—
Has one black, treason-guided hand
  Ever against that flag been raised.

Then should we speak but servile words,
  Or shall we hang our heads in shame?   70
Stand back of new-come foreign hordes,
  And fear our heritage to claim?

No! Stand erect and without fear,
  And for our foes let this suffice—
We've bought a rightful sonship here,   75
  And we have more than paid the price.

And yet, my brothers, well I know
  The tethered feet, the pinioned[4] wings,
The spirit bowed beneath the blow,
  The heart grown faint from wounds and stings;   80

The staggering force of brutish might,
  That strikes and leaves us stunned and dazed;
The long, vain waiting through the night
  To hear some voice for justice raised.

Full well I know the hour when hope   85
  Sinks dead, and 'round us everywhere
Hangs stifling darkness, and we grope
  With hands uplifted in despair.

Courage! Look out, beyond, and see
  The far horizon's beckoning span!   90

---

3. Crispus Attucks (1723?–1770), believed to have   Revolution.
been an escaped slave, was the first man to die in   4. Bound to prevent flying.
the Boston Massacre, a prelude to the American

Faith in your God-known destiny!
    We are a part of some great plan.

Because the tongues of Garrison
    And Phillips[5] now are cold in death,
Think you their work can be undone?   95
    Or quenched the fires lit by their breath?

Think you that John Brown's spirit stops?
    That Lovejoy[6] was but idly slain?
Or do you think those precious drops
    From Lincoln's heart were shed in vain?   100

That for which millions prayed and sighed,
    That for which tens of thousands fought,
For which so many freely died,
    God cannot let it come to naught.

                                    1913

Brothers

See! There he stands; not brave, but with an air
Of sullen stupor. Mark him well! Is he
Not more like brute than man? Look in his eye!
No light is there, none, save the light that shines
In the now glaring, and now shifting orbs   5
Of some wild animal in the hunter's trap.

    How came this beast in human shape and form?
Speak man!—We call you man because you wear
His shape—How are you thus? Are you not from
That docile, child-like, tender-hearted race   10
Which we have known three centuries? Not from
That more than faithful race which through three wars
Fed our dear wives and nursed our helpless babes
Without a single breach of trust? Speak out?

    I am, and am not.   15

    Then who, why are you?

    I am a thing not new, I am as old
As human nature. I am that which lurks,
Ready to spring whenever a bar is loosed;
The ancient trait which fights incessantly   20
Against restraint, balks at the upward climb;
The weight forever seeking to obey

---

5. Wendell Philips (1811–1884), antislavery orator. William Lloyd Garrison (1805–1879), crusading antislavery editor and orator.
6. Elijah P. Lovejoy (1802–1837), antislavery editor, killed by a proslavery mob in Alton, Illinois. John Brown (1800–1859) led an antislavery insurrection against the U.S. arsenal at Harpers Ferry, Virginia, resulting in his execution.

The law of downward pull,—and I am more:
The bitter fruit am I of planted seed,
The resultant, the inevitable end   25
Of evil forces and the powers of wrong.

   Lessons in degradation, taught and learned,
The memories of cruel sights and deeds,
The pent up bitterness, the unspent hate
Filtered through fifteen generations have   30
Sprung up and found in me sporadic life.
In me the muttered curse of dying men,
On me the stain of conquered women, and
Consuming me the fearful fires of lust,
Lit long ago by other hands than mine.   35
In me the down-crushed spirit, the hurled-back prayers
Of wretches now long dead,—their dire bequests,—
In me the echo of the stifled cry
Of children for their bartered mothers' breasts.
   I claim no race, no race claims me; I am   40
No more than human dregs; degenerate;
The monstrous offspring of the monster, Sin;
I am—just what I am—The race that fed
Your wives and nursed your babes would do the same
To-day, but I—   45

   Enough, the brute must die!
Quick! Chain him to that oak! It will resist
The fire much longer than this slender pine.
Now bring the fuel! Pile it 'round him! Wait!
Pile not so fast or high! or we shall lose   50
The agony and terror in his face.

And now the torch! Good fuel that! the flames
Already leap head-high. Ha! hear that shriek!
And there's another wilder than the first.
Fetch water! Water! Pour a little on   55
The fire, lest it should burn too fast. Hold so!
Now let it slowly blaze again. See there!
He squirms, he groans, his eyes bulge wildly out,
Searching around in vain appeal for help.
Another shriek, the last! Watch how the flesh   60
Grows crisp and hangs till, turned to ash, it sifts
Down through the coils of chain that hold erect
The ghastly frame against the bark-scorched tree.

   Stop! to each man no more than one man's share
You take that bone, and you this tooth; the chain   65
Let us divide its links; this skull, of course,
In fair division, to the leader comes.

   And now his fiendish crime has been avenged;
Let us back to our wives and children.—Say,

What did he mean by those last muttered words,   70
"Brothers in spirit, brothers in deed are we"?

                                                                  1916

The Creation

And God stepped out on space,
And he looked around and said:
I'm lonely—
I'll make me a world.

And far as the eye of God could see   5
Darkness covered everything,
Blacker than a hundred midnights
Down in a cypress swamp.

Then God smiled,
And the light broke,
And the darkness rolled up on one side,   10
And the light stood shining on the other,
And God said: That's good!

Then God reached out and took the light in his hands,
And God rolled the light around in his hands
Until he made the sun;   15
And he set that sun a-blazing in the heavens.
And the light that was left from making the sun
God gathered it up in a shining ball
And flung it against the darkness,   20
Spangling the night with the moon and stars.
Then down between
The darkness and the light
He hurled the world;
And God said: That's good!   25

Then God himself stepped down—
And the sun was on his right hand,
And the moon was on his left;
The stars were clustered about his head,
And the earth was under his feet.   30
And God walked, and where he trod
His footsteps hollowed the valleys out
And bulged the mountains up.

Then he stopped and looked and saw
That the earth was hot and barren.   35
So God stepped over to the edge of the world
And he spat out the seven seas—
He batted his eyes, and the lightnings flashed—
He clapped his hands, and the thunders rolled—

And the waters above the earth came down,
The cooling waters came down.

Then the green grass sprouted,
And the little red flowers blossomed,
The pine tree pointed his finger to the sky,
And the oak spread out his arms,   45
The lakes cuddled down in the hollows of the ground,
And the rivers ran down to the sea;
And God smiled again,
And the rainbow appeared,
And curled itself around his shoulder.   50

Then God raised his arm and he waved his hand
Over the sea and over the land,
And he said: Bring forth! Bring forth!
And quicker than God could drop his hand,
Fishes and fowls   55
And beasts and birds
Swam the rivers and the seas,
Roamed the forests and the woods,
And split the air with their wings.
And God said: That's good!   60

Then God walked around,
And God looked around
On all that he had made.
He looked at his sun,
And he looked at his moon,   65
And he looked at his little stars;
He looked on his world
With all its living things,
And God said: I'm lonely still.

Then God sat down—   70
On the side of a hill where he could think;
By a deep, wide river he sat down;
With his head in his hands,
God thought and thought,
Till he thought: I'll make me a man!   75

Up from the bed of the river
God scooped the clay;
And by the bank of the river
He kneeled him down;
And there the great God Almighty   80
Who lit the sun and fixed it in the sky,
Who flung the stars to the most far corner of the night,
Who rounded the earth in the middle of his hand;
This Great God,
Like a mammy bending over her baby,   85
Kneeled down in the dust

Toiling over a lump of clay
Till he shaped it in his own image;

Then into it he blew the breath of life,
And man became a living soul.   90
Amen.   Amen.

                                                        1920

My City

When I come down to sleep death's endless night,
     The threshold of the unknown dark to cross,
     What to me then will be the keenest loss,
When this bright world blurs on my fading sight?
Will it be that no more I shall see the trees   5
     Or smell the flowers or hear the singing birds
     Or watch the flashing streams or patient herds?
No, I am sure it will be none of these.
But, ah! Manhattan's sights and sounds, her smells,
     Her crowds, her throbbing force, the thrill that comes   10
From being of her a part, her subtile spells,
     Her shining towers, her avenues, her slums—
     O God! the stark, unutterable pity,
To be dead, and never again behold my city!

                                                        1923

The Autobiography of an Ex-Colored Man

Preface to the Original Edition of 1912

This vivid and startlingly new picture of conditions brought about by the
race question in the United States makes no special plea for the Negro, but
shows in a dispassionate, though sympathetic, manner conditions as they
actually exist between the whites and blacks to-day. Special pleas have already been made for and against the Negro in hundreds of books, but in
these books either his virtues or his vices have been exaggerated. This is
because writers, in nearly every instance, have treated the colored American as a *whole*; each has taken some one group of the race to prove his case.
Not before has a composite and proportionate presentation of the entire
race, embracing all of its various groups and elements, showing their relations with each other and to the whites, been made.

It is very likely that the Negroes of the United States have a fairly correct
idea of what the white people of the country think of them, for that opinion
has for a long time been and is still being constantly stated; but they are
themselves more or less a sphinx to the whites. It is curiously interesting
and even vitally important to know what are the thoughts of ten millions of

them concerning the people among whom they live. In these pages it is as though a veil had been drawn aside: the reader is given a view of the inner life of the Negro in America, is initiated into the "freemasonry," as it were, of the race.

These pages also reveal the unsuspected fact that prejudice against the Negro is exerting a pressure which, in New York and other large cities where the opportunity is open, is actually and constantly forcing an unascertainable number of fair-complexioned colored people over into the white race.

In this book the reader is given a glimpse behind the scenes of this race-drama which is being here enacted,—he is taken upon an elevation where he can catch a bird's-eye view of the conflict which is being waged.

THE PUBLISHERS
[Sherman, French & Company]

I

I know that in writing the following pages I am divulging the great secret of my life, the secret which for some years I have guarded far more carefully than any of my earthly possessions; and it is a curious study to me to analyze the motives which prompt me to do it. I feel that I am led by the same impulse which forces the un-found-out criminal to take somebody into his confidence, although he knows that the act is likely, even almost certain, to lead to his undoing. I know that I am playing with fire, and I feel the thrill which accompanies that most fascinating pastime; and, back of it all, I think I find a sort of savage and diabolical desire to gather up all the little tragedies of my life, and turn them into a practical joke on society.

And, too, I suffer a vague feeling of unsatisfaction, of regret, of almost remorse, from which I am seeking relief, and of which I shall speak in the last paragraph of this account.

I was born in a little town of Georgia a few years after the close of the Civil War. I shall not mention the name of the town, because there are people still living there who could be connected with this narrative. I have only a faint recollection of the place of my birth. At times I can close my eyes and call up in a dreamlike way things that seem to have happened ages ago in some other world. I can see in this half vision a little house—I am quite sure it was not a large one—I can remember that flowers grew in the front yard, and that around each bed of flowers was a hedge of vari-colored glass bottles stuck in the ground neck down. I remember that once, while playing around in the sand, I became curious to know whether or not the bottles grew as the flowers did, and I proceeded to dig them up to find out; the investigation brought me a terrific spanking, which indelibly fixed the incident in my mind. I can remember, too, that behind the house was a shed under which stood two or three wooden wash-tubs. These tubs were the earliest aversion of my life, for regularly on certain evenings I was plunged into one of them and scrubbed until my skin ached. I can remember to this day the pain caused by the strong, rank soap's getting into my eyes.

Back from the house a vegetable garden ran, perhaps seventy-five or one hundred feet; but to my childish fancy it was an endless territory. I can still recall the thrill of joy, excitement, and wonder it gave me to go on an exploring expedition through it, to find the blackberries, both ripe and green, that grew along the edge of the fence.

I remember with what pleasure I used to arrive at, and stand before, a little enclosure in which stood a patient cow chewing her cud, how I would occasionally offer her through the bars a piece of my bread and molasses, and how I would jerk back my hand in half fright if she made any motion to accept my offer.

I have a dim recollection of several people who moved in and about this little house, but I have a distinct mental image of only two: one, my mother; and the other, a tall man with a small, dark mustache. I remember that his shoes or boots were always shiny, and that he wore a gold chain and a great gold watch with which he was always willing to let me play. My admiration was almost equally divided between the watch and chain and the shoes. He used to come to the house evenings, perhaps two or three times a week; and it became my appointed duty whenever he came to bring him a pair of slippers and to put the shiny shoes in a particular corner; he often gave me in return for this service a bright coin, which my mother taught me to promptly drop in a little tin bank. I remember distinctly the last time this tall man came to the little house in Georgia; that evening before I went to bed he took me up in his arms and squeezed me very tightly; my mother stood behind his chair wiping tears from her eyes. I remember how I sat upon his knee and watched him laboriously drill a hole through a ten-dollar gold piece, and then tie the coin around my neck with a string. I have worn that gold piece around my neck the greater part of my life, and still possess it, but more than once I have wished that some other way had been found of attaching it to me besides putting a hole through it.

On the day after the coin was put around my neck my mother and I started on what seemed to me an endless journey. I knelt on the seat and watched through the train window the corn and cotton fields pass swiftly by until I fell asleep. When I fully awoke, we were being driven through the streets of a large city—Savannah. I sat up and blinked at the bright lights. At Savannah we boarded a steamer which finally landed us in New York. From New York we went to a town in Connecticut, which became the home of my boyhood.

My mother and I lived together in a little cottage which seemed to me to be fitted up almost luxuriously; there were horse-hair-covered chairs in the parlor, and a little square piano; there was a stairway with red carpet on it leading to a half second story; there were pictures on the walls, and a few books in a glass-doored case. My mother dressed me very neatly, and I developed that pride which well-dressed boys generally have. She was careful about my associates, and I myself was quite particular. As I look back now I can see that I was a perfect little aristocrat. My mother rarely went to anyone's house, but she did sewing, and there were a great many ladies coming to our cottage. If I was around they would generally call me, and ask me my name and age and tell my mother what a pretty boy I was. Some of them would pat me on the head and kiss me.

My mother was kept very busy with her sewing; sometimes she would have another woman helping her. I think she must have derived a fair income from her work. I know, too, that at least once each month she received a letter; I used to watch for the postman, get the letter, and run to her with it; whether she was busy or not, she would take it and instantly thrust it into her bosom. I never saw her read one of these letters. I knew later that they contained money and what was to her more than money. As busy as she generally was, she found time, however, to teach me my letters and figures and how to spell a number of easy words. Always on Sunday evenings she opened the little square piano and picked out hymns. I can recall now that whenever she played hymns from the book her *tempo* was always decidedly *largo*.[1] Sometimes on other evenings, when she was not sewing, she would play simple accompaniments to some old Southern songs which she sang. In these songs she was freer, because she played them by ear. Those evenings on which she opened the little piano were the happiest hours of my childhood. Whenever she started toward the instrument, I used to follow her with all the interest and irrepressible joy that a pampered pet dog shows when a package is opened in which he knows there is a sweet bit for him. I used to stand by her side and often interrupt and annoy her by chiming in with strange harmonies which I found on either the high keys of the treble or the low keys of the bass. I remember that I had a particular fondness for the black keys. Always on such evenings, when the music was over, my mother would sit with me in her arms, often for a very long time. She would hold me close, softly crooning some old melody without words, all the while gently stroking her face against my head; many and many a night I thus fell asleep. I can see her now, her great dark eyes looking into the fire, to where? No one knew but her. The memory of that picture has more than once kept me from straying too far from the place of purity and safety in which her arms held me.

At a very early age I began to thump on the piano alone, and it was not long before I was able to pick out a few tunes. When I was seven years old, I could play by ear all of the hymns and songs that my mother knew. I had also learned the names of the notes in both clefs, but I preferred not to be hampered by notes. About this time several ladies for whom my mother sewed heard me play and they persuaded her that I should at once be put under a teacher; so arrangements were made for me to study the piano with a lady who was a fairly good musician; at the same time arrangements were made for me to study my books with this lady's daughter. My music teacher had no small difficulty at first in pinning me down to the notes. If she played my lesson over for me, I invariably attempted to reproduce the required sounds without the slightest recourse to the written characters. Her daughter, my other teacher, also had her worries. She found that, in reading, whenever I came to words that were difficult or unfamiliar, I was prone to bring my imagination to the rescue and read from the picture. She has laughingly told me, since then, that I would sometimes substitute whole sentences and even paragraphs from what meaning I thought the illustrations conveyed. She said she not only was sometimes amused at the fresh

---

1. With a slow and dignified treatment (Italian).

treatment I would give an author's subject, but, when I gave some new and sudden turn to the plot of the story, often grew interested and even excited in listening to hear what kind of a denouement I would bring about. But I am sure this was not due to dullness, for I made rapid progress in both my music and my books.

And so for a couple of years my life was divided between my music and my school books. Music took up the greater part of my time. I had no playmates, but amused myself with games—some of them my own invention—which could be played alone. I knew a few boys whom I had met at the church which I attended with my mother, but I had formed no close friendships with any of them. Then, when I was nine years old, my mother decided to enter me in the public school, so all at once I found myself thrown among a crowd of boys of all sizes and kinds; some of them seemed to me like savages. I shall never forget the bewilderment, the pain, the heart-sickness, of that first day at school. I seemed to be the only stranger in the place; every other boy seemed to know every other boy. I was fortunate enough, however, to be assigned to a teacher who knew me; my mother made her dresses. She was one of the ladies who used to pat me on the head and kiss me. She had the tact to address a few words directly to me; this gave me a certain sort of standing in the class and put me somewhat at ease.

Within a few days I had made one staunch friend and was on fairly good terms with most of the boys. I was shy of the girls, and remained so; even now a word or look from a pretty woman sets me all a-tremble. This friend I bound to me with hooks of steel in a very simple way. He was a big awkward boy with a face full of freckles and a head full of very red hair. He was perhaps fourteen years of age; that is, four or five years older than any other boy in the class. This seniority was due to the fact that he had spent twice the required amount of time in several of the preceding classes. I had not been at school many hours before I felt that "Red Head"—as I involuntarily called him—and I were to be friends. I do not doubt that this feeling was strengthened by the fact that I had been quick enough to see that a big, strong boy was a friend to be desired at a public school; and, perhaps, in spite of his dullness, "Red Head" had been able to discern that I could be of service to him. At any rate there was a simultaneous mutual attraction.

The teacher had strung the class promiscuously around the walls of the room for a sort of trial heat for places of rank; when the line was straightened out, I found that by skillful maneuvering I had placed myself third and had piloted "Red Head" to the place next to me. The teacher began by giving us to spell the words corresponding to our order in the line. "Spell *first.*" "Spell *second.*" "Spell *third.*" I rattled off: "T-h-i-r-d, third," in a way which said: "Why don't you give us something hard?" As the words went down the line, I could see how lucky I had been to get a good place together with an easy word. As young as I was, I felt impressed with the unfairness of the whole proceeding when I saw the tailenders going down before *twelfth* and *twentieth,* and I felt sorry for those who had to spell such words in order to hold a low position. "Spell *fourth.*" "Red Head," with his hands clutched tightly behind his back, began bravely: "F-o-r-t-h." Like a flash a score of hands went up, and the teacher began saying: "No snapping of fingers, no snapping of fingers." This was the first word missed, and it seemed to me that some of the scholars were about to lose their senses; some were dancing up and down on one foot with a hand above their heads, the fingers working furiously, and joy beaming all over their faces; others stood still, their hands raised not so high, their fingers working less rapidly, and their faces expressing not quite so much happiness; there were still others who did not move or raise their hands, but stood with great wrinkles on their foreheads, looking very thoughtful.

The whole thing was new to me, and I did not raise my hand, but slyly whispered the letter "u" to "Red Head" several times. "Second chance," said the teacher. The hands went down and the class became quiet. "Red Head," his face now red, after looking beseechingly at the ceiling, then pitiably at the floor, began very haltingly: "F-u—" Immediately an impulse to raise hands went through the class, but the teacher checked it, and poor "Red Head," though he knew that each letter he added only took him farther out of the way, went doggedly on and finished: "—r-t-h." The handraising was now repeated with more hubbub and excitement than at first. Those who before had not moved a finger were now waving their hands above their heads. "Red Head" felt that he was lost. He looked very big and foolish, and some of the scholars began to snicker. His helpless condition went straight to my heart, and gripped my sympathies. I felt that if he failed, it would in some way be my failure. I raised my hand, and, under cover of the excitement and the teacher's attempts to regain order, I hurriedly shot up into his ear twice, quite distinctly: "F-o-u-r-t-h, f-o-u-r-t-h." The teacher tapped on her desk and said: "Third and last chance." The hands came down, the silence became oppressive. "Red Head" began: "F—" Since that day I have waited anxiously for many a turn of the wheel of fortune, but never under greater tension than when I watched for the order in which those letters would fall from "Red's" lips—"o-u-r-t-h." A sigh of relief and disappointment went up from the class. Afterwards, through all our school days, "Red Head" shared my wit and quickness and I benefited by his strength and dogged faithfulness.

There were some black and brown boys and girls in the school, and several of them were in my class. One of the boys strongly attracted my attention from the first day I saw him. His face was as black as night, but shone as though it were polished; he had sparkling eyes, and when he opened his mouth, he displayed glistening white teeth. It struck me at once as appropriate to call him "Shiny Face," or "Shiny Eyes," or "Shiny Teeth," and I spoke of him often by one of these names to the other boys. These terms were finally merged into "Shiny," and to that name he answered good-naturedly during the balance of his public school days.

"Shiny" was considered without question to be the best speller, the best reader, the best penman—in a word, the best scholar, in the class. He was very quick to catch anything, but, nevertheless, studied hard; thus he possessed two powers very rarely combined in one boy. I saw him year after year, on up into the high school, win the majority of the prizes for punctuality, deportment, essay writing, and declamation. Yet it did not take me long to discover that, in spite of his standing as a scholar, he was in some way looked down upon.

The other black boys and girls were still more looked down upon. Some of the boys often spoke of them as "niggers." Sometimes on the way home from school a crowd would walk behind them repeating:

"Nigger, nigger, never die,
Black face and shiny eye."

On one such afternoon one of the black boys turned suddenly on his tormentors and hurled a slate; it struck one of the white boys in the mouth, cutting a slight gash in his lip. At sight of the blood the boy who had thrown the slate ran, and his companions quickly followed. We ran after them pelting them with stones until they separated in several directions. I was very much wrought up over the affair, and went home and told my mother how one of the "niggers" had struck a boy with a slate. I shall never forget how she turned on me. "Don't you ever use that word again," she said, "and don't you ever bother the colored children at school. You ought to be ashamed of yourself." I did hang my head in shame, not because she had convinced me that I had done wrong, but because I was hurt by the first sharp word she had ever given me.

My school days ran along very pleasantly. I stood well in my studies, not always so well with regard to my behavior. I was never guilty of any serious misconduct, but my love of fun sometimes got me into trouble. I remember, however, that my sense of humor was so sly that most of the trouble usually fell on the head of the other fellow. My ability to play on the piano at school exercises was looked upon as little short of marvelous in a boy of my age. I was not chummy with many of my mates, but, on the whole, was about as popular as it is good for a boy to be.

One day near the end of my second term at school the principal came into our room and, after talking to the teacher, for some reason said: "I wish all of the white scholars to stand for a moment." I rose with the others. The teacher looked at me and, calling my name, said: "You sit down for the present, and rise with the others." I did not quite understand her, and questioned: "Ma'm?" She repeated, with a softer tone in her voice: "You sit down now, and rise with the others." I sat down dazed. I saw and heard nothing. When the others were asked to rise, I did not know it. When school was dismissed, I went out in a kind of stupor. A few of the white boys jeered me, saying: "Oh, you're a nigger too." I heard some black children say: "We knew he was colored." "Shiny" said to them: "Come along, don't tease him," and thereby won my undying gratitude.

I hurried on as fast as I could, and had gone some distance before I perceived that "Red Head" was walking by my side. After a while he said to me: "Le' me carry your books." I gave him my strap without being able to answer. When we got to my gate, he said as he handed me my books: "Say, you know my big red agate? I can't shoot with it any more. I'm going to bring it to school for you tomorrow." I took my books and ran into the house. As I passed through the hallway, I saw that my mother was busy with one of her customers; I rushed up into my own little room, shut the door, and went quickly to where my looking-glass hung on the wall. For an instant I was afraid to look, but when I did, I looked long and earnestly. I had often heard people say to my mother: "What a pretty boy you have!" I was accustomed to hear remarks about my beauty; but now, for the first time, I became conscious of it and recognized it. I noticed the ivory whiteness of my skin, the beauty of my mouth, the size and liquid darkness of my eyes, and how the long, black lashes that fringed and shaded them produced an effect that was strangely fascinating even to me. I noticed the softness and glossiness of my dark hair that fell in waves over my temples, making my forehead appear whiter than it really was. How long I stood there gazing at my image I do not know. When I came out and reached the head of the stairs, I heard the lady who had been with my mother going out. I ran downstairs and rushed to where my mother was sitting, with a piece of work in her hands. I buried my head in her lap and blurted out: "Mother, mother, tell me, am I a nigger?" I could not see her face, but I knew the piece of work dropped to the floor and I felt her hands on my head. I looked up into her face and repeated: "Tell me, mother, am I a nigger?" There were tears in her eyes and I could see that she was suffering for me. And then it was that I looked at her critically for the first time. I had thought of her in a childish way only as the most beautiful woman in the world; now I looked at her searching for defects. I could see that her skin was almost brown, that her hair was not so soft as mine, and that she did differ in some way from the other ladies who came to the house; yet, even so, I could see that she was very beautiful, more beautiful than any of them. She must have felt that I was examining her, for she hid her face in my hair and said with difficulty: "No, my darling, you are not a nigger." She went on: "You are as good as anybody; if anyone calls you a nigger, don't notice them." But the more she talked, the less was I reassured, and I stopped her by asking: "Well, mother, am I white? Are you white?" She answered tremblingly: "No, I am not white, but you—your father is one of the greatest men in the country—the best blood of the South is in you—" This suddenly opened up in my heart a fresh chasm of misgiving and fear, and I almost fiercely demanded: "Who is my father? Where is he?" She stroked my hair and said: "I'll tell you about him some day." I sobbed: "I want to know now." She answered: "No, not now."

Perhaps it had to be done, but I have never forgiven the woman who did it so cruelly. It may be that she never knew that she gave me a sword-thrust that day in school which was years in healing.

II

Since I have grown older I have often gone back and tried to analyze the change that came into my life after that fateful day in school. There did come a radical change, and, young as I was, I felt fully conscious of it, though I did not fully comprehend it. Like my first spanking, it is one of the few incidents in my life that I can remember clearly. In the life of everyone there is a limited number of unhappy experiences which are not written upon the memory, but stamped there with a die; and in long years after, they can be called up in detail, and every emotion that was stirred by them can be lived through anew; these are the tragedies of life. We may grow to include some of them among the trivial incidents of childhood—a broken toy, a promise made to us which was not kept, a harsh, heart-piercing word—but these, too, as well as the bitter experiences and disappointments of mature years, are the tragedies of life.

And so I have often lived through that hour, that day, that week, in which was wrought the miracle of my transition from one world into another; for I did indeed pass into another world. From that time I looked out through other eyes, my thoughts were colored, my words dictated, my actions limited by one dominating, all-pervading idea which constantly increased in force and weight until I finally realized in it a great, tangible fact.

And this is the dwarfing, warping, distorting influence which operates upon each and every colored man in the United States. He is forced to take his outlook on all things, not from the viewpoint of a citizen, or a man, or even a human being, but from the viewpoint of a *colored* man. It is wonderful to me that the race has progressed so broadly as it has, since most of its thought and all of its activity must run through the narrow neck of this one funnel.

And it is this, too, which makes the colored people of this country, in reality, a mystery to the whites. It is a difficult thing for a white man to learn what a colored man really thinks; because, generally, with the latter an additional and different light must be brought to bear on what he thinks; and his thoughts are often influenced by considerations so delicate and subtle that it would be impossible for him to confess or explain them to one of the opposite race. This gives to every colored man, in proportion to his intellectuality, a sort of dual personality; there is one phase of him which is disclosed only in the freemasonry of his own race. I have often watched with interest and sometimes with amazement even ignorant colored men under cover of broad grins and minstrel antics maintain this dualism in the presence of white men.

I believe it to be a fact that the colored people of this country know and understand the white people better than the white people know and understand them.

I now think that this change which came into my life was at first more subjective than objective. I do not think my friends at school changed so much toward me as I did toward them. I grew reserved, I might say suspicious. I grew constantly more and more afraid of laying myself open to some injury to my feelings or my pride. I frequently saw or fancied some slight where, I am sure, none was intended. On the other hand, my friends and teachers were, if anything different, more considerate of me; but I can remember that it was against this very attitude in particular that my sensitiveness revolted. "Red" was the only one who did not so wound me; up to this day I recall with a swelling heart his clumsy efforts to make me understand that nothing could change his love for me.

I am sure that at this time the majority of my white schoolmates did not understand or appreciate any differences between me and themselves; but there were a few who had evidently received instructions at home on the matter, and more than once they displayed their knowledge in word and action. As the years passed, I noticed that the most innocent and ignorant among the others grew in wisdom.

I myself would not have so clearly understood this difference had it not

been for the presence of the other colored children at school; I had learned
what their status was, and now I learned that theirs was mine. I had had no
particular like or dislike for these black and brown boys and girls; in fact, with
the exception of "Shiny," they had occupied very little of my thought; but I
do know that when the blow fell, I had a very strong aversion to being classed
with them. So I became something of a solitary. "Red" and I remained
inseparable, and there was between "Shiny" and me a sort of sympathetic
bond, but my intercourse with the others was never entirely free from a
feeling of constraint. I must add, however, that this feeling was confined
almost entirely to my intercourse with boys and girls of about my own age; I
did not experience it with my seniors. And when I grew to manhood, I found
myself freer with elderly white people than with those near my own age.

I was now about eleven years old, but these emotions and impressions
which I have just described could not have been stronger or more distinct
at an older age. There were two immediate results of my forced loneliness:
I began to find company in books, and greater pleasure in music. I made
the former discovery through a big, gilt-bound, illustrated copy of the
Bible, which used to lie in splendid neglect on the center table in our little
parlor. On top of the Bible lay a photograph album. I had often looked at
the pictures in the album, and one day, after taking the larger book down
and opening it on the floor, I was overjoyed to find that it contained what
seemed to be an inexhaustible supply of pictures. I looked at these pictures
many times; in fact, so often that I knew the story of each one without having to read the subject, and then, somehow, I picked up the thread of history on which are strung the trials and tribulations of the Hebrew children;
this I followed with feverish interest and excitement. For a long time King
David, with Samson a close second, stood at the head of my list of heroes;
he was not displaced until I came to know Robert the Bruce.[2] I read a
good portion of the Old Testament, all that part treating of wars and rumors of wars, and then started in on the New. I became interested in the
life of Christ, but became impatient and disappointed when I found that,
notwithstanding the great power he possessed, he did not make use of it
when, in my judgment, he most needed to do so. And so my first general
impression of the Bible was what my later impression has been of a number of modern books, that the authors put their best work in the first part,
and grew either exhausted or careless toward the end.

After reading the Bible, or those parts which held my attention, I began
to explore the glass-doored bookcase which I have already mentioned. I
found there *Pilgrim's Progress*, Peter Parley's *History of the United States*,
Grimm's *Household Stories*, *Tales of a Grandfather*, a bound volume of an
old English publication (I think it was called *The Mirror*), a little volume
called *Familiar Science*,[3] and somebody's *Natural Theology*, which last, of

2. Robert I (1274–1329), king of Scotland. David
(c. 1012–972 B.C.), biblical king of Israel. Samson
was a tragic biblical hero of great strength (Judges
13–16).
3. R. E. Peterson's *Familiar Science, or the Scientific Explanation of Common Things* (1851). *Pilgrim's Progress* (1678) is a prose religious allegory
by English author John Bunyan (1628–1688). "Parley's *History of the United States*": probably A *Picto-*

rial History of the United States (1844) by juvenile
writer Samuel G. Goodrich (1793–1860). *Household Stories* (1812–15) is a collection of fairy tales
by Wilhelm and Jacob Grimm. *Tales of a Grandfather* (1827–29) contains stories about the history of
Scotland by novelist Sir Walter Scott (1771–1832).
The Mirror Library series was published in the
1840s by Nathaniel Parker Willis.

course, I could not read, but which, nevertheless, I tackled, with the result of gaining a permanent dislike for all kinds of theology. There were several other books of no particular name or merit, such as agents sell to people who know nothing of buying books. How my mother came by this little library which, considering all things, was so well suited to me I never sought to know. But she was far from being an ignorant woman and had herself, very likely, read the majority of these books, though I do not remember ever seeing her with a book in her hand, with the exception of the Episcopal Prayer book. At any rate she encouraged in me the habit of reading, and when I had about exhausted those books in the little library which interested me, she began to buy books for me. She also regularly gave me money to buy a weekly paper which was then very popular for boys.

At this time I went in for music with an earnestness worthy of maturer years; a change of teachers was largely responsible for this. I began now to take lessons of the organist of the church which I attended with my mother; he was a good teacher and quite a thorough musician. He was so skillful in his instruction and filled me with such enthusiasm that my progress—these are his words—was marvelous. I remember that when I was barely twelve years old I appeared on a program with a number of adults at an entertainment given for some charitable purpose, and carried off the honors. I did more, I brought upon myself through the local newspapers the handicapping title of "infant prodigy."

I can believe that I did astonish my audience, for I never played the piano like a child; that is, in the "one-two-three" style with accelerated motion. Neither did I depend upon mere brilliancy of technique, a trick by which children often surprise their listeners; but I always tried to interpret a piece of music; I always played with feeling. Very early I acquired that knack of using the pedals, which makes the piano a sympathetic, singing instrument, quite a different thing from the source of hard or blurred sounds it so generally is. I think this was due not entirely to natural artistic temperament, but largely to the fact that I did not begin to learn the piano by counting out exercises, but by trying to reproduce the quaint songs which my mother used to sing, with all their pathetic turns and cadences.

Even at a tender age, in playing I helped to express what I felt by some of the mannerisms which I afterwards observed in great performers; I had not copied them. I have often heard people speak of the mannerisms of musicians as affectations adopted for mere effect; in some cases they may be so; but a true artist can no more play upon the piano or violin without putting his whole body in accord with the emotions he is striving to express than a swallow can fly without being graceful. Often when playing I could not keep the tears which formed in my eyes from rolling down my cheeks. Sometimes at the end or even in the midst of a composition, as big a boy as I was, I would jump from the piano, and throw myself sobbing into my mother's arms. She, by her caresses and often her tears, only encouraged these fits of sentimental hysteria. Of course, to counteract this tendency to temperamental excesses I should have been out playing ball or in swimming with other boys of my age; but my mother didn't know that. There was only once when she was really firm with me, making me do what she considered was best; I did not want to return to school after the unpleasant episode which I have related, and she was inflexible.

I began my third term, and the days ran along as I have already indicated. I had been promoted twice, and had managed each time to pull "Red" along with me. I think the teachers came to consider me the only hope of his ever getting through school, and I believe they secretly conspired with me to bring about the desired end. At any rate, I know it became easier in each succeeding examination for me not only to assist "Red," but absolutely to do his work. It is strange how in some things honest people can be dishonest without the slightest compunction. I knew boys at school who were too honorable to tell a fib even when one would have been just the right thing, but could not resist the temptation to assist or receive assistance in an examination. I have long considered it the highest proof of honesty in a man to hand his street-car fare to the conductor who had overlooked it.

One afternoon after school, during my third term, I rushed home in a great hurry to get my dinner and go to my music teacher's. I was never reluctant about going there, but on this particular afternoon I was impetuous. The reason of this was I had been asked to play the accompaniment for a young lady who was to play a violin solo at a concert given by the young people of the church, and on this afternoon we were to have our first rehearsal. At that time playing accompaniments was the only thing in music I did not enjoy; later this feeling grew into positive dislike. I have never been a really good accompanist because my ideas of interpretation were always too strongly individual. I constantly forced my *accelerandos* and *rubatos*[4] upon the soloist, often throwing the duet entirely out of gear.

Perhaps the reader has already guessed why I was so willing and anxious to play the accompaniment to this violin solo; if not—the violinist was a girl of seventeen or eighteen whom I had first heard play a short time before on a Sunday afternoon at a special service of some kind, and who had moved me to a degree which now I can hardly think of as possible. At present I do not think it was due to her wonderful playing, though I judge she must have been a very fair performer, but there was just the proper setting to produce the effect upon a boy such as I was; the half-dim church, the air of devotion on the part of the listeners, the heaving tremor of the organ under the clear wail of the violin, and she, her eyes almost closing, the escaping strands of her dark hair wildly framing her pale face, and her slender body swaying to the tones she called forth, all combined to fire my imagination and my heart with a passion, though boyish, yet strong and, somehow, lasting. I have tried to describe the scene; if I have succeeded, it is only half success, for words can only partially express what I wish to convey. Always in recalling that Sunday afternoon I am subconscious of a faint but distinct fragrance which, like some old memory-awakening perfume, rises and suffuses my whole imagination, inducing a state of reverie so airy as just to evade the powers of expression.

She was my first love, and I loved her as only a boy loves. I dreamed of

4. Departures from the tempo during performance (Italian). "Accelerandos": sections played with a gradual increase of speed (Italian).

her, I built air castles for her, she was the incarnation of each beautiful heroine I knew; when I played the piano, it was to her, not even music furnished an adequate outlet for my passion; I bought a new note-book and, to sing her praises, made my first and last attempts at poetry. I remember one day at school, after we had given in our notebooks to have some exercises corrected, the teacher called me to her desk and said: "I couldn't correct your exercises because I found nothing in your book but a rhapsody on somebody's brown eyes." I had passed in the wrong note-book. I don't think I have felt greater embarrassment in my whole life than I did at that moment. I was ashamed not only that my teacher should see this nakedness of my heart, but that she should find out that I had any knowledge of such affairs. It did not then occur to me to be ashamed of the kind of poetry I had written.

Of course, the reader must know that all of this adoration was in secret; next to my great love for this young lady was the dread that in some way she would find it out. I did not know what some men never find out, that the woman who cannot discern when she is loved has never lived. It makes me laugh to think how successful I was in concealing it all; within a short time after our duet all of the friends of my dear one were referring to me as her "little sweetheart," or her "little beau," and she laughingly encouraged it. This did not entirely satisfy me; I wanted to be taken seriously. I had definitely made up my mind that I should never love another woman, and that if she deceived me I should do something desperate—the great difficulty was to think of something sufficiently desperate—and the heartless jade,[5] how she led me on!

So I hurried home that afternoon, humming snatches of the violin part of the duet, my heart beating with pleasurable excitement over the fact that I was going to be near her, to have her attention placed directly upon me; that I was going to be of service to her, and in a way in which I could show myself to advantage—this last consideration has much to do with cheerful service—. The anticipation produced in me a sensation somewhat between bliss and fear. I rushed through the gate, took the three steps to the house at one bound, threw open the door, and was about to hang my cap on its accustomed peg of the hall rack when I noticed that that particular peg was occupied by a black derby hat. I stopped suddenly and gazed at this hat as though I had never seen an object of its description. I was still looking at it in open-eyed wonder when my mother, coming out of the parlor into the hallway, called me and said there was someone inside who wanted to see me. Feeling that I was being made a party to some kind of mystery, I went in with her, and there I saw a man standing leaning with one elbow on the mantel, his back partly turned toward the door. As I entered, he turned and I saw a tall, handsome, well-dressed gentleman of perhaps thirty-five; he advanced a step toward me with a smile on his face. I stopped and looked at him with the same feelings with which I had looked at the derby hat, except that they were greatly magnified. I looked at him from head to foot, but he was an absolute blank to me until my eyes rested on his slender, elegant polished shoes; then it seemed that indistinct and partly obliterated

5. A disreputable woman, a tart.

films of memory began, at first slowly, then rapidly, to unroll, forming a vague panorama of my childhood days in Georgia.

My mother broke the spell by calling me by name and saying: "This is your father."

"Father, father," that was the word which had been to me a source of doubt and perplexity ever since the interview with my mother on the subject. How often I had wondered about my father, who he was, what he was like, whether alive or dead, and, above all, why she would not tell me about him. More than once I had been on the point of recalling to her the promise she had made me, but I instinctively felt that she was happier for not telling me and that I was happier for not being told; yet I had not the slightest idea what the real truth was. And here he stood before me, just the kind of looking father I had wishfully pictured him to be; but I made no advance toward him; I stood there feeling embarrassed and foolish, not knowing what to say or do. I am not sure but that he felt pretty much the same. My mother stood at my side with one hand on my shoulder, almost pushing me forward, but I did not move. I can well remember the look of disappointment, even pain, on her face; and I can now understand that she could expect nothing else but that at the name "father" I should throw myself into his arms. But I could not rise to this dramatic, or, better, melodramatic, climax. Somehow I could not arouse any considerable feeling of need for a father. He broke the awkward tableau by saying: "Well, boy, aren't you glad to see me?" He evidently meant the words kindly enough, but I don't know what he could have said that would have had a worse effect; however, my good breeding came to my rescue, and I answered: "Yes, sir," and went to him and offered him my hand. He took my hand into one of his, and, with the other, stroked my head, saying that I had grown into a fine youngster. He asked me how old I was; which, of course, he must have done merely to say something more, or perhaps he did so as a test of my intelligence. I replied: "Twelve, sir." He then made the trite observation about the flight of time, and we lapsed into another awkward pause.

My mother was all in smiles; I believe that was one of the happiest moments of her life. Either to put me more at ease or to show me off, she asked me to play something for my father. There is only one thing in the world that can make music, at all times and under all circumstances, up to its general standard; that is a hand-organ, or one of its variations. I went to the piano and played something in a listless, half-hearted way. I simply was not in the mood. I was wondering, while playing, when my mother would dismiss me and let me go; but my father was so enthusiastic in his praise that he touched my vanity—which was great—and more than that; he displayed that sincere appreciation which always arouses an artist to his best effort, and, too, in an unexplainable manner, makes him feel like shedding tears. I showed my gratitude by playing for him a Chopin waltz with all the feeling that was in me. When I had finished, my mother's eyes were glistening with tears; my father stepped across the room, seized me in his arms, and squeezed me to his breast. I am certain that for that moment he was proud to be my father. He sat and held me standing between his knees while he talked to my mother. I, in the mean time, examined him with more curiosity, perhaps, than politeness. I interrupted the conversation by asking: "Mother, is he going to stay with us now?" I found it impossible to frame the word "father"; it was too new to me; so I asked the question through my mother. Without waiting for her to speak, my father answered: "I've got to go back to New York this afternoon, but I'm coming to see you again." I turned abruptly and went over to my mother, and almost in a whisper reminded her that I had an appointment which I should not miss; to my pleasant surprise she said that she would give me something to eat at once so that I might go. She went out of the room and I began to gather from off the piano the music I needed. When I had finished, my father, who had been watching me, asked: "Are you going?" I replied: "Yes, sir, I've got to go to practice for a concert." He spoke some words of advice to me about being a good boy and taking care of my mother when I grew up, and added that he was going to send me something nice from New York. My mother called, and I said good-bye to him and went out. I saw him only once after that.

I quickly swallowed down what my mother had put on the table for me, seized my cap and music, and hurried off to my teacher's house. On the way I could think of nothing but this new father, where he came from, where he had been, why he was here, and why he would not stay. In my mind I ran over the whole list of fathers I had become acquainted with in my reading, but I could not classify him. The thought did not cross my mind that he was different from me, and even if it had, the mystery would not thereby have been explained; for, notwithstanding my changed relations with most of my schoolmates, I had only a faint knowledge of prejudice and no idea at all how it ramified and affected our entire social organism. I felt, however, that there was something about the whole affair which had to be hid.

When I arrived, I found that she of the brown eyes had been rehearsing with my teacher and was on the point of leaving. My teacher, with some expressions of surprise, asked why I was late, and I stammered out the first deliberate lie of which I have any recollection. I told him that when I reached home from school, I found my mother quite sick, and that I had stayed with her awhile before coming. Then unnecessarily and gratuitously—to give my words force of conviction, I suppose—I added: "I don't think she'll be with us very long." In speaking these words I must have been comical; for I noticed that my teacher, instead of showing signs of anxiety or sorrow, half hid a smile. But how little did I know that in that lie I was speaking a prophecy!

She of the brown eyes unpacked her violin, and we went through the duet several times. I was soon lost to all other thoughts in the delights of music and love. I saw delights of love without reservation; for at no time of life is love so pure, so delicious, so poetic, so romantic, as it is in boyhood. A great deal has been said about the heart of a girl when she stands "where the brook and river meet," but what she feels is negative; more interesting is the heart of a boy when just at the budding dawn of manhood he stands looking wide-eyed into the long vistas opening before him; when he first becomes conscious of the awakening and quickening of strange desires and unknown powers; when what he sees and feels is still shadowy and mystical enough to be intangible, and, so, more beautiful; when his imagination is unsullied, and his faith new and whole—then it is that love wears a halo. The man who has not loved before he was fourteen has missed a foretaste of Elysium.[6]

When I reached home, it was quite dark and I found my mother without a light, sitting rocking in a chair, as she so often used to do in my childhood days, looking into the fire and singing softly to herself. I nestled close to her, and, with her arms around me, she haltingly told me who my father was—a great man, a fine gentleman—he loved me and loved her very much; he was going to make a great man of me. All she said was so limited by reserve and so colored by her feelings that it was but half truth; and so I did not yet fully understand.

III

Perhaps I ought not pass on in this narrative without mentioning that the duet was a great success, so great that we were obliged to respond with two encores. It seemed to me that life could hold no greater joy than it contained when I took her hand and we stepped down to the front of the stage bowing to our enthusiastic audience. When we reached the little dressing-room, where the other performers were applauding as wildly as the audience, she impulsively threw both her arms round me and kissed me, while I struggled to get away.

One day a couple of weeks after my father had been to see us, a wagon drove up to our cottage loaded with a big box. I was about to tell the men on the wagon that they had made a mistake, when my mother, acting darkly wise, told them to bring their load in; she had them unpack the box, and quickly there was evolved from the boards, paper, and other packing material a beautiful, brand-new, upright piano. Then she informed me that it was a present to me from my father. I at once sat down and ran my fingers over the keys; the full, mellow tone of the instrument was ravishing. I thought, almost remorsefully, of how I had left my father; but, even so, there momentarily crossed my mind a feeling of disappointment that the piano was not a grand. The new instrument greatly increased the pleasure of my hours of study and practice at home.

Shortly after this I was made a member of the boys' choir, it being found that I possessed a clear, strong soprano voice. I enjoyed the singing very much. About a year later I began the study of the pipe organ and the theory of music; and before I finished the grammar school, I had written out several simple preludes for organ which won the admiration of my teacher, and which he did me the honor to play at services.

The older I grew, the more thought I gave to the question of my mother's and my position, and what was our exact relation to the world in general. My idea of the whole matter was rather hazy. My study of United States history had been confined to those periods which were designated in my book as "Discovery," "Colonial," "Revolutionary," and "Constitutional." I now began to study about the Civil War, but the story was told in such a

---

6. In Greek mythology, the home of the blessed after death.

condensed and skipping style that I gained from it very little real information. It is a marvel how children ever learn any history out of books of that sort. And, too, I began now to read the newspapers; I often saw articles which aroused my curiosity, but did not enlighten me. But one day I drew from the circulating library a book that cleared the whole mystery, a book that I read with the same feverish intensity with which I had read the old Bible stories, a book that gave me my first perspective of the life I was entering; that book was *Uncle Tom's Cabin.*[7]

This work of Harriet Beecher Stowe has been the object of much unfavorable criticism. It has been assailed, not only as fiction of the most imaginative sort, but as being a direct misrepresentation. Several successful attempts have lately been made to displace the book from Northern school libraries. Its critics would brush it aside with the remark that there never was a Negro as good as Uncle Tom, nor a slave-holder as bad as Legree. For my part, I was never an admirer of Uncle Tom, nor of his type of goodness; but I believe that there were lots of old Negroes as foolishly good as he; the proof of which is that they knowingly stayed and worked the plantations that furnished sinews for the army which was fighting to keep them enslaved. But in these later years several cases have come to my personal knowledge in which old Negroes have died and left what was a considerable fortune to the descendants of their former masters. I do not think it takes any great stretch of the imagination to believe there was a fairly large class of slave-holders typified in Legree. And we must also remember that the author depicted a number of worthless if not vicious Negroes, and a slave-holder who was as much of a Christian and a gentleman as it was possible for one in his position to be; that she pictured the happy, singing, shuffling "darky" as well as the mother wailing for her child sold "down river."

I do not think it is claiming too much to say that *Uncle Tom's Cabin* was a fair and truthful panorama of slavery; however that may be, it opened my eyes as to who and what I was and what my country considered me; in fact, it gave me my bearing. But there was no shock; I took the whole revelation in a kind of stoical way. One of the greatest benefits I derived from reading the book was that I could afterwards talk frankly with my mother on all the questions which had been vaguely troubling my mind. As a result, she was entirely freed from reserve, and often herself brought up the subject, talking of things directly touching her life and mine and of things which had come down to her through the "old folks." What she told me interested and even fascinated me, and, what may seem strange, kindled in me a strong desire to see the South. She spoke to me quite frankly about herself, my father, and myself: she, the sewing girl of my father's mother; he, an impetuous young man home from college; I, the child of this unsanctioned love. She told me even the principal reason for our coming north. My father was about to be married to a young lady of another great Southern family. She did not neglect to add that another reason for our being in Connecticut was that he intended to give me an education and make a man of me. In none of her talks did she ever utter one word of complaint

7. Best-selling 1852 novel by Harriet Beecher Stowe (1811–1896).

against my father. She always endeavored to impress upon me how good he had been and still was, and that he was all to us that custom and the law would allow. She loved him; more, she worshiped him, and she died firmly believing that he loved her more than any other woman in the world. Perhaps she was right. Who knows?

All of these newly awakened ideas and thoughts took the form of a definite aspiration on the day I graduated from the grammar school. And what a day that was! The girls in white dresses, with fresh ribbons in their hair; the boys in new suits and creaky shoes; the great crowd of parents and friends; the flowers, the prizes and congratulations, made the day seem to me one of the greatest importance. I was on the program, and played a piano solo which was received by the audience with that amount of applause which I had come to look upon as being only the just due of my talent.

But the real enthusiasm was aroused by "Shiny." He was the principal speaker of the day, and well did he measure up to the honor. He made a striking picture, that thin little black boy standing on the platform, dressed in clothes that did not fit him any too well, his eyes burning with excitement, his shrill, musical voice vibrating in tones of appealing defiance, and his black face alight with such great intelligence and earnestness as to be positively handsome. What were his thoughts when he stepped forward and looked into that crowd of faces, all white with the exception of a score or so that were lost to view? I do not know, but I fancy he felt his loneliness. I think there must have rushed over him a feeling akin to that of a gladiator tossed into the arena and bade to fight for his life. I think that solitary little black figure standing there felt that for the particular time and place he bore the weight and responsibility of his race; that for him to fail meant general defeat; but he won, and nobly. His oration was Wendell Phillips's "Toussaint L'Ouverture,"[8] a speech which may now be classed as rhetorical—even, perhaps, bombastic; but as the words fell from "Shiny's" lips their effect was magical. How so young an orator could stir so great enthusiasm was to be wondered at. When, in the famous peroration,[9] his voice, trembling with suppressed emotion, rose higher and higher and then rested on the name "Toussaint L'Ouverture," it was like touching an electric button which loosed the pent-up feelings of his listeners. They actually rose to him.

I have since known of colored men who have been chosen as class orators in our leading universities, of others who have played on the varsity football and baseball teams, of colored speakers who have addressed great white audiences. In each of these instances I believe the men were stirred by the same emotions which actuated "Shiny" on the day of his graduation; and, too, in each case where the efforts have reached any high standard of excellence they have been followed by the same phenomenon of enthusiasm. I think the explanation of the latter lies in what is a basic, though often dormant, principle of the Anglo-Saxon heart, love of fair play. "Shiny," it is true, was what is so common in his race, a natural orator; but I doubt that

8. Leader of the Haitian slave revolt of the 1790s (c. 1743–1803). Phillips (1811–1884), renowned U.S. antislavery orator, celebrated L'Ouverture in his speech.
9. Conclusion of an oration.

any white boy of equal talent could have wrought the same effect. The sight of that boy gallantly waging with puny, black arms so unequal a battle touched the deep springs in the hearts of his audience, and they were swept by a wave of sympathy and admiration.

But the effect upon me of "Shiny's" speech was double; I not only shared the enthusiasm of his audience, but he imparted to me some of his own enthusiasm. I felt leap within me pride that I was colored; and I began to form wild dreams of bringing glory and honor to the Negro race. For days I could talk of nothing else with my mother except my ambitions to be a great man, a great colored man, to reflect credit on the race and gain fame for myself. It was not until years after that I formulated a definite and feasible plan for realizing my dreams.

I entered the high school with my class, and still continued my study of the piano, the pipe organ, and the theory of music. I had to drop out of the boys' choir on account of a changing voice; this I regretted very much. As I grew older, my love for reading grew stronger. I read with studious interest everything I could find relating to colored men who had gained prominence. My heroes had been King David, then Robert the Bruce; now Frederick Douglass was enshrined in the place of honor. When I learned that Alexandre Dumas[1] was a colored man, I re-read *Monte Cristo* and *The Three Guardsmen* with magnified pleasure. I lived between my music and books, on the whole a rather unwholesome life for a boy to lead. I dwelt in a world of imagination, of dreams and air castles—the kind of atmosphere that sometimes nourishes a genius, more often men unfitted for the practical struggles of life. I never played a game of ball, never went fishing or learned to swim; in fact, the only outdoor exercise in which I took any interest was skating. Nevertheless, though slender, I grew well formed and in perfect health. After I entered the high school, I began to notice the change in my mother's health, which I suppose had been going on for some years. She began to complain a little and to cough a great deal; she tried several remedies, and finally went to see a doctor; but though she was failing in health, she kept her spirits up. She still did a great deal of sewing, and in the busy seasons hired two women to help her. The purpose she had formed of having me go through college without financial worries kept her at work when she was not fit for it. I was so fortunate as to be able to organize a class of eight or ten beginners on the piano, and so start a separate little fund of my own. As the time for my graduation from the high school grew nearer, the plans for my college career became the chief subject of our talks. I sent for catalogues of all the prominent schools in the East and eagerly gathered all the information I could concerning them from different sources. My mother told me that my father wanted me to go to Harvard or Yale; she herself had a half desire for me to go to Atlanta University, and even had me write for a catalogue of that school. There were two reasons, however, that inclined her to my father's choice; the first, that at Harvard or Yale I should be near her; the second, that my father had promised to pay for a part of my college education.

---

1. French novelist and dramatist (1802–1870), author of *The Count of Monte Cristo* and *The Three Musketeers* (1844–45). Douglass (1818–1895), African American orator, editor, and civil rights leader.

Both "Shiny" and "Red" came to my house quite often of evenings, and we used to talk over our plans and prospects for the future. Sometimes I would play for them, and they seemed to enjoy the music very much. My mother often prepared sundry Southern dishes for them, which I am not sure but that they enjoyed more. "Shiny" had an uncle in Amherst, Mass., and he expected to live with him and work his way through Amherst College. "Red" declared that he had enough of school and that after he got his high school diploma, he would get a position in a bank. It was his ambition to become a banker and he felt sure of getting the opportunity through certain members of his family.

My mother barely had strength to attend the closing exercises of the high school when I graduated, and after that day she was seldom out of bed. She could no longer direct her work, and under the expense of medicines, doctors, and someone to look after her our college fund began to diminish rapidly. Many of her customers and some of the neighbors were very kind, and frequently brought her nourishment of one kind or another. My mother realized what I did not, that she was mortally ill, and she had me write a long letter to my father. For some time past she had heard from him only at irregular intervals; we never received an answer. In those last days I often sat at her bedside and read to her until she fell asleep. Sometimes I would leave the parlor door open and play on the piano, just loud enough for the music to reach her. This she always enjoyed.

One night, near the end of July, after I had been watching beside her for some hours, I went into the parlor and, throwing myself into the big arm chair, dozed off into a fitful sleep. I was suddenly aroused by one of the neighbors, who had come in to sit with her that night. She said: "Come to your mother at once." I hurried upstairs, and at the bedroom door met the woman who was acting as nurse. I noted with a dissolving heart the strange look of awe on her face. From my first glance at my mother I discerned the light of death upon her countenance. I fell upon my knees beside the bed and, burying my face in the sheets, sobbed convulsively. She died with the fingers of her left hand entwined in my hair.

I will not rake over this, one of the two sacred sorrows of my life; nor could I describe the feeling of unutterable loneliness that fell upon me. After the funeral I went to the house of my music teacher; he had kindly offered me the hospitality of his home for so long as I might need it. A few days later I moved my trunk, piano, my music, and most of my books to his home; the rest of my books I divided between "Shiny" and "Red." Some of the household effects I gave to "Shiny's" mother and to two or three of the neighbors who had been kind to us during my mother's illness; the others I sold. After settling up my little estate I found that, besides a good supply of clothes, a piano, some books and trinkets, I had about two hundred dollars in cash.

The question of what I was to do now confronted me. My teacher suggested a concert tour; but both of us realized that I was too old to be exploited as an infant prodigy and too young and inexperienced to go before the public as a finished artist. He, however, insisted that the people of the town would generously patronize a benefit concert; so he took up the matter and made arrangements for such an entertainment. A more than sufficient number of people with musical and elocutionary talent volunteered their services to make a program. Among these was my brown-eyed violinist. But our relations were not the same as they were when we had played our first duet together. A year or so after that time she had dealt me a crushing blow by getting married. I was partially avenged, however, by the fact that, though she was growing more beautiful, she was losing her ability to play the violin.

I was down on the program for one number. My selection might have appeared at that particular time as a bit of affectation, but I considered it deeply appropriate; I played Beethoven's[2] "Sonata Pathétique." When I sat down at the piano and glanced into the faces of the several hundreds of people who were there solely on account of love or sympathy for me, emotions swelled in my heart which enabled me to play the "Pathétique" as I could never again play it. When the last tone died away, the few who began to applaud were hushed by the silence of the others; and for once I played without receiving an encore.

The benefit yielded me a little more than two hundred dollars, thus raising my cash capital to about four hundred dollars. I still held to my determination of going to college; so it was now a question of trying to squeeze through a year at Harvard or going to Atlanta, where the money I had would pay my actual expenses for at least two years. The peculiar fascination which the South held over my imagination and my limited capital decided me in favor of Atlanta University; so about the last of September I bade farewell to the friends and scenes of my boyhood and boarded a train for the South.

IV

The farther I got below Washington, the more disappointed I became in the appearance of the country. I peered through the car windows, looking in vain for the luxuriant semi-tropical scenery which I had pictured in my mind. I did not find the grass so green, nor the woods so beautiful, nor the flowers so plentiful, as they were in Connecticut. Instead, the red earth partly covered by tough, scrawny grass, the muddy, straggling roads, the cottages of unpainted pine boards, and the clay-daubed huts imparted a "burnt up" impression. Occasionally we ran through a little white and green village that was like an oasis in a desert.

When I reached Atlanta, my steadily increasing disappointment was not lessened. I found it a big, dull, red town. This dull red color of that part of the South I was then seeing had much, I think, to do with the extreme depression of my spirits— no public squares, no fountains, dingy street-cars, and, with the exception of three or four principal thoroughfares, unpaved streets. It was raining when I arrived and some of these unpaved streets were absolutely impassable. Wheels sank to the hubs in red mire, and I actually stood for an hour and watched four or five men work to save a mule, which had stepped into a deep sink, from drowning, or, rather, suffocating in the mud. The Atlanta of today is a new city.

On the train I had talked with one of the Pullman car porters, a bright

2. Ludwig van Beethoven (1770–1827), German composer.

young fellow who was himself a student, and told him that I was going to Atlanta to attend school. I had also asked him to tell me where I might stop for a day or two until the University opened. He said I might go with him to the place where he stopped during his "lay-overs" in Atlanta. I gladly accepted his offer and went with him along one of those muddy streets until we came to a rather rickety looking frame house, which we entered. The proprietor of the house was a big, fat, greasy-looking brown-skin man. When I asked him if he could give me accommodations, he wanted to know how long I would stay. I told him perhaps two days, not more than three. In reply he said: "Oh, dat's all right den," at the same time leading the way up a pair of creaky stairs. I followed him and the porter to a room, the door of which the proprietor opened while continuing, it seemed, his remark, "Oh, dat's all right den," by adding: "You kin sleep in dat cot in de corner der. Fifty cents, please." The porter interrupted by saying: "You needn't collect from him now, he's got a trunk." This seemed to satisfy the man, and he went down, leaving me and my porter friend in the room. I glanced around the apartment and saw that it contained a double bed and two cots, two wash-stands, three chairs, and a time-worn bureau, with a looking-glass that would have made Adonis[3] appear hideous. I looked at the cot in which I was to sleep and suspected, not without good reasons, that I should not be the first to use the sheets and pillow-case since they had last come from the wash. When I thought of the clean, tidy, comfortable surroundings in which I had been reared, a wave of homesickness swept over me that made me feel faint. Had it not been for the presence of my companion, and that I knew this much of his history—that he was not yet quite twenty, just three years older than myself, and that he had been fighting his own way in the world, earning his own living and providing for his own education since he was fourteen—I should not have been able to stop the tears that were welling up in my eyes.

I asked him why it was that the proprietor of the house seemed unwilling to accommodate me for more than a couple of days. He informed me that the man ran a lodging house especially for Pullman porters, and, as their stays in town were not longer than one or two nights, it would interfere with his arrangements to have anyone stay longer. He went on to say: "You see this room is fixed up to accommodate four men at a time. Well, by keeping a sort of table of trips, in and out, of the men, and working them like checkers, he can accommodate fifteen or sixteen in each week and generally avoid having an empty bed. You happen to catch a bed that would have been empty for a couple of nights." I asked him where he was going to sleep. He answered: "I sleep in that other cot tonight; tomorrow night I go out." He went on to tell me that the man who kept the house did not serve meals, and that if I was hungry, we would go out and get something to eat.

We went into the street, and in passing the railroad station I hired a wagon to take my trunk to my lodging place. We passed along until, finally, we turned into a street that stretched away, up and down hill, for a mile or two; and here I caught my first sight of colored people in large numbers. I had seen little squads around the railroad stations on my way south, but

---

3. In Greek mythology, a handsome youth loved by the goddess Aphrodite.

here I saw a street crowded with them. They filled the shops and thronged the sidewalks and lined the curb. I asked my companion if all the colored people in Atlanta lived in this street. He said they did not and assured me that the ones I saw were of the lower class. I felt relieved, in spite of the size of the lower class. The unkempt appearance, the shambling, slouching gait and loud talk and laughter of these people aroused in me a feeling of almost repulsion. Only one thing about them awoke a feeling of interest; that was their dialect. I had read some Negro dialect and had heard snatches of it on my journey down from Washington; but here I heard it in all of its fullness and freedom. I was particularly struck by the way in which it was punctuated by such exclamatory phrases as "Lawd a mussy!" "G'wan, man!" "Bless ma soul!" "Look heah, chile!" These people talked and laughed without restraint. In fact, they talked straight from their lungs and laughed from the pits of their stomachs. And this hearty laughter was often justified by the droll humor of some remark. I paused long enough to hear one man say to another: "W'at's de mattah wid you an' yo' fr'en' Sam?" and the other came back like a flash: "Ma fr'en'? He ma fr'en'? Man! I'd go to his funeral jes' de same as I'd go to a minstrel show." I have since learned that this ability to laugh heartily is, in part, the salvation of the American Negro; it does much to keep him from going the way of the Indian.

The business places of the street along which we were passing consisted chiefly of low bars, cheap dry-goods and notion stores, barber shops, and fish and bread restaurants. We, at length, turned down a pair of stairs that led to a basement and I found myself in an eating-house somewhat better than those I had seen in passing; but that did not mean much for its excellence. The place was smoky, the tables were covered with oilcloth, the floor with sawdust, and from the kitchen came a rancid odor of fish fried over several times, which almost nauseated me. I asked my companion if this was the place where we were to eat. He informed me that it was the best place in town where a colored man could get a meal. I then wanted to know why somebody didn't open a place where respectable colored people who had money could be accommodated. He answered: "It wouldn't pay; all the respectable colored people eat at home, and the few who travel generally have friends in the towns to which they go, who entertain them." He added: "Of course, you could go in any place in the city; they wouldn't know you from white."

I sat down with the porter at one of the tables, but was not hungry enough to eat with any relish what was put before me. The food was not badly cooked; but the iron knives and forks needed to be scrubbed, the plates and dishes and glasses needed to be washed and well dried. I minced over what I took on my plate while my companion ate. When we finished, we paid the waiter twenty cents each and went out. We walked around until the lights of the city were lit. Then the porter said that he must get to bed and have some rest, as he had not had six hours' sleep since he left Jersey City. I went back to our lodging house with him.

When I awoke in the morning, there were, besides my newfound friend, two other men in the room, asleep in the double bed. I got up and dressed myself very quietly, so as not to awake anyone. I then drew from under the pillow my precious roll of greenbacks, took out a ten-dollar bill, and, very softly unlocking my trunk, put the remainder, about three hundred dollars, in the inside pocket of a coat near the bottom, glad of the opportunity to put it unobserved in a place of safety. When I had carefully locked my trunk, I tiptoed toward the door with the intention of going out to look for a decent restaurant where I might get something fit to eat. As I was easing the door open, my porter friend said with a yawn: "Hello! You're going out?" I answered him: "Yes." "Oh!" he yawned again, "I guess I've had enough sleep; wait a minute, I'll go with you." For the instant his friendship bored and embarrassed me. I had visions of another meal in the greasy restaurant of the day before. He must have divined my thoughts, for he went on to say: "I know a woman across town who takes a few boarders; I think we can go over there and get a good breakfast." With a feeling of mingled fears and doubts regarding what the breakfast might be, I waited until he had dressed himself.

When I saw the neat appearance of the cottage we entered, my fears vanished, and when I saw the woman who kept it, my doubts followed the same course. Scrupulously clean, in a spotless white apron and colored head-handkerchief, her round face beaming with motherly kindness, she was picturesquely beautiful. She impressed me as one broad expanse of happiness and good nature. In a few minutes she was addressing me as "chile" and "honey." She made me feel as though I should like to lay my head on her capacious bosom and go to sleep.

And the breakfast, simple as it was, I could not have had at any restaurant in Atlanta at any price. There was fried chicken, as it is fried only in the South, hominy boiled to the consistency where it could be eaten with a fork, and biscuits so light and flaky that a fellow with any appetite at all would have no difficulty in disposing of eight or ten. When I had finished, I felt that I had experienced the realization of, at least, one of my dreams of Southern life.

During the meal we found out from our hostess, who had two boys in school, that Atlanta University opened on that very day. I had somehow mixed my dates. My friend the porter suggested that I go out to the University at once and offered to walk over and show me the way. We had to walk because, although the University was not more than twenty minutes' distance from the center of the city, there were no streetcars running in that direction. My first sight of the school grounds made me feel that I was not far from home; here the red hills had been terraced and covered with green grass; clean gravel walks, well shaded, led up to the buildings; indeed, it was a bit of New England transplanted. At the gate my companion said he would bid me good-by, because it was likely that he would not see me again before his car went out. He told me that he would make two more trips to Atlanta and that he would come out and see me; that after his second trip he would leave the Pullman service for the winter and return to school in Nashville. We shook hands, I thanked him for all his kindness, and we said good-by.

I walked up to a group of students and made some inquiries. They directed me to the president's office in the main building. The president gave me a cordial welcome; it was more than cordial; he talked to me, not as the official head of a college, but as though he were adopting me into what was his large family, personally to look after my general welfare as well as my education. He seemed especially pleased with the fact that I had come to them all the way from the North. He told me that I could have come to the school as soon as I had reached the city and that I had better move my trunk out at once. I gladly promised him that I would do so. He then called a boy and directed him to take me to the matron, and to show me around afterwards. I found the matron even more motherly than the president was fatherly. She had me register, which was in effect to sign a pledge to abstain from the use of intoxicating beverages, tobacco, and profane language while I was a student in the school. This act caused me no sacrifice, as, up to that time, I was free from all three habits. The boy who was with me then showed me about the grounds. I was especially interested in the industrial building.

The sounding of a bell, he told me, was the signal for the students to gather in the general assembly hall, and he asked me if I would go. Of course I would. There were between three and four hundred students and perhaps all of the teachers gathered in the room. I noticed that several of the latter were colored. The president gave a talk addressed principally to newcomers; but I scarcely heard what he said, I was so much occupied in looking at those around me. They were of all types and colors, the more intelligent types predominating. The colors ranged from jet black to pure white, with light hair and eyes. Among the girls especially there were many so fair that it was difficult to believe that they had Negro blood in them. And, too, I could not help noticing that many of the girls, particularly those of the delicate brown shades, with black eyes and wavy dark hair, were decidedly pretty. Among the boys many of the blackest were fine specimens of young manhood, tall, straight, and muscular, with magnificent heads; these were the kind of boys who developed into the patriarchal "uncles" of the old slave regime.

When I left the University, it was with the determination to get my trunk and move out to the school before night. I walked back across the city with a light step and a light heart. I felt perfectly satisfied with life for the first time since my mother's death. In passing the railroad station I hired a wagon and rode with the driver as far as my stopping-place. I settled with my landlord and went upstairs to put away several articles I had left out. As soon as I opened my trunk, a dart of suspicion shot through my heart; the arrangement of things did not look familiar. I began to dig down excitedly to the bottom till I reached the coat in which I had concealed my treasure. My money was gone! Every single bill of it. I knew it was useless to do so, but I searched through every other coat, every pair of trousers, every vest, and even each pair of socks. When I had finished my fruitless search, I sat down dazed and heartsick. I called the landlord up and informed him of my loss; he comforted me by saying that I ought to have better sense than to keep money in a trunk and that he was not responsible for his lodgers' personal effects. His cooling words brought me enough to my senses to cause me to look and see if anything else was missing. Several small articles were gone, among them a black and gray necktie of odd design upon which my heart was set; almost as much as the loss of my money I felt the loss of my tie.

After thinking for a while as best I could, I wisely decided to go at once back to the University and lay my troubles before the president. I rushed breathlessly back to the school. As I neared the grounds, the thought came across me, would not my story sound fishy? Would it not place me in the position of an impostor or beggar? What right had I to worry these busy people with the results of my carelessness? If the money could not be recovered, and I doubted that it could, what good would it do to tell them about it? The shame and embarrassment which the whole situation gave me caused me to stop at the gate. I paused, undecided, for a moment; then turned and slowly retraced my steps, and so changed the whole course of my life.

If the reader has never been in a strange city without money or friends, it is useless to try to describe what my feelings were; he could not understand. If he has been, it is equally useless, for he understands more than words could convey. When I reached my lodgings, I found in the room one of the porters who had slept there the night before. When he heard what misfortune had befallen me, he offered many words of sympathy and advice. He asked me how much money I had left. I told him that I had ten or twelve dollars in my pocket. He said: "That won't last you very long here, and you will hardly be able to find anything to do in Atlanta. I'll tell you what you do, go down to Jacksonville and you won't have any trouble to get a job in one of the big hotels there, or in St. Augustine." I thanked him, but intimated my doubts of being able to get to Jacksonville on the money I had. He reassured me by saying: "Oh, that's all right. You express your trunk on through, and I'll take you down in my closet." I thanked him again, not knowing then what it was to travel in a Pullman porter's closet. He put me under a deeper debt of gratitude by lending me fifteen dollars, which he said I could pay back after I had secured work. His generosity brought tears to my eyes, and I concluded that, after all, there were some kind hearts in the world.

I now forgot my troubles in the hurry and excitement of getting my trunk off in time to catch the train, which went out at seven o'clock. I even forgot that I hadn't eaten anything since morning. We got a wagon—the porter went with me—and took my trunk to the express office. My new friend then told me to come to the station at about a quarter of seven and walk straight to the car where I should see him standing, and not to lose my nerve. I found my role not so difficult to play as I thought it would be, because the train did not leave from the central station, but from a smaller one, where there were no gates and guards to pass. I followed directions, and the porter took me on his car and locked me in his closet. In a few minutes the train pulled out for Jacksonville.

I may live to be a hundred years old, but I shall never forget the agonies I suffered that night. I spent twelve hours doubled up in the porter's basket for soiled linen, not being able to straighten up on account of the shelves for clean linen just over my head. The air was hot and suffocating and the smell of damp towels and used linen was sickening. At each lurch of the car over the none-too-smooth track I was bumped and bruised against the narrow walls of my narrow compartment. I became acutely conscious of the fact that I had not eaten for hours. Then nausea took possession of me, and at one time I had grave doubts about reaching my destination alive. If I had the trip to make again, I should prefer to walk.

V

The next morning I got out of the car at Jacksonville with a stiff and aching body. I determined to ask no more porters, not even my benefactor, about stopping-places; so I found myself on the street not knowing where to go. I walked along listlessly until I met a colored man who had the appearance of a preacher. I asked him if he could direct me to a respectable boarding-house for colored people. He said that if I walked along with him in the direction he was going, he would show me such a place: I turned and walked at his side. He proved to be a minister, and asked me a great many direct questions about myself. I answered as many as I saw fit to answer; the others I evaded or ignored. At length we stopped in front of a frame house, and my guide informed me that it was the place. A woman was standing in the doorway, and he called to her saying that he had brought her a new boarder. I thanked him for his trouble, and after he had urged upon me to attend his church while I was in the city, he went on his way.

I went in and found the house neat and not uncomfortable. The parlor was furnished with cane-bottomed chairs, each of which was adorned with a white crocheted tidy. The mantel over the fireplace had a white crocheted cover; a marble-topped center table held a lamp, a photograph album and several trinkets, each of which was set upon a white crocheted mat. There was a cottage organ in a corner of the room, and I noted that the lamp-racks upon it were covered with white crocheted mats. There was a matting on the floor, but a white crocheted carpet would not have been out of keeping. I made arrangements with the landlady for my board and lodging; the amount was, I think, three dollars and a half a week. She was a rather fine-looking, stout, brown-skin woman of about forty years of age. Her husband was a light-colored Cuban, a man about one half her size, and one whose age could not be guessed from his appearance. He was small in size, but a handsome black mustache and typical Spanish eyes redeemed him from insignificance.

I was in time for breakfast, and at the table I had the opportunity to see my fellow boarders. There were eight or ten of them. Two, as I afterwards learned, were colored Americans. All of them were cigar makers and worked in one of the large factories—cigar making is one trade in which the color line is not drawn. The conversation was carried on entirely in Spanish, and my ignorance of the language subjected me more to alarm than embarrassment. I had never heard such uproarious conversation; everybody talked at once, loud exclamations, rolling "*carambas*," menacing gesticulations with knives, forks, and spoons. I looked every moment for the clash of blows. One man was emphasizing his remarks by flourishing a cup in his hand, seemingly forgetful of the fact that it was nearly full of hot coffee. He ended by emptying it over what was, relatively, the only quiet man at the table excepting myself, bringing from him a volley of language which made the others appear dumb by comparison. I soon learned that in all of this clatter of voices and table utensils they were discussing purely ordinary affairs and arguing about mere trifles, and that not the least ill feeling was aroused. It was not long before I enjoyed the spirited chatter and *badinage* [4] at the table as much as I did my meals—and the meals were not bad.

I spent the afternoon in looking around the town. The streets were sandy, but were well-shaded by fine oak trees and far preferable to the clay roads of Atlanta. One or two public squares with green grass and trees gave the city a touch of freshness. That night after supper I spoke to my landlady and her husband about my intentions. They told me that the big winter hotels would not open within two months. It can easily be imagined what effect this news had on me. I spoke to them frankly about my financial condition and related the main fact of my misfortune in Atlanta. I modestly mentioned my ability to teach music and asked if there was any likelihood of my being able to get some scholars. My landlady suggested that I speak to the preacher who had shown me her house; she felt sure that through his influence I should be able to get up a class in piano. She added, however, that the colored people were poor, and that the general price for music lessons was only twenty-five cents. I noticed that the thought of my teaching white pupils did not even remotely enter her mind. None of this information made my prospects look much brighter.

The husband, who up to this time had allowed the woman to do most of the talking, gave me the first bit of tangible hope; he said that he could get me a job as a "stripper" in the factory where he worked, and that if I succeeded in getting some music pupils, I could teach a couple of them every night, and so make a living until something better turned up. He went on to say that it would not be a bad thing for me to stay at the factory and learn my trade as a cigar maker, and impressed on me that, for a young man knocking about the country, a trade was a handy thing to have. I determined to accept his offer and thanked him heartily. In fact, I became enthusiastic, not only because I saw a way out of my financial troubles, but also because I was eager and curious over the new experience I was about to enter. I wanted to know all about the cigar making business. This narrowed the conversation down to the husband and myself, so the wife went in and left us talking.

He was what is called a *regalía* [5] workman, and earned from thirty-five to forty dollars a week. He generally worked a sixty-dollar job; that is, he made cigars for which he was paid at the rate of sixty dollars per thousand. It was impossible for him to make a thousand in a week because he had to work very carefully and slowly. Each cigar was made entirely by hand. Each piece of filler and each wrapper had to be selected with care. He was able to make a bundle of one hundred cigars in a day, not one of which could be told from the others by any difference in size or shape, or even by any appreciable difference in weight. This was the acme of artistic skill in cigar making. Workmen of this class were rare, never more than three or four in one factory, and it was never necessary for them to remain out of work. There were men who made two, three, and four hundred cigars of the cheaper grades in a day; they had to be very fast in order to make a decent

---

4. Humorous banter or ridicule (French).   5. A large high-quality cigar.

week's wages. Cigar making was a rather independent trade; the men went to work when they pleased and knocked off when they felt like doing so. As a class the workmen were careless and improvident; some very rapid makers would not work more than three or four days out of the week, and there were others who never showed up at the factory on Mondays. "Strippers" were the boys who pulled the long stems from the tobacco leaves. After they had served at that work for a certain time they were given tables as apprentices.

All of this was interesting to me; and we drifted along in conversation until my companion struck the subject nearest his heart, the independence of Cuba. He was an exile from the island, and a prominent member of the Jacksonville Junta.[6] Every week sums of money were collected from juntas all over the country. This money went to buy arms and ammunition for the insurgents. As the man sat there nervously smoking his long, "green" cigar, and telling me of the Gómezes, both the white one and the black one, of Macéo and Bandera,[7] he grew positively eloquent. He also showed that he was a man of considerable education and reading. He spoke English excellently, and frequently surprised me by using words one would hardly expect from a foreigner. The first one of this class of words he employed almost shocked me, and I never forgot it; 'twas "ramify." We sat on the piazza until after ten o'clock. When we arose to go in to bed, it was with the understanding that I should start in the factory on the next day.

I began work the next morning seated at a barrel with another boy, who showed me how to strip the stems from the leaves, to smooth out each half leaf, and to put the "rights" together in one pile, and the "lefts" together in another pile on the edge of the barrel. My fingers, strong and sensitive from their long training, were well adapted to this kind of work, and within two weeks I was accounted the fastest "stripper" in the factory. At first the heavy odor of the tobacco almost sickened me, but when I became accustomed to it, I liked the smell. I was now earning four dollars a week, and was soon able to pick up a couple more by teaching a few scholars at night, whom I had secured through the good offices of the preacher I had met on my first morning in Jacksonville.

At the end of about three months, through my skill as a "stripper" and the influence of my landlord, I was advanced to a table and began to learn my trade; in fact, more than my trade; for I learned not only to make cigars, but also to smoke, to swear, and to speak Spanish. I discovered that I had a talent for languages as well as for music. The rapidity and ease with which I acquired Spanish astonished my associates. In a short time I was able not only to understand most of what was said at the table during meals, but to join in the conversation. I bought a method for learning the Spanish language, and with the aid of my landlord as a teacher, by constant practice with my fellow workmen, and by regularly reading the Cuban newspapers and finally some books of standard Spanish literature which were at the house, I was able in less than a year to speak like a native. In fact, it was my

6. Cuban exiles plotting the overthrow of the Spanish colonial government of the island.
7. Antonio Maceo (1845–1896) and his assistant, Quintin Banderas, were officers in the Cuban revolutionary armies of 1868–78 and 1893–98. Jose Miguel Gomez (1858–1921) and Maximo Gomez y Baez (1836–1905) were Cuban revolutionaries.

pride that I spoke better Spanish than many of the Cuban workmen at the factory.

After I had been in the factory a little over a year, I was repaid for all the effort I had put forth to learn Spanish by being selected as "reader." The "reader" is quite an institution in all cigar factories which employ Spanish-speaking workmen. He sits in the center of the large room in which the cigar makers work and reads to them for a certain number of hours each day all the important news from the papers and whatever else he may consider would be interesting. He often selects an exciting novel and reads it in daily installments. He must, of course, have a good voice, but he must also have a reputation among the men for intelligence, for being well-posted and having in his head a stock of varied information. He is generally the final authority on all arguments which arise, and in a cigar factory these arguments are many and frequent, ranging from the respective and relative merits of rival baseball clubs to the duration of the sun's light and energy— cigar making is a trade in which talk does not interfere with work. My position as "reader" not only released me from the rather monotonous work of rolling cigars, and gave me something more in accord with my tastes, but also added considerably to my income. I was now earning about twenty-five dollars a week, and was able to give up my peripatetic[8] method of giving music lessons. I hired a piano and taught only those who could arrange to take their lessons where I lived. I finally gave up teaching entirely, as what I made scarcely paid for my time and trouble. I kept the piano, however, in order to keep up my own studies, and occasionally I played at some church concert or other charitable entertainment.

Through my music teaching and my not absolutely irregular attendance at church I became acquainted with the best class of colored people in Jacksonville. This was really my entrance into the race. It was my initiation into what I have termed the freemasonry of the race. I had formulated a theory of what it was to be colored; now I was getting the practice. The novelty of my position caused me to observe and consider things which, I think, entirely escaped the young men I associated with; or, at least, were so commonplace to them as not to attract their attention. And of many of the impressions which came to me then I have realized the full import only within the past few years, since I have had a broader knowledge of men and history, and a fuller comprehension of the tremendous struggle which is going on between the races in the South.

It is a struggle; for though the black man fights passively, he nevertheless fights; and his passive resistance is more effective at present than active resistance could possibly be. He bears the fury of the storm as does the willow tree.

It is a struggle; for though the white man of the South may be too proud to admit it, he is, nevertheless, using in the contest his best energies; he is devoting to it the greater part of his thought and much of his endeavor. The South today stands panting and almost breathless from its exertions.

And how the scene of the struggle has shifted! The battle was first waged over the right of the Negro to be classed as a human being with a soul; later,

8. Walking or traveling from place to place.

as to whether he had sufficient intellect to master even the rudiments of learning; and today it is being fought out over his social recognition.

I said somewhere in the early part of this narrative that because the colored man looked at everything through the prism of his relationship to society as a *colored* man, and because most of his mental efforts ran through the narrow channel bounded by his rights and his wrongs, it was to be wondered at that he has progressed so broadly as he has. The same thing may be said of the white man of the South; most of his mental efforts run through one narrow channel; his life as a man and a citizen, many of his financial activities, and all of his political activities are impassably limited by the ever present "Negro question." I am sure it would be safe to wager that no group of Southern white men could get together and talk for sixty minutes without bringing up the "race question." If a Northern white man happened to be in the group, the time could be safely cut to thirty minutes. In this respect I consider the conditions of the whites more to be deplored than that of the blacks. Here, a truly great people, a people that produced a majority of the great historic Americans from Washington to Lincoln, now forced to use up its energies in a conflict as lamentable as it is violent.

I shall give the observations I made in Jacksonville as seen through the light of after years; and they apply generally to every Southern community. The colored people may be said to be roughly divided into three classes, not so much in respect to themselves as in respect to their relations with the whites. There are those constituting what might be called the desperate class—the men who work in the lumber and turpentine camps, the ex-convicts, the bar-room loafers are all in this class. These men conform to the requirements of civilization much as a trained lion with low muttered growls goes through his stunts under the crack of the trainer's whip. They cherish a sullen hatred for all white men, and they value life as cheap. I have heard more than one of them say: "I'll go to hell for the first white man that bothers me." Many who have expressed that sentiment have kept their word, and it is that fact which gives such prominence to this class; for in numbers it is only a small proportion of the colored people, but it often dominates public opinion concerning the whole race. Happily, this class represents the black people of the South far below their normal physical and moral condition, but in its increase lies the possibility of grave dangers. I am sure there is no more urgent work before the white South, not only for its present happiness, but for its future safety, than the decreasing of this class of blacks. And it is not at all a hopeless class; for these men are but the creatures of conditions, as much so as the slum and criminal elements of all the great cities of the world are creatures of conditions. Decreasing their number by shooting and burning them off will not be successful; for these men are truly desperate, and thoughts of death, however terrible, have little effect in deterring them from acts the result of hatred or degeneracy. This class of blacks hate everything covered by a white skin, and in return they are loathed by the whites. The whites regard them just about as a man would a vicious mule, a thing to be worked, driven, and beaten, and killed for kicking.

The second class, as regards the relation between blacks and whites, comprises the servants, the washerwomen, the waiters, the cooks, the coachmen, and all who are connected with the whites by domestic service. These may be generally characterized as simple, kind-hearted, and faithful; not over-fine in their moral deductions, but intensely religious, and relatively—such matters can be judged only relatively—about as honest and wholesome in their lives as any other grade of society. Any white person is "good" who treats them kindly, and they love him for that kindness. In return, the white people with whom they have to do regard them with indulgent affection. They come into close daily contact with the whites, and may be called the connecting link between whites and blacks; in fact, it is through them that the whites know the rest of their colored neighbors. Between this class of the blacks and the whites there is little or no friction.

The third class is composed of the independent workmen and tradesmen, and of the well-to-do and educated colored people; and, strange to say, for a directly opposite reason they are as far removed from the whites as the members of the first class I mentioned. These people live in a little world of their own; in fact, I concluded that if a colored man wanted to separate himself from his white neighbors, he had but to acquire some money, education, and culture, and to live in accordance. For example, the proudest and fairest lady in the South could with propriety—and it is what she would most likely do—go to the cabin of Aunt Mary, her cook, if Aunt Mary was sick, and minister to her comfort with her own hands; but if Mary's daughter, Eliza, a girl who used to run round my lady's kitchen, but who has received an education and married a prosperous young colored man, were at death's door, my lady would no more think of crossing the threshold of Eliza's cottage than she would of going into a bar-room for a drink.

I was walking down the street one day with a young man who was born in Jacksonville, but had been away to prepare himself for a professional life. We passed a young white man, and my companion said to me: "You see that young man? We grew up together; we have played, hunted, and fished together; we have even eaten and slept together; and now since I have come back home, he barely speaks to me." The fact that the whites of the South despise and ill-treat the desperate class of blacks is not only explainable according to the ancient laws of human nature, but it is not nearly so serious or important as the fact that as the progressive colored people advance, they constantly widen the gulf between themselves and their white neighbors. I think that the white people somehow feel that colored people who have education and money, who wear good clothes and live in comfortable houses, are "putting on airs," that they do these things for the sole purpose of "spiting the white folks," or are, at best, going through a sort of monkey-like imitation. Of course, such feelings can only cause irritation or breed disgust. It seems that the whites have not yet been able to realize and understand that these people in striving to better their physical and social surroundings in accordance with their financial and intellectual progress are simply obeying an impulse which is common to human nature the world over. I am in grave doubt as to whether the greater part of the friction in the South is caused by the whites' having a natural antipathy to Negroes as a race, or an acquired antipathy to Negroes in certain relations to themselves. However that may be, there is to my mind no more pathetic side of this many-sided question than the isolated position into which are forced the very colored people who most need and who could best appreciate sympathetic coöperation; and their position grows tragic when the effort is made to couple them, whether or no, with the Negroes of the first class I mentioned.

This latter class of colored people are well-disposed towards the whites, and always willing to meet them more than half-way. They, however, feel keenly any injustice or gross discrimination, and generally show their resentment. The effort is sometimes made to convey the impression that the better class of colored people fight against riding in "Jim Crow" cars because they want to ride with white people or object to being with humbler members of their own race. The truth is they object to the humiliation of being forced to ride in a *particular* car, aside from the fact that that car is distinctly inferior, and that they are required to pay full first-class fare. To say that the whites are forced to ride in the superior car is less than a joke. And, too, odd as it may sound, refined colored people get no more pleasure out of riding with offensive Negroes than anybody else would get.

I can realize more fully than I could years ago that the position of the advanced element of the colored race is often very trying. They are the ones among the blacks who carry the entire weight of the race question; it worries the others very little, and I believe the only thing which at times sustains them is that they know that they are in the right. On the other hand, this class of colored people get a good deal of pleasure out of life; their existence is far from being one long groan about their condition. Out of a chaos of ignorance and poverty they have evolved a social life of which they need not be ashamed. In cities where the professional and well-to-do class is large they have formed society—society as discriminating as the actual conditions will allow it to be; I should say, perhaps, society possessing discriminating tendencies which become rules as fast as actual conditions allow. This statement will, I know, sound preposterous, even ridiculous, to some persons; but as this class of colored people is the least known of the race it is not surprising. These social circles are connected throughout the country, and a person in good standing in one city is readily accepted in another. One who is on the outside will often find it a difficult matter to get in. I know personally of one case in which money to the extent of thirty or forty thousand dollars and a fine house, not backed up by a good reputation, after several years of repeated effort, failed to gain entry for the possessor. These people have their dances and dinners and card parties, their musicals, and their literary societies. The women attend social affairs dressed in good taste, and the men in dress suits which they own; and the reader will make a mistake to confound these entertainments with the "Bellman's Balls" and "Whitewashers' Picnics" and "Lime-kiln Clubs" with which the humorous press of the country illustrates "Cullud Sassiety."

Jacksonville, when I was there, was a small town, and the number of educated and well-to-do colored people was small: so this society phase of life did not equal what I have since seen in Boston, Washington, Richmond, and Nashville; and it is upon what I have more recently seen in these cities that I have made the observations just above. However, there were many comfortable and pleasant homes in Jacksonville to which I was often invited. I belonged to the literary society—at which we generally discussed the race question—and attended all of the church festivals and other charitable entertainments. In this way I passed three years which were not at all the least enjoyable of my life. In fact, my joy took such an exuberant turn that I fell in love with a young school teacher and began to have dreams of matrimonial bliss; but another turn in the course of my life brought these dreams to an end.

I do not wish to mislead my readers into thinking that I led a life in Jacksonville which would make copy for the hero of a Sunday-school library book. I was a hail fellow well met with all of the workmen at the factory, most of whom knew little and cared less about social distinctions. From their example I learned to be careless about money, and for that reason I constantly postponed and finally abandoned returning to Atlanta University. It seemed impossible for me to save as much as two hundred dollars. Several of the men at the factory were my intimate friends, and I frequently joined them in their pleasures. During the summer months we went almost every Monday on an excursion to a seaside resort called Pablo Beach. These excursions were always crowded. There was a dancing pavilion, a great deal of drinking, and generally a fight or two to add to the excitement. I also contracted the cigar maker's habit of riding around in a hack[9] on Sunday afternoons. I sometimes went with my cigar maker friends to public balls that were given at a large hall on one of the main streets. I learned to take a drink occasionally and paid for quite a number that my friends took; but strong liquors never appealed to my appetite. I drank them only when the company I was in required it, and suffered for it afterwards. On the whole, though I was a bit wild, I can't remember that I ever did anything disgraceful, or, as the usual standard for young men goes, anything to forfeit my claim to respectability.

At one of the first public balls I attended I saw the Pullman car porter who had so kindly assisted me in getting to Jacksonville. I went immediately to one of my factory friends and borrowed fifteen dollars with which to repay the loan my benefactor had made me. After I had given him the money, and was thanking him, I noticed that he wore what was, at least, an exact duplicate of my lamented black and gray tie. It was somewhat worn, but distinct enough for me to trace the same odd design which had first attracted my eye. This was enough to arouse my strongest suspicions, but whether it was sufficient for the law to take cognizance of I did not consider. My astonishment and the ironical humor of the situation drove everything else out of my mind.

These balls were attended by a great variety of people. They were generally given by the waiters of some one of the big hotels, and were often patronized by a number of hotel guests who came to "see the sights." The crowd was always noisy, but good-natured; there was much quadrille-dancing,[1] and a strong-lunged man called figures in a voice which did not confine itself to the limits of the hall. It is not worth the while for me to describe in detail how these people acted; they conducted themselves in

9. A vehicle for hire.　　　　　　　　　　1. A square dance performed by four couples.

about the same manner as I have seen other people at similar balls conduct themselves. When one has seen something of the world and human nature, one must conclude, after all, that between people in like stations of life there is very little difference the world over.

However, it was at one of these balls that I first saw the cake-walk.[2] There was a contest for a gold watch, to be awarded to the hotel head-waiter receiving the greatest number of votes. There was some dancing while the votes were being counted. Then the floor was cleared for the cake-walk. A half-dozen guests from some of the hotels took seats on the stage to act as judges, and twelve or fourteen couples began to walk for a sure enough, highly decorated cake, which was in plain evidence. The spectators crowded about the space reserved for the contestants and watched them with interest and excitement. The couples did not walk round in a circle, but in a square, with the men on the inside. The fine points to be considered were the bearing of the men, the precision with which they turned the corners, the grace of the women, and the ease with which they swung around the pivots. The men walked with stately and soldierly step, and the women with considerable grace. The judges arrived at their decision by a process of elimination. The music and the walk continued for some minutes; then both were stopped while the judges conferred; when the walk began again, several couples were left out. In this way the contest was finally narrowed down to three or four couples. Then the excitement became intense; there was much partisan cheering as one couple or another would execute a turn in extra elegant style. When the cake was finally awarded, the spectators were about evenly divided between those who cheered the winners and those who muttered about the unfairness of the judges. This was the cake-walk in its original form, and it is what the colored performers on the theatrical stage developed into the prancing movements now known all over the world, and which some Parisian critics pronounced the acme of poetic motion.

There are a great many colored people who are ashamed of the cake-walk, but I think they ought to be proud of it. It is my opinion that the colored people of this country have done four things which refute the oft-advanced theory that they are an absolutely inferior race, which demonstrate that they have originality and artistic conception, and, what is more, the power of creating that which can influence and appeal universally. The first two of these are the Uncle Remus stories, collected by Joel Chandler Harris, and the Jubilee songs, to which the Fisk singers[3] made the public and the skilled musicians of both America and Europe listen. The other two are ragtime music[4] and the cake-walk. No one who has traveled can question the world-conquering influence of ragtime, and I do not think it would be an exaggeration to say that in Europe the United States is popularly known better by ragtime than by anything else it has produced in a generation. In Paris they call it American music. The newspapers have al-

2. A dance developed from a contest in stylish walking; a cake was offered as a prize.
3. A nine-person traveling singing troupe founded in 1871 to raise funds for Fisk University. Harris (1848–1908), African American folklore collector, published his *Uncle Remus: His Songs and His Say-* ings in 1881. "Jubilee songs": southern African American religious folk songs.
4. African American instrumental musical style of the 1890s characterized by a syncopated melodic line and regularly accented accompaniment.

ready told how the practice of intricate cake-walk steps has taken up the time of European royalty and nobility. These are lower forms of art, but they give evidence of a power that will some day be applied to the higher forms. In this measure, at least, and aside from the number of prominent individuals the colored people of the United States have produced, the race has been a world influence; and all of the Indians between Alaska and Patagonia[5] haven't done as much.

Just when I was beginning to look upon Jacksonville as my permanent home and was beginning to plan about marrying the young school teacher, raising a family, and working in a cigar factory the rest of my life, for some reason, which I do not now remember, the factory at which I worked was indefinitely shut down. Some of the men got work in other factories in town; some decided to go to Key West and Tampa, others made up their minds to go to New York for work. All at once a desire like a fever seized me to see the North again and I cast my lot with those bound for New York.

VI

We steamed up into New York Harbor late one afternoon in spring. The last efforts of the sun were being put forth in turning the waters of the bay to glistening gold; the green islands on either side, in spite of their warlike mountings, looked calm and peaceful; the buildings of the town shone out in a reflected light which gave the city an air of enchantment; and, truly, it is an enchanted spot. New York City is the most fatally fascinating thing in America. She sits like a great witch at the gate of the country, showing her alluring white face and hiding her crooked hands and feet under the folds of her wide garments—constantly enticing thousands from far within, and tempting those who come from across the seas to go no farther. And all these become the victims of her caprice. Some she at once crushes beneath her cruel feet; others she condemns to a fate like that of galley slaves; a few she favors and fondles, riding them high on the bubbles of fortune; then with a sudden breath she blows the bubbles out and laughs mockingly as she watches them fall.

Twice I had passed through it, but this was really my first visit to New York; and as I walked about that evening, I began to feel the dread power of the city; the crowds, the lights, the excitement, the gaiety, and all its subtler stimulating influences began to take effect upon me. My blood ran quicker and I felt that I was just beginning to live. To some natures this stimulant of life in a great city becomes a thing as binding and necessary as opium is to one addicted to the habit. It becomes their breath of life; they cannot exist outside of it; rather than be deprived of it they are content to suffer hunger, want, pain, and misery; they would not exchange even a ragged and wretched condition among the great crowd for any degree of comfort away from it.

As soon as we landed, four of us went directly to a lodging house in Twenty-seventh Street, just west of Sixth Avenue. The house was run by a short, stout mulatto man, who was exceedingly talkative and inquisitive. In

5. A region of southern Argentina.

fifteen minutes he not only knew the history of the past life of each one of us, but had a clearer idea of what we intended to do in the future than we ourselves. He sought this information so much with an air of being very particular as to whom he admitted into his house that we tremblingly answered every question that he asked. When we had become located, we went out and got supper, then walked around until about ten o'clock. At that hour we met a couple of young fellows who lived in New York and were known to one of the members of our party. It was suggested we go to a certain place which was known by the proprietor's name. We turned into one of the cross streets and mounted the stoop of a house in about the middle of a block between Sixth and Seventh Avenues. One of the young men whom we had met rang a bell, and a man on the inside cracked the door a couple of inches; then opened it and let us in. We found ourselves in the hallway of what had once been a residence. The front parlor had been converted into a bar, and a half-dozen or so well-dressed men were in the room. We went in and after a general introduction had several rounds of beer. In the back parlor a crowd was sitting and standing around the walls of the room watching an exciting and noisy game of pool. I walked back and joined this crowd to watch the game, and principally to get away from the drinking party. The game was really interesting, the players being quite expert, and the excitement was heightened by the bets which were being made on the result. At times the antics and remarks of both players and spectators were amusing. When, at a critical point, a player missed a shot, he was deluged, by those financially interested in his making it, with a flood of epithets synonymous with "chump"; while from the others he would be jeered by such remarks as "Nigger, dat cue ain't no hoe-handle." I noticed that among this class of colored men the word "nigger" was freely used in about the same sense as the word "fellow," and sometimes as a term of almost endearment; but I soon learned that its use was positively and absolutely prohibited to white men.

I stood watching this pool game until I was called by my friends, who were still in the bar-room, to go upstairs. On the second floor there were two large rooms. From the hall I looked into the one on the front. There was a large, round table in the center, at which five or six men were seated playing poker. The air and conduct here were greatly in contrast to what I had just seen in the pool-room; these men were evidently the aristocrats of the place; they were well, perhaps a bit flashily, dressed and spoke in low modulated voices, frequently using the word "gentlemen"; in fact, they seemed to be practicing a sort of Chesterfieldian politeness[6] towards each other. I was watching these men with a great deal of interest and some degree of admiration when I was again called by the members of our party, and I followed them on to the back room. There was a door-keeper at this room, and we were admitted only after inspection. When we got inside, I saw a crowd of men of all ages and kinds grouped about an old billiard table, regarding some of whom, in supposing them to be white, I made no mistake. At first I did not know what these men were doing; they were using

6. A standard of urbane good manners represented by Philip Dormer Stanhope, fourth earl of Chesterfield (1694–1773).

terms that were strange to me. I could hear only a confusion of voices exclaiming: "Shoot the two!" "Shoot the four!" "Fate me! Fate me!" "I've got you fated!" "Twenty-five cents he don't turn!" This was the ancient and terribly fascinating game of dice, popularly known as "craps." I myself had played pool in Jacksonville—it is a favorite game among cigar makers—and I had seen others play cards; but here was something new. I edged my way in to the table and stood between one of my new-found New York friends and a tall, slender, black fellow, who was making side bets while the dice were at the other end of the table. My companion explained to me the principles of the game; and they are so simple that they hardly need to be explained twice. The dice came around the table until they reached the man on the other side of the tall, black fellow. He lost, and the latter said: "Gimme the bones."[7] He threw a dollar on the table and said: "Shoot the dollar." His style of play was so strenuous that he had to be allowed plenty of room. He shook the dice high above his head, and each time he threw them on the table, he emitted a grunt such as men give when they are putting forth physical exertion with a rhythmic regularity. He frequently whirled completely around on his heels, throwing the dice the entire length of the table, and talking to them as though they were trained animals. He appealed to them in short singsong phrases. "Come, dice," he would say. "Little Phoebe," "Little Joe," " 'Way down yonder in the cornfield." Whether these mystic incantations were efficacious or not I could not say, but, at any rate, his luck was great, and he had what gamblers term "nerve." "Shoot the dollar!" "Shoot the two!" "Shoot the four!" "Shoot the eight!" came from his lips as quickly as the dice turned to his advantage. My companion asked me if I had ever played. I told him no. He said that I ought to try my luck: that everybody won at first. The tall man at my side was waving his arms in the air, exclaiming: "Shoot the sixteen!" "Shoot the sixteen!" "Fate me!" Whether it was my companion's suggestion or some latent dare-devil strain in my blood which suddenly sprang into activity I do not know; but with a thrill of excitement which went through my whole body I threw a twenty-dollar bill on the table and said in a trembling voice: "I fate you."

I could feel that I had gained the attention and respect of everybody in the room, every eye was fixed on me, and the widespread question, "Who is he?" went around. This was gratifying to a certain sense of vanity of which I have never been able to rid myself, and I felt that it was worth the money even if I lost. The tall man, with a whirl on his heels and a double grunt, threw the dice; four was the number which turned up. This is considered as a hard "point" to make. He redoubled his contortions and his grunts and his pleadings to the dice; but on his third or fourth throw the fateful seven turned up, and I had won. My companion and all my friends shouted to me to follow up my luck. The fever was on me. I seized the dice. My hands were so hot that the bits of bone felt like pieces of ice. I shouted as loudly as I could: "Shoot it all!" but the blood was tingling so about my ears that I could not hear my own voice. I was soon "fated." I threw the dice—seven— I had won. "Shoot it all!" I cried again. There was a pause; the stake was

7. Dice.

more than one man cared to or could cover. I was finally "fated" by several men taking each a part of it. I then threw the dice again. Seven. I had won. "Shoot it all!" I shouted excitedly. After a short delay I was "fated." Again I rolled the dice. Eleven. Again I won. My friends now surrounded me and, much against my inclination, forced me to take down all of the money except five dollars. I tried my luck once more, and threw some small "point" which I failed to make, and the dice passed on to the next man.

In less than three minutes I had won more than two hundred dollars, a sum which afterwards cost me dearly. I was the hero of the moment and was soon surrounded by a group of men who expressed admiration for my "nerve" and predicted for me a brilliant future as a gambler. Although at the time I had no thought of becoming a gambler, I felt proud of my success. I felt a bit ashamed, too, that I had allowed my friends to persuade me to take down my money so soon. Another set of men also got around me and begged me for twenty-five or fifty cents to put them back into the game. I gave each of them something. I saw that several of them had on linen dusters,[8] and as I looked about, I noticed that there were perhaps a dozen men in the room similarly clad. I asked the fellow who had been my prompter at the dice table why they dressed in such a manner. He told me that men who had lost all the money and jewelry they possessed, frequently, in an effort to recoup their losses, would gamble away all their outer clothing and even their shoes; and that the proprietor kept on hand a supply of linen dusters for all who were so unfortunate. My informant went on to say that sometimes a fellow would become almost completely dressed and then, by a turn of the dice, would be thrown back into a state of semi-nakedness. Some of them were virtually prisoners and unable to get into the streets for days at a time. They ate at the lunch counter, where their credit was good so long as they were fair gamblers and did not attempt to jump their debts, and they slept around in chairs. They importuned friends and winners to put them back in the game, and kept at it until fortune again smiled on them. I laughed heartily at this, not thinking the day was coming which would find me in the same ludicrous predicament.

On passing downstairs I was told that the third and top floor of the house was occupied by the proprietor. When we passed through the bar, I treated everybody in the room—and that was no small number, for eight or ten had followed us down. Then our party went out. It was now about half past twelve, but my nerves were at such a tension that I could not endure the mere thought of going to bed. I asked if there was no other place to which we could go; our guides said yes, and suggested that we go to the "Club." We went to Sixth Avenue, walked two blocks, and turned to the west into another street. We stopped in front of a house with three stories and a basement. In the basement was a Chinese chop-suey restaurant. There was a red lantern at the iron gate to the areaway, inside of which the Chinaman's name was printed. We went up the steps of the stoop, rang the bell, and were admitted without any delay. From the outside the house bore a rather gloomy aspect, the windows being absolutely dark, but within, it was a veritable house of mirth. When we had passed through a small vestibule and

8. Long, loose-fitting linen coats.

reached the hallway, we heard mingled sounds of music and laughter, the clink of glasses, and the pop of bottles. We went into the main room and I was little prepared for what I saw. The brilliancy of the place, the display of diamond rings, scarf-pins, ear-rings, and breast-pins, the big rolls of money that were brought into evidence when drinks were paid for, and the air of gaiety that pervaded the place, all completely dazzled and dazed me. I felt positively giddy, and it was several minutes before I was able to make any clear and definite observations.

We at length secured places at a table in a corner of the room and, as soon as we could attract the attention of one of the busy waiters, ordered a round of drinks. When I had somewhat collected my senses, I realized that in a large back room into which the main room opened, there was a young fellow singing a song, accompanied on the piano by a short, thickset, dark man. After each verse he did some dance steps, which brought forth great applause and a shower of small coins at his feet. After the singer had responded to a rousing encore, the stout man at the piano began to run his fingers up and down the keyboard. This he did in a manner which indicated that he was master of a good deal of technique. Then he began to play; and such playing! I stopped talking to listen. It was music of a kind I had never heard before. It was music that demanded physical response, patting of the feet, drumming of the fingers, or nodding of the head in time with the beat. The barbaric harmonies, the audacious resolutions, often consisting of an abrupt jump from one key to another, the intricate rhythms in which the accents fell in the most unexpected places, but in which the beat was never lost, produced a most curious effect. And, too, the player—the dexterity of his left hand in making rapid octave runs and jumps was little short of marvelous; and with his right hand he frequently swept half the keyboard with clean-cut chromatics[9] which he fitted in so nicely as never to fail to arouse in his listeners a sort of pleasant surprise at the accomplishment of the feat.

This was ragtime music, then a novelty in New York, and just growing to be a rage, which has not yet subsided. It was originated in the questionable resorts about Memphis and St. Louis by Negro piano players who knew no more of the theory of music than they did of the theory of the universe, but were guided by natural musical instinct and talent. It made its way to Chicago, where it was popular some time before it reached New York. These players often improvised crude and, at times, vulgar words to fit the melodies. This was the beginning of the ragtime song. Several of these improvisations were taken down by white men, the words slightly altered, and published under the names of the arrangers. They sprang into immediate popularity and earned small fortunes, of which the Negro originators got only a few dollars. But I have learned that since that time a number of colored men, of not only musical talent, but training, are writing out their own melodies and words and reaping the reward of their work. I have learned also that they have a large number of white imitators and adulterators.

American musicians, instead of investigating ragtime, attempt to ignore

9. Series of twelve tones within an octave.

it, or dismiss it with a contemptuous word. But that has always been the course of scholasticism[1] in every branch of art. Whatever new thing the *people* like is pooh-poohed; whatever is *popular* is spoken of as not worth the while. The fact is, nothing great or enduring, especially in music, has ever sprung full-fledged and unprecedented from the brain of any master; the best that he gives to the world he gathers from the hearts of the people, and runs it through the alembic[2] of his genius. In spite of the bans which musicians and music teachers have placed upon it, the people still demand and enjoy ragtime. One thing cannot be denied; it is music which possesses at least one strong element of greatness: it appeals universally; not only the American, but the English, the French, and even the German people find delight in it. In fact, there is not a corner of the civilized world in which it is not known, and this proves its originality; for if it were an imitation, the people of Europe, anyhow, would not have found it a novelty. Anyone who doubts that there is a peculiar heel-tickling, smile-provoking, joy-awakening charm in ragtime needs only to hear a skillful performer play the genuine article to be convinced. I believe that it has its place as well as the music which draws from us sighs and tears.

I became so interested in both the music and the player that I left the table where I was sitting, and made my way through the hall into the back room, where I could see as well as hear. I talked to the piano player between the musical numbers and found out that he was just a natural musician, never having taken a lesson in his life. Not only could he play almost anything he heard, but he could accompany singers in songs he had never heard. He had, by ear alone, composed some pieces, several of which he played over for me; each of them was properly proportioned and balanced. I began to wonder what this man with such a lavish natural endowment would have done had he been trained. Perhaps he wouldn't have done anything at all; he might have become, at best, a mediocre imitator of the great masters in what they have already done to a finish, or one of the modern innovators who strive after originality by seeing how cleverly they can dodge about through the rules of harmony and at the same time avoid melody. It is certain that he would not have been so delightful as he was in ragtime.

I sat by, watching and listening to this man until I was dragged away by my friends. The place was now almost deserted; only a few stragglers hung on, and they were all the worse for drink. My friends were well up in this class. We passed into the street; the lamps were pale against the sky; day was just breaking. We went home and got into bed. I fell into a fitful sort of sleep, with ragtime music ringing continually in my ears.

VII

I shall take advantage of this pause in my narrative to describe more closely the "Club" spoken of in the latter part of the preceding chapter—to describe it as I afterwards came to know it, as an habitué.[3] I shall do this not only because of the direct influence it had on my life, but also because it

---

1. An insistence on traditional doctrines and methods.   2. A purifying still.
3. A person who frequents a certain place.

was at that time the most famous place of its kind in New York, and was well known to both white and colored people of certain classes.

I have already stated that in the basement of the house there was a Chinese restaurant. The Chinaman who kept it did an exceptionally good business; for chop-suey was a favorite dish among the frequenters of the place. It is a food that, somehow, has the power of absorbing alcoholic liquors that have been taken into the stomach. I have heard men claim that they could sober up on chop-suey. Perhaps that accounted, in some degree, for its popularity. On the main floor there were two large rooms: a parlor about thirty feet in length, and a large, square back room into which the parlor opened. The floor of the parlor was carpeted; small tables and chairs were arranged about the room; the windows were draped with lace curtains, and the walls were literally covered with photographs or lithographs of every colored man in America who had ever "done anything." There were pictures of Frederick Douglass and of Peter Jackson,[4] of all the lesser lights of the prize-fighting ring, of all the famous jockeys and the stage celebrities, down to the newest song and dance team. The most of these photographs were autographed and, in a sense, made a really valuable collection. In the back room there was a piano, and tables were placed around the wall. The floor was bare and the center was left vacant for singers, dancers, and others who entertained the patrons. In a closet in this room which jutted out into the hall the proprietor kept his buffet. There was no open bar, because the place had no liquor license. In this back room the tables were sometimes pushed aside, and the floor given over to general dancing. The front room on the next floor was a sort of private party room; a back room on the same floor contained no furniture and was devoted to the use of new and ambitious performers. In this room song and dance teams practiced their steps, acrobatic teams practiced their tumbles, and many other kinds of "acts" rehearsed their "turns." The other rooms of the house were used as sleeping-apartments.

No gambling was allowed, and the conduct of the place was surprisingly orderly. It was, in short, a center of colored Bohemians and sports.[5] Here the great prize fighters were wont to come, the famous jockeys, the noted minstrels, whose names and faces were familiar on every bill-board in the country; and these drew a multitude of those who love to dwell in the shadow of greatness. There were then no organizations giving performances of such order as are now given by several colored companies; that was because no manager could imagine that audiences would pay to see Negro performers in any other rôle than that of Mississippi River roustabouts; but there was lots of talent and ambition. I often heard the younger and brighter men discussing the time when they would compel the public to recognize that they could do something more than grin and cut pigeon-wings.[6]

Sometimes one or two of the visiting stage professionals, after being sufficiently urged, would go into the back room and take the places of the regu-

4. African American boxing champion (1861–1901).
5. Flashy, good-time people. "Bohemians": un-conventional, nonconforming people.
6. A dance step performed by jumping up and striking the legs together.

lar amateur entertainers, but they were very sparing with these favors, and the patrons regarded them as special treats. There was one man, a minstrel, who, whenever he responded to a request to "do something," never essayed anything below a reading from Shakespeare. How well he read I do not know, but he greatly impressed me; and I can say that at least he had a voice which strangely stirred those who heard it. Here was a man who made people laugh at the size of his mouth, while he carried in his heart a burning ambition to be a tragedian; and so after all he did play a part in a tragedy.

These notables of the ring, the turf, and the stage, drew to the place crowds of admirers, both white and colored. Whenever one of them came in, there were awe-inspired whispers from those who knew him by sight, in which they enlightened those around them as to his identity, and hinted darkly at their great intimacy with the noted one. Those who were on terms of approach immediately showed their privilege over others less fortunate by gathering around their divinity. I was, at first, among those who dwelt in darkness. Most of these celebrities I had never heard of. This made me an object of pity among many of my new associates. I soon learned, however, to fake a knowledge for the benefit of those who were greener than I; and, finally, I became personally acquainted with the majority of the famous personages who came to the "Club."

A great deal of money was spent here, so many of the patrons were men who earned large sums. I remember one night a dapper little brown-skin fellow was pointed out to me and I was told that he was the most popular jockey of the day, and that he earned $12,000 a year. This latter statement I couldn't doubt, for with my own eyes I saw him spending at about thirty times that rate. For his friends and those who were introduced to him he bought nothing but wine—in sporting circles, "wine" means champagne— and paid for it at five dollars a quart. He sent a quart to every table in the place with his compliments; and on the table at which he and his party were seated there were more than a dozen bottles. It was the custom at the "Club" for the waiter not to remove the bottles when champagne was being drunk until the party had finished. There were reasons for this; it advertised the brand of wine, it advertised that the party was drinking wine, and advertised how much they had bought. This jockey had won a great race that day, and he was rewarding his admirers for the homage they paid him, all of which he accepted with a fine air of condescension.

Besides the people I have just been describing, there was at the place almost every night one or two parties of white people, men and women, who were out sight-seeing, or slumming. They generally came in cabs; some of them would stay only for a few minutes, while others sometimes stayed until morning. There was also another set of white people who came frequently; it was made up of variety performers and others who delineated "darky characters"; they came to get their imitations first hand from the Negro entertainers they saw there.

There was still another set of white patrons, composed of women; these were not occasional visitors, but five or six of them were regular habituées. When I first saw them, I was not sure that they were white. In the first place, among the many colored women who came to the "Club" there were several just as fair; and, secondly, I always saw these women in company with colored men. They were all good-looking and well-dressed, and seemed to be women of some education. One of these in particular attracted my attention; she was an exceedingly beautiful woman of perhaps thirty-five; she had glistening copper-colored hair, very white skin, and eyes very much like Du Maurier's[7] conception of Trilby's "twin gray stars." When I came to know her, I found that she was a woman of considerable culture; she had traveled in Europe, spoke French, and played the piano well. She was always dressed elegantly, but in absolute good taste. She always came to the "Club" in a cab, and was soon joined by a well-set-up, very black young fellow. He was always faultlessly dressed; one of the most exclusive tailors in New York made his clothes, and he wore a number of diamonds in about as good taste as they could be worn in by a man. I learned that she paid for his clothes and his diamonds. I learned, too, that he was not the only one of his kind. More that I learned would be better suited to a book on social phenomena than to a narrative of my life.

This woman was known at the "Club" as the rich widow. She went by a very aristocratic-sounding name, which corresponded to her appearance. I shall never forget how hard it was for me to get over my feelings of surprise, perhaps more than surprise, at seeing her with her black companion; somehow I never exactly enjoyed the sight. I have devoted so much time to this pair, the "widow" and her companion, because it was through them that another decided turn was brought about in my life.

VIII

On the day following our night at the "Club" we slept until late in the afternoon; so late that beginning search for work was entirely out of the question. This did not cause me much worry, for I had more than three hundred dollars, and New York had impressed me as a place where there was lots of money and not much difficulty in getting it. It is needless to inform my readers that I did not long hold this opinion. We got out of the house about dark, went to a restaurant on Sixth Avenue and ate something, then walked around for a couple of hours. I finally suggested that we visit the same places we had been in the night before. Following my suggestion, we started first to the gambling house. The man on the door let us in without any question; I accredited this to my success of the night before. We went straight to the "crap" room, and I at once made my way to a table, where I was rather flattered by the murmur of recognition which went around. I played in up and down luck for three or four hours; then, worn with nervous excitement, quit, having lost about fifty dollars. But I was so strongly possessed with the thought that I would make up my losses the next time I played that I left the place with a light heart.

When we got into the street our party was divided against itself; two were for going home at once and getting to bed. They gave as a reason that we were to get up early and look for jobs. I think the real reason was that they had each lost several dollars in the game. I lived to learn that in the world of sport all men win alike, but lose differently; and so gamblers are rated, not

---

7. George Louis Du Maurier (1834–1896), English author of *Trilby* (1894), a popular novel about a famous singer.

by the way in which they win, but by the way in which they lose. Some men lose with a careless smile, recognizing that losing is a part of the game; others curse their luck and rail at fortune; and others, still, lose sadly; after each such experience they are swept by a wave of reform; they resolve to stop gambling and be good. When in this frame of mind it would take very little persuasion to lead them into a prayer-meeting. Those in the first class are looked upon with admiration; those in the second class are merely commonplace; while those in the third are regarded with contempt. I believe these distinctions hold good in all the ventures of life. After some minutes one of my friends and I succeeded in convincing the other two that a while at the "Club" would put us all in better spirits; and they consented to go, on our promise not to stay longer than an hour. We found the place crowded, and the same sort of thing going on which we had seen the night before. I took a seat at once by the side of the piano player, and was soon lost to everything except the novel charm of the music. I watched the performer with the idea of catching the trick, and during one of his intermissions I took his place at the piano and made an attempt to imitate him, but even my quick ear and ready fingers were unequal to the task on first trial.

We did not stay at the "Club" very long, but went home to bed in order to be up early the next day. We had no difficulty in finding work, and my third morning in New York found me at a table rolling cigars. I worked steadily for some weeks, at the same time spending my earnings between the "crap" game and the "Club." Making cigars became more and more irksome to me; perhaps my more congenial work as a "reader" had unfitted me for work at the table. And, too, the late hours I was keeping made such a sedentary occupation almost beyond the powers of will and endurance. I often found it hard to keep my eyes open and sometimes had to get up and move around to keep from falling asleep. I began to miss whole days from the factory, days on which I was compelled to stay at home and sleep.

My luck at the gambling table was varied; sometimes I was fifty to a hundred dollars ahead, and at other times I had to borrow money from my fellow workmen to settle my room rent and pay for my meals. Each night after leaving the dice game I went to the "Club" to hear the music and watch the gaiety. If I had won, this was in accord with my mood; if I had lost, it made me forget. I at last realized that making cigars for a living and gambling for a living could not both be carried on at the same time, and I resolved to give up the cigar making. This resolution led me into a life which held me bound more than a year. During that period my regular time for going to bed was somewhere between four and six o'clock in the mornings. I got up late in the afternoons, walked about a little, then went to the gambling house or the "Club." My New York was limited to ten blocks; the boundaries were Sixth Avenue from Twenty-third to Thirty-third Streets, with the cross streets one block to the west. Central Park was a distant forest, and the lower part of the city a foreign land. I look back upon the life I then led with a shudder when I think what would have been had I not escaped it. But had I not escaped it, I should have been no more unfortunate than are many young colored men who come to New York. During that dark period I became acquainted with a score of bright, intelligent young fellows who had come up to the great city with high hopes and ambitions and who had fallen under the spell of this under life, a spell they could not throw off. There was one popularly known as "the doctor"; he had had two years in the Harvard Medical School, but here he was, living this gas-light life, his will and moral sense so enervated and deadened that it was impossible for him to break away. I do not doubt that the same thing is going on now, but I have sympathy rather than censure for these victims, for I know how easy it is to slip into a slough from which it takes a herculean effort to leap.

I regret that I cannot contrast my views of life among colored people of New York; but the truth is, during my entire stay in this city I did not become acquainted with a single respectable family. I knew that there were several colored men worth a hundred or so thousand dollars each, and some families who proudly dated their free ancestry back a half-dozen generations. I also learned that in Brooklyn there lived quite a large colony in comfortable homes which they owned; but at no point did my life come in contact with theirs.

In my gambling experiences I passed through all the states and conditions that a gambler is heir to. Some days found me able to peel ten- and twenty-dollar bills from a roll, and others found me clad in a linen duster and carpet slippers. I finally caught up another method of earning money, and so did not have to depend entirely upon the caprices of fortune at the gaming table. Through continually listening to the music at the "Club," and through my own previous training, my natural talent and perseverance, I developed into a remarkable player of ragtime; indeed, I had the name at that time of being the best ragtime-player in New York. I brought all my knowledge of classic music to bear and, in so doing, achieved some novelties which pleased and even astonished my listeners. It was I who first made ragtime transcriptions of familiar classic selections. I used to play Mendelssohn's[8] "Wedding March" in a manner that never failed to arouse enthusiasm among the patrons of the "Club." Very few nights passed during which I was not asked to play it. It was no secret that the great increase in slumming visitors was due to my playing. By mastering ragtime I gained several things: first of all, I gained the title of professor. I was known as "the professor" as long as I remained in that world. Then, too, I gained the means of earning a rather fair livelihood. This work took up much of my time and kept me almost entirely away from the gambling table. Through it I also gained a friend who was the means by which I escaped from this lower world. And, finally, I secured a wedge which has opened to me more doors and made me a welcome guest than my playing of Beethoven and Chopin[9] could ever have done.

The greater part of the money I now began to earn came through the friend to whom I alluded in the foregoing paragraph. Among the other white "slummers" there came into the "Club" one night a clean-cut, slender, but athletic-looking man, who would have been taken for a youth had it not been for the tinge of gray about his temples. He was clean-shaven and had regular features, and all of his movements bore the indefinable but

---

8. Felix Mendelssohn (1809–1847), German composer.

9. Frederic Francois Chopin (1810–1849), Polish composer and pianist.

unmistakable stamp of culture. He spoke to no one, but sat languidly puffing cigarettes and sipping a glass of beer. He was the center of a great deal of attention; all of the old-timers were wondering who he was. When I had finished playing, he called a waiter and by him sent me a five-dollar bill. For about a month after that he was at the "Club" one or two nights each week, and each time after I had played, he gave me five dollars. One night he sent for me to come to his table; he asked me several questions about myself; then told me that he had an engagement which he wanted me to fill. He gave me a card containing his address and asked me to be there on a certain night.

I was on hand promptly and found that he was giving a dinner in his own apartments to a party of ladies and gentlemen and that I was expected to furnish the musical entertainment. When the grave, dignified man at the door let me in, the place struck me as being almost dark, my eyes had been so accustomed to the garish light of the "Club." He took my coat and hat, bade me take a seat, and went to tell his master that I had come. When my eyes were adjusted to the soft light, I saw that I was in the midst of elegance and luxury in a degree such as I had never seen; but not the elegance which makes one ill at ease. As I sank into a great chair, the subdued tone, the delicately sensuous harmony of my surroundings, drew from me a deep sigh of relief and comfort. How long the man was gone I do not know, but I was startled by a voice saying: "Come this way, if you please, sir," and I saw him standing by my chair. I had been asleep; and I awoke very much confused and a little ashamed, because I did not know how many times he may have called me. I followed him through into the diningroom, where the butler was putting the finishing touches to a table which already looked like a big jewel. The doorman turned me over to the butler, and I passed with the butler on back to where several waiters were busy polishing and assorting table utensils. Without being asked whether I was hungry or not, I was placed at a table and given something to eat. Before I had finished eating, I heard the laughter and talk of the guests who were arriving. Soon afterwards I was called in to begin my work.

I passed in to where the company was gathered and went directly to the piano. According to a suggestion from the host, I began with classic music. During the first number there was absolute quiet and appreciative attention, and when I had finished, I was given a round of generous applause. After that the talk and the laughter began to grow until the music was only an accompaniment to the chatter. This, however, did not disconcert me as it once would have done, for I had become accustomed to playing in the midst of uproarious noise. As the guests began to pay less attention to me, I was enabled to pay more to them. There were about a dozen of them. The men ranged in appearance from a girlish-looking youth to a big grizzled man whom everybody addressed as "Judge." None of the women appeared to be under thirty, but each of them struck me as being handsome. I was not long in finding out that they were all decidedly blasé. Several of the women smoked cigarettes, and with a careless grace which showed they were used to the habit. Occasionally a "Damn it!" escaped from the lips of some one of them, but in such a charming way as to rob it of all vulgarity. The most notable thing which I observed was that the reserve of the host increased in direct proportion with the hilarity of his guests. I thought that there was something going wrong which displeased him. I afterwards learned that it was his habitual manner on such occasions. He seemed to take cynical delight in watching and studying others indulging in excess. His guests were evidently accustomed to his rather non-participating attitude, for it did not seem in any degree to dampen their spirits.

When dinner was served, the piano was moved and the door left open, so that the company might hear the music while eating. At a word from the host I struck up one of my liveliest ragtime pieces. The effect was surprising, perhaps even to the host; the ragtime music came very near spoiling the party so far as eating the dinner was concerned. As soon as I began, the conversation suddenly stopped. It was a pleasure to me to watch the expression of astonishment and delight that grew on the faces of everybody. These were people—and they represented a large class—who were ever expecting to find happiness in novelty, each day restlessly exploring and exhausting every resource of this great city that might possibly furnish a new sensation or awaken a fresh emotion, and who were always grateful to anyone who aided them in their quest. Several of the women left the table and gathered about the piano. They watched my fingers and asked what kind of music it was that I was playing, where I had learned it, and a host of other questions. It was only by being repeatedly called back to the table that they were induced to finish their dinner. When the guests arose, I struck up my ragtime transcription of Mendelssohn's "Wedding March," playing it with terrific chromatic octave runs in the bass. This raised everybody's spirits to the highest point of gaiety, and the whole company involuntarily and unconsciously did an impromptu cake-walk. From that time on until the time of leaving they kept me so busy that my arms ached. I obtained a little respite when the girlish-looking youth and one or two of the ladies sang several songs, but after each of these it was "back to ragtime."

In leaving, the guests were enthusiastic in telling the host that he had furnished them the most unusual entertainment they had ever enjoyed. When they had gone, my millionaire friend—for he was reported to be a millionaire—said to me with a smile: "Well, I have given them something they've never had before." After I had put on my coat and was ready to leave, he made me take a glass of wine; he then gave me a cigar and twenty dollars in bills. He told me that he would give me lots of work, his only stipulation being that I should not play any engagements such as I had just filled for him, except by his instructions. I readily accepted the proposition, for I was sure that I could not be the loser by such a contract.

I afterwards played for him at many dinners and parties of one kind or another. Occasionally he "loaned" me to some of his friends. And, too, I often played for him alone at his apartments. At such times he was quite a puzzle to me until I became accustomed to his manners. He would sometimes sit for three or four hours hearing me play, his eyes almost closed, making scarcely a motion except to light a fresh cigarette, and never commenting one way or another on the music. At first I sometimes thought he had fallen asleep and would pause in playing. The stopping of the music always aroused him enough to tell me to play this or that; and I soon learned that my task was not to be considered finished until he got up from

his chair and said: "That will do." The man's powers of endurance in listening often exceeded mine in performing—yet I am not sure that he was
always listening. At times I became so oppressed with fatigue and sleepiness that it took almost superhuman effort to keep my fingers going; in fact,
I believe I sometimes did so while dozing. During such moments this man
sitting there so mysteriously silent, almost hid in a cloud of heavy-scented
smoke, filled me with a sort of unearthly terror. He seemed to be some
grim, mute, but relentless tyrant, possessing over me a supernatural power
which he used to drive me on mercilessly to exhaustion. But these feelings
came very rarely; besides, he paid me so liberally I could forget much.
There at length grew between us a familiar and warm relationship, and I
am sure he had a decided personal liking for me. On my part, I looked
upon him at that time as about all a man could wish to be.

The "Club" still remained my headquarters, and when I was not playing
for my good patron, I was generally to be found there. However, I no longer
depended on playing at the "Club" to earn my living; I rather took rank
with the visiting celebrities and, occasionally, after being sufficiently
urged, would favor my old and new admirers with a number or two. I say,
without any egotistic pride, that among my admirers were several of the
best-looking women who frequented the place, and who made no secret of
the fact that they admired me as much as they did my playing. Among
these was the "widow"; indeed, her attentions became so marked that one
of my friends warned me to beware of her black companion, who was generally known as a "bad man." He said there was much more reason to be
careful because the pair had lately quarreled and had not been together at
the "Club" for some nights. This warning greatly impressed me and I resolved to stop the affair before it should go any further; but the woman was
so beautiful that my native gallantry and delicacy would not allow me to
repulse her; my finer feelings entirely overcame my judgment. The warning also opened my eyes sufficiently to see that though my artistic temperament and skill made me interesting and attractive to the woman, she was,
after all, using me only to excite the jealousy of her companion and revenge herself upon him. It was this surly, black despot who held sway over
her deepest emotions.

One night, shortly afterwards, I went into the "Club" and saw the
"widow" sitting at a table in company with another woman. She at once
beckoned for me to come to her. I went, knowing that I was committing
worse than folly. She ordered a quart of champagne and insisted that I sit
down and drink with her. I took a chair on the opposite side of the table and
began to sip a glass of the wine. Suddenly I noticed by an expression on the
"widow's" face that something had occurred. I instinctively glanced
around and saw that her companion had just entered. His ugly look completely frightened me. My back was turned to him, but by watching the
"widow's" eyes I judged that he was pacing back and forth across the room.
My feelings were far from being comfortable; I expected every moment to
feel a blow on my head. She, too, was very nervous; she was trying hard to
appear unconcerned, but could not succeed in hiding her real feelings. I
decided that it was best to get out of such a predicament even at the expense of appearing cowardly, and I made a motion to rise. Just as I partly

turned in my chair, I saw the black fellow approaching; he walked directly to our table and leaned over. The "widow" evidently feared he was going to strike her, and she threw back her head. Instead of striking her he whipped out a revolver and fired; the first shot went straight into her throat. There were other shots fired, but how many I do not know; for the first knowledge I had of my surroundings and actions was that I was rushing through the chop-suey restaurant into the street. Just which streets I followed when I got outside I do not know, but I think I must have gone towards Eighth Avenue, then down towards Twenty-third Street and across towards Fifth Avenue. I traveled, not by sight, but instinctively. I felt like one fleeing in a horrible nightmare.

How long and far I walked I cannot tell; but on Fifth Avenue, under a light, I passed a cab containing a solitary occupant, who called to me, and I recognized the voice and face of my millionaire friend. He stopped the cab and asked: "What on earth are you doing strolling in this part of the town?" For answer I got into the cab and related to him all that had happened. He reassured me by saying that no charge of any kind could be brought against me; then added: "But of course you don't want to be mixed up in such an affair." He directed the driver to turn around and go into the park, and then went on to say: "I decided last night that I'd go to Europe tomorrow. I think I'll take you along instead of Walter." Walter was his valet. It was settled that I should go to his apartments for the rest of the night and sail with him in the morning.

We drove around through the park, exchanging only an occasional word. The cool air somewhat calmed my nerves and I lay back and closed my eyes; but still I could see that beautiful white throat with the ugly wound. The jet of blood pulsing from it had placed an indelible red stain on my memory.

IX

I did not feel at ease until the ship was well out of New York harbor; and, notwithstanding the repeated reassurances of my millionaire friend and my own knowledge of the facts in the case, I somehow could not rid myself of the sentiment that I was, in a great degree, responsible for the "widow's" tragic end. We had brought most of the morning papers aboard with us, but my great fear of seeing my name in connection with the killing would not permit me to read the accounts, although, in one of the papers, I did look at the picture of the victim, which did not in the least resemble her. This morbid state of mind, together with sea-sickness, kept me miserable for three or four days. At the end of that time my spirits began to revive, and I took an interest in the ship, my fellow passengers, and the voyage in general. On the second or third day out we passed several spouting whales, but I could not arouse myself to make the effort to go to the other side of the ship to see them. A little later we ran in close proximity to a large iceberg. I was curious enough to get up and look at it, and I was fully repaid for my pains. The sun was shining full upon it, and it glistened like a mammoth diamond, cut with a million facets. As we passed, it constantly changed its shape; at each different angle of vision it assumed new and astonishing forms of beauty. I watched it through a pair of glasses, seeking to verify my early conception of an iceberg—in the geographies of my grammar school days the pictures of icebergs always included a stranded polar bear, standing desolately upon one of the snowy crags. I looked for the bear, but if he was there, he refused to put himself on exhibition.

It was not, however, until the morning that we entered the harbor of Havre[1] that I was able to shake off my gloom. Then the strange sights, the chatter in an unfamiliar tongue, and the excitement of landing and passing the customs officials caused me to forget completely the events of a few days before. Indeed, I grew so lighthearted that when I caught my first sight of the train which was to take us to Paris, I enjoyed a hearty laugh. The toy-looking engine, the stuffy little compartment cars, with tiny, old-fashioned wheels, struck me as being extremely funny. But before we reached Paris my respect for our train rose considerably. I found that the "tiny" engine made remarkably fast time, and that the old-fashioned wheels ran very smoothly. I even began to appreciate the "stuffy" cars for their privacy. As I watched the passing scenery from the car window, it seemed too beautiful to be real. The bright-colored houses against the green background impressed me as the work of some idealistic painter. Before we arrived in Paris, there was awakened in my heart a love for France which continued to grow stronger, a love which to-day makes that country for me the one above all others to be desired.

We rolled into the station Saint Lazare about four o'clock in the afternoon and drove immediately to the Hôtel Continental. My benefactor, humoring my curiosity and enthusiasm, which seemed to please him very much, suggested that we take a short walk before dinner. We stepped out of the hotel and turned to the right into the rue de Rivoli. When the vista of the Place de la Concorde and the Champs Élysées[2] suddenly burst on me, I could hardly credit my own eyes. I shall attempt no such supererogatory[3] task as a description of Paris. I wish only to give briefly the impressions which that wonderful city made upon me. It impressed me as the perfect and perfectly beautiful city; and even after I had been there for some time, and seen not only its avenues and palaces, but its most squalid alleys and hovels, this impression was not weakened. Paris became for me a charmed spot, and whenever I have returned there, I have fallen under the spell, a spell which compels admiration for all of its manners and customs and justification of even its follies and sins.

We walked a short distance up the Champs Élysées and sat for a while in chairs along the sidewalk, watching the passing crowds on foot and in carriages. It was with reluctance that I went back to the hotel for dinner. After dinner we went to one of the summer theatres, and after the performance my friend took me to a large café on one of the Grands Boulevards. Here it was that I had my first glimpse of the French life of popular literature, so different from real French life. There were several hundred people, men and women, in the place drinking, smoking, talking, and listening to the music. My millionaire friend and I took seats at a table, where we sat smok-

---

1. A seaport in northwestern France.   3. Superfluous.
2. A famous and fashionable avenue in Paris.

ing and watching the crowd. It was not long before we were joined by two or three good-looking, well-dressed young women. My friend talked to them in French and bought drinks for the whole party. I tried to recall my high-school French, but the effort availed me little. I could stammer out a few phrases, but, very naturally, could not understand a word that was said to me. We stayed at the café a couple of hours, then went back to the hotel. The next day we spent several hours in the shops and at the tailor's. I had no clothes except what I had been able to gather together at my benefactor's apartments the night before we sailed. He bought me the same kind of clothes which he himself wore, and that was the best; and he treated me in every way as he dressed me, as an equal, not as a servant. In fact, I don't think anyone could have guessed that such a relation existed. My duties were light and few, and he was a man full of life and vigor, who rather enjoyed doing things for himself. He kept me supplied with money far beyond what ordinary wages would have amounted to. For the first two weeks we were together almost constantly, seeing the sights, sights old to him, but from which he seemed to get new pleasure in showing them to me. During the day we took in the places of interest, and at night the theatres and cafés. This sort of life appealed to me as ideal, and I asked him one day how long he intended to stay in Paris. He answered: "Oh, until I get tired of it." I could not understand how that could ever happen. As it was, including several short trips to the Mediterranean, to Spain, to Brussels, and to Ostend,[4] we did remain there fourteen or fifteen months. We stayed at the Hôtel Continental about two months of this time. Then my millionaire took apartments, hired a piano, and lived almost the same life he lived in New York. He entertained a great deal, some of the parties being a good deal more blasé than the New York ones. I played for the guests at all of them with an effect which to relate would be but a tiresome repetition to the reader. I played not only for the guests, but continued, as I used to do in New York, to play often for the host when he was alone. This man of the world, who grew weary of everything and was always searching for something new, appeared never to grow tired of my music; he seemed to take it as a drug. He fell into a habit which caused me no little annoyance; sometimes he would come in during the early hours of the morning and, finding me in bed asleep, would wake me up and ask me to play something. This, so far as I can remember, was my only hardship during my whole stay with him in Europe.

After the first few weeks spent in sight-seeing I had a great deal of time left to myself; my friend was often I did not know where. When not with him, I spent the day nosing about all the curious nooks and corners of Paris; of this I never grew tired. At night I usually went to some theatre, but always ended up at the big café on the Grands Boulevards. I wish the reader to know that it was not alone the gaiety which drew me there; aside from that I had a laudable purpose. I had purchased an English-French conversational dictionary, and I went there every night to take a language lesson. I used to get three or four of the young women who frequented the place at a table and buy beer and cigarettes for them. In return I received my lesson. I

---

4. Cities in Belgium.

got more than my money's worth, for they actually compelled me to speak the language. This, together with reading the papers every day, enabled me within a few months to express myself fairly well, and, before I left Paris, to have more than an ordinary command of French. Of course, every person who goes to Paris could not dare to learn French in this manner, but I can think of no easier or quicker way of doing it. The acquiring of another foreign language awoke me to the fact that with a little effort I could secure an added accomplishment as fine and as valuable as music; so I determined to make myself as much of a linguist as possible. I bought a Spanish newspaper every day in order to freshen my memory of that language, and, for French, devised what was, so far as I knew, an original system of study. I compiled a list which I termed "Three hundred necessary words." These I thoroughly committed to memory, also the conjugation of the verbs which were included in the list. I studied these words over and over, much as children of a couple of generations ago studied the alphabet. I also practiced a set of phrases like the following: "How?" "What did you say?" "What does the word —— mean?" "I understand all you say except ——." "Please repeat." "What do you call ——?" "How do you say ——?" These I called my working sentences. In an astonishingly short time I reached the point where the language taught itself—where I learned to speak merely by speaking. This point is the place which students taught foreign languages in our schools and colleges find great difficulty in reaching. I think the main trouble is that they learn too much of a language at a time. A French child with a vocabulary of two hundred words can express more spoken ideas than a student of French can with a knowledge of two thousand. A small vocabulary, the smaller the better, which embraces the common, everyday-used ideas, thoroughly mastered, is the key to a language. When that much is acquired the vocabulary can be increased simply by talking. And it is easy. Who cannot commit three hundred words to memory? Later I tried my method, if I may so term it, with German, and found that it worked in the same way.

I spent a good many evenings at the Opéra. The music there made me strangely reminiscent of my life in Connecticut; it was an atmosphere in which I caught a fresh breath of my boyhood days and early youth. Generally, in the morning after I had attended a performance, I would sit at the piano and for a couple of hours play the music which I used to play in my mother's little parlor.

One night I went to hear *Faust*.[5] I got into my seat just as the lights went down for the first act. At the end of the act I noticed that my neighbor on the left was a young girl. I cannot describe her either as to feature, or color of her hair, or of her eyes; she was so young, so fair, so ethereal, that I felt to stare at her would be a violation; yet I was distinctly conscious of her beauty. During the intermission she spoke English in a low voice to a gentleman and a lady who sat in the seats to her left, addressing them as father and mother. I held my program as though studying it, but listened to catch every sound of her voice. Her observations on the performance and the audience were so fresh and naïve as to be almost amusing. I gathered that

5. *Faust* (1859), an opera by French composer Charles Gounod (1818–1893).

she was just out of school, and that this was her first trip to Paris. I occasionally stole a glance at her, and each time I did so my heart leaped into my
throat. Once I glanced beyond to the gentleman who sat next to her. My
glance immediately turned into a stare. Yes, there he was, unmistakably,
my father! looking hardly a day older than when I had seen him some ten
years before. What a strange coincidence! What should I say to him? What
would he say to me? Before I had recovered from my first surprise, there
came another shock in the realization that the beautiful, tender girl at my
side was my sister. Then all the springs of affection in my heart, stopped
since my mother's death, burst out in fresh and terrible torrents, and I
could have fallen at her feet and worshiped her. They were singing the
second act, but I did not hear the music. Slowly the desolate loneliness of
my position became clear to me. I knew that I could not speak, but I would
have given a part of my life to touch her hand with mine and call her "sister." I sat through the opera until I could stand it no longer. I felt that I was
suffocating. Valentine's[6] love seemed like mockery, and I felt an almost
uncontrollable impulse to rise up and scream to the audience: "Here, here
in your very midst, is a tragedy, a real tragedy!" This impulse grew so strong
that I became afraid of myself, and in the darkness of one of the scenes I
stumbled out of the theatre. I walked aimlessly about for an hour or so, my
feelings divided between a desire to weep and a desire to curse. I finally
took a cab and went from café to café, and for one of the very few times in
my life drank myself into a stupor.

It was unwelcome news for me when my benefactor—I could not think
of him as employer—informed me that he was at last tired of Paris. This
news gave me, I think, a passing doubt as to his sanity. I had enjoyed life in
Paris, and, taking all things into consideration, enjoyed it wholesomely.
One thing which greatly contributed to my enjoyment was the fact that I
was an American. Americans are immensely popular in Paris; and this is
not due solely to the fact that they spend lots of money there, for they spend
just as much or more in London, and in the latter city they are merely
tolerated because they do spend. The Londoner seems to think that Americans are people whose only claim to be classed as civilized is that they have
money, and the regrettable thing about that is that the money is not English. But the French are more logical and freer from prejudices than the
British; so the difference of attitude is easily explained. Only once in Paris
did I have cause to blush for my American citizenship. I had become quite
friendly with a young man from Luxemburg whom I had met at the big
café. He was a stolid, slow-witted fellow, but, as we say, with a heart of gold.
He and I grew attached to each other and were together frequently. He was
a great admirer of the United States and never grew tired of talking to me
about the country and asking for information. It was his intention to try his
fortune there some day. One night he asked me in a tone of voice which
indicated that he expected an authoritative denial of an ugly rumor: "Did
they really burn a man alive in the United States?" I never knew what I
stammered out to him as an answer. I should have felt relieved if I could
even have said to him: "Well, only one."

---

6. The brother of Marguerite, the heroine of Gounod's *Faust*.

When we arrived in London, my sadness at leaving Paris was turned into despair. After my long stay in the French capital, huge, ponderous, massive London seemed to me as ugly a thing as man could contrive to make. I thought of Paris as a beauty spot on the face of the earth, and of London as a big freckle. But soon London's massiveness, I might say its very ugliness, began to impress me. I began to experience that sense of grandeur which one feels when he looks at a great mountain or a mighty river. Beside London Paris becomes a toy, a pretty plaything. And I must own that before I left the world's metropolis I discovered much there that was beautiful. The beauty in and about London is entirely different from that in and about Paris; and I could not but admit that the beauty of the French city seemed hand-made, artificial, as though set up for the photographer's camera, everything nicely adjusted so as not to spoil the picture; while that of the English city was rugged, natural, and fresh.

How these two cities typify the two peoples who built them! Even the sound of their names expresses a certain racial difference. Paris is the concrete expression of the gaiety, regard for symmetry, love of art, and, I might well add, of the morality of the French people. London stands for the conservatism, the solidarity, the utilitarianism, and, I might well add, the hypocrisy of the Anglo-Saxon. It may sound odd to speak of the morality of the French, if not of the hypocrisy of the English; but this seeming paradox impresses me as a deep truth. I saw many things in Paris which were immoral according to English standards, but the absence of hypocrisy, the absence of the spirit to do the thing if it might only be done in secret, robbed these very immoralities of the damning influence of the same evils in London. I have walked along the terrace cafés of Paris and seen hundreds of men and women sipping their wine and beer, without observing a sign of drunkenness. As they drank, they chatted and laughed and watched the passing crowds; the drinking seemed to be a secondary thing. This I have witnessed, not only in the cafés along the Grands Boulevards, but in the out-of-the-way places patronized by the working classes. In London I have seen in the "pubs" men and women crowded in stuffy little compartments, drinking seemingly only for the pleasure of swallowing as much as they could hold. I have seen there women from eighteen to eighty, some in tatters, and some clutching babes in their arms, drinking the heavy English ales and whiskies served to them by women. In the whole scene, not one ray of brightness, not one flash of gaiety, only maudlin joviality or grim despair. And I have thought, if some men and women will drink—and it is certain that some will—is it not better that they do so under the open sky, in the fresh air, than huddled together in some close, smoky room? There is a sort of frankness about the evils of Paris which robs them of much of the seductiveness of things forbidden, and with that frankness goes a certain cleanliness of thought belonging to things not hidden. London will do whatever Paris does, provided exterior morals are not shocked. As a result, Paris has the appearance only of being the more immoral city. The difference may be summed up in this: Paris practices its sins as lightly as it does its religion, while London practices both very seriously.

I should not neglect to mention what impressed me most forcibly during my stay in London. It was not St. Paul's nor the British Museum nor Westminster Abbey. It was nothing more or less than the simple phrase "Thank you," or sometimes more elaborated, "Thank you very kindly, sir." I was continually surprised by the varied uses to which it was put; and, strange to say, its use as an expression of politeness seemed more limited than any other. One night I was in a cheap music hall and accidentally bumped into a waiter who was carrying a tray-load of beer, almost bringing him to several shillings' worth of grief. To my amazement he righted himself and said: "Thank ye, sir," and left me wondering whether he meant that he thanked me for not completely spilling his beer, or that he would thank me for keeping out of his way.

I also found cause to wonder upon what ground the English accuse Americans of corrupting the language by introducing slang words. I think I heard more and more different kinds of slang during my few weeks' stay in London than in my whole "tenderloin"[7] life in New York. But I suppose the English feel that the language is theirs, and that they may do with it as they please without at the same time allowing that privilege to others.

My millionaire was not so long in growing tired of London as of Paris. After a stay of six or eight weeks we went across into Holland. Amsterdam was a great surprise to me. I had always thought of Venice as the city of canals; it had never entered my mind that I should find similar conditions in a Dutch town. I don't suppose the comparison goes far beyond the fact that there are canals in both cities—I have never seen Venice—but Amsterdam struck me as being extremely picturesque. From Holland we went to Germany, where we spent five or six months, most of the time in Berlin. I found Berlin more to my taste than London, and occasionally I had to admit that in some things it was superior to Paris.

In Berlin I especially enjoyed the orchestral concerts, and I attended a large number of them. I formed the acquaintance of a good many musicians, several of whom spoke of my playing in high terms. It was in Berlin that my inspiration was renewed. One night my millionaire entertained a party of men composed of artists, musicians, writers, and, for aught I know, a count or two. They drank and smoked a great deal, talked art and music, and discussed, it seemed to me, everything that ever entered man's mind. I could only follow the general drift of what they were saying. When they discussed music, it was more interesting to me; for then some fellow would run excitedly to the piano and give a demonstration of his opinions, and another would follow quickly, doing the same. In this way, I learned that, regardless of what his specialty might be, every man in the party was a musician. I was at the same time impressed with the falsity of the general idea that Frenchmen are excitable and emotional, and that Germans are calm and phlegmatic. Frenchmen are merely gay and never overwhelmed by their emotions. When they talk loud and fast, it is merely talk, while Germans get worked up and red in the face when sustaining an opinion, and in heated discussions are likely to allow their emotions to sweep them off their feet.

My millionaire planned, in the midst of the discussion on music, to have

7. A district of New York City below Forty-second Street and west of Broadway, noted for vice and corruption.

me play the "new American music" and astonish everybody present. The result was that I was more astonished than anyone else. I went to the piano and played the most intricate ragtime piece I knew. Before there was time for anybody to express an opinion on what I had done, a big bespectacled, bushy-headed man rushed over, and, shoving me out of the chair, exclaimed: "Get up! Get up!" He seated himself at the piano, and, taking the theme of my ragtime, played it through first in straight chords; then varied and developed it through every known musical form. I sat amazed. I had been turning classic music into ragtime, a comparatively easy task; and this man had taken ragtime and made it classic. The thought came across me like a flash—It can be done, why can't I do it? From that moment my mind was made up. I clearly saw the way of carrying out the ambition I had formed when a boy.

I now lost interest in our trip. I thought: "Here I am a man, no longer a boy, and what am I doing but wasting my time and abusing my talent? What use am I making of my gifts? What future have I before me following my present course?" These thoughts made me feel remorseful and put me in a fever to get to work, to begin to do something. Of course I know now that I was not wasting time; that there was nothing I could have done at that age which would have benefited me more than going to Europe as I did. The desire to begin work grew stronger each day. I could think of nothing else. I made up my mind to go back into the very heart of the South, to live among the people, and drink in my inspiration firsthand. I gloated over the immense amount of material I had to work with, not only modern ragtime, but also the old slave songs—material which no one had yet touched.

The more decided and anxious I became to return to the United States, the more I dreaded the ordeal of breaking with my millionaire. Between this peculiar man and me there had grown a very strong bond of affection, backed up by a debt which each owed to the other. He had taken me from a terrible life in New York and, by giving me the opportunity of traveling and of coming in contact with the people with whom he associated, had made me a polished man of the world. On the other hand, I was his chief means of disposing of the thing which seemed to sum up all in life that he dreaded— time. As I remember him now, I can see that time was what he was always endeavoring to escape, to bridge over, to blot out; and it is not strange that some years later he did escape it forever, by leaping into eternity.

For some weeks I waited for just the right moment in which to tell my patron of my decision. Those weeks were a trying time to me. I felt that I was playing the part of a traitor to my best friend. At length, one day he said to me: "Well, get ready for a long trip; we are going to Egypt, and then to Japan." The temptation was for an instant almost overwhelming, but I summoned determination enough to say: "I don't think I want to go." "What!" he exclaimed, "you want to go back to your dear Paris? You still think that the only spot on earth? Wait until you see Cairo and Tokio, you may change your mind." "No," I stammered, "it is not because I want to go back to Paris. I want to go back to the United States." He wished to know my reason, and I told him, as best I could, my dreams, my ambition, and my decision. While I was talking, he watched me with a curious, almost cynical, smile growing on his lips. When I had finished he put his hand on my shoulder—this was the first physical expression of tender regard he had ever shown me—and looking at me in a big-brotherly way, said: "My boy, you are by blood, by appearance, by education, and by tastes a white man. Now, why do you want to throw your life away amidst the poverty and ignorance, in the hopeless struggle, of the black people of the United States? Then look at the terrible handicap you are placing on yourself by going home and working as a Negro composer; you can never be able to get the hearing for your work which it might deserve. I doubt that even a white musician of recognized ability could succeed there by working on the theory that American music should be based on Negro themes. Music is a universal art; anybody's music belongs to everybody; you can't limit it to race or country. Now, if you want to become a composer, why not stay right here in Europe? I will put you under the best teachers on the Continent. Then if you want to write music on Negro themes, why, go ahead and do it."

We talked for some time on music and the race question. On the latter subject I had never before heard him express any opinion. Between him and me no suggestion of racial differences had ever come up. I found that he was a man entirely free from prejudice, but he recognized that prejudice was a big stubborn entity which had to be taken into account. He went on to say: "This idea you have of making a Negro out of yourself is nothing more than a sentiment; and you do not realize the fearful import of what you intend to do. What kind of a Negro would you make now, especially in the South? If you had remained there, or perhaps even in your club in New York, you might have succeeded very well; but now you would be miserable. I can imagine no more dissatisfied human being than an educated, cultured, and refined colored man in the United States. I have given more study to the race question in the United States than you may suppose, and I sympathize with the Negroes there; but what's the use? I can't right their wrongs, and neither can you; they must do that themselves. They are unfortunate in having wrongs to right, and you would be foolish to take their wrongs unnecessarily on your shoulders. Perhaps some day, through study and observation, you will come to see that evil is a force, and, like the physical and chemical forces, we cannot annihilate it; we may only change its form. We light upon one evil and hit it with all the might of our civilization, but only succeed in scattering it into a dozen other forms. We hit slavery through a great civil war. Did we destroy it? No, we only changed it into hatred between sections of the country: in the South, into political corruption and chicanery, the degradation of the blacks through peonage,[8] unjust laws, unfair and cruel treatment; and the degradation of the whites by their resorting to these practices, the paralyzation of the public conscience, and the ever over-hanging dread of what the future may bring. Modern civilization hit ignorance of the masses through the means of popular education. What has it done but turn ignorance into anarchy, socialism, strikes, hatred between poor and rich, and universal discontent? In like manner, modern philanthropy hit at suffering and disease through asylums and hospitals; it prolongs the sufferers' lives, it is true, but is, at the same time, sending down strains of insanity and weakness into future generations. My philosophy of life is this: make yourself as happy as possible,

---

8. A means of reducing to near-slavery blacks convicted of crimes who were unable to pay their fines.

and try to make those happy whose lives come in touch with yours; but to attempt to right the wrongs and ease the sufferings of the world in general is a waste of effort. You had just as well try to bail the Atlantic by pouring the water into the Pacific."

This tremendous flow of serious talk from a man I was accustomed to see either gay or taciturn so surprised and overwhelmed me that I could not frame a reply. He left me thinking over what he had said. Whatever was the soundness of his logic or the moral tone of his philosophy, his argument greatly impressed me. I could see, in spite of the absolute selfishness upon which it was based, that there was reason and common sense in it. I began to analyze my own motives, and found that they, too, were very largely mixed with selfishness. Was it more a desire to help those I considered my people, or more a desire to distinguish myself, which was leading me back to the United States? That is a question I have never definitely answered.

For several weeks longer I was in a troubled state of mind. Added to the fact that I was loath to leave my good friend was the weight of the question he had aroused in my mind, whether I was not making a fatal mistake. I suffered more than one sleepless night during that time. Finally, I settled the question on purely selfish grounds, in accordance with my million-aire's philosophy. I argued that music offered me a better future than any-thing else I had any knowledge of, and, in opposition to my friend's opinion, that I should have greater chances of attracting attention as a col-ored composer than as a white one. But I must own that I also felt stirred by an unselfish desire to voice all the joys and sorrows, the hopes and ambi-tions, of the American Negro, in classic musical form.

When my mind was fully made up, I told my friend. He asked me when I intended to start. I replied that I would do so at once. He then asked me how much money I had. I told him that I had saved several hundred dollars out of sums he had given me. He gave me a check for five hundred dollars, told me to write to him in care of his Paris bankers if I ever needed his help, wished me good luck, and bade me good-by. All this he did almost coldly; and I often wondered whether he was in a hurry to get rid of what he con-sidered a fool, or whether he was striving to hide deeper feelings.

And so I separated from the man who was, all in all, the best friend I ever had, except my mother, the man who exerted the greatest influence ever brought into my life, except that exerted by my mother. My affection for him was so strong, my recollections of him are so distinct, he was such a peculiar and striking character, that I could easily fill several chapters with reminiscences of him; but for fear of tiring the reader I shall go on with my narration.

I decided to go to Liverpool[9] and take ship for Boston. I still had an uneasy feeling about returning to New York; and in a few days I found myself aboard ship headed for home.

X

Among the first of my fellow-passengers of whom I took any particular notice was a tall, broad-shouldered, almost gigantic, colored man. His dark-

9. A British seaport.

brown face was clean-shaven; he was well-dressed and bore a decidedly distinguished air. In fact, if he was not handsome, he at least compelled admiration for his fine physical proportions. He attracted general attention as he strode the deck in a sort of majestic loneliness. I became curious to know who he was and determined to strike up an acquaintance with him at the first opportune moment. The chance came a day or two later. He was sitting in the smoking-room, with a cigar, which had gone out, in his mouth, reading a novel. I sat down beside him and, offering him a fresh cigar, said: "You don't mind my telling you something unpleasant, do you?" He looked at me with a smile, accepted the proffered cigar, and replied in a voice which comported perfectly with his size and appearance: "I think my curiosity overcomes any objections I might have." "Well," I said, "have you noticed that the man who sat at your right in the saloon during the first meal has not sat there since?" He frowned slightly without answering my question. "Well," I continued, "he asked the steward to remove him; and not only that, he attempted to persuade a number of the passengers to protest against your presence in the dining-saloon." The big man at my side took a long draw from his cigar, threw his head back, and slowly blew a great cloud of smoke toward the ceiling. Then turning to me he said: "Do you know, I don't object to anyone's having prejudices so long as those prejudices don't interfere with my personal liberty. Now, the man you are speaking of had a perfect right to change his seat if I in any way interfered with his appetite or his digestion. I should have no reason to complain if he removed to the farthest corner of the saloon, or even if he got off the ship; but when his prejudice attempts to move *me* one foot, one inch, out of the place where I am comfortably located, then I object." On the word "object" he brought his great fist down on the table in front of us with such a crash that everyone in the room turned to look. We both covered up the slight embarrassment with a laugh and strolled out on the deck.

We walked the deck for an hour or more, discussing different phases of the Negro question. In referring to the race I used the personal pronoun "we"; my companion made no comment about it, nor evinced any surprise, except to raise his eyebrows slightly the first time he caught the significance of the word. He was the broadest-minded colored man I have ever talked with on the Negro question. He even went so far as to sympathize with and offer excuses for some white Southern points of view. I asked him what were his main reasons for being so hopeful. He replied: "In spite of all that is written, said, and done, this great, big, incontrovertible fact stands out—the Negro is progressing, and that disproves all the arguments in the world that he is incapable of progress. I was born in slavery, and at emancipation was set adrift a ragged, penniless bit of humanity. I have seen the Negro in every grade, and I know what I am talking about. Our detractors point to the increase of crime as evidence against us; certainly we have progressed in crime as in other things; what less could be expected? And yet, in this respect, we are far from the point which has been reached by the more highly civilized white race. As we continue to progress, crime among us will gradually lose much of its brutal, vulgar, I might say healthy, aspect, and become more delicate, refined, and subtle. Then it will be less shocking and noticeable, although more dangerous to society." Then dropping his tone of irony, he continued with some show of eloquence: "But, above all, when I am discouraged and disheartened, I have this to fall back on: if there is a principle of right in the world, which finally prevails, and I believe that there is; if there is a merciful but justice-loving God in heaven, and I believe that there is, we shall win; for we have right on our side, while those who oppose us can defend themselves by nothing in the moral law, nor even by anything in the enlightened thought of the present age."

For several days, together with other topics, we discussed the race problem, not only of the United States, but as it affected native Africans and Jews. Finally, before we reached Boston, our conversation had grown familiar and personal. I had told him something of my past and much about my intentions for the future. I learned that he was a physician, a graduate of Howard University, Washington, and had done post-graduate work in Philadelphia; and this was his second trip abroad to attend professional courses. He had practiced for some years in the city of Washington, and though he did not say so, I gathered that his practice was a lucrative one. Before we left the ship, he had made me promise that I would stop two or three days in Washington before going on south.

We put up at a hotel in Boston for a couple of days and visited several of my new friend's acquaintances; they were all people of education and culture and, apparently, of means. I could not help being struck by the great difference between them and the same class of colored people in the South. In speech and thought they were genuine Yankees. The difference was especially noticeable in their speech. There was none of that heavy-tongued enunciation which characterizes even the best-educated colored people of the South. It is remarkable, after all, what an adaptable creature the Negro is. I have seen the black West Indian gentleman in London, and he is in speech and manners a perfect Englishman. I have seen natives of Haiti and Martinique[1] in Paris, and they are more Frenchy than a Frenchman. I have no doubt that the Negro would make a good Chinaman, with exception of the pigtail.

My stay in Washington, instead of being two or three days, was two or three weeks. This was my first visit to the national capital, and I was, of course, interested in seeing the public buildings and something of the working of the government; but most of my time I spent with the doctor among his friends and acquaintances. The social phase of life among colored people is more developed in Washington than in any other city in the country. This is on account of the large number of individuals earning good salaries and having a reasonable amount of leisure time to draw from. There are dozens of physicians and lawyers, scores of school teachers, and hundreds of clerks in the departments. As to the colored department clerks, I think it fair to say that in educational equipment they average above the white clerks of the same grade; for, whereas a colored college graduate will seek such a job, the white university man goes into one of the many higher vocations which are open to him.

In a previous chapter I spoke of social life among colored people; so there is no need to take it up again here. But there is one thing I did not

___

1. A republic and an island, respectively, in the Caribbean colonized by France.

mention: among Negroes themselves there is the peculiar inconsistency of a color question. Its existence is rarely admitted and hardly ever mentioned; it may not be too strong a statement to say that the greater portion of the race is unconscious of its influence; yet this influence, though silent, is constant. It is evidenced most plainly in marriage selection; thus the black men generally marry women fairer than themselves; while, on the other hand, the dark women of stronger mental endowment are very often married to light-complexioned men; the effect is a tendency toward lighter complexions, especially among the more active elements in the race. Some might claim that this is a tacit admission of colored people among themselves of their own inferiority judged by the color line. I do not think so. What I have termed an inconsistency is, after all, most natural; it is, in fact, a tendency in accordance with what might be called an economic necessity. So far as racial differences go, the United States puts a greater premium on color, or, better, lack of color, than upon anything else in the world. To paraphrase, "Have a white skin, and all things else may be added unto you."[2] I have seen advertisements in newspapers for waiters, bell-boys, or elevator men, which read: "Light-colored man wanted." It is this tremendous pressure which the sentiment of the country exerts that is operating on the race. There is involved not only the question of higher opportunity, but often the question of earning a livelihood; and so I say it is not strange, but a natural tendency. Nor is it any more a sacrifice of self-respect that a black man should give to his children every advantage he can which complexion of the skin carries than that the new or vulgar rich should purchase for their children the advantages which ancestry, aristocracy, and social position carry. I once heard a colored man sum it up in these words: "It's no disgrace to be black, but it's often very inconvenient."

Washington shows the Negro not only at his best, but also at his worst. As I drove around with the doctor, he commented rather harshly on those of the latter class which we saw. He remarked: "You see those lazy, loafing, good-for-nothing darkies; they're not worth digging graves for; yet they are the ones who create impressions of the race for the casual observer. It's because they are always in evidence on the street corners, while the rest of us are hard at work, and you know a dozen loafing darkies make a bigger crowd and a worse impression in this country than fifty white men of the same class. But they ought not to represent the race. We are the race, and the race ought to be judged by us, not by them. Every race and every nation should be judged by the best it has been able to produce, not by the worst."

The recollection of my stay in Washington is a pleasure to me now. In company with the doctor I visited Howard University, the public schools, the excellent colored hospital, with which he was in some way connected, if I remember correctly, and many comfortable and even elegant homes. It was with some reluctance that I continued my journey south. The doctor was very kind in giving me letters to people in Richmond and Nashville when I told him that I intended to stop in both of these cities. In Richmond a man who was then editing a very creditable colored newspaper gave me a great deal of his time and made my stay there of three or four days very

2. Luke 12:31: "But rather seek ye the kingdom of God; and all these things shall be added unto you."

pleasant. In Nashville I spent a whole day at Fisk University, the home of the "Jubilee Singers," and was more than repaid for my time. Among my letters of introduction was one to a very prosperous physician. He drove me about the city and introduced me to a number of people. From Nashville I went to Atlanta, where I stayed long enough to gratify an old desire to see Atlanta University again. I then continued my journey to Macon.

During the trip from Nashville to Atlanta I went into the smoking-compartment of the car to smoke a cigar. I was traveling in a Pullman, not because of an abundance of funds, but because through my experience with my millionaire a certain amount of comfort and luxury had become a necessity to me whenever it was obtainable. When I entered the car, I found only a couple of men there; but in a half-hour there were half a dozen or more. From the general conversation I learned that a fat Jewish-looking man was a cigar manufacturer, and was experimenting in growing Havana tobacco in Florida; that a slender bespectacled young man was from Ohio and a professor in some State institution in Alabama; that a white-mustached, well-dressed man was an old Union soldier who had fought through the Civil War; and that a tall, raw-boned, red-faced man, who seemed bent on leaving nobody in ignorance of the fact that he was from Texas, was a cotton planter.

In the North men may ride together for hours in a "smoker" and unless they are acquainted with each other never exchange a word; in the South men thrown together in such manner are friends in fifteen minutes. There is always present a warm-hearted cordiality which will melt down the most frigid reserve. It may be because Southerners are very much like French-men in that they must talk; and not only must they talk, but they must express their opinions.

The talk in the car was for a while miscellaneous—on the weather, crops, business prospects; the old Union soldier had invested capital in Atlanta, and he predicted that that city would soon be one of the greatest in the country. Finally the conversation drifted to politics; then, as a natural se-quence, turned upon the Negro question.

In the discussion of the race question the diplomacy of the Jew was something to be admired; he had the faculty of agreeing with everybody without losing his allegiance to any side. He knew that to sanction Negro oppression would be to sanction Jewish oppression and would expose him to a shot along that line from the old soldier, who stood firmly on the ground of equal rights and opportunity to all men; long traditions and busi-ness instincts told him when in Rome to act as a Roman. Altogether his position was a delicate one, and I gave him credit for the skill he displayed in maintaining it. The young professor was apologetic. He had had the same views as the G.A.R.[3] man; but a year in the South had opened his eyes, and he had to confess that the problem could hardly be handled any better than it was being handled by the Southern whites. To which the G.A.R. man responded somewhat rudely that he had spent ten times as many years in the South as his young friend and that he could easily under-stand how holding a position in a State institution in Alabama would bring

3. Grand Army of the Republic; the victorious federal army in the Civil War.

about a change of views. The professor turned very red and had very little more to say. The Texan was fierce, eloquent, and profane in his argument, and, in a lower sense, there was a direct logic in what he said, which was convincing; it was only by taking higher ground, by dealing in what Southerners call "theories," that he could be combated. Occasionally some one of the several other men in the "smoker" would throw in a remark to reinforce what he said, but he really didn't need any help; he was sufficient in himself.

In the course of a short time the controversy narrowed itself down to an argument between the old soldier and the Texan. The latter maintained hotly that the Civil War was a criminal mistake on the part of the North and that the humiliation which the South suffered during Reconstruction could never be forgotten. The Union man retorted just as hotly that the South was responsible for the war and that the spirit of unforgetfulness on its part was the greatest cause of present friction; that it seemed to be the one great aim of the South to convince the North that the latter made a mistake in fighting to preserve the Union and liberate the slaves. "Can you imagine," he went on to say, "what would have been the condition of things eventually if there had been no war, and the South had been allowed to follow its course? Instead of one great, prosperous country with nothing before it but the conquests of peace, a score of petty republics, as in Central and South America, wasting their energies in war with each other or in revolutions."

"Well," replied the Texan, "anything—no country at all—is better than having niggers over you. But anyhow, the war was fought and the niggers were freed; for it's no use beating around the bush, the niggers, and not the Union, was the cause of it; and now do you believe that all the niggers on earth are worth the good white blood that was spilt? You freed the nigger and you gave him the ballot, but you couldn't make a citizen out of him. He don't know what he's voting for, and we buy 'em like so many hogs. You're giving 'em education, but that only makes slick rascals out of 'em."

"Don't fancy for a moment," said the Northern man, "that you have any monopoly in buying ignorant votes. The same thing is done on a larger scale in New York and Boston, and in Chicago and San Francisco; and they are not black votes either. As to education's making the Negro worse, you might just as well tell me that religion does the same thing. And, by the way, how many educated colored men do you know personally?"

The Texan admitted that he knew only one, and added that he was in the penitentiary. "But," he said, "do you mean to claim, ballot or no ballot, education or no education, that niggers are the equals of white men?"

"That's not the question," answered the other, "but if the Negro is so distinctly inferior, it is a strange thing to me that it takes such tremendous effort on the part of the white man to make him realize it, and to keep him in the same place into which inferior men naturally fall. However, let us grant for sake of argument that the Negro is inferior in every respect to the white man; that fact only increases our moral responsibility in regard to our actions toward him. Inequalities of numbers, wealth, and power, even of intelligence and morals, should make no difference in the essential rights of men."

"If he's inferior and weaker, and is shoved to the wall, that's his own look-out," said the Texan. "That's the law of nature; and he's bound to go to the wall; for no race in the world has ever been able to stand competition with the Anglo-Saxon. The Anglo-Saxon race has always been and always will be the masters of the world, and the niggers in the South ain't going to change all the records of history."

"My friend," said the old soldier slowly, "if you have studied history, will you tell me, as confidentially between white men, what the Anglo-Saxon has ever done?"

The Texan was too much astonished by the question to venture any reply.

His opponent continued: "Can you name a single one of the great fundamental and original intellectual achievements which have raised man in the scale of civilization that may be credited to the Anglo-Saxon? The art of letters, of poetry, of music, of sculpture, of painting, of the drama, of architecture; the science of mathematics, of astronomy, of philosophy, of logic, of physics, of chemistry, the use of the metals, and the principles of mechanics, were all invented or discovered by darker and what we now call inferior races and nations. We have carried many of these to their highest point of perfection, but the foundation was laid by others. Do you know the only original contribution to civilization we can claim is what we have done in steam and electricity and in making implements of war more deadly? And there we worked largely on principles which we did not discover. Why, we didn't even originate the religion we use. We are a great race, the greatest in the world today, but we ought to remember that we are standing on a pile of past races, and enjoy our position with a little less show of arrogance. We are simply having our turn at the game, and we were a long time getting to it. After all, racial supremacy is merely a matter of dates in history. The man here who belongs to what is, all in all, the greatest race the world ever produced, is almost ashamed to own it. If the Anglo-Saxon is the source of everything good and great in the human race from the beginning, why wasn't the German forest the birthplace of civilization, rather than the valley of the Nile?"

The Texan was somewhat disconcerted, for the argument had passed a little beyond his limits, but he swung it back to where he was sure of his ground by saying: "All that may be true, but it hasn't got much to do with us and the niggers here in the South. We've got 'em here, and we've got 'em to live with, and it's a question of white man or nigger, no middle ground. You want us to treat niggers as equals. Do you want to see 'em sitting around in our parlors? Do you want to see a mulatto South? To bring it right home to you, would you let your daughter marry a nigger?"

"No, I wouldn't consent to my daughter's marrying a nigger, but that doesn't prevent my treating a black man fairly. And I don't see what fair treatment has to do with niggers sitting around in your parlors; they can't come there unless they're invited. Out of all the white men I know, only a hundred or so have the privilege of sitting around in my parlor. As to the mulatto South, if you Southerners have one boast that is stronger than another, it is your women; you put them on a pinnacle of purity and virtue and bow down in a chivalric worship before them; yet you talk and act as though, should you treat the Negro fairly and take the anti-inter-marriage laws off your statute books, these same women would rush into the arms of black lovers and husbands. It's a wonder to me that they don't rise up and resent the insult."

"Colonel," said the Texan, as he reached into his handbag and brought out a large flask of whisky, "you might argue from now until hell freezes over, and you might convince me that you're right, but you'll never convince me that I'm wrong. All you say sounds very good, but it's got nothing to do with facts. You can say what men ought to be, but they ain't that; so there you are. Down here in the South we're up against facts, and we're meeting 'em like facts. We don't believe the nigger is or ever will be the equal of the white man, and we ain't going to treat him as an equal; I'll be damned if we will. Have a drink." Everybody except the professor partook of the generous Texan's flask, and the argument closed in a general laugh and good feeling.

I went back into the main part of the car with the conversation on my mind. Here I had before me the bald, raw, naked aspects of the race question in the South; and, in consideration of the step I was just taking, it was far from encouraging. The sentiments of the Texan—and he expressed the sentiments of the South—fell upon me like a chill. I was sick at heart. Yet I must confess that underneath it all I felt a certain sort of admiration for the man who could not be swayed from what he held as his principles. Contrasted with him, the young Ohio professor was indeed a pitiable character. And all along, in spite of myself, I have been compelled to accord the same kind of admiration to the Southern white man for the manner in which he defends not only his virtues, but his vices. He knows that, judged by a high standard, he is narrow and prejudiced, that he is guilty of unfairness, oppression, and cruelty, but this he defends as stoutly as he would his better qualities. This same spirit obtains in a great degree among the blacks; they, too, defend their faults and failings. This they generally do whenever white people are concerned. And yet among themselves they are their own most merciless critics. I have never heard the race so terribly arraigned as I have by colored speakers to strictly colored audiences. It is the spirit of the South to defend everything belonging to it. The North is too cosmopolitan and tolerant for such a spirit. If you should say to an Easterner that Paris is a gayer city than New York, he would be likely to agree with you, or at least to let you have your own way; but to suggest to a South Carolinian that Boston is a nicer city to live in than Charleston would be to stir his greatest depths of argument and eloquence.

But to-day, as I think over that smoking-car argument, I can see it in a different light. The Texan's position does not render things so hopeless, for it indicates that the main difficulty of the race question does not lie so much in the actual condition of the blacks as it does in the mental attitude of the whites; and a mental attitude, especially one not based on truth, can be changed more easily than actual conditions. That is to say, the burden of the question is not that the whites are struggling to save ten million despondent and moribund people from sinking into a hopeless slough of ignorance, poverty, and barbarity in their very midst, but that they are unwilling to open certain doors of opportunity and to accord certain treatment to ten million aspiring, education-and-property-acquiring people. In a word, the difficulty of the problem is not so much due to the facts presented as to the hypothesis assumed for its solution. In this it is similar to the problem of the solar system. By a complex, confusing, and almost contradictory mathematical process, by the use of zigzags instead of straight lines, the earth can be proved to be the center of things celestial; but by an operation so simple that it can be comprehended by a schoolboy, its position can be verified among the other worlds which revolve about the sun, and its movements harmonized with the laws of the universe. So, when the white race assumes as a hypothesis that it is the main object of creation and that all things else are merely subsidiary to its well-being, sophism,[4] subterfuge, perversion of conscience, arrogance, injustice, oppression, cruelty, sacrifice of human blood, all are required to maintain the position, and its dealings with other races become indeed a problem, a problem which, if based on a hypothesis of common humanity, could be solved by the simple rules of justice.

When I reached Macon, I decided to leave my trunk and all my surplus belongings, to pack my bag, and strike out into the interior. This I did; and by train, by mule and ox-cart. I traveled through many counties. This was my first real experience among rural colored people, and all that I saw was interesting to me; but there was a great deal which does not require description at my hands; for log cabins and plantations and dialect-speaking "darkies" are perhaps better known in American literature than any other single picture of our national life. Indeed, they form an ideal and exclusive literary concept of the American Negro to such an extent that it is almost impossible to get the reading public to recognize him in any other setting; so I shall endeavor to avoid giving the reader any already overworked and hackneyed descriptions. This generally accepted literary ideal of the American Negro constitutes what is really an obstacle in the way of the thoughtful and progressive element of the race. His character has been established as a happy-go-lucky, laughing, shuffling, banjo-picking being, and the reading public has not yet been prevailed upon to take him seriously. His efforts to elevate himself socially are looked upon as a sort of absurd caricature of "white civilization." A novel dealing with colored people who lived in respectable homes and amidst a fair degree of culture and who naturally acted "just like white folks" would be taken in a comic-opera sense. In this respect the Negro is much in the position of a great comedian who gives up the lighter roles to play tragedy. No matter how well he may portray the deeper passions, the public is loath to give him up in his old character; they even conspire to make him a failure in serious work, in order to force him back into comedy. In the same respect, the public is not too much to be blamed, for great comedians are far more scarce than mediocre tragedians; every amateur actor is a tragedian. However, this very fact constitutes the opportunity of the future Negro novelist and poet to give the country something new and unknown, in depicting the life, the ambitions, the struggles,

4. A plausible but deceiving argument.

and the passions of those of their race who are striving to break the narrow limits of traditions. A beginning has already been made in that remarkable book by Dr. Du Bois, *The Souls of Black Folk.*[5]

Much, too, that I saw while on this trip, in spite of my enthusiasm, was disheartening. Often I thought of what my millionaire had said to me, and wished myself back in Europe. The houses in which I had to stay were generally uncomfortable, sometimes worse. I often had to sleep in a division or compartment with several other people. Once or twice I was not so fortunate as to find divisions; everybody slept on pallets on the floor. Frequently I was able to lie down and contemplate the stars which were in their zenith. The food was at times so distasteful and poorly cooked that I could not eat it. I remember that once I lived for a week or more on buttermilk, on account of not being able to stomach the fat bacon, the rank turniptops, and the heavy damp mixture of meal, salt, and water which was called corn bread. It was only my ambition to do the work which I had planned that kept me steadfast to my purpose. Occasionally I would meet with some signs of progress and uplift in even one of these back-wood settlements—houses built of boards, with windows, and divided into rooms; decent food, and a fair standard of living. This condition was due to the fact that there was in the community some exceptionally capable Negro farmer whose thrift served as an example. As I went about among these dull, simple people—the great majority of them hard working, in their relations with the whites submissive, faithful, and often affectionate, negatively content with their lot—and contrasted them with those of the race who had been quickened by the forces of thought, I could not but appreciate the logic of the position held by those Southern leaders who have been bold enough to proclaim against the education of the Negro. They are consistent in their public speech with Southern sentiment and desires. Those public men of the South who have not been daring or heedless enough to defy the ideals of twentieth-century civilization and of modern humanitarianism and philanthropy, find themselves in the embarrassing situation of preaching one thing and praying for another. They are in the position of the fashionable woman who is compelled by the laws of polite society to say to her dearest enemy: "How happy I am to see you!"

And yet in this respect how perplexing is Southern character; for, in opposition to the above, it may be said that the claim of the Southern whites that they love the Negro better than the Northern whites do is in a manner true. Northern white people love the Negro in a sort of abstract way, as a race; through a sense of justice, charity, and philanthropy, they will liberally assist in his elevation. A number of them have heroically spent their lives in this effort (and just here I wish to say that when the colored people reach the monument-building stage, they should not forget the men and women who went South after the war and founded schools for them). Yet, generally speaking, they have no particular liking for individuals of the race. Southern white people despise the Negro as a race, and will do nothing to aid in his elevation as such; but for certain individuals they have a

5. A collection of essays chiefly about African Americans in the South, written by W. E. B. Du Bois (1868–1963) in 1903.

strong affection, and are helpful to them in many ways. With these individual members of the race they live on terms of the greatest intimacy; they entrust to them their children, their family treasures, and their family secrets; in trouble they often go to them for comfort and counsel; in sickness they often rely upon their care. This affectionate relation between the Southern whites and those blacks who come into close touch with them has not been overdrawn even in fiction.

This perplexity of Southern character extends even to the intermixture of the races. That is spoken of as though it were dreaded worse than smallpox, leprosy, or the plague. Yet, when I was in Jacksonville, I knew several prominent families there with large colored branches, which went by the same name and were known and acknowledged as blood relatives. And what is more, there seemed to exist between these black brothers and sisters and uncles and aunts a decidedly friendly feeling.

I said above that Southern whites would do nothing for the Negro as a race. I know the South claims that it has spent millions for the education of the blacks, and that it has of its own free will shouldered this awful burden. It seems to be forgetful of the fact that these millions have been taken from the public tax funds for education, and that the law of political economy which recognizes the land owner as the one who really pays the taxes is not tenable. It would be just as reasonable for the relatively few land owners of Manhattan to complain that they had to stand the financial burden of the education of the thousands and thousands of children whose parents pay rent for tenements and flats. Let the millions of producing and consuming Negroes be taken out of the South, and it would be quickly seen how much less of public funds there would be to appropriate for education or any other purpose.

In thus traveling about through the country I was sometimes amused on arriving at some little railroad-station town to be taken for and treated as a white man, and six hours later, when it was learned that I was stopping at the house of the colored preacher or school teacher, to note the attitude of the whole town change. At times this led even to embarrassment. Yet it cannot be so embarrassing for a colored man to be taken for white as for a white man to be taken for colored; and I have heard of several cases of the latter kind.

All this while I was gathering material for work, jotting down in my notebook themes and melodies, and trying to catch the spirit of the Negro in his relatively primitive state. I began to feel the necessity of hurrying so that I might get back to some city like Nashville to begin my compositions and at the same time earn at least a living by teaching and performing before my funds gave out. At the last settlement in which I stopped I found a mine of material. This was due to the fact that "big meeting" was in progress. "Big meeting" is an institution something like camp-meeting, the difference being that it is held in a permanent church, and not in a temporary structure. All the churches of some one denomination—of course, either Methodist or Baptist—in a county, or, perhaps, in several adjoining counties, are closed, and the congregations unite at some centrally located church for a series of meetings lasting a week. It is really a social as well as a religious function. The people come in great numbers, making the trip, according to their financial status, in buggies drawn by sleek, fleet-footed mules, in ox-carts, or on foot. It was amusing to see some of the latter class trudging down the hot and dusty road, with their shoes, which were brand-new, strung across their shoulders. When they got near the church, they sat on the side of the road and, with many grimaces, tenderly packed their feet into those instruments of torture. This furnished, indeed, a trying test of their religion. The famous preachers come from near and far and take turns in warning sinners of the day of wrath. Food, in the form of those two Southern luxuries, fried chicken and roast pork, is plentiful, and no one need go hungry. On the opening Sunday the women are immaculate in starched stiff white dresses adorned with ribbons, either red or blue. Even a great many of the men wear streamers of vari-colored ribbons in the button-holes of their coats. A few of them carefully cultivate a forelock of hair by wrapping it in twine, and on such festive occasions decorate it with a nar-row ribbon streamer. Big meetings afford a fine opportunity to the younger people to meet each other dressed in their Sunday clothes, and much rus-tic courting, which is as enjoyable as any other kind, is indulged in.

This big meeting which I was lucky enough to catch was particularly well attended; the extra large attendance was due principally to two attrac-tions, a man by the name of John Brown, who was renowned as the most powerful preacher for miles around; and a wonderful leader of singing, who was known as "Singing Johnson." These two men were a study and a revelation to me. They caused me to reflect upon how great an influence their types have been in the development of the Negro in America. Both these types are now looked upon generally with condescension or con-tempt by the progressive element among the colored people; but it should never be forgotten that it was they who led the race from paganism and kept it steadfast to Christianity through all the long, dark years of slavery.

John Brown was a jet-black man of medium size, with a strikingly intelli-gent head and face, and a voice like an organ peal. He preached each night after several lesser lights had successively held the pulpit during an hour or so. As far as subject-matter is concerned, all of the sermons were alike: each began with the fall of man, ran through various trials and tribulations of the Hebrew children, on to the redemption by Christ, and ended with a fervid picture of the judgment day and the fate of the damned. But John Brown possessed magnetism and an imagination so free and daring that he was able to carry through what the other preachers would not attempt. He knew all the arts and tricks of oratory, the modulation of the voice to almost a whisper, the pause for effect, the rise through light, rapid-fire sentences to the terrific, thundering outburst of an electrifying climax. In addition, he had the intuition of a born theatrical manager. Night after night this man held me fascinated. He convinced me that, after all, eloquence consists more in the manner of saying than in what is said. It is largely a matter of tone pictures.

The most striking example of John Brown's magnetism and imagina-tion was his "heavenly march"; I shall never forget how it impressed me when I heard it. He opened his sermon in the usual way; then, proclaim-ing to his listeners that he was going to take them on the heavenly march, he seized the Bible under his arm and began to pace up and down the pulpit platform. The congregation immediately began with their feet a tramp, tramp, tramp, in time with the preacher's march in the pulpit, all the while singing in an undertone a hymn about marching to Zion. Suddenly he cried: "Halt!" Every foot stopped with the precision of a company of well-drilled soldiers, and the singing ceased. The morning star had been reached. Here the preacher described the beauties of that celestial body. Then the march, the tramp, tramp, tramp, and the singing were again taken up. Another "Halt!" They had reached the evening star. And so on, past the sun and moon—the intensity of religious emotion all the time increasing—along the milky way, on up to the gates of heaven. Here the halt was longer, and the preacher described at length the gates and walls of the New Jerusalem. Then he took his hearers through the pearly gates, along the golden streets, pointing out the glories of the city, pausing occasionally to greet some patriarchal members of the church, well-known to most of his listeners in life, who had had "the tears wiped from their eyes, were clad in robes of spotless white, with crowns of gold upon their heads and harps within their hands," and ended his march before the great white throne. To the reader this may sound ridiculous, but listened to under the circumstances, it was highly and effectively dramatic. I was a more or less sophisticated and non-religious man of the world, but the torrent of the preacher's words, moving with the rhythm and glowing with the eloquence of primitive poetry, swept me along, and I, too, felt like joining in the shouts of "Amen! Hallelujah!"

John Brown's powers in describing the delights of heaven were no greater than those in depicting the horrors of hell. I saw great, strapping fellows trembling and weeping like children at the "mourners' bench." His warnings to sinners were truly terrible. I shall never forget one expression that he used, which for originality and aptness could not be excelled. In my opinion, it is more graphic and, for us, far more expressive than St. Paul's "It is hard to kick against the pricks."[6] He struck the attitude of a pugilist and thundered out: "Young man, your arm's too short to box with God!"

Interesting as was John Brown to me, the other man, "Singing Johnson," was more so. He was a small, dark-brown, one-eyed man, with a clear, strong, high-pitched voice, a leader of singing, a maker of songs, a man who could improvise at the moment lines to fit the occasion. Not so striking a figure as John Brown, but, at "big meetings," equally important. It is indispensable to the success of the singing, when the congregation is a large one made up of people from different communities, to have someone with a strong voice who knows just what hymn to sing and when to sing it, who can pitch it in the right key, and who has all the leading lines committed to memory. Sometimes it devolves upon the leader to "sing down" a long-winded or uninteresting speaker. Committing to memory the leading lines of all the Negro spiritual songs is no easy task, for they run up into the hundreds. But the accomplished leader must know them all, because the congregation sings only the refrains and repeats; every ear in the church is fixed upon him, and if he becomes mixed in his lines or forgets them, the responsibility falls directly on his shoulders.

6. Cf. Acts 9:5: "It is hard for thee to kick against the pricks."

For example, most of these hymns are constructed to be sung in the following manner:

> Leader. *Swing low, sweet chariot.*
> Congregation. *Coming for to carry me home.*
> Leader. *Swing low, sweet chariot.*
> Congregation. *Coming for to carry me home.*
> Leader. *I look over yonder, what do I see?*
> Congregation. *Coming for to carry me home.*
> Leader. *Two little angels coming after me.*
> Congregation. *Coming for to carry me home. . . .*

The solitary and plaintive voice of the leader is answered by a sound like the roll of the sea, producing a most curious effect.

In only a few of these songs do the leader and the congregation start off together. Such a song is the well-known "Steal away to Jesus."

The leader and the congregation begin with part-singing:

> *Steal away, steal away,*
> *Steal away to Jesus;*
> *Steal away, steal away home,*
> *I ain't got long to stay here.*

Then the leader alone or the congregation in unison:

> *My Lord he calls me,*
> *He calls me by the thunder,*
> *The trumpet sounds within-a my soul.*

Then all together:

> *I ain't got long to stay here.*

The leader and the congregation again take up the opening refrain; then the leader sings three more leading lines alone, and so on almost *ad infinitum*. It will be seen that even here most of the work falls upon the leader, for the congregation sings the same lines over and over, while his memory and ingenuity are taxed to keep the songs going.

Generally the parts taken up by the congregation are sung in a three-part harmony, the women singing the soprano and a transposed tenor, the men with high voices singing the melody, and those with low voices a thundering bass. In a few of these songs, however, the leading part is sung in unison by the whole congregation, down to the last line, which is harmonized. The effect of this is intensely thrilling. Such a hymn is "Go down, Moses." It stirs the heart like a trumpet call.

"Singing Johnson" was an ideal leader, and his services were in great demand. He spent his time going about the country from one church to another. He received his support in much the same way as the preachers—part of a collection, food and lodging. All of his leisure time he devoted to originating new words and melodies and new lines for old songs. He always sang with his eyes—or, to be more exact, his eye—closed, indicating the *tempo* by swinging his head to and fro. He was a great judge of the proper hymn to sing at a particular moment; and I noticed several times, when the preacher reached a certain climax, or expressed a certain sentiment, that Johnson broke in with a line or two of some appropriate hymn. The speaker understood and would pause until the singing ceased.

As I listened to the singing of these songs, the wonder of their production grew upon me more and more. How did the men who originated them manage to do it? The sentiments are easily accounted for; they are mostly taken from the Bible; but the melodies, where did they come from? Some of them so weirdly sweet, and others so wonderfully strong. Take, for instance, "Go down, Moses." I doubt that there is a stronger theme in the whole musical literature of the world. And so many of these songs contain more than mere melody; there is sounded in them that elusive undertone, the note in music which is not heard with the ears. I sat often with the tears rolling down my cheeks and my heart melted within me. Any musical person who has never heard a Negro congregation under the spell of religious fervor sing these old songs has missed one of the most thrilling emotions which the human heart may experience. Anyone who without shedding tears can listen to Negroes sing "Nobody knows de trouble I see, Nobody knows but Jesus" must indeed have a heart of stone.

As yet, the Negroes themselves do not fully appreciate these old slave songs. The educated classes are rather ashamed of them and prefer to sing hymns from books. This feeling is natural; they are still too close to the conditions under which the songs were produced; but the day will come when this slave music will be the most treasured heritage of the American Negro.

At the close of the "big meeting" I left the settlement where it was being held, full of enthusiasm. I was in that frame of mind which, in the artistic temperament, amounts to inspiration. I was now ready and anxious to get to some place where I might settle down to work, and give expression to the ideas which were teeming in my head; but I strayed into another deviation from my path of life as I had it marked out, which led me upon an entirely different road. Instead of going to the nearest and most convenient railroad station, I accepted the invitation of a young man who had been present the closing Sunday at the meeting to drive with him some miles farther to the town in which he taught school, and there take the train. My conversation with this young man as we drove along through the country was extremely interesting. He had been a student in one of the Negro colleges—strange coincidence, in the very college, as I learned through him, in which "Shiny" was now a professor. I was, of course, curious to hear about my boyhood friend; and had it not been vacation time, and that I was not sure that I should find him, I should have gone out of my way to pay him a visit; but I determined to write to him as soon as the school opened. My companion talked to me about his work among the people, of his hopes and his discouragements. He was tremendously in earnest; I might say, too much so. In fact, it may be said that the majority of intelligent colored people are, in some degree, too much in earnest over the race question. They assume and carry so much that their progress is at times impeded and they are unable to see things in their proper proportions. In many instances a slight exercise of the sense of humor would save much anxiety of soul. Anyone who marks the general tone of editorials in colored newspapers is apt to be impressed with this idea. If the mass of Negroes took their present and future as seriously as do the most of their leaders, the race would be in no mental condition to sustain the terrible pressure which it undergoes; it would sink of its own weight. Yet it must be acknowledged that in the making of a race overseriousness is a far lesser failing than its reverse, and even the faults resulting from it lean toward the right.

We drove into the town just before dark. As we passed a large, unpainted church, my companion pointed it out as the place where he held his school. I promised that I would go there with him the next morning and visit awhile. The town was of that kind which hardly requires or deserves description; a straggling line of brick and wooden stores on one side of the railroad track and some cottages of various sizes on the other side constituted about the whole of it. The young school teacher boarded at the best house in the place owned by a colored man. It was painted, had glass windows, contained "store bought" furniture, an organ, and lamps with chimneys. The owner held a job of some kind on the railroad. After supper it was not long before everybody was sleepy. I occupied the room with the school teacher. In a few minutes after we got into the room he was in bed and asleep; but I took advantage of the unusual luxury of a lamp which gave light, and sat looking over my notes and jotting down some ideas which were still fresh in my mind. Suddenly I became conscious of that sense of alarm which is always aroused by the sound of hurrying footsteps on the silence of the night. I stopped work and looked at my watch. It was after eleven. I listened, straining every nerve to hear above the tumult of my quickening pulse. I caught the murmur of voices, then the gallop of a horse, then of another and another. Now thoroughly alarmed, I woke my companion, and together we both listened. After a moment he put out the light and softly opened the window-blind, and we cautiously peeped out. We saw men moving in one direction, and from the mutterings we vaguely caught the rumor that some terrible crime had been committed. I put on my coat and hat. My friend did all in his power to dissuade me from venturing out, but it was impossible for me to remain in the house under such tense excitement. My nerves would not have stood it. Perhaps what bravery I exercised in going out was due to the fact that I felt sure my identity as a colored man had not yet become known in the town.

I went out and, following the drift, reached the railroad station. There was gathered there a crowd of men, all white, and others were steadily arriving, seemingly from all the surrounding country. How did the news spread so quickly? I watched these men moving under the yellow glare of the kerosene lamps about the station, stern, comparatively silent, all of them armed, some of them in boots and spurs; fierce, determined men. I had come to know the type well, blond, tall, and lean, with ragged mustache and beard, and glittering gray eyes. At the first suggestion of daylight they began to disperse in groups, going in several directions. There was no extra noise or excitement, no loud talking, only swift, sharp words of command given by those who seemed to be accepted as leaders by mutual understanding. In fact, the impression made upon me was that everything was being done in quite an orderly manner. In spite of so many leaving, the crowd around the station continued to grow; at sunrise there were a great many women and children. By this time I also noticed some colored people; a few seemed to be going about customary tasks; several were standing on the outskirts of the crowd; but the gathering of Negroes usually seen in such towns was missing.

Before noon they brought him in. Two horsemen rode abreast; between them, half dragged, the poor wretch made his way through the dust. His hands were tied behind him, and ropes around his body were fastened to the saddle horns of his double guard. The men who at midnight had been stern and silent were now emitting that terror-instilling sound known as the "rebel yell." A space was quickly cleared in the crowd, and a rope placed about his neck, when from somewhere came the suggestion, "Burn him!" It ran like an electric current. Have you ever witnessed the transformation of human beings into savage beasts? Nothing can be more terrible. A railroad tie was sunk into the ground, the rope was removed, and a chain brought and securely coiled around the victim and the stake. There he stood, a man only in form and stature, every sign of degeneracy stamped upon his countenance. His eyes were dull and vacant, indicating not a single ray of thought. Evidently the realization of his fearful fate had robbed him of whatever reasoning power he had ever possessed. He was too stunned and stupefied even to tremble. Fuel was brought from everywhere, oil, the torch; the flames crouched for an instant as though to gather strength, then leaped up as high as their victim's head. He squirmed, he writhed, strained at his chains, then gave out cries and groans that I shall always hear. The cries and groans were choked off by the fire and smoke; but his eyes, bulging from their sockets, rolled from side to side, appealing in vain for help. Some of the crowd yelled and cheered, others seemed appalled at what they had done, and there were those who turned away sickened at the sight. I was fixed to the spot where I stood, powerless to take my eyes from what I did not want to see.

It was over before I realized that time had elapsed. Before I could make myself believe that what I saw was really happening, I was looking at a scorched post, a smoldering fire, blackened bones, charred fragments sifting down through coils of chain; and the smell of burnt flesh—human flesh—was in my nostrils.

I walked a short distance away and sat down in order to clear my dazed mind. A great wave of humiliation and shame swept over me. Shame that I belonged to a race that could be so dealt with; and shame for my country, that it, the great example of democracy to the world, should be the only civilized, if not the only state on earth, where a human being would be burned alive. My heart turned bitter within me. I could understand why Negroes are led to sympathize with even their worst criminals and to protect them when possible. By all the impulses of normal human nature they can and should do nothing less.

Whenever I hear protests from the South that it should be left alone to deal with the Negro question, my thoughts go back to that scene of brutality and savagery. I do not see how a people that can find in its conscience any excuse whatever for slowly burning to death a human being, or for tolerating such an act, can be entrusted with the salvation of a race. Of course, there are in the South men of liberal thought who do not approve lynching, but I wonder how long they will endure the limits which are placed upon free speech. They still cower and tremble before "Southern opinion." Even so late as the recent Atlanta riot[7] those men who were brave enough to speak a word in behalf of justice and humanity felt called upon, by way of apology, to preface what they said with a glowing rhetorical tribute to the Anglo-Saxon's superiority and to refer to the "great and impassable gulf" between the races "fixed by the Creator at the foundation of the world." The question of the relative qualities of the two races is still an open one. The reference to the "great gulf" loses force in face of the fact that there are in this country perhaps three or four million people with the blood of both races in their veins; but I fail to see the pertinency of either statement subsequent to the beating and murdering of scores of innocent people in the streets of a civilized and Christian city.

The Southern whites are in many respects a great people. Looked at from a certain point of view, they are picturesque. If one will put oneself in a romantic frame of mind, one can admire their notions of chivalry and bravery and justice. In this same frame of mind an intelligent man can go to the theatre and applaud the impossible hero, who with his single sword slays everybody in the play except the equally impossible heroine. So can an ordinary peace-loving citizen sit by a comfortable fire and read with enjoyment of the bloody deeds of pirates and the fierce brutality of Vikings. This is the way in which we gratify the old, underlying animal instincts and passions; but we should shudder with horror at the mere idea of such practices being realities in this day of enlightened and humanitarianized thought. The Southern whites are not yet living quite in the present age; many of their general ideas hark back to a former century, some of them to the Dark Ages. In the light of other days they are sometimes magnificent. Today they are often cruel and ludicrous.

How long I sat with bitter thoughts running through my mind I do not know; perhaps an hour or more. When I decided to get up and go back to the house, I found that I could hardly stand on my feet. I was as weak as a man who had lost blood. However, I dragged myself along, with the central idea of a general plan well fixed in my mind. I did not find my school teacher friend at home, so I did not see him again. I swallowed a few mouthfuls of food, packed my bag, and caught the afternoon train.

When I reached Macon, I stopped only long enough to get the main part of my luggage and to buy a ticket for New York. All along the journey I was occupied in debating with myself the step which I had decided to take. I argued that to forsake one's race to better one's condition was no less worthy an action than to forsake one's country for the same purpose. I finally made up my mind that I would neither disclaim the black race nor claim the white race; but that I would change my name, raise a mustache, and let the world take me for what it would; that it was not necessary for me to go about with a label of inferiority pasted across my forehead. All the while I

7. A bloody race riot in Atlanta, Georgia, in September 1906.

understood that it was not discouragement or fear or search for a larger field of action and opportunity that was driving me out of the Negro race. I knew that it was shame, unbearable shame. Shame at being identified with a people that could with impunity be treated worse than animals. For certainly the law would restrain and punish the malicious burning alive of animals.

So once again I found myself gazing at the towers of New York and wondering what future that city held in store for me.

XI

I have now reached that part of my narrative where I must be brief and touch only on important facts; therefore the reader must make up his mind to pardon skips and jumps and meager details.

When I reached New York, I was completely lost. I could not have felt more a stranger had I been suddenly dropped into Constantinople. [8] I knew not where to turn or how to strike out. I was so oppressed by a feeling of loneliness that the temptation to visit my old home in Connecticut was well-nigh irresistible. I reasoned, however, that unless I found my old music teacher, I should be, after so many years of absence, as much of a stranger there as in New York; and, furthermore, that in view of the step which I had decided to take, such a visit would be injudicious. I remembered, too, that I had some property there in the shape of a piano and a few books, but decided that it would not be worth what it might cost me to take possession.

By reason of the fact that my living expenses in the South had been very small, I still had nearly four hundred dollars of my capital left. In contemplation of this, my natural and acquired Bohemian tastes asserted themselves, and I decided to have a couple of weeks' good time before worrying seriously about the future. I went to Coney Island [9] and the other resorts, took in the pre-season shows along Broadway, and ate at firstclass restaurants; but I shunned the old Sixth Avenue district as though it were pest-infected. My few days of pleasure made appalling inroads upon what cash I had, and caused me to see that it required a good deal of money to live in New York as I wished to live and that I should have to find, very soon, some more or less profitable employment. I was sure that unknown, without friends or prestige, it would be useless to try to establish myself as a teacher of music; so I gave that means of earning a livelihood scarcely any consideration. And even had I considered it possible to secure pupils, as I then felt, I should have hesitated about taking up a work in which the chances for any considerable financial success are necessarily so small. I had made up my mind that since I was not going to be a Negro, I would avail myself of every possible opportunity to make a white man's success; and that, if it can be summed up in any one word, means "money."

I watched the "want" columns in the newspapers and answered a number of advertisements, but in each case found the positions were such as I could not fill or did not want. I also spent several dollars for "ads" which brought me no replies. In this way I came to know the hopes and disappointments of a large and pitiable class of humanity in this great city, the people who look for work through the newspapers. After some days of this sort of experience I concluded that the main difficulty with me was that I was not prepared for what I wanted to do. I then decided upon a course which, for an artist, showed an uncommon amount of practical sense and judgment. I made up my mind to enter a business college. I took a small room, ate at lunch counters, in order to economize, and pursued my studies with the zeal that I have always been able to put into any work upon which I set my heart. Yet, in spite of all my economy, when I had been at the school for several months, my funds gave out completely. I reached the point where I could not afford sufficient food for each day. In this plight I was glad to get, through one of the teachers, a job as an ordinary clerk in a downtown wholesale house. I did my work faithfully, and received a raise of salary before I expected it. I even managed to save a little money out of my modest earnings. In fact, I began then to contract the money fever, which later took strong possession of me. I kept my eyes open, watching for a chance to better my condition. It finally came in the form of a position with a house which was at the time establishing a South American department. My knowledge of Spanish was, of course, the principal cause of my good luck; and it did more for me: it placed me where the other clerks were practically put out of competition with me. I was not slow in taking advantage of the opportunity to make myself indispensable to the firm.

What an interesting and absorbing game is money-making! After each deposit at my savings-bank I used to sit and figure out, all over again, my principal and interest, and make calculations on what the increase would be in such and such time. Out of this I derived a great deal of pleasure. I denied myself as much as possible in order to swell my savings. As much as I enjoyed smoking, I limited myself to an occasional cigar, and that was generally of a variety which in my old days at the "Club" was known as a "Henry Mud." Drinking I cut out altogether, but that was no great sacrifice.

The day on which I was able to figure up a thousand dollars marked an epoch in my life. And this was not because I had never before had money. In my gambling days and while I was with my millionaire I handled sums running high up into the hundreds; but they had come to me like fairy godmother's gifts, and at a time when my conception of money was that it was made only to spend. Here, on the other hand, was a thousand dollars which I had earned by days of honest and patient work, a thousand dollars which I had carefully watched grow from the first dollar; and I experienced, in owning them, a pride and satisfaction which to me was an entirely new sensation. As my capital went over the thousand-dollar mark, I was puzzled to know what to do with it, how to put it to the most advantageous use. I turned down first one scheme and then another, as though they had been devised for the sole purpose of gobbling up my money. I finally listened to a friend who advised me to put all I had in New York real estate; and under his guidance I took equity in a piece of property on which stood a rickety old tenement-house. I did not regret following this friend's advice, for in something like six months I disposed of my equity for more than double my investment. From that time on I devoted myself to the study of New York real estate and watched for opportunities to make similar investments. In spite of two or three speculations which did not turn out well, I have been remarkably successful. Today I am the owner and part-owner of several flat-houses. I have changed my place of employment four times since returning to New York, and each change has been a decided advancement. Concerning the position which I now hold I shall say nothing except that it pays extremely well.

As my outlook on the world grew brighter, I began to mingle in the social circles of the men with whom I came in contact; and gradually, by a process of elimination, I reached a grade of society of no small degree of culture. My appearance was always good and my ability to play on the piano, especially ragtime, which was then at the height of its vogue, made me a welcome guest. The anomaly of my social position often appealed strongly to my sense of humor. I frequently smiled inwardly at some remark not altogether complimentary to people of color; and more than once I felt like declaiming: "I am a colored man. Do I not disprove the theory that one drop of Negro blood renders a man unfit?" Many a night when I returned to my room after an enjoyable evening, I laughed heartily over what struck me as the capital joke I was playing.

Then I met her, and what I had regarded as a joke was gradually changed into the most serious question of my life. I first saw her at a musical which was given one evening at a house to which I was frequently invited. I did not notice her among the other guests before she came forward and sang two sad little songs. When she began, I was out in the hallway, where many of the men were gathered; but with the first few notes I crowded with others into the doorway to see who the singer was. When I saw the girl, the surprise which I had felt at the first sound of her voice was heightened; she was almost tall and quite slender, with lustrous yellow hair and eyes so blue as to appear almost black. She was as white as a lily, and she was dressed in white. Indeed, she seemed to me the most dazzlingly white thing I had ever seen. But it was not her delicate beauty which attracted me most; it was her voice, a voice which made one wonder how tones of such passionate color could come from so fragile a body.

I determined that when the program was over, I would seek an introduction to her; but at the moment, instead of being the easy man of the world, I became again the bashful boy of fourteen, and my courage failed me. I contented myself with hovering as near her as politeness would permit; near enough to hear her voice, which in conversation was low, yet thrilling, like the deeper middle tones of a flute. I watched the men gather round her talking and laughing in an easy manner, and wondered how it was possible for them to do it. But destiny, my special destiny, was at work. I was standing near, talking with affected gaiety to several young ladies, who, however, must have remarked my preoccupation; for my second sense of hearing was alert to what was being said by the group of which the girl in white was the center, when I heard her say: "I think his playing of Chopin is exquisite." And one of my friends in the group replied: "You haven't met him? Allow me—" Then turning to me, "Old man, when you have a moment I wish you to meet Miss ———." I don't know what she said to me or what I said to her. I can remember that I tried to be clever, and experienced a growing conviction that I was making myself appear more and more idiotic. I am certain, too, that, in spite of my Italian-like complexion, I was as red as a beet.

Instead of taking the car, I walked home. I needed the air and exercise as a sort of sedative. I am not sure whether my troubled condition of mind was due to the fact that I had been struck by love or to the feeling that I had made a bad impression upon her.

As the weeks went by, and when I had met her several more times, I came to know that I was seriously in love; and then began for me days of worry, for I had more than the usual doubts and fears of a young man in love to contend with.

Up to this time I had assumed and played my rôle as a white man with a certain degree of nonchalance, a carelessness as to the outcome, which made the whole thing more amusing to me than serious; but now I ceased to regard "being a white man" as a sort of practical joke. My acting had called for mere external effects. Now I began to doubt my ability to play the part. I watched her to see if she was scrutinizing me, to see if she was looking for anything in me which made me differ from the other men she knew. In place of an old inward feeling of superiority over many of my friends I began to doubt myself. I began even to wonder if I really was like the men I associated with; if there was not, after all, an indefinable something which marked a difference.

But, in spite of my doubts and timidity, my affair progressed, and I finally felt sufficiently encouraged to decide to ask her to marry me. Then began the hardest struggle of my life, whether to ask her to marry me under false colors or to tell her the whole truth. My sense of what was exigent made me feel there was no necessity of saying anything; but my inborn sense of honor rebelled at even indirect deception in this case. But however much I moralized on the question, I found it more and more difficult to reach the point of confession. The dread that I might lose her took possession of me each time I sought to speak, and rendered it impossible for me to do so. That moral courage requires more than physical courage is no mere poetic fancy. I am sure I should have found it easier to take the place of a gladiator, no matter how fierce the Numidian[1] lion, than to tell that slender girl that I had Negro blood in my veins. The fact which I had at times wished to cry out, I now wished to hide forever.

During this time we were drawn together a great deal by the mutual bond of music. She loved to hear me play Chopin and was herself far from being a poor performer of his compositions. I think I carried her every new song that was published which I thought suitable to her voice, and played the accompaniment for her. Over these songs we were like two innocent children with new toys. She had never been anything but innocent; but my innocence was a transformation wrought by my love for her, love which melted away my cynicism and whitened my sullied soul and gave me back the wholesome dreams of my boyhood.

1. From Numidia, an ancient country in North Africa.

My artistic temperament also underwent an awakening. I spent many hours at my piano, playing over old and new composers. I also wrote several little pieces in a more or less Chopinesque style, which I dedicated to her. And so the weeks and months went by. Often words of love trembled on my lips, but I dared not utter them, because I knew they would have to be followed by other words which I had not the courage to frame. There might have been some other woman in my set whom I could have fallen in love with and asked to marry me without a word of explanation; but the more I knew this girl, the less could I find it in my heart to deceive her. And yet, in spite of this specter that was constantly looming up before me, I could never have believed that life held such happiness as was contained in those dream days of love.

One Saturday afternoon, in early June, I was coming up Fifth Avenue, and at the corner of Twenty-third Street I met her. She had been shopping. We stopped to chat for a moment, and I suggested that we spend half an hour at the Eden Musée.[2] We were standing leaning on the rail in front of a group of figures, more interested in what we had to say to each other than in the group, when my attention became fixed upon a man who stood at my side studying his catalogue. It took me only an instant to recognize in him my old friend "Shiny." My first impulse was to change my position at once. As quick as a flash I considered all the risks I might run in speaking to him, and most especially the delicate question of introducing him to her. I confess that in my embarrassment and confusion I felt small and mean. But before I could decide what to do, he looked around at me and, after an instant, quietly asked: "Pardon me; but isn't this—?" The nobler part in me responded to the sound of his voice and I took his hand in a hearty clasp. Whatever fears I had felt were quickly banished, for he seemed, at a glance, to divine my situation, and let drop no word that would have aroused suspicion as to the truth. With a slight misgiving I presented him to her and was again relieved of fear. She received the introduction in her usual gracious manner, and without the least hesitancy or embarrassment joined in the conversation. An amusing part about the introduction was that I was upon the point of introducing him as "Shiny," and stammered a second or two before I could recall his name. We chatted for some fifteen minutes. He was spending his vacation north, with the intention of doing four or six weeks' work in one of the summer schools; he was also going to take a bride back with him in the fall. He asked me about myself, but in so diplomatic a way that I found no difficulty in answering him. The polish of his language and the unpedantic manner in which he revealed his culture greatly impressed her; and after we had left the Musée she showed it by questioning me about him. I was surprised at the amount of interest a refined black man could arouse. Even after changes in the conversation she reverted several times to the subject of "Shiny." Whether it was more than mere curiosity I could not tell, but I was convinced that she herself knew very little about prejudice.

Just why it should have done so I do not know, but somehow the "Shiny"

2. A popular wax museum in downtown Manhattan.

incident gave me encouragement and confidence to cast the die of my fate. I reasoned, however, that since I wanted to marry her only, and since it concerned her alone, I would divulge my secret to no one else, not even her parents.

One evening, a few days afterwards, at her home we were going over some new songs and compositions when she asked me, as she often did, to play the Thirteenth Nocturne.[3] When I began, she drew a chair near to my right and sat leaning with her elbow on the end of the piano, her chin resting on her hand, and her eyes reflecting the emotions which the music awoke in her. An impulse which I could not control rushed over me, a wave of exultation, the music under my fingers sank almost to a whisper, and calling her for the first time by her Christian name, but without daring to look at her, I said: "I love you, I love you, I love you." My fingers were trembling so that I ceased playing. I felt her hand creep to mine, and when I looked at her, her eyes were glistening with tears. I understood, and could scarcely resist the longing to take her in my arms; but I remembered, re-membered that which has been the sacrificial altar of so much happiness— Duty; and bending over her hand in mine, I said: "Yes, I love you; but there is something more, too, that I must tell you." Then I told her, in what words I do not know, the truth. I felt her hand grow cold, and when I looked up, she was gazing at me with a wild, fixed stare as though I was some object she had never seen. Under the strange light in her eyes I felt that I was growing black and thick-featured and crimp-haired. She ap-peared not to have comprehended what I had said. Her lips trembled and she attempted to say something to me, but the words stuck in her throat. Then, dropping her head on the piano, she began to weep with great sobs that shook her frail body. I tried to console her, and blurted out incoherent words of love, but this seemed only to increase her distress, and when I left her, she was still weeping.

When I got into the street, I felt very much as I did the night after meet-ing my father and sister at the opera in Paris, even a similar desperate incli-nation to get drunk; but my self-control was stronger. This was the only time in my life that I ever felt absolute regret at being colored, that I cursed the drops of African blood in my veins and wished that I were really white. When I reached my rooms, I sat and smoked several cigars while I tried to think out the significance of what had occurred. I reviewed the whole his-tory of our acquaintance, recalled each smile she had given me, each word she had said to me that nourished my hope. I went over the scene we had just gone through, trying to draw from it what was in my favor and what was against me. I was rewarded by feeling confident that she loved me, but I could not estimate what was the effect upon her of my confession. At last, nervous and unhappy, I wrote her a letter, which I dropped into the mail-box before going to bed, in which I said:

> I understand, understand even better than you, and so I suffer even more than you. But why should either of us suffer for what neither of us is to blame for? If there is any blame, it belongs to me and I can only

3. A piano composition by Chopin.

make the old, yet strongest plea that can be offered, I love you; and I know that my love, my great love, infinitely overbalances that blame and blots it out. What is it that stands in the way of our happiness? It is not what you feel or what I feel; it is not what you are or what I am. It is what others feel and are. But, oh! is that a fair price? In all the endeavors and struggles of life, in all our strivings and longings, there is only one thing worth seeking, only one thing worth winning, and that is love. It is not always found; but when it is, there is nothing in all the world for which it can be profitably exchanged.

The second morning after, I received a note from her which stated briefly that she was going up into New Hampshire to spend the summer with relatives there. She made no reference to what had passed between us; nor did she say exactly when she would leave the city. The note contained no single word that gave me any clue to her feelings. I could gather hope only from the fact that she had written at all. On the same evening, with a degree of trepidation which rendered me almost frightened, I went to her house.

I met her mother, who told me that she had left for the country that very afternoon. Her mother treated me in her usual pleasant manner, which fact greatly reassured me; and I left the house with a vague sense of hope stirring in my breast, which sprang from the conviction that she had not yet divulged my secret. But that hope did not remain with me long. I waited one, two, three weeks, nervously examining my mail every day, looking for some word from her. All of the letters received by me seemed so insignificant, so worthless, because there was none from her. The slight buoyancy of spirit which I had felt gradually dissolved into gloomy heart-sickness. I became preoccupied; I lost appetite, lost sleep, and lost ambition. Several of my friends intimated to me that perhaps I was working too hard.

She stayed away the whole summer. I did not go to the house, but saw her father at various times, and he was as friendly as ever. Even after I knew that she was back in town, I did not go to see her. I determined to wait for some word or sign. I had finally taken refuge and comfort in my pride, pride which, I suppose, I came by naturally enough.

The first time I saw her after her return was one night at the theatre. She and her mother sat in company with a young man whom I knew slightly, not many seats away from me. Never did she appear more beautiful; and yet, it may have been my fancy, she seemed a trifle paler, and there was a suggestion of haggardness in her countenance. But that only heightened her beauty; the very delicacy of her charm melted down the strength of my pride. My situation made me feel weak and powerless, like a man trying with his bare hands to break the iron bars of his prison cell. When the performance was over, I hurried out and placed myself where, unobserved, I could see her as she passed out. The haughtiness of spirit in which I had sought relief was all gone, and I was willing and ready to undergo any humiliation.

Shortly afterward we met at a progressive card party, and during the evening we were thrown together at one of the tables as partners. This was really our first meeting since the eventful night at her house. Strangely enough, in spite of our mutual nervousness, we won every trick of the game, and one of our opponents jokingly quoted the old saw: "Lucky at cards, unlucky in love." Our eyes met and I am sure that in the momentary glance my whole soul went out to her in one great plea. She lowered her eyes and uttered a nervous little laugh. During the rest of the game I fully merited the unexpressed and expressed abuse of my various partners; for my eyes followed her wherever she was and I played whatever card my fingers happened to touch.

Later in the evening she went to the piano and began to play very softly, as to herself, the opening bars of the Thirteenth Nocturne. I felt that the psychic moment of my life had come, a moment which, if lost, could never be called back; and, in as careless a manner as I could assume, I sauntered over to the piano and stood almost bending over her. She continued playing, but, in a voice that was almost a whisper, she called me by my Christian name and said: "I love you, I love you. I love you." I took her place at the piano and played the Nocturne in a manner that silenced the chatter of the company both in and out of the room, involuntarily closing it with the major triad.

We were married the following spring, and went to Europe for several months. It was a double joy for me to be in France again under such conditions.

First there came to us a little girl, with hair and eyes dark like mine, but who is growing to have ways like her mother. Two years later there came a boy, who has my temperament, but is fair like his mother, a little golden-headed god, with a face and head that would have delighted the heart of an old Italian master. And this boy, with his mother's eyes and features, occupies an inner sanctuary of my heart; for it was for him that she gave all; and that is the second sacred sorrow of my life.

The few years of our married life were supremely happy, and perhaps she was even happier than I; for after our marriage, in spite of all the wealth of her love which she lavished upon me, there came a new dread to haunt me, a dread which I cannot explain and which was unfounded, but one that never left me. I was in constant fear that she would discover in me some shortcoming which she would unconsciously attribute to my blood rather than to a failing of human nature. But no cloud ever came to mar our life together; her loss to me is irreparable. My children need a mother's care, but I shall never marry again. It is to my children that I have devoted my life. I no longer have the same fear for myself of my secret's being found out, for since my wife's death I have gradually dropped out of social life; but there is nothing I would not suffer to keep the brand from being placed upon them.

It is difficult for me to analyze my feelings concerning my present position in the world. Sometimes it seems to me that I have never really been a Negro, that I have been only a privileged spectator of their inner life; at other times I feel that I have been a coward, a deserter, and I am possessed by a strange longing for my mother's people.

Several years ago I attended a great meeting in the interest of Hampton Institute [4] at Carnegie Hall. The Hampton students sang the old songs and

4. A school founded in Hampton, Virginia, for the training of African Americans and American Indians.

awoke memories that left me sad. Among the speakers were R. C. Ogden, ex-Ambassador Choate, and Mark Twain; but the greatest interest of the audience was centered in Booker T. Washington, [5] and not because he so much surpassed the others in eloquence, but because of what he represented with so much earnestness and faith. And it is this that all of that small but gallant band of colored men who are publicly fighting the cause of their race have behind them. Even those who oppose them know that these men have the eternal principles of right on their side, and they will be victors even though they should go down in defeat. Beside them I feel small and selfish. I am an ordinarily successful white man who has made a little money. They are men who are making history and a race. I, too, might have taken part in a work so glorious.

My love for my children makes me glad that I am what I am and keeps me from desiring to be otherwise; and yet, when I sometimes open a little box in which I still keep my fast yellowing manuscripts, the only tangible remnants of a vanished dream, a dead ambition, a sacrificed talent, I cannot repress the thought that, after all, I have chosen the lesser part, that I have sold my birthright for a mess of pottage.

1912

From The Book of American Negro Poetry

Preface

There is, perhaps, a better excuse for giving an Anthology of American Negro Poetry to the public than can be offered for many of the anthologies that have recently been issued. The public, generally speaking, does not know that there are American Negro poets—to supply this lack of information is, alone, a work worthy of somebody's effort.

Moreover, the matter of Negro poets and the production of literature by the colored people in this country involves more than supplying information that is lacking. It is a matter which has a direct bearing on the most vital of American problems.

A people may become great through many means, but there is only one measure by which its greatness is recognized and acknowledged. The final measure of the greatness of all peoples is the amount and standard of the literature and art they have produced. The world does not know that a people is great until that people produces great literature and art. No people that has produced great literature and art has ever been looked upon by the world as distinctly inferior.

The status of the Negro in the United States is more a question of national mental attitude toward the race than of actual conditions. And nothing will do more to change that mental attitude and raise his status than a demonstration of intellectual parity by the Negro through the production of literature and art.

---

5. African American educator, political leader, and author (1856–1915). Robert Curtis Ogden (1836–1913), educational reformer. Joseph Hodges Choate (1832–1917), political reformer and am-bassador to England. Mark Twain was the pen name of Samuel Langhorne Clemens (1835–1910), popular American humorist and author.

Is there likelihood that the American Negro will be able to do this? There is, for the good reason that he possesses the innate powers. He has the emotional endowment, the originality and artistic conception, and, what is more important, the power of creating that which has universal appeal and influence.

I make here what may appear to be a more startling statement by saying that the Negro has already proved the possession of these powers by being the creator of the only things artistic that have yet sprung from American soil and been universally acknowledged as distinctive American products. [1]

These creations by the American Negro may be summed up under four heads. The first two are the Uncle Remus stories, which were collected by Joel Chandler Harris, and the "spirituals" or slave songs, to which the Fisk Jubilee Singers[2] made the public and the musicians of both the United States and Europe listen. The Uncle Remus stories constitute the greatest body of folk lore that America has produced, and the "spirituals" the greatest body of folk song. I shall speak of the "spirituals" later because they are more than folk songs, for in them the Negro sounded the depths, if he did not scale the heights, of music.

The other two creations are the cakewalk and ragtime. [3] We do not need to go very far back to remember when cakewalking was the rage in the United States, Europe and South America. Society in this country and royalty abroad spent time in practicing the intricate steps. Paris pronounced it the "poetry of motion." The popularity of the cakewalk passed away but its influence remained. The influence can be seen today on any American stage where there is dancing.

The influence which the Negro has exercised on the art of dancing in this country has been almost absolute. For generations the "buck and wing" and the "stop-time" dances, which are strictly Negro, have been familiar to American theater audiences. A few years ago the public discovered the "turkey trot," the "eagle rock," "ballin' the jack,"[4] and several other varieties that started the modern dance craze. These dances were quickly followed by the "tango," a dance originated by the Negroes of Cuba and later transplanted to South America. (This fact is attested by no less authority than Vicente Blasco Ibañez[5] in his *Four Horsemen of the Apocalypse*.) Half the floor space in the country was then turned over to dancing, and highly paid exponents sprang up everywhere. The most noted, Mr. Vernon Castle, [6] and, by the way, an Englishman, never danced except to the music of a colored band, and he never failed to state to his audiences that most of his dances had long been done by "your colored people," as he put it.

1. This statement should probably be modified by the inclusion of American skyscraper architecture [Johnson's note, 1931 edition].
2. A nine-person traveling singing troupe founded in 1871 to raise funds for Fisk University. Harris (1848–1908) popularized African American folk tales in *Uncle Remus: His Songs and His Sayings* (1881).
3. African American instrumental musical style of the 1890s, characterized by a syncopated melodic line and regularly accented accompaniment.

"Cakewalk": a dance developed from an African American contest in stylish walking; a cake was offered as a prize.
4. African American dance steps that became popular with the white public in the late 19th and early 20th centuries.
5. Spanish novelist (1867–1928).
6. Castle (1887–1918) and his wife, Irene (1894–1969), revolutionized ballroom dancing in the 1910s by introducing the one-step, turkey trot, and Castle walk.

Any one who witnesses a musical production in which there is dancing cannot fail to notice the Negro stamp on all the movements; a stamp which even the great vogue of Russian dances that swept the country about the time of the popular dance craze could not affect. That peculiar swaying of the shoulders which you see done everywhere by the blond girls of the chorus is nothing more than a movement from the Negro dance referred to above, the "eagle rock." Occasionally the movement takes on a suggestion of the now outlawed "shimmy."[7]

As for Ragtime, I go straight to the statement that it is the one artistic production by which America is known the world over. It has been all-conquering. Everywhere it is hailed as "American music."

For a dozen years or so there has been a steady tendency to divorce Ragtime from the Negro; in fact, to take from him the credit of having originated it. Probably the younger people of the present generation do not know that Ragtime is of Negro origin. The change wrought in Ragtime and the way in which it is accepted by the country have been brought about chiefly through the change which has gradually been made in the words and stories accompanying the music. Once the text of all Ragtime songs was written in Negro dialect, and was about Negroes in the cabin or in the cotton field or on the levee or at a jubilee[8] or on Sixth Avenue or at a ball, and about their love affairs. Today, only a small proportion of Ragtime songs relate at all to the Negro. The truth is, Ragtime is now national rather than racial. But that does not abolish in any way the claim of the American Negro as its originator.

Ragtime music was originated by colored piano players in the questionable resorts of St. Louis, Memphis, and other Mississippi River towns. These men did not know any more about the theory of music than they did about the theory of the universe. They were guided by their natural musical instinct and talent, but above all by the Negro's extraordinary sense of rhythm. Any one who is familiar with Ragtime may note that its chief charm is not in melody, but in rhythms. These players often improvised crude and, at times, vulgar words to fit the music. This was the beginning of the Ragtime song.

Ragtime music got its first popular hearing at Chicago during the World's Fair[9] in that city. From Chicago it made its way to New York, and then started on its universal triumph.

The earliest Ragtime songs, like Topsy,[1] "jes' grew." Some of these earliest songs were taken down by white men, the words slightly altered or changed, and published under the names of the arrangers. They sprang into immediate popularity and earned small fortunes. The first to become widely known was "The Bully," a levee song which had been long used by roustabouts along the Mississippi. It was introduced in New York by Miss May Irwin,[2] and gained instant popularity. Another one of these "jes' grew" songs was one which for a while disputed for place with Yankee Doo-

7. Popular 1920s dance, characterized by shaking of the upper body, considered sexually suggestive.
8. A service of religious rejoicing.
9. World's Columbian Exhibition, held in 1893 to honor the first four hundred years of European settlement of America.

1. An orphaned slave girl in Harriet Beecher Stowe's *Uncle Tom's Cabin* (1852) who says of her past only that she "jes' grew."
2. Popular singer and Broadway performer in the 1890s.

dle; perhaps, disputes it even today. That song was "A Hot Time in the Old Town Tonight"; introduced and made popular by the colored regimental bands during the Spanish-American War.[3]

Later there came along a number of colored men who were able to transcribe the old songs and write original ones. I was, about that time, writing words to music for the music show stage in New York. I was collaborating with my brother, J. Rosamond Johnson, and the late Bob Cole. I remember that we appropriated about the last one of the old "jes' grew" songs. It was a song which had been sung for years all through the South. The words were unprintable, but the tune was irresistible, and belonged to nobody. We took it, re-wrote the verses, telling an entirely different story from the original, left the chorus as it was, and published the song, at first under the name of "Will Handy." It became very popular with college boys, especially at football games, and perhaps still is. The song was "Oh, Didn't He Ramble!"

In the beginning, and for quite a while, almost all of the Ragtime songs that were deliberately composed were the work of colored writers. Now, the colored composers, even in this particular field, are greatly outnumbered by the white.

The reader might be curious to know if the "jes' grew" songs have ceased to grow. No, they have not; they are growing all the time. The country has lately been flooded with several varieties of "The Blues." These "Blues," too, had their origin in Memphis, and the towns along the Mississippi. They are a sort of lament of a lover who is feeling "blue" over the loss of his sweetheart. The "Blues" of Memphis have been adulterated so much on Broadway that they have lost their pristine hue. But whenever you hear a piece of music which has a strain like this in it:

you will know you are listening to something which belonged originally to Beale Avenue, Memphis, Tennessee. The original "Memphis Blues," so far as it can be credited to a composer, must be credited to Mr. W. C. Handy,[4] a colored musician of Memphis.

As illustrations of the genuine Ragtime song in the making, I quote the words of two that were popular with the Southern colored soldiers in France. Here is the first:

Mah mammy's lyin' in her grave,
Mah daddy done run away,

---

3. An 1898 war that brought Cuban independence from Spain and transferred the Philippines, Puerto Rico, and Guam to U.S. possession.

4. William Christopher Handy (1873–1958), African American band leader and blues composer.

> Mah sister's married a gamblin' man,
>   An' I've done gone astray.
> Yes, I've done gone astray, po' boy,
>   An' I've done gone astray,
> Mah sister's married a gamblin' man,
>   An' I've done gone astray, po' boy.

These lines are crude, but they contain something of real poetry, of that elusive thing which nobody can define and that you can only tell is there when you feel it. You cannot read these lines without becoming reflective and feeling sorry for "Po' Boy."

Now, take in this word picture of utter dejection:

> I'm jes' as misabul as I can be,
> I'm unhappy even if I am free,
> I'm feelin' down, I'm feelin' blue;
> I wander 'round, don't know what to do.
> I'm go'n lay mah haid on de railroad line,
> Let de B. & O.[5] come and pacify mah min'.

These lines are, no doubt, one of the many versions of the famous "Blues." They are also crude, but they go straight to the mark. The last two lines move with the swiftness of all great tragedy.

In spite of the bans which musicians and music teachers have placed on it, the people still demand and enjoy Ragtime. In fact, there is not a corner of the civilized world in which it is not known and liked. And this proves its originality, for if it were an imitation, the people of Europe, at least, would not have found it a novelty. And it is proof of a more important thing, it is proof that Ragtime possesses the vital spark, the power to appeal universally, without which any artistic production, no matter how approved its form may be, is dead.

Of course, there are those who will deny that Ragtime is an artistic production. American musicians, especially, instead of investigating Ragtime, dismiss it with a contemptuous word. But this has been the course of scholasticism[6] in every branch of art. Whatever new thing the people like is pooh-poohed; whatever is popular is regarded as not worth while. The fact is, nothing great or enduring in music has ever sprung full-fledged from the brain of any master; the best he gives the world he gathers from the hearts of the people, and runs it through the alembic[7] of his genius.

Ragtime deserves serious attention. There is a lot of colorless and vicious imitation, but there is enough that is genuine. In one composition alone, "The Memphis Blues," the musician will find not only great melodic beauty, but a polyphonic[8] structure that is amazing.

It is obvious that Ragtime has influenced and, in a large measure, become our popular music; but not many would know that it has influenced even our religious music. Those who are familiar with gospel hymns can at once see this influence if they will compare the songs of thirty years ago, such as "In the Sweet Bye and Bye," "The Ninety and

---

5. Baltimore and Ohio railroad.
6. An insistence on traditional doctrines and methods.

7. A purifying still.
8. Making more than one sound at a time (as a piano).

Nine," etc., with the up-to-date, syncopated tunes that are sung in Sunday Schools, Christian Endeavor Societies,[9] Y.M.C.A.'s and like gatherings today.

Ragtime has not only influenced American music, it has influenced American life; indeed, it has saturated American life. It has become the popular medium for our national expression musically. And who can say that it does not express the blare and jangle and the surge, too, of our national spirit?

Any one who doubts that there is a peculiar heel-tickling, smile-provoking, joy-awakening, response-compelling charm in Ragtime needs only to hear a skillful performer play the genuine article, needs only to listen to its bizarre harmonies, its audacious resolutions often consisting of an abrupt jump from one key to another, its intricate rhythms in which the accents fall in the most unexpected places but in which the fundamental beat is never lost, in order to be convinced. I believe it has its place as well as the music which draws from us sighs and tears.

Now, these dances which I have referred to and Ragtime music may be lower forms of art, but they are evidence of a power that will some day be applied to the higher forms. And even now we need not stop at the Negro's accomplishment through these lower forms. In the "spirituals," or slave songs, the Negro has given America not only its only folk songs, but a mass of noble music. I never think of this music but that I am struck by the wonder, the miracle of its production. How did the men who originated these songs manage to do it? The sentiments are easily accounted for; they are, for the most part, taken from the Bible. But the melodies, where did they come from? Some of them so weirdly sweet, and others so wonderfully strong. Take, for instance, "Go Down, Moses"; I doubt that there is a stronger theme in the whole musical literature of the world.

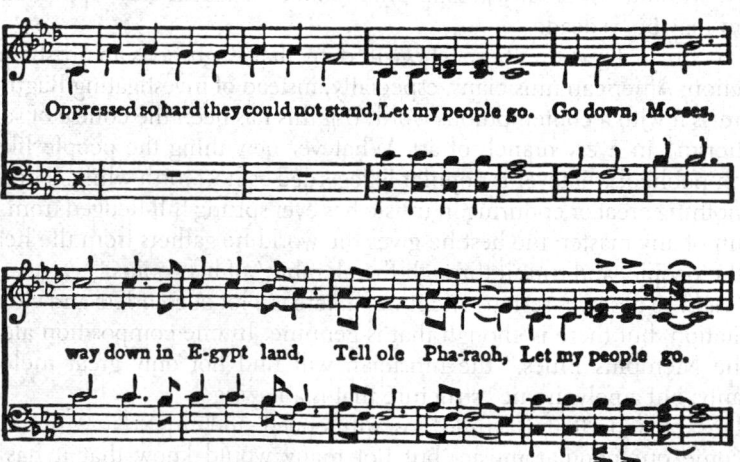

It is to be noted that whereas the chief characteristic of Ragtime is rhythm, the chief characteristic of the "spirituals" is melody. The melodies

9. Organizations formed to promote spiritual life among young people.

of "Steal Away to Jesus," "Swing Low Sweet Chariot," "Nobody Knows de Trouble I See," "I Couldn't Hear Nobody Pray," "Deep River," "O, Freedom Over Me," and many others of these songs possess a beauty that is— what shall I say? poignant. In the riotous rhythms of Ragtime the Negro expressed his irrepressible buoyancy, his keen response to the sheer joy of living; in the "spirituals" he voiced his sense of beauty and his deep religious feeling.

Naturally, not as much can be said for the words of these songs as for the music. Most of the songs are religious. Some of them are songs expressing faith and endurance and a longing for freedom. In the religious songs, the sentiments and often the entire lines are taken bodily from the Bible. However, there is no doubt that some of these religious songs have a meaning apart from the Biblical text. It is evident that the opening lines of "Go Down, Moses,"

> Go down, Moses,
>   'Way down in Egypt land;
> Tell old Pharaoh,
>   Let my people go.

have a significance beyond the bondage of Israel in Egypt.

The bulk of the lines to these songs, as is the case in all communal music, is made up of choral iteration[1] and incremental repetition of the leader's lines. If the words are read, this constant iteration and repetition are found to be tiresome; and it must be admitted that the lines themselves are often very trite. And, yet, there is frequently revealed a flash of real primitive poetry. I give the following examples;

> Sometimes I feel like an eagle in de air.

> You may bury me in de East,
> You may bury me in de West,
> But I'll hear de trumpet sound
>   In-a dat mornin'.

> I know de moonlight, I know de starlight;
>   I lay dis body down.
> I walk in de moonlight, I walk in de starlight;
>   I lay dis body down.
> I know de graveyard, I know de graveyard,
>   When I lay dis body down.
> I walk in de graveyard, I walk troo de graveyard
>   To lay dis body down.

> I lay in de grave an' stretch out my arms;
>   I lay dis body down.
> I go to de judgment in de evenin' of de day
>   When I lay dis body down.

1. Repetition by a chorus.

An' my soul an' yo soul will meet in de day
When I lay dis body down.

Regarding the line, "I lay in de grave an' stretch out my arms," Col.
Thomas Wentworth Higginson[2] of Boston, one of the first to give these
slave songs serious study, said: "Never, it seems to me, since man first lived
and suffered, was his infinite longing for peace uttered more plaintively
than in that line."

These Negro folk songs constitute a vast mine of material that has been
neglected almost absolutely. The only white writers who have in recent
years given adequate attention and study to this music, that I know of, are
Mr. H. E. Krehbiel and Mrs. Natalie Curtis Burlin.[3] We have our native
composers denying the worth and importance of this music, and trying to
manufacture grand opera out of so-called Indian themes.
    But there is a great hope for the development of this music, and that
hope is the Negro himself. A worthy beginning has already been made by
Burleigh, Cook, Johnson, and Dett.[4] And there will yet come great Negro
composers who will take this music and voice through it not only the soul
of their race, but the soul of America.
    And does it not seem odd that this greatest gift of the Negro has been the
most neglected of all he possesses? Money and effort have been expended
upon his development in every direction except this. This gift has been
regarded as a kind of side show, something for occasional exhibition;
wherein it is the touchstone, it is the magic thing, it is that by which the
Negro can bridge all chasms. No persons, however hostile, can listen to
Negroes singing this wonderful music without having their hostility melted
down.

This power of the Negro to suck up the national spirit from the soil and
create something artistic and original, which, at the same time, possesses
the note of universal appeal, is due to a remarkable racial gift of adaptability; it is more than adaptability, it is a transfusive quality. And the Negro has
exercised this transfusive[5] quality not only here in America, where the race
lives in large numbers, but in European countries, where the number has
been almost infinitesimal.
    Is it not curious to know that the greatest poet of Russia is Alexander
Pushkin, a man of African descent; that the greatest romancer of France is
Alexandre Dumas,[6] a man of African descent; and that one of the greatest
musicians of England is Coleridge-Taylor,[7] a man of African descent?
    The fact is fairly well known that the father of Dumas was a Negro of the
French West Indies, and that the father of Coleridge-Taylor was a native-

2. U.S. reformer (1823–1911) who was commander of the first black regiment in the Civil War.
3. Collectors of American folk songs from several
ethnic minorities.
4. Composer, arranger, choral leader (1882–1943).
Harry Thacker Burleigh (1866–1949), singer, composer, and arranger of spirituals. Will Marion Cook
(1869–1944), composer of musical comedies and

jazz orchestral director. John Rosamond Johnson
(1873–1954), brother of James Weldon, composer
of show tunes and arranger of spirituals.
5. The ability to transfer.
6. French novelist and dramatist (1802–1870).
Pushkin (1799–1837), Russian man of letters.
7. Samuel Coleridge-Taylor (1875–1912), English
composer.

born African; but the facts concerning Pushkin's African ancestry are not so familiar.

When Peter the Great[8] was Czar of Russia, some potentate presented him with a full-blooded Negro of gigantic size. Peter, the most eccentric ruler of modern times, dressed this Negro up in soldier clothes, christened him Hannibal,[9] and made him a special body-guard.

But Hannibal had more than size, he had brain and ability. He not only looked picturesque and imposing in soldier clothes, he showed that he had in him the making of a real soldier. Peter recognized this, and eventually made him a general. He afterwards ennobled him, and Hannibal, later, married one of the ladies of the Russian court. This same Hannibal was great-grandfather of Pushkin, the national poet of Russia, the man who bears the same relation to Russian literature that Shakespeare bears to English literature.

I know the question naturally arises: If out of the few Negroes who have lived in France there came a Dumas; and out of the few Negroes who have lived in England there came a Coleridge-Taylor; and if from the man who was at the time, probably, the only Negro in Russia there sprang that country's national poet, why have not the millions of Negroes in the United States with all the emotional and artistic endowment claimed for them produced a Dumas, or a Coleridge-Taylor, or a Pushkin?

The question seems difficult, but there is an answer. The Negro in the United States is consuming all of his intellectual energy in this grueling race-struggle. And the same statement may be made in a general way about the white South. Why does not the white South produce literature and art? The white South, too, is consuming all of its intellectual energy in this lamentable conflict. Nearly all of the mental efforts of the white South run through one narrow channel. The life of every Southern white man and all of his activities are impassably limited by the ever present Negro problem. And that is why, as Mr. H. L. Mencken[1] puts it, in all that vast region, with its thirty or forty million people and its territory as large as a half dozen Frances or Germanys, there is not a single poet, not a serious historian, not a creditable composer, not a critic good or bad, not a dramatist dead or alive.[2]

But, even so, the American Negro has accomplished something in pure literature. The list of those who have done so would be surprising both by its length and the excellence of the achievements. One of the great books written in this country since the Civil War is the work of a colored man, *The Souls of Black Folk*, by W. E. B. Du Bois.[3]

Such a list begins with Phillis Wheatley.[4] In 1761 a slave ship landed a cargo of slaves in Boston. Among them was a little girl seven or eight years of age. She attracted the attention of John Wheatley, a wealthy gentleman of Boston, who purchased her as a servant for his wife. Mrs. Wheatley was a

8. Peter I (1672–1725), ruled from 1682 to 1725.
9. After the North African general (247–183? B.C.) who made war on Rome.
1. Henry Louis Mencken (1880–1956), American editor, critic, and essayist.
2. This statement was quoted in 1921. The reader may consider for himself the changes wrought in the decade [Johnson's note, 1931 edition].
3. Author, editor, and social activist (1868–1963); published his collection of essays in 1903.
4. Author (c. 1753–1784) of the first book written by an African American (1773).

benevolent woman. She noticed the girl's quick mind and determined to give her opportunity for its development. Twelve years later Phillis published a volume of poems. The book was brought out in London, where Phillis was for several months an object of great curiosity and attention.

Phillis Wheatley has never been given her rightful place in American literature. By some sort of conspiracy she is kept out of most of the books, especially the text-books on literature used in the schools. Of course, she is not a *great* American poet—and in her day there were no great American poets—but she is an important American poet. Her importance, if for no other reason, rests on the fact that, save one, she is the first in order of time of all the women poets of America. And she is among the first of all American poets to issue a volume.

It seems strange that the books generally give space to a mention of Urian Oakes, President of Harvard College, and to quotations from the crude and lengthy elegy which he published in 1667; and print examples from the execrable versified version of the Psalms made by the New England divines, and yet deny a place to Phillis Wheatley.

Here are the opening lines from the elegy by Oakes, which is quoted from in most of the books on American literature:

> Reader, I am no poet, but I grieve.
> Behold here what that passion can do,
> That forced a verse without Apollo's leave,
> And whether the learned sisters would or no.

There was no need for Urian to admit what his handiwork declared. But this from the versified Psalms is still worse, yet it is found in the books:

> The Lord's song sing can we? being
> in stranger's land, then let
> lose her skill my right hand if I
> Jerusalem forget.

Anne Bradstreet[5] preceded Phillis Wheatley by a little over one hundred and twenty years. She published her volume of poems, *The Tenth Muse*, in 1650. Let us strike a comparison between the two. Anne Bradstreet was a wealthy, cultivated Puritan girl, the daughter of Thomas Dudley, Governor of Bay Colony. Phillis, as we know, was a Negro slave girl born in Africa. Let us take them both at their best and in the same vein. The following stanza is from Anne's poem entitled "Contemplation":

> While musing thus with contemplation fed,
> And thousand fancies buzzing in my brain,
> The sweet tongued Philomel percht o'er my head,
> And chanted forth a most melodious strain,
> Which rapt me so with wonder and delight,
> I judged my hearing better than my sight,
> And wisht me wings with her awhile to take my flight.

5. First published poet in North America (1612–1672).

And the following is from Phillis' poem entitled "Imagination":

> Imagination! who can sing thy force?
> Or who describe the swiftness of thy course?
> Soaring through air to find the bright abode,
> Th' empyreal palace of the thundering God,
> We on thy pinions can surpass the wind,
> And leave the rolling universe behind.
> From star to star the mental optics rove,
> Measure the skies, and range the realms above;
> There in one view we grasp the mighty whole,
> Or with new worlds amaze th' unbounded soul.

We do not think the black woman suffers much by comparison with the white. Thomas Jefferson said of Phillis: "Religion has produced a Phillis Wheatley, but it could not produce a poet; her poems are beneath contempt." It is quite likely that Jefferson's criticism was directed more against religion than against Phillis' poetry. On the other hand, General George Washington wrote her with his own hand a letter in which he thanked her for a poem which she had dedicated to him. He later received her with marked courtesy at his camp at Cambridge.

It appears certain that Phillis was the first person to apply to George Washington the phrase, "First in peace." The phrase occurs in her poem addressed to "His Excellency, General George Washington," written in 1775. The encomium, "First in war, first in peace, first in the hearts of his countrymen," was originally used in the resolutions presented to Congress on the death of Washington, December, 1799.

Phillis Wheatley's poetry is the poetry of the Eighteenth Century. She wrote when Pope and Gray[6] were supreme; it is easy to see that Pope was her model. Had she come under the influence of Wordsworth, Byron or Keats or Shelley,[7] she would have done greater work. As it is, her work must not be judged by the work and standards of a later day, but by the work and standards of her own day and her own contemporaries. By this method of criticism she stands out as one of the important characters in the making of American literature, without any allowances for her sex or her antecedents.

According to A *Bibliographical Checklist of American Negro Poetry*, compiled by Mr. Arthur A. Schomburg,[8] more than one hundred Negroes in the United States have published volumes of poetry ranging in size from pamphlets to books of from one hundred to three hundred pages. About thirty of these writers fill in the gap between Phillis Wheatley and Paul Laurence Dunbar.[9] Just here it is of interest to note that a Negro wrote and published a poem before Phillis Wheatley arrived in this country from Africa. He was Jupiter Hammon,[1] a slave belonging to a Mr. Lloyd of Queens Village, Long Island. In 1760 Hammon published a poem, eighty-

6. Alexander Pope (1688–1744) and Thomas Gray (1716–1771), English poets.
7. William Wordsworth (1770–1850); George Gordon, Lord Byron (1788–1824); John Keats (1795–1821); and Percy Bysshe Shelley (1792–1822), English Romantic poets.
8. African American bibliophile, book collector, and writer (1874–1938).
9. The most popular African American poet of his era (1872–1906).
1. New York poet (1711–1806?).

eight lines in length, entitled "An Evening Thought, Salvation by Christ, with Penettential Cries." In 1788 he published "An Address to Miss Phillis Wheatley, Ethiopian Poetess in Boston, who came from Africa at eight years of age, and soon became acquainted with the Gospel of Jesus Christ." These two poems do not include all that Hammon wrote.

The poets between Phillis Wheatley and Dunbar must be considered more in the light of what they attempted than of what they accomplished. Many of them showed marked talent, but barely a half dozen of them demonstrated even mediocre mastery of technique in the use of poetic material and forms. And yet there are several names that deserve mention. George M. Horton, Frances E. Harper, James M. Bell and Alberry A. Whitman,[2] all merit consideration when due allowances are made for their limitations in education, training and general culture. The limitations of Horton were greater than those of either of the others; he was born a slave in North Carolina in 1797, and as a young man began to compose poetry without being able to write it down. Later he received some instruction from professors of the University of North Carolina, at which institution he was employed as a janitor. He published a volume of poems, *The Hope of Liberty*, in 1829.

Mrs. Harper, Bell, and Whitman would stand out if only for the reason that each of them attempted sustained work. Mrs. Harper published her first volume of poems in 1854, but later she published "Moses, a Story of the Nile," a poem which ran to 52 closely printed pages. Bell in 1864 published a poem of 28 pages in celebration of President Lincoln's Emancipation Proclamation. In 1870 he published a poem of 32 pages in celebration of the ratification of the Fifteenth Amendment[3] to the Constitution. Whitman published his first volume of poems, a book of 253 pages, in 1877; but in 1884 he published "The Rape of Florida," an epic poem written in four cantos and done in the Spenserian stanza,[4] and which ran to 97 closely printed pages. The poetry of both Mrs. Harper and of Whitman had a large degree of popularity; one of Mrs. Harper's books went through more than twenty editions.

Of these four poets, it is Whitman who reveals not only the greatest imagination but also the more skillful workmanship. His lyric power at its best may be judged from the following stanza from the "Rape of Florida":

> "Come now, my love, the moon is on the lake;
> Upon the waters is my light canoe;
> Come with me, love, and gladsome oars shall make
> A music on the parting wave for you.
> Come o'er the waters deep and dark and blue;
> Come where the lilies in the marge have sprung,
> Come with me, love, for Oh, my love is true!"
> This is the song that on the lake was sung,
> The boatman sang it when his heart was young.

---

2. African Methodist Episcopal minister and author of long narrative verse (1851–1901). Horton (1797–1883?), slave-born poet from North Carolina. Harper (1825–1911), reformist lecturer and novelist. Bell (1826–1902), antislavery poet from the Midwest.

3. Ratified in 1870, it guaranteed voting rights to African American men.
4. A stanzaic pattern of poetry developed by Edmund Spenser in his epic *The Faerie Queene* (1590).

Some idea of Whitman's capacity for dramatic narration may be gained
from the following lines taken from "Not a Man, and Yet a Man," a poem
of even greater length than "The Rape of Florida."

> A flash of steely lightning from his hand,
> Strikes down the groaning leader of the band;
> Divides his startled comrades, and again
> Descending, leaves fair Dora's captors slain.
> Her, seizing then within a strong embrace,
> Out in the dark he wheels his flying pace;
>
> He speaks not, but with stalwart tenderness
> Her swelling bosom firm to his doth press;
> Springs like a stag that flees the eager hound,
> And like a whirlwind rustles o'er the ground.
> Her locks swim in disheveled wildness o'er
> His shoulders, streaming to his waist and more;
> While on and on, strong as a rolling flood,
> His sweeping footsteps part the silent wood.

It is curious and interesting to trace the growth of individuality and race
consciousness in this group of poets. Jupiter Hammon's verses were almost
entirely religious exhortations. Only very seldom does Phillis Wheatley
sound a native note. Four times in single lines she refers to herself as
"Afric's muse." In a poem of admonition addressed to the students at the
"University of Cambridge in New England" she refers to herself as follows:

> Ye blooming plants of human race divine,
> An Ethiop tells you 'tis your greatest foe.

But one looks in vain for some outburst or even complaint against the
bondage of her people, for some agonizing cry about her native land. In
two poems she refers definitely to Africa as her home, but in each instance
there seems to be under the sentiment of the lines a feeling of almost smug
contentment at her own escape therefrom. In the poem, "On Being
Brought from Africa to America," she says:

> 'Twas mercy brought me from my pagan land,
> Taught my benighted soul to understand
> That there's a God and there's a Saviour too;
> Once I redemption neither sought nor knew.
> Some view our sable race with scornful eye—
> "Their color is a diabolic dye."
> Remember, Christians, Negroes black as Cain,
> May be refined, and join th' angelic train.

In the poem addressed to the Earl of Dartmouth, she speaks of freedom
and makes a reference to the parents from whom she was taken as a child, a
reference which cannot but strike the reader as rather unimpassioned:

> Should you, my lord, while you peruse my song,
> Wonder from whence my love of Freedom sprung,

> Whence flow these wishes for the common good,
> By feeling hearts alone best understood;
> I, young in life, by seeming cruel fate
> Was snatch'd from Afric's fancy'd happy seat;
> What pangs excruciating must molest,
> What sorrows labor in my parents' breast?
> Steel'd was that soul and by no misery mov'd
> That from a father seiz'd his babe belov'd;
> Such, such my case. And can I then but pray
> Others may never feel tyrannic sway?

The bulk of Phillis Wheatley's work consists of poems addressed to people of prominence. Her book was dedicated to the Countess of Huntington, at whose house she spent the greater part of her time while in England. On his repeal of the Stamp Act,[5] she wrote a poem to King George III, whom she saw later; another poem she wrote to the Earl of Dartmouth, whom she knew. A number of her verses were addressed to other persons of distinction. Indeed, it is apparent that Phillis was far from being a democrat. She was far from being a democrat not only in her social ideas but also in her political ideas; unless a religious meaning is given to the closing lines of her ode to General Washington, she was a decided royalist:

> A crown, a mansion, and a throne that shine
> With gold unfading, Washington! be thine.

Nevertheless, she was an ardent patriot. Her ode to General Washington (1775), her spirited poem, "On Major General Lee" (1776), and her poem, "Liberty and Peace," written in celebration of the close of the war, reveal not only strong patriotic feeling but an understanding of the issues at stake. In her poem, "On Major General Lee," she makes her hero reply thus to the taunts of the British commander into whose hands he has been delivered through treachery:

> O arrogance of tongue!
> And wild ambition, ever prone to wrong!
> Believ'st thou, chief, that armies such as thine
> Can stretch in dust that heaven-defended line?
> In vain allies may swarm from distant lands,
> And demons aid in formidable bands.
> Great as thou art, thou shun'st the field of fame,
> Disgrace to Britain and the British name!
> When offer'd combat by the noble foe
> (Foe to misrule) why did the sword forego
> The easy conquest of the rebel-land?
> Perhaps TOO easy for thy martial hand.
> What various causes to the field invite!
> For plunder YOU, and we for freedom fight;
> Her cause divine with generous ardor fires,
> And every bosom glows as she inspires!

5. A means of raising revenue imposed on the American colonies by the English government in 1765.

Already thousands of your troops have fled
To the drear mansions of the silent dead:
Columbia, too, beholds with streaming eyes
Her heroes fall—'tis freedom's sacrifice!
So wills the power who with convulsive storms
Shakes impious realms, and nature's face deforms;
Yet those brave troops, innum'rous as the sands,
One soul inspires, one General Chief commands;
Find in your train of boasted heroes, one
To match the praise of Godlike Washington.
Thrice happy Chief in whom the virtues join,
And heaven taught prudence speaks the man divine.

What Phillis Wheatley failed to achieve is due in no small degree to her education and environment. Her mind was steeped in the classics; her verses are filled with classical and mythological allusions. She knew Ovid[6] thoroughly and was familiar with other Latin authors. She must have known Alexander Pope by heart. And, too, she was reared and sheltered in a wealthy and cultured family,—a wealthy and cultured Boston family; she never had the opportunity to learn life; she never found out her own true relation to life and to her surroundings. And it should not be forgotten that she was only about thirty years old when she died. The impulsion or the compulsion that might have driven her genius off the worn paths, out on a journey of exploration, Phillis Wheatley never received. But, whatever her limitations, she merits more than America has accorded her.

Horton, who was born three years after Phillis Wheatley's death, expressed in all of his poetry strong complaint at his condition of slavery and a deep longing for freedom. The following verses are typical of his style and his ability:

Alas! and am I born for this,
  To wear this slavish chain?
Deprived of all created bliss,
  Through hardship, toil, and pain?

Come, Liberty! thou cheerful sound,
  Roll through my ravished ears;
Come, let my grief in joys be drowned,
  And drive away my fears.

In Mrs. Harper we find something more than the complaint and the longing of Horton. We find an expression of a sense of wrong and injustice. The following stanzas are from a poem addressed to the white women of America:

You can sigh o'er the sad-eyed Armenian
  Who weeps in her desolate home.
You can mourn o'er the exile of Russia
  From kindred and friends doomed to roam.

6. Classical Roman poet (43 B.C.–A.D. 17?).

But hark! from our Southland are floating
   Sobs of anguish, murmurs of pain;
And women heart-stricken are weeping
   O'er their tortured and slain.

Have ye not, oh, my favored sisters,
   Just a plea, a prayer or a tear
For mothers who dwell 'neath the shadows
   Of agony, hatred and fear?

Weep not, oh, my well sheltered sisters,
   Weep not for the Negro alone,
But weep for your sons who must gather
   The crops which their fathers have sown.

Whitman, in the midst of "The Rape of Florida," a poem in which he related the taking of the State of Florida from the Seminoles,[7] stops and discusses the race question. He discusses it in many other poems; and he discusses it from many different angles. In Whitman we find not only an expression of a sense of wrong and injustice, but we hear a note of faith and a note also of defiance. For example, in the opening to Canto II of "The Rape of Florida":

Greatness by nature cannot be entailed;
It is an office ending with the man,—
Sage, hero, Saviour, tho' the Sire be hailed,
The son may reach obscurity in the van:
Sublime achievements know no patent plan,
Man's immortality's a book with seals,
And none but God shall open—none else can—
But opened, it the mystery reveals,—
Manhood's conquest of man to heaven's respect appeals.

Is manhood less because man's face is black?
Let thunders of the loosened seals reply!
Who shall the rider's restive steed turn back?
Or who withstand the arrows he lets fly
Between the mountains of eternity?
Genius ride forth! Thou gift and torch of heav'n!
The mastery is kindled in thine eye;
To conquest ride! thy bow of strength is giv'n—
The trampled hordes of caste before thee shall be driv'n!

'Tis hard to judge if hatred of one's race,
By those who deem themselves superior-born,
Be worse than that quiescence in disgrace,
Which only merits—and should only—scorn.
Oh, let me see the Negro night and morn,
Pressing and fighting in, for place and power!
All earth is place—all time th' auspicious hour,
While heaven leans forth to look, oh, will he quail or cower?

---

7. Native American group that waged war from 1832 to 1842 against the U.S. Army.

Ah! I abhor his protest and complaint!
His pious looks and patience I despise!
He can't evade the test, disguised as saint;
The manly voice of freedom bids him rise,
And shake himself before Philistine eyes!
And, like a lion roused, no sooner than
A foe dare come, play all his energies,
And court the fray with fury if he can;
For hell itself respects a fearless, manly man.

It may be said that none of these poets strike a deep native strain or sound a distinctly original note, either in matter or form. That is true; but the same thing may be said of all the American poets down to the writers of the present generation, with the exception of Poe and Walt Whitman.[8] The thing in which these black poets are mostly excelled by their contemporaries is mere technique.

Paul Laurence Dunbar stands out as the first poet from the Negro race in the United States to show a combined mastery over poetic material and poetic technique, to reveal innate literary distinction in what he wrote, and to maintain a high level of performance. He was the first to rise to a height from which he could take a perspective view of his own race. He was the first to see objectively its humor, its superstitions, its shortcomings; the first to feel sympathetically its heart-wounds, its yearnings, its aspirations, and to voice them all in a purely literary form.

Dunbar's fame rests chiefly on his poems in Negro dialect. This appraisal of him is, no doubt, fair; for in these dialect poems he not only carried his art to the highest point of perfection, but he made a contribution to American literature unlike what any one else had made, a contribution which, perhaps, no one else could have made. Of course, Negro dialect poetry was written before Dunbar wrote, most of it by white writers; but the fact stands out that Dunbar was the first to use it as a medium for the true interpretation of Negro character and psychology. And yet, dialect poetry does not constitute the whole or even the bulk of Dunbar's work. In addition to a large number of poems of a very high order done in literary English, he was the author of four novels and several volumes of short stories.

Indeed, Dunbar did not begin his career as a writer of dialect. I may be pardoned for introducing here a bit of reminiscence. My personal friendship with Paul Dunbar began before he had achieved recognition, and continued to be close until his death. When I first met him he had published a thin volume, *Oak and Ivy*,[9] which was being sold chiefly through his own efforts. *Oak and Ivy* showed no distinctive Negro influence, but rather the influence of James Whitcomb Riley.[1] At this time Paul and I were together every day for several months. He talked to me a great deal about his hopes and ambitions. In these talks he revealed that he had reached a realization of the possibilities of poetry in the dialect, together with a recognition of the fact that it offered the surest way by which he

---

8. U.S. poet (1819–1892). Edgar Allan Poe (1809–1849), U.S. poet, short-story writer, and literary critic.

9. Dunbar's first poetry collection (1893).

1. Indiana regionalist and dialect poet (1849–1916).

could get a hearing. Often he said to me: "I've got to write dialect poetry; it's the only way I can get them to listen to me." I was with Dunbar at the beginning of what proved to be his last illness. He said to me then: "I have not grown. I am writing the same things I wrote ten years ago, and am writing them no better." His self-accusation was not fully true; he had grown, and he had gained a surer control of his art, but he had not accomplished the greater things of which he was constantly dreaming; the public had held him to the things for which it had accorded him recognition. If Dunbar had lived he would have achieved some of those dreams, but even while he talked so dejectedly to me he seemed to feel that he was not to live. He died when he was only thirty-three.

It has a bearing on this entire subject to note that Dunbar was of unmixed Negro blood; so, as the greatest figure in literature which the colored race in the United States has produced, he stands as an example at once refuting and confounding those who wish to believe that whatever extraordinary ability an Aframerican shows is due to an admixture of white blood.

As a man, Dunbar was kind and tender. In conversation he was brilliant and polished. His voice was his chief charm, and was a great element in his success as a reader of his own works. In his actions he was impulsive as a child, sometimes even erratic; indeed, his intimate friends almost looked upon him as a spoiled boy. He was always delicate in health. Temperamentally, he belonged to that class of poets who Taine[2] says are vessels too weak to contain the spirit of poetry, the poets whom poetry kills, the Byrons, the Burnses, the De Mussets,[3] the Poes.

To whom may he be compared, this boy who scribbled his early verses while he ran an elevator, whose youth was a battle against poverty, and who, in spite of almost insurmountable obstacles, rose to success? A comparison between him and Burns is not unfitting. The similarity between many phases of their lives is remarkable, and their works are not incommensurable. Burns took the strong dialect of his people and made it classic; Dunbar took the humble speech of his people and in it wrought music.

Mention of Dunbar brings up for consideration the fact that, although he is the most outstanding figure in literature among the Aframericans of the United States, he does not stand alone among the Aframericans of the whole Western world. There are Plácido and Manzano in Cuba; Vieux and Durand in Haiti; Machado de Assis[4] in Brazil, and others still that might be mentioned, who stand on a plane with or even above Dunbar. Plácido and Machado de Assis rank as great in the literatures of their respective countries without any qualifications whatever. They are world figures in the literature of the Latin languages. Machado de Assis is somewhat handicapped in this respect by having as his tongue and medium the lesser known Portuguese, but Plácido, writing in the language of Spain, Mexico, Cuba and of almost the whole of South America, is universally known. His works have been republished in the original in Spain, Mexico and in most

2. Hippolyte Adolphe Taine (1828–1893), French literary critic and historian.
3. Louis Charles Alfred deMusset (1810–1857), French poet. Robert Burns (1759–1796), Scottish poet.
4. Brazilian short-story writer (1839–1908).

Plácido is the pen name of Gabriel de la Concepcion Valdes (1809–1844), Cuban poet and revolutionary. Juan Francisco Manzano (1797–1854), Cuban poet and autobiographer. Antonio Vieux, early-20th-century Haitian experimental poet.

of the Latin-American countries; several editions have been published in the United States; translations of his works have been made into French and German.

Plácido is in some respects the greatest of all the Cuban poets. In sheer genius and the fire of inspiration he surpasses his famous compatriot, Heredia.[5] Then, too, his birth, his life and his death ideally contained the tragic elements that go into the making of a halo about a poet's head. Plácido was born in Habana in 1809. The first months of his life were passed in a foundling asylum; indeed, his real name, Gabriel de la Concepcion Valdés, was in honor of its founder. His father took him out of the asylum, but shortly afterwards went to Mexico and died there. His early life was a struggle against poverty; his youth and manhood was a struggle for Cuban independence. His death placed him in the list of Cuban martyrs. On the twenty-seventh of June, 1844, he was lined up against a wall with ten others and shot by order of the Spanish authorities on a charge of conspiracy. In his short but eventful life he turned out work which bulks more than six hundred pages. During the few hours preceding his execution he wrote three of his best-known poems, among them his famous sonnet, "Mother, Farewell!"

Plácido's sonnet to his mother has been translated into every important language; William Cullen Bryant[6] did it in English; but in spite of its wide popularity, it is, perhaps, outside of Cuba the least understood of all Plácido's poems. It is curious to note how Bryant's translation totally misses the intimate sense of the delicate subtility of the poem. The American poet makes it a tender and loving farewell of a son who is about to die to a heartbroken mother; but that is not the kind of a farewell that Plácido intended to write or did write.

The key to the poem is in the first word, and the first word is the Spanish conjunction Si (if). The central idea, then, of the sonnet is, "If the sad fate which now overwhelms me should bring a pang to your heart, do not weep, for I die a glorious death and sound the last note of my lyre to you." Bryant either failed to understand or ignored the opening word, "If," because he was not familiar with the poet's history.

While Plácido's father was a Negro, his mother was a Spanish white woman, a dancer in one of the Habana theaters. At his birth she abandoned him to a foundling asylum, and perhaps never saw him again, although it is known that she outlived her son. When the poet came down to his last hours he remembered that somewhere there lived a woman who was his mother; that although she had heartlessly abandoned him; that although he owed her no filial duty, still she might, perhaps, on hearing of his sad end feel some pang of grief or sadness; so he tells her in his last words that he dies happy and bids her not to weep. This he does with nobility and dignity, but absolutely without affection. Taking into account these facts, and especially their humiliating and embittering effect upon a soul so sensitive as Plácido's, this sonnet, in spite of the obvious weakness of the sestet as compared with the octave, is a remarkable piece of work.

In considering the Aframerican poets of the Latin languages I am im-

5. Jose-Maria de Heredia (1842–1905), Cuban   6. U.S. poet and editor (1794–1878).
poet and journalist.

pelled to think that, as up to this time the colored poets of greater universality have come out of the Latin-American countries rather than out of the United States, they will continue to do so for a good many years. The reason for this I hinted at in the first part of this preface. The colored poet in the United States labors within limitations which he cannot easily pass over. He is always on the defensive or the offensive. The pressure upon him to be propagandic is well nigh irresistible. These conditions are suffocating to breadth and to real art in poetry. In addition he labors under the handicap of finding culture not entirely colorless in the United States. On the other hand, the colored poet of Latin America can voice the national spirit without any reservations. And he will be rewarded without any reservations, whether it be to place him among the great or declare him the greatest.

So I think it probable that the first world-acknowledged Aframerican poet will come out of Latin America. Over against this probability, of course, is the great advantage possessed by the colored poet in the United States of writing in the world-conquering English language.

This preface has gone far beyond what I had in mind when I started. It was my intention to gather together the best verses I could find by Negro poets and present them with a bare word of introduction. It was not my plan to make this collection inclusive nor to make the book in any sense a book of criticism. I planned to present only verses by contemporary writers; but, perhaps, because this is the first collection of its kind, I realized the absence of a starting-point and was led to provide one and to fill in with historical data what I felt to be a gap.

It may be surprising to many to see how little of the poetry being written by Negro poets today is being written in Negro dialect. The newer Negro poets show a tendency to discard dialect; much of the subject-matter which went into the making of traditional dialect poetry, 'possums, watermelons, etc., they have discarded altogether, at least, as poetic material. This tendency will, no doubt, be regretted by the majority of white readers; and, indeed, it would be a distinct loss if the American Negro poets threw away this quaint and musical folk speech as a medium of expression. And yet, after all, these poets are working through a problem not realized by the reader, and, perhaps, by many of these poets themselves not realized consciously. They are trying to break away from, not Negro dialect itself, but the limitations on Negro dialect imposed by the fixing effects of long convention.

The Negro in the United States has achieved or been placed in a certain artistic niche. When he is thought of artistically, it is as a happy-go-lucky, singing, shuffling, banjo-picking being or as a more or less pathetic figure. The picture of him is in a log cabin amid fields of cotton or along the levees. Negro dialect is naturally and by long association the exact instrument for voicing this phase of Negro life; and by that very exactness it is an instrument with but two full stops, humor and pathos. So even when he confines himself to purely racial themes, the Aframerican poet realizes that there are phases of Negro life in the United States which cannot be treated in the dialect either adequately or artistically. Take, for example, the phases rising out of life in Harlem, that most wonderful Negro city in the world. I do not deny that a Negro in a log cabin is more picturesque than a Negro in a Harlem flat, but the Negro in the Harlem flat is here, and he is but part of a group growing everywhere in the country, a group whose ideals are becoming increasingly more vital than those of the traditionally artistic group, even if its members are less picturesque.

What the colored poet in the United States needs to do is something like what Synge[7] did for the Irish; he needs to find a form that will express the racial spirit by symbols from within rather than by symbols from without, such as the mere mutilation of English spelling and pronunciation. He needs a form that is freer and larger than dialect, but which will still hold the racial flavor; a form expressing the imagery, the idioms, the peculiar turns of thought, and the distinctive humor and pathos, too, of the Negro, but which will also be capable of voicing the deepest and highest emotions and aspirations, and allow of the widest range of subjects and the widest scope of treatment.

Negro dialect is at present a medium that is not capable of giving expression to the varied conditions of Negro life in America, and much less is it capable of giving the fullest interpretation of Negro character and psychology. This is no indictment against the dialect as dialect, but against the mold of convention in which Negro dialect in the United States has been set. In time these conventions may become lost, and the colored poet in the United States may sit down to write in dialect without feeling that his first line will put the general reader in a frame of mind which demands that the poem be humorous or pathetic. In the meantime, there is no reason why these poets should not continue to do the beautiful things that can be done, and done best, in the dialect.

In stating the need for Aframerican poets in the United States to work out a new and distinctive form of expression I do not wish to be understood to hold any theory that they should limit themselves to Negro poetry, to racial themes; the sooner they are able to write *American* poetry spontaneously, the better. Nevertheless, I believe that the richest contribution the Negro poet can make to the American literature of the future will be the fusion into it of his own individual artistic gifts.

Not many of the writers here included, except Dunbar, are known at all to the general reading public; and there is only one of these who has a widely recognized position in the American literary world, William Stanley Braithwaite.[8] Mr. Braithwaite is not only unique in this respect, but he stands unique among all the Aframerican writers the United States has yet produced. He has gained his place, taking as the standard and measure for his work the identical standard and measure applied to American writers and American literature. He has asked for no allowances or rewards, either directly or indirectly, on account of his race.

Mr. Braithwaite is the author of two volumes of verses, lyrics of delicate and tenuous beauty. In his more recent and uncollected poems he shows himself more and more decidedly the mystic. But his place in American

7. John Middleton Synge (1871–1909), Irish dramatist whose works celebrate Irish traditions.   8. African American poet and editor (1878–1962).

literature is due more to his work as a critic and anthologist than to his work as a poet. There is still another rôle he has played, that of friend of poetry and poets. It is a recognized fact that in the work which preceded the present revival of poetry in the United States, no one rendered more unremitting and valuable service than Mr. Braithwaite. And it can be said that no future study of American poetry of this age can be made without reference to Braithwaite.

Two authors included in the book are better known for their work in prose than in poetry: W. E. B. Du Bois whose well-known prose at its best is, however, impassioned and rhythmical; and Benjamin Brawley[9] who is the author, among other works, of one of the best handbooks on the English drama that has yet appeared in America.

But the group of the new Negro poets, whose work makes up the bulk of this anthology, contains names destined to be known. Claude McKay,[1] although still quite a young man, has already demonstrated his power, breadth and skill as a poet. Mr. McKay's breadth is as essential a part of his equipment as his power and skill. He demonstrates mastery of the three when as a Negro poet he pours out the bitterness and rebellion in his heart in those two sonnet-tragedies, "If We Must Die" and "To the White Fiends," in a manner that strikes terror; and when as a cosmic poet he creates the atmosphere and mood of poetic beauty in the absolute, as he does in "Spring in New Hampshire" and "The Harlem Dancer." Mr. McKay gives evidence that he has passed beyond the danger which threatens many of the new Negro poets—the danger of allowing the purely polemical phases of the race problem to choke their sense of artistry.

Mr. McKay's earliest work is unknown in this country. It consists of poems written and published in his native Jamaica. I was fortunate enough to run across this first volume, and I could not refrain from reproducing here one of the poems written in the West Indian Negro dialect. I have done this not only to illustrate the widest range of the poet's talent and to offer a comparison between the American and the West Indian dialects, but on account of the intrinsic worth of the poem itself. I was much tempted to introduce several more, in spite of the fact that they might require a glossary, because however greater work Mr. McKay may do he can never do anything more touching and charming than these poems in the Jamaica dialect.

Fenton Johnson is a young poet of the ultra-modern school who gives promise of greater work than he has yet done. Jessie Fauset shows that she possesses the lyric gift, and she works with care and finish. Miss Fauset is especially adept in her translations from the French. Georgia Douglas Johnson[2] is a poet neither afraid nor ashamed of her emotions. She limits herself to the purely conventional forms, rhythms and rhymes, but through them she achieves striking effects. The principal theme of Mrs. Johnson's poems is the secret dread down in every woman's heart, the dread of the passing of youth and beauty, and with them love. An old theme, one which

9. Benjamin Griffith Brawley (1882–1939), college teacher and literary historian.
1. African American poet and novelist (1890–1948).
2. African American poet and playwright (1877–

1966). Fenton Johnson (1888–1958), African American playwright, poet, and short story writer. Jessie Fauset (1856?–1961), African American novelist and editor.

poets themselves have often wearied of, but which, like death, remains one of the imperishable themes on which is made the poetry that has moved men's hearts through all ages. In her ingenuously wrought verses, through sheer simplicity and spontaneousness, Mrs. Johnson often sounds a note of pathos or passion that will not fail to waken a response, except in those too sophisticated or cynical to respond to natural impulses. Of the half dozen or so colored women writing creditable verse, Anne Spencer[3] is the most modern and least obvious in her methods. Her lines are at times involved and turgid and almost cryptic, but she shows an originality which does not depend upon eccentricities. In her "Before the Feast of Shushan" she displays an opulence, the love of which has long been charged against the Negro as one of his naïve and childish traits, but which in art may infuse a much needed color, warmth and spirit of abandon into American poetry.

John W. Holloway,[4] more than any Negro poet writing in the dialect today, summons to his work the lilt, the spontaneity and charm of which Dunbar was the supreme master whenever he employed that medium. It is well to say a word here about the dialect poems of James Edwin Campbell.[5] In dialect, Campbell was a precursor of Dunbar. A comparison of his idioms and phonetics with those of Dunbar reveals great differences. Dunbar is a shade or two more sophisticated and his phonetics approach nearer to a mean standard of the dialects spoken in the different sections. Campbell is more primitive and his phonetics are those of the dialect as spoken by the Negroes of the sea islands off the coasts of South Carolina and Georgia, which to this day remains comparatively close to its African roots, and is strikingly similar to the speech of the uneducated Negroes of the West Indies. An error that confuses many persons in reading or understanding Negro dialect is the idea that it is uniform. An ignorant Negro of the uplands of Georgia would have almost as much difficulty in understanding an ignorant sea island Negro as an Englishman would have. Not even in the dialect of any particular section is a given word always pronounced in precisely the same way. Its pronunciation depends upon the preceding and following sounds. Sometimes the combination permits of a liaison so close that to the uninitiated the sound of the word is almost completely lost.

The constant effort in Negro dialect is to elide all troublesome consonants and sounds. This negative effort may be after all only positive laziness of the vocal organs, but the result is a softening and smoothing which makes Negro dialect so delightfully easy for singers.

Daniel Webster Davis[6] wrote dialect poetry at the time when Dunbar was writing. He gained great popularity, but it did not spread beyond his own race. Davis had unctuous humor, but he was crude. For illustration, note the vast stretch between his "Hog Meat" and Dunbar's "When de Co'n Pone's Hot," both of them poems on the traditional ecstasy of the Negro in contemplation of "good things" to eat.

It is regrettable that two of the most gifted writers included were cut off so early in life. R. C. Jamison and Joseph S. Cotter, Jr.,[7] died several years ago, both of them in their youth. Jamison was barely thirty at the time of his

---

3. African American poet (1882–1975).
4. African American poet (1865–1920?).
5. African American poet and journalist (1867–1896).

6. African American poet and orator (1862–1913).
7. African American poet (1895–1919). Roscoe C. Jamison wrote *Negro Soldiers and Other Poems* (1918).

death, but among his poems there is one, at least, which stamps him as a poet of superior talent and lofty inspiration. "The Negro Soldiers" is a poem with the race problem as its theme, yet it transcends the limits of race and rises to a spiritual height that makes it one of the noblest poems of the Great War. Cotter died a mere boy of twenty, and the latter part of that brief period he passed in an invalid state. Some months before his death he published a thin volume of verses which were for the most part written on a sick bed. In this little volume Cotter showed fine poetic sense and a free and bold mastery over his material. A reading of Cotter's poems is certain to induce that mood in which one will regretfully speculate on what the young poet might have accomplished had he not been cut off so soon.

As intimated above, my original idea for this book underwent a change in the writing of the introduction. I first planned to select twenty-five to thirty poems which I judged to be up to a certain standard, and offer them with a few words of introduction and without comment. In the collection, as it grew to be, that "certain standard" has been broadened if not lowered; but I believe that this is offset by the advantage of the wider range given the reader and the student of the subject.

I offer this collection without making apology or asking allowance. I feel confident that the reader will find not only an earnest for the future, but actual achievement. The reader cannot but be impressed by the distance already covered. It is a long way from the plaints of George Horton to the invectives of Claude McKay, from the obviousness of Frances Harper to the complexness of Anne Spencer. Much ground has been covered, but more will yet be covered. It is this side of prophecy to declare that the undeniable creative genius of the Negro is destined to make a distinctive and valuable contribution to American poetry. * * *

1921

PAUL LAURENCE DUNBAR
1872–1906

Dubbed the "Poet Laureate of the Negro race" by Booker T. Washington and praised by readers on both sides of the color line, Paul Laurence Dunbar was best known in his own time for his lively and genial verse in black dialect. Although he was not the first African American to write in this idiom, Dunbar demonstrated both the talent to "feel the Negro life aesthetically" and the craftsmanship to "express it lyrically," as the influential white critic William Dean Howells wrote in his introduction to Dunbar's *Lyrics of Lowly Life* (1896), the poet's best-selling book. Yet for all the unprecedented critical and commercial celebrity that Dunbar enjoyed during his relatively brief heyday, his place at the welcome table of twentieth-century literary criticism has often been challenged and sometimes denied. Although African American schools, cultural societies, and literary prizes were named in Dunbar's honor in the wake of his untimely death, during the last half-century Dunbar has frequently been treated as a cautionary example: a black artist co-opted by white media hype, a poet who by singing "serenely sweet" to whites only postponed the bitter realization resonant in his most poignant line: "I know why the caged bird sings."

A most unlikely candidate for literary fame in turn-of-the-century white supremacist America, Dunbar made his way to the top by remaking a regional persona into a racial one. The regional, or local color point of view, personified in a folksy, nostalgic celebrant of rural life and homely values, had charmed readers of American regional poetry and fiction since the end of the Civil War era. During the 1870s and 1880s, in the work of whites such as Irwin Russell and Joel Chandler Harris and blacks such as Daniel Webster Davis, the "old-time Negro," an entertaining blackface variant of the popular local color persona, began to make a name for himself in American literature. His peculiar dialect lent an air of apparent authenticity to the stories he told of quaint, amusing, and contentedly dependent blacks in the prewar and postwar South. Dunbar's poetry capitalized on the appeal that African American folk life in the South had to the sizable national reading audience won over by Harris and other cultivators of the plantation myth of benign southern race relations. A reading of Dunbar's most enduring poem, We Wear the Mask, suggests that he may well have been aware of the liability of allowing his own poetry to evoke an image of black folk that played on thoughtless prejudices and degrading stereotypes. But to tar all of Dunbar's dialect poetry with the brush of social accommodationism is to forget that wearing the mask let Dunbar "mouth with myriad subtleties" truths that whites refused to confront face to face.

Dunbar learned about African American rural folk from his parents, former Kentucky plantation slaves whose stories of their pre-Emancipation experiences gave the future writer much valuable material. A city dweller practically all his life, Dunbar was born in Dayton, Ohio, in 1872. After his parents' divorce when he was four years old, he grew up under the care of his watchful and encouraging mother, Matilda Glass Dunbar. Paul was an excellent student at Dayton High School; though the only African American in the school, he was elected president of his class and delivered the class's graduation poem in June 1891. Refused subsequent employment in Dayton newspaper and legal offices because of his color, Dunbar found a job as an elevator operator. Between calls he wrote poems and articles for various midwestern newspapers while studying his favorite poets: Tennyson, Shakespeare, Keats, Poe, Longfellow, and the Midwest's most famous regionalist, James Whitcomb Riley.

In 1893 Dunbar took out a loan to subsidize the printing of his first book, Oak and Ivy. This collection of fifty-six poems impressed many of the poet's early readers by its range of matter and mood and by the maturity of its technique. No one seems to have been bothered by the ease with which Dunbar could sound sentimental, even reactionary, about the pre-Emancipation South in the dialect poem Goin' Back while proclaiming elsewhere in the volume, in Ode to Ethiopia, his pride in his race's progress toward an expanding freedom. Six years later the poet hinted at a reason behind the double-voiced way he spoke about race—seemingly carefree when in black dialect, but more serious and brooding in standard English. In Sympathy, a self-revealing lament, Dunbar forecast his fate: like the song of a caged bird, his verse, although emanating from an intense desire for full artistic self-expression, would be deliberately misheard by whites as merely "a carol of joy or glee."

Dunbar's detractors have argued that he himself abetted this misevaluation by regaling his public with too many easygoing, uncritical portrayals of African American life and character in his dialect poetry. Dunbar's defenders answer that although the largest proportion of his verse was not in dialect, whites showed little interest in this side of the poet's talent. Inevitably constrained by the tastes of the times, Dunbar, like many of his literary contemporaries, white as well as black, tried to find ways to enlighten his audience without alienating them. Thus in his best dialect poems, such as *When Malindy Sings* and *An Ante-Bellum Sermon*, Dunbar paid tribute to the artistry inherent in black folk expression and, in the case of the dialect sermon, the subversiveness and social insight often hidden under the guise of simple down-home speech.

As the demand for his poetry grew, Dunbar cultivated literary friendships with prominent whites who in turn helped him publish and publicize his most famous volumes of poetry, *Majors and Minors* (1895) and *Lyrics of Lowly Life* (1896). Subsequent reading tours in the East not only enhanced Dunbar's popularity but also introduced him to the African American poet Alice Ruth Moore, whom he married in 1898. By that time, Dunbar had become an internationally acclaimed African American writer whose achievement earned him an appointment to a clerkship in the U.S. Library of Congress and an honorary Master of Arts degree from Atlanta University.

In 1898 Dunbar began to make a name for himself as a fiction writer. During the next six years he published four books of short stories and four novels. Although many of Dunbar's stories spoke frankly about racial injustice in the South, many more pandered to popular racist images of slaves and ex-slaves, causing some critics to wonder about the genuineness of the author's identification with people whom he seemed at times to champion and at other times to patronize. Dunbar's first three novels drew little on African American experience. But his final, important book, *The Sport of the Gods* (1903), addressed a major question for black America at the turn of the century—the advantages and disadvantages of migration from the rural South to the urban North. The motives behind this grim foray into urban realism also impelled Dunbar to publish *The Fourth of July and Race Outrages* in the *New York Times* in 1903, a sardonic attack on the myopic indifference of American patriotism to the race riots, lynchings, peonage, and disfranchisement of black voters in the South. By this time, however, Dunbar's steadily worsening health, brought on by heavy drinking and tuberculosis, together with his harried finances allowed him little time or energy to undertake serious new departures in his writing.

At the end of Dunbar's life, his self-described disciple James Weldon Johnson congratulated him on having taken dialect poetry as far as it could go, giving it what Johnson called in his autobiography *Along This Way* (1933), "the fullest measure of charm, tenderness, and beauty" possible. Johnson recalled that Dunbar's rueful reply to this compliment was simply, "I have never gotten to the things I really wanted to do."

Ode to Ethiopia

O Mother Race! to thee I bring
This pledge of faith unwavering,
    This tribute to thy glory.
I know the pangs which thou didst feel,
When Slavery crushed thee with its heel,   5
    With thy dear blood all gory.

Sad days were those—ah, sad indeed!
But through the land the fruitful seed
    Of better times was growing.
The plant of freedom upward sprung,   10
And spread its leaves so fresh and young—
    Its blossoms now are blowing.

On every hand in this fair land,
Proud Ethiope's swarthy children stand
  Beside their fairer neighbour;   15
The forests flee before their stroke,
Their hammers ring, their forges smoke,—
  They stir in honest labour.

They tread the fields where honour calls;
Their voices sound through senate halls   20
  In majesty and power.
To right they cling; the hymns they sing
Up to the skies in beauty ring,
  And bolder grow each hour.

Be proud, my Race, in mind and soul;   25
Thy name is writ on Glory's scroll
  In characters of fire.
High 'mid the clouds of Fame's bright sky
Thy banner's blazoned folds now fly,
  And truth shall lift them higher.   30

Thou hast the right to noble pride,
Whose spotless robes were purified
  By blood's severe baptism.
Upon thy brow the cross was laid,
And labour's painful sweat-beads made   35
  A consecrating chrism. [1]

No other race, or white or black,
When bound as thou wert, to the rack,
  So seldom stooped to grieving;
No other race, when free again,   40
Forgot the past and proved them men
  So noble in forgiving.

Go on and up! Our souls and eyes
Shall follow thy continuous rise;
  Our ears shall list thy story   45
From bards who from thy root shall spring,
And proudly tune their lyres to sing
  Of Ethiopia's glory.

                                                    1893

Worn Out

    You bid me hold my peace
      And dry my fruitless tears,
    Forgetting that I bear
      A pain beyond my years.

---

1. Sacramental oil.

You say that I should smile   5
    And drive the gloom away;
I would, but sun and smiles
    Have left my life's dark day.

All time seems cold and void,
    And naught but tears remain;   10
Life's music beats for me
    A melancholy strain.

I used at first to hope,
    But hope is past and gone;
And now without a ray   15
    My cheerless life drags on.

Like to an ash-stained hearth
    When all its fires are spent;
Like to an autumn wood
    By storm winds rudely shent, [1]—   20

So sadly goes my heart,
    Unclothed of hope and peace;
It asks not joy again,
    But only seeks release.

                                                       1893

A Negro Love Song

Seen my lady home las' night,
    Jump back, honey, jump back.
Hel' huh han' an' sque'z it tight,
    Jump back, honey, jump back.
Hyeahd huh sigh a little sigh,   5
Seen a light gleam f' om huh eye,
An' a smile go flittin' by—
    Jump back, honey, jump back.

Hyeahd de win' blow thoo de pine,
    Jump back, honey, jump back.   10
Mockin'-bird was singin' fine,
    Jump back, honey, jump back.
An' my hea't was beatin' so,
When I reached my lady's do',
Dat I couldn't ba' to go—   15
    Jump back, honey, jump back.

Put my ahm aroun' huh wais',
    Jump back, honey, jump back.
Raised huh lips an' took a tase,
    Jump back, honey, jump back.   20

1. Damaged.

Love me, honey, love me true?
Love me well ez I love you?
An' she answe'd, " 'Cose I do"—
    Jump back, honey, jump back.

                                                              1895

The Colored Soldiers

If the muse were mine to tempt it
    And my feeble voice were strong,
If my tongue were trained to measures,
    I would sing a stirring song.
I would sing a song heroic   5
    Of those noble sons of Ham, [1]
Of the gallant colored soldiers
    Who fought for Uncle Sam!

In the early days you scorned them,
    And with many a flip and flout   10
Said "These battles are the white man's,
    And the whites will fight them out."
Up the hills you fought and faltered,
    In the vales you strove and bled,
While your ears still heard the thunder   15
    Of the foes' advancing tread.

Then distress fell on the nation,
    And the flag was drooping low;
Should the dust pollute your banner?
    No! the nation shouted, No!   20
So when War, in savage triumph,
    Spread abroad his funeral pall—
Then you called the colored soldiers,
    And they answered to your call.

And like hounds unleashed and eager   25
    For the life blood of the prey,
Sprung they forth and bore them bravely
    In the thickest of the fray.
And where'er the fight was hottest,
    Where the bullets fastest fell,   30
There they pressed unblanched and fearless
    At the very mouth of hell.

Ah, they rallied to the standard
    To uphold it by their might;
None were stronger in the labors,   35
    None were braver in the fight.

---

1 In the Old Testament, the second of Noah's three sons, traditionally labeled the father of the black race.

From the blazing breach of Wagner
    To the plains of Olustee,[2]
They were foremost in the fight
    Of the battles of the free.   40

And at Pillow![3] God have mercy
    On the deeds committed there,
And the souls of those poor victims
    Sent to Thee without a prayer.
Let the fulness of Thy pity   45
    O'er the hot wrought spirits sway
Of the gallant colored soldiers
    Who fell fighting on that day!

Yes, the Blacks enjoy their freedom,
    And they won it dearly, too;   50
For the life blood of their thousands
    Did the southern fields bedew.
In the darkness of their bondage,
    In the depths of slavery's night,
Their muskets flashed the dawning,   55
    And they fought their way to light.

They were comrades then and brothers,
    Are they more or less to-day?
They were good to stop a bullet
    And to front the fearful fray.   60
They were citizens and soldiers,
    When rebellion raised its head;
And the traits that made them worthy,—
    Ah! those virtues are not dead.

They have shared your nightly vigils,   65
    They have shared your daily toil;
And their blood with yours commingling
    Has enriched the Southern soil.
They have slept and marched and suffered
    'Neath the same dark skies as you,   70
They have met as fierce a foeman,
    And have been as brave and true.

And their deeds shall find a record
    In the registry of Fame;
For their blood has cleansed completely   75
    Every blot of Slavery's shame.
So all honor and all glory
    To those noble sons of Ham—

---

2. Site of a Union defeat in Florida on February 20, 1863, where three black regiments distinguished themselves. At Fort Wagner, in South Carolina, a black Union regiment's bravery in defeat on July 18, 1863, earned widespread praise in the North.

3. Fort Pillow, in Tennessee, was the site of a massacre of black Union soldiers by Confederate forces on April 12, 1864.

The gallant colored soldiers
Who fought for Uncle Sam! 80

1895

An Ante-Bellum[1] Sermon

We is gathahed hyeah, my brothahs,
  In dis howlin' wildaness,
Fu' to speak some words of comfo't
  To each othah in distress.
An' we chooses fu' ouah subjic' 5
  Dis—we'll 'splain it by an' by;
"An' de Lawd said, 'Moses, Moses,'
  An' de man said, 'Hyeah am I.' "

Now ole Pher'oh, down in Egypt,
  Was de wuss man evah bo'n, 10
An' he had de Hebrew chillun
  Down dah wukin' in his co'n;
'Twell de Lawd got tiahed o' his foolin',
  An' sez he: "I'll let him know—
Look hyeah, Moses, go tell Pher'oh 15
  Fu' to let dem chillun go."

"An' ef he refuse to do it,
  I will make him rue de houah,[2]
Fu' I'll empty down on Egypt
  All de vials of my powah." 20
Yes, he did—an' Pher'oh's ahmy
  Wasn't wuth a ha'f a dime;
Fu' de Lawd will he'p his chillun,
  You kin trust him evah time.

An' yo' enemies may 'sail you 25
  In de back an' in de front;
But de Lawd is all aroun' you,
  Fu' to ba' de battle's brunt.
Dey kin fo'ge yo' chains an' shackles
  F'om de mountains to de sea; 30
But de Lawd will sen' some Moses
  Fu' to set his chillun free.

An' de lan' shall hyeah his thundah,
  Lak a blas' f'om Gab'el's[3] ho'n,
Fu' de Lawd of hosts is mighty 35
  When he girds his ahmor on.
But fu' feah some one mistakes me,
  I will pause right hyeah to say,

---

1. Before the U.S. Civil War (1861–65).
2. Hour.
3. In the Bible, Gabriel is the archangel of good news.

Dat I'm still a-preachin' ancient,
    I ain't talkin' 'bout to-day.   40

But I tell you, fellah christuns,
    Things'll happen mighty strange;
Now, de Lawd done dis fu' Isrul,
    An' his ways don't nevah change,
An' de love he showed to Isrul   45
    Wasn't all on Isrul spent;
Now don't run an' tell yo' mastahs
    Dat I's preachin' discontent.

'Cause I is n't; I 'se a-judgin'
    Bible people by deir ac's;   50
I 'se a-givin' you de Scriptuah,
    I 'se a-handin' you de fac's.
Cose ole Pher'oh b'lieved in slav'ry,
    But de Lawd he let him see,
Dat de people he put bref in,—   55
    Evah mothah's son was free.

An' dahs othahs thinks lak Pher'oh,
    But dey calls de Scriptuah liar,
Fu' de Bible says "a servant
    Is a-worthy of his hire."   60
An' you cain't git roun' nor thoo dat,
    An' you cain't git ovah it,
Fu' whatevah place you git in,
    Dis hyeah Bible too 'll fit.

So you see de Lawd's intention,   65
    Evah sence de worl' began,
Was dat His almighty freedom
    Should belong to evah man,
But I think it would be bettah,
    Ef I'd pause agin to say,   70
Dat I'm talkin' 'bout ouah freedom
    In a Bibleistic way.

But de Moses is a-comin',
    An' he's comin', suah and fas'
We kin hyeah his feet a-trompin',   75
    We kin hyeah his trumpit blas'.
But I want to wa'n you people,
    Don't you git too brigity;⁴
An' don't you git to braggin'
    'Bout dese things, you wait an' see.   80

But when Moses wif his powah
    Comes an' sets us chillun free,

---

4. Biggety, self-important.

We will praise de gracious Mastah[5]
　　Dat has gin us liberty;
An' we'll shout ouah halleluyahs,   85
　　On dat mighty reck'nin' day,
When we'se reco'nised ez citiz'[6]—
　　Huh uh! Chillun, let us pray!

1895

Ere Sleep Comes Down to Soothe the Weary Eyes

Ere sleep comes down to soothe the weary eyes,
　　Which all the day with ceaseless care have sought
The magic gold which from the seeker flies;
　　Ere dreams put on the gown and cap of thought,
And make the waking world a world of lies,—   5
　　Of lies most palpable, uncouth, forlorn,
That say life's full of aches and tears and sighs,—
　　Oh, how with more than dreams the soul is torn,
Ere sleep comes down to soothe the weary eyes.

Ere sleep comes down to soothe the weary eyes,   10
　　How all the griefs and heartaches we have known
Come up like pois'nous vapors that arise
　　From some base witch's caldron, when the crone,
To work some potent spell, her magic plies.
　　The past which held its share of bitter pain,   15
Whose ghost we prayed that Time might exorcise,
　　Comes up, is lived and suffered o'er again,
Ere sleep comes down to soothe the weary eyes.

Ere sleep comes down to soothe the weary eyes,
　　What phantoms fill the dimly lighted room;   20
What ghostly shades in awe-creating guise
　　Are bodied forth within the teeming gloom.
What echoes faint of sad and soul-sick cries,
　　And pangs of vague inexplicable pain
That pay the spirit's ceaseless enterprise,   25
　　Come thronging through the chambers of the brain,
Ere sleep comes down to soothe the weary eyes.

Ere sleep comes down to soothe the weary eyes,
　　Where ranges forth the spirit far and free?
Through what strange realms and unfamiliar skies   30
　　Tends her far course to lands of mystery?
To lands unspeakable—beyond surmise,
　　Where shapes unknowable to being spring,
Till, faint of wing, the Fancy fails and dies
　　Much wearied with the spirit's journeying,   35
Ere sleep comes down to soothe the weary eyes.

5. Jesus Christ.   6. Citizens.

Ere sleep comes down to soothe the weary eyes,
    How questioneth the soul that other soul,—
The inner sense which neither cheats nor lies,
    But self exposes unto self, a scroll   40
Full writ with all life's acts unwise or wise,
    In characters indelible and known;
So, trembling with the shock of sad surprise,
    The soul doth view its awful self alone,
Ere sleep comes down to soothe the weary eyes.   45

When sleep comes down to seal the weary eyes,
    The last dear sleep whose soft embrace is balm,
And whom sad sorrow teaches us to prize
    For kissing all our passions into calm,
Ah, then, no more we heed the sad world's cries,   50
    Or seek to probe th' eternal mystery,
Or fret our souls at long-withheld replies,
    At glooms through which our visions cannot see,
When sleep comes down to seal the weary eyes.

                                                                      1895

Not They Who Soar

Not they who soar, but they who plod
Their rugged way, unhelped, to God
Are heroes; they who higher fare,
And, flying, fan the upper air,
Miss all the toil that hugs the sod.   5
'Tis they whose backs have felt the rod,
Whose feet have pressed the path unshod,
May smile upon defeated care,
        Not they who soar.

High up there are no thorns to prod,   10
Nor boulders lurking 'neath the clod
To turn the keenness of the share,
For flight is ever free and rare;
But heroes they the soil who've trod,
        Not they who soar!   15

                                                                      1895

When Malindy Sings

G'way an' quit dat noise, Miss Lucy—
    Put dat music book away;
What's de use to keep on tryin'?
    Ef you practise twell you're gray,
You cain't sta't no notes a-flyin'   5
    Lak de ones dat rants and rings
F'om de kitchen to be big woods
    When Malindy sings.

You ain't got de nachel[1] o'gans
    Fu' to make de soun' come right,   10
You ain't got de tu'ns an' twistin's
    Fu' to make it sweet an' light.
Tell you one thing now, Miss Lucy,
    An' I'm tellin' you fu' true,
When hit comes to raal[2] right singin',   15
    'T ain't no easy thing to do.

Easy 'nough fu' folks to hollah,
    Lookin' at de lines an' dots,
When dey ain't no one kin sence it,
    An' de chune comes in, in spots;   20
But fu' real melojous music,
    Dat jes' strikes you' hea't and clings,
Jes' you stan' an' listen wif me
    When Malindy sings.

Ain't you nevah hyeahd Malindy?   25
    Blessed soul, tek up de cross!
Look hyeah, ain't you jokin', honey?
    Well, you don't know whut you los'.
Y' ought to hyeah dat gal a-wa'blin',
    Robins, la'ks, an' all dem things,   30
Heish dey moufs an' hides dey faces
    When Malindy sings.

Fiddlin' man jes' stop his fiddlin',
    Lay his fiddle on de she'f;
Mockin'-bird quit tryin' to whistle,   35
    'Cause he jes' so shamed hisse'f.
Folks a-playin' on de banjo
    Draps dey fingahs on de strings—
Bless yo' soul—fu'gits to move 'em,
    When Malindy sings.   40

She jes' spreads huh mouf and hollahs,
    "Come to Jesus,"[3] twell you hyeah
Sinnahs' tremblin' steps and voices,
    Timid-lak a-drawin' neah;
Den she tu'ns to "Rock of Ages,"[4]   45
    Simply to de cross she clings,
An' you fin' yo' teahs a-drappin'
    When Malindy sings.

Who dat says dat humble praises
    Wif de Master[5] nevah counts?   50
Heish yo' mouf, I hyeah dat music,
    Ez hit rises up an' mounts—

1. Natural.
2. Real.
3. A popular hymn.

4. A popular hymn.
5. Jesus Christ.

Floatin' by de hills an' valleys,
  Way above dis buryin' sod,
Ez hit makes its way in glory   55
  To de very gates of God!

Oh, hit's sweetah dan de music
  Of an edicated band;
An' hit's dearah dan de battle's
  Song o' triumph in de lan'.   60
It seems holier dan evenin'
  When de solemn chu'ch bell rings,
Ez I sit an' ca'mly listen
  While Malindy sings.

Towsah, stop dat ba'kin', hyeah me!   65
  Mandy, mek dat chile keep still;
Don't you hyeah de echoes callin'
  F'om de valley to de hill?
Let me listen, I can hyeah it,
  Th'oo de bresh of angels' wings,   70
Sof' an' sweet, "Swing Low, Sweet Chariot," [6]
  Ez Malindy sings.

                                              1895

We Wear the Mask

We wear the mask that grins and lies,
It hides our cheeks and shades our eyes,—
This debt we pay to human guile;
With torn and bleeding hearts we smile,
And mouth with myriad subtleties.   5

Why should the world be overwise,
In counting all our tears and sighs?
Nay, let them only see us, while
  We wear the mask.

We smile, but, O great Christ, our cries   10
To thee from tortured souls arise.
We sing, but oh the clay is vile
Beneath our feet, and long the mile;
But let the world dream otherwise,
  We wear the mask!   15

                                              1895

---

6. A Negro spiritual.

Little Brown Baby

Little brown baby wif spa'klin' eyes,
   Come to yo' pappy an' set on his knee.
What you been doin', suh—makin' san' pies?
   Look at dat bib—you's ez du'ty ez me.
Look at dat mouf—dat's merlasses, I bet;   5
   Come hyeah, Maria, an' wipe off his han's.
Bees gwine to ketch you an' eat you up yit,
   Bein' so sticky an' sweet—goodness lan's!

Little brown baby wif spa'klin' eyes,
   Who's pappy's darlin' an' who's pappy's chile?   10
Who is it all de day nevah once tries
   Fu' to be cross, er once loses dat smile?
Whah did you git dem teef? My, you's a scamp!
   Whah did dat dimple come f'om in yo' chin?
Pappy do' know you—I b'lieves you's a tramp;   15
   Mammy, dis hyeah's some ol' straggler got in!

Let's th'ow him outen de do' in de san',
   We do' want stragglers a-layin' 'roun' hyeah;
Let's gin him 'way to de big buggah-man;
   I know he's hidin' erroun' hyeah right ncah.   20
Buggah-man, buggah-man, come in de do',
   Hyeah's a bad boy you kin have fu' to eat.
Mammy an' pappy do' want him no mo',
   Swaller him down f'om his haid to his feet!

Dah, now, I t'ought dat you'd hug me up close.   25
   Go back, ol' buggah, you sha'n't have dis boy.
He ain't no tramp, ner no straggler, of co'se;
   He's pappy's pa'dner an' playmate an' joy.
Come to you' pallet now—go to yo' res';
   Wisht you could allus know ease an' cleah skies;   30
Wisht you could stay jes' a chile on my breas'—
   Little brown baby wif spa'klin' eyes!

                              1897

Her Thought and His

The gray of the sea, and the gray of the sky,
A glimpse of the moon like a half-closed eye.
The gleam on the waves and the light on the land,
A thrill in my heart,—and—my sweetheart's hand.

She turned from the sea with a woman's grace,   5
And the light fell soft on her upturned face,
And I thought of the flood-tide of infinite bliss
That would flow to my heart from a single kiss.

But my sweetheart was shy, so I dared not ask
For the boon, so bravely I wore the mask.   10
But into her face there came a flame:—
I wonder could she have been thinking the same?

                                                                        1899

A Cabin Tale

The Young Master Asks for a Story

Whut you say, dah? huh, uh! chile,
You's enough to dribe me wile.
Want a sto'y; jes' hyeah dat!
Whah' 'll I git a sto'y at?
Di'n' I tell you th'ee las' night?   5
Go 'way, honey, you ain't right.
I got somep'n' else to do,
'Cides jes' tellin' tales to you.
Tell you jes' one? Lem me see
Whut dat one's a-gwine to be.   10
When you's ole, yo membry fails;
Seems lak I do' know no tales.
Well, set down dah in dat cheer,
Keep still ef you wants to hyeah.
Tek dat chin up off yo' han's,   15
Set up nice now. Goodness lan's!
Hol' yo'se'f up lak yo' pa.
Bet nobidy evah saw
Him scrunched down lak you was den—
High-tone boys meks high-tone men.   20

    Once dey was a ole black bah,
Used to live 'roun' hyeah somewhah
In a cave. He was so big
He could ca'y off a pig
Lak you picks a chicken up,   25
Er yo' leetles' bit o' pup.
An' he had two gread big eyes,
Jes' erbout a saucer's size.
Why, dey looked lak balls o' fiah
Jumpin' 'roun' erpon a wiah   30
W'en dat bah was mad; an' laws!
But you ought to seen his paws!
Did I see 'em? How you 'spec
I's a-gwine to ricollec'
Dis hyeah ya'n I's try'n' to spin   35
Ef you keeps on puttin' in?
You keep still an' don't you cheep
Less I'll sen' you off to sleep.
Dis hyeah bah'd go trompin' 'roun'
Eatin' evahthing he foun';   40

No one couldn't have a fa'm
But dat bah 'u'd do 'em ha'm;
And dey couldn't ketch de scamp.
Anywhah he wan'ed to tramp.
Dah de scoun'el 'd mek his track,   45
Do his du't an' come on back.
He was sich a sly ole limb,
Traps was jes' lak fun to him.

   Now, down neah whah Mistah Bah
Lived, dey was a weasel dah;   50
But dey wasn't fren's a-tall
Case de weasel was so small.
An' de bah 'u'd, jes' fu' sass,
Tu'n his nose up w'en he'd pass.
Weasels's small o' cose, but my!   55
Dem air animiles is sly.
So dis hyeah one says, says he,
"I'll jes' fix dat bah, you see."
So he fixes up his plan
An' hunts up de fa'merman.   60
When de fa'mer see him come,
He 'mence lookin' mighty glum,
An' he ketches up a stick;
But de weasel speak up quick:
"Hol' on, Mistah Fa'mer man,   65
I wan' 'splain a little plan.
Ef you waits, I'll tell you whah
An' jes' how to ketch ol' Bah.
But I tell you now you mus'
Gin me one fat chicken fus'."   70
Den de man he scratch his haid,
Las' he say, "I'll mek de trade."
So de weasel et his hen,
Smacked his mouf and says, "Well, den,
Set yo' trap an' bait ternight,   75
An' I'll ketch de bah all right."
Den he ups an' goes to see
Mistah Bah, an' says, says he:
"Well, fren' Bah, we *ain't* been fren's,
But ternight ha'd feelin' en's.   80
Ef you ain't too proud to steal,
We kin git a splendid meal.
Cose I wouldn't come to you,
But it mus' be done by two;
Hit's a trap, but we kin beat   85
All dey tricks an' git de meat."
"Cose I's wif you," says de bah,
"Come on, weasel, show me whah."
Well, dey trots erlong ontwell
Dat air meat beginned to smell   90
In de trap. Den weasel say:
"Now you put yo' paw dis way

> While I hol' de spring back so,
> Den you grab de meat an' go."
> Well, de bah he had to grin   95
> Ez he put his big paw in,
> Den he juked up, but—kerbing!
> Weasel done let go de spring.
> "Dah now," says de weasel, "dah,
> I done cotched you, Mistah Bah!"   100
> O, dat bah did sno't and spout,
> Try'n' his bestes' to git out,
> But de weasel say, "Goo'-bye!
> Weasel small, but weasel sly."
> Den he tu'ned his back an' run   105
> Tol' de fa'mer whut he done.
> So de fa'mer come down dah,
> Wif a axe and killed de bah.
>
>   Dah now, ain't dat sto'y fine?
> Run erlong now, nevah min'.   110
> Want some mo', you rascal, you?
> No, suh! no, suh! dat'll do.

1899

Sympathy

> I know what the caged bird feels, alas!
>   When the sun is bright on the upland slopes;
> When the wind stirs soft through the springing grass,
> And the river flows like a stream of glass;
>   When the first bird sings and the first bud opes,   5
> And the faint perfume from its chalice [1] steals—
> I know what the caged bird feels!
>
> I know why the caged bird beats his wing
>   Till its blood is red on the cruel bars;
> For he must fly back to his perch and cling   10
> When he fain would be on the bough a-swing;
>   And a pain still throbs in the old, old scars
> And they pulse again with a keener sting—
> I know why he beats his wing!
>
> I know why the caged bird sings, ah me,   15
>   When his wing is bruised and his bosom sore,—
> When he beats his bars and he would be free;
> It is not a carol of joy or glee,
>   But a prayer that he sends from his heart's deep core,
> But a plea, that upward to Heaven he flings—   20
> I know why the caged bird sings!

1899

---

1. A cup-shaped flower.

Dinah Kneading Dough

I have seen full many a sight
Born of day or drawn by night:
Sunlight on a silver stream,
Golden lilies all a-dream,
Lofty mountains, bold and proud,   5
Veiled beneath the lacelike cloud;
But no lovely sight I know
Equals Dinah kneading dough.

Brown arms buried elbow-deep
Their domestic rhythm keep,   10
As with steady sweep they go
Through the gently yielding dough.
Maids may vaunt their finer charms—
Naught to me like Dinah's arms;
Girls may draw, or paint, or sew—   15
I love Dinah kneading dough.

Eyes of jet and teeth of pearl,
Hair, some say, too tight a-curl;
But the dainty maid I deem
Very near perfection's dream.   20
Swift she works, and only flings
Me a glance—the least of things.
And I wonder, does she know
That my heart is in the dough?

1899

The Haunted Oak

Pray why are you so bare, so bare,
  Oh, bough of the old oak-tree;
And why, when I go through the shade you throw,
  Runs a shudder over me?

My leaves were green as the best, I trow,[1]   5
  And sap ran free in my veins,
But I saw in the moonlight dim and weird
  A guiltless victim's pains.

I bent me down to hear his sigh;
  I shook with his gurgling moan,   10
And I trembled sore when they rode away,
  And left him here alone.

They'd charged him with the old, old crime,
  And set him fast in jail:

1. Believe.

901

Oh, why does the dog howl all night long,   15
    And why does the night wind wail?

He prayed his prayer and he swore his oath,
    And he raised his hand to the sky;
But the beat of hoofs smote on his ear,
    And the steady tread drew nigh.   20

Who is it rides by night, by night,
    Over the moonlit road?
And what is the spur that keeps the pace,
    What is the galling goad?

And now they beat at the prison door,   25
    "Ho, keeper, do not stay!
We are friends of him whom you hold within,
    And we fain would take him away

"From those who ride fast on our heels
    With mind to do him wrong;   30
They have no care for his innocence,
    And the rope they bear is long."

They have fooled the jailer with lying words,
    They have fooled the man with lies;
The bolts unbar, the locks are drawn,   35
    And the great door open flies.

Now they have taken him from the jail,
    And hard and fast they ride,
And the leader laughs low down in his throat,
    As they halt my trunk beside.   40

Oh, the judge, he wore a mask of black,
    And the doctor one of white,
And the minister, with his oldest son,
    Was curiously bedight. [2]

Oh, foolish man, why weep you now?   45
    'T is but a little space,
And the time will come when these shall dread
    The mem'ry of your face.

I feel the rope against my bark,
    And the weight of him in my grain,   50
I feel in the throe of his final woe
    The touch of my own last pain.

And never more shall leaves come forth
    On a bough that bears the ban;

2. Dressed.

I am burned with dread, I am dried and dead,   55
   From the curse of a guiltless man.

And ever the judge rides by, rides by,
   And goes to hunt the deer,
And ever another rides his soul
   In the guise of a mortal fear.   60

And ever the man he rides me hard,
   And never a night stays he;
For I feel his curse as a haunted bough,
   On the trunk of a haunted tree.

                                1903

Douglass

Ah, Douglass, we have fall'n on evil days,
   Such days as thou, not even thou didst know,
   When thee, the eyes of that harsh long ago
Saw, salient, at the cross of devious ways,
And all the country heard thee with amaze.   5
   Not ended then, the passionate ebb and flow,
   The awful tide that battled to and fro;
We ride amid a tempest of dispraise.

Now, when the waves of swift dissension swarm,
   And Honor, the strong pilot, lieth stark,   10
Oh, for thy voice high-sounding o'er the storm,
   For thy strong arm to guide the shivering bark,
The blast-defying power of thy form,
   To give us comfort through the lonely dark.

                                1903

Philosophy

I been t'inkin' 'bout de preachah; whut he said de othah night,
   'Bout hit bein' people's dooty, fu' to keep dey faces bright;
How one ought to live so pleasant dat ouah tempah never riles,
   Meetin' evahbody roun' us wid ouah very nicest smiles.

Dat's all right, I ain't a-sputin' not a t'ing dat soun's lak fac',   5
   But you don't ketch folks a-grinnin' wid a misery in de back;
An' you don't fin' dem a-smilin' w'en dey's hongry ez kin be,
   Leastways, dat's how human natur' allus seems to 'pear to me.

We is mos' all putty likely fu' to have our little cares,
   An' I think we's doin' fus' rate w'en we jes' go long and bears,   10
Widout breakin' up ouah faces in a sickly so't o' grin,
   W'en we knows dat in ouah innards we is p'intly mad ez sin.

Oh dey's times fu' bein' pleasant an' fu' goin' smilin' roun',
   'Cause I don't believe in people allus totin' roun' a frown,
But it's easy 'nough to titter w'en de stew is smokin' hot,   15
   But hit's mighty ha'd to giggle w'en dey's nuffin' in de pot.

1903

Black Samson of Brandywine [1]

"In the fight at Brandywine, Black Samson, a giant negro armed with a
scythe, sweeps his way through the red ranks. . . ."
     —C. M. SKINNER's *Myths and Legends of Our Own Land*

Gray are the pages of record,
   Dim are the volumes of eld;
Else had old Delaware told us
   More that her history held.
Told us with pride in the story,   5
   Honest and noble and fine,
More of the tale of my hero,
   Black Samson of Brandywine.

Sing of your chiefs and your nobles,
   Saxon and Celt and Gaul, [2]   10
Breath of mine ever shall join you,
   Highly I honor them all.
Give to them all of their glory,
   But for this noble of mine,
Lend him a tithe [3] of your tribute,   15
   Black Samson of Brandywine.

There in the heat of the battle,
   There in the stir of the fight,
Loomed he, an ebony giant,
   Black as the pinions [4] of night.   20
Swinging his scythe like a mower
   Over a field of grain,
Needless the care of the gleaners,
   Where he had passed amain. [5]

Straight through the human harvest,   25
   Cutting a bloody swath,
Woe to you, soldier of Briton!
   Death is abroad in his path.
Flee from the scythe of the reaper,
   Flee while the moment is thine,   30
None may with safety withstand him,
   Black Samson of Brandywine.

1. A creek in southeastern Pennsylvania, which was the site of a British victory in 1777 over the American Revolutionary Army.
2. One of the Celtic-speaking peoples of ancient France. The Saxons were a West Germanic people who invaded Britain in the 5th century A.D. The Celts were an ancient warlike Irish and Scottish people.
3. One-tenth.
4. Wings.
5. Furiously. "Gleaners": people who gather grain.

Was he a freeman or bondman?
Was he a man or a thing?
What does it matter? His brav'ry   35
Renders him royal—a king.
If he was only a chattel,[6]
Honor the ransom may pay
Of the royal, the loyal black giant
Who fought for his country that day.   40

Noble and bright is the story,
Worthy the touch of the lyre,[7]
Sculptor or poet should find it
Full of the stuff to inspire.
Beat it in brass and in copper,   45
Tell it in storied line,
So that the world may remember
Black Samson of Brandywine.

                                                                  1903

The Poet

He sang of life, serenely sweet,
With, now and then, a deeper note.
From some high peak, nigh yet remote,
He voiced the world's absorbing beat.

He sang of love when earth was young,   5
And Love, itself, was in his lays.
But ah, the world, it turned to praise
A jingle in a broken tongue.

                                                                  1903

The Fourth of July and Race Outrages

Belleville, Wilmington, Evansville, the Fourth of July, and Kishineff,[1] a curious combination and yet one replete with a ghastly humor. Sitting with closed lips over our own bloody deeds we accomplish the fine irony of a protest to Russia. Contemplating with placid eyes the destruction of all the Declaration of Independence and the Constitution stood for, we celebrate the thing which our own action proclaims we do not believe in.

But it is over and done. The Fourth is come and gone. The din has ceased and the smoke has cleared away. Nothing remains but the litter of all and a few reflections. The sky-rocket has ascended, the firecrackers have burst, the roman candles have sputtered, the "nigger chasers"—a pertinent American name—have run their courses, and we have celebrated the nation's birthday. Yes, and we black folks have celebrated.

6. Slave.
7. A small harp.
1. Sites of recent racial violence in Illinois, North Carolina, and Indiana, respectively, and of a pogrom against Jews in Moldavia, a province of Russia.

Dearborn Street and Armour Avenue[2] have been all life and light. Not even the Jews and the Chinaman have been able to outdo us in the display of loyalty. And we have done it all because we have not stopped to think just how little it means to us.

The papers are full of the reports of peonage[3] in Alabama. A new and more dastardly slavery there has arisen to replace the old. For the sake of reenslaving the Negro, the Constitution has been trampled under feet, the rights of man have been laughed out of court, and the justice of God has been made a jest and we celebrate.

Every wire, no longer in the South alone, brings us news of a new hanging or a new burning, some recent outrage against a helpless people, some fresh degradation of an already degraded race. One man sins and a whole nation suffers, and we celebrate.

Like a dark cloud, pregnant with terror and destruction, disenfranchisement has spread its wings over our brethren of the South. Like the same dark cloud, industrial prejudice glooms above us in the North. We may not work save when the new-come foreigner refuses to, and then they, high prized above our sacrificial lives, may shoot us down with impunity. And yet we celebrate.

With citizenship discredited and scored, with violated homes and long unheeded prayers, with bleeding hands uplifted, still sore and smarting from long beating at the door of opportunity, we raise our voices and sing, "My Country, 'Tis of Thee"; we shout and sing while from the four points of the compass comes our brothers' unavailing cry, and so we celebrate.

With a preacher, one who a few centuries ago would have sold indulgences to the murderers on St. Bartholomew's Day,[4] with such a preacher in a Chicago pulpit, jingling his thirty pieces of silver, distorting the number and nature of our crimes, excusing anarchy, apologizing for murder, and tearing to tatters the teachings of Jesus Christ while he cries, "Release unto us Barabbas,"[5] we celebrate.

But there are some who sit silent within their closed rooms and hear as from afar the din of joy come muffled to their ears as on some later day their children and their children's sons shall hear a nation's cry for succor in her need. Aye, there be some who on this festal day kneel in their private closets and with hands upraised and bleeding hearts cry out to God, if there still lives a God, "How long, O God, How long?"

1903

2. Streets in Chicago.
3. In parts of the late-19th-century South, a means of reducing to near-slavery blacks convicted of crimes who were unable to pay their fines.

4. The August 1572 massacre of Protestants by Catholics in Paris.
5. The murderer released by Pilate in exchange for a judgment of death against Jesus (Luke 23:18–25).

SUTTON E. GRIGGS

1872–1933

One of the most prolific African American prose writers of the early twentieth century, Sutton E. Griggs is, at the same time, among the least familiar to mainstream readers. Born in 1872 in Chatfield, Texas, to a prominent Baptist minister and his wife, Griggs was educated at Bishop College in that state and later at Richmond Theological Seminary (now Virginia Union University). Griggs himself became a Baptist minister and was assigned to churches in Virginia and Texas. The center of his religious activities for much of his career, however, was Tennessee. He not only headed a church for several years in Memphis but also held an administrative position with the education department of the National Baptist Convention in Nashville. Not coincidentally, both cities served as important bases for his literary work. For the first decade of the century, Griggs's books were released mainly by Orion Publishers in Nashville, a firm that he operated himself. Most of the remainder of his publications were issued by the National Public Welfare League, a social uplift organization that Griggs founded in Memphis.

When considering Griggs's writing, it is important to keep in mind that his ministerial activities served as his professional focus. Equally crucial is the fact that he worked primarily outside of mainstream white publishing channels. On the one hand, he thereby remained free of some of the constraints encountered by African American authors who sought and gained access to major white presses. On the other hand, Griggs had to distribute his own books and earned little money from them. Critics have suggested that both the style and the content of his writing reflect the intimate contact that Griggs maintained with the working-class black readers who were his primary audience. Indeed, the straightforward, spare language, melodramatic plots, and thin, often transparently figurative characterizations in his fiction might be attributed to his desire to appeal to a readership that varied widely in terms of formal education. However, we also see in his fiction—as we do, for instance, in Pauline Hopkins's *Contending Forces* and Charles W. Chesnutt's *The Marrow of Tradition*—the attempt to stretch the conventions of the contemporary popular novel to allow for an explicit political agenda. From the outset, his writing reflects his commitment both to protesting racism and to positing solutions—from the mundane to the speculative and even fantastic—to the daunting dilemmas that blacks faced. The extent to which we judge Griggs's work to be successful relates directly to how we both value the imaginative audacity of much of his writing and are willing to concede his relative lack of interest in psychological realism.

Griggs's literary reputation rests primarily on his five novels: *Imperium in Imperio* (1899), *Overshadowed* (1901), *Unfettered* (1902), *The Hindered Hand; or, The Reign of the Repressionist* (1905), and *Pointing the Way* (1908). In these books, Griggs occasionally voices militant black views that we rarely find in the work of his peers. As a result, some commentators have seen his novels—particularly, *Imperium in Imperio*—as foreshadowing such later fiction as John A. Williams's *Sons of Darkness, Sons of Light* (1969) and Sam Greenlee's *The Spook Who Sat by the Door* (1969), both of which dramatized aggressive nationalist responses to white racism. Ultimately, however, Griggs consistently endorses moderation and not the violence that some of his characters advocate.

From the outset of his literary career, Griggs was discouraged by the lack of support blacks gave his publications. Indeed, he claimed that he wrote *The Hindered Hand* primarily because the National Baptist Convention formally requested that he respond to Thomas Dixon's racist novel *The Leopard's Spots* (1902) and not because he was convinced that fiction was his most effective tool in fighting prejudice. And although he continued to attempt to reach black readers (and was a member of the all-black Niagara movement), he increasingly addressed himself to southern whites with his message of racial cooperation and interdependency. Griggs's final years were marked by extreme financial hardship; and when he died in Denison, Texas, in 1933, much of his work had already been forgotten.

From The Hindered Hand; or, The Reign of the Repressionist

"Princes shall come out of Egypt; Ethiopia shall
soon stretch out her hands unto God."[1]

[The following chapters depict the fate of Bud Harper and his wife, Foresta Crump,
two black southerners. Bud has been implicated in the murder of Alene Daleman,
the daughter of a prominent white man of their town, Almaville. As a result of the
subsequent risk to Bud and to protect Foresta from the unwanted sexual advances
of Arthur Daleman Jr., Alene's brother, the couple flees to Mississippi. Ramon
Mansford, who appears toward the end of chapter 20, was Alene's fiancé. He has
been attempting to track down Bud and Foresta.]

Chapter XIX

THE FUGITIVES FLEE AGAIN

When Bud Harper and Foresta, on the night following their elopement,
returned to Almaville, Bud took Foresta by her home to break the news to
her mother, leaving her at the gate, while he went to his home to tell his
mother. Finding a corpse in his house and noting the terror that his appearance seemed to inspire, Bud left and ran back to Foresta's home. In the
meantime Mrs. Crump had explained the situation to Foresta, who now
told Bud. With bowed heads and troubled hearts the three sat in deep study
as to what to do.

The white people were under the impression that Bud had committed
the murder. They had killed another man thinking that it was he. In case
they now apprehended him, would the popular feeling be that there was a
mistake in the lynching or a mistake as to Bud's having committed the
murder?

Bud felt fully able to demonstrate his innocence, but the ruthless mob
would hardly give him time to collect his evidence, he feared. Thus,
though innocent, he decided that it was best for him to leave Almaville and
remain in hiding for a time at least. Foresta asserted her determination to
go with him it mattered not where he went.

Bud gave to Foresta the privilege of choosing their exile. For a number
of years the condition of the Negroes in the cotton states farther South had
been weighing heavily on her mind. She had read how that under the
credit system, the country merchant, charging exorbitant prices for merchandise for which the crops stood as security, was causing the Negro
farmer to work from year to year only to sink deeper and deeper into debt.
She had read of the contract system under which ignorant Negroes, not
knowing the contents of the papers signed, practically sold themselves into
slavery, agreeing to work for a number of years for a mere pittance and
further agreeing to be locked up in a stockade at night and to pay for the
expense of a recapture in case they attempted to escape. She had heard
much of the practice of peonage, how that planters and contractors would
enter into collusion with magistrates and convict innocent Negroes of
crimes in order that they might get Negro laborers by the paying of fines

1. See Psalms 68:31 (King James Version).

908

assessed on these trumped up charges. She had read accounts of investigations of the prison system of the South, showing that the various states made the earning of money by the prisoners a prime consideration, and detailing how brutal overseers were wont to maltreat convicts leased to them by the state. These things coupled with the absence of reformatories for youths were destined, Foresta felt assured, to produce a harvest of criminals. What to her mind added to the hopelessness of the plight of the Negroes was the fact that an emigration agent[2] was required to pay such a heavy tax and stood in such a danger of bodily harm from the planters that nothing was being done toward pointing the inhabitants of the blighted regions to better lands.

Foresta concluded to choose Mississippi, a state in which conditions were in some respects so thoroughly forbidding, as their future home. Two things influenced her in making a choice, a desire to use her education for the amelioration of the ills of which she had heard so much and the thought that a land reputed to be so destitute of hope for the Negro would be searched last of all for Negro refugees. So the two had gone forth in the darkness and journeyed southward.

With money that Bud had saved they bought a small farm near Maulville, Mississippi. It was not long before Foresta's quiet influence was felt throughout that region. The whites who had been preying upon the more ignorant of the Negroes were not long in tracing this new influence to its source. It was agreed among them that the Fultons (for such was the name assumed by Bud and Foresta) were rather undesirable neighbors and a decision was reached to put them out of the way. The thousands of individual murders, and lynching by mobs, had so blunted the sensibility of these whites that they reached this decision without any qualms of conscience. Sidney Fletcher was agreed upon as the man to rid the settlement of Bud and Foresta.

On this particular afternoon, Foresta's hair was hanging down her back in girlish fashion. A small cap sat upon the top of her head, while a blue gingham apron protected her dress. She had finished the milking and was walking toward the house when Sidney Fletcher, the owner of a neighboring farm, approached her.

"Where has Tobe Stewart gone?" asked Fletcher, in a very gruff manner, inquiring about a Negro lad who had run away from him.

Foresta looked at him steadily without replying.

"You —— wench, you, you can't speak can you? You and that dad blasted man of yours have got the big head, anyway," said Fletcher, drawing his pistol and starting toward Foresta.

Foresta dropped her milk pail and ran into the house.

Fletcher took a seat on a bench in the yard and awaited the coming of Bud Harper, Foresta's husband, who was out hunting and was not due for some time yet.

Foresta stole out of the door on the other side of the house and reached a patch of woods without being observed by Sidney Fletcher. By a circuitous

2. Usually sent south by northern business interests, emigration agents sought to encourage blacks to migrate to the North, often with the promise of improved employment opportunities.

route she was able to place herself in Bud's pathway so as to intercept him before he reached home.

"Oh, Bud," said Foresta, greeting her husband, "Old Sid Fletcher is at our house waiting for you with a drawn revolver."

A frown came over Bud's face. "The jealous knave," said he. "Ever since we bought this farm he has had a dislike for me and I have been expecting trouble from him."

"Yes, Bud; but we must stay out of trouble. A colored man hasn't a dog's show in this part of the world."

Bud sat down on a stump and Foresta dropped at his feet.

"Let's stay away from home to-night. We have had trouble enough, Bud," said Foresta pleadingly.

Bud looked down on her tenderly, and said, "It is a shame for a peaceful, industrious man to have a home and not be able to go to it."

Just then Sidney Fletcher was seen coming in their direction.

"Get behind a tree; nobody knows what will take place," said Bud to Foresta. She obeyed and Bud now calmly awaited the approach of Sidney Fletcher.

When Fletcher got in shooting distance he deliberately opened fire on Bud. After the third shot Bud raised his gun to his shoulder and fired and Fletcher fell backward a corpse. Bud and Foresta now looked at each other aghast. They knew the penalty attached to the raising of a black hand against a white man, even when that man unjustly sought the life of the black.

Rushing to their humble little home, Bud and Foresta hastily gathered a few things into a bundle, seized whatever food there was in the house, armed themselves and went forth as fugitives, Foresta attiring herself in man's clothing. By day and by night, through fields and forest, swamp and morass, avoiding the sight of man the unhappy couple fled.

The news of the killing of Fletcher was not long in getting abroad and a mob of several hundred whites was soon organized to give chase. The news agencies acquainted the whole nation with the situation and day by day the millions of America scanned with eagerness and with sad forebodings the progress of the chase. Several Negroes who happened to be found in the pathway of the mob that was sweeping the country were shot down or hung according to the whim of the pursuers.

The two in turn relieved each other at watching, whenever the exhausted condition of one or the other imperatively demanded sleep. It became Foresta's time to sleep and the two took a position behind a huge fallen tree, Foresta reclining her head upon Bud's lap. Soon she was asleep, with Bud looking down in tenderness on her pretty face, now showing signs of the terrible strain that they were undergoing. Bud thought of his position as her protector and gnashed his teeth in the bitterness of his soul as he contemplated his utter helplessness. Hot tears coursed down his cheeks and, dropping on Foresta's face, awakened her.

Foresta, who had been having troubled dreams, quickly lifted her head from Bud's lap and looked about in terror. Turning toward him she saw his eyes reddened from weeping. She threw herself on his shoulder and the two now gave way to their feelings for the first time.

"We have one consolation, Bud. They can't destroy our love for one another, can they?" said Foresta.

Bud was too full of sorrow at the plight of the wife of his bosom to reply. A deep groan of anguish escaped his lips. He leaned back against the log, Foresta still clinging to his neck. After a while both of them from sheer exhaustion fell asleep.

Chapter XX

THE BLAZE

Little Melville Brant stamped his foot on the floor, looked defiantly at his mother, and said, in the whining tone of a nine-year old child,

"Mother, I want to go."

"Melville, I have told you this dozen times that you cannot go," responded the mother with a positiveness that caused the boy to feel that his chances were slim.

"You are always telling me to keep ahead of the other boys, and I can't even get up to some of them," whined Melville plaintively.

"What do you mean?" asked the mother.

"Ben Stringer is always a crowing over me. Every time I tell anything big he jumps in and tells what he's seen, and that knocks me out. He has seen a whole lots of lynchings. His papa takes him. I bet if my papa was living he would take me," said Melville.

"My boy, listen to your mother," said Mrs. Brant. "Nothing but bad people take part in or go to see those things. I want mother's boy to scorn such things, to be way above them."

"Well, I ain't. I want to see it. Ben Stringer ain't got no business being ahead of me," Melville said with vigor.

The shrieking of the train whistle caused the fever of interest to rise in the little boy.

"There's the train now, mother. Do let me go. I ain't never seen a darky burned."

"Burned!" exclaimed Mrs. Brant in horror.

Melville looked up at his mother as if pitying her ignorance.

"They are going to burn them. Sed Lonly heard his papa and Mr. Corkle talking about it, and it's all fixed up."

"My Heavenly Father!" murmured Mrs. Brant, horror struck.

The cheering of the multitude borne upon the air was now heard.

"Mother, I must go. You can beat me as hard as you want to after I do it. I can't let Ben Stringer be crowing over me. He'll be there."

Looking intently at his mother, Melville backed toward the door. Mrs. Brant rushed forward and seized him.

"I shall put you in the attic. You shall not see that inhuman affair."

To her surprise Melville did not resist, but meekly submitted to being taken up stairs and locked in the attic.

Knowing how utterly opposed his mother was to lynchings he had calculated upon her refusal and had provided for such a contingency. He fastened the attic door on the inside and took from a corner a stout stick and a rope which he had secreted there. Fastening the rope to the stick and placing the stick across the small attic window he succeeded in lowering himself to the ground. He ran with all the speed at his command and arrived at the railway station just in time to see the mob begin its march with Bud and Foresta toward the scene of the killing of Sidney Fletcher.

Arriving at the spot where Fletcher's body had been found, the mob halted and the leaders instituted the trial of the accused.

"Did you kill Mr. Sidney Fletcher?" asked the mob's spokesman of Bud.

"Can I explain the matter to you, gentlemen," asked Bud.

"We want you to tell us just one thing; did you kill Mr. Sidney Fletcher?"

"He tried to kill me," replied Bud.

"And you therefore killed him, did you?"

"Yes, sir. That's how it happened."

"You killed him, then?" asked the spokesman.

"I shot him, and if he died I suppose I must have caused it. But it was in self-defense."

"You hear that, do you. He has confessed," said the spokesman to his son who was the reporter of the world-wide news agency that was to give to the reading public an account of the affair.

"Well, we are ready to act," shouted the spokesman to the crowd.

Two men now stepped forward and reached the spokesman at about the same time.

"I got a fine place, with everything ready. I knew what you would need and I arranged for you," said one of the men.

"My place is nearer than his, and everything is as ready as it can be. I think I am entitled to it," said the other.

"You want the earth, don't you?" indignantly asked the first applicant of the second.

Ignoring this thrust the second applicant said to the spokesman,

"You know I have done all the dirty work here. If you all wanted anybody to stuff the ballot box or swear to false returns, I have been your man. I've put out of the way every biggety nigger that you sent me after. You know all this."

"You've been paid for it, too. Ain't you been to the legislature? Ain't you been constable? Haven't you captured prisoners and held 'um in secret till the governor offered rewards and then you have brung 'em forward? You have been well paid. But me, I've had none of the good things. I've done dirty work, too, don't you forget it. And now I want these niggers hung in my watermelon patch, so as to keep darkies out of nights, being as they are feart of hants, and you are here to keep me out of that little favor."

The dispute waxed so hot that it was finally decided that it was best to accept neither place.

"We want this affair to serve as a warning to darkies to never lift their hands against a white man, and it won't hurt to perform this noble deed where they will never forget it. I am commander to-day and I order the administration of justice to take place near the Negro church."

"Good! Good!" was the universal comment.

The crowd dashed wildly in the direction of the church, all being eager to get places where they could see best. The smaller boys climbed the trees so that they might see well the whole transaction. Two of the trees were decided upon for stakes and the boys who had chosen them had to come down. Bud was tied to one tree and Foresta to the other in such a manner that they faced each other. Wood was brought and piled around them and oil was poured on very profusely.

The mob decided to torture their victims before killing them and began on Foresta first. A man with a pair of scissors stepped up and cut off her hair and threw it into the crowd. There was a great scramble for bits of hair for souvenirs of the occasion. One by one her fingers were cut off and tossed into the crowd to be scrambled for. A man with a corkscrew came forward, ripped Foresta's clothing to her waist, bored into her breast with the corkscrew and pulled forth the live quivering flesh. Poor Bud her helpless husband closed his eyes and turned away his head to avoid the terrible sight. Men gathered about him and forced his eyelids open so that he could see all.

When it was thought that Foresta had been tortured sufficiently, attention was turned to Bud. His fingers were cut off one by one and the corkscrew was bored into his legs and arms. A man with a club struck him over the head, crushing his skull and forcing an eyeball to hang down from the socket by a thread. A rush was made toward Bud and a man who was a little ahead of his competitors snatched the eyeball as a souvenir.

After three full hours had been spent in torturing the two, the spokesman announced that they were now ready for the final act. The brother of Sidney Fletcher was called for and was given a match. He stood near his mutilated victims until the photographer present could take a picture of the scene. This being over the match was applied and the flames leaped up eagerly and encircled the writhing forms of Bud and Foresta.

When the flames had done their work and had subsided, a mad rush was made for the trees which were soon denuded of bark, each member of the mob being desirous, it seemed, of carrying away something that might testify to his proximity to so great a happening.

Little Melville Brant found a piece of the charred flesh in the ashes and bore it home.

"Ben Stringer aint got anything on me now," said he as he trudged along in triumph.

Entering by the rear he caught hold of the rope which he had left hanging, ascended to the attic window and crawled in.

The future ruler of the land!

On the afternoon of the lynching Ramon Mansford alighted from the train at Maulville in search of Bud and Foresta. He noted the holiday appearance of the crowd as it swarmed around the depot awaiting the going of the special trains that had brought the people to Maulville to see the lynching, and, not knowing the occasion that had brought them together, said within himself:

"This crowd looks happy enough. The South is indeed sunny and sunny are the hearts of its people."

At length he approached a man, who like himself seemed to be an onlooker. Using the names under which Mrs. Harper told him that Bud and Foresta were passing, he made inquiry of them. The man looked at him in amazement.

"You have just got in, have you?" Asked the man of Ramon.

"Yes," he replied.

"Haven't you been reading the papers?" further inquired the man.

"Not lately, I must confess; I have been so absorbed in unraveling a murder mystery (the victim being one very dear to me) that I have not read the papers for the last few days."

"We burned the people to-day that you are looking for."

"Burned them?" asked Ramon incredulously.

"Yes, burned them."

"The one crime!"[3] gasped Ramon.

"I understand you," said the man. "You want to know how we square the burning of a woman with the statement that we lynch for one crime in the South, heh?"

The shocked Ramon nodded affirmatively.

"That's all rot about one crime. We lynch niggers down here for anything. We lynch them for being sassy and sometimes lynch them on general principles. The truth of the matter is the real 'one crime' that paves the way for a lynching whenever we have the notion, is the crime of being black."

"Burn them! The one crime!" murmured Ramon, scarcely knowing what he said. With bowed head and hands clasped behind him he walked away to meditate.

"After all, do not I see to-day a gleam of light thrown on the taking away of my Alene? With murder and lawlessness rampant in the Southland, this section's woes are to be many. Who can say what bloody orgies Alene has escaped? Who can tell the contents of the storm cloud that hangs low over this section where the tragedy of the ages is being enacted? Alene, O Alene, my spirit longs for thee!"

Ramon took the train that night—not for Almaville, for he had not the heart to bear the terrible tidings to those helpless, waiting, simple folks, the parents of Bud and Foresta. He went North feeling that some day somehow he might be called upon to revisit the South as its real friend, but seeming foe. And he shuddered at the thought.

1905

3. A reference to rape.

ALICE MOORE DUNBAR NELSON

1875–1935

Born in New Orleans, Alice Ruth Moore attended the local public schools, graduated from Straight College (now Dillard University) in 1892, and began teaching in her hometown. An accomplished violinist, cellist, and mandolin player; an amateur actor; and a writer of local acclaim, the fair-skinned and spirited daughter of

Joseph and Patricia Moore was a leader among the African American intelligentsia even before her first book, *Violets and Other Tales* (1895), was published. One of her poems caught the fancy of another rising literary star, Paul Laurence Dunbar, who began a correspondence that led to their marriage. Ironically, Paul became famous for his dialect poetry and minstrel song writing while Alice was sometimes criticized because her work was so "nonracial." Perhaps her attitude is best summarized in a letter she wrote to Paul in May 1895:

> You ask my opinion about the Negro dialect in literature? Well, frankly, I believe in everyone following his own bent. If it be so that one has a special aptitude for dialect work why it is only right that dialect work should be a specialty. But if one should be like me—absolutely devoid of the ability to manage dialect, I don't see the necessity of cramming and forcing oneself into that plane because one is a Negro or a Southerner.

Apparently others shared the couple's respect for diversity, for Dodd, Mead & Company marketed Paul's *Poems of Cabin and Field* and Alice's second book, *The Goodness of St. Rocque* (1899), as companion pieces.

Dunbar Nelson's first two books are collections of poems, reviews, sketches, and short stories. She also gained distinction as an editor, a journalist, a literary critic, a scholar, and a teacher. Although two themes of great importance to her were race and gender, she tried to make a firm distinction between imaginative literature and journalism, reserving her explicit political discussions for the latter. This was not always workable, and as her poem *I Sit and Sew* shows, she occasionally violated her dictum. She joined the Local Color movement, but in focusing as she did on Creole culture, New Orleans, and other aspects of her personal experience and in experimenting with different prose forms, Dunbar Nelson consciously attempted to expand notions of African American life and literature.

As a scholar she often wrote on issues of curriculum and literature. Her master's thesis at Cornell on the influence of Milton upon Wordsworth has been cited by several scholars. Both *Masterpieces of Negro Eloquence* (1914) and the *Dunbar Speaker and Entertainer* (1920) demonstrate her concern with disseminating African American literature. As a teacher and a writer, she was increasingly active in politics and civic affairs, and after eighteen years on the Howard High School faculty in Wilmington, Delaware, Dunbar Nelson was fired because, despite a rule forbidding her school district's employees to engage in political activities, she participated in a social justice conference convened by then-senator Warren G. Harding. Dunbar Nelson published a series of regular columns in papers such as the Pittsburgh *Courier*, Washington *Eagle*, New York *Sun*, and the Chicago *Daily News*. She was a co-editor of the *A.M.E. Church Review*, and with her third husband, Robert Nelson, she owned and operated the *Wilmington Advocate*. When she died in 1935, she left manuscripts for several novels, screenplays, and a dairy. While most critical attention has focused on her youthful poetry and short stories, Dunbar Nelson's contributions over her lifetime were many and diverse.

Violets

I had not thought of violets of late,
The wild, shy kind that springs beneath your feet
In wistful April days, when lovers mate
And wander through the fields in raptures sweet.
And thought of violets meant florists' shops,   5

And bows and pins, and perfumed paper fine;
And garish lights, and mincing little fops [1]
And cabarets and songs, and deadening wine.

So far from sweet real things my thoughts had strayed,
I had forgot wide fields, and clear brown streams;   10
The perfect loveliness that God has made—
Wild violets shy and heaven-mounting dreams.
And now—unwittingly, you've made me dream
Of violets, and my soul's forgotten gleam.

                                                    1917

I Sit and Sew

I sit and sew—a useless task it seems,
My hands grown tired, my head weighed down with dreams—
The panoply of war, the martial tred of men,
Grim-faced, stern-eyed, gazing beyond the ken
Of lesser souls, whose eyes have not seen Death,   5
Nor learned to hold their lives but as a breath—
But—I must sit and sew.

I sit and sew—my heart aches with desire—
That pageant terrible, that fiercely pouring fire
On wasted fields, and writhing grotesque things   10
Once men. My soul in pity flings
Appealing cries, yearning only to go
There in that holocaust of hell, those fields of woe—
But—I must sit and sew.

The little useless seam, the idle patch;   15
Why dream I here beneath my homely thatch,
When there they lie in sodden mud and rain,
Pitifully calling me, the quick ones and the slain?
You need me, Christ! It is no roseate dream
That beckons me—this pretty futile seam,   20
It stifles me—God, must I sit and sew?

                                                    1920

April Is on the Way

April is on the way!
I saw the scarlet flash of a blackbird's wing
As he sang in the cold, brown February trees;
And children said that they caught a glimpse of the sky on a bird's
     wing from the far South.
(Dear God, was that a stark figure outstretched in the bare branches   5
     Etched brown against the amethyst sky?)

---

1. Men excessively concerned with their appearance, clothing, and manners.

April is on the way!
The ice crashed in the brown mud-pool under my tread,
The warning earth clutched my bloody feet with great fecund fingers.
I saw a boy rolling a hoop up the road,   10
His little bare hands were red with cold,
But his brown hair blew backward in the southwest wind.
(Dear God! He screamed when he saw my awful woe-spent eyes.)

April is on the way!
I met a woman in the lane;   15
Her burden was heavy as it is always, but today her step was light,
And a smile drenched the tired look away from her eyes.
(Dear God, she had dreams of vengeance for her slain mate,
Perhaps the west wind has blown the mist of hate from her heart,
The dead man was cruel to her, you know that, God.)   20

April is on the way!
My feet spurn the ground now; instead of dragging on the bitter road.
I laugh in my throat as I see the grass greening beside the patches of
      snow
(Dear God, those were wild fears. Can there be hate when the
      southwest wind is blowing?)

April is on the way!   25
The crisp brown hedges stir with the bustle of bird wings.
There is business of building, and songs from brown thrust throats
As the bird-carpenters make homes against Valentine Day.
(Dear God, could they build me a shelter in the hedge from the icy
      winds that will come with the dark?)

April is on the way!   30
I sped through the town this morning. The florist shops have put
      yellow flowers in the windows,
Daffodils and tulips and primroses, pale yellow flowers
Like the tips of her fingers when she waved me that frightened farewell.
And the women in the market have stuck pussy willows in the long
      necked bottles on their stands.
(Willow trees are kind, Dear God. They will not bear a body on their
      limbs.)   35

April is on the way!
The soul within me cried that all the husk of indifference to sorrow
      was but the crust of ice with which winter disguises life;
It will melt, and reality will burgeon forth like the crocuses in the glen.
(Dear God! Those thoughts were from long ago. When we read
      poetry after the day's toil, and got religion together at the revival
      meeting.)

April is on the way!   40
The infinite miracle of unfolding life in the brown February fields.
(Dear God, the hounds are baying!)
Murder and wasted love, lust and weariness, deceit and vainglory—
      what are they but the spent breath of the runner?

(God, you know he laid hairy red hands on the golden loveliness of
    her little daffodil body.)
Hate may destroy me, but from my brown limbs will bloom the
    golden buds with which we once spelled love.   45
(Dear God! How their light eyes glow into black pin points of hate!)

April is on the way!
Wars are made in April, and they sing at Easter time of the Resurrection.
Therefore I laugh in their faces.
(Dear God, give her the strength to join me before her golden petals
    are fouled in the slime!)   50
April is on the way!

                                              1927

Violets

I

"And she tied a bunch of violets with a tress of her pretty brown hair."

She sat in the yellow glow of the lamplight softly humming these words.
It was Easter evening, and the newly risen spring world was slowly sinking
to a gentle, rosy, opalescent slumber, sweetly tired of the joy which had
pervaded it all day. For in the dawn of the perfect morn, it had arisen,
stretched out its arms in glorious happiness to greet the Saviour and said its
hallelujahs, merrily trilling out carols of bird, and organ and flower-song.
But the evening had come, and rest.

There was a letter lying on the table, it read:

"Dear, I send you this little bunch of flowers as my Easter token. Perhaps
you may not be able to read their meaning, so I'll tell you. Violets, you
know, are my favorite flowers. Dear, little, human-faced things! They seem
always as if about to whisper a love-word; and then they signify that thought
which passes always between you and me. The orange blossoms—you
know their meaning;[1] the little pinks are the flowers you love; the evergreen leaf is the symbol of the endurance of our affection; the tube-roses I
put in, because once when you kissed and pressed me close in your arms, I
had a bunch of tube-roses on my bosom, and the heavy fragrance of their
crushed loveliness has always lived in my memory. The violets and pinks
are from a bunch I wore to-day, and when kneeling at the altar, during
communion, did I sin, dear, when I thought of you? The tube-roses and
orange-blossoms I wore Friday night; you always wished for a lock of my
hair, so I'll tie these flowers with them—but there, it is not stable enough;
let me wrap them with a bit of ribbon, pale blue, from that little dress I
wore last winter to the dance, when we had such a long, sweet talk in that
forgotten nook. You always loved that dress, it fell in such soft ruffles away
from the throat and bosom,—you called me your little forget-me-not, that
night. I laid the flowers away for awhile in our favorite book,—Byron[2]—just

---

1. Chastity and nuptials.
2. Perhaps the lover's name. It could also refer to
the author of the "favorite book"; perhaps Lord

Byron (George Gordon Byron) (1788–1824), English Romantic poet.

at the poem we loved best, and now I send them to you. Keep them always in remembrance of me, and if aught should occur to separate us, press these flowers to your lips, and I will be with you in spirit, permeating your heart with unutterable love and happiness."

II

It is Easter again. As of old, the joyous bells clang out the glad news of the resurrection. The giddy, dancing sunbeams laugh riotously in field and street; birds carol their sweet twitterings everywhere, and the heavy perfume of flowers scents the golden atmosphere with inspiring fragrance. One long, golden sunbeam steals silently into the white-curtained window of a quiet room, and lay athwart a sleeping face. Cold, pale, still, its fair, young face pressed against the satin-lined casket. Slender, white fingers, idle now, they that had never known rest; locked softly over a bunch of violets; violets and tube-roses in her soft, brown hair, violets in the bosom of her long, white gown; violets and tube-roses and orange-blossoms banked everywhere, until the air was filled with the ascending souls of the human flowers. Some whispered that a broken heart had ceased to flutter in that still, young form, and that it was a mercy for the soul to ascend on the slender sunbeam. To-day she kneels at the throne of heaven, where one year ago she had communed at an earthly altar.

III

Far away in a distant city, a man, carelessly looking among some papers, turned over a faded bunch of flowers tied with a blue ribbon and a lock of hair. He paused meditatively awhile, then turning to the regal-looking woman lounging before the fire, he asked:

"Wife, did you ever send me these?"

She raised her great, black eyes to his with a gesture of ineffable disdain, and replied languidly:

"You know very well I can't bear flowers. How could I ever send such sentimental trash to any one? Throw them into the fire."

And the Easter bells chimed a solemn requiem as the flames slowly licked up the faded violets. Was it merely fancy on the wife's part, or did the husband really sigh,—a long, quivering breath of remembrance?

1895

WILLIAM STANLEY BRAITHWAITE

1878–1962

William Stanley Braithwaite loved poetry and devoted his life to it as a poet, a critic, and an anthologist. Born in Boston, Massachusetts, to Emma DeWolfe and William Smith Braithwaite, young William was tutored at home to know French, the rituals of high tea, and the intricacies of the Church of England better than the names of the neighborhood children. Largely self-educated, he early developed an admiration for the British Romantics such as Keats and Blake, and his own poetry uses the traditional meters and forms of the nineteenth century. Yet he has been credited with "bullying and cajoling" American audiences into accepting the modernist and other unconventional poets. Braithwaite's sensitive reviews, perceptive analyses, and annual anthologies of magazine verse earned him recognition as a major figure in the revitalization of American poetry in the early twentieth century. Although he had appreciated and aided writers such as Paul Lawrence Dunbar, Langston Hughes, Countee Cullen, Nella Larsen, and James Weldon Johnson, it was not until he became a professor at Atlanta University that he knew and associated with many other African Americans.

Though he favorably reviewed the efforts of African Americans whose works clearly focused on black life and culture, Braithwaite wrote of subjects common to any culture. Knowing that his verse infuriated many proponents of an explicit expression of African American experience, he argued that the right and ability to "participate in the common ground of American authorship" ought not be influenced by an individual's racial heritage. He wanted to demonstrate that "a man of color was the equal of any other man in possession of the attributes that produced a literature of human thought and experience, and to force a recognition of this common capacity." Therefore, he vowed that he would not "treat in any phase, in any form, for any purpose, racial materials and racial experiences, until this recognition had been won, recorded and universally confirmed." Still, connections between his work and that of other African American writers can be glimpsed. For example, his literary aesthetics are comparable with those of Alice Dunbar Nelson, and the title of his first volume of poetry, *Lyrics of Life and Love* (1904), echoes that of Paul Lawrence Dunbar's *Lyrics of Lowly Life* published one year earlier. In addition to his poetry and anthologies, Braithwaite published at least two novels, a biography of the Brontës, and an autobiography titled *The House under Arcturus* (1940).

The Watchers

Two women on the lone wet strand
　(The wind's out with a will to roam)
The waves wage war on rocks and sand,
　(And a ship is long due home.)

The sea sprays in the women's eyes—　　　　　　　　　　　5
　(Hearts can writhe like the sea's wild foam)
Lower descend the tempestuous skies,
　(For the wind's out with a will to roam.)

"O daughter, thine eyes be better than mine,"
　(The waves ascend high as yonder dome)　　　　　　　10
"North or south is there never a sign?"
　(And a ship is long due home.)

They watched there all the long night through—
　(The wind's out with a will to roam)
Wind and rain and sorrow for two,—　　　　　　　　　　15
　(And heaven on the long reach home.)

1904

The House of Falling Leaves

I

Off our New England coast the sea to-night
Is moaning the full sorrow of its heart:
There is no will to comfort it apart
Since moon and stars are hidden from its sight.
And out beyond the furthest harbor-light   5
There runs a tide that marks not any chart
Wherewith man knows the ending and the start
Of that long voyage in the infinite.

If change and fate and hapless circumstance
May baffle and perplex the moaning sea,   10
And day and night in alternate advance
Still hold the primal Reasoning in fee,
Cannot my Grief be strong enough to chance
My voice across the tide I cannot see?

II

We go from house to house, from town to town,   15
And fill the distance full of smiles and words;
We take all pleasure that our strength affords
And care not if the sun be up or down.
The way of it no man has ever known—
But suddenly there is a snap of chords   20
Within the heart that sounds like hollow boards,—
We question every shadow that is thrown.

O to be near when the last word is said!
And see the last reflection in the eye—
For when the word is brought our friend is dead,   25
How bitter is the tear that will not dry,
Because so far away our steps are led
When Love should draw us close to say Good-bye!

III

Four seasons are there to the circling year:
Four houses where the dreams of men abide—   30
The stark and naked Winter without pride,
The Spring like a young maiden soft and fair;
The Summer like a bride about to bear
The issue of the love she deified;
And lastly, Autumn, on the turning tide   35
That ebbs the voice of nature to its bier.

Four houses with two spacious chambers each,
Named Birth and Death, wherein Time joys and grieves.

Is there no Fate so wise enough to teach
Into which door Life enters and retrieves?   40
What matter since his voice is out of reach,
And Sorrow fills My House of Falling Leaves!

IV

The House of Falling Leaves we entered in—
He and I—we entered in and found it fair;
At midnight some one called him up the stair,   45
And closed him in the Room I could not win.
Now must I go alone out in the din
Of hurrying days: for forth he cannot fare;
I must go on with Time, and leave him there
In Autumn's house where dreams will soon grow thin.   50

When Time shall close the door unto the house
And opens that of Winter's soon to be,
And dreams go moving through the ruined boughs—
He who went in comes out a Memory.
From his deep sleep no sound may e'er arouse,—   55
The moaning rain, nor wind-embattled sea.

1908

Sic Vita [1]

Heart free, hand free,
   Blue above, brown under
All the world to me
   Is a place of wonder.
Sun shine, moon shine,   5
   Stars, and winds a-blowing,
All into this heart of mine
   Flowing, flowing, flowing!

Mind free, step free,
   Days to follow after,   10
Joys of life sold to me
   For the price of laughter.
Girl's love, man's love,
   Love of work and duty,
Just a will of God's to prove   15
   Beauty, beauty, beauty!

1908

1. Such is life (Latin).

Turn Me to My Yellow Leaves

Turn me to my yellow leaves,
I am better satisfied;
There is nothing in me grieves—
That was never born—and died.
Let me be a scarlet flame   5
On a windy autumn morn,
I, who never had a name,
Nor from a breathing image born.
From the margin let me fall
Where the farthest stars sink down.   10
And the void consume me,—all
Into nothingness to drown.
Let me dream my dream entire,
Withered as an autumn leaf—
Let me have my vain desire,   15
Vain—as it is brief!

                                                       1948

Quiet Has a Hidden Sound

Beacon Hill[1]

Quiet has a hidden sound
Best upon a hillside street,
When the sunlight on the ground
Is luminous with heat.

Something teases one to peek   5
Behind the summer afternoon
And watch the shadowy legends leak
Off Time's unscalèd tune.

Just a common city street
Running up a city hill,   10
Filled with nothing but the heat
And houses standing still!

But where is silence castlèd,
Or stranger, the sunlight magic,
Than on this hillside, where the tread   15
Of summertime is tragic!

                                                       1948

---

1. Neighborhood in Boston, north of Boston Commons.

FENTON JOHNSON
1888–1958

Despite the widespread anthologizing of his poetry in collections of African American literature, Fenton Johnson remains one of the least-known black American writers. One probable reason for this neglect is that Johnson and his work fall into the crack in African American literary history between the authors active around the turn of the century and those identified with the New Negro Renaissance of the 1920s and 1930s. Ironically, his work is valuable in large measure precisely because it bridges in style and theme some of the most important defining characteristics of black writing in these two periods.

Born in Chicago on May 7, 1888, to Elijah H. and Jessie Taylor Johnson, Fenton was raised in a relatively well-to-do environment, attending local public schools before continuing his education at Northwestern University and in 1910 at the University of Chicago. After graduating from Chicago, he moved to Louisville to teach at a state university; but one year later, in his words "a year of abject poverty," he returned to Chicago, determined to pursue a literary career.

Johnson was a publishing author from a remarkably early age. His first poem appeared in a local newspaper in 1900, and his plays were produced at a Chicago theater when he was only nineteen. His initial volume of poetry, A Little Dreaming, was published in 1913. Around this time, he moved to New York, where he studied journalism at Columbia University. In this productive period, Johnson not only wrote for the Eastern Press Association and the New York News but also published (largely at his own expense) two more collections of verse, Visions of the Dusk (1915) and Songs of the Soil (1916). His return to Chicago in 1916 marked the beginning of his most intense editorial activity, as he produced two short-lived periodicals, Champion Magazine and Favorite Magazine. This period of his life came to a close in 1920, with the appearance of For the Highest Good and Tales of Darkest America, collections of essays and short stories, respectively. Though he lived until 1958 and continued to write poetry at least through the Depression, these two books represent Johnson's last major publications.

Like that of most black poets who came of age in the first decades of the twentieth century, Fenton Johnson's early work reveals the influence of Paul Laurence Dunbar as well as of the Romantic poets, to whom Dunbar himself owed a sizable debt. Accordingly, Johnson's first collection contains pieces written in conventional English as well as in black dialect. James Weldon Johnson and other critics single out The Vision of Lazarus, a long poem in blank verse; otherwise, A Little Dreaming was judged to be barely more than promising. In his second and third volumes, Fenton Johnson increasingly turns his energies toward capturing not just a distinctive black voice but also expressive African American cultural forms previously ignored by most writers, black and white. He was particularly captivated by spirituals, and the strongest titles in Visions of the Dusk and Songs of the Soil are informed by Johnson's immersion in this black folk form. The striking evolution of Johnson's verse was due both to the influence of such authors as Carl Sandberg and Edgar Lee Masters and to his involvement in the early Modernist poetry movement, based in Chicago and spearheaded by Harriet Monroe, with whom Johnson corresponded.

Although many pieces in his three volumes of verse merit serious attention, Johnson's reputation rests primarily on a small number of poems that he produced after World War I, such as Tired and The Scarlet Woman. Marked by a radical rejection of conventional rhymed structure, these works embrace the vernacular. Furthermore, their tone of world-weary resignation, bitterness, and despair stands out, even when read against the poetry of the early New Negro Renaissance.

Indeed, Sterling Brown suggests that the pessimism informing these pieces is directly related to Johnson's silence as a publishing author after 1920; and J. Saunders Redding contends that this later work contained a "theme and spirit with which America would have nothing to do." As Eugene Redmond observes, what is perhaps more important is the extent to which the fatalism of these poems partakes of the tone and mood found in some of the urban blues of the period. From this perspective, Fenton Johnson's role as a transitional figure in the African American literary tradition is even more interesting. In his use of folk forms such as the spiritual and the blues, he anticipates and perhaps even enables the subsequent work of such better-known authors as Jean Toomer, James Weldon Johnson, Langston Hughes, and Sterling Brown.

Singing Hallelujia

(A Negro Spiritual)

1

I went down to Jordan, [1]
  Singing, "Hallelujia!",
I went down to Jordan
  In the nighttime;
God of mine above me,   5
God of mine beneath me,
And the white robed angels
  Singing, "Hallelujia!"

2

I looked up to Heaven,
  Singing, "Hallelujia",   10
I looked up to Heaven
  In the nighttime;
God poured down His mercy,
Christ poured down His loving,
And the choir of angels   15
  Sang me, "Hallelujia!"

3

Threescore stood in Heaven,
  Singing, "Hallelujia",
Threescore stood in Heaven
  In the nighttime;   20
David[2] with his captains,
Jesus with His fishers,

1. A river in Palestine, identified in the Old Testament as that crossed by the Israelites on their way to the Promised Land. Crossing the Jordan often symbolizes entering Heaven.

2. In the Old Testament, the second king of Judah and Israel, the successor of Saul and father of Solomon; said to be the author of the Psalms.

And the white robed angels
Singing, "Hallelujia!"

4

Take me swift to Heaven,   25
Singing, "Hallelujia!"
Take me swift to Heaven
In the nighttime;
Seat me 'mid the lillies,
Crown me with the roses,   30
And let whiterobed angels
Sing me, "Hallelujia."

1915

Song of the Whirlwind

1

Oh, my God is in the whirlwind,
I am walking in the valley;
Lift me up, O Shining Father,
To the glory of the heavens,
I have seen a thousand troubles   5
On the journey men call living,
I have drunk a thousand goblets
From misfortune's bitter winepress,
But to Thee I cling forever,
God of Jacob, God of Rachel.[1]   10

2

Oh, my soul is in the whirlwind,
I am dying in the valley,
Oh, my soul is in the whirlwind
And my bones are in the valley;
At her spinning wheel is Mary   15
Spinning raiment of the lillies,
On her knees is Martha honey
Shining bright the golden pavement,
All the ninety nine[2] is waiting
For my coming, for my coming.   20

1915

My God in Heaven Said to Me

1

My God in Heaven said to me,
"Your mansion's ready in the sky,
Come home, my weary wanderer,

---

1. In the Old Testament, Jacob's second wife and the mother of Joseph and Benjamin. Jacob was the son of Isaac and grandson of Abraham. He fathered twelve sons, from whom descended the twelve tribes of Israel.
2. Refers to a biblical parable in which the shepherd leaves his ninety-nine sheep to locate the one that is lost (Luke 15:4–7 and Matthew 18:12–13).

And eat with Me the bread of life,
For I have slain the fatted calf,   5
For I have filled the honey bowl
And thou shalt always dwell with me.
Come home, my weary wanderer,"
My God in Heaven said to me.

2

And now I board the Gospel train,   10
For I am going home to-night
To meet my God on Jordan's coast.
My burdens to the wind I toss,
To-morrow freedom shall be mine;
A golden crown with burning stars,   15
And harp of David in my hand
That I may chant the Gospel tunes.

3

On God's plantation I shall dwell,
The overseer of happiness,
And dance with Israel[1] the dance   20
Of holiness and righteousness,
A thousand years with God to dwell
Is like a holiday below;
And Oh, my heart was glad to hear
My God in Heaven say to me,   25
"Your mansion's ready in the sky."

1915

The Lonely Mother

(A *Negro Spiritual*)

I

Oh, my mother's moaning by the river,
My poor mother's moaning by the river,
For her son who walks the earth in sorrow.
Long my mother's moaned beside the river,
And her tears have filled an angel's pitcher,   5
"Lord of Heaven, bring to me my honey,
Bring to me the darling of my bosom,
For a lonely mother by the river."

II

Cease, O mother, moaning by the river,
Cease, good mother, moaning by the river;   10
I have seen the star of Michael[1] shining
Michael shining at the Gates of Morning;
Row, O mighty Angel, down the twilight,

---

1. The Jewish or Hebrew people; figuratively the "chosen people" of God.
1. An Old Testament archangel represented as a warrior who appears to humans on various occasions; in Hebrew, the name means "who is like God."

Row until I find a lonely woman,
Swaying long beneath a tree of cypress,   15
Swaying for her son who walks in sorrow.

1916

Tired

I am tired of work; I am tired of building up somebody else's civilization.
Let us take a rest, M'Lissy Jane.
I will go down to the Last Chance Saloon, drink a gallon or two of
    gin, shoot a game or two of dice and sleep the rest of the night
    on one of Mike's barrels.
You will let the old shanty go to rot, the white people's clothes turn to
    dust, and the Calvary Baptist Church sink to the bottomless pit.
You will spend your days forgetting you married me and your nights
    hunting the warm gin Mike serves the ladies in the rear of the
    Last Chance Saloon.   5
Throw the children into the river; civilization has given us too many.
    It is better to die than to grow up and find that you are colored.
Pluck the stars out of the heavens. The stars mark our destiny. The
    stars marked my destiny.
I am tired of civilization.

1919

The Scarlet Woman

Once I was good like the Virgin Mary and the Minister's wife.
My father worked for Mr. Pullman[1] and white people's tips; but he
    died two days after his insurance expired.
I had nothing, so I had to go to work.
All the stock I had was a white girl's education and a face that
    enchanted the men of both races.
Starvation danced with me.   5
So when Big Lizzie, who kept a house for white men, came to me
    with tales of fortune that I could reap from the sale of my virtue
    I bowed my head to Vice.
Now I can drink more gin than any man for miles around.
Gin is better than all the water in Lethe.[2]

1922

---

1. George Pullman (1831–1897), inventor of the
modern railroad sleeping and dining cars and
founder of the Pullman Palace Car Company in
1865. Many black men found employment over
the years as Pullman porters.
2. In Greek mythology, the river of forgetfulness in
Hades, marking the boundary between life and
death.

Harlem Renaissance
1919–1940

A CULTURAL FLOWERING

Although the very existence of the Harlem Renaissance has been disputed, with some choosing to emphasize the national scope of the cultural phenomenon and thus downplaying its identification with one district in New York City, the term *Harlem Renaissance* has remained popular. It has remained so because most scholars and students agree that the 1920s was a decade of extraordinary creativity in the arts for black Americans and that much of that creativity found its focus in the activities of African Americans living in New York City, particularly in the district of Harlem.

Unquestionably, at least where the arts (including music and dance) are concerned, these years marked an especially brilliant moment in the history of blacks in America. In particular, the second half of the decade witnessed an outpouring of publications by African Americans that was unprecedented in its variety and scope, so that it clearly qualifies as a moment of renaissance, as such moments of unusually fertile cultural activity are often called. In poetry, fiction, drama, and the essay, as in music, dance, painting, and sculpture, African Americans worked not only with a new sense of confidence and purpose but also with a sense of achievement never before experienced by so many black artists in the long, troubled history of the peoples of African descent in North America.

Although the term *Harlem Renaissance* is convenient and defensible, it is important to remember that what took place in New York City was in many respects a heightened version of the unusual cultural productivity taking place elsewhere in the United States, especially in the major cities of the North. In addition, it is also important not to draw artificial lines between "serious" and "popular" art, although many of the renaissance creators certainly did so. Expressed in various ways, the creativity of black Americans undoubtedly came from a common source—the irresistible impulse of blacks to create boldly expressive art of a high quality as a primary response to their social conditions, as an affirmation of their dignity and humanity in the face of poverty and racism. What happened in the United States should also be linked to certain trends abroad. By the late 1920s, African and Caribbean students in Paris and progressive young intellectuals and artists in the West Indies were reading the work of black Americans as well as their own thinkers and creators and were taking the first tentative steps toward, in one instance, the Negritude movement, and in another, the flowering of literature in the British West Indies, perhaps best exemplified later in the century by the poetry and plays of Derek Walcott. Negritude was a movement, mainly among French-speaking black writers, that emphasized a distinctly African aesthetic.

Nevertheless, Harlem and New York were crucial to the movement in the United States. The history of the publication of books of poetry and novels, as well as the production of plays, attests to the fact that something new and significant was taking place. For example, when Harper & Brothers brought out Countee Cullen's first book of verse, *Color*, in 1925 in New York City, it was apparently the first book of poetry written by an African American to be published by a major American house since Dodd, Mead offered Paul Laurence Dunbar's books at the turn of the century (in 1922, Harcourt, Brace had published Claude McKay's *Harlem Shadows*, but McKay was born in Jamaica). In the same way, Jean Toomer's *Cane* was apparently the first book of fiction (sometimes called a novel, the work also contains poems and drama) by an American of African descent to appear from a New York publisher since Doubleday, Page announced the appearance of Charles Chesnutt's *The Colonel's Dream* in 1905. Certainly a new day had arrived for the black American writer in the 1920s in New York City.

MIGRATION NORTH

The cause or causes of a cultural renaissance are almost always difficult to trace precisely. However, New York City had become a magnet, perhaps the most powerful, for the thousands of blacks fleeing the South in the aftermath of the entrenchment of segregation following the end of the Reconstruction era, which itself followed the Civil War, and the segregationist rulings of the U.S. Supreme Court, notably the landmark case *Plessy v. Ferguson* in 1896, which endorsed separation in transportation. As legal segregation made living conditions for blacks in the South more and more intolerable, the widespread lynching of blacks bitterly underscored the extent to which they were powerless before the law and less than human in the eyes of many whites. Migration to the North increasingly seemed an absolute necessity for blacks seeking a better life for themselves and their children. In addition, swift industrial expansion in the North created a demand for labor that made many employers eager to recruit and hire black workers. This demand intensified when the United States entered World War I (1914–18) in 1917 and jobs previously held by white males, themselves now serving in the armed forces, became available to newcomers from the South.

While blacks settled in several northern cities, including Chicago, Philadelphia, and Cleveland, New York City was the destination of choice. Perhaps some migrants were enthralled by living in the largest, most cosmopolitan, and most renowned of American cities. More substantially, the district of Harlem had an additional attraction. Built originally to house middle-class and upper-middle-class whites, Harlem became available to blacks when it seemed clear that the area was seriously overbuilt; facing economic hardship, real estate interests among both races in effect conspired to break the exclusionary practices that had hitherto kept blacks out. Newcomers found grand avenues, broad sidewalks, and finely constructed houses that afforded blacks the chance to live in housing stock far superior in quality to anything available to them elsewhere in the United States. Harlem became home to all classes of blacks, including the leading writers and artists. As the national interest in African American culture grew, encouraged by a variety of factors, such as the growing popularity of jazz, blues, and dance, Harlem seemed well on its way to becoming, as the prominent writer and civil rights leader James Weldon Johnson put it, "the Negro capital of the world."

Harlem and New York quickly became the headquarters of many of the most important African American cultural and political national organizations, including the National Association for the Advancement of Colored People (NAACP), the National Urban League, and Marcus Garvey's Universal Negro Improvement Association. Also important was the effort of socialist groups to recruit blacks. Certain magazines and newspapers, based in Harlem, worked hard to stimulate a cultural wakening or renaissance. Of these, the most important was almost certainly the *Crisis*, edited by the brilliant scholar and propagandist W. E. B. Du Bois for the NAACP; *Opportunity*, edited by the urbane sociologist and cultural entrepreneur Charles S. Johnson for the National Urban League; the *Messenger*, edited by the socialist A. Philip Randolph and Chandler Owen; and Marcus Garvey's *Negro World*. Although the *Messenger* was proud of its radical leftist goals, there was little difference between the kinds of literature published in these journals. Each was dedicated to social and political progress and uplift for black Americans and to the development of literary and artistic traditions of which the typical readers might be proud. Du Bois and the *Crisis* took the lead in calling for a cultural renaissance among blacks that would prove the genius of black America to the greater world, and especially to white Americans, who presumably would be moved to treat blacks with greater justice and compassion. Indeed, between 1919 and 1926 the *Crisis* employed a literary editor, Jessie Fauset, a Phi Beta Kappa graduate of Cornell University who not only published four novels starting with *There Is Confusion* (1924) but also discovered and nurtured several younger writers.

THE NEW WRITERS

The first glimmerings of the new day in literature probably came not with the work of a black writer but with that of a white—*Three Plays for a Negro Theatre*, by Ridgely Torrence. James Weldon Johnson called the premiere of these plays in 1917 "the most important single event in the entire history of the Negro in the American Theatre." Overturning the tradition of depicting blacks in stereotypical minstrel forms, Torrence's plays featured black actors representing complex human emotions and yearnings; in this sense they anticipated not only plays of the 1920s about blacks such as *The Emperor Jones* (1920) and *All God's Chillun Got Wings* (1925) by the celebrated dramatist Eugene O'Neill but also the work of African American playwrights, poets, and fiction writers breaking with traditions that diminished and often insulted black humanity. Another landmark came in 1919, a year marked by several antiblack riots nationally, with the publication of the Jamaican-born poet Claude McKay's militant sonnet *If We Must Die*. Although the poem never alludes to race, to black readers it sounded a note of defiance against racism and racist violence unheard in black literature in many years. Then, in 1921, the musical review *Shuffle Along*, written and performed by blacks, brought to the stage novel styles of song, dance, and comedy that captivated blacks and whites alike and underscored the emergence of a new generation of black artistry.

In 1922, James Weldon Johnson's anthology of verse, *Book of American Negro Poetry*, emphasized the youthful promise of the new writers and established some of the terms of the emerging movement. In his preface, Johnson attacked dialect verse, which had dominated black American poetry until recently, and wrote of the need for the new black artists to find "a form expressing the imagery, the idioms, the peculiar turns of thought, and the distinctive humor and pathos" of African Americans that could nevertheless also give voice to "the deepest and highest emotions and aspirations" and the "widest range of subjects and the widest scope of treatment."

"What the colored poet in the United States needs to do," Johnson wrote, "is something like what Synge did for the Irish." Thus Johnson sought to link what was happening among blacks in the United States to the Irish Renaissance that had produced such internationally renowned figures as the poet William Butler Yeats and the playwright John Millington Synge. In alluding to "the racial spirit" he was identifying a counterpart to the so-called Celtic or Irish muse that was seen as quite distinct from the English literary imagination. In calling for a form "freer and larger than dialect," he challenged black writers to disentangle themselves from the stereotypes that had reached their highest form of art in the poetry of the African American writer Paul Laurence Dunbar, who had died in 1906. Above all, Johnson set the manipulation of language and other patterns of signification, not the overt assertion of political ideals, as the heart of the African American poetic enterprise. And he did so while reminding the young black writers, through his anthology, that they were also heirs to their own tradition—the tradition of African American literature from Phillis Wheatley in the eighteenth century down to his own work—on which they could draw with a measure of confidence as they moved into the future.

In Johnson's anthology and in Robert Kerlin's *Negro Poets and Their Poems* (1923) appeared the early work of many of the writers who would dominate the movement, including Countee Cullen and Langston Hughes. With very few exceptions, none of the younger writers of the movement saw himself or herself as part of the radical modernist strain of literature set in motion in America mainly through the efforts of poets such as Ezra Pound, T. S. Eliot, H. D., and Wallace Stevens or by the Irish writer James Joyce, whose novel *Ulysses* appeared in 1923. Such crucial tenets of radical modernism as a learned allusiveness and a necessary complexity of expression that demands an exclusive literary audience attracted few African American writers. Like most white poets of the age, most black poets were enthralled by traditional forms of verse as established by the major British and American Romantic poets and their admirers. Modernist verse that resembles the work of Pound, for example, would not appear until much later, and then on a highly restricted scale. Among major American poets after Whitman, only E. A. Robinson and Carl Sandburg would exert any particular degree of influence on the Harlem Renaissance. In part, this distance was owing, no doubt, to some inattentiveness on the part of the younger writers; in part, however, these writers were after a different business altogether. Most could not be completely taken, for example, by T. S. Eliot's epochal figuring of the entire modern world as a "Waste Land." For many of them, the 1920s was a decade of unrivaled optimism, and all through the generations of slavery and neo-slavery, black American culture had of necessity emphasized the power of endurance and survival, of love and laughter, as the only efficacious response to the painful circumstances surrounding their lives.

Even more important than Johnson's anthology as a text helping to define the emerging spirit of the movement was another anthology, albeit one of a far more varied sort: *The New Negro* (1925), edited by the Howard University professor Alain Locke. Locke's anthology combined essays, stories, poems, and artwork by older as well as younger writers, white as well as black, into a book that defined with incomparable clarity and flair the spirit of the Harlem Renaissance. Merging racial awareness with a desire for literary and artistic excellence, the text exuded a sense of confidence in the black world emerging from generations of repression in the United States, and in the spirit of Johnson's challenge, it conceived of black America as linked not only to other African-based cultural movements around the world but also to other movements, such as the Irish or Czech, that fused ethnic pride or nationalism with a desire for a fresh achievement and independence in art, culture, and politics.

Between the appearance of Johnson's anthology and Locke's, the publication of Jean Toomer's *Cane* independently illustrated several of the peculiar challenges and opportunities of the nascent movement. Opening with brief but hauntingly evocative portraits of the black South, then moving to a powerful rendition of blacks in northern cities, before returning to the South with a shrouded drama about a black northerner of troubled, fatalistic consciousness terrorized by the threat of violence at the hands of whites, *Cane* is a text that few of the young writers could resist. Technically, the work embraced certain principles of modernism and

even the avant-garde and yet is saturated with African American racial feeling offered now nostalgically, now militantly, but always in highly affecting language.
Quite apart from the fiction in the book, the poems included almost casually in the
volume were of a quality to challenge the best of the young Harlem writers, who
read *Cane* and saw Toomer as an authentic star.

Certainly the first important young writers birthed by the movement accepted
Toomer and his implicit challenge to them as an artist in this fashion. These writers
were Cullen, who had grown up in the city, and Hughes, who had spent most of his
youth in Kansas but had come to Columbia University as a student in 1921, ostensibly to be a student there but really, he later insisted, to be in Harlem. Cullen's *Color*
(1925) revealed an often dazzling lyrical facility that admitted racial feeling while
preserving its author's commitment to conservative poetic forms born of his passion
for English Romantic writers such as Keats and Shelley. Hughes, starting with his
collection *The Weary Blues* (1926), sometimes matched Cullen's lyrical intensity
but opened up a new front by advertising his worship of the blues and jazz, musical
forms seldom seen as compatible with formal poetry but that Hughes accepted as
perhaps the most authentic and moving expression in art of African American cultural feeling. The 1920s, it should be remembered, saw the rise of surpassingly accomplished musicians such as Bessie Smith, Louis Armstrong, and Duke
Ellington, whose artistry had a greater influence on the nation as a whole than the
work of any of the renaissance writers.

In addition to the timely and definitive appearance of Alain Locke's *The New
Negro*, a series of literary contests and dinners sponsored notably by *Opportunity*
magazine but also by the *Crisis*—and deliberately including some of the leading
white writers, editors, and publishers of the day—helped to set the stage for the high
phase of the movement in the second half of the decade. By the end of 1925, many
of the major young artists identified their careers with the fate of the movement.
The poet and novelist Arna Bontemps arrived from Los Angeles, as did the editor,
novelist, and critic Wallace Thurman; from Washington, D.C., came the Florida-
born Zora Neale Hurston, whose novel *Their Eyes Were Watching God* (1937),
although published after the end of the movement, should nevertheless be seen as
among its greatest achievements; the fiction writer Rudolph Fisher, by training a
physician, also saw himself as a serious writer; the artist and poet Gwendolyn Bennett came from Texas, drawn by the palpable sense of excitement in Harlem. A
little later, from New England, came the poet Helene Johnson and her cousin Dorothy West, notable as a writer of fiction and as an editor. These were only some of
the young artists drawn to Harlem by the renaissance there.

PATRONS AND FRIENDS

The deliberate courting and inclusion of leading whites in the Harlem Renaissance
have led to questions, at times acrimonious, about the role of patronage—that is,
white patronage—in the movement and even about the authenticity of the movement as an expression of African American culture if the renaissance depended so
heavily on the goodwill of whites. The truth probably is that such involvement was
important and even necessary to the movement, so deep was the historic chasm in
the United States between the races because of segregation and racist beliefs; if
books by blacks were to be published, something more than simple merit would
have to be involved. In particular, Charles S. Johnson of *Opportunity* and the National Urban League, seeing nothing but benefits in an association between blacks
and whites, worked assiduously and ingeniously to stimulate such contacts.

Perhaps the two leading white figures associated with the Harlem Renaissance
were Carl Van Vechten and Charlotte Osgood Mason. Van Vechten's interracial

parties broke new ground on the New York social scene, but he also used his influence as a fashionable novelist and critic to help launch certain careers, notably that of Langston Hughes. (Countee Cullen and a few other writers, however, were decidedly wary of Van Vechten's help.) Van Vechten's novel of Harlem life, *Nigger Heaven* (1926), became a best-seller, although many blacks were utterly alienated by the title. Through the dispensing of sums of money, Mason, an elderly woman of volatile temperament and sometimes arresting ideas, supported a number of black artists in this period, including Hurston, Hughes, and Locke; unlike Van Vechten, however, she did not hesitate to subject her beneficiaries to her powerful notions concerning parapsychology, the matchless force of folk culture, and the dangers of "civilization." In addition to Van Vechten and Mason, publishers and editors at houses such as Knopf; Macmillan; Harcourt, Brace; Macaulay; and Harper played a quieter but no less effective role in lowering the barriers between black writers and the major means of publication in the United States. The black writers eagerly seized these opportunities.

EMERGING CONFLICTS

Among the black writers themselves certain significant tensions became more serious as the movement grew. One such tension was occupational, in the sense that the writers and artists lived with the uneasy knowledge that their world was in crucial ways distinct from that of the masses of blacks, almost all of whom, as Langston Hughes once wryly observed, did not know that the Harlem Renaissance was going on. Another tension was generational—the growing antagonism between many of the older writers and editors and the younger set. James Weldon Johnson, among others of the old guard, had little difficulty with the new writers; his collection of prose pieces based on the black sermon, *God's Trombones* (1927), showed that he was still capable of innovative flights of creativity. However, the most powerful voice among the old guard, that of W. E. B. Du Bois, was less conciliatory. Increasingly disturbed by the apparent "immorality" of some of the new works, as well as by their lack of political seriousness, Du Bois organized in the *Crisis* a symposium, *The Negro in Art*, which appeared over several issues in 1926. Evidently dissatisfied with many of the responses, he openly criticized several of the new works. He was especially hard on Claude McKay's 1928 novel *Home to Harlem*, which Du Bois linked caustically with Van Vechten's *Nigger Heaven*, previously dismissed in the *Crisis* as "an affront to the hospitality of black folk and to the intelligence of white."

To most of the younger artists, including Thurman, Hughes, Hurston, and even the relatively conservative Cullen, the essence of the renaissance was freedom—freedom for them to create as they saw fit, without regard to politics. What freedom meant practically was another matter. Hughes expressed his freedom by insisting on racial commitment on the part of the black artist; Cullen expressed his own by abjuring jazz and blues verse in favor of conservative forms. In his landmark 1926 essay *The Negro Artist and the Racial Mountain*, Hughes insisted that the black artist must recognize that his or her link to Africa was a precious resource; Cullen preferred to suggest instead, as in his long poem *Heritage* (1925), that Africa was a source of confusion and ambivalence. Both, however, sought freedom from the political constraints that an older generation considered an essential part of the duty of the black artist. In 1926, many of the younger artists banded together to produce a new magazine, *Fire!!*, which promised "to burn up a lot of old, dead conventional Negro-white ideas of the past." Unfortunately, the magazine, weakly supported by the public and, indeed, by the artists themselves, lasted only one number.

DRAMA, POETRY, FICTION

Many of the younger writers were interested in the theater, but few made it a priority during the most important years of the Harlem Renaissance. The success of *Shuffle Along* in 1921 led to a vogue of such reviews and to many imitations of this compendium of song, dance, and humor. However, black involvement in more orthodox drama as part of the renaissance was far more restricted, and less attended by even provisional successes. Throughout the 1920s, the best-known dramas of black life were undoubtedly written by white artists such as Eugene O'Neill and Paul Green of North Carolina. The outstanding black talent was probably Willis Richardson, whose best-known play is *The Chip Woman's Fortune* (1923), the first serious play by an African American to be staged on Broadway. Richardson was, however, a resident of Washington, D.C., where he had been moved to write plays after seeing, in 1916, Angelina Weld Grimké's highly controversial *Rachel*, about racial persecution and its psychological effects. This controversy, about propaganda versus art, stimulated the theater in Washington but produced few new plays of quality.

In 1926, responding to this dearth of serious drama in New York involving blacks, Du Bois established the Krigwa Little Theatre movement. He asserted four basic principles: "The plays of a real Negro theatre must be: 1. *About us.* That is, they must have plots which reveal Negro life as it is. 2. *By us.* That is, they must be written by Negro authors who understand from birth and continual association just what it means to be a Negro today." The other principles called for the theater to be "*For us*"—catering mainly to black audiences, and "*Near us*"—that is, in a black neighborhood "near the masses of ordinary Negro people." The first two Krigwa productions, *Compromise* and *The Broken Banjo*, were by Willis Richardson, and Krigwa failed to inspire any important young New York playwrights. In the 1930s, Langston Hughes would emphasize drama with some success in his career, and his play about the South and miscegenation, *Mulatto* (1935), would have the longest run of any play by an African American on Broadway until Lorraine Hansberry's *A Raisin in the Sun* in the 1960s. Nevertheless, drama was almost certainly one of the weakest areas of achievement in the Harlem Renaissance.

Around 1928, the emphasis among the writers of the renaissance seemed to shift decisively away from poetry toward fiction. Poets such as Cullen, Hughes, Bontemps, Waring Cuney, Anne Spencer, and Helene Johnson continued to publish in magazines, but far fewer books of verse appeared; perhaps the only notable event of this sort was the appearance of Sterling Brown's folk-inflected *Southern Road* in 1932. In 1928 came Du Bois's novel *Dark Princess*, which was in large part his attempt to exemplify the idealistic, politically engaged fiction he preferred. More authentic that year to the mood of the age, however, were Rudolph Fisher's *The Walls of Jericho*; Nella Larsen's *Quicksand*, about one woman's chronic unhappiness with life and her descent into a self-imposed, tawdry marriage; and Claude McKay's epochal *Home to Harlem*, which celebrated the pleasures as well as the complexities of black urban life.

Still later in the renaissance came additional novels by McKay, Jessie Fauset, and Thurman, including the latter's *The Blacker the Berry* (1929), about skin-color fixation within the black community, a subject also of interest to Nella Larsen, as in her *Passing* (1929). In 1930 came Langston Hughes's *Not without Laughter*, about a young boy growing up in the Midwest. Arna Bontemps turned from poetry to write his first novel, *God Sends Sunday* (1931), based on the life of a beloved, fun-loving uncle whose approach to living contrasted with the strictness of Bontemps's Seventh Day Adventist religion. Also in 1931, the satirist George Schuyler, whose essay in the *Nation* in 1926, *The Negro-Art Hokum*, ridiculing African American race consciousness, had provoked Hughes's *Negro Artist and the Racial Mountain* there, published the satirical novel *Black No More*. Satire was prominent again in Wallace Thurman's novel *Infants of the Spring* (1932), in which several of the major figures of the renaissance are easily recognizable under their thin disguises, as Thurman lampooned many of the excesses and posturings of the Harlem Renaissance.

THE GREAT DEPRESSION AND THE DECLINE OF THE HARLEM RENAISSANCE

Although it is convenient and even accurate to include Hurston's lyrical 1937 novel about one woman's growth into mature self-confidence and self-fulfillment, *Their Eyes Were Watching God*, within the boundaries of the movement, it is also clear that by that year the movement was absolutely finished, although the talent of many of its writers was hardly exhausted. The Harlem Renaissance had been dependent in large part on a special prosperity in the publishing industry, the theater, and the art world. The crash of Wall Street in 1929 was the beginning of the end for the movement, which swiftly declined as the country lurched toward the Great Depression in the early 1930s. Conditions for blacks in New York City, and especially for blacks in Harlem, made a mockery of the heady enthusiasms that had led to the characterization of the 1920s as the Jazz Age, an era of reckless fun. Unemployment and the rise of crime (although the latter was mild compared with conditions a half-century later) damaged the image and the reality of Harlem as an artistic and cultural paradise. A civic explosion, often called the Harlem Riot of 1935, underscored the radically altered nature of the district and the lives of the people there.

The renaissance was over, to be revived in significantly different forms at later points in African American history. What did it achieve? Some critics, skeptical of the role of patronage and insistent on more militant and radical political approaches, have suggested that the cultural movement achieved little. Such a view may be short sighted, however. The art of the Harlem Renaissance—in poetry, fiction, drama, music, painting, and sculpture—represents a prodigious achievement for a people hardly more than a half-century removed from slavery and enmeshed in the chains of a dehumanizing segregation. In this movement, black American artists took stock of the lives and destinies of their people against the backdrop not only of the United States but also of the world. A sense of the modern overhangs the period, although the African American approach to the modern—insofar as one can speak of a single, collective African American approach—would be in many ways quite distinct from the pessimism and even despair of European attitudes to the same question.

In this period, black American artists laid the foundations for the representation of their people in the modern world, with a complexity and a self-knowledge that have proven durable even as the African American condition changed considerably with the unfolding of the twentieth century. The term *renaissance* is entirely appropriate, for in that decade or so a loose but united gathering of black artists, located most significantly in Harlem, rediscovered the ancient confidence and sense of destiny of their African ancestors and created a body of art on which future writers and musicians and artists might build and in which the masses of blacks could see their own faces and features accurately and lovingly reflected.

ARTHUR A. SCHOMBURG

1874–1938

As an adolescent, Arthur Schomburg was apparently told dismissively by one of his teachers that blacks had no history. In some respects, the urge to prove this teacher wrong drove the olive-skinned Puerto Rican youth to embrace wholeheartedly his African heritage. Schomburg went on to devote most of his life both to recovering as much of the history of the black peoples of the world as he could and to disseminating information that would discourage or even prevent such gross misstatements as that of his teacher. By the time of his death in 1938, he had amassed enough material to make the Schomburg Collection one of the major repositories of African American material in the world. In the process, he exerted a powerful influence on his contemporaries, particularly the young intelligentsia of Harlem. He left an enduring example and legacy to future generations of scholars, students, and readers interested in the African heritage.

Schomburg was born in San Juan, Puerto Rico, the son of a black laundress and a German merchant. After attending school in Puerto Rico and the Virgin Islands, he arrived in New York in 1891. He first developed his research skills while working as a clerk for a New York law firm; politically concerned, he also served as the secretary of Los Dos Antillas, an organization advocating Cuban and Puerto Rican independence. In 1906, he began work in the mail room of the Bankers Trust Company and was soon made chief of the foreign mailing department. He stayed with the company in that capacity until 1929. From his modest salary he not only supported himself and his large family but also built his remarkable collection of documents and drawings.

In 1911, he cofounded the Negro Society for Historical Research, serving as its secretary-treasurer and librarian for several years. By the time the American Negro Academy elected him president in 1922, Schomburg's collection had become fairly well known. In addition to lending out his materials, Schomburg regularly contributed articles to publications interested in African American culture. So enthusiastic was he about sharing his knowledge that he rarely turned down an invitation to lecture, even if it meant traveling at his own expense.

In 1926, on behalf of the New York Public Library, the Andrew Carnegie Corporation paid $10,000 for Schomburg's collection of five thousand books, three thousand manuscripts, and two thousand etchings and drawings. The collection included such prizes as manuscript poems by Paul Laurence Dunbar and original texts by Booker T. Washington. In 1932, another grant from the Carnegie Corporation enabled the New York Public Library to appoint Schomburg curator of his own collection at its 135th Street branch. In the essay printed here, Schomburg characteristically argues for the necessity of having and preserving a sense of one's history, especially when one belongs to a group whose history and humanity were routinely denied under slavery and segregation.

The Negro Digs Up His Past

The American Negro must remake his past in order to make his future. Though it is orthodox to think of America as the one country where it is unnecessary to have a past, what is a luxury for the nation as a whole becomes a prime social necessity for the Negro. For him, a group tradition must supply compensation for persecution, and pride of race the antidote for prejudice. History must restore what slavery took away, for it is the social damage of slavery that the present generations must repair and offset. So among the rising democratic millions we find the Negro thinking more collectively, more retrospectively than the rest, and apt out of the very pressure of the present to become the most enthusiastic antiquarian of them all.

Vindicating evidences of individual achievement have as a matter of fact been gathered and treasured for over a century: Abbé Gregoire's [1] liberal-minded book on Negro notables in 1808 was the pioneer effort; it has been followed at intervals by less known and often less discriminating compendiums of exceptional men and women of African stock. But this sort of thing was on the whole pathetically over-corrective, ridiculously over-laudatory; it was apologetics turned into biography. A true historical sense develops slowly and with difficulty under such circumstances. But today, even if for the ultimate purpose of group justification, history has become less a matter of argument and more a matter of record. There is the definite desire and determination to have a history, well documented, widely known at least within race circles, and administered as a stimulating and inspiring tradition for the coming generations.

Gradually as the study of the Negro's past has come out of the vagaries of rhetoric and propaganda and become systematic and scientific, three outstanding conclusions have been established:

First, that the Negro has been throughout the centuries of controversy an active collaborator, and often a pioneer, in the struggle for his own freedom and advancement. This is true to a degree which makes it the more surprising that it has not been recognized earlier.

Second, that by virtue of their being regarded as something "exceptional," even by friends and well-wishers, Negroes of attainment and genius have been unfairly disassociated from the group, and group credit lost accordingly.

Third, that the remote racial origins of the Negro, far from being what the race and the world have been given to understand, offer a record of credible group achievement when scientifically viewed, and more important still, that they are of vital general interest because of their bearing upon the beginnings and early development of human culture.

With such crucial truths to document and establish, an ounce of fact is worth a pound of controversy. So the Negro historian today digs under the spot where his predecessor stood and argued. Not long ago, the Public Library of Harlem housed a special exhibition of books, pamphlets, prints and old engravings, that simply said, to skeptic and believer alike, to scholar and schoolchild, to proud black and astonished white, "Here is the evidence." Assembled from the rapidly growing collections of the leading Negro book-collectors and research societies, there were in these cases, materials not only for the first true writing of Negro history, but for the rewriting of many important paragraphs of our common American history. Slow though it be, historical truth is no exception to the proverb.

---

1. Henri Gregoire (1750–1821), French author of *De la littératur des nègres, ou recherches sur leurs facultés intellectuelles, leurs qualité morales, et leur littérature* (1808).

Here among the rarities of early Negro Americana was Jupiter Hammon's[2] Address to the Negroes of the State of New York, edition of 1787,
with the first American Negro poet's famous "If we should ever get to
Heaven, we shall find nobody to reproach us for being black, or for being
slaves." Here was Phyllis Wheatley's Mss. poem of 1767 addressed to the
students of Harvard, her spirited encomiums upon George Washington
and the Revolutionary Cause,[3] and John Marrant's[4] St. John's Day eulogy
to the "Brothers of African Lodge No. 459" delivered at Boston in 1789.
Here too were Lemuel Haynes' Vermont commentaries on the American
Revolution and his learned sermons to his white congregation in Rutland,
Vermont, and the sermons of the year 1808 by the Rev. Absalom Jones of
St. Thomas Church, Philadelphia, and Peter Williams[5] of St. Philip's,
New York, pioneer Episcopal rectors who spoke out in daring and influen-
tial ways on the Abolition of the Slave Trade. Such things and many others
are more than mere items of curiosity: they educate any receptive mind.

Reinforcing these were still rarer items of Africana and foreign Negro
interest, the volumes of Juan Latino,[6] the best Latinist of Spain in the reign
of Philip V, incumbent of the chair of Poetry at the University of Granada,
and author of Poems printed there in 1573 and a book on the Escurial[7]
published 1576; the Latin and Dutch treatises of Jacobus Eliza Capitein, a
native of West Coast Africa and graduate of the University of Leyden, Gustavus Vassa's celebrated autobiography that supplied so much of the evidence in 1796 for Granville Sharpe's attack on slavery in the British
colonies, Julien Raymond's Paris exposé of the disabilities of the free people of color in the then (1791) French colony of Hayti, and Baron de Vastey's *Cry of the Fatherland*, the famous polemic by the secretary of
Christophe[8] that precipitated the Haytian struggle for independence. The
cumulative effect of such evidences of scholarship and moral prowess is too
weighty to be dismissed as exceptional.

But weightier surely than any evidence of individual talent and scholarship could ever be, is the evidence of important collaboration and significant pioneer initiative in social service and reform, in the efforts toward
race emancipation, colonization and race betterment. From neglected and
rust-spotted pages comes testimony to the black men and women who
stood shoulder to shoulder in courage and zeal, and often on a parity of
intelligence and talent, with their notable white benefactors. There was the
already cited work of Vassa that aided so materially the efforts of Granville
Sharpe, the record of Paul Cuffee,[9] the Negro colonization pioneer, associated so importantly with the establishment of Sierra Leone as a British
colony for the occupancy of free people of color in West Africa; the dra-

2. Poet (c. 1720–c. 1806).
3. Wheatley's (c. 1753–1784) poem to Harvard is
titled *To the University of Cambridge, in New England* and to Washington, *To His Excellency General Washington* (1776).
4. Born 1755.
5. Williams (c. 1780–1840). Haynes (1753–1833),
a New England minister popular with white and
black congregations, published his sermon *Universal Salvation* in 1806. Jones (c. 1746–1818).
6. Latino (c. 1518–1594).

7. A palace and monastery outside Madrid.
8. Henri Christophe (1767–1820), king of Haiti
from 1811 to 1820. Capitein (1717–1747), author
of *De Vocatione Ethnicorum* (1737) and a thesis defending slavery (1742). Vassa (c. 1745–1797), formerly named Olaudah Equiano, wrote his
autobiographical *Interesting Narrative* in 1789.
Granville Sharp (1735–1813), a leading British abolitionist. Vastey (d. 1820), author of *Le Cri de la
Patrie* (1815).
9. Cuffee (c. 1758–1817).

matic and history-making exposé of John Baptist Phillips,[1] African graduate of Edinburgh, who compelled through Lord Bathhurst in 1824 the enforcement of the articles of capitulation guaranteeing freedom to the
blacks of Trinidad. There is the record of the pioneer colonization project
of Rev. Daniel Coker in conducting a voyage of ninety expatriates to West
Africa in 1820, of the missionary efforts of Samuel Crowther in Sierra
Leone, first Anglican bishop of his diocese, and that of the work of John
Russwurm, a leader in the work and foundation of the American Colonization Society.

When we consider the facts, certain chapters of American history will
have to be reopened. Just as black men were influential factors in the campaign against the slave trade, so they were among the earliest instigators of
the abolition movement. Indeed there was a dangerous calm between the
agitation for the suppression of the slave trade and the beginning of the
campaign for emancipation. During that interval colored men were very
influential in arousing the attention of public men who in turn aroused the
conscience of the country. Continuously between 1808 and 1845, men
like Prince Saunders, Peter Williams, Absalom Jones, Nathaniel Paul, and
Bishops Varick and Richard Allen,[2] the founders of the two wings of African Methodism, spoke out with force and initiative, and men like Denmark Vesey (1822), David Walker (1828) and Nat Turner[3] (1831)
advocated and organized schemes for direct action. This culminated in the
generally ignored but important conventions of Free People of Color in
New York, Philadelphia and other centers, whose platforms and efforts are
to the Negro of as great significance as the nationally cherished memories
of Faneuil and Independence Halls.[4] Then with Abolition comes the better documented and more recognized collaboration of Samuel R. Ward,
William Wells Brown, Henry Highland Garnett, Martin Delany, Harriet
Tubman, Sojourner Truth, and Frederick Douglass[5] with their great colleagues, Tappan, Phillips, Sumner, Mott, Stowe and Garrison.[6]

But even this latter group[7] who came within the limelight of national
and international notice, and thus into open comparison with the best
minds of their generation, the public too often regards as a group of inspired illiterates, eloquent echoes of their Abolitionist sponsors. For a true
estimate of their ability and scholarship, however, one must go with the
antiquarian to the files of the *Anglo-African Magazine*, where page by page
comparisons may be made. Their writings show Douglass, McCune
Smith, Wells Brown, Delany, Wilmot Blyden and Alexander Crummell[8]

---

1. Phillips (1799–1851).
2. Allen (c. 1750–1831). Saunders (1775–1839).
Paul (1775–1834). James Varick (c. 1750–1827).
3. Turner (1800–1831) and Vesey (1767?–1822)
both led slave conspiracies to revolt in the South.
Walker (1785–1830) published his *Appeal to the
Colored Citizens of the World* in 1829.
4. Independence Hall (in Philadelphia) hosted
both the Second Constitutional Congress and the
federal convention of 1787. Faneuil Hall was the
meeting place for the participants in the Boston
Tea Party incident of 1773.
5. Brown (1815–1884), Garnet (1815–1882), Tubman (c. 1820–1913), Sojourner Truth (c. 1775–

1883), and Douglass (1818–1895) were escaped
slaves who joined Delany (1812–1885), a free man
of the North, in fighting slavery.
6. Arthur Tappan (1786–1865), Wendell Phillips
(1811–1884), Lucretia Mott (1793–1880), and William Lloyd Garrison (1805–1879) were prominent
abolitionists. Charles Sumner (1811–1874), an important Radical Republican during the Reconstruction Era. Harriet Beecher Stowe (1811–1896),
author of *Uncle Tom's Cabin*.
7. I.e., Ward, Brown, etc.
8. Crummell (1819–1898). James McCune Smith
(1813–1865). Blyden (1832–1912).

to have been as scholarly and versatile as any of the noted publicists with whom they were associated. All of them labored internationally in the cause of their fellows; to Scotland, England, France, Germany and Africa, they carried their brilliant offensive of debate and propaganda, and with this came instance upon instance of signal foreign recognition, from academic, scientific, public and official sources. Delany's *Principia of Ethnology* won public reception from learned societies, Pennington's[9] discourses an honorary doctorate from Heidelberg, Wells Brown's three year mission the entrée of the salons of London and Paris, and the tours of Frederick Douglass, receptions second only to Henry Ward Beecher's.[1]

After this great era of public interest and discussion, it was Alexander Crummell, who, with the reaction already setting in, first organized Negro brains defensively through the founding of the American Negro Academy in 1897 at Washington. A New York boy whose zeal for education had suffered a rude shock when refused admission to the Episcopal Seminary by Bishop Onderdonk, he had been befriended by John Jay[2] and sent to Cambridge University, England, for his education and ordination. On his return, he was beset with the idea of promoting race scholarship, and the Academy was the final result. It has continued ever since to be one of the bulwarks of our intellectual life, though unfortunately its members have had to spend too much of their energy and effort answering detractors and disproving popular fallacies. Only gradually have the men of this group been able to work toward pure scholarship. Taking a slightly different start, The Negro Society for Historical Research[3] was later organized in New York, and has succeeded in stimulating the collection from all parts of the world of books and documents dealing with the Negro. It has also brought together for the first time cooperatively in a single society African, West Indian and Afro-American scholars. Direct offshoots of this same effort are the extensive private collections[4] of Henry P. Slaughter of Washington, the Rev. Charles D. Martin of Harlem, of Arthur Schomburg of Brooklyn, and of the late John E. Bruce, who was the enthusiastic and far-seeing pioneer of this movement. Finally and more recently, the Association for the Study of Negro Life and History has extended these efforts into a scientific research project of great achievement and promise. Under the direction of Dr. Carter G. Woodson,[5] it has continuously maintained for nine years the publication of the learned quarterly, *The Journal of Negro History*, and with the assistance and recognition of two large educational foundations has maintained research and published valuable monographs in Negro history. Almost keeping pace with the work of scholarship has been the effort to popularize the results, and to place before Negro youth in the schools the true story of race vicissitude, struggle and accomplishment. So that quite largely now the ambition of Negro youth can be nourished on its own milk.

9. James Pennington (1809–1870).
1. A prominent abolitionist (1813–1887).
2. First U.S. Supreme Court chief justice (1745–1829). Benjamin T. Onderdonk (1791–1861).
3. Founded by Schomburg and John E. Bruce (1856–1924).
4. Schomburg's collection had been purchased by the New York Public Library in 1926, but he continued collecting materials and donating them to the library.
5. Woodson (1875–1950) began editing the *Journal of Negro History* in 1915. He founded Negro History Week, later Black History Month, in 1926.

Such work is a far cry from the puerile controversy and petty braggadocio with which the effort for race history first started. But a general as well as a racial lesson has been learned. We seem lately to have come at last to realize what the truly scientific attitude requires, and to see that the race issue has been a plague on both our historical houses, and that history cannot be properly written with either bias or counterbias. The blatant Caucasian racialist with his theories and assumptions of race superiority and dominance has in turn bred his Ethiopian counterpart—the rash and rabid amateur who has glibly tried to prove half of the world's geniuses to have been Negroes and to trace the pedigree of nineteenth century Americans from the Queen of Sheba. But fortunately to-day there is on both sides of a really common cause less of the sand of controversy and more of the dust of digging.

Of course, a racial motive remains—legitimately compatible with scientific method and aim. The work our race students now regard as important, they undertake very naturally to overcome in part certain handicaps of disparagement and omission too well-known to particularize. But they do so not merely that we may not wrongfully be deprived of the spiritual nourishment of our cultural past, but also that the full story of human collaboration and interdependence may be told and realized. Especially is this likely to be the effect of the latest and most fascinating of all of the attempts to open up the closed Negro past, namely the important study of African cultural origins and sources. The bigotry of civilization which is the taproot of intellectual prejudice begins far back and must be corrected at its source. Fundamentally it has come about from that depreciation of Africa which has sprung up from ignorance of her true rôle and position in human history and the early development of culture. The Negro has been a man without a history because he has been considered a man without a worthy culture. But a new notion of the cultural attainment and potentialities of the African stocks has recently come about, partly through the corrective influence of the more scientific study of African institutions and early cultural history, partly through growing appreciation of the skill and beauty and in many cases the historical priority of the African native crafts, and finally through the signal recognition which first in France and Germany, but now very generally, the astonishing art of the African sculptures has received. Into these fascinating new vistas, with limited horizons lifting in all directions, the mind of the Negro has leapt forward faster than the slow clearings of scholarship will yet safely permit. But there is no doubt that here is a field full of the most intriguing and inspiring possibilities. Already the Negro sees himself against a reclaimed background, in a perspective that will give pride and self-respect ample scope, and make history yield for him the same values that the treasured past of any people affords.

1925

ANGELINA WELD GRIMKÉ

1880–1958

Few writers of the Harlem Renaissance had a family history as poignant as that of Angelina Grimké. Her paternal great-aunts were southern white abolitionist women—Sarah Moore Grimké and her sister Angelina, who married Theodore Dwight Weld. In a rare example of such honesty, these two independent-minded daughters of a wealthy South Carolina slaveholder publicly acknowledged their ties to their brother Henry's sons Archibald Henry Grimké and Francis James Grimké, who had been born to a union between Henry Grimké and Nancy Weston, a slave on the Grimkés' Caneacre Plantation. Under the sponsorship of his two aunts, Archibald Grimké took his law degree from Harvard in 1874. In 1879, he married a white woman, Sarah E. Stanley (although her father, a prominent Boston clergyman, opposed the marriage). Angelina Weld Grimké was born to the couple the following year.

The strain of the marriage soon proved too much for Sarah Stanley, who abandoned Archibald and Angelina and never saw her daughter again. Angelina, pampered by her father and educated at such liberal institutions as Cushing Academy in Ashburnham, Massachusetts, and Carleton Academy in Northfield, Minnesota, seems to have grown up fairly sheltered from racial discrimination. However, her description of her play *Rachel* (first produced in 1916) indicates that at some point she certainly awoke to the reality of racism: "This is the first attempt to use the stage for race propaganda in order to enlighten the American people relating to the lamentable condition of ten millions of Colored citizens in this free republic."

Graduating from the Boston Normal School of Gymnastics in 1902, Grimké moved to Washington, D.C., where she taught English at the Armstrong Manual Training School until 1916. From there, she joined the faculty at the distinguished Dunbar High School, remaining there until shortly after her father's death in 1930. By that time, *Rachel* had been hailed, in the words of Alain Locke and Montgomery Gregory, as "apparently the first successful drama written by a Negro and interpreted by Negro actors." Frankly sentimental, it stressed the hurts of racism on middle-class blacks as well as the evil of lynching. Grimké also placed several of her delicate, traditional poems in magazines such as the *Crisis* and *Opportunity*, and in Countee Cullen's timely anthology *Caroling Dusk*. Her most important prose piece, *The Closing Door*, reiterates one of the themes of *Rachel* in its insistence on the immorality of bringing black children—particularly black males—into a world that does not want them and is likely to warp or destroy them. The story ends with a hysterical black woman killing the black boy to whom she has just given birth in order to prevent the possibility of his dying at the hands of a lynch mob at some future date.

In her important study of Grimké, Gloria Hull suggests that Grimké's adult life was one of chronic unhappiness because of an overdependence on her father and possible repression of homosexual desires. After her father's death, Grimké's sense of direction certainly seemed to leave her. She moved to New York, claiming that she intended to write, but nothing came of it. Apart from the friendship she kept up with the Washington poet Georgia Douglas Johnson, her remaining years seem to have been relatively desolate. Nevertheless, although her reputation rests mainly on a few lyric pieces repeatedly anthologized in collections of African American literature of the 1920s, that reputation seems likely to endure because of the refinement of her lyric sensibility and her consciousness as a woman and an artist in a literary culture then dominated by male writers.

A Winter Twilight

A silence slipping around like death,
Yet chased by a whisper, a sigh, a breath;
One group of trees, lean, naked and cold,
Inking their crest 'gainst a sky green-gold;
One path that knows where the corn flowers were;   5
Lonely, apart, unyielding, one fir;
And over it softly leaning down,
One star that I loved ere the fields went brown.

                                                    1923

The Black Finger

I have just seen a beautiful thing
        Slim and still,
Against a gold, gold sky,
        A straight cypress,
        Sensitive   5
        Exquisite,
A black finger
Pointing upwards.
Why, beautiful, still finger are you black?
And why are you pointing upwards?   10

                                                    1925

For the Candle Light

The sky was blue, so blue, that day,
And each daisy white, so white;
Oh! I knew that no more could rains fall gray,
And night again be night.

I knew! I knew! Well, if night is night,   5
And the gray skies grayly cry,
I have in a book, for the candle light,
A daisy, dead and dry.

                                                    1927

When the Green Lies Over the Earth

When the green lies over the earth, my dear,
A mantle of witching[1] grace,
When the smile and the tear of the young child year
Dimple across its face,
And then flee, when the wind all day is sweet   5

---

1. Bewitching or enchanting.

944

With the breath of growing things,
When the wooing bird lights on restless feet
And chirrups and trills and sings
　　　To his lady-love
　　　In the green above,   10
Then oh! my dear, when the youth's in the year,
Yours is the face that I long to have near,
　　　Yours is the face, my dear.

But the green is hiding your curls, my dear,
Your curls so shining and sweet;   15
And the gold-hearted daisies this many a year
Have bloomed and bloomed at your feet,
And the little birds just above your head
With their voices hushed, my dear,
For you have sung and have prayed and have pled   20
　　　This many, many a year.
　　　And the blossoms fall,
　　　On the garden wall,
And drift like snow on the green below.
　　　But the sharp thorn grows   25
　　　On the budding rose,
And my heart no more leaps at the sunset glow,
For oh! my dear, when the youth's in the year,
Yours is the face that I long to have near,
Yours is the face, my dear.   30

　　　　　　　　　　　　　　　　　　　　　　　　　1927

Tenebris[1]

There is a tree, by day,
That, at night,
Has a shadow,
A hand huge and black,
With fingers long and black.   5
　　　All through the dark,
Against the white man's house,
　　　In the little wind,
The black hand plucks and plucks
　　　At the bricks.   10
The bricks are the color of blood and very small.
　　　Is it a black hand,
　　　Or is it a shadow?

　　　　　　　　　　　　　　　　　　　　　　　　　1927

1. In darkness (Latin).

ANNE SPENCER

1882–1975

Of the poetry of the Harlem Renaissance, Anne Spencer's work is perhaps the most modernist, not least of all in its enigmatic, allusive quality and its emphasis on privacy of vision. She wrote sparingly but to distinct effect, much as she cultivated the garden at her home that became the focus of her life. Spencer and her husband, Edward, built the garden in the backyard of their home in Lynchburg, Virginia, where they settled in 1901, two years after their graduation from the Virginia Seminary. During those two years Anne Spencer (born Annie Bethel Bannister) had taught public school in the Bramwell, West Virginia, area, which she knew well. Her mother, Sarah Scales, had taken her there after separating from Anne's father in 1887.

Though she began writing poetry at the Virginia Seminary, Spencer did not publish until 1920, after James Weldon Johnson accidentally learned of her writing while staying at her home during a trip on NAACP business after local blacks decided to form a chapter of the organization. He cajoled Spencer into allowing *Before the Feast of Shushan* to be published in the *Crisis*. He also introduced her to the celebrated editor of *American Mercury* magazine, H. L. Mencken; but she rejected Mencken's help because she denied his right (as a nonpoet) to criticize her work. Although most of her verse is about nature, Spencer's best poetry, marked by the irony and some of the complexity typical of literary modernism, tends to be more concerned with gender than with race. The 1920s saw her publish in such magazines as *Survey Graphic, Palms, Opportunity,* and *Lyric* as well as in a number of important anthologies, including Johnson's *Book of American Negro Poetry* and Countee Cullen's *Caroling Dusk*. However, fewer than thirty of her poems were published during her lifetime, and only one of those, a tribute to Johnson called *For Jim, Easter Eve,* came after Johnson's untimely death in 1938.

After Johnson's death, fewer callers came to the Spencer home, which Claude McKay, W. E. B. Du Bois, Langston Hughes, Georgia Douglas Johnson, Paul Robeson, and many others had visited. Her husband's death in 1964 made Spencer a virtual recluse, and she allowed her beloved garden to fall into disrepair. She spent the last years of her life revising her poems in her own way, which often meant jotting down whatever alterations occurred to her on the scrap of paper nearest to hand. During her last illness in 1975, her friends, unable to make anything of these scraps, apparently discarded them. She died later that year in Lynchburg. Her home, its garden restored, has since been accorded the status of historic landmark. This is an entirely appropriate honor. Spencer's voice as a poet was distinctive, assured, and complex; it deserves further study and appreciation.

Before the Feast of Shushan [1]

Garden of Shushan!
After Eden, all terrace, pool, and flower recollect thee:
Ye weavers in saffron and haze and Tyrian purple, [2]
Tell yet what range in color wakes the eye;
Sorcerer, release the dreams born here when   5
Drowsy, shifting palm-shade enspells the brain;
And sound! ye with harp and flute ne'er essay
Before these star-noted birds escaped from paradise awhile to
Stir all dark, and dear, and passionate desire, till mine
Arms go out to be mocked by the softly kissing body of the
    wind—   10
Slave, send Vashti to her King!

The fiery wattles of the sun startle into flame
The marbled towers of Shushan:
So at each day's wane, two peers—the one in
Heaven, the other on earth—welcome with their   15
Splendor the peerless beauty of the Queen.

Cushioned at the Queen's feet and upon her knee
Finding glory for mine head,—still, nearly shamed
Am I, the King, to bend and kiss with sharp
Breath the olive-pink of sandaled toes between;   20
Or lift me high to the magnet of a gaze, dusky,
Like the pool when but the moon-ray strikes to its depth;
Or closer press to crush a grape 'gainst lips redder
Than the grape, a rose in the night of her hair;
Then—Sharon's Rose [3] in my arms.   25

And I am hard to force the petals wide;
And you are fast to suffer and be sad.
Is any prophet come to teach a new thing
Now in a more apt time?
Have him 'maze how you say love is sacrament;   30
How says Vashti, love is both bread and wine;
How to the altar may not come to break and drink,
Hulky flesh nor fleshly spirit!

I, thy lord, like not manna for meat as a Judahn; [4]
I, thy master, drink, and red wine, plenty, and when   35
I thirst. Eat meat, and full, when I hunger.
I, thy King, teach you and leave you, when I list.
No woman in all Persia sets out strange action

1. This reflective monologue is based on an incident in the Book of Esther (1:2–12): "When the
king Ahasuerus sat on the throne of his kingdom,
which was in Shushan the palace, . . . he made a
feast unto all his princes and his servants. . . . Also
Vashti the queen made a feast for the women in the
royal house which belonged to king Ahasuerus. On
the seventh day, when the heart of the king was
merry with wine, he commanded . . . the seven
chamberlains that served [him] to bring Vashti the
queen before the king with the crown royal, to
shew the people and the princes her beauty: for she
was fair to look on. But the queen Vashti refused to
come at the king's commandment by his chamberlains: therefore was the king very wroth, and his
anger burned in him."
2. Tyre was famous in antiquity for its purple dyes.
3. See Song of Solomon 2:1: "I am the rose of
Sharon, and the lily of the valleys."
4. See Exodus 16:13–36.

To confuse Persia's lord—
Love is but desire and thy purpose fulfillment;   40
I, thy King, so say!

1920

Dunbar[1]

Ah, how poets sing and die!
Make one song and Heaven takes it;
Have one heart and Beauty breaks it;
Chatterton, Shelley, Keats[2] and I—
Ah, how poets sing and die!   5

1920

At the Carnival

Gay little Girl-of-the-Diving-Tank,[1]
I desire a name for you,
Nice, as a right glove fits;
For you—who amid the malodorous
Mechanics of this unlovely thing,   5
Are darling of spirit and form.
I know you—a glance, and what you are
Sits-by-the-fire in my heart.
My Limousine-Lady[2] knows you, or
Why does the slant-envy of her eye mark   10
Your straight air and radiant inclusive smile?
Guilt pins a fig-leaf; Innocence is its own adorning.
The bull-necked man knows you—this first time
His itching flesh sees form divine and vibrant health
And thinks not of his avocation.   15
I came incuriously—
Set on no diversion save that my mind
Might safely nurse its brood of misdeeds
In the presence of a blind crowd.
The color of life was gray.   20
Everywhere the setting seemed right
For my mood.
Here the sausage and garlic booth
Sent unholy incense skyward;
There a quivering female-thing   25
Gestured assignations,[3] and lied
To call it dancing;
There, too, were games of chance

1. Paul Laurence Dunbar (1872–1906), the most
important African American poet at the turn of the
century; his *Lyrics of Lowly Life* was published in
1896.
2. Thomas Chatterton (1752–1770), Percy Bysshe
Shelley (1792–1822), and John Keats (1795–1821)

were English poets who, like Dunbar, died young.
1. A young woman who high dives into a water
tank at a carnival.
2. Wealthy woman.
3. Appointments for romantic meetings.

With chances for none;
But oh! Girl-of-the-Tank, at last!   30
Gleaming Girl, how intimately pure and free
The gaze you send the crowd,
As though you know the dearth of beauty
In its sordid life.
We need you—my Limousine-Lady,   35
The bull-necked man and I.
Seeing you here brave and water-clean,
Leaven for the heavy ones of earth,
I am swift to feel that what makes
The plodder glad is good; and   40
Whatever is good is God.
The wonder is that you are here;
I have seen the queer in queer places,
But never before a heaven-fed
Naiad[4] of the Carnival-Tank!   45
Little Diver, Destiny for you,
Like as for me, is shod in silence;
Years may seep into your soul
The bacilli of the usual and the expedient;
I implore Neptune[5] to claim his child today!   50

                                                  1923

Lady, Lady

Lady, Lady, I saw your face,
Dark as night withholding a star . . .
The chisel fell, or it might have been
You had borne so long the yoke of men.

Lady, Lady, I saw your hands,   5
Twisted, awry, like crumpled roots,
Bleached poor white in a sudsy tub,
Wrinkled and drawn from your rub-a-dub.

Lady, Lady, I saw your heart,
And altared[1] there in its darksome place   10
Were the tongues of flame the ancients knew,
Where the good God sits to spangle through.

                                                  1925

Letter to My Sister

It is dangerous for a woman to defy the gods;
To taunt them with the tongue's thin tip,
Or strut in the weakness of mere humanity,

---

4. Water nymph.   1. Enshrined, set on an altar.
5. Roman god of the sea. "Bacilli": bacteria.

Or draw a line daring them to cross;
The gods own the searing lightning,   5
The drowning waters, tormenting fears
And anger of red sins.

Oh, but worse still if you mince timidly—
Dodge this way or that, or kneel or pray,
Be kind, or sweat agony drops   10
Or lay your quick body over your feeble young;
If you have beauty or none, if celibate
Or vowed—the gods are Juggernaut, [1]
Passing over . . . over . . .

This you may do: 15
Lock your heart, then, quietly,
And lest they peer within,
Light no lamp when dark comes down
Raise no shade for sun;
Breathless must your breath come through   20
If you'd die and dare deny
The gods their god-like fun.

                                                   1927

The Wife-Woman [1]

Maker-of-Sevens [2] in the scheme of things
From earth to star;
Thy cycle holds whatever is fate, and
Over the border the bar.
Though rank and fierce the mariner   5
Sailing the seven seas,
He prays, as he holds his glass to his eyes,
Coaxing the Pleiades. [3]

I cannot love them; and I feel your glad
Chiding from the grave,   10
That my all was only worth at all, what
Joy to you it gave,
These seven links the *Law* [4] compelled
For the human chain—
I cannot love *them*; and *you*, oh,   15
Seven-fold months in Flanders [5] slain!

A jungle there, a cave here, bred six
And a million years,

1. A Hindu god; commonly, a large force or object
that crushes all that gets in its way.
1. The poem is written from the point of view of a
woman with seven children who has lost her husband in World War I.
2. The god of luck.
3. A cluster of stars named after the seven daugh-

ters of Atlas, although only six stars are visible.
4. From the Old Testament, particularly "Be fruitful, and multiply" (Genesis 1:28). "Seven links":
the speaker's children.
5. A region comprising western Belgium, northern
France, and southwestern Netherlands; the site of
prolonged fighting in World War I.

Sure and strong, mate for mate, such
Love as culture fears;   20
I gave you clear the oil and wine;
You saved me your hob[6] and hearth—
See how *even* life may be ere the
Sickle comes and leaves a swath.

But I can wait the seven of moons,   25
Or years I spare,
Hoarding the heart's plenty, nor spend
A drop, nor share—
So long but outlives a smile and
A silken gown;   30
Then gayly I reach up from my shroud,
And you, glory-clad, reach down.

                                                          1931

6. A shelf on the side of a fireplace used for keeping food warm.

JESSIE REDMON FAUSET
c. 1884–1961

When Langston Hughes credited Jessie Redmon Fauset with being (along with
Alain Locke and Charles S. Johnson) one of "the three people who mid-wifed the
so-called New Negro literature into being," he captured something of her central
importance to the Harlem Renaissance. Unfortunately, many critics have chosen to
dwell on Fauset's discovery or encouragement of writers such as Hughes, Claude
McKay, and Nella Larsen and ignored her own work. As brilliant an editor as she
was, Fauset was also, with four novels between 1924 and 1933, the most prolific
novelist of the Harlem Renaissance and a writer of genuine accomplishment as
well as ambition.

Born in a New Jersey suburb of Philadelphia to the Reverend Redmon Fauset
and his wife, Annie, Jessie Fauset grew up in a relatively poor but genteel family.
Educated in Philadelphia public schools, she graduated from the High School for
Girls in 1900. Although she hoped to attend the prestigious Bryn Mawr College,
that institution sidestepped the thorny issue of admitting a black by obtaining for
her a scholarship to Cornell University. Fauset was an excellent student. In 1905,
she became the first woman to graduate from Cornell with a Phi Beta Kappa key
and the first black woman in America to become a member of that society. Barred
from teaching in Philadelphia because of her race, she found a one-year position
with Douglass High School of Baltimore before moving on to Dunbar High School
in Washington, D.C., where she taught French and Latin until 1918. She then
devoted a year to completing her master's degree at the University of Pennsylvania.
About this time, Fauset also began to work for the *Crisis* (the organ of the NAACP)
under W. E. B. Du Bois. In October 1919, she became its literary editor, serving in
that capacity until 1926. Fauset was also important in the development of Du Bois's
The Brownies' Book, a children's monthly.

As a vehicle for literature, the *Crisis* was certainly at its best during Fauset's
seven-year tenure. As editor, she repeatedly demonstrated a flair for detecting literary talent and a capacity for hard work; at the same time, she produced her own

important essays and fiction. In 1926, for reasons that are not quite clear (including possibly the decline in the circulation of the magazine and a strain in her relationship with Du Bois), Fauset resigned her position, leaving the magazine altogether a year later. She returned to teaching (at DeWitt Clinton High School in New York) in 1927.

Fauset's first novel, *There Is Confusion*, was published in 1924 as a response to *Birthright* (1922), a book about blacks by T. S. Stribling, a white writer whose inadequate representation of the African American middle class, to which Fauset proudly belonged, made her determined to set the record straight. *Plum Bun: A Novel without a Moral* (1929) chronicles the complex story of Angela Murray, a light-skinned black whose attempt to pass for white makes up most of the story. Two other books followed, *The Chinaberry Tree: A Novel of American Life* (1931), regarded by many critics as perhaps Fauset's weakest literary achievement, and *Comedy, American Style* (1933), in which she experimented with the relationship between drama and narrative. In 1948, Hugh Gloster called this last novel "the most penetrating study of color mania in American fiction"; however, it has not appealed consistently to readers.

Fauset's 1929 marriage to Herbert E. Harris lasted until his death in 1958. They lived mainly in Montclair, New Jersey, but after Harris's death, Fauset returned to Philadelphia to live with her stepbrother, Earl Huff Fauset, until her death in 1961. Jessie Fauset's reputation is shrouded unfairly by a sense of her as having been snobbish both as an artist and as an individual, despite the testimony of sympathetic observers such as Langston Hughes. More attention should be paid to her intellectual and artistic energy, the high standards she set for herself as a writer, and the achievement of her fiction when read with sympathy for and understanding of the legitimate issues and complex narratives that characterize them.

As the critic Deborah McDowell has argued, *Plum Bun* may seem to be "just another novel of racial passing," but it rewards the attentive reader because of its rich texture and complicated meanings. In the end, its heroine comes to accept her ties to the African American world. This return to her origins caps a narrative that probes the relationship among money, power, and sexuality from an African American woman's perspective. As in almost all of Fauset's writing, the social milieu is the middle class, which she explores with wisdom and artistic deftness.

From Plum Bun: A Novel without a Moral [1]

From *Home*

CHAPTER I [BLACK PHILADELPHIA]

Opal Street, as streets go, is no jewel of the first water. [2] It is merely an imitation, and none too good at that. Narrow, unsparkling, uninviting, it stretches meekly off from dull Jefferson Street to the dingy, drab market which forms the north side of Oxford Street. It has no mystery, no allure, either of exclusiveness or of downright depravity; its usages are plainly significant,—an unpretentious little street lined with unpretentious little houses, inhabited for the most part by unpretentious little people.

The dwellings are three stories high, and contain six boxes called by

---

1. The title is taken from the nursery rhyme that serves as the epigraph for the novel: "To market, to market / To buy a Plum Bun; / Home again, Home again, / Market is done." *Plum Bun* is broken into five sections, each named after a word or phrase from the nursery rhyme. Included here are the two opening chapters of the first section.
2. No fine jewel. Opal Street is in Philadelphia.

courtesy, rooms—a "parlor," a midget of a dining-room, a larger kitchen and, above, a front bedroom seemingly large only because it extends for the full width of the house, a mere shadow of a bathroom, and another back bedroom with windows whose possibilities are spoiled by their outlook on sad and diminutive back-yards. And above these two, still two others built in similar wise.

In one of these houses dwelt a father, a mother and two daughters. Here, as often happens in a home sheltering two generations, opposite, unevenly matched emotions faced each other. In the houses of the rich the satisfied ambition of the older generation is faced by the overwhelming ambition of the younger. Or the elders may find themselves brought in opposition to the blank indifference and ennui of youth engendered by the realization that there remain no more worlds to conquer; their fathers having already taken all. In houses on Opal Street these niceties of distinction are hardly to be found; there is a more direct and concrete contrast. The satisfied ambition of maturity is a foil for the restless despair of youth.

Affairs in the Murray household were advancing towards this stage; yet not a soul in that family of four could have foretold its coming. To Junius and Mattie Murray, who had known poverty and homelessness, the little house on Opal Street represented the *ne plus ultra* [3] of ambition; to their daughter Angela it seemed the dingiest, drabbest chrysalis that had ever fettered the wings of a brilliant butterfly. The stories which Junius and Mattie told of difficulties overcome, of the arduous learning of trades, of the pitiful scraping together of infinitesimal savings, would have made a latter-day Iliad, [4] but to Angela they were merely a description of a life which she at any cost would avoid living. Somewhere in the world were paths which lead to broad thoroughfares, large, bright houses, delicate niceties of existence. Those paths Angela meant to find and frequent. At a very early age she had observed that the good things of life are unevenly distributed; merit is not always rewarded; hard labor does not necessarily entail adequate recompense. Certain fortuitous endowments, great physical beauty, unusual strength, a certain unswerving singleness of mind,—gifts bestowed quite blindly and disproportionately by the forces which control life,— these were the qualities which contributed toward a glowing and pleasant existence.

Angela had no high purpose in life; unlike her sister Virginia, who meant some day to invent a marvelous method for teaching the pianoforte, Angela felt no impulse to discover, or to perfect. True she thought she might become eventually a distinguished painter, but that was because she felt within herself an ability to depict which as far as it went was correct and promising. Her eye for line and for expression was already good and she had a nice feeling for color. Moreover she possessed the instinct for self-appraisal which taught her that she had much to learn. And she was sure that the knowledge once gained would flower in her case to perfection. But her gift was not for her the end of existence; rather it was an adjunct to a life which was to know light, pleasure, gaiety and freedom.

3. The highest point (Latin).
4. Ancient Greek epic poem (c. 700 B.C.) of the Trojan war, often attributed to Homer.

Freedom! That was the note which Angela heard oftenest in the melody of living which was to be hers. With a wildness that fell just short of unreasonableness she hated restraint. Her father's earlier days as coachman in a private family, his later successful, independent years as boss carpenter, her mother's youth spent as maid to a famous actress, all this was to Angela a manifestation of the sort of thing which happens to those enchained it might be by duty, by poverty, by weakness or by color.

Color or rather the lack of it seemed to the child the one absolute prerequisite to the life of which she was always dreaming. One might break loose from a too hampering sense of duty; poverty could be overcome; physicians conquered weakness; but color, the mere possession of a black or a white skin, that was clearly one of those fortuitous endowments of the gods. Gratitude was no strong ingredient in this girl's nature, yet very often early she began thanking Fate for the chance which in that household of four had bestowed on her the heritage of her mother's fair skin. She might so easily have been, like her father, black, or have received the melange[5] which had resulted in Virginia's rosy bronzeness and her deeply waving black hair. But Angela had received not only her mother's creamy complexion and her soft cloudy, chestnut hair, but she had taken from Junius the aquiline nose, the gift of some remote Indian ancestor which gave to his face and his eldest daughter's that touch of chiselled immobility.

It was from her mother that Angela learned the possibilities for joy and freedom which seemed to her inherent in mere whiteness. No one would have been more amazed than that same mother if she could have guessed how her daughter interpreted her actions. Certainly Mrs. Murray did not attribute what she considered her happy, busy, sheltered life on tiny Opal Street to the accident of her color; she attributed it to her black husband whom she had been glad and proud to marry. It is equally certain that that white skin of hers had not saved her from occasional contumely and insult. The famous actress for whom she had worked was aware of Mattie's mixed blood and, boasting temperament rather than refinement, had often dubbed her "white nigger."

Angela's mother employed her color very much as she practiced certain winning usages of smile and voice to obtain indulgences which meant much to her and which took nothing from anyone else. Then, too, she was possessed of a keener sense of humor than her daughter; it amused her when by herself to take lunch at an exclusive restaurant whose patrons would have been panic-stricken if they had divined the presence of a "colored" woman no matter how little her appearance differed from theirs. It was with no idea of disclaiming her own that she sat in orchestra seats which Philadelphia denied to colored patrons. But when Junius or indeed any other dark friend accompanied her she was the first to announce that she liked to sit in the balcony or gallery, as indeed she did; her infrequent occupation of orchestra seats was due merely to a mischievous determination to flout a silly and unjust law.

Her years with the actress had left their mark, a perfectly harmless and

5. A mixture or medley (French).

rather charming one. At least so it seemed to Junius, whose weakness was for the qualities known as "essentially feminine." Mrs. Murray loved pretty clothes, she liked shops devoted to the service of women; she enjoyed being even on the fringe of a fashionable gathering. A satisfaction that was almost ecstatic seized her when she drank tea in the midst of modishly gowned women in a stylish tea-room. It pleased her to stand in the foyer of a great hotel or of the Academy of Music and to be part of the whirling, humming, palpitating gaiety. She had no desire to be of these people, but she liked to look on; it amused and thrilled and kept alive some unquenchable instinct for life which thrived within her. To walk through Wanamaker's [6] on Saturday, to stroll from Fifteenth to Ninth Street on Chestnut, to have her tea in the Bellevue Stratford, to stand in the lobby of the St. James' fitting on immaculate gloves; all innocent, childish pleasures pursued without malice or envy contrived to cast a glamour over Monday's washing and Tuesday's ironing, the scrubbing of kitchen and bathroom and the fashioning of children's clothes. She was endowed with a humorous and pungent method of presentation; Junius, who had had the wit not to interfere with these little excursions and the sympathy to take them at their face value, preferred one of his wife's sparkling accounts of a Saturday's adventure in "passing" to all the tall stories told by cronies at his lodge.

Much of this pleasure, harmless and charming though it was, would have been impossible with a dark skin.

In these first years of marriage, Mattie, busied with the house and the two babies had given up those excursions. Later, when the children had grown and Junius had reached the stage where he could afford to give himself a half-holiday on Saturdays, the two parents inaugurated a plan of action which eventually became a fixed program. Each took a child, and Junius went off to a beloved but long since suspended pastime of exploring old Philadelphia, whereas Mattie embarked once more on her social adventures. It is true that Mattie accompanied by brown Virginia could not move quite as freely as when with Angela. But her maternal instincts were sound; her children, their feelings and their faith in her meant much more than the pleasure which she would have been first to call unnecessary and silly. As it happened the children themselves quite unconsciously solved the dilemma; Virginia found shopping tiring and stupid, Angela returned from her father's adventuring worn and bored. Gradually the rule was formed that Angela accompanied her mother and Virginia her father.

On such fortuities does life depend. Little Angela Murray, hurrying through Saturday morning's scrubbing of steps in order that she might have her bath at one and be with her mother on Chestnut Street at two, never realized that her mother took her pleasure among all these pale people because it was there that she happened to find it. It never occurred to her that the delight which her mother obviously showed in meeting friends on Sunday morning when the whole united Murray family came out of church was the same as she showed on Chestnut Street the previous Saturday, because she was finding the qualities which her heart craved, bustle,

6. A famous department store, now closed.

excitement and fashion. The daughter could not guess that if the economic status or the racial genius of colored people had permitted them to run modish hotels or vast and popular department stores her mother would have been there. She drew for herself certain clearly formed conclusions which her subconscious mind thus codified:

First, that the great rewards of life—riches, glamour, pleasure,—are for white-skinned people only. Secondly, that Junius and Virginia were denied these privileges because they were dark; here her reasoning bore at least an element of verisimilitude but she missed the essential fact that her father and sister did not care for this type of pleasure. The effect of her fallaciousness was to cause her to feel a faint pity for her unfortunate relatives and also to feel that colored people were to be considered fortunate only in the proportion in which they measured up to the physical standards of white people.

One Saturday excursion left a far-reaching impression. Mrs. Murray and Angela had spent a successful and interesting afternoon. They had browsed among the contents of the small exclusive shops in Walnut Street; they had had soda at Adams' on Broad Street and they were standing finally in the portico of the Walton Hotel deciding with fashionable and idle elegance what they should do next. A thin stream of people constantly passing threw an occasional glance at the quietly modish pair, the well-dressed, assured woman and the refined and no less assured daughter. The door-man knew them; it was one of Mrs. Murray's pleasures to proffer him a small tip, much appreciated since it was uncalled for. This was the atmosphere which she loved. Angela had put on her gloves and was waiting for her mother, who was drawing on her own with great care, when she glimpsed in the laughing, hurrying Saturday throng the figures of her father and of Virginia. They were close enough for her mother, who saw them too, to touch them by merely descending a few steps and stretching out her arm. In a second the pair had vanished. Angela saw her mother's face change— with trepidation she thought. She remarked: "It's a good thing Papa didn't see us, you'd have had to speak to him, wouldn't you?" But her mother, giving her a distracted glance, made no reply.

That night, after the girls were in bed, Mattie, perched on the arm of her husband's chair, told him about it. "I was at my old game of play-acting again today, June, passing you know, and darling, you and Virginia went by within arm's reach and we never spoke to you. I'm so ashamed."

But Junius consoled her. Long before their marriage he had known of his Mattie's weakness and its essential harmlessness. "My dear girl, I told you long ago that where no principle was involved, your passing means nothing to me. It's just a little joke; I don't think you'd be ashamed to acknowledge your old husband anywhere if it were necessary."

"I'd do that if people were mistaking me for a queen," she assured him fondly. But she was silent, not quite satisfied. "After all," she said with her charming frankness, "it isn't you, dear, who make me feel guilty. I really am ashamed to think that I let Virginia pass by without a word. I think I should feel very badly if she were to know it. I don't believe I'll ever let myself be quite as silly as that again."

But of this determination Angela, dreaming excitedly of Saturdays spent

in turning her small olive face firmly away from peering black countenances was, unhappily, unaware.

CHAPTER II [SUNDAYS]

Saturday came to be the day of the week for Angela, but her sister Virginia preferred Sundays. She loved the atmosphere of golden sanctity
which seemed to hover with a sweet glory about the stodgy, shabby little
dwelling. Usually she came downstairs first so as to enjoy by herself the
blessed "Sunday feeling" which, she used to declare, would have made it
possible for her to recognize the day if she had awakened to it even in
China. She was only twelve at this time, yet she had already developed a
singular aptitude and liking for the care of the home, and this her mother
gratefully fostered. Gradually the custom was formed of turning over to her
small hands all the duties of Sunday morning; they were to her a ritual.
First the kettle must be started boiling, then the pavement swept. Her father's paper must be carried up and left outside his door. Virginia found a
nameless and sweet satisfaction in performing these services.

She prepared the Sunday breakfast which was always the same,—bacon
and eggs, strong coffee with good cream for Junius, chocolate for the other
three and muffins. After the kettle had boiled and the muffins were mixed
it took exactly half an hour to complete preparations. Virginia always went
about these matters in the same way. She set the muffins in the oven, purs-
ing her lips and frowning a little just as she had seen her mother do; then
she went to the foot of the narrow, enclosed staircase and called "hoo-hoo"
with a soft rising inflection,—"last call to dinner," her father termed it. And
finally, just for those last few minutes before the family descended she went
into the box of a parlor and played hymns, old-fashioned and stately
tunes,—"How firm a foundation," "The spacious firmament on high,"
"Am I a soldier of the Cross." Her father's inflexible bass, booming down
the stairs, her mother's faint alto in thirds mingled with her own sweet treble; a shaft of sunlight, faint and watery in winter, strong and golden in
summer, shimmering through the room in the morning dusk completed
for the little girl a sensation of happiness which lay perilously near tears.

After breakfast came the bustle of preparing for church. Junius of course
had come down in complete readiness; but the others must change their
dresses; Virginia had mislaid her Sunday hair-ribbon again; Angela had discovered a rip in her best gloves and could not be induced to go down until
it had been mended. "Wait for me just a minute, Jinny dear, I can't go out
looking like this, can I?" She did not like going to church, at least not to
their church, but she did care about her appearance and she liked the lux-
uriousness of being "dressed up" on two successive days. At last the little
procession filed out, Mattie hoping that they would not be late, she did
hate it so; Angela thinking that this was a stupid way to spend Sunday and
wondering at just what period of one's life existence began to shape itself as
you wanted it. Her father's thoughts were inchoate; expressed they would
have revealed a patriarchal aspect almost biblical. He had been a poor boy,
homeless, a nobody, yet somehow he had contrived in his mid-forties to

attain to the status of a respectable citizen, house-owner, a good provider. He possessed a charming wife and two fine daughters, and as was befitting he was accompanying them to the house of the Lord. As for Virginia, no one to see her in her little red hat and her mother's cut-over blue coat could have divined how near she was to bursting with happiness. Father, mother and children, well-dressed, well-fed, united, going to church on a beautiful Sunday morning; there was an immense cosmic rightness about all this which she sensed rather than realized. She envied no one the incident of finer clothes or a larger home; this unity was the core of happiness, all other satisfactions must radiate from this one; greater happiness could be only a matter of degree but never of essence. When she grew up she meant to live the same kind of life; she would marry a man exactly like her father and she would conduct her home exactly as did her mother. Only she would pray very hard every day for five children, two boys and two girls and then a last little one,—it was hard for her to decide whether this should be a boy or a girl,—which should stay small for a long, long time. And on Sundays they would all go to church.

Intent on her dreaming she rarely heard the sermon. It was different with the hymns, for they constituted the main part of the service for her father, and she meant to play them again for him later in the happy, golden afternoon or the gray dusk of early evening. But first there were acquaintances to greet, friends of her parents who called them by their first names and who, in speaking of Virginia and Angela still said: "And these are the babies; my, how they grow! It doesn't seem as though it could be you, Mattie Ford, grown up and with children!"

On Communion Sundays the service was very late, and Angela would grow restless and twist about in her seat, but the younger girl loved the sudden, mystic hush which seemed to descend on the congregation. Her mother's sweetly merry face took on a certain childish solemnity, her father's stern profile softened into beatific expectancy. In the exquisite diction of the sacramental service there were certain words, certain phrases that almost made the child faint; the minister had a faint burr in his voice and somehow this lent a peculiar underlying resonance to his intonation; he half spoke, half chanted and when, picking up the wafer he began "For in the night" and then broke it, Virginia could have cried out with the ecstasy which filled her. She felt that those who partook of the bread and wine were somehow transfigured; her mother and father wore an expression of ineffable content as they returned to their seats and there was one woman, a middle-aged, mischief-making person, who returned from taking the sacrament, walking down the aisle, her hands clasped loosely in front of her and her face so absolutely uplifted that Virginia used to hasten to get within earshot of her after the church was dismissed, sure that her first words must savor of something mystic and holy. But her assumption proved always to be ill-founded.

The afternoon and the evening repeated the morning's charm but in a different key. Usually a few acquaintances dropped in; the parlor and dining-room were full for an hour or more of pleasant, harmless chatter. Mr. Henson, the policeman, a tall, yellow man with freckles on his nose and red "bad hair" would clap Mr. Murray on the back and exclaim "I tell you what, June,"—which always seemed to Virginia a remarkably daring way in which to address her tall, dignified father. Matthew Henson, a boy of sixteen, would inevitably be hovering about Angela who found him insufferably boresome and made no effort to hide her ennui. Mrs. Murray passed around rather hard cookies and delicious currant wine, talking stitches and patterns meanwhile with two or three friends of her youth with a frequent injection of "Mame, do you remember!"

Presently the house, emptied of all but the family, grew still again, dusk and the lamp light across the street alternately paneling the walls. Mrs. Murray murmured something about fixing a bite to eat, "I'll leave it in the kitchen if anybody wants it." Angela reflected aloud that she had still to get her Algebra or History or French as the case might be, but nobody moved. What they were really waiting for was for Virginia to start to play and finally she would cross the narrow absurdity of a room and stretching out her slim, brown hands would begin her version, a glorified one, of the hymns which they had sung in church that morning, and then the old favorites which she had played before breakfast. Even Angela, somewhat remote and difficult at first, fell into this evening mood and asked for a special tune or a repetition: "I like the way you play that, Jinny." For an hour or more they were as close and united as it is possible for a family to be.

At eight o'clock or thereabouts Junius said exactly as though it had not been in his thoughts all evening: "Play the 'Dying Christian,'[7] daughter." And Virginia, her treble sounding very childish and shrill against her father's deep, unyielding bass, began Pope's masterpiece on the death of a true believer. The magnificently solemn words: "Vital spark of heavenly flame," the strangely appropriate minor music filled the little house with an awesome beauty which was almost palpable. It affected Angela so that in sheer self-defence she would go out in the kitchen and eat her share of the cold supper set by her mother. But Mattie, although she never sang this piece, remained while her husband and daughter sang on. Death triumphant and mighty had no fears for her. It was inevitable, she knew, but she would never have to face it alone. When her husband died, she would die too, she was sure of it; and if death came to her first it would be only a little while before Junius would be there stretching out his hand and guiding her through all the rough, strange places just as years ago, when he had been a coachman to the actress for whom she worked, he had stretched out his good, honest hand and had saved her from a dangerous and equivocal position. She wiped away happy and grateful tears.

"The world recedes, it disappears," sang Virginia. But it made no difference how far it drifted away as long as the four of them were together; and they would always be together, her father and mother and she and Angela. With her visual mind she saw them proceeding endlessly through space; there were her parents, arm in arm, and she and—but tonight and other nights she could not see Angela; it grieved her to lose sight thus of her sister, she knew she must be there, but grope as she might she could not find her. And then quite suddenly Angela was there again, but a different Angela, not quite the same as in the beginning of the picture.

And suddenly she realized that she was doing four things at once and

---

7. "The Dying Christian to His Soul," by Alexander Pope (1688–1744).

each of them with all the intentness which she could muster; she was singing, she was playing, she was searching for Angela and she was grieving
because Angela as she knew her was lost forever.

"Oh Death, oh Death, where is thy sting!" the hymn ended triumphantly,—she and the piano as usual came out a little ahead of Junius
which was always funny. She said, "Where's Angela?" and knew what the
answer would be. "I'm tired, mummy! I guess I'll go to bed."

"You ought to, you got up so early and you've been going all day."

Kissing her parents good-night she mounted the stairs languidly, her
whole being pervaded with the fervid yet delicate rapture of the day.

1929

ALAIN LOCKE
1886–1954

The importance to the Harlem Renaissance of the March 1925 special issue of the
Survey Graphic, a national magazine devoted to sociology and social work, is hard
to overestimate. Paul Kellogg, editor of the magazine, had decided to devote that
entire number to the question of race and black New York. As special editor for this
project he chose Alain Locke, who subtitled the issue *Harlem: Mecca of the New
Negro* and imaginatively included a wide variety of articles, poems, stories, and
other pieces by writers such as Du Bois, James Weldon Johnson, Countee Cullen,
Langston Hughes, Claude McKay, Angelina Grimké, and Anne Spencer. The special issue was an extraordinary success. Eight months later, Locke brought out *The
New Negro*, an anthology including most of what had appeared in the *Survey
Graphic* (much of it revised) along with a good deal of new material, including
stunning artwork depicting blacks by the Bavarian artist Winold Reiss. Serving as a
coherent and articulate announcement of a new spirit among black Americans,
The New Negro was virtually the central text of the Harlem Renaissance.

The only son of a couple who belonged solidly to the black elite of Philadelphia,
Alain Locke excelled at Central High School and later (1902–04) at the Philadelphia School of Pedagogy, where his father taught. He then entered Harvard, from
which he graduated magna cum laude three years later, in 1907. In that year, he
became the first black American to be awarded a Rhodes scholarship (he remained
the only one for some sixty years). He earned a degree at Oxford in 1910, then spent
a year studying philosophy at the University of Berlin. In 1912, he returned to the
United States to begin teaching English, philosophy, and education at Howard
University. From 1916 to 1917, he worked to complete his doctoral thesis at Harvard, after which he became the chair of the philosophy department at Howard.
Except for a few months spent elsewhere, he remained at Howard for the rest of his
life.

Aside from *The New Negro*, Locke also edited *Plays of Negro Life* (1927, with
Montgomery Gregory), *Four Negro Poets* (1927), *The Negro in Art: A Pictorial Record of the Negro Artist and of the Negro Theme in Art* (1940), and *When Peoples
Meet, a Study in Race and Culture Contacts* (1942, with Bernhard J. Stern). But
perhaps more important than his own literary accomplishments was his influence
on the younger Harlem intellectuals. With remarkable skill and devotion, he directed their energies, helped them to be published, and put several of them (such
as Hughes, Hurston, and McKay) into contact with patrons—notably Mrs. Char-

lotte Osgood Mason, a wealthy, elderly white woman who provided financial and moral support for several struggling artists.

Locke died before completing what he considered to be his life's work—a comprehensive study of black American culture. (However, with the guidelines and the materials he left at his death, Margaret Just Butcher was able to publish *The Negro in American Culture* in 1956.) An indefatigable proponent of the role of art as a bridge between individuals and cultures, Locke was one of the most influential of the contemporary champions of the Harlem Renaissance. Although he clashed eventually with various people—including Toomer, McKay, and Hughes (over matters that range from changes in their texts made without permission to, in Hughes's case, personal betrayal)—perhaps no other senior intellectual matched his zeal in personally meeting and encouraging younger artists or his learning and cosmopolitanism in illuminating the question of race, notably where African American culture is concerned.

The New Negro

In the last decade something beyond the watch and guard of statistics has happened in the life of the American Negro and the three norns[1] who have traditionally presided over the Negro problem have a changeling in their laps. The Sociologist, the Philanthropist, the Race-leader are not unaware of the New Negro, but they are at a loss to account for him. He simply cannot be swathed in their formulæ. For the younger generation is vibrant with a new psychology; the new spirit is awake in the masses, and under the very eyes of the professional observers is transforming what has been a perennial problem into the progressive phases of contemporary Negro life.

Could such a metamorphosis have taken place as suddenly as it has appeared to? The answer is no; not because the New Negro is not here, but because the Old Negro had long become more of a myth than a man. The Old Negro, we must remember, was a creature of moral debate and historical controversy. His has been a stock figure perpetuated as an historical fiction partly in innocent sentimentalism, partly in deliberate reactionism. The Negro himself has contributed his share to this through a sort of protective social mimicry forced upon him by the adverse circumstances of dependence. So for generations in the mind of America, the Negro has been more of a formula than a human being—a something to be argued about, condemned or defended, to be "kept down," or "in his place," or "helped up," to be worried with or worried over, harassed or patronized, a social bogey or a social burden. The thinking Negro even has been induced to share this same general attitude, to focus his attention on controversial issues, to see himself in the distorted perspective of a social problem. His shadow, so to speak, has been more real to him than his personality. Through having had to appeal from the unjust stereotypes of his oppressors and traducers to those of his liberators, friends and benefactors he has had to subscribe to the traditional positions from which his case has been viewed. Little true social or self-understanding has or could come from such a situation.

1. The three fates in Norse mythology.

But while the minds of most of us, black and white, have thus burrowed in the trenches of the Civil War and Reconstruction, the actual march of development has simply flanked these positions, necessitating a sudden re-orientation of view. We have not been watching in the right direction; set North and South on a sectional axis, we have not noticed the East till the sun has us blinking.

Recall how suddenly the Negro spirituals revealed themselves; suppressed for generations under the stereotypes of Wesleyan hymn[2] harmony, secretive, half-ashamed, until the courage of being natural brought them out—and behold, there was folk-music. Similarly the mind of the Negro seems suddenly to have slipped from under the tyranny of social intimidation and to be shaking off the psychology of imitation and implied inferiority. By shedding the old chrysalis of the Negro problem we are achieving something like a spiritual emancipation. Until recently, lacking self-understanding, we have been almost as much of a problem to ourselves as we still are to others. But the decade[3] that found us with a problem has left us with only a task. The multitude perhaps feels as yet only a strange relief and a new vague urge, but the thinking few know that in the reaction the vital inner grip of prejudice has been broken.

With this renewed self-respect and self-dependence, the life of the Negro community is bound to enter a new dynamic phase, the buoyancy from within compensating for whatever pressure there may be of conditions from without. The migrant masses, shifting from countryside to city, hurdle several generations of experience at a leap, but more important, the same thing happens spiritually in the life-attitudes and self-expression of the Young Negro, in his poetry, his art, his education and his new outlook, with the additional advantage, of course, of the poise and greater certainty of knowing what it is all about. From this comes the promise and warrant of a new leadership. As one of them[4] has discerningly put it:

> We have tomorrow
> Bright before us
> Like a flame.
>
> Yesterday, a night-gone thing
> A sun-down name.
>
> And dawn today
> Broad arch above the road we came.
> We march!

This is what, even more than any "most creditable record of fifty years of freedom," requires that the Negro of today be seen through other than the dusty spectacles of past controversy. The day of "aunties," "uncles" and "mammies" is equally gone. Uncle Tom and Sambo have passed on, and even the "Colonel" and "George"[5] play barnstorm roles from which they

---

2. After Charles Wesley (1707–1788), English hymnist and brother of John Wesley, founder of Methodism.
3. The 1920s.

4. Langston Hughes (1902–1967). The following lines are from *Youth*.
5. Typical forms of interracial address during slavery and segregation.

escape with relief when the public spotlight is off. The popular melodrama has about played itself out, and it is time to scrap the fictions, garret the bogeys and settle down to a realistic facing of facts.

First we must observe some of the changes which since the traditional lines of opinion were drawn have rendered these quite obsolete. A main change has been, of course, that shifting of the Negro population which has made the Negro problem no longer exclusively or even predominantly Southern. Why should our minds remain sectionalized, when the problem itself no longer is? Then the trend of migration has not only been toward the North and the Central Midwest, but city-ward and to the great centers of industry—the problems of adjustment are new, practical, local and not peculiarly racial. Rather they are an integral part of the large industrial and social problems of our present-day democracy. And finally, with the Negro rapidly in process of class differentiation, if it ever was warrantable to regard and treat the Negro *en masse* it is becoming with every day less possible, more unjust and more ridiculous.

In the very process of being transplanted, the Negro is becoming transformed.

The tide of Negro migration, northward and city-ward, is not to be fully explained as a blind flood started by the demands of war industry coupled with the shutting off of foreign migration, or by the pressure of poor crops coupled with increased social terrorism in certain sections of the South and Southwest. Neither labor demand, the bollweevil[6] nor the Ku Klux Klan is a basic factor, however contributory any or all of them may have been. The wash and rush of this human tide on the beach line of the northern city centers is to be explained primarily in terms of a new vision of opportunity, of social and economic freedom, of a spirit to seize, even in the face of an extortionate and heavy toll, a chance for the improvement of conditions. With each successive wave of it, the movement of the Negro becomes more and more a mass movement toward the larger and the more democratic chance—in the Negro's case a deliberate flight not only from countryside to city, but from medieval America to modern.

Take Harlem as an instance of this. Here in Manhattan is not merely the largest Negro community in the world, but the first concentration in history of so many diverse elements of Negro life. It has attracted the African, the West Indian, the Negro American; has brought together the Negro of the North and the Negro of the South; the man from the city and the man from the town and village; the peasant, the student, the business man, the professional man, artist, poet, musician, adventurer and worker, preacher and criminal, exploiter and social outcast. Each group has come with its own separate motives and for its own special ends, but their greatest experience has been the finding of one another. Proscription and prejudice have thrown these dissimilar elements into a common area of contact and interaction. Within this area, race sympathy and unity have determined a further fusing of sentiment and experience. So what began in terms of segregation becomes more and more, as its elements mix and react, the laboratory of a great race-welding. Hitherto, it must be admitted that Amer-

---

6. A snout beetle notorious for destroying cotton crops.

ican Negroes have been a race more in name than in fact, or to be exact, more in sentiment than in experience. The chief bond between them has been that of a common condition rather than a common consciousness; a problem in common rather than a life in common. In Harlem, Negro life is seizing upon its first chances for group expression and self-determination. It is—or promises at least to be—a race capital. That is why our comparison is taken with those nascent centers of folk-expression and self-determination which are playing a creative part in the world today. Without pretense to their political significance, Harlem has the same role to play for the New Negro as Dublin has had for the New Ireland or Prague for the New Czechoslovakia.

Harlem, I grant you, isn't typical—but it is significant, it is prophetic. No sane observer, however sympathetic to the new trend, would contend that the great masses are articulate as yet, but they stir, they move, they are more than physically restless. The challenge of the new intellectuals among them is clear enough—the "race radicals" and realists who have broken with the old epoch of philanthropic guidance, sentimental appeal and protest. But are we after all only reading into the stirrings of a sleeping giant the dreams of an agitator? The answer is in the migrating peasant. It is the "man farthest down" who is most active in getting up. One of the most characteristic symptoms of this is the professional man, himself migrating to recapture his constituency after a vain effort to maintain in some Southern corner what for years back seemed an established living and clientele. The clergyman following his errant flock, the physician or lawyer trailing his clients, supply the true clues. In a real sense it is the rank and file who are leading, and the leaders who are following. A transformed and transforming psychology permeates the masses.

When the racial leaders of twenty years ago spoke of developing racepride and stimulating race-consciousness, and of the desirability of race solidarity, they could not in any accurate degree have anticipated the abrupt feeling that has surged up and now pervades the awakened centers. Some of the recognized Negro leaders and a powerful section of white opinion identified with "race work" of the older order have indeed attempted to discount this feeling as a "passing phase," an attack of "race nerves" so to speak, an "aftermath of the war," and the like. It has not abated, however, if we are to gauge by the present tone and temper of the Negro press, or by the shift in popular support from the officially recognized and orthodox spokesmen to those of the independent, popular, and often radical type who are unmistakable symptoms of a new order. It is a social disservice to blunt the fact that the Negro of the Northern centers has reached a stage where tutelage, even of the most interested and well-intentioned sort, must give place to new relationships, where positive self-direction must be reckoned with in ever increasing measure. The American mind must reckon with a fundamentally changed Negro.

The Negro too, for his part, has idols of the tribe to smash. If on the one hand the white man has erred in making the Negro appear to be that which would excuse or extenuate his treatment of him, the Negro, in turn, has too often unnecessarily excused himself because of the way he has been treated. The intelligent Negro of today is resolved not to make discrimina-

tion an extenuation for his shortcomings in performance, individual or collective; he is trying to hold himself at par, neither inflated by sentimental
allowances nor depreciated by current social discounts. For this he must
know himself and be known for precisely what he is, and for that reason he
welcomes the new scientific rather than the old sentimental interest. Sentimental interest in the Negro has ebbed. We used to lament this as the falling off of our friends; now we rejoice and pray to be delivered both from
self-pity and condescension. The mind of each racial group has had a bitter
weaning, apathy or hatred on one side matching disillusionment or resentment on the other; but they face each other today with the possibility at
least of entirely new mutual attitudes.

It does not follow that if the Negro were better known, he would be better liked or better treated. But mutual understanding is basic for any subsequent cooperation and adjustment. The effort toward this will at least have
the effect of remedying in large part what has been the most unsatisfactory
feature of our present stage of race relationships in America, namely the
fact that the more intelligent and representative elements of the two race
groups have at so many points got quite out of vital touch with one another.

The fiction is that the life of the races is separate, and increasingly so.
The fact is that they have touched too closely at the unfavorable and too
lightly at the favorable levels.

While inter-racial councils have sprung up in the South, drawing on forward elements of both races, in the Northern cities manual laborers may
brush elbows in their everyday work, but the community and business leaders have experienced no such interplay or far too little of it. These segments
must achieve contact or the race situation in America becomes desperate.
Fortunately this is happening. There is a growing realization that in social
effort the cooperative basis must supplant long-distance philanthropy, and
that the only safeguard for mass relations in the future must be provided in
the carefully maintained contacts of the enlightened minorities of both
race groups. In the intellectual realm a renewed and keen curiosity is replacing the recent apathy; the Negro is being carefully studied, not just
talked about and discussed. In art and letters, instead of being wholly
caricatured, he is being seriously portrayed and painted.

To all of this the New Negro is keenly responsive as an augury of a new
democracy in American culture. He is contributing his share to the new
social understanding. But the desire to be understood would never in itself
have been sufficient to have opened so completely the protectively closed
portals of the thinking Negro's mind. There is still too much possibility of
being snubbed or patronized for that. It was rather the necessity for fuller,
truer self-expression, the realization of the unwisdom of allowing social discrimination to segregate him mentally, and a counter-attitude to cramp
and fetter his own living—and so the "spite-wall" that the intellectuals built
over the "color-line" has happily been taken down. Much of this reopening
of intellectual contacts has centered in New York and has been richly fruitful not merely in the enlarging of personal experience, but in the definite
enrichment of American art and letters and in the clarifying of our common vision of the social tasks ahead.

The particular significance in the re-establishment of contact between the more advanced and representative classes is that it promises to offset some of the unfavorable reactions of the past, or at least to re-surface race contacts somewhat for the future. Subtly the conditions that are molding a New Negro are molding a new American attitude.

However, this new phase of things is delicate; it will call for less charity but more justice; less help, but infinitely closer understanding. This is indeed a critical stage of race relationships because of the likelihood, if the new temper is not understood, of engendering sharp group antagonism and a second crop of more calculated prejudice. In some quarters, it has already done so. Having weaned the Negro, public opinion cannot continue to paternalize. The Negro today is inevitably moving forward under the control largely of his own objectives. What are these objectives? Those of his outer life are happily already well and finally formulated, for they are none other than the ideals of American institutions and democracy. Those of his inner life are yet in process of formation, for the new psychology at present is more of a consensus of feeling than of opinion, of attitude rather than of program. Still some points seem to have crystallized.

Up to the present one may adequately describe the Negro's "inner objectives" as an attempt to repair a damaged group psychology and reshape a warped social perspective. Their realization has required a new mentality for the American Negro. And as it matures we begin to see its effects; at first, negative, iconoclastic, and then positive and constructive. In this new group psychology we note the lapse of sentimental appeal, then the development of a more positive self-respect and self-reliance; the repudiation of social dependence, and then the gradual recovery from hyper-sensitiveness and "touchy" nerves, the repudiation of the double standard of judgment with its special philanthropic allowances and then the sturdier desire for objective and scientific appraisal; and finally the rise from social disillusionment to race pride, from the sense of social debt to the responsibilities of social contribution, and offsetting the necessary working and common-sense acceptance of restricted conditions, the belief in ultimate esteem and recognition. Therefore the Negro today wishes to be known for what he is, even in his faults and shortcomings, and scorns a craven and precarious survival at the price of seeming to be what he is not. He resents being spoken of as a social ward or minor, even by his own, and to being regarded a chronic patient for the sociological clinic, the sick man of American Democracy. For the same reasons, he himself is through with those social nostrums and panaceas, the so-called "solutions" of his "problem," with which he and the country have been so liberally dosed in the past. Religion, freedom, education, money—in turn, he has ardently hoped for and peculiarly trusted these things; he still believes in them, but not in blind trust that they alone will solve his life-problem.

Each generation, however, will have its creed, and that of the present is the belief in the efficacy of collective effort, in race cooperation. This deep feeling of race is at present the mainspring of Negro life. It seems to be the outcome of the reaction to proscription and prejudice; an attempt, fairly successful on the whole, to convert a defensive into an offensive position, a handicap into an incentive. It is radical in tone, but not in purpose and only the most stupid forms of opposition, misunderstanding or persecution could make it otherwise. Of course, the thinking Negro has shifted a little toward the left with the world-trend, and there is an increasing group who affiliate with radical and liberal movements. But fundamentally for the present the Negro is radical on race matters, conservative on others, in other words, a "forced radical," a social protestant rather than a genuine radical. Yet under further pressure and injustice iconoclastic thought and motives will inevitably increase. Harlem's quixotic radicalisms call for their ounce of democracy today lest tomorrow they be beyond cure.

The Negro mind reaches out as yet to nothing but American wants, American ideas. But this forced attempt to build his Americanism on race values is a unique social experiment, and its ultimate success is impossible except through the fullest sharing of American culture and institutions. There should be no delusion about this. American nerves in sections unstrung with race hysteria are often fed the opiate that the trend of Negro advance is wholly separatist, and that the effect of its operation will be to encyst the Negro as a benign foreign body in the body politic. This cannot be—even if it were desirable. The racialism of the Negro is no limitation or reservation with respect to American life; it is only a constructive effort to build the obstructions in the stream of his progress into an efficient dam of social energy and power. Democracy itself is obstructed and stagnated to the extent that any of its channels are closed. Indeed they cannot be selectively closed. So the choice is not between one way for the Negro and another way for the rest, but between American institutions frustrated on the one hand and American ideals progressively fulfilled and realized on the other.

There is, of course, a warrantably comfortable feeling in being on the right side of the country's professed ideals. We realize that we cannot be undone without America's undoing. It is within the gamut of this attitude that the thinking Negro faces America, but with variations of mood that are if anything more significant than the attitude itself. Sometimes we have it taken with the defiant ironic challenge of McKay:[7]

> Mine is the future grinding down to-day
> Like a great landslip moving to the sea,
> Bearing its freight of débris far away
> Where the green hungry waters restlessly
> Heave mammoth pyramids, and break and roar
> Their eerie challenge to the crumbling shore.

Sometimes, perhaps more frequently as yet, it is taken in the fervent and almost filial appeal and counsel of Weldon Johnson's:

> O Southland, dear Southland!
> Then why do you still cling
> To an idle age and a musty page,
> To a dead and useless thing?[8]

7. Claude McKay (1889–1948), Harlem Renais-   8. From O Southland! (1907).
sance poet.

But between defiance and appeal, midway almost between cynicism and
hope, the prevailing mind stands in the mood of the same author's *To
America*,[9] an attitude of sober query and stoical challenge:

> How would you have us, as we are?
>   Or sinking 'neath the load we bear,
> Our eyes fixed forward on a star,
>   Or gazing empty at despair?
>
> Rising or falling? Men or things?
>   With dragging pace or footsteps fleet?
> Strong, willing sinews in your wings,
>   Or tightening chains about your feet?

More and more, however, an intelligent realization of the great discrepancy between the American social creed and the American social practice
forces upon the Negro the taking of the moral advantage that is his. Only
the steadying and sobering effect of a truly characteristic gentleness of spirit
prevents the rapid rise of a definite cynicism and counter-hate and a defiant
superiority feeling. Human as this reaction would be, the majority still deprecate its advent, and would gladly see it forestalled by the speedy amelioration of its causes. We wish our race pride to be a healthier, more positive
achievement than a feeling based upon a realization of the shortcomings of
others. But all paths toward the attainment of a sound social attitude have
been difficult; only a relatively few enlightened minds have been able as
the phrase puts it "to rise above" prejudice. The ordinary man has had
until recently only a hard choice between the alternatives of supine and
humiliating submission and stimulating but hurtful counter-prejudice.
Fortunately from some inner, desperate resourcefulness has recently
sprung up the simple expedient of fighting prejudice by mental passive resistance, in other words by trying to ignore it. For the few, this manna may
perhaps be effective, but the masses cannot thrive upon it.

Fortunately there are constructive channels opening out into which the
balked social feelings of the American Negro can flow freely.

Without them there would be much more pressure and danger than
there is. These compensating interests are racial but in a new and enlarged
way. One is the consciousness of acting as the advance-guard of the African
peoples in their contact with Twentieth Century civilization; the other, the
sense of a mission of rehabilitating the race in world esteem from that loss
of prestige for which the fate and conditions of slavery have so largely been
responsible. Harlem, as we shall see, is the center of both these movements; she is the home of the Negro's "Zionism."[1] The pulse of the Negro
world has begun to beat in Harlem. A Negro newspaper carrying news material in English, French and Spanish, gathered from all quarters of America, the West Indies and Africa has maintained itself in Harlem for over five
years. Two important magazines,[2] both edited from New York, maintain
their news and circulation consistently on a cosmopolitan scale. Under

---

9. Published in 1917.
1. An international movement aimed at securing a

homeland for the Jewish people.
2. Probably *Opportunity* and the *Crisis*.

American auspices and backing, three pan-African congresses have been held abroad for the discussion of common interests, colonial questions and the future cooperative development of Africa. In terms of the race question as a world problem, the Negro mind has leapt, so to speak, upon the parapets of prejudice and extended its cramped horizons. In so doing it has linked up with the growing group consciousness of the dark-peoples and is gradually learning their common interests. As one of our writers has recently put it: "It is imperative that we understand the white world in its relations to the non-white world." As with the Jew, persecution is making the Negro international.

As a world phenomenon this wider race consciousness is a different thing from the much asserted rising tide of color. Its inevitable causes are not of our making. The consequences are not necessarily damaging to the best interests of civilization. Whether it actually brings into being new Armadas of conflict or argosies[3] of cultural exchange and enlightenment can only be decided by the attitude of the dominant races in an era of critical change. With the American Negro, his new internationalism is primarily an effort to recapture contact with the scattered peoples of African derivation. Garveyism[4] may be a transient, if spectacular, phenomenon, but the possible role of the American Negro in the future development of Africa is one of the most constructive and universally helpful missions that any modern people can lay claim to.

Constructive participation in such causes cannot help giving the Negro valuable group incentives, as well as increased prestige at home and abroad. Our greatest rehabilitation may possibly come through such channels, but for the present, more immediate hope rests in the revaluation by white and black alike of the Negro in terms of his artistic endowments and cultural contributions, past and prospective. It must be increasingly recognized that the Negro has already made very substantial contributions, not only in his folk-art, music especially, which has always found appreciation, but in larger, though humbler and less acknowledged ways. For generations the Negro has been the peasant matrix of that section of America which has most undervalued him, and here he has contributed not only materially in labor and in social patience, but spiritually as well. The South has unconsciously absorbed the gift of his folk-temperament. In less than half a generation it will be easier to recognize this, but the fact remains that a leaven of humor, sentiment, imagination and tropic nonchalance has gone into the making of the South from a humble, unacknowledged source. A second crop of the Negro's gifts promises still more largely. He now becomes a conscious contributor and lays aside the status of a beneficiary and ward for that of a collaborator and participant in American civilization. The great social gain in this is the releasing of our talented group from the arid fields of controversy and debate to the productive fields of creative expression. The especially cultural recognition they win should in turn prove the key to that revaluation of the Negro which must precede or accompany any considerable further betterment of race relationships. But

3. Merchant ships. "Armadas": fleets of warships.
4. The Back to Africa movement of Marcus Garvey (1887–1940).

whatever the general effect, the present generation will have added the motives of self-expression and spiritual development to the old and still unfinished task of making material headway and progress. No one who
understandingly faces the situation with its substantial accomplishment or
views the new scene with its still more abundant promise can be entirely
without hope. And certainly, if in our lifetime the Negro should not be able
to celebrate his full initiation into American democracy, he can at least, on
the warrant of these things, celebrate the attainment of a significant and
satisfying new phase of group development, and with it a spiritual Coming
of Age.

1925

GEORGIA DOUGLAS JOHNSON
1886–1966

Although she never lived in Harlem, Georgia Douglas Johnson was almost universally regarded as the foremost poet among the women of the Harlem Renaissance
as well as among the most beloved because of her unstinting encouragement of the
younger writers, male and female. Johnson, a shy child, grew up in Rome, Georgia,
and Atlanta, where she was a favorite among her teachers. At the Atlanta University
Normal School, she overcame her loneliness by educating herself in the field of
music. She regarded the university as a haven and regretted having to leave it after
her graduation.

Douglas then taught in Marietta, Georgia, served as an assistant school principal
in Atlanta, and studied music at the Oberlin Conservatory and the Cleveland College of Music. She also wrote verse, but it was not until her marriage to Henry
Lincoln Johnson in 1903 that she began submitting poetry and short fiction to
newspapers and magazines. In 1910, the Johnsons moved to Washington, D.C.,
where Henry (a prominent Republican) was appointed recorder of deeds by President Taft in 1912. The Johnsons made their home (known as Halfway House) a
gathering place for black intellectuals in the capital. In 1918, Georgia Johnson published her first book, a slim collection of poems titled *The Heart of a Woman*. Despite praise from the best-known African American critic of poetry, William Stanley
Braithwaite, a number of readers took Johnson to task for her apparent lack of concern for the theme of race. In 1922, she responded with *Bronze: A Book of Verse*.
Dedicated entirely to racial themes, this volume enjoyed a friendlier critical reception. However, her main interest as a poet was clearly in romantic, sentimental, and
brief commentaries on the human condition.

After her husband's death in 1925, and partly in appreciation of his service to the
Republican Party, Calvin Coolidge appointed Johnson commissioner of conciliation in the Department of Labor. In 1928, she published her third volume of verse,
An Autumn Love Cycle, in which she returned to her favorite subject, the role of
love in the lives of women. In the years that followed, the energetic Johnson wrote
numerous short stories (many were never published), several well-received plays,
and four newspaper columns: *Homely Philosophy*, *Wise Sayings*, *Beauty Hints*, and
a column of interracial news for the *New York Amsterdam News*. For a while, she
even sponsored a lonely hearts club, to help people meet one another in the hope
of finding love. Her last book, *Share My World*, a small collection of poems, was

privately published in 1962. In 1965, Atlanta University conferred on her an honorary doctoral degree.

Although Johnson sometimes regretted that she never had either the time or the money to finish the many projects that were so important to her, she was nevertheless one of the most prolific writers of the Harlem Renaissance and one of its more memorable personalities.

The Heart of a Woman

The heart of a woman goes forth with the dawn,
As a lone bird, soft winging, so restlessly on,
Afar o'er life's turrets and vales does it roam
In the wake of those echoes the heart calls home.

The heart of a woman falls back with the night,   5
And enters some alien cage in its plight,
And tries to forget it has dreamed of the stars,
While it breaks, breaks, breaks on the sheltering bars.

                                                        1918

Youth

The dew is on the grasses, dear,
    The blush is on the rose,
And swift across our dial-youth,[1]
    A shifting shadow goes.

The primrose moments, lush with bliss,   5
    Exhale and fade away,
Life may renew the Autumn time,
    But nevermore the May!

                                                        1918

My Little Dreams

I'm folding up my little dreams
Within my heart tonight,
And praying I may soon forget
The torture of their sight.

For Time's deft fingers scroll my brow   5
With fell[2] relentless art—
I'm folding up my little dreams
Tonight, within my heart!

                                                        1918

1. I.e., sundial.   2. Cruel.

Lost Illusions

Oh, for the veils of my far away youth,
Shielding my heart from the blaze of the truth,
Why did I stray from their shelter and grow
Into the sadness that follows—to know!

Impotent atom[3] with desolate gaze   5
Threading the tumult of hazardous ways—
Oh, for the veils, for the veils of my youth
Veils that hung low o'er the blaze of the truth!

1922

I Want to Die While You Love Me[4]

I want to die while you love me,
    While yet you hold me fair,
While laughter lies upon my lips
    And lights are in my hair.

I want to die while you love me,   5
    And bear to that still bed,
Your kisses turbulent, unspent,
    To warm me when I'm dead.

I want to die while you love me,
    Oh, who would care to live   10
Till love has nothing more to ask
    And nothing more to give!

I want to die while you love me
    And never, never see
The glory of this perfect day   15
    Grow dim or cease to be.

1927

3. Puny individual.
4. Set to music (sung by Harry Burleigh for Victor Records), the poem became a popular song.

MARCUS GARVEY

1887–1940

Marcus Garvey, whose name continues to evoke the glorious "Back to Africa" slogan
with which it is inextricably linked, was easily the most controversial figure associated with Harlem in the 1920s. A hero to millions of blacks, he was scorned by
many of their other leaders and intellectuals. W. E. B. Du Bois clashed openly with
Garvey over basic questions of leadership; and even Wallace Thurman, who professed to admire him, once described Garvey as "composed of charlatan, moun-

tebank, saviour and fool." Many people who admired Garvey for his seemingly inexhaustible energy and vision were bewildered by his flamboyance and his equally apparent lack of business sense. No one can deny, however, that Garvey was a profound human force during the Harlem Renaissance, a mighty shaper of attitudes and molder of opinions concerning the rights and destiny of black Americans.

Born in St. Ann's Bay, Jamaica, Marcus Garvey had to quit school at the age of fourteen to help support his family. He found work as a printer's apprentice in Kingston, the capital of Jamaica. Moved by the economic and social inequities he saw all around him, he helped to lead a printer's union strike in 1907. Three years later, he founded *Garvey's Watchman*, a periodical that quickly failed. He moved on to Costa Rica, where, as a time keeper on a banana plantation, he indignantly witnessed the exploitation of black laborers by their lighter-skinned taskmasters. Further travels in Central America convinced him that wherever whites and blacks were found together, the whites were sure to be exploiting the blacks—a situation he was determined to change. In 1912, he traveled to London. While there, he read Booker T. Washington's *Up From Slavery* (1901), which changed his life. According to Garvey, after reading Washington's text he asked himself: " 'Where is the black man's government?' 'Where is his King and his kingdom?' 'Where is his president, his country, and his ambassador, his army, his navy, his men of big affairs?' I could not find them, and then I declared, 'I will help to make them.' "

With something approaching religious fervor, he returned to Jamaica in 1914. Later that year, he founded one of the most important organizations of the twentieth century, the Universal Negro Improvement Association (UNIA). Its principal objective, "the general uplift of the Negro peoples of the world," was identified at first with Garvey's struggle to provide Jamaicans with schools modeled on Washington's Tuskegee Institute in Alabama. Frustrated by his failure during the next two years to make progress toward his goals, Garvey traveled to the United States to raise money. Arriving in Harlem in 1916, he quickly decided to remain there. Within four years, he commanded a larger following than any other black leader in America. Much of the extraordinary growth of the UNIA is attributable to the success of *Negro World*, the weekly newspaper that Garvey founded in 1918 and in which many of his speeches and essays (usually brief) appeared. At one point, *Negro World* probably enjoyed a circulation of nearly a quarter million readers—although most statistics relating to the UNIA are impossible to verify.

The UNIA reached the zenith of its prestige and influence in 1920, with a remarkable international convention in Harlem. After the convention, which attracted some twenty-five thousand delegates, even Garvey's most hostile critics could no longer dismiss him as a marginal demagogue.

The tide began to turn, however, with the failure of one of Garvey's pet projects, the Black Star Line. The shipping line, for which the UNIA raised well over $500,000, had the threefold objective of making a profit, employing blacks in the important positions denied them in the traditionally white shipping industry, and serving as an economic means of transportation for blacks interested in escaping white oppression by moving to Africa, particularly to Liberia. But the line was a fiasco almost from its inception in 1919. By 1922, despite Garvey's attempts to raise money for it through a mail campaign, the Black Star Line was past saving. Garvey was arrested on a federal charge of mail fraud that same year and convicted in 1925. Sentenced to a five-year prison term, he served nearly three years before he was deported to Jamaica in 1927.

Garvey spent the remainder of his life vainly attempting to recover the prestige that he and the UNIA had lost. Ironically, opposed by the major colonial powers, he died in 1940 (of a stroke) without ever having set foot in Africa. Even after his death, the UNIA continued to plan for racial "uplift."

Marcus Garvey's achievement is difficult to evaluate. Despite his lack of organization, his occasional meetings with the Ku Klux Klan, who shared his racially exclusive views of society, and his failure to achieve many of his long-term goals, his gospel of race pride and race solidarity (key themes of the Harlem Renaissance) endures as a sustaining force in black cultures throughout the world.

Africa for the Africans

For five years the Universal Negro Improvement Association[1] has been advocating the cause of Africa for the Africans—that is, that the Negro peoples of the world should concentrate upon the object of building up for themselves a great nation in Africa.

When we started our propaganda toward this end several of the so-called intellectual Negroes who have been bamboozling the race for over half a century said that we were crazy, that the Negro peoples of the western world were not interested in Africa and could not live in Africa. One editor and leader went so far as to say at his so-called Pan-African Congress[2] that American Negroes could not live in Africa, because the climate was too hot. All kinds of arguments have been adduced by these Negro intellectuals against the colonization of Africa by the black race. Some said that the black man would ultimately work out his existence alongside of the white man in countries founded and established by the latter. Therefore, it was not necessary for Negroes to seek an independent nationality of their own. The old time stories of "African fever," "African bad climate," "African mosquitos," "African savages," have been repeated by these "brainless intellectuals" of ours as a scare against our people in America and the West Indies taking a kindly interest in the new program of building a racial empire of our own in our Motherland. Now that years have rolled by and the Universal Negro Improvement Association has made the circuit of the world with its propaganda, we find eminent statesmen and leaders of the white race coming out boldly advocating the cause of colonizing Africa with the Negroes of the western world. A year ago Senator MacCullum[3] of the Mississippi Legislature introduced a resolution in the House for the purpose of petitioning the Congress of the United States of America and the President to use their good influence in securing from the Allies sufficient territory in Africa in liquidation of the war debt, which territory should be used for the establishing of an independent nation for American Negroes. About the same time Senator France[4] of Maryland gave expression to a similar desire in the Senate of the United States. During a speech on the "Soldiers' Bonus," he said: "We owe a big debt to Africa and one which we have too long ignored. I need not enlarge upon our peculiar interest in the obligation to the people of Africa. Thousands of Americans have for years been contributing to the missionary work which has been carried out by the noble men and women who have been sent out in that field by the churches of America."

1. Founded by Garvey in 1916 with "the general uplift of the Negro peoples of the world" as its main objective.
2. W. E. B. Du Bois (1868–1963) organized the congress in 1919.

3. T. G. MacCallum, state senator for Mississippi (1932–36).
4. Joseph Irwin France (1873–1939), U.S. senator from 1917 to 1923.

Germany to the Front

This reveals a real change on the part of prominent statesmen in their attitude on the African question. Then comes another suggestion from Germany, for which Dr. Heinrich Schnee, a former Governor [5] of German East Africa, is author. This German statesman suggests in an interview given out in Berlin, and published in New York, that America takes over the mandatories of Great Britain and France in Africa for the colonization of American Negros. Speaking on the matter, he says, "As regards the attempt to colonize Africa with the surplus American colored population, this would in a long way settle the vexed problem, and under the plan such as Senator France has outlined, might enable France and Great Britain to discharge their duties to the United States, and simultaneously ease the burden of German reparations which is paralyzing economic life."

With expressions as above quoted from prominent world statesmen, and from the demands made by such men as Senators France and MacCullum, it is clear that the question of African nationality is not a farfetched one, but is as reasonable and feasible as was the idea of an American nationality.

A "Program" at Last

I trust that the Negro peoples of the world are now convinced that the work of the Universal Negro Improvement Association is not a visionary one, but very practical, and that it is not so far fetched, but can be realized in a short while if the entire race will only co-operate and work toward the desired end. Now that the work of our organization has started to bear fruit we find that some of these "doubting Thomases" of three and four years ago are endeavoring to mix themselves up with the popular idea of rehabilitating Africa in the interest of the Negro. They are now advancing spurious "programs" and in a short while will endeavor to force themselves upon the public as advocates and leaders of the African idea.

It is felt that those who have followed the career of the Universal Negro Improvement Association will not allow themselves to be deceived by these Negro opportunists who have always sought to live off the ideas of other people.

The Dream of a Negro Empire

It is only a question of a few more years when Africa will be completely colonized by Negroes, as Europe is by the white race. What we want is an independent African nationality, and if America is to help the Negro peoples of the world establish such a nationality, then we welcome the assistance.

It is hoped that when the time comes for American and West Indian Negroes to settle in Africa, they will realize their responsibility and their duty. It will not be to go to Africa for the purpose of exercising an overlordship over the natives, but it shall be the purpose of the Universal Negro Improvement Association to have established in Africa that brotherly co-

5. From 1912 to 1918.

operation which will make the interests of the African native and the American and West Indian Negro one and the same, that is to say, we shall enter into a common partnership to build up Africa in the interests of our race.

Oneness of Interests

Everybody knows that there is absolutely no difference between the native African and the American and West Indian Negroes, in that we are descendants from one common family stock. It is only a matter of accident that we have been divided and kept apart for over three hundred years, but it is felt that when the time has come for us to get back together, we shall do so in the spirit of brotherly love, and any Negro who expects that he will be assisted here, there or anywhere by the Universal Negro Improvement Association to exercise a haughty superiority over the fellows of his own race, makes a tremendous mistake. Such men had better remain where they are and not attempt to become in any way interested in the higher development of Africa.

The Negro has had enough of the vaunted practice of race superiority as inflicted upon him by others, therefore he is not prepared to tolerate a similar assumption on the part of his own people. In America and the West Indies, we have Negroes who believe themselves so much above their fellows as to cause them to think that any readjustment in the affairs of the race should be placed in their hands for them to exercise a kind of an autocratic and despotic control as others have done to us for centuries. Again I say, it would be advisable for such Negroes to take their hands and minds off the now popular idea of colonizing Africa in the interest of the Negro race, because their being identified with this new program will not in any way help us because of the existing feeling among Negroes everywhere not to tolerate the infliction of race or class superiority upon them, as is the desire of the self-appointed and self-created race leadership that we have been having for the last fifty years.

The Basis of an African Aristocracy

The masses of Negroes in America, the West Indies, South and Central America are in sympathetic accord with the aspirations of the native Africans. We desire to help them build up Africa as a Negro Empire, where every black man, whether he was born in Africa or in the Western world, will have the opportunity to develop on his own lines under the protection of the most favorable democratic institutions.

It will be useless, as before stated, for bombastic Negroes to leave America and the West Indies to go to Africa, thinking that they will have privileged positions to inflict upon the race that bastard aristocracy that they have tried to maintain in this Western world at the expense of the masses. Africa shall develop an aristocracy of its own, but it shall be based upon service and loyalty to race. Let all Negroes work toward that end. I feel that it is only a question of a few more years before our program will be accepted not only by the few statesmen of America who are now interested in it, but by the strong statesmen of the world, as the only solution to the great race problem. There is no other way to avoid the threatening war of the races that is bound to engulf all mankind, which has been prophesied by the world's greatest thinkers; there is no better method than by apportioning every race to its own habitat.

The time has really come for the Asiatics to govern themselves in Asia, as the Europeans are in Europe and the Western world, so also is it wise for the Africans to govern themselves at home, and thereby bring peace and satisfaction to the entire human family.

1923

The Future as I See It

It comes to the individual, the race, the nation, once in a life-time to decide upon the course to be pursued as a career. The hour has now struck for the individual Negro as well as the entire race to decide the course that will be pursued in the interest of our own liberty.

We who make up the Universal Negro Improvement Association have decided that we shall go forward, upward and onward toward the great goal of human liberty. We have determined among ourselves that all barriers placed in the way of our progress must be removed, must be cleared away for we desire to see the light of a brighter day.

The Negro Is Ready

The Universal Negro Improvement Association for five years has been proclaiming to the world the readiness of the Negro to carve out a pathway for himself in the course of life. Men of other races and nations have become alarmed at this attitude of the Negro in his desire to do things for himself and by himself. This alarm has become so universal that organizations have been brought into being here, there and everywhere for the purpose of deterring and obstructing this forward move of our race. Propaganda has been waged here, there and everywhere for the purpose of misinterpreting the intention of this organization; some have said that this organization seeks to create discord and discontent among the races; some say we are organized for the purpose of hating other people. Every sensible, sane and honest-minded person knows that the Universal Negro Improvement Association has no such intention. We are organized for the absolute purpose of bettering our condition, industrially, commercially, socially, religiously and politically. We are organized not to hate other men, but to lift ourselves, and to demand respect of all humanity. We have a program that we believe to be righteous; we believe it to be just, and we have made up our minds to lay down ourselves on the altar of sacrifice for the realization of this great hope of ours, based upon the foundation of righteousness. We declare to the world that Africa must be free, that the entire Negro race must be emancipated from industrial bondage, peonage and serfdom; we make no compromise, we make no apology in this our declaration. We do not desire to create offense on the part of other races, but we are determined that we shall be heard, that we shall be given the rights to which we are entitled.

The Propaganda of Our Enemies

For the purpose of creating doubts about the work of the Universal Negro Improvement Association, many attempts have been made to cast shadow and gloom over our work. They[1] have even written the most uncharitable things about our organization; they have spoken so unkindly of our effort, but what do we care? They spoke unkindly and uncharitably about all the reform movements that have helped in the betterment of humanity. They maligned the great movement of the Christian religion; they maligned the great liberation movements of America, of France, of England, of Russia; can we expect, then, to escape being maligned in this, our desire for the liberation of Africa and the freedom of four hundred million Negroes of the world?

We have unscrupulous men and organizations working in opposition to us. Some trying to capitalize the new spirit that has come to the Negro to make profit out of it to their own selfish benefit; some are trying to set back the Negro from seeing the hope of his own liberty, and thereby poisoning our people's mind against the motives of our organization; but every sensible far-seeing Negro in this enlightened age knows what propaganda means. It is the medium of discrediting that which you are opposed to, so that the propaganda of our enemies will be of little avail as soon as we are rendered able to carry to our peoples scattered throughout the world the true message of our great organization.

"Crocodiles" as Friends

Men of the Negro race, let me say to you that a greater future is in store for us; we have no cause to lose hope, to become faint-hearted. We must realize that upon ourselves depend our destiny, our future; we must carve out that future, that destiny, and we who make up the Universal Negro Improvement Association have pledged ourselves that nothing in the world shall stand in our way, nothing in the world shall discourage us, but opposition shall make us work harder, shall bring us closer together so that as one man the millions of us will march on toward that goal that we have set for ourselves. The new Negro shall not be deceived. The new Negro refuses to take advice from anyone who has not felt with him, and suffered with him. We have suffered for three hundred years, therefore we feel that the time has come when only those who have suffered with us can interpret our feelings and our spirit. It takes the slave to interpret the feelings of the slave; it takes the unfortunate man to interpret the spirit of his unfortunate brother; and so it takes the suffering Negro to interpret the spirit of his comrade. It is strange that so many people are interested in the Negro now, willing to advise him how to act, and what organizations he should join, yet nobody was interested in the Negro to the extent of not making him a slave

---

1. I.e., Garvey's opponents such as W. E. B. Du Bois.

for two hundred and fifty years, reducing him to industrial peonage and serfdom after he was freed; it is strange that the same people can be so interested in the Negro now, as to tell him what organization he should follow and what leader he should support.

Whilst we are bordering on a future of brighter things, we are also at our danger period, when we must either accept the right philosophy, or go down by following deceptive propaganda which has hemmed us in for many centuries.

Deceiving the People

There is many a leader of our race who tells us that everything is well, and that all things will work out themselves and that a better day is coming. Yes, all of us know that a better day is coming; we all know that one day we will go home to Paradise, but whilst we are hoping by our Christian virtues to have an entry into Paradise we also realize that we are living on earth, and that the things that are practiced in Paradise are not practiced here. You have to treat this world as the world treats you; we are living in a temporal, material age, an age of activity, an age of racial, national selfishness. What else can you expect but to give back to the world what the world gives to you, and we are calling upon the four hundred million Negroes of the world to take a decided stand, a determined stand, that we shall occupy a firm position; that position shall be an emancipated race and a free nation of our own. We are determined that we shall have a free country; we are determined that we shall have a flag; we are determined that we shall have a government second to none in the world.

An Eye for an Eye

Men may spurn the idea, they may scoff at it; the metropolitan press of this country may deride us; yes, white men may laugh at the idea of Negroes talking about government; but let me tell you there is going to be a government, and let me say to you also that whatsoever you give, in like measure it shall be returned to you.[2] The world is sinful, and therefore man believes in the doctrine of an eye for an eye, a tooth for a tooth.[3] Everybody believes that revenge is God's,[4] but at the same time we are men, and revenge sometimes springs up, even in the most Christian heart.

Why should man write down a history that will react against him? Why should man perpetrate deeds of wickedness upon his brother which will return to him in like measure? Yes, the Germans maltreated the French in the Franco-Prussian war of 1870, but the French got even with the Germans in 1918. It is history, and history will repeat itself. Beat the Negro, brutalize the Negro, kill the Negro, burn the Negro, imprison the Negro, scoff at the Negro, deride the Negro, it may come back to you one of these fine days, because the supreme destiny of man is in the hands of God. God

2. "For with the same measure that ye mete withal it shall be measured to you again" (Luke 6:38).
3. "Ye have heard that it hath been said, An eye for an eye, and a tooth for a tooth" (Matthew 5:38).
4. "To me belongeth vengeance, and recompence" (Deuteronomy 32:35).

is no respecter of persons, whether that person be white, yellow or black. Today the one race is up, tomorrow it has fallen; today the Negro seems to be the footstool of the other races and nations of the world; tomorrow the Negro may occupy the highest rung of the great human ladder.

But, when we come to consider the history of man, was not the Negro a power, was he not great once? Yes, honest students of history can recall the day when Egypt, Ethiopia and Timbuctoo towered in their civilizations, towered above Europe, towered above Asia. When Europe was inhabited by a race of cannibals, a race of savages, naked men, heathens and pagans, Africa was peopled with a race of cultured black men, who were masters in art, science and literature; men who were cultured and refined; men who, it was said, were like the gods. Even the great poets of old sang in beautiful sonnets of the delight it afforded the gods to be in companionship with the Ethiopians. Why, then, should we lose hope? Black men, you were once great; you shall be great again. Lose not courage, lose not faith, go forward. The thing to do is to get organized; keep separated and you will be exploited, you will be robbed, you will be killed. Get organized, and you will compel the world to respect you. If the world fails to give you consideration, because you are black men, because you are Negroes, four hundred millions of you shall, through organization, shake the pillars of the universe and bring down creation, even as Samson brought down the temple upon his head and upon the heads of the Philistines.[5]

An Inspiring Vision

So Negroes, I say, through the Universal Negro Improvement Association, that there is much to live for. I have a vision of the future, and I see before me a picture of a redeemed Africa, with her dotted cities, with her beautiful civilization, with her millions of happy children, going to and fro. Why should I lose hope, why should I give up and take a back place in this age of progress? Remember that you are men, that God created you Lords of this creation. Lift up yourselves, men, take yourselves out of the mire and hitch your hopes to the stars; yes, rise as high as the very stars themselves. Let no man pull you down, let no man destroy your ambition, because man is but your companion, your equal; man is your brother; he is not your lord; he is not your sovereign master.

We of the Universal Negro Improvement Association feel happy; we are cheerful. Let them connive to destroy us; let them organize to destroy us; we shall fight the more. Ask me personally the cause of my success, and I say opposition; oppose me, and I fight the more, and if you want to find out the sterling worth of the Negro, oppose him, and under the leadership of the Universal Negro Improvement Association he shall fight his way to victory, and in the days to come, and I believe not far distant, Africa shall reflect a splendid demonstration of the worth of the Negro, of the determination of the Negro, to set himself free and to establish a government of his own.

1923

5. Judges 16:29–30.

CLAUDE McKAY
1889–1948

Often regarded as the first major poet of the Harlem Renaissance, Claude McKay probably did more than anyone else to shape the trends that would later define that literary movement. More than any other writer of his time, he was able to satisfy and even inspire two major groups of black readers. Many African Americans were attracted to his poetry by its frequently explosive condemnations of bigotry and oppression, written invariably and ironically in such traditional poetic forms as the sonnet, McKay's favorite. Other readers, more easily moved by poetry in the genteel tradition, were also satisfied, even as they were often introduced at the same time to the power of race-conscious verse. These two groups sometimes seemed irreconcilable. Had it not been for McKay, they might have remained so in the renaissance. He helped to uncover some of the unifying principles underlying the major conflicting themes of the writers of the Harlem Renaissance.

Born September 15, 1889, Festus Claudius McKay was the youngest of the eleven children of Thomas and Ann McKay, members of the peasant class in Jamaica. McKay was raised in Sunny Ville, in Clarendon Parish, by a compassionate mother and a stern father who did his best to pass on to his children elements of the customs and traditions of the Ashanti, the West African people from whom he was descended, at least as he understood those customs and traditions. Repeatedly sharing with his children the story of his own father's enslavement by whites, Thomas McKay sought to instill in his offspring a suspicion of whites that would become particularly evident in his son Claude's writing. Other impressions from McKay's childhood that left an indelible mark on his literary productions include his profound respect for the sense of community he encountered among rural Jamaican farmers and a somewhat skeptical attitude toward religion encouraged by his older brother Uriah Theophilus, an elementary-school teacher.

At seventeen, McKay received government sponsorship to become an apprentice to a wheelwright and cabinetmaker in Brown's Town. At nineteen, he moved to Kingston (Jamaica's capital) and served as a police constable for less than a year before his sympathy for the criminals, whom he often considered the victims of an unjust colonial order, led him to return to Clarendon Parish. During the two years that followed, he was encouraged to write poetry in the Jamaican dialect by his most important mentor, Walter Jekyll, an English collector of island folklore with whom McKay had forged a close relationship. In 1912, Jekyll helped him to publish two books of poetry: *Songs of Jamaica* (with an introduction by Jekyll and melodies for six selections in an appendix) and *Constab Ballads*. *Songs of Jamaica* is primarily a celebration of the Jamaican peasants, with their relative freedom from bigotry; *Constab Ballads* centers more on Kingston and the contempt and exploitation encountered there by dark-skinned blacks at the hands of whites and mulattos. The books were respected enough for McKay to become the first black to receive the medal of the Jamaican Institute of Arts and Sciences, which came with a substantial cash award.

McKay, determined to use the prize money to finance an education at Booker T. Washington's Tuskegee Institute in Alabama, arrived in the United States in 1912, but he departed from Tuskegee in frustration at local conditions two months after his arrival. He went on to study agricultural science for two years at Kansas State College before he decided to resume his career as a writer. He left for Harlem.

Supporting himself at first as a waiter and a porter, McKay familiarized himself with the New York literary scene. He was soon befriended by such important white figures as the famed poet Edward Arlington Robinson and Waldo Frank, a Jewish radical novelist and cultural critic. His first break came in 1917, when Frank published two of his sonnets, *The Harlem Dancer* and *Invocation*, in the December issue of *The Seven Arts*, a highly respected avant-garde magazine. Short story writer Frank Harris, who published several of McKay's poems in *Pearson's*, another magazine, seems also to have made a major impression on the young poet. Unlike later black writers, McKay did not rely primarily on such periodicals as the *Crisis* and *Opportunity* as outlets for his verse. Though he wrote for black magazines on occasion, his most enduring literary ties were with white publications, particularly with the leftist magazines based in Greenwich Village. Indeed, Max Eastman, the dean of the American literary left in the early twentieth century, published McKay's *The Dominant White* in the April 1919 issue of *The Liberator* and nine more of his poems in the July issue. McKay later served on Eastman's editorial staff, contributing essays and reviews as well as poetry.

In 1919, McKay traveled to England, where he met George Bernard Shaw and worked for a time under Sylvia Pankhurst at *Workers Dreadnought*. C. K. Ogden included nearly two dozen of McKay's poems in the summer 1920 issue of *Cambridge Magazine*; and I. A. Richards, one of the foremost English literary critics of the century, wrote the preface for McKay's third book of verse, *Spring in New Hampshire*. According to Richards, McKay's was among "the best work that the present generation is producing" in Great Britain.

After his return to the United States in 1921, McKay continued to work for and contribute to a number of publications (including his fellow Jamaican Marcus Garvey's *Negro World*, until a political disagreement in 1922 severed their ties). In 1922, he published his most important collection of poetry, *Harlem Shadows*, which, in the opinion of some critics, virtually inaugurated the Harlem Renaissance. According to McKay, the book grew out of his urge to place the militant *If We Must Die*, his most famous poem, "inside of a book." The racial violence that racked America in the summer of 1919 had inspired the sonnet, which later served as one of the unofficial rallying cries of the Allied Forces in World War II, particularly after it was recited by Winston Churchill in a speech against the Nazis. Although the poem offers no internal evidence to suggest that it is about race, McKay had refrained from including it in *Spring in New Hampshire* (which was deeply admired by Countee Cullen and Langston Hughes) because of his express desire to avoid racial themes in that book. *Harlem Shadows*, however, marked a point of no return for several members of the literary set in Harlem, who saw in McKay's masterful treatment of racial issues evidence that a black writer's insights into matters of race could serve on more than an occasional basis as suitable subjects for poetry.

In 1923, in Moscow, McKay addressed the Fourth Congress of the Communist International and, as a black poet sympathetic to the Soviet cause, achieved instant popularity among the proletariat of the U.S.S.R. as well as with Communist Party officials. He was introduced to Trotsky and other leaders, and his poem *Petrograd: May Day, 1923* was published in translation in *Pravda*. Nevertheless, dismayed by the rigid ideological requirements of the Communist Party concerning all artistic productions, and perhaps a little tired of being treated as a novelty in the Soviet Union, he left for a stay of several years in France. While there, he produced his first novel, *Home to Harlem* (1928), and began work on his second, *Banjo*, which he completed during his travels in Spain and Morocco in 1929.

Home to Harlem was the first novel by an African American to become a bestseller. Reprinted five times in two months, it seems to have satisfied a consuming curiosity on the part of Americans for information about the nightlife—and the lowlife—of Harlem. The novel examines two characters, both of whom are seen by most critics as existing mainly for the purpose of taking the reader on a tour of Harlem. Jake is a hedonist who deserts the army to return to his beloved Harlem; he falls in love with a prostitute after she affectionately and surreptitiously returns the money he has paid her. Through Jake, the reader is introduced to Ray, a Haitian intellectual who envies Jake because his own desire to become a writer interferes with his enjoyment of life. Predictably, the stern W. E. B. Du Bois had little patience with McKay's presentation of Harlem. Du Bois declared that the book "for the most part nauseates me, and after the dirtier parts of its filth I feel distinctly like taking a bath." McKay's response was simply to accuse Du Bois of failing to make the proper distinction "between the task of propaganda and the work of art."

Banjo continues the story of Ray by matching him with a cagey version of Jake, nicknamed Banjo. The poor sales of this novel, which is set in Europe, support the argument that the success of *Home to Harlem* was based as much on its racy depiction of Harlem as on its artistic merit. McKay's third novel, *Banana Bottom* (1933), is generally regarded as his finest achievement in fiction. *Banana Bottom* tells the story of a Jamaican peasant girl, Bita Plant, who is rescued by the white missionaries Malcolm and Priscilla Craig after being raped. In taking refuge with the Craigs, however, Bita also becomes their prisoner and has their values (including an education in Britain) foisted on her. They even attempt to arrange her marriage. But Bita escapes and, overcoming the memory of rape, returns to the people in her native town of Jubilee. The critical reception of *Banana Bottom* was warm, but sometimes misguided; some reviewers seemed primarily captivated by its descriptions of lush tropical scenery. Like the rest of McKay's prose, except for *Home to Harlem, Banana Bottom* did not make much of an impression on the reading public of McKay's time. His collection of short stories, *Gingertown* (1932), did not fare any better.

In 1934, McKay returned to Harlem after twelve years of wandering through Europe and North Africa. He completed his autobiography, *A Long Way from Home*, three years later. His last book, a collection of essays titled *Harlem: Negro Metropolis*, followed in 1940. Neither book sold well. Through Ellen Tarry, a friend who wrote children's books, McKay became involved in the activities of Friendship House, a Catholic-sponsored community center in Harlem. Tarry's influence on McKay culminated in his conversion to Roman Catholicism in 1944, after he had moved to Chicago, where he spent the remainder of his life teaching classes at the Catholic Youth Organization.

When McKay died in 1948, the world lost the individual who, according to William Stanley Braithwaite, was possibly "the keystone of the new movement in racial poetic achievement." Unlike Countee Cullen, the other great figure of the Harlem Renaissance who treated racial themes in conventional poetic forms, Claude McKay was not at all concerned with living up to the intellectual, political, or social expectations of Du Bois or Alain Locke. In fact, he once referred to Locke's anthology, *The New Negro*, as a "remarkable chocolate soufflé of art and politics." Concerned with political consequences, McKay was a worker for social change; and subtle though his poetry indisputably is on some levels, he believed strongly that too many black poets had hidden behind lofty standards of poetic refinement to keep from offending white readers. He refused to mask his impatience with racism in this way. He managed to use traditional poetic forms as satisfying vehicles for the expression of that impatience; but at the same time, McKay refused to allow social relevance to become an excuse for the production of inferior art. McKay was a courageous thinker and writer who prized his intimate knowledge of all classes of people. His work rings with an authority and authenticity matched by that of few of his contemporaries.

Harlem Shadows

I hear the halting footsteps of a lass
   In Negro Harlem when the night lets fall
Its veil. I see the shapes of girls who pass
   To bend and barter at desire's call.
Ah, little dark girls who in slippered feet   5
Go prowling through the night from street to street!

Through the long night until the silver break
   Of day the little gray feet know no rest;
Through the lone night until the last snow-flake
   Has dropped from heaven upon the earth's white breast,   10
The dusky, half-clad girls of tired feet
Are trudging, thinly shod, from street to street.

Ah, stern harsh world, that in the wretched way
   Of poverty, dishonor and disgrace,
Has pushed the timid little feet of clay,   15
   The sacred brown feet of my fallen race!
Ah, heart of me, the weary, weary feet
In Harlem wandering from street to street.

                       1918

If We Must Die[1]

If we must die, let it not be like hogs
Hunted and penned in an inglorious spot,
While round us bark the mad and hungry dogs,
Making their mock at our accursed lot.
If we must die, O let us nobly die,   5
So that our precious blood may not be shed
In vain; then even the monsters we defy
Shall be constrained to honor us though dead!
O kinsmen! we must meet the common foe!
Though far outnumbered let us show us brave,   10
And for their thousand blows deal one deathblow!
What though before us lies the open grave?
Like men we'll face the murderous, cowardly pack,
Pressed to the wall, dying, but fighting back!

                       1919

To the White Fiends

   Think you I am not fiend and savage too?
   Think you I could not arm me with a gun
   And shoot down ten of you for every one

1. Written following the "Red Summer" of 1919, when antiblack riots broke out in several cities, notably Chicago. McKay later denied that the poem referred to blacks and whites specifically.

Of my black brothers murdered, burnt by you?
Be not deceived, for every deed you do   5
I could match—out-match: am I not Afric's son,
Black of that black land where black deeds are done?
But the Almighty from the darkness drew
My soul and said: Even thou shalt be a light
Awhile to burn on the benighted earth,   10
Thy dusky face I set among the white
For thee to prove thyself of higher worth;
Before the world is swallowed up in night,
To show thy little lamp: go forth, go forth!

1919

Africa

The sun sought thy dim bed and brought forth light,
The sciences were sucklings at thy breast;
When all the world was young in pregnant night
Thy slaves toiled at thy monumental best.
Thou ancient treasure-land, thou modern prize,   5
New peoples marvel at thy pyramids!
The years roll on, thy sphinx of riddle eyes
Watches the mad world with immobile lids.
The Hebrews humbled them [1] at Pharaoh's name.
Cradle of Power! Yet all things were in vain!   10
Honor and Glory, Arrogance and Fame!
They went. The darkness swallowed thee again.
Thou art the harlot, now thy time is done,
Of all the mighty nations of the sun.

1921

America

Although she feeds me bread of bitterness,
And sinks into my throat her tiger's tooth,
Stealing my breath of life, I will confess
I love this cultured hell that tests my youth!
Her vigor flows like tides into my blood,   5
Giving me strength erect against her hate.
Her bigness sweeps my being like a flood.
Yet as a rebel fronts a king in state,
I stand within her walls with not a shred
Of terror, malice, not a word of jeer.   10
Darkly I gaze into the days ahead,
And see her might and granite wonders there,

---

1. I.e., themselves. According to the Bible, Hebrew bondage in Egypt ended with the exodus led by Moses.

Beneath the touch of Time's unerring hand,
Like priceless treasures sinking in the sand.

1921

My Mother

The dawn departs, the morning is begun,
The Trades[1] come whispering from off the seas,
The fields of corn are golden in the sun,
The dark-brown tassels fluttering in the breeze;
The bell is sounding and children pass,   5
Frog-leaping, skipping, shouting, laughing shrill,
Down the red road, over the pasture-grass,
Up to the schoolhouse crumbling on the hill.
The older folk are at their peaceful toil,
Some pulling up the weeds, some plucking corn,   10
And others breaking up the sun-baked soil.
Float, faintly scented breeze, at early morn
Over the earth where mortals sow and reap—
Beneath its breast my mother lies asleep.

1921

Enslaved

Oh when I think of my long-suffering race,
For weary centuries despised, oppressed,
Enslaved and lynched, denied a human place
In the great life line of the Christian West;
And in the Black Land[2] disinherited,   5
Robbed in the ancient country of its birth,
My heart grows sick with hate, becomes as lead,
For this my race that has no home on earth.
Then from the dark depths of my soul I cry
To the avenging angel to consume   10
The white man's world of wonders utterly:
Let it be swallowed up in earth's vast womb,
Or upward roll as sacrificial smoke
To liberate my people from its yoke!

1921

The White House[3]

Your door is shut against my tightened face,
And I am sharp as steel with discontent;
But I possess the courage and the grace

---

1. I.e., trade winds; the easterly winds that predominate in the tropics and subtropics of the world.
2. Africa.

3. In *A Long Way from Home* (1937), McKay insisted that the title of this poem did not refer to the official residence of the U.S. president.

To bear my anger proudly and unbent.
The pavement slabs burn loose beneath my feet,   5
A chafing savage, down the decent street;
And passion rends my vitals as I pass,
Where boldly shines your shuttered door of glass.
Oh, I must search for wisdom every hour,
Deep in my wrathful bosom sore and raw,   10
And find in it the superhuman power
To hold me to the letter of your law!
Oh, I must keep my heart inviolate
Against the potent poison of your hate.

                                                    1922

Outcast

For the dim regions whence my fathers came
My spirit, bondaged by the body, longs.
Words felt, but never heard, my lips would frame;
My soul would sing forgotten jungle songs.
I would go back to darkness and to peace,   5
But the great western world holds me in fee,[4]
And I may never hope for full release
While to its alien gods I bend my knee.
Something in me is lost, forever lost,
Some vital thing has gone out of my heart,   10
And I must walk the way of life a ghost
Among the sons of earth, a thing apart;
For I was born, far from my native clime,
Under the white man's menace, out of time.

                                                    1922

St. Isaac's Church, Petrograd[5]

Bow down my soul in worship very low
And in the holy silences be lost.
Bow down before the marble Man of Woe,[6]
Bow down before the singing angel host.
What jewelled glory fills my spirit's eye,   5
What golden grandeur moves the depths of me!
The soaring arches lift me up on high,
Taking my breath with their rare symmetry.

Bow down my soul and let the wondrous light
Of beauty bathe thee from her lofty throne,   10
Bow down before the wonder of man's might.
Bow down in worship, humble and alone,

4. On condition of performing certain services.   (1917–24) and then Leningrad (1924–91).
5. St. Petersburg, Russia, once called Petrograd   6. A statue of Christ.

Bow lowly down before the sacred sight
Of man's Divinity alive in stone.

1925

From Home to Harlem

Chapter XVII. He Also Loved

It was in the winter of 1916 when I first came to New York to hunt for a job. I was broke. I was afraid I would have to pawn my clothes, and it was dreadfully cold. I didn't even know the right way to go about looking for a job. I was always timid about that. For five weeks I had not paid my rent. I was worried, and Ma Lawton, my landlady, was also worried. She had her bills to meet. She was a good-hearted old woman from South Carolina. Her face was all wrinkled and sensitive like finely-carved mahogany.

Every bed-space in the flat was rented. I was living in the small hall bedroom. Ma Lawton asked me to give it up. There were four men sleeping in the front room; two in an old, chipped-enameled brass bed, one on a davenport, and the other in a folding chair. The old lady put a little canvas cot in that same room, gave me a pillow and a heavy quilt, and said I should try and make myself comfortable there until I got work.

The cot was all right for me. Although I hate to share a room with another person and the fellows snoring disturbed my rest. Ma Lawton moved into the little room that I had had, and rented out hers—it was next to the front room—to a man and a woman.

The woman was above ordinary height, chocolate-colored. Her skin was smooth, too smooth, as if it had been pressed and fashioned out for ready sale like chocolate candy. Her hair was straightened out into an Indian Straight after the present style among Negro ladies. She had a mongoose sort of a mouth, with two top front teeth showing. She wore a long mink coat.

The man was darker than the woman. His face was longish, with the right cheek somewhat caved in. It was an interesting face, an attractive, salacious mouth, with the lower lip protruding. He wore a bottle-green peg-top suit, baggy at the hips. His coat hung loose from his shoulders and it was much longer than the prevailing style. He wore also a Mexican hat, and in his breast pocket he carried an Ingersoll watch attached to a heavy gold chain. His name was Jericho Jones, and they called him Jerco for short. And she was Miss Whicher—Rosalind Whicher.

Ma Lawton introduced me to them and said I was broke, and they were both awfully nice to me. They took me to a big feed of corned beef and cabbage at Burrell's on Fifth Avenue. They gave me a good appetizing drink of gin to commence with. And we had beer with the eats; not ordinary beer, either, but real Budweiser, right off the ice.

And as good luck sometimes comes pouring down like a shower, the next day Ma Lawton got me a job in the little free-lunch saloon right under her flat. It wasn't a paying job as far as money goes in New York, but I was glad to have it. I had charge of the free-lunch counter. You know the little

dry crackers that go so well with beer, and the cheese and fish and the potato salad. And I served, besides, spare-ribs and whole boiled potatoes and
corned beef and cabbage for those customers who could afford to pay for a
lunch. I got no wages at all, but I got my eats twice a day. And I made a few
tips, also. For there were about six big black men with plenty of money who
used to eat lunch with us, specially for our spare-ribs and sweet potatoes.
Each one of them gave me a quarter. I made enough to pay Ma Lawton for
my canvas cot.

Strange enough, too, Jerco and Rosalind took a liking to me. And sometimes they came and ate lunch perched up there at the counter, with Rosalind the only woman there, all made up and rubbing her mink coat against
the men. And when they got through eating, Jerco would toss a dollar bill
at me.

We got very friendly, we three. Rosalind would bring up squabs and
canned stuff from the German delicatessen in One Hundred and Twenty-
fifth Street, and sometimes they asked me to dinner in their room and gave
me good liquor.

I thought I was pretty well fixed for such a hard winter. All I had to do as
extra work was keeping the saloon clean. . . .

One afternoon Jerco came into the saloon with a man who looked pretty
near white. Of course, you never can tell for sure about a person's race in
Harlem, nowadays, when there are so many high-yallers floating round—
colored folks that would make Italian and Spanish people look like
Negroes beside them. But I figured out from his way of talking and acting
that the man with Jerco belonged to the white race. They went in through
the family entrance into the back room, which was unusual, for the family
room of a saloon, as you know, is only for women in the business and the
men they bring in there with them. Real men don't sit in a saloon here as
they do at home. I suppose it would be sissified. There's a bar for them to
lean on and drink and joke as long as they feel like.

The boss of the saloon was a little fidgety about Jerco and his friend sitting there in the back. The boss was a short pumpkin-bellied brown man, a
little bald off the forehead. Twice he found something to attend to in the
back room, although there was nothing at all there that wanted attending
to. . . . I felt better, and the boss, too, I guess, when Rosalind came along
and gave the family room its respectable American character. I served
Rosalind a Martini cocktail extra dry, and afterward all three of them, Rosalind, Jerco, and their friend, went up to Ma Lawton's.

The two fellows that slept together were elevator operators in a department store, so they had their Sundays free. On the afternoon of the Sunday
of the same week that the white-looking man had been in the saloon with
Jerco, I went upstairs to change my old shoes—they'd got soaking wet behind the counter—and I found Ma Lawton talking to the two elevator fellows.

The boys had given Ma Lawton notice to quit. They said they couldn't
sleep there comfortably together on account of the goings-on in Rosalind's
room. The fellows were members of the Colored Y. M. C. A. and were
queerly quiet and pious. One of them was studying to be a preacher. They
were the sort of fellows that thought going to cabarets a sin, and that parlor

socials were leading Harlem straight down to hell. They only went to
church affairs themselves. They had been rooming with Ma Lawton for
over a year. She called them her gentlemen lodgers.

Ma Lawton said to me: "Have you heard anything phony outa the next
room, dear?"

"Why, no, Ma," I said, "nothing more unusual than you can hear all
over Harlem. Besides, I work so late, I am dead tired when I turn in to bed,
so I sleep heavy."

"Well, it's the truth I do like that there Jerco an' Rosaline," said Ma Lawton. "They did seem quiet as lambs, although they was always havin' company. But Ise got to speak to them, 'cause I doana wanta lose ma young
mens. . . . But theys a real nice-acting couple. Jerco him treats me like him
was mah son. It's true that they doan work like all poah niggers, but they
pays that rent down good and prompt ehvery week."

Jerco was always bringing in ice-cream and cake or something for Ma
Lawton. He had a way about him, and everybody liked him. He was a sympathetic type. He helped Ma Lawton move beds and commodes and he
fixed her clothes lines. I had heard somebody talking about Jerco in the
saloon, however, saying that he could swing a mean fist when he got his
dander up, and that he had been mixed up in more than one razor cut-up.
He did have a nasty long razor scar on the back of his right hand.

The elevator fellows had never liked Rosalind and Jerco. The one who
was studying to preach Jesus said he felt pretty sure that they were an un-
godly-living couple. He said that late one night he had pointed out their
room to a woman that looked white. He said the woman looked suspicious.
She was perfumed and all powdered up and it appeared as if she didn't
belong among colored people.

"There's no sure telling white from high-yaller these days," I said.
"There are so many swell-looking quadroons and octoroons[1] of the
race."

But the other elevator fellow said that one day in the tenderloin section
he had run up against Rosalind and Jerco together with a petty officer of
marines. And that just put the lid on anything favorable that could be said
about them.

But Ma Lawton said: "Well, Ise got to run mah flat right an' try mah
utmost to please youall, but I ain't wanta dip mah nose too deep in a
lodger's affairs."

Late that night, toward one o'clock, Jerco dropped in at the saloon and
told me that Rosalind was feeling badly. She hadn't eaten a bite all day and
he had come to get a pail of beer, because she had asked specially for
draught beer. Jerco was worried, too.

"I hopes she don't get bad," he said. "For we ain't got a cent o' money.
Wese just in on a streak o' bad luck."

"I guess she'll soon be all right," I said.

The next day after lunch I stole a little time and went up to see Rosalind.
Ma Lawton was just going to attend to her when I let myself in, and she said
to me: "Now the poor woman is sick, poor chile, ahm so glad mah conscience is free and that I hadn't a said nothing evil t' her."

---

1. People of one-fourth and one-eighth African ancestry, respectively.

Rosalind was pretty sick. Ma Lawton said it was the grippe.[2] She gave Rosalind hot whisky drinks and hot milk, and she kept her feet warm with a hot-water bottle. Rosalind's legs were lead-heavy. She had a pain that pinched her side like a pair of pincers. And she cried out for thirst and begged for draught beer.

Ma Lawton said Rosalind ought to have a doctor. "You'd better go an' scares up a white one," she said to Jerco. "Ise nevah had no faith in these heah nigger doctors."

"I don't know how we'll make out without money," Jerco whined. He was sitting in the old Morris chair[3] with his head heavy on his left hand.

"You kain pawn my coat," said Rosalind. "Old man Greenbaum will give you two hundred down without looking at it."

"I won't put a handk'chief o' yourn in the hock shop," said Jerco. "You'll need you' stuff soon as you get better. Specially you' coat. You kain't go anywheres without it."

"S'posin' I don't get up again," Rosalind smiled. But her countenance changed suddenly as she held her side and moaned. Ma Lawton bent over and adjusted the pillows.

Jerco pawned his watch chain and his own overcoat, and called in a Jewish doctor from the upper Eighth Avenue fringe of the Belt.[4] But Rosalind did not improve under medical treatment. She lay there with a sad, tired look, as if she didn't really care what happened to her. Her lower limbs were apparently paralyzed. Jerco told the doctor that she had been sick unto death like that before. The doctor shot a lot of stuff into her system. But Rosalind lay there heavy and fading like a felled tree.

The elevator operators looked in on her. The student one gave her a Bible with a little red ribbon marking the chapter in St. John's Gospel about the woman taken in adultery.[5] He also wanted to pray for her recovery. Jerco wanted the prayer, but Rosalind said no. Her refusal shocked Ma Lawton, who believed in God's word.

The doctor stopped Rosalind from drinking beer. But Jerco slipped it in to her when Ma Lawton was not around. He said he couldn't refuse it to her when beer was the only thing she cared for. He had an expensive sweater. He pawned it. He also pawned their large suitcase. It was real leather and worth a bit of money.

One afternoon Jerco sat alone in the back room of the saloon and began to cry.

"I'd do anything. There ain't anything too low I wouldn't do to raise a little money," he said.

"Why don't you hock Rosalind's fur coat?" I suggested. "That'll give you enough money for a while."

"Gawd, no! I wouldn't touch none o' Rosalind's clothes. I jest kain't," he said. "She'll need them as soon as she's better."

"Well, you might try and find some sort of a job, then," I said.

---

2. Influenza.
3. Popular furniture style designed by English craftsman and poet William Morris (1834–1896).
4. I.e., the black belt, which then extended south to 125th Street.
5. "And the scribes and Pharisees brought unto [Jesus] a woman taken in adultery; and when they had set her in the midst, They say unto him, Master, . . . Moses in the law commanded us, that such should be stoned: but what sayest thou? . . . But Jesus . . . said unto them, He that is without sin among you, let him first cast a stone at her" (John 8:3–7).

"Me find a job? What kain I do? I ain't no good foh no job. I kain't work. I don't know how to ask for no job. I wouldn't know how. I wish I was a woman."

"Good God! Jerco," I said, "I don't see any way out for you but some sort of a job."

"What kain I do? What kain I do?" he whined. "I kain't do nothing. That's why I don't wanta hock Rosalind's fur coat. She'll need it soon as she's better. Rosalind's so wise about picking up good money. Just like that!" He snapped his fingers.

I left Jerco sitting there and went into the saloon to serve a customer a plate of corned beef and cabbage.

After lunch I thought I'd go up to see how Rosalind was making out. The door was slightly open, so I slipped in without knocking. I saw Jerco kneeling down by the open wardrobe and kissing the toe of one of her brown shoes. He started as he saw me, and looked queer kneeling there. It was a high old-fashioned wardrobe that Ma Lawton must have picked up at some sale. Rosalind's coat was hanging there, and it gave me a spooky feeling, for it looked so much more like the real Rosalind than the woman that was dozing there on the bed.

Her other clothes were hanging there, too. There were three gowns—a black silk, a glossy green satin, and a flimsy chiffon-like yellow thing. In a corner of the lowest shelf was a bundle of soiled champagne-colored silk stockings and in the other four pairs of shoes—one black velvet, one white kid, and another gold-finished. Jerco regarded the lot with dog-like affection.

"I wouldn't touch not one of her things until she's better," he said. "I'd sooner hock the shirt off mah back."

Which he was preparing to do. He had three expensive striped silk shirts, presents from Rosalind. He had just taken two out of the wardrobe and the other off his back, and made a parcel of them for old Greenbaum. . . . Rosalind woke up and murmured that she wanted some beer. . . .

A little later Jerco came to the saloon with the pail. He was shivering. His coat collar was turned up and fastened with a safety pin, for he only had an undershirt on.

"I don't know what I'd do if anything happens to Rosalind," he said. "I kain't live without her."

"Oh yes, you can," I said in a not very sympathetic tone. Jerco gave me such a reproachful pathetic look that I was sorry I said it.

The tall big fellow had turned into a scared, trembling baby. "You ought to buck up and hold yourself together," I told him. "Why, you ought to be game if you like Rosalind, and don't let her know you're down in the dumps."

"I'll try," he said. "She don't know how miserable I am. When I hooks up with a woman I treat her right, but I never let her know everything about me. Rosalind is an awful good woman. The straightest woman I ever had, honest."

I gave him a big glass of strong whisky.

Ma Lawton came in the saloon about nine o'clock that evening and said that Rosalind was dead. "I told Jerco we'd have to sell that theah coat to give the poah woman a decent fun'ral, an' he jest brokes down crying like a baby."

That night Ma Lawton slept in the kitchen and put Jerco in her little hall bedroom. He was all broken up. I took him up a pint of whisky.

"I'll nevah find another one like Rosalind," he said, "nevah!" He sat on an old black-framed chair in which a new yellow-varnished bottom had just been put. I put my hand on his shoulder and tried to cheer him up: "Buck up, old man. Never mind, you'll find somebody else." He shook his head. "Perhaps you didn't like the way me and Rosalind was living. But she was one naturally good woman, all good inside her."

I felt foolish and uncomfortable. "I always liked Rosalind, Jerco," I said, "and you, too. You were both awfully good scouts to me. I have nothing against her. I am nothing myself."

Jerco held my hand and whimpered: "Thank you, old top. Youse all right. Youse always been a regular fellar."

It was late, after two a. m. I went to bed. And, as usual, I slept soundly.

Ma Lawton was an early riser. She made excellent coffee and she gave the two elevator runners and another lodger, a porter who worked on Ellis Island, coffee and hot homemade biscuits every morning. The next morning she shook me abruptly out of my sleep.

"Ahm scared to death. Thar's moah tur'ble trouble. I kain't git in the barfroom and the hallway's all messy."

I jumped up, hauled on my pants, and went to the bathroom. A sickening purplish liquid coming from under the door had trickled down the hall toward the kitchen. I took Ma Lawton's rolling-pin and broke through the door.

Jerco had cut his throat and was lying against the bowl of the water-closet. Some empty coke papers[6] were on the floor. And he sprawled there like a great black boar in a mess of blood.

                                                                      1928

Harlem Runs Wild

Docile Harlem went on a rampage last week,[1] smashing stores and looting them and piling up destruction of thousands of dollars worth of goods. But the mass riot in Harlem was not a race riot. A few whites were jostled by colored people in the melee, but there was no manifest hostility between colored and white as such. All night until dawn on the Tuesday of the outbreak white persons, singly and in groups, walked the streets of Harlem without being molested. The action of the police was commendable in the highest degree. The looting was brazen and daring, but the police were restrained. In extreme cases, when they fired, it was into the air. Their restraint saved Harlem from becoming a shambles.

6. Drug paraphernalia. "Water-closet": toilet.
1. On March 19, 1935, Harlem erupted into violence. Bands of blacks, provoked by unprecedented levels of unemployment and racial discrimination, stormed the business places of white merchants. A few people were killed, many injured, and hundreds of thousands of dollars in property damage resulted.

The outbreak was spontaneous. It was directed against the stores exclusively. One Hundred and Twenty-fifth Street is Harlem's main street and the theatrical and shopping center of the colored thousands. Anything that starts there will flash through Harlem as quick as lightning. The alleged beating of a kid caught stealing a trifle[2] in one of the stores merely served to explode the smoldering discontent of the colored people against the Harlem merchants.

It would be too sweeping to assert that radicals incited the Harlem mass to riot and pillage. The *Young Liberators*[3] seized an opportune moment, but the explosion on Tuesday was not the result of Communist propaganda. There were, indeed, months of propaganda in it. But the propagandists are eager to dissociate themselves from Communists. Proudly they declare that they have agitated only in the American constitutional way for fair play for colored Harlem.

Colored people all over the world are notoriously the most exploitable material, and colored Harlem is no exception. The population is gullible to an extreme. And apparently the people are exploited so flagrantly because they invite and take it. It is their gullibility that gives to Harlem so much of its charm, its air of insouciance[4] and gaiety. But the façade of the Harlem masses' happy-go-lucky and hand-to-mouth existence has been badly broken by the Depression. A considerable part of the population can no longer cling even to the hand-to-mouth margin.

Wherever an ethnologically related group of people is exploited by others, the exploiters often operate on the principle of granting certain concessions as sops. In Harlem the exploiting group is overwhelmingly white. And it gives no sops. And so for the past two years colored agitators have exhorted the colored consumers to organize and demand of the white merchants a new deal: that they should employ Negroes as clerks in the colored community. These agitators are crude men, theoretically. They have little understanding of and little interest in the American labor movement, even from the most conservative trade-union angle. They address their audience mainly on the streets. Their following is not so big as that of the cultists and occultists. But it is far larger than that of the Communists.

One of the agitators is outstanding and picturesque. He dresses in turban and gorgeous robe. He has a bigger following than his rivals. He calls himself Sufi Abdul Hamid.[5] His organization is the Negro Industrial and Clerical Alliance. It was the first to start picketing the stores of Harlem demanding clerical employment for colored persons. Sufi Hamid achieved a little success. A few of the smaller Harlem stores engaged colored clerks. But on 125th Street the merchants steadfastly refused to employ colored clerical help. The time came when the Negro Industrial and Clerical Alliance felt strong enough to picket the big stores on 125th Street. At first the movement got scant sympathy from influential Negroes and the Harlem intelligentsia as a whole. Physically and mentally, Sufi Hamid is a different

---

2. Lino Rivera, a black adolescent, was caught stealing a knife from a white-owned store.
3. A radical socialist youth group.
4. Calm indifference.
5. Hamid (d. 1938) had a plan for economic ad-

vancement, encapsulated in the slogan "More Jobs for Negroes: Buy Where You Can Work?", which had met with considerable success in Chicago in 1930.

type. He does not belong. And moreover he used to excoriate the colored newspapers, pointing out that they would not support his demands on the bigger Harlem stores because they were carrying the stores' little ads.

Harlem was excited by the continued picketing and the resultant "incidents." Sufi Hamid won his first big support last spring when one of the most popular young men in Harlem, the Reverend Adam Clayton Powell, Jr. assistant pastor of the Abyssinian Church—the largest in Harlem—went on the picket line on 125th Street. This gesture set all Harlem talking and thinking and made the headlines of the local newspapers. It prompted the formation of a Citizens' League for Fair Play. The league was endorsed and supported by sixty-two organizations, among which were eighteen of the leading churches of Harlem. And at last the local press conceded some support.

One of the big stores capitulated and took on a number of colored clerks. The picketing of other stores was continued. And soon business was not so good as it used to be on 125th Street.

In the midst of the campaign Sufi Hamid was arrested. Sometime before his arrest a committee of Jewish Minute Men[6] had visited the Mayor and complained about an anti-Semitic movement among the colored people and the activities of a black Hitler in Harlem. The *Day* and the *Bulletin*, Jewish newspapers, devoted columns to the Harlem Hitler and anti-Semitism among Negroes. The articles were translated and printed in the Harlem newspapers under big headlines denouncing the black Hitler and his work.

On October 13 of last year Sufi Hamid was brought before the courts charged with disorderly conduct and using invective against the Jews. The witnesses against him were the chairman of the Minute Men and other persons more or less connected with the merchants. After hearing the evidence and defense, the judge decided that the evidence was biased and discharged Sufi Hamid. Meanwhile Sufi Hamid had withdrawn from the Citizens' League for Fair Play. He had to move from his headquarters and his immediate following was greatly diminished. An all-white Harlem Merchants' Association came into existence. Dissension divided the Citizens' League; the prominent members denounced Sufi Hamid and his organization.

In an interview last October Sufi Hamid told me that he had never styled himself the black Hitler. He said that once when he visited a store to ask for the employment of colored clerks, the proprietor remarked, "We are fighting Hitler in Germany." Sufi said that he replied, "We are fighting Hitler in Harlem." He went on to say that although he was a Moslem he had never entertained any prejudices against Jews as Jews. He was an Egyptian[7] and in Egypt the relations between Moslem and Jew were happier than in any other country. He was opposed to Hitlerism, for he had read Hitler's book, *Mein Kampf*,[8] and knew Hitler's attitude and ideas about all colored peoples. Sufi Hamid said that the merchants of Harlem spread the rumor

6. An organization devoted to combatting anti-Jewish activity.
7. Despite his claim, Hamid was an African American.

8. My struggle (German). Adolph Hitler (1889–1945) set forth his views on race, propaganda, politics, and other matters in this book.

of anti-Semitism among the colored people because they did not want to face the issue of giving them a square deal.

The Citizens' League continued picketing, and some stores capitulated. But the Leaguers began quarreling among themselves as to whether the clerks employed should be light-skinned or dark-skinned. Meanwhile the united white Harlem Merchants' Association was fighting back. In November the picketing committee was enjoined from picketing by Supreme Court Justice Samuel Rosenman. The court ruled that the Citizen's League was not a labor organization. It was the first time that such a case had come before the courts of New York. The chairman of the picketing committee remarked that "the decision would make trouble in Harlem."

One by one the colored clerks who had been employed in 125th Street stores lost their places. When inquiries were made as to the cause, the managements gave the excuse of slack business. The clerks had no organization behind them. Of the grapevine intrigue and treachery that contributed to the debacle of the movement, who can give the facts? They are as obscure and inscrutable as the composite mind of the Negro race itself. So the masses of Harlem remain disunited and helpless, while their would-be leaders wrangle and scheme and denounce one another to the whites. Each one is ambitious to wear the piebald mantle of Marcus Garvey.[9]

On Tuesday the crowds went crazy like the remnants of a defeated, abandoned, and hungry army. Their rioting was the gesture of despair of a bewildered, baffled, and disillusioned people.

1935

9. The leader of the United Negro Improvement Association (1887–1940).

ZORA NEALE HURSTON
1891–1960

Although all of her books appeared in the 1930s, Zora Neale Hurston was undoubtedly a product of the Harlem Renaissance as well as one of its most extraordinary writers. Some readers first encounter Hurston as a rather disconcerting figure in Langston Hughes's autobiography *The Big Sea* (1940), where Hughes depicts her as a somewhat eccentric, even occasionally bizarre character with the nerve to approach strangers in Harlem and measure their heads as part of an anthropological inquiry. In Wallace Thurman's roman à clef *Infants of the Spring* (1932), she appears as Sweetie Mae Carr, a woman who fundamentally cares nothing about art. For Alice Walker, however, as well as for thousands of Hurston's admirers, she is one of the greatest writers of the century. Walker has declared that if she were relegated to a desert island for the balance of her life with only ten books to sustain her, she "would choose, unhesitatingly, two of Zora's." Walker's choices, *Mules and Men* (1935) and *Their Eyes Were Watching God* (1937), are beyond question two of the finest achievements in African American literature.

Nevertheless, Hurston remains one of the more mysterious figures in that literature. In her autobiography, *Dust Tracks on a Road* (1942), she addressed the matter of her birth itself with characteristic aplomb: "This is all hearsay. Maybe some of the details of my birth as told me might be a little inaccurate, but it is pretty well established that I really did get born." For years, misled by Hurston herself, scholars set the year of her birth as 1901, when in fact she was born a decade earlier, on January 7, 1891. No scholar thus far has been able to account for this lost decade of Hurston's life. She was born and reared in Eatonville, Florida, the first black township to be incorporated in the United States. An extraordinary place by any reckoning, Hurston's hometown takes on an almost mythic quality in her fiction and autobiographical writing. In her view, the absence of whites not only kept Eatonville free of racism but also freed blacks to express themselves without reservation. She was also proud of her father's crucial role as mayor of and lawgiver to the town.

Despite the lively, comic stories of Eatonville, however, Hurston's childhood was far from perfect. Her parents' marriage was marred by tension, not least of all because of her father's many infidelities; and her mother died when Zora was only thirteen. When her father married again, she clashed repeatedly with her stepmother. Apparently, Hurston left school and was shuffled back and forth between relatives. Of the odd jobs she took to support herself in the years that followed, the most important took her away from Eatonville, when she became the personal maid of a kindly white actress in a traveling theatrical troupe. In Baltimore, Hurston left her employer and returned to school. She earned her high school diploma from Morgan Academy in 1918, then studied sporadically at Howard University between 1918 and 1924. In Washington, D.C., she came to know such literary figures as Alain Locke and Georgia Douglas Johnson. Locke paved the way for her migration to New York when he urged her to submit *Drenched in Light* to the editor of *Opportunity*, Charles S. Johnson, who published her story there in December 1924.

Arriving in New York City in 1925, Hurston soon established herself as one of the brightest of the young artists in Harlem. Her short play *Color Struck* (which would later appear in *Fire!!*, the magazine she cofounded with Hughes and a number of others) and her story *Spunk* (which appeared in the June 1925 issue of *Opportunity*) brought her to the attention of the novelist Fannie Hurst and the philanthropist Annie Nathan Meyer. Hurst hired Hurston as her personal secretary, and Meyer made it possible for Hurston to attend Barnard College.

While a student at Barnard, from which she graduated in 1928, she wrote a paper that her instructor passed on to Franz Boas, undoubtedly the foremost figure in anthropology in the United States at the time. Boas, then at Columbia University, was so impressed by her work that he convinced her to start graduate study in anthropology at Columbia. In turn, Hurston was thrilled by Boas's interest in the folktales (known to herself and the people who told them simply as "lies") that had kept her spellbound as a child in Eatonville. With a fourteen-hundred-dollar grant and Boas's intellectual and moral support, Hurston returned to her native South. Also important to Hurston's development as a folklorist was Charlotte Mason, the wealthy, elderly white woman who also befriended and aided Hughes and Alain Locke as well as other writers and artists.

With Mason's support, Hurston was able to gather the material that would later comprise *Mules and Men* (1935), generally regarded as the first collection of African American folklore to be compiled and published by an African American. *Mules and Men* received mixed reviews, with some black critics complaining that it was too easy on whites. According to Sterling A. Brown, for instance, Hurston's collection was "too pastoral" and would have been "nearer the truth" if it had been "more bitter." Nevertheless, the book was a popular success. Less successful was her second book of folklore, *Tell My Horse* (1938), which she began after joining the Depression-inspired Works Progress Administration in 1935. Many readers were disappointed to find that the purported collection of folklore actually emphasizes a comparison between the intraracial barriers in black America and those in the Caribbean and makes relatively short shrift of the delightful tales that had made her first collection so endearing.

Hurston's trip to the Caribbean in connection with research on this book was also important because during her stay there she completed her second and finest novel: *Their Eyes Were Watching God* (1937). Her first novel, *Jonah's Gourd Vine* (1934), had been well received both by the critics and the public. The story of John Pearson, a Baptist minister who is unable to remain faithful to his wife between sabbaths, *Jonah's Gourd Vine* is loosely modeled on the infidelities of Hurston's father, who was also a preacher. But as impressive as it is for a first novel, it probably prepared few readers for the book that was to follow. In its chronicle of Janie Crawford, a black woman who marries three times before she finds a man who is as concerned about her happiness as about his own, *Their Eyes Were Watching God* celebrates one individual's triumph over the limitations imposed on her mainly by sexism and poverty. Janie Crawford's ultimate attainment of contentment is based squarely on a mature understanding of life and of the acknowledgment of forces superior even to romantic love, which can blind women to the necessity of seeking emotional and intellectual independence as individuals in a complex world.

Throughout the 1930s, Hurston worked intermittently on musical productions that were generally based on the stories she collected in her travels. She also collaborated with Langston Hughes on the play *Mule Bone*. But a quarrel with Hughes kept the two from working together, and the play was never professionally staged during Hurston's lifetime. Her experience with the stage qualified her for a position as a drama instructor at the North Carolina College for Negroes at Durham, where she began working in 1939. Her third novel, *Moses, Man of the Mountain*, was published in November of that year. Most critics are perplexed by the book; typical of their ambivalent responses is the scholar Robert Hemenway's description of it as a "noble failure." Fascinating though this retelling of the Exodus story undoubtedly is, the transmuting of Israelites into African Americans and of Moses into a practitioner of hoodoo leaves many readers wondering whether Hurston was more interested in modernizing the biblical tale or parodying it. Nevertheless, *Moses, Man of the Mountain*, like the two novels before it, has proved attractive enough to have remained in print.

In fact, the only one of Hurston's novels not readily available is her last, *Seraph on the Suwanee* (1948), in which Hurston turns to the study of a fictional white woman, Arvay Henson. If many readers were surprised by this dramatic change in subject matter, Hurston herself had her reasons. In a letter to Carl Van Vechten she wrote, "I have hopes of breaking that old silly rule about Negroes not writing about white people." Her readers, though surprised, were probably not as troubled by her sudden breaking of that "silly" rule as her critics; and the book sold well despite many critics' fears that Hurston was perhaps turning her back on her race—a charge that was almost bound to be brought against her because of apparent inconsistencies in her views on race as she expressed them during the 1940s.

For Hurston, a new stage of her career and reputation began with the publication of her popular autobiography *Dust Tracks on a Road* in 1942, which led unquestionably to controversies and misconceptions concerning her. Even though Hurston's publisher had specifically requested an autobiography from her, he refused to publish the book she gave him because of several potentially objectionable passages in which Hurston indicts white America for its hypocrisy and racism. Without those passages, the book was published. *Dust Tracks on a Road* won Hurston the Anisfield-Wolf award for its contribution to the amelioration of race relations; it also won her the contempt of many black critics who considered it an unconscionably cheery portrayal of the life experience of a black woman in America. In other words, *Dust Tracks on a Road* failed (for these critics at least) precisely where *Their*

Eyes Were Watching God had succeeded. Nevertheless, Hurston found herself solicited for articles by numerous magazines. Soon she was appearing in such publications as the *Saturday Evening Post, Reader's Digest, American Mercury, World Telegram,* and *Negro Digest.* Her views were sometimes contradictory. In an article from 1943 she wrote that "the Jim Crow system works," but Hurston claimed just less than three years later that she was "all for the repeal of every Jim Crow law in the nation here and now." Ambivalence toward her deepened as the 1940s wore on, and she was probably relieved and a little surprised when *Seraph on the Suwanee* sold well.

But what might have been the beginning of a second phase in her career (it had been nearly a decade since the publication of her previous novel) was cut short by a personal calamity. In September 1948 Hurston was arrested on charges of having committed an immoral act with a ten-year-old boy. The fact that she had been out of the country when the crime was supposed to have taken place was not enough to keep the story out of the newspapers, and Hurston was humiliated. "My race," she wrote to Van Vechten, "has seen fit to destroy me without reason, and with the vilest tools conceived of by man so far." She never recovered from the incident, and wrote little in the remaining twelve years of her life. Discovered working as a cleaning woman in Florida in 1950, Hurston claimed unconvincingly that she was engaged in research for a piece she was planning to write about domestics.

Her brief stints of employment as librarian, reporter, and substitute teacher in the years that followed left her poor at her death in 1960, and her grave (in a segregated cemetery in Fort Pierce, Florida) was unmarked until 1973, when Alice Walker had a tombstone erected on the approximate location of the gravesite. The 1970s, in fact, saw a resurgence of interest in Hurston that continues to swell. Hurston has found a new audience, one composed of people, especially women, far more ready than her contemporaries to accept the complex wisdom of this woman who refused to be "tragically colored." For Hurston, that refusal entailed not a denial of her race, but a joyful affirmation of infinite possibility in the scope of her own life.

Sweat

It was eleven o'clock of a Spring night in Florida. It was Sunday. Any other night, Delia Jones would have been in bed for two hours by this time. But she was a washwoman, and Monday morning meant a great deal to her. So she collected the soiled clothes on Saturday when she returned the clean things. Sunday night after church, she sorted them and put the white things to soak. It saved her almost a half day's start. A great hamper in the bedroom held the clothes that she brought home. It was so much neater than a number of bundles lying around.

She squatted in the kitchen floor beside the great pile of clothes, sorting them into small heaps according to color, and humming a song in a mournful key, but wondering through it all where Sykes, her husband, had gone with her horse and buckboard.

Just then something long, round, limp and black fell upon her shoulders and slithered to the floor beside her. A great terror took hold of her. It softened her knees and dried her mouth so that it was a full minute before she could cry out or move. Then she saw that it was the big bull whip her husband liked to carry when he drove.

She lifted her eyes to the door and saw him standing there bent over with laughter at her fright. She screamed at him.

"Sykes, what you throw dat whip on me like dat? You know it would skeer me—looks just like a snake, an' you knows how skeered Ah is of snakes."

"Course Ah knowed it! That's how come Ah done it." He slapped his leg with his hand and almost rolled on the ground in his mirth. "If you such a big fool dat you got to have a fit over a earth worm or a string, Ah don't keer how bad Ah skeer you."

"You aint got no business doing it. Gawd knows it's a sin. Some day Ah'm gointuh drop dead from some of yo' foolishness. 'Nother thing, where you been wid mah rig? Ah feeds dat pony. He aint fuh you to be drivin' wid no bull whip."

"You sho is one aggravatin' nigger woman!" he declared and stepped into the room. She resumed her work and did not answer him at once. "Ah done tole you time and again to keep them white folks' clothes outa dis house."

He picked up the whip and glared down at her. Delia went on with her work. She went out into the yard and returned with a galvanized tub and set it on the washbench. She saw that Sykes had kicked all of the clothes together again, and now stood in her way truculently, his whole manner hoping, *praying*, for an argument. But she walked calmly around him and commenced to re-sort the things.

"Next time, Ah'm gointer kick 'em outdoors," he threatened as he struck a match along the leg of his corduroy breeches.

Delia never looked up from her work, and her thin, stooped shoulders sagged further.

"Ah aint for no fuss t'night Sykes. Ah just come from taking sacrament at the church house."

He snorted scornfully. "Yeah, you just come from de church house on a Sunday night, but heah you is gone to work on them clothes. You ain't nothing but a hypocrite. One of them amen-corner Christians—sing, whoop, and shout; then come home and wash white folks clothes on the Sabbath."

He stepped roughly upon the whitest pile of things, kicking them helter-skelter as he crossed the room. His wife gave a little scream of dismay, and quickly gathered them together again.

"Sykes, you quit grindin' dirt into these clothes! How can Ah git through by Sat'day if Ah don't start on Sunday?"

"Ah don't keer if you never git through. Anyhow, Ah done promised Gawd and a couple of other men, Ah aint gointer have it in mah house. Don't gimme no lip neither, else Ah'll throw 'em out and put mah fist up side yo' head to boot."

Delia's habitual meekness seemed to slip from her shoulders like a blown scarf. She was on her feet; her poor little body, her bare knuckly hands bravely defying the strapping hulk before her.

"Looka heah, Sykes, you done gone too fur. Ah been married to you fur fifteen years, and Ah been takin' in washin' fur fifteen years. Sweat, sweat, sweat! Work and sweat, cry and sweat, pray and sweat!"

"What's that got to do with me?" he asked brutally.

"What's it got to do with you, Sykes? Mah tub of suds is filled yo' belly with vittles more times than yo' hands is filled it. Mah sweat is done paid for this house and Ah reckon Ah kin keep on sweatin' in it."

She seized the iron skillet from the stove and struck a defensive pose, which act surprised him greatly, coming from her. It cowed him and he did not strike her as he usually did.

"Naw you won't," she panted, "that ole snaggle-toothed black woman you runnin' with aint comin' heah to pile up on *mah* sweat and blood. You aint paid for nothin' on this place, and Ah'm gointer stay right heah till Ah'm toted out foot foremost."

"Well, you better quit gittin' me riled up, else they'll be totin' you out sooner than you expect. Ah'm so tired of you Ah don't know whut to do. Gawd! how Ah hates skinny wimmen!"

A little awed by this new Delia, he sidled out of the door and slammed the back gate after him. He did not say where he had gone, but she knew too well. She knew very well that he would not return until nearly daybreak also. Her work over, she went on to bed but not to sleep at once. Things had come to a pretty pass!

She lay awake, gazing upon the debris that cluttered their matrimonial trail. Not an image left standing along the way. Anything like flowers had long ago been drowned in the salty stream that had been pressed from her heart. Her tears, her sweat, her blood. She had brought love to the union and he had brought a longing after the flesh. Two months after the wedding, he had given her the first brutal beating. She had the memory of his numerous trips to Orlando with all of his wages when he had returned to her penniless, even before the first year had passed. She was young and soft then, but now she thought of her knotty, muscled limbs, her harsh knuckly hands, and drew herself up into an unhappy little ball in the middle of the big feather bed. Too late now to hope for love, even if it were not Bertha it would be someone else. This case differed from the others only in that she was bolder than the others. Too late for everything except her little home. She had built it for her old days, and planted one by one the trees and flowers there. It was lovely to her, lovely.

Somehow, before sleep came, she found herself saying aloud: "Oh well, whatever goes over the Devil's back, is got to come under his belly. Sometime or ruther, Sykes, like everybody else, is gointer reap his sowing." After that she was able to build a spiritual earthworks against her husband. His shells could no longer reach her. *Amen.* She went to sleep and slept until he announced his presence in bed by kicking her feet and rudely snatching the covers away.

"Gimme some kivah heah, an' git yo' damn foots over on yo' own side! Ah oughter mash you in yo' mouf fuh drawing dat skillet on me."

Delia went clear to the rail without answering him. A triumphant indifference to all that he was or did.

The week was as full of work for Delia as all other weeks, and Saturday found her behind her little pony, collecting and delivering clothes.

It was a hot, hot day near the end of July. The village men on Joe

Clarke's porch even chewed cane listlessly. They did not hurl the cane-knots[1] as usual. They let them dribble over the edge of the porch. Even conversation had collapsed under the heat.

"Heah come Delia Jones," Jim Merchant said, as the shaggy pony came 'round the bend of the road toward them. The rusty buckboard was heaped with baskets of crisp, clean laundry.

"Yep," Joe Lindsay agreed. "Hot or col', rain or shine, jes ez reg'lar ez de weeks roll roun' Delia carries 'em an' fetches 'em on Sat'day."

"She better if she wanter eat," said Moss. "Syke Jones aint wuth de shot an' powder hit would tek tuh kill 'em. Not to *huh* he aint."

"He sho' aint," Walter Thomas chimed in. "It's too bad, too, cause she wuz a right pritty lil trick when he got huh. Ah'd uh mah'ied huh mahseff if he hadnter beat me to it."

Delia nodded briefly at the men as she drove past.

"Too much knockin' will ruin *any* 'oman. He done beat huh 'nough tuh kill three women, let 'lone change they looks," said Elijah Moseley. "How Syke kin stommuck dat big black greasy Mogul he's layin' roun' wid, gits me. Ah swear dat eight-rock[2] couldn't kiss a sardine can Ah done thowed out de back do' 'way las' yeah."

"Aw, she's fat, thass how come. He's allus been crazy 'bout fat women," put in Merchant. "He'd a' been tied up wid one long time ago if he could a' found one tuh have him. Did Ah tell yuh 'bout him come sidlin' roun' *mah* wife—bringin' her a basket uh peecans outa his yard fuh a present? Yeah, mah wife! She tol' him tuh take 'em right straight back home, cause Delia works so hard ovah dat washtub she reckon everything on de place taste lak sweat an' soapsuds. Ah jus' wisht Ah'd a' caught 'im 'roun' dere! Ah'd a' made his hips ketch on fiah down dat shell road."

"Ah know he done it, too. Ah sees 'im grinnin' at every 'oman dat passes," Walter Thomas said. "But even so, he useter eat some mighty big hunks uh humble pie tuh git dat lil' 'oman he got. She wuz ez pritty ez a speckled pup! Dat wuz fifteen yeahs ago. He useter be so skeered uh losin' huh, she could make him do some parts of a husband's duty. Dey never wuz de same in de mind."

"There oughter be a law about him," said Lindsay. "He aint fit tuh carry guts tuh a bear."

Clarke spoke for the first time. "Taint no law on earth dat kin make a man be decent if it aint in 'im. There's plenty men dat takes a wife lak dey do a joint uh sugar-cane. It's round, juicy an' sweet when dey gits it. But dey squeeze an' grind, squeeze an' grind an' wring tell dey wring every drop uh pleasure dat's in 'em out. When dey's satisfied dat dey is wrung dry, dey treats 'em jes lak dey do a cane-chew. Dey thows 'em away. Dey knows whut dey is doin' while dey is at it, an' hates theirselves fuh it but they keeps on hangin' after huh tell she's empty. Den dey hates huh fuh bein' a cane-chew an' in de way."

"We oughter take Syke an' dat stray 'oman uh his'n down in Lake Howell swamp an' lay on de rawhide till they cain't say Lawd a' mussy.' He allus wuz uh ovahbearin' niggah, but since dat white 'oman from up north done

---

1. The indigestible part of the sugarcane stalk.   2. The eight ball in pool, i.e., black.

teached 'im how to run a automobile, he done got too biggety to live—an' we oughter kill 'im," Old Man Anderson advised.

A grunt of approval went around the porch. But the heat was melting their civic virtue and Elijah Moseley began to bait Joe Clarke.

"Come on, Joe, git a melon outa dere an' slice it up for yo' customers. We'se all sufferin' wid de heat. De bear's done got *me!*"

"Thass right, Joe, a watermelon is jes' whut Ah needs tuh cure de ep-pizudicks,"[3] Walter Thomas joined forces with Moseley. "Come on dere, Joe. We all is steady customers an' you aint set us up in a long time. Ah chooses dat long, bowlegged Floridy favorite."

"A god, an' be dough. You all gimme twenty cents and slice way," Clarke retorted. "Ah needs a col' slice m'self. Heah, everybody chip in. Ah'll lend y'll mah meat knife."

The money was quickly subscribed and the huge melon brought forth. At that moment, Sykes and Bertha arrived. A determined silence fell on the porch and the melon was put away again.

Merchant snapped down the blade of his jackknife and moved toward the store door.

"Come on in, Joe, an' gimme a slab uh sow belly an' uh pound uh cof-fee—almost fuhgot 'twas Sat'day. Got to git on home." Most of the men left also.

Just then Delia drove past on her way home, as Sykes was ordering mag-nificently for Bertha. It pleased him for Delia to see.

"Git whutsoever yo' heart desires, Honey. Wait a minute, Joe. Give huh two botles uh strawberry soda-water, uh quart uh parched ground-peas, an' a block uh chewin' gum."

With all this they left the store, with Sykes reminding Bertha that this was his town and she could have it if she wanted it.

The men returned soon after they left, and held their watermelon feast.

"Where did Syke Jones git da 'oman from nohow?" Lindsay asked.

"Ovah Apopka.[4] Guess dey musta been cleanin' out de town when she lef'. She don't look lak a thing but a hunk uh liver wid hair on it."

"Well, she sho' kin squall," Dave Carter contributed. "When she gits ready tuh laff, she jes' opens huh mouf an' latches it back tuh de las' notch. No ole grandpa alligator down in Lake Bell ain't got nothin' on huh."

Bertha had been in town three months now. Sykes was still paying her room rent at Della Lewis'—the only house in town that would have taken her in. Sykes took her frequently to Winter Park to "stomps."[5] He still as-sured her that he was the swellest man in the state.

"Sho' you kin have dat lil' ole house soon's Ah kin git dat 'oman outa dere. Everything b'longs tuh me an' you sho' kin have it. Ah sho' 'bomi-nates uh skinny 'oman. Lawdy, you sho' is got one portly shape on you! You kin git *anything* you wants. Dis is *mah* town an' you sho' kin have it."

Delia's work-worn knees crawled over the earth in Gethsemane[6] and up

---

3. I.e., epizootic; any fast-spreading disease.
4. A town in Florida some ten miles from Hur-ston's birthplace, Eatonville.
5. Raucous dance parties.

6. The garden outside Jerusalem that was the scene of Jesus' agony and arrest (Matthew 26:36–57).

the rocks of Calvary many, many times during these months. She avoided the villagers and meeting places in her efforts to be blind and deaf. But Bertha nullified this to a degree, by coming to Delia's house to call Sykes out to her at the gate.

Delia and Sykes fought all the time now with no peaceful interludes. They slept and ate in silence. Two or three times Delia had attempted a timid friendliness, but she was repulsed each time. It was plain that the breaches must remain agape.

The sun had burned July to August. The heat streamed down like a million hot arrows, smiting all things living upon the earth. Grass withered, leaves browned, snakes went blind in shedding and men and dogs went mad. Dog days!

Delia came home one day and found Sykes there before her. She wondered, but started to go on into the house without speaking, even though he was standing in the kitchen door and she must either stoop under his arm or ask him to move. He made no room for her. She noticed a soap box beside the steps, but paid no particular attention to it, knowing that he must have brought it there. As she was stooping to pass under his outstretched arm, he suddenly pushed her backward, laughingly.

"Look in de box dere Delia, Ah done brung yuh somethin'!"

She nearly fell upon the box in her stumbling, and when she saw what it held, she all but fainted outright.

"Syke! Syke, mah Gawd! You take dat rattlesnake 'way from heah! You *gottuh*. Oh, Jesus, have mussy!"

"Ah aint gut tuh do nuthin' uh de kin'—fact is Ah aint got tuh do nothin' but die. Taint no use uh you puttin' on airs makin' out lak you skeered uh dat snake—he's gointer stay right heah tell he die. He wouldn't bite me cause Ah knows how tuh handle 'im. Nohow he wouldn't risk breakin' out his fangs 'gin yo' skinny laigs."

"Naw, now Syke, don't keep dat thing 'roun' heah tuh skeer me tuh death. You knows Ah'm even feared uh earth worms. Thass de biggest snake Ah evah did see. Kill 'im Syke, please."

"Doan ast me tuh do nothin' fuh yuh. Goin' 'roun' tryin' tuh be so damn asterperious.[7] Naw, Ah aint gonna kill it. Ah think uh damn sight mo' uh him dan you! Dat's a nice snake an' anybody doan lak 'im kin jes' hit de grit."

The village soon heard that Sykes had the snake, and came to see and ask questions.

"How de hen-fire did you ketch dat six-foot rattler, Syke?" Thomas asked.

"He's full uh frogs so he caint hardly move, thass how Ah eased up on 'm. But Ah'm a snake charmer an' knows how tuh handle 'em. Shux, dat aint nothin'. Ah could ketch one eve'y day if Ah so wanted tuh."

"Whut he needs is a heavy hick'ry club leaned real heavy on his head. Dat's de bes' way tuh charm a rattlesnake."

---

7. I.e., astorperious; haughty (probably a fusion of *Astor*, the name of a wealthy family, and *imperious*, or arrogant).

"Naw, Walt, y'll jes' don't understand dese diamon' backs lak Ah do," said Sykes in a superior tone of voice.

The village agreed with Walter, but the snake stayed on. His box remained by the kitchen door with its screen wire covering. Two or three days later it had digested its meal of frogs and literally came to life. It rattled at every movement in the kitchen or the yard. One day as Delia came down the kitchen steps she saw his chalky-white fangs curved like scimitars hung in the wire meshes. This time she did not run away with averted eyes as usual. She stood for a long time in the doorway in a red fury that grew bloodier for every second that she regarded the creature that was her torment.

That night she broached the subject as soon as Sykes sat down to the table.

"Syke, Ah wants you tuh take dat snake 'way fum heah. You done starved me an' Ah put up widcher, you done beat me an Ah took dat, but you done kilt all mah insides bringin' dat varmint heah."

Sykes poured out a saucer full of coffee and drank it deliberately before he answered her.

"A whole lot Ah keer 'bout how you feels inside uh out. Dat snake aint goin' no damn wheah till Ah gits ready fuh 'im tuh go. So fur as beatin' is concerned, yuh aint took near all dat you gointer take ef yuh stay 'roun' *me*."

Delia pushed back her plate and got up from the table. "Ah hates you, Sykes," she said calmly. "Ah hates you tuh de same degree dat Ah useter love yuh. Ah done took an' took till mah belly is full up tuh mah neck. Dat's de reason Ah got mah letter fum de church an' moved mah membership tuh Woodbridge—so Ah don't haftuh take no sacrament wid yuh. Ah don't wantuh see yuh 'roun' me atall. Lay 'roun' wid dat 'oman all yuh wants tuh, but gwan 'way fum me an' mah house. Ah hates yuh lak uh suck-egg dog."[8]

Sykes almost let the huge wad of corn bread and collard greens he was chewing fall out of his mouth in amazement. He had a hard time whipping himself up to the proper fury to try to answer Delia.

"Well, Ah'm glad you does hate me. Ah'm sho' tiahed uh you hangin' ontuh me. Ah don't want yuh. Look at yuh stringey ole neck! Yo' rawbony laigs an' arms is enough tuh cut uh man tuh death. You looks jes' lak de devvul's doll-baby tuh *me*. You cain't hate me no worse dan Ah hates you. Ah been hatin' *you* fuh years."

"Yo' ole black hide don't look lak nothin' tuh me, but uh passle uh wrinkled up rubber, wid yo' big ole yeahs flappin' on each side lak uh paih uh buzzard wings. Don't think Ah'm gointuh be run 'way fum mah house neither. Ah'm goin' tuh de white folks about *you*, mah young man, de very nex' time you lay yo' han's on me. Mah cup is done run ovah."[9] Delia said this with no signs of fear and Sykes departed from the house, threatening her, but made not the slightest move to carry out any of them.

That night he did not return at all, and the next day being Sunday, Delia

---

8. A dog that steals chicken eggs.   9. "My cup runneth over," Psalm 23:5.

was glad she did not have to quarrel before she hitched up her pony and drove the four miles to Woodbridge.

She stayed to the night service—"love feast"—which was very warm and full of spirit. In the emotional winds her domestic trials were borne far and wide so that she sang as she drove homeward,

> "Jurden [1] water, black an' col'
> Chills de body, not de soul
> An' Ah wantah cross Jurden in uh calm time."

She came from the barn to the kitchen door and stopped.

"Whut's de mattah, ol' satan, you aint kickin' up yo' racket?" She addressed the snake's box. Complete silence. She went on into the house with a new hope in its birth struggles. Perhaps her threat to go to the white folks had frightened Sykes! Perhaps he was sorry! Fifteen years of misery and suppression had brought Delia to the place where she would hope *anything* that looked towards a way over or through her wall of inhibitions.

She felt in the match safe behind the stove at once for a match. There was only one there.

"Dat niggah wouldn't fetch nothin' heah tuh save his rotten neck, but he kin run thew whut Ah brings quick enough. Now he done toted off nigh on tuh haff uh box uh matches. He done had dat 'oman heah in mah house, too."

Nobody but a woman could tell how she knew this even before she struck the match. But she did and it put her into a new fury.

Presently she brought in the tubs to put the white things to soak. This time she decided she need not bring the hamper out of the bedroom; she would go in there and do the sorting. She picked up the pot-bellied lamp and went in. The room was small and the hamper stood hard by the foot of the white iron bed. She could sit and reach through the bedposts—resting as she worked.

"Ah wantah cross Jurden in uh calm time." She was singing again. The mood of the "love feast" had returned. She threw back the lid of the basket almost gaily. Then, moved by both horror and terror, she sprang back toward the door. *There lay the snake in the basket!* He moved sluggishly at first, but even as she turned round and round, jumped up and down in an insanity of fear, he began to stir vigorously. She saw him pouring his awful beauty from the basket upon the bed, then she seized the lamp and ran as fast as she could to the kitchen. The wind from the open door blew out the light and the darkness added to her terror. She sped to the darkness of the yard, slamming the door after her before she thought to set down the lamp. She did not feel safe even on the ground, so she climbed up in the hay barn.

There for an hour or more she lay sprawled upon the hay a gibbering wreck.

Finally she grew quiet, and after that, coherent thought. With this, stalked through her a cold, bloody rage. Hours of this. A period of intro-

---

1. The river Jordan, mentioned in the Bible, signifies deliverance.

spection, a space of retrospection, then a mixture of both. Out of this an awful calm.

"Well, Ah done de bes' Ah could. If things aint right, Gawd knows taint mah fault."

She went to sleep—a twitch sleep—and woke up to a faint gray sky. There was a loud hollow sound below. She peered out. Sykes was at the wood-pile, demolishing a wire-covered box.

He hurried to the kitchen door, but hung outside there some minutes before he entered, and stood some minutes more inside before he closed it after him.

The gray in the sky was spreading. Delia descended without fear now, and crouched beneath the low bedroom window. The drawn shade shut out the dawn, shut in the night. But the thin walls held back no sound.

"Dat ol' scratch[2] is woke up now!" She mused at the tremendous whirr inside, which every woodsman knows, is one of the sound illusions. The rattler is a ventriloquist. His whirr sounds to the right, to the left, straight ahead, behind, close under foot—everywhere but where it is. Woe to him who guesses wrong unless he is prepared to hold up his end of the argument! Sometimes he strikes without rattling at all.

Inside, Sykes heard nothing until he knocked a pot lid off the stove while trying to reach the match safe in the dark. He had emptied his pockets at Bertha's.

The snake seemed to wake up under the stove and Sykes made a quick leap into the bedroom. In spite of the gin he had had, his head was clearing now.

"Mah Gawd!" he chattered, "ef Ah could on'y strack uh light!"

The rattling ceased for a moment as he stood paralyzed. He waited. It seemed that the snake waited also.

"Oh, fuh de light! Ah thought he'd be too sick"—Sykes was muttering to himself when the whirr began again, closer, right underfoot this time. Long before this, Sykes' ability to think had been flattened down to primitive instinct and he leaped—onto the bed.

Outside Delia heard a cry that might have come from a maddened chimpanzee, a stricken gorilla. All the terror, all the horror, all the rage that man possibly could express, without a recognizable human sound.

A tremendous stir inside there, another series of animal screams, the intermittent whirr of the reptile. The shade torn violently down from the window, letting in the red dawn, a huge brown hand seizing the window stick, great dull blows upon the wooden floor punctuating the gibberish of sound long after the rattle of the snake had abruptly subsided. All this Delia could see and hear from her place beneath the window, and it made her ill. She crept over to the four-o'clocks and stretched herself on the cool earth to recover.

She lay there. "Delia, Delia!" She could hear Sykes calling in a most despairing tone as one who expected no answer. The sun crept on up, and he called. Delia could not move—her legs were gone flabby. She never moved, he called, and the sun kept rising.

_____

2. A nickname of the devil; here refers to the serpent.

"Mah Gawd!" She heard him moan, "Mah Gawd fum Heben!" She heard him stumbling about and got up from her flower-bed. The sun was growing warm. As she approached the door she heard him call out hopefully, "Delia, is dat you Ah heah?"

She saw him on his hands and knees as soon as she reached the door. He crept an inch or two toward her—all that he was able, and she saw his horribly swollen neck and his one open eye shining with hope. A surge of pity too strong to support bore her away from that eye that must, could not, fail to see the tubs. He would see the lamp. Orlando with its doctors was too far. She could scarcely reach the Chinaberry tree, where she waited in the growing heat while inside she knew the cold river was creeping up and up to extinguish that eye which must know by now that she knew.

1926

How It Feels to Be Colored Me

I am colored but I offer nothing in the way of extenuating circumstances except the fact that I am the only Negro in the United States whose grandfather on the mother's side was *not* an Indian chief.

I remember the very day that I became colored. Up to my thirteenth year I lived in the little Negro town of Eatonville, Florida. It is exclusively a colored town. The only white people I knew passed through the town going to or coming from Orlando. The native whites rode dusty horses, the Northern tourists chugged down the sandy village road in automobiles. The town knew the Southerners and never stopped cane chewing when they passed. But the Northerners were something else again. They were peered at cautiously from behind curtains by the timid. The more venturesome would come out on the porch to watch them go past and got just as much pleasure out of the tourists as the tourists got out of the village.

The front porch might seem a daring place for the rest of the town, but it was a gallery seat for me. My favorite place was atop the gate-post. Proscenium box[1] for a born first-nighter. Not only did I enjoy the show, but I didn't mind the actors knowing that I liked it. I usually spoke to them in passing. I'd wave at them and when they returned my salute, I would say something like this: "Howdy-do-well-I-thank-you-where-you-goin'?" Usually automobile or the horse paused at this, and after a queer exchange of compliments, I would probably "go a piece of the way" with them, as we say in farthest Florida. If one of my family happened to come to the front in time to see me, of course negotiations would be rudely broken off. But even so, it is clear that I was the first "welcome-to-our-state" Floridian, and I hope the Miami Chamber of Commerce will please take notice.

During this period, white people differed from colored to me only in that they rode through town and never lived there. They liked to hear me "speak pieces" and sing and wanted to see me dance the parse-me-la, and gave me generously of their small silver for doing these things, which seemed strange to me for I wanted to do them so much that I needed brib-

---

1. The box seats in a theater on either side of and nearest to the stage.

ing to stop. Only they didn't know it. The colored people gave no dimes. They deplored any joyful tendencies in me, but I was their Zora neverthe- less. I belonged to them, to the nearby hotels, to the county—everybody's Zora.

But changes came in the family when I was thirteen, and I was sent to school in Jacksonville. I left Eatonville, the town of the oleanders, as Zora. When I disembarked from the river-boat at Jacksonville, she was no more. It seemed that I had suffered a sea change. I was not Zora of Orange County any more, I was now a little colored girl. I found it out in certain ways. In my heart as well as in the mirror, I became a fast[2] brown—war- ranted not to rub nor run.

But I am not tragically colored. There is no great sorrow dammed up in my soul, nor lurking behind my eyes. I do not mind at all. I do not belong to the sobbing school of Negrohood who hold that nature somehow has given them a lowdown dirty deal and whose feelings are all hurt about it. Even in the helter-skelter skirmish that is my life, I have seen that the world is to the strong regardless of a little pigmentation more or less. No, I do not weep at the world—I am too busy sharpening my oyster knife.[3]

Someone is always at my elbow reminding me that I am the grand- daughter of slaves. It fails to register depression with me. Slavery is sixty years in the past. The operation was successful and the patient is doing well, thank you. The terrible struggle that made me an American out of a potential slave said "On the line!" The Reconstruction said "Get set!"; and the generation before said "Go!" I am off to a flying start and I must not halt in the stretch to look behind and weep. Slavery is the price I paid for civili- zation, and the choice was not with me. It is a bully adventure and worth all that I have paid through my ancestors for it. No one on earth ever had a greater chance for glory. The world to be won and nothing to be lost. It is thrilling to think—to know that for any act of mine, I shall get twice as much praise or twice as much blame. It is quite exciting to hold the center of the national stage, with the spectators not knowing whether to laugh or to weep.

The position of my white neighbor is much more difficult. No brown specter pulls up a chair beside me when I sit down to eat. No dark ghost thrusts its leg against mine in bed. The game of keeping what one has is never so exciting as the game of getting.

I do not always feel colored. Even now I often achieve the unconscious Zora of Eatonville before the Hegira.[4] I feel most colored when I am thrown against a sharp white background.

For instance at Barnard. "Beside the waters of the Hudson" I feel my race. Among the thousand white persons, I am a dark rock surged upon, and overswept, but through it all, I remain myself. When covered by the waters, I am; and the ebb but reveals me again.

2. Colorfast.
3. An allusion to Shakespeare's *The Merry Wives of Windsor* 2.2.3–4: "Why, then the world's mine oys- ter, / Which I with sword will open."
4. In Islam, Mohammed's emigration from Mecca to Medina in A.D. 622; here, the journey to Jackson- ville.

Sometimes it is the other way around. A white person is set down in our midst, but the contrast is just as sharp for me. For instance, when I sit in the drafty basement that is The New World Cabaret with a white person, my color comes. We enter chatting about any little nothing that we have in common and are seated by the jazz waiters. In the abrupt way that jazz orchestras have, this one plunges into a number. It loses no time in circumlocutions, but gets right down to business. It constricts the thorax and splits the heart with its tempo and narcotic harmonies. This orchestra grows rambunctious, rears on its hind legs and attacks the tonal veil with primitive fury, rending it, clawing it until it breaks through to the jungle beyond. I follow those heathen—follow them exultingly. I dance wildly inside myself; I yell within, I whoop; I shake my assegai[5] above my head, I hurl it true to the mark *yeeeeooww!* I am in the jungle and living in the jungle way. My face is painted red and yellow and my body is painted blue. My pulse is throbbing like a war drum. I want to slaughter something—give pain, give death to what, I do not know. But the piece ends. The men of the orchestra wipe their lips and rest their fingers. I creep back slowly to the veneer we call civilization with the last tone and find the white friend sitting motionless in his seat, smoking calmly.

"Good music they have here," he remarks, drumming the table with his fingertips.

Music. The great blobs of purple and red emotion have not touched him. He has only heard what I felt. He is far away and I see him but dimly across the ocean and the continent that have fallen between us. He is so pale with his whiteness then and I am *so* colored.

At certain times I have no race, I am *me*. When I set my hat at a certain angle and saunter down Seventh Avenue, Harlem City, feeling as snooty as the lions in front of the Forty-Second Street Library,[6] for instance. So far as my feelings are concerned, Peggy Hopkins Joyce on the Boule Mich[7] with her gorgeous raiment, stately carriage, knees knocking together in a most aristocratic manner, has nothing on me. The cosmic Zora emerges. I belong to no race nor time. I am the eternal feminine with its string of beads.

I have no separate feeling about being an American citizen and colored. I am merely a fragment of the Great Soul that surges within the boundaries. My country, right or wrong.

Sometimes, I feel discriminated against, but it does not make me angry. It merely astonishes me. How *can* any deny themselves the pleasure of my company? It's beyond me.

But in the main, I feel like a brown bag of miscellany propped against a wall. Against a wall in company with other bags, white, red and yellow. Pour out the contents, and there is discovered a jumble of small things priceless and worthless. A first-water diamond,[8] an empty spool, bits of broken glass, lengths of string, a key to a door long since crumbled away, a rusty knife-blade, old shoes saved for a road that never was and never will

---

5. Spear.
6. The headquarters of the New York Public Library.
7. The elegant Boulevard St. Michel in Paris.
8. A diamond of the highest degree of fineness.

be, a nail bent under the weight of things too heavy for any nail, a dried flower or two still a little fragrant. In your hand is the brown bag. On the ground before you is the jumble it held—so much like the jumble in the bags, could they be emptied, that all might be dumped in a single heap and the bags refilled without altering the content of any greatly. A bit of colored glass more or less would not matter. Perhaps that is how the Great Stuffer of Bags filled them in the first place—who knows?

1928

The Gilded Six-Bits

It was a Negro yard around a Negro house in a Negro settlement that looked to the payroll of the G and G Fertilizer works for its support.

But there was something happy about the place. The front yard was parted in the middle by a sidewalk from gate to door-step, a sidewalk edged on either side by quart bottles driven neck down into the ground on a slant. A mess of homey flowers planted without a plan but blooming cheerily from their helter-skelter places. The fence and house were whitewashed. The porch and steps scrubbed white.

The front door stood open to the sunshine so that the floor of the front room could finish drying after its weekly scouring. It was Saturday. Everything clean from the front gate to the privy house. Yard raked so that the strokes of the rake would make a pattern. Fresh newspaper cut in fancy edge on the kitchen shelves.

Missie May was bathing herself in the galvanized washtub in the bedroom. Her dark-brown skin glistened under the soapsuds that skittered down from her wash rag. Her stiff young breasts thrust forward aggressively like broad-based cones with the tips lacquered in black.

She heard men's voices in the distance and glanced at the dollar clock on the dresser.

"Humph! Ah'm way behind time t'day! Joe gointer be heah 'fore Ah git mah clothes on if Ah don't make haste."

She grabbed the clean meal sack at hand and dried herself hurriedly and began to dress. But before she could tie her slippers, there came the ring of singing metal on wood. Nine[1] times.

Missie May grinned with delight. She had not seen the big tall man come stealing in the gate and creep up the walk grinning happily at the joyful mischief he was about to commit. But she knew that it was her husband throwing silver dollars in the door for her to pick up and pile beside her plate at dinner. It was this way every Saturday afternoon. The nine dollars hurled into the open door, he scurried to a hiding place behind the cape jasmine bush and waited.

Missie May promptly appeared at the door in mock alarm.

"Who dat chunkin' money in mah do'way?" She demanded. No answer from the yard. She leaped off the porch and began to search the shrubbery.

---

1. A number significant in mysticism.

She peeped under the porch and hung over the gate to look up and down the road. While she did this, the man behind the jasmine darted to the chinaberry tree. She spied him and gave chase.

"Nobody ain't gointer be chuckin' money at me and Ah not do 'em nothin'," she shouted in mock anger. He ran around the house with Missie May at his heels. She overtook him at the kitchen door. He ran inside but could not close it after him before she crowded in and locked with him in a rough and tumble. For several minutes the two were a furious mass of male and female energy. Shouting, laughing, twisting, turning, tussling, tickling each other in the ribs; Missie May clutching onto Joe and Joe trying, but not too hard, to get away.

"Missie May, take yo' hand out mah pocket!" Joe shouted out between laughs.

"Ah ain't, Joe, not lessen you gwine gimme whateve' it is good you got in yo' pocket. Turn it go, Joe, do Ah'll tear yo' clothes."

"Go on tear 'em. You de one dat pushes de needles round heah. Move yo' hand Missie May."

"Lemme git dat paper sack out yo' pocket. Ah bet its candy kisses."

"Tain't. Move yo' hand. Woman ain't go no business in a man's clothes nohow. Go way."

Missie May gouged way down and gave an upward jerk and triumphed.

"Unhhunh! Ah got it. It 'tis so candy kisses. Ah knowed you had somethin' for me in yo' clothes. Now Ah got to see whut's in every pocket you got."

Joe smiled indulgently and let his wife go through all of his pockets and take out the things that he had hidden there for her to find. She bore off the chewing gum, the cake of sweet soap, the pocket handkerchief as if she had wrested them from him, as if they had not been bought for the sake of this friendly battle.

"Whew! dat play-fight done got me all warmed up." Joe exclaimed. "Got me some water in de kittle?"

"Yo' water is on de fire and yo' clean things is cross de bed. Hurry up and wash yo'self and git changed so we kin eat. Ah'm hongry." As Missie said this, she bore the steaming kettle into the bedroom.

"You ain't hongry, sugar," Joe contradicted her. "Youse jes' a little empty. Ah'm de one whut's hongry. Ah could eat up camp meetin', back off 'ssociation, and drink Jurdan [2] dry. Have it on de table when Ah git out de tub."

"Don't you mess wid mah business, man. You git in yo' clothes. Ah'm a real wife, not no dress and breath. [3] Ah might not look lak one, but if you burn me, you won't git a thing but wife ashes."

Joe splashed in the bedroom and Missie May fanned around in the kitchen. A fresh red and white checked cloth on the table. Big pitcher of buttermilk beaded with pale drops of butter from the churn. Hot fried mullet, crackling bread, ham hock atop a mound of string beans and new potatoes, and perched on the window-sill a pone [4] of spicy potato pudding.

2. The Jordan River. "'Ssociation": a religious gathering.

3. Imitation wife.
4. Bread made without milk or eggs.

Very little talk during the meal but that little consisted of banter that pretended to deny affection but in reality flaunted it. Like when Missie May reached for a second helping of the tater pone. Joe snatched it out of her reach.

After Missie May had made two or three unsuccessful grabs at the pan, she begged, "Aw, Joe gimme some mo' dat tater pone."

"Nope, sweetenin' is for us men-folks. Y'all pritty lil frail eels don't need nothin' lak dis. You too sweet already."

"Please, Joe."

"Naw, naw. Ah don't want you to git no sweeter than whut you is already. We goin' down de road a lil piece t'night so you go put on yo' Sunday-go-to-meetin' things."

Missie May looked at her husband to see if he was playing some prank. "Sho nuff, Joe?"

"Yeah. We goin' to de ice cream parlor."

"Where de ice cream parlor at, Joe?"

"A new man done come heah from Chicago and he done got a place and took and opened it up for a ice cream parlor, and bein' as it's real swell, Ah wants you to be one de first ladies to walk in dere and have some set down."

"Do Jesus, Ah ain't knowed nothin' 'bout it. Who de man done it?"

"Mister Otis D. Slemmons, of spots and places—Memphis, Chicago, Jacksonville, Philadelphia and so on."

"Dat heavy-set man wid his mouth full of gold teethes?"

"Yeah. Where did you see 'im at?"

"Ah went down to de sto' tuh git a box of lye and Ah seen 'im standin' on de corner talkin' to some of de mens, and Ah come on back and went to scrubbin' de floor, and he passed and tipped his hat whilst Ah was scourin' de steps. Ah thought Ah never seen *him* befo'."

Joe smiled pleasantly. "Yeah, he's up to date. He got de finest clothes Ah ever seen on a colored man's back."

"Aw, he don't look no better in his clothes than you do in yourn. He got a puzzlegut on 'im and he so chuckle-headed, he got a pone behind his neck."

Joe looked down at his own abdomen and said wistfully, "Wisht Ah had a build on me lak he got. He ain't puzzle-gutted, honey. He jes' got a corp-eration. Dat make 'm look lak a rich white man. All rich mens is got some belly on 'em."

"Ah seen de pitchers of Henry Ford and he's a spare-built man and Rockefeller look lak he ain't got but one gut. But Ford and Rockefeller and dis Slemmons and all de rest kin be as many-gutted as dey please, Ah'm satisfied wid you jes' lak you is, baby. God took pattern after a pine tree and built you noble. Youse a pritty man, and if Ah knowed any way to make you mo' pritty still Ah'd take and do it."

Joe reached over gently and toyed with Missie May's ear. "You jes' say dat cause you love me, but Ah know Ah can't hold no light to Otis D. Slemmons. Ah ain't never been nowhere and Ah ain't got nothin' but you."

Missie May got on his lap and kissed him and he kissed back in kind. Then he went on. "All de womens is crazy 'bout 'im everywhere he go."

"How you know dat, Joe?"

"He tole us so hisself."

"Dat don't make it so. His mouf is cut cross-ways, ain't it? Well, he kin lie jes' lak anybody else."

"Good Lawd, Missie! You womens sho is hard to sense into things. He's got a five-dollar gold piece for a stick-pin and he got a ten-dollar gold piece on his watch chain and his mouf is jes' crammed full of gold teethes. Sho wisht it wuz mine. And whut make it so cool, he got money 'cumulated. And womens give it all to 'im."

"Ah don't see whut de womens see on 'im. Ah wouldn't give 'im a wink if de sheriff wuz after 'im."

"Well, he tole us how de white womens in Chicago give 'im all dat gold money. So he don't 'low nobody to touch it at all. Not even put dey finger on it. Dey tole 'im not to. You kin make 'miration at it, but don't tetch it."

"Whyn't he stay up dere where dey so crazy 'bout 'im?"

"Ah reckon dey done made 'im vast-rich and he wants to travel some. He say dey wouldn't leave 'im hit a lick of work. He got mo' lady people crazy 'bout him than he kin shake a stick at."

"Joe, Ah hates to see you so dumb. Dat stray nigger jes' tell y'all anything and y'all b'lieve it."

"Go 'head on now, honey and put on yo' clothes. He talkin' 'bout his pritty womens—Ah want 'im to see *mine*."

Missie May went off to dress and Joe spent the time trying to make his stomach punch out like Slemmons' middle. He tried the rolling swagger of the stranger, but found that his tall bone-and-muscle stride fitted ill with it. He just had time to drop back into his seat before Missie May came in dressed to go.

On the way home that night Joe was exultant. "Didn't Ah say ole Otis was swell? Can't he talk Chicago talk? Wuzn't dat funny whut he said when great big fat ole Ida Armstrong come in? He asted me, 'Who is dat broad wid de forte shake?' Dat's a new word. Us always thought forty was a set of figgers but he showed us where it means a whole heap of things. Sometimes he don't say forty, he jes' say thirty-eight and two and dat mean de same thing. Know whut he tole me when Ah wuz payin' for our ice cream? He say, 'Ah have to hand it to you, Joe. Dat wife of yours is jes' thirty-eight and two. Yessuh, she's forte!' Ain't he killin'?"

"He'll do in case of a rush. But he sho is got uh heap uh gold on 'im. Dat's de first time Ah ever seed gold money. It lookted good on him sho nuff, but it'd look a whole heap better on you."

"Who, me? Missie May youse crazy! Where would a po' man lak me git gold money from?"

Missie May was silent for a minute, then she said, "Us might find some goin' long de road some time. Us could."

"Who would be losin' gold money round heah? We ain't even seen none dese white folks wearin' no gold money on dey watch chain. You must be figgerin' Mister Packard or Mister Cadillac[5] goin' pass through heah."

"You don't know whut been lost 'round heah. Maybe somebody way back in memorial times lost they gold money and went on off and it ain't

5. Two lines of expensive cars.

never been found. And then if we wuz to find it, you could wear some 'thout havin' no gang of womens lak dat Slemmons say he got."

Joe laughed and hugged her. "Don't be so wishful 'bout me. Ah'm satisfied de way Ah is. So long as Ah be yo' husband, Ah don't keer 'bout nothin' else. Ah'd ruther all de other womens in de world to be dead than for you to have de toothache. Less we go to bed and git our night rest."

It was Saturday night once more before Joe could parade his wife in Slemmons' ice cream parlor again. He worked the night shift and Saturday was his only night off. Every other evening around six o'clock he left home, and dying dawn saw him hustling home around the lake where the challenging sun flung a flaming sword from east to west across the trembling water.

That was the best part of life—going home to Missie May. Their whitewashed house, the mock battle on Saturday, the dinner and ice cream parlor afterwards, church on Sunday nights when Missie outdressed any woman in town—all, everything was right.

One night around eleven the acid ran out at the G. and G. The foreman knocked off the crew and let the steam die down. As Joe rounded the lake on his way home, a lean moon rode the lake in a silver boat. If anybody had asked Joe about the moon on the lake, he would have said he hadn't paid it any attention. But he saw it with his feelings. It made him yearn painfully for Missie. Creation obsessed him. He thought about children. They had been married for more than a year now. They had money put away. They ought to be making little feet for shoes. A little boy child would be about right.

He saw a dim light in the bedroom and decided to come in through the kitchen door. He could wash the fertilizer dust off himself before presenting himself to Missie May. It would be nice for her not to know that he was there until he slipped into his place in bed and hugged her back. She always liked that.

He eased the kitchen door open slowly and silently, but when he went to set his dinner bucket on the table he bumped it into a pile of dishes, and something crashed to the floor. He heard his wife gasp in fright and hurried to reassure her.

"Iss me, honey. Don't get skeered."

There was a quick, large movement in the bedroom. A rustle, a thud, and a stealthy silence. The light went out.

What? Robbers? Murderers? Some varmint attacking his helpless wife, perhaps. He struck a match, threw himself on guard and stepped over the door-sill into the bedroom.

The great belt on the wheel of Time slipped and eternity stood still. By the match light he could see the man's legs fighting with his breeches in his frantic desire to get them on. He had both chance and time to kill the intruder in his helpless condition—half in and half out of his pants—but he was too weak to take action. The shapeless enemies of humanity that live in the hours of Time had waylaid Joe. He was assaulted in his weakness. Like Samson awakening after his haircut.[6] So he just opened his mouth and laughed.

6. See Judges 16:17, where Samson tells Delilah: "If I be shaven, then my strength will go from me, and I shall be like any other man."

The match went out and he struck another and lit the lamp. A howling wind raced across his heart, but underneath its fury he heard his wife sobbing and Slemmons pleading for his life. Offering to buy it with all that he had. "Please, suh, don't kill me. Sixty-two dollars at de sto'. Gold money."

Joe just stood. Slemmons looked at the window, but it was screened. Joe stood out like a rough-backed mountain between him and the door. Barring him from escape, from sunrise, from life.

He considered a surprise attack upon the big clown that stood there laughing like a chessy cat.[7] But before his fist could travel an inch, Joe's own rushed out to crush him like a battering ram. Then Joe stood over him.

"Git into yo' damn rags, Slemmons, and dat quick."

Slemmons scrambled to his feet and into his vest and coat. As he grabbed his hat, Joe's fury overrode his intentions and he grabbed at Slemmons with his left hand and struck at him with his right. The right landed. The left grazed the front of his vest. Slemmons was knocked a somersault into the kitchen and fled through the open door. Joe found himself alone with Missie May, with the golden watch charm clutched in his left fist. A short bit of broken chain dangled between his fingers.

Missie May was sobbing. Wails of weeping without words. Joe stood, and after awhile he found out that he had something in his hand. And then he stood and felt without thinking and without seeing with his natural eyes. Missie May kept on crying and Joe kept on feeling so much and not knowing what to do with all his feelings, he put Slemmons' watch charm in his pants pocket and took a good laugh and went to bed.

"Missie May, whut you cryin' for?"

"Cause Ah love you so hard and Ah know you don't love *me* no mo'."

Joe sank his face into the pillow for a spell then he said huskily, "You don't know de feelings of dat yet, Missie May."

"Oh Joe, honey, he said he wuz gointer give me dat gold money and he jes' kept on after me—"

Joe was very still and silent for a long time. Then he said, "Well, don't cry no mo', Missie May. Ah got yo' gold piece for you."

The hours went past on their rusty ankles. Joe still and quiet on one bed-rail and Missie May wrung dry of sobs on the other. Finally the sun's tide crept upon the shore of night and drowned all its hours. Missie May with her face stiff and streaked towards the window saw the dawn come into her yard. It was day. Nothing more. Joe wouldn't be coming home as usual. No need to fling open the front door and sweep off the porch, making it nice for Joe. Never no more breakfast to cook; no more washing and starching of Joe's jumper-jackets and pants. No more nothing. So why get up?

With this strange man in her bed, she felt embarrassed to get up and dress. She decided to wait till he had dressed and gone. Then she would get up, dress quickly and be gone forever beyond reach of Joe's looks and laughs. But he never moved. Red light turned to yellow, then white.

---

7. An allusion to the grinning Cheshire cat in Lewis Carroll's (1832–1898) *Alice's Adventures in Wonderland* (1865).

From beyond the no-man's land between them came a voice. A strange voice that yesterday had been Joe's.

"Missie May, ain't you gonna fix me no breakfus'?"

She sprang out of bed. "Yeah, Joe. Ah didn't reckon you wuz hongry."

No need to die today. Joe needed her for a few more minutes anyhow.

Soon there was a roaring fire in the cook stove. Water bucket full and two chickens killed. Joe loved fried chicken and rice. She didn't deserve a thing and good Joe was letting her cook him some breakfast. She rushed hot biscuits to the table as Joe took his seat.

He ate with his eyes on his plate. No laughter, no banter.

"Missie May, you ain't eatin' yo' breakfus'."

"Ah don't choose none, Ah thank yuh."

His coffee cup was empty. She sprang to refill it. When she turned from the stove and bent to set the cup beside Joe's plate, she saw the yellow coin on the table between them.

She slumped into her seat and wept into her arms.

Presently Joe said calmly, "Missie May, you cry too much. Don't look back lak Lot's wife and turn to salt."[8]

The sun, the hero of every day, the impersonal old man that beams as brightly on death as on birth, came up every morning and raced across the blue dome and dipped into the sea of fire every evening. Water ran down hill and birds nested.

Missie knew why she didn't leave Joe. She couldn't. She loved him too much, but she could not understand why Joe didn't leave her. He was polite, even kind at times, but aloof.

There were no more Saturday romps. No ringing silver dollars to stack beside her plate. No pockets to rifle. In fact the yellow coin in his trousers was like a monster hiding in the cave of his pockets to destroy her.

She often wondered if he still had it, but nothing could have induced her to ask nor yet to explore his pockets to see for herself. Its shadow was in the house whether or no.

One night Joe came home around midnight and complained of pains in the back. He asked Missie to rub him down with liniment. It had been three months since Missie had touched his body and it all seemed strange. But she rubbed him. Grateful for the chance. Before morning, youth triumphed and Missie exulted. But the next day, as she joyfully made up their bed, beneath her pillow she found the piece of money with the bit of chain attached.

Alone to herself, she looked at the thing with loathing, but look she must. She took it into her hands with trembling and saw first thing that it was no gold piece. It was a gilded half dollar. Then she knew why Slemmons had forbidden anyone to touch his gold. He trusted village eyes at a distance not to recognize his stick-pin as a gilded quarter, and his watch charm as a four-bit piece.

She was glad at first that Joe had left it there. Perhaps he was through with her punishment. They were man and wife again. Then another

---

8. According to Genesis 19:26, Lot's wife was turned to a pillar of salt for looking back on the destroyed city of Sodom.

thought came clawing at her. He had come home to buy from her as if she were any woman in the long house. Fifty cents for her love. As if to say that he could pay as well as Slemmons. She slid the coin into his Sunday pants pocket and dressed herself and left his house.

Halfway between her house and the quarters[9] she met her husband's mother, and after a short talk she turned and went back home. Never would she admit defeat to that woman who prayed for it nightly. If she had not the substance of marriage she had the outside show. Joe must leave *her*. She let him see she didn't want his old gold four-bits too.

She saw no more of the coin for some time though she knew that Joe could not help finding it in his pocket. But his health kept poor, and he came home at least every ten days to be rubbed.

The sun swept around the horizon, trailing its robes of weeks and days. One morning as Joe came in from work, he found Missie May chopping wood. Without a word he took the ax and chopped a huge pile before he stopped.

"You ain't got no business choppin' wood, and you know it."

"How come? Ah been choppin' it for de last longest."

"Ah ain't blind. You makin' feet for shoes."

"Won't you be glad to have a lil baby chile, Joe?"

"You know dat 'thout astin' me."

"Iss gointer be a boy chile and de very spit of you." "You reckon, Missie May?"

"Who else could it look lak?"

Joe said nothing, but he thrust his hand deep into his pocket and fingered something there.

It was almost six months later Missie May took to bed and Joe went and got his mother to come wait on the house.

Missie May delivered a fine boy. Her travail was over when Joe came in from work one morning. His mother and the old women were drinking great bowls of coffee around the fire in the kitchen.

The minute Joe came into the room his mother called him aside.

"How did Missie May make out?" he asked quickly.

"Who, dat gal? She strong as a ox. She gointer have plenty mo'. We done fixed her wid de sugar and lard to sweeten her for de nex' one."

Joe stood silent awhile.

"You ain't ast 'bout de baby, Joe. You oughter be mighty proud cause he sho is de spittin' image of yuh, son. Dat's yourn all right, if you never git another one, dat un is yourn. And you know Ah'm mighty proud too, son, cause Ah never thought well of you marryin' Missie May cause her ma used tuh fan her foot round right smart and Ah been mighty skeered dat Missie May was gointer git misput on her road."

Joe said nothing. He fooled around the house till late in the day then just before he went to work, he went and stood at the foot of the bed and asked his wife how she felt. He did this every day during the week.

On Saturday he went to Orlando to make his market. It had been a long time since he had done that.

9. The turpentine quarters, the dwellings in which the workers lived.

Meat and lard, meal and flour, soap and starch. Cans of corn and tomatoes. All the staples. He fooled around town for awhile and bought bananas and apples. Way after while he went around to the candy store.

"Hellow, Joe," the clerk greeted him. "Ain't seen you in a long time."

"Nope, Ah ain't been heah. Been round in spots and places."

"Want some of them molasses kisses you always buy?"

"Yessuh." He threw the gilded half dollar on the counter. "Will dat spend?"

"Whut is it, Joe? Well, I'll be doggone! A gold-plated four-bit piece. Where'd you git it, Joe?"

"Offen a stray nigger dat come through Eatonville. He had it on his watch chain for a charm—goin' round making out iss gold money. Ha ha! He had a quarter on his tie pin and it wuz all golded up too. Tryin' to fool people. Makin' out he so rich and everything. Ha! Ha! Tryin' to tole off folkses wives from home."

"How did you git it, Joe? Did he fool you, too?"

"Who, me? Naw suh! He ain't fooled me none. Know whut Ah done? He come round me wid his smart talk. Ah hauled off and knocked 'im down and took his old four-bits way from 'im. Gointer buy my wife some good ole lasses kisses wid it. Gimme fifty cents worth of dem candy kisses."

"Fifty cents buys a mighty lot of candy kisses, Joe. Why don't you split it up and take some chocolate bars, too. They eat good, too."

"Yessuh, dey do, but Ah wants all dat in kisses. Ah got a lil boy chile home now. Tain't a week old yet, but he kin suck a sugar tit and maybe eat one them kisses hisself."

Joe got his candy and left the store. The clerk turned to the next customer. "Wisht I could be like these darkies. Laughin' all the time. Nothin' worries 'em."

Back in Eatonville, Joe reached his own front door. There was the ring of singing metal on wood. Fifteen times. Missie May couldn't run to the door, but she crept there as quickly as she could.

"Joe Banks, Ah hear you chunkin' money in mah do'way. You wait till Ah got mah strength back and Ah'm gointer fix you for dat."

1933

Characteristics of Negro Expression

Drama

The Negro's universal mimicry is not so much a thing in itself as an evidence of something that permeates his entire self. And that thing is drama.

His very words are action words. His interpretation of the English language is in terms of pictures. One act described in terms of another. Hence the rich metaphor and simile.

The metaphor is of course very primitive. It is easier to illustrate than it is to explain because action came before speech. Let us make a parallel. Language is like money. In primitive communities actual goods, however bulky, are bartered for what one wants. This finally evolves into coin, the coin being not real wealth but a symbol of wealth. Still later even coin is abandoned for legal tender, and still later for checks in certain usages.

Every phase of Negro life is highly dramatized. No matter how joyful or how sad the case there is sufficient poise for drama. Everything is acted out. Unconsciously for the most part of course. There is an impromptu ceremony always ready for every hour of life. No little moment passes unadorned.

Now the people with highly developed languages have words for detached ideas. That is legal tender. "That-which-we-squat-on" has become "chair." "Groan-causer" has evolved into "spear" and so on. Some individuals even conceive of the equivalent of check words, like "ideation" and "pleonastic." Perhaps we might say that *Paradise Lost* and *Sartor Resartus*[1] are written in check words.

The primitive man exchanges descriptive words. His terms are all close fitting. Frequently the Negro, even with detached words in his vocabulary—not evolved in him but transplanted on his tongue by contact—must add action to it to make it do. So we have "chop-ax," "sitting-chair," "cookpot" and the like because the speaker has in his mind the picture of the object in use. Action. Everything illustrated. So we can say the white man thinks in a written language and the Negro thinks in hieroglyphics.

A bit of Negro drama familiar to all is the frequent meeting of two opponents who threaten to do atrocious murder one upon the other.

Who has not observed a robust young Negro chap posing upon a street corner, possessed of nothing but his clothing, his strength and his youth? Does he bear himself like a pauper? No, Louis XIV could be no more insolent in his assurance. His eyes say plainly "Female, halt!" His posture exults "Ah, female, I am the eternal male, the giver of life. Behold in my hot flesh all the delights of this world. Salute me, I am strength." All this with a languid posture, there is no mistaking his meaning.

A Negro girl strolls past the corner lounger. Her whole body panging[2] and posing. A slight shoulder movement that calls attention to her bust, that is all of a dare. A hippy undulation below the waist that is a sheaf of promises tied with conscious power. She is acting out. "I'm a darned sweet woman and you know it."

These little plays by strolling players are acted out daily in a dozen streets in a thousand cities, and no one ever mistakes the meaning.

Will to Adorn

The will to adorn is the second most notable characteristic in Negro expression. Perhaps his idea of ornament does not attempt to meet conventional standards, but it satisfies the soul of its creator.

In this respect the American Negro has done wonders to the English language. It has often been stated by etymologists that the Negro has introduced no African words to the language. This is true, but it is equally true

---

1. A combination of novel, essay, and autobiography written by Thomas Carlyle (1795–1881) in 1833. *Paradise Lost*, the most famous epic poem in the English language, is by John Milton (1608–1674).
2. As in pangs of hunger.

that he has made over a great part of the tongue to his liking and has his revision accepted by the ruling class. No one listening to a Southern white man talk could deny this. Not only has he softened and toned down strongly consonanted words like "aren't" to "aint" and the like, he has made new force words out of old feeble elements. Examples of this are "ham-shanked," "battle-hammed," "double-teen," "bodaciously," "muffle-jawed."

But the Negro's greatest contribution to the language is: (1) the use of metaphor and simile; (2) the use of the double descriptive; (3) the use of verbal nouns.

1. METAPHOR AND SIMILE

One at a time, like lawyers going to heaven.
You sho is propaganda.
Sobbing hearted.
I'll beat you till: (*a*) rope like okra, (*b*) slack like lime, (*c*) smell like onions.
Fatal for naked.
Kyting along.

That's a lynch.
That's a rope.
Cloakers—deceivers.
Regular as pig-tracks.
Mule blood—black molasses.
Syndicating—gossiping.
Flambeaux—cheap café (lighted by flambeaux).
To put yo'self on de ladder.

2. THE DOUBLE DESCRIPTIVE

High-tall.
Little-tee-ninchy (tiny).
Low-down.
Top-superior.
Sham-polish.
Lady-people.
Kill-dead.

Hot-boiling.
Chop-ax.
Sitting-chairs.
De watch wall.
Speedy-hurry.
More great and more better.

3. VERBAL NOUNS

She features somebody I know.
Funeralize.
Sense me into it.
Puts the shamery on him.
'Taint everybody you kin confidence.
I wouldn't friend with her.
Jooking—playing piano or guitar as

it is done in Jook-houses (houses of ill-fame).
Uglying away.
I wouldn't scorn my name all up on you.
Bookooing (beaucoup) around—showing off.

NOUNS FROM VERBS

Won't stand a broke.
She won't take a listen.
He won't stand straightening.

That is such a compliment.
That's a lynch.

The stark, trimmed phrases of the Occident seem too bare for the voluptuous child of the sun, hence the adornment. It arises out of the same impulse as the wearing of jewelry and the making of sculpture—the urge to adorn.

On the walls of the homes of the average Negro one always finds a glut of gaudy calendars, wall pockets and advertising lithographs. The sophisticated white man or Negro would tolerate none of these, even if they bore a likeness to the Mona Lisa. No commercial art for decoration. Nor the calendar nor the advertisement spoils the picture for this lowly man. He sees the beauty in spite of the declaration of the Portland Cement Works or the butcher's announcement. I saw in Mobile a room in which there was an over-stuffed mohair living-room suite, an imitation mahogany bed and chifferobe, a console victrola. The walls were gaily papered with Sunday supplements of the *Mobile Register*. There were seven calendars and three wall pockets. One of them was decorated with a lace doily. The mantelshelf was covered with a scarf of deep home-made lace, looped up with a huge bow of pink crêpe paper. Over the door was a huge lithograph showing the Treaty of Versailles being signed with a Waterman fountain pen.

It was grotesque, yes. But it indicated the desire for beauty. And decorating a decoration, as in the case of the doily on the gaudy wall pocket, did not seem out of place to the hostess. The feeling back of such an act is that there can never be enough of beauty, let alone too much. Perhaps she is right. We each have our standards of art, and thus are we all interested parties and so unfit to pass judgment upon the art concepts of others.

Whatever the Negro does of his own volition he embellishes. His religious service is for the greater part excellent prose poetry. Both prayers and sermons are tooled and polished until they are true works of art. The supplication is forgotten in the frenzy of creation. The prayer of the white man is considered humorous in its bleakness. The beauty of the Old Testament does not exceed that of a Negro prayer.

Angularity

After adornment the next most striking manifestation of the Negro is Angularity. Everything that he touches becomes angular. In all African sculpture and doctrine of any sort we find the same thing.

Anyone watching Negro dancers will be struck by the same phenomenon. Every posture is another angle. Pleasing, yes. But an effect achieved by the very means which an European strives to avoid.

The pictures on the walls are hung at deep angles. Furniture is always set at an angle. I have instances of a piece of furniture in the *middle* of a wall being set with one end nearer the wall than the other to avoid the simple straight line.

Asymmetry

Asymmetry is a definite feature of Negro art. I have no samples of true Negro painting unless we count the African shields, but the sculpture and carvings are full of this beauty and lack of symmetry.

It is present in the literature, both prose and verse. I offer an example of this quality in verse from Langston Hughes: [3]

> I aint gonna mistreat ma good gal any more,
> I'm just gonna kill her next time she makes me sore.

> I treats her kind but she don't do me right,
> She fights and quarrels most ever' night.

> I can't have no woman's got such low-down ways
> Cause de blue gum woman aint de style now'days.

> I brought her from the South and she's goin on back,
> Else I'll use her head for a carpet track.

It is the lack of symmetry which makes Negro dancing so difficult for white dancers to learn. The abrupt and unexpected changes. The frequent change of key and time are evidences of this quality in music. (Note the St. Louis Blues.)

The dancing of the justly famous Bo-Jangles and Snake Hips are excellent examples.

The presence of rhythm and lack of symmetry are paradoxical, but there they are. Both are present to a marked degree. There is always rhythm, but it is the rhythm of segments. Each unit has a rhythm of its own, but when the whole is assembled it is lacking in symmetry. But easily workable to a Negro who is accustomed to the break in going from one part to another, so that he adjusts himself to the new tempo.

Dancing

Negro dancing is dynamic suggestion. No matter how violent it may appear to the beholder, every posture gives the impression that the dancer will do much more. For example, the performer flexes one knee sharply, assumes a ferocious face mask, thrusts the upper part of the body forward with clenched fists, elbows taut as in hard running or grasping a thrusting blade. That is all. But the spectator himself adds the picture of ferocious assault, hears the drums and finds himself keeping time with the music and tensing himself for the struggle. It is compelling insinuation. That is the very reason the spectator is held so rapt. He is participating in the performance himself—carrying out the suggestions of the performer.

The difference in the two arts is: the white dancer attempts to express fully; the Negro is restrained, but succeeds in gripping the beholder by forcing him to finish the action the performer suggests. Since no art ever can express all the variations conceivable, the Negro must be considered the greater artist, his dancing is realistic suggestion, and that is about all a great artist can do.

---

3. Poet (1901–1967). The poem is his *Evil Woman* (1927).

Negro Folklore

Negro folklore is not a thing of the past. It is still in the making. Its great variety shows the adaptability of the black man: nothing is too old or too new, domestic or foreign, high or low, for his use. God and the Devil are paired, and are treated no more reverently than Rockefeller and Ford.[4] Both of these men are prominent in folklore, Ford being particularly strong, and they talk and act like good-natured stevedores or mill-hands. Ole Massa is sometimes a smart man and often a fool. The automobile is ranged alongside of the oxcart. The angels and the apostles walk and talk like section hands.[5] And through it all walks Jack, the greatest culture hero of the South; Jack beats them all—even the Devil, who is often smarter than God.

Culture Heroes

The Devil is next after Jack as a culture hero. He can out-smart everyone but Jack. God is absolutely no match for him. He is good-natured and full of humor. The sort of person one may count on to help out in any difficulty.

Peter the Apostle is the third in importance. One need not look far for the explanation. The Negro is not a Christian really. The primitive gods are not deities of too subtle inner reflection; they are hard-working bodies who serve their devotees just as laboriously as the suppliant serves them. Gods of physical violence, stopping at nothing to serve their followers. Now of all the apostles Peter is the most active. When the other ten fell back trembling in the garden, Peter wielded the blade on the posse.[6] Peter first and foremost in all action. The gods of no peoples have been philosophic until the people themselves have approached that state.

The rabbit, the bear, the lion, the buzzard, the fox are culture heroes from the animal world. The rabbit is far in the lead of all the others and is blood brother to Jack. In short, the trickster-hero[7] of West Africa has been transplanted to America.

John Henry is a culture hero in song, but no more so than Stacker Lee, Smokey Joe or Bad Lazarus. There are many, many Negroes who have never heard of any of the song heroes, but none who do not know John (Jack) and the rabbit.

EXAMPLES OF FOLKLORE AND THE MODERN CULTURE HERO

Why de Porpoise's Tail is on Crosswise

Now, I want to tell you 'bout de porpoise. God had done made de world and everything. He set de moon and de stars in de sky. He got de fishes of de sea, and de fowls of de air completed.

---

4. Henry Ford (1863–1947), U.S. automobile manufacturer. John D. Rockefeller (1839–1937), U.S. oil magnate.
5. Tracklayers for a railroad company.
6. John 18:10: "Then Simon Peter having a sword drew it, and smote the high priest's servant, and cut off his right ear."
7. The hero of many West African tales is frequently a trickster who prevails by using his wits, not physical force.

He made de sun and hung it up. Then He made a nice gold track for it to run on. Then He said, "Now, Sun, I got everything made but Time. That's up to you. I want you to start out and go round de world on dis track just as fast as you kin make it. And de time it takes you to go and come, I'm going to call day and night." De Sun went zoonin' on cross de elements. Now, de porpoise was hanging round there and heard God what he told de Sun, so he decided he'd take dat trip round de world hisself. He looked up and saw de Sun kytin' along, so he lit out too, him and dat Sun!

So de porpoise beat de Sun round de world by one hour and three minutes. So God said, "Aw naw, this aint gointer do! I didn't mean for nothin' to be faster than de Sun!" So God run dat porpoise for three days before he run him down and caught him, and took his tail off and put it on crossways to slow him up. Still he's de fastest thing in de water.

And dat's why de porpoise got his tail on crossways.

Rockefeller and Ford

Once John D. Rockefeller and Henry Ford was woofing at each other. Rockefeller told Henry Ford he could build a solid gold road round the world. Henry Ford told him if he would he would look at it and see if he liked it, and if he did he would buy it and put one of his tin liz-zies[8] on it.

Originality

It has been said so often that the Negro is lacking in originality that it has almost become a gospel. Outward signs seem to bear this out. But if one looks closely its falsity is immediately evident.

It is obvious that to get back to original sources is much too difficult for any group to claim very much as a certainty. What we really mean by origi-nality is the modification of ideas. The most ardent admirer of the great Shakespeare cannot claim first source even for him. It is his treatment of the borrowed material.

So if we look at it squarely, the Negro is a very original being. While he lives and moves in the midst of a white civilization, everything that he touches is re-interpreted for his own use. He has modified the language, mode of food preparation, practice of medicine, and most certainly the re-ligion of his new country, just as he adapted to suit himself the Sheik hair-cut made famous by Rudolph Valentino.

Everyone is familiar with the Negro's modification of the whites' musi-cal instruments, so that his interpretation has been adopted by the white man himself and then re-interpreted. In so many words, Paul Whiteman is giving an imitation of a Negro orchestra making use of white-invented mu-sical instruments in a Negro way. Thus has arisen a new art in the civilized

8. Small, cheap automobiles.

world, and thus has our so-called civilization come. The exchange and re-exchange of ideas between groups.

Imitation

The Negro, the world over, is famous as a mimic. But this in no way damages his standing as an original. Mimicry is an art in itself. If it is not, then all art must fall by the same blow that strikes it down. When sculpture, painting, dancing, literature neither reflect nor suggest anything in nature or human experience we turn away with a dull wonder in our hearts at why the thing was done. Moreover, the contention that the Negro imitates from a feeling of inferiority is incorrect. He mimics for the love of it. The group of Negroes who slavishly imitate is small. The average Negro glories in his ways. The highly educated Negro the same. The self-despisement lies in a middle class who scorns to do or be anything Negro. "That's just like a Nigger" is the most terrible rebuke one can lay upon this kind. He wears drab clothing, sits through a boresome church service, pretends to have no interest in the community, holds beauty contests, and otherwise apes all the mediocrities of the white brother. The truly cultured Negro scorns him, and the Negro "farthest down" is too busy "spreading his junk" in his own way to see or care. He likes his own things best. Even the group who are not Negroes but belong to the "sixth race," buy such records as "Shake dat thing" and "Tight lak dat." They really enjoy hearing a good bible-beater preach, but wild horses could drag no such admission from them. Their ready-made expression is: "We done got away from all that now." Some refuse to countenance Negro music on the grounds that it is nigger-ism, and for that reason should be done away with. Roland Hayes was thoroughly denounced for singing spirituals until he was accepted by white audiences. Langston Hughes is not considered a poet by this group because he writes of the man in the ditch, who is more numerous and real among us than any other.

But, this group aside, let us say that the art of mimicry is better developed in the Negro than in other racial groups. He does it as the mocking-bird does it, for the love of it, and not because he wishes to be like the one imitated. I saw a group of small Negro boys imitating a cat defecating and the subsequent toilet of the cat. It was very realistic, and they enjoyed it as much as if they had been imitating a coronation ceremony. The dances are full of imitations of various animals. The buzzard lope, walking the dog, the pig's hind legs, holding the mule, elephant squat, pigeon's wing, falling off the log, seabord (imitation of an engine starting), and the like.

Absence of the Concept of Privacy

It is said that Negroes keep nothing secret, that they have no reserve. This ought not to seem strange when one considers that we are an outdoor people accustomed to communal life. Add this to all-permeating drama and you have the explanation.

There is no privacy in an African village. Loves, fights, possessions are, to misquote Woodrow Wilson, "Open disagreements openly arrived at." [9] The community is given the benefit of a good fight as well as a good wedding. An audience is a necessary part of any drama. We merely go with nature rather than against it.

Discord is more natural than accord. If we accept the doctrine of the survival of the fittest there are more fighting honors than there are honors for other achievements. Humanity places premiums on all things necessary to its well-being, and a valiant and good fighter is valuable in any community. So why hide the light under a bushel? Moreover, intimidation is a recognized part of warfare the world over, and threats certainly must be listed under that head. So that a great threatener must certainly be considered an aid to the fighting machine. So then if a man or woman is a facile hurler of threats, why should he or she not show their wares to the community? Hence the holding of all quarrels and fights in the open. One relieves one's pent-up anger and at the same time earns laurels in intimidation. Besides, one does the community a service. There is nothing so exhilarating as watching well-matched opponents go into action. The entire world likes action, for that matter. Hence prizefighters become millionaires.

Likewise love-making is a biological necessity the world over and an art among Negroes. So that a man or woman who is proficient sees no reason why the fact should not be moot. He swaggers. She struts hippily about. Songs are built on the power to charm beneath the bed-clothes. Here again we have individuals striving to excel in what the community considers an art. Then if all of his world is seeking a great lover, why should he not speak right out loud?

It is all in a view-point. Love-making and fighting in all their branches are high arts, other things are arts among other groups where they brag about their proficiency just as brazenly as we do about these things that others consider matters for conversation behind closed doors. At any rate, the white man is despised by Negroes as a very poor fighter individually, and a very poor lover. One Negro, speaking of white men, said, "White folks is alright when dey gits in de bank and on de law bench, but dey sho' kin lie about wimmen folks."

I pressed him to explain. "Well you see, white mens makes out they marries wimmen to look at they eyes, and they know they gits em for just what us gits em for. 'Nother thing, white mens say they goes clear round de world and wins all de wimmen folks way from they men folks. Dat's a lie too. They don't win nothin, they buys em. Now de way I figgers it, if a woman don't want me enough to be wid me, 'thout I got to pay her, she kin rock right on, but these here white men don't know what do wid a woman when they gits her—dat's how come they gives they wimmen so much. They got to. Us wimmen works jus as hard as us does an come home an sleep wid us every night. They own wouldn't do it and its de mens fault. Dese white men done fooled theyself bout dese wimmen.

"Now me, I keeps me some wimmens all de time. Dat's whut dey wuz put here for—us mens to use. Dat's right now, Miss. Y'll wuz put here so us

9. From President Wilson's January 8, 1918, *Address to Congress*. The actual quotation is "Open covenants of peace, openly arrived at."

mens could have some pleasure. Course I don't run round like heap uh men folks. But if my ole lady go way from me and stay more'n two weeks, I got to git me somebody, aint I?"

The Jook

Jook is the word for a Negro pleasure house. It may mean a bawdy house. It may mean the house set apart on public works where the men and women dance, drink and gamble. Often it is a combination of all these.

In past generations the music was furnished by "boxes," another word for guitars. One guitar was enough for a dance; to have two was considered excellent. Where two were playing one man played the lead and the other seconded him. The first player was "picking" and the second was "framming," that is, playing chords while the lead carried the melody by dexterous finger work. Sometimes a third player was added, and he played a tom-tom effect on the low strings. Believe it or not, this is excellent dance music.

Pianos soon came to take the place of the boxes, and now player-pianos and victrolas are in all of the Jooks.

Musically speaking, the Jook is the most important place in America. For in its smelly, shoddy confines has been born the secular music known as blues, and on blues has been founded jazz. The singing and playing in the true Negro style is called "jooking."

The songs grow by incremental repetition as they travel from mouth to mouth and from Jook to Jook for years before they reach outside ears. Hence the great variety of subject-matter in each song.

The Negro dances circulated over the world were also conceived inside the Jooks. They too make the round of Jooks and public works before going into the outside world.

In this respect it is interesting to mention the Black Bottom. I have read several false accounts of its origin and name. One writer claimed that it got its name from the black sticky mud on the bottom of the Mississippi river. Other equally absurd statements gummed the press. Now the dance really originated in the Jook section of Nashville, Tennessee, around Fourth Avenue. This is a tough neighborhood known as Black Bottom—hence the name.

The Charleston is perhaps forty years old, and was danced up and down the Atlantic seaboard from North Carolina to Key West, Florida.

The Negro social dance is slow and sensuous. The idea in the Jook is to gain sensation, and not so much exercise. So that just enough foot movement is added to keep the dancers on the floor. A tremendous sex stimulation is gained from this. But who is trying to avoid it? The man, the woman, the time and the place have met. Rather, little intimate names are indulged in to heap fire on fire.

These too have spread to all the world.

The Negro theater, as built up by the Negro, is based on Jook situations, with women, gambling, fighting, drinking. Shows like "Dixie to Broadway" are only Negro in cast, and could just as well have come from pre-Soviet Russia.

Another interesting thing—Negro shows before being tampered with did not specialize in octoroon chorus girls. The girl who could hoist a Jook song from her belly and lam it against the front door of the theater was the lead, even if she were as black as the hinges of hell. The question was "Can she jook?" She must also have a good belly wobble, and her hips must, to quote a popular work song, "Shake like jelly all over and be so broad, Lawd, Lawd, and be so broad." So that the bleached chorus is the result of a white demand and not the Negro's.

The woman in the Jook may be nappy headed and black, but if she is a good lover she gets there just the same. A favorite Jook song of the past has this to say:

> *Singer:* It aint good looks dat takes you through dis world.
> *Audience:* What is it, good mama?
> *Singer:* Elgin movements[1] in your hips
> Twenty years guarantee.

And it always brought down the house too.

> Oh de white gal rides in a Cadillac,
> De yaller[2] gal rides de same,
> Black gal rides in a rusty Ford
> But she gits dere just de same.

The sort of woman her men idealize is the type that is put forth in the theater. The art-creating Negro prefers a not too thin woman who can shake like jelly all over as she dances and sings, and that is the type he put forth on the stage. She has been banished by the white producer and the Negro who takes his cue from the white.

Of course a black woman is never the wife of the upper class Negro in the North. This state of affairs does not obtain in the South, however. I have noted numerous cases where the wife was considerably darker than the husband. People of some substance, too.

This scornful attitude towards black women receives mouth sanction by the mud-sills.[3]

Even on the works and in the Jooks the black man sings disparagingly of black women. They say that she is evil. That she sleeps with her fists doubled up and ready for action. All over they are making a little drama of waking up a yaller wife and a black one.

A man is lying beside his yaller wife and wakes her up. She says to him, "Darling, do you know what I was dreaming when you woke me up?" He says, "No honey, what was you dreaming?" She says, "I dreamt I had done cooked you a big, fine dinner and we was setting down to eat out de same plate and I was setting on yo' lap jus huggin you and kissin you and you was so sweet."

Wake up a black woman, and before you kin git any sense into her she be done up and lammed you over the head four or five times. When you git

---

1. Like an Elgin watch.   3. The lowest members of a given community.
2. A light-skinned African American.

her quiet she'll say, "Nigger, know whut I was dreamin when you woke me up?"

You say, "No honey, what was you dreamin?" She says, "I dreamt you shook yo' rusty fist under my nose and I split yo' head open wid a ax."

But in spite of disparaging fictitious drama, in real life the black girl is drawing on his account at the commissary. Down in the Cypress Swamp[4] as he swings his ax he chants:

> Dat ole black gal, she keep on grumblin,
> New pair shoes, new pair shoes,
> I'm goint to buy her shoes and stockings
> Slippers too, slippers too.

Then adds aside: "Blacker de berry, sweeter de juice."

To be sure the black gal is still in power, men are still cutting and shooting their way to her pillow. To the queen of the Jook!

Speaking of the influence of the Jook, I noted that Mae West in "Sex" had much more flavor of the turpentine quarters[5] than she did of the white bawd. I know that the piece she played on the piano is a very old Jook composition. "Honey let yo' drawers hang low" had been played and sung in every Jook in the South for at least thirty-five years. It has always puzzled me why she thought it likely to be played in a Canadian bawdy house.

Speaking of the use of Negro material by white performers, it is astonishing that so many are trying it, and I have never seen one yet entirely realistic. They often have all the elements of the song, dance, or expression, but they are misplaced or distorted by the accent falling on the wrong element. Every one seems to think that the Negro is easily imitated when nothing is further from the truth. Without exception I wonder why the black-face comedians *are* black-face; it is a puzzle—good comedians, but darn poor niggers. Gershwin[6] and the other "Negro" rhapsodists come under this same axe. Just about as Negro as caviar or Ann Pennington's[7] athletic Black Bottom. When the Negroes who knew the Black Bottom in its cradle saw the Broadway version they asked each other, "Is you learnt dat *new* Black Bottom yet?" Proof that it was not *their* dance.

And God only knows what the world has suffered from the white damsels who try to sing Blues.

The Negroes themselves have sinned also in this respect. In spite of the goings up and down on the earth, from the original Fisk Jubilee Singers[8] down to the present, there has been no genuine presentation of Negro songs to white audiences. The spirituals that have been sung around the world are Negroid to be sure, but so full of musicians' tricks that Negro congregations are highly entertained when they hear their old songs so changed. They never use the new style songs, and these are never heard unless perchance some daughter or son has been off to college and returns with one of the old songs with its face lifted, so to speak.

4. In Florida.
5. Southern black rural communities where turpentine was made.
6. George Gershwin (1898–1937), U.S. composer

of "Rhapsody in Blue."
7. White dancer (1892–1971).
8. A celebrated 19th-century group of young singers who toured to raise funds for the university.

I am of the opinion that this trick style of delivery was originated by the Fisk Singers; Tuskeegee and Hampton followed suit and have helped spread this misconception of Negro spirituals. This Glee Club style has gone on so long and become so fixed among concert singers that it is considered quite authentic. But I say again, that not one concert singer in the world is singing the songs as the Negro song-makers sing them.

If anyone wishes to prove the truth of this let him step into some unfashionable Negro church and hear for himself.

To those who want to institute the Negro theater, let me say it is already established. It is lacking in wealth, so it is not seen in the high places. A creature with a white head and Negro feet struts the Metropolitan boards. The real Negro theater is in the Jooks and the cabarets. Self-conscious individuals may turn away the eye and say, "Let us search elsewhere for our dramatic art." Let 'em search. They certainly won't find it. Butter Beans and Susie, Bo-Jangles[9] and Snake Hips are the only performers of the real Negro school it has ever been my pleasure to behold in New York.

Dialect

If we are to believe the majority of writers of Negro dialect and the burnt-cork artists, Negro speech is a weird thing, full of "ams" and "Ises." Fortunately we don't have to believe them. We may go directly to the Negro and let him speak for himself.

I know that I run the risk of being damned as an infidel for declaring that nowhere can be found the Negro who asks "am it?" nor yet his brother who announces "Ise uh gwinter." He exists only for a certain type of writers and performers.

Very few Negroes, educated or not, use a clear clipped "I." It verges more or less upon "Ah." I think the lip form is responsible for this to a great extent. By experiment the reader will find that a sharp "I" is very much easier with a thin taut lip than with a full soft lip. Like tightening violin strings.

If one listens closely one will note too that a word is slurred in one position in the sentence but clearly pronounced in another. This is particularly true of the pronouns. A pronoun as a subject is likely to be clearly enunciated, but slurred as an object. For example: "You better not let me ketch yuh."

There is a tendency in some localities to add the "h" to "it" and pronounce it "hit." Probably a vestige of old English. In some localities "if" is "ef."

In story telling "so" is universally the connective. It is used even as an introductory word, at the very beginning of a story. In religious expression "and" is used. The trend in stories is to state conclusions; in religion, to enumerate.

I am mentioning only the most general rules in dialect because there are

9. Bill "Bojangles" Robinson (1876–1949) was a dance star of stage and screen. Jodie "Butterbeans" Edwards (1897–1967) and Susie Hawthorn were popular black entertainers known for their husband-and-wife sketches.

so many quirks that belong only to certain localities that nothing less than a volume would be adequate.

Now He told me, He said: "You got the three witnesses. One is water, one is spirit, and one is blood. And these three correspond with the three in heben—Father, Son, and Holy Ghost."

Now I ast Him about this lyin in sin and He give me a handful of seeds and He tole me to sow 'em in a bed and He tole me: "I want you to watch them seeds." The seeds come up about in places and He said: "Those seeds that come up, they died in the heart of the earth and quickened and come up and brought forth fruit. But those seeds that didn't come up, they died in the heart of the earth and rottened.

"And a soul that dies and quickens through my spirit they will live forever, but those that dont never pray, they are lost forever."

(Rev. JESSIE JEFFERSON.) [1]

1934

From Mules and Men

[*Negro Folklore*]

I was glad when somebody told me, "You may go and collect Negro folklore."

In a way it would not be a new experience for me. When I pitched head-foremost into the world I landed in the crib of negroism. From the earliest rocking of my cradle, I had known about the capers Brer Rabbit is apt to cut and what the Squinch Owl says from the house top. But it was fitting me like a tight chemise. I couldn't see it for wearing it. It was only when I was off in college, away from my native surroundings, that I could see myself like somebody else and stand off and look at my garment. Then I had to have the spy-glass of Anthropology to look through at that.

Dr. Boas [1] asked me where I wanted to work and I said, "Florida," and gave, as my big reason, that "Florida is a place that draws people—white people from all over the world, and Negroes from every Southern state surely and some from the North and West." So I knew that it was possible for me to get a cross section of the Negro South in the one state. And then I realized that I was new myself, so it looked sensible for me to choose familiar ground.

First place I aimed to stop to collect material was Eatonville, Florida.

And now, I'm going to tell you why I decided to go to my native village first. I didn't go back there so that the home folks could make admiration over me because I had been up North to college and come back with a diploma and a Chevrolet. I knew they were not going to pay either one of these items too much mind. I was just Lucy Hurston's daughter, Zora, and even if I had—to use one of our down-home expressions—had a Kaiser

---

1. A local minister observed by Hurston.
1. Franz Boas (1858–1952), father of American an-   thropology, who was a professor at Barnard College when Hurston was a student there (1925–28).

baby, and that's something that hasn't been done in this Country yet, I'd still be just Zora to the neighbors. If I had exalted myself to impress the town, somebody would have sent me word in a match-box that I had been up North there and had rubbed the hair off of my head against some college wall, and then come back there with a lot of form and fashion and outside show to the world. But they'd stand flat-footed and tell me that they didn't have me, neither my shampolish, to study 'bout. And that would have been that.

I hurried back to Eatonville because I knew that the town was full of material and that I could get it without hurt, harm or danger. As early as I could remember it was the habit of the men folks particularly to gather on the store porch of evenings and swap stories. Even the women folks would stop and break a breath with them at times. As a child when I was sent down to Joe Clarke's store, I'd drag out my leaving as long as possible in order to hear more.

Folk-lore is not as easy to collect as it sounds. The best source is where there are the least outside influences and these people, being usually underprivileged, are the shyest. They are most reluctant at times to reveal that which the soul lives by. And the Negro, in spite of his open-faced laughter, his seeming acquiescence, is particularly evasive. You see we are a polite people and we do not say to our questioner, "Get out of here!" We smile and tell him or her something that satisfies the white person because, knowing so little about us, he doesn't know what he is missing. The Indian resists curiosity by a stony silence. The Negro offers a featherbed resistance. That is, we let the probe enter, but it never comes out. It gets smothered under a lot of laughter and pleasantries.

The theory behind our tactics: "The white man is always trying to know into somebody else's business. All right, I'll set something outside the door of my mind for him to play with and handle. He can read my writing but he sho' can't read my mind. I'll put this play toy in his hand, and he will seize it and go away. Then I'll say my say and sing my song."

I knew that even I was going to have some hindrance among strangers. But here in Eatonville I knew everybody was going to help me. So below Palatka I began to feel eager to be there and I kicked the little Chevrolet right along.

I thought about the tales I had heard as a child. How even the Bible was made over to suit our vivid imagination. How the devil always out-smarted God and how that over-noble hero Jack or John—not *John Henry*, who occupies the same place in Negro folk-lore that Casey Jones does in white lore and if anything is more recent—outsmarted the devil. Brer Fox, Brer Deer, Brer 'Gator, Brer Dawg, Brer Rabbit, Ole Massa and his wife were walking the earth like natural men way back in the days when God himself was on the ground and men could talk with him. Way back there before God weighed up the dirt to make the mountains. When I was rounding Lily Lake I was remembering how God had made the world and the elements and people. He made souls for people, but he didn't give them out because he said:

"Folks ain't ready for souls yet. De clay ain't dry. It's de strongest thing Ah ever made. Don't aim to waste none thru loose cracks. And then men got to grow strong enough to stand it. De way things is now, if Ah give it out it would tear them shackly bodies to pieces. Bimeby, Ah give it out."

So folks went round thousands of years without no souls. All de time de soul-piece, it was setting 'round covered up wid God's loose raiment. Every now and then de wind would blow and hist up de cover and then de elements would be full of lightning and de winds would talk. So people told one 'nother that God was talking in de mountains.

De white man passed by it way off and he looked but he wouldn't go close enough to touch. De Indian and de Negro, they tipped by cautious too, and all of 'em seen de light of diamonds when de winds shook de cover, and de wind dat passed over it sung songs. De Jew come past and heard de song from de soul-piece then he kept on passin' and all of a sudden he grabbed up de soul-piece and hid it under his clothes, and run off down de road. It burnt him and tore him and throwed him down and lifted him up and toted him across de mountain and he tried to break loose but he couldn't do it. He kept on hollerin' for help but de rest of 'em run hid 'way from him. Way after while they come out of holes and corners and picked up little chips and pieces that fell back on de ground. So God mixed it up wid feelings and give it out to 'em. Way after while when He ketch dat Jew, He's goin' to 'vide things up more ekal'.

So I rounded Park Lake and came speeding down the straight stretch into Eatonville, the city of five lakes, three croquet courts, three hundred brown skins, three hundred good swimmers, plenty guavas, two schools, and no jail-house.

Before I enter the township, I wish to make acknowledgments to Mrs. R. Osgood Mason[2] of New York City. She backed my falling in a hearty way, in a spiritual way, and in addition, financed the whole expedition in the manner of the Great Soul that she is. The world's most gallant woman.

As I crossed the Maitland-Eatonville township line I could see a group on the store porch. I was delighted. The town had not changed. Same love of talk and song. So I drove on down there before I stopped. Yes, there was George Thomas, Calvin Daniels, Jack and Charlie Jones, Gene Brazzle, B. Moseley and "Seaboard." Deep in a game of Florida-flip. All of those who were not actually playing were giving advice—"bet straightening" they call it.

"Hello, boys," I hailed them as I went into neutral.

They looked up from the game and for a moment it looked as if they had forgotten me. Then B. Moseley said, "Well, if it ain't Zora Hurston!" Then everybody crowded around the car to help greet me.

"You gointer stay awhile, Zora?"

"Yep. Several months."

"Where you gointer stay, Zora?"

"With Mett and Ellis, I reckon."

"Mett" was Mrs. Armetta Jones, an intimate friend of mine since child-

---

2. Charlotte Mason (1854–1946), also known as "Godmother," who was Hurston's patron and confidant for several years, starting in 1927.

hood and Ellis was her husband. Their house stands under the huge camphor tree on the front street.

"Hello, heart-string," Mayor Hiram Lester yelled as he hurried up the
street. "We heard all about you up North. You back home for good, I
hope."

"Nope, Ah come to collect some old stories and tales and Ah know y'all
know a plenty of 'em and that's why Ah headed straight for home."

"What you mean, Zora, them big old lies we tell when we're jus' sittin'
around here on the store porch doin' nothin'?" asked B. Moseley.

"Yeah, those same ones about Ole Massa, and colored folks in heaven,
and—oh, y'all know the kind I mean."

"Aw shucks," exclaimed George Thomas doubtfully. "Zora, don't you
come here and tell de biggest lie first thing. Who you reckon want to read
all them old-time tales about Brer Rabbit and Brer Bear?"

"Plenty of people, George. They are a lot more valuable than you might
think. We want to set them down before it's too late."

"Too late for what?"

"Before everybody forgets all of 'em."

"No danger of that. That's all some people is good for—set 'round and lie
and murder groceries."

"Ah know one right now," Calvin Daniels announced cheerfully. "It's a
tale 'bout John and de frog."

"Wait till she gets out her car, Calvin. Let her get settled at 'Met's' and
cook a pan of ginger bread then we'll all go down and tell lies and eat ginger bread. Dat's de way to do. She's tired now from all dat drivin'."

"All right, boys," I agreed. "But Ah'll be rested by night. Be lookin' for
everybody."

So I unloaded the car and crowded it into Ellis' garage and got settled.
Armetta made me lie down and rest while she cooked a big pan of ginger
bread for the company we expected.

Calvin Daniels and James Moseley were the first to show up.

"Calvin, Ah sure am glad that you got here. Ah'm crazy to hear about
John and dat frog," I said.

"That's why Ah come so early so Ah could tell it to you and go. Ah got to
go over to Wood Bridge a little later on."

"Ah'm glad you remembered me first, Calvin."

"Ah always like to be good as my word, and Ah just heard about a toe-
party over to Wood Bridge tonight and Ah decided to make it."

"A toe-party! What on earth is that?"

"Come go with me and James and you'll see!"

"But, everybody will be here lookin' for me. They'll think Ah'm crazy—
tellin' them to come and then gettin' out and goin' to Wood Bridge myself.
But Ah certainly would like to go to that toe-party."

"Aw, come on. They kin come back another night. You gointer like this
party."

"Well, you tell me the story first, and by that time, Ah'll know what to
do."

"Ah, come on, Zora," James urged. "Git de car out. Calvin kin tell you
dat one while we're on de way. Come on, let's go to de toe-party."

"No, let 'im tell me this one first, then, if Ah go he can tell me some more on de way over."

James motioned to his friend. "Hurry up and tell it, Calvin, so we kin go before somebody else come."

"Aw, most of 'em ain't comin' nohow. They all 'bout goin' to Wood Bridge, too. Lemme tell you 'bout John and dis frog:

It was night and Ole Massa sent John, his favorite slave, down to the spring to get him a cool drink of water. He called John to him.

"John!"

"What you want, Massa?"

"John, I'm thirsty. Ah wants a cool drink of water, and Ah wants you to go down to de spring and dip me up a nice cool pitcher of water."

John didn't like to be sent nowhere at night, but he always tried to do everything Ole Massa told him to do, so he said, "Yessuh, Massa, Ah'll go git you some!"

Ole Massa said: "Hurry up, John, Ah'm mighty thirsty."

John took de pitcher and went on down to de spring. There was a great big ole bull frog settin' right on de edge of de spring, and when John dipped up de water de noise skeered de frog and he hollered and jumped over in de spring.

John dropped de water pitcher and tore out for de big house, hollerin' "Massa! Massa! A big ole booger[3] done got after me!"

Ole Massa told him, "Why, John, there's no such thing as a booger."

"Oh, yes it is, Massa. He down at dat Spring."

"Don't tell me, John. Youse just excited. Furthermore, you go git me dat water Ah sent you after."

"No, indeed, Massa, you and nobody else can't send me back there so dat booger kin git me."

Ole Massa begin to figger dat John musta seen somethin' sho nuff because John never had disobeyed him before, so he ast: "John, you say you seen a booger. What did it look like?"

John tole him, "Massa, he had two great big eyes lak balls of fire, and when he was standin' up he was sittin' down and when he moved, he moved by jerks, and he had most no tail."

Long before Calvin had ended his story James had lost his air of impatience.

"Now, Ah'll tell one," he said. "That is, if you so desire."

"Sure, Ah want to hear you tell 'em till daybreak if you will," I said eagerly.

"But where's the ginger bread?" James stopped to ask.

"It's out in the kitchen," I said. "Ah'm waiting for de others to come."

"Aw, naw, give us ours now. Them others may not get here before forty o'clock and Ah'll be done et mine and be in Wood Bridge. Anyhow Ah want a corner piece and some of them others will beat me to it."

So I served them with ginger bread and buttermilk.

3. A bogey man [Hurston's note].

"You sure going to Wood Bridge with us after Ah git thru tellin' this one?" James asked.

"Yeah, if the others don't show up by then," I conceded.

So James told the story about the man who went to Heaven from Johnstown.[4]

You know, when it lightnings, de angels is peepin' in de lookin' glass; when it thunders, they's rollin' out de rain-barrels; and when it rains, somebody done dropped a barrel or two and bust it.

One time, you know, there was going to be big doin's in Glory and all de angels had brand new clothes to wear and so they was all peepin' in the lookin' glasses, and therefore it got to lightning all over de sky. God tole some of de angels to roll in all de full rain barrels and they was in such a hurry that it was thunderin' from the east to the west and the zigzag lightning went to join the mutterin' thunder and, next thing you know, some of them angels got careless and dropped a whole heap of them rain barrels, and didn't it rain!

In one place they call Johnstown they had a great flood. And so many folks got drownded that it jus' look like Judgment day.

So some of de folks that got drownded in that flood went one place and some went another. You know, everything that happen, they got to be a nigger in it—and so one of de brothers in black went up to Heben from de flood.

When he got to the gate, Ole Peter let 'im in and made 'im welcome. De colored man was named John, so John ast Peter, says, "Is it dry in dere?"

Ole Peter tole 'im, "Why, yes it's dry in here. How come you ast that?"

"Well, you know Ah jus' come out of one flood, and Ah don't want to run into no mo'. Ooh, man! You ain't *seen* no water. You just oughter seen dat flood we had at Johnstown."

Peter says, "Yeah, we know all about it. Jus' go wid Gabriel and let him give you some new clothes."

So John went on off wid Gabriel and come back all dressed up in brand new clothes and all de time he was changin' his clothes he was tellin' Ole Gabriel all about dat flood, jus' like he didn't know already.

So when he come back from changin' his clothes, they give him a brand new gold harp and handed him to a gold bench and made him welcome. They was so tired of hearing about dat flood they was glad to see him wid his harp 'cause they figgered he'd get to playin' and forget all about it. So Peter tole him, "Now you jus' make yo'self at home and play all de music you please."

John went and took a seat on de bench and commenced to tune up his harp. By dat time, two angels come walkin' by where John was settin' so he throwed down his harp and tackled 'em.

"Say," he hollered, "Y'all want to hear 'bout de big flood Ah was in down on earth? Lawd, Lawd! It sho rained, and talkin' 'bout water!"

4. A town in Pennsylvania that was the site of the great flood of May 31, 1899, in which a dam broke and twenty-one hundred lives were lost.

Dem two angels hurried on off from 'im jus' as quick as they could.
He started to tellin' another one and he took to flyin'. Gab'ull went
over to 'im and tried to get 'im to take it easy, but John kept right on
stoppin' every angel dat he could find to tell 'im about dat flood of
water.

Way after while he went over to Ole Peter and said: "Thought you
said everybody would be nice and polite?"

Peter said, "Yeah, Ah said it. Ain't everybody treatin' you right?"

John said, "Naw. Ah jus' walked up to a man as nice and friendly as
Ah could and started to tell 'im 'bout all dat water Ah left back there in
Johnstown and instead of him turnin' me a friendly answer he said,
'Shucks! You ain't seen no water!' and walked off and left me standin'
by myself."

"Was he a *ole* man wid a crooked walkin' stick?" Peter ast John.

"Yeah."

"Did he have whiskers down to here?" Peter measured down to his
waist.

"He sho did," John tol' 'im.

"Aw shucks," Peter tol' im. "Dat was Ole Nora.[5] You can't tell *him*
nothin' 'bout no flood."

There was a lot of horn-honking outside and I went to the door. The
crowd drew up under the mothering camphor tree in four old cars. Everybody in boisterous spirits.

"Come on, Zora! Le's go to Wood Bridge. Great toe-party goin' on. All
kinds of 'freshments. We kin tell you some lies most any ole time. We never
run outer lies and lovin'. Tell 'em tomorrow night. Come on if you
comin'—le's go if you gwine."

So I loaded up my car with neighbors and we all went to Wood Bridge. It
is a Negro community joining Maitland on the north as Eatonville does on
the west, but no enterprising souls have ever organized it. They have no
schoolhouse, no post office, no mayor. It is lacking in Eatonville's feeling
of unity. In fact, a white woman lives there.

While we rolled along Florida No. 3, I asked Armetta where was the
shindig going to be in Wood Bridge. "At Edna Pitts' house," she told me.
"But she ain't givin' it by herself; it's for the lodge."

"Think it's gointer be lively?"

"Oh, yeah. Ah heard that a lot of folks from Altamonte and Longwood is
comin'. Maybe from Winter Park too."

We were the tail end of the line and as we turned off the highway we
could hear the boys in the first car doing what Ellis Jones called bookooing
before they even hit the ground. Charlie Jones was woofing[6] louder than
anybody else. "Don't y'all sell off dem pretty li'l pink toes befo' Ah git
dere."

Peter Stagg: "Save me de best one!"

Soddy Sewell: "Hey, you mullet heads! Get out de way there and let a
real man smoke them toes over."

5. Noah [Hurston's note].
6. Aimless talking [Hurston's note]. "Bookooing": loud talking, bullying, woofing. From French *beaucoup* [Hurston's note].

Gene Brazzle: "Come to my pick, gimme a vaseline brown!"

Big Willie Sewell: "Gimme any kind so long as you gimme more'n one."

Babe Brown, riding a running-board, guitar in hand, said, "Ah want a toe, but if it ain't got a good looking face on to it; don't bring de mess up."

When we got there the party was young. The house was swept and garnished, the refreshments on display, several people sitting around; but the spot needed some social juices to mix the ingredients. In other words, they had the carcass of a party lying around up until the minute Eatonville burst in on it. Then it woke up.

"Y'all done sold off any toes yet?" George Brown wanted to know.

Willie Mae Clarke gave him a certain look and asked him, "What's dat got to do with you, George Brown?" And he shut up. Everybody knows that Willie Mae's got the business with George Brown.

"Nope. We ain't had enough crowd, but I reckon we kin start now," Edna said. Edna and a sort of committee went inside and hung up a sheet across one end of the room. Then she came outside and called all of the young women inside. She had to coax and drag some of the girls.

"Oh, Ah'm shame-face-ted!" some of them said.

"Nobody don't want to buy *mah* ole rusty toe." Others fished around for denials from the male side.

I went on in with the rest and was herded behind the curtain.

"Say, what *is* this toe-party business?" I asked one of the girls. "Good gracious, Zora! Ain't you ever been to a toe-party before?"

"Nope. They don't have 'em up North where Ah been and Ah just got back today."

"Well, they hides all de girls behind a curtain and you stick out yo' toe. Some places you take off yo' shoes and some places you keep 'em on, but most all de time you keep 'em on. When all de toes is in a line, sticking out from behind de sheet they let de men folks in and they looks over all de toes and buys de ones they want for a dime. Then they got to treat de lady dat owns dat toe to everything she want. Sometime they play it so's you keep de same partner for de whole thing and sometime they fix it so they put de girls back every hour or so and sell de toes agin."

Well, my toe went on the line with the rest and it was sold five times during the party. Everytime a toe was sold there was a great flurry before the curtain. Each man eager to see what he had got, and whether the other men would envy him or ridicule him. One or two fellows ungallantly ran out of the door rather than treat the girls whose toe they had bought sight unseen.

Babe Brown got off on his guitar and the dancing was hilarious. There was plenty of chicken perleau[7] and baked chicken and fried chicken and rabbit. Pig feet and chitterlings and hot peanuts and drinkables. Everybody was treating wildly.

"Come on, Zora, and have a treat on me!" Charlie Jones insisted. "You done et chicken-ham and chicken-bosom wid every shag-leg[8] in Orange County *but* me. Come on and spend some of *my* money."

---

7. I.e., pilaf; a rice dish.   8. Fellow, slightly pejorative; akin to ne'er-do-well.

"Thanks, Charlie, but Ah got five helpin's of chicken inside already. Ah either got to get another stomach or quit eatin'."

"Quit eatin' then and go to thinking. Quit thinkin' and start to drinkin'. What you want?"

"Coca-Cola right off de ice, Charlie, and put some salt in it. Ah got a slight headache."

"Aw now, my money don't buy no sweet slop. Choose some coon dick."

"What is coon dick?"

"Aw, Zora, jus' somethin' to make de drunk come. Made out uh grape fruit juice, corn meal mash, beef bones and a few mo' things. Come on le's git some together. It might make our love come down."

As soon as we started over into the next yard where coon dick was to be had, Charlie yelled to the barkeep, "Hey, Seymore! fix up another quart of dat low wine—here come de boom!"

It was handed to us in a quart fruit jar and we went outside to try it.

The raw likker known locally as coon dick was too much. The minute it touched my lips, the top of my head flew off. I spat it out and "choosed" some peanuts. Big Willie Sewell said, "Come on, heartstring, and have some gospel-bird[9] on me. My money spends too." His Honor Hiram Lester, the Mayor, heard him and said, "There's no mo' chicken left, Willie. Why don't you offer her something she can get?"

"Well there *was* some chicken there when Ah passed the table a little while ago."

"Oh, so you offerin' her some chicken *was*. She can't eat that. What she want is some chicken *is*."

"Aw shut up, Hiram. Come on, Zora, le's go inside and make out we dancin'." We went on inside but it wasn't a party any more. Just some people herded together. The high spirits were simmering down and nobody had a dime left to cry so the toe-business suffered a slump. The heaped-up tables of refreshments had become shambles of chicken bones and empty platters anyway so that there was no longer any point in getting your toe sold, so when Columbus Montgomery said, "Le's go to Eatonville," Soddy Sewell jumped up and grabbed his hat and said, "I heard you buddy."

Eatonville began to move back home right then. Nearly everybody was packed in one of the five cars when the delegation from Altamonte arrived. Johnnie Barton and Georgia Burke. Everybody piled out again.

"Got yo' guitar wid you, Johnnie?"

"Man, you know Ah don't go nowhere unless Ah take my box wid me," said Johnnie in his starched blue shirt, collar pin with heart bangles hanging on each end and his cream pants with the black stripe. "And what make it so cool, Ah don't go nowhere unless I play it."

"And when you git to strowin' yo' mess and Georgy gits to singin' her alto, man it's hot as seven hells. Man, play dat 'Palm Beach'."

Babe Brown took the guitar and Johnnie Barton grabbed the piano stool. He sung. Georgia Burke and George Thomas singing about Polk County where the water taste like wine.

---

9. Chicken. Preachers are supposed to be fond of them [Hurston's note].

My heart struck sorrow, tears come running down.

At about the thirty-seventh verse, something about:

> Ah'd ruther be in Tampa with the Whip-poor-will,
> Ruther be in Tampa with the Whip-poor-will,
> Than to be 'round here—
> Honey with a hundred dollar bill,

I staggered sleepily forth to the little Chevrolet for Eatonville. The car was overflowing with passengers but I was so dull from lack of sleep that I didn't know who they were. All I knew is they belonged in Eatonville.

Somebody was woofing in my car about love and I asked him about his buddy—I don't know why now. He said, "Ah ain't got no buddy. They kilt my buddy so they could raise me. Jus' so Ah be yo' man Ah don't want no damn buddy. Ah hope they kill every man dat ever cried, 'titty-mamma' but me. Lemme be yo' kid."

Some voice from somewhere else in the car commented, "You sho' Lawd is gointer have a lot of hindrance."

Then somehow I got home and to bed and Armetta had Georgia syrup and waffles for breakfast.

1935

From Their Eyes Were Watching God

Chapter 1

[THE RETURN]

Ships at a distance have every man's wish on board. For some they come in with the tide. For others they sail forever on the horizon, never out of sight, never landing until the Watcher turns his eyes away in resignation, his dreams mocked to death by Time. That is the life of men.

Now, women forget all those things they don't want to remember, and remember everything they don't want to forget. The dream is the truth. Then they act and do things accordingly.

So the beginning of this was a woman and she had come back from burying the dead. Not the dead of sick and ailing with friends at the pillow and the feet. She had come back from the sodden and the bloated; the sudden dead, their eyes flung wide open in judgment.

The people all saw her come because it was sundown. The sun was gone, but he had left his footprints in the sky. It was the time for sitting on porches beside the road. It was the time to hear things and talk. These sitters had been tongueless, earless, eyeless conveniences all day long. Mules and other brutes had occupied their skins. But now, the sun and the bossman were gone, so the skins felt powerful and human. They became lords of sounds and lesser things. They passed notions through their mouths. They sat in judgment.

Seeing the woman as she was made them remember the envy they had stored up from other times. So they chewed up the back parts of their minds and swallowed with relish. They made burning statements with questions, and killing tools out of laughs. It was mass cruelty. A mood come alive. Words walking without masters; walking altogether like harmony in a song.

"What she doin' coming back here in dem overhalls? Can't she find no dress to put on?—Where's dat blue satin dress she left here in?—Where all dat money her husband took and died and left her?—What dat ole forty year ole 'oman doin' wid her hair swingin' down her back lak some young gal?—Where she left dat young lad of a boy she went off here wid?—Thought she was going to marry?—Where he left *her*?—What he done wid all her money?—Betcha he off wid some gal so young she ain't even got no hairs—why she don't stay in her class?—"

When she got to where they were she turned her face on the bander log and spoke. They scrambled a noisy "good evenin' " and left their mouths setting open and their ears full of hope. Her speech was pleasant enough, but she kept walking straight on to her gate. The porch couldn't talk for looking.

The men noticed her firm buttocks like she had grape fruits in her hip pockets; the great rope of black hair swinging to her waist and unraveling in the wind like a plume; then her pugnacious breasts trying to bore holes in her shirt. They, the men, were saving with the mind what they lost with the eye. The women took the faded shirt and muddy overalls and laid them away for remembrance. It was a weapon against her strength and if it turned out of no significance, still it was a hope that she might fall to their level some day.

But nobody moved, nobody spoke, nobody even thought to swallow spit until after her gate slammed behind her.

Pearl Stone opened her mouth and laughed real hard because she didn't know what else to do. She fell all over Mrs. Sumpkins while she laughed. Mrs. Sumpkins snorted violently and sucked her teeth.

"Humph! Y'all let her worry yuh. You ain't like me. Ah ain't got her to study 'bout. If she ain't got manners enough to stop and let folks know how she been makin' out, let her g'wan!"

"She ain't even worth talkin' after," Lulu Moss drawled through her nose. "She sits high, but she looks low. Dat's what Ah say 'bout dese ole women runnin' after young boys."

Pheoby Watson hitched her rocking chair forward before she spoke. "Well, nobody don't know if it's anything to tell or not. Me, Ah'm her best friend, and Ah don't know."

"Maybe us don't know into things lak you do, but we all know how she went 'way from here and us sho seen her come back. 'Tain't no use in your tryin' to cloak no ole woman lak Janie Starks, Pheoby, friend or no friend."

"At dat she ain't so ole as some of y'all dat's talking."

"She's way past forty to my knowledge, Pheoby."

"No more'n forty at de outside."

"She's 'way too old for a boy like Tea Cake."

"Tea Cake ain't been no boy for some time. He's round thirty his ownself."

"Don't keer what it was, she could stop and say a few words with us. She

act like we done done something to her," Pearl Stone complained. "She de
one been doin' wrong."

"You mean, you mad 'cause she didn't stop and tell us all her business.
Anyhow, what you ever know her to do so bad as y'all make out? The worst
thing Ah ever knowed her to do was taking a few years offa her age and dat
ain't never harmed nobody. Y'all makes me tired. De way you talkin' you'd
think de folks in dis town didn't do nothin' in de bed 'cept praise de Lawd.
You have to 'scuse me, 'cause Ah'm bound to go take her some supper."
Pheoby stood up sharply.

"Don't mind us," Lulu smiled, "just go right ahead, us can mind yo'
house for you till you git back. Mah supper is done. You bettah go see how
she feel. You kin let de rest of us know."

"Lawd," Pearl agreed, "Ah done scorched-up dat lil meat and bread too
long to talk about. Ah kin stay 'way from home long as Ah please. Mah
husband ain't fussy."

"Oh, er, Pheoby, if youse ready to go, Ah could walk over dere wid you,"
Mrs. Sumpkins volunteered. "It's sort of duskin' down dark. De booger
man might ketch yuh."

"Naw, Ah thank yuh. Nothin' couldn't ketch me dese few steps Ah'm
goin'. Anyhow mah husband tell me say no first class booger would have
me. If she got anything to tell yuh, you'll hear it."

Pheoby hurried on off with a covered bowl in her hands. She left the
porch pelting her back with unasked questions. They hoped the answers
were cruel and strange. When she arrived at the place, Pheoby Watson
didn't go in by the front gate and down the palm walk to the front door. She
walked around the fence corner and went in the intimate gate with her
heaping plate of mulatto rice. Janie must be round that side.

She found her sitting on the steps of the back porch with the lamps all
filled and the chimneys cleaned.

"Hello, Janie, how you comin'?"

"Aw, pretty good, Ah'm tryin' to soak some uh de tiredness and de dirt
outa mah feet." She laughed a little.

"Ah see you is. Gal, you sho looks *good*. You looks like youse yo' own
daughter." They both laughed. "Even wid dem overhalls on, you shows yo'
womanhood."

"G'wan! G'wan! You must think Ah brought yuh somethin'. When Ah
ain't brought home a thing but mahself."

"Dat's a gracious plenty. Yo' friends wouldn't want nothin' better."

"Ah takes dat flattery offa you, Pheoby, 'cause Ah know it's from de
heart." Janie extended her hand. "Good Lawd, Pheoby! ain't you never
goin' tuh gimme dat lil rations you brought me? Ah ain't had a thing on
mah stomach today exceptin' mah hand." They both laughed easily. "Give
it here and have a seat."

"Ah knowed you'd be hongry. No time to be huntin' stove wood after
dark. Mah mulatto rice[1] ain't so good dis time. Not enough bacon grease,
but Ah reckon it'll kill hongry."

"Ah'll tell you in a minute," Janie said, lifting the cover. "Gal, it's *too*
good! you switches a mean fanny round in a kitchen."

1. Rice and peas.

"Aw, dat ain't much to eat, Janie. But Ah'm liable to have something sho nuff good tomorrow, 'cause you done come."

Janie ate heartily and said nothing. The varicolored cloud dust that the sun had stirred up in the sky was settling by slow degrees.

"Here, Pheoby, take yo' ole plate. Ah ain't got a bit of use for a empty dish. Dat grub sho come in handy."

Pheoby laughed at her friend's rough joke. "Youse just as crazy as you ever was."

"Hand me dat wash-rag on dat chair by you, honey. Lemme scrub mah feet." She took the cloth and rubbed vigorously. Laughter came to her from the big road.

"Well, Ah see Mouth-Almighty is still sittin' in de same place. And Ah reckon they got *me* up in they mouth now."

"Yes indeed. You know if you pass some people and don't speak tuh suit 'em dey got tuh go way back in yo' life and see whut you ever done. They know mo' 'bout yuh than you do yo' self. An envious heart makes a treacherous ear. They done 'heard' 'bout you just what they hope done happened."

"If God don't think no mo' 'bout 'em then Ah do, they's a lost ball in de high grass."

"Ah hears what they say 'cause they just will collect round mah porch 'cause it's on de big road. Mah husband git so sick of 'em sometime he makes 'em all git for home."

"Sam is right too. They just wearin' out yo' sittin' chairs."

"Yeah, Sam say most of 'em goes to church so they'll be sure to rise in Judgment. Dat's de day dat every secret is s'posed to be made known. They wants to be there and hear it *all*."

"Sam is *too* crazy! You can't stop laughin' when youse round him."

"Uuh hunh. He says he aims to be there hisself so he can find out who stole his corn-cob pipe."

"Pheoby, dat Sam of your'n just won't quit! Crazy thing!"

"Most of dese zigaboos is so het up over yo' business till they liable to hurry theyself to Judgment to find out about you if they don't soon know. You better make haste and tell 'em 'bout you and Tea Cake gittin' married, and if he taken all yo' money and went off wid some young gal, and where at he is now and where at is all yo' clothes dat you got to come back here in overhalls."

"Ah don't mean to bother wid tellin' 'em nothin', Pheoby. 'Tain't worth de trouble. You can tell 'em what Ah say if you wants to. Dat's just de same as me 'cause mah tongue is in mah friend's mouf."

"If you so desire Ah'll tell 'em what you tell me to tell 'em."

"To start off wid, people like dem wastes up too much time puttin' they mouf on things they don't know nothin' about. Now they got to look into me loving Tea Cake and see whether it was done right or not! They don't know if life is a mess of corn-meal dumplings, and if love is a bed-quilt!"

"So long as they get a name to gnaw on they don't care whose it is, and what about, 'specially if they can make it sound like evil."

"If they wants to see and know, why they don't come kiss and be kissed? Ah could then sit down and tell 'em things. Ah been a delegate to de big 'ssociation of life. Yessuh! De Grand Lodge, de big convention of livin' is just where Ah been dis year and a half y'all ain't seen me."

They sat there in the fresh young darkness close together. Pheoby eager to feel and do through Janie, but hating to show her zest for fear it might be thought mere curiosity. Janie full of that oldest human longing—self revelation. Pheoby held her tongue for a long time, but she couldn't help moving her feet. So Janie spoke.

"They don't need to worry about me and my overhalls long as Ah still got nine hundred dollars in de bank. Tea Cake got me into wearing 'em—following behind him. Tea Cake ain't wasted up no money of mine, and he ain't left me for no young gal, neither. He give me every consolation in de world. He'd tell 'em so too, if he was here. If he wasn't gone."

Pheoby dilated all over with eagerness, "Tea Cake gone?"

"Yeah, Pheoby, Tea Cake is gone. And dat's de only reason you see me back here—cause Ah ain't got nothing to make me happy no more where Ah was at. Down in the Everglades there, down on the muck."

"It's hard for me to understand what you mean, de way you tell it. And then again Ah'm hard of understandin' at times."

"Naw, 'tain't nothin' lak you might think. So 'tain't no use in me telling you somethin' unless Ah give you de understandin' to go 'long wid it. Unless you see de fur, a mink skin ain't no different from a coon hide. Looka heah, Pheoby, is Sam waitin' on you for his supper?"

"It's all ready and waitin'. If he ain't got sense enough to eat it, dat's his hard luck."

"Well then, we can set right where we is and talk. Ah got the house all opened up to let dis breeze get a little catchin'.

"Pheoby, we been kissin'-friends for twenty years, so Ah depend on you for a good thought. And Ah'm talking to you from dat standpoint."

Time makes everything old so the kissing, young darkness became a monstropolous old thing while Janie talked.

Chapter 2

[PEAR TREE]

Janie saw her life like a great tree in leaf with the things suffered, things enjoyed, things done and undone. Dawn and doom was in the branches.

"Ah know exactly what Ah got to tell yuh, but it's hard to know where to start at.

"Ah ain't never seen mah papa. And Ah didn't know 'im if Ah did. Mah mama neither. She was gone from round dere long before Ah wuz big enough tuh know. Mah grandma raised me. Mah grandma and de white folks she worked wid. She had a house out in de back-yard and dat's where Ah wuz born. They was quality white folks up dere in West Florida. Named Washburn. She had four gran'chillun on de place and all of us played together and dat's how come Ah never called mah Grandma nothin' but Nanny, 'cause dat's what everybody on de place called her. Nanny used to ketch us in our devilment and lick every youngun on de place and Mis' Washburn did de same. Ah reckon dey never hit us ah lick amiss 'cause dem three boys and us two girls wuz pretty aggravatin', Ah speck.

"Ah was wid dem white chillun so much till Ah didn't know Ah wuzn't white till Ah was round six years old. Wouldn't have found it out then, but a man come long takin' pictures and without askin' anybody, Shelby, dat was de oldest boy, he told him to take us. Round a week later de man brought de picture for Mis' Washburn to see and pay him which she did, then give us all a good lickin'.

"So when we looked at de picture and everybody got pointed out there wasn't nobody left except a real dark little girl with long hair standing by Eleanor. Dat's where Ah wuz s'posed to be, but Ah couldn't recognize dat dark chile as me. So Ah ast, 'where is me? Ah don't see me.'

"Everybody laughed, even Mr. Washburn. Miss Nellie, de Mama of de chillun who come back home after her husband dead, she pointed to de dark one and said, 'Dat's you, Alphabet, don't you know yo' ownself?'

"Dey all useter call me Alphabet 'cause so many people had done named me different names. Ah looked at de picture a long time and seen it was mah dress and mah hair so Ah said:

"'Aw, aw! Ah'm colored!

"Den dey all laughed real hard. But before Ah seen de picture Ah thought Ah wuz just like de rest.

"Us lived dere havin' fun till de chillun at school got to teasin' me 'bout livin' in de white folks' back-yard. Dere wuz uh knotty head gal name Mayrella dat useter git mad every time she look at me. Mis' Washburn useter dress me up in all de clothes her gran'chillun didn't need no mo' which still wuz better'n whut de rest uh de colored chillun had. And then she useter put hair ribbon on mah head fuh me tuh wear. Dat useter rile Mayrella uh lot. So she would pick at me all de time and put some others up tuh do de same. They'd push me 'way from de ring plays and make out they couldn't play wid nobody dat lived on premises. Den they'd tell me not to be takin' on over mah looks 'cause they mama told 'em 'bout de hound dawgs huntin' mah papa all night long. 'Bout Mr. Washburn and de sheriff puttin' de bloodhounds on de trail tuh ketch mah papa for whut he done tuh mah mama. Dey didn't tell about how he wuz seen tryin' tuh git in touch wid mah mama later on so he could marry her. Naw, dey didn't talk dat part of it atall. Dey made it sound real bad so as tuh crumple mah feathers. None of 'em didn't even remember whut his name wuz, but dey all knowed de bloodhound part by heart. Nanny didn't love tuh see me wid mah head hung down, so she figgered it would be mo' better fuh me if us had uh house. She got de land and everything and then Mis' Washburn helped out uh whole heap wid things."

Pheoby's hungry listening helped Janie to tell her story. So she went on thinking back to her young years and explaining them to her friend in soft, easy phrases while all around the house, the night time put on flesh and blackness.

She thought awhile and decided that her conscious life had commenced at Nanny's gate. On a late afternoon Nanny had called her to come inside the house because she had spied Janie letting Johnny Taylor kiss her over the gatepost.

It was a spring afternoon in West Florida. Janie had spent most of the day under a blossoming pear tree in the back-yard. She had been spending every minute that she could steal from her chores under that tree for the last three days. That was to say, ever since the first tiny bloom had opened. It had called her to come and gaze on a mystery. From barren brown stems to glistening leaf-buds; from the leaf-buds to snowy virginity of bloom. It stirred her tremendously. How? Why? It was like a flute song forgotten in another existence and remembered again. What? How? Why? This singing she heard that had nothing to do with her ears. The rose of the world was breathing out smell. It followed her through all her waking moments and caressed her in her sleep. It connected itself with other vaguely felt matters that had struck her outside observation and buried themselves in her flesh. Now they emerged and quested about her consciousness.

She was stretched on her back beneath the pear tree soaking in the alto chant of the visiting bees, the gold of the sun and the panting breath of the breeze when the inaudible voice of it all came to her. She saw a dust-bearing bee sink into the sanctum of a bloom; the thousand sister-calyxes arch to meet the love embrace and the ecstatic shiver of the tree from root to tiniest branch creaming in every blossom and frothing with delight. So this was a marriage! She had been summoned to behold a revelation. Then Janie felt a pain remorseless sweet that left her limp and languid.

After a while she got up from where she was and went over the little garden field entire. She was seeking confirmation of the voice and vision, and everywhere she found and acknowledged answers. A personal answer for all other creations except herself. She felt an answer seeking her, but where? When? How? She found herself at the kitchen door and stumbled inside. In the air of the room were flies tumbling and singing, marrying and giving in marriage. When she reached the narrow hallway she was reminded that her grandmother was home with a sick headache. She was lying across the bed asleep so Janie tipped on out of the front door. Oh to be a pear tree—*any* tree in bloom! With kissing bees singing of the beginning of the world! She was sixteen. She had glossy leaves and bursting buds and she wanted to struggle with life but it seemed to elude her. Where were the singing bees for her? Nothing on the place nor in her grandma's house answered her. She searched as much of the world as she could from the top of the front steps and then went on down to the front gate and leaned over to gaze up and down the road. Looking, waiting, breathing short with impatience. Waiting for the world to be made.

Through pollinated air she saw a glorious being coming up the road. In her former blindness she had known him as shiftless Johnny Taylor, tall and lean. That was before the golden dust of pollen had beglamored his rags and her eyes.

In the last stages of Nanny's sleep, she dreamed of voices. Voices far-off but persistent, and gradually coming nearer. Janie's voice. Janie talking in whispery snatches with a male voice she couldn't quite place. That brought her wide awake. She bolted upright and peered out of the window and saw Johnny Taylor lacerating her Janie with a kiss.

"Janie!"

The old woman's voice was so lacking in command and reproof, so full of crumbling dissolution,—that Janie half believed that Nanny had not seen her. So she extended herself outside of her dream and went inside of the house. That was the end of her childhood.

Nanny's head and face looked like the standing roots of some old tree that had been torn away by storm. Foundation of ancient power that no longer mattered. The cooling palma christi leaves that Janie had bound about her grandma's head with a white rag had wilted down and become part and parcel of the woman. Her eyes didn't bore and pierce. They diffused and melted Janie, the room and the world into one comprehension.

"Janie, youse uh 'oman, now, so—"

"Naw, Nanny, naw Ah ain't no real 'oman yet."

The thought was too new and heavy for Janie. She fought it away.

Nanny closed her eyes and nodded a slow, weary affirmation many times before she gave it voice.

"Yeah, Janie, youse got yo' womanhood on yuh. So Ah mout ez well tell yuh what Ah been savin' up for uh spell. Ah wants to see you married right away."

"Me, married? Naw, Nanny, no ma'am! Whut Ah know 'bout uh husband?"

"Whut Ah seen just now is plenty for me, honey, Ah don't want no trashy nigger, no breath-and-britches, lak Johnny Taylor usin' yo' body to wipe his foots on."

Nanny's words made Janie's kiss across the gatepost seem like a manure pile after a rain.

"Look at me, Janie. Don't set dere wid yo' head hung down. Look at yo' ole grandma!" Her voice began snagging on the prongs of her feelings. "Ah don't want to be talkin' to you lak dis. Fact is Ah done been on mah knees to mah Maker many's de time askin' *please*—for Him not to make de burden too heavy for me to bear."

"Nanny, Ah just—Ah didn't mean nothin' bad."

"Dat's what makes me skeered. You don't mean no harm. You don't even know where harm is at. Ah'm ole now. Ah can't be always guidin' yo' feet from harm and danger. Ah wants to see you married right away."

"Who Ah'm goin' tuh marry off-hand lak dat? Ah don't know nobody."

"De Lawd will provide. He know Ah done bore de burden in de heat uh de day. Somebody done spoke to me 'bout you long time ago. Ah ain't said nothin' 'cause dat wasn't de way Ah placed you. Ah wanted yuh to school out and pick from a higher bush and a sweeter berry. But dat ain't yo' idea, Ah see."

"Nanny, who—who dat been askin' you for me?"

"Brother Logan Killicks. He's a good man, too."

"Naw, Nanny, no ma'am! Is dat whut he been hangin' round here for? He look like some ole skullhead in de grave yard."

The older woman sat bolt upright and put her feet to the floor, and thrust back the leaves from her face.

"So you don't want to marry off decent like, do yuh? You just wants to hug and kiss and feel around with first one man and then another, huh? You wants to make me suck de same sorrow yo' mama did, eh? Mah ole head ain't gray enough. Mah back ain't bowed enough to suit yuh!"

The vision of Logan Killicks was desecrating the pear tree, but Janie didn't know how to tell Nanny that. She merely hunched over and pouted at the floor.

"Janie."

"Yes, ma'am."

"You answer me when Ah speak. Don't you set dere poutin' wid me after all Ah done went through for you!"

She slapped the girl's face violently, and forced her head back so that their eyes met in struggle. With her hand uplifted for the second blow she saw the huge tear that welled up from Janie's heart and stood in each eye. She saw the terrible agony and the lips tightened down to hold back the cry and desisted. Instead she brushed back the heavy hair from Janie's face and stood there suffering and loving and weeping internally for both of them.

"Come to yo' Grandma, honey. Set in her lap lak yo' use tuh. Yo' Nanny wouldn't harm a hair uh yo' head. She don't want nobody else to do it neither if she kin help it. Honey, de white man is de ruler of everything as fur as Ah been able tuh find out. Maybe it's some place way off in de ocean where de black man is in power, but we don't know nothin' but what we see. So de white man throw down de load and tell de nigger man tuh pick it up. He pick it up because he have to, but he don't tote it. He hand it to his womenfolks. De nigger woman is de mule uh de world so fur as Ah can see. Ah been prayin' fuh it tuh be different wid you. Lawd, Lawd, Lawd!"

For a long time she sat rocking with the girl held tightly to her sunken breast. Janie's long legs dangled over one arm of the chair and the long braids of her hair swung low on the other side. Nanny half sung, half sobbed a running chant-prayer over the head of the weeping girl.

"Lawd have mercy! It was a long time on de way but Ah reckon it had to come. Oh Jesus! Do, Jesus! Ah done de best Ah could."

Finally, they both grew calm.

"Janie, how long you been 'lowin' Johnny Taylor to kiss you?"

"Only dis one time, Nanny. Ah don't love him at all. Whut made me do it is—oh, Ah don't know."

"Thank yuh, Massa Jesus."

"Ah ain't gointuh do it no mo', Nanny. Please don't make me marry Mr. Killicks."

" 'Tain't Logan Killicks Ah wants you to have, baby, it's protection. Ah ain't gittin' ole, honey. Ah'm *done* ole. One mornin' soon, now, de angel wid de sword is gointuh stop by here. De day and de hour is hid from me, but it won't be long. Ah ast de Lawd when you was uh infant in mah arms to let me stay here till you got grown. He done spared me to see de day. Mah daily prayer now is tuh let dese golden moments rolls on a few days longer till Ah see you safe in life."

"Lemme wait, Nanny, please, jus' a lil bit mo'."

"Don't think Ah don't feel wid you, Janie, 'cause Ah do. Ah couldn't love yuh no more if Ah had uh felt yo' birth pains mahself. Fact uh de matter, Ah loves yuh a whole heap more'n Ah do yo' mama, de one Ah did birth. But you got to take in consideration you ain't no everyday chile like most of 'em. You ain't got no papa, you might jus' as well say no mama, for de good she do yuh. You ain't got nobody but me. And mah head is ole and tilted towards de grave. Neither can you stand alone by yo'self. De thought uh you bein' kicked around from pillar tuh post is uh hurtin' thing. Every tear you drop squeezes a cup uh blood outa mah heart. Ah got tuh try and do for you befo' mah head is cold."

A sobbing sigh burst out of Janie. The old woman answered her with little soothing pats of the hand.

"You know, honey, us colored folks is branches without roots and that makes things come round in queer ways. You in particular. Ah was born back due in slavery so it wasn't for me to fulfill my dreams of whut a woman oughta be and to do. Dat's one of de hold-backs of slavery. But nothing can't stop you from wishin'. You can't beat nobody down so low till you can rob 'em of they will. Ah didn't want to be used for a work-ox and a brood-sow and Ah didn't want mah daughter used dat way neither. It sho wasn't mah will for things to happen lak they did. Ah even hated de way you was born. But, all de same Ah said thank God, Ah got another chance. Ah wanted to preach a great sermon about colored women sittin' on high, but they wasn't no pulpit for me. Freedom found me wid a baby daughter in mah arms, so Ah said Ah'd take a broom and a cook-pot and throw up a highway through de wilderness for her. She would expound what Ah felt. But somehow she got lost offa de highway and next thing Ah knowed here you was in de world."

* * *

1937

From Dust Tracks on a Road

Chapter X. Research

Research is formalized curiosity. It is poking and prying with a purpose. It is a seeking that he who wishes may know the cosmic secrets of the world and they that dwell therein.

I was extremely proud that Papa Franz [1] felt like sending me on that folk-lore search. As is well known, Dr. Franz Boas of the Department of Anthropology of Columbia University, is the greatest anthropologist alive, for two reasons. The first is his insatiable hunger for knowledge and then more knowledge; and the second is his genius for pure objectivity. He has no pet wishes to prove. His instructions are to go out and find what is there. He outlines his theory, but if the facts do not agree with it, he would not warp a jot or dot of the findings to save his theory. So knowing all this, I was proud that he trusted me. I went off in a vehicle made out of corona stuff. [2]

My first six months were disappointing. I found out later that it was not because I had no talents for research, but because I did not have the right approach. The glamor of Barnard College was still upon me. I dwelt in marble halls. I knew where the material was all right. But, I went about asking, in carefully accented Barnardese, "Pardon me, but do you know any folk-tales or folk-songs?" The men and women who had whole treasuries of material just seeping through their pores looked at me and shook their heads. No, they had never heard of anything like that around there. Maybe it was over in the next county. Why didn't I try over there? I did, and

---

1. Franz Boas (1858–1942), who convinced Hurston to begin graduate work in anthropology   at Columbia.
2. Left in an ecstatic mood.

got the selfsame answer. Oh, I got a few little items. But compared with what I did later, not enough to make a flea a waltzing jacket. Considering the mood of my going south, I went back to New York with my heart beneath my knees and my knees in some lonesome valley.

I stood before Papa Franz and cried salty tears. He gave me a good going over, but later I found that he was not as disappointed as he let me think. He knew I was green and feeling my oats,[3] and that only bitter disappointment was going to purge me. It did.

What I learned from him then and later, stood me in good stead when Godmother, Mrs. R. Osgood Mason,[4] set aside two hundred dollars a month for a two-year period for me to work.

My relations with Godmother were curious. Laugh if you will, but there was and is a psychic bond between us. She could read my mind, not only when I was in her presence, but thousands of miles away. Both Max Eastman and Richmond Barthe[5] have told me that she could do the same with them. But, the thing that delighted her was the fact that I was her only Godchild who could read her thoughts at a distance. Her old fingers were cramped and she could not write, but in her friend Cornelia Chapin's exact script, a letter would find me in Alabama, or Florida, or in the Bahama Islands and lay me by the heels for what I was *thinking*. "You have broken the law,"[6] it would accuse sternly. "You are dissipating your powers in things that have no real meaning," and go on to lacerate me. "Keep silent. Does a child in the womb speak?"

She was just as pagan as I. She had lived for years among the Plains Indians and had collected a beautiful book of Indian lore. Often when she wished to impress upon me my garrulity, she would take this book from the shelf and read me something of Indian beauty and restraint. Sometimes, I would feel like a rabbit at a dog convention. She would invite me to dinner at her apartment, 399 Park Avenue,[7] and then she, Cornelia Chapin, and Miss Chapin's sister, Mrs. Katherine Garrison Biddle would all hem me up and give me what for. When they had given me a proper straightening, and they felt that I saw the light, all the sternness would vanish, and I would be wrapped in love. A present of money from Godmother, a coat from Miss Chapin, a dress from Mrs. Biddle. We had a great deal to talk about because Cornelia Chapin was a sculptor, Katherine Biddle, a poet, and Godmother, an earnest patron of the arts.

Then too, she was Godmother to Miguel Covarrubias and Langston Hughes.[8] Sometimes all of us were there. She has several paintings by Covarrubias on her walls. She summoned us when one or the other of us returned from our labors. Miguel and I would exhibit our movies, and Godmother and the Chapin family, including brother Paul Chapin, would praise us and pan us, according as we had done. Godmother could be as tender as mother-love when she felt that you had been right spiritually. But anything in you, however clever, that felt like insincerity to her, called forth

---

3. Lively.
4. Charlotte Mason (1854–1946), patron of some of the leading figures of the Harlem Renaissance.
5. Barthé (1901–1989), African American sculptor. Eastman (1883–1969), U.S. editor and intellectual.
6. Mason's law of sincerity as defined in her strict doctrine of primitivism.
7. An elegant address in Manhattan.
8. Hughes (1902–1967), African American poet. Covarrubias (1904–1957), Mexican-born artist.

her well-known "That is nothing! It has no soul in it. You have broken the law!" Her tongue was a knout,[9] cutting off your outer pretenses, and bleeding your vanity like a rusty nail. She was merciless to a lie, spoken, acted or insinuated.

She was extremely human. There she was sitting up there at the table over capon, caviar and gleaming silver, eager to hear every word on every phase of life on a saw-mill "job."[1] I must tell the tales, sing the songs, do the dances, and repeat the raucous sayings and doings of the Negro farthest down. She is altogether in sympathy with them, because she says truthfully they are utterly sincere in living.

My search for knowledge of things took me into many strange places and adventures. My life was in danger several times. If I had not learned how to take care of myself in these circumstances, I could have been maimed or killed on most any day of the several years of my research work. Primitive minds are quick to sunshine and quick to anger. Some little word, look or gesture can move them either to love or to sticking a knife between your ribs. You just have to sense the delicate balance and maintain it.

In some instances, there is nothing personal in the killing. The killer wishes to establish a reputation as a killer, and you'll do as a sample. Some of them go around, making their announcements in singing:

> I'm going to make me a graveyard of my own,
> I'm going to make me a graveyard of my own,
> Oh, carried me down on de smoky road,
> Brought me back on de coolin' board,
> But I'm going to make me a graveyard of my own.[2]

And since the law is lax on these big saw-mill, turpentine and railroad "jobs,"[3] there is a good chance that they never will be jailed for it. All of these places have plenty of men and women who are fugitives from justice. The management asks no questions. They need help and they can't be bothered looking for a bug under every chip. In some places, the "law" is forbidden to come on the premises to hunt for malefactors who did their malefacting elsewhere. The wheels of industry must move, and if these men don't do the work, who is there to do it?

So if a man, or a woman, has been on the gang[4] for petty-thieving and mere mayhem, and is green with jealousy of the others who did the same amount of time for a killing and had something to brag about, why not look around for an easy victim and become a hero, too? I was nominated like that once in Polk County, Florida, and the only reason that I was not elected, was because a friend got in there and staved off old club-footed Death.

> Polk County! Ah!
> Where the water tastes like cherry wine.
> Where they fell great trees with ax and muscle.

---

9. A whiplike instrument of torture.
1. Socializing among black workers in the South.
2. This poem, like the others included in this selection, was probably a work song that Hurston had recorded.

3. Blacks were often employed in these industries. The turpentine industry was associated with the pine forests of Georgia and Florida. Blacks were hired as porters on the railroad.
4. I.e., chain gang.

These poets of the swinging blade! The brief, but infinitely graceful, dance of body and ax-head as it lifts over the head in a fluid arc, dances in air and rushes down to bite into the tree, all in beauty. Where the logs march into the mill with its smokestacks disputing with the elements, its boiler room reddening the sky, and its great circular saw screaming arrogantly as it attacks the tree like a lion making its kill. The log on the carriage coming to the saw. A growling grumble. Then contact! Yeelld-u-u-ow! And a board is laid shining and new on a pile. All day, all night. Rumble, thunder and grumble. Yee-ee-ow! Sweating black bodies, muscled like gods, working to feed the hunger of the great tooth. Polk County!

Polk County. Black men laughing and singing. They go down in the phosphate mines and bring up the wet dust of the bones of pre-historic monsters, to make rich land in far places, so that people can eat. But, all of it is not dust. Huge ribs, twenty feet from belly to backbone. Some old-time sea monster caught in the shallows in that morning when God said, "Let's make some more dry land. Stay there, great Leviathan![5] Stay there as a memory and a monument to Time." Shark-teeth as wide as the hand of a working man. Joints of backbone three feet high, bearing witness to the mighty monster of the deep when the Painted Land rose up and did her first dance with the morning sun. Gazing on these relics, forty thousand years old and more, one visualizes the great surrender to chance and change when these creatures were rocked to sleep and slumber by the birth of land.

Polk County. Black men from tree to tree among the lordly pines, a swift, slanting stroke to bleed the trees for gum. Paint, explosives, marine stores, flavors, perfumes, tone for a violin bow,[6] and many other things which the black men who bleed the trees never heard about.

Polk County. The clang of nine-pound hammers on railroad steel. The world must ride.

Hah! A rhythmic swing of the body, hammer falls, and another spike driven to the head in the tie.

> Oh, Mobile! Hank![7]
> Oh, Alabama! Hank!
> Oh, Fort Myers! Hank!
> Oh, in Florida! Hank!
> Oh, let's shake it! Hank!
> Oh, let's break it! Hank!
> Oh, let's shake it! Hank!
> Oh, just a hair! Hank!

The singing-liner cuts short his chant. The straw-boss[8] relaxes with a gesture of his hand. Another rail spiked down. Another offering to the soul of civilization whose other name is travel.

Polk County. Black men scrambling up ladders into orange trees. Singing, laughing, cursing, boasting of last night's love, and looking forward to

5. A sea monster; see, for example, Job 41:1.
6. Various products made from the sap of the pine tree.
7. The sound of a hammer hitting a railroad spike.
8. Member of a railroad crew who acts as boss.

the darkness again. They do not say embrace when they mean that they slept with a woman. A behind is a behind and not a form.[9] Nobody says anything about incompatibility when they mean it does not suit. No bones are made about being fed up.

> I got up this morning, and I knowed I didn't want it,
> Yea! Polk County!
> You don't know Polk County like I do
> Anybody been there, tell you the same thing, too.
> Eh, rider, rider!
> Polk County, where the water tastes like cherry wine.

Polk County. After dark, the jooks.[1] Songs are born out of feelings with an old beat-up piano, or a guitar for a mid-wife. Love made and unmade. Who put out dat lie, it was supposed to last forever? Love is when it is. No more here? Plenty more down the road. Take you where I'm going, woman? Hell no! Let every town furnish its own. Yeah, I'm going. Who care anything about no train fare? The railroad track is there, ain't it? I can count tires just like I been doing. I can ride de blind,[2] can't I?

> Got on de train didn't have no fare
> But I rode some
> Yes I rode some
> Got on de train didn't have no fare
> Conductor ast me what I'm doing there
> But I rode some.
> Yes I rode some.
>
> Well, he grabbed me by de collar and he led me to de door
> But I rode some
> Yes I rode some.
> Well, he grabbed me by de collar and he led me to de door
> He rapped me over de head with a forty-four
> But I rode some.
> Yes I rode some.

Polk County in the jooks. Dancing the square dance. Dancing the scronch. Dancing the belly-rub. Knocking the right hat off the wrong head, and backing it up with a switch-blade.

"Fan-foot, what you doing with my man's hat cocked on *your* nappy head? I know you want to see your Jesus. Who's a whore? Yeah I sleeps with my mens, but they pays me. I wouldn't be a fan-foot like you—just on de road somewhere. Runs up and down de road from job to job making pay-days. Don't nobody hold her! Let her jump on me! She pay her way on me, and I'll pay it off. Make time in old Bartow jail for her."

Maybe somebody stops the fight before the two switch-blades go to-gether. Maybe nobody can. A short, swift dash in. A lucky jab by one oppo-nent and the other one is dead. Maybe one gets a chill in the feet and leaps

---

9. Hurston is ridiculing genteel terms for parts of the human body.
1. I.e., jukeboxes, a term also used for nightclubs, saloons, and speakeasies.
2. Without paying.

out of the door. Maybe both get cut badly and back off. Anyhow, the fun of the place goes on. More dancing and singing and buying of drinks, parched peanuts, fried rabbit. Full drummy bass from the piano with weepy, intricate right-hand stuff. Singing the memories of Ella Wall, the Queen of love in the jooks of Polk County. Ella Wall, Planchita, Trottin' Liza.

It is a sad, parting song. Each verse ends up with:

> Quarters Boss![3] High Sheriff? Lemme git gone from here!
> Cold, rainy day, some old cold, rainy day
> I'll be back, some old cold, rainy day.
> Oh de rocks may be my pillow, Lawd!
> De sand may be my bed
> I'll be back some old cold, rainy day.

"Who run? What you running from the man for, nigger? Me, I don't aim to run a step. I ain't going to run unless they run me. I'm going to live anyhow until I die. Play me some music so I can dance! Aw, spank dat box,[4] man! ! Them white folks don't care nothing bout no nigger getting cut and kilt, nohow. They ain't coming in here. I done kilt me four and they ain't hung me yet. Beat dat box!"

"Yeah, but you ain't kilt no women, yet. They's mighty particular 'bout you killing up women."

"And I ain't killing none neither. I ain't crazy in de head. Nigger woman can kill all us men she wants to and they don't care. Leave us kill a woman and they'll run you just as long as you can find something to step on. I got good sense. I know I ain't got no show. De white mens and de nigger women is running this thing. Sing about old Georgy Buck[5] and let's dance off of it. Hit dat box!"

> Old Georgy Buck is dead
> Last word he said
> I don't want no shortening in my bread.
> Rabbit on de log
> Ain't got no dog
> Shoot him wid my rifle, bam! bam!

And the night, the pay night rocks on with music and gambling and laughter and dancing and fights. The big pile of cross-ties burning out in front simmers down to low ashes before sun-up, so then it is time to throw up all the likker you can't keep down and go somewhere and sleep the rest off, whether your knife has blood on it or not. That is, unless some strange, low member of your own race has gone and pimped to the white folks about something getting hurt. Very few of those kind are to be found.

That is the primeval flavor of the place, and as I said before, out of this primitive approach to things, I all but lost my life.

It was in a saw-mill jook in Polk County that I almost got cut to death.

---

3. The turpentine quarters—the dwellings in which the workers in the industry lived—were run by "bosses," usually white company representatives.

4. Play that guitar.
5. A traditional character in African American southern folklore.

Lucy really wanted to kill me. I didn't mean any harm. All I was doing was collecting songs from Slim, who used to be her man back up in West Florida before he ran off from her. It is true that she found out where he was after nearly a year, and followed him to Polk County and he paid her some slight attention. He was knocking the pad[6] with women, all around, and he seemed to want to sort of free-lance at it. But what he seemed to care most about was picking his guitar, and singing.

He was a valuable source of material to me, so I built him up a bit by buying him drinks and letting him ride in my car.

I figure that Lucy took a pick at me for three reasons. The first one was, her vanity was rubbed sore at not being able to hold her man. That was hard to own up to in a community where so much stress was laid on suiting. Nobody else had offered to shack up with her either. She was getting a very limited retail trade and Slim was ignoring the whole business. I had store-bought clothes, a lighter skin, and a shiny car, so she saw wherein she could use me for an alibi. So in spite of public knowledge of the situation for a year or more before I came, she was telling it around that I came and broke them up. She was going to cut everything off of me but "quit it."[7]

Her second reason was, because of my research methods I had dug in with the male community. Most of the women liked me, too. Especially her sworn enemy, Big Sweet. She was scared of Big Sweet, but she probably reasoned that if she cut Big Sweet's protégée it would be a slam on Big Sweet and build up her own reputation. She was fighting Big Sweet through me.

Her third reason was, she had been in little scraps and been to jail off and on, but she could not swear that she had ever killed anybody. She was small potatoes and nobody was paying her any mind. I was easy. I had no gun, knife or any sort of weapon. I did not even know how to do that kind of fighting.

Lucky for me, I had friended with Big Sweet. She came to my notice within the first week that I arrived on location. I heard somebody, a woman's voice "specifying"[8] up this line of houses from where I lived and asked who it was.

"Dat's Big Sweet" my landlady told me. "She got her foot up on somebody. Ain't she specifying?"

She was really giving the particulars. She was giving a "reading," a word borrowed from the fortune-tellers. She was giving her opponent lurid data and bringing him up to date on his ancestry, his looks, smell, gait, clothes, and his route through Hell in the hereafter. My landlady went outside where nearly everybody else of the four or five hundred people on the "job" were to listen to the reading. Big Sweet broke the news to him, in one of her mildest bulletins that his pa was a double-humpted camel and his ma was a grass-gut cow, but even so, he tore her wide open in the act of getting born, and so on and so forth. He was a bitch's baby out of a buzzard egg.

My landlady explained to me what was meant by "putting your foot up" on a person. If you are sufficiently armed—enough to stand off a panzer

6. Playing the field.
7. A plea for mercy.

8. Asking questions.

division[9]—and know what to do with your weapons after you get 'em, it is all right to go to the house of your enemy, put one foot up on his steps, rest one elbow on your knee and play in the family. That is another way of saying play the dozens, which also is a way of saying low-rate your enemy's ancestors and him, down to the present moment for reference, and then go into his future as far as your imagination leads you. But if you have no faith in your personal courage and confidence in your arsenal, don't try it. It is a risky pleasure. So then I had a measure of this Big Sweet.

"Hurt who?" Mrs. Bertha snorted at my fears. "Big Sweet? Humph! Tain't a man, woman nor child on this job going to tackle Big Sweet. If God send her a pistol she'll send him a man. She can handle a knife with anybody. She'll join hands and cut a duel. Dat Cracker Quarters Boss wears two pistols round his waist and goes for bad, but he won't break a breath with Big Sweet lessen he got his pistol in his hand. Cause if he start anything with her, he won't never get a chance to draw it. She ain't mean. She don't bother nobody. She just don't stand for no foolishness, dat's all."

Right away, I decided that Big Sweet was going to be my friend. From what I had seen and heard in the short time I had been there, I felt as timid as an egg without a shell. So the next afternoon when she was pointed out to me, I waited until she was well up the sawdust road to the Commissary,[1] then I got in my car and went that way as if by accident. When I pulled up beside her and offered her a ride, she frowned at me first, then looked puzzled, but finally broke into a smile and got in.

By the time we got to the Commissary post office we were getting along fine. She told everybody I was her friend. We did not go back to the Quarters at once. She carried me around to several places and showed me off. We made a date to go down to Lakeland come Saturday, which we did. By the time we sighted the Quarters on the way back from Lakeland, she had told me, "You sho is crazy!" Which is a way of saying I was witty. "I loves to friend with somebody like you. I aims to look out for you, too. Do your fighting for you. Nobody better not start nothing with you, do I'll get my switch-blade and go round de ham-bone looking for meat."

We shook hands and I gave her one of my bracelets. After that everything went well for me. Big Sweet helped me to collect material in a big way. She had no idea what I wanted with it, but if I wanted it, she meant to see to it that I got it. She pointed out people who knew songs and stories. She wouldn't stand for balkiness on their part. We held two lying contests, story-telling contests to you, and Big Sweet passed on who rated the prizes. In that way, there was no argument about it.

So when the word came to Big Sweet that Lucy was threatening me, she put her foot up on Lucy in a most particular manner and warned her against the try. I suggested buying a knife for defense, but she said I would certainly be killed that way.

"You don't know how to handle no knife. You ain't got dat kind of a sense. You wouldn't even know how to hold it to de best advantage. You would draw your arm way back to stop her, and whilst you was doing all dat,

9. Of the German army, consisting mainly of tanks, famous during World War II for its sudden attacks.
1. The local company store.

Lucy would run in under your arm and be done; cut you to death before you could touch her. And then again, when you sure 'nough fighting, it ain't enough to just stick 'em wid your knife. You got to ram it in to de hilt, then you pull *down*. They ain't no more trouble after dat. They's *dead*. But don't you bother 'bout no fighting. You ain't like me. You don't even sleep with no mens. I wanted to be a virgin one time, but I couldn't keep it up. I needed the money too bad. But I think it's nice for you to be like that. You just keep on writing down them lies. I'll take care of all de fighting. Dat'll make it more better, since we done made friends."

She warned me that Lucy might try to "steal" me. That is, ambush me, or otherwise attack me without warning. So I was careful. I went nowhere on foot without Big Sweet.

Several weeks went by, then I ventured to the jook alone. Big Sweet let it be known that she was not going. But later she came in and went over to the coon-can game[2] in the corner. Thinking I was alone, Lucy waited until things were in full swing and then came in with the very man to whom Big Sweet had given the "reading." There was only one door. I was far from it. I saw no escape for me when Lucy strode in, knife in hand. I saw sudden death very near that moment. I was paralyzed with fear. Big Sweet was in a crowd over in the corner, and did not see Lucy come in. But the sudden quiet of the place made her look around as Lucy charged. My friend was large and portly, but extremely light on her feet. She sprang like a lioness and I think the very surprise of Big Sweet being there when Lucy thought she was over at another party at the Pine Mill unnerved Lucy. She stopped abruptly as Big Sweet charged. The next moment, it was too late for Lucy to start again. The man who came in with Lucy tried to help her out, but two other men joined Big Sweet in the battle. It took on amazingly. It seemed that anybody who had any fighting to do, decided to settle-up then and there. Switch-blades, ice-picks and old-fashioned razors were out. One or two razors had already been bent back and thrown across the room, but our fight was the main attraction. Big Sweet yelled to me to run. I really ran, too. I ran out of the place, ran to my room, threw my things in the car and left the place. When the sun came up I was a hundred miles up the road, headed for New Orleans.

In New Orleans, I delved into Hoodoo, or sympathetic magic. I studied with the Frizzly Rooster, and all of the other noted "doctors." I learned the routines for making and breaking marriages; driving off and punishing enemies; influencing the minds of judges and juries in favor of clients; killing by remote control and other things. In order to work with these "two-headed" doctors, I had to go through an initiation with each. The routine varied with each doctor.

In one case it was not only elaborate, it was impressive. I lay naked for three days and nights on a couch, with my navel to a rattlesnake skin which had been dressed and dedicated to the ceremony. I ate no food in all that time. Only a pitcher of water was on a little table at the head of the couch so that my soul would not wander off in search of water and be attacked by

2. A two-handed card game, popular among African Americans in the South.

evil influences and not return to me. On the second day, I began to dream strange exalted dreams. On the third night, I had dreams that seemed real for weeks. In one, I strode across the heavens with lightning flashing from under my feet, and grumbling thunder following in my wake.

In this particular ceremony, my finger was cut and I became blood brother to the rattlesnake. We were to aid each other forever. I was to walk with the storm and hold my power, and get my answers to life and things in storms. The symbol of lightning was painted on my back. This was to be mine forever.

In another ceremony, I had to sit at the crossroads at midnight in complete darkness and meet the Devil, and make a compact. That was a long, long hour as I sat flat on the ground there alone and invited the King of Hell.

The most terrifying was going to a lonely glade in the swamp to get the black cat bone. The magic circle was made and all of the participants were inside. I was told that anything outside that circle was in deadly peril. The fire was built inside, the pot prepared and the black cat was thrown in with the proper ceremony and boiled until his bones fell apart. Strange and terrible monsters seemed to thunder up to that ring while this was going on. It took months for me to doubt it afterwards.

When I left Louisiana, I went to South Florida again, and from what I heard around Miami, I decided to go to the Bahamas. I had heard some Bahaman music and seen a Jumping Dance out in Liberty City and I was entranced.

This music of the Bahaman Negroes was more original, dynamic and African, than American Negro songs. I just had to know more. So without giving Godmother a chance to object, I sailed for Nassau.[3]

I loved the place the moment I landed. Then, that first night as I lay in bed, listening to the rustle of a coconut palm just outside my window, a song accompanied by string and drum broke out in full harmony. I got up and peeped out and saw four young men and they were singing Bellamina, led by Ned Isaacs.[4] I did not know him then, but I met him the next day. The song has a beautiful air, and the oddest rhythm.

> Bellamina, Bellamina!
> She come back in the harbor
> Bellamina, Bellamina
> She come back in the harbor
> Put Bellamina on the dock
> And paint Bellamina black! Black!
> Oh, put the Bellamina on the dock
> And paint Bellamina, black! Black!

I found out later that it was a song about a rum-running boat that had been gleaming white, but after it had been captured by the United States Coast Guard and released, it was painted black for obvious reasons.

That was my welcome to Nassau, and it was a beautiful one. The next day I got an idea of what prolific song-makers the Bahamans are. In that

---

3. Capital of the Bahamas.   4. A local singer.

West African accent grafted on the English of the uneducated Bahaman, I was told, "You do anything, we put you in sing." I walked carefully to keep out of "sing."

This visit to Nassau was to have far-reaching effects. I stayed on, ran to every Jumping Dance that I heard of, learned to "jump," collected more than a hundred tunes and resolved to make them known to the world.

On my return to New York in 1932, after trying vainly to interest others, I introduced Bahaman songs and dances to a New York audience at the John Golden Theater, and both the songs and the dances took on. The concert achieved its purpose. I aimed to show what beauty and appeal there was in genuine Negro material, as against the Broadway concept, and it went over.

Since then, there has been a sharp trend towards genuine Negro material. The dances aroused a tremendous interest in primitive Negro dancing. Hall Johnson took my group to appear with his singers at the Lewisohn Stadium that summer and built his "Run Lil' Chillun" [5] around them and the religious scene from my concert, "From Sun to Sin." That was not all, the dramatized presentation of Negro work-songs in that same concert aroused interest in them and they have been exploited by singers ever since.

I had no intention of making concert my field. I wanted to show the wealth and beauty of the material to those who were in the field and therefore I felt that my job was well done when it took on.

My group was invited to perform at the New School of Social Research; in the folk-dance carnival at the Vanderbilt Hotel in New York; at Nyack; at St. Louis; Chicago; Rollins College in Winter Park, Florida; Lake Wales; Sanford; Orlando; Constitution Hall, Washington, D.C.; and Daytona Beach, Florida.

Besides the finding of the dances and the music, two other important things happened to me in Nassau. One was, I lived through that terrible five-day hurricane of 1929. It was horrible in its intensity and duration. I saw dead people washing around on the streets when it was over. You could smell the stench from dead animals as well. More than three hundred houses were blown down in the city of Nassau alone.

Then I saw something else out there. I met Leon Walton Young. He is a grizzly, stocky black man, who is a legislator in the House. He represented the first district in the Bahamas and had done so for more than twenty years when I met him.

Leon Walton Young was either a great hero, or a black bounder, according to who was doing the talking. He was a great champion and a hero in the mouths of the lowly blacks of the islands and to a somewhat lesser degree to the native-born whites. He was a Bahaman for the Bahaman man and a stout fellow along those lines. To the English, who had been sent out to take the jobs of the natives, white and black, he was a cheeky dastard of a black colonial who needed to be put in his place. He was also too much for the mixed-blood Negroes of education and property, who were as preju-

---

5. This work by Johnson (1888–1970), African American composer and chorale leader, ran for 126 performances in New York in 1933.

diced against his color as the English. What was more, Leon Walton Young had no formal education, though I found him like George Schuyler[6] of New York to be better read than most people with college degrees. But did he, because of his lack of schooling, defer to the Negroes who had journeyed to London and Edinburgh? He most certainly did not, and what was more, he more than held his own in the hustings.

There was a much felt need for him to be put down, but those who put on the white armor of St. George to go out and slay the dragon always came back—not honorably dead on their shields—but splattered all over with mud and the seat of their pants torn and missing. A peasant mounted on a mule had unhorsed a cavalier and took his pants. The dance drums of Grantstown and Baintown would throb and his humbled opponents would be "put in sing."

He so humbled a governor, who tried to overawe Young by reminding him that he was "His Majesty's representative in these Islands" that the governor was recalled and sent to some peaceful spot in West Africa. Young had replied to that pompous statement with, "Yes, but if you continue your tactics out here you will make me forget it."

That was one of his gentlest thumps on the Governor's pride and prestige. His Majesty's Representative accused Young of having said publicly that he, the Governor, was a bum out of the streets of London, and to his eternal rage, Young more than admitted the statement. The English appointees and the high yellows shuddered at such temerity, but the local whites and the working blacks gloried in his spunk.

The humble Negroes of America are great songmakers, but the Bahaman is greater. He is more prolific and his tunes are better. Nothing is too big, or little, to be "put in sing." They only need discovery. They are much more original than the Calypso singers of Trinidad, as will be found the moment you put it to the proof.

I hear that now the Duke of Windsor[7] is their great hero. To them, he is "Our King." I would love to hear how he and his Duchess have been put in sing.

I enjoyed collecting the folk-tales and I believe the people from whom I collected them enjoyed the telling of them, just as much as I did the hearing. Once they got started, the "lies" just rolled and story-tellers fought for a chance to talk. It was the same with the songs. The one thing to be guarded against, in the interest of truth, was over-enthusiasm. For instance, if a song was going good, and the material ran out, the singer was apt to interpolate pieces of other songs into it. The only way you can know when that happens, is to know your material so well that you can sense the violation. Even if you do not know the song that is being used for padding, you can tell the change in rhythm and tempo. The words do not count. The subject matter in Negro folk-songs can be anything and go from love to work, to travel, to food, to weather, to fight, to demanding the return of a wig by a

6. Leading journalist (1895–1977) and author of *Black No More* (1931).
7. Edward VIII (1894–1972) abdicated the throne of England to marry an American divorcée, Wallis Simpson, who became the duchess of Windsor. From 1940 to 1945, Edward was the governor of the Bahamas.

woman who has turned unfaithful. The tune is the unity of the thing. And you have to know what you are doing when you begin to pass on that, because Negroes can fit in more words and leave out more and still keep the tune better than anyone I can think of.

One bit of research I did jointly for the Journal of Negro History and Columbia University, was in Mobile, Alabama. There I went to talk to Cudjo Lewis. That is the American version of his name. His African name was Kossola-O-Lo-Loo-Ay.

He arrived on the last load of slaves run into the United States and was the only Negro alive that came over on a slave ship. It happened in 1859 just when the fight between the South and the Abolitionists was moving toward the Civil War. He has died since I saw him.

I found him a cheerful, poetical old gentleman in his late nineties, who could tell a good story. His interpretation of the story of Jonah was marvelous.

He was a good Christian and so he pretended to have forgotten all of his African religion. He turned me off with the statement that his Nigerian religion was the same as Christianity. "We know it a God, you unner'stand, but we don't know He got a Son."

He told me in detail of the circumstances in Africa that brought about his slavery here. How the powerful Kingdom of Dahomey, finding the slave trade so profitable, had abandoned farming, hunting and all else to capture slaves to stock the barracoons[8] on the beach at Dmydah to sell to the slavers who came from across the ocean. How quarrels were manufactured by the King of Dahomey with more peaceful agricultural nations in striking distance of Dahomey in Nigeria and Gold Coast; how they were assaulted, completely wiped off the map, their names never to appear again, except when they were named in boastful chant before the King at one of his "customs" when his glory was being sung. The able-bodied who were captured were marched to Abomey, the capital city of Dahomey and displayed to the King, then put into the barracoons to await a buyer. The too old, the too young, the injured in battle were instantly beheaded and their heads smoked and carried back to the King. He paid off on heads, dead or alive. The skulls of the slaughtered were not wasted either. The King had his famous Palace of Skulls. The Palace grounds had a massive gate of skull-heads. The walls surrounding the grounds were built of skulls. You see, the Kings of Dahomey were truly great and mighty and a lot of skulls were bound to come out of their ambitions. While it looked awesome and splendid to him and his warriors, the sight must have been most grewsome and crude to Western eyes.

One thing impressed me strongly from this three months of association with Cudjo Lewis. The white people had held my people in slavery here in America. They had bought us, it is true and exploited us. But the inescapable fact that stuck in my craw, was: my people had *sold* me and the white people had bought me. That did away with the folklore I had been brought up on—that the white people had gone to Africa, waved a red handkerchief at the Africans and lured them aboard ship and sailed away. I know that

8. Enclosures for holding captives to be sold into slavery.

civilized money stirred up African greed. That wars between tribes were often stirred up by white traders to provide more slaves in the barracoons and all that. But, if the African princes had been as pure and as innocent as I would like to think, it could not have happened. No, my own people had butchered and killed, exterminated whole nations and torn families apart, for a profit before the strangers got their chance at a cut. It was a sobering thought. What is more, all that this Cudjo told me was verified from other historical sources. It impressed upon me the universal nature of greed and glory. Lack of power and opportunity passes off too often for virtue. If I were King, let us say, over the Western Hemisphere tomorrow, instead of who I am, what would I consider right and just? Would I put the cloak of Justice on my ambition and send her out a-whoring after conquests? It is something to ponder over with fear.

Cudjo's eyes were full of tears and memory of fear when he told me of the assault on his city and its capture. He said that his nation, the Takkoi, lived "three sleeps" from Dahomey. The attack came at dawn as the Takkoi were getting out of bed to go to their fields outside the city. A whooping horde of the famed Dahoman women warriors burst through the main gate, seized people as they fled from their houses and beheaded victims with one stroke of their big swords.

"Oh, oh! I runnee this way to that gate, but they there. I runnee to another one, but they there, too. All eight gates they there. Them women, they very strong. I nineteen years old, but they too strong for me. They take me and tie me. I don't know where my people at. I never see them no more."

He described the awful slaughter as the Amazons sacked the city. The clusters of human heads at their belts. The plight of those who fled through the gates to fall into the hands of the male warriors outside. How his King was finally captured and carried before the King of Dahomey, who had broken his rule and come on this expedition in person because of a grudge against the King of Takkoi, and how the vanquished monarch was led before him, bound.

"Now, that you have dared to send impudent words to me," the King of Dahomey said, "your country is conquered and you are before me in chains. I shall take you to Abomey."

"No," the King of Takkoi answered. "I am King in Takkoi. I will not go to Dahomey." He knew that he would be killed for a spectacle in Dahomey. He chose to die at home.

So two Dahoman warriors held each of his hands and an Amazon struck off his head.

Later, two representatives of a European power attended the customs of the King at Abomey, and told of seeing the highly polished skull of the King of Takkoi mounted in a beautiful ship-model. His name and his nation were mentioned in the chant to the glory of Dahomey. The skull was treated with the utmost respect, as the King of Dahomey would expect his to be treated in case he fell in battle. That was the custom in West Africa. For the same reason, no one of royal blood was sold into slavery. They were killed. There are no descendants of royal African blood among American Negroes for that reason. The Negroes who claim that they are descendants of royal African blood have taken a leaf out of the book of the white ancestor-hounds in America, whose folks went to England with William the Conqueror, got restless and caught the *Mayflower* for Boston, then feeling a romantic lack, rushed down the coast and descended from Pocahontas. From the number of her children, one is forced to the conclusion that that Pocahontas wasn't so poky, after all.

Kossola told me of the March to Abomey after the fall of Takkoi. How they were yoked by forked sticks and tied in a chain. How the Dahomans halted the march the second day in order to smoke the heads of the victims because they were spoiling. The prisoners had to watch the heads of their friends and relatives turning on long poles in the smoke. Abomey and the palace of the King and then the march to the coast and the barracoons. They were there sometime before a ship came to trade. Many, many tribes were there, each in a separate barracoon, lest they war among themselves. The traders could choose which tribe they wanted. When the tribe was decided upon, he was carried into the barracoon where that tribe was confined, the women were lined up on one side and the men on the other. He walked down between the lines and selected the individuals he wanted. They usually took an equal number.

He described the embarcation and the trip across the ocean in the *Chlotilde*, a fast sailing vessel built by the Maher brothers of Maine, who had moved to Alabama. They were chased by a British man-of-war on the look out for slavers, but the *Chlotilde* showed her heels. Finally the cargo arrived in Mobile. They were unloaded up the river,[9] the boat sunk, and the hundred-odd Africans began a four-year life of slavery.

"We so surprised to see mule and plow. We so surprised to see man pushee and mule pullee."

After the war, these Africans made a settlement of their own at Plateau, Alabama, three miles up the river from Mobile. They farmed and worked in the lumber mills and bought property. The descendants of these people are still there.

Kossola's great sorrow in America was the death of his favorite son, David, killed by a train. He refused to believe it was his David when he saw the body. He refused to let the bell be tolled for him.

"If dat my boy, where his head? No, dat not my David. Dat not my boy. My boy gone to Mobile. No, No! Don't ringee de bell for David. Dat not him."

But, finally his wife persuaded him that the headless body on the window blind was their son. He cried hard for several minutes and then said, "Ringee de bell."

His other great sorrow was that he had lost track of his folks in Africa.

"They don't know what become of Kossola. When you go there, you tellee where I at." He begged me. He did not know that his tribe was no more upon this earth, except for those who reached the barracoon at Dmydah. None of his family was in the barracoon. He had missed seeing their heads in the smoke, no doubt. It is easy to see how few would have looked on that sight too closely.

"I lonely for my folks. They don't know. Maybe they ask everybody go

9. I.e., the Mobile River, which runs through Mobile, Alabama. "Showed her heels": outran her pursuer.

there where Kossola. I know they hunt for me." There was a tragic catch in his voice like the whimper of a lost dog.

After seventy-five years, he still had that tragic sense of loss. That yearning for blood and cultural ties. That sense of mutilation. It gave me something to feel about.

Of my research in the British West Indies and Haiti, my greatest thrill was coming face to face with a Zombie and photographing her. This act had never happened before in the history of man. I mean the taking of the picture. I have said all that I know on the subject in the book, "Tell My Horse," which has been published also in England under the title "Voodoo Gods." I have spoken over the air on We the People on the subject, and the matter has been so publicized that I will not go into details here. But, it was a tremendous thrill, though utterly macabre.

I went Canzo in Voodoo ceremonies in Haiti and the ceremonies were both beautiful and terrifying.

I did not find them any more invalid than any other religion. Rather, I hold that any religion that satisfies the individual urge is valid for that person. It does satisfy millions, so it is true for its believers. The Sect Rouge, also known as the Cochon Gris (gray pig) and Ving Bra-Drig (from the sound of the small drum), a cannibalistic society there, has taken cover under the name of Voodoo, but the two things are in no wise the same. What is more, if science ever gets to the bottom of Voodoo in Haiti and Africa, it will be found that some important medical secrets, still unknown to medical science, give it its power, rather than the gestures of ceremony.

1942

NELLA LARSEN
1893–1964

Helga Crane, the protagonist of Nella Larsen's successful novel *Quicksand* (1928), bears a remarkable similarity to Larsen herself, especially in the fact that both women grew up as the only black member of a white family. Larsen's father, a black West Indian, is reported to have died two years after her birth; her mother, a Dane, married "a man of her own race and nationality" shortly thereafter. Larsen's childhood is so shrouded in mystery that a contemporary who attempted to sketch her biography labeled her "Madame X." She attended Fisk University (1909–10); audited classes at the University of Copenhagen (1910–12); and then began studying at the Lincoln School for Nurses in New York, where she completed the nursing program in 1915. She immediately went south to Alabama to serve as the head nurse at the John A. Andrew Hospital and Nurse Training School at Tuskegee Institute. She did not care for the South, however. Returning to New York a year later, she worked as assistant superintendent of nurses at Lincoln Hospital from 1916 to 1918 and then for the New York Department of Health.

In 1921, when Larsen left nursing to begin work in the New York Public Library system, she was put in charge of the children's room at the Countee Cullen Branch in Harlem. In October 1925, she took a year off from her job, ostensibly for health reasons. During this long convalescence, she wrote her first novel, *Quicksand*. With its rich symbolism and narrative complexity, *Quicksand* was an instant critical success when it appeared in 1928. Du Bois hailed it as "the best piece of fiction that

Negro America has produced since the heyday of Chesnutt." Larsen's second novel, *Passing* (1929), though not as warmly received as *Quicksand*, confirmed that she possessed superior potential as an artist. The story of two light-skinned blacks, Clare Kendry (who spends her adult life passing for white) and Irene Redfield, *Passing* demonstrated that Larsen was capable of sustaining a narrative not grounded in autobiography.

Why Larsen failed to produce any more novels in the remaining thirty-five years of her life is a matter of much speculation among scholars, who often cite two possible contributing factors. The first is the public charge of plagiarism brought in connection with her 1930 short story *Sanctuary*, which bore a striking resemblance to the story *Mrs. Adis* by Sheila Kaye-Smith, a contemporary writer. Larsen defended herself in an open letter to the magazine that had published the story, but seems never to have recovered from the accusation. Another contributing factor might have been the collapse around 1921 of her marriage to Dr. Elmer S. Imes, a physicist. When he headed south to take a position at Fisk, she spent a year traveling in Europe on a Guggenheim fellowship in preparation for a novel that never materialized. After they were divorced in 1933, Larsen was awarded alimony that enabled her to live without working until 1941; but this freedom produced no new novels. Imes's death in 1941 forced her to return to nursing.

During the last three decades of her life, Larsen became relatively reclusive. Circulating a rumor that she had left the United States for South America, she refused to correspond with most of her friends. In 1964, about five years before an upsurge of interest in women writers resulted in a reprinting of *Quicksand* and established Larsen as one of the central artists of the Harlem Renaissance, she was found dead in her New York apartment.

The following excerpt from *Quicksand* comprises the portion of the novel set in Denmark. Previously, Helga Crane had fled her position as an instructor at a black college in the South, after finding the atmosphere there stifling. She finds a stay in Harlem only somewhat more congenial, as she struggles with feelings of insecurity and confusion that spring from her childhood. Helga's mother, a Danish immigrant, had married a man of color from the West Indies, who soon left her after the birth of a daughter, Helga. Finally, Helga decides to go to Denmark to meet her relatives there.

From Quicksand

Chapter 12

[TO DENMARK]

Helga Crane felt no regret as the cliff-like towers[1] faded. The sight thrilled her as beauty, grandeur, of any kind always did, but that was all.

The liner drew out from churning slate-colored waters of the river into the open sea.[2] The small seething ripples on the water's surface became little waves. It was evening. In the western sky was a pink and mauve light, which faded gradually into a soft gray-blue obscurity. Leaning against the railing, Helga stared into the approaching night, glad to be at last alone, free of that great superfluity of human beings, yellow, brown, and black, which, as the torrid summer burnt to its close, had so oppressed her. No,

---

1. I.e., the tall buildings of Manhattan.
2. Crane is traveling by boat from New York to Denmark.

she hadn't belonged there. Of her attempt to emerge from that inherent aloneness which was part of her very being, only dullness had come, dullness and a great aversion.

Almost at once it was time for dinner. Somewhere a bell sounded. She turned and with buoyant steps went down. Already she had begun to feel happier. Just for a moment, outside the dining-salon, she hesitated, assailed with a tiny uneasiness which passed as quickly as it had come. She entered softly, unobtrusively. And, after all, she had had her little fear for nothing. The purser,[3] a man grown old in the service of the Scandinavian-American Line, remembered her as the little dark girl who had crossed with her mother years ago, and so she must sit at his table. Helga liked that. It put her at ease and made her feel important.

Everyone was kind in the delightful days which followed, and her first shyness under the politely curious glances of turquoise eyes of her fellow travelers soon slid from her. The old forgotten Danish of her childhood began to come, awkwardly at first, from her lips, under their agreeable tutelage. Evidently they were interested, curious, and perhaps a little amused about this Negro girl on her way to Denmark alone.

Helga was a good sailor, and mostly the weather was lovely with the serene calm of the lingering September summer, under whose sky the sea was smooth, like a length of watered silk, unruffled by the stir of any wind. But even the two rough days found her on deck, reveling like a released bird in her returned feeling of happiness and freedom, that blessed sense of belonging to herself alone and not to a race. Again, she had put the past behind her with an ease which astonished even herself. Only the figure of Dr. Anderson[4] obtruded itself with surprising vividness to irk her because she could get no meaning from that keen sensation of covetous exasperation that had so surprisingly risen within her on the night of the cabaret party. This question Helga Crane recognized as not entirely new; it was but a revival of the puzzlement experienced when she had fled so abruptly from Naxos[5] more than a year before. With the recollection of that previous flight and subsequent half-questioning a dim disturbing notion came to her. She wasn't, she couldn't be, in love with the man. It was a thought too humiliating, and so quickly dismissed. Nonsense! Sheer nonsense! When one is in love, one strives to please. Never, she decided, had she made an effort to be pleasing to Dr. Anderson. On the contrary, she had always tried, deliberately, to irritate him. She was, she told herself, a sentimental fool.

Nevertheless, the thought of love stayed with her, not prominent, definite; but shadowy, incoherent. And in a remote corner of her consciousness lurked the memory of Dr. Anderson's serious smile and gravely musical voice.

On the last morning Helga rose at dawn, a dawn outside old Copenhagen. She lay lazily in her long chair watching the feeble sun creeping over the ship's great green funnels with sickly light; watching the purply gray sky change to opal, to gold, to pale blue. A few other passengers, also early

---

3. An officer who takes care of financial matters on a ship.
4. Robert Anderson, once Crane's employer, arouses conflicting feelings of attraction and dis-

taste in her.
5. The school, headed by Anderson, where Crane had taught and from which she had abruptly resigned.

risen, excited by the prospect of renewing old attachments, of glad homecomings after long years, paced nervously back and forth. Now, at the last
moment, they were impatient, but apprehensive fear, too, had its place in
their rushing emotions. Impatient Helga Crane was not. But she *was* apprehensive. Gradually, as the ship drew into the lazier waters of the dock, she
became prey to sinister fears and memories. A deep pang of misgiving nauseated her at the thought of her aunt's husband, acquired since Helga's
childhood visit. Painfully, vividly, she remembered the frightened anger of
Uncle Peter's new wife, and looking back at her precipitate departure from
America, she was amazed at her own stupidity. She had not even considered the remote possibility that her aunt's husband might be like Mrs.
Nilssen.[6] For the first time in nine days she wished herself back in New
York, in America.

The little gulf of water between the ship and the wharf lessened. The
engines had long ago ceased their whirring, and now the buzz of conversation, too, died down. There was a sort of silence. Soon the welcoming
crowd on the wharf stood under the shadow of the great sea-monster, their
faces turned up to the anxious ones of the passengers who hung over the
railing. Hats were taken off, handkerchiefs were shaken out and frantically
waved. Chatter. Deafening shouts. A little quiet weeping. Sailors and laborers were yelling and rushing about. Cables were thrown. The gangplank was laid.

Silent, unmoving, Helga Crane stood looking intently down into
the gesticulating crowd. Was anyone waving to her? She couldn't
tell. She didn't in the least remember her aunt, save as a hazy pretty lady.
She smiled a little at the thought that her aunt, or anyone waiting there in
the crowd below, would have no difficulty in singling her out. But—had
she been met? When she descended the gangplank she was still uncertain
and was trying to decide on a plan of procedure in the event that she had
not. A telegram before she went through the customs? Telephone? A taxi?

But, again, she had all her fears and questionings for nothing. A smart
woman in olive-green came toward her at once. And, even in the fervent
gladness of her relief, Helga took in the carelessly trailing purple scarf and
correct black hat that completed the perfection of her aunt's costume, and
had time to feel herself a little shabbily dressed. For it was her aunt; Helga
saw that at once, the resemblance to her own mother was unmistakable.
There was the same long nose, the same beaming blue eyes, the same straying pale-brown hair so like sparkling beer. And the tall man with the fierce
mustache who followed carrying hat and stick must be Herr Dahl, Aunt
Katrina's husband. How gracious he was in his welcome, and how anxious
to air his faulty English, now that her aunt had finished kissing her and
exclaimed in Danish: "Little Helga! Little Helga! Goodness! But how you
have grown!"

Laughter from all three.

"Welcome to Denmark, to Copenhagen, to our home," said the new
uncle in queer, proud, oratorical English. And to Helga's smiling, grateful

6. Crane fears that Poul Dahl, the man whom her   Mrs. Nilssen had rejected Helga because of Helga's
Aunt Katrina has married, will be as cold to her as   color.
the new wife (Mrs. Nilssen) of her uncle Peter.

"Thank you," he returned: "Your trunks? Your checks?"[7] also in English, and then lapsed into Danish.

"Where in the world are the Fishers? We must hurry the customs."

Almost immediately they were joined by a breathless couple, a young gray-haired man and a fair, tiny, doll-like woman. It developed that they had lived in England for some years and so spoke English, real English, well. They were both breathless, all apologies and explanations.

"So early!" sputtered the man, Herr Fisher. "We inquired last night and they said nine. It was only by accident that we called again this morning to be sure. Well, you can imagine the rush we were in when they said eight! And of course we had trouble in finding a cab. One always does if one is late." All this in Danish. Then to Helga in English: "You see, I was especially asked to come because Fru Dahl didn't know if you remembered your Danish, and your uncle's English—well—"

More laughter.

At last, the customs having been hurried and a cab secured, they were off, with much chatter, through the toy-like streets, weaving perilously in and out among the swarms of bicycles.

It had begun, a new life for Helga Crane.

Chapter 13

[NEW LIFE]

She liked it, this new life. For a time it blotted from her mind all else. She took to luxury as the proverbial duck to water. And she took to admiration and attention even more eagerly.

It was pleasant to wake on that first afternoon, after the insisted-upon nap, with that sensation of lavish contentment and well-being enjoyed only by impecunious sybarites[8] waking in the houses of the rich. But there was something more than mere contentment and well-being. To Helga Crane it was the realization of a dream that she had dreamed persistently ever since she was old enough to remember such vague things as day-dreams and longings. Always she had wanted, not money, but the things which money could give, leisure, attention, beautiful surroundings. Things. Things. Things.

So it was more than pleasant, it was important, this awakening in the great high room which held the great high bed on which she lay, small but exalted. It was important because to Helga Crane it was the day, so she decided, to which all the sad forlorn past had led, and from which the whole future was to depend. This, then, was where she belonged. This was her proper setting. She felt consoled at last for the spiritual wounds of the past.

A discreet knocking on the tall paneled door sounded. In response to Helga's "Come in" a respectful rosy-faced maid entered and Helga lay for a long minute watching her adjust the shutters. She was conscious, too, of the girl's sly curious glances at her, although her general attitude was quite

7. I.e., baggage claim tickets.
8. People (such as Crane) who are devoted to expensive pleasures despite their lack of means.

correct, willing and disinterested. In New York, America, Helga would have resented this sly watching. Now, here, she was only amused. Marie, she reflected, had probably never seen a Negro outside the pictured pages of her geography book.

Another knocking. Aunt Katrina entered, smiling at Helga's quick, lithe spring from the bed. They were going out to tea, she informed Helga. What, the girl inquired, did one wear to tea in Copenhagen, meanwhile glancing at her aunt's dark purple dress and bringing forth a severely plain blue *crêpe* frock. But no! It seemed that that wouldn't at all do.

"Too sober," pronounced Fru Dahl. "Haven't you something lively, something bright?" And, noting Helga's puzzled glance at her own subdued costume, she explained laughingly: "Oh, I'm an old married lady, and a Dane. But you, you're young. And you're a foreigner, and different. You must have bright things to set off the color of your lovely brown skin. Striking things, exotic things. You must make an impression."

"I've only these," said Helga Crane, timidly displaying her wardrobe on couch and chairs. "Of course I intend to buy here. I didn't want to bring over too much that might be useless."

"And you were quite right too. Umm. Let's see. That black there, the one with the cerise and purple trimmings. Wear that."

Helga was shocked. "But for tea, Aunt! Isn't it too gay? Too—too—*outré?*" [9]

"Oh dear, no. Not at all, not for you. Just right." Then after a little pause she added: "And we're having people in to dinner tonight, quite a lot. Perhaps we'd better decide on our frocks now." For she was, in spite of all her gentle kindness, a woman who left nothing to chance. In her own mind she had determined the role that Helga was to play in advancing the social fortunes of the Dahls of Copenhagen, and she meant to begin at once.

At last, after much trying on and scrutinizing, it was decided that Marie should cut a favorite emerald-green velvet dress a little lower in the back and add some gold and mauve flowers, "to liven it up a bit," as Fru Dahl put it.

"Now that," she said, pointing to the Chinese red dressing-gown in which Helga had wrapped herself when at last the fitting was over, "suits you. Tomorrow we'll shop. Maybe we can get something that color. That black and orange thing there is good too, but too high. What a prim American maiden you are, Helga, to hide such a fine back and shoulders. Your feet are nice too, but you ought to have higher heels—and buckles."

Left alone, Helga began to wonder. She was dubious, too, and not a little resentful. Certainly she loved color with a passion that perhaps only Negroes and Gypsies know. But she had a deep faith in the perfection of her own taste, and no mind to be bedecked in flaunting flashy things. Still—she had to admit that Fru Dahl was right about the dressing-gown. It did suit her. Perhaps an evening dress. And she knew that she had lovely shoulders, and her feet *were* nice.

When she was dressed in the shining black taffeta with its bizarre trimmings of purple and cerise, Fru Dahl approved her and so did Herr Dahl.

9. Flashy (French).

Everything in her responded to his "She's beautiful; beautiful!" Helga
Crane knew she wasn't that, but it pleased her that he could think so, and
say so. Aunt Katrina smiled in her quiet, assured way, taking to herself her
husband's compliment to her niece. But a little frown appeared over the
fierce mustache, as he said, in his precise, faintly feminine voice: "She
ought to have ear-rings, long ones. Is it too late for Garborg's? We could
call up."

And call up they did. And Garborg, the jeweler, in Fredericksgaarde
waited for them. Not only were ear-rings bought, long ones brightly enameled, but glittering shoe-buckles and two great bracelets. Helga's sleeves
being long, she escaped the bracelets for the moment. They were wrapped
to be worn that night. The ear-rings, however, and the buckles came into
immediate use and Helga felt like a veritable savage as they made their
leisurely way across the pavement from the shop to the waiting motor. This
feeling was intensified by the many pedestrians who stopped to stare at the
queer dark creature, strange to their city. Her cheeks reddened, but both
Herr and Fru Dahl seemed oblivious of the stares or the audible whispers
in which Helga made out the one frequently recurring word "*sorte*," which
she recognized as the Danish word for "black."

Her Aunt Katrina merely remarked: "A high color becomes you, Helga.
Perhaps tonight a little rouge—" To which her husband nodded in agreement and stroked his mustache meditatively. Helga Crane said nothing.

They were pleased with the success she was at the tea, or rather the coffee—for no tea was served—and later at dinner. Helga herself felt like nothing so much as some new and strange species of pet dog being proudly
exhibited. Everyone was very polite and very friendly, but she felt the
massed curiosity and interest, so discreetly hidden under the polite greetings. The very atmosphere was tense with it. "As if I had horns, or three
legs," she thought. She was really nervous and a little terrified, but
managed to present an outward smiling composure. This was assisted by
the fact that it was taken for granted that she knew nothing or very little of
the language. So she had only to bow and look pleasant. Herr and Fru Dahl
did the talking, answered the questions. She came away from the coffee
feeling that she had acquitted herself well in the first skirmish. And, in spite
of the mental strain, she had enjoyed her prominence.

If the afternoon had been a strain, the evening was something more. It
was more exciting too. Marie had indeed "cut down" the prized green velvet, until, as Helga put it, it was "practically nothing but a skirt." She was
thankful for the barbaric bracelets, for the dangling ear-rings, for the beads
about her neck. She was even thankful for the rouge on her burning cheeks
and for the very powder on her back. No other woman in the stately pale-
blue room was so greatly exposed. But she liked the small murmur of wonder and admiration which rose when Uncle Poul brought her in. She liked
the compliments in the men's eyes as they bent over her hand. She liked
the subtle half-understood flattery of her dinner partners. The women too
were kind, feeling no need for jealousy. To them this girl, this Helga
Crane, this mysterious niece of the Dahls, was not to be reckoned seriously
in their scheme of things. True, she was attractive, unusual, in an exotic,
almost savage way, but she wasn't one of them. She didn't at all count.

Near the end of the evening, as Helga sat effectively posed on a red satin sofa, the center of an admiring group, replying to questions about America and her trip over, in halting, inadequate Danish, there came a shifting of the curious interest away from herself. Following the others' eyes, she saw that there had entered the room a tallish man with a flying mane of reddish blond hair. He was wearing a great black cape, which swung gracefully from his huge shoulders, and in his long, nervous hand he held a wide soft hat. An artist, Helga decided at once, taking in the broad streaming tie. But how affected! How theatrical!

With Fru Dahl he came forward and was presented. "Herr Olsen, Herr Axel Olsen." To Helga Crane that meant nothing. The man, however, interested her. For an imperceptible second he bent over her hand. After that he looked intently at her for what seemed to her an incredibly rude length of time from under his heavy drooping lids. At last, removing his stare of startled satisfaction, he wagged his leonine head approvingly.

"Yes, you're right. She's amazing. Marvelous," he muttered.

Everyone else in the room was deliberately not staring. About Helga there sputtered a little staccato murmur of manufactured conversation. Meanwhile she could think of no proper word of greeting to the outrageous man before her. She wanted, very badly, to laugh. But the man was as unaware of her omission as of her desire. His words flowed on and on, rising and rising. She tried to follow, but his rapid Danish eluded her. She caught only words, phrases, here and there. "Superb eyes . . . color . . . neck column . . . yellow . . . hair . . . alive . . . wonderful. . . ." His speech was for Fru Dahl. For a bit longer he lingered before the silent girl, whose smile had become a fixed aching mask, still gazing appraisingly, but saying no word to her, and then moved away with Fru Dahl, talking rapidly and excitedly to her and her husband, who joined them for a moment at the far side of the room. Then he was gone as suddenly as he had come.

"Who is he?" Helga put the question timidly to a hovering young army officer, a very smart captain just back from Sweden. Plainly he was surprised.

"Herr Olsen, Herr Axel Olsen, the painter. Portraits, you know."

"Oh," said Helga, still mystified.

"I guess he's going to paint you. You're lucky. He's queer. Won't do everybody."

"Oh, no. I mean, I'm sure you're mistaken. He didn't ask, didn't say anything about it."

The young man laughed. "Ha ha! That's good! He'll arrange that with Herr Dahl. He evidently came just to see you, and it's plain that he was pleased." He smiled, approvingly.

"Oh," said Helga again. Then at last she laughed. It was too funny. The great man hadn't addressed a word to her. Here she was, a curiosity, a stunt, at which people came and gazed. And was she to be treated like a secluded young miss, a Danish *frøkken*, [1] not to be consulted personally even on matters affecting her personally? She, Helga Crane, who almost all her life had looked after herself, was she now to be looked after by Aunt Katrina and her husband? It didn't seem real.

It was late, very late, when finally she climbed into the great bed after

1. I.e., *frøken*, title for an unmarried young woman.

having received an auntly kiss. She lay long awake reviewing the events of the crowded day. She was happy again. Happiness covered her like the lovely quilts under which she rested. She was mystified too. Her aunt's words came back to her. "You're young and a foreigner and—different." Just what did that mean, she wondered. Did it mean that the difference was to be stressed, accented? Helga wasn't so sure that she liked that. Hitherto all her efforts had been toward similarity to those about her.

"How odd," she thought sleepily, "and how different from America!"

Chapter 14

[TALK OF MARRIAGE]

The young officer had been right in his surmise. Axel Olsen was going to paint Helga Crane. Not only was he going to paint her, but he was to accompany her and her aunt on their shopping expedition. Aunt Katrina was frankly elated. Uncle Poul was also visibly pleased. Evidently they were not above kow-towing[2] to a lion. Helga's own feelings were mixed; she was amused, grateful, and vexed. It had all been decided and arranged without her, and, also, she was a little afraid of Olsen. His stupendous arrogance awed her.

The day was an exciting, not easily to be forgotten one. Definitely, too, it conveyed to Helga her exact status in her new environment. A decoration. A curio. A peacock. Their progress through the shops was an event; an event for Copenhagen as well as for Helga Crane. Her dark, alien appearance was to most people an astonishment. Some stared surreptitiously, some openly, and some stopped dead in front of her in order more fully to profit by their stares. *"Den Sorte"* dropped freely, audibly, from many lips.

The time came when she grew used to the stares of the population. And the time came when the population of Copenhagen grew used to her outlandish presence and ceased to stare. But at the end of that first day it was with thankfulness that she returned to the sheltering walls of the house on Maria Kirkplads.[3]

They were followed by numerous packages, whose contents all had been selected or suggested by Olsen and paid for by Aunt Katrina. Helga had only to wear them. When they were opened and the things spread out upon the sedate furnishings of her chamber, they made a rather startling array. It was almost in a mood of rebellion that Helga faced the fantastic collection of garments incongruously laid out in the quaint, stiff, pale old room. There were batik dresses in which mingled indigo, orange, green, vermilion, and black; dresses of velvet and chiffon in screaming colors, blood-red, sulfur-yellow, sea-green; and one black and white thing in striking combination. There was a black Manila shawl strewn with great scarlet and lemon flowers, a leopard-skin coat, a glittering opera-cape. There were turban-like hats of metallic silks, feathers and furs, strange jewelry, enameled or set with odd semi-precious stones, a nauseous Eastern perfume, shoes with dangerously high heels. Gradually Helga's perturbation subsided in the unusual pleasure of having so many new and expensive clothes at one time. She began to feel a little excited, incited.

2. Humbling themselves.   3. A Copenhagen street.

Incited. That was it, the guiding principle of her life in Copenhagen. She was incited to make an impression, a voluptuous impression. She was incited to inflame attention and admiration. She was dressed for it, subtly schooled for it. And after a little while she gave herself up wholly to the fascinating business of being seen, gaped at, desired. Against the solid background of Herr Dahl's wealth and generosity she submitted to her aunt's arrangement of her life to one end, the amusing one of being noticed and flattered. Intentionally she kept to the slow, faltering Danish. It was, she decided, more attractive than a nearer perfection. She grew used to the extravagant things with which Aunt Katrina chose to dress her. She managed, too, to retain that air of remoteness which had been in America so disastrous to her friendships. Here in Copenhagen it was merely a little mysterious and added another clinging wisp of charm.

Helga Crane's new existence was intensely pleasant to her; it gratified her augmented sense of self-importance. And it suited her. She had to admit that the Danes had the right idea. To each his own milieu. Enhance what was already in one's possession. In America Negroes sometimes talked loudly of this, but in their hearts they repudiated it. In their lives too. They didn't want to be like themselves. What they wanted, asked for, begged for, was to be like their white overlords. They were ashamed to be Negroes, but not ashamed to beg to be something else. Something inferior. Not quite genuine. Too bad!

Helga Crane didn't, however, think often of America, excepting in unfavorable contrast to Denmark. For she had resolved never to return to the existence of ignominy which the New World of opportunity and promise forced upon Negroes. How stupid she had been ever to have thought that she could marry and perhaps have children in a land where every dark child was handicapped at the start by the shroud of color! She saw, suddenly, the giving birth to little, helpless, unprotesting Negro children as a sin, an unforgivable outrage. More black folk to suffer indignities. More dark bodies for mobs to lynch. No, Helga Crane didn't think often of America. It was too humiliating, too disturbing. And she wanted to be left to the peace which had come to her. Her mental difficulties and questionings had become simplified. She now believed sincerely that there was a law of compensation, and that sometimes it worked. For all those early desolate years she now felt recompensed. She recalled a line that had impressed her in her lonely school-days, "The far-off interest of tears."

To her, Helga Crane, it had come at last, and she meant to cling to it. So she turned her back on painful America, resolutely shutting out the griefs, the humiliations, the frustrations, which she had endured there.

Her mind was occupied with other and nearer things.

The charm of the old city itself, with its odd architectural mixture of medievalism and modernity, and the general air of well-being which pervaded it, impressed her. Even in the so-called poor sections there was none of that untidiness and squalor which she remembered as the accompaniment of poverty in Chicago, New York, and the Southern cities of America. Here the door-steps were always white from constant scrubbings, the women neat, and the children washed and provided with whole clothing. Here were no tatters and rags, no beggars. But, then, begging, she learned, was an offense punishable by law. Indeed, it was unnecessary in a country where everyone considered it a duty somehow to support himself and his family by honest work; or, if misfortune and illness came upon one, everyone else, including the State, felt bound to give assistance, a lift on the road to the regaining of independence.

After the initial shyness and consternation at the sensation caused by her strange presence had worn off, Helga spent hours driving or walking about the city, at first in the protecting company of Uncle Poul or Aunt Katrina or both, or sometimes Axel Olsen. But later, when she had become a little familiar with the city, and its inhabitants a little used to her, and when she had learned to cross the streets in safety, dodging successfully the innumerable bicycles like a true Copenhagen, she went often alone, loitering on the long bridge which spanned the placid lakes, or watching the pageant of the blue-clad, sprucely tailored soldiers in the daily parade at Amielenborg Palace, or in the historic vicinity of the long, low-lying Exchange, a picturesque structure in picturesque surroundings, skirting as it did the great canal, which always was alive with many small boats, flying broad white sails and pressing close on the huge ruined pile of the Palace of Christiansborg.[4] There was also the Gammelstrand, the congregating-place of the venders of fish, where daily was enacted a spirited and interesting scene between sellers and buyers, and where Helga's appearance always roused lively and audible, but friendly, interest, long after she became in other parts of the city an accepted curiosity. Here it was that one day an old countrywoman asked her to what manner of mankind she belonged and at Helga's replying: "I'm a Negro," had become indignant, retorting angrily that, just because she was old and a countrywoman she could not be so easily fooled, for she knew as well as everyone else that Negroes were black and had woolly hair.

Against all this walking the Dahls had at first uttered mild protest. "But, Aunt dear, I have to walk, or I'll get fat," Helga asserted. "I've never, never in all my life, eaten so much." For the accepted style of entertainment in Copenhagen seemed to be a round of dinner-parties, at which it was customary for the hostess to tax the full capacity not only of her dining-room, but of her guests as well. Helga enjoyed these dinner-parties, as they were usually spirited affairs, the conversation brilliant and witty, often in several languages. And always she came in for a goodly measure of flattering attention and admiration.

There were, too, those popular afternoon gatherings for the express purpose of drinking coffee together, where between much talk, interesting talk, one sipped the strong and steaming beverage from exquisite cups fashioned of Royal Danish porcelain and partook of an infinite variety of rich cakes and smørrebrød. This smørrebrød, dainty sandwiches of an endless and tempting array, was distinctly a Danish institution. Often Helga wondered just how many of these delicious sandwiches she had consumed since setting foot on Denmark's soil. Always, wherever food was served, appeared the inevitable smørrebrød, in the home of the Dahls, in every other home that she visited, in hotels, in restaurants.

At first she had missed, a little, dancing, for, though excellent dancers, the Danes seemed not to care a great deal for that pastime, which so de-

---

4. Well-known sites in the middle of Copenhagen.

lightfully combines exercise and pleasure. But in the winter there was skating, solitary, or in gay groups. Helga liked this sport, though she was not very good at it. There were, however, always plenty of efficient and willing men to instruct and to guide her over the glittering ice. One could, too, wear such attractive skating-things.

But mostly it was with Axel Olsen that her thoughts were occupied. Brilliant, bored, elegant, urbane, cynical, worldly, he was a type entirely new to Helga Crane, familiar only, and that but little, with the restricted society of American Negroes. She was aware, too, that this amusing, if conceited, man was interested in her. They were, because he was painting her, much together. Helga spent long mornings in the eccentric studio opposite the Folkemuseum,[5] and Olsen came often to the Dahl home, where, as Helga and the man himself knew, he was something more than welcome. But in spite of his expressed interest and even delight in her exotic appearance, in spite of his constant attendance upon her, he gave no sign of the more personal kind of concern which—encouraged by Aunt Katrina's mild insinuations and Uncle Poul's subtle questionings—she had tried to secure. Was it, she wondered, race that kept him silent, held him back. Helga Crane frowned on this thought, putting it furiously from her, because it disturbed her sense of security and permanence in her new life, pricked her self-assurance.

Nevertheless she was startled when on a pleasant afternoon while drinking coffee in the Hotel Vivili, Aunt Katrina mentioned, almost casually, the desirability of Helga's making a good marriage.

"Marriage, Aunt dear!"

"Marriage," firmly repeated her aunt, helping herself to another anchovy and olive sandwich. "You are," she pointed out, "twenty-five."

"Oh, Aunt, I couldn't! I mean, there's nobody here for me to marry." In spite of herself and her desire not to be, Helga was shocked.

"Nobody?" There was, Fru Dahl asserted, Captain Frederick Skaargaard—and very handsome he was too—and he would have money. And there was Herr Hans Tietgen, not so handsome, of course, but clever and a good business man; he too would be rich, very rich, some day. And there was Herr Karl Pedersen, who had a good berth with the Landmands-bank and considerable shares in a prosperous cement-factory at Aalborg. There was, too, Christian Lende, the young owner of the new Odin Theater. Any of these Helga might marry, was Aunt Katrina's opinion. "And," she added, "others." Or maybe Helga herself had some ideas.

Helga had. She didn't, she responded, believe in mixed marriages, "between races, you know." They brought only trouble—to the children—as she herself knew but too well from bitter experience.

Fru Dahl thoughtfully lit a cigarette. Eventually, after a satisfactory glow had manifested itself, she announced: "Because your mother was a fool. Yes, she was! If she'd come home after she married, or after you were born, or even after your father—er—went off like that, it would have been different. If even she'd left you when she was here. But why in the world she should have married again, and a person like that, I can't see. She wanted to keep you, she insisted on it, even over his protest, I think. She loved you so much, she said.—And so she made you unhappy. Mothers, I suppose, are like that. Selfish. And Karen was always stupid. If you've got any brains at all they came from your father."

Into this Helga would not enter. Because of its obvious partial truths she felt the need for disguising caution. With a detachment that amazed herself she asked if Aunt Katrina didn't think, really, that miscegenation was wrong, in fact as well as principle.

"Don't," was her aunt's reply, "be a fool too, Helga. We don't think of those things here. Not in connection with individuals, at least." And almost immediately she inquired: "Did you give Herr Olsen my message about dinner tonight?"

"Yes, Aunt." Helga was cross, and trying not to show it.

"He's coming?"

"Yes, Aunt," with precise politeness.

"What about him?"

"I don't know. *What* about him?"

"He likes you?"

"I don't know. How can I tell that?" Helga asked with irritating reserve, her concentrated attention on the selection of a sandwich. She had a feeling of nakedness. Outrage.

Now Fru Dahl was annoyed and showed it. "What nonsense! Of course you know. Any girl does," and her satin-covered foot tapped, a little impatiently, the old tiled floor.

"Really, I don't know, Aunt," Helga responded in a strange voice, a strange manner, coldly formal, levelly courteous. Then suddenly contrite, she added: "Honestly, I don't. I can't tell a thing about him," and fell into a little silence. "Not a thing," she repeated. But the phrase, though audible, was addressed to no one. To herself.

She looked out into the amazing orderliness of the street. Instinctively she wanted to combat this searching into the one thing which, here, surrounded by all other things which for so long she had so positively wanted, made her a little afraid. Started vague premonitions.

Fru Dahl regarded her intently. It would be, she remarked with a return of her outward casualness, by far the best of all possibilities. Particularly desirable. She touched Helga's hand with her fingers in a little affectionate gesture. Very lightly.

Helga Crane didn't immediately reply. There was, she knew, so much reason—from one viewpoint—in her aunt's statement. She could only acknowledge it. "I know that," she told her finally. Inwardly she was admiring the cool, easy way in which Aunt Katrina had brushed aside the momentary acid note of the conversation and resumed her customary pitch. It took, Helga thought, a great deal of security. Balance.

"Yes," she was saying, while leisurely lighting another of those long, thin brown cigarettes which Helga knew from distressing experience to be incredibly nasty tasting, "it would be the ideal thing for you, Helga." She gazed penetratingly into the masked face of her niece and nodded, as though satisfied with what she saw there. "And you of course realize that you are a very charming and beautiful girl. Intelligent too. If you put your mind to it, there's no reason in the world why you shouldn't—" Abruptly she stopped, leaving her implication at once suspended and clear. Behind her there were footsteps. A small gloved hand appeared on her shoulder. In the short moment before turning to greet Fru Fischer she said quietly, meaningly: "Or else stop wasting your time, Helga."

Helga Crane said: "Ah, Fru Fischer. It's good to see you." She meant it. Her whole body was tense with suppressed indignation. Burning inside like the confined fire of a hot furnace. She was so harassed that she smiled in self-protection. And suddenly she was oddly cold. An intimation of things distant, but none the less disturbing, oppressed her with a faintly sick feeling. Like a heavy weight, a stone weight, just where, she knew, was her stomach.

Fru Fischer was late. As usual. She apologized profusely. Also as usual. And, yes, she would have some coffee. And some *smørrebrød.* Though she must say that the coffee here at the Vivili was atrocious. Simply atrocious. "I don't see how you stand it." And the place was getting so common, always so many Bolsheviks and Japs and things. And she didn't—"begging your pardon, Helga"—like that hideous American music they were forever playing, even if it was considered very smart. "Give me," she said, "the good old-fashioned Danish melodies of Gade and Heise.[6] 'Helios' is being performed with great success just now in England. But I suppose you know all about it, Helga. He's already told you. What?" This last was accompanied with an arch and insinuating smile.

A shrug moved Helga Crane's shoulders. Strange she'd never before noticed what a positively disagreeable woman Fru Fischer was. Stupid, too.

Chapter 15

[PROPOSAL]

Well into Helga's second year in Denmark, came an indefinite discontent. Not clear, but vague, like a storm gathering far on the horizon. It was long before she would admit that she was less happy than she had been during her first year in Copenhagen, but she knew that it was so. And this subconscious knowledge added to her growing restlessness and little mental insecurity. She desired ardently to combat this wearing down of her satisfaction with her life, with herself. But she didn't know how.

Frankly the question came to this: what was the matter with her? Was there, without her knowing it, some peculiar lack in her? Absurd. But she began to have a feeling of discouragement and hopelessness. Why couldn't she be happy, content, somewhere? Other people managed, somehow, to be. To put it plainly, didn't she know how? Was she incapable of it?

And then on a warm spring day came Anne's[7] letter telling of her coming marriage to Anderson, who retained still his shadowy place in Helga Crane's memory. It added, somehow, to her discontent, and to her growing dissatisfaction with her peacock's life. This, too, annoyed her.

6. Niels Wilhelm Gade (1817–1890), Peter Arnold Heise (1830–1890), and Carl August Nielsen (1865–1931), important modern Danish composers.
7. Anne Gray, Crane's friend, who disapproves of race mixing.

What, she asked herself, was there about that man which had the power always to upset her? She began to think back to her first encounter with him. Perhaps if she hadn't come away—She laughed. Derisively. "Yes, if I hadn't come away, I'd be stuck in Harlem. Working every day of my life. Chattering about the race problem."

Anne, it seemed, wanted her to come back for the wedding. This, Helga had no intention of doing. True, she had liked and admired Anne better than anyone she had ever known, but even for her she wouldn't cross the ocean.

Go back to America, where they hated Negroes! To America, where Negroes were not people. To America, where Negroes were allowed to be beggars only, of life, of happiness, of security. To America, where everything had been taken from those dark ones, liberty, respect, even the labor of their hands. To America, where if one had Negro blood, one mustn't expect money, education, or, sometimes, even work whereby one might earn bread. Perhaps she was wrong to bother about it now that she was so far away. Helga couldn't, however, help it. Never could she recall the shames and often the absolute horrors of the black man's existence in America without the quickening of her heart's beating and a sensation of disturbing nausea. It was too awful. The sense of dread of it was almost a tangible thing in her throat.

And certainly she wouldn't go back for any such idiotic reason as Anne's getting married to that offensive Robert Anderson. Anne was really too amusing. Just why, she wondered, and how had it come about that he was being married to Anne. And why did Anne, who had so much more than so many others—more than enough—want Anderson too? Why couldn't she— "I think," she told herself, "I'd better stop. It's none of my business. I don't care in the least. Besides," she added irrelevantly, "I hate such nonsensical soul-searching."

One night not long after the arrival of Anne's letter with its curious news, Helga went with Olsen and some other young folk to the great Circus, a vaudeville house, in search of amusement on a rare off night. After sitting through several numbers they reluctantly arrived at the conclusion that the whole entertainment was dull, unutterably dull, and apparently without alleviation, and so not to be borne. They were reaching for their wraps when out upon the stage pranced two black men, American Negroes undoubtedly, for as they danced and cavorted, they sang in the English of America an old ragtime song that Helga remembered hearing as a child, "Everybody Gives Me Good Advice."[8] At its conclusion the audience applauded with delight. Only Helga Crane was silent, motionless.

More songs, old, all of them old, but new and strange to that audience. And how the singers danced, pounding their thighs, slapping their hands together, twisting their legs, waving their abnormally long arms, throwing their bodies about with a loose ease! And how the enchanted spectators clapped and howled and shouted for more!

Helga Crane was not amused. Instead she was filled with a fierce hatred for the cavorting Negroes on the stage. She felt ashamed, betrayed, as if these pale pink and white people among whom she lived had suddenly

---

8. Written by Alfred Brian, Jams Kendiss, and Herman Paley.

been invited to look upon something in her which she had hidden away and wanted to forget. And she was shocked at the avidity at which Olsen beside her drank it in.

But later, when she was alone, it became quite clear to her that all along they had divined its presence, had known that in her was something, some characteristic, different from any that they themselves possessed. Else why had they decked her out as they had? Why subtly indicated that she was different? And they hadn't despised it. No, they had admired it, rated it as a precious thing, a thing to be enhanced, preserved. Why? She, Helga Crane, didn't admire it. She suspected that no Negroes, no Americans, did. Else why their constant slavish imitation of traits not their own? Why their constant begging to be considered as exact copies of other people? Even the enlightened, the intelligent ones demanded nothing more. They were all beggars like the motley crowd in the old nursery rhyme:

> Hark! Hark!
> The dogs do bark.
> The beggars are coming to town.
> Some in rags,
> Some in tags,
> And some in velvet gowns.

The incident left her profoundly disquieted. Her old unhappy question-ing mood came again upon her, insidiously stealing away more of the con-tentment from her transformed existence.

But she returned again and again to the Circus, always alone, gazing intently and solemnly at the gesticulating black figures, an ironical and si-lently speculative spectator. For she knew that into her plan for her life had thrust itself a suspensive conflict in which were fused doubts, rebellion, expediency, and urgent longings.

It was at this time that Axel Olsen asked her to marry him. And now Helga Crane was surprised. It was a thing that at one time she had much wanted, had tried to bring about, and had at last relinquished as impossible of achievement. Not so much because of its apparent hopelessness as be-cause of a feeling, intangible almost, that, excited and pleased as he was with her, her origin a little repelled him, and that, prompted by some im-pulse of racial antagonism, he had retreated into the fastness of a protecting habit of self-ridicule. A mordantly personal pride and sensitiveness deterred Helga from further efforts at incitation.

True, he had made, one morning, while holding his brush poised for a last, a very last stroke on the portrait, one admirably draped suggestion, speaking seemingly to the pictured face. Had he insinuated marriage, or something less—and easier? Or had he paid her only a rather florid compli-ment, in somewhat dubious taste? Helga, who had not at the time been quite sure, had remained silent, striving to appear unhearing.

Later, having thought it over, she flayed herself for a fool. It wasn't, she should have known, in the manner of Axel Olsen to pay florid compli-ments in questionable taste. And had it been marriage that he had meant, he would, of course, have done the proper thing. He wouldn't have stopped—or, rather, have begun—by making his wishes known to her when there was Uncle Poul to be formally consulted. She had been, she told herself, insulted. And a goodly measure of contempt and wariness was added to her interest in the man. She was able, however, to feel a gratifying sense of elation in the remembrance that she had been silent, ostensibly unaware of his utterance, and therefore, as far as he knew, not affronted.

This simplified things. It did away with the quandary in which the confession to the Dahls of such a happening would have involved her, for she couldn't be sure that they, too, might not put it down to the difference of her ancestry. And she could still go attended by him, and envied by others, to openings in Kongens Nytorv, to showings at the Royal Academy or Charlottenborg's Palace.[9] He could still call for her and Aunt Katrina of an afternoon or go with her to Magasin du Nord to select a scarf or a length of silk, of which Uncle Poul could say casually in the presence of interested acquaintances: "Um, pretty scarf"—or "frock"—"you're wearing, Helga. Is that the new one Olsen helped you with?"

Her outward manner toward him changed not at all, save that gradually she became, perhaps, a little more detached and indifferent. But definitely Helga Crane had ceased, even remotely, to consider him other than as someone amusing, desirable, and convenient to have about—if one was careful. She intended, presently, to turn her attention to one of the others. The decorative Captain of the Hussars, perhaps. But in the ache of her growing nostalgia, which, try as she might, she could not curb, she no longer thought with any seriousness on either Olsen or Captain Skaargaard. She must, she felt, see America again first. When she returned—

Therefore, where before she would have been pleased and proud at Olsen's proposal, she was now truly surprised. Strangely, she was aware also of a curious feeling of repugnance, as her eyes slid over his face, as smiling, assured, with just the right note of fervor, he made his declaration and request. She was astonished. Was it possible? Was it really this man that she had thought, even wished, she could marry?

He was, it was plain, certain of being accepted, as he was always certain of acceptance, of adulation, in any and every place that he deigned to honor with his presence. Well, Helga was thinking, that wasn't as much his fault as her own, her aunt's, everyone's. He was spoiled, childish almost.

To his words, once she had caught their content and recovered from her surprise, Helga paid not much attention. They would, she knew, be absolutely appropriate ones, and they didn't at all matter. They meant nothing to her—now. She was too amazed to discover suddenly how intensely she disliked him, disliked the shape of his head, the mop of his hair, the line of his nose, the tones of his voice, the nervous grace of his long fingers; disliked even the very look of his irreproachable clothes. And for some inexplicable reason, she was a little frightened and embarrassed, so that when he had finished speaking, for a short space there was only stillness in the small room, into which Aunt Katrina had tactfully had him shown. Even Thor, the enormous Persian, curled on the window ledge in the feeble late afternoon sun, had rested for the moment from his incessant purring under Helga's idly stroking fingers.

Helga, her slight agitation vanished, told him that she was surprised. The offer was, she said, unexpected. Quite.

9. King's New Square, in Copenhagen.

A little sardonically, Olsen interrupted her. He smiled too. "But of course I expected surprise. It is, is it not, the proper thing? And always you are proper, Frøkken Helga, always."

Helga, who had a stripped, naked feeling under his direct glance, drew herself up stiffly. Herr Olsen needn't, she told him, be sarcastic. She *was* surprised. He must understand that she was being quite sincere, quite truthful about that. Really, she hadn't expected him to do her so great an honor.

He made a little impatient gesture. Why, then, had she refused, ignored, his other, earlier suggestion?

At that Helga Crane took a deep indignant breath and was again, this time for an almost imperceptible second, silent. She had, then, been correct in her deduction. Her sensuous, petulant mouth hardened. That he should so frankly—so insolently, it seemed to her—admit his outrageous meaning was too much. She said, coldly: "Because, Herr Olsen, in my country the men, of my race, at least, don't make such suggestions to decent girls. And thinking that you were a gentleman, introduced to me by my aunt, I chose to think myself mistaken, to give you the benefit of the doubt."

"Very commendable, my Helga—and wise. Now you have your reward. Now I offer you marriage."

"Thanks," she answered, "thanks, awfully."

"Yes," and he reached for her slim cream hand, now lying quiet on Thor's broad orange and black back. Helga let it lie in his large pink one, noting their contrast. "Yes, because I, poor artist that I am, cannot hold out against the deliberate lure of you. You disturb me. The longing for you does harm to my work. You creep into my brain and madden me," and he kissed the small ivory hand. Quite decorously, Helga thought, for one so maddened that he was driven, against his inclination, to offer her marriage. But immediately, in extenuation, her mind leapt to the admirable casualness of Aunt Katrina's expressed desire for this very thing, and recalled the unruffled calm of Uncle Poul under any and all circumstances. It was, as she had long ago decided, security. Balance.

"But," the man before her was saying, "for me it will be an experience. It may be that with you, Helga, for wife, I will become great. Immortal. Who knows? I didn't want to love you, but I had to. That is the truth. I make of myself a present to you. For love." His voice held a theatrical note. At the same time he moved forward putting out his arms. His hands touched air. For Helga had moved back. Instantly he dropped his arms and took a step away, repelled by something suddenly wild in her face and manner. Sitting down, he passed a hand over his face with a quick, graceful gesture.

Tameness returned to Helga Crane. Her ironic gaze rested on the face of Axel Olsen, his leonine head, his broad nose—"broader than my own"—his bushy eyebrows, surmounting thick, drooping lids, which hid, she knew, sullen blue eyes. He stirred sharply, shaking off his momentary disconcertion.

In his assured, despotic way he went on: "You know, Helga, you are a contradiction. You have been, I suspect, corrupted by the good Fru Dahl, which is perhaps as well. Who knows? You have the warm impulsive nature of the women of Africa, but, my lovely, you have, I fear, the soul of a prostitute. You sell yourself to the highest buyer. I should of course be happy that it is I. And I am." He stopped, contemplating her, lost apparently, for the second, in pleasant thoughts of the future.

To Helga he seemed to be the most distant, the most unreal figure in the world. She suppressed a ridiculous impulse to laugh. The effort sobered her. Abruptly she was aware that in the end, in some way, she would pay for this hour. A quick brief fear ran through her, leaving in its wake a sense of impending calamity. She wondered if for this she would pay all that she'd had.

And, suddenly, she didn't at all care. She said, lightly, but firmly: "But you see, Herr Olsen, I'm not for sale. Not to you. Not to any white man. I don't at all care to be owned. Even by you."

The drooping lids lifted. The look in the blue eyes was, Helga thought, like the surprised stare of a puzzled baby. He hadn't at all grasped her meaning.

She proceeded, deliberately: "I think you don't understand me. What I'm trying to say is this, I don't want you. I wouldn't under any circumstances marry you," and since she was, as she put it, being brutally frank, she added: "Now."

He turned a little away from her, his face white but composed, and looked down into the gathering shadows in the little park before the house. At last he spoke, in a queer frozen voice: "You refuse me?"

"Yes," Helga repeated with intentional carelessness. "I refuse you."

The man's full upper lip trembled. He wiped his forehead, where the gold hair was now lying flat and pale and lusterless. His eyes still avoided the girl in the high-backed chair before him. Helga felt a shiver of compunction. For an instant she regretted that she had not been a little kinder. But wasn't it after all the greatest kindness to be cruel? But more gently, less indifferently, she said: "You see, I couldn't marry a white man. I simply couldn't. It isn't just you, not just personal, you understand. It's deeper, broader than that. It's racial. Some day maybe you'll be glad. We can't tell, you know; if we were married, you might come to be ashamed of me, to hate me, to hate all dark people. My mother did that."

"I have offered you marriage, Helga Crane, and you answer me with some strange talk of race and shame. What nonsense is this?"

Helga let that pass because she couldn't, she felt, explain. It would be too difficult, too mortifying. She had no words which could adequately, and without laceration to her pride, convey to him the pitfalls into which very easily they might step. "I might," she said, "have considered it once—when I first came. But you, hoping for a more informal arrangement, waited too long. You missed the moment. I had time to think. Now I couldn't. Nothing is worth the risk. We might come to hate each other. I've been through it, or something like it. I know. I couldn't do it. And I'm glad."

Rising, she held out her hand, relieved that he was still silent. "Good afternoon," she said formally. "It has been a great honor—"

"A tragedy," he corrected, barely touching her hand with his moist finger-tips.

"Why?" Helga countered, and for an instant felt as if something sinister and internecine [1] flew back and forth between them like poison.

1. Mutually destructive.

"I mean," he said, and quite solemnly, "that though I don't entirely understand you, yet in a way I do too. And—" He hesitated. Went on. "I think that my picture of you is, after all, the true Helga Crane. Therefore—a tragedy. For someone. For me? Perhaps."

"Oh, the picture!" Helga lifted her shoulders in a little impatient motion.

Ceremoniously Axel Olsen bowed himself out, leaving her grateful for the urbanity which permitted them to part without too much awkwardness. No other man, she thought, of her acquaintance could have managed it so well—except, perhaps, Robert Anderson.

"I'm glad," she declared to herself in another moment, "that I refused him. And," she added honestly, "I'm glad that I had the chance. He took it awfully well, though—for a tragedy." And she made a tiny frown.

The picture—she had never quite, in spite of her deep interest in him, and her desire for his admiration and approval, forgiven Olsen for that portrait. It wasn't, she contended, herself at all, but some disgusting sensual creature with her features. Herr and Fru Dahl had not exactly liked it either, although collectors, artists, and critics had been unanimous in their praise and it had been hung on the line at an annual exhibition, where it had attracted much flattering attention and many tempting offers.

Now Helga went in and stood for a long time before it, with its creator's parting words in mind: ". . . a tragedy . . . my picture is, after all, the true Helga Crane." Vehemently she shook her head. "It isn't, it isn't at all," she said aloud. Bosh! Pure artistic bosh and conceit. Nothing else. Anyone with half an eye could see that it wasn't, at all, like her.

"Marie," she called to the maid passing in the hall, "do you think this is a good picture of me?"

Marie blushed. Hesitated. "Of course, Frøkken, I know Herr Olsen is a great artist, but no, I don't like that picture. It looks bad, wicked. Begging your pardon, Frøkken."

"Thanks, Marie, I don't like it either."

Yes, anyone with half an eye could see that it wasn't she.

Chapter 16

[GOOD-BYE]

Glad though the Dahls may have been that their niece had had the chance of refusing the hand of Axel Olsen, they were anything but glad that she had taken that chance. Very plainly they said so, and quite firmly they pointed out to her the advisability of retrieving the opportunity, if, indeed, such a thing were possible. But it wasn't, even had Helga been so inclined, for, they were to learn from the columns of *Politikken*, Axel Olsen had gone off suddenly to some queer place in the Balkans. To rest, the newspapers said. To get Frøkken Crane out of his mind, the gossips said.

Life in the Dahl ménage[2] went on, smoothly as before, but not so pleasantly. The combined disappointment and sense of guilt of the Dahls and Helga colored everything. Though she had resolved not to think that they

2. Household.

felt that she had, as it were, "let them down," Helga knew that they did. They had not so much expected as hoped that she would bring down Olsen, and so secure the link between the merely fashionable set to which they belonged and the artistic one after which they hankered. It was of course true that there were others, plenty of them. But there was only one Olsen. And Helga, for some idiotic reason connected with race, had refused him. Certainly there was no use in thinking, even, of the others. If she had refused him, she would refuse any and all for the same reason. It was, it seemed, all-embracing.

"It isn't," Uncle Poul had tried to point out to her, "as if there were hundreds of mulattoes here. That, I can understand, might make it a little different. But there's only you. You're unique here, don't you see? Besides, Olsen had money and enviable position. Nobody'd dare to say, or even to think anything odd or unkind of you or him. Come now, Helga, it isn't this foolishness about race. Not here in Denmark. You've never spoken of it before. It can't be just that. You're too sensible. It must be something else. I wish you'd try to explain. You don't perhaps like Olsen?"

Helga had been silent, thinking what a severe wrench to Herr Dahl's ideas of decency was this conversation. For he had an almost fanatic regard for reticence, and a peculiar shrinking from what he looked upon as indecent exposure of the emotions.

"Just what is it, Helga?" he asked again, because the pause had grown awkward, for him.

"I can't explain any better then I have," she had begun tremulously, "it's just something—something deep down inside of me," and had turned away to hide a face convulsed by threatening tears.

But that, Uncle Poul had remarked with a reasonableness that was wasted on the miserable girl before him, was nonsense, pure nonsense.

With a shaking sigh and a frantic dab at her eyes, in which had come a despairing look, she had agreed that perhaps it was foolish, but she couldn't help it. "Can't you, won't you understand, Uncle Poul?" she begged, with a pleading look at the kindly worldly man who at that moment had been thinking that this strange exotic niece of his wife's was indeed charming. He didn't blame Olsen for taking it rather hard.

The thought passed. She was weeping. With no effort at restraint. Charming, yes. But insufficiently civilized. Impulsive. Imprudent. Selfish.

"Try, Helga, to control yourself," he had urged gently. He detested tears. "If it distresses you so, we won't talk of it again. You, of course, must do as you yourself wish. Both your aunt and I want only that you should be happy." He had wanted to make an end of this fruitless wet conversation.

Helga had made another little dab at her face with the scrap of lace and raised shining eyes to his face. She had said, with sincere regret: "You've been marvelous to me, you and Aunt Katrina. Angelic. I don't want to seem ungrateful. I'd do anything for you, anything in the world but this."

Herr Dahl had shrugged. A little sardonically he had smiled. He had refrained from pointing out that this was the only thing she could do for them, the only thing that they had asked of her. He had been too glad to be through with the uncomfortable discussion.

So life went on. Dinners, coffees, theaters, pictures, music, clothes.

More dinners, coffees, theaters, clothes, music. And that nagging aching for America increased. Augmented by the uncomfortableness of Aunt Katrina's and Uncle Poul's disappointment with her, that tormenting nostalgia grew to an unbearable weight. As spring came on with many gracious tokens of following summer, she found her thoughts straying with increasing frequency to Anne's letter and to Harlem, its dirty streets, swollen now, in the warmer weather, with dark, gay humanity.

Until recently she had had no faintest wish ever to see America again. Now she began to welcome the thought of a return. Only a visit, of course. Just to see, to prove to herself that there was nothing there for her. To demonstrate the absurdity of even thinking that there could be. And to relieve the slight tension here. Maybe when she came back—

Her definite decision to go was arrived at with almost bewildering suddenness. It was after a concert at which Dvořák's "New World Symphony"[3] had been wonderfully rendered. Those wailing undertones of "Swing Low, Sweet Chariot" were too poignantly familiar. They struck into her longing heart and cut away her weakening defenses. She knew at least what it was that had lurked formless and undesignated these many weeks in the back of her troubled mind. Incompleteness.

"I'm homesick, not for America, but for Negroes. That's the trouble."

For the first time Helga Crane felt sympathy rather than contempt and hatred for that father, who so often and so angrily she had blamed for his desertion of her mother. She understood, now, his rejection, his repudiation, of the formal calm her mother had represented. She understood his yearning, his intolerable need for the inexhaustible humor and the incessant hope of his own kind, his need for those things, not material, indigenous to all Negro environments. She understood and could sympathize with his facile surrender to the irresistible ties of race, now that they dragged at her own heart. And as she attended parties, the theater, the opera, and mingled with people on the streets, meeting only pale serious faces when she longed for brown laughing ones, she was able to forgive him. Also, it was as if in this understanding and forgiving she had come upon knowledge of almost sacred importance.

Without demur, opposition, or recrimination Herr and Fru Dahl accepted Helga's decision to go back to America. She had expected that they would be glad and relieved. It was agreeable to discover that she had done them less than justice. They were, in spite of their extreme worldliness, very fond of her, and would, as they declared, miss her greatly. And they did want her to come back to them, as they repeatedly insisted. Secretly they felt as she did, that perhaps when she returned—So it was agreed upon that it was only for a brief visit, "for your friend's wedding," and that she was to return in the early fall.

The last day came. The last good-byes were said. Helga began to regret that she was leaving. Why couldn't she have two lives, or why couldn't she be satisfied in one place? Now that she was actually off, she felt heavy at heart. Already she looked back with infinite regret at the two years in the

---

3. Antonin Dvořák (1841–1904), Czech composer, whose Symphony no. 9 (1893), *From the New World*, is rich in references to African American spirituals.

country which had given her so much, of pride, of happiness, of wealth, and of beauty.

Bells rang. The gangplank was hoisted. The dark strip of water widened. The running figures of friends suddenly grown very dear grew smaller, blurred into a whole, and vanished. Tears rose in Helga Crane's eyes, fear in her heart.

Good-bye Denmark! Good-bye. Good-bye!

1928

JEAN TOOMER
1894–1967

Although he never attained the lofty goals he set for himself, Jean Toomer was conspicuously a seeker, a man who viewed life as a search for the attainment of spiritual balance; Toomer apparently was interested in issues of race only insofar as they contributed to his achievement of inner peace. Claimed with equal passion by the race-conscious and the modernist camps for his groundbreaking work *Cane* (1923), Toomer spent his later years wondering why the reading public of his day failed to see that "*Cane* was a song of an end," a song that had helped Toomer to put the racial disquiet within himself to rest. With that turmoil behind him, it was only natural for a man of his spiritual temperament to remark, "Why people have expected me to write a second and a third and a fourth book like *Cane* is one of the queer misunderstandings of my life."

Toomer was born in Washington, D.C., in late 1894, to Nathan and Nina Pinchback Toomer. When Nathan, a farmer from Georgia, deserted his wife less than a year later, she moved with her son into the home of her parents, where Toomer spent most of his childhood. P. B. S. Pinchback, Toomer's remarkable maternal grandfather, had built a political career in Reconstruction Louisiana on his claim that he was black—although Jean Toomer himself would later assert that there was no proof in the matter. After the radical Republicans lost power and local whites regained control of the South, Pinchback could no longer reasonably expect to survive as a politician, and eventually settled in a white neighborhood in Washington, embittered by his fall from prominence.

In 1906, having remarried, Toomer's mother took him to live with her new husband in New Rochelle, New York. Toomer remained there until his mother's death in 1909, when he returned to Washington, D.C., to live with his grandparents, who were resettling from the middle-class white neighborhood where he had spent his boyhood to a black part of town. Attending the M Street High School, Toomer adapted quickly to his new environment. Toomer, who once described himself as descended from a mixture of "Scotch, Welsh, German, English, French, Dutch, Spanish, and some dark blood," apparently had the issue of race brought home to him personally for the first time in his life at this point. His reaction to the matter was to hold the United States responsible for living up to its image as a melting pot; rather than viewing himself as black or white, he stayed the issue of race by referring to himself as an American.

After graduating from high school, he devoted four years to higher education, but spent them at five different institutions (including the University of Wisconsin, the American College of Physical Training in Chicago, and the City College of New York) between 1914 and late 1917. He never remained anywhere long enough to take a degree, and he financed his education by taking all sorts of jobs: he sold cars, taught physical education, and worked in a shipyard.

His decision to become a writer came in 1919. With literary contacts such as Waldo Frank, Hart Crane, Edward Arlington Robinson, and Van Wyck Brooks impressed by his promise, he was not long in making a small reputation for himself. However, the turning point in his career came with a stay in Sparta, Georgia, in 1921, where he served as acting superintendent of a school for blacks. Out of the four months Toomer spent amid the rural blacks of Georgia grew *Cane*, which catapulted its author in 1923 into a position of prominence among the younger writers in the African American world.

Although *Cane* contains several poems and brief sketches that had already appeared in magazines, the overwhelming impression left by the book on its appearance was one of freshness and modernity. *Cane* comprises three sections. In the first part, Toomer depicts in overwhelmingly lyrical language the black folk of rural Georgia; in the second, he turns his attention to urban blacks, particularly those in Chicago and Washington, D.C.; and in the third section, a long, loosely autobiographical, dramatic piece titled *Kabnis*, he attempts to synthesize the preceding sections by depicting an urban black in a rural setting. Waldo Frank, who had first encouraged Toomer to collect his magazine pieces in book form, seemed to speak for the majority of critics in his highly laudatory introduction to the book. *Cane* was an unprecedented success, important enough not only to serve as the foundation of Toomer's career but also to sustain his reputation through a succession of failures.

Toomer had written other racially charged pieces before 1923. Of these, his best known was *Balo*, a one-act play included in the anthology *Plays of Negro Life* by Alain Locke and Montgomery Gregory. (Another play, *Natalie Mann*, and the short story "Withered Skins of Berries," though of interest to scholars, are probably as unfamiliar to the reading public as the philosophical and theological writings which followed from his pen.) After 1923, however, Toomer lost all interest in the issue of race. Indeed, he complained that Alain Locke had "tricked and misused" him by incorporating part of his work in his *The New Negro* in 1925.

With *Cane* and the racial tensions that had engendered it ostensibly behind him, Toomer began his long association with George I. Gurdjieff, an Armenian spiritualist who incorporated mysticism, yoga, Freudian psychoanalysis, and elements of dance into a system sometimes known as Unitism. Toomer, who had never shown a particular interest in religion, spent the summer of 1924 (and several later summers) at Gurdjieff's Institute for the Harmonious Development of Man in France; his goal in visiting the institute was apparently the attainment of "objective consciousness," a recognition of the self as a component in a larger whole. The themes of Unitism quickly began to dominate Toomer's writing. Working in the 1920s as a proselyte for Unitism in Harlem, Toomer temporarily attracted such people as Wallace Thurman, Aaron Douglas, and Nella Larsen as pupils. In all likelihood, however, they were drawn to Toomer less for bringing them Gurdjieff's message than for having written one of the most powerful texts of the Harlem Renaissance.

In 1932, Toomer married one of his white students, a writer named Margery Latimer, who died a year later during childbirth. He then married Marjorie Content, another white woman, in 1934. After they settled in Pennsylvania, Toomer formally broke with Gurdjieff and began to gain interest in the Society of Friends, though he did not become a Quaker until 1940.

In 1936, he wrote a long poem called *Blue Meridian* about the fusion of black-, white-, and red-skinned people into a new entity, the blue man. *Blue Meridian*, which appeared in *The New Caravan*, was the last major publication of Toomer's career. His studies *An Interpretation of Friends Worship* (1947) and *The Flavor of Man* (1949) appeared after his conversion to Quakerism. Much of the unpublished material that Toomer produced before turning his back on fiction and poetry in the mid-1940s has been collected in Darwin Turner's *The Wayward and the Seeking* (1980). Turner's objective was to cull the most interesting pieces from a body of work that Nellie Y. McKay has not unjustly called "largely didactic, tedious, and dull."

Even though Toomer insisted years before his death in 1967 that he was "of no particular race," his loss was deeply felt by the African American community. In the words of Arna Bontemps, Harlem had gone "quietly mad" when *Cane* appeared. If Toomer was indeed a one-book author, he was a one-book author of the first order. Many of the other luminaries of the Harlem Renaissance were more prolific, but few were more powerful as artists. Toomer once reflected: "Perhaps our lot on this earth is to seek and to search. Now and again we find just enough to enable us to carry on. I now doubt that any of us will completely find and be found in this life."

CANE [1]

Karintha

Her skin is like dusk on the eastern horizon,
O cant you see it, O cant you see it,
Her skin is like dusk on the eastern horizon
. . . When the sun goes down.

Men had always wanted her, this Karintha, even as a child, Karintha carrying beauty, perfect as dusk when the sun goes down. Old men rode her hobby-horse upon their knees. Young men danced with her at frolics when they should have been dancing with their grown-up girls. God grant us youth, secretly prayed the old men. The young fellows counted the time to pass before she would be old enough to mate with them. This interest of the male, who wishes to ripen a growing thing too soon, could mean no good to her.

Karintha, at twelve, was a wild flash that told the other folks just what it was to live. At sunset, when there was no wind, and the pine-smoke from over by the sawmill hugged the earth, and you couldnt see more than a few feet in front, her sudden darting past you was a bit of vivid color, like a black bird that flashes in light. With the other children one could hear, some distance off, their feet flopping in the two-inch dust. Karintha's running was a whir. It had the sound of the red dust that sometimes makes a spiral in the road. At dusk, during the hush just after the sawmill had closed down, and before any of the women had started their supper-getting-ready

---

1. *Cane* comprises three general sections. The first section is set in the rural South, with an emphasis on stories of individual women. The second section takes place, for the most part, in urban settings, such as Washington, D.C., and Chicago. The third section, *Kabnis*, is a drama set in a single locality in the South.

songs, her voice, high-pitched, shrill, would put one's ears to itching. But no one ever thought to make her stop because of it. She stoned the cows, and beat her dog, and fought the other children . . . Even the preacher, who caught her at mischief, told himself that she was as innocently lovely as a November cotton flower. Already, rumors were out about her. Homes in Georgia are most often built on the two-room plan. In one, you cook and eat, in the other you sleep, and there love goes on. Karintha had seen or heard, perhaps she had felt her parents loving. One could but imitate one's parents, for to follow them was the way of God. She played "home" with a small boy who was not afraid to do her bidding. That started the whole thing. Old men could no longer ride her hobby-horse upon their knees. But young men counted faster.

> Her skin is like dusk,
> O cant you see it,
> Her skin is like dusk,
> When the sun goes down.

Karintha is a woman. She who carries beauty, perfect as dusk when the sun goes down. She has been married many times. Old men remind her that a few years back they rode her hobby-horse upon their knees. Karintha smiles, and indulges them when she is in the mood for it. She has contempt for them. Karintha is a woman. Young men run stills [2] to make her money. Young men go to the big cities and run on the road. [3] Young men go away to college. They all want to bring her money. These are the young men who thought that all they had to do was to count time. But Karintha is a woman, and she has had a child. A child fell out of her womb onto a bed of pine-needles in the forest. Pine-needles are smooth and sweet. They are elastic to the feet of rabbits. . . . A sawmill was nearby. Its pyramidal sawdust pile smouldered. It is a year before one completely burns. Meanwhile, the smoke curls up and hangs in odd wraiths about the trees, curls up, and spreads itself out over the valley. . . . Weeks after Karintha returned home the smoke was so heavy you tasted it in water. Some one made a song:

> Smoke is on the hills. Rise up.
> Smoke is on the hills, O rise
> And take my soul to Jesus.

Karintha is a woman. Men do not know that the soul of her was a growing thing ripened too soon. They will bring their money; they will die not having found it out. . . . Karintha at twenty, carrying beauty, perfect as dusk when the sun goes down. Karintha . . .

> Her skin is like dusk on the eastern horizon,
> O cant you see it, O cant you see it,
> Her skin is like dusk on the eastern horizon
> . . . When the sun goes down.

Goes down . . .

---

2. Make liquor illegally.   3. Work for the railroad companies.

Reapers

Black reapers with the sound of steel on stones
Are sharpening scythes. I see them place the hones
In their hip-pockets as a thing that's done,
And start their silent swinging, one by one.
Black horses drive a mower through the weeds,   5
And there, a field rat, startled, squealing bleeds.
His belly close to ground. I see the blade,
Blood-stained, continue cutting weeds and shade.

November Cotton Flower

Boll-weevil's[1] coming, and the winter's cold,
Made cotton-stalks look rusty, seasons old,
And cotton, scarce as any southern snow,
Was vanishing; the branch, so pinched and slow,
Failed in its function as the autumn rake;   5
Drouth fighting soil had caused the soil to take
All water from the streams; dead birds were found
In wells a hundred feet below the ground—
Such was the season when the flower bloomed.
Old folks were startled, and it soon assumed   10
Significance. Superstition saw
Something it had never seen before:
Brown eyes that loved without a trace of fear,
Beauty so sudden for that time of year.

Becky

Becky was the white woman who had two Negro sons. She's dead; they've gone away. The pines whisper to Jesus. The Bible flaps its leaves with an aimless rustle on her mound.

Becky had one Negro son. Who gave it to her? Damn buck nigger, said the white folks' mouths. She wouldnt tell. Common, God-forsaken, insane white shameless wench, said the white folks' mouths. Her eyes were sunken, her neck stringy, her breasts fallen, till then. Taking their words, they filled her, like a bubble rising—then she broke. Mouth setting in a twist that held her eyes, harsh, vacant, staring. . . Who gave it to her? Low-down nigger with no self-respect, said the black folks' mouths. She wouldnt tell. Poor Catholic poor-white crazy woman, said the black folks' mouths. White folks and black folks built her cabin, fed her and her growing baby, prayed secretly to God who'd put His cross upon her and cast her out.

When the first was born, the white folks said they'd have no more to do with her. And black folks, they too joined hands to cast her out . . . The pines whispered to Jesus. . The railroad boss said not to say he said it, but

1. A beetle notorious for destroying crops.

she could live, if she wanted to, on the narrow strip of land between the railroad and the road. John Stone, who owned the lumber and the bricks, would have shot the man who told he gave the stuff to Lonnie Deacon, who stole out there at night and built the cabin. A single room held down to earth . . . O fly away to Jesus . . . by a leaning chimney . . .

Six trains each day rumbled past and shook the ground under her cabin. Fords, and horse- and mule-drawn buggies went back and forth along the road. No one ever saw her. Trainmen, and passengers who'd heard about her, threw out papers and food. Threw out little crumpled slips of paper scribbled with prayers, as they passed her eye-shaped piece of sandy ground. Ground islandized between the road and railroad track. Pushed up where a blue-sheen God[1] with listless eyes could look at it. Folks from the town took turns, unknown, of course, to each other, in bringing corn and meat and sweet potatoes. Even sometimes snuff . . . O thank y Jesus . . . Old David Georgia, grinding cane and boiling syrup, never went her way without some sugar sap. No one ever saw her. The boy grew up and ran around. When he was five years old as folks reckoned it, Hugh Jourdon saw him carrying a baby. "Becky has another son," was what the whole town knew. But nothing was said, for the part of man that says things to the likes of that had told itself that if there was a Becky, that Becky now was dead.

The two boys grew. Sullen and cunning . . . O pines, whisper to Jesus; tell Him to come and press sweet Jesus-lips against their lips and eyes . . . It seemed as though with those two big fellows there, there could be no room for Becky. The part that prayed wondered if perhaps she'd really died, and they had buried her. No one dared ask. They'd beat and cut a man who meant nothing at all in mentioning that they lived along the road. White or colored? No one knew, and least of all themselves. They drifted around from job to job. We, who had cast out their mother because of them, could we take them in? They answered black and white folks by shooting up two men and leaving town. "Godam the white folks; godam the niggers," they shouted as they left town. Becky? Smoke curled up from her chimney; she must be there. Trains passing shook the ground. The ground shook the leaning chimney. Nobody noticed it. A creepy feeling came over all who saw that thin wraith of smoke and felt the trembling of the ground. Folks began to take her food again. They quit it soon because they had a fear. Becky if dead might be a hant,[2] and if alive—it took some nerve even to mention it . . . O pines, whisper to Jesus . . .

It was Sunday. Our congregation had been visiting at Pulverton, and were coming home. There was no wind. The autumn sun, the bell from Ebenezer Church, listless and heavy. Even the pines were stale, sticky, like the smell of food that makes you sick. Before we turned the bend of the road that would show us the Becky cabin, the horses stopped stock-still, pushed back their ears, and nervously whinnied. We urged, then whipped them on. Quarter of a mile away thin smoke curled up from the leaning chimney . . . O pines, whisper to Jesus . . . Goose-flesh came on my skin

---

1. Perhaps the locomotive. 2. A ghost.

though there still was neither chill nor wind. Eyes left their sockets for the cabin. Ears burned and throbbed. Uncanny eclipse! fear closed my mind. We were just about to pass . . . Pines shout to Jesus! . . the ground trembled as a ghost train rumbled by. The chimney fell into the cabin. Its thud was like a hollow report, ages having passed since it went off. Barlo and I were pulled out of our seats. Dragged to the door that had swung open. Through the dust we saw the bricks in a mound upon the floor. Becky, if she was there, lay under them. I thought I heard a groan. Barlo, mumbling something, threw his Bible on the pile. (No one has ever touched it.) Somehow we got away. My buggy was still on the road. The last thing that I remember was whipping old Dan like fury; I remember nothing after that—that is, until I reached town and folks crowded round to get the true word of it.

Becky was the white woman who had two Negro sons. She's dead; they've gone away. The pines whisper to Jesus. The Bible flaps its leaves with an aimless rustle on her mound.

Face

Hair—
silver-gray,
like streams of stars,
Brows—
recurved canoes   5
quivered by the ripples blown by pain,
Her eyes—
mist of tears
condensing on the flesh below
And her channeled muscles   10
are cluster grapes of sorrow
purple in the evening sun
nearly ripe for worms.

Cotton Song

Come, brother, come. Lets lift it;
Come now, hewit! roll away!
Shackles fall upon the Judgment Day
But lets not wait for it.

God's body's got a soul,   5
Bodies like to roll the soul,
Cant blame God if we dont roll,
Come, brother, roll, roll!

Cotton bales are the fleecy way
Weary sinner's bare feet trod,   10
Softly, softly to the throne of God,
"We aint agwine t wait until th Judgment Day!

Nassur; nassur,
Hump.
Eoho, eoho, roll away!   15
We aint agwine t wait until th Judgment Day!"

God's body's got a soul,
Bodies like to roll the soul,
Cant blame God if we dont roll,
Come, brother, roll, roll!   20

Carma [1]

Wind is in the cane. Come along.
Cane leaves swaying, rusty with talk,
Scratching choruses above the guinea's squawk,
Wind is in the cane. Come along.

Carma, in overalls, and strong as any man, stands behind the old brown
mule, driving the wagon home. It bumps, and groans, and shakes as it
crosses the railroad track. She, riding it easy. I leave the men around the
stove to follow her with my eyes down the red dust road. Nigger woman
driving a Georgia chariot down an old dust road. Dixie Pike is what they
call it. Maybe she feels my gaze, perhaps she expects it. Anyway, she turns.
The sun, which has been slanting over her shoulder, shoots primitive rockets into her mangrove-gloomed, yellow flower face. Hi! Yip! God has left
the Moses-people [2] for the nigger. "Gedap." Using reins to slap the mule,
she disappears in a cloudy rumble at some indefinite point along the road.
(The sun is hammered to a band of gold. Pine-needles, like mazda, are
brilliantly aglow. No rain has come to take the rustle from the falling sweet-
gum leaves. Over in the forest, across the swamp, a sawmill blows its closing whistle. Smoke curls up. Marvelous web spun by the spider sawdust
pile. Curls up and spreads itself pine-high above the branch, a single silver
band along the eastern valley. A black boy . . . you are the most sleepiest
man I ever seed, Sleeping Beauty . . . cradled on a gray mule, guided by the
hollow sound of cowbells, heads for them through a rusty cotton field.
From down the railroad track, the chug-chug of a gas engine announces
that the repair gang is coming home. A girl in the yard of a whitewashed
shack not much larger than the stack of worn ties piled before it, sings. Her
voice is loud. Echoes, like rain, sweep the valley. Dusk takes the polish
from the rails. Lights twinkle in scattered houses. From far away, a sad
strong song. Pungent and composite, the smell of farmyards is the fragrance of the woman. She does not sing; her body is a song. She is in the
forest, dancing. Torches flare . . . juju men, greegree, [3] witch-doctors . . .
torches go out . . . The Dixie Pike has grown from a goat path in Africa.
                                                          Night.
Foxie, the bitch, slicks back her ears and barks at the rising moon.)

---

1. Or karma; the Hindu concept of the force of
destiny or faith.
2. Ancient Hebrews.

3. A charm, associated with Africa. "Juju men":
conjurers.

Wind is in the corn. Come along.
Corn leaves swaying, rusty with talk,
Scratching choruses above the guinea's squawk,
Wind is in the corn. Come along.

Carma's tale is the crudest melodrama. Her husband's in the gang.[4] And its her fault he got there. Working with a contractor, he was away most of the time. She had others. No one blames her for that. He returned one day and hung around the town where he picked up week-old boasts and rumors . . . Bane accused her. She denied. He couldnt see that she was becoming hysterical. He would have liked to take his fists and beat her. Who was strong as a man. Stronger. Words, like corkscrews, wormed to her strength. It fizzled out. Grabbing a gun, she rushed from the house and plunged across the road into a canebrake. . There, in quarter heaven shone the crescent moon . . . Bane was afraid to follow till he heard the gun go off. Then he wasted half an hour gathering the neighbor men. They met in the road where lamp-light showed tracks dissolving in the loose earth about the cane. The search began. Moths flickered the lamps. They put them out. Really, because she still might be live enough to shoot. Time and space have no meaning in a canefield. No more than the interminable stalks . . . Some one stumbled over her. A cry went up. From the road, one would have thought that they were cornering a rabbit or a skunk . . . It is difficult carrying dead weight through cane. They placed her on the sofa. A curious, nosey somebody looked for the wound. This fussing with her clothes aroused her. Her eyes were weak and pitiable for so strong a woman. Slowly, then like a flash, Bane came to know that the shot she fired, with averted head, was aimed to whistle like a dying hornet through the cane. Twice deceived, and one deception proved the other. His head went off. Slashed one of the men who'd helped, the man who'd stumbled over her. Now he's in the gang. Who was her husband. Should she not take others, this Carma, strong as a man, whose tale as I have told it is the crudest melodrama?

Wind is in the cane. Come along.
Cane leaves swaying, rusty with talk,
Scratching choruses above the guinea's squawk,
Wind is in the cane. Come along.

Song of the Son

Pour O pour that parting soul in song,
O pour it in the sawdust glow of night,
Into the velvet pine-smoke air to-night,
And let the valley carry it along.
And let the valley carry it along.   5

4. I.e., a chain gang.

O land and soil, red soil and sweet-gum tree,
So scant of grass, so profligate of pines,
Now just before an epoch's sun declines
Thy son, in time, I have returned to thee,
Thy son, I have in time returned to thee.   10

In time, for though the sun is setting on
A song-lit race of slaves, it has not set;
Though late, O soil, it is not too late yet
To catch thy plaintive soul, leaving, soon gone,
Leaving, to catch thy plaintive soul soon gone.   15

O Negro slaves, dark purple ripened plums,
Squeezed, and bursting in the pine-wood air,
Passing, before they stripped the old tree bare
One plum was saved for me, one seed becomes

An everlasting song, a singing tree,   20
Caroling softly souls of slavery,
What they were, and what they are to me,
Caroling softly souls of slavery.

Georgia Dusk

The sky, lazily disdaining to pursue
   The setting sun, too indolent to hold
   A lengthened tournament for flashing gold,
Passively darkens for night's barbecue,

A feast of moon and men and barking hounds,   5
   An orgy for some genius of the South
   With blood-hot eyes and cane-lipped scented mouth,
Surprised in making folk-songs from soul sounds.

The sawmill blows its whistle, buzz-saws stop,
   And silence breaks the bud of knoll and hill,   10
   Soft settling pollen where plowed lands fulfill
Their early promise of a bumper crop.

Smoke from the pyramidal sawdust pile
   Curls up, blue ghosts of trees, tarrying low
   Where only chips and stumps are left to show   15
The solid proof of former domicile.

Meanwhile, the men, with vestiges of pomp,
   Race memories of king and caravan,
   High-priests, an ostrich, and a juju-man, [1]
Go singing through the footpaths of the swamp.   20

1. A conjurer.

Their voices rise . . . the pine trees are guitars,
   Strumming, pine-needles fall like sheets of rain . . .
   Their voices rise . . . the chorus of the cane
Is caroling a vesper to the stars . . .

O singers, resinous and soft your songs   25
   Above the sacred whisper of the pines,
   Give virgin lips to cornfield concubines,
Bring dreams of Christ to dusky cane-lipped throngs.

Fern

Face flowed into her eyes. Flowed in soft cream foam and plaintive ripples, in such a way that wherever your glance may momentarily have rested, it immediately thereafter wavered in the direction of her eyes. The soft suggestion of down slightly darkened, like the shadow of a bird's wing might, the creamy brown color of her upper lip. Why, after noticing it, you sought her eyes, I cannot tell you. Her nose was aquiline, Semitic. If you have heard a Jewish cantor sing, if he has touched you and made your own sorrow seem trivial when compared with his, you will know my feeling when I follow the curves of her profile, like mobile rivers, to their common delta. They were strange eyes. In this, that they sought nothing—that is, nothing that was obvious and tangible and that one could see, and they gave the impression that nothing was to be denied. When a woman seeks, you will have observed, her eyes deny. Fern's eyes desired nothing that you could give her; there was no reason why they should withhold. Men saw her eyes and fooled themselves. Fern's eyes said to them that she was easy. When she was young, a few men took her, but got no joy from it. And then, once done, they felt bound to her (quite unlike their hit and run with other girls), felt as though it would take them a lifetime to fulfill an obligation which they could find no name for. They became attached to her, and hungered after finding the barest trace of what she might desire. As she grew up, new men who came to town felt as almost everyone did who ever saw her: that they would not be denied. Men were everlastingly bringing her their bodies. Something inside of her got tired of them, I guess, for I am certain that for the life of her she could not tell why or how she began to turn them off. A man in fever is no trifling thing to send away. They began to leave her, baffled and ashamed, yet vowing to themselves that some day they would do some fine thing for her: send her candy every week and not let her know whom it came from, watch out for her wedding-day and give her a magnificent something with no name on it, buy a house and deed it to her, rescue her from some unworthy fellow who had tricked her into marrying him. As you know, men are apt to idolize or fear that which they cannot understand, especially if it be a woman. She did not deny them, yet the fact was that they were denied. A sort of superstition crept into their consciousness of her being somehow above them. Being above them meant that she was not to be approached by anyone. She became a virgin. Now a virgin in a small southern town is by no means the usual thing, if you will believe me. That the sexes were made to mate is the practice of the

South. Particularly, black folks were made to mate. And it is black folks whom I have been talking about thus far. What white men thought of Fern I can arrive at only by analogy. They let her alone.

Anyone, of course, could see her, could see her eyes. If you walked up the Dixie Pike most any time of day, you'd be most like to see her resting listless-like on the railing of her porch, back propped against a post, head tilted a little forward because there was a nail in the porch post just where her head came which for some reason or other she never took the trouble to pull out. Her eyes, if it were sunset, rested idly where the sun, molten and glorious, was pouring down between the fringe of pines. Or maybe they gazed at the gray cabin on the knoll from which an evening folk-song was coming. Perhaps they followed a cow that had been turned loose to roam and feed on cotton-stalks and corn leaves. Like as not they'd settle on some vague spot above the horizon, though hardly a trace of wistfulness would come to them. If it were dusk, then they'd wait for the search-light of the evening train which you could see miles up the track before it flared across the Dixie Pike, close to her home. Wherever they looked, you'd follow them and then waver back. Like her face, the whole countryside seemed to flow into her eyes. Flowed into them with the soft listless cadence of Georgia's South. A young Negro, once, was looking at her, spellbound, from the road. A white man passing in a buggy had to flick him with his whip if he was to get by without running him over. I first saw her on her porch. I was passing with a fellow whose crusty numbness (I was from the North and suspected of being prejudiced and stuck-up) was melting as he found me warm. I asked him who she was. "That's Fern," was all that I could get from him. Some folks already thought that I was given to nosing around; I let it go at that, so far as questions were concerned. But at first sight of her I felt as if I heard a Jewish cantor sing. As if his singing rose above the unheard chorus of a folk-song. And I felt bound to her. I too had my dreams: something I would do for her. I have knocked about from town to town too much not to know the futility of mere change of place. Besides, picture if you can, this cream-colored solitary girl sitting at a tenement window looking down on the indifferent throngs of Harlem. Better that she listen to folk-songs at dusk in Georgia, you would say, and so would I. Or, suppose she came up North and married. Even a doctor or a lawyer, say, one who would be sure to get along—that is, make money. You and I know, who have had experience in such things, that love is not a thing like prejudice which can be bettered by changes of town. Could men in Washington, Chicago, or New York, more than the men of Georgia, bring her something left vacant by the bestowal of their bodies? You and I who know men in these cities will have to say, they could not. See her out and out a prostitute along State Street in Chicago. See her move into a southern town where white men are more aggressive. See her become a white man's concubine . . . . Something I must do for her. There was myself. What could I do for her? Talk, of course. Push back the fringe of pines upon new horizons. To what purpose? and what for? Her? Myself? Men in her case seem to lose their selfishness. I lost mine before I touched her. I ask you, friend (it makes no difference if you sit in the

Pullman[1] or the Jim Crow as the train crosses her road), what thoughts would come to you—that is, after you'd finished with the thoughts that leap into men's minds at the sight of a pretty woman who will not deny them; what thoughts would come to you, had you seen her in a quick flash, keen and intuitively, as she sat there on her porch when your train thundered by? Would you have got off at the next station and come back for her to take her where? Would you have completely forgotten her as soon as you reached Macon, Atlanta, Augusta, Pasadena, Madison, Chicago, Boston, or New Orleans? Would you tell your wife or sweetheart about a girl you saw? Your thoughts can help me, and I would like to know. Something I would do for her . . .

One evening I walked up the Pike on purpose, and stopped to say hello. Some of her family were about, but they moved away to make room for me. Damn if I knew how to begin. Would you? Mr. and Miss So-and-So, people, the weather, the crops, the new preacher, the frolic, the church benefit, rabbit and possum hunting, the new soft drink they had at old Pap's store, the schedule of the trains, what kind of town Macon was, Negro's migration north, bollweevils,[2] syrup, the Bible—to all these things she gave a yassur or nassur, without further comment. I began to wonder if perhaps my own emotional sensibility had played one of its tricks on me. "Lets take a walk," I at last ventured. The suggestion, coming after so long an isolation, was novel enough, I guess, to surprise. But it wasnt that. Something told me that men before me had said just that as a prelude to the offering of their bodies. I tried to tell her with my eyes. I think she understood. The thing from her that made my throat catch, vanished. Its passing left her visible in a way I'd thought, but never seen. We walked down the Pike with people on all the porches gaping at us. "Doesnt it make you mad?" She meant the row of petty gossiping people. She meant the world. Through a canebrake that was ripe for cutting, the branch was reached. Under a sweet-gum tree, and where reddish leaves had dammed the creek a little, we sat down. Dusk, suggesting the almost imperceptible procession of giant trees, settled with a purple haze about the cane. I felt strange, as I always do in Georgia, particularly at dusk. I felt that things unseen to men were tangibly immediate. It would not have surprised me had I had vision. People have them in Georgia more often than you would suppose. A black woman once saw the mother of Christ and drew her in charcoal on the courthouse wall . . . When one is on the soil of one's ancestors, most anything can come to one . . . From force of habit, I suppose, I held Fern in my arms— that is, without at first noticing it. Then my mind came back to her. Her eyes, unusually weird and open, held me. Held God. He flowed in as I've seen the countryside flow in. Seen men. I must have done something— what, I dont know, in the confusion of my emotion. She sprang up. Rushed some distance from me. Fell to her knees, and began swaying, swaying. Her body was tortured with something it could not let out. Like boiling sap it flooded arms and fingers till she shook them as if they burned her. It

---

1. Sleeping car on the railroad; blacks were gener-   2. Beetles notorious for destroying crops.
ally barred from these in the South.

found her throat, and spattered inarticulately in plaintive, convulsive sounds, mingled with calls to Christ Jesus. And then she sang, brokenly. A Jewish cantor singing with a broken voice. A child's voice, uncertain, or an old man's. Dusk hid her; I could hear only her song. It seemed to me as though she were pounding her head in anguish upon the ground. I rushed to her. She fainted in my arms.

There was talk about her fainting with me in the canefield. And I got one or two ugly looks from town men who'd set themselves up to protect her. In fact, there was talk of making me leave town. But they never did. They kept a watch-out for me, though. Shortly after, I came back North. From the train window I saw her as I crossed her road. Saw her on her porch, head tilted a little forward where the nail was, eyes vaguely focused on the sunset. Saw her face flow into them, the countryside and something that I call God, flowing into them . . . Nothing ever really happened. Nothing ever came to Fern, not even I. Something I would do for her. Some fine unnamed thing . . . And, friend, you? She is still living, I have reason to know. Her name, against the chance that you might happen down that way, is Fernie May Rosen.

Nullo

A spray of pine-needles,
Dipped in western horizon gold,
Fell onto a path.
Dry moulds of cow-hoofs.
In the forest.   5
Rabbits knew not of their falling,
Nor did the forest catch aflame.

Evening Song

Full moon rising on the waters of my heart,
Lakes and moon and fires,
Cloine tires,
Holding her lips apart.

Promises of slumber leaving shore to charm the moon,   5
Miracle made vesper-keeps,
Cloine sleeps,
And I'll be sleeping soon.

Cloine, curled like the sleepy waters where the moon-waves start,
Radiant, resplendently she gleams,   10
Cloine dreams,
Lips pressed against my heart.

Esther

1

Esther's hair falls in soft curls about her high-cheek-boned chalk-white
face. Esther's hair would be beautiful if there were more gloss to it. And if
her face were not prematurely serious, one would call it pretty. Her cheeks
are too flat and dead for a girl of nine. Esther looks like a little white child,
starched, frilled, as she walks slowly from her home towards her father's
grocery store. She is about to turn in Broad from Maple Street. White and
black men loafing on the corner hold no interest for her. Then a strange
thing happens. A clean-muscled, magnificent, black-skinned Negro,
whom she had heard her father mention as King Barlo, suddenly drops to
his knees on a spot called the Spittoon. White men, unaware of him, continue squirting tobacco juice in his direction. The saffron fluid splashes on
his face. His smooth black face begins to glisten and to shine. Soon, people
notice him, and gather round. His eyes are rapturous upon the heavens.
Lips and nostrils quiver. Barlo is in a religious trance. Town folks know it.
They are not startled. They are not afraid. They gather round. Some beg
boxes from the grocery stores. From old McGregor's notion shop. A coffin-
case is pressed into use. Folks line the curb-stones. Business men close
shop. And Banker Warply parks his car close by. Silently, all await the
prophet's voice. The sheriff, a great florid fellow whose leggings never meet
around his bulging calves, swears in three deputies. "Wall, y cant never tell
what a nigger like King Barlo might be up t." Soda bottles, five fingers full
of shine, [2] are passed to those who want them. A couple of stray dogs start a
fight. Old Goodlow's cow comes flopping up the street. Barlo, still as an
Indian fakir, [3] has not moved. The town bell strikes six. The sun slips in
behind a heavy mass of horizon cloud. The crowd is hushed and expectant.
Barlo's under jaw relaxes, and his lips begin to move.

"Jesus has been awhisperin strange words deep down, O way down deep,
deep in my ears."

Hums of awe and of excitement.

"He called me to His side an said, 'Git down on your knees beside me,
son, Ise gwine t whisper in your ears.'"

An old sister cries, "Ah, Lord."

"'Ise agwine t whisper in your ears,' he said, an I replied, 'Thy will be
done on earth as it is in heaven.'"

"Ah, Lord. Amen. Amen."

"An Lord Jesus whispered strange good words deep down, O way down
deep, deep in my ears. An He said, 'Tell em till you feel your throat on fire.'
I saw a vision. I saw a man arise, an he was big an black an powerful—"

Some one yells, "Preach it, preacher, preach it!"

"—but his head was caught up in the clouds. An while he was agazin at
th heavens, heart filled up with th Lord, some little white-ant biddies came

---

1. Esther's age in this section.
2. I.e., moonshine or illegal whisky.

3. Magician.

an tied his feet to chains. They led him t th coast, they led him t th sea, they led him across th ocean an they didnt set him free. The old coast didnt miss him, an th new coast wasnt free, he left the old-coast brothers, t give birth t you an me. O Lord, great God Almighty, t give birth t you an me."

Barlo pauses. Old gray mothers are in tears. Fragments of melodies are being hummed. White folks are touched and curiously awed. Off to themselves, white and black preachers confer as to how best to rid themselves of the vagrant, usurping fellow. Barlo looks as though he is struggling to continue. People are hushed. One can hear weevils[4] work. Dusk is falling rapidly, and the customary store lights fail to throw their feeble glow across the gray dust and flagging of the Georgia town. Barlo rises to his full height. He is immense. To the people he assumes the outlines of his visioned African. In a mighty voice he bellows:

"Brothers an sisters, turn your faces t th sweet face of the Lord, an fill your hearts with glory. Open your eyes an see th dawnin of th mornin light. Open your ears—"

Years afterwards Esther was told that at that very moment a great, heavy, rumbling voice actually was heard. That hosts of angels and of demons paraded up and down the streets all night. That King Barlo rode out of town astride a pitch-black bull that had a glowing gold ring in its nose. And that old Limp Underwood, who hated niggers, woke up next morning to find that he held a black man in his arms. This much is certain: an inspired Negress, of wide reputation for being sanctified, drew a portrait of a black madonna on the courthouse wall. And King Barlo left town. He left his image indelibly upon the mind of Esther. He became the starting point of the only living patterns that her mind was to know.

2

SIXTEEN

Esther begins to dream. The low evening sun sets the windows of McGregor's notion shop aflame. Esther makes believe that they really are aflame. The town fire department rushes madly down the road. It ruthlessly shoves black and white idlers to one side. It whoops. It clangs. It rescues from the second-story window a dimpled infant which she claims for her own. How had she come by it? She thinks of it immaculately. It is a sin to think of it immaculately. She must dream no more. She must repent her sin. Another dream comes. There is no fire department. There are no heroic men. The fire starts. The loafers on the corner form a circle, chew their tobacco faster, and squirt juice just as fast as they can chew. Gallons on top of gallons they squirt upon the flames. The air reeks with the stench of scorched tobacco juice. Women, fat chunky Negro women, lean scrawny white women, pull their skirts up above their heads and display the most ludicrous underclothes. The women scoot in all directions from the danger zone. She alone is left to take the baby in her arms. But what a baby! Black, singed, woolly, tobacco-juice baby—ugly as sin. Once held to her

---

4. I.e., boll weevils; beetles notorious for destroying crops.

breast, miraculous thing: its breath is sweet and its lips can nibble. She loves it frantically. Her joy in it changes the town folks' jeers to harmless jealousy, and she is left alone.

TWENTY-TWO

Esther's schooling is over. She works behind the counter of her father's grocery store. "To keep the money in the family," so he said. She is learning to make distinctions between the business and the social worlds. "Good business comes from remembering that the white folks dont divide the niggers, Esther. Be just as black as any man who has a silver dollar." Esther listlessly forgets that she is near white, and that her father is the richest colored man in town. Black folk who drift in to buy lard and snuff and flour of her, call her a sweet-natured, accommodating girl. She learns their names. She forgets them. She thinks about men. "I dont appeal to them. I wonder why." She recalls an affair she had with a little fair boy while still in school. It had ended in her shame when he as much as told her that for sweetness he preferred a lollipop. She remembers the salesman from the North who wanted to take her to the movies that first night he was in town. She refused, of course. And he never came back, having found out who she was. She thinks of Barlo. Barlo's image gives her a slightly stale thrill. She spices it by telling herself his glories. Black. Magnetically so. Best cotton picker in the county, in the state, in the whole world for that matter. Best man with his fists, best man with dice, with a razor. Promoter of church benefits. Of colored fairs. Vagrant preacher. Lover of all the women for miles and miles around. Esther decides that she loves him. And with a vague sense of life slipping by, she resolves that she will tell him so, whatever people say, the next time he comes to town. After the making of this resolution which becomes a sort of wedding cake for her to tuck beneath her pillow and go to sleep upon, she sees nothing of Barlo for five years. Her hair thins. It looks like the dull silk on puny corn ears. Her face pales until it is the color of the gray dust that dances with dead cotton leaves.

3

ESTHER IS TWENTY-SEVEN

Esther sells lard and snuff and flour to vague black faces that drift in her store to ask for them. Her eyes hardly see the people to whom she gives change. Her body is lean and beaten. She rests listlessly against the counter, too weary to sit down. From the street some one shouts, "King Barlo has come back to town." He passes her window, driving a large new car. Cut-out open.[5] He veers to the curb, and steps out. Barlo has made money on cotton during the war.[6] He is as rich as anyone. Esther suddenly is animate. She goes to her door. She sees him at a distance, the center of a group of credulous men. She hears the deep-bass rumble of his talk. The sun swings low. McGregor's windows are aflame again. Pale flame. A sharply dressed white girl passes by. For a moment Esther wishes that she

---

5. A car without a steel top.   6. World War I (1914–18).

might be like her. Not white; she has no need for being that. But sharp, sporty, with get-up about her. Barlo is connected with that wish. She mustnt wish. Wishes only make you restless. Emptiness is a thing that grows by being moved. "I'll not think. Not wish. Just set my mind against it." Then the thought comes to her that those purposeless, easy-going men will possess him, if she doesnt. Purpose is not dead in her, now that she comes to think of it. That loose women will have their arms around him at Nat Bowle's place tonight. As if her veins are full of fired sun-bleached southern shanties, a swift heat sweeps them. Dead dreams, and a forgotten resolution are carried upward by the flames. Pale flames. "They shant have him. Oh, they shall not. Not if it kills me they shant have him." Jerky, aflutter, she closes the store and starts home. Folks lazing on store windowsills wonder what on earth can be the matter with Jim Crane's gal, as she passes them. "Come to remember, she always was a little off, a little crazy, I reckon." Esther seeks her own room, and locks the door. Her mind is a pink meshbag filled with baby toes.

Using the noise of the town clock striking twelve to cover the creaks of her departure, Esther slips into the quiet road. The town, her parents, most everyone is sound asleep. This fact is a stable thing that comforts her. After sundown a chill wind came up from the west. It is still blowing, but to her it is a steady, settled thing like the cold. She wants her mind to be like that. Solid, contained, and blank as a sheet of darkened ice. She will not permit herself to notice the peculiar phosphorescent glitter of the sweet-gum leaves. Their movement would excite her. Exciting too, the recession of the dull familiar homes she knows so well. She doesnt know them at all. She closes her eyes, and holds them tightly. Wont do. Her being aware that they are closed recalls her purpose. She does not want to think of it. She opens them. She turns now into the deserted business street. The corrugated iron canopies and mule- and horse-gnawed hitching posts bring her a strange composure. Ghosts of the commonplaces of her daily life take stride with her and become her companions. And the echoes of her heels upon the flagging are rhythmically monotonous and soothing. Crossing the street at the corner of McGregor's notion shop, she thinks that the windows are a dull flame. Only a fancy. She walks faster. Then runs. A turn into a side street brings her abruptly to Nat Bowle's place. The house is squat and dark. It is always dark. Barlo is within. Quietly she opens the outside door and steps in. She passes through a small room. Pauses before a flight of stairs down which people's voices, muffled, come. The air is heavy with fresh tobacco smoke. It makes her sick. She wants to turn back. She goes up the steps. As if she were mounting to some great height, her head spins. She is violently dizzy. Blackness rushes to her eyes. And then she finds that she is in a large room. Barlo is before her.

"Well, I'm sholy damned—skuse me, but what, what brought you here, lil milk-white gal?"

"You." Her voice sounds like a frightened child's that calls homeward from some point miles away.

"Me?"

"Yes, you Barlo."

"This aint th place fer y. This aint th place fer y."

"I know. I know. But I've come for you."

"For me for what?"

She manages to look deep and straight into his eyes. He is slow at understanding. Guffaws and giggles break out from all around the room. A coarse woman's voice remarks, "So thats how the dictie niggers[7] does it." Laughs. "Mus give em credit fo their gall."

Esther doesnt hear. Barlo does. His faculties are jogged. She sees a smile, ugly and repulsive to her, working upward through thick licker fumes. Barlo seems hideous. The thought comes suddenly, that conception with a drunken man must be a mighty sin. She draws away, frozen. Like a somnambulist she wheels around and walks stiffly to the stairs. Down them. Jeers and hoots pelter bluntly upon her back. She steps out. There is no air, no street, and the town has completely disappeared.

Conversion

African Guardian of Souls,
Drunk with rum,
Feasting on a strange cassava,[1]
Yielding to new words and a weak palabra[2]
Of a white-faced sardonic god—   5
Grins, cries
Amen,
Shouts hosanna.

Portrait in Georgia

Hair—braided chestnut,
    coiled like a lyncher's rope,
Eyes—fagots,
Lips—old scars, or the first red blisters,
Breath—the last sweet scent of cane,   5
And her slim body, white as the ash
    of black flesh after flame.

Blood-Burning Moon[1]

1

Up from the skeleton stone walls, up from the rotting floor boards and the solid hand-hewn beams of oak of the pre-war cotton factory, dusk came. Up from the dusk the full moon came. Glowing like a fired pine-knot, it illumined the great door and soft showered the Negro shanties aligned

---

7. Educated blacks.
1. An edible, tuberous tropical root, served cooked or used as a starch or flour.

2. Word or talk (Spanish).
1. A reddish moon is said to portend a night of violence.

along the single street of factory town. The full moon in the great door was an omen. Negro women improvised songs against its spell.

Louisa sang as she came over the crest of the hill from the white folks' kitchen. Her skin was the color of oak leaves on young trees in fall. Her breasts, firm and up-pointed like ripe acorns. And her singing had the low murmur of winds in fig trees. Bob Stone, younger son of the people she worked for, loved her. By the way the world reckons things, he had won her. By measure of that warm glow which came into her mind at thought of him, he had won her. Tom Burwell, whom the whole town called Big Boy, also loved her. But working in the fields all day, and far away from her, gave him no chance to show it. Though often enough of evenings he had tried to. Somehow, he never got along. Strong as he was with hands upon the ax or plow, he found it difficult to hold her. Or so he thought. But the fact was that he held her to factory town more firmly than he thought for. His black balanced, and pulled against, the white of Stone, when she thought of them. And her mind was vaguely upon them as she came over the crest of the hill, coming from the white folks' kitchen. As she sang softly at the evil face of the full moon.

A strange stir was in her. Indolently, she tried to fix upon Bob or Tom as the cause of it. To meet Bob in the canebrake, as she was going to do an hour or so later, was nothing new. And Tom's proposal which she felt on its way to her could be indefinitely put off. Separately, there was no unusual significance to either one. But for some reason, they jumbled when her eyes gazed vacantly at the rising moon. And from the jumble came the stir that was strangely within her. Her lips trembled. The slow rhythm of her song grew agitant and restless. Rusty black and tan spotted hounds, lying in the dark corners of porches or prowling around back yards, put their noses in the air and caught its tremor. They began plaintively to yelp and howl. Chickens woke up and cackled. Intermittently, all over the countryside dogs barked and roosters crowed as if heralding a weird dawn or some ungodly awakening. The women sang lustily. Their songs were cotton-wads to stop their ears. Louisa came down into factory town and sank wearily upon the step before her home. The moon was rising towards a thick cloud-bank which soon would hide it.

> Red nigger moon. Sinner!
> Blood-burning moon. Sinner!
> Come out that fact'ry door.

2

Up from the deep dusk of a cleared spot on the edge of the forest a mellow glow arose and spread fan-wise into the low-hanging heavens. And all around the air was heavy with the scent of boiling cane. A large pile of cane-stalks lay like ribboned shadows upon the ground. A mule, harnessed to a pole, trudged lazily round and round the pivot of the grinder. Beneath a swaying oil lamp, a Negro alternately whipped out at the mule, and fed cane-stalks to the grinder. A fat boy waddled pails of fresh ground juice between the grinder and the boiling stove. Steam came from the copper boiling pan. The scent of cane came from the copper pan and drenched the forest and the hill that sloped to factory town, beneath its fragrance. It drenched the men in circle seated around the stove. Some of them chewed at the white pulp of stalks, but there was no need for them to, if all they wanted was to taste the cane. One tasted it in factory town. And from factory town one could see the soft haze thrown by the glowing stove upon the low-hanging heavens.

Old David Georgia stirred the thickening syrup with a long ladle, and ever so often drew it off. Old David Georgia tended his stove and told tales about the white folks, about moonshining and cotton picking, and about sweet nigger gals, to the men who sat there about his stove to listen to him. Tom Burwell chewed cane-stalk and laughed with the others till some one mentioned Louisa. Till some one said something about Louisa and Bob Stone, about the silk stockings she must have gotten from him. Blood ran up Tom's neck hotter than the glow that flooded from the stove. He sprang up. Glared at the men and said, "She's my gal." Will Manning laughed. Tom strode over to him. Yanked him up and knocked him to the ground. Several of Manning's friends got up to fight for him. Tom whipped out a long knife and would have cut them to shreds if they hadnt ducked into the woods. Tom had had enough. He nodded to Old David Georgia and swung down the path to factory town. Just then, the dogs started barking and the roosters began to crow. Tom felt funny. Away from the fight, away from the stove, chill got to him. He shivered. He shuddered when he saw the full moon rising towards the cloud-bank. He who didnt give a godam for the fears of old women. He forced his mind to fasten on Louisa. Bob Stone. Better not be. He turned into the street and saw Louisa sitting before her home. He went towards her, ambling, touched the brim of a marvelously shaped, spotted, felt hat, said he wanted to say something to her, and then found that he didnt know what he had to say, or if he did, that he couldnt say it. He shoved his big fists in his overalls, grinned, and started to move off.

"Youall want me, Tom?"

"Thats what us wants, sho, Louisa."

"Well, here I am—"

"An here I is, but that aint ahelpin none, all th same."

"You wanted to say something? . . ."

"I did that, sho. But words is like th spots on dice: no matter how y fumbles em, there's times when they jes wont come. I dunno why. Seems like th love I feels fo yo done stole m tongue. I got it now. Whee! Louisa, honey, I oughtnt tell y, I feel I oughtnt cause yo is young an goes t church an I has had other gals, but Louisa I sho do love y. Lil gal, Ise watched y from them first days when youall sat right here befo yo door befo th well an sang sometimes in a way that like t broke m heart. Ise carried y with me into th fields, day after day, an after that, an I sho can plow when yo is there, an I can pick cotton. Yassur! Come near beatin Barlo yesterday. I sho did. Yassur! An next year if ole Stone'll trust me, I'll have a farm. My own. My bales will buy yo what y gets from white folks now. Silk stockings an purple dresses— course I dont believe what some folks been whisperin as t how y gets them things now. White folks always did do for niggers what they likes. An they jes cant help alikin yo, Louisa. Bob Stone likes y. Course he does. But not th way folks is awhisperin. Does he, hon?"

"I dont know what you mean, Tom."

"Course y dont. Ise already cut two niggers. Had t hon, t tell em so. Niggers always tryin t make somethin out a nothin. An then besides, white folks aint up t them tricks so much nowadays. Godam better not be. Leastawise not with yo. Cause I wouldnt stand f it. Nassur."

"What would you do, Tom?"

"Cut him jes like I cut a nigger."

"No, Tom—"

"I said I would an there aint no mo to it. But that aint th talk f now. Sing, honey Louisa, an while I'm listenin t y I'll be makin love."

Tom took her hand in his. Against the tough thickness of his own, hers felt soft and small. His huge body slipped down to the step beside her. The full moon sank upward into the deep purple of the cloud-bank. An old woman brought a lighted lamp and hung it on the common well whose bulky shadow squatted in the middle of the road, opposite Tom and Louisa. The old woman lifted the well-lid, took hold the chain, and began drawing up the heavy bucket. As she did so, she sang. Figures shifted, restlesslike, between lamp and window in the front rooms of the shanties. Shadows of the figures fought each other on the gray dust of the road. Figures raised the windows and joined the old woman in song. Louisa and Tom, the whole street, singing:

> Red nigger moon. Sinner!
> Blood-burning moon. Sinner!
> Come out that fact'ry door.

3

Bob Stone sauntered from his veranda out into the gloom of fir trees and magnolias. The clear white of his skin paled, and the flush of his cheeks turned purple. As if to balance this outer change, his mind became consciously a white man's. He passed the house with its huge open hearth which, in the days of slavery, was the plantation cookery. He saw Louisa bent over that hearth. He went in as a master should and took her. Direct, honest, bold. None of this sneaking that he had to go through now. The contrast was repulsive to him. His family had lost ground. Hell no, his family still owned the niggers, practically. Damned if they did, or he wouldnt have to duck around so. What would they think if they knew? His mother? His sister? He shouldnt mention them, shouldnt think of them in this connection. There in the dusk he blushed at doing so. Fellows about town were all right, but how about his friends up North? He could see them incredible, repulsed. They didnt know. The thought first made him laugh. Then, with their eyes still upon him, he began to feel embarrassed. He felt the need of explaining things to them. Explain hell. They wouldnt understand, and moreover, who ever heard of a Southerner getting on his knees to any Yankee, or anyone. No sir. He was going to see Louisa tonight, and love her. She was lovely—in her way. Nigger way. What way was that?

Damned if he knew. Must know. He'd known her long enough to know. Was there something about niggers that you couldnt know? Listening to them at church didnt tell you anything. Looking at them didnt tell you anything. Talking to them didnt tell you anything—unless it was gossip, unless they wanted to talk. Of course, about farming, and licker, and craps—but those werent nigger. Nigger was something more. How much more? Something to be afraid of, more? Hell no. Who ever heard of being afraid of a nigger? Tom Burwell. Cartwell had told him that Tom went with Louisa after she reached home. No sir. No nigger had ever been with his girl. He'd like to see one try. Some position for him to be in. Him, Bob Stone, of the old Stone family, in a scrap with a nigger over a nigger girl. In the good old days . . . Ha! Those were the days. His family had lost ground. Not so much, though. Enough for him to have to cut through old Lemon's canefield by way of the woods, that he might meet her. She was worth it. Beautiful nigger gal. Why nigger? Why not, just gal? No, it was because she was nigger that he went to her. Sweet . . . The scent of boiling cane came to him. Then he saw the rich glow of the stove. He heard the voices of the men circled around it. He was about to skirt the clearing when he heard his own name mentioned. He stopped. Quivering. Leaning against a tree, he listened.

"Bad nigger. Yassur, he sho is one bad nigger when he gets started."

"Tom Burwell's been on th gang three times fo cuttin men."

"What y think he's agwine t do t Bob Stone?"

"Dunno yet. He aint found out. When he does—Baby!"

"Aint no tellin."

"Young Stone aint no quitter an I ken tell y that. Blood of th old uns in his veins."

"Thats right. He'll scrap, sho."

"Be gettin too hot f niggers round this away."

"Shut up, nigger. Y dont know what y talkin bout."

Bob Stone's ears burned as though he had been holding them over the stove. Sizzling heat welled up within him. His feet felt as if they rested on red-hot coals. They stung him to quick movement. He circled the fringe of the glowing. Not a twig cracked beneath his feet. He reached the path that led to factory town. Plunged furiously down it. Halfway along, a blindness within him veered him aside. He crashed into the bordering canebrake. Cane leaves cut his face and lips. He tasted blood. He threw himself down and dug his fingers in the ground. The earth was cool. Cane-roots took the fever from his hands. After a long while, or so it seemed to him, the thought came to him that it must be time to see Louisa. He got to his feet and walked calmly to their meeting place. No Louisa. Tom Burwell had her. Veins in his forehead bulged and distended. Saliva moistened the dried blood on his lips. He bit down on his lips. He tasted blood. Not his own blood; Tom Burwell's blood. Bob drove through the cane and out again upon the road. A hound swung down the path before him towards factory town. Bob couldnt see it. The dog loped aside to let him pass. Bob's blind rushing made him stumble over it. He fell with a thud that dazed him. The hound yelped. Answering yelps came from all over the countryside.

Chickens cackled. Roosters crowed, heralding the bloodshot eyes of southern awakening. Singers in the town were silenced. They shut their windows down. Palpitant between the rooster crows, a chill hush settled upon the huddled forms of Tom and Louisa. A figure rushed from the shadow and stood before them. Tom popped to his feet.

"Whats y want?"

"I'm Bob Stone."

"Yassur—an I'm Tom Burwell. Whats y want?"

Bob lunged at him. Tom side-stepped, caught him by the shoulder, and flung him to the ground. Straddled him.

"Let me up."

"Yassur—but watch yo doins,[2] Bob Stone."

A few dark figures, drawn by the sound of scuffle, stood about them. Bob sprang to his feet.

"Fight like a man, Tom Burwell, an I'll lick y."

Again he lunged. Tom side-stepped and flung him to the ground. Straddled him.

"Get off me, you godam nigger you."

"Yo sho has started somethin now. Get up."

Tom yanked him up and began hammering at him. Each blow sounded as if it smashed into a precious, irreplaceable soft something. Beneath them, Bob staggered back. He reached in his pocket and whipped out a knife.

"Thats my game, sho."

Blue flash, a steel blade slashed across Bob Stone's throat. He had a sweetish sick feeling. Blood began to flow. Then he felt a sharp twitch of pain. He let his knife drop. He slapped one hand against his neck. He pressed the other on top of his head as if to hold it down. He groaned. He turned, and staggered towards the crest of the hill in the direction of white town. Negroes who had seen the fight slunk into their homes and blew the lamps out. Louisa, dazed, hysterical, refused to go indoors. She slipped, crumbled, her body loosely propped against the woodwork of the well. Tom Burwell leaned against it. He seemed rooted there.

Bob reached Broad Street. White men rushed up to him. He collapsed in their arms.

"Tom Burwell. . . ."

White men like ants upon a forage rushed about. Except for the taut hum of their moving, all was silent. Shotguns, revolvers, rope, kerosene, torches. Two high-powered cars with glaring searchlights. They came together. The taut hum rose to a low roar. Then nothing could be heard but the flop of their feet in the thick dust of the road. The moving body of their silence preceded them over the crest of the hill into factory town. It flattened the Negroes beneath it. It rolled to the wall of the factory, where it stopped. Tom knew that they were coming. He couldnt move. And then he saw the search-lights of the two cars glaring down on him. A quick shock went through him. He stiffened. He started to run. A yell went up from the mob. Tom wheeled about and faced them. They poured down on him.

2. Actions.

They swarmed. A large man with dead-white face and flabby cheeks came to him and almost jabbed a gun-barrel through his guts.

"Hands behind y, nigger."

Tom's wrists were bound. The big man shoved him to the well. Burn him over it, and when the woodwork caved in, his body would drop to the bottom. Two deaths for a godam nigger. Louisa was driven back. The mob pushed in. Its pressure, its momentum was too great. Drag him to the factory. Wood and stakes already there. Tom moved in the direction indicated. But they had to drag him. They reached the great door. Too many to get in there. The mob divided and flowed around the walls to either side. The big man shoved him through the door. The mob pressed in from the sides. Taut humming. No words. A stake was sunk into the ground. Rotting floor boards piled around it. Kerosene poured on the rotting floor boards. Tom bound to the stake. His breast was bare. Nails' scratches let little lines of blood trickle down and mat into the hair. His face, his eyes were set and stony. Except for irregular breathing, one would have thought him already dead. Torches were flung onto the pile. A great flare muffled in black smoke shot upward. The mob yelled. The mob was silent. Now Tom could be seen within the flames. Only his head, erect, lean, like a blackened stone. Stench of burning flesh soaked the air. Tom's eyes popped. His head settled downward. The mob yelled. Its yell echoed against the skeleton stone walls and sounded like a hundred yells. Like a hundred mobs yelling. Its yell thudded against the thick front wall and fell back. Ghost of a yell slipped through the flames and out the great door of the factory. It fluttered like a dying thing down the single street of factory town. Louisa, upon the step before her home, did not hear it, but her eyes opened slowly. They saw the full moon glowing in the great door. The full moon, an evil thing, an omen, soft showering the homes of folks she knew. Where were they, these people? She'd sing, and perhaps they'd come out and join her. Perhaps Tom Burwell would come. At any rate, the full moon in the great door was an omen which she must sing to:

> Red nigger moon. Sinner!
> Blood-burning moon. Sinner!
> Come out that fact'ry door.

Seventh Street[1]

> Money burns the pocket, pocket hurts,
> Bootleggers in silken shirts,
> Ballooned, zooming Cadillacs,
> Whizzing, whizzing down the street-car tracks.

1. The stories and sketches in this section are set in Washington, D.C., except for *Bona and Paul*, which is set in Chicago.

Seventh Street is a bastard of Prohibition and the War.[2] A crude-boned, soft-skinned wedge of nigger life breathing its loafer air, jazz songs and love, thrusting unconscious rhythms, black reddish blood into the white and whitewashed wood of Washington. Stale soggy wood of Washington. Wedges rust in soggy wood . . . Split it! In two! Again! Shred it! . . . the sun. Wedges are brilliant in the sun; ribbons of wet wood dry and blow away. Black reddish blood. Pouring for crude-boned soft-skinned life, who set you flowing? Blood suckers of the War would spin in a frenzy of dizziness if they drank your blood. Prohibition would put a stop to it. Who set you flowing? White and whitewash disappear in blood. Who set you flowing? Flowing down the smooth asphalt of Seventh Street, in shanties, brick office buildings, theaters, drug stores, restaurants, and cabarets? Eddying on the corners? Swirling like a blood-red smoke up where the buzzards fly in heaven? God would not dare to suck black red blood. A Nigger God! He would duck his head in shame and call for the Judgment Day. Who set you flowing?

> Money burns the pocket, pocket hurts,
> Bootleggers in silken shirts,
> Ballooned, zooming Cadillacs,
> Whizzing, whizzing down the street-car tracks.

Rhobert

Rhobert wears a house, like a monstrous diver's helmet, on his head. His legs are banty-bowed and shaky because as a child he had rickets. He is way down. Rods of the house like antennae of a dead thing, stuffed, prop up in the air. He is way down. He is sinking. His house is a dead thing that weights him down. He is sinking as a diver would sink in mud should the water be drawn off. Life is a murky, wiggling, microscopic water that compresses him. Compresses his helmet and would crush it the minute that he pulled his head out. He has to keep it in. Life is water that is being drawn off.

> Brother, life is water that is being drawn off.
> Brother, life is water that is being drawn off.

The dead house is stuffed. The stuffing is alive. It is sinful to draw one's head out of live stuffing in a dead house. The propped-up antennæ would cave in and the stuffing be strewn . . shredded life-pulp . . in the water. It is sinful to have one's own head crushed. Rhobert is an upright man whose legs are banty-bowed and shaky because as a child he had rickets. The earth is round. Heaven is a sphere that surrounds it. Sink where you will. God is a Red Cross man with a dredge and a respiration-pump who's waiting for you at the opposite periphery. God built the house. He blew His breath into its stuffing. It is good to die obeying Him who can do these things. A futile something like the dead house wraps the live stuffing of the ques-

---

2. World War I.

tion: how long before the water will be drawn off? Rhobert does not care. Like most men who wear monstrous helmets, the pressure it exerts is enough to convince him of its practical infinity. And he cares not two straws as to whether or not he will ever see his wife and children again. Many a time he's seen them drown in his dreams and has kicked about joyously in the mud for days after. One thing about him goes straight to the heart. He has an Adam's-apple which strains sometimes as if he were painfully gulping great globules of air . . air floating shredded life-pulp. It is a sad thing to see a banty-bowed, shaky, ricket-legged man straining the raw insides of his throat against smooth air. Holding furtive thoughts about the glory of pulp-heads strewn in water. . He is way down. Down. Mud, coming to his banty knees, almost hides them. Soon people will be looking at him and calling him a strong man. No doubt he is for one who has had rickets. Lets give it to him. Lets call him great when the water shall have been all drawn off. Lets build a monument and set it in the ooze where he goes down. A monument of hewn oak, carved in nigger-heads. Lets open our throats, brother, and sing "Deep River"[1] when he goes down.

> Brother, Rhobert is sinking.
> Lets open our throats, brother,
> Lets sing Deep River when he goes down.

Avey

For a long while she was nothing more to me than one of those skirted beings whom boys at a certain age disdain to play with. Just how I came to love her, timidly, and with secret blushes, I do not know. But that I did was brought home to me one night, the first night that Ned wore his long pants. Us fellers were seated on the curb before an apartment house where she had gone in. The young trees had not outgrown their boxes then. V Street[1] was lined with them. When our legs grew cramped and stiff from the cold of the stone, we'd stand around a box and whittle it. I like to think now that there was a hidden purpose in the way we hacked them with our knives. I like to feel that something deep in me responded to the trees, the young trees that whinnied like colts impatient to be let free . . . On the particular night I have in mind, we were waiting for the top-floor light to go out. We wanted to see Avey leave the flat. This night she stayed longer than usual and gave us a chance to complete the plans of how we were going to stone and beat that feller on the top floor out of town. Ned especially had it in for him. He was about to throw a brick up at the window when at last the room went dark. Some minutes passed. Then Avey, as unconcerned as if she had been paying an old-maid aunt a visit, came out. I dont remember what she had on, and all that sort of thing. But I do know that I turned hot as bare pavements in the summertime at Ned's boast: "Hell, bet I could get her too if you little niggers weren't always spying and crabbing everything." I didnt say a word to him. It wasnt my way then. I just stood there like the others,

1. African-American spiritual.
1. A street passing through a densely populated

African American neighborhood in Washington, D.C.

and something like a fuse burned up inside of me. She never noticed us, but swung along lazy and easy as anything. We sauntered to the corner and watched her till her door banged to. Ned repeated what he'd said. I didnt seem to care. Sitting around old Mush-Head's bread box, the discussion began. "Hang if I can see how she gets away with it," Doc started. Ned knew, of course. There was nothing he didnt know when it came to women. He dilated on the emotional needs of girls. Said they werent much different from men in that respect. And concluded with the solemn avowal: "It does em good." None of us liked Ned much. We all talked dirt; but it was the way he said it. And then too, a couple of the fellers had sisters and had caught Ned playing with them. But there was no disputing the superiority of his smutty wisdom. Bubs Sanborn, whose mother was friendly with Avey's, had overheard the old ladies talking. "Avey's mother's ont her," he said. We thought that only natural and began to guess at what would happen. Some one said she'd marry that feller on the top floor. Ned called that a lie because Avey was going to marry nobody but him. We had our doubts about that, but we did agree that she'd soon leave school and marry some one. The gang broke up, and I went home, picturing myself as married.

Nothing I did seemed able to change Avey's indifference to me. I played basket-ball, and when I'd make a long clean shot she'd clap with the others, louder than they, I thought. I'd meet her on the street, and there'd be no difference in the way she said hello. She never took the trouble to call me by my name. On the days for drill, [2] I'd let my voice down a tone and call for a complicated maneuver when I saw her coming. She'd smile appreciation, but it was an impersonal smile, never for me. It was on a summer excursion down to Riverview that she first seemed to take me into account. The day had been spent riding merry-go-rounds, scenic-railways, and shoot-the-chutes. We had been in swimming and we had danced. I was a crack swimmer then. She didnt know how. I held her up and showed her how to kick her legs and draw her arms. Of course she didnt learn in one day, but she thanked me for bothering with her. I was also somewhat of a dancer. And I had already noticed that love can start on a dance floor. We danced. But though I held her tightly in my arms, she was way away. That college feller who lived on the top floor was somewhere making money for the next year. I imagined that she was thinking, wishing for him. Ned was along. He treated her until his money gave out. She went with another feller. Ned got sore. One by one the boys' money gave out. She left them. And they got sore. Every one of them but me got sore. This is the reason, I guess, why I had her to myself on the top deck of the *Jane Mosely* that night as we puffed up the Potomac, coming home. The moon was brilliant. The air was sweet like clover. And every now and then, a salt tang, a stale drift of sea-weed. It was not my mind's fault if it went romancing. I should have taken her in my arms the minute we were stowed in that old lifeboat. I dallied, dreaming. She took me in hers. And I could feel by the touch of it that it wasnt a man-to-woman love. It made me restless. I felt chagrined. I didnt know what it was, but I did know that I couldnt handle it. She ran her

2. Marching as part of the military training in high school.

fingers through my hair and kissed my forehead. I itched to break through her tenderness to passion. I wanted her to take me in her arms as I knew she had that college feller. I wanted her to love me passionately as she did him. I gave her one burning kiss. Then she laid me in her lap as if I were a child. Helpless. I got sore when she started to hum a lullaby. She wouldnt let me go. I talked. I knew damned well that I could beat her at that. Her eyes were soft and misty, the curves of her lips were wistful, and her smile seemed indulgent of the irrelevance of my remarks. I gave up at last and let her love me, silently, in her own way. The moon was brilliant. The air was sweet like clover, and every now and then, a salt tang, a stale drift of sea-weed . . .

The next time I came close to her was the following summer at Harpers Ferry. We were sitting on a flat projecting rock they give the name of Lover's Leap. Some one is supposed to have jumped off it. The river is about six hundred feet beneath. A railroad track runs up the valley and curves out of sight where part of the mountain rock had to be blasted away to make room for it. The engines of this valley have a whistle, the echoes of which sound like iterated gasps and sobs. I always think of them as crude music from the soul of Avey. We sat there holding hands. Our palms were soft and warm against each other. Our fingers were not tight. She would not let them be. She would not let me twist them. I wanted to talk. To explain what I meant to her. Avey was as silent as those great trees whose tops we looked down upon. She has always been like that. At least, to me. I had the notion that if I really wanted to, I could do with her just what I pleased. Like one can strip a tree. I did kiss her. I even let my hands cup her breasts. When I was through, she'd seek my hand and hold it till my pulse cooled down. Evening after evening we sat there. I tried to get her to talk about that college feller. She never would. There was no set time to go home. None of my family had come down. And as for hers, she didnt give a hang about them. The general gossips could hardly say more than they had. The boarding-house porch was always deserted when we returned. No one saw us enter, so the time was set conveniently for scandal. This worried me a little, for I thought it might keep Avey from getting an appointment in the schools. She didnt care. She had finished normal school.[3] They could give her a job if they wanted to. As time went on, her indifference to things began to pique me; I was ambitious. I left the Ferry earlier than she did. I was going off to college. The more I thought of it, the more I re-sented, yes, hell, thats what it was, her downright laziness. Sloppy indo-lence. There was no excuse for a healthy girl taking life so easy. Hell! she was no better than a cow. I was certain that she was a cow when I felt an udder in a Wisconsin stock-judging class. Among those energetic Swedes, or whatever they are, I decided to forget her. For two years I thought I did. When I'd come home for the summer she'd be away. And before she re-turned, I'd be gone. We never wrote; she was too damned lazy for that. But what a bluff I put up about forgetting her. The girls up that way, at least the

3. A teacher-training institution. Although a nor-mal school was not considered the equivalent of a four-year college, during the 1920s completion of a normal-school degree program was considered suf-ficient qualification for teaching in elementary or secondary schools.

ones I knew, havent got the stuff: they dont know how to love. Giving them-selves completely was tame beside just the holding of Avey's hand. One day I received a note from her. The writing, I decided, was slovenly. She wrote on a torn bit of note-book paper. The envelope had a faint perfume that I remembered. A single line told me she had lost her school and was going away. I comforted myself with the reflection that shame held no pain for one so indolent as she. Nevertheless, I left Wisconsin that year for good. Washington had seemingly forgotten her. I hunted Ned. Between curses, I caught his opinion of her. She was no better than a whore. I saw her mother on the street. The same old pinch-beck, jerky-gaited creature that I'd always known.

Perhaps five years passed. The business of hunting a job or something or other had bruised my vanity so that I could recognize it. I felt old. Avey and my real relation to her, I thought I came to know. I wanted to see her. I had been told that she was in New York. As I had no money, I hiked and bummed my way there. I got work in a ship-yard and walked the streets at night, hoping to meet her. Failing in this, I saved enough to pay my fare back home. One evening in early June, just at the time when dusk is most lovely on the eastern horizon, I saw Avey, indolent as ever, leaning on the arm of a man, strolling under the recently lit arc-lights of U Street.[4] She had almost passed before she recognized me. She showed no surprise. The puff over her eyes had grown heavier. The eyes themselves were still sleepy-large, and beautiful. I had almost concluded—indifferent. "You look older," was what she said. I wanted to convince her that I was, so I asked her to walk with me. The man whom she was with, and whom she never took the trouble to introduce, at a nod from her, hailed a taxi, and drove away. That gave me a notion of what she had been used to. Her dress was of some fine, costly stuff. I suggested the park, and then added that the grass might stain her skirt. Let it get stained, she said, for where it came from there are others.

I have a spot in Soldier's Home[5] to which I always go when I want the simple beauty of another's soul. Robins spring about the lawn all day. They leave their footprints in the grass. I imagine that the grass at night smells sweet and fresh because of them. The ground is high. Washington lies below. Its light spreads like a blush against the darkened sky. Against the soft dusk sky of Washington. And when the wind is from the South, soil of my homeland falls like a fertile shower upon the lean streets of the city. Upon my hill in Soldier's Home, I know the policeman who watches the place of nights. When I go there alone, I talk to him. I tell him I come there to find the truth that people bury in their hearts. I tell him that I do not come there with a girl to do the thing he's paid to watch out for. I look deep in his eyes when I say these things, and he believes me. He comes over to see who it is on the grass. I say hello to him. He greets me in the same way and goes off searching for other black splotches upon the lawn. Avey and I

---

4. A street passing through a densely populated   D.C.
African American neighborhood in Washington,   5. A park.

went there. A band in one of the buildings a fair distance off was playing a march. I wished they would stop. Their playing was like a tin spoon in one's mouth. I wanted the Howard Glee Club to sing "Deep River,"[6] from the road. To sing "Deep River, Deep River," from the road . . . Other than the first comments, Avey had been silent. I started to hum a folk-tune. She slipped her hand in mine. Pillowed her head as best she could upon my arm. Kissed the hand that she was holding and listened, or so I thought, to what I had to say. I traced my development from the early days up to the present time, the phase in which I could understand her. I described her own nature and temperament. Told how they needed a larger life for their expression. How incapable Washington was of understanding that need. How it could not meet it. I pointed out that in lieu of proper channels, her emotions had overflowed into paths that dissipated them. I talked, beautifully I thought, about an art that would be born, an art that would open the way for women the likes of her. I asked her to hope, and build up an inner life against the coming of that day. I recited some of my own things to her. I sang, with a strange quiver in my voice, a promise-song. And then I began to wonder why her hand had not once returned a single pressure. My old-time feeling about her laziness came back. I spoke sharply. My policeman friend passed by. I said hello to him. As he went away, I began to visualize certain possibilities. An immediate and urgent passion swept over me. Then I looked at Avey. Her heavy eyes were closed. Her breathing was as faint and regular as a child's in slumber. My passion died. I was afraid to move lest I disturb her. Hours and hours, I guess it was, she lay there. My body grew numb. I shivered. I coughed. I wanted to get up and whittle at the boxes of young trees. I withdrew my hand. I raised her head to waken her. She did not stir. I got up and walked around. I found my policeman friend and talked to him. We both came up, and bent over her. He said it would be all right for her to stay there just so long as she got away before the workmen came at dawn. A blanket was borrowed from a neighbor house. I sat beside her through the night. I saw the dawn steal over Washington. The Capitol dome looked like a gray ghost ship drifting in from sea. Avey's face was pale, and her eyes were heavy. She did not have the gray crimson-splashed beauty of the dawn. I hated to wake her. Orphan-woman . . .

Beehive

Within this black hive to-night
There swarm a million bees;
Bees passing in and out the moon,
Bees escaping out the moon,
Bees returning through the moon,   5
Silver bees intently buzzing,
Silver honey dripping from the swarm of bees
Earth is a waxen cell of the world comb,
And I, a drone,
Lying on my back,   10

6. Black American spiritual. Howard University is in Washington, D.C.

Lipping honey,
Getting drunk with silver honey,
Wish that I might fly out past the moon
And curl forever in some far-off farmyard flower.

Storm Ending

Thunder blossoms gorgeously above our heads,
Great, hollow, bell-like flowers,
Rumbling in the wind,
Stretching clappers to strike our ears . .
Full-lipped flowers   5
Bitten by the sun
Bleeding rain
Dripping rain like golden honey—
And the sweet earth flying from the thunder.

Theater

Life of nigger alleys, of pool rooms and restaurants and near-beer saloons
soaks into the walls of Howard Theater[1] and sets them throbbing jazz
songs. Black-skinned, they dance and shout above the tick and trill of
white-walled buildings. At night, they open doors to people who come in to
stamp their feet and shout. At night, road-shows volley songs into the mass-
heart of black people. Songs soak the walls and seep out to the nigger life of
alleys and near-beer saloons, of the Poodle Dog and Black Bear cabarets.
Afternoons, the house is dark, and the walls are sleeping singers until rehearsal begins. Or until John comes within them. Then they start throbbing to a subtle syncopation. And the space-dark air grows softly luminous.

John is the manager's brother. He is seated at the center of the theater,
just before rehearsal. Light streaks down upon him from a window high
above. One half his face is orange in it. One half his face is in shadow. The
soft glow of the house rushes to, and compacts about, the shaft of light.
John's mind coincides with the shaft of light. Thoughts rush to, and compact about it. Life of the house and of the slowly awakening stage swirls to
the body of John, and thrills it. John's body is separate from the thoughts
that pack his mind.

Stage-lights, soft, as if they shine through clear pink fingers. Beneath
them, hid by the shadow of a set, Dorris. Other chorus girls drift in. John
feels them in the mass. And as if his own body were the mass-heart of a
black audience listening to them singing, he wants to stamp his feet and
shout. His mind, contained above desires of his body, singles the girls out,
and tries to trace origins and plot destinies.

A pianist slips into the pit and improvises jazz. The walls awake. Arms of
the girls, and their limbs, which . . jazz, jazz . . by lifting up their tight street

---

1. In the African American section of Washington, D.C. The audiences and performers were also black.
"Near-beer saloons": establishments that sell low-proof or nonalcoholic beer.

skirts they set free, jab the air and clog the floor in rhythm to the music. (Lift your skirts, Baby, and talk t papa!) Crude, individualized, and yet . . . monotonous . . .

John: Soon the director will herd you, my full-lipped, distant beauties, and tame you, and blunt your sharp thrusts in loosely suggestive movements, appropriate to Broadway. (O dance!) Soon the audience will paint your dusk faces white, and call you beautiful.[2] (O dance!) Soon I . . . (O dance!) I'd like . . .

Girls laugh and shout. Sing discordant snatches of other jazz songs. Whirl with loose passion into the arms of passing show-men.

John: Too thick. Too easy. Too monotonous. Her whom I'd love I'd leave before she knew that I was with her. Her? Which? (O dance!) I'd like to . . .

Girls dance and sing. Men clap. The walls sing and press inward. They press the men and girls, they press John towards a center of physical ecstasy. Go to it, Baby! Fan yourself, and feed your papa! Put . . nobody lied . . and take . . when they said I cried over you. No lie! The glitter and color of stacked scenes, the gilt and brass and crimson of the house, converge towards a center of physical ecstasy. John's feet and torso and his blood press in. He wills thought to rid his mind of passion.

"All right, girls. Alaska. Miss Reynolds, please."

The director wants to get the rehearsal through with.

The girls line up. John sees the front row: dancing ponies. The rest are in shadow. The leading lady fits loosely in the front. Lack-life, monotonous. "One, two, three—" Music starts. The song is somewhere where it will not strain the leading lady's throat. The dance is somewhere where it will not strain the girls. Above the staleness, one dancer throws herself into it. Dorris. John sees her. Her hair, crisp-curled, is bobbed. Bushy, black hair bobbing about her lemon-colored face. Her lips are curiously full, and very red. Her limbs in silk purple stockings are lovely. John feels them. Desires her. Holds off.

John: Stage-door johnny; chorus-girl. No, that would be all right. Dictie,[3] educated, stuck-up; show-girl. Yep. Her suspicion would be stronger than her passion. It wouldn't work. Keep her loveliness. Let her go.

Dorris sees John and knows that he is looking at her. Her own glowing is too rich a thing to let her feel the slimness of his diluted passion.

"Who's that?" she asks her dancing partner.

"Th manager's brother. Dictie. Nothin doin, hon."

Dorris tosses her head and dances for him until she feels she has him. Then, withdrawing disdainfully, she flirts with the director.

Dorris: Nothin doin? How come? Aint I as good as him? Couldnt I have got an education if I'd wanted one? Dont I know respectable folks, lots of em, in Philadelphia and New York and Chicago? Aint I had men as

---

2. During the 1920s, producers and directors of all-black musical shows gave preference to African American females who were light skinned. Here, however, Toomer probably refers to a refusal by the predominantly white Broadway audience to accept African American beauty. Instead, the audience will instinctively consider the black dancers to be dusky-skinned whites. Then the audience can judge them beautiful while still believing that only whites are beautiful.

3. Educated, middle-class African American (slang); connotes being stuck-up or snobbish. "Stage-door johnny": a man who dates actresses, singers, and dancers (slang).

good as him? Better. Doctors an lawyers. Whats a manager's brother, anyhow?

Two steps back, and two steps front.

"Say, Mame, where do you get that stuff?"

"Whatshmean, Dorris?"

"If you two girls cant listen to what I'm telling you, I know where I can get some who can. Now listen."

Mame: Go to hell, you black bastard.

Dorris: Whats eatin at him, anyway?

"Now follow me in this, you girls. Its three counts to the right, three counts to the left, and then you shimmy[4]—"

John: —and then you shimmy. I'll bet she can. Some good cabaret, with rooms upstairs. And what in hell do you think you'd get from it? Youre going wrong. Here's right: get her to herself—(Christ, but how she'd bore you after the first five minutes)—not if you get her right she wouldnt. Touch her, I mean. To herself—in some room perhaps. Some cheap, dingy bedroom. Hell no. Cant be done. But the point is, brother John, it can be done. Get her to herself somewhere, anywhere. Go down in yourself—and she'd be calling you all sorts of asses while you were in the process of going down. Hold em, bud. Cant be done. Let her go. (Dance and I'll love you!) And keep her loveliness.

"All right now, Chicken Chaser.[5] Dorris and girls. Where's Dorris? I told you to stay on the stage, didnt I? Well? Now thats enough. All right. All right there, Professor?[6] All right. One, two, three—"

Dorris swings to the front. The line of girls, four deep, blurs within the shadow of suspended scenes. Dorris wants to dance. The director feels that and steps to one side. He smiles, and picks her for a leading lady, one of these days. Odd ends of stage-men emerge from the wings, and stare and clap. A crap game in the alley suddenly ends. Black faces crowd the rear stage doors. The girls, catching joy from Dorris, whip up within the footlights' glow. They forget set steps; they find their own. The director forgets to bawl them out. Dorris dances.

John: Her head bobs to Broadway. Dance from yourself. Dance! O just a little more.

Dorris' eyes burn across the space of seats to him.

Dorris: I bet he can love. Hell, he cant love. He's too skinny. His lips are too skinny. He wouldnt love me anyway, only for that. But I'd get a pair of silk stockings out of it. Red silk. I got purple. Cut it, kid. You cant win him to respect you that away. He wouldnt anyway. Maybe he would. Maybe he'd love. I've heard em say that men who look like him (what does he look like?) will marry if they love. O will you love me? And give me kids, and a home, and everything? (I'd like to make your nest, and honest, hon, I wouldnt run out on you.) You will if I make you. Just watch me.

Dorris dances. She forgets her tricks.[7] She dances.

Glorious songs are the muscles of her limbs.

And her singing is of canebrake loves and mangrove feastings.

---

4. A popular dance movement that emphasized an erotic vibration of the torso.
5. Another dance.

6. A nickname for a band leader or pianist.
7. Her practiced or stylized dance routine.

The walls press in, singing. Flesh of a throbbing body, they press close to John and Dorris. They close them in. John's heart beats tensely against her dancing body. Walls press his mind within his heart. And then, the shaft of light goes out the window high above him. John's mind sweeps up to follow it. Mind pulls him upward into dream.   Dorris dances . . . John dreams:

> Dorris is dressed in a loose black gown splashed with lemon ribbons. Her feet taper long and slim from trim ankles. She waits for him just inside the stage door. John, collar and tie colorful and flaring, walks towards the stage door. There are no trees in the alley. But his feet feel as though they step on autumn leaves whose rustle has been pressed out of them by the passing of a million satin slippers. The air is sweet with roasting chestnuts, sweet with bonfires of old leaves. John's melancholy is a deep thing that seals all senses but his eyes, and makes him whole.
>
> Dorris knows that he is coming. Just at the right moment she steps from the door, as if there were no door. Her face is tinted like the autumn alley. Of old flowers, or of a southern canefield, her perfume. "Glorious Dorris." So his eyes speak. And their sadness is too deep for sweet untruth. She barely touches his arm. They glide off with footfalls softened on the leaves, the old leaves powdered by a million satin slippers.
>
> They are in a room. John knows nothing of it. Only, that the flesh and blood of Dorris are its walls. Singing walls. Lights, soft, as if they shine through clear pink fingers. Soft lights, and warm.
>
> John reaches for a manuscript of his, and reads. Dorris, who has no eyes, has eyes to understand him. He comes to a dancing scene. The scene is Dorris. She dances. Dorris dances. Glorious Dorris. Dorris whirls, whirls, dances . . .

Dorris dances.
The pianist crashes a bumper chord. The whole stage claps. Dorris, flushed, looks quick at John. His whole face is in shadow. She seeks for her dance in it. She finds it a dead thing in the shadow which is his dream. She rushes from the stage. Falls down the steps into her dressing-room. Pulls her hair. Her eyes, over a floor of tears, stare at the whitewashed ceiling. (Smell of dry paste, and paint, and soiled clothing.) Her pal comes in. Dorris flings herself into the old safe arms, and cries bitterly.

"I told you nothin doin," is what Mame says to comfort her.

Her Lips Are Copper Wire

> whisper of yellow globes
> gleaming on lamp-posts that sway
> like bootleg licker[1] drinkers in the fog

---

1. Liquor illegally distilled, especially during Prohibition, a period during the 1920s and early 1930s when U.S. law prohibited the manufacture, transportation, sale, and possession of alcoholic beverages.

and let your breath be moist against me
like bright beads on yellow globes   5

telephone the power-house
that the main wires are insulate

(her words play softly up and down
dewy corridors of billboards)

then with your tongue remove the tape   10
and press your lips to mine
till they are incandescent

Calling Jesus

Her soul is like a little thrust-tailed dog that follows her, whimpering.
She is large enough, I know, to find a warm spot for it. But each night when
she comes home and closes the big outside storm door, the little dog is
left in the vestibule, filled with chills till morning. Some one . . . . eoho[1]
Jesus . . . soft as a cotton boll brushed against the milk-pod cheek of Christ,
will steal in and cover it that it need not shiver, and carry it to her where she
sleeps upon clean hay cut in her dreams.

When you meet her in the daytime on the streets, the little dog keeps
coming. Nothing happens at first, and then, when she has forgotten the
streets and alleys, and the large house where she goes to bed of nights, a soft
thing like fur begins to rub your limbs, and you hear a low, scared voice,
lonely, calling, and you know that a cool something nozzles moisture in
your palms. Sensitive things like nostrils, quiver. Her breath comes sweet as
honeysuckle whose pistils bear the life of coming song. And her eyes carry
to where builders find no need for vestibules, for swinging on iron hinges,
storm doors.

Her soul is like a little thrust-tailed dog, that follows her, whimpering.
I've seen it tagging on behind her, up streets where chestnut trees flowered,
where dusty asphalt had been freshly sprinkled with clean water. Up alleys
where niggers sat on low door-steps before tumbled shanties and sang and
loved. At night, when she comes home, the little dog is left in the vestibule,
nosing the crack beneath the big storm door, filled with chills till morning.
Some one . . . eoho Jesus . . . soft as the bare feet of Christ moving across
bales of southern cotton, will steal in and cover it that it need not shiver,
and carry it to her where she sleeps: cradled in dream-fluted cane.

1. Call.

Box Seat[1]

1

Houses are shy girls whose eyes shine reticently upon the dusk body of the street. Upon the gleaming limbs and asphalt torso of a dreaming nigger. Shake your curled wool-blossoms, nigger. Open your liver lips to the lean, white spring. Stir the root-life of a withered people. Call them from their houses, and teach them to dream.

Dark swaying forms of Negroes are street songs that woo virginal houses.

Dan Moore walks southward on Thirteenth Street. The low limbs of budding chestnut trees recede above his head. Chestnut buds and blossoms are wool he walks upon. The eyes of houses faintly touch him as he passes them. Soft girl-eyes, they set him singing. Girl-eyes within him widen upward to promised faces. Floating away, they dally wistfully over the dusk body of the street. Come on, Dan Moore, come on. Dan sings. His voice is a little hoarse. It cracks. He strains to produce tones in keeping with the houses' loveliness. Cant be done. He whistles. His notes are shrill. They hurt him. Negroes open gates, and go indoors, perfectly. Dan thinks of the house he's going to. Of the girl. Lips, flesh-notes of a forgotten song, plead with him . . .

Dan turns into a side-street, opens an iron gate, bangs it to. Mounts the steps, and searches for the bell. Funny, he cant find it. He fumbles around. The thought comes to him that some one passing by might see him, and not understand. Might think that he is trying to sneak, to break in.

Dan:[2] Break in. Get an ax and smash in. Smash in their faces. I'll show em. Break into an engine-house, steal a thousand horsepower fire truck. Smash in with the truck. I'll show em. Grab an ax and brain em. Cut em up. Jack the Ripper.[3] Baboon from the zoo. And then the cops come. "No, I aint a baboon. I aint Jack the Ripper. I'm a poor man out of work. Take your hands off me, you bull-necked bears. Look into my eyes. I am Dan Moore. I was born in a canefield. The hands of Jesus touched me. I am come to a sick world to heal it. Only the other day, a dope fiend brushed against me—Dont laugh, you mighty, juicy, meat-hook men. Give me your fingers and I will peel them as if they were ripe bananas."

Some one might think he is trying to break in. He'd better knock. His knuckles are raw bone against the thick glass door. He waits. No one comes. Perhaps they havent heard him. He raps again. This time, harder. He waits. No one comes. Some one is surely in. He fancies that he sees their shadows on the glass. Shadows of gorillas. Perhaps they saw him coming and dont want to let him in. He knocks. The tension of his arms makes the glass rattle. Hurried steps come towards him. The door opens.

"Please, you might break the glass—the bell—oh, Mr. Moore! I thought it must be some stranger. How do you do? Come in, wont you? Muriel?

---

1. Expensive theater seat usually located along a side wall. Box seats were considered the best seats in the theater; they were above stage level, and the closest were within arms' reach of the stage.
2. Throughout this story, a colon indicates that the thoughts, not the spoken words, of the character will follow.
3. The name given by newspapers to an unidentified individual in 19th-century London who killed and mutilated several prostitutes.

Yes. I'll call her. Take your things off, wont you? And have a seat in the parlor. Muriel will be right down. Muriel! Oh Muriel! Mr. Moore to see you. She'll be right down. You'll pardon me, wont you? So glad to see you."

Her eyes are weak. They are bluish and watery from reading newspapers. The blue is steel. It gimlets[4] Dan while her mouth flaps amiably to him.

Dan: Nothing for you to see, old mussel-head. Dare I show you? If I did, delirium would furnish you headlines for a month. Now look here. Thats enough. Go long, woman. Say some nasty thing and I'll kill you. Huh. Better damned sight not. Ta-ta, Mrs. Pribby.

Mrs. Pribby retreats to the rear of the house. She takes up a newspaper. There is a sharp click as she fits into her chair and draws it to the table. The click is metallic like the sound of a bolt being shot into place. Dan's eyes sting. Sinking into a soft couch, he closes them. The house contracts about him. It is a sharp-edged, massed, metallic house. Bolted. About Mrs. Pribby. Bolted to the endless rows of metal houses. Mrs. Pribby's house. The rows of houses belong to other Mrs. Pribbys. No wonder he couldn't sing to them.

Dan: What's Muriel doing here? God, what a place for her. Whats she doing? Putting her stockings on? In the bathroom. Come out of there, Dan Moore. People must have their privacy. Peeping-toms. I'll never peep. I'll listen. I like to listen.

Dan goes to the wall and places his ear against it. A passing street car and something vibrant from the earth sends a rumble to him. That rumble comes from the earth's deep core. It is the mutter of powerful underground races. Dan has a picture of all the people rushing to put their ears against walls, to listen to it. The next world-savior is coming up that way. Coming up. A continent sinks down. The new-world Christ will need consummate skill to walk upon the waters where huge bubbles burst . . . Thuds of Muriel coming down. Dan turns to the piano and glances through a stack of jazz music sheets. Ji-ji-bo, JI-JI-BO! . .

"Hello, Dan, stranger, what brought you here?"

Muriel comes in, shakes hands, and then clicks into a high-armed seat under the orange glow of a floor-lamp. Her face is fleshy. It would tend to coarseness but for the fresh fragrant something which is the life of it. Her hair like an Indian's. But more curly and bushed and vagrant. Her nostrils flare. The flushed ginger of her cheeks is touched orange by the shower of color from the lamp.

"Well, you havent told me, you havent answered my question, stranger. What brought you here?"

Dan feels the pressure of the house, of the rear room, of the rows of houses, shift to Muriel. He is light. He loves her. He is doubly heavy.

"Dont know, Muriel—wanted to see you—wanted to talk to you—to see you and tell you that I know what you've been through—what pain the last few months must have been—"

"Lets dont mention that."

"But why not, Muriel? I—"

"Please."

4. A gimlet is a small tool for piercing holes.

"But Muriel, life is full of things like that. One grows strong and beautiful in facing them. What else is life?"

"I dont know, Dan. And I dont believe I care. Whats the use? Lets talk about something else. I hear there's a good show at the Lincoln this week."

"Yes, so Harry was telling me. Going?"

"Tonight."

Dan starts to rise.

"I didnt know. I dont want to keep you."

"Its all right. You dont have to go till Bernice comes. And she wont be here till eight. I'm all dressed. I'll let you know."

"Thanks."

Silence. The rustle of a newspaper being turned comes from the rear room.

Muriel: Shame about Dan. Something awfully good and fine about him. But he dont fit in. In where? Me? Dan, I could love you if I tried. I dont have to try. I do. O Dan, dont you know I do? Timid lover, brave talker that you are. Whats the good of all you know if you dont know that? I wont let myself. I? Mrs. Pribby who reads newspapers all night wont. What has she got to do with me? She *is* me, somehow. No she's not. Yes she is. She is the town, and the town wont let me love you, Dan. Dont you know? You could make it let me if you would. Why wont you? Youre selfish. I'm not strong enough to buck it. Youre too selfish to buck it, for me. I wish you'd go. You irritate me. Dan, please go.

"What are you doing now, Dan?"

"Same old thing, Muriel. Nothing, as the world would have it. Living, as I look at things. Living as much as I can without—"

"But you cant live without money, Dan. Why dont you get a good job and settle down?"

Dan: Same old line. Shoot it at me, sister. Hell of a note, this loving business. For ten minutes of it youve got to stand the torture of an intolerable heaviness and a hundred platitudes. Well, damit, shoot on.

"To what? my dear. Rustling newspapers?"

"You mustnt say that, Dan. It isnt right. Mrs. Pribby has been awfully good to me."

"Dare say she has. Whats that got to do with it?"

"Oh, Dan, youre so unconsiderate and selfish. All you think of is yourself."

"I think of you."

"Too much—I mean, you ought to work more and think less. Thats the best way to get along."

"Mussel-heads get along, Muriel. There is more to you than that—"

"Sometimes I think there is, Dan. But I dont know. I've tried. I've tried to do something with myself. Something real and beautiful, I mean. But whats the good of trying? I've tried to make people, every one I come in contact with, happy—"

Dan looks at her, directly. Her animalism, still unconquered by zoo-restrictions and keeper-taboos, stirs him. Passion tilts upward, bringing with it the elements of an old desire. Muriel's lips become the flesh-notes of a futile, plaintive longing. Dan's impulse to direct her is its fresh life.

"Happy, Muriel? No, not happy. Your aim is wrong. There is no such thing as happiness. Life bends joy and pain, beauty and ugliness, in such a way that no one may isolate them. No one should want to. Perfect joy, or perfect pain, with no contrasting element to define them, would mean a monotony of consciousness, would mean death. Not happy, Muriel. Say that you have tried to make them create. Say that you have used your own capacity for life to cradle them. To start them upward-flowing. Or if you cant say that you have, then say that you will. My talking to you will make you aware of your power to do so. Say that you will love, that you will give yourself in love—"

"To you, Dan?"

Dan's consciousness crudely swerves into his passions. They flare up in his eyes. They set up quivers in his abdomen. He is suddenly over-tense and nervous.

"Muriel—"

The newspaper rustles in the rear room.

"Muriel—"

Dan rises. His arms stretch towards her. His fingers and his palms, pink in the lamplight, are glowing irons. Muriel's chair is close and stiff about her. The house, the rows of houses locked about her chair. Dan's fingers and arms are fire to melt and bars to wrench and force and pry. Her arms hang loose. Her hands are hot and moist. Dan takes them. He slips to his knees before her.

"Dan, you mustnt."

"Muriel—"

"Dan, really you mustnt. No, Dan. No."

"Oh, come, Muriel. Must I—"

"Shhh. Dan, please get up. Please. Mrs. Pribby is right in the next room. She'll hear you. She may come in. Dont, Dan. She'll see you—"

"Well then, lets go out."

"I cant. Let go, Dan. Oh, wont you please let go."

Muriel tries to pull her hands away. Dan tightens his grip. He feels the strength of his fingers. His muscles are tight and strong. He stands up. Thrusts out his chest. Muriel shrinks from him. Dan becomes aware of his crude absurdity. His lips curl. His passion chills. He has an obstinate desire to possess her.

"Muriel, I love you. I want you, whatever the world of Pribby says. Damn your Pribby. Who is she to dictate my love? I've stood enough of her. Enough of you. Come here."

Muriel's mouth works in and out. Her eyes flash and waggle. She wrenches her hands loose and forces them against his breast to keep him off. Dan grabs her wrists. Wedges in between her arms. Her face is close to him. It is hot and blue and moist. Ugly.

"Come here now."

"Dont, Dan. Oh, dont. What are you killing?"

"Whats weak in both of us and a whole litter of Pribbys. For once in your life youre going to face whats real, by God—"

A sharp rap on the newspaper in the rear room cuts between them. The rap is like cool thick glass between them. Dan is hot on one side. Muriel, hot on the other. They straighten. Gaze fearfully at one another. Neither moves. A clock in the rear room, in the rear room, the rear room, strikes eight. Eight slow, cool sounds. Bernice. Muriel fastens on her image. She smooths her dress. She adjusts her skirt. She becomes prim and cool. Rising, she skirts Dan as if to keep the glass between them. Dan, gyrating nervously above the easy swing of his limbs, follows her to the parlor door. Muriel retreats before him till she reaches the landing of the steps that lead upstairs. She smiles at him. Dan sees his face in the hall mirror. He runs his fingers through his hair. Reaches for his hat and coat and puts them on. He moves towards Muriel. Muriel steps backward up one step. Dan's jaw shoots out. Muriel jerks her arm in warning of Mrs. Pribby. She gasps and turns and starts to run. Noise of a chair scraping as Mrs. Pribby rises from it, ratchets down the hall. Dan stops. He makes a wry face, wheels round, goes out, and slams the door.

2

People come in slowly . . . mutter, laughs, flutter, wishadwash,[5] "I've changed my work-clothes—" . . . and fill vacant seats of Lincoln Theater. Muriel, leading Bernice who is a cross between a washerwoman and a blue-blood lady, a washer-blue, a washer-lady, wanders down the right aisle to the lower front box. Muriel has on an orange dress. Its color would clash with the crimson box-draperies, its color would contradict the sweet rose smile her face is bathed in, should she take her coat off. She'll keep it on. Pale purple shadows rest on the planes of her cheeks. Deep purple comes from her thick-shocked hair. Orange of the dress goes well with these. Muriel presses her coat down from around her shoulders. Teachers are not supposed to have bobbed hair.[6] She'll keep her hat on. She takes the first chair, and indicates that Bernice is to take the one directly behind her. Seated thus, her eyes are level with, and near to, the face of an imaginary man upon the stage. To speak to Berny she must turn. When she does, the audience is square upon her.

People come in slowly . . . "—for my Sunday-go-to-meeting dress. O glory God! O shout Amen!" . . . and fill vacant seats of Lincoln Theater. Each one is a bolt that shoots into a slot, and is locked there. Suppose the Lord should ask, where was Moses when the light went out? Suppose Gabriel should blow his trumpet![7] The seats are slots. The seats are bolted houses. The mass grows denser. Its weight at first is impalpable upon the box. Then Muriel begins to feel it. She props her arm against the brass box-rail, to ward it off. Silly. These people are friends of hers: a parent of a child she teaches, an old school friend. She smiles at them. They return her courtesy, and she is free to chat with Berny. Berny's tongue, started, runs on, and on. O washer-blue! O washer-lady!

Muriel: Never see Dan again. He makes me feel queer. Starts things he doesnt finish. Upsets me. I am not upset. I am perfectly calm. I am going to

---

5. The sounds made by a theater audience during the time before the curtain rises.
6. A short hairstyle of the 1920s that was considered fashionable and daring for women who re-

belled against the conservative custom of long hair.
7. The Christian concept that, at the end of the world, the angel Gabriel will blow a horn to announce Judgment Day.

enjoy the show. Good show. I've had some show! This damn tame thing. O Dan. Wont see Dan again. Not alone. Have Mrs. Pribby come in. She *was* in. Keep Dan out. If I love him, can I keep him out? Well then, I dont love him. Now he's out. Who is that coming in? Blind as a bat. Ding-bat. Looks like Dan. He mustnt see me. Silly. He cant reach me. He wont dare come in here. He'd put his head down like a goring bull and charge me. He'd trample them. He'd gore. He'd rape! Berny! He wont dare come in here.

"Berny, who was that who just came in? I havent my glasses."

"A friend of yours, a *good* friend so I hear. Mr. Daniel Moore, Lord."

"Oh. He's no friend of mine."

"No? I hear he is."

"Well, he isnt."

Dan is ushered down the aisle. He has to squeeze past the knees of seated people to reach his own seat. He treads on a man's corns. The man grumbles, and shoves him off. He shrivels close beside a portly Negress whose huge rolls of flesh meet about the bones of seat-arms. A soil-soaked fragrance comes from her. Through the cement floor her strong roots sink down. They spread under the asphalt streets. Dreaming, the streets roll over on their bellies, and suck their glossy health from them. Her strong roots sink down and spread under the river and disappear in blood-lines that waver south. Her roots shoot down. Dan's hands follow them. Roots throb. Dan's heart beats violently. He places his palms upon the earth to cool them. Earth throbs. Dan's heart beats violently. He sees all the people in the house rush to the walls to listen to the rumble. A new-world Christ is coming up. Dan comes up. He is startled. The eyes of the woman dont belong to her. They look at him unpleasantly. From either aisle, bolted masses press in. He doesnt fit. The mass grows agitant. For an instant, Dan's and Muriel's eyes meet. His weight there slides the weight on her. She braces an arm against the brass rail, and turns her head away.

Muriel: Damn fool; dear Dan, what did you want to follow me here for? Oh cant you ever do anything right? Must you always pain me, and make me hate you? I do hate you. I wish some one would come in with a horse-whip and lash you out. I wish some one would drag you up a back alley and brain you with the whip-butt.

Muriel glances at her wrist-watch.

"Quarter of nine. Berny, what time have you?"

"Eight-forty. Time to begin. Oh, look Muriel, that woman with the plume; doesnt she look good! They say she's going with, oh, whats his name. You know. Too much powder.[8] I can see it from here. Here's the orchestra now. O fine! Jim Clem at the piano!"

The men fill the pit. Instruments run the scale and tune. The saxophone moans and throws a fit. Jim Clem, poised over the piano, is ready to begin. His head nods forward. Opening crash. The house snaps dark. The curtain recedes upward from the blush of the footlights. Jazz overture is over. The first act is on.

Dan: Old stuff. Muriel—bored. Must be. But she'll smile and she'll clap. Do what youre bid, you she-slave. Look at her. Sweet, tame woman in a

---

8. Face powder, to make the skin seem lighter.

brass box seat. Clap, smile, fawn, clap. Do what youre bid. Drag me in with you. Dirty me. Prop me in your brass box seat. I'm there, am I not? because of you. He-slave. Slave of a woman who is a slave. I'm a damned sight worse than you are. I sing your praises, Beauty! I exalt thee, O Muriel! A slave, thou art greater than all Freedom because I love thee.

Dan fidgets, and disturbs his neighbors. His neighbors glare at him. He glares back without seeing them. The man whose corns have been trod upon speaks to him.

"Keep quiet, cant you, mister. Other people have paid their money besides yourself to see the show."

The man's face is a blur about two sullen liquid things that are his eyes. The eyes dissolve in the surrounding vagueness. Dan suddenly feels that the man is an enemy whom he has long been looking for.

Dan bristles. Glares furiously at the man.

"All right. All right then. Look at the show. I'm not stopping you."

"Shhh," from some one in the rear.

Dan turns around.

"Its that man there who started everything. I didnt say a thing to him until he tried to start something. What have I got to do with whether he has paid his money or not? Thats the manager's business. Do I look like the manager?"

"Shhhh. Youre right. Shhhh."

"Dont tell me to shhh. Tell him. That man there. He started everything. If what he wanted was to start a fight, why didnt he say so?"

The man leans forward.

"Better be quiet, sonny. I aint said a thing about fight, yet."

"Its a good thing you havent."

"Shhhh."

Dan grips himself. Another act is on. Dwarfs, dressed like prizefighters, foreheads bulging like boxing gloves, are led upon the stage. They are going to fight for the heavyweight championship. Gruesome. Dan glances at Muriel. He imagines that she shudders. His mind curves back into himself, and picks up tail-ends of experiences. His eyes are open, mechanically. The dwarfs pound and bruise and bleed each other, on his eyeballs.

Dan: Ah, but she was some baby! And not vulgar either. Funny how some women can do those things. Muriel dancing like that! Hell. She rolled and wabbled. Her buttocks rocked. She pulled up her dress and showed her pink drawers. Baby! And then she caught my eyes. Dont know what my eyes had in them. Yes I do. God, dont I though! Sometimes I think, Dan Moore, that your eyes could burn clean . . . burn clean . . . BURN CLEAN! . .

The gong rings. The dwarfs set to. They spar grotesquely, playfully, until one lands a stiff blow. This makes the other sore. He commences slugging. A real scrap is on. Time! The dwarfs go to their corners and are sponged and fanned off. Gloves bulge from their wrists. Their wrists are necks for the tight-faced gloves. The fellow to the right lets his eyes roam over the audience. He sights Muriel. He grins.

Dan: Those silly women arguing feminism. Here's what I should have said to them. "It should be clear to you women, that the proposition must be stated thus:

Me, horizontally above her.
Action: perfect strokes downward oblique.
Hence, man dominates because of limitation.
Or, so it shall be until women learn their stuff.

So framed, the proposition is a mental-filler, Dentist, I want gold teeth. It should become cherished of the technical intellect. I hereby offer it to posterity as one of the important machine-age designs. P.S. It should be noted, that because it *is* an achievement of this age, its growth and hence its causes, up to the point of maturity, antedate machinery. Ery . . ."

The gong rings. No fooling this time. The dwarfs set to. They clinch. The referee parts them. One swings a cruel upper-cut and knocks the other down. A huge head hits the floor. Pop! The house roars. The fighter, groggy, scrambles up. The referee whispers to the contenders not to fight so hard. They ignore him. They charge. Their heads jab like boxing-gloves. They kick and spit and bite. They pound each other furiously. Muriel pounds. The house pounds. Cut lips. Bloody noses. The referee asks for the gong. Time! The house roars. The dwarfs bow, are made to bow. The house wants more. The dwarfs are led from the stage.

Dan: Strange I never really noticed him before. Been sitting there for years. Born a slave. Slavery not so long ago. He'll die in his chair. Swing low, sweet chariot. Jesus will come and roll him down the river Jordan. Oh, come along, Moses, you'll get lost; stretch out your rod and come across. LET MY PEOPLE GO![9] Old man. Knows everyone who passes the corners. Saw the first horse-cars. The first Oldsmobile. And he was born in slavery. I did see his eyes. Never miss eyes. But they were bloodshot and watery. It hurt to look at them. It hurts to look in most people's eyes. He saw Grant and Lincoln. He saw Walt—old man, did you see Walt Whitman?[1] Did you see Walt Whitman! Strange force that drew me to him. And I went up to see. The woman thought I saw crazy. I told him to look into the heavens. He did, and smiled. I asked him if he knew what that rumbling is that comes up from the ground. Christ, what a stroke that was. And the jabbering idiots crowding around. And the crossing-cop leaving his job to come over and wheel him away . . .

The house applauds. The house wants more. The dwarfs are led back. But no encore. Must give the house something. The attendant comes out and announces that Mr. Barry, the champion, will sing one of his own songs, "for your approval." Mr. Barry grins at Muriel as he wabbles from the wing. He holds a fresh white rose, and a small mirror. He wipes blood from his nose. He signals Jim Clem. The orchestra starts. A sentimental love song, Mr. Barry sings, first to one girl, and then another in the audience. He holds the mirror in such a way that it flashes in the face of each one he sings to. The light swings around.

Dan: I am going to reach up and grab the girders of this building and pull them down. The crash will be a signal. Hid by the smoke and dust

---

9. "Swing Low, Sweet Chariot," "Roll, Jordan, Roll," and "Let My People Go" are African American spirituals that express hope for freedom on earth and in heaven.

1. A 19th-century American poet who voiced many ideas about democracy, brotherhood, and a new American race; he served as a nurse during the Civil War.

Dan Moore will arise. In his right hand will be a dynamo. In his left, a god's face that will flash white light from ebony. I'll grab a girder and swing it like a walking-stick. Lightning will flash. I'll grab its black knob and swing it like a crippled cane. Lightning . . . Some one's flashing . . . some one's flashing . . . Who in hell is flashing that mirror? Take it off me, godam you.

Dan's eyes are half blinded. He moves his head. The light follows. He hears the audience laugh. He hears the orchestra. A man with a high-pitched, sentimental voice is singing. Dan sees the dwarf. Along the mirror flash the song comes. Dan ducks his head. The audience roars. The light swings around to Muriel. Dan looks. Muriel is too close. Mr. Barry covers his mirror. He sings to her. She shrinks away. Nausea. She clutches the brass box-rail. She moves to face away. The audience is square upon her. Its eyes smile. Its hands itch to clap. Muriel turns to the dwarf and forces a smile at him. With a showy blare of orchestration, the song comes to its close. Mr. Barry bows. He offers Muriel the rose, first having kissed it. Blood of his battered lips is a vivid stain upon its petals. Mr. Barry offers Muriel the rose. The house applauds. Muriel flinches back. The dwarf steps forward, diffident; threatening. Hate pops from his eyes and crackles like a brittle heat about the box. The thick hide of his face is drawn in tortured wrinkles. Above his eyes, the bulging, tight-skinned brow. Dan looks at it. It grows calm and massive. It grows profound. It is a thing of wisdom and tenderness, of suffering and beauty. Dan looks down. The eyes are calm and luminous. Words come from them . . . Arms of the audience reach out, grab Muriel, and hold her there. Claps are steel fingers that manacle her wrists and move them forward to acceptance. Berny leans forward and whispers:

"Its all right. Go on—take it."

Words form in the eyes of the dwarf:

> Do not shrink. Do not be afraid of me.
> *Jesus*
> See how my eyes look at you.
> *the Son of God*
> I too was made in His image.
> *was once—*
> I give you the rose.

Muriel, tight in her revulsion, sees black, and daintily reaches for the offering. As her hand touches it, Dan springs up in his seat and shouts:
"JESUS WAS ONCE A LEPER!"

Dan steps down.

He is as cool as a green stem that has just shed its flower.

Rows of gaping faces strain towards him. They are distant, beneath him, impalpable. Squeezing out, Dan again treads upon the corn-foot man. The man shoves him.

"Watch where youre going, mister. Crazy or no, you aint going to walk over me. Watch where youre going there."

Dan turns, and serenely tweaks the fellow's nose. The man jumps up.

Dan is jammed against a seat-back. A slight swift anger flicks him. His fist hooks the other's jaw.

"Now you have started something. Aint no man living can hit me and get away with it. Come on on the outside."

The house, tumultuously stirring, grabs its wraps and follows the men.

The man leads Dan up a black alley. The alley-air is thick and moist with smells of garbage and wet trash. In the morning, singing niggers will drive by and ring their gongs . . . Heavy with the scent of rancid flowers and with the scent of fight. The crowd, pressing forward, is a hollow roar. Eyes of houses, soft girl-eyes, glow reticently upon the hubbub and blink out. The man stops. Takes off his hat and coat. Dan, having forgotten him, keeps going on.

Prayer

My body is opaque to the soul.
Driven of the spirit, long have I sought to temper it unto the spirit's
    longing,
But my mind, too, is opaque to the soul.
A closed lid is my soul's flesh-eye.
O Spirits of whom my soul is but a little finger,   5
Direct it to the lid of its flesh-eye.
I am weak with much giving.
I am weak with the desire to give more.
(How strong a thing is the little finger!)
So weak that I have confused the body with the soul,   10
And the body with its little finger.
(How frail is the little finger.)
My voice could not carry to you did you dwell in stars,
O Spirits of whom my soul is but a little finger . .

Harvest Song

I am a reaper whose muscles set at sundown. All my oats are cradled.
But I am too chilled, and too fatigued to bind them. And I hunger.

I crack a grain between my teeth. I do not taste it.
I have been in the fields all day. My throat is dry. I hunger.

My eyes are caked with dust of oatfields at harvest-time.   5
I am a blind man who stares across the hills, seeking stack'd fields of
    other harvesters.

It would be good to see them . . crook'd, split, and iron-ring'd handles
    of the scythes. It would be good to see them, dust-caked and
    blind. I hunger.

(Dusk is a strange fear'd sheath their blades are dull'd in.)
My throat is dry. And should I call, a cracked grain like the oats . . .
    eoho—

I fear to call. What should they hear me, and offer me their grain, oats,
     or wheat, or corn? I have been in the fields all day. I fear I could
     not taste it. I fear knowledge of my hunger.   10

My ears are caked with dust of oatfields at harvest-time.
I am a deaf man who strains to hear the calls of other harvesters whose
     throats are also dry.

It would be good to hear their songs . . reapers of the sweet-stalk'd
     cane, cutters of the corn . . even though their throats cracked and
     the strangeness of their voices deafened me.

I hunger. My throat is dry. Now that the sun has set and I am chilled, I
     fear to call. (Eoho, my brothers!)

I am a reaper. (Eoho!) All my oats are cradled. But I am too fatigued to
     bind them. And I hunger. I crack a grain. It has no taste to it. My
     throat is dry . . .   15

O my brothers, I beat my palms, still soft, against the stubble of my
     harvesting. (You beat your soft palms, too.) My pain is sweet.
     Sweeter than the oats or wheat or corn. It will not bring me
     knowledge of my hunger.

Bona and Paul [1]

1

   On the school gymnasium floor, young men and women are drilling.
They are going to be teachers, and go out into the world . . thud, thud . .
and give precision to the movements of sick people who all their lives
have been drilling. One man is out of step. In step. The teacher glares at
him. A girl in bloomers, seated on a mat in the corner because she has
told the director that she is sick, sees that the footfalls of the men are
rhythmical and syncopated. The dance of his blue-trousered limbs thrills
her.
   Bona: [2] He is a candle that dances in a grove swung with pale balloons.
   Columns of the drillers thud towards her. He is in the front row. He is in
no row at all. Bona can look close at him. His red-brown face—
   Bona: He is a harvest moon. He is an autumn leaf. He is a nigger. Bona!
But dont all the dorm girls say so? And dont you, when you are sane, say so?
Thats why I love— Oh, nonsense. You have never loved a man who didnt
first love you. Besides—
   Columns thud away from her. Come to a halt in line formation. Rigid.
The period bell rings, and the teacher dismisses them.
   A group collects around Paul. They are choosing sides for basket-ball.
Girls against boys. Paul has his. He is limbering up beneath the basket.

---

1. This story, set in Chicago, is the only story of the
second part not located in Washington, D.C.
2. Throughout this story, a colon indicates that the
thoughts, not the spoken words, of the character
will follow.

Bona runs to the girl captain and asks to be chosen. The girls fuss. The director comes to quiet them. He hears what Bona wants.

"But, Miss Hale, you were excused—"

"So I was, Mr. Boynton, but—"

"—you can play basket-ball, but you are too sick to drill."

"If you wish to put it that way."

She swings away from him to the girl captain.

"Helen, I want to play, and you must let me. This is the first time I've asked and I dont see why—"

"Thats just it, Bona. We have our team."

"Well, team or no team, I want to play and thats all there is to it."

She snatches the ball from Helen's hands, and charges down the floor.

Helen shrugs. One of the weaker girls says that she'll drop out. Helen accepts this. The team is formed. The whistle blows. The game starts. Bona, in center, is jumping against Paul. He plays with her. Out-jumps her, makes a quick pass, gets a quick return, and shoots a goal from the middle of the floor. Bona burns crimson. She fights, and tries to guard him. One of her team-mates advises her not to play so hard. Paul shoots his second goal.

Bona begins to feel a little dizzy and all in. She drives on. Almost hugs Paul to guard him. Near the basket, he attempts to shoot, and Bona lunges into his body and tries to beat his arms. His elbow, going up, gives her a sharp crack on the jaw. She whirls. He catches her. Her body stiffens. Then becomes strangely vibrant, and bursts to a swift life within her anger. He is about to give way before her hatred when a new passion flares at him and makes his stomach fall. Bona squeezes him. He suddenly feels stifled, and wonders why in hell the ring of silly gaping faces that's caked about him doesnt make way and give him air. He has a swift illusion that it is himself who has been struck. He looks at Bona. Whir. Whir. They seem to be human distortions spinning tensely in a fog. Spinning . . dizzy . . spinning . . . Bona jerks herself free, flushes a startling crimson, breaks through the bewildered teams, and rushes from the hall.

2

Paul is in his room of two windows.

Outside, the South-Side L[3] track cuts them in two.

Bona is one window. One window, Paul.

Hurtling Loop-jammed[4] L trains throw them in swift shadow.

Paul goes to his. Gray slanting roofs of houses are tinted lavender in the setting sun. Paul follows the sun, over the stock-yards where a fresh stench is just arising, across wheat lands that are still waving above their stubble, into the sun. Paul follows the sun to a pine-matted hillock in Georgia. He sees the slanting roofs of gray unpainted cabins tinted lavender. A Negress chants a lullaby beneath the mate-eyes of a southern planter. Her breasts are ample for the suckling of a song. She weans it, and sends it, curiously

---

3. Elevated train.
4. Crowded with passengers coming from the Loop, a section of downtown Chicago that was once the center of the shopping district.

weaving, among lush melodies of cane and corn. Paul follows the sun into himself in Chicago.

He is at Bona's window.

With his own glow he looks through a dark pane.

Paul's room-mate comes in.

"Say, Paul, I've got a date for you. Come on. Shake a leg, will you?"

His blond hair is combed slick. His vest is snug about him.

He is like the electric light which he snaps on.

"Whatdoysay, Paul? Get a wiggle on. Come on. We havent got much time by the time we eat and dress and everything."

His bustling concentrates on the brushing of his hair.

Art: What in hell's getting into Paul of late, anyway? Christ, but he's getting moony. Its his blood. Dark blood: moony. Doesnt get anywhere unless you boost it. You've got to keep it going—

"Say, Paul!"

—or it'll go to sleep on you. Dark blood; nigger? Thats what those jealous she-hens say. Not Bona though, or she . . from the South . . wouldnt want me to fix a date for him and her. Hell of a thing, that Paul's dark: youve got to always be answering questions.

"Say, Paul, for Christ's sake leave that window, cant you?"

"Whats it, Art?"

"Hell, I've told you about fifty times. Got a date for you. Come on."

"With who?"

Art: He didnt use to ask; now he does. Getting up in the air. Getting funny.

"Heres your hat. Want a smoke? Paul! Here. I've got a match. Now come on and I'll tell you all about it on the way to supper."

Paul: He's going to Life this time. No doubt of that. Quit your kidding. Some day, dear Art, I'm going to kick the living slats out of you, and you wont know what I've done it for. And your slats will bring forth Life . . beautiful woman . . .

Pure Food Restaurant.

"Bring me some soup with a lot of crackers, understand? And then a roast-beef dinner. Same for you, eh, Paul? Now as I was saying, you've got a swell chance with her. And she's game. Best proof: she dont give a damn what the dorm girls say about you and her in the gym, or about the funny looks that Boynton gives her, or about what they say about, well, hell, you know, Paul. And say, Paul, she's a sweetheart. Tall, not puffy and pretty, more serious and deep—the kind you like these days. And they say she's got a car. And say, she's on fire. But you know all about that. She got Helen to fix it up with me. The four of us—remember the last party? Crimson Gardens![5] Boy!"

Paul's eyes take on a light that Art can settle in.

5. A nightclub.

3

Art has on his patent-leather pumps and fancy vest. A loose fall coat is swung across his arm. His face has been massaged, and over a close shave, powdered. It is a healthy pink the blue of evening tints a purple pallor. Art is happy and confident in the good looks that his mirror gave him. Bubbling over with a joy he must spend now if the night is to contain it all. His bubbles, too, are curiously tinted purple as Paul watches them. Paul, contrary to what he had thought he would be like, is cool like the dusk, and like the dusk, detached. His dark face is a floating shade in evening's shadow. He sees Art, curiously. Art is a purple fluid, carbon-charged, that effervesces beside him. He loves Art. But is it not queer, this pale purple facsimile of a red-blooded Norwegian friend of his? Perhaps for some reason, white skins are not supposed to live at night. Surely, enough nights would transform them fantastically, or kill them. And their red passion? Night paled that too, and made it moony. Moony. Thats what Art thought of him. Bona didnt, even in the daytime. Bona, would she be pale? Impossible. Not that red glow. But the conviction did not set his emotion flowing.

"Come right in, wont you? The young ladies will be right down. Oh, Mr. Carlstrom, do play something for us while you are waiting. We just love to listen to your music. You play so well."

Houses, and dorm sitting-rooms are places where white faces seclude themselves at night. There is a reason . . .

Art sat on the piano and simply tore it down. Jazz. The picture of Our Poets hung perilously.

Paul: I've got to get the kid to play that stuff for me in the daytime. Might be different. More himself. More nigger. Different? There is. Curious, though.

The girls come in. Art stops playing, and almost immediately takes up a petty quarrel, where he had last left it, with Helen.

Bona, black-hair curled staccato, sharply contrasting with Helen's puffy yellow, holds Paul's hand. She squeezes it. Her own emotion supplements the return pressure. And then, for no tangible reason, her spirits drop. Without them, she is nervous, and slightly afraid. She resents this. Paul's eyes are critical. She resents Paul. She flares at him. She flares to poise and security.

"Shall we be on our way?"

"Yes, Bona, certainly."

The Boulevard is sleek in asphalt, and, with arc-lights and limousines, aglow. Dry leaves scamper behind the whir of cars. The scent of exploded gasoline that mingles with them is faintly sweet. Mellow stone mansions overshadow clapboard homes which now resemble Negro shanties in some southern alley. Bona and Paul, and Art and Helen, move along an island-like, far-stretching strip of leaf-soft ground. Above them, worlds of shadow-planes and solids, silently moving. As if on one of these, Paul looks down on Bona. No doubt of it: her face is pale. She is talking. Her words have no feel to them. One sees them. They are pink petals that fall upon velvet cloth. Bona is soft, and pale, and beautiful.

"Paul, tell me something about yourself—or would you rather wait?"

"I'll tell you anything you'd like to know."

"Not what I want to know, Paul; what you want to tell me."

"You have the beauty of a gem fathoms under sea."

"I feel that, but I dont want to be. I want to be near you. Perhaps I will be if I tell you something. Paul, I love you."

The sea casts up its jewel into his hands, and burns them furiously. To tuck her arm under his and hold her hand will ease the burn.

"What can I say to you, brave dear woman—I cant talk love. Love is a dry grain in my mouth unless it is wet with kisses."

"You would dare? right here on the Boulevard? before Arthur and Helen?"

"Before myself? I dare."

"Here then."

Bona, in the slim shadow of a tree trunk, pulls Paul to her. Suddenly she stiffens. Stops.

"But you have not said you love me."

"I cant—yet—Bona."

"Ach, you never will. Youre cold. Cold."

Bona: Colored; cold. Wrong somewhere.

She hurries and catches up with Art and Helen.

4

Crimson Gardens. Hurrah! So one feels. People . . . University of Chicago students, members of the stock exchange, a large Negro in crimson uniform who guards the door . . . had watched them enter. Had leaned towards each other over ash-smeared tablecloths and highballs and whispered: What is he, a Spaniard, an Indian, an Italian, a Mexican, a Hindu, or a Japanese? Art had at first fidgeted under their stares . . what are *you* looking at, you godam pack of owl-eyed hyenas? . . but soon settled into his fuss with Helen, and forgot them. A strange thing happened to Paul. Suddenly he knew that he was apart from the people around him. Apart from the pain which they had unconsciously caused. Suddenly he knew that people saw, not attractiveness in his dark skin, but difference. Their stares, giving him to himself, filled something long empty within him, and were like green blades sprouting in his consciousness. There was fullness, and strength and peace about it all. He saw himself, cloudy, but real. He saw the faces of the people at the tables round him. White lights, or as now, the pink lights of the Crimson Gardens gave a glow and immediacy to white faces. The pleasure of it, equal to that of love or dream, of seeing this. Art and Bona and Helen? He'd look. They were wonderfully flushed and beautiful. Not for himself; because they were. Distantly. Who were they, anyway? God, if he knew them. He'd come in with them. Of that he was sure. Come where? Into life? Yes. No. Into the Crimson Gardens. A part of life. A carbon bubble. Would it look purple if he went out into the night and looked at it? His sudden starting to rise almost upset the table.

"What in hell—pardon—whats the matter, Paul?"

"I forgot my cigarettes—"

"Youre smoking one."

"So I am. Pardon me."

The waiter straightens them out. Takes their order.

Art: What in hell's eating Paul? Moony aint the word for it. From bad to worse. And those godam people staring so. Paul's a queer fish. Doesnt seem to mind . . . He's my pal, let me tell you, you horn-rimmed owl-eyed hyena at that table, and a lot better than you whoever you are . . . Queer about him. I could stick up for him if he'd only come out, one way or the other, and tell a feller. Besides, a room-mate has a right to know. Thinks I wont understand. Said so. He's got a swell head when it comes to brains, all right. God, he's a good straight feller, though. Only, moony. Nut. Nuttish. Nuttery. Nutmeg . . . "What'd you say, Helen?"

"I was talking to Bona, thank you."

"Well, its nothing to get spiffy about."

"What? Oh, of course not. Please lets dont start some silly argument all over again."

"Well."

"Well."

"Now thats enough. Say, waiter, whats the matter with our order? Make it snappy, will you?"

Crimson Gardens. Hurrah! So one feels. The drinks come. Four high-balls. Art passes cigarettes. A girl dressed like a bareback rider in flaming pink, makes her way through tables to the dance floor. All lights are dimmed till they seem a lush afterglow of crimson. Spotlights the girl. She sings. "Liza, Little Liza Jane."

Paul is rosy before his window.

He moves, slightly, towards Bona.

With his own glow, he seeks to penetrate a dark pane.

Paul: From the South. What does that mean, precisely, except that you'll love or hate a nigger? Thats a lot. What does it mean except that in Chicago you'll have the courage to neither love or hate. A priori.[6] But it would seem that you have. Queer words, arent these, for a man who wears blue pants on a gym floor in the daytime. Well, never matter. You matter. I'd like to know you whom I look at. Know, not love. Not that knowing is a greater pleasure; but that I have just found the joy of it. You came just a month too late. Even this afternoon I dreamed. Tonight, along the Boulevard, you found me cold. Paul Johnson, cold! Thats a good one, eh, Art, you fine old stupid fellow, you! But I feel good! The color and the music and the song . . . . A Negress chants a lullaby beneath the mate-eyes of a southern planter. O song! . . . And those flushed faces. Eager brilliant eyes. Hard to imagine them as unawakened. Your own. Oh, they're awake all right. "And you know it too, dont you Bona?"

"What, Paul?"

"The truth of what I was thinking."

"I'd like to know I know—something of you."

---

6. In advance of the fact. A priori conclusions are judgments based on preconceived theories rather than on actual study and analysis.

"You will—before the evening's over. I promise it."

Crimson Gardens. Hurrah! So one feels. The bare-back rider balances agilely on the applause which is the tail of her song. Orchestral instruments warm up for jazz. The flute is a cat that ripples its fur against the deep-purring saxophone. The drum throws sticks. The cat jumps on the piano keyboard. Hi diddle, hi diddle, the cat and the fiddle. Crimson Gardens . . hurrah! . . jumps over the moon. Crimson Gardens! Helen . . O Eliza . . rabbit-eyes sparkling, plays up to, and tries to placate what she considers to be Paul's contempt. She always does that . . Little Liza Jane . . . Once home, she burns with the thought of what she's done. She says all manner of snidy things about him, and swears that she'll never go out again when he is along. She tries to get Art to break with him, saying, that if Paul, whom the whole dormitory calls a nigger, is more to him than she is, well, she's through. She does not break with Art. She goes out as often as she can with Art and Paul. She explains this to herself by a piece of information which a friend of hers had given her: men like him (Paul) can fascinate. One is not responsible for fascination. Not one girl had really loved Paul; he fascinated them. Bona didnt; only thought she did. Time would tell. And of course, *she* didn't. Liza . . . She plays up to, and tries to placate, Paul.

"Paul is so deep these days, and I'm so glad he's found some one to interest him."

"I dont believe I do."

The thought escapes from Bona just a moment before her anger at having said it.

Bona: You little puffy cat, I do. I do!

Dont I, Paul? Her eyes ask.

Her answer is a crash of jazz from the palm-hidden orchestra. Crimson Gardens is a body whose blood flows to a clot upon the dance floor. Art and Helen clot. Soon, Bona and Paul. Paul finds her a little stiff, and his mind, wandering to Helen (silly little kid who wants every highball spoon her hands touch, for a souvenir), supple, perfect little dancer, wishes for the next dance when he and Art will exchange.

Bona knows that she must win him to herself.

"Since when have men like you grown cold?"

"The first philosopher."

"I thought you were a poet—or a gym director."

"Hence, your failure to make love."

Bona's eyes flare. Water. Grow red about the rims. She would like to tear away from him and dash across the clotted floor.

"What do you mean?"

"Mental concepts rule you. If they were flush with mine—good. I dont believe they are."

"How do you know, Mr. Philosopher?"

"Mostly a priori."

"You talk well for a gym director."

"And you—"

"I hate you. Ou!"

She presses away. Paul, conscious of the convention in it, pulls her to him. Her body close. Her head still strains away. He nearly crushes her. She tries to pinch him. Then sees people staring, and lets her arms fall. Their eyes meet. Both, contemptuous. The dance takes blood from their minds and packs it, tingling, in the torsos of their swaying bodies. Passionate blood leaps back into their eyes. They are a dizzy blood clot on a gyrating floor. They know that the pink-faced people have no part in what they feel. Their instinct leads them away from Art and Helen, and towards the big uniformed black man who opens and closes the gilded exit door. The cloak-room girl is tolerant of their impatience over such trivial things as wraps. And slightly superior. As the black man swings the door for them, his eyes are knowing. Too many couples have passed out, flushed and fidgety, for him not to know. The chill air is a shock to Paul. A strange thing happens. He sees the Gardens purple, as if he were way off. And a spot is in the purple. The spot comes furiously towards him. Face of the black man. It leers. It smiles sweetly like a child's. Paul leaves Bona and darts back so quickly that he doesnt give the door-man a chance to open. He swings in. Stops. Before the huge bulk of the Negro.

"You're wrong."

"Yassur."

"Brother, you're wrong.

"I came back to tell you, to shake your hand, and tell you that you are wrong. That something beautiful is going to happen. That the Gardens are purple like a bed of roses would be at dusk. That I came into the Gardens, into life in the Gardens with one whom I did not know. That I danced with her, and did not know her. That I felt passion, contempt and passion for her whom I did not know. That I thought of her. That my thoughts were matches thrown into a dark window. And all the while the Gardens were purple like a bed of roses would be at dusk. I came back to tell you, brother, that white faces are petals of roses. That dark faces are petals of dusk. That I am going out and gather petals. That I am going out and know her whom I brought here with me to these Gardens which are purple like a bed of roses would be at dusk."

Paul and the black man shook hands.

When he reached the spot where they had been standing, Bona was gone.

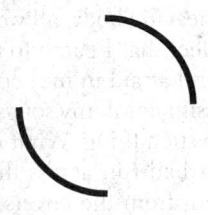

to Waldo Frank.[1]

Kabnis[2]

1

Ralph Kabnis, propped in his bed, tries to read. To read himself to sleep. An oil lamp[3] on a chair near his elbow burns unsteadily. The cabin room is spaced fantastically about it. Whitewashed hearth and chimney, black with sooty saw-teeth. Ceiling, patterned by the fringed globe of the lamp. The walls, unpainted, are seasoned a rosin yellow. And cracks between the boards are black. These cracks are the lips the night winds use for whispering. Night winds in Georgia are vagrant poets, whispering. Kabnis, against his will, lets his book slip down, and listens to them. The warm whiteness of his bed, the lamp-light, do not protect him from the weird chill of their song:

> White-man's land.
> Niggers,[4] sing.
> Burn, bear black children
> Till poor rivers bring
> Rest, and sweet glory
> In Camp Ground.[5]

Kabnis' thin hair is streaked on the pillow. His hand strokes the slim silk of his mustache. His thumb, pressed under his chin, seems to be trying to give squareness and projection to it. Brown eyes stare from a lemon face. Moisture gathers beneath his arm-pits. He slides down beneath the cover, seeking release.

Kabnis: Near me. Now. Whoever you are, my warm glowing sweetheart, do not think that the face that rests beside you is the real Kabnis. Ralph Kabnis is a dream. And dreams are faces with large eyes and weak chins and broad brows that get smashed by the fists of square faces. The body of the world is bull-necked. A dream is a soft face that fits uncertainly upon it . . . God, if I could develop that in words. Give what I know a bull-neck

<hr>

1. American author (1889–1967) who introduced Toomer's work and wrote a foreword for *Cane*.
2. At one time, Toomer prepared this work as a drama, with the hope that it would be produced on stage. Apparently it was once considered for production in a small playhouse, but there is no evidence that it was staged.
3. Although the story is set in the 20th century, Kabnis's cabin lacks electricity.
4. Here, suggests the subservient position of African Americans in "white-man's land."
5. A place where soldiers camp to rest during a march; here, symbolizes a resting place for blacks—probably in heaven. This is probably an original poem created in imitation of the spirituals.

and a heaving body, all would go well with me, wouldnt it, sweetheart? If I could feel that I came to the South to face it. If I, the dream (not what is weak and afraid in me) could become the face of the South. How my lips would sing for it, my songs being the lips of its soul. Soul. Soul hell. There aint no such thing. What in hell was that?

A rat had run across the thin boards of the ceiling. Kabnis thrusts his head out from the covers. Through the cracks, a powdery faded red dust sprays down on him. Dust of slavefields, dried, scattered . . . No use to read. Christ, if he only could drink himself to sleep. Something as sure as fate was going to happen. He couldnt stand this thing much longer. A hen, perched on a shelf in the adjoining room begins to tread. Her nails scrape the soft wood. Her feathers ruffle.

"Get out of that, you egg-laying bitch."

Kabnis hurls a slipper against the wall. The hen flies from her perch and cackles as if a skunk were after her.

"Now cut out that racket or I'll wring your neck for you."

Answering cackles arise in the chicken yard.

"Why in Christ's hell cant you leave me alone? Damn it, I wish your cackle would choke you. Choke every mother's son of them in this God-forsaken hole. Go away. By God I'll wring your neck for you if you dont. Hell of a mess I've got in: even the poultry is hostile. Go way. Go way. By God, I'll . . ."

Kabnis jumps from his bed. His eyes are wild. He makes for the door. Bursts through it. The hen, driving blindly at the windowpane, screams. Then flies and flops around trying to elude him. Kabnis catches her.

"Got you now, you she-bitch."

With his fingers about her neck, he thrusts open the outside door and steps out into the serene loveliness of Georgian autumn moonlight. Some distance off, down in the valley, a band of pine-smoke, silvered gauze, drifts steadily. The half-moon is a white child that sleeps upon the tree-tops of the forest. White winds croon its sleep-song:

> rock a-by baby . .
> Black mother sways, holding a white child on her bosom.
> when the bough bends . .
> Her breath hums through pine-cones.
> cradle will fall . .
> Teat moon-children at your breasts,
> down will come baby . .
> Black mother.[6]

Kabnis whirls the chicken by its neck, and throws the head away. Picks up the hopping body, warm, sticky, and hides it in a clump of bushes. He wipes blood from his hands onto the coarse scant grass.

Kabnis: Thats done. Old Chromo in the big house there will wonder whats become of her pet hen. Well, it'll teach her a lesson: not to make a hen-coop of my quarters. Quarters. Hell of a fine quarters, I've got. Five

---

6. Toomer alternates the familiar lines of a lullaby for children with lines of poetry describing the forest at night as a black mother nursing a white moon child.

years ago; look at me now. Earth's child. The earth my mother. God is a profligate red-nosed man about town.[7] Bastardy; me. A bastard son has got a right to curse his maker. God . . .

Kabnis is about to shake his fists heavenward. He looks up, and the night's beauty strikes him dumb. He falls to his knees. Sharp stones cut through his thin pajamas. The shock sends a shiver over him. He quivers. Tears mist his eyes. He writhes.

"God Almighty, dear God, dear Jesus, do not torture me with beauty. Take it away. Give me an ugly world. Ha, ugly. Stinking like unwashed niggers. Dear Jesus, do not chain me to myself and set these hills and valleys, heaving with folk-songs, so close to me that I cannot reach them. There is a radiant beauty in the night that touches and . . . tortures me. Ugh. Hell. Get up, you damn fool. Look around. Whats beautiful there? Hog pens and chicken yards. Dirty red mud. Stinking outhouse. Whats beauty anyway but ugliness if it hurts you? God, he doesnt exist, but nevertheless He is ugly. Hence, what comes from Him is ugly. Lynchers and business men, and that cockroach Hanby, especially. How come that he gets to be principal of a school? Of the school I'm driven to teach in? God's handiwork, doubtless. God and Hanby, they belong together. Two godam moral-spouters. Oh, no, I wont let that emotion come up in me. Stay down. Stay down, I tell you. O Jesus, Thou art beautiful . . . Come, Ralph, pull yourself together. Curses and adoration dont come from what is sane. This loneliness, dumbness, awful, intangible oppression is enough to drive a man insane. Miles from nowhere. A speck on a Georgia hillside. Jesus, can you imagine it—an atom of dust in agony on a hillside? Thats a spectacle for you. Come, Ralph, old man, pull yourself together."

Kabnis has stiffened. He is conscious now of the night wind, and of how it chills him. He rises. He totters as a man would who for the first time uses artificial limbs. As a completely artificial man would. The large frame house, squatting on brick pillars, where the principal of the school, his wife, and the boarding girls sleep, seems a curious shadow of his mind. He tries, but cannot convince himself of its reality. His gaze drifts down into the vale, across the swamp, up over the solid dusk bank of pines, and rests, bewildered-like, on the court-house tower. It is dull silver in the moonlight. White child that sleeps upon the top of pines. Kabnis' mind clears. He sees himself yanked beneath that tower. He sees white minds, with indolent assumption, juggle justice and a nigger . . . Somewhere, far off in the straight line of his sight, is Augusta. Christ, how cut off from everything he is. And hours, hours north, why not say a lifetime north? Washington sleeps. Its still, peaceful streets, how desirable they are. Its people whom he had always half-way despised. New York? Impossible. It was a fiction. He had dreamed it. An impotent nostalgia grips him. It becomes intolerable. He forces himself to narrow to a cabin silhouetted on a knoll about a mile away. Peace. Negroes within it are content. They farm. They sing. They love. They sleep. Kabnis wonders if perhaps they can feel him. If perhaps he gives them bad dreams. Things are so immediate in Georgia.

Thinking that now he can go to sleep, he reenters his room. He builds a fire in the open hearth. The room dances to the tongues of flames, and

7. A playboy. "Red-nosed": the result of excessive consumption of alcoholic beverages.

sings to the crackling and spurting of the logs. Wind comes up between the floor boards, through the black cracks of the walls.

Kabnis: Cant sleep. Light a cigarette. If that old bastard comes over here and smells smoke, I'm done for. Hell of a note, cant even smoke. The stillness of it: where they burn and hang men, you cant smoke. Cant take a swig of licker.[8] What do they think this is, anyway, some sort of temperance school? How did I ever land in such a hole? Ugh. One might just as well be in his grave. Still as a grave. Jesus, how still everything is. Does the world know how still it is? People make noise. They are afraid of silence. Of what lives, and God, of what dies in silence. There must be many dead things moving in silence. They come here to touch me. I swear I feel their fingers . . . Come, Ralph, pull yourself together. What in hell was that? Only the rustle of leaves, I guess. You know, Ralph, old man, it wouldnt surprise me at all to see a ghost. People dont think there are such things. They rationalize their fear, and call their cowardice science. Fine bunch, they are. Damit, that was a noise. And not the wind either. A chicken maybe. Hell, chickens dont wander around this time of night. What in hell is it?

A scraping sound, like a piece of wood dragging over the ground, is coming near.

"Ha, ha. The ghosts down this way havent got any chains to rattle, so they drag trees along with them. Thats a good one. But no joke, something is outside this house, as sure as hell. Whatever it is, it can get a good look at me and I cant see it. Jesus Christ!"

Kabnis pours water on the flames and blows his lamp out. He picks up a poker and stealthily approaches the outside door. Swings it open, and lurches into the night. A calf, carrying a yoke of wood, bolts away from him and scampers down the road.

"Well, I'm damned. This godam place is sure getting the best of me. Come, Ralph, old man, pull yourself together. Nights cant last forever. Thank God for that. Its Sunday already. First time in my life I've ever wanted Sunday to come. Hell of a day. And down here there's no such thing as ducking church. Well, I'll see Halsey and Layman, and get a good square meal. Thats something. And Halsey's a damn good feller. Cant talk to him, though. Who in Christ's world can I talk to? A hen. God. Myself . . . I'm going bats, no doubt of that. Come now, Ralph, go in and make yourself go to sleep. Come now . . in the door . . thats right. Put the poker down. There. All right. Slip under the sheets. Close your eyes. Think nothing . . a long time . . nothing, nothing. Dont even think nothing. Blank. Not even blank. Count. No, mustnt count. Nothing . . blank . . nothing . . blank . . space without stars in it. No, nothing . . nothing . .

Kabnis sleeps. The winds, like soft-voiced vagrant poets sing:

> White-man's land.
> Niggers, sing.
> Burn, bear black children
> Till poor rivers bring
> Rest, and sweet glory
> In Camp Ground.

8. Liquor.

2

The parlor of Fred Halsey's home. There is a seediness about it. It seems as though the fittings have given a frugal service to at least seven generations of middle-class shop-owners. An open grate burns cheerily in contrast to the gray cold changed autumn weather. An old-fashioned mantelpiece supports a family clock (not running), a figure or two in imitation bronze, and two small group pictures. Directly above it, in a heavy oak frame, the portrait of a bearded man. Black hair, thick and curly, intensifies the pallor of the high forehead. The eyes are daring. The nose, sharp and regular. The poise suggests a tendency to adventure checked by the necessities of absolute command. The portrait is that of an English gentleman who has retained much of his culture, in that money has enabled him to escape being drawn through a land-grubbing pioneer life. His nature and features, modified by marriage and circumstances, have been transmitted to his great-grandson, Fred. To the left of this picture, spaced on the wall, is a smaller portrait of the great-grandmother. That here there is a Negro strain, no one would doubt. But it is difficult to say in precisely what feature it lies. On close inspection, her mouth is seen to be wistfully twisted. The expression of her face seems to shift before one's gaze—now ugly, repulsive; now sad, and somehow beautiful in its pain. A tin wood-box rests on the floor below. To the right of the great-grandfather's portrait hangs a family group: the father, mother, two brothers, and one sister of Fred. It includes himself some thirty years ago when his face was an olive white, and his hair luxuriant and dark and wavy. The father is a rich brown. The mother, practically white. Of the children, the girl, quite young, is like Fred; the two brothers, darker. The walls of the room are plastered and painted green. An old upright piano is tucked into the corner near the window. The window looks out on a forlorn, box-like, whitewashed frame church. Negroes are gathering, on foot, driving questionable gray and brown mules, and in an occasional Ford, for afternoon service. Beyond, Georgia hills roll off into the distance, their dreary aspect heightened by the gray spots of unpainted one- and two-room shanties. Clumps of pine trees here and there are the dark points the whole landscape is approaching. The church bell tolls. Above its squat tower, a great spiral of buzzards reaches far into the heavens. An ironic comment upon the path that leads into the Christian land ... Three rocking chairs are grouped around the grate. Sunday papers scattered on the floor indicate a recent usage. Halsey, a well-built, stocky fellow, hair cropped close, enters the room. His Sunday clothes smell of wood and glue, for it is his habit to potter around his wagon-shop even on the Lord's day. He is followed by Professor Layman, tall, heavy, loose-jointed Georgia Negro, by turns teacher and preacher, who has traveled in almost every nook and corner of the state and hence knows more than would be good for anyone other than a silent man. Kabnis, trying to force through a gathering heaviness, trails in behind them. They slip into chairs before the fire.

Layman: Sholy[9] fine, Mr. Halsey, sholy fine. This town's right good at

9. Surely.

feedin folks, better'n most towns in th state, even for preachers, but I ken[1] say this beats um all. Yassur. Now aint that right, Professor[2] Kabnis?

Kabnis: Yes sir, this beats them all, all right—best I've had, and thats a fact, though my comparison doesnt carry far, y'know.

Layman: Hows that, Professor?

Kabnis: Well, this is my first time out—

Layman: For a fact. Aint seed you round so much. Whats th trouble? Dont like our folks down this away?

Halsey: Aint that, Layman. He aint like most northern niggers that way. Aint a thing stuck-up about him. He likes us, you an me, maybe all—its that red mud[3] over yonder—gets stuck in it an cant get out. (Laughs.) An then he loves th fire so, warm as its been. Coldest Yankee I've ever seen. But I'm goin t get him out now in a jiffy, eh, Kabnis?

Kabnis: Sure, I should say so, sure. Dont think its because I dont like folks down this way. Just the opposite, in fact. Theres more hospitality and everything. Its diff—that is, there's lots of northern exaggeration about the South. Its not half the terror they picture it. Things are not half bad, as one could easily figure out for himself without ever crossing the Mason and Dixie[4] line: all these people wouldnt stay down here, especially the rich, the ones that could easily leave, if conditions were so mighty bad. And then too, sometime back, my family were southerners y'know. From Georgia, in fact—

Layman: Nothin t feel proud about, Professor. Neither your folks nor mine.

Halsey (in a mock religious tone): Amen t that, brother Layman. Amen (turning to Kabnis, half playful, yet somehow dead in earnest). An Mr. Kabnis, kindly remember youre in th land of cotton—hell of a land. Th white folks get th boll; th niggers get th stalk. An dont you dare touch th boll, or even look at it. They'll swing y sho. (Laughs.)

Kabnis: But they wouldnt touch a gentleman—fellows, men like us three here—

Layman: Nigger's a nigger down this away, Professor. An only two dividins: good an bad. An even they aint permanent categories. They sometimes mixes um up when it comes t lynchin. I've seen um do it.

Halsey: Dont let th fear int y, though, Kabnis. This county's a good un. Aint been a stringin up I can remember. (Laughs.)

Layman: This is a good town an a good county. But theres some that makes up fer it.

Kabnis: Things are better now though since that stir about those peonage cases,[5] arent they?

Layman: Ever hear tell of a single shot killin moren one rabbit, Professor?

Kabnis: No, of course not, that is, but then—

Halsey: Now I know you werent born yesterday, sprung up so rapid like you aint heard of th brick thrown in th hornets' nest. (Laughs.)

Kabnis: Hardly, hardly, I know—

---

1. Can.
2. A term of respect by southern blacks for any male teacher on any grade level; sometimes also used to refer to preachers, pianists, and other educated or talented individuals.

3. In parts of Georgia the earth is typically red.
4. The imaginary Mason-Dixon line divides the North from the South.
5. Prisoners, especially black prisoners, who were leased to work, without pay, for white landowners.

Halsey: Course y do. (To Layman) See, northern niggers aint as dumb as they make out t be.

Kabnis (overlooking the remark): Just stirs them up to sting.

Halsey: T perfection. An put just like a professor should put it.

Kabnis: Thats what actually did happen?

Layman: Well, if it aint sos only because th stingers already movin jes as fast as they ken go. An been goin ever since I ken remember, an then some mo.[6] Though I dont usually make mention of it.

Halsey: Damn sight better not. Say, Layman, you come from where theyre always swarmin, dont y?

Layman: Yassur. I do that, sho. Dont want t mention it, but its a fact. I've seed th time when there werent no use t even stretch out flat upon th ground. Seen um shoot an cut a man t pieces who had died th night befo. Yassur. An they didnt stop when they found out he was dead—jes went on ahackin at him anyway.

Kabnis: What did you do? What did you say to them, Professor?

Layman: Thems th things you neither does a thing or talks about if y want t stay around this away, Professor.

Halsey: Listen t what he's tellin y, Kabnis. May come in handy some day.

Kabnis: Cant something be done? But of course not. This preacher-ridden race. Pray and shout. Theyre in the preacher's hands. Thats what it is. And the preacher's hands are in the white man's pockets.

Halsey: Present company always excepted.

Kabnis: The Professor knows I wasnt referring to him.

Layman: Preacher's a preacher anywheres you turn. No use exceptin.

Kabnis: Well, of course, if you look at it that way. I didnt mean— But cant something be done?

Layman: Sho. Yassur. An done first rate an well. Jes like Sam Raymon done it.

Kabnis: Hows that? What did he do?

Layman: Th white folks (reckon I oughtnt tell it) had jes knocked two others like you kill a cow—brained um with an ax, when they caught Sam Raymon by a stream. They was about t do fer him when he up an says, "White folks, I gotter die, I knows that. But wont y let me die in my own way?" Some was fer gettin after him, but th boss held um back an says, "Jes so longs th nigger dies—" An Sam fell down out his knees an prayed, "O Lord, Ise comin to y," and he up an jumps int th stream.

Singing from the church becomes audible. Above it, rising and falling in a plaintive moan, a woman's voice swells to shouting. Kabnis hears it. His face gives way to an expression of mingled fear, contempt, and pity. Layman takes no notice of it. Halsey grins at Kabnis. He feels like having a little sport with him.

Halsey: Lets go t church, eh, Kabnis?

Kabnis (seeking control): All right—no sir, not by a damn sight. Once a days enough for me. Christ, but that stuff gets to me. Meaning no reflection on you, Professor.

Halsey: Course not. Say, Kabnis, noticed y this morning. What'd y get up for an go out?

6. More.

Kabnis: Couldnt stand the shouting, and thats a fact. We dont have that sort of thing up North. We do, but, that is, some one should see to it that they are stopped or put out when they get so bad the preacher has to stop his sermon for them.

Halsey: Is that th way youall sit on sisters up North?

Kabnis: In the church I used to go to no one ever shouted—

Halsey: Lungs weak?

Kabnis: Hardly, that is—

Halsey: Yankees are right up t th minute in tellin folk how t turn a trick. They always were good at talkin.

Kabnis: Well, anyway, they should be stopped.

Layman: Thats right. Thats true. An its th worst ones in the community that comes int th church t shout. I've sort a made a study of it. You take a man what drinks, th biggest licker-head around will come int th church an yell th loudest. An th sister whats done wrong, an is always doin wrong, will sit down in th Amen corner[7] an swing her arms an shout her head off. Seems as if they cant control themselves out in th world; they cant control themselves in church. Now dont that sound logical, Professor?

Halsey: Reckon its as good as any. But I heard that queer cuss over yonder—y know him, dont y, Kabnis? Well, y ought t. He had a run-in with your boss th other day—same as you'll have if you don't walk th chalk-line. An th quicker th better. I hate that Hanby. Ornery bastard. I'll mash his mouth in one of these days. Well, as I was sayin, that feller, Lewis's name, I heard him sayin somethin about a stream whats dammed has got t cut loose somewheres. An that sounds good. I know th feelin myself. He strikes me as knowin a bucketful bout most things, that feller does. Seems like he doesnt want t talk, an does, sometimes, like Layman here. Damn queer feller, him.

Layman: Cant make heads or tails of him, an I've seen lots o queer possums in my day. Everybody's wonderin about him. White folks too. He'll have t leave here soon, thats sho. Always askin questions. An I aint seed his lips move once. Pokin round an notin somethin. Noted what I said th other day, an that werent fer notin down.

Kabnis: What was that?

Layman: Oh, a lynchin that took place bout a year ago. Th worst I know of round these parts.

Halsey: Bill Burnam?

Layman: Na. Mame Lamkins.

Halsey grunts, but says nothing.

The preacher's voice rolls from the church in an insistent chanting monotone. At regular intervals it rises to a crescendo note. The sister begins to shout. Her voice, high-pitched and hysterical, is almost perfectly attuned to the nervous key of Kabnis. Halsey notices his distress, and is amused by it. Layman's face is expressionless. Kabnis wants to hear the story of Mame Lamkins. He does not want to hear it. It can be no worse than the shouting.

Kabnis (his chair rocking faster): What about Mame Lamkins?

Halsey: Tell him, Layman.

---

7. A front area of the church, generally occupied by older female members of the congregation; so-called because of their practice of shouting *amen* as approval and exhortation of the preacher.

The preacher momentarily stops. The choir, together with the entire congregation, sings an old spiritual. The music seems to quiet the shouter. Her heavy breathing has the sound of evening winds that blow through pinecones. Layman's voice is uniformly low and soothing. A canebrake, murmuring the tale to its neighbor-road would be more passionate.

Layman: White folks know that niggers talk, an they dont mind jes so long as nothing comes of it, so here goes. She was in th family-way, Mame Lamkins was. They killed her in th street, an some white man seein th risin in her stomach as she lay there soppy in her blood like any cow, took an ripped her belly open, an th kid fell out. It was living; but a nigger baby aint supposed t live. So he jabbed his knife in it an stuck it t a tree. An then they all went away. [8]

Kabnis: Christ no! What had she done?

Layman: Tried t hide her husband when they was after him.

A shriek pierces the room. The bronze pieces on the mantel hum. The sister cries frantically: "Jesus, Jesus, I've found Jesus. O Lord, glory t God, one mo sinner is acomin home." At the height of this, a stone, wrapped round with paper, crashes through the window. Kabnis springs to his feet, terror-stricken. Layman is worried. Halsey picks up the stone. Takes off the wrapper, smooths it out, and reads: "You northern nigger, its time fer y t leave. Git along now." Kabnis knows that the command is meant for him. Fear squeezes him. Caves him in. As a violent external pressure would. Fear flows inside him. It fills him up. He bloats. He saves himself from bursting by dashing wildly from the room. Halsey and Layman stare stupidly at each other. The stone, the crumpled paper are things, huge things that weight them. Their thoughts are vaguely concerned with the texture of the stone, with the color of the paper. Then they remember the words, and begin to shift them about in sentences. Layman even construes them grammatically. Suddenly the sense of them comes back to Halsey. He grips Layman by the arm and they both follow after Kabnis.

A false dusk has come early. The countryside is ashen, chill. Cabins and roads and canebrakes whisper. The church choir, dipping into a long silence, sings:

> My Lord, what a mourning,
> My Lord, what a mourning,
> My Lord, what a mourning,
> When the stars begin to fall.

Softly luminous over the hills and valleys, the faint spray of a scattered star . . .

3

A splotchy figure drives forward along the cane- and corn-stalk hemmed-in road. A scarecrow replica of Kabnis, awkwardly animate. Fantastically plastered with red Georgia mud. It skirts the big house whose windows shine like mellow lanterns in the dusk. Its shoulder jogs against a sweet-

8. This is an account of an actual lynching, described by Walter White of the National Association for the Advancement of Colored People and by others.

gum tree. The figure caroms off against the cabin door, and lunges in. It slams the door as if to prevent some one entering after it.

"God Almighty, theyre here. After me. On me. All along the road I saw their eyes flaring from the cane. Hounds. Shouts. What in God's name did I run here for? A mud-hole trap. I stumbled on a rope. O God, a rope. Their clammy hands were like the love of death playing up and down my spine. Trying to trip my legs. To trip my spine. Up and down my spine. My spine . . . My legs . . . Why in hell didnt they catch me?"

Kabnis wheels around, half defiant, half numbed with a more immediate fear.

"Wanted to trap me here. Get out o there. I see you."

He grabs a broom from beside the chimney and violently pokes it under the bed. The broom strikes a tin wash-tub. The noise bewilders. He recovers.

"Not there. In the closet."

He throws the broom aside and grips the poker. Starts towards the closet door, towards somewhere in the perfect blackness behind the chimney.

"I'll brain you."

He stops short. The barks of hounds, evidently in pursuit, reach him. A voice, liquid in distance, yells, "Hi! Hi!"

"O God, theyre after me. Holy Father, Mother of Christ—hell, this aint no time for prayer—"

Voices, just outside the door:

"Reckon he's here."

"Dont see no light though."

The door is flung open.

Kabnis: Get back or I'll kill you.

He braces himself, brandishing the poker.

Halsey (coming in): Aint as bad as all that. Put that thing down.

Layman: Its only us, Professor. Nobody else after y.

Kabnis: Halsey. Layman. Close that door. Dont light that light. For godsake get away from there.

Halsey: Nobody's after y, Kabnis, I'm tellin y. Put that thing down an get yourself together.

Kabnis: I tell you they are. I saw them. I heard the hounds.

Halsey: These aint th days of hounds an Uncle Tom's Cabin,[9] feller. White folks aint in fer all them theatrics these days. Theys more direct than that. If what they wanted was t get y, theyd have just marched right in an took y where y sat. Somebodys down by th branch chasin rabbits an atreein possums.

A shot is heard.

Halsey: Got him, I reckon. Saw Tom goin out with his gun. Tom's pretty lucky most times.

He goes to the bureau and lights the lamp. The circular fringe is patterned on the ceiling. The moving shadows of the men are huge against the bare wall boards. Halsey walks up to Kabnis, takes the poker from his grip, and without more ado pushes him into a chair before the dark hearth.

---

9. One of the most dramatic incidents in Harriet Beecher Stowe's novel *Uncle Tom's Cabin* (1852) occurs when bloodhounds pursue a fleeing slave mother and her infant child who are trying to cross the frozen Ohio River to find freedom.

Halsey: Youre a mess. Here, Layman. Get some trash an start a fire.

Layman fumbles around, finds some newspapers and old bags, puts them in the hearth, arranges the wood, and kindles the fire. Halsey sets a black iron kettle where it soon will be boiling. Then takes from his hip-pocket a bottle of corn licker which he passes to Kabnis.

Halsey: Here. This'll straighten y out a bit.

Kabnis nervously draws the cork and gulps the licker down.

Kabnis: Ha. Good stuff. Thanks. Thank y, Halsey.

Halsey: Good stuff! Youre damn right. Hanby there dont think so. Wonder he doesnt come over t find out whos burnin his oil. Miserly bastard, him. Th boys what made this stuff—are y listenin t me, Kabnis? th boys what made this stuff have got th art down like I heard you say youd like t be with words. Eh? Have some, Layman?

Layman: Dont think I care for none, thank y jes th same, Mr. Halsey.

Halsey: Care hell. Course y care. Everybody cares around these parts. Preachers an school teachers an everybody. Here. Here, take it. Dont try that line on me.

Layman limbers up a little, but he cannot quite forget that he is on school ground.

Layman: Thats right. Thats true, sho. Shinin[1] is th only business what pays in these hard times.

He takes a nip, and passes the bottle to Kabnis. Kabnis is in the middle of a long swig when a rap sounds on the door. He almost spills the bottle, but manages to pass it to Halsey just as the door swings open and Hanby enters. He is a well-dressed, smooth, rich, black-skinned Negro who thinks there is no one quite so suave and polished as himself. To members of his own race, he affects the manners of a wealthy white planter. Or, when he is up North, he lets it be known that his ideas are those of the best New England tradition. To white men he bows, without ever completely humbling himself. Tradesmen in the town tolerate him because he spends his money with them. He delivers his words with a full consciousness of his moral superiority.

Hanby: Hum. Erer, Professor Kabnis, to come straight to the point: the progress of the Negro race is jeopardized whenever the personal habits and examples set by its guides and mentors fall below the acknowledged and hard-won standard of its average member. This institution, of which I am the humble president,[2] was founded, and has been maintained at a cost of great labor and untold sacrifice. Its purpose is to teach our youth to live better, cleaner, more noble lives. To prove to the world that the Negro race can be just like any other race. It hopes to attain this aim partly by the salutary examples set by its instructors. I cannot hinder the progress of a race simply to indulge a single member. I have thought the matter out beforehand, I can assure you. Therefore, if I find your resignation on my desk by tomorrow morning, Mr. Kabnis, I shall not feel obliged to call in the sheriff. Otherwise . . ."

Kabnis: A fellow can take a drink in his own room if he wants to, in the privacy of his own room.

---

1. Moonshining; the practice of making and selling liquor illegally (without paying tax to the government).
2. Principal.

Hanby: His room, but not the institution's room, Mr. Kabnis.

Kabnis: This is my room while I'm in it.

Hanby: Mr. Clayborn (the sheriff) can inform you as to that.

Kabnis: Oh, well, what do I care—glad to get out of this mudhole.

Hanby: I should think so from your looks.

Kabnis: You neednt get sarcastic about it.

Hanby: No, that is true. And I neednt wait for your resignation either, Mr. Kabnis.

Kabnis: Oh, you'll get that all right. Dont worry.

Hanby: And I should like to have the room thoroughly aired and cleaned and ready for your successor by tomorrow noon, Professor.

Kabnis (trying to rise): You can have your godam room right away. I dont want it.

Hanby: But I wont have your cursing.

Halsey pushes Kabnis back into his chair.

Halsey: Sit down, Kabnis, till I wash y.

Hanby (to Halsey): I would rather not have drinking men on the premises, Mr. Halsey. You will oblige me—

Halsey: I'll oblige you by stayin right on this spot, this spot, get me? till I get damned ready t leave.

He approaches Hanby. Hanby retreats, but manages to hold his dignity.

Halsey: Let me get you told right now, Mr. Samuel Hanby. Now listen t me. I aint no slick an span[3] slave youve hired, an dont y think it for a minute. Youve bullied enough about this town. An besides, wheres that bill youve been owin me? Listen t me. If I dont get it paid in by tmorrer noon, Mr. Hanby (he mockingly assumes Hanby's tone and manner), I shall feel obliged t call th sheriff. An that sheriff'll be myself who'll catch y in th road an pull y out your buggy an rightly attend t y. You heard me. Now leave him alone. I'm takin him home with me. I got it fixed. Before you came in. He's goin t work with me. Shapin shafts and buildin wagons'll make a man of him what nobody, y get me? what nobody can take advantage of. Thats all . . .

Halsey burrs off into vague and incoherent comment.

Pause. Disagreeable.

Layman's eyes are glazed on the spurting fire.

Kabnis wants to rise and put both Halsey and Hanby in their places. He vaguely knows that he must do this, else the power of direction will completely slip from him to those outside. The conviction is just strong enough to torture him. To bring a feverish, quick-passing flare into his eyes. To mutter words soggy in hot saliva. To jerk his arms upward in futile protest. Halsey, noticing his gestures, thinks it is water that he desires. He brings a glass to him. Kabnis slings it to the floor. Heat of the conviction dies. His arms crumple. His upper lip, his mustache, quiver. Rap! rap, on the door. The sounds slap Kabnis. They bring a hectic color to his cheeks. Like huge cold finger tips they touch his skin and goose-flesh it. Hanby strikes a commanding pose. He moves toward Layman. Layman's face is innocently immobile.

---

3. Possibly "spic and span," i.e., spotlessly clean.

Halsey: Whos there?

Voice: Lewis.

Halsey: Come in, Lewis. Come on in.

Lewis enters. He is the queer fellow who has been referred to. A tall wiry copper-colored man, thirty perhaps. His mouth and eyes suggest purpose guided by an adequate intelligence. He is what a stronger Kabnis might have been, and in an odd faint way resembles him. As he steps towards the others, he seems to be issuing sharply from a vivid dream. Lewis shakes hands with Halsey. Nods perfunctorily to Hanby, who has stiffened to meet him. Smiles rapidly at Layman, and settles with real interest on Kabnis.

Lewis: Kabnis passed me on the road. Had a piece of business of my own, and couldnt get here any sooner. Thought I might be able to help in some way or other.

Halsey: A good baths bout all he needs now. An somethin t put his mind t rest.

Lewis: I think I can give him that. That note was meant for me. Some Negroes have grown uncomfortable at my being here—

Kabnis: You mean, Mr. Lewis, some colored folks threw it? Christ Almighty!

Halsey: Thats what he means. An just as I told y. White folks more direct than that.

Kabnis: What are they after you for?

Lewis: Its a long story, Kabnis. Too long for now. And it might involve present company. (He laughs pleasantly and gestures vaguely in the direction of Hanby.) Tell you about it later on perhaps.

Kabnis: Youre not going?

Lewis: Not till my month's up.

Halsey: Hows that?

Lewis: I'm on a sort of contract with myself. (Is about to leave.) Well, glad its nothing serious—

Halsey: Come round t th shop sometime why dont y, Lewis? I've asked y enough. I'd like t have a talk with y. I aint as dumb as I look. Kabnis an me'll be in most any time. Not much work these days. Wish t hell there was. This burg[4] gets to me when there aint. (In answer to Lewis' question.) He's goin to work with me. Ya. Night air this side th branch[5] aint good fer him. (Looks at Hanby. Laughs.)

Lewis: I see . . .

His eyes turn to Kabnis. In the instant of their shifting, a vision of the life they are to meet. Kabnis, a promise of a soil-soaked beauty; uprooted, thinning out. Suspended a few feet above the soil whose touch would resurrect him.[6] Arm's length removed from him[7] whose will to help . . . There is a swift intuitive interchange of consciousness. Kabnis has a sudden need to rush into the arms of this man. His eyes call, "Brother." And then a savage, cynical twist-about within him mocks his impulse and strengthens him to repulse Lewis. His lips curl cruelly. His eyes laugh. They are glittering nee-

---

4. Town.
5. Of the river.
6. An allusion to the classical myth of a giant who regained full strength every time he came in con-

tact with the earth. To defeat him, Hercules must lift him from the ground.
7. Lewis.

dles, stitching. With a throbbing ache they draw Lewis to. Lewis brusquely wheels on Hanby.

Lewis: I'd like to see you, sir, a moment, if you dont mind.

Hanby's tight collar and vest effectively preserve him.

Hanby: Yes, erer, Mr. Lewis. Right away.

Lewis: See you later, Halsey.

Halsey: So long—thanks—sho hope so, Lewis.

As he opens the door and Hanby passes out, a woman, miles down the valley, begins to sing. Her song is a spark that travels swiftly to the near-by cabins. Like purple tallow flames, songs jet up. They spread a ruddy haze over the heavens. The haze swings low. Now the whole countryside is a soft chorus. Lord. O Lord . . . Lewis closes the door behind him. A flame jets out . . .

The kettle is boiling. Halsey notices it. He pulls the wash-tub from beneath the bed. He arranges for the bath before the fire.

Halsey: Told y them theatrics didnt fit a white man. Th niggers, just like I told y. An after him. Aint surprisin though. He aint bowed t none of them. Nassur. T nairy a one of them nairy an inch nairy a time. An only mixed when he was good an ready—

Kabnis: That song, Halsey, do you hear it?

Halsey: Thats a man. Hear me, Kabnis? A man—

Kabnis: Jesus, do you hear it.

Halsey: Hear it? Hear what? Course I hear it. Listen t what I'm tellin y. A man, get me? They'll get him yet if he dont watch out.

Kabnis is jolted into his fear.

Kabnis: Get him? What do you mean? How? Not lynch him?

Halsey: Na. Take a shotgun an shoot his eyes clear out. Well, anyway, it wasnt fer you, just like I told y. You'll stay over at th house an work with me, eh, boy? Good t get away from his nobs,[8] eh? Damn big stiff though, him. An youre not th first an I can tell y. (Laughs.)

He bustles and fusses about Kabnis as if he were a child. Kabnis submits, wearily. He has no will to resist him.

Layman (his voice is like a deep hollow echo): Thats right. Thats true, sho. Everybody's been expectin that th bust up was comin. Surprised um all y held on as long as y did. Teachin in th South aint th thing fer y. Nassur. You ought t be way back up North where sometimes I wish I was. But I've hung on down this away so long—

Halsey: An there'll never be no leavin time fer y.

4

A month has passed.

Halsey's work-shop. It is an old building just off the main street of Sempter.[9] The walls to within a few feet of the ground are of an age-worn cement mixture. On the outside they are considerably crumbled and peppered with what looks like musket-shot. Inside, the plaster has fallen away in great chunks, leaving the laths, grayed and cobwebbed, exposed. A sort of loft above the shop proper serves as a break-water for the rain and sunshine

8. A man of wealth and prominence, i.e., his high-
ness.

9. The name of the town.

which otherwise would have free entry to the main floor. The shop is filled
with old wheels and parts of wheels, broken shafts, and wooden litter. A
double door, midway the street wall. To the left of this, a workbench that
holds a vise and a variety of wood-work tools. A window with as many panes
broken as whole, throws light on the bench. Opposite, in the rear wall, a
second window looks out upon the back yard. In the left wall, a rickety
smoke-blackened chimney, and hearth with fire blazing. Smooth-worn
chairs grouped about the hearth suggest the village meeting-place. Several
large wooden blocks, chipped and cut and sawed on their upper surfaces
are in the middle of the floor. They are the supports used in almost any sort
of wagon-work. Their idleness means that Halsey has no worth-while job
on foot. To the right of the central door is a junk heap, and directly behind
this, stairs that lead down into the cellar. The cellar is known as "The
Hole." Besides being the home of a very old man, it is used by Halsey on
those occasions when he spices up the life of the small town.

Halsey, wonderfully himself in his work overalls, stands in the doorway
and gazes up the street, expectantly. Then his eyes grow listless. He
slouches against the smooth-rubbed frame. He lights a cigarette. Shifts his
position. Braces an arm against the door. Kabnis passes the window and
stoops to get in under Halsey's arm. He is awkward and ludicrous, like a
schoolboy in his big brother's new overalls. He skirts the large blocks on the
floor, and drops into a chair before the fire. Halsey saunters towards him.

Kabnis: Time f lunch.

Halscy: Ya.

He stands by the hearth, rocking backward and forward. He stretches his
hands out to the fire. He washes them in the warm glow of the flames. They
never get cold, but he warms them.

Kabnis: Saw Lewis up th street. Said he'd be down.

Halsey's eyes brighten. He looks at Kabnis. Turns away. Says nothing.
Kabnis fidgets. Twists his thin blue cloth-covered limbs.[1] Pulls closer to
the fire till the heat stings his shins. Pushes back. Pokes the burned logs.
Puts on several fresh ones. Fidgets. The town bell strikes twelve.

Kabnis: Fix it up f tnight?

Halsey: Leave it t me.

Kabnis: Get Lewis in?

Halsey: Tryin t.

The air is heavy with the smell of pine and resin. Green logs spurt and
sizzle. Sap trickles from an old pine-knot into the flames. Layman enters.
He carries a lunch-pail. Kabnis, for the moment, thinks that he is a day
laborer.

Layman: Evenin, gen'lemun.

Both: Whats say, Layman.

Layman squares a chair to the fire and droops into it. Several town fellows, silent unfathomable men for the most part, saunter in. Overalls.
Thick tan shoes. Felt hats marvelously shaped and twisted. One asks Halsey
for a cigarette. He gets it. The blacksmith, a tremendous black man, comes
in from the forge. Not even a nod from him. He picks up an axle and goes
out. Lewis enters. The town men look curiously at him. Suspicion and an

1. He is wearing overalls.

open liking contest for possession of their faces. They are uncomfortable. One by one they drift into the street.

Layman: Heard y was leavin, Mr. Lewis.

Kabnis: Months up, eh? Hell of a month I've got.

Halsey: Sorry y goin, Lewis. Just gettin acquainted like.

Lewis: Sorry myself, Halsey, in a way—

Layman: Gettin t like our town, Mr. Lewis?

Lewis: I'm afraid its on a different basis, Professor.

Halsey: An I've yet t hear about that basis. Been waitin long enough, God knows. Seems t me like youd take pity on a feller if nothin more.

Kabnis: Somethin that old black cockroach over yonder doesnt like, whatever it is.

Layman: Thats right. Thats right, sho.

Halsey: A feller dropped in here tother day an said he knew what you was about. Said you had queer opinions. Well, I could have told him you was a queer one, myself. But not th way he was driftin. Didnt mean anything by it, but just let drop he thought you was a little wrong up here—crazy, y'know. (Laughs.)

Kabnis: Y mean old Blodson? Hell, he's bats himself.

Lewis: I remember him. We had a talk. But what he found queer, I think, was not my opinions, but my lack of them. In half an hour he had settled everything: boll weevils, God, the World War.[2] Weevils and wars are the pests that God sends against the sinful. People are too weak to correct themselves: the Redeemer is coming back. Get ready, ye sinners, for the advent of Our Lord. Interesting, eh, Kabnis? but not exactly what we want.

Halsey: Y could have come t me. I've sho been after y enough. Most every time I've seen y.

Kabnis (sarcastically): Hows it y never came t us professors?

Lewis: I did—to one.

Kabnis: Y mean t say y got somethin from that celluloid-collar-eraser-cleaned old codger over in th mud hole?

Halsey: Rough on th old boy, aint he? (Laughs.)

Lewis: Something, yes. Layman here could have given me quite a deal, but the incentive to his keeping quiet is so much greater than anything I could have offered him to open up, that I crossed him off my mind. And you—

Kabnis: What about me?

Halsey: Tell him, Lewis, for godsake tell him. I've told him. But its somethin else he wants so bad I've heard him downstairs mumblin with th old man.

Lewis: The old man?

Kabnis: What about me? Come on now, you know so much.

Halsey: Tell him, Lewis. Tell it t him.

Lewis: Life has already told him more than he is capable of knowing. It has given him in excess of what he can receive. I have been offered. Stuff in his stomach curdled, and he vomited me.

Kabnis' face twitches. His body writhes.

---

2. I.e., World War I. "Boll weevils": insects that destroy cotton crops.

Kabnis: You know a lot, you do. How about Halsey?

Lewis: Yes . . . Halsey? Fits here. Belongs here. An artist in your way, arent you, Halsey?

Halsey: Reckon I am, Lewis. Give me th work and fair pay an I aint askin nothin better. Went over-seas an saw France; an I come back. Been up North; an I come back. Went t school; but there aint no books whats got th feel t them of them there tools. Nassur. An I'm atellin y.

A shriveled, bony white man passes the window and enters the shop. He carries a broken hatchet-handle and the severed head. He speaks with a flat, drawn voice to Halsey, who comes forward to meet him.

Mr. Ramsay: Can y fix this fer me, Halsey?

Halsey (looking it over): Reckon so, Mr. Ramsay. Here, Kabnis. A little practice fer y.

Halsey directs Kabnis, showing him how to place the handle in the vise, and cut it down. The knife hangs. Kabnis thinks that it must be dull. He jerks it hard. The tool goes deep and shaves too much off. Mr. Ramsay smiles brokenly at him.

Mr. Ramsay (to Halsey): Still breakin in the new hand, eh, Halsey? Seems like a likely enough faller once he gets th hang of it.

He gives a tight laugh at his own good humor. Kabnis burns red. The back of his neck stings him beneath his collar. He feels stifled. Through Ramsay, the whole white South weighs down upon him. The pressure is terrific. He sweats under the arms. Chill beads run down his body. His brows concentrate upon the handle as though his own life was staked upon the perfect shaving of it. He begins to out and out botch the job. Halsey smiles.

Halsey: He'll make a good un some of these days, Mr. Ramsay.

Mr. Ramsay: Y ought t know. Yer daddy was a good un before y. Runs in th family, seems like t me.

Halsey: Thats right, Mr. Ramsay.

Kabnis is hopeless. Halsey takes the handle from him. With a few deft strokes he shaves it. Fits it. Gives it to Ramsay.

Mr. Ramsay: How much on this?

Halsey: No charge, Mr. Ramsay.

Mr. Ramsay (going out): All right, Halsey. Come down an take it out in trade. Shoe-strings or something.

Halsey: Yassur, Mr. Ramsay.

Halsey rejoins Lewis and Layman. Kabnis, hangdog-fashion, follows him.

Halsey: They like y if y work fer them.

Layman: Thats right, Mr. Halsey. Thats right, sho.

The group is about to resume its talk when Hanby enters. He is all energy, bustle, and business. He goes direct to Kabnis.

Hanby: An axle is out in the buggy which I would like to have shaped into a crow-bar. You will see that it is fixed for me.

Without waiting for an answer, and knowing that Kabnis will follow, he passes out. Kabnis, scowling, silent, trudges after him.

Hanby (from the outside): Have that ready for me by three o'clock, young man. I shall call for it.

Kabnis (under his breath as he comes in): Th hell you say, you old black swamp-gut.

He slings the axle on the floor.

Halsey: Wheeee!

Layman, lunch finished long ago, rises, heavily. He shakes hands with Lewis.

Layman: Might not see y again befo y leave, Mr. Lewis. I enjoys t hear y talk. Y might have been a preacher. Maybe a bishop some day. Sho do hope t see y back this away again sometime, Mr. Lewis.

Lewis: Thanks, Professor. Hope I'll see you.

Layman waves a long arm loosely to the others, and leaves. Kabnis goes to the door. His eyes, sullen, gaze up the street.

Kabnis: Carrie K.'s comin with th lunch. Bout time.

She passes the window. Her red girl's-cap, catching the sun, flashes vividly. With a stiff, awkward little movement she crosses the doorsill and gives Kabnis one of the two baskets which she is carrying. There is a slight stoop to her shoulders. The curves of her body blend with this to a soft rounded charm. Her gestures are stiffly variant. Black bangs curl over the forehead of her oval-olive face. Her expression is dazed, but on provocation it can melt into a wistful smile. Adolescent. She is easily the sister of Fred Halsey.

Carrie K.: Mother says excuse her, brother Fred an Ralph, fer bein late.

Kabnis: Everythings all right an O.K., Carrie Kate. O.K. an all right.

The two men settle on their lunch. Carrie, with hardly a glance in the direction of the hearth, as is her habit, is about to take the second basket down to the old man, when Lewis rises. In doing so he draws her unwitting attention. Their meeting is a swift sunburst. Lewis impulsively moves towards her. His mind flashes images of her life in the southern town. He sees the nascent woman, her flesh already stiffening to cartilage, drying to bone. Her spirit-bloom, even now touched sullen, bitter. Her rich beauty fading . . . He wants to— He stretches forth his hands to hers. He takes them. They feel like warm cheeks against his palms. The sun-burst from her eyes floods up and haloes him. Christ-eyes, his eyes look to her. Fearlessly she loves into them. And then something happens. Her face blanches. Awkwardly she draws away. The sin-bogies[3] of respectable southern colored folks clamor at her: "Look out! Be a *good* girl. A *good* girl. Look out!" She gropes for her basket that has fallen to the floor. Finds it, and marches with a rigid gravity to her task of feeding the old man. Like the glowing white ash of burned paper, Lewis' eyelids, wavering, settle down. He stirs in the direction of the rear window. From the back yard, mules tethered to odd trees and posts blink dumbly at him. They too seem burdened with an impotent pain. Kabnis and Halsey are still busy with their lunch. They havent noticed him. After a while he turns to them.

Lewis: Your sister, Halsey, whats to become of her? What are you going to do for her?

Halsey: Who? What? What am I goin t do? . .

Lewis: What I mean is, what does she do down there?

Halsey: Oh. Feeds th old man. Had lunch, Lewis?

Lewis: Thanks, yes. You have never felt her, have you, Halsey? Well, no,

---

3. Disapproving looks.

I guess not. I dont suppose you can. Nor can she . . . Old man? Halsey, some one lives down there? I've never heard of him. Tell me—

Kabnis takes time from his meal to answer with some emphasis:

Kabnis: Theres lots of things you aint heard of.

Lewis: Dare say. I'd like to see him.

Kabnis: You'll get all th chance you want tnight.

Halsey: Fixin a little somethin up fer tnight, Lewis. Th three of us an some girls. Come round bout ten-thirty.

Lewis: Glad to. But what under the sun does he do down there?

Halsey: Ask Kabnis. He blows off t him every chance he gets.

Kabnis gives a grunting laugh. His mouth twists. Carrie returns from the cellar. Avoiding Lewis, she speaks to her brother.

Carrie K.: Brother Fred, father hasnt eaten now goin on th second week, but mumbles an talks funny, or tries t talk when I put his hands ont th food. He frightens me, an I dunno what t do. An oh, I came near fergettin, brother, but Mr. Marmon—he was eatin lunch when I saw him—told me t tell y that th lumber wagon busted down an he wanted y t fix it fer him. Said he reckoned he could get it t y after he ate.

Halsey chucks a half-eaten sandwich in the fire. Gets up. Arranges his blocks. Goes to the door and looks anxiously up the street. The wind whirls a small spiral in the gray dust road.

Halsey: Why didnt y tell me sooner, little sister?

Carrie K.: I fergot t, an just remembered it now, brother.

Her soft rolled words are fresh pain to Lewis. He wants to take her North with him What for? He wonders what Kabnis could do for her. What she could do for him. Mother him. Carrie gathers the lunch things, silently, and in her pinched manner, curtsies, and departs. Kabnis lights his after-lunch cigarette. Lewis, who has sensed a change, becomes aware that he is not included in it. He starts to ask again about the old man. Decides not to. Rises to go.

Lewis: Think I'll run along, Halsey.

Halsey: Sure. Glad t see y any time.

Kabnis: Dont forget tnight.

Lewis: Dont worry. I wont. So long.

Kabnis: So long. We'll be expectin y.

Lewis passes Halsey at the door. Halsey's cheeks form a vacant smile. His eyes are wide awake, watching for the wagon to turn from Broad Street into his road.

Halsey: So long.

His words reach Lewis halfway to the corner.

5

Night, soft belly of a pregnant Negress, throbs evenly against the torso of the South. Night throbs a womb-song to the South. Cane- and cotton-fields, pine forests, cypress swamps, sawmills, and factories are fecund at her touch. Night's womb-song sets them singing. Night winds are the breathing of the unborn child whose calm throbbing in the belly of a Negress sets them somnolently singing. Hear their song.

White-man's land.
Niggers, sing.
Burn, bear black children
Till poor rivers bring
Rest, and sweet glory
In Camp Ground.

Sempter's streets are vacant and still. White paint on the wealthier houses has the chill blue glitter of distant stars. Negro cabins are a purple blur. Broad Street is deserted. Winds stir beneath the corrugated iron canopies and dangle odd bits of rope tied to horse- and mule-gnawed hitching-posts. One store window has a light in it. Chesterfield cigarette and Chero-Cola cardboard advertisements are stacked in it. From a side door two men come out. Pause, for a last word and then say good night. Soon they melt in shadows thicker than they. Way off down the street four figures sway beneath iron awnings which form a sort of corridor that imperfectly echoes and jumbles what they say. A fifth form joins them. They turn into the road that leads to Halsey's workshop. The old building is phosphorescent above deep shade. The figures pass through the double door. Night winds whisper in the eaves. Sing weirdly in the ceiling cracks. Stir curls of shavings on the floor. Halsey lights a candle. A good-sized lumber wagon, wheels off, rests upon the blocks. Kabnis makes a face at it. An unearthly hush is upon the place. No one seems to want to talk. To move, lest the scraping of their feet . .

Halsey: Come on down this way, folks.

He leads the way. Stella follows. And close after her, Cora, Lewis, and Kabnis. They descend into the Hole. It seems huge, limitless in the candle light. The walls are of stone, wonderfully fitted. They have no openings save a small iron-barred window toward the top of each. They are dry and warm. The ground slopes away to the rear of the building and thus leaves the south wall exposed to the sun. The blacksmith's shop is plumb against the right wall. The floor is clay. Shavings have at odd times been matted into it. In the right-hand corner, under the stairs, two good-sized pine mattresses, resting on cardboard, are on either side of a wooden table. On this are several half-burned candles and an oil lamp. Behind the table, an irregular piece of mirror hangs on the wall. A loose something that looks to be a gaudy ball costume dangles from a near-by hook. To the front, a second table holds a lamp and several whiskey glasses. Six rickety chairs are near this table. Two old wagon wheels rest on the floor. To the left, sitting in a high-backed chair which stands upon a low platform, the old man. He is like a bust in black walnut. Gray-bearded. Gray-haired. Prophetic. Immobile. Lewis' eyes are sunk in him. The others, unconcerned, are about to pass on to the front table when Lewis grips Halsey and so turns him that the candle flame shines obliquely on the old man's features.

Lewis: And he rules over—

Kabnis: Th smoke an fire of th forge.

Lewis: Black Vulcan?[4] I wouldnt say so. That forehead. Great woolly

---

4. In Roman mythology, the blacksmith god; also the god of the hearth.

beard. Those eyes. A mute John the Baptist of a new religion—or a tongue-tied shadow of an old.

Kabnis: His tongue is tied all right, an I can vouch f that.

Lewis: Has he never talked to you?

Halsey: Kabnis wont give him a chance.

He laughs. The girls laugh. Kabnis winces.

Lewis: What do you call him?

Halsey: Father.[5]

Lewis: Good. Father what?

Kabnis: Father of hell.

Halsey: Father's th only name we have fer him. Come on. Lets sit down an get t th pleasure of the evenin.

Lewis: Father John[6] it is from now on . . .

Slave boy whom some Christian mistress taught to read the Bible. Black man who saw Jesus in the ricefields, and began preaching to his people. Moses- and Christ-words used for songs. Dead blind father of a muted folk who feel their way upward to a life that crushes or absorbs them. (Speak, Father!) Suppose your eyes could see, old man. (The years hold hands. O Sing!) Suppose your lips . . .

Halsey, does he never talk?

Halsey: Na. But sometimes. Only seldom. Mumbles. Sis says he talks—

Kabnis: I've heard him talk.

Halsey: First I've ever heard of it. You dont give him a chance. Sis says she's made out several words, mostly one—an like as not cause it was "sin."

Cora laughs in a loose sort of way. She is a tall, thin, mulatto woman. Her eyes are deep-set behind a pointed nose. Her hair is coarse and bushy. Seeing that Stella also is restless, she takes her arm and the two women move towards the table. They slip into chairs. Halsey follows and lights the lamp. He lays out a pack of cards. Stella sorts them as if telling fortunes. She is a beautifully proportioned, large-eyed, brown-skin girl. Except for the twisted line of her mouth when she smiles or laughs, there is about her no suggestion of the life she's been through. Kabnis, with great mock-solemnity, goes to the corner, takes down the robe, and dons it. He is a curious spectacle, acting a part, yet very real. He joins the others at the table. They are used to him. Lewis is surprised. He laughs. Kabnis shrinks and then glares at him with a furtive hatred. Halsey, bringing out a bottle of corn licker, pours drinks.

Halsey: Come on, Lewis. Come on, you fellers. Heres lookin at y.

Then, as if suddenly recalling something, he jerks away from the table and starts towards the steps.

Kabnis: Where y goin, Halsey?

Halsey: Where? Where y think? That oak beam in th wagon—

Kabnis: Come ere. Come ere. Sit down. What in hell's wrong with you fellers? You with your wagon. Lewis with his Father John. This aint th time fer foolin with wagons. Daytime's bad enough f that. Ere, sit down. Ere,

---

5. Not his biological father.
6. Probably an allusion to John the Baptist, with particular reference to John's ability to foretell the coming of the Savior.

Lewis, you too sit down. Have a drink. Thats right. Drink corn licker, love
th girls, an listen t th old man mumblin sin.

There seems to be no good-time spirit to the party. Something in the air
is too tense and deep for that. Lewis, seated now so that his eyes rest upon
the old man, merges with his source and lets the pain and beauty of the
South meet him there. White faces, pain-pollen, settle downward through
a cane-sweet mist and touch the ovaries of yellow flowers. Cotton-bolls
bloom, droop. Black roots twist in a parched red soil beneath a blazing sky.
Magnolias, fragrant, a trifle futile, lovely, far off . . . His eyelids close. A
force begins to heave and rise . . . Stella is serious, reminiscent.

Stella: Usall is brought up t hate sin worse than death—

Kabnis: An then before you have y eyes half open, youre made t love it if
y want t live.

Stella: Us never—

Kabnis: Oh, I know your story: that old prim bastard over yonder,[7] an
then old Calvert's office—

Stella: It wasnt them—

Kabnis: I know. They put y out of church, an then I guess th preacher
came around an asked f some. But thats your body. Now me—

Halsey (passing him the bottle): All right, kid, we believe y. Here, take
another. Wheres Clover, Stel?

Stella: You know how Jim is when he's just out th swamp. Done up in
shine[8] an wouldnt let her come. Said he'd bust her head open if she went
out.

Kabnis: Dont see why he doesnt stay over with Laura, where he belongs.

Stella: Ask him, an I reckon he'll tell y. More than you want.

Halsey: Th nigger hates th sight of a black woman worse than death.
Sorry t mix y up this way, Lewis. But y see how tis.

Lewis' skin is tight and glowing over the fine bones of his face. His lips
tremble. His nostrils quiver. The others notice this and smile knowingly at
each other. Drinks and smokes are passed around. They pay no never-
minds to him. A real party is being worked up. Then Lewis opens his eyes
and looks at them. Their smiles disperse in hot-cold tremors. Kabnis
chokes his laugh. It sputters, gurgles. His eyes flicker and turn away. He
tries to pass the thing off by taking a long drink which he makes considerable fuss over. He is drawn back to Lewis. Seeing Lewis' gaze still upon him,
he scowls.

Kabnis: Whatsha lookin at me for? Y want t know who I am? Well, I'm
Ralph Kabnis—lot of good its goin t do y. Well? Whatsha keep lookin for?
I'm Ralph Kabnis. Aint that enough f y? Want th whole family history? Its
none of your godam business, anyway. Keep off me. Do y hear? Keep off
me. Look at Cora. Aint she pretty enough t look at? Look at Halsey, or
Stella. Clover ought t be here an you could look at her. An love her. Thats
what you need. I know—

Lewis: Ralph Kabnis gets satisfied that way?

Kabnis: Satisfied? Say, quit your kiddin. Here, look at that old man
there. See him? He's satisfied. Do I look like him? When I'm dead I dont

7. Probably Hanby.   8. Intoxicated, drunk.

expect t be satisfied. Is that enough f y, with your godam nosin, or do you want more? Well, y wont get it, understand?

Lewis: The old man as symbol, flesh, and spirit of the past, what do you think he would say if he could see you? You look at him, Kabnis.

Kabnis: Just like any done-up preacher is what he looks t me. Jam some false teeth in his mouth and crank him, an youd have God Almighty spit in torrents all around th floor. Oh, hell, an he reminds me of that black cockroach over yonder. An besides, he aint my past. My ancestors were Southern blue-bloods—

Lewis: And black.

Kabnis: Aint much difference between blue an black.

Lewis: Enough to draw a denial from you. Cant hold them, can you? Master; slave. Soil; and the overarching heavens. Dusk; dawn. They fight and bastardize you. The sun tint of your cheeks, flame of the great season's multicolored leaves, tarnished, burned. Split, shredded: easily burned. No use . . .

His gaze shifts to Stella. Stella's face draws back, her breasts come towards him.

Stella: I aint got nothin f y, mister. Taint no use t look at me.

Halsey: Youre a queer feller, Lewis, I swear y are. Told y so, didnt I, girls? Just take him easy though, an he'll be ridin just th same as any Georgia mule, eh, Lewis? (Laughs.)

Stella: I'm goin t tell y somethin, mister. It aint t you, t th Mister Lewis what noses about. Its t somethin diffcrent, I dunno what. That old man there— maybe its him—is like m father used t look. He used t sing. An when he could sing no mo, they'd allus come f him an carry him t church an there he'd sit, befo th pulpit, aswayin an aleadin every song. A white man took m mother an it broke th old man's heart. He died; an then I didnt care what become of me, an I dont now. I dont care now. Dont get it in y head I'm some sentimental Susie askin for yo sop.[9] Nassur. But theres somethin t yo th others aint got. Boars an kids an fools—thats all I've known. Boars when their fever's up. When their fever's up they come t me. Halsey asks me over when he's off th job. Kabnis—it ud be a sin t play with him. He takes it out in talk.

Halsey knows that he has trifled with her. At odd things he has been inwardly penitent before her tasking him. But now he wants to hurt her. He turns to Lewis.

Halsey: Lewis, I got a little licker in me, an thats true. True's what I said. True. But th stuff just seems t wake me up an make my mind a man of me. Listen. You know a lot, queer as hell as y are, an I want t ask y some questions. Theyre too high fer them, Stella an Cora an Kabnis, so we'll just excuse em. A chat between ourselves. (Turns to the others.) You-all cant listen in on this. Twont interest y. So just leave th table t this gen'lemun an myself. Go long now.

Kabnis gets up, pompous in his robe, grotesquely so, and makes as if to go through a grand march with Stella. She shoves him off, roughly, and in a mood swings her body to the steps. Kabnis grabs Cora and parades

9. Food produced by sopping bread in gravy; here, charity or pity.

around, passing the old man, to whom he bows in mock-curtsy. He sweeps by the table, snatches the licker bottle, and then he and Cora sprawl on the mattresses. She meets his weak approaches after the manner she thinks Stella would use.

Halsey contemptuously watches them until he is sure that they are settled.

Halsey: This aint th sort o thing f me, Lewis, when I got work upstairs. Nassur. You an me has got things t do. Wastin time on common low-down women—say, Lewis, look at her now—Stella—aint she a picture? Common wench—na she aint, Lewis. You know she aint. I'm only tryin t fool y. I used t love that girl. Yassur. An sometimes when th moon is thick an I hear dogs up th valley barkin an some old woman fetches out her song, an th winds seem like th Lord made them fer t fetch an carry th smell o pine an cane, an there aint no big job on foot, I sometimes get t thinkin that I still do. But I want t talk t y, Lewis, queer as y are. Y know, Lewis, I went t school once. Ya. In Augusta. But it wasnt a regular school. Na. It was a pussy Sunday-school masqueradin under a regular name. Some goody-goody teachers from th North had come down t teach th niggers. If you was nearly white, they liked y. If you was black, they didnt. But it wasnt that—I was all right, y see. I couldnt stand em messin an pawin over m business like I was a child. So I cussed em out an left. Kabnis there ought t have cussed out th old duck over yonder an left. He'd a been a better man tday. But as I was sayin, I couldnt stand their ways. So I left an came here an worked with my father. An been here ever since. He died. I set in f myself. An its always been; give me a good job an sure pay an I aint far from being satisfied, so far as satisfaction goes. Prejudice is everywheres about this country. An a nigger aint in much standin anywheres. But when it comes t pottin round an doin nothin, with nothin bigger'n an ax-handle t hold a feller down, like it was a while back befo I got this job—that beam ought t be—but tmorrow mornin early's time enough f that. As I was sayin, I gets t thinkin. Play dumb naturally t white folks. I gets t thinkin. I used to subscribe t th *Literary Digest*[1] an that helped along a bit. But there werent nothing I could sink m teeth int. Theres lots I want t ask y, Lewis. Been askin y t come around. Couldnt get y. Cant get in much tnight. (He glances at the others. His mind fastens on Kabnis.) Say, tell me this, whats on your mind t say on that feller there? Kabnis' name. One queer bird ought t know another, seems like t me.

Licker has released conflicts in Kabnis and set them flowing. He pricks his ears, intuitively feels that the talk is about him, leaves Cora, and approaches the table. His eyes are watery, heavy with passion. He stoops. He is a ridiculous pathetic figure in his showy robe.

Kabnis: Talkin bout me. I know. I'm th topic of conversation everywhere theres talk about this town. Girls an fellers. White folks as well. An if its me youre talkin bout, guess I got a right t listen in. Whats sayin? Whats sayin bout his royal guts, the Duke? Whats sayin, eh?

Halsey (to Lewis): We'll take it up another time.

Kabnis: No nother time bout it. Now. I'm here now an talkin's just begun. I was born an bred in a family of orators, thats what I was.

1. A literary magazine published from 1890 to 1938.

Halsey: Preachers.

Kabnis: Na. Preachers hell. I didnt say wind-busters. Y misapprehended me. Y understand what that means, dont y? All right then, y misapprehended me. I didnt say preachers. I said orators. O R A T O R S. Born one an I'll die one. You understand me, Lewis. (He turns to Halsey and begins shaking his finger in his face.) An as f you, youre all right f choppin things from blocks of wood. I was good at that th day I ducked th cradle. An since then, I've been shapin words after a design that branded here. Know whats here? M soul. Ever heard o that? Th hell y have. Been shapin words t fit m soul. Never told y that before, did I? Thought I couldnt talk. I'll tell y. I've been shapin words; ah, but sometimes theyre beautiful an golden an have a taste that makes them fine t roll over with y tongue. Your tongue aint fit f nothin but t roll an lick hog-meat.

Stella and Cora come up to the table.

Halsey: Give him a shove there, will y, Stel?

Stella jams Kabnis in a chair. Kabnis springs up.

Kabnis: Cant keep a good man down. Those words I was tellin y about, they wont fit int th mold thats branded on m soul. Rhyme, y see? Poet, too. Bad rhyme. Bad poet. Somethin else youve learned tnight. Lewis dont know it all, an I'm atellin y. Ugh. Th form thats burned int my soul is some twisted awful thing that crept in from a dream, a godam nightmare, an wont stay still unless I feed it. An it lives on words. Not beautiful words. God Almighty no. Misshapen, split-gut, tortured, twisted words. Layman was feedin it back there that day you thought I ran out fearin things. White folks feed it cause their looks are words. Niggers, black niggers feed it cause theyre evil an their looks are words. Yallar niggers[2] feed it. This whole damn bloated purple country feeds it cause its goin down t hell in a holy avalanche of words. I want t feed th soul—I know what that is; th preachers dont—but I've got t feed it. I wish t God some lynchin white man ud stick his knife through it an pin it to a tree.[3] An pin it to a tree. You hear me? Thats a wish f y, you little snot-nosed pups who've been makin fun of me, an fakin that I'm weak. Me, Ralph Kabnis weak. Ha.

Halsey: Thats right, old man. There, there. Here, so much exertion merits a fittin reward. Help him t be seated, Cora.

Halsey gives him a swig of shine. Cora glides up, seats him, and then plumps herself down on his lap, squeezing his head into her breasts. Kabnis mutters. Tries to break loose. Curses. Cora almost stifles him. He goes limp and gives up. Cora toys with him. Ruffles his hair. Braids it. Parts it in the middle. Stella smiles contemptuously. And then a sudden anger sweeps her. She would like to lash Cora from the place. She'd like to take Kabnis to some distant pine grove and nurse and mother him. Her eyes flash. A quick tensioning throws her breasts and neck into a poised strain. She starts towards them. Halsey grabs her arm and pulls her to him. She struggles. Halsey pins her arms and kisses her. She settles, spurting like a pine-knot afire.

Lewis finds himself completely cut out. The glowing within him sub-

---

2. Lighter-skinned African Americans. "Black niggers": dark-skinned African Americans.

3. See the story of the lynching in section 2 of "Kabnis."

sides. It is followed by a dead chill. Kabnis, Carrie, Stella, Halsey, Cora, the old man, the cellar, and the work-shop, the southern town descend upon him. Their pain is too intense. He cannot stand it. He bolts from the table. Leaps up the stairs. Plunges through the work-shop and out into the night.

6

The cellar swims in a pale phosphorescence. The table, the chairs, the figure of the old man are amœba-like shadows which move about and float in it. In the corner under the steps, close to the floor, a solid blackness. A sound comes from it. A forcible yawn. Part of the blackness detaches itself so that it may be seen against the grayness of the wall. It moves forward and then seems to be clothing itself in odd dangling bits of shadow. The voice of Halsey, vibrant and deepened, calls.

Halsey: Kabnis. Cora. Stella.

He gets no response. He wants to get them up, to get on the job. He is intolerant of their sleepiness.

Halsey: Kabnis! Stella! Cora!

Gutturals, jerky and impeded, tell that he is shaking them.

Halsey: Come now, up with you.

Kabnis (sleepily and still more or less intoxicated): Whats th big idea? What in hell—

Halsey: Work. But never you mind about that. Up with you.

Cora: Ooooo! Look here, mister, I aint used t bein thrown int th street befo day.

Stella: Any bunk whats worked is worth in wages moren this. But come on. Taint no use t arger. [4]

Kabnis: I'll arger. Its preposterous—

The girls interrupt him with none too pleasant laughs.

Kabnis: Thats what I said. Know what it means, dont y? All right, then. I said its preposterous t root an artist out o bed at this ungodly hour, when there aint no use t it. You can start your damned old work. Nobody's stoppin y. But what we got t get up for? Fraid somebody'll see th girls leavin? Some sport, you are. I hand it t y.

Halsey: Up you get, all th same.

Kabnis: Oh, th hell you say.

Halsey: Well, son, seeing that I'm th kindhearted father, I'll give y chance t open your eyes. But up y get when I come down.

He mounts the steps to the work-shop and starts a fire in the hearth. In the yard he finds some chunks of coal which he brings in and throws on the fire. He puts a kettle on to boil. The wagon draws him. He lifts an oak-beam, fingers it, and becomes abstracted. Then comes to himself and places the beam upon the work-bench. He looks over some newly cut wooden spokes. He goes to the fire and pokes it. The coals are red-hot. With a pair of long prongs he picks them up and places them in a thick iron bucket. This he carries downstairs. Outside, darkness has given way to the

4. Argue.

impalpable grayness of dawn. This early morning light, seeping through the four barred cellar windows, is the color of the stony walls. It seems to be an emanation from them. Halsey's coals throw out a rich warm glow. He sets them on the floor, a safe distance from the beds.

Halsey: No foolin now. Come. Up with you.

Other than a soft rustling, there is no sound as the girls slip into their clothes. Kabnis still lies in bed.

Stella (to Halsey): Reckon y could spare us a light?

Halsey strikes a match, lights a cigarette, and then bends over and touches flame to the two candles on the table between the beds. Kabnis asks for a cigarette. Halsey hands him his and takes a fresh one for himself. The girls, before the mirror, are doing up their hair. It is bushy hair that has gone through some straightening process. Character, however, has not all been ironed out. As they kneel there, heavy-eyed and dusky, and throwing grotesque moving shadows on the wall, they are two princesses in Africa going through the early-morning ablutions of their pagan prayers. Finished, they come forward to stretch their hands and warm them over the glowing coals. Red dusk of a Georgia sunset, their heavy, coal-lit faces ... Kabnis suddenly recalls something.

Kabnis: Th old man talked last night.

Stella: And so did you.

Halsey: In your dreams.

Kabnis: I tell y, he did. I know what I'm talkin about. I'll tell y what he said. Wait now, lemme see.

Halsey: Look out, brother, th old man'll be getting int you by way o dreams. Come, Stel, ready? Cora? Coffee an eggs f both of you.

Halsey goes upstairs.

Stella: Gettin generous, aint he?

She blows the candles out. Says nothing to Kabnis. Then she and Cora follow after Halsey. Kabnis, left to himself, tries to rise. He has slept in his robe. His robe trips him. Finally, he manages to stand up. He starts across the floor. Half-way to the old man, he falls and lies quite still. Perhaps an hour passes. Light of a new sun is about to filter through the windows. Kabnis slowly rises to support upon his elbows. He looks hard, and internally gathers himself together. The side face of Father John is in the direct line of his eyes. He scowls at him. No one is around. Words gush from Kabnis.

Kabnis: You sit there like a black hound spiked to an ivory pedestal. An all night long I heard you murmurin that devilish word. They thought I didnt hear y, but I did. Mumblin, feedin that ornery thing thats livin on my insides. Father John. Father of Satan, more likely. What does it mean t you? Youre dead already. Death. What does it mean t you? To you who died way back there in th 'sixties. What are y throwin it in my throat for? Whats it goin t get y? A good smashin in th mouth, thats what. My fist'll sink int y black mush face clear t y guts—if y got any. Dont believe y have. Never seen signs of none. Death. Death. Sin an Death. All night long y mumbled death. (He forgets the old man as his mind begins to play with the word and its associations.) Death ... these clammy floors ... just like th place they used t stow away th worn-out, no-count niggers in th days of slavery . . . that was long ago; not so long ago . . . no windows (he rises higher on his elbows to verify this assertion. He looks around, and, seeing no one but the old man, calls.) Halsey! Halsey! Gone an left me. Just like a nigger. I thought he was a nigger all th time. Now I know it. Ditch y when it comes right down t it. Damn him anyway. Godam him. (He looks and re-sees the old man.) Eh, you? T hell with you too. What do I care whether you can see or hear? You know what hell is cause youve been there. Its a feelin an its ragin in my soul in a way that'll pop out of me an run you through, an scorch y, an burn an rip your soul. Your soul. Ha. Nigger soul. A gin soul that gets drunk on a preacher's words. An screams. An shouts. God Almighty, how I hate that shoutin. Where's th beauty in that? Gives a buzzard a windpipe an I'll bet a dollar t a dime th buzzard ud beat y to it. Aint surprisin th white folks hate y so. When you had eyes, did you ever see th beauty of th world? Tell me that. Th hell y did. Now dont tell me. I know y didnt. You couldnt have. Oh, I'm drunk an just as good as dead, but no eyes that have seen beauty ever lose their sight. You aint got no sight. If you had, drunk as I am, I hope Christ will kill me if I couldnt see it. Your eyes are dull and watery, like fish eyes. Fish eyes are dead eyes. Youre an old man, a dead fish man, an black at that. Theyve put y here t die, damn fool y are not t know it. Do y know how many feet youre under ground? I'll tell y. Twenty. An do y think you'll ever see th light of day again, even if you wasnt blind? Do y think youre out of slavery? Huh? Youre where they used t throw th worked-out, no-count slaves. On a damp clammy floor of a dark scum-hole. An they called that an infirmary. Th sons-a. . . . Why I can already see you toppled off that stool an stretched out on th floor beside me—not beside me, damn you, by yourself, with th flies buzzin an lickin God knows what they'd find on a dirty, black, foul-breathed mouth like yours . . .

Some one is coming down the stairs. Carrie, bringing food for the old man. She is lovely in her fresh energy of the morning, in the calm untested confidence and nascent maternity which rise from the purpose of her present mission. She walks to within a few paces of Kabnis.

Carrie K.: Brother says come up now, brother Ralph.

Kabnis: Brother doesnt know what he's talkin bout.

Carrie K.: Yes he does, Ralph. He needs you on th wagon.

Kabnis: He wants me on th wagon, eh? Does he think some wooden thing can lift me up? Ask him that.

Carrie K.: He told me t help y.

Kabnis: An how would you help me, child, dear sweet little sister?

She moves forward as if to aid him.

Carrie K.: I'm not a child, as I've more than once told you, brother Ralph, an as I'll show you now.

Kabnis: Wait, Carrie. No, thats right. Youre not a child. But twont do t lift me bodily. You dont understand. But its th soul of me that needs th risin.

Carrie K.: Youre a bad brother an just wont listen t me when I'm tellin y t go t church.

Kabnis doesnt hear her. He breaks down and talks to himself.

Kabnis: Great God Almighty, a soul like mine cant pin itself onto a wagon wheel an satisfy itself in spinnin round. Iron prongs an hickory sticks, an God knows what all . . . all right for Halsey . . . use him. Me? I get my life down in this scum-hole. Th old man an me—

Carrie K.: Has he been talkin?

Kabnis: Huh? Who? Him? No. Dont need to. I talk. An when I really talk, it pays th best of them t listen. Th old man is a good listener. He's deaf; but he's a good listener. An I can talk t him. Tell him anything.

Carrie K.: He's deaf an blind, but I reckon he hears, an sees too, from th things I've heard.

Kabnis: No. Cant. Cant I tell you. How's he do it?

Carrie K.: Dunno, except I've heard that th souls of old folks have a way of seein things.

Kabnis: An I've heard them call that superstition.

The old man begins to shake his head slowly. Carrie and Kabnis watch him, anxiously. He mumbles. With a grave motion his head nods up and down. And then, on one of the down-swings—

Father John (remarkably clear and with great conviction): Sin.

He repeats this word several times, always on the downward nodding. Surprised, indignant, Kabnis forgets that Carrie is with him.

Kabnis: Sin! Shut up. What do you know about sin, you old black bastard. Shut up, an stop that swayin an noddin your head.

Father John: Sin.

Kabnis tries to get up.

Kabnis: Didnt I tell y t shut up?

Carrie steps forward to help him. Kabnis is violently shocked at her touch. He springs back.

Kabnis: Carrie! What . . how . . Baby, you shouldnt be down here. Ralph says things. Doesnt mean to. But Carrie, he doesnt know what he's talkin about. Couldnt know. It was only a preacher's sin they knew in those old days, an that wasnt sin at all. Mind me, th only sin is whats done against th soul. Th whole world is a conspiracy t sin, especially in America, an against me. I'm th victim of their sin. I'm what sin is. Does he look like me? Have you ever heard him say th things youve heard me say? He couldnt if he had th Holy Ghost t help him. Dont look shocked, little sweetheart, you hurt me.

Father John: Sin.

Kabnis: Aw, shut up, old man.

Carrie K.: Leave him be. He wants t say somethin. (She turns to the old man.) What is it, Father?

Kabnis: Whatsha talkin t that old deaf man for? Come away from him.

Carrie K.: What is it, Father?

The old man's lips begin to work. Words are formed incoherently. Finally, he manages to articulate—

Father John: Th sin whats fixed . . . (Hesitates.)

Carrie K. (restraining a comment from Kabnis): Go on, Father.

Father John: . . . upon th white folks—

Kabnis: Suppose youre talkin about that bastard race thats roamin round th country. It looks like sin, if thats what y mean. Give us somethin new an up t date.

Father John:—f tellin Jesus—lies. O th sin th white folks 'mitted when they made th Bible lie.

Boom. Boom. BOOM! Thuds on the floor above. The old man sinks back into his stony silence. Carrie is wet-eyed. Kabnis, contemptuous.

Kabnis: So thats your sin. All these years t tell us that th white folks made th Bible lie. Well, I'll be damned. Lewis ought t have been here. You old black fakir—

Carrie K.: Brother Ralph, is that your best Amen?

She turns him to her and takes his hot cheeks in her firm cool hands. Her palms draw the fever out. With its passing, Kabnis crumples. He sinks to his knees before her, ashamed, exhausted. His eyes squeeze tight. Carrie presses his face tenderly against her. The suffocation of her fresh starched dress feels good to him. Carrie is about to lift her hands in prayer, when Halsey, at the head of the stairs, calls down.

Halsey: Well, well. Whats up? Aint you ever comin? Come on. Whats up down there? Take you all mornin t sleep off a pint? Youre weakenin, man, youre weakenin. Th axle an th beam's all ready waitin f y. Come on.

Kabnis rises and is going doggedly towards the steps. Carrie notices his robe. She catches up to him, points to it, and helps him take it off. He hangs it, with an exaggerated ceremony, on its nail in the corner. He looks down on the tousled beds. His lips curl bitterly. Turning, he stumbles over the bucket of dead coals. He savagely jerks it from the floor. And then, seeing Carrie's eyes upon him, he swings the pail carelessly and with eyes downcast and swollen, trudges upstairs to the work-shop. Carrie's gaze follows him till he is gone. Then she goes to the old man and slips to her knees before him. Her lips murmur, "Jesus, come."

Light streaks through the iron-barred cellar window. Within its soft circle, the figures of Carrie and Father John.

Outside, the sun arises from its cradle in the tree-tops of the forest. Shadows of pines are dreams the sun shakes from its eyes. The sun arises. Goldglowing child, it steps into the sky and sends a birth-song slanting down gray dust streets and sleepy windows of the southern town.

                                                                    1923

GEORGE SAMUEL SCHUYLER
1895–1977

Despite the historical value of George Schuyler's autobiography, *Black and Conservative* (1966), to scholars interested in the New York of Schuyler's youth and of his novel *Slaves Today* (1931) to those concerned with twentieth-century slavery in Liberia, Schuyler's literary reputation probably rests on two texts: the novel *Black No More; Being an Account of the Strange and Wonderful Workings of Science in the Land of the Free* (1931) and an essay, *The Negro-Art Hokum* (1926). *Black No More* was the first book-length satire on race by a black American, preceding Wallace Thurman's better-known *Infants of the Spring* by a year. The story of Dr. Crookman, a black man who has devised a process for the blanching of dark skins, the tale is a trenchant commentary on race relations in America, but cuts as mercilessly against blacks as it does against whites. *The Negro-Art Hokum* is important primarily for having provoked Langston Hughes's famous rejoinder, *The Negro Artist and the Racial Mountain* (both articles appeared in the *Nation* in June 1926); but it remains a lively and persuasive defense of the assimilationist position among African Americans, a position that has become unfashionable but continues to appeal to many blacks.

Schuyler's assimilationism appears to have been based on immense self-confidence. Throughout his life, he maintained that it was impossible for him to feel inferior to whites both because of his ancestors' participation in the Revolutionary War (one of his great-grandfathers served on the American side) and because his family had been free legally as far back as anyone had bothered to trace its genealogy. Born in Providence, Rhode Island, he moved with his family to Syracuse, New York, when he was three. He attended public school there until 1912, when he dropped out to join the army. Seven years later, he left the service as a first lieutenant. He spent a few years working at odd jobs in Syracuse and New York City before a short-lived flirtation with socialism brought him into contact with A. Philip Randolph, who, in 1923, hired him to work for the *Messenger*. Schuyler remained with Randolph as assistant editor until just after his marriage to a white woman, Josephine Cogdell, in 1928. Though he lived in New York, Schuyler worked much of his life for the *Pittsburgh Courier*, a popular black weekly newspaper for which he had begun to write columns in 1924. He stayed with the *Courier* in various capacities until 1966, by which time his controversial views, including the characterization of Martin Luther King Jr. as a "sable Typhoid Mary," had made him unpopular with *Courier* readers. While working for the *Courier*, however, he became almost as well known to the white world of journalism as he was to the black and, at one time, formed a close friendship with H. L. Mencken, on whose famously iconoclastic approach to journalism Schuyler clearly modeled his own work.

In the early 1950s, Schuyler joined the McCarthy camp; an intense animosity toward Communism remained one of the defining characteristics of his writing for the rest of his life. Later, in 1967, he began working for William Loeb's ultraconservative *Union Leader*, published in New Hampshire. That year, his only child, Phillipa Duke Schuyler, a concert pianist and classical composer, was killed while on an assignment in Vietnam for Loeb's publication. His wife died two years later.

Schuyler spent the remaining eight years of his life working as passionately as ever to propagate his own conservative beliefs. At his death, he was regarded by many blacks as something of a traitor to his race. Nevertheless, his reputation is secure as one of the most independent and vigorous writers in the history of African American literature.

The Negro-Art Hokum [1]

Negro art "made in America" is as non-existent as the widely advertised profundity of Cal Coolidge, the "seven years of progress" of Mayor Hylan, [2] or the reported sophistication of New Yorkers. Negro art there has been, is, and will be among the numerous black nations of Africa; but to suggest the possibility of any such development among the ten million colored people in this republic is self-evident foolishness. Eager apostles from Greenwich

1. For a reply to this article, see Langston Hughes's *The Negro Artist and the Racial Mountain*.
2. John F. Hylan (1868–1936), a mayor of New York City (1917–25). Calvin Coolidge (1872–1933), thirtieth U.S. president (1923–29), was known for the brevity of his speeches.

Village, Harlem, and environs proclaimed a great renaissance of Negro art just around the corner waiting to be ushered on the scene by those whose hobby is taking races, nations, peoples, and movements under their wing. New art forms expressing the "peculiar" psychology of the Negro were about to flood the market. In short, the art of Homo Africanus was about to electrify the waiting world. Skeptics patiently waited. They still wait.

True, from dark-skinned sources have come those slave songs based on Protestant hymns and Biblical texts known as the spirituals, work songs and secular songs of sorrow and tough luck known as the blues, that outgrowth of rag-time known as jazz (in the development of which whites have assisted), and the Charleston, an eccentric dance invented by the gamins[3] around the public market-place in Charleston, S.C. No one can or does deny this. But these are contributions of a caste in a certain section of the country. They are foreign to Northern Negroes, West Indian Negroes, and African Negroes. They are no more expressive or characteristic of the Negro race than the music and dancing of the Appalachian highlanders or the Dalmation[4] peasantry are expressive or characteristic of the Caucasian race. If one wishes to speak of the musical contributions of the peasantry of the South, very well. Any group under similar circumstances would have produced something similar. It is merely a coincidence that this peasant class happens to be of a darker hue than the other inhabitants of the land. One recalls the remarkable likeness of the minor strains of the Russian mujiks[5] to those of the Southern Negro.

As for the literature, painting, and sculpture of Aframericans—such as there is—it is identical in kind with the literature, painting, and sculpture of white Americans: that is, it shows more or less evidence of European influence. In the field of drama little of any merit has been written by and about Negroes that could not have been written by whites. The dean of the Aframerican literati is W. E. B. Du Bois, a product of Harvard and German universities; the foremost Aframerican sculptor is Meta Warwick Fuller, a graduate of leading American art schools and former student of Rodin, while the most noted Aframerican painter, Henry Ossawa Tanner,[6] is dean of American painters in Paris and has been decorated by the French Government. Now the work of these artists is no more "expressive of the Negro soul"—as the gushers put it—than are the scribblings of Octavus Cohen or Hugh Wiley.[7]

This, of course, is easily understood if one stops to realize that the Aframerican is merely a lampblacked Anglo-Saxon. If the European immigrant after two or three generations of exposure to our schools, politics, advertising, moral crusades, and restaurants becomes indistinguishable from the mass of Americans of the older stock (despite the influence of the foreign-language press), how much truer must it be of the sons of Ham[8] who have been subjected to what the uplifters call Americanism for the last

---

3. Street urchins.
4. Dalmatia is a region of Croatia.
5. Peasants.
6. Tanner (1859–1937). Du Bois (1868–1963), editor of the *Crisis* magazine. Fuller (1877–1963) attracted the attention of French sculptor Auguste Rodin (1840–1917) in her second year in Paris.

7. Cohen (1891–1959) and Wiley (1884–1969) were white writers who capitalized on existing stereotypes of blacks in their work.
8. According to one reading of the Bible (see, for example, Genesis 9:22–25 and 10:1), blacks were descendants of Ham.

three hundred years. Aside from his color, which ranges from very dark brown to pink, your American Negro is just plain American. Negroes and whites from the same localities in this country talk, think, and act about the same. Because a few writers with a paucity of themes have seized upon imbecilities of the Negro rustics and clowns and palmed them off as authentic and characteristic Aframerican behavior, the common notion that the black American is so "different" from his white neighbor has gained wide currency. The mere mention of the word "Negro" conjures up in the average white American's mind a composite stereotype of Bert Williams, Aunt Jemima, Uncle Tom, Jack Johnson, Florian Slappey,[9] and the various monstrosities scrawled by the cartoonists. Your average Aframerican no more resembles this stereotype than the average American resembles a composite of Andy Gump, Jim Jeffries, and a cartoon by Rube Goldberg.[1]

Again, the Africamerican is subject to the same economic and social forces that mold the actions and thoughts of the white Americans. He is not living in a different world as some whites and a few Negroes would have us believe. When the jangling of his Connecticut alarm clock gets him out of his Grand Rapids bed to a breakfast similar to that eaten by his white brother across the street; when he toils at the same or similar work in mills, mines, factories, and commerce alongside the descendants of Spartacus, Robin Hood, and Eric the Red;[2] when he wears similar clothing and speaks the same language with the same degree of perfection; when he reads the same Bible and belongs to the Baptist, Methodist, Episcopal, or Catholic church; when his fraternal affiliations also include the Elks, Masons, and Knights of Pythias; when he gets the same or similar schooling, lives in the same kind of houses, owns the same makes of cars (or rides in them), and nightly sees the same Hollywood version of life on the screen; when he smokes the same brands of tobacco, and avidly peruses the same puerile periodicals; in short, when he responds to the same political, social, moral, and economic stimuli in precisely the same manner as his white neighbor, it is sheer nonsense to talk about "racial differences" as between the American black man and the American white man. Glance over a Negro newspaper (it is printed in good Americanese) and you will find the usual quota of crime news, scandal, personals, and uplift to be found in the average white newspaper—which, by the way, is more widely read by the Negroes than is the Negro press. In order to satisfy the cravings of an inferiority complex engendered by the colorphobia of the mob, the readers of the Negro newspapers are given a slight dash of racialistic seasoning. In the homes of the black and white Americans of the same cultural and economic level one finds similar furniture, literature, and conversation. How, then, can the black American be expected to produce art and literature dissimilar to that of the white American?

Consider Coleridge-Taylor, Edward Wilmot Blyden, and Claude

9. One of Octavus Cohen's fictional creations. Williams (c. 1875–1922), a popular black entertainer who performed before black and white audiences wearing blackface makeup over his fairly light skin. Johnson (1878–1946), the first black heavyweight boxing champion of the world.
1. Goldberg (1883–1970), known for his cartoons of very complicated inventions designed to do simple things. Gump was a cartoon character created by Robert Sidney Smith and others. Jeffries (1875–1953), white champion boxer who at the end of his career lost to Jack Johnson.
2. Norse mariner (c. 950). Spartacus (d. 71 B.C.), Thracian leader of a slave rebellion.

McKay, the Englishmen; Pushkin, the Russian; Bridgewater, the Pole; Antar, the Arabian; Latino, the Spaniard; Dumas, *père* and *fils*, the Frenchmen; and Paul Laurence Dunbar, Charles W. Chestnutt, and James Weldon Johnson,[3] the Americans. All Negroes; yet their work shows the impress of nationality rather than race. They all reveal the psychology and culture of their environment—their color is incidental. Why should Negro artists of America vary from the national artistic norm when Negro artists in other countries have not done so? If we can foresee what kind of white citizens will inhabit this neck of the woods in the next generation by studying the sort of education and environment the children are exposed to now, it should not be difficult to reason that the adults of today are what they are because of the education and environment they were exposed to a generation ago. And that education and environment were about the same for blacks and whites. One contemplates the popularity of the Negro-art hokum and murmurs, "How come?"

This nonsense is probably the last stand of the old myth palmed off by Negrophobists for all these many years, and recently rehashed by the sainted Harding,[4] that there are "fundamental, eternal, and inescapable differences" between white and black Americans. That there are Negroes who will lend this myth a helping hand need occasion no surprise. It has been broadcast all over the world by the vociferous scions[5] of slaveholders, "scientists" like Madison Grant and Lothrop Stoddard,[6] and the patriots who flood the treasury of the Ku Klux Klan; and is believed, even today, by the majority of free, white citizens. On this baseless premise, so flattering to the white mob, that the blackamoor is inferior and fundamentally different, is erected the postulate that he must needs be peculiar; and when he attempts to portray life through the medium of art, it must of necessity be a peculiar art. While such reasoning may seem conclusive to the majority of Americans, it must be rejected with a loud guffaw by intelligent people.

1926

3. Prominent writer and civil rights leader (1871–1938). Samuel Coleridge-Taylor (1875–1912) (previous page), composer. Blyden (1882–1912) (previous page), educator and journalist. McKay (1891–1948), Jamaican-born poet whose *Harlem Shadows* appeared in 1922. Alexander Pushkin (1799–1837), author of verse novels, including *Eugene Onegin*. George Augustus Polgreen Bridgewater (1799–1860), concert violinist. Antar-bin Shedad (c. 500), Egyptian poet. Juan Latino "el negro" (1516–1597), African-born poet and professor. Alexandre Dumas père (1802–1870), author of *The*

Three Musketeers. Alexandre Dumas fils (1824–1895), author of *The Lady of the Camellias*. Dunbar (1872–1906), the foremost African American poet at the turn of the century. Chesnutt (1858–1932), author of *The Conjure Woman*.
4. Warren G. Harding (1865–1963), twenty-ninth U.S. president (1921–23).
5. Descendants.
6. Author of several white-supremacist texts (1883–1950). Grant (1865–1937), pro-white author, cofounder of the New York Zoological Society, opponent of easy immigration to the United States.

RUDOLPH FISHER

1897–1934

A skilled physician, brilliant writer, and musical arranger, as well as a remarkably witty and informed conversationalist, Rudolph Fisher was by many accounts probably the most intellectually gifted member of the Harlem Renaissance. The son of

Glendora Fisher and the Reverend John Wesley Fisher, he was born in Washington, D.C., but grew up in Providence, Rhode Island, where he graduated from Classical High School in 1915 with honors. Other honors came readily throughout the rest of his brief life. Attending Brown University as a prize scholar, he won an important award in German as a freshman, first prize in a prestigious speaking contest as a sophomore, and yet another major university award as a junior. Later, he wryly referred to Brown as "a most generous institution" that gave him "a great many prizes and scholarships, the degree of A.B. and A.M. in 1919 and 1920, and all of the keys—Phi Beta Kappa, Delta Sigma Rho and Sigma Xi. There was undoubtedly an oversupply that year."

The year 1924 was particularly eventful for Fisher: he took his M.D. (with highest honors) from Howard University Medical School, where he studied roentgenology (the diagnostic and therapeutic uses of x-rays); began his internship at Freedmen's Hospital in Washington, D.C.; and married Jane Ryder. In New York, he became a fellow of the National Research Council at Columbia University's College of Physicians and Surgeons. He specialized in roentgenology at Columbia for two years before opening his private practice in Harlem in 1927.

Despite the demands of his medical training, Fisher found time to write. In 1925, he published his first short story, The City of Refuge, in the prestigious Atlantic Monthly, which brought him instant fame among the Harlem literary set because of its vividly dramatic depiction of Harlem street life as seen through the consciousness of a southern migrant. In the next two years, he distributed his short fiction widely and in several other respected journals, including McClure's, Survey Graphic, Redbook, and Story Magazine. His essay The Caucasian Storms Harlem (1927) was the liveliest piece yet published on Harlem as a living cultural force. Fisher also published two novels: The Walls of Jericho (1928) and The Conjure Man Dies: A Mystery Tale of Dark Harlem (1932). The first was apparently written on a bet that Fisher could not create a unified narrative out of all the diverse elements of Harlem society. The second, The Conjure Man Dies, in which a doctor, John Archer, uses his medical expertise to help unravel a murder mystery, was hailed as the first black detective novel; he was the forerunner of Chester Himes and Ishmael Reed. This work was first produced in dramatic form at the Lafayette Theatre in 1936, more than a year after Fisher's untimely death from intestinal cancer, perhaps brought on by the machines he used in his medical practice.

Many critics have noted Fisher's consistent return to a handful of themes, including the conflicts between generations of African Americans and the values of settled Harlemites as opposed to those of black migrants fresh from the South or the Caribbean. This consistency may be seen in other ways. Certain characters in Jericho reappear in Conjure Man, and some characters in Conjure Man make it into certain of the later pieces of short fiction. Generally speaking, however, Fisher's treatment of such material improves with each return; one can only speculate about what he might have accomplished as a writer if he had not died so young.

The City of Refuge

I

Confronted suddenly by daylight, King Solomon Gillis stood dazed and blinking. The railroad station, the long, white-walled corridor, the impassible slot-machine, the terrifying subway train—he felt as if he had been caught up in the jaws of a steam-shovel, jammed together with other helpless lumps of dirt, swept blindly along for a time, and at last abruptly dumped.

There had been strange and terrible sounds: "New York! Penn Terminal[1]—all change!" "Pohter, hyer, pohter, suh?" Shuffle of a thousand soles, clatter of a thousand heels, innumerable echoes. Cracking rifleshots—no, snapping turnstiles. "Put a nickel in!" "Harlem? Sure. This side—next train." Distant thunder, nearing. The screeching onslaught of the fiery hosts of hell, headlong, breath-taking. Car doors rattling, sliding, banging open. "Say, wha' d'ye think this is, a baggage car?" Heat, oppression, suffocation—eternity—"Hundred'n turdy-fif[2] next!" More turnstiles. Jonah emerging from the whale.

Clean air, blue sky, bright sunlight.

Gillis set down his tan-cardboard extension-case and wiped his black, shining brow. Then slowly, spreadingly, he grinned at what he saw: Negroes at every turn; up and down Lenox Avenue, up and down One Hundred and Thirty-Fifth Street; big, lanky Negroes, short, squat Negroes; black ones, brown ones, yellow ones; men standing idle on the curb, women, bundle-laden, trudging reluctantly homeward, children rattletrapping about the sidewalks; here and there a white face drifting along, but Negroes predominantly, overwhelmingly everywhere. There was assuredly no doubt of his whereabouts. This was Negro Harlem.

Back in North Carolina Gillis had shot a white man and, with the aid of prayer and an automobile, probably escaped a lynching. Carefully avoiding the railroads, he had reached Washington in safety. For his car a Southwest bootlegger had given him a hundred dollars and directions to Harlem; and so he had come to Harlem.

Ever since a traveling preacher had first told him of the place, King Solomon Gillis had longed to come to Harlem. The Uggams were always talking about it; one of their boys had gone to France in the draft and, returning, had never got any nearer home than Harlem. And there were occasional "colored" newspapers from New York: newspapers that mentioned Negroes without comment, but always spoke of a white person as "So-and-so, white." That was the point. In Harlem, black was white. You had rights that could not be denied you; you had privileges, protected by law. And you had money. Everybody in Harlem had money. It was a land of plenty. Why, had not Mouse Uggam sent back as much as fifty dollars at a time to his people in Waxhaw?[3]

The shooting, therefore, simply catalyzed whatever sluggish mental reaction had been already directing King Solomon's fortunes toward Harlem. The land of plenty was more than that now: it was also the city of refuge.[4]

Casting about for direction, the tall newcomer's glance caught inevitably on the most conspicuous thing in sight, a magnificent figure in blue that stood in the middle of the crossing and blew a whistle and waved great

---

1. A major train station in Manhattan.
2. Or 135th Street, in central Harlem.
3. A town in south-central North Carolina.
4. See Numbers 35:11, where God instructs

Moses: "Appoint you cities to be cities of refuge for you; that the slayer may flee thither, which killeth any person at unawares." Later in the story, Gillis claims that the homicide was accidental.

white-gloved hands. The Southern Negro's eyes opened wide; his mouth opened wider. If the inside of New York had mystified him, the outside[5] was amazing him. For there stood a handsome, brass-buttoned giant directing the heaviest traffic Gillis had ever seen; halting unnumbered tons of automobiles and trucks and wagons and pushcarts and street-cars; holding them at bay with one hand while he swept similar tons peremptorily on with the other; ruling the wide crossing with supreme self-assurance; and he, too, was a Negro!

Yet most of the vehicles that leaped or crouched at his bidding carried white passengers. One of these overdrove bounds a few feet and Gillis heard the officer's shrill whistle and gruff reproof, saw the driver's face turn red and his car draw back like a threatened pup. It was beyond belief—impossible. Black might be white, but it couldn't be that white!

"Done died an' woke up in Heaven," thought King Solomon, watching, fascinated; and after a while, as if the wonder of it were too great to believe simply by seeing, "Cullud policemans!" he said, half aloud; then repeated over and over, with greater and greater conviction, "Even got cullud policemans—even got cullud—"

"Where y'want to go, big boy?"

Gillis turned. A little, sharp-faced yellow man was addressing him. "Saw you was a stranger. Thought maybe I could help y'out."

King Solomon located and gratefully extended a slip of paper. "Wha' dis hyeh at, please, suh?"

The other studied it a moment, pushing back his hat and scratching his head. The hat was a tall-crowned, unindented brown felt; the head was brown patent-leather, its glistening brush-back flawless save for a suspicious crimpiness near the clean-grazed edges.

"See that second corner? Turn to the left when you get there. Number forty-five's about halfway the block."

"Thank y', suh."

"You from—Massachusetts?"

"No, suh, Nawth Ca'lina."

"Is 'at so? You look like a Northerner. Be with us long?"

"Till I die," grinned the flattered King Solomon.

"Stoppin' there?"

"Reckon I is. Man in Washin'ton 'lowed I'd find lodgin' at dis address."

"Good enough. If y' don't, maybe I can fix y' up. Harlem's pretty crowded. This is me." He proffered a card.

"Thank y', suh," said Gillis, and put the card in his pocket.

The little yellow man watched him plod flat-footedly on down the street, long awkward legs never quite straightened, shouldered extension-case bending him sidewise, wonder upon wonder halting or turning him about. Presently, as he proceeded, a pair of bright-green stockings caught and held his attention. Tony, the storekeeper, was crossing the sidewalk with a bushel basket of apples. There was a collision; the apples rolled; Tony ex-

---

5. I.e., that part of New York which is aboveground. Gillis has spent his time to this point in subway stations, etc.

ploded; King Solomon apologized. The little yellow man laughed shortly, took out a notebook, and put down the address he had seen on King Solomon's slip of paper.

"Guess you're the shine[6] I been waitin' for," he surmised.

As Gillis, approaching his destination, stopped to rest, a haunting notion grew into an insistent idea. "Dat li'l yaller nigger was a sho' 'nuff gen'man to show me de road. Seem lak I knowed him befo'—" he pondered. That receding brow, that sharp-ridged, spreading nose, that tight upper lip over the two big front teeth, that chinless jaw—He fumbled hurriedly for the card he had not looked at and eagerly made out the name.

"Mouse Uggam, sho' 'nuff! Well, dog-gone!"

II

Uggam sought out Tom Edwards, once a Pullman porter, now prosperous proprietor of a cabaret, and told him:—

"Chief, I got him: a baby jess in from the land o' cotton and so dumb he thinks ante bellum's an old woman."

"Where d'you find him?"

"Where you find all the jay birds[7] when they first hit Harlem—at the subway entrance. This one come up the stairs, batted his eyes once or twice, an' froze to the spot—with his mouth open. Sure sign he's from 'way down behind the sun an' ripe f' the pluckin'."

Edwards grinned a gold-studded, fat-jowled grin. "Gave him the usual line, I suppose?"

"Didn't miss. An' he fell like a ton o' bricks. 'Course I've got him spotted, but damn 'f I know jess how to switch 'em on to him."

"Get him a job around a store somewhere. Make out you're befriendin' him. Get his confidence."

"Sounds good. Ought to be easy. He's from my state. Maybe I know him or some of his people."

"Make out you do, anyhow. Then tell him some fairy tales that'll switch your trade to him. The cops'll follow the trade. We could even let Froggy flop into some dumb white cop's hands and 'confess' where he got it. See?"

"Chief, you got a head, no lie."

"Don't lose no time. And remember, hereafter, it's better to sacrifice a little than to get squealed on. Never refuse a customer. Give him a little credit. Humor him along till you can get rid of him safe. You don't know what that guy that died may have said; you don't know who's on to you now. And if they get you—I don't know you."

"They won't get me," said Uggam.

King Solomon Gillis sat meditating in a room half the size of his hen-coop back home, with a single window opening into an airshaft.

An airshaft: cabbage and chitterlings cooking; liver and onions sizzling, sputtering; three player-pianos out-plunking each other; a man and woman calling each other vile things; a sick, neglected baby wailing; a phonograph broadcasting blues; dishes clacking; a girl crying heartbrokenly; waste

6. A black person (derogatory term used by whites).   7. Simpletons.

noises, waste odors of a score of families, seeing issue through a common channel; pollution from bottom to top—a sewer of sounds and smells.

Contemplating this, King Solomon grinned and breathed, "Doggone!" A little later, still gazing into the sewer, he grinned again. "Green stockin's," he said; "loud green!" The sewer gradually grew darker. A window lighted up opposite, revealing a woman in camisole and petticoat, arranging her hair. King Solomon, staring vacantly, shook his head and grinned yet again. "Even got culled policemans!" he mumbled softly.

III

Uggam leaned out of the room's one window and spat maliciously into the dinginess of the airshaft. "Damn glad you got him," he commented, as Gillis finished his story. "They's a thousand shines in Harlem would change places with you in a minute jess f' the honor of killin' a cracker."

"But, I didn't go to do it. 'Twas a accident."

"That's the only part to keep secret."

"Know whut dey done? Dey killed five o' Mose Joplin's hawses 'fo he lef'. Put groun' glass in de feed-trough. Sam Cheevers come up on three of 'em one night pizenin' his well. Bleesom beat Crinshaw out o' sixty acres o' lan' an' a year's crops. Dass jess how 't is. Soon's a nigger make a li'l sump'n he better git to leavin'. An' 'fo long ev'ybody's goin' be lef'!"

"Hope to hell they don't all come here."

The doorbell of the apartment rang. A crescendo of footfalls in the hallway culminated in a sharp rap on Gillis's door. Gillis jumped. Nobody but a policeman would rap like that. Maybe the landlady had been listening and had called in the law. It came again, loud, quick, angry. King Solomon prayed that the policeman would be a Negro.

Uggam stepped over and opened the door. King Solomon's apprehensive eyes saw framed therein, instead of a gigantic officer, calling for him, a little blot of a creature, quite black against even the darkness of the hallway, except for a dirty, wide-striped silk shirt, collarless, with the sleeves rolled up.

"Ah hahve bill fo' Mr. Gillis." A high, strongly accented Jamaican voice, with its characteristic singsong intonation, interrupted King Solomon's sigh of relief.

"Bill? Bill fo' me? What kin' o' bill?"

"Wan bushel appels. T'ree seventy-fife."

"Apples? I ain' bought no apples." He took the paper and read aloud, laboriously, "Antonio Gabrielli to K. S. Gillis, Doctor—"

"Mr. Gabrielli say, you not pays him, he send policemon."

"What I had to do wid 'is apples?"

"You bumps into him yesterday, no? Scatter appels everywhere—on de sidewalk, in de gutter. Kids pick up an' run away. Others all spoil. So you pays."

Gillis appealed to Uggam. "How 'bout it, Mouse?"

"He's a damn liar. Tony picked up most of 'em; I seen him. Lemme look at that bill—Tony never wrote this thing. This baby's jess playin' you for a sucker."

"Ain' had no apples, ain' payin' fo' none," announced King Solomon, thus prompted. "Didn't have to come to Harlem to git cheated. Plenty o' dat right wha' I come fum."

But the West Indian warmly insisted. "You cahn't do daht, mon. Whaht you t'ink, 'ey? Dis mon loose 'is appels an' 'is money too?"

"What diff'ence it make to you, nigger?"

"Who you call nigger, mon? Ah hahve you understahn'."—

"Oh, well, white folks, den. What all you got t' do wid dis hyeh, anyhow?"

"Mr. Gabrielli send me to collect bill!"

"How I know dat?"

"Do Ah not bring bill? You t'ink Ah steal t'ree dollar, 'ey?"

"Three dollars an' sebenty-fi'cent," corrected Gillis. " 'Nuther thing: wha' you ever see me befo'? How you know dis is me?"

"Ah see you, sure. Ah help Mr. Gabrielli in de store. When you knocks down de baskette appels, Ah see. Ah follow you. Ah know you comes in dis house."

"Oh, you does? An' how come you know my name an' flat an' room so good? How come dat?"

"Ah fin' out. Sometime Ah brings up here vegetables from de store."

"Humph! Mus' be workin' on shares."

"You pays, 'ey? You pays me or de policemon?"

"Wait a minute," broke in Uggam, who had been thoughtfully contemplating the bill. "Now listen, big shorty. You haul hips on back to Tony. We got your menu all right"—he waved the bill—"but we don't eat your kind o' cookin', see?"

The West Indian flared. "Whaht it is to you, 'ey? You can not mind your own business? Ah hahve not spik to you!"

"No, brother. But this is my friend, an' I'll be john-browned [8] if there's a monkey-chaser in Harlem can gyp him if I know it, see? Bes' thing f' you to do is catch air, toot sweet." [9]

Sensing frustration, the little islander demanded the bill back. Uggam figured he could use the bill himself, maybe. The West Indian hotly persisted; he even menaced. Uggam pocketed the paper and invited him to take it. Wisely enough, the caller preferred to catch air.

When he had gone, King Solomon sought words of thanks.

"Bottle it," said Uggam. "The point is this: I figger you got a job."

"Job? No I ain't! Wh' at?"

"When you show Tony this bill, he'll hit the roof and fire that monk."

"Wha ef he do?"

"Then you up 'n ask f' the job. He'll be too grateful to refuse. I know Tony some, an' I'll be there to put in a good word. See?"

King Solomon considered this. "Sho' needs a job, but ain' after stealin' none."

"Stealin'? 'T wouldn't be stealin'. Stealin' 's what that damn monkey-chaser tried to do from you. This would be doin' Tony a favor an' gettin' y'self out o' the barrel. What's the hold-back?"

---

8. After John Brown (1800–1859), leader of the raid on Harpers Ferry, who was executed.

9. Americanization of *tout de suite*, French for "immediately."

"What make you keep callin' him monkey-chaser?"

"West Indian. That's another thing. Any time y' can knife a monk, do it. They's too damn many of 'em here. They're an achin' pain."

"Jess de way white folks feels 'bout niggers."

"Damn that. How 'bout it? Y' want the job?"

"Hm—well—I'd ruther be a policeman."

"Policeman?" Uggam gasped.

"M—hm. Dass all I wants to be, a policeman, so I kin police all de white folks right plumb in jail!"

Uggam said seriously, "Well, y' might work up to that. But it takes time. An' y've got to eat while y're waitin'." He paused to let this penetrate. "Now, how 'bout this job at Tony's in the meantime? I should think y'd jump at it."

King Solomon was persuaded.

"Hm—well—reckon I does," he said slowly.

"Now y're tootin'!" Uggam's two big front teeth popped out in a grin of genuine pleasure. "Come on. Let's go."

IV

Spitting blood and crying with rage, the West Indian scrambled to his feet. For a moment he stood in front of the store gesticulating furiously and jabbering shrill threats and unintelligible curses. Then abruptly he stopped and took himself off.

King Solomon Gillis, mildly puzzled, watched him from Tony's doorway. "I jess give him a li'l shove," he said to himself, "an he roll' clean 'cross de sidewalk." And a little later, disgustedly, "Monkey-chaser!" he grunted, and went back to his sweeping.

"Well, big boy, how y' comin' on?"

Gillis dropped his broom. "Hay-o, Mouse. Wha' you been las' two-three days?"

"Oh, around. Gettin' on all right here? Had any trouble?"

"Deed I ain't—'ceptin' jess now I had to throw 'at li'l jigger out."

"Who? The monk?"

"M—hm. He sho' Lawd doan like me in his job. Look like he think I stole it from him, stiddy[1] him tryin' to steal from me. Had to push him down sho' 'nuff 'fo I could git rid of 'im. Den he run off talkin' Wes' Indi'-man an' shakin' his fis' at me."

"Ferget it." Uggam glanced about. "Where's Tony?"

"Boss man? He be back direckly."

"Listen—like to make two or three bucks a day extra?"

"Huh?"

"Two or three dollars a day more'n what you're gettin' already?"

"Ain' I near 'nuff in jail now?"

"Listen," King Solomon listened. Uggam hadn't been in France for nothing. Fact was, in France he'd learned about some valuable French medicine. He'd brought some back with him,—little white pills,—and while in Harlem had found a certain druggist who knew what they were

1. Instead of.

and could supply all he could use. Now there were any number of people who would buy and pay well for as much of this French medicine as Uggam could get. It was good for what ailed them, and they didn't know how to get it except through him. But he had no store in which to set up an agency and hence no single place where his customers could go to get what they wanted. If he had, he could sell three or four times as much as he did.

King Solomon was in a position to help him how, same as he had helped King Solomon. He would leave a dozen packages of the medicine—just small envelopes that could all be carried in a coat pocket—with King Solomon every day. Then he could simply send his customers to King Solomon at Tony's store. They'd make some trifling purchase, slip him a certain coupon which Uggam had given them, and King Solomon would wrap the little envelope of medicine with their purchase. Mustn't let Tony catch on, because he might object, and then the whole scheme would go gaflooey. Of course it wouldn't really be hurting Tony any. Wouldn't it increase the number of his customers?

Finally, at the end of each day, Uggam would meet King Solomon some place and give him a quarter for each coupon he held. There'd be at least ten or twelve a day—two and a half or three dollars plumb extra! Eighteen or twenty dollars a week!

"Dog-gone!" breathed Gillis.

"Does Tony ever leave you heer alone?"

"M—hm. Jess started dis mawnin'. Doan nobody much come round 'tween ten an' twelve, so he done took to doin' his buyin' right 'long 'bout dat time. Nobody hyeh but me fo' 'n hour or so."

"Good. I'll try to get my folks to come 'round here mostly while Tony's out, see?"

"I doan miss."

"Sure y' get the idea, now?" Uggam carefully explained it all again. By the time he had finished, King Solomon was wallowing in gratitude.

"Mouse, you sho' is been a friend to me. Why, 'f t had n' been fo' you—"

"Bottle it," said Uggam. "I'll be round to your room to-night with enough stuff for to-morrer, see? Be sure'n be there."

"Won't be nowha' else."

"An' remember, this is all jess between you 'n me."

"Nobody else but," vowed King Solomon.

Uggam grinned to himself as he went on his way. "Dumb Oscar![2] Wonder how much can we make before the cops nab him? French medicine—Hmph!"

V

Tony Gabrielli, an oblate Neapolitan of enormous equator, wabbled heavily out of his store and settled himself over a soap box.

Usually Tony enjoyed sitting out front thus in the evening, when his helper had gone home and his trade was slackest. He liked to watch the little Gabriellis playing over the sidewalk with the little Levys and Johnsons; the trios and quartettes of brightly dressed, dark-skinned girls merrily

2. Any stupid person (slang).

out for a stroll; the slovenly gaited, darker men, who eyed them up and down and commented to each other with an unsuppressed "Hot damn!" or "Oh, no, now!"

But to-night Tony was troubled. Something was different since the arrival of King Solomon Gillis. The new man had seemed to prove himself honest and trustworthy, it was true. Tony had tested him, as he always tested a new man, by apparently leaving him alone in charge for two or three mornings. Tony's store was a modification of the front rooms of his flat and was in direct communication with it by way of a glass-windowed door in the rear. Tony always managed to get back into his flat via the side-street entrance and watch the new man through this unobtrusive glass-windowed door. If anything excited his suspicion, like unwarranted interest in the cash register, he walked unexpectedly out of this door to surprise the offender in the act. Thereafter he would have no more such trouble. But he had not succeeded in seeing King Solomon steal even an apple.

What he had observed, however, was that the number of customers that came into the store during the morning's slack hour had pronouncedly increased in the last few days. Before, there had been three or four. Now there were twelve or fifteen. The mysterious thing about it was that their purchases totaled little more than those of the original three or four.

Yesterday and to-day Tony had elected to be in the store at the time when, on the other days, he had been out. But Gillis had not been over-charging or short-changing; for when Tony waited on the customers himself—strange faces all—he found that they bought something like a yeast cake or a five-cent loaf of bread. It was puzzling. Why should strangers leave their own neighborhoods and repeatedly come to him for a yeast cake or a loaf of bread? They were not new neighbors. New neighbors would have bought more variously and extensively and at different times of day. Living near by, they would have come in, the men often in shirtsleeves and slippers, the women in kimonos, with boudoir caps covering their lumpy heads. They would have sent in strange children for things like yeast cakes and loaves of bread. And why did not some of them come in at night when the new helper was off duty?

As for accosting Gillis on suspicion, Tony was too wise for that.

Patronage had a queer way of shifting itself in Harlem. You lost your temper and let slip a single "*nègre.*"[3] A week later you sold your business.

Spread over his soap box, with his pudgy hands clasped on his preposterous paunch, Tony sat and wondered. Two men came up, conspicuous for no other reason than that they were white. They displayed extreme nervousness, looking about as if afraid of being seen; and when one of them spoke to Tony it was in a husky, toneless, blowing voice, like the sound of a dirty phonograph record.

"Are you Antonio Gabrielli?"

"Yes, sure." Strange behavior for such lusty-looking fellows. He who had spoken unsmilingly winked first one eye then the other, and indicated by a gesture of his head that they should enter the store. His companion looked cautiously up and down the Avenue, while Tony, wondering what ailed them, rolled to his feet and puffingly led the way.

3. Nigger.

Inside, the spokesman snuffled, gave his shoulders a queer little hunch, and asked, "Can you fix us up, buddy?" The other glanced restlessly about the place as if he were constantly hearing unaccountable noises.

Tony thought he understood clearly now. "Booze, 'ey?" he smiled. "Sorry—I no got."

"Booze? Hell, no!" The voice dwindled to a throaty whisper. "Dope. Coke, milk, dice—anything. Name your price. Got to have it."

"Dope?" Tony was entirely at a loss. "What's a dis, dope?"

"Aw, lay off, brother. We're in on this. Here." He handed Tony a piece of paper. "Froggy gave us a coupon. Come on. You can't go wrong."

"I no got," insisted the perplexed Tony; nor could he be budged on that point.

Quite suddenly the manner of both men changed. "All right," said the first angrily, in a voice as robust as his body. "All right, you're clever, You no got. Well, you will get. You'll get twenty years!"

"Twenty year? Whadda you talk?"

"Wait a minute, Mac," said the second caller. "Maybe the wop's[4] on the level. Look here, Tony, we're officers, see? Policemen." He produced a badge. "A couple of weeks ago a guy was brought in dying for the want of a shot, see? Dope—he needed some dope—like this—in his arm. See? Well, we tried to make him tell us where he'd been getting it, but he was too weak. He croaked next day. Evidently he hadn't had money enough to buy any more.

"Well, this morning a little nigger that goes by the name of Froggy was brought into the precinct pretty well doped up. When he finally came to, he swore he got the stuff here at your store. Of course, we've just been trying to trick you into giving yourself away, but you don't bite. Now what's your game? Know anything about this?"

Tony understood. "I dunno," he said slowly; and then his own problem, whose contemplation his callers had interrupted, occurred to him. "Sure!" he exclaimed. "Wait. Maybeso I know somet'ing."

"All right. Spill it."

"I got a new man, work-a for me." And he told them what he had noted since King Solomon Gillis came.

"Sounds interesting. Where is this guy?"

"Here in da store—all day."

"Be here to-morrow?"

"Sure. All day."

"All right. We'll drop in to-morrow and give him the eye. Maybe he's our man."

"Sure. Come ten o'clock. I show you," promised Tony.

VI

Even the oldest and rattiest cabarets in Harlem have sense of shame enough to hide themselves under the ground—for instance, Edwards's.[5] To get into Edwards's you casually enter a dimly lighted corner saloon, apparently—only apparently—a subdued memory of brighter days. What

---

4. Derogatory term for an Italian.
5. Based on Edmond's Cellar, the cabaret made famous by singer Ethel Waters (1896–1977).

was once the family entrance is now a side entrance for ladies. Supporting yourself against close walls, you crouchingly descend a narrow, twisted staircase until, with a final turn, you find yourself in a glaring, long, low basement. In a moment your eyes become accustomed to the haze of tobacco smoke. You see men and women seated at wire-legged, white-topped tables, which are covered with half-empty bottles and glasses; you trace the slow-jazz accompaniment you heard as you came down the stairs to a pianist, a cornetist, and a drummer on a little platform at the far end of the room. There is a cleared space from the foot of the stairs, where you are standing, to the platform where this orchestra is mounted, and in it a tall brown girl is swaying from side to side and rhythmically proclaiming that she has the world in a jug and the stopper in her hand.[6] Behind a counter at your left sits a fat, bald, tea-colored Negro, and you wonder if this is Edwards—Edwards, who stands in with the police, with the political bosses, with the importers of wines and worse. A white-vested waiter hustles you to a seat and takes your order. The song's tempo changes to a quicker; the drum and the cornet rip out a fanfare, almost drowning the piano; the girl catches up her dress and begins to dance. . . .

Gillis's wondering eyes had been roaming about. They stopped.

"Look, Mouse!" he whispered. "Look a-yonder!"

"Look at what?"

"Dog-gone if it ain' de self-same gal!"

"Wha' d' ye mean, self-same girl?"

"Over yonder, wi' de green stockin's. Dass de gal made me knock over dem apples fust day I come to town. 'Member? Been wishin' I could see her ev'y sence."

"What for?" Uggam wondered.

King Solomon grew confidential. "Ain but two things in dis world, Mouse, I really wants. One is to be a policeman. Been wantin' dat ev'y sence I seen dat cullud traffic-cop dat day. Other is to git myse'f a gal lak dat one over yonder!"

"You'll do it," laughed Uggam, "if you live long enough."

"Who dat wid her?"

"How'n hell do I know?"

"He cullud?"

"Don't look like it. Why? What of it?"

"Hm—nuthin—"

"How many coupons y' got to-night?"

"Ten." King Solomon handed them over.

"Y'ought to've slipt 'em to me under the table, but it's all right now, long as we got this table to ourselves. Here's y' medicine for to-morrer."

"Wha'?"

"Reach under the table."

Gillis secured and pocketed the medicine.

"An' here's two-fifty for a good day's work." Uggam passed the money over. Perhaps he grew careless; certainly the passing this time was above the table, in plain sight.

"Thanks, Mouse."

6. From a popular blues song of the 1920s.

Two white men had been watching Gillis and Uggam from a table near by. In the tumult of merriment that rewarded the entertainer's most recent and daring effort, one of these men, with a word to the other, came over and took the vacant chair beside Gillis.

"Is your name Gillis?"

"Tain' nuthin' else."

Uggam's eyes narrowed.

The white man showed King Solomon a police officer's badge.

"You're wanted for dope-peddling. Will you come along without trouble?"

"Fo' what?"

"Violation of the narcotic law—dope-selling."

"Who—me?"

"Come on, now, lay off that stuff. I saw what happened just now myself." He addressed Uggam. "Do you know this fellow?"

"Nope. Never saw him before tonight."

"Didn't I just see him sell you something?"

"Guess you did. We happened to be sittin' here at the same table and got to talkin'. After a while I says I can't seem to sleep nights, so he offers me sump'n he says'll make me sleep, all right. I don't know what it is, but he says he uses it himself an' I offers to pay him what it cost him. That's how I come to take it. Guess he's got more in his pocket there now."

The detective reached deftly into the coat pocket of the dumbfounded King Solomon and withdrew a packet of envelopes. He tore off a corner of one, emptied a half-dozen tiny white tablets into his palm, and sneered triumphantly. "You'll make a good witness," he told Uggam.

The entertainer was issuing an ultimatum to all sweet mammas who dared to monkey around her loving man. Her audience was absorbed and delighted, with the exception of one couple—the girl with the green stockings and her escort. They sat directly in the line of vision of King Solomon's wide eyes, which, in the calamity that had descended upon him, for the moment saw nothing.

"Are you coming without trouble?"

Mouse Uggam, his friend. Harlem. Land of plenty. City of refuge—city of refuge. If you live long enough—

Consciousness of what was happening between the pair across the room suddenly broke through Gillis's daze like flame through smoke. The man was trying to kiss the girl and she was resisting. Gillis jumped up. The detective, taking the act for an attempt at escape, jumped with him and was quick enough to intercept him. The second officer came at once to his fellow's aid, blowing his whistle several times as he came.

People overturned chairs getting out of the way, but nobody ran for the door. It was an old crowd. A fight was a treat; and the tall Negro could fight.

"Judas Priest!"

"Did you see that?"

"Damn!"

White—both white. Five of Mose Joplin's horses. Poisoning a well. A year's crops. Green stockings—white—white—

"That's the time, papa!"

"Do it, big boy!"

"Good night!"

Uggam watched tensely, with one eye on the door. The second cop had blown for help—

Downing one of the detectives a third time and turning to grapple again with the other, Gillis found himself face to face with a uniformed black policeman.

He stopped as if stunned. For a moment he simply stared. Into his mind swept his own words like a forgotten song, suddenly recalled:—

"Cullud policemans!"

The officer stood ready, awaiting his rush.

"Even—got—cullud—policemans—"

Very slowly King Solomon's arms relaxed; very slowly he stood erect; and the grin that came over his features had something exultant about it.

1925

The Caucasian Storms Harlem

I

It might not have been such a jolt had my five years' absence from Harlem been spent otherwise. But the study of medicine includes no courses in cabareting; and, anyway, the Negro cabarets in Washington, where I studied, are all uncompromisingly black. Accordingly I was entirely unprepared for what I found when I returned to Harlem recently.

I remembered one place especially where my own crowd used to hold forth; and, hoping to find some old-timers there still, I sought it out one midnight. The old, familiar plunkety-plunk welcomed me from below as I entered. I descended the same old narrow stairs, came into the same smoke-misty basement, and found myself a chair at one of the ancient white-porcelain, mirror-smooth tables. I drew a deep breath and looked about, seeking familiar faces. "What a lot of 'fays![1] I thought, as I noticed the number of white guests. Presently I grew puzzled and began to stare, then I gaped—and gasped. I found myself wondering if this was the right place—if, indeed, this was Harlem at all. I suddenly became aware that, except for the waiters and members of the orchestra, I was the only Negro in the place.

After a while I left it and wandered about in a daze from night-club to night-club. I tried the Nest, Small's, Connie's Inn, the Capitol, Happy's, the Cotton Club. There was no mistake; my discovery was real and was repeatedly confirmed. No wonder my old crowd was not to be found in any of them. The best of Harlem's black cabarets have changed their names and turned white.

Such a discovery renders a moment's recollection irresistible. As irresistible as were the cabarets themselves to me seven or eight years ago. Just out of college in a town where cabarets were something only read about. A year

1. Short for "ofays," a derogatory term for whites.

of graduate work ahead. A Summer of rest at hand. Cabarets. Cabarets night after night, and one after another. There was no cover-charge then, and a fifteen-cent bottle of Whistle lasted an hour. It was just after the war[2]—the heroes were home—cabarets were the thing.

How the Lybia prospered in those happy days! It was the gathering place of the swellest Harlem set: if you didn't go to the Lybia, why, my dear, you just didn't belong. The people you saw at church in the morning you met at the Lybia at night. What romance in those war-tinged days and nights! Officers from Camp Upton,[3] with pretty maids from Brooklyn! Gay lieutenants, handsome captains—all whirling the lively onestep. Poor non-coms[4] completely ignored; what sensible girl wanted a corporal or even a sergeant? That white, old-fashioned house, standing alone in 138th street, near the corner of Seventh avenue—doomed to be torn down a few months thence—how it shook with the dancing and laughter of the dark merry crowds!

But the first place really popular with my friends was a Chinese restaurant in 136th street, which had been known as Hayne's Café and then became the Oriental. It occupied an entire house of three stories, and had carpeted floors and a quiet, superior air. There was excellent food and incredibly good tea and two unusual entertainers: a Cuban girl, who could so vary popular airs that they sounded like real music, and a slender little "brown" with a voice of silver and a way of singing a song that made you forget your food. One could dance in the Oriental if one liked, but one danced to a piano only, and wound one's way between linen-clad tables over velvety, noiseless floors.

Here we gathered: Fritz Pollard, All-American halfback,[5] selling Negro stock to prosperous Negro physicians; Henry Creamer and Turner Layton, who had written "After You've Gone" and a dozen more songs, and were going to write "Strut, Miss Lizzie;" Paul Robeson,[6] All-American end, on the point of tackling law, quite unaware that the stage would intervene; Preacher Harry Bragg, Harvard Jimmie MacLendon and a half a dozen others. Here at a little table, just inside the door, Bert Williams[7] had supper every night, and afterward sometimes joined us upstairs and sang songs with us and lampooned the Actors' Equity Association, which had barred him because of his color. Never did white guests come to the Oriental except as guests of Negroes. But the manager soon was stricken with a psychosis of some sort, became a black Jew, grew himself a bushy, square-cut beard, donned a skull-cap and abandoned the Oriental. And so we were robbed of our favorite resort, and thereafter became mere rounders.

II

Such places, those real Negro cabarets that we met in the course of our rounds! There was Edmonds' in Fifth avenue at 130th street. It was a sure-enough honky-tonk, occupying the cellar of a saloon. It was the social cen-

2. I.e., World War I. "Whistle": a beverage.
3. A military facility near Manhattan.
4. Noncommissioned officers.
5. In 1916 at Brown University. He was the first black professional football player (Akron Indians, 1919).
6. A distinguished football player at Rutgers before entering the Columbia University Law School in 1919 (1898–1976).
7. Popular black comedian and actor (c. 1874–1922).

ter of what was then, and still is, Negro Harlem's kitchen. Here a tall brown-skin girl, unmistakably the one guaranteed in the song to make a preacher lay his Bible down, used to sing and dance her own peculiar numbers, vesting them with her own originality. She was known simply as Ethel,[8] and was a genuine drawing-card. She knew her importance, too. Other girls wore themselves ragged trying to rise above the inattentive din of conversation, and soon, literally, yelled themselves hoarse; eventually they lost whatever music there was in their voices and acquired that familiar throaty roughness which is so frequent among blues singers, and which, though admired as characteristically African, is as a matter of fact nothing but a form of chronic laryngitis. Other girls did these things, but not Ethel. She took it easy. She would stride with great leisure and self-assurance to the center of the floor, stand there with a half-contemptuous nonchalance, and wait. All would become silent at once. Then she'd begin her song, genuine blues, which, for all their humorous lines, emanated tragedy and heartbreak:

> Woke up this mawnin'
> The day was dawnin'
> And I was sad and blue, so blue, Lord—
> Didn' have nobody
> To tell my troubles to—

It was Ethel who first made popular the song, "Tryin' to Teach My Good Man Right from Wrong," in the slow, meditative measures in which she complained:

> I'm gettin' sick and tired of my railroad man
> I'm gettin' sick and tired of my railroad man—
> Can't get him when I want him—
> I get him when I can.

It wasn't long before this song-bird escaped her dingy cage. Her name is a vaudeville attraction now, and she uses it all—Ethel Waters. Is there anyone who hasn't heard her sing "Shake That Thing!"?

A second place was Connor's in 135th street near Lenox avenue. It was livelier, less languidly sensuous, and easier to breathe in than Edmonds'. Like the latter, it was in a basement, reached by the typical narrow, head-long stairway. One of the girls there specialized in the Jelly-Roll song, and mad habitués[9] used to fling petitions of greenbacks at her feet—pretty nimble feet they were, too—when she sang that she loved 'em but she had to turn 'em down. Over in a corner a group of 'fays would huddle and grin and think they were having a wild time. Slumming. But they were still very few in those days.

And there was the Oriental, which borrowed the name that the former Hayne's Café had abandoned. This was beyond Lenox avenue on the south side of 135th street. An upstairs place, it was nevertheless as dingy as any of the cellars, and the music fairly fought its way through the babble and smoke to one's ears, suffering in transit weird and incredible distortion.

---

8. Ethel Waters (1896–1977). 9. Regular patrons.

The prize pet here was a slim, little lad, unbelievably black beneath his high-brown powder, wearing a Mexican bandit costume with a bright-colored head-dress and sash. I see him now, poor kid, in all his glory, shimmying for enraptured women, who marveled at the perfect control of his voluntary abdominal tremors. He used to let the women reach out and put their hands on his sash to palpate[1] those tremors—for a quarter.

Finally, there was the Garden of Joy, an open-air cabaret between 138th and 139th streets in Seventh avenue, occupying a plateau high above the sidewalk—a large, well-laid, smooth wooden floor with tables and chairs and a tinny orchestra, all covered by a propped-up roof, that resembled an enormous lampshade, directing bright light downward and outward. Not far away the Abysinnian Church used to hold its Summer camp-meetings in a great round circus-tent. Night after night there would arise the mingled strains of blues and spirituals, those peculiarly Negro forms of song, the one secular and the other religious, but both born of wretchedness in travail, both with their soarings of exultation and sinkings of despair. I used to wonder if God, hearing them both, found any real distinction.

There were the Lybia, then, and Hayne's, Connor's, the Oriental, Edmonds' and the Garden of Joy, each distinctive, standing for a type, some living up to their names, others living down to them, but all predominantly black. Regularly I made the rounds among these places and saw only incidental white people. I have seen them occasionally in numbers, but such parties were out on a lark. They weren't in their natural habitat and they often weren't any too comfortable.

But what of Barron's, you say? Certainly they were at home there. Yes, I know about Barron's. I have been turned away from Barron's because I was too dark to be welcome. I have been a member of a group that was told, "No more room," when we could see plenty of room. Negroes were never actually wanted in Barron's save to work. Dark skins were always discouraged or barred. In short, the fact about Barron's was this: it simply wasn't a Negro cabaret; it was a cabaret run by Negroes for whites. It wasn't even on the lists of those who lived in Harlem—they'd no more think of going there than of going to the Winter Garden Roof.[2] But these other places were Negro through and through. Negroes supported them, not merely in now-and-then parties, but steadily, night after night.

III

Now, however, the situation is reversed. It is I who go occasionally and white people who go night after night. Time and again, since I've returned to live in Harlem, I've been one of a party of four Negroes who went to this or that Harlem cabaret, and on each occasion we've been the only Negro guests in the place. The managers don't hesitate to say that it is upon these predominant white patrons that they depend for success. These places therefore are no longer mine but theirs. Not that I'm barred, any more than they were seven or eight years ago. Once known, I'm even welcome, just as some of them used to be. But the complexion of the place is theirs, not

---

1. Examine by touch.   2. A prominent Manhattan night club.

mine. I? Why, I am actually stared at, I frequently feel uncomfortable and out of place, and when I go out on the floor to dance I am lost in a sea of white faces. As another observer has put it to me since, time was when white people went to Negro cabarets to see how Negroes acted; now Negroes go to these same cabarets to see how white people act. Negro clubs have recently taken to hiring a place outright for a presumably Negro party; and even then a goodly percentage of the invited guests are white.

One hurries to account for this change of complexion as a reaction to the Negro invasion of Broadway not long since. One remembers "Shuffle Along"[3] of four years ago, the first Negro piece in the downtown district for many a moon. One says, "Oh yes, Negroes took their stuff to the whites and won attention and praise, and now the whites are seeking this stuff out on its native soil." Maybe. So I myself thought at first. But one looks for something of oppositeness in a genuine reaction. One would rather expect the reaction to the Negro invasion of Broadway to be apathy. One would expect that the same thing repeated under different names or in imitative fragments would meet with colder and colder reception, and finally with none at all.

A little recollection will show that just what one would expect was what happened. Remember "Shuffle Along's" successors: "Put and Take," "Liza," "Strut Miss Lizzie," "Runnin' Wild," and the others? True, none was so good as "Shuffle Along," but surely they didn't deserve all the roasting they got. "Liza" flared but briefly, during a holiday season. "Put and Take" was a loss, "Strut Miss Lizzie" strutted about two weeks, and the humor of "Runnin' Wild" was derided as Neo-Pleistocene. Here was reaction for you—wholesale withdrawal of favor. One can hardly conclude that such withdrawal culminated in the present swamping of Negro cabarets. People so sick of a thing would hardly go out of their way to find it.

And they *are* sick of it—in quantity at least. Only one Negro entertainment has survived this reaction of apathy in any permanent fashion. This is the series of revues built around the personality of Florence Mills.[4] Without that bright live personality the Broadway district would have been swept clean last season of all-Negro bills. Here is a girl who has triumphed over a hundred obstacles. Month after month she played obscure, unnoticed rôles with obscure, unknown dark companies. She was playing such a minor part in "Shuffle Along" when the departure of Gertrude Saunders, the craziest blues-singer on earth, unexpectedly gave her the spotlight. Florence Mills cleaned up. She cleaned up so thoroughly that the same public which grew weary of "Shuffle Along" and sick of its successors still had an eager ear for her. They have yet, and she neither wearies nor disappoints them. An impatient Broadway audience awaits her return from Paris, where she and the inimitable Josephine Baker[5] have been vying with each other as sensations. She is now in London on the way home, but London won't release her; the enthusiasm over her exceeds anything in the memory of the oldest reviewers.

3. A tremendously successful musical comedy (1921), created by Flournoy Miller, Aubrey Lyles, Noble Sissle, and Eubie Blake. It was the first dramatic success to be produced and performed entirely by African Americans.
4. Popular singer and dancer (1895–1927).
5. Dancer, singer, actress, and civil rights activist (1906–1975).

Florence Mills, moreover, is admired by her own people too, because, far from going to her head, her success has not made her forgetful. Not long ago, the rumor goes, she made a fabulous amount of money in the Florida real-estate boom, and what do you suppose she plans to do with it? Build herself an Italian villa somewhere up the Hudson? Not at all. She plans to build a first-rate Negro theatre in Harlem.

But that's Florence Mills. Others have encountered indifference. In vain has Eddie Hunter,[6] for instance, tried for a first-class Broadway showing, despite the fact that he himself has a new kind of Negro-comedian character to portray—the wise darkey, the "bizthniss man," the "fly" rascal who gets away with murder, a character who amuses by making a goat of others instead of by making a goat of himself. They say that some dozen Negro shows have met with similar denials. Yet the same people, presumably, whose spokesmen render these decisions flood Harlem night after night and literally crowd me off the dancing-floor. If this is a reaction, it is a reaction to a reaction, a swinging back of the pendulum from apathy toward interest. Maybe so. The cabarets may present only those special Negro features which have a particular and peculiar appeal, leaving out the high-yaller display that is merely feebly imitative. But a reaction to a reaction—that's differential calculus.

IV

Some think it's just a fad. White people have always more or less sought Negro entertainment as diversion. The old shows of the early nineteen hundreds, Williams and Walker[7] and Cole and Johnson, are brought to mind as examples. The howling success—literally that—of J. Leubrie Hill[8] around 1913 is another; on the road his "Darktown Follies" played in numerous white theatres. In Harlem it played at the black Lafayette and, behold, the Lafayette temporarily became white. And so now, it is held, we are observing merely one aspect of a meteoric phenomenon, which simply presents itself differently in different circumstances: Roland Hayes and Paul Robeson, Jean Toomer and Walter White, Charles Gilpin[9] and Florence Mills—"Green Thursday," "Porgy," "In Abraham's Bosom"[1]—Negro spirituals—the startling new African groups proposed for the Metropolitan Museum of Art. Negro stock is going up, and everybody's buying.

This doesn't sound unreasonable when it refers to certain things. Interest in the shows certainly presents many features of a fad. As in some epidemic fevers, there are sudden onset, swift contagion, brief duration, and a marked tendency to recur. Consider "Shuffle Along," for example, as a fad. Interest waned, as it will with fads. Disruption was hastened by internal dissension in the company: Sissle and Blake had written the songs and insisted on keeping the royalties therefrom, and Miller and Lyles had helped make the songs famous and contended that they too deserved a share of the

6. Popular black comedian (b. 1888), whose *How Come?* flopped in 1923.
7. Bert Williams and George Nash Walker formed an immensely popular vaudeville team in 1895.
8. Songwriter (1969–1916).

9. Actor (1878–1930). Hayes (1887–1976), singer. Toomer (1894–1967), author of *Cane.* White (1893–1955), writer and civil rights leader.
1. A 1926 play by white writer Paul Green. *Porgy* (1925), a novel by Du Bose Heyward.

proceeds. There was a deadlock and a split. "In Bamville" went one way and "Runnin' Wild"[2] another, but neither went the prosperous way of the parent fad, "Shuffle Along."

Meanwhile, Creamer and Layton, among others, had found that the fad no longer infected. But if America was barren ground was not Europe virgin soil?

So, while Creamer remained to run the Cotton Club, Layton packed off to England, where already Hayes had done admirably in recital and Robeson was becoming well known on the stage. Layton and his new partner, Tandy Johnstone,[3] were amazed at their success in England, and there they are at this writing. They earn more in a week there than they used to in many months over here. They have transplanted their fad into other susceptible communities—communities likely to become immune less swiftly. They are London vaudeville headliners, and their jazz has captivated the British. These entertainers will probably not soon lose that peculiar knack of striking a popular response. Turner Layton's father was for many years assistant director of music in the Washington public schools, and it is said that this imposing gentleman could get music out of a hall full of empty chairs. There may be something hereditary therefore in the way in which the most lifeless instrument responds to Turner's touch.

Followed Sissle and Blake to England, whence they have recently returned successful. Noble Sissle was the friend and companion of Jim Europe,[4] who organized the New York Clef Club and was the most popular Negro musician of his day. After Europe's unfortunate death, Sissle and Eubie Blake became an extremely popular vaudeville team. Earlier, Blake used to play the piano for house-parties and dances around Baltimore, and later played in cabarets. Certain of his Baltimore friends point to him proudly now, and well they may: the accuracy and agility with which his fingers scamper over the keyboard is always a breath-taking wonder. Sissle and Blake, too, have learned the lessons taught by struggle and disaster. Time was when the "Shuffle Along" company, coming to Washington from New York for a Sunday afternoon engagement at the world's best Negro theatre, the Lincoln, entered the town with all the triumphal glamor of a circus. Almost every principal in the show had his or her own automobile, and they weren't designed or painted with an eye for modest retirement. The principals drove down from New York in their cars, if you please; which was entirely their own business, of course. The point is that they *could*. Sissle and Blake, it appears, still can. Such is the profitable contagion of a fad.

Pending a contemplated reunion of these unusual teams, Miller and Lyles have been playing with various Broadway revues. These comical fellows are both college graduates, and eminently respectable and conservative in private life. It is, by the way, a noteworthy thing about all of these men, Creamer, Johnstone, Layton, Sissle, Blake, Miller, and Lyles, that one never hears the slightest murmur of social criticism about any one of

---

2. By Miller and Lyles. *In Bamville* was by Sissle and Blake.
3. Clarence "Tandy" Johnstone and J. Turner Layton Jr. were a highly successful vaudeville team

of the 1920s.
4. James Reese Europe (1881–1919), conductor and composer.

them. They have managed to conduct themselves off stage entirely above reproach. It is no accident that the private lives of these dark-skinned stars are so circumspect. It is part of the explanation of their success.

V

It is only a part, however; and the fadlike characteristics of their experience may be another part. It may be a season's whim, then, this sudden, contagious interest in everything Negro. If so, when I go into a familiar cabaret, or the place where a familiar cabaret used to be, and find it transformed and relatively colorless, I may be observing just one form that the season's whim has taken.

But suppose it is a fad—to say that explains nothing. How came the fad? What occasions the focusing of attention on this particular thing—rounds up and gathers these seasonal whims, and centers them about the Negro? Cabarets are peculiar, mind you. They're not like theatres and concert halls. You don't just go to a cabaret and sit back and wait to be entertained. You get out on the floor and join the pow-wow and help entertain yourself. Granted that white people have long enjoyed the Negro entertainment as a diversion, is it not something different, something more, when they bodily throw themselves into Negro entertainment in cabarets? "Now Negroes go to their own cabarets to see how white people act."

And what do we see? Why, we see them actually playing Negro games. I watch them in that epidemic Negroism, the Charleston. I look on and envy them. They camel and fish-tail and turkey, they geche and black-bottom and scronch, they skate and buzzard and mess-around[5]—and they do them all better than I! This interest in the Negro is an active and participating interest. It is almost as if a traveler from the North stood watching an African tribe-dance, then suddenly found himself swept wildly into it, caught in its tidal rhythm.

Willingly would I be an outsider in this if I could know that I read it aright—that out of this change in the old familiar ways some finer thing may come. Is this interest akin to that of the Virginians on the veranda of a plantation's big-house—sitting genuinely spellbound as they hear the lugubrious strains floating up from the Negro quarters? Is it akin to that of the African explorer, Stanley,[6] leaving a village far behind, but halting in spite of himself to catch the boom of its distant drum? Is it significant of basic human responses, the effect of which, once admitted, will extend far beyond cabarets? Maybe these Nordics at last have tuned in on our wavelength. Maybe they are at last learning to speak our language.

1927

---

5. Various popular dances.
6. Sir Henry Morgan Stanley (1841–1904), English explorer.

ERIC WALROND

1898–1966

Even before the publication of his only book, *Tropic Death*, in 1926, the Caribbean immigrant Eric Walrond had established himself as a member of the African American literary community of New York. Walrond had acquired valuable experience working for such publications as *Opportunity* and *Negro World*, and he had also contributed articles to *The New Republic, Current History*, and the *Independent*. Nevertheless, although *Tropic Death* was warmly received by critics and fellow artists, including W. E. B. Du Bois and Langston Hughes, the book did not sell well. Since then, Walrond's reputation as a writer has suffered. Recent critics have had relatively little to say about his writing, and even less about his life, which is yet to be adequately documented.

Not long after his birth in Georgetown, British Guiana, in 1898, Walrond and his mother were abandoned by his father. His mother soon left with young Eric for Barbados, where he attended St. Stephen's Boys' School in Black Rock. No one is certain exactly when Walrond's mother took him to the Panama Canal Zone in search of his father, but they settled in Colón around 1910. The attempt at a reconciliation between Walrond's parents proved a failure. After studying under a series of private tutors from 1913 to 1916, Walrond secured a position as a clerk at the health department in Cristobal. He also worked as a sports writer, a court reporter, and a general reporter for the *Panama Star and Herald*, before leaving for the United States in 1918.

Unable to find work with any of the Harlem newspapers upon his arrival, he decided to go back to school. Walrond attended the City College of New York for three years before spending a year studying creative writing at Columbia University. In 1921, he became owner and editor of the weekly *Brooklyn and Long Island Informer*, which did not flourish. About two years later, he began to devote most of his energy to Marcus Garvey's Universal Negro Improvement Association (UNIA). In addition to serving as an associate editor of Garvey's *Negro World*, Walrond contributed articles and short fiction to a number of other publications. During this time he wrote what is probably his most important article, *The New Negro Faces America* (*Current History*, 1923), in which he criticized the late Booker T. Washington's "old style leadership," Du Bois's intellectual elitism, and even Garvey's fondness for pageantry.

Growing more and more impatient with Garvey, who was arrested on a charge of mail fraud in 1922, Walrond left the UNIA to become the business manager of *Opportunity* magazine under Charles S. Johnson. While working for Johnson, he published *Tropic Death*, a collection of ten vivid stories that captured his intensely impressionistic style at its best as well as his eye for exotic details and his awareness of the power of violence. He remained with *Opportunity* for some months after the book was published, but left the United States in 1927, for Europe. Virtually nothing was heard from him during his European wanderings, though he is known to have spent some time in France. He was working on a book about the Panama Canal when he died in London in 1966.

The Wharf Rats

I

Among the motley crew recruited to dig the Panama Canal were artisans from the four ends of the earth. Down in the Cut[1] drifted hordes of Italians, Greeks, Chinese, Negroes—a hardy, sun-defying set of white, black and yellow men. But the bulk of the actual brawn for the work was supplied by the dusky peons of those coral isles in the Caribbean ruled by Britain, France and Holland.

At the Atlantic end of the Canal the blacks were herded in box car huts buried in the jungles of "Silver City"; in the murky tenements perilously poised on the narrow banks of Faulke's River; in the low, smelting cabins of Coco Té. The "Silver Quarters" harbored the inky ones, their wives and pickaninnies.[2]

As it grew dark the hewers at the Ditch, exhausted, half-asleep, naked but for wormy singlets,[3] would hum queer creole tunes, play on guitar or piccolo, and jig to the rhythm of the *coombia*. It was a *brujerial* chant, for *obeah*,[4] a heritage of the French colonial, honey-combed the life of the Negro laboring camps. Over smoking pots, on black, death-black nights legends of the bloodiest were recited till they became the essence of a sort of Negro Koran.[5] One refuted them at the price of one's breath. And to question the verity of the *obeah*, to dismiss or reject it as the ungodly rite of some lurid, crack-brained Islander was to be an accursed pale-face, dog of a white. And the *obeah* man, in a fury of rage, would throw a machette at the heretic's head or—worse—burn on his doorstep at night a pyre of Maubé bark or green Ganja weed.[6]

On the banks of a river beyond Cristobal,[7] Coco Té sheltered a colony of Negroes enslaved to the *obeah*. Near a roundhouse, daubed with smoke and coal ash, a river serenely flowed away and into the guava region, at the eastern tip of Monkey Hill. Across the bay from it was a sand bank—a rising out of the sea—where ships stopt for coal.

In the first of the six chinky cabins making up the family quarters of Coco Té lived a stout, pot-bellied St. Lucian,[8] black as the coal hills he mended, by the name of Jean Baptiste. Like a host of the native St. Lucian emigrants, Jean Baptiste forgot where the French in him ended and the English began. His speech was the petulant *patois*[9] of the unlettered French black. Still, whenever he lapsed into His Majesty's English, it was with a thick Barbadian bias.

A coal passer at the Dry Dock, Jean Baptiste was a man of intense piety. After work, by the glow of a red, setting sun, he would discard his crusted overalls, get in [his] starched *crocus bag*,[1] aping the Yankee foreman on the

---

1. The trench being dug for the Panama Canal, constructed between 1904 and 1914.
2. Black children (usually used derogatorily).
3. Men's jersey undershirts.
4. A type of sorcery. "Coombia": a local dance. "Brujerial": pertaining to practitioners of magic.
5. The central Islamic text, as recited by Mohammed (570–632).
6. Marijuana. "Maubé bark": usually used to make a beverage.
7. A seaport on the Atlantic side of the Panama Canal.
8. From the island of St. Lucia in the West Indies.
9. Here, an ungrammatical mixture of two or more languages.
1. A bag made from a grassy plant.

other side of the track in the "Gold Quarters," and loll on his coffee-vined porch. There, dozing in a bamboo rocker, Celestin, his second wife, a becomingly stout brown beauty from Martinique, chanted gospel hymns to him.

Three sturdy sons Jean Baptiste's first wife had borne him—Philip, the eldest, a good-looking, black fellow; Ernest, shifty, cunning; and Sandel, aged eight. Another boy, said to be wayward and something of a ne'er-do-well, was sometimes spoken of. But Baptiste, a proud, disdainful man, never once referred to him in the presence of his children. No vagabond son of his could eat from his table or sit at his feet unless he went to "meeting." In brief, Jean Baptiste was a religious man. It was a thrust at the omnipresent *obeah*. He went to "meeting."[2] He made the boys go, too. All hands went, not to the Catholic Church, where Celestin secretly worshiped, but to the English Plymouth Brethren in the Spanish city of Colon.

Stalking about like a ghost in Jean Baptiste's household was a girl, a black ominous Trinidad girl. Had Jean Baptiste been a man given to curiosity about the nature of women, he would have viewed skeptically Maffi's adoption by Celestin. But Jean Baptiste was a man of lofty unconcern, and so Maffi remained there, shadowy, obdurate.

And Maffi was such a hardworking *patois*[3] girl. From the break of day she'd be at the sink, brightening the tinware. It was she who did the chores which Madame congenitally shirked. And towards sundown, when the labor trains had emptied, it was she who scoured the beach for cockles for Jean Baptiste's epicurean[4] palate.

And as night fell, Maffi, a lone, black figure, would disappear in the dark to dream on top of a canoe hauled up on the mooning beach. An eternity Maffi'd sprawl there, gazing at the frosting of the stars and the glitter of the black sea.

A cabin away lived a family of Tortola mulattoes by the name of Boyce. The father was also a man who piously went to "meeting"—gaunt and hollow-cheeked. The eldest boy, Esau, had been a journeyman tailor for ten years; the girl next him, Ora, was plump, dark, freckled; others came— a string of ulcered[5] girls until finally a pretty, opaque one, Maura.

Of the Bantu[6] tribe Maura would have been a person to turn and stare at. Crossing the line into Cristobal or Colon—a city of rarefied gayety—she was often mistaken for a native *señorita* or an urbanized Cholo Indian[7] girl. Her skin was the reddish yellow of old gold and in her eyes there lurked the glint of mother-of-pearl. Her hair, long as a jungle elf's was jettish, untethered. And her teeth were whiter than the full-blooded black Philip's.

Maura was brought up, like the children of Jean Baptiste, in the Plymouth Brethren. But the Plymouth Brethren was a harsh faith to bring hemmed-in peasant children up in, and Maura, besides, was of a gentle romantic nature. Going to the Yankee commissary at the bottom of Eleventh and Front Streets, she usually wore a leghorn hat. With flowers be-

---

2. Religious service.
3. Here, humble.
4. Refined.
5. Pimply.

6. A member of any of the linguistically interrelated peoples of central and southern Africa.
7. A Native Mesoamerican people.

decking it, she'd look in it older, much older than she really was. Which was an impression quite flattering to her. For Maura, unknown to Philip, was in love—in love with San Tie, a Chinese half-breed, son of a wealthy canteen proprietor in Colon. But San Tie liked to go fishing and deer hunting up the Monkey Hill lagoon, and the object of his occasional visits to Coco Té was the eldest son of Jean Baptiste. And thus it was through Philip that Maura kept in touch with the young Chinese Maroon.[8]

One afternoon Maura, at her wit's end, flew to the shed roof to Jean Baptiste's kitchen.

"Maffi," she cried, the words smoky on her lips, "Maffi, when Philip come in to-night tell 'im I want fo' see 'im particular, yes?"

"*Sacre gache!*[9] All de time Philip, Philip!" growled the Trinidad girl, as Maura, in heartaching preoccupation, sped towards the lawn. "Why she no le' 'im alone, yes?" And with a spatter she flecked the hunk of lard on Jean Baptiste's stewing okras.

As the others filed up front after dinner that evening Maffi said to Philip, pointing to the cabin across the way, "She—she want fo' see yo'."

Instantly Philip's eyes widened. Ah, he had good news for Maura! San Tie, after an absence of six days, was coming to Coco Té Saturday to hunt on the lagoon. And he'd relish the joy that'd flood Maura's face as she glimpsed the idol of her heart, the hero of her dreams! And Philip, a true son of Jean Baptiste, loved to see others happy, ecstatic.

But Maffi's curious rumination checked him. "All de time, Maura, Maura, me can't understand it, yes. But no mind, me go stop it, *oui*,[1] me go stop it, so help me—"

He crept up to her, gently holding her by the shoulders.

"Le' me go, *sacre!*" She shook off his hands bitterly. "Le' me go—yo' go to yo' Maura." And she fled to her room, locking the door behind her.

Philip sighed. He was a generous, good-natured sort. But it was silly to try to enlighten Maffi. It wasn't any use. He could as well have spoken to the tattered torsos the lazy waves puffed up on the shores of Coco Té.

II

"Philip, come on, a ship is in—let's go." Ernest, the wharf rat, seized him by the arm.

"Come," he said, "let's go before it's too late. I want to get some money, yes."

Dashing out of the house the two boys made for the wharf. It was dusk. Already the Hindus in the bachelor quarters were mixing their *rotie*[2] and the Negroes in their singlets were smoking and cooling off. Night was rapidly approaching. Sunset, an iridescent bit of molten gold, was enriching the stream with its last faint radiance.

The boys stole across the lawn and made their way to the pier.

"Careful," cried Philip, as Ernest slid between a prong of oyster-crusted piles to a raft below, "careful, these shells cut wussah'n a knife."

---

8. A black descended from fugitive slaves of the 17th and 18th centuries and living in the West Indies and the Guianas.

9. A mild oath (French).
1. Yes (French).
2. A kind of flat bread common in India.

On the raft the boys untied a rowboat they kept stowed away under the dock, got into it and pushed off. The liner still had two hours to dock. Tourists crowded its decks. Veering away from the barnacled piles the boys eased out into the churning ocean.

It was dusk. Night would soon be upon them. Philip took the oars while Ernest stripped down to loin cloth.

"Come, Philip, let me paddle—" Ernest took the oars. Afar on the dusky sea a whistle echoed. It was the pilot's signal to the captain of port. The ship would soon dock.

The passengers on deck glimpsed the boys. It piqued their curiosity to see two black boys in a boat amid stream.

"All right, mistah," cried Ernest, "a penny, mistah."

He sprang at the guilder[3] as it twisted and turned through a streak of silver dust to the bottom of the sea. Only the tips of his crimson toes—a sherbet-like foam—and up he came with the coin between his teeth.

Deep sea gamin,[4] Philip off yonder, his mouth noisy with coppers, gargled, "This way, sah, as far as yo' like, mistah."

An old red-bearded Scot, in spats and mufti,[5] presumably a lover of the exotic in sport, held aloft a sovereign. A sovereign! Already red, and sore by virtue of the leaps and plunges in the briny swirl, Philip's eyes bulged at its yellow gleam.

"Ovah yah, sah—"

Off in a whirlpool the man tossed it. And like a garfish Philip took after it, a falling arrow in the stream. His body, once in the water, tore ahead. For a spell the crowd on the ship held its breath. "Where is he?" "Where is the nigger swimmer gone to?" Even Ernest, driven to the boat by the race for such an ornate prize, cold, shivering, his teeth chattering—even he watched with trembling and anxiety. But Ernest's concern was of a deeper kind. For there, where Philip had leaped, was Deathpool—a spawning place for sharks, for baracoudas!

But Philip rose—a brief gurgling sputter—a ripple on the sea—and the Negro's crinkled head was above the water.

"Hey!" shouted Ernest, "there, Philip! Down!"

And down Philip plunged. One—two—minutes. God, how long they seemed! And Ernest anxiously waited. But the bubble on the water boiled, kept on boiling—a sign that life still lasted! It comforted Ernest.

Suddenly Philip, panting, spitting, pawing, dashed through the water like a streak of lightning.

"Shark!" cried a voice aboard ship. "Shark! There he is, a great big one! Run, boy! Run for your life!"

From the edge of the boat Philip saw the monster as twice, thrice it circled the boat. Several times the shark made a dash for it endeavoring to strike it with its murderous tail.

The boys quietly made off. But the shark still followed the boat. It was a pale green monster. In the glittering dusk it seemed black to Philip. Fattened on the swill of the abattoir[6] nearby and the beef tossed from the

---

3. A Dutch coin.   5. Here, perhaps a kilt.
4. Vagabond boy, street urchin.   6. Slaughterhouse.

decks of countless ships in port it had become used to the taste of flesh and the smell of blood.

"Yo' know, Ernest," said Philip, as he made the boat fast to a raft, "one time I thought he wuz rubbin' 'gainst me belly. He wuz such a big able one. But it wuz wuth it, Ernie, it wuz wuth it—"

In his palm there was a flicker of gold. Ernest emptied his loin cloth and together they counted the money, dressed, and trudged back to the cabin.

On the lawn Philip met Maura. Ernest tipped his cap, left his brother, and went into the house. As he entered Maffi, pretending to be scouring a pan, was flushed and mute as a statue. And Ernest, starved, went in the dining room and for a long time stayed there. Unable to bear it any longer, Maffi sang out, "Ernest, whey Philip dey?"

"Outside—some whey—ah talk to Maura—"

"Yo' sure yo' no lie, Ernest?" she asked, suspended.

"Yes, up cose, I jes' lef' 'im 'tandin' out dey—why?"

"Nutton—"

He suspected nothing. He went on eating while Maffi tiptoed to the shed roof. Yes, confound it, there he was, near the stand-pipe, talking to Maura!

"Go stop *ee, oui*," she hissed impishly. "Go 'top ee, yes."

III

Low, shadowy, the sky painted Maura's face bronze. The sea, noisy, enraged, sent a blob of wind about her black, wavy hair. And with her back to the sea, her hair blew loosely about her face.

"D'ye think, d'ye think he really likes me, Philip?"

"I'm positive he do, Maura," vowed the youth.

And an ageing faith shone in Maura's eyes. No longer was she a silly, insipid girl. Something holy, reverent had touched her. And in so doing it could not fail to leave an impress of beauty. It was worshipful. And it mellowed, ripened her.

Weeks she had waited for word of San Tie. And the springs of Maura's life took on a noble ecstasy. Late at night, after the others had retired, she'd sit up in bed, dreaming. Sometimes they were dreams of envy. For Mama began to look with eyes of comparison upon the happiness of the Italian wife of the boss riveter at the Dry Dock—the lady on the other side of the railroad tracks in the "Gold Quarters" for whom she sewed—who got a fresh baby every year and who danced in a world of silks and satins. Yes, Maura had dreams, love dreams of San Tie, the flashy half-breed, son of a Chinese beer seller and a Jamaica Maroon, who had swept her off her feet by a playful wink of the eye.

"Tell me, Philip, does he work? Or does he play the lottery—what does he do, tell me!"

"I dunno," Philip replied with mock lassitude, "I dunno myself—"

"But it doesn't matter, Philip. I don't want to be nosy, see? I'm simply curious about everything that concerns him, see?"

Ah, but Philip wished to cherish Maura, to shield her, be kind to her. And so he lied to her. He did not tell her he had first met San Tie behind the counter of his father's saloon in the Colon tenderloin,[7] for he would have had to tell, besides, why he, Philip, had gone there. And that would have led him, a youth of meager guile, to Celestin Baptiste's mulish regard for anisette[8] which he procured her. He dared not tell her, well-meaning fellow that he was, what San Tie, a fiery comet in the night life of the district, had said to him the day before. "She sick in de head, yes," he had said. "Ah, me no dat saht o' man—don't she know no bettah, egh, Philip?" But Philip desired to be kindly, and hid it from Maura.

"What is to-day?" she cogitated, aloud, "Tuesday. You say he's comin' fo' hunt Saturday, Philip? Wednesday—four more days. I can wait. I can wait. I'd wait a million years fo' 'im, Philip."

But Saturday came and Maura, very properly, was shy as a duck. Other girls, like Hilda Long, a Jamaica brunette, the flower of a bawdy cabin up by the abattoir, would have been less genteel. Hilda would have caught San Tie by the lapels of his coat and in no time would have got him told.

But Maura was lowly, trepid, shy. To her he was a dream—a luxury to be distantly enjoyed. He was not to be touched. And she'd wait till he decided to come to her. And there was no fear, either, of his ever failing to come. Philip had seen to that. Had not he been the intermediary between them? And all Maura needed now was to sit back, and wait till San Tie came to her.

And besides, who knows, brooded Maura, San Tie might be a bashful fellow.

But when, after an exciting hunt, the Chinese mulatto returned from the lagoon, nodded stiffly to her, said good-by to Philip and kept on to the scarlet city, Maura was frantic.

"Maffi," she said, "tell Philip to come here quick—"

It was the same as touching a match to the *patois* girl's dynamite. "Yo' mek me sick," she said. "Go call he yo'self, yo' ole hag, yo' ole fire hag yo'." But Maura, flighty in despair, had gone on past the lawn.

"Ah go stop *ee, oui*," she muttered diabolically, "Ah go stop it, yes. This very night."

Soon as she got through lathering the dishes she tidied up and came out on the front porch.

It was a humid dusk, and the glowering sky sent a species of fly—bloody as a tick—buzzing about Jean Baptiste's porch. There he sat, rotund, and sleepy-eyed, rocking and languidly brushing the darting imps away.

"Wha' yo' gwine, Maffi?" asked Celestin Baptiste, fearing to wake the old man.

"Ovah to de Jahn Chinaman shop, mum," answered Maffi unheeding.

"Fi' what?"

"Fi' buy some wash blue, mum."

And she kept on down the road past the Hindu kiosk[9] to the Negro mess house.

---

7. District notorious for vice and graft.
8. A cordial flavored with anise seed.

9. Open pavillion. "Wash blue": bleachlike laundry additive that whitens clothes.

IV

"Oh, Philip," cried Maura, "I am so unhappy. Didn't he ask about me at all? Didn't he say he'd like to visit me—didn't he giv' yo' any message fo' me, Philip?"

The boy toyed with a blade of grass. His eyes were downcast. Sighing heavily he at last spoke. "No, Maura, he didn't ask about you."

"What, he didn't ask about me? Philip? I don't believe it! Oh, my God!"

She clung to Philip, mutely; her face, her breath coming warm and fast.

"I wish to God I'd never seen either of you," cried Philip.

"Ah, but wasn't he your friend, Philip? Didn't yo' tell me that?" And the boy bowed his head sadly.

"Answer me!" she screamed, shaking him. "Weren't you his friend?"

"Yes, Maura—"

"But you lied to me, Philip, you lied to me! You took messages from me—you brought back—lies!" Two *pearls*, large as pigeon's eggs, shone in Maura's burnished face.

"To think," she cried in a hollow sepulchral voice, "that I dreamed about a ghost, a man who didn't exist. Oh, God, why should I suffer like this? Why was I ever born? What did I do, what did my people do, to deserve such misery as this?"

She rose, leaving Philip with his head buried in his hands. She went into the night, tearing her hair, scratching her face, raving.

"Oh, how happy I was! I was a happy girl! I was so young and I had such merry dreams! And I wanted so little! I was carefree—"

Down to the shore of the sea she staggered, the wind behind her, the night obscuring her.

"Maura!" cried Philip, running after her. "Maura! come back!"

Great sheaves of clouds buried the moon, and the wind bearing up from the sea bowed the cypress and palm lining the beach.

"Maura—Maura—"

He bumped into some one, a girl, black, part of the dense pattern of the tropical night.

"Maffi," cried Philip, "have you seen Maura down yondah?"

The girl quietly stared at him. Had Philip lost his mind?

"Talk, no!" he cried, exasperated.

And his quick tones sharpened Maffi's vocal anger. Thrusting him aside, she thundered, "Think I'm she keeper! Go'n look fo' she yo'self. I is not she keeper! Le' me pass, move!"

Towards the end of the track he found Maura, heartrendingly weeping.

"Oh, don't cry, Maura! Never mind, Maura!"

He helped her to her feet, took her to the stand-pipe[1] on the lawn, bathed her temples and sat soothingly, uninterruptingly, beside her.

---

1. Public water faucet.

V

At daybreak the next morning Ernest rose and woke Philip.

He yawned, put on the loin cloth, seized a "cracked licker" skillet,[2] and stole cautiously out of the house. Of late Jean Baptiste had put his foot down on his sons' copper-diving proclivities. And he kept at the head of his bed a greased cat-o'-nine-tails which he would use on Philip himself if the occasion warranted.

"Come on, Philip, let's go—"

Yawning and scratching Philip followed. The grass on the lawn was bright and icy with the dew. On the railroad tracks the six o'clock labor trains were coupling. A rosy mist flooded the dawn. Out in the stream the tug *Exotic* snorted in a heavy fog.

On the wharf Philip led the way to the rafters below.

"Look out fo' that *crapeau*,[3] Ernest, don't step on him, he'll spit on you."

The frog splashed into the water. Prickle-backed crabs and oysters and myriad other shells spawned on the rotting piles. The boys paddled the boat. Out in the dawn ahead of them the tug puffed a path through the foggy mist. The water was chilly. Mist glistened on top of it. Far out, beyond the buoys, Philip encountered a placid, untroubled sea. The liner, a German tourist boat, was loaded to the bridge. The water was as still as a lake of ice.

"All right, Ernest, let's hurry—"

Philip drew in the oars. The *Kron Prinz Wilhelm* came near. Huddled in thick European coats, the passengers viewed from their lofty estate the spectacle of two naked Negro boys peeping up at them from a wiggly *bateau*.[4]

"Penny, mistah, penny, mistah!"

Somebody dropped a quarter. Ernest, like a shot, flew after it. Half a foot down he caught it as it twisted and turned in the gleaming sea. Vivified by the icy dip, Ernest was a raving wolf and the folk aboard dealt a lavish hand.

"Ovah, yah, mistah," cried Philip, "ovah, yah."

For a Dutch guilder Philip gave an exhibition of "cork." Under something of a ledge on the side of the boat he had stuck a piece of cork. Now, after his and Ernest's mouths were full of coins, he could afford to be extravagant and treat the Europeans to a game of West Indian "cork."

Roughly ramming the cork down in the water, Philip, after the fifteenth ram or so, let it go, and flew back, upwards, having thus "lost" it. It was Ernest's turn now, as a sort of end-man, to scramble forward to the spot where Philip had dug it down and "find" it; the first one to do so, having the prerogative, which he jealously guarded, of raining on the other a series of thundering leg blows. As boys in the West Indies Philip and Ernest had played it. Of a Sunday the Negro fishermen on the Barbadoes coast made a pagan rite of it. Many a Bluetown dandy got his spine cracked in a game of "cork."

With a passive interest the passengers viewed the proceedings. In a game

2. Frying pan with breakfast meats in it.   French).
3. Toad (French patois; *crapaud* in standard   4. Boat (French).

of "cork," the cork after a succession of "rammings" is likely to drift many feet away whence it was first "lost." One had to be an expert, quick, alert, to spy and promptly seize it as it popped up on the rolling waves. Once Ernest got it and endeavored to make much of the possession. But Philip, besides being two feet taller than he, was slippery as an eel, and Ernest, despite all the artful ingenuity at his command, was able to do no more than ineffectively beat the water about him. Again and again he tried, but to no purpose.

Becoming reckless, he let the cork drift too far away from him and Philip seized it.

He twirled it in the air like a crap shooter, and dug deep down in the water with it, "lost" it, then leaped back, briskly waiting for it to rise.

About them the water, due to the ramming and beating, grew restive. Billows sprang up; soaring, swelling waves sent the skiff nearer the shore. Anxiously Philip and Ernest watched for the cork to make its ascent.

It was all a bit vague to the whites on the deck, and an amused chuckle floated down to the boys.

And still the cork failed to come up.

"I'll go after it," said Philip at last, "I'll go and fetch it." And, from the edge of the boat he leaped, his body long and resplendent in the rising tropic sun.

It was a suction sea, and down in it Philip plunged. And it was lazy, too, and willful—the water. Ebony-black, it tugged and mocked. Old brass staves—junk dumped there by the retiring French—thick, yawping mud, barrel hoops, tons of obsolete brass, a wealth of slimy steel faced him. Did a "rammed" cork ever go that deep?

And the water, stirring, rising, drew a haze over Philip's eyes. Had a cuttlefish, an octopus, a nest of eels been routed? It seemed so to Philip, blindly diving, pawing. And the sea, the tide—touching the roots of Deathpool—tugged and tugged. His gathering hands stuck in mud. Iron staves bruised his shins. It was black down there. Impenetrable.

Suddenly, like a flash of lightning, a vision blew across Philip's brow. It was a soaring shark's belly. Drunk on the nectar of the deep, it soared above Philip—rolling, tumbling, rolling. It had followed the boy's scent with the accuracy of a diver's rope.

Scrambling to the surface, Philip struck out for the boat. But the sea, the depths of it wrested out of an æon's slumber, had sent it a mile from his diving point. And now, as his strength ebbed, a shark was at his heels.

"Shark! Shark!" was the cry that went up from the ship.

Hewing a lane through the hostile sea Philip forgot the cunning of the doddering beast and swam noisier than he needed to. Faster grew his strokes. His line was a straight, dead one. Fancy strokes and dives—giraffe leaps . . . he summoned into play. He shot out recklessly. One time he suddenly paused—and floated for a stretch. Another time he swam on his back, gazing at the chalky sky. He dived for whole lengths.

But the shark, a bloaty, stone-colored man-killer, took a shorter cut. Circumnavigating the swimmer it bore down upon him with the speed of a hurricane. Within adequate reach it turned, showed its gleaming belly, seizing its prey.

A fiendish gargle—the gnashing of bones—as the sea once more closed its jaws on Philip.

Some one aboard ship screamed. Women fainted. There was talk of a gun. Ernest, an oar upraised, capsized the boat as he tried to inflict a blow on the coursing, chop-licking maneater.

And again the fish turned. It scraped the waters with its deadly fins.

. . . .

At Coco Té, at the fledging of the dawn, Maffi, polishing the tinware, hummed an *obeah* melody

> Trinidad is a damn fine place
> But *obeah* down dey. . . .

Peace had come to her at last.

1926

MARITA BONNER

1899–1971

Among the best educated of the writers and artists of the Harlem Renaissance, Marita Odette Bonner (sometimes identified as Marieta Boner) was also one of the more versatile and talented.

Bonner never lived in Harlem, and seldom visited New York, but certainly left her mark on the literary movement. She was born in Brookline, Massachusetts, near Boston. After excelling as a student in Brookline High School, she entered Radcliffe College in nearby Cambridge in 1918. There she studied English and comparative literature (she would eventually become fluent in German) and made a name for herself as a singer. Admitted to an acclaimed and highly competitive writing seminar, she also laid, while at Radcliffe, the foundations for her literary career.

After receiving a bachelor's degree in 1922, Bonner taught for two years at the Bluefield Colored Institute in Bluefield, Virginia. Then, responding to the growing excitement among young African Americans about literature and culture, her writing began to mature with her move to Washington, D.C., in 1924 to teach at a high school. An important mentor was the poet Georgia Douglas Johnson, who welcomed Bonner to the celebrated weekly salon at her S Street home that at one time included Langston Hughes, Jean Toomer, Alain Locke, Willis Richardson, and most of the African American writers living in the district.

So multitalented was Bonner that she was able to win, in the 1920s, important prizes in the field of the essay, the short story, drama, and music. Her keen awareness of herself as a woman and an African American in an age of profound social change led to her remarkable landmark essay *On Being Young—a Woman—and Colored*, which appeared in December 1925 in the *Crisis*. Her dramatic writing, which included plays such as *The Pot Maker* (1927), *The Purple Flower* (1928), and *Exit: An Illusion* (1929), also brought her widespread recognition among black Americans as an important figure in the theater movement that included W. E. B. Du Bois and the Krigwa group in New York and Willis Richardson and other playwrights in Washington, D.C. In the 1920s, she also published several stories that further enhanced her reputation.

With her marriage in 1930 to an accountant, William Occomy, Bonner left Washington and settled in Chicago, where she lived for the rest of her life. In the following years she concentrated on the demands of her family, which included three children, but also wrote fiction, principally short stories, that responded to the realities of Chicago life, especially among black Americans living there. Around 1941, she more or less stopped writing, although to the end of her life she cherished literature and saw herself as a writer. In 1941, she resumed teaching, first at the Phillips High School in Chicago, and then, between 1950 and 1963, at the Doolittle School (also in Chicago), which served educationally deprived children. In 1971 she died following a fire at her Chicago home.

In almost everything she wrote, Bonner showed a keen interest in exploring the distance between the private, inner self of an individual and the suppositions about that individual generated by prejudices about race, class, and gender. She brought a special insight to her depictions of black feminine consciousness but never sought to limit herself to this subject. Her best stories, such as *Drab Rambles* (1927), *Tin Can* (1934), and *A Sealed Pod* (1936), are often presented as filtered through a complex, subjective consciousness; at their best, they fascinate the reader with their poetical and highly sensitive depictions of human character.

On Being Young—a Woman—and Colored

You start out after you have gone from kindergarten to sheepskin covered with sundry Latin phrases.

At least you know what you want life to give you. A career as fixed and as calmly brilliant as the North Star. The one real thing that money buys. Time. Time to do things. A house that can be as delectably out of order and as easily put in order as the doll-house of "playing-house" days. And of course, a husband you can look up to without looking down on yourself.

Somehow you feel like a kitten in a sunny catnip field that sees sleek, plump brown field mice and yellow baby chicks sitting coyly, side by side, under each leaf. A desire to dash three or four ways seizes you.

That's Youth.

But you know that things learned need testing—acid testing—to see if they are really after all, an interwoven part of you. All your life you have heard of the debt you owe "Your People" because you have managed to have the things they have not largely had.

So you find a spot where there are hordes of them—of course below the Line—to be your catnip field while you close your eyes to mice and chickens alike.

If you have never lived among your own, you feel prodigal. Some warm untouched current flows through them—through you—and drags you out into the deep waters of a new sea of human foibles and mannerisms; of a peculiar psychology and prejudices. And one day you find yourself entangled—enmeshed—pinioned in the seaweed of a Black Ghetto.

Not a Ghetto, placid like the Strasse[1] that flows, outwardly unperturbed and calm in a stream of religious belief, but a peculiar group. Cut off, flung

1. Street (German).

together, shoved aside in a bundle because of color and with no more in common.

Unless color is, after all, the real bond.

Milling around like live fish in a basket. Those at the bottom crushed into a sort of stupid apathy by the weight of those on top. Those on top leaping, leaping; leaping to scale the sides; to get out.

There are two "colored" movies, innumerable parties—and cards. Cards played so intensely that it fascinates and repulses at once.

Movies.

Movies worthy and worthless—but not even a low-caste spoken stage.

Parties, plentiful. Music and dancing and much that is wit and color and gaiety. But they are like the richest chocolate; stuffed costly chocolates that make the taste go stale if you have too many of them. That make plain whole bread taste like ashes.

There are all the earmarks of a group within a group. Cut off all around from ingress from or egress to other groups. A sameness of type. The smug self-satisfaction of an inner measurement; a measurement by standards known within a limited group and not those of an unlimited, seeing, world. . . . Like the blind, blind mice. Mice whose eyes have been blinded.

Strange longing seizes hold of you. You wish yourself back where you can lay your dollar down and sit in a dollar seat to hear voices, strings, reeds that have lifted the World out, up, beyond things that have bodies and walls. Where you can marvel at new marbles and bronzes and flat colors that will make men forget that things exist in a flesh more often than in spirit. Where you can sink your body in a cushioned seat and sink your soul at the same time into a section of life set before you on the boards for a few hours.

You hear that up at New York this is to be seen; that, to be heard.

You decide the next train will take you there.

You decide the next second that that train will not take you, nor the next—nor the next for some time to come.

For you know that—being a woman—you cannot twice a month or twice a year, for that matter, break away to see or hear anything in a city that is supposed to see and hear too much.

That's being a woman. A woman of any color.

You decide that something is wrong with a world that stifles and chokes; that cuts off and stunts; hedging in, pressing down on eyes, ears and throat. Somehow all wrong.

You wonder how it happens there that—say five hundred miles from the Bay State[2]—Anglo Saxon intelligence is so warped and stunted.

How judgment and discernment are bred out of the race. And what has become of discrimination? Discrimination of the right sort. Discrimination that the best minds have told you weighs shadows and nuances and spiritual differences before it catalogues. The kind they have taught you all of your life was best: that looks clearly past generalization and past appearance to dissect, to dig down to the real heart of matters. That casts aside

2. Massachusetts.

rapid summary conclusions, drawn from primary inference, as Daniel did the spiced meats.[3]

Why can't they then perceive that there is a difference in the glance from a pair of eyes that look, mildly docile, at "white ladies" and those that, impersonally and perceptively—aware of distinctions—see only women who happen to be white?

Why do they see a colored woman only as a gross collection of desires, all uncontrolled, reaching out for their Apollos and the Quasimodos[4] with avid indiscrimination?

Why unless you talk in staccato squawks—brittle as seashells—unless you "champ" gum—unless you cover two yards square when you laugh—unless your taste runs to violent colors—impossible perfumes and more impossible clothes—are you a feminine Caliban craving to pass for Ariel?[5]

An empty imitation of an empty invitation. A mime; a sham; a copy-cat. A hollow re-echo. A froth, a foam. A fleck of the ashes of superficiality?

Everything you touch or taste now is like the flesh of an unripe persimmon.

. . . Do you need to be told what that is being . . . ?

Old ideas, old fundamentals seem worm-eaten, out-grown, worthless, bitter; fit for the scrap-heap of Wisdom.

What you had thought tangible and practical has turned out to be a collection of "blue-flower" theories.

If they have not discovered how to use their accumulation of facts, they are useless to you in Their world.

Every part of you becomes bitter.

But—"In Heaven's name, do not grow bitter. Be bigger than they are"—exhort white friends who have never had to draw breath in a Jim-Crow train. Who have never had petty putrid insult dragged over them—drawing blood—like pebbled sand on your body where the skin is tenderest. On your body where the skin is thinnest and tenderest.

You long to explode and hurt everything white; friendly; unfriendly. But you know that you cannot live with a chip on your shoulder even if you can manage a smile around your eyes—without getting steely and brittle and losing the softness that makes you a woman.

For chips make you bend your body to balance them. And once you bend, you lose your poise, your balance, and the chip gets into you. The real you. You get hard.

. . . And many things in you can ossify . . .

And you know, being a woman, you have to go about it gently and quietly, to find out and to discover just what is wrong. Just what can be done.

You see clearly that they have acquired things.

Money; money. Money to build with, money to destroy. Money to swim in. Money to drown in. Money.

An ascendancy of wisdom. An incalculable hoard of wisdom in all fields, in all things collected from all quarters of humanity.

---

3. See Daniel 1:8–16, where he refused to "defile himself with the portion of the king's meat."
4. Quasimodo is the central character in Victor Hugo's novel *The Hunchback of Notre Dame*

(1831).
5. Savage and ugly trying to pass as noble and beautiful. Caliban and Ariel are characters in Shakespeare's *The Tempest*.

A stupendous mass of things.

Things.

So, too, the Greeks . . . Things.

And the Romans. . . .

And you wonder and wonder why they have not discovered how to handle deftly and skillfully, Wisdom, stored up for them—like the honey for the Gods on Olympus—since time unknown.

You wonder and you wonder until you wander out into Infinity, where—if it is to be found anywhere—Truth really exists.

The Greeks had possessions, culture. They were lost because they did not understand.

The Romans owned more than anyone else. Trampled under the heel of Vandals and Civilization, because they would not understand.

Greeks. Did not understand.

Romans. Would not understand.

"They." Will not understand.

So you find they have shut Wisdom up and have forgotten to find the key that will let her out. They have trapped, trammeled, lashed her to themselves with thews and thongs and theories. They have ransacked sea and earth and air to bring every treasure to her. But she sulks and will not work for a world with a whitish hue because it has snubbed her twin sister, Understanding.

You see clearly—off there is Infinity—Understanding. Standing alone, waiting for someone to really want her.

But she is so far out there is not way to snatch at her and really drag her in.

So—being a woman—you can wait.

You must sit quietly without a chip. Not sodden—and weighted as if your feet were cast in the iron of your soul. Not wasting strength in enervating gestures as if two hundred years of bonds and whips had really tricked you into nervous uncertainty.

But quiet; quiet. Like Buddha—who brown like I am—sat entirely at ease, entirely sure of himself; motionless and knowing, a thousand years before the white man knew there was so very much difference between feet and hands.

Motionless on the outside. But on the inside?

Silent.

Still . . . "Perhaps Buddha is a woman."

So you too. Still; quiet; with a smile, ever so slight, at the eyes so that Life will flow into and not by you. And you can gather, as it passes, the essences, the overtones, the tints, the shadows; draw understanding to yourself.

And then you can, when Time is ripe, swoop to your feet—at your full height—at a single gesture.

Ready to go where?

Why . . . Wherever God motions.

1925

STERLING A. BROWN

1901–1989

James Weldon Johnson seems to have spoken for the majority of modern African American critics when he declared that dialect poetry (most notably that of Paul Laurence Dunbar and his followers) was fundamentally limited to the expression of humor and pathos. However, his encounter with the dialect verse in Sterling A. Brown's *Southern Road* (1932) forced him to reevaluate the place of "the common, racy, living speech of the Negro" in literature—so much so that he finally found more to praise in Brown's dialect pieces than in the more traditional poems in the same volume. On the basis of that single collection of verse, Brown established himself as one of the two major folk poets of the Harlem Renaissance. His only important rival was Langston Hughes.

Brown was born in Washington, D.C., with advantages and options that were available to few blacks at the turn of the century. His father, Sterling Nelson Brown, who had counted Frederick Douglass and Paul Laurence Dunbar among his personal friends, was a well-published professor at Howard University. The young Brown attended Dunbar High School, where he encountered such teachers as Angelina Grimké and Jessie Redmon Fauset. He graduated from Williams College in 1922, then went on to take his master's degree from Harvard the following year. Nevertheless, he maintained throughout his life that his best teachers were the poor black folk of the South, particularly in the Lynchburg, Virginia, area, where he taught English at the Virginia Seminary for three years.

In 1929, Brown joined the faculty at Howard University. Three years later, when *Southern Road* appeared, he found himself popular with almost all the critics—except for his fellow English professors, who tended to look down on his passion for jazz and the blues. After he failed to find a publisher for his second collection of verse, *No Hiding Place*, Brown concentrated on the writing of criticism and the compiling of anthologies, including *The Negro in American Fiction* (1937), *Negro Poetry and Drama* (1937), and one of the most important compilations in African American history, *The Negro Caravan* (1941, edited with Arthur P. Davis and Ulysses Lee). He also devoted a good deal of energy to teaching; Brown later claimed that his students were his true legacy.

Although he remained at Howard until 1969, Brown spent three semesters teaching at Vassar College, where in 1945 he was offered a full-time position. That such a prestigious institution should invite an African American to join its faculty was shocking enough to be national news at the time. But Brown's devotion to Howard, where he was extremely popular with students, was such that he declined this offer. In 1971, Howard awarded him an honorary doctorate. In 1975, Brown at last published his second collection of verse, *The Last Ride of Wild Bill and Eleven Narratives; Southern Road* was also reprinted. Five years later, the poet Michael S. Harper brought out *The Collected Poems of Sterling A. Brown*, which included a good deal of the material from the rejected volume *No Hiding Place*. When Brown died in 1989, it was amid a revival of critical interest in his work that seems likely to endure.

Odyssey of Big Boy

Lemme be wid Casey Jones,[1]
   Lemme be wid Stagolee,[2]
Lemme be wid such like men
   When Death takes hol' on me,
     When Death takes hol' on me. . . .   5

Done skinned[3] as a boy in Kentucky hills,
   Druv steel dere as a man,
Done stripped tobacco in Virginia fiel's
   Alongst de River Dan,[4]
     Alongst de River Dan;   10

Done mined de coal in West Virginia,
   Liked dat job jes' fine,
Till a load o' slate curved roun' my head,
   Won't work in no mo' mine,
     Won't work in no mo' mine;   15

Done shocked de corn in Marylan',
   In Georgia done cut cane,
Done planted rice in South Caline,
   But won't do dat again,
     Do dat no mo' again.   20

Been roustabout in Memphis,
   Dockhand in Baltimore,
Done smashed up freight on Norfolk wharves,
   A fust class stevedore,
     A fust class stevedore. . . .   25

Done slung hash yonder in de North
   On de ole Fall River Line,
Done busted suds[5] in li'l New York,
   Which ain't no work o' mine—
     Lawd, ain't no work o' mine.   30

Done worked and loafed on such like jobs,
   Seen what dey is to see,
Done had my time wid a pint[6] on my hip
   An' a sweet gal on my knee,
     Sweet mommer on my knee: 35

Had stovepipe blond in Macon,
   Yaller gal in Marylan',
In Richmond had a choklit brown,

---

1. U.S. locomotive engineer and folk hero (1864–1900).
2. Also known as Stacker Lee (or Stackerlee), a prominent figure in African American folklore.
3. Hunted animals for their pelts.
4. A river in south-central Virginia.
5. I.e., worked as a dishwasher or launderer. "Fall River Line": a boat line from Fall River, Massachusetts, to New York.
6. Of liquor.

Called me huh monkey man—
  Huh big fool monkey man.   40

Had two fair browns in Arkansaw
  And three in Tennessee,
Had Creole gal in New Orleans,
  Sho Gawd did two time me—
    Lawd two time, fo' time me—   45

But best gal what I evah had
  Done put it over dem,
A gal in Southwest Washington
  At Four'n half and M[7]—
    Four'n half and M. . . .   50

Done took my livin' as it came,
  Done grabbed my joy, done risked my life;
Train done caught me on de trestle,[8]
  Man done caught me wid his wife,
    His doggone purty wife. . . .   55

I done had my women,
  I done had my fun;
Cain't do much complainin'
  When my jag[9] is done,
    Lawd, Lawd, my jag is done.   60

An' all dat Big Boy axes
  When time comes fo' to go,
Lemme be wid John Henry,[1] steel drivin' man,
  Lemme be wid old Jazzbo,
    Lemme be wid ole Jazzbo. . . .   65

                                  1927

Long Gone

I laks yo' kin' of lovin',
  Ain't never caught you wrong,
But it jes' ain' nachal
  Fo' to stay here long;

It jes' ain' nachal   5
  Fo' a railroad man,
With a itch fo' travelin'
  He cain't understan'. . . .

I looks at de rails,
  An' I looks at de ties,   10

7. On M Street, between Fourth and Fifth streets.   9. Spree.
8. Bridge.   1. A black folk hero.

An' I hears an ole freight
    Puffin' up de rise,

An' at nights on my pallet,
    When all is still,
I listens fo' de empties [1]   15
    Bumpin' up de hill;

When I oughta be quiet,
    I is got a itch
Fo' to hear de whistle blow
    Fo' de crossin' or de switch, [2]   20

An' I knows de time's a-nearin'
    When I got to ride,
Though it's homelike and happy
    At yo' side.

You is done all you could do   25
    To make me stay;
'Tain't no fault of yours I'se leavin'—
    I'se jes dataway.

I is got to see some people
    I ain't never seen,   30
Gotta highball thu some country
    Whah I never been.

I don't know which way I'm travelin'—
    Far or near,
All I knows fo' certain is   35
    I cain't stay here.

Ain't no call at all, sweet woman,
    Fo' to carry on—
Jes' my name and jes' my habit
    To be Long Gone. . . .   40

                1931

Southern Road

Swing dat hammer—hunh [1]—
Steady, bo';
Swing dat hammer—hunh—
Steady, bo';
Ain't no rush, bebby,   5
Long ways to go.

1. The empty, and therefore noisily rattling, train cars.
2. A device for diverting trains from one track to another.

1. The groan of the chain-gang worker as his hammer strikes.

Burner tore his—hunh—
Black heart away;[2]
Burner tore his—hunh—
Black heart away;   10
Got me life,[3] bebby,
An' a day.

Gal's on Fifth Street[4]—hunh—
Son done gone;
Gal's on Fifth Street—hunh—   15
Son done gone;
Wife's in de ward,[5] bebby,
Babe's not bo'n.

My ole man died—hunh—
Cussin' me;   20
My ole man died—hunh—
Cussin' me;
Ole lady rocks, bebby,
Huh misery.

Doubleshackled—hunh—   25
Guard behin';
Doubleshackled—hunh—
Guard behin';
Ball an' chain, bebby,
On my min'.   30

White man tells me—hunh—
Damn yo' soul;
White man tells me—hunh—
Damn yo' soul;
Got no need, bebby,   35
To be tole.

Chain gang nevah—hunh—
Let me go;
Chain gang nevah—hunh—
Let me go;   40
Po' los' boy, bebby,
Evahmo'. . . .

1931

---

2. I.e., he shot a man in the heart. "Burner": gun.   4. His daughter is now a prostitute.
3. I.e., he was sentenced to life imprisonment.   5. In the hospital.

Strong Men

The strong men keep coming on.
SANDBURG.[1]

They dragged you from homeland,
They chained you in coffles,[2]
They huddled you spoon-fashion in filthy hatches,
They sold you to give a few gentlemen ease.

They broke you in like oxen,   5
They scourged you,
They branded you,
They made your women breeders,
They swelled your numbers with bastards. . . .
They taught you the religion they disgraced.   10

You sang:
    Keep a-inchin' along
    Lak a po' inch worm. . . .

You sang:
    Bye and bye   15
    I'm gonna lay down dis heaby load. . . .

You sang:
    Walk togedder, chillen,
    Dontcha git weary. . . .
        The strong men keep a-comin' on   20
        The strong men git stronger.

They point with pride to the roads you built for them,
They ride in comfort over the rails you laid for them.
They put hammers in your hands
And said—Drive so much before sundown.   25

You sang:
    Ain't no hammah
    In dis lan',
    Strikes lak mine, bebby,
    Strikes lak mine.   30

They cooped you in their kitchens,
They penned you in their factories,
They gave you the jobs that they were too good for,
They tried to guarantee happiness to themselves
By shunting[3] dirt and misery to you.   35

You sang:
    Me an' muh baby gonna shine, shine
    Me an' muh baby gonna shine.

1. Carl Sandburg (1878–1967), American poet.   3. Shifting.
2. A group of slaves chained together.

The strong men keep a-comin' on
The strong men git stronger. . . .   40

They bought off some of your leaders
You stumbled, as blind men will . . .
They coaxed you, unwontedly [4] *soft-voiced. . . .*
You followed a way.
Then laughed as usual.   45

They heard the laugh and wondered;
Uncomfortable;
Unadmitting a deeper terror. . . .
          The strong men keep a-comin' on
          Gittin' stronger. . . .   50

What, from the slums
Where they have hemmed you,
What, from the tiny huts
They could not keep from you—
What reaches them   55
Making them ill at ease, fearful?
Today they shout prohibition at you
"Thou shalt not this"
"Thou shalt not that"
"Reserved for whites only"   60
You laugh.

One thing they cannot prohibit—
          The strong men . . . coming on
          The strong men gittin' stronger.
          Strong men. . . .   65
          Stronger. . . .

                                                              1931

Memphis Blues

1

          Nineveh, Tyre,
          Babylon, [1]
          Not much lef'
          Of either one.
          All dese cities   5
          Ashes and rust,
          De win' sing sperrichals
          Through deir dus' . . .
          Was another Memphis [2]
          Mongst de olden days,   10
          Done been destroyed

---

4. Unusually.
1. All three cities were threatened with divine

wrath at various points in the Old Testament.
2. On the Nile River in Egypt.

In many ways. . . .
Dis here Memphis[3]
It may go;
Floods may drown it;   15
Tornado blow;
Mississippi wash it
Down to sea—
Like de other Memphis in
History.   20

2

Watcha gonna do when Memphis on fire,
    Memphis on fire, Mistah Preachin' Man?
Gonna pray to Jesus and nebber tire,
    Gonna pray to Jesus, loud as I can,
        Gonna pray to my Jesus, oh, my Lawd!   25

Watcha gonna do when de tall flames roar,
    Tall flames roar, Mistah Lovin' Man?
Gonna love my brownskin better'n before—
    Gonna love my baby lak a do right man,
        Gonna love my brown baby, oh, my Lawd!   30

Watcha gonna do when Memphis falls down,
    Memphis falls down, Mistah Music Man?
Gonna plunk on dat box as long as it soun',
    Gonna plunk dat box fo' to beat de ban',
        Gonna tickle dem ivories, oh, my Lawd!   35

Watcha gonna do in de hurricane,
    In de hurricane, Mistah Workin' Man?
Gonna put dem buildings up again,
    Gonna put em up dis time to stan',
        Gonna push a wicked wheelbarrow, oh, my Lawd! 40

Watcha gonna do when Memphis near gone,
    Memphis near gone, Mistah Drinkin' Man?
Gonna grab a pint bottle of Mountain Corn,
    Gonna keep de stopper in my han',
        Gonna get a mean jag[4] on, oh, my Lawd!   45

Watcha gonna do when de flood roll fas',
    Flood roll fas', Mistah Gamblin' Man?
Gonna pick up my dice fo' one las' pass—
    Gonna fade my way to de lucky lan',
        Gonna throw my las' seven—oh, my Lawd!   50

---

3. On the Mississippi River in Tennessee.   4. Drinking spree.

3

Memphis go
By Flood or Flame;
Nigger won't worry
All de same—
Memphis go   55
Memphis come back,
Ain' no skin
Off de nigger's back.
All dese cities
Ashes, rust. . . .   60
De win' sing sperrichals
Through deir dus'.

1931

Slim Greer

Listen to the tale
Of Ole Slim Greer,
Waitines' devil
Waitin' here;

        Talkinges' guy   5
        An' biggest liar,
        With always a new lie
        On the fire.

Tells a tale
Of Arkansaw   10
That keeps the kitchen
In a roar;

        Tells in a long-drawled
        Careless tone,
        As solemn as a Baptist   15
        Parson's moan.

How he in Arkansaw
Passed for white,
An' he no lighter
Than a dark midnight.   20

        Found a nice white woman
        At a dance,
        Thought he was from Spain
        Or else from France;

Nobody suspicioned   25
Ole Slim Greer's race

But a Hill Billy, always
Roun' the place,

    Who called one day
    On the trustful dame   30
    An' found Slim comfy
    When he came.

The whites lef' the parlor
All to Slim
Which didn't cut   35
No ice with him,[1]

    An' he started a-tinklin'
    Some mo'nful blues,
    An' a-pattin' the time
    With No. Fourteen shoes.   40

The cracker listened
An' then he spat
An' said, "No white man
Could play like that. . . ."

    The white jane[2] ordered   45
    The tattler out;
    Then, female-like,
    Began to doubt,

Crept into the parlor
Soft as you please,   50
Where Slim was agitatin'
The ivories.

    Heard Slim's music—
    An' then, hot damn!
    Shouted sharp—"Nigger!"   55
    An' Slim said, "Ma'am?"

She screamed and the crackers
Swarmed up soon,
But found only echoes
Of his tune;   60

    'Cause Slim had sold out
    With lightnin' speed;
    "Hope I may die,[3] sir—
    Yes, indeed. . . ."

                   1931

1. I.e., which did not bother him.   3. A way of vouching for the truth of a tale.
2. Woman.

Tin Roof Blues

I'm goin' where de Southern crosses top de C. & O.[1]
I'm goin' where de Southern crosses top de C. & O.
I'm goin' down de country cause I cain't stay here no mo'.

Goin' where de Norfolk Western[2] curves jes' lak de river bends,
Where de Norfolk Western swing around de river bends,   5
Goin' where de people stacks up mo' lak friends.

Leave 'is dirty city, take my foot up in my hand,
Dis do-dirty city, take my foot up in my hand,
Git down to de livin' what a man kin understand.

Gang of dicties[3] here, an' de rest wants to git dat way,   10
Dudes an' dicties, others strive to git dat way,
Put pennies on de numbers from now unto de jedgement day.

I'm got de tin roof blues, got dese sidewalks on my mind,
De tin roof blues, dese lonesome sidewalks on my mind,
I'm goin' where de shingles covers people mo' my kind.   15

1931

Ma Rainey[1]

I

When Ma Rainey
Comes to town,
Folks from anyplace
Miles aroun',
From Cape Girardeau,   5
Poplar Bluff,[2]
Flocks in to hear
Ma do her stuff;
Comes flivverin'[3] in,
Or ridin' mules,   10
Or packed in trains,
Picknickin' fools. . . .
That's what it's like,
Fo' miles on down,
To New Orleans delta   15
An' Mobile[4] town,
When Ma hits
Anywheres aroun'.

---

1. The Southern and the C. & O. were both railroad lines.
2. Another railroad line.
3. Middle- and upper-class blacks.
1. Celebrated blues singer (1886–1939).
2. The seat of Butler County, in southeastern Missouri. Cape Girardeau is a city (and county) in southeastern Missouri.
3. Riding in a flivver, or a small, cheap automobile.
4. A seaport in Alabama.

II

Dey comes to hear Ma Rainey from de little river settlements,
From blackbottom[5] cornrows and from lumber camps;   20
Dey stumble in de hall, jes a-laughin' an' a-cacklin',
Cheerin' lak roarin' water, lak wind in river swamps.

An' some jokers keeps deir laughs a-goin' in de crowded aisles,
An' some folks sits dere waitin' wid deir aches an' miseries,
Till Ma comes out before dem, a-smilin' gold-toofed smiles   25
An' Long Boy ripples minors on de black an' yellow keys.[6]

III

O Ma Rainey,
Sing yo' song;
Now you's back
Whah you belong,   30
Git way inside us,
Keep us strong. . . .
O Ma Rainey,
Li'l an' low;
Sing us 'bout de hard luck   35
Roun' our do';
Sing us 'bout de lonesome road
We mus' go. . . .

IV

I talked to a fellow, an' the fellow say,
"She jes' catch hold of us, somekindaway.   40
She sang Backwater Blues one day:

   'It rained fo' days an' de skies was dark as night,
   Trouble taken place in de lowlands at night.

   'Thundered an' lightened an' the storm begin to roll
   Thousan's of people ain't got no place to go.   45

   'Den I went an' stood upon some high ol' lonesome hill,
   An' looked down on the place where I used to live.'

An' den de folks, dey natchally bowed dey heads an' cried,
Bowed dey heavy heads, shet dey moufs up tight an' cried,
An' Ma lef' de stage, an' followed some de folks outside."   50

Dere wasn't much more de fellow say:
She jes' gits hold of us dataway.

                                                  1932

---

5. Fertile land.
6. Plays songs on the piano in minor key signatures.

Cabaret

(1927, Black & Tan Chicago)[1]

Rich, flashy, puffy-faced,
Hebrew and Anglo-Saxon,
The overlords sprawl here with their glittering darlings.
The smoke curls thick, in the dimmed light
Surreptitiously, deaf-mute waiters   5
Flatter the grandees,[2]
Going easily over the rich carpets,
Wary lest they kick over the bottles[3]
Under the tables.

The jazzband unleashes its frenzy.   10

    Now, now,
    To it, Roger; that's a nice doggie,
    Show your tricks to the gentlemen.

The trombone belches, and the saxophone
Wails curdlingly, the cymbals clash,   15
The drummer twitches in an epileptic fit

    Muddy water
    Round my feet
    Muddy water

The chorus sways in.   20
The 'Creole Beauties from New Orleans'
(By way of Atlanta, Louisville, Washington, Yonkers,
With stop-overs they've used nearly all their lives)
Their creamy skin flushing rose warm,
O, *le bal des belles quarterounes!*[4]   25
Their shapely bodies naked save
For tattered pink silk bodices, short velvet tights,
And shining silver-buckled boots;
Red bandannas on their sleek and close-clipped hair;
To bring to mind (aided by the bottles under the tables)   30
Life upon the river—

    Muddy water, river sweet

(Lafitte the pirate, instead,
And his doughty[5] diggers of gold)

    There's peace and happiness there   35
    I declare

---

1. A reference to Duke Ellington's popular recording "Black and Tan Fantasy" (1927).
2. Patrons with money.
3. Liquor bottles, during Prohibition.
4. Oh, the ball of the beautiful quadroons

(French). A quadroon is a person of one-quarter
African ancestry.
5. Courageous and dependable. Jean Lafitte (c.
1780–c. 1825), French pirate.

(In Arkansas,
Poor half-naked fools,[6] *tagged with identification numbers,*
Worn out upon the levees,
Are carted back to the serfdom   40
They had never left before
And may never leave again)

   Bee—dap—ee—DOOP, dee—ba—dee—BOOP

The girls wiggle and twist

 Oh you too,   45
 Proud high-stepping beauties,
 Show your paces to the gentlemen.
 A prime filly, seh.
 What am I offered, gentlemen, gentlemen. . . .

  I've been away a year today   50
  To wander and roam
  I don't care if it's muddy there

(Now that the floods recede,
What is there left the miserable folk?
Oh time in abundance to count their losses,   55
There is so little else to count.)

  Still it's my home, sweet home

From the lovely throats
Moans and deep cries for home:
Nashville, Toledo, Spout Springs, Boston,   60
Creoles from Germantown;—
The bodies twist and rock;
The glasses are filled up again. . . .

(In Mississippi
The black folk huddle, mute, uncomprehending,   65
Wondering 'how come the good Lord
Could treat them this a way')

  shelter
  Down in the Delta*[7]*

Along the Yazoo[8]   70
The buzzards fly over, over, low,
Glutted, but with their scrawny necks stretching,
Peering still.)

  I've got my toes turned Dixie ways
  Round that Delta let me laze   75

6. Black prisoners in work gangs.   8. A river running through western Mississippi.
7. At the mouth of the Mississippi River.

The band goes mad, the drummer throws his sticks
At the moon, a *papier-mâché* moon,
The chorus leaps into weird posturings,
The firm-fleshed arms plucking at grapes to stain
Their coralled mouths; seductive bodies weaving   80
Bending, writhing, turning

       My heart cries out for
       M U D D Y   W A T E R

(Down in the valleys
The stench of the drying mud   85
Is a bitter reminder of death.)

       Dee da dee D A A A A H

       1932

Sporting Beasley

Good glory, give a look at Sporting Beasley
Strutting, oh my Lord.

    Tophat cocked one side his bulldog head,
    Striped four-in-hand,[1] and in his buttonhole
    A red carnation; Prince Albert coat[2]   5
    Form-fitting, corset like; vest snugly filled,
    Gray morning trousers, spotless and full-flowing,
    White spats[3] and a cane.

Step it, Mr. Beasley, oh step it till the sun goes down.

    Forget the snippy clerks you wait upon,   10
    Tread clouds of glory above the heads of pointing children,
    Oh, Mr. Peacock, before the drab barnfowl of the world.

    Forget the laughter when at the concert
    You paced down the aisle, your majesty,
    Down to Row A, where you pulled out your opera glasses.   15

Majesty. . . .

It's your turn now, Sporting Beasley,
Step it off.

    The world is a ragbag; the world
    Is full of heathens who haven't seen the light;   20
    Do it, Mr. Missionary.

1. A long necktie.
2. One of a number of fashionable 19th-century coat styles associated with the husband of Queen Victoria of Great Britain.
3. A short gaiter worn over the instep and fastened under the foot with a strap.

Great glory, give a look.

Oh Jesus, when this brother's bill falls due,[4]
When he steps off the chariot[5]
And flicks the dust from his patent leathers[6] with his silk
   handkerchief,   25
When he stands in front of the jasper gates, patting his tie,

And then paces in
Cane and knees working like well-oiled slow-timed pistons;

Lord help us, give a *look* at him.

Don't make him dress up in no night gown, Lord.   30
Don't put no fuss and feathers on his shoulders, Lord.

Let him know it's heaven.

Let him keep his hat, his vest, his elkstooth, and everything.

Let him have his spats and cane
Let him have his spats and cane.   35

                                      1932

Sam Smiley

I

The whites had taught him how to rip
   A Nordic belly with a thrust
Of bayonet,[1] had taught him how
   To transmute Nordic flesh to dust.

And a surprising fact had made   5
   Belated impress on his mind:
That shrapnel bursts and poison gas
   Were inexplicably color blind.

He picked up, from the difficult
   But striking lessons of the war,
Some truths that he could not forget,   10
   Though inconceivable before.

And through the lengthy vigils, stuck
   In never-drying stinking mud,
He was held up by dreams of one   15
   Chockfull of laughter, hot of blood.

4. I.e., when he dies.   6. Shoes.
5. That takes souls to heaven.   1. I.e., to attack German soldiers in World War I.

II

On the return Sam Smiley cheered
    The dirty steerage[2] with his dance,
Hot-stepping boy! Soon he would see
    The girl who beat all girls in France.   20

He stopped buckdancing[3] when he reached
    The shanties at his journey's end;
He found his sweetheart in the jail,
    And took white lightning[4] for his friend.

One night the woman whose full voice   25
    Had chortled so, was put away
Into a narrow gaping hole,[5]
    Sam sat beside till break of day.

He had been told what man it was
    Whose child the girl had had to kill,   30
Who best knew why her laugh was dumb,
    Who best knew why her blood was still.

And he remembered France, and how
    A human life was dunghill cheap,
And so he sent a rich white man   35
    His woman's company to keep.

III

The mob was in fine fettle, yet
    The dogs were stupid-nosed,[6] and day
Was far spent when the men drew round
    The scrawny woods where Smiley lay.   40

The oaken leaves drowsed prettily,
    The moon shone down benignly there;
And big Sam Smiley, King Buckdancer,
    Buckdanced on the midnight air.

1932   1975

2. The part of a ship designated for passengers with   5. A grave.
the cheapest tickets.   6. Slow to pick up Sam's scent. "Fettle": condi-
3. Dancing happily.   tion.
4. Cheap whiskey.

GWENDOLYN B. BENNETT
1902–1981

Poet, artist, and journalist of the Harlem Renaissance, Gwendolyn B. Bennett was
born in Giddings, Texas, in 1902—"unofficially" because that state denied official
birth certificates to blacks well into the twentieth century. Her parents soon took

her to Nevada, where they worked as teachers at an American Indian reservation until 1906 or 1907. They then moved to Washington, D.C., so that Bennett's father could study law. When the marriage failed, Gwendolyn's mother gained custody of her. However, her father kidnapped his eight-year-old daughter and dragged her into a nomadic life of hiding (mainly in Pennsylvania) that lasted until her junior year in high school, when they finally settled in Brooklyn.

An excellent student, Bennett became the first black member of the literary and dramatic societies in her high school, wrote the graduation speech and the lyrics to her graduation song, composed poetry, and took part in art competitions. After graduation, she studied fine arts at Columbia University and the Pratt Institute, where she earned a bachelor's degree in 1924. Having already established herself as a promising member of Harlem's literary and artistic set, she left New York for Washington, D.C., to teach art at Howard University. The next year, she won a $1000 scholarship from the Delta Sigma Theta sorority that enabled her to study art in Paris for a year. Returning to New York in the summer of 1926, she found the Harlem Renaissance in full swing and immediately found a prominent place in its ranks, especially with her poetry (*Heritage* had been published in 1923) and her illustrations for such magazines as *Opportunity*, the *Crisis*, and the short-lived *Fire!!* She also started a column called *The Ebony Flute*, which she described as a forum for "literary and social chit-chat," in Charles S. Johnson's *Opportunity*. This column aimed to satisfy anyone curious about the whereabouts, the recent accomplishments, or the plans of personalities such as the artist Aaron Douglas and the singer-actor Paul Robeson. Bennett kept her lively column going even after her return to Howard as an instructor. Indeed, the column lasted until May 1928, when Bennett accompanied her husband, Alfred Jackson, to Florida, where he wanted to establish a private medical practice.

Bennett soon found the rigid segregation of the South intolerable and convinced her husband to return to New York. Unfortunately, by this time the deepening Depression had virtually wiped out the Harlem Renaissance, and the death of her husband forced Bennett further away from the life of art. She managed to publish a few new poems and essays, but the demands of making a living began to consume most of her creative energy. She spent several years in government-sponsored positions before postwar anti-Communist hysteria claimed her—unfairly—as one of its victims. For a time she worked at the Consumers Union in Mount Vernon, New York, with the poet Helene Johnson; remarried, she spent the remainder of her life as a housewife and antiques dealer in Kutztown, Pennsylvania.

Some students of the Harlem Renaissance view Bennett as a figure whose literary reputation rests solely on her having been in the right place (Harlem) at the right time (the 1920s); but her poetry tells a different story—that of as lively an artistic intelligence and consciousness as possessed by many writers more prolific during the Harlem Renaissance.

Keenly aware as an artist of the grace and loveliness of people of African descent, especially women and girls, Bennett wrote lyrics that expressed her admiration in colorful ways. She was among the more judiciously race conscious of the Harlem writers, but her poetry quietly celebrated the physical and emotional qualities not always appreciated by blacks themselves in a time of intense segregation.

Heritage

I want to see the slim palm-trees,
Pulling at the clouds
With little pointed fingers. . . .

I want to see lithe Negro girls,   5
Etched dark against the sky
While sunset lingers.

I want to hear the silent sands,
Singing to the moon
Before the Sphinx-still face. . . .

I want to hear the chanting   10
Around a heathen fire
Of a strange black race.

I want to breathe the Lotus flow'r,
Sighing to the stars
With tendrils drinking at the Nile. . . .   15

I want to feel the surging
Of my sad people's soul
Hidden by a minstrel-smile.

                                                                  1923

To a Dark Girl

I love you for your brownness
And the rounded darkness of your breast.
I love you for the breaking sadness in your voice
And shadows where your wayward eye-lids rest.

Something of old forgotten queens   5
Lurks in the lithe abandon of your walk,
And something of the shackled slave
Sobs in the rhythm of your talk.

Oh, little brown girl, born for sorrow's mate,
Keep all you have of queenliness,   10
Forgetting that you once were slave,
And let your full lips laugh at Fate!

                                                                  1927

Sonnet—2

Some things are very dear to me—
Such things as flowers bathed by rain
Or patterns traced upon the sea
Or crocuses where snow has lain . . .
The iridescence of a gem,   5
The moon's cool opalescent light,
Azaleas and the scent of them,
And honeysuckles in the night.
And many sounds are also dear—

Like winds that sing among the trees   10
Or crickets calling from the weir[1]

Or Negroes humming melodies.
But dearer far than all surmise
Are sudden tear-drops in your eyes.

1927

Hatred

I shall hate you
Like a dart of singing steel
Shot through still air
At even-tide.
Or solemnly   5
As pines are sober
When they stand etched
Against the sky.
Hating you shall be a game
Played with cool hands   10
And slim fingers.
Your heart will yearn
For the lonely splendor
Of the pine tree;
While rekindled fires   15
In my eyes
Shall wound you like swift arrows.
Memory will lay its hands
Upon your breast
And you will understand   20
My hatred.

1927

1. A small dam in a river or stream.

WALLACE THURMAN

1902–1934

Of himself and his many roles in the Harlem Renaissance, the versatile and mercurial Wallace Thurman wrote in 1929: "Three years in Harlem have seen me become a New Negro (for no reason at all and without my consent), a poet (having had 2 poems published by generous editors), an editor (with a penchant for financially unsound publications), an exotic (see articles on Negro life and literature in *The Bookman, New Republic, Independent, World Tomorrow*, etc.), an actor (I was a denizen of Cat Fish Row in *Porgy*), a husband (having been married all of six months), a novelist (viz: *The Blacker the Berry*. Macaulay's, Feb. 1, 1929: $2.50), a playwright (being co-author of *Black Belt*). Now—what more could one do?"

Born and raised in Salt Lake City, Thurman attended the University of Utah before transferring to the University of Southern California in 1922. He supported himself in Los Angeles by working for the postal service (with Arna Bontemps) and writing a column called "Inklings" for a local black newspaper. He was apparently thinking of becoming a doctor when news of the Harlem Renaissance reached him. Hoping to spark a West Coast version of the movement, he founded the *Outlet*, a magazine that failed after half a year. Thurman moved to Harlem in 1925. He worked at first as both reporter and editor at *The Looking Glass*, then served as managing editor at the *Messenger*. In 1926, he improbably became circulation manager for *The World Tomorrow*, a religious magazine run by whites and aimed mainly at whites. That same year saw the first and only number of the ill-fated magazine *Fire!!*, the brainchild of Thurman, Langston Hughes, Bruce Nugent, Zora Neale Hurston, and others, who all agreed that Thurman should serve as editor. In 1928, Thurman started his own magazine, *Harlem: A Forum of Negro Life*, but it also failed after its first issue. In the meantime, he was hired at Macaulay's Publishing Company as the only black reader in any of the major publishing houses of New York.

In 1929, his first play, *Harlem: A Melodrama of Negro Life in Harlem*, written in collaboration with the white dramatist William Jourdan Rapp, reached Broadway. Also that year his first novel, *The Blacker the Berry*, was hailed as both a critical and a popular success. In part, the book examines the prejudices of the African American community against its darker-skinned members, an issue about which the dark-skinned Thurman was particularly sensitive. For sustained insight into Harlem life in the 1920s, however, Thurman's most important achievement is probably *Infants of the Spring* (1932), a roman à clef that mercilessly satirizes the Harlem Renaissance as a movement. His third and final novel, an exposé of hospital abuses called *The Interne* (1932), written in collaboration with the white author Abraham L. Furman, does not touch at all on racial issues and was generally disregarded by the Harlem community.

Thurman continued to work at Macaulay's until he was recruited by a filmmaker to write screenplays. Hired (reportedly) at an outrageously high salary, he moved back to California, where he wrote two scripts before a number of factors, including declining health and excessive drinking, led him to return to New York in 1934. There, he collapsed at a reunion party with his friends and was immediately hospitalized; he died a few months later of tuberculosis.

Langston Hughes captured some of the conflicts of Thurman's psychology when he wrote in 1940 that Thurman "wanted to be a *very* great writer, like Gorki or Thomas Mann, and he felt that he was merely a journalistic writer." Thurman compared his work with that of Proust, Melville, Tolstoy, and others and "found his own pages vastly wanting. So he contented himself by writing a great deal for money, laughing bitterly at his fabulously concocted 'true stories,' . . . drinking more and more gin, and then threatening to jump out of windows at people's parties and kill himself."

The chapter of *Infants of the Spring* presented here offers, albeit in a veiled and satirical way, one of the most illuminating contemporary views of the Harlem Renaissance. Here, in thinly disguised form, are most of the major personalities of the movement, including Langston Hughes, Zora Neale Hurston, Alain Locke, Countee Cullen, and Rudolph Fisher, who assemble in the apartment of the principal character, Raymond (who most resembles Thurman himself), to discuss the Renaissance.

From Infants of the Spring

Chapter XXI

[HARLEM SALON]

After Stephen's unexpected visit and their long conversation together, Raymond[1] seemed to have developed a new store of energy. For three days and nights, he had secluded himself in his room, and devoted all his time to the continuance of his novel. For three years it had remained a project. Now he was making rapid progress. The ease with which he could work once he set himself to it amazed him, and at the same time he was suspicious of this unexpected facility. Nevertheless, his novel was progressing, and he intended to let nothing check him.

In line with this resolution, he insisted that Paul[2] and Eustace hold their nightly gin parties without his presence, and they were also abjured to steer all company clear of his studio.

Stephen had gone upstate on a tutoring job, Lucille had not been in evidence since the donation party, and Raymond had made no attempt to get in touch with her. There was no one else in whom he had any interest. Aline and Janet he had dismissed from his mind, although Eustace and Paul had spent an entire dinner hour telling him of their latest adventures. Both had now left Aline's mother's house and were being supported by some white man, whom Aline had met at a downtown motion picture theater. They had an apartment in which they entertained groups of young colored boys on the nights their white protector was not in evidence.

Having withdrawn from every activity connected with Niggeratti Manor, Raymond had also forgotten that Dr. Parkes[3] had promised to communicate with him, concerning some mysterious idea, and he was taken by surprise when Eustace came into the room one morning, bearing a letter from Dr. Parkes.

"Well, I'm plucked," Raymond exclaimed.

"What's the matter?" Eustace queried.

"Will you listen to this?" He read the letter aloud.

"My dear Raymond:

I will be in New York on Thursday night. I want you to do me a favor. It seems to me that with the ever increasing number of younger Negro artists and intellectuals gathering in Harlem, some effort should be made to establish what well might become a distinguished salon. All of you engaged in creative work, should, I believe, welcome the chance to meet together once every fortnight, for the purpose of exchanging ideas and expressing and criticizing individual theories. This might prove to be both stimulating

---

1. Based on Thurman himself.
2. Probably based on Richard Bruce Nugent (1906–1987), a painter who also wrote fiction and was a professional actor.
3. Based on Dr. Alain Leroy Locke (1886–1954), champion of the Harlem Renaissance and editor of

The New Negro (1925). "Niggeratti Manor": Iolanthe Sydney's rooming house in Harlem, where Thurman and other figures of the Harlem Renaissance stayed at one time or another; Thurman and Zora Neal Hurston coined the term.

and profitable. And it might also bring into active being a concerted movement which would establish the younger Negro talent once and for all as a
vital artistic force. With this in mind, I would appreciate your inviting as
many of your colleagues as possible to your studio on Thursday evening. I
will be there to preside. I hope you are intrigued by the idea and willing to
cooperate. Please wire me your answer. Collect, of course.

Very sincerely yours,
Dr. A. L. Parkes."

"Are you any more good?" Raymond asked as he finished reading.

"Sounds like a great idea," Eustace replied enthusiastically.

"It *is* great. Too great to miss," Raymond acquiesced mischievously.
"Come on, let's get busy on the telephone."

Thursday night came and so did the young hopefuls. The first to arrive was
Sweetie May Carr.[4] Sweetie May was a short story writer, more noted for
her ribald wit and personal effervescence than for any actual literary work.
She was a great favorite among those whites who went in for Negro prodigies. Mainly because she lived up to their conception of what a typical
Negro should be. It seldom occurred to any of her patrons that she did this
with tongue in cheek. Given a paleface audience, Sweetie May would
launch forth into a saga of the little all-colored Mississippi town where she
claimed to have been born. Her repertoire of tales was earthy, vulgar and
funny. Her darkies always smiled through their tears, sang spirituals on the
slightest provocation, and performed buck dances when they should have
been working. Sweetie May was a master of southern dialect, and an able
raconteur, but she was too indifferent to literary creation to transfer to
paper that which she told so well. The intricacies of writing bored her, and
her written work was for the most part turgid and unpolished. But Sweetie
May knew her white folks.

"It's like this," she had told Raymond. "I have to eat. I also wish to finish
my education. Being a Negro writer these days is a racket and I'm going to
make the most of it while it lasts. Sure I cut the fool. But I enjoy it, too. I
don't know a tinker's damn about art. I care less about it. My ultimate ambition, as you know, is to become a gynecologist. And the only way I can
live easily until I have the requisite training is to pose as a writer of potential
ability. *Voila!* I get my tuition paid at Columbia. I rent an apartment and
have all the furniture contributed by kind hearted o'fays.[5] I receive bundles
of groceries from various sources several times a week . . . all accomplished
by dropping a discreet hint during an evening's festivities. I find queer
places for whites to go in Harlem . . . out of the way primitive churches,
sidestreet speakeasies. They fall for it. About twice a year I manage to sell a
story. It is acclaimed. I am a genius in the making. Thank God for this
Negro literary renaissance! Long may it flourish!"

Sweetie May was accompanied by two young girls, recently emigrated
from Boston. They were the latest to be hailed as incipient immortals.

---

4. Based loosely on Zora Neale Hurston (1891–
1960), author of *Mules and Men* and *Their Eyes*
Were Watching God.
5. Whites, a disparaging term.

Their names were Doris Westmore and Hazel Jamison.[6] Doris wrote short stories. Hazel wrote poetry. Both had become known through a literary contest fostered by one of the leading Negro magazines.[7] Raymond liked them more than he did most of the younger recruits to the movement. For one thing, they were characterized by a freshness and naïveté which he and his cronies had lost. And, surprisingly enough for Negro prodigies, they actually gave promise of possessing literary talent. He was most pleased to see them. He was also amused by their interest and excitement. A salon! A literary gathering! It was one of the civilized institutions they had dreamed of finding in New York, one of the things they had longed and hoped for.

As time passed, others came in. Tony Crews,[8] smiling and self-effacing, a mischievous boy, grateful for the chance to slip away from the backwoods college he attended. Raymond had never been able to analyze this young poet. His work was interesting and unusual. It was also spotty. Spasmodically he gave promise of developing into a first rate poet. Already he had published two volumes, prematurely, Raymond thought. Both had been excessively praised by whites and universally damned by Negroes. Considering the nature of his work this was to be expected. The only unknown quantity was the poet himself. Would he or would he not fulfill the promise exemplified in some of his work? Raymond had no way of knowing and even an intimate friendship with Tony himself had failed to enlighten him. For Tony was the most close-mouthed and cagey individual Raymond had ever known when it came to personal matters. He fended off every attempt to probe into his inner self and did this with such an unconscious and naive air that the prober soon came to one of two conclusions: Either Tony had no depth whatsoever, or else he was too deep for plumbing by ordinary mortals.

DeWitt Clinton,[9] the Negro poet laureate, was there, too, accompanied, as usual, by his *fideles achates*, David Holloway.[1] David had been acclaimed the most handsome Negro in Harlem by a certain group of whites. He was in great demand by artists who wished to paint him. He had become a much touted romantic figure. In reality he was a fairly intelligent school teacher, quite circumspect in his habits, a rather timid beau, who imagined himself to be bored with life.

Dr. Parkes finally arrived, accompanied by Carl Denny, the artist, and Carl's wife, Annette. Next to arrive was Cedric Williams,[2] a West Indian, whose first book, a collection of short stories with a Caribbean background, in Raymond's opinion, marked him as one of the three Negroes writing who actually had something to say, and also some concrete idea of style. Cedric was followed by Austin Brown, a portrait painter whom Raymond

6. Based on the poet Helene Johnson (1907–1995). Westmore is based on Johnson's cousin Dorothy West (b. 1908), author of *The Living Is Easy* (1948).
7. *Crisis* and *Opportunity* both sponsored literary contests in the 1920s.
8. Based on Langston Hughes (1902–1967); his two volumes of poetry in the 1920s were *The Weary Blues* (1926) and *Fine Clothes to the Jew* (1927).
9. Based on Countee Cullen (1903–1946), whose first collection of poetry, *Color*, appeared in 1925.
1. Based on Harold Jackman (1900–1960), whose

portrait (by Winold Reiss) had appeared in the "New Negro" issue of *Survey Graphic*. "*Fideles achates*": faithful Achates (Latin). Jackman was probably Cullen's closest friend and is, therefore, compared with Achates, Aeneas's most faithful companion in the *Aeneid*, a Roman epic poem by Virgil.
2. Based on Eric Walrond (1898–1966), author of *Tropic Death* (1926). The Dennys are based on Aaron (1898–1979) and Alta Douglas (c. 1899–1958).

personally despised, a Dr. Manfred Trout,[3] who practiced medicine and also wrote exceptionally good short stories, Glenn Madison, who was a Communist, and a long, lean professorial person, Allen Fenderson, who taught school and had ambitions to become a crusader modeled after W. E. B. Du Bois.

The roster was now complete. There was an hour of small talk and drinking of mild cocktails in order to induce ease and allow the various guests to become acquainted and voluble. Finally, Dr. Parkes ensconced himself in Raymond's favorite chair, where he could get a good view of all in the room, and clucked for order.

Raymond observed the professor closely. Paul's description never seemed more apt. He was a mother hen clucking at her chicks. Small, dapper, with sensitive features, graying hair, a dominating head, and restless hands and feet, he smiled benevolently at his brood. Then, in his best continental manner, which he had acquired during four years at European Universities, he began to speak.

"You are," he perorated, "the outstanding personalities in a new generation. On you depends the future of your race. You are not, as were your predecessors, concerned with donning armor, and clashing swords with the enemy in the public square. You are finding both an escape and a weapon in beauty, which beauty when created by you will cause the American white man to reestimate the Negro's value to his civilization, cause him to realize that the American black man is too valuable, too potential of utilitarian accomplishment, to be kept down-trodden and segregated.

"Because of your concerted storming up Parnassus,[4] new vistas will be spread open to the entire race. The Negro in the south will no more know peonage, Jim Crowism, or loss of the ballot, and the Negro everywhere in America will know complete freedom and equality.

"But," and here his voice took on a more serious tone, "to accomplish this, your pursuit of beauty must be vital and lasting. I am somewhat fearful of the decadent strain which seems to have filtered into most of your work. Oh, yes, I know you are children of the age and all that, but you must not, like your paleface contemporaries, wallow in the mire of post-Victorian license. You have too much at stake. You must have ideals. You should become . . . well, let me suggest your going back to your racial roots, and cultivating a healthy paganism based on African traditions.

"For the moment that is all I wish to say. I now want you all to give expression to your own ideas. Perhaps we can reach a happy mean for guidance."

He cleared his throat and leaned contentedly back in his chair. No one said a word. Raymond was full of contradictions, which threatened to ooze forth despite his efforts to remain silent. But he knew that once the ooze began there would be no stopping the flood, and he was anxious to hear what some of the others might have to say.

However, a glance at the rest of the people in the room assured him that most of them had not the slightest understanding of what had been said,

---

3. Based on Rudolph Fisher (1897–1934), whose *City of Refuge* appeared in the *Atlantic Monthly* (1925).

4. A mountain in central Greece, traditionally associated with the muses and artistic production.

nor any ideas on the subject, whatsoever. Once more Dr. Parkes clucked for discussion. No one ventured a word. Raymond could see that Cedric, like himself, was full of argument, and also like him, did not wish to appear contentious at such an early stage in the discussion. Tony winked at Raymond when he caught his eye, but the expression on his face was as inscrutable as ever. Sweetie May giggled behind her handkerchief. Paul amused himself by sketching the various people in the room. The rest were blank.

"Come, come, now," Dr. Parkes urged somewhat impatiently, "I'm not to do all the talking. What have you to say, DeWitt?"

All eyes sought out the so-called Negro poet laureate. For a moment he stirred uncomfortably in his chair, then in a high pitched, nasal voice proceeded to speak.

"I think, Dr. Parkes, that you have said all there is to say. I agree with you. The young Negro artist must go back to his pagan heritage for inspiration and to the old masters for form."

Raymond could not suppress a snort. For DeWitt's few words had given him a vivid mental picture of that poet's creative hours—eyes on a page of Keats, fingers on typewriter, mind frantically conjuring African scenes. And there would of course be a Bible nearby.

Paul had ceased being intent on his drawing long enough to hear "pagan heritage," and when DeWitt finished he inquired inelegantly:

"What old black pagan heritage?"

DeWitt gasped, surprised and incredulous.

"Why, from your ancestors."

"Which ones?" Paul pursued dumbly.

"Your African ones, of course." DeWitt's voice was full of disdain.

"What about the rest?"

"What rest?" He was irritated now.

"My German, English and Indian ancestors," Paul answered willingly. "How can I go back to African ancestors when their blood is so diluted and their country and times so far away? I have no conscious affinity for them at all."

Dr. Parkes intervened: "I think you've missed the point, Paul."

"And I," Raymond was surprised at the suddenness with which he joined in the argument, "think he has hit the nail right on the head. Is there really any reason why *all* Negro artists should consciously and deliberately dig into African soil for inspiration and material unless they actually wish to do so?"

"I don't mean that. I mean you should develop your inherited spirit."

DeWitt beamed. The doctor had expressed his own hazy theory. Raymond was about to speak again, when Paul once more took the bit between his own teeth.

"I ain't got no African spirit."

Sweetie May giggled openly at this, as did Carl Denny's wife, Annette. The rest looked appropriately sober, save for Tony, whose eyes continued to telegraph mischievously to Raymond. Dr. Parkes tried to squelch Paul with a frown. He should have known better.

"I'm not an African," the culprit continued. "I'm an American and a perfect product of the melting pot."

"That's nothing to brag about." Cedric spoke for the first time.

"And I think you're all on the wrong track." All eyes were turned toward this new speaker, Allen Fenderson. "Dr. Du Bois has shown us the way. We must be militant fighters. We must not hide away in ivory towers and prate of beauty. We must fashion cudgels and bludgeons rather than sensitive plants. We must excoriate the white man, and make him grant us justice. We must fight for complete social and political and economic equality."

"What we ought to do," Glenn Madison growled intensely, "is to join hands with the workers of the world and overthrow the present capitalistic régime. We are of the proletariat and must fight our battles allied with them, rather than singly and selfishly."

"All of us?" Raymond inquired quietly.

"All of us who have a trace of manhood and are more interested in the rights of human beings than in gin parties and neurotic capitalists."

"I hope you're squelched," Paul stage whispered to Raymond.

"And how!" Raymond laughed. Several joined in. Dr. Parkes spoke quickly to Fenderson, ignoring the remarks of the Communist.

"But, Fenderson . . . this is a new generation and must make use of new weapons. Some of us will continue to fight in the old way, but there are other things to be considered, too. Remember, a beautiful sonnet can be as effectual, nay even more effectual, than a rigorous hymn of hate."

"The man who would understand and be moved by a hymn of hate would not bother to read your sonnet and, even if he did, he would not know what it was all about."

"I don't agree. Your progress must be a boring in from the top, not a battle from the bottom. Convert the higher beings and the lower orders will automatically follow."

"Spoken like a true capitalistic minion," Glenn Madison muttered angrily.

Fenderson prepared to continue his argument, but he was forestalled by Cedric.

"What does it matter," he inquired diffidently, "what any of you do so long as you remain true to yourselves? There is no necessity for this movement becoming standardized. There is ample room for everyone to follow his own individual track. Dr. Parkes wants us all to go back to Africa and resurrect our pagan heritage, become atavistic. In this he is supported by Mr. Clinton. Fenderson here wants us all to be propagandists and yell at the top of our lungs at every conceivable injustice. Madison wants us all to take a cue from Leninism and fight the capitalistic bogey. Well . . . why not let each young hopeful choose his own path? Only in that way will anything at all be achieved."

"Which is just what I say," Raymond smiled gratefully at Cedric. "One cannot make movements nor can one plot their course. When the work of a given number of individuals during a given period is looked at in retrospect, then one can identify a movement and evaluate its distinguishing characteristics. Individuality is what we should strive for. Let each seek his own salvation. To me, a wholesale flight back to Africa or a wholesale allegiance to Communism or a wholesale adherence to an antiquated and for the most part ridiculous propagandistic program are all equally futile and unintelligent."

Dr. Parkes gasped and sought for an answer. Cedric forestalled him.

"To talk of an African heritage among American Negroes *is* unintelligent. It is only in the West Indies that you can find direct descendents from African ancestors. Your primitive instincts among all but the extreme proletariat have been ironed out. You're standardized Americans."

"Oh, no," Carl Denny interrupted suddenly. "You're wrong. It's in our blood. It's . . ." he fumbled for a word, "fixed. Why . . ." he stammered again, "remember Cullen's poem, *Heritage*:

> " 'So I lie who find no peace
> Night or day, no slight release
> From the unremittant beat
> Made by cruel padded feet
> Walking through my body's street.
> Up and down they go, and back,
> Treading out a jungle track.'⁵

"We're all like that. Negroes are the only people in America not standardized. The feel of the African jungle is in their blood. Its rhythms surge through their bodies. Look how Negroes laugh and dance and sing, all spontaneous and individual."

"Exactly," Dr. Parkes and DeWitt nodded assent.

"I have yet to see an intelligent or middle class American Negro laugh and sing and dance spontaneously. That's an illusion, a pretty sentimental fiction. Moreover your songs and dances are not individual. Your spirituals are mediocre folk songs, ignorantly culled from Methodist hymn books. There are white men who can sing them just as well as Negroes, if not better, should they happen to be untrained vocalists like Robeson, rather than highly trained technicians like Hayes.⁶ And as for dancing spontaneously and feeling the rhythms of the jungle . . . humph!"

Sweetie May jumped into the breach.

"I can do the Charleston better than any white person."

"I particularly stressed . . . intelligent people. The lower orders of any race have more vim and vitality than the illuminated tenth."

Sweetie May leaped to her feet.

"Why, you West Indian . . ."

"Sweetie, Sweetie," Dr. Parkes was shocked by her polysyllabic expletive.

Pandemonium reigned. The master of ceremonies could not cope with the situation. Cedric called Sweetie an illiterate southern hussy. She called him all types of profane West Indian monkey chasers. DeWitt and David were shocked and showed it. The literary doctor, the Communist and Fenderson moved uneasily around the room. Annette and Paul giggled. The two child prodigies from Boston looked on wide-eyed, utterly bewil-

---

5. Lines 64–70.
6. Roland Hayes (1887–1976), who studied music in Europe for two years. Paul Robeson (1898– 1976), who appeared in a number of musicals on and off Broadway.

dered and dismayed. Raymond leaned back in his chair, puffing on a cigarette, detached and amused. Austin, the portrait painter, audibly repeated
over and over to himself: "Just like niggers . . . just like niggers." Carl
Denny interposed himself between Cedric and Sweetie May. Dr. Parkes
clucked for civilized behavior, which came only when Cedric stalked angrily out of the room.

After the alien had been routed and peace restored, Raymond passed a
soothing cocktail. Meanwhile Austin and Carl had begun arguing about
painting. Carl did not possess a facile tongue. He always had difficulty for-
mulating in words the multitude of ideas which seethed in his mind. Austin, to quote Raymond, was an illiterate cad. Having examined one of
Carl's pictures on Raymond's wall, he had disparaged it. Raymond listened
attentively to their argument. He despised Austin mainly because he spent
most of his time imploring noted white people to give him a break by posing for a portrait. Having the gift of making himself pitiable, and having a
glib tongue when it came to expatiating on the trials and tribulations of
being a Negro, he found many sitters, all of whom thought they were encouraging a handicapped Negro genius. After one glimpse at the completed portrait, they invariably changed their minds.

"I tell you," he shouted, "your pictures are distorted and grotesque. Art is
art, I say. And art holds a mirror up to nature. No mirror would reflect a
man composed of angles.[7] God did not make man that way. Look at Sargent's[8] portraits. He was an artist."

"But he wasn't," Carl expostulated. "We . . . we of this age . . . we must
look at Matisse, Gauguin, Picasso and Renoir[9] for guidance. They get the
feel of the age. . . . They . . ."

"Are all crazy and so are you," Austin countered before Carl could proceed.

Paul rushed to Carl's rescue. He quoted Wilde in rebuttal: Nature imitates art,[1] then went on to blaspheme Sargent. Carl, having found some
words to express a new idea fermenting in his brain, forgot the argument at
hand, went off on a tangent and began telling the dazed Dr. Parkes about
the Negroid quality in his drawings. DeWitt yawned and consulted his
watch. Raymond mused that he probably resented having missed the
prayer meeting which he attended every Thursday night. In another corner
of the room the Communist and Fenderson had locked horns over the ultimate solution of the Negro problem. In loud voices each contended for his
own particular solution. Karl Marx and Lenin[2] were pitted against Du Bois
and his disciples. The writing doctor, bored to death, slipped quietly from
the room without announcing his departure or even saying good night.
Being more intelligent than most of the others, he had wisely kept silent.
Tony and Sweetie May had taken adjoining chairs, and were soon engaged

7. A reference to Cubism, an important trend
sweeping the art world at the time.
8. John Singer Sargent (1856–1925), American
painter.
9. Auguste Renoir (1841–1919), Henri Matisse
(1869–1954), Paul Gauguin (1848–1903), and
Pablo Picasso (1881–1973), all innovative painters.
1. A satiric slogan of the Art for Art's Sake move-

ment, with which Oscar Wilde (1856–1900) was
associated.
2. Pseudonym of Vladimir Ilyich Ulyanov (1870–
1924), Russian revolutionary leader and Soviet premier from 1918 to 1924. Marx (1818–1883), author
of The Communist Manifesto with Friedrich Engels.

in comparing their versions of original verses to the St. James Infirmary, [3] which Tony contended was soon to become as epical as the St. Louis Blues. Annette and Howard began gossiping about various outside personalities. The child prodigies looked from one to the other, silent, perplexed, uncomfortable, not knowing what to do or say. Dr. Parkes visibly recoiled from Carl's incoherent expository barrage, and wilted in his chair, willing but unable to effect a courteous exit. Raymond sauntered around the room, dispensing cocktails, chuckling to himself.

Such was the first and last salon.

1932

3. A blues number popularized by black entertainer Gladys Bentley.

ARNA BONTEMPS

1902–1973

Arna Wendell Bontemps was born in Alexandria, Louisiana, where his family remained for three years before his father, Paul Bontemps, threatened by two whites simply because they were drunk and he was black, decided that the South was no place to live. The Bontemps moved to Los Angeles. There, Arna's mother instilled in him a passion for literature, though his father, a brick mason, appears to have had little use for books. After Arna's mother died when he was twelve, a major influence on him was his Uncle Buddy, a hard-drinking, tale-telling, charismatic fellow who later would serve as a model for one of the central characters in Bontemps's first novel.

In 1917, Paul Bontemps, a devout Seventh Day Adventist, sent his son to the San Fernando Academy, a predominantly white boarding school run by the church. Bontemps recalled his father's parting advice to him—"Now don't go up there acting colored"—as one of the formative moments in his life. He later demanded: "How dare anyone, parent, schoolteacher, or merely literary critic, tell me not to act *colored?*" Bontemps went on to attend Pacific Union College, another church-run school, from which he was graduated in 1923. He worked briefly in the Los Angeles post office (with his friend Wallace Thurman) before responding to the call of Harlem and New York. In 1924, he began to teach at the Seventh Day Adventist Harlem Academy. First published in the *Crisis* in 1924, his poems soon won him a literary reputation and, in 1926 and 1927, three poetry prizes, awarded by *Opportunity* and the *Crisis.*

In 1926, he married a former student, Alberta Johnson. From the start, Bontemps's literary ambitions brought him into constant conflict with his superiors at the Harlem Academy. Against his will, he was sent in 1931 to Huntsville, Alabama, to teach at Oakwood Junior College, also run by the Adventists. Church officials were particularly distressed by the title and the tone of Bontemps's first novel, *God Sends Sunday* (1931). The story of Little Augie, a black jockey who enjoys fast living, *God Sends Sunday* received mixed reviews, with W. E. B. Du Bois criticizing it for its emphasis on the seamier side of black life. In 1932, Bontemps won yet another prize from *Opportunity,* this time for what would become his most anthologized short story, *A Summer Tragedy.* About this time, he began writing children's literature, collaborating with Langston Hughes on the highly successful *Popo and Fifina* (1932), a story set in Haiti.

Bontemps left Oakwood in 1934, first for Los Angeles and then for Chicago, where he finished what is perhaps his most respected work, the novel *Black Thunder*. Published in 1936, *Black Thunder* is the story of the aborted slave rebellion led by Gabriel Prosser in Virginia in 1800. Sterling A. Brown called it one of the six best African American novels ever written. *Drums at Dusk* (1939), the story of a slave rebellion in Haiti, and the last of Bontemps's novels, was much less successful.

In 1943, Bontemps received his master's degree in library science from the University of Chicago. Shortly thereafter, he became librarian at Fisk University in Nashville, where he remained, except for a few years at Yale and the University of Illinois, for the rest of his life. In addition to amassing enough material to make Fisk an important center for African American research, he continued to publish widely, producing literary anthologies, biographies, children's books, and a slender volume of poetry, *Personals* (1963). He died in 1973, while working on his autobiography.

Bontemps's poetry stands apart in the literature of the Harlem Renaissance because of its mainly meditative quality, behind which is the weight of his religious and spiritual interests. He was often hard pressed to reconcile these interests with either race pride or personal ambition as an artist but sought to do so because he never wished to repudiate the spiritual principles he had learned as a youth. His writing is characteristically graceful, serene, and yet intellectually challenging and independent. With few allusions to black folklore or other overt racial signs, his poems nevertheless convey a sense of his deep pride in his race and an intellectual and emotional integrity and confidence matched by few other writers.

Golgotha[1] Is a Mountain

Golgotha is a mountain, a purple mound
Almost out of sight.
One night they hanged two thieves there,
And another man.
Some women[2] wept heavily that night;   5
Their tears are flowing still. They have made a river;
Once it covered me.
Then the people went away and left Golgotha
Deserted.
Oh, I've seen many mountains: 10
Pale purple mountains melting in the evening mists and blurring
     on the borders of the sky.

I climbed old Shasta and chilled my hands in its summer snows.
I rested in the shadow of Popocatepetl and it whispered to me of
     daring prowess.
I looked upon the Pyrenees and felt the zest of warm exotic nights.
I slept at the foot of Fujiyama[3] and dreamed of legend and of death.   15
And I've seen other mountains rising from the wistful moors like the
     breasts of a slender maiden.

1. The skull or the hill of skulls (probably Aramaic); place where Jesus was crucified (Matthew 27:33–38).
2. "And many women were there beholding afar off, which followed Jesus from Galilee, ministering unto him" (Matthew 27:55).
3. Dormant volcano in central Japan. Shasta is a volcanic mountain in northern California. Popocatepetl is a volcano in south-central Mexico. The Pyrenees is a mountain range between Spain and France.

Who knows the mystery of mountains!
Some of them are awful, others are just lonely.

.   .   .

Italy has its Rome and California has San Francisco,
All covered with mountains.   20
Some think these mountains grew
Like ant hills
Or sand dunes.
That might be so—
I wonder what started them all!   25
Babylon is a mountain
And so is Nineveh, [4]
With grass growing on them;
Palaces and hanging gardens started them.
I wonder what is under the hills   30
In Mexico
And Japan!
There are mountains in Africa too.
Treasure is buried there:
Gold and precious stones   35
And moulded glory.
Lush grass is growing there
Sinking before the wind.
Black men are bowing.
Naked in that grass   40
Digging with their fingers.
I am one of them:
Those mountains should be ours.
It would be great
To touch the pieces of glory with our hands.   45
These mute unhappy hills,
Bowed down with broken backs,
Speak often one to another:
"A day is as a year," they cry,
"And a thousand years as one day."   50
We watched the caravan
That bore our queen [5] to the courts of Solomon;
And when the first slave traders came
We bowed our heads.
"Oh, Brothers, it is not long!   55
Dust shall yet devour the stones
But we shall be here when they are gone."
Mountains are rising all around me.
Some are so small they are not seen;
Others are large.   60
All of them get big in time and people forget
What started them at first.
Oh the world is covered with mountains!
Beneath each one there is something buried:

4. Cities threatened by divine destruction in the   5. I.e., Sheba (1 Kings 10:1–13).
Bible.

Some pile of wreckage that started it there.   65
Mountains are lonely and some are awful.

        .   .   .

One day I will crumble.
They'll cover my heap with dirt and that will make a mountain.
I think it will be Golgotha.

           1925

A Black Man Talks of Reaping

I have sown beside all waters in my day.
I planted deep, within my heart the fear
That wind or fowl would take the grain away.
I planted safe against this stark, lean year.

I scattered seed enough to plant the land   5
In rows from Canada to Mexico
But for my reaping only what the hand
Can hold at once is all that I can show.

Yet what I sowed and what the orchard yields
My brother's sons are gathering stalk and root,   10
Small wonder then my children glean in fields
They have not sown, and feed on bitter fruit.

           1926

Nocturne at Bethesda [1]

I thought I saw an angel flying low,
I thought I saw the flicker of a wing
Above the mulberry trees; but not again.
Bethesda sleeps. This ancient pool that healed
A host of bearded Jews does not awake.   5

This pool that once the angels troubled does not move.
No angel stirs it now, no Saviour comes
With healing in His hands to raise the sick
And bid the lame man leap upon the ground.

The golden days are gone. Why do we wait   10
So long upon the marble steps, blood
Falling from our open wounds? and why
Do our black faces search the empty sky?
Is there something we have forgotten? some precious thing
We have lost, wandering in strange lands?   15

1. "Now there is at Jerusalem by the sheep market a pool, which is called in the Hebrew tongue Bethesda, having five porches. In these lay a great multitude of impotent folk, of blind, halt, withered, waiting for the moving of the water. For an angel went down at a certain season into the pool, and troubled the water: whosoever then first after the troubling of the water stepped in was made whole of whatsoever disease he had" (John 5:2–4).

There was a day, I remember now,
I beat my breast and cried, "Wash me God,
Wash me with a wave of wind upon
The barley; O quiet One, draw near, draw near!
Walk upon the hills with lovely feet   20
And in the waterfall stand and speak.

"Dip white hands in the lily pool and mourn
Upon the harps still hanging in the trees
Near Babylon along the river's edge,
But oh, remember me, I pray, before   25
The summer goes and rose leaves lose their red."

The old terror takes my heart, the fear
Of quiet waters and of faint twilights.
There will be better days when I am gone
And healing pools where I cannot be healed.   30
Fragrant stars will gleam forever and ever
Above the place where I lie desolate.

Yet I hope, still I long to live.
And if there can be returning after death
I shall come back. But it will not be here;   35
If you want me you must search for me
Beneath the palms of Africa. Or if
I am not there then you may call to me
Across the shining dunes, perhaps I shall
Be following a desert caravan.   40

I may pass through centuries of death
With quiet eyes, but I'll remember still
A jungle tree with burning scarlet birds.
There is something I have forgotten, some precious thing.
I shall be seeking ornaments of ivory,   45
I shall be dying for a jungle fruit.

        You do not hear, Bethesda.
O still green water in a stagnant pool!
Love abandoned you and me alike.
There was a day you held a rich full moon   50
Upon your heart and listened to the words
Of men now dead and saw the angels fly.
There is a simple story on your face;
Years have wrinkled you. I know, Bethesda!
You are sad. It is the same with me.   55

                                                      1926

Southern Mansion

Poplars are standing there still as death
And ghosts of dead men
Meet their ladies walking
Two by two beneath the shade
And standing on the marble steps.   5

There is a sound of music echoing
Through the open door
And in the field there is
Another sound tinkling in the cotton:
Chains of bondmen dragging on the ground.   10

The years go back with an iron clank,
A hand is on the gate,
A dry leaf trembles on the wall.
Ghosts are walking.
They have broken roses down   15
And poplars stand there still as death.

                                          1931

Miracles

Doubt no longer miracles,
This spring day makes it plain
A man may crumble into dust
And straightway live again

A jug of water in the sun   5
Will easy turn to wine [1]
If love is stopping at the well
And love's brown arms entwine. [2]

And you who think him only man,
I tell you faithfully   10
That I have seen Christ clothed in rain
Walking on the sea. [3]

                                          1941

A Summer Tragedy

  Old Jeff Patton, the black share farmer, [1] fumbled with his bow tie. His
fingers trembled, and the high, stiff collar pinched his throat. A fellow loses
his hand for such vanities after thirty or forty years of simple life. Once a
year, or maybe twice if there's a wedding among his kin-folks, he may

---

1. An allusion to Jesus' miracle of changing water
into wine (John 2:3–9, 4:46).
2. According to John 4:5–28, Jesus encountered a
prostitute at Jacob's well in Samaria.

3. Matthew 14:25.
1. One who works others' lands for a share of the
crops.

spruce up; but generally fancy clothes do nothing but adorn the wall of the big room and feed the moths. That had been Jeff Patton's experience. He had not worn his stiff-bosomed shirt more than a dozen times in all his married life. His swallowtailed coat lay on the bed beside him, freshly brushed and pressed, but it was as full of holes as the overalls in which he worked on week days. The moths had used it badly. Jeff twisted his mouth into a hideous toothless grimace as he contended with the obstinate bow. He stamped his good foot and decided to give up the struggle.

"Jennie," he called.

"What's that, Jeff?" His wife's shrunken voice came out of the adjoining room like an echo. It was hardly bigger than a whisper.

"I reckon you'll have to he'p me wid this heah bow tie, baby," he said meekly. "Dog if I can hitch it up."

Her answer was not strong enough to reach him, but presently the old woman came to the door, feeling her way with a stick. She had a wasted, dead-leaf appearance. Her body, as scrawny and gnarled as a stringbean, seemed less than nothing in the ocean of frayed and faded petticoats that surrounded her. These hung an inch or two above the tops of her heavy, unlaced shoes and showed little grotesque piles where the stockings had fallen down from her negligible legs.

"You oughta could do a heap mo' wid a thing like that 'n me—beingst as you got yo' good sight."

"Looks like I *oughta* could," he admitted. "But ma fingers is gone democrat[2] on me. I get all mixed up in the looking glass an' can't tell whicha way to twist the devilish thing."

Jennie sat on the side of the bed and old Jeff Patton got down on one knee while she tied the bow knot. It was a slow and painful ordeal for each of them in this position. Jeff's bones cracked, his knee ached, and it was only after a half dozen attempts that Jennie worked a semblance of a bow into the tie.

"I got to dress maself now," the old woman whispered. "These is ma old shoes an' stockings, and I ain't so much as unwrapped ma dress."

"Well, don't worry 'bout me no mo', baby," Jeff said. "That 'bout finishes me. All I gotta do now is slip on that old coat 'n ves' an' I'll be fixed to leave."

Jennie disappeared again through the dim passage into the shed room. Being blind was no handicap to her in that black hole. Jeff heard the cane placed against the wall beside the door and knew that his wife was on easy ground. He put on his coat, took a battered top hat from the bed post, and hobbled to the front door. He was ready to travel. As soon as Jennie could get on her Sunday shoes and her old black silk dress, they would start.

Outside the tiny log house the day was warm and mellow with sunshine. A host of wasps was humming with busy excitement in the trunk of a dead sycamore. Gray squirrels were searching through the grass for hickory nuts and blue jays were in the trees, hopping from branch to branch. Pine woods stretched away to the left like a black sea. Among them were scattered scores of log houses like Jeff's, houses of black share farmers. Cows

---

2. I.e., his fingers seem to have developed minds of their own.

and pigs wandered freely among the trees. There was no danger of loss. Each farmer knew his own stock and knew his neighbor's as well as he knew his neighbor's children.

Down the slope to the right were the cultivated acres on which the colored folks worked. They extended to the river, more than two miles away, and they were today green with the unmade cotton crop. A tiny thread of a road, which passed directly in front of Jeff's place, ran through these green fields like a pencil mark.

Jeff, standing outside the door with his absurd hat in his left hand, surveyed the wide scene tenderly. He had been forty-five years on these acres. He loved them with the unexplained affection that others have for the countries to which they belong.

The sun was hot on his head, his collar still pinched his throat, and the Sunday clothes were intolerably hot. Jeff transferred the hat to his right hand and began fanning with it. Suddenly the whisper that was Jennie's voice came out of the shed room.

"You can bring the car round front whilst you's waitin'," it said feebly. There was a tired pause; then it added, "I'll soon be fixed to go."

"A'right, baby," Jeff answered. "I'll get it in a minute."

But he didn't move. A thought struck him that made his mouth fall open. The mention of the car brought to his mind, with new intensity, the trip he and Jennie were about to take. Fear came into his eyes; excitement took his breath. Lord, Jesus!

"Jeff . . . Oh Jeff," the old woman's whisper called.

He awakened with a jolt. "Hunh, baby?"

"What you doin'?"

"Nuthin. Jes studyin'. I jes been turnin' things round 'n round in ma mind."

"You could be gettin' the car," she said.

"Oh yes, right away, baby."

He started round to the shed, limping heavily on his bad leg. There were three frizzly chickens in the yard. All his other chickens had been killed or stolen recently. But the frizzly chickens had been saved somehow. That was fortunate indeed, for these curious creatures had a way of devouring "poison" from the yard and in that way protecting against conjure and bad luck and spells. But even the frizzly chickens seemed now to be in a stupor. Jeff thought they had some ailment; he expected all three of them to die shortly.

The shed in which the old model-T Ford stood was only a grass roof held up by four corner poles. It had been built by tremulous hands at a time when the little rattle-trap car had been regarded as a peculiar treasure. And, miraculously, despite wind and downpour, it still stood.

Jeff adjusted the crank and put his weight on it. The engine came to life with a sputter and bang that rattled the old car from radiator to tail light. Jeff hopped into the seat and put his foot on the accelerator. The sputtering and banging increased. The rattling became more violent. That was good. It was good banging, good sputtering and rattling, and it meant that the aged car was still in running condition. She could be depended on for this trip.

Again Jeff's thought halted as if paralyzed. The suggestion of the trip fell into the machinery of his mind like a wrench. He felt dazed and weak. He swung the car out into the yard, made a half turn, and drove around to the front door. When he took his hands off the wheel, he noticed that he was trembling violently. He cut off the motor and climbed to the ground to wait for Jennie.

A few moments later she was at the window, her voice rattling against the pane like a broken shutter.

"I'm ready, Jeff."

He did not answer, but limped into the house and took her by the arm. He led her slowly through the big room, down the step, and across the yard.

"You reckon I'd oughta lock the do'?" he asked softly.

They stopped and Jennie weighed the question. Finally she shook her head.

"Ne' mind the do'," she said. "I don't see no cause to lock up things."

"You right," Jeff agreed. "No cause to lock up."

Jeff opened the door and helped his wife into the car. A quick shudder passed over him. Jesus! Again he trembled.

"How come you shaking so?" Jennie whispered.

"I don't know," he said.

"You mus' be scairt, Jeff."

"No, baby, I ain't scairt."

He slammed the door after her and went around to crank up again. The motor started easily. Jeff wished that it had not been so responsive. He would have liked a few more minutes in which to turn things around in his head. As it was, with Jennie chiding him about being afraid, he had to keep going. He swung the car into the little pencilmark road and started off toward the river, driving very slowly, very cautiously.

Chugging across the green countryside, the small, battered Ford seemed tiny indeed. Jeff felt a familiar excitement, a thrill, as they came down the first slope to the immense levels on which the cotton was growing. He could not help reflecting that the crops were good. He knew what that meant, too; he had made forty-five of them with his own hands. It was true that he had worn out nearly a dozen mules, but that was the fault of old man Stevenson, the owner of the land. Major Stevenson had the odd notion that one mule was all a share farmer needed to work a thirty-acre plot. It was an expensive notion, the way it killed mules from overwork, but the old man held to it. Jeff thought it killed a good many share farmers as well as mules, but he had no sympathy for them. He had always been strong, and he had been taught to have no patience with weakness in men. Women or children might be tolerated if they were puny, but a weak man was a curse. Of course, his own children—

Jeff's thought halted there. He and Jennie never mentioned their dead children any more. And naturally he did not wish to dwell upon them in his mind. Before he knew it, some remark would slip out of his mouth and that would make Jennie feel blue. Perhaps she would cry. A woman like Jennie could not easily throw off the grief that comes from losing five grown children within two years. Even Jeff was still staggered by the blow. His memory had not been much good recently. He frequently talked to himself. And, although he had kept it a secret, he knew that his courage had left him. He was terrified by the least unfamiliar sound at night. He was reluctant to venture far from home in the daytime. And that habit of trembling when he felt fearful was now far beyond his control. Sometimes he became afraid and trembled without knowing what had frightened him. The feeling would just come over him like a chill.

The car rattled slowly over the dusty road. Jennie sat erect and silent, with a little absurd hat pinned to her hair. Her useless eyes seemed very large and very white in their deep sockets. Suddenly Jeff heard her voice, and he inclined his head to catch the words.

"Is we passed Delia Moore's house yet?" she asked.

"Not yet," he said.

"You must be drivin' mighty slow, Jeff."

"We jes as well take our time, baby."

There was a pause. A little puff of steam was coming out of the radiator of the car. Heat wavered above the hood. Delia Moore's house was nearly half a mile away. After a moment Jennie spoke again.

"You ain't really scairt, is you, Jeff?"

"Nah, baby, I ain't scairt."

"You know how we agreed—we gotta keep on goin'."

Jewels of perspiration appeared on Jeff's forehead. His eyes rounded, blinked, became fixed on the road.

"I don't know," he said with a shiver. "I reckon it's the only thing to do."

"Hm."

A flock of guinea fowls, pecking in the road, were scattered by the passing car. Some of them took to their wings; others hid under bushes. A blue jay, swaying on a leafy twig, was annoying a roadside squirrel. Jeff held an even speed till he came near Delia's place. Then he slowed down noticeably.

Delia's house was really no house at all, but an abandoned store building converted into a dwelling. It sat near a crossroads, beneath a single black cedar tree. There Delia, a catlike old creature of Jennie's age, lived alone. She had been there more years than anybody could remember, and long ago had won the disfavor of such women as Jennie. For in her young days Delia had been gayer, yellower, and saucier than seemed proper in those parts. Her ways with menfolks had been dark and suspicious. And the fact that she had had as many husbands as children did not help her reputation.

"Yonder's old Delia," Jeff said as they passed.

"What she doin'?"

"Jes sittin' in the do'," he said.

"She see us?"

"Hm," Jeff said. "Musta did."

That relieved Jennie. It strengthened her to know that her old enemy had seen her pass in her best clothes. That would give the old she-devil something to chew her gums and fret about, Jennie thought. Wouldn't she have a fit if she didn't find out? Old evil Delia! This would be just the thing for her. It would pay her back for being so evil. It would also pay her, Jennie thought, for the way she used to grin at Jeff—long ago when her teeth were good.

The road became smooth and red, and Jeff could tell by the smell of the air that they were nearing the river. He could see the rise where the road turned and ran along parallel to the stream. The car chugged on monotonously. After a long silent spell, Jennie leaned against Jeff and spoke.

"How many bale o' cotton you think we got standin'?" she said.

Jeff wrinkled his forehead as he calculated.

" 'Bout twenty-five, I reckon."

"How many you make las' year?"

"Twenty-eight," he said. "How come you ask that?"

"I's jes thinkin'," Jennie said quietly.

"It don't make a speck o' diff'ence though," Jeff reflected. "If we get much or if we get little, we still gonna be in debt to old man Stevenson when he gets through counting up agin us. It's took us a long time to learn that."

Jennie was not listening to these words. She had fallen into a trance-like meditation. Her lips twitched. She chewed her gums and rubbed her old gnarled hands nervously. Suddenly, she leaned forward, buried her face in the nervous hands, and burst into tears. She cried aloud in a dry, cracked voice that suggested the rattle of fodder on dead stalks. She cried aloud like a child, for she had never learned to suppress a genuine sob. Her slight old frame shook heavily and seemed hardly able to sustain such violent grief.

"What's the matter, baby?" Jeff asked awkwardly. "Why you cryin' like all that?"

"I's jes thinkin'," she said.

"So you the one what's scairt now, hunh?"

"I ain't scairt, Jeff. I's jes thinkin' 'bout leavin' eve'thing like this—eve'thing we been used to. It's right sad-like."

Jeff did not answer, and presently Jennie buried her face again and continued crying.

The sun was almost overhead. It beat down furiously on the dusty wagon path road, on the parched roadside grass, and the tiny battered car. Jeff's hands, gripping the wheel, became wet with perspiration; his forehead sparkled. Jeff's lips parted and his mouth shaped a hideous grimace. His face suggested the face of a man being burned. But the torture passed and his expression softened again.

"You mustn't cry, baby," he said to his wife. "We gotta be strong. We can't break down."

Jennie waited a few seconds, then said, "You reckon we oughta do it, Jeff? You reckon we oughta go 'head an' do it really?"

Jeff's voice choked; his eyes blurred. He was terrified to hear Jennie say the thing that had been in his mind all morning. She had egged him on when he had wanted more than anything in the world to wait, to reconsider, to think things over a little longer. Now *she* was getting cold feet. Actually, there was no need of thinking the question through again. It would only end in making the same painful decision once more. Jeff knew that. There was no need of fooling around longer.

"We jes as well to do like we planned," he said. "They ain't nuthin else for us now—it's the bes' thing."

Jeff thought of the handicaps, the near impossibility, of making another crop with his leg bothering him more and more each week. Then there was always the chance that he would have another stroke, like the one that had made him lame. Another one might kill him. The least it could do would be to leave him helpless. Jeff gasped . . . . Lord, Jesus! He could not bear to think of being helpless, like a baby, on Jennie's hands. Frail, blind Jennie.

The little pounding motor of the car worked harder and harder. The puff of steam from the cracked radiator became larger. Jeff realized that they were climbing a little rise. A moment later the road turned abruptly and he looked down upon the face of the river.

"Jeff."

"Hunh?"

"Is that the water I hear?"

"Hm. Tha's it."

"Well, which way you goin' now?"

"Down this-a way," he answered. "The road runs 'longside o' the water a lil piece."

She waited a while calmly. Then she said, "Drive faster."

"A'right, baby," Jeff said.

The water roared in the bed of the river. It was fifty or sixty feet below the level of the road. Between the road and the water there was a long smooth slope, sharply inclined. The slope was dry; the clay had been hardened by prolonged summer heat. The water below, roaring in a narrow channel, was noisy and wild.

"Jeff."

"Hunh?"

"How far you goin'?"

"Jes a lil piece down the road."

"You ain't scairt is you, Jeff?"

"Nah, baby," he said trembling. "I ain't scairt."

"Remember how we planned it, Jeff. We gotta do it like we said. Brave-like."

"Hm."

Jeff's brain darkened. Things suddenly seemed unreal, like figures in a dream. Thoughts swam in his mind foolishly, hysterically, like little blind fish in a pool within a dense cave. They rushed, crossed one another, jostled, collided, retreated, and rushed again. Jeff soon became dizzy. He shuddered violently and turned to his wife.

"Jennie, I can't do it. I can't." His voice broke pitifully.

She did not appear to be listening. All the grief had gone from her face. She sat erect, her unseeing eyes wide open, strained and frightful. Her glossy black skin had become dull. She seemed as thin and as sharp and bony as a starved bird. Now, having suffered and endured the sadness of tearing herself away from beloved things, she showed no anguish. She was absorbed with her own thoughts, and she didn't even hear Jeff's voice shouting in her ear.

Jeff said nothing more. For an instant there was light in his cavernous brain. That chamber was, for less than a second, peopled by characters he knew and loved. They were simple, healthy creatures, and they behaved in a manner that he could understand. They had quality. But since he had already taken leave of them long ago, the remembrance did not break his heart again. Young Jeff Patton was among them, the Jeff Patton of fifty years ago who went down to New Orleans with a crowd of country boys to the Mardi Gras doings. The gay young crowd—boys with candy-striped shirts and rouged brown girls in noisy silks—was like a picture in his head. Yet it did not make him sad. On that very trip Slim Burns had killed Joe Beasley—the crowd had been broken up. Since then Jeff Patton's world had been the Greenbrier Plantation. If there had been other Mardi Gras carnivals, he had not heard of them. Since then there had been no time; the years had fallen on him like waves. Now he was old, worn out. Another paralytic stroke like the one he had already suffered would put him on his back for keeps. In that condition, with a frail blind woman to look after him, he would be worse off than if he were dead.

Suddenly Jeff's hands became steady. He actually felt brave. He slowed down the motor of the car and carefully pulled off the road. Below, the water of the stream boomed, a soft thunder in the deep channel. Jeff ran the car onto the clay slope, pointed it directly toward the stream, and put his foot heavily on the accelerator. The little car leaped furiously down the steep incline toward the water. The movement was nearly as swift and direct as a fall. The two old black folks, sitting quietly side by side, showed no excitement. In another instant the car hit the water and dropped immediately out of sight.

A little later it lodged in the mud of a shallow place. One wheel of the crushed and upturned little Ford became visible above the rushing water.

1933

LANGSTON HUGHES

1902–1967

Langston Hughes enjoys a special relationship to the Harlem Renaissance for two reasons above all: he helped to define the spirit of the age, from a literary point of view, through his brilliant poetry and other writings during this era, in a career that continued to flourish when most of the other writers of the movement fell silent; and he also left behind him, in a section of his autobiography *The Big Sea* (1940), the finest first-person account of the renaissance, a treasure-trove of impressions and memories on which virtually all scholars and students of the cultural movement have depended in their own writings.

Hughes was among the first of the writers and artists drawn to Harlem by its promise as a center of African American cultural activity. Born in Joplin, Missouri, Hughes had grown up in Lawrence, Kansas, and Lincoln, Illinois, before going to high school in Cleveland, Ohio, and spending a year in Mexico, near Mexico City. In all these places he was part of a small, sometimes tiny community of blacks, to whom he was nevertheless profoundly attached from early in his life. Hughes was descended from a distinguished family. His maternal grandmother's first husband had died at Harpers Ferry fighting in John Brown's band; her second husband, Langston's maternal grandfather, had been prominent in Kansas politics during Reconstruction, before racism drove him from the field; and his brother, John Mercer Langston, had been one of the most famous black Americans of the nineteenth century, a congressman from Virginia and the founding dean of the law school of Howard University. However, Hughes's mother, Carrie Langston Hughes, and his father, James N. Hughes, separated not long after his birth. His father emigrated to Mexico, where he was successful in business. In contrast, Langston grew up lonely and near poverty in Lawrence, Kansas.

In September 1921, aided by his father, he arrived in New York ostensibly to attend Columbia University but really, he later claimed, to see Harlem. The previous June, he had published one of his greatest poems, *The Negro Speaks of Rivers*, in the *Crisis*, where his talent was immediately spotted by its brilliant literary editor, Jessie Fauset. Hughes lasted only one year at Columbia, where he did well but never felt comfortable. He took a succession of odd jobs, including stints as a delivery boy, vegetable farmer, and mess boy on a ship anchored up the Hudson River. In 1923, he sailed to Africa as a member of the crew of a merchant steamer; the following year he traveled the same way to Europe, where he jumped ship and spent several months in Paris working in the kitchen of a nightclub. Through all these jobs and adventures, Hughes continued to work on his poetry, which he published mainly in the *Crisis*. By 1924, his poetry showed the powerful influence of the blues and jazz. In fact, his poem *The Weary Blues* helped to launch his career when it won first prize in the poetry section of the 1925 literary contest organized by *Opportunity* magazine. Aided enthusiastically by Carl Van Vechten, who remained a friend all of Hughes's life, he won a book contract from Knopf and published *The Weary Blues*, his first collection of verse, in 1926.

Although Hughes's earliest influences as a mature poet came from Walt Whitman and Carl Sandburg ("my guiding star"), Claude McKay stood for him in the early 1920s as the embodiment of the cosmopolitan and yet racially confident and committed black poet Hughes hoped to be. Hughes was also indebted to older figures such as Du Bois and James Weldon Johnson, both of whom admired his work and aided him. Images and sentiments such as that in *Poem* ("The night is beautiful, / So the faces of my people") and *Dream Variations* ("Night coming tenderly / Black like me.") endeared his work to a wide range of African Americans, for whom he delighted in writing. His major step, encouraged in part by Sandburg's example (as in Sandburg's *Jazz Fantasies*, 1919) but anchored by his own near-worship of black music as the major form of art within the race, was his adaptation of traditional poetic forms first to jazz, then to the blues, in which Hughes sometimes used dialect but in a way radically different from that of earlier writers. In these steps Hughes was well served by his early experimentation with a loose form of rhyme that frequently gave way to an inventively rhythmic free verse ("Me an' ma baby's / Got two mo' ways, / Two mo' ways to do de buck!"). His landmark poem *The Weary Blues* was the first by any poet to make use of the basic blues form.

Even more radical experimentation with the blues form led to his next collection, *Fine Clothes to the Jew* (1927). Perhaps his finest single book of verse, *Fine Clothes* was also his least successful in terms of sales and, in the black press (though not the white), its critical reception. Several reviewers in black newspapers and magazines were distressed by Hughes's fearless and, to them, tasteless evocation of elements of lower-class black culture, including its sometimes raw eroticism, never before treated in serious poetry. The book was "about 100 pages of trash [reeking] of the gutter and sewer," wrote one man; another found the poems "insanitary, insipid and repulsing." These reviewers probably gave *Fine Clothes to the Jew* a harsher reception than that ever accorded any other book of American poetry, with the exception of Whitman's *Leaves of Grass*.

In response to his critics, Hughes was adamant about his determination to write about such people and to experiment with blues and jazz. The year before, 1926, he had published in the *Nation* an essay in defense of the freedom of the black writer, *The Negro Artist and the Racial Mountain.* "We younger Negro artists who create now intend to express our individual dark-skinned selves without fear or shame," he had declared. "We know we are beautiful. And ugly too." This essay quickly became a manifesto for many of the younger writers who also wished to assert their right to explore and exploit allegedly degraded aspects of black life. With most of these writers Hughes enjoyed a warm relationship; his modesty was matched by habits of generosity that endeared him to others.

Also in 1926, Hughes returned to school, this time at the historically black (although the faculty was almost entirely white) Lincoln University in Pennsylvania, from which he graduated in 1929. In 1927, his life took an extraordinary turn when he met Charlotte Osgood Mason, a wealthy, white patron of the arts then in her seventies, who had been led to Hughes by Alain Locke. In the next three years, Mason, who believed passionately in parapsychology, intuition, and folk culture, dominated Hughes's life with her gifts of money and her powerful advice about virtually every aspect of his life and art. She was directly involved in supervising the writing of his 1930 novel *Not without Laughter,* in which Hughes drew on his boyhood in Kansas to depict the life of a black child, Sandy, growing up in a representative midwestern African American home.

In 1930, in a dispute that involved Zora Neale Hurston, who was also being supported by Mason, the relationship between Hughes and his patron came to an explosive end. Hurt and baffled by Mason's rejection, in 1931 Hughes used money from a prize to spend several weeks recovering in Haiti. When he returned to the United States, he made a sharp turn toward the political left, although social and political consciousness, and an interest in socialism, had always been one feature of his verse. He published verse and essays in *New Masses,* a journal controlled by the Communist Party, and later that year began a tour of the South and the West designed to take poetry to the people, with Hughes reading his poems in churches and schools. In 1932, at the end of the tour, he boarded a ship in New York and sailed for the Soviet Union with a band of young African Americans invited to take part in a film about American race relations. For Hughes, the renaissance was long over, replaced by a sense of the need for political struggle and for an art that reflected this radical approach.

Unlike most of the writers of the renaissance, Hughes's career easily survived the end of that movement; there was never a year, or even a month or a week, when he did not produce art in keeping with his sense of himself as a thoroughly professional writer. In 1934, he published his first collection of short stories, the often acerbic and even embittered *The Ways of White Folks.* However, in the 1930s Hughes's main concern was probably the theater. His drama of miscegenation and the South, *Mulatto* (1935), became the longest running play by an African American on Broadway until Lorraine Hansberry's *A Raisin in the Sun* in the 1960s. Some of these plays were comedies, others were dramas of domestic African American life or were radical in their politics, as with Hughes's *Don't You Want to Be Free?,* which his Harlem Suitcase Theater staged in 1938.

With the start of World War II, Hughes returned to the political center. His first book of autobiography, *The Big Sea,* with its memorable portrait of the renaissance, appeared in 1940. In poetry, he revived his interest in some of his old themes and forms, including the blues, as in the verse collection *Shakespeare in Harlem* (1942). In 1943, in his weekly column for the Chicago *Defender,* he introduced one of his enduring fictional triumphs, the character Jesse B. Semple, or Simple, a Harlem everyman whose comic manner hardly obscured some of the serious themes raised by Hughes in relating Simple's exploits. In 1947, as lyricist for the Broadway musical *Street Scene,* with music by Kurt Weill, Hughes earned enough money to purchase a house in his beloved Harlem, where he lived for the rest of his life.

His output became prodigious. In addition to books of verse, including the bebop-shaped *Montage of a Dream Deferred* (1951), about a changing Harlem, fertile with humanity but in decline, he published another volume of autobiography, two more volumes of short stories, a second novel, about a dozen books for children, five books drawn from the Simple columns (which ran for twenty years), several plays and musicals (including pioneering examples of the gospel musical), a history of the NAACP, various libretti for operas and cantatas, and landmark anthologies of African American writing (notably *Poetry of the Negro*, 1949) and of African literature.

By the end of his life Hughes was almost everywhere recognized, because of his versatility and skill, as the most representative writer in the history of African American literature and also as probably the most original of all black American poets. He cherished and even encouraged the often-bestowed title of "Poet Laureate of the Negro Race," which captures the importance he placed on writing literature both about and for African Americans as well as the sense that he had accomplished the central goal of his life with almost unrivaled success. Maturing in the Harlem Renaissance, Hughes's career demonstrates the solidity of that movement as the main foundation of modern African American literature.

The Negro Speaks of Rivers

I've known rivers:
I've known rivers ancient as the world and older than the
    flow of human blood in human veins.

My soul has grown deep like the rivers.

I bathed in the Euphrates when dawns were young.
I built my hut near the Congo and it lulled me to sleep.   5
I looked upon the Nile and raised the pyramids above it.
I heard the singing of the Mississippi when Abe Lincoln
    went down to New Orleans,[1] and I've seen its muddy
    bosom turn all golden in the sunset.

I've known rivers:
Ancient, dusky rivers.

My soul has grown deep like the rivers.   10

                                                                        1921

Mother to Son

Well, son, I'll tell you:
Life for me ain't been no crystal stair.
It's had tacks in it,
And splinters,
And boards torn up,   5

---

1. Lincoln's determination to end slavery was said to have started when, as a young man, he visited New Orleans for the first time.

And places with no carpet on the floor—
Bare.
But all the time
I'se been a-climbin' on,
And reachin' landin's,   10
And turnin' corners,
And sometimes goin' in the dark
Where there ain't been no light.
So boy, don't you turn back.
Don't you set down on the steps   15
'Cause you finds it's kinder hard.
Don't you fall now—
For I'se still goin', honey,
I'se still climbin',
And life for me ain't been no crystal stair.   20

                                                      1922

Danse Africaine

The low beating of the tom-toms,
The slow beating of the tom-toms,
   Low . . . slow
   Slow . . . low—
   Stirs your blood.   5
    Dance!
A night-veiled girl
   Whirls softly into a
   Circle of light.
   Whirls softly . . . slowly,   10
Like a wisp of smoke around the fire—
   And the tom-toms beat,
   And the tom-toms beat,
And the low beating of the tom-toms
   Stirs your blood.   15

                                                 1922, 1926

Jazzonia

O, silver tree!
Oh, shining rivers of the soul!

In a Harlem cabaret
Six long-headed jazzers play.
A dancing girl whose eyes are bold   5
Lifts high a dress of silken gold.

Oh, singing tree!
Oh, shining rivers of the soul!

Were Eve's eyes
In the first garden   10
Just a bit too bold?
Was Cleopatra gorgeous
In a gown of gold?

Oh, shining tree!
Oh, silver rivers of the soul!   15

In a whirling cabaret
Six long-headed jazzers play.

                                                        1923

When Sue Wears Red

When Susanna Jones wears red
Her face is like an ancient cameo
Turned brown by the ages.

Come with a blast of trumpets,
    Jesus!   5

When Susanna Jones wears red
A queen from some time-dead Egyptian night
Walks once again.

Blow trumpets, Jesus!

And the beauty of Susanna Jones in red   10
Burns in my heart a love-fire sharp like pain.

Sweet silver trumpets,
    Jesus!

                                              1923, 1926

Dream Variations

To fling my arms wide
In some place of the sun,
To whirl and to dance
Till the white day is done.
Then rest at cool evening   5
Beneath a tall tree
While night comes on gently,
    Dark like me—
That is my dream!

To fling my arms wide   10
In the face of the sun,
Dance! Whirl! Whirl!

Till the quick day is done.
Rest at pale evening . . .
A tall, slim tree . . .   15
Night coming tenderly
  Black like me.

                                              1924, 1926

The Weary Blues

Droning a drowsy syncopated tune,
Rocking back and forth to a mellow croon,
  I heard a Negro play.
Down on Lenox Avenue [1] the other night
By the pale dull pallor of an old gas light   5
  He did a lazy sway. . . .
  He did a lazy sway. . . .
To the tune o' those Weary Blues.
With his ebony hands on each ivory key
He made that poor piano moan with melody.   10
  O Blues!
Swaying to and fro on his rickety stool
He played that sad raggy tune like a musical fool.
  Sweet Blues!
Coming from a black man's soul.   15
  O Blues!
In a deep song voice with a melancholy tone
I heard that Negro sing, that old piano moan—
  "Ain't got nobody in all this world,
  Ain't got nobody but ma self.
  I's gwine to quit ma frownin'   20
  And put ma troubles on the shelf."
Thump, thump, thump, went his foot on the floor.
He played a few chords then he sang some more—
  "I got the Weary Blues
  And I can't be satisfied.   25
  Got the Weary Blues
  And can't be satisfied—
  I ain't happy no mo'
  And I wish that I had died."
And far into the night he crooned that tune.   30
The stars went out and so did the moon.
The singer stopped playing and went to bed
While the Weary Blues echoed through his head.
He slept like a rock or a man that's dead.

1923   1925

---

1. Major Harlem thoroughfare, now Adam Clayton Powell Boulevard.

I, Too

I, too, sing America.

I am the darker brother.
They send me to eat in the kitchen
When company comes,
But I laugh,   5
And eat well,
And grow strong.

Tomorrow,
I'll be at the table
When company comes.   10
Nobody'll dare
Say to me,
"Eat in the kitchen,"
Then.

Besides,   15
They'll see how beautiful I am
And be ashamed—

I, too, am America.

                                                    1925, 1959

A House in Taos [1]

Rain

Thunder of the Rain God:
   And we three
   Smitten by beauty.

Thunder of the Rain God: 5
   And we three
   Weary, weary.

Thunder of the Rain God:
   And you, she, and I
   Waiting for nothingness.   10

Do you understand the stillness
   Of this house
   In Taos
Under the thunder of the Rain God?

---

1. A town in New Mexico noted as an artists' colony. Hughes had not yet visited the town.

Sun   15

That there should be a barren garden
About this house in Taos
Is not so strange,
But that there should be three barren hearts
In this one house in Taos—   20
Who carries ugly things to show the sun?

Moon

Did you ask for the beaten brass of the moon?
We can buy lovely things with money,
You, she, and I,   25
Yet you seek,
As though you could keep,
This unbought loveliness of moon.

Wind

Touch our bodies, wind.   30
Our bodies are separate, individual things.
Touch our bodies, wind,
But blow quickly
Through the red, white, yellow skins
Of our bodies   35
To the terrible snarl,
Not mine,
Not yours,
Not hers,
But all one snarl of souls.   40
Blow quickly, wind,
Before we run back
Into the windlessness—
With our bodies—
Into the windlessness   45
Of our house in Taos.

                                                              1926

Homesick Blues

De railroad bridge's
A sad song in de air.
De railroad bridge's
A sad song in de air.
Ever time de trains pass   5
I wants to go somewhere.

I went down to de station.
Ma heart was in ma mouth.
Went down to de station.
Heart was in ma mouth.   10

Lookin' for a box car
To roll me to de South.

Homesick blues, Lawd,
'S a terrible thing to have.
Homesick blues is   15
A terrible thing to have.
To keep from cryin'
I opens ma mouth an' laughs.

1926

Po' Boy Blues

When I was home de
Sunshine seemed like gold.
When I was home de
Sunshine seemed like gold.
Since I come up North de   5
Whole damn world's turned cold.

I was a good boy,
Never done no wrong.
Yes, I was a good boy,
Never done no wrong,
But this world is weary   10
An' de road is hard an' long.

I fell in love with
A gal I thought was kind.
Fell in love with
A gal I thought was kind.   15
She made me lose ma money
An' almost lose ma mind.

Weary, weary,
Weary early in de morn.
Weary, weary,   20
Early, early in de morn.
I's so weary
I wish I'd never been born.

1926

Gypsy Man

Ma man's a gypsy
Cause he never does come home.
Ma man's a gypsy,—
He never does come home.
I'm gonna be a gypsy woman   5
Fer I can't stay here alone.

Once I was in Memphis,
I mean Tennessee.
Once I was in Memphis,
Said Tennessee.   10
But I had to leave cause
Nobody there was good to me.

I met a yellow papa,
He took ma last thin dime.
Met a yellow papa,   15
He took ma last thin dime.
I give it to him cause I loved him
But I'll have mo' sense next time.

Love, Oh, love is
Such a strange disease.   20
Love, Oh, love is
Such a strange disease.
When it hurts yo' heart you
Sho can't find no ease.

                                                    1926

Lament over Love

I hope my child'll
Never love a man.
I say I hope my child'll
Never love a man.
Love can hurt you   5
Mo'n anything else can.

I'm goin' down to the river
An' I ain't goin' there to swim;
Down to the river,
Ain't goin' there to swim.   10
My true love's left me
And I'm goin' there to think about him.

Love is like whiskey,
Love is like red, red wine.
Love is like whiskey,   15
Like sweet red wine.
If you want to be happy
You got to love all the time.

I'm goin' up in a tower
Tall as a tree is tall,   20
Up in a tower
Tall as a tree is tall.
Gonna think about my man—
And let my fool self fall.

                                               1926, 1959

Red Silk Stockings

Put on yo' red silk stockings,
Black gal.
Go out an' let de white boys
Look at yo' legs.

Ain't nothin' to do for you, nohow,   5
Round this town,—
You's too pretty.
Put on yo' red silk stockings, gal,
An' tomorrow's chile'll
Be a high yaller.   10

Go out an' let de white boys
Look at yo' legs.

1927

Bad Man

I'm a bad, bad man
Cause everbody tells me so.
I'm a bad, bad man.
Everbody tells me so.
I takes ma meanness and ma licker   5
Everwhere I go.

I beats ma wife an'
I beats ma side gal too.
Beats ma wife an'
Beats ma side gal too.   10
Don't know why I do it but
It keeps me from feelin' blue.

I'm so bad I
Don't even want to be good.
So bad, bad I   15
Don't even want to be good.
I'm goin' to de devil an'
I wouldn't go to heaben if I could.

1927

Song for a Dark Girl

Way Down South in Dixie
    (Break the heart of me)
They hung my black young lover
    To a cross roads tree.

Way Down South in Dixie   5
    (Bruised body high in air)
I asked the white Lord Jesus
    What was the use of prayer.

Way Down South in Dixie
    (Break the heart of me)   10
Love is a naked shadow
    On a gnarled and naked tree.

1927

Gal's Cry for a Dying Lover

Heard de owl a hootin',
Knowed somebody's 'bout to die.
Heard de owl a hootin',
Knowed somebody's 'bout to die.
Put ma head un'neath de kiver,   5
Started in to moan an' cry.

Hound dawg's barkin'
Means he's gonna leave this world.
Hound dawg's barkin'
Means he's gonna leave this world.   10
O, Lawd have mercy
On a po' black girl.

Black an' ugly
But he sho do treat me kind.
I'm black an' ugly   15
But he sho do treat me kind.
High-in-heaben Jesus,
Please don't take this man o' mine.

1927

Hard Daddy

I went to ma daddy,
Says Daddy I have got the blues.
Went to ma daddy,
Says Daddy I have got the blues.
Ma daddy says, Honey,   5
Can't you bring no better news?

I cried on his shoulder but
He turned his back on me.
Cried on his shoulder but
He turned his back on me.   10
He said a woman's cryin's
Never gonna bother me.

I wish I had wings to
Fly like the eagle flies.
Wish I had wings to   15
Fly like the eagle flies.
I'd fly on ma man an'
I'd scratch out both his eyes.

                                        1927, 1955

Sylvester's Dying Bed

I woke up this mornin'
'Bout half-past three.
All the womens in town
Was gathered round me.

Sweet gals was a-moanin',   5
"Sylvester's gonna die!"
And a hundred pretty mamas
Bowed their heads to cry.

I woke up little later
'Bout half-past fo',   10
The doctor 'n' undertaker's
Both at ma do'.

Black gals was a-beggin',
"You can't leave us here!"
Brown-skins cryin', "Daddy!   15
Honey! Baby! Don't go, dear!"

But I felt ma time's a-comin',
And I know'd I's dyin' fast
I seed the River Jerden [1]
A-creepin' muddy past—   20
But I's still Sweet Papa 'Vester,
Yes, sir! Long as life do last!

So I hollers, "Com'ere, babies,
Fo' to love yo' daddy right!"
And I reaches up to hug 'em—   25
When the Lawd put out the light.

Then everything was darkness
In a great . . . big . . . night.

                                        1931

1. I.e., Jordan; a river in Israel, which is crossed to reach the Promised Land.

Ballad of the Landlord

Landlord, landlord,
My roof has sprung a leak.
Don't you 'member I told you about it
Way last week?

Landlord, landlord,   5
These steps is broken down.
When you come up yourself
It's a wonder you don't fall down.

Ten Bucks you say I owe you?
Ten Bucks you say is due?   10
Well, that's Ten Bucks more'n I'll pay you
Till you fix this house up new.

What? You gonna get eviction orders?
You gonna cut off my heat?
You gonna take my furniture and   15
Throw it in the street?

Um-huh! You talking high and mighty.
Talk on—till you get through.
You ain't gonna be able to say a word
If I land my fist on you.   20

Police! Police!
Come and get this man!
He's trying to ruin the government
And overturn the land!

Copper's whistle!   25
Patrol bell!
Arrest.

Precinct Station.
Iron cell.
Headlines in press: 30

MAN THREATENS LANDLORD

TENANT HELD NO BAIL

JUDGE GIVES NEGRO 90 DAYS IN COUNTY JAIL

                                                      1940, 1955

Juke Box Love Song

I could take the Harlem night
and wrap around you,
Take the neon lights and make a crown,
Take the Lenox Avenue busses,
Taxis, subways,   5
And for your love song tone their rumble down.
Take Harlem's heartbeat,
Make a drumbeat,
Put it on a record, let it whirl,
And while we listen to it play,   10
Dance with you till day—
Dance with you, my sweet brown Harlem girl.

                                           1950, 1959

Dream Boogie

Good morning, daddy!
Ain't you heard
The boogie-woogie [1] rumble
Of a dream deferred?

Listen closely: 5
You'll hear their feet
Beating out and beating out a—

   You think
   It's a happy beat?

Listen to it closely: 10
Ain't you heard
something underneath
like a—

   What did I say?

Sure,   15
I'm happy!
Take it away!

   Hey, pop!
   Re-bop!
   Mop!   20

   Y-e-a-h!

                                           1951, 1959

1. A style of dancing and music; in the South, also slang for a case of syphilis.

Harlem

What happens to a dream deferred?

Does it dry up
like a raisin in the sun?
Or fester like a sore—
And then run?   5
Does it stink like rotten meat?
Or crust and sugar over—
like a syrupy sweet?

Maybe it just sags
like a heavy load.   10

Or does it explode?

1951, 1959

Motto

I play it cool
And dig all jive.
That's the reason
I stay alive.

My motto,   5
As I live and learn,
is:
*Dig And Be Dug
In Return.*

1951, 1967

The Negro Artist and the Racial Mountain [1]

One of the most promising of the young Negro poets said to me once, "I want to be a poet—not a Negro poet," meaning, I believe, "I want to write like a white poet"; meaning subconsciously, "I would like to be a white poet"; meaning behind that, "I would like to be white." And I was sorry the young man said that, for no great poet has ever been afraid of being himself. And I doubted then that, with his desire to run away spiritually from his race, this boy would ever be a great poet. But this is the mountain standing in the way of any true Negro art in America—this urge within the race toward whiteness, the desire to pour racial individuality into the mold of American standardization, and to be as little Negro and as much American as possible.

But let us look at the immediate background of this young poet. His fam-

---

1. The essay originally appeared in *The Nation* in response to George S. Schuyler's essay *The Negro-Art Hokum*, which was printed in *The Nation* the week before.

ily is of what I suppose one would call the Negro middle class: people who are by no means rich yet never uncomfortable nor hungry—smug, contented, respectable folk, members of the Baptist church. The father goes to work every morning. He is a chief steward at a large white club. The mother sometimes does fancy sewing or supervises parties for the rich families of the town. The children go to a mixed school. In the home they read white papers and magazines. And the mother often says "Don't be like niggers" when the children are bad. A frequent phrase from the father is, "Look how well a white man does things." And so the word white comes to be unconsciously a symbol of all virtues. It holds for the children beauty, morality, and money. The whisper of "I want to be white" runs silently through their minds. This young poet's home is, I believe, a fairly typical home of the colored middle class. One sees immediately how difficult it would be for an artist born in such a home to interest himself in interpreting the beauty of his own people. He is never taught to see that beauty. He is taught rather not to see it, or if he does, to be ashamed of it when it is not according to Caucasian patterns.

For racial culture the home of a self-styled "high-class" Negro has nothing better to offer. Instead there will perhaps be more aping of things white than in a less cultured or less wealthy home. The father is perhaps a doctor, lawyer, landowner, or politician. The mother may be a social worker, or a teacher, or she may do nothing and have a maid. Father is often dark but he has usually married the lightest woman he could find. The family attend a fashionable church where few really colored faces are to be found. And they themselves draw a color line. In the North they go to white theaters and white movies. And in the South they have at least two cars and house "like white folks." Nordic manners, Nordic faces, Nordic hair, Nordic art (if any), and an Episcopal heaven. A very high mountain indeed for the would-be racial artist to climb in order to discover himself and his people.

But then there are the low-down folks, the so-called common element, and they are the majority—may the Lord be praised! The people who have their hip of gin on Saturday nights and are not too important to themselves or the community, or too well fed, or too learned to watch the lazy world go round. They live on Seventh Street in Washington or State Street in Chicago and they do not particularly care whether they are like white folks or anybody else. Their joy runs, bang! into ecstasy. Their religion soars to a shout. Work maybe a little today, rest a little tomorrow. Play awhile. Sing awhile. O, let's dance! These common people are not afraid of spirituals, as for a long time their more intellectual brethren were, and jazz is their child. They furnish a wealth of colorful, distinctive material for any artist because they still hold their own individuality in the face of American standardizations. And perhaps these common people will give to the world its truly great Negro artist, the one who is not afraid to be himself. Whereas the better-class Negro would tell the artist what to do, the people at least let him alone when he does appear. And they are not ashamed of him—if they know he exists at all. And they accept what beauty is their own without question.

Certainly there is, for the American Negro artist who can escape the restrictions the more advanced among his own group would put upon him, a great field of unused material ready for his art. Without going outside his race, and even among the better classes with their "white" culture and conscious American manners, but still Negro enough to be different, there is sufficient matter to furnish a black artist with a lifetime of creative work. And when he chooses to touch on the relations between Negroes and whites in this country with their innumerable overtones and undertones surely, and especially for literature and the drama, there is an inexhaustible supply of themes at hand. To these the Negro artist can give his racial individuality, his heritage of rhythm and warmth, and his incongruous humor that so often, as in the Blues, becomes ironic laughter mixed with tears. But let us look again at the mountain.

A prominent Negro clubwoman in Philadelphia paid eleven dollars to hear Raquel Meller sing Andalusian popular songs. But she told me a few weeks before she would not think of going to hear "that woman," Clara Smith,[2] a great black artist, sing Negro folksongs. And many an upper-class Negro church, even now, would not dream of employing a spiritual in its services. The drab melodies in white folks' hymnbooks are much to be preferred. "We want to worship the Lord correctly and quietly. We don't believe in 'shouting.' Let's be dull like the Nordics," they say, in effect.

The road for the serious black artist, then, who would produce a racial art is most certainly rocky and the mountain is high. Until recently he received almost no encouragement for his work from either white or colored people. The fine novels of Chesnutt[3] go out of print with neither race noticing their passing. The quaint charm and humor of Dunbar's[4] dialect verse brought to him, in his day, largely the same kind of encouragement one would give a sideshow freak (A colored man writing poetry! How odd!) or a clown (How amusing!).

The present vogue in things Negro, although it may do as much harm as good for the budding colored artist, has at least done this: it has brought him forcibly to the attention of his own people among whom for so long, unless the other race had noticed him beforehand, he was a prophet with little honor. I understand that Charles Gilpin[5] acted for years in Negro theaters without any special acclaim from his own, but when Broadway gave him eight curtain calls, Negroes, too, began to beat a tin pan in his honor. I know a young colored writer, a manual worker by day, who had been writing well for the colored magazines for some years, but it was not until he recently broke into the white publications and his first book was accepted by a prominent New York publisher that the "best" Negroes in his city took the trouble to discover that he lived there. Then almost immediately they decided to give a grand dinner for him. But the society ladies

2. Major blues singer (1885–1935). "Andalusian": from a region of Spain.
3. Charles Chesnutt (1858–1932), author of three novels, The House behind the Cedars (1900), The Marrow of Tradition (1901), and The Colonel's Dream (1905); a biography of Frederick Douglass; and two short story collections, The Conjure Woman (1899) and The Wife of His Youth and Other Stories of the Color Line (1899).
4. Paul Laurence Dunbar (1872–1906), poet and author of the novel Sport of the Gods (1907).
5. American actor (1878–1930).

were careful to whisper to his mother that perhaps she'd better not come. They were not sure she would have an evening gown.[6]

The Negro artist works against an undertow of sharp criticism and misunderstanding from his own group and unintentional bribes from the whites. "Oh, be respectable, write about nice people, show how good we are," say the Negroes. "Be stereotyped, don't go too far, don't shatter our illusions about you, don't amuse us too seriously. We will pay you," say the whites. Both would have told Jean Toomer not to write Cane.[7] The colored people did not praise it. The white people did not buy it. Most of the colored people who did read Cane hate it. They are afraid of it. Although the critics gave it good reviews the public remained indifferent. Yet (excepting the work of Du Bois) Cane contains the finest prose written by a Negro in America. And like the singing of Robeson,[8] it is truly racial.

But in spite of the Nordicized Negro intelligentsia and the desires of some white editors we have an honest American Negro literature already with us. Now I await the rise of the Negro theater. Our folk music, having achieved world-wide fame, offers itself to the genius of the great individual American composer who is to come. And within the next decade I expect to see the work of a growing school of colored artists who paint and model the beauty of dark faces and create with new technique the expressions of their own soul-world. And the Negro dancers who will dance like flame and the singers who will continue to carry our songs to all who listen—they will be with us in even greater numbers tomorrow.

Most of my own poems are racial in theme and treatment, derived from the life I know. In many of them I try to grasp and hold some of the meanings and rhythms of jazz. I am as sincere as I know how to be in these poems and yet after every reading I answer questions like these from my own people: Do you think Negroes should always write about Negroes? I wish you wouldn't read some of your poems to white folks. How do you find anything interesting in a place like a cabaret? Why do you write about black people? You aren't black. What makes you do so many jazz poems?

But jazz to me is one of the inherent expressions of Negro life in America; the eternal tom-tom beating in the Negro soul—the tom-tom of revolt against weariness in a white world, a world of subway trains, and work, work, work; the tom-tom of joy and laughter, and pain swallowed in a smile. Yet the Philadelphia clubwoman is ashamed to say that her race created it and she does not like me to write about it. The old subconscious "white is best" runs through her mind. Years of study under white teachers, a lifetime of white books, pictures, and papers, and white manners, morals, and Puritan standards made her dislike the spirituals. And now she turns up her nose at jazz and all its manifestations—likewise almost everything else distinctly racial. She doesn't care for the Winold Reiss[9] portraits of Negroes because they are "too Negro." She does not want a true picture of herself from anybody. She wants the artist to flatter her, to make the white world

6. This incident, which happened to Hughes himself in 1925, is related in his autobiography The Big Sea (1940).
7. A 1923 collection of short stories and poetry about the rural South and the urban North.
8. Paul Robeson (1898–1976), actor and singer.

W. E. B. Du Bois (1868–1963) helped found the NAACP and edited its journal, Crisis, from 1910 to 1934; he is best known for The Souls of Black Folk (1903).
9. Portrait painter (1886–1953).

believe that all Negroes are as smug and as near white in soul as she wants
to be. But, to my mind, it is the duty of the younger Negro artist, if he
accepts any duties at all from outsiders, to change through the force of his
art that old whispering "I want to be white," hidden in the aspirations of
his people, to "Why should I want to be white? I am a Negro—and beautiful"?

So I am ashamed for the black poet who says, "I want to be a poet, not a
Negro poet," as though his own racial world were not as interesting as any
other world. I am ashamed, too, for the colored artist who runs from the
painting of Negro faces to the painting of sunsets after the manner of the
academicians because he fears the strange un-whiteness of his own features. An artist must be free to choose what he does, certainly, but he must
also never be afraid to do what he might choose.

Let the blare of Negro jazz bands and the bellowing voice of Bessie
Smith[1] singing Blues penetrate the closed ears of the colored near-
intellectuals until they listen and perhaps understand. Let Paul Robeson
singing "Water Boy," and Rudolph Fisher writing about the streets of Harlem, and Jean Toomer holding the heart of Georgia in his hands, and
Aaron Douglas[2] drawing strange black fantasies cause the smug Negro
middle class to turn from their white, respectable, ordinary books and papers to catch a glimmer of their own beauty. We younger Negro artists who
create now intend to express our individual dark-skinned selves without
fear or shame. If white people are pleased we are glad. If they are not, it
doesn't matter. We know we are beautiful. And ugly too. The tom-tom
cries and the tom-tom laughs. If colored people are pleased we are glad. If
they are not, their displeasure doesn't matter either. We build our temples
for tomorrow, strong as we know how, and we stand on top of the mountain, free within ourselves.

1926

The Blues I'm Playing[1]

I

Oceola Jones, pianist, studied under Philippe in Paris. Mrs. Dora Ellsworth[2] paid her bills. The bills included a little apartment on the Left
Bank and a grand piano. Twice a year Mrs. Ellsworth came over from New
York and spent part of her time with Oceola in the little apartment. The
rest of her time abroad she usually spent at Biarritz or Juan les Pins,[3] where
she would see the new canvases of Antonio Bas, young Spanish painter
who also enjoyed the patronage of Mrs. Ellsworth. Bas and Oceola, the
woman thought, both had genius. And whether they had genius or not, she
loved them, and took good care of them.

1. Blues singer (1894–1937).
2. Artist and educator (1899–1979). Fisher (1897–
1934), author of two novels, The Walls of Jericho
(1928) and The Conjure Man Dies (1932).
1. This short story was first published in Hughes's
The Ways of White Folks (1934).

2. Probably based on Charlotte Mason (1854–
1946), patron of Hughes and other leading figures
of the Harlem Renaissance.
3. Fashionable resort towns on the Mediterranean
in southwestern France.

Poor dear lady, she had no children of her own. Her husband was dead. And she had no interest in life now save art, and the young people who created art. She was very rich, and it gave her pleasure to share her richness with beauty. Except that she was sometimes confused as to where beauty lay—in the youngsters or in what they made, in the creators or the creation. Mrs. Ellsworth had been known to help charming young people who wrote terrible poems, blue-eyed young men who painted awful pictures. And she once turned down a garlic-smelling soprano-singing girl who, a few years later, had all the critics in New York at her feet. The girl was so sallow. And she really needed a bath, or at least a mouth wash, on the day when Mrs. Ellsworth went to hear her sing at an East Side settlement house. Mrs. Ellsworth had sent a small check and let it go at that—since, however, living to regret bitterly her lack of musical acumen in the face of garlic.

About Oceola, though, there had been no doubt. The Negro girl had been highly recommended to her by Ormond Hunter, the music critic, who often went to Harlem to hear the church concerts there, and had thus listened twice to Oceola's playing.

"A most amazing tone," he had told Mrs. Ellsworth, knowing her interest in the young and unusual. "A flare for the piano such as I have seldom encountered. All she needs is training—finish, polish, a repertoire."

"Where is she?" asked Mrs. Ellsworth at once. "I will hear her play."

By the hardest,[4] Oceola was found. By the hardest, an appointment was made for her to come to East 63rd Street and play for Mrs. Ellsworth. Oceola had said she was busy every day. It seemed that she had pupils, rehearsed a church choir, and played almost nightly for colored house parties or dances. She made quite a good deal of money. She wasn't tremendously interested, it seemed, in going way downtown to play for some elderly lady she had never heard of, even if the request did come from the white critic, Ormond Hunter, via the pastor of the church whose choir she rehearsed, and to which Mr. Hunter's maid belonged.

It was finally arranged, however. And one afternoon, promptly on time, black Miss Oceola Jones rang the door bell of white Mrs. Dora Ellsworth's grey stone house just off Madison. A butler who actually wore brass buttons opened the door, and she was shown upstairs to the music room. (The butler had been warned of her coming.) Ormond Hunter was already there, and they shook hands. In a moment, Mrs. Ellsworth came in, a tall stately gray-haired lady in black with a scarf that sort of floated behind her. She was tremendously intrigued at meeting Oceola, never having had before amongst all her artists a black one. And she was greatly impressed that Ormond Hunter should have recommended the girl. She began right away, treating her as a protegee; that is, she began asking her a great many questions she would not dare ask anyone else at first meeting, except a protegee. She asked her how old she was and where her mother and father were and how she made her living and whose music she liked best to play and was she married and would she take one lump or two in her tea, with lemon or cream?

After tea, Oceola played. She played the Rachmaninoff *Prelude in C*

4. With the greatest effort.

Sharp Minor. She played from the Liszt *Études.* She played the *St. Louis Blues.* She played Ravel's [5] *Pavanne pour une Enfante Défunte.* And then she said she had to go. She was playing that night for a dance in Brooklyn for the benefit of the Urban League. [6]

Mrs. Ellsworth and Ormond Hunter breathed, "How lovely!"

Mrs. Ellsworth said, "I am quite overcome, my dear. You play so beautifully." She went on further to say, "You must let me help you. Who is your teacher?"

"I have none now," Oceola replied. "I teach pupils myself. Don't have time any more to study—nor money either."

"But you must have time," said Mrs. Ellsworth, "and money, also. Come back to see me on Tuesday. We will arrange it, my dear."

And when the girl had gone, she turned to Ormond Hunter for advice on piano teachers to instruct those who already had genius, and need only to be developed.

II

Then began one of the most interesting periods in Mrs. Ellsworth's whole experience in aiding the arts. The period of Oceola. For the Negro girl, as time went on, began to occupy a greater and greater place in Mrs. Ellsworth's interests, to take up more and more of her time, and to use up more and more of her money. Not that Oceola ever asked for money, but Mrs. Ellsworth herself seemed to keep thinking of so much more Oceola needed.

At first it was hard to get Oceola to need anything. Mrs. Ellsworth had the feeling that the girl mistrusted her generosity, and Oceola did—for she had never met anybody interested in pure art before. Just to be given things for *art's sake* seemed suspicious to Oceola.

That first Tuesday, when the colored girl came back at Mrs. Ellsworth's request, she answered the white woman's questions with a why-look in her eyes.

"Don't think I'm being personal, dear," said Mrs. Ellsworth, "but I must know your background in order to help you. Now, tell me . . ."

Oceola wondered why on earth the woman wanted to help her. However, since Mrs. Ellsworth seemed interested in her life's history, she brought it forth so as not to hinder the progress of the afternoon, for she wanted to get back to Harlem by six o'clock.

Born in Mobile in 1903. Yes, m'am, she was older than she looked. Papa had a band, that is her step-father. Used to play for all the lodge turn-outs, picnics, dances, barbecues. You could get the best roast pig in the world in Mobile. Her mother used to play the organ in church, and when the deacons bought a piano after the big revival, her mama played that, too. Oceola played by ear for a long while until her mother taught her notes. Oceola played an organ, also, and a cornet.

5. Maurice Ravel (1875–1937), Sergei Rachmaninoff (1873–1943), and Franz Liszt (1811–1886), all noted European composers. "St. Louis Blues" was composed by W. C. Handy (1873–1958), an African American.

6. The National Urban League was founded in 1911 to help the large numbers of blacks moving from rural areas to major cities.

"My, my," said Mrs. Ellsworth.

"Yes, m'am," said Oceola. She had played and practiced on lots of instruments in the South before her step-father died. She always went to band rehearsals with him.

"And where was your father, dear?" asked Mrs. Ellsworth.

"My step-father had the band," replied Oceola. Her mother left off playing in the church to go with him traveling in Billy Kersands'[7] Minstrels. He had the biggest mouth in the world, Kersands did, and used to let Oceola put both her hands in it at a time and stretch it. Well, she and her mama and step-papa settled down in Houston. Sometimes her parents had jobs and sometimes they didn't. Often they were hungry, but Oceola went to school and had a regular piano-teacher, an old German woman, who gave her what technique she had today.

"A fine old teacher," said Oceola. "She used to teach me half the time for nothing. God bless her."

"Yes," said Mrs. Ellsworth. "She gave you an excellent foundation."

"Sure did. But my step-papa died, got cut, and after that Mama didn't have no more use for Houston so we moved to St. Louis. Mama got a job playing for the movies in a Market Street theater, and I played for a church choir, and saved some money and went to Wilberforce.[8] Studied piano there, too. Played for all the college dances. Graduated. Came to New York and heard Rachmaninoff and was crazy about him. Then Mama died, so I'm keeping the little flat myself. One room is rented out."

"Is she nice?" asked Mrs. Ellsworth, "your roomer?"

"It's not a she," said Oceola. "He's a man. I hate women roomers."

"Oh!" said Mrs. Ellsworth. "I should think all roomers would be terrible."

"He's right nice," said Oceola. "Name's Pete Williams."

"What does he do?" asked Mrs. Ellsworth.

"A Pullman porter," replied Oceola, "but he's saving money to go to Med school. He's a smart fellow."

But it turned out later that he wasn't paying Oceola any rent.

That afternoon, when Mrs. Ellsworth announced that she had made her an appointment with one of the best piano teachers in New York, the black girl seemed pleased. She recognized the name. But how, she wondered, would she find time for study, with her pupils and her choir, and all. When Mrs. Ellsworth said that she would cover her *entire* living expenses, Oceola's eyes were full of that why-look, as though she didn't believe it.

"I have faith in your art, dear," said Mrs. Ellsworth, at parting. But to prove it quickly, she sat down that very evening and sent Oceola the first monthly check so that she would no longer have to take in pupils or drill choirs or play at house parties. And so Oceola would have faith in art, too.

That night Mrs. Ellsworth called up Ormond Hunter and told him what she had done. And she asked if Mr. Hunter's maid knew Oceola, and if she supposed that that man rooming with her were anything to her. Ormond Hunter said he would inquire.

7. Minstrel star (1842–1915).   8. A traditionally black university in Xenia, Ohio.

Before going to bed, Mrs. Ellsworth told her housekeeper to order a book called "Nigger Heaven"[9] on the morrow, and also anything else Brentano's had about Harlem. She made a mental note that she must go up there sometime, for she had never yet seen that dark section of New York; and now that she had a Negro protegee, she really ought to know something about it. Mrs. Ellsworth couldn't recall ever having known a single Negro before in her whole life, so she found Oceola fascinating. And just as black as she herself was white.

Mrs. Ellsworth began to think in bed about what gowns would look best on Oceola. Her protegee would have to be well-dressed. She wondered, too, what sort of a place the girl lived in. And who that man was who lived with her. She began to think that really Oceola ought to have a place to herself. It didn't seem quite respectable. . . .

When she woke up in the morning, she called her car and went by her dressmaker's. She asked the good woman what kind of colors looked well with black; not black fabrics, but a black skin.

"I have a little friend to fit out," she said.

"A *black* friend?" said the dressmaker.

"A black friend," said Mrs. Ellsworth.

III

Some days later Ormond Hunter reported on what his maid knew about Oceola. It seemed that the two belonged to the same church, and although the maid did not know Oceola very well, she knew what everybody said about her in the church. Yes, indeedy! Oceola were a right nice girl, for sure, but it certainly were a shame she were giving all her money to that man what stayed with her and what she was practically putting through college so he could be a doctor.

"Why," gasped Mrs. Ellsworth, "the poor child is being preyed upon."

"It seems to me so," said Ormond Hunter.

"I must get her out of Harlem," said Mrs. Ellsworth, "at once. I believe it's worse than Chinatown."

"She might be in a more artistic atmosphere," agreed Ormond Hunter. "And with her career launched, she probably won't want that man anyhow."

"She won't need him," said Mrs. Ellsworth. "She will have her art."

But Mrs. Ellsworth decided that in order to increase the rapprochement between art and Oceola, something should be done now, at once. She asked the girl to come down to see her the next day, and when it was time to go home, the white woman said, "I have a half-hour before dinner. I'll drive you up. You know I've never been to Harlem."

"All right," said Oceola. "That's nice of you."

But she didn't suggest the white lady's coming in, when they drew up before a rather sad-looking apartment house in 134th Street. Mrs. Ellsworth had to ask could she come in.

"I live on the fifth floor," said Oceola, "and there isn't any elevator."

9. The 1926 novel about Harlem by Carl Van Vechten (1880–1964).

"It doesn't matter, dear," said the white woman, for she meant to see the inside of this girl's life, elevator or no elevator.

The apartment was just as she thought it would be. After all, she had read Thomas Burke on Limehouse.[1] And here was just one more of those holes in the wall, even if it was five stories high. The windows looked down on slums. There were only four rooms, small as maids' rooms, all of them. An upright piano almost filled the parlor. Oceola slept in the dining-room. The roomer slept in the bed-chamber beyond the kitchen.

"Where is he, darling?"

"He runs on the road all summer," said the girl. "He's in and out."

"But how do you breathe in here?" asked Mrs. Ellsworth. "It's so small. You must have more space for your soul, dear. And for a grand piano. Now, in the Village[2] . . ."

"But I don't want to move yet. I promised my roomer he could stay till fall."

"Why till fall?"

"He's going to Meharry then."

"To marry?"

"Meharry, yes m'am. That's a colored Medicine school in Nashville."

"Colored? Is it good?"

"Well, it's cheap," said Oceola. "After he goes, I don't mind moving."

"But I wanted to see you settled before I go away for the summer."

"When you come back is all right. I can do till then."

"Art is long," reminded Mrs. Ellsworth, "and time is fleeting, my dear."

"Yes, m'am," said Oceola, "but I gets nervous if I start worrying about time."

So Mrs. Ellsworth went off to Bar Harbor for the season, and left the man with Oceola.

IV

That was some years ago. Eventually art and Mrs. Ellsworth triumphed. Oceola moved out of Harlem. She lived in Gay Street west of Washington Square where she met Genevieve Taggard, and Ernestine Evans,[3] and two or three sculptors, and a cat-painter who was also a protegee of Mrs. Ellsworth. She spent her days practicing, playing for friends of her patron, going to concerts, and reading books about music. She no longer had pupils or rehearsed the choir, but she still loved to play for Harlem house parties—for nothing—now that she no longer needed the money, out of sheer love of jazz. This rather disturbed Mrs. Ellsworth, who still believed in art of the old school, portraits that really and truly looked like people, poems about nature, music that had soul in it, not syncopation. And she felt the dignity of art. Was it in keeping with genius, she wondered, for Oceola to have a studio full of white and colored people every Saturday night (some of them actually drinking gin *from bottles*) and dancing to the most tomtom-like music she had ever heard coming out of a grand piano?

1. A poor district in the East End of London.
2. I.e., Greenwich Village, in Manhattan.
3. Author, journalist, editor, and literary critic.

Washington Square is in the heart of Greenwich Village. Taggard (1894–1948), poet, biographer, and editor.

She wished she could lift Oceola up bodily and take her away from all that, for art's sake.

So in the spring, Mrs. Ellsworth organized weekends in the up-state mountains where she had a little lodge and where Oceola could look from the high places at the stars, and fill her soul with the vastness of the eternal, and forget about jazz. Mrs. Ellsworth really began to hate jazz—especially on a grand piano.

If there were a lot of guests at the lodge, as there sometimes were, Mrs. Ellsworth might share the bed with Oceola. Then she would read aloud Tennyson or Browning[4] before turning out the light, aware all the time of the electric strength of that brown-black body beside her, and of the deep drowsy voice asking what the poems were about. And then Mrs. Ellsworth would feel very motherly toward this dark girl whom she had taken under her wing on the wonderful road of art, to nurture and love until she became a great interpreter of the piano. At such times the elderly white woman was glad her late husband's money, so well invested, furnished her with a large surplus to devote to the needs of her protegees, especially to Oceola, the blackest—and most interesting of all.

Why the most interesting?

Mrs. Ellsworth didn't know, unless it was that Oceola really was talented, terribly alive, and that she looked like nothing Mrs. Ellsworth had ever been near before. Such a rich velvet black, and such a hard young body! The teacher of the piano raved about her strength.

"She can stand a great career," the teacher said. "She has everything for it."

"Yes," agreed Mrs. Ellsworth, thinking, however, of the Pullman porter at Meharry, "but she must learn to sublimate her soul."

So for two years then, Oceola lived abroad at Mrs. Ellsworth's expense. She studied with Philippe, had the little apartment on the Left Bank, and learned about Debussy's[5] African background. She met many black Algerian and French West Indian students, too, and listened to their interminable arguments ranging from Garvey to Picasso to Spengler to Jean Cocteau,[6] and thought they all must be crazy. Why did they or anybody argue so much about life or art? Oceola merely lived—and loved it. Only the Marxian students seemed sound to her for they, at least, wanted people to have enough to eat. That was important, Oceola thought, remembering, as she did, her own sometimes hungry years. But the rest of the controversies, as far as she could fathom, were based on air.

Oceola hated most artists, too, and the word *art* in French or English. If you wanted to play the piano or paint pictures or write books, go ahead! But why talk so much about it? Montparnasse[7] was worse in that respect than the Village. And as for the cultured Negroes who were always saying art would break down color lines, art could save the race and prevent lynch-

---

4. Either Robert Browning (1812–1889) or Elizabeth Barrett Browning (1806–1861), both English poets. Alfred, Lord Tennyson (1809–1892), English poet.
5. Claude Debussy (1862–1918), French composer.
6. French writer, filmmaker, and painter (1889–

1963). Marcus Garvey (1887–1940), founder of the Universal Negro Improvement Association. Pablo Picasso (1881–1973), Spanish painter and sculptor. Oswald Spengler (1880–1936), German philosopher.
7. A bohemian district in Paris.

ings![8] "Bunk!" said Oceola. "My ma and pa were both artists when it came to making music, and the white folks ran them out of town for being dressed up in Alabama. And look at the Jews! Every other artist in the world's a Jew, and still folks hate them."

She thought of Mrs. Ellsworth (dear soul in New York), who never made uncomplimentary remarks about Negroes, but frequently did about Jews. Of little Menuhin[9] she would say, for instance, "He's a *genius*—not a Jew," hating to admit his ancestry.

In Paris, Oceola especially loved the West Indian ball rooms where the black colonials danced the beguin. And she liked the entertainers at Bricktop's.[1] Sometimes late at night there, Oceola would take the piano and beat out a blues for Brick and the assembled guests. In her playing of Negro folk music, Oceola never doctored it up, or filled it full of classical runs, or fancy falsities. In the blues she made the bass notes throb like tom-toms, the trebles cry like little flutes, so deep in the earth and so high in the sky that they understood everything. And when the night club crowd would get up and dance to her blues, and Bricktop would yell, "Hey! Hey!" Oceola felt as happy as if she were performing a Chopin[2] étude for the nicely gloved Oh's and Ah-ers in a Crillon salon.

Music, to Oceola, demanded movement and expression, dancing and living to go with it. She liked to teach, when she had the choir, the singing of those rhythmical Negro spirituals that possessed the power to pull colored folks out of their seats in the amen corner and make them prance and shout in the aisles for Jesus. She never liked those fashionable colored churches where shouting and movement were discouraged and looked down upon, and where New England hymns instead of spirituals were sung. Oceola's background was too well-grounded in Mobile, and Billy Kersands' Minstrels, and the Sanctified churches[3] where religion was a joy, to stare mystically over the top of a grand piano like white folks and imagine that Beethoven had nothing to do with life, or that Schubert's[4] love songs were only sublimations.

Whenever Mrs. Ellsworth came to Paris, she and Oceola spent hours listening to symphonies and string quartettes and pianists. Oceola enjoyed concerts, but seldom felt, like her patron, that she was floating on clouds of bliss. Mrs. Ellsworth insisted, however, that Oceola's spirit was too moved for words at such times—therefore she understood why the dear child kept quiet. Mrs. Ellsworth herself was often too moved for words, but never by pieces like Ravel's *Bolero* (which Oceola played on the phonograph as a dance record) or any of the compositions of *les Six*.[5]

What Oceola really enjoyed most with Mrs. Ellsworth was not going to

8. Possible reference to the views of Alain Locke (1886–1954), editor of *The New Negro* (1925).
9. Yehudi Menuhin (b. 1916), U.S. violinist.
1. A club named after Ada "Bricktop" Smith (1894–1984), American singer whose European career started in Paris at *Le Grand Duc* (where Hughes had worked as a dishwasher in 1924). "Beguin": or beguine, a popular Cuban dance.
2. Frederic Chopin (1810–1849), Polish composer and pianist. His beautiful *études* are known for their difficulty.
3. Group of Fundamentalist Christian churches

that emphasized music and self-expression.
4. Franz Schubert (1797–1828), Austrian composer. Ludwig van Beethoven (1770–1827), German composer.
5. The six (French); an innovative group of French composers, including George Auric, Louis Durey, Arthur Honneger, Darius Milhaud, Francis Poulenc, and Germaine Taillefer. "Bolero": the revolutionary result of a ballet Ravel was commissioned to write in 1928, known for its obsessively repetitive and rhythmical structure.

concerts, but going for trips on the little river boats in the Seine; or riding out to old chateaux in her patron's hired Renault; or to Versailles, and listening to the aging white lady talk about the romantic history of France, the wars and uprising, the loves and intrigues of princes and kings and queens, about guillotines and lace handkerchiefs, snuff boxes and daggers. For Mrs. Ellsworth had loved France as a girl, and had made a study of its life and lore. Once she used to sing simple little French songs rather well, too. And she always regretted that her husband never understood the lovely words—or even tried to understand them.

Oceola learned the accompaniments for all the songs Mrs. Ellsworth knew and sometimes they tried them over together. The middle-aged white woman loved to sing when the colored girl played, and she even tried spirituals. Often, when she stayed at the little Paris apartment, Oceola would go into the kitchen and cook something good for late supper, maybe an oyster soup, or fried apples and bacon. And sometimes Oceola had pigs' feet.

"There's nothing quite so good as a pig's foot," said Oceola, "after playing all day."

"Then you must have pigs' feet," agreed Mrs. Ellsworth.

And all this while Oceola's development at the piano blossomed into perfection. Her tone became a singing wonder and her interpretations warm and individual. She gave a concert in Paris, one in Brussels, and another in Berlin. She got the press notices all pianists crave. She had her picture in lots of European papers. And she came home to New York a year after the stock market crashed and nobody had any money—except folks like Mrs. Ellsworth who had so much it would be hard to ever lose it all.

Oceola's one time Pullman porter, now a coming doctor, was graduating from Meharry that spring. Mrs. Ellsworth saw her dark protegee go South to attend his graduation with tears in her eyes. She thought that by now music would be enough, after all those years under the best teachers, but alas, Oceola was not yet sublimated, even by Philippe. She wanted to see Pete.

Oceola returned North to prepare for her New York concert in the fall. She wrote Mrs. Ellsworth at Bar Harbor that her doctor boy-friend was putting in one more summer on the railroad, then in the autumn he would intern at Atlanta. And Oceola said that he had asked her to marry him. Lord, she was happy!

It was a long time before she heard from Mrs. Ellsworth. When the letter came, it was full of long paragraphs about the beautiful music Oceola had within her power to give the world. Instead, she wanted to marry and be burdened with children! Oh, my dear, my dear!

Oceola, when she read it, thought she had done pretty well knowing Pete this long and not having children. But she wrote back that she didn't see why children and music couldn't go together. Anyway, during the present depression, it was pretty hard for a beginning artist like herself to book a concert tour—so she might just as well be married awhile. Pete, on his last run in from St. Louis, had suggested that they have the wedding Christmas in the South. "And he's impatient, at that. He needs me."

This time Mrs. Ellsworth didn't answer by letter at all. She was back in town in late September. In November, Oceola played at Town Hall. The critics were kind, but they didn't go wild. Mrs. Ellsworth swore it was because of Pete's influence on her protegee.

"But he was in Atlanta," Oceola said.

"His spirit was here," Mrs. Ellsworth insisted. "All the time you were playing on that stage, he was here, the monster! Taking you out of yourself, taking you away from the piano."

"Why, he wasn't," said Oceola. "He was watching an operation in Atlanta."

But from then on, things didn't go well between her and her patron. The white lady grew distinctly cold when she received Oceola in her beautiful drawing room among the jade vases and amber cups worth thousands of dollars. When Oceola would have to wait there for Mrs. Ellsworth, she was afraid to move for fear she might knock something over—that would take ten years of a Harlemite's wages to replace, if broken.

Over the tea cups, the aging Mrs. Ellsworth did not talk any longer about the concert tour she had once thought she might finance for Oceola, if no recognized bureau took it up. Instead, she spoke of that something she believed Oceola's fingers had lost since her return from Europe. And she wondered why any one insisted on living in Harlem.

"I've been away from my own people so long," said the girl, "I want to live right in the middle of them again."

Why, Mrs. Ellsworth wondered farther, did Oceola, at her last concert in a Harlem church, not stick to the classical items listed on the program. Why did she insert one of her own variations on the spirituals, a syncopated variation from the Sanctified Church, that made an old colored lady rise up and cry out from her pew, "Glory to God this evenin'! Yes! Hallelujah! Whooo-oo!" right at the concert? Which seemed most undignified to Mrs. Ellsworth, and unworthy of the teachings of Philippe. And furthermore, why was Pete coming up to New York for Thanksgiving? And who had sent him the money to come?

"Me," said Oceola. "He doesn't make anything interning."

"Well," said Mrs. Ellsworth, "I don't think much of him." But Oceola didn't seem to care what Mrs. Ellsworth thought, for she made no defense.

Thanksgiving evening, in bed, together in a Harlem apartment, Pete and Oceola talked about their wedding to come. They would have a big one in a church with lots of music. And Pete would give her a ring. And she would have on a white dress, light and fluffy, not silk. "I hate silk," she said. "I hate expensive things." (She thought of her mother being buried in a cotton dress, for they were all broke when she died. Mother would have been glad about her marriage.) "Pete," Oceola said, hugging him in the dark, "let's live in Atlanta, where there are lots of colored people, like us."

"What about Mrs. Ellsworth?" Pete asked. "She coming down to Atlanta for our wedding?"

"I don't know," said Oceola.

"I hope not, 'cause if she stops at one of them big hotels, I won't have you going to the back door to see her. That's one thing I hate about the South— where there're white people, you have to go to the back door."

"Maybe she can stay with us," said Oceola. "I wouldn't mind."

"I'll be damned," said Pete. "You want to get lynched?"

But it happened that Mrs. Ellsworth didn't care to attend the wedding, anyway. When she saw how love had triumphed over art, she decided she could no longer influence Oceola's life. The period of Oceola was over. She would send checks, occasionally, if the girl needed them, besides, of course, something beautiful for the wedding, but that would be all. These things she told her the week after Thanksgiving.

"And Oceola, my dear, I've decided to spend the whole winter in Europe. I sail on December eighteenth. Christmas—while you are marrying—I shall be in Paris with my precious Antonio Bas. In January, he has an exhibition of oils in Madrid. And in the spring, a new young poet is coming over whom I want to visit Florence, to really know Florence. A charming white-haired boy from Omaha whose soul has been crushed in the West. I want to try to help him. He, my dear, is one of the few people who live for their art—and nothing else. . . . Ah, such a beautiful life! . . . You will come and play for me once before I sail?"

"Yes, Mrs. Ellsworth," said Oceola, genuinely sorry that the end had come. Why did white folks think you could live on nothing but art? Strange! Too strange! Too strange!

V

The Persian vases in the music room were filled with long-stemmed lilies that night when Oceola Jones came down from Harlem for the last time to play for Mrs. Dora Ellsworth. Mrs. Ellsworth had on a gown of black velvet, and a collar of pearls about her neck. She was very kind and gentle to Oceola, as one would be to a child who has done a great wrong but doesn't know any better. But to the black girl from Harlem, she looked very cold and white, and her grand piano seemed like the biggest and heaviest in the world—as Oceola sat down to play it with the technique for which Mrs. Ellsworth had paid.

As the rich and aging white woman listened to the great roll of Beethoven sonatas and to the sea and moonlight of the Chopin nocturnes, as she watched the swaying dark strong shoulders of Oceola Jones, she began to reproach the girl aloud for running away from art and music, for burying herself in Atlanta and love—love for a man unworthy of lacing up her boot straps, as Mrs. Ellsworth put it.

"You could shake the stars with your music, Oceola. Depression or no depression, I could make you great. And yet you propose to dig a grave for yourself. Art is bigger than love."

"I believe you, Mrs. Ellsworth," said Oceola, not turning away from the piano. "But being married won't keep me from making tours, or being an artist."

"Yes, it will," said Mrs. Ellsworth. "He'll take all the music out of you."

"No, he won't," said Oceola.

"You don't know, child," said Mrs. Ellsworth, "what men are like."

"Yes, I do," said Oceola simply. And her fingers began to wander slowly

up and down the keyboard, flowing into the soft and lazy syncopation of a
Negro blues, a blues that deepened and grew into rollicking jazz, then into
an earth-throbbing rhythm that shook the lilies in the Persian vases of Mrs.
Ellsworth's music room. Louder than the voice of the white woman who
cried that Oceola was deserting beauty, deserting her real self, deserting
her hope in life, the flood of wild syncopation filled the house, then sank
into the slow and singing blues with which it had begun.

The girl at the piano heard the white woman saying, "Is this what I spent
thousands of dollars to teach you?"

"No," said Oceola simply. "This is mine. . . . Listen! . . . How sad and gay
it is. Blue and happy—laughing and crying. . . . How white like you and
black like me. . . . How much like a man. . . . And how like a woman. . . .
Warm as Pete's mouth. . . . These are the blues. . . . I'm playing."

Mrs. Ellsworth sat very still in her chair looking at the lilies trembling
delicately in the priceless Persian vases, while Oceola made the bass notes
throb like tomtoms deep in the earth.

> O, if I could holler

sang the blues,

> Like a mountain jack,
> I'd go up on de mountain

sang the blues,

> And call my baby back.

"And I," said Mrs. Ellsworth rising from her chair, "would stand looking
at the stars."

1934

From The Big Sea

When the Negro Was in Vogue

The 1920's were the years of Manhattan's black Renaissance. It began
with Shuffle Along, Running Wild, and the Charleston.[1] Perhaps some
people would say even with The Emperor Jones, Charles Gilpin, and the
tom-toms at the Provincetown.[2] But certainly it was the musical revue,
Shuffle Along, that gave a scintillating send-off to that Negro vogue in Manhattan, which reached its peak just before the crash of 1929, the crash that

1. A popular dance that swept the nation in the
1920s. Shuffle Along, a 1921 musical comedy created by Flournoy Miller, Aubrey Lyles, Eubie
Blake, and Noble Sissle, was a tremendous success
in New York. Runnin' Wild, another musical revue
by Miller and Lyles, is often credited with introducing New York to the Charleston in 1923.
2. I.e., the Provincetown Playhouse. The Emperor
Jones, by white playwright Eugene O'Neill, premiered in 1920. Gilpin (1878–1930), black actor,
had the title role.

sent Negroes, white folks, and all rolling down the hill toward the Works Progress Administration.[3]

Shuffle Along was a honey of a show. Swift, bright, funny, rollicking, and gay, with a dozen danceable, singable tunes. Besides, look who were in it: The now famous choir director, Hall Johnson, and the composer, William Grant Still, were a part of the orchestra. Eubie Blake and Noble Sissle wrote the music and played and acted in the show. Miller and Lyles were the comics. Florence Mills skyrocketed to fame in the second act. Trixie Smith sang "He May Be Your Man But He Comes to See Me Sometimes." And Caterina Jarboro, now a European prima donna, and the internationally celebrated Josephine Baker[4] were merely in the chorus. Everybody was in the audience—including me. People came back to see it innumerable times. It was always packed.

To see *Shuffle Along* was the main reason I wanted to go to Columbia.[5] When I saw it, I was thrilled and delighted. From then on I was in the gallery of the Cort Theatre every time I got a chance. That year, too, I saw Katharine Cornell in *A Bill of Divorcement*, Margaret Wycherly in *The Verge*, Maugham's *The Circle* with Mrs. Leslie Carter, and the Theatre Guild production of Kaiser's *From Morn Till Midnight*.[6] But I remember *Shuffle Along* best of all. It gave just the proper push—a pre-Charleston kick—to that Negro vogue of the 20's, that spread to books, African sculpture, music, and dancing.

Put down the 1920's for the rise of Roland Hayes, who packed Carnegie Hall, the rise of Paul Robeson in New York and London, of Florence Mills over two continents, of Rose McClendon in Broadway parts that never measured up to her, the booming voice of Bessie Smith and the low moan of Clara on thousands of records, and the rise of that grand comedienne of song, Ethel Waters, singing: "Charlie's elected now! He's in right for sure!" Put down the 1920's for Louis Armstrong and Gladys Bentley[7] and Josephine Baker.

White people began to come to Harlem in droves. For several years they packed the expensive Cotton Club on Lenox Avenue. But I was never there, because the Cotton Club was a Jim Crow club for gangsters and monied whites. They were not cordial to Negro patronage, unless you were a celebrity like Bojangles.[8] So Harlem Negroes did not like the Cotton Club and never appreciated its Jim Crow policy in the very heart of their dark community. Nor did ordinary Negroes like the growing influx of whites toward Harlem after sundown, flooding the little cabarets and bars where formerly only colored people laughed and sang, and where now the strangers were given the best ringside tables to sit and stare at the Negro customers—like amusing animals in a zoo.

The Negroes said: "We can't go downtown and sit and stare at you in

3. One of Franklin Roosevelt's programs for economic recovery from the Great Depression. "Crash of 1929": the stock market crash that ushered in the Depression.
4. All African Americans involved in music or theater who became famous in the 1920s.
5. Hughes attended Columbia University in New York from 1921 to 1922.
6. All plays that were hits on Broadway during the 1921–22 season.
7. All African American singers, actors, or musicians famous in the 1920s.
8. Bill "Bojangles" Robinson (1876–1949), dancer.

your clubs. You won't even let us in your clubs." But they didn't say it out loud—for Negroes are practically never rude to white people. So thousands of whites came to Harlem night after night, thinking the Negroes loved to have them there, and firmly believing that all Harlemites left their houses at sundown to sing and dance in cabarets, because most of the whites saw nothing but the cabarets, not the houses.

Some of the owners of Harlem clubs, delighted at the flood of white patronage, made the grievous error of barring their own race, after the manner of the famous Cotton Club. But most of these quickly lost business and folded up, because they failed to realize that a large part of the Harlem attraction for downtown New Yorkers lay in simply watching the colored customers amuse themselves. And the smaller clubs, of course, had no big floor shows or a name band like the Cotton Club, where Duke Ellington[9] usually held forth, so, without black patronage, they were not amusing at all.

Some of the small clubs, however, had people like Gladys Bentley, who was something worth discovering in those days, before she got famous, acquired an accompanist, specially written material, and conscious vulgarity. But for two or three amazing years, Miss Bentley sat, and played a big piano all night long, literally all night, without stopping—singing songs like "The St. James Infirmary,"[1] from ten in the evening until dawn, with scarcely a break between the notes, sliding from one song to another, with a powerful and continuous underbeat of jungle rhythm. Miss Bentley was an amazing exhibition of musical energy—a large, dark, masculine lady, whose feet pounded the floor while her fingers pounded the keyboard—a perfect piece of African sculpture, animated by her own rhythm.

But when the place where she played became too well known, she began to sing with an accompanist, became a star, moved to a larger place, then downtown, and is now in Hollywood. The old magic of the woman and the piano and the night and the rhythm being one is gone. But everything goes, one way or another. The '20's are gone and lots of fine things in Harlem night life have disappeared like snow in the sun— since it became utterly commercial, planned for the downtown tourist trade, and therefore dull.

The lindy-hoppers[2] at the Savoy even began to practice acrobatic routines, and to do absurd things for the entertainment of the whites, that probably never would have entered their heads to attempt merely for their own effortless amusement. Some of the lindy-hoppers had cards printed with their names on them and became dance professors teaching the tourists. Then Harlem nights became show nights for the Nordics.[3]

Some critics say that that is what happened to certain Negro writers, too—that they ceased to write to amuse themselves and began to write to amuse and entertain white people, and in so doing distorted and overcolored their material, and left out a great many things they thought would

9. Composer, pianist, and bandleader (1899–1974).
1. Words and music by Joe Primrose (1930), but possibly known in the 1890s as "Gambler's Blues."
2. Those who dance the Lindy-hop, named after the celebrated 1927 transatlantic solo flight of Charles Lindbergh.
3. Whites.

offend their American brothers of a lighter complexion. Maybe—since Negroes have writer-racketeers, as has any other race. But I have known almost all of them, and most of the good ones have tried to be honest, write honestly, and express their world as they saw it.

All of us know that the gay and sparkling life of the so-called Negro Renaissance of the '20's was not so gay and sparkling beneath the surface as it looked. Carl Van Vechten, in the character of Byron in *Nigger Heaven*,[4] captured some of the bitterness and frustration of literary Harlem that Wallace Thurman later so effectively poured into his *Infants of the Spring*[5]— the only novel by a Negro about that fantastic period when Harlem was in vogue.

It was a period when, at almost every Harlem uppercrust dance or party, one would be introduced to various distinguished white celebrities there as guests. It was a period when almost any Harlem Negro of any social importance at all would be likely to say casually: "As I was remarking the other day to Heywood—," meaning Heywood Broun. Or: "As I said to George—," referring to George Gershwin.[6] It was a period when local and visiting royalty were not at all uncommon in Harlem. And when the parties of A'Lelia Walker,[7] the Negro heiress, were filled with guests whose names would turn any Nordic social climber green with envy. It was a period when Harold Jackman,[8] a handsome young Harlem school teacher of modest means, calmly announced one day that he was sailing for the Riviera for a fortnight, to attend Princess Murat's[9] yachting party. It was a period when Charleston preachers opened up shouting churches as sideshows for white tourists. It was a period when at least one charming colored chorus girl, amber enough to pass for a Latin American, was living in a pent house, with all her bills paid by a gentleman whose name was banker's magic on Wall Street. It was a period when every season there was at least one hit play on Broadway acted by a Negro cast. And when books by Negro authors were being published with much greater frequency and much more publicity than ever before or since in history. It was a period when white writers wrote about Negroes more successfully (commercially speaking) than Negroes did about themselves. It was the period (God help us!) when Ethel Barrymore appeared in blackface in *Scarlet Sister Mary!*[1] It was the period when the Negro was in vogue.

I was there. I had a swell time while it lasted. But I thought it wouldn't last long. (I remember the vogue for things Russian, the season the Chauve-Souris[2] first came to town.) For how could a large and enthusiastic number of people be crazy about Negroes forever? But some Harlemites

4. Van Vechten's 1926 novel set in Harlem.
5. A satirical novel of 1932.
6. U.S. composer (1898–1937). Broun (1888–1939), celebrated literary and dramatic critic of the *New York Tribune*.
7. Daughter (1885–1932) of Sarah Breedlove "Madame C. J." Walker, the first African American woman to become a millionaire. Through sales of her hair-straightening "preparations," Sarah Walker was able to leave a fortune of at least $2 million to her daughter, who became the central

socialite of Harlem.
8. A Harlem schoolteacher (1900–1960) and close friend of Countee Cullen.
9. A Princess Violette Murat visited Harlem regularly around 1928.
1. A 1928 folk comedy based on a novel by Julia Peterkin (1880–1961), a white writer. Barrymore (1879–1959), U.S. actress.
2. A Russian troupe that presented programs of dance, drama, songs, and tableaux in New York City from 1922 to 1923.

thought the millennium had come. They thought the race problem had at last been solved through Art plus Gladys Bentley. They were sure the New Negro would lead a new life from then on in green pastures of tolerance created by Countee Cullen, Ethel Waters, Claude McKay, Duke Ellington, Bojangles, and Alain Locke.[3]

I don't know what made any Negroes think that—except that they were mostly intellectuals doing the thinking. The ordinary Negroes hadn't heard of the Negro Renaissance. And if they had, it hadn't raised their wages any. As for all those white folks in the speakeasies and night clubs of Harlem— well, maybe a colored man could find *some* place to have a drink that the tourists hadn't yet discovered.

Then it was that house-rent parties began to flourish—and not always to raise the rent either. But, as often as not, to have a get-together of one's own, where you could do the black-bottom with no stranger behind you trying to do it, too. Non-theatrical, non-intellectual Harlem was an unwilling victim of its own vogue. It didn't like to be stared at by white folks. But perhaps the downtowners never knew this—for the cabaret owners, the entertainers, and the speakeasy proprietors treated them fine—as long as they paid.

The Saturday night rent parties that I attended were often more amusing than any night club, in small apartments where God knows who lived— because the guests seldom did—but where the piano would often be augmented by a guitar, or an odd cornet, or somebody with a pair of drums walking in off the street. And where awful bootleg whiskey and good fried fish or steaming chitterling were sold at very low prices. And the dancing and singing and impromptu entertaining went on until dawn came in at the windows.

These parties, often termed whist parties or dances, were usually announced by brightly colored cards stuck in the grille of apartment house elevators. Some of the cards were highly entertaining in themselves:

We got yellow girls, we've got black and tan
Will you have a good time? - YEAH MAN !

𝔄 𝔖𝔬𝔠𝔦𝔞𝔩 𝔚𝔥𝔦𝔰𝔱 𝔓𝔞𝔯𝔱𝔶
—GIVEN BY—
MARY WINSTON
147 West 145th Street   Apt. 5

SATURDAY EVE., MARCH 19th, 1932

GOOD MUSIC   REFRESHMENTS

---

3. Editor (1886–1954) of *The New Negro* (1927). Cullen (1903–1946), author of *Color* (1925). McKay (1889–1948), Jamaican-born poet whose *Harlem Shadows* (1922) is sometimes considered the first major achievement of the Harlem Renaissance.

H U R R A Y

COME AND SEE WHAT IS IN STORE FOR YOU AT THE

TEA CUP PARTY

GIVEN BY MRS. VANDERBILT SMITH

at 409 EDGECOMBE AVENUE
NEW YORK CITY

Apartment 10-A

on Thursday evening, January 23rd, 1930

at 8:30 P. M.

ORIENTAL - GYPSY - SOUTHERN MAMMY -
STARLIGHT
and other readers will be present

Music and Talent   —   —   Refreshments Served

Ribbons-Maws and Trotters A Specialty

Fall in line, and watch your step, For there'll be
Lots of Browns with plenty of Pep At

A Social Whist Party

Given by

Lucille & Minnie

149 West 117th Street, N. Y. Gr. floor, W,

Saturday Evening, Nov. 2nd 1929

Refreshments Just It   Music Won't Quit

If Sweet Mamma is running wild, and you are looking
for a Do-right child, just come around and
linger awhile at a

SOCIAL WHIST PARTY

GIVEN BY

PINKNEY & EPPS

260 West 129th Street   Apartment 10

SATURDAY EVENING, JUNE 9, 1928

GOOD MUSIC   REFRESHMENTS

Railroad Men's Ball

AT CANDY'S PLACE

FRIDAY, SATURDAY & SUNDAY,

April 29-30, May 1, 1927

Black Wax, says change your mind and say they
do and he will give you a hearing, while MEAT
HOUSE SLIM, laying in the bin
killing all good men.

L. A. VAUGH, *President*

OH BOY   OH JOY

The Eleven Brown Skins

of the

Evening Shadow Social Club

are giving their

Second Annual St. Valentine Dance

Saturday evening, Feb. 18th, 1928

At 129 West 136th Street, New York City

Good Music   Refreshments Served

Subscription   **25 Cents**

---

*Some wear pajamas, some wear pants, what does it matter
just so you can dance, at*

A Social Whist Party

GIVEN BY

Mr. & Mrs. BROWN

AT 258 W. 115TH STREET, APT. 9

SATURDAY EVE., SEPT. 14, 1929

The music is sweet and everything good to eat!

Almost every Saturday night when I was in Harlem I went to a house-rent party. I wrote lots of poems about house-rent parties, and ate thereat many a fried fish and pig's foot—with liquid refreshments on the side. I met ladies' maids and truck drivers, laundry workers and shoe shine boys, seamstresses and porters. I can still hear their laughter in my ears, hear the soft slow music, and feel the floor shaking as the dancers danced.

Harlem Literati

The summer of 1926, I lived in a rooming house on 137th Street, where Wallace Thurman and Harcourt Tynes[4] also lived. Thurman was then managing editor of the *Messenger*, a Negro magazine that had a curious career. It began by being very radical, racial, and socialistic, just after the war. I believe it received a grant from the Garland Fund[5] in its early days. Then it later became a kind of Negro society magazine and a plugger for Negro business, with photographs of prominent colored ladies and their nice homes in it. A. Phillip Randolph, now President of the Brotherhood of Sleeping Car Porters, Chandler Owen, and George S. Schuyler were connected with it. Schuyler's editorials, à la Mencken,[6] were the most interesting things in the magazine, verbal brickbats that said sometimes one thing, sometimes another, but always vigorously. I asked Thurman what kind of magazine the *Messenger* was, and he said it reflected the policy of whoever paid off best at the time.

Anyway, the *Messenger* bought my first short stories. They paid me ten dollars a story. Wallace Thurman wrote me that they were very bad stories, but better than any others they could find, so he published them.

Thurman had recently come from California to New York. He was a strangely brilliant black boy, who had read everything, and whose critical mind could find something wrong with everything he read. I have no critical mind, so I usually either like a book or don't. But I am not capable of liking a book and then finding a million things wrong with it, too—as Thurman was capable of doing.

Thurman had read so many books because he could read eleven lines at a time. He would get from the library a great pile of volumes that would have taken me a year to read. But he would go through them in less than a week, and be able to discuss each one at great length with anybody. That was why, I suppose, he was later given a job as a reader at Macaulay's—the only Negro reader, so far as I know, to be employed by any of the larger publishing firms.

Later Thurman became a ghost writer for *True Story*, and other publications, writing under all sorts of fantastic names, like Ethel Belle Mandrake or Patrick Casey. He did Irish and Jewish and Catholic "true confessions." He collaborated with William Jordan Rapp[7] on plays and novels. Later he

4. A friend of Thurman's. "House on 137th Street": the rooming house appears in Thurman's *Infants of the Spring* as "Niggerati Manor."
5. The American Fund for Public Service, established in 1920 by Charles Garland.
6. Henry Louis Mencken (1880–1956), prominent Baltimore essayist, critic, and editor, who was a friend of Schuyler's. Randolph (1889–1976) and

Owen (1889–1967), editors at the *Messenger*, who hired Schuyler as a writer in 1923. Schuyler (1895–1977), conservative black writer.
7. White playwright (1895–1942), editor of *True Story* magazine. The only work certain to be a collaboration of Thurman and Rapp is the play *Harlem* (1929).

ghosted books. In fact, this quite dark young Negro is said to have written *Men, Women, and Checks*.

Wallace Thurman wanted to be a great writer, but none of his own work ever made him happy. *The Blacker the Berry*, [8] his first book, was an important novel on a subject little dwelt upon in Negro fiction—the plight of the very dark Negro woman, who encounters in some communities a double wall of color prejudice within and without the race. His play, *Harlem*, considerably distorted for box office purposes, was, nevertheless, a compelling study—and the only one in the theater—of the impact of Harlem on a Negro family fresh from the South. And his *Infants of the Spring*, a superb and bitter study of the bohemian fringe of Harlem's literary and artistic life, is a compelling book.

But none of these things pleased Wallace Thurman. He wanted to be a *very* great writer, like Gorki or Thomas Mann,[9] and he felt that he was merely a journalistic writer. His critical mind, comparing his pages to the thousands of other pages he had read, by Proust, Melville, Tolstoy, Galsworthy, Dostoyevski, Henry James, Sainte-Beauve, Taine, Anatole France,[1] found his own pages vastly wanting. So he contented himself by writing a great deal for money, laughing bitterly at his fabulously concocted "true stories," creating two bad motion pictures[2] of the "Adults Only" type for Hollywood, drinking more and more gin, and then threatening to jump out of windows at people's parties and kill himself.

During the summer of 1926, Wallace Thurman, Zora Neale Hurston, Aaron Douglas, John P. Davis, Bruce Nugent, Gwendolyn Bennett,[3] and I decided to publish "a Negro quarterly of the arts" to be called *Fire*—the idea being that it would burn up a lot of the old, dead conventional Negro-white ideas of the past, *épater le bourgeois*[4] into a realization of the existence of the younger Negro writers and artists, and provide us with an outlet for publication not available in the limited pages of the small Negro magazines then existing, the *Crisis*, *Opportunity*, and the *Messenger*—the first two being house organs of inter-racial organizations, and the latter being God knows what.

Sweltering summer evenings we met to plan *Fire*. Each of the seven of us agreed to give fifty dollars to finance the first issue. Thurman was to edit it, John P. Davis to handle the business end, and Bruce Nugent to take charge of distribution. The rest of us were to serve as an editorial board to collect material, contribute our own work, and act in any useful way that we could. For artists and writers, we got along fine and there were no quarrels. But October came before we were ready to go to press. I had to return to Lincoln,[5] John Davis to Law School at Harvard, Zora Hurston to her

---

8. Published in 1929.
9. German novelist (1875–1955). Maxim Gorki was the pen name of Russian writer Aleksey Maksimovich Pyeshkov (1868–1936).
1. Pen name of French novelist and essayist Jacques Antole Francois Thibault (1844–1924). Marcel Proust (1871–1922), French novelist. Herman Melville (1819–1891), U.S. writer. Leo Tolstoy (1828–1910), Russian novelist and social critic. John Galsworthy (1867–1933), English novelist. Fyodor Dostoyevski (1821–1881), Russian novelist. James (1843–1916), U.S. novelist and

critic. Charles Augustin Sainte-Beuve (1804–1869), French critic and poet. Hippolyte Adolphe Taine (1828–1893), French critic and historian.
2. *Tomorrow's Children* (1934) and *High School Girl* (1935).
3. Poet (1902–1981). Hurston (1891–1960), novelist and folklore collector. Douglas (1898–1979), artist. Davis (1905–1973), lawyer and prominent leftist. Nugent (1906–1987), illustrator and writer.
4. Shock the middle class (French).
5. I.e., Lincoln University in Pennsylvania.

studies at Barnard, from whence she went about Harlem with an anthropologist's ruler, measuring heads for Franz Boas.[6]

Only three of the seven had contributed their fifty dollars, but the others faithfully promised to send theirs out of tuition checks, wages, or begging. Thurman went on with the work of preparing the magazine. He got a printer. He planned the layout. It had to be on good paper, he said, worthy of the drawings of Aaron Douglas. It had to have beautiful type, worthy of the first Negro art quarterly. It had to be what we seven young Negroes dreamed our magazine would be—so in the end it cost almost a thousand dollars, and nobody could pay the bills.

I don't know how Thurman persuaded the printer to let us have all the copies to distribute, but he did. I think Alain Locke, among others, signed notes guaranteeing payments. But since Thurman was the only one of the seven of us with a regular job, for the next three or four years his checks were constantly being attached and his income seized to pay for *Fire*. And whenever I sold a poem, mine went there, too—to *Fire*.

None of the older Negro intellectuals would have anything to do with *Fire*. Dr. DuBois[7] in the *Crisis* roasted it. The Negro press called it all sorts of bad names, largely because of a green and purple story by Bruce Nugent, in the Oscar Wilde[8] tradition, which we had included. Rean Graves, the critic for the *Baltimore Afro-American*, began his review by saying: "I have just tossed the first issue of *Fire* into the fire." Commenting upon various of our contributors, he said: "Aaron Douglas who, in spite of himself and the meaningless grotesqueness of his creations, has gained a reputation as an artist, is permitted to spoil three perfectly good pages and a cover with his pen and ink hudge pudge. Countee Cullen has written a beautiful poem in his 'From a Dark Tower,' but tries his best to obscure the thought in superfluous sentences. Langston Hughes displays his usual ability to say nothing in many words."

So *Fire* had plenty of cold water thrown on it by the colored critics. The white critics (except for an excellent editorial in the *Bookman* for November, 1926) scarcely noticed it at all. We had no way of getting it distributed to bookstands or news stands. Bruce Nugent took it around New York on foot and some of the Greenwich Village bookshops put it on display, and sold it for us. But then Bruce, who had no job, would collect the money and, on account of salary, eat it up before he got back to Harlem.

Finally, irony of ironies, several hundred copies of *Fire* were stored in the basement of an apartment where an actual fire occurred and the bulk of the whole issue was burned up. Even after that Thurman had to go on paying the printer.

Now *Fire* is a collector's item, and very difficult to get, being mostly ashes.

That taught me a lesson about little magazines. But since white folks had

---

6. German-born American anthropologist (1858–1942).
7. W. E. B. Du Bois (1868–1963), African American writer, editor of *Crisis*, and cofounder of the NAACP.

8. Irish playwright (1854–1900), a proponent of the Art for Art's Sake movement. "Green and purple story": the first installment of a novel called *Smoke, Lilies and Jade*.

them, we Negroes thought we could have one, too. But we didn't have the money.

Wallace Thurman laughed a long bitter laugh. He was a strange kind of fellow, who liked to drink gin, but *didn't* like to drink gin; who liked being a Negro, but felt it a great handicap; who adored bohemianism, but thought it wrong to be a bohemian. He liked to waste a lot of time, but he always felt guilty wasting time. He loathed crowds, yet he hated to be alone. He almost always felt bad, yet he didn't write poetry.

Once I told him if I could feel as bad as he did *all* the time, I would surely produce wonderful books. But he said you had to know how to *write*, as well as how to feel bad. I said I didn't have to know how to feel bad, because, every so often, the blues just naturally overtook me, like a blind beggar with an old guitar:

> *You don't know,*
> *You don't know my mind—*
> *When you see me laughin',*
> *I'm laughin' to keep from cryin'.* [9]

About the future of Negro literature Thurman was very pessimistic. He thought the Negro vogue had made us all too conscious of ourselves, had flattered and spoiled us, and had provided too many easy opportunities for some of us to drink gin and more gin, on which he thought we would always be drunk. With his bitter sense of humor, he called the Harlem literati, the "niggerati."

Of this "niggerati," Zora Neale Hurston was certainly the most amusing. Only to reach a wider audience, need she ever write books—because she is a perfect book of entertainment in herself. In her youth she was always getting scholarships and things from wealthy white people, some of whom simply paid her just to sit around and represent the Negro race for them, she did it in such a racy fashion. She was full of side-splitting anecdotes, humorous tales, and tragicomic stories, remembered out of her life in the South as a daughter of a travelling minister of God. She could make you laugh one minute and cry the next. To many of her white friends, no doubt, she was a perfect "darkie," in the nice meaning they give the term— that is a naïve, childlike, sweet, humorous, and highly colored Negro.

But Miss Hurston was clever, too—a student who didn't let college give her a broad *a* and who had great scorn for all pretensions, academic or otherwise. That is why she was such a fine folk-lore collector,[1] able to go among the people and never act as if she had been to school at all. Almost nobody else could stop the average Harlemite on Lenox Avenue and measure his head with a strange-looking, anthropological device and not get bawled out for the attempt, except Zora, who used to stop anyone whose head looked interesting, and measure it.

When Miss Hurston graduated from Barnard she took an apartment in West 66th Street near the park, in that row of Negro houses there. She moved in with no furniture at all and no money, but in a few days friends had given her everything, from decorative silver birds, perched atop the

---

9. Hughes later titled a collection of his short stories *Laughing to Keep from Crying* (1952).

1. Hurston published two such collections: *Mules
and Men* (1935) and *Tell My Horse* (1938).

linen cabinet, down to a footstool. And on Saturday night, to christen the place, she had a *hand*-chicken dinner, since she had forgotten to say she needed forks.

She seemed to know almost everybody in New York. She had been a secretary to Fannie Hurst,[2] and had met dozens of celebrities whose friendship she retained. Yet she was always having terrific ups-and-downs about money. She tells this story on herself, about needing a nickel to go downtown one day and wondering where on earth she would get it. As she approached the subway, she was stopped by a blind beggar holding out his cup.

"Please help the blind! Help the blind! A nickel for the blind!"

"I need money worse than you today," said Miss Hurston, taking five cents out of his cup. "Lend me this! Next time, I'll give it back." And she went on downtown.

Harlem was like a great magnet for the Negro intellectual, pulling him from everywhere. Or perhaps the magnet was New York—but once in New York, he had to live in Harlem, for rooms were hardly to be found elsewhere unless one could pass for white or Mexican or Eurasian and perhaps live in the Village—which always seemed to me a very arty locale, in spite of the many real artists and writers who lived there. Only a few of the New Negroes lived in the Village, Harlem being their real stamping ground.

The wittiest of these New Negroes of Harlem, whose tongue was flavored with the sharpest and saltiest humor, was Rudolph Fisher, whose stories appeared in the *Atlantic Monthly*. His novel, *Walls of Jericho*,[3] captures but slightly the raciness of his own conversation. He was a young medical doctor and X-ray specialist, who always frightened me a little, because he could think of the most incisively clever things to say—and I could never think of anything to answer. He and Alain Locke together were great for intellectual wise-cracking. The two would fling big and witty words about with such swift and punning innuendo that an ordinary mortal just sat and looked wary for fear of being caught in a net of witticisms beyond his cultural ken. I used to wish I could talk like Rudolph Fisher. Besides being a good writer, he was an excellent singer, and had sung with Paul Robeson during their college days. But I guess Fisher was too brilliant and too talented to stay long on this earth. During the same week, in December, 1934, he and Wallace Thurman both died.

Thurman died of tuberculosis in the charity ward at Bellevue Hospital, having just flown back to New York from Hollywood.

Downtown

Downtown there were many interesting parties in those days, too, to which I was sometimes bidden. I remember one at Florine Stettheimer's, another at V. F. Calverton's,[4] and another at Bob Chandler's, where the walls were hung with paintings and Louise Helstrom served the drinks. Paul Haakon, who was a kid then whom Louise had "discovered" some-

2. U.S. fiction writer (1899–1968).
3. Published in 1928. Fisher (1897–1934), short story writer and novelist. His *The City of Refuge* was the first short story by an African American to be accepted at the prestigious *Atlantic Monthly*.
4. Left-oriented editor (1900–1940) of *The Anthology of American Negro Literature* (1929) and *Modern Quarterly* magazine.

where, danced and everybody Oh'ed and Ah'ed, and said what a beautiful young artist! What an artist! But later when nobody was listening, Paul Haakon said to me: "Some baloney—I'm no artist. I'm in vaudeville!"

I remember also a party at Jake Baker's, somewhere on the lower East Side near the river, where I do not recall any whites being present except Mr. Baker himself. Jake Baker then had one of the largest erotic libraries in New York, ranging from the ancient to the modern, the classic to the vulgar, the *Kama Sutra* to T. R. Smith's anthology of *Poetica Erotica*.[5] But since Harlemites are not very familiar with erotic books, Mr. Baker was never able to get the party started. His gathering took on the atmosphere of the main reading room at the public library with everybody hunched over a book—trying to find out what white folks say about love when they really come to the point.

I remember also a big cocktail party for Ernestine Evans at the Ritz, when she had got a new job with some publishing firm and they were celebrating her addition to the staff. Josephine Herbst[6] was there and we had a long talk near the hors-d'œuvres, and I liked Josephine Herbst very much. Also I recall a dinner party for Claire Spencer at Colin McPhee's and Jane Belo's in the village, where Claire Spencer told about a thrilling night flight over Manhattan Island in a monoplane and also another party in the Fifties for Rebecca West,[7] who knew a lot of highly amusing gossip about the Queen of Rumania. I remember well, too, my first party after a Broadway opening, the one Horace Liveright gave for Paul Robeson and Fredi Washington,[8] following the premiere of Jim Tully's *Black Boy*.[9] And there was one grand New Year's Eve fête at the Alfred A. Knopf's[1] on Fifth Avenue, where I met Ethel Barrymore and Jascha Heifetz,[2] and everybody was in tails but me, and all I had on was a blue serge suit—which didn't seem to matter to anyone—for Fifth Avenue was not nearly so snooty about clothes as Washington's Negro society.[3]

Downtown at Charlie Studin's parties, at Arthur and Mrs. Springarn's,[4] Eddie Wasserman's, at Muriel Draper's, or Rita Romilly's, one would often meet almost as many Negro guests as in Harlem. But only Carl Van Vechten's parties were so Negro that they were reported as a matter of course in the colored society columns, just as though they occurred in Harlem instead of West 55th Street, where he and Fania Marinoff then lived in a Peter Whiffle[5] apartment, full of silver fishes and colored glass balls and ceiling-high shelves of gaily-bound books.

Not only were there interesting Negroes at Carl Van Vechten's parties, ranging from famous writers to famous tap dancers, but there were always many other celebrities of various colors and kinds, old ones and new ones from Hollywood, Broadway, London, Paris or Harlem. I remember one party when Chief Long Lance of the cinema did an Indian war dance,

5. Published in 1927. The *Kama Sutra* is a Hindu text on love and marriage.
6. "Proletarian" novelist of the 1930s (1897–1969).
7. Pen name of English novelist Cicily Andrews (1892–1983).
8. Prominent African American actress (1903–1994), who starred in the 1934 film *Imitation of Life*. Liveright (1886–1933), New York publisher.
9. By Tully and Frank Dazey. It opened in 1926.
1. Publisher Alfred and his wife, Blanche.

2. U.S. violinist (1901–1987).
3. In *The Big Sea*, Hughes depicted black society in Washington, D.C., where he lived in 1925, as particularly snobbish.
4. Arthur (1878–1971), lawyer, and his wife, Marian, were supporters of the NAACP.
5. Title character in a 1922 novel by Van Vechten. Marinoff (1887–1971), Russian-born actress, who was married to Van Vechten.

while Adelaide Hall of *Blackbirds*[6] played the drums, and an international assemblage crowded around to cheer.

At another of Mr. Van Vechten's parties, Bessie Smith sang the blues. And when she finished, Margarita D'Alvarez of the Metropolitan Opera arose and sang an aria. Bessie Smith did not know D'Alvarez, but, liking her voice, she went up to her when she had ceased and cried: "Don't let nobody tell you you can't sing!"

Carl Van Vechten and A'Lelia Walker were great friends, and at each of their parties many of the same people were to be seen, but more writers were present at Carl Van Vechten's. At cocktail time, or in the evening, I first met at his house Somerset Maugham, Hugh Walpole, Fannie Hurst, Witter Bynner, Isa Glenn, Emily Clark, William Seabrook, Arthur Davison Ficke, Louis Untermeyer, and George Sylvester Viereck.[7]

Mr. Viereck cured me of a very bad habit I used to have of thinking I had to say something nice to every writer I met concerning his work. Upon being introduced to Mr. Viereck, I said, "I like your books."

He demanded: "Which one?"

And I couldn't think of a single one.

Of course, at Mr. Van Vechten's parties there were always many others who were not writers: Lawrence Langner and Armina Marshall of the Theatre Guild, Eugene Goossens, Jane Belo, who married Colin McPhee and went to Bali to live, beautiful Rose Rolanda, who married Miguel Covarrubias, Lilyan Tashman, who died, Horace Liveright, Blanche Dunn, Ruben Mamoulian, Marie Doro, Nicholas Muray, Madame Helena Rubinstein, Richmond Barthe, Salvador Dali, Waldo Frank, Dudley Murphy, and often Dorothy Peterson, a charming colored girl who had grown up mostly in Puerto Rico, and who moved with such poise among these colorful celebrities that I thought when I first met her she was a white girl of the grande monde, slightly sun-tanned. But she was a Negro teacher of French and Spanish, who later got a leave of absence from her school work to play Cain's Gal in *The Green Pastures*.

Being interested in the Negro problem in various parts of the world, Dorothy Peterson once asked Dali if he knew anything about Negroes.

"Everything!" Dali answered. "I've met Nancy Cunard!"

Speaking of celebrities, one night as one of Carl Van Vechten's parties was drawing to a close, Rudolph Valentino[8] called, saying that he was on his way. That was the only time I have ever seen the genial Van Vechten hospitality waver. He told Mr. Valentino the party was over. It seems that our host was slightly perturbed at the thought of so celebrated a guest coming into a party that had passed its peak. Besides, he told the rest of us, movie stars usually expect a lot of attention—and it was too late in the evening for such extended solicitude now.

Carl Van Vechten once wrote a book called *Parties*.[9] But it is not nearly so amusing as his own parties. Once he gave a gossip party, where everybody was at liberty to go around the room repeating the worst things they

6. A series of musical reviews between 1926 and 1939 arranged by Will Vodery and staged by Lew Leslie, often featuring singer Hall.
7. Novelist and playwright (1884–1962). Walpole (1884–1941), New Zealand-born English novelist.

Ficke (1883–1945), poet and critic. Untermeyer (1885–1977), U.S. poet and editor.
8. Pseudonym of silent screen actor Rudolpho d'Antonguolla (1895–1926).
9. Published in 1930.

could make up or recall about each other to their friends on opposite sides of the room—who were sure to go right over and tell them all about it.

At another party of his (but this was incidental) the guests were kept in a constant state of frightful expectancy by a lady standing in the hall outside Mr. Van Vechten's door, who announced that she was waiting for her husband to emerge from the opposite apartment, where he was visiting another woman. When I came to the party, I saw her standing grimly there. It was her full intention to kill her husband, she said. And she displayed to Mrs. Van Vechten's maids the pistol in her handbag.

At intervals during the evening, the woman in the hall would receive coffee from the Van Vechten party to help her maintain her vigil. But the suspense was not pleasant. I kept feeling goose pimples on my body and hearing a gun in my mind. Finally someone suggested phoning the apartment across the way to inform the erring husband of the fate awaiting him if he came out. Perhaps this was done. I don't know. But I learned later that the woman waited until dawn and then went home. No husband emerged from the silent door, so her gun was not fired.

Once when Mr. Van Vechten gave a bon voyage party in the Prince of Wales suite aboard the Cunarder on which he was sailing, as the champagne flowed, Nora Holt, the scintillating Negro blonde entertainer de luxe from Nevada, sang a ribald ditty called, "My Daddy Rocks Me With One Steady Roll." As she ceased, a well-known New York matron cried ecstatically, with tears in her eyes: "My dear! Oh, my dear! How beautifully you sing Negro spirituals!"

Carl Van Vechten moved about filling glasses and playing host with the greatest of zest at his parties, while his tiny wife, Fania Marinoff, looking always very pretty and very gay, when the evening grew late would sometimes take Mr. Van Vechten severely to task for his drinking—before bidding the remaining guests good night and retiring to her bed.

Now, Mr. Van Vechten has entirely given up drinking (as well as writing books and smoking cigarettes) in favor of photography. Although his parties are still gaily liquid for those who wish it, he himself is sober as a judge, but not as solemn.

For several pleasant years, he gave an annual birthday party for James Weldon Johnson, young Alfred A. Knopf, Jr., and himself, for their birthdays fall on the same day.[1] At the last of these parties the year before Mr. Johnson died, on the Van Vechten table there were three cakes, one red, one white, and one blue—the colors of our flag. They honored a Gentile, a Negro, and a Jew—friends and fellow-Americans. But the differences of race did not occur to me until days later, when I thought back about the three colors and the three men.

Carl Van Vechten is like that party. He never talks grandiloquently about democracy or Americanism. Nor makes a fetish of those qualities. But he lives them with sincerity—and humor.

Perhaps that is why *his* parties were reported in the Harlem press.

1940

---

1. June 17.

From The Best of Simple [1]

Feet Live Their Own Life

"If you want to know about my life," said Simple as he blew the foam from the top of the newly filled glass the bartender put before him, "don't look at my face, don't look at my hands. Look at my feet and see if you can tell how long I been standing on them."

"I cannot see your feet through your shoes," I said.

"You do not need to see through my shoes," said Simple. "Can't you tell by the shoes I wear—not pointed, not rocking-chair, not French-toed, not nothing but big, long, broad, and flat—that I been standing on these feet a long time and carrying some heavy burdens? They ain't flat from standing at no bar, neither, because I always sets at a bar. Can't you tell that? You know I do not hang out in a bar unless it has stools, don't you?"

"That I have observed," I said, "but I did not connect it with your past life."

"Everything I do is connected up with my past life," said Simple. "From Virginia to Joyce, from my wife to Zarita, from my mother's milk to this glass of beer, everything is connected up."

"I trust you will connect up with that dollar I just loaned you when you get paid," I said. "And who is Virginia? You never told me about her."

"Virginia is where I was borned," said Simple. "I *would* be borned in a state named after a woman. From that day on, women never give me no peace."

"You, I fear, are boasting. If the women were running after you as much as you run after them, you would not be able to sit here on this bar stool in peace. I don't see any women coming to call you out to go home, as some of these fellows' wives do around here."

"Joyce better not come in no bar looking for me," said Simple. "That is why me and my wife busted up—one reason. I do not like to be called out of no bar by a female. It's a man's perogative to just set and drink sometimes."

"How do you connect that prerogative with your past?" I asked.

"When I was a wee small child," said Simple, "I had no place to set and think in, being as how I was raised up with three brothers, two sisters, seven cousins, one married aunt, a common-law uncle, and the minister's grandchild—and the house only had four rooms. I never had no place just to set and think. Neither to set and drink—not even much my milk before some hongry child snatched it out of my hand. I were not the youngest, neither a girl, nor the cutest. I don't know why, but I don't think nobody liked me much. Which is why I was afraid to like anybody for a long time myself. When I did like somebody, I was full-grown and then I picked out the wrong woman because I had no practice in liking anybody before that. We did not get along."

---

1. Jesse B. Semple, better known as Simple, is a character developed by Hughes in 1943 as a feature of his weekly column in the Chicago *Defender* newspaper. The exploits of Simple, a kind of Harlem everyman, became the most popular aspect of the column and the basis of five collections of sketches edited by Hughes: *Simple Speaks His Mind* (1950), *Simple Takes a Wife* (1953), *Simple Stakes a Claim* (1957), *The Best of Simple* (1961), and *Simple's Uncle Sam* (1965).

"Is that when you took to drink?"

"Drink took to me," said Simple. "Whiskey just naturally likes me but beer likes me better. By the time I got married I had got to the point where a cold bottle was almost as good as a warm bed, especially when the bottle could not talk and the bed-warmer could. I do not like a woman to talk to me too much—I mean about me. Which is why I like Joyce. Joyce most in generally talks about herself."

"I am still looking at your feet," I said, "and I swear they do not reveal your life to me. Your feet are no open book."

"You have eyes but you see not,"[2] said Simple. "These feet have stood on every rock from the Rock of Ages[3] to 135th and Lenox. These feet have supported everything from a cotton bale to a hongry woman. These feet have walked ten thousand miles working for white folks and another ten thousand keeping up with colored. These feet have stood at altars, crap tables, free lunches, bars, graves, kitchen doors, betting windows, hospital clinics, WPA[4] desks, social security railings, and in all kinds of lines from soup lines to the draft. If I just had four feet, I could have stood in more places longer. As it is, I done wore out seven hundred pairs of shoes, eighty-nine tennis shoes, twelve summer sandals, also six loafers. The socks that these feet have bought could build a knitting mill. The corns I've cut away would dull a German razor. The bunions I forgot would make you ache from now till Judgment Day. If anybody was to write the history of my life, they should start with my feet."

"Your feet are not all that extraordinary," I said. "Besides, everything you are saying is general. Tell me specifically some one thing your feet have done that makes them different from any other feet in the world, just one."

"Do you see that window in that white man's store across the street?" asked Simple. "Well, this right foot of mine broke out that window in the Harlem riots[5] right smack in the middle. Didn't no other foot in the world break that window but mine. And this left foot carried me off running as soon as my right foot came down. Nobody else's feet saved me from the cops that night but these two feet right here. Don't tell me these feet ain't had a life of their own."

"For shame," I said, "going around kicking out windows. Why?"

"Why?" said Simple. "You have to ask my great-great-grandpa why. He must of been simple—else why did he let them capture him in Africa and sell him for a slave to breed my great-grandpa in slavery to breed my grandpa in slavery to breed my pa to breed me to look at that window and say, 'It ain't mine! Bam-mmm-mm-m!' and kick it out?"

"This bar glass is not yours either," I said. "Why don't you smash it?"

"It's got my beer in it," said Simple.

Just then Zarita came in wearing her Thursday-night rabbit-skin coat. She didn't stop at the bar, being dressed up, but went straight back to a booth. Simple's hand went up, his beer went down, and the glass back to its wet spot on the bar.

---

2. An allusion to any of a number of biblical passages, e.g., Psalm 115:5: "Eyes have they, but they see not."
3. From the hymn "Rock of Ages (Cleft for Me)."

4. The Works Progress Administration, one of President Franklin D. Roosevelt's New Deal programs.
5. Of August 1943.

"Excuse me a minute," he said, sliding off the stool.

Just to give him pause, the dozens, that old verbal game of maligning a friend's female relatives, came to mind. "Wait," I said. "You have told me about what to ask your great-great-grandpa. But I want to know what to ask your great-great-grand*ma*."

"I don't play the dozens that far back," said Simple, following Zarita into the smoky juke-box blue of the back room.

A Toast to Harlem

Quiet can seem unduly loud at times. Since nobody at the bar was saying a word during a lull in the bright blues-blare of the Wishing Well's usually overworked juke box, I addressed my friend Simple.

"Since you told me last night you are an Indian, explain to me how it is you find yourself living in a furnished room in Harlem, my brave buck, instead of on a reservation?"

"I am a colored Indian," said Simple.

"In other words, a Negro."

"A Black Foot Indian, daddy-o, not a red one. Anyhow, Harlem is the place I always did want to be. And if it wasn't for landladies, I would be happy. That's a fact! I love Harlem."

"What is it you love about Harlem?"

"It's so full of Negroes," said Simple. "I feel like I got protection."

"From what?"

"From white folks," said Simple. "Furthermore, I like Harlem because it belongs to me."

"Harlem does not belong to you. You don't own the houses in Harlem. They belong to white folks."

"I might not own 'em," said Simple, "but I live in 'em. It would take an atom bomb to get me out."

"Or a depression," I said.

"I would not move for no depression. No, I would not go back down South, not even to Baltimore. I am in Harlem to stay! You say the houses ain't mine. Well, the sidewalk is—and don't nobody push me off. The cops don't even say, 'Move on,' hardly no more. They learned something from them Harlem riots. They used to beat your head right in public, but now they only beat it after they get you down to the stationhouse. And they don't beat it then if they think you know a colored congressman."

"Harlem has a few Negro leaders," I said.

"Elected by my *own* vote," said Simple. "Here I ain't scared to vote— that's another thing I like about Harlem. I also like it because we've got subways and it does not take all day to get downtown, neither are you Jim Crowed[6] on the way. Why, Negroes is running some of these subway trains. This morning I rode the A Train down to 34th Street. There were a Negro driving it, making ninety miles a hour. That cat *were really driving* that train! Every time he flew by one of them local stations looks like he was saying, 'Look at me! This train is mine!' That cat were gone, ole man.

6. Racially segregated.

Which is another reason why I like Harlem! Sometimes I run into Duke Ellington[7] on 125th Street and I say, 'What you know there, Duke?' Duke says, 'Solid, ole man.' He does not know me from Adam, but he speaks. One day I saw Lena Horne[8] coming out of the Hotel Theresa and I said, 'Hubba! Hubba!' Lena smiled. Folks is friendly in Harlem. I feel like I got the world in a jug and the stopper in my hand! So drink a toast to Harlem!"

Simple lifted his glass of beer:

> "Here's to Harlem!
> They say Heaven is Paradise.
> If Harlem ain't Heaven,
> Then a mouse ain't mice!"

"Heaven is a state of mind," I commented.

"It sure is *mine*," said Simple, draining his glass. "From Central Park to 179th, from river to river, Harlem is mine! Lots of white folks is scared to come up here, too, after dark."

"That is nothing to be proud of," I said.

"I am sorry white folks is scared to come to Harlem, but I am scared to go around some of *them*. Why, for instant, in my home town once before I came North to live, I was walking down the street when a white woman jumped out of her door and said, 'Boy, get away from here because I am scared of you.'

"I said, 'Why?'

"She said, 'Because you are black.'

"I said, 'Lady, I am scared of you because you are white.' I went on down the street, but I kept wishing I was blacker—so I could of scared that lady to death. So help me, I did. Imagine somebody talking about they is scared of me because I am black! I got more reason to be scared of white folks than they have of me."

"Right," I said.

"The white race drug me over here from Africa, slaved me, freed me, lynched me, starved me during the depression, Jim Crowed me during the war—then they come talking about they is scared of me! Which is why I am glad I have got one spot to call my own where I hold sway—Harlem. Harlem, where I can thumb my nose at the world!"

"You talk just like a Negro nationalist," I said.

"What's that?"

"Someone who wants Negroes to be on top."

"When everybody else keeps me on the *bottom*, I don't see why I shouldn't want to be on top. I will, too, someday."

"That's the spirit that causes wars," I said.

"I would not mind a war if I could win it. White folks fight, lynch, and enjoy themselves."

"There you go," I said. "That old *race-against-race* jargon. There'll never be peace that way. The world tomorrow ought to be a world where everybody gets along together. The least we can do is extend a friendly hand."

---

7. Composer and musician (1899–1974).   8. Singer and actress (b. 1917).

"Every time I extend my hand I get put back in my place. You know them poetries about the black cat that tried to be friendly with the white one:

> "*The black cat said to the white cat,*
> '*Let's sport around the town.*'
> *The white cat said to the black cat,*
> '*You better set your black self down!*' "

"Unfriendliness of that nature should not exist," I said. "Folks ought to live like neighbors."

"You're talking about what ought to be. But as long as what *is* is—and Georgia is Georgia—I will take Harlem for mine. At least, if trouble comes, I will have *my own window* to shoot from."

"I refuse to argue with you any more," I said. "What Harlem ought to hold out to the world from its windows is a friendly hand, not a belligerent attitude."

"It will not be my attitude I will have out my window," said Simple.

Jealousy

"That Joyce," said Simple, "is not a drinking woman—for which I love her. But if she wasn't my girl friend, I swear she would make me madder than she do sometimes."

"What's come off between you and Joyce now?" I asked.

"She has upset me," said Simple.

"How?"

"One night last week when we come out of the subway, it was sleeting too hard to walk and we could not get a cab for love nor money. So Joyce condescends to stop in the Whistle and Rest with me and have a beer. If I had known what was in there, I would of kept on to Paddy's, where they don't have nothing but a juke box."

"What was in there?"

"A trio," said Simple. "They was humming and strumming up a breeze with the bass just a-thumping, piano trilling, and electric guitar vibrating with every string overcharged. They was playing off-bop.[9] Now, I do not care much for music, and Joyce does not care much for beer. So after I had done had from four to six and she had had two, I said, 'Let's go.' Joyce said, 'No, baby! I want to stay awhile more.'

"Now that were the first time I have ever heard Joyce say she wants to set in a bar.

"I said, 'What ails you?'

"Joyce said, 'I *love* his piano playing.'

"I said, 'You sure it ain't the piano *player* you love?' He were a slick-headed cat that looked like a shmoo[1] and had a part in his teeth.

"Joyce said, 'Don't insinuate.'

"I said, 'Before you sin, *you* better wait. It looks like to me that piano

9. A variation on be-bop, or the new jazz music of the 1940s.

1. A fictitious animal in one of the popular comic strips of the era.

player is eying you mighty hard. He'd best keep his eyes on them keys, else I will close one and black the other, also be-bop his chops.'

"Joyce says, Huh! It is about time you got a little jealous of me, Jess. Sometimes I think you take me for granted. But I *do* like that man's music.'

" 'Are you sure it's his music you like?' I says. 'As flirtatious as you is this evening, your middle name ought to be Frisky.'

" 'Don't put me in no class with Zarita,' says Joyce right out of the clear skies. 'I am no bar-stool hussy'—which kinder took me back because I did not know Joyce had any information about Zarita. A man can't do nothing even once without Harlem and his brother knowing it. Somebody has been talking, or else Joyce is getting too well acquainted with some of my friends—like you."

"I never mention your personal affairs to anyone," I said, "least of all to Joyce, whom I scarcely know except through your introduction."

"Well, anyhow," said Simple, "I did not wish to argue. I says to her, 'I ignore that remark.'

"Joyce says, 'I ignore you.' And turned her back to me and cupped her ear to the music.

" 'Don't rile me, woman,' I says. 'Come out of here and lemme take you home. You know we have to work in the morning.'

" 'Work does not cross your mind,' says Joyce, turning around, 'when you're setting up drinking beer all by yourself—so you say—at Paddy's. I do not see why you have to mention work to *me* when I am enjoying *myself*. The way that man plays "Stardust"[2] sends me. I swear it do. Sends me. Sends me!'

" 'Be yourself, Joyce,' I said. 'Put your coat around your shoulders. Are you high? We are going home.'

"I took Joyce out of there. And by Saturday, to tell the truth, I had forgot all about it. Come the week end, I says, 'Let's walk a little, honey. Which movie do you want to see?'

"Joyce says, 'I do not want to see a picture, daddy. They are all alike. Let's go to the Whistle and Rest Bar.'

" 'O.K.,' I said, because I knowed every Friday they change the music behind that bar. They had done switched to a great big old corn-fed blues man who looked like Ingagi, hollered like a mountain-jack, and almost tore a guitar apart. He were singing:

> *Where you goin', Mr. Spider,*
> *Walking up the wall?*
> *Spider said, I'm goin'*
> *To get my ashes hauled.*

The joint were jumping—rocking, rolling, whooping, hollering, and stomping. It was a far cry from 'Stardust' to that spider walking up the wall.

"When I took Joyce in and she did not see her light-dark shmoo with the conked crown curved over the piano smearing riffs,[3] she said, 'Is this the same place we was at last time?'

---

2. A song by Hoagy Carmichael and Mitchell Parish.

3. Melodic phrases. "Conked": artificially straightened hair.

"I said, 'Sure, baby! What's the matter? Don't you like blues?'
"Joyce said, 'You know I never did like blues. I am from the North.'
" 'North what?' I said. 'Carolina?'
" 'I thought this was a refined cocktail lounge,' says Joyce, turning up her nose. 'But I see I was in error. It's a low dive. Let's go on downtown and catch John Garfield after all.'
" 'No, no, no. No *after all* for me,' I said. 'Here we are—and here we stay right in this bar till *I* get ready to go. . . . Waiter, a beer! . . . Anyhow, I do not see why *you* would want to see John Garfield. Garfield does not conk his hair. Neither is he light black. Neither does he play "Stardust." ' '
" 'You are acting just like a Negro,' says Joyce.
" 'It's my Indian blood,' I admitted."

1961

COUNTEE CULLEN

1903–1946

In their adherence to a traditional poetic format, on the one hand, and their troubled perception of the issue of race, on the other, the lines "Yet do I marvel at this curious thing: / To make a poet black, and bid him sing!" may rightly serve as the signature couplet for the brilliant poet Countee Cullen, who produced some of the most haunting lyrics of the Harlem Renaissance. An African American determined to succeed in the white-dominated field of literature, Cullen was probably the figure from the Harlem Renaissance who most closely corresponded to Alain Locke's idea of the New Negro. Because he wanted to succeed as a poet not by innovation but by an adherence to the traditional standards and practices of English verse, Cullen shied away from being labeled a racial writer; yet he won his greatest poetic renown for his most race-conscious lyrics. His determined resistance to the theme that proved most fruitful for him is clear in one of his most frequently quoted remarks: "I find that I am actuated by a strong sense of race consciousness. This grows upon me, I find, as I grow older, and although I struggle against it, it colors my writing, I fear, in spite of everything I can do." Ambivalent though he may have been toward the most fruitful theme in his own writing, many people were impressed by his power as an artist. In the mid-1920s, none of the younger Harlem poets, not even Langston Hughes, seemed more promising to Harlem readers than Countee Cullen.

Cullen's own origins were long shrouded in mystery. However, it now seems clear that shortly after his birth in 1903 to Elizabeth Lucas in Louisville, Kentucky, Cullen was left in the care of Elizabeth Porter, who may have been his paternal grandmother. Cullen remained at Porter's New York residence until her death in 1918, at which time he was taken into the home of Reverend Frederick Cullen, pastor of the prominent Salem Methodist Episcopal church in Harlem, and his wife, Carolyn. With strong ties to the NAACP and the National Urban League, the Cullens were deeply interested in race matters. Their adopted son, grateful for their kindness but more romantic than either of his foster parents, later described life with the religious couple as a constant posing of the problem of "reconciling a Christian upbringing with a pagan inclination." Cullen excelled as a student and as a poet at the predominantly white De Witt Clinton High School, from which he graduated in 1922, and then at New York University. While there, he won prizes in the Witter Bynner Poetry Contest (open to all American undergraduate college students) in 1923, 1924, and 1925. In 1925 he was graduated Phi Beta Kappa and then began work on his master's degree at Harvard. Also that year, his first volume of poetry, *Color*, was published. His *Threnody for a Brown Girl* won him the John Reed Memorial Prize from *Poetry* magazine and his *Two Moods of Love* the Spingarn Award from the *Crisis*. He also took prizes in contests sponsored by *Palms* and *Opportunity*. The eminent literary critic Irving Babbit hailed Cullen's *Ballad of the Brown Girl* as the finest poem of its type ever written by an American.

In 1927, after returning to New York to begin working for Charles S. Johnson as assistant editor at *Opportunity*, Cullen published two more books of poetry, *Copper Sun* and *The Ballad of the Brown Girl: An Old Ballad Retold*. These books reflected his absolute commitment to conservative forms. At Harvard he had studied poetry composition under Robert Hillyard, who required his pupils to master the Spenserian stanza, rime royal, terza rima, and other conventional poetic forms. Like Claude McKay, Cullen felt most at ease when he was working within a fairly rigid structure; he had virtually no use for dialect verse, or blues and jazz as influences on poetry.

Throughout the 1920s he garnered several honors. Cullen received the Harmon Foundation Literary Award in 1927, when he published his invaluable anthology of African American poetry, *Caroling Dusk*. His influence grew with the appearance of his column, "The Dark Tower," in *Opportunity* magazine. In 1928, Cullen received a Guggenheim fellowship. That year, he also married Nina Yolande Du Bois, daughter of W. E. B. Du Bois, in perhaps the single most spectacular event of the Harlem Renaissance. More than one thousand guests and a host of onlookers witnessed this wedding at Reverend Cullen's Harlem church. The marriage, however, was a failure. Cullen left for Europe without his bride only two months after the ceremony and formalized the divorce from Paris in 1930.

By this time, his career as a writer also was in decline. *The Black Christ and Other Poems* appeared in 1929, but left his many admirers wondering about the future of a poet who had once seemed the brightest talent of the Harlem Renaissance. Cullen's only novel, *One Way to Heaven* (1932), was also a disappointment. One of its two plots concerns the relationship between Mattie Johnson, who works as a maid in Harlem, and a one-armed Texas con man, Sam Lucas, who supports himself by moving from town to town and faking his conversion to Christianity. The other plot focuses on Constancia Brandon, Mattie's wealthy black employer, who hosts literary gatherings of pretentious people who rarely read anything. These two plots seem fundamentally unrelated; according to the acerbic Rudolph Fisher, Cullen was guilty of "exhibiting a lovely pastel and cartoon on the same frame." Cullen went on to collaborate with Harry Hamilton in adapting the novel to the stage, but it was never produced professionally.

In 1934, Cullen turned to teaching French and English to support himself when he took a position at the Frederick Douglass Junior High School in New York. A year later, he brought out his *The Medea and Some Poems*, based on his translation of Euripides; but this effort did virtually nothing to revive his career as a writer. Later came two collections of children's stories, *The Lost Zoo* (1940) and *My Lives and How I Lost Them* (1942). The last major artistic endeavor of Cullen's life was a collaboration with Arna Bontemps that resulted in the dramatization of Bontemps's novel *God Sends Sunday* as *St. Louis Woman*. Unfortunately for Cullen, several members of the black cultural elite objected to it for its emphasis on life among the African American lower class. Cullen considered this criticism unjust and was deeply hurt by it. He died suddenly, only two and a half months before *St. Louis Woman* was finally produced in New York. After his death came *On These I Stand:*

TABLEAU   1305

An Anthology of the Best Poems of Countee Cullen, a collection Cullen himself had arranged.

One of Cullen's main admirers, James Weldon Johnson, noted: "Cullen himself has declared that, in the sense of wishing for consideration or allowances on account of race or of recognizing for himself any limitation to 'racial' themes and forms, he has no desire or intention of being a Negro poet. In this he is not only within his right; he is right. Yet, strangely, it is because Cullen revolts against these 'racial' limitations—technical and spiritual—that the best of his poetry is motivated by race." The truth seems to be that Cullen was as gifted as any writer of the Harlem Renaissance and that in his vacillations and insecurities he mirrored enduring truths about the psychological state of many African Americans. Some of his poems are utterly unforgettable, so capable was he of setting down in precise language the subtle feelings that made him one of the most intriguing writers in African American literature.

Yet Do I Marvel

I doubt not God is good, well-meaning, kind,
And did He stoop to quibble could tell why
The little buried mole continues blind,
Why flesh that mirrors Him must some day die,
Make plain the reason tortured Tantalus[1]   5
Is baited by the fickle fruit, declare
If merely brute caprice dooms Sisyphus[2]
To struggle up a never-ending stair.
Inscrutable His ways are, and immune
To catechism[3] by a mind too strewn   10
With petty cares to slightly understand
What awful brain compels His awful hand.
Yet do I marvel at this curious thing:
To make a poet black, and bid him sing!

                                                              1925

Tableau

(For Donald Duff)

Locked arm in arm they cross the way,
    The black boy and the white,
The golden splendor of the day,
    The sable pride of night.

From lowered blinds the dark folk stare,   5
    And here the fair folk talk,
Indignant that these two should dare
    In unison to walk.

1. In Greek myth, he was punished after death by being placed by a pool of water that retreated whenever he stooped to drink and under trees whose branches lurched upward whenever he reached for their fruit.

2. His punishment after death was to spend eternity struggling to roll uphill a boulder that forever rolled back upon him.
3. Understanding.

Oblivious to look and word
  They pass, and see no wonder   10
That lightning brilliant as a sword
  Should blaze the path of thunder.

                                                     1925

Incident

(For Eric Walrond) [1]

Once riding in old Baltimore,
  Heart-filled, head-filled with glee,
I saw a Baltimorean
  Keep looking straight at me.

Now I was eight and very small,   5
  And he was no whit bigger,
And so I smiled, but he poked out
  His tongue, and called me, "Nigger."

I saw the whole of Baltimore
  From May until December;   10
Of all the things that happened there
  That's all that I remember.

                                                     1925

Saturday's Child [1]

Some are teethed on a silver spoon,
  With the stars strung for a rattle;
I cut my teeth as the black raccoon—
  For implements of battle.

Some are swaddled in silk and down,   5
  And heralded by a star; [2]
They swathed my limbs in a sackcloth gown
  On a night that was black as tar.

For some, godfather and goddame
  The opulent fairies be;   10
Dame Poverty gave me my name,
  And Pain godfathered me.

For I was born on Saturday—
  "Bad time for planting a seed,"
Was all my father had to say,   15
  And, "One mouth more to feed."

---

1. Author (1898–1966), who wrote *Tropic Death* (1926).
1. According to a popular nursery rhyme, "Satur-day's child works hard for his living."
2. According to Matthew 2:7–10, Jesus' birth was accompanied by the appearance of a new star.

Death cut the strings that gave me life,
And handed me to Sorrow,
The only kind of middle wife
My folks could beg or borrow.   20

                                                                1925

The Shroud of Color

(For Llewellyn Ransom)

"Lord, being dark," I said, "I cannot bear
The further touch of earth, the scented air;
Lord, being dark, forewilled to that despair
My color shrouds me in, I am as dirt
Beneath my brother's heel; there is a hurt   5
In all the simple joys which to a child
Are sweet; they are contaminate, defiled
By truths of wrongs the childish vision fails
To see; too great a cost this birth entails.
I strangle in this yoke drawn tighter than   10
The worth of bearing it, just to be man.
I am not brave enough to pay the price
In full; I lack the strength to sacrifice.
I who have burned my hands upon a star,
And climbed high hills at dawn to view the far   15
Illimitable wonderments of earth,
For whom all cups have dripped the wine of mirth,
For whom the sea has strained her honeyed throat
Till all the world was sea, and I a boat
Unmoored, on what strange quest I willed to float;   20
Who wore a many-colored coat[1] of dreams,
Thy gift, O Lord—I whom sun-dabbled streams
Have washed, whose bare brown thighs have held the sun
Incarcerate until his course was run,[2]
I who considered man a high-perfected   25
Glass where loveliness could lie reflected,
Now that I sway athwart Truth's deep abyss,
Denuding man for what he was and is,
Shall breath and being so inveigle me
That I can damn my dreams to hell, and be   30
Content, each new-born day, anew to see
The steaming crimson vintage of my youth
Incarnadine[3] the altar-slab of Truth?

Or hast Thou, Lord, somewhere I cannot see,
A lamb imprisoned in a bush for me?[4]   35

---

1. An allusion to Joseph's coat of many colors (Genesis 37:3).
2. Bathed in the sun from morning to night.
3. Stain red.

4. Just as Abraham was about to sacrifice his son, Isaac, God stopped him and told him to slaughter a ram caught in the bushes nearby instead (Genesis 22:12–13).

Not so? Then let me render one by one
Thy gifts, while still they shine; some little sun
Yet gilds these thighs; my coat, albeit worn,
Still hold its colors fast; albeit torn,
My heart will laugh a little yet, if I   40
May win of Thee this grace, Lord: on this high
And sacrificial hill 'twixt earth and sky,
To dream still pure all that I loved, and die.
There is no other way to keep secure
My wild chimeras,[5] grave-locked against the lure   45
Of Truth, the small hard teeth of worms, yet less
Envenomed than the mouth of Truth, will bless
Them into dust and happy nothingness.
Lord, Thou art God; and I, Lord, what am I
But dust? With dust my place. Lord, let me die."   50

Across the earth's warm, palpitating crust
I flung my body in embrace; I thrust
My mouth into the grass and sucked the dew,
Then gave it back in tears my anguish drew;
So hard I pressed against the ground, I felt   55
The smallest sandgrain like a knife, and smelt
The next year's flowering; all this to speed
My body's dissolution, fain to feed
The worms. And so I groaned, and spent my strength
Until, all passion spent, I lay full length   60
And quivered like a flayed and bleeding thing.

So lay till lifted on a great black wing
That had no mate nor flesh-apparent trunk
To hamper it; with me all time had sunk
Into oblivion; when I awoke   65
The wing hung poised above two cliffs that broke
The bowels of the earth in twain, and cleft
The seas apart. Below, above, to left,
To right, I saw what no man saw before:
Earth, hell, and heaven; sinew, vein, and core.   70
All things that swim or walk or creep or fly,
All things that live and hunger, faint and die,
Were made majestic then and magnified
By sight so clearly purged and deified.
The smallest bug that crawls was taller than   75
A tree, the mustard seed loomed like a man.
The earth that writhes eternally with pain
Of birth, and woe of taking back her slain,
Laid bare her teeming bosom to my sight,
And all was struggle, gasping breath, and fight.   80
A blind worm here dug tunnels to the light,
And there a seed, racked with heroic pain,
Thrust eager tentacles to sun and rain;
It climbed; it died; the old love conquered me

5. Imaginings; traditionally, a mythical creature having a lion's head, a goat's body, and a serpent's tail.

To weep the blossom it would never be.   85
But here a bud won light; it burst and flowered
Into a rose whose beauty challenged, "Coward!"
There was no thing alive save only I
That held life in contempt and longed to die.
And still I writhed and moaned, "The curse, the curse,   90
Than animated death, can death be worse?"

"Dark child of sorrow, mine no less, what art
Of mine can make thee see and play thy part?
The key to all strange things is in thy heart." [6]

What voice was this that coursed like liquid fire   95
Along my flesh, and turned my hair to wire?

I raised my burning eyes, beheld a field
All multitudinous with carnal yield,
A grim ensanguined [7] mead whereon I saw
Evolve the ancient fundamental law [8]   100
Of tooth and talon, fist and nail and claw.
There with the force of living, hostile hills
Whose clash the hemmed-in vale with clamor fills,
With greater din contended fierce majestic wills
Of beast with beast, of man with man, in strife   105
For love of what my heart despised, for life
That unto me at dawn was now a prayer
For night, at night a bloody heart-wrung tear
For day again; for *this*, these groans
From tangled flesh and interlocked bones.   110
And no thing died that did not give
A testimony that it longed to live.
Man, strange composite blend of brute and god,
Pushed on, nor backward glanced where last he trod:
He seemed to mount a misty ladder flung   115
Pendant from a cloud, yet never gained a rung
But at his feet another tugged and clung.
My heart was still a pool of bitterness,
Would yield nought else, nought else confess.
I spoke (although no form was there   120
To see, I knew an ear was there to hear),
"Well, let them fight; they *can* whose flesh is fair."

Crisp lightning flashed; a wave of thunder shook
My wing; a pause, and then a speaking, "Look."

I scarce dared trust my ears or eyes for awe   125
Of what they heard, and dread of what they saw;
For, privileged beyond degree, this flesh
Beheld God and His heaven in the mesh
Of Lucifer's revolt, [9] saw Lucifer

6. At this point, the speaker in the poem is cast
along the lines of a biblical prophet, such as Ezekiel, and presented with divine visions.
7. Bloodied.

8. I.e., of evolution, or survival of the fittest.
9. It is widely believed that Lucifer (the name of
the morning star as well as of Satan) led a revolt
against God just before the world was created.

Glow like the sun, and like a dulcimer   130
I heard his sin-sweet voice break on the yell
Of God's great warriors: Gabriel,
Saint Clair and Michael, Israfel and Raphael.
And strange it was to see God with His back
Against a wall, to see Christ hew and hack   135
Till Lucifer, pressed by the mighty pair,
And losing inch by inch, clawed at the air
With fevered wings; then, lost beyond repair,
He tricked a mass of stars [1] into his hair;
He filled his hands with stars, crying as he fell,   140
"A star's a star although it burns in hell."
So God was left to His divinity,
Omnipotent at that most costly fee.

There was a lesson here, but still the clod
In me was sycophant unto the rod,   145
And cried, "Why mock me thus? Am I a god?"

"One trial more: this failing, then I give
You leave to die; no further need to live."

Now suddenly a strange wild music smote
A chord long impotent in me; a note   150
Of jungles, primitive and subtle, throbbed
Against my echoing breast, and tom-toms sobbed
In every pulse-beat of my frame. The din
A hollow log bound with a python's skin
Can make wrought every nerve to ecstasy,   155
And I was wind and sky again, and sea,
And all sweet things that flourish, being free.

Till all at once the music changed its key.

And now it was of bitterness and death,
The cry the lash extorts, the broken breath   160
Of liberty enchained; and yet there ran
Through all a harmony of faith in man,
A knowledge all would end as it began.
All sights and sounds and aspects of my race
Accompanied this melody, kept pace   165
With it; with music all their hopes and hates
Were charged, not to be downed by all the fates.
And somehow it was borne upon my brain
How being dark, and living through the pain
Of it, is courage more than angels have. I knew   170
What storms and tumults lashed the tree that grew
This body that I was, this cringing I
That feared to contemplate a changing sky,
This that I grovelled, whining, "Let me die,"
While others struggled in Life's abattoir. [2]   175

1. The fallen third of the host of heaven that Satan   2. Slaughterhouse.
is reported to have enlisted on his side of the battle.

The cries of all dark people near or far
Were billowed over me, a mighty surge
Of suffering in which my puny grief must merge
And lose itself; I had no further claim to urge
For death; in shame I raised my dust-grimed head,   180
And though my lips moved not, God knew I said,
"Lord, not for what I saw in flesh or bone
Of fairer men; not raised on faith alone;
Lord, I will live persuaded by mine own.
I cannot play the recreant[3] to these;   185
My spirit has come home, that sailed the doubtful seas."
With the whiz of a sword that severs space,
The wing dropped down at a dizzy pace,
And flung me on my hill flat on my face;
Flat on my face I lay defying pain,   190
Glad of the blood in my smallest vein,
And in my hands I clutched a loyal dream,
Still spitting fire, bright twist and coil and gleam,
And chiseled like a hound's white tooth.
"Oh, I will match you yet," I cried, "to truth."   195

Right glad I was to stoop to what I once had spurned,
Glad even unto tears; I laughed aloud; I turned
Upon my back, and though the tears for joy would run,
My sight was clear; I looked and saw the rising sun.

                                                        1925

Heritage

(For Harold Jackman)[1]

What is Africa to me:
Copper sun or scarlet sea,
Jungle star or jungle track,
Strong bronzed men, or regal black
Women from whose loins I sprang   5
When the birds of Eden sang?
One three centuries removed
From the scenes his fathers loved,
Spicy grove, cinnamon tree,[2]
What is Africa to me?   10

So I lie, who all day long
Want no sound except the song
Sung by wild barbaric birds
Goading massive jungle herds,
Juggernauts of flesh that pass   15
Trampling tall defiant grass
Where young forest lovers lie,

---

3. Traitor.   2. Despite this line, the cinnamon tree is not na-
1. A Harlem schoolteacher (1900–1960), probably   tive to Africa.
Cullen's closest friend.

Plighting troth beneath the sky.
So I lie, who always hear,
Though I cram against my ear   20
Both my thumbs, and keep them there,
Great drums throbbing through the air.
So I lie, whose fount of pride,
Dear distress, and joy allied,
Is my somber flesh and skin,   25
With the dark blood dammed within
Like great pulsing tides of wine
That, I fear, must burst the fine
Channels of the chafing net
Where they surge and foam and fret.   30

Africa? A book one thumbs
Listlessly, till slumber comes.
Unremembered are her bats
Circling through the night, her cats
Crouching in the river reeds,   35
Stalking gentle flesh that feeds
By the river brink; no more
Does the bugle-throated roar
Cry that monarch[3] claws have leapt
From the scabbards where they slept.   40
Silver snakes that once a year
Doff the lovely coats you wear,
Seek no covert in your fear
Lest a mortal eye should see;
What's your nakedness to me?   45
Here no leprous flowers rear
Fierce corollas[4] in the air;
Here no bodies sleek and wet,
Dripping mingled rain and sweat,
Tread the savage measures of   50
Jungle boys and girls in love.
What is last year's snow to me,
Last year's anything? The tree
Budding yearly must forget
How its past arose or set—   55
Bough and blossom, flower, fruit,
Even what shy bird with mute
Wonder at her travail there,
Meekly labored in its hair.
One three centuries removed   60
From the scenes his fathers loved,
Spicy grove, cinnamon tree,
What is Africa to me?

So I lie, who find no peace
Night or day, no slight release   65
From the unremittant beat

---

3. Lion, king of the jungle.   4. The petals collectively.

Made by cruel padded feet
Walking through my body's street.
Up and down they go, and back,
Treading out a jungle track.   70
So I lie, who never quite
Safely sleep from rain at night—
I can never rest at all
When the rain begins to fall;
Like a soul gone mad with pain   75
I must match its weird refrain;
Ever must I twist and squirm,
Writhing like a baited worm,
While its primal measures drip
Through my body, crying, "Strip!   80
Doff this new exuberance.
Come and dance the Lover's Dance!"
In an old remembered way
Rain works on me night and day.

Quaint, outlandish heathen gods   85
Black men fashion out of rods,
Clay, and brittle bits of stone,
In a likeness like their own,
My conversion came high-priced;
I belong to Jesus Christ,   90
Preacher of humility;
Heathen gods are naught to me.

Father, Son, and Holy Ghost,
So I make an idle boast;
Jesus of the twice-turned cheek,   95
Lamb of God, although I speak
With my mouth thus, in my heart
Do I play a double part.
Ever at Thy glowing altar
Must my heart grow sick and falter,   100
Wishing He I served were black,
Thinking then it would not lack
Precedent of pain to guide it,
Let who would or might deride it;
Surely then this flesh would know   105
Yours had borne a kindred woe.
Lord, I fashion dark gods, too,
Daring even to give You
Dark despairing features where,
Crowned with dark rebellious hair,   110
Patience wavers just so much as
Mortal grief compels, while touches
Quick and hot, of anger, rise
To smitten cheek and weary eyes.
Lord, forgive me if my need   115
Sometimes shapes a human creed.
All day long and all night through,

One thing only must I do:
Quench my pride and cool my blood,
Lest I perish in the flood.   120
Lest a hidden ember set
Timber that I thought was wet
Burning like the dryest flax,
Melting like the merest wax,
Lest the grave restore its dead.   125
Not yet has my heart or head
In the least way realized
They and I are civilized.

                                                              1925

To John Keats, [1] Poet, at Spring Time

(For Carl Van Vechten) [2]

I cannot hold my peace, John Keats;
There never was a spring like this;
It is an echo, that repeats
My last year's song and next year's bliss.
I know, in spite of all men say   5
Of Beauty, you have felt her most.
Yea, even in your grave her way
Is laid. Poor, troubled, lyric ghost,
Spring never was so fair and dear
As Beauty makes her seem this year.   10

I cannot hold my peace, John Keats,
I am as helpless in the toil
Of Spring as any lamb that bleats
To feel the solid earth recoil
Beneath his puny legs. Spring beats   15
Her tocsin [3] call to those who love her,
And lo! the dogwood petals cover
Her breast with drifts of snow, and sleek
White gulls fly screaming to her, and hover
About her shoulders, and kiss her cheek,   20
While white and purple lilacs muster
A strength that bears them to a cluster
Of color and odor; for her sake
All things that slept are now awake.

And you and I, shall we lie still,   25
John Keats, while Beauty summons us?
Somehow I feel your sensitive will
Is pulsing up some tremulous
Sap road of a maple tree, whose leaves
Grow music as they grow, since your   30
Wild voice is in them, a harp that grieves

---

1. English Romantic poet (1795–1821).   3. An alarm sounded on a bell.
2. Writer and photographer (1880–1964).

For life that opens death's dark door.
Though dust, your fingers still can push
The Vision Splendid to a birth,
Though now they work as grass in the hush   35
Of the night on the broad sweet page of the earth.

"John Keats is dead," they say, but I
Who hear your full insistent cry
In bud and blossom, leaf and tree,
Know John Keats still writes poetry.   40
And while my head is earthward bowed
To read new life sprung from your shroud,
Folks seeing me must think it strange
That merely spring should so derange
My mind. They do not know that you,   45
John Keats, keep revel with me, too.

                                                        1925

From the Dark Tower

(To Charles S. Johnson) [1]

We shall not always plant while others reap
The golden increment of bursting fruit,
Not always countenance, abject and mute,
That lesser men should hold their brothers cheap;
Not everlastingly while others sleep   5
Shall we beguile their limbs with mellow flute, [2]
Not always bend to some more subtle brute;
We were not made eternally to weep.

The night whose sable breast relieves the stark,
White stars is no less lovely being dark,   10
And there are buds that cannot bloom at all
In light, but crumple, piteous, and fall;
So in the dark we hide the heart that bleeds,
And wait, and tend our agonizing seeds.

                                                        1927

1. Founder and editor of *Opportunity* magazine   2. Relax them with music.
(1893–1956).

HELENE JOHNSON

1907–1995

The youngest of the poets associated with the Harlem Renaissance, Helen Johnson
(her pen name, Helene, was suggested to her by an aunt) was born in Boston, where
she attended public schools and, for a time, Boston University. She came to New
York in 1926 for *Opportunity* magazine's annual award ceremony for the winners
of its poetry contest, in which she had earned honorable mention, and stayed.

When she moved into the only apartment building in mid-Manhattan that allowed black tenants, another tenant was Zora Neale Hurston, and the two quickly became friends. Johnson was also helped by her closeness to her cousin Dorothy West and later to Gwendolyn Bennett, both prominent figures in the Harlem Renaissance.

Johnson's early years in New York were the most productive of her life. She published work in numerous magazines and anthologies, including *Opportunity, Vanity Fair, Fire!!,* and Cullen's *Caroling Dusk.* However, with her marriage (to William Warner Hubbell) and particularly after the birth of her daughter, Abigail, in 1940, Johnson wrote less. After she and her husband separated, Johnson returned to Massachusetts for some years before failing health brought her back to Manhattan, where she died. Of her own writings, she largely agreed with her critics in seeing the two dozen or so poems that she published in the late 1920s and early 1930s as her strongest work. Her poetry is marked by an often lovely lyricism in which a genteel sensuality and a usually muted expression of racial pride are blended.

Poem

Little brown boy,
Slim, dark, big-eyed,
Crooning love songs to your banjo
Down at the Lafayette [1]
Gee, boy, I love the way you hold your head,   5
High sort of and a bit to one side,
Like a prince, a jazz prince. And I love
Your eyes flashing, and your hands,
And your patent-leathered feet,

And your shoulders jerking the jig-wa. [2]   10
And I love your teeth flashing,
And the way your hair shines in the spotlight
Like it was the real stuff.
Gee, brown boy, I loves you all over.
I'm glad I'm a jig. [3] I'm glad I can   15
Understand your dancin' and your
Singin', and feel all the happiness
And joy and don't-care in you.
Gee, boy, when you sing, I can close my ears
And hear tomtoms just as plain.   20
Listen to me, will you, what do I know
About tomtoms? But I like the word, sort of,
Don't you? It belongs to us.
Gee, boy, I love the way you hold your head,
And the way you sing and dance,   25
And everything.
Say, I think you're wonderful. You're
All right with me,
You are.

1927

1. The Lafayette Theatre on 132nd Street and Seventh Avenue in New York. 2. A dance.
3. A black person.

Sonnet to a Negro in Harlem

You are disdainful and magnificent—
Your perfect body and your pompous gait,
Your dark eyes flashing solemnly with hate,
Small wonder that you are incompetent
To imitate those whom you so despise—   5
Your shoulders towering high above the throng,
Your head thrown back in rich, barbaric song,
Palm trees and mangoes stretched before your eyes.
Let others toil and sweat for labor's sake
And wring from grasping hands their meed [1] of gold.   10
Why urge ahead your supercilious feet?
Scorn will efface each footprint that you make.
I love your laughter arrogant and bold.
You are too splendid for this city street.

                                                                1927

Remember Not

Remember not the promises we made
In this same garden many moons ago.
You must forget them. I would have it so.
Old vows are like old flowers as they fade
And vaguely vanish in a feeble death.   5
There is no reason why your hands should clutch
At pretty yesterdays. There is not much
Of beauty in me now. And though my breath
Is quick, my body sentient, my heart
Attuned to romance as before, you must   10
Not, through mistaken chivalry, pretend
To love me still. There is no mortal art
Can overcome Time's deep, corroding rust.
Let Love's beginning expiate Love's end.

                                                                1931

Invocation

Let me be buried in the rain
In a deep, dripping wood,
Under the warm wet breast of Earth
Where once a gnarled tree stood.
And paint a picture on my tomb   5
With dirt and a piece of bough
Of a girl and a boy beneath a round, ripe moon
Eating of love with an eager spoon
And vowing an eager vow.

1. Reward.

1317

And do not keep my plot mowed smooth   10
And clean as a spinster's bed,
But let the weed, the flower, the tree,
Riotous, rampant, wild and free,
Grow high above my head.

1931

Realism, Naturalism, Modernism

1940-1960

The two decades between 1940 and 1960 comprise a watershed epoch in African American letters, though we could use Ralph Ellison's comment about jazz criticism to capture the essence of this period: it "exist[s] in a curious state of history and prehistory simultaneously." Conventionally plotted in terms of literary giants who authored legendary works, a more complete history of this period would reveal a broad swath of literary activity that cannot be contained in traditional categories of genre, mode, and subject. For example, the rich and complex store of writings that blacks contributed to magazines has seldom found its way into the familiar syntheses of this period's currents and crosscurrents; yet many black magazines, such as *Crisis*, *Opportunity*, and *The Negro Quarterly*, gave a hearing as well as small financial incentives to black writers who were otherwise closed out of mass circulation magazines.

By the same token, standard literary histories, which tend to focus exclusively on the traditional genres of narrative, poetry, and drama in their "high-cultural" varieties, obscure the range of popular cultural forms in which African American writers achieved considerable successes. Chester Himes and Frank Yerby, for instance, were among the few writers of the period whose ambitions ran to popular fiction. After publishing two serious novels to respectable notice, Himes turned to writing detective stories that were widely successful in France, though less so in the United States. Similarly, Yerby aspired to write what most of his critics regarded, invidiously, as "pulp" or "escape" fiction. Yerby preferred to categorize his more than thirty popular novels, including the best-selling *The Foxes of Harrow* (1946), as "costume novels" and defended their importance to readers who needed occasional "escape" from the "sprawling messiness" and "shapelessness of modern existence." Judging from the texts that have achieved canonical status, however, these were times that called not for escape from but for confrontation with life in all its "sprawling messiness."

MIGRATION, DESEGREGATION, AND SOCIAL CHANGE

African American writers certainly found a sprawling mess of raw material from which to draw during the years between 1940 and 1960, from the atomic explosions and fascism of World War II to social revolution and many other cataclysms in between. Among the events marking these decades are the second wave of the Great Migration from South to North that sent approximately five and a half mil-

lion black people from impoverished farms and hamlets into the major war industries, dubbed by Franklin D. Roosevelt the Arsenal of Democracy; Truman's creation of the Commission on Civil Rights in 1947; the fall of colonialism, which
ended European domination of Africa and resulted in the establishment of numerous independent republics, among them Ghana, Nigeria, Senegal, and Algeria; the
U.S. Supreme Court's May 1954 ruling on *Brown v. the Topeka Board of Education*, which desegregated public schools; and, ironically, in the Cradle of the Confederacy, the Montgomery, Alabama, Bus Boycott in December 1955, ushering in
what came to be called the "nonviolent protest movement." Led by the young Martin Luther King Jr., the movement succeeded in tumbling the walls of the U.S.
system of apartheid and the "separate but equal" laws that buttressed it.

But this list of public events cannot be separated from the social, political, and
cultural currents it reflected and influenced. No consideration of the Great Migration, for example, is complete without a discussion of the labor conflicts, class antagonisms, and housing discrimination it created or, for that matter, without a
discussion of the explosion of a black urban street culture that transformed mainstream white culture. The vogue of the zoot suit, which crossed racial lines to be
imitated by white youth, along with many elements of "bop" or "hip talk," must
also be noted. Termed by some the "new poetry of the proletariat," this language of
hip, which resulted from a people's movement from southern rural plantations into
the cities of the north, introduced a distinctly urban idiom into the American language. This new black urban aesthetic, in which some have seen resistance to racial
discrimination, is arguably one of the most significant developments in the history
of African American culture. Even without hip talk, an urban sensibility defines the
literature that African Americans produced between 1940 and 1960. It is saturated
with the signs, sights, and sounds of the city, beginning in 1940 with Richard
Wright's publishing sensation *Native Son*.

URBAN REALISM

At least in strictly literary terms, Wright's novel christened the decade in 1940. A
Book-of-the-Month Club selection, *Native Son* made Wright the first African
American writer to receive both critical acclaim and commercial success simultaneously. Close on the heels of Wright's success, other African American writers
garnered recognition and prestige from a predominantly white literary world that
had historically been stingy in awarding its favors to black writers. Margaret Walker
won the Yale Younger Poets Award for *For My People* in 1942; Gwendolyn Brooks,
the Pulitzer Prize for *Annie Allen* in 1950; Ralph Ellison, the National Book Award
for *Invisible Man* in 1952; and closing out the era was Lorraine Hansberry's stunning New York Drama Critics Circle Award for *A Raisin in the Sun* in 1959.

In the minds of many, to Wright was owed much of the credit for paving the way
for these successes as well as for creating publishing opportunities for many black
writers, directly and indirectly. The support and assistance he gave black writers is
well documented. He helped James Baldwin win a Rosenwald Fellowship; read
and encouraged the poetry of Margaret Walker; favorably reviewed Chester
Himes's first novel, *If He Hollers Let Him Go*; and helped Gwendolyn Brooks to
place her first volume of poetry, *A Street in Bronzeville*. But critics such as Irving
Howe have claimed for Wright much more than this. Invoking the rhetoric of mil-
lenialism, Howe proclaimed: "The day *Native Son* appeared, American culture
was changed forever. . . . It made impossible a repetition of the old lies. . . . [Wright]
brought out into the open, as no one ever had before, the hatred, fear and violence
that have crippled and may yet destroy our culture."

Standard histories and chronologies of African American literature have agreed with the spirit if not the letter of Howe's judgment of Richard Wright's *Native Son* and its impact on African American letters of the post–World War II era. According to John Henrik Clarke, for example, "After the emergence of Richard Wright, the period of indulgence for Negro writers was over. . . . The era of the patronized and pampered black writer had at last come to an end." Presumably, the era to which Clarke referred was the Harlem Renaissance.

This 1920s and 1930s efflorescence of activity in all branches of the arts, the Harlem Renaissance, has tended to be judged harshly in most retrospective accounts of the period, including Wright's own famous assessment in *Blueprint for Negro Writing*. Indeed Clark could have taken his wording directly from Wright's famous opening statement: "Generally speaking, Negro writing in the past has been confined to humble novels, poems, and plays, prim and decorous ambassadors who went a-begging to white America. They entered the court of American public opinion dressed in the knee pants of servility, curtsying to show that the Negro was not inferior." Alain Locke, the self-appointed dean of Harlem Renaissance letters, published his *Spiritual Truancy* in the same issue of *New Challenge* (Fall 1937) in which Wright's *Blueprint* appeared. There he described Harlem Renaissance writers as "aesthetic wastrels," given to a decadent and "exhibitionist flair." While they should have addressed themselves to the "people themselves," he continued, they played to a "gallery of faddist negrophiles." To the "present younger generation of Negro writers," Locke issued the vague challenge to discover the "undiscovered and dormant" "group soul." And reinforcing Wright's manifesto, Locke called for black writers to forsake bourgeois privilege and comfort for the larger rewards—literary and social alike—of the collective good.

At least in his early and critically most significant work, Wright, in effect, rose to execute his own blueprint by rejecting what Locke saw as the "decadent aestheticism" of Harlem Renaissance writers and by turning to the "nourishing" formula of Marxism and social protest. He sent "the word" into battle and stamped his vision of African American culture on this new and necessary era in African American letters. Despite its urban, "secular" impulses, that vision was actually an extension of the didactic, declamatory utterances found in the black sermon and historically linked to the narratives of enslavement. In other words, although Wright defied his grandmother's Seventh-Day Adventist religion (as Bigger did the "old time" religion of his mother in *Native Son*), he was wed no less to the Protestant passions of testifying and truth telling in his portrait of a young modern man alienated in the city. Few critics have observed this tension in Wright. The opinion widely shared, then as now, was that Wright's *Native Son* had single-handedly birthed and shaped a new agenda, establishing for African American writing a center of gravity that combined a gritty urban realism with a "lyrical" naturalism that documented the harsh realities of urban living for black Americans.

Both the novel and *How Bigger Was Born*, the essay that explained the genesis of his famous character, go far to document the attraction that the Chicago School of Urban Sociology held for Wright. According to its theories, Bigger Thomas is the victim of a raw environmental determinism, a "juvenile delinquent" mired in the unforgiving straits of urban blight and deprivation. It was Wright's mission to document these conditions, a documentation that came to be regarded as perhaps the highest form of "social protest."

Social protest certainly did not originate with Wright—a current of social consciousness had long flowed through African American letters. It was there in the narratives of enslavement and in the Harlem Renaissance debates. Du Bois's write-in symposium, "The Negro in Art: How Shall He Be Portrayed," generated a controversy about the relative merits of "art" versus "propaganda" or "protest," and Langston Hughes's famous manifesto *The Negro Artist and the Racial Mountain* kept alive debates over what aspects of black American experience were suitable for literary treatment, in what proportions and aesthetic forms. But with the emergence of Richard Wright, the battle over the contents and aesthetics of African American writing seemed momentarily to be won and decided: black art and "social protest" must be synonymous. This elevation of protest to a category of aesthetic value far outlived the decade of the 1940s and came to be reflexively applied to a range of writers as diverse as William Attaway, Chester Himes, Frank Yerby, and Ann Petry.

Despite their differences, they are often linked together in what some critics have termed the "Wright School." To yoke these writers together as direct descendants of Wright who simply cribbed from him their themes and techniques is misleading. To be sure, recognizable elements of realism and naturalism are to be found in their work, but they all brought to these traditions their own distinctive variations, blending them with a variety of narrative forms and modes, from both popular and nonpopular genres. Despite these and other qualifications, the twin ideas of Richard Wright as the literary lodestone of the 1940s (a view based almost solely on the success of Native Son) and protest fiction as the narrative mode of black writers, and thus a racial litmus test, have been difficult to dislodge.

The imprint of Wright's early style shows most plainly in the writings of another Mississippi-born writer, William Attaway, who became friends with Wright while both were involved in the Federal Writers' Project of Illinois. Attaway's second and most accomplished novel, Blood on the Forge, was published in 1941, the same year as Wright's Twelve Million Black Voices, and like Wright's phototext, it dramatized the Great Migration from the agrarian South to the industrial North just after World War I. Blood on the Forge was rated one of the most complex treatments of the exploitation of black American workers caught in the maw of northern steel mills and locked in a losing competition with white and immigrant labor in a market that pitted each group against the other.

Chester Himes's association with the labor movement also figures in his two most significant novels of the 1940s: The Lonely Crusade (1947), an account of a labor organizer who fights against racial discrimination in the unions, and If He Hollers Let Him Go (1945), the best known and most successful, the story of an educated, northern Negro set against poor southern whites in a Los Angeles shipyard during war time. Accused of raping a white woman, the protagonist is ultimately defeated by the powerful and intractable tradition of sexual racism.

Largely on the basis of its urban setting and naturalistic mode, Ann Petry's first novel, The Street (1946), is frequently likened to Native Son. While the comparison is apt, it overlooks those aspects of Petry's novel that not only set it apart from Wright's but might also be read as a radical negation of Native Son. At the end of The Street, when the female protagonist bludgeons to death a man who has tried to exploit her, Petry can be said to redress the murders of two women in Native Son, which are figured as essential to Bigger Thomas's emergent creativity. But more important, to insist too rigidly on Petry's indebtedness to Wright is to overlook the impressive artistry of Petry's own work. Not just in The Street but also in The Narrows and Country Place, Petry makes masterful use of pacing and suspense, of details of scenery, and of concealed narration that move her beyond any narrow notions of naturalism as well as beyond the category of social protest. To read her novels in the context of her era is to be apprised of stylistic continuities she shares with such 1920s and 1930s writers as Nella Larsen and Jessie Fauset.

This notion, then, of Wright as progenitor of a new era in African American letters ignores much that is significant about the two decades of this section, both in terms of literary productivity and in terms of the zeitgeist in which it participated. Make no mistake. Black American writing was indeed shifting away from the expression of black middle-class ideals that Wright had harshly indicted and giving way to those of the black working class. But class consciousness was not the only order of business in the 1940s literary world, or Richard Wright the only agent of change.

Due largely to the effects of the Depression many black writers found the brutal realism and naturalism that quickened Wright's socially conscious art essential to their own literary goals and philosophies, but others found social realism both philosophically limited and aesthetically restrictive, including Ralph Ellison. In his 1941 essay *Recent Negro Fiction*, published in *New Masses*, Ellison had made large, enthusiastic claims for *Native Son* as forerunner and literary paradigm. In his words, it "represent[ed] the take-off in a leap which promise[d] to carry over a whole tradition, and mark[ed] the merging of the imaginative depiction of American Negro life into the broad stream of American literature." But by the time he published *Invisible Man*, a little more than ten years later, Ellison had distanced himself from this early opinion, and *Native Son* seemed no longer to mark for the Negro writer a "path which he might follow to reach maturity."

ELLISON AND BLACK MODERNIST FICTION

Many critics attribute the turn away from Wright's brand of urban realism as a turn toward a vision of integration as a social ideal. Indeed, as the 1940s drew to a close, writers—among them, Petry, Zora Neale Hurston, Willard Motley—who came of age during the Depression demonstrated this "integrationist" temper by turning to what some critics have inadequately termed "non-Negro" or nonracial subject matter. So labeled simply because of an absence of black characters and black urban settings, this fiction included Petry's novels *Country Place* (1947) and *The Narrows* (1953), set in New England. While some critics have commended this shift and have seen it as evidence of artistic maturation beyond the urban realism and sociological determinism of her first novel, others regard both these novels as much less riveting and powerful than *The Street*. For most critics, though, the turn from urban realism had more to do with the exhaustion of the mode itself.

The publication of James Baldwin's essay *Everybody's Protest Novel* (1949) in the *Partisan Review* contributed to that opinion, although it did little injury to Wright's status overall. It took the success of *Invisible Man* to give further impetus to those writers already wrestling with and wriggling out from under the narrative straitjacket of realism and naturalism. As Ellison put it in *Brave Words for a Startling Occasion*, his address at the ceremony of the National Book Award in 1952, "the very 'facts' which the naturalists assumed would make us free have lost the power to protect us from despair." He went on to state that the "tight well-made Jamesian novel" and the "hard boiled" novel alike were "too restricted to contain the experience which I knew. The diversity of American life with its extreme fluidity and openness seemed too vital and alive to be caught for more than the briefest instant" by these forms. Without naming either Wright or his alleged "descendants," Ellison admitted that, in the course of writing *Invisible Man*, he was "forced to conceive of a novel unburdened by the narrow naturalism which has led, after so many triumphs, to the final and unrelieved despair which marks so much of our current fiction." As a result, his novel reflected what Ellison described as a more "experimental attitude," designed to combine a commitment to "social responsibility" with a studied attention to the novel as a form. This latter effort, Ellison maintained, was fueled for him as much by reading Marx, Malraux, Freud, Eliot, Pound, Stein, and Hemingway as by reading Richard Wright, James Baldwin, and Langston Hughes and by listening to the blues and jazz.

It is a critical commonplace that with *Invisible Man*, African American writers came to grips with the aims and provocations of modernism. But, of course, if that concept is used to refer to rigorous attention to stylistic detail, to distortions of "reality," to fragmentation of the human image, then Jean Toomer's *Cane* (1923) and

Nella Larsen's *Quicksand* and *Passing* (1929) would have to be considered precursors to Ellison's *Invisible Man* as would Langston Hughes's *The Weary Blues* (1926), Melvin Tolson's *Libretto for the Republic of Liberia*, and Gwendolyn Brooks's *Anniad* or *In the Mecca*. If we move beyond the confines of African American letters, when and where to draw the modernist map gets still more complicated. Although not technically considered modernist, Emily Dickinson's poetry and Herman Melville's fiction are not easily eliminated from the rubric, which thus shows itself as a timeless disposition, casting a crooked shape that defies straight-line delineation and accounting.

However it is mapped, few would deny that Ellison belongs squarely within its borders. For being situated there, he suffered severe attacks from critics who found his acknowledged indebtedness to the Western modernist tradition necessarily opposed to African American cultural values. His critics objected most to those resonances in Ellison of writers, Ezra Pound chief among them, whose work has been associated with fascism, racism, and elitism. Ellison sustained one of his most stinging blows from Irving Howe, who, in a famous essay, *Black Boys and Native Sons*, condemned both Ellison and Baldwin for failing to be "protest writers," an ideal he saw embodied most perfectly in Richard Wright.

Ellison's equally famous response to Howe, *The World and the Jug*, riffed on Howe's family metaphors to reject the notion of Richard Wright as literary father. Drawing a controversial distinction, Ellison explained that while "one can do nothing about choosing one's relatives, one can, as artist, choose one's 'ancestors.' Wright was . . . a 'relative'; Hemingway an 'ancestor.' " Even given this pronouncement, it would be a mistake to read Ellison's words as a rejection of African American influences, for *Invisible Man* draws on black lore and legend, spirituals, and the blues. Indeed, in the very prologue of the novel, the protagonist listens to Louis Armstrong's "What Did I Do to Be So Black and Blue." With this and other rich allusions, he mixes writings and references from the American Renaissance, especially those that establish the cultural pluralism that makes "America" and defies any notions of national unity and consensus.

Despite the mutually supportive relationship that they enjoyed in the beginnings of James Baldwin's career, Baldwin too tried to dissociate himself from the vision of Richard Wright, although his first novel, *Go Tell It on the Mountain* (1953), thematically fusing religious fundamentalism, collective guilt, and the psychodynamics of family life, owes much to Wright's own brand of naturalism. Similarly, Baldwin's most celebrated essays are steeped in the fiery rhetoric of Protestantism and "truth telling" that Wright could not renounce.

The plots of African American literary history based on prose forms of socialist realism and focused on the public quarrels between Wright, Baldwin, and Ellison constitute a "brotherhood" narrative from which women are exiled. As the critic Mary Helen Washington has put it, "the real 'invisible man' of the 1950s was the black woman." Gwendolyn Brooks's *Maud Martha* and Paule Marshall's *Brown Girl, Brownstones* (1959) were two exceptions to an era in which the contributions of black women in prose fiction went largely unnoticed, except in passing. And even Brooks's novel *Maud Martha*, following on the heels of *Annie Allen*, her Pulitzer Prize–winning volume of poems and published a year after Ellison's in 1953, received only belittling treatment that ensured its critical neglect.

POETRY

The poetry published between 1940 and 1960 defies the categories and complicates the debates that issue from too keen a focus on this period's narrative forms. When we confront the poetry of Gwendolyn Brooks and her most highly regarded contemporaries—Margaret Walker, Melvin Tolson, and Robert Hayden—the bearded debates about realism and naturalism versus modernism, protest versus "quiescence," quickly show their threadbare edges. Critics have been slow, however, to leave these debates behind.

The last lines of *For My People*, the title poem of Margaret Walker's prizewinning volume, are frequently quoted to support the premise that Walker keeps a militant protest tradition alive: "Let the martial songs be written, let the dirges disappear. Let a race of men now rise and take control!" But these lines provide far from a total summary of the volume. Little critical attention has focused on the folk ballads of the volume's second half, and even less on its studied language, drawn from biblical poetry and Southern Baptist preaching. Breathless stanzaic forms and word collages in the first half of the volume have been likened to Whitman; its free verse, to Carl Sandburg; and the folk ballads of the volume's second half, to Sterling Brown's *Southern Road*.

A similar confluence runs through Gwendolyn Brooks's first volume of poetry, *A Street in Bronzeville* (1945). What Brooks herself describes as "folksy narrative" in the volume's ballads runs alongside the conventions of Italian and English sonnet forms employed in *Gay Chaps at the Bar*, the sonnet sequence on World War II. Again, because the first part of the volume focuses on poor blacks in the kitchenettes and vacant lots of Chicago's South Side, Brooks has been linked to Richard Wright and to the realism and naturalism associated with his art. Praised for taking her poetry to the ghetto streets of Chicago and capturing its sounds and rhythms, its smells of "onion fumes," of garbage "ripening in the hall," *A Street in Bronzeville* widens its frame beyond Bronzeville to touch on the global realities of war and the spreading shadow of fascism.

Brooks describes *Annie Allen* (1949), for which she won the Pulitzer Prize, as an extensive experiment, written to "*prove* that [she] could write *well*." The experiment resulted, in her view, in "some rather artificial poetry," especially the *Anniad*, which she judged "just an exercise, just an exercise." Few have concurred with Brooks's opinion that *Annie Allen* is merely an exercise in conventional poetics. While she demonstrated technical surety with a range of conventional poetic forms—the lyric, ballad, sonnet—she also showed a willingness to challenge them, especially the gendered limitations of the traditional sonnet form.

Writing in an era when American poetry was highly intellectualized and academic, Brooks's studied attention to form and technical craftsmanship links her with Melvin Tolson and Robert Hayden. The three are frequently grouped together as poets conscious of technique and fluent with such modern experimental poets as Hart Crane, Eliot, and Yeats. Unlike Brooks, however, Tolson and Hayden are disparaged as library poets who read without discrimination and self-consciously paraded their schooling in their verse. Such an assessment seems much more befitting Tolson than Hayden, whose poetry, however densely allusive and studiously attentive to craft, is full of passionate simplicity, much derived from black folk history.

Critics generally consider Tolson's first volume, *Rendezvous with America* (1944), the most "accessible" of Tolson's work, while noting that its elite and mannered form and close-lipped control seem inconsistent with its rebellious and populist convictions, although the opening sections of *Rendezvous* show him engaging Whitman's populist vision as well as Emily Dickinson's compressed syntax and understatement. An academic who admitted to reading and absorbing the techniques of Eliot, Pound, Yeats, Baudelaire, and all those he termed "the great moderns," Tolson described modernism as a "historical inevitability," observing that "When T. S. Eliot published *The Waste Land* in 1922 . . . the victory of the moderns was complete. . . . The modern idiom is here to stay—like modern physics." For statements such as these and for the erudition of his poems, Tolson's severest critics dismiss the learned aspects of his work as intellectual exhibition that reached its outer limits in *Libretto for the Republic of Liberia* (1953).

When Tolson published *Rendezvous with America*, World War II was reducing the cities of Europe to rubble. For *The Idols of the Tribe*, one of the volume's most successful poems, he chose as the epigraph a passage from Hitler's *Mein Kampf*: "A State which, in the epoch of race poisoning, dedicates itself to the cherishing of its best racial elements, must some day be master of the world." Tolson's war sonnets in this first volume invite comparison to Brooks's sonnet sequence at the end of *A Street in Bronzeville*. In addition to this thematic connection, both employ forms and imagery from popular culture—Tolson, the propaganda of World War II poster art; Brooks, the rough-riding heroic cowboy (or "chap"), a cultural figure that gave way to the image of the American soldier-as-hero.

The careers of Brooks, Hayden, Tolson, and Walker had their beginnings in the 1940s, but their poetic output extended through to the Black Arts movement of the 1960s and beyond. Still other poets, Langston Hughes, for example, who had their beginnings in the Harlem Renaissance, likewise spilled over into the 1940–60 period and beyond. Hughes published three volumes of poetry in the 1940s and two in the 1950s, including his jazz-influenced *Montage of a Dream Deferred* (1951), which contains *Harlem*, one of his most anthologized poems. The poem's haunting, opening question, "What happens to a dream deferred?" is one of the most popular lines in all of African American poetry. From its line "Does it dry up like a raisin in the sun?" Lorraine Hansberry took the title of her play *A Raisin in the Sun* (1959).

DRAMA

While Hansberry's *Raisin in the Sun* began the longest run on Broadway of any drama written by a black American up to that time, throughout the 1930s and 1940s blacks were increasingly found to have appeal and significance as dramatic subjects, capable of attracting the playgoing public and ensuring a sizable financial return. The establishment of the American Negro Theater (ANT) in 1940 made that decade unusual in African American theater history. Conceived as an experimental community theater in Harlem, the ANT produced several original scripts in its roughly ten-year existence, including *On Striver's Row*, its inaugural production, written by Abram Hill, one of the theater's founders. *Native Son: A Biography of a Young American* (1941) by Richard Wright and Paul Green, the stage adaptation of Wright's *Native Son*, produced by Orson Welles's Mercury Theater, enjoyed a short run on Broadway. Langston Hughes continued playwrighting with *The Sun Do Move* (1942) and *Simply Heavenly* (1957), the latter, based on his book *Simple Takes a Wife* (1957). James Baldwin's *The Amen Corner* opened at Howard University in 1956, and Alice Childress's *Trouble in Mind* won an Obie Award in 1955 for best original off-Broadway play.

Only ten plays written totally or partly by black Americans were produced on Broadway from 1926 until 1959, when Hansberry's *A Raisin in the Sun* took the theater establishment by storm, winning the New York Drama Critics Award over entries by such long-established playwrights as Eugene O'Neill and Tennessee Williams. Though written at a moment when visions of an integrated society were brought closer to reality by such landmark decisions as *Brown v. the Topeka Board of Education* and the success of the Montgomery Bus Boycott, *A Raisin in the Sun* anticipated many of the concerns of what would come to be the Black Arts movement, for example, Hansberry's explorations of the African roots of African American identity and culture. But in the opinions of Hansberry's detractors, such concerns constituted mere gestures in a drama whose dominant impulses were integrationist and integrationist at a time when even James Baldwin had given up on the promises of a racially integrated America. Returning to his signature poetics of apocalypse, he had asked why any black American would want to be integrated into a burning house, since that would be tantamount to death. Or as he put it to his biographer, Fern Eckman: "I don't want to be fitted into this society . . . I would rather be *dead*. In fact, there's no difference between being fitted into this society and *dying*."

PROPHETS OF A NEW DAY

Making similar use of apocalyptic imagery, other black writers served notice that yet another era in black letters was emerging. Importantly, the apocalypse they heralded was not in Baldwin's Old Testament scheme but one that would be the work of their own hands. In the famous words of one of their idols, Malcolm X, whom they called the "fire prophet," they would force revolution "by any means necessary." These writers would come to be the "prophets of a new day," to borrow the title of Margaret Walker's volume of verse. One such self-styled prophet was Amiri Baraka (LeRoi Jones), whose poem *Black Art*, from his volume *Black Magic Poetry*, set much of the pace, form, and violent tone of the "new" black literature of the 1960s.

> We want "poems that kill."
> Assassin poems, Poems that shoot
> guns. Poems that wrestle cops into alleys
> and take their weapons leaving them dead
> with tongues pulled out and sent to Ireland.

Baraka's desire for "killing poems" hearkened back to Richard Wright's desire for "words as weapons," for art in the service of a struggle for human liberation.

While some writers of the previous generation resisted the aesthetics and ideology of these new prophets, others, most notably Margaret Walker and Gwendolyn Brooks, sought a rapprochement. Brooks's involvement in poetry workshops with the Blackstone Rangers, a Chicago youth gang, and her expressed desire to get poetry, in her words, into "tavern atmosphere[s], on street corners," and in prisons are examples of this outreach. This new activism was reflected in Brooks's decision to leave her New York publishers and have her work published by black publishers, especially Broadside Press. From this period came several volumes, including *In the Mecca* (1968), *Riot* (1969), *Family Pictures* (1970), and *The Near-Johannesburg Boy, and Other Poems* (1986).

Because black writers of the 1940–60 generation had earned their stripes, so to speak, in the American market of letters and had garnered a considerable degree of public success and recognition, it could be said that they opened a frontier on the future that the Harlem Renaissance generation had barely begun to perceive. Though it would be wrong here to posit a narrative of progress in which every round of writers gets "higher and higher," it seems plausible to argue that 1940–60 constitutes the first full literary fruit of African American culture. Unlike their Harlem Renaissance predecessors, the writers of this period were certain of one fundamental thing: America was not always ready to make good on its democratic claims. At the same time, democracy could neither anticipate nor impede the production of black letters. With this generation of writers, black readers in particular were summoned to confront new literary realities, a bracing new tenor of change, whose echoes we occasionally hear as far away from its source as David Bradley's *Chaneysville Incident* (1981). This 1940–60 generation offers quite likely our most powerful cluster of texts and propositions in the post–World War II period.

MELVIN B. TOLSON

1900?–1966

If this anthology does nothing more than recover the works of Melvin B. Tolson to a wider audience, that alone will justify its existence. Reading Tolson allows one to explore modernist poetics from an African American cultural stance. Like Ralph Ellison and Gwendolyn Brooks, Tolson grew up on an American frontier; like Langston Hughes, he witnessed the later stages of the civil rights movement; and like modernist practitioners before him, he exploited poetic traditions.

Born February 6, 1900, in Moberly, Missouri, to the Reverend Alonzo Tolson and Lera Hurt Tolson, Tolson was raised in a Methodist Episcopal household, with a father who had taught himself classical languages. As the reverend took different churches, the Tolsons moved around a circuit of small midwestern towns. It was in the local newspaper of Oskaloosa, Iowa, that Tolson, fourteen years old, published his first poem, on the sinking of the *Titanic*. Tolson moved with his family in 1916 to Kansas City, Missouri, where he was elected senior class poet. He spent one year at Fisk University, but transferred the next to Lincoln University in Lincoln, Pennsylvania; there he acquired impressive skills in debating and public speaking and met his future wife, Ruth Southall. They were married on January 29, 1922, and a year and a half later, Tolson graduated with a bachelor's degree. Shortly thereafter, Melvin B. Tolson Jr. was born, the first of their four children.

Throughout the 1920s, Tolson taught at Wiley College in Marshall, Texas, where he coached the debating team and published adventure stories in the Wiley *Wild Cat*. With the advent of the Depression, he moved his family to his parents' home in Kansas City, and during a 1931–32 sabbatical from Wiley, he enrolled in a master's program in comparative literature at Columbia University in New York City, producing a thesis on the Harlem Renaissance. During that year, Tolson began writing his first book of poems, *Gallery of Harlem Portraits*, or *Harlem Gallery*, which was not published until 1965. Still, throughout the 1930s, poems from the volume appeared in *Arts Quarterly*, *Modern Monthly*, and *Modern Quarterly*. In New York, Tolson met important figures such as literary critic and editor V. F. Calverton, who described him in *Current History* as "a bright vivid writer who attains his best effects by understatement rather than overstatement, and who catches in a line or a stanza what most of his contemporaries have failed to capture in pages or volumes."

Tolson's fearless attitude toward controversy and his spirited defense of his religious and social views drew not only fire but also an invitation to publish in the *Pittsburgh Courier*. From 1937 to 1944 he wrote a weekly column, "Caviar and Cabbages," for the *Washington Tribune*. In the column, whose topics ranged from national politics to popular culture, Tolson attacked the class pretensions and lack of racial pride of the black middle class. His poem *Dark Symphony* won first place in a 1939 national poetry contest sponsored by Chicago's American Negro Exposition. When the *Atlantic Monthly* published the poem in 1941, the magazine's editor at the time, Mary Lou Chamberlain, so admired it that, upon moving to Dodd, Mead, she urged Tolson to produce a volume for her to publish. *Rendezvous with*

America, which includes *Dark Symphony,* was the result, and the book quickly saw three editions, from 1944 on. Tolson left Wiley College in 1947 for Langston University in Langston, Oklahoma; that same year he was named poet laureate of the West African nation of Liberia by its president, William S. V. Tubman, the son of Harriet Tubman. Perhaps the poet's most ambitious work, *The Libretto for the Republic of Liberia* was commissioned that year; he completed it in 1953 for the 1956 Liberian centennial. Tolson was subsequently admitted to the Liberian Knighthood of the Order of the Star of Africa.

While the 1950s and 1960s would bring Tolson increasing successes—among them, *Poetry*'s Bess Hokin Prize for his 1951 poem *E. & O.E.,* an honorary doctorate from Lincoln University in 1965, and a chair in the humanities at the Tuskegee Institute—none of these honors, perhaps, generated more excitement for Tolson than his being elected mayor of the town of Langston for four consecutive terms in the 1950s. But as Tolson's visibility grew, his health declined. In 1966 he died of abdominal cancer.

As nearly any of the eight sections of *The Libretto* will attest, Tolson stands with the best of the American modernists. Allen Tate, a champion of the New Criticism, suggested in his preface to the first publication of the poem that Tolson was in a direct line of poetic descent from Hart Crane. If Tate is right, then the poem itself marks the intersection of several disparate strands—modernist stylistics superimposed on an English pindaric ode about an African political moment by an African American artist. Unfortunately, Tate's tone, as he concludes, is somewhat condescending: "In the end I found that I was reading *Libretto for the New Republic of Liberia* not because Mr. Tolson is a Negro but because he is a poet, not because the poem has a 'Negro subject,' but because it is about the world of all men. And this subject is not merely asserted; it is embodied in a rich and complex language, and realized in terms of the poetic imagination," which terms Tate himself does not address at any length. But uttered nearly a half century ago, Tate's words were considered crucial simply because a celebrated and canonical poet-critic had written them about a noncanonical poet and his strange, difficult work. Today *Libretto* remains an underread poem "by a Negro" that gives an initial clue to its meaning by allusive indirection. The poem opens on "do," the first tone of the diatonic scale, running through successive tones—re, mi, fa, sol, la, ti—and, of course, back to do, completing the octave in solfeggio. Prefacing each stanza of the opening section with an abrupt inquiry—"Liberia?"—the narrative persona suggests that this "singing" will not be easy: "No micro-footnote in a bunioned book / Homed by a pedant / With a gelded look: / You are / The ladder of survival dawn men saw / In the quicksilver sparrow that slips / The eagle's claw!" With a massive web of allusions that run a global gamut of linguistic, textual, and cultural referents, this libretto points to "No waste land yet, nor yet a destooled elite." After so long a time, Countee Cullen's black bard exacts a stern revenge. The poem, as indeed the entire canon of Melvin Tolson, offers itself as one of the formidable poetic challenges of the modernist era.

An Ex-Judge at the Bar

Bartender, make it straight and make it two—
One for the you in me and the me in you.
Now let us put our heads together: one
Is half enough for malice, sense, or fun.

I know, Bartender, yes, I know when the Law   5
Should wag its tail or rip with fang and claw.
When Pilate [1] washed his hands, that neat event
Set for us judges a Caesarean precedent.

What I shall tell you now, as man is man,
You'll find in neither Bible nor Koran.   10
It happened after my return from France
At the bar in Tony's Lady of Romance.

We boys drank pros and cons, sang *Dixie*; and then,
The bar a Sahara, we pledged to meet again.
But lo, on the bar there stood in naked scorn   15
The Goddess Justice, like September Morn.

Who blindfolds Justice on the courthouse roof
While the lawyers weave the sleight-of-hand of proof?
I listened, Bartender, with my heart and head,
As the Goddess Justice unbandaged her eyes and said: 20

"To make the world safe for Democracy,
You lost a leg in Flanders fields—*oui*, [2] *oui?*
To gain the judge's seat, you twined the noose
That swung the Negro higher than a goose."

Bartender, who has dotted every *i?*   25
Crossed every *t?* Put legs on every *y?*
Therefore, I challenged her: "Lay on, Macduff, [3]
And damned be him who first cries, 'Hold, enough!' "

The boys guffawed, and Justice began to laugh
Like a maniac on a broken phonograph.   30
Bartender, make it straight and make it three—
One for the Negro . . . one for you and me.

1944

---

1. Pontius Pilate was the judge in the trial and execution of Jesus. See Matthew 27:24: "When Pilate saw that he could prevail nothing, but that rather a tumult was made, he took water, and washed his hands before the multitude, saying, I am innocent of the blood of this just person [i.e., Jesus]: see ye to it."
2. Yes (French).
3. In Shakespeare's *Macbeth* 5.10; Macduff, the thane of Fife, slays Macbeth.

Dark Symphony

I. Allegro Moderato[1]

Black Crispus Attucks[2] taught
           Us how to die
Before white Patrick Henry's[3] bugle breath
Uttered the vertical
           Transmitting cry: 5
"Yea, give me liberty or give me death."

Waifs of the auction block,
           Men black and strong
The juggernauts of despotism withstood,
Loin-girt with faith that worms   10
           Equate the wrong
And dust is purged to create brotherhood.

No Banquo's[4] ghost can rise
           Against us now,
Aver we hobnailed Man beneath the brute,   15
Squeezed down the thorns of greed
           On Labor's brow,
Garroted lands and carted off the loot.

II. Lento Grave[5]

The centuries-old pathos in our voices
Saddens the great white world,   20
And the wizardry of our dusky rhythms
Conjures up shadow-shapes of ante-bellum years:

Black slaves singing *One More River to Cross*
In the torture tombs of slave-ships,
Black slaves singing *Steal Away to Jesus*   25
In jungle swamps,
Black slaves singing *The Crucifixion*
In slave-pens at midnight,
Black slaves singing *Swing Low, Sweet Chariot*
In cabins of death,   30
Black slaves singing *Go Down, Moses*
In the canebrakes of the Southern Pharaohs.

III. Andante Sostenuto[6]

They tell us to forget
           The Golgotha[7] we tread . . .

1. Moderately lively (Italian). This and the titles to the other sections are directions for the performance of music.
2. An escaped slave who was killed by the British in the Boston Massacre, March 5, 1770, a prelude to the American Revolutionary War.
3. Virginia-born patriot (1736–1799) whose orator-ical skills fueled the American Revolution.
4. In Shakespeare's *Macbeth*, the murdered lord whose ghost haunts the guilty Macbeth.
5. Slowly and solemnly (Italian).
6. Moderately slowly and sustained (Italian).
7. Or the hill of Calvary, where Jesus was cruci-fied.

We who are scourged with hate,   35
A price upon our head.
They who have shackled us
Require of us a song,
They who have wasted us
Bid us condone the wrong.   40

They tell us to forget
Democracy is spurned.
They tell us to forget
The Bill of Rights is burned.
Three hundred years we slaved,   45
We slave and suffer yet:
Though flesh and bone rebel,
They tell us to forget!

Oh, how can we forget
Our human rights denied?   50
Oh, how can we forget
Our manhood crucified?
When Justice is profaned
And plea with curse is met,
When Freedom's gates are barred,   55
Oh, how can we forget?

IV. Tempo Primo [8]

The New Negro strides upon the continent
In seven-league boots . . .
The New Negro
Who sprang from the vigor-stout loins   60
Of Nat Turner, gallows-martyr for Freedom,
Of Joseph Cinquez, Black Moses of the Amistad Mutiny,
Of Frederick Douglass, oracle of the Catholic Man,
Of Sojourner Truth, eye and ear of Lincoln's legions,
Of Harriet Tubman, [9] Saint Bernard of the Underground
     Railroad.   65

The New Negro
Breaks the icons of his detractors,
Wipes out the conspiracy of silence,
Speaks to *his* America:

"My history-moulding ancestors   70
Planted the first crops of wheat on these shores,
Built ships to conquer the seven seas,
Erected the Cotton Empire,
Flung railroads across a hemisphere,
Disemboweled the earth's iron and coal,   75

---

8. In the time of the opening movement (Italian).
9. An escaped slave (c. 1820–1913) who helped
hundreds of other slaves escape to freedom in the
North. Turner (1800–1831) led his fellow slaves in
a revolt against his master and other local whites.

Cinquez, or Cinqué, led an 1839 mutiny on board
The Amistad, a slave ship. Douglass (1817–1895),
African American abolitionist, writer, and orator.
Truth (c. 1797–1883), African American abolition-
ist and religious orator.

Tunneled the mountains and bridged rivers,
Harvested the grain and hewed forests,
Sentineled the Thirteen Colonies,
Unfurled Old Glory at the North Pole, [1]
Fought a hundred battles for the Republic."   80

The New Negro:
His giant hands fling murals upon high chambers,
His drama teaches a world to laugh and weep,
His music leads continents captive,
His voice thunders the Brotherhood of Labor,   85
His science creates seven wonders,
His Republic of Letters challenges the Negro-baiters.

The New Negro,
Hard-muscled, Fascist-hating, Democracy-ensouled,
Strides in seven-league boots   90
Along the Highway of Today
Toward the Promised Land of Tomorrow!

V. Larghetto [2]

None in the Land can say
To us black men Today:
You send the tractors on their bloody path,   95
And create Okies for *The Grapes of Wrath.*
You breed the slum that breeds a *Native Son* [3]
To damn the good earth Pilgrim Fathers won.

None in the Land can say
To us black men Today: 100
You dupe the poor with rags-to-riches tales,
And leave the workers empty dinner pails.
You stuff the ballot box, and honest men
Are muzzled by your demagogic din.

None in the Land can say   105
To us black men Today:
You smash stock markets with your coined blitzkriegs, [4]
And make a hundred million guinea pigs.
You counterfeit our Christianity,
And bring contempt upon Democracy.   110

None in the Land can say
To us black men Today:
You prowl when citizens are fast asleep,
And hatch Fifth Column [5] plots to blast the deep

1. Reference to Matthew Henson (1866–1955), African American explorer and co-discoverer, with Robert Peary, of the North Pole.
2. Somewhat slowly (Italian).
3. Richard Wright's novel (1939) about Bigger Thomas, a young African American living in the northern ghettos. John Steinbeck's novel *The Grapes of Wrath* (1939) is about an Oklahoma fam-ily's trek westward looking for farmwork.
4. Lightning wars (German, literal trans.); sudden attacks made by Germany against Poland and France during World War II.
5. Franco (fascist) sympathizers in Madrid during the Spanish Civil War (1936–39); more generally, a group who acts traitorously out of secret sympathy with an enemy of their country.

Foundations of the State and leave the Land   115
A vast Sahara with a Fascist brand.

VI. Tempo di Marcia[6]

Out of abysses of Illiteracy,
Through labyrinths of Lies,
Across waste lands of Disease . . .
We advance!   120

Out of dead-ends of Poverty,
Through wildernesses of Superstition,
Across barricades of Jim Crowism[7] . . .
We advance!

With the Peoples of the World . . .   125
We advance!

                                                     1944

A Legend of Versailles[1]

Lloyd George and Woodrow Wilson and Clemenceau—
The Big Three: England, America, and France—
Met at Versailles. The Tiger ached to know
About the myth to end war's dominance.

"One moment, gentlemen," the Tiger said,   5
"Do you really want a lasting peace?" And then
Lloyd George assented with his shaggy head
And Woodrow Wilson, nodding, chafed his chin.

"The price of such a peace is great. We must give
Up secret cartels, spheres of power and trade;   10
Tear down our tariff walls; let lesser breeds live
As equals; scrap the empires we have made."

The gentlemen protested, "You go too far."
The Tiger shouted, "You don't mean peace, but war!"

                                                     1944

6. In march time (Italian).
7. Legal system that promoted racial segregation;
first enacted by southern legislatures in 1865 to separate blacks from whites on public transportation.
1. A reference to the peace conference held at Versailles, France (site of the 17th-century palace built
for Louis XIV), after World War I, from January to
June 1919. The main treaty negotiators were the so-
called Big Four: Lloyd George (Britain); Woodrow
Wilson (United States); Georges Clemenceau
(France); and Vittorio Emanuele Orlando (Italy),
known as the Tiger. The treaty assigned responsibility for the war to Germany, imposed reparation
payments on it, reduced its military powers, and
took away its overseas colonies.

Libretto for the Republic of Liberia

Do

Liberia?
No micro-footnote in a bunioned book
Homed by a pedant
With a gelded look:
You are   5
The ladder of survival dawn men saw
In the quicksilver sparrow that slips [1]
The eagle's claw!

Liberia?
No side-show barker's bio-accident,   10
No corpse of a soul's errand [2]
To the Dark Continent:
You are
The lightning rod of Europe, Canaan's key,
The rope across the abyss, [3]   15
Mehr licht for the Africa-To-Be!

Liberia?
No haply black [4] man's X
Fixed to a Magna Charta without a magic-square [5]
By Helon's leprous hand, to haunt and vex: [6] 20
You are
The Orient of Colors everywhere,
The oasis of Tahoua, the salt bar of Harrar,
To trekkers in saharas, in sierras, with Despair!

Liberia?   25
No oil-boiled Barabas,
No Darwin's bulldog for ermined flesh,
No braggart Lamech, no bema's Ananias:
You are
Libertas flayed and naked by the road [7] 30
To Jericho, for a people's five score years
Of bones for manna, for balm an alien goad! [8]

Liberia?
No pimple on the chin of Africa,
No brass-lipped cicerone of Big Top democracy, 35
No lamb to tame a lion with a baa:

1. Cf. Dryden, All for Love, II, i: ". . . upon my eagle's wings / I bore this wren, till I was tired of soaring, / and now he mounts above me." [All notes for this selection are Tolson's—Editor.]
2. Cf. Raleigh, The Soul's Errand.
3. V. Nietzsche, Thus Spake Zarathustra.
4. Cf. Shakespeare, Othello, III, iii: "Haply, for I am black . . ."
5. Magic-square: a symbol of equality. The diagram consists of a number of small squares each containing a number. The numbers are so arranged that the sum of those in each of the various rows is the same. Cf. Thomson, The City of Dreadful Night, XXI, 1061.
6. Cf. Willis, The Leper.
7. The motto of Liberia: "The love of liberty brought us here."
8. Cf. Carlyle: "God has put into every white man's hand a whip to flog a black man."

You are
Black Lazarus risen from the White Man's grave,[9]
Without a road to Downing Street,
Without a hemidemisemiquaver in an Oxford stave!   40

Liberia?
No Cobra Pirate of the Question Mark,[1]
No caricature[2] with a mimic flag
And golden joys to fat the shark:[3]
You are   45
American genius uncrowned in Europe's charnel-house.[4]
Leave fleshpots for the dogs and apes; for Man
The books whose head is golden[5] espouse!

Liberia?
No waste land yet, nor yet a destooled[6] elite,   50
No merry-andrew, an Ed-dehebi[7] at heart,
With St. Paul's root and Breughel's cheat:
You are
The iron nerve[8] of lame and halt and blind,
Liberia and not Liberia,   55
A moment of the conscience of mankind![9]

Re

The Good Gray Bard in Timbuktu[1] chanted:
"Brow tron lo—eta ne a ne won oh gike!"[2]

---

9. Cf. the tavern scenes in Boulton's comic opera, *The Sailor's Farewell*.

1. *Cobra Pirate.* V. Hardy, *Les Grands Etapes de l'Histoire du Maroc*, 50–54. *The Question Mark.* The shape of the map of Africa dramatizes two schools of thought among native African scholars. To the Christian educator, Dr. James E. Kwegyir Aggrey, it is a moral interrogation point that challenges the white world. According to Dr. Nnamdi Azikiwe, the leader of the nationalistic movement on the West Coast, foreigners consider it "a hambone designed by destiny for the carving-knife of European imperialism." I have found very fruitful the suggestions and criticisms of Professor Diana Pierson, the Liberian, and Dr. Akiki Nyabongo, the Ugandian. I now know that the Question Mark is rough water between Scylla and Charybdis.

2. Cf. Bismarck: "They [Negroes] appear to me to be a caricature of the white man."

3. Cf. Shakespeare, *Henry IV*, III, i: "A foutra for the world and worldlings base! / I speak of Africa and golden joys."

4. Cf. Emerson: "While European genius is symbolized by some majestic Corinne crowned in the capitol at Rome, American genius finds its true type in the poor negro soldier lying in the trenches by the Potomac with his spelling book in one hand and his musket in the other." V. Maran, *Batouala*, 9: "Civilization, civilization, pride of the Europeans and charnel-house of innocents, Rabindranath Tagore, the Hindu poet, once, at Tokio, told what you are! You have built your kingdom on corpses."

5. *The books whose head is golden.* Cf. Rossetti, *Mary's Girlhood*.

6. *Destooled.* On the Gold Coast the "Stool" is the symbol of the soul of the nation, its Magna Charta. In 1900, Sir Frederick Hodgson, Governor of the Gold Coast, demanded that the Ashantis surrender their "Stool." They immediately declared war. "Destooling" is a veto exercised by the sovereign people over unpopular rulers.

7. *Ed-dehebi:* "The Master of Gold." He was the conqueror of Songhai, with its fabulous gold mines.

8. *The iron nerve.* Cf. Tennyson, *Ode on the Death of the Duke of Wellington*.

9. V. the address of Anatole France at the bier of Emile Zola.

1. Cf. *A Memoir of Tennyson*, Vol. I, 46, the letter of Arthur Hallam to William Gladstone on the Timbuktu prize poem: "I consider Tennyson as promising fair to be the greatest poet of our generation, perhaps of our century." V. Delafosse, *Les Noirs de L'Afrique*. The Schomburg Collection, in Harlem, contains many rare items on the civilization at Timbuktu. Dr. Lorenzo Turner's *Africanism in the Gullah Dialects*, by tracing West Coast derivatives to their Arabic and Moslem and Portuguese cultural roots, has revealed the catholicity and sophistication of African antiquity and exploded the theory of the Old English origin of the Gullah dialects.

2. I am informed that variations of this *eironeia* or mockery may be found in scores of African languages. It means here: "The world is too large—that's why we do not hear everything." Cf. Pliny, *Historia Naturalis*, II: "There is always something new from Africa." Also Swift: "So geographers, in Afric maps, / With savage pictures fill their gaps . . ."

Before Liberia was, Songhai was: before
America set the raw foundling on Africa's   60
Doorstep, before the Genoese diced west,
Burnt warriors and watermen of Songhai
Tore into *bizarreries* the uniforms of Portugal
And sewed an imperial quilt of tribes.

In Milan and Mecca, in Balkh and Bombay,   65
Sea lawyers in the eyeservice of sea kings
Mixed liquors with hyperboles to cure deafness.
Europe bartered Africa crucifixes for red ivory,
Gewgaws for black pearls,[3] *pierres d'aigris* for green gold:
Soon the rivers and roads became clog almanacs!   70

The Good Gray Bard in Timbuktu chanted:
"Wanawake wanazaa ovyo! Kazi yenu wazungu!"[4]

Black Askia's fetish was his people's health:
The world his world, he gave the Bengal light
Of Books the Inn of Court in Songhai. *Beba mzigo!*[5]   75
The law of empathy set the market price,
Scaled the word and deed: the gravel-blind saw
Deserts give up the ghost to green pastures!

Solomon in all his glory had no Oxford,
Alfred the Great no University of Sankoré:[6]   80
Footloose professors,[7] chimney sweeps of the skull,
From Europe and Asia; youths, souls in one skin,[8]
Under white scholars like El-Akit, under
Black humanists like Bagayogo. *Karibu wee!*[9]

The Good Gray Bard in Timbuktu chanted: 85
"Europe is an empty python in hiding grass!"

Lia![1] *Lia!* The river Wagadu, the river Bagana,
Became dusty metaphors where white ants ate canoes,
And the locust Portuguese raped the maiden crops,
And the sirocco Spaniard razed the city-states,   90
And the leopard Saracen bolted his scimitar into
The jugular vein of Timbuktu. *Dieu seul est grand!*[2]

3. *Black pearls.* V. Shakespeare, *Two Gentlemen of Verona*, V, i. Also *Othello*, II, i: "Well prais'd! How if she be black and witty?" Mr. J. A. Rogers treats the subject and time and place adequately in *Sex and Race.*
4. *Wanawake wanazaa ovyo:* "The women keep having children right and left." *Kazi yenu wazungu:* "It's the work of you white men."
5. *Beba mzigo:* "Lift the loads." This *repetend* is tacked on *ex tempore* to ballads growing out of a diversity of physical and spiritual experiences.
6. V. Du Bois, *The World and Africa*, a book to which I am deeply indebted for facts.
7. The nomadic pedagogues gathered at Timbuktu are not to be confused with the *vagantes* of the *Carmina Burana.*
8. *Souls in one skin.* V. Firdousi, *The Dream of*

Dakiki, I, A.
9. *Karibu wee.* Among primitives hospitality is a thing poetic—and apostolic. *Jogoo linawika: Karibu wee.* "The rooster crows: Welcome!" *Mbuzi wanalia: Karibu wee.* "The goats bleat: Welcome."
1. *Lia.* The word means "weep" and seems to follow the patterns of "*otototoi*" in the Aeschylean chorus.
2. *Dieu seul est grand.* These first words of Massillon's exordium, delivered at the magnificent funeral of Louis XIV, brought the congregation to its feet in the cathedral. For an account of the destruction of Timbuktu, see the *Tarikh el-Fettach.* The *askia* Issahak, in a vain attempt to stop the Spanish renegades at Tondibi, used cows as Darius had used elephants against the Macedonian phalanx.

And now the hyenas whine among the barren bones
Of the seventeen sun sultans of Songhai,
And hooded cobras, hoodless mambas, hiss   95
In the gold caverns of Falémé and Bambuk,
And puff adders, hook scorpions, whisper
In the weedy corridors of Sankoré. *Lia! Lia!*

The Good Gray Bard chants no longer in Timbuktu:
"The maggots fat on yeas and nays of nut empires!"[3]   100

Mi

Before the bells of Yankee capital
Tolled for the feudal glory of the South
And Frederick Douglass's Vesuvian mouth
Erupted amens crushing Copperheads,

Old Robert Finley, Jehovah's Damasias,   105
Swooped into Pennsylvania Avenue
To pinion Henry Clay, the shuttlecock,
And Bushrod Washington, whose family name

Dwarfed signatures of blood: his magnet Yea
Drew Lawyer Key, the hymnist primed to match   110
A frigate's guns, and Bishop Meade, God's purse,
And Doctor Torrey, the People's clock: they eagled

The gospel for the wren Republic in
Supreme Court chambers. That decision's cash
And credit bought a balm for conscience, verved   115
Black Pilgrim Fathers to Cape Mesurado,

Where sun and fever, brute and vulture, spelled
The idioms of their faith in whited bones.
No linguist of the Braille of prophecy ventured:
The rubber from Liberia shall arm   120

Free peoples and her airport hinterlands
Let loose the winging grapes of wrath[4] *upon*
The Desert Fox's cocained nietzscheans
A goosestep from the Gateway of the East!

Fa

A fabulous mosaic log,   125
        the Bola boa lies
        gorged to the hinges of his jaws,
        eyeless, yet with eyes . . .

in the interlude of peace.

3. *Nut empires.* Cf. Sagittarius, *New Statesman and Nation*, May 1, 1948, the poem entitled "Pea-Nuts": "The sun of Empire will not set / While Empire nuts abound."
4. The airfields of Liberia sent 17,000 bombers a month against Rommel's *Afrika Korps.*

The beaked and pouched assassin sags 130
  on to his corsair rock,
and from his talons swim the blood-
red feathers of a cock . . .

in the interlude of peace.

The tawny typhoon striped with black 135
  torpors in grasses tan:
a doomsday cross, his paws uprear
the leveled skull of a man . . .

in the interlude of peace

Sol

White Pilgrims, turn your trumpets west! 140
Black Pilgrims, *shule, agrah,*[5] nor tread
The Skull of another's stairs![6]

This is the horned American[7]
Dilemma: yet, this too, O Christ,
This too, O Christ, will pass! 145

The brig *Elizabeth* flaunts her stern
At auction blocks with the eyes of Cain[8]
And down-the-river sjamboks.[9]

This is the Middle Passage: here
Gehenna hatchways vomit up 150
The debits of pounds of flesh.

This is the Middle Passage: here
The sharks wax fattest and the stench
Goads God to hold His nose!

Elijah Johnson, his *Tygers heart*[1] 155
In the whale's belly, flenses midnight:
"How long? How long? How long?"

5. *Shule, agrah:* "Move, my heart." Cf. Sharp, *Shule, Shule, Shule, Agrah.* It is a refrain from old Gaelic ballads.
6. *Skull:* "gulgoleth," a place of torment and martyrdom. *Another's stairs.* Cf. Rossetti, *Dante at Verona,* the epigraph from *Paradiso,* XVII: "Yea, thou shalt learn how salt his food who fares / Upon another's bread—how steep his path / Who treadeth up and down another's stairs."
7. V. Myrdal, *An American Dilemma.* Cf. Aptheker, *The Negro People in America.* Also Cox, *Race, Caste and Class.*
8. *Auction blocks.* Cf. Rolfe, *Diary, 1619:* "About the last of August came a Dutch man of warre that sold us twenty negars." Also Field, *Freedom Is More than a Word:* "And the Negroes have been in this country longer, on the average, than their white neighbors; they first came to this country on a ship called the 'Jesus' one year before the 'Mayflower' . . ." *With the eyes of Cain.* Cf. Watson, *The World in Armor.*
9. Cf. John Davis, *Travels,* the chapter on a slave hanging alive on a gibbet in South Carolina: ". . . the negur lolled out his tongue, his eyes starting from their sockets, and for three long days his only cry was Water! Water! Water!" *Sjamboks.* Cf. Padmore, *Africa:* "The Africans are housed like cattle in a compound . . . they are guarded by foremen armed with the sjambok, a hide whip—the symbol of South African civilization."
1. *Tygers heart:* Greene's allusion to "the onely Shake-scene."

A dark age later the answer dawns
When whitecap pythons thrash upon
The molar teeth of reefs   160

And hallelujahs quake the brig
From keel to crow's-nest and tomtoms gibber
In cosmic *deepi-talki.* [2]

Elijah feels the Forty Nights'
Octopus reach up to drag his mind   165
Into man's genesis.

He hears the skulls plowed under [3] cry:
"*Griots,* [4] the quick owe the quick and dead.
A man owes man to man!"

"*Seule de tous les continents,*" [5] the parrots   170
chatter, "*l'Afrique n'a pas d'histoire!*"
Mon petit doigt me l'a dit:

"Africa is a rubber ball;
the harder you dash it to the ground,
the higher it will rise.   175

"A lie betrays its mother tongue.
The Eye said, 'Ear, the Belly is
the foremost of the gods.'

"Fear makes a gnarl a cobra's head.
One finger cannot kill a louse.   180
The seed waits for the lily.

"No fence's legs are long enough.
The lackey licks the guinea's boot
till holes wear in the tongue.

"A camel on its knees solicits   185
the ass's load. Potbellies cook
no meals for empty maws.

"When skins are dry the flies go home.
Repentance is a peacock's tail.
The cock is yolk and feed.   190

2. Cf. LaVarre: "My black companions had two
languages: *deepitalki,* a secret language no white
man understands; and *talki-talki,* a concoction of
many languages and idioms which I understood."
3. *Skulls plowed under.* Cf. Sharp, *The Last Aborig-
inal.*
4. *Griots:* "living encyclopedias." Giryama, Bantu,
Amharic, Swahili, Yoruba, Vai, Thonga, Zulu,
Jaba, Sudanese—these tribal scholars speak, with
no basic change in idea and image, from line 173
to 214. The Africans have their *avant garde* in oral
literature. Sometimes one of these bards becomes
esoteric and sneers in a council of chiefs a line like
this: "The snake walks on its belly." And thus elder
statesmen are often puzzled by more than the
seven ambiguities. Delafosse feared that the mass
production technics introduced by missionaries
and traders would contaminate art for art's sake in
Africa.
5. These words of Guernier are no longer *ex cathe-
dra:* the scope of a native culture is vertical—not
horizontal.

"Three steps put man one step ahead.
The rich man's weights are not the poor
man's scales. To each his coole.

"A stinkbug[6] should not peddle perfume.
The tide that ebbs will flow again.   195
A louse that bites is in

"the inner shirt. An open door
sees both inside and out. The saw that severs the topmost limb

"comes from the ground. God saves the black
man's soul but not his buttocks from   200
the white man's lash. The mouse

"as artist paints a mouse that chases
a cat. The diplomat's lie is fat
at home and lean abroad.

"It is the grass that suffers when   205
two elephants fight. The white man solves
between white sheets his black

"problem. Where would the rich cream be
without skim milk? The eye can cross
the river in a flood.   210

"Law is a rotten tree; black man, rest
thy weight elsewhere, or like the goat
outrun the white man's stink!"

Elijah broods: "The fevers hoed
Us under at Sherbro. Leopard saints   215
Puked us from Bushrod Beach

"To Providence Island, where John Mill,
The mulatto trader, fended off
The odds that bait the hook.

"The foxes have holes, the birds have nests,[7]   220
And I have found a place to lay
My head, Lord of Farewells!"

And every ark awaits its raven,
Its vesper dove with an olive-leaf,
Its rainbow over Ararat.[8]   225

---

6. *A stinkbug.* Cf. Kipling, *the White Man's Burden.*
7. Cf. Matthew VIII, xx.
8. V. *New York Times,* "Journey to Ararat," April

17, 1949. Cf. Maill's translation of a poem by an
officer in the hospital at Erivan: "Here is Mount
Ararat. It has a brooding look . . . / One would think
it was waiting to be set free."

La

Glaciers had shouldered down
The cis-Saharan snows,
Shoved antelope and lion
Past *Uaz-Oîriet* [9] floes.

Leopard, elephant, ape,   230
Rhinoceros and giraffe
Jostled in odysseys
To Africa: siamang laugh

And curse impaled the frost
As Northmen brandished paws   235
And shambled Europe-ward,
Gnashing Cerberean jaws.

After *netami lennowak,* [1]
A white man spined with dreams [2]
Came to cudgel parrot scholars   240
And slay philistine schemes.

"The lion's teeth, the eagle's
Talons, shall break!" declared
Prophet Jehudi Ashmun, [3]
Christening the bones that dared.   245

When the black bat's ultima smote
His mate in the yoke, he felt
The seven swords' *pis aller* [4]
Twist in his heart at the hilt.

He said: "My Negro kinsmen,   250
America is my mother,
Liberia is my wife,
And Africa my brother."

Ti

O Calendar of the Century,
red-letter the Republic's birth!   255
O Hallelujah,
oh, let no *Miserere* [5]
venom the spinal cord of Afric earth!
Selah!

---

9. *Uaz-Oîrit.* "The Very Green," the ancient Egyptian name for the Mediterranean.
1. *Netami lennowak:* "the first men."
2. Cf. Virgil, *Aeneid,* IV, 625: "*Exoriare aliquis!*"
3. *Prophet Jehudi Ashmun.* Lincoln University, the oldest Negro institution of its kind in the world, was founded as Ashmun Institute. The memory of the white pilgrim survives in old Ashmun Hall and in the Greek and Latin inscriptions cut in stones sacred to Lincoln men. The annual Lincoln-Liberian dinner is traditional, and two of the graduates have been ministers to Liberia.
4. V. Apollinaire, *La Chanson du Mal-Aimé,* the fifth and sixth sections.
5. *Miserere.* Cf. Newman, *The Definition of a Gentleman:* ". . . we attended the Tenebrae, at the Sestine, for the sake of the Miserere . . ."

"Ecce homo!"   260
the blind men cowled in azure[6] rant
before the Capitol,
between the Whale and Elephant,[7]
where no longer stands Diogenes' hearse
readied for the ebony mendicant,   265
nor weeping widow Europe with her hands
making the multitudinous seas incarnadine
or earth's *massebôth*[8] worse:
O Great White World, thou boy of tears,[9] omega hounds
lap up the alpha laugh and *du-haut-en-bas* curse.   270
Selah!

O Africa, Mother of Science
... *lachen mit yastchekes*[1] ...
What dread hand,[2]
to make tripartite one august event,[3]   275
sundered Gondwanaland?
What dread grasp crushed your biceps and
back upon the rack
chaos of chance and change
fouled in Malebolgean isolation?   280
What dread *elboga* shoved your soul
into the *tribulum* of retardation?
melamin or melanin dies to the world and dies:
Rome casketed herself in Homeric hymns.
Man's culture in barb and Arab lies:[4]   285
The Jordan flows into the Tiber,[5]
the Yangtze into the Thames,
the Ganges into the Mississippi, the Niger
into the Seine.
Judge of the Nations, spare us: yet,   290
fool latins, alumni of one school,
on Clochan-na-n'all,[6] say *Phew*
... *Lest we forget! Lest we forget!* ...
to dusky peers of Roman, Greek, and Jew.
Selah!   295

Elders of Agâ's House,[7] keening
at the Eagles' feast, cringing
before the Red Slayer, shrinking
from the blood on Hubris' pall—

---

6. *Cowled in azure*: the cloak of deceit and false humility. Cf. Hafiz, *The Divan (Odes)*, V, translated by Bicknell.
7. *Whale and Elephant*: the symbols Jefferson used to designate Great Britain with her navy under Nelson and France with her army under Napoleon. V. Anderson, *Liberia*, X.
8. *Massebôth*: "sacred pillars." Cf. Genesis, XXVIII, xviii. Also the J author.
9. *Thou boy of tears*. Cf. Shakespeare, *Coriolanus*, V, v.
1. *Lachen mit vastchekes*: "laughing with needles being stuck in you"; ghetto laughter.
2. Cf. Blake, *The Tiger*.

3. Cf. Hardy, *The Convergence of the Twain*.
4. V. Pycraft, *Animals of the World*, 1941–1942. A *fortiori*, the American trotter is "a combination of barb and Arab on English stock."
5. V. Christy, *The Asian Legacy and American Life*. This book contains vital facts on Oriental influences in the New Poetry. What I owe the late Professor Arthur E. Christy, a favorite teacher, is not limited to the concept of "the shuttle ceaselessly weaving the warp and weft of the world's cultural fabric."
6. *Clochan-na-n'all*: "the blind men's steppingstones." Cf. Ferguson, *The Welshmen of Tirawley*.
7. V. Aeschylus, *Agamemnon*.

carked by cracks of myriad curbs,[8]   300
hitherto, against the Wailing Wall
of Ch'in,[9] the blind men cried:
All cultures crawl
walk hard
fall,   305
flout
under classes under
Lout,
enmesh in ethos, in *masôreth,*[1] the poet's flesh,
intone the Mass of the class as the requiem of the mass,   310
serve *adola mentis*[2] till the crack of will,
castle divorcee[3] Art in a blue-blood moat,
read the flesh of grass
into bulls and bears,
let Brahmin pens kill   315
Everyman the Goat,
write Culture's epitaph in *Notes* upstairs.
O *Cordon Sanitaire,*
thy brain's tapeworm, extract, thy eyeball's mote!
Selah!   320

Between pavilions
small and great
sentineled from capital to stylobate
by crossbow, harquebus, cannon, or Pegasus' bomb[4]
... and none went in and none went out[5] *...*   325
hitherto the State,[6]
in spite of Sicilian Vespers, stout
from slave, feudal, bourgeois, or soviet grout,
has hung its curtain[7]—scrim, foulard, pongee,
silk, lace, or iron—helled in by Sancho's fears[8]   330
of the bitter hug of the Great Fear,[9] Not-To-Be—
oscuro Luzbel,[1]
with no bowels of mercy,[2]
in the starlight[3]
de las canteras sin auroras.   335
Behind the curtain, aeon after aeon,

---

8. Cf. Shakespeare, *Coriolanus,* I, i, 67–76. See also Mr. Traversi's essay on this phase of the play.
9. I came across these words somewhere: "The Ch'in emperor built the Great Wall to keep out Mongolian enemies from the north and burned the books of China to destroy intellectual enemies from within."
1. Cf. Akiba: "*Masôreth* is a fence for the sayings of the fathers."
2. *Adola mentis.* V. Bacon, *Novum Organum.*
3. *Divorcee Art.* Cf. Gourmont: "*Car je crois que l'art est par essence, absolument inintelligible au peuple.*"
4. *Pegasus' bomb.* Cf. Dobson, *On the Future of Poetry.*
5. V. Joshua VI, i.
6. Cf. Treitschke: "The State is Power. Of so unusual a type is its power, that it has no power to limit its power. Hence no treaty, when it becomes inconvenient, can be binding; hence the very notion of arbitration is absurd; hence war is a part of the Divine order." Contrast this idea with Lincoln's premise that the people can establish either a republic of wolves or a democracy of lambs, as instanced in the poem *The Dictionary of the Wolf.* Cf. Bismarck: "The clause *rebus sic stantis* is understood in all treaties."
7. *Curtain.* Cf. Crile, *A Mechanistic View of War and Peace, 1915:* "France [is] a nation of forty million with a deep-rooted grievance and an iron curtain at its frontier."
8. *Sancho's fears.* V. Cervantes, *Don Quixote de la Mancha,* Part II, translated by Peter Motteux, the episode of the letter: "To Don Sancho Pança, Governor of the Island of Barataria, to be delivered into his own hands, or those of his secretary."
9. *The Great Fear.* V. Madelin, *French Revolution,* 69.
1. Alberti, *Sobre los Angeles.*
2. Cf. the aphorism: "*La politique n'a pas d'entrailles.*"
3. Cf. Meredith, *Lucifer in Starlight.*

he who doubts the white book's colophon
is Truth's, if not Laodicean, wears
the black flower[4] T of doomed Laocoön.
Before hammer and sickle or swastika, two
worlds existed: the Many, the Few.
They sat at Delos', at Vienna's, at Yalta's, ado:
Macbeth, without three rings,[5] as host
to Banquo's ghost.
Selah!

Like some gray ghoul from Alcatraz,
old Profit, the bald rake *paseq*,[6] wipes the bar,
polishes the goblet vanity,
leers at the tigress Avarice
as
she harlots roués from afar:[7]
swallowtails unsaved by loincloths,
famed enterprises prophesying war,[8]
hearts of rags *(Hanorish tharah sharinas)* souls of chalk,[9]
laureates with sugary grace in zinc buckets of verse,[1]
myths rattled by the blueprint's talk,
ists potted and pitted by a feast,
Red Ruin's skeleton horsemen, four abreast[2]
. . . galloping . . .
Marx, the exalter, would not know his East
. . . galloping . . .
nor Christ, the Leveler,[3] His West.
Selah!

O Age of Tartuffe
. . . *a lighthouse with no light atop* . . .
O Age, *pesiq*,[4] O Age,
kinks internal and global stinks
fog the bitter black estates of Buzzard and Og.[5]
A Dog, I'd rather be, o sage, a Monkey or a Hog.[6]

340

345

350

355

360

365

---

4. Cf. Hawthorne, *The Scarlet Letter:* "The black flower of civilized society, a prison."
5. V. Boccaccio, *The Three Rings.* Cf. Lessing, *Nathan the Wise.*
6. *Paseq:* "divider." This is a vertical line that occurs about 480 times in our Hebrew Bible. Although first mentioned in the *Midrash Rabba* in the eleventh century, it is still the most mysteriuos sign in the literature.
7. Cf. Cavafy, *Waiting for the Barbarians.*
8. *Famed enterprises.* V. Erasmus, *The Praise of Folly,* "Soldiers and Philosophers," *in toto,* the revised translation by John Wilson.
9. *Hearts of rags . . . souls of chalk:* Whitman's epithets for the "floating mass" that vote early and often for bread and circuses. *Hanorish tharah sharinas:* "Man is a being of varied, manifold, and inconstant nature." V. Della Mirandola, *Oration on the Dignity of Man.* Cf. Cunha: "The fantasy of universal suffrage [is] the Hercules' club of our dignity."
1. *Zinc buckets of verse.* V. Pasternak, *Definition of Poetry. Sugary grace.* Cf. Martial, *To a Rival Poet.*
2. Cf. Tennyson, *Idylls of the King:* "Red Ruin, and the breaking up of laws." V. Revelation VI. Cf.

Jouve, *La Resurrection des Morts.* See the White Horse, the Red Horse, the Black Horse, and the fourth horse, the worst: "*Tu es jaune et ta forme coule à ta charpente / Sur le tonneau ajouré de tes côtes / Les lambeaux verts tombent plus transparents / La queue est chauve et le bassin a des béquilles / Pour le stérile va-et-vient de la violence . . .*"
3. *The Leveler.* V. The Acts V, xxxii–xxxvi.
4. *Pesiq:* "divided." V. Fuchs, *Pesiq ein Glossenzeichen.* It seems to me that this linguistic symbol gives us a concrete example of the teleological—perhaps the only one. By an accident of *a priori* probability, the sign in itself indicates both cause and effect, and the index of the relationship is served synchronously by either *paseq* or *pasiq.* Of course the protagonist of the poem uses them for his own purpose on another level.
5. *Bitter black estates.* Cf. Petrarca, *The Spring Returns, but Not to Him Returns,* translated by Auslander. *Buzzard.* V. Dryden, *The Hind and the Panther.* Og. V. Tate, *Second Part of Absalom and Achitophel,* the passage inserted by Dryden.
6. V. Rochester, *Satyr against Mankind.* Cf. Cocteau, *Le Cap de Bonne Espérance:* "*J'ai mal d'être homme.*"

O Peoples of the Brinks,　　370
come with the hawk's resolve,
the skeptic's optic nerve, the prophet's *tele* verve
and Oedipus' guess, to solve
the riddle of
the Red Enigma and the White Sphinx.　　375
Selah!

O East . . . *el grito de Dolores* [7] . . . O West,
pacts, disemboweled, crawl off to die;
white books, *fiers instants promis à la faux,* [8]
in sick bay choke on mulligan truth and lie;　　380
the knife of Rousseau hacks the anatomy
of the fowl necessity;
dead eyes accuse red Desfourneau, [9]
whose sit-down strike gives High-Heels vertigo;
the wind blows through the keyhole [1]　　385
and the fettered pull down the shades;
while *il santo* and *pero* [2] hone phillipics,
Realpolitik explodes the hand grenades
faits accomplis
in the peace of parades;　　390
caught in the blizzard *divide et impera,*
the little gray cattle [3] cower
before the Siamese wolves,
pomp and power;
Esperanto trips the heels of Greek;　　395
in brain-sick lands, [4] the pearls too rich for swine
the claws of the anonymous seek; [5]
the case Caesarean, Lethean brew
nor instruments obstetrical at hand,
the midwife of the old disenwombs the new.　　400
Selah!

The *Höhere* [6] of Gaea's children
is beyond the *dérèglement de tous les sens,* is beyond
gold fished from cesspools, the *galerie des rois,* [7]
the seeking of cows, *apartheid,* [8] Sisyphus' despond,　　405

---

7. The watchword of Hidalgo, "Captain General of America."
8. Cf. Muselli, *Ballade de Contradiction: "Fiers instants promis à la faux, / Eclairs sombres au noir domaine!"*
9. Cf. Camus, *The Artist as Witness of Freedom:* M. Desfourneau's ". . . demands were clear. He naturally wanted a bonus for each execution, which is customary in any enterprise. But, more important, he vigorously demanded that he be given . . . an administrative status. Thus came to an end, beneath the weight of history, one of the last of our liberal professions. . . . Almost everywhere else in the world, executioners have already been installed in ministerial chairs. They have merely substituted the rubber stamp for the axe."
1. Cf. Nietzsche, *Thus Spoke Zarathustra,* 232.
2. *Il Santo and Pero:* respectively, the nicknames of Nietzsche and Trotsky—the first innocently ironical, the second ironically innocent.
3. Cf. the remark of Nicholas I to a harassed minister of war: "We have plenty of little gray cattle." the Czar had in mind the Russian peasant.
4. *Brain-sick lands.* V. Meredith, *On the Danger of War.*
5. In the fable of Antisthenes, when the hares demanded equality for all, the lions said: "Where are your claws?" Cf. Martial, *Epigram XII,* 93: *"Dic mihi, si fias tu leo, qualis eris?"*
6. *Höhere.* Cf. Petronius: *"Proecipitandus est liber spiritus."*
7. In the Gilded Era, cynics said of Babcock: "He fished for gold in every stinking cesspool." *Galerie des rois.* Cf. Verlaine, *Nocturne Parisien,* the reference to the twenty-eight statues of French kings.
8. *The seeking of cows:* this is the literal meaning of the word "battle" among the ancient Aryans who ravaged the Indo-Gangetic plains. The backwardness of their culture is attested by their failure to fumigate and euphemize their war aims. *Apartheid:* the South African system of multi-layered segregation.

the Ilande intire of itselfe with *die Schweine* in mud,
the potter's wheel that stocks the potter's field,
Kchesinskaja's balcony with epitaphs in blood,
deeds hostile all, O Caton,[9] to hostile eyes,
the breaking of foreheads against the walls,[1]   410
gazing at navels, thinking with thighs

The *Höhere* of God's stepchildren
is beyond the sabotaged world,[2] is beyond
das Diktat der Menschenverachtung,[3]
la muerte sobre el esqueleto de la nada,   415
the pelican's breast rent red to feed the young,[4]
summer's third-class ticket, the *Revue des morts,*[5]
the skulls trepanned[6] to hold ideas plucked from dung,
Dives' crumbs in the church of the unchurched,
absurd life shaking its ass's ears among[7]   420
the colors of vowels and Harrar blacks[8]
with Nessus shirts from Europe on their backs

The *Höhere* of X's children
is beyond Heralds' College, the *filets d'Arachné,*[9] is beyond
maggot democracy, the *Mal éternel,*[1] the Bells of Ys,   425
the doddering old brigades with aorist medicines of poetry,
the *Orizaba* with its Bridge of Sighs,
the *oasis d'horreur dans un déserte d'ennui,*[2]
the girasol rocks of Secunderabad,[3]
Yofan's studio and *Shkola Nenavisti,*[4]   430
the *otototoi*[5]—in Crimson Tapestries—of the *hoi polloi,*
Euboean[6] defeats
in the Sausage Makers' bout
the fool himself himself finds out
and in the cosmos of his chaos   435
repeats.
Selah!

9. *Deeds hostile all:* these words are from the *Chorus to Ajax,* by Sophocles, which Mr. Forrestal apparently read just before his death. *O Caton:* Cato the Younger committed suicide in 46 B.C. He had spent the previous night reading Plato's *Phaedo.* Cf. Lamartine, *Le Désespoir.*
1. *The walls:* "economic doctrines." The figure is Blok's.
2. *Sabotaged world.* Cf. Salmon, *Age de l'Humanité.*
3. V. Mitscherlich and Mielke, *Doctors of Infamy,* translated by Norden. Cf. Grotius, *De Jure Belli et Pacis,* "Prolegomena," XVIII: ". . . a people which violates the Laws of Nature and Nations, beats down the bulwark of its own tranquillity for future time."
4. Cf. Ronsard, *Le Bocage.* Also Musset, *La Nuit de mai.*
5. V. Gautier, *Vieux de la vieille,* the reference to Raffet's *nocturne* showing Napoleon's spirit reviewing spectral troops.
6. Plekhanov had Alexander II in mind when he used the trepan figure.
7. V. Cendrars, *Éloge de la vie dangereuse.*
8. Rimbaud, in a town near the Red Sea, looked toward Khartoum and wrote: "*Leur Gordon est un*

idiot, leur Wolseley un âne, et toutés leurs entreprises une suite insensée d'absurdités et de déprédations." But fifty years later, when the Black Shirts entered Harrar, the ex-poet who plotted with Menelik against Italy was not there to hear Vittorio Mussolini's poetic account: "I still remember the effect produced on a small group of Galla tribesmen massed around a man in black clothes. I dropped an aerial bomb right in the center, and the group opened up like a flowering rose. It was most entertaining."
9. *Filets d'Arachné.* Cf. Chénier, *Qui? moi? de Phébus te dicter les leçons?*
1. *Mal éternel.* Cf. Lisle, *Dies irae.*
2. Cf. Baudelaire, *Le Voyage.*
3. V. Robinson, the Preface to *The Story of Medicine.*
4. *Yofan's studio:* Napoleon's old residence by the Kremlin wall. *Shkola Nenavisti:* a Berlin film on a Dublin subject in a Moscow theater.
5. *Otototoi.* See Gilbert Murray's Notes to Aeschylus.
6. Cf. Ovid, *Tristia,* quoted by Montaigne in *Of Three Commerces.* "Whoever of the Grecian fleet has escaped the Caphearean rocks ever takes care to steer clear from those of the Euboean sea."

The *Höhere* of one's pores *En Masse*[7]
... Christians, Jews, *ta ethne* ...makes as apishly
brazen as the brag and brabble of brass   440
the flea's fiddling
on the popinjay,
the pollack's pout
in the net's hurray,
the jerboa's feat   445
in the fawn and the flout
of
Quai d'Orsay,
White House,
Kremlin,   450
Downing Street.
Again black Aethiop[8] reaches at the sun, O Greek.
Things-as-they-are-for-us, *nullius in verba,*[9]
speak!
O East, O West,   455
on tenotomy bent,
Chang's tissue is
Eng's ligament!
Selah!

Between Yesterday's wars   460
now hot now cold
the grief-in-grain[1] of Man
dripping dripping dripping
from the Cross of Iron
dripping   465
drew jet vampires
of the Skull;
Between Yesterday's wills of Tanaka, between
golden goblet and truckling trull
and the ires   470
of rivers red with the reflexes of fires,
the ferris wheel
of race, of caste, of class
dumped and alped cadavers till the ground
fogged the Pleiades with Gila rot: Today the mass,   475
the Beast with a Maginot Line in its Brain,
the staircase Avengers of base alloy,[2]
the *vile canaille—Gorii!*[3]—the *Bastard-rasse,*
the *uomo qualyque,* the *hoi barbaroi,*

---

7. Cf. Lamartine: *"Il faut . . . Avec l'humanité t'u-nir par chaque pore."* Cf. Hugo, the Preface to *Les Contemplations:* "When I speak to you of myself, I am speaking to you of you." And again, Romains: *"Il faut bien qu'un jour on soit l'humanité!"*
8. *Black Aethiop.* Cf. Shakespeare, *Pericles,* II, ii: "A knight of Sparta, my renowned father, / And the device he bears upon his shield / Is a black Aethiop, reaching at the sun; / The word, 'Lux tua vita mihi'."
9. *Nullius in verba.* V. Lyons, *The Royal Society.*
1. *Grief-in-grain.* The "grain" I have in mind in

this figure consists of the dried female bodies of a scale insect found on cacti in Mexico and Central America. The dye is red and unfading. Cf. Henley, *To James McNeill Whistler, in toto.*
2. Cf. Cavafy, *The Footsteps.*
3. *Gorii.* The voyage of the Carthaginian general Hanno carried him as far as what is now Liberia. The aborigines he saw were called *Gorii,* which later Greek and Latin scholars turned into "go-rilla." However, to Hanno's interpreter and in the Wolof language today, the expression means "These too are men."

the *raya* in the *Oeil de Boeuf,*[4] 480
the *vsechelovek*, the *descamisados,*[5] the *hoi polloi*,
the Raw from the Coliseum of the Cooked,[6]
Il Duce's Whore,[7] Vardaman's Hound—
unparadised nobodies with maps of Nowhere[8]
ride the merry-go-round! 485
Selah!

Do

a *pelageya* in *as seccas*[9] the old she-fox today
eyes dead letters mouth a hole in a privy
taschunt a corpse's in a mud-walled troy of *jagunços*[1]
(naze naze desu ka servant de dakar) (el grito de yara)[2] 490
cackles among the garbage cans of mummy truths
o frontier saints bring out your dead[3]

the aria of the old *sookin sin* breaks my shoulders[4]
lasciatemi morire o africa *(maneno matupu)*[5]
the fat of fame didn't outlast a night in hog's wash[6] 495
nor geneva's church nor the savage's ten pounds[7]
for stratford's poor (bles be ye man for jesvs sake)
here one singeth[8] *per me si va nella città dolente*

bclow the triumvirate flag & tongue & mammon
while *blut und boden* play the anthemn *iron masters gold*[9] 500
ruble shilling franc yen lira baht and dime
brass-knuckled *(la légalité nous tue)*[1] and iron-toed

4. *Raya.* In the Turkish conquest of the Southern Slavs, the maltreated people became *raya* or cattle. Conquest salves its conscience with contempt. Among the *raya* for five hundred years, the ballads of the wandering *guslars* kept freedom alive. *Oeil de Boeuf*: a waiting room at Versailles. Cf. Dobson, *On a Fan That Belonged to the Marquise de Pompadour.*
5. *Vsechelovek*: "universal man." In spite of its global image, this concept has a taint of *blut und boden.* Ever since Dostoevski, in a eulogy on Pushkin, identified the latter's genius with *vsechelovek*, the term has created pros and cons. Cf. the Latin: "Paul is a Roman and not a Roman." *Descamisados*: "the shirtless ones."
6. The line was suggested by the history of the *Crudes* and *Asados* of Uruguay.
7. *Il Duce's Whore.* V. *Ciano Diaries 1939–43*, edited by Gibson. This is one of the "many instances of the vast contempt in which Il Duce held his people."
8. Cf. Milton, the outline of *Adam Unparadised.*
9. *Pelageya*: the wench of the Draft Constitution. V. Gogol, *Dead Souls. As seccas*: the devastating periodic droughts of Brazil.
1. *Taschunt.* Cf. Frobenius, *African Genesis,* 47 (Faber & Faber, Ltd.): "He felt that he had a thabuscht." A *mudwalled troy of jaguncos*: the home of Maciel's fanatics.
2. *Naze naze desu ka.* V. Mailer, *The Naked and the Dead*, the diary of Major Ishimara, 247. Also Apollinaire, *Les Soupirs du Servant de Dakar. El grito de yara*: the watchword at Manzanillo, October 16, 1869.
3. Cf. Francia: ". . . now I know that bullets are the best saints you can have on the frontiers." *Bring out your dead*: the cry of the bellman walking by night in

front of the deadcart. V. Defoe, *Journal of the Plague Year.*
4. *Aria.* Cf. Ludwig: "Dictatorship is always an aria, never an opera." *Sookin sin.* V. Duranty, *One Life, One Kopeck,* 3. *Breaks my shoulders.* Cf. Baudelaire: *"Pour ne pas sentir l'horrible fardeau du temps qui brise vos épaules et vous penche vers terre, il faut vous enivrer sans trêve."*
5. *Lasciatemi morire.* V. Monteverdi, *Lament of Arianna.* Cf. Mendelssohn, *Aria from Elijah:* "O Lord, take away my life, for I am not better than my fathers." See also Mecaenas: *"Debilem, facito manu, / Debilem pede, coxâ; / Lubricos quate dentes: / Vita dum superset, bene est . . ." Maneno matupu:* "empty words," an epithet used in *deepitalki*—not *talki-talki.*
6. *Hog's Wash*: a London newspaper edited by Daniel Isaac Eaton during the "Anti-Jacobin Terror." Its name was an ironical allusion to Burke's epithet, "the swinish multitude."
7. *Savage's ten pounds.* Cf. Voltaire, *Irene*, the preliminary letter: "Shakespeare is a savage with sparks of genius in a dreadful darkness of night." See Shakespeare's will and epitaph.
8. *Here one singeth.* Cf. *Aucassin and Nocolete*, translated by Andrew Lang, the warning *aubade*, or "dawn song," of the sentinel on the tower above the trysting place.
9. When Croesus showed Solon his gold, the sage said: "Sir, if any other come that hath better iron than you, he will be master of all this gold."
1. *La légalité nous tue.* Muraviev, the Hangman, when he was governor-general of Poland, wrung this cry from the people.

wage armageddon in the temple of *dieu et l'état*
o earl of queensberry o last christian on the cross

vexilla regis prodeunt inferni what is man f.r.a.i. *tò tí*[2]   505
(a professor of metaphysicotheologicocosmonigology[3]
a tooth puller a pataphysicist in a cloaca of error[4]
a belly's wolf a skull's tabernacle a #13 with stars[5]
a muses' darling a busie bee *de sac et de corde*[6]
a neighbor's bed-shaker a walking hospital on the walk)[7]   510
lincoln walks the midnight epoch of the ant-hill[8]
and barbaric yawps shatter the shoulder-knots[9] of white peace
jai hind (dawn comes up like thunder)[1] *pakinstan zindabad*
britannia rules the waves *my pokazhem meeru*[2]
the world is my parish[3] *muhammad rasulu 'llah*   515
hara ga hette iru oh yeah *higashi no kazeame*[4]

naïfs pray for a guido's scale of good and evil to match
worldmusic's sol-fa syllables (*o do de do de do de*)[5]
worldmathematics' arabic and roman figures
worldscience's greek and latin symbols   520
the letter killeth five hundred global tongues
before esperanto garrotes voläpuk *vanitas vanitatum*

o majesty-dwarf'd brothers *en un solo espasmo sexual*[6]
ye have mock'd the golden rules of eleven sons of god
smitten to rubble *ein feste burg*[7] for a few acres of snow   525
buried the open sesame *satya bol gat hai*[8] among dry bones
wasted the balm *assalamu aleykum*[9] on lice and maggots
snarled the long spoon for the scaly horror

pin-pricks precede blitzkriegs *mala' oun el yom yomek*[1]
idiots carol happy dashes in st. innocent's[2] little acre   530

2. *Vexilla regis prodeunt inferni*. Cf. Dante, *Inferno*, Canto XXXIV. *Tò tí*: "What is it?" This was
the old gadfly's everlasting question.
3. Cf. Boileau, *Satires*, IV, 5–10.
4. *Tooth Puller*: "*Tiradentes*," the nickname of the
first martyr of Brazilian independence. *A cloaca of
error*. See Pascal's doctrine of the Thinking Reed.
Cf. Jarry, *Gestes et Opinions du Dr. Pataphysicien*.
5. A *belly's wolf*. Cf. Beaumont and Fletcher,
Woman Pleased. Also Malley: "Religion is a process
of turning your skull into a tabernacle, not of going
up to Jerusalem once a year." *#13 with stars*: James
Wilkinson, American general and secret Spanish
agent, who sought to establish an empire in the
Southwest under his own sword and sceptre.
6. Orlov in a letter to Golonin branded Muraviev
as "*un homme de sac et de corde.*"
7. *The Walk*: the *Peripatos* of the Lyceum.
8. *Epoch of the ant-hill*. V. Amiel, *Journal*: "The
age of great men is going . . ."
9. *Shoulder-knots*. Cf. Swift, *A Tale of the Tub*, II.
1. *Dawn comes up like thunder*. Cf. Kipling, *Man-
dalay*.
2. *My pokazhem meeru*: "We'll show the whole
world."
3. *The world is my parish*: Wesley's announcement
of his mission.
4. *Hara ga hette iru*: "The belly has shrunken."
Higashi no kazeame: the code words all Japanese
embassies had received by mid-November, 1941.

This phrase—"East wind rain"—was to be repeated
in a short-wave news broadcast in case of a rupture
in Japanese-American relations.
5. *O do de do de do de*. V. Shakespeare, *King Lear*,
III, iv.
6. V. Newman, *The Dream of Gerontius*. Cf. Silva:
"*Juan lanas, el mozo de esquina, / Es ab-
solutamente igual / Al Emperador de la China; /
Los dos son un mismo animal.*"
7. V. Luther: "*Ein feste Burg ist unser Gott / Ein
gute Wehr und Waffen.*" Voltaire looked upon the
Seven Years' War as the devastation of Europe to
settle whether England or France should win "a
few acres of snow" in Canada.
8. *Satya bol gat hai*: "In truth lies salvation."
9. *Assalamu aleykum*: "Peace to you."
1. Cf. Napoleon's words to Czar Alexander at Til-
sit, June 22, 1807: "If they want peace, nations
should avoid the pin-pricks that precede cannon-
shots." *Mala' oun el yom yomek*. It is said that Taha
Shanin, the Dongolawi, as he plunged his spear
into General Gordon, cried: "O cursèd one, your
time has come!"
2. *St. Innocent's*. Cf. Browne, *Hydriotaphia or Urn
Burial*. Also Job XIV, vii. The hag Today in the
poem says the idiots have a word for it. In China it
means "Kong Hi Sing Yen"; in Africa, "Happy
Dashes"; in America, "Merry Christmas." Cf.
F.P.A., *For the Other 364 Days*: "Christmas is over
and Business is Business."

of rags and bones without brasses black and red[3]
booby mouths looted of the irritating parenthesis[4]
patrol skulls unhonored by a cromwell's pike
snaggleteeth glutted *in sudori vultus alieni*

o sweet chariot[5] these aesop's flies without mirth   535
these *oh-mono* without music in greed's akeldama[6]
are one with the great auk of the north star
mouldy rolls of noah's ark and wall street
nuclei fed to demogorgon's mill[7]
alms for oblivion raindrops minus h_2o 540

o's without figures on ice the sun licks
pebbles let fall in the race of a night sea
jockeyed by beaufort no. 12
iotas of the *yod* of god in a rolls royce[8]
the seven trumpets of today's baby boys summon peace[9]   545
and the walls come tumblin' down (christ sleeps)[1]

and no mourners go crying *dam-bid-dam*[2]
about the ex-streets of scarlet letters
only the souls of hyenas whining *teneo te africa*[3]
only the blind men gibbering *mboagan*[4] in greek   550
against sodom's pillars of salt
below the mountain of rodinsmashedstatues *aleppe*[5]

. . . .

Tomorrow[6] . . . O . . . Tomorrow,
Where is the glory of the *mestizo* Pharaoh?
The Mahdi's tomb of the foul deed?   555

3. *Brasses black and red.* Cf. Newbolt, *He Fell among Thieves.* Also his *Clifton Chapel,* the inscription which gives an epitome of two or three brasses in the Chapel: " '*Qui procul hinc,*' the legend's writ— / The frontier-grave is far away— / '*Qui ante diem periit: / Sed miles, sed pro patria'.*"
4. *Irritating parenthesis:* Cunha's figure for the problem of miscegenation. V. Cunha, *Os Sertoes,* II, ii, 108–110.
5. *O sweet chariot:* I have in mind the Negro spiritual.
6. *Oh-mono:* "high-muck-a-mucks." *Greed's akeldama.* V. The Acts I, xv–xxi.
7. *Demogorgon's mill.* Cf. Shelley, *Prometheus Unbound.*
8. *God in a rolls royce:* Father Divine. Some years ago in a jeremiad issued from one of his "heavens" he announced that he had reduced the Mayor of New York City "to a tittle of a jot" during the Harlem riot.
9. *The seven trumpets.* Cf. Joshua VI, viii. *Today's baby boys:* the code words for the A-bombs. The day after it was proved at Alamagordo, New Mexico, that the weapon worked, the late Henry L. Stimson, then secretary of war, received the message: "Baby boy born today mother and child doing well."
1. In the days of the Norman King Stephen, men

cried out that "Christ and His saints slept."
2. *Dam-bid-dam:* "blood for blood." This was the way the Saadists phrased the idea of talion at the Abbasiya mausoleum of Nokrashy Pasha. Cf. Leviticus XXIV, xvii–xxi.
3. *Souls of hyenas:* another reference to the bloody Muraview, "this loathsome figure with a bulldog's face and a hyena's soul." The phrase is from Kucharzewski. *Teneo te Africa:* the words uttered by Caesar when he stumbled and fell on touching the shore of Africa. Cf. Suetonius, *Lives of the Caesars.*
4. *Mboagan:* "death."
5. *Rodinsmashedstatues.* The twisted version of the hag Today keeps her from seeing that only the hands of the statues have been chopped off; and thus she misses the apocalypse in the Rodin image, the magnetic needle of whose compass pivots toward the Africa-To-Be (*Höhere* and *Khopirā*), set as the goal, by the protagonist, in the first section. For an elucidation of this transitional Janus-faced image, see Lajos Egri, *The Art of Dramatic Writing,* 30–31. *Aleppe.* Cf. Dante, *Inferno,* Canto VII: "*Pape Satan! pape, aleppe!*"
6. *Tomorrow.* V. Blake, *The Bard.* Cf. Rimbaud: "*Je vais dévoiler tous les mystères . . . mort, naissance, avenir, passé, cosmogonie, néant.*" Also Goethe, *Faust,* 7433: "Enough, the poet is not bound by time."

Black Clitus of the fatal verse[7] and Hamlet's arras?
   The cesspool of the reef of gold?[8]
   Der Schwarze Teufel, Napoleon's savior?[9]
   The Black Virgin of Creation's Hell Hole?[1]
   Tomorrow . . . O . . . Tomorrow,   560
   Where is Jugurtha the dark Iago?
   The witches' Sabbath of sleeping sickness?
   The *Nye ke mi* eyeless in the River of Blood?
   The Tagus that imitates the Congo?[2]
   The *Mein Kampf of kitab al sudan wa'lbidan?*[3]   565
   The black albatross about the white man's neck?
   O Tomorrow,
Where is the graven image *pehleh* of *Nash Barin?*[4]
   Their white age of their finest black hour?
   The forged minute book of ebony Hirsch?   570
The chattel whose Rock vies with the Rime of the upstart Crow?[5]
   Ppt. knows.[6]

. . . .

The Futurafrique, the *chef d'oeuvre* of Liberian
   Motors slips through the traffic
   swirl of axial Parsifal-Feirefiz[7]   575
   Square, slithers past the golden
   statues of the half-brothers as
   brothers, with *cest prace*[8] . . .
The Futurafrique, the accent on youth and speed
   and beauty, escalades the   580
   Mount Sinai of Tubman University, the vistas of which
   bloom with co-eds from seven
   times seven lands . . .
The Futurafrique, windows periscopic, idles past   585

7. *The fatal verse.* Alexander the Great made Black Clitus, "his best beloved," King of Bactria and commander of his celebrated cavalry, which synchronized with the Macedonian phalanx to deliver a battle's one-two punch. Dropsica, Clitus' mother, was Alexander's nurse. During the Persian campaign, a furious argument broke out at the king's supper table. He snatched a spear from a soldier and ran it through Clitus as he came from behind a curtain shouting a verse from Euripides' *Andromache:* "In Greece, alas, how ill things ordered are!" V. Plutarch, *Lives,* "Alexander." Cf. Shakespeare, *Hamlet,* III, iv.
8. The epithet African intellectuals give to Johánnesburg.
9. The German army's nickname for General Dumas, who rescued Napoleon from the Mamelukes by riding a stallion into a mosque in Cairo. The general's astounding feats kept him from getting a marshal's baton. He never recovered from the blow.
1. Cf. Xenophanes: "Men have always made their gods in their own images—the Greeks like Greeks, the Ethiopians like Ethiopians." Again Professor Christy's figure of "the world's cultural fabric" is evidenced in the statues of the Black Virgin Mary and Negro saints which were common in Germany and Latin Europe, as well as northern Africa, dur-

ing the Middle Ages. The stained glass of the Cathedral at Chartres has portraits in ebony. *Creation's Hell Hole:* the name the Italians gave the Danakil Desert.
2. Cf. Moog, *Um Rio imita o Rheno.* Moog created his symbol to suggest the heavy German settlement in Rio Grande do Sul. The line indicates a historical parallel when 10,000 Negroes gathered in Lisbon and threatened to outnumber the whites.
3. *Kitab al sudan wa'lbidan:* "the superiority of the black race over the white." Before the swastika gave Nordicism the Stuka, an Arab scholar, Al-Jahiz, issued his racist theory in reverse: another instance of similarity in dissimilarity.
4. *Pehleh:* "money." *Nash Barin:* before the October Revolution, this expression meant "Our Master" or God. I don't know its present meaning. Cf. I Timothy VI, v. Also Milton, *Paradise Lost,* 678.
5. *The chattel:* "Tariq." *Rock:* Gibraltar was named for this black general and ex-slave. *The Rime of the upstart Crow.* Cf. Shakespeare, *Sonnet LV:* "Not marble, nor the gilded monuments / Of princes, shall outlive this powerful rime."
6. *Ppt. knows.* V. Swift, *Journal to Stella,* March 15, 1712.
7. *Parsifal-Feirefiz.* Cf. Eschenbach, *Parsifal.* Also Du Bois, *The World and Africa,* X.
8. *Cest prace:* "all honor to labor."

the entrance to the 70A subway[9] station, volplanes into the
aria of Swynnerton Avenue,
zooms by the Zorzor[1] Monu-
ment, zigzags between the fac-   590
tory   hierarchies,   rockets
upcountry and backcountry,
arcs the ad-libbing soapy blue
harbor crossroads of Waldorf
Astorias at anchor, atom fueled   595
and burnished in ports of the
six seagirt worlds . . .
The Futurafrique strokes the thigh of Mount Bar-
clay and skis toward the Good-
lowe   Straightaway,   whose   600
coloratura sunset is the alpen-
glow of cultures in the Shovel-
head Era of the Common Man
        . . .
The Futurafrique glitters past bronze Chomolungma, odic
memorial to Matilda New-   605
port—on and on and on, out-
racing the supercoach of the
Momolu Bukere Black-Hound
winging along the seven-lane
Equatorial Highway toward   610
Khopirû[2] . . .
The Futurafrique, flight-furbished ebony astride
velvet-paved miles, vies with
the sunflower magnificence of
the Oriens, challenges the   615
snow-lily diadem of the Europa
        . . .
The Futurafrique, with but a scintilla of its Niagara
power, slices Laubach Park,
eclipses the Silver Age Gibbet
of Shikata-gai-nai,[3] beyond the   620

9. 70A subway. V. Wilson, Liberia, for many of these references.
1. The Zorzor twins were miracle-workers in iron, see line 273.
2. Khopirû: "To Be." The concept embraces the Eternity of Thence, which, free from blind necessity, contains the good life.
3. Shikata-gai-nai: "It cannot be helped." This is the stoicism with which Japanese villagers meet the earth convulsions of sacred Fujiyama. In other lands it is fate, kismet, predestination, artistries of Circumstance, economic determinism, necessitari-anism—from Aeschylus' Nemesis to Chénier's filets d'Arachné. Sometimes it takes the form of the so-phistry, human nature does not change. As a hidden premise it blocks the kinetic; it confuses the feral with the societal and leads to petitio principii. History, then, remains a Heraclitean continuum of a world flaring up and dying down as "it always was, is, and shall be." Some moderns have turned this

ancient seesaw figure of a crude dialectics into a lo-comotive of history. In the poem, however, the flux of men and things is set forth in symbols whose mo-tions are vertical-circular, horizontal-circular, and rectilinear. In spite of the diversity of phenomena, the underlying unity of the past is represented by the ferris wheel; the present by the merry-go-round; and the future by the automobile, the train, the ship, and the aeroplane. I placed the ship image in the middle of the images of swifter vehicles to indi-cate the contradiction in the essence of things, the struggle of opposites, which mankind will face even in Khopirû and Höhere. By the Law of Relativity, history will always have its silver age as well as its golden, and each age will contain some of the other's metal. Because of these upward and onward lags and leaps, it is not an accident that Liberia reaches her destination, the Parliament of African Peoples, after the aerial symbol. Cf. Meredith, The World's Advance, the figure of the reeling spiral.

ars of Phidias;[4] on and on,
herds only blears of rotor masts
rouletting, estates only rococo
decks and sails swirling, the
Futurafrique, the Oriens, the   625
Auster, the Americus, the
Europa, rend space, gut time,
arrowing past tiering Nidaba,[5]
glissading side by side, into the
cosmopolis of Höhere—the by-   630
gone habitat of mumbo jumbo
and blue tongue, of sasswood-
bark jury and tsetse fly, aeons
and aeons before the Unhappie
Wright of the Question Mark   635
crossed the Al Sirat!
The United Nations Limited volts over the untenanted, untitled grave of Black
Simoom, the red Chaka of *ruse
de guerre*, the Cheops of pyra-   640
mids with the skulls of Pygmy
and Britisher, Boer and Arab
. . .
The United Nations Limited careers across Seretse
Khama's Bechuanaland, yester-
day and yesterday and yesterday   645
after the body of Livingstone
kneeled its trek in dry salt from
Lake Bangeula to the sabbath
of Westminster Abbey . . .650
The United Nations Limited horseshoe-curves Stan-   650
ley Falls, sheens the surrealistic
harlotry of the mirage-veiled
Sahara, quakes the dinosaurian
teeth bolted in the jaws of Tibes-
ti, zoom-zooms through the   655
Ptolemaic Subterane like a sil-
ver sirocco . . .
The United Nations Limited, stream-phrased and air-
chamoised   and   sponge-
cushioned, telescopes the poly   660
genetic metropolises polychro-
matic between Casablanco and
Mafeking, Freetown and Addis
Ababa!

The Bula Matadi, diesel-engined, fourfold-decked,   665
swan-sleek, glides like an ice-
ballet skater out of the Bight of
Benin, the lily lyricism of

4. *Ars of Phidias.* Cf. Rodin: "Beyond Phidias   5. *Nidaba.* Cf. Dr. Samuel Noah Kramer's transla-
sculpture will never advance." Also Shakespeare,   tion of a Sumerian tablet in the Museum of the An-
Troilus and Cressida: "The baby figure of the giant   cient Orient: "You have exalted Nidaba, the queen
mass / Of things to come."   of the places of learning."

whose ivory and gold figurines
  larked space oneness on the   670
  shelf ice of avant-garde Art . . .
The Bula Matadi swivels past isled Ribat, where, in
  a leaden age's iliads, the Black
  Messiah and his Black Puri-
  tans, exsected by Sodoms and   675
  Gomorrahs, daunted doxy
  doubts with skeletons of dharna
    . . .
The Bula Matadi skirrs up the Niger, with her Khufu
  cargo from Tel Aviv and Hiro-
  shima, Peiping and San Salva-   680
  dor, Monrovia and Picayune!

Le Premier des Noirs,[6] of Pan-African Airways, whirs
  beyond the copper cordilleran
  climaxes of glass skyscrapers on
  pavonine Cape Mesurado . . .   685
Le Premier des Noirs meteors beyond the Great White
  Way of Kpandemai, aglitter
  with the ebony beau monde
    . . .
Le Premier des Noirs waltzes across Lake Chad, curv-
  ets above the Fifth Cataract,   690
  wantons with the friar stars of
  the Marra Mountains, eagles its
  steeple-nosed prow toward the
  Very Black and the iron cur-
  tainless Kremlin![7]   695

The Parliament of African Peoples plants the winged
  lex scripta of its New Order on
  Roberts Avenue, in Bunker
  Hill, Liberia . . .
The Parliament of African Peoples pinnacles Novus   700
  Homo in the Ashmun Interna-
  tional House,[8] where, free and
  joyful again, all mankind
  unites, without heralds of earth
  and water[9] . . .   705
The Parliament of African Peoples churns with magic
  potions, monsoon spirits, zonal
  oscillations, kinetic credenda,
  apocalyptic projects—shudder-
  ing at its own depth,[1] shudder-   710
  ing as if Shakespeare terrified
  Shakespeare . . .

6. Le Premier des Noirs. When Napoleon became First Consul, Toussaint L'Ouverture addressed him in this manner: "From the First of the Blacks to the First of the Whites."
7. The Very Black: "Qim-Oîrit," or the Red Sea. V.
Maspero, The Dawn of Civilization, I.
8. Cf. Beethoven, Ninth Symphony, "Finale."
9. Heralds of earth and water: ancient symbols of submission.
1. In this phrase Hugo was describing Hugo.

The Parliament of African Peoples, chains riven in an
 age luminous with alpha ray
 ideas, rives the cycle of years   715
 lean and fat, poises the scales of
 Head and Hand, gives Science
 dominion over Why and Art
 over How, bids Man cross the
 bridge of Bifrost and drink   720
 draughts of rases from verved
 and loined apes of God with
 leaves of grass and great audiences . . .
The Parliament of African Peoples, After the Deluge,   725
 wipes out the zymotic zombi
 cult of God's wounds, exscinds
 the fetid fetish Zu'lkadah, bans
 the genocidal *Siyáfa*,[2] enroots
 the Kiowa anthemn *Geh Tai*   730
 Gea[3] . . .
The Parliament of African Peoples pedestals a new gold-
 en calendar of Höhere and
 quickens the death-in-life of
 the unparadised with the olive   735
 alpenstocks of the Violent
 Men[4] . . .
The Parliament of African Peoples decrees the Zu'l-
 hijyah of Everyman and etern-
 izes *Afrika sikelél' iAfrika*[5] . . .   740
The Parliament of African Peoples hormones the Iscar-
 iot- cuckolded Four Freedoms,
 upholsters warehoused *unto*
 each according as any one has
 need, keystones italics ushered   745
 in by epee Pros and Cons In-
 corruptible, banishes cicerones
 of the witch hunt under the
 aegis of Flag and Cross, while
 the tiered galleries and televi-   750
 sion continents hosanna the
 Black Jews from the cis-Dana-
 kil Desert, the Ashantis from
 the Great Sierra Nile, the Hot-
 tentots from Bushland, the   755
 Mpongwes from the Cameroon
 Peoples' Republic, the Pygmies
 from the United States of Outer
 Ubangi . . .
The Parliament of African Peoples signets forever the   760
 Recessional of Europe and

2. *Siyáfa:* "We Die."
3. *Geh Tai Gea:* "All Is Well."
4. *The Violent Men:* the stigmatized advocates of
the Declaration of Independence in the First and
Second Continental Congresses. V. Mèigs, *The Vi-*
olent Men.
5. *Afrika sikelél' iAfrika:* "Africa save Africa."

trumpets the abolition of itself:
and no nation uses *Felis leo* or
Aquila heliaca as the emblem
of *blut und boden;* and the   765
hyenas whine no more among
the barren bones of the seventeenth sunset sultans of Songhai; and the deserts that gave up
the ghost to green pastures   770
chant in the ears and teeth of
the Dog, in the Rosh Hashana
of the Afric calends: *"Honi soit
qui mal y pense!"*

1953

The Birth of John Henry [1]

The night John Henry is born an ax
of lightning splits the sky,
and a hammer of thunder pounds the earth,
and the eagles and panthers cry!

John Henry—he says to his Ma and Pa: 5
"Get a gallon of barleycorn. [2]
I want to start right, like a he-man child,
the night that I am born!"

Says: "I want some ham hocks, ribs, and jowls,
a pot of cabbage and greens;   10
some hoecakes, [3] jam, and buttermilk,
a platter of pork and beans!"

John Henry's Ma—she wrings her hands,
and his Pa—he scratches his head.
John Henry—he curses in giraffe-tall words,   15
flops over, and kicks down the bed.

He's burning mad, like a bear on fire—
so he tears to the riverside.
As he stoops to drink, Old Man River gets scared
and runs upstream to hide!   20

Some say he was born in Georgia—O Lord!
Some say in Alabam.
But it's writ on the rock at the Big Bend Tunnel:
"Lousyana was my home. So scram!"

1965

---

1. A legendary figure from African American ballads and folklore. In the story, John Henry competed with a steam-powered drill to drive railroad
spikes; he won the contest but died from exhaustion.
2. Whiskey made from barley.
3. Cornmeal cakes.

Satchmo[1]

King Oliver[2] of New Orleans
has kicked the bucket, but he left behind
old Satchmo with his red-hot horn
to syncopate the heart and mind.
The honky-tonks in Storyville   5
have turned to ashes, have turned to dust,
but old Satchmo is still around
like Uncle Sam's IN GOD WE TRUST.

Where, oh, where is Bessie Smith[3]
with her heart as big as the blues of truth?   10
Where, oh, where is Mister Jelly Roll[4]
with his Cadillac and diamond tooth?
Where, oh, where is Papa Handy[5]
with his blue notes a-dragging from bar to bar?
Where, oh, where is bulletproof Leadbelly   15
with his tall tales and 12-string guitar?

1965

1. The title of American jazz musician Louis Armstrong's (1901–1971) autobiography.
2. New Orleans–born bandleader (1885–1938), whose King Oliver Creole Band was considered the greatest jazz band of its day. Armstrong stated that Oliver was his true idol.
3. American blues singer (1894–1937), known as the Empress of the Blues.
4. Ferdinand "Jelly Roll" Morton (1885–1941), American jazz pianist.
5. William Christopher Handy (1873–1958), American composer known as the Father of the Blues.

DOROTHY WEST

b. 1907

In the biographical remarks that accompanied the second publication of her short story *An Unimportant Man*, Dorothy West wrote, "I have no ability nor desire to be other than a writer, though the fact is I whistle beautifully." West was born on June 2, 1907, to Rachel Pease West and Isaac Christopher West in Boston, Massachusetts, where she attended Girls' Latin School and Boston University. Hers has been a long and varied writing career, which spans more than seventy years, if we count the short story she wrote at age seven. When she was barely fifteen she was selling stories to the *Boston Post*. And before she was eighteen, already living in New York, West had won second place in the national competition sponsored by *Opportunity* magazine, an honor she shared with Zora Neale Hurston. The winning story, *The Typewriter*, was later included in Edward O'Brien's *The Best Short Stories of 1926*.

A friend of such luminaries as Countee Cullen, Langston Hughes, Claude McKay, and Wallace Thurman, Dorothy West judged them and herself harshly for "degenerat[ing] through [their] vices" and for failing, in general, to live up to their promise. Thus, in what many consider the waning days of the Harlem Renaissance and in the lean years of the Depression, West used personal funds to start *Challenge*, a literary quarterly, hoping to recapture some of this failed promise. She served as its editor from 1934–1937. The last issue of the magazine appeared in the spring of 1937 and was followed by *New Challenge* in the fall of that same year. The renamed journal listed Dorothy West and Marian Minus as coeditors and Richard

Wright as associate editor; it included Wright's famous and influential essay *Blueprint for Negro Writing* and Ralph Ellison's first published piece, *Creative and Cultural Lag.*

The shift from *Challenge* to *New Challenge* can perhaps best be summed up in Wallace Thurman's observation to West that *Challenge* had been too "high schoolish" and "pink tea." Whether *Challenge* was to *New Challenge* what pink tea was to red is debatable, but West has admitted that *New Challenge* became associated with a strict Communist Party line, which she found increasingly difficult to toe. Despite her resistance to this turn in the journal's emphases, *New Challenge*, under West's editorship, encouraged and published submissions that explored the desperate conditions of the black working class.

Because of her involvement with *Challenge* and her early associations with the figures and events that gave the period its singular status and acclaim, West is now generally designated the "last surviving member of the Harlem Renaissance." The bulk of her writing, however, actually began to be published long after what most literary historians consider the height of the movement.

During the Depression, West worked as a bit actress in the original 1929 production of DuBose Heyward's *Porgy* and in 1932–33, she spent time in the Soviet Union as a member of a group of intellectuals, including Langston Hughes, invited to make a film about black life in the United States. The film was never made. West worked briefly as a welfare investigator in Harlem and then, until the mid-1940s, for the WPA Federal Writers' Project.

Many of the more than sixty short stories written throughout her career were published in the *New York Daily News*. The first to appear there was *Jack in the Pot* (retitled *Jackpot* by the editors), which won the Blue Ribbon Fiction contest. Despite her success with the short story, West is best known for her novel, *The Living Is Easy*, the first three chapters of which are printed here. Published in 1948, the novel has been praised for its engaging portrayal of Cleo Judson, the unscrupulous and manipulative woman who brings ruin on herself as well as the members of her family who fall under her domination and control. But the novel has also earned West high marks for its treatment of the class snobbery, insularity, and all-around shallowness of the New England black bourgeoisie, whom West has termed the "genteel poor."

New evaluations of West's works followed the 1982 reprint of *The Living Is Easy* by the Feminist Press and placed the novel in both an emergent women's tradition, focused on the development of female power and autonomy, and in an American tradition that includes Theodore Dreiser and Sinclair Lewis.

For the past forty-plus years, Dorothy West has lived on Martha's Vineyard, contributing since 1968 a generous sampling of occasional pieces and columns to its newspaper, the *Vineyard Gazette*. Her long-awaited novel *The Wedding* received strong notices when it was published in 1995; *The Richer, the Poorer, Sketches and Reminiscences* was published the same year.

From The Living Is Easy

From *Part One*

CHAPTER 1.
[CLEO]

"Walk up," hissed Cleo, somewhat fiercely.

Judy was five, and her legs were fat, but she got up steam and propelled her small stout body along like a tired scow straining in the wake of a racing sloop. She peeped at her mother from under the expansive brim of her leghorn straw. She knew what Cleo would look like. Cleo looked mad.

Cleo swished down the spit-spattered street with her head in the air and her sailor aslant her pompadour. Her French heels rapped the sidewalk smartly, and her starched skirt swayed briskly from her slender buttocks. Through the thin stuff of her shirtwaist her golden shoulders gleamed, and were tied to the rest of her torso with the immaculate straps of her camisole, chemise, and summer shirt, which were banded together with tiny gold-plated safety pins. One gloved hand gave ballast to Judy, the other gripped her pocketbook.

This large patent-leather pouch held her secret life with her sisters. In it were their letters of obligation, acknowledging her latest distribution of money and clothing and prodigal advice. The instruments of the concrete side of her charity, which instruments never left the inviolate privacy of her purse, were her credit books, showing various aliases and unfinished payments, and her pawnshop tickets, the expiration dates of which had mostly come and gone, constraining her to tell her husband, with no intent of irony, that another of her diamonds had gone down the drain.

The lesser items in Cleo's pocketbook were a piece of chamois, lightly sprinkled with talcum powder, and only to be used in extreme necessity if there was no eye to observe this public immodesty, a lollipop for Judy in case she got tiresome, an Irish-linen handkerchief for elegance, a cotton square if Judy stuck up her mouth, and a change purse with silver, half of which Cleo, clandestinely and without conscience, had shaken out of Judy's pig bank.

Snug in the bill compartment of the bag were forty-five dollars, which she had come by more or less legitimately after a minor skirmish with her husband on the matter of renting a ten-room house.

She had begun her attack in the basement kitchen of their landlady's house, a brownstone dwelling in the South End section of Boston. Judy had been sent upstairs to play until bedtime, and Bart had been basking in the afterglow of a good dinner. Ten years before, he had brought his bride to this address, where they had three furnished rooms and the use of the kitchen and the clothesline at a rent which had never increased from its first modest figure. Here, where someone else was responsible for the up-keep, Bart intended to stay and save his money until he was rich enough to spend it.

Cleo had bided her time impatiently. Now Judy was nearing school age. She had no intention of sending her to school in the South End. Whenever she passed these schools at recess time, she would hustle Judy out of sight and sound. "Little knotty-head niggers," she would mutter unkindly, while Judy looked shocked because "nigger" was a bad-word.

These midget comedians made Cleo feel that she was back in the Deep South. Their accents prickled her scalp. Their raucous laughter soured the sweet New England air. Their games were reminiscent of all the whooping and hollering she had indulged in before her emancipation. These r'aring-tearing young ones had brought the folkways of the South to the classrooms of the North. Their numerical strength gave them the brass to mock their timid teachers and resist attempts to make them conform to the Massachu-setts pattern. Those among them who were born in Boston fell into the customs of their southern-bred kin before they were old enough to know that a Bostonian, black or white, should consider himself a special species of fish.

The nicer colored people, preceded by a similar class of whites, were moving out of the South End, so prophetically named with this influx of black cotton-belters. For years these northern Negroes had lived next door to white neighbors and taken pride in proximity. They viewed their southern brothers with alarm, and scattered all over the city and its suburbs to escape this plague of their own locusts.

Miss Althea Binney, Judy's private teacher, who for the past three years had been coming four mornings weekly to give Judy the benefit of her accent and genteel breeding, and to get a substantial lunch that would serve as her principal meal of the day, had told Cleo of a house for rent to colored on a street abutting the Riverway, a boulevard which touched the storied Fens [1] and the arteries of sacred Brookline.

On the previous night, Thea's brother, Simeon, the impoverished owner and editor of the Negro weekly, *The Clarion*, had received a telephone call from a Mr. Van Ryper, who succinctly advised him that he would let his ten-room house for thirty-five dollars monthly to a respectable colored family. Notice to this effect was to be inserted in the proper column of the paper.

Thea, *The Clarion's* chronicler of social events, had urged Simeon to hold the notice until Cleo had had first chance to see the house. Cleo had been so grateful that she had promised Thea an extravagant present, though Thea could better have used her overdue pay that Cleo had spent in an irresistible moment in a department store.

The prospect of Judy entering school in Brookline filled her with awe. There she would rub shoulders with children whose parents took pride in sending them to public school to learn how a democracy functions. This moral obligation discharged, they were then sent to private school to fulfill their social obligation to themselves.

"It's like having a house drop in our laps," said Cleo dramatically. "We'd be fools, Mr. Judson, to let this opportunity pass."

"What in the name of common sense," Bart demanded, "do we want with a ten-room house? We'd rattle around like three pills in a box, paying good money for unused space. What's this Jack the Ripper want for rent?"

"Fifty dollars," Cleo said easily, because the sum was believable and she saw a chance to pocket something for herself.

"That's highway robbery," said Bart, in an aggrieved voice. It hurt him to think that Cleo would want him to pay that extravagant rent month after month and year after year until they all landed in the poorhouse.

"Hold on to your hat," Cleo said coolly. "I never knew a man who got so hurt in his pocketbook. Don't think I want the care of a three-story house. I wasn't born to work myself to the bone. It's Judy I'm thinking of. I won't have her starting school with hoodlums. Where's the common sense in paying good money to Thea if you want your daughter to forget everything she's learned?"

---

1. Or the Fenway, a parkway that stretches through Brookline, a town adjacent to Boston famous for its wealthy homes, estates, and apartment buildings.

Bart had never seen the sense in paying Thea Binney to teach his daughter to be a Bostonian when two expensive doctors of Cleo's uncompromising choosing could bear witness to her tranquil Boston birth. But he did not want Cleo to think that he was less concerned with his child's upbringing than she.

Slowly an idea took shape in his mind. "I'll tell you how I figure we can swing the rent without strain. We can live on one floor and let the other two. If we got fifteen dollars a floor, our part would be plain sailing."

"Uh huh," said Cleo agreeably.

He studied her pleasant expression with suspicion. It wasn't like her to consent to anything without an argument.

"You better say what you want to say now," he advised her.

"Why, I like a house full of people," she said dreamily. "I've missed it ever since I left the South. Mama and Pa and my three sisters made a good-size family. As long as I'm the boss of the house, I don't care how many people are in it."

"Well, of course," he said cautiously, "strangers won't be like your own flesh. Matter of fact, you don't want to get too friendly with tenants. It encourages them to fall behind with the rent."

"I tell you what," she said brilliantly, "we can rent furnished rooms instead of flats. Then there won't be any headaches with poor payers. It's easier to ask a roomer to pack his bag and go than it is to tell a family to pack their furniture."

He saw the logic of that and nodded sagely. "Ten to one a roomer's out all day at work. You don't get to see too much of them. But when you let flats to families, there's bound to be children. No matter how they fell behind, I couldn't put people with children on the sidewalk. It wouldn't set right on my conscience."

Cleo said quietly, "I'd have banked my life on your saying that." For a moment tenderness flooded her. But the emotion embarrassed her. She said briskly: "You remind me of Pa. One of us had a sore tooth, Mama would tell us to go to sleep and forget it. But Pa would nurse us half the night, keeping us awake with kindness."

He accepted the dubious compliment with a modest smile. Then the smile froze into a grimace of pain. He had been hurt in his pocketbook.

"It'll take a pretty penny to furnish all those extra bedrooms. We don't want to bite off more than we can chew. Don't know but what unfurnished flats would be better, after all. We could pick settled people without any children to make me chicken-hearted."

She stared at him like an animal at bay. Little specks of green began to glow in her gray eyes, and her lips pulled away from her even teeth. Bart started back in bewilderment.

"You call yourself a businessman," she said passionately. "You run a big store. You take in a lot of money. But whenever I corner you for a dime, it's like pulling teeth to get it out of you. You always have the same excuse. You need every dollar to buy bananas. And when I say, What's the sense of being in business if you can't enjoy your cash, you always say, In business you have to spend money to make money. Now when I try to advise you to buy a few measly sticks of bedroom furniture, a man who spends thousands of dollars on fruit, you balk like a mule at a racetrack."

He rubbed his mustache with his forefinger. "I see what you mean," he conceded. "I try to keep my store filled with fruit. I can't bear to see an empty storeroom. I guess you got a right to feel the same way about a house. In the long run it's better to be able to call every stick your own than have half your rooms dependent on some outsider's furniture."

She expelled a long breath. "That's settled then."

He thought it prudent to warn her. "We'll have to economize to the bone while we're furnishing that house."

She rolled her eyes upward. "We'll even eat bones if you say so."

He answered quietly: "You and the child will never eat less than the best as long as I live. And all my planning is to see to it that you'll never know want when I'm gone. No one on earth will ever say that I wasn't a good provider. That's my pride, Cleo. Don't hurt it when you don't have to."

"Well, I guess you're not the worst husband in the world," she acknowledged softly, and added slowly, "And I guess I'm the kind of wife God made me." But she did not like the echo of that in her ears. She said quickly, "And you can like it or lump it."

Bart took out an impressive roll of bills, peeled off a few of the lesser ones, and laid them on the table. The sight of the bank roll made Cleo sick with envy. There were so many things she could do with it. All Mr. Judson would do with it was buy more bananas.

She sighed and counted her modest pile. There were only forty-five dollars.

"It's five dollars short," she said frigidly.

"Yep," he said complacently. "I figure if this Jack the Ripper wants fifty dollars he'll take forty-five if he knows he'll get it every month on the dot. And if he ever goes up five dollars on the rent, we still won't be paying him any more than he asked for in the first place. In business, Cleo, I've learned to stay on my toes. You've got to get up with the early birds to get ahead of me."

CHAPTER 2.
[CLEO'S HIGH JINKS]

Her eyes flew open. The birds were waking in the Carolina woods. Cleo always got up with them. There were never enough hours in a summer day to extract the full joy of being alive. She tumbled out of the big old-fashioned bed. Small Serena stirred, then lay still again on her share of the pillow. At the foot of the bed, Lily and Charity nestled together.

She stared at her three younger sisters, seeing the defenselessness of their innocent sleep. The bubbling mischief in her made her take one of Lily's long braids and double knot it with one of Charity's. She looked back at Serena, who tried so hard to be a big girl and never let anyone help her dress. She picked up Serena's little drawers and turned one leg inside out.

She was almost sorry she would be far away when the fun began. She could picture Lily and Charity leaping to the floor from opposite sides of the bed, and their heads snapping back, and banging together. As for Serena, surprise would spread all over her solemn face when she stepped into one leg of her drawers and found the other leg closed to her. She would start all over again, trying her other foot this time, only to find she had stepped into the same kettle of hot water. She would wrassle for fifteen minutes, getting madder and madder. Cleo had to clap her hand to her mouth to hush her giggles.

She would get a whipping for it. Mama would never see the joke. Mama would say it was mean to tease your sisters. You had to walk a chalkline to please her.

Sometimes Cleo tried to walk a chalkline, but after a little while, keeping to the strait and narrow made her too nervous. At home, there was nothing to do except stay around. Away from home, there were trees to climb, and boys to fight, and hell to raise with Josie Beauchamp.

She climbed out of the open window and dropped to the ground at the moment that Josie Beauchamp was quietly creeping down the stairs of her magnificent house. Some day Cleo was going to live in a fine house, too. And maybe some day Josie was going to be as poor as church mice.

They met by their tree, at the foot of which they had buried their symbols of friendship. Josie had buried her gold ring because she loved it best of everything, and Cleo best of everybody. Cleo had buried Lily's doll, mostly because it tickled her to tell her timid sister that she had seen a big rat dragging it under the house. Lily had taken a long stick and poked around. But every time it touched something, Lily had jumped a mile.

Cleo and Josie wandered over the Beauchamp place, their bare feet drinking in the dew, their faces lifted to feel the morning. Only the birds were abroad, their vivid splashes of color, the brilliant outpouring of their waking songs filling the eye and ear with summer's intoxication.

They did not talk. They had no words to express their aliveness. They wanted none. Their bodies were their eloquence. Clasping hands, they began to skip, too impatient of meeting the morning to walk toward it any longer. Suddenly Cleo pulled her hand away and tapped Josie on the shoulder. They should have chosen who was to be "It." But Cleo had no time for counting out. The wildness was in her, the unrestrained joy, the desire to run to the edge of the world and fling her arms around the sun, and rise with it, through time and space, to the center of everywhere.

She was swift as a deer, as mercury, with Josie running after her, falling back, and back, until Josie broke the magic of the morning with her exhausted cry, "Cleo, I can't catch you."

"Nobody can't never catch me," Cleo exulted. But she spun around to wait for Josie. The little sob in Josie's throat touched the tenderness she always felt toward those who had let her show herself the stronger.

They wandered back toward Josie's house, for now the busyness of the birds had quieted to let the human toilers take over the morning. Muted against the white folks' sleeping, the Negro voices made velvet sounds. The field hands and the house servants diverged toward their separate spheres, the house servants settling their masks in place, the field hands waiting for the overseer's eye before they stooped to servility.

Cleo and Josie dawdled before the stables. The riding horses whinnied softly, thrusting their noses to the day. Josie's pony nuzzled her hand, wanting to hear his name dripping in honey. And Cleo moved away. Anybody could ride an old pony. She wanted to ride General Beauchamp's roan stallion, who shied at any touch but his master's.

She marched back to Josie. "Dare me to ride the red horse," she challenged. Her eyes were green as they bored into Josie's, the gray gone under in her passion.

"No," said Josie, desperately trying not to flounder in the green sea. "He'd throw you and trample you. He'd kill you dead."

"He can't tromp me! I ain't ascairt of nothing alive. I dare you to dare me. I double dare you!"

"I won't, I won't! I'm bad, but I'm not wicked."

"I'm not wicked neither! I just ain't a coward."

She streaked to the stall and flung open the barrier. The wild horse smelled her wildness. Her green eyes locked with his red-flecked glare. Their wills met, clashed, and would not yield. The roan made a savage sound in his throat, his nostrils flared, his great sides rippled. He lowered his head to lunge. But Cleo was quicker than he was. She grasped his mane, leaped on his broad neck, slid down his back, and dug her heels in his flanks.

"Giddap, red horse!" she cried.

He flung back his head, reared, and crashed out of the stall, with Josie screeching and sobbing and sidestepping just in time.

Cleo hung on for ten minutes, ten minutes of dazzling flight to the sun. She felt no fear, feeling only the power beneath her and the power inside her, and the rush of wind on which she and the roan were riding. When she was finally thrown, she landed unhurt in a clover field. It never occurred to her to feel for broken bones. She never doubted that she had a charmed life. Her sole mishap was a minor one. She had split the seat of her drawers.

She got up and brushed off her pinafore, in a fever now to get home and brag to her sisters. She knew that she ought to let Josie see that she was still alive. The riderless horse would return, and Josie would never tell who had ridden him off. But she would be tormented by fear for as long as Cleo stayed away.

Josie would not want to eat, no matter what fancy things the white folks had for breakfast. She would not want to ride in her pony cart, no matter how pretty a picture she made. She would not want to go calling with her stylish mother, not even if she was let to wear the dress that came all the way from Paris. On this bright day the sun had darkened for Josie, and nobody but Cleo could make it shine again.

The four sisters sat around the kitchen table, eating their salt pork and biscuit and hominy, slupping down their buttermilk. Charity was nine, two years younger than Cleo, Lily was eight, Serena four. Their faces were tear-streaked. Cleo's was not, though she was the one who had got the whipping. Mama couldn't keep track of the times she had tanned Cleo's hide, trying to bring her up a Christian. But the Devil was trying just as hard in the other direction.

There Cleo was this morning, looking square in Mama's eye, telling her she must have been sleepwalking again. Couldn't remember getting dressed or tying her sisters' braids together. Just remembered coming awake in a clover field. Mama had tried to beat the truth out of her, but Cleo wouldn't budge from her lie. Worst of all, she wouldn't cry and show remorse. Finally Mama had to put away the strap because her other children looked as if they would die if she didn't.

They couldn't bear to see Cleo beaten. She was their oldest sister, their protector. She wasn't afraid of the biggest boy or the fiercest dog, or the meanest teacher. She could sass back. She could do anything. They accepted her teasing and tormenting as they accepted the terrors of night. Night was always followed by day, and made day seem more wonderful.

Mama stood by the hearth, feeling helpless in her mind. Cleo was getting too big to beat, but she wasn't a child that would listen to reason. Whatever she didn't want to hear went in one ear and out the other. She was old enough to be setting an example for her sisters. And all they saw her do was devilment.

With a long blackened fireplace stick Mama carefully tilted the lid of the three-legged skillet to see if her corn bread was done. The rest of Pa's noon dinner—the greens, the rice, the hunk of fresh pork—was waiting in his bucket. Gently she let the lid drop, and began to work the skillet out of its covering of coals that had been charred down from the oak wood. As the skillet moved forward, the top coals dislodged. Their little plunking sounds were like the tears plopping in Mama's heart.

Sulkily Cleo spooned the hominy she hated because she mustn't make Mama madder by leaving it. Mama bleached her corn in lye water made from fireplace ashes. Pa spit tobacco juice in those ashes. He spit to the side, and Mama took her ashes from the center, but that didn't make them seem any cleaner. Mama thought everything about Pa was wonderful, even his spit.

Cleo made a face at Mama's back, and then her face had to smile a little bit as she watched the dimples going in and out of Mama's round arms. You could almost touch their softness with your eyes. A flush lay just under the surface, giving them a look of tender warmth. For all the loving in Mama's arms, she had no time for it all day. Only at night, when her work was done, and her children in bed, you knew by Mama's silver laughter that she was finding time for Pa.

Mama loved Pa better than anyone. And what was left over from loving him was divided among her daughters. Divided even, Mama said whenever Cleo asked her. Never once would Mama say she loved one child the most.

On their straggling way to the mill with Pa's dinner, Cleo told her sisters about her wild ride. They were bewitched by her fanciful telling. Timid Lily forgot to watch where she was walking. Her toes uncurled. She snatched up a stick and got astride it.

Serena clung to Charity's hand to keep herself from flying. Cleo was carrying her away, and she wanted to feel the ground again. She wanted to take Pa his dinner, and go back home and play house.

Charity saw a shining prince on a snow-white charger. The prince rode toward her, dazzling her eyes with light, coming nearer and nearer, leaning to swoop her up in his arms. And Cleo, looking at Charity's parted lips and the glowing eyes, thought that Charity was seeing her riding the red horse into the sun.

Her triumphant tale, in which she did not fall, but grandly dismounted to General Beauchamp's applause, came to its thrilling conclusion. She turned and looked at Lily scornfully, because a stick was not a horse. Lily felt foolish, and let the stick fall, and stepped squish on an old fat worm. Serena freed her hand. Released from Cleo's spell, she felt independent again. Charity's shining prince vanished, and there was only Cleo, walking ahead as usual, forgetting to take back the bucket she had passed to Charity.

Pa was waiting in the shade, letting the toil pour off him in perspiration. His tired face lightened with love when they reached him. He opened his dinner bucket and gave them each a taste. Nothing ever melted so good in their mouths as a bite of Pa's victuals.

He gave them each a copper, too, though he could hardly spare it, what with four of them to feed and Mama wanting yard goods and buttons and ribbons to keep herself feeling proud of the way she kept her children. Time was, he gave them kisses for toting his bucket. But the day Cleo brazenly said, I don't want a kiss, I want a copper, the rest of them shamefacedly said it after her. Most times Pa had a struggle to dig down so deep. Four coppers a day, six days a week, was half a day's pay gone up in smoke for candy.

Pa couldn't bring himself to tell Mama. She would have wrung out of him that Cleo had been the one started it. And Cleo was his eldest. A man who loved his wife couldn't help loving his first-born best, the child of his fiercest passion. When that first-born was a girl, she could trample on his heart, and he would swear on a stack of Bibles that it didn't hurt.

The sisters put their coppers in their pinafore pockets and skipped back through the woods.

Midway Cleo stopped and pointed to a towering oak. "You all want to bet me a copper I can't swing by my feet from up in that tree?"

Lily clapped her hands to her eyes. "I doesn't want to bet you," she implored. "I ain't fixing to see you fall."

Serena said severely, "You bust your neck, you see if Mama don't bust it again."

Charity said tremulously, "Cleo, what would us do if our sister was dead?"

Cleo saw herself dressed up fine as Josie Beauchamp, stretched out in a coffin with her sisters sobbing beside it, and Pa with his Sunday handkerchief holding his tears, and Mama crying, I loved you best, Cleo. I never said it when you were alive. And I'm sorry, sorry, I waited to say it after you were gone.

"You hold my copper, Charity. And if I die, you can have it."

Lily opened two of her fingers and peeped through the crack. "Cleo, I'll give you mine if you don't make me see you hanging upside down." It was one thing to hear Cleo tell about herself. It was another thing to see her fixing to kill herself.

"Me, too," said Serena, with a little sob, more for the copper than for Cleo, whom she briefly hated for compelling unnecessary sacrifice.

"You can have mine," said Charity harshly. Her sweet tooth ached for a peppermint stick, and she almost wished that Cleo was dead.

Cleo flashed them all an exultant smile. She had won their money with-

out trying. She had been willing to risk her neck to buy rich Josie Beauchamp some penny candy. Now that it was too late to retrieve Josie Beauchamp's lost hours of anxiety, Cleo wanted to carry her a bag of candy, so
that when Josie got through with being glad, and got mad, she wouldn't
stay mad too long.

She held out her hand. Each tight fist poised over her palm, desperately
clung aloft, then slowly opened to release the bright coin that was to have
added a special sweetness to the summer day.

Cleo couldn't bear to see their woe-begone faces. She felt frightened,
trapped by their wounded eyes. She had to do something to change their
expressions.

"I'll do a stunt for you," she said feverishly. "I'll swing by my hands. It
ain't nothing to be ascairt to see. You watch."

Quickly, agilely she climbed the tree and hung by her hands. Wildly,
wildly she swung, to make them forget she had taken their money, to let
them see how wonderful she was.

Then a boy came by, just an ordinary knotted-headed, knobby-kneed
boy. He looked at her and laughed, because to him a girl carrying on so
crazy cut a funny figure. She wanted to kill him. He made her feel silly.
She climbed down, and she knew he was watching her, watching the split
in her drawers.

When she reached the ground, she whirled to face him, and found his
feet waving in front of her. He was walking on his hands. And her sisters
were squealing with delight. They had seen her walk on her hands a thousand times. What was there so wonderful about watching a boy?

She flung herself upon him, and they fought like dogs, the coppers lost
irrecoverably. Her sisters circled them, crying and wringing their hands.
She had to win, no matter how. She bent her head and butted him in the
groin, where the weakness of boys was—the contradictory delicacy.

The fight was knocked out of him. He lay very still, his hands shielding
his innocent maleness from further assault, and the blood on his lips where
his anguished teeth had sunk in.

Her sisters fluttered around him. They felt no pride for her victory. Instead they pitied him. She watched them with wonder. What was there to
being a boy? What was there to being a man? Men just worked. That was
easier than what women did. It was women who did the lying awake, the
planning, the sorrowing, the scheming to stretch a dollar. That was the
hard part, the head part. A woman had to think all the time. A woman had
to be smart.

Her sisters weren't smart. They thought Pa was the head of the house.
They didn't know the house was run by the beat of Mama's heart. There
was an awful lonesomeness in Cleo when Mama went across the river to
Grandma's. She did not want to be bad then. She wanted to be good so
God would send Mama back safe. But she was wildly bad again the moment Mama returned. She could not bear the way she felt inside, like
laughing and crying and kissing Mama's face.

She never kissed Mama. Kisses were silly. Pa kissed Mama when he
came home from work. There was sweat on him from his labor, but Mama
lifted her mouth to his. His mustache prickled against her lips, but Mama
did not pull away.

Looking at her sisters, standing above the suffering boy, she saw in each some likeness of Mama—in Charity the softness and roundness, the flush just under the thin skin, the silver laughter; in Lily the doe eyes, liquid and vulnerable, the plaited hair that kept escaping in curls; in small Serena the cherry-red mouth, the dimpled cheeks. She knew that she looked like Pa. Everyone said so. Everyone said she was a beauty. What was wrong with their seeing? How could looking like Pa, with his sweat and his stained mustache, make anybody a beauty? Sometimes she would stare at herself in Mama's mirror and stick out her tongue.

Now, seeing her sisters, with their tender faces turned toward the boy, a terrible sorrow assailed her. Some day they would all grow up. They would all get married and go away. They would never live together again, nor share the long bright busy days. Mama, too, would go. Mama would die. Didn't she always say that her side of the family were not long livers? They were dead before they were fifty. Dead with their loveliness alive in their still, smooth faces. When Mama was gone in a last luminous moment, there would be the look of her and the silver laughter in the children she had blessed with her resemblance.

So long as her sisters were within sight and sound, they were the mirrors in which she would see Mama. They would be her remembering of her happy, happy childhood.

She flung herself down on the ground, and her torture was worse than the boy's. For hers was spiritual suffering and immeasurable frustration. All her terror of the future, all her despair at knowing that nothing lasts—that sisters turn into wives, that men take their women and ride away, that childhood is no longer than a summer day—were in her great dry sobs.

The boy staggered to his feet in complete alarm. He thought he had hurt her in some dreadful way mysterious to girls, her breast, her belly where the babies grew. Her father would skin him alive. He made a limping dash across the road and the trees closed in.

Then her sisters knelt beside her, letting their soothing fingers caress her face. Her sobbing quieted. She jumped up and began to turn cartwheels. A wildness was in her. She was going to turn cartwheels all the way home, heretofore an impossible feat.

Mama was in the doorway, watching her hurtle down a dusty road, seeing a girl eleven years old turning upside down, showing her drawers. Mama got the strap again and laid it on hard and heavy. Cleo just grinned, and wouldn't wipe the grin off, even with the whole of her on fire and hurting. Mama couldn't bear such impudence from her own flesh and blood. She let the strap fall and sat down and cried.

Mama didn't know what made Cleo so wild. Cleo got more of her attention than all of her other children put together. God help her when she grew up. God help the man who married her. God help her sisters not to follow in her footsteps. Better for her sisters if Cleo had never been born.

Somewhere in Springfield, Massachusetts, at that moment, Bart Judson, a grown man, a businessman, too interested in the Almighty Dollar to give any thought to a wife, was certainly giving no thought to an eleven-year-old hell-raiser way down South. But for Bart, whose inescapable destiny this unknown hoyden was to be, it might have been better if her sisters had never been born.

CHAPTER 3.
[CLEO GOES NORTH]

Cleo arrived in Springfield three years later. She and Josie reached their teens within a month of each other. Cleo became the Kennedy kitchen help and caught her hair up in a bright bandana to keep it out of the cooking. Josie caught her hair up, too, but with pins and combs in the fashion. She put on a long dress and learned to pour tea in the parlor. Cleo learned to call her Miss Josephine, and never said anything that was harder.

Providence appeared as an elderly spinster, a northern lady seeking sun for her sciatica. Cleo's way home lay past her boarding place. She was entranced by Cleo's beauty as she returned from work, her hair flying free, the color still staining her cheeks from the heat of the cookstove and the fire in her heart, and her eyes sea-green from her sullen anger at working in the white folks' kitchen.

Miss Peterson, hating to see this sultry loveliness ripen in the amoral atmosphere of the South, urged Mama to let her take Cleo North. Mama considered it an answer to prayer. With Cleo getting so grown, Mama's heart stayed in her mouth. She didn't know what minute Cleo might disgrace herself. The wildness in the child might turn to wantonness in the girl. And that would kill Pa. Better for him if she sent Cleo North with this strict-looking spinster.

Cleo considered going North an adventure. Miss Josephine, who had never been outside of Carolina, would turn green with envy. In her secret sessions with her heartsick sisters, Cleo promised to send for them as soon as she got rich. She did not know how she was going to do it, but this boastful promise was more important than the performance.

She had thought she was going to night school when she reached the North. But her conscientious custodian, seeing that Cleo looked just as vividly alive in Springfield as she had looked in South Carolina, decided against permitting her to walk down darkened streets alone. There were too many temptations along the way in the guise of coachmen and butlers and porters.

Cleo's time, between her easy chores, was spent in training her tongue to a northern twist, in learning to laugh with a minimum show of teeth, and in memorizing a new word in the dictionary every day.

The things that Cleo never had to be taught were how to hold her head high, how to scorn sin with men, and how to keep her left hand from knowing what her right hand was doing.

She saw Bart Judson six months after her arrival, on one of the few occasions that she was let out of her cloister. This brief encounter, with a plate-glass window between them, made no impression on either participant. The wheels of their inseparable destiny were revolving slowly. For shortly thereafter Bart was to be on his way to Boston. And not for five years more was Cleo to follow, and then with no knowledge that Bart Judson had preceded her.

As they stared disinterestedly at each other, he seeing only a pretty, half-grown, countrified girl, she seeing only a shirt-sleeved man with a mustache, and neither recognizing Fate, the disappointed goddess had half a mind to change their charted course. Then with habitual perversity thought better of it.

Cleo had come to a halt before a store front, where an exquisite pile of polished fruit was arrayed on a silver tray, the sole and eye-compelling window display. Two men were busy inside the store, one, a fair-skinned man whom Cleo mistook for white and the proprietor, was waiting on the customer, the other man, obviously the colored help, was restocking the counters. The colored man stared briefly, as did Cleo. Then her eyes moved to a wide arch which made convenient access to an ice-cream parlor next door.

Two retail stores on busy State Street was the distance Virginia-born Bart had come in his lucky boots on his way to the banana docks of the Boston Market. Cleo, with ten cents burning a hole in her pocket and her throat parched for a fancy dish of ice cream, slowly walked away, because she wasn't certain that the owner wanted colored customers. And, as a matter of fact, Bart didn't.

When he and Cleo met five years later, again it was pure chance. But this time Fate flung them headlong at each other, and for Bart, at least, there was no mistaking that he had met the woman he wanted for his wife.

Cleo was sent to Boston by the relatives of her Springfield benefactress when the old lady's lingering illness was inevitably leading her to the grave. The relatives rallied around her, for there were always cases of elderly people deciding to leave their estates to faithful servants. They arrived *en masse*, for there were cases, too, of elderly people deciding that one devoted relative was more deserving than the rest.

They overflowed the small house. There was no room for Cleo, and also no need, for the women industriously cooked and cleaned, went errands, and wrote letters. One of the letters was to a Boston friend of Miss Peterson, who knew Cleo slightly from her occasional visits to Springfield. She was importuned to give shelter to this young Negro girl. With Christian charity, she promptly did so.

She shared her home with a nephew, whom she had raised and educated. The young man, coming of age, was not grateful. He wanted to get married. He intended to leave home. He was so obdurate about these matters that his aunt, Miss Boorum, was nearly resigned to spending her declining years alone, regretting the sacrifice that had caused her spinsterhood.

Cleo seemed a light in the gathering gloom. She was southern, she was colored. From what Miss Boorum had read of southern colored people they were devoted to what they quaintly called "my white folks," and quite disdainful of their own kind, often referring to them as "niggers." They liked to think of themselves as an integral part of the family, and preferred to die in its bosom rather than any place else. It was to be hoped that Cleo would show the same sterling loyalty.

In Boston Cleo settled into the same routine that she had endured in Springfield. She was indifferent to the change. One old white woman looked just like any other old white woman to her. Only difference was Miss Boorum wore false teeth that slipped up and down when she talked. She paid the same five dollars a month, the sum that Cleo had been receiving, obliquely, since she was sixteen. It was not considered wages. The amount was not the thing that mattered so much as the spirit that prompted it. Though Cleo's duties were similar to a servant's, she was considered a ward. She was fed and clothed, and given a place at table and a chair in the parlor, except when there was company. At such times she put on an apron, held her proud head above the level of everybody's eyes, and wished they would all drop dead.

Both her Springfield and Boston protectresses felt that Cleo was better off without money. Each month Miss Boorum, as had her predecessor, sent five dollars to Mama affixed to a little note in an aging hand full of fancy flourishes that Mama spent a day deciphering. These custodians of Cleo's character had no wish to teach her to save. Nothing, they knew, is a greater inducement to independent action than knowing where you can put your hand on a bit of cash.

Their little notes reported to Mama on Cleo's exemplary behavior. But Cleo was neither good nor bad. She was in a state of suspension. She knew she was paying penance for all the joyous wildness of her childhood. She had been exiled to learn the discipline that Mama's punishments had not taught her. She did not mind these years of submission any more than she had minded Mama strapping her. If you were bad, you got punished. But you had had your fun. And that was what counted. These meek years would not last forever. The follies of childhood were sweet sins that did not merit eternal damnation. This was the period of instruction that was preparing her for adulthood. Yet she knew she was not changing. She was merely learning guile.

She was going to run away the minute she got her bearings in Boston, leaving a sassy note saying, Thank you for nothing. Good-bye and good riddance. If I never see you again, that will be too soon.

Then she was going on the stage. She was going to sing and dance. That would be wickeder than anything she had ever done, but almost as much fun as there had been in the Carolina woods. Pa would disown her, and Mama would pray for her soul. But she would fix up the house for Mama with furniture and running water, and buy her some store clothes and a horse to hitch the buggy to in place of Pa's old mule.

She sat in Miss Boorum's parlor, reading Little Women[2] aloud, looking demure and gray-eyed, hearing the richness of her own voice, being thrilled by its velvet sound, and seeing herself singing and kicking her heels on a stage in a swirl of lace petticoats. The only thing was she wasn't going to have any partner. She wasn't going to sing an old love-song with any greasy-haired coon. She wasn't going to dance any cakewalk[3] with him either, and let his sweaty hand ruin her fancy costumes.

Miss Boorum's nephew, looking at Cleo across the table, was profoundly disturbed by his emotions. He, too, had heard about Negroes. He had heard mostly about Negro women, and the information was correct. Desire was growing in his loins and there was nothing he could do to stop it. All he could do was try to keep it from spreading to his heart.

He talked no more of marriage now, nor of moving away. He rarely went out in the evening. He gloomed about the house, staring moodily at Cleo. Miss Boorum supposed he was beset by the jealous fear that her ward

2. By Louisa May Alcott, an extremely popular children's book published in 1868–69. It details the daily lives of four girls in a 19th-century New England family.
3. A dance of exaggerated strutting movements, thought to have been originated on plantations by slaves mimicking white overseers and masters. It was usually performed in competitions in which the best dancer won a cake.

would supplant him in her affections. To punish him for the pain he had caused her, she made his ears ring with Cleo's praises. Cleo supposed he was jealous, too, as the Springfield relatives had been, and took a wicked delight in tormenting him by being her most appealing in his presence.

Mama died. The letter came. Nobody down home had sense enough to send a telegram. Mama was buried by the time the letter reached Boston. She died bearing a dead child. Pa had just as good as killed her.

Cleo hadn't seen Mama since she was fourteen. Mama standing in the station saying, "God watch between me and thee, while we are absent one from another." Mama with the flush in her face from her fast-beating heart, and the tears held tight in her searching doe eyes, her coral lip trembling between her white teeth, and her arms reaching out, the rounded arms with dimples. Mama was dead, and the lid was shut down. Now Mama could never say, Cleo, I loved you best of all my children.

Cleo's grief was an inward thing that gave her a look of such purity that Miss Boorum's nephew was even further enmeshed. The enchantment of knowing that she was no one's was monstrous. He was seduced by her chastity. He would never be free as long as he knew he could be her first lover. Until he could see the face of her purity replaced by the face of surrender, her image would lie on his lids to torment him.

He grew thin and wan. Cleo looked at him and thought indifferently that he was coming down with something, and hoped it wouldn't be catching.

Miss Boorum's nephew began his campaign. He bought Cleo a bicycle. Ostensibly it was to solace her sorrow. Actually it was because he could not afford to deck her in diamonds.

He did not ride with her, nor would he instruct her in the intricacies of balance. Subconsciously he had the bloody hope that she would break every bone in her body and destroy her beauty, if not herself.

She pedaled away as easily as if she had been cycling all her life, for she still did not know there was anything she was incapable of doing. In Norumbega Park she sped around a curve and rode unromantically into Mr. Judson's stomach.

The impact sent them sprawling on either side of the path, with the shiny new bicycle rearing like a bucking horse, flinging itself against a boulder, and smashing itself to pieces.

Because she had not long lost Mama, and now she had lost her new bicycle, Cleo burst into heartbroken howls. Her heretofore unshed tears flowed in a torrent. Mr. Judson sat and rubbed his upset stomach and felt himself drowning helplessly in her welling eyes and tumbled hair.

When she could speak, she sobbed accusations. Why didn't he look where he was going? Why hadn't he jumped out of her way? Look at her brand-new bicycle. Who did he think was going to get her another one?

He was, Mr. Judson assured her gallantly. He helped her to her feet, though she fought him all the way, jerking and twisting out of his unexploring hands. He asked her for her name and address, and she gave them to him defiantly. She knew this poor darky didn't have one thin dime to lay against another, but if he wanted to talk big, let him back up his promise. He told her his name, and she forgot it immediately. What did she want to know his name for? She wasn't going to give him a bicycle.

He offered to see her home. She refused so vehemently that he pictured her parents as martinets, and supposed that the courtship, on which he had decided the minute he got back his breath, would be long and hazardous.

She took the poor wreck of her bicycle and pushed off unaided. It was a painful journey, and she was often admonished to get a horse. She reached home footsore and furious. Miss Boorum's nephew flew to the door, for Cleo rang the bell so sharply that the unhappy young man had the rather pleasurable foreboding that a policeman had brought bad tidings.

It was Cleo. He had never seen her in a wild moment, and he was further undone. For now he saw her with all her aliveness, her dark hair streaming, her eyes sparking green stars, the blood in her cheeks with the tear streaks and dust streaks, and her apple breasts betraying the pulse of her angry heart. He knew God was punishing him for his desire to see her dead by sending her back more alive than ever.

That night Miss Boorum's nephew and Mr. Judson tossed and turned in their restless sleep, while Cleo slept like a rock from all the air she had imbibed on the long ride and the long walk.

Mr. Judson was ardently in love. Why it had come upon him like this, he could not have explained, except that he had reached the age for it. He had distrusted women until now. He thought all they saw in a man was his pocketbook. When they asked him flattering questions, he imagined they were prying into his affairs, trying to find out how much he had that they would have if they married him. Artfully he had sidestepped them all, spending his days in such hard work that sleep came easily, and there were no wakeful hours of aching loins. On Sunday afternoons he strolled in the city's parks.

His excursions into society were infrequent and unsuccessful. He did not look like a rich man, for he wore a disguise of ancient suits to confuse the predatory. He did not resemble a Bostonian. His tongue was soft and liquid. He was dark. He was unimpressed by backgrounds. He made it plain that if you were a State House attendant, you were only a porter to him, no matter how many of your forebears had been freeborn.

The men with whom he had daily contact were unpretentious rich men, the bankers, the brokers, the shipowners, the heads of wholesale houses. When he moved among colored men, he was slightly contemptuous, though he thought he was merely bored. He had been in business for himself since he was ten, and was never wholly able to understand anyone who was content to let someone else be the boss man.

Bart bought the finest bicycle he could find in Boston and dispatched it next day, with a crate of oranges and two handsome hands of bananas that he hoped would impress Cleo's parents.

He called the following Sunday, and was surprised to find that Cleo worked in service, but rather pleased. She ought to consider herself a lucky girl to be courted by a man of substance. Miss Boorum, herself, showed him into the parlor, and sat down with a colored man for the first time in her life. Though she had not seen through her nephew, she saw through Bart immediately. He was in love with Cleo. This did not surprise her. It was typical of colored men.

Her nephew, hearing a male voice below with a Negro flavor, came down from his study in acute anxiety. Here was the stranger his common sense had commanded to come. Here was the man who would set him

THE LIVING IS EASY

free. And his eyes were hot with hatred. Bart saw the young man's anguish. He saw that Cleo did not see it. Nor Miss Boorum. He had to get Cleo out of this house before the fever in the young man's eyes spread to his loins. He could not let her be lost in one wanton night. Or her image would lie on his eyelids for the rest of his life.

All the next day he worried like a hen with one helpless chick. When his picture-making grew too intolerable, he washed off his surface sweat and went to Miss Boorum's. He approached the house by way of the alley, hoping to find Cleo in the kitchen, where he could talk unheard. He had better luck than he bargained for. She was in the clothes yard. She had clothes-pins in her mouth, and was too surprised to take them out.

He began to whisper fiercely, and she only heard half of what he said, for he kept jerking his head around to see who might be coming. He told her hurriedly and harriedly that she was in great danger, a wolf was abroad in Miss Boorum's nephew's clothing. She was not safe, and never would be safe, so long as she stayed within reach of his clutches. She was too young to be alone in Boston. She had no mother to guide her. She needed a good man's protection. She needed a husband. He would marry her today if she would have him. If she would have him, he would apply for a license today and marry her at City Hall at nine o'clock on Thursday morning.

If he had proposed to her any other way, if he had courted her for a longer time, she might have refused him, out of sheer contrariness. He had not frightened her with his fears. She felt that she could subdue any man with her scorn. But she wanted to get away. She couldn't stand seeing Miss Boorum's nephew moping around like a half-sick dog if woman hankering was what ailed him. If he ever came hankering after her, she'd stab him dead with an ice-pick. And no man on earth, let alone a white man, was worth going to hell for.

She was still so wrapped up in murderous thoughts and daring Miss Boorum's demoralized nephew to come within a foot of her that she married Bart without thinking about it. When she found herself in her marriage bed, she let him know straightaway that she had no intention of renouncing her maidenhood for one man if she had married to preserve it from another.

Bart had expected that he would have to lead her to love with patience. He was a man of vigor and could wait without wasting for Cleo's awakening. Some part of him was soothed and satisfied by the fact of his right to cherish her. It did not torment him to lie beside her and know that he could not possess her. He threw his energy into buying and selling. For he loved his fruit almost as much as he loved his wife. There was rich satisfaction in seeing it ripen, seeing the downiness on it, the blush on it, feeling the firmness of its flesh.

When Cleo was twenty, their sex battle began. It was not a savage fight. She did not struggle against his superior strength. She found a weapon that would cut him down quickly and cleanly. She was nice. Neither her mouth nor her body moved to meet his. The open eyes were wide with mocking at the busyness below. There was no moment when everything in her was wrenched and she was one with the man who could submerge her in himself.

Five years later, she conceived a child on a night when her body's hunger broke down her controlled resistance. For there was no real abhorrence of sex in her. Her need of love was as urgent as her aliveness indicated. But her perversity would not permit her to weaken. She would not face the knowledge that she was incomplete in herself.

Yet now, as she walked toward the trolley stop, she was determined not to live another year without her sisters.

1948

RICHARD WRIGHT
1908–1960

A summary of Richard Wright's life is captured in the title of an early critical article on his work: "Juvenile Delinquent Becomes Famous Writer." Born in 1908 on a plantation near Natchez, Mississippi, Wright's life conformed to the stock pattern of the American success myth. From his impoverished and educationally barren early years to his achievement as a favored literary touchstone and ancestor figure, the details of Wright's life constitute the stuff of legends.

Wright's early life gave him bitter preparation for the intellectual outlook and the acute social and political consciousness of his writing. Shuttled from relative to relative, after his mother's partial paralysis forced her to place him and his brother temporarily in an orphanage, Wright lived a time with his grandmother and aunt, whose religious fanaticism stunted Wright's education but not his passion for encyclopedic reading. Working in Memphis as an errand boy, Wright fed his obsession, subverting Jim Crow laws by forging the now famous note to the public librarian: "Dear Madam: Will you please let this nigger boy have some books by H. L. Mencken?" Although Wright also read the fiction of Theodore Dreiser, Sherwood Anderson, and Sinclair Lewis and shared their indictments of middle-class babbitry, it was Mencken's work that first inspired Wright's own literary ambitions and focused his aspirations as a stylist. From Mencken's A Book of Prefaces, Wright sensed a man "fighting, fighting with words . . . using words as a weapon . . . as one would use a club." Wright would later supplement this early reading with the work of experimentalists and modernists such as Marcel Proust, Henry James, and Gertrude Stein, whose character Melanctha from Three Lives Wright considered one of the few credible portraits of an African American by a white author.

In 1927 Wright migrated to Chicago, along with masses of other blacks who fled the racism, poverty, and lynch law of the rural South only to find the cities of the urban North, as he put it, "sprawling centers of steel and stone" as cold and unyielding as the South. Disabused of his expectation that life in the North "could be lived with dignity," Wright turned to Communism and began to find a literary voice and ideological affinity in the leftist political ferment of the 1930s. In 1936 he served as literary adviser and press agent for the Negro Federal Theatre of Chicago and became involved in dramatic productions. A year later he broke with the Communist Party, largely because of its attempts to control his freedom as a writer. The final break with the party came in 1942, again over artistic freedom, but more important, because of the party's weak position on discrimination in the armed forces during World War II. The break became public and official in 1944 when he published excerpts of I Tried to Be a Communist in Atlantic Monthly, but it was far from precipitous. Well up to the publication of Twelve Million Black Voices (1941), Wright had tried to sharpen his conception of literary form and to work out the relationship between the techniques of fiction and the tenets of Marxism. He attended meetings of the Chicago John Reed Club, churned out proletarian poems for such Communist journals as *Partisan Review* and *New Masses*, and served as chief Harlem correspondent for the *Daily Worker*.

It followed logically from these experiences that Wright would attempt to outline a literary theory for black American writers. The result was *Blueprint for Negro Writing*. Published in the inaugural issue of *New Challenge* (1937)—a magazine Wright coedited with Dorothy West and Marian Minus—*Blueprint*, was, like Langston Hughes's earlier *The Negro Artist and the Racial Mountain*, a manifesto and declaration of independence from what he judged to be bourgeois literary forms and agenda long dominant in black letters. Distancing himself from the writings of the Harlem Renaissance, which he dismissed as "humble novels, poems, and plays," written by "prim and decorous ambassadors who went a-begging to white America," Wright urged black writers to embrace a Marxist conception of reality and society, which offered, in his judgment, the "maximum degree of freedom in thought and feeling . . . for the Negro writer."

Wright executed his own blueprint in *Uncle Tom's Children* (1938), a collection of four novellas set in the Jim Crow South. At times, the stories are flawed by Marxist propagandizing, melodrama, ponderous didacticism, and improbable plots. Nevertheless, they show some of the major influences on Wright's fiction: naturalism, Marxism, and Freudianism. Also palpably present is the black folk tradition, with which Wright had a love-hate relationship that lasted throughout his career.

Long Black Song is one of the few works by Wright written from the perspective of a woman. It is believed to be based on the tragedy of his uncle Hoskins, a successful bar owner in Elaine, Arkansas, who was murdered by whites who wanted his business and his land. Critics have often praised its somber lyricism, reminiscent of Jean Toomer's *Blood Burning Moon*, a tale of an interracial triangle, but only recently have they begun to notice that *Long Black Song* fits a pattern dominant in Wright's work: women figure merely to be subsumed under larger political and philosophical themes. In this story, as novelist and critic Sherley Anne Williams notes, Wright represents the rape of Sarah not as a violation of *her* body but rather as an affront to her *husband's* pride and masculinity.

Uncle Tom's Children brought Wright first prize in a competition among writers of the WPA Federal Writers' Project as well as a Guggenheim Fellowship, which enabled him to work exclusively on his writing. Despite its success, however, Wright was harshly critical of the collection. Characterizing it as a sentimental work, which "even bankers' daughters could read and weep over and feel good about," he vowed that his next novel would be one "so hard and deep that [readers] would have to face it without the consolation of tears." That next novel was *Native Son*, which contained extremities of violence and horror not likely to inspire anything but fear. Indeed *Fear* was, significantly, the title Wright gave to the first of the book's three parts.

Native Son is widely considered Wright's most monumental achievement in fiction. In a now famous overstatement, critic Irving Howe declared, "The day *Native Son* appeared, American culture was changed forever." Whether one accepts Howe's judgment or not, it is certain that *Native Son* is not only the novel that established Richard Wright as a major twentieth century writer but also the novel whose mix of urban realism, sociological theory, and naturalistic determinism helped to define and influence almost the entire sweep of African American fiction of the post–World War II era.

But *Native Son* is also the work that defined Wright as a major literary talent and one that limited the critical response to his work to virtually a single category. The book earned Wright the reputation as a protest writer who dared to expose the stresses and pathologies of the urban ghettos. It also made him the first African American writer to receive both critical acclaim and commercial success simultaneously. Published by Harper & Brothers, Native Son was a Book-of-the-Month Club selection. It sold two hundred thousand copies inside of three weeks, breaking a twenty-year sales record for Harper's and beating out John Steinbeck's Pulitzer Prize–winning novel The Grapes of Wrath as number one best-seller.

Wright's fame following the publication of Native Son led to extensive lecturing and travel. He spoke around the country and, in 1942, was awarded the NAACP's Spingarn Medal, then the most prestigious award for achievements by any African American in the country. A successful stage production of Native Son (1941), adapted by Wright, toured the country after a brief Broadway run.

Native Son combined the determinism of naturalism with the grittiness of socialist realism that Wright drew from the works of such writers as James T. Farrell and Theodore Dreiser. Dreiser's An American Tragedy, to which Native Son is frequently compared, had an especial impact on Wright's literary development and philosophical outlook. He would later write in Black Boy, his autobiography: "I was overwhelmed. . . . It would have been impossible for me to have told anyone what I derived from these novels. All my life has shaped me for the realism, the naturalism of the modern novel." Of course, by the time Wright made that statement, the turbulence of modernism, which had revolutionized so many of the arts in America, was an established fact of literary life, but realism and naturalism remained vital forces in his work.

While he was clearly influenced by these traditions, however, Wright, as his more perceptive critics have noted, was also influenced by the tradition of the Gothic romance, employed by such nineteenth-century American writers as Nathaniel Hawthorne and Edgar Allan Poe. Still others have noted that the language of symbolism in Wright's work brings him closer to the tradition of modernism than is generally acknowledged.

But whatever modernist elements can be found in Wright's work are certainly obscured by the signs of his investments in the Chicago School of Urban Sociology and the deterministic slants of its theories. He acknowledged that the Chicago School provided him the explanatory concepts and theoretical frameworks for his fiction. Indeed the Chicago School provided the shaping apparatus not only for Native Son but for Twelve Million Black Voices as well. Published a year after Native Son, in 1941, Twelve Million Black Voices was subtitled "A Folk History of the American Negro." Based on photographs culled from the Farm Security Administration files, the book features Wright's running commentary throughout the text, explaining the crippling effects of the Great Migration on southern blacks. In an idea that structured his entire text, Wright supposed that the forces affecting black life in the North, as in the South, were all attributable to property ownership. "The Lords of the Land" in the agrarian South and the "Bosses of Buildings" in the industrial North were alike in exacting a heavy toll of oppression and death from blacks who were "landless upon the land" in the South and constricted in kitchenette apartments in the North.

Such crude Marxist analysis is mitigated by a passion and lyricism that Wright was able to sustain through to the publication of his autobiography Black Boy, published in 1945. Hailed as a masterpiece, Black Boy, which included the formerly published essay The Ethics of Living Jim Crow, was praised for its achievement of a tautness and lyric intensity generally smothered in Wright's work by ideological abstractions. Writing in the militant spirit of Frederick Douglass's 1845 Narrative and drawing on a number of slave narrative conventions, Wright fashioned a myth of self that conformed to the stock pattern of the American myth of the "self-made man," of which Benjamin Franklin's Autobiography and Douglass's Narrative are prototypical examples. When he reviewed the book, Ralph Ellison cheered Wright as a "black boy singing lustily as he probes his own grievous wound" and predicted that the book would "do much to redefine the problem of the Negro and American Democracy."

Following the publication of *Black Boy*, Wright moved to Paris, where he remained until his death in 1960. There he became involved with Jean-Paul Sartre, Simone de Beauvoir, Albert Camus, and other members of *Les Temps Modernes* who are inaccurately credited with influencing the existentialist philosophy of Wright's novel *The Outsider* (1953). Some critics suggest that Wright's traumatic childhood in Mississippi made him a "home-grown" existentialist and that he had actually begun to incorporate the philosophy into his writing as early as 1944 when his short story *The Man Who Lived Underground* appeared in the anthology *Cross Section*. In both *The Outsider* and *The Man Who Lived Underground*, Wright also indulges his lifelong fascination with the conventions of such popular genres as detective stories and dime novels.

Wright traveled throughout Europe and Africa in the 1950s and continued to be prolific in a variety of forms. His association with the poets and novelists of the Negritude movement, including Leopold Senghor and Aime Cesaire, with whom he founded *Presence Africaine*, enabled Wright to see the social and psychological effects of material oppression in global perspective. *Black Power: A Record of Reactions in a Land of Pathos* (1954) and *White Man Listen!* (1957) resulted from his extensive travels in Africa, where he observed third world peoples buckling under the weight of colonialism. In addition to *Black Power* and *White Man Listen!*, Wright published *Savage Holiday* (1954) and *The Long Dream* (1958). Despite this prodigious output during the 1950s critics generally agree that Wright's career as serious literary artist ended in 1946, when he left the United States. They argue that while France liberated Wright as a person, it shackled his creative expression, dulling the vivid memories of his childhood and early life, deadening his ear to the rhythms and cadences of black American speech, all of which he had captured so compellingly in such works as *The Ethics of Living Jim Crow* and *Black Boy*. The result was contrived and artificial work, full of windy abstractions.

Wright's embrace of black nationalism formed a bridge connecting Wright himself to the Black Aesthetic critics and writers of the late 1960s who claimed Wright as a favored ancestor without whose *Native Son* no viable African American literary tradition would have been possible. Like most critics before them, the black aestheticians designated Wright a "protest" writer par excellence, finding in his work the "clenched militancy" that Irving Howe had praised at the expense of Ralph Ellison and James Baldwin.

The full extent and importance of Wright's artistic contributions to African American literature are still being assessed in light of the contemporary editions of his work that restore expurgated passages originally perceived to be too raw and sexually explicit for American reading audiences of the time. The restored passages of *Native Son*, for example, now lead critics to underline the homoerotic aspects of that novel, only hinted at in the original. Similarly, only the first part of Wright's autobiography was published in 1945. Describing his experiences in the South, it appeared under the title *Black Boy*. The second part focused on Wright's life in Chicago and was posthumously published as *American Hunger* in 1977. The new Library of America edition brings the two parts together for the first time. Finally, the restoration of lengthy editorial cuts to *The Outsider* provides a stronger sense of the style, which Wright called "poetic realism," toward which he was groping in this work.

Even without these invaluable new editions of Wright's work, it would continue to be read. *Native Son* made sure of that. If he had produced nothing else, Wright's reputation would have been secure. While critics have disagreed—often bitterly—over the artistic merits of *Native Son*, none denies its power. Though compromised by ideological commitments and marred by overwriting, *Black Son*, with its class consciousness, its exploration of sexual racism and social dislocation, and its rejection of the dominant discourse on race, guarantees Wright's place in the world of letters.

Blueprint for Negro Writing

1) *The Role of Negro Writing: Two Definitions*

Generally speaking, Negro writing in the past has been confined to humble novels, poems, and plays, prim and decorous ambassadors who went a-begging to white America. They entered the Court of American Public Opinion dressed in the knee-pants of servility, curtsying to show that the Negro was not inferior, that he was human, and that he had a life comparable to that of other people. For the most part these artistic ambassadors were received as though they were French poodles who do clever tricks.

White America never offered these Negro writers any serious criticism. The mere fact that a Negro could write was astonishing. Nor was there any deep concern on the part of white America with the role Negro writing should play in American culture; and the role it did play grew out of accident rather than intent or design. Either it crept in through the kitchen in the form of jokes; or it was the fruits of that foul soil which was the result of a liason between inferiority-complexed Negro "geniuses" and burnt-out white Bohemians with money.

On the other hand, these often technically brilliant performances by Negro writers were looked upon by the majority of literate Negroes as something to be proud of. At best, Negro writing has been something external to the lives of educated Negroes themselves. That the productions of their writers should have been something of a guide in their daily living is a matter which seems never to have been raised seriously.

Under these conditions Negro writing assumed two general aspects: 1) It became a sort of conspicuous ornamentation, the hallmark of "achievement." 2) It became the voice of the educated Negro pleading with white America for justice.

Rarely was the best of this writing addressed to the Negro himself, his needs, his sufferings, his aspirations. Through misdirection, Negro writers have been far better to others than they have been to themselves. And the mere recognition of this places the whole question of Negro writing in a new light and raises a doubt as to the validity of its present direction.

2) *The Minority Outlook*

Somewhere in his writings Lenin [1] makes the observation that oppressed minorities often reflect the techniques of the bourgeoisie more brilliantly

---

1. Vladimir Ilyich Ulyanov (1870–1924), Communist theorist and founder of the Bolshevik Party. He was the leader of the newly formed Soviet Union until his death.

than some sections of the bourgeoisie themselves. The psychological importance of this becomes meaningful when it is recalled that oppressed minorities, and especially the petty bourgeois sections of oppressed minorities, strive to assimilate the virtues of the bourgeoisie in the assumption that by doing so they can lift themselves into a higher social sphere. But not only among the oppressed petty bourgeoisie does this occur. The workers of a minority people, chafing under exploitation, forge organizational forms of struggle to better their lot. Lacking the handicaps of false ambition and property, they have access to a wide social vision and a deep social consciousness. They display a greater freedom and initiative in pushing their claims upon civilization than even do the petty bourgeoisie. Their organizations show greater strength, adaptability, and efficiency than any other group or class in society.

That Negro workers, propelled by the harsh conditions of their lives, have demonstrated this consciousness and mobility for economic and political action there can be no doubt. But has this consciousness been reflected in the work of Negro writers to the same degree as it has in the Negro workers' struggle to free Herndon and the Scottsboro Boys,[2] in the drive toward unionism, in the fight against lynching? Have they as creative writers taken advantage of their unique minority position?

The answer decidedly is *no*. Negro writers have lagged sadly, and as time passes the gap widens between them and their people.

How can this hiatus be bridged? How can the enervating effects of this long standing split be eliminated?

In presenting questions of this sort an attitude of self-consciousness and self-criticism is far more likely to be a fruitful point of departure than a mere recounting of past achievements. An emphasis upon tendency and experiment, a view of society as something becoming rather than as something fixed and admired is the one which points the way for Negro writers to stand shoulder to shoulder with Negro workers in mood and outlook.

3) A Whole Culture

There is, however, a culture of the Negro which is his and has been addressed to him; a culture which has, for good or ill, helped to clarify his consciousness and create emotional attitudes which are conducive to action. This culture has stemmed mainly from two sources: 1) the Negro church; 2) and the folklore of the Negro people.

It was through the portals of the church that the American Negro first entered the shrine of western culture. Living under slave conditions of life,

2. Nine black youths tried for the alleged rape of two white women in 1931 in Alabama. All were convicted, and all but one were sentenced to death, despite expert medical testimony that no rape had occurred. Subsequent U.S. Supreme Court decisions (1932 and 1935) reversed the convictions. In further proceedings in Alabama from 1935 to 1937, four of the Scottsboro Nine were once again convicted, resulting in prison terms ranging from seventy-five years to life. Charges against the remaining five were dropped. The case was used by the Communist Party to shore up its support, as it fought the NAACP for the opportunity to represent the defendants. Angelo Herndon was the lead figure in what was, along with the trial of the Scottsboro Boys, one of the most celebrated criminal trials in African American history. Born in Ohio, Herndon was a member of the Communist Party. For organizing an antidiscrimination march in Georgia, he was convicted in 1933 of inciting insurrection and sentenced to a twenty-year prison term under a one-hundred-year-old slave law. The U.S. Supreme Court reversed this decision in 1937.

bereft of his African heritage, the Negroes' struggle for religion on the plantations between 1820–60 assumed the form of a struggle for human rights. It remained a relatively revolutionary struggle until religion began to serve as an antidote for suffering and denial. But even today there are millions of American Negroes whose only sense of a whole universe, whose only relation to society and man, and whose only guide to personal dignity comes through the archaic morphology of Christian salvation.

It was, however, in a folklore moulded out of rigorous and inhuman conditions of life that the Negro achieved his most indigenous and complete expression. Blues, spirituals, and folk tales recounted from mouth to mouth; the whispered words of a black mother to her black daughter on the ways of men; the confidential wisdom of a black father to his black son; the swapping of sex experiences on street corners from boy to boy in the deepest vernacular; work songs sung under blazing suns—all these formed the channels through which the racial wisdom flowed.

One would have thought that Negro writers in the last century of striving at expression would have continued and deepened this folk tradition, would have tried to create a more intimate and yet a more profoundly social system of artistic communication between them and their people. But the illusion that they could escape through individual achievement the harsh lot of their race swung Negro writers away from any such path. Two separate cultures sprang up: one for the Negro masses, unwritten and unrecognized; and the other for the sons and daughters of a rising Negro bourgeoisie, parasitic and mannered.

Today the question is: Shall Negro writing be for the Negro masses, moulding the lives and consciousness of those masses toward new goals, or shall it continue begging the question of the Negroes' humanity?

4) The Problem of Nationalism in Negro Writing

In stressing the difference between the role Negro writing failed to play in the lives of the Negro people, and the role it should play in the future if it is to serve its historic function; in pointing out the fact that Negro writing has been addressed in the main to a small white audience rather than to a Negro one, it should be stated that no attempt is being made here to propagate a specious and blatant nationalism. Yet the nationalist character of the Negro people is unmistakable. Psychologically this nationalism is reflected in the whole of Negro culture, and especially in folklore.

In the absence of fixed and nourishing forms of culture, the Negro has a folklore which embodies the memories and hopes of his struggle for freedom. Not yet caught in paint or stone, and as yet but feebly depicted in the poem and novel, the Negroes' most powerful images of hope and despair still remain in the fluid state of daily speech. How many John Henrys[3] have lived and died on the lips of these black people? How many mythical heroes in embryo have been allowed to perish for lack of husbanding by alert intelligence?

---

3. A legendary figure from African American ballads and folklore. In the story, John Henry competed with a steam-powered drill to drive railroad spikes. He won the contest but died from exhaustion.

Negro folklore contains, in a measure that puts to shame more deliberate forms of Negro expression, the collective sense of Negro life in America. Let those who shy at the nationalist implications of Negro life look
at this body of folklore, living and powerful, which rose out of a unified
sense of a common life and a common fate. Here are those vital beginnings of a recognition of value in life as it is *lived*, a recognition that
marks the emergence of a new culture in the shell of the old. And at the
moment this process starts, at the moment when a people begin to realize
a *meaning* in their suffering, the civilization that engenders that suffering
is doomed.

The nationalist aspects of Negro life are as sharply manifest in the social
institutions of Negro people as in folklore. There is a Negro church, a
Negro press, a Negro social world, a Negro sporting world, a Negro business world, a Negro school system, Negro professions; in short, a Negro way
of life in America. The Negro people did not ask for this, and deep down,
though they express themselves through their institutions and adhere to
this special way of life, they do not want it now. This special existence was
forced upon them from without by lynch rope, bayonet and mob rule.
They accepted these negative conditions with the inevitability of a tree
which must live or perish in whatever soil it finds itself.

The few crumbs of American civilization which the Negro has got from
the tables of capitalism have been through these segregated channels.
Many Negro institutions are cowardly and incompetent; but they are all
that the Negro has. And, in the main, any move, whether for progress or
reaction, must come through these institutions for the simple reason that
all other channels are closed. Negro writers who seek to mould or influence the consciousness of the Negro people must address their messages to
them through the ideologies and attitudes fostered in this warping way of
life.

5) The Basis and Meaning of Nationalism in Negro Writing

The social institutions of the Negro are imprisoned in the Jim Crow[4]
political system of the South, and this Jim Crow political system is in turn
built upon a plantation-feudal economy. Hence, it can be seen that the
emotional expression of group-feeling which puzzles so many whites and
leads them to deplore what they call "black chauvinism" is not a morbidly
inherent trait of the Negro, but rather the reflex expression of a life whose
roots are imbedded deeply in Southern soil.

Negro writers must accept the nationalist implications of their lives, not
in order to encourage them, but in order to change and transcend them.
They must accept the concept of nationalism because, in order to transcend it, they must *possess* and *understand* it. And a nationalist spirit in
Negro writing means a nationalism carrying the highest possible pitch of
social consciousness. It means a nationalism that knows its origins, its limitations; that is aware of the dangers of its position; that knows its ultimate
aims are unrealizable within the framework of capitalist America; a nation-

4. System of social segregation in the U.S. South during the late 19th and the 20th centuries.

ism whose reason for being lies in the simple fact of self-possession and in the consciousness of the interdependence of people in modern society.

For purposes of creative expression it means that the Negro writer must realize within the area of his own personal experience those impulses which, when prefigured in terms of broad social movements, constitute the stuff of nationalism.

For Negro writers even more so than for Negro politicians, nationalism is a bewildering and vexing question, the full ramifications of which cannot be dealt with here. But among Negro workers and the Negro middle class the spirit of nationalism is rife in a hundred devious forms; and a simple literary realism which seeks to depict the lives of these people devoid of wider social connotations, devoid of the revolutionary significance of these nationalist tendencies, must of necessity do a rank injustice to the Negro people and alienate their possible allies in the struggle for freedom.

6) Social Consciousness and Responsibility

The Negro writer who seeks to function within his race as a purposeful agent has a serious responsibility. In order to do justice to his subject matter, in order to depict Negro life in all of its manifold and intricate relationships, a deep, informed, and complex consciousness is necessary; a consciousness which draws for its strength upon the fluid lore of a great people, and moulds this lore with the concepts that move and direct the forces of history today.

With the gradual decline of the moral authority of the Negro church, and with the increasing irresolution which is paralyzing Negro middle class leadership, a new role is devolving upon the Negro writer. He is being called upon to do no less than create values by which his race is to struggle, live and die.

By his ability to fuse and make articulate the experiences of men, because his writing possesses the potential cunning to steal into the inmost recesses of the human heart, because he can create the myths and symbols that inspire a faith in life, he may expect either to be consigned to oblivion, or to be recognized for the valued agent he is.

This raises the question of the personality of the writer. It means that in the lives of Negro writers must be found those materials and experiences which will create a meaningful picture of the world today. Many young writers have grown to believe that a Marxist analysis of society presents such a picture. It creates a picture which, when placed before the eyes of the writer, should unify his personality, organize his emotions, buttress him with a tense and obdurate will to change the world.

And, in turn, this changed world will dialectically change the writer. Hence, it is through a Marxist conception of reality and society that the maximum degree of freedom in thought and feeling can be gained for the Negro writer. Further, this dramatic Marxist vision, when consciously grasped, endows the writer with a sense of dignity which no other vision can give. Ultimately, it restores to the writer his lost heritage, that is, his role as a creator of the world in which he lives, and as a creator of himself.

Yet, for the Negro writer, Marxism is but the starting point. No theory of life can take the place of life. After Marxism has laid bare the skeleton of society, there remains the task of the writer to plant flesh upon those bones out of his will to live. He may, with disgust and revulsion, say *no* and depict the horrors of capitalism encroaching upon the human being. Or he may, with hope and passion, say *yes* and depict the faint stirrings of a new and emerging life. But in whatever social voice he chooses to speak, whether positive or negative, there should always be heard or *over*-heard his faith, his necessity, his judgement.

His vision need not be simple or rendered in primer-like terms; for the life of the Negro people is not simple. The presentation of their lives should be simple, yes; but all the complexity, the strangeness, the magic wonder of life that plays like a bright sheen over the most sordid existence, should be there. To borrow a phrase from the Russians, it should have a *complex simplicity*. Eliot, Stein, Joyce, Proust, Hemingway, and Anderson; Gorky, Barbusse, Nexo, and Jack London[5] no less than the folklore of the Negro himself should form the heritage of the Negro writer. Every iota of gain in human thought and sensibility should be ready grist for his mill, no matter how far-fetched they may seem in their immediate implications.

7) The Problem of Perspective

What vision must Negro writers have before their eyes in order to feel the impelling necessity for an about face? What angle of vision can show them all the forces of modern society in process, all the lines of economic development converging toward a distant point of hope? Must they believe in some "ism"?

They may feel that only dupes believe in "isms"; they feel with some measure of justification that another commitment means only another disillusionment. But anyone destitute of a theory about the meaning, structure and direction of modern society is a lost victim in a world he cannot understand or control.

But even if Negro writers found themselves through some "ism," how would that influence their writing? Are they being called upon to "preach"? To be "salesmen"? To "prostitute" their writing? Must they "sully" themselves? Must they write "propaganda"?

No; it is a question of awareness, of consciousness; it is, above all, a question of perspective.

Perspective is that part of a poem, novel, or play which a writer never puts directly upon paper. It is that fixed point in intellectual space where a writer stands to view the struggles, hopes, and sufferings of his people. There are times when he may stand too close and the result is a blurred vision. Or he may stand too far away and the result is a neglect of important things.

5. American writer (1876–1916). T. S. Eliot (1888–1965), American poet, playwright, and literary critic. Gertrude Stein (1874–1946), American-born author who later settled in Paris, where her home became the social center for a group of American and European artists. James Joyce (1882–1941), Irish novelist and poet. Marcel Proust (1871–1922), French novelist, essayist, and critic. Ernest Hemingway (1899–1961), American writer. Sherwood Anderson (1876–1941), American writer. Maxim Gorky (1868–1935), Russian prose writer and playwright. Henri Barbusse (1874–1935), French novelist and journalist. Martin Anderson Nexo (1869–1954), Danish novelist.

Of all the problems faced by writers who as a whole have never allied themselves with world movements, perspective is the most difficult of achievement. At its best, perspective is a pre-conscious assumption, something which a writer takes for granted, something which he wins through his living.

A Spanish writer recently spoke of living in the heights of one's time. Surely, perspective means just *that*.

It means that a Negro writer must learn to view the life of a Negro living in New York's Harlem or Chicago's South Side with the consciousness that one-sixth of the earth surface belongs to the working class. It means that a Negro writer must create in his readers' minds a relationship between a Negro woman hoeing cotton in the South and the men who loll in swivel chairs in Wall Street and take the fruits of her toil.

Perspective for Negro writers will come when they have looked and brooded so hard and long upon the harsh lot of their race and compared it with the hopes and struggles of minority peoples everywhere that the cold facts have begun to tell them something.

8) *The Problem of Theme*

This does not mean that a Negro writer's sole concern must be with rendering the social scene; but if his conception of the life of his people is broad and deep enough, if the sense of the *whole* life he is seeking is vivid and strong in him, then his writing will embrace all those social, political, and economic forms under which the life of his people is manifest.

In speaking of theme one must necessarily be general and abstract; the temperament of each writer moulds and colors the world he sees. Negro life may be approached from a thousand angles, with no limit to technical and stylistic freedom.

Negro writers spring from a family, a clan, a class, and a nation; and the social units in which they are bound have a story, a record. Sense of theme will emerge in Negro writing when Negro writers try to fix this story about some pole of meaning, remembering as they do so that in the creative process meaning proceeds *equally* as much from the contemplation of the subject matter as from the hopes and apprehensions that rage in the heart of the writer.

Reduced to its simplest and most general terms, theme for Negro writers will rise from understanding the meaning of their being transplanted from a "savage" to a "civilized" culture in all of its social, political, economic, and emotional implications. It means that Negro writers must have in their consciousness the foreshortened picture of the *whole*, nourishing culture from which they were torn in Africa, and of the long, complex (and for the most part, unconscious) struggle to regain in some form and under alien conditions of life a *whole* culture again.

It is not only this picture they must have, but also a knowledge of the social and emotional milieu that gives it tone and solidity of detail. Theme for Negro writers will emerge when they have begun to feel the meaning of the history of their race as though they in one life time had lived it themselves throughout all the long centuries.

9) *Autonomy of Craft*

For the Negro writer to depict this new reality requires a greater discipline and consciousness than was necessary for the so-called Harlem school[6] of expression. Not only is the subject matter dealt with far more meaningful and complex, but the new role of the writer is qualitatively different. The Negro writers' new position demands a sharper definition of the status of his craft, and a sharper emphasis upon its functional autonomy.

Negro writers should seek through the medium of their craft to play as meaningful a role in the affairs of men as do other professionals. But if their writing is demanded to perform the social office of other professions, then the autonomy of craft is lost and writing detrimentally fused with other interests. The limitations of the craft constitute some of its greatest virtues. If the sensory vehicle of imaginative writing is required to carry too great a load of didactic material, the artistic sense is submerged.

The relationship between reality and the artistic image is not always direct and simple. The imaginative conception of a historical period will not be a carbon copy of reality. Image and emotion possess a logic of their own. A vulgarized simplicity constitutes the greatest danger in tracing the reciprocal interplay between the writer and his environment.

Writing has its professional autonomy; it should complement other professions, but it should not supplant them or be swamped by them.

10) *The Necessity for Collective Work*

It goes without saying that these things cannot be gained by Negro writers if their present mode of isolated writing and living continues. This isolation exists *among* Negro writers as well as *between* Negro and white writers. The Negro writers' lack of thorough integration with the American scene, their lack of a clear realization among themselves of their possible role, have bred generation after generation of embittered and defeated literati.

Barred for decades from the theater and publishing houses, Negro writers have been *made* to feel a sense of difference. So deep has this white-hot iron of exclusion been burnt into their hearts that thousands have all but lost the desire to become identified with American civilization. The Negro writers' acceptance of this enforced isolation and their attempt to justify it is but a defense-reflex of the whole special way of life which has been rammed down their throats.

This problem, by its very nature, is one which must be approached contemporaneously from *two* points of view. The ideological unity of Negro writers and the alliance of that unity with all the progressive ideas of our day is the primary prerequisite for collective work. On the shoulders of white writers and Negro writers alike rest the responsibility of ending this mistrust and isolation.

By placing cultural health above narrow sectional prejudices, liberal writers of all races can help to break the stony soil of aggrandizement out of

6. Designation given those writers who took their subject matter from the black working classes and their language from the rhythms and inflections of black speech.

which the stunted plants of Negro nationalism grow. And, simultaneously, Negro writers can help to weed out these choking growths of reactionary nationalism and replace them with hardier and sturdier types.

These tasks are imperative in light of the fact that we live in a time when the majority of the most basic assumptions of life can no longer be taken for granted. Tradition is no longer a guide. The world has grown huge and cold. Surely this is the moment to ask questions, to theorize, to speculate, to wonder out of what materials can a human world be built.

Each step along this unknown path should be taken with thought, care, self-consciousness, and deliberation. When Negro writers think they have arrived at something which smacks of truth, humanity, they should want to test it with others, feel it with a degree of passion and strength that will enable them to communicate it to millions who are groping like themselves.

Writers faced with such tasks can have no possible time for malice or jealousy. The conditions for the growth of each writer depend too much upon the good work of other writers. Every first rate novel, poem, or play lifts the level of consciousness higher.

1937

The Ethics of Living Jim Crow, [1] an Autobiographical Sketch

I

My first lesson in how to live as a Negro came when I was quite small. We were living in Arkansas. Our house stood behind the railroad tracks. Its skimpy yard was paved with black cinders. Nothing green ever grew in that yard. The only touch of green we could see was far away, beyond the tracks, over where the white folks lived. But cinders were good enough for me and I never missed the green growing things. And anyhow, cinders were fine weapons. You could always have a nice hot war with huge black cinders. All you had to do was crouch behind the brick pillars of a house with your hands full of gritty ammunition. And the first woolly black head you saw pop out from behind another row of pillars was your target. You tried your very best to knock it off. It was great fun.

I never fully realized the appalling disadvantages of a cinder environment till one day the gang to which I belonged found itself engaged in a war with the white boys who lived beyond the tracks. As usual we laid down our cinder barrage, thinking that this would wipe the white boys out. But they replied with a steady bombardment of broken bottles. We doubled our cinder barrage, but they hid behind trees, hedges, and the sloping embankments of their lawns. Having no such fortifications, we retreated to the brick pillars of our homes. During the retreat a broken milk bottle caught me behind the ear, opening a deep gash which bled profusely. The sight of blood pouring over my face completely demoralized our ranks. My fellow-combatants left me standing paralyzed in the center of the yard, and scur-

---

1. System of social segregation in the U.S. South.

ried for their homes. A kind neighbor saw me and rushed me to a doctor, who took three stitches in my neck.

I sat brooding on my front steps, nursing my wound and waiting for my mother to come from work. I felt that a grave injustice had been done me. It was all right to throw cinders. The greatest harm a cinder could do was leave a bruise. But broken bottles were dangerous; they left you cut, bleeding, and helpless.

When night fell, my mother came from the white folks' kitchen. I raced down the street to meet her. I could just feel in my bones that she would understand. I knew she would tell me exactly what to do next time. I grabbed her hand and babbled out the whole story. She examined my wound, then slapped me.

"How come yuh didn't hide?" she asked me. "How come yuh awways fightin'?"

I was outraged, and bawled. Between sobs I told her that I didn't have any trees or hedges to hide behind. There wasn't a thing I could have used as a trench. And you couldn't throw very far when you were hiding behind the brick pillars of a house. She grabbed a barrel stave, dragged me home, stripped me naked, and beat me till I had a fever of one hundred and two. She would smack my rump with the stave, and, while the skin was still smarting, impart to me gems of Jim Crow wisdom. I was never to throw cinders any more. I was never to fight any more wars. I was never, never, under any conditions, to fight *white* folks again. And they were absolutely right in clouting me with the broken milk bottle. Didn't I know she was working hard every day in the hot kitchens of the white folks to make money to take care of me? When was I ever going to learn to be a good boy? She couldn't be bothered with my fights. She finished by telling me that I ought to be thankful to God as long as I lived that they didn't kill me.

All that night I was delirious and could not sleep. Each time I closed my eyes I saw monstrous white faces suspended from the ceiling, leering at me.

From that time on, the charm of my cinder yard was gone. The green trees, the trimmed hedges, the cropped lawns grew very meaningful, became a symbol. Even today when I think of white folks, the hard, sharp outlines of white houses surrounded by trees, lawns, and hedges are present somewhere in the background of my mind. Through the years they grew into an overreaching symbol of fear.

It was a long time before I came in close contact with white folks again. We moved from Arkansas to Mississippi. Here we had the good fortune not to live behind the railroad tracks, or close to white neighborhoods. We lived in the very heart of the local Black Belt. There were black churches and black preachers; there were black schools and black teachers; black groceries and black clerks. In fact, everything was so solidly black that for a long time I did not even think of white folks, save in remote and vague terms. But this could not last forever. As one grows older one eats more. One's clothing costs more. When I finished grammar school I had to go to work. My mother could no longer feed and clothe me on her cooking job.

There is but one place where a black boy who knows no trade can get a job, and that's where the houses and faces are white, where the trees, lawns, and hedges are green. My first job was with an optical company in Jackson,

Mississippi. The morning I applied I stood straight and neat before the boss, answering all his questions with sharp yessirs and nosirs. I was very careful to pronounce my *sirs* distinctly, in order that he might know that I was polite, that I knew where I was, and that I knew he was a *white* man. I wanted that job badly.

He looked me over as though he were examining a prize poodle. He questioned me closely about my schooling, being particularly insistent about how much mathematics I had had. He seemed very pleased when I told him I had had two years of algebra.

"Boy, how would you like to try to learn something around here?" he asked me.

"I'd like it fine, sir," I said, happy. I had visions of "working my way up." Even Negroes have those visions.

"All right," he said. "Come on."

I followed him to the small factory.

"Pease," he said to a white man of about thirty-five, "this is Richard. He's going to work for us."

Pease looked at me and nodded.

I was then taken to a white boy of about seventeen.

"Morrie, this is Richard, who's going to work for us."

"Whut yuh sayin' there, boy!" Morrie boomed at me.

"Fine!" I answered.

The boss instructed these two to help me, teach me, give me jobs to do, and let me learn what I could in my spare time.

My wages were five dollars a week.

I worked hard, trying to please. For the first month I got along O.K. Both Pease and Morrie seemed to like me. But one thing was missing. And I kept thinking about it. I was not learning anything and nobody was volunteering to help me. Thinking they had forgotten that I was to learn something about the mechanics of grinding lenses, I asked Morrie one day to tell me about the work. He grew red.

"Whut yuh tryin' t' do, nigger, git smart?" he asked.

"Naw; I ain' tryin' t' git smart," I said.

"Well, don't, if yuh know whut's good for yuh!"

I was puzzled. Maybe he just doesn't want to help me, I thought. I went to Pease.

"Say, are you crazy, you black bastard?" Pease asked me, his gray eyes growing hard.

I spoke out, reminding him that the boss had said I was to be given a chance to learn something.

"Nigger, you think you're *white*, don't you?"

"Naw, sir!"

"Well, you're acting mighty like it!"

"But, Mr. Pease, the boss said . . ."

Pease shook his fist in my face.

"This is a *white* man's work around here, and you better watch yourself!"

From then on they changed toward me. They said goodmorning no more. When I was just a bit slow in performing some duty, I was called a lazy black son-of-a-bitch.

Once I thought of reporting all this to the boss. But the mere idea of what would happen to me if Pease and Morrie should learn that I had "snitched" stopped me. And after all, the boss was a white man, too. What was the use?

The climax came at noon one summer day. Pease called me to his workbench. To get to him I had to go between two narrow benches and stand with my back against a wall.

"Yes, sir," I said.

"Richard, I want to ask you something," Pease began pleasantly, not looking up from his work.

"Yes, sir," I said again.

Morrie came over, blocking the narrow passage between the benches. He folded his arms, staring at me solemnly.

I looked from one to the other, sensing that something was coming.

"Yes, sir," I said for the third time.

Pease looked up and spoke very slowly.

"Richard, *Mr.* Morrie here tells me you called me *Pease*."

I stiffened. A void seemed to open up in me. I knew this was the showdown.

He meant that I had failed to call him *Mr.* Pease. I looked at Morrie. He was gripping a steel bar in his hands. I opened my mouth to speak, to protest, to assure Pease that I had never called him simply *Pease*, and that I had never had any intentions of doing so, when Morrie grabbed me by the collar, ramming my head against the wall.

"Now, be careful, nigger!" snarled Morrie, baring his teeth. "*I* heard yuh call 'im *Pease!* 'N' if yuh say yuh didn't, yuh're callin' me a *lie*, see?" He waved the steel bar threateningly.

If I had said: No, sir, Mr. Pease, I never called you *Pease*, I would have been automatically calling Morrie a liar. And if I had said: Yes, sir, Mr. Pease, I called you *Pease*, I would have been pleading guilty to having uttered the worst insult that a Negro can utter to a southern white man. I stood hesitating, trying to frame a neutral reply.

"Richard, I asked you a question!" said Pease. Anger was creeping into his voice.

"I don't remember calling you *Pease*, Mr. Pease," I said cautiously. "And if I did, I sure didn't mean . . ."

"You black son-of-a-bitch! You called me *Pease*, then!" he spat, slapping me till I bent sideways over a bench. Morrie was on top of me, demanding:

"Didn't yuh call 'im *Pease?* If yuh say yuh didn't, I'll rip yo' gut string loose with this bar, yuh black granny dodger! Yuh can't call a white man a lie 'n' git erway with it, you black son-of-a-bitch!"

I wilted. I begged them not to bother me. I knew what they wanted. They wanted me to leave.

"I'll leave," I promised. "I'll leave right *now*."

They gave me a minute to get out of the factory. I was warned not to show up again, or tell the boss.

I went.

When I told the folks at home what had happened, they called me a fool. They told me that I must never again attempt to exceed my boundaries.

When you are working for white folks, they said, you got to "stay in your place" if you want to keep working.

II

My Jim Crow education continued on my next job, which was portering in a clothing store. One morning, while polishing brass out front, the boss and his twenty-year-old son got out of their car and half dragged and half kicked a Negro woman into the store. A policeman standing at the corner looked on, twirling his nightstick. I watched out of the corner of my eye, never slackening the strokes of my chamois upon the brass. After a few minutes, I heard shrill screams coming from the rear of the store. Later the woman stumbled out, bleeding, crying, and holding her stomach. When she reached the end of the block, the policeman grabbed her and accused her of being drunk. Silently, I watched him throw her into a patrol wagon.

When I went to the rear of the store, the boss and his son were washing their hands at the sink. They were chuckling. The floor was bloody and strewn with wisps of hair and clothing. No doubt I must have appeared pretty shocked, for the boss slapped me reassuringly on the back.

"Boy, that's what we do to niggers when they don't want to pay their bills," he said, laughing.

His son looked at me and grinned.

"Here, hava cigarette," he said.

Not knowing what to do, I took it. He lit his and held the match for me. This was a gesture of kindness, indicating that even if they had beaten the poor old woman, they would not beat me if I knew enough to keep my mouth shut.

"Yes, sir," I said, and asked no questions.

After they had gone, I sat on the edge of a packing box and stared at the bloody floor till the cigarette went out.

That day at noon, while eating in a hamburger joint, I told my fellow Negro porters what had happened. No one seemed surprised. One fellow, after swallowing a huge bite, turned to me and asked:

"Huh! Is tha' all they did t' her?"

"Yeah. Wasn't tha' enough?" I asked.

"Shucks! Man, she's a lucky bitch!" he said, burying his lips deep into a juicy hamburger. "Hell, it's a wonder they didn't lay her when they got through."

III

I was learning fast, but not quite fast enough. One day, while I was delivering packages in the suburbs, my bicycle tire was punctured. I walked along the hot, dusty road, sweating and leading my bicycle by the handlebars.

A car slowed at my side.

"What's the matter, boy?" a white man called.

I told him my bicycle was broken and I was walking back to town.

"That's too bad," he said. "Hop on the running board."

He stopped the car. I clutched hard at my bicycle with one hand and clung to the side of the car with the other.

"All set?"

"Yes, sir," I answered. The car started.

It was full of young white men. They were drinking. I watched the flask pass from mouth to mouth.

"Wanna drink, boy?" one asked.

I laughed as the wind whipped my face. Instinctively obeying the freshly planted precepts of my mother, I said:

"Oh, no!"

The words were hardly out of my mouth before I felt something hard and cold smash me between the eyes. It was an empty whisky bottle. I saw stars, and fell backwards from the speeding car into the dust of the road, my feet becoming entangled in the steel spokes of my bicycle. The white men piled out and stood over me.

"Nigger, ain' yuh learned no better sense'n tha' yet?" asked the man who hit me. "Ain' yuh learned t' say *sir* t' a white man yet?"

Dazed, I pulled to my feet. My elbows and legs were bleeding. Fists doubled, the white man advanced, kicking my bicycle out of the way.

"Aw, leave the bastard alone. He's got enough," said one.

They stood looking at me. I rubbed my shins, trying to stop the flow of blood. No doubt they felt a sort of contemptuous pity, for one asked:

"Yuh wanna ride t' town now, nigger? Yuh reckon yuh know enough t' ride now?"

"I wanna walk," I said, simply.

Maybe it sounded funny. They laughed.

"Well, walk, yuh black son-of-a-bitch!"

When they left they comforted me with:

"Nigger, yuh sho better be damn glad it wuz us yuh talked t' tha' way. Yuh're a lucky bastard, 'cause if yuh'd said tha' t' somebody else, yuh might've been a dead nigger now."

IV

Negroes who have lived South know the dread of being caught alone upon the streets in white neighborhoods after the sun has set. In such a simple situation as this the plight of the Negro in America is graphically symbolized. While white strangers may be in these neighborhoods trying to get home, they can pass unmolested. But the color of a Negro's skin makes him easily recognizable, makes him suspect, converts him into a defenseless target.

Late one Saturday night I made some deliveries in a white neighborhood. I was pedaling my bicycle back to the store as fast as I could, when a police car, swerving toward me, jammed me into the curbing.

"Get down and put up your hands!" the policemen ordered.

I did. They climbed out of the car, guns drawn, faces set, and advanced slowly.

"Keep still!" they ordered.

I reached my hands higher. They searched my pockets and packages.

They seemed dissatisfied when they could find nothing incriminating. Finally, one of them said:

"Boy, tell your boss not to send you out in white neighborhoods after sundown."

As usual, I said:

"Yes, sir."

V

My next job was as hall-boy in a hotel. Here my Jim Crow education broadened and deepened. When the bell-boys were busy, I was often called to assist them. As many of the rooms in the hotel were occupied by prostitutes, I was constantly called to carry them liquor and cigarettes. These women were nude most of the time. They did not bother about clothing, even for bell-boys. When you went into their rooms, you were supposed to take their nakedness for granted, as though it startled you no more than a blue vase or a red rug. Your presence awoke in them no sense of shame, for you were not regarded as human. If they were alone, you could steal side-long glimpses at them. But if they were receiving men, not a flicker of your eyelids could show. I remember one incident vividly. A new woman, a huge, snowy-skinned blonde, took a room on my floor. I was sent to wait upon her. She was in bed with a thick-set man; both were nude and uncovered. She said she wanted some liquor and slid out of bed and waddled across the floor to get her money from a dresser drawer. I watched her.

"Nigger, what in hell you looking at?" the white man asked me, raising himself upon his elbows.

"Nothing," I answered, looking miles deep into the blank wall of the room.

"Keep your eyes where they belong, if you want to be healthy!" he said.

"Yes, sir."

VI

One of the bell-boys I knew in this hotel was keeping steady company with one of the Negro maids. Out of a clear sky the police descended upon his home and arrested him, accusing him of bastardy. The poor boy swore he had had no intimate relations with the girl. Nevertheless, they forced him to marry her. When the child arrived, it was found to be much lighter in complexion than either of the two supposedly legal parents. The white men around the hotel made a great joke of it. They spread the rumor that some white cow must have scared the poor girl while she was carrying the baby. If you were in their presence when this explanation was offered, you were supposed to laugh.

VII

One of the bell-boys was caught in bed with a white prostitute. He was castrated and run out of town. Immediately after this all the bell-boys and hall-boys were called together and warned. We were given to understand that the boy who had been castrated was a "mighty, mighty lucky bastard."

We were impressed with the fact that next time the management of the hotel would not be responsible for the lives of "trouble-makin' niggers." We were silent.

VIII

One night, just as I was about to go home, I met one of the Negro maids. She lived in my direction, and we fell in to walk part of the way home together. As we passed the white night-watchman, he slapped the maid on her buttock. I turned around, amazed. The watchman looked at me with a long, hard, fixed-under stare. Suddenly he pulled his gun and asked:

"Nigger, don't yuh like it?"

I hesitated.

"I asked yuh don't yuh like it?" he asked again, stepping forward.

"Yes, sir," I mumbled.

"Talk like it, then!"

"Oh, yes, sir!" I said with as much heartiness as I could muster.

Outside, I walked ahead of the girl, ashamed to face her. She caught up with me and said:

"Don't be a fool! Yuh couldn't help it!"

This watchman boasted of having killed two Negroes in self-defense.

Yet, in spite of all this, the life of the hotel ran with an amazing smoothness. It would have been impossible for a stranger to detect anything. The maids, the hall-boys, and the bell-boys were all smiles. They had to be.

IX

I had learned my Jim Crow lessons so thoroughly that I kept the hotel job till I left Jackson for Memphis. It so happened that while in Memphis I applied for a job at a branch of the optical company. I was hired. And for some reason, as long as I worked there, they never brought my past against me.

Here my Jim Crow education assumed quite a different form. It was no longer brutally cruel, but subtly cruel. Here I learned to lie, to steal, to dissemble. I learned to play that dual role which every Negro must play if he wants to eat and live.

For example, it was almost impossible to get a book to read. It was assumed that after a Negro had imbibed what scanty schooling the state furnished he had no further need for books. I was always borrowing books from men on the job. One day I mustered enough courage to ask one of the men to let me get books from the library in his name. Surprisingly, he consented. I cannot help but think that he consented because he was a Roman Catholic and felt a vague sympathy for Negroes, being himself an object of hatred. Armed with a library card, I obtained books in the following manner: I would write a note to the librarian, saying: "Please let this nigger boy have the following books." I would then sign it with the white man's name.

When I went to the library, I would stand at the desk, hat in hand, looking as unbookish as possible. When I received the books desired I would take them home. If the books listed in the note happened to be out, I would sneak into the lobby and forge a new one. I never took any chances guessing with the white librarian about what the fictitious white man would want to read. No doubt if any of the white patrons had suspected that some of the volumes they enjoyed had been in the home of a Negro, they would not have tolerated it for an instant.

The factory force of the optical company in Memphis was much larger than that in Jackson, and more urbanized. At least they liked to talk, and would engage the Negro help in conversation whenever possible. By this means I found that many subjects were taboo from the white man's point of view. Among the topics they did not like to discuss with Negroes were the following: American white women; the Ku Klux Klan; France, and how Negro soldiers fared while there; French women; Jack Johnson; the entire northern part of the United States; the Civil War; Abraham Lincoln; U. S. Grant; General Sherman; Catholics; the Pope; Jews; the Republican Party; slavery; social equality; Communism; Socialism; the 13th and 14th Amendments to the Constitution;[2] or any topic calling for positive knowledge or manly self-assertion on the part of the Negro. The most accepted topics were sex and religion.

There were many times when I had to exercise a great deal of ingenuity to keep out of trouble. It is a southern custom that all men must take off their hats when they enter an elevator. And especially did this apply to us blacks with rigid force. One day I stepped into an elevator with my arms full of packages. I was forced to ride with my hat on. Two white men stared at me coldly. Then one of them very kindly lifted my hat and placed it upon my armful of packages. Now the most accepted response for a Negro to make under such circumstances is to look at the white man out of the corner of his eye and grin. To have said: "Thank you!" would have made the white man *think* that you *thought* you were receiving from him a personal service. For such an act I have seen Negroes take a blow in the mouth. Finding the first alternative distasteful, and the second dangerous, I hit upon an acceptable course of action which fell safely between these two poles. I immediately—no sooner than my hat was lifted—pretended that my packages were about to spill, and appeared deeply distressed with keeping them in my arms. In this fashion I evaded having to acknowledge his service, and, in spite of adverse circumstances, salvaged a slender shred of personal pride.

How do Negroes feel about the way they have to live? How do they discuss it when alone among themselves? I think this question can be answered in a single sentence. A friend of mine who ran an elevator once told me:

"Lawd, man! Ef it wuzn't fer them polices 'n' them ol' lynch-mobs, there wouldn't be nothin' but uproar down here!"

1937

<hr/>

2. The Thirteenth Amendment (proclaimed December 18, 1865) abolished slavery and involuntary servitude, and the Fourteenth Amendment (proclaimed July 28, 1868) made American blacks citizens of the United States. Jack Johnson (1879–1946), black American heavyweight fighter who won the championship title in 1908.

Long Black Song

I

Go t sleep, baby
Papas gone t town
Go t sleep, baby
The suns goin down
Go t sleep, baby
Yo candys in the sack
Go t sleep, baby
Papas comin back
. . .

Over and over she crooned, and at each lull of her voice she rocked the wooden cradle with a bare black foot. But the baby squalled louder, its wail drowning out the song. She stopped and stood over the cradle, wondering what was bothering it, if its stomach hurt. She felt the diaper; it was dry. She lifted it up and patted its back. Still it cried, longer and louder. She put it back into the cradle and dangled a string of red beads before its eyes. The little black fingers clawed them away. She bent over, frowning, murmuring: "Whut's the mattah, chile? Yuh wan some watah?" She held a dripping gourd to the black lips, but the baby turned its head and kicked its legs. She stood a moment, perplexed. Whuts wrong wid tha chile? She ain never carried on like this this tima day. She picked it up and went to the open door. "See the sun, baby?" she asked, pointing to a big ball of red dying between the branches of trees. The baby pulled back and strained its round black arms and legs against her stomach and shoulders. She knew it was tired; she could tell by the halting way it opened its mouth to draw in air. She sat on a wooden stool, unbuttoned the front of her dress, brought the baby closer and offered it a black teat. "Don baby wan suppah?" It pulled away and went limp, crying softly, piteously, as though it would never stop. Then it pushed its fingers against her breasts and wailed. Lawd, chile, whut yuh wan? Yo ma cant help yuh less she knows whut yuh wan. Tears gushed; four white teeth flashed in red gums; the little chest heaved up and down and round black fingers stretched floorward. Lawd, chile, whuts wrong wid yuh? She stooped slowly, allowing her body to be guided by the downward tug. As soon as the little fingers touched the floor the wail quieted into a broken sniffle. She turned the baby loose and watched it crawl toward a corner. She followed and saw the little fingers reach for the tail-end of an old eight-day clock. "Yuh wan tha ol clock?" She dragged the clock into the center of the floor. The baby crawled after it, calling, "Ahh!" Then it raised its hands and beat on top of the clock Bink! Bink! Bink! "Naw, yuhll hurt yo hans!" She held the baby and looked around. It cried and struggled. "Wait, baby!" She fetched a small stick from the top of a rickety dresser. "Here," she said, closing the little fingers about it. "Beat wid this, see?" She heard each blow landing squarely on top of the clock Bang! Bang! Bang! And with each bang the baby smiled and said, "Ahh!" Mabbe thall keep yuh quiet erwhile. Mabbe Ah kin git some res now. She stood in the doorway. Lawd, tha chiles a pain! She mus be teethin. Er something . . .

She wiped sweat from her forehead with the bottom of her dress and looked out over the green fields rolling up the hillsides. She sighed, fighting a feeling of loneliness. Lawd, its sho hard t pass the days wid Silas gone. Been mos a week now since he took the wagon outta here. Hope ain nothin wrong. He mus be buyin a heapa stuff there in Colwatah t be stayin all this time. Yes; maybe Silas would remember and bring that five-yard piece of red calico she wanted. Oh, Lawd! Ah *hope* he don fergit it!

She saw green fields wrapped in the thickening gloam. It was as if they had left the earth, those fields, and were floating slowly skyward. The afterglow lingered, red, dying, somehow tenderly sad. And far away, in front of her, earth and sky met in a soft swoon of shadow. A cricket chirped, sharp and lonely; and it seemed she could hear it chirping long after it had stopped. Silas oughta c mon soon. Ahm tireda staying here by mahsef.

Loneliness ached in her. She swallowed, hearing Bang! Bang! Bang! Tom been gone t war mos a year now. N tha ol wars over n we ain heard nothin yit. Lawd, don let Tom be dead! She frowned into the gloam and wondered about that awful war so far away. They said it was over now. Yeah, Gawd had t stop em fo they killed everbody. She felt that merely to go so far away from home was a kind of death in itself. Just to go that far away was to be killed. Nothing good could come from men going miles across the seas to fight. N how come they wanna kill each other? How come they wanna make blood? Killing was not what men ought to do. Shucks! she thought.

She sighed, thinking of Tom, hearing Bang! Bang! Bang! She saw Tom, saw his big black smiling face; her eyes went dreamily blank, drinking in the red afterglow. Yes, God; it could have been Tom instead of Silas who was having her now. Yes; it could have been Tom she was loving. She smiled and asked herself, Lawd, Ah wondah how would it been wid Tom? Against the plush sky she saw a white bright day and a green cornfield and she saw Tom walking in his overalls and she was with Tom and he had his arm about her waist. She remembered how weak she had felt feeling his fingers sinking into the flesh of her hips. Her knees had trembled and she had had a hard time trying to stand up and not just sink right there to the ground. Yes; that was what Tom had wanted her to do. But she had held Tom up and he had held her up; they had held each other up to keep from slipping to the ground there in the green cornfield. Lawd! Her breath went and she passed her tongue over her lips. But that was not as exciting as that winter evening when the grey skies were sleeping and she and Tom were coming home from church down dark Lover's Lane. She felt the tips of her teats tingling and touching the front of her dress as she remembered how he had crushed her against him and hurt her. She had closed her eyes and was smelling the acrid scent of dry October leaves and had gone weak in his arms and had felt she could not breathe any more and had torn away and run, run home. And that sweet ache which had frightened her then was stealing back to her loins now with the silence and the cricket calls and the red afterglow and Bang! Bang! Bang! Lawd, Ah wondah how would it been wid Tom?

She stepped out on the porch and leaned against the wall of the house. Sky sang a red song. Fields whispered a green prayer. And song and prayer were dying in silence and shadow. Never in all her life had she been so much alone as she was now. Days were never so long as these days; and nights were never so empty as these nights. She jerked her head impatiently, hearing Bang! Bang! Bang! Shucks! she thought. When Silas had gone something had ebbed so slowly that at first she had not noticed it. Now she felt all of it as though the feeling had no bottom. She tried to think just how it had happened. Yes; there had been all her life the long hope of white bright days and the deep desire of dark black nights and then Silas had gone. Bang! Bang! Bang! There had been laughter and eating and singing and the long gladness of green cornfields in summer. There had been cooking and sewing and sweeping and the deep dream of sleeping grey skies in winter. Always it had been like that and she had been happy. But no more. The happiness of those days and nights, of those green cornfields and grey skies had started to go from her when Tom had gone to war. His leaving had left an empty black hole in her heart, a black hole that Silas had come in and filled. But not quite. Silas had not quite filled that hole. No; days and nights were not as they were before.

She lifted her chin, listening. She had heard something, a dull throb like she had heard that day Silas had called her outdoors to look at the airplane. Her eyes swept the sky. But there was no plane. Mabbe its behin the house? She stepped into the yard and looked upward through paling light. There were only a few big wet stars trembling in the east. Then she heard the throb again. She turned, looking up and down the road. The throb grew louder, droning; and she heard Bang! Bang! Bang! There! A car! Wondah whuts a car doin comin out here? A black car was winding over a dusty road, coming toward her. Mabbe some white mans bringing Silas home wida loada goods? But, Lawd, Ah *hope* its no trouble! The car stopped in front of the house and a white man got out. Wondah whut he wans? She looked at the car, but could not see Silas. The white man was young; he wore a straw hat and had no coat. He walked toward her with a huge black package under his arm.

"Well, howre yuh today, Aunty?"

"Ahm well. How yuh?"

"Oh, so-so. Its sure hot today, hunh?"

She brushed her hand across her forehead and sighed.

"Yeah; it is kinda warm."

"You busy?"

"Naw, Ah ain doin nothin."

"I've got something to show you. Can I sit here, on your porch?"

"Ah reckon so. But, Mistah, Ah ain got no money."

"Havent you sold your cotton yet?"

"Silas gone t town wid it now."

"Whens he coming back?"

"Ah don know. Ahm waitin fer im."

She saw the white man take out a handkerchief and mop his face. Bang! Bang! Bang! He turned his head and looked through the open doorway, into the front room.

"Whats all that going on in there?"

She laughed.

"Aw, thas jus Ruth."

"Whats she doing?"

"She beatin tha ol clock."

"Beating a *clock*?"

She laughed again.

"She wouldn't go t sleep so Ah give her tha ol clock t play wid."

The white man got up and went to the front door; he stood a moment looking at the black baby hammering on the clock. Bang! Bang! Bang!

"But why let her tear your clock up?"

"It ain no good."

"You could have it fixed."

"We ain got no money t be fixin no clocks."

"Havent you got a clock?"

"Naw."

"But how do you keep time?"

"We git erlong widout time."

"But how do you know when to get up in the morning?"

"We jus git up, thas all."

"But how do you know what time it is when you get up?"

"We git up wid the sun."

"And at night, how do you tell when its night?"

"It gits dark when the sun goes down."

"Havent you ever had a clock?"

She laughed and turned her face toward the silent fields.

"Mistah, we don need no clock."

"Well, this beats everything! I dont see how in the world anybody can live without time."

"We jus don need no time, Mistah."

The white man laughed and shook his head; she laughed and looked at him. The white man was funny. Jus lika lil boy. Astin how do Ah know when t git up in the mawnin! She laughed again and mused on the baby, hearing Bang! Bang! Bang! She could hear the white man breathing at her side; she felt his eyes on her face. She looked at him; she saw he was looking at her breasts. Hes jus lika lil boy. Acks like he cant understan *nothin!*

"But you need a clock," the white man insisted. "Thats what Im out here for. Im selling clocks and graphophones. The clocks are made right into the graphophones, a nice sort of combination, hunh? You can have music and time all at once. Ill show you . . ."

"Mistah, we don need no clock!"

"You dont have to buy it. It wont cost you anything just to look."

He unpacked the big black box. She saw the strands of his auburn hair glinting in the afterglow. His back bulged against his white shirt as he stooped. He pulled out a square brown graphophone. She bent forward, looking. Lawd, but its pretty! She saw the face of a clock under the horn of the graphophone. The gilt on the corners sparkled. The color in the wood glowed softly. It reminded her of the light she saw sometimes in the baby's eyes. Slowly she slid a finger over a beveled edge; she wanted to take the box into her arms and kiss it.

"Its eight o'clock," he said.

"Yeah?"

"It only costs fifty dollars. And you dont have to pay for it all at once. Just five dollars down and five dollars a month."

She smiled. The white man was just like a little boy. Jus lika chile. She saw him grinding the handle of the box.

"Just listen to this," he said.

There was a sharp, scratching noise; then she moved nervously, her body caught in the ringing coils of music.

When the trumpet of the Lord shall sound . . .

She rose on circling waves of white bright days and dark black nights.

. . . and time shall be no more . . .

Higher and higher she mounted.

And the morning breaks . . .

Earth fell far behind, forgotten.

. . . eternal, bright and fair . . .

Echo after echo sounded.

When the saved of the earth shall gather . . .

Her blood surged like the long gladness of summer.

. . . over on the other shore . . .

Her blood ebbed like the deep dream of sleep in winter.

And when the roll is called up yonder . . .

She gave up, holding her breath.

I'll be there [1] *. . .*

A lump filled her throat. She leaned her back against a post, trembling, feeling the rise and fall of days and nights, of summer and winter; surging, ebbing, leaping about her, beyond her, far out over the fields to where earth and sky lay folded in darkness. She wanted to lie down and sleep, or else leap up and shout. When the music stopped she felt herself coming back, being let down slowly. She sighed. It was dark now. She looked into the doorway. The baby was sleeping on the floor. Ah gotta git up n put tha chile t bed, she thought.

"Wasnt that pretty?"

"It wuz pretty, awright."

"When do you think your husbands coming back?"

"Ah don know, Mistah."

She went into the room and put the baby into the cradle. She stood again in the doorway and looked at the shadowy box that had lifted her up and carried her away. Crickets called. The dark sky had swallowed up the earth, and more stars were hanging, clustered, burning. She heard the white man sigh. His face was lost in shadow. She saw him rub his palms over his forehead. Hes jus lika lil boy.

"Id like to see your husband tonight," he said. "Ive got to be in Lilydale at six o'clock in the morning and I wont be back through here soon. I got to pick up my buddy over there and we're heading North."

She smiled into the darkness. He was just like a little boy. A little boy selling clocks.

"Yuh sell them things alla time?" she asked.

---

1. From "When the Roll Is Called Up Yonder," an American hymn by James M. Black.

"Just for the summer," he said. "I go to school in winter. If I can make enough money out of this Ill go to Chicago to school this fall . . ."

"Whut yuh gonna be?"

"*Be?* What do you mean?"

"Whut yuh goin t school fer?"

"Im studying science."

"Whuts tha?"

"Oh, er . . ." He looked at her. "Its about why things are as they are."

"Why things is as they *is?*"

"Well, its something like that."

"How come yuh wanna study tha?"

"Oh, you wouldnt understand."

She sighed.

"Naw, Ah guess Ah wouldnt."

"Well, I reckon Ill be getting along," said the white man. "Can I have a drink of water?"

"Sho. But we ain got nothin but well-watah, n yuhll have t come n git."

"Thats all right."

She slid off the porch and walked over the ground with bare feet. She heard the shoes of the white man behind her, falling to the earth in soft whispers. It was black dark now. She led him to the well, groped her way, caught the bucket and let it down with a rope; she heard a splash and the bucket grew heavy. She drew it up, pulling against its weight, throwing one hand over the other, feeling the cool wet of the rope on her palms.

"Ah don git watah outta here much," she said, a little out of breath. "Silas gits the watah mos of the time. This buckets too heavy fer me."

"Oh, wait! Ill help!"

His shoulder touched hers. In the darkness she felt his warm hands fumbling for the rope.

"Where is it?"

"Here."

She extended the rope through the darkness. His fingers touched her breasts.

"Oh!"

She said it in spite of herself. He would think she was thinking about that. And he was a white man. She was sorry she had said that.

"Wheres the gourd?" he asked. "Gee, its dark!"

She stepped back and tried to see him.

"Here."

"I cant see!" he said, laughing.

Again she felt his fingers on the tips of her breasts. She backed away, saying nothing this time. She thrust the gourd out from her. Warm fingers met her cold hands. He had the gourd. She heard him drink; it was the faint, soft music of water going down a dry throat, the music of water in a silent night. He sighed and drank again.

"I was thirsty," he said. "I hadnt had any water since noon."

She knew he was standing in front of her; she could not see him, but she felt him. She heard the gourd rest against the wall of the well. She turned, then felt his hands full on her breasts. She struggled back.

"Naw, Mistah!"

"Im not going to hurt you!"

White arms were about her, tightly. She was still. But hes a *white* man. A *white* man. She felt his breath coming hot on her neck and where his hands held her breasts the flesh seemed to knot. She was rigid, poised; she swayed backward, then forward. She caught his shoulders and pushed.

"Naw, naw . . . Mistah, Ah cant do that!"

She jerked away. He caught her hand.

"Please . . ."

"Lemme go!"

She tried to pull her hand out of his and felt his fingers tighten. She pulled harder, and for a moment they were balanced, one against the other. Then he was at her side again, his arms about her.

"I wont hurt you! I wont hurt you . . ."

She leaned backward and tried to dodge his face. Her breasts were full against him; she gasped, feeling the full length of his body. She held her head far to one side; she knew he was seeking her mouth. His hands were on her breasts again. A wave of warm blood swept into her stomach and loins. She felt his lips touching her throat and where he kissed it burned.

"Naw, naw . . ."

Her eyes were full of the wet stars and they blurred, silver and blue. Her knees were loose and she heard her own breathing; she was trying to keep from falling. But hes a *white* man! A *white* man! Naw! Naw! And still she would not let him have her lips; she kept her face away. Her breasts hurt where they were crushed against him and each time she caught her breath she held it and while she held it it seemed that if she would let it go it would kill her. Her knees were pressed hard against his and she clutched the upper parts of his arms, trying to hold on. Her loins ached. She felt her body sliding.

"Gawd . . ."

He helped her up. She could not see the stars now; her eyes were full of the feeling that surged over her body each time she caught her breath. He held her close, breathing into her ear; she straightened, rigidly, feeling that she had to straighten or die. And then her lips felt his and she held her breath and dreaded ever to breathe again for fear of the feeling that would sweep down over her limbs. She held tightly, hearing a mounting tide of blood beating against her throat and temples. Then she gripped him, tore her face away, emptied her lungs in one long despairing gasp and went limp. She felt his hand; she was still, taut, feeling his hand, then his fingers. The muscles in her legs flexed and she bit her lips and pushed her toes deep into the wet dust by the side of the well and tried to wait and tried to wait until she could wait no longer. She whirled away from him and a streak of silver and blue swept across her blood. The wet ground cooled her palms and knee-caps. She stumbled up and ran, blindly, her toes flicking warm, dry dust. Her numbed fingers grabbed at a rusty nail in the post at the porch and she pushed ahead of hands that held her breasts. Her fingers found the door-facing; she moved into the darkened room, her hands before her. She touched the cradle and turned till her knees hit the bed. She went over, face down, her fingers trembling in the crumpled folds of his shirt. She moved and moved again and again, trying to keep ahead of the warm flood of blood that sought to catch her. A liquid metal covered her and she rode on the curve of white bright days and dark black nights and the surge of the long gladness of summer and the ebb of the deep dream of sleep in winter till a high red wave of hotness drowned her in a deluge of silver and blue that boiled her blood and blistered her flesh *bang-bangbang* . . .

II

"Yuh bettah go," she said.

She felt him standing by the side of the bed, in the dark. She heard him clear his throat. His belt-buckle tinkled.

"Im leaving that clock and graphophone," he said.

She said nothing. In her mind she saw the box glowing softly, like the light in the baby's eyes. She stretched out her legs and relaxed.

"You can have it for forty instead of fifty. Ill be by early in the morning to see if your husbands in."

She said nothing. She felt the hot skin of her body growing steadily cooler.

"Do you think hell pay ten on it? Hell only owe thirty then."

She pushed her toes deep into the quilt, feeling a night wind blowing through the door. Her palms rested lightly on top of her breasts.

"Do you think hell pay ten on it?"

"Hunh?"

"Hell pay ten, wont he?"

"Ah don know," she whispered.

She heard his shoe hit against a wall; footsteps echoed on the wooden porch. She started nervously when she heard the roar of his car; she followed the throb of the motor till she heard it when she could hear it no more, followed it till she heard it roaring faintly in her ears in the dark and silent room. Her hands moved on her breasts and she was conscious of herself, all over; she felt the weight of her body resting heavily on shucks. She felt the presence of fields lying out there covered with night. She turned over slowly and lay on her stomach, her hands tucked under her. From somewhere came a creaking noise. She sat upright, feeling fear. The wind sighed. Crickets called. She lay down again, hearing shucks rustle. Her eyes looked straight up in the darkness and her blood sogged. She had lain a long time, full of a vast peace, when a far away tinkle made her feel the bed again. The tinkle came through the night; she listened, knowing that soon she would hear the rattle of Silas' wagon. Even then she tried to fight off the sound of Silas' coming, even then she wanted to feel the peace of night filling her again; but the tinkle grew louder and she heard the jangle of a wagon and the quick trot of horses. Thas Silas! She gave up and waited. She heard horses neighing. Out of the window bare feet whispered in the dust, then crossed the porch, echoing in soft booms. She closed her eyes and saw Silas come into the room in his dirty overalls as she had seen him come in a thousand times before.

"Yuh sleep, Sarah?"

She did not answer. Feet walked across the floor and a match scratched. She opened her eyes and saw Silas standing over her with a lighted lamp. His hat was pushed far back on his head and he was laughing.

"Ah reckon yuh thought Ah wuznt never comin back, hunh? Cant yuh wake up? See, Ah got that red cloth yuh wanted . . ." He laughed again and threw the red cloth on the mantel.

"Yuh hongry?" she asked.

"Naw, Ah kin make out till mawnin." Shucks rustled as he sat on the edge of the bed. "Ah got two hundred n fifty fer mah cotton."

"Two hundred n fifty?"

"Nothin different! N guess whut Ah done?"

"Whut?"

"Ah bought ten mo acres o lan. Got em from ol man Burgess. Paid im a hundred n fifty dollahs down. Ahll pay the res next year ef things go erlong awright. Ahma have t git a man t hep me nex spring . . ."

"Yuh mean hire somebody?"

"Sho, hire somebody! Whut yuh think? Ain tha the way the white folks do? Ef yuhs gonna git anywheres yuhs gotta do just like they do." He paused. "Whut yuh been doin since Ah been gone?"

"Nothin. Cookin, cleanin, n . . ."

"How Ruth?"

"She awright." She lifted her head. "Silas, yuh git any lettahs?"

"Naw. But Ah heard Tom wuz in town."

"In *town*?"

She sat straight up.

"Yeah, thas whut the folks wuz sayin at the sto."

"Back from the war?"

"Ah ast erroun t see ef Ah could fin im. But Ah couldnt."

"Lawd, Ah wish hed c mon home."

"Them white folks sho's glad the wars over. But things wuz kinda bad there in town. Everwhere Ah looked wuznt nothin but black n white soljers. N them white folks beat up a black soljer yistiddy. He wuz jus in from France. Wuz still wearin his soljers suit. They claimed he sassed a white woman . . ."

"Who wuz he?"

"Ah don know. Never saw im befo."

"Yuh see An Peel?"

"Naw."

"Silas!" she said reprovingly.

"Aw, Sarah, Ah jus couldnt git out there."

"Whut else yuh bring sides the cloth?"

"Ah got yuh some high-top shoes." He turned and looked at her in the dim light of the lamp. "Woman, ain yuh glad Ah bought yuh some shoes n cloth?" He laughed and lifted his feet to the bed. "Lawd, Sarah, yuhs sho sleepy, ain yuh?"

"Bettah put tha lamp out, Silas . . ."

"Aw . . ." He swung out of the bed and stood still for a moment. She watched him, then turned her face to the wall.

"Whuts that by the windah?" he asked.

She saw him bending over and touching the graphophone with his fingers.

"Thasa graphophone."

"Where yuh git it from?"

"A man lef it here."

"When he bring it?"

"Today."

"But how come he t leave it?"

"He says hell be out here in the mawnin t see ef yuh wans t buy it."

He was on his knees, feeling the wood and looking at the gilt on the edges of the box. He stood up and looked at her.

"Yuh ain never said yuh wanted one of these things."

She said nothing.

"Where wuz the man from?"

"Ah don know."

"He white?"

"Yeah."

He put the lamp back on the mantel. As he lifted the globe to blow out the flame, his hand paused.

"Whos hats this?"

She raised herself and looked. A straw hat lay bottom upwards on the edge of the mantel. Silas picked it up and looked back to the bed, to Sarah.

"Ah guess its the white mans. He must a lef it . . ."

"Whut he doin *in our room?*"

"He wuz talkin t me bout tha graphophone."

She watched him go to the window and stoop again to the box. He picked it up, fumbled with the price-tag and took the box to the light.

"Whut this thing cos?"

"Forty dollahs."

"But its marked fifty here."

"Oh, Ah means he said fifty . . ."

He took a step toward the bed.

"Yuh lyin t me!"

"Silas!"

He heaved the box out of the front door; there was a smashing, tinkling noise as it bounded off the front porch and hit the ground.

"Whut in hell yuh lie t me fer?"

"Yuh broke the box!"

"Ahma break yo Gawddam neck ef yuh don stop lyin t me!"

"Silas, Ah ain lied t yuh!"

"Shut up, Gawddammit! Yuh did!"

He was standing by the bed with the lamp trembling in his hand. She stood on the other side, between the bed and the wall.

"How come yuh tell me tha thing cos *forty* dollahs when it cos *fifty?*"

"Thas whut he tol me."

"How come he take *ten* dollahs off fer yuh?"

"He ain took nothin off fer me, Silas!"

"Yuh lyin t me! N yuh lied t me bout Tom, too!"

She stood with her back to the wall, her lips parted, looking at him silently, steadily. Their eyes held for a moment. Silas looked down, as though he were about to believe her. Then he stiffened.

"Whos this?" he asked, picking up a short yellow pencil from the crumpled quilt.

She said nothing. He started toward her.

"Yuh wan me t take mah raw-hide whip n make yuh talk?"

"Naw, naw, Silas! Yuh wrong! He wuz figgerin wid tha pencil!"

He was silent a moment, his eyes searching her face.

"Gawddam yo black soul t hell, don yuh try lyin t me! Ef yuh start layin wid white men Ahll hoss-whip yuh t a incha yo life. Shos theres a Gawd in Heaven Ah will! From sunup t sundown Ah works mah guts out t pay them white trash bastards whut Ah owe em, n then Ah comes n fins they been in mah house! Ah cant go into their houses, n yuh know Gawddam well Ah cant! They don have no mercy on no black folks; wes just like dirt under their feet! Fer ten years Ah slaves lika dog t git mah farm free, givin ever penny Ah kin t em, n then Ah comes n fins they been in mah house . . ." He was speechless with outrage. "Ef yuh wans t eat at mah table yuhs gonna keep them white trash bastards out, yuh hear? Tha white ape kin come n git tha damn box n Ah ain gonna pay im a cent! He had no bisness leavin it here, n yuh had no bisness lettin im! Ahma tell tha sonofabitch something when he comes out here in the mawnin, so hep me Gawd! Now git back in tha bed!"

She slipped beneath the quilt and lay still, her face turned to the wall. Her heart thumped slowly and heavily. She heard him walk across the floor in his bare feet. She heard the bottom of the lamp as it rested on the mantel. She stiffened when the room darkened. Feet whispered across the floor again. The shucks rustled from Silas' weight as he sat on the edge of the bed. She was still, breathing softly. Silas was mumbling. She felt sorry for him. In the darkness it seemed that she could see the hurt look on his black face. The crow of a rooster came from far away, came so faintly that it seemed she had not heard it. The bed sank and the shucks cried out in dry whispers; she knew Silas had stretched out. She heard him sigh. Then she jumped because he jumped. She could feel the tenseness of his body; she knew he was sitting bolt upright. She felt his hands fumbling jerkily under the quilt. Then the bed heaved amid a wild shout of shucks and Silas' feet hit the floor with a loud boom. She snatched herself to her elbows, straining her eyes in the dark, wondering what was wrong now. Silas was moving about, cursing under his breath.

"Don wake Ruth up!" she whispered.

"Ef yuh say one mo word t me Ahma slap yuh inter a black spasm!"

She grabbed her dress, got up and stood by the bed, the tips of her fingers touching the wall behind her. A match flared in yellow flame; Silas' face was caught in a circle of light. He was looking downward, staring intently at a white wad of cloth balled in his hand. His black cheeks were hard, set; his lips were tightly pursed. She looked closer; she saw that the white cloth was a man's handkerchief. Silas' fingers loosened; she heard the handkerchief hit the floor softly, damply. The match went out.

"Yuh little bitch!"

Her knees gave. Fear oozed from her throat to her stomach. She moved in the dark toward the door, struggling with the dress, jamming it over her head. She heard the thick skin of Silas' feet swish across the wooden planks.

"Ah got mah raw-hide whip n Ahm takin yuh t the barn!"

She ran on tiptoe to the porch and paused, thinking of the baby. She shrank as something whined through air. A red streak of pain cut across the small of her back and burned its way into her body, deeply.

"Silas!" she screamed.

She grabbed for the post and fell in dust. She screamed again and crawled out of reach.

"Git t the barn, Gawddammit!"

She scrambled up and ran through the dark, hearing the baby cry. Behind her leather thongs hummed and feet whispered swiftly over the dusty ground.

"Cmere, yuh bitch! Cmere, Ah say!"

She ran to the road and stopped. She wanted to go back and get the baby, but she dared not. Not as long as Silas had that whip. She stiffened, feeling that he was near.

"Yuh jus as well c mon back n git yo beatin!"

She ran again, slowing now and then to listen. If she only knew where he was she would slip back into the house and get the baby and walk all the way to Aunt Peel's.

"Yuh ain comin back in mah house till Ah beat yuh!"

She was sorry for the anger she knew he had out there in the field. She had a bewildering impulse to go to him and ask him not to be angry; she wanted to tell him that there was nothing to be angry about; that what she had done did not matter; that she was sorry; that after all she was his wife and still loved him. But there was no way she could do that now; if she went to him he would whip her as she had seen him whip a horse.

"Sarah! Sarah!"

His voice came from far away. Ahm goin git Ruth. Back through dust she sped, going on her toes, holding her breath.

"Saaaarah!"

From far off his voice floated over the fields. She ran into the house and caught the baby in her arms. Again she sped through dust on her toes. She did not stop till she was so far away that his voice sounded like a faint echo falling from the sky. She looked up; the stars were paling a little. Mus be gittin near mawnin. She walked now, letting her feet sink softly into the cool dust. The baby was sleeping; she could feel the little chest swelling against her arm. She looked up again; the sky was solid black. Its gittin near mawnin. Ahma take Ruth t An Peels. N mabbe Ahll fin Tom . . . But she could not walk all that distance in the dark. Not now. Her legs were tired. For a moment a memory of surge and ebb rose in her blood; she felt her legs straining, upward. She sighed. Yes, she would go to the sloping hillside back of the garden and wait until morning. Then she would slip away. She stopped, listening. She heard a faint, rattling noise. She imagined Silas' kicking or throwing the smashed graphophone. Hes mad! Hes sho mad! Aw, Lawd! . . . She stopped stock still, squeezing the baby till it whimpered. What would happen when that white man came out in the morning? She had forgotten him. She

would have to head him off and tell him. Yeah, cause Silas jus mad ernuff t kill! Lawd, hes mad ernuff t kill!

III

She circled the house widely, climbing a slope, groping her way, holding the baby high in her arms. After awhile she stopped and wondered
where on the slope she was. She remembered there was an elm tree near
the edge; if she could find it she would know. She groped farther, feeling
with her feet. Ahm gittin los! And she did not want to fall with the baby.
Ahma stop here, she thought. When morning came she would see the car
of the white man from this hill and she would run down the road and tell
him to go back; and then there would be no killing. Dimly she saw in her
mind a picture of men killing and being killed. White men killed the black
and black men killed the white. White men killed the black men because
they could, and the black men killed the white men to keep from being
killed. And killing was blood. Lawd, Ah wish Tom wuz here. She shuddered, sat on the ground and watched the sky for signs of morning. Mabbe
Ah oughta walk on down the road? Naw . . . Her legs were tired. Again she
felt her body straining. Then she saw Silas holding the white man's handkerchief. She heard it hit the floor, softly, damply. She was sorry for what
she had done. Silas was as good to her as any black man could be to a black
woman. Most of the black women worked in the fields as croppers. But
Silas had given her her own home, and that was more than many others
had done for their women. Yes, she knew how Silas felt. Always he had said
he was as good as any white man. He had worked hard and saved his money
and bought a farm so he could grow his own crops like white men. Silas
hates white folks! Lawd, he sho hates em!

The baby whimpered. She unbuttoned her dress and nursed her in the
dark. She looked toward the east. There! A tinge of grey hovered. It wont be
long now. She could see ghostly outlines of trees. Soon she would see the
elm, and by the elm she would sit till it was light enough to see the road.

The baby slept. Far off a rooster crowed. Sky deepened. She rose and
walked slowly down a narrow, curving path and came to the elm tree.
Standing on the edge of a slope, she saw a dark smudge in a sea of shifting
shadows. That was her home. Wondah how come Silas didnt light the
lamp? She shifted the baby from her right hip to her left, sighed, struggled
against sleep. She sat on the ground again, caught the baby close and
leaned against the trunk of a tree. Her eye-lids drooped and it seemed that a
hard cold hand caught hold of her right leg—or was it her left leg? she did
not know which—and began to drag her over a rough litter of shucks and
when she strained to see who it was that was pulling her no one was in sight
but far ahead was darkness and it seemed that out of the darkness some
force came and pulled her like a magnet and she went sliding along over a
rough bed of screeching shucks and it seemed that a wild fear made her
want to scream but when she opened her mouth to scream she could not
scream and she felt she was coming to a wide black hole and again she
made ready to scream and then it was too late for she was already over the
wide black hole falling falling falling . . .

She awakened with a start and blinked her eyes in the sunshine. She found she was clutching the baby so hard that it had begun to cry. She got to her feet, trembling from fright of the dream, remembering Silas and the white man and Silas' running her out of the house and the white man's coming. Silas was standing in the front yard; she caught her breath. Yes, she had to go and head that white man off! Naw! She could not do that, not with Silas standing there with that whip in his hand. If she tried to climb any of those slopes he would see her surely. And Silas would never forgive her for something like that. If it were anybody but a white man it would be different.

Then, while standing there on the edge of the slope looking wonderingly at Silas striking the whip against his overall-leg—and then, while standing there looking—she froze. There came from the hills a distant throb. Lawd! The baby whimpered. She loosened her arms. The throb grew louder, droning. Hes comin fas! She wanted to run to Silas and beg him not to bother the white man. But he had that whip in his hand. She should not have done what she had done last night. This was all her fault. Lawd, ef anything happens t im its mah blame . . . Her eyes watched a black car speed over the crest of a hill. She should have been out there on the road instead of sleeping here by the tree. But it was too late now. Silas was standing in the yard; she saw him turn with a nervous jerk and sit on the edge of the porch. He was holding the whip stiffly. The car came to a stop. A door swung open. A white man got out. Thas im! She saw another white man in the front seat of the car. N thats his buddy . . . The white man who had gotten out walked over the ground, going to Silas. They faced each other, the white man standing up and Silas sitting down; like two toy men they faced each other. She saw Silas point the whip to the smashed graphophone. The white man looked down and took a quick step backward. The white man's shoulders were bent and he shook his head from left to right. Then Silas got up and they faced each other again; like two dolls, a white doll and a black doll, they faced each other in the valley below. The white man pointed his finger into Silas' face. Then Silas' right arm went up; the whip flashed. The white man turned, bending, flinging his hands to shield his head. Silas' arm rose and fell, rose and fell. She saw the white man crawling in dust, trying to get out of reach. She screamed when she saw the other white man get out of the car and run to Silas. Then all three were on the ground, rolling in dust, grappling for the whip. She clutched the baby and ran. Lawd! Then she stopped, her mouth hanging open. Silas had broken loose and was running toward the house. She knew he was going for his gun.

"Silas!"

Running, she stumbled and fell. The baby rolled in the dust and bawled. She grabbed it up and ran again. The white men were scrambling for their car. She reached level ground, running. Hell be killed! Then again she stopped. Silas was on the front porch, aiming a rifle. One of the white men was climbing into the car. The other was standing, waving his arms, shouting at Silas. She tried to scream, but choked; and she could not scream till she heard a shot ring out.

"Silas!"

One of the white men was on the ground. The other was in the car. Silas was aiming again. The car started, running in a cloud of dust. She fell to her knees and hugged the baby close. She heard another shot, but the car was roaring over the top of the southern hill. Fear was gone now. Down the slope she ran. Silas was standing on the porch, holding his gun and looking at the fleeing car. Then she saw him go to the white man lying in dust and stoop over him. He caught one of the man's legs and dragged the body into the middle of the road. Then he turned and came slowly back to the house. She ran, holding the baby, and fell at his feet.

"Siiilas!"

IV

"Git up, Sarah!"

His voice was hard and cold. She lifted her eyes and saw blurred black feet. She wiped tears away with dusty fingers and pulled up. Something took speech from her and she stood with bowed shoulders. Silas was standing still, mute; the look on his face condemned her. It was as though he had gone far off and had stayed a long time and had come back changed even while she was standing there in the sunshine before him. She wanted to say something, to give herself. She cried.

"Git the chile up, Sarah!"

She lifted the baby and stood waiting for him to speak, to tell her something to change all this. But he said nothing. He walked toward the house. She followed. As she attempted to go in, he blocked the way. She jumped to one side as he threw the red cloth outdoors to the ground. The new shoes came next. Then Silas heaved the baby's cradle. It hit the porch and a rocker splintered; the cradle swayed for a second, then fell to the ground, lifting a cloud of brown dust against the sun. All of her clothes and the baby's clothes were thrown out.

"Silas!"

She cried, seeing blurred objects sailing through the air and hearing them hit softly in the dust.

"Git yo things n go!"

"Silas."

"Ain no use yuh sayin *nothin* now!"

"But theyll kill yuh!"

"There ain nothin Ah kin do. N there ain nothin yuh kin do. Yuh done done too Gawddam much awready. Git you things n go!"

"Theyll kill yuh, Silas!"

He pushed her off the porch.

"GIT YO THINGS N GO T AN PEELS!"

"Les *both* go, Silas!"

"Ahm stayin here till they come back!"

She grabbed his arm and he slapped her hand away. She dropped to the edge of the porch and sat looking at the ground.

"Go way," she said quietly. "Go way fo they comes. Ah didnt mean no harm . . ."

"Go way fer whut?"

"Theyll *kill* yuh . . ."

"It don make no difference." He looked out over the sunfilled fields. "Fer ten years Ah slaved mah life out t git mah farm free . . ." His voice broke off. His lips moved as though a thousand words were spilling silently out of his mouth, as though he did not have breath enough to give them sound. He looked to the sky, and then back to the dust. "Now, its all gone. *Gone* . . . Ef Ah run erway, Ah ain got nothin. Ef Ah stay n fight, Ah ain got nothin. It don make no difference which way Ah go. Gawd! Gawd, Ah wish alla them white folks wuz dead! *Dead*, Ah tell yuh! Ah wish Gawd would kill em *all!*"

She watched him run a few steps and stop. His throat swelled. He lifted his hands to his face; his fingers trembled. Then he bent to the ground and cried. She touched his shoulders.

"Silas!"

He stood up. She saw he was staring at the white man's body lying in the dust in the middle of the road. She watched him walk over to it. He began to talk to no one in particular; he simply stood over the dead white man and talked out of his life, out of a deep and final sense that now it was all over and nothing could make any difference.

"The white folks ain never gimme a chance! They ain never give no black man a chance! There ain nothin in yo whole life yuh kin keep from em! They take yo lan! They take yo freedom! They take yo women! N then they take yo life!" He turned to her, screaming. "N then Ah gits stabbed in the back by mah own blood! When mah eyes is on the white folks to keep em from killin me, mah own blood trips me up!" He knelt in the dust again and sobbed; after a bit he looked to the sky, his face wet with tears. "Ahm gonna be hard like they is! So hep me, Gawd, Ah'm gonna be *hard!* When they come fer me Ah'm gonna *be* here! N when they git me outta here theys gonna *know* Ahm gone! Ef Gawd lets me live Ahm gonna make em *feel* it!" He stopped and tried to get his breath. "But, Lawd, Ah don wanna be this way! It don mean nothin! Yuh die ef yuh fight! Yuh die ef yuh don fight! Either way yuh die n it don mean nothin . . ."

He was lying flat on the ground, the side of his face deep in dust. Sarah stood nursing the baby with eyes black and stony. Silas pulled up slowly and stood again on the porch.

"Git on t An Peels, Sarah!"

A dull roar came from the south. They both turned. A long streak of brown dust was weaving down the hillside.

"Silas!"

"Go on cross the fiels, Sarah!"

"We kin *both* go! Git the hosses!"

He pushed her off the porch, grabbed her hand, and led her to the rear of the house, past the well, to where a path led up a slope to the elm tree.

"Silas!"

"Yuh git on fo they ketch yuh too!"

Blind from tears, she went across the swaying fields, stumbling over blurred grass. It ain no use! She knew it was now too late to make him change his mind. The calves of her legs knotted. Suddenly her throat tightened, aching. She stopped, closed her eyes and tried to stem a flood of sorrow that drenched her. Yes, killing of white men by black men and killing of black men by white men went on in spite of the hope of white bright days and the desire of dark black nights and the long gladness of green cornfields in summer and the deep dream of sleeping grey skies in winter. And when killing started it went on, like a red river flowing. Oh, she felt sorry for Silas! Silas . . . He was following that long river of blood. Lawd, how come he wans t stay there like tha? And he did not want to die; she knew he hated dying by the way he talked of it. Yet he followed the old river of blood, knowing that it meant nothing. He followed it, cursing and whimpering. But he followed it. She stared before her at the dry, dusty grass. Somehow, men, black men and white men, land and houses, green cornfields and grey skies, gladness and dreams, were all a part of that which made life good. Yes, somehow, they were linked, like the spokes in a spinning wagon wheel. She felt they were. She knew they were. She felt it when she breathed and knew it when she looked. But she could not say how; she could not put her finger on it and when she thought hard about it it became all mixed up, like milk spilling suddenly. Or else it knotted in her throat and chest in a hard aching lump, like the one she felt now. She touched her face to the baby's face and cried again.

There was a loud blare of auto horns. The growing roar made her turn round. Silas was standing, seemingly unafraid, leaning against a post of the porch. The long line of cars came speeding in clouds of dust. Silas moved toward the door and went in. Sarah ran down the slope a piece, coming again to the elm tree. Her breath was slow and hard. The cars stopped in front of the house. There was a steady drone of motors and drifting clouds of dust. For a moment she could not see what was happening. Then on all sides white men with pistols and rifles swarmed over the fields. She dropped to her knees, unable to take her eyes away, unable it seemed to breathe. A shot rang out. A white man fell, rolling over, face downward.

"Hes gotta gun!"

"Git back!"

"Lay down!"

The white men ran back and crouched behind cars. Three more shots came from the house. She looked, her head and eyes aching. She rested the baby in her lap and shut her eyes. Her knees sank into the dust. More shots came, but it was no use looking now. She knew it all by heart. She could feel it happening even before it happened. There were men killing and being killed. Then she jerked up, being compelled to look.

"Burn the bastard out!"

"Set the sonofabitch on fire!"

"Cook the coon!"

"Smoke im out!"

She saw two white men on all fours creeping past the well. One carried a gun and the other a red tin can. When they reached the back steps the one with the tin can crept under the house and crept out again. Then both rose and ran. Shots. One fell. A yell went up. A yellow tongue of fire licked out from under the back steps.

"Burn the nigger!"

"C mon out, nigger, n git yos!"

She watched from the hill-slope; the back steps blazed. The white men
fired a steady stream of bullets. Black smoke spiraled upward in the sunshine. Shots came from the house. The white men crouched out of sight,
behind their cars.

"Make up yo mind, nigger!"

"C mon out er burn, yuh black bastard!"

"Yuh think yuhre white now, nigger?"

The shack blazed, flanked on all sides by whirling smoke filled with flying sparks. She heard the distant hiss of flames. White men were crawling
on their stomachs. Now and then they stopped, aimed, and fired into the
bulging smoke. She looked with a tense numbness; she looked, waiting for
Silas to scream, or run out. But the house crackled and blazed, spouting
yellow plumes to the blue sky. The white men shot again, sending a hail of
bullets into the furious pillars of smoke. And still she could not see Silas
running out, or hear his voice calling. Then she jumped, standing. There
was a loud crash; the roof caved in. A black chimney loomed amid crumbling wood. Flames roared and black smoke billowed, hiding the house.
The white men stood up, no longer afraid. Again she waited for Silas,
waited to see him fight his way out, waited to hear his call. Then she
breathed a long, slow breath, emptying her lungs. She knew now. Silas had
killed as many as he could and had stayed on to burn, had stayed without a
murmur. She filled her lungs with a quick gasp as the walls fell in; the
house was hidden by eager plumes of red. She turned and ran with the
baby in her arms, ran blindly across the fields, crying, "Naw, Gawd!"

1938

The Man Who Lived Underground

I've got to hide, he told himself. His chest heaved as he waited, crouching in a dark corner of the vestibule. He was tired of running and dodging.
Either he had to find a place to hide, or he had to surrender. A police car
swished by through the rain, its siren rising sharply. They're looking for me
all over . . . He crept to the door and squinted through the fogged plate
glass. He stiffened as the siren rose and died in the distance. Yes, he had to
hide, but where? He gritted his teeth. Then a sudden movement in the
street caught his attention. A throng of tiny columns of water snaked into
the air from the perforations of a manhole cover. The columns stopped
abruptly, as though the perforations had become clogged; a gray spout of
sewer water jutted up from underground and lifted the circular metal
cover, juggled it for a moment, then let it fall with a clang.

He hatched a tentative plan: he would wait until the siren sounded far
off, then he would go out. He smoked and waited, tense. At last the siren
gave him his signal; it wailed, dying, going away from him. He stepped to
the sidewalk, then paused and looked curiously at the open manhole, half
expecting the cover to leap up again. He went to the center of the street and
stooped and peered into the hole, but could see nothing. Water rustled in
the black depths.

He started with terror; the siren sounded so near that he had the idea that he had been dreaming and had awakened to find the car upon him. He dropped instinctively to his knees and his hands grasped the rim of the manhole. The siren seemed to hoot directly above him and with a wild gasp of exertion he snatched the cover far enough off to admit his body. He swung his legs over the opening and lowered himself into watery darkness. He hung for an eternal moment to the rim by his finger tips, then he felt rough metal prongs and at once he knew that sewer workmen used these ridges to lower themselves into manholes. Fist over fist, he let his body sink until he could feel no more prongs. He swayed in dank space; the siren seemed to howl at the very rim of the manhole. He dropped and was washed violently into an ocean of warm, leaping water. His head was battered against a wall and he wondered if this were death. Frenziedly his fingers clawed and sank into a crevice. He steadied himself and measured the strength of the current with his own muscular tension. He stood slowly in water that dashed past his knees with fearful velocity.

He heard a prolonged scream of brakes and the siren broke off. Oh, God! They had found him! Looming above his head in the rain a white face hovered over the hole. "How did this damn thing get off?" he heard a policeman ask. He saw the steel cover move slowly until the hole looked like a quarter moon turned black. "Give me a hand here," someone called. The cover clanged into place, muffling the sights and sounds of the upper world. Knee-deep in the pulsing current, he breathed with aching chest, filling his lungs with the hot stench of yeasty rot.

From the perforations of the manhole cover, delicate lances of hazy violet sifted down and wove a mottled pattern upon the surface of the streaking current. His lips parted as a car swept past along the wet pavement overhead, its heavy rumble soon dying out, like the hum of a plane speeding through a dense cloud. He had never thought that cars could sound like that; everything seemed strange and unreal under here. He stood in darkness for a long time, knee-deep in rustling water, musing.

The odor of rot had become so general that he no longer smelled it. He got his cigarettes, but discovered that his matches were wet. He searched and found a dry folder in the pocket of his shirt and managed to strike one; it flared weirdly in the wet gloom, glowing greenishly, turning red, orange, then yellow. He lit a crumpled cigarette; then, by the flickering light of the match, he looked for support so that he would not have to keep his muscles flexed against the pouring water. His pupils narrowed and he saw to either side of him two steaming walls that rose and curved inward some six feet above his head to form a dripping, mouse-colored dome. The bottom of the sewer was a sloping V-trough. To the left, the sewer vanished in ashen fog. To the right was a steep down-curve into which water plunged.

He saw now that had he not regained his feet in time, he would have been swept to death, or had he entered any other manhole he would have probably drowned. Above the rush of the current he heard sharper juttings of water; tiny streams were spewing into the sewer from smaller conduits. The match died; he struck another and saw a mass of debris sweep past him and clog the throat of the down-curve. At once the water began rising rapidly. Could he climb out before he drowned? A long hiss sounded and the debris was sucked from sight; the current lowered. He understood now what had made the water toss the manhole cover; the down-curve had become temporarily obstructed and the perforations had become clogged.

He was in danger; he might slide into a down-curve; he might wander with a lighted match into a pocket of gas and blow himself up; or he might contract some horrible disease . . . Though he wanted to leave, an irrational impulse held him rooted. To the left, the convex ceiling swooped to a height of less than five feet. With cigarette slanting from pursed lips, he waded with taut muscles, his feet sloshing over the slimy bottom, his shoes sinking into spongy slop, the slate-colored water cracking in creamy foam against his knees. Pressing his flat left palm against the lowered ceiling, he struck another match and saw a metal pole nestling in a niche of the wall. Yes, some sewer workman had left it. He reached for it, then jerked his head away as a whisper of scurrying life whisked past and was still. He held the match close and saw a huge rat, wet with slime, blinking beady eyes and baring tiny fangs. The light blinded the rat and the frizzled head moved aimlessly. He grabbed the pole and let it fly against the rat's soft body; there was shrill piping and the grizzly body splashed into the dun-colored water and was snatched out of sight, spinning in the scuttling stream.

He swallowed and pushed on, following the curve of the misty cavern, sounding the water with the pole. By the faint light of another manhole cover he saw, amid loose wet brick, a hole with walls of damp earth leading into blackness. Gingerly he poked the pole into it; it was hollow and went beyond the length of the pole. He shoved the pole before him, hoisted himself upward, got to his hands and knees, and crawled. After a few yards he paused, struck to wonderment by the silence; it seemed that he had traveled a million miles away from the world. As he inched forward again he could sense the bottom of the dirt tunnel becoming dry and lowering slightly. Slowly he rose and to his astonishment he stood erect. He could not hear the rustling of the water now and he felt confoundingly alone, yet lured by the darkness and silence.

He crept a long way, then stopped, curious, afraid. He put his right foot forward and it dangled in space; he drew back in fear. He thrust the pole outward and it swung in emptiness. He trembled, imagining the earth crumbling and burying him alive. He scratched a match and saw that the dirt floor sheered away steeply and widened into a sort of cave some five feet below him. An old sewer, he muttered. He cocked his head, hearing a feathery cadence which he could not identify. The match ceased to burn.

Using the pole as a kind of ladder, he slid down and stood in darkness. The air was a little fresher and he could still hear vague noises. Where was he? He felt suddenly that someone was standing near him and he turned sharply, but there was only darkness. He poked cautiously and felt a brick wall; he followed it and the strange sounds grew louder. He ought to get out of here. This was crazy. He could not remain here for any length of time; there was no food and no place to sleep. But the faint sounds tantalized him; they were strange but familiar. Was it a motor? A baby crying? Music? A siren? He groped on, and the sounds came so clearly that he could feel the pitch and timbre of human voices. Yes, singing! That was it! He listened with open mouth. It was a church service. Enchanged, he groped toward the waves of melody.

Jesus, take me to your home above
And fold me in the bosom of Thy love . . .

The singing was on the other side of a brick wall. Excited, he wanted to watch the service without being seen. Whose church was it? He knew most of the churches in this area above ground, but the singing sounded too strange and detached for him to guess. He looked to the left, to the right, down to the black dirt, then upward and was startled to see a bright sliver of light slicing the darkness like the blade of a razor. He struck one of his two remaining matches and saw rusty pipes running along an old concrete ceiling. Photographically he located the exact position of the pipes in his mind. The match flame sank and he sprang upward; his hands clutched a pipe. He swung his legs and tossed his body onto the bed of pipes and they creaked, swaying up and down; he thought that the tier was about to crash, but nothing happened. He edged to the crevice and saw a segment of black men and women, dressed in white robes, singing, holding tattered songbooks in their black palms. His first impulse was to laugh, but he checked himself.

What was he doing? He was crushed with a sense of guilt. Would God strike him dead for that? The singing swept on and he shook his head, disagreeing in spite of himself. They oughtn't to do that, he thought. But he could think of no reason *why* they should not do it. Just singing with the air of the sewer blowing in on them . . . He felt that he was gazing upon something abysmally obscene, yet he could not bring himself to leave.

After a long time he grew numb and dropped to the dirt. Pain throbbed in his legs and a deeper pain, induced by the sight of those black people groveling and begging for something they could never get, churned in him. A vague conviction made him feel that those people should stand unrepentant and yield no quarter in singing and praying, yet *he* had run away from the police, had pleaded with them to believe in *his* innocence. He shook his head, bewildered.

How long had he been down here? He did not know. This was a new kind of living for him; the intensity of feelings he had experienced when looking at the church people sing made him certain that he had been down here a long time, but his mind told him that the time must have been short. In this darkness the only notion he had of time was when a match flared and measured time by its fleeting light. He groped back through the hole toward the sewer and the waves of song subsided and finally he could not hear them at all. He came to where the earth hole ended and he heard the noise of the current and time lived again for him, measuring the moments by the wash of water.

The rain must have slackened, for the flow of water had lessened and came only to his ankles. Ought he to go up into the streets and take his chances on hiding somewhere else? But they would surely catch him. The mere thought of dodging and running again from the police made him tense. No, he would stay and plot how to elude them. But what could he do down here? He walked forward into the sewer and came to another manhole cover; he stood beneath it, debating. Fine pencils of gold spilled suddenly from the little circles in the manhole cover and trembled on the surface of the current. Yes, street lamps . . . It must be night . . .

He went forward for about a quarter of an hour, wading aimlessly, poking the pole carefully before him. Then he stopped, his eyes fixed and intent. What's that? A strangely familiar image attracted and repelled him. Lit by the yellow stems from another manhole cover was a tiny nude body of a baby snagged by debris and half-submerged in water. Thinking that the baby was alive, he moved impulsively to save it, but his roused feelings told him that it was dead, cold, nothing, the same nothingness he had felt while watching the men and women singing in the church. Water blossomed about the tiny legs, the tiny arms, the tiny head, and rushed onward. The eyes were closed, as though in sleep; the fists were clenched, as though in protest; and the mouth gaped black in a soundless cry.

He straightened and drew in his breath, feeling that he had been staring for all eternity at the ripples of veined water skimming impersonally over the shriveled limbs. He felt as condemned as when the policemen had accused him. Involuntarily he lifted his hand to brush the vision away, but his arm fell listlessly to his side. Then he acted; he closed his eyes and reached forward slowly with the soggy shoe of his right foot and shoved the dead baby from where it had been lodged. He kept his eyes closed, seeing the little body twisting in the current as it floated from sight. He opened his eyes, shivered, placed his knuckles in the sockets, hearing the water speed in the somber shadows.

He tramped on, sensing at times a sudden quickening in the current as he passed some conduit whose waters were swelling the stream that slid by his feet. A few minutes later he was standing under another manhole cover, listening to the faint rumble of noises above ground. Streetcars and trucks, he mused. He looked down and saw a stagnant pool of gray-green sludge; at intervals a balloon pocket rose from the scum, glistening a bluish-purple, and burst. Then another. He turned, shook his head, and tramped back to the dirt cave by the church, his lips quivering.

Back in the cave, he sat and leaned his back against a dirt wall. His body was trembling slightly. Finally his senses quieted and he slept. When he awakened he felt stiff and cold. He had to leave this foul place, but leaving meant facing those policemen who had wrongly accused him. No, he could not go back aboveground. He remembered the beating they had given him and how he had signed his name to a confession, a confession which he had not even read. He had been too tired when they had shouted at him, demanding that he sign his name; he had signed it to end his pain.

He stood and groped about in the darkness. The church singing had stopped. How long had he slept? He did not know. But he felt refreshed and hungry. He doubled his fist nervously, realizing that he could not make a decision. As he walked about he stumbled over an old rusty iron pipe. He picked it up and felt a jagged edge. Yes, there was a brick wall and he could dig into it. What would he find? Smiling, he groped to the brick wall, sat, and began digging idly into damp cement. I can't make any noise, he cautioned himself. As time passed he grew thirsty, but there was no water. He had to kill time or go aboveground. The cement came out of the wall easily; he extracted four bricks and felt a soft draft blowing into his face. He stopped, afraid. What was beyond? He waited a long time and nothing happened; then he began digging again, soundlessly, slowly; he enlarged the hole and crawled through into a dark room and collided with another wall. He felt his way to the right; the wall ended and his fingers toyed in space, like the antennae of an insect.

He fumbled on and his feet struck something hollow, like wood. What's this? He felt with his fingers. Steps . . . He stooped and pulled off his shoes and mounted the stairs and saw a yellow chink of light shining and heard a low voice speaking. He placed his eye to a keyhole and saw the nude waxen figure of a man stretched out upon a white table. The voice, low-pitched and vibrant, mumbled indistinguishable words, neither rising nor falling. He craned his neck and squinted to see the man who was talking, but he could not locate him. Above the naked figure was suspended a huge glass container filled with a blood-red liquid from which a white rubber tube dangled. He crouched closer to the door and saw the tip end of a black object lined with pink satin. A coffin, he breathed. This is an undertaker's establishment . . . A fine-spun lace of ice covered his body and he shuddered. A throaty chuckle sounded in the depths of the yellow room.

He turned to leave. Three steps down it occurred to him that a light switch should be nearby; he felt along the wall, found an electric button, pressed it, and a blinding glare smote his pupils so hard that he was sightless, defenseless. His pupils contracted and he wrinkled his nostrils at a peculiar odor. At once he knew that he had been dimly aware of this odor in the darkness, but the light had brought it sharply to his attention. Some kind of stuff they use to embalm, he thought. He went down the steps and saw piles of lumber, coffins, and a long workbench. In one corner was a tool chest. Yes, he could use tools, could tunnel through walls with them. He lifted the lid of the chest and saw nails, a hammer, a crowbar, a screwdriver, a light bulb, and a long length of electric wire. Good! He would lug these back to his cave.

He was about to hoist the chest to his shoulders when he discovered a door behind the furnace. Where did it lead? He tried to open it and found it securely bolted. Using the crowbar so as to make no sound, he pried the door open; it swung on creaking hinges, outward. Fresh air came to his face and he caught the faint roar of faraway sound. Easy now, he told himself. He widened the door and a lump of coal rattled toward him. A coalbin . . . Evidently the door led into another basement. The roaring noise was louder now, but he could not identify it. Where was he? He groped slowly over the coal pile, then ranged in darkness over a gritty floor. The roaring noise seemed to come from above him, then below. His fingers followed a wall until he touched a wooden ridge. A door, he breathed.

The noise died to a low pitch; he felt his skin prickle. It seemed that he was playing a game with an unseen person whose intelligence outstripped his. He put his ear to the flat surface of the door. Yes, voices . . . Was this a prize fight stadium? The sound of the voices came near and sharp, but he could not tell if they were joyous or despairing. He twisted the knob until he heard a soft click and felt the springy weight of the door swinging toward him. He was afraid to open it, yet captured by curiosity and wonder. He jerked the door wide and saw on the far side of the basement a furnace glowing red. Ten feet away was still another door, half ajar. He crossed and peered through the door into an empty, high-ceilinged corridor that terminated in a dark complex of shadow. The belling voices rolled about him and his eagerness mounted. He stepped into the corridor and the voices swelled louder. He crept on and came to a narrow stairway leading circularly upward; there was no question but that he was going to ascend those stairs.

Mounting the spiraled staircase, he heard the voices roll in a steady wave, then leap to crescendo, only to die away, but always remaining audible. Ahead of him glowed red letters: E—X—I—T. At the top of the steps he paused in front of a black curtain that fluttered uncertainly. He parted the folds and looked into a convex depth that gleamed with clusters of shimmering lights. Sprawling below him was a stretch of human faces, tilted upward, chanting, whistling, screaming, laughing. Dangling before the faces, high upon a screen of silver, were jerking shadows. A movie, he said with slow laughter breaking from his lips.

He stood in a box in the reserved section of a movie house and the impulse he had had to tell the people in the church to stop their singing seized him. These people were laughing at their lives, he thought with amazement. They were shouting and yelling at the animated shadows of themselves. His compassion fired his imagination and he stepped out of the box, walked out upon thin air, walked on down to the audience; and, hovering in the air just above them, he stretched out his hand to touch them . . . His tension snapped and he found himself back in the box, looking down into the sea of faces. No; it could not be done; he could not awaken them. He sighed. Yes, these people were children, sleeping in their living, awake in their dying.

He turned away, parted the black curtain, and looked out. He saw no one. He started down the white stone steps and when he reached the bottom he saw a man in trim blue uniform coming toward him. So used had he become to being underground that he thought that he could walk past the man, as though he were a ghost. But the man stopped. And he stopped.

"Looking for the men's room, sir?" the man asked, and, without waiting for an answer, he turned and pointed. "This way, sir. The first door to your right."

He watched the man turn and walk up the steps and go out of sight. Then he laughed. What a funny fellow! He went back to the basement and stood in the red darkness, watching the glowing embers in the furnace. He went to the sink and turned the faucet and the water flowed in a smooth silent stream that looked like a spout of blood. He brushed the mad image from his mind and began to wash his hands leisurely, looking about for the usual bar of soap. He found one and rubbed it in his palms until a rich lather bloomed in his cupped fingers, like a scarlet sponge. He scrubbed and rinsed his hands meticulously, then hunted for a towel; there was none. He shut off the water, pulled off his shirt, dried his hands on it; when he put it on again he was grateful for the cool dampness that came to his skin.

Yes, he was thirsty; he turned on the faucet again, bowled his fingers and when the water bubbled over the brim of his cupped palms, he drank in long, slow swallows. His bladder grew tight; he shut off the water, faced the wall, bent his head, and watched a red stream strike the floor. His nostrils wrinkled against acrid wisps of vapor; though he had tramped in the waters of the sewer, he stepped back from the wall so that his shoes, wet with sewer slime, would not touch his urine.

He heard footsteps and crawled quickly into the coalbin. Lumps rattled noisily. The footsteps came into the basement and stopped. Who was it? Had someone heard him and come down to investigate? He waited, crouching, sweating. For a long time there was silence, then he heard the clang of metal and a brighter glow lit the room. Somebody's tending the furnace, he thought. Footsteps came closer and he stiffened. Looming before him was a white face lined with coal dust, the face of an old man with watery blue eyes. Highlights spotted his gaunt cheekbones, and he held a huge shovel. There was a screechy scrape of metal against stone, and the old man lifted a shovelful of coal and went from sight.

The room dimmed momentarily, then a yellow glare came as coal flared at the furnace door. Six times the old man came to the bin and went to the furnace with shovels of coal, but not once did he lift his eyes. Finally he dropped the shovel, mopped his face with a dirty handkerchief, and sighed: "Wheeew!" He turned slowly and trudged out of the basement, his footsteps dying away.

He stood, and lumps of coal clattered down the pile. He stepped from the bin and was startled to see the shadowy outline of an electric bulb hanging above his head. Why had not the old man turned it on? Oh, yes . . . He understood. The old man had worked here for so long that he had no need for light; he had learned a way of seeing in his dark world, like those sightless worms that inch along underground by a sense of touch.

His eyes fell upon a lunch pail and he was afraid to hope that it was full. He picked it up; it was heavy. He opened it. *Sandwiches!* He looked guiltily around; he was alone. He searched farther and found a folder of matches and a half-empty tin of tobacco; he put them eagerly into his pocket and clicked off the light. With the lunch pail under his arm, he went through the door, groped over the pile of coal, and stood again in the lighted basement of the undertaking establishment. I've got to get those tools, he told himself. And turn off that light. He tiptoed back up the steps and switched off the light; the invisible voice still droned on behind the door. He crept down and, seeing with his fingers, opened the lunch pail and tore off a piece of paper bag and brought out the tin and spilled grains of tobacco into the makeshift concave. He rolled it and wet it with spittle, then inserted one end into his mouth and lit it: he sucked smoke that bit his lungs. The nicotine reached his brain, went out along his arms to his finger tips, down to his stomach, and over all the tired nerves of his body.

He carted the tools to the hole he had made in the wall. Would the noise of the falling chest betray him? But he would have to take a chance; he had to have those tools. He lifted the chest and shoved it; it hit the dirt on the other side of the wall with a loud clatter. He waited, listening; nothing happened. Head first, he slithered through and stood in the cave. He grinned, filled with a cunning idea. Yes, he would now go back into the basement of the undertaking establishment and crouch behind the coal pile and dig another hole. Sure! Fumbling, he opened the tool chest and extracted a crowbar, a screwdriver, and a hammer; he fastened them securely about his person.

With another lumpish cigarette in his flexed lips, he crawled back through the hole and over the coal pile and sat, facing the brick wall. He jabbed with the crowbar and the cement sheered away; quicker than he thought, a brick came loose. He worked an hour; the other bricks did not come easily. He sighed, weak from effort. I ought to rest a little, he thought. I'm hungry. He felt his way back to the cave and stumbled along the wall till he came to the tool chest. He sat upon it, opened the lunch pail, and took out two thick sandwiches. He smelled them. Pork chops . . . His mouth watered. He closed his eyes and devoured a sandwich, savoring the smooth rye bread and juicy meat. He ate rapidly, gulping down lumpy mouthfuls that made him long for water. He ate the other sandwich and found an apple and gobbled that up too, sucking the core till the last trace of flavor was drained from it. Then, like a dog, he ground the meat bones with his teeth, enjoying the salty, tangy marrow. He finished and stretched out full length on the ground and went to sleep. . . .

. . . His body was washed by cold water that gradually turned warm and he was buoyed upon a stream and swept out to sea where waves rolled gently and suddenly he found himself walking upon the water how strange and delightful to walk upon the water and he came upon a nude woman holding a nude baby in her arms and the woman was sinking into the water holding the baby above her head and screaming *help* and he ran over the water to the woman and he reached her just before she went down and he took the baby from her hands and stood watching the breaking bubbles where the woman sank and he called *lady* and still no answer yes dive down there and rescue that woman but he could not take this baby with him and he stooped and laid the baby tenderly upon the surface of the water expecting it to sink but it floated and he leaped into the water and held his breath and strained his eyes to see through the gloomy volume of water but there was no woman and he opened his mouth and called *lady* and the water bubbled and his chest ached and his arms were tired but he could not see the woman and he called again *lady lady* and his feet touched sand at the bottom of the sea and his chest felt as though it would burst and he bent his knees and propelled himself upward and water rushed past him and his head bobbed out and he breathed deeply and looked around where was the baby the baby was gone and he rushed over the water looking for the baby calling *where is it* and the empty sky and sea threw back his voice *where is it* and he began to doubt that he could stand upon the water and then he was sinking and as he struggled the water rushed him downward spinning dizzily and he opened his mouth to call for help and water surged into his lungs and he choked . . .

He groaned and leaped erect in the dark, his eyes wide. The images of terror that thronged his brain would not let him sleep. He rose, made sure that the tools were hitched to his belt, and groped his way to the coal pile and found the rectangular gap from which he had taken the bricks. He took out the crowbar and hacked. Then dread paralyzed him. How long had he slept? Was it day or night now? He had to be careful. Someone might hear him if it were day. He hewed softly for hours at the cement, working silently. Faintly quivering in the air above him was the dim sound of yelling voices. Crazy people, he muttered. They're still there in that movie . . .

Having rested, he found the digging much easier. He soon had a dozen bricks out. His spirits rose. He took out another brick and his fingers fluttered in space. Good! What lay ahead of him? Another basement? He made the hole larger, climbed through, walked over an uneven floor and felt a metal surface. He lighted a match and saw that he was standing behind a furnace in a basement; before him, on the far side of the room, was a door. He crossed and opened it; it was full of odds and ends. Daylight spilled from a window above his head.

Then he was aware of a soft, continuous tapping. What was it? A clock? No, it was louder than a clock and more irregular. He placed an old empty box beneath the window, stood upon it, and looked into an areaway. He eased the window up and crawled through; the sound of the tapping came clearly now. He glanced about; he was alone. Then he looked upward at a series of window ledges. The tapping identified itself. That's a typewriter, he said to himself. It seemed to be coming from just above. He grasped the ridges of a rain pipe and lifted himself upward; through a half-inch opening of window he saw a doorknob about three feet away. No, it was not a doorknob; it was a small circular disk made of stainless steel with many fine markings upon it. He held his breath; an eerie white hand, seemingly detached from its arm, touched the metal knob and whirled it, first to the left, then to the right. It's a safe! . . . Suddenly he could see the dial no more; a huge metal door swung slowly toward him and he was looking into a safe filled with green wads of paper money, rows of coins wrapped in brown paper, and glass jars and boxes of various sizes. His heart quickened. Good Lord! The white hand went in and out of the safe, taking wads of bills and cylinders of coins. The hand vanished and he heard the muffled click of the big door as it closed. Only the steel dial was visible now. The typewriter still tapped in his ears, but he could not see it. He blinked, wondering if what he had seen was real. There was more money in that safe than he had seen in all his life.

As he clung to the rain pipe, a daring idea came to him and he pulled the screwdriver from his belt. If the white hand twirled that dial again, he would be able to see how far to left and right it spun and he would have the combination! His blood tingled. I can scratch the numbers right here, he thought. Holding the pipe with one hand, he made the sharp edge of the screwdriver bite into the brick wall. Yes, he could do it. Now, he was set. Now, he had a reason for staying here in the underground. He waited for a long time, but the white hand did not return. Goddamn! Had he been more alert, he could have counted the twirls and he would have had the combination. He got down and stood in the areaway, sunk in reflection.

How could he get into that room? He climbed back into the basement and saw wooden steps leading upward. Was that the room where the safe stood? Fearing that the dial was now being twirled, he clambered through the window, hoisted himself up the rain pipe, and peered; he saw only the naked gleam of the steel dial. He got down and doubled his fists. Well, he would explore the basement. He returned to the basement room and mounted the steps to the door and squinted through the keyhole; all was dark, but the tapping was still somewhere near, still faint and directionless. He pushed the door in; along one wall of a room was a table piled with radios and electrical equipment. A radio shop, he muttered.

Well, he could rig up a radio in his cave. He found a sack, slid the radio into it, and slung it across his back. Closing the door, he went down the steps and stood again in the basement, disappointed. He had not solved the problem of the steel dial and he was irked. He set the radio on the floor and again hoisted himself through the window and up the rain pipe and squinted; the metal door was swinging shut. Goddamn! He's worked the combination again. If I had been patient, I'd have had it! How could he get into that room? He *had* to get into it. He could jimmy the window, but it would be much better if he could get in without any traces. To the right of him, he calculated, should be the basement of the building that held the safe; therefore, if he dug a hole right *here*, he ought to reach his goal.

He began a quiet scraping; it was hard work, for the bricks were not damp. He eventually got one out and lowered it softly to the floor. He had to be careful; perhaps people were beyond this wall. He extracted a second layer of brick and found still another. He gritted his teeth, ready to quit. I'll dig one more, he resolved. When the next brick came out he felt air blowing into his face. He waited to be challenged, but nothing happened.

He enlarged the hole and pulled himself through and stood in quiet darkness. He scratched a match to flame and saw steps; he mounted and peered through a keyhole: Darkness . . . He strained to hear the typewriter, but there was only silence. Maybe the office had closed? He twisted the knob and swung the door in; a frigid blast made him shiver. In the shadows before him were halves and quarters of hogs and lambs and steers hanging from metal hooks on the low ceiling, red meat encased in folds of cold white fat. Fronting him was frost-coated glass from behind which came indistinguishable sounds. The odor of fresh raw meat sickened him and he backed away. A meat market, he whispered.

He ducked his head, suddenly blinded by light. He narrowed his eyes; the red-white rows of meat were drenched in yellow glare. A man wearing a crimson-spotted jacket came in and took down a bloody meat cleaver. He eased the door to, holding it ajar just enough to watch the man, hoping that the darkness in which he stood would keep him from being seen. The man took down a hunk of steer and placed it upon a bloody wooden block and bent forward and whacked with the cleaver. The man's face was hard, square, grim; a jet of mustache smudged his upper lip and a glistening cowlick of hair fell over his left eye. Each time he lifted the cleaver and brought it down upon the meat, he let out a short, deep-chested grunt. After he had cut the meat, he wiped blood off the wooden block with a sticky wad of gunny sack and hung the cleaver upon a hook. His face was proud as he placed the chunk of meat in the crook of his elbow and left.

The door slammed and the light went off; once more he stood in shadow. His tension ebbed. From behind the frosted glass he heard the man's voice: "Forty-eight cents a pound, ma'am." He shuddered, feeling that there was something he had to do. But what? He stared fixedly at the cleaver, then he sneezed and was terrified for fear that the man had heard him. But the door did not open. He took down the cleaver and examined the sharp edge smeared with cold blood. Behind the ice-coated glass a cash register rang with a vibrating, musical tinkle.

Absent-mindedly holding the meat cleaver, he rubbed the glass with his thumb and cleared a spot that enabled him to see into the front of the store. The shop was empty, save for the man who was now putting on his hat and coat. Beyond the front window a wan sun shone in the streets; people passed and now and then a fragment of laughter or the whir of a speeding auto came to him. He peered closer and saw on the right counter of the shop a mosquito netting covering pears, grapes, lemons, oranges, bananas, peaches, and plums. His stomach contracted.

The man clicked out the light and he gritted his teeth, muttering, Don't lock the icebox door . . . The man went through the door of the shop and locked it from the outside. Thank God! Now, he would eat some more! He waited, trembling. The sun died and its rays lingered on in the sky, turning the streets to dusk. He opened the door and stepped inside the shop. In reverse letters across the front window was: NICK'S FRUITS AND MEATS. He laughed, picked up a soft ripe yellow pear and bit into it; juice squirted; his mouth ached as his saliva glands reacted to the acid of the fruit. He ate three pears, gobbled six bananas, and made away with several oranges, taking a bite out of their tops and holding them to his lips and squeezing them as he hungrily sucked the juice.

He found a faucet, turned it on, laid the cleaver aside, pursed his lips under the stream until his stomach felt about to burst. He straightened and belched, feeling satisfied for the first time since he had been underground. He sat upon the floor, rolled and lit a cigarette, his bloodshot eyes squinting against the film of drifting smoke. He watched a patch of sky turn red, then purple; night fell and he lit another cigarette, brooding. Some part of him was trying to remember the world he had left, and another part of him did not want to remember it. Sprawling before him in his mind was his wife, Mrs. Wooten for whom he worked, the three policemen who had picked him up . . . He possessed them now more completely than he had ever possessed them when he had lived aboveground. How this had come about he could not say, but he had no desire to go back to them. He laughed, crushed the cigarette, and stood up.

He went to the front door and gazed out. Emotionally he hovered between the world aboveground and the world underground. He longed to go out, but sober judgment urged him to remain here. Then impulsively he pried the lock loose with one swift twist of the crowbar; the door swung outward. Through the twilight he saw a white man and a white woman coming toward him. He held himself tense, waiting for them to pass; but they came directly to the door and confronted him.

"I want to buy a pound of grapes," the woman said.

Terrified, he stepped back into the store. The white man stood to one side and the woman entered.

"Give me a pound of dark ones," the woman said.

The white man came slowly forward, blinking his eyes.

"Where's Nick?" the man asked.

"Were you just closing?" the woman asked.

"Yes, ma'am," he mumbled. For a second he did not breathe, then he mumbled again: "Yes, ma'am."

"I'm sorry," the woman said.

The street lamps came on, lighting the store somewhat. Ought he run? But that would raise an alarm. He moved slowly, dreamily, to a counter and lifted up a bunch of grapes and showed them to the woman.

"Fine," the woman said. "But isn't that more than a pound?"

He did not answer. The man was staring at him intently.

"Put them in a bag for me," the woman said, fumbling with her purse.

"Yes, ma'am."

He saw a pile of paper bags under a narrow ledge; he opened one and put the grapes in.

"Thanks," the woman said, taking the bag and placing a dime in his dark palm.

"Where's Nick?" the man asked again. "At supper?"

"Sir? Yes, sir," he breathed.

They left the store and he stood trembling in the doorway. When they were out of sight, he burst out laughing and crying. A trolley car rolled noisily past and he controlled himself quickly. He flung the dime to the pavement with a gesture of contempt and stepped into the warm night air. A few shy stars trembled above him. The look of things was beautiful, yet he felt a lurking threat. He went to an unattended newsstand and looked at a stack of papers. He saw a headline: HUNT NEGRO FOR MURDER.

He felt that someone had slipped up on him from behind and was stripping off his clothes; he looked about wildly, went quickly back into the store, picked up the meat cleaver where he had left it near the sink, then made his way through the icebox to the basement. He stood for a long time, breathing heavily. They know I didn't do anything, he muttered. But how could he prove it? He had signed a confession. Though innocent, he felt guilty, condemned. He struck a match and held it near the steel blade, fascinated and repelled by the dried blotches of blood. Then his fingers gripped the handle of the cleaver with all the strength of his body, he wanted to fling the cleaver from him, but he could not. The match flame wavered and fled; he struggled through the hole and put the cleaver in the sack with the radio. He was determined to keep it, for what purpose he did not know.

He was about to leave when he remembered the safe. Where was it? He wanted to give up, but felt that he ought to make one more try. Opposite the last hole he had dug, he tunneled again, plying the crowbar. Once he was so exhausted that he lay on the concrete floor and panted. Finally he made another hole. He wriggled through and his nostrils filled with the fresh smell of coal. He struck a match; yes, the usual steps led upward. He tiptoed to a door and eased it open. A fair-haired white girl stood in front of a steel cabinet, her blue eyes wide upon him. She turned chalky and gave a high-pitched scream. He bounded down the steps and raced to his hole and clambered through, replacing the bricks with nervous haste. He paused, hearing loud voices.

"What's the matter, Alice?"

"A man . . ."

"What man? Where?"

"A man was at that door . . ."

"Oh, nonsense!"

"He was looking at me through the door!"

"Aw, you're dreaming."

"I *did* see a man!"

The girl was crying now.

"There's nobody here."

Another man's voice sounded.

"What is it, Bob?"

"Alice says she saw a man in here, in that door!"

"Let's take a look."

He waited, poised for flight. Footsteps descended the stairs.

"There's nobody down here."

"The window's locked."

"And there's no door."

"You ought to fire that dame."

"Oh, I don't know. Women are that way."

"She's too hysterical."

The men laughed. Footsteps sounded again on the stairs. A door slammed. He sighed, relieved that he had escaped. But he had not done what he had set out to do; his glimpse of the room had been too brief to determine if the safe was there. He had to know. Boldly he groped through the hole once more; he reached the steps and pulled off his shoes and tiptoed up and peered through the keyhole. His head accidentally touched the door and it swung silently in a fraction of an inch; he saw the girl bent over the cabinet, her back to him. Beyond her was the safe. He crept back down the steps, thinking exultingly: I found it!

Now he had to get the combination. Even if the window in the areaway was locked and bolted, he could gain entrance when the office closed. He scoured through the holes he had dug and stood again in the basement where he had left the radio and the cleaver. Again he crawled out of the window and lifted himself up the rain pipe and peered. The steel dial showed lonely and bright, reflecting the yellow glow of an unseen light. Resigned to a long wait, he sat and leaned against a wall. From far off came the faint sounds of life aboveground; once he looked with a baffled expression at the dark sky. Frequently he rose and climbed the pipe to see the white hand spin the dial, but nothing happened. He bit his lip with impatience. It was not the money that was luring him, but the mere fact that he could get it with impunity. Was the hand now twirling the dial? He rose and looked, but the white hand was not in sight.

Perhaps it would be better to watch continuously? Yes; he clung to the pipe and watched the dial until his eyes thickened with tears. Exhausted, he stood again in the areaway. He heard a door being shut and he clawed up the pipe and looked. He jerked tense as a vague figure passed in front of him. He stared unblinkingly, hugging the pipe with one hand and holding the screwdriver with the other, ready to etch the combination upon the wall. His ears caught: *Dong . . . Dong . . . Dong . . . Dong . . . Dong . . . Dong . . . Dong . . .* Seven o'clock, he whispered. Maybe they were closing now?

What kind of a store would be open as late as this? he wondered. Did any-one live in the rear? Was there a night watchman? Perhaps the safe was *already* locked for the night! Goddamn! While he had been eating in that shop, they had locked up everything . . . Then, just as he was about to give up, the white hand touched the dial and turned it once to the right and stopped at six. With quivering fingers, he etched 1—R—6 upon the brick wall with the tip of the screwdriver. The hand twirled the dial twice to the left and stopped at two, and he engraved 2—L—2 upon the wall. The dial was spun four times to the right and stopped at six again; he wrote 4—R—6. The dial rotated three times to the left and was centered straight up and down; he wrote 3—L—0. The door swung open and again he saw the piles of green money and the rows of wrapped coins. I got it, he said grimly.

Then he was stone still, astonished. There were two hands now. A right hand lifted a wad of green bills and deftly slipped it up the sleeve of a left arm. The hands trembled; again the right hand slipped a packet of bills up the left sleeve. He's stealing, he said to himself. He grew indignant, as if the money belonged to him. Though *he* had planned to steal the money, he despised and pitied the man. He felt that his stealing the money and the man's stealing were two entirely different things. He wanted to steal the money merely for the sensation involved in getting it, and he had no inten-tion whatever of spending a penny of it; but he knew that the man who was now stealing it was going to spend it, perhaps for pleasure. The huge steel door closed with a soft click.

Though angry, he was somewhat satisfied. The office would close soon. I'll clean the place out, he mused. He imagined the entire office staff cring-ing with fear; the police would question everyone for a crime they had not committed, just as they had questioned him. And they would have no idea of how the money had been stolen until they discovered the holes he had tunneled in the walls of the basements. He lowered himself and laughed mischievously, with the abandoned glee of an adolescent.

He flattened himself against the wall as the window above him closed with rasping sound. He looked; somebody was bolting the window securely with a metal screen. That won't help you, he snickered to himself. He clung to the rain pipe until the yellow light in the office went out. He went back into the basement, picked up the sack containing the radio and cleaver, and crawled through the two holes he had dug and groped his way into the basement of the building that held the safe. He moved in slow motion, breathing softly. Be careful now, he told himself. There might be a night watchman . . . . In his memory was the combination written in bold white characters as upon a blackboard. Eel-like he squeezed through the last hole and crept up the steps and put his hand on the knob and pushed the door in about three inches. Then his courage ebbed; his imagination wove dangers for him.

Perhaps the night watchman was waiting in there, ready to shoot. He dangled his cap on a forefinger and poked it past the jamb of the door. If anyone fired, they would hit his cap; but nothing happened. He widened the door, holding the crowbar high above his head, ready to beat off an assailant. He stood like that for five minutes; the rumble of a streetcar brought him to himself. He entered the room. Moonlight floated in from a side window. He confronted the safe, then checked himself. Better take a look around first . . . He stepped about and found a closed door. Was the night watchman in there? He opened it and saw a washbowl, a faucet, and a commode. To the left was still another door that opened into a huge dark room that seemed empty; on the far side of that room he made out the shadow of still another door. Nobody's here, he told himself.

He turned back to the safe and fingered the dial; it spun with ease. He laughed and twirled it just for fun. Get to work, he told himself. He turned the dial to the figures he saw on the blackboard of his memory; it was so easy that he felt that the safe had not been locked at all. The heavy door eased loose and he caught hold of the handle and pulled hard, but the door swung open with a slow momentum of its own. Breathless, he gaped at wads of green bills, rows of wrapped coins, curious glass jars full of white pellets, and many oblong green metal boxes. He glanced guiltily over his shoulder; it seemed impossible that someone should not call to him to stop.

They'll be surprised in the morning, he thought. He opened the top of the sack and lifted a wad of compactly tied bills; the money was crisp and new. He admired the smooth, clean-cut edges. The fellows in Washington sure know how to make this stuff, he mused. He rubbed the money with his fingers, as though expecting it to reveal hidden qualities. He lifted the wad to his nose and smelled the fresh odor of ink. Just like any other paper, he mumbled. He dropped the wad into the sack and picked up another. Holding the bag, he thought and laughed.

There was in him no sense of possessiveness; he was intrigued with the form and color of the money, with the manifold reactions which he knew that men aboveground held toward it. The sack was one-third full when it occurred to him to examine the denominations of the bills; without realizing it, he had put many wads of one-dollar bills into the sack. Aw, nuts, he said in disgust. Take the big ones . . . He dumped the one-dollar bills onto the floor and swept all the hundred-dollar bills he could find into the sack, then he raked in rolls of coins with crooked fingers.

He walked to a desk upon which sat a typewriter, the same machine which the blond girl had used. He was fascinated by it; never in his life had he used one of them. It was a queer instrument of business, something beyond the rim of his life. Whenever he had been in an office where a girl was typing, he had almost always spoken in whispers. Remembering vaguely what he had seen others do, he inserted a sheet of paper into the machine; it went in lopsided and he did not know how to straighten it. Spelling in a soft diffident voice, he pecked out his name on the keys: *freddaniels*. He looked at it and laughed. He would learn to type correctly one of these days.

Yes, he would take the typewriter too. He lifted the machine and placed it atop the bulk of money in the sack. He did not feel that he was stealing, for the cleaver, the radio, the money, and the typewriter were all on the same level of value, all meant the same thing to him. They were the serious toys of the men who lived in the dead world of sunshine and rain he had left, the world that had condemned him, branded him guilty.

But what kind of a place is this? He wondered. What was in that dark room to his rear? He felt for his matches and found that he had only one left. He leaned the sack against the safe and groped forward into the room, encountering smooth, metallic objects that felt like machines. Baffled, he touched a wall and tried vainly to locate an electric switch. Well, he *had* to strike his last match. He knelt and struck it, cupping the flame near the floor with his palms. The place seemed to be a factory, with benches and tables. There were bulbs with green shades spaced about the tables; he turned on a light and twisted it low so that the glare was limited. He saw a half-filled packet of cigarettes and appropriated it. There were stools at the benches and he concluded that men worked here at some trade. He wandered and found a few half-used folders of matches. If only he could find more cigarettes! But there were none.

But what kind of a place was this? On a bench he saw a pad of paper captioned: PEER'S—MANUFACTURING JEWELERS. His lips formed an "O," then he snapped off the light and ran back to the safe and lifted one of the glass jars and stared at the tiny white pellets. Gingerly he picked up one and found that it was wrapped in tissue paper. He peeled the paper and saw a glittering stone that looked like glass, glinting white and blue sparks. Diamonds, he breathed.

Roughly he tore the paper from the pellets and soon his palm quivered with precious fire. Trembling, he took all four glass jars from the safe and put them into the sack. He grabbed one of the metal boxes, shook it, and heard a tiny rattle. He pried off the lid with the screwdriver. Rings! Hundreds of them . . . Were they worth anything? He scooped up a handful and jets of fire shot fitfully from the stones. These are diamonds too, he said. He pried open another box. Watches! A chorus of soft, metallic ticking filled his ears. For a moment he could not move, then he dumped all the boxes into the sack.

He shut the safe door, then stood looking around, anxious not to overlook anything. Oh! He had seen a door in the room where the machines were. What was in there? More valuables? He re-entered the room, crossed the floor, and stood undecided before the door. He finally caught hold of the knob and pushed the door in; the room beyond was dark. He advanced cautiously inside and ran his fingers along the wall for the usual switch, then he was stark still. *Something had moved in the room!* What was it? Ought he to creep out, taking the rings and diamonds and money? Why risk what he already had? He waited and the ensuing silence gave him confidence to explore further. Dare he strike a match? Would not a match flame make him a good target? He tensed again as he heard a faint sigh; he was now convinced that there was something alive near him, something that lived and breathed. On tiptoe he felt slowly along the wall, hoping that he would not collide with anything. Luck was with him; he found the light switch.

No; don't turn the light on . . . Then suddenly he realized that he did not know in what direction the door was. Goddamn! He had to turn the light on or strike a match. He fingered the switch for a long time, then thought of an idea. He knelt upon the floor, reached his arm up to the switch and flicked the button, hoping that if anyone shot, the bullet would go above his head. The moment the light came on he narrowed his eyes to see quickly. He sucked in his breath and his body gave a violent twitch and was still. In front of him, so close that it made him want to bound up and scream, was a human face.

He was afraid to move lest he touch the man. If the man had opened his eyes at that moment, there was no telling what he might have done. The man—long and rawboned—was stretched out on his back upon a little cot, sleeping in his clothes, his head cushioned by a dirty pillow; his face, clouded by a dark stubble of beard, looked straight up to the ceiling. The man sighed, and he grew tense to defend himself; the man mumbled and turned his face away from the light. I've got to turn off that light, he thought. Just as he was about to rise, he saw a gun and cartridge belt on the floor at the man's side. Yes, he would take the gun and cartridge belt, not to use them, but just to keep them, as one takes a memento from a country fair. He picked them up and was about to click off the light when his eyes fell upon a photograph perched upon a chair near the man's head; it was the picture of a woman, smiling, shown against a background of open fields; at the woman's side were two young children, a boy and a girl. He smiled indulgently; he could send a bullet into that man's brain and time would be over for him . . .

He clicked off the light and crept silently back into the room where the safe stood; he fastened the cartridge belt about him and adjusted the holster at his right hip. He strutted about the room on tiptoe, lolling his head nonchalantly, then paused abruptly pulled the gun, and pointed it with grim face toward an imaginary foe. "Boom!" he whispered fiercely. Then he bent forward with silent laughter. That's just like they do it in the movies, he said.

He contemplated his loot for a long time, then got a towel from the washroom and tied the sack securely. When he looked up he was momentarily frightened by his shadow looming on the wall before him. He lifted the sack, dragged it down the basement steps, lugged it across the basement, gasping for breath. After he had struggled through the hole, he clumsily replaced the bricks, then tussled with the sack until he got it to the cave. He stood in the dark, wet with sweat, brooding about the diamonds, the rings, the watches, the money; he remembered the singing in the church, the people yelling in the movie, the dead baby, the nude man stretched out upon the white table . . . He saw these items hovering before his eyes and felt that some dim meaning linked them together, that some magical relationship made them kin. He stared with vacant eyes, convinced that all of these images, with their tongueless reality, were striving to tell him something . . .

Later, seeing with his fingers, he untied the sack and set each item neatly upon the dirt floor. Exploring, he took the bulb, the socket, and the wire out of the tool chest; he was elated to find a double socket at one end of the wire. He crammed the stuff into his pockets and hoisted himself upon the rusty pipes and squinted into the church; it was dim and empty. Somewhere in this wall were live electric wires; but where? He lowered himself, groped and tapped the wall with the butt of the screwdriver, listening vainly for hollow sounds. I'll just take a chance and dig, he said.

For an hour he tried to dislodge a brick, and when he struck a match, he found that he had dug a depth of only an inch! No use in digging here, he sighed. By the flickering light of a match, he looked upward, then lowered his eyes, only to glance up again, startled. Directly above his head, beyond the pipes, was a wealth of electric wiring. I'll be damned, he snickered.

He got an old dull knife from the chest and, seeing again with his fingers, separated the two strands of wire and cut away the insulation. Twice he received a slight shock. He scraped the wiring clean and managed to join the two twin ends, then screwed in the bulb. The sudden illumination blinded him and he shut his lids to kill the pain in his eyeballs. I've got that much done, he thought jubilantly.

He placed the bulb on the dirt floor and the light cast a blatant glare on the bleak clay walls. Next he plugged one end of the wire that dangled from the radio into the light socket and bent down and switched on the button; almost at once there was the harsh sound of static, but no words or music. Why won't it work? he wondered. Had he damaged the mechanism in any way? Maybe it needed grounding? Yes . . . He rummaged in the tool chest and found another length of wire, fastened it to the ground of the radio, and then tied the opposite end to a pipe. Rising and growing distinct, a slow strain of music entranced him with its measured sound. He sat upon the chest, deliriously happy.

Later he searched again in the chest and found a half-gallon can of glue; he opened it and smelled a sharp odor. Then he recalled that he had not even looked at the money. He took a wad of green bills and weighed it in his palm, then broke the seal and held one of the bills up to the light and studied it closely. *The United States of America will pay to the bearer on demand one hundred dollars,* he read in slow speech; then: *This note is legal tender for all debts, public and private. . . .* He broke into a musing laugh, feeling that he was reading of the doings of people who lived on some far-off planet. He turned the bill over and saw on the other side of it a delicately beautiful building gleaming with paint and set amidst green grass. He had no desire whatever to count the money; it was what it stood for—the various currents of life swirling aboveground—that captivated him. Next he opened the rolls of coins and let them slide from their paper wrappings to the ground; the bright, new gleaming pennies and nickles and dimes piled high at his feet, a glowing mound of shimmering copper and silver. He sifted them through his fingers, listening to their tinkle as they struck the conical heap.

Oh, yes! He had forgotten. He would now write his name on the typewriter. He inserted a piece of paper and poised his fingers to write. But what was his name? He stared, trying to remember. He stood and glared about the dirt cave, his name on the tip of his lips. But it would not come to him. Why was he here? Yes, he had been running away from the police. But why? His mind was blank. He bit his lips and sat again, feeling a vague terror. But why worry? He laughed, then pecked slowly: *itwasalonghotday.* He was determined to type the sentence without making any mistakes. How did one make capital letters? He experimented and luckily discovered how to lock the machine for capital letters and then shift it back to lower case. Next he discovered how to make spaces, then he wrote neatly and correctly: *It was a long hot day.* Just why he selected that sentence he did not know; it was merely the ritual of performing the thing that appealed to him. He took the sheet out of the machine and looked around with stiff neck and hard eyes and spoke to an imaginary person:

"Yes, I'll have the contracts ready tomorrow."

He laughed. That's just the way they talk, he said. He grew weary of the game and pushed the machine aside. His eyes fell upon the can of glue, and a mischievous idea bloomed in him, filling him with nervous eagerness. He leaped up and opened the can of glue, then broke the seals on all the wads of money. I'm going to have some wallpaper, he said with a luxurious, physical laugh that made him bend at the knees. He took the towel with which he had tied the sack and balled it into a swab and dipped it into the can of glue and dabbed glue onto the wall; then he pasted one green bill by the side of another. He stepped back and cocked his head. Jesus! That's funny . . . He slapped his thighs and guffawed. He had triumphed over the world aboveground! He was free! If only people could see this! He wanted to run from this cave and yell his discovery to the world.

He swabbed all the dirt walls of the cave and pasted them with green bills; when he had finished the walls blazed with a yellow-green fire. Yes, this room would be his hide-out; between him and the world that had branded him guilty would stand this mocking symbol. He had not stolen the money; he had simply picked it up, just as a man would pick up firewood in a forest. And that was how the world aboveground now seemed to him, a wild forest filled with death.

The walls of money finally palled on him and he looked about for new interests to feed his emotions. The cleaver! He drove a nail into the wall and hung the bloody cleaver upon it. Still another idea welled up. He pried open the metal boxes and lined them side by side on the dirt floor. He grinned at the gold and fire. From one box he lifted up a fistful of ticking gold watches and dangled them by their gleaming chains. He stared with an idle smile, then began to wind them up; he did not attempt to set them at any given hour, for there was no time for him now. He took a fistful of nails and drove them into the papered walls and hung the watches upon them, letting them swing down by their glittering chains, trembling and ticking busily against the backdrop of green with the lemon sheen of the electric light shining upon the metal watch casings, converting the golden disks into blobs of liquid yellow. Hardly had he hung up the last watch than the idea extended itself; he took more nails from the chest and drove them into the green paper and took the boxes of rings and went from nail to nail and hung up the golden bands. The blue and white sparks from the stones filled the cave with brittle laughter, as though enjoying his hilarious secret. People certainly can do some funny things, he said to himself.

He sat upon the tool chest, alternately laughing and shaking his head soberly. Hours later he became conscious of the gun sagging at his hip and he pulled it from the holster. He had seen men fire guns in movies, but somehow his life had never led him into contact with firearms. A desire to feel the sensation others felt in firing came over him. But someone might hear . . . Well, what if they did? They would not know where the shot had come from. Not in their wildest notions would they think that it had come from under the streets! He tightened his fingers on the trigger; there was a deafening report and it seemed that the entire underground had caved in upon his eardrums; and in the same instant there flashed an orange-blue spurt of flame that died quickly but lingered on as a vivid after-image. He smelled the acrid stench of burnt powder filling his lungs and he dropped the gun abruptly.

The intensity of his feelings died and he hung the gun and cartridge belt upon the wall. Next he lifted the jars of diamonds and turned them bottom upward, dumping the white pellets upon the ground. One by one he picked them up and peeled the tissue paper from them and piled them in a neat heap. He wiped his sweaty hands on his trousers, lit a cigarette, and commenced playing another game. He imagined that he was a rich man who lived aboveground in the obscene sunshine and he was strolling through a park of a summer morning, smiling, nodding to his neighbors, sucking an after-breakfast cigar. Many times he crossed the floor of the cave, avoiding the diamonds with his feet, yet subtly gauging his footsteps so that his shoes, wet with sewer slime, would strike the diamonds at some undetermined moment. After twenty minutes of sauntering, his right foot smashed into the heap and diamonds lay scattered in all directions, glinting with a million tiny chuckles of icy laughter. Oh, shucks, he mumbled in mock regret, intrigued by the damage he had wrought. He continued walking, ignoring the brittle fire. He felt that he had a glorious victory locked in his heart.

He stooped and flung the diamonds more evenly over the floor and they showered rich sparks, collaborating with him. He went over the floor and trampled the stones just deep enough for them to be faintly visible, as though they were set delicately in the prongs of a thousand rings. A ghostly light bathed the cave. He sat on the chest and frowned. Maybe *any*thing's right, he mumbled. Yes, if the world as men had made it was right, then anything else was right, any act a man took to satisfy himself, murder, theft, torture.

He straightened with a start. What was happening to him? He was drawn to these crazy thoughts, yet they made him feel vaguely guilty. He would stretch out upon the ground, then get up; he would want to crawl again through the holes he had dug, but would restrain himself; he would think of going again up into the streets, but fear would hold him still. He stood in the middle of the cave, surrounded by green walls and a laughing floor, trembling. He was going to do something, but what? Yes, he was afraid of himself, afraid of doing some nameless thing.

To control himself, he turned on the radio. A melancholy piece of music rose. Brooding over the diamonds on the floor was like looking up into a sky full of restless stars; then the illusion turned into its opposite: he was high up in the air looking down at the twinkling lights of a sprawling city. The music ended and a man recited news events. In the same attitude in which he had contemplated the city, so now, as he heard the cultivated tone, he looked down upon land and sea as men fought, as cities were razed, as planes scattered death upon open towns, as long lines of trenches wavered and broke. He heard the names of generals and the names of mountains and the names of countries and the names and numbers of divisions that were in action on different battle fronts. He saw black smoke billowing from the stacks of warships as they neared each other over wastes of water and he heard their huge guns thunder as red-hot shells screamed across the surface of night seas. He saw hundreds of planes wheeling and droning in the sky and heard the clatter of machine guns as they fought each other and he saw planes falling in plumes of smoke and blaze of fire. He saw steel tanks rumbling across fields of ripe wheat to meet other tanks and there was a loud clang of steel as numberless tanks collided. He saw troops with fixed bayonets charging in waves against other troops who held fixed bayonets and men groaned as steel ripped into their bodies and they went down to die . . . The voice of the radio faded and he was staring at the diamonds on the floor at his feet.

He shut off the radio, fighting an irrational compulsion to act. He walked aimlessly about the cave, touching the walls with his finger tips. Suddenly he stood still. *What was the matter with him?* Yes, he knew . . . It was these walls; these crazy walls were filling him with a wild urge to climb out into the dark sunshine aboveground. Quickly he doused the light to banish the shouting walls, then sat again upon the tool chest. Yes, he was trapped. His muscles were flexed taut and sweat ran down his face. He knew now that he could not stay here and he could not go out. He lit a cigarette with shaking fingers; the match flame revealed the green-papered walls with militant distinctness; the purple on the gun barrel glinted like a threat; the meat cleaver brooded with its eloquent splotches of blood; the mound of silver and copper smoldered angrily; the diamonds winked at him from the floor; and the gold watches ticked and trembled, crowning time the king of consciousness, defining the limits of living . . . The match blaze died and he bolted from where he stood and collided brutally with the nails upon the walls. The spell was broken. He shuddered, feeling that, in spite of his fear, sooner or later he would go up into that dead sunshine and somehow say something to somebody about all this.

He sat again upon the tool chest. Fatigue weighed upon his forehead and eyes. Minutes passed and he relaxed. He dozed, but his imagination was alert. He saw himself rising, wading again in the sweeping water of the sewer; he came to a manhole and climbed out and was amazed to discover that he had hoisted himself into a room filled with armed policemen who were watching him intently. He jumped awake in the dark; he had not moved. He sighed, closed his eyes, and slept again; this time his imagination designed a scheme of protection for him. His dreaming made him feel that he was standing in a room watching over his own nude body lying stiff and cold upon a white table. At the far end of the room he saw a crowd of people huddled in a corner, afraid of his body. Though lying dead upon the table, he was standing in some mysterious way at his side, warding off the people, guarding his body, and laughing to himself as he observed the situation. *They're scared of me,* he thought.

He awakened with a start, leaped to his feet, and stood in the center of the black cave. It was a full minute before he moved again. He hovered between sleeping and waking, unprotected, a prey of wild fears. He could neither see nor hear. One part of him was asleep; his blood coursed slowly and his flesh was numb. On the other hand he was roused to a strange, high pitch of tension. He lifted his fingers to his face, as though about to weep. Gradually his hands lowered and he struck a match, looking about, expect-

ing to see a door through which he could walk to safety; but there was no
door, only the green walls and the moving floor. The match flame died and
it was dark again.

Five minutes later he was still standing when the thought came to him
that he had been asleep. Yes . . . But he was not yet fully awake; he was still
queerly blind and deaf. How long had he slept? Where was he? Then suddenly he recalled the green-papered walls of the cave and in the same instant he heard loud singing coming from the church beyond the wall. Yes,
they woke me up, he muttered. He hoisted himself and lay atop the bed of
pipes and brought his face to the narrow slit. Men and women stood here
and there between pews. A song ended and a young black girl tossed back
her head and closed her eyes and broke plaintively into another hymn:

> Glad, glad, glad, oh, so glad
> I got Jesus in my soul . . .

Those few words were all she sang, but what her words did not say, her
emotions said as she repeated the lines, varying the mood and tempo, making her tone express meanings which her conscious mind did not know.
Another woman melted her voice with the girl's, and then an old man's
voice merged with that of the two women. Soon the entire congregation
was singing:

> Glad, glad, glad, oh, so glad
> I got Jesus in my soul . . .

They're wrong, he whispered in the lyric darkness. He felt that their
search for a happiness they could never find made them feel that they had
committed some dreadful offense which they could not remember or understand. He was now in possession of the feeling that had gripped him
when he had first come into the underground. It came to him in a series of
questions: Why was this sense of guilt so seemingly innate, so easy to come
by, to think, to feel, so verily physical? It seemed that when one felt this
guilt one was retracing in one's feelings a faint pattern designed long
before; it seemed that one was always trying to remember a gigantic shock
that had left a haunting impression upon one's body which one could not
forget or shake off, but which had been forgotten by the conscious mind,
creating in one's life a state of eternal anxiety.

He had to tear himself away from this; he got down from the pipes. His
nerves were so taut that he seemed to feel his brain pushing through his
skull. He felt that he had to do something, but he could not figure out what
it was. Yet he knew that if he stood here until he made up his mind, he
would never move. He crawled through the hole he had made in the brick
wall and the exertion afforded him respite from tension. When he entered
the basement of the radio store, he stopped in fear, hearing loud voices.

"Come on, boy! Tell us what you did with the radio!"

"Mister, I didn't steal the radio! I swear!"

He heard a dull thumping sound and he imagined a boy being struck
violently.

"Please, mister!"

"Did you take it to a pawn shop?"

"No, sir! I didn't steal the radio! I got a radio at home," the boy's voice pleaded hysterically. "Go to my home and look!"

There came to his ears the sound of another blow. It was so funny that he had to clap his hand over his mouth to keep from laughing out loud. They're beating some poor boy, he whispered to himself, shaking his head. He felt a sort of distant pity for the boy and wondered if he ought to bring back the radio and leave it in the basement. No. Perhaps it was a good thing that they were beating the boy; perhaps the beating would bring to the boy's attention, for the first time in his life, the secret of his existence, the guilt that he could never get rid of.

Smiling, he scampered over a coal pile and stood again in the basement of the building where he had stolen the money and jewelry. He lifted himself into the areaway, climbed the rain pipe, and squinted through a two-inch opening of window. The guilty familiarity of what he saw made his muscles tighten. Framed before him in a bright tableau of daylight was the night watchman sitting upon the edge of a chair, stripped to the waist, his head sagging forward, his eyes red and puffy. The watchman's face and shoulders were stippled with red and black welts. Back of the watchman stood the safe, the steel door wide open showing the empty vault. Yes, they think he did it, he mused.

Footsteps sounded in the room and a man in a blue suit passed in front of him, then another, then still another. Policemen, he breathed. Yes, they were trying to make the watchman confess, just as they had once made him confess to a crime he had not done. He stared into the room, trying to recall something. Oh . . . Those were the same policemen who had beaten him, had made him sign that paper when he had been too tired and sick to care. Now, they were doing the same thing to the watchman. His heart pounded as he saw one of the policemen shake a finger into the watchman's face.

"Why don't you admit it's an inside job, Thompson?" the policeman said.

"I've told you all I know," the watchman mumbled through swollen lips.

"But nobody was here but you!" the policeman shouted.

"I was sleeping," the watchman said. "It was wrong, but I was sleeping all that night!"

"Stop telling us that lie!"

"It's the truth!"

"When did you get the combination?"

"I don't know how to open the safe," the watchman said.

He clung to the rain pipe, tense; he wanted to laugh, but he controlled himself. He felt a great sense of power; yes, he could go back to the cave, rip the money off the walls, pick up the diamonds and rings, and bring them here and write a note, telling them where to look for their foolish toys. No . . . What good would that do? It was not worth the effort. The watchman was guilty; although he was not guilty of the crime of which he had been accused, he was guilty, had always been guilty. The only thing that worried him was that the man who had been really stealing was not being accused. But he consoled himself: they'll catch him sometime during his life.

He saw one of the policemen slap the watchman across the mouth.

"Come clean, you bastard!"

"I've told you all I know," the watchman mumbled like a child.

One of the police went to the rear of the watchman's chair and jerked it from under him; the watchman pitched forward upon his face.

"Get up!" a policeman said.

Trembling, the watchman pulled himself up and sat limply again in the chair.

"Now, are you going to talk?"

"I've told you all I know," the watchman gasped.

"Where did you hide the stuff?"

"I didn't take it!"

"Thompson, your brains are in your feet," one of the policemen said. "We're going to string you up and get them back into your skull."

He watched the policemen clamp handcuffs on the watchman's wrists and ankles; then they lifted the watchman and swung him upside-down and hoisted his feet to the edge of a door. The watchman hung, head down, his eyes bulging. They're crazy, he whispered to himself as he clung to the ridges of the pipe.

"You going to talk?" a policeman shouted into the watchman's ear.

He heard the watchman groan.

"We'll let you hang there till you talk, see?"

He saw the watchman close his eyes.

"Let's take 'im down. He passed out," a policeman said.

He grinned as he watched them take the body down and dump it carelessly upon the floor. The policeman took off the handcuffs.

"Let 'im come to. Let's get a smoke," a policeman said.

The three policemen left the scope of his vision. A door slammed. He had an impulse to yell to the watchman that he could escape through the hole in the basement and live with him in the cave. But he wouldn't understand, he told himself. After a moment he saw the watchman rise and stand, swaying from weakness. He stumbled across the room to a desk, opened a drawer, and took out a gun. He's going to kill himself, he thought, intent, eager, detached, yearning to see the end of the man's actions. As the watchman stared vaguely about he lifted the gun to his temple; he stood like that for some minutes, biting his lips until a line of blood etched its way down a corner of his chin. No, he oughtn't do that, he said to himself in a mood of pity.

"Don't!" he half whispered and half yelled.

The watchman looked wildly about; he had heard him. But it did not help; there was a loud report and the watchman's head jerked violently and he fell like a log and lay prone, the gun clattering over the floor.

The three policemen came running into the room with drawn guns. One of the policemen knelt and rolled the watchman's body over and stared at a ragged, scarlet hole in the temple.

"Our hunch was right," the kneeling policeman said. "He was guilty, all right."

"Well, this ends the case," another policeman said.

"He knew he was licked," the third one said with grim satisfaction.

He eased down the rain pipe, crawled back through the holes he had made, and went back into his cave. A fever burned in his bones. He had to act, yet he was afraid. His eyes stared in the darkness as though propped open by invisible hands, as though they had become lidless. His muscles were rigid and he stood for what seemed to him a thousand years.

When he moved again his actions were informed with precision, his muscular system reinforced from a reservoir of energy. He crawled through the hole of earth, dropped into the gray sewer current, and sloshed ahead. When his right foot went forward at a street intersection, he fell backward and shot down into water. In a spasm of terror his right hand grabbed the concrete ledge of a down-curve and he felt the streaking water tugging violently at his body. The current reached his neck and for a moment he was still. He knew that if he moved clumsily he would be sucked under. He held onto the ledge with both hands and slowly pulled himself up. He sighed, standing once more in the sweeping water, thankful that he had missed death.

He waded on through sludge, moving with care, until he came to a web of light sifting down from a manhole cover. He saw steel hooks running up the side of the sewer wall; he caught hold and lifted himself and put his shoulder to the cover and moved it an inch. A crash of sound came to him as he looked into a hot glare of sunshine through which blurred shapes moved. Fear scalded him and he dropped back into the pallid current and stood paralyzed in the shadows. A heavy car rumbled past overhead, jarring the pavement, warning him to stay in his world of dark light, knocking the cover back into place with an imperious clang.

He did not know how much fear he felt, for fear claimed him completely; yet it was not a fear of the police or of people, but a cold dread at the thought of the actions he knew he would perform if he went out into that cruel sunshine. His mind said no; his body said yes; and his mind could not understand his feelings. A low whine broke from him and he was in the act of uncoiling. He climbed upward and heard the faint honking of auto horns. Like a frantic cat clutching a rag, he clung to the steel prongs and heaved his shoulder against the cover and pushed it off halfway. For a split second his eyes were drowned in the terror of yellow light and he was in a deeper darkness than he had ever known in the underground.

Partly out of the hole, he blinked, regaining enough sight to make out meaningful forms. An odd thing was happening: No one was rushing forward to challenge him. He had imagined the moment of his emergence as a desperate tussle with men who wanted to cart him off to be killed; instead, life froze about him as the traffic stopped. He pushed the cover aside, stood, swaying in a world so fragile that he expected it to collapse and drop him into some deep void. But nobody seemed to pay him heed. The cars were now swerving to shun him and the gaping hole.

"Why in hell don't you put up a red light, dummy?" a raucous voice yelled.

He understood; they thought that he was a sewer workman. He walked toward the sidewalk, weaving unsteadily through the moving traffic.

"Look where you're going, nigger!"

"That's right! Stay there and get killed!"

"You blind, you bastard?"

"Go home and sleep your drunk off!"

A policeman stood at the curb, looking in the opposite direction. When he passed the policeman, he feared that he would be grabbed, but nothing happened. Where was he? Was this real? He wanted to look about to get his bearings, but felt that something awful would happen to him if he did. He wandered into a spacious doorway of a store that sold men's clothing and saw his reflection in a long mirror: his cheekbones protruded from a hairy black face; his greasy cap was perched askew upon his head and his eyes were red and glassy. His shirt and trousers were caked with mud and hung loosely. His hands were gummed with a black stickiness. He threw back his head and laughed so loudly that passers-by stopped and stared.

He ambled on down the sidewalk, not having the merest notion of where he was going. Yet, sleeping within him, was the drive to go somewhere and say something to somebody. Half an hour later his ears caught the sound of spirited singing.

The Lamb, the Lamb, the Lamb
I hear thy voice a-calling
The Lamb, the Lamb, the Lamb
I feel thy grace a-falling

A church! He exclaimed. He broke into a run and came to brick steps leading downward to a subbasement. This is it! The church into which he had peered. Yes, he was going in and tell them. What? He did not know; but, once face to face with them, he would think of what to say. Must be Sunday, he mused. He ran down the steps and jerked the door open; the church was crowded and a deluge of song swept over him.

The Lamb, the Lamb, the Lamb
Tell me again your story
The Lamb, the Lamb, the Lamb
Flood my soul with your glory

He stared at the singing faces with a trembling smile.

"Say!" he shouted.

Many turned to look at him, but the song rolled on. His arm was jerked violently.

"I'm sorry, Brother, but you can't do that in here," a man said.

"But, mister!"

"You can't act rowdy in God's house," the man said.

"He's filthy," another man said.

"But I want to tell 'em," he said loudly.

"He stinks," someone muttered.

The song had stopped, but at once another one began.

Oh, wondrous sight upon the cross
Vision sweet and divine
Oh, wondrous sight upon the cross
Full of such love sublime

He attempted to twist away, but other hands grabbed him and rushed him into the doorway.

"Let me alone!" he screamed, struggling.

"Get out!"

"He's drunk," somebody said. "He ought to be ashamed!"

"He acts crazy!"

He felt that he was failing and he grew frantic.

"But, mister, let me tell—"

"Get away from this door, or I'll call the police!"

He stared, his trembling smile fading in a sense of wonderment.

"The police," he repeated vacantly.

"Now, get!"

He was pushed toward the brick steps and the door banged shut. The waves of song came.

Oh, wondrous sight, wondrous sight
Lift my heavy heart above
Oh, wondrous sight, wondrous sight
Fill my weary soul with love

He was smiling again now. Yes, the police . . . That was it! Why had he not thought of it before? The idea had been deep down in him, and only now did it assume supreme importance. He looked up and saw a street sign: COURT STREET—HARTSDALE AVENUE. He turned and walked northward, his mind filled with the image of the police station. Yes, that was where they had beaten him, accused him, and had made him sign a confession of his guilt. He would go there and clear up everything, make a statement. What statement? He did not know. He was the statement, and since it was all so clear to him, surely he would be able to make it clear to others.

He came to the corner of Hartsdale Avenue and turned westward. Yeah, there's the station . . . A policeman came down the steps and walked past him without a glance. He mounted the stone steps and went through the door, paused; he was in a hallway where several policemen were standing, talking, smoking. One turned to him.

"What do you want, boy?"

He looked at the policeman and laughed.

"What in hell are you laughing about?" the policeman asked.

He stopped laughing and stared. His whole being was full of what he wanted to say to them, but he could not say it.

"Are you looking for the Desk Sergeant?"

"Yes, sir," he said quickly; then: "Oh, no, sir."

"Well, make up your mind, now."

Four policemen grouped themselves around him.

"I'm looking for the men," he said.

"What men?"

Peculiarly, at that moment he could not remember the names of the policemen; he recalled their beating him, the confession he had signed, and how he had run away from them. He saw the cave next to the church, the money on the walls, the guns, the rings, the cleaver, the watches, and the diamonds on the floor.

"They brought me here," he began.

"When?"

His mind flew back over the blur of the time lived in the underground blackness. He had no idea of how much time had elapsed, but the intensity of what had happened to him told him that it could not have transpired in a short space of time, yet his mind told him that time must have been brief.

"It was a long time ago." He spoke like a child relating a dimly remembered dream. "It was a long time," he repeated, following the promptings of his emotions. "They beat me . . . I was scared . . . I ran away."

A policeman raised a finger to his temple and made a derisive circle.

"Nuts," the policeman said.

"Do you know what place this is, boy?"

"Yes, sir. The police station," he answered sturdily, almost proudly.

"Well, who do you want to see?"

"The men," he said again, feeling that surely they knew the men. "You know the men," he said in a hurt tone.

"What's your name?"

He opened his lips to answer and no words came. He had forgotten. But what did it matter if he had? It was not important.

"Where do you live?"

Where did he live? It had been so long ago since he had lived up here in this strange world that he felt it was foolish even to try to remember. Then for a moment the old mood that had dominated him in the underground surged back. He leaned forward and spoke eagerly.

"They said I killed the woman."

"What woman?" a policeman asked.

"And I signed a paper that said I was guilty," he went on, ignoring their questions. "Then I ran off . . ."

"Did you run off from an institution?"

"No, sir," he said, blinking and shaking his head. "I came from under the ground. I pushed off the manhole cover and climbed out . . ."

"All right, now," a policeman said, placing an arm about his shoulder. "We'll send you to the psycho and you'll be taken care of."

"Maybe he's a Fifth Columnist!"[1] a policeman shouted.

There was laughter and, despite his anxiety, he joined in. But the laughter lasted so long that it irked him.

"I got to find those men," he protested mildly.

"Say, boy, what have you been drinking?"

"Water," he said. "I got some water in a basement."

"Were the men you ran away from dressed in white, boy?"

---

1. I.e., a communist.

"No, sir," he said brightly. "They were men like you."

An elderly policeman caught hold of his arm.

"Try and think hard. Where did they pick you up?"

He knitted his brows in an effort to remember, but he was blank inside. The policeman stood before him demanding logical answers and he could no longer think with his mind; he thought with his feelings and no words came.

"I was guilty," he said. "Oh, no, sir. I wasn't then, I mean, mister!"

"Aw, talk sense. Now, where did they pick you up?"

He felt challenged and his mind began reconstructing events in reverse; his feelings ranged back over the long hours and he saw the cave, the sewer, the bloody room where it was said that a woman had been killed.

"Oh, yes, sir," he said, smiling. "I was coming from Mrs. Wooten's."

"Who is she?"

"I work for her."

"Where does she live?"

"Next door to Mrs. Peabody, the woman who was killed."

The policemen were very quiet now, looking at him intently.

"What do you know about Mrs. Peabody's death, boy?"

"Nothing, sir. But they said I killed her. But it doesn't make any difference. I'm guilty!"

"What are you talking about, boy?"

His smile faded and he was possessed with memories of the underground; he saw the cave next to the church and his lips moved to speak. But how could he say it? The distance between what he felt and what these men meant was vast. Something told him, as he stood there looking into their faces, that he would never be able to tell them, that they would never believe him even if he told them.

"All the people I saw was guilty," he began slowly.

"Aw, nuts," a policeman muttered.

"Say," another policeman said, "that Peabody woman was killed over on Winewood. That's Number Ten's beat."

"Where's Number Ten?" a policeman asked.

"Upstairs in the swing room," someone answered.

"Take this boy up, Sam," a policeman ordered.

"O.K. Come along, boy."

An elderly policeman caught hold of his arm and led him up a flight of wooden stairs, down a long hall, and to a door.

"Squad Ten!" the policeman called through the door.

"What?" a gruff voice answered.

"Someone to see you!"

"About what?"

The old policeman pushed the door in and then shoved him into the room.

He stared, his lips open, his heart barely beating. Before him were the three policemen who had picked him up and had beaten him to extract the confession. They were seated about a small table, playing cards. The air was blue with smoke and sunshine poured through a high window, lighting up fantastic smoke shapes. He saw one of the policemen look up; the policeman's face was tired and a cigarette dropped limply from one corner of his mouth and both of his fat, puffy eyes were squinting and his hands gripped his cards.

"Lawson!" the man exclaimed.

The moment the man's name sounded he remembered the names of all of them: Lawson, Murphy, and Johnson. How simple it was. He waited, smiling, wondering how they would react when they knew that he had come back.

"Looking for me?" the man who had been called Lawson mumbled, sorting his cards. "For what?"

So far only Murphy, the red-headed one, had recognized him.

"Don't you-all remember me?" he blurted, running to the table.

All three of the policemen were looking at him now. Lawson, who seemed the leader, jumped to his feet.

"Where in hell have you been?"

"Do you know 'im, Lawson?" the old policeman asked.

"Huh?" Lawson frowned. "Oh, yes. I'll handle 'im." The old policeman left the room and Lawson crossed to the door and turned the key in the lock. "Come here, boy," he ordered in a cold tone.

He did not move; he looked from face to face. Yes, he would tell them about his cave.

"He looks batty to me," Johnson said, the one who had not spoken before.

"Why in hell did you come back here?" Lawson said.

"I—I just didn't want to run away no more," he said. "I'm all right, now." He paused; the men's attitude puzzled him.

"You've been hiding, huh?" Lawson asked in a tone that denoted that he had not heard his previous words. "You told us you were sick, and when we left you in the room, you jumped out of the window and ran away."

Panic filled him. Yes, they were indifferent to what he would say! They were waiting for him to speak and they would laugh at him. He had to rescue himself from this bog; he had to force the reality of himself upon them.

"Mister, I took a sackful of money and pasted it on the walls . . ." he began.

"I'll be damned," Lawson said.

"Listen," said Murphy, "let me tell you something for your own good. We don't want you, see? You're free, free as air. Now go home and forget it. It was all a mistake. We caught the guy who did the Peabody job. He wasn't colored at all. He was an Eyetalian."

"Shut up!" Lawson yelled. "Have you no sense!"

"But I want to tell 'im," Murphy said.

"We can't let this crazy fool go," Lawson exploded. "He acts nuts, but this may be a stunt . . ."

"I was down in the basement," he began in a childlike tone, as though repeating a lesson learned by heart; "and I went into a movie . . ." His voice failed. He was getting ahead of his story. First, he ought to tell them about the singing in the church, but what words could he use? He looked at them appealingly. "I went into a shop and took a sackful of money and diamonds and watches and rings . . . I didn't steal 'em; I'll give 'em all back. I just took 'em to play with . . ." He paused, stunned by their disbelieving eyes.

Lawson lit a cigarette and looked at him coldly.

"What did you do with the money?" he asked in a quiet, waiting voice.

"I pasted the hundred-dollar bills on the walls."

"What walls?" Lawson asked.

"The walls of the dirt room," he said, smiling, "the room next to the church. I hung up the rings and the watches and I stamped the diamonds into the dirt . . ." He saw that they were not understanding what he was saying. He grew frantic to make them believe, his voice tumbled on eagerly. "I saw a dead baby and a dead man . . ."

"Aw, you're nuts," Lawson snarled, shoving him into a chair.

"But, mister . . ."

"Johnson, where's the paper he signed?" Lawson asked.

"What paper?"

"The confession, fool!"

Johnson pulled out his billfold and extracted a crumpled piece of paper.

"Yes, sir, mister," he said, stretching forth his hand. "That's the paper I signed . . ."

Lawson slapped him and he would have toppled had his chair not struck a wall behind him. Lawson scratched a match and held the paper over the flame; the confession burned down to Lawson's fingertips.

He stared, thunderstruck; the sun of the underground was fleeing and the terrible darkness of the day stood before him. They did not believe him, but he *had* to make them believe him!

"But, mister . . ."

"It's going to be all right, boy," Lawson said with a quiet, soothing laugh. "I've burned your confession, see? You didn't sign anything." Lawson came close to him with the black ashes cupped in his palm. "You don't remember a thing about this, do you?"

"Don't you-all be scared of me," he pleaded, sensing their uneasiness. "I'll sign another paper, if you want me to. I'll show you the cave."

"What's your game, boy?" Lawson asked suddenly.

"What are you trying to find out?" Johnson asked.

"Who sent you here?" Murphy demanded.

"Nobody sent me, mister," he said. "I just want to show you the room . . ."

"Aw, he's plumb bats," Murphy said. "Let's ship 'im to the psycho."

"No," Lawson said. "He's playing a game and I wish to God I knew what it was."

There flashed through his mind a definite way to make them believe him; he rose from the chair with nervous excitement.

"Mister, I saw the night watchman blow his brains out because you accused him of stealing," he told them. "But he didn't steal the money and diamonds. I took 'em."

Tigerishly Lawson grabbed his collar and lifted him bodily.

"*Who told you about that?*"

"Don't get excited, Lawson," Johnson said. "He read about it in the papers."

Lawson flung him away.

"He couldn't have," Lawson said, pulling papers from his pocket. "I haven't turned in the reports yet."

"Then how *did* he find out?" Murphy asked.

"Let's get out of here," Lawson said with quick resolution. "Listen, boy, we're going to take you to a nice, quiet place, see?"

"Yes, sir," he said. "And I'll show you the underground."

"Goddamn," Lawson muttered, fastening the gun at his hip. He narrowed his eyes at Johnson and Murphy. "Listen," he spoke just above a whisper, "say nothing about this, you hear?"

"O.K.," Johnson said.

"Sure," Murphy said.

Lawson unlocked the door and Johnson and Murphy led him down the stairs. The hallway was crowded with policemen.

"What have you got there, Lawson?"

"What did he do, Lawson?"

"He's psycho, ain't he, Lawson?"

Lawson did not answer; Johnson and Murphy led him to the car parked at the curb, pushed him into the back seat. Lawson got behind the steering wheel and the car rolled forward.

"What's up, Lawson?" Murphy asked.

"Listen," Lawson began slowly, "we tell the papers that he spilled about the Peabody job, then he escapes. The Wop is caught and we tell the papers that we steered them wrong to trap the real guy, see? Now this dope shows up and acts nuts. If we let him go, he'll squeal that we framed him, see?"

"I'm all right, mister," he said, feeling Murphy's and Johnson's arm locked rigidly into his. "I'm guilty . . . I'll show you everything in the underground. I laughed and laughed . . ."

"Shut that fool up!" Lawson ordered.

Johnson tapped him across the head with a blackjack and he fell back against the seat cushion, dazed.

"Yes, sir," he mumbled. "I'm all right."

The car sped along Hartsdale Avenue, then swung onto Pine Street and rolled to State Street, then turned south. It slowed to a stop, turned in the middle of a block, and headed north again.

"You're going around in circles, Lawson," Murphy said.

Lawson did not answer; he was hunched over the steering wheel. Finally he pulled the car to a stop at a curb.

"Say, boy, tell us the truth," Lawson asked quietly. "Where did you hide?"

"I didn't hide, mister."

The three policemen were staring at him now; he felt that for the first time they were willing to understand him.

"Then what happened?"

"Mister, when I looked through all of those holes and saw how people were living, I loved 'em . . ."

"Cut out that crazy talk!" Lawson snapped. "Who sent you back here?"

"Nobody, mister."

"Maybe he's talking straight," Johnson ventured.

"All right," Lawson said. "Nobody hid you. Now, tell us *where* you hid."

"I went underground . . ."

"What goddamn underground do you keep talking about?"

"I just went . . ." He paused and looked into the street, then pointed to a manhole cover. "I went down in there and stayed."

"In the *sewer?*"

"Yes, sir."

The policemen burst into a sudden laugh and ended quickly. Lawson swung the car around and drive to Woodside Avenue; he brought the car to a stop in front of a tall apartment building.

"What're we going to do, Lawson?" Murphy asked.

"I'm taking him up to my place," Lawson said. "We've got to wait until night. There's nothing we can do now."

They took him out of the car and led him into a vestibule.

"Take the steps," Lawson muttered.

They led him up four flights of stairs and into the living room of a small apartment. Johnson and Murphy let go of his arms and he stood uncertainly in the middle of the room.

"Now, listen, boy," Lawson began, "forget those wild lies you've been telling us. Where did you hide?"

"I just went underground, like I told you."

The room rocked with laughter. Lawson went to a cabinet and got a bottle of whisky; he placed glasses for Johnson and Murphy. The three of them drank.

He felt that he could not explain himself to them. He tried to muster all the sprawling images that floated in him; the images stood out sharply in his mind, but he could not make them have the meaning for others that they had for him. He felt so helpless that he began to cry.

"He's nuts, all right," Johnson said. "All nuts cry like that."

Murphy crossed the room and slapped him.

"Stop that raving!"

A sense of excitement flooded him; he ran to Murphy and grabbed his arm.

"Let me show you the cave," he said. "Come on, and you'll see!"

Before he knew it a sharp blow had clipped him on the chin; darkness covered his eyes. He dimly felt himself being lifted and laid out on the sofa. He heard low voices and struggled to rise, but hard hands held him down. His brain was clearing now. He pulled to a sitting posture and stared with glazed eyes. It had grown dark. How long had he been out?

"Say, boy," Lawson said soothingly, "will you show us the underground?"

His eyes shone and his heart swelled with gratitude. Lawson believed him! He rose, glad; he grabbed Lawson's arm, making the policeman spill whisky from the glass to his shirt.

"Take it easy, goddammit," Lawson said.

"Yes, sir."

"O.K. We'll take you down. But you'd better be telling us the truth, you hear?"

He clapped his hands in wild joy.

"I'll show you everything!"

He had triumphed at last! He would now do what he had felt was compelling him all along. At last he would be free of his burden.

"Take 'im down," Lawson ordered.

They led him down to the vestibule; when he reached the sidewalk he saw that it was night and a fine rain was falling.

"It's just like when I went down," he told them.

"What?" Lawson asked.

"The rain," he said, sweeping his arm in a wide arc. "It was raining when I went down. The rain made the water rise and lift the cover off."

"Cut it out," Lawson snapped.

They did not believe him now, but they would. A mood of high selflessness throbbed in him. He could barely contain his rising spirits. They would see what he had seen; they would feel what he had felt. He would lead them through all the holes he had dug and . . . He wanted to make a hymn, prance about in physical ecstasy, throw his arm about the policemen in fellowship.

"Get into the car," Lawson ordered.

He climbed in and Johnson and Murphy sat at either side of him; Lawson slid behind the steering wheel and started the motor.

"Now, tell us where to go," Lawson said.

"It's right around the corner from where the lady was killed," he said.

The car rolled slowly and he closed his eyes, remembering the song he had heard in the church, the song that had brought him to such a high pitch of terror and pity. He sang softly, lolling is head:

> *Glad, glad, glad, oh, so glad*
> *I got Jesus in my soul . . .*

"Mister," he said, stopping his song, "you ought to see how funny the rings look on the wall." He giggled. "I fired a pistol, too. Just once, to see how it felt."

"What do you suppose he's suffering from?" Johnson asked.

"Delusions of grandeur, maybe," Murphy said.

"Maybe it's because he lives in a white man's world," Lawson said.

"Say, boy, what did you eat down there?" Murphy asked, prodding Johnson anticipatorily with his elbow.

"Pears, oranges, bananas, and pork chops," he said.

The car filled with laughter.

"You didn't eat any watermelon?" Lawson asked, smiling.

"No, sir," he answered calmly. "I didn't see any."

The three policemen roared harder and louder.

"Boy, you're sure some case," Murphy said, shaking his head in wonder.

The car pulled to a curb.

"All right, boy," Lawson said. "Tell us where to go."

He peered through the rain and saw where he had gone down. The streets, save for a few dim lamps glowing softly through the rain, were dark and empty.

"Right there, mister," he said, pointing.

"Come on; let's take a look," Lawson said.

"Well, suppose he did hide down there," Johnson said, "what is that supposed to prove?"

"I don't believe he hid down there," Murphy said.

"It won't hurt to look," Lawson said. "Leave things to me."

Lawson got out of the car and looked up and down the street.

He was eager to show them the cave now. If he could show them what he had seen, then they would feel what he had felt and they in turn would show it to others and those others would feel as they had felt, and soon everybody would be governed by the same impulse of pity.

"Take 'im out," Lawson ordered.

Johnson and Murphy opened the door and pushed him out; he stood trembling in the rain, smiling. Again Lawson looked up and down the street; no one was in sight. The rain came down hard, slanting like black wires across the wind-swept air.

"All right," Lawson said. "Show us."

He walked to the center of the street, stopped and inserted a finger in one of the tiny holes of the cover and tugged, but he was too weak to budge it.

"Did you really go down in there, boy?" Lawson asked; there was a doubt in his voice.

"Yes, sir. Just a minute. I'll show you."

"Help 'im get that damn thing off," Lawson said.

Johnson stepped forward and lifted the cover; it clanged against the wet pavement. The hole gaped round and black.

"I went down in there," he announced with pride.

Lawson gazed at him for a long time without speaking, then he reached his right hand to his holster and drew his gun.

"Mister, I got a gun just like that down there," he said, laughing and looking into Lawson's face. "I fired it once then hung it on the wall. I'll show you."

"Show us how you went down," Lawson said quietly.

"I'll go down first, mister, and then you-all can come after me, hear?" he spoke like a little boy playing a game.

"Sure, sure," Lawson said soothingly. "Go ahead. We'll come."

He looked brightly at the policemen; he was bursting with happiness. He bent down and placed his hands on the rim of the hole and sat on the edge, his feet dangling into watery darkness. He heard the familiar drone of the gray current. He lowered his body and hung for a moment by his fingers, then he went downward on the steel prongs, hand over hand, until he reached the last rung. He dropped and his feet hit the water and he felt the stiff current trying to suck him away. He balanced himself quickly and looked back upward at the policemen.

"Come on, you-all!" he yelled, casting his voice above the rustling at his feet.

The vague forms that towered above him in the rain did not move. He laughed, feeling that they doubted him. But, once they saw the things he had done, they would never doubt again.

"Come on! The cave isn't far!" he yelled. "But be careful when your feet hit the water, because the current's pretty rough down here!"

Lawson still held the gun. Murphy and Johnson looked at Lawson quizzically.

"What are we going to do, Lawson?" Murphy asked.

"We are not going to follow that crazy nigger down into that sewer, are we?" Johnson asked.

"Come on, you-all!" he begged in a shout.

He saw Lawson raise the gun and point it directly at him. Lawson's face twitched, as though he were hesitating.

Then there was a thunderous report and a streak of fire ripped through his chest. He was hurled into the water, flat on his back. He looked in amazement at the blurred white faces looming above him. They shot me, he said to himself. The water flowed past him, blossoming in foam about his arms, his legs, and his head. His jaw sagged and his mouth gaped soundless. A vast pain gripped his head and gradually squeezed out consciousness. As from a great distance he heard hollow voices.

"What did you shoot him for, Lawson?"

"I had to."

"Why?"

"You've got to shoot his kind. They'd wreck things."

As though in a deep dream, he heard a metallic clank; they had replaced the manhole cover, shutting out forever the sound of wind and rain. From overhead came the muffled roar of a powerful motor and the swish of a speeding car. He felt the strong tide pushing him slowly into the middle of the sewer, turning him about. For a split second there hovered before his eyes the glittering cave, the shouting walls, and the laughing floor . . . Then his mouth was full of thick, bitter water. The current spun him around. He sighed and closed his eyes, a whirling object rushing alone in the darkness, veering, tossing, lost in the heart of the earth.

1942

From Black Boy

Chapter XIII

[BOOKLIST]

One morning I arrived early at work and went into the bank lobby where the Negro porter was mopping. I stood at a counter and picked up the Memphis *Commercial Appeal* and began my free reading of the press. I came finally to the editorial page and saw an article dealing with one H. L. Mencken.[1] I knew by hearsay that he was the editor of the *American Mercury*, but aside from that I knew nothing about him. The article was a furi-

---

1. H(enry) L(ouis) Mencken (1880–1956), American editor and critic; founder and editor (1924–33) of the *American Mercury*, he wrote essays of vitriolic social criticism.

ous denunciation of Mencken, concluding with one, hot, short sentence:
Mencken is a fool.

I wondered what on earth this Mencken had done to call down upon
him the scorn of the South. The only people I had ever heard denounced
in the South were Negroes, and this man was not a Negro. Then what ideas
did Mencken hold that made a newspaper like the *Commercial Appeal* cas-
tigate him publicly? Undoubtedly he must be advocating ideas that the
South did not like. Were there, then, people other than Negroes who criticized the South? I knew that during the Civil War the South had hated
northern whites, but I had not encountered such hate during my life.
Knowing no more of Mencken than I did at that moment, I felt a vague
sympathy for him. Had not the South, which had assigned me the role of a
non-man, cast at him its hardest words?

Now, how could I find out about this Mencken? There was a huge library near the riverfront, but I knew that Negroes were not allowed to patronize its shelves any more than they were the parks and playgrounds of
the city. I had gone into the library several times to get books for the white
men on the job. Which of them would now help me to get books? And how
could I read them without causing concern to the white men with whom I
worked? I had so far been successful in hiding my thoughts and feelings
from them, but I knew that I would create hostility if I went about this
business of reading in a clumsy way.

I weighed the personalities of the men on the job. There was Don, a Jew;
but I distrusted him. His position was not much better than mine and I
knew that he was uneasy and insecure; he had always treated me in an
offhand, bantering way that barely concealed his contempt. I was afraid to
ask him to help me to get books; his frantic desire to demonstrate a racial
solidarity with the whites against Negroes might make him betray me.

Then how about the boss? No, he was a Baptist and I had the suspicion
that he would not be quite able to comprehend why a black boy would
want to read Mencken. There were other white men on the job whose attitudes showed clearly that they were Kluxers[2] or sympathizers, and they
were out of the question.

There remained only one man whose attitude did not fit into an anti-
Negro category, for I had heard the white men refer to him as a "Pope
lover." He was an Irish Catholic and was hated by the white Southerners. I
knew that he read books, because I had got him volumes from the library
several times. Since he, too, was an object of hatred, I felt that he might
refuse me but would hardly betray me. I hesitated, weighing and balancing
the imponderable realities.

One morning I paused before the Catholic fellow's desk.

"I want to ask you a favor," I whispered to him.

"What is it?"

"I want to read. I can't get books from the library. I wonder if you'd let
me use your card?"

He looked at me suspiciously.

2. I.e., members of the Ku Klux Klan.

"My card is full most of the time," he said.

"I see," I said and waited, posing my question silently.

"You're not trying to get me into trouble, are you, boy?" he asked, staring at me.

"Oh, no, sir."

"What book do you want?"

"A book by H. L. Mencken."

"Which one?"

"I don't know. Has he written more than one?"

"He has written several."

"I didn't know that."

"What makes you want to read Mencken?"

"Oh, I just saw his name in the newspaper," I said.

"It's good of you to want to read," he said. "But you ought to read the right things."

I said nothing. Would he want to supervise my reading?

"Let me think," he said. "I'll figure out something."

I turned from him and he called me back. He stared at me quizzically.

"Richard, don't mention this to the other white men," he said.

"I understand," I said. "I won't say a word."

A few days later he called me to him.

"I've got a card in my wife's name," he said. "Here's mine."

"Thank you, sir."

"Do you think you can manage it?"

"I'll manage fine," I said.

"If they suspect you, you'll get in trouble," he said.

"I'll write the same kind of notes to the library that you wrote when you sent me for books," I told him. "I'll sign your name."

He laughed.

"Go ahead. Let me see what you get," he said.

That afternoon I addressed myself to forging a note. Now, what were the names of books written by H. L. Mencken? I did not know any of them. I finally wrote what I thought would be a foolproof note: *Dear Madam: Will you please let this nigger boy*—I used the word "nigger" to make the librarian feel that I could not possibly be the author of the note—*have some books by H. L. Mencken?* I forged the white man's name.

I entered the library as I had always done when on errands for whites, but I felt that I would somehow slip up and betray myself. I doffed my hat, stood a respectful distance from the desk, looked as unbookish as possible, and waited for the white patrons to be taken care of. When the desk was clear of people, I still waited. The white librarian looked at me.

"What do you want, boy?"

As though I did not possess the power of speech, I stepped forward and simply handed her the forged note, not parting my lips.

"What books by Mencken does he want?" she asked.

"I don't know, ma'am," I said, avoiding her eyes.

"Who gave you this card?"

"Mr. Falk," I said.

"Where is he?"

"He's at work, at the M—— Optical Company," I said. "I've been in here for him before."

"I remember," the woman said. "But he never wrote notes like this."

Oh, God, she's suspicious. Perhaps she would not let me have the books? If she had turned her back at that moment, I would have ducked out the door and never gone back. Then I thought of a bold idea.

"You can call him up, ma'am," I said, my heart pounding.

"You're not using these books, are you?" she asked pointedly.

"Oh, no, ma'am. I can't read."

"I don't know what he wants by Mencken," she said under her breath.

I knew now that I had won; she was thinking of other things and the race question had gone out of her mind. She went to the shelves. Once or twice she looked over her shoulder at me, as though she was still doubtful. Finally she came forward with two books in her hand.

"I'm sending him two books," she said. "But tell Mr. Falk to come in next time, or send me the names of the books he wants. I don't know what he wants to read."

I said nothing. She stamped the card and handed me the books. Not daring to glance at them, I went out of the library, fearing that the woman would call me back for further questioning. A block away from the library I opened one of the books and read a title: A *Book of Prefaces*. I was nearing my nineteenth birthday and I did not know how to pronounce the word "preface." I thumbed the pages and saw strange words and strange names. I shook my head, disappointed. I looked at the other book; it was called *Prejudices*. I knew what that word meant; I had heard it all my life. And right off I was on guard against Mencken's books. Why would a man want to call a book *Prejudices*? The word was so stained with all my memories of racial hate that I could not conceive of anybody using it for a title. Perhaps I had made a mistake about Mencken? A man who had prejudices must be wrong.

When I showed the books to Mr. Falk, he looked at me and frowned.

"That librarian might telephone you," I warned him.

"That's all right," he said. "But when you're through reading those books, I want you to tell me what you get out of them."

That night in my rented room, while letting the hot water run over my can of pork and beans in the sink, I opened *A Book of Prefaces* and began to read. I was jarred and shocked by the style, the clear, clean, sweeping sentences. Why did he write like that? And how did one write like that? I pictured the man as a raging demon, slashing with his pen, consumed with hate, denouncing everything American, extolling everything European or German, laughing at the weaknesses of people, mocking God, authority. What was this? I stood up, trying to realize what reality lay behind the meaning of the words . . . . Yes, this man was fighting, fighting with words. He was using words as a weapon, using them as one would use a club. Could words be weapons? Well, yes, for here they were. Then, maybe, perhaps, I could use them as a weapon? No. It frightened me. I read on and what amazed me was not what he said, but how on earth anybody had the courage to say it.

Occasionally I glanced up to reassure myself that I was alone in the room. Who were these men about whom Mencken was talking so passionately? Who was Anatole France? Joseph Conrad? Sinclair Lewis, Sherwood Anderson, Dostoevski, George Moore, Gustave Flaubert, Maupassant, Tolstoy, Frank Harris, Mark Twain, Thomas Hardy, Arnold Bennett, Stephen Crane, Zola, Norris, Gorky, Bergson, Ibsen, Balzac, Bernard Shaw, Dumas, Poe, Thomas Mann, O. Henry, Dreiser, H. G. Wells, Gogol, T. S. Eliot, Gide, Baudelaire, Edgar Lee Masters, Stendhal, Turgenev, Huneker, Nietzsche, and scores of others? Were these men real? Did they exist or had they existed? And how did one pronounce their names?

I ran across many words whose meanings I did not know, and I either looked them up in a dictionary or, before I had a chance to do that, encountered the word in a context that made its meaning clear. But what strange world was this? I concluded the book with the conviction that I had somehow overlooked something terribly important in life. I had once tried to write, had once reveled in feeling, had let my crude imagination roam, but the impulse to dream had been slowly beaten out of me by experience. Now it surged up again and I hungered for books, new ways of looking and seeing. It was not a matter of believing or disbelieving what I read, but of feeling something new, of being affected by something that made the look of the world different.

As dawn broke I ate my pork and beans, feeling dopey, sleepy. I went to work, but the mood of the book would not die; it lingered, coloring everything I saw, heard, did. I now felt that I knew what the white men were feeling. Merely because I had read a book that had spoken of how they lived and thought, I identified myself with that book. I felt vaguely guilty. Would I, filled with bookish notions, act in a manner that would make the whites dislike me?

I forged more notes and my trips to the library became frequent. Reading grew into a passion. My first serious novel was Sinclair Lewis's *Main Street*. It made me see my boss, Mr. Gerald, and identify him as an American type. I would smile when I saw him lugging his golf bags into the office. I had always felt a vast distance separating me from the boss, and now I felt closer to him, though still distant. I felt now that I knew him, that I could feel the very limits of his narrow life. And this had happened because I had read a novel about a mythical man called George F. Babbitt.

The plots and stories in the novels did not interest me so much as the point of view revealed. I gave myself over to each novel without reserve, without trying to criticize it; it was enough for me to see and feel something different. And for me, everything was something different. Reading was like a drug, a dope. The novels created moods in which I lived for days. But I could not conquer my sense of guilt, my feeling that the white men around me knew that I was changing, that I had begun to regard them differently.

Whenever I brought a book to the job, I wrapped it in newspaper—a habit that was to persist for years in other cities and under other circumstances. But some of the white men pried into my packages when I was absent and they questioned me.

"Boy, what are you reading those books for?"

"Oh, I don't know, sir."

"That's deep stuff you're reading, boy."

"I'm just killing time, sir."

"You'll addle your brains if you don't watch out."

I read Dreiser's *Jennie Gerhardt* and *Sister Carrie* and they revived in me a vivid sense of my mother's suffering; I was overwhelmed. I grew silent, wondering about the life around me. It would have been impossible for me to have told anyone what I derived from these novels, for it was nothing less than a sense of life itself. All my life had shaped me for the realism, the naturalism of the modern novel, and I could not read enough of them.

Steeped in new moods and ideas, I bought a ream of paper and tried to write; but nothing would come, or what did come was flat beyond telling. I discovered that more than desire and feeling were necessary to write and I dropped the idea. Yet I still wondered how it was possible to know people sufficiently to write about them? Could I ever learn about life and people? To me, with my vast ignorance, my Jim Crow station in life, it seemed a task impossible of achievement. I now knew what being a Negro meant. I could endure the hunger. I had learned to live with hate. But to feel that there were feelings denied me, that the very breath of life itself was beyond my reach, that more than anything else hurt, wounded me. I had a new hunger.

In buoying me up, reading also cast me down, made me see what was possible, what I had missed. My tension returned, new, terrible, bitter, surging, almost too great to be contained. I no longer *felt* that the world about me was hostile, killing; I *knew* it. A million times I asked myself what I could do to save myself, and there were no answers. I seemed forever condemned, ringed by walls.

I did not discuss my reading with Mr. Falk, who had lent me his library card; it would have meant talking about myself and that would have been too painful. I smiled each day, fighting desperately to maintain my old behavior, to keep my disposition seemingly sunny. But some of the white men discerned that I had begun to brood.

"Wake up there, boy!" Mr. Olin said one day.

"Sir!" I answered for the lack of a better word.

"You act like you've stolen something," he said.

I laughed in the way I knew he expected me to laugh, but I resolved to be more conscious of myself, to watch my every act, to guard and hide the new knowledge that was dawning within me.

If I went north, would it be possible for me to build a new life then? But how could a man build a life upon vague, unformed yearnings? I wanted to write and I did not even know the English language. I bought English grammars and found them dull. I felt that I was getting a better sense of the language from novels than from grammars. I read hard, discarding a writer as soon as I felt that I had grasped his point of view. At night the printed page stood before my eyes in sleep.

Mrs. Moss, my landlady, asked me one Sunday morning:

"Son, what is this you keep on reading?"

"Oh, nothing. Just novels."

"What you get out of 'em?"

"I'm just killing time," I said.

"I hope you know your own mind," she said in a tone which implied that she doubted if I had a mind.

I knew of no Negroes who read the books I liked and I wondered if any Negroes ever thought of them. I knew that there were Negro doctors, lawyers, newspapermen, but I never saw any of them. When I read a Negro newspaper I never caught the faintest echo of my preoccupation in its pages. I felt trapped and occasionally, for a few days, I would stop reading. But a vague hunger would come over me for books, books that opened up new avenues of feeling and seeing, and again I would forge another note to the white librarian. Again I would read and wonder as only the naïve and unlettered can read and wonder, feeling that I carried a secret, criminal burden about with me each day.

That winter my mother and brother came and we set up housekeeping, buying furniture on the installment plan, being cheated and yet knowing no way to avoid it. I began to eat warm food and to my surprise found that regular meals enabled me to read faster. I may have lived through many illnesses, and survived them, never suspecting that I was ill. My brother obtained a job and we began to save toward the trip north, plotting our time, setting tentative dates for departure. I told none of the white men on the job that I was planning to go north; I knew that the moment they felt I was thinking of the North they would change toward me. It would have made them feel that I did not like the life I was living, and because my life was completely conditioned by what they said or did, it would have been tantamount to challenging them.

I could calculate my chances for life in the South as a Negro fairly clearly now.

I could fight the southern whites by organizing with other Negroes, as my grandfather had done. But I knew that I could never win that way; there were many whites and there were but few blacks. They were strong and we were weak. Outright black rebellion could never win. If I fought openly I would die and I did not want to die. News of lynchings were frequent.

I could submit and live the life of a genial slave, but that was impossible. All of my life had shaped me to live by my own feelings and thoughts. I could make up to Bess and marry her and inherit the house. But that, too, would be the life of a slave; if I did that, I would crush to death something within me, and I would hate myself as much as I knew the whites already hated those who had submitted. Neither could I ever willingly present myself to be kicked, as Shorty had done. I would rather have died than do that.

I could drain off my restlessness by fighting with Shorty and Harrison. I had seen many Negroes solve the problem of being black by transferring their hatred of themselves to others with a black skin and fighting them. I would have to be cold to do that, and I was not cold and I could never be.

I could, of course, forget what I had read, thrust the whites out of my mind, forget them; and find release from anxiety and longing in sex and alcohol. But the memory of how my father had conducted himself made that course repugnant. If I did not want others to violate my life, how could I voluntarily violate it myself?

I had no hope whatever of being a professional man. Not only had I been so conditioned that I did not desire it, but the fulfillment of such an ambition was beyond my capabilities. Well-to-do Negroes lived in a world that was almost as alien to me as the world inhabited by whites.

What, then, was there? I held my life in my mind, in my consciousness each day, feeling at times that I would stumble and drop it, spill it forever. My reading had created a vast sense of distance between me and the world in which I lived and tried to make a living, and that sense of distance was increasing each day. My days and nights were one long, quiet, continuously contained dream of terror, tension, and anxiety. I wondered how long I could bear it.

Chapter XVI

[CHICAGO]

In the spring I took the postal examination again. Time had somewhat repaired the ravages of hunger and I was able to meet the required physical weight. We moved to a larger apartment. My increased pay made better food possible. I was happy in my own way.

Working nights, I spent my days in experimental writing, filling endless pages with stream-of-consciousness Negro dialect, trying to depict the dwellers of the Black Belt as I felt and saw them. My reading in sociology had enabled me to discern many strange types of Negro characters, to identify many modes of Negro behavior; and what moved me above all was the frequency of mental illness, that tragic toll that the urban environment exacted of the black peasant. Perhaps my writing was more an attempt at understanding than self-expression. A need that I did not comprehend made me use words to create religious types, criminal types, the warped, the lost, the baffled; my pages were full of tension, frantic poverty, and death.

But something was missing in my imaginative efforts; my flights of imagination were too subjective, too lacking in reference to social action. I hungered for a grasp of the framework of contemporary living, for a knowledge of the forms of life about me, for eyes to see the bony structures of personality, for theories to light up the shadows of conduct.

While sorting mail in the post office, I met a young Irish chap whose sensibilities amazed me. We would take a batch of mail in our fingers and, while talking in low monotones out of the sides of our mouths, toss them correctly into their designated holes and suddenly our hands would be empty and we would have no memory of having worked. Most of the clerks could work in this automatic manner. The Irish chap and I had read a lot in common and we laughed at the same sacred things. He was as cynical as I was regarding uplift and hope, and we were proud of having escaped what we called the "childhood disease of metaphysical fear." I was introduced to the Irish chap's friends and we formed a "gang" of Irish, Jewish, and Negro wits who poked fun at government, the masses, statesmen, and political parties. We assumed that all people were good to the degree to which they amused us, or to the extent to which we could make them objects of laughter. We ridiculed all ideas of protest, of organized rebellion or revolution. We felt that all businessmen were thoroughly stupid and that no other group was capable of rising to challenge them. We sneered at voting, for we felt that the choice between one political crook and another was too small for serious thought. We believed that man should live by hard facts alone, and we had so long ago put God out of our minds that we did not even discuss Him.

During this cynical period I met a Negro literary group on Chicago's South Side; it was composed of a dozen or more boys and girls, all of whom possessed academic learning, economic freedom, and vague ambitions to write. I found them more formal in manner than their white counterparts; they wore stylish clothes and were finicky about their personal appearance. I had naïvely supposed that I would have much in common with them, but I found them preoccupied with twisted sex problems. Coming from a station in life which they no doubt would have branded "lower class," I could not understand why they were so all-absorbed with sexual passion. I was encountering for the first time the full-fledged Negro Puritan invert—the emotionally sick—and I discovered that their ideas were but excuses for sex, leads to sex, hints at sex, substitutes for sex. In speech and action they strove to act as un-Negro as possible, denying the racial and material foundations of their lives, accepting their class and racial status in ways so oblique that one had the impression that no difficulties existed for them. Though I had never had any assignments from a college professor, I had made much harder and more prolonged attempts at self-expression than any of them. Swearing love for art, they hovered on the edge of Bohemian life. Always friendly, they could never be anybody's friend; always reading, they could really never learn; always boasting of their passions, they could never really feel and were afraid to live.

The one group I met during those exploring days whose lives enthralled me was the Garveyites, an organization of black men and women who were forlornly seeking to return to Africa. Theirs was a passionate rejection of America, for they sensed with that directness of which only the simple are capable that they had no chance to live a full human life in America. Their lives were not cluttered with ideas in which they could only half believe; they could not create illusions which made them think they were living when they were not; their daily lives were too nakedly harsh to permit of camouflage. I understood their emotions, for I partly shared them.

The Garveyites had embraced a totally racialistic outlook which endowed them with a dignity that I had never seen before in Negroes. On the walls of their dingy flats were maps of Africa and India and Japan, pictures of Japanese generals and admirals, portraits of Marcus Garvey in gaudy regalia, the faces of colored men and women from all parts of the world. I gave no credence to the ideology of Garveyism; it was, rather, the emotional dynamics of its adherents that evoked my admiration. Those Garveyites I knew could never understand why I liked them but would never follow them, and I pitied them too much to tell them that they could never achieve their goal, that Africa was owned by the imperial powers of Europe, that their lives were alien to the mores of the natives of Africa, that they were people of the West and would forever be so until they either merged with the West or perished. It was when the Garveyites spoke fervently of building their own country, of someday living within the boundaries of a culture of their own making, that I sensed the passionate hunger of their lives, that I caught a glimpse of the potential strength of the American Negro.

Rumors of unemployment came, but I did not listen to them. I heard of the organizational efforts of the Communist party among the Negroes of the South Side, but Communist activities were too remote to strike my mind with any degree of vividness. Whenever I met a person whom I suspected of being a Communist, I talked to him affably but from an emotional distance. I sensed that something terrible was beginning to happen in the world, but I tried to shut it out of my mind by reading and writing.

When the time came for my appointment as a regular clerk, I was told that no appointments would be made for the time being. The volume of mail dropped. My hours of work dwindled. My paychecks grew small. Food became scarce at home. The hunger I thought I had left behind returned. One winter afternoon, in 1929, en route to work from the library, I passed a newsstand on which papers blazed:

STOCKS CRASH—BILLIONS FADE

Most of what I had seen in newspapers had never concerned me, so why should this? Newspapers reported the doings in a life I did not share. But the volume of mail fell so low that I worked but one or two nights a week. In the post-office canteen the boys stood about and talked.

"The cops beat up some demonstrators today."

"The Reds had a picket line around the City Hall."

"Wall Street's cracking down on the country."

"Surplus production's throwing millions out of work."

"There're more than two million unemployed."

"They don't count. They're always out of work."

"Read Karl Marx and get the answer, boys."

"There'll be a revolution if this keeps up."

"Hell, naw. Americans are too dumb to make a revolution."

The post-office job ended and again I was out of work. I could no longer think that the tides of economics were not my concern. But how could I have had any possible say in how the world had been run? I had grown up in complete ignorance of what created jobs. Having been thrust out of the world because of my race, I had accepted my destiny by not being curious about what shaped it.

The following summer I was again called for temporary duty in the post office, and the work lasted into the winter. Aunt Cleo succumbed to a severe cardiac condition and, hard on the heels of her illness, my brother developed stomach ulcers. To rush my worries to a climax, my mother also became ill. I felt that I was maintaining a private hospital. Finally the post-office work ceased altogether and I haunted the city for jobs. But when I went into the streets in the morning I saw sights that killed my hope for the rest of the day. Unemployed men loitered in doorways with blank looks in their eyes, sat dejectedly on front steps in shabby clothing, congregated in sullen groups on street corners, and filled all the empty benches in the parks of Chicago's South Side.

Luck of a sort came when a distant cousin of mine, who was a superintendent in a Negro burial society, offered me a position on his staff as an agent. The thought of selling insurance policies to ignorant Negroes disgusted me.

"Well, if you don't sell them, somebody else will," my cousin told me. "You've got to eat, haven't you?"

During that year I worked for several burial and insurance societies that operated among Negroes, and I received a new kind of education. I found that the burial societies, with some exceptions, were mostly "rackets." Some of them conducted their businesses legitimately, but there were many that exploited the ignorance of their black customers.

I was paid under a system that netted me fifteen dollars for every dollar's worth of new premiums that I placed upon the company's books, and for every dollar's worth of old premiums that lapsed I was penalized fifteen dollars. In addition, I was paid a commission of ten per cent on total premiums collected, but during the depression it was extremely difficult to persuade a black family to buy a policy carrying even a dime premium. I considered myself lucky if, after subtracting lapses from new business, there remained fifteen dollars that I could call my own.

This "gambling" method of remuneration was practiced by some of the burial companies because of the tremendous "turnover" in policyholders, and the companies had to have a constant stream of new business to keep afloat. Whenever a black family moved or suffered a slight reverse in fortune, it usually let its policy lapse and later bought another policy from some other company.

Each day now I saw how the Negro in Chicago lived, for I visited hundreds of dingy flats filled with rickety furniture and ill-clad children. Most of the policyholders were illiterate and did not know that their policies carried clauses severely restricting their benefit payments, and, as an insurance agent, it was not my duty to tell them.

After tramping the streets and pounding on doors to collect premiums, I was dry, strained, too tired to read or write. I hungered for relief and, as a salesman of insurance to many young black girls, I found it. There were many comely black housewives who, trying desperately to keep up their insurance payments, were willing to make bargains to escape paying a ten-cent premium. I had a long, tortured affair with one girl by paying her ten-cent premium each week. She was an illiterate black child with a baby whose father she did not know. During the entire period of my relationship with her, she had but one demand to make of me: She wanted me to take her to a circus. Just what significance circuses had for her, I was never able to learn.

After I had been with her one morning—in exchange for the dime premium—I sat on the sofa in the front room and began to read a book I had with me. She came over shyly.

"Lemme see that," she said.

"What?" I asked.

"That book," she said.

I gave her the book; she looked at it intently. I saw that she was holding it upside down.

"What's in here you keep reading?" she asked.

"Can't you really read?" I asked.

"Naw," she giggled. "You know I can't read."

"You can read *some*," I said.

"Naw," she said.

I stared at her and wondered just what a life like hers meant in the scheme of things, and I came to the conclusion that it meant absolutely nothing. And neither did my life mean anything.

"How come you looking at me that way for?" she asked.

"Nothing."

"You don't talk much."

"There isn't much to say."

"I wished Jim was here," she sighed.

"Who's Jim?" I asked, jealous. I knew that she had other men, but I resented her mentioning them in my presence.

"Just a friend," she said.

I hated her then, then hated myself for coming to her.

"Do you like Jim better than you like me?" I asked.

"Naw. Jim just likes to talk."

"Then why do you be with me, if you like Jim better?" I asked, trying to make an issue and feeling a wave of disgust because I wanted to.

"You all right," she said, giggling. "I like you."

"I could kill you," I said.

"What?" she exclaimed.

"Nothing," I said, ashamed.

"Kill me, you said? You crazy, man," she said.

"Maybe I am," I muttered, angry that I was sitting beside a human being to whom I could not talk, angry with myself for coming to her, hating my wild and restless loneliness.

"You oughta go home and sleep," she said. "You tired."

"What do you ever think about?" I demanded harshly.

"Lotta things."

"What, for example?"

"You," she said, smiling.

"You know I mean just one dime to you each week," I said.

"Naw, I thinka lotta you."

"Then what do you think?"

" 'Bout how you talk when you talk. I wished I could talk like you," she said seriously.

"Why?" I taunted her.

"When you gonna take me to a circus?" she demanded suddenly.

"You ought to be in a circus," I said.

"I'd like it," she said, her eyes shining.

I wanted to laugh, but her words sounded so sincere that I could not laugh.

"There's no circus in town," I said.

"I bet there is and you won't tell me 'cause you don't wanna take me," she said, pouting.

"But there's no circus in town, I tell you!"

"When will one come?"

"I don't know."

"Can't you read it in the papers?" she asked.

"There's nothing in the papers about a circus."

"There is," she said. "If I could read, I'd find it."

I laughed and she was hurt.

"There *is* a circus in town," she said stoutly.

"There's no circus in town," I said. "But if you want to learn to read, then I'll teach you."

She nestled at my side, giggling.

"See that word?" I said, pointing.

"Yeah."

"That's an 'and,' " I said.

She doubled, giggling.

"What's the matter?" I asked.

She rolled on the floor, giggling.

"What's so funny?" I demanded.

"You," she giggled. "You so funny."

I rose.

"The hell with you," I said.

"Don't you go and cuss me now," she said. "I don't cuss you."

"I'm sorry," I said.

I got my hat and went to the door.

"I'll see you next week?" she asked.

"Maybe," I said.

When I was on the sidewalk, she called to me from a window.

"You promised to take me to a circus, remember?"

"Yes." I walked close to the window. "What is it you like about a circus?"

"The animals," she said simply.

I felt that there was a hidden meaning, perhaps, in what she had said; but I could not find it. She laughed and slammed the window shut.

Each time I left her I resolved not to visit her again. I could not talk to her; I merely listened to her passionate desire to see a circus. She was not calculating; if she liked a man, she just liked him. Sex relations were the only relations she had ever had; no others were possible with her, so limited was her intelligence.

Most of the other agents also had their bought girls and they were extremely anxious to keep other agents from tampering with them. One day a new section of the South Side was given to me as a part of my collection area and the agent from whom the territory had been taken suddenly became very friendly with me.

"Say, Wright," he asked, "did you collect from Ewing at——Champlain Avenue yet?"

"Yes," I answered, after consulting my book.

"How did you like her?" he asked, staring at me.

"She's a good-looking number," I said.

"You had anything to do with her yet?" he asked.

"No, but I'd like to," I said, laughing.

"Look," he said. "I'm a friend of yours."

"Since when?" I countered.

"No, I'm really a friend," he said.

"What's on your mind?"

"Listen, that gal's sick," he said seriously.

"What do you mean?"

"She's got the clap," he said. "Keep away from her. She'll lay with anybody."

"Gee, I'm glad you told me," I said.

"You had your eye on her, didn't you?" he asked.

"Yes, I did," I said.

"Leave her alone," he said. "She'll get you down."

That night I told my cousin what the agent had said about Miss Ewing. My cousin laughed.

"That gal's all right," he said. "That agent's been fooling around with her. He told you she had a disease so that you'd be scared to bother her. He was protecting her from you."

That was the way the black women were regarded by the black agents. Some of the agents were vicious; if they had claims to pay to a sick black woman and if the woman was able to have sex relations with them, they would insist upon it, using the claim money as a bribe. If the woman refused, they would report to the office that the woman was a malingerer. The average black woman would submit because she needed the money badly.

As an insurance agent, it was necessary for me to take part in one swindle. It appears that the burial society had originally issued a policy that was—from their point of view—too liberal in its provisions, and the officials decided to exchange the policies then in the hands of their clients for other policies carrying stricter clauses; of course, this had to be done in a manner that would not allow the policyholder to know that his policy was being switched, that he was being swindled. I did not like it, but there was only one thing I could do to keep from being a party to it: I could quit and starve. But I did not feel that being honest was worth the price of starvation.

The swindle worked in this way. In my visits to the homes of policyholders to collect premiums, I was accompanied by the superintendent who claimed to the policyholder that he was making a routine inspection. The policyholder, usually an illiterate black woman, would dig up her policy from the bottom of a trunk or a chest and hand it to the superintendent. Meanwhile I would be marking the woman's premium book, an act which would distract her from what the superintendent was doing. The superintendent would exchange the old policy for a new one which was identical in color, serial number, and beneficiary, but which carried much smaller payments. It was dirty work and I wondered how I could stop it. And when I could think of no safe way I would curse myself and the victims and forget about it. (The black owners of the burial societies were leaders in the Negro communities and were respected by whites.)

As I went from house to house collecting money, I saw black men mounted upon soapboxes at street corners, bellowing about bread, rights, and revolution. I liked their courage, but I doubted their wisdom. The speakers claimed that Negroes were angry, that they were about to rise and join their white fellow workers to make a revolution. I was in and out of

many Negro homes each day and I knew that the Negroes were lost, ignorant, sick in mind and body. I saw that a vast distance separated the agitators
from the masses, a distance so vast that the agitators did not know how to
appeal to the people they sought to lead.

Some mornings I found leaflets on my steps telling of China, Russia, and
Germany; on some days I witnessed as many as five thousand jobless
Negroes, led by Communists, surging through the streets. I would watch
them with an aching heart, firmly convinced that they were being duped;
but if I had been asked to give them another solution for their problems, I
would not have known how.

It became a habit of mine to visit Washington Park of an afternoon after
collecting a part of my premiums, and I would wander through crowds of
unemployed Negroes, pausing here and there to sample the dialectic or
indignation of Communist speakers. What I heard and saw baffled and angered me. The Negro Communists were deliberately careless in their personal appearance, wearing their shirt collars turned in to make V's at their
throats, wearing their caps—they wore caps because Lenin had worn caps—
with the visors turned backward, tilted upward at the nape of their necks.
Many of their mannerisms, pronunciations, and turns of speech had been
consciously copied from white Communists whom they had recently met.
While engaged in conversation, they stuck their thumbs in their suspenders or put their left hands into their shirt bosoms or hooked their thumbs
into their back pockets as they had seen Lenin or Stalin do in photographs.
Though they did not know it, they were naïvely practicing magic; they
thought that if they acted like the men who had overthrown the czar, then
surely they ought to be able to win their freedom in America.

In speaking they rolled their "r's" in Continental style, pronouncing
"party" as "parrrtee," stressing the last syllable, having picked up the habit
from white Communists. "Comrades" became "cumrrades," and "distribute," which they had known how to pronounce all their lives, was twisted
into "distrrribuuute," with the accent on the last instead of the second syllable, a mannerism which they copied from Polish Communist immigrants
who did not know how to pronounce the word. Many sensitive Negroes
agreed with the Communist program but refused to join their ranks because of the shabby quality of those Negroes whom the Communists had
already admitted to membership.

When speaking from the platform, the Negro Communists, eschewing
the traditional gestures of the Negro preacher—as though they did not possess the strength to develop their own style of Communist preaching—
stood straight, threw back their heads, brought the edge of the right palm
down hammerlike into the outstretched left palm in a series of jerky motions to pound their points home, a mannerism that characterized Lenin's
method of speaking. When they walked, their stride quickened; all the
peasant hesitancy of their speech vanished as their voices became clipped,
terse. In debate they interrupted their opponents in a tone of voice that was
an octave higher, and if their opponents raised their voices to be heard, the
Communists raised theirs still higher until shouts rang out over the park.
Hence, the only truth that prevailed was that which could be shouted and
quickly understood.

Their emotional certainty seemed buttressed by access to a fund of knowledge denied to ordinary men, but a day's observation of their activities was sufficient to reveal all their thought processes. An hour's listening disclosed the fanatical intolerance of minds sealed against new ideas, new facts, new feelings, new attitudes, new hints at ways to live. They denounced books they had never read, people they had never known, ideas they could never understand, and doctrines whose names they could not pronounce. Communism, instead of making them leap forward with fire in their hearts to become masters of ideas and life, had frozen them at an even lower level of ignorance than had been theirs before they met Communism.

When Hoover threatened to drive the bonus marchers from Washington, one Negro Communist speaker said:

"If he drives the bonus marchers out of Washington, the people will rise up and make a revolution!"

I went to him, determined to get at what he really meant.

"You know that even if the United States Army actually kills the bonus marchers, there'll be no revolution," I said.

"You don't know the indignation of the masses!" he exploded.

"But you don't seem to know what it takes to make a revolution," I explained. "Revolutions are rare occurrences."

"You underestimate the masses," he told me.

"No, I know the masses of Negroes very well," I said. "But I don't believe that a revolution is pending. Revolutions come through concrete historical processes . . . ."

"You're an intellectual," he said, smiling disdainfully.

A few days later, after Hoover had had the bonus marchers driven from Washington at the point of bayonets, I accosted him:

"What about that revolution you predicted if the bonus marchers were driven out?" I asked.

"The prerequisite conditions did not exist," he shrugged and muttered.

I left him, wondering why he felt it necessary to make so many ridiculous overstatements. I could not refute the general Communist analysis of the world; the only drawback was that their world was just too simple for belief. I liked their readiness to act, but they seemed lost in folly, wandering in a fantasy. For them there was no yesterday or tomorrow, only the living moment of today; their only task was to annihilate the enemy that confronted them in any manner possible.

At times their speeches, glowing with rebellion, were downright offensive to lowly, hungry Negroes. Once a Negro Communist speaker, inveighing against religion, said:

"There ain't no goddamn God! If there is, I hereby challenge Him to strike me dead!"

He paused dramatically before his vast black audience for God to act, but God declined. He then pulled out his watch.

"Maybe God didn't hear me!" he yelled. "I'll give Him two more minutes!" Then, with sarcasm: "Mister God, kill me!"

He waited, looking mockingly at his watch. The audience laughed uneasily.

"I'll tell you where to find God," the speaker went on in a hard, ranting voice. "When it rains at midnight, take your hat, turn it upside down on a floor in a dark room, and you'll have God!"

I had to admit that I had never heard atheism of so militant a nature; but the Communist speaker seemed to be amusing and frightening the people more than he was convincing them.

"If there is a God up there in that empty sky," the speaker roared on, "I'll reach up there and grab Him by His beard and jerk Him down here on this hungry earth and cut His throat!" He wagged his head. "Now, let God dare me!"

The audience was shocked into silence for a moment, then it yelled with delight. I shook my head and walked away. That was not the way to destroy people's outworn beliefs . . . They were acting like irresponsible children . . .

I was now convinced that they did not know the complex nature of Negro life, did not know how great was the task to which they had set themselves. They had rejected the state of things as they were, and that seemed to me to be the first step toward embracing a creative attitude toward life. I felt that it was not until one wanted the world to be different that one could look at the world with will and emotion. But these men had rejected what was before their eyes without quite knowing what they had rejected and why.

I felt that the Negro could not live a full, human life under the conditions imposed upon him by America; and I felt, too, that America, for different reasons, could not live a full, human life. It seemed to me, then, that if the Negro solved his problem, he would be solving infinitely more than his problem alone. I felt certain that the Negro could never solve his problem until the deeper problem of American civilization had been faced and solved. And because the Negro was the most cast-out of all the outcast people in America, I felt that no other group in America could tackle this problem of what our American lives meant so well as the Negro could.

But, as I listened to the Communist Negro speakers, I wondered if the Negro, blasted by three hundred years of oppression, could possibly cast off his fear and corruption and rise to the task. Could the Negro ever possess himself, learn to know what had happened to him in relation to the aspirations of Western society? It seemed to me that for the Negro to try to save himself he would have to forget himself and try to save a confused, materialistic nation from its own drift toward self-destruction. Could the Negro accomplish this miracle? Could he take up his bed and walk?

Election time was nearing and a Negro Republican precinct captain asked me to help him round up votes. I had no interest in the candidates, but I needed the money. I went from door to door with the precinct captain and discovered that the whole business was one long process of bribery, that people voted for three dollars, for the right to continue their illicit trade in sex or alcohol. On election day I went into the polling booth and drew the curtain behind me and unfolded my ballots. As I stood there the sordid implications of politics flashed through my mind. "Big Bill" Thompson headed the local Republican machine and I knew that he was using the Negro vote to control the city hall; in turn, he was engaged in vast

political deals of which the Negro voters, political innocents, had no notion. With my pencil I wrote in a determined scrawl across the face of the
ballots:

I PROTEST THIS FRAUD

I knew that my gesture was futile. But I wanted somebody to know that
out of that vast sea of ignorance in the Black Belt there was at least one
person who knew the game for what it was. I collected my ten dollars and
went home.

The depression deepened and I could not sell insurance to hungry
Negroes. I sold my watch and scouted for cheaper rooms; I found a rotting
building and rented an apartment in it. The place was dismal; plaster was
falling from the walls; the wooden stairs sagged. When my mother saw it,
she wept. I felt bleak. I had not done what I had come to the city to do.

One morning I rose and my mother told me that there was no food for
breakfast. I knew that the city had opened relief stations, but each time I
thought of going into one of them I burned with shame. I sat for hours,
fighting hunger, avoiding my mother's eyes. Then I rose, put on my hat
and coat, and went out. As I walked toward the Cook County Bureau of
Public Welfare to plead for bread, I knew that I had come to the end of
something.

1945

CHESTER B. HIMES

1909–1984

Born on July 29, 1909, in Jefferson City, Missouri, Chester B. Himes was the
youngest of three sons of schoolteachers. Himes spent his early years in several
places, including Mississippi. After graduating from high school in 1926, he sustained a serious back injury; a disability pension allowed him to enroll at Ohio State
University in Columbus, but after a single semester, Himes left the university, according to one source withdrawn for disciplinary reasons, according to another "depressed by the white environment." In any event, Himes entered the work force at
the bottom—as a bellhop and hustler—and soon launched a very different kind of
career. Arrested in 1928 for armed robbery, he was sentenced to twenty years in the
Ohio State Penitentiary. Like other celebrated black prisoners, among them Malcolm X, George Jackson, Etheridge Knight, and Eldridge Cleaver, Himes apparently changed course during his confinement and became an apprentice writer. In
fact, his first story, *Crazy in the Stir*, appeared in *Esquire* in 1934, while he was still
in prison. That same year, one of Himes's most widely read early stories, *To What
Red Hell?* was published, taking its cue from a 1930 prison fire that had killed 320
convicts. His 1955 novel, *Cast the First Stone*, was also based on his prison experience.

By the time of his release in 1936, Himes had published in various venues; in
addition to *Esquire*, his stories had appeared in *The Pittsburgh Courier* and *The
Afro-American*, among other newspapers and journals. Himes spent a brief period
on the West Coast, working in the shipyards of Los Angeles and San Francisco. His
first novels, *If He Hollers Let Him Go* (1945) and *Lonely Crusade* (1947), both take

their inspiration from these years. A failed marriage, unsuccessful love, racism, and underemployment all worked to drive him out of American society. In 1953, Himes left the United States for Europe. Until his death in 1984, he would make only brief trips back, usually to New York City.

Though in the shadow of Richard Wright, as were many black writers of the period, Himes was actually quite celebrated within French literary and intellectual circles, especially for his detective novels. The French translation of the first novel in his series, *For Love of Imabelle*, appeared in 1957, and in 1958 Himes won the Grand Prix Policier. Set in Harlem, the novels featured characters named Coffin Ed Johnson and Gravedigger Jones, after the tradition of hard-boiled heroes such as Dashiell Hammet's Sam Spade and Raymond Chandler's Philip Marlowe. Much of Himes's work, especially *If He Hollers*, with its depiction of the difficult circumstances of black life, owes a profound debt to Richard Wright. Himes's two autobiographies—*The Quality of Hurt* and *My Life of Absurdity*—were published in 1972 and 1976, respectively. Other work includes *Third Generation* (1954), *The Primitive* (1955), *Pinktoes* (1961), and *Cotton Comes to Harlem* (1965), later made into a successful film.

Perhaps among the least read of the postwar writers, Chester Himes, after twenty years of European living and certain material success, apparently remained American to the core, never quite working out his existential dilemma. In *My Life of Absurdity*, Himes writes: "I travelled through Europe trying desperately to find a life into which I would fit; and my determination stemmed from my desire to succeed without America. . . . I never found a place where I even began to fit, due in great part to my inability to learn any foreign language and my antagonism toward all white people, who, I thought, treated me as an inferior." A web of contradictions, Himes spent a good deal of his life among "all white people." As we might anticipate, his varied writings reflect the intense conflicts within Chester Himes himself.

Salute to the Passing

When Dick Small pushed through the service hall into the main dining room, he sensed an exasperation in the general mood of the diners with that surety of feeling which twenty years as headwaiter at the Park Manor Hotel had bestowed on him. The creased, careful smile adorning his brown face knotted with self reproach. He should have been there sooner.

His roving gaze searched quickly for flaws in the service. There was fat Mr. McLaughlin knuckling the table impatiently as he awaited—Dick was quite sure that it was broiled lobster that Mr. McLaughlin was so impatiently awaiting. And Mrs. Shipley was frowning with displeasure at the dirty dishes which claimed her elbow room as she endeavored to lean closer to her boon companion, Mrs. Hamilton, and impart in a theatrical whisper a choice morsel of spicy gossip—Dick had no doubt that it was both choice and spicy. When Mr. Lyons lifted his glass to take another sip of iced water, he found to his extreme annoyance that there was no more iced water to be sipped, and even from where he stood, Dick could see Mr. Lyons' forbearance abruptly desert him.

The white-jacketed colored waiters showed a passable alacrity, Dick observed without censor. But direction was lacking. The captain, heavy-footed and slow, plodded about in a stew of indecision.

Dick clapped his hands. "Fill those glasses for that deuce there," he directed the busboy who had sprung to his side. "Take an ashstand to the party at that center table. Clear up those ladies." He left the busboy spinning in his tracks; turned to the captain who came rushing over. "I'll take it over now, son. You slip into a white jacket and bring in Mr. McLaughlin's lobster."

His presence was established and the wrinkles of exasperation ironed smoothly out.

The captain nodded and flashed white teeth, relieved. He turned away, turned back. "Chief, Mr. Erskine has a party of six for six-thirty. I gave it to Pat. Here's the bill of fare." He gave Dick a scrawled note.

Dick pocketed the note and for an instant he stood quite still in the center of the room, head cocked to one side as if deferentially listening. A hum of cultured voices engaged in leisurely conversation; the gentle clatter of silver on fine china, the slight scrape of a chair, the tinkle of ice in glasses, the aroma of hot coffee and savory, well-cooked food, the sight of unhurried dining and hurried service, all blended into an atmosphere ineffably dear to his heart. For directing the service of this dining room in a commendable manner was the ultimate aim of his life. It was as much a part of him as the thin spot in his meticulously brushed hair or the habitual immaculateness of the tuxedoes which draped his slight, spright frame. He was one of the last of his kind, the black headwaiter, a passing American institution.

But the press of duty left no time for idle reflection. He went to Mr. Erskine's table and scanned the setup. After a moment's study, he leaned across the table and aligned a fork, smoothed an infinitesimal wrinkle from the linen, shifted the near candlestick just a wee bit to the left. Then he rocked back on his heels and allowed his eyes to smile. He was pleased.

He nodded commendation to Pat, tan and lanky, who was spooning ice cubes into the upturned glasses, and Pat acknowledged it with his roguish grin.

"Here's the bill of fare, Pat." His voice was quick and crisp. "Put your cocktails on ice and have everything prepared by a quarter after six."

Glancing at the wall clock he noticed that it was already nearly six. He stepped away, wondering detachedly at the cause for the early rush, circled an unoccupied table and came back, frowning slightly. "This is usually Mrs. Van Denter's table, Pat. Why did the captain decide to put that party of six here?"

"Cap called the desk, chief," Pat explained. "They said Mrs. Van Denter had gone into the country to spend a week with her sister."

"You know how contrary she is. Been that way for twenty years to my knowing, ever since her husband died and . . ." he caught himself and stopped abruptly, ashamed of himself. . . . "Put your reserved card on, Pat." A snap had come into his voice. "Always put your reserved card on first, then . . ."

The sight of Mrs. Van Denter coming through the entrance archway choked him. She made straight for her table, ploughing everyone aside who got in her way. This evening she looked slightly forbidding, her grayish, stoutish, sixtyish appearance looking rockier than ever and the tight seam of her mouth carrying an overload of obstinacy. At first glance he thought that she had had a Martini too many, but as she lumbered closer with her elephantine directness, he decided that it came from her disposition instead of her digestion.

Perhaps she and her sister had had a rift, he reflected, bowing to her with more than his customary deference. "How are you this evening, Mrs. Van Denter?" he smiled. After a brief pause he began an apology, "I am very sorry to have to change you, Mrs. Van Denter, but the captain was under the impression that you were in the country. . . ."

She brushed him aside and aimed her solid body for the table on which Pat had just placed the reserved sign. He turned quickly to follow her, his mouth momentarily slack. There was the hint of a race. But she won.

And for all of the iced glasses and party silver and crimped napkins and bowl of roses and engraved name cards at each plate, for all of the big black-lettered sign which read, Reserved, staring up into her face, she reached for the nearest chair, pulled it out and planted her plump body into it with sickening finality. Then she reached for an iced glass.

Dick placed a menu card before her and signaled Pat to take her order, his consternation under control now so that his actions registered no more than a natural desire to serve. He picked up the bowl of flowers and the reserved card and placed them on another table, then moved casually away in both thought and body.

At the third table he stopped for a moment to address the stately, white-haired lady seated there. "How do you do, Mrs. Hughes. And this is your sister, Mrs. Walpole, of Boston, I am sure.

"We're delighted to have you with us again, Mrs. Walpole. I remember quite well when you visited us before."

Mrs. Hughes smiled cordially and Mrs. Walpole said, "I've been here several times before."

"But I was referring to your last visit; it was in August three years ago."

"What a remarkable memory," Mrs. Walpole murmured.

Dick allowed himself a moment's complacence. Why have a memory if he couldn't share it? But when he moved away it carried him deeper into the past, when the black man was America's principal servant and the black headwaiter the pampered protégé of millionaires and royalty among his own people. Not that he had ever let it go to his head, he quickly amended. Not in his thirty years of service had he once gotten out of his place. The reflection brought a glow of pride. But it was quickly followed by the disturbing thought that now was an era of change. The black headwaiter was giving way to white hostesses, foreigners, to all sorts of people who claimed to be servants. He was saddened by the thought. Would there ever again be a black man as big as a black headwaiter? he asked himself. A black man who could serve a Senator's steak and have a fellow lodge member appointed to a position in Washington, who could stop a busy industrialist and save a Negro school. . . .

When he spoke again his voice was brusk. "Clear that table!" he ordered a busboy as if he alone was to blame for the change of things.

A party of seven at a center table demanded his personal attention and he was cheered again. "Good evening, Mr. and Mrs. Seedle," he greeted the elderly hosts, knowing that they would not consider the service sufficient until he made his appearance. "And how is this young gentleman?" he inquired of the seven-year-old smart aleck seated beside them.

"I'm all right, Dick," the boy replied, "but I'm no gentleman 'cause gramma just said so. . . ."

"Arnold!" Mrs. Seedle rebuked.

"Fill these glasses," Dick directed a busy waiter to hide his smile, then filled them himself before the startled waiter had a chance to protest.

He looked about for a busboy. Seeing none at hand, he hurried across the room, irritation lumping in his face.

"What's the matter with you, are you deaf?" he demanded, shaking the boy's shoulder.

"No sir, I—I—er—"

"Go get the salad tray and present it to that party of seven," he snapped, then hurried away in his loping gait to greet Mrs. Collar, eighty and cross, who hesitated undecidedly under the entrance archway.

"It's a rather nasty night, Mrs. Collar," he remarked by way of greeting, seating her in a corner nook. "It doesn't seem to be able to make up its mind whether to rain or sleet, but I feel that it will clear up by tomorrow."

Mrs. Collar looked up at him over the rim of her ancient spectacles. "That isn't any encouragement to me," she replied in her harsh, unconciliatory voice. "I'm going out *tonight*."

Confusion took the smoothness out of Dick's speech. "I—er, I wouldn't be surprised if it cleared up very shortly. It seems . . ."

"Well, make up your mind!" she snapped, scanning the menu.

He smiled deprecatingly, signaling to a waiter. "I'm afraid I'd make a poor weather-man."

"You should concentrate your efforts on the service," she advised sharply.

He turned away from her, reproached, and started kitchenward to recruit more waiters from the room service department. He just must have more waiters, the management should realize that. . . . Something about one of the waiters on duty halted him. He glanced down, glanced up again. "What kind of polish do you use, son?" he inquired disarmingly.

"Paste," the waiter replied, unthinkingly.

He let his gaze drop meaningly to the waiter's unshined shoes. "Try liquid next time, son," he suggested, passing on through the service hall into the kitchen.

Beyond the range, over by the elevator, where the room service was stationed, a waiter lounged indolently by a table and yelled at the closed elevator doors, "Knock-knock!"

Dick drew up quietly behind him, heard the slightly muffled reply from within the elevator, "Who's there?"

"Mr. Small!" Dick said crisply.

The waiter jumped. His hand flew up and knocked over a glass of water on the clean linen. The elevator doors popped open, emitting two other waiters in an impressive hurry.

"If you fellows don't care to work—" he began.

But they did care to work. He rushed them into the dining room. Following, he quickly scanned the sidestand, exploring for negligence. But the pitchers were filled and the butter was iced. The silver was neatly arranged in the drawers. A slight expression of commendation came into his smile. Busboys such as that would make good waiters some day.

Then his thoughts turned back to the guests. Without any question, he realized that these people were his life. They took up his time, his thoughts, his energy. He was interested in them, interested in their private lives and their individual prosperity. His most vital emotions derived coloring from theirs; when they were pleased, he was pleased, when they were hurt, he was hurt, when they failed or prospered in their respective endeavors it had a personal bearing on the course of his life. Each day, as he stood looking over them, he received some quality of character from them which instilled in him a certain dignity.

Now his gaze drifted slowly from face to face, reading the feelings and emotions of each with an uncanny perception. For a moment his cup was filled to overflowing. He felt a bond between himself and these people, the age-old bond between servant and master.

There were Tommy and Jackie Rightmire, the polo playing twins, he noticed with a glow of pride for their achievements. And several tables distant, he saw their sister dining with a Spanish count whom he had never been quite able to admire.

Then suddenly Mrs. Andrews came through the entrance archway and beat a hard-heeled, determined path straight toward the rear of the room where Mr. Andrews, her spouse, and a Mrs. Winnings, a comely divorcee, were dining together behind the slight screen of a rear column. Mrs. Andrews was older than her husband, and showed it, and reputedly was very jealous of his affections.

Knowing this, Dick's compelling thought was to avoid catastrophe, for catastrophe it would be, he sincerely felt, should she chance upon her husband's animated tête-à-tête. He headed her off just in time.

"Right this way, Mrs. Andrews," he began, pulling a chair from a conspicuously placed center table.

"No, no, not that," she refused with a gesture, "I want something remote, quiet. I'm expecting a friend." Her eyes dared him to think more than that which she had explicitly stated, which, he was fully cognizant, it was not his prerogative to do.

"Then this will be just the thing for you," he purred smoothly, seating her across the dining room from her husband with her back toward him and the column between them.

"Thank you, this will be just fine." She smiled, pleased, and he had the feeling of a golfer who has just scored a hole in one.

Strolling casually away, he noticed Mrs. Van Denter preparing to leave and went over to her table. "Was your dinner enjoyable, Madame?" he inquired, bowing again with slightly exaggerated deference.

Dinner, enjoyable or not, had not softened the stone of Mrs. Van Denter's face. "Dick," she snapped, "I find your obsequiousness a bit repugnant." Then she plodded smilelessly away.

He upbraided himself. That was twice in one day that he had drawn criticism. But there was no time to explore into the causes, for the table of two women needed clearing. He went in search of a busboy.

The boy whom he found was a greenhorn. Although it was his second day on the job he was still shy about approaching people and taking their plates. So he slipped up behind the nearer lady, a thin, overly made-up widow with a lashing voice, and reached from behind her for her plate. She had just leaned forward to whisper when she saw his stealthily reaching hand.

"Oh!" she gasped, her sharp mouth going slack like a fish's.

The boy went panicky, fearing that he had offended her. He snatched at the plate in a hurry to get away. But the thin lady jerked it away from him, spilling a bone to the table. By this time the boy was frightened. He grabbed again for the plate.

The lady twisted angrily around in her chair. "Let go!" she shrieked.

The boy released it and jumped backward, his nostrils flaring, his eyes white-rimmed in his black face.

"Always taking my plate before I'm finished!" the lady shrilled caustically.

The boy kept backing away from her and at a safe distance turned and hurried toward the kitchen doorway. Dick started after him, intending to school him in the manner of clearing tables, but by the time he reached the kitchen the boy was downstairs changing into his street clothes. He sent the captain down to bring him back, but he was too frightened to try again.

"Well, he wouldn't have made a waiter, anyway," Dick remarked, and added philosophically, "Good servants are born servants. Take my father; he was his master's butler. A field hand won't make a good servant. . . ." But noticing that a raised window was annoying a stag party of four in the rear corner, he broke off and hurried over to close it.

Afterwards he paused in a half-bow, inquiring solicitously, "Are you being taken care of, gentlemen?"

On closer observation he saw that they were all drunk and not gentlemen after all.

"That's a good looking tux, boy," one remarked. "Where'd you get it? Steal it?"

"No sir, I purchased it. . . ."

"What makes you black?" another cut in. A laugh spurted.

Dick's smile was constant. "God did, gentlemen," he said and moved away.

At a center table a high pressure voice was saying, "Just talked to the Governor. He said. . . ." Dick turned his glance obliquely and noticed a late-comer pull out a chair opposite a comely young matron. Why, of course, that was her husband, but she was the one who signed the checks, and who was the other woman he had seen him with the other day?

The sight of old Mr. Woodford standing in the entrance archway snapped his line of thought before he could recall and he hurried forward to meet him.

"And how are you this evening, Mr. Woodford, sir?" he greeted, then added without awaiting a reply, knowing there would be none, "Right this way, sir. I reserved your table for you."

He received Mr. Woodford's grudging nod and led the way rearward, head cocked and arms swinging, recalling reluctantly the time when Mr. Woodford had been genial and talkative and worth many millions. Since the stock crash he had been broke and now he was glum, with blood-shot eyes from drinking too much.

When he moved away his actions were slowed, groggy, as if he had taken a severe beating. The old order was passing, he told himself, suddenly realizing that in a very short time he would be beyond the sixty mark. Sixty was old for a waiter in a busy hotel. . . . He shook himself as if awakening from a bad dream, stepped forward with a brave show of energy.

Perhaps he wasn't looking, perhaps he could not see, but he bumped into a busboy with a loaded tray. China crashed on the tiled floor, silver rang. The sudden shatter shook the room. He patted the stooping boy on the shoulder, the unusual show of feeling leaving the boy slightly flustered, turned quickly away, head held high, refusing to notice the shattered crockery. By his refusal to notice it, he averted attention.

But by now the dinner rush was gradually subsiding. Dick was first made aware of it by the actions of his waiters. They had begun to move about with a languor which bespoke of liberal tips. He glanced at the clock. It was eight-thirty.

He released the first shift with the ironic suggestion, "Don't disappoint your money, boys."

Watching their happy departure, he was aware that before the hour passed they would be hanging over their favorite bar. A frown of disapproval crossed his face. Well, it was their business, but the first one that stepped into this dining room with the smell of liquor on his breath would be immediately discharged, he promised himself.

Then his attention was drawn to a drunken party at a center table. Overflow from the bar, no doubt. His frown deepened. The coarseness of their speech and actions spread a personal humiliation within him. He always pictured the guests as infallible criterions of gentility, and it hurt him to be disappointed.

Some one of the party made a risqué remark and everyone laughed. The nearby waiter smothered his laugh in a napkin.

Dick rushed over and chastened him with a severe voice. "Take that napkin from your face! Get some side towels and use them. And don't ever let me catch you using a napkin in that manner." His harshness was an outlet.

He moved toward the side windows, trying to stifle the buildup of emotion in his mind. The guests were always right, and a waiter was always impersonal in action and in thought, no matter what occurred—that was the one rigid rule in the waiters' code. But now it helped him but a very little. He decided that he must be tired.

George, tall and dark-skinned, passed him. He noticed that George needed new tuxedo trousers. He didn't say anything, for he knew also that George had a high-yellow woman who took most of his money. It wouldn't be long now before George would need another job.

But he thought no more about it for he had just noticed Mr. Spivat, half-owner of the hotel, dining alone at a wall table. He went over and spoke to him. "Nasty weather we're having, Mr. Spivat."

"Yes, it is, Dick," Mr. Spivat replied absently, scanning the late edition.

The window behind Mr. Spivat drew Dick's gaze. He looked out into the dark night. Park foliage across the street was a thick blackness, wet in the sleet and rain. On a distant summit, the Museum was a chiseled stone block in white light, hanging from the starless night by invisible strings. Street lights in the foreground showed a stone wall bordering the park, a strip of sidewalk, slushy pavement. A car turned the corner, its headlights stabbing into the darkness. The purr of a motor sounded faintly as it passed; the red tail light bobbed lingeringly into the bog of distant darkness. Dick stared into the void after it, feeling very tired. He thought of a chicken farm in the country where he could get off of his feet. But he knew that he would never be satisfied away from a dining room. With a vague, undefined regret, he thought of his son who was now a young doctor and not making anything at it. Nowadays colored boys didn't want to be servants, he reflected with his nearest approach to bitterness. Perhaps it was for the best, who knew? A father couldn't live his son's life. But to head a lineage of headwaiters—He sighed.

When he turned back, traces of an inner weariness showed in the edges of his smile, making it ragged. But his eyes were as sharp as ever. They lingered a moment on the slightly hobbling white-coated figure of Bishop. A little stooped was Bishop, a little paunched, a little gray, with a moon face and soiled eyes and rough skin of midnight blue. A good name, Bishop, a descriptive name, Dick thought with a half smile.

He noticed Bishop lurch once and followed him into the kitchen, overtaking him at the pantry. He spun him about and sniffed his breath, catching the scent of mints and a very faint odor of alcohol.

"You haven't been drinking again, have you, Bishop?" he asked sharply.

Bishop forced a laugh as if to dispel such an idea. "Nosuh, Chief. Been rubbin' my leg with rubbin' alcohol. That's what you smell. My neuritis[1] is troublin' me a lot."

Dick nodded sympathetically. "You need to watch your diet, Bishop," he advised. "Go home when you serve that dessert."

Bishop bobbed his head, rubbing his hands together. "Thank you, Chief."

Following him back into the dining room, Dick noticed that it was Mr. Spivat whom he was serving. He frowned, trying to recall whether he or the captain had assigned him to Mr. Spivat. He certainly wouldn't have if he had known how badly he was limping for Mr. Spivat was convinced, anyway, that the majority of Negro waiters drank too much. And Bishop did appear drunk.

It all happened so quickly that Dick couldn't move.

Bishop's right leg buckled as he placed the cream pitcher. He jacknifed forward on his knee. Cream flew in a thin sheet over the front of Mr. Spivat's dark blue suit.

Mr. Spivat blanched, then ripened like a russet apple. He got slowly to his feet, controlling himself.

Dick was there in three swift strides, applying a cold damp towel to Mr. Spivat's suit. "Clean up, George," he directed the other waiter, trying to avert the drama which he felt engulfing them. "Sorry, Mr. Spivat, sir.

---

1. Painful nerve inflammation.

Sorry, sir. The boy's got a bad case of neuritis; it's very bad during this nasty weather. I'll lay him off until it gets better."

But cold damp towels could not help Mr. Spivat's suit, nor expressions of sorrow allay his quiet rage. "Dick, see that this man gets his money, and if I ever see him in this hotel again I'll fire the whole bunch of you. I have no tolerance for a drunken waiter."

Dick motioned Bishop from the dining room and followed behind. He had the checker make out a requisition for Bishop's pay and had another waiter take it out to the *maître de hôtel's* office. It was for an even thirteen dollars.

Bishop stood at a respectful distance, his shoulders drooping, his whole body sagging, wordless and very sad. Dick could not meet the dog-like plea of his eyes. He knew that Bishop had liked serving Mr. Spivat. He recalled how Bishop and Mr. Spivat used to talk baseball during the season.

After a time Bishop said irrelevantly, a slight protest in his voice, "I got seven kids."

Dick looked down at Bishop's feet. Big feet they were, with broken arches from shouldering heavy trays on adamant concrete. Big and flat and knotty. He felt in his pockets, discovered a twenty-dollar bill. He pressed it into Bishop's hand.

"I wasn't drunk, Chief. Nosuh, I swear I wasn't," Bishop said.

Dick wanted to believe that, but he couldn't. Bishop as a rule didn't eat mints; he didn't like sweets of any kind. But mints would help kill the odor of whiskey on his breath. He sighed. He knew that Bishop would drink. There was very little of the likes and dislikes and habits of all his waiters, of their family affairs and personal lives, that he did not know.

"Accidents will happen, son," he said. "Yours just cost you your job. Try not to let it happen again. If there's anything I can do for you, let me know. Anything reasonable. And even if it isn't reasonable, come and let me say so." He stood quite still for a moment, his face weary.

Then he shook it all from his mind. He blinked his eyes clear of the picture of a dejected black face, donned his creased, careful smile and pushed through the service hall into the dining room, his head cocked to one side as if deferentially listening.

It required a special effort.

1937

ANN PETRY

b. 1911

Students of her fiction see the blighted landscape of the inner city and the false fronts of rural New England as the boundaries of Ann Petry's art, but such a schema quickly breaks down on closer inspection of her rich corpus, which includes three novels (*The Street*, 1946; *Country Place*, 1947; and *The Narrows*, 1953), one collection of short stories (*Miss Muriel and Other Stories*, 1971), and four children's books.

Ann Petry was born on October 12, 1911, in Old Saybrook, Connecticut, to a middle-class family. Her father was a pharmacist and owned a drugstore in town. Her mother was licensed to practice chiropody in 1915. Convinced that she could write when she created a slogan for a perfume advertisement while still in high school, Petry began her writing career in earnest following a brief stint as a pharmacist in her hometown. In the late 1930s, she served a kind of apprenticeship as a journalist for two Harlem newspapers, *The Amsterdam News* and *The People's Voice*. This experience rubbed her face in the gritty world of Harlem's poverty, violence, crime, and economic exploitation, which worked its way into her early fiction and gave it its compelling edge. Her first published short story, *On Saturday the Siren Sounds at Noon*, appeared in *Crisis* in 1943. The editor at *Crisis* found *Like a Winding Sheet*, printed here, similarly engrossing and published it in 1945. Collected in Martha Foley's *Best American Stories of 1946, Like a Winding Sheet* brought Petry national attention and a Houghton Mifflin Literary Fellowship Award to complete her best-known novel, *The Street* (1946), the first by a black woman to sell more than a million copies.

Inspired by a newspaper story of an apartment house superintendent who taught a young boy to steal letters from mailboxes, *The Street* aimed, according to Petry, to "show how simply and easily the environment can change the course of a person's life." It is precisely for treating the power of a corrosive urban environment on Lutie Johnson that *The Street* has linked Petry, in the minds of many critics, to Richard Wright.

While there are obvious and valid comparisons to be made between *The Street* and *Native Son*, exaggerating the links between Wright and Petry obscures perhaps the most salient and critical distinction between them: the sexual politics of race and the racial politics of gender. As critic Calvin Hernton observes, until *The Street* "no one had made a thesis of the debilitating mores of economic, racial and sexual violence let loose against black women in their new urban ghetto environment." Unlike *Native Son*, which projects its anxieties about black masculinity onto a phallicized Bigger Thomas, *The Street* focuses on the thwarted and naive efforts of a young black woman to secure a decent living for herself and her son. Petry closely documents the effects of the ghetto on a black woman and shows a critical sensitivity to woman as spectacle, as a body to be looked at and made the object of male sexual desire and exploitation. This particular achievement of *The Street* must be set against the perception in *Native Son* that the objectification, rape, and dismemberment of women are preconditions of Bigger's rising manhood.

In her second novel, *Country Place* (1947), which has been likened to Sherwood Anderson's *Winesburg, Ohio*, and Sinclair Lewis's *Main Street*, Petry shifts her focus from Harlem to Monmouth, Connecticut. Petry wrote *Country Place*, as she explained to critic James O'Brien, "because I happened to have been in a small town in Connecticut during a hurricane—I decided to write about that violent, devastating storm and its effect on the town and the people who lived there." But such a description hardly begins to capture the novel's intricate weaving of strands of class conflict, bloodlines, and social respectability. Petry reworks many of these same themes in *The Narrows*, a novel about the tabooed and ultimately tragic relationship between a black man and a white woman. Petry does not skirt the history of sexual and racial politics that weighs on their relationship, a history that makes her cry of rape and his subsequent lynching inevitable. In both *Country Place* and *The Narrows*, Petry turned to what critics have inadequately termed non-Negro or New England subject matter. While some see this shift as evidence of artistic maturation beyond the urban realism of *The Street*, others regard both these New England novels as less powerful than *The Street*.

Petry joins the urban and rural scenes in *Miss Muriel and Other Stories*. Prominent in this diverse collection are those stories in which Petry experiments with the point of view of precocious introspective child narrators. Set variously in Harlem, small-town New York, and Connecticut, these stories show Petry's deft manipulation of psychology. Petry's interest in children as fictional subjects has extended to the publication of four children's books, including *Harriet Tubman: Conductor on the Underground Railway* (1955) and *Tituba of Salem Village* (1964). In a *Hornbook* essay on children's literature, published in 1965, Petry described her driving motivations as writer: "Over and over again, I have said: These are people.... Look at them and remember them. Remember for what a long, long time black people have been in this country, have been part of America; a sturdy, indestructible, wonderful part of America, woven into its heart and into its soul."

Like a Winding Sheet [1]

He had planned to get up before Mae did and surprise her by fixing breakfast. Instead he went back to sleep and she got out of bed so quietly he didn't know she wasn't there beside him until he woke up and heard the queer soft gurgle of water running out of the sink in the bathroom.

He knew he ought to get up but instead he put his arms across his forehead to shut the afternoon sunlight out of his eyes, pulled his legs up close to his body, testing them to see if the ache was still in them.

Mae had finished in the bathroom. He could tell because she never closed the door when she was in there and now the sweet smell of talcum powder was drifting down the hall and into the bedroom. Then he heard her coming down the hall.

"Hi, babe," she said affectionately.

"Hum," he grunted, and moved his arms away from his head, opened one eye.

"It's a nice morning."

"Yeah," he rolled over and the sheet twisted around him, outlining his thighs, his chest. "You mean afternoon, don't ya?"

Mae looked at the twisted sheet and giggled. "Looks like a winding sheet," she said. "A shroud—." Laughter tangled with her words and she had to pause for a moment before she could continue. "You look like a huckleberry—in a winding sheet—"

"That's no way to talk. Early in the day like this," he protested.

He looked at his arms silhouetted against the white of the sheets. They were inky black by contrast and he had to smile in spite of himself and he lay there smiling and savouring the sweet sound of Mae's giggling.

"Early?" She pointed a finger at the alarm clock on the table near the bed, and giggled again. "It's almost four o'clock. And if you don't spring up out of there you're going to be late again."

"What do you mean 'again'?"

"Twice last week. Three times the week before. And once the week before and—"

"I can't get used to sleeping in the day time," he said fretfully. He pushed his legs out from under the covers experimentally. Some of the ache had gone out of them but they weren't really rested yet. "It's too light for good sleeping. And all that standing beats the hell out of my legs."

---

1. A sheet in which a corpse is wrapped.

"After two years you oughtta be used to it," Mae said.

He watched her as she fixed her hair, powdered her face, slipping into a pair of blue denim overalls. She moved quickly and yet she didn't seem to hurry.

"You look like you'd had plenty of sleep," he said lazily. He had to get up but he kept putting the moment off, not wanting to move, yet he didn't dare let his legs go completely limp because if he did he'd go back to sleep. It was getting later and later but the thought of putting his weight on his legs kept him lying there.

When he finally got up he had to hurry and he gulped his breakfast so fast that he wondered if his stomach could possibly use food thrown at it at such a rate of speed. He was still wondering about it as he and Mae were putting their coats on in the hall.

Mae paused to look at the calendar. "It's the thirteenth," she said. Then a faint excitement in her voice. "Why it's Friday the thirteenth." She had one arm in her coat sleeve and she held it there while she stared at the calendar. "I oughtta stay home," she said. "I shouldn't go outta the house."

"Aw don't be a fool," he said. "Today's payday. And payday is a good luck day everywhere, any way you look at it." And as she stood hesitating he said, "Aw, come on."

And he was late for work again because they spent fifteen minutes arguing before he could convince her she ought to go to work just the same. He had to talk persuasively, urging her gently and it took time. But he couldn't bring himself to talk to her roughly or threaten to strike her like a lot of men might have done. He wasn't made that way.

So when he reached the plant he was late and he had to wait to punch the time clock because the day shift workers were streaming out in long lines, in groups and bunches that impeded his progress.

Even now just starting his work-day his legs ached. He had to force himself to struggle past the out-going workers, punch the time clock, and get the little cart he pushed around all night because he kept toying with the idea of going home and getting back in bed.

He pushed the cart out on the concrete floor, thinking that if this was his plant he'd make a lot of changes in it. There were too many standing up jobs for one thing. He'd figure out some way most of 'em could be done sitting down and he'd put a lot more benches around. And this job he had—this job that forced him to walk ten hours a night, pushing this little cart, well, he'd turn it into a sittin-down job. One of those little trucks they used around railroad stations would be good for a job like this. Guys sat on a seat and the thing moved easily, taking up little room and turning in hardly any space at all, like on a dime.

He pushed the cart near the foreman. He never could remember to refer to her as the forelady even in his mind. It was funny to have a woman for a boss in a plant like this one.

She was sore about something. He could tell by the way her face was red and her eyes were half shut until they were slits. Probably been out late and didn't get enough sleep. He avoided looking at her and hurried a little, head down, as he passed her though he couldn't resist stealing a glance at her out of the corner of his eyes. He saw the edge of the light colored slacks she wore and the tip end of a big tan shoe.

"Hey, Johnson!" the woman said.

The machines had started full blast. The whirr and the grinding made the building shake, made it impossible to hear conversations. The men and women at the machines talked to each other but looking at them from just a little distance away they appeared to be simply moving their lips because you couldn't hear what they were saying. Yet the woman's voice cut across the machine sounds—harsh, angry.

He turned his head slowly. "Good Evenin', Mrs. Scott," he said and waited.

"You're late again."

"That's right. My legs were bothering me."

The woman's face grew redder, angrier looking. "Half this shift comes in late," she said. "And you're the worst one of all. You're always late. Whatsa matter with ya?"

"It's my legs," he said. "Somehow they don't ever get rested. I don't seem to get used to sleeping days. And I just can't get started."

"Excuses. You guys always got excuses," her anger grew and spread. "Every guy comes in here late always has an excuse. His wife's sick or his grandmother died or somebody in the family had to go to the hospital," she paused, drew a deep breath. "And the niggers are the worse. I don't care what's wrong with your legs. You get in here on time. I'm sick of you niggers—"

"You got the right to get mad," he interrupted softly. "You got the right to cuss me four ways to Sunday but I ain't letting nobody call me a nigger."

He stepped closer to her. His fists were doubled. His lips were drawn back in a thin narrow line. A vein in his forehead stood out swollen, thick.

And the woman backed away from him, not hurriedly but slowly—two, three steps back.

"Aw, forget it," she said. "I didn't mean nothing by it. It slipped out. It was an accident." The red of her face deepened until the small blood vessels in her cheeks were purple. "Go on and get to work," she urged. And she took three more slow backward steps.

He stood motionless for a moment and then turned away from the red lipstick on her mouth made him remember that the foreman was a woman. And he couldn't bring himself to hit a woman. He felt a curious tingling in his fingers and he looked down at his hands. They were clenched tight, hard, ready to smash some of those small purple veins in her face.

He pushed the cart ahead of him, walking slowly. When he turned his head, she was staring in his direction, mopping her forehead with a dark blue handkerchief. Their eyes met and then they both looked away.

He didn't glance in her direction again but moved past the long work benches, carefully collecting the finished parts, going slowly and steadily up and down, back and forth the length of the building and as he walked he forced himself to swallow his anger, get rid of it.

And he succeeded so that he was able to think about what had happened without getting upset about it. An hour went by but the tension stayed in his hands. They were clenched and knotted on the handles of the cart as though ready to aim a blow.

And he thought he should have hit her anyway, smacked her hard in the face, felt the soft flesh of her face give under the hardness of his hands. He tried to make his hands relax by offering them a description of what it would have been like to strike her because he had the queer feeling that his hands were not exactly a part of him any more—they had developed a separate life of their own over which he had no control. So he dwelt on the pleasure his hands would have felt—both of them cracking at her, first one and then the other. If he had done that his hands would have felt good now—relaxed, rested.

And he decided that even if he'd lost his job for it he should have let her have it and it would have been a long time, maybe the rest of her life before she called anybody else a nigger.

The only trouble was he couldn't hit a woman. A woman couldn't hit back the same way a man did. But it would have been a deeply satisfying thing to have cracked her narrow lips wide open with just one blow, beautifully timed and with all his weight in back of it. That way he would have gotten rid of all the energy and tension his anger had created in him. He kept remembering how his heart had started pumping blood so fast he had felt it tingle even in the tips of his fingers.

With the approach of night fatigue nibbled at him. The corners of his mouth dropped, the frown between his eyes deepened, his shoulders sagged; but his hands stayed tight and tense. As the hours dragged by he noticed that the women workers had started to snap and snarl at each other. He couldn't hear what they said because of the sound of the machines but he could see the quick lip movements that sent words tumbling from the sides of their mouths. They gestured irritably with their hands and scowled as their mouths moved.

Their violent jerky motions told him that it was getting close on to quitting time but somehow he felt that the night still stretched ahead of him, composed of endless hours of steady walking on his aching legs. When the whistle finally blew he went on pushing the cart, unable to believe that it had sounded. The whirring of the machines died away to a murmur and he knew then that he'd really heard the whistle. He stood still for a moment filled with a relief that made him sigh.

Then he moved briskly, putting the cart in the store room, hurrying to take his place in the line forming before the paymaster. That was another thing he'd change, he thought. He'd have the pay envelopes handed to the people right at their benches so there wouldn't be ten or fifteen minutes lost waiting for the pay. He always got home about fifteen minutes late on payday. They did it better in the plant where Mae worked, brought the money right to them at their benches.

He stuck his pay envelope in his pants' pocket and followed the line of workers heading for the subway in a slow moving stream. He glanced up at the sky. It was a nice night, the sky looked packed full to running over with stars. And he thought if he and Mae would go right to bed when they got home from work they'd catch a few hours of darkness for sleeping. But they never did. They fooled around—cooking and eating and listening to the radio and he always stayed in a big chair in the living room and went almost but not quite to sleep and when they finally got to bed it was five or six in the morning and daylight was already seeping around the edges of the sky.

He walked slowly, putting off the moment when he would have to plunge into the crowd hurrying toward the subway. It was a long ride to Harlem and tonight the thought of it appalled him. He paused outside an all-night restaurant to kill time, so that some of the first rush of workers would be gone when he reached the subway.

The lights in the restaurant were brilliant, enticing. There was life and motion inside. And as he looked through the window he thought that everything within range of his eyes gleamed—the long imitation marble counter, the tall stools, the white porcelain topped tables and especially the big metal coffee urn right near the window. Steam issued from its top and a gas flame flickered under it—a lively, dancing, blue flame.

A lot of the workers from his shift—men and women—were lining up near the coffee urn. He watched them walk to the porcelain topped tables carrying steaming cups of coffee and he saw that just the smell of the coffee lessened the fatigue lines in their faces. After the first sip their faces softened, they smiled, they began to talk and laugh.

On a sudden impulse he shoved the door open and joined the line in front of the coffee urn. The line moved slowly. And as he stood there the smell of the coffee, the sound of the laughter and of the voices, helped dull the sharp ache in his legs.

He didn't pay any attention to the girl who was serving the coffee at the urn. He kept looking at the cups in the hands of the men who had been ahead of him. Each time a man stepped out of the line with one of the thick white cups the fragrant steam got in his nostrils. He saw that they walked carefully so as not to spill a single drop. There was a froth of bubbles at the top of each cup and he thought about how he would let the bubbles break against his lips before he actually took a big deep swallow.

Then it was his turn. "A cup of coffee," he said, just as he had heard the others say.

The girl looked past him, put her hands up to her head and gently lifted her hair away from the back of her neck, tossing her head back a little. "No more coffee for awhile," she said.

He wasn't certain he'd heard her correctly and he said, "What?" blankly. "No more coffee for awhile," she repeated.

There was silence behind him and then uneasy movement. He thought someone would say something, ask why or protest, but there was only silence and then a faint shuffling sound as though the men standing behind him had simultaneously shifted their weight from one foot to the other.

He looked at her without saying anything. He felt his hands begin to tingle and the tingling went all the way down to his finger tips so that he glanced down at them. They were clenched tight, hard, into fists. Then he looked at the girl again. What he wanted to do was hit her so hard that the scarlet lipstick on her mouth would smear and spread over her nose, her chin, out toward her cheeks; so hard that she would never toss her head again and refuse a man a cup of coffee because he was black.

He estimated the distance across the counter and reached forward, balancing his weight on the balls of his feet, ready to let the blow go. And then his hands fell back down to his sides because he forced himself to lower them, to unclench them and make them dangle loose. The effort took his breath away because his hands fought against him. But he couldn't hit her.

He couldn't even now bring himself to hit a woman, not even this one, who had refused him a cup of coffee with a toss of her head. He kept seeing the gesture with which she had lifted the length of her blond hair from the back of her neck as expressive of her contempt for him.

When he went out the door he didn't look back. If he had he would have seen the flickering blue flame under the shiny coffee urn being extinguished. The line of men who had stood behind him lingered a moment to watch the people drinking coffee at the tables and then they left just as he had without having had the coffee they wanted so badly. The girl behind the counter poured water in the urn and swabbed it out and as she waited for the water to run out she lifted her hair gently from the back of her neck and tossed her head before she began making a fresh lot of coffee.

But he walked away without a backward look, his head down, his hands in his pockets, raging at himself and whatever it was inside of him that had forced him to stand quiet and still when he wanted to strike out.

The subway was crowded and he had to stand. He tried grasping an overhead strap and his hands were too tense to grip it. So he moved near the train door and stood there swaying back and forth with the rocking of the train. The roar of the train beat inside his head, making it ache and throb, and the pain in his legs clawed up into his groin so that he seemed to be bursting with pain and he told himself that it was due to all that anger-born energy that had piled up in him and not been used and so it had spread through him like a poison—from his feet and legs all the way up to his head.

Mae was in the house before he was. He knew she was home before he put the key in the door of the apartment. The radio was going. She had it tuned up loud and she was singing along with it.

"Hello, Babe," she called out as soon as he opened the door.

He tried to say "hello" and it came out half a grunt and half sigh.

"You sure sound cheerful," she said.

She was in the bedroom and he went and leaned against the door jamb. The denim overalls she wore to work were carefully draped over the back of a chair by the bed. She was standing in front of the dresser, tying the sash of a yellow housecoat around her waist and chewing gum vigorously as she admired her reflection in the mirror over the dresser.

"What sa matter?" she said. "You get bawled out by the boss or somep'n?"

"Just tired," he said slowly. "For God's sake do you have to crack that gum like that?"

"You don't have to lissen to me," she said complacently. She patted a curl in place near the side of her head and then lifted her hair away from the back of her neck, ducking her head forward and then back.

He winced away from the gesture. "What you got to be always fooling with your hair for?" he protested.

"Say, what's the matter with you, anyway?" she turned away from the mirror to face him, put her hands on her hips. "You ain't been in the house two minutes and you're picking on me."

He didn't answer her because her eyes were angry and he didn't want to quarrel with her. They'd been married too long and got along too well and so he walked all the way into the room and sat down in the chair by the bed and stretched his legs out in front of him, putting his weight on the heels of his shoes, leaning way back in the chair, not saying anything.

"Lissen," she said sharply. "I've got to wear those overalls again tomorrow. You're going to get them all wrinkled up leaning against them like that."

He didn't move. He was too tired and his legs were throbbing now that he had sat down. Besides the overalls were already wrinkled and dirty, he thought. They couldn't help but be for she'd worn them all week. He leaned further back in the chair.

"Come on, get up," she ordered.

"Oh, what the hell," he said wearily and got up from the chair. "I'd just as soon live in a subway. There'd be just as much place to sit down."

He saw that her sense of humor was struggling with her anger. But her sense of humor won because she giggled.

"Aw, come on and eat," she said. There was a coaxing note in her voice. "You're nothing but a old hungry nigger trying to act tough and—" she paused to giggle and then continued, "You—"

He had always found her giggling pleasant and deliberately said things that might amuse her and then waited, listening for the delicate sound to emerge from her throat. This time he didn't even hear the giggle. He didn't let her finish what she was saying. She was standing close to him and that funny tingling started in his finger tips, went fast up his arms and sent his fist shooting straight for her face.

There was the smacking sound of soft flesh being struck by a hard object and it wasn't until she screamed that he realized he had hit her in the mouth—so hard that the dark red lipstick had blurred and spread over her full lips, reaching up toward the tip of her nose, down toward her chin, out toward her cheeks.

The knowledge that he had struck her seeped through him slowly and he was appalled but he couldn't drag his hands away from her face. He kept striking her and he thought with horror that something inside him was holding him, binding him to this act, wrapping and twisting about him so that he had to continue it. He had lost all control over his hands. And he groped for a phrase, a word, something to describe what this thing was like that was happening to him and he thought it was like being enmeshed in a winding sheet—that was it—like a winding sheet. And even as the thought formed in his mind his hands reached for her face again and yet again.

1945

From The Street

Chapter I

[THE APARTMENT]

There was a cold November wind blowing through 116th Street.[1] It rattled the tops of garbage cans, sucked window shades out through the top of

---

1. In Harlem.

opened windows and set them flapping back against the windows; and it drove most of the people off the street in the block between Seventh and Eighth Avenues except for a few hurried pedestrians who bent double in an effort to offer the least possible exposed surface to its violent assault.

It found every scrap of paper along the street—theater throwaways, announcements of dances and lodge meetings, the heavy waxed paper that loaves of bread had been wrapped in, the thinner waxed paper that had enclosed sandwiches, old envelopes, newspapers. Fingering its way along the curb, the wind set the bits of paper to dancing high in the air, so that a barrage of paper swirled into the faces of the people on the street. It even took time to rush into doorways and areaways and find chicken bones and pork-chop bones and pushed them along the curb.

It did everything it could to discourage the people walking along the street. It found all the dirt and dust and grime on the sidewalk and lifted it up so that the dirt got into their noses, making it difficult to breathe; the dust got into their eyes and blinded them; and the grit stung their skins. It wrapped newspaper around their feet entangling them until the people cursed deep in their throats, stamped their feet, kicked at the paper. The wind blew it back again and again until they were forced to stoop and dislodge the paper with their hands. And then the wind grabbed their hats, pried their scarves from around their necks, stuck its fingers inside their coat collars, blew their coats away from their bodies.

The wind lifted Lutie Johnson's hair away from the back of her neck so that she felt suddenly naked and bald, for her hair had been resting softly and warmly against her skin. She shivered as the cold fingers of the wind touched the back of her neck, explored the sides of her head. It even blew her eyelashes away from her eyes so that her eyeballs were bathed in a rush of coldness and she had to blink in order to read the words on the sign swaying back and forth over her head.

Each time she thought she had the sign in focus, the wind pushed it away from her so that she wasn't certain whether it said three rooms or two rooms. If it was three, why, she would go in and ask to see it, but if it said two—why, there wasn't any point. Even with the wind twisting the sign away from her, she could see that it had been there for a long time because its original coat of white paint was streaked with rust where years of rain and snow had finally eaten the paint off down to the metal and the metal had slowly rusted, making a dark red stain like blood.

It was three rooms. The wind held it still for an instant in front of her and then swooped it away until it was standing at an impossible angle on the rod that suspended it from the building. She read it rapidly. Three rooms, steam heat, parquet floors, respectable tenants. Reasonable.

She looked at the outside of the building. Parquet floors here meant that the wood was so old and so discolored no amount of varnish or shellac would conceal the scars and the old scraped places, the years of dragging furniture across the floors, the hammer blows of time and children and drunks and dirty, slovenly women. Steam heat meant a rattling, clanging noise in radiators early in the morning and then a hissing that went on all day.

Respectable tenants in these houses where colored people were allowed to live included anyone who could pay the rent, so some of them would be drunk and loud-mouthed and quarrelsome; given to fits of depression when they would curse and cry violently, given to fits of equally violent elation. And, she thought, because the walls would be flimsy, why, the good people, the bad people, the children, the dogs, and the godawful smells would all be wrapped up together in one big package—the package that was called respectable tenants.

The wind pried at the red skullcap on her head, and as though angered because it couldn't tear it loose from its firm anchorage of bobby pins, the wind blew a great cloud of dust and ashes and bits of paper into her face, her eyes, her nose. It smacked against her ears as though it were giving her a final, exasperated blow as proof of its displeasure in not being able to make her move on.

Lutie braced her body against the wind's attack determined to finish thinking about the apartment before she went in to look at it. Reasonable— now that could mean almost anything. On Eighth Avenue it meant tene- ments—ghastly places not fit for humans. On St. Nicholas Avenue it meant high rents for small apartments; and on Seventh Avenue it meant great big apartments where you had to take in roomers in order to pay the rent. On this street it could mean almost anything.

She turned and faced the wind in order to estimate the street. The build- ings were old with small slit-like windows, which meant the rooms were small and dark. In a street running in this direction there wouldn't be any sunlight in the apartments. Not ever. It would be hot as hell in summer and cold in winter. "Reasonable" here in this dark, crowded street ought to be about twenty-eight dollars, provided it was on a top floor.

The hallways here would be dark and narrow. Then she shrugged her shoulders, for getting an apartment where she and Bub would be alone was more important than dark hallways. The thing that really mattered was get- ting away from Pop and his raddled[2] women, and anything was better than that. Dark hallways, dirty stairs, even roaches on the walls. Anything. Any- thing. Anything.

Anything? Well, almost anything. So she turned toward the entrance of the building and as she turned, she heard someone clear his or her throat. It was so distinct—done as it was on two notes, the first one high and then the grunting expiration of breath on a lower note—that it came to her ears quite clearly under the sound of the wind rattling the garbage cans and slapping at the curtains. It was as though someone had said "hello," and she looked up at the window over her head.

There was a faint light somewhere in the room she was looking into and the enormous bulk of a woman was silhouetted against the light. She half- closed her eyes in order to see better. The woman was very black, she had a bandanna knotted tightly around her head, and Lutie saw, with some sur- prise, that the window was open. She began to wonder how the woman could sit by an open window on a cold, windy night like this one. And she didn't have on a coat, but a kind of loose-looking cotton dress—or at least it must be cotton, she thought, for it had a clumsy look—bulky and wrinkled.

"Nice little place, dearie. Just ring the Super's bell and he'll show it to you."

---

2. Worn out, broken down.

The woman's voice was rich. Pleasant. Yet the longer Lutie looked at her, the less she liked her. It wasn't that the woman had been sitting there all along staring at her, reading her thoughts, pushing her way into her very mind, for that was merely annoying. But it was understandable. She probably didn't have anything else to do; perhaps she was sick and the only pleasure she got out of life was in watching what went on in the street outside her window. It wasn't that. It was the woman's eyes. They were as still and as malignant as the eyes of a snake. She could see them quite plainly—flat eyes that stared at her—wandering over her body, inspecting and appraising her from head to foot.

"Just ring the Super's bell, dearie," the woman repeated.

Lutie turned toward the entrance of the building without answering, thinking about the woman's eyes. She pushed the door open and walked inside and stood there nodding her head. The hall was dark. The low-wattage bulb in the ceiling shed just enough light so that you wouldn't actually fall over—well, a piano that someone had carelessly left at the foot of the stairs; so that you could see the outlines of—oh, possibly an elephant if it were dragged in from the street by some enterprising tenant.

However, if you dropped a penny, she thought, you'd have to get down on your hands and knees and scrabble around on the cracked tile floor before you could ever hope to find it. And she was wrong about being able to see an elephant or a piano because the hallway really wasn't wide enough to admit either one. The stairs went up steeply—dark high narrow steps. She stared at them fascinated. Going up stairs like those you ought to find a newer and more intricate—a much-involved and perfected kind of hell at the top—the very top.

She leaned over to look at the names on the mail boxes. Henry Lincoln Johnson lived here, too, just as he did in all the other houses she'd looked at. Either he or his blood brother. The Johnsons and the Jacksons were mighty prolific. Then she grinned, thinking who am I to talk, for I, too, belong to that great tribe, that mighty mighty tribe of Johnsons. The bells revealed that the Johnsons had roomers—Smith, Roach, Anderson— holy smoke! even Rosenberg. Most of the names were inked in over the mail boxes in scrawling handwriting—the letters were big and bold on some of them. Others were written in pencil; some printed in uneven scraggling letters where names had been scratched out and other names substituted.

There were only two apartments on the first floor. And if the Super didn't live in the basement, why, he would live on the first floor. There it was printed over One A. One A must be the darkest apartment, the smallest, most unrentable apartment, and the landlord would feel mighty proud that he'd given the Super a first-floor apartment.

She stood there thinking that it was really a pity they couldn't somehow manage to rent the halls, too. Single beds. No. Old army cots would do. It would bring in so much more money. If she were a landlord, she'd rent out the hallways. It would make it so much more entertaining for the tenants. Mr. Jones and wife could have cots number one and two; Jackson and girl friend could occupy number three. And Rinaldi, who drove a cab nights, could sublet the one occupied by Jackson and girl friend.

She would fill up all the cots—row after row of them. And when the tenants who had apartments came in late at night, they would have the added pleasure of checking up on the occupants. Jackson not home yet but girl friend lying in the cot alone—all curled up. A second look, because the lack of light wouldn't show all the details, would reveal—ye gods, why, what's Rinaldi doing home at night! Doggone if he ain't tucked up cozily in Jackson's cot with Jackson's girl friend. No wonder she looked contented. And the tenants who had apartments would sit on the stairs just as though the hall were a theater and the performance about to start—they'd sit there waiting until Jackson came home to see what he'd do when he found Rinaldi tucked into his cot with his girl friend. Rinaldi might explain that he thought the cot was his for sleeping and if the cot had blankets on it did not he, too, sleep under blankets; and if the cot had girl friend on it, why should not he, too, sleep with girl friend?

Instead of laughing, she found herself sighing. Then it occurred to her that if there were only two apartments on the first floor and the Super occupied one of them, then the occupant of the other apartment would be the lady with the snake's eyes. She looked at the names on the mail boxes. Yes. A Mrs. Hedges lived in One B. The name was printed on the card—a very professional-looking card. Obviously an extraordinary woman with her bandanna on her head and her sweet, sweet voice. Perhaps she was a snake charmer and she sat in her window in order to charm away at the snakes, the wolves, the foxes, the bears that prowled and loped and crawled on their bellies through the jungle of 116th Street.

Lutie reached out and rang the Super's bell. It made a shrill sound that echoed and re-echoed inside the apartment and came back out into the hall. Immediately a dog started a furious barking that came closer and closer as he ran toward the door of the apartment. Then the weight of his body landed against the door and she drew back as he threw himself against the door. Again and again until the door began to shiver from the impact of his weight. There was the horrid sound of his nose snuffing up air, trying to get her scent. And then his weight hurled against the door again. She retreated toward the street door, pausing there with her hand on the knob. Then she heard heavy footsteps, the sound of a man's voice threatening the dog, and she walked back toward the apartment.

She knew instantly by his faded blue overalls that the man who opened the door was the Super. The hot fetid air from the apartment in back of him came out into the hall. She could hear the faint sound of steam hissing in the radiators. Then the dog tried to plunge past the man and the man kicked the dog back into the apartment. Kicked him in the side until the dog cringed away from him with its tail between its legs. She heard the dog whine deep in its throat and then the murmur of a woman's voice—a whispering voice talking to the dog.

"I came to see about the apartment—the three-room apartment that's vacant," she said.

"It's on the top floor. You wanta look at it?"

The light in the hall was dim. Dim like that light in Mrs. Hedges' apartment. She pulled her coat around her a little tighter. It's this bad light, she thought. Somehow the man's eyes were worse than the eyes of the woman sitting in the window. And she told herself that it was because she was so tired; that was the reason she was seeing things, building up pretty pictures in people's eyes.

He was a tall, gaunt man and he towered in the doorway, looking at her. It isn't the bad light, she thought. It isn't my imagination. For after his first quick furtive glance, his eyes had filled with a hunger so urgent that she was instantly afraid of him and afraid to show her fear.

But the apartment—did she want the apartment? Not in this house where he was super; not in this house where Mrs. Hedges lived. No. She didn't want to see the apartment—the dark, dirty three rooms called an apartment. Then she thought of where she lived now. Those seven rooms where Pop lived with Lil, his girl friend. A place filled with roomers. A place spilling over with Lil.

There seemed to be no part of it that wasn't full of Lil. She was always swallowing coffee in the kitchen; trailing through all seven rooms in housecoats that didn't quite meet across her lush, loose bosom; drinking beer in tall glasses and leaving the glasses in the kitchen sink so the foam dried in a crust around the rim—the dark red of her lipstick like an accent mark on the crust; lounging on the wide bed she shared with Pop and only God knows who else; drinking gin with the roomers until late at night.

And what was far more terrifying giving Bub a drink on the sly; getting Bub to light her cigarettes for her. Bub at eight with smoke curling out of his mouth.

Only last night Lutie slapped him so hard that Lil cringed away from her dismayed; her housecoat slipping even farther away from the fat curve of her breasts. "Jesus!" she said. "That's enough to make him deaf. What's the matter with you?"

But did she want to look at the apartment? Night after night she'd come home from work and gone out right after supper to peer up at the signs in front of the apartment houses in the neighborhood, looking for a place just big enough for her and Bub. A place where the rent was low enough so that she wouldn't come home from work some night to find a long sheet of white paper stuck under the door; "These premises must be vacated by ——" better known as an eviction notice. Get out in five days or be tossed out. Stand by and watch your furniture pile up on the sidewalk. If you could call those broken beds, wornout springs, old chairs with the stuffing crawling out from under, chipped porcelain-topped kitchen table, flimsy kitchen chairs with broken rungs—if you could call those things furniture. That was an important point—now could you call fire-cracked china from the five-and-dime, and red-handled knives and forks and spoons that were bent and coming apart, could you really call those things furniture?

"Yes," she said firmly. "I want to look at the apartment."

"I'll get a flashlight," he said and went back into his apartment, closing the door behind him so that it made a soft, sucking sound. He said something, but she couldn't hear what it was. The whispering voice inside the apartment stopped and the dog was suddenly quiet.

Then he was back at the door, closing it behind him so it made the same soft, sucking sound. He had a long black flashlight in his hand. And she went up the stairs ahead of him thinking that the rod of its length was almost as black as his hands. The flashlight was a shiny black—smooth and gleaming faintly as the light lay along its length. Whereas the hand that held it was flesh—dull, scarred, worn flesh—no smoothness there. The knuckles were knobs that stood out under the skin, pulled out from hauling ashes, shoveling coal.

But not apparently from using a mop or a broom, for, as she went up and up the steep flight of stairs, she saw that they were filthy, with wastepaper, cigarette butts, the discarded wrappings from packages of snuff, pink ticket stubs from the movie houses. On the landings there were empty gin and whiskey bottles.

She stopped looking at the stairs, stopped peering into the corners of the long hallways, for it was cold, and she began walking faster trying to keep warm. As they completed a flight of stairs and turned to walk up another hall, and then started climbing another flight of stairs, she was aware that the cold increased. The farther up they went, the colder it got. And in summer she supposed it would get hotter and hotter as you went up until when you reached the top floor your breath would be cut off completely.

The halls were so narrow that she could reach out and touch them on either side without having to stretch her arms any distance. When they reached the fourth floor, she thought, instead of her reaching out for the walls, the walls were reaching out for her—bending and swaying toward her in an effort to envelop her. The Super's footsteps behind her were slow, even, steady. She walked a little faster and apparently without hurrying, without even increasing his pace, he was exactly the same distance behind her. In fact his heavy footsteps were a little nearer than before.

She began to wonder how it was that she had gone up the stairs first, why was she leading the way? It was all wrong. He was the one who knew the place, the one who lived here. He should have gone up first. How had he got her to go up the stairs in front of him? She wanted to turn around and see the expression on his face, but she knew if she turned on the stairs like this, her face would be on a level with his; and she wouldn't want to be that close to him.

She didn't need to turn around, anyway; he was staring at her back, her legs, her thighs. She could feel his eyes traveling over her—estimating her, summing her up, wondering about her. As she climbed up the last flight of stairs, she was aware that the skin on her back was crawling with fear. Fear of what? she asked herself. Fear of him, fear of the dark, of the smells in the halls, the high steep stairs, of yourself? She didn't know, and even as she admitted that she didn't know, she felt sweat start pouring from her armpits, dampening her forehead, breaking out in beads on her nose.

The apartment was in the back of the house. The Super fished another flashlight from his pocket which he handed to her before he bent over to unlock the door very quietly. And she thought, everything he does, he does quietly.

She played the beam of the flashlight on the walls. The rooms were small. There was no window in the bedroom. At least she supposed it was the bedroom. She walked over to look at it, and then went inside for a better look. There wasn't a window—just an air shaft and a narrow one at that. She looked around the room, thinking that by the time there was a bed and a chest of drawers in it there'd be barely space enough to walk around in. At that she'd probably bump her knees every time she went past the corner of the bed. She tried to visualize how the room would look and began to wonder why she had already decided to take this room for herself.

It might be better to give it to Bub, let him have a real bedroom to himself for once. No, that wouldn't do. He would swelter in this room in summer. It would be better to have him sleep on the couch in the living room, at least he'd get some air, for there was a window out there, though it wasn't a very big one. She looked out into the living room, trying again to see the window, to see just how much air would come through, how much light there would be for Bub to study by when he came home from school, to determine, too, the amount of air that would reach into the room at night when the window was open, and he was sleeping curled up on the studio couch.

The Super was standing in the middle of the living room. Waiting for her. It wasn't anything that she had to wonder about or figure out. It wasn't by any stretch of the imagination something she had conjured up out of thin air. It was a simple fact. He was waiting for her. She knew it just as she knew she was standing there in that small room. He was holding his flashlight so the beam fell down at his feet. It turned him into a figure of neverending tallness. And his silent waiting and his appearance of incredible height appalled her.

With the light at his feet like that, he looked as though his head must end somewhere in the ceiling. He simply went up and up into darkness. And he radiated such desire for her that she could feel it. She told herself she was a fool, an idiot, drunk on fear, on fatigue and gnawing worry. Even while she thought it, the hot, choking awfulness of his desire for her pinioned her there so that she couldn't move. It was an aching yearning that filled the apartment, pushed against the walls, plucked at her arms.

She forced herself to start walking toward the kitchen. As she went past him, it seemed to her that he actually did reach one long arm out toward her, his body swaying so that its exaggerated length almost brushed against her. She really couldn't be certain of it, she decided, and resolutely turned the beam of her flashlight on the kitchen walls.

It isn't possible to read people's minds, she argued. Now the Super was probably not even thinking about her when he was standing there like that. He probably wanted to get back downstairs to read his paper. Don't kid yourself, she thought, he probably can't read, or if he can, he probably doesn't spend any time at it. Well—listen to the radio. That was it, he probably wanted to hear his favorite program and she had thought he was filled with the desire to leap upon her. She was as bad as Granny. Which just went on to prove you couldn't be brought up by someone like Granny without absorbing a lot of nonsense that would spring at you out of nowhere, so to speak, and when you least expected it. All those tales about things that people sensed before they actually happened. Tales that had been handed down and down and down until, if you tried to trace them back, you'd end up God knows where—probably Africa. And Granny had them all at the tip of her tongue.

Yet would wanting to hear a radio program make a man look quite like that? Impatiently she forced herself to inspect the kitchen; holding the light on first one wall, then another. It was no better and no worse than she had anticipated. The sink was battered; and the gas stove was a little rusted. The faint smell of gas that hovered about it suggested a slow, incurable leak somewhere in its connections.

Peering into the bathroom, she saw that the fixtures were old-fashioned and deeply chipped. She thought Methuselah himself might well have taken baths in the tub. Certainly it looked ancient enough, though he'd have had to stick his beard out in the hall while he washed himself, for the place was far too small for a man with a full-grown beard to turn around in. She presumed because there was no window that the vent pipe would serve as a source of nice, fresh, clean air.

One thing about it the rent wouldn't be very much. It couldn't be for a place like this. Tiny hall. Bathroom on the right, kitchen straight ahead; living room to the left of the hall and you had to go through the living room to get to the bedroom. The whole apartment would fit very neatly into just one good-sized room.

She was conscious that all the little rooms smelt exactly alike. It was a mixture that contained the faint persistent odor of gas, of old walls, dusty plaster, and over it all the heavy, sour smell of garbage—a smell that seeped through the dumb-waiter shaft. She started humming under her breath, not realizing she was doing it. It was an old song that Granny used to sing. "Ain't no restin' place for a sinner like me. Like me. Like me." It had a nice recurrent rhythm. "Like me. Like me." The humming increased in volume as she stood there thinking about the apartment.

There was a queer, muffled sound from the Super in the living room. It startled her so she nearly dropped the flashlight. "What was that?" she said sharply, thinking, My God, suppose I'd dropped it, suppose I'd been left standing here in the dark of this little room and he'd turned out his light. Suppose he'd started walking toward me, nearer and nearer in the dark. And I could only hear his footsteps, couldn't see him, but could hear him coming closer until I started reaching out in the dark trying to keep him away from me, trying to keep him from touching me—and then—then my hands found him right in front of me— At the thought she gripped the flashlight so tightly that the long beam of light from it started wavering and dancing over the walls so that the shadows moved—shadow from the light fixture overhead, shadow from the tub, shadow from the very doorway itself—shifting, moving back and forth.

"I cleared my throat," the Super said. His voice had a choked, unnatural sound as though something had gone wrong with his breathing.

She walked out into the hall, not looking at him; opened the door of the apartment and stepping over the threshold, still not looking at him, said, "I've finished looking."

He came out and turned the key in the lock. He kept his back turned toward her so that she couldn't have seen the expression on his face even if she'd looked at him. The lock clicked into place, smoothly. Quietly. She stood there not moving, waiting for him to start down the hall toward the stairs, thinking, Never, so help me, will he walk down those stairs in back of me.

When he didn't move, she said, "You go first." Then he made a slight motion toward the stairs with his flashlight indicating that she was to precede him. She shook her head very firmly.

"Think you'll take it?" he asked.

"I don't know yet. I'll think about it going down."

When he finally started down the hall, it seemed to her that he had stood there beside her for days, weeks, months, willing her to go down the stairs first. She followed him, thinking, It wasn't my imagination when I got that feeling at the sight of him standing there in the living room; otherwise, why did he have to go through all that rigamarole of my going down the stairs ahead of him? Like going through the motions of a dance; you first; no, you first; but you see, you'll spoil the pattern if you don't go first; but I won't go first, you go first; but no, it'll spoil the—

She was aware that they'd come up the stairs much faster than they were going down. Was she going to take the apartment? The price wouldn't be too high from the looks of it and by being careful she and Bub could manage—by being very, very careful. White paint would fix the inside of it up; not exactly fix it up, but keep it from being too gloomy, shove the darkness back a little.

Then she thought, Layers and layers of paint won't fix that apartment. It would always smell; finger marks and old stains would come through the paint; the very smell of the wood itself would eventually win out over the paint. Scrubbing wouldn't help any. Then there were these dark, narrow halls, the long flights of stairs, the Super himself, that woman on the first floor.

Or she could go on living with Pop. And Lil. Bub would learn to like the taste of gin, would learn to smoke, would learn in fact a lot of other things that Lil could teach him—things that Lil would think it amusing to teach him. Bub at eight could get a liberal education from Lil, for she was home all day and Bub got home from school a little after three.

You've got a choice a yard wide and ten miles long. You can sit down and twiddle your thumbs while your kid gets a free education from your father's blowsy girl friend. Or you can take this apartment. The tall gentleman who is the superintendent is supposed to rent apartments, fire the furnace, sweep the halls, and that's as far as he's supposed to go. If he tries to include making love to the female tenants, why, this is New York City in the year 1944, and as yet there's no grass growing in the streets and the police force still functions. Certainly you can holler loud enough so that if the gentleman has some kind of dark designs on you and tries to carry them out, a cop will eventually rescue you. That's that.

As for the lady with the snake eyes, you're supposed to be renting the top-floor apartment and if she went with the apartment the sign out in front would say so. Three rooms and snake charmer for respectable tenant. No extra charge for the snake charmer. Seeing as the sign didn't say so, it stood to reason if the snake charmer tried to move in, she could take steps—whatever the hell that meant.

Her high-heeled shoes made a clicking noise as she went down the stairs, and she thought, Yes, take steps like these. It was all very well to reason lightheartedly like that; to kid herself along—there was no explaining away the instinctive, immediate fear she had felt when she first saw the Super. Granny would have said, "Nothin' but evil, child. Some folks so full of it you can feel it comin' at you—oozin' right out of their skins."

She didn't believe things like that and yet, looking at his tall, gaunt figure going down that last flight of stairs ahead of her, she half-expected to see horns sprouting from behind his ears; she wouldn't have been greatly surprised if, in place of one of the heavy work shoes on his feet, there had been a cloven hoof that twitched and jumped as he walked so slowly down the stairs.

Outside the door of his apartment, he stopped and turned toward her.

"What's the rent?" she asked, not looking at him, but looking past him at the One A printed on the door of his apartment. The gold letters were filled with tiny cracks, and she thought that in a few more years they wouldn't be distinguishable from the dark brown of the door itself. She hoped the rent would be so high she couldn't possibly take it.

"Twenty-nine fifty."

He wants me to take it, she thought. He wants it so badly that he's bursting with it. She didn't have to look at him to know it; she could feel him willing it. What difference does it make to him? Yet it was of such obvious importance that if she hesitated just a little longer, he'd be trembling. No, she decided, not that apartment. Then she thought Bub would look cute learning to drink gin at eight.

"I'll take it," she said grimly.

"You wanta leave a deposit?" he asked.

She nodded, and he opened his door, standing aside to let her go past him. There was a dim light burning in the small hall inside and she saw that the hall led into a living room. She didn't wait for an invitation, but walked on into the living room. The dog had been lying near the radio that stood under a window at the far side of the room. He got up when he saw her, walking toward her with his head down, his tail between his legs; walking as though he were drawn toward her irresistibly, even though he knew that at any moment he would be forced to stop. Though he was a police dog, his hair had such a worn, rusty look that he resembled a wolf more than a dog. She saw that he was so thin, his great haunches and the small bones of his ribs were sharply outlined against his skin. As he got nearer to her, he got excited and she could hear his breathing.

"Lie down," the Super said.

The dog moved back to the window, shrinking and walking in such a way that she thought if he were human he'd walk backward in order to see and be able to dodge any unexpected blow. He lay down calmly enough and looked at her, but he couldn't control the twitching of his nose; he looked, too, at the Super as though he were wondering if he could possibly cross the room and get over to her without being seen.

The Super sat down in front of an old office desk, found a receipt pad, picked up a fountain pen and, carefully placing a blotter in front of him, turned toward her. "Name?" he asked.

She swallowed an impulse to laugh. There was something so solemn about the way he'd seated himself, grasping the pen firmly, moving the pad in front of him to exactly the right angle, opening a big ledger book whose pages were filled with line after line of heavily inked writing that she thought he's acting like a big businessman about to transact a major deal.

"Mrs. Lutie Johnson. Present address 2370 Seventh Avenue." Opening her pocketbook she took out a ten-dollar bill and handed it to him. Ten whole dollars that it had taken a good many weeks to save. By the time she had moved in here and paid the balance which would be due on the rent, her savings would have disappeared. But it would be worth it to be living in a place of her own.

He wrote with a painful slowness, concentrating on each letter, having difficulty with the numbers twenty-three seventy. He crossed it out and bit his lip. "What was that number?" he asked.

"Twenty-three seventy," she repeated, thinking perhaps it would be simpler to write it down for him. At the rate he was going, it would take him all of fifteen minutes to write ten dollars and then figure out the difference between ten dollars and twenty-nine dollars which would in this case constitute that innocuous looking phrase, "the balance due." She shouldn't be making fun of him; very likely he had taught himself to read and write after spending a couple of years in grammar school where he undoubtedly didn't learn anything. He looked to be in his fifties, but it was hard to tell.

It irritated her to stand there and watch him go through the slow, painful process of forming the letters. She wanted to get out of the place, to get back to Pop's house, plan the packing, get hold of a moving man. She looked around the room idly. The floor was uncarpeted—a terrible-looking floor. Rough and splintered. There was a sofa against the long wall; its upholstery marked by a greasy line along the back. All the people who had sat on it from the time it was new until the time it had passed through so many hands it finally ended up here must have ground their heads along the back of it.

Next to the sofa there was an overstuffed chair and she drew her breath in sharply as she looked at it, for there was a woman sitting in it, and she had thought that she and the dog and the Super were the only occupants of the room. How could anyone sit in a chair and melt into it like that? As she looked, the shapeless small dark woman in the chair got up and bowed to her without speaking.

Lutie nodded her head in acknowledgment of the bow, thinking, That must be the woman I heard whispering. The woman sat down in the chair again. Melting into it. Because the dark brown dress she wore was almost the exact shade of the dark brown of the upholstery and because the overstuffed chair swallowed her up until she was scarcely distinguishable from the chair itself. Because, too, of a shrinking withdrawal in her way of sitting as though she were trying to take up the least possible amount of space. So that after bowing to her Lutie completely forgot the woman was in the room, while she went on studying its furnishings.

No pictures, no rugs, no newspapers, no magazines, nothing to suggest anyone had ever tried to make it look homelike. Not quite true, for there was a canary huddled in an ornate birdcage in the corner. Looking at it, she thought, Everything in the room shrinks: the dog, the woman, even the canary, for it had only one eye open as it perched on one leg. Opposite the sofa an overornate table shone with varnish. It was a very large table with intricately carved claw feet and looking at it she thought, That's the kind of big ugly furniture white women love to give to their maids. She turned to look at the shapeless little woman because she was almost certain the table was hers.

The woman must have been looking at her, for when Lutie turned the woman smiled; a toothless smile that lingered while she looked from Lutie to the table.

"When you want to move in?" the Super asked, holding out the receipt.

"This is Tuesday—do you think you could have the place ready by Friday?"

"Easy," he said. "Some special color you want it painted?"

"White. Make all the rooms white," she said, studying the receipt. Yes, he had it figured out correctly—balance due, nineteen fifty. He had crossed out his first attempt at the figures. Evidently nines were hard for him to make. And his name was William Jones. A perfectly ordinary name. A highly suitable name for a superintendent. Nice and normal. Easy to remember. Easy to spell. Only the name didn't fit him. For he was obviously unusual, extraordinary, abnormal. Everything about him was the exact opposite of his name. He was standing up now looking at her, eating her up with his eyes.

She took a final look around the room. The whispering woman seemed to be holding her breath; the dog was dying with the desire to growl or whine, for his throat was working. The canary, too, ought to be animated with some desperate emotion, she thought, but he had gone quietly to sleep. Then she forced herself to look directly at the Super. A long hard look, malignant, steady, continued. Thinking, That'll fix you, Mister William Jones, but, of course, if it was only my imagination upstairs, it isn't fair to look at you like this. But just in case some dark leftover instinct warned me of what was on your mind—just in case it made me know you were snuffing on my trail, slathering, slobbering after me like some dark hound of hell seeking me out, tonguing along in back of me, this look, my fine feathered friend, should give you much food for thought.

She closed her pocketbook with a sharp, clicking final sound that made the Super's eyes shift suddenly to the ceiling as though seeking out some pattern in the cracked plaster. The dog's ears straightened into sharp points; the canary opened one eye and the whispering woman almost showed her gums again, for her mouth curved as though she were about to smile.

Lutie walked quickly out of the apartment, pushed the street door open and shivered as the cold air touched her. It had been hot in the Super's apartment, and she paused a second to push her coat collar tight around her neck in an effort to make a barrier against the wind howling in the street outside. Now that she had this apartment, she was just one step farther up on the ladder of success. With the apartment Bub would be standing a better chance, for he'd be away from Lil.

Inside the building the dog let out a high shrill yelp. Immediately she headed for the street, thinking he must have kicked it again. She paused for a moment at the corner of the building, bracing herself for the full blast of the wind that would hit her head-on when she turned the corner.

"Get fixed up, dearie?" Mrs. Hedges' rich voice asked from the street-floor window.

She nodded at the bandannaed head in the window and flung herself into the wind, welcoming its attack, aware as she walked along that the woman's hard flat eyes were measuring her progress up the street.

1946

ROBERT HAYDEN

1913–1982

Born Asa Bundy Sheffey on August 4, 1913, in Detroit, Michigan, Robert Hayden grew up in a slum neighborhood called Paradise Valley, which he would later memorialize in *Elegies for Paradise Valley* (1978). Asa and Gladys Ruth Finn Sheffey separated soon after his birth, and their child became the foster son of neighbors Sue Ellen Westerfield and William Hayden. As a teenager, Hayden was embroiled in an ongoing family drama that shuttled him emotionally between the Haydens and his mother, who lived next door. Actually, Ruth Sheffey moved in with the Haydens for a time, as the two women and the son were often allied against the father. At other times, this triangle of desire and antagonism pitted the Haydens and Robert against his mother. This complicated fabric of intimate relations helped shape the sensitive personality of the boy, who also suffered from a severe sight impairment that kept him from participating in sports and games but did not prevent his becoming an avid reader. Hayden as a poet would take full advantage of that reading, whose richness is translated into the body of his work. Perhaps his most significant achievement was the idea that "black experience" illuminated the human predicament, as he, not unlike Melvin Tolson, adapted modernist notions of technical precision and polish to the historical context of African American life.

In spite of the poverty and strife in which he grew up, Hayden's foster parents provided him with whatever advantages they could. He graduated from Detroit Northern High School in 1932 and, on a scholarship arranged by the Hayden family's caseworker, matriculated at Detroit City College, later renamed Wayne State University. During his undergraduate years, Hayden acted in a Langston Hughes play, which led to his meeting the celebrated writer and showing him some early poems. Hughes pronounced them "derivative." Between 1936 and 1938, Hayden worked with Detroit's Federal Writers' Project, conducting research in local black history and folklore.

In 1940 Hayden published *Heart-Shape in the Dust*, his first book of poems, and married concert pianist and aspiring composer Erma Morris. *Heart-Shape in the Dust* deals with subjects of protest, as in *These Are My People*, which takes up the story of the Scottsboro Boys. Other poems from this volume include *Gabriel*, about the nineteenth-century slave insurrectionist Gabriel Prosser, and *Bacchanale*, which is written in the rhythms of a folk song. He enrolled in the graduate program in English literature at the University of Michigan in 1942; that year his and Erma's only child, Maia, was born. While at Michigan, he studied with visiting professor W. H. Auden; Hayden would later recall this encounter as a "strategic experience" in his life, as Auden showed him his poetic strengths and weaknesses "in ways no one else before had done." Though Hayden was already a student of the craft, having admired the poetry of Harlem Renaissance writers Hughes, Countee Cullen, and Jean Toomer as well as that of Elinor Wiley, Edna St. Vincent Millay, Sara

Teasdale, Carl Sandburg, and Hart Crane, Auden would lead the apprentice poet to find his own voice and to explore his feelings. Hayden continued to write through graduate school and twice received the Hopwood Prize for student poetry. He took a master's degree in English in 1944 and stayed at Michigan for two years as a teaching fellow, the first black member of the English department.

Hayden's second book, *Black Spear*, appeared in 1942; and though still the work of an apprentice, it, along with *Heart-Shape in the Dust*, shows Hayden's passionate, lifelong interest in African American history as well as his taste for radical politics. Critics have concluded that the major stylistic influence on *Black Spear* is Stephen Vincent Benét's Civil War epic *John Brown's Body* (1928). If, as one critic suggests, Hayden's narrator in *Black Spear* was calling for a poet to sing the "black-skinned epic, epic with the black spear," that volume represents one of the first appearances of Hayden as poet-historiographer and especially as poet-historiographer of the African sojourn in the New World. *Middle Passage*, among Hayden's best-known works, was first published in the journal *Phylon* in 1945. Characterized by multiple voices and a dialogue between narrative and lyric, the poem offers Hayden's version of a rebellion aboard the slave ship *Amistad*, focusing especially on the legendary African mutineer Cinque. Along with *Runagate Runagate* and *Frederick Douglass, Middle Passage* is one of three major history poems by Hayden from the 1940s.

In 1946 Hayden accepted a professorship in English literature at Fisk University in Nashville, where he would remain for more than twenty years. At Fisk he met writer and head librarian Arna Bontemps; together they edited the anthology *Poetry of the Negro* (1949). With another Fisk colleague, art curator Myron O'Higgins, Hayden published a small poetry collection entitled *The Lion and the Archer* (1948), which included *Homage to the Empress of the Blues*, Hayden's paean to blues singer Bessie Smith.

While Hayden published consistently across the decades, including *Figure of Time* in the 1950s, the 1960s brought him both international recognition and controversy. First issued by Dutch publisher Paul Bremen, *Ballad of Remembrance* (1962) was thematically arranged around an assortment of topics, from black history and Mexico to human quest and autobiographical issues. *Ballad* won the grand prize for poetry at the First World Festival of Negro Arts at Dakar, Senegal, West Africa, in 1966; an American version of the book came out that year as *Selected Poems*.

But in 1966, too, the Black Writers' Conference was convened on the Fisk campus. Hayden's art—subtle, intellectual, firmly situated in the academy—was not what the young black nationalists had in mind, mainly because it did not promote an aesthetic that furthered the cause of black revolution, and they did not hold back from saying so. Gwendolyn Brooks's work also came in for such criticism. Though Brooks's poetry did eventually take a different turn, Hayden refused to be pressured. Four years later, after returning to the University of Michigan as a professor of English, Hayden explored the 1966 event in *Words in the Mourning Time*. Several poems in *Mourning* deal explicitly with the idea of liberation—*Soledad; The Dream*; and *El Hajj Malik El-Shabazz*, a tribute to Malcolm X. *The Night Blooming Cereus* (1972) was seen by some as Hayden's retreat from black history into a world of private symbolism; others felt it showed a successful coexistence of Hayden the symbolist with Hayden the historicist. After publishing *Angle of Ascent: New and Selected Poems* in 1975, Hayden was appointed consultant in poetry to the Library of Congress in 1976, the first black American artist to receive that honor. At work on a new collection, he died of a heart ailment in Ann Arbor, in February 1982.

Nearly anywhere that one turns in the Hayden canon, one is struck by the elegant concision of line and contour, by sentences honed by a "hard precision of thought," to quote Ezra Pound, and by a vision of human possibility that bet its whole hand on the redemptive occasions of the future. It is difficult to believe that the sixties radicals could have mistaken this beat, for example, that evokes the shade of Frederick Douglass:

> When it is finally ours, this freedom, this liberty, this beautiful
> and terrible thing, needful to man as air,
> usable as earth . . .
> this man, superb in love and logic, this man
> shall be remembered.

Perhaps we could say, with a good deal of justification, that these lines are not unfitting for Hayden himself.

The Diver

Sank through easeful
azure. Flower
creatures flashed and
shimmered there—
lost images   5
fadingly remembered.
Swiftly descended
into canyon of cold
nightgreen emptiness.
Freefalling, weightless   10
as in dreams of
wingless flight,
plunged through infra-
space and came to
the dead ship,   15
carcass that swarmed with
voracious life.
Angelfish, their
lively blue and
yellow prised from   20
darkness by the
flashlight's beam,
thronged her portholes.
Moss of bryozoans [1]
blurred, obscured her   25
metal. Snappers,
gold groupers explored her,
fearless of bubbling
manfish. I entered
the wreck, awed by her silence,   30
feeling more keenly
the iron cold.

1. Small aquatic animals.

With flashlight probing
fogs of water
saw the sad slow   35
dance of gilded
chairs, the ectoplasmic[2]
swirl of garments,
drowned instruments
of buoyancy,   40
drunken shoes. Then
livid gesturings,
eldritch[3] hide and
seek of laughing
faces. I yearned to   45
find those hidden
ones, to fling aside
the mask and call to them,
yield to rapturous
whisperings, have   50
done with self and
every dinning[4]
vain complexity.
Yet in languid
frenzy strove, as   55
one freezing fights off
sleep desiring sleep;
strove against the
cancelling arms that
suddenly surrounded   60
me, fled the numbing
kisses that I craved.
Reflex of life-wish?
Respirator's brittle
belling? Swam from   65
the ship somehow;
somehow began the
measured rise.

                                                                          1962

Homage to the Empress of the Blues[1]

Because there was a man somewhere in a candystripe silk shirt,
gracile[2] and dangerous as a jaguar and because a woman moaned
for him in sixty-watt gloom and mourned him Faithless Love
Twotiming Love Oh Love Oh Careless Aggravating Love,

She came out on the stage in yards of pearls, emerging like   5
a favorite scenic view, flashed her golden smile and sang.

2. I.e., having to do with the materialization of   1. I.e., Bessie Smith (1894–1937), American blues
spirits and movement of objects without contact.   singer.
3. Ghostly.   2. Slender.
4. Loud.

Because grey laths[3] began somewhere to show from underneath
torn hurdygurdy[4] lithographs of dollfaced heaven;
and because there were those who feared alarming fists of snow
on the door and those who feared the riot-squad of statistics,   10

She came out on the stage in ostrich feathers, beaded satin,
and shone that smile on us and sang.

1962

Middle Passage[1]

I

Jesús, Estrella, Esperanza, Mercy:[2]

Sails flashing to the wind like weapons,
sharks following the moans the fever and the dying;
horror the corposant and compass rose.[3]

Middle Passage: 5
          voyage through death
                    to life upon these shores.

"10 April 1800—
Blacks rebellious. Crew uneasy. Our linguist says
their moaning is a prayer for death,   10
ours and their own. Some try to starve themselves.
Lost three this morning leaped with crazy laughter
to the waiting sharks, sang as they went under."

Desire, Adventure, Tartar, Ann:

Standing to America, bringing home   15
black gold, black ivory, black seed.

> *Deep in the festering hold thy father lies,*
> *of his bones New England pews are made,*
> *those are altar lights that were his eyes.*[4]

Jesus   Saviour   Pilot   Me   20
Over   Life's   Tempestuous   Sea[5]

We pray that Thou wilt grant, O Lord,
safe passage to our vessels bringing
heathen souls unto Thy chastening.

---

3. Strips of wood or metal used as supports in building.
4. Barrel organ or similar musical instrument played by turning a crank.
1. The journey across the Atlantic from Africa to the Americas aboard slave ships.
2. Names of slave ships. "*Estrella*": star (Spanish). "*Esperanza*": hope (Spanish).

3. Circle printed on a map showing compass directions. "Corposant": a fiery light that can appear on the decks of ships during electrical storms.
4. An allusion to Shakespeare's *The Tempest* 1.2.-399–401: "Full fathom five thy father lies; / Of his bones are coral made; / Those are pearls that were his eyes."
5. Lines from a Protestant hymn.

Jesus   Saviour   25

"8 bells. I cannot sleep, for I am sick
with fear, but writing eases fear a little
since still my eyes can see these words take shape
upon the page & so I write, as one
would turn to exorcism. 4 days scudding,[6]   30
but now the sea is calm again. Misfortune
follows in our wake like sharks (our grinning
tutelary[7] gods). Which one of us
has killed an albatross?[8] A plague among
our blacks—Ophthalmia: blindness—& we   35
have jettisoned the blind to no avail.
It spreads, the terrifying sickness spreads.
Its claws have scratched sight from the Capt.'s eyes
& there is blindness in the fo'c'sle[9]
& we must sail 3 weeks before we come   40
to port."

           What port awaits us, Davy Jones'
           or home? I've heard of slavers drifting, drifting,
           playthings of wind and storm and chance, their crews
           gone blind, the jungle hatred   45
           crawling up on deck.

Thou   Who   Walked   On   Galilee

"Deponent[1] further sayeth *The Bella J*
left the Guinea Coast
with cargo of five hundred blacks and odd   50
for the barracoons[2] of Florida:

"That there was hardly room 'tween-decks for half
the sweltering cattle stowed spoon-fashion there;
that some went mad of thirst and tore their flesh
and sucked the blood: 55

"That Crew and Captain lusted with the comeliest
of the savage girls kept naked in the cabins;
that there was one they called The Guinea Rose
and they cast lots and fought to lie with her:

"That when the Bo's'n piped all hands,[3] the flames   60
spreading from starboard already were beyond
control, the negroes howling and their chains
entangled with the flames:

6. Running rapidly before the wind.
7. Guardian.
8. Sea bird thought to bring good luck; to kill one
is considered a bad omen. An allusion to Samuel
Taylor Coleridge's *The Rime of the Ancient Mariner.*

9. I.e., forecastle; sailors' quarters aboard a ship.
1. One who gives evidence.
2. Slave quarters.
3. I.e., when the boatswain (petty officer) signaled
to all the crew.

"That the burning blacks could not be reached,
that the Crew abandoned ship,   65
leaving their shrieking negresses behind,
that the Captain perished drunken with the wenches:

"Further Deponent sayeth not."

    Pilot   Oh   Pilot   Me

II

Aye, lad, and I have seen those factories,   70
Gambia, Rio Pongo, Calabar;[4]
have watched the artful mongos[5] baiting traps
of war wherein the victor and the vanquished

Were caught as prizes for our barracoons.
Have seen the nigger kings whose vanity   75
and greed turned wild black hides of Fellatah,
Mandingo, Ibo, Kru[6] to gold for us.

And there was one—King Anthracite we named him—
fetish face beneath French parasols
of brass and orange velvet, impudent mouth   80
whose cups were carven skulls of enemies:

He'd honor us with drum and feast and conjo[7]
and palm-oil-glistening wenches deft in love,
and for tin crowns that shone with paste,
red calico and German-silver trinkets   85

Would have the drums talk war and send
his warriors to burn the sleeping villages
and kill the sick and old and lead the young
in coffles[8] to our factories.

Twenty years a trader, twenty years,   90
for there was wealth aplenty to be harvested
from those black fields, and I'd be trading still
but for the fevers melting down my bones.

III

Shuttles in the rocking loom of history,
the dark ships move, the dark ships move,   95
their bright ironical names
like jests of kindness on a murderer's mouth;
plough through thrashing glister toward
fata morgana's[9] lucent melting shore,

4. A city in southeast Nigeria. Gambia is a west   6. African tribes.
African nation. Rio Pongo is an east African water-   7. Dance.
way.   8. Trains of slaves fastened together.
5. Africans.   9. A mirage.

weave toward New World littorals [1] that are   100
mirage and myth and actual shore.

Voyage through death,
                    voyage whose chartings are unlove.

A charnel stench, effluvium of living death
spreads outward from the hold,   105
where the living and the dead, the horribly dying,
lie interlocked, lie foul with blood and excrement.

> *Deep in the festering hold thy father lies,*
> *the corpse of mercy rots with him,*
> *rats eat love's rotten gelid eyes.*   110

> *But, oh, the living look at you*
> *with human eyes whose suffering accuses you,*
> *whose hatred reaches through the swill of dark*
> *to strike you like a leper's claw.*

> *You cannot stare that hatred down*   115
> *or chain the fear that stalks the watches*
> *and breathes on you its fetid scorching breath;*
> *cannot kill the deep immortal human wish,*
> *the timeless will.*

> "But for the storm that flung up barriers   120
> of wind and wave, *The Amistad,* [2] señores,
> would have reached the port of Príncipe in two,
> three days at most; but for the storm we should
> have been prepared for what befell.
> Swift as the puma's leap it came. There was   125
> that interval of moonless calm filled only
> with the water's and the rigging's usual sounds,
> then sudden movement, blows and snarling cries
> and they had fallen on us with machete
> and marlinspike. It was as though the very   130
> air, the night itself were striking us.
> Exhausted by the rigors of the storm,
> we were no match for them. Our men went down
> before the murderous Africans. [3] Our loyal
> Celestino ran from below with gun   135
> and lantern and I saw, before the cane-
> knife's wounding flash, Cinquez,
> that surly brute who calls himself a prince,
> directing, urging on the ghastly work.
> He hacked the poor mulatto down, and then   140
> he turned on me. The decks were slippery
> when daylight finally came. It sickens me
> to think of what I saw, of how these apes
> threw overboard the butchered bodies of

1. Shores.
2. "Friendship"; a Spanish ship carrying fifty-three
illegally obtained slaves out of Havana, Cuba, in
July 1839.

3. During the mutiny the Africans, led by a man
called Cinqué, or Cinquez, killed the captain, his
slave Celestino, and the mate, but spared the two
slave owners.

our men, true Christians all, like so much jetsam.   145
Enough, enough. The rest is quickly told:
Cinquez was forced to spare the two of us
you see to steer the ship to Africa,
and we like phantoms doomed to rove the sea
voyaged east by day and west by night,   150
deceiving them, hoping for rescue,
prisoners on our own vessel, till
at length we drifted to the shores of this
your land, America, where we were freed
from our unspeakable misery. Now we   155
demand, good sirs, the extradition of
Cinquez and his accomplices to La
Havana.[4] And it distresses us to know
there are so many here who seem inclined
to justify the mutiny of these blacks.   160
We find it paradoxical indeed
that you whose wealth, whose tree of liberty
are rooted in the labor of your slaves
should suffer the august John Quincy Adams[5]
to speak with so much passion of the right   165
of chattel slaves to kill their lawful masters
and with his Roman rhetoric weave a hero's
garland for Cinquez. I tell you that
we are determined to return to Cuba
with our slaves and there see justice done. Cinquez—   170
or let us say 'the Prince'—Cinquez shall die."

The deep immortal human wish,
the timeless will:

Cinquez its deathless primaveral image,
life that transfigures many lives.   175

Voyage through death
            to life upon these shores.

1962

O Daedalus,[1] Fly Away Home

(For Maia and Julie)

Drifting night in the Georgia pines,
coonskin drum and jubilee banjo.
Pretty Malinda, dance with me.

4. *The Amistad* reached Long Island Sound after
two months, where it was detained by the American ship *Washington*; the slaves were imprisoned,
and the owners were freed. The owners began litigation to force the slaves' return to Havana to be
tried for murder.
5. The case reached the Supreme Court in 1841;
the Africans were defended by former president
John Quincy Adams, and the court released the

thirty-seven survivors to Africa.
1. In Greek mythology, Daedalus and his son,
Icarus, were imprisoned by the Minotaur in a labyrinth (designed by Daedalus himself). He made
wings of wax and feathers so he and Icarus could
escape, but when Icarus flew too close to the sun,
the wax binding together the wings melted and he
fell into the sea and drowned. Daedalus escaped to
Sicily.

Night is juba, night is conjo.[2]
    Pretty Malinda, dance with me.   5

Night is an African juju[3] man
weaving a wish and a weariness together
    to make two wings.

    O fly away home fly away

Do you remember Africa?   10

    O cleave the air fly away home

My gran, he flew back to Africa,
 just spread his arms and
    flew away home.

Drifting night in the windy pines;   15
night is a laughing, night is a longing.
    Pretty Malinda, come to me.

Night is a mourning juju man
weaving a wish and a weariness together
    to make two wings.   20

    O fly away home fly away

                    1962

Runagate[1] Runagate

I

Runs falls rises stumbles on from darkness into darkness
and the darkness thicketed with shapes of terror
and the hunters pursuing and the hounds pursuing
and the night cold and the night long and the river
to cross and the jack-muh-lanterns beckoning beckoning   5
and blackness ahead and when shall I reach that somewhere
morning and keep on going and never turn back and keep on going
      Runagate
          Runagate
              Runagate   10

Many thousands rise and go
many thousands crossing over

                O mythic North
                O star-shaped yonder Bible city

---

2. "Conjo" and "juba" are dances.   belief.
3. Endowed with magical powers; a West African   1. Runaway (archaic).

Some go weeping and some rejoicing   15
some in coffins and some in carriages
some in silks and some in shackles

       Rise and go or fare you well

No more auction block for me
no more driver's lash for me   20

    If you see my Pompey, 30 yrs of age,
    new breeches, plain stockings, negro shoes;
    if you see my Anna, likely young mulatto
    branded E on the right cheek, R^2 on the left,
    catch them if you can and notify subscriber.   25
    Catch them if you can, but it won't be easy.
    They'll dart underground when you try to catch them,
    plunge into quicksand, whirlpools, mazes,
    turn into scorpions when you try to catch them.

And before I'll be a slave   30
I'll be buried in my grave

    North star and bonanza gold
    I'm bound for the freedom, freedom-bound
    and oh Susyanna don't you cry for me

          Runagate   35

          Runagate

II

Rises from their anguish and their power,

        Harriet Tubman, [3]

        woman of earth, whipscarred,
        a summoning, a shining   40

        Mean to be free

And this was the way of it, brethren brethren,
way we journeyed from Can't to Can.
Moon so bright and no place to hide,
the cry up and the patterollers[4] riding,   45
hound dogs belling in bladed air.
And fear starts a-murbling, Never make it,
we'll never make it. *Hush that now,*
and she's turned upon us, levelled pistol

---

2. The letters *ER* stand for Elizabeth Regina, or Elizabeth I of England.
3. Slave-born American abolitionist (1820?–1913), who helped hundreds of enslaved African Americans escape through the Underground Railroad.
4. White patrollers of southern plantations whose job was to prevent slaves from escaping.

glinting in the moonlight: 50
Dead folks can't jaybird-talk, she says;
you keep on going now or die, she says.

Wanted   Harriet Tubman   alias The General
alias Moses   Stealer of Slaves
In league with Garrison   Alcott   Emerson   55
Garrett   Douglass   Thoreau   John Brown[5]

Armed and known to be Dangerous

Wanted   Reward   Dead or Alive

Tell me, Ezekiel, oh tell me do you see
mailed Jehovah[6] coming to deliver me?   60

Hoot-owl calling in the ghosted air,
five times calling to the hands in the air.
Shadow of a face in the scary leaves,
shadow of a voice in the talking leaves:

Come ride-a my train   65

Oh that train, ghost-story train
through swamp and savanna movering movering,
over trestles of dew, through caves of the wish,
Midnight Special on a sabre track movering movering,
first stop Mercy and the last Hallelujah.   70

Come ride-a my train

Mean mean mean to be free.

                                                                   1962

Frederick Douglass[1]

When it is finally ours, this freedom, this liberty, this beautiful
and terrible thing, needful to man as air,
usable as earth; when it belongs at last to all,
when it is truly instinct, brain matter, diastole, systole,[2]
reflex action; when it is finally won; when it is more   5
than the gaudy mumbo jumbo of politicians:
this man, this Douglass, this former slave, this Negro

5. U.S. abolitionist (1800–1859), hanged for treason after planning a slave rebellion and leading a
raid on Harpers Ferry. William Lloyd Garrison
(1805–1879), American abolitionist and social reformer. Amos Bronson Alcott (1799–1888), American educator and philosopher. Ralph Waldo
Emerson (1803–1882), American philosopher.
Thomas Garrett (1789–1871), American abolitionist, instrumental in the Underground Railroad.
Frederick Douglass (1817?–1895), American abolitionist and statesman. Henry David Thoreau
(1817–1862), American author.
6. God (Hebrew). Ezekiel is an Old Testament
prophet.
1. Slave-born American abolitionist and statesman
(1817?–1895).
2. The regular contraction of the heart that pushes
the blood outward into the blood vessels. "Diastole": the rhythmic dilation and relaxation of the
heart during which it fills with blood.

beaten to his knees, exiled, visioning a world
where none is lonely, none hunted, alien,
this man, superb in love and logic, this man   10
shall be remembered. Oh, not with statues' rhetoric,
not with legends and poems and wreaths of bronze alone,
but with the lives grown out of his life, the lives
fleshing his dream of the beautiful, needful thing.

                                                              1962

A Ballad of Remembrance

Quadroon[1] mermaids, Afro angels, black saints
balanced upon the switchblades of that air
and sang. Tight streets unfolding to the eye
like fans of corrosion and elegiac lace
crackled with their singing: Shadow of time. Shadow of blood.   5

Shadow, echoed the Zulu king, dangling
from a cluster of balloons. Blood,
whined the gun-metal priestess, floating
over the courtyard where dead men diced.

What will you have? she inquired, the sallow vendeuse[2]   10
of prepared tarnishes and jokes of nacre and ormolu,[3]
what but those gleamings, oldrose[4] graces,
manners like scented gloves? Contrived ghosts
rapped to metronome clack of lavalieres.[5]

Contrived illuminations riding a threat   15
of river, masked Negroes wearing chameleon
satins gaudy now as a fortuneteller's
dream of disaster, lighted the crazy flopping
dance of love and hate among joys, rejections.

Accommodate, muttered the Zulu king,   20
toad on a throne of glaucous[6] poison jewels.
Love, chimed the saints and the angels and the mermaids.
Hate, shrieked the gun-metal priestess
from her spiked bellcollar curved like a fleur-de-lis:[7]

As well have a talon as a finger, a muzzle as a mouth,   25
as well have a hollow as a heart. And she pinwheeled
away in coruscations[8] of laughter, scattering
those others before her like foil stars.

---

1. A person having one-quarter black ancestry.
2. Vendor (French, feminine).
3. An alloy of copper, tin, and zinc that looks like gold. "Nacre": mother-of-pearl.
4. Grayish.
5. Ornamental pendants. "Metronome": an instrument that marks off an exact tempo by a series of clicks.

6. Sea green.
7. A stylized iris; armorial symbol of French royalty. "Bellcollar": device used to torture slaves, especially women suspected of having an abortion, in which case the collar remained on their necks until they had a child.
8. Sparkles of light.

But the dance continued—now among metaphorical
doors, coffee cups floating poised   30
hysterias, decors of illusion; now among
mazurka[9] dolls offering death's-heads
of cocaine roses and real violets.

Then you arrived, meditative, ironic,
richly human; and your presence was shore where I rested   35
released from the hoodoo[1] of that dance, where I spoke
with my true voice again.

And therefore this is not only a ballad of remembrance
for the down-South arcane city[2] with death
in its jaws like gold teeth and archaic cusswords;   40
not only a token for the troubled generous friends
held in the fists of that schizoid city like flowers,
but also, Mark Van Doren,[3]
a poem of remembrance, a gift, a souvenir for you.   45

1962

Mourning Poem for the Queen of Sunday

Lord's lost Him His mockingbird,
His fancy warbler;
Satan sweet-talked her,
four bullets hushed her.
Who would have thought   5
she'd end that way?

Four bullets hushed her. And the world a-clang with evil.
Who's going to make old hardened sinner men tremble now
and the righteous rock?
Oh who and oh who will sing Jesus down   10
to help with struggling and doing without and being colored
all through blue Monday?
Till way next Sunday?

All those angels
in their cretonne[1] clouds and finery   15
the true believer saw
when she rared back her head and sang,
all those angels are surely weeping.
Who would have thought
she'd end that way?   20

Four holes in her heart. The gold works wrecked.
But she looks so natural in her big bronze coffin
among the Broken Hearts and Gates-Ajar,

9. Polish dance.   3. American man of letters (1894–1972), a friend
1. Syncretistic blend of African and Christian reli-   of Hayden's.
gious beliefs; also called *voodoo.*   1. White.
2. New Orleans during Mardi Gras.

it's as if any moment she'd lift her head
from its pillow of chill gardenias   25
and turn this quiet into shouting Sunday
and make folks forget what she did on Monday.

Oh, Satan sweet-talked her,
and four bullets hushed her.
Lord's lost Him His diva,   30
His fancy warbler's gone.
Who would have thought,
who would have thought she'd end that way?

1962

Soledad[1]

(And I, I am no longer of that world)

Naked, he lies in the blinded room
chainsmoking, cradled by drugs, by jazz
as never by any lover's cradling flesh.

Miles Davis coolly blows for him:
O *pena negra*,[2] sensual Flamenco[3] blues;   5
the red clay foxfire voice of Lady Day[4]

(lady of the pure black magnolias)
sobsings her sorrow and loss and fare you well,
dryweeps the pain his treacherous jailers

have released him from for a while.   10
His fears and his unfinished self
await him down in the anywhere streets.

He hides on the dark side of the moon,
takes refuge in a stained-glass cell,
flies to a clockless country of crystal.   15

Only the ghost of Lady Day knows where
he is. Only the music. And he swings
oh swings: beyond complete immortal now.

1970

1. Aloneness or loneliness (Spanish).
2. Oh dark pain (Spanish).
3. A southern Spanish music and dance.

4. Billie Holiday (1915–1959), American jazz
singer whose career was eventually ended by drug
addiction.

El-Hajj Malik El-Shabazz[1]
(Malcolm X)

O masks and metamorphoses of Ahab, Native Son

I

The icy evil that struck his father down
and ravished his mother into madness
trapped him in violence of a punished self
struggling to break free.

As Home Boy, as Dee-troit Red,   5
he fled his name, became the quarry of
his own obsessed pursuit.

He conked his hair and Lindy-hopped,[2]
zoot-suited[3] jiver, swinging those chicks
in the hot rose and reefer glow.   10

His injured childhood bullied him.
He skirmished in the Upas trees[4]
and cannibal flowers of the American Dream—

but could not hurt the enemy
powered against him there.   15

II

Sometimes the dark that gave his life
its cold satanic sheen would shift
a little, and he saw himself
floodlit and eloquent;

yet how could he, "Satan" in The Hole,   20
guess what the waking dream foretold?

Then false dawn of vision came;
he fell upon his face before
a racist Allah[5] pledged to wrest him from
the hellward-thrusting hands of Calvin's[6] Christ—   25

to free him and his kind
from Yakub's[7] white-faced treachery.
He rose redeemed from all but prideful anger,

1. Arabic name of Malcolm X, African American religious and political leader, assassinated in 1965, purportedly by Black Muslims, from whom he had split in 1963.
2. Jitter-bugged; danced energetically. "Conked": straightened.
3. Wearing a zootsuit, or a man's suit with baggy, tight-cuffed trousers and an oversized jacket; popular in the 1940s.
4. Tropical trees whose milky sap is used for arrow poison.
5. God (Arabic).
6. John Calvin (1509–1564), French Protestant theologian who taught the doctrine of predestination.
7. In the teachings of the Nation of Islam in the United States, Yakub is a black man embittered toward God who creates an evil race of white men as a revenge against his fellow blacks and God.

though adulterate attars[8] could not cleanse
him of the odors of the pit.   30

III

Asalam alaikum! [9]

He X'd his name, became his people's anger,
exhorted them to vengeance for their past;
rebuked, admonished them,

their scourger who   35
would shame them, drive them from
the lush ice gardens of their servitude.

Asalam alaikum!

Rejecting Ahab, he was of Ahab's tribe.
"Strike through the mask!"   40

IV

Time. "The martyr's time," he said.
Time and the karate killer,
knifer, gunman. Time that brought
ironic trophies as his faith

twined sparking round the bole,   45
the fruit of neo-Islam.
"The martyr's time."

But first, the ebb time pilgrimage
toward revelation, hejira to
his final metamorphosis;   50

Labbayk! [1] *Labbayk!*

He fell upon his face before
Allah the raceless in whose blazing Oneness all
were one. He rose renewed renamed, became
much more than there was time for him to be.   55

                                                              1970

A Letter from Phillis Wheatley[1]

London, 1773

Dear Obour[2]
        Our crossing was without
event. I could not help, at times,
reflecting on that first—my Destined—
voyage long ago (I yet   5
have some remembrance of its Horrors)
and marvelling at God's Ways.
        Last evening, her Ladyship[3] presented me
to her illustrious Friends.
I scarce could tell them anything   10
of Africa, though much of Boston
and my hope of Heaven. I read
my latest Elegies to them.
"O Sable[4] Muse!" the Countess cried,
embracing me, when I had done.   15
I held back tears, as is my wont,
and there were tears in Dear
Nathaniel's[5] eyes.
        At supper—I dined apart
like captive Royalty—   20
the Countess and her Guests promised
signatures affirming me
True Poetess, albeit once a slave.
Indeed, they were most kind, and spoke,
moreover, of presenting me   25
at Court (I thought of Pocahontas[6])—
an Honor, to be sure, but one,
I should, no doubt, as Patriot decline.
        My health is much improved;
I feel I may, if God so Wills,   30
entirely recover here.
Idyllic England! Alas, there is
no Eden without its Serpent. Under
the chiming Complaisance I hear him Hiss;
I see his flickering tongue   35
when foppish would-be Wits
murmur of the Yankee Pedlar
and his Cannibal Mockingbird.[7]
        Sister, forgive th'intrusion of

1. American poet (1753–1784), born in Africa and brought to the United States in slavery to work for John and Susannah Wheatley. When she was nineteen, she published *Poems on Various Subjects, Religious, and Moral*, which bore a prefatory testament by many prominent Boston citizens assuring the public that a female slave had indeed written the enclosed poems.
2. I.e., Tanner, a young, free black man who was one of Wheatley's few friends.
3. The countess of Huntington, one of many Londoners who knew and loved Wheatley.
4. Black; an allusion to Wheatley's term *sable race* in her poem *On Being Brought from Africa to America*.
5. John and Susannah Wheatley's son, who accompanied Phillis to England.
6. A Native American princess (1595–1617), who is the heroine of a folk tale that recounts how she saved the life of Captain John Smith. She married Englishman John Rolfe, who presented her to the British court in 1616.
7. Insulting references to John Wheatley and Phillis herself, whose poetry's detractors found her work "merely imitative."

my Sombreness—Nocturnal Mood   40
I would not share with any save
your trusted Self. Let me disperse,
in closing, such unseemly Gloom
by mention of an Incident
you may, as I, consider Droll: 45
Today, a little Chimney Sweep,
his face and hands with soot quite Black,
staring hard at me, politely asked:
"Does you, M'lady, sweep chimneys too?"
I was amused, but dear Nathaniel   50
(ever Solicitous) was not.
    I pray the Blessings of our Lord
and Saviour Jesus Christ be yours
Abundantly. In His Name.

                    Phillis   55
                    1978

RALPH ELLISON

1914–1994

Ralph Ellison, who at mid-century would single-handedly rewrite the American novel as an *African American* adventure in fiction, was born in Oklahoma City on March 1, 1914. Years later Ellison would write that the frontier spirit of Oklahoma, which had achieved statehood in only 1907, had fostered in him a sense of human possibility that he considered the very essence of American democracy. Ellison's father, small businessman Lewis Alfred Ellison, died in 1917, when Ellison was three; Ellison and his brother were raised by their mother, Ida Millsap, who moved the family into the parsonage of a local church. There, young Ralph, already an avid reader, was exposed to a wider world of books and popular magazines, *Vanity Fair* and *Literary Digest*, for example, brought home by his mother from the white households in which she worked as a domestic. Years later, such glimpses into a world beyond his own would evoke these memories:

> You might say that my environment was extended by these slender threads into the worlds of white families. . . . These magazines and recordings . . . spoke to me of a life that was broader and more interesting and although it was not really a part of my own life, I never thought they were not for me because I happened to be a Negro. They were things which spoke of a world which I could some day make my own.

An early interest in music developed into one of the great passions of Ellison's life and one of the great presences in his writing. During his years at the Frederick Douglass School in Oklahoma City, which he entered in 1920, Ellison studied music theory and acquired working knowledge of several brass instruments, including the trumpet. Oklahoma City was at that time, along with Kansas City, a rich experimental music scene, and Ellison heard many jazz greats, notably King Oliver and the Old Blue Devils Band. Wanting to become a versatile musician, Ellison decided to obtain conservatory training and so entered the Tuskegee Institute on a state scholarship in 1933. At Tuskegee he was inspired by two fine teachers: William L. Dawson, director of the a cappella choir, and Hazel Harrison, a concert pianist. A sophomore-year course in the English novel introduced him to another brilliant teacher, Morteza Sprague, who in turn introduced him to the powerful influence of Eliot's *Waste Land*. Truly a Renaissance man, Ellison soon added the study of sculpture to his impressive arts repertoire.

Despite the richness of this education, Ellison left Tuskegee at the end of his junior year not just because confusion over his scholarship left him unable to pay his full tuition but also because he found Tuskegee anti-intellectual and overly accommodationist, and he could not rest easy with the state of race relations in Alabama. That same year, Ellison embarked on a pilgrimage to New York City, not unlike that of the unnamed protagonist of *Invisible Man*. In New York and living at the Harlem YMCA, he renewed his acquaintance with Alain Locke (whom he'd met during one of the philosopher's visits to Tuskegee) and was introduced to Langston Hughes. Hughes in turn would provide the young man entree to Richard Wright, who was soon to begin editing the Marxist literary magazine *New Challenge*. Stimulated by their common interest in literature, Wright and Ellison were bound for an instant friendship. For Wright, Ellison offered relief from the unpleasant working atmosphere in the Harlem bureau of the *Daily Worker*; for Ellison, Wright was an informal teacher and mentor. Some of Ellison's early reviews and short fiction were submitted, with Wright's encouragement, for publication in the *New Challenge*.

His mother's death in 1937 interrupted Ellison's New York apprenticeship. Grieving, Ellison spent seven months in Ohio with his brother, Herbert, during which time he hunted and read. Having withdrawn temporarily from the challenge of the great city, Ellison emerged from his depression with a clear purpose: he would return to New York and become a writer. But the late 1930s in the United States were hardly an auspicious time for creative work among black intellectuals, especially as the Depression had depleted the patronage that had fed the Harlem Renaissance during the 1920s. Aspiring writers could either take on low-paying jobs, which would leave them just barely enough time to develop their craft, or they could find employment with the Federal Writers' Project, in which case a bit more space could be freed up for creativity. With Wright's help, Ellison was able to do the latter, working for $103 a month collecting facts and folklore for books on African Americans. Ellison's experience interviewing Harlem residents, rather like Du Bois's interviewing black Philadelphians at the turn of the century, deepened his appreciation for folk tales and offered themes for his fiction. Doubtless, the creative synthesis in *Invisible Man*—between the folk and the modern, the city and the country, the psychic and the archetypal—had its roots, in part, in Ellison's work with the Writers' Project.

Between 1938 and 1944, Ellison produced some fifty-seven articles and eight stories, as he reported on the 1943 Harlem riot for the *New York Post* and offered commentary on other significant political events of the day. Although Ellison, along with other black intellectuals of the time, was deeply attracted to Marxism, it was his doubting the ideology that in part allowed him to write his celebrated novel. Ellison's reflections on the inadequacy of Marxism for art arose out of careful consideration of texts by Marx, Engels, and Malraux but also from his friendship with Richard Wright. Close enough to Wright to be able to see *Native Son* emerge from the typewriter, Ellison, as essays in *Shadow and Act* attest, sustained mixed feelings toward his friend's magnum opus and eventually concluded that Wright's career itself gave the lie to black psychopathology as black personality's first and only truth: Wright himself was refined, interesting, and life affirming, while the protagonist of *Native Son*, Bigger Thomas, embodied the terrible spectacle of stunted modern man—devoid of imagination and purely victimized by negative social forces. Rejecting Wright's theory of naturalism, as well as radical Marxist cant, Ellison turned his attention toward a world different from Wright's fictional creation for much of his inspiration: the blues, jazz, and the tragicomedy of everyday life, as seen in tales like *Sweet Monkey*. To affirm himself, his mother, and the old men who told stories in barber shops, Ellison had to depart, quite radically, from *Native Son* and the tenets that it had deployed.

Even though World War II ended the Depression by gearing up the nation's war machine, it did little to resolve the paradoxical status of African Americans. Could one really wage war against fascist evil from the swollen ranks of a segregated armed force? Ellison did not think so, and so he joined the Merchant Marine in 1943, serving as a cook until 1945. During the war years, Ellison met Fanny McConnell, whom he would marry in 1946. On sick leave in 1945, he wrote the following words: "I am an invisible man." Ellison nearly threw out the page, but not before attempting to imagine what kind of soul would say such a thing. Within seven years, he knew. And so did the world.

It is difficult to imagine any response to *Invisible Man* short of praise. Sure enough, on its debut in 1952 it was hailed by critics as proof that the black writer had arrived. Ellison's newfound golden status among black intellectuals, however, was marred by displeasure from the Left, where some were not happy with an apparently ironic portrait of the Communist Party contained in a chapter called "The Brotherhood"; others felt that the novel was devoid of the radical political message that black artists should communicate. Critic Oliver O. Killens, for example, called the book a "vicious distortion of Negro life," claiming that the "Negro people need-[ed] Ralph Ellison's *Invisible Man* like [they] need[ed] a hole in the head or a stab in the back." Responses like Killens's demonstrated the extent to which Ellison had threatened the ideological stranglehold that had so long prevailed over the study of African American life and thought. Ellison's acceptance speech for the 1953 National Book Award acknowledged the "rhetorical canniness" of black American speech, the accents of its "rich babble" as heard in *Invisible Man*, and spoke of the novel's effort to go beyond immediate literary predecessors like Wright and Hemingway as well as to draw on the ancestral figures of Melville and Twain, whose situating of race as a matter of importance in fiction loomed large over any writer dealing with that topic in the twentieth century.

Though a 1965 *Book Week* poll of two hundred critics voted *Invisible Man* "the most distinguished American novel written since World War II," controversy again surrounded the book late in the decade, as a young generation of black nationalists took issue with Ellison's stance on black rebellion, particularly with his treatment of the character of Ras the Destroyer. Earlier in the 1960s, white critic Irving Howe had confronted Ellison and James Baldwin for evading what he saw as the mission of the black intellectual—to foreground and protest victimization, to avoid taking comfort from the promises of Western civilization. Ellison responded with his essay *The World and the Jug*, anthologized here, in which he spoke out against the pigeonholing of artists by race and called down the limitations of such expectations as Howe's.

Why does *Invisible Man* evoke such passionate, antagonistic responses? In part, the answer lies in its brilliant use of intertextual and cultural nuance and maneuver, from Dante to Louis Armstrong to German *lieder* to Eliot to the slave auction to Dostoevsky. In part, it arises out of the text's ability to simultaneously fit into and challenge any number of theoretical grids, from the American novel since World War II to the African American novel, from problems of canon formation to questions about minority and postcolonial discourse. *Invisible Man* defined the historic moment of mid-twentieth-century America and forced a reconsideration of the powers of writing. As fresh today as it was in 1952, it eschews the liabilities of pathos and opens before its readership, particularly its African American readership, a new and different order of inquiry: What is the value of self-knowledge?

Over the years, Ellison taught at Bard College, the University of Chicago, and New York University, where he was the Albert Schweitzer Professor of the Humanities. In 1986 he published *Going to the Territory*, a book of essays and stories. When Ralph Ellison died of cancer on April 16, 1994, he left behind a second, unfinished novel.

From Invisible Man

Prologue

I am an invisible man. No, I am not a spook like those who haunted Edgar Allan Poe; nor am I one of your Hollywood-movie ectoplasms. I am a man of substance, of flesh and bone, fiber and liquids—and I might even be said to possess a mind. I am invisible, understand, simply because people refuse to see me. Like the bodiless heads you see sometimes in circus sideshows, it is as though I have been surrounded by mirrors of hard, distorting glass. When they approach me they see only my surroundings, themselves, or figments of their imagination—indeed, everything and anything except me.

Nor is my invisibility exactly a matter of a biochemical accident to my epidermis. That invisibility to which I refer occurs because of a peculiar disposition of the eyes of those with whom I come in contact. A matter of the construction of their *inner* eyes, those eyes with which they look through their physical eyes upon reality. I am not complaining, nor am I protesting either. It is sometimes advantageous to be unseen, although it is most often rather wearing on the nerves. Then too, you're constantly being bumped against by those of poor vision. Or again, you often doubt if you really exist. You wonder whether you aren't simply a phantom in other people's minds. Say, a figure in a nightmare which the sleeper tries with all his strength to destroy. It's when you feel like this that, out of resentment, you begin to bump people back. And, let me confess, you feel that way most of the time. You ache with the need to convince yourself that you do exist in the real world, that you're a part of all the sound and anguish, and you strike out with your fists, you curse and you swear to make them recognize you. And, alas, it's seldom successful.

One night I accidentally bumped into a man, and perhaps because of the near darkness he saw me and called me an insulting name. I sprang at him, seized his coat lapels and demanded that he apologize. He was a tall blond man, and as my face came close to his he looked insolently out of his blue eyes and cursed me, his breath hot in my face as he struggled. I pulled his chin down sharp upon the crown of my head, butting him as I had seen the West Indians do, and I felt his flesh tear and the blood gush out, and I yelled, "Apologize! Apologize!" But he continued to curse and struggle, and I butted him again and again until he went down heavily, on his knees, profusely bleeding. I kicked him repeatedly, in a frenzy because he still uttered insults though his lips were frothy with blood. Oh yes, I kicked him! And in my outrage I got out my knife and prepared to slit his throat, right there beneath the lamplight in the deserted street, holding him in the collar with one hand, and opening the knife with my teeth—when it occurred to me that the man had not *seen* me, actually; that he, as far as he knew, was in the midst of a walking nightmare! And I stopped the blade, slicing the air as I pushed him away, letting him fall back to the street. I stared at him hard as the lights of a car stabbed through the darkness. He lay there, moaning on the asphalt; a man almost killed by a phantom. It unnerved me. I was both disgusted and ashamed. I was like a drunken man myself, wavering about on weakened legs. Then I was amused: Something in this man's thick head had sprung out and beaten him within an inch of his life. I began to laugh at this crazy discovery. Would he have awakened at the point of death? Would Death himself have freed him for wakeful living? But I didn't linger. I ran away into the dark, laughing so hard I feared I might rupture myself. The next day I saw his picture in the *Daily News*, beneath a caption stating that he had been "mugged." Poor fool, poor blind fool, I thought with sincere compassion, mugged by an invisible man!

Most of the time (although I do not choose as I once did to deny the violence of my days by ignoring it) I am not so overtly violent. I remember that I am invisible and walk softly so as not to awaken the sleeping ones. Sometimes it is best not to awaken them; there are few things in the world as dangerous as sleepwalkers. I learned in time though that it is possible to carry on a fight against them without their realizing it. For instance, I have been carrying on a fight with Monopolated Light & Power for some time now. I use their service and pay them nothing at all, and they don't know it. Oh, they suspect that power is being drained off, but they don't know where. All they know is that according to the master meter back there in their power station a hell of a lot of free current is disappearing somewhere into the jungle of Harlem. The joke, of course, is that I don't live in Harlem but in a border area. Several years ago (before I discovered the advantages of being invisible) I went through the routine process of buying service and paying their outrageous rates. But no more. I gave up all that, along with my apartment, and my old way of life: That way based upon the fallacious assumption that I, like other men, was visible. Now, aware of my invisibility, I live rent-free in a building rented strictly to whites, in a section of the basement that was shut off and forgotten during the nineteenth century, which I discovered when I was trying to escape in the night from Ras the Destroyer. But that's getting too far ahead of the story, almost to the end, although the end is in the beginning and lies far ahead.

The point now is that I found a home—or a hole in the ground, as you will. Now don't jump to the conclusion that because I call my home a "hole" it is damp and cold like a grave; there are cold holes and warm holes. Mine is a warm hole. And remember, a bear retires to his hole for the winter and lives until spring; then he comes strolling out like the Easter chick breaking from its shell. I say all this to assure you that it is incorrect to assume that, because I'm invisible and live in a hole, I am dead. I am neither dead nor in a state of suspended animation. Call me Jack-the-Bear,[1] for I am in a state of hibernation.

1. The title of a 1940 recording by jazz musician Duke Ellington (1899–1974) and his orchestra.

My hole is warm and full of light. Yes, *full* of light. I doubt if there is a brighter spot in all New York than this hole of mine, and I do not exclude Broadway. Or the Empire State Building on a photographer's dream night. But that is taking advantage of you. Those two spots are among the darkest of our whole civilization—pardon me, our whole *culture* (an important distinction, I've heard)—which might sound like a hoax, or a contradiction, but that (by contradiction, I mean) is how the world moves: Not like an arrow, but a boomerang. (Beware of those who speak of the *spiral* of history; they are preparing a boomerang. Keep a steel helmet handy.) I know; I have been boomeranged across my head so much that I now can see the darkness of lightness. And I love light. Perhaps you'll think it strange that an invisible man should need light, desire light, love light. But maybe it is exactly because I *am* invisible. Light confirms my reality, gives birth to my form. A beautiful girl once told me of a recurring nightmare in which she lay in the center of a large dark room and felt her face expand until it filled the whole room, becoming a formless mass while her eyes ran in bilious jelly up the chimney. And so it is with me. Without light I am not only invisible, but formless as well; and to be unaware of one's form is to live a death. I myself, after existing some twenty years, did not become alive until I discovered my invisibility.

That is why I fight my battle with Monopolated Light & Power. The deeper reason, I mean: It allows me to feel my vital aliveness. I also fight them for taking so much of my money before I learned to protect myself. In my hole in the basement there are exactly 1,369 lights. I've wired the entire ceiling, every inch of it. And not with fluorescent bulbs, but with the older, more-expensive-to-operate kind, the filament type. An act of sabotage, you know. I've already begun to wire the wall. A junk man I know, a man of vision, has supplied me with wire and sockets. Nothing, storm or flood, must get in the way of our need for light and ever more and brighter light. The truth is the light and light is the truth. When I finish all four walls, then I'll start on the floor. Just how that will go, I don't know. Yet when you have lived invisible as long as I have you develop a certain ingenuity. I'll solve the problem. And maybe I'll invent a gadget to place my coffee pot on the fire while I lie in bed, and even invent a gadget to warm my bed—like the fellow I saw in one of the picture magazines who made himself a gadget to warm his shoes! Though invisible, I am in the great American tradition of tinkers. That makes me kin to Ford, Edison and Franklin. Call me, since I have a theory and a concept, a "thinker-tinker." Yes, I'll warm my shoes; they need it, they're usually full of holes. I'll do that and more.

Now I have one radio-phonograph; I plan to have five. There is a certain acoustical deadness in my hole, and when I have music I want to *feel* its vibration, not only with my ear but with my whole body. I'd like to hear five recordings of Louis Armstrong[2] playing and singing "What Did I Do to Be so Black and Blue"—all at the same time. Sometimes now I listen to Louis while I have my favorite dessert of vanilla ice cream and sloe gin. I pour the red liquid over the white mound, watching it glisten and the vapor rising as

2. African American jazz musician (1900–1971).

Louis bends that military instrument into a beam of lyrical sound. Perhaps I like Louis Armstrong because he's made poetry out of being invisible. I think it must be because he's unaware that he *is* invisible. And my own grasp of invisibility aids me to understand his music. Once when I asked for a cigarette, some jokers gave me a reefer, which I lighted when I got home and sat listening to my phonograph. It was a strange evening. Invisibility, let me explain, gives one a slightly different sense of time, you're never quite on the beat. Sometimes you're ahead and sometimes behind. Instead of the swift and imperceptible flowing of time, you are aware of its nodes, those points where time stands still or from which it leaps ahead. And you slip into the breaks and look around. That's what you hear vaguely in Louis' music.

Once I saw a prizefighter boxing a yokel. The fighter was swift and amazingly scientific. His body was one violent flow of rapid rhythmic action. He hit the yokel a hundred times while the yokel held up his arms in stunned surprise. But suddenly the yokel, rolling about in the gale of boxing gloves, struck one blow and knocked science, speed and footwork as cold as a well-digger's posterior. The smart money hit the canvas. The long shot got the nod. The yokel had simply stepped inside of his opponent's sense of time. So under the spell of the reefer I discovered a new analytical way of listening to music. The unheard sounds came through, and each melodic line existed of itself, stood out clearly from all the rest, said its piece, and waited patiently for the other voices to speak. That night I found myself hearing not only in time, but in space as well. I not only entered the music but descended, like Dante, into its depths. And *beneath the swiftness of the hot tempo there was a slower tempo and a cave and I entered it and looked around and heard an old woman singing a spiritual as full of* Weltschmerz [3] *as flamenco, and beneath that lay a still lower level on which I saw a beautiful girl the color of ivory pleading in a voice like my mother's as she stood before a group of slaveowners who bid for her naked body, and below that I found a lower level and a more rapid tempo and I heard someone shout:*

"*Brothers and sisters, my text this morning is the 'Blackness of Blackness.'* "

And a congregation of voices answered: "*That blackness is most black, brother, most black . . .*"

"*In the beginning . . .*"

"*At the very start,*" *they cried.*

"*. . . there was blackness . . .*"

"*Preach it . . .*"

"*. . . and the sun . . .*"

"*The sun, Lawd . . .*"

"*. . . was bloody red . . .*"

"*Red . . .*"

"*Now black is . . .*" *the preacher shouted.*

"*Bloody . . .*"

"*I said black is . . .*"

"*Preach it, brother . . .*"

3. Sadness or world weariness (German).

"... an' black ain't ..."

"Red, Lawd, red: He said it's red!"

"Amen, brother ..."

"Black will git you ..."

"Yes, it will ..."

"Yes, it will ..."

"... an' black won't ..."

"Naw, it won't!"

"It do ..."

"It do, Lawd ..."

"... an' it don't."

"Halleluiah ..."

"... It'll put you, glory, glory, Oh my Lawd, in the WHALE'S BELLY."

"Preach it, dear brother ..."

"... an' make you tempt ..."

"Good God a-mighty!"

"Old Aunt Nelly!"

"Black will make you ..."

"Black ..."

"... or black will un-make you."

"Ain't it the truth, Lawd?"

And at that point a voice of trombone timbre screamed at me, "Git out of here, you fool! Is you ready to commit treason?"

And I tore myself away, hearing the old singer of spirituals moaning, "Go curse your God, boy, and die."

I stopped and questioned her, asked her what was wrong.

"I dearly loved my master, son," she said.

"You should have hated him," I said.

"He gave me several sons," she said, "and because I loved my sons I learned to love their father though I hated him too."

"I too have become acquainted with ambivalence," I said. "That's why I'm here."

"What's that?"

"Nothing, a word that doesn't explain it. Why do you moan?"

"I moan this way 'cause he's dead," she said.

"Then tell me, who is that laughing upstairs?"

"Them's my sons. They glad."

"Yes, I can understand that too," I said.

"I laughs too, but I moans too. He promised to set us free but he never could bring hisself to do it. Still I loved him ..."

"Loved him? You mean ...?"

"Oh yes, but I loved something else even more."

"What more?"

"Freedom."

"Freedom," I said. "Maybe freedom lies in hating."

"Naw, son, it's in loving. I loved him and give him the poison and he withered away like a frost-bit apple. Them boys woulda tore him to pieces with they homemade knives."

"A mistake was made somewhere," I said, "I'm confused." And I wished to *say other things, but the laughter upstairs became too loud and moan-like for me and I tried to break out of it, but I couldn't. Just as I was leaving I felt an urgent desire to ask her what freedom was and went back. She sat with her head in her hands, moaning softly; her leather-brown face was filled with sadness.*

"Old woman, what is this freedom you love so well?" I asked around a corner of my mind.

She looked surprised, then thoughtful, then baffled. "I done forgot, son. It's all mixed up. First I think it's one thing, then I think it's another. It gits my head to spinning. I guess now it ain't nothing but knowing how to say what I got up in my head. But it's a hard job, son. Too much is done happen to me in too short a time. Hit's like I have a fever. Ever' time I starts to walk my head gits to swirling and I falls down. Or if it ain't that, it's the boys; they gits to laughing and wants to kill up the white folks. They's bitter, that's what they is . . ."

"But what about freedom?"

"Leave me 'lone, boy; my head aches!"

I left her, feeling dizzy myself. I didn't get far.

Suddenly one of the sons, a big fellow six feet tall, appeared out of nowhere and struck me with his fist.

"What's the matter, man?" I cried.

"You made Ma cry!"

"But how?" I said, dodging a blow.

"Askin' her them questions, that's how. Git outa here and stay, and next time you got questions like that, ask yourself!"

He held me in a grip like cold stone, his fingers fastening upon my wind-pipe until I thought I would suffocate before he finally allowed me to go. I stumbled about dazed, the music beating hysterically in my ears. It was dark. My head cleared and I wandered down a dark narrow passage, thinking I heard his footsteps hurrying behind me. I was sore, and into my being had come a profound craving for tranquillity, for peace and quiet, a state I felt I could never achieve. For one thing, the trumpet was blaring and the rhythm was too hectic. A tom-tom beating like heart-thuds began drowning out the trumpet, filling my ears. I longed for water and I heard it rushing through the cold mains my fingers touched as I felt my way, but I couldn't stop to search because of the footsteps behind me.

"Hey, Ras," I called. "Is it you, Destroyer? Rinehart?"

No answer, only the rhythmic footsteps behind me. Once I tried crossing the road, but a speeding machine struck me, scraping the skin from my leg as it roared past.

Then somehow I came out of it, ascending hastily from this underworld of sound to hear Louis Armstrong innocently asking,

> *What did I do*
> *To be so black*
> *And blue?*

At first I was afraid; this familiar music had demanded action, the kind of which I was incapable, and yet had I lingered there beneath the surface I might have attempted to act. Nevertheless, I know now that few really listen to this music. I sat on the chair's edge in a soaking sweat, as though each of my 1,369 bulbs had every one become a klieg light[4] in an individual setting for a third degree with Ras and Rinehart in charge. It was exhausting—as though I had held my breath continuously for an hour under the terrifying serenity that comes from days of intense hunger. And yet, it was a strangely satisfying experience for an invisible man to hear the silence of sound. I had discovered unrecognized compulsions of my being—even though I could not answer "yes" to their promptings. I haven't smoked a reefer since, however; not because they're illegal, but because to *see* around corners is enough (that is not unusual when you are invisible). But to hear around them is too much; it inhibits action. And despite Brother Jack and all that sad, lost period of the Brotherhood, I believe in nothing if not in action.

Please, a definition: A hibernation is a covert preparation for a more overt action.

Besides, the drug destroys one's sense of time completely. If that happened, I might forget to dodge some bright morning and some cluck would run me down with an orange and yellow street car, or a bilious bus! Or I might forget to leave my hole when the moment for action presents itself.

Meanwhile I enjoy my life with the compliments of Monopolated Light & Power. Since you never recognize me even when in closest contact with me, and since, no doubt, you'll hardly believe that I exist, it won't matter if you know that I tapped a power line leading into the building and ran it into my hole in the ground. Before that I lived in the darkness into which I was chased, but now I see. I've illuminated the blackness of my invisibility—and vice versa. And so I play the invisible music of my isolation. The last statement doesn't seem just right, does it? But it is; you hear this music simply because music is heard and seldom seen, except by musicians. Could this compulsion to put invisibility down in black and white be thus an urge to make music of invisibility? But I am an orator, a rabble rouser—Am? I *was*, and perhaps shall be again. Who knows? All sickness is not unto death, neither is invisibility.

I can hear you say, "What a horrible, irresponsible bastard!" And you're right. I leap to agree with you. I am one of the most irresponsible beings that ever lived. Irresponsibility is part of my invisibility; any way you face it, it is a denial. But to whom can I be responsible, and why should I be, when you refuse to see me? And wait until I reveal how truly irresponsible I am. Responsibility rests upon recognition, and recognition is a form of agreement. Take the man whom I almost killed: Who was responsible for that near murder—I? I don't think so, and I refuse it. I won't buy it. You can't give it to me. *He* bumped *me, he* insulted *me.* Shouldn't he, for his own personal safety, have recognized my hysteria, my "danger potential"? He, let us say, was lost in a dream world. But didn't *he* control that dream world—which, alas, is only too real!—and didn't *he* rule me out of it? And if he had yelled for a policeman, wouldn't *I* have been taken for the offending one? Yes, yes, yes! Let me agree with you, I was the irresponsible one;

4. Powerful arc light once widely used when filming motion pictures.

for I should have used my knife to protect the higher interests of society. Some day that kind of foolishness will cause us tragic trouble. All dreamers and sleepwalkers must pay the price, and even the invisible victim is responsible for the fate of all. But I shirked that responsibility; I became too snarled in the incompatible notions that buzzed within my brain. I was a coward . . .

But what did *I* do to be so blue? Bear with me.

Chapter 1

[BATTLE ROYAL]

It goes a long way back, some twenty years. All my life I had been looking for something, and everywhere I turned someone tried to tell me what it was. I accepted their answers too, though they were often in contradiction and even self-contradictory. I was naïve. I was looking for myself and asking everyone except myself questions which I, and only I, could answer. It took me a long time and much painful boomeranging of my expectations to achieve a realization everyone else appears to have been born with: That I am nobody but myself. But first I had to discover that I am an invisible man!

And yet I am no freak of nature, nor of history. I was in the cards, other things having been equal (or unequal) eighty-five years ago. I am not ashamed of my grandparents for having been slaves. I am only ashamed of myself for having at one time been ashamed. About eighty-five years ago they were told that they were free, united with others of our country in everything pertaining to the common good, and, in everything social, separate like the fingers of the hand. And they believed it. They exulted in it. They stayed in their place, worked hard, and brought up my father to do the same. But my grandfather is the one. He was an odd old guy, my grandfather, and I am told I take after him. It was he who caused the trouble. On his death-bed he called my father to him and said, "Son, after I'm gone I want you to keep up the good fight. I never told you, but our life is a war and I have been a traitor all my born days, a spy in the enemy's country ever since I give up my gun back in the Reconstruction.[5] Live with your head in the lion's mouth. I want you to overcome 'em with yeses, undermine 'em with grins, agree 'em to death and destruction, let 'em swoller you till they vomit or bust wide open." They thought the old man had gone out of his mind. He had been the meekest of men. The younger children were rushed from the room, the shades drawn and the flame of the lamp turned so low that it sputtered on the wick like the old man's breathing. "Learn it to the younguns," he whispered fiercely; then he died.

But my folks were more alarmed over his last words than over his dying. It was as though he had not died at all, his words caused so much anxiety. I was warned emphatically to forget what he had said and, indeed, this is the first time it has been mentioned outside the family circle. It had a tremendous effect upon me, however. I could never be sure of what he meant.

5. Period of readjustment (1865–77) following the Civil War; black civil and political rights were highly contested at this time.

Grandfather had been a quiet old man who never made any trouble, yet on his deathbed he had called himself a traitor and a spy, and he had spoken of his meekness as a dangerous activity. It became a constant puzzle which lay unanswered in the back of my mind. And whenever things went well for me I remembered my grandfather and felt guilty and uncomfortable. It was as though I was carrying out his advice in spite of myself. And to make it worse, everyone loved me for it. I was praised by the most lily-white men of the town. I was considered an example of desirable conduct—just as my grandfather had been. And what puzzled me was that the old man had defined it as *treachery*. When I was praised for my conduct I felt a guilt that in some way I was doing something that was really against the wishes of the white folks, that if they had understood they would have desired me to act just the opposite, that I should have been sulky and mean, and that that really would have been what they wanted, even though they were fooled and thought they wanted me to act as I did. It made me afraid that some day they would look upon me as a traitor and I would be lost. Still I was more afraid to act any other way because they didn't like that at all. The old man's words were like a curse. On my graduation day I delivered an oration in which I showed that humility was the secret, indeed, the very essence of progress. (Not that I believed this—how could I, remembering my grandfather?—I only believed that it worked.) It was a great success. Everyone praised me and I was invited to give the speech at a gathering of the town's leading white citizens. It was a triumph for our whole community.

It was in the main ballroom of the leading hotel. When I got there I discovered that it was on the occasion of a smoker, and I was told that since I was to be there anyway I might as well take part in the battle royal to be fought by some of my schoolmates as part of the entertainment. The battle royal came first.

All of the town's big shots were there in their tuxedoes, wolfing down the buffet foods, drinking beer and whiskey and smoking black cigars. It was a large room with a high ceiling. Chairs were arranged in neat rows around three sides of a portable boxing ring. The fourth side was clear, revealing a gleaming space of polished floor. I had some misgivings over the battle royal, by the way. Not from a distaste for fighting, but because I didn't care too much for the other fellows who were to take part. They were tough guys who seemed to have no grandfather's curse worrying their minds. No one could mistake their toughness. And besides, I suspected that fighting a battle royal might detract from the dignity of my speech. In those pre-invisible days I visualized myself as a potential Booker T. Washington.[6] But the other fellows didn't care too much for me either, and there were nine of them. I felt superior to them in my way, and I didn't like the manner in which we were all crowded together into the servants' elevator. Nor did they like my being there. In fact, as the warmly lighted floors flashed past the elevator we had words over the fact that I, by taking part in the fight, had knocked one of their friends out of a night's work.

We were led out of the elevator through a rococo hall into an anteroom

---

6. Slave-born American educator (1856–1915), founder of the Tuskegee Institute in Alabama, an industrial training school. He emphasized the pri-ority of economic equality for African Americans over social equality.

and told to get into our fighting togs. Each of us was issued a pair of boxing gloves and ushered out into the big mirrored hall, which we entered looking cautiously about us and whispering, lest we might accidentally be heard above the noise of the room. It was foggy with cigar smoke. And already the whiskey was taking effect. I was shocked to see some of the most important men of the town quite tipsy. They were all there—bankers, lawyers, judges, doctors, fire chiefs, teachers, merchants. Even one of the more fashionable pastors. Something we could not see was going on up front. A clarinet was vibrating sensuously and the men were standing up and moving eagerly forward. We were a small tight group, clustered together, our bare upper bodies touching and shining with anticipatory sweat; while up front the big shots were becoming increasingly excited over something we still could not see. Suddenly I heard the school superintendent, who had told me to come, yell, "Bring up the shines, gentlemen! Bring up the little shines!"

We were rushed up to the front of the ballroom, where it smelled even more strongly of tobacco and whiskey. Then we were pushed into place. I almost wet my pants. A sea of faces, some hostile, some amused, ringed around us, and in the center, facing us, stood a magnificent blonde—stark naked. There was dead silence. I felt a blast of cold air chill me. I tried to back away, but they were behind me and around me. Some of the boys stood with lowered heads, trembling. I felt a wave of irrational guilt and fear. My teeth chattered, my skin turned to goose flesh, my knees knocked. Yet I was strongly attracted and looked in spite of myself. Had the price of looking been blindness, I would have looked. The hair was yellow like that of a circus kewpie doll, the face heavily powdered and rouged, as though to form an abstract mask, the eyes hollow and smeared a cool blue, the color of a baboon's butt. I felt a desire to spit upon her as my eyes brushed slowly over her body. Her breasts were firm and round as the domes of East Indian temples, and I stood so close as to see the fine skin texture and beads of pearly perspiration glistening like dew around the pink and erected buds of her nipples. I wanted at one and the same time to run from the room, to sink through the floor, or go to her and cover her from my eyes and the eyes of the others with my body; to feel the soft thighs, to caress her and destroy her, to love her and murder her, to hide from her, and yet to stroke where below the small American flag tattooed upon her belly her thighs formed a capital V. I had a notion that of all in the room she saw only me with her impersonal eyes.

And then she began to dance, a slow sensuous movement; the smoke of a hundred cigars clinging to her like the thinnest of veils. She seemed like a fair bird-girl girdled in veils calling to me from the angry surface of some gray and threatening sea. I was transported. Then I became aware of the clarinet playing and the big shots yelling at us. Some threatened us if we looked and others if we did not. On my right I saw one boy faint. And now a man grabbed a silver pitcher from a table and stepped close as he dashed ice water upon him and stood him up and forced two of us to support him as his head hung and moans issued from his thick bluish lips. Another boy began to plead to go home. He was the largest of the group, wearing dark red fighting trunks much too small to conceal the erection which projected from him as though in answer to the insinuating low-registered moaning of the clarinet. He tried to hide himself with his boxing gloves.

And all the while the blonde continued dancing, smiling faintly at the big shots who watched her with fascination, and faintly smiling at our fear. I noticed a certain merchant who followed her hungrily, his lips loose and drooling. He was a large man who wore diamond studs in a shirtfront which swelled with the ample paunch underneath, and each time the blonde swayed her undulating hips he ran his hand through the thin hair of his bald head and, with his arms upheld, his posture clumsy like that of an intoxicated panda, wound his belly in a slow and obscene grind. This creature was completely hypnotized. The music had quickened. As the dancer flung herself about with a detached expression on her face, the men began reaching out to touch her. I could see their beefy fingers sink into the soft flesh. Some of the others tried to stop them and she began to move around the floor in graceful circles, as they gave chase, slipping and sliding over the polished floor. It was mad. Chairs went crashing, drinks were spilt, as they ran laughing and howling after her. They caught her just as she reached a door, raised her from the floor, and tossed her as college boys are tossed at a hazing, and above her red, fixed-smiling lips I saw the terror and disgust in her eyes, almost like my own terror and that which I saw in some of the other boys. As I watched, they tossed her twice and her soft breasts seemed to flatten against the air and her legs flung wildly as she spun. Some of the more sober ones helped her to escape. And I started off the floor, heading for the anteroom with the rest of the boys.

Some were still crying and in hysteria. But as we tried to leave we were stopped and ordered to get into the ring. There was nothing to do but what we were told. All ten of us climbed under the ropes and allowed ourselves to be blindfolded with broad bands of white cloth. One of the men seemed to feel a bit sympathetic and tried to cheer us up as we stood with our backs against the ropes. Some of us tried to grin. "See that boy over there?" one of the men said. "I want you to run across at the bell and give it to him right in the belly. If you don't get him, I'm going to get you. I don't like his looks." Each of us was told the same. The blindfolds were put on. Yet even then I had been going over my speech. In my mind each word was as bright as flame. I felt the cloth pressed into place, and frowned so that it would be loosened when I relaxed.

But now I felt a sudden fit of blind terror. I was unused to darkness. It was as though I had suddenly found myself in a dark room filled with poisonous cottonmouths. I could hear the bleary voices yelling insistently for the battle royal to begin.

"Get going in there!"

"Let me at that big nigger!"

I strained to pick up the school superintendent's voice, as though to squeeze some security out of that slightly more familiar sound.

"Let me at those black sonsabitches!" someone yelled.

"No, Jackson, no!" another voice yelled. "Here, somebody, help me hold Jack."

"I want to get at that ginger-colored nigger. Tear him limb from limb," the first voice yelled.

I stood against the ropes trembling. For in those days I was what they called ginger-colored, and he sounded as though he might crunch me between his teeth like a crisp ginger cookie.

Quite a struggle was going on. Chairs were being kicked about and I could hear voices grunting as with a terrific effort. I wanted to see, to see more desperately than ever before. But the blindfold was tight as a thick skin-puckering scab and when I raised my gloved hands to push the layers of white aside a voice yelled, "Oh, no you don't, black bastard! Leave that alone!"

"Ring the bell before Jackson kills him a coon!" someone boomed in the sudden silence. And I heard the bell clang and the sound of the feet scuffing forward.

A glove smacked against my head. I pivoted, striking out stiffly as someone went past, and felt the jar ripple along the length of my arm to my shoulder. Then it seemed as though all nine of the boys had turned upon me at once. Blows pounded me from all sides while I struck out as best I could. So many blows landed upon me that I wondered if I were not the only blindfolded fighter in the ring, or if the man called Jackson hadn't succeeded in getting me after all.

Blindfolded, I could no longer control my motions. I had no dignity. I stumbled about like a baby or a drunken man. The smoke had become thicker and with each new blow it seemed to sear and further restrict my lungs. My saliva became like hot bitter glue. A glove connected with my head, filling my mouth with warm blood. It was everywhere. I could not tell if the moisture I felt upon my body was sweat or blood. A blow landed hard against the nape of my neck. I felt myself going over, my head hitting the floor. Streaks of blue light filled the black world behind the blindfold. I lay prone, pretending that I was knocked out, but felt myself seized by hands and yanked to my feet. "Get going, black boy! Mix it up!" My arms were like lead, my head smarting from blows. I managed to feel my way to the ropes and held on, trying to catch my breath. A glove landed in my mid-section and I went over again, feeling as though the smoke had become a knife jabbed into my guts. Pushed this way and that by the legs milling around me, I finally pulled erect and discovered that I could see the black, sweat-washed forms weaving in the smoky-blue atmosphere like drunken dancers weaving to the rapid drumlike thuds of blows.

Everyone fought hysterically. It was complete anarchy. Everybody fought everybody else. No group fought together for long. Two, three, four, fought one, then turned to fight each other, were themselves attacked. Blows landed below the belt and in the kidney, with the gloves open as well as closed, and with my eye partly opened now there was not so much terror. I moved carefully, avoiding blows, although not too many to attract attention, fighting from group to group. The boys groped about like blind, cautious crabs crouching to protect their mid-sections, their heads pulled in short against their shoulders, their arms stretched nervously before them, with their fists testing the smoke-filled air like the knobbed feelers of hypersensitive snails. In one corner I glimpsed a boy violently punching the air and heard him scream in pain as he smashed his hand against a ring post. For a second I saw him bent over holding his hand, then going down as a blow caught his unprotected head. I played one group against the other, slipping in and throwing a punch then stepping out of range while pushing the others into the melee to take the blows blindly aimed at me. The smoke was agonizing and there were no rounds, no bells at three minute intervals to relieve our exhaustion. The room spun round me, a swirl of lights, smoke, sweating bodies surrounded by tense white faces. I bled from both nose and mouth, the blood spattering upon my chest.

The men kept yelling, "Slug him, black boy! Knock his guts out!" "Uppercut him! Kill him! Kill that big boy!"

Taking a fake fall, I saw a boy going down heavily beside me as though we were felled by a single blow, saw a sneaker-clad foot shoot into his groin as the two who had knocked him down stumbled upon him. I rolled out of range, feeling a twinge of nausea.

The harder we fought the more threatening the men became. And yet, I had begun to worry about my speech again. How would it go? Would they recognize my ability? What would they give me?

I was fighting automatically when suddenly I noticed that one after another of the boys was leaving the ring. I was surprised, filled with panic, as though I had been left alone with an unknown danger. Then I understood. The boys had arranged it among themselves. It was the custom for the two men left in the ring to slug it out for the winner's prize. I discovered this too late. When the bell sounded two men in tuxedoes leaped into the ring and removed the blindfold. I found myself facing Tatlock, the biggest of the gang. I felt sick at my stomach. Hardly had the bell stopped ringing in my ears than it clanged again and I saw him moving swiftly toward me. Thinking of nothing else to do I hit him smash on the nose. He kept coming, bringing the rank sharp violence of stale sweat. His face was a black blank of a face, only his eyes alive—with hate of me and aglow with a feverish terror from what had happened to us all. I became anxious. I wanted to deliver my speech and he came at me as though he meant to beat it out of me. I smashed him again and again, taking his blows as they came. Then on a sudden impulse I struck him lightly and as we clinched, I whispered, "Fake like I knocked you out, you can have the prize."

"I'll break your behind," he whispered hoarsely.

"For *them?*"

"For *me*, sonofabitch!"

They were yelling for us to break it up and Tatlock spun me half around with a blow, and as a joggled camera sweeps in a reeling scene, I saw the howling red faces crouching tense beneath the cloud of blue-gray smoke. For a moment the world wavered, unraveled, flowed, then my head cleared and Tatlock bounced before me. That fluttering shadow before my eyes was his jabbing left hand. Then falling forward, my head against his damp shoulder, I whispered,

"I'll make it five dollars more."

"Go to hell!"

But his muscles relaxed a trifle beneath my pressure and I breathed, "Seven?"

"Give it to your ma," he said, ripping me beneath the heart.

And while I still held him I butted him and moved away. I felt myself bombarded with punches. I fought back with hopeless desperation. I wanted to deliver my speech more than anything else in the world, because I felt that only these men could judge truly my ability, and now this stupid clown was ruining my chances. I began fighting carefully now, moving in to punch him and out again with my greater speed. A lucky blow to his chin and I had him going too—until I heard a loud voice yell, "I got my money on the big boy."

Hearing this, I almost dropped my guard. I was confused: Should I try to win against the voice out there? Would not this go against my speech, and was not this a moment for humility, for nonresistance? A blow to my head as I danced about sent my right eye popping like a jack-in-the-box and settled my dilemma. The room went red as I fell. It was a dream fall, my body languid and fastidious as to where to land, until the floor became impatient and smashed up to meet me. A moment later I came to. An hypnotic voice said FIVE emphatically. And I lay there, hazily watching a dark red spot of my own blood shaping itself into a butterfly, glistening and soaking into the soiled gray world of the canvas.

When the voice drawled TEN I was lifted up and dragged to a chair. I sat dazed. My eye pained and swelled with each throb of my pounding heart and I wondered if now I would be allowed to speak. I was wringing wet, my mouth still bleeding. We were grouped along the wall now. The other boys ignored me as they congratulated Tatlock and speculated as to how much they would be paid. One boy whimpered over his smashed hand. Looking up front, I saw attendants in white jackets rolling the portable ring away and placing a small square rug in the vacant space surrounded by chairs. Perhaps, I thought, I will stand on the rug to deliver my speech.

Then the M.C. called to us, "Come on up here boys and get your money."

We ran forward to where the men laughed and talked in their chairs, waiting. Everyone seemed friendly now.

"There it is on the rug," the man said. I saw the rug covered with coins of all dimensions and a few crumpled bills. But what excited me, scattered here and there, were the gold pieces.

"Boys, it's all yours," the man said. "You get all you grab."

"That's right, Sambo," a blond man said, winking at me confidentially.

I trembled with excitement, forgetting my pain. I would get the gold and the bills, I thought. I would use both hands. I would throw my body against the boys nearest me to block them from the gold.

"Get down around the rug now," the man commanded, "and don't anyone touch it until I give the signal."

"This ought to be good," I heard.

As told, we got around the square rug on our knees. Slowly the man raised his freckled hand as we followed it upward with our eyes.

I heard, "These niggers look like they're about to pray!"

Then, "Ready," the man said. "Go!"

I lunged for a yellow coin lying on the blue design of the carpet, touching it and sending a surprised shriek to join those rising around me. I tried frantically to remove my hand but could not let go. A hot, violent force tore through my body, shaking me like a wet rat. The rug was electrified. The hair bristled up on my head as I shook myself free. My muscles jumped, my nerves jangled, writhed. But I saw that this was not stopping the other boys. Laughing in fear and embarrassment, some were holding back and scooping up the coins knocked off by the painful contortions of the others. The men roared above us as we struggled.

"Pick it up, goddamnit, pick it up!" someone called like a bass-voiced parrot. "Go on, get it!"

I crawled rapidly around the floor, picking up the coins, trying to avoid the coppers and to get greenbacks and the gold. Ignoring the shock by laughing, as I brushed the coins off quickly, I discovered that I could contain the electricity—a contradiction, but it works. Then the men began to push us onto the rug. Laughing embarrassedly, we struggled out of their hands and kept after the coins. We were all wet and slippery and hard to hold. Suddenly I saw a boy lifted into the air, glistening with sweat like a circus seal, and dropped, his wet back landing flush upon the charged rug, heard him yell and saw him literally dance upon his back, his elbows beating a frenzied tattoo upon the floor, his muscles twitching like the flesh of a horse stung by many flies. When he finally rolled off, his face was gray and no one stopped him when he ran from the floor amid booming laughter.

"Get the money," the M.C. called. "That's good hard American cash!"

And we snatched and grabbed, snatched and grabbed. I was careful not to come too close to the rug now, and when I felt the hot whiskey breath descend upon me like a cloud of foul air I reached out and grabbed the leg of a chair. It was occupied and I held on desperately.

"Leggo, nigger! Leggo!"

The huge face wavered down to mine as he tried to push me free. But my body was slippery and he was too drunk. It was Mr. Colcord, who owned a chain of movie houses and "entertainment palaces." Each time he grabbed me I slipped out of his hands. It became a real struggle. I feared the rug more than I did the drunk, so I held on, surprising myself for a moment by trying to topple *him* upon the rug. It was such an enormous idea that I found myself actually carrying it out. I tried not to be obvious, yet when I grabbed his leg, trying to tumble him out of the chair, he raised up roaring with laughter, and, looking at me with soberness dead in the eye, kicked me viciously in the chest. The chair leg flew out of my hand and I felt myself going and rolled. It was as though I had rolled through a bed of hot coals. It seemed a whole century would pass before I would roll free, a century in which I was seared through the deepest levels of my body to the fearful breath within me and the breath seared and heated to the point of explosion. It'll all be over in a flash, I thought as I rolled clear. It'll all be over in a flash.

But not yet, the men on the other side were waiting, red faces swollen as though from apoplexy as they bent forward in their chairs. Seeing their fingers coming toward me I rolled away as a fumbled football rolls off the receiver's fingertips, back into the coals. That time I luckily sent the rug sliding out of place and heard the coins ringing against the floor and the boys scuffling to pick them up and the M.C. calling, "All right, boys, that's all. Go get dressed and get your money."

I was limp as a dish rag. My back felt as though it had been beaten with wires.

When we had dressed the M.C. came in and gave us each five dollars, except Tatlock, who got ten for being last in the ring. Then he told us to leave. I was not to get a chance to deliver my speech, I thought. I was going out into the dim alley in despair when I was stopped and told to go back. I returned to the ballroom, where the men were pushing back their chairs and gathering in groups to talk.

The M.C. knocked on a table for quiet. "Gentlemen," he said, "we almost forgot an important part of the program. A most serious part, gentlemen. This boy was brought here to deliver a speech which he made at his graduation yesterday . . ."

"Bravo!"

"I'm told that he is the smartest boy we've got out there in Greenwood. I'm told that he knows more big words than a pocket-sized dictionary."

Much applause and laughter.

"So now, gentlemen, I want you to give him your attention."

There was still laughter as I faced them, my mouth dry, my eye throbbing. I began slowly, but evidently my throat was tense, because they began shouting, "Louder! Louder!"

"We of the younger generation extol the wisdom of that great leader and educator," I shouted, "who first spoke these flaming words of wisdom: 'A ship lost at sea for many days suddenly sighted a friendly vessel. From the mast of the unfortunate vessel was seen a signal: "Water, water; we die of thirst!" The answer from the friendly vessel came back: "Cast down your bucket where you are." The captain of the distressed vessel, at last heeding the injunction, cast down his bucket, and it came up full of fresh sparkling water from the mouth of the Amazon River.' And like him I say, and in his words, 'To those of my race who depend upon bettering their condition in a foreign land, or who underestimate the importance of cultivating friendly relations with the Southern white man, who is his next-door neighbor, I would say: "Cast down your bucket where you are"—cast it down in making friends in every manly way of the people of all races by whom we are surrounded . . .' "

I spoke automatically and with such fervor that I did not realize that the men were still talking and laughing until my dry mouth, filling up with blood from the cut, almost strangled me. I coughed, wanting to stop and go to one of the tall brass, sand-filled spittoons to relieve myself, but a few of the men, especially the superintendent, were listening and I was afraid. So I gulped it down, blood, saliva and all, and continued. (What powers of endurance I had during those days! What enthusiasm! What a belief in the rightness of things!) I spoke even louder in spite of the pain. But still they talked and still they laughed, as though deaf with cotton in dirty ears. So I spoke with greater emotional emphasis. I closed my ears and swallowed blood until I was nauseated. The speech seemed a hundred times as long as before, but I could not leave out a single word. All had to be said, each memorized nuance considered, rendered. Nor was that all. Whenever I uttered a word of three or more syllables a group of voices would yell for me to repeat it. I used the phrase "social responsibility" and they yelled:

"What's that word you say, boy?"

"Social responsibility," I said.

"What?"

"Social . . ."

"Louder."

". . . responsibility."

"More!"

"Respon—"

"Repeat!"

"—sibility."

The room filled with the uproar of laughter until, no doubt distracted by having to gulp down my blood, I made a mistake and yelled a phrase I had often seen denounced in newspaper editorials, heard debated in private.

"Social . . ."

"What?" they yelled.

". . . equality—"

The laughter hung smokelike in the sudden stillness. I opened my eyes, puzzled. Sounds of displeasure filled the room. The M.C. rushed forward. They shouted hostile phrases at me. But I did not understand.

A small dry mustached man in the front row blared out, "Say that slowly, son!"

"What, sir?"

"What you just said!"

"Social responsibility, sir," I said.

"You weren't being smart, were you, boy?" he said, not unkindly.

"No, sir!"

"You sure that about 'equality' was a mistake?"

"Oh, yes, sir," I said. "I was swallowing blood."

"Well, you had better speak more slowly so we can understand. We mean to do right by you, but you've got to know your place at all times. All right, now, go on with your speech."

I was afraid. I wanted to leave but I wanted also to speak and I was afraid they'd snatch me down.

"Thank you, sir," I said, beginning where I had left off, and having them ignore me as before.

Yet when I finished there was a thunderous applause. I was surprised to see the superintendent come forth with a package wrapped in white tissue paper, and, gesturing for quiet, address the men.

"Gentlemen, you see that I did not overpraise this boy. He makes a good speech and some day he'll lead his people in the proper paths. And I don't have to tell you that that is important in these days and times. This is a good, smart boy, and so to encourage him in the right direction, in the name of the Board of Education I wish to present him a prize in the form of this . . ."

He paused, removing the tissue paper and revealing a gleaming calfskin brief case.

". . . in the form of this first-class article from Shad Whitmore's shop."

"Boy," he said, addressing me, "take this prize and keep it well. Consider it a badge of office. Prize it. Keep developing as you are and some day it will be filled with important papers that will help shape the destiny of your people."

I was so moved that I could hardly express my thanks. A rope of bloody saliva forming a shape like an undiscovered continent drooled upon the leather and I wiped it quickly away. I felt an importance that I had never dreamed.

"Open it and see what's inside," I was told.

My fingers a-tremble, I complied, smelling the fresh leather and finding an official-looking document inside. It was a scholarship to the state college for Negroes. My eyes filled with tears and I ran awkwardly off the floor.

I was overjoyed; I did not even mind when I discovered that the gold pieces I had scrambled for were brass pocket tokens advertising a certain make of automobile.

When I reached home everyone was excited. Next day the neighbors came to congratulate me. I even felt safe from grandfather, whose deathbed curse usually spoiled my triumphs. I stood beneath his photograph with my brief case in hand and smiled triumphantly into his stolid black peasant's face. It was a face that fascinated me. The eyes seemed to follow everywhere I went.

That night I dreamed I was at a circus with him and that he refused to laugh at the clowns no matter what they did. Then later he told me to open my brief case and read what was inside and I did, finding an official envelope stamped with the state seal; and inside the envelope I found another and another, endlessly, and I thought I would fall of weariness. "Them's years," he said. "Now open that one." And I did and in it I found an engraved document containing a short message in letters of gold. "Read it," my grandfather said. "Out loud!"

"To Whom It May Concern," I intoned. "Keep This Nigger-Boy Running."

I awoke with the old man's laughter ringing in my ears.

(It was a dream I was to remember and dream again for many years after. But at that time I had no insight into its meaning. First I had to attend college.)

* * *

Epilogue

So there you have all of it that's important. Or at least you *almost* have it. I'm an invisible man and it placed me in a hole—or showed me the hole I was in, if you will—and I reluctantly accepted the fact. What else could I have done? Once you get used to it, reality is as irresistible as a club, and I was clubbed into the cellar before I caught the hint. Perhaps that's the way it had to be; I don't know. Nor do I know whether accepting the lesson has placed me in the rear or in the *avant-garde. That,* perhaps, is a lesson for history, and I'll leave such decisions to Jack and his ilk while I try belatedly to study the lesson of my own life.

Let me be honest with you—a feat which, by the way, I find of the utmost difficulty. When one is invisible he finds such problems as good and evil, honesty and dishonesty, of such shifting shapes that he confuses one with the other, depending upon who happens to be looking through him at the time. Well, now I've been trying to look through myself, and there's a risk in it. I was never more hated than when I tried to be honest. Or when, even as just now I've tried to articulate exactly what I felt to be the truth. No one was satisfied—not even I. On the other hand, I've never been more loved and appreciated than when I tried to "justify" and affirm someone's mistaken beliefs; or when I've tried to give my friends the incorrect, absurd answers they wished to hear. In my presence they could talk and agree with themselves, the world was nailed down, and they loved it. They received a feeling of security. But here was the rub: Too often, in order to justify *them*, I had to take myself by the throat and choke myself until my eyes bulged and my tongue hung out and wagged like the door of an empty house in a high wind. Oh, yes, it made them happy and it made me sick. So I became ill of affirmation, of saying "yes" against the nay-saying of my stomach—not to mention my brain.

There is, by the way, an area in which a man's feelings are more rational than his mind, and it is precisely in that area that his will is pulled in several directions at the same time. You might sneer at this, but I know now. I was pulled this way and that for longer than I can remember. And my problem was that I always tried to go in everyone's way but my own. I have also been called one thing and then another while no one really wished to hear what I called myself. So after years of trying to adopt the opinions of others I finally rebelled. I am an *invisible* man. Thus I have come a long way and returned and boomeranged a long way from the point in society toward which I originally aspired.

So I took to the cellar; I hibernated. I got away from it all. But that wasn't enough. I couldn't be still even in hibernation. Because, damn it, there's the mind, the *mind*. It wouldn't let me rest. Gin, jazz and dreams were not enough. Books were not enough. My belated appreciation of the crude joke that had kept me running, was not enough. And my mind revolved again and again back to my grandfather. And, despite the farce that ended my attempt to say "yes" to Brotherhood, I'm still plagued by his deathbed advice . . . Perhaps he hid his meaning deeper than I thought, perhaps his anger threw me off—I can't decide. Could he have meant—hell, he *must* have meant the principle, that we were to affirm the principle on which the country was built and not the men, or at least not the men who did the violence. Did he mean say "yes" because he knew that the principle was greater than the men, greater than the numbers and the vicious power and all the methods used to corrupt its name? Did he mean to affirm the principle, which they themselves had dreamed into being out of the chaos and darkness of the feudal past, and which they had violated and compromised to the point of absurdity even in their own corrupt minds? Or did he mean that we had to take the responsibility for all of it, for the men as well as the principle, because we were the heirs who must use the principle because no other fitted our needs? Not for the power or for vindication, but because we, with the given circumstance of our origin, could only thus find transcendence? Was it that we of all, we, most of all, had to affirm the principle, the plan in whose name we had been brutalized and sacrificed—not because we would always be weak nor because we were afraid or opportunistic, but because we were older than they, in the sense of what it took to live in the world with others and because they had exhausted in us, some—not much, but some—of the human greed and smallness, yes, and the fear and superstition that had kept them running. (Oh, yes, they're running too, running all over themselves.) Or was it, did he mean that we should affirm the principle because we, through no fault of our own, were linked to all the others in the loud, clamoring semi-visible world, that world seen only as a fertile field for exploitation by Jack and his kind, and with condescension by Norton[7] and his, who were tired of being the mere pawns in the futile game of "making history?" Had he seen that for these too we had to say "yes" to the principle, lest they turn upon us to destroy both it and us?

"Agree 'em to death and destruction," grandfather had advised. Hell, weren't they their own death and their own destruction except as the principle lived in them and in us? And here's the cream of the joke: Weren't we *part of them* as well as apart from them and subject to die when they died? I can't figure it out; it escapes me. But what do *I* really want, I've asked myself. Certainly not the freedom of a Rinehart or the power of a Jack, nor simply the freedom not to run. No, but the next step I couldn't make, so I've remained in the hole.

I'm not blaming anyone for this state of affairs, mind you; nor merely crying *mea culpa*. The fact is that you carry part of your sickness within you, at least I do as an invisible man. I carried my sickness and though for a long time I tried to place it in the outside world, the attempt to write it down shows me that at least half of it lay within me. It came upon me slowly, like that strange disease that affects those black men whom you see turning slowly from black to albino, their pigment disappearing as under the radiation of some cruel, invisible ray. You go along for years knowing something is wrong, then suddenly you discover that you're as transparent as air. At first you tell yourself that it's all a dirty joke, or that it's due to the "political situation." But deep down you come to suspect that you're yourself to blame, and you stand naked and shivering before the millions of eyes who look through you unseeingly. *That* is the real soul-sickness, the spear in the side, the drag by the neck through the mob-angry town, the Grand Inquisition, the embrace of the Maiden, the rip in the belly with the guts spilling out, the trip to the chamber with the deadly gas that ends in the oven so hygienically clean—only it's worse because you continue stupidly to live. But live you must, and you can either make passive love to your sickness or burn it out and go on to the next conflicting phase.

Yes, but what *is* the next phase? How often have I tried to find it! Over and over again I've gone up above to seek it out. For, like almost everyone else in our country, I started out with my share of optimism. I believed in hard work and progress and action, but now, after first being "for" society and then "against" it, I assign myself no rank or any limit, and such an attitude is very much against the trend of the times. But my world has become one of infinite possibilities. What a phrase—still it's a good phrase and a good view of life, and a man shouldn't accept any other; that much I've learned underground. Until some gang succeeds in putting the world in a strait jacket, its definition is possibility. Step outside the narrow borders of what men call reality and you step into chaos—ask Rinehart, he's a mas-

---

7. A white philanthropist whom the invisible man guides around his college and its environs. When he inadvertently allows Norton to meet the black sharecropper Jim Trueblood, who has committed incest with his daughter, the invisible man incurs the wrath of Dr. Bledsoe, the college president.

ter of it—or imagination. That too I've learned in the cellar, and not by deadening my sense of perception; I'm invisible, not blind.

No indeed, the world is just as concrete, ornery, vile and sublimely wonderful as before, only now I better understand my relation to it and it to me. I've come a long way from those days when, full of illusion, I lived a public life and attempted to function under the assumption that the world was solid and all the relationships therein. Now I know men are different and that all life is divided and that only in division is there true health. Hence again I have stayed in my hole, because up above there's an increasing passion to make men conform to a pattern. Just as in my nightmare, Jack and the boys are waiting with their knives, looking for the slightest excuse to . . . well, to "ball the jack," and I do not refer to the old dance step, although what they're doing is making the old eagle rock dangerously.

Whence all this passion toward conformity anyway?—diversity is the word. Let man keep his many parts and you'll have no tyrant states. Why, if they follow this conformity business they'll end up by forcing me, an invisible man, to become white, which is not a color but the lack of one. Must I strive toward colorlessness? But seriously, and without snobbery, think of what the world would lose if that should happen. America is woven of many strands; I would recognize them and let it so remain. It's "winner take nothing" that is the great truth of our country or of any country. Life is to be lived, not controlled; and humanity is won by continuing to play in face of certain defeat. Our fate is to become one, and yet many—This is not prophecy, but description. Thus one of the greatest jokes in the world is the spectacle of the whites busy escaping blackness and becoming blacker every day, and the blacks striving toward whiteness, becoming quite dull and gray. None of us seems to know who he is or where he's going.

Which reminds me of something that occurred the other day in the subway. At first I saw only an old gentleman who for the moment was lost. I knew he was lost, for as I looked down the platform I saw him approach several people and turn away without speaking. He's lost, I thought, and he'll keep coming until he sees me, then he'll ask his direction. Maybe there's an embarrassment in it if he admits he's lost to a strange white man. Perhaps to lose a sense of *where* you are implies the danger of losing a sense of *who* you are. That must be it, I thought—to lose your direction is to lose your face. So here he comes to ask his direction from the lost, the invisible. Very well, I've learned to live without direction. Let him ask.

But then he was only a few feet away and I recognized him; it was Mr. Norton. The old gentleman was thinner and wrinkled now but as dapper as ever. And seeing him made all the old life live in me for an instant, and I smiled with tear-stinging eyes. Then it was over, dead, and when he asked me how to get to Centre Street, I regarded him with mixed feelings.

"Don't you know me?" I said.

"Should I?" he said.

"You see me?" I said, watching him tensely.

"Why, of course—Sir, do you know the way to Centre Street?"

"So. Last time it was the Golden Day, now it's Centre Street. You've retrenched, sir. But don't you really know who I am?"

"Young man, I'm in a hurry," he said, cupping a hand to his ear. "Why should I know you?"

"Because I'm your destiny."

"My destiny, did you say?" He gave me a puzzled stare, backing away. "Young man, are you well? Which train did you say I should take?"

"I didn't say," I said, shaking my head. "Now, aren't you ashamed?"

"Ashamed? ASHAMED!" he said indignantly.

I laughed, suddenly taken by the idea. "Because, Mr. Norton, if you don't know *where* you are, you probably don't know *who* you are. So you came to me out of shame. You are ashamed, now aren't you?"

"Young man, I've lived too long in this world to be ashamed of anything. Are you light-headed from hunger? How do you know my name?"

"But I'm your destiny, I made you. Why shouldn't I know you?" I said, walking closer and seeing him back against a pillar. He looked around like a cornered animal. He thought I was mad.

"Don't be afraid, Mr. Norton," I said. "There's a guard down the platform there. You're safe. Take any train; they all go to the Golden D—"

But now an express had rolled up and the old man was disappearing quite spryly inside one of its doors. I stood there laughing hysterically. I laughed all the way back to my hole.

But after I had laughed I was thrown back on my thoughts—how had it all happened? And I asked myself if it were only a joke and I couldn't answer. Since then I've sometimes been overcome with a passion to return into that "heart of darkness" across the Mason-Dixon line, but then I remind myself that the true darkness lies within my own mind, and the idea loses itself in the gloom. Still the passion persists. Sometimes I feel the need to reaffirm all of it, the whole unhappy territory and all the things loved and unlovable in it, for all of it is part of me. Till now, however, this is as far as I've ever gotten, for all life seen from the hole of invisibility is absurd.

So why do I write, torturing myself to put it down? Because in spite of myself I've learned some things. Without the possibility of action, all knowledge comes to one labeled "file and forget," and I can neither file nor forget. Nor will certain ideas forget me; they keep filing away at my lethargy, my complacency. Why should I be the one to dream this nightmare? Why should I be dedicated and set aside—yes, if not to at least *tell* a few people about it? There seems to be no escape. Here I've set out to throw my anger into the world's face, but now that I've tried to put it all down the old fascination with playing a role returns, and I'm drawn upward again. So that even before I finish I've failed (maybe my anger is too heavy; perhaps, being a talker, I've used too many words). But I've failed. The very act of trying to put it all down has confused me and negated some of the anger and some of the bitterness. So it is that now I denounce and defend, or feel prepared to defend. I condemn and affirm, say no and say yes, say yes and say no. I denounce because though implicated and partially responsible, I have been hurt to the point of abysmal pain, hurt to the point of invisibility. And I defend because in spite of all I find that I love. In order to get some of it down I *have* to love. I sell you no phony forgiveness, I'm a desperate man—but too much of your life will be lost, its meaning lost, unless you approach it as much through love as through hate. So I approach it through division. So I denounce and I defend and I hate and I love.

Perhaps that makes me a little bit as human as my grandfather. Once I thought my grandfather incapable of thoughts about humanity, but I was wrong. Why should an old slave use such a phrase as, "This and this or this has made me more human," as I did in my arena speech? Hell, he never had any doubts about his humanity—that was left to his "free" offspring. He accepted his humanity just as he accepted the principle. It was his, and the principle lives on in all its human and absurd diversity. So now having tried to put it down I have disarmed myself in the process. You won't believe in my invisibility and you'll fail to see how any principle that applies to you could apply to me. You'll fail to see it even though death waits for both of us if you don't. Nevertheless, the very disarmament has brought me to a decision. The hibernation is over. I must shake off the old skin and come up for breath. There's a stench in the air, which, from this distance underground, might be the smell either of death or of spring—I hope of spring. But don't let me trick you, there *is* a death in the smell of spring and in the smell of thee as in the smell of me. And if nothing more, invisibility has taught my nose to classify the stenches of death.

In going underground, I whipped it all except the mind, the *mind*. And the mind that has conceived a plan of living must never lose sight of the chaos against which that pattern was conceived. That goes for societies as well as for individuals. Thus, having tried to give pattern to the chaos which lives within the pattern of your certainties, I must come out, I must emerge. And there's still a conflict within me: With Louis Armstrong one half of me says, "Open the window and let the foul air out," while the other says, "It was good green corn before the harvest." Of course Louie was kidding, *he* wouldn't have thrown old Bad Air out, because it would have broken up the music and the dance, when it was the good music that came from the bell of old Bad Air's horn that counted. Old Bad Air is still around with his music and his dancing and his diversity, and I'll be up and around with mine. And, as I said before, a decision has been made. I'm shaking off the old skin and I'll leave it here in the hole. I'm coming out, no less invisible without it, but coming out nevertheless. And I suppose it's damn well time. Even hibernations can be overdone, come to think of it. Perhaps that's my greatest social crime, I've overstayed my hibernation, since there's a possibility that even an invisible man has a socially responsible role to play.

"Ah," I can hear you say, "so it was all a build-up to bore us with his buggy jiving. He only wanted us to listen to him rave!" But only partially true: Being invisible and without substance, a disembodied voice, as it were, what else could I do? What else but try to tell you what was really happening when your eyes were looking through? And it is this which frightens me:

Who knows but that, on the lower frequencies, I speak for you?

1952

Change the Joke and Slip the Yoke [1]

Stanley Edgar Hyman's essay on the relationship between Negro American literature and Negro American folklore concerns matters in which my own interest is such that the very news of his piece aroused my enthusiasm. Yet after reading it I find that our conceptions of the way in which folk tradition gets into literature—and especially into the novel; our conceptions of just what is *Negro* and what is *American* in Negro American folklore; and our conceptions of a Negro American writer's environment—are at such odds that I must disagree with him all along the way. And since much of his essay is given over so generously to aspects of my own meager writings, I am put in the ungrateful—and embarrassing—position of not only evaluating some of his statements from that highly dubious (but privileged) sanctuary provided by one's intimate knowledge of one's personal history, but of questioning some of his readings of my own novel by consulting the text.

Archetypes, like taxes, seem doomed to be with us always, and so with literature, one hopes; but between the two there must needs be the living human being in a specific texture of time, place and circumstance; who must respond, make choices, achieve eloquence and create specific works of art. Thus I feel that Hyman's fascination with folk tradition and the pleasure of archetype-hunting leads to a critical game that ignores the specificity of literary works. And it also causes him to blur the distinction between various archetypes and different currents of American folklore, and, generally, to oversimplify the American tradition.

Hyman's favorite archetypical figure is the trickster, but I see a danger here. From a proper distance *all* archetypes would appear to be tricksters and confidence men; part-God, part-man, no one seems to know he-she-its true name, because he-she-it is protean with changes of pace, location and identity. Further, the trickster is everywhere and anywhere at one and the same time, and, like the parts of some dismembered god, is likely to be found on stony as well as on fertile ground. Folklore is somewhat more stable, in its identity if not in its genealogy; but even here, if we are to discuss *Negro* American folklore let us not be led astray by interlopers.

Certainly we should not approach Negro folklore through the figure Hyman calls the " 'darky' entertainer." For even though such performers as he mentions appear to be convenient guides, they lead us elsewhere, into a Cthonic [2] labyrinth. The role with which they are identified is not, despite its "blackness," Negro American (indeed, Negroes are repelled by it); it does not find its popularity among Negroes but among whites; and although it resembles the role of the clown familiar to Negro variety-house

1. This essay originated in the form of a letter in which, from Rome, I expressed my reactions to a lecture which Stanley Edgar Hyman, an old friend and intellectual sparring partner, was preparing for what was to be the first of the Ludwig Lewisohn lectures at Brandeis University. Hyman wrote back suggesting that I work up my ideas as part of a publishable debate, and the two essays were presented in *Partisan Review*, Spring 1958. They were titled "The Negro Writer in America: An Exchange," and they are apt to yield their maximum return when read together. Hyman's part of the exchange, which is a most useful discussion of the Negro American's relation to the folk tradition, appears in his book of essays and reviews, "The Promised End," published by The World Publishing Company, 1963 [Ellison's note].

2. Of the dark gods of the underworld of Greek mythology.

audiences, it derives not from the Negro but from the Anglo-Saxon branch of American folklore. In other words, this "'darky' entertainer" is white. Nevertheless, it might be worth while to follow the trail for a while, even though we seem more interested in interracial warfare than the question of literature.

These entertainers are, as Hyman explains, professionals, who in order to enact a symbolic role basic to the underlying drama of American society assume a ritual mask—the identical mask and role taken on by white minstrel men when *they* depicted comic Negroes. Social changes occurring since the 1930's have made for certain modifications (Rochester operates in a different climate of rhetoric, say, than did Stepin Fetchit[3]) but the mask, stylized and iconic, was once required of anyone who would act the role—even those Negroes whose natural coloration should, for any less ritualistic purposes at least, have made it unnecessary.

Nor does the role, which makes use of Negro idiom, songs, dance motifs and word-play, grow out of the Negro American sense of the comic (although we too have our comedy of blackness), but out of the white American's Manichean[4] fascination with the symbolism of blackness and whiteness expressed in such contradictions as the conflict between the white American's Judeo-Christian morality, his democratic political ideals and his daily conduct—indeed in his general anti-tragic approach to experience.

Being "highly pigmented," as the sociologists say, it was our Negro "misfortune" to be caught up associatively in the negative side of this basic dualism of the white folk mind, and to be shackled to almost everything it would repress from conscience and consciousness. The physical hardships and indignities of slavery were benign compared with this continuing debasement of our image. Because these things are bound up with their notion of chaos it is almost impossible for many whites to consider questions of sex, women, economic opportunity, the national identity, historic change, social justice—even the "criminality" implicit in the broadening of freedom itself—without summoning malignant images of black men into consciousness.

In the Anglo-Saxon branch of American folklore and in the entertainment industry (which thrives on the exploitation and debasement of all folk materials), the Negro is reduced to a negative sign that usually appears in a comedy of the grotesque and the unacceptable. As Constance Rourke[5] has made us aware, the action of the early minstrel show—with its Negro-deprived choreography, its ringing of banjos and rattling of bones, its voices cackling jokes in pseudo-Negro dialect, with its nonsense songs, its bright costumes and sweating performers—constituted a ritual of exorcism. Other white cultures had their gollywogs and blackamoors but the fact of Negro slavery went to the moral heart of the American social drama and here the Negro was too real for easy fantasy, too serious to be dealt with in anything

---

3. Actor and comedian (b. 1902) who portrayed the stereotype of an unsophisticated, subservient black man; the first black actor to receive feature billing. Rochester, Jack Benny's "handy man," was played by Eddie Anderson (1906–1977).
4. Dualistic; a reference to the religious system of the Persian prophet Manes (c. 216–276), whose basic doctrine posited a conflict between light and dark.
5. American biographer and cultural critic (1885–1941).

less than a national art. The mask was an inseparable part of the national iconography. Thus even when a Negro acted in an abstract role the national implications were unchanged. His costume made use of the "sacred" symbolism of the American flag—with red and white striped pants and coat and with stars set in a field of blue for a collar—but he could appear only with his hands gloved in white and his face blackened with burnt cork or greasepaint.

This mask, this willful stylization and modification of the natural face and hands, was imperative for the evocation of that atmosphere in which the fascination of blackness could be enjoyed, the comic catharsis achieved. The racial identity of the performer was unimportant, the mask was the thing (the "thing" in more ways than one) and its function was to veil the humanity of Negroes thus reduced to a sign, and to repress the white audience's awareness of its moral identification with its own acts and with the human ambiguities pushed behind the mask.

Hyman sees the comic point of the contemporary Negro's performance of the role as arising from the circumstance that a skilled man of intelligence is parodying a subhuman grotesque; this is all very kind, but when we move in from the wide-ranging spaces of the archetype for a closer inspection we see that the specific rhetorical situation involves the self-humiliation of the "sacrificial" figure, and that a psychological dissociation from this symbolic self-maiming is one of the powerful motives at work in the audience. Motives of race, status, economics and guilt are always clustered here. The comic point is inseparable from the racial identity of the performer—as is clear in Hyman's example from Wright's *Black Boy*—who by assuming the group-debasing role for gain not only substantiates the audience's belief in the "blackness" of things black, but relieves it, with dreamlike efficiency, of its guilt by accepting the very profit motive that was involved in the designation of the Negro as national scapegoat in the first place. There are all kinds of comedy: here one is reminded of the tribesman in *Green Hills of Africa* [6] who hid his laughing face in shame at the sight of a gun-shot hyena jerking out its own intestines and eating them, in Hemingway's words, "with relish."

Down at the deep dark bottom of the melting pot, where the private is public and the public private, where black is white and white black, where the immoral becomes moral and the moral is anything that makes one feel good (or that one has the power to sustain), the white man's relish is apt to be the black man's gall.

It is not at all odd that this black-faced figure of white fun is for Negroes a symbol of everything they rejected in the white man's thinking about race, in themselves and in their own group. When he appears, for example, in the guise of Nigger Jim, the Negro is made uncomfortable. Writing at a time when the blackfaced minstrel was still popular, and shortly after a war which left even the abolitionists weary of those problems associated with the Negro, Twain fitted Jim into the outlines of the minstrel tradition, and it is from behind this stereotype mask that we see Jim's dignity and human capacity—and Twain's complexity—emerge. Yet it is his source in this same

6. Novel (1935) by American writer Ernest Hemingway (1899–1961).

tradition which creates that ambivalence between his identification as an adult and parent and his "boyish" naïveté, and which by contrast makes Huck, with his street-sparrow sophistication, seem more adult. Certainly it upsets a Negro reader, and it offers a less psychoanalytical explanation of the discomfort which lay behind Leslie Fiedler's thesis concerning the relation of Jim and Huck in his essay "Come Back to the Raft Ag'in, Huck Honey!"[7]

A glance at a more recent fictional encounter between a Negro adult and a white boy, that of Lucas Beauchamp and Chick Mallison in Faulkner's *Intruder in the Dust*,[8] will reinforce my point. For all the racial and caste differences between them, Lucas holds the ascendency in his mature dignity over the youthful Mallison and refuses to lower himself in the comic duel of status forced on him by the white boy whose life he has saved. Faulkner was free to reject the confusion between manhood and the Negro's caste status which is sanctioned by white Southern tradition, but Twain, standing closer to the Reconstruction[9] and to the oral tradition, was not so free of the white dictum that Negro males must be treated either as boys or "uncles"—never as men. Jim's friendship for Huck comes across as that of a boy for another boy rather than as the friendship of an adult for a junior; thus there is implicit in it not only a violation of the manners sanctioned by society for relations between Negroes and whites, there is a violation of our conception of adult maleness.

In Jim the extremes of the private and the public come to focus, and before our eyes an "archetypal" figure gives way before the realism implicit in the form of the novel. Here we have, I believe, an explanation in the novel's own terms of that ambiguity which bothered Fiedler. Fiedler was accused of mere sensationalism when he named the friendship homosexual, yet I believe him so profoundly disturbed by the manner in which the deep dichotomies symbolized by blackness and whiteness are resolved that, forgetting to look at the specific form of the novel, he leaped squarely into the middle of that tangle of symbolism which he is dedicated to unsnarling, and yelled out his most terrifying name for chaos. Other things being equal, he might have called it "rape," "incest," "parricide" or—"miscegenation." It is ironic that what to a Negro appears to be a lost fall in Twain's otherwise successful wrestle with the ambiguous figure in black face is viewed by a critic as a symbolic loss of sexual identity. Surely for literature there is some rare richness here.

Although the figure in black face looks suspiciously homegrown, Western and Calvinist to me, Hyman identifies it as being related to an archetypical trickster figure, originating in Africa. Without arguing the point I shall say only that if it *is* a trickster, its adjustment to the contours of "white" symbolic needs is far more intriguing than its alleged origins, for it tells us something of the operation of American values as modulated by folklore and literature. We are back once more to questions of order and

---

7. The references in this paragraph are to Mark Twain's *Adventures of Huckleberry Finn* (1885), in which Huck, a white boy, and runaway slave Jim raft down the Mississippi River. As noted in the following paragraphs, Fiedler examined what he saw as the homoeroticism in Huck and Jim's friendship.

8. William Faulkner's 1948 novel. This and his collection of stories *Go Down, Moses* (1942) comprise his fullest treatment of African American life in the South.

9. The period of adjustment (1865–77) following the Civil War, a time during which black civil and political rights were highly contested.

chaos, illusion and reality, nonentity and identity.

The trickster, according to Karl Kerenyi (in a commentary included in Paul Radin's study, *The Trickster*[1]), represents a personification of the body

> which is . . . never wholly subdued, ruled by lust and hunger, forever running into pain and injury, cunning and stupid in action. Disorder belonging to the totality of life . . . the spirit of this disorder is the trickster. His function in an archaic society, or rather the function of his mythology, of the tales told about him, is to add disorder to order and to make a whole, to render possible, within the fixed bounds of what is permitted, an experience of what is not permitted. . . .

But ours is no archaic society (although its archaic elements exert far more influence in our lives than we care to admit), and it is an ironic reversal that in what is regarded as the most "open" society in the world, the license of the black trickster figure is limited by the rigidities of racial attitudes, by political expediencies, and by the guilt bound up with the white compulsion to identify with the ever-present man of flesh and blood whose irremediable features have been expropriated for "immoral" purposes. Hyman, incidentally, would have found in Louis Armstrong[2] a much better example of the trickster, his medium being music rather than words and pantomime. Armstrong's clownish license and intoxicating powers are almost Elizabethan; he takes liberties with kings, queens and presidents; emphasizes the physicality of his music with sweat, spittle and facial contortions; he performs the magical feat of making romantic melody issue from a throat of gravel; and some few years ago was recommending to all and sundry his personal physic, "Pluto Water," as a purging way to health, happiness and international peace.

When the white man steps behind the mask of the trickster his freedom is circumscribed by the fear that he is not simply miming a personification of his disorder and chaos but that he will become in fact that which he intends only to symbolize; that he will be trapped somewhere in the mystery of hell (for there is a mystery in the whiteness of blackness, the innocence of evil and the evil of innocence, though, being initiates, Negroes express the joke of it in the blues) and thus lose that freedom which, in the fluid, "traditionless," "classless" and rapidly changing society, he would recognize as the white man's alone.

Here another ironic facet of the old American problem of identity crops up. For out of the counterfeiting of the black American's identity there arises a profound doubt in the white man's mind as to the authenticity of his own image of himself. He, after all, went into the business when he refused the king's shilling and revolted. He had put on a mask of his own, as it were; and when we regard our concern with identity in the light of what Robert Penn Warren has termed the "intentional" character of our national beginnings, a quotation from W. B. Yeats[3] proves highly meaningful:

---

1. Anthropologist Paul Radin's *The Trickster: A Study in American Indian Mythology* (1956) is a widely read collection of Winnebago trickster stories. Kerenyi's essay is titled *The Trickster in Relation to Greek Mythology.*

2. African American jazz musician (1900–1971).
3. Irish poet, playwright, and philosopher (1865–1939). Warren (1905–1989), American poet, novelist, teacher, and literary critic.

There is a relation between discipline and the theatrical sense. If we cannot imagine ourselves as different from what we are and assume the second self, we cannot impose a discipline upon ourselves, though we may accept one from others. Active virtue, as distinct from the passive acceptance of a current code, is the wearing of a mask. It is the condition of an arduous full life.

For the ex-colonials, the declaration of an American identity meant the assumption of a mask, and it imposed not only the discipline of national self-consciousness, it gave Americans an ironic awareness of the joke that always lies between appearance and reality, between the discontinuity of social tradition and that sense of the past which clings to the mind. And perhaps even an awareness of the joke that society is man's creation, not God's. Americans began their revolt from the English fatherland when they dumped the tea into the Boston Harbor, masked as Indians, and the mobility of the society created in this limitless space has encouraged the use of the mask for good and evil ever since. As the advertising industry, which is dedicated to the creation of masks, makes clear, that which cannot gain authority from tradition may borrow it with a mask. Masking is a play upon possibility and ours is a society in which possibilities are many. When American life is most American it is apt to be most theatrical.

And it is this which makes me question Hyman's designation of the "smart man playing dumb" role as primarily Negro, if he means by "conflict situations" those in which racial pressure is uppermost. Actually it is a role which Negroes share with other Americans, and it might be more "Yankee" than anything else. It is a strategy common to the culture, and it is reinforced by our anti-intellectualism, by our tendency toward conformity and by the related desire of the individual to be left alone; often simply by the desire to put more money in the bank. But basically the strategy grows out of our awareness of the joke at the center of the American identity. Said a very dark Southern friend of mine in laughing reply to a white businessman who complained of his recalcitrance in a bargaining situation, "I know, you thought I was colored, didn't you." It is across this joke that Negro and white Americans regard one another. The white American has charged the Negro American with being without past or tradition (something which strikes the white man with a nameless horror), just as he himself has been so charged by European and American critics with a nostalgia for the stability once typical of European cultures; and the Negro knows that both were "mammy-made" right here at home. What's more, each secretly believes that he alone knows what is valid in the American experience, and that the other knows he knows but will not admit it, and each suspects the other of being at bottom a phony.

The white man's half-conscious awareness that his image of the Negro is false makes him suspect the Negro of always seeking to take him in, and assume his motives are anger and fear—which very often they are. On his side of the joke the Negro looks at the white man and finds it difficult to believe that the "grays"—a Negro term for white people—can be so absurdly self-deluded over the true interrelatedness of blackness and whiteness. To him the white man seems a hypocrite who boasts of a pure identity while standing with his humanity exposed to the world.

Very often, however, the Negro's masking is motivated not so much by fear as by a profound rejection of the image created to usurp his identity. Sometimes it is for the sheer joy of the joke; sometimes to challenge those who presume, across the psychological distance created by race manners, to know his identity. Nonetheless, it is in the American grain. Benjamin Franklin, the practical scientist, skilled statesman and sophisticated lover, allowed the French to mistake him for Rousseau's Natural Man.[4] Hemingway poses as a non-literary sportsman, Faulkner as a farmer; Abe Lincoln allowed himself to be taken for a simple country lawyer—until the chips were down. Here the "darky" act makes brothers of us all. America is a land of masking jokers. We wear the mask for purposes of aggression as well as for defense; when we are projecting the future and preserving the past. In short, the motives hidden behind the mask are as numerous as the ambiguities the mask conceals.

My basic quarrel with Hyman is not over his belief in the importance of the folk tradition, nor over his interest in archetypes; but that when he turns to specific works of literature he tends to distort their content to fit his theory. Since he refers so generously to my own novel, let us take it as a case in point. So intense is Hyman's search for archetypical forms that he doesn't see that the narrator's grandfather in Invisible Man is no more involved in a "darky" act than was Ulysses in Polyphemus' cave.[5] Nor is he so much a "smart-man-playing-dumb" as a weak man who knows the nature of his oppressor's weakness. There is a good deal of spite in the old man, as there comes to be in his grandson, and the strategy he advises is a kind of jiujitsu of the spirit, a denial and rejection through agreement. Samson,[6] eyeless in Gaza, pulls the building down when his strength returns; politically weak, the grandfather has learned that conformity leads to a similar end, and so advises his children. Thus his mask of meekness conceals the wisdom of one who has learned the secret of saying the "yes" which accomplishes the expressive "no." Here, too, is a rejection of a current code and a denial become metaphysical. More important to the novel is the fact that he represents the ambiguity of the past for the hero, for whom his sphinxlike deathbed advice poses a riddle which points the plot in the dual direction which the hero will follow throughout the novel.

Certainly B. P. Rinehart[7] (the P. is for "Proteus," the B. for "Bliss") would seem the perfect example of Hyman's trickster figure. He is a cunning man who wins the admiration of those who admire skulduggery and know-how; an American virtuoso of identity who thrives on chaos and swift change; he is greedy, in that his masquerade is motivated by money as well as by the sheer bliss of impersonation; he is godlike, in that he brings new techniques—electric guitars, etc.—to the service of God, and in that there are many men in his image while he is himself unseen; he is phallic in his

4. Jean-Jacques Rousseau (1712–1778), Swiss-French philosopher, saw civilization as a fall from humanity's natural goodness. Late in 1776, Franklin (1706–1790) sailed to France as a diplomat for the new American republic and paved the way for French recognition of the United States in 1778.
5. In Homer's Odyssey the cyclops Polyphemus imprisoned Odysseus and his men in a cave; they escaped by giving Polyphemus wine, blinding him when he was drunk, and hiding under his sheep as they left the cave.
6. Judge of Israel whose long hair symbolized the covenant with God that gave him great strength. Delilah cut his hair, which enabled the Philistines to blind and chain him. When his hair grew back and his strength returned, Samson pulled down the temple walls, in the process killing his captors and himself (Judges 13–16).
7. Character in Ellison's Invisible Man (1952) who assumes many different roles.

role of "lover"; as a numbers runner he is a bringer of manna and a worker of miracles, in that he transforms (for winners, of course) pennies into dollars, and thus he feeds (and feeds on) the poor. Indeed, one could extend this list in the manner of much myth-mongering criticism until the fiction dissolved into anthropology, but Rinehart's role in the formal structure of the narrative is to suggest to the hero a mode of escape from Ras, and a means of applying, in yet another form, his grandfather's cryptic advice to his own situation. One could throw Rinehart among his literary betters and link him with Mann's Felix Krull, the Baron Clappique of Malraux's *Man's Fate*[8] and many others, but that would be to make a game of criticism and really say nothing.

The identity of fictional characters is determined by the implicit realism of the form, not by their relation to tradition; they are what they do or do not do. Archetypes are timeless, novels are time-haunted. Novels achieve timelessness through time. If the symbols appearing in a novel link up with those of universal myth they do so by virtue of their emergence from the specific texture of a specific form of social reality. The final act of *Invisible Man* is not that of a concealment in darkness in the Anglo-Saxon connotation of the word, but that of a voice issuing its little wisdom out of the substance of its own inwardness—after having undergone a transformation from ranter to writer. If, by the way, the hero is pulling a "darky art" in this, he certainly is not a smart man playing dumb. For the novel, his memoir, is one long, loud rant, howl and laugh. Confession, not concealment, is his mode. His mobility is dual; geographical, as Hyman points out, but, more importantly, it is intellectual. And in keeping with the reverse English of the plot, and with the Negro American conception of blackness, his movement vertically downward (not into a "sewer," Freud[9] notwithstanding, but into a coal cellar, a source of heat, light, power and, through association with the character's motivation, self-perception) is a process of *rising* to an understanding of his human condition. He gets his restless mobility not so much from the blues or from sociology but from the circumstance that he appears in a literary form which has time and social change as its special province. Besides, restlessness of the spirit is an American condition that transcends geography, sociology and past condition of servitude.

Discussions of folk tradition and literature which slight the specific literary forms involved seem to me questionable. Most of the writers whom Hyman mentions are novelists, workers in a form which has absorbed folk tradition into its thematic structures, its plots, symbolism and rhetoric; and which has its special way with folklore as it has with manners, history, sociology and psychology. Besides, novelists in our time are more likely to be inspired by reading novels than by their acquaintance with any folk tradition.

I use folklore in my work not because I am Negro, but because writers like Eliot and Joyce[1] made me conscious of the literary value of my folk

8. A 1933 novel about the Chinese revolution of the 1920s by André Malraux (1901–1976), French man of letters and political figure. It features the enigmatic Baron de Clappique, who has a talent for disguise. Thomas Mann (1875–1955), German writer, published the picaresque comedy Confes-

sions of Felix Krull, Confidence Man in 1954.
9. Sigmund Freud (1856–1939), Austrian psychiatrist and founder of psychoanalysis.
1. James Joyce (1882–1941), Irish novelist. T. S. Eliot (1888–1965), U.S.-born English poet and critic.

inheritance. My cultural background, like that of most Americans, is dual (my middle name, sadly enough, is Waldo).

I knew the trickster Ulysses just as early as I knew the wily rabbit of Negro American lore, and I could easily imagine myself a pint-sized Ulysses but hardly a rabbit, no matter how human and resourceful or Negro. And a little later I could imagine myself as Huck Finn (I so nicknamed my brother) but not, though I racially identified with him, as Nigger Jim, who struck me as a white man's inadequate portrait of a slave.

My point is that the Negro American writer is also an heir of the human experience which is literature, and this might well be more important to him than his living folk tradition. For me, at least, in the discontinuous, swiftly changing and diverse American culture, the stability of the Negro American folk tradition became precious as a result of an act of literary discovery. Taken as a whole, its spirituals along with its blues, jazz and folk tales, it has, as Hyman suggests, much to tell us of the faith, humor and adaptability to reality necessary to live in a world which has taken on much of the insecurity and blues-like absurdity known to those who brought it into being. For those who are able to translate its meanings into wider, more precise vocabularies it has much to offer indeed. Hyman performs a service when he makes us aware that Negro American folk tradition constitutes a valuable source for literature, but for the novelist, of any cultural or racial identity, his form is his greatest freedom and his insights are where he finds them.

1958

The World and the Jug [1]

> What runs counter to the revolutionary
> convention is, in revolutionary histories,
> suppressed more imperiously than embar-
> rassing episodes in private memoirs, and
> by the same obscure forces. . . .
> —ANDRÉ MALRAUX

I

First, three questions: Why is it so often true that when critics confront the American as *Negro* they suddenly drop their advanced critical armament and revert with an air of confident superiority to quite primitive modes of analysis? Why is it that sociology-oriented critics seem to rate literature so far below politics and ideology that they would rather kill a novel

1. "The World and the Jug" is actually a combination of two separate pieces. The first, bearing the original title, was written at the suggestion of Myron Kolatch of *The New Leader*, who was interested in my reactions, via telephone, to an essay by Irving Howe titled "Black Boys and Native Sons," which appeared in the Autumn 1963 issue of Howe's magazine, *Dissent*.

Usually such a reply would have appeared in the same magazine in which the original essay was published, but in this instance, and since it hadn't occurred to me to commit my reactions to paper, they went to the editor who asked for them. The second section of the essay, originally entitled, "A Rejoinder," was written after Irving Howe had consented to reply, in *The New Leader*, of February 3, 1964, to my attack. There is, unfortunately, too little space here to do justice to Howe's arguments, and it is recommended that the interested reader consult Mr. Howe's book of essays, *A World More Attractive*—a book worthy of his attention far beyond the limits of our exchange—published by Horizon Press in 1963 [Ellison's note].

than modify their presumptions concerning a given reality which it seeks in its own terms to project? Finally, why is it that so many of those who would tell us the meaning of Negro life never bother to learn how varied it really is?

These questions are aroused by "Black Boys and Native Sons," an essay by Irving Howe, the well-known critic and editor of *Dissent*, in the Autumn 1963 issue of that magazine. It is a lively piece, written with something of the Olympian authority that characterized Hannah Arendt's "Reflections on Little Rock" in the Winter 1959 *Dissent* (a dark foreshadowing of the Eichmann blowup). And in addition to a hero, Richard Wright, it has two villains, James Baldwin[2] and Ralph Ellison, who are seen as "black boys" masquerading as false, self-deceived "native sons." Wright himself is given a diversity of roles (all conceived by Howe): He is not only the archetypal and true-blue black boy—the "honesty" of his famous autobiography established this for Howe—but the spiritual father of Ellison, Baldwin and all other Negroes of literary bent to come. Further, in the platonic sense he is his own father and the culture hero who freed Ellison and Baldwin to write more "modulated" prose.

Howe admires Wright's accomplishments, and is frankly annoyed by the more favorable evaluation currently placed upon the works of the younger men. His claims for *Native Son* are quite broad:

> The day [it] appeared, American culture was changed forever . . . it made impossible a repetition of the old lies . . . it brought into the open . . . the fear and violence that have crippled and may yet destroy our culture. . . . A blow at the white man, the novel forced him to recognize himself as an oppressor. A blow at the black man, the novel forced him to recognize the cost of his submission. *Native Son* assaulted the most cherished of American vanities: the hope that the accumulated injustices of the past would bring with it no lasting penalties, the fantasy that in his humiliation the Negro somehow retained a sexual potency . . . that made it necessary to envy and still more to suppress him. Speaking from the black wrath of retribution, Wright insisted that history can be a punishment. He told us the one thing even the most liberal whites preferred not to hear: that Negroes were far from patient or forgiving, that they were scarred by fear, that they hated every moment of their suppression even when seeming most acquiescent, and that often enough they hated *us*, the decent and cultivated white men who from complicity or neglect shared in the responsibility of their plight. . . .

There are also negative criticisms: that the book is "crude," "melodramatic" and marred by "claustrophobia" of vision, that its characters are "cartoons," etc. But these defects Howe forgives because of the book's "clenched militancy." One wishes he had stopped there. For in his zeal to champion Wright, it is as though he felt it necessary to stage a modern version of the Biblical myth of Noah, Ham, Shem and Japheth (based originally, I'm told, on a castration ritual), with first Baldwin and then Ellison

---

2. African American author (1924–1987). Wright (1908–1960), African American author.

acting out the impious role of Ham:[3] Baldwin by calling attention to Noah-Wright's artistic nakedness in his famous essays, "Everybody's Protest Novel" (1949) and "Many Thousands Gone" (1951); Ellison by rejecting "narrow naturalism" as a fictional method, and by alluding to the "diversity, fluidity and magical freedom of American life" on that (for him at least) rather magical occasion when he was awarded the National Book Award. Ellison also offends by having the narrator of *Invisible Man* speak of his life (Howe either missing the irony or assuming that *I* did) as one of "infinite possibilities" while living in a hole in the ground.

Howe begins by attacking Baldwin's rejection in "Everybody's Protest Novel" of the type of literature he labeled "protest fiction" (*Uncle Tom's Cabin* and *Native Son*[4] being prime examples), and which he considered incapable of dealing adequately with the complexity of Negro experience. Howe, noting that this was the beginning of Baldwin's career, sees the essay's underlying motive as a declaration of Baldwin's intention to transcend "the sterile categories of 'Negroness,'" whether those enforced by the white world or those defensively erected by the Negroes themselves. No longer mere victim or rebel, the Negro would stand free in a self-achieved humanity. As Baldwin put it some years later, he hoped to 'prevent himself from becoming merely a Negro; or even, merely, a Negro writer.'" Baldwin's elected agency for self-achievement would be the novel—as it turns out, it was the essay *and* the novel—but the novel, states Howe, "is an inherently ambiguous genre: it strains toward formal autonomy and can seldom avoid being public gesture."

I would have said that it is *always* a public gesture, though not necessarily a political one. I would also have pointed out that the American Negro novelist is himself "inherently ambiguous." As he strains toward self-achievement as artist (and here he can only "integrate" and free himself), he moves toward fulfilling his dual potentialities as Negro and American. While Howe agrees with Baldwin that "literature and sociology are not one and the same," he notes nevertheless that, "it is equally true that such statements hardly begin to cope with the problem of how a writer's own experience affects his desire to represent human affairs in a work of fiction." Thus Baldwin's formula evades "through rhetorical sweep, the genuinely difficult issue of the relationship between social experience and literature." And to Baldwin's statement that one writes "out of one thing only—one's own experience" (I would have added, for the novelist, this qualification: one's own experience as understood and ordered through one's knowledge of self, culture and literature), Howe, appearing suddenly in blackface, replies with a rhetorical sweep of his own:

> What, then, was the experience of a man with a black skin, what could it be here in this country? How could a Negro put pen to paper, how could he so much as think or breathe, without some impulsion to protest, be it harsh or mild, political or private, released or buried?" . . .

3. After his son Ham saw him naked and drunk in his tent, Noah cursed Ham and his descendants and made them slaves to those of his two brothers, who had covered their father with a garment.

4. Richard Wright's 1940 novel. Harriet Beecher Stowe's *Uncle Tom's Cabin* (1852) aroused much northern indignation against slavery.

The "sociology" of his existence forms a constant pressure on his literary work, and not merely in the way this might be true of any writer, but with a pain and ferocity that nothing could remove.

I must say that this brought a shock of recognition. Some twelve years ago, a friend argued with me for hours that I could not possibly write a novel because my experience as a Negro had been too excruciating to allow me to achieve that psychological and emotional distance necessary to artistic creation. Since he "knew" Negro experience better than I, I could not convince him that he might be wrong. Evidently Howe feels that unrelieved suffering is the only "real" Negro experience, and that the true Negro writer must be ferocious.

But there is also an American Negro tradition which teaches one to deflect racial provocation and to master and contain pain. It is a tradition which abhors as obscene any trading on one's own anguish for gain or sympathy; which springs not from a desire to deny the harshness of existence but from a will to deal with it as men at their best have always done. It takes fortitude to be a man and no less to be an artist. Perhaps it takes even more if the black man would be an artist. If so, there are no exemptions. It would seem to me, therefore, that the question of how the "sociology of his existence" presses upon a Negro writer's work depends upon how much of his life the individual writer is able to transform into art. What moves a writer to eloquence is less meaningful than what he makes of it. How much, by the way, do we know of Sophocles'[5] wounds?

One unfamiliar with what Howe stands for would get the impression that when he looks at a Negro he sees not a human being but an abstract embodiment of living hell. He seems never to have considered that American Negro life (and here he is encouraged by certain Negro "spokesmen") is, for the Negro who must live it, not only a burden (and not always that) but also a *discipline*—just as any human life which has endured so long is a discipline teaching its own insights into the human condition, its own strategies of survival. There is a fullness, even a richness here; and here *despite* the realities of politics, perhaps, but nevertheless here and real. Because it is *human* life. And Wright, for all of his indictments, was no less its product than that other talented Mississippian, Leontyne Price.[6] To deny in the interest of revolutionary posture that such possibilities of human richness exist for others, even in Mississippi, is not only to deny us our humanity but to betray the critic's commitment to social reality. Critics who do so should abandon literature for politics.

For even as his life toughens the Negro, even as it brutalizes him, sensitizes him, dulls him, goads him to anger, moves him to irony, sometimes fracturing and sometimes affirming his hopes; even as it shapes his attitudes toward family, sex, love, religion; even as it modulates his humor, tempers his joy—it *conditions* him to deal with his life and with himself. Because it is *his* life and no mere abstraction in someone's head. He must live it and try consciously to grasp its complexity until he can change it; must live it *as* he changes it. He is no mere product of his socio-political

5. Greek tragic poet (c. 496–406 B.C.).
6. African American soprano and eminent opera singer (b. 1927).

predicament. He is a product of the interaction between his racial predicament, his individual will and the broader American cultural freedom in which he finds his ambiguous existence. Thus he, too, in a limited way, is his own creation.

In his loyalty to Richard Wright, Howe considers Ellison and Baldwin guilty of filial betrayal because, in their own work, they have rejected the path laid down by Native Son, phonies because, while actually "black boys," they pretend to be mere American writers trying to react to something of the pluralism of their predicament.

In his myth Howe takes the roles of both Shem and Japheth, trying mightily (his face turned backward so as not to see what it is he's veiling) to cover the old man's bare belly, and then becoming Wright's voice from beyond the grave by uttering the curses which Wright was too ironic or too proud to have uttered himself, at least in print:

> In response to Baldwin and Ellison, Wright would have said (I virtually quote the words he used in talking to me during the summer of 1958) that only through struggle could men with black skins, and for that matter, all the oppressed of the world, achieve their humility. It was a lesson, said Wright, with a touch of bitterness yet not without kindness, that the younger writers would have to learn in their own way and their own time. All that has happened since bears him out.

What, coming eighteen years after Native Son and thirteen years after World War II, does this rather limp cliché mean? Nor is it clear what is meant by the last sentence—or is it that today Baldwin has come to out-Wrighting Richard? The real questions seem to be: How does the Negro writer participate as a writer in the struggle for human freedom? To whom does he address his work? What values emerging from Negro experience does he try to affirm?

I started with the primary assumption that men with black skins, having retained their humanity before all of the conscious efforts made to dehumanize them, especially following the Reconstruction,[7] are unquestionably human. Thus they have the obligation of freeing themselves—whoever their allies might be—by depending upon the validity of their own experience for an accurate picture of the reality which they seek to change, and for a gauge of the values they would see made manifest. Crucial to this view is the belief that their resistance to provocation, their coolness under pressure, their sense of timing and their tenacious hold on the ideal of their ultimate freedom are indispensable values in the struggle, and are at least as characteristic of American Negroes as the hatred, fear and vindictiveness which Wright chose to emphasize.

Wright believed in the much abused idea that novels are "weapons"—the counterpart of the dreary notion, common among most minority groups, that novels are instruments of good public relations. But I believe that true novels, even when most pessimistic and bitter, arise out of an impulse to celebrate human life and therefore are ritualistic and ceremonial

---

7. Period of adjustment (1865–77) following the Civil War, during which black political and civil rights were highly contested.

at their core. Thus they would preserve as they destroy, affirm as they reject.

In *Native Son*, Wright began with the ideological proposition that what whites think of the Negro's reality is more important than what Negroes themselves know it to be. Hence Bigger Thomas was presented as a near-subhuman indictment of white oppression. He was designed to shock whites out of their apathy and end the circumstances out of which Wright insisted Bigger emerged. Here environment is all—and interestingly enough, environment conceived solely in terms of the physical, the non-conscious. Well, cut off my legs and call me Shorty! Kill my parents and throw me on the mercy of the court as an orphan! Wright could imagine Bigger, but Bigger could not possibly imagine Richard Wright. Wright saw to that.

But without arguing Wright's right to his personal vision, I would say that he was himself a better argument for my approach than Bigger was for his. And so, to be fair and as inclusive as Howe, is James Baldwin. Both are true Negro Americans, and both affirm the broad possibility of personal realization which I see as a saving aspect of American life. Surely, this much can be admitted without denying the injustice which all three of us have protested.

Howe is impressed by Wright's pioneering role and by the ". . . enormous courage, the discipline of self-conquest required to conceive Bigger Thomas. . . ." And earlier: "If such younger novelists as Baldwin and Ralph Ellison were able to move beyond Wright's harsh naturalism toward more supple modes of fiction, that was only possible because Wright had been there first, courageous enough to release the full weight of his anger."

It is not for me to judge Wright's courage, but I must ask just why it was possible for me to write as I write "only" because Wright released his anger? Can't I be allowed to release my own? What does Howe know of my acquaintance with violence, or the shape of my courage or the intensity of my anger? I suggest that my credentials are at least as valid as Wright's, even though he began writing long before I did, and it is possible that I have lived through and committed even more violence than he. Howe must wait for an autobiography before he can be responsibly certain. Everybody wants to tell us what a Negro is, yet few wish, even in a joke, to be one. But if you would tell me who I am, at least take the trouble to discover what I have been.

Which brings me to the most distressing aspect of Howe's thinking: his Northern white liberal version of the white Southern myth of absolute separation of the races. He implies that Negroes can only aspire to contest other Negroes (this at a time when Baldwin has been taking on just about everyone, including Hemingway, Faulkner and the United States Attorney General!), and must wait for the appearance of a Black Hope before they have the courage to move. Howe is so committed to a sociological vision of society that he apparently cannot see (perhaps because he is dealing with Negroes—although not because he would suppress us socially or politically, for in fact he is anxious to end such suppression) that whatever the efficiency of segregation as a socio-political arrangement, it has been far from absolute on the level of *culture*. Southern whites cannot walk, talk, sing, conceive of laws or justice, think of sex, love, the family or freedom without responding to the presence of Negroes.

Similarly, no matter how strictly Negroes are segregated socially and politically, on the level of the imagination their ability to achieve freedom is limited only by their individual aspiration, insight, energy and will. Wright was able to free himself in Mississippi because he had the imagination and the will to do so. He was as much a product of his reading as of his painful experiences, and he made himself a writer by subjecting himself to the writer's discipline—as he understood it. The same is true of James Baldwin, who is not the product of a Negro store-front church but of the library, and the same is true of me.

Howe seems to see segregation as an opaque steel jug with the Negroes inside waiting for some black messiah to come along and blow the cork. Wright is his hero and he sticks with him loyally. But if we are in a jug it is transparent, not opaque, and one is allowed not only to see outside but to read what is going on out there; to make identifications as to values and human quality. So in Macon County, Alabama, I read Marx, Freud, T. S. Eliot, Pound, Gertrude Stein and Hemingway.[8] Books which seldom, if ever, mentioned Negroes were to release me from whatever "segregated" idea I might have had of my human possibilities. I was freed not by propagandists or by the example of Wright—I did not know him at the time and was earnestly trying to learn enough to write a symphony and have it performed by the time I was twenty-six, because Wagner had done so and I admired his music—but by composers, novelists, and poets who spoke to me of more interesting and freer ways of life.

These were works which, by fulfilling themselves as works of art, by being satisfied to deal with life in terms of their own sources of power, were able to give me a broader sense of life and possibility. Indeed, I understand a bit more about myself as Negro because literature has taught me something of my identity as Western man, as political being. It has also taught me something of the cost of being an individual who aspires to conscious eloquence. It requires real poverty of the imagination to think that this can come to a Negro *only* through the example of *other Negroes*, especially after the performance of the slaves in re-creating themselves, in good part, out of the images and myths of the Old Testament Jews.

No, Wright was no spiritual father of mine, certainly in no sense I recognize—nor did he pretend to be, since he felt that I had started writing too late. It was Baldwin's career, not mine, that Wright proudly advanced by helping him attain the Eugene Saxton Fellowship,[9] and it was Baldwin who found Wright a lion in his path. Being older and familiar with quite different lions in quite different paths, I simply stepped around him.

But Wright was a friend for whose magazine I wrote my first book review

8. American novelist and short story writer (1899–1961). Karl Marx (1818–1883), German social philosopher and theorist of modern socialism and communism. Sigmund Freud (1856–1939), Austrian psychiatrist and founder of psychoanalysis. Eliot (1888–1965), U.S.-born English poet and critic. Ezra Pound (1885–1972), American poet, critic, and translator. Stein (1874–1946), American expatriate and author.
9. At Wright's request, Baldwin mailed him the first sixty pages of his first novel, *In My Father's House*, which Wright liked enough to arrange the award for Baldwin. Baldwin was unable to complete the novel during the tenure of the fellowship.

and short story, and a personal hero in the same way Hot Lips Paige and Jimmy Rushing[1] were friends and heroes. I felt no need to attack what I considered the limitations of his vision because I was quite impressed by what he had achieved. And in this, although I saw with the black vision of Ham, I was, I suppose, as pious as Shem and Japheth. Still I would write my own books and they would be in themselves, implicitly, criticisms of Wright's; just as all novels of a given historical moment form an argument over the nature of reality and are, to an extent, criticisms each of the other.

While I rejected Bigger Thomas as any *final* image of Negro personality, I recognized *Native Son* as an achievement; as one man's essay in defining the human condition as seen from a specific Negro perspective at a given time in a given place. And I was proud to have known Wright and happy for the impact he had made upon our apathy. But Howe's ideas notwithstanding, history is history, cultural contacts ever mysterious, and taste exasperatingly personal. Two days after arriving in New York I was to read Malraux's *Man's Fate* and *The Days of Wrath*,[2] and after these how could I be impressed by Wright as an ideological novelist. Need my skin blind me to all other values? Yet Howe writes:

> When Negro liberals write that despite the prevalence of bias there has been an improvement in the life of their people, such statements are reasonable and necessary. But what have these to do with the way Negroes feel, with the power of the memories they must surely retain? About this we know very little and would be well advised not to nourish preconceptions, for their feelings may well be closer to Wright's rasping outbursts than to the more modulated tones of the younger Negro novelists. *Wright remembered*, and what he remembered other Negroes must also have remembered. And in that way he kept faith with the experience of the boy who had fought his way out of the depths, to speak for those who remained there.

Wright, for Howe, is the genuine article, the authentic Negro writer, and his tone the only authentic tone. But why strip Wright of his individuality in order to criticize other writers. He had his memories and I have mine, just as I suppose Irving Howe has his—or has Marx spoken the final word for him? Indeed, very early in *Black Boy*,[3] Wright's memory and his contact with literature come together in a way revealing, at least to the eye concerned with Wright the literary man, that his manner of keeping faith with the Negroes who remained in the depths is quite interesting:

> (After I had outlived the shocks of childhood, after the habit of reflection had been born in me, I used to mull over the strange absence of real kindness in Negroes, how unstable was our tenderness, how lacking in genuine passion we were, how void of great hope, how timid our joy, how bare our traditions, how hollow our memories, how lacking we were in those intangible sentiments that bind man to man and how shallow was even our despair. After I had learned other ways of life I

---

1. Jazz singer (1903–1972). Oran "Hot Lips" Page (1908–1954), jazz trumpeter and singer.
2. Novels by French author and political figure

André Malraux (1901–1976).
3. Wright's 1945 autobiography.

used to brood upon the unconscious irony of those who felt that Negroes led so passional an existence! I saw that what had been taken for our emotional strength was our negative confusions, our flights, our fears, our frenzy under pressure.

(Whenever I thought of the essential bleakness of black life in America, I knew that Negroes had never been allowed to catch the full spirit of Western civilization, that they lived somehow in it but not of it. And when I brooded upon the cultural barrenness of black life, I wondered if clean, positive tenderness, love, honor, loyalty and the capacity to remember were native with man. I asked myself if these human qualities were not fostered, won, struggled and suffered for, preserved in ritual from one generation to another.)

Must I be condemned because my sense of Negro life was quite different? Or because for me keeping faith would never allow me to even raise such a question about any segment of humanity? *Black Boy* is not a sociological case history but an autobiography, and therefore a work of art shaped by a writer bent upon making an ideological point. Doubtlessly, this was the beginning of Wright's exile, the making of a decision which was to shape his life and writing thereafter. And it is precisely at this point that Wright is being what I would call, in Howe's words, "literary to a fault."

For just as *How Bigger Was Born* is Wright's Jamesian preface to *Native Son*, the passage quoted above is his paraphrase of Henry James' catalogue of those items of a high civilization which were absent from American life during Hawthorne's[4] day, and which seemed so necessary in order for the novelist to function. This, then, was Wright's list of those items of high humanity which he found missing among Negroes. Thank God, I have never been quite that literary.

How awful that Wright found the facile answers of Marxism before he learned to use literature as a means for discovering the forms of American Negro humanity. I could not and cannot question their existence, I can only seek again and again to project that humanity as I see it and feel it. To me Wright as *writer* was less interesting than the enigma he personified: that he could so dissociate himself from the complexity of his background while trying so hard to improve the condition of black men everywhere; that he could be so wonderful an example of human possibility but could not for ideological reasons depict a Negro as intelligent, as creative or as dedicated as himself.

In his effort to resuscitate Wright, Irving Howe would designate the role which Negro writers are to play more rigidly than any Southern politician—and for the best of reasons. We must express "black" anger and "clenched militancy"; most of all we should not become too interested in the problems of the art of literature, even though it is through these that we seek our individual identities. And between writing well and being ideologically militant, we must choose militancy.

4. Nathaniel Hawthorne (1804–1864), American novelist and short story writer. James (1843–1916), American novelist and critic.

Well, it all sounds quite familiar and I fear the social order which it forecasts more than I do that of Mississippi. Ironically, during the 1940s it was one of the main sources of Wright's rage and frustration.

II

I am sorry Irving Howe got the impression that I was throwing bean-balls when I only meant to pitch him a hyperbole. It would seem, however, that he approves of angry Negro writers only until one questions his ideas; then he reaches for his honor, cries "misrepresentation" and "distortion," and charges the writer with being both out of control of himself and with fashioning a "strategy calculated to appeal, ready-made, to the preconceptions of the liberal audience." Howe implies that there are differences between us which I disguised in my essay, yet whatever the validity of this attempt at long-distance psychoanalysis, it was not his honor which I questioned but his thinking; not his good faith but his critical method.

And the major differences which these raised between us I tried to describe. They are to be seen by anyone who reads Howe's "Black Boys and Native Sons" not as a collection of thematically related fragments but as the literary exposition of a considered point of view. I tried to interpret this essay in the light of the impact it made upon my sense of life and literature, and I judged it through its total form—just as I would have Howe base his judgments of writers and their circumstances on as much of what we know about the actual complexity of men living in a highly pluralistic society as is possible. I realize that the *un*common sense of a critic, his special genius, is a gift to be thankful for whenever we find it. The very least I expected of Howe, though, was that he would remember his *common* sense, that he would not be carried away by that intellectual abandon, that lack of restraint, which seizes those who regard blackness as an absolute and who see in it a release from the complications of the real world.

Howe is interested in militant confrontation and suffering, yet evidently he recognizes neither when they involve some act of his own. He *really* did not know the subject was loaded. Very well, but I was brought into the booby-trapped field of his assumptions and finding myself in pain, I did not choose to "hold back from the suffering" inflicted upon me there. Out of an old habit I yelled—without seeking Howe's permission, it is true—where it hurt the most. For oddly enough, I found it far less painful to have to move to the back of a Southern bus, or climb to the peanut gallery of a movie house—matters about which I could do nothing except walk, read, hunt, dance, sculpt, cultivate ideas, or seek other uses for my time—than to tolerate concepts which distorted the actual reality of my situation or my reactions to it.

I could escape the reduction imposed by unjust laws and customs, but not that imposed by ideas which defined me as no more than the *sum* of those laws and customs. I learned to outmaneuver those who interpreted my silence as submission, my efforts at self-control as fear, my contempt as awe before superior status, my dreams of faraway places and room at the top of the heap as defeat before the barriers of their stifling, provincial world. And my struggle became a desperate battle which was usually fought, though not always, in silence; a guerrilla action in a larger war in which I found some of the most treacherous assaults against me committed by those who regarded themselves either as neutrals, as sympathizers, or as disinterested military advisers.

I recall this not in complaint, for thus was I disciplined to endure the absurdities of both conscious and unconscious prejudice, to resist racial provocation and, before the ready violence of brutal policemen, railroad "bulls," and casual white citizens, to hold my peace and bide my time. Thus was I forced to evaluate my own self-worth, and the narrow freedom in which it existed, against the power of those who would destroy me. In time I was to leave the South, although it has never left me, and the interests which I discovered there became my life.

But having left the South I did not leave the battle—for how could I leave Howe? He is a man of words and ideas, and since I, too, find my identity in the world of ideas and words, where would I flee? I still endure the nonsense of fools with a certain patience, but when a respected critic distorts my situation in order to feel comfortable in the abstractions he would impose upon American reality, then it is indeed "in accordance with my nature" to protest. Ideas are important in themselves, perhaps, but when they are interposed between me and my sense of reality I feel threatened; they are too elusive, they move with missile speed and are too often fired from altitudes rising high above the cluttered terrain upon which I struggle. And too often those with a facility for ideas find themselves in the councils of power representing me at the double distance of racial alienation and inexperience.

Taking leave of Howe for a moment—for his lapse is merely symptomatic—let me speak generally. Many of those who write of Negro life today seem to assume that as long as their hearts are in the right place they can be as arbitrary as they wish in their formulations. Others seem to feel that they can air with impunity their most private Freudian fantasies as long as they are given the slightest camouflage of intellectuality and projected as "Negro." They have made of the no-man's land created by segregation a territory for infantile self-expression and intellectual anarchy. They write as though Negro life exists only in light of their belated regard, and they publish interpretations of Negro experience which would not hold true for their own or for any other form of human life.

Here the basic unity of human experience that assures us of some possibility of empathic and symbolic identification with those of other backgrounds is blasted in the interest of specious political and philosophical conceits. Prefabricated Negroes are sketched on sheets of paper and superimposed upon the Negro community; then when someone thrusts his head through the page and yells, "Watch out there, Jack, there're people living under here," they are shocked and indignant. I am afraid, however, that we shall hear much more of such protest as these interpositions continue. And I predict this, not out of any easy gesture of militancy (and what an easy con-game for ambitious, publicity-hungry Negroes this stance of "militancy" has become!) but because as Negroes express increasingly their irritation in this critical area, many of those who make so lightly with our image shall find their own subjected to a most devastating scrutiny.

One of the most insidious crimes occurring in this democracy is that of designating another, politically weaker, less socially acceptable, people as the receptacle for one's own self-disgust, for one's own infantile rebellions, for one's own fears of, and retreats from, reality. It is the crime of reducing the humanity of others to that of a mere convenience, a counter in a banal game which involves no apparent risk to ourselves. With us Negroes it started with the appropriation of our freedom and our labor; then it was our music, our speech, our dance and the comic distortion of our image by burnt-corked, cotton-gloved corn-balls yelling, "Mammy!" And while it would be futile, non-tragic, and un-Negro American to complain over the processes through which we have become who and what we are, it is perhaps permissible to say that the time for such misappropriations ran out long ago.

For one thing, Negro American consciousness is not a product (as so often seems true of so many American groups) of a will to historical forgetfulness. It is a product of our memory, sustained and constantly reinforced by events, by our watchful waiting, and by our hopeful suspension of final judgment as to the meaning of our grievances. For another, most Negroes recognize themselves as themselves despite what others might believe them to be. Thus, although the sociologists tell us that thousands of light-skinned Negroes become white each year undetected, most Negroes can spot a paper-thin "white Negro" every time simply because those who masquerade missed what others were forced to pick up along the way: discipline—a discipline which these heavy thinkers would not undergo even if guaranteed that combined with their own heritage it would make of them the freest of spirits, the wisest of men and the most sublime of heroes.

The rhetorical strategy of my original reply was not meant, as Howe interprets it, to strike the stance of a "free artist" against the "ideological critic," although I do recognize that I can be free only to the extent that I detect error and grasp the complex reality of my circumstances and work to dominate it through the techniques which are my means of confronting the world. Perhaps I am only free enough to recognize those tendencies of thought which, actualized, would render me even less free.

Even so, I did not intend to take the stance of the "knowing Negro writer" against the "presuming white intellectual." While I am without doubt a Negro, and a writer, I am also an *American* writer, and while I am more knowing than Howe where my own life and its influences are concerned, I took the time to question his presumptions as one responsible for contributing as much as he is capable to the clear perception of American social reality. For to think unclearly about that segment of reality in which I find my existence is to do myself violence. To allow others to go unchallenged when they distort that reality is to participate not only in that distortion but to accept, as in this instance, a violence inflicted upon the art of criticism. And if I am to recognize those aspects of my role as writer which do not depend primarily upon my racial identity, if I am to fulfill the writer's basic responsibilities to his craft, then surely I must insist upon the maintenance of a certain level of precision in language, a maximum correspondence between the form of a piece of writing and its content, and between words and ideas and the things and processes of his world.

Whatever my role as "race man" (and it knocks me out whenever anyone, black or white, tries to tell me—and the white Southerners have no monopoly here—how to become their conception of a "good Negro"), I am as writer no less a custodian of the American language than is Irving Howe. Indeed, to the extent that I am a writer—I lay no claims to being a thinker—the American language, including the Negro idiom, is all that I have. So let me emphasize that my reply to Howe was neither motivated by racial defensiveness nor addressed to his own racial identity.

It is fortunate that it was not, for considering how Howe identifies himself in this instance, I would have missed the target, which would have been embarrassing. Yet it would have been an innocent mistake, because in situations such as this many Negroes, like myself, make a positive distinction between "whites" and "Jews." Not to do so could be either offensive, embarrassing, unjust or even dangerous. If I would know who I am and preserve who I am, then I must see others distinctly whether they see me so or no. Thus I feel uncomfortable whenever I discover Jewish intellectuals writing as though *they* were guilty of enslaving my grandparents, or as though the *Jews* were responsible for the system of segregation. Not only do they have enough troubles of their own, as the saying goes, but Negroes know this only too well.

The real guilt of such Jewish intellectuals lies in their facile, perhaps unconscious, but certainly unrealistic, identification with what is called the "power structure." Negroes call that "passing for white." Speaking personally, both as writer and as Negro American, I would like to see the more positive distinctions between whites and Jewish Americans maintained. Not only does it make for a necessary bit of historical and social clarity, at least where Negroes are concerned, but I consider the United States freer politically and richer culturally because there are Jewish Americans to bring it the benefit of their special forms of dissent, their humor and their gift for ideas which are based upon the uniqueness of their experience. The diversity of American life is often painful, frequently burdensome and always a source of conflict, but in it lies our fate and our hope.

To Howe's charge that I found his exaggerated claims for Richard Wright's influence upon my own work presumptuous, I plead guilty. Was it necessary to impose a line of succession upon Negro writers simply because Howe identified with Wright's cause? And why, since he grasps so readily the intentional absurdity of my question regarding his relationship to Marx, couldn't he see that the notion of an intellectual or artistic succession based upon color or racial background is no less absurd than one based upon a common religious background? (*Of course, Irving, I know that you haven't believed in final words for twenty years—not even your own—and I know, too, that the line from Marx to Howe is as complex and as dialectical as that from Wright to Ellison. My point was to try to see to it that certain lapses in your thinking did not become final.*) In fact, this whole exchange would never have started had I not been dragged into the discussion. Still, if Howe could take on the role of man with a "black skin," why shouldn't I assume the role of critic-of-critic?

But how surprising are Howe's ideas concerning the ways of controversy. Why, unless of course he holds no respect for his opponent, should a

polemicist be expected to make things *hard* for himself? As for the "preconceptions of the liberal audience," I had not considered them, actually, except as they appear in Howe's own thinking. Beyond this I wrote for anyone
who might hesitate to question his formulations, especially very young
Negro writers who might be bewildered by the incongruity of such ideas
coming from such an authority. Howe himself rendered complicated rhetorical strategies unnecessary by lunging into questionable territory with
his flanks left so unprotected that any schoolboy sniper could have routed
him with a bird gun. Indeed, his reaction to my reply reminds me of an
incident which occurred during the 1937 Recession[5] when a companion
and I were hunting the country outside Dayton, Ohio.

There had been a heavy snowfall and we had just put up a covey of quail
from a thicket which edged a field when, through the rising whirr of the
rocketing, snow-shattering birds, we saw, emerging from a clump of trees
across the field, a large, red-faced, mackinawed farmer, who came running
toward us shouting and brandishing a rifle. I could see strands of moisture
tearing from his working mouth as he came on, running like a bear across
the whiteness, the brown birds veering and scattering before him; and
standing there against the snow, a white hill behind me and with no tree
nor foxhole for cover I felt as exposed as a Black Muslim caught at a meeting of the K.K.K.[6]

He had appeared as suddenly as the quail, and although the rifle was not
yet to his shoulder, I was transfixed, watching him zooming up to become
the largest, loudest, most aggressive-sounding white man I'd seen in my
life, and I was, quite frankly, afraid. Then I was measuring his approach to
the crunching tempo of his running and praying silently that he'd come
within range of my shotgun before he fired; that I would be able to do what
seemed necessary for me to do; that, shooting from the hip with an old
twelve-gauge shotgun, I could stop him before he could shoot either me or
my companion; and that, though stopped effectively, he would be neither
killed, nor blinded, nor maimed.

It was a mixed-up prayer in an icy interval which ended in a smoking
fury of cursing, when, at a warning from my companion, the farmer suddenly halted. Then we learned that the reckless man had meant only to
warn us off of land which was not even his but that of a neighbor—my companion's foster father. He stood there between the two shotguns pointing
short-ranged at his middle, his face quite drained of color now by the realization of how close to death he'd come, sputtering indignantly that we'd
interpreted his rifle, which wasn't loaded, in a manner other than he'd intended. He truly did not realize that situations can be more loaded than
guns and gestures more eloquent than words.

Fortunately, words are not rifles, but perhaps Howe is just as innocent of
the rhetorical eloquence of situations as the farmer. He does not see that
the meaning which emerges from his essay is not determined by isolated
statements, but by the juxtaposition of those statements in a context which

---

5. From 1937 to 1938 there was a severe recession,
during which time the percentage of industries registering decline was 97 to 100 percent.
6. Ku Klux Klan; a secret organization directed

against blacks, Catholics, Jews, and the foreign
born. "Black Muslim": a member of a U.S. black
nationalist religious movement.

creates a larger statement. Or that contributing to the judgment rendered by that larger statement is the one in which it is uttered. When Howe pits Baldwin and Ellison against Wright and then gives Wright the better of the argument by using such emotionally weighted terms as "remembered" and "kept faith," the implication to me is that Baldwin and Ellison did *not* remember or keep faith with those who remained behind. If this be true, then I think that in this instance "villain" is not too strong a term.

Howe is not the first writer given to sociological categories who has had unconscious value judgments slip into his "analytical" or "scientific" descriptions. Thus I can believe that his approach was meant to be "analytic, not exhortatory; descriptive, not prescriptive." The results, however, are something else again. And are we to believe that he simply does not recognize rhetoric when he practices it? That when he asks, "what *could* [his italics] the experience of a man with a black skin be . . ." etc., he thinks he is describing a situation as viewed by each and every Negro writer rather than expressing, yes, and in the mode of "exhortation," the views of Irving Howe? Doesn't he recognize that just as the anti-Negro stereotype is a command to Negroes to mold themselves in its image, there sounds through his descriptive "thus it is" the command "thus you become"? And doesn't he realize that in this emotion-charged area definitive description is, in effect, prescription? If he does not, how then can we depend upon his "analysis" of politics or his reading of fiction?

Perhaps Howe could relax his views concerning the situation of the writers with a "black skin" if he examined some of the meanings which he gives to the word "Negro." He contends that I "cannot help being caught up with *the idea* of the Negro," but I have never said that I could or wished to do so—only Howe makes a problem for me here. When he uses the term "Negro" he speaks of it as a "stigma," and again, he speaks of "Negroness" as a "sterile category." He sees the Negro writer as experiencing a "constant pressure upon his literary work" from the "sociology of his existence . . . not merely in the way this might be true of any writer, but with a *pain* and *ferocity* that nothing could remove."[7]

Note that this is a condition arising from a *collective* experience which leaves no room for the individual writer's unique existence. It leaves no room for that intensity of personal anguish which compels the artist to seek relief by projecting it into the world in conjunction with other things; that anguish which might take the form of an acute sense of inferiority for one, homosexuality for another, an overwhelming sense of the absurdity of human life for still another. Nor does it leave room for the experience that might be caused by humiliation, by a harelip, by a stutter, by epilepsy—indeed, by any and everything in this life which plunges the talented individual into solitude while leaving him the will to transcend his condition through art. The individual Negro writer must create out of his own special needs and through his own sensibilities, and these alone. Otherwise, all those who suffer in anonymity would be creators.

Howe makes of "Negroness" a metaphysical condition, one that is a state of irremediable agony which all but engulfs the mind. Happily, the view

7. Italics mine [Ellison's note].

from inside the skin is not so dark as it appears to be from Howe's remote position, and therefore my view of "Negroness" is neither his nor that of the exponents of *negritude*. It is not skin color which makes a Negro American but cultural heritage as shaped by the American experience, the social and political predicament; a sharing of that "concord of sensibilities" which the group expresses through historical circumstance and through which it has come to constitute a subdivision of the larger American culture. Being a Negro American has to do with the memory of slavery and the hope of emancipation and the betrayal by allies and the revenge and contempt inflicted by our former masters after the Reconstruction, and the myths, both Northern and Southern, which are propagated in justification of that betrayal. It involves, too, a special attitude toward the waves of immigrants who have come later and passed us by.

It has to do with a special perspective on the national ideals and the national conduct, and with a tragicomic attitude toward the universe. It has to do with special emotions evoked by the details of cities and countrysides, with forms of labor and with forms of pleasure; with sex and with love, with food and with drink, with machines and with animals; with climates and with dwellings, with places of worship and places of entertainment; with garments and dreams and idioms of speech; with manners and customs, with religion and art, with life styles and hoping, and with that special sense of predicament and fate which gives direction and resonance to the Freedom Movement.[8] It involves a rugged initiation into the mysteries and rites of color which makes it possible for Negro Americans to suffer the injustice which race and color are used to excuse without losing sight of either the humanity of those who inflict that injustice or the motives, rational or irrational, out of which they act. It imposes the uneasy burden and occasional joy of a complex double vision, a fluid, ambivalent response to men and events which represents, at its finest, a profoundly civilized adjustment to the cost of being human in this modern world.

More important, perhaps, being a Negro American involves a *willed* (who wills to be a Negro? *I* do!) affirmation of self as against all outside pressures—an identification with the group as extended through the individual self which rejects all possibilities of escape that do not involve a basic resuscitation of the original American ideals of social and political justice. And those white Negroes (and I do not mean Norman Mailer's[9] dream creatures) are Negroes too—if they wish to be.

Howe's defense against my charge that he sees unrelieved suffering as the basic reality of Negro life is to quote favorable comments from his review of *Invisible Man*. But this does not cancel out the restricted meaning which he gives to "Negroness," or his statement that "the sociology of [the Negro writer's] existence forms a constant pressure with a *pain* and *ferocity* that nothing could remove." He charges me with unfairness for writing that he believes ideological militancy is more important than writing well, yet he tells us that "there may of course be times when one's obligation as a

---

8. The civil rights movement of the 1960s.   9. American writer (b. 1923).

human being supersedes one's obligation as a writer. . . ." I think that the writer's obligation in a struggle as broad and abiding as the one we are engaged in, which involves not merely Negroes but all Americans, is best carried out through his role as writer. And if he chooses to stop writing and take to the platform, then it should be out of personal choice and not under pressure from would-be managers of society.

Howe plays a game of pitty-pat with Baldwin and Ellison. First he throws them into the pit for lacking Wright's "pain," "ferocity," "memory," "faithfulness" and "clenched militance," then he pats them on the head for the quality of their writing. If he would see evidence of this statement, let him observe how these terms come up in his original essay when he traces Baldwin's move toward Wright's position. Howe's rhetoric is weighted against "more modulated tones" in favor of "rasping outbursts," the Baldwin of *Another Country* becomes "a voice of anger, rasping and thrusting," and he is no longer "held back" by the "proprieties of literature." The character of Rufus in that novel displays a "ferocity" quite new in Baldwin's fiction, and Baldwin's essays gain resonance from "the tone of unrelenting protest . . . from [their] very anger, even the violence," etc. I am afraid that these are "good" terms in Howe's essay and they led to part of my judgment.

In defense of Wright's novel *The Long Dream*, Howe can write:

> . . . This book has been attacked for presenting Negro life in the South through "old-fashioned" images of violence, but [and now we have "prescription"] one ought to hesitate before denying the relevance of such images or joining in the criticism of their use. *For Wright was perhaps justified* in not paying attention to the changes that have occurred in the South these past few decades. [1]

If this isn't a defense, if not of bad writing at least of an irresponsible attitude toward good writing, I simply do not understand the language. I find it astonishing advice, since novels exist, since the fictional spell comes into existence precisely through the care which the novelist gives to selecting the details, the images, the tonalities, the specific social and psychological processes of specific characters in specific milieus at specific points in time. Indeed, it is one of the main tenets of the novelist's morality that he should write of that which he knows, and this is especially crucial for novelists who deal with a society as mobile and rapidly changing as ours. To justify ignoring this basic obligation is to encourage the downgrading of literature in favor of other values, in this instance "anger," "protest" and "clenched militancy." Novelists create not simply out of "memory" but out of memory modified, extended, transformed by social change. For a novelist to heed such advice as Howe's is to commit an act of artistic immorality. Amplify this back through society and the writer's failure could produce not order but chaos.

Yet Howe proceeds on the very next page of his essay to state, with no sense of contradiction, that Wright failed in some of the stories which comprise *Eight Men* ("The Man Who Lived Underground" was first pub-

1. Italics mine [Ellison's note].

lished, by the way, in 1944) because he needed the "accumulated material of circumstance." If a novelist ignores social change, how can he come by the "accumulated material of circumstance"? Perhaps if Howe could grasp the full meaning of that phrase he would understand that Wright did not report in *Black Boy* much of his life in Mississippi, and he would see that Ross Barnett[2] is not the whole state, that there is also a Negro Mississippi which is much more varied than that which Wright depicted.

For the critic there simply exists no substitute for the knowledge of history and literary tradition. Howe stresses Wright's comment that when he went into rooms where there were naked white women he felt like a "nonman . . . doubly cast out." But had Howe thought about it he might have questioned this reaction, since most young men would have been delighted with the opportunity to study, at first hand, women usually cloaked in an armor of taboos. I wonder how Wright felt when he saw Negro women acting just as shamelessly? Clearly this was an ideological point, not a factual report. And anyone aware of the folk sources of Wright's efforts to create literature would recognize that the situation is identical with that of the countless stories which Negro men tell of the male slave called in to wash the mistress' back in the bath, of the Pullman porter invited in to share the beautiful white passenger's favors in the berth, of the bellhop seduced by the wealthy blond guest.

It is interesting that Howe should interpret my statement about Mississippi as evidence of a loss of self-control. So allow me to repeat it coldly: I fear the implications of Howe's ideas concerning the Negro writer's role as actionist more than I do the State of Mississippi. Which is not to deny the viciousness which exists there but to recognize the degree of freedom which also exists there precisely because the repression is relatively crude, or at least it was during Wright's time, and it left the world of literature alone. William Faulkner lived neither in Jefferson nor Frenchman's Bend but in Oxford. He, too, was a Mississippian, just as the boys who helped Wright leave Jackson were the sons of a Negro college president. Both Faulkner and these boys must be recognized as part of the social reality of Mississippi. I said nothing about Ross Barnett, and I certainly did not say that Howe was a "cultural authoritarian," so he should not spread his honor so thin. Rather, let him look to the implications of his thinking.

Yes, and let him learn more about the South and about Negro Americans if he would speak with authority. When he points out that "the young Ralph Ellison, even while reading these great writers, could not in Macon County attend the white man's school or movie house," he certainly appears to have me cornered. But here again he does not know the facts and he underplays choice and will. I rode freight trains to Macon County, Alabama, during the Scottsboro trial because I desired to study with the Negro conductor-composer William L. Dawson,[3] who was, and probably still is, the greatest classical musician in that part of the country. I had no need to

2. Governor of Mississippi during the early civil rights era (1960–64).
3. Musician and composer (1898–1971), who directed the Tuskegee Institute choir for many years.

"Scottsboro trial": in 1931 nine black youths were indicted at Scottsboro, Alabama, on charges of having raped two white girls in a freight car passing through Alabama.

attend a white university when the master I wished to study with was available at Tuskegee. Besides, why should I have wished to attend the white state-controlled university where the works of the great writers might not have been so easily available.

As for the movie-going, it is ironic but nonetheless true that one of the few instances where "separate but equal" was truly separate and equal was in a double movie house in the town of Tuskegee, where Negroes and whites were accommodated in parallel theaters, entering from the same street level through separate entrances and with the Negro side viewing the same pictures shortly after the showing for whites had begun. It was a product of social absurdity and, of course, no real relief from our resentment over the restriction of our freedom, but the movies were just as enjoyable or boring. And yet, is not knowing the facts more interesting, even as an isolated instance, and more stimulating to real thought than making abstract assumptions? I went to the movies to see pictures, not to be with whites. I attended a certain college because what I wanted was there. What is more, I *never* attended a white school from kindergarten through my three years of college, and yet, like Howe, I have taught and lectured for some years now at Northern, predominantly white, colleges and universities.

Perhaps this counts for little, changes little of the general condition of society, but it *is* factual and it does form a part of my sense of reality because, though it was not a part of Wright's life, it is my own. And if Howe thinks mine is an isolated instance, let him do a bit of research.

I do not really think that Howe can make a case for himself by bringing up the complimentary remarks which he made about *Invisible Man*. I did not quarrel with them in 1952, when they were first published, and I did not quarrel with them in my reply. His is the right of any critic to make judgment of a novel, and I do not see the point of arguing that I achieved an aesthetic goal if it did not work for him. I can only ask that my fiction be judged as art; if it fails, it fails aesthetically, not because I did or did not fight some ideological battle. I repeat, however, that Howe's strategy of bringing me into the public quarrel between Baldwin and Wright was inept. I simply did not belong in the conflict, since I knew, even then, that protest is *not* the source of the inadequacy characteristic of most novels by Negroes, but the simple failure of craft, bad writing; the desire to have protest perform the difficult tasks of art; the belief that racial suffering, social injustice or ideologies of whatever mammy-made variety, is enough. I know, also, that when the work of Negro writers has been rejected they have all too often protected their egos by blaming racial discrimination, while turning away from the fairly obvious fact that good art—and Negro musicians are ever present to demonstrate this—commands attention of itself, whatever the writer's politics or point of view. And they forget that publishers will publish almost anything which is written with even a minimum of competency, and that skill is developed by hard work, study and a conscious assault upon one's own fear and provincialism.

I agree with Howe that protest is an element of all art, though it does not necessarily take the form of speaking for a political or social program. It might appear in a novel as a technical assault against the styles which have gone before, or as protest against the human condition. If *Invisible Man* is even "apparently" free from "the ideological and emotional penalties suffered by Negroes in this country," it is because I tried to the best of my ability to transform these elements into art. My goal was not to escape, or hold back, but to work through; to transcend, as the blues transcend the painful conditions with which they deal. The protest is there, not because I was helpless before my racial condition, but because I *put* it there. If there is anything "miraculous" about the book it is the result of hard work undertaken in the belief that the work of art is important in itself, that it is a social action in itself.

I cannot hope to persuade Irving Howe to this view, for it seems quite obvious that he believes there are matters more important than artistic scrupulousness. I will point out, though, that the laws of literary form exert their validity upon all those who write, and that it is his slighting of the formal necessities of his essay which makes for some of our misunderstanding. After reading his reply, I gave in to my ear's suggestion that I had read certain of his phrases somewhere before, and I went to the library, where I discovered that much of his essay was taken verbatim from a review in the *Nation* of May 10, 1952, and that another section was published verbatim in the *New Republic* of February 13, 1962; the latter, by the way, being in its original context a balanced appraisal and warm farewell to Richard Wright.

But when Howe spliced these materials together with phrases from an old speech of mine, swipes at the critics of the *Sewanee* and *Kenyon* reviews (journals in which I have never published), and the Baldwin-Wright quarrel, the effect was something other than he must have intended. A dialectical transformation into a new quality took place and despite the intention of Howe's content, the form made its own statement. If he would find the absurdities he wants me to reduce to a quotation, he will really have to read his essay whole. One gets the impression that he did a paste-and-scissors job and, knowing what he intended, knowing how the separated pieces had operated by themselves, did not bother to read very carefully their combined effect. It could happen to anyone; nevertheless, I'm glad he is not a scientist or a social engineer.

I do not understand why Howe thinks I said anything on the subject of writing about "Negro experience" in a manner which excludes what he calls "plight and protest"; he must have gotten his Negroes mixed. But as to answering his question concerning the "ways a Negro writer can achieve personal realization apart from the common effort of his people to win their full freedom," I suggest that he ask himself in what way shall a Negro writer achieve personal realization (as writer) *after* his people shall have won their full freedom? The answer appears to be the same in both instances: He will have to go it alone! He must suffer alone even as he shares the suffering of his group, and he must write alone and pit his talents against the standards set by the best practitioners of the craft, both past and present, in any case. For the writer's real way of sharing the experience of his group is to convert its mutual suffering into lasting value. Is Howe suggesting, incidentally, that Heinrich Heine[4] did not exist?

His question is silly, really, for there is no such thing as "full freedom" (Oh, how Howe thirsts and hungers for the absolute for Negroes!), just as the notion of an equality of talent is silly. I am a Negro who once played trumpet with a certain skill, but alas, I am no Louis Armstrong or Clark Terry. Willie Mays[5] has realized himself quite handsomely as an individual despite coming from an impoverished Negro background in oppressive Alabama; and Negro Americans, like most Americans who know the value of baseball, exult in his success. I am, after all, only a minor member, not the whole damned tribe; in fact, most Negroes have never heard of me. I could shake the nation for a while with a crime or with indecent disclosures, but my pride lies in earning the right to call myself quite simply "writer." Perhaps if I write well enough the children of today's Negroes will be proud that I did, and so, perhaps, will Irving Howe's.

Let me end with a personal note: Dear Irving, I have no objections to being placed beside Richard Wright in any estimation which is based not upon the irremediable ground of our common racial identity, but upon the quality of our achievements as writers. I respected Wright's work and I knew him, but this is not to say that he "influenced" me as significantly as you assume. Consult the text! I *sought out* Wright because I had read Eliot, Pound, Gertrude Stein and Hemingway, and as early as 1940 Wright viewed me as a potential rival, partially, it is true, because he feared I would allow myself to be used against him by political manipulators who were not Negro and who envied and hated him. But perhaps you will understand when I say he did not influence me if I point out that while one can do nothing about choosing one's relatives, one can, as artist, choose one's "ancestors." Wright was, in this sense, a "relative"; Hemingway an "ancestor." Langston Hughes,[6] whose work I knew in grade school and whom I knew before I knew Wright, was a "relative"; Eliot, whom I was to meet only many years later, and Malraux and Dostoievsky and Faulkner, were "ancestors"—if you please or don't please!

Do you still ask why Hemingway was more important to me than Wright? Not because he was white, or more "accepted." But because he appreciated the things of this earth which I love and which Wright was too driven or deprived or inexperienced to know: weather, guns, dogs, horses, love *and* hate and impossible circumstances which to the courageous and dedicated could be turned into benefits and victories. Because he wrote with such precision about the processes and techniques of daily living that I could keep myself and my brother alive during the 1937 Recession by following his descriptions of wing-shooting; because he knew the difference between politics and art and something of their true relationship for

4. German-born Jewish poet (1797–1856), who was politically exiled because of his liberal sympathies; he left for Paris in 1831.
5. Professional baseball player (b. 1931). Terry (b.

1920), African American jazz trumpeter.
6. African American poet and author (1902–1967).

the writer. Because all that he wrote—and this is very important—was imbued with a spirit beyond the tragic with which I could feel at home, for it was very close to the feeling of the blues, which are, perhaps, as close as Americans can come to expressing the spirit of tragedy. (And if you think Wright knew anything about the blues, listen to a "blues" he composed with Paul Robeson singing, a *most* unfortunate collaboration!; and read his introduction to Paul Oliver's *Blues Fell This Morning*. [7]) But most important, because Hemingway was a greater artist than Wright, who although a Negro like myself, and perhaps a great man, understood little if anything of these, at least to me, important things. Because Hemingway loved the American language and the joy of writing, making the flight of birds, the loping of lions across an African plain, the mysteries of drink and moonlight, the unique styles of diverse peoples and individuals come alive on the page. Because he was in many ways the true father-as-artist of so many of us who came to writing during the late thirties.

I will not dwell upon Hemingway's activities in Spain or during the liberation in Paris, [8] for you know all of that. I will remind you, however, that any writer takes what he needs to get his own work done from wherever he finds it. I did not need Wright to tell me how to be a Negro, or how to be angry or to express anger—Joe Louis [9] was doing that very well—or even to teach me about socialism; my mother had canvassed for the socialists, not the communists, the year I was born. No, I had been a Negro for twenty-two or twenty-three years when I met Wright, and in more places and under a greater variety of circumstances than he had then known. He was generously helpful in sharing his ideas and information, but I needed instruction in other values and I found them in the works of other writers—Hemingway was one of them, T. S. Eliot initiated the search.

I like your part about Chekhov [1] arising from his sickbed to visit the penal colony at Sakhalin Island. It was, as you say, a noble act. But shouldn't we remember that it was significant only because Chekhov was *Chekhov*, the great writer? You compliment me truly, but I have not written so much or so well, even though I *have* served a certain apprenticeship in the streets and even touch events in the Freedom Movement in a modest way. But I can also recall the story of a certain writer who succeeded with a great fanfare of publicity in having a talented murderer released from prison. It made for another very short story which ended quite tragically—though not for the writer: A few months after his release the man killed the mother of two young children. I also know of another really quite brilliant writer who, under the advice of certain wise men who were then managing the consciences of artists, abandoned the prison of his writing to go to Spain, where he was allowed to throw away his life defending a worthless hill. I have not heard his name in years but I remember it vividly; it was Christopher Cauldwell, *né* Christopher St. John Sprigg. [2] There are many

7. A history and criticism of blues music (1960) by Oliver (b. 1927), a British lecturer on art and folk music who has written extensively on jazz. Robeson (1898–1976), an African American actor and singer, was controversial for his leftwing politics.
8. On August 26, 1944, the German occupation of Paris ended.

9. American boxer (1914–1981).
1. Anton Chekhov (1860–1904), Russian short story writer, dramatist, and physician.
2. British aviator, publisher, journalist, literary theorist, poet, and author of crime novels and nonfiction (1907–1937).

such stories, Irving. It's heads you win, tails you lose, and you are quite right about my not following Baldwin, who is urged on by a nobility—or is it a demon—quite different from my own. It has cost me quite a pretty penny, indeed, but then I was always poor and not (and I know this is a sin in our America) too uncomfortable.

Dear Irving, I am still yakking on and there's many a thousand gone, but I assure you that no Negroes are beating down my door, putting pressure on me to join the Negro Freedom Movement, for the simple reason that they realize that I am enlisted for the duration. Such pressure is coming only from a few disinterested "military advisers," since Negroes want no more fairly articulate would-be Negro leaders cluttering up the airways. For, you see, my Negro friends recognize a certain division of labor among the members of the tribe. Their demands, like that of many whites, are that I publish more novels—and here I am remiss and vulnerable perhaps. You will recall what the Talmud[3] has to say about the trees of the forest and the making of books, etc. But then, Irving, they recognize what you have not allowed yourself to see; namely, that my reply to your essay is in itself a small though necessary action in the Negro struggle for freedom. You should not feel unhappy about this or think that I regard you either as dishonorable or an enemy. I hope, rather, that you will come to view this exchange as an act of, shall we say, "antagonistic co-operation"?

                                                                                    1963, 1964

3. Body of Jewish civil and religious law.

MARGARET WALKER
b. 1915

When Margaret Walker's first volume of poetry, *For My People*, was published in 1942, it was only the second volume of American poetry published by a black woman for more than two decades (Georgia Douglass Johnson's *The Heart of a Woman and Other Poems* had been published in 1918). *For My People* launched Walker's career, which spans several decades, extending from the waning days of the Harlem Renaissance in the 1930s to the Black Arts movement of the 1960s and beyond. In the foreword to *For My People*, Stephen Vincent Benét praised Walker's poetry for its "controlled intensity of emotion and [its] language that, at times, even when it is most modern, has something of the surge of biblical poetry." Walker would have heard these biblical overtones in the sermons of her father, a minister in the Methodist Episcopal Church in Alabama and Mississippi. It is little wonder, then, that the Bible and the black sermonic tradition influence so much of Walker's writing and that the title poem of *For My People* has been likened to a sermon.

Walker was born July 7, 1915, in Birmingham, Alabama, to Reverend Sigismund C. Walker and Marion Dozier Walker who instilled in her a love of scholarship, music, and the church. She was exposed early to the classics of English and American literature, reading widely in poetry from Shakespeare to John Greenleaf Whittier to Countee Cullen and Langston Hughes. She credits Hughes—both his life and his poetry—with profoundly influencing her ambitions and her development as a writer.

While a student at Northwestern University, Walker worked for the WPA Federal Writers' Project, where she became friends with Richard Wright, enjoying a three-year collaboration and exchange that she describes as a strictly "literary" relationship, a "rare and once-in-a-lifetime association." Wright read and responded to Walker's poetry, and she helped with his revisions of *Almos' a Man* and the posthumously published *Lawd Today*. After leaving Chicago, Walker assisted Wright in the research for *Native Son*, sending him newspaper clippings about Robert Nixon, a young black man accused of rape in Chicago, who partly inspired Wright's depiction of Bigger Thomas. Their friendship and literary collaboration ended abruptly, and Walker has explained some of the underlying reasons in a recent and controversial book, *Richard Wright: A Daemonic Genius*.

From Chicago, Walker went to the University of Iowa Writers' Workshop where she finished *For My People*, which won the Yale University Younger Poet's Award in 1942. Critic Eugenia Collier described the title poem as community property, a "signature piece" for black audiences:

> We knew the poem. It was ours. . . .And as [it] moved on, rhythmically piling image after image of our lives, making us know again the music wrenched from our slave agony, the religious faith, the toil and confusion and hopelessness, the strength to endure in spite of it all, [it] went on mirroring our collective selves, [and] we cried out in deep response.

Despite its success, *For My People* marked the end of Walker's published efforts for roughly twenty years. After receiving her master's degree, she married and began a teaching career. Her novel *Jubilee* broke the silence in 1966. *Jubilee* is most frequently read as a response to the nostalgic fantasies about slavery found in white fiction that recreates the antebellum and Reconstruction South—especially Margaret Mitchell's popular *Gone with the Wind*. Two volumes of poetry followed: *Prophets for a New Day* (1970) and *October Journey* (1973). *Prophets for a New Day* features poems on the black freedom struggle from Nat Turner's rebellion to the civil rights movement. Its cover a montage of photographs of Martin Luther King Jr. and Malcolm X, *Prophets for a New Day* addresses the need for leadership in chaotic times and the despair of a community that finds a worthy leader, only to be deprived of his guidance by an assassin's bullet. Published by Broadside Press, the volume also represent's Walker's decision, like that of Gwendolyn Brooks, to support black independent publishers dedicated, as the word *broadside* suggests, to forceful verbal attack, to militance on the page.

Few disagree that Margaret Walker's reputation rests largely on the poems in *For My People*. Stephen Vincent Benét's original judgment of them still rings true: "These poems keep on talking to you after the book is shut because . . . Walker has made living and passionate speech."

For My People

For my people everywhere singing their slave songs repeatedly: their
   dirges and their ditties and their blues and jubilees, praying their
   prayers nightly to an unknown god, bending their knees humbly to an
   unseen power;

For my people lending their strength to the years, to the gone years and
   the now years and the maybe years, washing ironing cooking scrubbing sewing mending hoeing plowing digging planting pruning

patching dragging along never gaining never reaping never knowing
and never understanding.

For my playmates in the clay and dust and sand of Alabama backyards
playing baptizing and preaching and doctor and jail and soldier and
school and mama and cooking and playhouse and concert and store
and hair and Miss Choomby and company;

For the cramped bewildered years we went to school to learn to know
the reasons why and the answers to and the people who and the
places where and the days when, in memory of the bitter hours when
we discovered we were black and poor and small and different and
nobody cared and nobody wondered and nobody understood;

For the boys and girls who grew in spite of these things to be Man and
Woman, to laugh and dance and sing and play and drink their wine
and religion and success, to marry their playmates and bear children
and then die of consumption and anemia and lynching;

For my people thronging 47th Street in Chicago and Lenox Avenue in
New York and Rampart Street in New Orleans, lost disinherited dispossessed and happy people filling the cabarets and taverns and other
people's pockets needing bread and shoes and milk and land and
money and something—something all our own;

For my people walking blindly spreading joy, losing time being lazy,
sleeping when hungry, shouting when burdened, drinking when
hopeless, tied and shackled and tangled among ourselves by the unseen creatures who tower over us omnisciently and laugh;

For my people blundering and groping and floundering in the dark of
churches and schools and clubs and societies, associations and councils and committees and conventions, distressed and disturbed and
deceived and devoured by money-hungry glory-craving leeches,
preyed on by facile force of state and fad and novelty, by false prophet
and holy believer;

For my people standing staring trying to fashion a better way from confusion, from hypocrisy and misunderstanding, trying to fashion a
world that will hold all the people, all the faces, all the adams and
eves and their countless generations;

Let a new earth rise. Let another world be born. Let a bloody peace be
written in the sky. Let a second generation full of courage issue forth;
let a people loving freedom come to growth. Let a beauty full of healing and a strength of final clenching be the pulsing in our spirits and
our blood. Let the martial songs be written, let the dirges disappear.
Let a race of men now rise and take control.

1937, 1942

Poppa Chicken

Poppa was a sugah daddy
Pimping in his prime;
All the gals for miles around
Walked to Poppa's time.

Poppa Chicken owned the town,   5
Give his women hell;
All the gals on Poppa's time
Said that he was swell.

Poppa's face was long and black;
Poppa's grin was broad.   10
When Poppa Chicken walked the streets
The gals cried Lawdy! Lawd!

Poppa Chicken made his gals
Toe his special line:
"Treat 'em rough and make 'em say   15
Poppa Chicken's fine!"

Poppa Chicken toted guns;
Poppa wore a knife.
One night Poppa shot a guy
Threat'ning Poppa's life.   20

Poppa done his time in jail
Though he got off light;
Bought his pardon in a year;
Come back out in might.

Poppa walked the streets this time,   25
Gals around his neck.
And everybody said the jail
Hurt him nary speck.

Poppa smoked his long cigars—
Special Poppa brands—   30
Rocks all glist'ning in his tie;
On his long black hands.

Poppa lived without a fear;
Walked without a rod.
Poppa cussed the coppers out;   35
Talked like he was God.

Poppa met a pretty gal;
Heard her name was Rose;
Took one look at her and soon
Bought her pretty clothes.   40

One night she was in his arms,
In walked her man Joe.

All he done was look and say,
"Poppa's got to go."

Poppa Chicken still is hot   45
Though he's old and gray,
Walking round here with his gals
Pimping every day.

1942

For Malcolm X

All you violated ones with gentle hearts;
You violent dreamers whose cries shout heartbreak;
Whose voices echo clamors of our cool capers,
And whose black faces have hollowed pits for eyes.
All you gambling sons and hooked children and bowery bums   5
Hating white devils and black bourgeoisie,
Thumbing your noses at your burning red suns,
Gather round this coffin and mourn your dying swan.

Snow-white moslem head-dress around a dead black face!
Beautiful were your sand-papering words against our skins!   10
Our blood and water pour from your flowing wounds.
You have cut open our breasts and dug scalpels in our brains.
When and Where will another come to take your holy place?
Old man mumbling in his dotage, or crying child, unborn?

1970

Prophets for a New Day

1
As the Word came to prophets of old,
As the burning bush spoke to Moses,
And the fiery coals cleansed the lips of Isaiah;
As the wheeling cloud in the sky
Clothed the message of Ezekiel;   5
So the Word of fire burns today
On the lips of our prophets in an evil age—
Our sooth-sayers and doom-tellers and doers of the Word.
So the Word of the Lord stirs again
These passionate people toward deliverance.   10
As Amos, Shepherd of Tekoa spoke
To the captive children of Judah, [1]

1. This stanza makes many references to the Old
Testament of the Bible. Moses saw a vision of an
angel in a burning bush and was compelled by God
to return to Egypt to deliver the Israelites from
bondage (Exodus 3:2–10). Isaiah (8th century B.C.)
prophesied the destruction and redemption of Israel. Ezekiel (6th century B.C.), prophet who had a
vision of God as wheels within wheels (Ezekiel
1:4–18). Amos (8th century B.C.), a prophet from
Tekoa (a small town just south of Jerusalem), was
the first prophet to proclaim God as ruler of the
universe. Judah, the fourth son of Jacob, saved Joseph's life by proposing that his brother be sold into
slavery rather than be murdered (Genesis 37:26–
27). He is also the ancestor of the tribe of Judah
(one of the twelve tribes of Israel).

Preaching to the dispossessed and the poor,
So today in the pulpits and the jails,
On the highways and in the byways,   15
A fearless shepherd speaks at last
To his suffering weary sheep.

2

So, kneeling by the river bank
Comes the vision to a valley of believers
So in flaming flags of stars in the sky   20
And in the breaking dawn of a blinding sun
The lamp of truth is lighted in the Temple
And the oil of devotion is burning at midnight
So the glittering censer in the Temple
Trembles in the presence of the priests   25
And the pillars of the door-posts move
And the incense rises in smoke
And the dark faces of the sufferers
Gleam in the new morning
The complaining faces glow   30
And the winds of freedom begin to blow
While the Word descends on the waiting World below.

3

A beast is among us.
His mark is on the land.
His horns and his hands and his lips are gory with our blood.   35
He is War and Famine and Pestilence
He is Death and Destruction and Trouble
And he walks in our houses at noonday
And devours our defenders at midnight.
He is the demon who drives us with whips of fear   40
And in his cowardice
He cries out against liberty
He cries out against humanity
Against all dignity of green valleys and high hills
Against clean winds blowing through our living;   45
Against the broken bodies of our brothers.
He has crushed them with a stone.
He drinks our tears for water
And he drinks our blood for wine;
He eats our flesh like a ravenous lion   50
And he drives us out of the city
To be stabbed on a lonely hill.

1970

GWENDOLYN BROOKS

b. 1917

The following observation from Gwendolyn Brooks's 1972 autobiography, *Report from Part One*, outlines several of the many motives that have marked the poet's long, distinguished career:

> My aim, in my next future, is to write poems that will somehow successfully "call" . . . all black people: black people in taverns, black people in alleys, black people in gutters, schools, offices, factories, prisons, the consulate; I wish to reach black people in pulpits, black people in mines, on farms, on thrones; not always to "teach"—I shall wish often to entertain, to illumine. My newish voice will not be an imitation of the contemporary young black voice, which I so admire, but an adaptation of today's Gwendolyn Brooks' voice.

And indeed, the poet, shifting after three decades from Harper & Row to Broadside Press (Detroit) and Third World Press (Chicago), continues into the 1990s to write the elegant spare rhythms that have characterized her poetry all along. True to her wish to reach a wide audience, her thin, handsome volumes are affordable—*Primer for Blacks* and *Black Love* sold in 1981 for less than $5. Though this distribution strategy has made it difficult for academics to get hold of Brooks's poetry for the classroom, it proves her passionate commitment to making her work available to black people everywhere and underscores her belief that poetry is not the sole province of the privileged, educated few.

One of two children of schoolteacher Keziah Corinne Wims and janitor David Anderson Brooks, Gwendolyn Brooks was born in Topeka, Kansas, in 1917. Five weeks after her birth, the family moved to Chicago, where she has spent most of her life. Brooks published her first poem at thirteen, in *American Child* magazine. Fonder at fourteen of paper dolls than parties and in possession at sixteen of a critique of her poems from poet and novelist James Weldon Johnson, Brooks graduated from high school in 1935, by which time she was already a regular contributor to the weekly variety column of the *Chicago Defender*. In 1936 she graduated from Wilson Junior College and then worked for a short time as a maid and secretary to one Dr. E. N. French. A spiritual adviser who hawked charms and potions to the unfortunate, this "doctor" appears to have informed the image of Prophet Williams in the poet's powerful 1960s epic *In the Mecca*. Brooks joined Chicago's NAACP Youth Council in 1938; there she met Henry Lowington Blakely II, whom she married the following year.

Shortly after the birth of her first child, in October 1940, Brooks met the "elegant rebel" and resident of the city's Gold Coast, Inez Cunningham Stark Boulton. Boulton came to the South Side "to instruct a class of Negro would-be poets, in the very *buckle* of the Black Belt." Armed with subscriptions to *Poetry* magazine for the class, Boulton would count among her students more than a few who would later publish books, articles, fiction, poems, and criticism. In her autobiography, Brooks discusses her teacher's pedagogical strategies, but it appears that Boulton did not regard herself so much as an instructor as "a friend who loved poetry and respected [the students'] interest in it." The poetry workshop—often quite rigorous—exposed Brooks to a wide variety of reading, in modernist verse particularly; but if Brooks's own teacherly strategies at Chicago's Columbia College some years later took their cue from Boulton's example, then Boulton's students were grounded in a range of styles, from Petrarchan and Shakespearean sonnets, through the ballad and iambic pentameter, to free verse.

After winning the Midwestern Writers' Conference poetry award in 1943, Brooks was approached by Emily Morison of Knopf for a book of poems. Morison read a batch on various subjects—love, war, nature, patriotism, prejudice—and then told Brooks that she would like to see more of the "Negro poems." Brooks gathered nineteen poems on the subject, but somewhat put off by Morison, she sent the bundle to Elizabeth Lawrence at Harper. A *Street in Bronzeville* was published in 1945. It would be followed by *Annie Allen* (1949), winner of the 1950 Pulitzer Prize; *Maud Martha* (1953); and *The Bean Eaters* (1961). As she observed, Brooks's poetry of this period is solidly based in the stuff of everyday life: "As for my husband and myself, our own best parties were given at 623 East 63rd Street, our most exciting kitchenette . . . right on the corner . . . of 63rd and Champlain, above a real-estate agency. If you wanted a poem, you had only to look out a window. There was material always, walking or running, fighting or screaming or singing." It was in this famed kitchenette that Brooks hosted a party for her friend and mentor Langston Hughes; once, he dropped in unexpectedly, and Brooks and Blakely shared with him a meal of mustard greens, ham hocks, and candied sweet potatoes.

Hughes died in 1967, the year of the Second Black Writers' Conference at Nashville's Fisk University. "A general energy, an electricity, in look, walk, speech, gesture" underscored the proceedings, according to Brooks, who reported that she had never before seen "such insouciance, such live firmness, such confident vigor." Here Brooks was exposed to cultural activists and artists such as Don L. Lee (Haki Madhubuti), Imamu Amiri Baraka, Larry Neal, and A. B. Spelman, among others, who would fashion the outline of a new black cultural nationalism. After the Fisk conference, Brooks reported: "If it hadn't been for these young people, these young writers who influenced me, I wouldn't know what I know about this society. By associating with them, I know who I am." Much of Brooks's subsequent activity was inspired by her experience at Fisk, including the creative writing class that she conducted with some of Chicago's Blackstone Rangers, a teenage gang. In 1968, she published *In the Mecca*, with its brilliant closing pieces: the "sermons" on the Warpland.

Across the years and volumes, Brooks's poetry has struck readers with several distinctive traits: a stunning juxtaposition of disparate objects and words, notably in *The Anniad* and *In the Mecca*; a masterful control of rhyme and meter; sophisticated use of formal and thematic irony, as in *We Real Cool*; and the delicate but striking translation of public events into memorable poetic details. Though Brooks's recent poetry shows something of a different innovation and though the results may not be as uniformly impressive as the earlier work, the poet's primary concern—to hammer out a portrait of and for African Americans—remains unaltered.

Any attempt to outline Gwendolyn Brooks's career would be incomplete without at least brief mention of the prose fiction *Maud Martha* (1953). A female subject's ruminations before, during, and after World War II, the work should be read *with* the poetry, not apart from it. Not only is *Maud Martha* one of the few works by a black woman writer written between the Harlem Renaissance and the civil rights era but it also offers a point of view not marked by the ideological debates of the postwar years. *Maud Martha*'s ugliness—the ugliness of racism, classism, and sexism—is "made in America" and must be solved there as well. But as unflinching is its view of one woman's life, so beautiful and muscular is its lyricism. The marvel of this text is that it narrates the most difficult, or unspeakable, of human failings—those that occur on the level of intimacy—through the finely tuned sensibility and contemplations of its protagonist. It is a generous, sensitive, and tough contribution to a remarkable body of work by a major modern American poet.

kitchenette building

We are things of dry hours and the involuntary plan,
Grayed in, and gray. "Dream" makes a giddy sound, not strong
Like "rent," "feeding a wife," "satisfying a man."

But could a dream send up through onion fumes
Its white and violet, fight with fried potatoes   5
And yesterday's garbage ripening in the hall,
Flutter, or sing an aria down these rooms

Even if we were willing to let it in,
Had time to warm it, keep it very clean,
Anticipate a message, let it begin?   10

We wonder. But not well! not for a minute!
Since Number Five is out of the bathroom now,
We think of lukewarm water, hope to get in it.

                                                          1945

the mother

Abortions will not let you forget.
You remember the children you got that you did not get,
The damp small pulps with a little or with no hair,
The singers and workers that never handled the air.
You will never neglect or beat   5
Them, or silence or buy with a sweet.
You will never wind up the sucking-thumb
Or scuttle off ghosts that come.
You will never leave them, controlling your luscious sigh,
Return for a snack of them, with gobbling mother-eye.   10

I have heard in the voices of the wind the voices of my dim killed
    children.
I have contracted. I have eased
My dim dears at the breasts they could never suck.
I have said, Sweets, if I sinned, if I seized
Your luck   15
And your lives from your unfinished reach,
If I stole your births and your names,
Your straight baby tears and your games,
Your stilted or lovely loves, your tumults, your marriages, aches, and
    your deaths,
If I poisoned the beginnings of your breaths,   20
Believe that even in my deliberateness I was not deliberate.
Though why should I whine,
Whine that the crime was other than mine?—
Since anyhow you are dead.
Or rather, or instead,   25
You were never made.

But that too, I am afraid,
Is faulty: oh, what shall I say, how is the truth to be said?
You were born, you had body, you died.
It is just that you never giggled or planned or cried.   30

Believe me, I loved you all.
Believe me, I knew you, though faintly, and I loved, I loved you
All.

                                                              1945

a song in the front yard

I've stayed in the front yard all my life.
I want a peek at the back
Where it's rough and untended and hungry weed grows.
A girl gets sick of a rose.

I want to go in the back yard now   5
And maybe down the alley,
To where the charity children play.
I want a good time today.

They do some wonderful things.
They have some wonderful fun.   10
My mother sneers, but I say it's fine
How they don't have to go in at quarter to nine.
My mother, she tells me that Johnnie Mae
Will grow up to be a bad woman.
That George'll be taken to Jail soon or late   15
(On account of last winter he sold our back gate).

But I say it's fine. Honest, I do.
And I'd like to be a bad woman, too,
And wear the brave stockings of night-black lace
And strut down the streets with paint on my face.   20

                                                              1945

Sadie and Maud

Maud went to college.
Sadie stayed at home.
Sadie scraped life
With a fine-tooth comb.

She didn't leave a tangle in.   5
Her comb found every strand.
Sadie was one of the livingest chits [1]
In all the land.

1. Pert young girls.

Sadie bore two babies
Under her maiden name.   10
Maud and Ma and Papa
Nearly died of shame.

When Sadie said her last so-long
Her girls struck out from home.
(Sadie had left as heritage   15
Her fine-tooth comb.)

Maud, who went to college,
Is a thin brown mouse.
She is living all alone
In this old house.   20

1945

the vacant lot

Mrs. Coley's three-flat brick
Isn't here any more.
All done with seeing her fat little form
Burst out of the basement door;
And with seeing her African son-in-law   5
(Rightful heir to the throne)
With his great white strong cold squares of teeth
And his little eyes of stone;
And with seeing the squat fat daughter
Letting in the men   10
When majesty has gone for the day—
And letting them out again.

1945

the preacher: ruminates behind the sermon

I think it must be lonely to be God.
Nobody loves a master. No. Despite
The bright hosannas, [1] bright dear-Lords, and bright
Determined reverence of Sunday eyes.

Picture Jehovah [2] striding through the hall   5
Of His importance, creatures running out
From servant-corners to acclaim, to shout
Appreciation of His merit's glare.

But who walks with Him?—dares to take His arm,
To slap Him on the shoulder, tweak His ear,   10
Buy Him a Coca-Cola or a beer,
Pooh-pooh His politics, call Him a fool?

1. Songs of praise.   2. God (Hebrew).

Perhaps—who knows?—He tires of looking down.
Those eyes are never lifted. Never straight.
Perhaps sometimes He tires of being great   15
In solitude. Without a hand to hold.

1945

The Sundays of Satin-Legs Smith

Inamoratas, [1] with an approbation,
Bestowed his title. Blessed his inclination.)

He wakes, unwinds, elaborately: a cat
Tawny, reluctant, royal. He is fat
And fine this morning. Definite. Reimbursed.   5

He waits a moment, he designs his reign,
That no performance may be plain or vain.
Then rises in a clear delirium.

He sheds, with his pajamas, shabby days.
And his desertedness, his intricate fear, the   10
Postponed resentments and the prim precautions.

Now, at his bath, would you deny him lavender
Or take away the power of his pine?
What smelly substitute, heady as wine,
Would you provide? life must be aromatic.   15
There must be scent, somehow there must be some.
Would you have flowers in his life? suggest
Asters? a Really Good geranium?
A white carnation? would you prescribe a Show
With the cold lilies, formal chrysanthemum   20
Magnificence, poinsettias, and emphatic
Red of prize roses? might his happiest
Alternative (you muse) be, after all,
A bit of gentle garden in the best
Of taste and straight tradition? Maybe so.   25
But you forget, or did you ever know,
His heritage of cabbage and pigtails,
Old intimacy with alleys, garbage pails,
Down in the deep (but always beautiful) South
Where roses blush their blithest (it is said)   30
And sweet magnolias put Chanel [2] to shame.

No! He has not a flower to his name.
Except a feather one, for his lapel.
Apart from that, if he should think of flowers
It is in terms of dandelions or death.   35
Ah, there is little hope. You might as well—

---

1. Women with whom one has had an intimate re-   2. A perfume created by Coco Chanel, Parisian
lation.   fashion designer.

Unless you care to set the world a-boil
And do a lot of equalizing things,
Remove a little ermine, say, from kings,
Shake hands with paupers and appoint them men,   40
For instance—certainly you might as well
Leave him his lotion, lavender and oil.

Let us proceed. Let us inspect, together
With his meticulous and serious love,
The innards of this closet. Which is a vault   45
Whose glory is not diamonds, not pearls,
Not silver plate with just enough dull shine.
But wonder-suits in yellow and in wine,
Sarcastic green and zebra-striped cobalt.
All drapes. With shoulder padding that is wide   50
And cocky and determined as his pride;
Ballooning pants that taper off to ends
Scheduled to choke precisely.
                                  Here are hats
Like bright umbrellas; and hysterical ties   55
Like narrow banners for some gathering war.

People are so in need, in need of help.
People want so much that they do not know.

Below the tinkling trade of little coins
The gold impulse not possible to show   60
Or spend. Promise piled over and betrayed.

These kneaded limbs receive the kiss of silk.
Then they receive the brave and beautiful
Embrace of some of that equivocal wool.
He looks into his mirror, loves himself—   65
The neat curve here; the angularity
That is appropriate at just its place;
The technique of a variegated grace.

Here is all his sculpture and his art
And all his architectural design.   70
Perhaps you would prefer to this a fine
Value of marble, complicated stone.
Would have him think with horror of baroque,
Rococo.[3] You forget and you forget.

He dances down the hotel steps that keep   75
Remnants of last night's high life and distress.
As spat-out purchased kisses and spilled beer.
He swallows sunshine with a secret yelp.
Passes to coffee and a roll or two.

3. An artistic style originating in 18th-century France characterized by elaborate ornamentation. "Baroque": a style in art and architecture typified by elaborate and ornate scrolls, curves, and symmetrical ornamentation.

Has breakfasted.   80
    Out. Sounds about him smear,
Become a unit. He hears and does not hear
The alarm clock meddling in somebody's sleep;
Children's governed Sunday happiness;
The dry tone of a plane; a woman's oath;   85
Consumption's [4] spiritless expectoration;
An indignant robin's resolute donation
Pinching a track through apathy and din;
Restaurant vendors weeping; and the L [5]
That comes on like a slightly horrible thought.   90

Pictures, too, as usual, are blurred.
He sees and does not see the broken windows
Hiding their shame with newsprint; little girl
With ribbons decking wornness, little boy
Wearing the trousers with the decentest patch,   95
To honor Sunday; women on their way
From "service," temperate holiness arranged
Ably on asking faces; men estranged
From music and from wonder and from joy
But far familiar with the guiding awe   100
Of foodlessness.
                    He loiters.
                                Restaurant vendors
Weep, or out of them rolls a restless glee.
The Lonesome Blues, the Long-lost Blues, I Want A   105
Big Fat Mama. Down these sore avenues
Comes no Saint-Saëns, no piquant elusive Grieg,
And not Tschaikovsky's wayward eloquence
And not the shapely tender drift of Brahms. [6]
But could he love them? Since a man must bring   110
To music what his mother spanked him for
When he was two: bits of forgotten hate,
Devotion: whether or not his mattress hurts:
The little dream his father humored: the thing
His sister did for money: what he ate   115
For breakfast—and for dinner twenty years
Ago last autumn: all his skipped desserts.

The pasts of his ancestors lean against
Him. Crowd him. Fog out his identity.
Hundreds of hungers mingle with his own,   120
Hundreds of voices advise so dexterously
He quite considers his reactions his,
Judges he walks most powerfully alone,
That everything is—simply what it is.

But movie-time approaches, time to boo   125
The hero's kiss, and boo the heroine

4. I.e., tuberculosis's.   1921), French. Edvard Grieg (1843–1907), Norwe-
5. I.e., the elevated train that runs through Chi-   gian. Piotr Tchaikovsky (1840–1893), Russian. Jo-
cago.   hannes Brahms (1833–1897), German.
6. All composers. Camille Saint-Saëns (1835–

Whose ivory and yellow it is sin
For his eye to eat of. The Mickey Mouse,
However, is for everyone in the house.

Squires his lady to dinner at Joe's Eats.   130
His lady alters as to leg and eye,
Thickness and height, such minor points as these,
From Sunday to Sunday. But no matter what
Her name or body positively she's
In Queen Lace stockings with ambitious heels   135
That strain to kiss the calves, and vivid shoes
Frontless and backless, Chinese fingernails,
Earrings, three layers of lipstick, intense hat
Dripping with the most voluble of veils.
Her affable extremes are like sweet bombs   140
About him, whom no middle grace or good
Could gratify. He had no education
In quiet arts of compromise. He would
Not understand your counsels on control, nor
Thank you for your late trouble.   145
          At Joe's Eats
You get your fish or chicken on meat platters.
With coleslaw, macaroni, candied sweets,
Coffee and apple pie. You go out full.
(The end is—isn't it?—all that really matters.)   150

          And even and intrepid come
          The tender boots of night to home.

          Her body is like new brown bread
          Under the Woolworth mignonette. [7]
          Her body is a honey bowl   155
          Whose waiting honey is deep and hot.
          Her body is like summer earth,
          Receptive, soft, and absolute . . .

                                        1945

                    Maxie Allen

          Maxie Allen always taught her
          Stipendiary little daughter
          To thank her Lord and lucky star
          For eye that let her see so far,
          For throat enabling her to eat   5
          Her Quaker Oats and Cream-of-Wheat,
          For tongue to tantrum for the penny,
          For ear to hear the haven't-any,
          For arm to toss, for leg to chance,
          For heart to hanker for romance.   10

7. A plant known for its dainty and fragrant white flowers.

Sweet Annie tried to teach her mother
There was somewhat of something other.
And whether it was veils and God
And whistling ghosts to go unshod
Across the broad and bitter sod,   15
Or fleet love stopping at her foot
And giving her its never-root
To put into her pocket-book,
Or just a deep and human look,
She did not know; but tried to tell.   20

Her mother thought at her full well,
In inner voice not like a bell
(Which though not social has a ring
Akin to wrought bedevilling)
But like an oceanic thing: 25
    What do you guess I am?
    You've lots of jacks and strawberry jam.
And you don't have to go to bed, I remark,
With two dill pickles in the dark,
Nor prop what hardly calls you honey   30
And gives you only a little money.

                                                    1949

The Rites for Cousin Vit

Carried her unprotesting out the door.
Kicked back the casket-stand. But it can't hold her,
That stuff and satin aiming to enfold her,
The lid's contrition nor the bolts before.
Oh oh. Too much. Too much. Even now, surmise,   5
She rises in the sunshine. There she goes,
Back to the bars she knew and the repose
In love-rooms and the things in people's eyes.
Too vital and too squeaking. Must emerge.
Even now she does the snake-hips with a hiss,   10
Slops the bad wine across her shantung,[1] talks
Of pregnancy, guitars and bridgework, walks
In parks or alleys, comes haply on the verge
Of happiness, haply hysterics. Is.

                                                    1949

The Children of the Poor[1]

1

People who have no children can be hard:
Attain a mail[2] of ice and insolence:

---

1. Garment of the heavy, irregular, partly silk fabric called "shantung."
1. This sonnet sequence features both Petrarchan
and Shakespearean sonnet forms.
2. Armor usually made of metal links.

Need not pause in the fire, and in no sense
Hesitate in the hurricane to guard.
And when wide world is bitten and bewarred   5
They perish purely, waving their spirits hence
Without a trace of grace or of offense
To laugh or fail, diffident, wonder-starred.
While through a throttling dark we others hear
The little lifting helplessness, the queer   10
Whimper-whine; whose unridiculous
Lost softness softly makes a trap for us.
And makes a curse. And makes a sugar of
The malocclusions,[3] the inconditions of love.

2

What shall I give my children? who are poor,   15
Who are adjudged the leastwise of the land,
Who are my sweetest lepers, who demand
No velvet and no velvety velour;
But who have begged me for a brisk contour,
Crying that they are quasi, contraband   20
Because unfinished, graven by a hand
Less than angelic, admirable or sure.
My hand is stuffed with mode, design, device.
But I lack access to my proper stone.
And plenitude or plan shall not suffice   25
Nor grief nor love shall be enough alone
To ratify my little halves who bear
Across an autumn freezing everywhere.

3

And shall I prime my children, pray, to pray?
Mites, come invade most frugal vestibules   30
Spectered with crusts of penitents' renewals
And all hysterics arrogant for a day.
Instruct yourselves here is no devil to pay.
Children, confine your lights in jellied rules;
Resemble graves; be metaphysical mules;   35
Learn Lord will not distort nor leave the fray.
Behind the scurryings of your neat motif
I shall wait, if you wish: revise the psalm
If that should frighten you: sew up belief
If that should tear: turn, singularly calm   40
At forehead and at fingers rather wise,
Holding the bandage ready for your eyes.

4

First flight. Then fiddle. Ply the slipping string
With feathery sorcery; muzzle the note
With hurting love; the music that they wrote   45
Bewitch, bewilder. Qualify to sing
Threadwise. Devise no salt, no hempen[4] thing

---

3. Faulty closure, usually in the coming together   4. Resembling hemp, a coarse fiber often used for
of the teeth.   ropes.

For the dear instrument to bear. Devote
The bow to silks and honey. Be remote
A while from malice and from murdering.   50
But first to arms, to armor. Carry hate
In front of you and harmony behind.
Be deaf to music and to beauty blind.
Win war. Rise bloody, maybe not too late
For having first to civilize a space   55
Wherein to play your violin with grace.

5

When my dears die, the festival-colored brightness
That is their motion and mild repartee
Enchanted, a macabre mockery
Charming the rainbow radiance into tightness   60
And into a remarkable politeness
That is not kind and does not want to be,
May not they in the crisp encounter see
Something to recognize and read as rightness?
I say they may, so granitely discreet,   65
The little crooked questionings inbound,
Concede themselves on most familiar ground,
Cold an old predicament of the breath:
Adroit, the shapely prefaces complete,
Accept the universality of death.   70

6

Life for my child is simple, and is good.
He knows his wish. Yes, but that is not all.
Because I know mine too.
And we both want joy of undeep and unabiding things,
Like kicking over a chair or throwing blocks out of a window   75
Or tipping over an icebox pan
Or snatching down curtains or fingering an electric outlet
Or a journey or a friend or an illegal kiss.
No. There is more to it than that.
It is that he has never been afraid.   80
Rather, he reaches out and to the chair falls with a beautiful crash,
And the blocks fall, down on the people's heads,
And the water comes slooshing sloppily out across the floor.
And so forth.
Not that success, for him, is sure, infallible.   85
But never has he been afraid to reach.
His lesions are legion.
But reaching is his rule.

1949

The Lovers of the Poor

arrive. The Ladies from the Ladies' Betterment
   League
Arrive in the afternoon, the late light slanting
In diluted gold bars across the boulevard brag
Of proud, seamed faces with mercy and murder hinting
Here, there, interrupting, all deep and debonair,   5
The pink paint on the innocence of fear;
Walk in a gingerly manner up the hall.
Cutting with knives served by their softest care,
Served by their love, so barbarously fair.
Whose mothers taught: You'd better not be cruel!   10
You had better not throw stones upon the wrens!
Herein they kiss and coddle and assault
Anew and dearly in the innocence
With which they baffle nature. Who are full,
Sleek, tender-clad, fit, fiftyish, a-glow, all   15
Sweetly abortive, hinting at fat fruit,
Judge it high time that fiftyish fingers felt
Beneath the lovelier planes of enterprise.
To resurrect. To moisten with milky chill.
To be a random hitching-post or plush.   20
To be, for wet eyes, random and handy hem.
      Their guild is giving money to the poor.
The worthy poor. The very very worthy
And beautiful poor. Perhaps just not too swarthy?
Perhaps just not too dirty nor too dim   25
Nor—passionate. In truth, what they could wish
Is—something less than derelict or dull.
Not staunch enough to stab, though, gaze for gaze!
God shield them sharply from the beggar-bold!
The noxious needy ones whose battle's bald   30
Nonetheless for being voiceless, hits one down.
      But it's all so bad! and entirely too much for them.
The stench; the urine, cabbage, and dead beans,
Dead porridges of assorted dusty grains,
The old smoke, *heavy* diapers, and, they're told,   35
Something called chitterlings.[1] The darkness. Drawn
Darkness, or dirty light. The soil that stirs.
The soil that looks the soil of centuries.
And for that matter the *general* oldness. Old
Wood. Old marble. Old tile. Old old old.   40
Not homekind Oldness! Not Lake Forest, Glencoe.[2]
Nothing is sturdy, nothing is majestic,
There is no quiet drama, no rubbed glaze, no
Unkillable infirmity of such
A tasteful turn as lately they have left,   45
Glencoe, Lake Forest, and to which their cars
Must presently restore them. When they're done

---

1. The small intestines of animals, mainly hogs, especially fried or boiled.   2. Prosperous suburbs north of Chicago.

With dullards and distortions of this fistic [3]
Patience of the poor and put-upon.
                They've never seen such a make-do-ness as   50
Newspaper rugs before! In this, this "flat,"
Their hostess is gathering up the oozed, the rich
Rugs of the morning (tattered! the bespattered. . . .)
Readies to spread clean rugs for afternoon.
Here is a scene for you. The Ladies look,   55
In horror, behind a substantial citizenness
Whose trains clank out across her swollen heart.
Who, arms akimbo, almost fills a door.
All tumbling children, quilts dragged to the floor
And tortured thereover, potato peelings, soft-   60
Eyed kitten, hunched-up, haggard, to-be-hurt.
                Their League is allotting largesse to the Lost.
But to put their clean, their pretty money, to put
Their money collected from delicate rose-fingers
Tipped with their hundred flawless rose-nails seems . . .   65
                They own Spode, Lowestoft, candelabra,
Mantels, and hostess gowns, and sunburst clocks,
Turtle soup, Chippendale, red satin "hangings,"
Aubussons and Hattie Carnegie. [4] They Winter
In Palm Beach; cross the Water [5] in June; attend,   70
When suitable, the nice Art Institute;
Buy the right books in the best bindings; saunter
On Michigan, [6] Easter mornings, in sun or wind.
Oh Squalor! This sick four-story hulk, this fiber
With fissures everywhere! Why, what are bringings   75
Of loathe-love largesse? What shall peril hungers
So old old, what shall flatter the desolate?
Tin can, blocked fire escape and chitterling
And swaggering seeking youth and the puzzled wreckage
Of the middle passage, [7] and urine and stale shames   80
And, again, the porridges of the underslung
And children children children. Heavens! That
Was a rat, surely, off there, in the shadows? Long
And long-tailed? Gray? The Ladies from the Ladies'
Betterment League agree it will be better   85
To achieve the outer air that rights and steadies,
To hie to a house that does not holler, to ring
Bells elsetime, better presently to cater
To no more Possibilities, to get
Away. Perhaps the money can be posted.   90
Perhaps they two may choose another Slum!
Some serious sooty half-unhappy home!—
Where loathe-love likelier may be invested.
                Keeping their scented bodies in the center
Of the hall as they walk down the hysterical hall,   95

3. Having to do with boxing or fighting with the   American designer of the 1950s.
fists.   5. I.e., travel to Europe.
4. Symbols of wealth. "Spode" and "Lowestoft":   6. Prosperous Chicago avenue.
English fine china. "Chippendale": 18th-century   7. An allusion to the passage of slaves from Africa
English furniture. "Aubussons": 18th-century   across the Atlantic to America and the West Indies.
French rugs. Hattie Carnegie was a fashionable

They allow their lovely skirts to graze no wall,
Are off at what they manage of a canter,
And, resuming all the clues of what they were,
Try to avoid inhaling the laden air.

1960

We Real Cool

The Pool Players.
Seven at the Golden Shovel.

We real cool. We
Left school. We

Lurk late. We   5
Strike straight. We

Sing sin. We
Thin gin. We

Jazz June. We
Die soon.   10

1960

The Chicago *Defender* Sends a Man to Little Rock [1]

Fall, 1957

In Little Rock the people bear
Babes, and comb and part their hair
And watch the want ads, put repair
To roof and latch. While wheat toast burns
A woman waters multiferns.   5

Time upholds or overturns
The many, tight, and small concerns.

In Little Rock the people sing
Sunday hymns like anything,
Through Sunday pomp and polishing.   10

And after testament and tunes,
Some soften Sunday afternoons
With lemon tea and Lorna Doones.

I forecast
And I believe   15
Come Christmas Little Rock will cleave

1. Federal intervention was necessary to implement school desegregation in Little Rock.

To Christmas tree and trifle, weave,
From laugh and tinsel, texture fast.

In Little Rock is baseball; Barcarolle.[2]
That hotness in July . . . the uniformed figures raw and
   implacable   20
And not intellectual,
Batting the hotness or clawing the suffering dust.
The Open Air Concert, on the special twilight green . . .
When Beethoven is brutal or whispers to lady-like air.
Blanket-sitters are solemn, as Johann[3] troubles to lean   25
To tell them what to mean. . . .

There is love, too, in Little Rock. Soft women softly
Opening themselves in kindness,
Or, pitying one's blindness,
Awaiting one's pleasure   30
In azure
Glory with anguished rose at the root. . . .
To wash away old semi-discomfitures.
They re-teach purple and unsullen blue.
The wispy soils go. And uncertain   35
Half-havings have they clarified to sures.

In Little Rock they know
Not answering the telephone is a way of rejecting life,
That it is our business to be bothered, is our business
To cherish bores or boredom, be polite   40
To lies and love and many-faceted fuzziness.

I scratch my head, massage the hate-I-had.
I blink across my prim and pencilled pad.
The saga I was sent for is not down.
Because there is a puzzle in this town.   45
The biggest News I do not dare
Telegraph to the Editor's chair:
"They are like people everywhere."

The angry Editor would reply
In hundred harryings of Why.   50

And true, they are hurling spittle, rock,
Garbage and fruit in Little Rock.
And I saw coiling storm a-writhe
On bright madonnas. And a scythe
Of men harassing brownish girls.   55
(The bows and barrettes in the curls
And braids declined away from joy.)

I saw a bleeding brownish boy. . . .

2. A Venetian gondolier's song with a rhythm suggestive of rowing.
3. Johann Sebastian Bach (1685–1750), German
organist and composer. Ludwig van Beethoven
(1770–1827), German composer noted for his innovative symphonies.

The lariat lynch-wish I deplored.

The loveliest lynchee was our Lord.   60

1960

A Lovely Love

Lillian's

Let it be alleys. Let it be a hall
Whose janitor javelins epithet and thought
To cheapen hyacinth darkness that we sought
And played we found, rot, make the petals fall.
Let it be stairways, and a splintery box   5
Where you have thrown me, scraped me with your kiss,
Have honed me, have released me after this
Cavern kindness, smiled away our shocks.
That is the birthright of our lovely love
In swaddling clothes. Not like that Other one.   10
Not lit by any fondling star above.
Not found by any wise men, either. Run.
People are coming. They must not catch us here
Definitionless in this strict atmosphere.

1960

Malcolm X

For Dudley Randall

Original.
Ragged-round.
Rich-robust.

He had the hawk-man's eyes.
We gasped. We saw the maleness.   5
The maleness raking out and making guttural the air
and pushing us to walls.

And in a soft and fundamental hour
a sorcery devout and vertical
beguiled the world.   10

He opened us—
who was a key,

who was a man.

1968

Two Dedications

I

THE CHICAGO PICASSO

August 15, 1967

"Mayor Daley[1] tugged a white ribbon, loosing the blue percale wrap.
A hearty cheer went up as the covering slipped off the big steel
sculpture that looks at once like a bird and a woman."
—CHICAGO SUN-TIMES

(Seiji Ozawa[2] leads the Symphony.
The Mayor smiles.
And 50,000 See.)

Does man love Art? Man visits Art, but squirms.
Art hurts. Art urges voyages—
and it is easier to stay at home,
the nice beer ready.
        In commonrooms
we belch, or sniff, or scratch.
Are raw.

But we must cook ourselves and style ourselves for Art, who
is a requiring courtesan.
We squirm.
We do not hug the Mona Lisa.
We
may touch or tolerate
an astounding fountain, or a horse-and-rider.
At most, another Lion.

Observe the tall cold of a Flower
which is as innocent and as guilty,
as meaningful and as meaningless as any
other flower in the western field.

II

THE WALL

August 27, 1967

For Edward Christmas

"The side wall of a typical slum building on the corner of 43rd and
Langley became a mural communicating black dignity. . . ."
—EBONY

A drumdrumdrum.
Humbly we come.

1. Richard Joseph Daley (1902–1976), Democratic mayor of Chicago from 1955 to 1976.
2. Seiji Ozawa (b. 1935), Japanese conductor who joined the New York Philharmonic in 1961 and became the music director of the Boston Symphony Orchestra in 1973.

South of success and east of gloss and glass are   25
sandals;
flowercloth;
grave hoops of wood or gold, pendant
from black ears, brown ears, reddish-brown
and ivory ears;   30

black boy-men.
Black
boy-men on roofs fist out "Black Power!" Val,
a little black stampede
in African   35
images of brass and flowerswirl,
fists out "Black Power!"—tightens pretty eyes,
leans back on mothercountry and is tract,
is treatise through her perfect and tight teeth.

Women in wool hair chant their poetry.   40
Phil Cohran gives us messages and music
made of developed bone and polished and honed cult.
It is the Hour of tribe and of vibration,
the day-long Hour. It is the Hour
of ringing, rouse, of ferment-festival.   45

On Forty-third and Langley
black furnaces resent ancient
legislatures
of ploy and scruple and practical gelatin.
They keep the fever in,   50
fondle the fever.

All
worship the Wall.

I mount the rattling wood. Walter
says, "She is good." Says, "She   55
our Sister is." In front of me
hundreds of faces, red-brown, brown, black, ivory,
yield me hot trust, their yea and their Announcement
that they are ready to rile the high-flung ground.
Behind me, Paint.   60
Heroes.
No child has defiled
the Heroes of this Wall this serious Appointment
this still Wing
this Scald this Flute this heavy Light this Hinge.   65

An emphasis is paroled.
The old decapitations are revised,
the dispossessions beakless.

And we sing.

                                        1968

Riot

A riot is the language of the unheard.
—MARTIN LUTHER KING

John Cabot,[1] out of Wilma, once a Wycliffe,
all whitebluerose below his golden hair,
wrapped richly in right linen and right wool,
almost forgot his Jaguar and Lake Bluff;
almost forgot Grandtully (which is The   5
Best Thing That Ever Happened To Scotch); almost
forgot the sculpture at the Richard Gray
and Distelheim; the kidney pie at Maxim's,
the Grenadine de Boeuf at Maison Henri.

Because the Negroes were coming down the street.   10

Because the Poor were sweaty and unpretty
(not like Two Dainty Negroes in Winnetka[2])
and they were coming toward him in rough ranks.
In seas. In windsweep. They were black and loud.
And not detainable. And not discreet.   15

Gross. Gross. "*Que tu es grossier!*"[3] John Cabot
itched instantly beneath the nourished white
that told his story of glory to the World.
"Don't let It touch me! the blackness! Lord!" he whispered
to any handy angel in the sky.   20
But, in a thrilling announcement, on It drove
and breathed on him: and touched him. In that breath
the fume of pig foot, chitterling[4] and cheap chili,
malign, mocked John. And, in terrific touch, old
averted doubt jerked forward decently,   25
cried "Cabot! John! You are a desperate man,
and the desperate die expensively today."

John Cabot went down in the smoke and fire
and broken glass and blood, and he cried "Lord!
Forgive these nigguhs that know not what they do."   30

1969

---

1. The Cabot family has been prominent in America since the early 18th century; their fortune was initially based on trading in rum, slaves, and opium.

2. Prosperous Chicago suburb.
3. How crude you are! (French).
4. The small intestines of animals, especially fried or boiled.

The Third Sermon on the Warpland

Phoenix
"In Egyptian mythology, a bird which
lived for five hundred years and then
consumed itself in fire, rising renewed
from the ashes."
—WEBSTER

The earth is a beautiful place.
Watermirrors and things to be reflected.
Goldenrod across the little lagoon.

The Black Philosopher says
"Our chains are in the keep of the Keeper   5
in a labeled cabinet
on the second shelf by the cookies,
sonatas, the arabesques. . . .
There's a rattle, sometimes.
You do not hear it who mind only   10
cookies and crunch them.
You do not hear the remarkable music—'A
Death Song For You Before You Die.'
If you could hear it
you would make music too.   15
The *black*blues."

West Madison Street.
In "Jessie's Kitchen"
nobody's eating Jessie's Perfect Food.
Crazy flowers   20
cry up across the sky, spreading
and hissing *This is*
it.

The young men run.

They will not steal Bing Crosby but will steal   .   25
Melvin Van Peebles[1] who made Lillie
a thing of Zampoughi a thing of red wiggles and trebles
(and I know there are twenty wire stalks sticking out of her head
as her underfed haunches jerk jazz).

A clean riot is not one in which little rioters   30
long-stomped, long-straddled, BEANLESS
but knowing no Why
go steal in hell
a radio, sit to hear James Brown
and Mingus, Young-Holt, Coleman, John, on V.O.N.,[2]   35
and sun themselves in Sin.

---

1. An African American director whose independent film *The Night the Sun Came Out* was made
in the 1960s. It grossed more than $10 million,
opening the way for further independent African
American film ventures. He recorded "Lilly Done

the Zampoughi" on the album *Brer Soul.* Bing
Crosby (1903–1977), one of the first great romantic
crooners and, subsequently, motion picture star.
2. Album label based in Detroit. These lines make
up a catalog of black musicians.

However, what
is going on
is going on.

Fire.   40
That is their way of lighting candles in the darkness.
A White Philosopher said
"It is better to light one candle than curse the darkness." [3]
        These candles curse—
inverting the deeps of the darkness.   45

GUARD HERE, GUNS LOADED.
The young men run.
The children in ritual chatter
scatter upon
their Own and old geography.   50

The Law comes sirening across the town.

A woman is dead.
Motherwoman.
She lies among the boxes
(that held the haughty hats, the Polish sausages)   55
in newish, thorough, firm virginity
as rich as fudge is if you've had five pieces.
Not again shall she
partake of steak
on Christmas mornings, nor of nighttime   60
chicken and wine at Val Gray Ward's
nor say
of Mr. Beetley, Exit Jones, Junk Smith
nor neat New-baby Williams (man-to-many)
"He treat me right."   65

That was a gut gal.

"We'll do an us!" yells Yancey, a twittering twelve.
"Instead of your deathintheafternoon,
kill 'em, bull!
kill 'em, bull!"   70

The Black Philosopher blares
"I tell you, exhaustive black integrity
would assure a blackless America. . . ."

Nine die, Sun-Times will tell
and will tell too   75
in small black-bordered oblongs "Rumor? check it
at 744-4111."

A Poem to Peanut.
"Coooooool!" purrs Peanut. Peanut is

3. The motto of the Christopher Society, a Catholic lay organization.

Richard—a Ranger[4] and a gentleman.   80
A Signature. A Herald. And a Span.
This Peanut will not let his men explode.
And Rico will not.
Neither will Sengali.
Nor Bop nor Jeff, Geronimo nor Lover.   85
These merely peer and purr,
and pass the Passion over.
The Disciples stir
and thousandfold confer
with ranging Rangermen;   90
mutual in their "Yeah!—
this AIN'T all upinheah!"

"But WHY do These People offend *themselves?*" say they
who say also "It's time.
It's time to help   95
These People."

Lies are told and legends made.
Phoenix rises unafraid.

The Black Philosopher will remember:
"There they came to life and exulted,   100
the hurt mute.
Then it was over.

The dust, as they say, settled."

    1969

Young Heroes

I

KEORAPETSE KGOSITSILE (WILLIE)

He is very busy with his looking.
To look, he knows, is to involve
subject and suppliant.
He looks at life—
moves life into his hands—   5
saying
Art is life worked with: is life
wheedled, or whelmed:
assessed:
clandestine, but evoked.   10

Look! Look to *this* page!
A horror here

---

4. Member of a Chicago gang, the Blackstone Rangers, for whom Brooks ran a poetry workshop. Richard "Peanut" Washington was a leader of the Rangers.

walks toward you in working clothes.
   He sees
hellishness among the half-men.   15
He sees
pellmelling loneliness in the
center of grouphood.
He sees
lenient dignity. He   20
sees pretty flowers under blood.

He teaches dolls and dynamite.
Because he knows
there is a scientific thinning of our ranks.
Not merely Medgar Malcolm Martin and Black
    Panthers,[1]   25
but Susie. Cecil Williams. Azzie Jane.
He teaches
strategy and the straight aim;
black volume;
might of mind, black flare—   30
volcanoing merit, black
herohood.

Black total.

   He is no kitten Traveler
and no poor Knower of himself.   35

   Blackness
is a going to essences and to unifyings.

"MY NAME IS AFRIKA"!
   Well, every fella's a Foreign Country.

This Foreign Country speaks to You.   40

II

TO DON AT SALAAM

I like to see you lean back in your chair
so far you have to fall but do not—
your arms back, your fine hands
in your print pockets.
Beautiful. Impudent.   45
Ready for life.
A tied storm.

I like to see you wearing your boy smile
whose tribute is for two of us or three.

1. A U.S. black militant organization active in the
1960s and 1970s, whose open conflict with the police led to many of its leaders being killed or imprisoned. Medgar Wiley Evers (1925–1963), Malcolm
X (1925–1965), and Martin Luther King Jr. (1929–
1968), despite differences of political philosophy,
were all martyred while actively engaged in the
civil rights movement.

Sometimes in life   50
things seem to be moving
and they are not
and they are not
there.
You are there.   55

Your voice is the listened-for music.
Your act is the consolation.

I like to see you living in the world.

III

WALTER BRADFORD

Just As You Think You're "Better Now"
Something Comes To The Door.   60
It's a Wilderness, Walter.
It's a Whirlpool or Whipper.

THEN you have to revise the messages;
and, pushing through roars of the Last Trombones of seduction,
the deft orchestration,   65
settle the sick ears to hear and to heed and to hold;
the sick ears a-plenty.

It's Walter-work, Walter.
——Not overmuch for
brick-fitter, brick-MAKER, and wave-   70
outwitter;
whip-stopper.

Not overmuch for a
Tree-planting Man.

Stay.   75

                                                           1970

when you have forgotten Sunday: the love story

——And when you have forgotten the bright bedclothes on a
        Wednesday and a Saturday,
And most especially when you have forgotten Sunday—
When you have forgotten Sunday halves in bed,
Or me sitting on the front-room radiator in the limping afternoon
Looking off down the long street   5
To nowhere,
Hugged by my plain old wrapper of no-expectation
And nothing-I-have-to-do and I'm-happy-why?
And if-Monday-never-had-to-come—
When you have forgotten that, I say,   10

And how you swore, if somebody beeped the bell,
And how my heart played hopscotch if the telephone rang;
And how we finally went in to Sunday dinner,
That is to say, went across the front room floor to the ink-spotted
    table in the southwest corner
To Sunday dinner, which was always chicken and noodles   15
Or chicken and rice
And salad and rye bread and tea
And chocolate chip cookies—
I say, when you have forgotten that,
When you have forgotten my little presentiment   20
That the war would be over before they got to you;
And how we finally undressed and whipped out the light and flowed
    into bed,
And lay loose-limbed for a moment in the week-end
Bright bedclothes,
Then gently folded into each other—   25
When you have, I say, forgotten all that,
Then you may tell,
Then I may believe
You have forgotten me well.

                                                            1981

Maud Martha

1. description of Maud Martha

What she liked was candy buttons, and books, and painted music (deep blue, or delicate silver) and the west sky, so altering, viewed from the steps of the back porch; and dandelions.

She would have liked a lotus, or China asters or the Japanese Iris, or meadow lilies—yes, she would have liked meadow lilies, because the very word meadow made her breathe more deeply, and either fling her arms or want to fling her arms, depending on who was by, rapturously up to whatever was watching in the sky. But dandelions were what she chiefly saw. Yellow jewels for everyday, studding the patched green dress of her back yard. She liked their demure prettiness second to their everydayness; for in that latter quality she thought she saw a picture of herself, and it was comforting to find that what was common could also be a flower.

And could be cherished! To be cherished was the dearest wish of the heart of Maud Martha Brown, and sometimes when she was not looking at dandelions (for one would not be looking at them all the time, often there were chairs and tables to dust or tomatoes to slice or beds to make or grocery stores to be gone to, and in the colder months there were no dandelions at all), it was hard to believe that a thing of only ordinary allurements—if the allurements of any flower could be said to be ordinary—was as easy to love as a thing of heart-catching beauty.

Such as her sister Helen! who was only two years past her own age of seven, and was almost her own height and weight and thickness. But oh, the long lashes, the grace, the little ways with the hands and feet.

2. spring landscape: detail

The school looked solid. Brownish-red brick, dirty cream stone trim. Massive chimney, candid, serious. The sky was gray, but the sun was making little silver promises somewhere up there, hinting. A wind blew. What sort of June day was this? It was more like the last days of November. It was more than rather bleak; still, there were these little promises, just under cover; whether they would fulfill themselves was anybody's guess.

Up the street, mixed in the wind, blew the children, and turned the corner onto the brownish-red brick school court. It was wonderful. Bits of pink, of blue, white, yellow, green, purple, brown, black, carried by jerky little stems of brown or yellow or brown-black, blew by the unhandsome gray and decay of the double-apartment buildings, past the little plots of dirt and scanty grass that held up their narrow brave banners: PLEASE KEEP OFF THE GRASS—NEWLY SEEDED. There were lives in the buildings. Past the tiny lives the children blew. Cramp, inhibition, choke—they did not trouble themselves about these. They spoke shrilly of ways to fix curls and pompadours, of "nasty" boys and "sharp" boys, of Joe Louis,[1] of ice cream, of bicycles, of baseball, of teachers, of examinations, of Duke Ellington, of Bette Davis.[2] They spoke—or at least Maud Martha spoke—of the sweet potato pie that would be served at home.

It was six minutes to nine; in one minute the last bell would ring. "Come on! You'll be late!" Low cries. A quickening of steps. A fluttering of brief cases. Inevitably, though, the fat girl, who was forced to be nonchalant, who pretended she little cared whether she was late or not, who would *not* run! (Because she would wobble, would lose her dignity.) And inevitably the little fellows in knickers, ten, twelve, thirteen years old, nonchalant just for the fun of it—who lingered on the red bricks, throwing balls to each other, or reading newspapers and comic books, or punching each other half playfully.

But eventually every bit of the wind managed to blow itself in, and by five minutes after nine the school court was bare. There was not a hot cap nor a bow ribbon anywhere.

3. love and gorillas

so the gorilla really did escape!

She was sure of it, now that she was awake. For she was awake. This was awakeness. Stretching, curling her fingers, she was still rather protected by the twists of thin smoky stuff from the too sudden onslaught of the red draperies with white and green flowers on them, and the picture of the mother and dog loving a baby, and the dresser with blue paper flowers on it. But that she was now awake in all earnest she could not doubt.

That train—a sort of double-deck bus affair, traveling in a blue-lined half dark. Slow, that traveling. Slow. More like a boat. It came to a stop before the gorilla's cage. The gorilla, lying back, his arms under his head, one leg

---

1. African American boxer (1914–1981), who was the heavyweight champion from 1937 to 1949.
2. American actress (1905–1989). Duke Ellington (1899–1974), African American jazz composer, orchestra leader, and pianist.

resting casually across the other, watched the people. Then he rose, lumbered over to the door of his cage, peered, clawed at his bars, shook his bars. All the people on the lower deck climbed to the upper deck.

But why would they not get off?

"Motor trouble!" called the conductor. "Motor trouble! And the gorilla, they think, will escape!"

But why would not the people get off?

Then there was flaring green and there was red and there was redorange, and she was in the middle of it, her few years many times added to, doubtless, for she was treated as an adult. All the people were afraid, but no one would get off.

All the people wondered if the gorilla would escape.

Awake, she knew he had.

She was safe, but the others—were they eaten? and if so had he begun on the heads first? and could he eat such things as buttons and watches and hair? or would he first tear those away?

Maud Martha got up, and on her way to the bathroom cast a glance toward her parents' partly open door. Her parents were close together. Her father's arm was around her mother.

Why, how lovely!

For she remembered last night. Her father stamping out grandly, dressed in his nicest suit and hat, and her mother left alone. Later, she and Helen and Harry had gone out with their mother for a "night hike."

How she loved a "hike." Especially in the evening, for then everything was moody, odd, deliciously threatening, always hunched and ready to close in on you but never doing so. East of Cottage Grove you saw fewer people, and those you did see had, all of them (how strange, thought Maud Martha), white faces. Over there that matter of mystery and hunchedness was thicker, a hundredfold.

Shortly after they had come in, Daddy had too. The children had been sent to bed, and off Maud Martha had gone to her sleep and her gorilla. (Although she had not known that in the beginning, oh no!) In the deep deep night she had waked, just a little, and had called "Mama." Mama had said, "Shut up!"

The little girl did not mind being told harshly to shut up when her mother wanted it quiet so that she and Daddy could love each other.

Because she was very *very* happy that their quarrel was over and that they would once again be nice.

Even though while the loud hate or silent cold was going on, Mama was so terribly sweet and good to her.

4. death of Grandmother

They had to sit in a small lobby, waiting for the nurses to change Gramma.

"She can't control herself," explained Maud Martha's mother.

Oh what a thing! What a thing.

When finally they could be admitted, Belva Brown, Maud Martha and Harry tiptoed into the lackluster room, single file.

Gramma lay in what seemed to Maud Martha a wooden coffin. Boards had been put up on either side of the bed to keep the patient from harming herself. All the morning, a nurse confided, Ernestine Brown had been trying to get out of the bed and go home.

They looked in the coffin. Maud Martha felt sick. That was not her Gramma. Couldn't be. Elongated, pulpy-looking face. Closed eyes; lashes damp-appearing, heavy lids. Straight flat thin form under a dark gray blanket. And the voice thick and raw. "Hawh—hawh—hawh." Maud Martha was frightened. But she mustn't show it. She spoke to the semi-corpse.

"Hello, Gramma. This is Maudie." After a moment, "Do you know me, Gramma?"

"Hawh—"

"Do you feel better? Does anything hurt you?"

"Hawh—" Here Gramma slightly shook her head. She did not open her eyes, but apparently she could understand whatever they said. And maybe, thought Maud Martha, what we are not saying.

How alone they were, how removed from this woman, this ordinary woman who had suddenly become a queen, for whom presently the most interesting door of them all would open, who, lying locked in boards with her "hawhs," yet towered, triumphed over them, while they stood there asking the stupid questions people ask the sick, out of awe, out of half horror, half envy.

"I never saw anybody die before," thought Maud Martha. "But I'm seeing somebody die now."

What was that smell? When would her mother go? She could not stand much more. What was that smell? She turned her gaze away for a while. To look at the other patients in the room, instead of at Gramma! The others were white women. There were three of them, two wizened ones, who were asleep, a stout woman of about sixty, who looked insane, and who was sitting up in bed, wailing, "Why don't they come and bring me a bedpan? Why don't they? Nobody brings me a bedpan." She clutched Maud Martha's coat hem, and stared up at her with glass-bright blue eyes, begging, "Will you tell them to bring me a bedpan? Will you?" Maud Martha promised, and the weak hand dropped.

"Poor dear," said the stout woman, glancing tenderly at Gramma.

When they finally left the room and the last "hawh," Maud Martha told a nurse passing down the hall just then about the woman who wanted the bedpan. The nurse tightened her lips. "Well, she can keep on wanting," she said, after a moment's indignant silence. "That's all they do, day long, night long—whine for the bedpan. We can't give them the bedpan every two minutes. Just forget it, Miss."

They started back down the long corridor. Maud Martha put her arm around her mother.

"Oh Mama," she whimpered, "she—she looked awful. I had no idea. I never saw such a horrible—creature—" A hard time she had, keeping the tears back. And as for her brother, Harry had not said a word since entering the hospital.

When they got back to the house, Papa was receiving a telephone message. Ernestine Brown was dead.

She who had taken the children of Abraham Brown to the circus, and who had bought them pink popcorn, and Peanut Crinkle candy, who had laughed—that Ernestine was dead.

5. you're being so good, so kind

Maud Martha looked the living room over. Nicked old upright piano. Sag-seat leather armchair. Three or four straight chairs that had long ago given up the ghost of whatever shallow dignity they may have had in the beginning and looked completely disgusted with themselves and with the Brown family. Mantel with scroll decorations that usually seemed rather elegant but which since morning had become unspeakably vulgar, impossible.

There was a small hole in the sad-colored rug, near the sofa. Not an outrageous hole. But she shuddered. She dashed to the sofa, maneuvered it till the hole could not be seen.

She sniffed a couple of times. Often it was said that colored people's houses necessarily had a certain heavy, unpleasant smell. Nonsense, that was. Vicious—and nonsense. But she raised every window.

Here was the theory of racial equality about to be put into practice, and she only hoped she would be equal to being equal.

No matter how taut the terror, the fall proceeds to its dregs. . . .

At seven o'clock her heart was starting to make itself heard, and with great energy she was assuring herself that, though she liked Charles, though she admired Charles, it was only at the high school that she wanted to see Charles.

This was no Willie or Richard or Sylvester coming to call on her. Neither was she Charles's Sally or Joan. She was the whole "colored" race, and Charles was the personalization of the entire Caucasian plan.

At three minutes to eight the bell rang, hesitantly. Charles! No doubt regretting his impulse already. No doubt regarding, with a rueful contempt, the outside of the house, so badly in need of paint. Those rickety steps. She retired into the bathroom. Presently she heard her father go to the door; her father—walking slowly, walking patiently, walking unafraid, as if about to let in a paper boy who wanted his twenty cents, or an insurance man, or Aunt Vivian, or no more than Woodette Williams, her own silly friend.

What was this she was feeling now? Not fear, not fear. A sort of gratitude! It sickened her to realize it. As though Charles, in coming, gave her a gift. Recipient and benefactor.

It's so good of you.

You're being so good.

6. at the Regal

The applause was quick. And the silence—final.

That was what Maud Martha, sixteen and very erect, believed, as she manipulated herself through a heavy outflowing crowd in the lobby of the Regal Theatre on Forty-seventh and South Park.

She thought of fame, and of that singer, that Howie Joe Jones, that tall oily brown thing with hair set in thickly pomaded waves, with cocky teeth, eyes like thin glass. With—a Voice. A Voice that Howie Joe's publicity described as "rugged honey." She had not been favorably impressed. She had not been able to thrill. Not even when he threw his head back so that his waves dropped low, shut his eyes sweetly, writhed, thrust out his arms (really *gave* them to the world) and thundered out, with passionate seriousness, with deep meaning, with high purpose—

—Sa-WEET sa-oooo
Jaust-a YOOOOOOO—

Maud Martha's brow wrinkled. The audience had applauded. Had stamped its strange, hilarious foot. Had put its fingers in its mouth—whistled. Had sped a shininess up to its eyes. But now part of it was going home, as she was, and its face was dull again. It had not been helped. Not truly. Not well. For a hot half hour it had put that light gauze across its little miseries and monotonies, but now here they were again, ungauzed, self-assertive, cancerous as ever. The audience had gotten a fairy gold. And it was not going to spend the rest of its life, or even the rest of the night, being grateful to Howie Joe Jones. No, it would not make plans to raise a hard monument to him.

She swung out of the lobby, turned north.

The applause was quick.

But the silence was final, so what was the singer's profit?

Money.

You had to admit Howie Joe Jones was making money. Money that was raced to the track, to the De Lisa, to women, to the sellers of cars; to Capper and Capper, to Henry C. Lytton and Company for those suits in which he looked like an upright corpse. She read all about it in the columns of the Chicago *Defender's* gossip departments.

She had never understood how people could parade themselves on a stage like that, exhibit their precious private identities; shake themselves about; be very foolish for a thousand eyes.

She was going to keep herself to herself. She did not want fame. She did not want to be a "star."

To create—a role, a poem, picture, music, a rapture in stone: great. But not for her.

What she wanted was to donate to the world a good Maud Martha. That was the offering, the bit of art, that could not come from any other.

She would polish and hone that.

7. Tim

Oh, how he used to wriggle!—do little mean things! do great big wonderful things! and laugh laugh laugh.

He had shaved and he had scratched himself through the pants. He had lain down and ached for want of a woman. He had married. He had wiped out his nostrils with bits of tissue paper in the presence of his wife and his wife had turned her head, quickly, but politely, to avoid seeing them as they dropped softly into the toilet, and floated. He had had a big stomach and an alarmingly loud laugh. He had been easy with the ain'ts and sho-nuffs. He had been drunk one time, only one time, and on that occasion had done the Charleston in the middle of what was then Grand Boulevard and is now South Park, at four in the morning. Here was a man who had absorbed the headlines in the *Tribune,* studied the cartoons in *Collier's* and the *Saturday Evening Post.*

These facts she had known about her Uncle Tim. And she had known that he liked sweet potato pie. But what were the facts that she had not known, that his wife, her father's sister Nannie, had not known? The things that nobody had known.

Maud Martha looked down at the gray clay lying hard-lipped, cold, defi-nitely not about to rise and punch off any alarm clock, on the tufted white satin that was at once so beautiful and so ghastly. I must tell them, she thought, as she walked back to her seat, I must let Helen and Harry know how I want to be arranged in my casket; I don't want my head straight up like that; I want my head turned a little to the right, so my best profile will be showing; and I want my left hand resting on my breast, nicely; and I want my hair plain, not waved—I don't want to look like a gray clay doll.

It all came down to gray clay.

Then just what was important? What had been important about this life, this Uncle Tim? Was the world any better off for his having lived? A little, perhaps. Perhaps he had stopped his car short once, and saved a dog, so that another car could kill it a month later. Perhaps he had given some little street wretch a nickel's worth of peanuts in its unhappy hour, and that little wretch would grow up and forget Uncle Tim but all its life would carry in its heart an anonymous, seemingly underivative softness for man-kind. Perhaps. Certainly he had been good to his wife Nannie. She had never said a word against him.

But how important was this, what was the real importance of this, what would—God say? Oh, no! What she would rather mean was, what would Uncle Tim say, if he could get back?

Maud Martha looked at Aunt Nannie. Aunt Nannie had put too much white powder on her face. Was it irreverent, Maud Martha wondered, to be able to think of powdering your face for a funeral, when you were the new widow? Not in this case, she decided, for (she remembered this other thing about him) Uncle Tim, whose nose was always oily, had disliked an oily nose. Aunt Nannie was being brave. As yet she had not dropped a tear. But then, her turn at the casket had not come.

A large woman in a white uniform and white stockings and low-heeled white shoes was playing "We Shall Understand It Better By and By" at the organ, almost inaudibly (with a little jazz roll in her bass). How gentle the music was, how suggestive. Maud Martha saw people, after having all but knocked themselves out below, climbing up the golden, golden stairs, to a throne where sat Jesus, or the Almighty God; who promptly opened a Book, similar to the arithmetic book she had had in grammar school, turned to the back, and pointed out—the Answers! And the people, poor little things, nodding and cackling among themselves—"So that was it all the time! that is what I should have done!" "But—so simple! so *easy!* I should just have turned here! instead of there!" How wonderful! Was it true? Were people to get the Answers in the sky? Were people really going to understand It better by and by? When it was too late?

8. *home*

What had been wanted was this always, this always to last, the talking softly on this porch, with the snake plant in the jardiniere [3] in the southwest corner, and the obstinate slip from Aunt Eppie's magnificent Michigan fern at the left side of the friendly door. Mama, Maud Martha and Helen rocked slowly in their rocking chairs, and looked at the late afternoon light on the lawn, and at the emphatic iron of the fence and at the poplar tree. These things might soon be theirs no longer. Those shafts and pools of light, the tree, the graceful iron, might soon be viewed possessively by different eyes.

Papa was to have gone that noon, during his lunch hour, to the office of the Home Owners' Loan. If he had not succeeded in getting another extension, they would be leaving this house in which they had lived for more than fourteen years. There was little hope. The Home Owners' Loan was hard. They sat, making their plans.

"We'll be moving into a nice flat somewhere," said Mama. "Somewhere on South Park, or Michigan, or in Washington Park Court." Those flats, as the girls and Mama knew well, were burdens on wages twice the size of Papa's. This was not mentioned now.

"They're much prettier than this old house," said Helen. "I have friends I'd just as soon not bring here. And I have other friends that wouldn't come down this far for anything, unless they were in a taxi."

Yesterday, Maud Martha would have attacked her. Tomorrow she might. Today she said nothing. She merely gazed at a little hopping robin in the tree, her tree, and tried to keep the fronts of her eyes dry.

"Well, I do know," said Mama, turning her hands over and over, "that I've been getting tireder and tireder of doing that firing. From October to April, there's firing to be done."

"But lately we've been helping, Harry and I," said Maud Martha. "And sometimes in March and April and in October, and even in November, we could build a little fire in the fireplace. Sometimes the weather was just right for that."

She knew, from the way they looked at her, that this had been a mistake. They did not want to cry.

But she felt that the little line of white, somewhat ridged with smoked purple, and all that cream-shot saffron, would never drift across any western sky except that in back of this house. The rain would drum with as sweet a dullness nowhere but here. The birds on South Park were mechanical birds, no better than the poor caught canaries in those "rich" women's sun parlors.

3. A large, decorative stand or pot for plants.

"It's just going to kill Papa!" burst out Maud Martha. "He loves this house! He *lives* for this house!"

"He lives for us," said Helen. "It's us he loves. He wouldn't want the house, except for us."

"And he'll have us," added Mama, "wherever."

"You know," Helen sighed, "if you want to know the truth, this is a relief. If this hadn't come up, we would have gone on, just dragged on, hanging out here forever."

"It might," allowed Mama, "be an act of God. God may just have reached down, and picked up the reins."

"Yes," Maud Martha cracked in, "that's what you always say—that God knows best."

Her mother looked at her quickly, decided the statement was not suspect, looked away.

Helen saw Papa coming. "There's Papa," said Helen.

They could not tell a thing from the way Papa was walking. It was that same dear little staccato walk, one shoulder down, then the other, then repeat, and repeat. They watched his progress. He passed the Kennedys', he passed the vacant lot, he passed Mrs. Blakemore's. They wanted to hurl themselves over the fence, into the street, and shake the truth out of his collar. He opened his gate—the gate—and still his stride and face told them nothing.

"Hello," he said.

Mama got up and followed him through the front door. The girls knew better than to go in too.

Presently Mama's head emerged. Her eyes were lamps turned on.

"It's all right," she exclaimed. "He got it. It's all over. Everything is all right."

The door slammed shut. Mama's footsteps hurried away.

"I think," said Helen, rocking rapidly, "I think I'll give a party. I haven't given a party since I was eleven. I'd like some of my friends to just casually see that we're homeowners."

9. Helen

What she remembered was Emmanuel; laughing, glinting in the sun; kneeing his wagon toward them, as they walked tardily home from school. Six years ago.

"How about a ride?" Emmanuel had hailed.

She had, daringly—it was not her way, not her native way—made a quip. A "sophisticated" quip. "Hi, handsome!" Instantly he had scowled, his dark face darkening.

"I don't mean you, you old black gal," little Emmanuel had exclaimed. "I mean Helen."

He had meant Helen, and Helen on the reissue of the invitation had climbed, without a word, into the wagon and was off and away.

Even now, at seventeen—high school graduate, mistress of her fate, and a ten-dollar-a-week file clerk in the very Forty-seventh Street lawyer's office where Helen was a fifteen-dollar-a-week typist—as she sat on Helen's bed and watched Helen primp for a party, the memory hurt. There was no consolation in the thought that not now and not then would she have *had* Emmanuel "off a Christmas tree." For the basic situation had never changed. Helen was still the one they wanted in the wagon, still "the pretty one," "the dainty one." The lovely one.

She did not know what it was. She had tried to find the something that must be there to imitate, that she might imitate it. But she did not know what it was. I wash as much as Helen does, she thought. My hair is longer and thicker, she thought. I'm much smarter. I read books and newspapers and old folks like to talk with me, she thought.

But the kernel of the matter was that, in spite of these things, she was poor, and Helen was still the ranking queen, not only with the Emmanuels of the world, but even with their father—their mother—their brother. She did not blame the family. It was not their fault. She understood. They could not help it. They were enslaved, were fascinated, and they were not at all to blame.

Her noble understanding of their blamelessness did not make any easier to bear such a circumstance as Harry's springing to open a door so that Helen's soft little hands might not have to cope with the sullyings of a doorknob, or running her errands, to save the sweet and fine little feet, or shouldering Helen's part against Maud Martha. Especially could these items burn when Maud Martha recalled her comradely rompings with Harry, watched by the gentle Helen from the clean and gentle harbor of the porch: take the day, for example, when Harry had been chased by those five big boys from Forty-first and Wabash, cursing, smelling, beastlike boys! with bats and rocks, and little stones that were more worrying than rocks; on that occasion out Maud Martha had dashed, when she saw from the front-room window Harry, panting and torn, racing for home; out she had dashed and down into the street with one of the smaller porch chairs held high over her head, and while Harry gained first the porch and next the safety side of the front door she had swung left, swung right, clouting a head here, a head there, and screaming at the top of her lungs, "Y' leave my brother alone! Y' leave my brother alone!" And who had washed those bloody wounds, and afterward vaselined them down? Really—in spite of everything she could not understand why Harry had to hold open doors for Helen, and calmly let them slam in her, Maud Martha's, his friend's, face.

It did not please her either, at the breakfast table, to watch her father drink his coffee and contentedly think (oh, she knew it!), as Helen started on her grapefruit, how daintily she ate, how gracefully she sat in her chair, how pure was her robe and unwrinkled, how neatly she had arranged her hair. Their father preferred Helen's hair to Maud Martha's (Maud Martha knew), which impressed him, not with its length and body, but simply with its apparent untamableness; for he would never get over that zeal of his for order in all things, in character, in housekeeping, in his own labor, in grooming, in human relationships. Always he had worried about Helen's homework, Helen's health. And now that boys were taking her out, he believed not one of them worthy of her, not one of them good enough to receive a note of her sweet voice: he insisted that she be returned before midnight. Yet who was it who sympathized with him in his decision to remain, for the rest of his days, the simple janitor! when everyone else was urging him to get out, get prestige, make more money? Who was it who sympathized with him in his almost desperate love for this old house? Who followed him about, emotionally speaking, loving this, doting on that? The kitchen, for instance, that was not beautiful in any way! The walls and ceilings, that were cracked. The chairs, which cried when people sat in them. The tables, that grieved audibly if anyone rested more than two fingers upon them. The huge cabinets, old and tired (when you shut their doors or drawers there was a sick, bickering little sound). The radiators, high and hideous. And underneath the low sink coiled unlovely pipes, that Helen said made her think of a careless woman's underwear, peeping out. In fact, often had Helen given her opinion, unasked, of the whole house, of the whole "hulk of rotten wood." Often had her cool and gentle eyes sneered, gently and coolly, at her father's determination to hold his poor estate. But take that kitchen, for instance! Maud Martha, taking it, saw herself there, up and down her seventeen years, eating apples after school; making sweet potato tarts; drawing, on the pathetic table, the horse that won her the sixth grade prize; getting her hair curled for her first party, at that stove; washing dishes by summer twilight, with the back door wide open; making cheese and peanut butter sandwiches for a picnic. And even crying, crying in that pantry, when no one knew. The old sorrows brought there!—now dried, flattened out, breaking into interesting dust at the merest look. . . .

"You'll never get a boy friend," said Helen, fluffing on her Golden Peacock powder, "if you don't stop reading those books."

10. first beau

He had a way of putting his hands on a Woman. Light, but perforating. Passing by, he would touch the Woman's hair, he would give the Woman's hair a careless, and yet deliberate, caress, working down from the top to the ends, then gliding to the chin, then lifting the chin till the poor female's eyes were forced to meet his, then proceeding down the neck. Maud Martha had watched this technique time after time, privately swearing that if he ever tried it on her she would settle him soon enough. Finally he had tried it, and a sloppy feeling had filled her, and she had not settled him at all. Not that she was thereafter, like the others, his to command, flatter, neglect, swing high, swing low, smooth with a grin, wrinkle with a scowl, just as his fancy wished. For Russell lacked—what? He was—nice. He was fun to go about with. He was decorated inside and out. He did things, said things, with a flourish. That was what he was. He was a flourish. He was a dazzling, long, and sleepily swishing flourish. "He will never be great," Maud Martha thought. "But he wouldn't be hurt if anybody told him that—if possible to choose from two, he would without hesitation choose being grand."

There he sat before her, in a sleeveless yellow-tan sweater and white, open-collared sport shirt, one leg thrust sexily out, fist on that hip, brown eyes ablaze, chin thrust up at her entrance as if it were to give her greeting, devil-like smile making her blink.

11. second beau

And—don't laugh—he wanted a dog.

A picture of the English country gentleman. Roaming the rustic hill. He had not yet bought a pipe. He would immediately.

There already was the herringbone tweed. (Although old sensuousness, old emotional daring broke out at the top of the trousers, where there was that gathering, that kicked-back yearning toward the pleat!) There was the tie a man might think about for an hour before entering that better shop, in order to be able to deliberate only a sharp two minutes at the counter, under the icy estimate of the salesman. Here were the socks, here was the haircut, here were the shoes. The educated smile, the slight bow, the faint imperious nod. He belonged to the world of the university.

He was taking a number of loose courses on the Midway.

His scent was withdrawn, expensive, as he strode down the worn carpet of her living room, as though it were the educated green of the Midway.

He considered Parrington's *Main Currents in American Thought*. He had not mastered it. Only recently, he announced, had he learned of its existence. "Three volumes of the most reasonable approaches!—Yet there are chaps on that campus—*young!*—younger than I am—who read it years ago, who know it, who have had it for themselves for years, who have been seeing it on their fathers' shelves since infancy. They heard it discussed at the dinner table when they were four. As a ball is to me, so Parrington is to them. They've been kicking him around for years, like a *foot*ball!"

The idea agitated. His mother had taken in washing. She had had three boys, whom she sent to school clean but patched-up. Just so they were clean, she had said. That was all that mattered, she had said. She had said "ain't." She had said, "I ain't stud'n you." His father—he hadn't said anything at all.

He himself had had a paper route. Had washed windows, cleaned basements, sanded furniture, shoveled snow, hauled out trash and garbage for the neighbors. He had worked before that, running errands for people when he was six. What chance did he have, he mused, what chance was there for anybody coming out of a set of conditions that never allowed for the prevalence of sensitive, and intellectual, yet almost frivolous, dinner-table discussions of Parrington across four-year-old heads?

Whenever he left the Midway, said David McKemster, he was instantly depressed. East of Cottage Grove, people were clean, going somewhere that mattered, not talking unless they had something to say. West of the Midway, they leaned against buildings and their mouths were opening and closing very fast but nothing important was coming out. What did they know about Aristotle?[4] The unhappiness he felt over there was physical. He wanted to throw up. There was a fence on Forty-seventh and—Champlain? Langley? Forestville?—he forgot what; broken, rotten, trying to lie down; and passing it on a windy night or on a night when it was drizzling, he felt lost, lapsed, negative, untended, extinguished, broken and lying down too—unappeasable. And looking up in those kitchenette windows,

4. Greek philosopher and scientist (384–322 B.C.).

where the lights were dirty through dirty glass—they *could* wash the windows—was not at all "interesting" to him as it probably was to those guys at the university who had—who had—

Made a football out of Parrington.

Because he knew what it was. He knew it was a mess! He knew it wasn't "colorful," "exotic," "fascinating."

He wanted a dog. A good dog. No mongrel. An apartment—well-furnished, containing a good bookcase, filled with good books in good bindings. He wanted a phonograph, and records. The symphonies. And Yehudi Menuhin.[5] He wanted some good art. These things were not extras. They went to make up a good background. The kind of background those guys had.

12. Maud Martha and New York

The name "New York" glittered in front of her like the silver in the shops on Michigan Boulevard. It was silver, and it was solid, and it was remote: it was behind glass, it was behind bright glass like the silver in the shops. It was not for her. Yet.

When she was out walking, and with grating iron swish a train whipped by, off, above, its passengers were always, for her comfort, New York-bound. She sat inside with them. She leaned back in the plush. She sped, past farms, through tiny towns, where people slept, kissed, quarreled, ate midnight snacks; unfortunate folk who were not New York-bound and never would be.

Maud Martha loved it when her magazines said "New York," described "good" objects there, wonderful people there, recalled fine talk, the bristling or the creamy or the tactfully shimmering ways of life. They showed pictures of rooms with wood paneling, softly glowing, touched up by the compliment of a spot of auburn here, the low burn of a rare binding there. There were ferns in these rooms, and Chinese boxes; bits of dreamlike crystal; a taste of leather. In the advertisement pages, you saw where you could buy six Italian plates for eleven hundred dollars—and you must hurry, for there was just the one set; you saw where you could buy antique French bisque figurines (pale blue and gold) for—for— Her whole body become a hunger, she would pore over these pages. The clothes interested her, too; especially did she care for the pictures of women wearing carelessly, as if they were rags, dresses that were plain but whose prices were not. And the foolish food (her mother's description) enjoyed by New Yorkers fascinated her. They paid ten dollars for an eight-ounce jar of Russian caviar; they ate things called anchovies, and capers; they ate little diamond-shaped cheeses that paprika had but breathed on; they ate bitter-almond macaroons; they ate papaya packed in rum and syrup; they ate peculiar sauces, were free with honey, were lavish with butter, wine and cream.

She bought the New York papers downtown, read of the concerts and plays, studied the book reviews, was intent over the announcements of auctions. She liked the sound of "Fifth Avenue," "Town Hall," "B. Altman,"

5. American violinist and concert virtuoso (b. 1916).

"Hammacher Schlemmer." She was on Fifth Avenue whenever she wanted to be, and she it was who rolled up, silky or furry, in the taxi, was assisted out, and stood, her next step nebulous, before the theaters of the thousand lights, before velvet-lined impossible shops; she it was.

New York, for Maud Martha, was a symbol. Her idea of it stood for what she felt life ought to be. Jeweled. Polished. Smiling. Poised. Calmly rushing! Straight up and down, yet graceful enough.

She thought of them drinking their coffee there—or tea, as in England. It was afternoon. Lustrous people glided over perfect floors, correctly smiling. They stopped before a drum table, covered with heavy white—and bearing a silver coffee service, old (in the better sense) china, a platter of orange and cinnamon cakes (or was it nutmeg the cakes would have in them?), sugar and cream, a Chinese box, one tall and slender flower. Their host or hostess poured, smiling too, nodding quickly to this one and that one, inquiring gently whether it should be sugar, or cream, or both, or neither. (She was teaching herself to drink coffee with neither.) All was *very* gentle. The voices, no matter how they rose, or even sharpened, had fur at the base. The steps never bragged, or grated in any way on any ear—not that they could very well, on so good a Persian rug, or deep soft carpeting. And the drum table stood in front of a screen, a Japanese one, perhaps, with rich and mellow, bread-textured colors. The people drank and nibbled, while they discussed the issues of the day, sorting, rejecting, revising. Then they went home, quietly, elegantly. They retired to homes not one whit less solid or embroidered than the home of their host or hostess.

What she wanted to dream, and dreamed, was her affair. It pleased her to dwell upon color and soft bready textures and light, on a complex beauty, on gemlike surfaces. What was the matter with that? Besides, who could safely swear that she would never be able to make her dream come true for herself? Not altogether, then!—but slightly?—in some part?

She was eighteen years old, and the world waited. To caress her.

13. low yellow

I know what he is thinking, thought Maud Martha, as she sat on the porch in the porch swing with Paul Phillips. He is thinking that I am all right. That I am really all right. That I will do.

And I am glad of that, because my whole body is singing beside him. And when you feel like that beside a man you ought to be married to him. I am what he would call—sweet.

But I am certainly not what he would call pretty. Even with all this hair (which I have just assured him, in response to his question, is not "natural," is not good grade or anything like good grade) even with whatever I have that puts a dimple in his heart, even with these nice ears, I am still, definitely, not what he can call pretty if he remains true to what his idea of pretty has always been. Pretty would be a little cream-colored thing with curly hair. Or at the very lowest pretty would be a little curly-haired thing the color of cocoa with a lot of milk in it. Whereas, I am the color of cocoa straight, if you can be even that "kind" to me.

He wonders, as we walk in the street, about the thoughts of the people who look at us. Are they thinking that he could do no better than—me? Then he thinks, Well, hmp! Well, huh!—all the little good-lookin' dolls that have wanted *him*—all the little sweet high-yellows that have ambled slowly past *his* front door—What he would like to tell those secretly snickering ones!—That any day out of the week he can do better than this black gal.

And by my own admission my hair is absolutely knappy.

"Fatherhood," said Paul, "is not exactly in my line. But it would be all right to have a couple or so of kids, good-looking, in my pocket, so to speak."

"I am not a pretty woman," said Maud Martha. "If you married a pretty woman, you could be the father of pretty children. Envied by people. The father of beautiful children."

"But I don't know," said Paul. "Because my features aren't fine. They aren't regular. They're heavy. They're real Negro features. I'm light, or at least I can claim to be a sort of low-toned yellow, and my hair has a teeny crimp. But even so I'm not handsome."

No, there would be little "beauty" getting born out of such a union.

Still, mused Maud Martha, I am what he would call—sweet, and I am good, and he will marry me. Although, he will be thinking, that's what he always says about letting yourself get interested in these incorruptible virgins, that so often your manhood will not let you concede defeat, and before you know it, you have let them steal you, put an end, perhaps, to your career.

He will fight, of course. He will decide that he must think a long time before he lets that happen here.

But in the end I'll hook him, even while he's wondering how this marriage will cramp him or pinch at him—at him, admirer of the gay life, spiffy clothes, beautiful yellow girls, natural hair, smooth cars, jewels, night clubs, cocktail lounges, class.

14. everybody will be surprised

"Of course," said Paul, "we'll have to start small. But it won't be very long before everybody will be surprised."

Maud Martha smiled.

"Your apartment, eventually, will be a dream. The *Defender* will come and photograph it." Paul grinned when he said that, but quite literally he believed it. Since he had decided to go ahead and marry her, he meant to "do it up right." People were going to look at his marriage and see only things to want. He was going to have a swanky flat. He and Maudie were going to dress well. They would entertain a lot.

"Listen," said Paul eagerly, "at a store on Forty-third and Cottage they're selling four rooms of furniture for eighty-nine dollars."

Maud Martha's heart sank.

"We'll go look at it tomorrow," added Paul.

"Paul—do you think we'll have a hard time finding a nice place—when the time comes?"

"No. I don't think so. But look here. I think we ought to plan on a stove-heated flat. We could get one of those cheap."

"Oh, I wouldn't like that. I've always lived in steam."

"I've always lived in stove—till a year ago. It's just as warm. And about fifteen dollars cheaper."

"Then what made your folks move to steam, then?"

"Ma wanted to live on a better-looking street. But we can't think about foolishness like that, when we're just starting out. Our flat will be hot stuff; the important thing is the flat, not the street; we can't study about foolishness like that; but our flat will be hot stuff. We'll have a swell flat."

"When you have stove heat, you have to have those ugly old fat black pipes stretching out all over the room."

"You don't just have to have long ones."

"I don't want any ones."

"You can have a little short one. And the new heaters they got look like radios. You'll like 'em."

Maud Martha silently decided she wouldn't, and resolved to hold out firmly against stove-heated flats. No stove-heated flats. And no basements. You got T.B. in basements.

"If you think a basement would be better—" began Paul.

"I don't," she interrupted.

"Basements are cheap too."

Was her attitude unco-operative? Should she be wanting to sacrifice more, for the sake of her man? A procession of pioneer women strode down her imagination; strong women, bold; praiseworthy, faithful, stout-minded; with a stout light beating in the eyes. Women who could stand low temperatures. Women who would toil eminently, to improve the lot of their men. Women who cooked. She thought of herself, dying for her man. It was a beautiful thought.

15. *the kitchenette*

Their home was on the third floor of a great gray stone building. The two rooms were small. The bedroom was furnished with a bed and dresser, old-fashioned, but in fair condition, and a faded occasional chair. In the kitchen were an oilcloth-covered table, two kitchen chairs, one folding chair, a cabinet base, a brown wooden icebox, and a three-burner gas stove. Only one of the burners worked, the housekeeper told them. The janitor would fix the others before they moved in. Maud Martha said she could fix them herself.

"Nope," objected Paul. "The janitor'll do it. That's what they pay him for." There was a bathroom at the end of the hall, which they would have to share with four other families who lived on the floor.

The housekeeper at the kitchenette place did not require a reference. . . . The *Defender* would never come here with cameras.

Still, Maud Martha was, at first, enthusiastic. She made plans for this home. She would have the janitor move the bed and dresser out, tell Paul to buy a studio couch, a desk chest, a screen, a novelty chair, a white Venetian blind for the first room, and a green one for the kitchen, since the wallpaper there was green (with little red fishes swimming about). Perhaps they could even get a rug. A green one. And green drapes for the windows.

Why, this *might* even turn out to be their dream apartment. It was small, but wonders could be wrought here. They could open up an account at L. Fish Furniture Store, pay a little every month. In that way, they could have the essentials right away. Later, they could get a Frigidaire. A baby's bed, when one became necessary, could go behind the screen, and they would have a pure living room.

Paul, after two or three weeks, told her sheepishly that kitchenettes were not so bad. Theirs seemed "cute and cozy" enough, he declared, and for his part, he went on, he was ready to "camp right down" until the time came to "build." Sadly, however, by that time Maud Martha had lost interest in the place, because the janitor had said that the Owner would not allow the furniture to be disturbed. Tenants moved too often. It was not worth the Owner's financial while to make changes, or to allow tenants to make them. They would have to be satisfied with "the apartment" as it was.

Then, one month after their installation, the first roach arrived. Ugly, shiny, slimy, slick-moving. She had rather see a rat—well, she had rather see a mouse. She had never yet been able to kill a roach. She could not bear to touch one, with foot or stick or twisted paper. She could only stand helpless, frozen, and watch the slick movement suddenly appear and slither, looking doubly evil, across the mirror, before which she had been calmly brushing her hair. And why? Why was he here? For she was scrubbing with water containing melted American Family soap and Lysol every other day.

And these things—roaches, and having to be satisfied with the place as it was—were not the only annoyances that had to be reckoned with. She was becoming aware of an oddness in color and sound and smell about her, the color and sound and smell of the kitchenette building. The color was gray, and the smell and sound had taken on a suggestion of the properties of color, and impressed one as gray, too. The sobbings, the frustrations, the small hates, the large and ugly hates, the little pushing-through love, the boredom, that came to her from behind those walls (some of them beaver-board) via speech and scream and sigh—all these were gray. And the smells of various types of sweat, and of bathing and bodily functions (the bathroom was always in use, someone was always in the bathroom) and of fresh or stale love-making, which rushed in thick fumes to your nostrils as you walked down the hall, or down the stairs—these were *gray*.

There was a whole lot of grayness here.

16. *the young couple at home*

Paul had slept through most of the musicale. Three quarters of the time his head had been a heavy knot on her shoulder. At each of her attempts to remove it, he had waked up so suddenly, and had given her a look of such childlike fierceness, that she could only smile.

Now on the streetcar, however—the car was in the garage—he was not sleepy, and he kept "amusing" Maud Martha with little "tricks," such as cocking his head archly and winking at her, or digging her slyly in the ribs, or lifting her hand to his lips, and blowing on it softly, or poking a finger under her chin and raising it awkwardly, or feeling her muscle, then putting her hand on his muscle, so that she could tell the difference. Such as that. "Clowning," he called it. And because he felt that he was making her happy, she tried not to see the uncareful stares and smirks of the other passengers—uncareful and insultingly consolatory. He sat playfully upon part of her thigh. He gently kicked her toe.

Once home, he went immediately to the bathroom. He did not try to mask his need, he was obvious and direct about it.

"He could make," she thought, "a comment or two on what went on at the musicale. Or some little joke. It isn't that I'm unreasonable or stupid. But everything can be done with a little grace. I'm sure of it."

When he came back, he yawned, stretched, smeared his lips up and down her neck, assured her of his devotion, and sat down on the bed to take off his shoes. She picked up *Of Human Bondage*, [6] and sat at the other end of the bed.

"Snuggle up," he invited.

"I thought I'd read awhile."

"I guess I'll read awhile, too," he decided, when his shoes were off and had been kicked into the kitchen. She got up, went to the shoes, put them in the closet. He grinned at her merrily. She was conscious of the grin, but refused to look at him. She went back to her book. He settled down to his. His was a paper-backed copy of *Sex in the Married Life*. [7]

There he sat, slouched down, terribly absorbed, happy in his sock feet, curling his toes inside the socks.

"I want you to read this book," he said, "—but at the right times: one chapter each night before retiring." He reached over, pinched her on the buttock.

She stood again. "Shall I make some cocoa?" she asked pleasantly. "And toast some sandwiches?"

"Say, I'd like that," he said, glancing up briefly.

She toasted rye strips spread with pimento cheese and grated onion. She made cocoa.

They ate, drank, and read together. She read *Of Human Bondage*. He read *Sex in the Married Life*. They were silent.

Five minutes passed. She looked at him. He was asleep. His head had fallen back, his mouth was open—it was a good thing there were no flies— his ankles were crossed. And the feet!—pointing confidently out (no one would harm them). *Sex in the Married Life* was about to slip to the floor. She did not stretch out a hand to save it.

Once she had taken him to a library. While occupied with the card cases she had glanced up, had observed that he, too, was busy among the cards. "Do you want a book?" "No-o. I'm just curious about something. I wondered if there could be a man in the world named Bastard. Sure enough, there is."

Paul's book fell, making a little clatter. But he did not wake up, and she did not get up.

6. Novel by British writer Somerset Maugham (1874–1965).
7. Perhaps *Sex in Married Life: A Practical Hand-* *book for Men and Women* (1938, 1965), by George Ryley Scott.

17. Maud Martha spares the mouse

There. She had it at last. The weeks it had devoted to eluding her, the tricks, the clever hide-and-go-seeks, the routes it had in all sobriety devised, together with the delicious moments it had, undoubtedly, laughed up its sleeve—all to no ultimate avail. She had that mouse.

It shook its little self, as best it could, in the trap. Its bright black eyes contained no appeal—the little creature seemed to understand that there was no hope of mercy from the eternal enemy, no hope of reprieve or postponement—but a fine small dignity. It waited. It looked at Maud Martha.

She wondered what else it was thinking. Perhaps that there was not enough food in its larder. Perhaps that little Betty, a puny child from the start, would not, now, be getting fed. Perhaps that, now, the family's seasonal house-cleaning, for lack of expert direction, would be left undone. It might be regretting that young Bobby's education was now at an end. It might be nursing personal regrets. No more the mysterious shadows of the kitchenette, the uncharted twists, the unguessed halls. No more the sweet delights of the chase, the charms of being unsuccessfully hounded, thrown at.

Maud Martha could not bear the little look.

"Go home to your children," she urged. "To your wife or husband." She opened the trap. The mouse vanished.

Suddenly, she was conscious of a new cleanness in her. A wide air walked in her. A life had blundered its way into her power and it had been hers to preserve or destroy. She had not destroyed. In the center of that simple restraint was—creation. She had created a piece of life. It was wonderful.

"Why," she thought, as her height doubled, "why, I'm good! I am *good.*"

She ironed her aprons. Her back was straight. Her eyes were mild, and soft with a godlike loving-kindness.

18. we're the only colored people here

When they went out to the car there were just the very finest bits of white powder coming down with an almost comical little ethereal hauteur, to add themselves to the really important, piled-up masses of their kind.

And it wasn't cold.

Maud Martha laughed happily to herself. It was pleasant out, and tonight she and Paul were very close to each other.

He held the door open for her—instead of going on around to the driving side, getting in, and leaving her to get in at her side as best she might. When he took this way of calling her "lady" and informing her of his love she felt precious, protected, delicious. She gave him an excited look of gratitude. He smiled indulgently.

"Want it to be the Owl again?"

"Oh, no no, Paul. Let's not go there tonight. I feel too good inside for that. Let's go downtown?"

She had to suggest that with a question mark at the end, always. He usually had three protests. Too hard to park. Too much money. Too many white folks. And tonight she could almost certainly expect a no, she feared, because he had come out in his blue work shirt. There was a spot of apricot juice on the collar, too. His shoes were not shined. . . . But he nodded!

"We've never been to the World Playhouse," she said cautiously. "They have a good picture. I'd feel rich in there."

"You really wanta?"

"Please?"

"Sure."

It wasn't like other movie houses. People from the Studebaker Theatre which, as Maud Martha whispered to Paul, was "all-locked-arms" with the World Playhouse, were strolling up and down the lobby, laughing softly, smoking with gentle grace.

"There must be a play going on in there and this is probably an intermission," Maud Martha whispered again.

"I don't know why you feel you got to whisper," whispered Paul. "Nobody else is whispering in here." He looked around, resentfully, wanting to see a few, just a few, colored faces. There were only their own.

Maud Martha laughed a nervous defiant little laugh; and spoke loudly. "There certainly isn't any reason to whisper. Silly, huh."

The strolling women were cleverly gowned. Some of them had flowers or flashers in their hair. They looked—cooked. Well cared-for. And as though they had never seen a roach or a rat in their lives. Or gone without heat for a week. And the men had even edges. They were men, Maud Martha thought, who wouldn't stoop to fret over less than a thousand dollars.

"We're the only colored people here," said Paul.

She hated him a little. "Oh, hell. Who in hell cares."

"Well, what I want to know is, where do you pay the damn fares."

"There's the box office. Go on up."

He went on up. It was closed.

"Well," sighed Maud Martha, "I guess the picture has started already. But we can't have missed much. Go on up to that girl at the candy counter and ask her where we should pay our money."

He didn't want to do that. The girl was lovely and blonde and cold-eyed, and her arms were akimbo, and the set of her head was eloquent. No one else was at the counter.

"Well. We'll wait a minute. And see—"

Maud Martha hated him again. Coward. She ought to flounce over to the girl herself—show him up. . . .

The people in the lobby tried to avoid looking curiously at two shy Negroes wanting desperately not to seem shy. The white women looked at the Negro woman in her outfit with which no special fault could be found, but which made them think, somehow, of close rooms, and wee, close lives. They looked at her hair. They liked to see a dark colored girl with long, long hair. They were always slightly surprised, but agreeably so, when they did. They supposed it was the hair that had got her that yellowish, good-looking Negro man.

The white men tried not to look at the Negro man in the blue work shirt, the Negro man without a tie.

An usher opened a door of the World Playhouse part and ran quickly down the few steps that led from it to the lobby. Paul opened his mouth.

"Say, fella. Where do we get the tickets for the movie?"

The usher glanced at Paul's feet before answering. Then he said coolly, but not unpleasantly, "I'll take the money."

They were able to go in.

And the picture! Maud Martha was so glad that they had not gone to the Owl! Here was technicolor, and the love story was sweet. And there was classical music that silvered its way into you and made your back cold. And the theater itself! It was no palace, no such Great Shakes as the Tivoli out south, for instance (where many colored people went every night). But you felt good sitting there, yes, good, and as if, when you left it, you would be going home to a sweet-smelling apartment with flowers on little gleaming tables; and wonderful silver on night-blue velvet, in chests; and crackly sheets; and lace spreads on such beds as you saw at Marshall Field's. Instead of back to your kit'n't apt., with the garbage of your floor's families in a big can just outside your door, and the gray sound of little gray feet scratching away from it as you drag up those flights of narrow complaining stairs.

Paul pressed her hand. Paul said, "We oughta do this more often."

And again. "We'll have to do this more often. And go to plays, too. I mean at that Blackstone, and Studebaker."

She pressed back, smiling beautifully to herself in the darkness. Though she knew that once the spell was over it would be a year, two years, more, before he would return to the World Playhouse. And he might never go to a real play. But she was learning to love moments. To love moments for themselves.

When the picture was over, and the lights revealed them for what they were, the Negroes stood up among the furs and good cloth and faint perfume, looked about them eagerly. They hoped they would meet no cruel eyes. They hoped no one would look intruded upon. They had enjoyed the picture so, they were so happy, they wanted to laugh, to say warmly to the other outgoers, "Good, huh? Wasn't it swell?"

This, of course, they could not do. But if only no one would look intruded upon. . . .

19. if you're light and have long hair

Came the invitation that Paul recognized as an honor of the first water, and as sufficient indication that he was, at last, a social somebody. The invitation was from the Foxy Cats Club, the club of clubs. He was to be present, in formal dress, at the Annual Foxy Cats Dawn Ball. No chances were taken: "Top hat, white tie and tails" hastily followed the "Formal dress," and that elucidation was in bold type.

Twenty men were in the Foxy Cats Club. All were good-looking. All wore clothes that were rich and suave. All "handled money," for their number consisted of well-located barbers, policemen, "government men" and men with a lucky touch at the tracks. Certainly the Foxy Cats Club was not a representative of that growing group of South Side organizations devoted to moral and civic improvements, or to literary or other cultural pursuits. If that had been so, Paul would have chucked his bid (which was black and silver, decorated with winking cat faces) down the toilet with a yawn. "That kind of stuff" was hardly understood by Paul, and was always dismissed with an airy "dicty," "hincty" or "high-falutin'." But no. The Foxy Cats devoted themselves solely to the business of being "hep," and each year they spent hundreds of dollars on their wonderful Dawn Ball, which did not begin at dawn, but was scheduled to end at dawn. "Ball," they called the frolic, but it served also the purposes of party, feast and fashion show. Maud Martha, watching him study his invitation, watching him lift his chin, could see that he considered himself one of the blessed.

Who—what kind soul had recommended him!

"He'll have to take me," thought Maud Martha. "For the envelope is addressed 'Mr. and Mrs.,' and I opened it. I guess he'd like to leave me home. At the Ball, there will be only beautiful girls, or real stylish ones. There won't be more than a handful like me. My type is not a Foxy Cat favorite. But he can't avoid taking me—since he hasn't yet thought of words or ways strong enough, and at the same time soft enough—for he's kind: he doesn't like to injure—to carry across to me the news that he is not to be held permanently by my type, and that he can go on with this marriage only if I put no ropes or questions around him. Also, he'll want to humor me, now that I'm pregnant."

She would need a good dress. That, she knew, could be a problem, on his grocery clerk's pay. He would have his own expenses. He would have to rent his topper and tails, and he would have to buy a fine tie, and really excellent shoes. She knew he was thinking that on the strength of his appearance and sophisticated behavior at this Ball might depend his future admission (for why not dream?) to *membership*, actually, in the Foxy Cats Club!

"I'll settle," decided Maud Martha, "on a plain white princess-style thing and some blue and black satin ribbon. I'll go to my mother's. I'll work miracles at the sewing machine.

"On that night, I'll wave my hair. I'll smell faintly of lily of the valley."

The main room of the Club 99, where the Ball was held, was hung with green and yellow and red balloons, and the thick pillars, painted to give an effect of marble, and stretching from floor to ceiling, were draped with green and red and yellow crepe paper. Huge ferns, rubber plants and bowls of flowers were at every corner. The floor itself was a decoration, golden, glazed. There was no overhead light; only wall lamps, and the bulbs in these were romantically dim. At the back of the room, standing on a furry white rug, was the long banquet table, dressed in damask, accented by groups of thin silver candlesticks bearing white candles, and laden with lovely food: cold chicken, lobster, candied ham fruit combinations, potato salad in a great gold dish, corn sticks, a cheese fluff in spiked tomato cups, fruit cake, angel cake, sunshine cake. The drinks were at a smaller table nearby, behind which stood a genial mixologist, quick with maraschino cherries, and with lemon, ice and liquor. Wines were there, and whiskey, and rum, and eggnog made with pure cream.

Paul and Maud Martha arrived rather late, on purpose. Rid of their wraps, they approached the glittering floor. Bunny Bates's orchestra was playing Ellington's "Solitude."

Paul, royal in rented finery, was flushed with excitement. Maud Martha looked at him. Not very tall. Not very handsomely made. But there was that extraordinary quality of maleness. Hiding in the body that was not *too* yellow, waiting to spring out at her, surround her (she liked to think)—that maleness. The Ball stirred her. The Beauties, in their gorgeous gowns, bustling, supercilious; the young men, who at other times most unpleasantly blew their noses, and darted surreptitiously into alleys to relieve themselves, and sweated and swore at their jobs, and scratched their more intimate parts, now smiling, smooth, overgallant; the drowsy lights; the smells of food and flowers, the smell of Murray's pomade, the body perfumes, natural and superimposed; the sensuous heaviness of the wine-colored draperies at the many windows; the music, now steamy and slow, now as clear and fragile as glass, now raging, passionate, now moaning and thickly gray. The Ball made toys of her emotions, stirred her variously. But she was anxious to have it end, she was anxious to be at home again, with the door closed behind herself and her husband. Then, he might be warm. There might be more than the absent courtesy he had been giving her of late. Then, he might be the tree she had a great need to lean against, in this "emergency." There was no telling what dear thing he might say to her, what little gem let fall.

But, to tell the truth, his behavior now was not very promising of gems to come. After their second dance he escorted her to a bench by the wall, left her. Trying to look nonchalant, she sat. She sat, trying not to show the inferiority she did not feel. When the music struck up again, he began to dance with someone red-haired and curved, and white as a white. Who was she? He had approached her easily, he had taken her confidently, he held her and conversed with her as though he had known her well for a long, long time. The girl smiled up at him. Her gold-spangled bosom was pressed—was pressed against that maleness—

A man asked Maud Martha to dance. He was dark, too. His mustache was small.

"Is this your first Foxy Cats?" he asked.

"What?" Paul's cheek was on that of Gold-Spangles.

"First Cats?"

"Oh. Yes." Paul and Gold-Spangles were weaving through the noisy twisting couples, were trying, apparently, to get to the reception hall.

"Do you know that girl? What's her name?" Maud Martha asked her partner, pointing to Gold-Spangles. Her partner looked, nodded. He pressed her closer.

"That's Maella. That's Maella."

"Pretty, isn't she?" She wanted him to keep talking about Maella. He nodded again.

"Yep. She has 'em howling along the stroll, all right, all right."

Another man, dancing past with an artificial redhead, threw a whispered word at Maud Martha's partner, who caught it eagerly, winked. "Solid, ol' man," he said. "Solid, Jack." He pressed Maud Martha closer. "You're a babe," he said. "You're a real babe." He reeked excitingly of tobacco, liquor, pinesoap, toilet water, and Sen Sen.

Maud Martha thought of her parents' back yard. Fresh. Clean. Smokeless. In her childhood, a snowball bush had shone there, big above the dandelions. The snowballs had been big, healthy. Once, she and her sister and brother had waited in the back yard for their parents to finish readying themselves for a trip to Milwaukee. The snowballs had been so beautiful, so fat and startlingly white in the sunlight, that she had suddenly loved home a thousand times more than ever before, and had not wanted to go to Milwaukee. But as the children grew, the bush sickened. Each year the snowballs were smaller and more dispirited. Finally a summer came when there were no blossoms at all. Maud Martha wondered what had become of the bush. For it was not there now. Yet she, at least, had never seen it go.

"Not," thought Maud Martha, "that they love each other. It oughta be that simple. Then I could lick it. It oughta be that easy. But it's my color that makes him mad. I try to shut my eyes to that, but it's no good. What I am inside, what is really me, he likes okay. But he keeps looking at my color, which is like a wall. He has to jump over it in order to meet and touch what I've got for him. He has to jump away up high in order to see it. He gets awful tired of all that jumping."

Paul came back from the reception hall. Maella was clinging to his arm. A final cry of the saxophone finished that particular slice of the blues. Maud Martha's partner bowed, escorted her to a chair by a rubber plant, bowed again, left.

"I could," considered Maud Martha, "go over there and scratch her upsweep down. I could spit on her back. I could scream. 'Listen,' I could scream, 'I'm making a baby for this man and I mean to do it in peace.' "

But if the root was sour what business did she have up there hacking at a leaf?

20. a birth

After dinner, they washed dishes together. Then they undressed, and Paul got in bed, and was asleep almost instantly. She went down the long public hall to the bathroom, in her blue chenille robe. On her way back down the squeezing dark of the hall she felt—something softly separate in her. Back in the bedroom, she put on her gown, then stepped to the dresser to smear her face with cold cream. But when she turned around to get in the bed she couldn't move. Her legs cramped painfully, and she had a tremendous desire to eliminate which somehow she felt she would never be able to gratify.

"Paul!" she cried. As though in his dreams he had been waiting to hear that call, and that call only, he was up with a bound.

"I can't move."

He rubbed his eyes.

"Maudie, are you kidding?"

"I'm not kidding, Paul. I can't move."

He lifted her up and laid her on the bed, his eyes stricken.

"Look here, Maudie. Do you think you're going to have that baby to-night?"

"No—no. These are just what they call 'false pains.' I'm not going to have the baby tonight. Can you get—my gown off?"

"Sure. Sure."

But really he was afraid to touch her. She lay nude on the bed for a few moments, perfectly still. Then all of a sudden motion came to her. Whereas before she had not been able to move her legs, now she could not keep them still.

"Oh, my God," she prayed aloud. "Just let my legs get still five minutes." God did not answer the prayer.

Paul was pacing up and down the room in fright.

"Look here. I don't think those are false pains. I think you're going to have that baby tonight."

"Don't say that, Paul," she muttered between clenched teeth. "I'm not going to have the baby tonight."

"I'm going to call your mother."

"Don't do that, Paul. She can't stand to see things like this. Once she got a chance to see a stillborn baby, but she fainted before they even un-wrapped it. She can't stand to see things like this. False pains, that's all. Oh, God, why don't you let me keep my legs still!"

She began to whimper in a manner that made Paul want to vomit. His thoughts traveled to the girl he had met at the Dawn Ball several months before. Cool. Sweet. Well-groomed. Fair.

"You're going to have that baby *now.* I'm going down to call up your mother and a doctor."

"DON'T YOU GO OUT OF HERE AND LEAVE ME ALONE! Damn. DAMN!"

"All right. All right. I won't leave you alone. I'll get the woman next door to come in. But somebody's got to get a doctor here."

"Don't you sneak out! Don't you *sneak* out!" She was pushing down with her stomach now. Paul, standing at the foot of the bed with his hands in his pockets, saw the creeping insistence of what he thought was the head of the child.

"Oh, my Lord!" he cried. "It's coming! It's coming!"

He walked about the room several times. He went to the dresser and began to brush his hair. She looked at him in speechless contempt. He went out of the door, and ran down the three flights of stairs two or three steps at a time. The telephone was on the first floor. No sooner had he picked up the receiver than he heard Maud Martha give what he was sure could *only* be called a "bloodcurdling scream." He bolted up the stairs, saw her wriggling on the bed, said softly, "Be right back," and bolted down again. First he called his mother's doctor, and begged him to come right over. Then he called the Browns.

"Get her to the hospital!" shouted Belva Brown. "You'll have to get her to the hospital right away!"

"I can't. She's having the baby now. She isn't going to let anybody touch her. I tell you, she's having the baby."

"Don't be a fool. Of course she can get to the hospital. Why, she mustn't have it there in the house! I'm coming over there. I'll take her myself. Be sure there's plenty of gas in that car."

He tried to reach his mother. She was out—had not returned from a revival meeting.

When Paul ran back up the stairs, he found young Mrs. Cray, who lived in the front apartment of their floor, attending his shrieking wife.

"I heard 'er yellin', and thought I'd better come in, seein' as how you all is so confused. Got a doctor comin'?"

Paul sighed heavily. "I just called one. Thanks for coming in. This—this came on all of a sudden, and I don't think I know what to do."

"Well, the thing to do is get a doctor right off. She's goin' to have the baby soon. Call *my* doctor." She gave him a number. "Whichever one gets here first can work on her. Ain't no time to waste."

Paul ran back down the stairs and called the number. "What's the doctor's address?" he yelled up. Mrs. Cray yelled it down. He went out to get the doctor personally. He was glad of an excuse to escape. He was sick of hearing Maudie scream. He had had no idea that she could scream that kind of screaming. It was awful. How lucky he was that he had been born a man. How lucky he was that he had been born a man!

Belva arrived in twenty minutes. She was grateful to find another woman present. She had come to force Maud Martha to start for the hospital, but a swift glance told her that the girl would not leave her bed for many days. As she said to her husband and Helen later on, "The baby was all ready to spill out."

When her mother came in the door Maud Martha tightened her lips, temporarily forgetful of her strange pain. (But it wasn't pain. It was something else.) "Listen. If you're going to make a fuss, go on out. I'm having enough trouble without you making a fuss over everything."

Mrs. Cray giggled encouragingly. Belva said bravely, "I'm not going to make a fuss. You'll see. Why, there's nothing to make a fuss *about*. You're just going to have a baby, like millions of other women. Why should I make a fuss?"

Maud Martha tried to smile but could not quite make it. The sensations were getting grindingly sharp. She screamed longer and louder, explaining breathlessly in between times, "I just can't help it. Excuse me."

"Why, go on and scream," urged Belva. "You're supposed to scream. That's your privilege. I'm sure *I* don't mind." Her ears were splitting, and over and over as she stood there looking down at her agonized daughter, she said to herself, "Why doesn't the doctor come? Why doesn't the doctor come? I know I'm going to faint." She and Mrs. Cray stood, one on each side of the bed, purposelessly holding a sheet over Maud Martha, under which they peeped as seldom as they felt was safe. Maud Martha kept asking, "Has the head come?" Presently she felt as though her whole body were having a bowel movement. The head came. Then, with a little difficulty, the wide shoulders. Then easily, with soft and slippery smoothness, out slipped the rest of the body and the baby was born. The first thing it did was sneeze.

Maud Martha laughed as though she could never bear to stop. "Listen to him sneeze. My little baby. Don't let him drown, Mrs. Cray." Mrs. Cray looked at Maud Martha, because she did not want to look at the baby. "How you know it's a him?" Maud Martha laughed again.

Belva also refused to look at the baby. "See, Maudie," she said, "see how brave I was? The baby is born, and I didn't get nervous or faint or anything. Didn't I tell you?"

"Now isn't that nice," thought Maud Martha. "Here I've had the baby, and she thinks I should praise her for having stood up there and looked on." Was it, she suddenly wondered, as hard to watch suffering as it was to bear it?

Five minutes after the birth, Paul got back with Mrs. Cray's doctor, a large silent man, who came in swiftly, threw the sheet aside without saying a word, cut the cord. Paul looked at the new human being. It appeared gray and greasy. Life was hard, he thought. What had he done to deserve a stillborn child? But there it was, lying dead.

"It's dead, isn't it?" he asked dully.

"Oh, get out of here!" cried Mrs. Cray, pushing him into the kitchen and shutting the door.

"Girl," said the doctor. Then grudgingly, "Fine girl."

"Did you hear what the doctor said, Maudie?" chattered Belva. "You've got a daughter, the doctor says." The doctor looked at her quickly.

"Say, you'd better go out and take a walk around the block. You don't look so well."

Gratefully, Belva obeyed. When she got back, Mrs. Cray and the doctor had oiled and dressed the baby—dressed her in an outfit found in Maud Martha's top dresser drawer. Belva looked at the newcomer in amazement.

"Well, she's a little beauty, isn't she!" she cried. She had not expected a handsome child.

Maud Martha's thoughts did not dwell long on the fact of the baby. There would be all her life long for that. She preferred to think, now, about how well she felt. Had she ever in her life felt so well? She felt well enough to get up. She folded her arms triumphantly across her chest, as another young woman, her neighbor to the rear, came in.

"Hello, Mrs. Barksdale!" she hailed. "Did you hear the news? I just had a baby, and I feel strong enough to go out and shovel coal! Having a baby is *nothing*, Mrs. Barksdale. Nothing at all."

"Aw, yeah?" Mrs. Barksdale smacked her gum admiringly. "Well, from what I heard back there a while ago, didn't seem like it was nothing. Girl, I didn't know anybody *could* scream that loud." Maud Martha tittered. Oh, she felt fine. She wondered why Mrs. Barksdale hadn't come in while the screaming was going on; she had missed it all.

People. Weren't they sweet. She had never said more than "Hello, Mrs. Barksdale" and "Hello, Mrs. Cray" to these women before. But as soon as something happened to her, in they trooped. People were sweet.

The doctor brought the baby and laid it in the bed beside Maud Martha. Shortly before she had heard it in the kitchen—a bright delight had flooded through her upon first hearing that part of Maud Martha Brown Phillips expressing itself with a voice of its own. But now the baby was quiet and returned its mother's stare with one that seemed equally curious and mystified but perfectly cool and undisturbed.

21. posts

People have to choose something decently constant to depend on, thought Maud Martha. People must have something to lean on.

But the love of a single person was not enough. Not only was personal love itself, however good, a thing that varied from week to week, from second to second, but the parties to it were likely, for example, to die, any minute, or otherwise be parted, or destroyed. At any time.

Not alone was the romantic love of a man and a woman fallible, but the breadier love between parents and children; brothers; animals; friend and friend. Those too could not be heavily depended on.

Could be nature, which had a seed, or root, or an element (what do you want to call it) of constancy, under all that system of change. Of course, to say "system" at all implied arrangement, and therefore some order of constancy.

Could be, she mused, a marriage. The marriage shell, not the romance, or love, it might contain. A marriage, the plainer, the more plateaulike, the better. A marriage made up of Sunday papers and shoeless feet, baking powder biscuits, baby baths, and matinees and laundrymen, and potato plants in the kitchen window.

Was, perhaps, the whole life of man a dedication to this search for something to lean upon, and was, to a great degree, his "happiness" or "unhappiness" written up for him by the demands or limitations of what he chose for that work?

For work it was. Leaning was a work.

22. tradition and Maud Martha

What she had wanted was a solid. She had wanted shimmering form; warm, but hard as stone and as difficult to break. She had wanted to found—tradition. She had wanted to shape, for their use, for hers, for his, for little Paulette's, a set of falterless customs. She had wanted stone: here she was, being wife to *him*, salving him, in every way considering and replenishing him—in short, here she was celebrating Christmas night by passing pretzels and beer.

He had done his part, was his claim. He had, had he not? lugged in a Christmas tree. So he had waited till early Christmas morning, when a tree was cheap; so he could not get the lights to burn; so the tinsel was insufficient and the gold balls few. He had promised a tree and he had gotten a tree, and that should be enough for everybody. Furthermore, Paulette had her blocks, her picture book, her doll buggy and her doll. So the doll's left elbow was chipped: more than that would be chipped before Paulette was through! And if the doll buggy was not like the Gold Coast[8] buggies, that was too bad; that was too, too bad for Maud Martha, for Paulette. Here he was, whipping himself to death daily, that Maud Martha's stomach and Paulette's stomach might receive bread and milk and navy beans with tomato catsup, and he was taken to task because he had not furnished, in addition, a velvet-lined buggy with white-walled wheels! Oh yes that *was*

8. Slang term for the wealthy, lakeside, residential area of Chicago.

what Maud Martha wanted, for her precious princess daughter, and no use denying. But she could just get out and work, that was all. She could just get out and grab herself a job and buy some of these beans and buggies. And in the meantime, she could just help entertain his friends. She was his wife, and he was the head of the family, and on Christmas night the least he could do, by God, and *would* do, by God, was stand his friends a good mug of beer. And to heck with, in fact, to hell with, her fruitcakes and coffees. Put Paulette to bed.

At Home, the buying of the Christmas tree was a ritual. Always it had come into the Brown household four days before Christmas, tall, but not too tall, and not too wide. Tinsel, bulbs, little Santa Clauses and snowmen, and the pretty gold and silver and colored balls did not have to be renewed oftener than once in five years because after Christmas they were always put securely away, on a special shelf in the basement, where they rested for a year. Black walnut candy, in little flat white sheets, crunchy, accompanied the tree, but it was never eaten until Christmas eve. Then, late at night, a family decorating party was held, Maud Martha, Helen and Harry giggling and teasing and occasionally handing up a ball or Santa Claus, while their father smiled benignly over all and strung and fitted and tinseled, and their mother brought in the black walnut candy and steaming cups of cocoa with whipped cream, and plain shortbread. And everything peaceful, sweet!

And there were the other customs. Easter customs. In childhood, never till Easter morning was "the change" made, the change from winter to spring underwear. Then, no matter how cold it happened to be, off came the heavy trappings and out, for Helen and Maud Martha, were set the new little patent leather shoes and white socks, the little b.v.d.'s and light petticoats, and for Harry, the new brown oxfords, and white shorts and sleeveless undershirts. The Easter eggs had always been dyed the night before, and in the morning, before Sunday school, the Easter baskets, full of chocolate eggs and candy bunnies and cotton bunnies, were handed round, but not eaten from until after Sunday school, and even then not much!—because there was more candy coming, and dyed eggs, too, to be received (and eaten on the spot) at the Sunday School Children's Easter Program, on which every one of them recited until Maud Martha was twelve.

What of October customs?—of pumpkins yellowly burning; of polished apples in a water-green bowl; of sheets for ghost costumes, surrendered up by Mama with a sigh?

And birthdays, with their pink and white cakes and candles, strawberry ice cream, and presents wrapped up carefully and tied with wide ribbons: whereas here was this man, who never considered giving his own mother a birthday bouquet, and dropped in his wife's lap a birthday box of drugstore candy (when he thought of it) wrapped in the drugstore green.

The dinner table, at home, was spread with a white white cloth, cheap but white and very white, and whatever was their best in china sat in cheerful dignity, firmly arranged, upon it. This man was not a lover of tablecloths, he could eat from a splintery board, he could eat from the earth.

She passed round Blatz, and inhaled the smoke of the guests' cigarettes, and watched the soaked tissue that had enfolded the corner Chicken Inn's burned barbecue drift listlessly to her rug. She removed from her waist the arm of Chuno Jones, Paul's best friend.

23. *kitchenette folks*

Of the people in her building, Maud Martha was most amused by Oberto, who had the largest flat of all, a three-roomer on the first floor.

Oberto was a happy man. He had a nice little going grocery store. He had his health. And, most important, he had his little lovely wife Marie.

Some folks did not count Marie among his blessings. She never got up before ten. Oberto must prepare his breakfast or go breakfastless. As a rule, he made only coffee, leaving one cup of it in the pot for her. At ten or after, in beautiful solitude, she would rise, bathe and powder for an hour, then proceed to the kitchen, where she heated that coffee, fried bacon and eggs for herself, and toasted raisin bread.

Marie dusted and swept infrequently, scrubbed only when the floors were heavy with dirt and grease. Her meals were generally underdone or burned. She sent the laundry out every week, but more often than not left the clothes (damp) in the bag throughout the week, spilling them out a few minutes before she expected the laundryman's next call, that the bag might again be stuffed with dirty clothes and carried off. Oberto's shirts were finished at the laundry. Underwear he wore rough-dried. Her own clothes, however, she ironed with regularity and care.

Such domestic sins were shocking enough. But people accused her of yet more serious crimes. It was well thought on the south side that Oberto's wife was a woman of affairs, barely taking time to lay one down before she gathered up another. It was rumored, too, but not confirmed, that now and then she was obliged to make quiet calls of business on a certain Madame Lomiss, of Thirty-fourth and Calumet.

But Oberto was happy. The happiest man, he argued, in his community. True enough, Wilma, the wife of Magnicentius, the Thirty-ninth Street barber, baked rolls of white and fluffy softness. But Magnicentius himself could not deny that Wilma was a filthy woman, and wore stockings two days, at least, before she washed them. He even made no secret of the fact that she went to bed in ragged, dire, cotton nightgowns.

True, too, Viota, the wife of Leon, the Coca-Cola truck driver, not only ironed her husband's shirts, but did all the laundry work herself, beginning early every Monday morning—scrubbing the sheets, quilts, blankets, and slip covers with her own hefty hand. But Leon himself could not deny that Viota was a boisterous, big woman with a voice of wonderful power, and eyes of pink-streaked yellow and a nose that never left off sniffing.

Who, further, would question the truth that Nathalia, the wife of John the laundryman, kept her house shining, and smelling of Lysol and Gold Dust at all times, and that every single Saturday night she washed down the white walls of her perfect kitchen? But verily who (of an honorable tongue) could deny that the active-armed Nathalia had little or no acquaintance with the deodorant qualities of Mum, Hush, or Quiet?

Remembering Nathalia, and remembering Wilma and Viota, Oberto thanked his lucky stars that he had had sense enough to marry his dainty little Marie, who spoke in modulated tones (almost in a whisper), who wore filmy black nightgowns, who bathed always once and sometimes twice a day in water generously treated with sweet bath crystals, and fluffed herself all over with an expensive lavender talcum, and creamed her arms and legs with a rosy night cream, and powdered her face, that was reddish brown (like an Indian's!) with a stuff that the movie stars preferred, and wore clothes out of *Vogue* and *Harper's Bazaar*, and favored Kleenex, and dressed her hair in a smart upsweep, and pinned silver flowers at her ears, and used My Sin perfume.

He loved to sit and watch her primp before the glass.

She didn't know whether she liked a little or a lot (a person could not always tell) the white woman married to a West Indian who lived in the third-floor kitchenette next Maud Martha's own. Through the day and night this woman, Eugena Banks, sang over and over again—varying the choruses, using what undoubtedly were her own improvisations, for they were very bad—the same popular song. Maud Martha had her own ideas about popular songs. "A popular song," thought she, "especially if it's one of the old, soft ones, is beautiful, sometimes, and seems to touch your mood exactly. But the touch is usually not full. You rise up with a popular song, but it isn't able to rise as high, once it has you started, as you are; by the time you've risen as high as it can take you you can't bear to stop, and you swell up and up and up till you're swelled to bursting. The popular music has long ago given up and left you."

This woman would come over, singing or humming her popular song, to see Maud Martha, wanting to know what special technique was to be used in dealing with a Negro man; a Negro man was a special type man; she knew that there should be, indeed, that there had to be, a special technique to be used with this type man, but what? And after all, there should be more than—than singing across the sock washing, the cornbread baking, the fish frying. No, she had not expected wealth, no—but he had seemed so exciting! so primitive!—life with a Negro man had looked, from the far side, like adventure—and the nights *were* good; but there were precious few of the nights, because he stayed away for days (though when he came back he was "very swell" and would hang up a picture or varnish a chair or let her make him some crêpes suzette, which she had always made so well).

Her own mother would not write to her; and she was, Mrs. Eugena Banks whined, beginning to wonder if it had not all been a mistake; could she not go back to Dayton? could she not begin again?

Then there was Clement Lewy, a little boy at the back, on the second floor.

Lewy life was not terrifically tossed. Saltless, rather. Or like an unmixed batter. Lumpy.

Little Clement's mother had grown listless after the desertion. She looked as though she had been scrubbed, up and down, on the washing board, doused from time to time in gray and noisome water. But little Clement looked alert, he looked happy, he was always spirited. He was in second grade. He did his work, and had always been promoted. At home he sang. He recited little poems. He told his mother little stories wound out of the air by himself. His mother glanced at him once in a while. She would have been proud of him if she had had the time.

She started toward her housemaid's work each morning at seven. She left a glass of milk and a bowl of dry cereal and a dish of prunes on the table, and set the alarm clock for eight. At eight little Clement punched off the alarm, stretched, got up, washed, dressed, combed, brushed, ate his breakfast. It was quiet in the apartment. He hurried off to school. At noon he returned from school, opened the door with his key. It was quiet in the apartment. He poured himself a second glass of milk, got more prunes, and ate a slice—"just one slice," his mother had cautioned—of bread and butter. He went back to school. At three o'clock he returned from school, opened the door with his key. It was quiet in the apartment. He got a couple of graham crackers out of the cookie can. He drew himself a glass of water. He changed his clothes. Then he went out to play, leaving behind him the two rooms. Leaving behind him the brass beds, the lamp with the faded silk tassel and frayed cord, the hooked oven door, the cracks in the walls and the quiet. As he played, he kept a lookout for his mother, who usually arrived at seven, or near that hour. When he saw her rounding the corner, his little face underwent a transformation. His eyes lashed into brightness, his lips opened suddenly and became a smile, and his eyebrows climbed toward his hairline in relief and joy.

He would run to his mother and almost throw his little body at her. "Here I am, mother! Here I am! Here I am!"

There was, or there had been, Richard—whose weekly earnings as a truck driver for a small beverage concern had dropped, slyly, from twenty-five, twenty-three, twenty-one, to sixteen, fifteen, twelve, while his weekly rent remained what it was (the family of five lived in one of the one-room apartments, a whole dollar cheaper than such a two-room as Paul and Maud Martha occupied); his family food and clothing bills had not dropped; and altogether it had been too much, the never having enough to buy Pabst or Ninety Proof for the boys, the being scared to death to offer a man a couple of cigarettes for fear your little supply, and with it your little weak-kneed nonchalance, might be exhausted before the appearance of your next pay envelope (pink, and designated elaborately on the outside, "Richard"), the coming back at night, every night, to a billowy diaper world, a wife with wild hair, twin brats screaming, and writhing, and wetting their crib, and a third brat, leaping on, from, and about chairs and table with repeated Hi-yo Silvers, and the sitting down to a meal never quite adequate, never quite—despite all your sacrifices, your inability to "treat" your friends, your shabby rags, your heartache. . . . It was altogether too much, so one night he had simply failed to come home.

There was an insane youth of twenty, twice released from Dunning. He had a smooth tan face, overlaid with oil. His name was Binnie. Or perhaps it was Bennie, or Benjamin. But his mother lovingly called him "Binnie." Binnie strode the halls, with huge eyes, direct and annoyed. He strode, and played "catch" with a broken watch, which was attached to a long string wound around his left arm. There was no annoyance in his eyes when he spoke to Maud Martha, though, and none in his nice voice. He was very fond of Maud Martha. Once, when she answered a rap on the door, there he was, and he pushed in before she could open her mouth. He had on a new belt, he said. "My Uncle John gave it to me," he said. "So my pants won't fall down." He walked about the apartment, after closing the door with a careful sneer. He touched things. He pulled a petal from a pink rose with savage anger, then kissed it with a tenderness that was more terrible than the anger; briskly he rapped on the table, turned suddenly to stare at her, to see if she approved of what he was doing—she smiled uncertainly; he saw the big bed, fingered it, sat on it, got up, kicked it. He opened a dresser drawer, took out a ruler. "This is ni-ice—but I won't take it" (with firm decision, noble virtue). "I'll put it back." He spoke of his aunt, his Uncle John's wife Octavia. "She's ni-ice—you know, she can even call me, and I don't even get mad." With another careful sneer, he opened the door. He went out.

Mrs. Teenie Thompson. Fifty-three; and pepper whenever she talked of the North Shore people who had employed her as housemaid for ten years. "She went to huggin' and kissin' of me—course I got to receive it—I got to work for 'em. But they think they got me thinkin' they love me. Then I'm supposed to kill my silly self slavin' for 'em. To be worthy of their love. These old whi' folks. They jive you, honey. Well, I jive 'em just like they jive me. They can't beat me jivin'. They'll have to jive much, to come any-where *near* my mark in jivin'."

About one of the one-roomers, a little light woman flitted. She was thin and looked ill. Her hair, which was long and of a strangely flat blackness, hung absolutely still, no matter how much its mistress moved. If anyone passed her usually open door, she would nod cheerily, but she rarely spoke. Chiefly you would see her flitting, in a faded blue rayon housecoat, touch-ing this, picking up that, adjusting, arranging, posing prettily. She was Mrs. Whitestripe. Mr. Whitestripe was a dark and dapper young man of me-dium height, with a small soot-smear of a mustache. The Whitestripes were the happiest couple Maud Martha had ever met. They were soft-spoken, kind to each other, were worried about each other. "Now you watch that cough now, Coopie!" For that was what she called him. "Here, take this Rem, here, take this lemon juice." "You wrap up good, now, you put on that scarf, Coo!" For that was what he called her. Or (rushing out of the door in his undershirt, one shoe off) "Did I hear you stumble down there, Coo? Did I hear you hurt your knee?" Often, visiting them, you were em-barrassed, because it was obvious that you were interrupting the progress of a truly great love; even as you conversed, there they would be, kissing or patting each other, or gazing into each other' eyes. Most fitting was it that adjacent to their "domicile" was the balcony of the building. Unfortu-nately, it was about two inches wide. Three pressures of a firm foot, and the little balcony would crumble downward to mingle with other dust. The Whitestripes never sat on it, but Maud Martha had no doubt that often on summer evenings they would open the flimsy "French" door, and stand there gazing out, thinking of what little they knew about Romeo and Juliet, their arms about each other.

"It is such a beautiful story," sighed Maud Martha once, to Paul.

"What is?"

"The love story of the Whitestripes."

"Well, I'm no 'Coopie' Whitestripe," Paul had observed, sharply, "so you can stop mooning. I'll never be a 'Coopie' Whitestripe."

"No," agreed Maud Martha. "No, you never will."

The one-roomer next the Whitestripes was occupied by Maryginia Washington, a maiden of sixty-eight, or sixty-nine, or seventy, a be-crutched, gnarled, bleached lemon with smartly bobbed white hair; who claimed, and proudly, to be an "indirect" descendant of the first President of the United States; who loathed the darker members of her race but did rather enjoy playing the *grande dame*, a hobbling, denture-clacking version, for their benefit, while they played, at least in her imagination, Top-sys—and did rather enjoy advising them, from time to time, to apply lightening creams to the horror of their flesh—"because they ain't no sense in lookin' any worser'n you have to, is they, dearie?"

In the fifth section, on the third floor, lived a Woman of Breeding. Her name was Josephine Snow. She was too much of a Woman of Breeding to allow the title "Madame" to vulgarize her name, but certain inhabitants of the building had all they could do to keep from calling her "Madame Snow," and eventually they relaxed, and called her that as a matter of course, behind her back.

Madame Snow was the color of soured milk, about sixty, and very superior to her surroundings—although she was not a Maryginia Washington. She had some sort of mysterious income, for although she had lived for seven years in "Gappington Arms" (the name given the building by the tenants, in dubious honor of the autocratic lady owner) no one had ever seen her go out to work. She rarely went anywhere. She went to church no more than once a month, and she sent little Clement Lewy and other children in the building to the store. She maintained a standard rate of pay; no matter how far the errand runner had to go, nor how heavily-loaded he was to be upon his return, she paid exactly five cents. It is hardly necessary to add that the identity of her runner was seldom the same for two days straight, and that a runner had to be poverty-stricken indeed before he searched among the paper nameplates downstairs and finally rang, with a disgruntled scowl, the bell of Miss Josephine Alberta Snow, Apt. 3E, who, actually, had been graduated from Fisk University.

What the source or size of Josephine's income was nobody knew. Her one-room apartment, although furnished with the same type of scarred brass bed and scratched dresser with which the other apartments were favored (for all her seven years), had received rich touches from her cultured hands. Her walls were hung with tapestry, strange pictures, china and il-luminated poems. She had "lived well," as these things declared, and it was evident that she meant to go on "living well," Gappington Arms or no Gap-pington Arms.

This lady did the honors of the teacup and cookie crock each afternoon, with or without company. She would spread a large stool with a square of lace, deck it with a low bowl of artificial flowers, a teacup or teacups, the pot of tea, sugar, cream and lemon, and the odd-shaped crock of sweet crackers.

On indoor weekdays she wore always the same dress—a black sateen thing that fell to her ankles and rose to her very chin. On the Sundays she condescended to go to church, she wore a pink lace, winter and summer, which likewise embraced her from ankle to chin. She charmed the neighborhood with that latter get-up, too, on those summer afternoons when the heat drove her down from her third-floor quarters to the little porch, with its one chair. There she would sit, frightening everyone, panting, fanning, and glaring at old Mr. Neville, the caretaker's eighty-two-year-old father, if he came out and so much as dared to look, with an eyeful of timid covetousness, at the single porch chair over which her bottom flowed (for she was a large lady). Then there was nothing for poor old Mr. Neville to do but sit silently on the hard stone steps—split, and crawling with ants and worse—chew his tobacco, glance peculiarly from time to time at that large pink lady, that pink and yellow lady, fanning indignantly at him.

As for the other tenants, they did not know what to say to Miss Snow after they had exchanged the time of day with her. Some few had attempted the tossing of sallies her way, centered in politics, the current murders, or homely philosophy, wanting to draw her out. But they very soon saw they would have to leave off all that, because it was too easy to draw her out. She would come out so far as to almost knock them down. She had a tremendous impatience with other people's ideas—unless those happened to be exactly like hers; even then, often as not, she gave hurried, almost angry, affirmative, and flew on to emphatic illuminations of her own. Then she would settle back in her chair, nod briskly a few times, as if to say, "Now! Now we are finished with it." What could be done? What was there further to be said?

24. an encounter

They went to the campus Jungly Hovel, a reedy-boothed place. Inside, before you saw anything, really, you got this impression of straw and reed. There were vendor outlets in the booths, and it could be observed what a struggle the management had had, trying to settle on something that was not out-and-out low, and that yet was not out-and-out highborn. In a weak moment someone had included Borden's Boogie Hoogie Woogie.

Maud Martha had gone to hear the newest young Negro author speak, at Mandel Hall on the University campus, and whom had she run into, coming out, but David McKemster. Outside, David McKemster had been talking seriously with a tall, dignified old man. When he saw her, he gravely nodded. He gravely waved. She decided to wait for him, not knowing whether that would be agreeable to him or not. After all, this was the University world, this was his element. Perhaps he would feel she did not belong here, perhaps he would be cold to her.

He certainly was cold to her. Free of the dignified old man, he joined her, walked with her down Fifty-ninth Street, past the studious gray buildings, west toward Cottage Grove. He yawned heartily at every sixth or seventh step.

"I'll put you on a streetcar," he said. "God, I'm tired."

Then nothing more was said by him, or by her—till they met a young white couple, going east. David's face lit up. These were his good, good friends. He introduced them as such to Maud Martha. Had they known about the panel discussion? No, they had not. Tell him, when had they seen Mary, Mary Ehreburg? Say, he had seen Metzger Freestone tonight. Ole Metzger. (He lit a cigarette.) Say, he had had dinner with the Beefy Godwins and Jane Wather this evening. Say, what were they doing tomorrow night? Well, what about going to the Adamses' tomorrow night? (He took excited but carefully sophisticated puffs.) Yes, they would go to the Adamses' tomorrow night. They would get Dora, and all go to the Adamses'. Say, how about going to Power's for a beer, tonight, if they had nothing else to do? Here he glanced at his companion—how to dispose of her! Well, no "how" about it, the disposal would have to be made. But first he had better buy her a coffee. That would pacify her. "Power'll still be up—prob'ly spraw*l*ing on that white rug of his, with Parrington in front of 'im," laughed David. It was, Maud Martha observed, one of the conceits of David McKemster that he did not have to use impeccable English all the time. Sometimes it was permissible to make careful slips. These must be, however, when possible, sandwiched in between thick hunks of the most rational, particularistic, critical, and intellectually aloof discourse. "But first let's go to the Jungly Hovel and have coffee with Mrs. Phillips," said David McKemster.

So off to the Jungly Hovel. They went into one of the booths and ordered.

The strange young man's face was pleasant when it smiled; the jaw was a little forward; Maud Martha was reminded of Pat O'Brien, the movie star. He kept looking at her; when he looked at her his eyes were somewhat agape; "Well!" they seemed to exclaim—"Well! and what have we here!" The girl, who was his fiancée, it turned out—"Stickie"—had soft pink coloring, summer-blue eyes, was attractive. She had, her soft pink notwithstanding, that brisk, thriving, noisy, "oh-so-American" type of attractiveness. She was confidential, she communicated everything except herself, which was precisely the thing her eyes, her words, her nods, her suddenly whipped-off laughs assured you she *was* communicating. She leaned healthily across the table; her long, lovely dark hair swung at you; her bangs came right out to meet you, and her face and forefinger did too (she emphasized, robustly, some point). But herself stayed stuck to the back of her seat, and was shrewd, and "took in," and contemplated, not quite warmly, everything.

"And there was this young—man. Twenty-one or two years old, wasn't he, Maudie?" David looked down at his guest. When they sat, their heights were equal, for his length was in the legs. But he thought he was looking down at her, and she was very willing to concede that that was what he was doing, for the immediate effect of the look was to make her sit straight as a stick. "Really quite, really most am*az*ing. Didn't you think, Maudie? Has written a book. Seems well-read chap, seems to know a lot about—a lot about—"

"Everything," supplied Maud Martha furiously.

"Well—yes." His brows gathered. He stabbed "Stickie" with a well-made gaze of seriousness, sober economy, doubt—mixed. "PRESENT things," he emphasized sharply. "He's very impressed by, he's all adither about—current plays in New York—Kafka.[9] *That* sawt of thing," he ended. His "sawt" was not sarcastic. Our position is hardly challenged, it implied. We are still on top of the wave, it implied. We who know about Aristotle, Plato, who weave words like anachronism, transcendentalist, cosmos, metaphysical, corollary, integer, monarchical, into our breakfast speech as a matter of course—

"And he disdains the universities!"

"Is he in school?" asked "Stickie," leaning: on the answer to that would depend—so much.

"Oh, no," David assured her, smiling. "He was pretty forceful on that point. There is nothing in the schools for *him*, he has decided. What are degrees, he asks contemptously." You see? David McKemster implied. This upstart, this, this brazen emissary, this rash representative from the ranks of the intellectual *nouveau riche.*[1] So he was brilliant. So he could outchatter me. So intellectuality was his oyster. So he has kicked—not Parrington—but Joyce, maybe, around like a football. But he is not rooted in Aristotle, in Plato, in Aeschylus, in Epictetus.[2] In all those Goddamn Greeks. As we are. Aloud, David skirted some of this—"Aristotle," he said, "is probably Greek to him." "Stickie" laughed quickly, stopped. Pat O'-Brien smiled lazily; leered.

The waitress brought coffee, four lumps of sugar wrapped in pink paper, hot mince pie.

25. the self-solace

Sonia Johnson got together her towels and soap. She scrubbed out her bowls. She mixed her water.

Maud Martha, waiting, was quiet. It was pleasant to let her mind go blank. And here in the beauty shop that was not a difficult thing to do. For the perfumes in the great jars, to be sold for twelve dollars and fifty cents an ounce and one dollar a dram, or seven dollars and fifty cents an ounce and one dollar a dram, the calendars, the bright signs extolling the virtues of Lily cologne (Made by the Management), the limp lengths of detached human hair, the pile of back-number *Vogues* and *Bazaars*, the earrings and clasps and beaded bags, white blouses—the "side line"—these things did not force themselves into the mind and make a disturbance there. One was and was not aware of them. Could sit here and think, or not think, of problems. Think, or not. One did not have to, if one wished not.

"If she burns me today—if she yanks at my hair—if she calls me sweetheart or dahlin'—"

Sonia Johnson parted the hangings that divided her reception room from her workrooms. "Come on back, baby doll."

9. Franz Kafka (1883–1924), novelist and short story writer known for his experimental prose.
1. Newly rich (French); often used to suggest vulgar excess.

2. Greek philosopher of the Stoic period (A.D. 50?–130). Plato (c. 428?–c. 348 B.C.), Greek philosopher. Aeschylus (524?–456 B.C.), Greek dramatist and writer of tragedies.

But just then the bell tinkled, and in pushed a young white woman, wearing a Persian lamb coat, and a Persian lamb cap with black satin ribbon swirled capably in a soft knot at the back.

"Yes," thought Maud Martha, "it's legitimate. It's November. It's not cold, but it's cool. You can wear your new fur now and not be laughed at by too many people."

The young white woman introduced herself to Mrs. Johnson as Miss Ingram, and said that she had new toilet waters, a make-up base that was so good it was "practically impossible," and a new lipstick.

"No make-up bases," said Sonia. "And no toilet water. We create our own."

"This new lipstick, this new shade," Miss Ingram said, taking it out of a smart little black bag, "is just the thing for your customers. For their dark complexions."

Sonia Johnson looked interested. She always put herself out to be kind and polite to these white salesmen and saleswomen. Some beauticians were brusque. They were almost insulting. They were glad to have the whites at their mercy, if only for a few moments. They made them crawl. Then they applied the whiplash. Then they sent the poor creatures off— with no orders. Then they laughed and laughed and laughed, a terrible laughter. But Sonia Johnson was not that way. She liked to be kind and polite. She liked to be merciful. She did not like to take advantage of her power. Indeed, she felt it was better to strain, to bend far back, to spice one's listening with the smooth smile, the quick and attentive nod, the well-timed "sure" or "uh-huh." She was against this eye-for-eye-tooth-for-tooth stuff.

Maud Martha looked at Miss Ingram's beautiful legs, wondered where she got the sheer stockings that looked like bare flesh at the same time that they did not, wondered if Miss Ingram knew that in the "Negro group" there were complexions whiter than her own, and other complexions, brown, tan, yellow, cream, which could not take a dark lipstick and keep their poise. Maud Martha picked up an ancient *Vogue*, turned the pages.

"What's the lipstick's name?" Sonia Johnson asked.

"Black Beauty," Miss Ingram said, with firm-lipped determination. "You won't regret adding it to your side line, I assure you, Madam."

"What's it sell for?"

"A dollar and a half. Let me leave you—say, ten—and in a week I'll come back and find them all gone, and you'll be here clamoring for more, I know you will. I'll leave ten."

"Well. Okay."

"That's fine, Madam. Now, I'll write down your name and address—"

Sonia rattled them off for her. Miss Ingram wrote them down. Then she closed her case.

"Now, I'll take just five dollars. Isn't that reasonable? You don't pay the rest till they're all sold. Oh, I know you're going to be just terribly pleased. And your customers too, Mrs. Johnson."

Sonia opened her cash drawer and took out five dollars for Miss Ingram. Miss Ingram brightened. The deal was closed. She pushed back a puff of straw-colored hair that had slipped from under her Persian lamb cap and fallen over the faint rose of her cheek.

"I'm mighty glad," she confided, "that the cold weather is in. I love the cold. It was awful, walking the streets in that nasty old August weather. And even September was rather close this year, didn't you think?"

Sonia agreed. "Sure was."

"People," confided Miss Ingram, "think this is a snap job. It ain't. I work like a nigger to make a few pennies. A few lousy pennies."

Maud Martha's head shot up. She did not look at Miss Ingram. She stared intently at Sonia Johnson. Sonia Johnson's sympathetic smile remained. Her eyes turned, as if magnetized, toward Maud Martha; but she forced her smile to stay on. Maud Martha went back to *Vogue*. "For," she thought, "I must have been mistaken. I was afraid I heard that woman say 'nigger.' Apparently not. Because of course Mrs. Johnson wouldn't let her get away with it. In her own shop." Maud Martha closed *Vogue*. She began to consider what she herself might have said, had she been Sonia Johnson, and had the woman really said "nigger." I wouldn't curse. I wouldn't holler. I'll bet Mrs. Johnson would do both those things. And I could understand her wanting to, all right. I would be gentle in a cold way. I would give her, not a return insult—directly, at any rate!—but information. I would get it across to her that—" Maud Martha stretched. "But I wouldn't insult her." Maud Martha began to take the hairpins out of her hair. "I'm glad, though, that she didn't say it. She's pretty and pleasant. If she had said it, I would feel all strained and tied up inside, and I would feel that it was my duty to help Mrs. Johnson get it settled, to help clear it up in some way. I'm too relaxed to fight today. Sometimes fighting is interesting. Today, it would have been just plain old ugly duty."

"Well, I wish you success with Black Beauty," Miss Ingram said, smiling in a tired manner, as she buttoned the top button of her Persian lamb. She walked quickly out of the door. The little bell tinkled charmingly.

Sonia Johnson looked at her customer with thoughtful narrowed eyes. She walked over, dragged a chair up close. She sat. She began to speak in a dull level tone.

"You know, why I didn't catch her up on that, is—our people is got to stop feeling so sensitive about these words like 'nigger' and such. I often think about this, and how these words like 'nigger' don't mean to some of these here white people what our people *think* they mean. Now, 'nigger,' for instance, means to them something bad, or slavey-like, or low. They don't mean anything against me. I'm a Negro, not a 'nigger.' Now, a white man can be a 'nigger,' according to their meaning for the word, just like a colored man can. So why should I go getting all stepped up about a thing like that? Our people is got to stop getting all stepped up about every little thing, especially when it don't amount to nothing. . . ."

"You mean to say," Maud Martha broke in, "that that woman really did say 'nigger'?"

"Oh, yes, she said it, all right, but like I'm telling—"

"Well! At first, I thought she said it, but then I decided I must have been mistaken, because you weren't getting after her."

"Now that's what I'm trying to explain to you, dearie. Sure, I could have got all hot and bothered, and told her to clear out of here, or cussed her daddy, or something like that. But what would be the point, when, like I say, that word 'nigger' can mean one of them just as fast as one of us, and in fact it don't mean us, and in fact we're just too sensitive and all? What would be the point? Why make enemies? Why go getting all hot and bothered all the time?"

Maud Martha stared steadily into Sonia Johnson's irises. She said nothing. She kept on staring into Sonia Johnson's irises.

26. Maud Martha's tumor

As she bent over Paulette, she felt a peculiar pain in her middle, at the right. She touched the spot. There it was. A knot, hard, manipulable, the proscription of her doom.

At first, she could only be weak (as the pain grew sharper and sharper). Then she was aware of creeping fear; fear of the operating table, the glaring instruments, the cold-faced nurses, the relentlessly submerging ether, the chokeful awakening, the pain, the ensuing cancer, the ensuing death.

Then she thought of her life. Decent childhood, happy Christmases; some shreds of romance, a marriage, pregnancy and the giving birth, her growing child, her experiments in sewing, her books, her conversations with her friends and enemies.

"It hasn't been bad," she thought.

"It's been interesting," she thought, as she put Paulette in the care of Mrs. Maxawanda Barksdale and departed for the doctor's.

She looked at the trees, she looked at the grass, she looked at the faces of the passers-by. It had been interesting, it had been rather good, and it was still rather good. But really, she was ready. Since the time had come, she was ready. Paulette would miss her for a long time, Paul for less, but really, their sorrow was their business, not hers. Her business was to descend into the deep cool, the salving dark, to be alike indifferent to the good and the not-good.

"And what," asked Dr. Williams, "did you do yesterday that was out of line with your regular routine?" He mashed her here, tapped there.

She remembered.

"Why, I was doing the bends."

"Doing—"

"The bends. Exercising. With variations. I lay on the bed, also, and keeping my upper part absolutely still, I raised my legs up, then lowered them, twenty times."

"Is this a nightly custom of yours?"

"No. Last night was the first time I had done it since before my little girl was born."

"Three dollars, please."

"You mean—I'm not going to die."

She bounced down the long flight of tin-edged stairs, was shortly claimed by the population, which seemed proud to have her back. An old woman, bent, shriveled, smiled sweetly at her.

She was already on South Park. She jumped in a jitney and went home.

27. Paul in the 011 Club

The 011 Club did not like it so much, your buying only a beer. . . .

Do you want to get into the war? Maud Martha "thought at" Paul, as, over their wine, she watched his eye-light take leave of her. To get into the war, perhaps. To be mixed up in peculiar, hooped adventure, adventure dominant, entire, ablaze with bunched and fidgeting color, pageantry, thrilling with the threat of danger—through which he would come without so much as a bruised ankle.

The baby was getting darker all the time! She knew that he was tired of his wife, tired of his living quarters, tired of working at Sam's, tired of his two suits.

He is ever so tired, she thought.

He had no money, no car, no clothes, and he had not been put up for membership in the Foxy Cats Club.

Something should happen. He was not on show. She knew that he believed he had been born to invade, to occur, to confront, to inspire the flapping of flags, to panic people. To wear, but carelessly, a crown. What could give him his chance, illuminate his gold?—be a happening?

She looked about, about at these, the people he would like to impress. The real people. It was Sunday afternoon and they were dressed in their best. It was May, and for hats the women wore gardens and birds. They wore tight-fitting prints, or flounced satin, or large-flowered silk under the coats they could not afford but bought anyhow. Their hair was intricately curled, or it was sedately marcelled. Some of it was hennaed. Their escorts were in broad-shouldered suits, and sported dapper handkerchiefs. Their hair was either slicked back or very close-cut. All spoke in subdued tones. There were no roughnecks here. These people knew what whiskies were good, what wine was "the thing" with this food, that food, what places to go, how to dance, how to smoke, how much stress to put on love, how to dress, when to curse, and did not indulge (for the most part) in homosexuality but could discuss it without eagerness, distaste, curiosity—without anything but ennui. These, in her husband's opinion, were the real people. And this was the real place. The manner of the waitresses toward the patrons, by unspoken agreement, was just this side of insulting. They seemed to have something to prove. They wanted you to know, to be *sure* that they were as good as you were and maybe a lot better. They did not want you to be misled by the fact that on a Sunday afternoon, instead of silk and little foxes, they wore white uniforms and carried trays and picked up (rapidly) tips.

A flame-colored light flooded the ceiling in the dining foyer. (But there was a blue-red-purple note in the bar.) On the east wall of the dining foyer, painted against a white background, was an unclothed lady, with a careless bob, challenging nipples, teeth-revealing smile; her arms were lifted, to call attention to "all"—and she was standing behind a few huge leaves of sleepy color and amazing design. On the south wall was painted one of those tropical ladies clad in carefully careless sarong, and bearing upon her head with great ease and glee a platter of fruit—apples, spiky pineapple, bananas. . . .

She watched the little dreams of smoke as they spiraled about his hand, and she thought about happenings. She was afraid to suggest to him that, to most people, nothing at all "happens." That most people merely live from day to day until they die. That, after he had been dead a year, doubtless

fewer than five people would think of him oftener than once a year. That
there might even come a year when no one on earth would think of him at
all.

28. brotherly love

Maud Martha was fighting with a chicken. The nasty, nasty mess. It had
been given a bitter slit with the bread knife and the bread knife had been
biting in that vomit-looking interior for almost five minutes without being
able to detach certain resolute parts from their walls. The bread knife had it
all to do, as Maud Martha had no intention of putting her hand in there.
Another hack—another hack—STUFF! Splat in her eye. She leaped at the
faucet.

She thought she had praise coming to her. She was doing this job with
less stomach-curving than ever before. She thought of the times before the
war, when there were more chickens than people wanting to buy them,
and butchers were happy to clean them, and even cut them up. None of
that now. In those happy, happy days—if she had opened up a chicken and
seen it all unsightly like this, and smelled it all smelly, she would have
scooped up the whole batch of slop and rushed it to the garbage can. Now
meat was jewelry and she was practically out of Red Points. You were lucky
to find a chicken. She had to be as brave as she could.

People could do this! people could cut a chicken open, take out the
mess, with bare hands or a bread knife, pour water in, as in a bag, pour
water out, shake the corpse by neck or by legs, free the straggles of water.
Could feel that insinuating slipping bone, survey that soft, that headless
death. The *faint*hearted could do it. But if the chicken were a man!—cold
man with no head or feet and with all the little feath—er, hairs to be pulled,
and the intestines loosened and beginning to ooze out, and the gizzard yet
to be grabbed and the stench beginning to rise! And yet the chicken was a
sort of person, a respectable individual, with its own kind of dignity. The
difference was in the knowing. What was unreal to you, you could deal
with violently. If chickens were ever to be safe, people would have to live
with them, and know them, see them loving their children, finishing the
evening meal, arranging jealousy.

When the animal was ready for the oven Maud Martha smacked her lips
at the thought of her meal.

29. millinery

"Looks lovely on you," said the manager. "Makes you look—" What?
Beautiful? Charming? Glamorous? Oh no, oh no, she could not stoop to the
usual lies; not today; her coffee had been too strong, had not set right; and
there had been another fight at home, for her daughter continued to insist
on gallivanting about with that Greek—a Greek!—not even a Jew, which,
though revolting enough, was at least becoming fashionable, was "timely."
Oh, not today would she cater to these nigger women who tried on every hat
in her shop, who used no telling what concoctions of smelly grease on the
heads that integrity, straightforwardness, courage, would certainly have kept
kinky. She started again—"Makes you look—" She stopped.

"How much is the hat?" Maud Martha asked.

"Seven ninety-nine."

Maud Martha rose, went to the door.

"Wait, wait," called the hat woman, hurrying after her. She smiled at Maud Martha. When she looked at Maud Martha, it was as if God looked; it was as if—

"Now just how much, Madam, had you thought you would prefer to pay?"

"Not a cent over five."

"Five? Five, dearie? You expect to buy a hat like this for five dollars? This, this straw that you can't even get any more and which I showed you only because you looked like a lady of taste who could appreciate a good value?"

"Well," said Maud Martha, "thank you." She opened the door.

"Wait, wait," shrieked the hat woman. Good-naturedly, the escaping customer hesitated again. "Just a moment," ordered the hat woman coldly. "I'll speak to the—to the owner. He might be willing to make some slight reduction, since you're an old customer. I remember you. You've been in here several times, haven't you?"

"I've never been in the store before." The woman rushed off as if she had heard nothing. She rushed off to consult with the owner. She rushed off to appeal to the boxes in the back room.

Presently the hat woman returned.

"Well. The owner says it'll be a crying shame, but seeing as how you're such an old customer he'll make a reduction. He'll let you have it for five. Plus tax, of course!" she added chummily; they had, always, more appreciation when, after one of these "reductions," you added that.

"I've decided against the hat."

"What? Why, you told—But, you said—"

Maud Martha went out, tenderly closed the door.

"Black—oh, black—" said the hat woman to her hats—which, on the slender stands, shone pink and blue and white and lavender, showed off their tassels, their sleek satin ribbons, their veils, their flower coquettes.

30. at the Burns-Coopers'

It was a little red and white and black woman who appeared in the doorway of the beautiful house in Winnetka.

About, thought Maud Martha, thirty-four.

"I'm Mrs. Burns-Cooper," said the woman, "and after this, well, it's all right this time, because it's your first time, but after this time always use the back entrance."

There is a pear in my icebox, and one end of rye bread. Except for three Irish potatoes and a cup of flour and the empty Christmas boxes, there is absolutely nothing on my shelf. My husband is laid off. There is newspaper on my kitchen table instead of oilcloth. I can't find a filing job in a hurry. I'll smile at Mrs. Burns-Cooper and hate her just some.

"First, you have the beds to make," said Mrs. Burns-Cooper. "You either change the sheets or air the old ones for ten minutes. I'll tell you about the changing when the time comes. It isn't any special day. You are to pull my

sheets, and pat and pat and pull till all's tight and smooth. Then shake the
pillows into the slips, carefully. Then punch them in the middle.

"Next, there is the washing of the midnight snack dishes. Next, there is
the scrubbing. Now, I know that your other ladies have probably wanted
their floors scrubbed after dinner. I'm different. I like to enjoy a bright
clean floor all the day. You can just freshen it up a little before you leave in
the evening, if it needs a few more touches. Another thing. I disapprove of
mops. You can do a better job on your knees.

"Next is dusting. Next is vacuuming—that's for Tuesdays and Fridays.
On Wednesdays, ironing and silver cleaning.

"Now about cooking. You're very fortunate in that here you have only
the evening meal to prepare. Neither of us has breakfast, and I always step
out for lunch. Isn't that lucky?"

"It's quite a kitchen, isn't it?" Maud Martha observed. "I mean, big."

Mrs. Burns-Cooper's brows raced up in amazement.

"Really? I hadn't thought so. I'll bet"—she twinkled indulgently—
"you're comparing it to your *own* little kitchen." And why do that, her light
eyes laughed. Why talk of beautiful mountains and grains of alley sand in
the same breath?

"Once," mused Mrs. Burns-Cooper, "I had a girl who botched up the
kitchen. Made a botch out of it. But all I had to do was just sort of cock my
head and say, 'Now, now, Albertine!' Her name was Albertine. Then she'd
giggle and scrub and scrub and she was so sorry about trying to take advantage."

It was while Maud Martha was peeling potatoes for dinner that Mrs.
Burns-Cooper laid herself out to prove that she was not a snob. Then it was
that Mrs. Burns-Cooper came out to the kitchen and, sitting, talked and
talked at Maud Martha. In my college days. At the time of my debut. The
imported lace on my lingerie. My brother's rich wife's Stradivarius.[3] When
I was in Madrid. The charm of the Nile. Cost fifty dollars. Cost one hundred dollars. Cost one thousand dollars. Shall I mention, considered Maud
Martha, my own social triumphs, my own education, my travels to Gary
and Milwaukee and Columbus, Ohio? Shall I mention my collection of
fancy pink satin bras? She decided against it. She went on listening, in silence, to the confidences until the arrival of the lady's mother-in-law (large-
eyed, strong, with hair of a mighty white, and with an eloquent, angry
bosom). Then the junior Burns-Cooper was very much the mistress, was
stiff, cool, authoritative.

There was no introduction, but the elder Burns-Cooper boomed,
"Those potato parings are entirely too thick!"

The two of them, richly dressed, and each with that health in the face
that bespeaks, or seems to bespeak, much milk drinking from earliest childhood, looked at Maud Martha. There was no remonstrance; no firing!
They just looked. But for the first time, she understood what Paul endured
daily. For so—she could gather from a Paul-word here, a Paul-curse there—
his Boss! when, squared, upright, terribly upright, superior to the President,
commander of the world, he wished to underline Paul's lacks, to indicate
soft shock, controlled incredulity. As his boss looked at Paul, so these peo-

---

3. A rare and expensive violin.

ple looked at her. As though she were a child, a ridiculous one, and one that ought to be given a little shaking, except that shaking was—not quite the thing, would not quite do. One held up one's finger (if one did anything), cocked one's head, was arch. As in the old song, one hinted, "Tut tut! now now! come come!" Metal rose, all built, in one's eye.

I'll never come back, Maud Martha assured herself, when she hung up her apron at eight in the evening. She knew Mrs. Burns-Cooper would be puzzled. The wages were very good. Indeed, what could be said in explanation? Perhaps that the hours were long. I couldn't explain *my* explanation, she thought.

One walked out from that almost perfect wall, spitting at the firing squad. What difference did it make whether the firing squad understood or did not understand the manner of one's retaliation or why one had to retaliate?

Why, one was a human being. One wore clean nightgowns. One loved one's baby. One drank cocoa by the fire—or the gas range—come the evening, in the wintertime.

31. on Thirty-fourth Street

Maud Martha went east on Thirty-fourth Street, headed for Cottage Grove. It was August, and Thirty-fourth Street was all in bloom. The blooms, in their undershirts, sundresses and diapers, were hanging over porches and fence stiles and strollers, and were even bringing chairs out to the rims of the sidewalks.

At the corner of Thirty-fourth and Cottage Grove, a middle-aged blind man on a three-legged stool picked at a scarred guitar. The five or six patched and middle-aged men around him sang in husky, low tones, which carried the higher tone—ungarnished, insistent, at once a question and an answer—of the instrument.

Those men were going no further—and had gone nowhere. Tragedy.

She considered that word. On the whole, she felt, life was more comedy than tragedy. Nearly everything that happened had its comic element, not too well buried, either. Sooner or later one could find something to laugh at in almost every situation. That was what, in the last analysis, could keep folks from going mad. The truth was, if you got a good Tragedy out of a lifetime, one good, ripping tragedy, thorough, unridiculous, bottom-scraping, *not* the issue of human stupidity, you were doing, she thought, very well, you were doing well.

32. Mother comes to call

Mama came, bringing two oranges, nine pecans, a Hershey bar and a pear.

Mama explained that one of the oranges was for Maud Martha, one was for Paulette. The Hershey bar was for Paulette. The pear was for Maud Martha, for it was not, Mama said, a very good pear. Four of the pecans were for Maud Martha, four were for Paulette, one was for Paul.

Maud Martha spread her little second-hand table—a wide tin band was wound beneath the top, for strength—with her finest wedding gift, a really good white luncheon cloth. She brought out white coffee cups and saucers, sugar, milk, and a little pink pot of cocoa. She brought a plate of frosted gingerbread. Mother and daughter sat down to Tea.

"And how is Helen? I haven't seen her in two weeks. When I'm over there to see you, she's always out."

"Helen doesn't like to come here much," said Mama, nodding her head over the gingerbread. "Not enough cinnamon in this but very good. She says it sort of depresses her. She wants you to have more things."

"I like nutmeg better than cinnamon. I have a lot of things. I have more than she has. I have a husband, a nice little girl, and a clean home of my own."

"A kitchenette of your own," corrected Mama, "without even a private bathroom. I think Paul could do a little better, Maud Martha."

"It's hard to find even a kitchenette."

"Nothing beats a trial but a failure. Helen thinks she's going to marry Doctor Williams."

"Our own family doctor. Not our own family doctor!"

"She says her mind's about made up."

"But he's over fifty years old."

"She says he's steady, not like the young ones she knows, and kind, and will give her a decent home."

"And what do you say?"

"I say, it's a hard cold world and a woman had better do all she can to help herself get along as long as what she does is honest. It isn't as if she didn't like Doctor Williams."

"She always did, yes. Ever since we were children, and he used to bring her licorice sticks, and forgot to bring any to me, except very seldom."

"It isn't as if she merely sold herself. She'll try to make him happy, I'm sure. Helen was always a good girl. And in any marriage, the honeymoon is soon over."

"What does Papa say?"

"He's thinking of changing doctors."

"It hasn't been a hard cold world for you, Mama. You've been very lucky. You've had a faithful, homecoming husband, who bought you a house, not the best house in town, but a house. You have, most of the time, plenty to eat, you have enough clothes so that you can always be clean. And you're strong as a horse."

"It certainly has been a hard season," said Belva Brown. "I don't know when we've had to burn so much coal in October before."

"I'm thinking of Helen."

"What about Helen, dear?"

"It's funny how some people are just charming, just pretty, and others, born of the same parents, are just not."

"You've always been wonderful, dear."

They looked at each other.

"I always say you make the best cocoa in the family."

"I'm never going to tell my secret."

"That girl down at the corner, next to the parsonage—you know?—is going to have another baby."

"The third? And not her husband's *either*?"

"Not her husband's either."
"Did Mrs. Whitfield get all right?"
"No, she'll have to have the operation."

33. tree leaves leaving trees

Airplanes and games and dolls and books and wagons and blackboards
and boats and guns and bears and rabbits and pandas and ducks, and dogs
and cats and gray elephants with black howdahs and rocking chairs and
houses and play dishes and scooters and animal hassocks, and trains and
trucks and yo-yos and telephones and balls and jeeps and jack-in-the-boxes
and puzzles and rocking horses.
    And Santa Claus.

> Round, ripe, rosy,
> As the stories said.
> And white, it fluffed out from his chin,
> It laughed about his head.

And there were the children. Many groups of them, for this was a big
department store. Santa pushed out plump ho-ho-ho's! He patted the children's cheeks, and if a curl was golden and sleek enough he gave it a bit of
a tug, and sometimes he gave its owner a bit of a hug. And the children's
Christmas wants were almost torn out of them.
    It was very merry and much as the children had dreamed.
    Now came little Paulette. When the others had been taken care of. Her
insides scampering like mice. And, leaving her eyeballs, diamonds and
stars.
    Santa Claus.
    Suddenly she was shy.
    Maud Martha smiled, gave her a tiny shove, spoke as much to Santa
Claus as to her daughter.
    "Go on. There he is. You've wanted to talk to him all this time. Go on.
Tell Santa what you want for Christmas."
    "No."
    Another smile, another shove, with some impatience, with some severity
in it. And Paulette was off.
    "Hello!"
    Santa Claus rubbed his palms together and looked vaguely out across the
Toy Department.
    He was unable to see either mother or child.
    "I want," said Paulette, "a wagon, a doll, a big ball, a bear and a tricycle
with a horn."
    "Mister," said Maud Martha, "my little girl is talking to you."
    Santa Claus's neck turned with hard slowness, carrying his unwilling
face with it.
    "Mister," said Maud Martha.
    "And what—do you want for Christmas." No question mark at the end.
    "I want a wagon, a doll, a bear, a big ball, and a tricycle with a horn."
    Silence. Then, "Oh." Then, "Um-hm."
    Santa Claus had taken care of Paulette.

"And some candy and some nuts and a seesaw and bow and arrow."

"Come on, baby."

"But I'm not through, Mama."

"Santa Claus is through, hon."

Outside, there was the wonderful snow, high and heavy, crusted with blue twinkles. The air was quiet.

"Certainly is a nice night," confided Mama.

"Why didn't Santa Claus like me?"

"Baby, of course he liked you."

"He didn't like me. Why didn't he like me?"

"It maybe seemed that way to you. He has a lot on his mind, of course."

"He liked the other children. He smiled at them and shook their hands."

"He maybe got tired of smiling. Sometimes even I get—"

"He didn't look at me, he didn't shake *my* hand."

"Listen, child. People don't have to kiss you to show they like you. Now you know Santa Claus liked you. What have I been telling you? Santa Claus loves every child, and on the night before Christmas he brings them swell presents. Don't you remember, when you told Santa Claus you wanted the ball and bear and tricycle and doll he said 'Um-hm'? That meant he's going to bring you all those. You watch and see. Christmas'll be here in a few days. You'll wake up Christmas morning and find them and then you'll know Santa Claus loved *you* too."

Helen, she thought, would not have twitched, back there. Would not have yearned to jerk trimming scissors from purse and jab jab jab that evading eye. Would have gathered her fires, patted them, rolled them out, and blown on them. Because it really would not have made much difference to Helen. Paul would have twitched, twitched awfully, might have cursed, but after the first tough cough-up of rage would forget, or put off studious perusal indefinitely.

She could neither resolve nor dismiss. There were these scraps of baffled hate in her, hate with no eyes, no smile and—this she especially regretted, called her hungriest lack—not much voice.

Furtively, she looked down at Paulette. Was Paulette believing her? Surely she was not going to begin to think tonight, to try to find out answers tonight. She hoped the little creature wasn't ready. She hoped there hadn't been enough for that. She wasn't up to coping with—Some other night, not tonight.

Feeling her mother's peep, Paulette turned her face upward. Maud Martha wanted to cry.

Keep her that land of blue!

Keep her those fairies, with witches always killed at the end, and Santa every winter's lord, kind, sheer being who never perspires, who never does or says a foolish or ineffective thing, who never looks grotesque, who never has occasion to pull the chain and flush the toilet.

34. back from the wars!

There was Peace, and her brother Harry was back from the wars, and well.

And it was such a beautiful day!

The weather was bidding her bon voyage.

She did not have to tip back the shade of her little window to know that
outside it was bright, because the sunshine had broken through the dark
green of that shade and was glorifying every bit of her room. And the air
crawling in at the half-inch crack was like a feather, and it tickled her
throat, it teased her lashes, it made her sit up in bed and stretch, and zip the
dark green shade up to the very top of the window—and made her whisper,
What, *what*, am I to do with all of this life?

And exactly what was one to do with it all? At a moment like this one was
ready for anything, was not afraid of anything. If one were down in a dark
cool valley one could stick arms out and presto! they would be wings cutting away at the higher layers of air. At a moment like this one could think
even of death with a sharp exhilaration, feel that death was a part of life:
that life was good and death would be good too.

Maud Martha, with her daughter, got out-of-doors.

She did not need information, or solace, or a guidebook, or a sermon—
not in this sun!—not in this blue air!

. . . They "marched," they battled behind her brain—the men who had
drunk beer with the best of them, the men with two arms off and two legs
off, the men with the parts of faces. Then her guts divided, then her eyes
swam under frank mist.

And the Negro press (on whose front pages beamed the usual representations of womanly Beauty, pale and pompadoured) carried the stories of the
latest of the Georgia and Mississippi lynchings. . . .

But the sun was shining, and some of the people in the world had been
left alive, and it was doubtful whether the ridiculousness of man would
ever completely succeed in destroying the world or, in fact, the basic equa-
nimity of the least and commonest flower: for would its kind not come up
again in the spring? come up, if necessary, among, between, or out of—
beastly inconvenient!—the smashed corpses lying in strict composure, in
that hush infallible and sincere.

And was not this something to be thankful for?

And, in the meantime, while people did live they would be grand, would
be glorious and brave, would have nimble hearts that would beat and beat.
They would even get up nonsense, through wars, through divorce, through
evictions and jiltings and taxes.

And, in the meantime, she was going to have another baby.

The weather was bidding her bon voyage.

1953

JAMES BALDWIN

1924–1987

All of James Baldwin's writings bear some stamp of his assertion that "all art is a
kind of confession," that all artists, if they are to survive, are forced, at last, to tell the
whole story, to "vomit the anguish up." But in Baldwin's work, such confession was

not merely a self-indulgent form of personal catharsis. With elegance and artful-
ness, he pierced the historic block in America's racial consciousness by linking the
most intimate areas of his own experience with the broadest questions of national
and global destiny.

Baldwin returned compulsively to those events of his early life that seared themselves in his imagination: the struggles with poverty; the humiliation of police brutality; the strangling religious indoctrination; but most of all, the estrangement from
his stepfather, David Baldwin, an embittered, authoritarian lay preacher steeped in
the Old Testament gospel of sinners in the hands of an angry God. Baldwin inherited that tradition, serving a brief time as a child evangelist in a store-front church in
Harlem. Although he left the Church and renounced Christianity, he often
conceded that he never left the pulpit, and the spirit of evangelism in his writings
bears him out. Baldwin possessed the consciousness of a moralist, shaped by an Old
Testament certainty of right and wrong, sin and transgression, and the New Testament promise of resurrection and redemption. This sermonic rhetoric of sin, damnation, and repentance pours through Baldwin's writings and mixes with the lyrics
of the spirituals, blues, and gospel, creating a prose that demands the reader's attentive ear as much as eye, for the pace, cadences, rhythms, accents, and timbres are
often lost in print. His immersion in black biblical rhetoric earned Baldwin the
rightful title of latter-day Jeremiah, never more apparent than in *The Fire Next Time*
(1963), a collection judged by many to be his finest. In *Down at the Cross: Letter
from a Region in My Mind,* Baldwin utters one of his most famous prophecies: "If
we do not dare everything, the fulfillment of that prophecy, re-created from the
Bible in song by a slave, is upon us: God gave Noah the rainbow sign, No more
water, the fire next time!" In the 1960s, he was to see his prophecies come continually to pass in the uprisings that erupted all over urban America, leaving whole
communities under piles of ash and rubble.

Born on August 2, 1924, in Harlem, which he described as a "southern community displaced in the streets of New York," Baldwin was the out-of-wedlock son of
Emma Berdis Jones. When she married David Baldwin, three years later, he
adopted James, who was never to feel a sense of security or belonging in the family.
Baldwin escaped from his stepfather's hatred and the harshness of his home in reading, claiming that by age thirteen he had read most of the books in the two Harlem
libraries and had had to move on to the New York Public Library on Forty-second
Street.

Baldwin began his literary apprenticeship at the age of twelve when he published
a short story about the Spanish revolution in a church newspaper. He found support for his writing in his high school's literary club, directed by Countee Cullen,
and served as editor of the school newspaper, the *Douglass Pilot*. After high school,
he continued to write, publishing his first book review (on Maxim Gorky) in 1946
at age twenty-two. His subsequent reviews for the *New Leader* on "the Negro problem" prompted Robert Warshow to commission a piece on Harlem for *Commentary*, the publishing arm of the American Jewish Committee. Titled *The Harlem
Ghetto*, the controversial essay on black anti-Semitism launched Baldwin's career
as a writer and garnered him numerous invitations from other magazines.

With characteristic candor, Baldwin admits to writing in an "attempt to be loved.
It seemed the only way to another world." But the passage to that "other" world that
writing provided seemed restricted by Baldwin's experience with racism and homophobia, a situation that compelled him to move to Paris in November 1948, a year
after his mentor, Richard Wright, made the same transatlantic trek.

During Baldwin's days as a fledgling writer in New York, Wright had encouraged
him, helping him to secure the Eugene F. Saxton fellowship for work on his first
novel, *Go Tell It on the Mountain*. Again, in Paris, Wright introduced Baldwin to

the editors of *Zero* magazine, in which Baldwin published one of his most influential essays, *Everybody's Protest Novel* (1949). Best known for its attack on protest fiction, the essay examines Harriet Beecher Stowe's *Uncle Tom's Cabin* and Richard Wright's *Native Son* as examples of the limitations and excesses of ideological fiction. Appearing simultaneously in New York's *Partisan Review*, the essay sparked intense debate on both sides of the Atlantic and was widely perceived as a spiteful and ungrateful personal attack on Richard Wright. Although the essay resulted in a breach between Wright and Baldwin that was never healed, it further established Baldwin's reputation as a major American writer and essayist in the Emersonian tradition and a polemicist in the tradition of Thomas Paine and W. E. B. Du Bois.

Many, including Baldwin himself, have interpreted his relationship with Wright, and the estrangement that followed, as an Oedipal struggle of fathers and sons. Certainly, this struggle figures as one of the major obsessions of Baldwin's life and work and is at the heart of his first full-length work, *Go Tell It on the Mountain*. Published in 1953 to excellent reviews, the novel was originally titled "In My Father's House" and is a semiautobiographical story of a young man's coming-of-age, repressed and choked by his father's religious fundamentalism and its puritanical regime.

The relationship between the father, Gabriel, and Johnny, his son, recalls that of the biblical Abraham and Ishmael. As the rejected "bastard" within the home, Baldwin saw his position as that of Ishmael, the son of the bondwoman. Like many African American writers before him, Baldwin seized on the story of Ishmael, the archetypal outcast, not only as a metaphor for his own life but as a metaphor for the collective lives of blacks dispossessed within America.

Many agree that *Go Tell It on the Mountain* is Baldwin's most technically accomplished and narratively disciplined novel, although most conclude that his true *metier* was not the novel. Though Baldwin published six other novels over his career—*Giovanni's Room* (1956), *Another Country* (1962), *Tell Me How Long This Train's Been Gone* (1968), *If Beale Street Could Talk* (1974), and *Just above My Head* (1979)—his essays were invariably praised at the expense of his fiction. Those collected in *Notes of a Native Son* (1955), *Nobody Knows My Name* (1961), and *The Fire Next Time* (1963), won Baldwin a popularity and acclaim as the "conscience of the nation," who brought to racial discourse a passion and honesty that demanded notice. Baldwin's knife-edged criticism of the failed promises of American democracy, and the consequent social injustices, is unrelenting and demonstrates a piercing understanding of the function of blacks in the white racial imagination, especially the function of black males.

In *The Black Boy Looks at the White Boy*, a response to Norman Mailer's essay *The White Negro*, Baldwin made some of his most trenchant pronouncements on the subject. "To be an American Negro male," he wrote, "is also to be a kind of walking phallic symbol; which means that one pays, in one's own personality, for the sexual insecurity of others." He expanded these insights in essays and interviews throughout his career—*Preservation of Innocence, Here Be Dragons, The Male Prison*—analyzing the inextricable connection between sex and race in America. He speculated that if America ever transcended its racial antagonisms, it would then have to confront its Protestant Puritan legacy, complete with its taboos against sex and the flesh. He understood that, in terms of violence and discrimination, black Americans have borne the historical brunt of American sexual anxieties, the very same anxieties that serve a cultural agenda of compulsory heterosexuality. This agenda has, in turn, created the homosexual as outcast to shore up an enfeebled masculine identity. In *Go the Way Your Blood Beats*, a 1984 interview with Richard Goldstein, Baldwin argued that macho men need "faggots" whom they have created "in order to act out a sexual fantasy on the body of another man and not take any responsibility for it." In both *Giovanni's Room* (1956) and *Another Country*

(1962), he waged a twin assault on such racial and sexual intolerance and, somewhat sentimentally, dramatized blackness and homosexuality as liberating influences.

Baldwin had a long and varied career in which, in addition to essays and novels, he produced plays, scripts, short stories, and children's books; but he was at his artistic summit in those works that he published during the 1950s and early 1960s. Almost nothing pertaining to race relations and social turbulence escaped Baldwin's pen during this period, although he addressed a range of other subjects, including homosexuality in Andre Gide's novel *Madeleine*, William Faulkner and desegregation, and the ideology of racial separatism espoused by the Black Muslims.

Neither racial separatism nor segregation could Baldwin easily abide. By his account, photographs of Dorothy Counts being spat upon as she tried to integrate a Charlotte, North Carolina, school convinced him to join the civil rights struggle; and after nearly a decade in France, he returned to the United States in 1957.

Baldwin became a national figure in the movement, traveling to the South and producing acid social commentaries that were published in such mass-circulation magazines as *Commentary*, *Partisan Review*, and *Esquire* and later collected in *Nobody Knows My Name* and *The Fire Next Time*. These essays, along with those in the first collection, *Notes of a Native Son*, are Baldwin at his best, by most critical accounts. Some have suggested, perhaps too pattly, that, taken together, these three collections move backward from a New Testament optimism to an Old Testament gloom and record the stages in Baldwin's growing disillusionment with the American racial situation. While *Notes of a Native Son* and *Nobody Knows My Name* register hope that blacks would be integrated into an American society where the healing force of love abounded, *The Fire Next Time* shows evidence that all belief in the redemptive possibilities of love is shattered.

Later collections found Baldwin's prophetic stance unshaken. In *No Name in the Street* (1972), he returned to the Old Testament to offer the curse of Job's friend Bildad as an object lesson for America. Bildad foretold the doom that would befall the wicked of his generation: "His remembrance shall perish from the earth, and he shall have no name in the street" (Job 18:17). Closing on a characteristically apocalyptic note, Baldwin prophesied yet more violence and bloodshed for an America heedless of the lessons of its own history and shackled to myths, shibboleths, and primitive reflexes that had too long defined race relations in America: "There will be bloody actions all over the world for years to come; but the Western party is over, and the white man's sun has set. Period."

After his civil rights involvement, Baldwin returned to Europe, where he lived, except for brief trips to the United States, until his death on November 30, 1987, in St. Paul de Vence. In an interview with Quincy Troupe weeks before his death, Baldwin said, "No true account really of black life can be held, can be contained, in the American vocabulary. As it is, the only way that you can deal with it is by doing great violence to the assumptions on which the vocabulary is based. What I tried to do, or to interpret and make clear, was that no society can smash the social contract and be exempt from the consequences, and the consequences are chaos for everybody in the society."

Many critics allege that, by the end of his career, Baldwin was spouting rhetoric that compromised the moral persuasion and authority that had made his earlier works so powerful and compelling. Others charged that the line between his artistic preoccupations and his own personal and psychic life had become embarrassingly blurred. Still others observed that, in resorting to abstract sociological categories, Baldwin was flattening what had once been a richly complicated view of race and racialism in America and thus committing the same ideological excesses he had once condemned in Richard Wright. Still, whatever the criticisms, few will deny that Baldwin played a shaping role in the definition of post–World War II African American literature and had a stunning impact on American cultural life.

Everybody's Protest Novel

In *Uncle Tom's Cabin*,[1] that cornerstone of American social protest fiction, St. Clare, the kindly master, remarks to his coldly disapproving Yankee cousin, Miss Ophelia, that, so far as he is able to tell, the blacks have been turned over to the devil for the benefit of the whites in this world— however, he adds thoughtfully, it may turn out in the next. Miss Ophelia's reaction is, at least, vehemently right-minded: "This is perfectly horrible!" she exclaims. "You ought to be ashamed of yourselves!"

Miss Ophelia, as we may suppose, was speaking for the author; her exclamation is the moral, neatly framed, and incontestable like those improving mottoes sometimes found hanging on the walls of furnished rooms. And, like these mottoes, before which one invariably flinches, recognizing an insupportable, almost an indecent glibness, she and St. Clare are terribly in earnest. Neither of them questions the medieval morality from which their dialogue springs: black, white, the devil, the next world—posing its alternatives between heaven and the flames—were realities for them as, of course, they were for their creator. They spurned and were terrified of the darkness, striving mightily for the light; and considered from this aspect, Miss Ophelia's exclamation, like Mrs. Stowe's novel, achieves a bright, almost a lurid significance, like the light from a fire which consumes a witch. This is the more striking as one considers the novels of Negro oppression written in our own, more enlightened day, all of which say only: "This is perfectly horrible! You ought to be ashamed of yourselves!" (Let us ignore, for the moment, those novels of oppression written by Negroes, which add only a raging, near-paranoiac postscript to this statement and actually reinforce, as I hope to make clear later, the principles which activate the oppression they decry.)

Uncle Tom's Cabin is a very bad novel, having, in its self-righteous, virtuous sentimentality, much in common with *Little Women*.[2] Sentimentality, the ostentatious parading of excessive and spurious emotion, is the mark of dishonesty, the inability to feel; the wet eyes of the sentimentalist betray his aversion to experience, his fear of life, his arid heart; and it is always, therefore, the signal of secret and violent inhumanity, the mask of cruelty. *Uncle Tom's Cabin*—like its multitudinous, hard-boiled descendants—is a catalogue of violence. This is explained by the nature of Mrs. Stowe's subject matter, her laudable determination to flinch from nothing in presenting the complete picture; an explanation which falters only if we pause to ask whether or not her picture is indeed complete; and what constriction or failure of perception forced her to so depend on the description of brutality—unmotivated, senseless—and to leave unanswered and unnoticed the only important question: what it was, after all, that moved her people to such deeds.

1. Harriet Beecher Stowe's antislavery novel, published in 1851–52. A runaway best-seller, this novel played a major role in the debate over slavery in the decade before the Civil War.

2. Novel by Louisa May Alcott, published in 1868–69. Extremely popular children's book detailing the daily lives of four girls in a 19th-century New England family.

But this, let us say, was beyond Mrs. Stowe's powers; she was not so much a novelist as an impassioned pamphleteer; her book was not intended to do anything more than prove that slavery was wrong; was, in fact, perfectly horrible. This makes material for a pamphlet but it is hardly enough for a novel; and the only question left to ask is why we are bound still within the same constriction. How is it that we are so loath to make a further journey than that made by Mrs. Stowe, to discover and reveal something a little closer to the truth?

But that battered word, truth, having made its appearance here, confronts one immediately with a series of riddles and has, moreover, since so many gospels are preached, the unfortunate tendency to make one belligerent. Let us say, then, that truth, as used here, is meant to imply a devotion to the human being, his freedom and fulfillment; freedom which cannot be legislated, fulfillment which cannot be charted. This is the prime concern, the frame of reference; it is not to be confused with a devotion to Humanity which is too easily equated with a devotion to a Cause; and Causes, as we know, are notoriously blood-thirsty. We have, as it seems to me, in this most mechanical and interlocking of civilizations, attempted to lop this creature down to the status of a time-saving invention. He is not, after all, merely a member of a Society or a Group or a deplorable conundrum to be explained by Science. He is—and how old-fashioned the words sound!—something more than that, something resolutely indefinable, unpredictable. In overlooking, denying, evading his complexity—which is nothing more than the disquieting complexity of ourselves—we are diminished and we perish; only within this web of ambiguity, paradox, this hunger, danger, darkness, can we find at once ourselves and the power that will free us from ourselves. It is this power of revelation which is the business of the novelist, this journey toward a more vast reality which must take precedence over all other claims. What is today parroted as his Responsibility—which seems to mean that he must make formal declaration that he is involved in, and affected by, the lives of other people and to say something improving about this somewhat self-evident fact—is, when he believes it, his corruption and our loss; moreover, it is rooted in, interlocked with and intensifies this same mechanization. Both *Gentleman's Agreement* and *The Postman Always Rings Twice* [3] exemplify this terror of the human being, the determination to cut him down to size. And in *Uncle Tom's Cabin* we may find foreshadowing of both: the formula created by the necessity to find a lie more palatable than the truth has been handed down and memorized and persists yet with a terrible power.

It is interesting to consider one more aspect of Mrs. Stowe's novel, the method she used to solve the problem of writing about a black man at all. Apart from her lively procession of field hands, house niggers, Chloe, Topsy, etc.—who are the stock, lovable figures presenting no problem—she has only three other Negroes in the book. These are the important ones and two of them may be dismissed immediately, since we have only the author's word that they are Negro and they are, in all other respects, as

3. A 1946 film directed by Tay Garnett, based on a novel of the same name by James M. Cain. An example of *film noir*, it takes a critical look at the pernicious consequences of the American dream.

Gentleman's Agreement is a 1947 film directed by Elia Kazan, based on a novel of the same name by Laura Hobson; one of the first films to openly attack anti-Semitism.

white as she can make them. The two are George and Eliza, a married couple with a wholly adorable child—whose quaintness, incidentally, and whose charm, rather put one in mind of a darky bootblack doing a buck and wing to the clatter of condescending coins. Eliza is a beautiful, pious hybrid, light enough to pass—the heroine of *Quality*[4] might, indeed, be her reincarnation—differing from the genteel mistress who has overseered her education only in the respect that she is a servant. George is darker, but makes up for it by being a mechanical genius, and is, moreover, sufficiently un-Negroid to pass through town, a fugitive from his master, disguised as a Spanish gentleman, attracting no attention whatever beyond admiration. They are a race apart from Topsy. It transpires by the end of the novel, through one of those energetic, last-minute convolutions of the plot, that Eliza has some connection with French gentility. The figure from whom the novel takes its name, Uncle Tom, who is a figure of controversy yet, is jet-black, wooly-haired, illiterate; and he is phenomenally forbearing. He has to be; he is black; only through this forbearance can he survive or triumph. (*Cf.* Faulkner's preface to *The Sound and the Fury*:[5] These others were not Compsons. They were black:—They endured.) His triumph is metaphysical, unearthly; since he is black, born without the light, it is only through humility, the incessant mortification of the flesh, that he can enter into communion with God or man. The virtuous rage of Mrs. Stowe is motivated by nothing so temporal as a concern for the relationship of men to one another—or, even, as she would have claimed, by a concern for their relationship to God—but merely by a panic of being hurled into the flames, of being caught in traffic with the devil. She embraced this merciless doctrine with all her heart, bargaining shamelessly before the throne of grace: God and salvation becoming her personal property, purchased with the coin of her virtue. Here, black equates with evil and white with grace; if, being mindful of the necessity of good works, she could not cast out the blacks—a wretched, huddled mass, apparently, claiming, like an obsession, her inner eye—she could not embrace them either without purifying them of sin. She must cover their intimidating nakedness, robe them in white, the garments of salvation; only thus could she herself be delivered from ever-present sin, only thus could she bury, as St. Paul demanded, "the carnal man, the man of the flesh."[6] Tom, therefore, her only black man, has been robbed of his humanity and divested of his sex. It is the price for that darkness with which he has been branded.

Uncle Tom's Cabin, then, is activated by what might be called a theological terror, the terror of damnation; and the spirit that breathes in this book, hot, self-righteous, fearful, is not different from that spirit of medieval times which sought to exorcize evil by burning witches; and is not different from that terror which activates a lynch mob. One need not, indeed, search for examples so historic or so gaudy; this is a warfare waged daily in the heart, a warfare so vast, so relentless and so powerful that the interracial handshake or the interracial marriage can be as crucifying as the public hanging or the secret rape. This panic motivates our cruelty, this fear of the dark makes it

4. A 1946 novel by Cid Ricketts Sumner.
5. Novel (1929) by William Faulkner (1897–1962).
6. Probably from St. Paul's first letter to the Corin-
thians, one of two canonical letters Paul addressed to his congregation in Corinth (see Romans 8:7–8). St. Paul was an early Christian missionary and Christianity's first theologian.

impossible that our lives shall be other than superficial; this, interlocked with and feeding our glittering, mechanical, inescapable civilization which has put to death our freedom.

This, notwithstanding that the avowed aim of the American protest novel is to bring greater freedom to the oppressed. They are forgiven, on the strength of these good intentions, whatever violence they do to language, whatever excessive demands they make of credibility. It is, indeed, considered the sign of a frivolity so intense as to approach decadence to suggest that these books are both badly written and wildly improbable. One is told to put first things first, the good of society coming before niceties of style or characterization. Even if this were incontestable—for what exactly is the "good" of society?—it argues an insuperable confusion, since literature and sociology are not one and the same; it is impossible to discuss them as if they were. Our passion for categorization, life neatly fitted into pegs, has led to an unforeseen, paradoxical distress; confusion, a breakdown of meaning. Those categories which were meant to define and control the world for us have boomeranged us into chaos; in which limbo we whirl, clutching the straws of our definitions. The "protest" novel, so far from being disturbing, is an accepted and comforting aspect of the American scene, ramifying that framework we believe to be so necessary. Whatever unsettling questions are raised are evanescent, titillating; remote, for this has nothing to do with us, it is safely ensconced in the social arena, where, indeed, it has nothing to do with anyone, so that finally we receive a very definite thrill of virtue from the fact that we are reading such a book at all. This report from the pit reassures us of its reality and its darkness and of our own salvation; and "As long as such books are being published," an American liberal once said to me, "everything will be all right."

But unless one's ideal of society is a race of neatly analyzed, hard-working ciphers, one can hardly claim for the protest novels the lofty purpose they claim for themselves or share the present optimism concerning them. They emerge for what they are: a mirror of our confusion, dishonesty, panic, trapped and immobilized in the sunlit prison of the American dream. They are fantasies, connecting nowhere with reality, sentimental; in exactly the same sense that such movies as The Best Years of Our Lives or the works of Mr. James M. Cain[7] are fantasies. Beneath the dazzling pyrotechnics of these current operas one may still discern, as the controlling force, the intense theological preoccupations of Mrs. Stowe, the sick vacuities of The Rover Boys.[8] Finally, the aim of the protest novel becomes something very closely resembling the zeal of those alabaster missionaries to Africa to cover the nakedness of the natives, to hurry them into the pallid arms of Jesus and thence into slavery. The aim has now become to reduce all Americans to the compulsive, bloodless dimensions of a guy named Joe.

It is the peculiar triumph of society—and its loss—that it is able to convince those people to whom it has given inferior status of the reality of this decree; it has the force and the weapons to translate its dictum into fact, so

---

7. Novelist and journalist (1892–1977) known primarily for novels about criminals and those on the fringe of society. The Best Years of Our Lives (1946) is an Academy Award–winning William Wyler film, based on Glory for Me by MacKinley Kantor, which examines the difficulties faced by World War II veterans when they returned to their jobs and families.
8. Series of books for boys by Edward Stratemeyer published 1899–1916 under the pseudonym Arthur M. Winfield.

that the allegedly inferior are actually made so, insofar as the societal realities are concerned. This is a more hidden phenomenon now than it was in the days of serfdom, but it is no less implacable. Now, as then, we find ourselves bound, first without, then within, by the nature of our categorization. And escape is not effected through a bitter railing against this trap; it is as though this very striving were the only motion needed to spring the trap upon us. We take our shape, it is true, within and against that cage of reality bequeathed us at our birth; and yet it is precisely through our dependence on this reality that we are most endlessly betrayed. Society is held together by our need; we bind it together with legend, myth, coercion, fearing that without it we will be hurled into that void, within which, like the earth before the Word was spoken, the foundations of society are hidden. From this void—ourselves—it is the function of society to protect us; but it is only this void, our unknown selves, demanding, forever, a new act of creation, which can save us—"from the evil that is in the world." With the same motion, at the same time, it is this toward which we endlessly struggle and from which, endlessly, we struggle to escape.

It must be remembered that the oppressed and the oppressor are bound together within the same society; they accept the same criteria, they share the same beliefs, they both alike depend on the same reality. Within this cage it is romantic, more, meaningless, to speak of a "new" society as the desire of the oppressed, for that shivering dependence on the props of reality which he shares with the *Herrenvolk*[9] makes a truly "new" society impossible to conceive. What is meant by a new society is one in which inequalities will disappear, in which vengeance will be exacted; either there will be no oppressed at all, or the oppressed and the oppressor will change places. But, finally, as it seems to me, what the rejected desire is, is an elevation of status, acceptance within the present community. Thus, the African, exile, pagan, hurried off the auction block and into the fields, fell on his knees before that God in Whom he must now believe; who had made him, but not in His image. This tableau, this impossibility, is the heritage of the Negro in America: *Wash me*, cried the slave to his Maker, *and I shall be whiter, whiter than snow!* For black is the color of evil; only the robes of the saved are white. It is this cry, implacable on the air and in the skull, that he must live with. Beneath the widely published catalogue of brutality—bringing to mind, somehow, an image, a memory of church-bells burdening the air—is this reality which, in the same nightmare notion, he both flees and rushes to embrace. In America, now, this country devoted to the death of the paradox—which may, therefore, be put to death by one—his lot is as ambiguous as a tableau by Kafka.[1] To flee or not, to move or not, it is all the same; his doom is written on his forehead, it is carried in his heart. In *Native Son*,[2] Bigger Thomas stands on a Chicago street corner watching airplanes flown by white men racing against the sun and "Goddamn" he says, the bitterness bubbling up like blood, remembering a million indignities, the terrible, rat-infested house, the humiliation of home-relief, the intense, aimless, ugly bickering, hating it; hatred smoul-

9. Master race (German).
1. Franz Kafka (1883–1924), German-speaking Jewish novelist, known for his often disturbing por-

trayals of a surreal reality that conspires against lonely and confused individuals.
2. A 1940 novel by Richard Wright.

ders through these pages like sulphur fire. All of Bigger's life is controlled, defined by his hatred and his fear. And later, his fear drives him to murder and his hatred to rape; he dies, having come, through this violence, we are told, for the first time, to a kind of life, having for the first time redeemed his manhood. Below the surface of this novel there lies, as it seems to me, a continuation, a complement of that monstrous legend it was written to destroy. Bigger is Uncle Tom's descendant, flesh of his flesh, so exactly opposite a portrait that, when the books are placed together, it seems that the contemporary Negro novelist and the dead New England woman are locked together in a deadly, timeless battle; the one uttering merciless exhortations, the other shouting curses. And, indeed, within this web of lust and fury, black and white can only thrust and counter-thrust, long for each other's slow, exquisite death; death by torture, acid, knives and burning; the thrust, the counter-thrust, the longing making the heavier that cloud which blinds and suffocates them both, so that they go down into the pit together. Thus has the cage betrayed us all, this moment, our life, turned to nothing through our terrible attempts to insure it. For Bigger's tragedy is not that he is cold or black or hungry, not even that he is American, black; but that he has accepted a theology that denies him life, that he admits the possibility of his being sub-human and feels constrained, therefore, to battle for his humanity according to those brutal criteria bequeathed him at his birth. But our humanity is our burden, our life; we need not battle for it; we need only to do what is infinitely more difficult—that is, accept it. The failure of the protest novel lies in its rejection of life, the human being, the denial of his beauty, dread, power, in its insistence that it is his categorization alone which is real and which cannot be transcended.

1949

Many Thousands Gone

It is only in his music, which Americans are able to admire because a protective sentimentality limits their understanding of it, that the Negro in America has been able to tell his story. It is a story which otherwise has yet to be told and which no American is prepared to hear. As is the inevitable result of things unsaid, we find ourselves until today oppressed with a dangerous and reverberating silence; and the story is told, compulsively, in symbols and signs, in hieroglyphics; it is revealed in Negro speech and in that of the white majority and in their different frames of reference. The ways in which the Negro has affected the American psychology are betrayed in our popular culture and in our morality; in our estrangement from him is the depth of our estrangement from ourselves. We cannot ask: what do we *really* feel about him—such a question merely opens the gates on chaos. What we really feel about him is involved with all that we feel about everything, about everyone, about ourselves.

The story of the Negro in America is the story of America—or, more precisely, it is the story of Americans. It is not a very pretty story: the story of a people is never very pretty. The Negro in America, gloomily referred to as that shadow which lies athwart our national life, is far more than that. He is a series of shadows, self-created, intertwining, which now we helplessly battle. One may say that the Negro in America does not really exist except in the darkness of our minds.

This is why his history and his progress, his relationship to all other Americans, has been kept in the social arena. He is a social and not a personal or a human problem; to think of him is to think of statistics, slums, rapes, injustices, remote violence; it is to be confronted with an endless cataloguing of losses, gains, skirmishes; it is to feel virtuous, outraged, helpless, as though his continuing status among us were somehow analogous to disease—cancer, perhaps, or tuberculosis—which must be checked, even though it cannot be cured. In this arena the black man acquires quite another aspect from that which he has in life. We do not know what to do with him in life; if he breaks our sociological and sentimental image of him we are panic-stricken and we feel ourselves betrayed. When he violates this image, therefore, he stands in the greatest danger (sensing which, we uneasily suspect that he is very often playing a part for our benefit); and, what is not always so apparent but is equally true, we are then in some danger ourselves—hence our retreat or our blind and immediate retaliation.

Our dehumanization of the Negro then is indivisible from our dehumanization of ourselves: the loss of our own identity is the price we pay for our annulment of his. Time and our own force act as our allies, creating an impossible, a fruitless tension between the traditional master and slave. Impossible and fruitless because, literal and visible as this tension has become, it has nothing to do with reality.

Time has made some changes in the Negro face. Nothing has succeeded in making it exactly like our own, though the general desire seems to be to make it blank if one cannot make it white. When it has become blank, the past as thoroughly washed from the black face as it has been from ours, our guilt will be finished—at least it will have ceased to be visible, which we imagine to be much the same thing. But, paradoxically, it is we who prevent this from happening; since it is we, who, every hour that we live, reinvest the black face with our guilt; and we do this—by a further paradox, no less ferocious—helplessly, passionately, out of an unrealized need to suffer absolution.

Today, to be sure, we know that the Negro is not biologically or mentally inferior; there is no truth in those rumors of his body odor or his incorrigible sexuality; or no more truth than can be easily explained or even defended by the social sciences. Yet, in our most recent war, his blood was segregated[1] as was, for the most part, his person. Up to today we are set at a division, so that he may not marry our daughters or our sisters, nor may he—for the most part—eat at our tables or live in our houses. Moreover, those who do, do so at the grave expense of a double alienation: from their own people, whose fabled attributes they must either deny or, worse, cheapen and bring to market; from us, for we require of them, when we accept them, that they at once cease to be Negroes and yet not fail to remember what being a Negro means—to remember, that is, what it means to us. The threshold of insult is higher or lower, according to the people

---

1. During World War II, there was hysteria about the consequences of contaminating white soldiers with infusions of black blood.

involved, from the bootblack in Atlanta to the celebrity in New York. One must travel very far, among saints with nothing to gain or outcasts with nothing to lose, to find a place where it does not matter—and perhaps a word or a gesture or simply a silence will testify that it matters even there.

For it means something to be a Negro, after all, as it means something to have been born in Ireland or in China, to live where one sees space and sky or to live where one sees nothing but rubble or nothing but high buildings. We cannot escape our origins, however hard we try, those origins which contain the key—could we but find it—to all that we later become. What it means to be a Negro is a good deal more than this essay can discover; what it means to be a Negro in America can perhaps be suggested by an examination of the myths we perpetuate about him.

Aunt Jemima and Uncle Tom are dead, their places taken by a group of amazingly well-adjusted young men and women, almost as dark, but ferociously literate, well-dressed and scrubbed, who are never laughed at, who are not likely ever to set foot in a cotton or tobacco field or in any but the most modern of kitchens. There are others who remain, in our odd idiom, "underprivileged"; some are bitter and these come to grief; some are unhappy, but, continually presented with the evidence of a better day soon to come, are speedily becoming less so. Most of them care nothing whatever about race. They want only their proper place in the sun and the right to be left alone, like any other citizen of the republic. We may all breathe more easily. Before, however, our joy at the demise of Aunt Jemima and Uncle Tom approaches the indecent, we had better ask whence they sprang, how they lived? Into what limbo have they vanished?

However inaccurate our portraits of them were, these portraits do suggest, not only the conditions, but the quality of their lives and the impact of this spectacle on our consciences. There was no one more forbearing than Aunt Jemima, no one stronger or more pious or more loyal or more wise; there was, at the same time, no one weaker or more faithless or more vicious and certainly no one more immoral. Uncle Tom, trustworthy and sexless, needed only to drop the title "Uncle" to become violent, crafty, and sullen, a menace to any white woman who passed by. They prepared our feast tables and our burial clothes; and, if we could boast that we understood them, it was far more to the point and far more true that they understood us. They were, moreover, the only people in the world who did; and not only did they know us better than we knew ourselves, but they knew us better than we knew them. This was the piquant flavoring to the national joke, it lay behind our uneasiness as it lay behind our benevolence: Aunt Jemima and Uncle Tom, our creations, at the last evaded us; they had a life—their own, perhaps a better life than ours—and they would never tell us what it was. At the point where we were driven most privately and painfully to conjecture what depths of contempt, what heights of indifference, what prodigies of resilience, what untamable superiority allowed them so vividly to endure, neither perishing nor rising up in a body to wipe us from the earth, the image perpetually shattered and the word failed. The black man in our midst carried murder in his heart, he wanted vengeance. We carried murder too, we wanted peace.

In our image of the Negro breathes the past we deny, not dead but living yet and powerful, the beast in our jungle of statistics. It is this which defeats us, which continues to defeat us, which lends to interracial cocktail parties their rattling, genteel, nervously smiling air: in any drawing room at such a gathering the beast may spring, filling the air with flying things and an unenlightened wailing. Wherever the problem touches there is confusion, there is danger. Wherever the Negro face appears a tension is created, the tension of a silence filled with things unutterable. It is a sentimental error, therefore, to believe that the past is dead; it means nothing to say that it is all forgotten, that the Negro himself has forgotten it. It is not a question of memory. Oedipus[2] did not remember the thongs that bound his feet; nevertheless the marks they left testified to that doom toward which his feet were leading him. The man does not remember the hand that struck him, the darkness that frightened him, as a child; nevertheless, the hand and the darkness remain with him, indivisible from himself forever, part of the passion that drives him wherever he thinks to take flight.

The making of an American begins at that point where he himself rejects all other ties, any other history, and himself adopts the vesture of his adopted land. This problem has been faced by all Americans throughout our history—in a way it *is* our history—and it baffles the immigrant and sets on edge the second generation until today. In the case of the Negro the past was taken from him whether he would or no; yet to forswear it was meaningless and availed him nothing, since his shameful history was carried, quite literally, on his brow. Shameful; for he was heathen as well as black and would never have discovered the healing blood of Christ had not we braved the jungles to bring him these glad tidings. Shameful; for, since our role as missionary had not been wholly disinterested, it was necessary to recall the shame from which we had delivered him in order more easily to escape our own. As he accepted the alabaster Christ and the bloody cross—in the bearing of which he would find his redemption, as, indeed, to our outraged astonishment, he sometimes did—he must, henceforth, accept that image we then gave him of himself: having no other and standing, moreover, in danger of death should he fail to accept the dazzling light thus brought into such darkness. It is this quite simple dilemma that must be borne in mind if we wish to comprehend his psychology.

However we shift the light which beats so fiercely on his head, or *prove*, by victorious social analysis, how his lot has changed, how we have both improved, our uneasiness refuses to be exorcized. And nowhere is this more apparent than in our literature on the subject—"problem" literature when written by whites, "protest" literature when written by Negroes—and nothing is more striking than the tremendous disparity of tone between the two creations. *Kingsblood Royal* bears, for example, almost no kinship to *If He Hollers Let Him Go,*[3] though the same reviewers praised them both for what were, at bottom, very much the same reasons. These reasons may be

2. In Greek mythology, the son of Laius and Jocasta, king and queen of Thebes, but raised by the king of Corinth. Oedipus later returns to Thebes and unwittingly kills his father and marries his mother.
3. A 1945 novel by black American writer Chester

Himes, which examines the discrimination against a black worker in a California defense plant. *Kingsblood Royal* is a 1947 novel by white author Sinclair Lewis, which explores the intricacies of racial prejudice.

suggested, far too briefly but not at all unjustly, by observing that the presupposition is in both novels exactly the same: black is a terrible color with which to be born into the world.

Now the most powerful and celebrated statement we have yet had of what it means to be a Negro in America is unquestionably Richard Wright's *Native Son*. The feeling which prevailed at the time of its publication was that such a novel, bitter, uncompromising, shocking, gave proof, by its very existence, of what strides might be taken in a free democracy; and its indisputable success, proof that Americans were now able to look full in the face without flinching the dreadful facts. Americans, unhappily, have the most remarkable ability to alchemize all bitter truths into an innocuous but piquant confection and to transform their moral contradictions, or public discussion of such contradictions, into a proud decoration, such as are given for heroism on the field of battle. Such a book, we felt with pride, could never have been written before—which was true. Nor could it be written today. It bears already the aspect of a landmark; for Bigger and his brothers have undergone yet another metamorphosis; they have been accepted in baseball leagues and by colleges hitherto exclusive; and they have made a most favorable appearance on the national screen. We have yet to encounter, nevertheless, a report so indisputably authentic, or one that can begin to challenge this most significant novel.

It is, in a certain American tradition, the story of an unremarkable youth in battle with the force of circumstance; that force of circumstance which plays and which has played so important a part in the national fables of success or failure. In this case the force of circumstance is not poverty merely but color, a circumstance which cannot be overcome, against which the protagonist battles for his life and loses. It is, on the surface, remarkable that this book should have enjoyed among Americans the favor it did enjoy; no more remarkable, however, than that it should have been compared, exuberantly, to Dostoevsky, though placed a shade below Dos Passos, Dreiser, and Steinbeck;[4] and when the book is examined, its impact does not seem remarkable at all, but becomes, on the contrary, perfectly logical and inevitable.

We cannot, to begin with, divorce this book from the specific social climate of that time: it was one of the last of those angry productions, encountered in the late twenties and all through the thirties, dealing with the inequities of the social structure of America. It was published one year before our entry into the last world war—which is to say, very few years after the dissolution of the WPA and the end of the New Deal[5] and at a time when bread lines and soup kitchens and bloody industrial battles were bright in everyone's memory. The rigors of that unexpected time filled us not only with a genuinely bewildered and despairing idealism—so that, be-

---

4. John Steinbeck (1902–1968), American novelist, most famous for *The Grapes of Wrath* (1939). Fyodor Mikhailovich Dostoevsky (1821–1881), Russian novelist whose work often dealt with the downtrodden and neglected. John Dos Passos (1896–1970), American novelist whose books often portrayed the unfortunate by-products of materialism and exploitation. Theodore Dreiser (1871–1945), American novelist who combined his talent for journalism with his concern for individuals struggling against hostile circumstances.
5. President Franklin Roosevelt's program of economic relief and legislative reforms in response to the Great Depression of the 1930s. "WPA": Works Projects Administration, created in 1935 by Roosevelt to provide useful public work for the unemployed; part of the New Deal.

cause there at least was *something* to fight for, young men went off to die in Spain—but also with a genuinely bewildered self-consciousness. The Negro, who had been during the magnificent twenties a passionate and delightful primitive, now became, as one of the things we were most self-conscious about, our most oppressed minority. In the thirties, swallowing Marx[6] whole, we discovered the Worker and realized—I should think with some relief—that the aims of the Worker and the aims of the Negro were one. This theorem—to which we shall return—seems now to leave rather too much out of account; it became, nevertheless, one of the slogans of the "class struggle" and the gospel of the New Negro.

As for this New Negro, it was Wright who became his most eloquent spokesman; and his work, from its beginning, is most clearly committed to the social struggle. Leaving aside the considerable question of what relationship precisely the artist bears to the revolutionary, the reality of man as a social being is not his only reality and that artist is strangled who is forced to deal with human beings solely in social terms; and who has, moreover, as Wright had, the necessity thrust on him of being the representative of some thirteen million people. It is a false responsibility (since writers are not congressmen) and impossible, by its nature, of fulfillment. The unlucky shepherd soon finds that, so far from being able to feed the hungry sheep, he has lost the wherewithal for his own nourishment: having not been allowed—so fearful was his burden, so present his audience!—to re-create his own experience. Further, the militant men and women of the thirties were not, upon examination, significantly emancipated from their antecedents, however bitterly they might consider themselves estranged or however gallantly they struggled to build a better world. However they might extol Russia, their concept of a better world was quite helplessly American and betrayed a certain thinness of imagination, a suspect reliance on suspect and badly digested formulae, and a positively fretful romantic haste. Finally, the relationship of the Negro to the Worker cannot be summed up, nor even greatly illuminated, by saying that their aims are one. It is true only insofar as they both desire better working conditions and useful only insofar as they unite their strength as workers to achieve these ends. Further than this we cannot in honesty go.

In this climate Wright's voice first was heard and the struggle which promised for a time to shape his work and give it purpose also fixed it in an ever more unrewarding rage. Recording his days of anger he has also nevertheless recorded, as no Negro before him had ever done, that fantasy Americans hold in their minds when they speak of the Negro: that fantastic and fearful image which we have lived with since the first slave fell beneath the lash. This is the significance of *Native Son* and also, unhappily, its overwhelming limitation.

Native Son begins with the *Brring!* of an alarm clock in the squalid Chicago tenement where Bigger and his family live. Rats live there too, feeding off the garbage, and we first encounter Bigger in the act of killing one. One

6. Karl Marx (1818–1883), German revolutionary leader, social philosopher, and political economist; founder of modern socialism.

may consider that the entire book, from that harsh *Brring!* to Bigger's weak "Good-by" as the lawyer, Max, leaves him in the death cell, is an extension, with the roles inverted, of this chilling metaphor. Bigger's situation and Bigger himself exert on the mind the same sort of fascination. The premise of the book is, as I take it, clearly conveyed in these first pages: we are confronting a monster created by the American republic and we are, through being made to share his experience, to receive illumination as regards the manner of his life and to feel both pity and horror at his awful and inevitable doom. This is an arresting and potentially rich idea and we would be discussing a very different novel if Wright's execution had been more perceptive and if he had not attempted to redeem a symbolical monster in social terms.

One may object that it was precisely Wright's intention to create in Bigger a social symbol, revelatory of social disease and prophetic of disaster. I think, however, that it is this assumption which we ought to examine more carefully. Bigger has no discernible relationship to himself, to his own life, to his own people, nor to any other people—in this respect, perhaps, he is most American—and his force comes, not from his significance as a social (or anti-social) unit, but from his significance as the incarnation of a myth. It is remarkable that, though we follow him step by step from the tenement room to the death cell, we know as little about him when this journey is ended as we did when it began; and, what is even more remarkable, we know almost as little about the social dynamic which we are to believe created him. Despite the details of slum life which we are given, I doubt that anyone who has thought about it, disengaging himself from sentimentality, can accept this most essential premise of the novel for a moment. Those Negroes who surround him, on the other hand, his hard-working mother, his ambitious sister, his poolroom cronies, Bessie, might be considered as far richer and far more subtle and accurate illustrations of the ways in which Negroes are controlled in our society and the complex techniques they have evolved for their survival. We are limited, however, to Bigger's view of them, part of a deliberate plan which might not have been disastrous if we were not also limited to Bigger's perceptions. What this means for the novel is that a necessary dimension has been cut away; this dimension being the relationship that Negroes bear to one another, that depth of involvement and unspoken recognition of shared experience which creates a way of life. What the novel reflects—and at no point interprets—is the isolation of the Negro within his own group and the resulting fury of impatient scorn. It is this which creates its climate of anarchy and unmotivated and unapprehended disaster; and it is this climate, common to most Negro protest novels, which has led us all to believe that in Negro life there exists no tradition, no field of manners, no possibility of ritual or intercourse, such as may, for example, sustain the Jew even after he has left his father's house. But the fact is not that the Negro has no tradition but that there has as yet arrived no sensibility sufficiently profound and tough to make this tradition articulate. For a tradition expresses, after all, nothing more than the long and painful experience of a people; it comes out of the battle waged to maintain their integrity or, to put it more simply, out of their struggle to survive. When we speak of the Jewish tradition we are speaking of centuries of exile and persecution, of the strength which endured and the sensibility which discovered in it the high possibility of the moral victory.

This sense of how Negroes live and how they have so long endured is hidden from us in part by the very speed of the Negro's public progress, a progress so heavy with complexity, so bewildering and kaleidoscopic, that he dare not pause to conjecture on the darkness which lies behind him; and by the nature of the American psychology which, in order to apprehend or be made able to accept it, must undergo a metamorphosis so profound as to be literally unthinkable and which there is no doubt we will resist until we are compelled to achieve our own identity by the rigors of a time that has yet to come. Bigger, in the meanwhile, and all his furious kin, serve only to whet the notorious national taste for the sensational and to reinforce all that we now find it necessary to believe. It is not Bigger whom we fear, since his appearance among us makes our victory certain. It is the others, who smile, who go to church, who give no cause for complaint, whom we sometimes consider with amusement, with pity, even with affection—and in whose faces we sometimes surprise the merest arrogant hint of hatred, the faintest, withdrawn, speculative shadow of contempt—who make us uneasy; whom we cajole, threaten, flatter, fear; who to us remain unknown, though we are not (we feel with both relief and hostility and with bottomless confusion) unknown to them. It is out of our reaction to these hewers of wood and drawers of water that our image of Bigger was created.

It is this image, living yet, which we perpetually seek to evade with good works; and this image which makes of all our good works an intolerable mockery. The "nigger," black, benighted, brutal, consumed with hatred as we are consumed with guilt, cannot be thus blotted out. He stands at our shoulders when we give our maid her wages, it is his hand which we fear we are taking when struggling to communicate with the current "intelligent" Negro, his stench, as it were, which fills our mouths with salt as the monument is unveiled in honor of the latest Negro leader. Each generation has shouted behind him, Nigger! as he walked our streets; it is he whom we would rather our sisters did not marry; he is banished into the vast and wailing outer darkness whenever we speak of the "purity" of our women, of the "sanctity" of our homes, of "American" ideals. What is more, he knows it. He is indeed the "native son": he is the "nigger." Let us refrain from inquiring at the moment whether or not he actually exists; for we believe that he exists. Whenever we encounter him amongst us in the flesh, our faith is made perfect and his necessary and bloody end is executed with a mystical ferocity of joy.

But there is a complementary faith among the damned which involves their gathering of the stones with which those who walk in the light shall stone them; or there exists among the intolerably degraded the perverse and powerful desire to force into the arena of the actual those fantastic crimes of which they have been accused, achieving their vengeance and their own destruction through making the nightmare real. The American image of the Negro lives also in the Negro's heart; and when he has surrendered to this image life has no other possible reality. Then he, like the

white enemy with whom he will be locked one day in mortal struggle, has
no means save this of asserting his identity. This is why Bigger's murder of
Mary can be referred to as an "act of creation" and why, once this murder
has been committed, he can feel for the first time that he is living fully and
deeply as a man was meant to live. And there is, I should think, no Negro
living in America who has not felt, briefly or for long periods, with anguish
sharp or dull, in varying degrees and to varying effect, simple, naked and
unanswerable hatred; who has not wanted to smash any white face he may
encounter in a day, to violate, out of motives of the cruelest vengeance,
their women, to break the bodies of all white people and bring them low, as
low as that dust into which he himself has been and is being trampled; no
Negro, finally, who has not had to make his own precarious adjustment to
the "nigger" who surrounds him and to the "nigger" in himself.

Yet the adjustment must be made—rather, it must be attempted, the tension perpetually sustained—for without this he has surrendered his birthright as a man no less than his birthright as a black man. The entire
universe is then peopled only with his enemies, who are not only white
men armed with rope and rifle, but his own far-flung and contemptible
kinsmen. Their blackness is his degradation and it is their stupid and passive endurance which makes his end inevitable.

Bigger dreams of some black man who will weld all blacks together into
a mighty fist, and feels, in relation to his family, that perhaps they had to
live as they did precisely because none of them had ever done anything,
right or wrong, which mattered very much. It is only he who, by an act of
murder, has burst the dungeon cell. He has made it manifest that *he* lives
and that his despised blood nourishes the passions of a man. He has forced
his oppressors to see the fruit of that oppression: and he feels, when his
family and his friends come to visit him in the death cell, that they should
not be weeping or frightened, that they should be happy, *proud* that he has
dared, through murder and now through his own imminent destruction, to
redeem their anger and humiliation, that he has hurled into the spiritless
obscurity of their lives the lamp of his passionate life and death. Henceforth, they may remember Bigger—who has died, as we may conclude, for
them. But they do not feel this; they only know that he has murdered two
women and precipitated a reign of terror; and that now he is to die in the
electric chair. They therefore weep and are honestly frightened—for which
Bigger despises them and wishes to "blot" them out. What is missing in his
situation and in the representation of his psychology—which makes his situation false and his psychology incapable of development—is any revelatory apprehension of Bigger as one of the Negro's realities or as one of the
Negro's roles. This failure is part of the previously noted failure to convey
any sense of Negro life as a continuing and complex group reality. Bigger,
who cannot function therefore as a reflection of the social illness, having,
as it were, no society to reflect, likewise refuses to function on the loftier
level of the Christ-symbol. His kinsmen are quite right to weep and be
frightened, even to be appalled: for it is not his love for them or for himself
which causes him to die, but his hatred and his self-hatred; he does not
redeem the pains of a despised people, but reveals, on the contrary, nothing more than his own fierce bitterness at having been born one of them. In

this also he is the "native son," his progress determinable by the speed with which the distance increases between himself and the auction-block and all that the auction-block implies. To have penetrated this phenomenon, this inward contention of love and hatred, blackness and whiteness, would have given him a stature more nearly human and an end more nearly tragic; and would have given us a document more profoundly and genuinely bitter and less harsh with an anger which is, on the one hand, exhibited and, on the other hand, denied.

Native Son finds itself at length so trapped by the American image of Negro life and by the American necessity to find the ray of hope that it cannot pursue its own implications. This is why Bigger must be at the last redeemed, to be received, if only by rhetoric, into that community of phantoms which is our tenaciously held ideal of the happy social life. It is the socially conscious whites who receive him—the Negroes being capable of no such objectivity—and we have, by way of illustration, that lamentable scene in which Jan, Mary's lover, forgives him for her murder; and, carrying the explicit burden of the novel, Max's long speech to the jury. This speech, which really ends the book, is one of the most desperate performances in American fiction. It is the question of Bigger's humanity which is at stake, the relationship in which he stands to all other Americans—and, by implication, to all people—and it is precisely this question which it cannot clarify, with which it cannot, in fact, come to any coherent terms. He is the monster created by the American republic, the present awful sum of generations of oppression; but to say that he is a monster is to fall into the trap of making him subhuman and he must, therefore, be made representative of a way of life which is real and human in precise ratio to the degree to which it seems to us monstrous and strange. It seems to me that this idea carries, implicitly, a most remarkable confession: that is, that Negro life is in fact as debased and impoverished as our theology claims; and, further, that the use to which Wright puts this idea can only proceed from the assumption—not entirely unsound—that Americans, who evade, so far as possible, all genuine experience, have therefore no way of assessing the experience of others and no way of establishing themselves in relation to any way of life which is not their own. The privacy or obscurity of Negro life makes that life capable, in our imaginations, of producing anything at all; and thus the idea of Bigger's monstrosity can be presented without fear of contradiction, since no American has the knowledge or authority to contest it and no Negro has the voice. It is an idea, which, in the framework of the novel, is dignified by the possibility it promptly affords of presenting Bigger as the herald of disaster, the danger signal of a more bitter time to come when not Bigger alone but all his kindred will rise, in the name of the many thousands who have perished in fire and flood and by rope and torture, to demand their rightful vengeance.

But it is not quite fair, it seems to me, to exploit the national innocence in this way. The idea of Bigger as a warning boomerangs not only because it is quite beyond the limit of probability that Negroes in America will ever achieve the means of wreaking vengeance upon the state but also because it cannot be said that they have any desire to do so. Native Son does not convey the altogether savage paradox of the American Negro's situation, of which the social reality which we prefer with such hopeful superficiality to study is but, as it were, the shadow. It is not simply the relationship of oppressed to oppressor, of master to slave, nor is it motivated merely by hatred; it is also, literally and morally, a *blood* relationship, perhaps the most profound reality of the American experience, and we cannot begin to unlock it until we accept how very much it contains of the force and anguish and terror of love.

Negroes are Americans and their destiny is the country's destiny. They have no other experience besides their experience on this continent and it is an experience which cannot be rejected, which yet remains to be embraced. If, as I believe, no American Negro exists who does not have his private Bigger Thomas living in the skull, then what most significantly fails to be illuminated here is the paradoxical adjustment which is perpetually made, the Negro being compelled to accept the fact that this dark and dangerous and unloved stranger is part of himself forever. Only this recognition sets him in any wise free and it is this, this necessary ability to contain and even, in the most honorable sense of the word, to *exploit* the "nigger," which lends to Negro life its high element of the ironic and which causes the most well-meaning of their American critics to make such exhilarating errors when attempting to understand them. To present Bigger as a warning is simply to reinforce the American guilt and fear concerning him, it is most forcefully to limit him to that previously mentioned social arena in which he has no human validity, it is simply to condemn him to death. For he has always been a warning, he represents the evil, the sin and suffering which we are compelled to reject. It is useless to say to the courtroom in which this heathen sits on trial that he is their responsibility, their creation, and his crimes are theirs; and that they ought, therefore, to allow him to live, to make articulate to himself behind the walls of prison the meaning of his existence. The meaning of his existence has already been most adequately expressed, nor does anyone wish, particularly not in the name of democracy, to think of it any more; as for the possibility of articulation, it is this possibility which above all others we most dread. Moreover, the courtroom, judge, jury, witnesses and spectators, recognize immediately that Bigger is their creation and they recognize this not only with hatred and fear and guilt and the resulting fury of self-righteousness but also with that morbid fullness of pride mixed with horror with which one regards the extent and power of one's wickedness. They know that death is his portion, that he runs to death; coming from darkness and dwelling in darkness, he must be, as often as he rises, banished, lest the entire planet be engulfed. And they know, finally, that they do not wish to forgive him and that he does not wish to be forgiven; that he dies, hating them, scorning that appeal which they cannot make to that irrecoverable humanity of his which cannot hear it; and that he *wants* to die because he glories in his hatred and prefers, like Lucifer, rather to rule in hell than serve in heaven.

For, bearing in mind the premise on which the life of such a man is based, *i.e.*, that black is the color of damnation, this is his only possible end. It is the only death which will allow him a kind of dignity or even, however horribly, a kind of beauty. To tell this story, no more than a single aspect of the story of the "nigger," is inevitably and richly to become involved with the force of life and legend, how each perpetually assumes the guise of the other, creating that dense, many-sided and shifting reality which is the world we live in and the world we make. To tell his story is to begin to liberate us from his image and it is, for the first time, to clothe this phantom with flesh and blood, to deepen, by our understanding of him and his relationship to us, our understanding of ourselves and of all men.

But this is not the story which *Native Son* tells, for we find here merely, repeated in anger, the story which we have told in pride. Nor, since the implications of this anger are evaded, are we ever confronted with the actual or potential significance of our pride; which is why we fall, with such a positive glow of recognition, upon Max's long and bitter summing up. It is addressed to those among us of good will and it seems to say that, though there are whites and blacks among us who hate each other, we will not; there are those who are betrayed by greed, by guilt, by blood lust, but not we; we will set our faces against them and join hands and walk together into that dazzling future when there will be no white or black. This is the dream of all liberal men, a dream not at all dishonorable, but, nevertheless, a dream. For, let us join hands on this mountain as we may, the battle is elsewhere. It proceeds far from us in the heat and horror and pain of life itself where all men are betrayed by greed and guilt and blood-lust and where no one's hands are clean. Our good will, from which we yet expect such power to transform us, is thin, passionless, strident: its roots, examined, lead us back to our forebears, whose assumption it was that the black man, to become truly human and acceptable, must first become like us. This assumption once accepted, the Negro in America can only acquiesce in the obliteration of his own personality, the distortion and debasement of his own experience, surrendering to those forces which reduce the person to anonymity and which make themselves manifest daily all over the darkening world.

1951

Stranger in the Village

From all available evidence no black man had ever set foot in this tiny Swiss village before I came. I was told before arriving that I would probably be a "sight" for the village; I took this to mean that people of my complexion were rarely seen in Switzerland, and also that city people are always something of a "sight" outside of the city. It did not occur to me—possibly because I am an American—that there could be people anywhere who had never seen a Negro.

It is a fact that cannot be explained on the basis of the inaccessibility of the village. The village is very high, but it is only four hours from Milan and three hours from Lausanne. It is true that it is virtually unknown. Few people making plans for a holiday would elect to come here. On the other hand, the villagers are able, presumably, to come and go as they please— which they do: to another town at the foot of the mountain, with a population of approximately five thousand, the nearest place to see a movie or go to the bank. In the village there is no movie house, no bank, no library, no theater; very few radios, one jeep, one station wagon; and, at the moment, one typewriter, mine, an invention which the woman next door to me here had never seen. There are about six hundred people living here, all Catholic—I conclude this from the fact that the Catholic church is open all year round, whereas the Protestant chapel, set off on a hill a little removed from the village, is open only in the summertime when the tourists arrive. There are four or five hotels, all closed now, and four or five *bistros*,[1] of which, however, only two do any business during the winter. These two do not do a great deal, for life in the village seems to end around nine or ten o'clock. There are a few stores, butcher, baker, *épicerie*,[2] a hardware store, and a money-changer—who cannot change travelers' checks, but must send them down to the bank, an operation which takes two or three days. There is something called the *Ballet Haus*,[3] closed in the winter and used for God knows what, certainly not ballet, during the summer. There seems to be only one schoolhouse in the village, and this for the quite young children; I suppose this to mean that their older brothers and sisters at some point descend from these mountains in order to complete their education—possibly, again, to the town just below. The landscape is absolutely forbidding, mountains towering on all four sides, ice and snow as far as the eye can reach. In this white wilderness, men and women and children move all day, carrying washing, wood, buckets of milk or water, sometimes skiing on Sunday afternoons. All week long boys and young men are to be seen shoveling snow off the rooftops, or dragging wood down from the forest in sleds.

The village's only real attraction, which explains the tourist season, is the hot spring water. A disquietingly high proportion of these tourists are cripples, or semi-cripples, who come year after year—from other parts of Switzerland, usually—to take the waters. This lends the village, at the height of the season, a rather terrifying air of sanctity, as though it were a lesser Lourdes.[4] There is often something beautiful, there is always something awful, in the spectacle of a person who has lost one of his faculties, a faculty he never questioned until it was gone, and who struggles to recover it. Yet people remain people, on crutches or indeed on deathbeds; and wherever I passed, the first summer I was here, among the native villagers or among the lame, a wind passed with me—of astonishment, curiosity, amusement, and outrage. That first summer I stayed two weeks and never intended to return. But I did return in the winter, to work; the village offers, obviously, no distractions whatever and has the further advantage of being extremely cheap. Now it is winter again, a year later, and I am here again. Everyone in the village knows my name, though they scarcely ever use it, knows that I come from America—though, this, apparently, they will never really believe: black men come from Africa—and everyone knows that I am the friend of the son of a woman who was born here, and that I am staying in their chalet. But I remain as much a stranger today as I was the first day I arrived, and the children shout *Neger!*[5] *Neger!* as I walk along the streets.

It must be admitted that in the beginning I was far too shocked to have

---

1. Bar or café (French).
2. Grocery store (French).
3. Ballet house (German, literal trans.).
4. A town in southwest France, which is the site of a famous Catholic shrine.
5. Negro (German).

any real reaction. In so far as I reacted at all, I reacted by trying to be pleas-ant—it being a great part of the American Negro's education (long before he goes to school) that he must make people "like" him. This smile-and-the-world-smiles-with-you routine worked about as well in this situation as it had in the situation for which it was designed, which is to say that it did not work at all. No one, after all, can be liked whose human weight and complexity cannot be, or has not been, admitted. My smile was simply an-other unheard-of phenomenon which allowed them to see my teeth—they did not, really, see my smile and I began to think that, should I take to snarling, no one would notice any difference. All of the physical character-istics of the Negro which had caused me, in America, a very different and almost forgotten pain were nothing less than miraculous—or infernal—in the eyes of the village people. Some thought my hair was the color of tar, that it had the texture of wire, or the texture of cotton. It was jocularly sug-gested that I might let it all grow long and make myself a winter coat. If I sat in the sun for more than five minutes some daring creature was certain to come along and gingerly put his fingers on my hair, as though he were afraid of an electric shock, or put his hand on my hand, astonished that the color did not rub off. In all of this, in which it must be conceded there was the charm of genuine wonder and in which there was certainly no element of intentional unkindness, there was yet no suggestion that I was human: I was simply a living wonder.

I knew that they did not mean to be unkind, and I know it now; it is necessary, nevertheless, for me to repeat this to myself each time that I walk out of the chalet. The children who shout Neger! have no way of knowing the echoes this sound raises in me. They are brimming with good humor and the more daring swell with pride when I stop to speak with them. Just the same, there are days when I cannot pause and smile, when I have no heart to play with them; when, indeed, I mutter sourly to myself, exactly as I muttered on the streets of a city these children have never seen, when I was no bigger than these children are now: Your mother was a nigger. Joyce[6] is right about history being a nightmare—but it may be the night-mare from which no one can awaken. People are trapped in history and history is trapped in them.

There is a custom in the village—I am told it is repeated in many vil-lages—of "buying" African natives for the purpose of converting them to Christianity. There stands in the church all year round a small box with a slot for money, decorated with a black figurine, and into this box the villag-ers drop their francs. During the carnaval which precedes Lent,[7] two vil-lage children have their faces blackened—out of which bloodless darkness their blue eyes shine like ice—and fantastic horsehair wigs are placed on their blond heads; thus disguised, they solicit among the villagers for money for the missionaries in Africa. Between the box in the church and the blackened children, the village "bought" last year six or eight African natives. This was reported to me with pride by the wife of one of the bistro

6. James Joyce (1882–1941), Irish novelist and poet.
7. A time of penitence observed by Christians that begins on Ash Wednesday and ends on Easter;

sometimes observed by fasting. "Carnaval": or car-nival, celebrated before Lent and similar to Mardi Gras.

owners and I was careful to express astonishment and pleasure at the solicitude shown by the village for the souls of black folk. The *bistro* owner's wife beamed with a pleasure far more genuine than my own and seemed to feel that I might now breathe more easily concerning the souls of at least six of my kinsmen.

I tried not to think of these so lately baptized kinsmen, of the price paid for them, or the peculiar price they themselves would pay, and said nothing about my father, who having taken his own conversion too literally never, at bottom, forgave the white world (which he described as heathen) for having saddled him with a Christ in whom, to judge at least from their treatment of him, they themselves no longer believed. I thought of white men arriving for the first time in an African village, strangers there, as I am a stranger here, and tried to imagine the astounded populace touching their hair and marveling at the color of their skin. But there is a great difference between being the first white man to be seen by Africans and being the first black man to be seen by whites. The white man takes the astonishment as tribute, for he arrives to conquer and to convert the natives, whose inferiority in relation to himself is not even to be questioned; whereas I, without a thought of conquest, find myself among a people whose culture controls me, has even, in a sense, created me, people who have cost me more in anguish and rage than they will ever know, who yet do not even know of my existence. The astonishment with which I might have greeted them, should they have stumbled into my African village a few hundred years ago, might have rejoiced their hearts. But the astonishment with which they greet me today can only poison mine.

And this is so despite everything I may do to feel differently, despite my friendly conversations with the *bistro* owner's wife, despite their three-year-old son who has at last become my friend, despite the *saluts* and *bonsoirs*[8] which I exchange with people as I walk, despite the fact that I know that no individual can be taken to task for what history is doing, or has done. I say that the culture of these people controls me—but they can scarcely be held responsible for European culture. America comes out of Europe, but these people have never seen America, nor have most of them seen more of Europe than the hamlet at the foot of their mountain. Yet they move with an authority which I shall never have; and they regard me, quite rightly, not only as a stranger in their village but as a suspect latecomer, bearing no credentials, to everything they have—however unconsciously—inherited.

For this village, even were it incomparably more remote and incredibly more primitive, is the West, the West onto which I have been so strangely grafted. These people cannot be, from the point of view of power, strangers anywhere in the world; they have made the modern world, in effect, even if they do not know it. The most illiterate among them is related, in a way that I am not, to Dante, Shakespeare, Michelangelo, Aeschylus, Da Vinci, Rembrandt, and Racine; the cathedral at Chartres[9] says something to them

8. Good evenings (French). "*Saluts*": greetings (French).
9. A city in western France. Dante (1265–1321), Italian poet. William Shakespeare (1564–1616), English poet and playwright. Michelangelo (1475–1564), Italian sculptor and painter. Aeschylus (525–456 B.C.), Athenian tragic dramatist. Leonardo da Vinci (1452–1519), Italian sculptor, painter, and scientist. Rembrandt (1607–1669), Dutch painter. Jean Racine (1639–1695), French tragic poet and dramatist.

which it cannot say to me, as indeed would New York's Empire State Building, should anyone here ever see it. Out of their hymns and dances come Beethoven and Bach.[1] Go back a few centuries and they are in their full glory—but I am in Africa, watching the conquerors arrive.

The rage of the disesteemed is personally fruitless, but it is also absolutely inevitable; this rage, so generally discounted, so little understood even among the people whose daily bread it is, is one of the things that makes history. Rage can only with difficulty, and never entirely, be brought under the domination of the intelligence and is therefore not susceptible to any arguments whatever. This is a fact which ordinary representatives of the *Herrenvolk*,[2] having never felt this rage and being unable to imagine it, quite fail to understand. Also, rage cannot be hidden, it can only be dissembled. This dissembling deludes the thoughtless, and strengthens rage and adds, to rage, contempt. There are, no doubt, as many ways of coping with the resulting complex of tensions as there are black men in the world, but no black man can hope ever to be entirely liberated from this internal warfare—rage, dissembling, and contempt having inevitably accompanied his first realization of the power of white men. What is crucial here is that, since white men represent in the black man's world so heavy a weight, white men have for black men a reality which is far from being reciprocal; and hence all black men have toward all white men an attitude which is designed, really, either to rob the white man of the jewel of his naïveté, or else to make it cost him dear.

The black man insists, by whatever means he finds at his disposal, that the white man cease to regard him as an exotic rarity and recognize him as a human being. This is a very charged and difficult moment, for there is a great deal of will power involved in the white man's naïveté. Most people are not naturally reflective any more than they are naturally malicious, and the white man prefers to keep the black man at a certain human remove because it is easier for him thus to preserve his simplicity and avoid being called to account for crimes committed by his forefathers, or his neighbors. He is inescapably aware, nevertheless, that he is in a better position in the world than black men are, nor can he quite put to death the suspicion that he is hated by black men therefore. He does not wish to be hated, neither does he wish to change places, and at this point in his uneasiness he can scarcely avoid having recourse to those legends which white men have created about black men, the most usual effect of which is that the white man finds himself enmeshed, so to speak, in his own language which describes hell, as well as the attributes which lead one to hell, as being as black as night.

Every legend, moreover, contains its residuum of truth, and the root function of language is to control the universe by describing it. It is of quite considerable significance that black men remain, in the imagination, and in over-whelming numbers in fact, beyond the disciplines of salvation; and this despite the fact that the West has been "buying" African natives for centuries. There is, I should hazard, an instantaneous necessity to be di-

---

1. Johann Sebastian Bach (1685–1750), German composer and instrumentalist. Ludwig van Beetho-   ven (1770–1827), German composer.
2. Master race (German).

vorced from this so visibly unsaved stranger, in whose heart, moreover, one cannot guess what dreams of vengeance are being nourished; and, at the same time, there are few things on earth more attractive than the idea of the unspeakable liberty which is allowed the unredeemed. When, beneath the black mask, a human being begins to make himself felt one cannot escape a certain awful wonder as to what kind of human being it is. What one's imagination makes of other people is dictated, of course, by the laws of one's own personality and it is one of the ironies of black-white relations that, by means of what the white man imagines the black man to be, the black man is enabled to know who the white man is.

I have said, for example, that I am as much a stranger in this village today as I was the first summer I arrived, but this is not quite true. The villagers wonder less about the texture of my hair than they did then, and wonder rather more about me. And the fact that their wonder now exists on another level is reflected in their attitudes and in their eyes. There are the children who make those delightful, hilarious, sometimes astonishingly grave overtures of friendship in the unpredictable fashion of children; other children, having been taught that the devil is a black man, scream in genuine anguish as I approach. Some of the older women never pass without a friendly greeting, never pass, indeed, if it seems that they will be able to engage me in conversation; other women look down or look away or rather contemptuously smirk. Some of the men drink with me and suggest that I learn how to ski—partly, I gather, because they cannot imagine what I would look like on skis—and want to know if I am married, and ask questions about my *métier*. But some of the men have accused *le sale nègre*[3]— behind my back—of stealing wood and there is already in the eyes of some of them that peculiar, intent, paranoiac malevolence which one sometimes surprises in the eyes of American white men when, out walking with their Sunday girl, they see a Negro male approach.

There is a dreadful abyss between the streets of this village and the streets of the city in which I was born, between the children who shout *Neger!* today and those who shouted *Nigger!* yesterday—the abyss is experience, the American experience. The syllable hurled behind me today expresses, above all, wonder: I am a stranger here. But I am not a stranger in America and the same syllable riding on the American air expresses the war my presence has occasioned in the American soul.

For this village brings home to me this fact: that there was a day, and not really a very distant day, when Americans were scarcely Americans at all but discontented Europeans, facing a great unconquered continent and strolling, say, into a marketplace and seeing black men for the first time. The shock this spectacle afforded is suggested, surely, by the promptness with which they decided that these black men were not really men but cattle. It is true that the necessity on the part of the settlers of the New World of reconciling their moral assumptions with the fact—and the necessity—of slavery enhanced immensely the charm of this idea, and it is also true that this idea expresses, with a truly American bluntness, the attitude which to varying extents all masters have had toward all slaves.

3. The dirty nigger (French). "*Métier*": profession (French).

But between all former slaves and slave-owners and the drama which begins for Americans over three hundred years ago at Jamestown,[4] there are at least two differences to be observed. The American Negro slave could not suppose, for one thing, as slaves in past epochs had supposed and often done, that he would ever be able to wrest the power from his master's hands. This was a supposition which the modern era, which was to bring about such vast changes in the aims and dimensions of power, put to death; it only begins, in unprecedented fashion, and with dreadful implications, to be resurrected today. But even had this supposition persisted with undiminished force, the American Negro slave could not have used it to lend his condition dignity, for the reason that this supposition rests on another: that the slave in exile yet remains related to his past, has some means—if only in memory—of revering and sustaining the forms of his former life, is able, in short, to maintain his identity.

This was not the case with the American Negro slave. He is unique among the black men of the world in that his past was taken from him, almost literally, at one blow. One wonders what on earth the first slave found to say to the first dark child he bore. I am told that there are Haitians able to trace their ancestry back to African kings, but any American Negro wishing to go back so far will find his journey through time abruptly arrested by the signature on the bill of sale which served as the entrance paper for his ancestor. At the time—to say nothing of the circumstances—of the enslavement of the captive black man who was to become the American Negro, there was not the remotest possibility that he would ever take power from his master's hands. There was no reason to suppose that his situation would ever change, nor was there, shortly, anything to indicate that his situation had ever been different. It was his necessity, in the words of E. Franklin Frazier,[5] to find a "motive for living under American culture or die." The identity of the American Negro comes out of this extreme situation, and the evolution of this identity was a source of the most intolerable anxiety in the minds and the lives of his masters.

For the history of the American Negro is unique also in this: that the question of his humanity, and of his rights therefore as a human being, became a burning one for several generations of Americans, so burning a question that it ultimately became one of those used to divide the nation. It is out of this argument that the venom of the epithet *Nigger!* is derived. It is an argument which Europe has never had, and hence Europe quite sincerely fails to understand how or why the argument arose in the first place, why its effects are so frequently disastrous and always so unpredictable, why it refuses until today to be entirely settled. Europe's black possessions remained—and do remain—in Europe's colonies, at which remove they represented no threat whatever to European identity. If they posed any problem at all for the European conscience, it was a problem which remained comfortingly abstract: in effect, the black man, *as a man*, did not exist for Europe. But in America, even as a slave, he was an inescapable

---

4. Established (1607) in present-day Virginia, the site of the first permanent English settlement in the New World and the place where the first blacks landed in 1619.

5. Black educator and sociologist (1894–1962), a prolific writer on the black family and the development of a black middle class.

part of the general social fabric and no American could escape having an attitude toward him. Americans attempt until today to make an abstraction of the Negro, but the very nature of these abstractions reveals the tremendous effects the presence of the Negro has had on the American character.

When one considers the history of the Negro in America it is of the greatest importance to recognize that the moral beliefs of a person, or a people, are never really as tenuous as life—which is not moral—very often causes them to appear; these create for them a frame of reference and a necessary hope, the hope being that when life has done its worst they will be enabled to rise above themselves and to triumph over life. Life would scarcely be bearable if this hope did not exist. Again, even when the worst has been said, to betray a belief is not by any means to have put oneself beyond its power; the betrayal of a belief is not the same thing as ceasing to believe. If this were not so there would be no moral standards in the world at all. Yet one must also recognize that morality is based on ideas and that all ideas are dangerous—dangerous because ideas can only lead to action and where the action leads no man can say. And dangerous in this respect: that confronted with the impossibility of remaining faithful to one's beliefs, and the equal impossibility of becoming free of them, one can be driven to the most inhuman excesses. The ideas on which American beliefs are based are not, though Americans often seem to think so, ideas which originated in America. They came out of Europe. And the establishment of democracy on the American continent was scarcely as radical a break with the past as was the necessity, which Americans faced, of broadening this concept to include black men.

This was, literally, a hard necessity. It was impossible, for one thing, for Americans to abandon their beliefs, not only because these beliefs alone seemed able to justify the sacrifices they had endured and the blood that they had spilled, but also because these beliefs afforded them their only bulwark against a moral chaos as absolute as the physical chaos of the continent it was their destiny to conquer. But in the situation in which Americans found themselves, these beliefs threatened an idea which, whether or not one likes to think so, is the very warp and woof of the heritage of the West, the idea of white supremacy.

Americans have made themselves notorious by the shrillness and the brutality with which they have insisted on this idea, but they did not invent it; and it has escaped the world's notice that those very excesses of which Americans have been guilty imply a certain, unprecedented uneasiness over the idea's life and power, if not, indeed, the idea's validity. The idea of white supremacy rests simply on the fact that white men are the creators of civilization (the present civilization, which is the only one that matters; all previous civilizations are simply "contributions" to our own) and are therefore civilization's guardians and defenders. Thus it was impossible for Americans to accept the black man as one of themselves, for to do so was to jeopardize their status as white men. But not so to accept him was to deny his human reality, his human weight and complexity, and the strain of denying the overwhelmingly undeniable forced Americans into rationalizations so fantastic that they approached the pathological.

At the root of the American Negro problem is the necessity of the American white man to find a way of living with the Negro in order to be able to live with himself. And the history of this problem can be reduced to the means used by Americans—lynch law and law, segregation and legal acceptance, terrorization and concession—either to come to terms with this necessity, or to find a way around it, or (most usually) to find a way of doing both these things at once. The resulting spectacle, at once foolish and dreadful, led someone to make the quite accurate observation that "the Negro-in-America is a form of insanity which overtakes white men."

In this long battle, a battle by no means finished, the unforeseeable effects of which will be felt by many future generations, the white man's motive was the protection of his identity; the black man was motivated by the need to establish an identity. And despite the terrorization which the Negro in America endured and endures sporadically until today, despite the cruel and totally inescapable ambivalence of his status in his country, the battle for his identity has long ago been won. He is not a visitor to the West, but a citizen there, an American; as American as the Americans who despise him, the Americans who fear him, the Americans who love him—the Americans who became less than themselves, or rose to be greater than themselves by virtue of the fact that the challenge he represented was inescapable. He is perhaps the only black man in the world whose relationship to white men is more terrible, more subtle, and more meaningful than the relationship of bitter possessed to uncertain possessor. His survival depended, and his development depends, on his ability to turn his peculiar status in the Western world to his own advantage and, it may be, to the very great advantage of that world. It remains for him to fashion out of his experience that which will give him sustenance, and a voice.

The cathedral at Chartres, I have said, says something to the people of this village which it cannot say to me; but it is important to understand that this cathedral says something to me which it cannot say to them. Perhaps they are struck by the power of the spires, the glory of the windows; but they have known God, after all, longer than I have known him, and in a different way, and I am terrified by the slippery bottomless well to be found in the crypt, down which heretics were hurled to death, and by the obscene, inescapable gargoyles jutting out of the stone and seeming to say that God and the devil can never be divorced. I doubt that the villagers think of the devil when they face a cathedral because they have never been identified with the devil. But I must accept the status which myth, if nothing else, gives me in the West before I can hope to change the myth.

Yet, if the American Negro has arrived at his identity by virtue of the absoluteness of his estrangement from his past, American white men still nourish the illusion that there is some means of recovering the European innocence, of returning to a state in which black men do not exist. This is one of the greatest errors Americans can make. The identity they fought so hard to protect has, by virtue of that battle, undergone a change: Americans are as unlike any other white people in the world as it is possible to be. I do not think, for example, that it is too much to suggest that the American vision of the world—which allows so little reality, generally speaking, for any of the darker forces in human life, which tends until today to paint moral issues in glaring black and white—owes a great deal to the battle waged by Americans to maintain between themselves and black men a human separation which could not be bridged. It is only now beginning to be borne in on us—very faintly, it must be admitted, very slowly, and very much against our will—that this vision of the world is dangerously inaccurate, and perfectly useless. For it protects our moral high-mindedness at the terrible expense of weakening our grasp of reality. People who shut their eyes to reality simply invite their own destruction, and anyone who insists on remaining in a state of innocence long after that innocence is dead turns himself into a monster.

The time has come to realize that the interracial drama acted out on the American continent has not only created a new black man, it has created a new white man, too. No road whatever will lead Americans back to the simplicity of this European village where white men still have the luxury of looking on me as a stranger. I am not, really, a stranger any longer for any American alive. One of the things that distinguishes Americans from other people is that no other people has ever been so deeply involved in the lives of black men, and vice versa. This fact faced, with all its implications, it can be seen that the history of the American Negro problem is not merely shameful, it is also something of an achievement. For even when the worst has been said, it must also be added that the perpetual challenge posed by this problem was always, somehow, perpetually met. It is precisely this black-white experience which may prove of indispensable value to us in the world we face today. This world is white no longer, and it will never be white again.

1953

Notes of a Native Son

On the 29th of July, in 1943, my father died. On the same day, a few hours later, his last child was born. Over a month before this, while all our energies were concentrated in waiting for these events, there had been, in Detroit, one of the bloodiest race riots of the century. A few hours after my father's funeral, while he lay in state in the undertaker's chapel, a race riot broke out in Harlem. On the morning of the 3rd of August, we drove my father to the graveyard through a wilderness of smashed plate glass.

The day of my father's funeral had also been my nineteenth birthday. As we drove him to the graveyard, the spoils of injustice, anarchy, discontent, and hatred were all around us. It seemed to me that God himself had devised, to mark my father's end, the most sustained and brutally dissonant of codas. And it seemed to me, too, that the violence which rose all about us as my father left the world had been devised as a corrective for the pride of his eldest son. I had declined to believe in that apocalypse which had been central to my father's vision; very well, life seemed to be saying, here is something that will certainly pass for an apocalypse until the real thing comes along. I had inclined to be contemptuous of my father for the conditions of his life, for the conditions of our lives. When his life had ended I began to wonder about that life and also, in a new way, to be apprehensive about my own.

I had not known my father very well. We had got on badly, partly because we shared, in our different fashions, the vice of stubborn pride. When he was dead I realized that I had hardly ever spoken to him. When he had been dead a long time I began to wish I had. It seems to be typical of life in America, where opportunities, real and fancied, are thicker than anywhere else on the globe, that the second generation has no time to talk to the first. No one, including my father, seems to have known exactly how old he was, but his mother had been born during slavery. He was of the first generation of free men. He, along with thousands of other Negroes, came North after 1919 and I was part of that generation which had never seen the landscape of what Negroes sometimes call the Old Country.

He had been born in New Orleans and had been a quite young man there during the time that Louis Armstrong, a boy, was running errands for the dives and honky-tonks of what was always presented to me as one of the most wicked of cities—to this day, whenever I think of New Orleans, I also helplessly think of Sodom and Gomorrah.[1] My father never mentioned Louis Armstrong,[2] except to forbid us to play his records; but there was a picture of him on our wall for a long time. One of my father's strong-willed female relatives had placed it there and forbade my father to take it down. He never did, but he eventually maneuvered her out of the house and when, some years later, she was in trouble and near death, he refused to do anything to help her.

He was, I think, very handsome. I gather this from photographs and from my own memories of him, dressed in his Sunday best and on his way to preach a sermon somewhere, when I was little. Handsome, proud, and ingrown, "like a toe-nail," somebody said. But he looked to me, as I grew older, like pictures I had seen of African tribal chieftains: he really should have been naked, with war-paint on and barbaric mementos, standing among spears. He could be chilling in the pulpit and indescribably cruel in his personal life and he was certainly the most bitter man I have ever met; yet it must be said that there was something else in him, buried in him, which lent him his tremendous power and, even, a rather crushing charm. It had something to do with his blackness, I think—he was very black—with his blackness and his beauty, and with the fact that he knew that he was black but did not know that he was beautiful. He claimed to be proud of his blackness but it had also been the cause of much humiliation and it had fixed bleak boundaries to his life. He was not a young man when we were growing up and he had already suffered many kinds of ruin; in his outrageously demanding and protective way he loved his children, who were black like him and menaced, like him; and all these things sometimes showed in his face when he tried, never to my knowledge with any success, to establish contact with any of us. When he took one of his children on his knee to play, the child always became fretful and began to cry; when he tried to help one of us with our homework the absolutely unabating tension which emanated from him caused our minds and our tongues to become paralyzed, so that he, scarcely knowing why, flew into a rage and the child,

---

1. Cities of ancient Palestine; according to Genesis 19:24–28, they were destroyed by fire because of vice and corruption.

2. Jazz trumpeter and singer (1900–1971), who was famous for his innovative playing style and gravelly voice.

not knowing why, was punished. If it ever entered his head to bring a surprise home for his children, it was, almost unfailingly, the wrong surprise and even the big watermelons he often brought home on his back in the summertime led to the most appalling scenes. I do not remember, in all those years, that one of his children was ever glad to see him come home. From what I was able to gather of his early life, it seemed that this inability to establish contact with other people had always marked him and had been one of the things which had driven him out of New Orleans. There was something in him, therefore, groping and tentative, which was never expressed and which was buried with him. One saw it most clearly when he was facing new people and hoping to impress them. But he never did, not for long. We went from church to smaller and more improbable church, he found himself in less and less demand as a minister, and by the time he died none of his friends had come to see him for a long time. He had lived and died in an intolerable bitterness of spirit and it frightened me, as we drove him to the graveyard through those unquiet, ruined streets, to see how powerful and overflowing this bitterness could be and to realize that this bitterness now was mine.

When he died I had been away from home for a little over a year. In that year I had had time to become aware of the meaning of all my father's bitter warnings, had discovered the secret of his proudly pursed lips and rigid carriage: I had discovered the weight of white people in the world. I saw that this had been for my ancestors and now would be for me an awful thing to live with and that the bitterness which had helped to kill my father could also kill me.

He had been ill a long time—in the mind, as we now realized, reliving instances of his fantastic intransigence in the new light of his affliction and endeavoring to feel a sorrow for him which never, quite, came true. We had not known that he was being eaten up by paranoia, and the discovery that his cruelty, to our bodies and our minds, had been one of the symptoms of his illness was not, then, enough to enable us to forgive him. The younger children felt, quite simply, relief that he would not be coming home anymore. My mother's observation that it was he, after all, who had kept them alive all these years meant nothing because the problems of keeping children alive are not real for children. The older children felt, with my father gone, that they could invite their friends to the house without fear that their friends would be insulted or, as had sometimes happened with me, being told that their friends were in league with the devil and intended to rob our family of everything we owned. (I didn't fail to wonder, and it made me hate him, what on earth we owned that anybody else would want.)

His illness was beyond all hope of healing before anyone realized that he was ill. He had always been so strange and had lived, like a prophet, in such unimaginably close communion with the Lord that his long silences which were punctuated by moans and hallelujahs and snatches of old songs while he sat at the living-room window never seemed odd to us. It was not until he refused to eat because, he said, his family was trying to poison him that my mother was forced to accept as a fact what had, until then, been only an unwilling suspicion. When he was committed, it was discovered that he had tuberculosis and, as it turned out, the disease of his mind allowed the disease of his body to destroy him. For the doctors could not force him to eat, either, and, though he was fed intravenously, it was clear from the beginning that there was no hope for him.

In my mind's eye I could see him, sitting at the window, locked up in his terrors; hating and fearing every living soul including his children who had betrayed him, too, by reaching towards the world which had despised him. There were nine of us. I began to wonder what it could have felt like for such a man to have had nine children whom he could barely feed. He used to make little jokes about our poverty, which never, of course, seemed very funny to us; they could not have seemed very funny to him, either, or else our all too feeble response to them would never have caused such rages. He spent great energy and achieved, to our chagrin, no small amount of success in keeping us away from the people who surrounded us, people who had all-night rent parties to which we listened when we should have been sleeping, people who cursed and drank and flashed razor blades on Lenox Avenue. He could not understand why, if they had so much energy to spare, they could not use it to make their lives better. He treated almost everybody on our block with a most uncharitable asperity and neither they, nor, of course, their children were slow to reciprocate.

The only white people who came to our house were welfare workers and bill collectors. It was almost always my mother who dealt with them, for my father's temper, which was at the mercy of his pride, was never to be trusted. It was clear that he felt their very presence in his home to be a violation: this was conveyed by his carriage, almost ludicrously stiff, and by his voice, harsh and vindictively polite. When I was around nine or ten I wrote a play which was directed by a young, white schoolteacher, a woman, who then took an interest in me, and gave me books to read and, in order to corroborate my theatrical bent, decided to take me to see what she somewhat tactlessly referred to as "real" plays. Theater-going was forbidden in our house, but, with the really cruel intuitiveness of a child, I suspected that the color of this woman's skin would carry the day for me. When, at school, she suggested taking me to the theater, I did not, as I might have done if she had been a Negro, find a way of discouraging her, but agreed that she should pick me up at my house one evening. I then, very cleverly, left all the rest to my mother, who suggested to my father, as I knew she would, that it would not be very nice to let such a kind woman make the trip for nothing. Also, since it was a schoolteacher, I imagine that my mother countered the idea of sin with the idea of "education," which word, even with my father, carried a kind of bitter weight.

Before the teacher came my father took me aside to ask *why* she was coming, what *interest* she could possibly have in our house, in a boy like me. I said I didn't know but I, too, suggested that it had something to do with education. And I understood that my father was waiting for me to say something—I didn't quite know what; perhaps that I wanted his protection against this teacher and her "education." I said none of these things and the teacher came and we went out. It was clear, during the brief interview in our living room, that my father was agreeing very much against his will and that he would have refused permission if he had dared. The fact that he did not dare caused me to despise him: I had no way of knowing that he was facing in that living room a wholly unprecedented and frightening situation.

Later, when my father had been laid off from his job, this woman became very important to us. She was really a very sweet and generous woman and went to a great deal of trouble to be of help to us, particularly during one awful winter. My mother called her by the highest name she knew: she said she was a "christian." My father could scarcely disagree but during the four or five years of our relatively close association he never trusted her and was always trying to surprise in her open, Midwestern face the genuine, cunningly hidden, and hideous motivation. In later years, particularly when it began to be clear that this "education" of mine was going to lead me to perdition, he became more explicit and warned me that my white friends in high school were not really my friends and that I would see, when I was older, how white people would do anything to keep a Negro down. Some of them could be nice, he admitted, but none of them were to be trusted and most of them were not even nice. The best thing was to have as little to do with them as possible. I did not feel this way and I was certain, in my innocence, that I never would.

But the year which preceded my father's death had made a great change in my life. I had been living in New Jersey, working in defense plants, working and living among southerners, white and black. I knew about the south, of course, and about how southerners treated Negroes and how they expected them to behave, but it had never entered my mind that anyone would look at me and expect *me* to behave that way. I learned in New Jersey that to be a Negro meant, precisely, that one was never looked at but was simply at the mercy of the reflexes the color of one's skin caused in other people. I acted in New Jersey as I had always acted, that is as though I thought a great deal of myself—I had to *act* that way—with results that were, simply, unbelievable. I had scarcely arrived before I had earned the enmity, which was extraordinarily ingenious, of all my superiors and nearly all my co-workers. In the beginning, to make matters worse, I simply did not know what was happening. I did not know what I had done, and I shortly began to wonder what *anyone* could possibly do, to bring about such unanimous, active, and unbearably vocal hostility. I knew about jim-crow[3] but I had never experienced it. I went to the same self-service restaurant three times and stood with all the Princeton boys before the counter, waiting for a hamburger and coffee; it was always an extraordinarily long time before anything was set before me; but it was not until the fourth visit that I learned that, in fact, nothing had ever been set before me: I had simply picked something up. Negroes were not served there, I was told, and they had been waiting for me to realize that I was always the only Negro present. Once I was told this, I determined to go there all the time. But now they were ready for me and, though some dreadful scenes were subsequently enacted in that restaurant, I never ate there again.

It was the same story all over New Jersey, in bars, bowling alleys, diners,

3. Systematic supression and segregation of blacks.

places to live. I was always being forced to leave, silently, or with mutual imprecations. I very shortly became notorious and children giggled behind me when I passed and their elders whispered or shouted—they really believed that I was mad. And it did begin to work on my mind, of course; I began to be afraid to go anywhere and to compensate for this I went places to which I really should not have gone and where, God knows, I had no desire to be. My reputation in town naturally enhanced my reputation at work and my working day became one long series of acrobatics designed to keep me out of trouble. I cannot say that these acrobatics succeeded. It began to seem that the machinery of the organization I worked for was turning over, day and night, with but one aim: to eject me. I was fired once, and contrived, with the aid of a friend from New York, to get back on the payroll; was fired again, and bounced back again. It took a while to fire me for the third time, but the third time took. There were no loopholes anywhere. There was not even any way of getting back inside the gates.

That year in New Jersey lives in my mind as though it were the year during which, having an unsuspected predilection for it, I first contracted some dread, chronic disease, the unfailing symptom of which is a kind of blind fever, a pounding in the skull and fire in the bowels. Once this disease is contracted, one can never be really carefree again, for the fever, without an instant's warning, can recur at any moment. It can wreck more important things than race relations. There is not a Negro alive who does not have this rage in his blood—one has the choice, merely, of living with it consciously or surrendering to it. As for me, this fever has recurred in me, and does, and will until the day I die.

My last night in New Jersey, a white friend from New York took me to the nearest big town, Trenton, to go to the movies and have a few drinks. As it turned out, he also saved me from, at the very least, a violent whipping. Almost every detail of that night stands out very clearly in my memory. I even remember the name of the movie we saw because its title impressed me as being so patly ironical. It was a movie about the German occupation of France, starring Maureen O'Hara and Charles Laughton and called *This Land Is Mine*. I remember the name of the diner we walked into when the movie ended: it was the "American Diner." When we walked in the counterman asked what we wanted and I remember answering with the casual sharpness which had become my habit: "We want a hamburger and a cup of coffee, what do you think we want?" I do not know why, after a year of such rebuffs, I so completely failed to anticipate his answer, which was, of course, "We don't serve Negroes here." This reply failed to discompose me, at least for the moment. I made some sardonic comment about the name of the diner and we walked out into the streets.

This was the time of what was called the "brown-out," when the lights in all American cities were very dim. When we re-entered the streets something happened to me which had the force of an optical illusion, or a nightmare. The streets were very crowded and I was facing north. People were moving in every direction but it seemed to me, in that instant, that all of the people I could see, and many more than that, were moving toward me, against me, and that everyone was white. I remember how their faces gleamed. And I felt, like a physical sensation, a *click* at the nape of my neck as though some interior string connecting my head to my body had been cut. I began to walk. I heard my friend call after me, but I ignored him. Heaven only knows what was going on in his mind, but he had the good sense not to touch me—I don't know what would have happened if he had—and to keep me in sight. I don't know what was going on in my mind, either; I certainly had no conscious plan. I wanted to do something to crush these white faces, which were crushing me. I walked for perhaps a block or two until I came to an enormous, glittering, and fashionable restaurant in which I knew not even the intercession of the Virgin would cause me to be served. I pushed through the doors and took the first vacant seat I saw, at a table for two, and waited.

I do not know how long I waited and I rather wonder, until today, what I could possibly have looked like. Whatever I looked like, I frightened the waitress who shortly appeared, and the moment she appeared all of my fury flowed towards her. I hated her for her white face, and for her great, as-tounded, frightened eyes. I felt that if she found a black man so frightening I would make her fright worth-while.

She did not ask me what I wanted, but repeated, as though she had learned it somewhere, "We don't serve Negroes here." She did not say it with the blunt, derisive hostility to which I had grown so accustomed, but, rather, with a note of apology in her voice, and fear. This made me colder and more murderous than ever. I felt I had to do something with my hands. I wanted her to come close enough for me to get her neck between my hands.

So I pretended not to have understood her, hoping to draw her closer. And she did step a very short step closer, with her pencil poised incongru-ously over her pad, and repeated the formula: ". . . don't serve Negroes here."

Somehow, with the repetition of that phrase, which was already ringing in my head like a thousand bells of a nightmare, I realized that she would never come any closer and that I would have to strike from a distance. There was nothing on the table but an ordinary water-mug half full of water, and I picked this up and hurled it with all my strength at her. She ducked and it missed her and shattered against the mirror behind the bar. And, with that sound, my frozen blood abruptly thawed, I returned from wherever I had been, I *saw*, for the first time, the restaurant, the people with their mouths open, already, as it seemed to me, rising as one man, and I realized what I had done, and where I was, and I was frightened. I rose and began running for the door. A round, potbellied man grabbed me by the nape of the neck just as I reached the doors and began to beat me about the face. I kicked him and got loose and ran into the streets. My friend whispered, "*Run!*" and I ran.

My friend stayed outside the restaurant long enough to misdirect my pursuers and the police, who arrived, he told me, at once. I do not know what I said to him when he came to my room that night. I could not have said much. I felt, in the oddest, most awful way, that I had somehow be-trayed him. I lived it over and over and over again, the way one relives an automobile accident after it has happened and one finds oneself alone and safe. I could not get over two facts, both equally difficult for the imagina-

tion to grasp, and one was that I could have been murdered. But the other
was that I had been ready to commit murder. I saw nothing very clearly but
I did see this: that my life, my *real* life, was in danger, and not from anything other people might do but from the hatred I carried in my own heart.

II

I had returned home around the second week in June—in great haste
because it seemed that my father's death and my mother's confinement
were both but a matter of hours. In the case of my mother, it soon became
clear that she had simply made a miscalculation. This had always been her
tendency and I don't believe that a single one of us arrived in the world, or
has since arrived anywhere else, on time. But none of us dawdled so intolerably about the business of being born as did my baby sister. We sometimes amused ourselves, during those endless, stifling weeks, by picturing
the baby sitting within in the safe, warm dark, bitterly regretting the necessity of becoming a part of our chaos and stubbornly putting it off as long as
possible. I understood her perfectly and congratulated her on showing such
good sense so soon. Death, however, sat as purposefully at my father's bedside as life stirred within my mother's womb and it was harder to understand why he so lingered in that long shadow. It seemed that he had bent,
and for a long time, too, all of his energies towards dying. Now death was
ready for him but my father held back.

All of Harlem, indeed, seemed to be infected by waiting. I had never
before known it to be so violently still. Racial tensions throughout this
country were exacerbated during the early years of the war, partly because
the labor market brought together hundreds of thousands of ill-prepared
people and partly because Negro soldiers, regardless of where they were
born, received their military training in the south. What happened in defense plants and army camps had repercussions, naturally, in every Negro
ghetto. The situation in Harlem had grown bad enough for clergymen, policemen, educators, politicians, and social workers to assert in one breath
that there was no "crime wave" and to offer, in the very next breath, suggestions as to how to combat it. These suggestions always seemed to involve
playgrounds, despite the fact that racial skirmishes were occurring in the
playgrounds, too. Playground or not, crime wave or not, the Harlem police
force had been augmented in March, and the unrest grew—perhaps, in
fact, partly as a result of the ghetto's instinctive hatred of policemen. Perhaps the most revealing news item, out of the steady parade of reports of
muggings, stabbings, shootings, assaults, gang wars, and accusations of police brutality, is the item concerning six Negro girls who set upon a white
girl in the subway because, as they all too accurately put it, she was stepping on their toes. Indeed she was, all over the nation.

I had never before been so aware of policemen, on foot, on horseback,
on corners, everywhere, always two by two. Nor had I ever been so aware of
small knots of people. They were on stoops and on corners and in doorways, and what was striking about them, I think, was that they did not seem
to be talking. Never, when I passed these groups, did the usual sound of a

curse or a laugh ring out and neither did there seem to be any hum of gossip. There was certainly, on the other hand, occurring between them communication extraordinarily intense. Another thing that was striking was the unexpected diversity of the people who made up these groups. Usually, for example, one would see a group of sharpies standing on the street corner, jiving the passing chicks; or a group of older men, usually, for some reason, in the vicinity of a barber shop, discussing baseball scores, or the numbers, or making rather chilling observations about women they had known. Women, in a general way, tended to be seen less often together—unless they were church women, or very young girls, or prostitutes met together for an unprofessional instant. But that summer I saw the strangest combinations: large, respectable, churchly matrons standing on the stoops or the corners with their hair tied up, together with a girl in sleazy satin whose face bore the marks of gin and the razor, or heavy-set, abrupt, no-nonsense older men, in company with the most disreputable and fanatical "race" men, or these same "race" men with the sharpies, or these sharpies with the churchly women. Seventh Day Adventists and Methodists and Spiritualists seemed to be hobnobbing with Holyrollers and they were all, alike, entangled with the most flagrant disbelievers; something heavy in their stance seemed to indicate that they had all, incredibly, seen a common vision, and on each face there seemed to be the same strange, bitter shadow.

The churchly women and the matter-of-fact, no-nonsense men had children in the Army. The sleazy girls they talked to had lovers there, the sharpies and the "race" men had friends and brothers there. It would have demanded an unquestioning patriotism, happily as uncommon in this country as it is undesirable, for these people not to have been disturbed by the bitter letters they received, by the newspaper stories they read, not to have been enraged by the posters, then to be found all over New York, which described the Japanese as "yellow-bellied Japs." It was only the "race" men, to be sure, who spoke ceaselessly of being revenged—how this vengeance was to be exacted was not clear—for the indignities and dangers suffered by Negro boys in uniform; but everybody felt a directionless, hopeless bitterness, as well as that panic which can scarcely be suppressed when one knows that a human being one loves is beyond one's reach, and in danger. This helplessness and this gnawing uneasiness does something, at length, to even the toughest mind. Perhaps the best way to sum all this up is to say that the people I knew felt, mainly, a peculiar kind of relief when they knew that their boys were being shipped out of the south, to do battle overseas. It was, perhaps, like feeling that the most dangerous part of a dangerous journey had been passed and that now, even if death should come, it would come with honor and without the complicity of their countrymen. Such a death would be, in short, a fact with which one could hope to live.

It was on the 28th of July, which I believe was a Wednesday, that I visited my father for the first time during his illness and for the last time in his life. The moment I saw him I knew why I had put off this visit so long. I had told my mother that I did not want to see him because I hated him. But this was not true. It was only that I *had* hated him and I wanted to hold on to this hatred. I did not want to look on him as a ruin: it was not a ruin I had hated. I imagine that one of the reasons people cling to their hates so stubbornly is because they sense, once hate is gone, that they will be forced to deal with pain.

We traveled out to him, his older sister and myself, to what seemed to be the very end of a very Long Island. It was hot and dusty and we wrangled, my aunt and I, all the way out, over the fact that I had recently begun to smoke and, as she said, to give myself airs. But I knew that she wrangled with me because she could not bear to face the fact of her brother's dying. Neither could I endure the reality of her despair, her unstated bafflement as to what had happened to her brother's life, and her own. So we wrangled and I smoked and from time to time she fell into a heavy reverie. Covertly, I watched her face, which was the face of an old woman; it had fallen in, the eyes were sunken and lightless; soon she would be dying, too.

In my childhood—it had not been so long ago—I had thought her beautiful. She had been quick-witted and quick-moving and very generous with all the children and each of her visits had been an event. At one time one of my brothers and myself had thought of running away to live with her. Now she could no longer produce out of her handbag some unexpected and yet familiar delight. She made me feel pity and revulsion and fear. It was awful to realize that she no longer caused me to feel affection. The closer we came to the hospital the more querulous she became and at the same time, naturally, grew more dependent on me. Between pity and guilt and fear I began to feel that there was another me trapped in my skull like a jack-in-the-box who might escape my control at any moment and fill the air with screaming.

She began to cry the moment we entered the room and she saw him lying there, all shriveled and still, like a little black monkey. The great, gleaming apparatus which fed him and would have compelled him to be still even if he had been able to move brought to mind, not beneficence, but torture; the tubes entering his arm made me think of pictures I had seen when a child, of Gulliver, tied down by the pygmies on that island.[4] My aunt wept and wept, there was a whistling sound in my father's throat; nothing was said; he could not speak. I wanted to take his hand, to say something. But I do not know what I could have said, even if he could have heard me. He was not really in that room with us, he had at last really embarked on his journey; and though my aunt told me that he said he was going to meet Jesus, I did not hear anything except that whistling in his throat. The doctor came back and we left, into that unbearable train again, and home. In the morning came the telegram saying that he was dead. Then the house was suddenly full of relatives, friends, hysteria, and confusion and I quickly left my mother and the children to the care of those impressive women, who, in Negro communities at least, automatically appear at times of bereavement armed with lotions, proverbs, and patience, and an ability to cook. I went downtown. By the time I returned, later the same day, my mother had been carried to the hospital and the baby had been born.

---

4. A reference to Jonathan Swift's *Gulliver's Travels* (1726).

III

For my father's funeral I had nothing black to wear and this posed a nagging problem all day long. It was one of those problems, simple, or impossible of solution, to which the mind insanely clings in order to avoid the mind's real trouble. I spent most of that day at the downtown apartment of a girl I knew, celebrating my birthday with whiskey and wondering what to wear that night. When planning a birthday celebration one naturally does not expect that it will be up against competition from a funeral and this girl had anticipated taking me out that night, for a big dinner and a night club afterwards. Sometime during the course of that long day we decided that we would go out anyway, when my father's funeral service was over. I imagine I decided it, since, as the funeral hour approached, it became clearer and clearer to me that I would not know what to do with myself when it was over. The girl, stifling her very lively concern as to the possible effects of the whiskey on one of my father's chief mourners, concentrated on being conciliatory and practically helpful. She found a black shirt for me somewhere and ironed it and, dressed in the darkest pants and jacket I owned, and slightly drunk, I made my way to my father's funeral.

The chapel was full, but not packed, and very quiet. There were, mainly, my father's relatives, and his children, and here and there I saw faces I had not seen since childhood, the faces of my father's one-time friends. They were very dark and solemn now, seeming somehow to suggest that they had known all along that something like this would happen. Chief among the mourners was my aunt, who had quarreled with my father all his life; by which I do not mean to suggest that her mourning was insincere or that she had not loved him. I suppose that she was one of the few people in the world who had, and their incessant quarreling proved precisely the strength of the tie that bound them. The only other person in the world, as far as I knew, whose relationship to my father rivaled my aunt's in depth was my mother, who was not there.

It seemed to me, of course, that it was a very long funeral. But it was, if anything, a rather shorter funeral than most, nor, since there were no overwhelming, uncontrollable expressions of grief, could it be called—if I dare to use the word—successful. The minister who preached my father's funeral sermon was one of the few my father had still been seeing as he neared his end. He presented to us in his sermon a man whom none of us had ever seen—a man thoughtful, patient, and forbearing, a Christian inspiration to all who knew him, and a model for his children. And no doubt the children, in their disturbed and guilty state, were almost ready to believe this; he had been remote enough to be anything and, anyway, the shock of the incontrovertible, that it was really our father lying up there in that casket, prepared the mind for anything. His sister moaned and this grief-stricken moaning was taken as corroboration. The other faces held a dark, non-committal thoughtfulness. This was not the man they had known, but they had scarcely expected to be confronted with *him*; this was, in a sense deeper than questions of fact, the man they had not known, and the man they had not known may have been the real one. The real man, whoever he had been, had suffered and now he was dead: this was all that was sure and all that mattered now. Every man in the chapel hoped that when his hour came he, too, would be eulogized, which is to say forgiven, and that all of his lapses, greeds, errors, and strayings from the truth would be invested with coherence and looked upon with charity. This was per-haps the last thing human beings could give each other and it was what they demanded, after all, of the Lord. Only the Lord saw the midnight tears, only He was present when one of His children, moaning and wring-ing hands, paced up and down the room. When one slapped one's child in anger the recoil in the heart reverberated through heaven and became part of the pain of the universe. And when the children were hungry and sullen and distrustful and one watched them, daily, growing wilder, and further away, and running headlong into danger, it was the Lord who knew what the charged heart endured as the strap was laid to the backside; the Lord alone who knew what one *would* have said if one had had, like the Lord, the gift of the living word. It was the Lord who knew of the impossibility every parent in that room faced: how to prepare the child for the day when the child would be despised and how to *create* in the child—by what means?—a stronger antidote to this poison than one had found for oneself. The avenues, side streets, bars, billiard halls, hospitals, police stations, and even the playgrounds of Harlem—not to mention the houses of correction, the jails, and the morgue—testified to the potency of the poison while re-maining silent as to the efficacy of whatever antidote, irresistibly raising the question of whether or not such an antidote existed; raising, which was worse, the question of whether or not an antidote was desirable; perhaps poison should be fought with poison. With these several schisms in the mind and with more terrors in the heart than could be named, it was better not to judge the man who had gone down under an impossible burden. It was better to remember: *Thou knowest this man's fall; but thou knowest not his wrassling.*

While the preacher talked and I watched the children—years of chang-ing their diapers, scrubbing them, slapping them, taking them to school, and scolding them had had the perhaps inevitable result of making me love them, though I am not sure I knew this then—my mind was busily breaking out with a rash of disconnected impressions. Snatches of popular songs, indecent jokes, bits of books I had read, movie sequences, faces, voices, political issues—I thought I was going mad; all these impressions sus-pended, as it were, in the solution of the faint nausea produced in me by the heat and liquor. For a moment I had the impression that my alcoholic breath, inefficiently disguised with chewing gum, filled the entire chapel. Then someone began singing one of my father's favorite songs and, abruptly, I was with him, sitting on his knee, in the hot, enormous, crowded church which was the first church we attended. It was the Abys-sinia Baptist Church on 138th Street. We had not gone there long. With this image, a host of others came. I had forgotten, in the rage of my growing up, how proud my father had been of me when I was little. Apparently, I had had a voice and my father had liked to show me off before the mem-bers of the church. I had forgotten what he had looked like when he was pleased but now I remembered that he had always been grinning with plea-sure when my solos ended. I even remembered certain expressions on his face when he teased my mother—had he loved her? I would never know. And when had it all begun to change? For now it seemed that he had not always been cruel. I remembered being taken for a haircut and scraping my knee on the footrest of the barber's chair and I remembered my father's face as he soothed my crying and applied the stinging iodine. Then I remembered our fights, fights which had been of the worst possible kind because my technique had been silence.

I remembered the one time in all our life together when we had really spoken to each other.

It was on a Sunday and it must have been shortly before I left home. We were walking, just the two of us, in our usual silence, to or from church. I was in high school and had been doing a lot of writing and I was, at about this time, the editor of the high school magazine. But I had also been a Young Minister and had been preaching from the pulpit. Lately, I had been taking fewer engagements and preached as rarely as possible. It was said in the church, quite truthfully, that I was "cooling off."

My father asked me abruptly, "You'd rather write than preach, wouldn't you?"

I was astonished at his question—because it was a real question. I answered, "Yes."

That was all we said. It was awful to remember that that was all we had *ever* said.

The casket now was opened and the mourners were being led up the aisle to look for the last time on the deceased. The assumption was that the family was too overcome with grief to be allowed to make this journey alone and I watched while my aunt was led to the casket and, muffled in black, and shaking, led back to her seat. I disapproved of forcing the children to look on their dead father, considering that the shock of his death, or, more truthfully, the shock of death as a reality, was already a little more than a child could bear, but my judgment in this matter had been overruled and there they were, bewildered and frightened and very small, being led, one by one, to the casket. But there is also something very gallant about children at such moments. It has something to do with their silence and gravity and with the fact that one cannot help them. Their legs, somehow, seem *exposed*, so that it is at once incredible and terribly clear that their legs are all they have to hold them up.

I had not wanted to go to the casket myself and I certainly had not wished to be led there, but there was no way of avoiding either of these forms. One of the deacons led me up and I looked on my father's face. I cannot say that it looked like him at all. His blackness had been equivocated by powder and there was no suggestion in that casket of what his power had or could have been. He was simply an old man dead, and it was hard to believe that he had ever given anyone either joy or pain. Yet, his life filled that room. Further up the avenue his wife was holding his newborn child. Life and death so close together, and love and hatred, and right and wrong, said something to me which I did not want to hear concerning man, concerning the life of man.

After the funeral, while I was downtown desperately celebrating my birthday, a Negro soldier, in the lobby of the Hotel Braddock, got into a

fight with a white policeman over a Negro girl. Negro girls, white policemen, in or out of uniform, and Negro males—in or out of uniform—were
part of the furniture of the lobby of the Hotel Braddock and this was certainly not the first time such an incident had occurred. It was destined,
however, to receive an unprecedented publicity, for the fight between the
policeman and the soldier ended with the shooting of the soldier. Rumor,
flowing immediately to the streets outside, stated that the soldier had been
shot in the back, an instantaneous and revealing invention, and that the
soldier had died protecting a Negro woman. The facts were somewhat different—for example, the soldier had not been shot in the back, and was not
dead, and the girl seems to have been as dubious a symbol of womanhood
as her white counterpart in Georgia usually is, but no one was interested in
the facts. They preferred the invention because this invention expressed
and corroborated their hates and fears so perfectly. It is just as well to remember that people are always doing this. Perhaps many of those legends,
including Christianity, to which the world clings began their conquest of
the world with just some such concerted surrender to distortion. The effect, in Harlem, of this particular legend was like the effect of a lit match in
a tin of gasoline. The mob gathered before the doors of the Hotel Braddock
simply began to swell and to spread in every direction, and Harlem exploded.

The mob did not cross the ghetto lines. It would have been easy, for
example, to have gone over Morningside Park on the west side or to have
crossed the Grand Central railroad tracks at 125th Street on the east side, to
wreak havoc in white neighborhoods. The mob seems to have been mainly
interested in something more potent and real than the white face, that is, in
white power, and the principal damage done during the riot of the summer
of 1943 was to white business establishments in Harlem. It might have
been a far bloodier story, of course, if, at the hour the riot began, these
establishments had still been open. From the Hotel Braddock the mob
fanned out, east and west along 125th Street, and for the entire length of
Lenox, Seventh, and Eighth avenues. Along each of these avenues, and
along each major side street—116th, 125th, 135th, and so on—bars, stores,
pawnshops, restaurants, even little luncheonettes had been smashed open
and entered and looted—looted, it might be added, with more haste than
efficiency. The shelves really looked as though a bomb had struck them.
Cans of beans and soup and dog food, along with toilet paper, corn flakes,
sardines and milk tumbled every which way, and abandoned cash registers
and cases of beer leaned crazily out of the splintered windows and were
strewn along the avenues. Sheets, blankets, and clothing of every description formed a kind of path, as though people had dropped them while running. I truly had not realized that Harlem *had* so many stores until I saw
them all smashed open; the first time the word *wealth* ever entered my
mind in relation to Harlem was when I saw it scattered in the streets. But
one's first, incongruous impression of plenty was countered immediately
by an impression of waste. None of this was doing anybody any good. It
would have been better to have left the plate glass as it had been and the
goods lying in the stores.

It would have been better, but it would also have been intolerable, for

Harlem had needed something to smash. To smash something is the ghetto's chronic need. Most of the time it is the members of the ghetto who smash each other, and themselves. But as long as the ghetto walls are standing there will always come a moment when these outlets do not work. That summer, for example, it was not enough to get into a fight on Lenox Avenue, or curse out one's cronies in the barber shops. If ever, indeed, the violence which fills Harlem's churches, pool halls, and bars erupts outward in a more direct fashion, Harlem and its citizens are likely to vanish in an apocalyptic flood. That this is not likely to happen is due to a great many reasons, most hidden and powerful among them the Negro's real relation to the white American. This relation prohibits, simply, anything as uncomplicated and satisfactory as pure hatred. In order really to hate white people, one has to blot so much out of the mind—and the heart—that this hatred itself becomes an exhausting and self-destructive pose. But this does not mean, on the other hand, that love comes easily: the white world is too powerful, too complacent, too ready with gratuitous humiliation, and, above all, too ignorant and too innocent for that. One is absolutely forced to make perpetual qualifications and one's own reactions are always canceling each other out. It is this, really, which has driven so many people mad, both white and black. One is always in the position of having to decide between amputation and gangrene. Amputation is swift but time may prove that the amputation was not necessary—or one may delay the amputation too long. Gangrene is slow, but it is impossible to be sure that one is reading one's symptoms right. The idea of going through life as a cripple is more than one can bear, and equally unbearable is the risk of swelling up slowly, in agony, with poison. And the trouble, finally, is that the risks are real even if the choices do not exist.

"But as for me and my house," my father had said, "we will serve the Lord."[5] I wondered, as we drove him to his resting place, what this line had meant for him. I had heard him preach it many times. I had preached it once myself, proudly giving it an interpretation different from my father's. Now the whole thing came back to me, as though my father and I were on our way to Sunday school and I were memorizing the golden text: *And if it seem evil unto you to serve the Lord, choose you this day whom you will serve; whether the gods which your fathers served that were on the other side of the flood, or the gods of the Amorites, in whose land ye dwell: but as for me and my house, we will serve the Lord.* I suspected in these familiar lines a meaning which had never been there for me before. All of my father's texts and songs, which I had decided were meaningless, were arranged before me at his death like empty bottles, waiting to hold the meaning which life would give them for me. This was his legacy: nothing is ever escaped. That bleakly memorable morning I hated the unbelievable streets and the Negroes and whites who had, equally, made them that way. But I knew that it was folly, as my father would have said, this bitterness was folly. It was necessary to hold on to the things that mattered. The dead man mattered, the new life mattered; blackness and whiteness did not matter; to believe that they did was to acquiesce in one's own destruction. Hatred, which

5. Joshua 24:15.

could destroy so much, never failed to destroy the man who hated and this was an immutable law.

It began to seem that one would have to hold in the mind forever two ideas which seemed to be in opposition. The first idea was acceptance, the acceptance, totally without rancor, of life as it is, and men as they are: in the light of this idea, it goes without saying that injustice is a commonplace. But this did not mean that one could be complacent, for the second idea was of equal power: that one must never, in one's own life, accept these injustices as commonplace but must fight them with all one's strength. This fight begins, however, in the heart and it now had been laid to my charge to keep my own heart free of hatred and despair. This intimation made my heart heavy and, now that my father was irrecoverable, I wished that he had been beside me so that I could have searched his face for the answers which only the future would give me now.

1955

Sonny's Blues

I read about it in the paper, in the subway, on my way to work. I read it, and I couldn't believe it, and I read it again. Then perhaps I just stared at it, at the newsprint spelling out his name, spelling out the story. I stared at it in the swinging lights of the subway car, and in the faces and bodies of the people, and in my own face, trapped in the darkness which roared outside.

It was not to be believed and I kept telling myself that, as I walked from the subway station to the high school. And at the same time I couldn't doubt it. I was scared, scared for Sonny. He became real to me again. A great block of ice got settled in my belly and kept melting there slowly all day long, while I taught my classes algebra. It was a special kind of ice. It kept melting, sending trickles of ice water all up and down my veins, but it never got less. Sometimes it hardened and seemed to expand until I felt my guts were going to come spilling out or that I was going to choke or scream. This would always be at a moment when I was remembering some specific thing Sonny had once said or done.

When he was about as old as the boys in my classes his face had been bright and open, there was a lot of copper in it; and he'd had wonderfully direct brown eyes, and great gentleness and privacy. I wondered what he looked like now. He had been picked up, the evening before, in a raid on an apartment downtown, for peddling and using heroin.

I couldn't believe it: but what I mean by that is that I couldn't find any room for it anywhere inside me. I had kept it outside me for a long time. I hadn't wanted to know. I had had suspicions, but I didn't name them, I kept putting them away. I told myself that Sonny was wild, but he wasn't crazy. And he'd always been a good boy, he hadn't ever turned hard or evil or disrespectful, the way kids can, so quick, so quick, especially in Harlem. I didn't want to believe that I'd ever see my brother going down, coming to nothing, all that light in his face gone out, in the condition I'd already seen so many others. Yet it had happened and here I was, talking about algebra to a lot of boys who might, every one of them for all I knew, be popping off needles every time they went to the head.[1] Maybe it did more for them than algebra could.

I was sure that the first time Sonny had ever had horse,[2] he couldn't have been much older than these boys were now. These boys, now, were living as we'd been living then, they were growing up with a rush and their heads bumped abruptly against the low ceiling of their actual possibilities. They were filled with rage. All they really knew were two darknesses, the darkness of their lives, which was now closing in on them, and the darkness of the movies, which had blinded them to that other darkness, and in which they now, vindictively, dreamed, at once more together than they were at any other time, and more alone.

When the last bell rang, the last class ended, I let out my breath. It seemed I'd been holding it for all that time. My clothes were wet—I may have looked as though I'd been sitting in a steam bath, all dressed up, all afternoon. I sat alone in the classroom a long time. I listened to the boys outside, downstairs, shouting and cursing and laughing. Their laughter struck me for perhaps the first time. It was not the joyous laughter which—God knows why—one associates with children. It was mocking and insular, its intent was to denigrate. It was disenchanted, and in this, also, lay the authority of their curses. Perhaps I was listening to them because I was thinking about my brother and in them I heard my brother. And myself.

One boy was whistling a tune, at once very complicated and very simple, it seemed to be pouring out of him as though he were a bird, and it sounded very cool and moving through all that harsh, bright air, only just holding its own through all those other sounds.

I stood up and walked over to the window and looked down into the courtyard. It was the beginning of the spring and the sap was rising in the boys. A teacher passed through them every now and again, quickly, as though he or she couldn't wait to get out of that courtyard, to get those boys out of their sight and off their minds. I started collecting my stuff. I thought I'd better get home and talk to Isabel.

The courtyard was almost deserted by the time I got downstairs. I saw this boy standing in the shadow of a doorway, looking just like Sonny. I almost called his name. Then I saw that it wasn't Sonny, but somebody we used to know, a boy from around our block. He'd been Sonny's friend. He'd never been mine, having been too young for me, and, anyway, I'd never liked him. And now, even though he was a grown-up man, he still hung around that block, still spent hours on the street corners, was always high and raggy. I used to run into him from time to time and he'd often work around to asking me for a quarter or fifty cents. He always had some real good excuse, too, and I always gave it to him, I don't know why.

But now, abruptly, I hated him. I couldn't stand the way he looked at me, partly like a dog, partly like a cunning child. I wanted to ask him what the hell he was doing in the school courtyard.

He sort of shuffled over to me, and he said, "I see you got the papers. So you already know about it."

1. Bathroom. 2. Heroin.

"You mean about Sonny? Yes, I already know about it. How come they didn't get you?"

He grinned. It made him repulsive and it also brought to mind what he'd looked like as a kid. "I wasn't there. I stay away from them people."

"Good for you." I offered him a cigarette and I watched him through the smoke. "You come all the way down here just to tell me about Sonny?"

"That's right." He was sort of shaking his head and his eyes looked strange, as though they were about to cross. The bright sun deadened his damp dark brown skin and it made his eyes look yellow and showed up the dirt in his kinked hair. He smelled funky. I moved a little away from him and I said, "Well, thanks. But I already know about it and I got to get home."

"I'll walk you a little ways," he said. We started walking. There were a couple of kids still loitering in the courtyard and one of them said good-night to me and looked strangely at the boy beside me.

"What're you going to do?" he asked me. "I mean, about Sonny?"

"Look. I haven't seen Sonny for over a year, I'm not sure I'm going to do anything. Anyway, what the hell can I do?"

"That's right," he said quickly, "ain't nothing you can do. Can't much help old Sonny no more, I guess."

It was what I was thinking and so it seemed to me he had no right to say it.

"I'm surprised at Sonny, though," he went on—he had a funny way of talking, he looked straight ahead as though he were talking to himself—"I thought Sonny was a smart boy, I thought he was too smart to get hung."

"I guess he thought so too," I said sharply, "and that's how he got hung. And now about you? You're pretty goddamn smart, I bet."

Then he looked directly at me, just for a minute. "I ain't smart," he said. "If I was smart, I'd have reached for a pistol a long time ago."

"Look. Don't tell me your sad story, if it was up to me, I'd give you one."

Then I felt guilty—guilty, probably, for never having supposed that the poor bastard had a story of his own, much less a sad one, and I asked, quickly, "What's going to happen to him now?"

He didn't answer this. He was off by himself some place. "Funny thing," he said, and from his tone we might have been discussing the quickest way to get to Brooklyn, "when I saw the papers this morning, the first thing I asked myself was if I had anything to do with it. I felt sort of responsible."

I began to listen more carefully. The subway station was on the corner, just before us, and I stopped. He stopped, too. We were in front of a bar and he ducked slightly, peering in, but whoever he was looking for didn't seem to be there. The juke box was blasting away with something black and bouncy and I half watched the barmaid as she danced her way from the juke box to her place behind the bar. And I watched her face as she laughingly responded to something someone said to her, still keeping time to the music. When she smiled one saw the little girl, one sensed the doomed, still-struggling woman beneath the battered face of the semi-whore.

"I never give Sonny nothing," the boy said finally, "but a long time ago I come to school high and Sonny asked me how it felt." He paused, I couldn't bear to watch him, I watched the barmaid, and I listened to the music which seemed to be causing the pavement to shake. "I told him it felt great." The music stopped, the barmaid paused and watched the juke box until the music began again. "It did."

All this was carrying me some place I didn't want to go. I certainly didn't want to know how it felt. It filled everything, the people, the houses, the music, the dark, quicksilver barmaid, with menace; and this menace was their reality.

"What's going to happen to him now?" I asked again.

"They'll send him away some place and they'll try to cure him." He shook his head. "Maybe he'll even think he's kicked the habit. Then they'll let him loose"—he gestured, throwing his cigarette into the gutter. "That's all."

"What do you mean, that's *all?*"

But I knew what he meant.

"I *mean,* that's *all.*" He turned his head and looked at me, pulling down the corners of his mouth. "Don't you know what I mean?" he asked, softly.

"How the hell *would* I know what you mean?" I almost whispered it, I don't know why.

"That's right," he said to the air, "how would *he* know what I mean?" He turned toward me again, patient and calm, and yet I somehow felt him shaking, shaking as though he were going to fall apart. I felt that ice in my guts again, the dread I'd felt all afternoon; and again I watched the barmaid, moving about the bar, washing glasses, and singing. "Listen. They'll let him out and then it'll just start all over again. That's what I mean."

"You mean—they'll let him out. And then he'll just start working his way back in again. You mean he'll never kick the habit. Is that what you mean?"

"That's right," he said, cheerfully. "*You* see what I mean."

"Tell me," I said it last, "why does he want to die? He must want to die, he's killing himself, why does he want to die?"

He looked at me in surprise. He licked his lips. "He don't want to die. He wants to live. Don't nobody want to die, ever."

Then I wanted to ask him—too many things. He could not have answered, or if he had, I could not have borne the answers. I started walking. "Well, I guess it's none of my business."

"It's going to be rough on old Sonny," he said. We reached the subway station. "This is your station?" he asked. I nodded. I took one step down. "Damn!" he said, suddenly. I looked up at him. He grinned again. "Damn it if I didn't leave all my money home. You ain't got a dollar on you, have you? Just for a couple of days, is all."

All at once something inside gave and threatened to come pouring out of me. I didn't hate him any more. I felt that in another moment I'd start crying like a child.

"Sure," I said. "Don't sweat." I looked in my wallet and didn't have a dollar, I only had a five. "Here," I said. "That hold you?"

He didn't look at it—he didn't want to look at it. A terrible, closed look came over his face, as though he were keeping the number on the bill a secret from him and me. "Thanks," he said, and now he was dying to see me go. "Don't worry about Sonny. Maybe I'll write him or something."

"Sure," I said. "You do that. So long."

"Be seeing you," he said. I went on down the steps.

And I didn't write Sonny or send him anything for a long time. When I finally did, it was just after my little girl died, he wrote me back a letter which made me feel like a bastard.

Here's what he said:

> Dear brother,
>
> You don't know how much I needed to hear from you. I wanted to write you many a time but I dug how much I must have hurt you and so I didn't write. But now I feel like a man who's been trying to climb up out of some deep, real deep and funky hole and just saw the sun up there, outside. I got to get outside.
>
> I can't tell you much about how I got here. I mean I don't know how to tell you. I guess I was afraid of something or I was trying to escape from something and you know I have never been very strong in the head (smile) I'm glad Mama and Daddy are dead and can't see what's happened to their son and I swear if I'd known what I was doing I would never have hurt you so, you and a lot of other fine people who were nice to me and who believed in me.
>
> I don't want you to think it had anything to do with me being a musician. It's more than that. Or maybe less than that. I can't get anything straight in my head down here and I try not to think about what's going to happen to me when I get outside again. Sometime I think I'm going to flip and *never* get outside and sometime I think I'll come straight back. I tell you one thing, though, I'd rather blow my brains out than go through this again. But that's what they all say, so they tell me. If I tell you when I'm coming to New York and if you could meet me, I sure would appreciate it. Give my love to Isabel and the kids and I was sure sorry to hear about little Gracie. I wish I could be like Mama and say the Lord's will be done, but I don't know it seems to me that trouble is the one thing that never does get stopped and I don't know what good it does to blame it on the Lord. But maybe it does some good if you believe it.
>
> Your brother,
> Sonny

Then I kept in constant touch with him and I sent him whatever I could and I went to meet him when he came back to New York. When I saw him many things I thought I had forgotten came flooding back to me. This was because I had begun, finally, to wonder about Sonny, about the life that Sonny lived inside. This life, whatever it was, had made him older and thinner and it had deepened the distant stillness in which he had always moved. He looked very unlike my baby brother. Yet, when he smiled, when we shook hands, the baby brother I'd never known looked out from the depths of his private life, like an animal waiting to be coaxed into the light.

"How you been keeping?" he asked me.

"All right. And you?"

"Just fine." He was smiling all over his face. "It's good to see you again."

"It's good to see you."

The seven years' difference in our ages lay between us like a chasm: I wondered if these years would ever operate between us as a bridge. I was remembering, and it made it hard to catch my breath, that I had been there when he was born; and I had heard the first words he had ever spoken. When he started to walk, he walked from our mother straight to me. I caught him just before he fell when he took the first steps he ever took in this world.

"How's Isabel?"

"Just fine. She's dying to see you."

"And the boys?"

"They're fine, too. They're anxious to see their uncle."

"Oh, come on. You know they don't remember me."

"Are you kidding? Of course they remember you."

He grinned again. We got into a taxi. We had a lot to say to each other, far too much to know how to begin.

As the taxi began to move, I asked, "You still want to go to India?"

He laughed. "You still remember that. Hell, no. This place is Indian enough for me."

"It used to belong to them," I said.

And he laughed again. "They damn sure knew what they were doing when they got rid of it."

Years ago, when he was around fourteen, he'd been all hipped on the idea of going to India. He read books about people sitting on rocks, naked, in all kinds of weather, but mostly bad, naturally, and walking barefoot through hot coals and arriving at wisdom. I used to say that it sounded to me as though they were getting away from wisdom as fast as they could. I think he sort of looked down on me for that.

"Do you mind," he asked, "if we have the driver drive alongside the park? On the west side—I haven't seen the city in so long."

"Of course not," I said. I was afraid that I might sound as though I were humoring him, but I hoped he wouldn't take it that way.

So we drove along, between the green of the park and the stony, lifeless elegance of hotels and apartment buildings, toward the vivid, killing streets of our childhood. These streets hadn't changed, though housing projects jutted up out of them now like rocks in the middle of a boiling sea. Most of the houses in which we had grown up had vanished, as had the stores from which we had stolen, the basements in which we had first tried sex, the rooftops from which we had hurled tin cans and bricks. But houses exactly like the houses of our past yet dominated the landscape, boys exactly like the boys we once had been found themselves smothering in these houses, came down into the streets for light and air and found themselves encircled by disaster. Some escaped the trap, most didn't. Those who got out always left something of themselves behind, as some animals amputate a leg and leave it in the trap. It might be said, perhaps, that I had escaped, after all, I was a school teacher; or that Sonny had, he hadn't lived in Harlem for years. Yet, as the cab moved uptown through streets which seemed, with a rush, to darken with dark people, and as I covertly studied Sonny's face, it came to me that what we both were seeking through our separate cab windows was that part of ourselves which had been left behind. It's always at the hour of trouble and confrontation that the missing member aches.

We hit 110th Street and started rolling up Lenox Avenue. And I'd known this avenue all my life, but it seemed to me again, as it had seemed on the day I'd first heard about Sonny's trouble, filled with a hidden menace which was its very breath of life.

"We almost there," said Sonny.

"Almost." We were both too nervous to say anything more.

We live in a housing project. It hasn't been up long. A few days after it was up it seemed uninhabitably new, now, of course, it's already rundown. It looks like a parody of the good, clean, faceless life—God knows the people who live in it do their best to make it a parody. The beat-looking grass lying around isn't enough to make their lives green, the hedges will never hold out the streets, and they know it. The big windows fool no one, they aren't big enough to make space out of no space. They don't bother with the windows, they watch the TV screen instead. The playground is most popular with the children who don't play at jacks, or skip rope, or roller skate, or swing, and they can be found in it after dark. We moved in partly because it's not too far from where I teach, and partly for the kids; but it's really just like the houses in which Sonny and I grew up. The same things happen, they'll have the same things to remember. The moment Sonny and I started into the house I had the feeling that I was simply bringing him back into the danger he had almost died trying to escape.

Sonny has never been talkative. So I don't know why I was sure he'd be dying to talk to me when supper was over the first night. Everything went fine, the oldest boy remembered him, and the youngest boy liked him, and Sonny had remembered to bring something for each of them; and Isabel, who is really much nicer than I am, more open and giving, had gone to a lot of trouble about dinner and was genuinely glad to see him. And she's always been able to tease Sonny in a way that I haven't. It was nice to see her face so vivid again and to hear her laugh and watch her make Sonny laugh. She wasn't, or, anyway, she didn't seem to be, at all uneasy or embarrassed. She chatted as though there were no subject which had to be avoided and she got Sonny past his first, faint stiffness. And thank God she was there, for I was filled with that icy dread again. Everything I did seemed awkward to me, and everything I said sounded freighted with hidden meaning. I was trying to remember everything I'd heard about dope addiction and I couldn't help watching Sonny for signs. I wasn't doing it out of malice. I was trying to find out something about my brother. I was dying to hear him tell me he was safe.

"Safe!" my father grunted, whenever Mama suggested trying to move to a neighborhood which might be safer for children. "Safe, hell! Ain't no place safe for kids, nor nobody."

He always went on like this, but he wasn't, ever, really as bad as he sounded, not even on weekends, when he got drunk. As a matter of fact, he was always on the lookout for "something a little better," but he died before he found it. He died suddenly, during a drunken weekend in the middle of the war, when Sonny was fifteen. He and Sonny hadn't ever got on too well. And this was partly because Sonny was the apple of his father's eye. It was because he loved Sonny so much and was frightened for him, that he was always fighting with him. It doesn't do any good to fight with Sonny. Sonny just moves back, inside himself, where he can't be reached. But the principal reason that they never hit it off is that they were so much alike. Daddy was big and rough and loud-talking, just the opposite of Sonny, but they both had—that same privacy.

Mama tried to tell me something about this, just after Daddy died. I was home on leave from the army.

This was the last time I ever saw my mother alive. Just the same, this picture gets all mixed up in my mind with pictures I had of her when she was younger. The way I always see her is the way she used to be on a Sunday afternoon, say, when the old folks were talking after the big Sunday dinner. I always see her wearing pale blue. She'd be sitting on the sofa. And my father would be sitting in the easy chair, not far from her. And the living room would be full of church folks and relatives. There they sit, in chairs all around the living room, and the night is creeping up outside, but nobody knows it yet. You can see the darkness growing against the window-panes and you hear the street noises every now and again, or maybe the jangling beat of a tambourine from one of the churches close by, but it's real quiet in the room. For a moment nobody's talking, but every face looks darkening, like the sky outside. And my mother rocks a little from the waist, and my father's eyes are closed. Everyone is looking at something a child can't see. For a minute they've forgotten the children. Maybe a kid is lying on the rug, half asleep. Maybe somebody's got a kid in his lap and is absent-mindedly stroking the kid's head. Maybe there's a kid, quiet and big-eyed, curled up in a big chair in the corner. The silence, the darkness coming, and the darkness in the faces frightens the child obscurely. He hopes that the hand which strokes his forehead will never stop—will never die. He hopes that there will never come a time when the old folks won't be sitting around the living room, talking about where they've come from, and what they've seen, and what's happened to them and their kinfolk.

But something deep and watchful in the child knows that this is bound to end, is already ending. In a moment someone will get up and turn on the light. Then the old folks will remember the children and they won't talk any more that day. And when light fills the room, the child is filled with darkness. He knows that every time this happens he's moved just a little closer to that darkness outside. The darkness outside is what the old folks have been talking about. It's what they've come from. It's what they endure. The child knows that they won't talk any more because if he knows too much about what's happened to *them*, he'll know too much too soon, about what's going to happen to *him*.

The last time I talked to my mother, I remember I was restless. I wanted to get out and see Isabel. We weren't married then and we had a lot to straighten out between us.

There Mama sat, in black, by the window. She was humming an old church song, *Lord, you brought me from a long ways off.* Sonny was out somewhere. Mama kept watching the streets.

"I don't know," she said, "if I'll ever see you again, after you go off from here. But I hope you'll remember the things I tried to teach you."

"Don't talk like that," I said, and smiled. "You'll be here a long time yet."

She smiled, too, but she said nothing. She was quiet for a long time. And I said, "Mama, don't you worry about nothing. I'll be writing all the time, and you be getting the checks. . . ."

"I want to talk to you about your brother," she said, suddenly. "If anything happens to me he ain't going to have nobody to look out for him."

"Mama," I said, "ain't nothing going to happen to you or Sonny. Sonny's all right. He's a good boy and he's got good sense."

"It ain't a question of his being a good boy," Mama said, "nor of his having good sense. It ain't only the bad ones, nor yet the dumb ones that gets sucked under." She stopped, looking at me. "Your Daddy once had a brother," she said, and she smiled in a way that made me feel she was in pain. "You didn't never know that, did you?"

"No," I said, "I never knew that," and I watched her face.

"Oh, yes," she said, "your Daddy had a brother." She looked out of the window again. "I know you never saw your Daddy cry. But I did—many a time, through all these years."

I asked her, "What happened to his brother? How come nobody's ever talked about him?"

This was the first time I ever saw my mother look old.

"His brother got killed," she said, "when he was just a little younger than you are now. I knew him. He was a fine boy. He was maybe a little full of the devil, but he didn't mean nobody no harm."

Then she stopped and the room was silent, exactly as it had sometimes been on those Sunday afternoons. Mama kept looking out into the streets.

"He used to have a job in the mill," she said, "and, like all young folks, he just liked to perform on Saturday nights. Saturday nights, him and your father would drift around to different place, go to dances and things like that, or just sit around with people they knew, and your father's brother would sing, he had a fine voice, and play along with himself on his guitar. Well, this particular Saturday night, him and your father was coming home from some place, and they were both a little drunk and there was a moon that night, it was bright like day. Your father's brother was feeling kind of good, and he was whistling to himself, and he had his guitar slung over his shoulder. They was coming down a hill and beneath them was a road that turned off from the highway. Well, your father's brother, being always kind of frisky, decided to run down this hill, and he did, with that guitar banging and clanging behind him, and he ran across the road, and he was making water behind a tree. And your father was sort of amused at him and he was still coming down the hill, kind of slow. Then he heard a car motor and that same minute his brother stepped from behind the tree, into the road, in the moonlight. And he started to cross the road. And your father started to run down the hill, he says he don't know why. This car was full of white men. They was all drunk, and when they seen your father's brother they let out a great whoop and holler and they aimed the car straight at him. They was having fun, they just wanted to scare him, the way they do sometimes, you know. But they was drunk. And I guess the boy, being drunk, too, and scared, kind of lost his head. By the time he jumped it was too late. Your father says he heard his brother scream when the car rolled over him, and he heard the wood of that guitar when it give, and he heard them strings go flying, and he heard them white men shouting, and the car kept on a-going and it ain't stopped till this day. And, time your father got down the hill, his brother weren't nothing but blood and pulp."

Tears were gleaming on my mother's face. There wasn't anything I could say.

"He never mentioned it," she said, "because I never let him mention it before you children. Your Daddy was like a crazy man that night and for many a night thereafter. He says he never in his life seen anything as dark as that road after the lights of that car had gone away. Weren't nothing, weren't nobody on that road, just your Daddy and his brother and that busted guitar. Oh, yes. Your Daddy never did really get right again. Till the day he died he weren't sure but that every white man he saw was the man that killed his brother."

She stopped and took out her handkerchief and dried her eyes and looked at me.

"I ain't telling you all this," she said, "to make you scared or bitter or to make you hate nobody. I'm telling you this because you got a brother. And the world ain't changed."

I guess I didn't want to believe this. I guess she saw this in my face. She turned away from me, toward the window again, searching those streets.

"But I praise my Redeemer," she said at last, "that He called your Daddy home before me. I ain't saying it to throw no flowers at myself, but, I declare, it keeps me from feeling too cast down to know I helped your father get safely through this world. Your father always acted like he was the roughest, strongest man on earth. And everybody took him to be like that. But if he hadn't had *me* there—to see his tears!"

She was crying again. Still, I couldn't move. I said, "Lord, Lord, Mama, I didn't know it was like that."

"Oh, honey," she said, "there's a lot that you don't know. But you are going to find it out." She stood up from the window and came over to me. "You got to hold on to your brother," she said, "and don't let him fall, no matter what it looks like is happening to him and no matter how evil you gets with him. You going to be evil with him many a time. But don't you forget what I told you, you hear?"

"I won't forget," I said. "Don't you worry, I won't forget. I won't let nothing happen to Sonny."

My mother smiled as though she were amused at something she saw in my face. Then, "You may not be able to stop nothing from happening. But you got to let him know you's *there*."

Two days later I was married, and then I was gone. And I had a lot of things on my mind and I pretty well forgot my promise to Mama until I got shipped home on a special furlough for her funeral.

And, after the funeral, with just Sonny and me alone in the empty kitchen, I tried to find out something about him.

"What do you want to do?" I asked him.

"I'm going to be a musician," he said.

For he had graduated, in the time I had been away, from dancing to the juke box to finding out who was playing what, and what they were doing with it, and he had bought himself a set of drums.

"You mean, you want to be a drummer?" I somehow had the feeling that being a drummer might be all right for other people but not for my brother Sonny.

"I don't think," he said, looking at me very gravely, "that I'll ever be a good drummer. But I think I can play a piano."

I frowned. I'd never played the role of the older brother quite so seriously before, had scarcely ever, in fact, *asked* Sonny a damn thing. I sensed myself in the presence of something I didn't really know how to handle, didn't understand. So I made my frown a little deeper as I asked: "What kind of musician do you want to be?"

He grinned. "How many kinds do you think there are?"

"Be *serious*," I said.

He laughed, throwing his head back, and then looked at me. "I *am* serious."

"Well, then, for Christ's sake, stop kidding around and answer a serious question. I mean, do you want to be a concert pianist, you want to play classical music and all that, or—or what?" Long before I finished he was laughing again. "For Christ's *sake*, Sonny!"

He sobered, but with difficulty. "I'm sorry. But you sound so—*scared!*" and he was off again.

"Well, you may think it's funny now, baby, but it's not going to be so funny when you have to make your living at it, let me tell you *that*." I was furious because I knew he was laughing at me and I didn't know why.

"No," he said, very sober now, and afraid, perhaps, that he'd hurt me, "I don't want to be a classical pianist. That isn't what interests me. I mean"— he paused, looking hard at me, as though his eyes would help me to understand, and then gestured helplessly, as though perhaps his hand would help—"I mean, I'll have a lot of studying to do, and I'll have to study *everything*, but, I mean, I want to play *with*—jazz musicians." He stopped. "I want to play jazz," he said.

Well, the word had never before sounded as heavy, as real, as it sounded that afternoon in Sonny's mouth. I just looked at him and I was probably frowning a real frown by this time. I simply couldn't see why on earth he'd want to spend his time hanging around nightclubs, clowning around on bandstands, while people pushed each other around a dance floor. It seemed—beneath him, somehow. I had never thought about it before, had never been forced to, but I suppose I had always put jazz musicians in a class with what Daddy called "good-time people."

"Are you *serious*?"

"Hell, *yes*, I'm serious."

He looked more helpless than ever, and annoyed, and deeply hurt.

I suggested, helpfully: "You mean—like Louis Armstrong?"[3]

---

3. Jazz musician and singer (1900–1971).

His face closed as though I'd struck him. "No. I'm not talking about none of that old-time, down home crap."

"Well, look, Sonny, I'm sorry, don't get mad. I just don't altogether get it, that's all. Name somebody—you know, a jazz musician you admire."

"Bird."

"Who?"

"Bird! Charlie Parker![4] Don't they teach you nothing in the goddamn army?"

I lit a cigarette. I was surprised and then a little amused to discover that I was trembling. "I've been out of touch," I said. "You'll have to be patient with me. Now. Who's this Parker character?"

"He's just one of the greatest jazz musicians alive," said Sonny, sullenly, his hands in his pockets, his back to me. "Maybe *the* greatest," he added, bitterly, "that's probably why *you* never heard of him."

"All right," I said, "I'm ignorant. I'm sorry. I'll go out and buy all the cat's records right away, all right?"

"It don't," said Sonny, with dignity, "make any difference to me. I don't care what you listen to. Don't do me no favors."

I was beginning to realize that I'd never seen him so upset before. With another part of my mind I was thinking that this would probably turn out to be one of those things kids go through and that I shouldn't make it seem important by pushing it too hard. Still, I didn't think it would do any harm to ask: "Doesn't all this take a lot of time? Can you make a living at it?"

He turned back to me and half leaned, half sat, on the kitchen table. "Everything takes time," he said, "and—well, yes, sure, I can make a living at it. But what I don't seem to be able to make you understand is that it's the only thing I want to do."

"Well, Sonny," I said, gently, "you know people can't always do exactly what they *want* to do—"

"No, I don't know that," said Sonny, surprising me. "I think people *ought* to do what they want to do, what else are they alive for?"

"You getting to be a big boy," I said desperately, "it's time you started thinking about your future."

"I'm thinking about my future," said Sonny, grimly. "I think about it all the time."

I gave up. I decided, if he didn't change his mind, that we could always talk about it later. "In the meantime," I said, "you got to finish school." We had already decided that he'd have to move in with Isabel and her folks. I knew this wasn't the ideal arrangement because Isabel's folks are inclined to be dicty[5] and they hadn't especially wanted Isabel to marry me. But I didn't know what else to do. "And we have to get you fixed up at Isabel's."

There was a long silence. He moved from the kitchen table to the window. "That's a terrible idea. You know it yourself."

"Do you have a *better* idea?"

He just walked up and down the kitchen for a minute. He was as tall as I

4. Charlie "Bird" Parker (1920–1955), saxophonist   5. Snobbish, bossy.
and jass innovator, one of the developers of bebop.

was. He had started to shave. I suddenly had the feeling that I didn't know him at all.

He stopped at the kitchen table and picked up my cigarettes. Looking at me with a kind of mocking, amused defiance, he put one between his lips. "You mind?"

"You smoking already?"

He lit the cigarette and nodded, watching me through the smoke. "I just wanted to see if I'd have the courage to smoke in front of you." He grinned and blew a great cloud of smoke to the ceiling. "It was easy." He looked at my face. "Come on, now. I bet you was smoking at my age, tell the truth."

I didn't say anything but the truth was on my face, and he laughed. But now there was something very strained in his laugh. "Sure. And I bet that ain't all you was doing."

He was frightening me a little. "Cut the crap," I said. "We already decided that you was going to go and live at Isabel's. Now what's got into you all of a sudden?"

"*You* decided it," he pointed out. "*I* didn't decide nothing." He stopped in front of me, leaning against the stove, arms loosely folded. "Look, brother. I don't want to stay in Harlem no more, I really don't." He was very earnest. He looked at me, then over toward the kitchen window. There was something in his eyes I'd never seen before, some thoughtfulness, some worry all his own. He rubbed the muscle of one arm. "It's time I was getting out of here."

"Where do you want to *go*, Sonny?"

"I want to join the army. Or the navy, I don't care. If I say I'm old enough, they'll believe me."

Then I got mad. It was because I was so scared. "You must be crazy. You goddamn fool, what the hell do you want to go and join the *army* for?"

"I just told you. To get out of Harlem."

"Sonny, you haven't even finished *school*. And if you really want to be a musician, how do you expect to study if you're in the *army?*"

He looked at me, trapped, and in anguish. "There's ways. I might be able to work out some kind of deal. Anyway, I'll have the G.I. Bill[6] when I come out."

"*If* you come out." We stared at each other. "Sonny, please. Be reasonable. I know the setup is far from perfect. But we got to do the best we can."

"I ain't learning nothing in school," he said. "Even when I go." He turned away from me and opened the window and threw his cigarette out into the narrow alley. I watched his back. "At least, I ain't learning nothing you'd want me to learn." He slammed the window so hard I thought the glass would fly out, and turned back to me. "And I'm sick of the stink of these garbage cans!"

"Sonny," I said, "I know how you feel. But if you don't finish school now, you're going to be sorry later that you didn't." I grabbed him by the shoulders. "And you only got another year. It ain't so bad. And I'll come

6. Popular name for the Serviceman's Readjustment Act of 1944, which provided World War II veterans up to four years of educational and vocational training at government expense.

back and I swear I'll help you do *whatever* you want to do. Just try to put up with it till I come back. Will you please do that? For me?"

He didn't answer and he wouldn't look at me.

"Sonny. You hear me?"

He pulled away. "I hear you. But you never hear anything *I* say."

I didn't know what to say to that. He looked out of the window and then back at me. "OK," he said, and sighed. "I'll try."

Then I said, trying to cheer him up a little, "They got a piano at Isabel's. You can practice on it."

And as a matter of fact, it did cheer him up for a minute. "That's right," he said to himself. "I forgot that." His face relaxed a little. But the worry, the thoughtfulness, played on it still, the way shadows play on a face which is staring into the fire.

But I thought I'd never hear the end of that piano. At first, Isabel would write me, saying how nice it was that Sonny was so serious about his music and how, as soon as he came in from school, or wherever he had been when he was supposed to be at school, he went straight to that piano and stayed there until suppertime. And, after supper, he went back to that piano and stayed there until everybody went to bed. He was at the piano all day Saturday and all day Sunday. Then he bought a record player and started playing records. He'd play one record over and over again, all day long sometimes, and he'd improvise along with it on the piano. Or he'd play one section of the record, one chord, one change, one progression, then he'd do it on the piano. Then back to the record. Then back to the piano.

Well, I really don't know how they stood it. Isabel finally confessed that it wasn't like living with a person at all, it was like living with sound. And the sound didn't make any sense to her, didn't make any sense to any of them— naturally. They began, in a way, to be afflicted by this presence that was living in their home. It was as though Sonny were some sort of god, or monster. He moved in an atmosphere which wasn't like theirs at all. They fed him and he ate, he washed himself, he walked in and out of their door; he certainly wasn't nasty or unpleasant or rude, Sonny isn't any of those things; but it was as though he were all wrapped up in some cloud, some fire, some vision all his own; and there wasn't any way to reach him.

At the same time, he wasn't really a man yet, he was still a child, and they had to watch out for him in all kinds of ways. They certainly couldn't throw him out. Neither did they dare to make a great scene about that piano be- cause even they dimly sensed, as I sensed, from so many thousands of miles away, that Sonny was at that piano playing for his life.

But he hadn't been going to school. One day a letter came from the school board and Isabel's mother got it—there had, apparently, been other letters but Sonny had torn them up. This day, when Sonny came in, Isa- bel's mother showed him the letter and asked where he'd been spending his time. And she finally got it out of him that he'd been down in Green- wich Village, with musicians and other characters, in a white girl's apart- ment. And this scared her and she started to scream at him and what came up, once she began—though she denies it to this day—was what sacrifices they were making to give Sonny a decent home and how little he appreciated it.

Sonny didn't play the piano that day. By evening, Isabel's mother had calmed down but then there was the old man to deal with, and Isabel herself. Isabel says she did her best to be calm but she broke down and started crying. She says she just watched Sonny's face. She could tell, by watching him, what was happening with him. And what was happening was that they penetrated his cloud, they had reached him. Even if their fingers had been a thousand times more gentle than human fingers ever are, he could hardly help feeling that they had stripped him naked and were spitting on that nakedness. For he also had to see that his presence, that music, which was life or death to him, had been torture for them and that they had endured it, not at all for his sake, but only for mine. And Sonny couldn't take that. He can take it a little better today than he could then but he's still not very good at it and, frankly, I don't know anybody who is.

The silence of the next few days must have been louder than the sound of all the music ever played since time began. One morning, before she went to work, Isabel was in his room for something and she suddenly realized that all of his records were gone. And she knew for certain that he was gone. And he was. He went as far as the navy would carry him. He finally sent me a postcard from some place in Greece and that was the first I knew that Sonny was still alive. I didn't see him any more until we were both back in New York and the war had long been over.

He was a man by then, of course, but I wasn't willing to see it. He came by the house from time to time, but we fought almost every time we met. I didn't like the way he carried himself, loose and dreamlike all the time, and I didn't like his friends, and his music seemed to be merely an excuse for the life he led. It sounded just that weird and disordered.

Then we had a fight, a pretty awful fight, and I didn't see him for months. By and by I looked him up, where he was living, in a furnished room in the Village, and I tried to make it up. But there were lots of other people in the room and Sonny just lay on his bed, and he wouldn't come downstairs with me, and he treated these other people as though they were his family and I weren't. So I got mad and then he got mad, and then I told him that he might just as well be dead as live the way he was living. Then he stood up and he told me not to worry about him any more in life, that he *was* dead as far as I was concerned. Then he pushed me to the door and the other people looked on as though nothing were happening, and he slammed the door behind me. I stood in the hallway, staring at the door. I heard somebody laugh in the room and then the tears came to my eyes. I started down the steps, whistling to keep from crying, I kept whistling to myself, *You going to need me, baby, one of these cold, rainy days.*

I read about Sonny's trouble in the spring. Little Grace died in the fall. She was a beautiful little girl. But she only lived a little over two years. She died of polio and she suffered. She had a slight fever for a couple of days, but it didn't seem like anything and we just kept her in bed. And we would certainly have called the doctor, but the fever dropped, she seemed to be all right. So we thought it had just been a cold. Then, one day, she was up, playing, Isabel was in the kitchen fixing lunch for the two boys when they'd come in from school, and she heard Grace fall down in the living room. When you have a lot of children you don't always start running when one of them falls, unless they start screaming or something. And, this time, Grace was quiet. Yet, Isabel says that when she heard that *thump* and then that silence, something happened in her to make her afraid. And she ran to the living room and there was little Grace on the floor, all twisted up, and the reason she hadn't screamed was that she couldn't get her breath. And when she did scream, it was the worst sound, Isabel says, that she'd ever heard in all her life, and she still hears it sometimes in her dreams. Isabel will sometimes wake me up with a low, moaning, strangled sound and I have to be quick to awaken her and hold her to me and where Isabel is weeping against me seems a mortal wound.

I think I may have written Sonny the very day that little Grace was buried. I was sitting in the living room in the dark, by myself, and I suddenly thought of Sonny. My trouble made his real.

One Saturday afternoon, when Sonny had been living with us, or, anyway, been in our house, for nearly two weeks, I found myself wandering aimlessly about the living room, drinking from a can of beer, and trying to work up the courage to search Sonny's room. He was out, he was usually out whenever I was home, and Isabel had taken the children to see their grandparents. Suddenly I was standing still in front of the living room window, watching Seventh Avenue. The idea of searching Sonny's room made me still. I scarcely dared to admit to myself what I'd be searching for. I didn't know what I'd do if I found it. Or if I didn't.

On the sidewalk across from me, near the entrance to a barbecue joint, some people were holding an old-fashioned revival meeting. The barbecue cook, wearing a dirty white apron, his conked[7] hair reddish and metallic in the pale sun, and a cigarette between his lips, stood in the doorway, watching them. Kids and older people paused in their errands and stood there, along with some older men and a couple of very tough-looking women who watched everything that happened on the avenue, as though they owned it, or were maybe owned by it. Well, they were watching this, too. The revival was being carried on by three sisters in black, and a brother. All they had were their voices and their Bibles and a tambourine. The brother was testifying[8] and while he testified two of the sisters stood together, seeming to say, amen, and the third sister walked around with the tambourine outstretched and a couple of people dropped coins into it. Then the brother's testimony ended and the sister who had been taking up the collection dumped the coins into her palm and transferred them to the pocket of her long black robe. Then she raised both hands, striking the tambourine against the air, and then against one hand, and she started to sing. And the two other sisters and the brother joined in.

It was strange, suddenly, to watch, though I had been seeing these street meetings all my life. So, of course, had everybody else down there. Yet, they paused and watched and listened and I stood still at the window. *"Tis*

---

7. Straightened and greased.   8. Publicly professing belief.

the old ship of Zion," they sang, and the sister with the tambourine kept a steady, jangling beat, *"it has rescued many a thousand!"* Not a soul under the sound of their voices was hearing this song for the first time, not one of them had been rescued. Nor had they seen much in the way of rescue work being done around them. Neither did they especially believe in the holiness of the three sisters and the brother, they knew too much about them, knew where they lived, and how. The woman with the tambourine, whose voice dominated the air, whose face was bright with joy, was divided by very little from the woman who stood watching her, a cigarette between her heavy, chapped lips, her hair a cuckoo's nest, her face scarred and swollen from many beatings, and her black eyes glittering like coal. Perhaps they both knew this, which was why, when, as rarely, they addressed each other, they addressed each other as Sister. As the singing filled the air the watching, listening faces underwent a change, the eyes focusing on something within; the music seemed to soothe a poison out of them; and time seemed, nearly, to fall away from the sullen, belligerent, battered faces, as though they were fleeing back to their first condition, while dreaming of their last. The barbecue cook half shook his head and smiled, and dropped his cigarette and disappeared into his joint. A man fumbled in his pockets for change and stood holding it in his hand impatiently, as though he had just remembered a pressing appointment further up the avenue. He looked furious. Then I saw Sonny, standing on the edge of the crowd. He was carrying a wide, flat notebook with a green cover, and it made him look, from where I was standing, almost like a schoolboy. The coppery sun brought out the copper in his skin, he was very faintly smiling, standing very still. Then the singing stopped, the tambourine turned into a collection plate again. The furious man dropped in his coins and vanished, so did a couple of the women, and Sonny dropped some change in the plate, looking directly at the woman with a little smile. He started across the avenue, toward the house. He has a slow, loping walk, something like the way Harlem hipsters walk, only he's imposed on this his own half-beat. I had never really noticed it before.

I stayed at the window, both relieved and apprehensive. As Sonny disappeared from my sight, they began singing again. And they were still singing when his key turned in the lock.

"Hey," he said.

"Hey, yourself. You want some beer?"

"No. Well, maybe." But he came up to the window and stood beside me, looking out. "What a warm voice," he said.

They were singing *If I could only hear my mother pray again!*

"Yes," I said, "and she can sure beat that tambourine."

"But what a terrible song," he said, and laughed. He dropped his notebook on the sofa and disappeared into the kitchen. "Where's Isabel and the kids?"

"I think they went to see their grandparents. You hungry?"

"No." He came back into the living room with his can of beer. "You want to come some place with me tonight?"

I sensed, I don't know how, that I couldn't possibly say no. "Sure. Where?"

He sat down on the sofa and picked up his notebook and started leafing through it. "I'm going to sit in with some fellows in a joint in the Village."

"You mean, you're going to play, tonight?"

"That's right." He took a swallow of his beer and moved back to the window. He gave me a sidelong look. "If you can stand it."

"I'll try," I said.

He smiled to himself and we both watched as the meeting across the way broke up. The three sisters and the brother, heads bowed, were singing *God be with you till we meet again.* The faces around them were very quiet. Then the song ended. The small crowd dispersed. We watched the three women and the lone man walk slowly up the avenue.

"When she was singing before," said Sonny, abruptly, "her voice reminded me for a minute of what heroin feels like sometimes—when it's in your veins. It makes you feel sort of warm and cool at the same time. And distant. And—and sure." He sipped his beer, very deliberately not looking at me. I watched his face. "It makes you feel—in control. Sometimes you've got to have that feeling."

"Do you?" I sat down slowly in the easy chair.

"Sometimes." He went to the sofa and picked up his notebook again. "Some people do."

"In order," I asked, "to play?" And my voice was very ugly, full of contempt and anger.

"Well"—he looked at me with great, troubled eyes, as though, in fact, he hoped his eyes would tell me things he could never otherwise say—"they *think* so. And *if* they think so—!"

"And what do *you* think?" I asked.

He sat on the sofa and put his can of beer on the floor. "I don't know," he said, and I couldn't be sure if he were answering my question or pursuing his thoughts. His face didn't tell me. "It's not so much to *play.* It's to *stand* it, to be able to make it at all. On any level." He frowned and smiled: "In order to keep from shaking to pieces."

"But these friends of yours," I said, "they seem to shake themselves to pieces pretty goddamn fast."

"Maybe." He played with the notebook. And something told me that I should curb my tongue, that Sonny was doing his best to talk, that I should listen. "But of course you only know the ones that've gone to pieces. Some don't—or at least they haven't *yet* and that's just about all *any* of us can say." He paused. "And then there are some who just live, really, in hell, and they know it and they see what's happening and they go right on. I don't know." He sighed, dropped the notebook, folded his arms. "Some guys, you can tell from the way they play, they on something *all* the time. And you can see that, well, it makes something real for them. But of course," he picked up his beer from the floor and sipped it and put the can down again, "they *want* to, too, you've got to see that. Even some of them that say they don't—*some,* not all."

"And what about you?" I asked—I couldn't help it. "What about you? Do *you* want to?"

He stood up and walked to the window and remained silent for a long time. Then he sighed. "Me," he said. Then: "While I was downstairs before, on my way here, listening to that woman sing, it struck me all of a sudden how much suffering she must have had to go through—to sing like that. It's *repulsive* to think you have to suffer that much."

I said: "But there's no way not to suffer—is there, Sonny?"

"I believe not," he said and smiled, "but that's never stopped anyone from trying." He looked at me. "Has it?" I realized, with this mocking look, that there stood between us, forever, beyond the power of time or forgiveness, the fact that I had held silence—so long!—when he had needed human speech to help him. He turned back to the window. "No, there's no way not to suffer. But you try all kinds of ways to keep from drowning in it, to keep on top of it, and to make it seem—well, like *you*. Like you did something, all right, and now you're suffering for it. You know?" I said nothing. "Well you know," he said, impatiently, "why *do* people suffer? Maybe it's better to do something to give it a reason, *any* reason."

"But we just agreed," I said, "that there's no way not to suffer. Isn't it better, then, just to—take it?"

"But nobody just takes it," Sonny cried, "that's what I'm telling you! *Everybody* tries not to. You're just hung up on the *way* some people try—it's not *your* way!"

The hair on my face began to itch, my face felt wet. "That's not true," I said, "that's not true. I don't give a damn what other people do, I don't even care how they suffer. I just care how *you* suffer." And he looked at me. "Please believe me," I said, "I don't want to see you—die—trying not to suffer."

"I won't," he said, flatly, "die trying not to suffer. At least, not any faster than anybody else."

"But there's no need," I said, trying to laugh, "is there? in killing yourself."

I wanted to say more, but I couldn't. I wanted to talk about will power and how life could be—well, beautiful. I wanted to say that it was all within; but was it? or, rather, wasn't that exactly the trouble? And I wanted to promise that I would never fail him again. But it would all have sounded—empty words and lies.

So I made the promise to myself and prayed that I would keep it.

"It's terrible sometimes, inside," he said, "that's what's the trouble. You walk these streets, black and funky and cold, and there's not really a living ass to talk to, and there's nothing shaking, and there's no way of getting it out—that storm inside. You can't talk it and you can't make love with it, and when you finally try to get with it and play it, you realize *nobody's* listening. So *you've* got to listen. You got to find a way to listen."

And then he walked away from the window and sat on the sofa again, as though all the wind had suddenly been knocked out of him. "Sometimes you'll do *anything* to play, even cut your mother's throat." He laughed and looked at me. "Or your brother's." Then he sobered. "Or your own." Then: "Don't worry. I'm all right now and I think I'll *be* all right. But I can't forget—where I've been. I don't mean just the physical place I've been, I mean where I've *been*. And *what* I've been."

"What have you been, Sonny?" I asked.

He smiled—but sat sideways on the sofa, his elbow resting on the back, his fingers playing with his mouth and chin, not looking at me. "I've been something I didn't recognize, didn't know I could be. Didn't know anybody could be." He stopped, looking inward, looking helplessly young, looking old. "I'm not talking about it now because I feel *guilty* or anything like that—maybe it would be better if I did, I don't know. Anyway, I can't really talk about it. Not to you, not to anybody," and now he turned and faced me. "Sometimes, you know, and it was actually when I was most *out* of the world, I felt that I was in it, that I was *with* it, really, and I could play or I didn't really have to *play*, it just came out of me, it was there. And I don't know how I played, thinking about it now, but I know I did awful things, those times, sometimes, to people. Or it wasn't that I *did* anything to them—it was that they weren't real." He picked up the beer can; it was empty; he rolled it between his palms: "And other times—well, I needed a fix, I needed to find a place to lean, I needed to clear a space to *listen*—and I couldn't find it, and I—went crazy, I did terrible things to *me*, I was terrible *for* me." He began pressing the beer can between his hands, I watched the metal begin to give. It glittered, as he played with it, like a knife, and I was afraid he would cut himself, but I said nothing. "Oh well. I can never tell you. I was all by myself at the bottom of something, stinking and sweating and crying and shaking, and I smelled it, you know? *my* stink, and I thought I'd die if I couldn't get away from it and yet, all the same, I knew that everything I was doing was just locking me in with it. And I didn't know," he paused, still flattening the beer can, "I didn't know, I still *don't* know, something kept telling me that maybe it was good to smell your own stink, but I didn't think that *that* was what I'd been trying to do—and—who can stand it?" and he abruptly dropped the ruined beer can, looking at me with a small, still smile, and then rose, walking to the window as though it were the lodestone rock. I watched his face, he watched the avenue. "I couldn't tell you when Mama died—but the reason I wanted to leave Harlem so bad was to get away from drugs. And then, when I ran away, that's what I was running from—really. When I came back, nothing had changed, *I* hadn't changed, I was just—older." And he stopped, drumming with his fingers on the windowpane. The sun had vanished, soon darkness would fall. I watched his face. "It can come again," he said, almost as though speaking to himself. Then he turned to me. "It can come again," he repeated. "I just want you to know that."

"All right," I said, at last. "So it can come again, All right."

He smiled, but the smile was sorrowful. "I had to try to tell you," he said.

"Yes," I said. "I understand that."

"You're my brother," he said, looking straight at me, and not smiling at all.

"Yes," I repeated, "yes. I understand that."

He turned back to the window, looking out. "All that hatred down there," he said, "all that hatred and misery and love. It's a wonder it doesn't blow the avenue apart."

We went to the only nightclub on a short, dark street, downtown. We squeezed through the narrow, chattering, jam-packed bar to the entrance of the big room, where the bandstand was. And we stood there for a moment, for the lights were very dim in this room and we couldn't see. Then, "Hello, boy," said a voice and an enormous black man, much older than Sonny or myself, erupted out of all that atmospheric lighting and put an arm around Sonny's shoulder. "I been sitting right here," he said, "waiting for you."

He had a big voice, too, and heads in the darkness turned toward us.

Sonny grinned and pulled a little away, and said, "Creole, this is my brother. I told you about him."

Creole shook my hand. "I'm glad to meet you, son," he said, and it was clear that he was glad to meet me *there*, for Sonny's sake. And he smiled, "You got a real musician in *your* family," and he took his arm from Sonny's shoulder and slapped him, lightly, affectionately, with the back of his hand.

"Well. Now I've heard it all," said a voice behind us. This was another musician, and a friend of Sonny's, a coal-black, cheerful-looking man, built close to the ground. He immediately began confiding to me, at the top of his lungs, the most terrible things about Sonny, his teeth gleaming like a lighthouse and his laugh coming up out of him like the beginning of an earthquake. And it turned out that everyone at the bar knew Sonny, or almost everyone; some were musicians, working there, or nearby, or not working, some were simply hangers-on, and some were there to hear Sonny play. I was introduced to all of them and they were all very polite to me. Yet, it was clear that, for them, I was only Sonny's brother. Here, I was in Sonny's world. Or, rather: his kingdom. Here, it was not even a question that his veins bore royal blood.

They were going to play soon and Creole installed me, by myself, at a table in a dark corner. Then I watched them, Creole, and the little black man, and Sonny, and the others, while they horsed around, standing just below the bandstand. The light from the bandstand spilled just a little short of them and, watching them laughing and gesturing and moving about, I had the feeling that they, nevertheless, were being most careful not to step into that circle of light too suddenly: that if they moved into the light too suddenly, without thinking, they would perish in flame. Then, while I watched, one of them, the small, black man, moved into the light and crossed the bandstand and started fooling around with his drums. Then— being funny and being, also, extremely ceremonious—Creole took Sonny by the arm and led him to the piano. A woman's voice called Sonny's name and a few hands started clapping. And Sonny, also being funny and being ceremonious, and so touched, I think, that he could have cried, but neither hiding it nor showing it, riding it like a man, grinned, and put both hands to his heart and bowed from the waist.

Creole then went to the bass fiddle and a lean, very bright-skinned brown man jumped up on the bandstand and picked up his horn. So there they were, and the atmosphere on the bandstand and in the room began to change and tighten. Someone stepped up to the microphone and announced them. Then there were all kinds of murmurs. Some people at the bar shushed others. The waitress ran around, frantically getting in the last orders, guys and chicks got closer to each other, and the lights on the bandstand, on the quartet, turned to a kind of indigo. Then they all looked different there. Creole looked about him for the last time, as though he were

making certain that all his chickens were in the coop, and then he—
jumped and struck the fiddle. And there they were.

All I know about music is that not many people ever really hear it. And
even then, on the rare occasions when something opens within, and the
music enters, what we mainly hear, or hear corroborated, are personal, private, vanishing evocations. But the man who creates the music is hearing
something else, is dealing with the roar rising from the void and imposing
order on it as it hits the air. What is evoked in him, then, is of another order,
more terrible because it has no words, and triumphant, too, for that same
reason. And his triumph, when he triumphs, is ours. I just watched Sonny's
face. His face was troubled, he was working hard, but he wasn't with it. And
I had the feeling that, in a way, everyone on the bandstand was waiting for
him, both waiting for him and pushing him along. But as I began to watch
Creole, I realized that it was Creole who held them all back. He had them
on a short rein. Up there, keeping the beat with his whole body, wailing on
the fiddle, with his eyes half closed, he was listening to everything, but he
was listening to Sonny. He was having a dialogue with Sonny. He wanted
Sonny to leave the shoreline and strike out for the deep water. He was
Sonny's witness that deep water and drowning were not the same thing—he
had been there, and he knew. And he wanted Sonny to know. He was waiting for Sonny to do the things on the keys which would let Creole know
that Sonny was in the water.

And, while Creole listened, Sonny moved, deep within, exactly like
someone in torment. I had never before thought of how awful the relationship must be between the musician and his instrument. He has to fill it,
this instrument, with the breath of life, his own. He has to make it do what
he wants it to do. And a piano is just a piano. It's made out of so much wood
and wires and little hammers and big ones, and ivory. While there's only so
much you can do with it, the only way to find this out is to try; to try and
make it do everything.

And Sonny hadn't been near a piano for over a year. And he wasn't on
much better terms with his life, not the life that stretched before him now.
He and the piano stammered, started one way, got scared, stopped; started
another way, panicked, marked time, started again; then seemed to have
found a direction, panicked again, got stuck. And the face I saw on Sonny
I'd never seen before. Everything had been burned out of it, and, at the
same time, things usually hidden were being burned in, by the fire and fury
of the battle which was occurring in him up there.

Yet, watching Creole's face as they neared the end of the first set, I had
the feeling that something had happened, something I hadn't heard. Then
they finished, there was scattered applause, and then, without an instant's
warning, Creole started into something else, it was almost sardonic, it was
Am I Blue. [9] And, as though he commanded, Sonny began to play. Something began to happen. And Creole let out the reins. The dry, low, black
man said something awful on the drums, Creole answered, and the drums
talked back. Then the horn insisted, sweet and high, slightly detached perhaps, and Creole listened, commenting now and then, dry, and driving,

9. Jazz standard; Billie Holliday made a famous recording of it.

beautiful and calm and old. Then they all came together again, and Sonny was part of the family again. I could tell this from his face. He seemed to have found, right there beneath his fingers, a damn brand-new piano. It seemed that he couldn't get over it. Then, for awhile, just being happy with Sonny, they seemed to be agreeing with him that brand-new pianos certainly were a gas.

Then Creole stepped forward to remind them that what they were playing was the blues. He hit something in all of them, he hit something in me, myself, and the music tightened and deepened, apprehension began to beat the air. Creole began to tell us what the blues were all about. They were not about anything very new. He and his boys up there were keeping it new, at the risk of ruin, destruction, madness, and death, in order to find new ways to make us listen. For, while the tale of how we suffer, and how we are delighted, and how we may triumph is never new, it always must be heard. There isn't any other tale to tell, it's the only light we've got in all this darkness.

And this tale, according to that face, that body, those strong hands on those strings, has another aspect in every country, and a new depth in every generation. Listen, Creole seemed to be saying, listen. Now these are Sonny's blues. He made the little black man on the drums know it, and the bright, brown man on the horn. Creole wasn't trying any longer to get Sonny in the water. He was wishing him Godspeed. Then he stepped back, very slowly, filling the air with the immense suggestion that Sonny speak for himself.

Then they all gathered around Sonny and Sonny played. Every now and again one of them seemed to say, amen. Sonny's fingers filled the air with life, his life. But that life contained so many others. And Sonny went all the way back, he really began with the spare, flat statement of the opening phrase of the song. Then he began to make it his. It was very beautiful because it wasn't hurried and it was no longer a lament. I seemed to hear with what burning he had made it his, with what burning we had yet to make it ours, how we could cease lamenting. Freedom lurked around us and I understood, at last, that he could help us to be free if we would listen, that he would never be free until we did. Yet, there was no battle in his face now. I heard what he had gone through, and would continue to go through until he came to rest in earth. He had made it his: that long line, of which we knew only Mama and Daddy. And he was giving it back, as everything must be given back, so that, passing through death, it can live forever. I saw my mother's face again, and felt, for the first time, how the stones of the road she had walked on must have bruised her feet. I saw the moonlit road where my father's brother died. And it brought something else back to me, and carried me past it, I saw my little girl again and felt Isabel's tears again, and I felt my own tears begin to rise. And I was yet aware that this was only a moment, that the world waited outside, as hungry as a tiger, and that trouble stretched above us, longer than the sky.

Then it was over. Creole and Sonny let out their breath, both soaking wet, and grinning. There was a lot of applause and some of it was real. In the dark, the girl came by and I asked her to take drinks to the bandstand. There was a long pause, while they talked up there in the indigo light and after awhile I saw the girl put a Scotch and milk on top of the piano for

Sonny. He didn't seem to notice it, but just before they started playing again, he sipped from it and looked toward me, and nodded. Then he put it back on top of the piano. For me, then, as they began to play again, it glowed and shook above my brother's head like the very cup of trembling.[1]

1957

1. See Isaiah 51:17, 22.

BOB KAUFMAN

1925–1986

Born on April 18, 1925, in New Orleans to an Orthodox Jewish father and a mother of African descent, Bob Kaufman has been referred to as the "black Rimbaud" of the Beat poets. Some think of him as the Beat movement's "unsung Patriarch"; and for sure, he is not frequently included in the roll call of bad boys that embraces the likes of Ferlinghetti, Kerouac, Rexroth, Burrows, Ginsberg, and Corso, whose works, *Howl*, *On the Road*, and *Naked Lunch*, among others, have generally been accepted as the leading benchmarks of this alternative American culture that sprang up among the bars and gay places of San Francisco in the 1950s and 1960s. But inspired by the musical innovations of Charlie Parker, Dizzy Gillespie, and Miles Davis, Kaufman fashioned a poetry that was decidedly modernist in its irrational, surrealist, and Dadaistic appeal. Some have even attributed the term *Beat* to Kaufman and his fine sense of word play. One critic suggests that Kaufman's poetic practice adapts the "harmonic complexities and spontaneous inventions of bebop to poetic euphony and meter," employing "the jargon of bebop and the improvisational structure" of this musical genre in the interest of poetic discourse. The "quintessential jazz poet," Kaufman also borrowed some of his licks from jazz singer and songwriter King Pleasure. But his repertoire of heroes showed a considerable catholicity of taste as it included the literary figures Walt Whitman, Hart Crane, Albert Camus, and Guillaume Apollinaire. Kaufman's poetry crosses the thematic range of Beat concerns—madness, poverty, spontaneity, and the search for holiness. Superimposed on Kaufman's metrical innovations, these influences combine to make the poet an invigorating radical and unconventional voice.

One of the younger of thirteen siblings, Kaufman searched at length for a system of values, a basis for belief, and found it, in part, in an eventual strong identification with the philosophy of Buddhism. After attending elementary school in New Orleans, he left home at about the seventh or eighth grade for a life at sea and spent twenty years in the U.S. Merchant Marines, during which time he acquired a taste for literature. In the late 1950s, he settled in San Francisco, with his wife, Eileen. One of the key figures of the burgeoning literary scene on the West Coast, he produced at least two classic works of the Beat school—a broadside titled *Abomunist Manifesto* (1959) and *Solitudes Crowded with Loneliness* (1965). The former, "an indictment of contemporary society," might be taken as a programmatic statement of Beat intent and purpose, though we would be hard pressed to think of the original Beatniks as "programmatic" in any rigorous sense. One poem from *Solitudes*— *Bagel Shop Jazz*, its title resonating across disparate cultures—won the poet the Guiness Poetry Award and appeared in the fourth volume of the *Guiness Book of Poetry* in 1961. Kaufman's *Golden Sardine* appeared in 1967. *Crootey Song*, from this collection, is said to have abandoned "language altogether in an attempt to reproduce a bebop scat improvisation."

For almost a decade following the publication of *Golden Sardine*, Kaufman, it is said, did not speak a word, but he dramatically breached his silence on the day that the Vietnam War ended. Over the next few years, Kaufman wrote new poems that were collected in *The Ancient Rain: Poems 1956–1978* (1981). But in 1978, Kaufman renounced both writing and speech and withdrew once again into a silent place. A target of police harrassment, a user of drugs, and no stranger to madness and its anguish, Kaufman died on a Sunday morning, January 12, 1986, in San Francisco. It is not difficult to trace the cutting edge of his poetry down to the succeeding generation of black nationalists and the Black Arts movement of the sixties, especially in the chanting poems of LeRoi Jones's and Larry Neal's important anthology *Black Fire.*

Walking Parker [1] Home

Sweet beats of jazz impaled on slivers of wind
Kansas Black Morning/ First Horn Eyes/
Historical sound pictures on New Bird wings
People shouts/ boy alto dreams/ Tomorrow's
Gold belled pipe of stops and future Blues Times   5
Lurking Hawkins/ shadows of Lester/[2] realization
Bronze fingers—brain extensions seeking trapped sounds
Ghetto thoughts/ bandstand courage/ solo flight
Nerve-wracked suspicions of newer songs and doubts
New York altar city/ black tears/ secret disciples   10
Hammer horn pounding soul marks on unswinging gates
Culture gods/ mob sounds/ visions of spikes
Panic excursions to tribal Jazz wombs and transfusions
Heroin nights of birth/ and soaring/ over boppy new ground.
Smothered rage covering pyramids of notes spontaneously
      exploding   15
Cool revelations/ shrill hopes/ beauty speared into greedy ears
Birdland [3] nights on bop mountains, windy saxophone revolutions
Dayrooms of junk/ and melting walls and circling vultures/
Money cancer/ remembered pain/ terror flights/
Death and indestructible existence   20

In that Jazz corner of life
Wrapped in a mist of sound
His legacy, our Jazz-tinted dawn
Wailing his triumphs of oddly begotten dreams
Inviting the nerveless to feel once more   25
That fierce dying of humans consumed
In raging fires of Love.

                                                                      1965

Grandfather Was Queer, Too

He was first seen in a Louisiana bayou,
Playing chess with an intellectual lobster.

1. Charlie Parker (1920–1955), African American jazz musician.
2. Coleman Hawkins and Lester Young were prominent African American jazz musicians.
3. Legendary New York City jazz club.

They burned his linoleum house alive
And sent that intellectual off to jail.
He wrote home every day, to no avail.   5
Grandfather had cut out, he couldn't raise the bail.

Next seen, skiing on some dusty Texas road,
An intellectual's soul hung from his ears,
Discussing politics with an unemployed butterfly.
They hung that poor butterfly, poor butterfly.   10
Grandfather had cut out, he couldn't raise the bail.

Next seen on the Arizona desert, walking,
Applying soothing poultices to the teeth
Of an aching mountain.
Dentists all over the state brought gauze balls,   15
Bandaged the mountain, buried it at sea.
Grandfather had cut out, he couldn't raise the bail.

Next seen in California, the top part,
Arranging a marriage, mating trees,
Crossing a rich redwood and a black pine.   20
He was exposed by the Boy Scouts of America.
The trees were arrested on a vag charge.[1]
Grandfather cut out, he couldn't raise the bail.

Now I have seen him here. He is beat.
His girlfriend has green ears;   25
She is twenty-three months pregnant.
I kissed them both:
Live happily ever after.

                                                    1965

Jail Poems

1

I am sitting in a cell with a view of evil parallels,
Waiting thunder to splinter me into a thousand me's.
It is not enough to be in one cage with one self;
I want to sit opposite every prisoner in every hole.
Doors roll and bang, every slam a finality, bang!   5
The junkie disappeared into a red noise, stoning out his hell.
The odored wino congratulates himself on not smoking,
Fingerprints left lying on black inky gravestones,
Noises of pain seeping through steel walls crashing
Reach my own hurt. I become part of someone forever.   10
Wild accents of criminals are sweeter to me than hum of cops,
Busy battening down hatches of human souls; cargo
Destined for ports of accusations, harbors of guilt.
What do policemen eat, Socrates,[1] still prisoner, old one?

1. Vagrancy charge.
1. Ancient Greek teacher and philosopher (470–
399 B.C.), who was charged with the corruption of
youth; he was sentenced to die by drinking hemlock.

2

Painter, paint me a crazy jail, mad water-color cells.   15
Poet, how old is suffering? Write it in yellow lead.
God, make me a sky on my glass ceiling. I need stars now,
To lead through this atmosphere of shrieks and private hells,
Entrances and exits, in . . . out . . . up . . . down, the civic seesaw.
Here—me—now—hear—me—now—always here somehow.   20

3

In a universe of cells—who is not in jail? Jailers.
In a world of hospitals—who is not sick? Doctors.
A golden sardine is swimming in my head.
Oh we know some things, man, about some things
Like jazz and jails and God.   25
Saturday is a good day to go to jail.

4

Now they give a new form, quivering jelly-like,
That proves any boy can be president of Muscatel.[2]
They are mad at him because he's one of Them.
Gray-speckled unplanned nakedness; stinking   30
Fingers grasping toilet bowl. Mr. America wants to bathe.
Look! On the floor, lying across America's face—
A real movie star featured in a million newsreels.
What am I doing—feeling compassion?
When he comes out of it, he will help kill me.   35
He probably hates living.

5

Nuts, skin bolts, clanking in his stomach, scrambled.
His society's gone to pieces in his belly, bloated.
See the·great American windmill, tilting at itself,
Good solid stock, the kind that made America drunk.   40
Success written all over his street-streaked ass.
Successful-type success, forty home runs in one inning.
Stop suffering, Jack, you can't fool us. We know.
This is the greatest country in the world, ain't it?
He didn't make it. Wino in Cell 3.   45

6

There have been too many years in this short span of mine.
My soul demands a cave of its own, like the Jain[3] god;
Yet I must make it go on, hard like jazz, glowing
In this dark plastic jungle, land of long night, chilled.
My navel is a button to push when I want inside out.   50
Am I not more than a mass of entrails and rough tissue?
Must I break my bones? Drink my wine-diluted blood?
Should I dredge old sadness from my chest?
Not again,
All those ancient balls of fire, hotly swallowed, let them lie.   55
Let me spit breath mists of introspection, bits of me,
So that when I am gone, I shall be in the air.

2. Sweet fortified wine made from Muscat grapes.
3. One who practices the Indian religion of Jain-   ism, which teaches that salvation can be achieved through knowledge, faith, and good conduct.

7

Someone whom I am is no one.
Something I have done is nothing.
Someplace I have been is nowhere.　　　　60
I am not me.
What of the answers
I must find questions for?
All these strange streets
I must find cities for,　　　　65
Thank God for beatniks.

8

All night the stink of rotting people,
Fumes rising from pyres of live men,
Fill my nose with gassy disgust,
Drown my exposed eyes in tears.　　　　70

9

Traveling God salesmen, bursting my ear drum
With the dullest part of a good sexy book,
Impatient for Monday and adding machines.

10

Yellow-eyed dogs whistling in evening.

11

The baby came to jail today.　　　　75

12

One more day to hell, filled with floating glands.

13

The jail, a huge hollow metal cube
Hanging from the moon by a silver chain.
Someday Johnny Appleseed is going to chop it down.

14

Three long strings of light　　　　80
Braided into a ray.

15

I am apprehensive about my future;
My past has turned its back on me.

16

Shadows I see, forming on the wall,
Pictures of desires protected from my own eyes.　　　　85

17

After spending all night constructing a dream,
Morning came and blinded me with light.
Now I seek among mountains of crushed eggshells
For the God damned dream I never wanted.

18
Sitting here writing things on paper,   90
Instead of sticking the pencil into the air.

19
The Battle of Monumental Failures raging,
Both hoping for a good clean loss.

20
Now I see the night, silently overwhelming day.

21
Caught in imaginary webs of conscience,   95
I weep over my acts, yet believe.

22
Cities should be built on one side of the street.

23
People who can't cast shadows
Never die of freckles.

24
The end always comes last.   100

25
We sat at a corner table,
Devouring each other word by word,
Until nothing was left, repulsive skeletons.

26
I sit here writing, not daring to stop,
For fear of seeing what's outside my head.   105

27
There, Jesus, didn't hurt a bit, did it?

28
I am afraid to follow my flesh over those narrow
Wide hard soft female beds, but I do.

29
Link by link, we forged the chain.
Then, discovering the end around our necks,   110
We bugged out.

30
I have never seen a wild poetic loaf of bread,
But if I did, I would eat it, crust and all.

31
From how many years away does a baby come?

32
Universality, duality, totality . . . . one.   115

33
The defective on the floor, mumbling,
Was once a man who shouted across tables.

34
Come, help flatten a raindrop.

Written in San Francisco City Prison
Cell 3, 1959

1965

Unanimity Has Been Achieved, Not a Dot Less for Its Accidentalness

Raga[1] of the drum, the drum the drum the drum the drum, the
    heartbeat
Raga of hold, raga of fold, raga of root, raga of crest, raga before
    coming,
Raga of lip, raga of brass, raga of ultimate come with yesterday, raga
    of a parched tongue-walked lip, raga of yellow, raga of mellow,
    raga of new, raga of old, raga of blue, raga of gold, raga of air
    spinning into itself,
I ring against slate and shell and wood and stone and leaf and bone
And towered holes and floors and eyes—against lone is lorn & rock &
    dust & flattened ball & solitudes of air & breath & hair & skin
    fed halves & wholes & bulls & calves & mad & soul & new &
    old & silence & saves & fall wall & water falling & fling my eye
    to sky & tingle & tangle.   5
I sing a mad raga, I sing a mad raga, a glad raga for the ringing bell I
    sing.
A man fishing with old clothes line, shouting bass drum
Sometimes in extravagant moments of shock of unrehearsed
    curiosity, I crawl outside myself, sneaking out through the eyes,
    one blasé, one surprised, until I begin to feel my own
    strangeness; shyly I give up the ghost and go back in until next
    time.

I can remember four times when I was not crying & once when I was
    not laughing.
I am kneaded by a million black fingers & nothing about me
    improves.   10
Gothic brain surgeons, weeping over the remains of destroyed love
    machines.
Diggers, corkscrewing cleanly in, exhilerausted, into the mind mine,
    impaled on edgeless shafts of subtle reminiscence,
    green-walking across the belts and ties.
Slanted dark-walked time, wet with ages of dryness,

---

1. Ancient traditional melodic patterns in Indian music, often used as the basis for improvisation.

Raga of insignificance & blessed hopelessness.
Raga of sadness, of madness, of green screamed dreams, mile-deep
    eyes.   15

The greatest men have gone unknown: Buddha was the
    twenty-fourth.
A beggar is the body of a God-ness, come to shoot movies with his
    eye,
Movies of people who do not beg, ragged, broke eagles, hummed
    into the wheels turning, some in, others out, rarely ever in or
    out, or vice versa, half open.
A string begins where a man ends a string, a man begins where a
    string ends. A man bereft of string falls all walls, becomes a
    screamed baby, raved.

                                                                  1981

War Memoir: Jazz, Don't Listen to It at Your Own Risk

In the beginning, in the wet
Warm dark place,
Straining to break out, clawing at strange cables
Hearing her screams, laughing
"Later we forgot ourselves, we didn't know"   5
Some secret jazz
Shouted, wait, don't go.
Impatient, we came running, innocent
Laughing blobs of blood and faith.
To this mother, father world   10
Where laughter seems out of place
So we learned to cry, pleased
They pronounced human.
The secret jazz blew a sigh
Some familiar sound shouted wait   15
Some are evil, some will hate.
"Just Jazz, blowing it's top again"
So we rushed and laughed.
As we pushed and grabbed
While Jazz blew in the night   20
Suddenly we were too busy to hear a sound
We were busy shoving mud in men's mouths,
Who were busy dying on living ground
Busy earning medals, for killing children on deserted streetcorners
Occupying their fathers, raping their mothers, busy humans were   25
Busy burning Japanese in atomicolorcinescope
With stereophonic screams,
What one-hundred-percent red-blooded savage would waste
    precious time
Listening to Jazz, with so many important things going on
But even the fittest murderers must rest   30
So we sat down on our blood-soaked garments,
And listened to Jazz
                        lost, steeped in all our dreams
We were shocked at the sound of life, long gone from our own

We were indignant at the whistling, thinking, singing, beating,
    swinging
Living sound, which mocked us, but let us feel sweet life again   35
We wept for it, hugged, kissed it, loved it, joined it, we drank it,
Smoked it, ate with it, slept with it
We made our girls wear it for lovemaking
Instead of silly lace gowns,
Now in those terrible moments, when the dark memories come   40
The secret moments to which we admit no one
When guiltily we crawl back in time, reaching away from ourselves
We hear a familiar sound,
Jazz, scratching, digging, bluing, swinging jazz,
And we listen   45
And we feel
And live.

1981

LORRAINE HANSBERRY

1930–1965

When *A Raisin in the Sun* debuted at the Ethel Barrymore Theater in March 1959, Lorraine Hansberry became the first black woman to have a play produced on Broadway. When it went on to win the New York Drama Critics Circle award for Best Play of the Year, beating out Tennessee Williams's *Sweet Bird of Youth* and Eugene O'Neill's *A Touch of the Poet*, Hansberry became the youngest writer and first black to achieve that distinction. Running for 538 performances, *A Raisin in the Sun* broke yet another record as the longest running play by an African American on Broadway.

Since its first appearance, the popularity of *A Raisin in the Sun* with American audiences has never waned, and its impact on modern drama has been consistently noted. The play has been hailed a classic and often placed in that small inner circle of American dramas that includes Arthur Miller's *Death of a Salesman*, Tennessee Williams's *The Glass Menagerie*, and Eugene O'Neill's *Long Day's Journey into Night*.

Originally titling the play "The Crystal Stair," after a line from Langston Hughes's *Mother to Son*, Hansberry finally settled on a line from *Harlem*, another Hughes poem: "What happens to a dream deferred? / Does it dry up / like a raisin in the sun. . . . *Or does it explode?*" In its dramatization of deferred dreams that ever threaten to explode, *A Raisin in the Sun* has been likened to Richard Wright's *Native Son*. Beginning with the sound of the alarm clock that opens the play, some note, the play bears a striking resemblance to Wright's novel. Others press the comparison still further to suggest that *A Raisin in the Sun* is to black drama what Richard Wright's *Native Son* is to the black novel.

Born May 19, 1930, on the South Side of Chicago, Lorraine Vivian Hansberry was the youngest of four children of Carl A. Hansberry and Nanny Perry Hansberry. She enjoyed a comfortable, middle-class existence, and the prominence of her family in Chicago, as well as national, black political circles brought her into contact with such figures as Paul Robeson; Duke Ellington; and Walter White, novelist and former secretary of the NAACP. Her uncle Leo Hansberry, distinguished professor of African history at Howard University, is credited with influencing the Pan-

African dimension of Hansberry's work, which in turn globalized her commitments to black liberation struggles.

Hansberry became personally acquainted with struggles for social and political change when her family challenged Chicago's restrictive real estate covenants and became a test case for integrated housing in 1938, when Hansberry was eight years old. As Hansberry describes it, "howling mobs surrounded [our] house," throwing bricks in protest against the move. Hansberry's father eventually won the case in a historic 1940 Supreme Court decision (Hansberry vs. Lee).

Hansberry's interests in drama were sparked when she wandered into a rehearsal of Sean O'Casey's Juno and the Paycock, while a student at the University of Wisconsin. Dissatisfied with the Wisconsin curriculum, she left for New York in 1950, where she worked as a reporter for Robeson's radical black newspaper, Freedom, writing reviews and essays, and eventually becoming associate editor. She was actively involved in peace and freedom movements, marching on picket lines and protesting against the domination of a white power elite. It was while marching on a picket line that she met Robert Nemiroff, whom she married in 1953 and with whom she maintained a strong artistic relationship even after their separation and subsequent divorce. The year she married, Hansberry resigned from Freedom to pursue her ambitions as a playwright.

While the forces that collaborated to create A Raisin in the Sun are multiple, Hansberry could not have chosen a more propitious moment to dramatize the role of racial discrimination in deferring the dreams of a black family for decent housing. The play appeared five years after Brown vs. the Board of Education, the Supreme Court's landmark decision on school desegregation; four years after the Montgomery Bus Boycott; and on the eve of the student sit-in movement. For these reasons, Amiri Baraka called A Raisin in the Sun the "quintessential civil rights drama."

Her commitments to social commentary, but not to agitprop, led Hansberry to employ the conventional realism of the well-made play, a style that other classic American dramatists had used to full effect, but one that seemed already anachronistic by 1959. Hansberry described her work as "genuine realism," which she distinguished from naturalism:

> Naturalism tends to take the world as it is and say: this is what it is, this is how it happens, it is "true" because we see it everyday in life that way—you know, you simply photograph the garbage can. But in realism—I think the artist who is creating the realistic work imposes on it not only what is but what is *possible* . . . because that is part of reality too.

While critics have been almost uniform in their praise of Hansberry and of the impact of A Raisin in the Sun on modern drama, others have taken issue with her work, going so far as to suggest that her vision and expectations as a dramatist were shaped by whites, and especially white males, who constitute the elite world of Broadway, theater critics, and the white theater-going public.

Although many of its self-styled militant vanguard were stringent in their criticism of A Raisin in the Sun—some dismissing it as nonthreatening "kitchen melodrama," others as "assimilationist," others as a sellout to the white power structure, still others as a fable of a rejected strategy of "passive resistance"—Hansberry's play actually paved the way for the black theater movement of the 1960s. Amiri Baraka later admitted this and reversed his early opinion that the play was a period piece with outdated topical concerns. He praised it for its "profoundly imposing stature, continuing relevance, and pointed social analysis."

Hansberry sold the film rights for A Raisin in the Sun to Columbia Pictures in 1959, and in an effort to preserve the play's artistic integrity, she wrote the screenplay. Although Columbia heavily censored the script, especially scenes judged to be too critical of the dominant culture, the film was nominated for best screenplay of the year by the Screenwriters' Guild.

The success of *A Raisin in the Sun* brought Hansberry celebrity status, which expanded her role as activist and spokesperson for black causes. She organized support for the Student Non-Violent Coordinating Committee (SNCC) and wrote the text for *The Movement: Documentary of a Struggle for Equality*, a book prepared by the SNCC that consisted of graphic photographs of lynchings and savage beatings of civil rights demonstrators. Her work with the SNCC, as well as her criticism of the House Un-American Activities Committee, undoubtedly contributed to Hansberry's classification by the FBI as a member of "black nationalist hate groups."

Hansberry's unwavering and uncompromising political stances contribute to an understanding of her second play, *The Sign in Sidney Brustein's Window*. Produced in 1964, it follows a Jewish intellectual's vacillation between disenchantment and political conviction. In a letter to an admirer in China, Hansberry discussed one force behind the writing of the play: "I am working on a play which presumes to try and examine something of the nature of commitment. It happens to be, in my opinion, one of the leading problems before my generation here: what to identify with, what to become involved in; what to take a stand on; what, if you will, even to believe in at all."

Sidney Brustein enjoyed neither the critical acclaim nor the commercial success of *A Raisin in the Sun*, a fact that has been widely attributed to the intellectual content of the play and the subtle complexity of the characters. In part, an attack on the then fashionable ideas of existentialism and the theater of the absurd, *The Sign in Sidney Brustein's Window* challenged the bankrupt assumption that struggles for social change were pointless. In an unpublished play, *The Arrival of Mr. Todog*, Hansberry satirized Samuel Beckett's play *Waiting for Godot*, registering her sense of the spiritual bankruptcy in its ideas, which American intellectuals of the time were taking warmly to their bosom. Despite the poor reception that greeted *Sidney Brustein*, Hansberry's supporters rallied to keep the play alive and managed to keep it open for 101 performances. The play closed the day Hansberry died of cancer, on January 12, 1965.

At the time of her death, Hansberry was at work on a play about Mary Wollstonecraft, an eighteenth-century feminist, along with two other plays, which were eventually edited and published by her ex-husband and literary executor, Robert Nemiroff: *Les Blancs* and *What Use Are Flowers?* A third television drama, *The Drinking Gourd*, commissioned but not produced by NBC, was posthumously published in 1972. Scenes from the script were included in Nemiroff's play *To Be Young, Gifted and Black*, also the title he gave the series of Hansberry's autobiographical writings, letters, and plays he compiled and published in 1969. Subtitled *Lorraine Hansberry in Her Own Words*, *To Be Young, Gifted and Black* has been criticized for revealing too little about Hansberry and for possibly censoring or diluting the radical feminist vision found in early planning notes for her plays and evident in such unpublished essays as *Simone De Beauvoir and The Second Sex: An American Commentary, 1957*.

By the time she wrote the essay on de Beauvoir, Hansberry was coming out as a lesbian and ending her marriage. In several letters to *The Ladder*, an early lesbian publication, she analyzed the political connections between homophobia and anti-feminism, as well as the economic and psychological factors that pressure lesbians into marriage.

While Hansberry produced much in her short life of both aesthetic and social significance, it is *A Raisin in the Sun* that critics single out from among her versatile contributions. In 1989, in celebration of the play's twenty-fifth anniversary, *A Raisin in the Sun* was staged with restorations of scenes and passages omitted from the original production. Time had not diminished the enthusiasm the play has long enjoyed. Critics praised its expanded version as a "bristling, unqualified triumph." While preparing for a documentary film on the black theater movement, Woodie King Jr. found that more than forty of the sixty playwrights interviewed professed to being influenced or aided, or both, by Lorraine Hansberry and her work, a tribute earning her a place in the firmament of classic American drama.

A Raisin in the Sun

What happens to a dream deferred?
Does it dry up
Like a raisin in the sun?
Or fester like a sore—
And then run?
Does it stink like rotten meat?
Or crust and sugar over—
Like a syrupy sweet?

Maybe it just sags
Like a heavy load.

Or does it explode?
—LANGSTON HUGHES

CAST OF CHARACTERS

RUTH YOUNGER
TRAVIS YOUNGER
WALTER LEE YOUNGER (BROTHER)
BENEATHA YOUNGER
LENA YOUNGER (MAMA)

JOSEPH ASAGAI
GEORGE MURCHISON
KARL LINDNER
BOBO
MOVING MEN

Act I

SCENE ONE

The Younger living room would be a comfortable and well-ordered room if it were not for a number of indestructible contradictions to this state of being. Its furnishings are typical and undistinguished and their primary feature now is that they have clearly had to accommodate the living of too many people for too many years—and they are tired. Still, we can see that at some time, a time probably no longer remembered by the family (except perhaps for MAMA) *the furnishings of this room were actually selected with care and love and even hope—and brought to this apartment and arranged with taste and pride.*

That was a long time ago. Now the once loved pattern of the couch upholstery has to fight to show itself from under acres of crocheted doilies and couch covers which have themselves finally come to be more important than the upholstery. And here a table or a chair has been moved to disguise the worn places in the carpet; but the carpet has fought back by showing its weariness, with depressing uniformity, elsewhere on its surface.

Weariness has, in fact, won in this room. Everything has been polished, washed, sat on, used, scrubbed too often. All pretenses but living itself have long since vanished from the very atmosphere of this room.

Moreover, a section of this room, for it is not really a room unto itself, though the landlord's lease would make it seem so, slopes backward to provide a small kitchen area, where the family prepares the meals that are eaten in the living room proper, which must also serve as dining room. The single window that has been provided for these "two" rooms is located in this kitchen area. The sole natural light the family may enjoy in the course of a day is only that which fights its way through this little window.

At left, a door leads to a bedroom which is shared by MAMA *and her daughter,* BENEATHA. *At right, opposite, is a second room (which in the beginning of the life of this apartment was probably a breakfast room) which serves as a bedroom for* WALTER *and his wife,* RUTH.

Time: Sometime between World War II and the present.

Place: Chicago's Southside.

At Rise: It is morning dark in the living room. TRAVIS *is asleep on the make-down bed at center. An alarm clock sounds from within the bedroom at right, and presently* RUTH *enters from that room and closes the door behind her. She crosses sleepily toward the window. As she passes her sleeping son she reaches down and shakes him a little. At the window she raises the shade and a dusky Southside morning light comes in feebly. She fills a pot with water and puts it on to boil. She calls to the boy, between yawns, in a slightly muffled voice.*

RUTH *is about thirty. We can see that she was a pretty girl, even exceptionally so, but now it is apparent that life has been little that she expected, and disappointment has already begun to hang in her face. In a few years, before thirty-five even, she will be known among her people as a "settled woman."*

She crosses to her son and gives him a good, final, rousing shake.

RUTH: Come on now, boy, it's seven thirty! [*Her son sits up at last, in a stupor of sleepiness.*] I say hurry up, Travis! You ain't the only person in the world got to use a bathroom! [*The child, a sturdy, handsome little boy of ten or eleven, drags himself out of the bed and almost blindly takes his towels and "today's clothes" from drawers and a closet and goes out to the bathroom, which is in an outside hall and which is shared by another family or families on the same floor.* RUTH *crosses to the bedroom door at right and opens it and calls in to her husband.*] Walter Lee! . . . It's after seven thirty! Lemme see you do some waking up in there now! [*She waits.*] You better get up from there, man! It's after seven thirty I tell you. [*She waits again.*] All right, you just go ahead and lay there and next thing you know Travis be finished and Mr. Johnson'll be in there and you'll be fussing and cussing round here like a mad man! And be late too! [*She waits, at the end of patience.*] Walter Lee—it's time for you to get up!

[*She waits another second and then starts to go into the bedroom, but is apparently satisfied that her husband has begun to get up. She stops, pulls the door to, and returns to the kitchen area. She wipes her face with a moist cloth and runs her fingers through her sleep-disheveled hair in a vain effort and ties an apron around her housecoat. The bedroom door at right opens and her husband stands in the doorway in his pajamas, which are rumpled and mismated. He is a lean, intense young man in his middle thirties, inclined to quick nervous movements and erratic speech habits—and always in his voice there is a quality of indictment.*]

WALTER: Is he out yet?

RUTH: What you mean *out?* He ain't hardly got in there good yet.

WALTER: [*Wandering in, still more oriented to sleep than to a new day.*] Well, what was you doing all that yelling for if I can't even get in there yet? [*Stopping and thinking.*] Check coming today?

RUTH: They *said* Saturday and this is just Friday and I hopes to God you ain't going to get up here first thing this morning and start talking to me 'bout no money—'cause I 'bout don't want to hear it.

WALTER: Something the matter with you this morning?

RUTH: No—I'm just sleepy as the devil. What kind of eggs you want?

WALTER: Not scrambled. [RUTH *starts to scramble eggs.*] Paper come? [RUTH *points impatiently to the rolled up* Tribune *on the table, and he gets it and spreads it out and vaguely reads the front page.*] Set off another bomb yesterday.

RUTH: [*Maximum indifference.*] Did they?

WALTER: [*Looking up.*] What's the matter with you?

RUTH: Ain't nothing the matter with me. And don't keep asking me that this morning.

WALTER: Ain't nobody bothering you. [*Reading the news of the day absently again.*] Say Colonel McCormick is sick.

RUTH: [*Affecting tea-party interest.*] Is he now? Poor thing.

WALTER: [*Sighing and looking at his watch.*] Oh, me. [*He waits.*] Now what is that boy doing in that bathroom all this time? He just going to have to start getting up earlier. I can't be late to work on account of him fooling around in there.

RUTH: [*Turning on him.*] Oh, no he ain't going to be getting up no earlier no such thing! It ain't his fault that he can't get to bed no earlier nights 'cause he got a bunch of crazy good-for-nothing clowns sitting up running their mouths in what is supposed to be his bedroom after ten o'-clock at night . . .

WALTER: That's what you mad about, ain't it? The things I want to talk about with my friends just couldn't be important in your mind, could they?

[*He rises and finds a cigarette in her handbag on the table and crosses to the little window and looks out, smoking and deeply enjoying this first one.*]

RUTH: [*Almost matter of factly, a complaint too automatic to deserve emphasis.*] Why you always got to smoke before you eat in the morning?

WALTER: [*At the window.*] Just look at 'em down there . . . Running and racing to work . . . [*He turns and faces his wife and watches her a moment at the stove, and then, suddenly.*] You look young this morning, baby.

RUTH: [*Indifferently.*] Yeah?

WALTER: Just for a second—stirring them eggs. It's gone now—just for a second it was—you looked real young again. [*Then, drily.*] It's gone now—you look like yourself again.

RUTH: Man, if you don't shut up and leave me alone.

WALTER: [*Looking out to the street again.*] First thing a man ought to learn in life is not to make love to no colored woman first thing in the morning. You all some evil people at eight o'clock in the morning.

[TRAVIS *appears in the hall doorway, almost fully dressed and quite wide awake now, his towels and pajamas across his shoulders. He opens the door and signals for his father to make the bathroom in a hurry.*]

TRAVIS: [*Watching the bathroom.*] Daddy, come on!

[WALTER *gets his bathroom utensils and flies out to the bathroom.*]

RUTH: Sit down and have your breakfast, Travis.

TRAVIS: Mama, this is Friday. [*Gleefully.*] Check coming tomorrow, huh?

RUTH: You get your mind off money and eat your breakfast.

TRAVIS: [*Eating.*] This is the morning we supposed to bring the fifty cents to school.

RUTH: Well, I ain't got no fifty cents this morning.

TRAVIS: Teacher say we have to.

RUTH: I don't care what teacher say. I ain't got it. Eat your breakfast, Travis.

TRAVIS: I *am* eating.

RUTH: Hush up now and just eat!

[*The boy gives her an exasperated look for her lack of understanding, and eats grudgingly.*]

TRAVIS: You think Grandmama would have it?

RUTH: No! And I want you to stop asking your grandmother for money, you hear me?

TRAVIS: [*Outraged.*] Gaaaleee! I don't ask her, she just gimme it sometimes!

RUTH: Travis Willard Younger—I got too much on me this morning to be—

TRAVIS: Maybe Daddy—

RUTH: Travis!

[*The boy hushes abruptly. They are both quiet and tense for several seconds.*]

TRAVIS: [*Presently.*] Could I maybe go carry some groceries in front of the supermarket for a little while after school then?

RUTH: Just hush, I said. [TRAVIS *jabs his spoon into his cereal bowl viciously, and rests his head in anger upon his fists.*] If you through eating, you can get over there and make up your bed.

[*The boy obeys stiffly and crosses the room, almost mechanically, to the bed and more or less carefully folds the covering. He carries the bedding into his mother's room and returns with his books and cap.*]

TRAVIS: [*Sulking and standing apart from her unnaturally.*] I'm gone.

RUTH: [*Looking up from the stove to inspect him automatically.*] Come here. [*He crosses to her and she studies his head.*] If you don't take this comb and fix this here head, you better! [TRAVIS *puts down his books with a great sigh of oppression, and crosses to the mirror. His mother mutters under her breath about his "slubbornness."*] 'Bout to march out of here with that head looking just like chickens slept in it! I just don't know

where you get your slubborn ways . . . And get your jacket, too. Looks
chilly out this morning.

TRAVIS: [*With conspicuously brushed hair and jacket.*] I'm gone.

RUTH: Get carfare and milk money—[*Waving one finger.*]—and not a single penny for no caps, you hear me?

TRAVIS: [*With sullen politeness.*] Yes'm.

[*He turns in outrage to leave. His mother watches after him as in his
frustration he approaches the door almost comically. When she
speaks to him, her voice has become a very gentle tease.*]

RUTH: [*Mocking; as she thinks he would say it.*] Oh, Mama makes me so
mad sometimes, I don't know what to do! [*She waits and continues to his
back as he stands stock-still in front of the door.*] I wouldn't kiss that
woman good-bye for nothing in this world this morning! [*The boy finally
turns around and rolls his eyes at her, knowing the mood has changed and
he is vindicated; he does not, however, move toward her yet.*] Not for nothing in this world! [*She finally laughs aloud at him and holds out her arms
to him and we see that it is a way between them, very old and practiced. He
crosses to her and allows her to embrace him warmly but keeps his face
fixed with masculine rigidity. She holds him back from her presently and
looks at him and runs her fingers over the features of his face. With utter
gentleness—*] Now—whose little old angry man are you?

TRAVIS: [*The masculinity and gruffness start to fade at last.*] Aw gaalee—
Mama . . .

RUTH: [*Mimicking.*] Aw—gaaaaalleeeee, Mama! [*She pushes him, with
rough playfulness and finality, toward the door.*] Get on out of here or
you going to be late.

TRAVIS: [*In the face of love, new aggressiveness.*] Mama, could I *please* go
carry groceries?

RUTH: Honey, it's starting to get so cold evenings.

WALTER: [*Coming in from the bathroom and drawing a make-believe gun
from a make-believe holster and shooting at his son.*] What is it he wants
to do?

RUTH: Go carry groceries after school at the supermarket.

WALTER: Well, let him go . . .

TRAVIS: [*Quickly, to the ally.*] I *have* to—she won't gimme the fifty
cents . . .

WALTER: [*To his wife only.*] Why not?

RUTH: [*Simply, and with flavor.*] 'Cause we don't have it.

WALTER: [*To RUTH only.*] What you tell the boy things like that for?
[*Reaching down into his pants with a rather important gesture.*] Here,
son—

[*He hands the boy the coin, but his eyes are directed to his wife's.
TRAVIS takes the money happily.*]

TRAVIS: Thanks, Daddy.

[*He starts out. RUTH watches both of them with murder in her eyes.
WALTER stands and stares back at her with defiance, and suddenly
reaches into his pocket again on an afterthought.*]

WALTER: [*Without even looking at his son, still staring hard at his wife.*] In fact, here's another fifty cents . . . Buy yourself some fruit today—or take a taxicab to school or something!

TRAVIS: Whoopee—

[*He leaps up and clasps his father around the middle with his legs, and they face each other in mutual appreciation; slowly* WALTER LEE *peeks around the boy to catch the violent rays from his wife's eyes and draws his head back as if shot.*]

WALTER: You better get down now—and get to school, man.

TRAVIS: [*At the door.*] O.K. Good-bye.

[*He exits.*]

WALTER: [*After him, pointing with pride.*] That's *my* boy. [*She looks at him in disgust and turns back to her work.*] You know what I was thinking 'bout in the bathroom this morning?

RUTH: No.

WALTER: How come you always try to be so pleasant!

RUTH: What is there to be pleasant 'bout!

WALTER: You want to know what I was thinking 'bout in the bathroom or not!

RUTH: I know what you thinking 'bout.

WALTER: [*Ignoring her.*] 'Bout what me and Willy Harris was talking about last night.

RUTH: [*Immediately—a refrain.*] Willy Harris is a good-for-nothing loud mouth.

WALTER: Anybody who talks to me has got to be a good-for-nothing loud mouth, ain't he? And what you know about who is just a good-for-nothing loud mouth? Charlie Atkins was just a "good-for-nothing loud mouth" too, wasn't he! When he wanted me to go in the dry-cleaning business with him. And now—he's grossing a hundred thousand a year. A hundred thousand dollars a year! You still call *him* a loud mouth!

RUTH: [*Bitterly.*] Oh, Walter Lee . . .

[*She folds her head on her arms over the table.*]

WALTER: [*Rising and coming to her and standing over her.*] You tired, ain't you? Tired of everything. Me, the boy, the way we live—this beat-up hole—everything. Ain't you? [*She doesn't look up, doesn't answer.*] So tired—moaning and groaning all the time, but you wouldn't do nothing to help, would you? You couldn't be on my side that long for nothing, could you?

RUTH: Walter, please leave me alone.

WALTER: A man needs for a woman to back him up . . .

RUTH: Walter—

WALTER: Mama would listen to you. You know she listen to you more than she do me and Bennie. She think more of you. All you have to do is just sit down with her when you drinking your coffee one morning and talking 'bout things like you do and—[*He sits down beside her and demonstrates graphically what he thinks her methods and tone should be.*]— you just sip your coffee, see, and say easy like that you been thinking 'bout that deal Walter Lee is so interested in, 'bout the store and all, and sip some more coffee, like what you saying ain't really that important to you— And the next thing you know, she be listening good and asking you questions and when I come home—I can tell her the details. This ain't no fly-by-night proposition, baby. I mean we figured it out, me and Willy and Bobo.

RUTH: [*With a frown.*] Bobo?

WALTER: Yeah. You see, this little liquor store we got in mind cost seventy-five thousand and we figured the initial investment on the place be 'bout thirty thousand, see. That be ten thousand each. Course, there's a couple of hundred you got to pay so's you don't spend your life just waiting for them clowns to let your license get approved—

RUTH: You mean graft?

WALTER: [*Frowning impatiently.*] Don't call it that. See there, that just goes to show you what women understand about the world. Baby, don't *nothing* happen for you in this world 'less you pay *somebody* off!

RUTH: Walter, leave me alone! [*She raises her head and stares at him vigorously—then says, more quietly.*] Eat your eggs, they gonna be cold.

WALTER: [*Straightening up from her and looking off.*] That's it. There you are. Man say to his woman: I got me a dream. His woman say: Eat your eggs. [*Sadly, but gaining in power.*] Man say: I got to take hold of this here world, baby! And a woman will say: Eat your eggs and go to work. [*Passionately now.*] Man say: I got to change my life, I'm choking to death, baby! And his woman say—[*In utter anguish as he brings his fists down on his thighs.*]—Your eggs is getting cold!

RUTH: [*Softly.*] Walter, that ain't none of our money.

WALTER: [*Not listening at all or even looking at her.*] This morning, I was lookin' in the mirror and thinking about it . . . I'm thirty-five years old; I been married eleven years and I got a boy who sleeps in the living room—[*Very, very quietly.*]—and all I got to give him is stories about how rich white people live . . .

RUTH: Eat your eggs, Walter.

WALTER: *Damn my eggs . . . damn all the eggs that ever was!*

RUTH: Then go to work.

WALTER: [*Looking up at her.*] See—I'm trying to talk to you 'bout myself— [*Shaking his head with the repetition.*]—and all you can say is eat them eggs and go to work.

RUTH: [*Wearily.*] Honey, you never say nothing new. I listen to you every day, every night and every morning, and you never say nothing new. [*Shrugging.*] So you would rather *be* Mr. Arnold than be his chauffeur. So—I would *rather* be living in Buckingham Palace.

WALTER: That is just what is wrong with the colored woman in this world . . . Don't understand about building their men up and making 'em feel like they somebody. Like they can do something.

RUTH: [*Drily, but to hurt.*] There *are* colored men who do things.

WALTER: No thanks to the colored woman.

RUTH: Well, being a colored woman, I guess I can't help myself none.

    [*She rises and gets the ironing board and sets it up and attacks a huge pile of rough-dried clothes, sprinkling them in preparation for the ironing and then rolling them into tight fat balls.*]

WALTER: [*Mumbling.*] We one group of men tied to a race of women with small minds.

[*His sister* BENEATHA *enters. She is about twenty, as slim and intense as her brother. She is not as pretty as her sister-in-law, but her lean, almost intellectual face has a handsomeness of its own. She wears a bright-red flannel nightie, and her thick hair stands wildly about her head. Her speech is a mixture of many things; it is different from the rest of the family's insofar as education has permeated her sense of English—and perhaps the Midwest rather than the South has finally—at last—won out in her inflection; but not altogether, because over all of it is a soft slurring and transformed use of vowels which is the decided influence of the Southside. She passes through the room without looking at either* RUTH *or* WALTER *and goes to the outside door and looks, a little blindly, out to the bathroom. She sees that it has been lost to the Johnsons. She closes the door with a sleepy vengeance and crosses to the table and sits down a little defeated.*]

BENEATHA: I am going to start timing those people.

WALTER: You should get up earlier.

BENEATHA: [*Her face in her hands. She is still fighting the urge to go back to bed.*] Really—would you suggest dawn? Where's the paper?

WALTER: [*Pushing the paper across the table to her as he studies her almost clinically, as though he has never seen her before.*] You a horrible-looking chick at this hour.

BENEATHA: [*Drily.*] Good morning, everybody.

WALTER: [*Senselessly.*] How is school coming?

BENEATHA: [*In the same spirit.*] Lovely. Lovely. And you know, biology is the greatest. [*Looking up at him.*] I dissected something that looked just like you yesterday.

WALTER: I just wondered if you've made up your mind and everything.

BENEATHA: [*Gaining in sharpness and impatience.*] And what did I answer yesterday morning—and the day before that?

RUTH: [*From the ironing board, like someone disinterested and old.*] Don't be so nasty, Bennie.

BENEATHA: [*Still to her brother.*] And the day before that and the day before that!

WALTER: [*Defensively.*] I'm interested in you. Something wrong with that? Ain't many girls who decide—

WALTER *and* BENEATHA: [*In unison.*] —"to be a doctor."
      [*Silence.*]

WALTER: Have we figured out yet just exactly how much medical school is going to cost?

RUTH: Walter Lee, why don't you leave that girl alone and get out of here to work?

BENEATHA: [*Exits to the bathroom and bangs on the door.*] Come on out of there, please!
      [*She comes back into the room.*]

WALTER: [*Looking at his sister intently.*] You know the check is coming tomorrow.

BENEATHA: [*Turning on him with a sharpness all her own.*] That money belongs to Mama, Walter, and it's for her to decide how she wants to use it. I don't care if she wants to buy a house or a rocket ship or just nail it up somewhere and look at it. It's hers. Not ours—*hers.*

WALTER: [*Bitterly.*] Now ain't that fine! You just got your mother's inter-est at heart, ain't you, girl? You such a nice girl—but if Mama got that money she can always take a few thousand and help you through school too—can't she?

BENEATHA: I have never asked anyone around here to do anything for me!

WALTER: No! And the line between asking and just accepting when the time comes is big and wide—ain't it it!

BENEATHA: [*With fury.*] What do you want from me, Brother—that I quit school or just drop dead, which!

WALTER: I don't want nothing but for you to stop acting holy 'round here. Me and Ruth done made some sacrifices for you—why can't you do something for the family?

RUTH: Walter, don't be dragging me in it.

WALTER: You are in it— Don't you get up and go work in somebody's kitchen for the last three years to help put clothes on her back?

RUTH: Oh, Walter—that's not fair . . .

WALTER: It ain't that nobody expects you to get on your knees and say thank you, Brother; thank you, Ruth; thank you, Mama—and thank you, Travis, for wearing the same pair of shoes for two semesters—

BENEATHA: [*Dropping to her knees.*] Well—I *do*—all right?—thank every-body . . . and forgive me for ever wanting to be anything at all . . . forgive me, forgive me!

RUTH: Please stop it! Your mama'll hear you.

WALTER: Who the hell told you you had to be a doctor? If you so crazy 'bout messing 'round with sick people—then go be a nurse like other women—or just get married and be quiet . . .

BENEATHA: Well—you finally got it said . . . It took you three years but you finally got it said. Walter, give up; leave me alone—it's Mama's money.

WALTER: *He was my father, too!*

BENEATHA: So what? He was mine, too—and Travis' grandfather—but the insurance money belongs to Mama. Picking on me is not going to make her give it to you to invest in any liquor stores—[*Underbreath, dropping into a chair.*]—and I for one say, God bless Mama for that!

WALTER: [*To* RUTH.] See—did you hear? Did you hear!

RUTH: Honey, please go to work.

WALTER: Nobody in this house is ever going to understand me.

BENEATHA: Because you're a nut.

WALTER: Who's a nut?

BENEATHA: You—you are a nut. Thee is mad, boy.

WALTER: [*Looking at his wife and his sister from the door, very sadly.*] The world's most backward race of people, and that's a fact.

BENEATHA: [*Turning slowly in her chair.*] And then there are all those prophets who would lead us out of the wilderness—[WALTER *slams out of the house.*]—into the swamps!

RUTH: Bennie, why you always gotta be pickin' on your brother? Can't you be a little sweeter sometimes? [*Door opens.* WALTER *walks in.*]

WALTER: [*To Ruth.*] I need some money for carfare.

RUTH: [*Looks at him, then warms; teasing, but tenderly.*] Fifty cents? [*She goes to her bag and gets money.*] Here, take a taxi.

[*WALTER exits. MAMA enters. She is a woman in her early sixties, full-bodied and strong. She is one of those women of a certain grace and beauty who wear it so unobtrusively that it takes a while to notice. Her dark-brown face is surrounded by the total whiteness of her hair, and, being a woman who has adjusted to many things in life and overcome many more, her face is full of strength. She has, we can see, wit and faith of a kind that keep her eyes lit and full of interest and expectancy. She is, in a word, a beautiful woman. Her bearing is perhaps most like the noble bearing of the women of the Hereros[1] of Southwest Africa—rather as if she imagines that as she walks she still bears a basket or a vessel upon her head. Her speech, on the other hand, is as careless as her carriage is precise—she is inclined to slur everything—but her voice is perhaps not so much quiet as simply soft.*]

MAMA: Who that 'round here slamming doors at this hour?

[*She crosses through the room, goes to the window, opens it, and brings in a feeble little plant growing doggedly in a small pot on the window sill. She feels the dirt and puts it back out.*]

RUTH: That was Walter Lee. He and Bennie was at it again.

MAMA: My children and they tempers. Lord, if this little old plant don't get more sun than it's been getting it ain't never going to see spring again. [*She turns from the window.*] What's the matter with you this morning, Ruth? You looks right peaked. You aiming to iron all them things? Leave some for me. I'll get to 'em this afternoon. Bennie honey, it's too drafty for you to be sitting 'round half dressed. Where's your robe?

BENEATHA: In the cleaners.

MAMA: Well, go get mine and put it on.

BENEATHA: I'm not cold, Mama, honest.

MAMA: I know—but you so thin . . .

BENEATHA: [*Irritably.*] Mama, I'm not cold.

MAMA: [*Seeing the make-down bed as TRAVIS has left it.*] Lord have mercy, look at that poor bed. Bless his heart—he tries, don't he?

[*She moves to the bed TRAVIS has sloppily made up.*]

RUTH: No—he don't half try at all 'cause he knows you going to come along behind him and fix everything. That's just how come he don't know how to do nothing right now—you done spoiled that boy so.

MAMA: Well—he's a little boy. Ain't supposed to know 'bout housekeeping. My baby, that's what he is. What you fix for his breakfast this morning?

RUTH: [*Angrily.*] I feed my son, Lena!

MAMA: I ain't meddling—[*Underbreath; busy-bodyish.*] I just noticed all last week he had cold cereal, and when it starts getting this chilly in the fall a child ought to have some hot grits or something when he goes out in the cold—

---

1. Nomadic people of a region of eastern Namibia.

RUTH: [*Furious.*] I gave him hot oats—is that all right!

MAMA: I ain't meddling. [*Pause.*] Put a lot of nice butter on it? [RUTH *shoots her an angry look and does not reply.*] He likes lots of butter.

RUTH: [*Exasperated.*] Lena—

MAMA: [*To* BENEATHA. MAMA *is inclined to wander conversationally sometimes.*] What was you and your brother fussing 'bout this morning?

BENEATHA: It's not important, Mama.

> [*She gets up and goes to look out at the bathroom, which is apparently free, and she picks up her towels and rushes out.*]

MAMA: What was they fighting about?

RUTH: Now you know as well as I do.

MAMA: [*Shaking her head.*] Brother still worrying hisself sick about that money?

RUTH: You know he is.

MAMA: You had breakfast?

RUTH: Some coffee.

MAMA: Girl, you better start eating and looking after yourself better. You almost thin as Travis.

RUTH: Lena—

MAMA: Un-hunh?

RUTH: What are you going to do with it?

MAMA: Now don't you start, child. It's too early in the morning to be talking about money. It ain't Christian.

RUTH: It's just that he got his heart set on that store—

MAMA: You mean that liquor store that Willy Harris want him to invest in?

RUTH: Yes—

MAMA: We ain't no business people, Ruth. We just plain working folks.

RUTH: Ain't nobody business people till they go into business. Walter Lee say colored people ain't never going to start getting ahead till they start gambling on some different kinds of things in the world—investments and things.

MAMA: What done got into you, girl? Walter Lee done finally sold you on investing.

RUTH: No. Mama, something is happening between Walter and me. I don't know what it is—but he needs something—something I can't give him any more. He needs this chance, Lena.

MAMA: [*Frowning deeply.*] But liquor, honey—

RUTH: Well—like Walter say—I spec people going to always be drinking themselves some liquor.

MAMA: Well—whether they drinks it or not ain't none of my business. But whether I go into business selling it to 'em *is*, and I don't want that on my ledger this late in life. [*Stopping suddenly and studying her daughter-in-law.*] Ruth Younger, what's the matter with you today? You look like you could fall over right there.

RUTH: I'm tired.

MAMA: Then you better stay home from work today.

RUTH: I can't stay home. She'd be calling up the agency and screaming at them, "My girl didn't come in today—send me somebody! My girl didn't come in!" Oh, she just have a fit . . .

MAMA: Well, let her have it. I'll just call her up and say you got the flu—

RUTH: [*Laughing.*] Why the flu?

MAMA: 'Cause it sounds respectable to 'em. Something white people get, too. They know 'bout the flu. Otherwise they think you been cut up or something when you tell 'em you sick.

RUTH: I got to go in. We need the money.

MAMA: Somebody would of thought my children done all but starved to death the way they talk about money here late. Child, we got a great big old check coming tomorrow.

RUTH: [*Sincerely, but also self-righteously.*] Now that's your money. It ain't got nothing to do with me. We all feel like that—Walter and Bennie and me—even Travis.

MAMA: [*Thoughtfully, and suddenly very far away.*] Ten thousand dollars—

RUTH: Sure is wonderful.

MAMA: Ten thousand dollars.

RUTH: You know what you should do, Miss Lena? You should take yourself a trip somewhere. To Europe or South America or someplace—

MAMA: [*Throwing up her hands at the thought.*] Oh, child!

RUTH: I'm serious. Just pack up and leave! Go on away and enjoy yourself some. Forget about the family and have yourself a ball for once in your life—

MAMA: [*Drily.*] You sound like I'm just about ready to die. Who'd go with me? What I look like wandering 'round Europe by myself?

RUTH: Shoot—these here rich white women do it all the time. They don't think nothing of packing up they suitcases and piling on one of them big steamships and—swoosh!—they gone, child.

MAMA: Something always told me I wasn't no rich white woman.

RUTH: Well—what are you going to do with it then?

MAMA: I ain't rightly decided. [*Thinking. She speaks now with emphasis.*] Some of it got to be put away for Beneatha and her schoolin'—and ain't nothing going to touch that part of it. Nothing. [*She waits several seconds, trying to make up her mind about something, and looks at* RUTH *a little tentatively before going on.*] Been thinking that we maybe could meet the notes on a little old two-story somewhere, with a yard where Travis could play in the summertime, if we use part of the insurance for a down payment and everybody kind of pitch in. I could maybe take on a little day work again, few days a week—

RUTH: [*Studying her mother-in-law furtively and concentrating on her ironing, anxious to encourage without seeming to.*] Well, Lord knows, we've put enough rent into this here rat trap to pay for four houses by now . . .

MAMA: [*Looking up at the words "rat trap" and then looking around and leaning back and sighing—in a suddenly reflective mood—*] "Rat trap"— yes, that's all it is. [*Smiling.*] I remember just as well the day me and Big Walter moved in here. Hadn't been married but two weeks and wasn't planning on living here no more than a year. [*She shakes her head at the dissolved dream.*] We was going to set away, little by little, don't you know, and buy a little place out in Morgan Park. We had even picked out the house. [*Chuckling a little.*] Looks right dumpy today. But Lord, child, you should know all the dreams I had 'bout buying that house and fixing it up and making me a little garden in the back—[*She waits and stops smiling.*] And didn't none of it happen.

[*Dropping her hands in a futile gesture.*]

RUTH: [*Keeps her head down, ironing.*] Yes, life can be a barrel of disappointments, sometimes.

MAMA: Honey, Big Walter would come in here some nights back then and slump down on that couch there and just look at the rug, and look at me and look at the rug and then back at me—and I'd know he was down then . . . really down. [*After a second very long and thoughtful pause; she is seeing back to times that only she can see.*] And then, Lord, when I lost that baby—little Claude—I almost thought I was going to lose Big Walter too. Oh, that man grieved hisself! He was one man to love his children.

RUTH: Ain't nothin' can tear at you like losin' your baby.

MAMA: I guess that's how come that man finally worked hisself to death like he done. Like he was fighting his own war with this here world that took his baby from him.

RUTH: He sure was a fine man, all right. I always liked Mr. Younger.

MAMA: Crazy 'bout his children! God knows there was plenty wrong with Walter Younger—hard-headed, mean, kind of wild with women—plenty wrong with him. But he sure loved his children. Always wanted them to have something—be something. That's where Brother gets all these notions, I reckon. Big Walter used to say, he'd get right wet in the eyes sometimes, lean his head back with the water standing in his eyes and say, "Seem like God didn't see fit to give the black man nothing but dreams—but He did give us children to make them dreams seem worth while." [*She smiles.*] He could talk like that, don't you know.

RUTH: Yes, he sure could. He was a good man, Mr. Younger.

MAMA: Yes, a fine man—just couldn't never catch up with his dreams, that's all.

[BENEATHA *comes in, brushing her hair and looking up to the ceiling, where the sound of a vacuum cleaner has started up.*]

BENEATHA: What could be so dirty on that woman's rugs that she has to vacuum them every single day?

RUTH: I wish certain young women 'round here who I could name would take inspiration about certain rugs in a certain apartment I could also mention.

BENEATHA: [*Shrugging.*] How much cleaning can a house need, for Christ's sakes.

MAMA: [*Not liking the Lord's name used thus.*] Bennie!

RUTH: Just listen to her—just listen!

BENEATHA: Oh, God!

MAMA: If you use the Lord's name just one more time—

BENEATHA: [*A bit of a whine.*] Oh, Mama—

RUTH: Fresh—just fresh as salt, this girl!

BENEATHA: [*Drily.*] Well—if the salt loses its savor—

MAMA: Now that will do. I just ain't going to have you 'round here reciting the scriptures in vain—you hear me?

BENEATHA: How did I manage to get on everybody's wrong side by just walking into a room?

RUTH: If you weren't so fresh—
BENEATHA: Ruth, I'm twenty years old.
MAMA: What time you be home from school today?
BENEATHA: Kind of late. [*With enthusiasm.*] Madeline is going to start my guitar lessons today.
[MAMA *and* RUTH *look up with the same expression.*]
MAMA: Your *what* kind of lessons?
BENEATHA: Guitar.
RUTH: Oh, Father!
MAMA: How come you done taken it in your mind to learn to play the guitar?
BENEATHA: I just want to, that's all.
MAMA: [*Smiling.*] Lord, child, don't you know what to do with yourself? How long it going to be before you get tired of this now—like you got tired of that little play-acting group you joined last year? [*Looking at* RUTH.] And what was it the year before that?
RUTH: The horseback-riding club for which she bought that fifty-five-dollar riding habit that's been hanging in the closet ever since!
MAMA: [*To* BENEATHA.] Why you got to flit so from one thing to another, baby?
BENEATHA: [*Sharply.*] I just want to learn to play the guitar. Is there anything wrong with that?
MAMA: Ain't nobody trying to stop you. I just wonders sometimes why you has to flit so from one thing to another all the time. You ain't never done nothing with all that camera equipment you brought home—
BENEATHA: I don't flit! I—I experiment with different forms of expression—
RUTH: Like riding a horse?
BENEATHA: —People have to express themselves one way or another.
MAMA: What is it you want to express?
BENEATHA: [*Angrily.*] Me! [MAMA *and* RUTH *look at each other and burst into raucous laughter.*] Don't worry—I don't expect you to understand.
MAMA: [*To change the subject.*] Who you going out with tomorrow night?
BENEATHA: [*With displeasure.*] George Murchison again.
MAMA: [*Pleased.*] Oh—you getting a little sweet on him?
RUTH: You ask me, this child ain't sweet on nobody but herself—[*Under-breath.*] Express herself!
[*They laugh.*]
BENEATHA: Oh—I like George all right, Mama. I mean I like him enough to go out with him and stuff, but—
RUTH: [*For devilment.*] What does *and stuff* mean?
BENEATHA: Mind your own business.
MAMA: Stop picking at her now, Ruth. [*A thoughtful pause, and then a suspicious sudden look at her daughter as she turns in her chair for emphasis.*] What *does* it mean?
BENEATHA: [*Wearily.*] Oh, I just mean I couldn't ever really be serious about George. He's—he's so shallow.
RUTH: Shallow—what do you mean he's shallow? He's *Rich!*
MAMA: Hush, Ruth.
BENEATHA: I know he's rich. He knows he's rich, too.

RUTH: Well—what other qualities a man got to have to satisfy you, little girl?

BENEATHA: You wouldn't even begin to understand. Anybody who married Walter could not possibly understand.

MAMA: [*Outraged.*] What kind of way is that to talk about your brother?

BENEATHA: Brother is a flip—let's face it.

MAMA: [*To* RUTH, *helplessly.*] What's a flip?

RUTH: [*Glad to add kindling.*] She's saying he's crazy.

BENEATHA: Not crazy. Brother isn't really crazy yet—he—he's an elaborate neurotic.

MAMA: Hush your mouth!

BENEATHA: As for George. Well. George looks good—he's got a beautiful car and he takes me to nice places and, as my sister-in-law says, he is probably the richest boy I will ever get to know and I even like him sometimes—but if the Youngers are sitting around waiting to see if their little Bennie is going to tie up the family with the Murchisons, they are wasting their time.

RUTH: You mean you wouldn't marry George Murchison if he asked you someday? That pretty, rich thing? Honey, I knew you was odd—

BENEATHA: No I would not marry him if all I felt for him was what I feel now. Besides, George's family wouldn't really like it.

MAMA: Why not?

BENEATHA: Oh, Mama—The Murchisons are honest-to-God-real-*live*-rich colored people, and the only people in the world who are more snobbish than rich white people are rich colored people. I thought everybody knew that. I've met Mrs. Murchison. She's a scene!

MAMA: You must not dislike people 'cause they well off, honey.

BENEATHA: Why not? It makes just as much sense as disliking people 'cause they are poor, and lots of people do that.

RUTH: [*A wisdom-of-the-ages manner. To* MAMA.] Well, she'll get over some of this—

BENEATHA: Get over it? What are you talking about, Ruth? Listen, I'm going to be a doctor. I'm not worried about who I'm going to marry yet—if I ever get married.

MAMA *and* RUTH: If!

MAMA: Now, Bennie—

BENEATHA: Oh, I probably will . . . but first I'm going to be a doctor, and George, for one, still thinks that's pretty funny. I couldn't be bothered with that. I am going to be a doctor and everybody around here better understand that!

MAMA: [*Kindly.*] 'Course you going to be a doctor, honey, God willing.

BENEATHA: [*Drily.*] God hasn't got a thing to do with it.

MAMA: Beneatha—that just wasn't necessary.

BENEATHA: Well—neither is God. I get sick of hearing about God.

MAMA: Beneatha!

BENEATHA: I mean it! I'm just tired of hearing about God all the time. What has He got to do with anything? Does he pay tuition?

MAMA: You 'bout to get your fresh little jaw slapped!

RUTH: That's just what she needs, all right!

BENEATHA: Why? Why can't I say what I want to around here, like everybody else?

MAMA: It don't sound nice for a young girl to say things like that—you
wasn't brought up that way. Me and your father went to trouble to get
you and Brother to church every Sunday.

BENEATHA: Mama, you don't understand. It's all a matter of ideas, and
God is just one idea I don't accept. It's not important. I am not going out
and be immoral or commit crimes because I don't believe in God. I
don't even think about it. It's just that I get tired of Him getting credit for
all the things the human race achieves through its own stubborn effort.
There simply is no blasted God—there is only man and it is he who
makes miracles!

[MAMA *absorbs this speech, studies her daughter and rises slowly and
crosses to* BENEATHA *and slaps her powerfully across the face. After,
there is only silence and the daughter drops her eyes from her
mother's face, and* MAMA *is very tall before her.*]

MAMA: Now—you say after me, in my mother's house there is still God.
[*There is a long pause and* BENEATHA *stares at the floor wordlessly.* MAMA
repeats the phrase with precision and cool emotion.] In my mother's
house there is still God.

BENEATHA: In my mother's house there is still God.
[A *long pause.*]

MAMA: [*Walking away from* BENEATHA, *too disturbed for triumphant posture. Stopping and turning back to her daughter.*] There are some ideas
we ain't going to have in this house. Not long as I am at the head of this
family.

BENEATHA: Yes, ma'am.
[MAMA *walks out of the room.*]

RUTH: [*Almost gently, with profound understanding.*] You think you a
woman, Bennie—but you still a little girl. What you did was childish—so
you got treated like a child.

BENEATHA: I see. [*Quietly.*] I also see that everybody thinks it's all right for
Mama to be a tyrant. But all the tyranny in the world will never put a
God in the heavens!
[*She picks up her books and goes out.*]

RUTH: [*Goes to* MAMA's *door.*] She said she was sorry.

MAMA: [*Coming out, going to her plant.*] They frightens me, Ruth. My
children.

RUTH: You got good children, Lena. They just a little off sometimes—but
they're good.

MAMA: No—there's something come down between me and them that
don't let us understand each other and I don't know what it is. One done
almost lost his mind thinking 'bout money all the time and the other
done commence to talk about things I can't seem to understand in no
form or fashion. What is it that's changing, Ruth?

RUTH: [*Soothingly, older than her years.*] Now . . . you taking it all too
seriously. You just got strong-willed children and it takes a strong woman
like you to keep 'em in hand.

MAMA: [*Looking at her plant and sprinkling a little water on it.*] They spirited all right, my children. Got to admit they got spirit—Bennie and Walter. Like this little old plant that ain't never had enough sunshine or nothing—and look at it . . .

[*She has her back to* RUTH, *who has had to stop ironing and lean against something and put the back of her hand to her forehead.*]

RUTH: [*Trying to keep* MAMA *from noticing.*] You . . . sure . . . loves that little old thing, don't you? . . .

MAMA: Well, I always wanted me a garden like I used to see sometimes at the back of the houses down home. This plant is close as I ever got to having one. [*She looks out of the window as she replaces the plant.*] Lord, ain't nothing as dreary as the view from this window on a dreary day, is there? Why ain't you singing this morning, Ruth? Sing that "No Ways Tired." That song always lifts me up so—[*She turns at last to see that* RUTH *has slipped quietly into a chair, in a state of semiconsciousness.*] Ruth! Ruth honey—what's the matter with you . . . Ruth!

[*Curtain.*]

SCENE TWO

It is the following morning; a Saturday morning, and house cleaning is in progress at the Youngers. Furniture has been shoved hither and yon and MAMA *is giving the kitchen-area walls a washing down.* BENEATHA, *in dungarees, with a handkerchief tied around her face, is spraying insecticide into the cracks in the walls. As they work, the radio is on and a Southside disk-jockey program is inappropriately filling the house with a rather exotic saxophone blues.* TRAVIS, *the sole idle one, is leaning on his arms, looking out of the window.*

TRAVIS: Grandmama, that stuff Bennie is using smells awful. Can I go downstairs, please?

MAMA: Did you get all them chores done already? I ain't seen you doing much.

TRAVIS: Yes'm—finished early. Where did Mama go this morning?

MAMA: [*Looking at* BENEATHA.] She had to go on a little errand.

TRAVIS: Where?

MAMA: To tend to her business.

TRAVIS: Can I go outside then?

MAMA: Oh, I guess so. You better stay right in front of the house, though . . . and keep a good lookout for the postman.

TRAVIS: Yes'm. [*He starts out and decides to give his aunt* BENEATHA *a good swat on the legs as he passes her.*] Leave them poor little old cockroaches alone, they ain't bothering you none.

[*He runs as she swings the spray gun at him both viciously and playfully.* WALTER *enters from the bedroom and goes to the phone.*]

MAMA: Look out there, girl, before you be spilling some of that stuff on that child!

TRAVIS: [*Teasing.*] That's right—look out now!

[*He exits.*]

BENEATHA: [*Drily.*] I can't imagine that it would hurt him—it has never hurt the roaches.

MAMA: Well, little boys' hides ain't as tough as Southside roaches.

WALTER: [*Into phone.*] Hello—Let me talk to Willy Harris.

MAMA: You better get over there behind the bureau. I seen one marching out of there like Napoleon yesterday.

WALTER: Hello, Willy? It ain't come yet. It'll be here in a few minutes. Did the lawyer give you the papers?

BENEATHA: There's really only one way to get rid of them, Mama—

MAMA: How?

BENEATHA: Set fire to this building.

WALTER: Good. Good. I'll be right over.

BENEATHA: Where did Ruth go, Walter?

WALTER: I don't know.

    [*He exits abruptly.*]

BENEATHA: Mama, where did Ruth go?

MAMA: [*Looking at her with meaning.*] To the doctor, I think.

BENEATHA: The doctor? What's the matter? [*They exchange glances.*] You don't think—

MAMA: [*With her sense of drama.*] Now I ain't saying what I think. But I ain't never been wrong 'bout a woman neither.

    [*The phone rings.*]

BENEATHA: [*At the phone.*] Hay-lo . . . [*Pause, and a moment of recognition.*] Well—when did you get back! . . . And how was it? . . . Of course I've missed you—in my way . . . This morning? No . . . house cleaning and all that and Mama hates it if I let people come over when the house is like this . . . You *have?* Well, that's different . . . What is it— Oh, what the hell, come on over . . . Right, see you then.

    [*She hangs up.*]

MAMA: [*Who has listened vigorously, as is her habit.*] Who is that you inviting over here with this house looking like this? You ain't got the pride you was born with!

BENEATHA: Asagai doesn't care how houses look, Mama—he's an intellectual.

MAMA: *Who?*

BENEATHA: Asagai—Joseph Asagai. He's an African boy I met on campus. He's been studying in Canada all summer.

MAMA: What's his name?

BENEATHA: Asagai, Joseph. Ah-sah-guy . . . He's from Nigeria.

MAMA: Oh, that's the little country that was founded by slaves way back . . .

BENEATHA: No, Mama—that's Liberia.

MAMA: I don't think I never met no African before.

BENEATHA: Well, do me a favor and don't ask him a whole lot of ignorant questions about Africans. I mean, do they wear clothes and all that—

MAMA: Well, now, I guess if you think we so ignorant 'round here maybe you shouldn't bring your friends here—

BENEATHA: It's just that people ask such crazy things. All anyone seems to know about when it comes to Africa is Tarzan—

MAMA: [*Indignantly.*] Why should I know anything about Africa?

BENEATHA: Why do you give money at church for the missionary work?

MAMA: Well, that's to help save people.

BENEATHA: You mean save them from *heathenism*—

MAMA: [*Innocently.*] Yes.

BENEATHA: I'm afraid they need more salvation from the British and the French.

> [RUTH *comes in forlornly and pulls off her coat with dejection. They both turn to look at her.*]

RUTH: [*Dispiritedly.*] Well, I guess from all the happy faces—everybody knows.

BENEATHA: You pregnant?

MAMA: Lord have mercy, I sure hope it's a little old girl. Travis ought to have a sister.

> [BENEATHA *and* RUTH *give her a hopeless look for this grandmotherly enthusiasm.*]

BENEATHA: How far along are you?

RUTH: Two months.

BENEATHA: Did you mean to? I mean did you plan it or was it an accident?

MAMA: What do you know about planning or not planning?

BENEATHA: Oh, Mama.

RUTH: [*Wearily.*] She's twenty years old, Lena.

BENEATHA: Did you plan it, Ruth?

RUTH: Mind your own business.

BENEATHA: It is my business—where is he going to live, on the *roof*? [*There is silence following the remark as the three women react to the sense of it.*] Gee—I didn't mean that, Ruth, honest. Gee, I don't feel like that at all. I—I think it is wonderful.

RUTH: [*Dully.*] Wonderful.

BENEATHA: Yes—really.

MAMA: [*Looking at* RUTH, *worried.*] Doctor say everything going to be all right?

RUTH: [*Far away.*] Yes—she says everything is going to be fine . . .

MAMA: [*Immediately suspicious.*] "She"— What doctor you went to?

> [RUTH *folds over, near hysteria.*]

MAMA: [*Worriedly hovering over* RUTH.] Ruth honey—what's the matter with you—you sick?

> [RUTH *has her fists clenched on her thighs and is fighting hard to suppress a scream that seems to be rising in her.*]

BENEATHA: What's the matter with her, Mama?

MAMA: [*Working her fingers in* RUTH's *shoulder to relax her.*] She be all right. Women gets right depressed sometimes when they get her way. [*Speaking softly, expertly, rapidly.*] Now you just relax. That's right . . . just lean back, don't think 'bout nothing at all . . . nothing at all—

RUTH: I'm all right . . .

> [*The glassy-eyed look melts and then she collapses into a fit of heavy sobbing. The bell rings.*]

BENEATHA: Oh, my God—that must be Asagai.

MAMA: [*To* RUTH.] Come on now, honey. You need to lie down and rest awhile . . . then have some nice hot food.

[*They exit,* RUTH's *weight on her mother-in-law.* BENEATHA, *herself profoundly disturbed, opens the door to admit a rather dramatic-looking young man with a large package.*]

ASAGAI: Hello, Alaiyo—

BENEATHA: [*Holding the door open and regarding him with pleasure.*] Hello . . . [*Long pause.*] Well—come in. And please excuse everything. My mother was very upset about my letting anyone come here with the place like this.

ASAGAI: [*Coming into the room.*] You look disturbed too . . . Is something wrong?

BENEATHA: [*Still at the door, absently.*] Yes . . . we've all got acute ghetto-itus. [*She smiles and comes toward him, finding a cigarette and sitting.*] So—sit down! How was Canada?

ASAGAI: [*A sophisticate.*] Canadian.

BENEATHA: [*Looking at him.*] I'm very glad you are back.

ASAGAI: [*Looking back at her in turn.*] Are you really?

BENEATHA: Yes—very.

ASAGAI: Why—you were quite glad when I went away. What happened?

BENEATHA: You went away.

ASAGAI: Ahhhhhhhh.

BENEATHA: Before—you wanted to be so serious before there was time.

ASAGAI: How much time must there be before one knows what one feels?

BENEATHA: [*Stalling this particular conversation. Her hands pressed together, in a deliberately childish gesture.*] What did you bring me?

ASAGAI: [*Handing her the package.*] Open it and see.

BENEATHA: [*Eagerly opening the package and drawing out some records and the colorful robes of a Nigerian woman.*] Oh, Asagai! . . . You got them for me! . . . How beautiful . . . and the records too! [*She lifts out the robes and runs to the mirror with them and holds the drapery up in front of herself.*]

ASAGAI: [*Coming to her at the mirror.*] I shall have to teach you how to drape it properly. [*He flings the material about her for the moment and stands back to look at her.*] Ah—Oh-pay-gay-day, oh-gbah-mu-shay. [*A Yoruba exclamation for admiration.*] You wear it well . . . very well . . . mutilated hair and all.

BENEATHA: [*Turning suddenly.*] My hair—what's wrong with my hair?

ASAGAI: [*Shrugging.*] Were you born with it like that?

BENEATHA: [*Reaching up to touch it.*] No . . . of course not.

[*She looks back to the mirror, disturbed.*]

ASAGAI: [*Smiling.*] How then?

BENEATHA: You know perfectly well how . . . as crinkly as yours . . . that's how.

ASAGAI: And it is ugly to you that way?

BENEATHA: [*Quickly.*] Oh, no—not ugly . . . [*More slowly, apologetically.*] But it's so hard to manage when it's, well—raw.

ASAGAI: And so to accommodate that—you mutilate it every week?

BENEATHA: It's not mutilation!

ASAGAI: [*Laughing aloud at her seriousness.*] Oh . . . please! I am only teasing you because you are so very serious about these things. [*He stands back from her and folds his arms across his chest as he watches her pulling at her hair and frowning in the mirror.*] Do you remember the first time you met me at school? . . . [*He laughs.*] You came up to me and you said—and I thought you were the most serious little thing I had ever seen—you said: [*He imitates her.*] "Mr. Asagai—I want very much to talk with you. About Africa. You see, Mr. Asagai, I am looking for my *identity!*"
       [*He laughs.*]

BENEATHA: [*Turning to him, not laughing.*] Yes—
       [*Her face is quizzical, profoundly disturbed.*]

ASAGAI: [*Still teasing and reaching out and taking her face in his hands and turning her profile to him.*] Well . . . it is true that this is not so much a profile of a Hollywood queen as perhaps a queen of the Nile—[*A mock dismissal of the importance of the question.*] But what does it matter? Assimilationism is so popular in your country.

BENEATHA: [*Wheeling, passionately, sharply.*] I am not an assimilationist!

ASAGAI: [*The protest hangs in the room for a moment and* ASAGAI *studies her, his laughter fading.*] Such a serious one. [*There is a pause.*] So—you like the robes? You must take excellent care of them—they are from my sister's personal wardrobe.

BENEATHA: [*With incredulity.*] You—you sent all the way home—for me?

ASAGAI: [*With charm.*] For you—I would do much more . . . Well, that is what I came for. I must go.

BENEATHA: Will you call me Monday?

ASAGAI: Yes . . . We have a great deal to talk about. I mean about identity and time and all that.

BENEATHA: Time?

ASAGAI: Yes. About how much time one needs to know what one feels.

BENEATHA: You never understood that there is more than one kind of feeling which can exist between a man and a woman—or, at least, there should be.

ASAGAI: [*Shaking his head negatively but gently.*] No. Between a man and a woman there need be only one kind of feeling. I have that for you . . . Now even . . . right this moment . . .

BENEATHA: I know—and by itself—it won't do. I can find that anywhere.

ASAGAI: For a woman it should be enough.

BENEATHA: I know—because that's what it says in all the novels that men write. But it isn't. Go ahead and laugh—but I'm not interested in being someone's little episode in America or—[*With feminine vengeance.*]— one of them! [ASAGAI *has burst into laughter again.*] That's funny as hell, huh!

ASAGAI: It's just that every American girl I have known has said that to me. White—black—in this you are all the same. And the same speech, too!

BENEATHA: [*Angrily.*] Yuk, yuk, yuk!

ASAGAI: It's how you can be sure that the world's most liberated women are not liberated at all. You all talk about it too much!
       [MAMA *enters and is immediately all social charm because of the presence of a guest.*]

BENEATHA: Oh—Mama—this is Mr. Asagai.

MAMA: How do you do?

ASAGAI: [*Total politeness to an elder.*] How do you do, Mrs. Younger. Please forgive me for coming at such an outrageous hour on a Saturday.

MAMA: Well, you are quite welcome. I just hope you understand that our house don't always look like this. [*Chatterish.*] You must come again. I would love to hear all about—[*Not sure of the name.*]—your country. I think it's so sad the way our American Negroes don't know nothing about Africa 'cept Tarzan and all that. And all that money they pour into these churches when they ought to be helping you people over there drive out them French and Englishmen done taken away your land.

[*The mother flashes a slightly superior look at her daughter upon completion of the recitation.*]

ASAGAI: [*Taken aback by this sudden and acutely unrelated expression of sympathy.*] Yes . . . yes . . .

MAMA: [*Smiling at him suddenly and relaxing and looking him over.*] How many miles is it from here to where you come from?

ASAGAI: Many thousands.

MAMA: [*Looking at him as she would* WALTER.] I bet you don't half look after yourself, being away from your mama either. I spec you better come 'round here from time to time and get yourself some decent home-cooked meals . . .

ASAGAI: [*Moved.*] Thank you. Thank you very much. [*They are all quiet, then*—] Well . . . I must go. I will call you Monday, Alaiyo.

MAMA: What's that he call you?

ASAGAI: Oh—"Alaiyo." I hope you don't mind. It is what you would call a nickname, I think. It is a Yoruba word. I am a Yoruba.

MAMA: [*Looking at* BENEATHA.] I—I thought he was from—

ASAGAI: [*Understanding.*] Nigeria is my country. Yoruba is my tribal origin—

BENEATHA: You didn't tell us what Alaiyo means . . . for all I know, you might be calling me Little Idiot or something . . .

ASAGAI: Well . . . let me see . . . I do not know how just to explain it . . . The sense of a thing can be so different when it changes languages.

BENEATHA: You're evading.

ASAGAI: No—really it is difficult . . . [*Thinking.*] It means . . . it means One for Whom Bread—Food—Is Not Enough. [*He looks at her.*] Is that all right?

BENEATHA: [*Understanding, softly.*] Thank you.

MAMA: [*Looking from one to the other and not understanding any of it.*] Well . . . that's nice . . . You must come see us again—Mr.—

ASAGAI: Ah-sah-guy . . .

MAMA: Yes . . . Do come again.

ASAGAI: Good-bye.

[*He exits.*]

MAMA: [*After him.*] Lord, that's a pretty thing just went out here! [*Insinuatingly, to her daughter.*] Yes, I guess I see why we done commence to get so interested in Africa 'round here. Missionaries my aunt Jenny!

[*She exits.*]

BENEATHA: Oh, Mama! . . .

[*She picks up the Nigerian dress and holds it up to her in front of the mirror again. She sets the headdress on haphazardly and then notices her hair again and clutches at it and then replaces the headdress and frowns at herself. Then she starts to wriggle in front of the mirror as she thinks a Nigerian woman might.* TRAVIS *enters and regards her.*]

TRAVIS: You cracking up?

BENEATHA: Shut up.

[*She pulls the headdress off and looks at herself in the mirror and clutches at her hair again and squinches her eyes as if trying to imagine something. Then, suddenly, she gets her raincoat and kerchief and hurriedly prepares for going out.*]

MAMA: [*Coming back into the room.*] She's resting now. Travis, baby, run next door and ask Miss Johnson to please let me have a little kitchen cleanser. This here can is empty as Jacob's kettle.

TRAVIS: I just came in.

MAMA: Do as you told. [*He exits and she looks at her daughter.*] Where you going?

BENEATHA: [*Halting at the door.*] To become a queen of the Nile!

[*She exits in a breathless blaze of glory.* RUTH *appears in the bedroom doorway.*]

MAMA: Who told you to get up?

RUTH: Ain't nothing wrong with me to be lying in no bed for. Where did Bennie go?

MAMA: [*Drumming her fingers.*] Far as I could make out—to Egypt. [RUTH *just looks at her.*] What time is it getting to?

RUTH: Ten twenty. And the mailman going to ring that bell this morning just like he done every morning for the last umpteen years.

[TRAVIS *comes in with the cleanser can.*]

TRAVIS: She say to tell you that she don't have much.

MAMA: [*Angrily.*] Lord, some people I could name sure is tight-fisted! [*Directing her grandson.*] Mark two cans of cleanser down on the list there. If she that hard up for kitchen cleanser, I sure don't want to forget to get her none!

RUTH: Lena—maybe the woman is just short on cleanser—

MAMA: [*Not listening.*] —Much baking powder as she done borrowed from me all these years, she could of done gone into the baking business!

[*The bell sounds suddenly and sharply and all three are stunned—serious and silent—mid-speech. In spite of all the other conversations and distractions of the morning, this is what they have been waiting for, even* TRAVIS, *who looks helplessly from his mother to his grandmother.* RUTH *is the first to come to life again.*]

RUTH: [*To* TRAVIS.] Get down them steps, boy!

[TRAVIS *snaps to life and flies out to get the mail.*]

MAMA: [*Her eyes wide, her hand to her breast.*] You mean it done really come?

RUTH: [*Excited.*] Oh, Miss Lena!

MAMA: [*Collecting herself.*] Well . . . I don't know what we all so excited about 'round here for. We known it was coming for months.

RUTH: That's a whole lot different from having it come and being able to hold it in your hands . . . a piece of paper worth ten thousand dollars

. . . [TRAVIS *bursts back into the room. He holds the envelope high above his head, like a little dancer, his face is radiant and he is breathless. He moves to his grandmother with sudden slow ceremony and puts the envelope into her hands. She accepts it, and then merely holds it and looks at it.*] Come on! Open it . . . Lord have mercy, I wish Walter Lee was here!

TRAVIS: Open it, Grandmama!

MAMA: [*Staring at it.*] Now you all be quiet. It's just a check.

RUTH: Open it . . .

MAMA: [*Still staring at it.*] Now don't act silly . . . We ain't never been no people to act silly 'bout no money—

RUTH: [*Swiftly.*] We ain't never had none before—*open it!*

[MAMA *finally makes a good strong tear and pulls out the thin blue slice of paper and inspects it closely. The boy and his mother study it raptly over* MAMA's *shoulders.*]

MAMA: Travis! [*She is counting off with doubt.*] Is that the right number of zeros.

TRAVIS: Yes'm . . . ten thousand dollars. Gaalee, Grandmama, you rich.

MAMA: [*She holds the check away from her, still looking at it. Slowly her face sobers into a mask of unhappiness.*] Ten thousand dollars. [*She hands it to* RUTH.] Put it away somewhere, Ruth. [*She does not look at* RUTH; *her eyes seem to be seeing something somewhere very far off.*] Ten thousand dollars they give you. Ten thousand dollars.

TRAVIS: [*To his mother, sincerely.*] What's the matter with Grandmama— don't she want to be rich?

RUTH: [*Distractedly.*] You go on out and play now, baby. [TRAVIS *exits.* MAMA *starts wiping dishes absently, humming intently to herself.* RUTH *turns to her, with kind exasperation.*] You've gone and got yourself upset.

MAMA: [*Not looking at her.*] I spec if it wasn't for you all . . . I would just put that money away or give it to the church or something.

RUTH: Now what kind of talk is that. Mr. Younger would just be plain mad if he could hear you talking foolish like that.

MAMA: [*Stopping and staring off.*] Yes . . . he sure would. [*Sighing.*] We got enough to do with that money, all right. [*She halts then, and turns and looks at her daughter-in-law hard;* RUTH *avoids her eyes and* MAMA *wipes her hands with finality and starts to speak firmly to* RUTH.] Where did you go today, girl?

RUTH: To the doctor.

MAMA: [*Impatiently.*] Now, Ruth . . . you know better than that. Old Doctor Jones is strange enough in his way but there ain't nothing 'bout him make somebody slip and call him "she"—like you done this morning.

RUTH: Well, that's what happened—my tongue slipped.

MAMA: You went to see that woman, didn't you?

RUTH: [*Defensively, giving herself away.*] What woman you talking about?

MAMA: [*Angrily.*] That woman who—

[WALTER *enters in great excitement.*]

WALTER: Did it come?

MAMA: [*Quietly.*] Can't you give people a Christian greeting before you start asking about money?

WALTER: [*To* RUTH.] Did it come? [RUTH *unfolds the check and lays it quietly before him, watching him intently with thoughts of her own.* WALTER *sits down and grasps it close and counts off the zeros.*] Ten thousand dollars—[*He turns suddenly, frantically to his mother and draws some papers out of his breast pocket.*] Mama—look. Old Willy Harris put everything on paper—

MAMA: Son—I think you ought to talk to your wife . . . I'll go on out and leave you alone if you want—

WALTER: I can talk to her later— Mama, look—

MAMA: Son—

WALTER: WILL SOMEBODY PLEASE LISTEN TO ME TODAY!

MAMA: [*Quietly.*] I don't 'low no yellin' in this house, Walter Lee, and you know it—[WALTER *stares at them in frustration and starts to speak several times.*] And there ain't going to be no investing in no liquor stores. I don't aim to have to speak on that again.

     [*A long pause.*]

WALTER: Oh—so you don't aim to have to speak on that again? So *you* have decided . . . [*Crumpling his papers.*] Well, *you* tell that to my boy tonight when you put him to sleep on the living-room couch . . . [*Turning to* MAMA *and speaking directly to her.*] Yeah—and tell it to my wife, Mama, tomorrow when she has to go out of here to look after somebody else's kids. And tell it to *me*, Mama, every time we need a new pair of curtains and I have to watch *you* go out and work in somebody's kitchen. Yeah, you tell me then!

     [WALTER *starts out.*]

RUTH: Where you going?

WALTER: I'm going out!

RUTH: Where?

WALTER: Just out of this house somewhere—

RUTH: [*Getting her coat.*] I'll come too.

WALTER: I don't want you to come!

RUTH: I got something to talk to you about, Walter.

WALTER: That's too bad.

MAMA: [*Still quietly.*] Walter Lee—[*She waits and he finally turns and looks at her.*] Sit down.

WALTER: I'm a grown man, Mama.

MAMA: Ain't nobody said you wasn't grown. But you still in my house and my presence. And as long as you are—you'll talk to your wife civil. Now sit down.

RUTH: [*Suddenly.*] Oh, let him go on out and drink himself to death! He makes me sick to my stomach! [*She flings her coat against him.*]

WALTER: [*Violently.*] And you turn mine too, baby! [RUTH *goes into their bedroom and slams the door behind her.*] That was my greatest mistake—

MAMA: [*Still quietly.*] Walter, what is the matter with you?

WALTER: Matter with me? Ain't nothing the matter with *me*!

MAMA: Yes there is. Something eating you up like a crazy man. Something more than me not giving you this money. The past few years I been watching it happen to you. You get all nervous acting and kind of wild in the eyes—[WALTER *jumps up impatiently at her words.*] I said sit there now, I'm talking to you!

WALTER: Mama—I don't need no nagging at me today.

MAMA: Seem like you getting to a place where you always tied up in some kind of knot about something. But if anybody ask you 'bout it you just yell at 'em and bust out the house and go out and drink somewheres. Walter Lee, people can't live with that. Ruth's a good, patient girl in her way—but you getting to be too much. Boy, don't make the mistake of driving that girl away from you.

WALTER: Why—what she do for me?

MAMA: She loves you.

WALTER: Mama—I'm going out. I want to go off somewhere and be by myself for a while.

MAMA: I'm sorry 'bout your liquor store, son. It just wasn't the thing for us to do. That's what I want to tell you about—

WALTER: I got to go out, Mama—
     [*He rises.*]

MAMA: It's dangerous, son.

WALTER: What's dangerous?

MAMA: When a man goes outside his home to look for peace.

WALTER: [*Beseechingly.*] Then why can't there never be no peace in this house then?

MAMA: You done found it in some other house?

WALTER: No—there ain't no woman! Why do women always think there's a woman somewhere when a man gets restless. [*Coming to her.*] Mama—Mama—I want so many things . . .

MAMA: Yes, son—

WALTER: I want so many things that they are driving me kind of crazy . . . Mama—look at me.

MAMA: I'm looking at you. You a good-looking boy. You got a job, a nice wife, a fine boy and—

WALTER: A job. [*Looks at her.*] Mama, a job? I open and close car doors all day long. I drive a man around in his limousine and I say, "Yes, sir; no, sir; very good, sir; shall I take the Drive, sir?" Mama, that ain't no kind of job . . . that ain't nothing at all. [*Very quietly.*] Mama, I don't know if I can make you understand.

MAMA: Understand what, baby?

WALTER: [*Quietly.*] Sometimes it's like I can see the future stretched out in front of me—just plain as day. The future, Mama. Hanging over there at the edge of my days. Just waiting for me—a big, looming blank space—full of *nothing*. Just waiting for *me*. [*Pause.*] Mama—sometimes when I'm downtown and I pass them cool, quiet-looking restaurants where them white boys are sitting back and talking 'bout things . . . sitting there turning deals worth millions of dollars . . . sometimes I see guys don't look much older than me—

MAMA: Son—how come you talk so much 'bout money?

WALTER: [*With immense passion.*] Because it is life, Mama!

MAMA: [*Quietly.*] Oh—[*Very quietly.*] So now it's life. Money is life. Once upon a time freedom used to be life—now it's money. I guess the world really do change . . .

WALTER: No—it was always money, Mama. We just didn't know about it.

MAMA: No . . . something has changed. [*She looks at him.*] You something new, boy. In my time we was worried about not being lynched and getting to the North if we could and how to stay alive and still have a pinch of dignity too . . . Now here come you and Beneatha—talking 'bout things we ain't never even thought about hardly, me and your daddy. You ain't satisfied or proud of nothing we done. I mean that you had a home; that we kept you out of trouble till you was grown; that you don't have to ride to work on the back of nobody's streetcar— You my children—but how different we done become.

WALTER: You just don't understand, Mama, you just don't understand.

MAMA: Son—do you know your wife is expecting another baby? [WALTER stands, stunned, and absorbs what his mother has said.] That's what she wanted to talk to you about. [WALTER sinks down into a chair.] This ain't for me to be telling—but you ought to know. [She waits.] I think Ruth is thinking 'bout getting rid of that child.

WALTER: [Slowly understanding.] No—no—Ruth wouldn't do that.

MAMA: When the world gets ugly enough—a woman will do anything for her family. The part that's already living.

WALTER: You don't know Ruth, Mama, if you think she would do that.

[RUTH opens the bedroom door and stands there a little limp.]

RUTH: [Beaten.] Yes I would too, Walter. [Pause.] I gave her a five-dollar down payment.

[There is total silence as the man stares at his wife and the mother stares at her son.]

MAMA: [Presently.] Well — [Tightly.] Well — son, I'm waiting to hear you say something . . . I'm waiting to hear how you be your father's son. Be the man he was . . . [Pause.] Your wife say she going to destroy your child. And I'm waiting to hear you talk like him and say we a people who give children life, not who destroys them—[She rises.] I'm waiting to see you stand up and look like your daddy and say we done give up one baby to poverty and that we ain't going to give up nary another one . . . I'm waiting.

WALTER: Ruth—

MAMA: If you a son of mine, tell her! [WALTER turns, looks at her and can say nothing. She continues, bitterly.] You . . . you are a disgrace to your father's memory. Somebody get me my hat.

[Curtain.]

Act II

SCENE ONE

Time: Later the same day.

At rise: RUTH *is ironing again. She has the radio going. Presently* BENEA-THA's *bedroom door opens and* RUTH's *mouth falls and she puts down the iron in fascination.*

RUTH: What have we got on tonight!

BENEATHA: [Emerging grandly from the doorway so that we can see her thoroughly robed in the costume ASAGAI brought.] You are looking at what a well-dressed Nigerian woman wears—[She parades for RUTH, her hair

completely hidden by the headdress; she is coquettishly fanning herself
with an ornate oriental fan, mistakenly more like Butterfly than any
Nigerian that ever was.] Isn't it beautiful? [*She promenades to the radio*
and, with an arrogant flourish, turns off the good loud blues that is play-
ing.] Enough of this assimilationist junk! [RUTH *follows her with her*
eyes as she goes to the phonograph and puts on a record and turns and
waits ceremoniously for the music to come up. Then, with a shout—]
OCOMOGOSIAY!

> [RUTH *jumps. The music comes up, a lovely Nigerian melody.* BENEA-
> THA *listens, enraptured, her eyes far away—"back to the past." She*
> *begins to dance.* RUTH *is dumbfounded.*]

RUTH: What kind of dance is that?

BENEATHA: A folk dance.

RUTH: [*Pearl Bailey.*][2] What kind of folks do that, honey?

BENEATHA: It's from Nigeria. It's a dance of welcome.

RUTH: Who you welcoming?

BENEATHA: The men back to the village.

RUTH: Where they been?

BENEATHA: How should I know—out hunting or something. Anyway, they
are coming back now . . .

RUTH: Well, that's good.

BENEATHA: [*With the record.*]
Alundi, alundi
Alundi alunya
Jop pu a jeepua
Ang gu soooooooooo

Ai yai yae . . .
Ayehaye—alundi . . .
> [WALTER *comes in during this performance; he has obviously been*
> *drinking. He leans against the door heavily and watches his sister, at*
> *first with distaste. Then his eyes look off—"back to the past"—as he*
> *lifts both his fists to the roof, screaming.*]

WALTER: YEAH . . . AND ETHIOPIA STRETCH FORTH HER
HANDS AGAIN! . . .

RUTH: [*Drily, looking at him.*] Yes—and Africa sure is claiming her own
tonight. [*She gives them both up and starts ironing again.*]

WALTER: [*All in a drunken, dramatic shout.*] Shut up! . . . I'm digging
them drums . . . them drums move me! . . . [*He makes his weaving way to*
his wife's face and leans in close to her.] In my heart of hearts— [*He*
thumps his chest.]—I am much warrior!

RUTH: [*Without even looking up.*] In your heart of hearts you are much
drunkard.

WALTER: [*Coming away from her and starting to wander around the room,*
shouting.] Me and Jomo . . . [*Intently, in his sister's face. She has stopped*
dancing to watch him in this unknown mood.] That's my man, Kenyatta.
[*Shouting and thumping his chest.*] FLAMING SPEAR! HOT DAMN!

2. American singer, dancer, actor, and author (1918–1990).

[*He is suddenly in possession of an imaginary spear and actively spearing enemies all over the room.*] OCOMOGOSIAY . . . THE LION IS WAKING . . . OWIMOWEH! [*He pulls his shirt open and leaps up on a table and gestures with his spear. The bell rings.* RUTH *goes to answer.*]

BENEATHA: [*To encourage* WALTER, *thoroughly caught up with this side of him.*] OCOMOGOSIAY, FLAMING SPEAR!

WALTER: [*On the table, very far gone, his eyes pure glass sheets. He sees what we cannot, that he is a leader of his people, a great chief, a descendant of Chaka, and that the hour to march has come.*] Listen, my black brothers—

BENEATHA: OCOMOGOSIAY!

WALTER: —Do you hear the waters rushing against the shores of the coastlands—

BENEATHA: OCOMOGOSIAY!

WALTER: —Do you hear the screeching of the cocks in yonder hills beyond where the chiefs meet in council for the coming of the mighty war—

BENEATHA: OCOMOGOSIAY!

WALTER: —Do you hear the beating of the wings of the birds flying low over the mountains and the low places of our land—

[RUTH *opens the door.* GEORGE MURCHISON *enters.*]

BENEATHA: OCOMOGOSIAY!

WALTER: —Do you hear the singing of the women, singing the war songs of our fathers to the babies in the great houses . . . singing the sweet war songs? OH, DO YOU HEAR, MY BLACK BROTHERS!

BENEATHA: [*Completely gone.*] We hear you, Flaming Spear—

WALTER: Telling us to prepare for the greatness of the time—[*To* GEORGE.] Black Brother!

[*He extends his hand for the fraternal clasp.*]

GEORGE: Black Brother, hell!

RUTH: [*Having had enough, and embarrassed for the family.*] Beneatha, you got company—what's the matter with you? Walter Lee Younger, get down off that table and stop acting like a fool . . .

[WALTER *comes down off the table suddenly and makes a quick exit to the bathroom.*]

RUTH: He's had a little to drink . . . I don't know what her excuse is.

GEORGE: [*To* BENEATHA.] Look honey, we're going *to* the theatre—we're not going to be *in* it . . . so go change, huh?

RUTH: You expect this boy to go out with you looking like that?

BENEATHA: [*Looking at* GEORGE.] That's up to George. If he's ashamed of his heritage—

GEORGE: Oh, don't be so proud of yourself, Bennie—just because you look eccentric.

BENEATHA: How can something that's natural be eccentric?

GEORGE: That's what being eccentric means—being natural. Get dressed.

BENEATHA: I don't like that, George.

RUTH: Why must you and your brother make an argument out of everything people say?

BENEATHA: Because I hate assimilationist Negroes!

RUTH: Will somebody please tell me what assimila-who-ever means!

GEORGE: Oh, it's just a college girl's way of calling people Uncle Toms—but that isn't what it means at all.

RUTH: Well, what does it mean?

BENEATHA: [*Cutting* GEORGE *off and staring at him as she replies to* RUTH.] It means someone who is willing to give up his own culture and submerge himself completely in the dominant, and in this case, *oppressive* culture!

GEORGE: Oh, dear, dear, dear! Here we go! A lecture on the African past! On our Great West African Heritage! In one second we will hear all about the great Ashanti empires; the great Songhay civilizations; and the great sculpture of Bénin[3]—and then some poetry in the Bantu—and the whole monologue will end with the word *heritage!* [*Nastily.*] Let's face it, baby, your heritage is nothing but a bunch of raggedy-assed spirituals and some grass huts!

BENEATHA: *Grass huts!* [RUTH *crosses to her and forcibly pushes her toward the bedroom.*] See there . . . you are standing there in your splendid ignorance talking about people who were the first to smelt iron on the face of the earth! [RUTH *is pushing her through the door.*] The Ashanti were performing surgical operations when the English—[RUTH *pulls the door to, with* BENEATHA *on the other side, and smiles graciously at* GEORGE. BENEATHA *opens the door and shouts the end of the sentence defiantly at* GEORGE.]—were still tatooing themselves with blue dragons . . . [*She goes back inside.*]

RUTH: Have a seat, George. [*They both sit.* RUTH *folds her hands rather primly on her lap, determined to demonstrate the civilization of the family.*] Warm, ain't it? I mean for September. [*Pause.*] Just like they always say about Chicago weather: If it's too hot or cold for you, just wait a minute and it'll change. [*She smiles happily at this cliché of clichés.*] Everybody say it's got to do with them bombs and things they keep setting off. [*Pause.*] Would you like a nice cold beer?

GEORGE: No, thank you. I don't care for beer. [*He looks at his watch.*] I hope she hurries up.

RUTH: What time is the show?

GEORGE: It's an eight-thirty curtain. That's just Chicago, though. In New York standard curtain time is eight forty.
          [*He is rather proud of this knowledge.*]

RUTH: [*Properly appreciating it.*] You get to New York a lot?

GEORGE: [*Offhand.*] Few times a year.

RUTH: Oh—that's nice. I've never been to New York.
          [WALTER *enters. We feel he has relieved himself, but the edge of unreality is still with him.*]

WALTER: New York ain't got nothing Chicago ain't. Just a bunch of hustling people all squeezed up together—being "Eastern."
          [*He turns his face into a screw of displeasure.*]

---

3. Bronze and brass royal sculptures produced in Benin (now part of Nigeria) in the 14th to 17th centuries. The Ashanti empires were the strongest political organization in West Africa during the time of the European slave trade. The Songhay civilizations were the largest and longest-lasting political group in West Africa before the advent of European trade.

GEORGE: Oh—you've been?

WALTER: *Plenty* of times.

RUTH: [*Shocked at the lie.*] Walter Lee Younger!

WALTER: [*Staring her down.*] Plenty! [*Pause.*] What we got to drink in this house? Why don't you offer this man some refreshment. [*To* GEORGE.] They don't know how to entertain people in this house, man.

GEORGE: Thank you—I don't really care for anything.

WALTER: [*Feeling his head; sobriety coming.*] Where's Mama?

RUTH: She ain't come back yet.

WALTER: [*Looking* MURCHISON *over from head to toe, scrutinizing his carefully casual tweed sports jacket over cashmere V-neck sweater over soft eyelet shirt and tie, and soft slacks, finished off with white buckskin shoes.*] Why all you college boys wear them fairyish-looking white shoes?

RUTH: Walter Lee!

[GEORGE MURCHISON *ignores the remark.*]

WALTER: [*To* RUTH.] Well, they look crazy as hell—white shoes, cold as it is.

RUTH: [*Crushed.*] You have to excuse him—

WALTER: No he don't! Excuse me for what? What you always excusing me for! I'll excuse myself when I needs to be excused! [*A pause.*] They look as funny as them black knee socks Beneatha wears out of here all the time.

RUTH: It's the college *style*, Walter.

WALTER: Style, hell. She looks like she got burnt legs or something!

RUTH: Oh, Walter—

WALTER: [*An irritable mimic.*] Oh, Walter! Oh, Walter! [*To* MURCHISON.] How's your old man making out? I understand you all going to buy that big hotel on the Drive? [*He finds a beer in the refrigerator, wanders over to* MURCHISON, *sipping and wiping his lips with the back of his hand, and straddling a chair backwards to talk to the other man.*] Shrewd move. Your old man is all right, man. [*Tapping his head and half winking for emphasis.*] I mean he knows how to operate. I mean he thinks *big*, you know what I mean, I mean for a *home*, you know? But I think he's kind of running out of ideas now. I'd like to talk to him. Listen, man, I got some plans that could turn this city upside down. I mean I think like he does. *Big.* Invest big, gamble big, hell, lose *big* if you have to, you know what I mean. It's hard to find a man on this whole Southside who understands my kind of thinking—you dig? [*He scrutinizes* MURCHISON *again, drinks his beer, squints his eyes and leans in close, confidential, man to man.*] Me and you ought to sit down and talk sometimes, man. Man, I got me some ideas . . .

GEORGE: [*With boredom.*] Yeah—sometimes we'll have to do that, Walter.

WALTER: [*Understanding the indifference, and offended.*] Yeah—well, when you get the time, man. I know you a busy little boy.

RUTH: Walter, please—

WALTER: [*Bitterly, hurt.*] I know ain't nothing in this world as busy as you colored college boys with your fraternity pins and white shoes . . .

RUTH: [*Covering her face with humiliation.*] Oh, Walter Lee—

WALTER: I see you all all the time—with the books tucked under your
   arms—going to your [British A—a mimic.] "clahsses." And for what!
   What the hell you learning over there? Filling up your heads—[Count-
   ing off on his fingers.]—with the sociology and the psychology—but they
   teaching you how to be a man? How to take over and run the world?
   They teaching you how to run a rubber plantation or a steel mill? Naw—
   just to talk proper and read books and wear white shoes . . .
GEORGE: [Looking at him with distaste, a little above it all.] You're all
   wacked up with bitterness, man.
WALTER: [Intently, almost quietly, between the teeth, glaring at the boy.]
   And you—ain't you bitter, man? Ain't you just about had it yet? Don't
   you see no stars gleaming that you can't reach out and grab? You
   happy?—You contented son-of-a-bitch—you happy? You got it made?
   Bitter? Man, I'm a volcano. Bitter? Here I am a giant—surrounded by
   ants! Ants who can't even understand what it is the giant is talking about.
RUTH: [Passionately and suddenly.] Oh, Walter—ain't you with nobody!
WALTER: [Violently.] No! 'Cause ain't nobody with me! Not even my own
   mother!
RUTH: Walter, that's a terrible thing to say!
   [BENEATHA enters, dressed for the evening in a cocktail dress and ear-
   rings.]
GEORGE: Well—hey, you look great.
BENEATHA: Let's go, George. See you all later.
RUTH: Have a nice time.
GEORGE: Thanks. Good night. [To WALTER, sarcastically.] Good night,
   Prometheus.⁴
   [BENEATHA and GEORGE exit.]
WALTER: [To RUTH.] Who is Prometheus?
RUTH: I don't know. Don't worry about it.
WALTER: [In fury, pointing after GEORGE.] See there—they get to a point
   where they can't insult you man to man—they got to go talk about some-
   thing ain't nobody never heard of!
RUTH: How do you know it was an insult? [To humor him.] Maybe
   Prometheus is a nice fellow.
WALTER: Prometheus! I bet there ain't even no such thing! I bet that sim-
   ple-minded clown—
RUTH: Walter—
   [She stops what she is doing and looks at him.]
WALTER: [Yelling.] Don't start!
RUTH: Start what?
WALTER: Your nagging! Where was I? Who was I with? How much
   money did I spend?
RUTH: [Plaintively.] Walter Lee—why don't we just try to talk about
   it . . .
WALTER: [Not listening.] I been out talking with people who understand
   me. People who care about the things I got on my mind.

4. In Greek mythology, a Titan who stole fire from   rock and sent an eagle to eat his liver, which grew
Mount Olympus and gave it to humankind. As   back daily.
punishment for the theft, Zeus chained him to a

RUTH: [*Wearily.*] I guess that means people like Willy Harris.

WALTER: Yes, people like Willy Harris.

RUTH: [*With a sudden flash of impatience.*] Why don't you all just hurry up and go into the banking business and stop talking about it!

WALTER: Why? You want to know why? 'Cause we all tied up in a race of people that don't know how to do nothing but moan, pray and have babies!

    [*The line is too bitter even for him and he looks at her and sits down.*]

RUTH: Oh, Walter . . . [*Softly.*] Honey, why can't you stop fighting me?

WALTER: [*Without thinking.*] Who's fighting you? Who even cares about you?

    [*This line begins the retardation of his mood.*]

RUTH: Well—[*She waits a long time, and then with resignation starts to put away her things.*] I guess I might as well go on to bed . . . [*More or less to herself.*] I don't know where we lost it . . . but we have . . . [*Then, to him.*] I—I'm sorry about this new baby, Walter. I guess maybe I better go on and do what I started . . . I guess I just didn't realize how bad things was with us . . . I guess I just didn't really realize— [*She starts out to the bedroom and stops.*] You want some hot milk?

WALTER: Hot milk?

RUTH: Yes—hot milk.

WALTER: Why hot milk?

RUTH: 'Cause after all that liquor you come home with you ought to have something hot in your stomach.

WALTER: I don't want no milk.

RUTH: You want some coffee then?

WALTER: No, I don't want no coffee. I don't want nothing hot to drink. [*Almost plaintively.*] Why you always trying to give me something to eat?

RUTH: [*Standing and looking at him helplessly.*] What else can I give you, Walter Lee Younger?

    [*She stands and looks at him and presently turns to go out again. He lifts his head and watches her going away from him in a new mood which began to emerge when he asked her "Who cares about you?"*]

WALTER: It's been rough, ain't it, baby? [*She hears and stops but does not turn around and he continues to her back.*] I guess between two people there ain't never as much understood as folks generally thinks there is. I mean like between me and you—[*She turns to face him.*] How we gets to the place where we scared to talk softness to each other. [*He waits, thinking hard himself.*] Why you think it got to be like that? [*He is thoughtful, almost as a child would be.*] Ruth, what is it gets into people ought to be close?

RUTH: I don't know, honey. I think about it a lot.

WALTER: On account of you and me, you mean? The way things are with us. The way something done come down between us.

RUTH: There ain't so much between us, Walter . . . Not when you come to me and try to talk to me. Try to be with me . . . a little even.

WALTER: [*Total honesty.*] Sometimes . . . sometimes . . . I don't even know how to try.

RUTH: Walter—

WALTER: Yes?

RUTH: [*Coming to him, gently and with misgiving, but coming to him.*] Honey . . . life don't have to be like this. I mean sometimes people can do things so that things are better . . . You remember how we used to talk when Travis was born . . . about the way we were going to live . . . the kind of house . . . [*She is stroking his head.*] Well, it's all starting to slip away from us . . .

[MAMA *enters, and* WALTER *jumps up and shouts at her.*]

WALTER: Mama, where have you been?

MAMA: My—them steps is longer than they used to be. Whew! [*She sits down and ignores him.*] How you feeling this evening, Ruth?

[RUTH *shrugs, disturbed some at having been prematurely interrupted and watching her husband knowingly.*]

WALTER: Mama, where have you been all day?

MAMA: [*Still ignoring him and leaning on the table and changing to more comfortable shoes.*] Where's Travis?

RUTH: I let him go out earlier and he ain't come back yet. Boy, is he going to get it!

WALTER: Mama!

MAMA: [*As if she has heard him for the first time.*] Yes, son?

WALTER: Where did you go this afternoon?

MAMA: I went downtown to tend to some business that I had to tend to.

WALTER: What kind of business?

MAMA: You know better than to question me like a child, Brother.

WALTER: [*Rising and bending over the table.*] Where were you, Mama? [*Bringing his fists down and shouting.*] Mama, you didn't go do something with that insurance money, something crazy?

[*The front door opens slowly, interrupting him, and* TRAVIS *peeks his head in, less than hopefully.*]

TRAVIS: [*To his mother.*] Mama, I—

RUTH: "Mama I" nothing! You're going to get it, boy! Get on in that bedroom and get yourself ready!

TRAVIS: But I—

MAMA: Why don't you all never let the child explain hisself.

RUTH: Keep out of it now, Lena.

[MAMA *clamps her lips together, and* RUTH *advances toward her son menacingly.*]

RUTH: A thousand times I have told you not to go off like that—

MAMA: [*Holding out her arms to her grandson.*] Well—at least let me tell him something. I want him to be the first one to hear . . . Come here, Travis. [*The boy obeys, gladly.*] Travis—[*She takes him by the shoulder and looks into his face.*]—you know that money we got in the mail this morning?

TRAVIS: Yes'm—

MAMA: Well—what you think your grandmama gone and done with that money?

TRAVIS: I don't know, Grandmama.

MAMA: [*Putting her finger on his nose for emphasis.*] She went out and she bought you a house! [*The explosion comes from* WALTER *at the end of the revelation and he jumps up and turns away from all of them in a fury.* MAMA *continues, to* TRAVIS.] You glad about the house? It's going to be yours when you get to be a man.

TRAVIS: Yeah—I always wanted to live in a house.

MAMA: All right, gimme some sugar then—[TRAVIS *puts his arms around her neck as she watches her son over the boy's shoulder. Then, to* TRAVIS, *after the embrace.*] Now when you say your prayers tonight, you thank God and your grandfather—'cause it was him who give you the house— in his way.

RUTH: [*Taking the boy from* MAMA *and pushing him toward the bedroom.*] Now you get out of here and get ready for your beating.

TRAVIS: Aw, Mama—

RUTH: Get on in there—[*Closing the door behind him and turning radiantly to her mother-in-law.*] So you went and did it!

MAMA: [*Quietly, looking at her son with pain.*] Yes, I did.

RUTH: [*Raising both arms classically.*] Praise God! [*Looks at* WALTER *a moment, who says nothing. She crosses rapidly to her husband.*] Please, honey—let me be glad . . . you be glad too. [*She has laid her hands on his shoulders, but he shakes himself free of her roughly, without turning to face her.*] Oh, Walter . . . a home . . . a home. [*She comes back to* MAMA.] Well—where is it? How big is it? How much it going to cost?

MAMA: Well—

RUTH: When we moving?

MAMA: [*Smiling at her.*] First of the month.

RUTH: [*Throwing back her head with jubilance.*] Praise God!

MAMA: [*Tentatively, still looking at her son's back turned against her and* RUTH.] It's—it's a nice house too . . . [*She cannot help speaking directly to him. An imploring quality in her voice, her manner, makes her almost like a girl now.*] Three bedrooms—nice big one for you and Ruth . . . Me and Beneatha still have to share our room, but Travis have one of his own— and [*With difficulty.*] I figure if the—new baby—is a boy, we could get one of them double-decker outfits . . . And there's a yard with a little patch of dirt where I could maybe get to grow me a few flowers . . . And a nice big basement . . .

RUTH: Walter honey, be glad—

MAMA: [*Still to his back, fingering things on the table.*] 'Course I don't want to make it sound fancier than it is . . . It's just a plain little old house—but it's made good and solid—and it will be *ours*. Walter Lee—it makes a difference in a man when he can walk on floors that belong to him . . .

RUTH: Where is it?

MAMA: [*Frightened at this telling.*] Well—well—it's out there in Clybourne Park—

[RUTH's *radiance fades abruptly, and* WALTER *finally turns slowly to face his mother with incredulity and hostility.*]

RUTH: Where?

MAMA: [*Matter-of-factly.*] Four o six Clybourne Street, Clybourne Park.

RUTH: Clybourne Park? Mama, there ain't no colored people living in Clybourne Park.

MAMA: [*Almost idiotically.*] Well, I guess there's going to be some now.

WALTER: [*Bitterly.*] So that's the peace and comfort you went out and bought for us today!

MAMA: [*Raising her eyes to meet his finally.*] Son—I just tried to find the nicest place for the least amount of money for my family.

RUTH: [*Trying to recover from the shock.*] Well—well—'course I ain't one never been 'fraid of no crackers,[5] mind you—but—well, wasn't there no other houses nowhere?

MAMA: Them houses they put up for colored in them areas way out all seem to cost twice as much as other houses. I did the best I could.

RUTH: [*Struck senseless with the news, in its various degrees of goodness and trouble, she sits a moment, her fists propping her chin in thought, and then she starts to rise, bringing her fists down with vigor, the radiance spreading from cheek to cheek again.*] Well—well!—All I can say is—if this is my time in life—my time—to say good-bye—[*And she builds with momentum as she starts to circle the room with an exuberant, almost tearfully happy release.*]—to these Goddamned cracking walls!—[*She pounds the walls.*]—and these marching roaches!—[*She wipes at an imaginary army of marching roaches.*]—and this cramped little closet which ain't now or never was no kitchen! . . . then I say it loud and good, Hallelujah! and good-bye misery . . . I don't never want to see your ugly face again! [*She laughs joyously, having practically destroyed the apartment, and flings her arms up and lets them come down happily, slowly, reflectively, over her abdomen, aware for the first time perhaps that the life therein pulses with happiness and not despair.*] Lena?

MAMA: [*Moved, watching her happiness.*] Yes, honey?

RUTH: [*Looking off.*] Is there—is there a whole lot of sunlight?

MAMA: [*Understanding.*] Yes, child, there's a whole lot of sunlight.

[*Long pause.*]

RUTH: [*Collecting herself and going to the door of the room* TRAVIS *is in.*] Well—I guess I better see 'bout Travis. [*To* MAMA.] Lord, I sure don't feel like whipping nobody today!

[*She exits.*]

MAMA: [*The mother and son are left alone now and the mother waits a long time, considering deeply, before she speaks.*] Son—you—you understand what I done, don't you? [WALTER *is silent and sullen.*] I—I just seen my family falling apart today . . . just falling to pieces in front of my eyes . . . We couldn't of gone on like we was today. We was going backwards 'stead of forwards—talking 'bout killing babies and wishing each other was dead . . . When it gets like that in life—you just got to do something different, push on out and do something bigger . . . [*She waits.*] I wish you say something, son . . . I wish you'd say how deep inside you you think I done the right thing—

WALTER: [*Crossing slowly to his bedroom door and finally turning there and speaking measuredly.*] What you need me to say you done right for?

5. Whites (slang).

You the head of this family. You run our lives like you want to. It was your money and you did what you wanted with it. So what you need for me to say it was all right for? [*Bitterly, to hurt her as deeply as he knows is possible.*] So you butchered up a dream of mine—you—who always talking 'bout your children's dreams . . .

MAMA: Walter Lee—

[*He just closes the door behind him.* MAMA *sits alone, thinking heavily.*]

[*Curtain.*]

SCENE TWO

Time: Friday night. A few weeks later.

At rise: Packing crates mark the intention of the family to move. BENEATHA *and* GEORGE *come in, presumably from an evening out again.*

GEORGE: O.K. . . . O.K., whatever you say . . . [*They both sit on the couch. He tries to kiss her. She moves away.*] Look, we've had a nice evening; let's not spoil it, huh? . . .

[*He again turns her head and tries to nuzzle in and she turns away from him, not with distaste but with momentary lack of interest; in a mood to pursue what they were talking about.*]

BENEATHA: I'm *trying* to talk to you.

GEORGE: We always talk.

BENEATHA: Yes—and I love to talk.

GEORGE: [*Exasperated; rising.*] I know it and I don't mind it sometimes . . . I want you to cut it out, see—The moody stuff, I mean. I don't like it. You're a nice-looking girl . . . all over. That's all you need, honey, forget the atmosphere. Guys aren't going to go for the atmosphere—they're going to go for what they see. Be glad for that. Drop the Garbo[6] routine. It doesn't go with you. As for myself, I want a nice—[*Groping.*]—simple [*Thoughtfully.*]—sophisticated girl . . . not a poet—O.K.?

[*She rebuffs him again and he starts to leave.*]

BENEATHA: Why are you angry?

GEORGE: Because this is stupid! I don't go out with you to discuss the nature of "quiet desperation" or to hear all about your thoughts—because the world will go on thinking what it thinks regardless—

BENEATHA: Then why read books? Why go to school?

GEORGE: [*With artificial patience, counting on his fingers.*] It's simple. You read books—to learn facts—to get grades—to pass the course—to get a degree. That's all—it has nothing to do with thoughts.

[*A long pause.*]

BENEATHA: I see. [*A longer pause as she looks at him.*] Good night, George.

[GEORGE *looks at her a little oddly, and starts to exit. He meets* MAMA *coming in.*]

GEORGE: Oh—hello, Mrs. Younger.

6. Greta Garbo (1905–1990), Swedish-born American actor known for her reclusiveness.

MAMA: Hello, George, how you feeling?
GEORGE: Fine—fine, how are you?
MAMA: Oh, a little tired. You know them steps can get you after a day's work. You all have a nice time tonight?
GEORGE: Yes—a fine time. Well, good night.
MAMA: Good night. [*He exits.* MAMA *closes the door behind her.*] Hello, honey. What you sitting like that for?
BENEATHA: I'm just sitting.
MAMA: Didn't you have a nice time?
BENEATHA: No.
MAMA: No? What's the matter?
BENEATHA: Mama, George is a fool—honest. [*She rises.*]
MAMA: [*Hustling around unloading the packages she has entered with. She stops.*] Is he, baby?
BENEATHA: Yes.
     [BENEATHA *makes up* TRAVIS' *bed as she talks.*]
MAMA: You sure?
BENEATHA: Yes.
MAMA: Well—I guess you better not waste your time with no fools.
     [BENEATHA *looks up at her mother, watching her put groceries in the refrigerator. Finally she gatheres up her things and starts into the bedroom. At the door she stops and looks back at her mother.*]
BENEATHA: Mama—
MAMA: Yes, baby—
BENEATHA: Thank you.
MAMA: For what?
BENEATHA: For understanding me this time.
     [*She exits quickly and the mother stands, smiling a little, looking at the place where* BENEATHA *just stood.* RUTH *enters.*]
RUTH: Now don't you fool with any of this stuff, Lena—
MAMA: Oh, I just thought I'd sort a few things out.
     [*The phone rings.* RUTH *answers.*]
RUTH: [*At the phone.*] Hello—Just a minute. [*Goes to door.*] Walter, it's Mrs. Arnold. [*Waits. Goes back to the phone. Tense.*] Hello. Yes, this is his wife speaking . . . He's lying down now. Yes . . . well, he'll be in tomorrow. He's been very sick. Yes—I know we should have called, but we were so sure he'd be able to come in today. Yes—yes, I'm very sorry. Yes . . . Thank you very much. [*She hangs up.* WALTER *is standing in the doorway of the bedroom behind her.*] That was Mrs. Arnold.
WALTER: [*Indifferently.*] Was it?
RUTH: She said if you don't come in tomorrow that they are getting a new man . . .
WALTER: Ain't that sad—ain't that crying sad.
RUTH: She said Mr. Arnold has had to take a cab for three days . . . Walter, you ain't been to work for three days! [*This is a revelation to her.*] Where you been, Walter Lee Younger? [WALTER *looks at her and starts to laugh.*] You're going to lose your job.
WALTER: That's right . . .
RUTH: Oh, Walter, and with your mother working like a dog every day—

WALTER:　That's sad too— Everything is sad.

MAMA:　What you been doing for these three days, son?

WALTER:　Mama—you don't know all the things a man what got leisure can find to do in this city . . . What's this—Friday night? Well—Wednesday I borrowed Willy Harris' car and I went for a drive . . . just me and myself and I drove and drove . . . Way out . . . way past South Chicago, and I parked the car and I sat and looked at the steel mills all day long. I just sat in the car and looked at them big black chimneys for hours. Then I drove back and I went to the Green Hat. [*Pause.*] And Thursday— Thursday I borrowed the car again and I got in it and I pointed it the other way and I drove the other way—for hours—way, way up to Wisconsin, and I looked at the farms. I just drove and looked at the farms. Then I drove back and I went to the Green Hat. [*Pause.*] And today—today I didn't get the car. Today I just walked. All over the Southside. And I looked at the Negroes and they looked at me and finally I just sat down on the curb at Thirty-ninth and South Parkway and I just sat there and watched the Negroes go by. And then I went to the Green Hat. You all sad? You all depressed? And you know where I am going right now—
　　[RUTH *goes out quietly.*]

MAMA:　Oh, Big Walter, is this the harvest of our days?

WALTER:　You know what I like about the Green Hat? [*He turns the radio on and a steamy, deep blues pours into the room.*] I like this little cat they got there who blows a sax . . . He blows. He talks to me. He ain't but 'bout five feet tall and he's got a conked[7] head and his eyes is always closed and he's all music—

MAMA:　[*Rising and getting some papers out of her handbag.*] Walter—

WALTER:　And there's this other guy who plays the piano . . . and they got a sound. I mean they can work on some music . . . They got the best little combo in the world in the Green Hat . . . You can just sit there and drink and listen to them three men play and you realize that don't nothing matter worth a damn, but just being there—

MAMA:　I've helped do it to you, haven't I, son? Walter, I been wrong.

WALTER:　Naw—you ain't never been wrong about nothing, Mama.

MAMA:　Listen to me, now. I say I been wrong, son. That I been doing to you what the rest of the world been doing to you. [*She stops and he looks up slowly at her and she meets his eyes pleadingly.*] Walter—what you ain't never understood is that I ain't got nothing, don't own nothing, ain't never really wanted nothing that wasn't for you. There ain't nothing as precious to me . . . There ain't nothing worth holding on to, money, dreams, nothing else—if it means—if it means it's going to destroy my boy. [*She puts her papers in front of him and he watches her without speaking or moving.*] I paid the man thirty-five hundred dollars down on the house. That leaves sixty-five hundred dollars. Monday morning I want you to take this money and take three thousand dollars and put it in a savings account for Beneatha's medical schooling. The rest you put in a checking account—with your name on it. And from now on any penny that come out of it or that go in it is for you to look after. For you to decide. [*She drops her hands a little helplessly.*] It ain't much, but it's all

---

7. Chemically straightened hair.

I got in the world and I'm putting it in your hands. I'm telling you to be
the head of this family from now on like you supposed to be.

WALTER: [*Stares at the money.*] You trust me like that, Mama?

MAMA: I ain't never stop trusting you. Like I ain't never stop loving you.
[*She goes out, and* WALTER *sits looking at the money on the table as
the music continues in its idiom, pulsing in the room. Finally, in a
decisive gesture, he gets up, and, in mingled joy and desperation,
picks up the money. At the same moment,* TRAVIS *enters for bed.*]

TRAVIS: What's the matter, Daddy? You drunk?

WALTER: [*Sweetly, more sweetly than we have ever known him.*] No,
Daddy ain't drunk. Daddy ain't going to never be drunk again. . . .

TRAVIS: Well, good night, Daddy.
[*The father has come from behind the couch and leans over, embracing his son.*]

WALTER: Son, I feel like talking to you tonight.

TRAVIS: About what?

WALTER: Oh, about a lot of things. About you and what kind of man you
going to be when you grow up. . . . Son—son, what do you want to be
when you grow up?

TRAVIS: A bus driver.

WALTER: [*Laughing a little.*] A what? Man, that ain't nothing to want to
be!

TRAVIS: Why not?

WALTER: 'Cause, man—it ain't big enough—you know what I mean.

TRAVIS: I don't know then. I can't make up my mind. Sometimes Mama
asks me that too. And sometimes when I tell you I just want to be like
you—she says she don't want me to be like that and sometimes she says
she does. . . .

WALTER: [*Gathering him up in his arms.*] You know what, Travis? In
seven years you going to be seventeen years old. And things is going to be
very different with us in seven years, Travis. . . . One day when you are
seventeen I'll come home—home from my office downtown somewhere—

TRAVIS: You don't work in no office, Daddy.

WALTER: No—but after tonight. After what your daddy gonna do tonight,
there's going to be offices—a whole lot of offices. . . .

TRAVIS: What you gonna do tonight, Daddy?

WALTER: You wouldn't understand yet, son, but your daddy's gonna make
a transaction . . . a business transaction that's going to change our lives.
. . . That's how come one day when you 'bout seventeen years old I'll
come home and I'll be pretty tired, you know what I mean, after a day of
conferences and secretaries getting things wrong the way they do . . .
'cause an executive's life is hell, man—[*The more he talks the farther
away he gets.*] And I'll pull the car up on the driveway . . . just a plain
black Chrysler, I think, with white walls—no—black tires. More elegant.
Rich people don't have to be flashy . . . though I'll have to get something
a little sportier for Ruth—maybe a Cadillac convertible to do her shopping in. . . . And I'll come up the steps to the house and the gardener will
be clipping away at the hedges and he'll say, "Good evening, Mr.
Younger." And I'll say, "Hello, Jefferson, how are you this evening?" And

I'll go inside and Ruth will come downstairs and meet me at the door and we'll kiss each other and she'll take my arm and we'll go up to your room to see you sitting on the floor with the catalogues of all the great schools in America around you. . . . All the great schools in the world! And—and I'll say, all right son—it's your seventeenth birthday, what is it you've decided? . . . Just tell me where you want to go to school and you'll go. Just tell me, what it is you want to be—and you'll *be* it. . . . Whatever you want to be—Yessir! [*He holds his arms open for* TRAVIS.] You just name it, son . . . [TRAVIS *leaps into them.*] and I hand you the world!

[WALTER's *voice has risen in pitch and hysterical promise and on the last line he lifts* TRAVIS *high.*]

[*Blackout.*]

SCENE THREE

Time: Saturday, moving day, one week later.

Before the curtain rises, RUTH's *voice, a strident, dramatic church alto, cuts through the silence.*

It is, in the darkness, a triumphant surge, a penetrating statement of expectation: "Oh, Lord, I don't feel no ways tired! Children, oh, glory hallelujah!"

As the curtain rises we see that RUTH *is alone in the living room, finishing up the family's packing. It is moving day. She is nailing crates and tying cartons.* BENEATHA *enters, carrying a guitar case, and watches her exuberant sister-in-law.*

RUTH: Hey!

BENEATHA: [*Putting away the case.*] Hi.

RUTH: [*Pointing at a package.*] Honey—look in that package there and see what I found on sale this morning at the South Center. [RUTH *gets up and moves to the package and draws out some curtains.*] Lookahere—hand-turned hems!

BENEATHA: How do you know the window size out there?

RUTH: [*Who hadn't thought of that.*] Oh— Well, they bound to fit something in the whole house. Anyhow, they was too good a bargain to pass up. [RUTH *slaps her head, suddenly remembering something.*] Oh, Bennie—I meant to put a special note on that carton over there. That's your mama's good china and she wants 'em to be very careful with it.

BENEATHA: I'll do it.

[BENEATHA *finds a piece of paper and starts to draw large letters on it.*]

RUTH: You know what I'm going to do soon as I get in that new house?

BENEATHA: What?

RUTH: Honey—I'm going to run me a tub of water up to here . . . [*With her fingers practically up to her nostrils.*] And I'm going to get in it—and I am going to sit . . . and sit . . . and sit in that hot water and the first person who knocks to tell *me* to hurry up and come out—

BENEATHA: Gets shot at sunrise.

RUTH: [*Laughing happily.*] You said it, sister! [*Noticing how large* BENEA-
THA *is absent-mindedly making the note.*] Honey, they ain't going to read
that from no airplane.

BENEATHA: [*Laughing herself.*] I guess I always think things have more
emphasis if they are big, somehow.

RUTH: [*Looking up at her and smiling.*] You and your brother seem to
have that as a philosophy of life. Lord, that man—done changed so
'round here. You know—you know what we did last night? Me and Walter Lee?

BENEATHA: What?

RUTH: [*Smiling to herself.*] We went to the movies. [*Looking at* BENEATHA
to see if she understands.] We went to the movies. You know the last time
me and Walter went to the movies together?

BENEATHA: No.

RUTH: Me neither. That's how long it been. [*Smiling again.*] But we went
last night. The picture wasn't much good, but that didn't seem to matter.
We went—and we held hands.

BENEATHA: Oh, Lord!

RUTH: We held hands—and you know what?

BENEATHA: What?

RUTH: When we come out of the show it was late and dark and all the
stores and things was closed up . . . and it was kind of chilly and there
wasn't many people on the streets . . . and we was still holding hands, me
and Walter.

BENEATHA: You're killing me.

[WALTER *enters with a large package. His happiness is deep in him;
he cannot keep still with his new-found exuberance. He is singing
and wiggling and snapping his fingers. He puts his package in a corner and puts a phonograph record, which he has brought in with
him, on the record player. As the music comes up he dances over to*
RUTH *and tries to get her to dance with him. She gives in at last to his
raunchiness and in a fit of giggling allows herself to be drawn into his
mood and together they deliberately burlesque an old social dance of
their youth.*]

BENEATHA: [*Regarding them a long time as they dance, then drawing in
her breath for a deeply exaggerated comment which she does not particularly mean.*] Talk about—olddddddddddd-fashioneddddddddd—Negroes!

WALTER: [*Stopping momentarily.*] What kind of Negroes?

[*He says this in fun. He is not angry with her today, nor with anyone.
He starts to dance with his wife again.*]

BENEATHA: Old-fashioned.

WALTER: [*As he dances with* RUTH.] You know, when these *New Negroes*
have their convention—[*Pointing at his sister.*]—that is going to be the
chairman of the Committee on Unending Agitation. [*He goes on dancing, then stops.*] Race, race, race! . . . Girl, I do believe you are the first
person in the history of the entire human race to successfully brainwash
yourself. [BENEATHA *breaks up and he goes on dancing. He stops again,
enjoying his tease.*] Damn, even the N double A C P takes a holiday
sometimes! [BENEATHA *and* RUTH *laugh. He dances with* RUTH *some more*

and starts to laugh and stops and pantomimes someone over an operating table.] I can just see that chick someday looking down at some poor cat on an operating table before she starts to slice him, saying . . . [*Pulling his sleeves back maliciously.*] "By the way, what are your views on civil rights down there? . . ."

     [*He laughs at her again and starts to dance happily. The bell sounds.*]

BENEATHA: Sticks and stones may break my bones but . . . words will never hurt me!

     [BENEATHA *goes to the door and opens it as* WALTER *and* RUTH *go on with the clowning.* BENEATHA *is somewhat surprised to see a quiet-looking middle-aged white man in a business suit holding his hat and a briefcase in his hand and consulting a small piece of paper.*]

MAN: Uh—how do you do, miss. I am looking for a Mrs.—[*He looks at the slip of paper.*] Mrs. Lena Younger?

BENEATHA: [*Smoothing her hair with slight embarrassment.*] Oh—yes, that's my mother. Excuse me [*She closes the door and turns to quiet the other two.*] Ruth! Brother! Somebody's here. [*Then she opens the door. The* MAN *casts a curious quick glance at all of them.*] Uh—come in please.

MAN: [*Coming in.*] Thank you.

BENEATHA: My mother isn't here just now. Is it business?

MAN: Yes . . . well, of a sort.

WALTER: [*Freely, the Man of the House.*] Have a seat. I'm Mrs. Younger's son. I look after most of her business matters.

     [RUTH *and* BENEATHA *exchange amused glances.*]

MAN: [*Regarding* WALTER, *and sitting.*] Well—My name is Karl Lindner . . .

WALTER: [*Stretching out his hand.*] Walter Younger. This is my wife— [RUTH *nods politely.*]—and my sister.

LINDNER: How do you do.

WALTER: [*Amiably, as he sits himself easily on a chair, leaning with interest forward on his knees and looking expectantly into the newcomer's face.*] What can we do for you, Mr. Lindner!

LINDNER: [*Some minor shuffling of the hat and briefcase on his knees.*] Well—I am a representative of the Clybourne Park Improvement Association—

WALTER: [*Pointing.*] Why don't you sit your things on the floor?

LINDNER: Oh—yes. Thank you. [*He slides the briefcase and hat under the chair.*] And as I was saying—I am from the Clybourne Park Improvement Association and we have had it brought to our attention at the last meeting that you people—or at least your mother—has bought a piece of residential property at—[*He digs for the slip of paper again.*]—four o six Clybourne Street . . .

WALTER: That's right. Care for something to drink? Ruth, get Mr. Lindner a beer.

LINDNER: [*Upset for some reason.*] Oh—no, really. I mean thank you very much, but no thank you.

RUTH: [*Innocently.*] Some coffee?

LINDNER: Thank you, nothing at all.

    [BENEATHA *is watching the man carefully.*]

LINDNER: Well, I don't know how much you folks know about our organization. [*He is a gentle man; thoughtful and somewhat labored in his manner.*] It is one of these community organizations set up to look after—oh, you know, things like block upkeep and special projects and we also have what we call our New Neighbors Orientation Committee . . .

BENEATHA: [*Drily.*] Yes—and what do they do?

LINDNER: [*Turning a little to her and then returning the main force to* WALTER.] Well—it's what you might call a sort of welcoming committee, I guess. I mean they, we, I'm the chairman of the committee—go around and see the new people who move into the neighborhood and sort of give them the lowdown on the way we do things out in Clybourne Park.

BENEATHA: [*With appreciation of the two meanings, which escape* RUTH *and* WALTER.] Un-huh.

LINDNER: And we also have the category of what the association calls— [*He looks elsewhere.*]—uh—special community problems . . .

BENEATHA: Yes—and what are some of those?

WALTER: Girl, let the man talk.

LINDNER: [*With understated relief.*] Thank you. I would sort of like to explain this thing in my own way. I mean I want to explain to you in a certain way.

WALTER: Go ahead.

LINDNER: Yes. Well. I'm going to try to get right to the point. I'm sure we'll all appreciate that in the long run.

BENEATHA: Yes.

WALTER: Be still now!

LINDNER: Well—

RUTH: [*Still innocently.*] Would you like another chair—you don't look comfortable.

LINDNER: [*More frustrated than annoyed.*] No, thank you very much. Please. Well—to get right to the point I—[*A great breath, and he is off at last.*] I am sure you people must be aware of some of the incidents which have happened in various parts of the city when colored people have moved into certain areas—[BENEATHA *exhales heavily and starts tossing a piece of fruit up and down in the air.*] Well—because we have what I think is going to be a unique type of organization in American community life—not only do we deplore that kind of thing—but we are trying to do something about it. [BENEATHA *stops tossing and turns with a new and quizzical interest to the man.*] We feel—[*gaining confidence in his mission because of the interest in the faces of the people he is talking to.*]—we feel that most of the trouble in this world, when you come right down to it—[*He hits his knee for emphasis.*]—most of the trouble exists because people just don't sit down and talk to each other.

RUTH: [*Nodding as she might in church, pleased with the remark.*] You can say that again, mister.

LINDNER: [*More encouraged by such affirmation.*] That we don't try hard enough in this world to understand the other fellow's problem. The other guy's point of view.

RUTH: Now that's right.

    [BENEATHA *and* WALTER *merely watch and listen with genuine interest.*]

LINDNER: Yes—that's the way we feel out in Clybourne Park. And that's why I was elected to come here this afternoon and talk to you people. Friendly like, you know, the way people should talk to each other and see if we couldn't find some way to work this thing out. As I say, the whole business is a matter of *caring* about the other fellow. Anybody can see that you are a nice family of folks, hard working and honest I'm sure. [BENEATHA *frowns slightly, quizzically, her head tilted regarding him.*] Today everybody knows what it means to be on the outside of *something.* And of course, there is always somebody who is out to take the advantage of people who don't always understand.

WALTER: What do you mean?

LINDNER: Well—you see our community is made up of people who've worked hard as the dickens for years to build up that little community. They're not rich and fancy people; just hard-working, honest people who don't really have much but those little homes and a dream of the kind of community they want to raise their children in. Now, I don't say we are perfect and there is a lot wrong in some of the things they want. But you've got to admit that a man, right or wrong, has the right to want to have the neighborhood he lives in a certain kind of way. And at the moment the overwhelming majority of our people out there feel that people get along better, take more of a common interest in the life of the community, when they share a common background. I want you to believe me when I tell you that race prejudice simply doesn't enter into it. It is a matter of the people of Clybourne Park believing, rightly or wrongly, as I say, that for the happiness of all concerned that our Negro families are happier when they live in their *own* communities.

BENEATHA: [*With a grand and bitter gesture.*] This, friends, is the Welcoming Committee!

WALTER: [*Dumfounded, looking at* LINDNER.] Is this what you came marching all the way over here to tell us?

LINDNER: Well, now we've been having a fine conversation. I hope you'll hear me all the way through.

WALTER: [*Tightly.*] Go ahead, man.

LINDNER: You see—in the face of all things I have said, we are prepared to make your family a very generous offer . . .

BENEATHA: Thirty pieces and not a coin less!

WALTER: Yeah?

LINDNER: [*Putting on his glasses and drawing a form out of the briefcase.*] Our association is prepared, through the collective effort of our people, to buy the house from you at a financial gain to your family.

RUTH: Lord have mercy, ain't this the living gall!

WALTER: All right, you through?

LINDNER: Well, I want to give you the exact terms of the financial arrangement—

WALTER: We don't want to hear no exact terms of no arrangements. I want to know if you got any more to tell us 'bout getting together?

LINDNER: [*Taking off his glasses.*] Well—I don't suppose that you feel . . .

WALTER: Never mind how I feel—you got any more to say 'bout how people ought to sit down and talk to each other? . . . Get out of my house, man.

[*He turns his back and walks to the door.*]

LINDNER: [*Looking around at the hostile faces and reaching and assembling his hat and briefcase.*] Well—I don't understand why you people are reacting this way. What do you think you are going to gain by moving into a neighborhood where you just aren't wanted and where some elements—well—people can get awful worked up when they feel that their whole way of life and everything they've ever worked for is threatened.

WALTER: Get out.

LINDNER: [*At the door, holding a small card.*] Well—I'm sorry it went like this.

WALTER: Get out.

LINDNER: [*Almost sadly regarding* WALTER.] You just can't force people to change their hearts, son.

[*He turns and put his card on a table and exits.* WALTER *pushes the door to with stinging hatred, and stands looking at it.* RUTH *just sits and* BENEATHA *just stands. They say nothing.* MAMA *and* TRAVIS *enter.*]

MAMA: Well—this all the packing got done since I left out of here this morning. I testify before God that my children got all the energy of the dead. What time the moving men due?

BENEATHA: Four o'clock. You had a caller, Mama.

[*She is smiling, teasingly.*]

MAMA: Sure enough—who?

BENEATHA: [*Her arms folded saucily.*] The Welcoming Committee.

[WALTER *and* RUTH *giggle.*]

MAMA: [*Innocently.*] Who?

BENEATHA: The Welcoming Committee. They said they're sure going to be glad to see you when you get there.

WALTER: [*Devilishly.*] Yeah, they said they can't hardly wait to see your face. [*Laughter.*]

MAMA: [*Sensing their facetiousness.*] What's the matter with you all?

WALTER: Ain't nothing the matter with us. We just telling you 'bout the gentleman who came to see you this afternoon. From the Clybourne Park Improvement Association.

MAMA: What he want?

RUTH: [*In the same mood as* BENEATHA *and* WALTER.] To welcome you, honey.

WALTER: He said they can't hardly wait. He said the one thing they don't have, that they just *dying* to have out there is a fine family of colored people! [*To* RUTH *and* BENEATHA.] Ain't that right!

RUTH *and* BENEATHA: [*Mockingly.*] Yeah! He left his card in case—

[*They indicate the card, and* MAMA *picks it up and throws it on the floor—understanding and looking off as she draws her chair up to the table on which she has put her plant and some sticks and some cord.*]

MAMA: Father, give us strength. [*Knowingly—and without fun.*] Did he threaten us?

BENEATHA: Oh—Mama—they don't do it like that any more. He talked Brotherhood. He said everybody ought to learn how to sit down and hate each other with good Christian fellowship.

[*She and* WALTER *shake hands to ridicule the remark.*]

MAMA: [*Sadly.*] Lord, protect us . . .

RUTH: You should hear the money those folks raised to buy the house from us. All we paid and then some.

BENEATHA: What they think we going to do—eat 'em?

RUTH: No, honey, marry 'em.

MAMA: [*Shaking her head.*] Lord, Lord, Lord . . .

RUTH: Well—that's the way the crackers crumble. Joke.

BENEATHA: [*Laughingly noticing what her mother is doing.*] Mama, what are you doing?

MAMA: Fixing my plant so it won't get hurt none on the way . . .

BENEATHA: Mama, you going to take *that* to the new house?

MAMA: Un-huh—

BENEATHA: That raggedy-looking old thing?

MAMA: [*Stopping and looking at her.*] It expresses *me.*

RUTH: [*With delight, to* BENEATHA.] So there, Miss Thing!

[WALTER *comes to* MAMA *suddenly and bends down behind her and squeezes her in his arms with all his strength. She is overwhelmed by the suddenness of it and, though delighted, her manner is like that of* RUTH *with* TRAVIS.]

MAMA: Look out now, boy! You make me mess up my thing here!

WALTER: [*His face lit, he slips down on his knees beside her, his arms still about her.*] Mama . . . you know what it means to climb up in the chariot?

MAMA: [*Gruffly, very happy.*] Get on away from me now . . .

RUTH: [*Near the gift-wrapped package, trying to catch* WALTER's *eye.*] Psst—

WALTER: What the old song say, Mama . . .

RUTH: Walter— Now?

[*She is pointing at the package.*]

WALTER: [*Speaking the lines, sweetly, playfully, in his mother's face.*]
          I got wings . . . you got wings . . .
          All God's Children got wings[8] . . .

MAMA: Boy—get out of my face and do some work . . .

WALTER: When I get to heaven gonna put on my wings,
          Gonna fly all over God's heaven . . .

BENEATHA: [*Teasingly, from across the room.*] Everybody talking 'bout heaven ain't going there!

WALTER: [*To* RUTH, *who is carrying the box across to them.*] I don't know, you think we ought to give her that . . . Seems to me she ain't been very appreciative around here.

MAMA: [*Eying the box, which is obviously a gift.*] What is that?

---

8. Black spiritual; also the title of a controversial 1923 play by Eugene O'Neill about a racially mixed marriage.

WALTER: [*Taking it from* RUTH *and putting it on the table in front of* MAMA.] Well—what you all think? Should we give it to her?

RUTH: Oh—she was pretty good today.

MAMA: I'll good you—
[*She turns her eyes to the box again.*]

BENEATHA: Open it, Mama.
[*She stands up, looks at it, turns and looks at all of them, and then presses her hands together and does not open the package.*]

WALTER: [*Sweetly.*] Open it, Mama. It's for you. [MAMA *looks in his eyes. It is the first present in her life without its being Christmas. Slowly she opens her package and lifts out, one by one, a brand-new sparkling set of gardening tools.* WALTER *continues, prodding.*] Ruth made up the note—read it . . .

MAMA: [*Picking up the card and adjusting her glasses.*] "To our own Mrs. Miniver[9]—Love from Brother, Ruth and Beneatha." Ain't that lovely . . .

TRAVIS: [*Tugging at his father's sleeve.*] Daddy, can I give her mine now?

WALTER: All right, son. [TRAVIS *flies to get his gift.*] Travis didn't want to go in with the rest of us, Mama. He got his own. [*Somewhat amused.*] We don't know what it is . . .

TRAVIS: [*Racing back in the room with a large hatbox and putting it in front of his grandmother.*] Here!

MAMA: Lord have mercy, baby. You done gone and bought your grandmother a hat?

TRAVIS: [*Very proud.*] Open it!
[*She does and lifts out an elaborate, but very elaborate, wide gardening hat, and all the adults break up at the sight of it.*]

RUTH: Travis, honey, what is that?

TRAVIS: [*Who thinks it is beautiful and appropriate.*] It's a gardening hat! Like the ladies always have on in the magazines when they work in their gardens.

BENEATHA: [*Giggling fiercely.*] Travis—we were trying to make Mama Mrs. Miniver—not Scarlett O'Hara!

MAMA: [*Indignantly.*] What's the matter with you all! This here is a beautiful hat! [*Absurdly.*] I always wanted me one just like it!
[*She pops it on her head to prove it to her grandson, and the hat is ludicrous and considerably oversized.*]

RUTH: Hot dog! Go, Mama!

WALTER: [*Doubled over with laughter.*] I'm sorry, Mama—but you look like you ready to go out and chop you some cotton sure enough!
[*They all laugh except* MAMA, *out of deference to* TRAVIS' *feelings.*]

MAMA: [*Gathering the boy up to her.*] Bless your heart—this is the prettiest hat I ever owned— [WALTER, RUTH *and* BENEATHA *chime in—noisily, festively and insincerely congratulating* TRAVIS *on his gift.*] What are we all standing around here for? We ain't finished packin' yet. Bennie, you ain't packed one book.
[*The bell rings.*]

---

9. Title character in a 1942 film starring Greer Garson about life in wartime London.

BENEATHA: That couldn't be the movers . . . it's not hardly two good yet—
  [BENEATHA *goes into her room.* MAMA *starts for door.*]
WALTER: [*Turning, stiffening.*] Wait—wait—I'll get it.
  [*He stands and looks at the door.*]
MAMA: You expecting company, son?
WALTER: [*Just looking at the door.*] Yeah—yeah . . .
  [MAMA *looks at* RUTH, *and they exchange innocent and unfrightened glances.*]
MAMA: [*Not understanding.*] Well, let them in, son.
BENEATHA: [*From her room.*] We need some more string.
MAMA: Travis—you run to the hardware and get me some string cord.
  [MAMA *goes out and* WALTER *turns and looks at* RUTH. TRAVIS *goes to a dish for money.*]
RUTH: Why don't you answer the door, man?
WALTER: [*Suddenly bounding across the floor to her.*] 'Cause sometimes it hard to let the future begin! [*Stooping down in her face.*]
    I got wings! You got wings!
    All God's children got wings!
  [*He crosses to the door and throws it open. Standing there is a very slight little man in a not too prosperous business suit and with haunted frightened eyes and a hat pulled down tightly, brim up, around his forehead.* TRAVIS *passes between the men and exits.* WALTER *leans deep in the man's face, still in his jubilance.*]
    When I get to heaven gonna put on my wings,
    Gonna fly all over God's heaven . . .
  [*The little man just stares at him.*]
    Heaven—
  Suddenly he stops and looks past the little man into the empty hallway.] Where's Willy, man?
BOBO: He ain't with me.
WALTER: [*Not disturbed.*] Oh—come on in. You know my wife.
BOBO: [*Dumbly, taking off his hat.*] Yes—h'you, Miss Ruth.
RUTH: [*Quietly, a mood apart from her husband already, seeing* BOBO.]
  Hello, Bobo.
WALTER: You right on time today . . . Right on time. That's the way! [*He slaps* BOBO *on his back.*] Sit down . . . lemme hear.
  [RUTH *stands stiffly and quietly in back of them, as though somehow she senses death, her eyes fixed on her husband.*]
BOBO: [*His frightened eyes on the floor, his hat in his hands.*] Could I please get a drink of water, before I tell you about it, Walter Lee?
  [WALTER *does not take his eyes off the man.* RUTH *goes blindly to the tap and gets a glass of water and brings it to* BOBO.]
WALTER: There ain't nothing wrong, is there?
BOBO: Lemme tell you—
WALTER: Man—didn't nothing go wrong?
BOBO: Lemme tell you—Walter Lee. [*Looking at* RUTH *and talking to her more than to* WALTER.] You know how it was. I got to tell you how it was. I mean first I got to tell you how it was all the way . . . I mean about the money I put in, Walter Lee . . .
WALTER: [*With taut agitation now.*] What about the money you put in?

BOBO: Well—it wasn't much as we told you—me and Willy—[*He stops.*] I'm sorry, Walter. I got a bad feeling about it. I got a real bad feeling about it . . .

WALTER: Man, what you telling me about all this for? . . . Tell me what happened in Springfield . . .

BOBO: Springfield.

RUTH: [*Like a dead woman.*] What was supposed to happen in Springfield?

BOBO: [*To her.*] This deal that me and Walter went into with Willy— Me and Willy was going to go down to Springfield and spread some money 'round so's we wouldn't have to wait so long for the liquor license . . . That's what we were going to do. Everybody said that was the way you had to do, you understand, Miss Ruth?

WALTER: Man—what happened down there?

BOBO: [*A pitiful man, near tears.*] I'm trying to tell you, Walter.

WALTER: [*Screaming at him suddenly.*] THEN TELL ME, GODDAMMIT . . . WHAT'S THE MATTER WITH YOU?

BOBO: Man . . . I didn't go to no Springfield, yesterday.

WALTER: [*Halted, life hanging in the moment.*] Why not?

BOBO: [*The long way, the hard way to tell.*] 'Cause I didn't have no reasons to . . .

WALTER: Man, what are you talking about!

BOBO: I'm talking about the fact that when I got to the train station yesterday morning—eight o'clock like we planned . . . Man—*Willy didn't never show up.*

WALTER: Why . . . where was he . . . where is he?

BOBO: That's what I'm trying to tell you . . . I don't know . . . I waited six hours . . . I called his house . . . and I waited . . . six hours . . . I waited in that train station six hours . . . [*Breaking into tears.*] That was all the extra money I had in the world . . . [*Looking up at* WALTER *with the tears running down his face.*] Man, Willy is gone.

WALTER: Gone, what you mean Willy is gone? Gone where? You mean he went by himself. You mean he went off to Springfield by himself— to take care of getting the license—[*Turns and looks anxiously at* RUTH.] You mean maybe he didn't want too many people in on the business down there? [*Looks to* RUTH *again, as before.*] You know Willy got his own ways. [*Looks back to* BOBO.] Maybe you was late yesterday and he just went on down there without you. Maybe—maybe—he's been callin' you at home tryin' to tell you what happened or something. Maybe—maybe—he just got sick. He's somewhere—he's got to be somewhere. We just got to find him—me and you got to find him. [*Grabs* BOBO *senselessly by the collar and starts to shake him.*] We got to!

BOBO: [*In sudden angry, frightened agony.*] What's the matter with you, Walter! *When a cat take off with your money he don't leave you no maps!*

WALTER: [*Turning madly, as though he is looking for* WILLY *in the very room.*] Willy! . . . Willy . . . don't do it . . . Please don't do it . . . Man, not with that money . . . Man, please, not with that money . . . Oh, God . . . Don't let it be true . . . [*He is wandering around, crying out for* WILLY

and looking for him or perhaps for help from God.] Man . . . I trusted you
. . . Man, I put my life in your hands . . . [*He starts to crumple down on the
floor as* RUTH *just covers her face in horror.* MAMA *opens the door and
comes into the room, with* BENEATHA *behind her.*] Man . . . [*He starts to
pound the floor with his fists, sobbing wildly.*] That money is made out of
my father's flesh . . .

BOBO: [*Standing over him helplessly.*] I'm sorry, Walter . . . [*Only* WAL-
TER's *sobs reply.* BOBO *puts on his hat.*] I had my life staked on this deal,
too . . .
          [*He exits.*]

MAMA: [*To* WALTER.] Son—[*She goes to him, bends down to him, talks to
his bent head.*] Son . . . Is it gone? Son, I gave you sixty-five hundred
dollars. Is it gone? All of it? Beneatha's money too?

WALTER: [*Lifting his head slowly.*] Mama . . . I never . . . went to the bank
at all . . .

MAMA: [*Not wanting to believe him.*] You mean . . . your sister's school
money . . . you used that too . . . Walter? . . .

WALTER: Yessss! . . . All of it . . . It's all gone . . . [*There is total silence.
RUTH stands with her face covered with her hands;* BENEATHA *leans forlornly against a wall, fingering a piece of red ribbon from the mother's gift.*
MAMA *stops and looks at her son without recognition and then, quite without thinking about it, starts to beat him senselessly in the face.* BENEATHA
goes to them and stops it.]

BENEATHA: Mama!
          [MAMA *stops and looks at both of her children and rises slowly and
          wanders vaguely, aimlessly away from them.*]

MAMA: I seen . . . him . . . night after night . . . come in . . . and look at that
rug . . . and then look at me . . . the red showing in his eyes . . . the veins
moving in his head . . . I seen him grow thin and old before he was forty
. . . working and working and working like somebody's old horse . . .
killing himself . . . and you—you give it all away in a day . . .

BENEATHA: Mama—

MAMA: Oh, God . . . [*She looks up to Him.*] Look down here—and show
me the strength.

BENEATHA: Mama—

MAMA: [*Folding over.*] Strength . . .

BENEATHA: [*Plaintively.*] Mama . . .

MAMA: Strength!

[*Curtain.*]

Act III

An hour later.

At curtain, there is a sullen light of gloom in the living room, gray light not
unlike that which began the first scene of Act I. At left we can see WALTER
within his room, alone with himself. He is stretched out on the bed, his shirt
out and open, his arms under his head. He does not smoke, he does not cry

*out, he merely lies there, looking up at the ceiling, much as if he were alone
in the world.*

In the living room BENEATHA *sits at the table, still surrounded by the now
almost ominous packing crates. She sits looking off. We feel that this is a
mood struck perhaps an hour before, and it lingers now, full of the empty
sound of profound disappointment. We see on a line from her brother's bedroom the sameness of their attitudes. Presently the bell rings and* BENEATHA
rises without ambition or interest in answering. It is ASAGAI, *smiling broadly,
striding into the room with energy and happy expectation and conversation.*

ASAGAI: I came over . . . I had some free time. I thought I might help with
the packing. Ah, I like the look of packing crates! A household in preparation for a journey! It depresses some people . . . but for me . . . it is
another feeling. Something full of the flow of life, do you understand?
Movement, progress . . . It makes me think of Africa.

BENEATHA: Africa!

ASAGAI: What kind of a mood is this? Have I told you how deeply you
move me?

BENEATHA: He gave away the money, Asagai . . .

ASAGAI: Who gave away what money?

BENEATHA: The insurance money. My brother gave it away.

ASAGAI: Gave it away?

BENEATHA: He made an investment! With a man even Travis wouldn't
have trusted.

ASAGAI: And it's gone?

BENEATHA: Gone!

ASAGAI: I'm very sorry . . . And you, now?

BENEATHA: Me? . . . Me? . . . Me I'm nothing . . . Me. When I was very
small . . . we used to take our sleds out in the wintertime and the only
hills we had were the ice-covered stone steps of some houses down the
street. And we used to fill them in with snow and make them smooth and
slide down them all day . . . and it was very dangerous you know . . . far
too steep . . . and sure enough one day a kid named Rufus came down
too fast and hit the sidewalk . . . and we saw his face just split open right
there in front of us . . . And I remember standing there looking at his
bloody open face thinking that was the end of Rufus. But the ambulance
came and they took him to the hospital and they fixed the broken bones
and they sewed it all up . . . and the next time I saw Rufus he just had a
little line down the middle of his face . . . I never got over that . . .
    [WALTER *sits up, listening on the bed. Throughout this scene it is im-
    portant that we feel his reaction at all times, that he visibly respond to
    the words of his sister and* ASAGAI.]

ASAGAI: What?

BENEATHA: That that was what one person could do for another, fix him
up—sew up the problem, make him all right again. That was the most
marvelous thing in the world . . . I wanted to do that. I always thought it
was the one concrete thing in the world that a human being could do.
Fix up the sick, you know—and make them whole again. This was truly
being God . . .

ASAGAI: You wanted to be God?

BENEATHA: No—I wanted to cure. It used to be so important to me. I
wanted to cure. It used to matter. I used to care. I mean about people
and how their bodies hurt . . .

ASAGAI: And you've stopped caring?

BENEATHA: Yes—I think so.

ASAGAI: Why?

> [WALTER rises, goes to the door of his room and is about to open it,
> then stops and stands listening, leaning on the door jamb.]

BENEATHA: Because it doesn't seem deep enough, close enough to what
ails mankind—I mean this thing of sewing up bodies or administering
drugs. Don't you understand? It was a child's reaction to the world. I
thought that doctors had the secret to all the hurts. . . . That's the way a
child sees things—or an idealist.

ASAGAI: Children see things very well sometimes—and idealists even better.

BENEATHA: I know that's what you think. Because you are still where I left
off—you still care. This is what you see for the world, for Africa. You with
the dreams of the future will patch up all Africa—you are going to cure
the Great Sore of colonialism with Independence——

ASAGAI: Yes!

BENEATHA: Yes—and you think that one word is the penicillin of the
human spirit: "Independence!" But then what?

ASAGAI: That will be the problem for another time. First we must get
there.

BENEATHA: And where does it end?

ASAGAI: End? Who even spoke of an end? To life? To living?

BENEATHA: An end to misery!

ASAGAI: [Smiling.] You sound like a French intellectual.

BENEATHA: No! I sound like a human being who just had her future taken
right out of her hands! While I was sleeping in my bed in there, things
were happening in this world that directly concerned me—and nobody
asked me, consulted me—they just went out and did things—and
changed my life. Don't you see there isn't any real progress, Asagai, there
is only one large circle that we march in, around and around, each of us
with our own little picture—in front of us—our own little mirage that we
think is the future.

ASAGAI: That is the mistake.

BENEATHA: What?

ASAGAI: What you just said—about the circle. It isn't a circle—it is simply
a long line—as in geometry, you know, one that reaches into infinity.
And because we cannot see the end—we also cannot see how it changes.
And it is very odd but those who see the changes are called "idealists"—
and those who cannot, or refuse to think, they are the "realists." It is very
strange, and amusing too, I think.

BENEATHA: You—you are almost religious.

ASAGAI: Yes . . . I think I have the religion of doing what is necessary in the
world—and of worshipping man—because he is so marvelous, you see.

BENEATHA: Man is foul! And the human race deserves its misery!

ASAGAI: You see: *you* have become the religious one in the old sense. Already, and after such a small defeat, you are worshipping despair.

BENEATHA: From now on, I worship the truth—and the truth is that people are puny, small and selfish. . . .

ASAGAI: Truth? Why is it that you despairing ones always think that only you have the truth? I never thought to see *you* like that. You! Your brother made a stupid, childish mistake—and you are grateful to him. So that now you can give up the ailing human race on account of it. You talk about what good is struggle; what good is anything? Where are we all going? And why are we bothering?

BENEATHA: *And you cannot answer it!* All your talk and dreams about Africa and Independence. Independence and then what? What about all the crooks and petty thieves and just plain idiots who will come into power to steal and plunder the same as before—only now they will be black and do it in the name of the new Independence— You cannot answer that.

ASAGAI: [*Shouting over her.*] *I live the answer!* [*Pause.*] In my village at home it is the exceptional man who can even read a newspaper . . . or who ever *sees* a book at all. I will go home and much of what I will have to say will seem strange to the people of my village . . . But I will teach and work and things will happen, slowly and swiftly. At times it will seem that nothing changes at all . . . and then again . . . the sudden dramatic events which make history leap into the future. And then quiet again. Retrogression even. Guns, murder, revolution. And I even will have moments when I wonder if the quiet was not better than all that death and hatred. But I will look about my village at the illiteracy and disease and ignorance and I will not wonder long. And perhaps . . . perhaps I will be a great man . . . I mean perhaps I will hold on to the substance of truth and find my way always with the right course . . . and perhaps for it I will be butchered in my bed some night by the servants of empire . . .

BENEATHA: *The martyr!*

ASAGAI: . . . or perhaps I shall live to be a very old man, respected and esteemed in my new nation . . . And perhaps I shall hold office and this is what I'm trying to tell you, Alaiyo; perhaps the things I believe now for my country will be wrong and outmoded, and I will not understand and do terrible things to have things my way or merely to keep my power. Don't you see that there will be young men and women, not British soldiers then, but my own black countrymen . . . to step out of the shadows some evening and slit my then useless throat? Don't you see they have always been there . . . that they always will be. And that such a thing as my own death will be an advance? They who might kill me even . . . actually replenish me!

BENEATHA: Oh, Asagai, I know all that.

ASAGAI: Good! Then stop moaning and groaning and tell me what you plan to do.

BENEATHA: Do?

ASAGAI: I have a bit of a suggestion.

BENEATHA: What?

ASAGAI: [*Rather quietly for him.*] That when it is all over—that you come home with me—

BENEATHA: [*Slapping herself on the forehead with exasperation born of misunderstanding.*] Oh—Asagai—at this moment you decide to be romantic!

ASAGAI: [*Quickly understanding the misunderstanding.*] My dear, young creature of the New World—I do not mean across the city—I mean across the ocean; home—to Africa.

BENEATHA: [*Slowly understanding and turning to him with murmured amazement.*] To—to Nigeria?

ASAGAI: Yes! . . . [*Smiling and lifting his arms playfully.*] Three hundred years later the African Prince rose up out of the seas and swept the maiden back across the middle passage over which her ancestors had come—

BENEATHA: [*Unable to play.*] Nigeria?

ASAGAI: Nigeria. Home. [*Coming to her with genuine romantic flippancy.*] I will show you our mountains and our stars; and give you cool drinks from gourds and teach you the old songs and the ways of our people—and, in time, we will pretend that—[*Very softly.*]—you have only been away for a day—

[*She turns her back to him, thinking. He swings her around and takes her full in his arms in a long embrace which proceeds to passion.*]

BENEATHA: [*Pulling away.*] You're getting me all mixed up—

ASAGAI: Why?

BENEATHA: Too many things—too many things have happened today. I must sit down and think. I don't know what I feel about anything right this minute.

[*She promptly sits down and props her chin on her fist.*]

ASAGAI: [*Charmed.*] All right, I shall leave you. No—don't get up. [*Touching her, gently, sweetly.*] Just sit awhile and think . . . Never be afraid to sit awhile and think. [*He goes to door and looks at her.*] How often I have looked at you and said, "Ah—so this is what the New World hath finally wrought . . ."

[*He exits.* BENEATHA *sits on alone. Presently* WALTER *enters from his room and starts to rummage through things, feverishly looking for something. She looks up and turns in her seat.*]

BENEATHA: [*Hissingly.*] Yes—just look at what the New World hath wrought! . . . Just look! [*She gestures with bitter disgust.*] There he is! *Monsieur le petit bourgeois noir*[1]—himself! There he is—Symbol of a Rising Class! Entrepreneur! Titan of the system! [WALTER *ignores her completely and continues frantically and destructively looking for something and hurling things to the floor and tearing things out of their place in his search.* BENEATHA *ignores the eccentricity of his actions and goes on with the monologue of insult.*] Did you dream of yachts on Lake Michigan, Brother? Did you see yourself on that Great Day sitting down at the Conference Table, surrounded by all the mighty bald-headed men in

---

1. Mr. Black Bourgeoisie (French).

America? All halted, waiting, breathless, waiting for your pronouncements on industry? Waiting for you—Chairman of the Board? [WALTER *finds what he is looking for—a small piece of white paper—and pushes it in his pocket and puts on his coat and rushes out without ever having looked at her. She shouts after him.*] I look at you and I see the final triumph of stupidity in the world!

> [*The door slams and she returns to just sitting again.* RUTH *comes quickly out of* MAMA's *room.*]

RUTH: Who was that?

BENEATHA: Your husband.

RUTH: Where did he go?

BENEATHA: Who knows—maybe he has an appointment at U.S. Steel.

RUTH: [*Anxiously, with frightened eyes.*] You didn't say nothing bad to him, did you?

BENEATHA: Bad? Say anything bad to him? No—I told him he was a sweet boy and full of dreams and everything is strictly peachy keen, as the ofay[2] kids say!

> [MAMA *enters from her bedroom. She is lost, vague, trying to catch hold, to make some sense of her former command of the world, but it still eludes her. A sense of waste overwhelms her gait; a measure of apology rides on her shoulders. She goes to her plant, which has remained on the table, looks at it, picks it up and takes it to the window sill and sits it outside, and she stands and looks at it a long moment. Then she closes the window, straightens her body with effort and turns around to her children.*]

MAMA: Well—ain't it a mess in here, though? [*A false cheerfulness, a beginning of something.*] I guess we all better stop moping around and get some work done. All this unpacking and everything we got to do. [RUTH *raises her head slowly in response to the sense of the line; and* BENEATHA *in similar manner turns very slowly to look at her mother.*] One of you all better call the moving people and tell 'em not to come.

RUTH: Tell 'em not to come?

MAMA: Of course, baby. Ain't no need in 'em coming all the way here and having to go back. They charges for that too. [*She sits down, fingers to her brow, thinking.*] Lord, ever since I was a little girl, I always remembers people saying, "Lena—Lena Eggleston, you aims too high all the time. You needs to slow down and see life a little more like it is. Just slow down some." That's what they always used to say down home—"Lord, that Lena Eggleston is a high-minded thing. She'll get her due one day!"

RUTH: No, Lena . . .

MAMA: Me and Big Walter just didn't never learn right.

RUTH: Lena, no! We gotta go. Bennie—tell her . . . [*She rises and crosses to* BENEATHA *with her arms outstretched.* BENEATHA *doesn't respond.*] Tell her we can still move . . . the notes ain't but a hundred and twenty-five a month. We got four grown people in this house—we can work . . .

MAMA: [*To herself.*] Just aimed too high all the time—

RUTH: [*Turning and going to* MAMA *fast—the words pouring out with ur-*

2. White (slang).

gency and desperation.] Lena—I'll work . . . I'll work twenty hours a day in all the kitchens in Chicago . . . I'll strap my baby on my back if I have to and scrub all the floors in America and wash all the sheets in America if I have to—but we got to move . . . We got to get out of here . . .

[MAMA *reaches out absently and pats* RUTH's *hand.*]

MAMA: No—I sees things differently now. Been thinking 'bout some of the things we could do to fix this place up some. I seen a second-hand bureau over on Maxwell Street just the other day that could fit right there. [*She points to where the new furniture might go.* RUTH *wanders away from her.*] Would need some new handles on it and then a little varnish and then it look like something brand-new. And—we can put up them new curtains in the kitchen . . . Why this place be looking fine. Cheer us all up so that we forget trouble ever came . . . [*To* RUTH.] And you could get some nice screens to put up in your room round the baby's bassinet . . . [*She looks at both of them, pleadingly.*] Sometimes you just got to know when to give up some things . . . and hold on to what you got.

[WALTER *enters from the outside, looking spent and leaning against the door, his coat hanging from him.*]

MAMA: Where you been, son?

WALTER: [*Breathing hard.*] Made a call.

MAMA: To who, son?

WALTER: To The Man.

MAMA: What man, baby?

WALTER: The Man, Mama. Don't you know who The Man is?

RUTH: Walter Lee?

WALTER: *The Man.* Like the guys in the streets say—The Man. Captain Boss—Mistuh Charley . . . Old Captain Please Mr. Bossman . . .

BENEATHA: [*Suddenly.*] Lindner!

WALTER: That's right! That's good. I told him to come right over.

BENEATHA: [*Fiercely, understanding.*] For what? What do you want to see him for!

WALTER: [*Looking at his sister.*] We going to do business with him.

MAMA: What you talking 'bout, son?

WALTER: Talking 'bout life, Mama. You all always telling me to see life like it is. Well—I laid in there on my back today . . . and I figured it out. Life just like it is. Who gets and who don't get. [*He sits down with his coat on and laughs.*] Mama, you know it's all divided up. Life is. Sure enough. Between the takers and the "tooken." [*He laughs.*] I've figured it out finally. [*He looks around at them.*] Yeah. Some of us always getting "tooken." [*He laughs.*] People like Willy Harris, they don't never get "tooken." And you know why the rest of us do? 'Cause we all mixed up. Mixed up bad. We get to looking 'round for the right and the wrong; and we worry about it and cry about it and stay up nights trying to figure out 'bout the wrong and the right of things all the time . . . And all the time, man, them takers is out there operating, just taking and taking. Willy Harris? Shoot—Willy Harris don't even count. He don't even count in the big scheme of things. But I'll say one thing for old Willy Harris . . . he's taught me something. He's taught me to keep my eye on what counts in this world. Yeah—[*Shouting out a little.*] Thanks, Willy!

RUTH: What did you call that man for, Walter Lee?

WALTER: Called him to tell him to come on over to the show. Gonna put
on a show for the man. Just what he wants to see. You see, Mama, the
man came here today and he told us that them people out there where
you want us to move—well they so upset they willing to pay us not to
move out there. [*He laughs again.*] And—and oh, Mama—you would of
been proud of the way me and Ruth and Bennie acted. We told him to
get out . . . Lord have mercy! We told the man to get out. Oh, we was
some proud folks this afternoon, yeah. [*He lights a cigarette.*] We were
still full of that old-time stuff . . .

RUTH: [*Coming toward him slowly.*] You talking 'bout taking them people's money to keep us from moving in that house?

WALTER: I ain't just talking 'bout it, baby—I'm telling you that's what's
going to happen.

BENEATHA: Oh, God! Where is the bottom! Where is the real honest-to-
God bottom so he can't go any farther!

WALTER: See—that's the old stuff. You and that boy that was here today.
You all want everybody to carry a flag and a spear and sing some marching songs, huh? You wanna spend your life looking into things and trying
to find the right and the wrong part, huh? Yeah. You know what's going
to happen to that boy someday—he'll find himself sitting in a dungeon,
locked in forever—and the takers will have the key! Forget it, baby!
There ain't no causes—there ain't nothing but taking in this world, and
he who takes most is smartest—and it don't make a damn bit of difference *how.*

MAMA: You making something inside me cry, son. Some awful pain inside me.

WALTER: Don't cry, Mama. Understand. That white man is going to walk
in that door able to write checks for more money than we ever had. It's
important to him and I'm going to help him . . . I'm going to put on the
show, Mama.

MAMA: Son—I come from five generations of people who was slaves and
sharecroppers—but ain't nobody in my family never let nobody pay 'em
no money that was a way of telling us we wasn't fit to walk the earth. We
ain't never been that poor. [*Raising her eyes and looking at him.*] We
ain't never been that dead inside.

BENEATHA: Well—we are dead now. All the talk about dreams and sunlight that goes on in this house. All dead.

WALTER: What's the matter with you all! I didn't make this world! It
was give to me this way! Hell, yes, I want me some yachts someday!
Yes, I want to hang some real pearls 'round my wife's neck. Ain't she
supposed to wear no pearls? Somebody tell me—tell me, who decides which women is suppose to wear pearls in this world. I tell you
I am a *man*—and I think my wife should wear some pearls in this
world!

    [*This last line hangs a good while and* WALTER *begins to move about
the room. The word "Man" has penetrated his consciousness; he
mumbles it to himself repeatedly between strange agitated pauses as
he moves about.*]

MAMA: Baby, how you going to feel on the inside?

WALTER: Fine! . . . Going to feel fine . . . a man . . .

MAMA: You won't have nothing left then, Walter Lee.

WALTER: [*Coming to her.*] I'm going to feel fine, Mama. I'm going to look that son-of-a-bitch in the eyes and say—[*He falters.*]—and say, "All right, Mr. Lindner—[*He falters even more.*]—that's your neighborhood out there. You got the right to keep it like you want. You got the right to have it like you want. Just write the check and—the house is yours." And, and I am going to say—[*His voice almost breaks.*] And you—you people just put the money in my hand and you won't have to live next to this bunch of stinking niggers! . . . [*He straightens up and moves away from his mother, walking around the room.*] Maybe—maybe I'll just get down on my black knees . . . [*He does so;* RUTH *and* BENNIE *and* MAMA *watch him in frozen horror.*] Captain, Mistuh, Bossman. [*He starts crying.*] A-hee-hee-hee! [*Wringing his hands in profoundly anguished imitation.*] Yassss-suh! Great White Father, just gi' ussen de money, fo' God's sake, and we's ain't gwine come out deh and dirty up yo' white folks neighbor-hood . . .

   [*He breaks down completely, then gets up and goes into the bed-room.*]

BENEATHA: That is not a man. That is nothing but a toothless rat.

MAMA: Yes—death done come in this here house. [*She is nodding, slowly, reflectively.*] Done come walking in my house On the lips of my chil-dren. You what supposed to be my beginning again. You—what sup-posed to be my harvest. [*To* BENEATHA.] You—you mourning your brother?

BENEATHA: He's no brother of mine.

MAMA: What you say?

BENEATHA: I said that that individual in that room is no brother of mine.

MAMA: That's what I thought you said. You feeling like you better than he is today? [BENEATHA *does not answer.*] Yes? What you tell him a minute ago? That he wasn't a man? Yes? You give him up for me? You done wrote his epitaph too—like the rest of the world? Well, who give you the privilege?

BENEATHA: Be on my side for once! You saw what he just did, Mama! You saw him—down on his knees. Wasn't it you who taught me—to despise any man who would do that. Do what he's going to do.

MAMA: Yes—I taught you that. Me and your daddy. But I thought I taught you something else too . . . I thought I taught you to love him.

BENEATHA: Love him? There is nothing left to love.

MAMA: There is always something left to love. And if you ain't learned that, you ain't learned nothing. [*Looking at her.*] Have you cried for that boy today? I don't mean for yourself and for the family 'cause we lost the money. I mean for him; what he been through and what it done to him. Child, when do you think is the time to love somebody the most; when they done good and made things easy for everybody? Well then, you ain't through learning—because that ain't the time at all. It's when he's at his lowest and can't believe in hisself 'cause the world done whipped him so. When you starts measuring somebody, measure him right, child, measure him right. Make sure you done taken into account what hills and valleys he come through before he got to wherever he is.

[TRAVIS *bursts into the room at the end of the speech, leaving the door open.*]

TRAVIS: Grandmama—the moving men are downstairs! The truck just pulled up.

MAMA: [*Turning and looking at him.*] Are they, baby? They downstairs?

[*She sighs and sits.* LINDNER *appears in the doorway. He peers in and knocks lightly, to gain attention, and comes in. All turn to look at him.*]

LINDNER: [*Hat and briefcase in hand.*] Uh—hello . . . [RUTH *crosses mechanically to the bedroom door and opens it and lets it swing open freely and slowly as the lights come up on* WALTER *within, still in his coat, sitting at the far corner of the room. He looks up and out through the room to* LINDNER.]

RUTH: He's here.

[*A long minute passes and* WALTER *slowly gets up.*]

LINDNER: [*Coming to the table with efficiency, putting his briefcase on the table and starting to unfold papers and unscrew fountain pens.*] Well, I certainly was glad to hear from you people. [WALTER *has begun the trek out of the room, slowly and awkwardly, rather like a small boy, passing the back of his sleeve across his mouth from time to time.*] Life can really be so much simpler than people let it be most of the time. Well—with whom do I negotiate? You, Mrs. Younger, or your son here? [MAMA *sits with her hands folded on her lap and her eyes closed as* WALTER *advances.* TRAVIS *goes close to* LINDNER *and looks at the papers curiously.*] Just some official papers, sonny.

RUTH: Travis, you go downstairs.

MAMA: [*Opening her eyes and looking into* WALTER'S.] No. Travis, you stay right here. And you make him understand what you doing, Walter Lee. You teach him good. Like Willy Harris taught you. You show where our five generations done come to. Go ahead, son—

WALTER: [*Looks down into his boy's eyes.* TRAVIS *grins at him merrily and* WALTER *draws him beside him with his arm lightly around his shoulders.*] Well, Mr. Lindner. [BENEATHA *turns away.*] We called you—[*There is a profound, simple groping quality in his speech.*]—because, well, me and my family [*He looks around and shifts from one foot to the other.*] Well— we are very plain people . . .

LINDNER: Yes—

WALTER: I mean—I have worked as a chauffeur most of my life—and my wife here, she does domestic work in people's kitchens. So does my mother. I mean—we are plain people . . .

LINDNER: Yes, Mr. Younger—

WALTER: [*Really like a small boy, looking down at his shoes and then up at the man.*] And—uh—well, my father, well, he was a laborer most of his life.

LINDNER: [*Absolutely confused.*] Uh, yes—

WALTER: [*Looking down at his toes once again.*] My father almost beat a
man to death once because this man called him a bad name or something, you know what I mean?

LINDNER: No, I'm afraid I don't.

WALTER: [*Finally straightening up.*] Well, what I mean is that we come
from people who had a lot of pride. I mean—we are very proud people.
And that's my sister over there and she's going to be a doctor—and we are
very proud—

LINDNER: Well—I am sure that is very nice, but—

WALTER: [*Starting to cry and facing the man eye to eye.*] What I am telling
you is that we called you over here to tell you that we are very proud and
that this is—this is my son, who makes the sixth generation of our family
in this country, and that we have all thought about your offer and we
have decided to move into our house because my father—my father—he
earned it. [MAMA *has her eyes closed and is rocking back and forth as
though she were in church, with her head nodding the amen yes.*] We
don't want to make no trouble for nobody or fight no causes—but we will
try to be good neighbors. That's all we got to say. [*He looks the man absolutely in the eyes.*] We don't want your money.

[*He turns and walks away from the man.*]

LINDNER: [*Looking around at all of them.*] I take it then that you have
decided to occupy.

BENEATHA: That's what the man said.

LINDNER: [*To* MAMA *in her reverie.*] Then I would like to appeal to you,
Mrs. Younger. You are older and wiser and understand things better I am
sure . . .

MAMA: [*Rising.*] I am afraid you don't understand. My son said we was
going to move and there ain't nothing left for me to say. [*Shaking her
head with double meaning.*] You know how these young folks is nowadays, mister. Can't do a thing with 'em. Good-bye.

LINDNER: [*Folding up his materials.*] Well—if you are that final about
it . . . There is nothing left for me to say. [*He finishes. He is almost
ignored by the family, who are concentrating on* WALTER LEE. *At the
door* LINDNER *halts and looks around.*] I sure hope you people know
what you're doing.

[*He shakes his head and exits.*]

RUTH: [*Looking around and coming to life.*] Well, for God's sake—if the
moving men are here—LET'S GET THE HELL OUT OF HERE!

MAMA: [*Into action.*] Ain't it the truth! Look at all this here mess. Ruth,
put Travis' good jacket on him . . . Walter Lee, fix your tie and tuck your
shirt in, you look just like somebody's hoodlum. Lord have mercy, where
is my plant? [*She flies to get it amid the general bustling of the family,
who are deliberately trying to ignore the nobility of the past moment.*] You
all start on down . . . Travis child, don't go empty-handed . . . Ruth,
where did I put that box with my skillets in it? I want to be in charge of it
myself . . . I'm going to make us the biggest dinner we ever ate tonight
. . . Beneatha, what's the matter with them stockings? Pull them things
up, girl . . .

[*The family starts to file out as two moving men appear and begin to carry out the heavier pieces of furniture, bumping into the family as they move about.*]

BENEATHA: Mama, Asagai—asked me to marry him today and go to Africa—

MAMA: [*In the middle of her getting-ready activity.*] He did? You ain't old enough to marry nobody—[*Seeing the moving men lifting one of her chairs precariously.*] Darling, that ain't no bale of cotton, please handle it so we can sit in it again. I had that chair twenty-five years . . .

[*The movers sigh with exasperation and go on with their work.*]

BENEATHA: [*Girlishly and unreasonably trying to pursue the conversation.*] To go to Africa, Mama—be a doctor in Africa . . .

MAMA: [*Distracted.*] Yes, baby—

WALTER: Africa! What he want you to go to Africa for?

BENEATHA: To practice there . . .

WALTER: Girl, if you don't get all them silly ideas out your head! You better marry yourself a man with some loot . . .

BENEATHA: [*Angrily, precisely as in the first scene of the play.*] What have you got to do with who I marry!

WALTER: Plenty. Now I think George Murchison—

[*He and* BENEATHA *go out yelling at each other vigorously;* BENEATHA *is heard saying that she would not marry* GEORGE MURCHISON *if he were Adam and she were Eve, etc. The anger is loud and real till their voices diminish.* RUTH *stands at the door and turns to* MAMA *and smiles knowingly.*]

MAMA: [*Fixing her hat at last.*] Yeah—they something all right, my children . . .

RUTH: Yeah—they're something. Let's go, Lena.

MAMA: [*Stalling, starting to look around at the house.*] Yes—I'm coming. Ruth—

RUTH: Yes?

MAMA: [*Quietly, woman to woman.*] He finally come into his manhood today, didn't he? Kind of like a rainbow after the rain . . .

RUTH: [*Biting her lip lest her own pride explode in front of* MAMA.] Yes, Lena.

[WALTER'*s voice calls for them raucously.*]

MAMA: [*Waving* RUTH *out vaguely.*] All right, honey—go on down. I be down directly.

[RUTH *hesitates, then exits.* MAMA *stands, at last alone in the living room, her plant on the table before her as the lights start to come down. She looks around at all the walls and ceilings and suddenly, despite herself, while the children call below, a great heaving thing rises in her and she puts her fist to her mouth, takes a final desperate look, pulls her coat about her, pats her hat and goes out. The lights dim down. The door opens and she comes back in, grabs her plant, and goes out for the last time.*]

[*Curtain.*]
1959

The Black Arts Movement

1960–1970

The 1960s was a time of dramatic social upheaval at home and of costly military engagement abroad. The proud, optimistic sense of global leadership and domestic tranquillity that characterized post–World War II America was shattered during the decade by black civil rights and white youth movements that polarized various populations of the United States. Youth squared off against age; southern whites dug in their heels against blacks seeking civil rights; zealous northerners challenged the Deep South's cherished system of racial segregation.

The tragic costs of an undeclared war in Vietnam were broadcast into the nation's living rooms each evening with the six o'clock news. Americans saw dazed, contorted faces of young men writhing in pain and terrifying files of body bags holding the corpses of those who had already perished in the jungles of Indochina. The conflict in Southeast Asia known as the Vietnam War (or the Second Indochina War) was a contest between an American client state known as the Republic of Vietnam (South Vietnam) and a Soviet-supported state called the Democratic Republic of Vietnam (North Vietnam), led by Ho Chi Minh. The division between these mutually exclusive provinces had its origin in an accord signed in Geneva immediately following the French defeat in 1954 (during the First Indochina War) at the town of Dien Bien Phu. The war of the 1960s, which escalated to immense proportions, was defined by the American White House and Pentagon as a military mission to curb the spread of communism in Southeast Asia. When the last of the U.S. troops withdrew in 1975, more than fifty-seven thousand Americans had been killed in combat and more than three hundred thousand were casualties.

In national politics, the decade was launched by Democratic Senator John F. Kennedy's successful campaign for the presidency in 1960. His opponent was Republican nominee Richard M. Nixon, who had served two terms as vice president for Dwight D. Eisenhower. Kennedy was the youngest person and the only Roman Catholic ever elected to the presidency. His youth, decisiveness, charisma, idealism, political savvy, and good looks brought national and international prestige and esteem. He and his wife, Jackie, transformed the bland, amiable atmosphere of the Eisenhower years into a sophisticated and enchanting political milieu that, in later years, was popularly compared to King Arthur's court at Camelot.

But after such ebullient and hopeful beginnings, the 1960s quickly produced international diplomatic crises such as the ill-fated Bay of Pigs invasion of Cuba in 1961 and the Cuban Missile Crisis in 1962. The years following brought disruptive civil rights and Black Power agitation, national mourning for the deaths of slain leaders (John Kennedy, 1963; Malcolm X, 1965; Martin Luther King Jr., 1968;

Robert Kennedy, 1968), monumental military expenditure for an unpopular war, and unprecedented generational factionalism and revolt. The decade ended with Richard Nixon firmly in control of the White House, having captured the presidency in 1968 by vowing to restore law and order to a nation dispirited by urban riots, antiwar demonstrations, and too many American deaths.

THE CIVIL RIGHTS MOVEMENT

Like the presidency, the civil rights and Black Power movements of the 1960s dissolved from energetic idealism and communal hopefulness to sullen and at times dictatorial cynicism. The movement for black civil rights offers a striking example.

In 1960, four black college students inaugurated the modern black civil rights sit-in movement by occupying seats at a segregated lunch counter in the downtown Woolworth's store of Greensboro, North Carolina. Joseph McNeill, Ezell Blair, Franklin McCain, and David Richardson were all students at North Carolina State University. They believed that nonviolent, direct action protest by African Americans was a moral and effective means of securing guaranteed constitutional rights for black America. Martin Luther King Jr., the African American Baptist minister, had made such a belief popular during the Montgomery, Alabama, bus boycott of the mid-1950s. As a young leader himself, King had invoked the doctrines of civil disobedience and passive resistance so effectively used by Gandhi during the fight against British colonialism in India. By the time of the Greensboro sit-in, King was already acknowledged one of the most effective black civil rights leaders and orators of all time. The young students in North Carolina, like much of the rest of the country, admired and endorsed King's Christian strategies of black liberation. And the world as a whole acknowledged King's magisterial leadership when he received the Nobel Peace Prize in 1964.

In North Carolina in 1960, Woolworth's capitulated. Its lunch counter was desegregated. The heroic spirit displayed by the Greensboro Four and the many others who joined their protest galvanized black youth across the nation. Nonviolence, civil disobedience, Christian love, and moral suasion became the norms for a sit-in movement that enlisted hundreds of thousands of high school and university students. The courage and energy of these students inspired adults, especially national civil rights leaders, to heighten their demands for "Freedom Now!" Nonviolence and love seemed to be keys to successful struggle.

By the end of the decade, however, the African American freedom struggle had encountered bitter frustration and violent setbacks. Despite the passage of the 1964 and 1968 Civil Rights Acts, and the 1965 Voting Rights Act, the U.S. government repeatedly refused to enforce the laws of the land. Resistant whites shot, bombed, beat, and viciously harassed black freedom seekers and applied cruel economic sanctions to any who dared to speak out for citizenship rights. Southern policemen, National Guard forces, and state troopers violently assaulted demonstrators with complete impunity. And white vigilantes orchestrated a reign of terror that sometimes seemed akin to the martial horror and intimidation of the Third Reich.

MALCOLM X AND THE NATION OF ISLAM

The seemingly state-sanctioned violent denial of African American citizenship rights focused new attention on the pronouncements, publications, and institutional leadership and programs of the Nation of Islam, known popularly as the Black Muslims. Endorsing the leadership of Elijah Muhammad—who was born in Sandersville, Georgia, in 1897, with the name Elijah Poole—the Nation had its origins in a religious cult founded in Detroit during the 1930s by a mysterious peddler named W. D. Fard. Elijah Muhammad, whose family migrated to Detroit in search of economic opportunity, became Fard's chief lieutenant and carried his preachments to Chicago, where he founded the second Temple of Islam. Through the years, the Nation grew in popularity, principally among the African American working class. By 1960, the Black Muslims boasted a membership of at least a hundred thousand, carrying out work in more than ninety temples (some of them based in prisons) across the land.

The Nation's most charismatic representative was Minister Malcolm X Shabazz of the influential Temple Number 7 in Harlem. Malcolm X's brilliant and fearless oratory and his deft leadership awakened the working-class masses of African Americans to "Mr. Muhammad's Message." Not surprisingly, Malcolm X drew incredible fire from the reactionary white forces and publications of the United States. When he summoned more than four thousand Muslims to a New York police precinct to protest the beating and arrest of a Nation member, the New York commissioner of police remarked that the young minister had "too much power for any one man."

Business enterprises of the Nation (restaurants, cafés, boutiques, schools, and technical services from plumbing to newspaper publishing) were admired by an emergent black nationalism of the 1960s. The appeal of the Black Muslims to black lower- and working-class audiences seemed admirable. In combination with Malcolm X's fierce rhetoric of black self-pride and black resistance to the brainwashing and violent deracination by whites of the so-called Negro, Muslims' rehabilitation of black ex-convicts, drug addicts, pimps, hustlers, gamblers, and alcoholics was considered by black nationalists a model of community activism.

Black people in America, according to black nationalists of the 1960s, had to redeem themselves. No better example than the Muslims seemed to exist for a separatist agenda in which African Americans would undertake their own economic, moral, social, religious, and political regeneration as a "nation within a nation" in America. The Black Muslims displayed astute financial management, ascetic self-discipline, effective public relations, and uncanny zeal for reform among their predominantly black male membership.

Though few in the Black Power or Black Arts movements actually joined the Nation of Islam, the Muslims' rejection of "slave names" and substitution of "African" designations was widespread in black militant circles. The Nation of Islam, moreover, was not without its own art. *Orgena* and *The Trial* were immensely popular agit-prop Muslim entertainments, both written by Louis X of Boston's famous Temple Number 10. They are rousing propaganda pageants meant to forward antiwhite feeling and black self-pride dogma. Today, Louis X is known as Minister Louis Farrakhan.

The important Black Arts poet Sonia Sanchez was, for a brief time, a member of the Nation and a proselyte for its programs. And virtually no black activist of the sixties escaped entirely the influence of the Nation's newspaper, *Muhammad Speaks*. The paramilitary appeal of the Nation's Fruit of Islam guard of lean and dangerous-looking black men was commensurate with militant male allure. On street corners dispensing the message or in cafés where their famous "bean pies" were sold in vast quantities, neatly attired and fiercely zealous Black Muslims were icons of black self-empowerment.

It was the assassination of Malcolm X, along with the strong belief that his death resulted from Muslim internal politics, that cast (and still casts) the Nation of Islam into disrepute among many black Americans. By the mid-sixties, Malcolm X had in many ways transcended the religious and cultic parochialism of the Black Muslims. His travels to Africa and the Middle East and his study of orthodox Islam made him controversial among the dedicated disciples of Elijah Muhammad. Malcolm refused to be silenced on national matters such as the assassination of President John F. Kennedy, scandalously proclaiming to the horror of a grieving nation: "The chickens have come home to roost!" He insisted that the type of violence America was visiting on black people at home and "colored subjects" abroad had returned to kill Kennedy. Malcolm also refused to be silent about his own leader's sexual affairs with secretaries in the Nation of Islam. Mr. Muhammad, in flagrant disregard of the Nation's preachments on sexual abstemiousness and marital fidelity, had fathered more than one child out of wedlock.

Malcolm X's fearless honesty was so admired by black nationalists at the time of his death that they could not excuse any organization—not even one so populous and popular as the Nation of Islam—that might have been complicitous in his murder. Malcolm was courageous and enterprising enough by the mid-1960s to establish the Organization of Afro-American Unity (OAAU), a group devoted to the ideal of international liberation and the empowerment of people of color against global capitalism. But Malcolm's time with the organization was too short to guarantee it growth or influence in the world. The OAAU existed far more in name and idea than in concrete membership or accomplishments. Still, Malcolm's passionate and open resistance to what he perceived as attempts by American whites to eradicate African Americans became a model for the Black Power movement, one sorely needed in the face of the mounting terror being visited upon African Americans seeking justice.

BLACK POWER

Birmingham, Alabama's commissioner of public safety, Eugene "Bull" Connor—who fought all efforts at integration in 1963—turned fire hoses and police dogs on nonviolent demonstrators, while his troops clubbed women and children alike into bloody unconsciousness. Elected southern officials—governors, mayors, registrars, and school superintendents—endlessly temporized, refusing to obey the law and integrate public facilities. White lawlessness and violence led, eventually, to a Black Power revolt.

Organizations such as the Congress of Racial Equality (CORE) and the Student Nonviolent Coordinating Committee (SNCC), which had since their founding propagated integrationist ideals, transformed themselves almost overnight into stridently revolutionary cadres. When James Meredith, who had integrated the University of Mississippi in 1962, was wounded during the first day of his self-proclaimed March Against Fear in 1966, a number of civil rights organizations agreed to continue Meredith's march. In Greenwood, Mississippi, one of the rest stops for the march, Stokeley Carmichael of SNCC leapt to the stage and gave a rousing speech in which he called not for love and forbearance, but for "Black Power." The meaning of the phrase was as mysterious to Carmichael (who ceaselessly altered its definitions) as to the country at large. But the spirit motivating it was as clear as the fingers of a clenched fist. Young black America was fed up with sitting in. The time had arrived for militant, outgoing, radical activism and revolt.

The most controversial representation of Black Power during the 1960s, however, was not Carmichael (who, as a result of his pandering to the media was sometimes mocked as "Starmichael") but the Black Panther Party for Self-Defense. Founded in Oakland, California, in 1966 by Huey Newton and Bobby Seale, the Black Panthers adopted a sober uniform of black leather jackets and stylish berets. They declared themselves revolutionaries and announced their intention to bring Black Power to black people by any means necessary. Constructing a party agenda from an eclectic range of sources such as the Black Muslim preachments of Malcolm X, the teachings of Mao Tse-tung, and the anticolonialist writings of West Indian Frantz Fanon, the Panthers openly displayed their dedication to a gospel of the gun.

As a kind of paramilitary gang, the Black Panthers were most effective in scaring the living daylights out of white America. They also, however, brought a naive, romantic pride to urban black Americans in need of strongmen heroes after the destructive riots that tore apart inner-city America during the mid-sixties. The fires of Watts (Los Angeles), Hough (Cleveland), and downtown Detroit during America's "long hot summers" from 1964 to 1968 left a legacy of despair and a palpable need for something to believe in. Federal funds were poured into hastily conceived "renewal" projects, while the Panthers postured militarily and promised land, bread, peace, and power to the people. But the slaying of black leaders such as Medgar Evers (1963), Malcolm X (1965), and Martin Luther King Jr. (1968) only heightened urban America's sense of despair. To many black Americans, the Panthers seemed like an army of light.

Almost from the start, party members became involved in a series of violent confrontations with the police. After Bobby Seale and Huey Newton were arrested and imprisoned, ex-convict Eldridge Cleaver assumed leadership of the party. In 1968 he published his fugitive musings on the condition of the nation in the best-selling *Soul on Ice*. That same year, he announced his candidacy for president of the United States.

THE NEW LEFT

The white youth movement of the 1960s also witnessed a continuous retreat from idealism and studied reform. The emergence of the movement is usually dated from the 1962 Port Huron, Michigan, convention at which Students for a Democratic Society (SDS) was founded. At Port Huron, SDS proclaimed that it represented a New Left in American politics. During the 1960s, this New Left was responsible for much of the country's antiwar energy and campus revolt. The New Left sought to establish communication with the international peace movement, Third World revolutionary leaders, and working-class organizations across the United States. Its courageously romantic goals were meant to reform America radically, giving birth to an intellectual and utopian new order.

Arising from the leadership of the New Left, a brilliant group of women activists articulated their own liberation agenda. When Betty Friedan's *The Feminine Mystique* appeared in 1963, there were already locally organized groups dedicated to raising the consciousness of American women. Young and courageous, the women who gave birth to the women's liberation movement not only burned restrictive undergarments in public but also refused subservience to male ideals. In 1966 they established one of the most powerful social advocacy forums in the United States: the National Organization for Women (NOW).

But peaceful, intelligent, egalitarian reform was no more the result of white youth initiatives than of black liberation efforts. Continual confrontations with police, state troopers, and the National Guard and the implacable resilience of old American ways of profit and oppression frustrated the New Left elite. Brutality against the country's youth was especially horrifying at the 1968 National Democratic Convention in Chicago, where the police force of Mayor Richard Daley mercilessly clubbed hundreds of chanting demonstrators under the very lenses of recording television cameras.

After myriad battles and frustrations, the reformist New Left gave way to more strident factions, and *revolution* replaced *reform* in the vocabulary of the SDS breakaway group known as the Weathermen. The Weathermen were young radicals who cultivated underground identities and believed in strategic bombings as a means of bringing down the old American order. In 1970, several members of the group blew themselves up in a freak explosion. Not surprisingly, as such underground, occasionally violent activity increased, so did government surveillance and the policing of rebellious, dissident, or revolutionary groups and individuals. By 1970 it had reached a point of illegal wiretapping, relentless harassment, invasion of privacy, and deeply problematic jailing, all of which bore the collective title COINTELPRO, for Counterintelligence and Propaganda. This state-sanctioned response to radicalism was overseen by the Federal Bureau of Investigation, the Office of the Attorney General, and the Justice Department. It had the blessing of President Nixon.

The sturdy Cold War patriotism and balanced budgets of the Eisenhower years of the 1950s were but golden memories when the sixties came to a close. In their preteens, the youth of the 1960s swooned to the quavering voice and gyrating hips of Elvis Presley's rockabilly "Hound Dog." Later, they went wild with the Beatles and responded passionately to the folk-rock didacticism of Bob Dylan. Certainly, the 1967 Summer of Love in San Francisco's Haight-Ashbury district was youth's most concentrated display of earnest alternative camaraderie, not to mention drugged fogginess. By the decade's very end, however, passion for the new, the reformist, and the madcap had seriously diminished. Indeed, the decade's youth had grown sharply discouraged by the minimal social and academic gains they had achieved. So in August 1969 they basked nude in the sun or danced crazily in the rain at the three-day Woodstock Music and Art Fair in Bethel, New York. Woodstock's sex, drugs, music, and love—shared by more than three hundred thousand participants—seemed symptomatic of a narcotic, hedonistic withdrawal by the nation's young from the conservative, law-and-order politics of an era's conclusion.

THE BLACK ARTS MOVEMENT

Properly speaking, a *movement* is a continuous, collective effort to bring about fundamental social reform. It is a collaborative rather than an individualistic enterprise. No matter how many factions are involved, there is always a common objective. The black freedom struggle of the 1960s was such a movement. Its objective was to transform the manner in which black people in the United States of America were defined and treated. And African American writers and artists, as a vital sector of the movement, sought to transform the manner in which black Americans were represented or portrayed in literature and the arts.

In accord with their definition of themselves as participants in a movement, African American writers and artists turned to the African American masses for their inspiration and defined their goals in broadly collective social and political terms. Their objective was to create works that would be—in the words of Maulana Karenga—"functional, collective, and committing." Hence, the Black Arts of the 1960s proposed to create politically engaged expression as a corollary to the new black spirit of the decade. The writer Larry Neal described the project as follows:

> The Black Arts Movement is radically opposed to any concept of the artist that alienates him from his community. Black Art is the aesthetic and spiritual sister of the Black Power concept. As such, it envisions an art that speaks directly to the needs and aspirations of Black America. . . . The Black Arts and the Black Power concept both relate broadly to the Afro-American's desire for self-determination and nationhood. Both concepts are nationalistic.

The oratory of the civil rights and Black Power movements was delivered by ministers and black church-affiliated leaders accustomed to inspiring mass congregations with "the Word." This oratory was complemented and seasoned by the folk wisdom, plain speaking, and sharp directness of such unschooled leaders of the struggle as Fannie Lou Hamer, who co-founded the Mississippi Freedom Democratic Party. Finally, words and wisdom of the struggle were shaped by the argot, linguistic creativity, and musical tastes of countless young black workers who traveled America's rural hamlets and urban ghettos in efforts to end three hundred years of white American oppression. The emulations of such mass speech and musical referents, as the critic Stephen Henderson has claimed, was a central characteristic of the New Black Poetry produced during the 1960s.

THE NEW BLACK POETRY

Poetry was the creative genre that saw the most accomplished, experimental, and distinguished work by the black artists of the sixties. Because poetry normally requires far less time to compose than prose genres such as the novel or short story, it was ideally suited to the felt immediacy of struggle characteristic of Black Arts and Black Power advocates and adherents. The Black Arts movement believed that occasional, performative, musical, authentic, and affective sounds of a black voice committed to struggle could serve as persuasive and effective weapons in the campaign to liberate a black nation. Hence, Black Arts practitioners sought to combine the African American vernacular resonances of sermons, popular music, and black mass "speech" into a rousing new form of poetry. Their verse was free, conversational, jazzy, and bluesy, as in the early efforts of Quincy Troupe and Sonia Sanchez. In its experimental variety, however, it could work like the best black vernacular linguistic and musical strategies and appropriate "standard" American forms such as the rhythms of the East Village Beatnik. No one was more competent in this combination of the experimental and the vernacular than Amiri Baraka (LeRoi Jones), whose volume *Black Magic Poetry, 1961–1967* (1969) is one of the finest products of the African American creative energies of the 1960s. The traditions of African oral praise poetry and of the public performative style of the African griot were combined with African American liberation themes in all the work of the poet Etheridge Knight. Knight's recitations of his poems from memory to black audiences were prime instances of an art and artist as "functional, committed, and committing." The temptation, though, with the call for black spontaneous vernacular overflow of emotion, was that many 1960s practitioners failed to refine their emotions in tranquillity before giving utterance to them. Bombast and outright silliness could result from casual or hasty refusals to take seriously the mission of a black vernacular poetry of music and voice.

THE BLACK ARTS MOVEMENT AND FICTION

In his classic *The Souls of Black Folk*, W. E. B. Du Bois speaks of a veil that black Americans are forced to live behind in the United States. What Du Bois means is that black Americans have never been able to enjoy the serenity, choices, opportunities, or benefits of "normal" (read "white") everyday life in America. There is always, even in the seemingly normal comings and goings of black American life, therefore, a hidden or veiled African remainder. This veiled African remainder is a kind of defensive survival strategy against alienation. The fiction written by black Americans has not dealt at length with this African sounding of the veil. In the 1960s, only the short stories of the tragically short-lived Henry Dumas took up themes of Africa. His work resonated with the overt attention to Africa found in the poetical rhythms and nationalist politics of the Black Arts movement. Yet Dumas's stories were often only roughly polished polemics. Hidden or obscured by the more powerful presence of poetry and drama, there were, however, novels and stories that reflect what might be thought of as the "deep structure" of the 1960s.

One such work was John A. Williams's popular and engaging novel *The Man Who Cried I Am* (1967). The novel offers a tale of the always endangered position of the black spokesperson, writer, or artist who seeks to expose inequities of American life. Its protagonist, Max Reddick, is a man under sentence of death; he is dying of a cancer that represents white America's return on Max's efforts to tell a black and honest truth about his native land. Max is also an object of surveillance and policing commensurate with COINTELPRO and FBI tactics deployed against Black Power and the New Left. Max might be thought of as Black Art in exile, sustaining a precarious European existence and perishing under the evil hands of powerful white American "counterintelligence." Williams's novel captures the undercurrent of paranoia and pessimism that always haunts revolutionary moments. Definitely a product of the deeper, psychological recesses of the Black Arts veil, it is a cautionary tale with elements of a black *roman à clef*.

The work of James Alan McPherson, who had only recently graduated from college when the sixties were in their heyday, represents a revolutionary moment "beyond the veil." Adopting the aesthetics of Ralph Ellison, McPherson was nonetheless able to craft short stories into extraordinary black vernacular songs. While almost every page of his work reveals a concern for the criteria of "high art," his stories ironically emerge with an air of vernacular purity. Trains, Pullman porters, dining cars, "Negro service" on the American rails, survival discipline of black men riding the blinds—these are as critically black American in their resonance as the blues themselves. The "solo song" for Doc in McPherson's short story is clearly blues. Ultimately, the story is about undermining (and unmanning) the polished survival strategies of an elegant black trainman by a "rule book" of white power. What makes the story blues, of course, is the omniscient narrator, one of Doc's progeny. He is an aspiring tyro after the high "art" of the vernacular—an art that will avoid dismissal or "firing" by white rules.

THE REACH OF THE BLACK ARTS MOVEMENT

From the work of the poet Phillis Wheatley to the extraordinary productions of the former poet laureate of the United States, Rita Dove, African American poetical forms have provided expressive outlets for a people who often could not afford the time and luxury of the Great American Novel or the full-length drama. Black poetry during the sixties was adopted by elementary school students, university professors, working wives and mothers, community activists, prison inmates, barber shop aficionados, athletes, and "trained" poets alike to express a new pride of the times.

There scarcely seemed to be a need for a class of professional interpreters or critics to make clear what Don L. Lee "really meant to say" in the poems of *Think Black.* Black poetry was an art of everyday use during the 1960s.

The Black Arts movement was, indisputably, committed to a goal of black mass communication. Poems and dramas created by 1960s writers did not seek to dazzle the intellect with difficult allusions to Western mythology. Nor did they ponderously rehearse abstract philosophical wisdom. Instead, the products of the Black Arts movement were blazingly simple in language and virtually impossible to misunderstand. For example, Nikki Giovanni writes as follows in her early effort *Poem for Black Boys*:

> Where are your heroes, my little Black ones
> You are the indian you so disdainfully shoot
> Not the big bad sheriff on his faggoty white
>   horse
> You should play run-away-slave
>   or Mau Mau
> These are more in line with your history
> Ask your mothers for a Rap Brown gun
> Santa just may comply if you wish hard enough
>   Ask for CULLURD instead of Monopoly
> DO NOT SIT IN DO NOT FOLLOW KING
>   GO DIRECTLY TO STREETS
> This is a game you can win.

And Amiri Baraka, a principal architect of the Black Arts, stated in one of his early works:

> We have awaited the coming of a natural
> phenomenon. Mystics and romantics,
> knowledgeable
> workers
> of the land.
> But none has come.
> (Repeat)
>   but none has come.
> Will the machinegunners please step forward?

Baraka began his artistic career among the Beat generation of the 1950s, living in Greenwich Village and associating with such figures as Allen Ginsberg, Gary Snyder, Jack Kerouac, and Charles Olson. But the poet made a rapid transition when he went uptown to Harlem and established the Black Arts Repertory Theatre/ School in 1965. Baraka's artistic output and his literary-critical, social, and political influence on the Black Arts easily outstripped that of any other black writer of the period. His drama *Dutchman* was a powerful artistic model for the new Black Aesthetic (a set of prescriptive formulas for artistic creation best defended by the critic Addison Gayle Jr.), and it has withstood subsequent literary-critical and literary-theoretical scrutiny.

Several senior black American authors during the 1960s such as Gwendolyn Brooks, Robert Hayden, and Dudley Randall joined their efforts to those of the Black Arts movement. Brooks and Randall welcomed the new energies of the young black creators and provided publishing venues for their work and offered sound guidelines for their enterprise. Though Hayden made known his disagreement with the more prescriptive, racialistic demands of the Black Arts movement, his work was nevertheless shaped and energized during the 1960s by the renewed sense of black history. The distance is immense between poems found in Hayden's *Heartshape in the Dust* (1940) and the mighty resonances of *Middle Passage*. During his term at the Library of Congress as poet in residence, Hayden graciously welcomed the new spokesperson of the Black Arts. Other senior black writers and critics were not so adaptable. Some of them roundly condemned the new creative moment as a demagogic black departure from the universal standards of art and culture. Novelist Ralph Ellison and man of letters J. Saunders Redding were in the very forefront of such detractors.

THE BLACK ARTS MOVEMENT AND AFRICA

Still, among black Americans involved with culture, scholarship, and the arts, there was a shared sense of a new black world coming into existence in the United States. The resources pouring into black urban communities from the War on Poverty, a new sense of equal opportunities waiting just down the road, the opening of doors onto new endeavors brought about by affirmative action programs—all these combined to add ebullience to the Black Arts movement. But the "new" black personhood was *not* to be a replica of white American humanity. Instead, the Black Arts turned to Africa for inspiration, wisdom, and a sense of black origins with which to construct what Don L. Lee called "the way of the new world." In his poem *The Primitive*, Lee writes:

> taken from the
> shores of Mother Africa:
> the savages they thought
> we were—
> they being the real savages.
> to save us. (from what?)
> our happiness, our love, each other?
> their bible for
> our land. (introduction to economics)
> christianized us.
> raped our minds with:
> T.V. & straight hair,
> Reader's Digest & bleaching creams,
> tarzan & jungle jim,
> used cars & used homes,
> reefers & napalm,
> european history & promises.
> Those alien concepts
> of whi-teness,
> the being of what
> is not.
> against our nature
> this weapon called
> civilization—
> they brought us here—
> to drive us mad.
> (like them)

The treatment of Africa as a subject in all genres of Black Arts writing is a direct result of the black nationalist impulse to construct a myth of origins for Africans in America. A homeland and an imagined common culture are minimal requirements for nationalism. An Africa of both the mind and the imagination was welcomed by the Black Arts and Black Power movements. The geographical Africa of the 1960s was a continent in transition, moving from colonial domination to independence. In 1960 alone, seventeen African states received their independence.

African American artistic and literary history are full of statements of longing for Africa, plans for blacks to emigrate from the United States back to an African "homeland," programs of reform or revolution that will produce an "African" way of life in the Americas. But the reality of the continent before the 1960s was a sobering condition of white domination. Foregrounded were images of white colonial administrators and their lieutenants poised with whips in hand—literally, ideologically, or metaphorically—over the naked backs of African subordinates. Early experiments in black migration to Africa such as the Liberian and Sierra Leone projects did not substantially alter the subordinate status of Africa in even the most romantic black nationalist's imagination. At an imaginative level, however, black writers and thinkers such as Phillis Wheatley, Martin Delaney, Wylmot Blyden, Marcus Garvey, Melvin Tolson, Countee Cullen, Julian Mayfield, and others from the eighteenth to the twentieth century have projected fanciful and idyllic representations of Africa as a place of hope and promise for black Americans. It was not until the 1960s, though, that such images seemed to coexist with a new spatial reality. Independent African "nations" were sending representatives—finely garbed and carrying diplomatic power—to the United Nations.

Writers, scholars, and artists of the Black Arts movement hailed their African homeland in the 1960s as a thriving zone of black independence and rich cultural promise that would take its place in global leadership. Sonia Sanchez, Amiri Baraka, Larry Neal, Hoyt Fuller, Nikki Giovanni, and others actually traveled to Africa, making a journey back to their origins that became critical for their efforts to frame a new and liberated African American identity. These writers returned from their African journeys equipped not only with new vocabularies and images but also with fresh perspectives and enthusiastic accounts from African intellectuals and activists. They also returned with new styles of dress, movement, and song to incorporate into performative black American poetry and the new black drama. Dramatist Paul Carter Harrison named this dramaturgy of the Black Arts movement the "drama of Nommo." Nommo invokes West African philosophical and aesthetic concerns with the power of the spoken word.

The Drama of Nommo

The plays of Amiri Baraka and Ed Bullins fit Harrison's definition. They are dramas that speak African American spirit and intent into words. In their conversational, black, slice-of-life fashion, they move decisively away from the cardboard "protest" tradition of an integrationist poetics. Bullins's and Baraka's characters have no interest whatsoever in securing a place in white America as they know it. Rather, the aim of the dramas is clearly a revolution of black will, insight, energy, and awareness. This revolution is predicated on an exposed, speaking performance and sounding of everyday black American reality under the weight of white American racism. Nommo's characters are not adaptable to a Shakespearean or heroic stage. For they are paradoxically "average" actors trapped in an American racial allegory. This allegory of passionate self-revelation drives them either to simple self-dissolution or to the apocalypse.

Like many dramas of the 1960s, the works of Baraka and Bullins seek through vernacular tonalities and portrayal of "low" African American life in the throes of oppression to speak a new spirit of black liberation. Audiences are challenged to bring to the theater a ready ear for discordant truths, a capacity for understanding black life as spoken liberation. Black Arts drama, at its best, is the idea of black mass liberation. It is a celebration of the "ordinary" black self rendered in the form of empathetic, memorable, speaking characters. Like Black Arts poetry, the drama of Nommo drew on the talents of African Americans across a wide ideological and aesthetic spectrum, from the elegant avant garde of Adrienne Kennedy to the one-act exemplar of Sonia Sanchez. In the 1960s, Broadway and Off-Broadway resounded with the extraordinary energy of the black spoken word. And in some ways, this dramatic forum of black thought was not unlike that moment during the Harlem Renaissance of the 1920s when black dramatic hits such as *Shuffle Along* drew black poets such as Langston Hughes from the Midwest to New York to try their hand at "black art." Both moments gesture toward the type of instructive, public staging of significant social manners, mores, and grievances envisioned by Greek dramatists long ago.

The Attitude toward Colonialism

The apparent success of black Africa in overthrowing white domination seemed to offer a model of "decolonization"—a freeing of the black mind as well as spaces for black occupancy. The work of the West Indian intellectual and psychiatrist Frantz Fanon offered brilliantly dramatic accounts of this overthrow. Fanon's *The Wretched of the Earth* became a Black Power and Black Arts movement handbook for imagining the transformation of black American urban ghettos into empowered, self-dependent realms for a black national "good life." The music, dress, and rituals of Africa were incorporated by African Americans into their daily lives. The Afro hairstyle, kente cloth shirts and dresses, and African expressive cultural productions for home aesthetics became far more prominent among all classes of African Americans during the 1960s than at any previous moment in black history. The assertion "We Are an African People!" became almost conventional wisdom in the Black Arts.

The reality of African neocolonialism—the continuing exploitation of the masses of Africa by former white rulers in league with puppet representatives among a black African neocolonial "leadership"—was seldom recognized, analyzed, or condemned by American black nationalists looking for "home." Nevertheless, the introduction of African intellectual, cultural, and imaginative matters into the works of Black Power and the Black Arts shifted the very definition of *modernism* as it was articulated by the West.

By dealing openly with European colonialism, imperialism, and cultural domination, Black Power and the Black Arts, in their university guise as "black studies," revealed the ghost in the machine of Western dominance. Cultural erasure by force was the absolute corollary to colonialism's actual physical conquest. Such cultural erasure, misinterpretation, and perversion of the truths of other people's lives were the West's most important strategies in proclaiming its own "modern" superiority and artistic greatness. Colonialism's cultural erasures—particularly with respect to Africa—seemed far more causal to some Black Arts workers such as Addison Gayle Jr. than "civilization," genius, or talent in the West's ranking of itself as superiorly modern. Never before the 1960s had so many African Americans looked on the realities of what the scholar Chancellor Williams calls the "destruction of African civilization." Never before had so many turned attention to African history as the very foundation of the West, a foundation carefully revealed by historians such as Cheik Anta Diop, John Henrik Clarke, Vincent Harding, and others. Afrocentrism's most viable modern roots lie in the Black Arts and Black Power movements.

One way of distinguishing the literary, artistic, and intellectual production of African Americans before the 1960s from the Black Arts movements is to note the very different orientation toward Africa of the sixties. No longer was Africa a dream deferred or a sign of shame. In the sixties, Africa became among African Americans a linguistic badge of honor: a source of artistic, intellectual, and cultural pride.

For the Black Arts, an insistence that African Americans were really "just Americans"—that is to say, merely white Americans in blackface—was at best ignorant. At worst, it was an invitation to black national suicide. Unlike many of their predecessors, workers in the Black Power and Black Arts movements were not motivated by an integrationist poetics that urged African American writers and artists to sound and write and dance and sing and perform in accordance with the best, the most modern, examples of Western thought and culture. For the Black Arts understood that the best of Western thought and culture was inseparable from the brutality of Western colonialism and imperialism. The Black Arts were far more interested in correcting the erasures of Africa than in imitating the "masterpieces" of the West. The Black Arts intended Africa to become part of a new aesthetic, a new way of being black in the world of the Americas.

ANCESTORS OF THE BLACK ARTS

It is fair to say that beyond their African internationalism, the Black Arts and Black Power movements also differed from past generations of African American artistic and intellectual thought in their celebration and cultivation of a black mass audience. Not content merely to emulate existing (read "white American") protocols for art and intellectual creativity, the Black Arts set out both to win and to half-create a black audience for their productions. Such an audience had been dreamed of only by a select few 1960s predecessors. Langston Hughes, as his biographer Arnold Rampersad has demonstrated, was far more the model for the artistic and intellectual creativity championed by the sixties than either W. E. B. Du Bois or, certainly, Ralph Ellison.

Like Hughes, Black Arts workers wished to construct performances, essays, books, dramas and stories that would have the feel of the black majority. They wanted their work to be experimental, musical, vernacularly in harmony with the "dream life" of the masses. Hence, the Black Arts movement, to use Rampersad's phrase for Hughes's aesthetic practice, self-consciously put a "ceiling" on its intelligence. This is not to say that the movement dumbed itself down. After all, ceilings can be lofty when seen from the ground.

Like Hughes, the Black Arts wished to give back, in newly creative form, the beauty it discovered in the black majority. Again like Hughes, the Black Arts deemed political as well as spiritual liberation and joy an essential part of its mission. To tell a black truth to white power was a central goal of the Black Arts. Perhaps the dated cast of many 1960s productions has to do with the simple, time-bound, committed black mass political aims of their creators.

The spiritual, intellectual, and educational state of the black nation is the best indication of how well Black Art is doing in America, or so the Black Arts movement believed. That is one reason the Black Arts were so deeply annoyed with pronouncements such as those of Ralph Ellison, who claimed art and experience represented incommensurate orders of existence. For Ellison, art is above and beyond the world of everyday experience, and the black artist has no obligation to engage directly in the liberation struggles of the black majority. Furthermore, the successful artist for Ellison is one who moves according to the black formal models of artistic "greatness" that the West has to offer. Dragging along his "kit bag" of black vernacular seasonings, Ellison's black artist strives to out-Hemingway Hemingway and out–Mark Twain Samuel Clemens himself. Ellison roundly denounced both Black Power and the Black Arts. And the Black Arts and Black Power returned the discourtesy.

Richard Wright, by contrast, produced analyses of the black situation in the United States that are as relevant to the black masses of the 1990s as they were for the black southern urban migrant population described in Native Son. Wright and Langston Hughes—in both their vernacular orientation and their awareness of mass liberation struggles for modernity—are far closer to the agendas of Black Arts and Black Power than Ellison and his latter-day disciples.

PUBLISHING

The Black Arts movement was productive not only of new publishing ventures such as Dudley Randall's Broadside Press, Chicago's Third World Press, and Washington's Drum and Spear Press, but also of new periodicals such as the Journal of Black Poetry, Amistad, Black Books Bulletin, Soulbook, and Negro Digest (subsequently retitled Black World and then First World). Major American publishers such as Random House, Doubleday, McGraw-Hill, and William Morrow, sensing market possibilities in a new Black Art, began to sign African American writers to lucrative contracts. They also began to comb their archives for out-of-print black works to provide new editions of books such as Jean Toomer's Cane. It was virtually impossible to enter a commercial bookstore in the late 1960s without encountering newly minted paperback editions of works by African American writers.

However, the novelty and revisionist ideals of the Black Arts also produced more than a little confusion. Nothing like the Black Arts movement had occurred in American history. Hence, the movement had to improvise, improvise, improvise. The results sometimes included ludicrously bombastic and banal critical proclamations in the name of "the revolution." There was also a great deal of sheer nonsense issued in the sacred name of the Black Arts; much of it was consumed, in fact, by white readers eager for a fix on the revolution. (Such cravings became known as "radical chic.") There was a good measure of masculine parading and ideological misdirection. Finally, there was the repetition, with a vengeance, of a virtually patented rhetoric of African American anti-Semitism.

CONTROVERSIES OF THE BLACK ARTS MOVEMENT

Anti-Semitism

Baraka's lines from Black Art that read, "We want poems / like fists beating niggers out of Jocks / or dagger poems in the slimy bellies / of the owner-jews," are calculated to shock readers into breathlessness. They are as scandalous in intent, if not nearly so filled with mordant wit, as the title of Langston Hughes's second volume of poetry, Fine Clothes to the Jew. Hughes's title refers to the necessity for urban black ghetto dwellers to trade their clothing to Jewish pawnshop owners to pay their rent and buy food. The rhetoric of anti-Semitism among African Americans is, in the last instance, a shorthand for a bizarre Anglo-American economics of race, space, and money.

This Anglo-American economics pits two minorities (African Americans and Jews) against each other. In an essay titled *The Harlem Ghetto*, James Baldwin states the matter as follows:

> The structure of the American commonwealth has trapped both these minorities into attitudes of perpetual hostility. They do not dare trust each other—the Jew because he feels he must climb higher on the American social ladder and has, so far as he is concerned, nothing to gain from identifying with any minority even more unloved than he; while the Negro is in the even less tenable position of not really daring to trust anyone.

Baldwin suggests that the majority of wealth in the United States is controlled by a minute fraction of the Anglo-American population. This wealthy white economic elite has a vested interest in keeping all minorities in stereotypical roles, warring with one another and blind to their exploitation and exclusions. Since Jews, who own many businesses in the black urban ghetto, are white, they become catalytic not only for the release of black contempt, but also for that minority warfare welcomed by Anglo-America.

Among lower- and working-class blacks, then, *Jew* becomes what Stephen Henderson in *Understanding the New Black Poetry* calls a "mascon word": a word that, like a sponge, absorbs the animus, bare intuition, disappointment, stereotypes, and rank feelings of American racial economics. Mascon utterances are shorthand ways of encompassing vast ranges of experience—in the case of blacks and Jews, experiences of oppression. Baraka, Haki Madhubuti, and Carolyn Rodgers all employ the anti-Semitic rhetoric of black America's long and materially troubled relationship with Jews. In so doing, they follow the paths of the Nation of Islam and its proselytes, who have long credited world Jewry with quite improbable powers of control, exploitation, and general malfeasance. Of course, for the Black Muslims, the word *Jew* also signals a power or force standing in opposition to the world triumph of Islam. For the Black Arts movement, the Jew— like the Negro leader or the Negro jock of Baraka's *Black Art*—is simply one of the immediate, tangible, white forces of black life. Like the sycophantic and disgusting Negro leader, the Jew must be removed from occupancy if the space of a black good life is to be achieved.

But the anti-Semitism of the Black Arts movement is scarcely more devastating or inhumane than the economic, social, political, and educational conditions from which the Black Arts hoped to rescue the black American majority. Whiteness in general was the enemy of the Black Arts movement. *Jew* was a word marking a material and ideological manifestation of American whiteness with which the black majority has been forced to contend for generations.

Misogyny, Homophobia

Subsequent generations have not been slow to identify the clear misogyny and ugly homophobia of the Black Arts movement. These were sad accompaniments of earnest ventures. They resulted, at least in part, from the inescapable, paramilitary, social-realist bravado of male leaders in the Black Arts. Yet it is also accurate to note that Amiri Baraka was one of the first black artists in the twentieth century, other than James Baldwin, to air the theme of African American homosexuality, as he did in his plays *The Baptism* (1967) and *The Toilet* (1967). And such emergent black women writers as Sonia Sanchez, June Jordan, Carolyn Rodgers, Nikki Giovanni, Jayne Cortez, and Mari Evans took second place to none where women's issues in the Black Arts were concerned. If there were leading proponents of the Black Aesthetic to be reckoned with, black women artists and their specifically womanist themes were in the front ranks. Like Diane Nash, Kathleen Cleaver, Arthurine Lucy, Ella Baker, and Angela Davis in the arena of civil rights and Black Power politics, black women artists were respected spokespersons of the Black Arts movement. No one can discount their part in shaping the splendid emergence of African American women's creativity during the past two decades.

THE BLACK ARTS MOVEMENT AND THE ACADEMY

In criticism and scholarship, the Black Arts movement gained strength not only from new journals and publishers but also from newly established black studies programs on American university campuses. Critics such as Darwin Turner, Addison Gayle Jr., George Kent, Ama Bontemps, Eugenia Collier, and Carolyn Fowler were all academically trained and university affiliated. In a number of instances, such scholars had started their careers studying English and Euro-American literature and criticism. Their conversion to Black Aesthetic doctrines produced an interestingly hybrid scholarship, as exemplified by Kent's *Blackness and the Adventure of Western Culture* and Gayle's *The Black Situation.* These monographs are replete with New Critical interpretations of texts and Western philosophical and literary allusions. The subjects of the work, however, are indubitably black. Grounded, at least in part, in a traditional New Criticism, Gayle and Kent adhered in many ways to the radical imperatives of an emerging black art.

A combination of flamboyant polemical excess and original, direct, accessible plain speaking marked the labors of the Black Arts movement. Many of the movement's most controversial claims, institutions, and products were short lived. But the creative and critical dreams of new black artistic forms were endorsed by emergent literatures and critical traditions around the world. In the United States alone, Native American, Chicano and Chicana, and gay and lesbian writers, critics, and scholars have acknowledged—either directly or by implication—their enormous debt to the strategies, authors, and works of the Black Arts movement. Unlike the social impulses of the decade, therefore, the Black Aesthetic did not end with a solipsistic whimper. Rather, it continues to enrich artistic traditions and critical debate that will enliven the twenty-first century.

MARI EVANS

Born in Toledo, Ohio, Mari Evans is one of the most energetic and respected poets of the Black Arts movement. The eloquent simplicity of her lyrics perfectly complements the directness of her themes. She writes preeminently of loss—a lost Africa, lost love, failed relationships between black women and black men. But she is also a blues philosopher insofar as she feels such losses summon from us the courage to struggle, to continue in the face of adversity and pain. She works with the themes of African liberation and comes, eventually, to embrace Africa and the third world as ideal subjects.

After attending college at the University of Toledo, Evans established her credentials in theater, media production, and the literary arts. Always an aspiring writer, she also had ambitions as a teacher and scholar. Her various posts as a professor of literature and creative writing have carried her from Indiana University to Northwestern University and the State University of New York at Albany. She has served as a visiting professor at Washington University and Cornell University.

Her television show *The Black Experience,* broadcast in the late 1960s and early

1970s by WTTV in Indianapolis, helped to bring her to the attention of the African American community and, in turn, helped to focus her energy and attention on the unique problems of the black community. She has written of the show, which she both produced and directed, that it "attempted to answer the question posed by some anonymous poet: 'Who will show me myself?' " For the past two decades, Evans has explored the language, history, and concerns of the black community in works ranging from children's books and dramas to collections of poetry and an important and timely anthology of black women's writing.

Her volume *I Am a Black Woman*, whose title poem first appeared in *Negro Digest*, links the themes of black enslavement and impoverishment with the global oppression of the wretched. Claims for freedom and justice for blacks in the United States are joined with protest against the imperialistic oppression of the Vietnamese people and the subjugation of people of color generally. In the collection, Evans vindicates the lives of the poor, particularly poor black women who work in white homes as domestics. Such historical figures as Malcolm X and Martin Luther King feature prominently in the poems.

Evans's anthology, *Black Women Writers, 1950–1980*, is a richly informed compendium that remains an invaluable critical resource.

Status Symbol

i
Have Arrived
  i am the
New Negro
  i   5
am the result of
President Lincoln
World War 1
and Paris
the   10
Red Ball Express [1]
white drinking fountains
sitdowns and
sit-ins
Federal Troops   15
Marches on Washington
and
prayer meetings . . . .
today
They hired me   20
it
is a status
job . . . . .
along
with my papers   25
They
gave me my
Status Symbol . . .

1. Title of a 1952 film starring Sidney Poitier as a member of a famous trucking unit among U.S. troops in the Korean War.

the
key   30
to the
White
Locked
JOHN

                                                                1964

I Am a Black Woman

I am a black woman
the music of my song
some sweet arpeggio of tears
is written in a minor key
and I   5
can be heard humming in the night
Can be heard
                humming
in the night.

I saw my mate leap screaming to the sea   10
and I/with these hands/cupped the lifebreath
from my issue in the canebrake
I lost Nat's [1] swinging body in a rain of tears
and heard my son scream all the way from Anzio [2]
for Peace he never knew. . . . I   15
learned Da Nang and Pork Chop Hill [3]
in anguish
Now my nostrils know the gas
and these trigger tire/d fingers
seek the softness in my warrior's beard   20

I
am a black woman
tall as a cypress
strong
beyond all definition still   25
defying place
and time
and circumstance
    assailed
        impervious   30
            indestructible
Look
    on me and be
renewed

                                                                1969

1. Nat Turner, Virginia slave who was executed in 1831 for leading a slave revolt.
2. A fishing town in Italy, which was the site of a sustained attack by the Germans on Allied forces in World War II.
3. The site of one of the last battles of the Korean War; it was ultimately abandoned by U.N. forces after multiple attacks by the North Koreans. Da Nang was a major American base in South Vietnam.

HOYT FULLER

1923–1981

Called by Addison Gayle Jr. "the voice of young black writers across the country who dared to differ . . . with . . . the mainstream of American literature," Hoyt Fuller was a forceful critic of Western standards, practices, and awards in the arts and cultural practices of the United States. Born in Detroit, Fuller graduated from Wayne State University, where he majored in literature and journalism. Relentless in his pursuit of inequities of representation and reward where black America was concerned, Fuller sought to convince all black writers and cultural workers to formulate new African-inspired values and models of creativity.

When Fuller assumed editorship of the journal *Negro Digest*, the little magazine was devoted to collecting stories and news releases on black social, political, and athletic activities across the country. In 1970, after a few years as editor, Fuller changed the name of the journal to *Black World*. This name change reflected the editor's commitment to making his own work and that of the journal an arm of the new Black Aesthetic. Fuller himself wrote reviews and scathing denunciations of what he considered egregious Western cultural erasures of black art and achievements. He published poems, essays, short stories, and forums by the new workers in the Black Arts and black power movements. Such writers as John A. Williams, Mari Evans, Etheridge Knight, Carolyn Fowler, Carolyn Rodgers, and Alice Walker found their bylines in *Black World*.

When *Black World* was threatened with discontinuation by Johnson Publishing Company, masses of black people assembled in the street outside the company's Chicago office and burned copies of *Ebony*, its glossy black bourgeoisie magazine. But as pressures from the police and U.S. counterintelligence forces mounted, Johnson's hand against *Black World* was strengthened; the magazine went out of circulation in the mid-1970s.

However, Fuller, joined by a committed group of black activists, founded a successor journal named *First World*. Volunteering time, money, and professional skills, the *First World* collective often found itself sleeping on the floor of Fuller's Atlanta home and planning revolution over the only meal they could afford—pizza. The Atlanta home became an African mecca in the midst of a reactionary storm blowing across the land.

Black colleges and universities in Atlanta—always bastions of learning and respectability—refused to hire Fuller to teach. So he journeyed to Ithaca, New York, to teach at Cornell University. Much of his salary was plied back into the work of *First World*.

In the book *Journey to Africa*, Fuller wrote cogently about one of the most significant times of his life. This autobiographical work anticipates the efforts of Alex Haley's *Roots* by several years. Fuller's account consists of three essays that outline the work of Pan-Africanism. Commencing with the observation that being "American" has often entailed a search for roots in Europe, Fuller describes how as a very young man he sought out African origins. In this quest, he joined such earlier Pan-Africanists as George Padmore and W. E. B. Du Bois.

Journey to Africa was released by Third World Press of Chicago, one of the new publishing venues of the Black Arts movement. An inspired editor and enthusiastic supporter of the Black Arts, Fuller served as an elder statesman for such cultural organizations as the Organization of Black American Culture (OBAC) in Chicago. He was also a key organizer for various Pan-African festivals and celebrations both in the United States and in Africa. An indefatigable proponent for the emergence of a new African people in the Americas, he was found dead of a heart attack on an Atlanta street in 1981.

In his obituary for Fuller, historian Robert Harris proclaimed, "He challenged us to document and to preserve Afro-American culture, the bedrock of our experience in this country and informed at its source by Africa."

Towards a Black Aesthetic

The black revolt is as palpable in letters as it is in the streets, and if it has not yet made its impact upon the Literary Establishment, then the nature of the revolt itself is the reason. For the break between the revolutionary black writers and the "literary mainstream" is, perhaps of necessity, cleaner and more decisive than the noisier and more dramatic break between the black militants and traditional political and institutional structures. Just as black intellectuals have rejected the NAACP,[1] on the one hand, and the two major political parties, on the other, and gone off in search of new and more effective means and methods of seizing power, so revolutionary black writers have turned their backs on the old "certainties" and struck out in new, if uncharted, directions. They have begun the journey toward a black aesthetic.

The road to that place—if it exists at all—cannot, by definition, lead through the literary mainstreams. Which is to say that few critics will look upon the new movement with sympathy, even if a number of publishers might be daring enough to publish the works which its adherents produce. The movement will be reviled as "racism-in-reverse," and its writers labeled "racists," opprobrious terms which are flung lightly at black people now that the piper is being paid for all the long years of rejection and abuse which black people have experienced at the hands of white people—with few voices raised in objection.

Is this too harsh and sweeping a generalization? White people might think so; black people will not; which is a way of stating the problem and the prospect before us. Black people are being called "violent" these days, as if violence is a new invention out of the ghetto. But violence against the black minority is in-built in the established American society. There is no need for the white majority to take to the streets to clobber the blacks, although there certainly is *enough* of that; brutalization is inherent in all the customs and practices which bestow privileges on the whites and relegate the blacks to the status of pariahs.

These are old and well-worn truths which hardly need repeating. What is new is the reaction to them. Rapidly now, black people are turning onto that uncertain road, and they are doing so with the approval of all kinds of fellow-travellers who ordinarily are considered "safe" for the other side. In the fall 1967 issue of the *Journal of the National Medical Association* (all-black), for example, Dr. Charles A. De Leon of Cleve-

---

1. National Association for the Advancement of Colored People, founded in New York in 1909 to empower and enfranchise African Americans.

land, Ohio, explained why the new turn is necessary: "If young Negroes are to avoid the unnecessary burden of self-hatred (via identification with the aggressor) they will have to develop a keen faculty for identifying, fractionating out, and rejecting the absurdities of the conscious as well as the unconscious white racism in American society from what is worthwhile in it."

Conscious and unconscious white racism is everywhere, infecting all the vital areas of national life. But the revolutionary black writer, like the new breed of militant activist, has decided that white racism will no longer exercise its insidious control over his work. If the tag of "racist" is one the white critic will hang on him in dismissing him, then he is more than willing to bear that. He is not going to separate literature from life.

But just how widespread is white racism—conscious and unconscious—in the realm of letters? In a review of Gwendolyn Brooks's [2] *Selected Poems* in the old *New York Herald Tribune Book Week* back in October 1963, poet Louis Simpson began by writing that the Chicago poet's book of poems "contains some lively pictures of Negro life," an ambiguous enough opener which did not necessarily suggest a literary putdown. But Mr. Simpson's next sentence dispelled all ambiguity. "I am not sure it is possible for a Negro to write well without making us aware he is a Negro," he wrote. "On the other hand, if being a Negro is the only subject, the writing is not important."

All the history of American race relations is contained in that appraisal, despite its disingenuousness. It is civilized, urbane, gentle and elegant; and it is arrogant, condescending, presumptuous and racist. To most white readers, no doubt, Mr. Simpson's words, if not his assessment, seemed eminently sensible; but it is all but impossible to imagine a black reader not reacting to the words with unalloyed fury.

Both black and white readers are likely to go to the core of Mr. Simpson's statement, which is: "if being a Negro is the only subject, the writing is not important." The white reader will, in all probability, find that clear and acceptable enough; indeed, he is used to hearing it. "Certainly," the argument might proceed, "to be important, writing must have *universal values, universal implications*; it cannot deal exclusively with Negro problems." The plain but unstated assumption being, of course, that there are no "universal values" and no "universal implications" in Negro life.

Mr. Simpson is a greatly respected American poet, a winner of the Pulitzer Prize for poetry, as is Miss Brooks, and it will be considered the depth of irresponsibility to accuse him of the viciousness of racism. He is probably the gentlest and most compassionate of men. Miss Brooks, who met Mr. Simpson at the University of California not many months after the review was published, reported that the gentleman was most kind and courteous to her. There is no reason to doubt it. The essential point here is not the presence of overt hostility; it is the absence of clarity of vision. The glass through which black life is viewed by white Americans is, inescapably (it is

2. African American author, poet, and lecturer (b. 1917).

a matter of extent), befogged by the hot breath of history. True "objectivity" where race is concerned is as rare as a necklace of Hope diamonds.[3]

In October 1967, a young man named Jonathan Kozol published a book called *Death at an Early Age*, which is an account of his experiences as a teacher in a predominantly Negro elementary school in Boston. Mr. Kozol broke with convention in his approach to teaching and incurred the displeasure of a great many people, including the vigilant policeman father of one of his few white pupils. The issue around which the young teacher's opponents seemed to rally was his use of a Langston Hughes poem in his classroom. Now the late Langston Hughes was a favorite target of some of the more aggressive right-wing pressure groups during his lifetime, but it remained for an official of the Boston School Committee to come to the heart of the argument against the poet. Explaining the opposition to the poem used by Mr. Kozol, the school official said that "no poem by any Negro author can be considered permissible if it involves suffering."

There is a direct connecting line between the school official's rejection of Negro poetry which deals with suffering and Mr. Simpson's facile dismissal of writing about Negroes "only." Negro life, which is characterized by suffering imposed by the maintenance of white privilege in America, must be denied validity and banished beyond the pale. The facts of Negro life accuse white people. In order to look at Negro life unflinchingly, the white viewer either must relegate it to the realm of the subhuman, thereby justifying an attitude of indifference, or else the white viewer must confront the imputation of guilt against him. And no man who considers himself humane wishes to admit complicity in crimes against the human spirit.

There is a myth abroad in American literary criticism that Negro writing has been favored by a "double standard" which judges it less stringently. The opposite is true. No one will seriously dispute that, on occasions, critics have been generous to Negro writers, for a variety of reasons; but there is no evidence that generosity has been the rule. Indeed, why should it be assumed that literary critics are more sympathetic to blacks than are other white people? During any year, hundreds of mediocre volumes of prose and poetry by white writers are published, little noted, and forgotten. At the same time, the few creative works by black writers are seized and dissected and, if not deemed of the "highest" literary quality, condemned as still more examples of the failure of black writers to scale the rare heights of literature. And the condemnation is especially strong for those black works which have not screened their themes of suffering, redemption and triumph behind frail façades of obscurity and conscious "universality."

Central to the problem of the irreconcilable conflict between the black writer and the white critic is the failure of recognition of a fundamental and obvious truth of American life—that the two races are residents of two separate and naturally antagonistic worlds. No manner of well-meaning rhetoric about "one country" and "one people," and even about the two races' long joint-occupancy of this troubled land, can obliterate the high,

---

3. Largest known blue diamond (112 karats); found in India and now held at the Smithsonian.

thick dividing walls which hate and history have erected—and maintain— between them. The breaking down of those barriers might be a goal, worthy or unworthy (depending on viewpoint), but the reality remains. The world of the black outsider, however much it approximates and parallels and imitates the world of the white insider, by its very nature is inheritor and generator of values and viewpoints which threaten the insiders. The outsiders' world, feeding on its own sources, fecundates and vibrates, stamping its progeny with its very special ethos, its insuperably logical bias.

The black writer, like the black artist generally, has wasted much time and talent denying a propensity every rule of human dignity demands that he possess, seeking an identity that can only do violence to his sense of self. Black Americans are, for all practical purposes, colonized in their native land, and it can be argued that those who would submit to subjection without struggle deserve to be enslaved. It is one thing to accept the guiding principles on which the American republic ostensibly was founded; it is quite another thing to accept the prevailing practices which violate those principles.

The rebellion in the streets is the black ghetto's response to the vast distance between the nation's principles and its practices. But that rebellion has roots which are deeper than most white people know; it is many-veined, and its blood has been sent pulsating to the very heart of black life. Across this country, young black men and women have been infected with a fever of affirmation. They are saying, "We are black and beautiful," and the ghetto is reacting with a liberating shock of realization which transcends mere chauvinism. They are rediscovering their heritage and their history, seeing it with newly focused eyes, struck with the wonder of that strength which has enabled them to endure and, in spirit, to defeat the power of prolonged and calculated oppression. After centuries of being told, in a million different ways, that they were not beautiful, and that whiteness of skin, straightness of hair, and aquilineness of features constituted the only measures of beauty, black people have revolted. The trend has not yet reached the point of avalanche, but the future can be clearly seen in the growing number of black people who are snapping off the shackles of imitation and are wearing their skin, their hair, and their features "natural" and with pride. In a poem called "Nittygritty," which is dedicated to poet LeRoi Jones,[4] Joseph Bevans Bush put the new credo this way:

> . . . We all gonna come from behind those
> Wigs and start to stop using those
> Standards of beauty which can never
> Be a frame for our reference; wash
> That excess grease out of our hair,
> Come out of that bleach bag and get
> Into something meaningful to us as
> Nonwhite people—Black people . . .

4. Amiri Baraka: poet, educator, editor, political activist, and award-winning playwright (b. 1934).

If the poem lacks the resonances of William Shakespeare, that is intentional. The "great bard of Avon" has only limited relevance to the revolutionary spirit raging in the ghetto. Which is not to say that the black revolutionaries reject the "universal" statements inherent in Shakespeare's works; what they do reject, however, is the literary assumption that the style and language and the concerns of Shakespeare establish the appropriate limits and "frame of reference" for black poetry and people. This is above and beyond the doctrine of revolution to which so many of the brighter black intellectuals are committed, that philosophy articulated by the late Frantz Fanon[5] which holds that, in the time of revolutionary struggle, the traditional Western liberal ideals are not merely irrelevant but they must be assiduously opposed. The young writers of the black ghetto have set out in search of a black aesthetic, a system of isolating and evaluating the artistic works of black people which reflect the special character and imperatives of black experiencee.

That was the meaning and intent of poet-playwright LeRoi Jones' aborted Black Arts Theater in Harlem in 1965, and it is the generative idea behind such later groups and institutions as Spirit House in Newark, the Black House in San Francisco, the New School of Afro-American Thought in Washington, D.C., the Institute for Black Studies in Los Angeles, Forum '66 in Detroit, and the Organization of Black American Culture in Chicago. It is a serious quest, and the black writers themselves are well aware of the possibility that what they seek is, after all, beyond codifying. They are fully aware of the dual nature of their heritage, and of the subleties and complexities; but they are even more aware of the terrible reality of their outsideness, of their political and economic powerlessness, and of the desperate racial need for unity. And they have been convinced, over and over again, by the irrefutable facts of history and by the cold intransigence of the privileged white majority that the road to solidarity and strength leads inevitably through reclamation and indoctrination of black art and culture.

In Chicago, the Organization of Black American Culture[6] has moved boldly toward a definition of a black aesthetic. In the writers' workshop sponsored by the group, the writers are deliberately striving to invest their work with the distinctive styles and rhythms and colors of the ghetto, with those peculiar qualities which, for example, characterize the music of a John Coltrane or a Charlie Parker or a Ray Charles.[7] Aiming toward the publication of an anthology which will manifest this aesthetic, they have established criteria by which they measure their own work and eliminate from consideration those poems, short stories, plays, essays and sketches which do not adequately reflect the black experience. What the sponsors of the workshop most hope for in this delicate and dangerous experiment is the emergence of new black critics who will be able to articulate and expound the new aesthetic and eventually set in motion the long overdue assault against the restrictive assumptions of the white critics.

It is not that the writers of OBAC have nothing to start with. That there

---

5. Martinican psychiatrist and author of several important critiques of racism and colonialism (1925–1961).

6. A nonprofit writers' workshop in Chicago founded by Fuller.

7. African American jazz musicians.

exists already a mystique of blackness even some white critics will agree. In the November 1967 issue of *Esquire* magazine, for instance, George Frazier, a white writer who is not in the least sympathetic with the likes of LeRoi Jones, nevertheless did a commendable job of identifying elements of the black mystique. Discussing "the Negro's immense style, a style so seductive that it's little wonder that black men are, as Shakespeare put it in *The Two Gentlemen of Verona*, 'pearls in beauteous ladies' eyes,'" Mr. Frazier singled out the following examples:

"The formal daytime attire (black sack coats and striped trousers) the Modern Jazz Quartet wore when appearing in concert; the lazy amble with which Jimmy Brown used to return to the huddle; the delight the late 'Big Daddy' Lipscomb took in making sideline tackles in full view of the crowd and the way, after crushing a ball carrier to the ground, he would chivalrously assist him to his feet; the constant cool of 'Satchel' Paige; the chic of Bobby Short; the incomparable grace of John Bubbles—things like that are style and they have nothing whatsoever to do with ability (although the ability, God wot, is there, too). It is not that there are no white men with style, for there is Fred Astaire, for one, and Cary Grant, for another, but that there are so very, very few of them. Even in the dock, the black man has an air about him—Adam Clayton Powell, so blithe, so self-possessed, so casual, as contrasted with Tom Dodd, sanctimonious, whining, an absolute disgrace. What it is that made Miles Davis and Cassius Clay, Sugar Ray Robinson and Archie Moore and Ralph Ellison and Sammy Davis, Jr. seem so special was their style. . . .

"And then, of course, there is our speech.

"For what nuances, what plays of light and shade, what little sharpnesses our speech has are almost all of them, out of the black world—the talk of Negro musicians and whores and hoodlums and whatnot. 'Cool' and all the other words in common currency came out of the mouths of Negroes.

"'We love you madly,' said Duke Ellington, and now the phrase is almost a cliché. But it is a quality of the Negro's style—that he is forever creative, forever more stylish. There was a night when, as I stood with Duke Ellington outside the Hickory House, I looked up at the sky and said, 'I hope it's a good day tomorrow. I want to wake up early.'

"'Any day I wake up,' said Ellington, 'is a good day.'

"And that was style."

Well, yes. . . .

Black critics have the responsibility of approaching the works of black writers assuming these qualities to be present, and with the knowledge that white readers—and white critics—cannot be expected to recognize and to empathize with the subtleties and significance of black style and technique. They have the responsibility of rebutting the white critics and of putting things in the proper perspective. Within the past few years, for example, Chicago's white critics have given the backs of their hands to worthy works by black playwrights, part of their criticism directly attributable to their ignorance of the intricacies of black style and black life. Oscar Brown, Jr.'s rockingly soulful *Kicks and Company* was panned for many of the wrong reasons; and Douglas Turner Ward's two plays, *Day of Absence* and *Happy Ending*, were tolerated as labored and a bit tasteless. Both Brown and Ward had dealt satirically with race relations, and there were not many black people in the audiences who found themselves in agreement with the critics. It is the way things are—but not the way things will continue to be if the OBAC writers and those similarly concerned elsewhere in America have anything to say about it.

1968

MALCOLM X
(EL-HAJJ MALIK EL-SHABAZZ)
1925–1965

Malcolm X was born Malcolm Little in Omaha, Nebraska, to Earl Little, a black man who championed the nationalist, back-to-Africa doctrines of Marcus Garvey. Malcolm's father was murdered by resentful whites, and his family came to depend entirely upon the widow, Louise. Under the stress of impossible family responsibilities and sharply limited finances, Malcolm's mother suffered a nervous breakdown and was placed in a mental asylum. The family came apart.

Malcolm, after a successful middle-school career, headed for Boston. There he enjoyed a life of heady and sometimes criminal activity. Moving to New York in the bustling 1940s, he quickly became part of a black urban scene rife with underworld number runners, jazz musicians, masterful hustlers, and budding comedians such as Redd Foxx.

Malcolm was soon engaged in life outside the law and was later arrested and imprisoned for burglary in Massachusetts at the Charlestown State Prison from 1946 to 1952. It was in prison that he underwent a conversion to the doctrines of the Lost-Found Nation of Islam in America and its charismatic leader, the Honorable Elijah Muhammad. Upon his release from prison, Malcolm became a member of the Nation of Islam—popularly known as the Black Muslims.

Not surprisingly, given his verbal and oratorical skills, Malcolm became famous as the chief spokesperson for the Honorable Elijah, but fell into disfavor when he described the assassination of John F. Kennedy as commensurate with America's traditional history of armed violence. Tensions between Malcolm and Elijah grew to a fever pitch, and Malcolm recanted his earlier advocacy for the Black Muslims. In 1964 he traveled to Mecca and returned home to establish the Organization of Afro-American Unity. In February 1965, he was assassinated at the Audubon Ballroom in Harlem, a murder in which the Black Muslims have long been vaguely and controversially implicated.

Malcolm X's nationalist preachings and his sheer magnetism of style and courage in the face of white power and pomposity endeared him to a generation of Black Power advocates in search of a role model. A man of powerful intellectual abilities, Malcolm became legendary, and he was revered by African Americans who believed that their destiny in America depended largely on a profound education in and commitment to the roots of their culture. *The Autobiography of Malcolm X*, written in conjunction with Alex Haley, became a best-seller in 1964, the year that it was published. It remains a classic of American autobiography and has received worldwide acclaim and extensive scholarly attention.

From The Autobiography of Malcolm X

Chapter Eleven

SAVED

I did write to Elijah Muhammad. [1] He lived in Chicago at that time, at 6116 South Michigan Avenue. At least twenty-five times I must have written that first one-page letter to him, over and over. I was trying to make it both legible and understandable. I practically couldn't read my handwriting myself; it shames even to remember it. My spelling and my grammar were as bad, if not worse. Anyway, as well as I could express it, I said I had been told about him by my brothers and sisters, and I apologized for my poor letter.

Mr. Muhammad sent me a typed reply. It had an all but electrical effect upon me to see the signature of the "Messenger of Allah." After he welcomed me into the "true knowledge," he gave me something to think about. The black prisoner, he said, symbolized white society's crime of keeping black men oppressed and deprived and ignorant, and unable to get decent jobs, turning them into criminals.

He told me to have courage. He even enclosed some money for me, a five-dollar bill. Mr. Muhammad sends money all over the country to prison inmates who write to him, probably to this day.

Regularly my family wrote to me, "Turn to Allah . . . pray to the East."

The hardest test I ever faced in my life was praying. You understand. My comprehending, my believing the teachings of Mr. Muhammad had only required my mind's saying to me, "That's right!" or "I never thought of that."

But bending my knees to pray—that *act*—well, that took me a week.

You know what my life had been. Picking a lock to rob someone's house was the only way my knees had ever been bent before.

I had to force myself to bend my knees. And waves of shame and embarrassment would force me back up.

Of evil to bend its knees, admitting its guilt, to implore the forgiveness of God, is the hardest thing in the world. It's easy for me to see and to say that now. But then, when I was the personification of evil, I was going through it. Again, again, I would force myself back down into the praying-to-Allah posture. When finally I was able to make myself stay down—I didn't know what to say to Allah.

For the next years, I was the nearest thing to a hermit in the Norfolk Prison Colony. [2] I never have been more busy in my life. I still marvel at how swiftly my previous life's thinking pattern slid away from me, like snow off a roof. It is as though someone else I knew of had lived by hustling and crime. I would be startled to catch myself thinking in a remote way of my earlier self as another person.

The things I felt, I was pitifully unable to express in the one-page letter

---

1. Muhammad (1897–1975) was the leader of the Nation of Islam during Malcolm's lifetime.
2. Malcolm was arrested and convicted of multiple counts of burglary in 1946. He served a total of six years at Norfolk and two other Massachusetts prisons.

that went every day to Mr. Elijah Muhammad. And I wrote at least one more daily letter, replying to one of my brothers and sisters. Every letter I received from them added something to my knowledge of the teachings of Mr. Muhammad. I would sit for long periods and study his photographs.

I've never been one for inaction. Everything I've ever felt strongly about, I've done something about. I guess that's why, unable to do anything else, I soon began writing to people I had known in the hustling world, such as Sammy the Pimp, John Hughes, the gambling house owner, the thief Jumpsteady, and several dope peddlers. I wrote them all about Allah and Islam and Mr. Elijah Muhammad. I had no idea where most of them lived. I addressed their letters in care of the Harlem or Roxbury bars and clubs where I'd known them.

I never got a single reply. The average hustler and criminal was too un-educated to write a letter. I have known many slick, sharp-looking hustlers, who would have you think they had an interest in Wall Street; privately, they would get someone else to read a letter if they received one. Besides, neither would I have replied to anyone writing me something as wild as "the white man is the devil."

What certainly went on the Harlem and Roxbury wires was that Detroit Red[3] was going crazy in stir, or else he was trying some hype to shake up the warden's office.

During the years that I stayed in the Norfolk Prison Colony, never did any official directly say anything to me about those letters, although, of course, they all passed through the prison censorship. I'm sure, however, they monitored what I wrote to add to the files which every state and federal prison keeps on the conversion of Negro inmates by the teachings of Mr. Elijah Muhammad.

But at that time, I felt that the real reason was that the white man knew that he was the devil.

Later on, I even wrote to the Mayor of Boston, to the Governor of Massachusetts, and to Harry S. Truman. They never answered; they probably never even saw my letters. I handscratched to them how the white man's society was responsible for the black man's condition in this wilderness of North America.

It was because of my letters that I happened to stumble upon starting to acquire some kind of a homemade education.

I became increasingly frustrated at not being able to express what I wanted to convey in letters that I wrote, especially those to Mr. Elijah Muhammad. In the street, I had been the most articulate hustler out there—I had commanded attention when I said something. But now, trying to write simple English, I not only wasn't articulate, I wasn't even functional. How would I sound writing in slang, the way I would *say* it, something such as, "Look, daddy, let me pull your coat about a cat, Elijah Muhammad—"

Many who today hear me somewhere in person, or on television, or those who read something I've said, will think I went to school far beyond the eighth grade. This impression is due entirely to my prison studies.

---

3. Malcolm's nickname while a hustler in New York and Boston during the early to mid 1940s.

It had really begun back in the Charlestown Prison, when Bimbi[4] first made me feel envy of his stock of knowledge. Bimbi had always taken charge of any conversations he was in, and I had tried to emulate him. But every book I picked up had few sentences which didn't contain anywhere from one to nearly all of the words that might as well have been in Chinese. When I just skipped those words, of course, I really ended up with little idea of what the book said. So I had come to the Norfolk Prison Colony still going through only book-reading motions. Pretty soon, I would have quit even these motions, unless I had received the motivation that I did.

I saw that the best thing I could do was get hold of a dictionary—to study, to learn some words. I was lucky enough to reason also that I should try to improve my penmanship. It was sad. I couldn't even write in a straight line. It was both ideas together that moved me to request a dictionary along with some tablets and pencils from the Norfolk Prison Colony school.

I spent two days just riffling uncertainly through the dictionary's pages. I'd never realized so many words existed! I didn't know *which* words I needed to learn. Finally, just to start some kind of action, I began copying.

In my slow, painstaking, ragged handwriting, I copied into my tablet everything printed on that first page, down to the punctuation marks.

I believe it took me a day. Then, aloud, I read back, to myself, everything I'd written on the tablet. Over and over, aloud, to myself, I read my own handwriting.

I woke up the next morning, thinking about those words—immensely proud to realize that not only had I written so much at one time, but I'd written words that I never knew were in the world. Moreover, with a little effort, I also could remember what many of these words meant. I reviewed the words whose meanings I didn't remember. Funny thing, from the dictionary first page right now, that "aardvark" springs to my mind. The dictionary had a picture of it, a long-tailed, long-eared, burrowing African mammal, which lives off termites caught by sticking out its tongue as an anteater does for ants.

I was so fascinated that I went on—I copied the dictionary's next page. And the same experience came when I studied that. With every succeeding page, I also learned of people and places and events from history. Actually the dictionary is like a miniature encyclopedia. Finally the dictionary's A section had filled a whole tablet—and I went on into the B's. That was the way I started copying what eventually became the entire dictionary. It went a lot faster after so much practice helped me to pick up handwriting speed. Between what I wrote in my tablet, and writing letters, during the rest of my time in prison I would guess I wrote a million words.

I suppose it was inevitable that as my word-base broadened, I could for the first time pick up a book and read and now begin to understand what the book was saying. Anyone who has read a great deal can imagine the new world that opened. Let me tell you something: from then until I left that prison, in every free moment I had, if I was not reading in the library, I was reading on my bunk. You couldn't have gotten me out of books with a

---

4. Fellow inmate at Charlestown State Prison; Bimbi encouraged Malcolm to begin correspondence courses.

wedge. Between Mr. Muhammad's teachings, my correspondence, my visitors—usually Ella and Reginald[5]—and my reading of books, months passed without my even thinking about being imprisoned. In fact, up to then, I never had been so truly free in my life.

The Norfolk Prison Colony's library was in the school building. A variety of classes was taught there by instructors who came from such places as Harvard and Boston universities. The weekly debates between inmate teams were also held in the school building. You would be astonished to know how worked up convict debaters and audiences would get over subjects like "Should Babies Be Fed Milk?"

Available on the prison library's shelves were books on just about every general subject. Much of the big private collection that Parkhurst[6] had willed to the prison was still in crates and boxes in the back of the library— thousands of old books. Some of them looked ancient: covers faded, old-time parchment-looking binding. Parkhurst, I've mentioned, seemed to have been principally interested in history and religion. He had the money and the special interest to have a lot of books that you wouldn't have in general circulation. Any college library would have been lucky to get that collection.

As you can imagine, especially in a prison where there was heavy emphasis on rehabilitation, an inmate was smiled upon if he demonstrated an unusually intense interest in books. There was a sizable number of well-read inmates, especially the popular debaters. Some were said by many to be practically walking encyclopedias. They were almost celebrities. No university would ask any student to devour literature as I did when this new world opened to me, of being able to read and *understand*.

I read more in my room than in the library itself. An inmate who was known to read a lot could check out more than the permitted maximum number of books. I preferred reading in the total isolation of my own room.

When I had progressed to really serious reading, every night at about ten P.M. I would be outraged with the "lights out." It always seemed to catch me right in the middle of something engrossing.

Fortunately, right outside my door was a corridor light that cast a glow into my room. The glow was enough to read by, once my eyes adjusted to it. So when "lights out" came, I would sit on the floor where I could continue reading in that glow.

At one-hour intervals the night guards paced past every room. Each time I heard the approaching footsteps, I jumped into bed and feigned sleep. And as soon as the guard passed, I got back out of bed onto the floor area of that light-glow, where I would read for another fifty-eight minutes—until the guard approached again. That went on until three or four every morning. Three or four hours of sleep a night was enough for me. Often in the years in the streets I had slept less than that.

The teachings of Mr. Muhammad stressed how history had been "whitened"—when white men had written history books, the black man simply

---

5. Malcolm's sister and brother; both worked hard to convert him to Islam.
6. Millionaire who left his library to the Norfolk State Prison; Norfolk was considered a relatively enlightened, "intellectuals'" prison.

had been left out. Mr. Muhammad couldn't have said anything that would have struck me much harder. I had never forgotten how when my class, me and all of those whites, had studied seventh-grade United States history back in Mason, the history of the Negro had been covered in one paragraph, and the teacher had gotten a big laugh with his joke, "Negroes' feet are so big that when they walk, they leave a hole in the ground."

This is one reason why Mr. Muhammad's teachings spread so swiftly all over the United States, among *all* Negroes, whether or not they became followers of Mr. Muhammad. The teachings ring true—to every Negro. You can hardly show me a black adult in America—or a white one, for that matter—who knows from the history books anything like the truth about the black man's role. In my own case, once I heard of the "glorious history of the black man," I took special pains to hunt in the library for books that would inform me on details about black history.

I can remember accurately the very first set of books that really impressed me. I have since bought that set of books and I have it at home for my children to read as they grow up. It's called *Wonders of the World*. It's full of pictures of archeological finds, statues that depict, usually, non-European people.

I found books like Will Durant's *Story of Civilization*. I read H. G. Wells' *Outline of History*. *Souls of Black Folk* by W. E. B. Du Bois[7] gave me a glimpse into the black people's history before they came to this country. Carter G. Woodson's *Negro History*[8] opened my eyes about black empires before the black slave was brought to the United States, and the early Negro struggles for freedom.

J. A. Rogers' three volumes of *Sex and Race*[9] told about race-mixing before Christ's time; about Aesop being a black man who told fables; about Egypt's Pharaohs; about the great Coptic Christian Empires; about Ethiopia, the earth's oldest continuous black civilization, as China is the oldest continuous civilization.

Mr. Muhammad's teaching about how the white man had been created led me to *Findings In Genetics* by Gregor Mendel.[1] (The dictionary's G section was where I had learned what "genetics" meant.) I really studied this book by the Austrian monk. Reading it over and over, especially certain sections, helped me to understand that if you started with a black man, a white man could be produced; but starting with a white man, you never could produce a black man—because the white chromosome is recessive. And since no one disputes that there was but one Original Man, the conclusion is clear.

During the last year or so, in the *New York Times*, Arnold Toynbee[2] used the word "bleached" in describing the white man. His words were:

7. Du Bois's *Souls of Black Folk* (1903) contains a detailed analysis of social and economic relations in the post-Reconstruction South. Will and Ariel Durant's *Story of Civilization* is an 11-volume treatise published between 1935 and 1975. Wells's *Outline of History, being a plain history of life and mankind*, was published in two volumes in 1920.
8. *The Negro in Our History* was first published in 1927; Woodson, an African American historian, founded *The Journal of Negro History* in 1916.

9. Rogers's 3-volume *Sex and Race* (1900) dealt with the subject of race mixing in the old and new worlds.
1. Gregor Johann Mendel (1822–1884), considered the father of modern genetics, arrived at his theories by studying plant hybridization.
2. English historian (1889–1975) who published extensively on world history, with an emphasis on European and Asian histories.

"White (i.e. bleached) human beings of North European origin. . . ."
Toynbee also referred to the European geographic area as only a peninsula
of Asia. He said there is no such thing as Europe. And if you look at the
globe, you will see for yourself that America is only an extension of Asia.
(But at the same time Toynbee is among those who have helped to bleach
history. He has written that Africa was the only continent that produced no
history. He won't write that again. Every day now, the truth is coming to
light.)

I never will forget how shocked I was when I began reading about slavery's total horror. It made such an impact upon me that it later became one
of my favorite subjects when I became a minister of Mr. Muhammad's.
The world's most monstrous crime, the sin and the blood on the white
man's hands, are almost impossible to believe. Books like the one by Frederick Olmsted[3] opened my eyes to the horrors suffered when the slave was
landed in the United States. The European woman, Fannie Kimball, who
had married a Southern white slaveowner, described how human beings
were degraded. Of course I read *Uncle Tom's Cabin*.[4] In fact, I believe
that's the only novel I have ever read since I started serious reading.

Parkhurst's collection also contained some bound pamphlets of the Abolitionist Anti-Slavery Society of New England. I read descriptions of atrocities, saw those illustrations of black slave women tied up and flogged with
whips; of black mothers watching their babies being dragged off, never to
be seen by their mothers again; of dogs after slaves, and of the fugitive slave
catchers, evil white men with whips and clubs and chains and guns. I read
about the slave preacher Nat Turner,[5] who put the fear of God into the
white slavemaster. Nat Turner wasn't going around preaching pie-in-the-
sky and "non-violent" freedom for the black man. There in Virginia one
night in 1831, Nat and seven other slaves started out at his master's home
and through the night they went from one plantation "big house" to the
next, killing, until by the next morning 57 white people were dead and Nat
had about 70 slaves following him. White people, terrified for their lives,
fled from their homes, locked themselves up in public buildings, hid in the
woods, and some even left the state. A small army of soldiers took two
months to catch and hang Nat Turner. Somewhere I have read where Nat
Turner's example is said to have inspired John Brown[6] to invade Virginia
and attack Harper's Ferry nearly thirty years later, with thirteen white men
and five Negroes.

I read Herodotus, "the father of History,"[7] or, rather, I read about him.

3. Frederick Law Olmsted (1822–1903), antislavery journalist, spent 14 months traveling throughout the slave states. His observations were recorded
in a trilogy: *Journey to the Seaboard Slave States*
(1856); *A Journey Through Texas* (1857); and *A
Journey in the Back Country* (1860). In 1861
Olmsted published *The Cotton Kingdom*, which
was based on his three earlier volumes. He is usually remembered as a designer of public parks, including New York City's Central Park.
4. The novel by abolitionist Harriet Beecher
Stowe (1811–1896) was first published in 1852.
5. Slave (1800–1831) who led his followers in the
most serious slave insurrection of the antebellum
South, in Virginia's Southampton County in August 1831. A confession was allegedly obtained
from Turner while in prison, and he was hanged on
November 11, 1831.
6. Brown (1800–1859) raided Harpers Ferry, a
government armory and arsenal, in an attempt to
free the slaves. The eighteen men who marched
with Brown included five blacks. A week after the
raid, Brown and four of the surviving men were
tried and convicted. Brown was hanged on December 2, 1859.
7. Herodotus, 5th-century B.C. Greek who introduced the idea of *History*, meaning a record of past
events, to Western literature. He was dubbed the
Father of History by the Roman Cicero.

And I read the histories of various nations, which opened my eyes gradually, then wider and wider, to how the whole world's white men had indeed acted like devils, pillaging and raping and bleeding and draining the whole world's non-white people. I remember, for instance, books such as Will Durant's *The Story of Oriental Civilization*, and Mahatma Gandhi's[8] accounts of the struggle to drive the British out of India.

Book after book showed me how the white man had brought upon the world's black, brown, red, and yellow peoples every variety of the sufferings of exploitation. I saw how since the sixteenth century, the so-called "Christian trader" white man began to ply the seas in his lust for Asian and African empires, and plunder, and power. I read, I saw, how the white man never has gone among the non-white peoples bearing the Cross in the true manner and spirit of Christ's teachings—meek, humble, and Christ-like.

I perceived, as I read, how the collective white man had been actually nothing but a piratical opportunist who used Faustian machinations to make his own Christianity his initial wedge in criminal conquests. First, always "religiously," he branded "heathen" and "pagan" labels upon ancient non-white cultures and civilizations. The stage thus set, he then turned upon his non-white victims his weapons of war.

I read how, entering India—half a *billion* deeply religious brown people—the British white man, by 1759, through promises, trickery and manipulations, controlled much of India through Great Britain's East India Company. The parasitical British administration kept tentacling out to half of the sub-continent. In 1857, some of the desperate people of India finally mutinied—and, excepting the African slave trade, nowhere has history recorded any more unnecessary bestial and ruthless human carnage than the British suppression of the non-white Indian people.

Over 115 million African blacks—close to the 1930's population of the United States—were murdered or enslaved during the slave trade. And I read how when the slave market was glutted, the cannibalistic white powers of Europe next carved up, as their colonies, the richest areas of the black continent. And Europe's chancelleries for the next century played a chess game of naked exploitation and power from Cape Horn to Cairo.

Ten guards and the warden couldn't have torn me out of those books. Not even Elijah Muhammad could have been more eloquent than those books were in providing indisputable proof that the collective white man had acted like a devil in virtually every contact he had with the world's collective non-white man. I listen today to the radio, and watch television, and read the headlines about the collective white man's fear and tension concerning China. When the white man professes ignorance about why the Chinese hate him so, my mind can't help flashing back to what I read, there in prison, about how the blood forebears of this same white man raped China at a time when China was trusting and helpless. Those original white "Christian traders" sent into China millions of pounds of opium. By 1839, so many of the Chinese were addicts that China's desperate government destroyed twenty thousand chests of opium. The first Opium War

8. Gandhi (1869–1948) led India in its long struggle for independence from Britain, which finally
came in 1947. He developed his belief in nonviolent protest and religious tolerance while working
as a barrister in South Africa in his early years.
Gandhi was assassinated in 1948.

was promptly declared by the white man. Imagine! Declaring *war* upon someone who objects to being narcotized! The Chinese were severely beaten, with Chinese-invented gunpowder.

The Treaty of Nanking made China pay the British white man for the destroyed opium: forced open China's major ports to British trade; forced China to abandon Hong Kong; fixed China's import tariffs so low that cheap British articles soon flooded in, maiming China's industrial development.

After a second Opium War, the Tientsin Treaties legalized the ravaging opium trade, legalized a British-French-American control of China's customs. China tried delaying that Treaty's ratification; Peking was looted and burned.

"Kill the foreign white devils!" was the 1901 Chinese war cry in the Boxer Rebellion. Losing again, this time the Chinese were driven from Peking's choicest areas. The vicious, arrogant white man put up the famous signs, "Chinese and dogs not allowed."

Red China after World War II closed its doors to the Western white world. Massive Chinese agricultural, scientific, and industrial efforts are described in a book that *Life* magazine recently published. Some observers inside Red China have reported that the world never has known such a hate-white campaign as is now going on in this non-white country where, present birth-rates continuing, in fifty more years Chinese will be half the earth's population. And it seems that some Chinese chickens will soon come home to roost, with China's recent successful nuclear tests.

Let us face reality. We can see in the United Nations a new world order being shaped, along color lines—an alliance among the non-white nations. America's U.N. Ambassador Adlai Stevenson complained not long ago that in the United Nations "a skin game" was being played. He was right. He was facing reality. A "skin game" *is* being played. But Ambassador Stevenson sounded like Jesse James accusing the marshal of carrying a gun. Because who in the world's history ever has played a worse "skin game" than the white man?

Mr. Muhammad, to whom I was writing daily, had no idea of what a new world had opened up to me through my efforts to document his teachings in books.

When I discovered philosophy, I tried to touch all the landmarks of philosophical development. Gradually, I read most of the old philosophers, Occidental and Oriental. The Oriental philosophers were the ones I came to prefer; finally, my impression was that most Occidental philosophy had largely been borrowed from the Oriental thinkers. Socrates, for instance, traveled in Egypt. Some sources even say that Socrates was initiated into some of the Egyptian mysteries. Obviously Socrates got some of his wisdom among the East's wise men.

I have often reflected upon the new vistas that reading opened to me. I knew right there in prison that reading had changed forever the course of my life. As I see it today, the ability to read awoke inside me some long dormant craving to be mentally alive. I certainly wasn't seeking any degree, the way a college confers a status symbol upon its students. My homemade education gave me, with every additional book that I read, a little bit more sensitivity to the deafness, dumbness, and blindness that was afflicting the black race in America. Not long ago, an English writer telephoned me from London, asking questions. One was, "What's your alma mater?" I told him, "Books." You will never catch me with a free fifteen minutes in which I'm not studying something I feel might be able to help the black man.

Yesterday I spoke in London, and both ways on the plane across the Atlantic I was studying a document about how the United Nations proposes to insure the human rights of the oppressed minorities of the world. The American black man is the world's most shameful case of minority oppression. What makes the black man think of himself as only an internal United States issue is just a catch-phrase, two words, "civil rights." How is the black man going to get "civil rights" before first he wins his *human* rights? If the American black man will start thinking about his *human* rights, and then start thinking of himself as part of one of the world's great peoples, he will see he has a case for the United Nations.

I can't think of a better case! Four hundred years of black blood and sweat invested here in America, and the white man still has the black man begging for what every immigrant fresh off the ship can take for granted the minute he walks down the gangplank.

But I'm digressing. I told the Englishman that my alma mater was books, a good library. Every time I catch a plane, I have with me a book that I want to read—and that's a lot of books these days. If I weren't out here every day battling the white man, I could spend the rest of my life reading, just satisfying my curiosity—because you can hardly mention anything I'm not curious about. I don't think anybody ever got more out of going to prison than I did. In fact, prison enabled me to study far more intensively than I would have if my life had gone differently and I had attended some college. I imagine that one of the biggest troubles with colleges is there are too many distractions, too much panty-raiding, fraternities, and boola-boola and all of that. Where else but in a prison could I have attacked my ignorance by being able to study intensely sometimes as much as fifteen hours a day?

Schopenhauer, Kant, Nietzsche,[9] naturally, I read all of those. I don't respect them; I am just trying to remember some of those whose theories I soaked up in those years. These three, it's said, laid the groundwork on which the Fascist and Nazi philosophy was built. I don't respect them because it seems to me that most of their time was spent arguing about things that are not really important. They remind me of so many of the Negro "intellectuals," so-called, with whom I have come in contact—they are always arguing about something useless.

Spinoza[1] impressed me for a while when I found out that he was black. A black Spanish Jew. The Jews excommunicated him because he advocated a pantheistic[2] doctrine, something like the "allness of God," or

9. German philosophers: Schopenhauer (1788–1860) argued that humans could liberate themselves through a negation of the will; Kant (1724–1804) argued that knowledge rests upon a priori judgments; Nietzsche (1844–1900) was a critic of rationalism, Christianity, and accepted standards of morality.

1. Dutch Jewish philosopher (1632–1677), an exponent of rationalism.
2. Of a system that "supposes God and Nature, or God and the whole Universe, to be one and the same Substance, one Universal Being; insomuch that Men's Souls are only Modifications of the divine Substance" (*OED*).

"God in everything." The Jews read their burial services for Spinoza, meaning that he was dead as far as they were concerned; his family was run out of Spain, they ended up in Holland, I think.

I'll tell you something. The whole stream of Western philosophy has now wound up in a cul-de-sac. The white man has perpetrated upon himself, as well as upon the black man, so gigantic a fraud that he has put himself into a crack. He did it through his elaborate, neurotic necessity to hide the black man's true role in history.

And today the white man is faced head on with what is happening on the Black Continent, Africa. Look at the artifacts being discovered there, that are proving over and over again, how the black man had great, fine, sensitive civilizations before the white man was out of the caves. Below the Sahara, in the places where most of America's Negroes' foreparents were kidnapped, there is being unearthed some of the finest craftsmanship, sculpture and other objects, that has ever been seen by modern man. Some of these things now are on view in such places as New York City's Museum of Modern Art. Gold work of such fine tolerance and workmanship that it has no rival. Ancient objects produced by black hands . . . refined by those black hands with results that no human hand today can equal.

History has been so "whitened" by the white man that even the black professors have known little more than the most ignorant black man about the talents and rich civilizations and cultures of the black man of millenniums ago. I have lectured in Negro colleges and some of these brainwashed black Ph.D.'s, with their suspenders dragging the ground with degrees, have run to the white man's newspapers calling me a "black fanatic." Why, a lot of them are fifty years behind the times. If I were president of one of these black colleges, I'd hock the campus if I had to, to send a bunch of black students off digging in Africa for more, more and more proof of the black race's historical greatness. The white man now is in Africa digging and searching. An African elephant can't stumble without falling on some white man with a shovel. Practically every week, we read about some great new find from Africa's lost civilizations. All that's new is white science's attitude. The ancient civilizations of the black man have been buried on the Black Continent all the time.

Here is an example: a British anthropologist named Dr. Louis S. B. Leakey is displaying some fossil bones—a foot, part of a hand, some jaws, and skull fragments. On the basis of these, Dr. Leakey has said it's time to rewrite completely the history of man's origin.

This species of man lived 1,818,036 years before Christ. And these bones were found in Tanganyika. In the Black Continent.

It's a crime, the lie that has been told to generations of black men and white men both. Little innocent black children, born of parents who believed that their race had no history. Little black children seeing, before they could talk, that their parents considered themselves inferior. Innocent black children growing up, living out their lives, dying of old age—and all of their lives ashamed of being black. But the truth is pouring out of the bag now.

Two other areas of experience which have been extremely formative in my life since prison were first opened to me in the Norfolk Prison Colony.

For one thing, I had my first experiences in opening the eyes of my brain-washed black brethren to some truths about the black race. And, the other: when I had read enough to know something, I began to enter the Prison Colony's weekly debating program—my baptism into public speaking.

I have to admit a sad, shameful fact. I had so loved being around the white man that in prison I really disliked how Negro convicts stuck together so much. But when Mr. Muhammad's teachings reversed my attitude toward my black brothers, in my guilt and shame I began to catch every chance I could to recruit for Mr. Muhammad.

You have to be careful, very careful, introducing the truth to the black man who has never previously heard the truth about himself, his own kind, and the white man. My brother Reginald had told me that all Muslims experienced this in their recruiting for Mr. Muhammad. The black brother is so brainwashed that he may even be repelled when he first hears the truth. Reginald advised that the truth had to be dropped only a little bit at a time. And you had to wait a while to let it sink in before advancing the next step.

I began first telling my black brother inmates about the glorious history of the black man—things they never had dreamed. I told them the horrible slavery-trade truths that they never knew. I would watch their faces when I told them about that, because the white man had completely erased the slaves' past, a Negro in America can never know his true family name, or even what tribe he was descended from: the Mandingos, the Wolof, the Scrcr, the Fula, the Fanti, the Ashanti,[3] or others. I told them that some slaves brought from Africa spoke Arabic, and were Islamic in their religion. A lot of these black convicts still wouldn't believe it unless they could see that a white man had said it. So, often, I would read to these brothers selected passages from white men's books. I'd explain to them that the real truth was known to some white men, the scholars; but there had been a conspiracy down through the generations to keep the truth from black men.

I would keep close watch on how each one reacted. I always had to be careful. I never knew when some brainwashed black imp, some dyed-in-the-wool Uncle Tom, would nod at me and then go running to tell the white man. When one was ripe—and I could tell—then away from the rest, I'd drop it on him, what Mr. Muhammed taught: "The white man is the devil."

That would shock many of them—until they started thinking about it.

This is probably as big a single worry as the America prison system has today—the way the Muslim teachings, circulated among all Negroes in the country, are converting new Muslims among black men in prison, and black men are in prison in far greater numbers than their proportion in the population.

The reason is that among all Negroes the black convict is the most perfectly preconditioned to hear the words, "the white man is the devil."

You tell that to any Negro. Except for those relatively few "integration"-mad so-called "intellectuals," and those black men who are

3. Many slaves brought to the Americas came from these West African tribes.

otherwise fat, happy, and deaf, dumb, and blinded, with their crumbs from the white man's rich table, you have struck a nerve center in the American black man. He may take a day to react, a month, a year; he may never respond, openly; but of one thing you can be sure—when he thinks about his own life, he is going to see where, to him, personally, the white man sure has acted like a devil.

And, as I say, above all Negroes, the black prisoner. Here is a black man caged behind bars, probably for years, put there by the white man. Usually the convict comes from among those bottom-of-the-pile Negroes, the Negroes who through their entire lives have been kicked about, treated like children—Negroes who never have met one white man who didn't either take something from them or do something to them.

You let this caged-up black man start thinking, the same way I did when I first heard Elijah Muhammad's teachings: let him start thinking how, with better breaks when he was young and ambitious he might have been a lawyer, a doctor, a scientist, anything. You let this caged-up black man start realizing, as I did, how from the first landing of the first slave ship, the millions of black men in America have been like sheep in a den of wolves. That's why black prisoners become Muslims so fast when Elijah Muhammad's teachings filter into their cages by way of other Muslim convicts. "The white man is the devil" is a perfect echo of that black convict's life-long experience.

I've told how debating was a weekly event there at the Norfolk Prison Colony. My reading had my mind like steam under pressure. Some way, I had to start telling the white man about himself to his face. I decided I could do this by putting my name down to debate.

Standing up and speaking before an audience was a thing that through-out my previous life never would have crossed my mind. Out there in the streets, hustling, pushing dope, and robbing, I could have had the dreams from a pound of hashish and I'd never have dreamed anything so wild as that one day I would speak in coliseums and arenas, at the greatest American universities, and on radio and television programs, not to mention speaking all over Egypt and Africa and in England.

But I will tell you that, right there, in the prison, debating, speaking to a crowd, was as exhilarating to me as the discovery of knowledge through reading had been. Standing up there, the faces looking up at me, the things in my head coming out of my mouth, while my brain searched for the next best thing to follow what I was saying, and if I could sway them to my side by handling it right, then I had won the debate—once my feet got wet, I was gone on debating. Whichever side of the selected subject was assigned to me, I'd track down and study everything I could find on it. I'd put myself in my opponent's place and decide how I'd try to win if I had the other side; and then I'd figure a way to knock down those points. And if there was any way in the world, I'd work into my speech the devilishness of the white man.

"Compulsory Military Training—Or None?" That's one good chance I got unexpectedly, I remember. My opponent flailed the air about the Ethiopians throwing rocks and spears at Italian airplanes, "proving" that compulsory military training was needed. I said the Ethiopians' black flesh had been splattered against trees by bombs the Pope in Rome had blessed, and the Ethiopians would have thrown even their bare bodies at the airplanes because they had seen that they were fighting the devil incarnate.

They yelled "foul," that I'd made the subject a race issue. I said it wasn't race, it was a historical fact, that they ought to go and read Pierre van Paassen's *Days of Our Years*,[4] and something not surprising to me, that book, right after the debate, disappeared from the prison library. It was right there in prison that I made up my mind to devote the rest of my life to telling the white man about himself—or die. In a debate about whether or not Homer had ever existed, I threw into those white faces the theory that Homer only symbolized how white Europeans kidnapped black Africans, then blinded them so that they could never get back to their own people. (Homer and Omar and *Moor*, you see, are related terms; it's like saying Peter, Pedro, and *petra*, all three of which mean rock.) These blinded Moors the Europeans taught to sing about the Europeans' glorious accomplishments. I made it clear that was the devilish white man's idea of kicks. Aesop's *Fables*—another case in point. "Aesop" was only the Greek name for an Ethiopian.

Another hot debate I remember I was in had to do with the identity of Shakespeare. No color was involved there; I just got intrigued over the Shakespearean dilemma. The King James translation of the Bible is considered the greatest piece of literature in English. Its language supposedly represents the ultimate in using the King's English. Well, Shakespeare's language and the Bible's language are one and the same. They say that from 1604 to 1611, King James got poets to translate, to write the Bible. Well, if Shakespeare existed, he was then the top poet around. But Shakespeare is nowhere reported connected with the Bible. If he existed, why didn't King James use him? And if he did use him, why is it one of the world's best kept secrets?

I know that many say that Francis Bacon was Shakespeare. If that is true, why would Bacon have kept it secret? Bacon wasn't royalty, when royalty sometimes used the *nom de plume* because it was "improper" for royalty to be artistic or theatrical. What would Bacon have had to lose? Bacon, in fact, would have had everything to gain.

In the prison debates I argued for the theory that King James himself was the real poet who used the *nom de plume* Shakespeare. King James was brilliant. He was the greatest king who ever sat on the British throne. Who else among royalty, in his time, would have had the giant talent to write Shakespeare's works? It was he who poetically "fixed" the Bible—which in itself and its present King James version has enslaved the world.

When my brother Reginald visited, I would talk to him about new evidence I found to document the Muslim teachings. In either volume 43 or 44 of The Harvard Classics, I read Milton's *Paradise Lost*. The devil,

4. Van Paassen was a Dutch-born American journalist; *Days of Our Years* (1939) is his memoir, beginning with his youth in The Netherlands, his family's relocation to Canada, and his journalism career, which took him to Europe, the Middle East, and Africa during World War II. Probably because of his early religious training, Van Paassen's observations on religious practices are the most insightful aspect of the book.

kicked out of Paradise, was trying to regain possession. He was using the forces of Europe, personified by the Popes, Charlemagne, Richard the Lionhearted, and other knights. I interpreted this to show that the Europeans were motivated and led by the devil, or the personification of the devil. So Milton and Mr. Elijah Muhammad were actually saying the same thing.

I couldn't believe it when Reginald began to speak ill of Elijah Muhammad. I can't specify the exact things he said. They were more in the nature of implications against Mr. Muhammad—the pitch of Reginald's voice, or the way that Reginald looked, rather than what he said.

It caught me totally unprepared. It threw me into a state of confusion. My blood brother, Reginald, in whom I had so much confidence, for whom I had so much respect, the one who had introduced me to the Nation of Islam. I couldn't believe it! And now Islam meant more to me than anything I ever had known in my life. Islam and Mr. Elijah Muhammad had changed my whole world.

Reginald, I learned, had been suspended from the Nation of Islam by Elijah Muhammad. He had not practiced moral restraint. After he had learned the truth, and had accepted the truth, and the Muslim laws, Reginald was still carrying on improper relations with the then secretary of the New York Temple. Some other Muslim who learned of it had made charges against Reginald to Mr. Muhammad in Chicago, and Mr. Muhammad had suspended Reginald.

When Reginald left, I was in torment. That night, finally, I wrote to Mr. Muhammad, trying to defend my brother, appealing for him. I told him what Reginald was to me, what my brother meant to me.

I put the letter into the box for the prison censor. Then all the rest of that night, I prayed to Allah. I don't think anyone ever prayed more sincerely to Allah. I prayed for some kind of relief from my confusion.

It was the next night, as I lay on my bed, I suddenly, with a start, became aware of a man sitting beside me in my chair. He had on a dark suit, I remember. I could see him as plainly as I see anyone I look at. He wasn't black, and he wasn't white. He was light-brown-skinned, an Asiatic cast of countenance, and he had oily black hair.

I looked right into his face.

I didn't get frightened. I knew I wasn't dreaming. I couldn't move, I didn't speak, and he didn't. I couldn't place him racially—other than that I knew he was a non-European. I had no idea whatsoever who he was. He just sat there. Then, suddenly as he had come, he was gone.

Soon, Mr. Muhammad sent me a reply about Reginald. He wrote, "If you once believed in the truth, and now you are beginning to doubt the truth, you didn't believe the truth in the first place. What could make you doubt the truth other than your own weak self?"

That struck me. Reginald was not leading the disciplined life of a Muslim. And I knew that Elijah Muhammad was right, and my blood brother was wrong. Because right is right, and wrong is wrong. Little did I then realize the day would come when Elijah Muhammad would be accused by his own sons as being guilty of the same acts of immorality that he judged Reginald and so many others for.

But at that time, all of the doubt and confusion in my mind was removed. All of the influence that my brother had wielded over me was broken. From that day on, as far as I am concerned, everything that my brother Reginald has done is wrong.

But Reginald kept visiting me. When he had been a Muslim, he had been immaculate in his attire. But now, he wore things like a T-shirt, shabby-looking trousers, and sneakers. I could see him on the way down. When he spoke, I heard him coldly. But I would listen. He was my blood brother.

Gradually, I saw the chastisement of Allah—what Christians would call "the curse"—come upon Reginald. Elijah Muhammad said that Allah was chastising Reginald—and that anyone who challenged Elijah Muhammad would be chastened by Allah. In Islam we were taught that as long as one didn't know the truth, he lived in darkness. But once the truth was accepted, and recognized, he lived in light, and whoever would then go against it would be punished by Allah.

Mr. Muhammad taught that the five-pointed star stands for justice, and also for the five senses of man. We were taught that Allah executes justice by working upon the five senses of those who rebel against His Messenger, or against His truth. We were taught that this was Allah's way of letting Muslims know His sufficiency to defend His Messenger against any and all opposition, as long as the Messenger himself didn't deviate from the path of truth. We were taught that Allah turned the minds of any defectors into turmoil. I thought truly that it was Allah doing this to my brother.

The letter, I think from my brother Philbert, told me that Reginald was with them in Detroit. I heard no more about Reginald until one day, weeks later, Ella visited me; she told me that Reginald was at her home in Roxbury, sleeping. Ella said she had heard a knock, she had gone to the door, and there was Reginald, looking terrible. Ella said she had asked, "Where did you come from?" And Reginald had told her he came from Detroit. She said she asked him, "How did you get here?" And he had told her, "I walked."

I believed he *had* walked. I believed in Elijah Muhammad, and he had convinced us that Allah's chastisement upon Reginald's mind had taken away Reginald's ability to gauge distance and time. There is a dimension of time with which we are not familiar here in the West. Elijah Muhammad said that under Allah's chastisement the five senses of a man can be so deranged by those whose mental powers are greater than his that in five minutes his hair can turn snow white. Or he will walk nine hundred miles as he might walk five blocks.

In prison, since I had become a Muslim, I had grown a beard. When Reginald visited me, he nervously moved about in his chair; he told me that each hair of my beard was a snake. Everywhere, he saw snakes.

He next began to believe that he was the "Messenger of Allah." Reginald went around in the streets of Roxbury, Ella reported to me, telling people that he had some divine power. He graduated from this to saying that he was Allah.

He finally began saying he was *greater* than Allah.

Authorities picked up Reginald, and he was put into an institution. They couldn't find what was wrong. They had no way to understand Allah's chastisement. Reginald was released. Then he was picked up again, and was put into another institution.

Reginald is in an institution now. I know where, but I won't say. I would not want to cause him any more trouble than he has already had.

I believe, today, that it was written, it was meant, for Reginald to be used for one purpose only: as a bait, as a minnow to reach into that ocean of blackness where I was, to save me.

I cannot understand it any other way.

After Elijah Muhammad himself was later accused as a very immoral man, I came to believe that it wasn't a divine chastisement upon Reginald, but the pain he felt when his own family totally rejected him for Elijah Muhammad, and this hurt made Reginald turn insanely upon Elijah Muhammad.

It's impossible to dream, or to see, or to have a vision of someone whom you never have seen before—and to see him exactly as he is. To see someone, and to see him exactly as he looks, is to have a pre-vision.

I would later come to believe that my pre-vision was of Master W. D. Fard,[5] the Messiah, the one whom Elijah Muhammad said had appointed him—Elijah Muhammad—as His Last Messenger to the black people of North America.

My last year in prison was spent back in the Charlestown Prison. Even among the white inmates, the word had filtered around. Some of those brainwashed black convicts talked too much. And I know that the censors had reported on my mail. The Norfolk Prison Colony officials had become upset. They used as a reason for my transfer that I refused to take some kind of shots, an inoculation or something.

The only thing that worried me was that I hadn't much time left before I would be eligible for parole-board consideration. But I reasoned that they might look at my representing and spreading Islam in another way: instead of keeping me in they might want to get me out.

I had come to prison with 20/20 vision. But when I got sent back to Charlestown, I had read so much by the lights-out glow in my room at the Norfolk Prison Colony that I had astigmatism and the first pair of the eyeglasses that I have worn ever since.

I had less maneuverability back in the much stricter Charlestown Prison. But I found that a lot of Negroes attended a Bible class, and I went there.

Conducting the class was a tall, blond, blue-eyed (a perfect "devil") Harvard Seminary student. He lectured, and then he starred in a question-and-answer session. I don't know which of us had read the Bible more, he or I, but I had to give him credit; he really was heavy on his religion. I puzzled and puzzled for a way to upset him, and to give those Negroes present something to think and talk about and circulate.

Finally, I put up my hand; he nodded. He had talked about Paul.

---

5. Reference to Wali D. Fard, the founder of the Nation of Islam.

I stood up and asked, "What color was Paul?" And I kept talking, with pauses, "He had to be black . . . because he was a Hebrew and the original Hebrews were black . . . weren't they?"

He had started flushing red. You know the way white people do. He said "Yes."

I wasn't through yet. "What color was Jesus . . . he was Hebrew, too . . . wasn't he?"

Both the Negro and the white convicts had sat bolt upright. I don't care how tough the convict, be he brainwashed black Christian, or a "devil" white Christian, neither of them is ready to hear anybody saying Jesus wasn't white. The instructor walked around. He shouldn't have felt bad. In all of the years since, I never have met any intelligent white man who would try to insist that Jesus was white. How could they? He said, "Jesus was brown."

I let him get away with that compromise.

Exactly as I had known it would, almost overnight the Charlestown convicts, black and white, began buzzing with the story. Wherever I went, I could feel the nodding. And anytime I got a chance to exchange words with a black brother in stripes, I'd say, "My man! You ever heard about somebody named Mr. Elijah Muhammad?"

1964

JOHN ALFRED WILLIAMS

b. 1925

John A. Williams was born in Hinds County, near Jackson, Mississippi. He earned his bachelor's degree from Syracuse University. During World War II, Williams served in the navy, an experience that later became symbolic capital for his novel *Captain Blackman* (1972). He has worked for CBS and NBC and for *Newsweek, Ebony,* and *Jet* magazines and has taught at the College of the Virgin Islands, Sarah Lawrence College, the University of California at Santa Barbara, and elsewhere. From 1973 to 1977, he served as distinguished professor of English at the City University of New York. Currently, he teaches at Rutgers University's Newark Campus.

Williams is by any measure a contrarian. Indeed, one of the most inexplicable moments of his career came when his 1962 nomination for the prestigious Prix de Rome was rejected by the American Academy of Arts and Letters, a rejection Williams took extremely personally and publicly. This peculiar moment finds its fictional reflection in *The Man Who Cried I Am* (1967). Friend and admirer of Richard Wright and Chester Himes, Williams has produced both romantically plotted popular novels and hard-edged journalistic essays denouncing the pervasiveness of white racism across the globe. His fictional prose is always fast moving and psychologically gripping. During the Black Arts movement, Williams was an outspoken and deeply informed sharer of a new vision of the possibilities for African life in the United States. Williams's most famous novel, *The Man Who Cried I Am,* deals with black male writers who are trying to navigate issues of politics, race, and international society. Max Reddick, the protagonist, is dying of colon cancer. Two other characters, Harry Ames and Marion Dawes, are literary reincarnations of Richard Wright and James Baldwin, respectively.

An uncompromising critic of the racial inequities of the American world, Williams's presentation on exile and the black American writer at the Black Writers Conference at Medgar Evers University in 1996 was a shrewd update of his insights in *The Man Who Cried I Am.*

From The Man Who Cried I Am

1

AMSTERDAM

[IN AN OUTDOOR CAFE]

It was a late afternoon in the middle of May and Max Reddick was sitting in an outdoor cafe on the Leidseplein toying with a Pernod. The factories and shops were closing and traffic streamed from Leidsestraat onto the Plein.[1] There were many bicycle riders. Through eyes that had been half glazed over for several days with alcohol, Librium[2] and morphine, Max looked appreciatively at the female cyclists. The men were so average. He quickly dismissed them. The girls were something else again, big-legged and big-buttocked. (Very much like African women, Max thought.) They pedaled past, their chins held high, their knees promising for fractions of seconds only, a flash of white above the stockingtops and then, the view imminent, the knees rushed up and obscured all view. Once in a while Max would see a girl pedaling saucily, not caring if her knees blocked out the sights above or not. Max would think: Go, baby!

The cafe was empty. That was a good sign. It meant that the people Max used to know in Amsterdam, the painters, writers and sculptors, the composers and song-and-dance men who were the year-round Black Peters for the Dutch, the jazzmen, were working well. They would be out later and drink Genever[3] or beer until they became high, wanted to talk about their work or go make love. Maybe they would go up to the Kring,[4] if they were members or honored guests, and play four-ball billiards while eating fresh herring. It was time for the fresh herring, the green herring.

Max glanced at the sky. God! he thought. It was like a clear highnoon sky in New York. No night would appear here until nine, but daybreak would come galloping up at close to three in the morning. He finished his Pernod and twisted to find the waiter, raising his hand at the same time. He felt something *squish* as he moved, and the meaning of the feeling caught at his voice. "*Ober,*"[5] he said, then more loudly, "*Ober.*" The waiter, clad in a red jacket, black tie and black pants looked up with a smile. This was a new face, a new American. A little older than many others, and a sick look about him at that! Painter, writer, sculptor, jazz musician, dancer . . . ?

"Pernod," Max said. The waiter nodded and retreated to the bar. Max felt a sharp, gouging pain and he gripped his glass tightly. Water came to his eyes and he felt sweat pop out on his forehead. "Goddamn," he whis-

---

1. Square, esplanade, or piazza (Dutch). "Leidse-straat": Leiden Street (Dutch).
2. Tranquilizer.
3. Holland gin.
4. Circle, district, area, or orbit (Dutch, Afrikaans).
5. Waiter (Dutch).

pered. When the pain subsided, he rose and went to the men's room inside the cafe.

When he came out he noticed that the fresh Pernod was already on his table and he said *"Dank U"* to the waiter. That phrase he remembered, as he remembered others in French, German, Spanish, Italian, but he could barely put a sentence together in them. He sat down again, glancing at his watch. Where was she?

She had told him in their exchange of polite letters that she had returned to the gallery. If that was so, she should be passing the cafe at any moment, passing with that long, springy stride, so strange because she was small and not thin, passing with her hair billowing back over her shoulders. He had seen her pass many, many times. Before. Before, when he had sat deep inside the cafe watching, and would only call to her when she was almost out of sight. "Lost your cool then, man," he now whispered to himself. "You ba-lew it!" He always thought of the canals when he thought of her. Now they would be reflecting with aching clarity the marvelous painter's sky. The barges and boats would be on the way in, and soon the ducks and swans would be tucking their necks in to sleep. He had to sleep soon, too; it might prolong his life. A few days more.

Ah yes, he thought, *you Dutch motherfuckers. I've returned.* "A Dutch man o' warre that sold us twenty negars," John Rolfe wrote, *Well, you-all, I bring myself. Free! Three hundred and forty-five years after Jamestown.*[6] *Now . . . how's that for the circle come full?*

He did not really care about the Dutch except that she was Dutch. She was thirty-five now, fourteen years younger than he. Would she still be as blond? (How he had hated that robust blondness at first after the malnourished black of Africa. The blondness had been so much like that of the Swedish blondes, jazz freaks who lived on jazz concerts, who saw the black musicians in their staged cool postures; but how he had been attracted to it as well!) Did he love her still—billowing blond hair; sturdy swimmer's legs; long, sinewy stride on such a small body and all? (And all? What was all? A memory. Nineteen years old.) He supposed he did love her, transposed, a bit bleached out, in a clinical way, the way you'd discuss it in an analyst's office. *Anal,* he thought, *list.* Shit list. Man, am I on that! But he did want to tell her he was sorry; tell her why it hadn't worked. He was glad he was still on his feet and able to move about. If he had stayed in the hospital in New York, it would have happened, his dying, and somehow she would have learned about it. No. Stand on two feet and tell her you had her mixed up with someone who happened nineteen years ago.

No pity. Didn't want that. Perhaps by that time, back in New York, he would have had it, and taken to the winds to watch her and try to comfort her when she cried. She would cry. He would have—you *are* drunk, he told himself, signaling for another drink.

The first time in his life he had ever had Pernod was in a bedbug-ridden flat in the East Village[7] between Christmas and New Year's. The East Village was just the East Side then. He had drunk it straight and had crossed

6. One of the first settlements in Virginia; the first "cargo" of African slaves arrived in Jamestown aboard a Dutch ship in 1619. Rolfe (1585–1622),   English colonist who married Pocahontas.
7. In New York City.

the street to a party where a painter with a penchant for teen-agers was displaying portraits of rhinoceroses with the words MAU MAU [8] stitched between their legs. As far as Max knew, the painter was still doing rhinoceroses, marrying young girls or knocking them up and leaving them. When last heard from he was doing a trumpet solo in an Athens nightclub—"Saints"—which was the only number he knew, and the Greeks loved him because he was black, because he skipped and danced when he blew, and because he always reminded them of the spring festival when they put on blackface and roamed the streets drunk. There was no more screwing atop the hills in celebration of Oestra. Now the Greeks did it in bed, just like everybody else, nearly. Maybe Max hated that painter so much for so long, not because he was a phony, but because, when he went home that night from the East Village, he felt as though he had a steel-jacketed slug between his eyes. After some time at home, his phone had rung. It was the girl who had sent him fleeing into the streets to get drunk. But everything was all right, after that call. Pernod. What could he associate Scotch with? Bourbon? Gin? Cognac? Beer? There was always something.

Where *is* she? He would hate to go to her house, but he would if he had to. Maybe he shouldn't have come. Maybe he should have gone right back out to Orly and returned to the hospital in New York. Comfort at least. But he *was* here and he hadn't been any drunker than usual when he decided to come by train. There were only three places to go after Harry Ames [9] dropped dead—another section of Paris, New York or Amsterdam. Hell, he planned to go to Amsterdam anyway. Who was he shucking, himself, *now*? It really hurt to think of old Harry going like that. He should have been drunk and stroking and grinding and talking trash in some broad's ear. He always said he wanted to go like that.

Then he thought he saw her and he came half out of his chair, but it was someone else. He sat down slowly. How would it go anyway? She would be walking with that stride that made her seem even smaller, it was so long. He would call out. She would stop, for his voice would be the most familiar of all voices. Unbelievingly she would come near the table. He would not rise, merely sit there and motion to a chair with a smile on his face. (Haw! Haw! Surprise, surprise!) He would have a drink in his hand, perhaps even the one he was holding.

The stride was not the same: he fitted it into the one he remembered watching in Holland, Spain, France, Puerto Rico, St. Thomas, Manhattan, East Hampton, Vermont, Mexico . . . There was something sad about her stride now. The heels of her shoes still rapped sharply on the pavement and the face, that small face with the cheekbones riding high along the sides, was still ready for the smile, the bright, lyrical *"Daaag!"* And that wise body, curving with motion. Her hair was darker, yes, like gold left too long in the open.

"Margrit! [Lillian!] Margrit! [Lillian!] Margrit! [Lillian!]," he shouted, coming out of his chair like a shot, the pain grabbing deeply at his rectum,

8. A Kenyan revolutionary group made up mostly of the Kikuyu people. The group was dedicated to self-rule and recovering land from European colonizers.
9. Fictitious African American writer, somewhat modeled after Richard Wright.

and he was halfway across the street, all the while fighting the urge to grab himself, tear himself inside out.

And she stopped. Her mouth sprang open. Her dark blue eyes went bulging. With the deepest part of the eye he saw her start impulsively toward him, but she caught herself and stood waving as a leaf in some slight, capricious wind. He stopped too, out of pain and uncertainty; he had blown his lines again. But when he stopped she moved forward. On she came, the bright face ready to brighten even more, the stride now full, heel-rapping, confident. He stood waving, surprised at his own lack of cool, aghast at the waterfall of love he had thought dammed.

"Mox, Mox, it *is* you?" she said.

That goddamn broad A, he thought, but he said, "Yes." His arms trembled at his sides. Should he open them and put them around her? Should he simply stand and wait, then wilt when she placed hers around him? Signals. As she approached, her right hand darted out before her, thumb extended ludicrously in the air. Resigned, he took it, shook it gently and placed his left hand over hers. He led her to the table. "Please sit." It pained him to look at her figure. She wore a blue sweater which, no matter how loose it might have been, would have shown her breasts to tender and exciting advantage; they were always so white and fragile, so vulnerable. Her hips were fuller now. Time does do its work. And her swimmer's legs, big-calved and just short of being too heavily ankled, still made him itch to stroke them from top to—

He looked into Margrit's clear blue eyes. He moved his hand up her arm. Quite suddenly his eyes grew wet with remembering and even as he turned his head to fake a cough, he knew that the Pernod had helped to bring the tears on. "Whiskey," Max said to the waiter, who was watching them. Give her something quick, Max thought, before she starts remembering and runs away. Remembers the bad things.

But she was remembering some things already. She looked at him directly, head on, unblinking, without fear or remorse or pity—without, goddamn it, he thought, *anything*. But hell, he had never been able to decipher her looks, not once except when she cried. God, make me sober—no drunker. ". . . and another Pernod," he called, fingering with surprise the half-full glass already in his hand. He took a deep breath and fought down a rising pain. "How are you?" he said.

"Okay, Mox. You? Hi."

"Fine. Okay. Hi yourself."

"When did you come?"

"Today. About three hours ago."

"Are you well?"

"I—never better." He patted her hand.

"You look sick." She smiled her thanks at the waiter who placed the drinks before them.

"No. Just tired. Took the train from Paris."

"Paris? Harry died, didn't he? It was in *De Arbeiderspers* and *Het Parool* [1] and some other papers. Were you there?"

---

1. *The Watchword* (Dutch). *"De Arbeiderspers"*: *The Workers' Press* (Dutch).

Max smiled. The Europeans. The goddamn Europeans with their Black Peters and Black Madonnas and blackface celebrations. Five hundred years of guilt transposed into something like vague concern for anyone with a black skin. But Harry was loved more in Europe—and hated too—but not more than back home. There was some kind of balance here that the New York *Times* and the Chicago *Sun-Times* and the "Skibbidum Times" could never have when it came to Harry Ames. He spoke: "I was just a bit too late. We were to have drinks that day—"

"Oh, Mox, it must have been awful for you."

He felt angry. "Hell, it was all right! Harry was my friend, like a brother. But he had to go. We all have to go. He went quick. Didn't hurt at all. I'm all right. You know me."

Margrit bent her head and studied her Scotch. It was a very expensive alcohol. Genever would have been all right for her, even though in New York she had come to like Scotch. Yes, she knew. Harry's death had hurt Max. There was a time when he never admitted anything, but then, she thought, there was another time when he did. She stole a look at him. Yes, he was still handsome. He was graying evenly through his hair and moustache, but the lines in his square face had deepened, as if cut by a tired sculptor creating a hardness to offset the wide, soft eyes. But the eyes (how that soft look had deceived her!) were red, the almost amber-colored pupils diffused as though in the process of melting. He *isn't* well! she thought with a shock. "How long are you here?"

Max drank from the unfinished Pernod and then sipped from the other. "Not long. I wanted to tell you something, Margrit. Margrit, baby, I have news for you!"

His voice had risen and gone spinning loudly into space. She looked at him with cautious eyes. She knew the waiter and bartender and the customers who were coming in now were used to *Neger uitbundigheid*, Negro exuberance; they smiled at it. It was the image they had.

"What is your news, Mox?" Margrit was suddenly irritated. She and Max had spent so much time talking about images. "Is it good news? You have come all this way to tell me?" She smiled thinly. "Are you to be married?"

He rose and touched her shoulder. Automatically she lent support to his unsteady fingers. "Will you wait until I return? I have to pee." He giggled. She smiled. But as soon as he had left her, she turned to watch him. Something was the matter.

Max wavered to the men's room again. A vicious cycle. If he didn't drink, he wouldn't have to urinate. To urinate was to suffer the most intense pain. But, if he didn't drink he would have to take either the pills or the morphine tucked into the pouch of the jock strap he was wearing. He had thrown the cup away. The morphine got the pain right by the balls he thought, with a weak chuckle, but it didn't let him operate the way he had to during the day. But then the pain was growing every day. It gripped him at the most inopportune moments and left him breathless, weak, and with his eyes watering. *Jesus Christ!* he moaned, leaning against a wall which for a few seconds seemed to have vanished altogether. Did Herod[2] ever have it

---

2. King of Judea who, according to the New Testament, tried to murder Jesus by ordering the death of all children under the age of two in Bethlehem.

so bad? He pushed himself away from the wall and went into one of the stalls. Clean. At least the Dutch wouldn't give him as many germs as the French. He took out the cotton and looked at it. It was soaked through with dark red blood. Almost came through that time, he thought, and pulled a roll of fresh cotton from his pocket and tore off a piece. This he pushed gently into place. While sitting, he pulled at the jock strap and looked at the plastic five-cc syringe and at the morphine itself. He felt his breast pocket to see if the needle was still there. Not now, later. The pain subsided.

He returned to the table and without looking at her said, "Margrit, I'm sorry. Easy to say. Said it before, but believe me, I am sorry. Late, I know. Don't want anything. I can't want anything, not even you again. I just wanted to see you and say that."

"Well . . ." She wanted to say that it was all right, but she knew it wasn't and he knew it too. Then she wanted to reach across the table and slap him as hard as she could. *Sorry!* But the black Americans were all the same: they walked away from things mumbling, "Sorry." Sorry! After a moment, the bitterness ebbed. "But you look tired. Maybe you should get some rest. If you like, we can talk later [more sorry!]. Where are you staying?"

Come full circle on the Dutch, he was thinking as she spoke. He knew he was giving her answers. ("Yes, a little tired. Don't know where I'll be staying. Maybe the American. Do it up right. Last trip, Ducks, ho?")

"One more drink," he said aloud. "Then I'll get my bag and go to the hotel. If you have dinner with me. In that corner. You know." He rushed on, not wanting her to decline. "You know where we sat for four hours just watching people pass . . ."

Margrit thought, Yes, I know, I remember, I remember, and the waiters trying to rush us, and it seemed as if the sun would never come down.

". . . and maybe after dinner we can find Roger and some of the other guys. How are they doing? Do you see them often?" He paused. He didn't give a damn about Roger or the others. It was too late. "Will you, will you have dinner?"

"No more drinks then," she said.

"All right." He breathed deeply in relief.

"I will get your bag," she said.

"No you won't," he said. Then with sudden vehemence he said, "Will you *stop* doing things for me!"

Unruffled she said, "Mox, you will walk across the street to the hotel and get your room. I will touch up a bit, call a taxi and get your bag. The driver will help me and the hotel boys will help me. Give me the ticket." She held out her hand for the ticket as his hands went limply into pocket after pocket. Finally he found it. Taking it she said, "You don't look well. I am worried."

"How can you be worried?"

She hunched her shoulders. "I just am. Please go."

"All right, Maggie." He sucked in his breath quickly. The pain. She was right. Let her get the goddamn bag. Get to the hotel. Fast! Get off your feet. Take a pill.

"What is it?" she asked.

"A belch. I had to belch."

"Happy New Year, then."

"Thanks. Shall we go now?"

He paid the waiter and they left. "It will not be long," she said.

"All right. Maggie?"

"What?"

"I am truly sorry."

"Shut up, Mox," she said, not unpleasantly. "I will not be long."

He wondered if her apartment was the same. It overlooked one of the canals, had high ceilings and dark musty hallways. And cats. One was a striped, swollen brown that padded softly about the rooms. The other was a sleek young black with a triangle of white on the face, a female. He had watched them lick each other's backs and play, but there had been no catting between them, only with the other cats that gathered on the rooftops at night. Max wondered if the walls were still thick with the paintings of friends, or if the bedroom was the same, with the windows to the east so that as soon as the sun took a notion to rise, *whop!* daylight in the room. And in that room, he thought, discovering without surprise that he had the key to his hotel room in his hand and that he was following the bellman, she would be touching herself up a bit.

Suddenly he wanted to listen to someone else's rhythms; his own were sonorous, too labored. He paused. There was something he wanted, something . . . Ah, a paper. He had just picked up the *Tribune* when he saw, out of the corner of his eye, another Negro. How the eye catches color in a country where there is so little! Or how that same eye catches no color—an albino in Africa—where color abounds. Kiss my ass, Max thought, drawing back without knowing why, Alfonse Edwards.

2

AMSTERDAM

[MEMORIES, MARGRIT, MORPHINE]

He sat waist-deep in the lukewarm water of his bath and watched it turn slowly from a clear to pinkish color. He could hear the trams ringing their bells as they pulled off from the stop in front of the hotel. Why, he wondered, couldn't Alfonse Edwards be in Amsterdam too? What instinct (Negroes not only had that good old natural rhythm, but instinct too) had made him draw back? True, he had *not* liked Edwards from the first, from Nigeria. Even less since he had been with Harry when Harry died.

Edwards had told it like this:

He and Harry were walking out of Rue de Berri and paused at the corner waiting for a traffic light to change. Harry had gone down just like an FFI caught in the crossfire of snipers. Max imagined that crowds gathered and someone finally recognized that dark round face, the bitterness on it suddenly replaced by surprise, and shouted, *"Le M'sieu Ames, le romancier américain."*[3]

3. Mr. Ames, the American novelist (French).

"Boom, like that," Edwards had said in Paris, his lean face suggesting rather than actually possessing sorrow. Max remembered that even then he wondered just why Harry would bother with a type like that. He must have been getting senile. Edwards was a black Ivy Leaguer. Close-cropped hair, for he *wanted* Europeans to know that he was American. The other Negroes let their hair grow long and bushy—nappy—in order to be mistaken for Africans. Not Edwards. American all the way. Red white and black.

So, anyway, there was Harry down in the street at the corner where the Rue de Berri runs into the Champs-Elysées, with the Arc de Triomphe humped up through the noon haze. Harry was down and didn't get up and later there was Edwards describing his death: "Boom, like that," and Max also thought then, These hippies, Ivy League or Watermelon League, they never learn. English is limiting but it's all we know well, and there are times and places when it should be used, such as when describing how Harry died. Harry would never die "Boom, like that."

Why not? Because he was too goddamned evil. And why else not? Because.

Max had taken the morphine as much for the shock of Harry's death as for the pain. He stood at the rear of the small, hastily assembled crowd within the walls of Cimetière du Montparnasse. Edwards was there. Charlotte, Harry's wife was there, a few Americans, like Iris Stapleton of the nightclubs, painters and writers. There were some Africans, a few Indians. And it was only twenty hours after Harry had died. Very few of them had been summoned by Charlotte. The papers had announced his death, and they had come unbidden. Max stood there drunk with the drug, sick with pain and shock, and suddenly he noticed that Michelle Bouilloux, even more isolated from the small crowd than himself, was staring at him. He *thought* she was staring. Max turned back to listen once more to the eulogies. When he turned again to Michelle, he let his eyes roam; her husband wasn't there. She seemed to have moved closer to him, and now he knew she was staring from under her veil. And she was doing something with her hands, he couldn't tell what, because she was wearing black gloves and moving her hands against the background of a black suit. Then she took off one glove and one startlingly white hand showed, and one of its fingers curled back and forth at him. Her eyes seemed to come through the veil. Max thought, Ah, Michelle, Michelle, he's dead. The eulogies were over. The crowd started to break up. Michelle threw one glance at Charlotte, who even now was approaching Max, snatched up her veil displaying a glint of red hair, pointed fiercely to herself, then stumbled toward the gate. "Please join us, Max," Charlotte said. Alfonse Edwards was standing at her shoulder.

"No," Max said. He had seen enough men cremated in tanks, the bodies curling and snapping and frying in their own juices. He wasn't going to sit in anybody's anteroom and wait for Harry to be cooked down to ashes. "But why?" he croaked as the others, not invited to wait for the Harry-fry, gathered behind her and Edwards. "Why couldn't you let him lay around a little while so people could come and look at him. He'd like that."

"Oh, Max, shut up," Charlotte said, turning from him. Edwards paused before turning, and there was nothing in his look and yet everything. "To hell with you too," Max said and left, caught a taxi, picked up his bag and took the train to Amsterdam.

Why else not? Michelle Bouilloux. He glanced at his watch. M. Bouilloux would be home now. Maybe not. Maybe he hadn't seen her at the funeral at all. Hell, he wasn't sure of anything anymore except that he had a great, raging pain in the ass. And then, having thought of Charlotte, he admitted to himself for the first time that he had hated the hell out of her ever since he had known her. She had run Harry out of one marriage and into another with her. She understood, she had said. But it faded, of course, that understanding. She demanded more and more time from the great man (and he had had times of greatness, but America pretended not to see them, and Harry *wanted* America to acknowledge his greatness. But America had said in essence: *We may study you in freshman English anthologies, and if we ever arrive at the point where we show our fear or admit that we are guilty and ignore that guilt, we will study you first, Harry Ames!*). Charlotte had been a pain in the ass (Ho! Ho!). Always when things were rough, she made a point of reminding Harry how much she had given up to marry him: family, friends, a whole culture. And Harry had always countered by saying, "Tough titty. You can go. I didn't want you because you're white. Go." But Charlotte never went. She stayed and sulked, and sulked even more when things were going well. She was, after all, a mediocre person when it came to dealing with the things Harry juggled with ease: history, politics, economics, people. Charlotte could only deal with herself. When had sulking turned to hatred?

Michelle. No, long before Michelle. Max looked at his watch again. He would call her. He placed the call and lay back. Great pills, absolutely fantastic pills. Margrit would be coming soon, too. Not too soon. She would give him a chance to rest a little. Damn her anyway. When the phone rang he said, "Max. Michelle?"

"Yes. How is Margrit?"

God*damn* these women, he thought. "All right. We are having dinner in a little while. Listen," he said speaking carefully, "I have not been well. It is nothing serious. But did I imagine that you were signaling me at the funeral?"

"Yes, I would see you. It is most urgent. It is about Harry."

Max mashed out his cigarette.

"It is about Harry," she said again.

"What, what about Harry?" Then he said, "Edwards?"

"Tonight by express, I will come to Rotterdam. From there the other train to Leiden. Will you meet me tomorrow?"

"What address?"

She gave him the address and quickly rang off. Max lay back once more and closed his eyes. What in the hell was going on? Why didn't he leave well enough alone. Harry wasn't going to revert to flesh and blood. Charlotte. I bet she enjoyed thinking about him cooking and curling behind that wall. Got her kicks every stinking minute it took.

Margrit. Even if he wanted Margrit back he couldn't have her. Maybe it was good it went the way it did. He would have hated to have her around now, twenty-four hours a day, shuttling between the house and the hospital, doing with a smile the tasks that every nurse he'd had frowned at.

He had dressed and was dozing on the bed when Margrit called from the lobby. He felt better and smiled as he straightened his tie. The old Margrit would have walked briskly through the lobby, taken the lift and come up to the room and talked while he dressed. And he would not have dressed until afterward.

He took a deep breath, patted his things into place and went downstairs. She had said she would be at the table. "What table?" he had almost asked, but he remembered in time. *The* table, of course.

She smiled up at him. "You got your bag all right, I see."

"Sure," he said, sliding over the seat to the window side. What was she talking about? Of course he had his bag. Then he remembered. When had he slept? When he woke he went directly to his bag, opened it, took out a fresh shirt and underwear. He hadn't even remembered that when he entered the room he had been without his bag. Jesus, he thought, Jesus Christ. "Drink?" he said.

"Yes, of course."

He smiled and looked across the street at the side entrances of the Stads-schouwburg[4] and thought once again that Amsterdam was the one city he could have lived in other than New York. Idly he watched a Surinamer[5] saunter down the street, past their window. Traffic was much thinner now, not so many bicycles, not so many cars; there were many people walking. "It remains constant, doesn't it?"

Margrit turned to the window—she had been looking at him. "The same, you mean? Yes, nearly so."

"Fantastic place." He marveled as they sipped their drinks, how in Amsterdam, except when you headed a little south, all that was new had been built around the old, had not overwhelmed the narrow, steeply gabled houses, nor the canals. Suddenly, he wished he were younger and starting all over again.

"What is the matter, Mox?"

"Nothing, Margrit. Hi. It's good to see you again. Why haven't you married some lucky Dutchman?"

"I haven't been waiting for you," she said.

"I didn't want you to. I didn't think you would."

"And you, Mox, who do you see now?"

"I'm kind of a fugitive."

"Fugi—"

"I'm not seeing anyone."

"Oh. Oh, I don't believe that, Mox."

He laughed. The pill and the liquor were making him high very fast. "I didn't think you would, but it is the truth."

She snorted. "You have had an amputation then."

---

4. The town theater (Dutch).
5. A person from the South American country of Surinam (formerly known as Dutch Guiana).

"Yes." He glanced around the huge dining room. The tables and chairs were a rich, warm brown, the white tablecloths crisp and stiff. An elderly man was sitting at the reading table, poring over the papers from the racks.

"You are with the same magazine, Mox?"

He looked up quickly. He had forgotten that too. "No," he said.

"What are you doing?"

He looked at her with exasperation, then remembered that she wasn't his wife anymore, and that he had no right to be exasperated with her. But she had seen the look. "Or shouldn't I ask?"

"I've taken a leave," he said. "Tired."

"Yes," she said, turning once again to the window, her hair trailing a soft gold, "you were always tired, Mox."

Max signaled the waiter for more drinks. He supposed he was always tired. Bored, that's what brought it on, bored with all of it, the predictability of wars, the behavior of statesmen, cabdrivers, most men, most women. Bored because writing books had become, finally, unexciting; bored because The Magazine too, and all the people connected with it, did their work and lived by formulae. He was bored with New Deals and Square Deals and New Frontiers and Great Societies; suspicious of the future, untrusting of the past. He was sure of one thing: that he was; that he existed. The pain in his ass told him so.

"I guess I was always tired. Tired when I was born, maybe."

"That's what you always said."

"See? Nothing new. How's Roger?"

"Roger? Roger is still Roger, what else?"

"Still macking[6] in his own intellectual way?"

"Still what—?"

"Macking. Macking. Oh, Margrit, you know what macking is."

"But no, I don't."

"We talked about it," he insisted. Shut your mouth, he told himself.

"No, we didn't."

"Okay, okay. Roger's still the same, that means he's macking."

"Have it your way."

"Thanks."

Roger was not an ordinary macker; he gave a little more than most Negroes in Europe who were thus engaged between books or articles or showings or jazz engagements. Roger gave his women laughs and little peeks at Kafka, Mann, Wright, Jami of Samarkand, the suppressed Books of Enoch; and he talked in ringing poetic tones of Wardell Gray, Bird, Pres; of Fats Navarro and the early Miles, and then, shifting pace, breaking it down into a long, smooth lope, he would go into Kant, Kierkegaard, Spinoza and Walter Van Tilburg Clark's[7] philosophical handling of *The Ox-bow Incident*; he studied Hausa and Swahili and planned to get into Yoruba, Ga and Ibo[8]—oh, Max remembered, Roger macked with finesse. After all this, *then* he would get the money from a Parisienne, a stacked female Swede or Dane or Hollander, and for dessert, he would climb

---

6. Exploiting or pimping women.   8. African languages.
7. Famous authors, musicians, and philosophers.

aboard, down periscope and sail that sub. Roger worked at macking. He gave something Mack the Knife never had time for. The others, the pussy carried them away. They could be starving, but the pussy came first. Always the pussy.

They ordered dinner. It was after nine and the night was descending slowly. Midway through, she said, "Do you want to see him?"

"See who?"

"Roger." She hated it when he was this way, his mind slipping from one thing to another so quickly that she could never follow it. She had noticed that he had ordered chopped sirloin well done, the vegetables well cooked and creamed potatoes. Not unusual, only the way he kept jabbing his fork into the food to see just how well done it was.

"Yes. And tell me, do you know a guy, Negro, named Alfonse Edwards?"

"Sure."

Max's gorge rose. What does *that* mean, he asked silently, *Sure.*

"What's his hype now? I mean is he really writing, or has he become a painter or a sculptor or a tourist?"

Margrit was on her third drink and she broke into laughter. "Tourist," she echoed. "Tourist."

"Yeah, so what's he really do?" You can get out of New York, Max thought, but you couldn't get New York out of you; you felt better knowing where a guy's pigeonhole is.

"I tell you they say he is a writer."

Max sagged in his seat then. For the moment he was feeling so good that he wondered if the doctor wasn't wrong. Then he remembered the long session in the doctor's office after the first biopsy. That long session while Margrit was working happily in the gallery in New York. Anyway, he felt good. But they were talking of Edwards. What in the world would he be doing in Holland? Writing? Who, Edwards? He hadn't talked to him about writing in Paris. Why not? When Harry was too busy to talk writing, they turned to him—Max. The younger fellows remembered that once Max had been considered better than Harry, a fact that made Harry sullen for over two years. They turned to Max when Harry was addressing the various Pan-African[9] conferences or busy at something else. *That* was one of the odd things: Edwards had not in any way explained himself lately. A hipster would, somehow, with a casual turn of phrase, a word, a couple of words dropped here or there, let you pick up the pieces and complete your puzzle. A hipster knew how to play the game. No one came up to you and said, My name is Rinky-Dink and I'm a landscape artist. Anybody hip, they dropped signals and you got them. Most of the world went that way.

"What's he written?"

"They say he's working on a couple of novels, and he does articles."

"Yeah?"

"Yes."

Okay, he thought. Edwards a writer? I know what he *was*, but is he now? Max went on thinking. No, with his background he isn't just sitting around

9. A movement that originated at the end of the 18th century with the creation of black states such as Sierra Leone (1787) and Haiti (1804); its pri-   mary goal was to unify Africa for Africans and all identifiable descendants.

Europe starving between books and articles waiting for race riots to break out in the States so he can interpret them for the European press. How long until the next race riot? Edwards in Nigeria, Edwards in Europe.

Dessert, coffee and cognac, and then Margrit asked, pushing back the silence that had fallen, "What is the matter, Mox? Won't you tell me?"

He glanced up, tempted to ask her to go with him tomorrow to meet Michelle in case it became too hard for him. They'd gotten along well, the two of them. But then he thought, To hell with her. I'll go alone. He'd rent a car; it would be better than a train. He could stop and pull over and lie down if he had to. He could change the cotton if it felt too messy. It would be awkward on a train—he remembered the trip from Paris—and worse on a bus. "I told you," he said. "I'm tired."

"There is more than that this time. You won't tell me?"

"No."

"Is it bad?"

"Maggie, it was bad when I was born."

"You mean born black?"

"If you choose."

Margrit said, "Somehow, this conversation sounds like so many we had when we were together."

Max laughed and took her hand. "It does, doesn't it? Ah, Margrit. It's all a bit too much for old Max. Tell me now about Edwards. Does he come up here often? Has Roger cleared him of being a U.S. Government fink? Roger has a nose for that, you know. And Edwards did work for the government in Nigeria."

"They all say he does not work for your government any more, but they don't like him. He starts trouble. He picks fights for nothing. No one likes him. The tables become quiet on the Leidseplein when he is in town. I don't know who his friends are. Roger talks to him sometimes."

"Did he ever talk about Harry Ames?"

"Not to me, and I don't know anyone who ever mentioned his talking about Harry. What is it, Mox? What is going on?"

He said, "I don't know," and looked down at her hand. White, beginning to wrinkle, the wedding band on the right hand. He looked at the hand and pressed it. He too was wondering what was going on. Little pieces sometimes fell into place with a bang. Her voice drifted with a question. He answered it. She spoke again and he answered, but he was back in Paris, his very first time there, on leave from the *Century* and the Korean War was three years old.

He had been working, as usual. (Third novel, fourth novel?) From time to time he paused and looked out on the Paris rooftops, a hodgepodge of color against the blue summer sky. The phone rang. Harry.

"Hey, man, listen. Get right over here, can you? Tell you what's going on: just got a call from Senator Braden's number-one boy. That's right. Is he a faggot, do you know? Anyway, he's coming over to talk about some of my opinions I've put out over coffee at the cafe. He sounded real ominous, you know? After that business with that rotten magazine. I don't want to talk to nobody unless I got a witness. Make a million dollars that way.

Come on over and listen to some of this shit. Goddamn Government won't let me alone, I tell you, Max, a man with pen and paper is dangerous, but don't let him be black too—that's a hundred times worse. Make it in fifteen? Go, Max. See you."

When Max arrived, Harry was rubbing his hands in glee. "Those people really think they're pretty sharp. They can scare the pants off the whole of the United States, but they can't scare Harry Ames. Shit, I come from Mississippi; the rest of America can't begin to compare to the crackers they make down there. Where shall I put you? Sure wish that tape recorder was working. All this Philips stuff they got here in Europe, I don't know, man. Don't like General Electric and can't stand Westinghouse, but they gotta have something. Take that Calvados[1] and get behind that closet curtain. That's it. Wait. That Calvados stinks. Oh, hell, take the Scotch, but don't drink too much of it, you bastard. No! Not like that! Max, don't be such a goddamn clown. You drink all that Scotch and Charlotte's going to pitch a bitch . . ."

Sipping the Scotch, Max had peeked out at Michael Sheldon. He was a handsome young man, polite, sure of himself. Max saw Harry's eyes glittering with false cheeriness; Harry behaved just as a shark must behave when it has come across a choice morsel.

"In foreign countries, particularly those with strong attractions to communism," Sheldon began, "we'd like all Americans to be careful in their criticisms. Now, you, Mr. Ames, have been rather harsh on us."

"I have?" Harry asked innocently. "I don't remember. Do you have an example?"

Sheldon pulled some cards from his pocket. "This is one of your quotes: 'Senator Braden's Committee has driven Americans into the far corners of fear.' Another: 'America ought to try communism, just once.' "

Harry said, "On the second one, I thought I said, if everything else fails, America ought to try communism of some kind because capitalism, hand in hand with the American dream, just doesn't work; there are too many people deprived of their rights to vote and to work. That's what I said."

"But there were others," Sheldon said, and he read them back with measured, self-confident cadence. The phrases sounded familiar to Max. Who at the cafe would turn Harry's words over to the U.S. Government?

"What do you want me to do?" Harry was asking.

"We'd appreciate it if you weren't so critical. Publicly. You're only hurting yourself. The alternative is trouble, pure and simple." Sheldon smiled. The Senator's assistant reminded Max of every upper echelon vice-squad cop he'd ever seen. The face was regular, the hair combed just right, the shoes were shined and he wore a dark blue suit, of course.

"No," Harry said. "I plead freedom of speech. I'll speak my mind wherever I am and whenever I choose to. We're in France now, not America."

Sheldon stood up. "Your mouth, Ames, can be made to stay shut."

Harry taunted, "L'il ol' white boy."

"That's your whole problem, this race thing."

"L'il ol' white boy."

1. A French apple brandy.

"Bolton Warren thought he was pretty tough, too, but we got him down to Washington. He took the stand but he didn't say too much. We adjourned, took him to another room, read him the material in his dossier, and he hasn't stopped talking to us yet."

Max waited while Harry roved through the past with Warren. Warren had gone to Spain to be in the Brigades[2] and had had heavy flirtations with the Party,[3] but who the hell hadn't?

"Are you threatening me, Sheldon?"

"In the name of Senator Braden's Committee, I warn you that your passport may be revoked if you continue the way you are."

"That's what is going to happen if I don't stop my coffeehouse chatterings?"

Sheldon smiled and widened his stance. "Look at it like this, Ames. My visit can be official or unofficial. I was passing through Paris anyway. It's up to you. But remember your former affiliations with the Party; remember your affairs with several white ladies of some reputation before you left America. Further, don't count on the French so much. They are becoming less and less enchanted with you. A word to the wise should be sufficient. The French, for all their slogans, are becoming modern. Liberty, yes; equality, yes, of a sort; fraternity—with their women—highly questionable."

A cherubic smile spread slowly over Harry's face. "You'd reveal all my sordid affairs, would you?"

"Only if we had to and only to the right people."

"Gee," Harry said, and Max recognized the word as the prelude to the ultimate put-on. "I wonder if you'd do me a favor. You've really got me by the balls, Sheldon. You know Max Reddick, the *other* American Negro writer? Let's face it, Warren's over the hill, so that leaves Max the *other* Negro writer, right? Copacetic as we used to say. Anyway, look there in that closet will you, behind the curtain?" Sheldon did not move. "Max is behind that curtain, you bastard, and he's heard every word you said. In fact, he has taped them and taken them down in shorthand. Didn't know Max knew shorthand, did you? Well, he's one of them bright colored folks. Max!"

Hastily Max had set down the bottle of Scotch and sauntered through the curtain. "Hiya, Sheldon, what's new?"

Sheldon had left quickly and angrily, threatening to destroy them both if ever they stepped foot in the States again. They had laughed for fifteen minutes until Harry remembered to look at the Scotch. When he did, he cried, "Max, you greedy sonofabitch, I'm gonna catch hell! There's nothing left in the budget for Scotch for a whole month! You bastard, oh, you rotten black bastard! Did you see the look on that boy's face? Skin me, man, *skin* me!" And they had smacked palms ringingly.

It wasn't funny later. Later, Max and Harry reasoned that if Michael Sheldon was interested, someone else was too, the fink at the cafe. So, it had all started with a U.S. Government agency and worked its way down to Braden and his committee. And the Spanish Government managed to let Harry know that it wasn't at all happy about the series of articles he had

2. I.e., to fight in the Spanish Civil War.   3. I.e., the Communist Party.

written on the Franco[4] regime. A number of West Africans had started to cut Harry dead because of what he said about them. And generally, the Communists of Europe distrusted him. After all, he had quit the American Communist Party. Harry wrote about all of them; he talked about them. He danced barefoot on a hot stove lid, but no one knew it then.

Max and Margrit were walking now along the Singel.[5] His pace was slow and Margrit had slowed to match it. There were no flowers out that time of night. He was tiring and he had to get up early, but now they were going to see Roger. The pain was coming again in long, stomach-turning spasms.

"We'll take a cab back from Roger's," Max threw in. He watched Margrit nod. "Isn't your boyfriend going to be a little upset with you tonight?"

"Yes," she said, "he is, but he will understand."

"Oh, yeah," he said, thinking to himself with humor, You bitch, Margrit.

3

[PICTURE OF THE WRITER]

When Roger Wilkinson opened his door, to Max Reddick he was the picture of the writer as a failure. Max pushed Margrit forward into a dingy flat, and he shook hands with Roger who seemed both surprised and embarrassed by the unannounced visit.

But Roger broke into a smile and said, "Sit down, you folks, if you can find a chair. You lookin' pretty tired, Max. You been down to Paris? For the funeral? Yeah?" He was rustling through some bottles. "Ain't got much here. A little beer, some Genever." Roger smiled through his reddish beard. "How'd you find me? You see I've moved." He'd always left his places of residence a mystery. "I'm into my thing," he would explain, and vanish, and in Europe, the black artists went along with your wish to be left alone, most of the time. Until you started to make it, then they came back to bug you back into failure. "You should have let me know you were coming," Roger said.

"Ah, well," Max said, accepting a beer. "What's new?"

Roger cleared his throat loudly and glanced around the room. "You know, man, the same old thing. Trying to make it, you know."

Max nodded. Roger had been in Europe a long time. He had written three novels, which he had been unable to sell. Roger was wound up in himself, Max had concluded. Roger for Roger.

"Articles?" Max asked. Roger was one of those writers who, whenever race riots broke out back home, was summoned hastily by the local magazine or newspaper editors to explain what was going on. *"Le célèbre écrivain noir américain Roger Wilkinson explique pourquoi les noirs des Etats Unis[6] . . ."* With a photo of Roger bearded and pensive, *artistic*, surveying the accompanying three-column picture of rioters.

---

4. Francisco Franco (1892–1975), soldier, politician, and leader of the rebel forces that defeated the Republicans in the Spanish Civil War (1936–39); dictator of Spain from 1939 to 1975.
5. Canal, boulevard, promenade, or avenue

(Dutch).
6. The celebrated black American writer Roger Wilkinson explains why the blacks in the United States . . . (French).

"Well, they keep me in bread. But here in Holland, man, getting money out of Hans Brinker is like forcing your way into Fort Knox. They tight with the change, man. Tight."

"Yeah-yeah," Max said. He had known Roger back in the States. Then Roger had come to Europe. To be free. He'd returned to New York briefly then back to Europe for good. He knew all the European capitals, having lived in them at one time or another, until he settled in Amsterdam. He would have preferred Scandinavia; the women were the most handsome in Europe. But it was too cold.

"Listen," Max said. "I'm not in town for long. Just came up to see Margrit. Have to get back home."

"You're not going to stay a while, Max? What a drag, man. Really."

"Yeah. Do you know Alfonse Edwards?"

Roger feigned drawing away from an unwholesome object. "*That* cat! Well, yes and well, no. I mean I'm not up tight with him; no one is. I see him around when he's in town. That's about all."

"Do you know where he's staying?"

"I hear he's in a hotel. What's happening, Max?"

"I don't know. Margrit tells me he's writing."

Roger drew a dirty fingernail through his beard. His hair was very thick, but no one would mistake him for an African; his complexion was too light. "I *guess* he writes. I've *heard* that he writes. He loads up a car with articles and drives around Europe selling them to papers and magazines. You know, crap all *pre*pared, and about half of it plagiarized. I mean, these people over here just don't know."

"Does he make it, like that?"

"He must. Always wearing some boss shit and got some fine fox on his arm. He *must* be making it."

"Yeah," Max said.

"—and he eats very well," Roger added.

"Is he a fink?"

"A fink. No, man, he's just got his hype going and it's working. If the government planted a fink, wouldn't they make him to be one of the boys, you know, not sharp, an artist, starving, trying to get all the pussy he can. Now, Edwards, he's just a little bit away from everybody. Uncle Sam don't work that way. In the middle, right in the middle."

Margrit was watching Max. What is the matter with him, she wondered. The hand with which he was holding the beer glass trembled suddenly, and Max casually lowered it to the table. But Margrit had seen it. She wished she could be glad he was ill, but she could not; she had got over the past and had even been pleased to see him again. She never thought she would be. She was still attracted to him; the mystery that seemed to be him when they first met to a substantial extent was still there. Perhaps in a way the reason for that *was* because of that big, ponderously walking Negro who led a column of liberating black Americans through the streets of Groningen.[7] Groningen was a city you left just as soon as you realized that the

---

7. In northeastern Netherlands.

people in it were more German than Dutch. He had walked, Margrit remembered, with a wide step, and there was a grin on his face and chocolate bars were sticking out from his pockets. She had broken loose from her parents and, with a group of other small children who waved the tiny American flags their parents had kept hidden, had raced into the street. The big black man picked her up and laughed, gave her candy and put her down again. Max had said, once when she talked about that day, "Well, the world starts whirling for different people for different reasons and at different times. I'll thank that guy if I ever see him."

"More beer?" Roger asked. "Man, I'm really sorry I didn't know you were coming. We coulda turned one on."

"Your first book, we'll turn one one. You'll be coming home then, I guess?"

"Yeah, I guess it would be time enough then."

Max thought back to when he had ever thought to quit writing. All the time. Roger never thought about it and should have quit a long time ago. After a while, Max thought, all the talk of writing, all the advice, is nothing if you haven't got it yourself. With Harry, they seldom talked about writing or even other writers. That was mostly because they were always talking about women or The Problem at home. It was also because Harry was secretive with his French and British and American writer friends if they were the good ones. Max never knew just who they were; they would show up at a party, and by the way Harry talked with them Max would know that they had been friends for a long time. Harry didn't really like to share things. Like Roger, still looking very young, but starting to age in a strange, distant sort of way, didn't like to share himself either. And chances were, Max mused, that Roger did have a bottle tucked back somewhere, for a very special piece of ass that he had to impress. He didn't bring the bottle out because he had to have his revenge for the invasion of his privacy. In that privacy, Max knew, he was picking dried snot out of his nose, rubbing it into his pants and thinking hard thoughts on a world that refused to read his works. Mostly, he was feeling sorry for himself, whether as a Negro or a writer, Max didn't know. As a Negro, he hadn't suffered, hadn't Armied in the South, hadn't been hungry, and he had never gone south of Manhattan. Roger's Negro anger was ersatz; ersatz, but useful. If he hadn't been Negro, he would have had no reason on earth to raise his voice, or to want to write.

"Listen," Roger was saying. "Shall we look for Edwards' hotel?"

Max spun the glass between his thumb and forefinger. "Maybe tomorrow."

"But I thought you were leaving, like, *zap!*"

"I have to take care of a few things first. Tomorrow morning I've got something to do and then we'll see."

"Where you staying?" Roger asked, sliding his eyes toward Margrit.

"The American," Max said, rising, catching pain midway up, but shuffling in his step so they wouldn't see.

"That's boss," Roger said. His smile was twisted. "One of these days, baby, one of these days."

"Got to stay with it," Max mumbled.

"See you tomorrow? We can have a taste on the Plein. I'll stop by the hotel, okay?"

"Well, yeah, okay, maybe late in the afternoon." Max started through the door after Margrit, then paused. "None of my business. But I talk to your father pretty often. Scribble a note so I can take it back with me. Something?"

Roger's face became blank, then stiff. He shook his head. Max knew that talk of Roger's father, for some reason, was off limits. "No, man, nothing."

"Okay, Roger," Max said. He reached into his wallet. This cat was just too much. Max thought of all the time he'd wasted with Roger. He found the check. "Catch, baby, he sent you a few bills. With love." Max swung his arm in a soft arc and the check tumbled up out of his hand, twisted once or twice and started its green and white descent to the floor. "He's very sick," Max said, watching the check and Roger's face at the same time. "He doesn't think you're a writer at all. He thinks you're pretending; he thinks you're afraid to go home and take your lumps with the rest of the spades." Roger's hand was snapping at the check now. "Don't call me at the hotel, Roger, I'll call *you*."

"Hey, man," Roger was saying as Max closed the door after him; his last view was that of Roger scrambling around on the floor for the check.

"You were hard on him," Margrit said, holding his arm.

"Screw 'im. Christ, why did I have to wait until now to start telling people the way they are? Look, a cab. I don't feel like walking."

"All right."

They passed a herring stand. Max stopped. "Shall we have eel or the green herring?"

"Whichever you want, Mox."

He shook his head. "Neither." They walked to the cabs parked beneath the trees. They were just down the street from the Anna Frank House,[8] and that part of Amsterdam always did strange things to him; it made him sad and it made him angry. It also made him aware of what so easily could be at home.

"Mox, why are you so thin?"

The cab rolled easily over the cobblestones; it passed the couples lingering over the edges of the canals. Max suddenly felt frightened. There would be a billion other nights in Amsterdam as soft as this one, filled with the odor of sea and old bricks and tarred wood pilings; and there would be the smell of food, drifting gently down upon the street from those Vermeer[9] kitchens; there would be young men and young women, unjaded as yet, talking about loving one another.

I don't want to miss it! Max thought, I don't want to miss any of it! I want to live forever and ever and ever and ever . . .

"Mox . . ."

"Oh! That last trip to Africa, I guess. It was kind of rough."

"Thanks for the card." They were at her house now. The cab had

---

8. The house in Amsterdam in which Anne Frank (1929–1945), a Jew, and her family hid during the Nazi occupation. She died in a concentration camp, but her diary survived and was published in 1947.

9. Jan Vermeer (1632–1675), Dutch painter noted for interior genre scenes.

stopped. Margrit got out. For a second she waited, then she knew that Max was going on to the hotel. She spoke to the driver in Dutch. "I will see you tomorrow?"

"In the afternoon, Maggie. Shall I meet you in the hotel?"

"What is wrong with the morning?"

"You have to work."

"I would take it off."

"I have something to do. In Leiden."

"Do you want me to go with you?"

She was bending, peering into the cab, and Max could smell her perfume.

"Thanks, no. Business."

"Good night, Mox."

"Good night, Maggie."

She closed the door. "American," Max said, and slumped back in the seat, his eyes half closed. The driver nodded. "She telled," he said.

"Okay," Max said. "Fine."

1967

MARTIN LUTHER KING JR.

1929–1968

Martin Luther King's *Letter from Birmingham Jail* was written in 1963 while King was serving a jail sentence for participating in demonstrations in Birmingham, Alabama. The eloquent testimony was in large part a response to eight white "liberal" Alabama clergymen who had collectively drafted an open letter early in 1963 that addressed King's particular engagement in the civil rights movement. They entreated with King to limit his battle for integration to local and federal courts and cautioned him that his peaceful/pacifist resistance could serve to incite further civil disturbance and rioting. Dr. King wanted to suggest to such critics that a Christianity that in any way sanctioned racial oppression and prejudice was morally bankrupt and that the demands of the gospel transcended the social mores of the South.

The title of the piece (which was written on scraps of paper provided to King by the jail's black trustees) was chosen to evoke the memory of the apostle Paul, who was jailed many times for the sake of Jesus. In 1956, Dr. King had preached a sermon entitled "Paul's Letter to American Christians." The sermon contained most of the points found in his own *Letter*, including the central tenet that segregation contradicted America's democratic faith and religious heritage.

Letter from Birmingham Jail was instrumental in galvanizing U.S. public opinion around issues of black civil rights. King himself believed that it was indispensable in helping him and others to conceptualize the 1963 March on Washington and that it influenced the legislation that allowed the 1963 Civil Rights Bill to come into being. The letter was widely circulated by the national and international media; not surprisingly, it shook the conscience of the United States.

With the publication of the *Letter from Birmingham Jail* came an enormous outpouring of support for the civil rights struggle from myriad organizations and individuals. Finances were suddenly available, and coalitions of a new type were forged. For instance, soon after absorbing the import of the letter, the leadership of the National Council of Churches urged its thirty-one member denominations to initiate "nationwide organizations against racial discrimination."

Letter from Birmingham Jail

MY DEAR FELLOW CLERGYMEN:

While confined here in the Birmingham city jail, I came across your recent statement calling my present activities "unwise and untimely." Seldom do I pause to answer criticism of my work and ideas. If I sought to answer all the criticisms that cross my desk, my secretaries would have little time for anything other than such correspondence in the course of the day, and I would have no time for constructive work. But since I feel that you are men of genuine good will and that your criticisms are sincerely set forth, I want to try to answer your statement in what I hope will be patient and reasonable terms.

I think I should indicate why I am here in Birmingham, since you have been influenced by the view which argues against "outsiders coming in." I have the honor of serving as president of the Southern Christian Leadership Conference, an organization operating in every southern state, with headquarters in Atlanta, Georgia. We have some eighty-five affiliated organizations across the South, and one of them is the Alabama Christian Movement for Human Rights. Frequently we share staff, educational, and financial resources with our affiliates. Several months ago the affiliate here in Birmingham asked us to be on call to engage in a nonviolent direct-action program if such were deemed necessary. We readily consented, and when the hour came we lived up to our promise. So I, along with several members of my staff, am here because I was invited here. I am here because I have organizational ties here.

But more basically, I am in Birmingham because injustice is here. Just as the prophets of the eighth century B.C. left their villages and carried their "thus saith the Lord" far beyond the boundaries of their home towns, and just as the Apostle Paul left his village of Tarsus and carried the gospel of Jesus Christ to the far corners of the Greco-Roman world, so am I compelled to carry the gospel of freedom beyond my own home town. Like Paul, I must constantly respond to the Macedonian call for aid.

Moreover, I am cognizant of the interrelatedness of all communities and states. I cannot sit idly by in Atlanta and not be concerned about what happens in Birmingham. Injustice anywhere is a threat to justice everywhere. We are caught in an inescapable network of mutuality, tied in a single garment of destiny. Whatever affects one directly, affects all indirectly. Never again can we afford to live with the narrow, provincial "outside agitator" idea. Anyone who lives inside the United States can never be considered an outsider anywhere within its bounds.

You deplore the demonstrations taking place in Birmingham. But your statement, I am sorry to say, fails to express a similar concern for the conditions that brought about the demonstrations. I am sure that none of you would want to rest content with the superficial kind of social analysis that deals merely with effects and does not grapple with underlying causes. It is unfortunate that demonstrations are taking place in Birmingham, but it is even more unfortunate that the city's white power structure left the Negro community with no alternative.

In any nonviolent campaign there are four basic steps: collection of the facts to determine whether injustices exist; negotiation; self-purification; and direct action. We have gone through all these steps in Birmingham. There can be no gainsaying the fact that racial injustice engulfs this community. Birmingham is probably the most thoroughly segregated city in the United States. Its ugly record of brutality is widely known. Negroes have experienced grossly unjust treatment in the courts. There have been more unsolved bombings of Negro homes and churches in Birmingham than in any other city in the nation. These are the hard, brutal facts of the case. On the basis of these conditions, Negro leaders sought to negotiate with the city fathers. But the latter consistently refused to engage in good-faith negotiation.

Then, last September, came the opportunity to talk with leaders of Birmingham's economic community. In the course of the negotiations, certain promises were made by the merchants—for example, to remove the stores' humiliating racial signs. On the basis of these promises, the Reverend Fred Shuttlesworth and the leaders of the Alabama Christian Movement for Human Rights agreed to a moratorium on all demonstrations. As the weeks and months went by, we realized that we were the victims of a broken promise. A few signs, briefly removed, returned; the others remained.

As in so many past experiences, our hopes had been blasted, and the shadow of deep disappointment settled upon us. We had no alternative except to prepare for direct action, whereby we would present our very bodies as a means of laying our case before the conscience of the local and the national community. Mindful of the difficulties involved, we decided to undertake a process of self-purification. We began a series of workshops on nonviolence, and we repeatedly asked ourselves: "Are you able to accept blows without retaliating?" "Are you able to endure the ordeal of jail?" We decided to schedule our direct-action program for the Easter season, realizing that except for Christmas, this is the main shopping period of the year. Knowing that a strong economic-withdrawal program would be the by-product of direct action, we felt that this would be the best time to bring pressure to bear on the merchants for the needed change.

Then it occurred to us that Birmingham's mayoral election was coming up in March, and we speedily decided to postpone action until after election day. When we discovered that the Commissioner of Public Safety, Eugene "Bull" Connor, had piled up enough votes to be in the run-off, we decided again to postpone action until the day after the run-off so that the demonstrations could not be used to cloud the issues. Like many others, we wanted to see Mr. Connor defeated, and to this end we endured postponement after postponement. Having aided in this community need, we felt that our direct-action program could be delayed no longer.

You may well ask, "Why direct action? Why sit-ins, marches, and so forth? Isn't negotiation a better path?" You are quite right in calling for negotiation. Indeed, this is the very purpose of direct action. Nonviolent direct action seeks to create such a crisis and foster such a tension that a community which has constantly refused to negotiate is forced to confront the issue. It seeks so to dramatize the issue that it can no longer be ignored. My citing the creation of tension as part of the work of the nonviolent-resister may sound rather shocking. But I must confess that I am not afraid of the word "tension." I have earnestly opposed violent tension, but there is a type of constructive, nonviolent tension which is necessary for growth. Just as Socrates felt that it was necessary to create a tension in the mind so that individuals could rise from the bondage of myths and half-truths to the unfettered realm of creative analysis and objective appraisal, so must we see the need for nonviolent gadflies to create the kind of tension in society that will help men rise from the dark depths of prejudice and racism to the majestic heights of understanding and brotherhood.

The purpose of our direct-action program is to create a situation so crisis-packed that it will inevitably open the door to negotiation. I therefore concur with you in your call for negotiation. Too long has our beloved Southland been bogged down in a tragic effort to live in monologue rather than dialogue.

One of the basic points in your statement is that the action that I and my associates have taken in Birmingham is untimely. Some have asked: "Why didn't you give the new city administration time to act?" The only answer that I can give to this query is that the new Birmingham administration must be prodded about as much as the outgoing one, before it will act. We are sadly mistaken if we feel that the election of Albert Boutwell as mayor will bring the millennium to Birmingham. While Mr. Boutwell is a much more gentle person than Mr. Connor, they are both segregationists, dedicated to maintenance of the status quo. I have hoped that Mr. Boutwell will be reasonable enough to see the futility of massive resistance to desegregation. But he will not see this without pressure from devotees of civil rights. My friends, I must say to you that we have not made a single gain in civil rights without determined legal and nonviolent pressure. Lamentably, it is an historical fact that privileged groups seldom give up their privileges voluntarily. Individuals may see the moral light and voluntarily give up their unjust posture; but, as Reinhold Niebuhr[1] has reminded us, groups tend to be more immoral than individuals.

We know through painful experience that freedom is never voluntarily given by the oppressor; it must be demanded by the oppressed. Frankly, I have yet to engage in a direct-action campaign that was "well timed" in the view of those who have not suffered unduly from the disease of segregation. For years now I have heard the word "Wait!" It rings in the ear of every Negro with piercing familiarity. This "Wait" has almost always meant "Never." We must come to see, with one of our distinguished jurists, that "justice too long delayed is justice denied."

We have waited for more than 340 years for our constitutional and God-given rights. The nations of Asia and Africa are moving with jetlike speed

_____
1. American Protestant theologian (1892–1971).

toward gaining political independence, but we still creep at horse-and-buggy pace toward gaining a cup of coffee at a lunch counter. Perhaps it is easy for those who have never felt the stinging darts of segregation to say, "Wait." But when you have seen vicious mobs lynch your mothers and fathers at will and drown your sisters and brothers at whim; when you have seen hate-filled policemen curse, kick, and even kill your black brothers and sisters; when you see the vast majority of your twenty million Negro brothers smothering in an airtight cage of poverty in the midst of an affluent society; when you suddenly find your tongue twisted and your speech stammering as you seek to explain to your six-year-old daughter why she can't go to the public amusement park that has just been advertised on television, and see tears welling up in her eyes when she is told that Funtown is closed to colored children, and see ominous clouds of inferiority beginning to form in her little mental sky, and see her beginning to distort her personality by developing an unconscious bitterness toward white people; when you have to concoct an answer for a five-year-old son who is asking, "Daddy, why do white people treat colored people so mean?"; when you take a cross-country drive and find it necessary to sleep night after night in the uncomfortable corners of your automobile because no motel will accept you; when you are humiliated day in and day out by nagging signs reading "white" and "colored"; when your first name becomes "nigger," your middle name becomes "boy" (however old you are) and your last name becomes "John," and your wife and mother are never given the respected title "Mrs."; when you are harried by day and haunted by night by the fact that you are a Negro, living constantly at tiptoe stance, never quite knowing what to expect next, and are plagued with inner fears and outer resentments; when you are forever fighting a degenerating sense of "nobodiness"—then you will understand why we find it difficult to wait. There comes a time when the cup of endurance runs over, and men are no longer willing to be plunged into the abyss of despair. I hope, sirs, you can understand our legitimate and unavoidable impatience.

You express a great deal of anxiety over our willingness to break laws. This is certainly a legitimate concern. Since we so diligently urge people to obey the Supreme Court's decision of 1954 outlawing segregation in the public schools, at first glance it may seem rather paradoxical for us consciously to break laws. One may well ask: "How can you advocate breaking some laws and obeying others?" The answer lies in the fact that there are two types of laws: just and unjust. I would be the first to advocate obeying just laws. One has not only a legal but a moral responsibility to obey just laws. Conversely, one has a moral responsibility to disobey unjust laws. I would agree with St. Augustine[2] that "an unjust law is no law at all."

Now, what is the difference between the two? How does one determine whether a law is just or unjust? A just law is a man-made code that squares with the moral law or the law of God. An unjust law is a code that is out of harmony with the moral law. To put it in the terms of St. Thomas Aquinas:[3] An unjust law is a human law that is not rooted in eternal law and

<hr/>

2. Early Christian church father (354–430).
3. Christian philosopher and theologian (1225–1274).

natural law. Any law that uplifts human personality is just. Any law that degrades human personality is unjust. All segregation statutes are unjust because segregation distorts the soul and damages the personality. It gives the segregator a false sense of superiority and the segregated a false sense of inferiority. Segregation, to use the terminology of the Jewish philosopher Martin Buber,[4] substitutes an "I-it" relationship for an "I-thou" relationship and ends up relegating persons to the status of things. Hence segregation is not only politically, economically, and sociologically unsound, it is morally wrong and sinful. Paul Tillich[5] has said that sin is separation. Is not segregation an existential expression of man's tragic separation, his awful estrangement, his terrible sinfulness? Thus it is that I can urge men to obey the 1954 decision of the Supreme Court, for it is morally right; and I can urge them to disobey segregation ordinances, for they are morally wrong.

Let us consider a more concrete example of just and unjust laws. An unjust law is a code that a numerical or power majority group compels a minority group to obey but does not make binding on itself. This is *difference* made legal. By the same token, a just law is a code that a majority compels a minority to follow and that it is willing to follow itself. This is *sameness* made legal.

Let me give another explanation. A law is unjust if it is inflicted on a minority that, as a result of being denied the right to vote, had no part in enacting or devising the law. Who can say that the legislature of Alabama which set up that state's segregation laws was democratically elected? Throughout Alabama all sorts of devious methods are used to prevent Negroes from becoming registered voters, and there are some counties in which, even though Negroes constitute a majority of the population, not a single Negro is registered. Can any law enacted under such circumstances be considered democratically structured?

Sometimes a law is just on its face and unjust in its application. For instance, I have been arrested on a charge of parading without a permit. Now, there is nothing wrong in having an ordinance which requires a permit for a parade. But such an ordinance becomes unjust when it is used to maintain segregation and to deny citizens the First-Amendment privilege of peaceful assembly and protest.

I hope you are able to see the distinction I am trying to point out. In no sense do I advocate evading or defying the law, as would the rabid segregationist. That would lead to anarchy. One who breaks an unjust law must do so openly, lovingly, and with a willingness to accept the penalty. I submit that an individual who breaks a law that conscience tells him is unjust, and who willingly accepts the penalty of imprisonment in order to arouse the conscience of the community over its injustice, is in reality expressing the highest respect for law.

Of course, there is nothing new about this kind of civil disobedience. It was evidenced sublimely in the refusal of Shadrach, Meshach, and Abednego to obey the laws of Nebuchadnezzar,[6] on the ground that a higher

---

moral law was at stake. It was practiced superbly by the early Christians, who were willing to face hungry lions and the excruciating pain of chopping blocks rather than submit to certain unjust laws of the Roman Empire. To a degree, academic freedom is a reality today because Socrates practiced civil disobedience.[7] In our own nation, the Boston Tea Party represented a massive act of civil disobedience.

We should never forget that everything Adolf Hitler did in Germany was "legal" and everything the Hungarian freedom fighters[8] did in Hungary was "illegal." It was "illegal" to aid and comfort a Jew in Hitler's Germany. Even so, I am sure that, had I lived in Germany at the time, I would have aided and comforted my Jewish brothers. If today I lived in a Communist country where certain principles dear to the Christian faith are suppressed, I would openly advocate disobeying that country's anti-religious laws.

I must make two honest confessions to you, my Christian and Jewish brothers. First, I must confess that over the past few years I have been gravely disappointed with the white moderate. I have almost reached the regrettable conclusion that the Negro's great stumbling block in his stride toward freedom is not the White Citizen's Counciler[9] or the Ku Klux Klanner, but the white moderate, who is more devoted to "order" than to justice; who prefers a negative peace which is the absence of tension to a positive peace which is the presence of justice; who constantly says, "I agree with you in the goal you seek, but I cannot agree with your methods of direct action"; who paternalistically believes he can set the timetable for another man's freedom; who lives by a mythical concept of time and who constantly advises the Negro to wait for a "more convenient season." Shallow understanding from people of good will is more frustrating than absolute misunderstanding from people of ill will. Lukewarm acceptance is much more bewildering than outright rejection.

I had hoped that the white moderate would understand that law and order exist for the purpose of establishing justice and that when they fail in this purpose they become the dangerously structured dams that block the flow of social progress. I had hoped that the white moderate would understand that the present tension in the South is a necessary phase of the transition from an obnoxious negative peace, in which the Negro passively accepted his unjust plight, to a substantive and positive peace, in which all men will respect the dignity and worth of human personality. Actually, we who engage in nonviolent direct action are not the creators of tension. We merely bring to the surface the hidden tension that is already alive. We bring it out in the open, where it can be seen and dealt with. Like a boil that can never be cured so long as it is covered up but must be opened with all its ugliness to the natural medicines of air and light, injustice must be exposed, with all the tension its exposure creates, to the light of human conscience and the air of national opinion, before it can be cured.

In your statement you assert that our actions, even though peaceful,

---

7. The ancient Greek philosopher Socrates was tried by the Athenians for corrupting their youth through his skeptical, questioning manner of teaching. He refused to change his ways and was condemned to death.
8. In the anti-Communist revolution of 1956,
which was quickly put down by Soviet forces.
9. That is, a member of a southern organization formed to combat the implementation of the Brown v. the Board of Education decision on the integration of schools.

must be condemned because they precipitate violence. But is this a logical assertion? Isn't this like condemning a robbed man because his possession of money precipitated the evil act of robbery? Isn't this like condemning Socrates because his unswerving commitment to truth and his philosophical inquiries precipitated the act by the misguided populace in which they made him drink hemlock? Isn't this like condemning Jesus because his unique God-consciousness and never-ceasing devotion to God's will precipitated the evil act of crucifixion? We must come to see that, as the federal courts have consistently affirmed, it is wrong to urge an individual to cease his efforts to gain his basic constitutional rights because the quest may precipitate violence. Society must protect the robbed and punish the robber.

I had also hoped that the white moderate would reject the myth concerning time in relation to the struggle for freedom. I have just received a letter from a white brother in Texas. He writes: "All Christians know that the colored people will receive equal rights eventually, but it is possible that you are in too great a religious hurry. It has taken Christianity almost two thousand years to accomplish what it has. The teachings of Christ take time to come to earth." Such an attitude stems from a tragic misconception of time, from the strangely irrational notion that there is something in the very flow of time that will inevitably cure all ills. Actually, time itself is neutral; it can be used either destructively or constructively. More and more I feel that the people of ill will have used time much more effectively than have the people of good will. We will have to repent in this generation not merely for the hateful words and actions of the bad people, but for the appalling silence of the good people. Human progress never rolls in on wheels of inevitability; it comes through the tireless efforts of men willing to be co-workers with God, and without this hard work, time itself becomes an ally of the forces of social stagnation. We must use time creatively, in the knowledge that the time is always ripe to do right. Now is the time to make real the promise of democracy and transform our pending national elegy into a creative psalm of brotherhood. Now is the time to lift our national policy from the quicksand of racial injustice to the solid rock of human dignity.

You speak of our activity in Birmingham as extreme. At first I was rather disappointed that fellow clergymen would see my nonviolent efforts as those of an extremist. I began thinking about the fact that I stand in the middle of two opposing forces in the Negro community. One is a force of complacency, made up in part of Negroes who, as a result of long years of oppression, are so drained of self-respect and a sense of "somebodiness" that they have adjusted to segregation; and in part of a few middle-class Negroes who, because of a degree of academic and economic security and because in some ways they profit by segregation, have become insensitive to the problems of the masses. The other force is one of bitterness and hatred, and it comes perilously close to advocating violence. It is expressed in the various black nationalist groups that are springing up across the nation, the largest and best-known being Elijah Muhammad's Muslim movement. [1] Nourished by the Negro's frustration over the continued existence

1. That is, the Nation of Islam.

of racial discrimination, this movement is made up of people who have lost faith in America, who have absolutely repudiated Christianity, and who have concluded that the white man is an incorrigible "devil."

I have tried to stand between these two forces, saying that we need emulate neither the "do-nothingism" of the complacent nor the hatred and despair of the black nationalist. For there is the more excellent way of love and nonviolent protest. I am grateful to God that, through the influence of the Negro church, the way of nonviolence became an integral part of our struggle.

If this philosophy had not emerged, by now many streets of the South would, I am convinced, be flowing with blood. And I am further convinced that if our white brothers dismiss as "rabblerousers" and "outside agitators" those of us who employ nonviolent direct action, and if they refuse to support our nonviolent efforts, millions of Negroes will, out of frustration and despair, seek solace and security in black-nationalist ideologies—a development that would inevitably lead to a frightening racial nightmare.

Oppressed people cannot remain oppressed forever. The yearning for freedom eventually manifests itself, and that is what has happened to the American Negro. Something within has reminded him of his birthright of freedom, and something without has reminded him that it can be gained. Consciously or unconsciously, he has been caught up by the Zeitgeist, [2] and with his black brothers of Africa and his brown and yellow brothers of Asia, South America, and the Caribbean, the United States Negro is moving with a sense of great urgency toward the promised land of racial justice. If one recognizes this vital urge that has engulfed the Negro community, one should readily understand why public demonstrations are taking place. The Negro has many pent-up resentments and latent frustrations, and he must release them. So let him march; let him make prayer pilgrimages to the city hall; let him go on freedom rides—and try to understand why he must do so. If his repressed emotions are not released in nonviolent ways, they will seek expression through violence; this is not a threat but a fact of history. So I have not said to my people, "Get rid of your discontent." Rather, I have tried to say that this normal and healthy discontent can be channeled into the creative outlet of nonviolent direct action. And now this approach is being termed extremist.

But though I was initially disappointed at being categorized as an extremist, as I continued to think about the matter I gradually gained a measure of satisfaction from the label. Was not Jesus an extremist for love: "Love your enemies, bless them that curse you, do good to them that hate you, and pray for them which despitefully use you, and persecute you." Was not Amos an extremist for justice: "Let justice roll down like waters and righteousness like an ever-flowing stream." Was not Paul an extremist for the Christian gospel: "I bear in my body the marks of the Lord Jesus." Was not Martin Luther an extremist: "Here I stand; I cannot do otherwise, so help me God." And John Bunyan: [3] "I will stay in jail to the end of my days before I make a butchery of my conscience." And Abraham Lincoln:

2. The spirit of the times.
3. English preacher and author (1628–1688); Amos was an Old Testament prophet; Paul a New

Testament apostle; Luther (1483–1546), German Protestant reformer.

"This nation cannot survive half slave and half free." And Thomas Jefferson: "We hold these truths to be self-evident, that all men are created equal. . . ." So the question is not whether we will be extremists, but what kind of extremists we will be. Will we be extremists for hate or for love? Will we be extremists for the preservation of injustice or for the extension of justice? In that dramatic scene on Calvary's hill three men were crucified. We must never forget that all three were crucified for the same crime—the crime of extremism. Two were extremists for immorality, and thus fell below their environment. The other, Jesus Christ, was an extremist for love, truth, and goodness, and thereby rose above his environment. Perhaps the South, the nation, and the world are in dire need of creative extremists.

I had hoped that the white moderate would see this need. Perhaps I was too optimistic; perhaps I expected too much. I suppose I should have realized that few members of the oppressor race can understand the deep groans and passionate yearnings of the oppressed race, and still fewer have the vision to see that injustice must be rooted out by strong, persistent, and determined action. I am thankful, however, that some of our white brothers in the South have grasped the meaning of this social revolution and committed themselves to it. They are still all too few in quantity, but they are big in quality. Some—such as Ralph McGill, Lillian Smith, Harry Golden, James McBridge Dabbs, Ann Braden, and Sarah Patton Boyle— have written about our struggle in eloquent and prophetic terms. Others have marched with us down nameless streets of the South. They have languished in filthy, roach-infested jails, suffering the abuse and brutality of policemen who view them as "dirty nigger-lovers." Unlike so many of their moderate brothers and sisters, they have recognized the urgency of the moment and sensed the need for powerful "action" antidotes to combat the disease of segregation.

Let me take note of my other major disappointment. I have been so greatly disappointed with the white church and its leadership. Of course, there are some notable exceptions. I am not unmindful of the fact that each of you has taken some significant stands on this issue. I commend you, Reverend Stallings, for your Christian stand on this past Sunday, in welcoming Negroes to your worship service on a nonsegregated basis. I commend the Catholic leaders of this state for integrating Spring Hill College several years ago.

But despite these notable exceptions, I must honestly reiterate that I have been disappointed with the church. I do not say this as one of those negative critics who can always find something wrong with the church. I say this as a minister of the gospel, who loves the church; who was nurtured in its bosom; who has been sustained by its spiritual blessings and who will remain true to it as long as the cord of life shall lengthen.

When I was suddenly catapulted into the leadership of the bus protest in Montgomery, Alabama, a few years ago,[4] I felt we would be supported by the white church. I felt that the white ministers, priests, and rabbis of the

----

4. The boycott began in December 1955, when Rosa Parks refused to move to the Negro section of a bus.

South would be among our strongest allies. Instead, some have been out-right opponents, refusing to understand the freedom movement and mis-representing its leaders; all too many others have been more cautious than courageous and have remained silent behind the anesthetizing security of stainedglass windows.

In spite of my shattered dreams, I came to Birmingham with the hope that the white religious leadership of this community would see the justice of our cause and, with deep moral concern, would serve as the channel through which our just grievances could reach the power structure. I had hoped that each of you would understand. But again I have been disap-pointed.

I have heard numerous southern religious leaders admonish their wor-shipers to comply with a desegregation decision because it is the law, but I have longed to hear white ministers declare: "Follow this decree because integration is morally right and because the Negro is your brother." In the midst of blatant injustices inflicted upon the Negro, I have watched white churchmen stand on the sideline and mouth pious irrelevancies and sanc-timonious trivialities. In the midst of a mighty struggle to rid our nation of racial and economic injustice, I have heard many ministers say: "Those are social issues, with which the gospel has no real concern." And I have watched many churches commit themselves to a completely otherworldly religion which makes a strange, un-Biblical distinction between body and soul, between the sacred and the secular.

I have traveled the length and breadth of Alabama, Mississippi, and all the other southern states. On sweltering summer days and crisp autumn mornings I have looked at the South's beautiful churches with their lofty spires pointing heavenward. I have beheld the impressive outlines of her massive religious-education buildings. Over and over I have found myself asking: "What kind of people worship here? Who is their God? Where were their voices when the lips of Governor Barnett dripped with words of interposition and nullification? Where were they when Governor Wallace gave a clarion call for defiance and hatred?[5] Where were their voices of support when bruised and weary Negro men and women decided to rise from the dark dungeons of complacency to the bright hills of creative pro-test?"

Yes, these questions are still in my mind. In deep disappointment I have wept over the laxity of the church. But be assured that my tears have been tears of love. There can be no deep disappointment where there is not deep love. Yes, I love the church. How could I do otherwise? I am in the rather unique position of being the son, the grandson, and the great-grandson of preachers. Yes, I see the church as the body of Christ. But, oh! How we have blemished and scarred that body through social neglect and through fear of being nonconformists.

There was a time when the church was very powerful—in the time when the early Christians rejoiced at being deemed worthy to suffer for what they believed. In those days the church was not merely a thermometer that re-

5. George Wallace (1919–), then governor of Ala-bama, opposed admission of black students to the University of Alabama. Ross Barnett (1898–1988), governor of Mississippi, opposed James Meredith's admission to the University of Mississippi.

corded the ideas and principles of popular opinion; it was a thermostat that transformed the mores of society. Whenever the early Christians entered a town, the people in power became disturbed and immediately sought to convict the Christians for being "disturbers of the peace" and "outside agitators." But the Christians pressed on, in the conviction that they were "a colony of heaven," called to obey God rather than man. Small in number, they were big in commitment. They were too God-intoxicated to be "astronomically intimidated." By their effort and example they brought an end to such ancient evils as infanticide and gladiatorial contests.

Things are different now. So often the contemporary church is a weak, ineffectual voice with an uncertain sound. So often it is an arch-defender of the status quo. Far from being disturbed by the presence of the church, the power structure of the average community is consoled by the church's silent—and often even vocal—sanction of things as they are.

But the judgment of God is upon the church as never before. If today's church does not recapture the sacrificial spirit of the early church, it will lose its authenticity, forfeit the loyalty of millions, and be dismissed as an irrelevant social club with no meaning for the twentieth century. Every day I meet young people whose disappointment with the church has turned into outright disgust.

Perhaps I have once again been too optimistic. Is organized religion too inextricably bound to the status quo to save our nation and the world? Perhaps I must turn my faith to the inner spiritual church, the church within the church, as the true *ekklesia* [6] and the hope of the world. But again I am thankful to God that some noble souls from the ranks of organized religion have broken loose from the paralyzing chains of conformity and joined us as active partners in the struggle for freedom. They have left their secure congregations and walked the streets of Albany, Georgia, with us. They have gone down the highways of the South on tortuous rides for freedom. Yes, they have gone to jail with us. Some have been dismissed from their churches, have lost the support of their bishops and fellow ministers. But they have acted in the faith that right defeated is stronger than evil triumphant. Their witness has been the spiritual salt that has preserved the true meaning of the gospel in these troubled times. They have carved a tunnel of hope through the dark mountain of disappointment.

I hope the church as a whole will meet the challenge of this decisive hour. But even if the church does not come to the aid of justice, I have no despair about the future. I have no fear about the outcome of our struggle in Birmingham, even if our motives are at present misunderstood. We will reach the goal of freedom in Birmingham and all over the nation, because the goal of America is freedom. Abused and scorned though we may be, our destiny is tied up with America's destiny. Before the pilgrims landed at Plymouth, we were here. Before the pen of Jefferson etched the majestic words of the Declaration of Independence across the pages of history, we were here. For more than two centuries our forebears labored in this country without wages; they made cotton king; they built the homes of their masters while suffering gross injustice and shameful humiliation—and yet

6. The Greek New Testament word for the early Christian church.

out of a bottomless vitality they continued to thrive and develop. If the inexpressible cruelties of slavery could not stop us, the opposition we now face will surely fail. We will win our freedom because the sacred heritage of our nation and the eternal will of God are embodied in our echoing demands.

Before closing I feel impelled to mention one other point in your statement that has troubled me profoundly. You warmly commended the Birmingham police force for keeping "order" and "preventing violence." I doubt that you would have so warmly commended the police force if you had seen its dogs sinking their teeth into unarmed, nonviolent Negroes. I doubt that you would so quickly commend the policemen if you were to observe their ugly and inhumane treatment of Negroes here in the city jail; if you were to watch them push and curse old Negro women and young Negro girls; if you were to see them slap and kick old Negro men and young boys; if you were to observe them, as they did on two occasions, refuse to give us food because we wanted to sing our grace together. I cannot join you in your praise of the Birmingham police department.

It is true that the police have exercised a degree of discipline in handling the demonstrators. In this sense they have conducted themselves rather "nonviolently" in public. But for what purpose? To preserve the evil system of segregation. Over the past few years I have consistently preached that nonviolence demands that the means we use must be as pure as the ends we seek. I have tried to make clear that it is wrong to use immoral means to attain moral ends. But now I must affirm that it is just as wrong, or perhaps even more so, to use moral means to preserve immoral ends. Perhaps Mr. Connor and his policemen have been rather nonviolent in public, as was Chief Pritchett in Albany, Georgia, but they have used the moral means of nonviolence to maintain the immoral end of racial injustice. As T. S. Eliot has said, "The last temptation is the greatest treason: To do the right deed for the wrong reason."[7]

I wish you had commended the Negro sit-inners and demonstrators of Birmingham for their sublime courage, their willingness to suffer, and their amazing discipline in the midst of great provocation. One day the South will recognize its real heroes. They will be the James Merediths,[8] with the noble sense of purpose that enables them to face jeering and hostile mobs, and with the agonizing loneliness that characterizes the life of the pioneer. They will be old, oppressed, battered Negro women, symbolized in a seventy-two-year-old woman in Montgomery, Alabama, who rose up with a sense of dignity and with her people decided not to ride segregated buses, and who responded with ungrammatical profundity to one who inquired about her weariness: "My feets is tired, but my soul is at rest." They will be the young high school and college students, the young ministers of the gospel and a host of their elders, courageously and nonviolently sitting in at lunch counters and willingly going to jail for conscience' sake. One day the South will know that when these disinherited children of God sat down at lunch counters, they were in reality standing up for what is best in the American dream and for the most sacred values in our Judaeo-Chris-

7. From Eliot's verse play *Murder in the Cathedral.*

8. First black to enroll at the University of Mississippi.

tian heritage, thereby bringing our nation back to those great wells of democracy which were dug deep by the founding fathers in their formulation of the Constitution and the Declaration of Independence.

Never before have I written so long a letter. I'm afraid it is much too long to take your precious time. I can assure you that it would have been much shorter if I had been writing from a comfortable desk, but what else can one do when he is alone in a narrow jail cell, other than write long letters, think long thoughts, and pray long prayers?

If I have said anything in this letter that overstates the truth and indicates an unreasonable impatience, I beg you to forgive me. If I have said anything that understates the truth and indicates my having a patience that allows me to settle for anything less than brotherhood, I beg God to forgive me.

I hope this letter finds you strong in the faith. I also hope that circumstances will soon make it possible for me to meet each of you, not as an integrationist or a civil-rights leader but as a fellow clergyman and a Christian brother. Let us all hope that the dark clouds of racial prejudice will soon pass away and the deep fog of misunderstanding will be lifted from our fear-drenched communities, and in some not too distant tomorrow the radiant stars of love and brotherhood will shine over our great nation with all their scintillating beauty.

Yours for the cause of Peace and Brotherhood,
MARTIN LUTHER KING, JR.
1964

ETHERIDGE KNIGHT
1931–1985

Etheridge Knight was born in Corinth, Mississippi, on April 19, 1931. As an adolescent, he was partner to men who frequented juke joints, pool halls, bars, and underground poker games. It was in this robust black male environment, where talk was highly valued, that Knight honed his skills as a performer of black toasts—long, rhyming, humorous verbal performances that require extraordinary memory and deft oratorical ability. Knight became addicted to drugs at an early age and never freed himself from the influence of narcotics. He served in the U.S. Army from 1947 to 1951.

Knight was arrested for robbery in 1960 and sentenced to eight years in prison. At the Indiana State Prison in Michigan City, the verbal abilities learned in his youth did not desert him. He began writing poems that won acclaim from such established African American artists as Dudley Randall and Gwendolyn Brooks. It was Randall, during repeated visits to the prison, who convinced Knight that he had unusual talent and deserved public recognition.

In 1968, Knight's volume *Poems from Prison* was published by Randall's newly established Broadside Press. Joining the world of Black Arts poets, Knight met and was briefly married to poet Sonia Sanchez. The marriage proved both difficult and unsatisfactory as a result of Knight's drug addiction. Still, Knight was charismatic, energetic, and hugely successful, receiving national acclaim and never abandoning his practice of reciting his work from memory.

His *Belly Song and Other Poems* (1973) is one of the most significant volumes to emerge from the Black Arts movement. Knight was an inspiration to all those who felt poetry should be a functional and communal art with a strong oral artist in the middle of the circle. In *Understanding the New Black Poetry*, Stephen Henderson notes that Knight's poetry helped shape the values of the Attica Penitentiary inmates who rebelled during the 1970s and that his work increased the self-esteem of the "wretched of the earth" in its pithy insistence on the dignity of every human life.

The Idea of Ancestry

I

Taped to the wall of my cell are 47 pictures: 47 black
faces: my father, mother, grandmothers (1 dead), grand
fathers (both dead), brothers, sisters, uncles, aunts,
cousins (1st & 2nd), nieces, and nephews. They stare
across the space at me sprawling on my bunk. I know   5
their dark eyes, they know mine. I know their style,
they know mine. I am all of them, they are all of me;
they are farmers, I am a thief, I am me, they are thee.

I have at one time or another been in love with my mother,
1 grandmother, 2 sisters, 2 aunts (1 went to the asylum),   10
and 5 cousins. I am now in love with a 7 yr old niece
(she sends me letters written in large block print, and
her picture is the only one that smiles at me).

I have the same name as 1 grandfather, 3 cousins, 3 nephews,
and 1 uncle. The uncle disappeared when he was 15, just took   15
off and caught a freight (they say). He's discussed each year
when the family has a reunion, he causes uneasiness in
the clan, he is an empty space. My father's mother, who is 93
and who keeps the Family Bible with everybody's birth dates
(and death dates) in it, always mentions him. There is no   20
place in her Bible for "whereabouts unknown."

II

Each Fall the graves of my grandfathers call me, the brown
hills and red gullies of mississippi send out their electric
messages, galvanizing my genes. Last yr/like a salmon quitting
the cold ocean—leaping and bucking up his birthstream/I   25
hitchhiked my way from L.A. with 16 caps [1] in my pocket and a
monkey on my back, and I almost kicked it with the kinfolks.
I walked barefooted in my grandmother's backyard / I smelled the old
land and the woods / I sipped cornwhiskey from fruit jars with the
    men /
I flirted with the women / I had a ball till the caps ran out   30

---

1. A reference to units of heroin sold on the street to addicts.

and my habit came down. That night I looked at my grandmother
and split / my guts were screaming for junk / but I was almost
contented / I had almost caught up with me.
   The next day in Memphis I cracked a croaker's crib[2] for a fix.

This yr there is a gray stone wall damming my stream, and when   35
the falling leaves stir my genes, I pace my cell or flop on my bunk
and stare at 47 black faces across the space. I am all of them,
they are all of me, I am me, they are thee, and I have no sons
to float in the space between.

                                                   1968

Hard Rock Returns to Prison from the Hospital for the Criminal Insane

Hard Rock was "known not to take no shit
From nobody," and he had the scars to prove it:
Split purple lips, lumped ears, welts above
His yellow eyes, and one long scar that cut
Across his temple and plowed through a thick   5
Canopy of kinky hair.

The WORD was that Hard Rock wasn't a mean nigger
Anymore, that the doctors had bored a hole in his head,
Cut out part of his brain, and shot electricity
Through the rest. When they brought Hard Rock back,   10
Handcuffed and chained, he was turned loose,
Like a freshly gelded stallion, to try his new status.
And we all waited and watched, like indians at a corral,
To see if the WORD was true.

As we waited we wrapped ourselves in the cloak   15
Of his exploits: "Man, the last time, it took eight
Screws to put him in the Hole."[1] "Yeah, remember when he
Smacked the captain with his dinner tray?" "He set
The record for time in the Hole—67 straight days!"
"Ol Hard Rock! man, that's one crazy nigger."   20
And then the jewel of a myth that Hard Rock had once bit
A screw on the thumb and poisoned him with syphilitic spit.

The testing came, to see if Hard Rock was really tame.
A hillbilly called him a black son of a bitch
And didn't lose his teeth, a screw who knew Hard Rock   25
From before shook him down and barked in his face.
And Hard Rock did *nothing.* Just grinned and looked silly,
His eyes empty like knot holes in a fence.

And even after we discovered that it took Hard Rock
Exactly 3 minutes to tell you his first name,   30

---

2. A drug seller's home.   1. Solitary confinement. "Screws": prison guards.

We told ourselves that he had just wised up,
Was being cool; but we could not fool ourselves for long,
And we turned away, our eyes on the ground. Crushed.
He had been our Destroyer,[2] the doer of things
We dreamed of doing but could not bring ourselves to do,   35
The fears of years, like a biting whip,
Had cut grooves too deeply across our backs.

1968

For Black Poets Who Think of Suicide

Black Poets should live—not leap
From steel bridges (Like the white boys do.
Black Poets should *live*—not lay
Their necks on railroad tracks (like the white boys do.
Black Poets should seek—but not search too much   5
In sweet dark caves, nor hunt for snipe [1]
Down psychic trails (like the white boys do.

For Black Poets belong to Black People. Are
The Flutes of Black Lovers. Are
The Organs of Black Sorrows. Are   10
The Trumpets of Black Warriors.
Let All Black poets die as trumpets,
And be buried in the dust of marching feet.

1969

2. A reference to Ras the Destroyer, a central figure of Rastafarianism.

1. A marsh bird characterized by a long straight
bill; it is common to England.

ADDISON GAYLE JR.

1932–1991

A graduate of New York's City College and a prolific editor of works dedicated to the spirit of the Black Aesthetic, Addison Gayle was born in Newport News, Virginia. He served in the United States Air Force before completing his undergraduate education at the City University of New York. After receiving a Master's degree in literature from the University of California at Los Angeles in 1966, Gayle returned to his adopted home of Manhattan to begin an influential career as a college professor, literary critic, and national spokesperson for the Black Arts. He taught English at Bernard M. Baruch College of the City University of New York for twenty-five years, becoming a Distinguished Professor during the 1980s.

Early in his graduate study, Gayle dedicated himself to compiling invaluable documents of criticism and theory devoted to the literature and culture of African Americans. Within a short period of time, he had transformed this dedication into a product, publishing *Black Expression* (1969) and the inimitable collection titled *The Black Aesthetic* (1971). *The Black Aesthetic* is, arguably, the theoretical bible of the Black Arts movement.

In *The Black Aesthetic*, which is a collection of essays by various authors arranged under the headings "Theory," "Music," "Drama," and "Fiction," Gayle sets forth his own manifesto for the Black Arts. Uncompromising in his belief that the term "universal" was a shallow masquerade for Western standards, Gayle challenged a tradition of criticism and academic work which, in his words, strangled black cultural and literary creativity. The West's offensive strategy was found in the popularization of negative images, myths, and symbols of Africa and African American life in the United States. Therefore, the committed black writer was enjoined by Gayle to accept the proposition that "Black is beautiful" and to craft images commensurate with this proposition—positive images of a real African American life of struggle and achievement. Gayle envisioned the role of the black artist as "providing us with images based on our own lives." He also encouraged black artists to "wage war against every institution which influences the actions of black people." Gayle's ability to formulate his critical polemics in an elegant, almost eighteenth-century prose made him a formidable opponent of the status quo in American letters.

Addison Gayle was an essayist and orator par excellence. During the 1960s and 1970s, no single spokesperson for the Black Arts other than Amiri Baraka drew more fire from mainstream white literary critics than Gayle. It is impossible to understand or appreciate the Black Arts movement—or the recent advance of African American literary studies in the United States—without a knowledge of the extensive, informed, and engaging corpus of Addison Gayle Jr.

The Black Aesthetic

Introduction

A new note, discernible even to the most biased observer, was sounded in the art of black people during the nineteen fifties and sixties. "I will go on judging and elucidating novels and plays and poetry by Negroes according to what general powers I possess," writes Richard Gilman, "but the kind of Negro *writing* I have been talking about, the act of creation of the self in the face of the self's historic denial by our society, seems to me to be at this point beyond my right to intrude."[1]

Some critics, less amenable to conversion than Gilman, would have us believe that only two elements separate the present-day black artist from his forerunner. One such element is anger! ". . . Negro writers are demonstrating the responsibility of the artist to the disciplines and traditions of art and literature . . . ," writes Herbert Hill;[2] "simple protest and anger are not enough and rhetoric will not be useful in masking the inadequacies of literary craftsmanship." The other is black nationalism, which, according to Robert Bone, "for all its militancy is politically Utopian."[3]

The element of black anger is neither new nor, as Herbert Hill would have us believe, passé. The black artist in the American society who creates without interjecting a note of anger is creating not as a black man, but as an American. For anger in black art is as old as the first utterances by black men on American soil:

---

1. In the late 1960s and early 1970s, Gilman wrote a series of essays in which he examined the role that race plays in the understanding of literature.
2. Hill, critic, author, essayist, former secretary of the NAACP and faculty member of the New School for Social Research, edited and wrote the introduction to *Anger and Beyond: Negro Writers in the United States* (1966).
3. Bone is best known for *The Negro Novel in America* (1965), which discusses the impact of race on the artistic potential of African Americans.

> "If I had-a my way,
> I'd tear this building down
> Great God, then, if I had-a my way
> If I had-a my way, little children
> If I had-a my way,
> I'd tear this building down. . . ."

As old as Frances Ellen Watkins,[4] who made one demand of her undertaker:

> "I ask no monument, proud and high
> To arrest the gaze of the passer-by,
> All that my yearning spirit craves
> Is bury me not in a land of slaves."

Nowhere does anger reach more intensive expression than in DuBois,[5] who strikes a note that has found accord in the breast of contemporary black artists:

> "I hate them, oh!
> I hate them well,
> I hate them, Christ!
> As I hate hell!
> If I were God,
> I'd sound their knell
> This day."

Neither is black nationalism a new element in black life or black art. In 1836, ". . . some of the delegates [at the National Negro Convention]," writes Philip S. Foner, "were convinced that Canadian colonization was still the most urgent business at hand. Others felt that it was necessary to concentrate upon building a better social order in the United States. . . . One group doubted the efficacy of associating with any set of white abolitionists, and advocated restricting the convention to Negro membership. Another, convinced of the inability to achieve equality for Negroes in existing institutions, favored continuing the establishment of separate schools and churches for the Negro people."[6] This sentiment reaches dramatic form in the fiction of Martin Delaney, *Blake, or the Huts of America* (1859); Sutton Griggs, *Imperium in Imperio* (1899); and DuBois, *Dark Princess* (1928).[7]

Again, animosity against the inept, sterile critiques of American academicians—so prevalent in black critical writings today—is not new. As early

4. Crusading African American abolitionist, poet, novelist, essayist, and orator (1825–1911).

5. Among the most prominent American intellectuals of the 20th century, Du Bois (1868–1963) wrote poetry, novels, essays, and journalism; in addition, he was a founder of the NAACP and played an active and often controversial role in American politics.

6. Foner (1910–), a historian of the political "left," has written widely on African American history,

Marxism, socialism, and the American labor movement.

7. Delany's (1812–1885) novel *Blake* details the travails of a slave named Henry. Sutton Griggs (1872–1933) wrote extensively about the relationship between African and white Americans. Du Bois's *Dark Princess* is, in Du Bois's own words, a "romance with a message"; it tells the story of a black medical student forced out of his studies by racism.

as 1900, Pauline Hopkins[8] realized that art was ". . . of great value to any people as a preserver of manners and customs—religious, political, and social. It is a record of growth and development from generation to generation. No one will do this for us; we must ourselves develop the men and women who will faithfully portray the inmost thoughts and feelings of the Negro with all the fire and romance which lie dormant in our history. . . ." Twenty-two years later, William Pickens[9] was more direct: "It is not simply that the white story teller will not do full justice to the humanity of the black race; *he cannot.*" William Stanley Braithwaite,[1] an American critic in every essential, quotes from an article in the *Independent Magazine* (1925): "The white writer seems to stand baffled before the enigma, and so he expends all his energies on dialect and in general on the Negro's minstrel characteristics. . . . We shall have to look to the Negro himself to go all the way. It is quite likely that no white man can do it. *It is reasonable to suppose that his white psychology will get in the way.*" (Italics mine)

Nevertheless, there is a discernible element in black art today that is new, and Hoyt W. Fuller[2] has come closest to pointing it out: "The Negro revolt is as palpable in letters as it is in the streets." Change revolt to war, and the characteristics that distinguish the old art from the new are readily apparent. The serious black artist of today is at war with the American society as few have been throughout American history. Too often, as Richard Wright[3] noted, the black (artists) ". . . entered the court of American public opinion dressed in the knee pants of servility, curtsying to show that the Negro was not inferior, that he was human, and that he had a life comparable to other people." They waged war not against the society but against the societal laws and mores that barred *them* from equal membership. They were, in the main, anxious to become Americans, to share in the fruits of the country's economic system and to surrender their history and culture to a universal melting pot. They were men of another era who believed in the American dream more fervently than their white contemporaries. They saw the nation as a land of innocence, young enough to hold out promises of maturing into a nation of freedom, justice, and equality. The days of innocence have passed. The child has become the adult, and instead of improving with age, she has grown increasingly worse. Yesterday America was evil personified in her youth; today she is evil personified in adulthood.

The dimensions of the black artist's war against the society are highly visible. At the core of black art in the past was a vendetta against the South. The black novel, from William Wells Brown[4] to Richard Wright, was concerned primarily with southern tyranny and injustice. Often the North escaped with no more than a rap on the knuckles. "Northern white people," wrote James Weldon Johnson[5] in *The Autobiography of an Ex-Coloured Man* (1912), "love the Negro in a sort of abstract way, as a race; through a

---

8. Hopkins (1859–1930), one of the first writers, black or white, to introduce racial themes into the traditional 19th-century novel.
9. Pickens (1881–1954), educator, orator, editor, and civil rights leader.
1. Braithwaite (1878–1962), poet, critic, anthologist, editor, essayist, and biographer, helped popularize the work of many African American authors.

2. Black activist intellectual (1923–1981).
3. Wright (1908–1960), deeply influential African American writer of the mid 20th century.
4. Brown (1815–1884), slave-born novelist, most famous for *Clotel* (1853), a melodramatic story of miscegenation.
5. African American novelist, poet, essayist (1871–1938); also active in the NAACP.

sense of justice, charity, and philanthropy, they will liberally assist in his elevation. . . ."

With the exception of writers such as Dunbar and Chesnutt,[6] who viewed the black man's exodus from South to North as an exchange of one hell for another, black writers spoke of the North as the new Canaan,[7] of northern whites as a different breed of man from their southern counterparts. Is it any wonder that black people, falling sway to increasing southern tyranny, began, in 1917, the exodus that swelled the urban areas of America in the sixties and seventies?

"I've seen them come dark/wondering/wide-eyed/dreaming/out of Penn Station . . . ," writes Langston Hughes,[8] "but the trains are late. The gates open/but there're bars/at each gate." The bars were erected by northern, not southern, whites. Black people had run away from white terrorism in Savannah in 1904 and Atlanta in 1906, only to experience white terrorism in Ohio in 1904, Illinois in 1908, and New York in 1935. The evenhanded treatment of blacks North and South made little imprint upon Negro leaders who, then as now, were more willing to combat injustices down south than up north.

The task of pointing out northern duplicity was left to the black artist, and no writer was more effective in this undertaking than Richard Wright. When Wright placed Bigger Thomas and Mr. Dalton[9] in a northern setting and pointed up the fact that Bigger's condition resulted from Dalton's hypocrisy, he opened a Pandora's box of problems for white liberals and Negro leaders, neither of whom could bring themselves to share his vision. Dalton is a white liberal philanthropist who, although donating money to "Negro uplift organizations," owns the slums in which Bigger Thomas is forced to live. His control of the young black man is more despotic than that of the southern plantation owner over blacks in the South: for him, the weapons of control are economic, social, and political.

He is more sagacious and dishonest than his southern counterpart; he has discovered a way to "keep the nigger in his place" without such aids as signs and restrictive covenants. He has constructed a cosmology that allows him to pose as a humanitarian on the one hand, while he sets about defining the black man's limitations on the other. His most cherished symbol of the black man is Uncle Tom; and he remains enamored of Nigger Jim,[1] the black everyboy toward whom he feels paternalistic. Like Theodore Gross,[2] he is able to share with Joel Chandler Harris[3] ". . . the fears, laughter, and anger of the Negro"; and he is equally convinced with Gross that Harris ". . . contributed the most popular Negro characters to American

6. Charles Chesnutt (1858–1932), short story writer; many of his works deal with the folk elements of African American culture. Paul Laurence Dunbar (1872–1906), the son of former slaves; famed as a poet, especially for his experiments with vernacular forms.
7. A region of Palestine west of Jordan, considered by the ancient Israelites as the "promised land."
8. African American poet, novelist, short story writer, and essayist (1902–1967); one of the most prominent and influential of the writers of the Harlem Renaissance
9. Bigger Thomas is the protagonist of Richard Wright's Native Son (1940); Mr. Dalton is his land-

lord and employer.
1. Slave hero of Twain's Adventures of Huckleberry Finn. Uncle Tom is a character in Harriet Beecher Stowe's Uncle Tom's Cabin (1852), famous for his devotion to his white master and for his submitting to—rather than fighting against—the evil actions of Simon Legree.
2. Gross (1930–), critic, editor, academic; during the 1970s he was embroiled in controversies about the availability of education to the underprivileged.
3. Harris (1848–1908), American journalist and author, known for his adaptations of African American folk stories in the Uncle Remus tales.

fiction—Uncle Remus, Balaam, Ananias, and Mingo . . ."—characters whom he, too, believes to be representative of the race.

Thomas Nelson Page, Thomas Dixon, and Hinton Helper might create, for Southerners, the image of the black man as ". . . a degenerate, inferior, irresponsible, and bestial creature 'transformed by the exigency of war from a chattel to be bought and sold into a possible beast to be feared and guarded.' " Dalton, however, will not accept this image. Such portraits of black men disturb his humanitarian (read sexual) ideal of the black man. "In an effort to make Hell endurable," Robert Bone writes of James Baldwin,[4] "Baldwin attempts to spiritualize his sexual rebellion. Subjectively, I have no doubt, he is convinced that he has found God. Not the white God of his black father, but a darker deity who dwells in the heart of carnal mystery. . . . The stranger the sex partner, the better the orgasm, for it violates a stronger taboo." Bone's inability to come to grips with the sexual aspects of Baldwin's novels, reveals more about Bone than it does about Baldwin.

At the least, it reveals a great deal about the Daltons of the North. In order to protect the Marys of the earth (Dalton's daughter in *Native Son*), they have defined the black man in the most negative terms possible. To the northern mind, Nigger Jim and Uncle Tom are opposite ends of the same pole; the young boy and the old man are both eunuchs, paternalistic wards who, one step removed from the jungle, are capable of limited, prescribed salvation. The inability of the Daltons to see the black man as other than an impotent sexual force accounts for much of the negative criticism by white writers about black literature; it also accounts for the sexually impotent black men who people the novels of William Styron and Norman Mailer.[5]

The liberal ideology—both social and literary—of the northern Daltons has become the primary target of the Afro-American writer and critic. In the novels of John A. Williams, Sam Greenlee, Cecil Brown, and Ishmael Reed, the criticism of Don L. Lee, Ron Wellburn, LeRoi Jones, and Hoyt Fuller,[6] to name but a few, the liberal shibboleths are called into question. The Daltons are brought before the bar of black public opinion and revealed for the modern-day plantation owners they are.

There is another, more important aspect to this war. The black artist of the past worked with the white public in mind. The guidelines by which he measured his production was its acceptance or rejection by white people. To be damned by a white critic and disavowed by a white public was reason enough to damn the artist in the eyes of his own people. The invisible censor, white power, hovered over him in the sanctuary of his private room—whether at the piano or the typewriter—and, like his black brothers, he debated about what he could say to the world without bringing censure upon himself. The mannerisms he had used to survive in the society outside, he now brought to his art; and, to paraphrase Richard Wright, he was forced to figure out how to sound each note and how to write down each word.

---

4. Baldwin (1924–1987), African American writer, known for his novels and plays, and especially for his incisive personal/political essays indicting the racism of American society.
5. Styron and Mailer, white American novelists known for controversial essays and fiction; Styron, especially, came in for much criticism for his *Confessions of Nat Turner* (1967).
6. African American writers prominent during the 1960s and beyond.

The result was usually an artistic creation filled with half-truths. His works were always seasoned with the proper amount of anger—an anger that dared not reach the explosive level of calling for total demolition of the American society—and condescension; condescension that meant he would assure his audience, at some point in the production, that he believed in the principles of Americanism. To return to Richard Wright, he was not ". . . ever expected to speak honestly about the problem. [He had to] wrap it up in myth, legend, morality, folklore, niceties, and plain lies."

Speaking honestly is a fundamental principle of today's black artist. He has given up the futile practice of speaking to whites, and has begun to speak to his brothers. Ofttimes, as in essays in this anthology, he points up the wide disparity between the pronouncements of liberal intellectuals and their actions. Yet his purpose is not to convert the liberals (one does not waste energy on the likes of Selden Rodman, Irving Howe, Theodore Gross, Louis Simpson, Herbert Hill, or Robert Bone), but instead to point out to black people the true extent of the control exercised upon them by the American society, in the hope that a process of de-Americanization will occur in every black community in the nation.

The problem of the de-Americanization of black people lies at the heart of the Black Aesthetic. "After the Egyptian and Indian, the Greek and Roman, the Teuton and Mongolian," wrote DuBois in 1903, "the Negro is a sort of seventh son, born with a veil, and gifted with second sight in this American world—a world which yields him no true self-consciousness, but only lets him see himself through the revelation of the other world. It is a peculiar sensation, this double consciousness, this sense of always looking at one's self through the eyes of others, of measuring one's soul by the tape of a world that looks on in amused contempt and pity. One ever feels his twoness—an American, a Negro; two souls, two thoughts, two unreconciled strivings; two warring ideals in one dark body, whose dogged strength alone keeps it from being torn asunder."

In 1961 the old master resolved the psychic tension in his own breast by leaving the country that had rewarded his endeavors with scorn and oppression. His denunciations of America and his exodus back to the land of his forefathers provide an appropriate symbol of the black man who de-Americanized himself.

His act proclaimed to black men the world over that the price for becoming an American was too high. It meant, at the least, to desert one's heritage and culture; at the most, to become part of all ". . . that has been instrumental in wanton destruction of life, degradation of dignity, and contempt for the human spirit." To be an American is to be opposed to humankind, against the dignity of the individual, and against the striving in man for compassion and tenderness: to be an American is to lose one's humanity.

What else is one to make of My Lai, Vietnam? A black soldier has been charged with joining his white compatriots in the murder of innocent Vietnamese women and children. How far has the Americanization of black men progressed when a southern black man stands beside white men and shoots down, not the enemies of his people, but the niggers of American construction?

To understand this incident and what must be done to correct it is to understand the Black Aesthetic. A critical methodology has no relevance to the black community unless it aids men in becoming better than they are. Such an element has been sorely lacking in the critical canons handed down from the academies by the Aristotelian Critics, the Practical Critics, the Formalistic Critics, and the New Critics. Each has this in common: it aims to evaluate the work of art in terms of *its* beauty and not in terms of the transformation from ugliness to beauty that the work of art demands from its audience.

The question for the black critic today is not how beautiful is a melody, a play, a poem, or a novel, but how much more beautiful has the poem, melody, play, or novel made the life of a single black man? How far has the work gone in transforming an American Negro into an African-American or black man? The Black Aesthetic, then, as conceived by this writer, is a corrective—a means of helping black people out of the polluted mainstream of Americanism, and offering logical, reasoned arguments as to why he should not desire to join the ranks of a Norman Mailer or a William Styron. To be an American writer is to be an American, and, for black people, there should no longer be honor attached to either position.

To paraphrase Saunders Redding,[7] I have been enclothed with no authority to speak for others. Therefore, it is not my intention, in this introduction, to speak for the contributors to this anthology. Few of them may share my views; a great many may find them reprehensible. These are independent artists who demand the right to think for themselves and who, rightfully so, will resist the attempt by anyone—black or white—to articulate positions in their names.

Each has his own idea of the Black Aesthetic, of the function of the black artist in the American society and of the necessity for new and different critical approaches to the artistic endeavors of black artists. Few, I believe, would argue with my assertion that the black artist, due to his historical position in America at the present time, is engaged in a war with this nation that will determine the future of black art. Likewise, there are few among them—and here again this is only conjecture—who would disagree with the idea that unique experiences produce unique cultural artifacts, and that art is a product of such cultural experiences. To push this thesis to its logical conclusion, unique art derived from unique cultural experiences mandates unique critical tools for evaluation. Further than this, agreement need not go!

One final note: Less than a decade ago, anthologies on black writing were edited almost exclusively by whites. Today, there is a noticeable difference: the white academician edits an anthology and calls upon a black man to write the introduction. The editor then declares that his anthology "represents the best of black literature" or that he has chosen those works "which rank with the best in American artistic production."

This editor makes no such farcical and nonsensical claims. Represented in this anthology is not the best critical thought on the subject of the Black Aesthetic, but critical thought that is among the best. This anthology is not

---

7. J. Saunders Redding (1906–1988), novelist, essayist, historian, and critic; his *To Make a Poet Black* was the first critical and historical account of black literature undertaken by an African American.

definitive and does not claim to be. The first of its kind to treat of this subject, it is meant as an incentive to young black critics to scan the pages of *The Black World* [*Negro Digest*], *Liberator Magazine, Soulbook, Journal of Negro Poetry, Amistad, Umbra,* and countless other black magazines, and anthologize the thousands of essays that no single anthology could possibly cover.

Many writers whose claim to recognition is equal to that of the other contributors and the editor have been left out of this anthology. This could not be helped. Perhaps it can be rectified. Instead of being content to write introduction for white editors, perhaps our serious black artists will edit anthologies themselves. If this is done, the present renaissance in black letters will escape the fate of its predecessor in the nineteen twenties, and endure. Then and only then will the revolution in black letters gain viability and continue right on!

1971

AMIRI BARAKA

b. 1934

Amiri Baraka was the American writer of the 1950s and 1960s who most effectively bridged the sometimes precarious territory between African American revisionary movements and other cultural and political movements. Without doubt, Baraka has been influential in the development of contemporary black letters, succeeding and building upon the work of such major figures as W. E. B. Du Bois and Richard Wright.

Born LeRoi Jones in Newark, New Jersey, to middle-class parents who would gladly have seen him become a doctor or lawyer, Baraka did extremely well in his studies and graduated at the age of 15. During his teenage years, he was an uneasy spirit. Reflecting back on this stage of his life, he remarked, "When I was in high school I used to drink a lot of wine, throw bottles around, walk down the street in women's clothes just because I couldn't find anything to satisfy myself."

In 1952 Baraka enrolled at Howard University in Washington, D.C. Not surprisingly, given the depth and restlessness of his intellect, he quickly found the college atmosphere claustrophobic, and by 1954 he had flunked out. Baraka's merciless critique of what he saw as the university's bourgeois pretentiousness reveals the direction of his political thought even as an undergraduate. Before leaving Howard, however, Baraka benefited from the tutelage of several famous black scholars, including E. Franklin Frazier, Nathan Scott Jr., and Sterling A. Brown. Extracurricular sessions with writer, critic, and jazz buff Brown taught Baraka and some of his lucky fellow students the ecstasies, themes, techniques, and able practitioners of African American music. Brown knew African American musical traditions and was more than generous in passing them on to young tyros such as Baraka and A. B. Spellman.

After Howard, Baraka joined the air force and served three years in Puerto Rico. In 1957 he was dishonorably discharged; he then moved to New York's Greenwich Village, where the Beat scene was in full swing, with writers such as Gregory Corso and Allen Ginsberg "howling" their audiences into a new consciousness, while Ornette Coleman, Thelonius Monk, Wilbur Ware, John Coltrane, and other principals of the "new music" reeducated jazz lovers to the music's infinite possibilities.

During the next few years, Baraka established his reputation as a music critic, writing about jazz for *Downbeat, Metronome,* and the *Jazz Review.* Along with Hettie Roberta Cohen, a white Jewish woman whom he married in 1958, he founded *Yugen,* an art magazine that featured the poetry of Beat writers. By the late 1950s his own poetry began attracting critical attention; his first volume, *Preface to a Twenty Volume Suicide Note,* appeared in 1961 from a publishing firm he had helped to establish. *Preface* was enthusiastically received by many who appreciated its technical innovations. By the late 1950s and early 1960s, Baraka's reputation had grown to the extent that he gained the moniker "King of the Village," a nickname influenced by the French meaning of his birth name, LeRoi.

Baraka's 1959 poem *January 1 1959: Fidel Castro,* inspired the New York chapter of the Fair Play for Cuba Committee to invite the poet to visit Cuba, which he did in 1960. In *The Autobiography of LeRoi Jones* (1984), he commented about the experience, "Cuba split me open," and went on to add that the trip was "a turning point in my life." During his stay in Cuba, he encountered third world political artists and intellectuals who challenged the status of his art and his political convictions. Furthermore, they questioned his allegiance to America and tabbed him a "cowardly bourgeoisie individualist."

In *Cuba Libre* (1961), Baraka responded to such criticism: "Look, why jump on me? . . . I'm in complete agreement with you. I'm a poet . . . what can I do? I write, that's all, I'm not even interested in politics." The Mexican poet Jaime Shelly sharply retorted, saying, "You want to cultivate your soul? In that ugliness you live in, you want to cultivate your soul? Well, we've got millions of starving people to feed, and that moves me enough to make poems out of." Struck by the power and starkness of such arguments, Baraka began to forsake his literary bohemianism and embrace black nationalism.

During these transitional years, Baraka changed his name from LeRoi Jones to Amiri Baraka. He wrote essays, including a collection titled *Home;* a second poetry volume, *The Dead Lecturer;* and many plays, including *The Slave, The Toilet,* and *Dutchman. Dutchman* was widely celebrated; Norman Mailer, for instance, claimed that it was "the best play in America." The play garnered the 1964 Obie award for the best Off-Broadway production and made Baraka a national sensation.

Dutchman's opening stage direction, which states that the "subway is heaped in modern myth," signals the manner in which the play interrogates the mythologies that fuel American perceptions about race and gender. Lula and Clay embody many of the social dimensions that these mythologies give rise to. *Dutchman* toys with stereotypes, implicitly probing the interplay between "authentic" identity and that determined by a social script underwritten by elite whites. Neither Clay nor his antagonistic counterpart, Lula, can withstand the socially sanctioned stereotyping imposed upon them. The result of this is that their interaction becomes nearly farcical. The play can be seen as a modern parable of the encounter between white and black America: an encounter in which the consequences for African Americans are dire.

Critic Carl Brucker suggests that the play's underground setting connotes "incarceration," "damnation," and "entombment" and that it "could be emblematic of the subconscious." He goes on to suggest that the play's setting and title "remind the audience of the packed holds of Dutch slave traders, which brought the first African to Jamestown; the historic Underground Railroad, which helped slaves escape the South; and the legendary *Flying Dutchman,* the cursed phantom ship that endlessly sails the seas." Brucker also claims that "the biblical parallels to the story of Adam and Eve are obvious. In *Dutchman,* Lula tempts Clay to come out from behind his assimilationist facade, to lower the disguise that is his only protection against white society's racist anger."

Dutchman polarized its audience. While some praised its "power," "freshness," and "deadly wit," others were offended by its bawdiness and its depiction of the role that white presence plays in the racial conundrum. Baraka responded to such criticism in these terms: "Lula . . . is not meant to represent white people—as some critics have thought—but America itself . . . the spirit of America. . . . The play is about the difficulty of becoming and remaining a man in America. . . . Manhood—black or white—is not wanted here."

An admirer of Malcolm X and a convert to that leader's revolutionary political doctrines of black nationalism, Baraka was shocked into action by Malcolm's assassination in 1965. Abandoning and repudiating his Greenwich Village lifestyle, beliefs, wife and two children, and friends, he headed uptown to Harlem.

In Harlem, Baraka established the Black Arts Repertory/School. His productions from the mid-sixties through the end of the decade were avowedly nationalist, dedicated to a new Black Aesthetic. In 1966 Baraka moved to Newark, where he established the arts institution known as "Spirit House." *Tales*, a collection of impressionistic and sometimes surreal short fiction, appeared in 1967. Becoming active as a political organizer in Newark by the end of the decade, Baraka was enormously influential in the election of the city's first black mayor, Kenneth Gibson. He also had a hand in founding the National Black Political Assembly.

Baraka's influence on and his prolific contributions to the Black Arts movement ensure the importance of the 1960s in black art and culture in any history of modern American letters. *Black Fire: An Anthology of Afro-American Writing* (1968), which Baraka co-edited with Larry Neal, is a veritable handbook of the themes, techniques, and personalities of the Black Aesthetic. Moving fluidly and with profound wit and deep social commitment across genres and social identities, Amiri Baraka has bestowed a profound legacy on African American creativity.

Preface to a Twenty Volume Suicide Note

(For Kellie Jones, born 16 May 1959)

Lately, I've become accustomed to the way
The ground opens up and envelopes me
Each time I go out to walk the dog.
Or the broad edged silly music the wind
Makes when I run for a bus . . .   5

Things have come to that.

And now, each night I count the stars,
And each night I get the same number.
And when they will not come to be counted,
I count the holes they leave.   10

Nobody sings anymore.

And then last night, I tiptoed up
To my daughter's room and heard her
Talking to someone, and when I opened
The door, there was no one there . . .   15
Only she on her knees, peeking into

Her own clasped hands.

1961

In Memory of Radio

Who has ever stopped to think of the divinity of Lamont Cranston? [1]
(Only Jack Kerouac, that I know of: & me.
The rest of you probably had on WCBS and Kate Smith, [2]
Or something equally unattractive.)

What can I say?   5
It is better to have loved and lost
Than to put linoleum in your living rooms?

Am I a sage or something?
Mandrake's [3] hypnotic gesture of the week?
(Remember, I do not have the healing powers of Oral Roberts . . .   10
I cannot, like F. J. Sheen, [4] tell you how to get saved & rich!
I cannot even order you to gaschamber satori like Hitler or Goody
        Knight [5]

& Love is an evil word.
Turn it backwards/see, see what I mean?
An evol word. & besides   15
who understands it?
I certainly wouldn't like to go out on that kind of limb.

Saturday mornings we listened to *Red Lantern* & his undersea folk.
At 11, *Let's Pretend*/& we did/& I, the poet, still do, Thank God!

What was it he used to say (after the transformation, when he was
        safe   20
& invisible & the unbelievers couldn't throw stones?) "Heh, heh,
        heh,
Who knows what evil lurks in the hearts of men? The Shadow
        knows."

O, yes he does
O, yes he does.
An evil word it is,   25
This Love.

                                                                        1961

---

1. A character in the popular mystery radio series *The Shadow* of the 1930s and beyond. Cranston's alter ego, "The Shadow," brought evil-doers to justice.
2. Popular singer (1909–1986). Kerouac (1922–1969), principal writer of the Beat generation.
3. Radio character—a magician.
4. American Roman Catholic bishop (1895–1979) who broadcast his conservative ideas on radio and television. Roberts (b. 1918), evangelist who preached on both radio and television.
5. Goodwin Knight (1869–1970), attorney and Republican politician. "Satori": enlightenment in Zen Buddhism.

A Poem for Black Hearts

For Malcolm's[1] eyes, when they broke
the face of some dumb white man, For
Malcolm's hands raised to bless us
all black and strong in his image
of ourselves, For Malcolm's words   5
fire darts, the victor's tireless
thrusts, words hung above the world
change as it may, he said it, and
for this he was killed, for saying,
and feeling, and being///change, all   10
collected hot in his heart, For Malcolm's
heart, raising us above our filthy cities,
for his stride, and his beat, and his address
to the grey monsters of the world, For Malcolm's
pleas for your dignity, black men, for your life,   15
black man, for the filling of your minds
with righteousness, For all of him dead and
gone and vanished from us, and all of him which
clings to our speech black god of our time.
For all of him, and all of yourself, look up,   20
black man, quit stuttering and shuffling, look up,
black man, quit whining and stooping, for all of him,
For Great Malcolm a prince of the earth, let nothing in us rest
until we avenge ourselves for his death, stupid animals
that killed him, let us never breathe a pure breath if   25
we fail, and white men call us faggots till the end of
the earth.

                                                              1969

I don't love you

Whatever you've given me, whiteface glass
to look through, to find another there, another
what motherfucker? another bread tree mad at its
sacredness, and the law of some dingaling god, cold
as ice cucumbers, for the shouters and the wigglers,   5
and what was the world to the words of slick nigger fathers,
too depressed to explain why they could not appear to be men.

The bread fool. The don'ts of this white hell. The crashed eyes
of dead friends, standing at the bar, eyes focused on actual ugliness.

I don't love you. Who is to say what that will mean. I don't   10
love you, expressed the train, moves, and uptown days later
we look up and breathe much easier

I don't love you

                                                              1969

---

1. Malcolm X (1925–1965), deeply influential African American minister and activist.

Three Movements and a Coda

THE QUALITY OF NIGHT THAT YOU HATE MOST IS ITS
   BLACK
AND ITS STARTEETH EYES, AND STICKS ITS STICKY
   FINGERS
IN YOUR EARS. RED NIGGER EYES LOOKING UP FROM A
   BLACK HOLE.
RED NIGGER LIPS TURNING KILLER GEOMETRY, LIKE HIS
   EYES ROLL UP
LIKE HE THOUGHT RELIGION WAS BEBOP.   5
               LIKE HE THOUGHT RELIGION WAS
               BEBOP . . . SIXTEEN KILLERS ON A
               LIVE MAN'S CHEST . . .
                          THE LONE RANGER
IS DEAD.   10
THE SHADOW[1]
IS DEAD.
ALL YOUR HEROES ARE DYING. J. EDGAR HOOVER WILL
SOON BE DEAD. YOUR MOTHER WILL DIE. LYNDON
   JOHNSON.[2]
                          these are natural   15
                          things. No one is
                          threatening anybody
                          thats just the way life
                          is,
                          boss.   20
Red Spick talking to you from a foxhole very close to the
Vampire Nazis' lines. I can see a few Vampire Nazis moving very
   quickly
back and forth under the heavy smoke. I hear, and perhaps you do, in
the background, the steady deadly cough of mortars, and the light
   shatter
of machine guns.   25

BANZAI!! BANZAI!! BANZAI!! BANZAI!! BANZAI!!

Came running out of the drugstore window with
an electric alarm clock, and then dropped the motherfucker
and broke it. Go get somethin' else. Take everything in there.
Look in the cashregister. TAKE THE MONEY. TAKE THE
   MONEY. YEH.   30
TAKE IT ALL. YOU DONT HAVE TO CLOSE THE DRAWER.
   COME ON MAN, I SAW
A TAPE RECORDER BACK THERE.

1. A popular mystery radio series of the 1930s and beyond. Lamont Cranston's alter ego, "The Shadow," brought evil-doers to justice.
2. Democratic politician (1908–1973) who be- came president of the United States after John F. Kennedy was assassinated in 1963. Hoover (1895–1972), director of the FBI from 1924 until his death.

These are the words of lovers.
Of dancers, of dynamite singers
These are songs if you have the   35
music

1969

SOS

Calling black people
Calling all black people, man woman child
Wherever you are, calling you, urgent, come in
Black People, come in, wherever you are, urgent, calling
you, calling all black people   5
calling all black people, come in, black people, come
on in.

1969

Black Art

Poems are bullshit unless they are
teeth or trees or lemons piled
on a step. Or black ladies dying
of men leaving nickel hearts
beating them down. Fuck poems   5
and they are useful, wd they shoot
come at you, love what you are,
breathe like wrestlers, or shudder
strangely after pissing. We want live
words of the hip world live flesh &   10
coursing blood. Hearts Brains
Souls splintering fire. We want poems
like fists beating niggers out of Jocks
or dagger poems in the slimy bellies
of the owner-jews. [1] Black poems to   15
smear on girdlemamma mulatto bitches
whose brains are red jelly stuck
between 'lizabeth taylor's [2] toes. Stinking
Whores! We want "poems that kill."
Assassin poems, Poems that shoot   20
guns. Poems that wrestle cops into alleys
and take their weapons leaving them dead
with tongues pulled out and sent to Ireland. Knockoff
poems for dope selling wops [3] or slick halfwhite
politicians Airplane poems, rrrrrrrrrrrrrrrr   25
rrrrrrrrrrrrrrr . . . tuhtuhtuhtuhtuhtuhtuhtuhtuh
. . . rrrrrrrrrrrrrrrr . . . Setting fire and death to
whities ass. Look at the Liberal

1. Anti-Semitic rhetoric most likely directed at
Jewish proprietors in black communities. Baraka
suspected that Jewish liberals were politically opportunistic.

2. American actress (b. 1932) known for her on-
screen and off-screen romances.
3. A pejorative term for those of Italian descent.

Spokesman for the jews clutch his throat
& puke himself into eternity . . . rrrrrrrr   30
There's a negroleader pinned to
a bar stool in Sardi's[4] eyeballs melting
in hot flame Another negroleader
on the steps of the white house one
kneeling between the sheriff's thighs   35
negotiating cooly for his people.
Agggh . . . stumbles across the room . . .
Put it on him, poem. Strip him naked
to the world! Another bad poem cracking
steel knuckles in a jewlady's mouth   40
Poem scream poison gas on beasts in green berets
Clean out the world for virtue and love,
Let there be no love poems written
until love can exist freely and
cleanly. Let Black People understand   45
that they are the lovers and the sons
of lovers and warriors and sons
of warriors Are poems & poets &
all the loveliness here in the world

We want a black poem. And a   50
Black World.
Let the world be a Black Poem
And Let All Black People Speak This Poem
Silently
or LOUD   55

1969

The Invention of Comics

I am a soul in the world: in
the world of my soul the whirled
light from the day
the sacked land
of my father.   5

In the world, the sad
nature of
myself. In myself
nature is sad. Small
prints of the day. Its   10
small dull fires. Its
sun, like a greyness
smeared on the dark.

The day of my soul, is
the nature of that   15
place. It is a landscape. Seen

---

4. A fashionable after-theater spot in Manhattan.

from the top of a hill. A
grey expanse; dull fires
throbbing on its seas.

The man's soul, the complexion   20
of his life. The menace
of its greyness. The
fire, throbs, the sea
moves. Birds shoot
from the dark. The edge   25
of the waters lit
darkly for the moon.

And the moon, from the soul. Is
the world, of the man. The man
and his sea, and its moon, and   30
the soft fire throbbing. Kind
death. O
my dark and sultry
love.

                                        1971

Dutchman

CHARACTERS

CLAY, twenty-year-old Negro
LULA, thirty-year-old white woman
RIDERS OF COACH, white and black
YOUNG NEGRO
CONDUCTOR

In the flying underbelly of the city. Steaming hot, and summer on top, out-side. Underground. The subway heaped in modern myth.

Opening scene is a man sitting in a subway seat, holding a magazine but looking vacantly just above its wilting pages. Occasionally he looks blankly toward the window on his right. Dim lights and darkness whistling by against the glass. (Or paste the lights, as admitted props, right on the subway windows. Have them move, even dim and flicker. But give the sense of speed. Also stations, whether the train is stopped or the glitter and activity of these stations merely flashes by the windows.)

The man is sitting alone. That is, only his seat is visible, though the rest of the car is outfitted as a complete subway car. But only his seat is shown. There might be, for a time, as the play begins, a loud scream of the actual train. And it can recur throughout the play, or continue on a lower key once the dialogue starts.

The train slows after a time, pulling to a brief stop at one of the stations. The man looks idly up, until he sees a woman's face staring at him through the window; when it realizes that the man has noticed the face, it begins very premeditatedly to smile. The man smiles too, for a moment, without a trace of self-consciousness. Almost an instinctive though undesirable response. Then a kind of awkwardness or embarrassment sets in, and the man makes to look away, is further embarrassed, so he brings back his eyes to where the face was, but by now the train is moving again, and the face would seem to be left behind by the way the man turns his head to look back through the other windows at the slowly fading platform. He smiles then; more comfortably confident, hoping perhaps that his memory of this brief encounter will be pleasant. And then he is idle again.

Scene I

Train roars. Lights flash outside the windows.

LULA *enters from the rear of the car in bright, skimpy summer clothes and sandals. She carries a net bag full of paper books, fruit, and other anonymous articles. She is wearing sunglasses, which she pushes up on her forehead from time to time.* LULA *is a tall, slender, beautiful woman with long red hair hanging straight down her back, wearing only loud lipstick in somebody's good taste. She is eating an apple, very daintily. Coming down the car toward* CLAY.

She stops beside CLAY's *seat and hangs languidly from the strap, still managing to eat the apple. It is apparent that she is going to sit in the seat next to* CLAY, *and that she is only waiting for him to notice her before she sits.*

CLAY *sits as before, looking just beyond his magazine, now and again pulling the magazine slowly back and forth in front of his face in a hopeless effort to fan himself. Then he sees the woman hanging there beside him and he looks up into her face, smiling quizzically.*

LULA: Hello.
CLAY: Uh, hi're you?
LULA: I'm going to sit down. . . . O.K.?
CLAY: Sure.
LULA: [*Swings down onto the seat, pushing her legs straight out as if she is very weary.*] Oooof! Too much weight.
CLAY: Ha, doesn't look like much to me. [*Leaning back against the window, a little surprised and maybe stiff.*]
LULA: It's so anyway.
        [*And she moves her toes in the sandals, then pulls her right leg up on the left knee, better to inspect the bottoms of the sandals and the back of her heel. She appears for a second not to notice that* CLAY *is sitting next to her or that she has spoken to him just a second before.* CLAY *looks at the magazine, then out the black window. As he does this, she turns very quickly toward him.*]
        Weren't you staring at me through the window?
CLAY: [*Wheeling around and very much stiffened.*] What?
LULA: Weren't you staring at me through the window? At the last stop?

CLAY: Staring at you? What do you mean?

LULA: Don't you know what staring means?

CLAY: I saw you through the window . . . if that's what it means. I don't know if I was staring. Seems to me you were staring through the window at me.

LULA: I was. But only after I'd turned around and saw you staring through that window down in the vicinity of my ass and legs.

CLAY: Really?

LULA: Really. I guess you were just taking those idle potshots. Nothing else to do. Run your mind over people's flesh.

CLAY: Oh boy. Wow, now I admit I was looking in your direction. But the rest of that weight is yours.

LULA: I suppose.

CLAY: Staring through train windows is weird business. Much weirder than staring very sedately at abstract asses.

LULA: That's why I came looking through the window . . . so you'd have more than that to go on. I even smiled at you.

CLAY: That's right.

LULA: I even got into this train, going some other way than mine. Walked down the aisle . . . searching you out.

CLAY: Really? That's pretty funny.

CLAY: [Cocking his head from one side to the other, embarrassed and trying to make some comeback, but also intrigued by what the woman is saying . . . even the sharp city coarseness of her voice, which is still a kind of gentle sidewalk throb.] Really? I look like all that?

LULA: Not all of it. [She feints a seriousness to cover an actual somber tone.] I lie a lot. [Smiling.] It helps me control the world.

CLAY: [Relieved and laughing louder than the humor.] Yeah, I bet.

LULA: But it's true, most of it, right? Jersey? Your bumpy neck?

CLAY: How'd you know all that? Huh? Really, I mean about Jersey . . . and even the beard. I met you before? You know Warren Enright?

LULA: You tried to make it with your sister when you were ten. [CLAY leans back hard against the back of the seat, his eyes opening now, still trying to look amused.] But I succeeded a few weeks ago. [She starts to laugh again.]

CLAY: What're you talking about? Warren tell you that? You're a friend of Georgia's?

LULA: I told you I lie. I don't know your sister. I don't know Warren Enright.

CLAY: You mean you're just picking these things out of the air?

LULA: Is Warren Enright a tall skinny black black boy with a phony English accent?

CLAY: I figured you knew him.

LULA: But I don't. I just figured you would know somebody like that. [Laughs.]

CLAY: Yeah, yeah.

LULA: You're probably on your way to his house now.

CLAY: That's right.

LULA: [Putting her hand on CLAY's closest knee, drawing it from the knee

*up to the thigh's hinge, then removing it, watching his face very closely,
and continuing to laugh, perhaps more gently than before.*] Dull, dull,
dull. I bet you think I'm exciting.

CLAY: You're O.K.

LULA: Am I exciting you now?

CLAY: Right. That's not what's supposed to happen?

LULA: That's pretty funny. . . . God, you're dull.

CLAY: Well, I'm sorry, lady, but I really wasn't prepared for party talk.

LULA: No, you're not. What are you prepared for? [*Wrapping the apple
core in a Kleenex and dropping it on the floor.*]

CLAY: [*Takes her conversation as pure sex talk. He turns to confront her
squarely with this idea.*] I'm prepared for anything. How about you?

LULA: [*Laughing loudly and cutting it off abruptly.*] What do you think
you're doing?

CLAY: What?

LULA: You think I want to pick you up, get you to take me somewhere and
screw me, huh?

CLAY: Is that the way I look?

LULA: You look like you been trying to grow a beard. That's exactly what
you look like. You look like you live in New Jersey with your parents and
are trying to grow a beard. That's what. You look like you've been reading Chinese poetry and drinking lukewarm sugarless tea.

[*Laughs, uncrossing and recrossing her legs.*]
You look like death eating a soda cracker.

LULA: How do I know?

[*She returns her hand, without moving it, then takes it away and
plunges it in her bag to draw out an apple.*]
You want this?

CLAY: Sure.

LULA: [*She gets one out of the bag for herself.*] Eating apples together is
always the first step. Or walking up uninhabited Seventh Avenue in the
twenties on weekends. [*Bites and giggles, glancing at* CLAY *and speaking
in loose sing-song.*] Can get you involved . . . boy! Get us involved. Um-
huh. [*Mock seriousness.*] Would you like to get involved with me, Mister
Man?

CLAY: [*Trying to be as flippant as* LULA, *whacking happily at the apple.*]
Sure. Why not? A beautiful woman like you. Huh, I'd be a fool not to.

LULA: And I bet you're sure you know what you're talking about. [*Taking
him a little roughly by the wrist, so he cannot eat the apple, then shaking
the wrist.*] I bet you're sure of almost everything anybody ever asked you
about . . . right? [*Shakes his wrist harder.*] Right?

CLAY: Yeah, right. . . . Wow, you're pretty strong, you know? Whatta you,
a lady wrestler or something?

LULA: What's wrong with lady wrestlers? And don't answer because you
never knew any. Huh. [*Cynically.*] That's for sure. They don't have any
lady wrestlers in that part of Jersey. That's for sure.

CLAY: Hey, you still haven't told me how you know so much about me.

LULA: I told you I didn't know anything about *you* . . . you're a well-known
type.

CLAY: Really?

LULA: Or at least I know the type very well. And your skinny English friend too.

CLAY: Anonymously?

LULA: [*Settles back in seat, single-mindedly finishing her apple and humming snatches of rhythm and blues song.*] What?

CLAY: Without knowing us specifically?

LULA: Oh boy. [*Looking quickly at* CLAY.] What a face. You know, you could be a handsome man.

CLAY: I can't argue with you.

LULA: [*Vague, off-center response.*] What?

CLAY: [*Raising his voice, thinking the train noise has drowned part of his sentence.*] I can't argue with you.

LULA: My hair is turning gray. A gray hair for each year and type I've come through.

CLAY: Why do you want to sound so old?

LULA: But it's always gentle when it starts. [*Attention drifting.*] Hugged against tenements, day or night.

CLAY: What?

LULA: [*Refocusing.*] Hey, why don't you take me to that party you're going to?

CLAY: You must be a friend of Warren's to know about the party.

LULA: Wouldn't you like to take me to the party? [*Imitates clinging vine.*] Oh, come on, ask me to your party.

CLAY: Of course I'll ask you to come with me to the party. And I'll bet you're a friend of Warren's.

LULA: Why not be a friend of Warren's? Why not? [*Taking his arm.*] Have you asked me yet?

CLAY: How can I ask you when I don't know your name?

LULA: Are you talking to my name?

CLAY: What is it, a secret?

LULA: I'm Lena the Hyena.

CLAY: The famous woman poet?

LULA: Poetess! The same!

CLAY: Well, you know so much about me . . . what's my name?

LULA: Morris the Hyena.

CLAY: The famous woman poet?

LULA: The same. [*Laughing and going into her bag.*] You want another apple?

CLAY: Can't make it, lady. I only have to keep one doctor away a day.

LULA: I bet your name is . . . something like . . . uh, Gerald or Walter. Huh?

CLAY: God, no.

LULA: Lloyd, Norman? One of those hopeless colored names creeping out of New Jersey. Leonard? Gag. . . .

CLAY: Like Warren?

LULA: Definitely. Just exactly like Warren. Or Everett.

CLAY: Gag. . . .

LULA: Well, for sure, it's not Willie.

CLAY: It's Clay.

LULA: Clay? Really? Clay what?

CLAY: Take your pick. Jackson, Johnson, or Williams.

LULA: Oh, really? Good for you. But it's got to be Williams. You're too
pretentious to be a Jackson or Johnson.

CLAY: Thass right.

LULA: But Clay's O.K.

CLAY: So's Lena.

LULA: It's Lula.

CLAY: Oh?

LULA: Lula the Hyena.

CLAY: Very good.

LULA: [Starts laughing again.] Now you say to me, "Lula, Lula, why don't
you go to this party with me tonight?" It's your turn, and let those be your
lines.

CLAY: Lula, why don't you go to this party with me tonight, Huh?

LULA: Say my name twice before you ask, and no huh's.

CLAY: Lula, Lula, why don't you go to this party with me tonight?

LULA: I'd like to go, Clay, but how can you ask me to go when you barely
know me?

CLAY: That is strange, isn't it?

LULA: What kind of reaction is that? You're supposed to say, "Aw, come
on, we'll get to know each other better at the party."

CLAY: That's pretty corny.

LULA: What are you into anyway? [Looking at him half sullenly but still
amused.] What thing are you playing at, Mister? Mister Clay Williams?
[Grabs his thigh, up near the crotch.] What are you thinking about?

CLAY: Watch it now, you're gonna excite me for real.

LULA: [Taking her hand away and throwing her apple core through the
window.] I bet. [She slumps in the seat and is heavily silent.]

CLAY: I thought you knew everything about me? What happened?
[LULA looks at him, then looks slowly away, then over where the other
aisle would be. Noise of the train. She reaches in her bag and pulls
out one of the paper books. She puts it on her leg and thumbs the
pages listlessly. CLAY cocks his head to see the title of the book. Noise
of the train. LULA flips pages and her eyes drift. Both remain silent.]
Are you going to the party with me, Lula?

LULA: [Bored and not even looking.] I don't even know you.

CLAY: You said you know my type.

LULA: [Strangely irritated.] Don't get smart with me, Buster. I know you
like the palm of my hand.

CLAY: The one you eat the apples with?

LULA: Yeh. And the one I open doors late Saturday evening with. That's
my door. Up at the top of the stairs. Five flights. Above a lot of Italians
and lying Americans. And scrape carrots with. Also . . . [Looks at him.]
the same hand I unbutton my dress with, or let my skirt fall down. Same
hand. Lover.

CLAY: Are you angry about anything? Did I say something wrong?

LULA: Everything you say is wrong. [Mock smile.] That's what makes you
so attractive. Ha. In that funnybook jacket with all the buttons. [More

animated, taking hold of his jacket.] What've you got that jacket and tie on in all this heat for? And why're you wearing a jacket and tie like that? Did your people ever burn witches or start revolutions over the price of tea? Boy, those narrow-shoulder clothes come from a tradition you ought to feel oppressed by. A three-button suit. What right do you have to be wearing a three-button suit and striped tie? Your grandfather was a slave, he didn't go to Harvard.

CLAY: My grandfather was a night watchman.

LULA: And you went to a colored college where everybody thought they were Averell Harriman.[1]

CLAY: All except me.

LULA: And who did you think you were? Who do you think you are now?

CLAY: [*Laughs as if to make light of the whole trend of the conversation.*] Well, in college I thought I was Baudelaire.[2] But I've slowed down since.

LULA: I bet you never once thought you were a black nigger. [*Mock serious, then she howls with laughter.* CLAY *is stunned but after initial reaction, he quickly tries to appreciate the humor.* LULA *almost shrieks.*] A black Baudelaire.

CLAY: That's right.

LULA: Boy, are you corny. I take back what I said before. Everything you say is not wrong. It's perfect. You should be on television.

CLAY: You act like you're on television already.

LULA: That's because I'm an actress.

CLAY: I thought so.

LULA: Well, you're wrong. I'm no actress. I told you I always lie. I'm nothing, honey, and don't you ever forget it. [*Lighter.*] Although my mother was a Communist. The only person in my family ever to amount to anything.

CLAY: My mother was a Republican.

LULA: And your father voted for the man rather than the party.

CLAY: Right!

LULA: Yea for him. Yea, yea for him.

CLAY: Yea!

LULA: And yea for America where he is free to vote for the mediocrity of his choice! Yea!

CLAY: Yea!

LULA: And yea for both your parents who even though they differ about so crucial a matter as the body politic still forged a union of love and sacrifice that was destined to flower at the birth of the noble Clay . . . what's your middle name?

CLAY: Clay.

LULA: A union of love and sacrifice that was destined to flower at the birth of the noble Clay Clay Williams. Yea! And most of all yea yea for you, Clay Clay. The Black Baudelaire! Yes! [*And with knifelike cynicism.*] My Christ. My Christ.

---

1. Democratic politician, businessman, and author (1891–1986).   2. French Symbolist poet (1821–1867).

CLAY: Thank you, ma'am.

LULA: May the people accept you as a ghost of the future. And love you, that you might not kill them when you can.

CLAY: What?

LULA: You're a murderer, Clay, and you know it. [*Her voice darkening with significance.*] You know goddamn well what I mean.

CLAY: I do?

LULA: So we'll pretend the air is light and full of perfume.

CLAY: [*Sniffing at her blouse.*] It is.

LULA: And we'll pretend the people cannot see you. That is, the citizens. And that you are free of your own history. And I am free of my history. We'll pretend that we are both anonymous beauties smashing along through the city's entrails. [*She yells as loud as she can.*] GROOVE! [*Black.*]

Scene II

Scene is the same as before, though now there are other seats visible in the car. And throughout the scene other people get on the subway. There are maybe one or two seated in the car as the scene opens, though neither CLAY *nor* LULA *notices them.* CLAY's *tie is open.* LULA *is hugging his arm.*

CLAY: The party!

LULA: I know it'll be something good. You can come in with me, looking casual and significant. I'll be strange, haughty, and silent, and walk with long slow strides.

CLAY: Right.

LULA: When you get drunk, pat me once, very lovingly on the flanks, and I'll look at you cryptically, licking my lips.

CLAY: It sounds like something we can do.

LULA: You'll go around talking to young men about your mind, and to old men about your plans. If you meet a very close friend who is also with someone like me, we can stand together, sipping our drinks and exchanging codes of lust. The atmosphere will be slithering in love and half-love and very open moral decision.

CLAY: Great. Great.

LULA: And everyone will pretend they don't know your name, and then . . . [*She pauses heavily.*] later, when they have to, they'll claim a friendship that denies your sterling character.

CLAY: [*Kissing her neck and fingers.*] And then what?

LULA: Then? Well, then we'll go down the street, late night, eating apples and winding very deliberately toward my house.

CLAY: Deliberately?

LULA: I mean, we'll look in all the shopwindows, and make fun of the queers. Maybe we'll meet a Jewish Buddhist and flatten his conceits over some very pretentious coffee.

CLAY: In honor of whose God?

LULA: Mine.

CLAY: Who is . . . ?

LULA: Me . . . and you?

CLAY: A corporate Godhead.
LULA: Exactly. Exactly. [*Notices one of the other people entering.*]
CLAY: Go on with the chronicle. Then what happens to us?
LULA: [*A mild depression, but she still makes her description triumphant and increasingly direct.*] To my house, of course.
CLAY: Of course.
LULA: And up the narrow steps of the tenement.
CLAY: You live in a tenement?
LULA: Wouldn't live anywhere else. Reminds me specifically of my novel form of insanity.
CLAY: Up the tenement stairs.
LULA: And with my apple-eating hand I push open the door and lead you, my tender big-eyed prey, into my . . . God, what can I call it . . . into my hovel.
CLAY: Then what happens?
LULA: After the dancing and games, after the long drinks and long walks, the real fun begins.
CLAY: Ah, the real fun. [*Embarrassed, in spite of himself.*] Which is . . . ?
LULA: [*Laughs at him.*] Real fun in the dark house. Hah! Real fun in the dark house, high up above the street and the ignorant cowboys. I lead you in, holding your wet hand gently in my hand . . .
CLAY: Which is not wet?
LULA: Which is dry as ashes.
CLAY: And cold?
LULA: Don't think you'll get out of your responsibility that way. It's not cold at all. Your Fascist! Into my dark living room. Where we'll sit and talk endlessly, endlessly.
CLAY: About what?
LULA: About what? About your manhood, what do you think? What do you think we've been talking about all this time?
CLAY: Well, I didn't know it was that. That's for sure. Every other thing in the world but that. [*Notices another person entering, looks quickly, almost involuntarily up and down the car, seeing the other people in the car.*] Hey, I didn't even notice when those people got on.
LULA: Yeah, I know.
CLAY: Man, this subway is slow.
LULA: Yeah, I know.
CLAY: Well, go on. We were talking about my manhood.
LULA: We still are. All the time.
CLAY: We were in your living room.
LULA: My dark living room. Talking endlessly.
CLAY: About my manhood.
LULA: I'll make you a map of it. Just as soon as we get to my house.
CLAY: Well, that's great.
LULA: One of the things we do while we talk. And screw.
CLAY: [*Trying to make his smile broader and less shaky.*] We finally got there.
LULA: And you'll call my rooms black as a grave. You'll say, "This place is like Juliet's tomb."
CLAY: [*Laughs.*] I might.

LULA: I know. You've probably said it before.

CLAY: And is that all? The whole grand tour?

LULA: Not all. You'll say to me very close to my face, many, many times, you'll say, even whisper, that you love me.

CLAY: Maybe I will.

LULA: And you'll be lying.

CLAY: I wouldn't lie about something like that.

LULA: Hah. It's the only kind of thing you will lie about. Especially if you think it'll keep me alive.

CLAY: Keep you alive? I don't understand.

LULA: [*Bursting out laughing, but too shrilly.*] Don't understand? Well, don't look at me. It's the path I take, that's all. Where both feet take me when I set them down. One in front of the other.

CLAY: Morbid. Morbid. You sure you're not an actress? All that self-aggrandizement.

LULA: Well, I told you I wasn't an actress . . . but I also told you I lie all the time. Draw your own conclusions.

CLAY: Morbid. Morbid. You sure you're not an actress? All scribed? There's no more?

LULA: I've told you all I know. Or almost all.

CLAY: There's no funny parts?

LULA: I thought it was all funny.

CLAY: But you mean peculiar, not ha-ha.

LULA: You don't know what I mean.

CLAY: Well, tell me the almost part then. You said almost all. What else? I want the whole story.

LULA: [*Searching aimlessly through her bag. She begins to talk breathlessly, with a light and silly tone.*] All stories are whole stories. All of 'em. Our whole story . . . nothing but change. How could things go on like that forever? Huh?

  [*Slaps him on the shoulder, begins finding things in her bag, taking them out and throwing them over her shoulder into the aisle.*]

Except I do go on as I do. Apples and long walks with deathless intelligent lovers. But you mix it up. Look out the window, all the time. Turning pages. Change change change. Till, shit, I don't know you. Wouldn't, for that matter. You're too serious. I bet you're even too serious to be psychoanalyzed. Like all those Jewish poets from Yonkers,[3] who leave their mothers looking for other mothers, or others' mothers, on whose baggy tits they lay their fumbling heads. Their poems are always funny, and all about sex.

CLAY: They sound great. Like movies.

LULA: But you change. [*Blankly.*] And things work on you till you hate them.

  [*More people come into the train. They come closer to the couple, some of them not sitting, but swinging drearily on the straps, staring at the two with uncertain interest.*]

---

3. A city in southeastern New York. Perhaps a reference to Allen Ginsberg's poetry, especially his collection *Kaddish and Other Poems* (1961).

CLAY: Wow. All these people, so suddenly. They must all come from the same place.

LULA: Right. That they do.

CLAY: Oh? You know about them too?

LULA: Oh yeah. About them more than I know about you. Do they frighten you?

CLAY: Frighten me? Why should they frighten me?

LULA: 'Cause you're an escaped nigger.

CLAY: Yeah?

LULA: 'Cause you crawled through the wire and made tracks to my side.

CLAY: Wire?

LULA: Don't they have wire around plantations?

CLAY: You must be Jewish. All you can think about is wire. Plantations didn't have any wire. Plantations were big open whitewashed places like heaven, and everybody on 'em was grooved to be there. Just strummin' and hummin' all day.

LULA: Yes, yes.

CLAY: And that's how the blues was born.

LULA: Yes, yes. And that's how the blues was born. [*Begins to make up a song that becomes quickly hysterical. As she sings she rises from her seat, still throwing things out of her bag into the aisle, beginning a rhythmical shudder and twistlike wiggle, which she continues up and down the aisle, bumping into many of the standing people and tripping over the feet of those sitting. Each time she runs into a person she lets out a very vicious piece of profanity, wiggling and stepping all the time.*] And that's how the blues was born. Yes. Yes. Son of a bitch, get out of the way. Yes. Quack. Yes. Yes. And that's how the blues was born. Ten little niggers sitting on a limb, but none of them ever looked like him. [*Points to* CLAY, *returns toward the seat, with her hands extended for him to rise and dance with her.*] And that's how blues was born. Yes. Come on, Clay. Let's do the nasty. Rub bellies. Rub bellies.

CLAY: [*Waves his hands to refuse. He is embarrassed, but determined to get a kick out of the proceedings.*] Hey, what was in those apples? Mirror, mirror on the wall, who's the fairest one of all? Snow White, baby, and don't you forget it.

LULA: [*Grabbing for his hands, which he draws away.*] Come on, Clay. Let's rub bellies on the train. The nasty. The nasty. Do the gritty grind, like your ol' rag-head mammy. Grind till you lose your mind. Shake it, shake it, shake it, shake it! OOOOweeee! Come on, Clay. Let's do the choo-choo train shuffle, the navel scratcher.

CLAY: Hey, you coming on like the lady who smoked up her grass skirt.

LULA: [*Becoming annoyed that he will not dance, and becoming more animated as if to embarrass him still further.*] Come on, Clay . . . let's do the thing. Uhh! Uhh! Clay! Clay! You middle-class black bastard. Forget your social-working mother for a few seconds and let's knock stomachs. Clay, you liver-lipped white man. You would-be Christian. You ain't no nigger, you're just a dirty white man. Get up, Clay. Dance with me, Clay.

CLAY: Lula! Sit down, now. Be cool.

LULA: [*Mocking him, in wild dance.*] Be cool. Be cool. That's all you
know . . . shaking that wildroot cream-oil on your knotty head, jackets
buttoning up to your chin, so full of white man's words. Christ. God. Get
up and scream at these people. Like scream meaningless shit in these
hopeless faces. [*She screams at people in train, still dancing.*] Red trains
cough Jewish underwear for keeps! Expanding smells of silence. Gravy
snot whistling like sea birds. Clay. Clay, you got to break out. Don't sit
there dying the way they want you to die. Get up.

CLAY: Oh, sit the fuck down. [*He moves to restrain her.*] Sit down, goddamn it.

LULA: [*Twisting out of his reach.*] Screw yourself, Uncle Tom. Thomas
Woolly-head.

     [*Begins to dance a kind of jig, mocking* CLAY *with loud forced
humor.*]

     There is Uncle Tom . . . I mean, Uncle Thomas Woolly-Head. With old
white matted mane. He hobbles on his wooden cane. Old Tom. Old
Tom. Let the white man hump his ol' mama, and he jes' shuffle off in
the woods and hide his gentle gray head. Ol' Thomas Woolly-Head.

     [*Some of the other riders are laughing now. A drunk gets up and joins*
LULA *in her dance, singing, as best he can, her "song."* CLAY *gets up
out of his seat and visibly scans the faces of the other riders.*]

CLAY: Lula! Lula!

     [*She is dancing and turning, still shouting as loud as she can. The
drunk too is shouting, and waving his hands wildly.*]

     Lula . . . you dumb bitch. Why don't you stop it? [*He rushes half stum-
bling from his seat, and grabs one of her flailing arms.*]

LULA: Let me go! You black son of a bitch. [*She struggles against him.*]
Let me go! Help!

     [CLAY *is dragging her towards her seat, and the drunk seeks to inter-
fere. He grabs* CLAY *around the shoulders and begins wrestling with
him.* CLAY *clubs the drunk to the floor without releasing* LULA, *who is
still screaming.* CLAY *finally gets her to the seat and throws her into it*]

CLAY: Now you shut the hell up. [*Grabbing her shoulders.*] Just shut up.
You don't know what you're talking about. You don't know anything. So
just keep your stupid mouth closed.

LULA: You're afraid of white people. And your father was. Uncle Tom Big
Lip!

CLAY: [*Slaps her as hard as he can, across the mouth.* LULA's *head bangs
against the back of the seat. When she raises it again,* CLAY *slaps her
again.*] Now shut up and let me talk.

     [*He turns toward the other riders, some of whom are sitting on the
edge of their seats. The drunk is on one knee, rubbing his head, and
singing softly the same song. He shuts up too when he sees* CLAY
*watching him. The others go back to newspapers or stare out the win-
dows.*]

     Shit, you don't have any sense, Lula, nor feelings either. I could murder
you now. Such a tiny ugly throat. I could squeeze it flat, and watch
you turn blue, on a humble. For dull kicks. And all these weak-faced

ofays[4] squatting around here, staring over their papers at me. Murder them too. Even if they expected it. That man there . . . [*Points to well-dressed man.*] I could rip that *Times* right out of his hand, as skinny and middle-classed as I am, I could rip that paper out of his hand and just as easily rip out his throat. It takes no great effort. For what? To kill you soft idiots? You don't understand anything but luxury.

LULA: You fool!

CLAY: [*Pushing her against the seat.*] I'm not telling you again, Tallulah Bankhead![5] Luxury. In your face and your fingers. You telling me what I ought to do. [*Sudden scream frightening the whole coach.*] Well, don't! Don't you tell me anything! If I'm a middle-class fake white man . . . let me be. And let me be in the way I want. [*Through his teeth*] I'll rip your lousy breasts off! Let me be who I feel like being. Uncle Tom. Thomas. Whoever. It's none of your business. You don't know anything except what's there for you to see. An act. Lies. Device. Not the pure heart, the pumping black heart. You don't ever know that. And I sit here, in this buttoned-up suit, to keep myself from cutting all your throats. I mean wantonly. You great liberated whore! You fuck some black man, and right away you're an expert on black people. What a lotta shit that is. The only thing you know is that you come if he bangs you hard enough. And that's all. The belly rub? You wanted to do the belly rub? Shit, you don't even know how. You don't know how. That ol' dipty-dip shit you do, rolling your ass like an elephant. That's not my kind of belly rub. Belly rub is not Queens. Belly rub is dark places, with big hats and overcoats held up with one arm. Belly rub hates you. Old bald-headed four-eyed ofays popping their fingers . . . and don't know yet what they're doing. They say, "I love Bessie Smith."[6] And don't even understand that Bessie Smith is saying, "Kiss my ass, kiss my black unruly ass." Before love, suffering, desire, anything you can explain, she's saying, and very plainly, "Kiss my black ass." And if you don't know that, it's you that's doing the kissing.

Charlie Parker?[7] Charlie Parker. All the hip white boys scream for Bird. And Bird saying, "Up your ass, feeble-minded ofay! Up your ass." And they sit there talking about the tortured genius of Charlie Parker. Bird would've played not a note of music if he just walked up to East Sixty-seventh Street and killed the first ten white people he saw. Not a note! And I'm the great would-be poet. Yes. That's right! Poet. Some kind of bastard literature . . . all it needs is a simple knife thrust. Just let me bleed you, you loud whore, and one poem vanished. A whole people of neurotics, struggling to keep from being sane. And the only thing that would cure the neurosis would be your murder. Simple as that. I mean if I murdered you, then other white people would begin to understand me. You understand? No. I guess not. If Bessie Smith had killed some white people she wouldn't have needed that music. She could have talked very

---

4. A derogatory term for white people. "On a humble": immediately, without hesitation.
5. Southern actress (1902–1968) whose acting was considered by many to be banal.

6. Blues and jazz singer (1898–1937).
7. Jazz saxophonist (1920–1955); he was called "Bird."

straight and plain about the world. No metaphors. No grunts. No wiggles in the dark of her soul. Just straight two and two are four. Money. Power. Luxury. Like that. All of them. Crazy niggers turning their backs on sanity. When all it needs is that simple act. Murder. Just murder! Would make us all sane. [*Suddenly weary.*]

Ahhh. Shit. But who needs it? I'd rather be a fool. Insane. Safe with my words, and no deaths, and clean, hard thoughts, urging me to new conquests. My people's madness. Hah! That's a laugh. My people. They don't need me to claim them. They got legs and arms of their own. Personal insanities. Mirrors. They don't need all those words. They don't need any defense. But listen, though, one more thing. And you tell this to your father, who's probably the kind of man who needs to know at once. So he can plan ahead. Tell him not to preach so much rationalism and cold logic to these niggers. Let them alone. Let them sing curses at you in code and see your filth as simple lack of style. Don't make the mistake, through some irresponsible surge of Christian charity, of talking too much about the advantages of Western rationalism, or the great intellectual legacy of the white man, or maybe they'll begin to listen. And then, maybe one day, you'll find they actually do understand exactly what you are talking about, all these fantasy people. All these blues people. And on that day, as sure as shit, when you really believe you can "accept" them into your fold, as half-white trusties late of the subject peoples. With no more blues, except the very old ones, and not a watermelon in sight, the great missionary heart will have triumphed, and all of those ex-coons will be stand-up Western men, with eyes for clean hard useful lives, sober, pious and sane, and they'll murder you. They'll murder you, and have very rational explanations. Very much like your own. They'll cut your throats, and drag you out to the edge of your cities so the flesh can fall away from your bones, in sanitary isolation.

LULA: [*Her voice takes on a different, more businesslike quality.*] I've heard enough.

CLAY: [*Reaching for his books.*] I bet you have. I guess I better collect my stuff and get off this train. Looks like we won't be acting out that little pageant you outlined before.

LULA: No. We won't. You're right about that, at least. [*She turns to look quickly around the rest of the car.*]

All right! [*The others respond.*]

CLAY: [*Bending across the girl to retrieve his belongings.*]

Sorry, baby, I don't think we could make it. [*As he is bending over her, the girl brings up a small knife and plunges it into* CLAY's *chest. Twice. He slumps across her knees, his mouth working stupidly.*]

LULA: Sorry is right. [*Turning to the others in the car who have already gotten up from their seats.*]

Sorry is the rightest thing you've said. Get this man off me! Hurry, now! [*The others come and drag* CLAY's *body down the aisle.*]

Open the door and throw his body out. [*They throw him off.*]

And all of you get off at the next stop.

[LULA *busies herself straightening her things. Getting everything in order. She takes out a notebook and makes a quick scribbling note.*

*Drops it in her bag. The train apparently stops and all the others get
off, leaving her alone in the coach.*
    Very soon a YOUNG NEGRO *of about twenty comes into the coach,
with a couple of books under his arm. He sits a few seats in back of*
LULA. *When he is seated she turns and gives him a long slow look. He
looks up from his book and drops the book on his lap. Then an old
Negro* CONDUCTOR *comes into the car, doing a sort of restrained soft
shoe, and half mumbling the words of some song. He looks at the*
YOUNG MAN, *briefly, with a quick greeting.*]
CONDUCTOR: Hey, brother!
YOUNG MAN: Hey. [*The* CONDUCTOR *continues down the aisle with his little dance and the mumbled song.* LULA *turns to stare at him and follows
his movements down the aisle. The* CONDUCTOR *tips his hat when he
reaches her seat, and continues out the car.*]
                                  [*Curtain.*]
                                    1964

The Revolutionary Theatre

The Revolutionary Theatre should force change; it should be change.
(All their faces turned into the lights and you work on them black nigger
magic, and cleanse them at having seen the ugliness. And if the beautiful
see themselves, they will love themselves.) We are preaching virtue again,
but by that to mean NOW, toward what seems the most constructive use of
the world.

The Revolutionary Theatre must EXPOSE! Show up the insides of
these humans, look into black skulls. White men will cower before this
theatre because it hates them. Because they themselves have been trained
to hate. The Revolutionary Theatre must hate them for hating. For presuming with their technology to deny the supremacy of the Spirit. They
will all die because of this.

The Revolutionary Theatre must teach them their deaths. It must crack
their faces open to the mad cries of the poor. It must teach them about
silence and the truths lodged there. It must kill any God anyone names
except Common Sense. The Revolutionary Theatre should flush the fags
and murders out of Lincoln's face.

It should stagger through our universe correcting, insulting, preaching,
spitting craziness—but a craziness taught to us in our most rational moments. People must be taught to trust true scientists (knowers, diggers, odd-
balls) and that the holiness of life is the constant possibility of widening the
consciousness. And they must be incited to strike back against *any* agency
that attempts to prevent this widening.

The Revolutionary Theatre must Accuse and Attack anything that can
be accused and attacked. It must Accuse and Attack because it is a theatre
of Victims. It looks at the sky with the victims' eyes, and moves the victims
to look at the strength in their minds and their bodies.

Clay, in *Dutchman*, Ray in *The Toilet*, Walker in *The Slave*, are all victims. In the Western sense they could be heroes. But the Revolutionary

Theatre, even if it is Western, must be anti-Western. It must show horrible coming attractions of *The Crumbling of the West*. Even as Artaud[1] designed *The Conquest of Mexico*, so we must design *The Conquest of White Eye*, and show the missionaries and wiggly Liberals dying under blasts of concrete. For sound effects, wild screams of joy, from all the peoples of the world.

The Revolutionary Theatre must take dreams and give them a reality. It must isolate the ritual and historical cycles of reality. But it must be food for all those who need food, and daring propaganda for the beauty of the Human Mind. It is a political theatre, a weapon to help in the slaughter of these dim-witted fatbellied white guys who somehow believe that the rest of the world is here for them to slobber on.

This should be a theatre of World Spirit. Where the spirit can be shown to be the most competent force in the world. Force. Spirit. Feeling. The language will be anybody's, but tightened by the poet's backbone. And even the language must show what the facts are in this consciousness epic, what's happening. We will talk about the world, and the preciseness with which we are able to summon the world will be our art. Art is method. And art, "like any ashtray or senator," remains in the world. Wittgenstein[2] said ethics and aesthetics are one. I believe this. So the Broadway theatre is a theatre of reaction whose ethics, like its aesthetics, reflect the spiritual values of this unholy society, which sends young crackers all over the world blowing off colored people's heads. (In some of these flippy Southern towns they even shoot up the immigrants' Favorite Son, be it Michael Schwerner[3] or JFKennedy.)

The Revolutionary Theatre is shaped by the world, and moves to reshape the world, using as its force the natural force and perpetual vibrations of the mind in the world. We are history and desire, what we are, and what any experience can make us.

It is a social theatre, but all theatre is social theatre. But we will change the drawing rooms into places where real things can be said about a real world, or into smoky rooms where the destruction of Washington can be plotted. The Revolutionary Theatre must function like an incendiary pencil planted in Curtis Lemay's[4] cap. So that when the final curtain goes down brains are splattered over the seats and the floor, and bleeding nuns must wire SOS's to Belgians with gold teeth.[5]

Our theatre will show victims so that their brothers in the audience will be better able to understand that they are the brothers of victims, and that they themselves are victims if they are blood brothers. And what we show must cause the blood to rush, so that pre-revolutionary temperaments will be bathed in this blood, and it will cause their deepest souls to move, and they will find themselves tensed and clenched, even ready to die, at what

---

1. Antonin Artaud (1896–1948), French actor, producer, playwright, and poet. In his abstract play *The Conquest of Mexico*, Hernando Cortés and the colonial Spaniards are defeated.
2. Ludwig Wittgenstein (1889–1951), Austrian philosopher.
3. White civil rights worker who was killed in 1964, along with two other workers (one white, one black), in Mississippi.
4. Former member of the Joint Chiefs of Staff and author of *America Is in Danger* (1968), in which he criticized U.S. military and diplomatic policy.
5. Perhaps a reference to Catholic missionaries who worked in the Congo when it was a Belgian colony.

the soul has been taught. We will scream and cry, murder, run through the streets in agony, if it means some soul will be moved, moved to actual life understanding of what the world is, and what it ought to be. We are preaching virtue and feeling, and a natural sense of the self in the world. All men live in the world, and the world ought to be a place for them to live.

What is called the imagination (from image, magi, magic, magician, etc.) is a practical vector from the soul. It stores all data, and can be called on to solve all our "problems." The imagination is the projection of ourselves past our sense of ourselves as "things." Imagination (Image) is all possibility, because from the image, the initial circumscribed energy, any use (idea) is possible. And so begins that image's use in the world. Possibility is what moves us.

The popular white man's theatre like the popular white man's novel shows tired white lives, and the problems of eating white sugar, or else it herds bigcaboosed blondes onto huge stages in rhinestones and makes believe they are dancing or singing. WHITE BUSINESSMEN OF THE WORLD, DO YOU WANT TO SEE PEOPLE REALLY DANCING AND SINGING??? ALL OF YOU GO UP TO HARLEM AND GET YOURSELF KILLED. THERE WILL BE DANCING AND SINGING, THEN, FOR REAL!! (In *The Slave*, Walker Vessels, the black revolutionary, wears an armband, which is the insignia of the attacking army—a big red-lipped minstrel, grinning like crazy.)

The liberal white man's objection to the theatre of the revolution (if he is "hip" enough) will be on aesthetic grounds. Most white Western artists do not need to be "political," since usually, whether they know it or not, they are in complete sympathy with the most repressive social forces in the world today. There are more junior birdmen fascists running around the West today disguised as Artists than there are disguised as fascists. (But then, that word, *Fascist*, and with it, *Fascism*, has been made obsolete by the words *America* and *Americanism*.) The American Artist usually turns out to be just a super-Bourgeois, because, finally, all he has to show for his sojourn through the world is "better taste" than the Bourgeois—many times not even that.

Americans will hate the Revolutionary Theatre because it will be out to destroy them and whatever they believe is real. American cops will try to close the theatres where such nakedness of the human spirit is paraded. American producers will say the revolutionary plays are filth, usually because they will treat human life as if it were actually happening. American directors will say that the white guys in the plays are too abstract and cowardly ("don't get me wrong . . . I mean aesthetically . . .") and they will be right.

The force we want is of twenty million spooks storming America with furious cries and unstoppable weapons. We want actual explosions and actual brutality: AN EPIC IS CRUMBLING and we must give it the space and hugeness of its actual demise. The Revolutionary Theatre, which is now peopled with victims, will soon begin to be peopled with new kinds of heroes—not the weak Hamlets debating whether or not they are ready to die for what's on their minds, but men and women (and minds) digging out from under a thousand years of "high art" and weak-faced dalliance.

We must make an art that will function so as to call down the actual wrath of world spirit. We are witch doctors and assassins, but we will open a place for the true scientists to expand our consciousness. This is a theatre of assault. The play that will split the heavens for us will be called THE DE-STRUCTION OF AMERICA. The heroes will be Crazy Horse, Denmark Vesey, Patrice Lumumba,[6] and not history, not memory, not sad sentimental groping for a warmth in our despair; these will be new men, new heroes, and their enemies most of you who are reading this.

1969

6. African nationalist leader (1925–1961) who was the first prime minister of the Democratic Republic of the Congo (now Zaire). Crazy Horse (1849– 1877), Ogala Sioux war chief. Vessey (1767–1822), leader of a failed 1822 slave revolt in South Carolina.

SONIA SANCHEZ
b. 1934

One of the most admired and respected poets of the Black Arts movement, Sonia Sanchez was born in Birmingham, Alabama, and was reared in Harlem. After graduating from Hunter College in 1955, she began work on behalf of the Congress of Racial Equality. Her early ideals were integrationist; however, after hearing a powerful speech by Malcolm X—on a rainy Sunday afternoon in New York during the early 1960s—she became a vernacular poet for the African American masses.

In the late sixties, Sanchez helped to forward the movement for black studies at San Francisco State College. There, the black studies movement met its first severe challenges: the administrators and board of trustees worked hard to discredit the program. Eventually, under the leadership of S. I. Hayakawa, black studies was eliminated—a whole department was closed down. Sanchez, Nathan Hare, and others were in the forefront of the resistance to such actions. The San Francisco State black studies model—with its strong and legitimate demands for departmental autonomy and nonstandardized curricula—was in some ways the diametrical opposite of Yale's more accommodationist black studies project.

In the 1970s, Sanchez headed the Afro-American Studies Program at Amherst College, frequently confronting the hostility or indifference of the college's president and deans. Later in the decade, she became a well-known spokesperson for the Nation of Islam. She was idealistic when she entered the Nation in 1972, but she was literally evicted from its Chicago offices in 1975. Afterward, she taught as a visiting professor in African American studies and English at the University of Pennsylvania.

Sanchez has never separated her work as an essayist, poet, short story writer, and dramatist from her life as an academic, teacher, and critic. Her extensive travels have included visits to Cuba, China, and Scandinavia. Certainly Sanchez's most remarkable quality is her dazzling performative style. She does not read her works in the manner of, say, a slow-paced professor of British literature. Rather, she invokes the vocal intonations of Africa and African America in performance, moving audiences to call/response interaction that can make the rafters of the largest auditoriums ring.

Beginning with the slim volume *Homecoming* (1969), her work has progressed through dozens of collections of verse, dramas, children's books, and critical and familiar essays. A more recent volume, *homegirls & handgrenades* (1984), received the American Book Award in 1985. Speaking in a voice that resounds with the blues beat of late-night worrying and the early-morning energy of revolution, Sanchez's poems maintain a freshness and attraction almost unmatched by those of any other poet of the Black Arts movement.

homecoming

i have been a
way so long
once after college
i returned tourist
style to watch all   5
the niggers killing
themselves with
3 for oners[1]
with
needles   10
that
cd
not support
their
stutters.   15
               now woman
i have returned
leaving behind me
all those hide and
seek faces peeling   20
with freudian dreams.
this is for real.
               black
       niggers
               my beauty.   25
baby.
i have learned it
ain't like they say
in the newspapers.

                                        1969

poem at thirty

it is midnight
no magical bewitching
hour for me
i know only that
i am here waiting   5
remembering that
once as a child

---

1. A method of selling heroin to new users; the discount offering is a means of expanding the market by creating new addicts.

i walked two
miles in my sleep.
did i know   10
then where i
was going?
traveling. i'm
always traveling.
i want to tell   15
you about me
about nights on a
brown couch when
i wrapped my
bones in lint and   20
refused to move.
no one touches
me anymore.
father do not
send me out   25
among strangers.
you you black man
stretching scraping
the mold from your body.
here is my hand.   30
i am not afraid
of the night.

                                                    1969

for our lady

yeh.
        billie. [1]   if someone
had loved u like u
shud have been loved
ain't no tellin what   5
kinds of songs
                u wud have swung
gainst this country's wite mind.
or what kinds of lyrics
                wud have pushed us from   10
our blue / nites.
                yeh.   billie.
if some blk / man
                had reallee
made u feel   15
                permanentlee warm.
ain't no tellen
                where the jazz of yo / songs.
                wud have led us.

                                                    1969

1. Billie Holiday (1915–1959), jazz vocalist, was frequently referred to as Lady Day.

Summer Words of a Sistuh Addict

the first day i shot dope
was on a sunday.
       i had just come
home from church
       got mad at my motha   5
cuz she got mad at me. u dig?
       went out. shot up
behind a feelen against her.
       it felt good.
gooder than dooing it. yeah.   10
       it was nice.
i did it. uh huh. i did it.   uh. huh.
i want to do it again. it felt so gooooood.
       and as the sistuh
       sits in her silent /   15
       remembered / high
       someone leans for
       ward gently asks her:
       sistuh.
       did u   20
       finally
       learn how to hold yo / mother?
and the music of the day
       drifts in the room
to mingle with the sistuh's young tears.   25
       and we all sing.

                        1969

From A Blues Book for Blue Black Magical Women

From *Part Three*

PRESENT

1

This woman vomiting her
hunger over the world
this melancholy woman forgotten
before memory came
this yellow movement bursting forth like   5
coltrane's[1] melodies all mouth
buttocks moving like palm trees,
this honeycoatedalabamianwoman
raining rhythms of blue/black/smiles
this yellow woman carrying beneath her breasts   10
pleasures without tongues
this woman whose body weaves

---

1. John Coltrane (1926–1967), jazz saxophonist.

desert patterns,
this woman, wet with wandering,
reviving the beauty of forests and winds   15
is telling you secrets
gather up your odors and listen
as she sings the mold from memory.

                       there is no place
for a soft/black/woman.   20
there is no smile green enough or
summertime words warm enough to allow my growth.
and in my head
i see my history
standing like a shy child   25
and i chant lullabies
as i ride my past on horseback
tasting the thirst of yesterday tribes
hearing the ancient / black / woman
me, singing   hay-hay-hay-hay-ya-ya-ya   30
                  hay-hay-hay-hay-ya-ya-ya.
like a slow scent
beneath the sun
           and i dance my
creation and my grandmothers gathering   35
from my bones like great wooden birds
spread their wings
while their long / legged / laughter
stretches the night.
             and i taste the   40
seasons of my birth. mangoes. papayas.
drink my woman / coconut / milks
stalk the ancient grandfathers
sipping on proud afternoons
walk with a song round my waist   45
tremble like a new / born / child troubled
with new breaths
             and my singing
becomes the only sound of a
blue / black / magical / woman. walking.   50
womb ripe. walking. loud with mornings. walking
making pilgrimage to herself. walking.

                                             1974

ED BULLINS

b. 1935

Considered one of the most prolific and influential playwrights, producers, essayists, and short story writers of the Black Arts movement, Ed Bullins was born in Philadelphia, Pennsylvania, to Bertha Marie Queen and Edward Bullins. Shortly after quitting high school, Bullins joined the navy but later returned to Philadelphia to complete his secondary education. His writing career began in 1958 when he entered Los Angeles City College and began reading extensively and writing short stories. However, it was not until 1964, when Bullins enrolled in the creative writing program at San Francisco State College, that he began to write plays.

In the mid-1960s, unable to find anyone in San Francisco who was willing to produce his plays, Bullins formed several theater companies and produced his work himself, in lofts, coffeehouses, and bars. In 1967, after reading some of Bullins's work, director Robert Macbeth invited the playwright to join the newly established New Lafayette Theatre in Harlem. Bullins's first works, produced in 1968 at the New Lafayette, *Three Plays by Ed Bullins* (*The Electronic Nigger; A Son, Come Home*; and *Clara's Ole Man*), were quite successful and won him the Vernon Rice Drama Desk Award. Bullins remained a central figure to the New Lafayette until the company's demise in 1972. In 1973, Bullins served as the playwright-in-residence at the American Place Theatre, also in New York City; and for the next ten years, he was on staff at the Public Theatre's New York Shakespeare Festival.

The recipient of two Guggenheim fellowships; three Rockefeller grants; an honorary doctorate from Columbia College in Chicago; and Obie awards for *In New England Winter* (1971), *The Fabulous Miss Marie* (1971), and *The Taking of Miss Janie* (1975), Bullins has greatly influenced American theater and literature. His work, characterized by a disdain for ineffective political rhetoric as a substitute for action, most often examines the lives of black people in inner-city ghettos and offers the audience the opportunity to interact verbally with the actors.

Beginning in 1965 with his first short play, *How Do You Do?*, Bullins has written more than fifty plays, over forty of which have been professionally produced. His work has progressed through a book of short stories, *The Hungered One, Early Writings* (1971); dozens of plays, including *In the Wine Time* (1969) and *Goin'a Buffalo* (1969); two children's plays, *I Am Lucy Terry* (1976) and *The Mystery of Phyllis Wheatley* (1976); and the books for two musicals, *Sepia Star* (1977) and *Storyville* (1977). He currently resides in the San Francisco area.

In *Goin'a Buffalo*, Bullins questions the meaning of love and loyalty. The characters are essentially alone and in search of the one person that they can trust. However, they are often unaware of the consequences of their actions. Bullins explores the contradictions between the promise of the American Dream and the reality of the lives of black Americans. He focuses on the efforts of street people to transcend the brutally harsh realities of their existence.

Goin'a Buffalo: A Tragifantasy

> Sometimes . . .
> I'd like to be
> a Stranger in town . . .
> Sort'a mysterious.
> Strange tales would be
> told about me . . .
> And they would be
> FANTASTIC!
> —MARTIN P. ABRAMSON

CAST OF CHARACTERS

CURT: *29 years old.*
RICH: *28 years old.*
PANDORA: *22 years old.* CURT's *wife.*
ART: *23 years old.*
MAMMA TOO TIGHT: *20 years old.*
SHAKY: *36 years old.* MAMMA TOO
TIGHT's *man.*

PIANO PLAYER.
BASS PLAYER.
DRUMMER.
BARTENDER.
DEENY.
BOUNCER.
CUSTOMERS.
SHOWGIRL.
VOICE.

Act I

SCENE I

This play is about some black people: CURT, PANDORA, ART, RICH, *and* SHAKY, *though* MAMMA TOO TIGHT *is white. The remainder of the cast is interracial, but two of the musicians are black and if* DEENY, *the* BOUNCER *and one of the* CUSTOMERS *are white, there might be added tensions. But it is left to the director's imagination to match the colors to the portrayals.*

Time: Early 1960's, late evening in January.

Scene: A court apartment in Los Angeles in the West Adams district. The room is done in white—white ceiling, white walls, white overly elaborate furniture—but a red wall-to-wall carpet covers the floor. A wall bed is raised. Upstairs, two doorless entrances stand on each side of the head of the bed. The right entrance is to the kitchen; the backstage area that represents the kitchen is shielded by a filmy curtain, and the actors' dim silhouettes are seen when the area is lighted. The left entrance will be raised and off stage right at the head of a short flight of stairs and a platform which leads into the combination bathroom-dressing-room—closet. When the actors are within this area, their shadows will be cast upon the wall fronting the stairs. And when the bed is lowered a scarlet spread is shown.

Within the interior of the front room the light is a mixture of red, blues, and violet, with crimson shadows bordering the edges of the stage to create the illusion of a world afire, with this pocket of atmosphere an oasis.

A telefunken, turned very low, plays the local jazz station, and CURT *and* RICH *lean over a chess board.* CURT *squats upon a stool, and, facing him across the coffee table and chess board,* RICH, *a stocky, brooding man, studies his next move, seated on the edge of the couch. Each has an empty beer bottle and a glass close at hand.*

CURT: I just about have you up tight, Rich.

RICH: [*Annoyed.*] Awww . . . Curt, man . . . don't try and hustle me!

CURT: [*Looks at him.*] Did I say somethin' to upset you, man?

    [RICH *shakes his head and curses to himself. A shadow appears at head of stairs and pauses as if the figure is listening for conversation. Then* PANDORA *enters—a beautiful black girl wearing tight white pants, a crimson blouse, and black boots—and slowly descends the stairs while looking at the men. She crosses behind them and walks toward the kitchen.* RICH *looks a second at her behind, but drops his gaze when* CURT *begins tapping the chess board with a finger nail.* CURT *gives no discernible attention to* PANDORA. *She enters the kitchen; a light goes on.*]

CURT: [*Staring at* RICH.] This game's somethin' else . . . man.

RICH: [*Studies board, looks up at* CURT, *and concentrates upon the board again. Mutters to himself.*] Ain't this somethin' else though . . . [*Looking up.*] You almost got my ass, man.

CURT: [*Mocking.*] I have got your ass, Rich.

RICH: [*Half-hearted.*] Awww . . . man . . . why don't you go fuck yourself? [*He places hand upon a piece.*]

CURT: [*Warning and placing hand upon one of his pieces.*] Wouldn't do that if I were you, good buddy.

RICH: [*Frowns and takes hand from board. He shakes head and mumbles, then curses his own caution.*] Sheeet! [*He makes move.*] Let's see what you're goin' ta do with that, man!

CURT: [*Deliberately.*] Checkmate!

RICH: [*Half rising.*] What you say, Curt?

CURT: [*Toneless.*] Checkmate, man.

    [CURT *looks toward the rear of the apartment; the faucet has been turned on, and in the kitchen* PANDORA *leisurely crosses the entrance doorway.*]

CURT: WE'RE READY FOR ANOTHER ONE, PANDORA!

PANDORA: [*Off.*] Already?

CURT: That's what I said, baby!

PANDORA: [*Crosses doorway again.*] Okay.

RICH: [*Mumbles and studies chessboard.*] Well . . . I'll be goddamned. [*Faucet sound goes off.*]

PANDORA: [*Off.*] You don't need fresh glasses, da ya? [*Sound of refrigerator opening.*]

CURT: [*Surely.*] NO, PANDORA, JUST THE BEER!

PANDORA: [*Raising voice.*] Okay . . . Okay . . . wait a fuckin' minute, will ya? Be right there! [*Rattles of bottles.*]

CURT: [*Glowering toward the kitchen, then staring at* RICH *who sits stoop-shouldered.*] How 'bout another one, Rich?

    [RICH *reaches into pocket and brings out a small roll and pulls off two bills and places them beside* CURT's *glass. He mutters to himself.*]

RICH: I wonder why in the fuck I didn't see that?

PANDORA: [*With a cross expression, enters carrying two bottles of Miller's Highlife.*] Just because you're pissed off at the world don't take it out on me! What'ta hell ya think ya got 'round here, maid service? [CURT *stands to meet her; she slows. Whining.*] Awww . . . Curt . . . [*A knock comes from backstage; relieved, she looks at* CURT.] I wonder who would be knocking at the kitchen door, honey?

CURT: [*Reaches down, palms and pockets the money.*] There's only one way to be sure, sugar. [*Sits down, looks at* RICH.] You clean, man?

RICH: [*Nods.*] Yeah . . . Curt.

CURT: [*Nods to* PANDORA *as the knock sounds again.*] Just watch your mouth, pretty baby . . . it's goin' ta get you in trouble one of these days, ya know. [PANDORA *places bottles on the edge of the table and briskly goes to open back door.*]

PANDORA: Maybe it's little Mamma already.

CURT: [*Mostly to himself.*] She wouldn't come around to the back door for nobody. [*Disregards the noise of the kitchen door's lock snapping back and the rattle of the night chain being fixed in its hasp.*] I have the black men this time, right, Rich?

RICH: [*Reaching for the beer.*] Yeah.

ART: [*Off.*] Hello, is Curt home? My name's Art. I ran into Curt this afternoon and he told me to drop by.

PANDORA: [*Off.*] Just a minute . . . I'll see. [*The sound of the door closing is heard, and* PANDORA *returns to the main room.*] Curt . . . Curt?

CURT: [*Setting up his chess pieces; in a bored voice.*] Yeah, baby?

PANDORA: There's a guy named Art out here who says you told him to drop around.

CURT: [*Not looking at her but down at the board.*] Invite him in, baby. [PANDORA *exits.*]

RICH: Is this the guy?

CURT: [*Nods, in low voice.*] Never a dull moment . . . right, Rich?

RICH: [*Sarcastic.*] Yeah. We're really in ta somethin', man.

[*The music changes during the remainder of this scene. "Delilah" and "Parisian Thoroughfare" as recorded by Max Roach and Clifford Brown play. These will be the themes for the scenes between* ART *and* PANDORA, *except when other music is necessary to stress altering moods. If Act I extends long enough, "Sketches of Spain" by Miles Davis*[1] *is to be played also, but "Delilah" should be replayed during* PANDORA's *box scene.*]

PANDORA: [*Off.*] Just a minute.

[*Noise of the lock and chain.*]

ART: Good evening.

[*She leads him into the living room.* RICH *has poured beer for* CURT *and himself; he stands and saunters to the radio as if to change stations, but turns after* ART *has passed behind him and sizes up the stranger from the rear.*]

CURT: [*Stands.*] Hey, good buddy! You found the place okay, huh?

ART: [*Pleased by greeting.*] Yeah, it wasn't so hard to find but I guess I came around to the wrong door.

---

1. Jazz trumpter (1926–1991) who recorded the album *Sketches of Spain* (1959–60) with arranger-conductor Gil Evans. Roach, a drummer, and Brown, a trumpeter, were co-leaders of a jazz band in the 1950s.

CURT: [*With a wave.*] Awww . . . that's okay. One's good as the other. It's better to come in that way if you're walkin' from Washington Boulevard. You live somewhere 'round there, don't ya?

ART: [*Hesitant.*] Well . . . I did.

CURT: [*Gesturing.*] Here, I want you to meet my wife and a buddy of mine. [*Introducing* PANDORA.] This is my wife, Pandora . . . and . . .

PANDORA: [*Smiles brightly.*] We already met, kinda. He told me his name at the door.

CURT: [*Ignoring* PANDORA.] . . . and this is Rich.

RICH: [*Remains in same spot.* ART *turns and* RICH *gives him a casual salute.*] What's happen'n, brother?

CURT: [*To* PANDORA *and* RICH.] This is a guy I met in jail. [*Introduces* ART.] Art Garrison. [*Shows* ART *a seat on the couch, downstage from* RICH.] Yeah, Art was one of the best young cons on Tier Three . . . [*To* PANDORA.] Get my boy here a drink, baby.

PANDORA: [*Starts for kitchen.*] You drink beer, Art?

ART: Sure . . . that sounds great.

PANDORA: [*Over her shoulder.*] We got some scotch, if you want it.

ART: No, thanks.

[RICH *sits, makes opening move, not looking at* ART.]

CURT: [*To* RICH.] Yeah, if it wasn't for Art here I wouldn't be sittin' here.

RICH: [*Bored.*] Yeah?

CURT: This is the kid who banged Scooter aside the jaw during the riot last summer in the joint.

RICH: [*Sounding more enthused.*] Yeah . . . you were doin' a stretch down at county jail when that happened, weren't you?

CURT: Yeah, man. I was there bigger den shit. [*Takes seat.*] Yeah, that paddy[2] mathafukker, Scooter, was comin' down on me with an ice pick, man . . . we had all been rumblin' up and down the cell block and I slipped on somethin' wet . . . I think it was Cory's blood 'cause Miles and his boys had stomped the mathafukker so good . . .

[*During the telling of the incident,* PANDORA *stands framed in the kitchen doorway, watching the men.*]

CURT: And I went to look up and all I could see was that gray-eyed mathafukkin' Scooter comin' at me with that ice pick of his . . . He reached down and grabbed my shirt front and drew back his arm and WHAMMO . . . [*Indicating* ART.] just like a bat out'ta hell my boy here had scored on the sucker's jaw.

ART: [*Pleased.*] Well . . . I couldn't let that white sonna bitch do you in, man.

RICH: [*Dryly.*] What was the beef about, man?

CURT: Well you know Miles goes for the Muslims though he ain't one hisself. Now the Muslims were in a hassle at the joint with the guards and the big people on top because of their religious beliefs, dig?

RICH: [*Interested.*] What do you mean?

CURT: Well the guards didn't want them havin' their meetin's 'cause they said they were organizing' and plottin'. And the Muslims wanted

2. Irish man or police officer (slang).

some of the chow changed 'cause they don't eat the same kind'a food
we do.

RICH: Yeah!

CURT: So while this was all goin' on, Cory . . . a young, wise nigger who
thinks he's in ta something' . . . well he started agitatin' and signifyin'
bout who the Muslims think they was. And what made it so rank was a lot
of the ofays, ya know, Charles, the white man, start in sayin' things they
had held back before, so Miles and some of the boys got together one day
and caught that little jive-sucker Cory outside his cell block and stomped
him so bad the deck was greasy wit' his blood, man. That's when the shit
started really goin' down, right there, man. Bumpy, Cory's cousin come
runnin' up, man, and that big nigger kicked Miles square in the nuts and
laid out two of his boys before the rest of them got themselves together.
By that time some of the whiteys come runnin' up and a few more of
Miles's boys. Yeah, the whole shit started right there where Cory lay almost done in . . .

RICH: Yeah . . . I heard a couple of cats got stabbed, man.

CURT: Yeah, man, it was pretty scary for a while, mostly black cons against
white ones except for the studs who just tried to stay out of the shit and
the Uncle Toms . . . those Toms we were really out to cool.

RICH: [Heated.] Yeah, you should have done those mathafukkers in!

CURT: Even the guards wouldn't come into the cell block and break it up
at first . . . a whole lot of shit went down that day. [Looking at ART.] I owe
my boy here a lot for that day.

ART: [Embarrassed.] Yeah, man, I would have liked to have stayed out of
it but I couldn't.

CURT: Yeah, Art. I us'ta wonder about that . . . [A two-beat pause.] How
could you just go about your business and stay in the middle all the time
in that place when so much crap was goin' down?

ART: I just stayed out of everything, that's all.

CURT: But didn't you care about anything, man? Didn't you feel anything
when that shit was happen'n to you?

ART: Yeah, I cared but I just didn't let it bother me too much. I just froze
up on everything that tried to get in and not too much touched me.

PANDORA: [From doorway.] Talk about somebody bein' cold!

CURT: [Having noticed her in doorway for first time, stares at ART.] But you
don't know how I appreciate what you did, man. It wasn't your fight,
man. You weren't takin' sides. You were one of the quiet guys waitin' for
trial who just kept his mouth shut and minded his own business.

ART: I never do try and take sides in stir, just serve my time and forget
about it, that's all.

[PANDORA has moved out of the doorway.]

CURT: Well, I'm glad you did that time, man, and if there's anything I can
ever . . .

RICH: [Interrupting.] What were you in for, Art?

[CURT takes a drink of his beer, lights a cigarette and blows smoke
across the table above the two men's heads. PANDORA drops something made of glass in the kitchen and curses.]

ART: Well . . . I was waiting for trial . . . attempted murder.

RICH: That's a tough one to have on your rap sheet.

ART: Yeah, it doesn't do your record or you any good, especially when it ain't for money.

CURT: [*Finally makes answering chess move.*] It was over a broad, wasn't it?

ART: [*Lights a cigarette, offers* RICH *a light but is refused.*] Yeah. I guess girls are my main weakness.

RICH: [*With unlit cigarette dangling from his lips, makes move.*] How much time did you do?

ART: Waited on my trial for nine months at county when the husband of the girl dropped the charges and left town.

CURT: [*Replies to move.*] That's who you shot, the girl's husband?

ART: [*His eyes following game.*] Yeah.

RICH: [*Moves quickly.*] You pretty good with a gun?

ART: [*Caught up in game.*] I can usually hold one without it blowing my foot off.

RICH: [*Sharply.*] Any simple ass can do that! I asked you are you any good with one!

[*The three men are fixed in tableau for a three-beat interval:* ART *strains forward from his seat and is about to speak.*]

CURT: [*To* RICH *as he makes his move.*] This move's goin' ta show ya to stop fuckin' with Curt the Kid, good buddy.

[*Noise of refrigerator opening and slamming, and* PANDORA *enters with a bottle and a glass. She pours beer for* ART *and sets the glass down beside him as the men all look at the chessboard.*]

PANDORA: [*In a light mood.*] Sorry I took so long, Art. I just dropped the supper. [*To* CURT.] Honey, the beans are all messed up. Little Mamma won't have anything to eat 'cept eggs.

CURT: [*Not looking at her.*] Didn't want no fuckin' beans anyhow! And I know Mamma Too Tight don't want any either . . . what kind'a shit is that . . . givin' that broad beans on her first night on the streets?

PANDORA: [*Defensively.*] That's all we got, honey . . . You know we won't have any spendin' money until Deeny pays me.

RICH: Why don't you have a seat, Pan?

PANDORA: I gotta finish cleanin' the kitchen . . . I don't want no roaches 'round here. Last place we had we had to split 'cause the roaches took it over. The little mathafukkers got mo' of the food than Curt or me. Soon as I bring in a little money to get some food with . . . [CURT *looks at her sharply but she is turned toward* RICH *and* ART.] there's mo' of them little mathafukkers there than your eyes could see. And I put too much time in fixin' this pad up nice the way it is to have them little mathafukkers move in on me and try to take it over.

CURT: You better finish up, sweetcake, so I can take you to work. [*The term sweetcake is used with derision and seldom with affection.* PANDORA *picks up* CURT's *empty bottles and exits.*]

CURT: Your move, Richie.

RICH: Are you sure, man?

CURT: Just ask Art, he's been watchin' the game.

ART: Well, I ain't in it, man.

RICH: That's right, you ain't in it.

CURT: [*Watching* ART's *face.*] Yeah, it's your move, Richie, babe.

RICH: [*To* ART.] That was pretty nice of that girl's ole man to let you off, Art.

ART: Nawh . . . he wanted his ole lady to leave the state with him so he had to drop the charges against me to let her off the hook too.

RICH: She was in it too, huh?

ART: She shot him with me.

CURT: You play this game, Art?

ART: Yeah, some. But I haven't had much practice lately.

CURT: Well, this one's about over.

RICH: [*Snorts.*] Sheeet!

CURT: Maybe you'd like ta play the winner.

RICH: [*Grimacing before making hesitant move.*] Where ya livin' now, Art?

ART: I just got locked out of my room.

RICH: Yeah, Curt said you wanted to make some money.

ART: [*Intensely.*] I have to, man. I'm really on my ass.

CURT: Check!

RICH: [*Makes move.*] Not yet, sucker.

ART: I gotta get out of this town.

RICH: You got a car, ain't ya?

CURT: [*Moves.*] Not long now, Rich.

ART: Yeah, that's about all I got. A car and a suitcase. I've also gotten more jail time in this town than in my whole life, and I've been halfway round the world and all over this country.

RICH: [*Moves and acts angry.*] Yeah, L.A.'s no fuckin' good, man. If I was off parole now I would get the first thing on wheels out of here. How bout you, Curt? If you weren't out on bail wouldn't you make it?

     [CURT *doesn't answer. Stage left, a knock sounds and* PANDORA *comes out of the kitchen striding toward the entrance which serves as the front door to the apartment.*]

PANDORA: That must be little Mamma.

CURT: Sure hope it is . . . I would really like to see that little broad.

PANDORA: [*Peers through window.*] Yeah, there's that chick. [*Calling outside in jocular way.*] Hey, broad, what they doin' lettin' you out'ta jail? [*An indistinct shout and a laugh comes from outside.*]

CURT: [*To* RICH.] Checkmate, man!

     [*Lights lower to blacken the stage.*]

Act I

SCENE II

When the lights go up MAMMA TOO TIGHT *and* SHAKY *sit upon the lowered bed. Faintly reflecting a glow, the bedspread gives them the appearance of sitting upon smoldering coals.* MAMMA TOO TIGHT, *a small, voluptuous girl, is dressed well. Her shift complements her creamy complexion and full-blown build.* SHAKY *is nondescript but dresses in expensive casual clothes.*

CURT, RICH, *and* ART *sit in the same area, stage right, facing the bed, forming the lower lip of a half-moon, and* PANDORA *has changed to a black cocktail dress and sits upon the stairs to the bathroom. She faces front with a bit of red ruffled slip peeking beneath and around her black stockinged legs.*

They all eat chicken from cardboard containers and reach for beers and cigarettes. The light in the kitchen is off, and the radio plays.

ART: Thanks again, Curt . . . if you hadn't invited me to eat I don't know what I'd do . . . probably had to drive downtown on what little gas I got and eat at one of those Rescue Missions.

MAMMA TOO TIGHT: [*Nudging* SHAKY *in the ribs.*] Well, I'll be damned . . . Ole Curt done saved himself a soul . . .

SHAKY: [*Slow and languid.*] Easy, baby, you gonna make me spill my beer.

MAMMA TOO TIGHT: What you know 'bout eatin' at Rescue Missions, boy?

PANDORA: [*Interjecting.*] You better stop callin' that guy ah boy, Mamma . . . ha ha . . . girl . . . you got mo' gall.

RICH: [*Drinking beer.*] Yeah, Mamma, how fuckin' big do boys grow where you come from?

CURT: [*With food in mouth.*] Forget about it, Art, glad to have ya. One more don't mean a thing.

PANDORA: Listen to that, Mamma Too Tight . . . [*Mocking.*] "One mo' mouf don't mean a thing." . . . We eat beans all week and when you and Curt's friends come in we play big shit! . . . And call out for food and beer.

[CURT, SHAKY, *and* ART *stop eating.* CURT *stares at* PANDORA *and* ART *holds his plate like it is hot and he is trying not to drop it on the floor.* SHAKY *eyes* MAMMA TOO TIGHT *and gives a mean scowl.* MAMMA *has seen the look on* CURT's *face before.* RICH *goes on enjoying his meal.*]

MAMMA: [*In a jolly tone, to* PANDORA.] Girl, you don't have ta tell me a thing . . . these here men think that money can be just picked up off a them pavements out there like chewin' gum paper . . . until they got ta get out there for themselves. [*She swings off the bed and shows flashes of lingerie.*] Like this pretty boy here with the fuzz on his face. [*She approaches* ART *and stands so her hips from a prominent profile to* CURT's *line of vision.*] He ain't even eatin' no mo' . . . and Curt's not either, honey. What I tell ya? These men are somethin' else. So weak from plottin' what we should be doin' to bring some money in that they can't eat themselves. [*Puts her plate on coffee table.*] I knows that Curt is a big strong man . . . he's always lettin' Pan know. [*Strong dialect.*] So he don't need no help from us frail ass women but maybe ole fuzzy wuzzy face here needs some help. [*Her audience is in better humor once more. To* ART.] You wants Mamma Too Tight to feeds him some food, baby boy?

SHAKY: Cut out the Magnolia act. Everything wears thin, Queenie!

MAMMA: [*Sudden anger.*] Don't you call me no fuckin' Queenie!

SHAKY: [*Sarcastic.*] Anything you say, baby.

[PANDORA *guffaws at* SHAKY's *tone.*]

PANDORA: [*Mimicking* MAMMA's *drawl.*] But ain't dat you name, hooneee?

[MAMMA *ignores* SHAKY *and* PANDORA, *picks drumstick from plate and offers it to* ART *who frowns, and pulls it away and puts it to her mouth imitating a mother feeding a reluctant child. Finally,* ART *smiles at her as* SHAKY *speaks.*]

SHAKY: Why don' chou lighten up, woman!

MAMMA: Lighten up? . . . Damn . . . man . . . I ain't here ten minutes before I see your face and you tell *me* to lighten up! I been with you since I hit the streets at noon and you still checkin' up on me . . . don't worry, man . . . I'm goin' ta get right ta work.

SHAKY: [*Slow and languid.*] I know that, baby.

MAMMA: [*To* PANDORA.] Girl you should of seen Shaky . . . ha ha ha . . . almost swept me off my feet, girl. Said he loved me and really missed me so much the last ninety days that he almost went out of his mind . . . ha ha . . . [*Coyly.*] I was so embarrassed and impressed, girl, I liked to have blushed and nearly peed on myself like a sixteen-year-old girl. [*Change of voice.*] But the ole sonna bitch didn't fool me none with that shit . . . The only thing he missed was that good steady money!

CURT: [*Picqued.*] Why don't you check yourself, Mamma!

MAMMA: [*Waving* CURT'*s threat off and returning to the edge of the bed.*] But, girl, he sho threw some lovin' on me . . . hee heee . . . sheeet, I should go away again after this afternoon. [PANDORA *laughs throughout.*] Ummm . . . chile . . . I nearly thought I was on that honeymoon I never had.

PANDORA: You should after that routine, baby.

MAMMA: And then when the sun start goin' down and things got really gettin' romantic, girl . . . this mathafukker says . . .

[*Lights lower; spot on bed.* SHAKY *speaks the line.*]

SHAKY: I want you to bring in a yard tonight, baby.

[MAMMA *resumes speech. Bed spot off; colored spot on* MAMMA.]

MAMMA: You what, man?

[*Colored spot off; bed spot on.*]

SHAKY: A hundred stone cold dollars, baby. Tonight, baby!

[*Spot off; lights go up.*]

MAMMA: [*To* PANDORA.] And girl, do you know what I said?

PANDORA: Yeah, I know what you said.

MAMMA: That's right, baby, I said to Shaky, "How do you want them daddy . . . in fives or tens?"

[*Laughter halts the speeches; the glasses are filled and fingers cleaned of chicken grease and cigarettes lit.*]

CURT: [*To* SHAKY.] Don't let Mamma try and fool you . . . she wanted to see you so bad . . . everytime Pan us'ta go visit her she would say to Pan, "How's that ole dirty Shaky doin?"

MAMMA: Yeah, I'd ask . . . cause I'd be wonderin' why ain't the mathafukker down here.

SHAKY: Now, let's not go into that again, baby.

CURT: Yeah, Mamma . . . you know what's happen'n behind that. You know why Shaky didn't come down . . . you never can tell when they might have a warrant out on him or somethin' and keep him too. You remember what happened at court, don't cha?

MAMMA: Yeah, I remember. How can I forget? The judge said for Shaky to leave the court cause every time I'm on trial he's in the back row hangin' round and that last ole woman judge said she knew who Shaky was an' she'd like to put him behind bars instead of me . . . but comin' down to visit me in jail is different, Curt!

SHAKY: [*Pleading.*] Now, baby . . .

CURT: Listen, Mamma . . . how old are you?

MAMMA: Twenty.

CURT: That means you're a big girl now, a woman who should be able to understand things, right?

MAMMA: Yeah, but . . .

CURT: [*Cutting.*] Right! Now listen, baby . . . and listen hard . . . now how many times you been busted?

MAMMA: Thirty-three times . . . but I only fell this once for more than ten days and that was because I got that new fuckin' woman judge. I got the best record in town of any broad on the block I know. Pandora's rap sheet is worse than mine and I was on the block two years before she was.

CURT: Exactly, baby. Now if you didn't have an old man like Shaky out there workin' for you, you'd be out of business and servin' some big time . . . right? Wouldn't that be a drag to be servin' some grand theft time behind givin' up a little body! Pan ain't been snatched since before we were married . . . ain't that right, Pandora? See there? Now let me tell you, baby, and listen hard. [*Intensely.*] A self-respectin' man won't let his ole lady stay in jail. If he can't get the bail for her or the juice to pay off somebody downtown like Shaky done you to have your time cut to one third . . . [*Disgust.*] he's a punk! And any broad that even looks at the jive-sucker should get her funky ass run into the ground like a piece of scum!

MAMMA: [*On defensive.*] I know all that, Curt, but I got so lonely down there. Nothin' down there but broads and most of them are butches.

PANDORA: Mamma . . . don't even talk about it. Makes cold chills run up my back just thinkin' bout it.

CURT: Yeah, we know it was hard, baby, but you can't afford to lose your old man by his gettin' busted behind a jail visit. That would be a stone trick, Mamma. Nothin' but a hummer . . . Right?

MAMMA: Awww . . . Curt, you try and make it sound so smooth.

PANDORA: He can really make it do that, girl.

RICH: [*Finishes drinking the last of his beer.*] Hey, Shaky, I want you to take a walk with me, okay?

SHAKY: [*Standing slowly and visibly rocking.*] Yeah, man. [*To* MAMMA.] I'll see you back at the house, baby. Watch yourself.

MAMMA: I'll probably be in early, Shaky. Unless I catch somethin' good.

[RICH *and* SHAKY *exit by the front door.* PANDORA *accompanies them and checks the outside before they step out.*]

MAMMA: Sheeet, Pandora, I thought Shaky was the Chicken Delight man when he knocked. I wasn't here ten minutes before he was knockin' on the door to see if I had my ride to the club. Didn't even think about feedin' me. [*Soulful.*] Just give me some good lovin' ta show me where it's at.

PANDORA: These men are somethin' else, girl . . . 'spect a girl to go out'ta here on an empty stomach and turn all kinds of tricks . . . but Curt and me did have some beans for you, girl, but I dropped them.

MAMMA: Well, I'm glad you did.

CURT: [*Packing away chessboard.*] I told her you didn't want no beans, Mamma.

MAMMA: I got too many beans in the joint.

PANDORA: [*Peeved.*] Well that's what I had for you, chick.

MAMMA: [*To* ART.] Hey, pretty baby, why you so quiet?

ART: Oh, I ain't got much to say, I guess.

CURT: This is my boy Art, Mamma. I introduced you when you came in.

MAMMA: [*Sultry.*] I know his name . . . ha ha . . . I just want to know his game, dat's all. Hey, fuzz face, what's yo game? Is you kinda fuzzy wuzzy 'round the edges?

ART: I'm sorry . . . I don't know . . .

CURT: Awww . . . he's okay, Mamma . . . he was in the joint with me. He's just quiet, that's all. Reads too much . . . somethin' you should do more of.

PANDORA: Why should she? Ain't heard of nobody gettin' no money readin'.

MAMMA: [*To* ART.] Now I know your name, fuzzy boy, now you say my name.

ART: [*Surprise.*] Your name?

MAMMA: Yeah. Say MAMMA TOO TIGHT!

ART: I know your name.

MAMMA: But I want you to say it.

ART: I don't have to with you broadcasting it all over the place ever since you been here.

MAMMA: [*Cross.*] You must think you're wise, man.

ART: [*In low, even voice.*] I am, you big-mouthed bitch and I want you to stop jivin' with me.

[PANDORA *giggles.* CURT *looks on enjoying the surprise showing on* MAMMA's *face.*]

MAMMA: Well . . . 'scuse me, tiger. [*Walks over to* ART *and sits beside him.*] Aww . . . forget it. I always act this way, ask Pan and Curt. 'Specially when I'm ah little bit loaded . . . Hey, Pandora, your friend here ain't got no sense of humor.

PANDORA: Nawh . . . he's too much like Curt. Serious. That's why they probably get along so good, girl . . . they probably made for each other. [*The girls laugh.*]

CURT: C'mon, Pan . . . it's almost time for you to go to work. Deeny will be callin' nex' thing and that's one mathafukker I don't even want to see much less talk to. Go on and get the stuff.

[PANDORA *exits through the bathroom door.*]

MAMMA: [*To* ART.] You want to know why they call me Mamma Too Tight, pretty baby?

CURT: If Shaky ever heard you callin' my boy that that he'd break your arm, Mamma.

MAMMA: Yeah, he might. But Shaky ain't where nothin's shakin' at the moment. . . . Just out givin' Rich a fix . . .

CURT: Both of you bitches talk too much!

MAMMA: [*To* ART.] You know what, fuzz wuzz? I sho wish I had a lil fuzzy wuzzy like you up there some of those cold nights in the joint. [*She gets up and walks to stand before the men. She plays it strictly for laughs, swinging her hips to the radio music, and singsongs in a hearty, brazen voice like one of the old-time red hot mamma's. Singing.*] Why do they call me what they call me, baby. When what they call me is my name.

ART: [*Dryly.*] I have suspicions but I'm not positive.

MAMMA: [*Ridiculing, but friendly.*] You have suspicions as every little fuzzy wuzzy does but let me tell you . . . because my real name is Quee-nie Mack! Queenie Bell Mack! Ain't that some shit? No self-respectin' whore in the world can go 'round with a name like that unless she's in Mississippi . . . sheet . . . Queenie!

ART: So you named yourself Mamma Too . . .

MAMMA: [*Cutting.*] No! It just happened. I don't know how. I just woke up one day with my name that way . . . And I like it that way . . . it's me! [*Turning toward* ART.] Don't you think it fits, honey?

ART: I think it really does.

MAMMA: Damn right it does. It makes me feel so alive. That's why I'm glad to be out . . .

CURT: [*Yelling.*] Hey, Pandora!

MAMMA: Man, but it's so good to be high again. It's so good to be free.

[PANDORA *enters from the bathroom and descends the stairs and places a cardboard box on the table as the lights blacken briefly and the music rises.*]

Act I

SCENE III

As the lights go up and the music lowers, the scene has shifted. CURT *and* PANDORA *sit upon the couch, across from* ART, *and* MAMMA TOO TIGHT *has taken the stool* CURT *was seated on. Uncovered, the box waits in the center of the table.* CURT *is licking a brown cigarette as the theme plays.*

CURT: Yeah. We want to make some money, Art, so we can get out of this hole. [*Lights the cigarette and inhales fiercely. Drops head. Two-beat pause. In strained voice, holding smoke back.*] We're makin' it to Buffalo, man. You hip to Buffalo?

ART: No, I don't think so . . .

CURT: [*Takes another drag.*] It's a good little hustlin' town, I hear. I got a case comin' up here for passin' some bad paper, ya know, forgin' payroll checks . . . and when I get the money to make restitution and give the people downtown some juice, ya know, man, pay them off, I'm makin' it East. But I need some grand theft dough.

ART: But won't you get some time with your record?

CURT: Nawh. Probably not. You see, I'm a good thief. I take money by my wits . . . ya know, with a pen or by talkin' some sucker out of it. It's only seldom that I'm forced to really take any money by force. If I make full restitution for these checks and fix my lawyer up and the other people downtown, I'll get probation. They'll reduce it to a misdemeanor and breakin' probation for somethin' like that ain't nothin' . . . besides, Buffalo's a long way away, man.

PANDORA: [*Receiving cigarette from* CURT.] It's supposed to be a good little town. A different scene entirely. I'm due for a good scene for a change.

CURT: Yeah, but we have to get that juice money first, baby. We gotta get us some long money.

MAMMA: Any place is better than L.A. but I heard that Buffalo is really boss.

PANDORA: [*Languid.*] It sho is, baby.

MAMMA: I wonder if I could get Shaky to go?

CURT: Sure you could, Mamma. He can get connections to deal his stuff there just like here. That's the idea. When we make our hit and split out of here we're gon'a take as many as we can with us. You know, set up a kinda organization.

PANDORA: [*Passing cigarette to* MAMMA.] They really got respect for cats from the coast back there.

ART: [*Getting caught up in the mood.*] Yeah, they really do . . . when I . . .

PANDORA: [*Cutting speech.*] With me workin' on the side and with Curt dealin' we'd be on our feet in no time.

CURT: We want to be on our feet when we get there, baby.

ART: And that's where I come in, right?

CURT: Right, good buddy.

MAMMA: [*Handing cigarette to* ART.] Here, baby.

ART: [*Waving it away.*] So what's on your mind, Curt?

MAMMA: [*Extending cigarette.*] I said here, baby, I just don't like to hold this thing and see all this bread go up in ashes.

ART: I don't want any.

[*A three-beat stop, all caught in tableau staring at* ART, *then* PANDORA *snickers and breaks into a tittering laugh, looking at* CURT.]

PANDORA: [*Ridicule.*] You and your friends, Curt . . . I thought . . .

CURT: [*Heated.*] Shut up, bitch . . . you talk too much!

PANDORA: [*Rising anger.*] Why shouldn't I when you bring some square-all little . . . [CURT *slaps her; she jumps to her feet and spins to claw him but* CURT *lunges forward and slaps her again, causing her to trip backwards across the edge of the coffee table. From the floor, removing one of her shoes.*] Goddamn you Curt . . . [*She begins to crawl to her knees and* CURT *moves around the table after her. Then* ART *steps between them and pushes* CURT *backward on the couch. Surprise is upon* CURT's *face and* MAMMA TOO TIGHT *seems frozen in place.*]

CURT: What the fuck's goin' on, man?

ART: [*Low.*] Don't hit her any more, Curt.

CURT: [*Incredulous.*] What? . . . Man, are you payin' this woman's bills . . . have you got any papers on her?

PANDORA: [*To* CURT.] Are you payin' my bills, mathafukker?

CURT: [*Rising to attack* PANDORA; ART *blocks his way.*] I've told you to keep your mouth . . . [*To* ART *when he won't let him pass.*] Now listen,

Art, you're like a brother to me but you don't know what's goin' down, man.

ART: Why don't we all sit down and try and relax, Curt? Why don't you do it for me, huh? As a favor. I'm sorry for buttin' into your business between you and your ole lady but somethin' just happens to me, man, when I see a guy hit a girl.

[*After a minute,* CURT *is soothed and sits upon the couch again, glaring at* PANDORA *who holds her shoe like a weapon.*]

MAMMA: [*Partially recovered.*] Oh, man, I just hit the streets and this is what I run into . . .

CURT: [*Intense, to* ART.] What are you doin', man? Squarin' out on me? Man, I've went a long way . . .

ART: [*Leaning forward.*] Well, look, Curt . . . I can split . . .

[CURT *stands and looks down on* ART. *Changing expression,* PANDORA *makes a move for the box but* CURT *waves her hand away.*]

CURT: No, I don't think you better try that, Art. [*Pause.*] Tell me, Art. Why don't you want to smoke any marijuana?

ART: Why don't . . . I don't understand why you should ask me that.

CURT: Is your playin' hero for Pandora a game to cover up somethin', man?

[MAMMA *is clutching herself as if she has returned to the womb.*]

MAMMA: Oh . . . shit shit shit . . . shit . . . just today . . . just today they cut me loose . . . just today.

PANDORA: [*No longer angry, placing hand on* CURT's *arm.*] Easy, baby, I think he's okay.

CURT: You would!

ART: Now, look, man, I don't put down anybody for doin' what they want but just don't hassle me!

PANDORA: [*Hostile, to* ART.] Cool it, baby, you're in some deep trouble now.

MAMMA: Oh, goddamn . . . why can't I just be plain ass Queenie Bell Mack?

CURT: [*Low.*] What's happen'n, brother?

ART: I just don't get high . . . that's all . . .

MAMMA: [*Nearly screaming.*] Neither does J. Edgar Hoover, sucker, but he don't come in here pretend'n to be no friend!

PANDORA: [*Enraged, fearful of losing control, to* MAMMA.] Shut up, bitch! This is Curt and our place. We got mo' to lose than just our ass. Just shut on up!

[MAMMA *looks almost like a small girl with wide, moist eyes.*]

CURT: For the last time, Art, tell me somethin'.

ART: I just don't . . .

[PANDORA *stands and moves in front of* CURT. *The coffee table separates them from* ART, *but she leans over.*]

PANDORA: [*To* CURT, *behind her.*] He's all right, honey. If he were a cop he'd be smokin' stuff right along with us . . . you know that . . .

ART: [*Bewildered.*] A cop! . . .

PANDORA: [*Sarcastic.*] He's just a little square around the edges, Curt . . . [*Silence, then to* ART.] But why, honey?

ART: [*Shrugging sheepishly.*] I had a bad experience once behind pot,
    that's all.

    [MAMMA *cackles until* CURT *stops her.*]

MAMMA: He had a bad experience . . . hee hee hee . . . ha ha ha . . . He
    had . . .

CURT: [*Menace.*] Pan has already told you to check yourself, woman, he's
    still my friend.

PANDORA: What was it all about, man . . . can you tell us about it?

ART: I'd rather not . . .

CURT: [*Cutting.*] We know you'd rather not but . . .

PANDORA: [*Cutting.*] Now look, Art, you're not givin' us much of a break
    . . . we don't want to act like this but we got a lot of the future riding on
    what happens in the nex' few days. Why don't you tell us?

ART: I would but it don't seem that much . . .

CURT: [*Not so threatening.*] But it is, Art!

PANDORA: C'mon, trust me. Can't you say anything? We've gone more
    than half- . . .

CURT: Stop rankin' him, will ya!

PANDORA: I'm only doin' it for you!

    [*Silence as* CURT *and* PANDORA *stare at each other.*]

ART: Yeah, I'll talk about it . . . [CURT *sits.* PANDORA *moves around the table
    closer to* ART. *The cigarette has been dropped by* MAMMA *beside the box.
    "Delilah" plays.*] You see . . . it was about three years ago. I shipped out
    on a freighter . . . ya know, one of those scows that fly the Panamanian or
    Liberian flag but don't really belong to any country . . .

MAMMA: [*In small girl's voice.*] Ain't they Americans?

ART: Well, in a way. They belong to American corporations and the busi-
    nessmen don't want to pay high taxes on 'em. They're pretty ratty. [PAN-
    DORA *makes a seat on the floor between the men.*] Well I went on a
    four-month cruise, ya know, to ports around the West Indies and then to
    North Africa.

MAMMA: Wow . . . that sounds gassy . . . I wish . . .

PANDORA: [*Cutting.*] Mamma!

ART: Well I been blowin' weed since I was about twelve . . .

MAMMA: [*Ridicule.*] Ha ha ha . . . since he was twelve . . .

    [PANDORA *and* CURT *frown at her and she huddles in her seat and
    looks cold.*]

ART: . . . and everything was cool. I smoked it when I ran into it and
    never thought about it much unless someone turned me on. But in
    Tangier it was about as easy to get as a bottle of beer. Man, I had a
    ball all the while I was over there and before I left I bought a big bag.
    [*Showing with his hands.*] This big for about five bucks. All the way
    back on my night watches I just smoked grass and just thought of what
    the guys on my corner back home would say when I would pull out a
    joint or two and just give it to them. Prices back East are about triple
    what they are here, so you can guess what it was worth . . . And all the
    broads I would make . . . you know how it goes . . . take a broad up to
    your room and smoke a little weed and if you have anything goin' for
    you at all, man, that's it.

PANDORA: [*Disgust.*] Yeah, there's a lot of stupid broads in this world.

ART: [*Sensing the reduced tension.*] And I could still sell some when my
money got low and come out beautiful. I was really feeling good about
that grass, Curt. Well this tub docks in Philly about 1:00 A.M. and I have
to leave ship and when I get to the station I find that my train don't leave
until two the next afternoon. I got my pay and my belongings, so I stash
most of my bags in a locker at the station, the bag of weed is in one but I
have about half a dozen joints on me. Now I know Philly a little. I know
where there's an after-hour joint so I grab a cab and go over there. The
place is jumpin' . . . they're havin' a fish fry, and I start in drinkin' and
talkin' to girls but none of them are listen'n 'cept for seven bucks for
them and three for the management for rentin' one of the upstairs
rooms, and I ain't buyin' no cock . . . not in the States . . .

PANDORA: Well, I'm glad of that. I can take squares but not tricks, baby.

CURT: [*To* PANDORA.] You still runnin' your mouth, ain't you?

ART: So I start talkin' with some guy and he tells me of a place he knows
'cross town that's better than this one. He looks okay to me. A blood.
Dressed real sharp with a little goatee and everything. I had been talkin'
to him about bein' out to sea and since he don't try and con me into a
crap game and is buyin' one drink for every one of mine, I don't give a
damn where we go cause I got the whole night to kill.

MAMMA: Oh wow . . . I know this is the bad part . . .

PANDORA: Listen, Mamma.

MAMMA: [*Turning her face away.*] I don't like to hear bad things.

ART: So we drinkin' bottles of beer and drivin' up Broad Street in Philly in
his old wreck of a Buick and I think how it would be nice to turn on and
get really loaded before we get where we're goin'. So I reach for my
pocket but it's wintertime and I got on a pea jacket and sweaters and I
have trouble gettin' to my pocket. And while I was lookin' I start in
laughin'.

CURT: Laughin'?

ART: Yeah. I start wonderin' what would happen if this was a cop I was
with and the idea was just too much. So funny. So I started in laughin'.
And the guy asks me what I was laughin' at and I said I was just laughin'
about him bein' a cop. And he said that he was and how did I know.
[*Two-beat pause.*] I don't know how I got out of that car or away from
him. But soon after I was pukin' my guts up, and I threw those joints into
a sewer and they wouldn't go down 'cause snow and ice was cloggin' it
up. And I was stompin' on 'em so they would go down and gettin' sick
and after a while my feet were all covered with ice and snow and puke
and marijuana . . . Ya know . . . I had nearly twenty bucks worth of dope
frozen to the soles of my shoes.

MAMMA: [*Seriously.*] Awww . . . no, man . . . I can't stand any more.

PANDORA: [*Giggling.*] That's the best trip I've been on this week, Art.

ART: Nawh, really . . . baby. And the bag . . . I left it in a locker. Not the
one I used but another empty one.

MAMMA: Those janitors must'a naturally been happy the next day.

ART: Yeah, they must have been but I couldn't even think of the stuff for a
long time without wanting to heave up my guts.

CURT: That must'a been pretty scary, man.

[PANDORA *has reached over and gotten the cigarette and relit it.*]

PANDORA: [*Offering it to* ART.] Now it's time to get back on the horse, cowboy.

ART: [*Placing hand on stomach.*] I don't think I can.

MAMMA: You'll never think about that time in Philly again after the first
drag, baby.

CURT: C'mon, man, you're already one of us. Do you think I'd bring you
in if I thought you'd be a square?

PANDORA: Don't say that, Curt. He's not. Somethin' like what happened
to him can mess up your mind about things. [*She stands over him and
puffs on the cigarette. Staring at him.*] Now don't think about anything
. . . just look into my eyes. [*She inhales once more and gives the cigarette
to* ART.] Now, here, put it in your mouth.

ART: [*Takes it and puts to lips.*] I can do it all right but I just don't
want to.

PANDORA: [*Staring.*] Look into my eyes and inhale. Don't think about it
being in your hand. [ART *inhales and looks at her.*] All the way down now
and hold it.

MAMMA: Don't ever say you don't believe in witches, boy.

CURT: Cool it, Mamma!

PANDORA: Now one more drag, Art.

[ART *takes another puff and hands the reefer to* CURT. ART *has a great
grin on his face.*]

ART: So that's what's in Pandora's box.

[*Lights change.*]

PANDORA: [*Fantasy.*] Among other things, Art. Among other things. But
those have been lies you've been told about bad things comin' out of
Pandora's box.

MAMMA: Most people think that a girl's box is in other places.

PANDORA: Nothin' can be found bad in there either. People only bring
evil there with them. They only look for evil there. The sick . . .

ART: What do you mean by sick?

PANDORA: The come freaks, that's who. The queers who buy sex from a
woman.

MAMMA: [*Bitterly.*] Yeah, they say we're wrong but they're the queers . . .
payin' for another person's body.

CURT: [*In euphoria, musing.*] Art, my man, we're goin'a Buffalo . . . goin'
one day real soon.

PANDORA: [*Repulsion.*] Some of them are real nice-lookin' cats. Not old
with fat greasy bellies. Real nice-lookin' studs. [*Bitterly.*] Those are the
real queers you have ta watch. They want ta hurt women.

MAMMA: You hip ta that, baby? Those muscle cats, you know, muscle
queens . . . always wantin' ta freak out on ya.

ART: And that's all that comes out of Pandora's box?

[CURT *pulls a nickel-plated revolver out of the box.*]

CURT: No. Right now this is the most important thing. There's always
something new in there. [*Handing gun to* ART.] Feel it, brother.

[ART *takes the gun. He is caught up in the music and with his new
friends.*]

ART: It's a good one.

MAMMA: Look how it shines.

[*Lights change.*]

ART: [*Dreamlike.*] Yeah . . . like Pandora's eyes.

[*Lights change.*]

PANDORA: [*Fantasy.*] Nothin' bad comes out of me or from my box, baby. Nothin' bad. You can believe that. It's all in what you bring to us.

[*Lights change.*]

MAMMA: That's wha's happen'n, baby.

CURT: It's yours now, Art, as much yours as mine. Can you handle it, brother?

ART: [*Looking at* PANDORA *and taking a new reefer.*] If that's my job, brother.

[*The cigarette has been replaced by a new one and others are in the hands of the group;* PANDORA *drags in deeply.*]

PANDORA: Buffalo's goin'a be a gas.

[*The phone rings from the dressing room and* CURT *goes to answer. His shadow can be seen upon the wall at the top of the stairs.*]

CURT: [*Off.*] Yeah, Deeny . . . yeah yeah yeah . . . yeah, man, . . . yeah.

MAMMA: Who ever heard of a telephone in the toilet?

PANDORA: It's in the dressing room next to the bathroom, Mamma.

MAMMA: Sho is strange . . . Hey, are you goin'a Buffalo too, fuzz wuzz?

ART: It looks that way.

PANDORA: [*Smiling.*] I think I'll like that, Art. I think that'll be nice.

[*A knock sounds at the front door.* CURT'S *shadow hangs up the phone and retreats farther into the area.*]

CURT: [*Off.*] Pandora! Move! Goddamn it! Get a move on!

[ART *stands as* PANDORA *jumps to her feet. He has a cross expression as he looks toward the dressing room entrance.*]

ART: [*To* PANDORA.] Can I help you?

[PANDORA *shakes her head.*]

ART: Is there anything I can do?

PANDORA: No, I don't think anybody can do anything, especially you. [*She places the gun and the marijuana in the box and hurries up the stairs. The knock comes again.*]

MAMMA: [*Still seated, toward door.*] Just a minute!

[ART *watches* PANDORA *enters dressing room.*]

MAMMA: You want to get the door, Art?

ART: I learned once never to open another man's door.

[PANDORA *and* CURT, *in coats, come from the dressing room;* PANDORA *has her costumes in her arms.* MAMMA TOO TIGHT *gets up and walks downstage.*]

CURT: That fuckin' Deeny wants you to rehearse some new music before your act, Pan.

PANDORA: Sonna bitch! Always late payin' somebody and always wantin' you to work your ass off.

CURT: Is your car parked far, Art?

ART: Not too far.

MAMMA: [*Looking out window.*] It's only Rich.

CURT: Good. He can stay here and watch the phone while we're at the

club. First, we'll stop and get you some gas, Art, and then you can take us
to the Strip Club.

PANDORA: Is your car big enough to get us all to the Strip Club on Western, Art?

ART: It'll even get us as far as Buffalo, Pandora.

    [*They exit.* RICH *enters, turns in doorway and is seen talking to some-
one outside. Then he shuts door, saunters gracefully across the room,
and turns the radio off. Lights dim out as he sprawls upon the
couch.*]

CURTAIN

Act II

*The curtain opens showing the Strip Club, or rather the suggested represen-
tation of a cheap night club in the Wilshire area of Los Angeles, featuring
"Bronze" stripteasers. But the effect should be directed toward the illusions of
time, place, and matter. Reality is questionable here. The set should be
painted in lavish phony hues except for the bare brown floor. Seeing the set
the female audience should respond with: "gorgeous, lovely, marvelous, delightful," and similar banalities. The men should wonder if the habitat of
whores is not indeed the same as the region of their creatures of private myth,
dream, and fantasy.*

    *A rotating color wheel, in front of the major lights, should turn constantly
throughout this scene, giving an entire spectrum of altering colored shadows.
Additional colored lights and spots should be used to stress mood changes
and the violence of the ending scene.*

    *A musician plays randomly at the piano. He is tall, wearing a dark suit
with an open-necked dark shirt. The* BARTENDER, *wiry with his head shaven
clean, sweeps the floor and empties ash trays. A few* CUSTOMERS *sit and
watch the musician, and, later, the group, as the show hasn't begun.*

    *The voice which is heard at the close of this act can be that of a customer.
Two other musicians enter and climb upon the stage.*

PIANO PLAYER: [*Joking, to* BASS PLAYER *seated at piano.*] Hey, man, they
lookin' for bass players all up and down the street but you cats are all
bangin' out chords on out-of-tune pianos.

BASS PLAYER: What's happen'n, man? Say . . . listen to this . . . [*He plays a
couple of frames.*] What about that, man . . . huh?

PIANO PLAYER: Man, like I said . . . you're a damn good bass man . . .

BASS PLAYER: [*Getting up.*] What you say about somebody lookin' for bass
men? . . . Man! Turn me on. I wouldn't be here in this trap if I knew
where one of those gigs were.

DRUMMER: [*Seated, working up a beat.*] Yeah, man, they need you like
they need me.

PIANO: [*Wryly.*] How's it feel to keep gettin' replaced by a juke box?

    [BASS PLAYER *begins working with* DRUMMER. PIANO PLAYER *strikes a
few chords, then lights a cigarette.*]

BASS: Hey, where's Stew and Ronny? I want to practice those new charts
before Pandora gets in.

PIANO: [*Blowing smoke out.*] They quit.

BASS: [*Halting.*] What?

DRUMMER: Deeny wouldn't pay them this afternoon and pushed the new charts on them. They didn't want to learn new scores, not getting paid the money owed them, so they quit.

BASS: Just like that . . . they quit?

PIANO: This is our last night here, too. Deeny's in trouble with the union. No more gigs here until the hearin'.

BASS: Awww, man . . . there's always some shit with that jive-ass sucker. Is we gettin' our bread from Deeny tonight?

DRUMMER: Who knows? He don't have to pay until the last performance, and the union says stay on the gig until tonight.

BASS: We always gettin' put in some cross . . .

PIANO: Yeah, man. But juke boxes don't go on strike and Deeny knows we know it, so let's take care of business.

BASS: Man, don't tell me that . . . the broads can't dance to no juke box.

PIANO: [*Seriously.*] Why not, man?

BASS: It just ain't done, man. No machine ain't never goin'a take a musician's play from him when it comes to providin' music for shows.

PIANO: Don't believe it, baby . . . in a couple of mo' years they'll find a way. Broads will be shakin' their cans to canned music just as good as to your playin' or mine and the customers will be payin' even higher prices . . . nobody wins, man. Least of all us. C'mon, let's hit it . . .

[*He begins playing "Delilah" as* PANDORA, MAMMA TOO TIGHT, *and* CURT *make their entrances. The girls wave at the musicians and stop at the bar, then move to a table near the bandstand.* PANDORA *places her costumes on an empty chair of a nearby table.* CURT *stands with his back to the bar.*]

PIANO: Okay. That's better . . . c'mon . . . Cook! . . .

BASS: [*Not enthused, to* MAMMA *who waves again.*] Hey, pretty girl . . .

[ART *walks in, saunters to the cigarette machine;* CURT *joins the girls.*]

CURT: Hey, I wonder where everybody's at.

DRUMMER: [*Stopping, followed by others.*] Hey . . . hey . . . what's the use of this fuckin' shit . . . ?

PIANO: What's happen'n now, man?

[DRUMMER *hops from stage.*]

MAMMA: Damn . . . Stew and Ronny must be late, Pan.

PANDORA: [*To* BARTENDER.] What happened to your boss, Deeny, Chico?

[BARTENDER *ignores her.*]

DRUMMER: [*To* PIANO PLAYER.] Not a thing, man . . . everything's cool . . . [*Goes to bar, to* BARTENDER.] Hey, Chico. Give me a screwdriver and charge it to your boss.

BARTENDER: Deeny ain't in the charity business, baby.

[ART *sits down with his friends. One of the* CUSTOMERS *leaves.*]

PANDORA: [*To* BARTENDER.] Yeah, baby, give me the usual and give my friends what they want. Put it on my tab.

DRUMMER: [*To* BARTENDER.] You let me and Deeny worry about that, cool breeze. Give me a screwdriver like I said.

[BARTENDER *goes behind bar and begins mixing* DRUMMER's *drink.*]

BARTENDER: [*Sullenly, to* PANDORA.] When you gonna take care of that tab, sweetcake?

PANDORA: [*Angry.*] When your fuckin' boss pays me, mister! Now get us our drinks, please!

CURT: [*To* BASS PLAYER *who stands beside instrument.*] Where's Deeny?

[PIANO PLAYER *has gotten off of stage and talks to* DRUMMER *at the bar. A* CUSTOMER *goes to jukebox and looks over the selections.*]

PIANO: What's happen'n, man? We got to make this gig . . . that's what the union says.

DRUMMER: Fuck the union.

BASS: [*To* CURT.] It's a mystery to me, Curt.

MAMMA: [*To* BASS PLAYER.] That number's a gassy one, honey. Pan's gonna work by that, ain't she?

BASS: Looks that way, Mamma, if anybody works at all tonight.

PIANO: [*To* DRUMMER.] Awww, man . . . you know I know how you feel . . .

DRUMMER: Well, just don't run that crap down to me. I'm just fed up. The union screws you out of your dues and the clubs fuck you every chance they get . . .

PIANO: It ain't exactly that way . . . now if . . .

MAMMA: Don't you like Pan's new number, Art?

[ART *doesn't answer. The* CUSTOMER *drops a coin into the jukebox and punches a selection; "Something Cool" sung by June Christie*[3] *is played.*]

PANDORA: [*To* ART *and* MAMMA.] Can't come in here one day without some shit goin' down. Where's the brass so I can rehearse?

MAMMA: They better get here soon, honey. It'll be too late after a while.

BASS: [*To* PANDORA.] Forget about it, Pan. They ain't no brass tonight.

DRUMMER: [*To* PIANO PLAYER.] Well I know all that, but it's no use rehearsin' without any brass and if this is our last night anyhow . . .

CURT: [*Rising and going to the bar.*] You said this is the last night, man?

PANDORA: [*To* BASS PLAYER.] NO BRASS!

MAMMA: [*To* ART.] You hear what he said?

BASS: [*Putting down instrument.*] Hey, fix me a C.C. and ginger ale, Chico!

[CUSTOMER *who played record goes to the bar and sits down.*]

PANDORA: [*To* BARTENDER.] Hey, what about our drinks, man?

BARTENDER: Okay, Pandora . . . just a minute.

CURT: Hey, fellas . . . what's goin' down?

[*The musicians tell* CURT *about the trouble as the scene plays on in center stage at the table. The conversations should overlap as they have but become increasingly rapid and confusing if necessary. After the musicians are served the* BARTENDER *takes the orders at* PANDORA's *table as* CURT *continues to talk at the bar.*]

PANDORA: Shit . . . no brass . . . musicians quittin' . . . I ain't got no job no more.

3. Jazz and cabaret singer popular in the 1950s and 1960s.

MAMMA: Yeah. It don't look so good but perhaps Deeny can do somethin' when he comes in . . .

PANDORA: Deeny . . . shit . . . Deeny . . . all he can do! . . . [*Furious, searching for words.*] Why, shit, woman! Deeny can't even do numbers and shit cucumbers!

ART: Thanks for the drink, Pan.

PANDORA: Is that all you can do, man? Say thank you?

ART: No. It's not the only thing.

[MAMMA *gets up and goes over to the* BASS PLAYER *who drops out of the conversation between* CURT, *the other two musicians, and the* BARTENDER. *Another* CUSTOMER *leaves, leaving only one sitting upon a stool, attempting to get the* BARTENDER'S *attention.*]

BARTENDER: Well look, man, I only work here. You better settle that with Deeny.

[*Behind the bar the phone rings. The* BARTENDER *answers.*]

CURT: If that's Deeny I want to talk to him.

BARTENDER: Hey, man, I'm talkin' on the phone.

DRUMMER: Let me talk to the mathafukker! [*He tries to reach across the bar.*]

BARTENDER: [*Backing off.*] Hey, cool it! Wait!

PIANO: [*Grabbing* DRUMMER'S *arm.*] Hold it, man!

DRUMMER: Take your fuckin' hands off me, baby!

BARTENDER: Wait, I said.

CURT: Tell Deeny I'm waitin' for him.

[DRUMMER *breaks away from* PIANO PLAYER *and begins around the bar.* BARTENDER *reaches under bar for a weapon.*]

BARTENDER: [*Shouts.*] Wait!

[*The scene freezes in tableau except for the* BARTENDER, PANDORA, *and* CURT. *Lights go down to purples and deep shadow shades as an eerie spot plays upon the table. Occasionally from the shadows voices are heard.*]

BARTENDER: [*In shadows.*] Okay, Deeny. I'll be expectin' ya.

PANDORA: [*To* ART.] So he's comin'.

ART: Yeah, no need to wait for very long now.

PANDORA: What else can you do, Art?

ART: What else can I do except say thank you, you mean?

PANDORA: Yeah. That's what I mean.

ART: I can wait, Pandora.

PANDORA: [*Jolly.*] What's the good of waitin' when things have ta be done? Is that why you have to eat at Rescue Missions and get favors from friends, baby? Cause you waitin'? Tell me. What are you waitin' on, Art?

ART: Me? I'm just waitin' so I won't jump into somethin' too fast and I think you should do the same.

PANDORA: I didn't know you gave out advice too. But I wish I could take some of it. Ya see, we're already in the middle of some deep shit . . . There just ain't time to sit back and cool it, honey . . .

ART: [*Disregarding the ridicule in her voice, soothing.*] Yes you can . . . just sit back and look around and wait a while. You don't have to do anything

. . . baby, the whole world will come to you if you just sit back and be ready for it.

PANDORA: [*Serious.*] I wish I could. But so much has to be done and we keep fallin' behind.

BARTENDER: [*In shadows.*] Now what can I do, man? Deeny left with Pete and he said he'd be right back and for you guys to practice with the girls.

[*One of the* CUSTOMERS *who walked out enters with a* SHOW GIRL. *She is dark and thin and pretty in a tinseled way. They stop in the shadows and whisper and the girl separates from him, enters the light, passes through and heads toward the dressing rooms in the rear. The* CUSTOMER *takes a seat at the bar. He is engulfed by shadows and becomes frozen in place like the others.*]

PANDORA: [*Nodding to* SHOW GIRL *as she passes.*] Hi, Cookie. I really dig that dress, baby.

ART: Things can always get worse, Pan.

PANDORA: Oh, you're one of those? How can they? Just lost my job. This was to keep me goin' until you guys turned up somethin' big and I didn't even get paid from the last two weeks so I know this just means another great big zero.

ART: What do you think will happen now?

PANDORA: I don't know . . . the job Curt's got planned can't be pulled off until three more days and in a week we got to have all our money together for the restitution and juice . . . not to mention the goin' away money. And I'm not even goin'a get paid for this gig.

ART: Haven't you got any now?

PANDORA: Just a couple of hundred but we can't go into that. Got to hold onto it. We wouldn't eat if we didn't have to. We got to hold on to every cent.

BARTENDER: [*In shadows.*] Do you want that scotch with anything?

[DRUMMER *momentarily breaks out of position.*]

DRUMMER: I ain't finished talkin' yet, Chico.

BARTENDER: Just a minute, man.

[MAMMA *breaks out of position and goes to* PANDORA.]

MAMMA: Lend me a dime, Pan. I got to call Shaky.

PANDORA: [*Fishing in her oversized purse.*] You got somethin' workin', baby?

MAMMA: Yeah. Slim's gonna get somethin' from Shaky.

PANDORA: That's workin'.

[*She gives* MAMMA *a coin.* MAMMA *enters the shadows and walks to the rear of the club.* PANDORA *notices* ART *looking at her.*]

PANDORA: Forget about her. Shaky's got her up tight. All you could do is play young lover a little. You can't support her habit, Art.

ART: She can't have a habit if she's just hit the street.

PANDORA: She's got one. What do you think they came in high on? In a couple more days she'll be hooked as bad as before. Shaky'll see to that.

ART: What does she do it for?

PANDORA: What does . . . ? Awww, man . . . what kinda question is that? I thought you knew somethin', baby.

ART: I tried to ask an honest question, Pan.

PANDORA:　Is it an honest question when you don't have anything to go by to compare her experience with yours?

ART:　I don't know. Is it?

PANDORA:　Do you know how it feels havin' somebody paw all over you every day?

ART:　Well, no . . .

PANDORA:　Then you don't know that she has to use that stuff to put off the reality of it happen'n?

ART:　Oh, I see.

PANDORA:　[Bitter.] Yeah, you see. Do you see her givin' up her body every day and murdering herself every day? Is that what the world has brought to her, Art? That's all she can look forward to each day . . . killin' herself with that needle by inches. She has her fix, and maybe a bust and she has keepin' her man. She just takes her fixes to get through the day and Shaky keeps her on it so she'll need him more.

ART:　That's too bad.

PANDORA:　Wait a minute, Art. Don't sing no sad songs for that woman, you understand? She's not askin' for your pity. She's a real woman in some ways and she won't let you take it away from her by your pity. She'd spit on your pity.

ART:　[Annoyed.] And you?
　　　[Lights change.]

PANDORA:　[Fantasy.] And me? . . . Well I ain't no whore . . . I'm just makin' this money so Curt and me can get on our feet. One day we gonna own property and maybe some businesses when we get straight . . . and out of this town.

ART:　In Buffalo?

PANDORA:　Maybe if we decide to stay there but I'm really an entertainer. I'll show you my act one day and Curt's got a good mind. He's a good hustler but he's givin' that up after a while. He can be anything he wants.
　　　[Lights change.]

ART:　What does he want?

PANDORA:　He wants what I want.

ART:　How do you know?

PANDORA:　He tells me . . . We talk about it all the time.

ART:　Can you be sure?

PANDORA:　Sure?

ART:　Yeah . . . like Mamma's sure she'll always get her fix and her bail paid.

PANDORA:　You little smooth-faced punk . . . wha . . .

ART:　[Cutting.] Some guys are really lucky.

PANDORA:　Kiss my ass, sucker!

ART:　Curt and Shaky are really into something.

PANDORA:　Yeah! Because they're men!

ART:　Is that what bein' a man is, bein' lucky?

PANDORA:　No. It's from gettin' what you want.

ART:　And how do you get what you want, Pan?

PANDORA:　You go after it.

ART:　And after you have it.

PANDORA: Then maybe it's yours and you can do whatever you want with it.

ART: And what if I wanted you, Pandora?

PANDORA: [*Three-beat pause.*] You don't have enough to give me, Art. What could you give me that would make things better for me?

ART: I'm not a giver, Pan. I'm a taker.

[*Lights go up evenly. Figures become animated and resume activities. The* BARTENDER *pours drinks and nods to grumbling musicians and to* CURT. *A* CUSTOMER *goes to jukebox and drops coin in. "Parisian Thoroughfare" plays. The* SHOW GIRL, *in thin robe, revealing skimpy costume, walks from the rear and takes a seat beside the* CUSTOMER *she entered with.* MAMMA TOO TIGHT *goes to the table and sits.*]

MAMMA: [*Brightly.*] What you guys been talkin' bout so long?

PANDORA: Nothin' much, why?

MAMMA: Oh nothin' . . . just thought I'd ask. But the way you and old fuzz wuzz was goin' at it and lookin' at each other . . .

PANDORA: Looks can't hurt you, Mamma, but your big mouth can.

MAMMA: [*Fake surprise.*] Pan . . . I didn't mean . . .

PANDORA: I'm sure you didn't, Mamma!

MAMMA: [*Now hurt.*] Now listen, Pan. If you can't take a little teasin' . . . What's wrong with you? This is my first day home and you been on my ass all the time. Girl . . . you been the best friend I ever had, but lighten up.

PANDORA: Awww, Mamma . . . let's not you and me start in actin' flaky . . .

ART: Would you like a drink, Mamma?

MAMMA: [*Pleased.*] Yeah . . . but you can't pry Chico from behind that bar.

[ART *stands and places hand upon* MAMMA's *shoulder.*]

ART: That's okay. Just sit. [*He goes to bar and stands beside* CURT *who has his back to him, drinking and brooding.*]

MAMMA: [*To* PANDORA.] Hey, he's so nice.

PANDORA: See . . . I told you I wasn't tryin' to steal your little playmate.

MAMMA: [*Serious.*] If I didn't know I was kiddin' I wouldn't take that, Pan.

PANDORA: You wouldn't? . . . Well, I wasn't kiddin', broad!

MAMMA: [*Half rising.*] Hey, check yourself, girl. This is me! Remember? Mamma Too Tight. Don't you know me? Lil ole Queenie Bell Mack from Biloxi, Mississippi.

PANDORA: Okay. Sit down before you trip over yourself. I know who you are.

MAMMA: [*Sitting.*] And I know you too, baby. Remember I was the one who was there those times so many yesterdays ago. Remember? I was there with you holding your hand in those dark, little lonely rooms all them nights that your man was out on a job . . . Remember how we shivered together, girl? Remember how we cried together each time he got busted and sent away again . . . I'm your friend, baby . . . and you actin' like this to me?

PANDORA: [*Genuine.*] I'm sorry, Mamma. It's just that Art. He's different. Everything seems different when he's around.

MAMMA: I think I know what you mean, Pan. I think I know . . .

[*Lights dim; color wheel still throws pastel shadows.* CURT *and* ART *stand in spot at end of bar. In the shadows there are rustles from the other people and lighted cigarettes arc through the gloom toward mouths which suck at them like spiders draining fireflies.* CURT *turns.*]

CURT: Hey, Art. Sorry to put you through all this hassle but some bad shit is goin' down, man. I'm really gettin' worried . . . If things keep breakin' bad like this . . .

ART: Don't worry about me, Curt. I'm just along for the ride. Try and get yourself together. It don't matter to me what you have to go through to get yourself straight, man. Just work it on out.

[*Spot off* ART *and* CURT. *Spot on* SHOW GIRL *and* CUSTOMER.]

CUSTOMER: How 'bout it, sugar?

SHOW GIRL: Are you kiddin', man?

CUSTOMER: [*Whining.*] Well christ . . . twenty-five bucks . . . what's it lined with . . . gold or somethin'?

SHOW GIRL: You see those two broads over at that table?

[*Lights on* PANDORA *and* MAMMA.]

CUSTOMER: Yeah. You suggestin' that I hit on them?

SHOW GIRL: Yeah. Do that. The one in the black dress won't even speak to you unless you're ready to leave a hundred or more . . . and besides . . . she has to like your type first. The other one might consider it for fifty.

CUSTOMER: Who's the girl in the black dress?

[*Lights change.*]

SHOW GIRL: That's *Pandora.* She headlines the Revue. You have to give her twenty bucks just to get her phone number. So why don't you go hit on her?

[*Lights off. Spot on* BARTENDER.]

BARTENDER: You call yourselves artists and then you want me to bleed for you? What kinda crap is that?

DRUMMER: [*In shadows.*] Listen you jive-time whiskey-pourer. We are artists and I don't care what you call us or how you bleed. It's cats like you and your boss who make us all the time have to act like thugs, pimps and leeches to just make it out here in this world.

BARTENDER: So why ya tellin' me? So make it some other way?

PIANO PLAYER: [*In shadows.*] It's just impossible to talk to you people . . . it's just impossible to be heard any more.

[*Spot off* BARTENDER. *Spot on* CURT *and* ART.]

CURT: Yeah . . . when I first met her, Art. You should of seen her. It was in a joint somethin' like this . . .

[*Light off; spot picks up* PANDORA *standing in the door looking younger, nervous.* CURT *crosses stage to meet her as he speaks.*]

CURT: [*Entering light.*] She was just eighteen . . . had the prettiest little pair of tits poking right out at me . . . sharp enough to put your eyes out. [*He takes* PANDORA *in his arms and kisses her violently. She resists but he is overwhelming.*]

PANDORA: [*Young voice.*] I beg your pardon, mister.

CURT: I said that you're beautiful . . . that I want you . . . that you are mine forever . . . that it will always be this way for you, for you are mine. [*He brutally subdues her. Her hair falls across her face. Her face has that expression that prisoners' sometimes have when they are shifted without prior explanation from an old cell to an unfamiliar cell, equally as old.*]

PANDORA: Are you the man I'm to love?

CURT: [*Dragging her into the shadows.*] Don't talk of something you'll never know anything about . . .

[*They speak from the shadows now, facing the audience.*]

PANDORA: I can't love you? I can't love if I even wanted . . . ?

CURT: You are mine . . . my flesh . . . my body . . . you are in my keeping.

PANDORA: Is it so much to ask for . . . just to be your woman?

CURT: You will do as I say . . . your flesh, your soul, your spirit is at my command . . . I possess you . . .

PANDORA: First there were others . . . now there is you . . . always the same for me . . .

[*Lights change.*]

CURT: [*In shadows, walking toward* ART.] Yeah . . . she was ready . . . has always been.

[*Spot on* ART. CURT *enters light.*]

ART: Pandora's a beautiful girl, Curt. You're lucky, man, to have her. I envy you.

CURT: Thanks, Art.

ART: Don't mention it, don't mention it at all.

[*Lights go down. Come up with* SHAKY *sitting at the table with* MAMMA *and* PANDORA.]

SHAKY: What's happen'n, baby?

MAMMA: Nothin' yet, Shaky. Give me time. The joint ain't even open yet.

SHAKY: Don't take too long, woman.

MAMMA: Give me time, Shaky. Why you got to come on so strong, man? You know I always take care of business. You know I got to get used to it again. Didn't I set up that thing between you and Slim?

SHAKY: Yeah, baby. But that's my department. You take care of business on your side of the street. [*The* BASS PLAYER *comes over to the table. To* BASS PLAYER.] Let's take a walk, poppa.

BASS: After you, Shake Shake.

MAMMA: I'll be here, Shaky.

SHAKY: Let's hope you're either here or there . . . okay?

MAMMA: Shaky . . . you're goin' too fast. Don't push me so hard.

SHAKY: [*Leaving.*] Tonight, baby. One hundred stone cold dollars, baby.

[*Light on* SHOW GIRL *and* CUSTOMER.]

SHOW GIRL: They're alone. Why not now?

CUSTOMER: Okay . . . okay . . . twenty-five you get . . . after the show tonight.

[*Lights off; spot on* CURT *and* ART.]

CURT: When I saw you in action, Art, I said to myself I could really use that kid. Man, you're like a little brother to me now, man. I watch the

way you act around people. You think on your feet and study them like a
good gambler does. You're like me in a lot of ways. Man, we're a new
breed, ya know. Renegades. Rebels. There's no rules for us . . . we make
them as we break them.

ART: Sounds kind'a romantic, Curt.

CURT: And why shouldn't it? Man, this ain't a world we built so why
should we try and fit in it? We have to make it over the best we can . . .
and we are the ones to do it. We are, man, we are!

[*Spot on* MAMMA.]

MAMMA: I don't know why I'm this way . . . I just am. Is it because my
name is different and I am different? Is it because I talk like a spade?

PANDORA: [*From shadows.*] Take a look at that! Just because this white
broad's been hangin' out with us for a couple of years she's goin' ta
blame that bad talk on us.

[*Light on table.*]

PANDORA: [*To* MAMMA.] When you brought your funky ass from Mississippi woman we couldn't even understand you . . . sheeet . . . we taught
you how to speak if anything!

MAMMA: [*Out at audience.*] All I know is that I'm here and that's where
I'm at . . . and I'll be here until somethin' happens . . . I wish Shaky
wouldn't push me so . . . I want to be good for him . . . I want him to be
my man and care about me a little . . .

[ART *brings* MAMMA *her drink.* CURT *sits with him at the table.*]

CURT: [*To* PANDORA.] Don't look so pissed off, honcy.

PANDORA: Why shouldn't I? Everything's gone wrong.

[CURT *stands and takes* PANDORA'*s arm.*]

CURT: C'mere, baby. Let me talk to you. [*They walk into the shadows.*]

ART: Just saw Shaky. He didn't stay long.

MAMMA: Nawh. He's gone to take care of some business. Wants me to stay
here and take care of mine.

ART: I guess that's what you should do then.

MAMMA: Should I? He's rushin' me too fast, that's what he's doin'. He
knows I take a little time gettin' right inside before I can go back to work
but he's pushin' me. It's Curt's and Pan's fault . . . they're desparate for
money and they're pressin' Shaky.

ART: Maybe you should try and talk to him or to Curt.

MAMMA: It wouldn't do any good!

ART: It wouldn't? If you were my girl I'd listen to what you had to say.

MAMMA: Oh, man, knock off the bullshit!

ART: But I would, really.

MAMMA: [*Hesitant.*] You would? I bet you're full of shit.

ART: Sure I would. I look young but I know what you need . . . and I know
what you want.

MAMMA: [*Giggling.*] You do? [*Peering over her glass.*] What do I need and
want, fuzz wuzz?

ART: Understanding.

MAMMA: What?

ART: [*Soft.*] Understanding.

MAMMA: Sheeet . . .

ART: [*Softer.*] Understanding.
        [*Lights down; spot on* CURT *and* PANDORA.]
PANDORA: I'm gettin' fed up with this shit, Curt. We seem to be goin'
        backwards, not forward.
CURT: I know that, baby. But things will get straightened out. You know it
        has to. When the job . . .
PANDORA: [*Cutting.*] The job! Yeah . . . it better be somethin', Curt, or
        you're in some big trouble . . . We're both in some big trouble . . . what'd
        I do without you?
CURT: If anything happens, baby . . . let Art take care of things . . .
PANDORA: Art?
CURT: Yeah.
PANDORA: [*Afraid.*] But I'm your woman, remember?
CURT: He's like a little brother to me. I've already spoken to him about it
        . . . you can get a real gig in a show or somethin' and share an apartment
        with him. He'll look out for you while I'm away. Go up to Frisco and
        wait for me . . . Art's got a head and he can look after things until I get out
        . . . then things will be okay again. But that's if the worst happens and we
        don't get the juice money . . .
PANDORA: [*Struck.*] You think that much of him, Curt?
CURT: I told you he's like my brother, baby. I've been waitin' a long time
        for a real cat to come along . . . we're on our way now . . .
        [*Lights lower; spot on table as* SHAKY *enters.*]
SHAKY: [*To* ART.] Hey, what you say your name was?
ART: [*Smiling, holding out his hand.*] It's Art, Shaky, you know I met . . .
SHAKY: [*Cutting.*] Yeah, I know . . . what you doin' takin' up my ole lady's
        time?
        [BASS PLAYER *enters.*]
ART: I was only sittin' here and bought her a drink. She rode over in my
        car with Curt and Pan.
SHAKY: That's what I mean, man . . . takin' up her time.
MAMMA: Shaky . . . stop it! He wasn't doin' nothin' . . . he's a friend of
        Curt's and . . .
SHAKY: Shut up!
MAMMA: You don't understand . . .
        [*He slaps her.* ART *grabs his arm and pushes him sprawling across a*
        chair. SHAKY *regains his balance and begins to lunge but is caught by*
        CURT.]
CURT: Hey, cool it, man! What's goin' on?
SHAKY: This little punk friend of yours doesn't like what I do with my
        woman.
BASS PLAYER: Why don't you forget it, Shaky. If it had been me I would of
        done the same thing. Forget it. It ain't worth it.
MAMMA: [*Scared.*] He don't understand.
SHAKY: You'll see what I understand when we get home, bitch!
ART: [*Putting out his hand.*] I'm sorry, man. It was my fault. I had . . .
        [SHAKY *knocks* ART'*s hand aside and turns, being led toward the door*
        by the musician.]
SHAKY: [*To* ART.] I'll see you later.

CURT: Hey, Shaky. C'mere, man. It don't mean nothin'.

[*They exit.* PANDORA *takes a seat.* CURT *goes to the bar and answers the questions of the musicians and the* BARTENDER. *The* SHOW GIRL *goes to the rear of the club and the* CUSTOMER *orders another drink.*]

MAMMA: He just don't understand . . . he can't understand and he can't give me any understanding . . .

PANDORA: Who don't understand, Mamma?

MAMMA: Shaky . . . he just don't understand . . . he should try and understand me more.

PANDORA: Girl, you so stoned you're not makin' any sense. He understands, Mamma. He understands you perfectly.

MAMMA: He can't, Pan. He can't or I wouldn't feel this way about him now.

ART: Maybe you're changin'.

PANDORA: Oh, man, you're full of it!

ART: You're cynical but not that hard, Pandora.

PANDORA: Man, I've seen it all. I don't have to be hard . . . I just use what I know.

ART: Have you seen everything, Pan?

PANDORA: Yes!

ART: Then you've seen me before?

PANDORA: [*Staring.*] Yeah . . . I've seen you before. There's a you standin' on every corner with his hands in his pockets and his fly half unzipped . . . there's a you in every drunk tank in every city . . . there's a you sniffin' around moochin' drinks and kissin' ass and thinkin' he's a make-out artist. Yeah . . . I've seen you before, punk!

MAMMA: He just don't understand . . .

ART: No, you've never seen me before, Pandora. I'm goin'a tell you something.

PANDORA: [*Sarcastic.*] What are you goin'a tell me, Art?

ART: That I'm goin'a change your life.

PANDORA: What?

[*Lights go up with a startling flash.* DEENY *and the* BOUNCER, *Pete, enter.* DEENY, *in black glasses, sports an ascot and a cummerbund under his sport coat. In the thin dress she entered in, the* SHOW GIRL *walks from the rear and takes a seat beside the* CUSTOMER. MAMMA TOO TIGHT *stands and* CURT *nearly bowls over a* CUSTOMER *on his way to meet* DEENY *in center stage in front of* PANDORA's *table.* PANDORA *jumps to her feet beside* MAMMA, *followed by* ART.]

CURT: Deeny!

[*The* BASS PLAYER *enters, and the* DRUMMER *and* PIANO PLAYER *hurry over. Behind the bar the* BARTENDER *stands tensed; the* BASS PLAYER *climbs upon the stage and begins zippering his bass fiddle into its cloth bag.*]

DEENY: Keep it, Curt! I don't want to hear it. I just come from the union and I've taken all the crap I'm gonna . . . the show's closed.

[*Chorus of yells.*]

CURT: Deeny, what you take us for?

PANDORA: Hey, man . . . let's go in the back and talk . . .

DRUMMER: [*Pushing his way around the* PIANO PLAYER.] Yeah, Deeny, I want to talk to you!

DEENY: I just don't want to hear it from any of you. Okay? . . . Okay! Now everybody . . . this club is closin'. Ya hear? Everybody out inside of ten minutes . . . understand? This is my property. Get off it inside of ten minutes or I'm callin' the cops . . . your things and you out . . . hit the street . . . that means everybody!

[*Another chorus of yells from nearly everyone. The* CUSTOMERS *hurry out the exit and the* SHOW GIRL *joins the group.*]

BASS PLAYER: [*To other musicians.*] Hey, fellas, I'm splittin' . . . what about you?

[MAMMA *turns and goes over to him.*]

DRUMMER: Man, what about my pay?

DEENY: Take your bitchin' to the union, fellah. They instigated this hassle.

PANDORA: We don't know nothin' bout no union, Deeny . . .

DEENY: [*Sarcastic.*] I know you don't, sugar. But you girls should get organized . . . try to get paid hourly and get off the quota system and you'd . . .

CURT: Watch your mouth, mathafukker!

BOUNCER: You'd better watch yours!

DEENY: [*To* BARTENDER.] Hey, Chico, call the cops! You just can't reason with some jerks! Call them now!

[*The* BARTENDER *dials.*]

PANDORA: [*To* CURT.] What we gonna do, baby . . . ?

CURT: Quiet!

PANDORA: But your case, honey . . .

BARTENDER: [*On phone.*] Yeah . . . there's trouble at the Strip Club on Western . . . yeah . . .

[DEENY *tries to push his way past but* CURT *blocks him. The* BOUNCER *moves to shove* CURT *out of the way but* ART *steps in as the four confront each other, and the girls back off. The* PIANO PLAYER *has coaxed the* DRUMMER *to join the* BASS PLAYER *upon the stage, packing away his equipment. At a run, the* SHOW GIRL *rushes to the rear of the club as the* BARTENDER *hangs up the phone. As the other musicians pack up, the* PIANO PLAYER *comes back to the group.*]

PIANO: Deeny, you just can't do this. This ain't right about us. We stuck by you for below scale wages, riskin' our own necks with the union to keep you in business, until you got on your feet. And still we never got paid on time. Now I hear you gonna put some names in here and clean up on the rep we made for you.

BOUNCER: Shut up, mister. You're not supposed to be here right now, remember?

PANDORA: [*Furious.*] You owe me for two and a half weeks, man!

DEENY: [*Trying to get by again.*] Sorry, baby. Come around some time and maybe we can work out somethin'.

CURT: I know why you doin' this, Deeny. Don't pull that union shit on me! You want all the girls to work for you . . . on the block like tramps for ten and fifteen dollars a trick. Pan, Mamma, and all the other broads. I'd die before I'd let you put my woman on the street for ten tricks a day. Why you got to be so fuckin' greedy, man? You ain't right! You already got six girls now.

BOUNCER: Just say he has taste and discrimination, Curt. You know he wants your old lady because . . .

DEENY: [*Cutting.*] Shut up all of you! And are you goin' to get out of my way?

MAMMA: [*From bandstand.*] Deeny. Who you think you are?

DEENY: [*To* MAMMA.] You know who I am, you stupid country cunt. And if you want to stay on the streets and keep that junkie ole man of yours cool, just keep your mouth out of this! That way you won't get your legs broke and . . .

CURT: [*Cutting.*] I know why you doin' this, Deeny.

[SHAKY *enters. The* SHOW GIRL *rushes from the rear with costumes in arms and exits, speaking to no one.*]

SHAKY: Did I hear somebody say they gonna break Mamma's legs?

[*There is general bedlam with shouts and near screaming.*]

DRUMMER: [*Exiting.*] I'm goin' ta take this farther than to the union, Deeny!

BOUNCER: You can take it to your mother, punk!

[DRUMMER *drops equipment and lunges toward* BOUNCER *but* PIANO PLAYER *grabs him and holds.* BASS PLAYER *helps.*]

BASS PLAYER: [*Exiting with* DRUMMER.] Hey, Deeny, you're wrong! You're dead wrong, man!

PIANO: [*To* CURT *and* PANDORA.] Cool it. Let's all split. This ain't nothin' but a big bust. [*It becomes suddenly quiet and the* BARTENDER, *a club in hand, comes around the bar and stands behind* CURT *and* ART. SHAKY *stands to the side of* DEENY *and the* BOUNCER. MAMMA *is on the bandstand, wide-eyed, and* PANDORA *is downstage glowering at her enemies. Leaving.*] I'll see you guys. [*Seeing* SHAKY.] Hey, man. It ain't worth it.

SHAKY: I'll get in touch with you, okay?

PIANO: C'mon, man. I don't like what I see.

SHAKY: Make it! Be a good friend and make it.

[PIANO PLAYER *exits. It is even more quiet. Very low, from somewhere outside, the theme is heard as each group eyes the other and tenses.*]

PANDORA: [*Spitting it out, violent as unexpected spit spattering a face.*] Fuck you, Deeny! Fuck you! Fuck you! *Fuck you!*

DEENY: [*Frenzied.*] You little trampy bitch . . . you . . .

[CURT *smashes him in the mouth as he reaches for* PANDORA. DEENY *falls back beside the table, grabs a glass and hurls it into* CURT's *face, shattering it.* CURT *launches himself upon him and pummels* DEENY *to the floor. Meanwhile, the* BOUNCER *and* ART *fight in center stage.* SHAKY *is struck almost immediately from behind by the* BARTENDER's *club.* ART, *seeing the* BARTENDER *advancing on* CURT's *rear, breaks away and desperately kicks out at the* BARTENDER. *With a screech he doubles over and grabs his groin. The* BOUNCER *seizes* ART *from behind, about the throat, in an armlock, and begins strangling him.* PANDORA, *who has taken off her shoes after kicking* DEENY *several times as* CURT *beats him upon the floor, attacks the* BOUNCER *from*

*behind and repeatedly strikes him about the head with her shoe heels.
The* BOUNCER *loosens his grip on* ART *and grabs* PANDORA *and
punches her. She falls.* ART, *gasping, reaches down for the* BAR-
TENDER'*s dropped club, picks it up and turns and beats the* BOUNCER
to the floor. All the while MAMMA TOO TIGHT *screams. With face
bloodied from splintered glass,* CURT *has beaten* DEENY *into unconsciousness and staggers over and pulls* PANDORA *up. Sirens, screeches,
and slamming car doors are heard from outside. Shouts.*]

CURT: [*Towing* PANDORA.] C'mon, Art! Pull yourself together. The cops
are here.

[ART *staggers over to* SHAKY *and tries to lift him but he is too weak.*
MAMMA, *crying and screaming, jumps from the bandstand and pulls
at* SHAKY.]

CURT: [*Heading for the rear.*] He's too heavy, Art. Leave him. Grab
Mamma and let's get out the back way. Move! C'mon, man, move!

[*Dazed, but following orders,* ART *grabs* MAMMA'*s arms and struggles
with her.*]

MAMMA: [*Resisting.*] No! No! I can't leave him like that!

CURT: [*Exiting.*] Bring her, Art. Out the back way to the car.

MAMMA: [*Being dragged out by* ART.] My first day out . . . my first day . . .

[*They exit and immediately the stage blackens, then the rumble of
running feet.*]

VOICE: CHRIST! [*More heavy running, then stop.*] Hey, call a couple of
ambulances . . . Emergency!

CURTAIN

Act III

SCENE I

Time: Three days later. Afternoon.

Scene: CURT'*s apartment. He and* RICH *play chess as in Act I. The bed is
lowered and* MAMMA TOO TIGHT *sleeps with the covers pulled up to her chin
as if she is cold. The radio is off and the California sunshine glistens in the
clean room. The room looks sterile, unlived-in and motel-like without the
lighting of the first act.*

CURT *wears two band-aids upon his face, one upon his forehead, the other
on the bridge of his nose.*

CURT: [*Bored.*] It'll be mate in two moves, Rich. Do you want to play it
out?

RICH: Nawh, man. I ain't up to it.

CURT: [*Sitting back.*] The last three day have just taken everything out of
me, man.

RICH: Yeah. They been pretty rough. [CURT *stands, stretches, and walks
across the stage.*] Hey, man. Is there any more beer?

CURT: Nawh. Pan and Art's bringing some in with them when they come.

RICH: [*Muttering.*] Yeah . . . when they get here.

CURT: [*Noticing* RICH'*s tone.*] What did you say, man?

RICH: Oh. Nothin', man.

CURT: [*Sharply.*] You're a liar . . . I heard what you said!

RICH: [*Sullen.*] I ain't goin'a be many more of them liars, Curt.

CURT: [*Gesturing.*] Awww, man. Forget it . . . you know how I feel with Deeny in a coma from his concussion for the past three days and me not knowin' if he's goin' to press charges finally or die.

RICH: Yeah, man. I'm a bit edgy myself. Forget about what I said.

[CURT *returns to the couch and sprawls back.*]

CURT: But I'd like to know what you meant by it, Rich.

RICH: [*Seeing no way out.*] Now, Curt. You and I been friends since we were young punks stealin' hub caps and tires together, right? Remember that time you, me and the guys gang-banged that Pachuco broad? . . . And the Dog Town boys came up and we had that big rumble and they killed Sparky?

CURT: [*Sensing something coming.*] How can I forget it . . . I served my first stretch behind it for stabbin' that Mexican kid, Manuel.

RICH: Yeah. That was a good time ago and Manuel ain't no kid no more . . .

CURT: Yeah. But, tell me. What do you have to say, good buddy?

RICH: [*Pausing, then serious.*] It's about this guy Art and Pandora, man.

CURT: What do you mean, man?

RICH: Man . . . I don't mean there's anything goin' on yet . . . but each afternoon he's taken Pandora out for the past three days they been gettin' back later . . . and . . .

CURT: And what, Rich?

RICH: And the way she looks at him, Curt.

CURT: [*Disgusted and angry.*] Awww, man . . . I thought I knew you better.

RICH: Well I told you that I didn't think that they were doin' anything really.

CURT: But, what? That he drives her up to Sunset Strip to keep her dates with the big tricks . . . you know how much dough she brings back, man?

RICH: [*Resolutely.*] Yeah, man. Sometimes over a hundred dollars for one trick.

CURT: So you can't hurry those people for that kinda bread, man.

RICH: [*Trying to be understood.*] But I wasn't talkin' about the tricks, Curt. I don't think they're holdin' back any money on you.

CURT: Then what are you talkin' 'bout?

RICH: About that little jive-ass square gettin' next to your woman, that's what!

CURT: Now listen, Rich. We're friends and all that but that little jive-ass square as you call him is just like a brother to me . . . and we been in some tighter things than you and me will ever be in.

RICH: [*Obviously hurt.*] Well, forget it!

CURT: No, let's not forget it. You're accusing my wife of jivin' around on me. You know that Pan's the straightest broad you'll ever find. That's why I married her. You know if we couldn't have gotten another man that she would have gone on the job and been as good as most men. She and I are a team. What could she gain by messin' 'round on me with my ace buddy?

RICH: Forget it, I said.

CURT: Nawh, Rich. I don't want to. I know what's really buggin' you. Ever since Shaky got busted at the Club and they found all that smack on him you been buggin' Mamma to be your woman 'cause you know that with Shaky's record he won't be hittin' the streets again for at least ten years. But you're wrong on two counts cause we're bailin' out Shaky tonight and takin' him with us and Mamma don't want you cause she wants Art but he don't go for her.

RICH: [Getting to his feet.] I'll see you, man. Between your broad and that cat you can't think any more! [CURT reaches for RICH's shirt front; RICH throws his hands off.] Take it easy, Curt. You already won a close one this week. And your guardian angel ain't round to sneak-punch people.
      [CURT stares at him and steps back.]

MAMMA: [From bed.] Hey, what's all that shoutin' about?

CURT: Nothin', baby. Rich and I are just crackin' jokes.

MAMMA: [Sitting up.] Curt, I wonder if . . .

CURT: No, Mamma. You can't have no fix. Remember what I told you? You don't turn no tricks in town cause you're hot behind Shaky's bust so you don't need any heroin, right? You're on holiday and besides, you're full of codeine now . . . that's enough . . .

MAMMA: But I would be good if I could get some. I wouldn't worry about Shaky so much and I'd feel . . .

CURT: You just come out of the joint clean, Mamma. You don't need anything but to keep cool.

MAMMA: [Pouting.] But I got the sixteen hundred dollars that Shaky had stashed at our pad. I could buy it okay, Curt.

CURT: Forget it. That money is with the other bread. We all takin' a trip with that. Besides . . . Shaky had over two thousand bucks worth of stuff in the pad and we sellin' it tonight so we can bail him out so he can leave with us . . .
      [MAMMA jumps out of bed in a thin gown.]

MAMMA: [Delighted.] You are? Then he'll be home soon?

CURT: Yeah. Then we all make it before Deeny comes out of his coma or croaks. Now get back in bed before Rich grabs you!

MAMMA: [Playful.] Rich, you better not. Shaky will be home soon.

RICH: [Teasing.] Sheeet, woman. I don't care about old ass Shaky. C'mon, baby, why don't you get yourself a young stud?

MAMMA: [Getting in bed.] When I get one it won't be you.

RICH: [Serious.] Then who?

CURT: [Mutters.] I told Art and Pan that we need the car this evening to drop off the stuff. After that it'll be time to get ready for the job.

RICH: [Bitterly, to MAMMA.] So he's got to you, too.

MAMMA: Nobody's got to me. What'chou talkin' 'bout, Rich? Art's been stayin' over to Shaky and my place for the last couple of nights while I stayed here. How can he get . . .

RICH: [Cutting.] How did you know I was talkin' about Art?

MAMMA: Cause you got Art on the brain, that's why!

CURT: I thought we dropped that, Rich.

RICH: [*To* MAMMA.] If you're goin'a get somebody young . . . get a man
. . . not some little book-readin' faggot . . .

MAMMA: [*Red-faced, to* RICH.] Oh, go fuck yourself, man! [*She covers her
head.*]

RICH: Okay, man. We got a lot to do tonight, so I'll lay off.

        [*Through the back curtain the outside kitchen door can be seen open-
        ing. Dusk is come and* ART *enters first with a large bag;* PANDORA
        *follows, closes the door, and purposely bumps against him as she
        passes. She wears dark glasses, her pants, and boots.*]

ART: Hey, you almost made me drop this! Where should I put it?

        [PANDORA *enters front room smiling.*]

PANDORA: Hi, honey. Hello, Rich. [*She walks over to* CURT, *kisses him,
and places money in his hand.*]

CURT: Hey, pretty baby. [*He pulls her to him, gives her an extended kiss,
and breaks it, looking over* PANDORA's *shoulders at* RICH *who looks away.*]

CURT: Everything okay?

PANDORA: Smooth as Silky Sullivan.

        [*In the kitchen* ART *is taking items from the bag.* CURT *hands back the
        money to* PANDORA.]

CURT: Here, Pan, put this in the box with the rest.

PANDORA: Okay. [*She walks past bed and looks down.*] What's wrong with
Mamma?

CURT: Rich's been tryin' to love her up.

RICH: She won't go for my program, baby.

PANDORA: [*Entering the kitchen.*] That's too bad . . . you better cultivate
some charm, Rich.

RICH: Yeah, that's what's happen'n. I'm not one of the lucky ones . . .
some people don't need it.

PANDORA: [*Going to* ART.] Let me take in the beer, Art. You put the frozen
food in the refrigerator and the canned things in the cupboard.

        [ART *pulls her to him and kisses her.*]

PANDORA: [*Taking breath.*] Hand me the glasses, will ya?

        [*They kiss again, she responding this time, then she pushes him away
        and begins fixing beer for* CURT *and* RICH.]

CURT: Hey, Mamma. You want any beer?

MAMMA: [*Under the cover.*] No, no.

        [PANDORA *serves* CURT *and* RICH, *then climbs the stairs and enters the
        dressing room.* ART *comes out of the kitchen.*]

RICH: How you feel, Art?

ART: Okay. Hollywood's an interesting place. First job I ever had just drivin' somebody around.

CURT: Hope it's your last, Art. With this job tonight and my cut from sellin' Shaky's heroin we'll be just about in. Might even go into business
back East.

ART: Yeah? I hope so.

CURT: We already got almost twenty-four hundred with Shaky's money
we found at his place and the bread we've been able to hustle the last few
days. After tonight we'll be set.

RICH: Yeah. After tonight you'll be set.

CURT: [*Looking at* RICH.] It's too bad you won't come with us, Rich. But your share will fix you up out here okay.

RICH: Fix me up? Ha ha . . . I'll probably shoot that up in smack inside of several months . . . but if I make it I'll probably be lookin' you up in two more years when my probation's up. No use ruin'n a good thing. When I cut this town loose I want to be clean. I just hope all goes well with you.

ART: [*Smiling.*] Why shouldn't it?

CURT: Yeah, Rich, why shouldn't it?

RICH: Funny things happen to funny-style people, ya know.

CURT: Yeah. Too bad you won't be comin' along . . . we need a clown in our show.

[RICH *watches* ART *studying the chess game.*]

RICH: Do you see anything I missed, good buddy?

ART: Oh. I don't know.

RICH: You know I seldom beat Curt. Why don't you play him?

ART: [*Still looking at board.*] Maybe I will when we find time.

CURT: What would you have done from there, Art?

ART: It's according to what side I'm on.

CURT: You have the black. White's going to mate you in two moves.

ART: He is?

RICH: Yeah. He is.

[ART *reaches over and picks up the black king.*]

ART: Most kings need a queen to be most powerful but others do the best they can. [*He places the king upon another square.*] That's what I'd do, Rich.

CURT: [*Perceiving.*] Yeah. I see . . . I see . . .

RICH: Say, why'd you move there? . . . He can't move now . . . he can't put himself in check . . .

ART: [*As* RICH *stares at him.*] Yeah, Rich?

CURT: [*Matter-of-factly.*] A stalemate.

RICH: [*Muttering.*] I should of seen that. [*To* ART.] How did you . . . why . . .

ART: When you play the game you look for any break you can make.

CURT: We should play sometime, Art.

ART: I'm looking forward to it, Curt. But you name the time.

CURT: [*Standing.*] I'll do that. Hey, Pandora! We got to go!

[PANDORA *comes to the top of the stairs. She has changed into a simple dress.*]

PANDORA: We goin' some place?

CURT: I got to drop Shaky's stuff off and go down to the bail bondsman and the lawyer. I want you to drive. C'mon, Rich. Pan will sit in the car down the street in the next block and you and me will walk up the street talkin' about baseball, understand? On the corner of Adams and Crenshaw we'll meet a man and hit a grand slam.

RICH: Yeah, I hope so, brother.

CURT: It's trip time from here on in, baby.

PANDORA: [*Excited.*] Wait until I get my coat.

CURT: [*In good humor.*] Let's go, woman. It's eighty degrees outside and we might be the hottest thing in L.A. but it just ain't that warm. Let's go, now. See you, Art. [*Going to* ART.] Oh, I almost forgot the car keys.

ART: [*Handing him the keys.*] See you guys.

CURT: [*Hands keys to* PANDORA.] You'll watch the phone, okay?

ART: Sure, good buddy, I'll see to the phone.

CURT: If Mamma wakes up and wants a fix don't give in to her.

ART: I'll try not to.

CURT: [*Serious.*] I mean it, Art.

ART: [*Smiling.*] I'm dead serious, man.

PANDORA: See you later, Art.

ART: See you later, Pan. Good-bye, Curt. Good-bye, Rich.

> [*The trio exit and* ART *goes to the radio and switches it on. It plays the theme as he enters the kitchen and gets himself a beer. He comes from the kitchen drinking from the bottle and climbs the bathroom stairs. His shadow is seen lifting and then dialing. His voice is muffled by the music and by his whisper; nothing is understood. After the shadow hangs up,* ART *returns to the living room and descends the stairs. He sits upon the bed and shakes* MAMMA TOO TIGHT.]

MAMMA: [*Being shaken.*] Huh? I don't want any beer. [ART *shakes her once more. She uncovers her head.*] Oh, Art. It's you. Where's everybody? [*He doesn't answer, looks at her. Evening comes and the room blackens.*] I'm glad you woke me. I always like to talk to you but I guess I bug you since you don't say too much to me. Why ain't you sayin' nothin' now? [*Three-beat pause.*]

ART: [*Laughing.*] Ha ha ha . . . ha ha . . . Ma-ma Too Tight! . . . ha ha ha . . .

MAMMA: You said it! Sometimes you have such a nice look on your face and now . . . you look different . . . [*Pause.*] like you so happy you could scream . . . You never looked at me like this before, Art, never. [*In total blackness as the music plays.*] You said Shaky wouldn't be back? . . . You won't? . . . I don't care as long as you don't go away . . . You know . . . you understand me. It's like you can look inside my head . . . Oh how did you know? Just a little bit? More? You say I can have a fix any time I want? . . . Oh! . . . You understand me, don't cha? Don't let Curt know . . . you say don't worry about Curt . . . don't care what anybody thinks or says except you? [*Silence, pause.*] Oh I feel so good now . . . I didn't know but I was hoping . . . I didn't know, honey . . . Oh, Art! . . . Ahhhh . . . now I can feel you oozing out of me . . . and I'm glad so glad . . . it's good . . .

Act III

SCENE II

PANDORA *leans against the kitchen door as the lights go up. The atmosphere of the first act is recreated by the lights and music. The bed has been put up and* ART *sits upon the couch.* PANDORA *has been crying and what can be seen of her face around her dark glasses appears shocked.*
She walks to the center of the room and faces ART.

PANDORA: Art . . . Art . . . they got them. They got Curt and Rich . . . with all that stuff on them. The cops were waitin' on them. They busted them with all those narcotics . . . we'll never see them again.

ART: [*Rising.*] We're hot, Pandora. We got to get out of town.

PANDORA: They got 'em, don't you hear me, Art? What can we do?

ART: Nothin' . . . we got to make it before Curt or Rich break and the cops are kickin' that door in.

PANDORA: You said nothin'? But we . . . what do you mean? We got to do somethin'! [*Crying.*] We can't just let it happen to them . . . we got to do somethin' like Curt would do if it was one of us . . . Art! Art! Don't just stand there! Do . . .

    [*He slaps her viciously, knocking off her glasses, exposing her blackened eyes.*]

ART: [*Commanding.*] Get a hold on yourself, Pandora. You've had a bad experience. [*She holds her face and looks dazed.*] Now listen to me. Mamma has gone over to her place to pack and as soon as she gets back we're all leaving.

PANDORA: [*Dazed.*] Mamma is packin'? . . . Did Curt tell her to pack?

ART: You know he didn't. Now as soon as she gets here I want us to be packed, okay?

PANDORA: But . . . Art . . . packed . . . where we goin'?

ART: To Buffalo, baby. Where else?

PANDORA: To Buffalo?

ART: That's what I said. Now go up in your dressing room and get your suit case . . . [*A knock comes from the front door.*] That's Mamma already . . . we're runnin' late, woman. C'mon, get a move on. [*He shoves her.*] Move! Get a move on, Pandora! [*She stumbles over the first step, catches her balance and begins climbing.* ART *looks after her.*] Oh . . . Pandora . . . [*She turns and looks vacantly at him.*] Don't forget your box!

    [*As she turns and climbs the last steps* ART *saunters to the radio as the knock sounds again. Instantaneously, as he switches the radio off, the stage is thrown in complete blackness.*]

                  1969

ELDRIDGE CLEAVER

b. 1935

Born in Wabbeseka, Arkansas, to Thelma and Leroy Eldridge Cleaver, Eldridge Cleaver was convicted in 1954 of drug possession. This began what one commentator describes as a "twelve-year cycle of assorted prison terms at Soledad, Folsom, and San Quentin." Like Malcolm X, Cleaver converted to the Black Muslim faith while in prison and devoted much of his incarceration to self-education.

Upon his release from prison, Cleaver became a writer for *Ramparts* magazine, there publishing portions of an autobiographical novella titled *Black Moochie* (completed in exile in 1969). By 1967, he had become the minister of information of the Black Panther Party for Self-Defense. His best-selling book, *Soul on Ice* (1968), made him one of the foremost revolutionary celebrities of the 1960s. Not unaware of the nature of American showmanship, Cleaver worked rather like a black revolutionary P. T. Barnum, even declaring his candidacy for the presidency in 1968. Fleeing criminal charges from a shoot-out with the Oakland (California) police, he spent much of the 1970s abroad, residing in Cuba, Algeria, and Europe. Upon his return to the United States, Cleaver announced his miraculous rebirth as a fundamentalist Christian.

The style, tone, and ideology of the writings in *Soul on Ice* were influential for aspiring young revolutionary writers of the Black Arts movement. And high school and college teachers alike introduced Cleaver's writings to their classes as powerful examples of a new, ardent black male primitivism.

From Soul on Ice

The Primeval Mitosis [1]

And the Lord God caused a deep sleep to fall upon Adam, and he slept: and he took one of his ribs, and closed up the flesh instead thereof; And the rib, which the Lord God had taken from man, made he a woman, and brought her unto the man. And Adam said, This is now bone of my bones, and flesh of my flesh: she shall be called Woman, because she was taken out of Man.

—GENESIS 2:21–23

It is as if in the evolution of sex a particle one day broke away from an X-chromosome, and thereafter in relation to X-chromosomes could produce only an incomplete female—the creature we now call the male! It is to this original chromosomal deficiency that all the various troubles to which the male falls heir can be traced.

—ASHLEY MONTAGU, [2] *The Natural Superiority of Women*

I think that *any* submerged class is going to be more accustomed to sexuality than a leisure class. A leisure class may be more *preoccupied* with sexuality; but a submerged class is going to be more drenched in it.

You see, the upper classes are obsessed with sex, but they contain very little of it themselves. They use up much too much sex in their manipulations of power. In effect, they exchange sex for power. So they restrict themselves in their sexuality—whereas the submerged classes have to take their desires for power and plow them back into sex.

—NORMAN MAILER, [3] *The Presidential Papers*

The roots of heterosexuality are buried in that evolutionary choice made long ago in some misty past—but not so remote that it can't be reached with the long arm of the mind—by some unknown forerunner of Homo sapiens. Struggling up from some murky swamp, some stagnant mudhole, some peaceful meadow, that unknown ancestor of Man/Woman, by some weird mitosis of the essence, divided its Unitary Self in half—into the male and female hemispheres of the Primeval Sphere. These hemispheres evolved into what we know today as man and woman.

When the Primeval Sphere divided itself, it established a basic tension of

1. A process of cell division.
2. Well-known British anthropologist (b. 1905) who has published numerous studies and social commentaries.

3. Pulitzer Prize–winning author (b. 1923) who was characterized as "the prophet of hip" because of his classic essay *The White Negro*.

attraction, a dynamic magnetism of opposites—the Primeval Urge—which exerts an irresistible attraction between the male and female hemispheres, ever tending to fuse them back together into a unity in which the male and female realize their true nature—the lost unity of the Primeval Sphere. This is the eternal and unwavering motivation of the male and female hemispheres, of man and woman, to transcend the Primeval Mitosis and achieve supreme identity in the Apocalyptic Fusion.

Each half of the human equation, the male and female hemispheres of the Primeval Sphere, must prepare themselves for the fusion by achieving a Unitary Sexual Image, i.e., a heterosexual identity free from the mutually exclusive, antagonistic, antipodal impediments of homosexuality (the product of the fissure of society into antagonistic classes and a dying culture and civilization alienated from its biology).

Man's continual striving for a Unitary Sexual Image, which can only be achieved in a Unitary Society, becomes a basic driving force of the Class Struggle, which is, in turn, the dynamic of history. The quest for the Apocalyptic Fusion will find optimal conditions only in a Classless Society, the absence of classes being the *sine qua non*[4] for the existence of a Unitary Society in which the Unitary Sexual Image can be achieved.

Each social structure projects onto the screen of possibility the images of the highest type of male and female sexual identities realizable within the limits of that society. The people within that society are motivated and driven, by the perennial quest for Apocalyptic Fusion, to achieve this highest identity, or as close as they can come to the perfection of the Unitary Sexual Image. All impediments to realization of this image become sources of alienation, obstacles in the way of the Self seeking to realize its ultimate identity.

Since each society projects its own sexual image, the Unitary Society will project a Unitary Sexual Image. We can thus postulate, following the model of Marx,[5] that in ancient communal society, which was not cleft into antagonistic classes, there existed a Unitary Society in which a Unitary Sexual Image was in natural coincidence with the way of life of the people. This is the lost innocence of the Garden of Eden.

The Class Society projects a fragmented sexual image. Each class projects a sexual image coinciding with its class-function in society. And since its class-function will differ from that of other classes, its sexual image will differ also and in the same proportion. The source of the fragmentation of the Self in Class Society lies in the alienation between the function of man's Mind and the function of his Body. Man as thinker performs an Administrative Function in society. Man as doer performs a Brute Power Function. These two basic functions I symbolize, when they are embodied in living men functioning in society, as the Omnipotent Administrator and the Supermasculine Menial.

Since all men are created equal, when the Self is fragmented by the operation of the laws and forces of Class Society, men in the elite classes usurp the controlling and Administrative Function of the society as a

4. The one thing that is absolutely necessary (Latin).
5. Karl Marx (1818–1883), German social and ec-

onomic philosopher whose writings inspired 20th-century communism.

whole—i.e., they usurp the administrative component in the nature and biology of the men in the classes below them. Administrative power is concentrated at the apex of society, in the Godhead of the society (pharaoh, king, president, chairman). Administrative power beneath the apex is delegated. Those in classes to which no administrative power has been delegated have the administrative component in their personalities suppressed, alienated, denied expression. Those who have usurped the Administrative Function we shall call the Omnipotent Administrators. Struggling among themselves for higher positions in the administrative hierarchy, they repudiate the component of Brute Power in themselves, claim no kinship with it, and project it onto the men in the classes below them.

All the males in the classes beneath *the* Omnipotent Administrator, or Godhead of the society, are alienated from the administrative component in themselves in proportion to their distance from the apex. That is, they perceive their alienation in terms of their distance from the apex. This perception of their alienation, in terms of the apex, is an illusion. In fact, their alienation must be measured by their distance from the attainment of a Unitary Sexual Image, the take-off stage for the Apocalyptic Fusion. Generally, in a fragmented Class Society, the basic impulse of Omnipotent Administrators is to despise their bodies and glorify their minds.

Those who have been assigned the Brute Power Function we shall call the Supermasculine Menials. They are alienated from their minds. For them the mind counts only insofar as it enables them to receive, understand, and carry out the will of the Omnipotent Administrators.

The Class Society has a built-in bias, which tends to perpetuate the social system. The Omnipotent Administrators, wishing to preserve what they perceive as their superior position and way of life, have, from a class point of view and also on an individual level, a negative reaction toward any influence in the society that tends to increase the number of males qualified to fulfill the functions of administration. When it comes to anything that will better the lot of those beneath him, the Omnipotent Administrator starts with a basic "anti" reflex. Any liberality he might show is an indication of the extent to which he has suppressed his "anti" reflex, and is itself a part of his lust for omnipotence. His liberality is, in fact, charity.

The Supermasculine Menial clearly realizes that the superiority of the Omnipotent Administrators over him is based upon the development of their minds and the power they command as a result. Hence, he starts with a "pro" reflex. He is, for example, pro-universal education at public expense.

Weakness, frailty, cowardice, and effeminacy are, among other attributes, associated with the Mind. Strength, brute power, force, virility, and physical beauty are associated with the Body. Thus the upper classes, or Omnipotent Administrators, are perennially associated with physical weakness, decay, underdeveloped bodies, effeminacy, sexual impotence, and frigidity. Virility, strength, and power are associated with the lower classes, the Supermasculine Menials.

In feudal society, the men of the nobility, who were Omnipotent Administrators by Divine Right, are generally considered to have been weak, delicate, and effeminate, with the affectations of demonstrative homosexuals. The serfs and peasants are considered to have been physically strong, sturdy, hearty, fecund—"supermasculine."

The image of the Omnipotent Administrator, that he is markedly effeminate and delicate by reason of his explicit repudiation and abdication of his body in preference for his mind, is decisive for the image of the woman of the elite classes. *Even though her man is effeminate, she is required to possess and project an image that is in sharp contrast to his, more sharply feminine than his, so that the effeminate image of her man can still, by virtue of the sharp contrast in degrees of femininity, be perceived as masculine.* Therefore, she becomes "Ultrafeminine."

In order to project an image of Ultrafemininity, the women of the elite repudiate and abdicate the Domestic Function of the female (which is, in the female, the counterpart of the function of Brute Power in the male). To enhance her image and to increase her femininity, the domestic component of her nature is projected onto the women in the classes beneath her, and the femininity of the women below is correspondingly decreased. In effect, a switch is made: the woman of the elite absorbs into her being the femininity of the woman below her, and she extirpates her domestic component; the woman below absorbs the elite woman's cast-off domestic component and relinquishes her own femininity. The elite woman thus becomes *Ultrafeminine* while the woman below becomes *Subfeminine*. For the purposes of social imagery, the woman below becomes an Amazon.

Thus, a most weird and complex dialectic of inversion is established in Class Society. The Omnipotent Administrator is launched on a perpetual search for his alienated body, for affirmation of his unstable masculinity. He becomes a worshiper of physical prowess, or he may come to despise the body and everything associated with it. Fearing impotence, impotence being implicit in his negation and abdication of his Body, his profoundest need is for evidence of his virility. His opposite, the Body, the Supermasculine Menial, is a threat to his self-concept (and to compound it all, this perceived threat and resultant fear is reinforced decisively by the fact that the men beneath him are a threat to him *in reality*, because their life goal is to destroy his Omnipotence over them). He views them as his enemies and inferiors, men of a lesser breed than himself and his kind. He despises, hates them. Yet, because of the infirmity in his image and being which moves him to worship masculinity and physical prowess, the Omnipotent Administrator cannot help but covertly, and perhaps in an extremely sublimated guise, envy the bodies and strength of the most alienated men beneath him—those furthest from the apex of administration—because the men most alienated from the mind, least diluted by admixture of the Mind, will be perceived as the most masculine manifestations of the Body: the Supermasculine Menials. (This is precisely the root, the fountainhead, of the homosexuality that is perennially associated with the Omnipotent Administrator.) The dialectic of the Supermasculine Menial is the converse of that of the Omnipotent Administrator. The Supermasculine Menial has an infirmity of the brain because of his alienation from his mind.

Because he despises weakness of the body in himself, the Omnipotent Administrator will have a secret or subconscious aversion to the women of his own class, because of the Ultrafemininity which they have developed to counterbalance his effeminacy. At the same time, he will surpass himself in his efforts to conceal his aversion and make believe that the very opposite is true. He thus makes an icon of his woman and, literally, worships her. He pays obeisance to Her ritualistically while in the chapel of Her presence. Enshrining Her on a pedestal, he goes off seeking confirmation of his insecure masculinity elsewhere. Since the women of the elite tend to become the same, i.e., to project a homogeneous image of Ultrafemininity, they cannot, in the end, satisfy his psychic need—the confirmation of his masculinity. Strength gauges its own potency through a confrontation with other strength. To test it, he must go where it is. He may become addicted to a masculine imaged sport, become a big-game hunter, outdoorsman, mountain climber. He may find satisfaction enough from some outlet as to have no problem at all which he is aware of as a sexual infirmity. He may be unaware of his impotence because he is blinded by his dazzling success and superiority in another field.

But in his quest for confirmation of his masculinity, a quest which he usually perceives as a search for sexual satisfaction and new conquests, his attention is attracted, with the force of the pull of gravity, to the potent Bodies in the classes beneath him, to the strength. He may sexually exploit the white-collar Bodies at the office; then, on his descent toward the Power Source, he may be drawn to the blue-collar Bodies in the plant. If these Bodies leave him still in the clutches of his lust and insecurity, he will bore deeper and deeper into the lower strata until he finds his sexual Balm of Gilead.[6] There is a Pandora's box of sexual aberrations here.

The Body is tropical, warm, hot: Fire! It is soft, pleasing to the touch, luscious to the kiss. The blood is hot. Muscles are strength. *The basic motion of the women of the elite is flight from their bodies.* The weakness of the female body when contrasted to the strength of the male body is an obvious attribute of femininity as manifested in social imagery. Thus, to enhance and emphasize the femininity of her image—which is mandatory in order that she present a sharp feminine contrast to the effeminate image of her man, the Omnipotent Administrator—she seeks to increase the weakness of her body and stamp out all traces of strength, to differentiate it further from the effeminate form of her man. An appearance of strength in her body is called *ugly.*

Having projected her strength, her domestic component, onto the women beneath her, she achieves an image of frailty, weakness, helplessness, delicacy, daintiness. Silks, ruffles, frills, bangles, and laces are her element. In the realm of sex, because the act of sexual intercourse is both a physical and mental process, a joint venture between the Mind and the Body, her basic contradiction is that she is physically inadequate while mentally voracious, with her mind in extreme conflict with her body. The mechanism of her orgasm, which begins in her body and ends in the psychic depths of her mind, becomes short-circuited in the struggle between her mind and her body.

Sitting at the foot of her bed, like the mute Sphinx on the bank of the

---

6. Healing or comfort. Gilead, a region of ancient Palestine, was known for its medicines and healing herbs (Jeremiah 8:22).

Nile, is the Ogre of Frigidity. She is terrified, because of the quality of her life, by the prospect of becoming a life-termer in the prison of frigidity. Her basic fear is frigidity, the state in which her frantic search for Ultrafemininity collides with an icepack death of the soul: where the fire in her body is extinguished by the ice in her mind. The psychic core of her sensuality, the male-seeking pole of her Female Principle, the trigger of the mechanism of her orgasm, moves beyond the reach or range of the effeminate clitoris of her man. Frigid, cold, icy, ice. Arctic. Antarctic. At the end of her flight from her body is a sky-high wall of ice. (If a lesbian is anything she is a frigid woman, a frozen cunt, with a warp and a crack in the wall of her ice.)

In proportion to the intensity of the Ultrafeminine's fear and feel of the ice is her psychic lust for the flame, for the heat of the fire: the Body. The Ultrafeminine, seeking sexual satisfaction, finds only physical exhaustion in the bed of the Omnipotent Administrator, and the odds are against her finding psychic satisfaction there. Her "psychic bridegroom" is the Supermasculine Menial. The Omnipotent Administrator, having repudiated and abdicated his body, his masculine component which he has projected onto the men beneath him, cannot present his woman, the Ultrafeminine, with an image of masculinity capable of penetrating into the psychic depths where the treasure of her orgasm is buried. The sexual act being a joint venture of the Mind and Body, though he satisfy her body and sap its strength, he cannot touch that magic spot in her mind which triggers the mechanism of her orgasm. Bereft of psychic satisfaction, and inhibited by social conventions and mores from embarking on a quest for her sexual fulfillment, yet performing her function as a mother and wife to the Omnipotent Administrator, the Ultrafeminine becomes a psychic celibate.

At the nth degree of the Ultrafeminine's scale of psychic lust (the contours of which few men or women throughout their entire lives ever in fact explore, resort being had to the forms of sublimation) stands the walking phallus symbol of the Supermasculine Menial. Though she may never have had a sexual encounter with a Supermasculine Menial, she is fully convinced that he can fulfill her physical need. It will be no big thing for him to do since he can handle those Amazons down there with him, with his strong body, rippling muscles, his strength and fire, the driving force of his spine, the thrust of his hips and the fiery steel of his rod. But what wets the Ultrafeminine's juice is that she is allured and tortured by the secret, intuitive knowledge that he, her psychic bridegroom, can blaze through the wall of her ice, plumb her psychic depths, test the oil of her soul, melt the iceberg in her brain, touch her inner sanctum, detonate the bomb of her orgasm, and bring her sweet release.

The chip on the Supermasculine Menial's shoulder is the fact that he has been robbed of his mind. In an uncannily effective manner, the society in which he lives has assumed in its very structure that he, minus a mind, is the embodiment of Brute Power. The bias and reflex of the society are against the cultivation or even the functioning of his mind, and it is borne in upon him from all sides that the society is actually deaf, dumb, and blind to his mind. The products of his mind, unless they are very closely associated with his social function of Brute Power, are resented and held in contempt by society as a whole. The further away from Brute Power his mental productions stand, the more emphatically will they be rejected and scorned by society, and treated as upstart invasions of the realm of the Omnipotent Administrator. His thoughts count for nothing. He doesn't run, regulate, control, or administer anything. Indeed, he is himself regulated, manipulated, and controlled by the Omnipotent Administrators. The struggle of his life is for the emancipatioon of his mind, to receive recognition for the products of his mind, and official recognition of the fact that he has a mind.

In his society, the Mind has been adjudged superior to the Body, and he knows that he is the Body and the Omnipotent Administrator is the Mind. It's Mind over matter, and the Body is matter. He may despise the Omnipotent Administrator for his physical weakness and envy him for his mind; or he may despise his own body and idolize the weak body of the Omnipotent Administrator. He may even strive to attain a weak physical image himself in order to identify with the image of the Omnipotent Administrator. The people at the base of society, where the Supermasculine Menial is, are well known for their reflex of attempting to conform to the style, pattern, manners, and habits of the upper classes, of the Omnipotent Administrators and Ultrafeminines. Just how this works itself out is a problem for analysis by sociologists and social psychologists on the mass level, and the headshrinkers and nutcrackers on the individual level. What we are outlining here is a perspective from which such analysis might best be approached.

The psychic bride of the Supermasculine Menial is the Ultrafeminine. She is his "dream girl." She, the delicate, weak, helpless Ultrafeminine, exerts a magnetic attraction upon him. When he compares her with his own woman, the strong, self-reliant Amazon, lust for her burns in his brain. He recoils from the excess of strength injected into the Amazon by the Domestic Function she performs. Also, since standards of beauty are set by the elite, the Ultrafeminine personifies the official standard of feminine beauty of society as a whole. Influenced by and imbued with this official standard of beauty, while at the same time surrounded by Amazons who do not embody this standard and who are in fact clashing with it, the Supermasculine Menial develops an obsessive yearning and lust for sexual contact with the Ultrafeminine. These yearnings are compounded by the fact that on the whole they are foredoomed to remain unfulfilled. The society has arranged things so that the Supermasculine Menial and the Ultrafeminine are not likely to have access or propinquity to each other conducive to stimulating sexual involvement. In fact, it has not been rare for the Supermasculine Menial and the Ultrafeminine to be severely persecuted, if not put to death, for such sexual contact.

The Amazon is in a peculiar position. Just as her man has been deprived of his manhood, so she has been deprived of her full womanhood. Society has decreed that the Ultrafeminine, the woman of the elite, is the goddess on the pedestal. The Amazon is the personification of the rejected domestic component, the woman on whom "dishpan hands" seem not out of character. The worship and respect which both the Omnipotent Adminis-

trator and the Supermasculine Menial lavish upon the image of the Ultrafeminine is a source of deep vexation to the Amazon. She envies the
pampered, powderpuff existence of the Ultrafeminine and longs to incorporate these elements into her own life. Alienated from the feminine component of her nature, her reinforced domestic component is an awesome
burden and shame of which she longs to be free.

The Amazon finds it difficult to respect the Supermasculine menial.
She sees him essentially as only half a man, an incomplete man. Having no
sovereignty over himself, he hasn't that sovereignty over her which our traditional patriarchal myths lead her to believe he should have. On a still
deeper level, the urges and needs of the Amazon's psyche move her toward
the source of power, toward the receptacle of sovereignty—an attraction
motivated by the Primeval Urge to transcend the Primeval Mitosis. When
the Primeval Sphere split into the male and female hemispheres, the attribute of sovereignty was reposited in the male hemisphere, and this attribute
exercises a magnetic attraction upon the female hemisphere. Usurping the
Supermasculine Menial's mind, the Omnipotent Administrator usurped
all sovereignty; and because of his monopoly on sovereignty, he is the psychic bridegroom of the Amazon. In another sense, however, being also attracted to the body of the Supermasculine Menial, the Amazon is lost
between two worlds.

In net effect, then, there will exist in Class Society two sets of competing
images. Contending for the crown of masculinity is one image based on
the Body and another based on the Mind; contending for the crown of
femininity is one image based on weak, helpless Ultrafemininity and another based on the strong, self-reliant attributes of the Amazon. In a society
with a racially homogeneous population, in which the people at the top are
racially the same as the ones at the bottom, the competing images are not
mutually exclusive. A Supermasculine Menial, for instance, who acquires
the training of an Omnipotent Administrator, can become a member of
the elite and function accordingly—assuming the existence of some vertical social mobility, which is not, of course, always the case. But even if he is
prevented from ascending the social ladder in fact, a Supermasculine Menial can at least imagine himself doing so without first having to transcend
any biological barriers. Likewise, an Omnipotent Administrator can descend the social ladder, develop his muscles, and hoe the row with the
coolest serf on the manor. The women, too, can descend or ascend, depending on the merits, without having to breach a biological chain.

But in a society where there exists a racial caste system, where the people
at the top are sharply distinguished from those at the bottom by race as well
as social image, then the two sets of competing images can come to be
considered mutually exclusive. The gulf between the Mind and the Body
will seem to coincide with the gulf between the two races. At that point, the
fear of biological miscegenation is transposed into social imagery; and
since the distinction between the two races is founded in biology, the social
distinction between Mind and Body is made sacred. Any attempt by the
Supermasculine Menial to heal his wound and reclaim his mind will be
viewed as a malignant desire to transcend the laws of nature by mixing,
"mongrelizing," miscegenating. Coming from the other side, if a member

of the elite should attempt to bridge the gulf, it will be conceived as the rankest form of degeneracy and treason to caste. Deep-seated fears and emotions, which are in fact connected with biological traits and are part of a mechanism to aid racial and ethnic survival, are harnessed to social images and thereby transformed into weapons of the Class Struggle. Race fears are weapons in the struggle between the Omnipotent Administrator and the Supermasculine Menial for control of sexual sovereignty.

The Supermasculine Menial and the Amazon are the least alienated from the biological chain, although their minds—especially the Supermasculine Menials'!—are in a general state of underdevelopment. Still, they are the wealth of a nation, an abundant supply of unexhausted, undessenced human raw material upon which the future of the society depends and with which, through the implacable march of history to an ever broader base of democracy and equality, the society will renew and transform itself.

1968

A. B. SPELLMAN
b. 1935

A. B. Spellman was born in North Carolina; both his parents (Alfred and Rosa Spellman) were teachers. He graduated from Howard University in 1958 and moved to New York, where he became involved with the Beat generation and decided to become a writer. Though he has authored only a single book of poems, *The Beautiful Days* (1965), Spellman's influence has been keenly felt by those who profited from his work as an editor of experimental magazines; jazz critic; and instructor of poetry, creative writing, African American literature, culture, and jazz at Rutgers University, Harvard University, Morehouse College and Emory University.

Spellman's study *Four Lives in the Bebop Business* (1966), with its engaging evocations of Herbie Nichols, Jackie McLean, Ornette Coleman, and Cecil Taylor, demonstrates the conjunction of musical knowledge and poetical dedication to the sound of the masses that characterized the Black Arts movement. *Did John's Music Kill Him?* is one of the most outstanding of the many Black Arts poems that paid homage to the genius of tenor saxophonist John Coltrane.

Did John's[1] Music Kill Him?

      in the morning part
      of evening he would stand
      before his crowd. the voice
      would call his name &
      redlight fell around him.   5
      jimmy'd bow a quarter hour
      till Mccoy fed block chords

1. John Coltrane (1926–1967), avant-garde jazz saxophonist.

to his stroke, elvin's[2] thunder
roll & eric's[3] scream. then john.

then john. *little old lady*   10
had a nasty mouth. *summertime*
when the war is. *africa* ululating[4]
a line bunched up like itself
into knots paints beauty black.

trane's horn had words in it   15
i know when i sleep sober & dream
those dreams i duck in the world
of sun & shadow. yet even in the day john
& a little grass put them on me clear
as tomorrow in a glass enclosure.   20

kill me john my life eats
life. The thing that beats out of
me happens in a vat enclosed
& fermenting & wanting to explode
like your song.   25

         so beat john's death words down
         on me in the darker part
         of evening. the black light issued
         from him in the pit he made
         around us. worms came clear   30
         to me where i thought i had been
         brilliant. o john death will
         not contain you death
         will not contain you

         1969

2. The members of Coltrane's quartet. Jimmy Gar-rison (1934–1976), double bass player. McCoy Tyner (b. 1938), pianist. Elvin Jones (b. 1927), drummer.

3. Eric Dolphy (1928–1964), jazz clarinetist, saxo-phonist, and flutist who sometimes played with Coltrane.
4. Shrill, wordless wailing.

JAYNE CORTEZ
b. 1936

Jayne Cortez is celebrated for her performance style, in which she converts the the written poetical text into a score for her jazz-influenced vocalizations. To hear Cortez read her most volatile poems is akin to listening to a Greek chorus rebuke the cosmos. Her poetry is a protest against dehumanizing poverty, imperialism, and political repression.

Cortez was born in Fort Huachuca, Arizona, where her father was stationed on an army base. She began her writing and acting careers in Los Angeles. In 1964 she co-founded the Watts Repertory Theatre, for which she served as artistic director from 1964 to 1970. In 1972 Cortez formed her own publishing company, Bola Press. She was a teacher and writer-in-residence at Rutgers University from 1977 to

1983. Cortez has traveled and read her poetry throughout the Caribbean, Latin America, Africa, and Europe. She has produced stunning recordings of many of her works, among them *There It Is* (1982) and *Maintain Control* (1986). Her books of poetry include *Pisstained Stairs and the Monkey Man's Wares* (1969) and *Festivals and Funerals* (1971).

Cortez has been praised for her ability to combine speech with jazz and blues music traditions. Her *Pisstained Stairs* displays an identification with the working class and underclass and an admiration for black historic figures and musicians. In *Festivals and Funerals*, Cortez combines African language and folk elements with musical traditions in an expression of resistance to colonialism and imperialism. Cortez's son, Denardo, from her first marriage, to jazz musician Ornette Coleman, is an accomplished drummer who accompanies her on many of her performances.

How Long Has Trane[1] Been Gone

Tell me about the good things
you clappin & laughin

Will you remember
or will you forget

Forget about the good things   5
like Blues & Jazz being black
Yeah Black Music
all about you

And the musicians that
write & play about you   10
a black brother groanin
a black sister moanin
& beautiful black children
ragged . . . underfed laughin
not knowin   15

Will you remember their names
or do they have no names
no lives—only products
to be used when you wanna
dance fuck & cry   20

You takin—they givin
You livin—they
creating starving dying
trying to make a better tomorrow
Giving you & your children a history   25
But what do you care about
history—Black History
and John Coltrane
No

---

1. John Coltrane (1926–1967), avant-garde jazz saxophonist.

All you wanna do   30
is pat your foot
sip a drink & pretend
with your head bobbin up & down
What do you care about acoustics
bad microphones or out-of-tune pianos   35
& noise
You the club owners & disc jockeys
made a deal didn't you
a deal about Black Music
& you really don't give   40
a shit long as you take

        There was a time
when KGFJ[2] played all black music
from Bird to Johnny Ace[3]
on show after show   45
but what happened
I'll tell you what happened
they divided black music
doubled the money
& left us split again   50
is what happened

John Coltrane's dead & some
of you
have yet to hear him play
How long how long has that Trane been gone   55

and how many more Tranes will go
before you understand your life
John Coltrane who had the whole of
life wrapped up in B flat
John Coltrane like Malcolm[4]   60
True image of Black Masculinity

Now tell me about the good things
I'm telling you about
John Coltrane

A name that should ring   65
throughout the projects mothers
Mothers with sons
who need John Coltrane
Need the warm arm of his music
like words from a Father   70
words of Comfort
words of Africa
words of Welcome
How long how long has that Trane been gone

2. Radio station in Los Angeles.
3. Perhaps Johnny Hodges (1907–1970), one of
Coltrane's favorite saxophonists. Charlie "Bird"
Parker (1920–1955), influential jazz saxophonist of
the 1940s and 1950s.
4. Malcolm X (1925–1965), powerful black leader
of the early 1960s.

John palpatating love notes   75
in a lost-found nation
within a nation
His music resounding discovery
signed Always
John Coltrane   80

Rip those dead white people off
your walls Black People
black people whose walls
should be a hall
A Black Hall Of Fame   85
so our children will know
will know & be proud
Proud to say I'm from Parker City—Coltrane City—Ornette City
Pharoah City living on Holiday street next to
James Brown⁵ park in the State of Malcolm   90

How Long
how long
will it take for you to understand
that Tranes been gone
riding in a portable radio   95
next to your son whose lonely
Who walks walks walks into nothing
no city no state no home no Nothing
how long
How long   100
Have black people been gone

                                                               1969

5. Popular soul singer (b. 1928). Ornette Coleman   who played in Coltrane's quartet from 1965 to
(b. 1930), innovator of the free jazz style developed   1967. Billie Holiday (1915–1959), jazz singer.
in the 1960s. Pharoah Sanders, tenor saxophonist

LARRY NEAL

1937–1981

Music critic, pianist and flutist, literary commentator, theoretician of the Black
Arts, screenwriter, dramatist, journal editor, and university lecturer, Larry Neal
filled his life with captivating poetry and sinewy criticism. Upon his death from a
heart attack in 1981, the African American community was robbed of a dynamic
and powerful spokesperson.

After graduating from Lincoln University (in Pennsylvania), Neal pursued gradu-
ate studies in politics and folklore at the University of Pennsylvania. Moving to
Manhattan in the 1960s, he became arts editor for the *Liberator* magazine and,
eventually, the magazine's principal editor. In 1968 he edited, with Amiri Baraka,
Black Fire: An Anthology of Afro-American Writing, which captured the spirit of the
Black Arts movement. The anthology was for the 1960s what Alain Locke's *The
New Negro* was for the 1920s—an invaluable handbook of theory, criticism, and
creative examples of the black arts. Neal asserted that the Black Arts movement was

the "spiritual sister" of the Black Power movement; it was a wedding of art and politics. In 1969 Neal and Baraka collaborated with A. B. Spellman on *Trippin': A Need for Change.*

Neal achieved his reputation as a suave spokesperson for Black Aesthetics through his poetry and arts commentary. His first volume of poetry, *Black Booga-loo: Notes on Black Liberation* (1969), is rife with jazz allusions; his second volume, *Hoodoo Hollerin' Bebop Ghosts* (1971), is resonant with black folk figures, whom Neal first encountered in boyhood and later studied in graduate school.

Neal's first play, *The Glorious Monster in the Bell of the Horn* (1976), has been termed a "lyric drama" that expresses the aspirations of black artists and the black middle class. An introspective work, its emphasis is on individual choice and personal responsibility. In contrast, *In an Upstate Motel* (1981) conveys a sense of hopelessness found in much of the existential drama of the time.

Neal's critical style is tough, informed, and contentious. Indeed, his poetry is meant to be issued or performed by some glorious monster in the bell of a jazz musician's horn. To read his analyses of African American art and culture is to encounter one of the most intelligent and urbane voices of the Black Arts movement.

The Black Arts Movement

1

The Black Arts Movement is radically opposed to any concept of the artist that alienates him from his community. Black Art is the aesthetic and spiritual sister of the Black Power concept. As such, it envisions an art that speaks directly to the needs and aspirations of Black America. In order to perform this task, the Black Arts Movement proposes a radical reordering of the western cultural aesthetic. It proposes a separate symbolism, mythology, critique, and iconology. The Black Arts and the Black Power concept both relate broadly to the Afro-American's desire for self-determination and nationhood. Both concepts are nationalistic. One is concerned with the relationship between art and politics; the other with the art of politics.

Recently, these two movements have begun to merge: the political values inherent in the Black Power concept are now finding concrete expression in the aesthetics of Afro-American dramatists, poets, choreographers, musicians, and novelists. A main tenet of Black Power is the necessity for Black people to define the world in their own terms. The Black artist has made the same point in the context of aesthetics. The two movements postulate that there are in fact and in spirit two Americas—one black, one white. The Black artist takes this to mean that his primary duty is to speak to the spiritual and cultural needs of Black people. Therefore, the main thrust of this new breed of contemporary writers is to confront the contradictions arising out of the Black man's experience in the racist West. Currently, these writers are re-evaluating western aesthetics, the traditional role of the writer, and the social function of art. Implicit in this re-evaluation is the need to develop a "black aesthetic." It is the opinion of many Black writers, I among them, that the Western aesthetic has run its course: it is impossible to construct anything meaningful within its decaying structure. We advocate a cultural revolution in art and ideas. The cultural values inherent in western history must either be radicalized or destroyed, and we will probably find that even radicalization is impossible. In fact, what is needed is a whole new system of ideas. Poet Don L. Lee expresses it:

> . . . We must destroy Faulkner, dick, jane, and other perpetuators of evil. It's time for DuBois, Nat Turner, and Kwame Nkrumah. As Frantz Fanon[1] points out; destroy the culture and you destroy the people. This must not happen. Black artists are culture stabilizers; bringing back old values, and introducing new ones. Black Art will talk to the people and with the will of the people stop impending "protective custody."

The Black Arts Movement eschews "protest" literature. It speaks directly to Black people. Implicit in the concept of "protest" literature, as Brother Knight[2] has made clear, is an appeal to white morality:

> Now any Black man who masters the technique of his particular art form, who adheres to the white aesthetic, and who directs his work toward a white audience is, in one sense, protesting. And implicit in the act of protest is the belief that a change will be forthcoming once the masters are aware of the protestor's "grievance" (the very word connotes begging, supplications to the gods). Only when that belief has faded and protestings end, will Black art begin.

Brother Knight also has some interesting statements about the development of a "Black aesthetic":

> Unless the Black artist establishes a "Black aesthetic" he will have no future at all. To accept the white aesthetic is to accept and validate a society that will not allow him to live. The Black artist must create new forms and new values, sing new songs (or purify old ones); and along with other Black authorities, he must create a new history, new symbols, myths and legends (and purify old ones by fire). And the Black artist, in creating his own aesthetic, must be accountable for it only to the Black people. Further, he must hasten his own dissolution as an individual (in the Western sense)—painful though the process may be, having been breast-fed the poison of "individual experience."

When we speak of a "Black aesthetic" several things are meant. First, we assume that there is already in existence the basis for such an aesthetic. Essentially, it consists of an African-American cultural tradition. But this aesthetic is finally, by implication, broader than that tradition. It encompasses most of the useable elements of Third World culture. The motive behind the Black aesthetic is the destruction of the white thing, the destruction of white ideas, and white ways of looking at the world. The new

1. Martinican psychiatrist (1925–1961), author of several important critiques of racism and colonialism. William Faulkner (1897–1962), modernist writer from Mississippi. W. E. B. Du Bois (1865–1963), scholar, editor of Crisis (1909–34), and co-founder of the NAACP. Turner (1800–1831), leader of an 1831 slave rebellion in Virginia. Nkrumah (1909–1972), first president of independent Ghana. 2. Etheridge Knight (1931–1985), contemporary poet.

aesthetic is mostly predicated on an Ethics which asks the question: whose vision of the world is finally more meaningful, ours or the white oppressors'? What is truth? Or more precisely, whose truth shall we express, that of the oppressed or of the oppressors? These are basic questions. Black intellectuals of previous decades failed to ask them. Further, national and international affairs demand that we appraise the world in terms of our own interests. It is clear that the question of human survival is at the core of contemporary experience. The Black artist must address himself to this reality in the strongest terms possible. In a context of world upheaval, ethics and aesthetics must interact positively and be consistent with the demands for a more spiritual world. Consequently, the Black Arts Movement is an ethical movement. Ethical, that is, from the viewpoint of the oppressed. And much of the oppression confronting the Third World and Black America is directly traceable to the Euro-American cultural sensibility. This sensibility, anti-human in nature, has, until recently, dominated the psyches of most Black artists and intellectuals; it must be destroyed before the Black creative artist can have a meaningful role in the transformation of society.

It is this natural reaction to an alien sensibility that informs the cultural attitudes of the Black Arts and the Black Power movement. It is a profound ethical sense that makes a Black artist question a society in which art is one thing and the actions of men another. The Black Arts Movement believes that your ethics and your aesthetics are one. That the contradictions between ethics and aesthetics in western society is symptomatic of a dying culture.

The term "Black Arts" is of ancient origin, but it was first used in a positive sense by LeRoi Jones:

> We are unfair
> And unfair
> We are black magicians
> Black arts we make
> in black labs of the heart
>
> The fair are fair
> and deathly white
>
> The day will not save them
> And we own the night

There is also a section of the poem "Black Dada Nihilismus" that carries the same motif. But a fuller amplification of the nature of the new aesthetics appears in the poem "Black Art":

> Poems are bullshit unless they are
> teeth or trees or lemons piled
> on a step. Or black ladies dying
> of men leaving nickel hearts
> beating them down. Fuck poems
> and they are useful, would they shoot
> come at you, love what you are,

>   breathe like wrestlers, or shudder
>   strangely after peeing. We want live
>   words of the hip world, live flesh &
>   coursing blood. Hearts and Brains
>   Souls splintering fire. We want poems
>   like fists beating niggers out of Jocks
>   or dagger poems in the slimy bellies
>   of the owner-jews . . .

Poetry is a concrete function, an action. No more abstractions. Poems are physical entities: fists, daggers, airplane poems, and poems that shoot guns. Poems are transformed from physical objects into personal forces:

>   . . . Put it on him poem. Strip him naked
>   to the world. Another bad poem cracking
>   steel knuckles in a jewlady's mouth
>   Poem scream poison gas on breasts in green berets . . .

Then the poem affirms the integral relationship between Black Art and Black people:

>   . . . Let Black people understand
>   that they are the lovers and the sons
>   of lovers and warriors and sons
>   of warriors Are poems & poets &
>   all the loveliness here in the world

It ends with the following lines, a central assertion in both the Black Arts Movement and the philosophy of Black Power:

>   We want a black poem. And a
>   Black World.
>   Let the world be a Black Poem
>   And let All Black People Speak This Poem
>   Silently
>   or LOUD

The poem comes to stand for the collective conscious and unconscious of Black America—the real impulse in back of the Black Power movement, which is the will toward self-determination and nationhood, a radical reordering of the nature and function of both art and the artist.

2

In the spring of 1964, LeRoi Jones, Charles Patterson, William Patterson, Clarence Reed, Johnny Moore, and a number of other Black artists opened the Black Arts Repertoire Theatre School. They produced a number of plays including Jones' *Experimental Death Unit # One*, *Black Mass*, *Jello*, and *Dutchman*. They also initiated a series of poetry readings and concerts. These activities represented the most advanced tendencies in the movement and were of excellent artistic quality. The Black Arts School came under immediate attack by the New York power structure. The Establishment, fearing Black creativity, did exactly what it was expected to do—it attacked the theatre and all of its values. In the meantime, the school was granted funds by OEO[3] though HARYOU-ACT. Lacking a cultural program itself, HARYOU turned to the only organization which addressed itself to the needs of the community. In keeping with its "revolutionary" cultural ideas, the Black Arts Theatre took its programs into the streets of Harlem. For three months, the theatre presented plays, concerts, and poetry readings to the people of the community. Plays that shattered the illusions of the American body politic, and awakened Black people to the meaning of their lives.

Then the hawks from the OEO moved in and chopped off the funds. Again, this should have been expected. The Black Arts Theatre stood in radical opposition to the feeble attitudes about culture of the "War On Poverty"[4] bureaucrats. And later, because of internal problems, the theatre was forced to close. But the Black Arts group proved that the community could be served by a valid and dynamic art. It also proved that there was a definite need for a cultural revolution in the Black community.

With the closing of the Black Arts Theatre, the implications of what Brother Jones and his colleagues were trying to do took on even more significance. Black Art groups sprang up on the West Coast and the idea spread to Detroit, Philadelphia, Jersey City, New Orleans, and Washington, D.C. Black Arts movements began on the campuses of San Francisco State College, Fisk University, Lincoln University, Hunter College in the Bronx, Columbia University, and Oberlin College. In Watts, after the rebellion, Maulana Karenga welded the Black Arts Movement into a cohesive cultural ideology which owed much to the work of LeRoi Jones. Karenga sees culture as the most important element in the struggle for self-determination:

> Culture is the basis of all ideas, images and actions. To move is to move culturally, i.e. by a set of values given to you by your culture. Without a culture Negroes are only a set of reactions to white people. The seven criteria for culture are:
> 1. Mythology
> 2. History
> 3. Social Organization
> 4. Political Organization
> 5. Economic Organization
> 6. Creative Motif
> 7. Ethos

In drama, LeRoi Jones represents the most advanced aspects of the movement. He is its prime mover and chief designer. In a poetic essay entitled "The Revolutionary Theatre," he outlines the iconology of the movement:

3. Office of Equal Opportunity.
4. Part of President Lyndon Johnson's "Great Society," a program of domestic policy reform.

The Revolutionary Theatre should force change: it should be change. (All their faces turned into the lights and you work on them black nigger magic, and cleanse them at having seen the ugliness. And if the beautiful see themselves, they will love themselves.) We are preaching virtue again, but by that to mean NOW, toward what seems the most constructive use of the word.

The theatre that Jones proposes is inextricably linked to the Afro-American political dynamic. And such a link is perfectly consistent with Black America's contemporary demands. For theatre is potentially the most social of all of the arts. It is an integral part of the socializing process. It exists in direct relationship to the audience it claims to serve. The decadence and inanity of the contemporary American theatre is an accurate reflection of the state of American society. Albee's[5] *Who's Afraid of Virginia Woolf?* is very American: sick white lives in a homosexual hell hole. The theatre of white America is escapist, refusing to confront concrete reality. Into this cultural emptiness come the musicals, an up-tempo version of the same stale lives. And the use of Negroes in such plays as *Hello Dolly* and *Hallelujah Baby* does not alter their nature; it compounds the problem. These plays are simply hipper versions of the minstrel show. They present Negroes acting out the hang-ups of middle-class white America. Consequently, the American theatre is a palliative prescribed to bourgeois patients who refuse to see the world as it is. Or, more crucially, as the world sees them. It is no accident, therefore, that the most "important" plays come from Europe—Brecht, Weiss, and Ghelderode.[6] And even these have begun to run dry.

The Black Arts theatre, the theatre of LeRoi Jones, is a radical alternative to the sterility of the American theatre. It is primarily a theatre of the Spirit, confronting the Black man in his interaction with his brothers and with the white thing.

Our theatre will show victims so that their brothers in the audience will be better able to understand that they are the brothers of victims, and that they themselves are blood brothers. And what we show must cause the blood to rush, so that prerevolutionary temperaments will be bathed in this blood, and it will cause their deepest souls to move, and they will find themselves tensed and clenched, even ready to die, at what the soul has been taught. We will scream and cry, murder, run through the streets in agony, if it means some soul will be moved, moved to actual life understanding of what the world is, and what it ought to be. We are preaching virtue and feeling, and a natural sense of the self in the world. All men live in the world, and the world ought to be a place for them to live.

The victims in the world of Jones' early plays are Clay, murdered by the white bitch-goddess in *Dutchman*, and Walker Vessels, the revolutionary

5. Edward Albee's *Who's Afraid of Virginia Woolf?* opened on Broadway in 1962. The play received mixed reviews and inspired rumors that it was really about homosexuals.

6. Michel de Ghelderode (1898–1962), Belgian playwright. Bertolt Brecht (1898–1956), German socialist playwright. Peter Weiss (b. 1916), German-Swiss playwright.

in *The Slave*. Both of these plays present Black men in transition. Clay, the middle-class Negro trying to get himself a little action from Lula, digs himself and his own truth only to get murdered after telling her like it really is:

> Just let me bleed you, you loud whore, and one poem vanished. A whole people neurotics, struggling to keep from being sane. And the only thing that would cure the neurosis would be your murder. Simple as that. I mean if I murdered you, then other white people would understand me. You understand? No. I guess not. If Bessie Smith[7] had killed some white people she wouldn't needed that music. She could have talked very straight and plain about the world. Just straight two and two are four. Money. Power. Luxury. Like that. All of them. Crazy niggers turning their back on sanity. When all it needs is that simple act. Just murder. Would make us all sane.

But Lula understands, and she kills Clay first. In a perverse way it is Clay's nascent knowledge of himself that threatens the existence of Lula's idea of the world. Symbolically, and in fact, the relationship between Clay (Black America) and Lula (white America) is rooted in the historical castration of black manhood. And in the twisted psyche of white America, the Black man is both an object of love and hate. Analogous attitudes exist in most Black Americans, but for decidedly different reasons. Clay is doomed when he allows himself to participate in Lula's "fantasy" in the first place. It is the fantasy to which Frantz Fanon alludes in *The Wretched of the Earth* and *Black Skins, White Mask*: the native's belief that he can acquire the oppressor's power by acquiring his symbols, one of which is the white woman. When Clay finally digs himself it is too late.

Walker Vessels, in *The Slave*, is Clay reincarnated as the revolutionary confronting problems inherited from his contact with white culture. He returns to the home of his ex-wife, a white woman, and her husband, a literary critic. The play is essentially about Walker's attempt to destroy his white past. For it is the past, with all of its painful memories, that is really the enemy of the revolutionary. It is impossible to move until history is either recreated or comprehended. Unlike Todd, in Ralph Ellison's *Invisible Man*, Walker cannot fall outside history. Instead, Walker demands a confrontation with history, a final shattering of bullshit illusions. His only salvation lies in confronting the physical and psychological forces that have made him and his people powerless. Therefore, he comes to understand that the world must be restructured along spiritual imperatives. But in the interim it is basically a question of *who* has power:

> EASLEY. You're so wrong about everything. So terribly, sickeningly wrong. What can you change? What do you hope to change? Do you think Negroes are better people than whites . . . that they can govern a society *better* than whites? That they'll be more judicious or more tolerant? Do you think they'll make fewer mistakes? I mean really, if the Western white man has proved one thing . . . it's the futility of modern society. So the have-not peoples become the haves. Even so, will that

---

7. Blues singer and innovator of blues jazz (1894–1937).

change the essential functions of the world? Will there be more love or
beauty in the world . . . more knowledge . . . because of it?

WALKER.   Probably. Probably there will be more . . . if more people
have a chance to understand what it is. But that's not even the point. It
comes down to baser human endeavor than any social-political thinking. What does it matter if there's more love or beauty? Who the fuck
cares? Is that what the Western ofay thought while he was ruling . . .
that his rule somehow brought more love and beauty into the world?
Oh, he might have thought that concomitantly, while sipping a gin
rickey and scratching his ass . . . but that was not ever the point. Not
even on the Crusades. The point is that you had your chance, darling,
now these other folks have theirs. *Quietly.* Now they have theirs.

EASLEY.   God, what an ugly idea.

   This confrontation between the black radical and the white liberal is
symbolic of larger confrontations occurring between the Third World and
Western society. It is a confrontation between the colonizer and the colonized, the slavemaster and the slave. Implicit in Easley's remarks is the belief that the white man is culturally and politically superior to the Black
Man. Even though Western society has been traditionally violent in its relation with the Third World, it sanctimoniously deplores violence or self
assertion on the part of the enslaved. And the Western mind, with clever
rationalizations, equates the violence of the oppressed with the violence of
the oppressor. So that when the native preaches self-determination, the
Western white man cleverly misconstrues it to mean hate of *all* white men.
When the Black political radical warns his people not to trust white politicians of the left and the right, but instead to organize separately on the basis
of power, the white man cries: "racism in reverse." Or he will say, as many
of them do today: "We deplore both white and black racism." As if the two
could be equated.
   There is a minor element in *The Slave* which assumes great importance
in a later play entitled *Jello*. Here I refer to the emblem of Walker's army: a
red-mouthed grinning field slave. The revolutionary army has taken one of
the most hated symbols of the Afro-American past and radically altered its
meaning.[8] This is the supreme act of freedom, available only to those who
have liberated themselves psychically. Jones amplifies this inversion of emblem and symbol in *Jello* by making Rochester (Ratfester) of the old Jack
Benny (Penny) program[9] into a revolutionary nationalist. Ratfester, ordinarily the supreme embodiment of the Uncle Tom Clown, surprises Jack
Penny by turning on the other side of the nature of the Black man. He
skillfully, and with an evasive black humor, robs Penny of all of his money.

8. In Jones' study of Afro-American music, *Blues
People*, we find the following observation: ". . .
Even the adjective *funky*, which once meant to
many Negroes merely a stink (usually associated
with sex), was used to qualify the music as meaningful (the word became fashionable and is now almost useless). The social implication, then, was
that even the old stereotype of a distinctive Negro

smell that white America subscribed to could be
turned against white America. For this smell now,
real or not, was made a valuable characteristic of
'Negro-ness.' And 'Negro-ness,' by the fifties, for
many Negroes (and whites) was the only strength
left to American culture" [Neal's note].
9. *The Jack Benny Show* was a popular television
variety show of the 1950s.

But Ratfester's actions are "moral." That is to say, Ratfester is getting his back pay; payment of a long over-due debt to the Black man. Ratfester's sensibilities are different from Walker's. He is *blues people* smiling and shuffling while trying to figure out how to destroy the white thing. And like the blues man, he is the master of the understatement. Or in the Afro-American folk tradition, he is the signifying Monkey, Shine, and Stagolee all rolled into one. There are no stereotypes any more. History has killed Uncle Tom. Because even Uncle Tom has a breaking point beyond which he will not be pushed. Cut deeply enough into the most docile Negro, and you will find a conscious murderer. Behind the lyrics of the blues and the shuffling porter loom visions of white throats being cut and cities burning.

Jones' particular power as a playwright does not rest solely on his revolutionary vision, but is instead derived from his deep lyricism and spiritual outlook. In many ways, he is fundamentally more a poet than a playwright. And it is his lyricism that gives body to his plays. Two important plays in this regard are *Black Mass* and *Slave Ship*. *Black Mass* is based on the Muslim myth of Yacub. According to this myth, Yacub, a Black scientist, developed the means of grafting different colors of the Original Black Nation until a White Devil was created. In *Black Mass*, Yacub's experiments produce a raving White Beast who is condemned to the coldest regions of the North. The other magicians implore Yacub to cease his experiments. But he insists on claiming the primacy of scientific knowledge over spiritual knowledge. The sensibility of the White Devil is alien, informed by lust and sensuality. The Beast is the consummate embodiment of evil, the beginning of the historical subjugation of the spiritual world.

Black Mass takes place in some pre-historical time. In fact, the concept of time, we learn, is the creation of an alien sensibility, that of the Beast. This is a deeply weighted play, a colloquy on the nature of man, and the relationship between legitimate spiritual knowledge and scientific knowledge. It is LeRoi Jones' most important play mainly because it is informed by a mythology that is wholly the creation of the Afro-American sensibility.

Further, Yacub's creation is not merely a scientific exercise. More fundamentally, it is the aesthetic impulse gone astray. The Beast is created merely for the sake of creation. Some artists assert a similar claim about the nature of art. They argue that art need not have a function. It is against this decadent attitude toward art—ramified throughout most of Western society—that the play militates. Yacub's real crime, therefore, is the introduction of a meaningless evil into a harmonious universe. The evil of the Beast is pervasive, corrupting everything and everyone it touches. What was beautiful is twisted into an ugly screaming thing. The play ends with destruction of the holy place of the Black Magicians. Now the Beast and his descendants roam the earth. An off-stage voice chants a call for the Jihad to begin. It is then that myth merges into legitimate history, and we, the audience, come to understand that all history is merely someone's version of mythology.

Slave Ship presents a more immediate confrontation with history. In a series of expressionistic tableaux it depicts the horrors and the madness of the Middle Passage.[1] It then moves through the period of slavery, early

---

1. The voyage across the Atlantic from Africa to the Americas by slave ships.

attempts at revolt, tendencies toward Uncle Tom-like reconciliation and betrayal, and the final act of liberation. There is no definite plot (LeRoi calls it a pageant), just a continuous rush of sound, groans, screams, and souls wailing for freedom and relief from suffering. This work has special affinities with the New Music of Sun Ra, John Coltrane, Albert Ayler, and Ornette Coleman.[2] Events are blurred, rising and falling in a stream of sound. Almost cinematically, the images flicker and fade against a heavy back-drop of rhythm. The language is spare, stripped to the essential. It is a play which almost totally eliminates the need for a text. It functions on the basis of movements and energy—the dramatic equivalent of the New Music.[3]

Slave Ship's energy is, at base, ritualistic. As a matter of fact, to see the play any other way is to miss the point. All the New York reviewers, with the possible exception of John Lahr, were completely cut off from this central aspect of the play when it was performed at the Brooklyn Academy under the brilliant direction of Gilbert Moses. One of the prime motivations behind the work is to suck the audience into a unique and very precise universe. The episodes of this "pageant" do not appear as strict interpretations of history. Rather, what we are digging is ritualized history. That is, history that allows emotional and religious participation on the part of the audience. And, like all good ritual, its purpose is to make the audience stronger, more sensitive to the historical realities that have shaped our lives and the lives of our ancestors. The play acts to extend memory. For black people to forget the realities posed by *Slave Ship* is to fall prey to an existential paralysis. History, like the blues, demands that we witness the painful events of our prior lives; and that we either confront these painful events or be destroyed by them.

3

LeRoi Jones is the best known and the most advanced playwright of the movement, but he is not alone. There are other excellent playwrights who express the general mood of the Black Arts ideology. Among them are Ron Milner, Ed Bullins, Ben Caldwell, Jimmy Stewart, Joe White, Charles Patterson, Charles Fuller, Aisha Hughes, Carol Freeman, and Jimmy Garrett.

Ron Milner's *Who's Got His Own* is of particular importance. It strips bare the clashing attitudes of a contemporary Afro-American family. Milner's concern is with legitimate manhood and morality. The family in *Who's Got His Own* is in search of its conscience, or more precisely its own definition of life. On the day of his father's death, Tim and his family are forced to examine the inner fabric of their lives: the lies, self-deceits, and sense of powerlessness in a white world. The basic conflict, however, is internal. It is rooted in the historical search for black manhood. Tim's mother is representative of a generation of Christian Black women who have implicitly understood the brooding violence lurking in their men. And with this understanding, they have interposed themselves between

2. Avant-garde jazz saxophonist (b. 1930). Sun Ra (1915–1993), jazz pianist. Coltrane (1926–1967), jazz saxophonist. Ayler (1936–1970), free-form tenor saxophonist.
3. Avant-garde jazz style developed in the early 1960s.

their men and the object of that violence—the white man. Thus unable to direct his violence against the oppressor, the Black man becomes more frustrated and the sense of powerlessness deepens. Lacking the strength to be a man in the white world, he turns against his family. So the oppressed, as Fanon explains, constantly dreams violence against his oppressor, while killing his brother on fast weekends.

Tim's sister represents the Negro woman's attempt to acquire what Eldridge Cleaver calls "ultrafemininity." That is, the attributes of her white upper-class counterpart. Involved here is a rejection of the body-oriented life of the working class Black man, symbolized by the mother's traditional religion. The sister has an affair with a white upper-class liberal, ending in abortion. There are hints of lesbianism, i.e., a further rejection of the body. The sister's life is a pivotal factor in the play. Much of the stripping away of falsehood initiated by Tim is directed at her life, which they have carefully kept hidden from the mother.

Tim is the product of the new Afro-American sensibility, informed by the psychological revolution now operative within Black America. He is a combination ghetto soul brother and militant intellectual, very hip and slightly flawed himself. He would change the world, but without comprehending the particular history that produced his "tyrannical" father. And he cannot be the man his father was—not until he truly understands his father. He must understand why his father allowed himself to be insulted daily by the "honky" types on the job; why he took a demeaning job in the "shit-house"; and why he spent on his family the violence that he should have directed against the white man. In short, Tim must confront the history of his family. And that is exactly what happens. Each character tells his story, exposing his falsehood to the other until a balance is reached.

Who's Got His Own is not the work of an alienated mind. Milner's main thrust is directed toward unifying the family around basic moral principles, toward bridging the "generation gap." Other Black playwrights, Jimmy Garrett for example, see the gap was unbridgeable.

Garrett's *We Own the Night* takes place during an armed insurrection. As the play opens we see the central characters defending a section of the city against attacks by white police. Johnny, the protagonist, is wounded. Some of his Brothers intermittently fire at attacking forces, while others look for medical help. A doctor arrives, forced at gun point. The wounded boy's mother also comes. She is a female Uncle Tom who berates the Brothers and their cause. She tries to get Johnny to leave. She is hysterical. The whole idea of Black people fighting white people is totally outside of her orientation. Johnny begins a vicious attack on his mother, accusing her of emasculating his father—a recurring theme in the sociology of the Black community. In Afro-American literature of previous decades the strong Black mother was the object of awe and respect. But in the new literature her status is ambivalent and laced with tension. Historically, Afro-American women have had to be the economic mainstays of the family. The oppressor allowed them to have jobs while at the same time limiting the economic mobility of the Black man. Very often, therefore, the woman's aspirations and values are closely tied to those of the white power structure and not to those of her man. Since he cannot provide for his family the way

white men do, she despises his weakness, tearing into him at every opportunity until, very often, there is nothing left but a shell.

The only way out of this dilemma is through revolution. It either must
be an actual blood revolution, or one that psychically redirects the energy
of the oppressed. Milner is fundamentally concerned with the latter and
Garrett with the former. Communication between Johnny and his mother
breaks down. The revolutionary imperative demands that men step outside
the legal framework. It is a question of erecting *another* morality. The old
constructs do not hold up, because adhering to them means consigning
oneself to the oppressive reality. Johnny's mother is involved in the old constructs. Manliness is equated with white morality. And even though she
claims to love her family (her men), the overall design of her ideas are
against black manhood. In Garrett's play the mother's morality manifests
itself in a deep-seated hatred of Black men; while in Milner's work the
mother understands, but holds her men back.

The mothers that Garrett and Milner see represent the Old Spirituality—the Faith of the Fathers of which DuBois spoke. Johnny and Tim represent the New Spirituality. They appear to be a type produced by the
upheavals of the colonial world of which Black America is a part. Johnny's
assertion that he is a criminal is remarkably similar to the rebel's comments
in Aimé Césaire's[4] play, *Les Armes Miraculouses (The Miraculous Weapons)*. In that play the rebel, speaking to his mother, proclaims: "My name—
an offense; my Christian name—humiliation; my status—a rebel; my age—
the stone age." To which the mother replies: "My race—the human race.
My religion—brotherhood." The Old Spirituality is generalized. It seeks to
recognize Universal Humanity. The New Spirituality is specific. It begins
by seeing the world from the concise point-of-view of the colonialized.
Where the Old Spirituality would live with oppression while ascribing to
the oppressors an innate goodness, the New Spirituality demands a radical
shift in point-of-view. The colonialized native, the oppressed must, of necessity, subscribe to a *separate* morality. One that will liberate him and his
people.

The assault against the Old Spirituality can sometimes be humorous. In
Ben Caldwell's play, *The Militant Preacher*, a burglar is seen slipping into
the home of a wealthy minister. The preacher comes in and the burglar
ducks behind a large chair. The preacher, acting out the role of the suppli-
cant minister begins to moan, praying to De Lawd for understanding.

In the context of today's politics, the minister is an Uncle Tom, mouthing platitudes against self-defense. The preacher drones in a self-pitying
monologue about the folly of protecting oneself against brutal policemen.
Then the burglar begins to speak. The preacher is startled, taking the burglar's voice for the voice of God. The burglar begins to play on the
preacher's old time religion. He *becomes* the voice of God insulting and
goading the preacher on until the preacher's attitudes about protective violence change. The next day the preacher emerges militant, gun in hand,
sounding like Reverend Cleage[5] in Detroit. He now preaches a new gos-

---

4. Martinican playwright, poet, and politician   5. Leader of the Black Messiah movement in the
(b.1913).   1960s.

pel—the gospel of the gun, an eye for an eye. The gospel is preached in the rhythmic cadences of the old Black church. But the content is radical. Just as Jones inverted the symbols in *Jello,* Caldwell twists the rhythms of the Uncle Tom preacher into the language of the new militancy.

These plays are directed at problems within Black America. They begin with the premise that there is a well defined Afro-American audience. An audience that must see itself and the world in terms of its own interests. These plays, along with many others, constitute the basis for a viable movement in the theatre—a movement which takes as its task a profound reevaluation of the Black man's presence in America. The Black Arts Movement represents the flowering of a cultural nationalism that has been suppressed since the 1920's. I mean the "Harlem Renaissance"—which was essentially a failure. It did not address itself to the mythology and the life-styles of the Black community. It failed to take roots, to link itself concretely to the struggles of that community, to become its voice and spirit. Implicit in the Black Arts Movement is the idea that Black people, however dispersed, constitute a *nation* within the belly of white America. This is not a new idea. Garvey said it and the Honorable Elijah Muhammad[6] says it now. And it is on this idea that the concept of Black Power is predicated.

Afro-American life and history is full of creative possibilities, and the movement is just beginning to perceive them. Just beginning to understand that the most meaningful statements about the nature of Western society must come from the Third World of which Black America is a part. The thematic material is broad, ranging from folk heroes like Shine and Stagolee to historical figures like Marcus Garvey and Malcolm X. And then there is the struggle for Black survival, the coming confrontation between white America and Black America. If art is the harbinger of future possibilities, what does the future of Black America portend?

1968

6. Leader of the Nation of Islam from the early 1930s until his death in 1975. Marcus Garvey (1887–1940), pioneer of black nationalism and founder of the Universal Negro Improvement Association, which advocated the return to Africa.

MAULANA KARENGA
b. 1941

Maulana Karenga achieved prominence during the 1960s as the chair of Us, a cultural and social change organization. An activist-scholar of national and international reputation, Karenga has participated in academic and organizational projects in Africa, Asia, Latin America, the Caribbean and Europe. Moreover, Karenga and Us played vanguard roles in the founding and development of the movements for Black Power, black studies, black student unions, black independent schools, and Black Arts. More recently, Karenga has played a similar major role in the development of Afrocentric theory, ancient Egyptian studies within black studies, rites of passage programs for youth, and national black united front structures; in addition, he served as an executive committee member and author of the *Mission Statement* of the Million Man March/Day of Absence.

Karenga is currently professor and chair of the Department of Black Studies and chair of the President's Task Force on Multicultural Education and Campus Diversity at California State University, Long Beach. He is chairman of The Organization Us, director of the African American Cultural Center and the Kawaida Institute of Pan-African Studies, Los Angeles. Notably Karenga is the creator of Kwanzaa, a seven-day (December 16–January 1) African American and Pan-African holiday which is celebrated by millions throughout the world African community. Moreover, he is the author of numerous scholarly articles and ten books, including *Introduction to Black Studies; Kwanzaa: A Celebration of Family, Community and Culture; Selections from the Husia: Sacred Wisdom of Ancient Egypt;* and *Kawaida Theory: A Communitarian African Philosophy.*

Maulana Karenga's statement of purpose for the Black Arts movement, anthologized here, is judged by many as the clearest and most accessible statement of Black Aesthetic aims and was widely distributed during the 1960s and afterward.

Black Art: Mute Matter Given Force and Function

Black art, like everything else in the black community, must respond positively to the reality of revolution.

It must become and remain a part of the revolutionary machinery that moves us to change quickly and creatively. We have always said, and continue to say, that the battle we are waging now is the battle for the minds of Black people, and that if we lose this battle, we cannot win the violent one. It becomes very important then, that art plays the role it should play in Black survival and not bog itself down in the meaningless madness of the Western world wasted. In order to avoid this madness, black artists and those who wish to be artists must accept the fact that what is needed is an aesthetic, a black aesthetic, that is a criteria for judging the validity and/or the beauty of a work of art.

Pursuing this further, we discover that all art can be judged on two levels—on the social level and on the artistic level. In terms of the artistic level, we will be brief in talking about this, because the artistic level involves a consideration of form and feeling, two things which obviously involve more technical consideration and terminology than we have space, time or will to develop adequately here. Let it be enough to say that the artistic consideration, although a necessary part, is not sufficient. What completes the picture is that social criteria for judging art. And it is this criteria that is the most important criteria. For all art must reflect and support the Black Revolution, and any art that does not discuss and contribute to the revolution is invalid, no matter how many lines and spaces are produced in proportion and symmetry and no matter how many sounds are boxed in or blown out and called music.

All we do and create, then, is based on tradition and reason, that is to say, on foundation and movement. For we begin to build on traditional foundation, but it is out of movement, that is experience, that we complete our creation. Tradition teaches us, Leopold Senghor[1] tells us, that all African art has at least three characteristics: that is, it is functional, collective and

---

1. Léopold Sédar Senghor (b. 1906), long-time president of Senegal (1960–80), poet, and co-founder of the Negritude movement in the 1930s.

committing or committed. Since this is traditionally valid, it stands to reason that we should attempt to use it as the foundation for a rational construction to meet our present day needs. And by no mere coincidence we find that the criteria is not only valid, but inspiring. That is why we say that all Black art, irregardless of any technical requirements, must have three basic characteristics which make it revolutionary. In brief, it must be functional, collective and committing. It must be functional, that is *useful*, as we cannot accept the false doctrine of "art for art's sake." For, in fact, there is no such thing as "art for art's sake." All art reflects the value system from which it comes. For if the artist created only for himself and not for others, he would lock himself up somewhere and paint or write or play just for himself. But he does not do that. On the contrary, he invites us over, even *insists* that we come to hear him or to see his work; in a word, he expresses a need for our evaluation and/or appreciation and our evaluation cannot be a favorable one if the work of art is not first functional, that is, useful.

So what, then, is the use of art—our art, Black art? Black art must expose the enemy, praise the people and support the revolution. It must be like LeRoi Jones'[2] poems that are assassins' poems, poems that kill and shoot guns and "wrassle cops into alleys taking their weapons, leaving them dead with tongues pulled out and sent to Ireland." It must be functional like the poem of another revolutionary poet from "US," Clyde Halisi, who described the Master's words as "Sun Genies, dancing through the crowd snatching crosses and St. Christopher's from around niggers' necks and passing the white gapped legs in their minds to Simbas[3] to be disposed of."

Or, in terms of painting, we do not need pictures of oranges in a bowl or trees standing innocently in the midst of a wasteland. If we must paint oranges and trees, let our guerrillas be eating those oranges for strength and using those trees for cover. We need new images, and oranges in a bowl or fat white women smiling lewdly cannot be those images. All material is mute until the artist gives it a message, and that message must be a message of revolution. Then we have destroyed "art for art's sake," which is of no use anyhow, and have developed art for all our sake, art for Mose the miner, Sammy the shoeshine boy, T.C. the truck driver and K.P. the unwilling soldier.

In conclusion, the real function of art is to make revolution, using its own medium.

The second characteristic of Black art is that it must be collective. In a word, it must be from the people and must be returned to the people in a form more beautiful and colorful than it was in real life. For that is what art is: everyday life given more form and color. And in relationship to that, the Black artist can find no better subject than Black People themselves, and the Black artist who does not choose or develop this subject will find himself unproductive. For no one is any more than the context to which he owes his existence, and if an artist owes his existence to the Afroamerican context, then he also owes his art to that context and therefore must be held accountable to the people of that context. To say that art must be collective, however, raises four questions. Number one, the question of populari-

---

2. (Amiri Baraka) (b. 1934). African American poet, educator, editor, political activist, and award-winning playwright.

3. Swahili for Young Lions, the Youth Movement in US Organization [Karenga's note].

zation versus elevation; two, personality versus individuality; three, diversity in unity; and four, freedom *to* versus freedom *from*.

The question of popularization versus elevation is an old one; what it really seeks to do is to ask and to answer the question whether or not art should be lowered to the level of the people or the people raised to the level of art. Our contention is that if art is from the people, and for the people, there is no question of raising people to art or lowering art to the people, for they are one and the same thing. As we said previously—art is everyday life given more form and color. And what one seeks to do then is to use art as a means of educating the people, and being educated by them, so that it is a mutual exchange rather than a one-way communication. Art and people must develop at the same time and for the same reason. It must move with the masses and be moved by the masses.

For we should not demand that our people go to school to learn to appreciate art, but that an artist go to school formally or informally to learn new and better techniques of expressing his appreciation for the people and all they represent and his disdain for anything and everything that threatens or hinders their existence. Then and only then can both the artist and the people move forward with a positive pace rooted to the reality of revolution.

The second question raised is the question of personality versus individuality. Now this question is one of how much the emphasis on collective art destroys the individuality of the artist. We say that individualism is a luxury that we cannot afford, moreover, individualism is, in effect, nonexistent. For since no one is any more than the context to which he owes his existence, he has no individuality, only personality. Individuality by definition is "me" in spite of everyone, and personality is "me" in relation to everyone. The one, a useless isolation and the other an important involvement. We have heard it even said that the individual is like an atom, that which can no longer be reduced, or the essence of humanity. However, aside from this being a rather strained analogy, it does not prove that a man who wants to be an individual can stand alone. For the atom itself is a part of a molecule and cannot exist without interdependence, and even then, it is at best a simple theoretical construction for the convenience of conversation. We say that there is no virtue in a false independence, but there is value in a real interdependence.

The third question raised with regard to collective art is an extension of the second one, and that is, does unity preclude diversity? Our answer to that is an emphatic, "NO," for there can be and is unity in diversity, even as there can be diversity in unity. What one seeks, however, is not a standardization of every move or creation, but a framework in which one can create and avoid the European gift of trial and error. [4] One can seek the reality of the concept of diversity in unity or unity in diversity in listening to a Trippin ensemble. [5] In a Trippin ensemble the "leader" sets the pace and oth-

4. Karenga is apparently signifying on the privilege of trial and error that is granted to white Americans and often denied to African Americans.
5. Trippin is our word for what white boys and others call jazz. In line with our obsession with self-determination which demands new definitions and nomenclature, we reject the word jazz, for jazz is taken from the white word, jazzy, i.e. sexy, because that is what he thought our music was. We call it Trippin because that is what we do when we play it or listen to it [Karenga's note].

ers come in, or go out, as it pleases them, but in the end they all come to a very dynamic and overwhelmingly harmonious conclusion. So it is with our dance—two partners dance together the same dance and yet they provide us with a demonstration of that which is unique in each of them. But that is not individuality—that is personality. For it is an expression of uniqueness, not isolation from, but in relation to, each other and the collective experience that they both have shared.

The last question is one of freedom *to* versus freedom *from*. This is really a political question, or social one, and is one that raises contradiction for the artist who rejects the social interpretation of art. However, when he demands freedom to do something or freedom from the restriction that prohibits his doing something, he is asking for a socio-political right, and that, as we said, makes art social first and aesthetic second. Art does not exist in the abstract just like freedom does not exist in the abstract. It is not an independent living thing; it lives through us and through the meaning and message we give it. And an artist may have any freedom to do what he wishes as long as it does not take the freedom from the people to be protected from those images, words and sounds that are negative to their life and development. The people give us the freedom from isolation and alienation and random searching for subject matter and artists, in view of this, must not ask for freedom to deny this, but on the contrary must praise the people for this. In conclusion, the concept of collective art can best be expressed in the African proverb showing the interdependence of all by saying, "One hand washes the other."

The final thing that is characteristic of Black art is that it must be committing. It must commit us to revolution and change. It must commit us to a future that is ours. In a word, it must commit us to all that is US-yesterday, today and the sunrise of tomorrow. It must tell us like Halisi's poem, "Maulana and Word Magic," that we must give up the past or be found out and exposed, "as the notes of a new day come tripping through searching each one's heart for any traces of Peyton Place."[6] It must commit us to the fact that the earth is ours and the fullness thereof. As LeRoi Jones says, "You can't steal nothing from the white man. He's already stole it, he owes you anything you want, even his life." So, "Black People take the shit you want, take their lives if need, but get what you want, what you need. Dance up and down the street, turn all the music up." This is commitment to the struggle, a commitment that includes the artist and the observer. We cannot let each other rest; there is so much to do, and we all know we have done so little. Art will revive us, inspire us, give us enough courage to face another disappointing day. It must not teach us resignation. For all our art must contribute to revolutionary change and if it does not, it is invalid.

Therefore, we say the blues are invalid; for they teach resignation, in a word acceptance of reality—and we have come to change reality. We will not submit to the resignation of our fathers who lost their money, their women, and their lives and sat around wondering "what did they do to be so black and blue." We will say again with Brother LeRoi, "We are lovers and the sons of lovers, and warriors and the sons of warriors." Therefore, we

6. Early television soap opera synonymous with tangled, illicit, love affairs.

will love—and unwillingly though necessarily, make war, revolutionary war. We will not cry for those things that are gone, but find meaning in those things that remain with us. Perhaps people will object violently to the idea that the blues are invalid, but one should understand that they are not invalid historically. They will always represent a very beautiful, musical and psychological achievement of our people; but today they are not functional because they do not commit us to the struggle of today and tomorrow, but keep us in the past. And whatever we do, we cannot remain in the past, for we have too much at stake in the present. And we find our future much too much rewarding to be rejected.

Let our art remind us of our distaste for the enemy, our love for each other, and our commitment to the revolutionary struggle that will be fought with the rhythmic reality of a permanent revolution.

1968

HAKI R. MADHUBUTI
b. 1942

Writer, publisher, literary critic, and community activist, Haki R. Madhubuti began his creative career by printing poems on single sheets and selling them at barbershops, beauty salons, and other gathering places in the African American community. His style is not unlike that of the direct, commonsense prose Benjamin Franklin used in his *Poor Richard's Almanac*. It seeks to delight and to teach black people the pleasures and perils of their situation in America. Scarcely intended for the consumption of academic critics or white undergraduate English majors, Madhubuti's sometimes rollickingly simple lines have drawn sharp comment from those who maintain that poetry must be dense and incomprehensible.

Born in Arkansas, raised in Detroit, and transplanted to Chicago, Madhubuti was one of that city's champions of the Black Aesthetic, establishing both the Third World Press and the Institute for Positive Education as ways of forwarding a new conception of poetry and education in the United States. He was also one of the founding members of Chicago's Organization of Black American Culture.

In early volumes such as *Think Black* (1967), *Black Pride* (1968), and *Don't Cry, Scream* (1969), Madhubuti explores themes and feelings that have been common currency among African Americans for generations. His humorous puncturing of false ideals (*Back Again, Home*) and his clever line arrangements (*Malcolm Spoke / who listened?*) give these volumes the feeling of a wise, street-corner speaking voice, reminding readers of things they have always known but were reluctant to express as poetry.

As a critic of black literature and culture, Madhubuti writes in a vernacular, didactic prose that follows a single line of argument and evaluation: if you are not for the Black Arts and Black Power revolutions, then you are against black American interests. His essays in *Dynamite Voices I* (1971) understandably made traditional academic critics extremely uncomfortable because he defined the best critics as established creative writers who were confident in their own work and suggested that most other literary critics were frustrated writers-turned-hatchet men.

As his influence grew and his endeavors expanded, Madhubuti became increasingly visionary in tone and increasingly disparaging of the social and artistic directions of African America. His hortatory voice of the post–Black Aesthetic years has tended to be far less lauded than his more passionate early work.

Back Again, Home

(Confessions of an ex-executive)

Pains of insecurity surround me;
  shined shoes,
  conservative suits,
  button down shirts with silk ties.
  bi-weekly payroll.   5

Ostracized, but not knowing why;
  executive haircut,
  clean shaved,
  "yes" instead of "yeah" and "no" instead of "naw",
  hours, nine to five. (after five he's alone)   10

"Doing an excellent job, keep it up;"
  promotion made—semi-monthly payroll,
  very quiet—never talks,
  budget balanced—saved the company money,
  quality work—production tops.   15
  He looks sick. (but there is a smile in his eyes)

He resigned, we wonder why;
  let his hair grow—a mustache too,
  out of a job—broke and hungry,
  friends are coming back—bring food,   20
  not quiet now—trying to speak,
  what did he say?

"Back Again,"

BLACK AGAIN,

Home."   25
              1967

Introduction [to *Think Black*]

    I was born into slavery in Feb. of 1942. In the spring of that same year 110,000 persons of Japanese descent were placed in protective custody by the white people of the United States. Two out of every three of these were American citizens by birth; the other third were aliens forbidden by law to be citizens. No charges had been filed against these people nor had any hearing been held. The removal of these people was on racial or ancestral grounds only. World War II, the war against racism; yet no Germans or other enemy aliens were placed in protective custody. There should have been Japanese writers directing their writings toward Japanese audiences.
    Black. Poet. Black poet am I. This should leave little doubt in the minds of anyone as to which is first. Black art is created from black forces that live within the body. These forces can be lost at any time as in the case of Louis

Lomax, Frank Yerby and Ralph Ellison. Direct and meaningful contact
with black people will act as energizers for the black forces. Black art will
elevate and enlighten our people and lead them toward an awareness of
self, i.e., their blackness. It will show them mirrors. Beautiful symbols. And
will aid in the destruction of anything nasty and detrimental to our advancement as a people. Black art is a reciprocal art. The black writer learns
from his people and because of his insight and "know how" he is able to
give back his knowledge to the people in a manner in which they can identify, learn and gain some type of mental satisfaction, e.g., rage or happiness.
We must destroy Faulkner, dick, jane, and other perpetuators of evil. It's
time for Du Bois, Nat Turner and Kwame Nkrumah. As Frantz Fanon
points out: destroy the culture and you destroy people. This must not happen. Black artists are culture stabilizers; bringing back old values, and introducing new ones. Black art will talk to the people and with the will of
the people stop the impending "protective custody."

              America calling.
              negroes.
              can you dance?
              play foot/baseball?
              nanny?   5
              cook?
              needed now. negroes
              who can entertain
              ONLY.
              others not   10
              wanted.
              (& are considered extremely dangerous.)
                                                            1967

                    The Long Reality

              What Viet Nam means to me,
              rice fields and muddy streets
              where children resist-
                        as a "manchild" should,
              where mothers sell and a country seeks,   5
              where death and unclaimed freedom weeps

              With Buddha majority and Catholic rule
              that Bible again, that golden fool,
              how many niggers have you killed today,
              dying for emancipation—   10
                        away, away?

              Napalm in Viet Nam,
                        Congress here,
              come black brothers
              the message is clear-   15
                    America is in tears

crying her pleas of broken promises and
                 hypocrisies

Viet-brothers come give us a hand
we fight for freedom,   20
               we fight for land.

Give me my forty acres.
give me my mule.
               broken promises and hypocrisies
where death died and claimed freedom flees.   25

                                    1967

Malcolm Spoke / who listened?

(this poem is for my consciousness too)

he didn't say
wear yr / blackness in
outer garments
& blk / slogans fr / the top 10.

he was fr a long   5
line of super-cools,
       doo-rag lovers &
       revolutionary pimps.
u are playing that
high-yellow game in blackface   10
minus the straighthair.
now
it's nappy-black
& air conditioned volkswagens
with undercover whi   15
te girls who studied faulkner at
smith
& are authorities on "militant"
knee / grows
selling u at jew town rates: [1]   20
       niggers with wornout tongues
       three for a quarter / or will consider a trade

the double-breasted hipster
has been replaced with a
dashiki wearing rip-off   25
who went to city college
majoring in physical education.

animals come in all colors.
dark meat will roast as fast as whi-te meat

---

1. A pejorative phrase directed at the Jewish economic establishments in African American communities.

especially in
the unitedstatesofamerica's
new
self-cleaning ovens.

if we don't listen.

1969

a poem to complement other poems

change.
life if u were a match i wd light u into something beauti-
    ful. change.
change.
for the better into a realreal together thing. change, from   5
    a make believe
nothing on corn meal and water. change.
change. from the last drop to the first, maxwellhouse
    did. change.
change was a programmer for IBM, thought him was a   10
    brown computor. change.
colored is something written on southern out-
    houses. change.
grayhound did, i mean they got rest rooms on buses.
    change.   15
change.
change nigger.
saw a nigger hippy, him wanted to be different. changed.
saw a nigger liberal, him wanted to be different.
    changed.   20
saw a nigger conservative, him wanted to be different.
    changed.
niggers don't u know that niggers are different. change.
a doublechange. nigger wanted a double zero in front of
    his name; a license to kill,   25
niggers are licensed to be killed. change. a negro: some-
    thing pigs eat.
change. i say change into a realblack righteous aim. like
    i don't play
saxophone but that doesn't mean i don't dig 'trane.'[1]   30
    change.
change.
hear u coming but yr / steps are too loud. change. even a
    lamp post changes nigger.
change, stop being an instant yes machine. change.   35
niggers don't change they just grow. that's a change;
    bigger & better niggers.
change, into a necessary blackself.
change, like a gas meter gets higher.

1. John Coltrane (1926–1967), influential jazz saxophonist.

change, like a blues song talking about a righteous to-   40
    morrow.
change, like a tax bill getting higher.
change, like a good sister getting better.
change, like knowing wood will burn. change.
know the realenemy.   45
change,
change nigger: standing on the corner, thought him was
            cool. him still
        standing there. it's winter time, him cool.
change,   50
know the realenemy.
change: him wanted to be a TV star. him is. ten o'clock
        news.
    wanted, wanted. nigger stole some lemon & lime
        popsicles,   55
        thought them were diamonds.
change nigger change.
know the realenemy.
change: is u is or is u aint. change. now now change. for
        the better change.   60
    read a change. live a change. read a blackpoem.
        change. be the realpeople.
    change. blackpoems
will change:
know the realenemy. change. know the realenemy. change   65
    yr / enemy change know the real
change know the realenemy change, change, know the
    realenemy, the realenemy, the real
realenemy change your the enemies / change your change
    your change your enemy change   70
your enemy. know the realenemy, the world's enemy.
    know them know them know them the
realenemy   change your enemy   change your change
    change change your enemy change change
change change your change change change.   75
your
mind nigger.

                                1969

NIKKI GIOVANNI

b. 1943

Born in Knoxville, Tennessee, and given the name Yolande Cornelia Giovanni Jr.,
Nikki Giovanni was one of the first Black Arts movement poets to achieve stardom.
Her unabashed advocacy of murderous militancy as a proper black response to
white oppression brought her instant fame. She appeared on talk shows, received
honorary degrees, and brushed off with consummate ease inquiries about incompatibility between her fame as a poet and her avowedly revolutionary intentions to
destroy white America.

In rapid succession between 1967 and 1970, Giovanni produced three volumes of poetry that were avidly read by black audiences. *Black Feeling* (1967), *Black Judgment* (1968), and *Re: Creation* (1970) were immediate hits on the United States black poetry charts. Quickly, the boldness of Giovanni's revolutionary proclamations and the accessibility of her simple nostrums made her name a household word. She went on to produce a recording of her poetical musings called *Truth Is on Its Way* (1971). Her performance was backed up by a New York religious choir, and the work enjoyed great success. Giovanni, who displayed not only an entrepreneurial spirit but also a deft awareness of the Black Aesthetic claim that poetry cannot be divorced from music in the African American tradition, made several more albums of her poetry read in musical settings.

By the early 1970s, Giovanni had realized that what the critic Arthur P. Davis called the "new poetry of black hate" had exhausted its market, and she produced a surprising collection of love poems called *My House* (1972). In subsequent years, she has written verse for children, continued teaching literature and creative writing, and been the subject of academic dissertations. Still, her earliest, revolutionary verse is the work of hers that remains most resonant in American memory.

For Saundra

i wanted to write
a poem
that rhymes
but revolution doesn't lend
itself to be-bopping   5

then my neighbor
who thinks i hate
asked—do you ever write
tree poems—i like trees
so i thought   10
i'll write a beautiful green tree poem
peeked from my window
to check the image
noticed the school yard was covered
with asphalt   15
no green—no trees grow
in manhattan

then, well, i thought the sky
i'll do a big blue sky poem
but all the clouds have winged   20
low since no-Dick[1] was elected

so i thought again
and it occurred to me
maybe i shouldn't write
at all   25
but clean my gun
and check my kerosene supply

1. I.e., Richard M. Nixon (1913–1994), thirty-seventh president of the United States

perhaps these are not poetic
times
at all   30
                                                                     1968

Beautiful Black Men

(with compliments and apologies to all not mentioned by name)

i wanta say just gotta say something
bout those beautiful beautiful beautiful outasight
black men
with they afros
walking down the street   5
is the same ol danger
but a brand new pleasure

sitting on stoops, in bars, going to offices
running numbers, watching for their whores
preaching in churches, driving their hogs   10
walking their dogs, winking at me
in their fire red, lime green, burnt orange
royal blue tight tight pants that hug
what i like to hug

jerry butler, wilson pickett, the impressions   15
temptations, mighty mighty sly[1]
don't have to do anything but walk
on stage
and i scream and stamp and shout
see new breed men in breed alls   20
dashiki suits with shirts that match
the lining that compliments the ties
that smile at the sandals
where dirty toes peek at me
and i scream and stamp and shout   25
for more beautiful beautiful beautiful
black men with outasight afros

                                                                     1968

Nikki-Rosa

childhood remembrances are always a drag
if you're Black
you always remember things like living in Woodlawn[1]
with no inside toilet

1. Musical artists and groups popular in the 1960s. Butler (b. 1939), rhythm and blues singer. Pickett (b. 1941), soul singer. The Impressions was a soul group. The Temptations was a Motown group. Sly Stone (b. 1944), lead singer of the soul, funk, and rock group Sly and the Family Stone.
1. Black suburb of Cincinnati.

and if you become famous or something   5
they never talk about how happy you were to have your mother
all to yourself and
how good the water felt when you got your bath from one of those
big tubs that folk in chicago barbecue in
and somehow when you talk about home   10
it never gets across how much you
understood their feelings
as the whole family attended meetings about Hollydale
and even though you remember
your biographers never understand   15
your father's pain as he sells his stock
and another dream goes
and though you're poor it isn't poverty that
concerns you
and though they fought a lot   20
it isn't your father's drinking that makes any difference
but only that everybody is together and you
and your sister have happy birthdays and very good christmasses
and I really hope no white person ever has cause to write about me
because they never understand Black love is Black wealth and
    they'll   25
probably talk about my hard childhood and never understand that
all the while I was quite happy

                                  1968

JAMES ALAN McPHERSON

b. 1943

Hailed by many as one of the most gifted short story writers to emerge during the 1960s and 1970s, James Alan McPherson was born and raised by James and Mabel McPherson in Savannah, Georgia. He briefly attended Morgan State University before receiving a B.A. degree from Morris Brown College in Atlanta. In 1965, McPherson was recruited by Harvard University Law School, and during the same year his second short story, *Gold Coast*, was awarded first prize in a fiction contest sponsored by the *Atlantic Monthly*. After completing his law degree and later earning an M.F.A. from the Writer's Workshop at the University of Iowa, he continued to produce prize-winning fiction. McPherson has been an instructor of creative writing and African American literature at the University of Iowa (1968–69), the University of Santa Cruz (1969), Morgan State University (1969–70), and the University of Virginia (1976–81).

McPherson is largely known for his short stories. In them he often presents interpersonal differences that cannot be bridged or overcome. Many of McPherson's stories involve the culture that surrounds trains, which he is able to vividly convey, perhaps in part because he worked his way through college as a waiter aboard the Great Northern Railroad.

Hue and Cry: Short Stories earned McPherson a National Institute of Arts and Letters grant in 1970, a Rockefeller grant that same year, and a Guggenheim fellowship two years later. McPherson later won a Pulitzer Prize for his collection *Elbow Room* and was awarded a MacArthur Foundation grant in 1981.

Although McPherson's stories deal intimately with issues of race and class, he attempts always to highlight the universality of his characters' predicaments. Of his own work, McPherson hopes that it can be read as "about people, all kinds of people. . . . As a matter of fact, certain of them happen to be white; but I have tried to keep the color part of most of them far in the background, where these things should be rightly kept."

A Solo Song: For Doc

I

So you want to know this business, youngblood? So you want to be a Waiter's Waiter? The Commissary gives you a book with all the rules and tells you to learn them. And you do, and think that is all there is to it. A big, thick black book. Poor youngblood.

Look at me. I am a Waiter's Waiter. I know all the moves, all the pretty, fine moves that big book will never teach you. I built this railroad with my moves; and so did Sheik Beasley and Uncle T. Boone and Danny Jackson, and so did Doc Craft. That book they made you learn came from our moves and from our heads. There was a time when six of us, big men, danced at the same time in that little Pantry without touching and shouted orders to the sweating paddies[1] in the kitchen. There was a time when they *had* to respect us because our sweat and our moves supported them. We knew the service and the paddies, even the green dishwashers, knew that we did and didn't give us the crap they pull on you.

Do you know how to sneak a Blackplate to a nasty cracker?[2] Do you know how to rub asses with five other men in the Pantry getting their orders together and still know that you are a man, just like them? Do you know how to bullshit while you work and keep the paddies in their places with your bullshit? Do you know how to breathe down the back of an old lady's dress to hustle a bigger tip?

No. You are summer stuff, youngblood. I am old, my moves are not so good any more, but I know this business. The Commissary hires you for the summer because they don't want to let anyone get as old as me on them. I'm sixty-three, but they can't fire me: I'm in the Union. They can't lay me off for fucking up: I know this business too well. And so they hire you, youngblood, for the summer when the tourists come, and in September you go away with some tips in your pocket to buy pussy and they wait all winter for me to die. I am dying, youngblood, and so is this business. Both of us will die together. There'll always be summer stuff like you, but the big men, the big trains, are dying every day and everybody can see it. And nobody but us who are dying with them gives a damn.

Look at the big picture at the end of the car, youngblood. That's the man who built this road. He's in your history books. He's probably in that big black bible you read. He was a great man. He hated people. He didn't want

---

1. Those of Irish descent; from "Paddy," a nickname for Patrick.
2. A poor white southerner. "Blackplate": African American cuisine that includes dumplings, baked grits, scrambled pork brains, chittlins, cornbread, and fried catfish.

to feed them but the government said he had to. He didn't want to hire me, but he needed me to feed the people. I know this, youngblood, and that is why that book is written for you and that is why I have never read it. That is why you get nervous and jump up to polish the pepper and salt shakers when the word comes down the line that an inspector is getting on at the next stop. That is why you warm the toast covers for every cheap old lady who wants to get coffee and toast and good service for sixty-five cents and a dime tip. You know that he needs you only for the summer and that hundreds of youngbloods like you want to work this summer to buy that pussy in Chicago and Portland and Seattle. The man uses you, but he doesn't need you. But me he needs for the winter, when you are gone, and to teach you something in the summer about this business you can't get from that big black book. He needs me and he knows it and I know it. That is why I am sitting here when there are tables to be cleaned and linen to be changed and silver to be washed and polished. He needs me to die. That is why I am taking my time. I know it. And I will take his service with me when I die, just like the Sheik did and like Percy Fields did, and like Doc.

Who are they? Why do I keep talking about them? Let me think about it. I guess it is because they were the last of the Old School, like me. We made this road. We got a million miles of walking up and down these cars under our feet. Doc Craft was the Old School, like me. He was a Waiter's Waiter. He danced down these aisles with us and swung his tray with the roll of the train, never spilling in all his trips a single cup of coffee. He could carry his tray on two fingers, or on one and a half if he wanted, and he knew all the tricks about hustling tips there are to know. He could work anybody. The girls at the Northland in Chicago knew Doc, and the girls at the Haverville in Seattle, and the girls at the Step-Inn in Portland and all the girls in Winnipeg knew Doc Craft.

But wait. It is just 1:30 and the first call for dinner is not until 5:00. You want to kill some time; you want to hear about the Old School and how it was in my day. If you look in that black book you would see that you should be polishing silver now. Look out the window; this is North Dakota, this is Jerry's territory. Jerry, the Unexpected Inspector. Shouldn't you polish the shakers or clean out the Pantry or squeeze oranges, or maybe change the linen on the tables? Jerry Ewald is sly. The train may stop in the middle of this wheatfield and Jerry may get on. He lives by that book. He knows where to look for dirt and mistakes. Jerry Ewald, the Unexpected Inspector. He knows where to look; he knows how to get you. He got Doc.

Now you want to know about him, about the Old School. You have even put aside your book of rules. But see how you keep your finger in the pages as if the book was more important than what I tell you. That's a bad move, and it tells on you. You will be a waiter. But you will never be a Waiter's Waiter. The Old School died with Doc, and the very last of it is dying with me. What happened to Doc? Take your finger out of the pages, youngblood, and I will tell you about a kind of life these rails will never carry again.

When your father was a boy playing with himself behind the barn, Doc was already a man and knew what the thing was for. But he got tired of using it when he wasn't much older than you, and he set his mind on making money. He had no skills. He was black. He got hungry. On Christmas Day in 1916, the story goes, he wandered into the Chicago stockyards and over to a dining car waiting to be connected up to the main train for the Chicago-to-San Francisco run. He looked up through the kitchen door at the chef storing supplies for the kitchen and said: "I'm hungry."

"What do you want *me* to do about it?" the Swede chef said.

"I'll work," said Doc.

That Swede was Chips Magnusson, fresh off the boat and lucky to be working himself. He did not know yet that he should save all extra work for other Swedes fresh off the boat. He later learned this by living. But at that time he considered a moment, bit into one of the fresh apples stocked for apple pie, chewed considerably, spit out the seeds and then waved the black on board the big train. "You can eat all you want," he told Doc. "But you work all I tell you."

He put Doc to rolling dough for the apple pies and the train began rolling for Doc. It never stopped. He fell in love with the feel of the wheels under his feet clicking against the track and he got the rhythm of the wheels in him and learned, like all of us, how to roll with them and move with them. After that first trip Doc was never at home on the ground. He worked everything in the kitchen from putting out dough to second cook, in six years. And then, when the Commissary saw that he was good and would soon be going for one of the chef's spots they saved for the Swedes, they put him out of the kitchen and told him to learn this waiter business; and told him to learn how to bullshit on the other side of the Pantry. He was almost thirty, youngblood, when he crossed over to the black side of the Pantry. I wasn't there when he made his first trip as a waiter, but from what they tell me of that trip I know that he was broke in by good men. Pantryman was Sheik Beasley, who stayed high all the time and let the waiters steal anything they wanted as long as they didn't bother his reefers. Danny Jackson, who was black and knew Shakespeare before the world said he could work with it, was second man. Len Dickey was third, Reverend Hendricks was fourth, and Uncle T. Boone, who even in those early days could not straighten his back, ran fifth. Doc started in as sixth waiter, the "mule." They pulled some shit on him at first because they didn't want somebody fresh out of a paddy kitchen on the crew. They messed with his orders, stole his plates, picked up his tips on the sly, and made him do all the dirty work. But when they saw that he could take the shit without getting hot and when they saw that he was set on being a waiter, even though he was older than most of them, they settled down and began to teach him this business and all the words and moves and slickness that made it a good business.

His real name was Leroy Johnson, I think, but when Danny Jackson saw how cool and neat he was in his moves, and how he handled the plates, he began to call him "the Doctor." Then the Sheik, coming down from his high one day after missing the lunch and dinner service, saw how Doc had taken over his station and collected fat tips from his tables by telling the passengers that the Sheik had had to get off back along the line because of a heart attack. The Sheik liked that because he saw that Doc understood crackers and how they liked nothing better than knowing that a nigger had died on the job, giving them service. The Sheik was impressed. And he was not an easy man to impress because he knew too much about life and had to stay high most of the time. And when Doc would not split the tips with him, the Sheik got mad at first and called Doc a barrel of motherfuckers and some other words you would not recognize. But he was impressed. And later that night, in the crew car when the others were gambling and drinking and bullshitting about the women they had working the corners for them, the Sheik came over to Doc's bunk and said: "You're a crafty motherfucker."

"Yeah?" says Doc.

"Yeah," says the Sheik, who did not say much. "You're a crafty mother-fucker but I like you." Then he got into the first waiter's bunk and lit up again. But Reverend Hendricks, who always read his Bible before going to sleep and who always listened to anything the Sheik said because he knew the Sheik only said something when it was important, heard what was said and remembered it. After he put his Bible back in his locker, he walked over to Doc's bunk and looked down at him. "Mister Doctor Craft," the Reverend said. "Youngblood Doctor Craft."

"Yeah?" says Doc.

"Yeah," says Reverend Hendricks. "That's who you are."

And that's who he was from then on.

II

I came to the road away from the war. This was after '41, when people at home were looking for Japs under their beds every night. I did not want to fight because there was no money in it and I didn't want to go overseas to work in a kitchen. The big war was on and a lot of soldiers crossed the country to get to it, and as long as a black man fed them on trains he did not have to go to that war. I could have got a job in a Chicago factory, but there was more money on the road and it was safer. And after a while it got into your blood so that you couldn't leave it for anything. The road got into my blood the way it got into everybody's; the way going to the war got in the blood of redneck farm boys and the crazy Polacks from Chicago. It was all right for them to go to the war. They were young and stupid. And they died that way. I played it smart. I was almost thirty-five and I didn't want to go. But I took *them* and fed them and gave them good times on their way to the war, and for that I did not have to go. The soldiers had plenty of money and were afraid not to spend it all before they got to the ships on the Coast. And we gave them ways to spend it on the trains.

Now in those days there was plenty of money going around and everybody stole from everybody. The kitchen stole food from the company and the company knew it and wouldn't pay good wages. There were no rules in those days, there was no black book to go by and nobody said what you couldn't eat or steal. The paddy cooks used to toss boxes of steaks off the train in the Chicago yards for people at the restaurants there who paid them, cash. These were the days when ordinary people had to have red stamps or blue stamps to get powdered eggs and white lard to mix with red powder to make their own butter.

The stewards stole from the company and from the waiters; the waiters stole from the stewards and the company and from each other. I stole. Doc stole. Even Reverend Hendricks put his Bible far back in his locker and stole with us. You didn't want a man on your crew who didn't steal. He made it bad for everybody. And if the steward saw that he was a dummy and would never get to stealing, he wrote him up for something and got him off the crew so as not to slow down the rest of us. We had a redneck cracker steward from Alabama by the name of Casper who used to say: "*Jesus Christ!* I ain't got time to hate you niggers, I'm making so much money." He used to keep all his cash at home under his bed in a cardboard box because he was afraid to put it in the bank.

Doc and Sheik Beasley and me were on the same crew together all during the war. Even in those days, as young as we were, we knew how to be Old Heads. We organized for the soldiers. We had to wear skullcaps all the time because the crackers said our hair was poison and didn't want any of it to fall in their food. The Sheik didn't mind wearing one. He kept reefers in his and used to sell them to the soldiers for double what he paid for them in Chicago and three times what he paid the Chinamen in Seattle. That's why we called him the Sheik. After every meal the Sheik would get in the linen closet and light up. Sometimes he wouldn't come out for days. Nobody gave a damn, though; we were all too busy stealing and working. And there was more for us to get as long as he didn't come out.

Doc used to sell bootlegged booze to the soldiers; that was his specialty. He had redcaps in the Chicago stations telling the soldiers who to ask for on the train. He was an open operator and had to give the steward a cut, but he still made a pile of money. That's why that old cracker always kept us together on his crew. We were the three best moneymakers he ever had. That's something you should learn, youngblood. They can't love you for being you. They only love you if you make money for them. All that talk these days about integration and brotherhood, that's a lot of bullshit. The man will love you as long as he can make money with you. I made money. And old Casper had to love me in the open although I knew he called me a nigger at home when he had put that money in his big cardboard box. I know he loved me on the road in the wartime because I used to bring in the biggest moneymakers. I used to handle the girls.

Look out that window. See all that grass and wheat? Look at that big farm boy cutting it. Look at that burnt cracker on that tractor. He probably has a wife who married him because she didn't know what else to do. Back during wartime the girls in this part of the country knew what to do. They got on the trains at night.

You can look out that window all day and run around all the stations when we stop, but you'll never see a black man in any of these towns. You know why, youngblood? These farmers hate you. They still remember when their girls came out of these towns and got on the trains at night. They've been running black men and dark Indians out of these towns for years. They hate anything dark that's not that way because of the sun. Right now there are big farm girls with hair under their arms on the corners in San Francisco, Chicago, Seattle and Minneapolis who got started on these cars back during wartime. The farmers still remember that and they hate you and me for it. But it wasn't for me they got on. Nobody wants a stiff, smelly farm girl when there are sporting women to be got for a dollar in the cities. It was for the soldiers they got on. It was just business to me. But they hate you and me anyway.

I got off in one of these towns once, a long time after the war, just to get a drink while the train changed engines. Everybody looked at me and by the time I got to a bar there were ten people on my trail. I was drinking a fast one when the sheriff came in the bar.

"What are you doing here?" he asks me.

"Just getting a shot," I say.

He spit on the floor. "How long you plan to be here?"

"I don't know," I say, just to be nasty.

"There ain't no jobs here," he says.

"I wasn't looking," I say.

"We don't want you here."

"I don't give a good goddamn," I say.

He pulled his gun on me. "All right, coon, back on the train," he says.

"Wait a minute," I tell him. "Let me finish my drink."

He knocked my glass over with his gun. "You're finished *now*," he says. "Pull your ass out of here *now!*"

I didn't argue.

I was the night man. After dinner it was my job to pull the cloths off the tables and put paddings on. Then I cut out the lights and locked both doors. There was a big farm girl from Minot named Hilda who could take on eight or ten soldiers in one night, white soldiers. These white boys don't know how to last. I would stand by the door and when the soldiers came back from the club car they would pay me and I would let them in. Some of the girls could make as much as one hundred dollars in one night. And I always made twice as much. Soldiers don't care what they do with their money. They just have to spend it.

We never bothered with the girls ourselves. It was just business as far as we were concerned. But there was one dummy we had with us once, a boy from the South named Willie Joe something who handled the dice. He was really hot for one of these farm girls. He used to buy her good whiskey and he hated to see her go in the car at night to wait for the soldiers. He was a real dummy. One time I heard her tell him: "It's all right. They can have my body. I know I'm black inside. *Jesus*, I'm so black inside I wisht I was black all over!"

And this dummy Willie Joe said: "Baby, *don't you ever change!*"

I knew we had to get rid of him before he started trouble. So we had the steward bump him off the crew as soon as we could find a good man to handle the gambling. That old redneck Casper was glad to do it. He saw what was going on.

But you want to hear about Doc, you say, so you can get back to your reading. What can I tell you? The road got into his blood? He liked being a waiter? You won't understand this, but he did. There were no Civil Rights or marches or riots for something better in those days. In those days a man found something he liked to do and liked it from then on because he couldn't help himself. What did he like about the road? He liked what I liked: the money, owning the car, running it, telling the soldiers what to do, hustling a bigger tip from some old maid by looking under her dress and laughing at her, having all the girls at the Haverville Hotel waiting for us to come in for stopover, the power we had to beat them up or lay them if we wanted. He liked running free and not being married to some bitch who would spend his money when he was out of town or give it to some stud. He liked getting drunk with the boys up at Andy's, setting up the house and then passing out from drinking too much, knowing that the boys would get him home.

I ran with that one crew all during wartime and they, Doc, the Sheik and Reverend Hendricks, had taken me under their wings. I was still a young-blood then, and Doc liked me a lot. But he never said that much to me; he was not a talker. The Sheik had taught him the value of silence in things that really matter. We roomed together in Chicago at Mrs. Wright's place in those days. Mrs. Wright didn't allow women in the rooms and Doc liked that, because after being out for a week and after stopping over in those hotels along the way, you get tired of women and bullshit and need your privacy. We weren't like you. We didn't need a woman every time we got hard. We knew when we had to have it and when we didn't. And we didn't spend all our money on it, either. You youngbloods think the way to get a woman is to let her see how you handle your money. That's stupid. The way to get a woman is to let her see how you handle other women. But you'll never believe that until it's too late to do you any good.

Doc knew how to handle women. I can remember a time in a Winnipeg hotel how he ran a bitch out of his room because he had enough of it and did not need her any more. I was in the next room and heard everything.

"Come on, Doc," the bitch said. "Come on honey, let's do it one more time."

"Hell no," Doc said. "I'm tired and I don't want to any more."

"How can you say you're tired?" the bitch said. "How can you say you're tired when you didn't go but two times?"

"I'm tired of it," Doc said, "because I'm tired of you. And I'm tired of you because I'm tired of it and bitches like you in all the towns I been in. You drain a man. And I know if I beat you, you'll still come back when I hit you again. *That's* why I'm tired. I'm tired of having things around I don't care about."

"What *do* you care about, Doc?" the bitch said.

"I don't know," Doc said. "I guess I care about moving and being some-where else when I want to be. I guess I care about going out, and coming in to wait for the time to go out again."

"You crazy, Doc," the bitch said.

"Yeah?" Doc said. "I guess I'm crazy all right."

Later that bitch knocked on my door and I did it for her because she was just a bitch and I knew Doc wouldn't want her again. I don't think he ever wanted a bitch again. I never saw him with one after that time. He was just a little over fifty then and could have still done whatever he wanted with women.

The war ended. The farm boys who got back from the war did not spend money on their way home. They did not want to spend any more money on women, and the girls did not get on at night any more. Some of them went into the cities and turned pro. Some of them stayed in the towns and married the farm boys who got back from the war. Things changed on the road. The Commissary started putting that book of rules together and told us to stop stealing. They were losing money on passengers now because of the airplanes and they began to really tighten up and started sending inspectors down along the line to check on us. They started sending in spotters,[3] too. One of them caught that redneck Casper writing out a check for two dollars less than he had charged the spotter. The Commissary got him in on the rug for it. I wasn't there, but they told me he said to the General Superintendent: "Why are you getting on me, a white man, for a lousy son-of-a-bitching two bucks? There's niggers out there been stealing for *years!*"

"Who?" the General Superintendent asked.

And Casper couldn't say anything because he had that cardboard box full of money still under his bed and knew he would have to tell how he got it if any of us was brought in. So he said nothing.

"Who?" the General Superintendent asked him again.

"Why, all them nigger waiters steal, *everybody knows that!*"

"And the cooks, what about them?" the Superintendent said.

"They're white," said Casper.

They never got the story out of him and he was fired. He used the money to open a restaurant someplace in Indiana and I heard later that he started a branch of the Klan in his town. One day he showed up at the station and told Doc, Reverend Hendricks and me: "I'll see you boys get *yours.* Damn if I'm takin' the rap for you niggers."

We just laughed in his face because we knew he could do nothing to us through the Commissary. But just to be safe we stopped stealing so much. But they did get the Sheik, though. One day an inspector got on in the mountains just outside of Whitefish and grabbed him right out of that linen closet. The Sheik had been smoking in there all day and he was high and laughing when they pulled him off the train.

That was the year we got in the Union. The crackers and Swedes finally let us in after we paid off. We really stopped stealing and got organized and there wasn't a damn thing the company could do about it, although it tried like hell to buy us out. And to get back at us, they put their heads together and began to make up that big book of rules you keep your finger in. Still, *we* knew the service and they had to write the book the way we gave the service and at first there was nothing for the Old School men to learn. We got seniority through the Union, and as long as we gave the service and didn't steal, they couldn't touch us. So they began changing the rules, and sending us notes about the service. Little changes at first, like how the initials on the doily should always face the customer, and how the silver should be taken off the tables between meals. But we were getting old and set in our old service, and it got harder and harder learning all those little changes. And we had to learn new stuff all the time because there was no telling when an inspector would get on and catch us giving bad service. It was hard as hell. It was hard because we knew that the company was out to

---

3. Spies or detectives, especially those hired by a company to keep watch on employees.

break up the Old School. The Sheik was gone, and we knew that Reverend Hendricks or Uncle T. or Danny Jackson would go soon because they stood for the Old School, just like the Sheik. But what bothered us most was knowing that they would go for Doc first, before anyone else, because he loved the road so much.

Doc was over sixty-five then and had taken to drinking hard when we were off. But he never touched a drop when we were on the road. I used to wonder whether he drank because being a Waiter's Waiter was getting hard or because he had to do something until his next trip. I could never figure it. When we had our layovers he would spend all his time in Andy's, setting up the house. He had no wife, no relatives, not even a hobby. He just drank. Pretty soon the slicksters at Andy's got to using him for a good thing. They commenced putting the touch on him because they saw he was getting old and knew he didn't have far to go, and they would never have to pay him back. Those of us who were close to him tried to pull his coat, but it didn't help. He didn't talk about himself much, he didn't talk much about anything that wasn't related to the road; but when I tried to hip him once about the hustlers and how they were closing in on him, he just took another shot and said:

"I don't need no money. Nobody's jiving me. I'm jiving them. You know I can still pull in a hundred in tips in one trip. I *know* this business."

"Yeah, I know, Doc," I said. "But how many more trips can you make before you have to stop?"

"I ain't never gonna stop. Trips are all I know and I'll be making them as long as these trains haul people."

"That's just it," I said. "They don't *want* to haul people any more. The planes do that. The big roads want freight now. Look how they hired youngbloods just for the busy seasons just so they won't get any seniority in the winter. Look how all the Old School waiters are dropping out. They got the Sheik, Percy Fields just lucked up and died before they got to *him*, they almost got Reverend Hendricks. Even *Uncle T.* is going to retire! And they'll get us too."

"Not me," said Doc. "I know my moves. This old fox can still dance with a tray and handle four tables at the same time. I can still bait a queer and make the old ladies tip big. There's no waiter better than me and I know it."

"Sure, Doc," I said. "I know it too. But please save your money. Don't be a dummy. There'll come a day when you just can't get up to go out and they'll put you on the ground for good."

Doc looked at me like he had been shot. "Who taught you the moves when you were just a raggedy-ass waiter?"

"You did, Doc," I said.

"Who's always the first man down in the yard at train-time?" He threw down another shot. "Who's there sitting in the car every tenth morning while you other old heads are still at home pulling on your longjohns?"

I couldn't say anything. He was right and we both knew it.

"I have to go out," he told me. "Going out is my whole life, I wait for that tenth morning. I ain't never missed a trip and I don't mean to."

What could I say to him, youngblood? What can I say to you? He had to go out, not for the money; it was in his blood. You have to go out too, but it's for the money you go. You hate going out and you love coming in. He loved going out and he hated coming in. Would *you* listen if I told you to stop spending your money on pussy in Chicago? Would he listen if I told him to save *his* money? To stop setting up the bar at Andy's? No. Old men are just as bad as young men when it comes to money. They can't think. They always try to buy what they should have for free. And what they buy, after they have it, is nothing.

They called Doc into the Commissary and the doctors told him he had lumbago[4] and a bad heart and was weak from drinking too much, and they wanted him to get down for his own good. He wouldn't do it. Tesdale, the General Superintendent, called him in and told him that he had enough years in the service to pull down a big pension and that the company would pay for a retirement party for him, since he was the oldest waiter working, and invite all the Old School waiters to see him off, if he would come down. Doc said no. He knew that the Union had to back him. He knew that he could ride as long as he made the trains on time and as long as he knew the service. And he knew that he could not leave the road.

The company called in its lawyers to go over the Union contract. I wasn't there, but Len Dickey was in on the meeting because of his office in the Union. He told me about it later. Those fat company lawyers took the contract apart and went through all their books. They took the seniority clause apart word by word, trying to figure a way to get at Doc. But they had written it airtight back in the days when the company *needed* waiters, and there was nothing in it about compulsory retirement. Not a word. The paddies in the Union must have figured that waiters didn't *need* a new contract when they let us in, and they had let us come in under the old one thinking that all waiters would die on the job, or drink themselves to death when they were still young, or die from buying too much pussy, or just quit when they had put in enough time to draw a pension. But *nothing* in the whole contract could help them get rid of Doc Craft. They were sweating, they were working so hard. And all the time Tesdale, the General Superintendent, was calling them sons-of-bitches for not earning their money. But there was nothing the company lawyers could do but turn the pages of their big books and sweat and promise Tesdale that they would find some way if he gave them more time.

The word went out from the Commissary: "Get Doc." The stewards got it from the assistant superintendents: "Get Doc." Since they could not get him to retire, they were determined to catch him giving bad service. He had more seniority than most other waiters, so they couldn't bump him off our crew. In fact, all the waiters with more seniority than Doc were on the crew with him. There were four of us from the Old School: me, Doc, Uncle T. Boone, and Danny Jackson. Reverend Hendricks wasn't running regular any more; he was spending all his Sundays preaching in his Church on the South Side because he knew what was coming and wanted to have something steady going for him in Chicago when his time came. Fifth and sixth men on that crew were two hardheads who had read the

_____

4. Rheumatism of the lower back.

book. The steward was Crouse, and he really didn't want to put the screws to Doc but he couldn't help himself. Everybody wants to work. So Crouse started in to riding Doc, sometimes about moving too fast, sometimes about not moving fast enough. I was on the crew, I saw it all. Crouse would seat four singles at the same table, on Doc's station, and Doc had to take care of all four different orders at the same time. He was seventy-three, but that didn't stop him, knowing this business the way he did. It just slowed him down some. But Crouse got on him even for that and would chew him out in front of the passengers, hoping that he'd start cursing and bother the passengers so that they would complain to the company. It never worked, though. Doc just played it cool. He'd look into Crouse's eyes and know what was going on. And then he'd lay on his good service, the only service he knew, and the passengers would see how good he was with all that age on his back and they would get mad at the steward, and leave Doc a bigger tip when they left.

The Commissary sent out spotters to catch him giving bad service. These were pale-white little men in glasses who never looked you in the eye, but who always felt the plate to see if it was warm. And there were the old maids, who like that kind of work, who would order shrimp or crabmeat cocktails or celery and olive plates because they knew how the rules said these things had to be made. And when they came, when Doc brought them out, they would look to see if the oyster fork was stuck into the thing, and look out the window a long time.

"Ain't no use trying to fight it," Uncle T. Boone told Doc in the crew car one night, "the black waiter is *doomed*. Look at all the good restaurants, the class restaurants in Chicago. *You* can't work in them. Them white waiters got those jobs sewed up fine."

"I can be a waiter anywhere," says Doc. "I know the business and I like it and I can do it anywhere."

"The black waiter is doomed," Uncle T. says again. "The whites is taking over the service in the good places. And when they run you off of here, you won't have no place to go."

"They won't run me off of here," says Doc. "As long as I give the right service they can't touch me."

"You're a goddamn *fool!*" says Uncle T. "You're a nigger and you ain't got no right except what the Union says you have. And that ain't worth a damn because when the Commissary finally gets you, those niggers won't lift a finger to help you."

"Leave off him," I say to Boone. "If anybody ought to be put off it's you. You ain't had your back straight for thirty years. You even make the crackers sick the way you keep bowing and folding your hands and saying, 'Thank you, Mr. Boss.' Fifty years ago that would of got you a bigger tip," I say, "but now it ain't worth a shit. And every time you do it the crackers hate you. And every time I see you serving with that skullcap on I hate you. The Union said we didn't have to wear them *eighteen years ago!* Why can't you take it off?"

Boone just sat on his bunk with his skullcap in his lap, leaning against his big belly. He knew I was telling the truth and he knew he wouldn't change. But he said: "That's the trouble with the Negro waiter today. He ain't got no humility. And as long as he don't have humility, he keeps losing the good jobs."

Doc had climbed into the first waiter's bunk in his longjohns and I got in the second waiter's bunk under him and lay there. I could hear him breathing. It had a hard sound. He wasn't well and all of us knew it.

"Doc?" I said in the dark.

"Yeah?"

"Don't mind Boone, Doc. He's a dead man. He just don't know it."

"We all are," Doc said.

"Not you," I said.

"What's the use? He's right. They'll get me in the end."

"But they ain't done it yet."

"They'll get me. And they know it and I know it. I can even see it in old Crouse's eyes. He knows they're gonna get me."

"Why don't you get a woman?"

He was quiet. "What can I do with a woman now, that I ain't already done too much?"

I thought for a while. "If you're on the ground, being with one might not make it so bad."

"I hate women," he said.

"You ever try fishing?"

"No."

"You want to?"

"No," he said.

"You can't keep *drinking*."

He did not answer.

"Maybe you could work in town. In the Commissary."

I could hear the big wheels rolling and clicking along the tracks and I knew by the smooth way we were moving that we were almost out of the Dakota flatlands. Doc wasn't talking. "Would you like that?" I thought he was asleep. "Doc, would you like that?"

"Hell no," he said.

"You have to try *something!*"

He was quiet again. "I know," he finally said.

III

Jerry Ewald, the Unexpected Inspector, got on in Winachee that next day after lunch and we knew that he had the word from the Commissary. He was cool about it: he laughed with the steward and the waiters about the old days and his hard gray eyes and shining glasses kept looking over our faces as if to see if we knew why he had got on. The two hardheads were in the crew car stealing a nap on company time. Jerry noticed this and could have caught them, but he was after bigger game. We all knew that, and we kept talking to him about the days of the big trains and looking at his white hair and not into the eyes behind his glasses because we knew what was there. Jerry sat down on the first waiter's station and said to Crouse: "Now I'll have some lunch. Steward, let the headwaiter bring me a menu."

Crouse stood next to the table where Jerry sat, and looked at Doc, who had been waiting between the tables with his tray under his arm. The way the rules say. Crouse looked sad because he knew what was coming. Then Jerry looked directly at Doc and said: "Headwaiter Doctor Craft, bring me a menu."

Doc said nothing and he did not smile. He brought the menu. Danny Jackson and I moved back into the hall to watch. There was nothing we could do to help Doc and we knew it. He was the Waiter's Waiter, out there by himself, hustling the biggest tip he would ever get in his life. Or losing it.

"Goddamn," Danny said to me. "Now let's sit on the ground and talk about how *kings* are gonna get fucked."

"Maybe not," I said. But I did not believe it myself because Jerry is the kind of man who lies in bed all night, scheming. I knew he had a plan.

Doc passed us on his way to the kitchen for water and I wanted to say something to him. But what was the use? He brought the water to Jerry. Jerry looked him in the eye. "Now, Headwaiter," he said. "I'll have a bowl of onion soup, a cold roast beef sandwich on white, rare, and a glass of iced tea."

"Write it down," said Doc. He was playing it right. He knew that the new rules had stopped waiters from taking verbal orders.

"Don't be so professional, Doc," Jerry said. "It's me, one of the *boys.*"

"You have to write it out," said Doc, "it's in the black book."

Jerry clicked his pen and wrote the order out on the check. And handed it to Doc. Uncle T. followed Doc back into the Pantry.

"He's gonna get you, Doc," Uncle T. said. "I knew it all along. You know why? The Negro waiter ain't got no more humility."

"Shut the fuck up, Boone!" I told him.

"You'll see," Boone went on. "You'll see I'm right. There ain't a thing Doc can do about it, either. We're gonna lose all the good jobs."

We watched Jerry at the table. He saw us watching and smiled with his gray eyes. Then he poured some of the water from the glass on the linen cloth and picked up the silver sugar bowl and placed it right on the wet spot. Doc was still in the Pantry. Jerry turned the silver sugar bowl around and around on the linen. He pressed down on it some as he turned. But when he picked it up again, there was no dark ring on the wet cloth. We had polished the silver early that morning, according to the book, and there was not a dirty piece of silver to be found in the whole car. Jerry was drinking the rest of the water when Doc brought out the polished silver soup tureen, underlined with a doily and a breakfast plate, with a shining soup bowl underlined with a doily and a breakfast plate, and a bread-and-butter plate with six crackers; not four or five or seven, but six, the number the Commissary had written in the black book. He swung down the aisle of the car between the two rows of white tables and you could not help but be proud of the way he moved with the roll of the train and the way that tray was like a part of his arm. It was good service. He placed everything neat, with all company initials showing, right where things should go.

"Shall I serve up the soup?" he asked Jerry.

"Please," said Jerry.

Doc handled that silver soup ladle like one of those Chicago Jew tailors handles a needle. He ladled up three good-sized spoonfuls from the tureen and then laid the wet spoon on an extra bread-and-butter plate on the side of the table, so he would not stain the cloth. Then he put a napkin over the wet spot Jerry had made and changed the ashtray for a prayer-card because every good waiter knows that nobody wants to eat a good meal looking at an ashtray.

"You know about the spoon plate, I see," Jerry said to Doc.

"I'm a waiter," said Doc. "I know."

"You're a damn good waiter," said Jerry.

Doc looked Jerry square in the eye. "I know," he said slowly.

Jerry ate a little of the soup and opened all six of the cracker packages. Then he stopped eating and began to look out the window. We were passing through his territory, Washington State, the country he loved because he was the only company inspector in the state and knew that once he got through Montana he would be the only man the waiters feared. He smiled and then waved for Doc to bring out the roast beef sandwich.

But Doc was into his service now and cleared the table completely. Then he got the silver crumb knife from the Pantry and gathered all the cracker crumbs, even the ones Jerry had managed to get in between the salt and pepper shakers.

"You want the tea with your sandwich, or later?" he asked Jerry.

"Now is fine," said Jerry, smiling.

"You're doing good," I said to Doc when he passed us on his way to the Pantry. "He can't touch you or nothing."

He did not say anything.

Uncle T. Boone looked at Doc like he wanted to say something too, but he just frowned and shuffled out to stand next to Jerry. You could see that Jerry hated him. But Jerry knew how to smile at everybody, and so he smiled at Uncle T. while Uncle T. bent over the table with his hands together like he was praying, and moved his head up and bowed it down.

Doc brought out the roast beef, proper service. The crock of mustard was on a breakfast plate, underlined with a doily, initials facing Jerry. The lid was on the mustard and it was clean, like it says in the book, and the little silver service spoon was clean and polished on a bread-and-butter plate. He set it down. And then he served the tea. You think you know the service, youngblood, all of you do. But you don't. Anybody can serve, but not everybody can become a part of the service. When Doc poured that pot of hot tea into that glass of crushed ice, it was like he was pouring it through his own fingers; it was like he and the tray and the pot and the glass and all of it was the same body. It was a beautiful move. It was fine service. The iced tea glass sat in a shell dish, and the iced tea spoon lay straight in front of Jerry. The lemon wedge Doc put in a shell dish half-full of crushed ice with an oyster fork stuck into its skin. Not in the meat, mind you, but squarely under the skin of that lemon, and the whole thing lay in a pretty curve on top of that crushed ice.

Doc stood back and waited. Jerry had been watching his service and was impressed. He mixed the sugar in his glass and sipped. Danny Jackson and I were down the aisle in the hall. Uncle T. stood behind Jerry, bending over, his arms folded, waiting. And Doc stood next to the table, his tray under his arm looking straight ahead and calm because he had given good service and knew it. Jerry sipped again.

"Good tea," he said. "Very good tea."

Doc was silent.

Jerry took the lemon wedge off the oyster fork and squeezed it into the glass, and stirred, and sipped again. "*Very* good," he said. Then he drained the glass. Doc reached over to pick it up for more ice but Jerry kept his hand on the glass. "Very good service, Doc," he said. "But you served the lemon wrong."

Everybody was quiet. Uncle T. folded his hands in the praying position. "How's that?" said Doc.

"The service was wrong," Jerry said. He was not smiling now.

"How could it be? I been giving that same service for years, right down to the crushed ice for the lemon wedge."

"That's just it, Doc," Jerry said. "The lemon wedge. You served it wrong."

"Yeah?" said Doc.

"Yes," said Jerry, his jaws tight. "Haven't you seen the new rule?"

Doc's face went loose. He knew now that they had got him.

"Haven't you *seen* it?" Jerry asked again.

Doc shook his head.

Jerry smiled that hard, gray smile of his, the kind of smile that says: "I have always been the boss and I am smiling this way because I know it and can afford to give you something." "Steward Crouse," he said. "Steward Crouse, go get the black bible for the headwaiter."

Crouse looked beaten too. He was sixty-three and waiting for his pension. He got the bible.

Jerry took it and turned directly to the very last page. He knew where to look. "Now, Headwaiter," he said, "*listen* to this." And he read aloud: "Memorandum Number 22416. From: Douglass A. Tesdale, General Superintendent of Dining Cars. To: Waiters, Stewards, Chefs of Dining Cars. Attention: As of 7/9/65 the proper service for iced tea will be (a) Fresh brewed tea in teapot, poured over crushed ice at table; iced tea glass set in shell dish (b) Additional ice to be immediately available upon request after first glass of tea (c) Fresh lemon wedge will be served on bread-and-butter plate, no doily, with times of oyster fork stuck into *meat* of lemon." Jerry paused.

"Now you know, Headwaiter," he said.

"Yeah," said Doc.

"But why didn't you know before?"

No answer.

"This notice came out last week."

"I didn't check the book yet," said Doc.

"But that's a rule. Always check the book before each trip. *You* know that, Headwaiter."

"Yeah," said Doc.

"Then that's *two* rules you missed."

Doc was quiet.

"Two rules you didn't read," Jerry said. "You're slowing down, Doc."

"I know," Doc mumbled.

"You want some time off to rest?"

Again Doc said nothing.

"I think you need some time on the ground to rest up, don't you?"

Doc put his tray on the table and sat down in the seat across from Jerry. This was the first time we had ever seen a waiter sit down with a customer, even an inspector. Uncle T., behind Jerry's back, began waving his hands, trying to tell Doc to get up. Doc did not look at him.

"You *are* tired, aren't you?" said Jerry.

"I'm just resting my feet," Doc said.

"Get up, Headwaiter," Jerry said. "You'll have plenty of time to do that. I'm writing you up."

But Doc did not move and just continued to sit there. And all Danny and I could do was watch him from the back of the car. For the first time I saw that his hair was almost gone and his legs were skinny in the baggy white uniform. I don't think Jerry expected Doc to move. I don't think he really cared. But then Uncle T. moved around the table and stood next to Doc, trying to apologize for him to Jerry with his eyes and bowed head. Doc looked at Uncle T. and then got up and went back to the crew car. He left his tray on the table. It stayed there all that evening because none of us, not even Crouse or Jerry or Uncle T., would touch it. And Jerry didn't try to make any of us take it back to the Pantry. He understood at least that much. The steward closed down Doc's tables during dinner service, all three settings of it. And Jerry got off the train someplace along the way, quiet, like he had got on.

After closing down the car we went back to the crew quarters and Doc was lying on his bunk with his hands behind his head and his eyes open. He looked old. No one knew what to say until Boone went over to his bunk and said: "I feel bad for you, Doc, but all of us are gonna get it in the end. The railroad waiter is *doomed.*"

Doc did not even notice Boone.

"I could of told you about the lemon but he would of got you on something else. It wasn't no use. Any of it."

"Shut the fuck up, Boone!" Danny said. "The one thing that really hurts is that a crawling son-of-a-bitch like you will be riding when all the good men are gone. Dummies like you and these two hardheads will be working your asses off reading that damn bible and never know a goddamn thing about being a waiter. *That* hurts like a *motherfucker!*"

"It ain't my fault if the colored waiter is doomed," said Boone. "It's your fault for letting go your humility and letting the whites take over the good jobs."

Danny grabbed the skullcap off Boone's head and took it into the bathroom and flushed it down the toilet. In a minute it was half a mile away and soaked in old piss on the tracks. Boone did not try to fight, he just sat on his bunk and mumbled. He had other skullcaps. No one said anything to Doc, because that's the way real men show that they care. You don't talk. Talking makes it worse.

IV

What else is there to tell you, youngblood? They made him retire. He didn't try to fight it. He was beaten and he knew it; not by the service, but by a book. *That book*, that *bible* you keep your finger stuck in. That's not a good way for a man to go. He should die in the service. He should die doing the things he likes. But not by a book.

All of us Old School men will be beaten by it. Danny Jackson is gone now, and Reverend Hendricks put in for his pension and took up preaching, full-time. But Uncle T. Boone is still riding. They'll get *me* soon enough, with that book. But it will never get you because you'll never be a waiter, or at least a Waiter's Waiter. You read too much.

Doc got a good pension and he took it directly to Andy's. And none of the boys who knew about it knew how to refuse a drink on Doc. But none of us knew how to drink with him knowing that we would be going out again in a few days, and he was on the ground. So a lot of us, even the drunks and hustlers who usually hang around Andy's, avoided him whenever we could. There was nothing to talk about any more.

He died five months after he was put on the ground. He was seventy-three and it was winter. He froze to death wandering around the Chicago yards early one morning. He had been drunk, and was still steaming when the yard crew found him. Only the few of us left in the Old School know what he was doing there.

I am sixty-three now. And I haven't decided if I should take my pension when they ask me to go or continue to ride. I *want* to keep riding, but I know that if I do, Jerry Ewald or Harry Silk or Jack Tate will get me one of these days. I could get down if I wanted: I have a hobby and I am too old to get drunk by myself. I couldn't drink with you, youngblood. We have nothing to talk about. And after a while you would get mad at me for talking anyway, and keeping you from your pussy. You are tired already. I can see it in your eyes and in the way you play with the pages of your rule book.

I know it. And I wonder why I should keep talking to you when you could never see what I see or understand what I understand or know the real difference between my school and yours. I wonder why I have kept talking this long when all the time I have seen that you can hardly wait to hit the city to get off this thing and spend your money. You have a good story. But you will never remember it. Because all this time you have had pussy in your mind, and your fingers in the pages of that black bible.

1970

QUINCY TROUPE

b. 1943

Quincy Troupe was born in New York City. After attending Grambling College (now Grambling State University) in Louisiana, he moved to Los Angeles, where he earned a journalism degree and became a member of the Watts Writers' movement. In 1968, Troupe published the anthology *Watts Poets: A Book of New Poetry and Essays*; he later issued the impressive collection *Giant Talk: An Anthology of*

Third World Writings (1975) in conjunction with Rainer Schulte. Always a partisan of African American music, Troupe has over the years produced poems of rhythmic subtlety and shrewd vernacular insight. He has published two collections of poetry: *Embryo Poems, 1967–1971* and *Snake-Back Solos: Selected Poems, 1969–1977* (which won the American Book Award in 1980). Troupe has also worked as an editor for the periodicals *Shrewd* and *Confrontation: A Journal of Third World Literature and American Rag* and has taught creative writing and African American and third world literature at the University of California at Los Angeles, Ohio University, the University of California at Berkeley, the University of Ghana at Legion, and the City University of New York.

In Texas Grass

all along the rail
road tracks of texas
old train cars lay
rusted & overturned
like new african governments 5
long forgotten by the people
who built & rode them
till they couldn't run no more,
they remind me of old race horses
who ve been put out to pasture 10
amongst the weeds
rain sleet & snow
till they die, rot away
like photos fading
in grandma s picture book, 15
of old black men in mississippi / texas
who sit on dilapidated porches,
that fall away
like dead man s skin,

like white peoples eyes, 20
& on the peeling photos,
old men sit sad-eyed
waiting, waiting for
worm dust, thinking of
the master & his long forgotten 25
promise of 40 acres & a mule,[1]
& even now, if you pass across
this bleeding flesh ever-
changing landscape,
you will see the fruited 30
countryside, stretching, stretching,
old black men, & young black men,
sitting on porches
waiting, waiting for rusted
trains in texas grass 35

1975

---

1. After the Civil War, freed slaves were promised forty acres and a mule to help them start their new lives; generally, the promise was not kept.

Conversation Overheard

the way they saw it

for Earl Driver, my brother

most people in the world stumble
or drive around 24 hours everyday on a treadmill;
they never move forward one inch;
                their lives attempt
to scale the absurdities on television;   5
"no money down all we want is your life!"
says the commercial on the idiot tube
but my love asks me, why are these people walking
around believing that the television is the bible?
and how many of them that voted for   10
tricky dick nixon[1] ever seen / touched
his living / dead flesh, how many of them
know that agnew[2] has toejam between his toes
after he lies all day on t.v.?
selling suntan lotion with foul breath   15
thats supposed to make you
a tennis champion, or a golf pro,
or an ohjaysimpson selling chevrolet cars
and running backwards a hundred years
for a touch-back; orangejuicesimpson,   20
eye thought you said—in college—you wanted
to be a social worker and help underprivileged
children like yourself
                is that you on t.v. tryin'
to outrun a corvette on the salt-lake flats!?   25
in full football gear with a football
tucked under your brain / your fingers
tryin' to hold on to those "pretty little
green ones," is that you overjoyedsimpson!?
oh well, maybe you will become a movie star   30
and play sad cow / boys like big jim; a lover?
naw, they'll never let you play a lover, cause
they're grooming broadway joe namath[3] for that,
anyway, what are these people looking for
that stumble in place on the treadmill?   35
that kill themselves with five cadillacs—
while millions of people are starving—
in their ten car garages
with only two people—themselves—
in their family, who wear 25 diamond rings   40
on five stubby fingers
and have 1000 silk suits in their closets
along with 2000 pairs of alligator shoes

1. Richard Milhous Nixon (1913–1994), thirty-seventh president of the United States; resigned from office after the Watergate scandal.
2. Spiro Agnew (b. 1918), vice president under Nixon.
3. Football quarterback (b. 1943), one of the sport's first superstars. Jim Brown (line 31), black football superstar.

that come alive at night and eat up the soggy
brains of their owners, who have spacious   45
bookshelves with no books on those shelves
and flash hopalong cassidy[4] smiles
out the side of they mouths sayin;
"everything is everything, and
gimme-limme what cha got ta spare"   50
what is that growing in the test tube in washington
how much makeup does elizabeth taylor wear
how many corsets, how many facelifts has
zsa zsa gabor[5] had, who made up this standard
for beauty anyway? how many movies will linda   55
kasabian[6] make, how many books will she write?
how come they chained those beautiful black
panther ladies in los angeles and let mansons
tribe of women[7] walk into the courtroom unchained
how many newspapers did the l.a. times sell   60
for their shit / winning coverage
of angela davis[8]
who is that faggot with a snake for a face
who is that judge with his head blown off
why is his head blown off   65
who is that drunk with that time bomb
ticking in his pocket
why is that beautiful brother lying dead
in that shot up / bloody chicago deathroom
why hasn't the police shot up   70
the klu klux klan, the minutemen
the white citizens committee, the birch society[9]
what was the algiers motel and sharpsville[1] all about
who are the 600 families that rule the world
and play chess games of war with whole countries   75
why is the hour so late and filled with blood
murders, suicides, mad-dogs and com freaks,
why are these people dancing and singing on this
        treadmill!!??
oh well, eye guess these stupid motherfuckers
will be dancing and singing on this treadmill   80
for some millions of years to come,
what can a truth seeking poet like me do about it
but go down to the corner

4. Popular fictitious cowboy hero; a character in many 1930s films and a 1950s television series.
5. Taylor and Gabor are glamorous Hollywood stars.
6. A co-conspirator in the Charles Manson murders. In return for immunity, she became a witness for the prosecution and later starred in a film about Manson's trial.
7. A group of women who committed murder for Charles Manson. "Black panther ladies": women involved in the Black Panther Party who had been arrested.
8. Social activist of the 1960s (b. 1944) who was involved in the Student Nonviolent Coordinating Committee, the Black Panthers, and the Commu-

nist Party. A warrant for her arrest was issued in 1970 because her guns were used in a criminal act. Although she went underground, she was found and imprisoned. At her trial she was acquitted of all charges.
9. Organizations and societies that promote white supremacy, segregation, and/or right-wing politics.
1. A town in South Africa where in 1960 white police officers opened fire on individuals participating in a Pan-African Congress protest; seventy-two people were killed and two hundred were injured. "Algiers motel": during the 1967 Detroit riots, three black men were killed by sniper fire at the motel; the police involved in the incident were acquitted.

> suck in the freshness of some breeze then
> go home and make love to my woman   85

1975

Impressions / of Chicago; For Howlin' Wolf[1]

1

the wind / blade cutting in
& out swinging in over the lake
slicing white foam from the tips
of delicate fingers
that danced & weaved   5
under the sunken light / night;
this wind / blade was so sharp & cold
it'd cut a four-legged mosquito into fours
while a hungry lion slept on the wings of some chittlins[2]
slept within the blues of a poem that was forming   10

we came in the sulphuric night drinkin' old crow
while a buzzard licked its beak atop the head of richard nixon
while gluttonous daly[3] ate hundreds of pigs that were his ego
while daddy-o played bop on the box
came to the bituminous breath of chicago   15
howling with three million voices of pain

& this is the music;
the kids of chicago have eyes that are older
                 than the deepest pain in the world
& they run with feet bared over south / side streets   20
shimmering with a billion shivers of glass
razors that never seem to cut their feet;
they dance in & out of the traffic,
the friday night smells of fish
the scoobedoo sounds   25
of bo didely[4]

2

these streets belong to the dues payers
to the blues players drinkin whiskey on satdaynight
muddy waters & the wolfman howlin smokestack lightnin[5]
now many more years down in the bottom   30
no place to go moanin' for my baby
a spoonful of evil
back door man

---

1. Chester A. Burnett (1910–1976), Chicago blues musician of the 1950s who punctuated his singing by howling.
2. The small intestines of animals, usually pigs, which are added to soups, used as sausage casings, or fried in batter.
3. Richard Daley (1902–1976), long-time mayor of Chicago. Nixon (1913–1994), thirty-seventh president of the United States.
4. Blues and rock musician (b. 1928).
5. The title of one of Howlin' Wolf's albums. Waters (1915–1983), blues musician whose work influenced early rock and roll.

all night long how many more years
down in the bottom built for comfort

1975

CAROLYN M. RODGERS

b. 1945

One of the founders of the Third World Press, Carolyn Rodgers is a native of Chicago who received her B.A. degree from Roosevelt University. Her serious commitment to creative writing was an outgrowth of attendance at workshops in her native city conducted by the Organization of Black American Culture and by Gwendolyn Brooks. Rodgers has written: "I've been compared to Phillis Wheatley. But I like to think of myself as a female Langston Hughes and a quasi Zora N. Hurston. I'm probably not as good as either, but I have my aspirations."

Indeed, her aspirations for a vernacular poetical voice that reflects the language and activities of everyday life in African America are abundantly apparent in her first volumes of poetry *Paper Soul* (1968) and *Songs of a Black Bird* (1969), both published by Third World Press. Rodgers writes about overheard conversations, radio banalities, revolutionary pretensions, and the discords of black love. Her poems are full of wit, though her tone can rise to a fiercely revolutionary pitch. And she is not averse to employing obscenities if her subject—such as brutal white oppression of blacks in America—seems to deserve such language. Subsequent to her rise in the Black Arts movement, Rodgers turned to more personal and religious themes, recanting her more militant views in the volume *how i got ovah: New and Selected Poems* (1975).

Jesus Was Crucified

or, It Must be Deep (an epic pome)

i was sick
and my motha called me
tonight yeah, she did she
sd she was sorri
i was sick, but what   5
  she wanted tuh tell
me was that i shud pray or
have her (hunky) preacher
pray for me. she sd. i
had too much hate in me   10
she sd u know the way yuh think is
got a lots to do
wid the way u feel, and i
agreed, told her i WAS angry a lot THESE days
and maybe my insides was too and she sd   15
    why it's somethin wrong wid yo mind girl
that's what it is
            and i sd yes, i was aware a lot

lately and she sd if she had evah known educashun
woulda mad me crazi, she woulda neva sent me to   20
school (college that is)
she sd the way i worked my fingers to the bone in
this white mans factori to make u a de-cent some-
bodi and here u are actin not like decent folks
                talkin bout hatin white folks & revolution   25
& such and runnin round wid NegroEs
        WHO CURSE IN PUBLIC!!!! (she sd)
THEY COMMUNIST GIRL!!! DON'T YUH KNOW THAT???
    DON'T YUH READ*THE NEWSPAPERS?????
                            (and i sd)   30
i don't believe—(and she sd) U DON'T BELIEVE IN GOD
                    NO MO DO U?????
u wudn't raised that way! U gon die and go tuh HELL
and i sd i hoped it wudn't be NO HUNKIES there
and she sd   35
what do u mean, there is some good white people and some
bad ones, just like there is negroes
and i says i had neva seen ONE (wite good that is) but
she sd negroes ain't readi, i knows this and
deep in yo heart you do too and i sd yes u right   40
negroes ain't readi and she sd
why just the utha day i was in the store and there was
uh negro packin clerk put uh colored woman's ice cream
in her grocery bag widout wun of them "don't melt" bags
        and the colored ladi sd to the colored clerk   45
"how do u know mah ice cream ain't gon tuh melt befo I
git home."
            clerk sd. "i don't" and took the ice cream
            back out and put it in wun of them "stay hard"
            bags,   50
and me and that ladi sd see see, ne-groes don't treat
nobody right why that clerk packin groceries was un
grown main, acted mad, white folks wudn't treat yuh that
way. why when i went tuh the BANK the otha day to deposit some MONEY   55
this white man helped me fast and nice. u gon die girl
and go tuh hell if yuh hate white folks. i sd, me and
my friends could dig it . . . hell, that is
she sd du u pray? i sd sorta when i hear Coltrane[1] and
she sd if yuh read yuh bible it'll show u read genesis   60
revelation and she couldn't remember the otha chapter
i should read but she sd what was in the Bible was
happnin now, fire & all and she sd just cause i didn't
        believe the bible don't make it not true
                    (and i sd)   65
    just cause she believed the bible didn't make it true
and she sd it is it is and deep deep down
in yo heart u know it's true
                    (and i sd)

---

1. Avant-garde jazz saxophonist (1926–1967).

it must be d   70
       eeeep
she sd i mon pray fuh u tuh be saved. i sd thank yuh.
    but befo she hung up my motha sd
    well girl, if yuh need me call me
i hope we don't have to straighten the truth out no mo.   75
i sd i hoped we didn't too
            (it was 10 P.M. when she called)
she sd, i got tuh go so i can git up early tomorrow
and go tuh the social security board to clarify my
record cause i need my money.   80
work hard for 30 yrs. and they don't want tuh give me
$28.00 once every two weeks.
       i sd yeah . . .
don't let em nail u wid no technicalities
    git yo checks . . . (then i sd)   85

    catch yuh later on jesus, i mean motha!

       it must be
              deeeeep . . .
                            1969

It Is Deep

(don't never forget the bridge
that you crossed over on)

Having tried to use the
witch cord
that erases the stretch of
thirty-three blocks
and tuning in the voice which   5
    woodenly stated that the
    talk box was "disconnected"

My mother, religiously girdled in
her god, slipped on some love, and
laid on my bell like a truck,   10
blew through my door warm wind from the south
concern making her gruff and tight-lipped
    and scared
that her "baby" was starving.
she, having learned, that disconnection results from   15
             non-payment of bill (s).

She did not
recognize the poster of the
grand le-roi [1] (al) cat on the wall
had never even seen the book of   20

1. LeRoi Jones, who changed his name to Amiri Baraka.

Black poems that I have written
thinks that I am under the influence of
                communists
when I talk about Black as anything
other than something ugly to kill it befo it grows   25
        in any impression she would not be
considered "relevant" or "Black"
                                but
there she was, standing in my room
not loudly condemning that day and   30
not remembering that I grew hearing her
curse the factory where she "cut uh slave"
and the cheap j-boss[2] wouldn't allow a union,
not remembering that I heard the tears when
they told her a high school diploma was not enough,   35
and here now, not able to understand, what she had
been forced to deny, still—

she pushed into my kitchen so
she could open my refrigerator to see
what I had to eat, and pressed fifty   40
bills in my hand saying "pay the talk bill and buy
some food; you got folks who care about you . . ."

My mother, religious-negro, proud of
having waded through a storm, is very obviously,
a sturdy Black bridge that I   45
crossed over, on.

                                                        1969

For Sistuhs Wearin' Straight Hair

    me?
    i never could keep my edges and kitchen
    straight
    even after
    supercool / straighterPerm had burned   5
    whiteness onto my scalp
    my edges and kitchen didn't
    ever get the message that they
    was not supposed to go back home.
    oh yeah. edges and kitchens   10
    will tell that they know where
    they nat'chal home is at!

                                                        1969

2. I.e., Jewish boss.

Literature since 1970

LOOKING BACK: INFLUENCES OF THE 1960s

One cannot provide an overview of African American literature of the 1970s and 1980s without first looking back at the preceding decades. Out of the 1950s civil rights movement and the 1960s Black Power movement, racism in the United States had emerged as a major political and social issue. Liberation movements in African nations such as Nigeria and Kenya as well as the Vietnam War raised the consciousness of many African Americans about the relationship between imperialism, colonialism, and racism. The Black Arts movement, the cultural arm of the Black Power movement, not only recuperated writers such as Frantz Fanon and Richard Wright but also emphasized black folk forms as bases for art. African American culture could thus be looked to as a legitimate culture with its own ideas, forms, and styles rather than as a pathology or a derivation of European American culture. As African American writers of the 1960s increasingly saw blacks rather than whites as their primary audience, they began to explore with a new intensity their own culture, history, and communities.

Yet despite all this collective exploration, the 1960s was not a monolithic period in African American literary history. Though the most visible writings were cultural nationalist in tone, several major writers of the sixties such as Ishmael Reed and Adrienne Kennedy questioned the Black Arts movement's tendency to ascribe to all blacks the same backgrounds, desires, and goals. Women writers such as June Jordan challenged the cultural nationalists' painting of blackness almost entirely in male terms. Southern writers such as Tom Dent and Alice Walker questioned the Black Arts movement's assumption that the urban Northeast was the only place where "real" black people lived. Homosexual writers such as Audre Lorde protested the ways in which lesbians and gays fell outside the cultural nationalist definition of "blackness." Immigrant writers such as Paule Marshall reminded readers that U.S. African American culture was not the only black culture, and the experiences both of travelers to newly liberated African and Caribbean nations and of immigrants from those countries to the United States made it increasingly clear that the concept of blackness was neither simple nor fixed. In effect, the cultural nationalist emphasis on a single blackness led to one of the most important and inspirational questions of black literary production in the contemporary period: What, in fact, does "blackness" mean?

In essence, there was no sharp delineation between the 1960s and 1970s, either politically or culturally. True, by the early seventies, the tone of U.S. political life began to change as the Vietnam War wound down and the antiwar movements disbanded. Exhausted from "the decade for death," as Alice Walker characterized the 1960s in *Meridian* (1976), the major black movements of the 1960s shifted gears in the 1970s, becoming more local and less national. Nonetheless, black uprisings such as the Attica Prison revolt (1971) continued into the seventies. Likewise, black "events" such as the celebrated trial of Angela Davis, the African American communist revolutionary accused of taking part in an attempted courtroom escape in which four people were killed, took place in 1971–72. And in the community too, black voices continued to demand a hearing in the decades following the 1960s, the most dramatic examples being the 1980 Miami uprising in response to police brutality and the 1993 South Central Los Angeles reaction to the Rodney King hearings.

As important, the civil rights movement and the antiwar effort helped to generate other major movements in the early 1970s. Especially in the western United States, other peoples of color—Asian Americans, Chicanos, Native Americans—sought equality through their own nationalist endeavors and helped to forge the rising debates about multiculturalism. In addition, the contemporary women's movement, ignited a decade before by such manifestos as Betty Friedan's *The Feminine Mystique* (1963), gained center stage in the politics of the United States, especially in relation to reproductive rights and sexual violence.

Among the most important pieces of legislation of the 1960s was the Civil Rights Act of 1964, which, while it profoundly affected class formations in African American communities, did so often unpredictably. Though its ban on discrimination because of a person's race, color, national origin, religion, or sex opened up the racialized society of the United States, one of the most significant effects in the 1970s and 1980s was the increasing separation of middle-class professional blacks from working-class African Americans, a subject that would be a central issue in African American writing of the time. More and more, middle-class blacks lived in different communities and went to different schools, churches, and the like from working class and poor blacks. Still, the Civil Rights Act and the black power movement's demands for black studies paved the way for a small number of African Americans to enter historically white universities such as Harvard, Cornell, Princeton, Yale, the University of California, and Columbia. That movement into the universities was extremely important. Until this point, few African American writers had received critical attention in mainstream institutions. Now blacks themselves developed African American studies programs and concentrated on scholarship related directly to African Americans. Without doubt, the presence of African Americans in the academy, both as teachers and as students, would change the study of American literature.

Critical trends that distinguished the 1960s from the 1970s are (1) the remapping of African American cultural and social history, much of which had been neglected, distorted, or hidden; (2) the exploration of African American folk forms; (3) the attention to African American women as writers both creative and scholarly, an attention demanded by their presence in every literary genre; (4) the acknowledgment of the multiplicity of African American identities; and (5) the increased participation of African Americans in framing the study of American literature.

MOVING FORWARD: EXCAVATING THE PAST

The excavation of black history and literature from the perspective of African Americans resulted in scholarship that laid the bases for important literary works. In the early seventies, historical studies such as John Blassingame's *The Slave Community: Plantation Life in the Ante-Bellum South* (1972) and Gerda Lerner's *Black Women in White America* (1973) revised the understanding of blacks' roles in American history. Literary anthologies such as Houston Baker's *Black Literature in America* (1971) and Mary Helen Washington's *Black-Eyed Susans: Classic Stories by and about Black Women* (1975) pointed to the long-neglected traditions of black literatures. Not surprisingly, creative writers were central to this excavation. Ernest Gaines's folk autobiography *The Autobiography of Miss Jane Pittman* (1971), which was made into a TV movie in 1973, and Alex Haley's *Roots* (1976), which became an unprecedentedly popular TV miniseries, highlighted the importance of understanding slavery and made a case for the study of the "peculiar institution" in America's schools. In *In Search of Our Mothers' Gardens* (1974), Alice Walker reclaimed the legacy of southern black women by focusing on their art forms, such as quilting, gardening, and storytelling; at the same time, she suggested a new approach to the writings of Phillis Wheatley, the celebrated eighteenth-century African American poet. Walker also helped to revive the reputation of Harlem Renaissance writer Zora Neale Hurston, an effort that led to the republication and valorization of Hurston's works. And Toni Morrison helped guide to publication *The Black Book* (1971), a scrapbook of African American history that included such folk forms as recipes as well as the coverage of historical events.

Such writing, of course, did more than merely excavate the history of blacks in America. While earlier writers, white and black, had dismissed slavery as shameful, African American writers of the contemporary period focused on the slave era as a way of understanding the present. Notable examples are Gaines's *Autobiography of Miss Jane Pittman*, Gayle Jones's *Corregidora* (1975), Charles Johnson's *Oxherding Tale* (1982) and *Middle Passage* (1989), Toni Morrison's *Song of Solomon* (1977) and *Beloved* (1987), Sherley Anne Williams's *Dessa Rose* (1986), and Gloria Naylor's *Mama Day* (1988) as well as the poetry in Jay Wright's *Death as History* (1967) and Rita Dove's *Thomas and Beulah* (1986). Slavery was no longer seen as something that African Americans wanted to forget. Nor was it only one story. Past literatures concentrated on plantation slavery, although that was not the primary form of slavery in the United States. Morrison focused on a small Kentucky farm in *Beloved*, while Williams in *Dessa Rose* told the story of the trek west taken by some slaves to gain freedom. In *Oxherding Tale* and *Middle Passage*, Johnson explored within the context of slavery the Enlightenment ideas of freedom and citizenship. In addition to these new books, many nineteenth-century texts were reissued, for example, the slave narratives and novels of William Wells Brown and the poetry, fiction, and essays of Frances Harper. As well, the focus on history as a means of understanding the present would result in Orlando Patterson's *Slavery and Social Death* (1982) and Paul Gilroy's *The Black Atlantic* (1993), in which slavery was studied not only as a unique experience of African Americans but also as a central component of the development of modernity in the West.

It is important to note that African American writers of the 1970s and 1980s did not produce traditionally linear historical novels such as Margaret Walker's *Jubilee* (1966); rather, their novels, poems, plays, and essays remapped the past and sought in it that which would give meaning to the present. As critic Wilhemina Lubiano points out, Toni Morrison's opus, from *The Bluest Eye* (1970) to *Jazz* (1992), "remaps the terrain of African American cultural and social history and allows for a community of the imagination . . . which interrupts the ideology that produces the kind of world we inhabit." That remapping is also true of Alice Walker's novels, even as she extends that terrain in her last three works to Africa. Ishmael Reed's *Mumbo Jumbo* (1972) and *Flight to Canada* (1976) are not only satirical treatments of the present but also revisions of the great black texts on slavery. David Bradley's *The Chaneysville Incident* (1981) relates the present condition of African Americans to an understanding of their past in a small town, while Paule Marshall's *The Chosen Place, the Timeless People* (1969) and *Praisesong for the Widow* (1983) map connections between the African past and the New World. Dramatist August Wilson's cycle of plays explores a central issue facing African Americans in each decade of the twentieth century, thus remembering and revising that history, while his fellow Pittsburgh writer John Wideman's *Homewood Trilogy* (1981–83) revolves around the descendants of Sybila Owens, his great-great-great-grandmother, who escaped slavery and in the 1850s settled in Homewood, the black section of Pittsburgh.

AFRICAN INFLUENCES

Another return to the past was seen in the influence of Africa on the works of many contemporary writers. Though few texts are actually situated in Africa (Walker's Africa section in *The Color Purple, The Temple of My Familiar,* and *Possessing the Secret of Joy* and Johnson's *Middle Passage* being exceptions), such novels as Morrison's *Beloved,* Gloria Naylor's *Mama Day,* Paule Marshall's *The Chosen Place, the Timeless People,* Ntozake Shange's *Sassafrass, Cypress and Indigo,* Ishmael Reed's *Mumbo Jumbo,* and Audre Lorde's and Jay Wright's poetry incorporate African belief systems and rituals still central to African American life. Contemporary writers also pointed to the significant role current African writers played in their own compositions. Alice Walker notes in an early interview that Okop'ptek's *Song of Lowino* is her favorite modern poem and that she has been influenced by Elechi Amadi's *The Concubine* as well as by Camera Laye, Ayi Kwei Armah, and Bessie Head. Also influential have been Chinua Achebe, Ngugi wa Thiong'o, Sembene Ousmane, Flora Nwapa, Buchi Emecheta, Ama Ata Aidoo, and Wole Soyinka, the first African writer to receive the Nobel Prize for literature.

Many contemporary African American writers have preserved and drawn on a sense of distinctive African American cosmologies and mythologies. Central to the works of the 1970s and 1980s is the significance of the ancestor. Morrison's evocation in *Beloved* of the importance of "rememory" in the construction of a people (which includes both the living and those who have "passed on"), Alice Walker's recuperation of her ancestors in *The Color Purple,* Gloria Naylor's characterization of Mama Day in the novel of that name, John Wideman's use of dream time as a continuum rather than a segmentation of time—all are fictional representations of spiritual/cultural rituals.

USING BLACK CULTURE

Language

As well as increased attention to the importance of Africa, black writers began paying more heed to controversial issues of language and social identity. In her poetry, her novel *His Own Where* (1970), written entirely in black English, and in essays such as *White English/Black English* (1972) and *Nobody Mean More to Me Than You and the Future Life of Willie Jordan* (1985), June Jordan analyzed the relationships between power and black languages. In her Pulitzer Prize–winning *The Color Purple* (1982), Alice Walker demonstrated the rich potential of black English that her literary ancestory Zora Neale Hurston had sought to preserve. Walker's novel would help to galvanize scholarly interest in black English not as a deficient form of standard English but as a language in its own right. That focus would greatly influence the study of Caribbean literatures and of the creolizations that New World blacks have forged. Such use of language had been forecast in Paule Marshall's *Brown Girl, Brownstones* (1959) as well as in the poetry of Jamaica's premier poet Louise Bennett. By the 1990s scholarly studies as well as college courses would focus on "nation languages" in their own right, and African Caribbean writers such as Derek Walcott, Jamaica Kincaid, Michelle Cliff, and Opal Palmer Adisa would become important in the African American literary canon.

As was true of earlier writers, contemporary poets and novelists continued to use African American musical forms as the bases of their work. Playwright August Wilson and poet, novelist, and playwright Sherley Anne Williams drew on the healing power of the blues for their exploration of black cultural forms. Poets Michael Harper and Quincy Troupe consistently used the structures of jazz as the bases of their complex poems, while Al Young wrote many lyrical musical memoirs. Novel-

son and poet, novelist, and playwright Sherley Anne Williams drew on the healing power of the blues for their exploration of black cultural forms. Poets Michael Harper and Quincy Troupe consistently used the structures of jazz as the bases of their complex poems, while Al Young wrote many lyrical musical memoirs. Novelist Gloria Naylor employed the formal qualities of a jazz suite for her fourth novel, *Bailey's Cafe* (1992), while the very title of Toni Morrison's most recent novel, *Jazz*, points to the layered rhythms of freedom and improvisation crucial to its composition. And like 1960s poets who used rhythm 'n' blues as the basis for their forms, young poets in the 1980s and 1990s have drawn on the rhythms of rap music.

The Oral Tradition

Early-twentieth-century African American writers such as Zora Neale Hurston, Sterling Brown, and Langston Hughes had drawn on the black oral tradition for inspiration. In the 1970s, writers intensified the focus on what began to be called the "vernacular." Toni Cade Bambara used the black traditions of oral storytelling, what she calls the "kitchen tradition," in her stories. In one particularly interesting formulation, Toni Morrison pointed out that making black literature was not just a matter of dropping the "g's" but rather the linguistic embodying of particular values. Some of her prose contains gaps—actual spaces between words—which invite reader participation in much the same way a black preacher's pauses allow his congregation to respond. Increasingly, writers use the call/response patterns so central to the vernacular and have invented what Morrison calls "unorthodox novelistic techniques" such as the chorus to elicit group participation. Public acceptance of black cultural forms has been dramatic. For example, Jesse Jackson's speech at the 1988 Democratic convention not only used the call/response patterns of the oral tradition, but also drew on the image of the quilt as a metaphor for a complex, connected fabric of cultural constructs.

A central trope of the oral tradition is that of signifying, what Henry Louis Gates Jr. defines as "repetition and revision, or repetition with a signal difference," a quality as well of jazz. That quality is, of course, not new in African American literature, as the works of Zora Neale Hurston so aptly demonstrate. In the 1970s and 1980s, however, writers self-consciously played with language in their texts. Ishmael Reed's *Mumbo Jumbo* is itself a search for an apparent contradiction, "The Talking Book." Reed's double entendres are complex signifying; they play with language at the crux of the black oral *and* literary traditions. As Gates demonstrates in his critical study *The Signifying Monkey* (1988), black texts "talk" to other black texts and the art of signifying is simultaneously oral and literary. Such "talking back" has certainly increased because black writers now have access to their literary predecessors. Walker's *The Color Purple* speaks back to Hurston's *Their Eyes Were Watching God*. Naylor, who was able to study African American literature in a way that writers of the 1930s and 1940s could not, tells us that reading Morrison's *The Bluest Eye* in college gave her the authority to enter the forbidden terrain of prose. Naylor's second novel, *Linden Hills* (1985), is a tribute to her knowledge not only of Dante's *Inferno* but also of works by Hurston, Morrison, and Walker.

CONTEMPORARY AFRICAN AMERICAN WOMEN WRITERS

Another dramatic difference in literary production between the 1960s and the 1970s was the explosion of works by African American women novelists, as a result of the intersection of two movements—the black movement and the women's movement. Certainly, the increased visibility of African American women writers exemplifies the relationship between political movements and literary canons. Earlier women writers such as Jessie Fauset, Nella Larsen, Zora Neale Hurston, Ann

become literary artists; rather, it was that the cultural ethos was ready to accept them as writers who were engaging in the valid exploration of central social/political and literary issues.

Many African American women writers, such as June Jordan, Audre Lorde, and Alice Walker, had been major actors in both the civil rights and the women's movements. In the early 1970s, they began to explore the racism in the women's movement and the sexism in the black. The year 1970 was critical for African American women writers. In that year, Maya Angelou's autobiography *I Know Why the Caged Bird Sings* was published, and its success signaled the existence of a market for works by black women. The anthology *The Black Women* (1970), edited by Toni Cade (later Bambara), critiqued the predominantly male cultural nationalist movement and the predominantly white women's movement even as it gathered the points of view of many different contemporary African American women. That same year, Alice Walker, Toni Morrison, and June Jordan, women whose writings would become increasingly important, published their first novels, respectively, *The Third Life of Grange Copeland, The Bluest Eye,* and *His Own Where.* Set in different times and places—Morrison's featured a small midwestern town in the 1940s; Walker's spanned the first sixty years of the twentieth century in rural Georgia; Jordan's was set in contemporary New York City—these novels shifted the focus from that of a monolithic black community to that of specific black communities. In so doing, they refused all-encompassing definitions of the black community or the black man or the black woman and emphasized the concept of difference that would be so central to the literature and criticism of the seventies and the eighties.

These first novels also critique the 1960s in their concern with relationships between black women and men rather than with relations between blacks and whites or the black-white wars in northern cities so typical of the focus of black male writers from Richard Wright in the 1940s to LeRoi Jones in the 1960s. By concentrating on the relationships within black communities, these authors confirmed that it was to blacks that they were addressing their work. Rather than idealizing black communities, as so many writings of the 1960s had attempted to do, African American women writers of the 1970s articulated the complexities of African American culture and history; at the same time, they demonstrated how black communities had also deeply internalized racist stereotypes that radically affected their definitions for and expectations of women and men.

In exploring gender issues, these writers also introduced new themes into African American literature, such as motherhood, mother/daughter relationships, women's friendships, and the relationship between sexuality and spirituality in African American cosmologies. In *Sula,* her second novel, Morrison's central character tests the conventional definition of good and evil in relation to women by insisting that she exists primarily as and for herself—not to be a mother or to be the lover of men. While Morrison worked with the idea that "black women have always been both the harbor and the ship," Walker, in her second novel, *Meridian,* explored the relationship of motherhood to revolution and wondered whether the nurturing and protecting qualities of motherhood might in fact be necessary qualities for a revolutionary. Unlike many white women writers of this period, African American women writers related the personal issues of their communities to global political issues. In effect, they insisted that personal and political issues could not be separated into exclusive categories.

One genre that clearly demonstrated the relationship between the personal and the political was writing for children. Contemporary African American women writers both resisted restrictive definitions of motherhood and insisted on the voices of black children in the literature they produced for this young audience. Celebrated poet Lucille Clifton has published more than sixteen books for children, many of them focusing on the adventures of Everett Anderson. Rosa Guy's trilogy for young adults focuses on two Harlem families and is unique in its exploration of the sexuality of black girls. Virginia Hamilton, the premier black woman writer of children's literature, has published fifteen books for children, including the celebrated *The Planet of Junior Brown* (1971) and *The People Could Fly* (1985), a children's version of the black folktale that some slaves could fly back to Africa, the basis of Toni Morrison's *Song of Solomon*. Joyce Carol Thomas has also written many children's and adolescents' books about life in Oklahoma and on the West Coast. Her *Gathering of Flowers: Stories about Being Young in America* (1990) is a classic. Since the 1960s, June Jordan has produced much children's literature. Indeed, one of her first publications was her children's anthology *The Voice of the Children* (1970), followed by *His Own Where* (1971). She has also written a children's biography of civil rights activist Fannie Lou Hamer (1972) as well as *Kimako's Story* (1981), a fictional account of a contemporary black girl's growing up. Alice Walker has published two works for children: a biography of Langston Hughes in 1974 and her beautifully illustrated *To Hell with Dying* (1990). Sherley Anne Williams's *Working Cotton* (1992), based on her poetry collection *Peacock Poems* (1975), tells the story of one day in the life of a migrant worker family.

Important too to this period is the recognition that black women writers excelled in genres other than the novel or the short story. Essayists such as Alice Walker, in *In Search of Our Mothers' Gardens*, and June Jordan, in *Civil Wars* (1981) and *On Call* (1985), analyzed topics from the Vietnam War to the civil rights movement, from the art of quilting to the appointment of Clarence Thomas to the Supreme Court. Poetry collections such as Jordan's *Things I Do in the Dark* (1977), Audre Lorde's *The Black Unicorn* (1978), Lucille Clifton's *Good News about the Earth* (1972), Ntozake Shange's *Nappy Edges* (1978), and Sherley Anne Williams's *Peacock Poems* (1985) mined black women's voices as well as forms such as the quilt, the blues, the journal, and the letter. Shange's award-winning play *for colored girls who have considered suicide/when the rainbow is enuf* (1977) unleashed debates in the black community about sexism even as it opened the way for later black women playwrights such as Alexis de Veaux and Anna Devere Smith.

The writings of African American women in the 1970s would also prepare the ground for literary scholarship on black women writers of the past as well as for the development of black feminist criticism. By the late 1970s, partly because of the entrance of a small but significant number of black women into mainstream white universities where they witnessed the absence of their histories, ideas, and concerns, and partly as a result of the literary/scholarly activism of writers such as Morrison, Walker, and Barbara Smith, scholars began to excavate a long-forgotten black women's history and literature and to read and teach postcolonial women writers such as Bessie Head and Maryse Conde. And while few Americans in 1970 would have been able to name a prominent black woman writer, in 1992 books by three African American women—Terry McMillan, Toni Morrison, and Alice Walker—would appear simultaneously on the *New York Times* best-seller list. Also by the early 1990s, scholarship on writers such as Morrison, the first African American to be awarded the Nobel Prize for literature, and Walker, the first African American woman to win the Pulitzer Prize for fiction, had multiplied a hundredfold.

By focusing on sexuality as a major issue in black thought and life, African American women writers helped to generate interest in the neglected area of lesbian writing. Barbara Smith's anthology of black lesbian writing, *Home Girls* (1983), Audre Lorde's collection of essays, *Sister Outsider* (1984), and her automythobiography, *Zami* (1982), as well as her poetry collections provided theoretical grounding for the exploration of black lesbian thought and expression. At the same time,

Walker's *Color Purple* included a black lesbian relationship at its center, and Gloria Naylor told the story of a black lesbian couple in *Women of Brewster Place*. As a result, analyses of sexual preference and of homophobia within black communities became a major topic of inquiry.

BROADENING HORIZONS

Caught up in the whirl of change generated by black women writers, African American men also began to explore their own generational relationships. Writers such as John Wideman and Clarence Major have credited African American women authors with establishing constructs within which they too could explore relationships to their fathers, mothers, sisters, brothers, and lovers, rather than primarily to the "white man." And while there had been acknowledged black homosexual writers such as James Baldwin, sexuality per se had not been the topic on which they wrote; black homosexual men in the 1980s and 1990s such as Essex Hemphill would in their poetry, novels, and essays focus on the specific condition of being a gay black man in America.

By destabilizing the idea of a monolithic "blackness," African American women writers also called attention to issues of class. Early-twentieth-century writers such as Alain Locke, W. E. B. Du Bois, Jessie Fauset, Nella Larsen, Ann Petry, and Dorothy West had looked carefully at class consciousness among African Americans; but as the century progressed, concerns about class were more and more eclipsed by sorrow and anger over racism. Class, though, reasserted itself as a topic of literature after the 1960s. Walker in her first three novels presented different class positions: a sharecropper's family in *The Third Life of Grange Copeland*, a small-town southern family in *Meridian*, and in *The Color Purple* a landed southern black family at the turn of the century. Still, it was not until the early 1980s that critics noticed that Walker, Morrison, and Naylor were critiquing class positions in the African American community. Sherley Anne Williams in the essay *Roots of Privilege: New Black Fiction* (1985) noted the resurgence of middle-class concerns in African American women's fiction when she reviewed Andrea Lee's *Sarah Phillips*, Gloria Naylor's *Linden Hills*, and Ntozake Shange's *Betsy Brown*. She could also have included the devastating analysis of class differences among blacks in Toni Morrison's *Song of Solomon* and *Tar Baby* (1981). While 1970s African American women's novels tended to be set in the small town and village, Naylor explored the lives of underclass urban black women in *The Women of Brewster Place* and of middle-class blacks in *Linden Hills*. Black male writers such as Darryl Pickniny in *High Cotton* (1992) highlighted the dilemmas of upwardly mobile black men. Carolivia Herron's *Thereafter, Johnnie* (1991), one of the great novels of the 1990s, used the history of a black middle-class family as the basis for her apocalyptic prophecy of the decline of "the American empire."

African American writers have also used profitably the insights of other cultural traditions. Like his jazz musician counterpart John Coltrane, Charles Johnson incorporated into his *Oxherding Tale* elements of Eastern philosophy. Ernest Gaines's first novel, *Catherine Carmier*, is modeled on the Russian novelist Turgenev's *Fathers and Sons*. Alice Walker's use of the letter in *The Color Purple* speaks to the epistolary beginnings of the English novel. Charles Fuller's Pulitzer Prize–winning play *A Soldier's Story* is influenced by Herman Melville's *Billy Budd*. Gloria Naylor's *Mama Day* is clearly based on a text that resonates throughout Caribbean literature—Shakespeare's *The Tempest*. Rita Dove uses elements of German culture in her collection *Museum* and places the story of Demeter and Persephone in a modern context in *Mother Love* (1995). Toni Morrison's *Beloved* has been characterized by some critics as a revision of works by nineteenth-century

American writers Harriet Beecher Stowe and Mark Twain. Ishmael Reed's works have been influenced by American horror films and detective stories. And Octavia Butler and Samuel Delaney write in the tradition of science fiction and fantasy. In the 1990s Walter Mosley's writings extended African American literature into the genre of the hard-boiled mystery, and Terri McMillan's novels made black romance stories a central part of U.S. publishing successes. Each of these writers had a novel translated into a popular movie. As Henry Louis Gates Jr. points out in his introduction to *Black Literature and Literary Theory* (1984), black writers have been educated in schools that taught almost exclusively texts of the Western literary tradition. What they have done with such texts is to refigure them through the "differences" of black figurative language.

While a clear development of the contemporary period has been the broadening of subjects that African American writers felt free to explore, from homosexuality to the psyches of white characters, there has also arisen a counteracting tendency, which some call Afrocentricity—a tendency that recalls 1960s concepts of blackness and that draws to some extent on the Back to Africa movement of Marcus Garvey in the 1920s. Molefi Kete Asante's book *Afrocentricity: The Theory of Social Change* (1980) has been the bible of this movement. Responding to "race power" as the central idea in European thought since Bartolomeo de las Casas, Asante calls for a scholarship based on Africa as the center of civilization. Although his ideas have not been widely accepted by black scholars, Asante is clearly popular among young writers. Whether his philosophy is a response to African American discomfort with the multiplicity of identities currently so favored in the Academy or to the tremendous economic and social stress felt by many black communities will undoubtedly be a topic for African American writers of the future.

CONTEMPORARY AFRICAN AMERICAN SCHOLARSHIP

Another decisive characteristic of the contemporary period has been the increase of scholarship on African American writers and especially an increase of scholarship by African American writers. In an essay in Addison Gayle's *The Black Aesthetic* (1971), African American critic Darwin Turner lamented the fact that while black poets and novelists were beginning to be recognized, the African American critic remained largely unseen. By the early 1980s, however, African American critics were becoming more visible and were beginning to affect the study of African American literature. Books such as Gayle's *The Way of the New World: The Black Novel in America* (1975), Robert Stepto's *Behind the Veil: A Study of Afro-American Narrative* (1979), Houston Baker's *The Journey Back: Issues in Black Literature and Criticism* (1980), Barbara Christian's *Black Women Novelists: The Development of a Tradition, 1892–1976* (1980), and Donald Gibson's *The Politics of Literary Expression: A Study of Major Black Writers* (1981) are examples of the variety of critical studies in this period. As well, anthologies of critical essays such as Roseann Bell, Bettye Fisher, and Beverley Guy Sheftall's *Sturdy Black Bridges: Visions of Black Women in Literature* (1979); Dexter Fisher and Robert Stepto's *Afro-American Literature: The Reconstruction of Instruction* (1979); Henry Louis Gates Jr.'s *Black Literature and Literary Theory*; Michael Harper and Robert Stepto's *Chants of Saints: A Gathering of Afro-American Literature, Art, and Scholarship* (1979); and R. Baxter Miller's *Black American Literature and Humanism* (1978) suggested different approaches to teaching and theorizing about black literatures.

As was true in the nineteenth and early twentieth centuries, creative writers have also contributed to the body of critical texts produced by and about African American writers. Practically every contemporary writer in this anthology has either written essays that recovered older writers, illuminated the relationship between the

African American oral tradition and African American literatures, and/or crafted literary theories in the area of race and feminism. Most recently, Toni Morrison's collection of critical essays *Playing in the Dark* (1992) articulated the theory that the construction of whiteness, and therefore of "white" texts such as Melville's *Moby Dick* and Hawthorne's gothic romances, is based on the anxieties European Americans felt about the African presence in America.

By the mid-1980s, literary theory had also become an important aspect of the study of black literature. Critics of African American literature engaged in readings from the wide range of perspectives that existed in the academy, such as formalism, Marxism, psychoanalysis, poststructuralism, and feminism, even as they attempted to create theories that took into account the "differences" of black texts. Because black literature was often studied in interdisciplinary programs such as African American, ethnic, and women's studies, the criticism of the 1980s was often placed within a historical, cultural, or materialist context. In *Blues, Ideology, and Afro-American Literature: A Vernacular Theory*, Houston Baker used the blues, a major motif in African American culture, as a basis for reading African American literature, while in *Reconstructing Womanhood*, Hazel Carby used a materialist approach to read black women's literature of the nineteenth century. In *Signifying Monkey*, Henry Louis Gates Jr. employed a folk myth central among "New World" blacks, the West African trickster figure, as a means of "lift[ing] the discourse of signifyin(g) from the vernacular to the discourse of literary discourse," thereby attempting "to locate and identify how the black tradition had theorized about itself."

This emphasis on interdisciplinarity in African American studies also contributed to the development of cultural studies, a diverse interdisciplinary field that sees culture not as a static "canon" or "tradition" but as the emerging and dynamic product of a network of antagonistic power relations. Not surprisingly, cultural studies have been profoundly concerned with African American culture. African American cultural critics such as bell hooks, Shelby Steele, Michele Wallace, Toni Morrison, Ishmael Reed, and Cornel West, whose book *Race Matters* was a bestseller, are now seen, even by the mainstream literary establishment, as public intellectuals. Recently, major journals such as *The Atlantic Monthly* and *The New Republic* have featured essays on the rise of the Public Black Intellectual.

Ironically, while black scholars have been largely responsible for the increased attention given African American literature in the academy and in popular culture, their small numbers may soon decrease. During the 1980s and early 1990s, the number of black Ph.D.s, which peaked in the mid 1970s, declined. Whether the literary critical discourses to which African Americans have been central will continue to develop is of concern. Though African American literatures have survived, even flourished, in the worst of times, the African American critic's presence in the academy may well determine whether and how these literatures will be studied in the twenty-first century United States.

ALBERT MURRAY

b. 1916

Albert Murray's career as a writer has been distinguished by his insistent drive to create, in fiction and nonfiction, the literary equivalents of blues and jazz. Murray the modernist has undertaken this project under the auspices of Eliot, Hemingway, Joyce, Faulkner, and especially Thomas Mann—all highly conscious writers who employ mythic patterns and a wide range of intellectual and artistic references to give their writing the peculiar weight and force that define a vital aspect of the modern. But Murray wears these influences lightly. In a voice unmistakably his own, he brings to life the little-explored aspect of African American experience that views the shortfalls and tragedies of life in much the way they are regarded in blues-idiom music, where trouble is taken for granted ("Trouble, trouble," one blues song says, "I've had it all my days") but where defeat is never conceded. Murray's heroes learn to regard their lives as fairy tales and romances in which, whether they receive official recognition or not, they achieve a style of living and loving and making art that transcends the bounds of officialdom. Ultimately, they achieve a way of life—even in the violent briar patches of segregated America—which, like the music of Louis Armstrong and Duke Ellington, is the envy of the world.

Born on May 12, 1916, in Nokomis, Alabama, Albert Lee Murray was adopted soon after birth by sharecropper, dockworker, railway crosstie cutter, and sawmill hand Hugh Murray and homemaker Mattie (James) Murray. Murray grew up in Magazine Point, outside of Mobile, where he discovered a world at once stiflingly provincial and open to possibility. In his fiction and essays, Mobile is an international city comparable to New Orleans, having its own complex transportation systems, by land and by sea; its own Mardi Gras; and a culture where a wide variety of types of blacks, whites, and Indians interacted. At Mobile County Training School, Murray fell under the influence of the principal, Benjamin Francis Baker, who regarded him as part of the New Negro Movement, the "Talented Tenth," whose goals involved loyalty to past and future generations of African Americans and the will to assume leadership on a broad scale. Winning recognition in basketball, baseball, football and track and field—and as the best all-around student—Murray received a scholarship to attend college and enrolled at the Tuskegee Institute in September 1935.

At Tuskegee, Murray undertook an intense program of literary studies, reading assigned texts along with unassigned new works by such critics as Edmund Wilson and Morton Zabel, which encouraged and enhanced his study of the literary moderns. He also tuned in to the national radio broadcasts of Duke Ellington, Earl Hines, and other jazz masters whose work was fast becoming a consuming passion. Though they did not become close friends until later, Murray the undergraduate was aware of another ambitious reader at Tuskegee, music major Ralph Ellison.

Murray pursued graduate study at the University of Michigan before returning to Tuskegee Institute (in 1942), where he taught English and directed theatrical productions. In 1943, he enlisted in the air force. He served through World War II and continued, in active and inactive service at home and abroad, until his retirement as a major in 1962. Between stints of active service, he received his master's degree from New York University (in 1948) and taught at Tuskegee. After retiring from the air force, Murray settled in New York City, where he worked as a writer and as an occasional visiting professor—at Colgate, Barnard, Columbia, Emory, the University of Massachusetts at Boston, Washington and Lee, and elsewhere.

In 1970, when Murray was fifty-four years old, he published his first book, *The Omni-Americans*, a compendium of essays and reviews that challenged the prevailing social-scientific view of Negro Americans as marginal victims of white racism by asserting the wholeness and the defiant stylishness of blacks who are, in Murray's formulation, in some ways *the* quintessentially representative American group: not just Afro- or African Americans but *Omni*-Americans. Most social science on the question of race, said Murray, was best regarded as "social science fiction." *South to a Very Old Place* (1971), the book that Murray speaks of as his favorite, is a novel-cum-travelog in which the author takes off from Harlem to retrace his southern roads and highways while investigating the state of race relations (including the art and rhetoric along the color line) after the civil rights revolution. *The Hero and the Blues* (1973) collects lectures on jazz, blues, and literature that Murray had delivered the previous year at the University of Missouri. *Stomping the Blues* (1976) was begun as a picture book on jazz and then expanded into a comprehensive aesthetic of the music in its "Saturday night" setting, where it drives the blues off the dance floor (to stomp the blues) and heralds the revelry that also defines blues-idiom music. *Good Morning, Blues* (1985), the autobiography of Count Basie as told to Murray, presents the story of "the boy from Red Bank" who became a piano sensation and then bandleader on the Kansas City Southwest circuit before his music and fame traveled around the world. In this book, as in the others, the emphasis is on heroic accomplishment in the face of what can appear to be unpromising odds.

Murray's latest collection of essays, *The Blue Devils of Nada* (1996), gathers his pieces on Romare Bearden, Duke Ellington, and Ernest Hemingway and on the processes of writing the Basie book (that four-fisted piano collaboration). This book also studies riff-style artistic expression in a world infected with entropy (or meaningless randomness)—infested with "the blue devils of nada." (Of course the "blue devils" are, like blues music itself, ironically named insofar as they represent not only misery and wretchedness in blue but also the Blue Devil bomber-pilotlike warriors, ever on duty against the misery and wretchedness associated with blue moods.) According to this philosopher of the music, the best way to fight the blues is with the blues!

Sometime in the mid 1940s, Murray began a novel. (A letter from his close friend Ralph Ellison wondered if the two of them would publish their novels in the same year, 1952, when *Invisible Man* appeared.) One section of it appeared in *New World Writing*, 1953, as "The Luzana Cholly Kick." Working on it off and on between other projects, Murray released part one of the novel as *Train Whistle Guitar* in 1974. So far two more installments have appeared: *The Spyglass Tree* (1991) and *The Seven League Boots* (1996). This trilogy comprises an eloquent "lyrical reminiscence" by a highly intelligent and winning narrator whose nickname, appropriately enough, is Scooter.

In *Train Whistle*, Scooter remembers the Deep South of the 1920s not as a Gothic prison house but as an enthralling and at times bewildering scene of adventures. This first novel, and indeed the entire trilogy, concerns problems of history and memory in a culture where official schoolbook history is one thing (and a powerful thing it can be) while the versions of the past traded by adults in the barbershop and in the front room at home are something else again. Of course, Scooter, like his maker, will need both the "learned" and the vernacular traditions: good book training and the dirty dozens, both.

The *Spyglass Tree* takes Scooter to a college strongly resembling Tuskegee, where his dorm room replaces his hometown's chinaberry tree as a lookout post from which to gain perspective on the widening world. Perspective, along with history and memory, is a concern throughout the Scooter trilogy. *The Seven League*

Boots retells, in riff choruslike recapitulations, stories narrated in the first two books as it pushes forward the saga of Scooter, now a recent college graduate, who is hired, during the Swing Era, as bass player in the band of the legendary itinerant jazz musician/composer Bossman, the "Emperor of Syncopation," who looks a lot like Duke Ellington.

In addition to his work as a writer, Murray has recently been a major figure in the institutionalization of jazz through his work with the Smithsonian, in Washington, D.C., and especially with Lincoln Center, in New York City. Working with Wynton Marsalis, Rob Gibson, and Stanley Crouch, Murray has provided intellectual leadership to Lincoln Center's jazz department, championing against all doubters the idea that jazz is a fine art form whose values of resiliency, improvisation, and individuality, all within a group context, mark it as *the* quintessential American art form and *the* music of the century.

Train Whistle Guitar

[*History Lessons*]

It was as if you had been born hearing and knowing about trains and train whistles, and the same was also true of sawmills and sawmill whistles. I already knew how to mark the parts of the day by sawmill whistles long before I learned to read time as such from the face of a clock.

Sometimes, probably having heard the earliest morning sawmill whistles in my sleep as you sometimes hear neighborhood roosters crowing for daybreak, I used to wake up and lie listening long enough to hear the first-shift hands passing by outside. That was when the daytime fireman relieved the night fireman, and it was also the time when you could hear the logging crews that came that way going to work on that part of Mobile River and Three Mile Creek. These were the putt-boat pilots and the raftmen, some of whom were also skiffboatmen. And there were also the boom men, who used to wear their turned down hip boots (which I also used to call magellan boots and isthmus of panama boots) to and from home, carrying their peavies and hook-and-jam poles angling across their shoulders as pike men did in story books and also as railroad crosstie cutters used to carry their crosscut saws and broadaxes to and from the timber woods.

It was the head day-shift fireman who always blew the next whistle, and that was when the main-shift hands would be coming by. So that was when what you heard passing was not only the log carriage experts like, say, old Sawmill Turner, for instance; but also the shed and the yard crews, including the timekeepers and tallymen. But I was usually asleep again by then, and when I woke up for good it would be time to get up and be ready before the first school bell rang.

It would be full daylight then, and by the time you finished breakfast, the first lumber trucks would be grinding their way up out of Sawdust Bottom. And when you heard the next gear shift, that meant they were finally up the hill and leveling off into our flat but somewhat sandy and rutty road to come whining by the gate. Then the next gearstroke meant that they were ready to pick up speed to fade on away because they had turned onto Buckshaw Road, which was macadamized like Telegraph Road even before the

Cochrane Bridge was built and they finally paved it with asphalt like the Chickasaw Highway and made it a part of US 90.

•

From September through the fall and winter and spring the next thing after the first lumber trucks was always the first school bell. So from then on it was as if you didn't really hear either the sawmills or train whistles (or even boat whistles) anymore until after three o'clock. Because during that part of every day except Saturday and Sunday, everything you did was part of the also and also that school bells and school bell times were all about. Such as singing in 70-degree Fahrenheit schoolroom unison: *Good morning to you good morning to you good morning dear teacher good morning to you.* With your scrubbed hands on the pencil tray desk for roll call and fingernail inspection, with your hair trimmed and combed and brushed and your head erect, your back straight, your shoulders square and your eyes on the exemplary pre-lesson neatness of the janitor-washed blackboard with its semi-permanent border design and theme of the month and motto of the month and chalk colored checkerboard calendar.

Good solo teacher talk morning dear children.

Good unison-pupil response-chant morning dear teacher.

A very good morning from toothpaste smiles and rainbow ribbons and oilcloth book satchels and brown bag sandwich smells to you Miss So and Miss So and Miss So and So and Miss So-So and Miss So On and Miss So Forth to Miss Metcalf.

Then (when the first kitten mitten mornings of steaming breath and glittering wayside ponds were outside once more) also: *Old Jack Frost is a funny old fellow when the wind begins he begins to bellow. He bites little children on their nose. He bites little children on their toes. He makes little girls say Oh! Oh! Oh! And he makes little boys say Ouch! Ouch! Ouch! He makes little pointed-ats wring hands and blow fingers and say Oh! Oh! Oh! And he makes little nodded-and-smiled-ats shake fists and say Ouch! Ouch! Ouch! He makes little sugar and spice and everything nice girls say —! —! — ! And he makes little frogs and snails and puppydogtail boys (but not Scooter and not Little Buddy Marshall and not old Cateye Gander Gallagher the Gallinipper) say ——! ——! ——!*

But sometimes (especially during afternoon quiet sessions) you could still hear the syrup-green sawdust whine of the log carriage even from that far away, and I could hardly wait to get back home to my own play sawmill, which millwright that I already was I had built complete with boom, rafts, conveyer ramp, carriage, slab and sawdust pile, stacking yard, dry kiln and planer shed, long before the time came to go to school that first year. Because in the summertime in those days I almost always used to become a hard rolling sawmill man as soon as Buckshaw whistle used to blow for high noon no matter what else I was supposed to be at the time. Because that was when you could sit at the sawhorse table outside under the chinaberry tree stripped to the waist like a stacking yard hand, eating new corn and pole beans (or snap beans or string beans) plus new red-skinned potatoes; or butterbeans plus okra; or green (shelled) blackeye peas plus okra; or crowder peas plus okra; along with the very thinnest of all shortening-rich golden crusted corners of cornbread. Not to mention the yellow-flecked mellowness of the home churned buttermilk of those days. Or the homemade lemonade or fresh ice-tea. Especially when you could drink it from your very own quart-size fruit jar not only as if you had been stacking lumber all the morning but also as if all the good cooking in your napkin-covered slat basket had been prepared by your honey brown good-looking wife or woman, who had put on her frilly starched baby doll gingham dress and brought it to where she now sat beside you fanning away the flies in the stacking yard shade.

But all of that was before Miss Lexine Metcalf, and her blue and green and yellow globe revolving on its tilted axis with its North and South Poles, and its Eastern and Western Hemispheres, and its equator plus its Torrid and North Temperate and South Temperate and Frigid Zones and its continents and its oceans and seas and gulfs and great lakes and rivers and basins, and its mountain ranges and plains and deserts and oases, and its islands and peninsulas and archipelagos and capes and horns and straits.

Because from then on (what with her sandtable igloos and wigwams and thatched huts and mud huts and caravan tents and haciendas and chalets and chinese paper houses with lanterns; and what with her bulletin board costumes of many lands and her teacher's desk that could become the Roundtable from which armor-clad knights errant set forth to do battle with dragons and blackboard problems; what with her window box plants that could become Robin Hood's forest and what with her magic pointer that could change everyday Gasoline Point schoolgirls into Cinderellas and Sleeping Beauties and you into Prince Charming or Roland or Siegfried or Sinbad or Ulysses and your Buster Brown shoes or your Keds into Seven League Boots) I was to become a schoolboy above and beyond everything else, for all the absolutely indispensable times I was still to play hooky with Little Buddy Marshall.

What with Miss Lexine Metcalf with whose teacher-pronunciation my given name finally became the classroom equivalent not only of Scooter but also of the other nickname Mama used to call me which was Man which was to say Mama's Man which was to say Mama's Little Man which was to say Mama's Big Man; because Miss Lexine Metcalf was the one who also said it looking at you as if to let you know that she was also calling you what Miss Tee had always called you, which was her mister. *My Mister. Hello My Mister. This is My Mister. Show them My Mister.*

What with Miss Lexine Metcalf who came to be the one who was there in the classroom. But what also with Miss Tee, from whom had already come ABC blocks and ABC picture books and wax crayon coloring sets, and was the one for whom you learned your first numbers, and who was also the one who said: *This is My Mister who can write his name all by himself. Show them My Mister. This is My Mister who can do addition and subtraction all by himself. Show them My Mister. And show them how My Mister can also recite from the Reader all by himself. The cat said not I. The dog said not I. The little red hen said I will and she did. The little choo choo going up the hill said I think I can I think I can I thought I could I thought I could. Because it tried and it did.*

•

Sometimes a thin gray, ghost-whispering mid-winter drizzle would begin while you were still at school, and not only would it settle in for the rest of the mist-blurred, bungalow-huddled afternoon, but it would still be falling after dark as if it would continue throughout the night; and even as you realized that such was the easiest of all times to get your homework (even when it was arithmetic) done (no matter what kind of schoolboy you were) you also knew as who hasn't always known that it was also and also the very best of all good times to be where grown folks were talking again, especially when there were the kind of people visiting who always came because there was somebody there from out of town and you could stay up listening beyond your usual time to be in bed.

Their cane bottom chairs and hide bottom chairs and rocking chairs plus stools always formed the same old family-cozy semi-circle before the huge open hearth, and from your place in the chimney corner you could see the play of the firelight against their faces and also watch their tale-time shadows moving against the newspaper wallpaper walls and the ceiling. Not even the best of all barbershops were ever to surpass the best of such nights at home.

They would be talking and rocking and smoking and sometimes drinking, and, aware of the roof sanding, tree-shivering night weather outside, I would be listening, and above us on the scalloped mantlepiece was the old fashioned pendulum clock, which was Papa's heirloom from that ancestral mansion of ante-bellum columns and gingham crisp kitchens in which his mulatto grandmother had herself been an inherited slave until Sherman's March to the Sea[1] but which I still remember as the Mother Goose clock; because it ticked and tocked and ticked and tocked and tocked and struck not only the hours but also the quarter-hours with the soft clanging sound you remember when you remember fairy tale steeples and the rainbow colors of nursery rhyme cobwebs; because it hickory dickory docked and clocked like a brass spoon metronome above the steel blue syncopation of guitar string memories; because it hockey-tock rocked to jangle like such honky tonk piano mallets as echo midnight freight train distances beyond patch-quilt horizons and bedside windowpanes.

Sometimes it would be obvious enough that they were only telling the tallest tales and the most outrageous lies they could either remember or fabricate, and sometimes you could be every bit as certain that their primary purpose was to spell out as precisely as possible the incontestable facts and most reliable figures involved in the circumstance under consideration. But when you listened through the meshes of the Mother Goose clock you already knew long before you came to recognize any necessity to understand (not to mention explain) that no matter which one they said or even believed they were doing they were almost always doing it at least a little of both. (Because even as the Mother Goose clock was measuring the

---

1. General William Tecumseh Sherman's destructive "March to the Sea," from Atlanta to Savannah in late 1864, divided the Confederacy in two and played a major role in its defeat.

hours and minutes of ordinary days and nights and time tables its tictocula-
tion created that fabulous once upon a time spell under which you also
knew that the Jacksonville of the section gang song for instance was really a
make-believe place even though you could find it by moving your finger to
the right from Pensacola and across Tallahassee on the map of Florida—
just as you could find Kansas City by tracing left from St. Louis on the map
of Missouri.)

Sometimes there would also be such winter-delicious things as paper-
shell pecans and chinquapins[2] and fresh roasted peanuts to pass around in
Mama's pinestraw bowl-basket, and sometimes there was homemade
blackberry wine or muscadine wine,[3] and sometimes when it was really a
very very special occasion Miss Alzenia Nettleton, who was once a cook in
the Governor's Mansion, would either send or bring one of her mouth-
melting sweet potato pones. Sometimes when it was blizzard weather there
would be a big cast-iron pot of lye hominy (which is something I didn't
learn to like until later on), and on some of the best nights the main reason
everybody was there in the first place was that it was hog-killing-time
weather and somebody had brought Mama the makings of a feast of chitterlings and/or middlings,[4] but of course when that happened the best of the
talking seldom if ever got started until the eating was almost over.

Uncle Jerome would always be there unless there was a fruit boat to be
unloaded that night, clearing his throat even when he was not going to say
anything, squinting his eyes and making a face and clearing again and
swallowing and stretching and rolling his chin because he was a preacher.
Because although he had been a longshoreman for the last twenty some
odd years and a field hand for some thirty odd years before that, he was
supposed to have the Call, although he had never been called by any congregation to be the pastor of any church.

Sometimes Mister Doc Donahue the Dock Hand would also be there.
But they wouldn't be drinking just wine with him there. Because leather
bellied stevedore[5] that he was he always said that wine was for women and
children and Christmas morning fruitcake, and he would get up and get
the longshoreman's knapsack he always carried along with his cargo hook
and bring out a brown crockery jug of corn whiskey, which always made
Papa look over at Mama and get just about tickled to death. They would be
passing it around, pouring against the light of the fire, and there would be
that aroma then, which I always used to enjoy as much as the smell of
warm cigar ashes and freshly opened Prince Albert tobacco cans.

They would talk on and on, and then (when somebody mentioned
something about the weather itself and somebody else said Yeah but talking about some weather) you could always tell you were going to hear
about the great Juvember Storm again, and sometimes that would be what
they spent the rest of the night telling about, each one telling it as he remembered it from where he was at the time, with Uncle Jerome telling his
as if it all had been something happening in the Bible, although nobody,

2. Nuts from a small tree related to the chestnut.
3. Wine made from grapes of a vine common to
the southeastern United States.
4. Pork or bacon cut from between the shoulders
of the hog. "Chitterlings": the small intestines of
pigs cooked for food.
5. Loader and unloader of ship cargo.

not even he, ever claimed that it had actually stormed for forty days and forty nights. But Uncle Jerome always pointed out that everything under the sun was in the Bible including automobiles, because old Ezekiel saw the wheel in the middle of the wheel, and what was an airship but a horseless chariot in the sky, and if somebody didn't cut in on him he would stand up and begin walking the floor and preaching another one of his sermons.

Everybody had his own way of telling about it, but no matter how many parts were added you always saw the main part the same way: rivers and creeks rising and overflowing the back country, washing houses off their foundations and sometimes completely away; bales of cotton and barrels of flour and molasses and cans of lard floating out of warehouses and scattering through the swamps; horses neighing and cows lowing and trying to swim but drowning because (so they used to say) their behinds sucked in so much water; people living in barns and hay lofts and paddling everywhere in skiff boats, people camping in lean-to tent cities in the hills like hobos. People camping on the bluffs like Indians, people camping on timber rafts like the early settlers; trains not running because not only were the tracks washed out but in some places whole spans of bridges had been swept loose. . . .

Then afterwards, there was the epidemic during which even more perished than during the storm itself. But all of that was always a part of the storm story also. And that was when Uncle Jerome always used to say God was warning sinners that He could do it again although He had promised that it would be the fire next time, and he would get up and start clearing his throat and making faces and walking the floor again and then he would go on to show you how even in the almighty act of bringing the flood again God had also brought the fire next time after all. Because what so many many people had suffered and died from was the FEVER, which meant that they were being consumed in a fire more terrible than brimstone! Mess around with mortal man born in sin and shaped in inequity but Gentlemen Sir don't you never start trying to mess with God.

But Papa, whose given name was Whit probably for Whitley but maybe for Whitney and so was sometimes called Papa Whit and sometimes Unka Whit, who had not been inside a church except to attend somebody's funeral since he was baptized thirty some odd years ago, would then take another swallow from his whiskey glass and wipe his mouth and wink at Mister Doc the Dock Hand and look over at Mama because he knew good and well she was going to be scandalized to mortification and say Amen God sure did work a mysterious way His wonders or His blessings or whichever it was to bestow because that was the same storm that had made more good paying jobs for our folks in that country than anything else till the war came.

What I always used to call Papa was Papoo and he used to call me his little gingerbrown papoose boy, which may have been why I called him Papoo in the first place. He himself was as white as any out and out white man I have ever seen in my life. And no wonder either, because not only was he said to be a whole lot more than just half white, it was also said quite accurately that he was acknowledged by most of his white blood relatives much more readily than he himself was ever willing to acknowledge any of them (except when it came to such legal matters as clearing titles to property inherited in common). I myself once overheard Mama telling Aunt Callie the Cat Callahan that the main reason we had moved down into Mobile County when the war boom came was to get away from Papa's white kinfolks in the country. And another time I heard her telling Miss Sadie Womack about how red Papa's ears used to turn when the white people back in the country used to see him driving her into town in the buckboard[6] and pretend that they thought she was not his wife but only one of his black field hands.

Papa himself never talked about white people as such. But sometimes when they were talking about hard times, somebody would get him to tell about some of the things he had seen and done during those times when he had to go off somewhere and pass for white to get a job. That was something to hear about also, and one time when I was telling Little Buddy Marshall about it the next day, he said: Everybody say, don't care how much of his skin and his keen nose and his flat ass Mister Whit might have got from the whitefolks, he got his mother-wit from the getting place. That's how come you don't never catch nobody calling him no old shit-colored peckerwood behind his back.

There was also that time with that white man downtown by the marine store on Government Street. He and Papa knew each other and they were laughing and talking and I was having a good time looking in store windows, and I went looking all the way up to the sporting goods store, and when I came back they were talking about a job; and the man said something about something both of them had been doing somewhere, and that brought up something else, and I heard the man say Papa was a fool for being a durned ole niggie when he could be a wyat man. Hell Whit you as wyat as I am any durned day of the week be durned if you ain't, and Papa just shook his head and said You don't understand, Pete.

Midwinter nights around the fireplace was one of the times when Soldier Boy Crawford used to tell about crossing the Atlantic Ocean and about the mines and the torpedoes and the submarines, and then about the French places he had been to, and sometimes he would mix in a lot of French words with what he was saying such as bonjour come on tally voo and such as sand meal killing my trees easy to Paree and such as donay me unbootay cornyak silver plate and such as voo lay voo zig zig and so on, screwing up his face and narrowing his shoulders as well as his eyes and wiggling his fingers as if he were playing the words as notes on a musical instrument.

When you heard him talking about France in the barbershop he was usually telling either about the Argonne Forest or the Hindenburg Line[7] or about French women whom he called frog women. But what he used to talk mostly about at the fireside was the kind of farming country they had over there, especially the wine making country. And he would also tell about the mountain country and the churches which he said had the finest

---

6. Four-wheeled open carriage.
7. Along a "line" from Lens in northern France to Rheims in the northeast, consolidated German forces stemmed Allied advances to the west during World War I. "Argonne Forest": in northeastern France, a wooded region that was a major battleground during World War I.

bells and the keenest steeples and the prettiest windows in the world: Talking about some stain glass church windows y'all ain't seen no stain glass church windows y'all ain't seen no church statues and I ain't talking about no wood I'm talking about natural stone nine hundred years old.

What he used to tell about Paris at such times was mostly about the buildings and the streets with the cafes on the sidewalk and the parks and the cabarets, and that was also when he used to tell about eating horse meat, snails and frogs legs (but not about the pissoirs and the bidets and best of all the poules[8] from whom came french kissing). He would always say Gay Paree was the best city in the world, and that was also when he would always say A man is a man over there and if somebody said as somebody as often as not did that a man ain't nothing but a man nowhere, you knew he was going to say Yeah but that ain't what I'm talking about, what I'm talking about is somewhere you can go anywhere you big enough to go and do anything you big enough to do and have yourself some of anything you got the money to pay for. That's what I'm talking about.

Soldier Boy Crawford, (who during blizzard weather also used to wear his woolen wraparound leggings along with his Army coat and overseas cap and who also had a steel helmet that looked like a wash basin but which he called his doughboy hat and who was said to have brought back a German Luger plus some hand grenades plus a bayonet, a musette bag[9] and a gas mask too because he for one was never going to let them catch him with his pants down if he could help it) was the main one who used to tell me and Little Buddy Marshall about all of the things Luzana Cholly had done during the war. Because old Luze himself never did talk about any of that, not even when you asked him about it. Sometimes he used to say he was going to save it and tell us about it when we were old enough to understand it, and sometimes he would answer one or two questions about something, say, like how far Big Bertha could shoot, and how the Chau-Chau automatic rifle worked and things like that. But you could never get him to sit down and tell about the actual fighting like Soldier Boy Crawford did. Once you got Soldier Boy Crawford worked up he was subject to fight the whole war all over again.

The rain that was falling then would be crackling down on the shingles of the gabled roof of that house, and the fire in the hearth would sparkle as Papa poked it, and I would be in my same chair in my same place in the corner; and sometimes they would be telling about some of the same old notorious rounders and roustabouts that the guitar players and the piano players made up songs about. Especially if Mister Doc Donahue was there, because he was the one who could always remember something else about old John Henry, who went with blue steel sparks, and old John Hardy, who went with greased lightning. Once he held the floor all night just describing how old Stagolee shot and killed Billy Lyons, and what happened at that famous trial.

Mister Doc Donahue was also the one who used to tell about how old

8. Prostitutes; literally, hens (French). "Pissoirs": public urinals. "Bidets": French-style toilets.

9. Small leather or canvas shoulderbag used by soldiers or travelers.

Robert Charles declared war on the city of New Orleans and fought the whole police force all by himself with his own special homemade bullets. But the best of all the old so-called outlaws he used to tell about was always the one from Alabama named Railroad Bill. Who was so mean when somebody crossed him and so tricky that most people believed that there was something supernatural about him. He was the one that no jail could hold overnight and no bloodhounds could track beyond a certain point. Because he worked a mojo [1] on them that nobody ever heard of before or since. And the last time he broke jail, they had the best bloodhounds in the whole state there to track him. But the next morning they found them all tied together in a fence corner near the edge of the swamp, not even barking anymore, just whining, and when they got them untangled they were ruined forever, couldn't scent a polecat and wouldn't even run a rabbit; and nobody ever saw or came near hide nor hair of old Railroad Bill from that time on.

Naturally the whitefolks claimed they caught him and lynched him; but everybody knew better. The whitefolks were always claiming something like that. They claimed that they had caught old Pancho Villa and hung him for what he had done out in New Mexico; and they claimed that they had hemmed up old Robert Charles in a steeple and burned him alive; and they also claimed that Jessie Willard had salivated old Jack Johnson [2] down in Havana that time! Well, they could go around bragging about how the great white hope had put the big black menace back in his place and proved white supremacy all they wanted to, but everybody knew that Jack Johnson who was married to a white woman had to trade his world championship in for his American citizenship, and thirty thousand dollars to get back in the USA and there was a picture in every barbershop which showed him letting himself be counted out, lying shading his eyes from the Cuban sun, lying with his legs propped like somebody lying on the front porch; and as for Jessie Willard, everybody knew he couldn't even stand up to Jack Dempsey, [3] who was the same Jack Dempsey who brought back old John L. Sullivan's color line because he didn't ever intend to get caught in the same ring with the likes of Jack Johnson, Sam Langford or even somebody like Harry Wills, not even with a submachine gun. Everybody knew that.

The whitefolks claimed that they had finally caught up with old Railroad Bill at some crossroads store somewhere and had slipped up on him while he was sitting in the middle of the floor sopping molasses with his gun lying off to one side, and they swore that they had blown the back of his head off with a double barrel charge of triple-ought buckshot. But in the first place Railroad Bill didn't eat molasses, and in the second place he didn't have to break into any store to get something to eat. Because folks kept him in plenty of rations everywhere he went by putting out buckets of it in certain special places for him mostly along the Railroad which was what his name was all about; and in the third place he must have broken into more than fifty stores by that time and he just plain didn't rob a store in the broad open daylight, not and then sit down in the middle of the floor and eat right

---

1. A spell; witchcraft.
2. American prizefighter (1878–1946), first black world heavyweight champion (1908–15).

3. American prizefighter (1895–1983), heavyweight champion from 1919 to 1926.

there, and in the fourth place there was at least a dozen other mobs in at least a dozen other places all claiming that they had been the ones who laid him low, each one of them telling a completely different tale about how and when and where it all happened. Some claimed that they had hung him upside down on the drawbridge and then riddled him and left what was left of him there for the buzzards. But they never settled on which bridge.

I didn't know very much about history then. Which was what all that about Uncle Walt and the bloodhounds was all about too. Because I knew even while it was happening that it wasn't just happening then. I didn't know very much about historical cause and effect then, but I knew enough to realize that when something happened it was a part of something that had been going on before, and I wasn't surprised at all that time when I was awakened in the middle of the night and got up and saw Uncle Walt sitting by the fire in Papa's clothes talking about how he had made his way through Tombigbee Swamp. He slept in Uncle Jerome's bed and Uncle Jerome slept on a pallet in front of the fireplace. They put ointment on the bruises and rubbed his joints down in Sloan's Liniment, and he slept all day the next day and all the day after that too, telling about it again the second night by the fire with his feet soaking in a tub of hot salt water, and I could see it all and I was in it too, and it was me running through the swamps, hearing them barking, coming, and it was me who swam across the creek and was running wet and freezing in the soggy shoes all the next day. Hungry and cold but not stopping even when I didn't hear them anymore, and not hopping a freight either, because they would be looking for you to do that. It was me who made my way because I knew that country like the Indians knew it, and I knew the swamps and the streams like the old keelboat men and I knew the towns and villages like a post rider, and then it was me who was long gone like a Natchez Trace[4] bandit.

I saw Uncle Walt sitting there in the firelight not afraid but careful, talking about how he was going to make it across the Mason-Dixon,[5] and I didn't really know anything at all about whatever it was he had done or hadn't done, and I still don't know what it was, but I knew that whatever it was it was trouble, and I said It's like once upon a time back then. Because that's what Mama always said, who knew it from her grandfather, who was Uncle Walt's grandfather too, who knew it from his father when there was no hope of foot rest this side of Canada, which was also called Canaan, which was the Promised Land, and I also knew that all of that was about something called the Underground Railroad, which ran from the House of Bondage to the land of Jubilo.[6]

They were always talking about freedom and citizenship, and that was something else that Uncle Jerome used to start preaching about. He had all kinds of sermons ready for times like that. Sometimes he would be talking

4. An old road connecting Natchez, Mississippi, with Nashville, Tennessee.
5. Boundary between Pennsylvania and Maryland, before the Civil War seen as the division between free and slave states.
6. The North; Heaven. "The Underground Railroad": secret network that helped southern slaves reach the North or Canada in the years before the Civil War.

about children of Israel, and sometimes it would be the walls of Jericho, and sometimes it would be the big handwriting on the wall which was also the BIG HAND writing on the wall which was also the Big Hand writing on the WAR. That was when he used to say that the color of freedom was blue. The Union Army came dressed in blue. The big hand that signed the freedom papers signed them in blue ink which was also blood. The very sky itself was blue, limitless *(and gentlemen, sir, before I'd be a slave, I'll be buried in my grave). And I said My name is Jack the Rabbit and my home is in the briarpatch.*

Sometimes he would also say that the freedom road was a road through the wilderness and sometimes it wasn't any road at all because there never was any royal road to freedom for anybody (so don't you let nobody turn you round. And don't you let nobody know too much about your business either. And I said Call me Jack the Bear on my way somewhere).

Then it would be Education again. They didn't ever get tired of talking about that, the old folks telling about how they learned to spell and write back in the old days when they used to use slate tablets and the old Blueback Webster. The old days when they used to have to hold school whenever and wherever they could. Whenever they could spare the time from working the crops and wherever the teacher could find a place to shelter them. Whenever there was a teacher.

Then later on I was the one they meant when they said the young generation was the hope and glory. Because I had come that far in school by then; and sometimes it was Geography and sometimes it was History, and sometimes I had to tell about it, and sometimes I had to get the book and read it to them. Especially when it was about the Revolutionary War. Sometimes I had to read about Columbus too, and sometimes it would also be the explorers and the early settlers. But most of the time what they wanted to hear about was how the original thirteen colonies became the first thirteen states and who said what and who did what during that time and how the Constitution was made and who the first Presidents were and what they did.

That was also when I used to love to recite the Declaration of Independence, and the Gettysburg Address for them; and I could also recite the Preamble to the Constitution and part of the Emancipation Proclamation; and I could also quote from the famous speeches of Patrick Henry and James Otis and Citizen Tom Paine; and I knew all kinds of sayings from *Poor Richard's Almanac.*

That boy can just about preach that thing right now, Mister Jeff Jefferson said one night after I had recited the William Lloyd Garrison and Frederick Douglass parts from the National Negro History Week pageant.

That boy can talk straight out of the dictionary when he want to, Mister Big Martin said looking at me but talking to everybody.

It just do you good to hear that kind of talk.

Whitefolks need to hear some talk like that.

The whitefolks the very one said all that, Jeff.

What kind of whitefolks talking like that?

Histry-book whitefolks.

What kind of histry-book whitefolks?

Whitefolks in that same book that child reading.

I ain't never heard no whitefolks believing nothing like that in all of my born days.

Whitefolks printed that book, didn't they?

I don't care who printed that book, that's *freedom* talk.

Well, the histry book whitefolks got up the Constitution, didn't they?

Yeah, and there was some histry book blackfolks in there somewhere too, you can just about bet on that. There was a jet-black roustabout right in there with old Christopher Columbus, and the very first one to try to climb that bunker hill was a mean black son-of-a-gun from Boston.[7] Ain't nothing never happened and wasn't some kind of a black hand mixed up in it somewhere. You just look at it close enough. The very first ones to come up with iron was them royal black Ethiopians.

You right about that, Mister Big Martin said, ain't nobody going to dispute you about that.

I know I'm right, Mister Jeff said, And I still say these whitefolks need to hear some of that kind of gospel. These ain't no histry book whitefolks around here and this ain't no histry. This ain't nothing but just a plain old everyday mess!

Trying to keep the black man down.

All whitefolks ain't like that, Phil.

Yeah, but them that is.

And some of us too, Jesus, Miss Minnie Ridley Stovall said, Lord the truth is the light, and some of us just ain't ready yet.

Amen, Mister Big Martin said.

Amen? Mister Phil Motley said. What you mean Amen?

That's what I want to know, Mister Jeff Jefferson said.

I mean the truth is the light just like Minnie say.

I done told you, Miss Minnie Ridley Stovall said.

Well ain't none of these peckerwoods around here ready for nothing neither, but just look at them. That's some truth for the light too.

Yeah but I still say some of us still ain't learned how to stick together yet.

Now Big'un, you know good and well that can get to be a horse of another color, Mister Doc Donahue said. I for one don't never intend to be sticking with any and everybody coming along because he say he one of us. You know better than that.

That's why I say *some* of us, Jesus, Miss Minnie Ridley Stovall said.

That's all right about all that, Mister Big Martin said. I'm talking about when you talking about going up against that stone wall. I want us to be ready. I'm talking about Stonewall Jackson. I'm talking about Jericho. That's what I'm talking about.

Well, we talking about the same thing then, Mister Phil Motley said.

That's all right about your Stonewall Jackson too, Mister Jeff Jefferson said, and your Vardaman and your Pitchfork Ben and all the rest of them. This child right here is getting old Stonewall Jackson's water ready.

They were all laughing then. Because everybody in Gasoline Point knew

---

7. Crispus Attucks (1723?–1770), former slave, among the first men to die in the Boston Massacre.

how Shorty Hollingsworth had met his waterloo and got the name Hot Water Shorty. His wife had come up behind him and dashed a pot of scalding lye water down the seat of his pants while he was sitting on the front steps cleaning his shotgun and bragging about what he was going to do if she didn't have his supper on the table in the next five minutes. He had yelled, dropped his shotgun and lit out across the barbwire fence and hadn't stopped until he was chin deep in Three Mile Creek. He had a new name from then on and he also had a new reputation: he could outrun a striped-assed ape.

Uncle Jerome said I was learning about verbs and adverbs and proverbs; and he preached his sermon on the dictionary that time, and he had his own special introduction to the principles of grammar: A noun is someone or something; a pronoun is anything or anybody; a verb is tells and does and is; an adverb is anyhow, anywhere, anytime; an adjective is number and nature; a preposition is relationship; and conjunction is membership; and interjection is the spirit of energy.

Then that time when Aunt Sue was visiting us from Atmore, old Mayfield Turner was there. Old Sawmill Turner, the log carriage expert, who Mama said had been trying to marry Aunt Sue for more than seventeen years, which meant that he had started before she married her first husband (she was visiting us because she had just separated from her fourth husband). Old Sawmill was wearing his blue pinstripe, tailor-made suit and his Edwin Clapp shoes and smelling like the barbershop and sitting cross-legged like Henry Ford; and every time he took a puff on his White Owl, he flashed his diamond ring like E. Berry Wall. Sometimes when they were talking about him behind his back they used to give him names like John D. Rockefeller Turner and J. P. Morgan Turner and Jay Gould Turner[8] because he also sported pearl gray kidskin gloves, and he was always talking about stocks and bonds and worrying about the National Debt.

I was reading about Valley Forge[9] that night, and I knew he was there just as I knew that Mister Lige and Miss Emma Tolliver and Bro Mark Simpkins and his wife, Miss Willeen were all there, because they were always the first ones to come by to see Aunt Sue when she was in town. But at first the only ones that I was really conscious of were Miss Lula Crayton and Miss Liza Jefferson, because every time I paused Miss Lula Crayton kept saying Tribulation tribulation trials and tribulation, and Miss Ida Jefferson would respond one time as if she were hearing some new gossip, and the next time as if I were reading the Bible itself (saying Honey don't tell me, saying Lord have mercy Jesus).

Then I happened to glance up and see old Sawmill again, and he had stopped puffing on his cigar. He was leaning forward with his hand under his chin, his eyes closed, his lips moving, repeating everything I was reading, word for word. He had forgotten all about Aunt Sue, for the time being at least. I was reading about how the Redcoats were wining and dining and

---

8. Appended to "Turner" are the names of American financial tycoons of the late 19th and early 20th centuries.
9. Southeastern Pennsylvania location of the Revolutionary Army headquarters from late 1777 to mid 1778; severe winter weather caused much suffering.

dancing warm in Philadelphia while the ragtag bobtail Continental Army was starving and freezing in makeshift huts and hovels, and about how General George Washington himself had to get out and personally whip slackers and stragglers and would-be deserters back into the ranks with the flat of his sword. All of which was what Give me liberty or give me death really meant, which was why whenever you talked about following in the footsteps of our great American forefathers you were also talking about the bloody tracks the half barefooted troops left in the snow that fateful winter.

Everytime I glanced up I could see old Sawmill Turner still leaning forward toward me, his lips still moving, the tip of his cigar gone to ash. Then when I came to the end of the chapter and closed the book, he stood up and stepped out; into the center of the semi-circle as Uncle Jerome always did. I'm a histry scholar myself, he said. I been a histry scholar ever since I first saw all of them seals and emblems down at the post office when I was a little boy back in Lowdnes County. Then he ran his hand down into his pocket and pulled out a fat roll of brand-new greenbacks, which he held against his chest like a deck of gambling cards. He peeled off a crisp one-dollar bill and held it up and said, Old George Washington is number one because he was first in war and first in peace and first in the hearts of his countrymen. He got it started.

And old Abe Lincoln. *(He held up a five-dollar bill.)* Came along later on and had to save the Union. Old Alexander Hamilton didn't get to be the President, but he was in there amongst them when they started talking about how they were going to handle the money, and here he is. *(He pulled off a ten-dollar bill.)* And here's old Tom Jefferson. *(Off came a twenty-dollar bill.)* Now he was a educated man and he knowed exactly what to do with his book learning. And then you come on up to old Ulysses S. Grant. (He held up a fifty-dollar bill without even pausing.) He was the one old Abe Lincoln himself had to send for when the going got tight, and later on they made him the eighteenth President.

He held up the fifty-dollar bill long enough for everybody to see that it really was a fifty-dollar bill and then he held up a hundred-dollar bill and said, Old Ben Franklin didn't ever even want to be the President. But old Ben Franklin left just as big a mark in histry as any of them. They didn't put him up there on no one-hundred-dollar bill for nothing. Old Ben Franklin was one of the smartest men they had back in them days, and everybody give him his due respect. Old Ben Franklin told them a lot of good points about how to put them clauses in the Constitution. He was just about the first one they thought about when they had to send somebody across the water to do some official business for the Government with them fast talking Frenchmen. And talking about being cunning, old Ben Franklin was the one that took a kite and a Cocola bottle and stole naked lightning.

He came and stood in front of my chair then. This boy is worth more than one hundred shares of gilt-edged preferred, and the good part about it is we all going to be drawing down interest on him. Then he handed me a five-dollar bill as crisp as the one he had held up before, and told me to buy myself a fountain pen; and he told Mama he was going to be the one to stake me to all the ink and paper I needed as long as I stayed in school. All I had to do was show him my report card.

All I could do was say thank you, and I said I would always do my best. And Miss Lula Crayton said Amen. And Miss Liza Jefferson said God bless the lamb and God bless you Mayfield Turner. Then before anybody else could say anything he excused himself and Aunt Sue walked him to the door and he put on his alpaca topcoat, his black Homburg hat and his Wall Street gloves and was gone.

All Mama could do was wipe her eyes, and all Papa could do was look at the floor and shake his head and smile. But Uncle Jerome was on his feet again, saying he was talking about the word made manifest for Manifest Destiny;[1] and I knew he was going to take over where Sawmill Turner had left off and preach a whole sermon with me in it that night. And so did everybody else, and they were looking at me as if I really had become the Lamb or something. So I looked at the mantlepiece, and I heard the Mother Goose clock and outside there was the Valley Forge bitter wind in the turret-tall chinaberry tree.

1974

1. In the 19th century, a doctrine that the United States had both the right and the duty to expand across North America.

MAYA ANGELOU
b. 1928

In an interview with African American critic Claudia Tate, Maya Angelou proclaimed, "All my work is meant to say, 'You may encounter many defeats but you must not be defeated." In fact, the encountering may be the very experience which creates the vitality and the power to endure."

The career of Maya Angelou is a testament both to her vitality and to her power to endure. Angelou has expressed her talents as a dancer, singer, producer, composer, journalist, actor, and teacher, as well as a writer. Beginning with *I Know Why the Caged Bird Sings* (1970), which was nominated for a National Book Award, she has chronicled her various careers in four other autobiographical volumes. Angelou has also published five volumes of poetry: *Just Give Me a Cool Drink of Water 'for I Diie* (1971), which was nominated for a Pulitzer Prize, *Oh Pray My Wings Are Gonna Fit Me Well* (1975), *And Still I Rise* (1978), *Shaker Why Don't You Sing* (1983), *Now Sheba Sings the Song* (1987), and *I Shall Not Be Moved* (1990). Chosen by President Bill Clinton to read at his inauguration on January 21, 1993, Angelou was both the first African American and the first woman poet to be so honored.

Born Marguerite Annie Johnson on April 4, 1926, in St. Louis, Angelou's childhood was one of frequent, difficult moves. Her divorced parents, Vivian Baxter and Bailey Johnson, sent her and her brother, Bailey, back and forth between St. Louis and Stamps, Arkansas, where her paternal grandmother lived, then finally to San Francisco to settle with their mother. It was her ten years in Arkansas that provided Angelou with the experiences that would be the core of her immensely popular autobiography, *I Know Why the Caged Bird Sings*.

In that volume Angelou describes what it meant to be a black girl in Arkansas, a geographical area rarely portrayed in African American literature. One vivid example was the treatment she received from the ironically named dentist Dr. Lincoln, who refused to treat her seriously decayed teeth because she was black. Angelou reflects: "It seems terribly unfair to have a toothache and a headache and to have to bear at the same time the heavy burden of Blackness." However, the racism of the South was exceeded by the trauma of her being raped at age eight by her mother's boyfriend. After naming her assailant, Angelou had to endure the horror of the trial and the subsequent murder of her rapist by her uncles. Feeling that her words had the power to kill, she descended into silence for the next five years. The writer who was later to state, "I write for the Black voice and any ear which can hear it," spent many years unable to speak herself, but listening to the voices around her and absorbing them.

Despite the difficulties of her early life, Angelou's autobiographies and poetry are full of references to the positive, life-affirming values, particularly courage, of the African American community in which she grew up. Her grandmother, Annie Henderson, of Stamps, embodied for this injured child strength in the face of adversity. Through the Depression and despite racism and sexism, Henderson's ability to keep her general store solvent and her pride intact excited her granddaughter's admiration. Another resilient southern woman, Mrs. Flowers, the aristocrat of black Stamps, helped Angelou regain her voice through afternoons of reading and reciting literary classics.

These experiences in the South provided Angelou with the "power to endure" her adolescent years in California. *I Know Why the Caged Bird Sings* recounts her headlong rush into maturity as she became the first African American streetcar conductor in San Francisco and graduated from Mission High School at sixteen only to deliver a son one month later. Throughout the second volume of her autobiography, *Gather Together in My Name* (1974), Angelou weathers difficulties with men and with jobs, including a week's stint with prostitution and a flirtation with drugs.

In the third volume of her autobiography, *Singin' and Swingin' and Gettin' Merry Like Christmas* (1976), Angelou begins her life as a dancer and joins the European touring cast of *Porgy and Bess*. During the period covered by this book, 1950 to 1955, she also tried to achieve middle-class marital respectability when she married an ex-sailor. But guilt over leaving her child for the exciting world of a professional touring company led her to deep depression.

Writing and political activism were sources of recuperation for her. In *The Heart of a Woman* (1981), Angelou relates her growing commitment to writing and her involvement in the civil rights movement of the 1960s. She moved to Brooklyn to learn the craft of writing from her friend John Oliver Killens, who introduced her to the Harlem Writers Guild and to writers such as Paule Marshall and James Baldwin. During this time, she met Martin Luther King Jr. and became the Southern Christian Leadership Conferences' northern coordinator. She also appeared as the White Queen in Jean Genet's play *The Blacks* and, when she moved to Egypt in 1960, became the editor of the English-language *Arab Observer*.

Angelou's travels are the subject of her last autobiographical volume, *All God's Children Need Traveling Shoes* (1984). In this book she tells of her quest to understand Africa during a stay in Ghana and of her decision to return to the southern United States for the first time since her childhood. Not surprisingly, her sojourn in Africa helped her to understand herself both as an African and as an American.

Until recently, Angelou's poems have received less critical attention than her autobiographies; however, she has been writing poetry steadily for years. Many of her poems explore the vicissitudes of love and the pleasures and difficulties of being an African American. The volume *And Still I Rise* challenges the reader to struggle against the forces of death. Angelou has also written for television—the PBS series *Black, Blues, Black* (1968) and a teleplay of *Caged Bird*—and for the screen— *Georgia, Georgia* (1971) and *Sister, Sister* (1979). She received a Tony nomination for best supporting actress in the television series *Roots*.

More than a dozen colleges and universities have awarded Angelou honorary degrees, including Smith College, Mills College, and the University of Arkansas. In 1981, she accepted a lifetime appointment as the first Reynolds Professor of American Studies at Wake Forest University.

Still I Rise

You may write me down in history
With your bitter, twisted lies,
You may trod me in the very dirt
But still, like dust, I'll rise.

Does my sassiness upset you?   5
Why are you beset with gloom?
'Cause I walk like I've got oil wells
Pumping in my living room.

Just like moons and like suns,
With the certainty of tides,   10
Just like hopes springing high,
Still I'll rise.

Did you want to see me broken?
Bowed head and lowered eyes?
Shoulders falling down like teardrops,   15
Weakened by my soulful cries.

Does my haughtiness offend you?
Don't you take it awful hard
'Cause I laugh like I've got gold mines
Diggin' in my own back yard.   20

You may shoot me with your words,
You may cut me with your eyes,
You may kill me with your hatefulness,
But still, like air, I'll rise.

Does my sexiness upset you?   25
Does it come as a surprise
That I dance like I've got diamonds
At the meeting of my thighs?

Out of the huts of history's shame
I rise   30
Up from a past that's rooted in pain
I rise
I'm a black ocean, leaping and wide,
Welling and swelling I bear in the tide.
Leaving behind nights of terror and fear   35
I rise
Into a daybreak that's wondrously clear

I rise
Bringing the gifts that my ancestors gave,
I am the dream and the hope of the slave.   40
I rise
I rise
I rise.

1978

My Arkansas

There is a deep brooding
in Arkansas.
Old crimes like moss pend
from poplar trees.
The sullen earth   5
is much too
red for comfort.

Sunrise seems to hesitate
and in that second
lose its   10
incandescent aim, and
dusk no more shadows
than the noon.
The past is brighter yet.

Old hates and   15
ante-bellum[1] lace, are rent
but not discarded.
Today is yet to come
in Arkansas.
It writhes. It writhes in awful   20
waves of brooding.

1978

From I Know Why the Caged Bird Sings

Chapter 15

[MRS. FLOWERS]

For nearly a year, I sopped around the house, the Store, the school and
the church, like an old biscuit, dirty and inedible. Then I met, or rather got
to know, the lady who threw me my first life line.

Mrs. Bertha Flowers was the aristocrat of Black Stamps. She had the
grace of control to appear warm in the coldest weather, and on the Arkansas summer days it seemed she had a private breeze which swirled around,
cooling her. She was thin without the taut look of wiry people, and her

---

1. Existing before the Civil War.

printed voile dresses and flowered hats were as right for her as denim overalls for a farmer. She was our side's answer to the richest white woman in
town.

Her skin was a rich black that would have peeled like a plum if snagged,
but then no one would have thought of getting close enough to Mrs. Flowers to ruffle her dress, let along snag her skin. She didn't encourage familiarity. She wore gloves too.

I don't think I ever saw Mrs. Flowers laugh, but she smiled often. A slow
widening of her thin black lips to show even, small white teeth, then the
slow effortless closing. When she chose to smile on me, I always wanted to
thank her. The action was so graceful and inclusively benign.

She was one of the few gentlewomen I have ever known, and has remained throughout my life the measure of what a human being can be.

Momma[1] had a strange relationship with her. Most often when she
passed on the road in front of the Store, she spoke to Momma in that soft
yet carrying voice, "Good day, Mrs. Henderson." Momma responded with
"How you, Sister Flowers?"

Mrs. Flowers didn't belong to our church, nor was she Momma's familiar.[2] Why on earth did she insist on calling her Sister Flowers? Shame
made me want to hide my face. Mrs. Flowers deserved better than to
be called Sister. Then, Momma left out the verb. Why not ask, "How *are*
you, *Mrs.* Flowers?" With the unbalanced passion of the young, I hated
her for showing her ignorance to Mrs. Flowers. It didn't occur to me
for many years that they were as alike as sisters, separated only by formal
education.

Although I was upset, neither of the women was in the least shaken by
what I thought an unceremonious greeting. Mrs. Flowers would continue
her easy gait up the hill to her little bungalow, and Momma kept on shelling peas or doing whatever had brought her to the front porch.

Occasionally, though, Mrs. Flowers would drift off the road and down to
the Store and Momma would say to me, "Sister, you go on and play." As I
left I would hear the beginning of an intimate conversation. Momma persistently using the wrong verb, or none at all.

"Brother and Sister Wilcox is sho'ly the meanest—" "Is," Momma? "Is"?
Oh, please, not "is," Momma, for two or more. But they talked, and from
the side of the building where I waited for the ground to open up and swallow me, I heard the soft-voiced Mrs. Flowers and the textured voice of my
grandmother merging and melting. They were interrupted from time to
time by giggles that must have come from Mrs. Flowers (Momma never
giggled in her life). Then she was gone.

She appealed to me because she was like people I had never met personally. Like women in English novels who walked the moors (whatever they
were) with their loyal dogs racing at a respectful distance. Like the women
who sat in front of roaring fireplaces, drinking tea incessantly from silver
trays full of scones and crumpets. Women who walked over the "heath"
and read morocco-bound[3] books and had two last names divided by a hy-

1. Angelou called her grandmother "Momma."
2. A member of one's family or someone as close

as family.
3. Leather-bound.

phen. It would be safe to say that she made me proud to be Negro, just by being herself.

She acted just as refined as whitefolks in the movies and books and she was more beautiful, for none of them could have come near that warm color without looking gray by comparison.

It was fortunate that I never saw her in the company of powhitefolks. For since they tend to think of their whiteness as an evenizer, I'm certain that I would have had to hear her spoken to commonly as Bertha, and my image of her would have been shattered like the unmendable Humpty-Dumpty.

One summer afternoon, sweet-milk[4] fresh in my memory, she stopped at the Store to buy provisions. Another Negro woman of her health and age would have been expected to carry the paper sacks home in one hand, but Momma said, "Sister Flowers, I'll send Bailey up to your house with these things."

She smiled that slow dragging smile, "Thank you, Mrs. Henderson. I'd prefer Marguerite, though." My name was beautiful when she said it. "I've been meaning to talk to her, anyway." They gave each other age-group looks.

Momma said, "Well, that's all right then. Sister, go and change your dress. You going to Sister Flowers's."

The chifforobe[5] was a maze. What on earth did one put on to go to Mrs. Flowers' house? I knew I shouldn't put on a Sunday dress. It might be sacrilegious. Certainly not a house dress, since I was already wearing a fresh one. I chose a school dress, naturally. It was formal without suggesting that going to Mrs. Flowers' house was equivalent to attending church.

I trusted myself back into the Store.

"Now, don't you look nice." I had chosen the right thing, for once.

"Mrs. Henderson, you make most of the children's clothes, don't you?"

"Yes, ma'am. Sure do. Store-bought clothes ain't hardly worth the thread it take to stitch them."

"I'll say you do a lovely job, though, so neat. That dress looks professional."

Momma was enjoying the seldom-received compliments. Since everyone we knew (except Mrs. Flowers, of course) could sew competently, praise was rarely handed out for the commonly practiced craft.

"I try, with the help of the Lord, Sister Flowers, to finish the inside just like I does the outside. Come here, Sister."

I had buttoned up the collar and tied the belt, apronlike, in back. Momma told me to turn around. With one hand she pulled the strings and the belt fell free at both sides of my waist. Then her large hands were at my neck, opening the button loops. I was terrified. What was happening?

"Take it off, Sister." She had her hands on the hem of the dress.

"I don't need to see the inside, Mrs. Henderson, I can tell . . ." But the dress was over my head and my arms were stuck in the sleeves. Momma said, "That'll do. See here, Sister Flowers, I French-seams[6] around the armholes." Through the cloth film, I saw the shadow approach. "That

---

4. Milk that has had sugar added to it.
5. Combination bureau and wardrobe.

6. Stitches the seam on both sides of the fabric so that no raw edges are exposed.

makes it last longer. Children these days would bust out of sheet-metal clothes. They so rough."

"That is a very good job, Mrs. Henderson. You should be proud. You can put your dress back on, Marguerite."

"No ma'am. Pride is a sin. And 'cording to the Good Book, it goeth before a fall."

"That's right. So the Bible says. It's a good thing to keep in mind."

I wouldn't look at either of them. Momma hadn't thought that taking off my dress in front of Mrs. Flowers would kill me stone dead. If I had refused, she would have thought I was trying to be "womanish" and might have remembered St. Louis.[7] Mrs. Flowers had known that I would be embarrassed and that was even worse. I picked up the groceries and went out to wait in the hot sunshine. It would be fitting if I got a sunstroke and died before they came outside. Just dropped dead on the slanting porch.

There was a little path beside the rocky road, and Mrs. Flowers walked in front swinging her arms and picking her way over the stones.

She said, without turning her head, to me, "I hear you're doing very good school work, Marguerite, but that it's all written. The teachers report that they have trouble getting you to talk in class." We passed the triangular farm on our left and the path widened to allow us to walk together. I hung back in the separate unasked and unanswerable questions.

"Come and walk along with me, Marguerite." I couldn't have refused even if I wanted to. She pronounced my name so nicely. Or more correctly, she spoke each word with such clarity that I was certain a foreigner who didn't understand English could have understood her.

"Now no one is going to make you talk—possibly no one can. But bear in mind, language is man's way of communicating with his fellow man and it is language alone which separates him from the lower animals." That was a totally new idea to me, and I would need time to think about it.

"Your grandmother says you read a lot. Every chance you get. That's good, but not good enough. Words mean more than what is set down on paper. It takes the human voice to infuse them with the shades of deeper meaning."

I memorized the part about the human voice infusing words. It seemed so valid and poetic.

She said she was going to give me some books and that I not only must read them, I must read them aloud. She suggested that I try to make a sentence sound in as many different ways as possible.

"I'll accept no excuse if you return a book to me that has been badly handled." My imagination boggled at the punishment I would deserve if in fact I did abuse a book of Mrs. Flowers'. Death would be too kind and brief.

The odors in the house surprised me. Somehow I had never connected Mrs. Flowers with food or eating or any other common experience of common people. There must have been an outhouse, too, but my mind never recorded it.

The sweet scent of vanilla had met us as she opened the door.

"I made tea cookies this morning. You see, I had planned to invite you

---

7. Angelou had been raped in St. Louis by her mother's boyfriend.

for cookies and lemonade so we could have this little chat. The lemonade is in the icebox."

It followed that Mrs. Flowers would have ice on an ordinary day, when most families in our town bought ice late on Saturdays only a few times during the summer to be used in the wooden ice-cream freezers.

She took the bags from me and disappeared through the kitchen door. I looked around the room that I had never in my wildest fantasies imagined I would see. Browned photographs leered or threatened from the walls and the white, freshly done curtains pushed against themselves and against the wind. I wanted to gobble up the room entire and take it to Bailey, who would help me analyze and enjoy it.

"Have a seat, Marguerite. Over there by the table." She carried a platter covered with a tea towel. Although she warned that she hadn't tried her hand at baking sweets for some time, I was certain that like everything else about her the cookies would be perfect.

They were flat round wafers, slightly browned on the edges and butter-yellow in the center. With the cold lemonade they were sufficient for childhood's lifelong diet. Remembering my manners, I took nice little lady-like bites off the edges. She said she had made them expressly for me and that she had a few in the kitchen that I could take home to my brother. So I jammed one whole cake in my mouth and the rough crumbs scratched the insides of my jaws, and if I hadn't had to swallow, it would have been a dream come true.

As I ate she began the first of what we later called "my lessons in living." She said that I must always be intolerant of ignorance but understanding of illiteracy. That some people, unable to go to school, were more educated and even more intelligent than college professors. She encouraged me to listen carefully to what country people called mother wit. That in those homely sayings was couched the collective wisdom of generations.

When I finished the cookies she brushed off the table and brought a thick, small book from the bookcase. I had read A Tale of Two Cities[8] and found it up to my standards as a romantic novel. She opened the first page and I heard poetry for the first time in my life.

"It was the best of times and the worst of times . . ." Her voice slid in and curved down through and over the words. She was nearly singing. I wanted to look at the pages. Were they the same that I had read? Or were there notes, music, lined on the pages, as in a hymn book? Her sounds began cascading gently. I knew from listening to a thousand preachers that she was nearing the end of her reading, and I hadn't really heard, heard to understand, a single word.

"How do you like that?"

It occurred to me that she expected a response. The sweet vanilla flavor was still on my tongue and her reading was a wonder in my ears. I had to speak.

I said, "Yes, ma'am." It was the least I could do, but it was the most also.

"There's one more thing. Take this book of poems and memorize one for me. Next time you pay me a visit, I want you to recite."

8. A novel about the French revolution, by English writer Charles Dickens (1812–1870).

I have tried often to search behind the sophistication of years for the enchantment I so easily found in those gifts. The essence escapes but its aura remains. To be allowed, no, invited, into the private lives of strangers, and to share their joys and fears, was a chance to exchange the Southern bitter wormwood for a cup of mead with Beowulf or a hot cup of tea and milk with Oliver Twist.[9] When I said aloud, "It is a far, far better thing that I do, than I have ever done . . ." tears of love filled my eyes at my selflessness.

On that first day, I ran down the hill and into the road (few cars ever came along it) and had the good sense to stop running before I reached the Store.

I was liked, and what a difference it made. I was respected not as Mrs. Henderson's grandchild or Bailey's sister but for just being Marguerite Johnson.

Childhood's logic never asks to be proved (all conclusions are absolute). I didn't question why Mrs. Flowers had singled me out for attention, nor did it occur to me that Momma might have asked her to give me a little talking to. All I cared about was that she had made tea cookies for *me* and read to *me* from her favorite book. It was enough to prove that she liked me.

Momma and Bailey were waiting inside the Store. He said, "My, what did she give you?" He had seen the books, but I held the paper sack with his cookies in my arms shielded by the poems.

Momma said, "Sister, I know you acted like a little lady. That do my heart good to see settled people take to you all. I'm trying my best, the Lord knows, but these days . . ." Her voice trailed off. "Go on in and change your dress."

In the bedroom it was going to be a joy to see Bailey receive his cookies. I said, "By the way, Bailey, Mrs. Flowers sent you some tea cookies—"

Momma shouted, "What did you say, Sister? You, Sister, what did you say?" Hot anger was crackling in her voice.

Bailey said, "She said Mrs. Flowers sent me some—"

"I ain't talking to you, Ju." I heard the heavy feet walk across the floor toward our bedroom. "Sister, you heard me. What's that you said?" She swelled to fill the doorway.

Bailey said, "Momma." His pacifying voice—"Momma, she—"

"You shut up, Ju. I'm talking to your sister."

I didn't know what sacred cow I had bumped, but it was better to find out than to hang like a thread over an open fire. I repeated, "I said, 'Bailey, by the way, Mrs. Flowers sent you—' "

"That's what I thought you said. Go on and take off your dress. I'm going to get a switch."

At first I thought she was playing. Maybe some heavy joke that would end with "You sure she didn't send me something?" but in a minute she was back in the room with a long, ropy, peach-tree switch, the juice smelling bitter at having been torn loose. She said, "Get down on your knees. Bailey, Junior, you come on, too."

The three of us knelt as she began, "Our Father, you know the tribula-

<hr />

9. Eponymous character in Dickens's 1838 novel. "Wormwood": bitter or grievous thing, after the oil of the artemesia plant. "Mead": fermented drink of water, honey, malt, and yeast. "Beowulf": eponymous hero of an 8th-century English epic.

tions of your humble servant. I have with your help raised two grown boys. Many's the day I thought I wouldn't be able to go on, but you gave me the strength to see my way clear. Now, Lord, look down on this heavy heart today. I'm trying to raise my son's children in the way they should go, but, oh, Lord, the Devil try to hinder me on every hand. I never thought I'd live to hear cursing under this roof, what I try to keep dedicated to the glorification of God. And cursing out of the mouths of babes. But you said, in the last days brother would turn against brother, and children against their parents. That there would be a gnashing of teeth and a rendering of flesh. Father, forgive this child, I beg you, on bended knee."

I was crying loudly now. Momma's voice had risen to a shouting pitch, and I knew that whatever wrong I had committed was extremely serious. She had even left the Store untended to take up my case with God. When she finished we were all crying. She pulled me to her with one hand and hit me only a few times with the switch. The shock of my sin and the emotional release of her prayer had exhausted her.

Momma wouldn't talk right then, but later in the evening I found that my violation lay in using the phrase "by the way." Momma explained that "Jesus was the Way, the Truth and the Light," and anyone who says "by the way" is really saying, "by Jesus," or "by God" and the Lord's name would not be taken in vain in her house.

When Bailey tried to interpret the words with: "Whitefolks use 'by the way' to mean while we're on the subject," Momma reminded us that "whitefolks' mouths were most in general loose and their words were an abomination before Christ."

Chapter 16

["MAM"]

Recently a white woman from Texas, who would quickly describe herself as a liberal, asked me about my hometown. When I told her that in Stamps my grandmother had owned the only Negro general merchandise store since the turn of the century, she exclaimed, "Why, you were a debutante." Ridiculous and even ludicrous. But Negro girls in small Southern towns, whether poverty-stricken or just munching along on a few of life's necessities, were given as extensive and irrelevant preparations for adulthood as rich white girls shown in magazines. Admittedly the training was not the same. While white girls learned to waltz and sit gracefully with a tea cup balanced on their knees, we were lagging behind, learning the mid-Victorian values with very little money to indulge them. (Come and see Edna Lomax spending the money she made picking cotton on five balls of ecru tatting thread. Her fingers are bound to snag the work and she'll have to repeat the stitches time and time again. But she knows that when she buys the thread.)

We were required to embroider and I had trunkfuls of colorful dishtowels, pillowcases, runners and handkerchiefs to my credit. I mastered the art of crocheting and tatting, and there was a lifetime's supply of dainty doilies that would never be used in sacheted dresser drawers. It went without saying that all girls could iron and wash, but the finer touches around the home, like setting a table with real silver, baking roasts and cooking vegetables without meat, had to be learned elsewhere. Usually at the source of those habits. During my tenth year, a white woman's kitchen became my finishing school.

Mrs. Viola Cullinan was a plump woman who lived in a three-bedroom house somewhere behind the post office. She was singularly unattractive until she smiled, and then the lines around her eyes and mouth which made her look perpetually dirty disappeared, and her face looked like the mask of an impish elf. She usually rested her smile until late afternoon when her women friends dropped in and Miss Glory, the cook, served them cold drinks on the closed-in porch.

The exactness of her house was inhuman. This glass went here and only here. That cup had its place and it was an act of impudent rebellion to place it anywhere else. At twelve o'clock the table was set. At 12:15 Mrs. Cullinan sat down to dinner (whether her husband had arrived or not). At 12:16 Miss Glory brought out the food.

It took me a week to learn the difference between a salad plate, a bread plate and a dessert plate.

Mrs. Cullinan kept up the tradition of her wealthy parents. She was from Virginia. Miss Glory, who was a descendant of slaves that had worked for the Cullinans, told me her history. She had married beneath her (according to Miss Glory). Her husband's family hadn't had their money very long and what they had "didn't 'mount to much."

As ugly as she was, I thought privately, she was lucky to get a husband above or beneath her station. But Miss Glory wouldn't let me say a thing against her mistress. She was very patient with me, however, over the housework. She explained the dishware, silverware and servants' bells.

The large round bowl in which soup was served wasn't a soup bowl, it was a tureen. There were goblets, sherbet glasses, ice-cream glasses, wine glasses, green glass coffee cups with matching saucers, and water glasses. I had a glass to drink from, and it sat with Miss Glory's on a separate shelf from the others. Soup spoons, gravy boat, butter knives, salad forks and carving platter were additions to my vocabulary and in fact almost represented a new language. I was fascinated with the novelty, with the fluttering Mrs. Cullinan and her Alice-in-Wonderland house.

Her husband remains, in my memory, undefined. I lumped him with all the other white men that I had ever seen and tried not to see.

On our way home one evening, Miss Glory told me that Mrs. Cullinan couldn't have children. She said that she was too delicate-boned. It was hard to imagine bones at all under those layers of fat. Miss Glory went on to say that the doctor had taken out all her lady organs. I reasoned that a pig's organs included the lungs, heart and liver, so if Mrs. Cullinan was walking around without those essentials, it explained why she drank alcohol out of unmarked bottles. She was keeping herself embalmed.

When I spoke to Bailey about it, he agreed that I was right, but he also informed me that Mr. Cullinan had two daughters by a colored lady and that I knew them very well. He added that the girls were the spitting image of their father. I was unable to remember what he looked like, although I had just left him a few hours before, but I thought of the Coleman girls. They were very light-skinned and certainly didn't look very much like their mother (no one ever mentioned Mr. Coleman).

My pity for Mrs. Cullinan preceded me the next morning like the Cheshire cat's smile. Those girls, who could have been her daughters, were beautiful. They didn't have to straighten their hair. Even when they were caught in the rain, their braids still hung down straight like tamed snakes. Their mouths were pouty little cupid's bows. Mrs. Cullinan didn't know what she missed. Or maybe she did. Poor Mrs. Cullinan.

For weeks after, I arrived early, left late and tried very hard to make up for her barrenness. If she had had her own children, she wouldn't have had to ask me to run a thousand errands from her back door to the back door of her friends. Poor old Mrs. Cullinan.

Then one evening Miss Glory told me to serve the ladies on the porch. After I set the tray down and turned toward the kitchen, one of the women asked, "What's your name, girl?" It was the speckled-faced one. Mrs. Cullinan said, "She doesn't talk much. Her name's Margaret."

"Is she dumb?"

"No. As I understand it, she can talk when she wants to but she's usually quiet as a little mouse. Aren't you, Margaret?"

I smiled at her. Poor thing. No organs and couldn't even pronounce my name correctly.

"She's a sweet little thing, though."

"Well, that may be, but the name's too long. I'd never bother myself. I'd call her Mary if I was you."

I fumed into the kitchen. That horrible woman would never have the chance to call me Mary because if I was starving I'd never work for her. I decided I wouldn't pee on her if her heart was on fire. Giggles drifted in off the porch and into Miss Glory's pots. I wondered what they could be laughing about.

Whitefolks were so strange. Could they be talking about me? Everybody knew that they stuck together better than the Negroes did. It was possible that Mrs. Cullinan had friends in St. Louis who heard about a girl from Stamps being in court and wrote to tell her. Maybe she knew about Mr. Freeman.[1]

My lunch was in my mouth a second time and I went outside and relieved myself on the bed of four-o'clocks. Miss Glory thought I might be coming down with something and told me to go on home, that Momma would give me some herb tea, and she'd explain to her mistress.

I realized how foolish I was being before I reached the pond. Of course Mrs. Cullinan didn't know. Otherwise she wouldn't have given me the two nice dresses that Momma cut down, and she certainly wouldn't have called me a "sweet little thing." My stomach felt fine, and I didn't mention anything to Momma.

That evening I decided to write a poem on being white, fat, old and without children. It was going to be a tragic ballad. I would have to watch her carefully to capture the essence of her loneliness and pain.

1. A reference to Angelou's rape and the subsequent trial of Mr. Freeman.

The very next day, she called me by the wrong name. Miss Glory and I were washing up the lunch dishes when Mrs. Cullinan came to the doorway. "Mary?"

Miss Glory asked, "Who?"

Mrs. Cullinan, sagging a little, knew and I knew. "I want Mary to go down to Mrs. Randall's and take her some soup. She's not been feeling well for a few days."

Miss Glory's face was a wonder to see. "You mean Margaret, ma'am. Her name's Margaret."

"That's too long. She's Mary from now on. Heat that soup from last night and put it in the china tureen and, Mary, I want you to carry it carefully."

Every person I knew had a hellish horror of being "called out of his name." It was a dangerous practice to call a Negro anything that could be loosely construed as insulting because of the centuries of their having been called niggers, jigs, dinges, blackbirds, crows, boots and spooks.

Miss Glory had a fleeting second of feeling sorry for me. Then as she handed me the hot tureen she said, "Don't mind, don't pay that no mind. Sticks and stones may break your bones, but words . . . You know, I been working for her for twenty years."

She held the back door open for me. "Twenty years. I wasn't much older than you. My name used to be Hallelujah. That's what Ma named me, but my mistress give me 'Glory,' and it stuck. I likes it better too."

I was in the little path that ran behind the houses when Miss Glory shouted, "It's shorter too."

For a few seconds it was a tossup over whether I would laugh (imagine being named Hallelujah) or cry (imagine letting some white woman rename you for her convenience). My anger saved me from either outburst. I had to quit the job, but the problem was going to be how to do it. Momma wouldn't allow me to quit for just any reason.

"She's a peach. That woman is a real peach." Mrs. Randall's maid was talking as she took the soup from me, and I wondered what her name used to be and what she answered to now.

For a week I looked into Mrs. Cullinan's face as she called me Mary. She ignored my coming late and leaving early. Miss Glory was a little annoyed because I had begun to leave egg yolk on the dishes and wasn't putting much heart in polishing the silver. I hoped that she would complain to our boss, but she didn't.

Then Bailey solved my dilemma. He had me describe the contents of the cupboard and the particular plates she liked best. Her favorite piece was a casserole shaped like a fish and the green glass coffee cups. I kept his instructions in mind, so on the next day when Miss Glory was hanging out clothes and I had again been told to serve the old biddies on the porch, I dropped the empty serving tray. When I heard Mrs. Cullinan scream, "Mary!" I picked up the casserole and two of the green glass cups in readiness. As she rounded the kitchen door I let them fall on the tiled floor.

I could never absolutely describe to Bailey what happened next, because each time I got to the part where she fell on the floor and screwed up her ugly face to cry, we burst out laughing. She actually wobbled around on the floor and picked up shards of the cups and cried, "Oh, Momma. Oh, dear Gawd. It's Momma's china from Virginia. Oh, Momma, I sorry."

Miss Glory came running in from the yard and the women from the porch crowded around. Miss Glory was almost as broken up as her mistress. "You mean to say she broke our Virginia dishes? What we gone do?"

Mrs. Cullinan cried louder, "That clumsy nigger. Clumsy little black nigger."

Old speckled-face leaned down and asked, "Who did it, Viola? Was it Mary? Who did it?"

Everything was happening so fast I can't remember whether her action preceded her words, but I know that Mrs. Cullinan said, "Her name's Margaret, goddamn it, her name's Margaret." And she threw a wedge of the broken plate at me. It could have been the hysteria which put her aim off, but the flying crockery caught Miss Glory right over her ear and she started screaming.

I left the front door wide open so all the neighbors could hear.

Mrs. Cullinan was right about one thing. My name wasn't Mary.

1970

PAULE MARSHALL

b. 1929

Paule Marshall wrote the novel that most black feminist critics consider to be the beginning of contemporary African American women's writings. *Brown Girl, Brownstones* was published in 1959 to fine critical reviews but without much fanfare since most African American literature of the time focused mainly on black manhood. Since then *Brown Girl, Brownstones* has been claimed by well-known African American woman writers such as Alice Walker and Ntozake Shange as important to their own literary development, because it portrayed black women's centrality within the context of a specifically black culture. Not as well known as other major African American women writers, Marshall has maintained her uniqueness over the years and has tended in the United States to fall between the cracks of many categories: African American, Caribbean, third world, woman. She has, however, been celebrated by what are now called postcolonialist critics, from India, West Africa, South America, the Caribbean.

Born April 9 in Stuyvesant Heights (now Bedford Stuyvesant), New York, the daughter of Ada and Samuel Burke, Marshall grew up in an immigrant community confronted by racism and the challenge of maintaining a Caribbean identity while succeeding in the capitalist culture of the United States. Not surprisingly, the themes of colonialism; immigration; the lure of American materialism; racism; African, Caribbean, African American cultures; and the importance of women's voices in the intersection of these cultures are central to Marshall's works. These include four novels—*Brown Girl, Brownstones* (1959), *The Chosen Place, the Timeless People* (1969), *Praisesong for the Widow* (1983), and *Daughters* (1991)—as well as her collection of novellas, *Clap Hands and Sing* (1961); her short stories; and her much-quoted essay, *The Making of a Writer: From the Poets in the Kitchen* (1983). In *Poets in the Kitchen* Marshall traces the powerful influence that her mother and her friends had on her writing. By claiming these supposedly "ordinary" women as her primary literary mentors, Marshall emphasizes the artistry of the oral tradition, so much a part of Caribbean culture, as well as the African belief that the day-to-day rituals of life are the bases of art. Years before the discussions of black English with which we are familiar today, discussions generated to some extent by Alice Walker's *The Color Purple* (1982), Marshall demonstrated how blacks in the diaspora imbued the King's English with their own values and aesthetics. In *Brown Girl, Brownstones*, Marshall dug into American stereotypes of gender and race through her complex characterizations of the apparently domineering Silla, the supposedly weak Deighton, and their brown daughter Selina. Written against the ideological position that the black family was deviant, the evolving position that West Indians were a model minority, as well as the 1950s American belief that women were to be submissive, Marshall's first novel questioned American concepts of womanhood and manhood.

In addition to her education in "the workshop of the kitchen," Marshall read nineteenth- and early-twentieth-century novelists Charles Dickens, Thomas Mann, and Joseph Conrad and from them learned much about rendering characters, especially in relation to culture and setting. Although she graduated from Brooklyn College in 1953 with a degree in English, Marshall at that time had read only two African American writers: Paul Lawrence Dunbar and Richard Wright. During the 1950s, she was especially influenced by two other African American thinkers: Ralph Ellison, whose *Shadow and Act* (1964) she has called her "literary bible," and James Baldwin, whose essays were especially influential to her both as a writer and as a thinker. Like many other African American women she did not encounter earlier African American women writers until the late 1960s, when she read Zora Neale Hurston, Dorothy West, and Gwendolyn Brooks, whose *Maud Martha* (1953) she would call "the finest portrayal of an African American woman in the novel to date and one which had a decided influence on [my] work."

After completing college, Marshall sought work as a journalist, at a time when most professional black women were to be teachers or social workers. It was during her employment at a small black magazine, *Our World*, afraid that she might end up a hack writer, that she began writing *Brown Girl, Brownstones*, not so much for publication as to "unravel [her] own knots." The writing of that novel, which she called an "exhilarating experience," converted her into a fiction writer. But she did not anticipate the resistance to her becoming a writer from her first husband, Kenneth Marshall, whom she had married in 1950 and with whom she had a son. Although he was proud that she wrote, he seriously objected to her decision to write in a friend's apartment, feeling that it would lead to her neglecting their child. From that experience Marshall learned what other contemporary American women writers such as Tillie Olsen in *Silences* (1978) and Alice Walker in *One Child of One's Own* would later write about—that motherhood and authorship are often seen in this society as antithetical.

As a journalist, Marshall traveled to the Caribbean and South America, the settings of *Clap Hands and Sing* (1961). Comprising four novellas—*Barbados, Brooklyn, British Guiana,* and *Brazil*—this collection is the first to trace the connections between black cultures in various parts of the Western Hemisphere. In her second novel, Marshall continued her focus on the world outside the United States. Her monumental *The Chosen Place, the Timeless People* is primarily set in the Caribbean and was called by Jamaican poet Edward Braithwaite "a truly third world novel," for it explores the hidden complexities of the relationship between the supposedly underdeveloped world and the developed worlds.

Marshall's first two novels as well as her stories of the 1960s were ahead of their time in that they clearly focused on the variety of black communities, and on black women, at a time when black cultural nationalism fostered a monolithic view of blacks as urban African American and male. Although her novels received fine reviews, Marshall did not become well known. While she received many awards, including a Guggenheim fellowship and a National Endowment for the Arts fellowship, she had difficulty making a living as a writer. During the 1970s she taught creative writing at universities such as Yale and Columbia and remarried, living part of the time in Haiti and part of the time in the United States. Perhaps as a result of her complicated life, she did not publish her third novel, *Praisesong for the Widow*, until 1982.

Praisesong for the Widow features a very unlikely heroine, Avey Johnson, an African American middle-class, middle-aged woman who has achieved the American Dream but feels her "dis-ease" with it. Marshall's portrayal of Avey's journey from dis-ease to health is a praise song, an African ritual. At the same time *Praisesong*, like Marshall's other novels, is concerned with the ways in which American materialism threatens black cultural wholeness. *Praisesong* also completes a journey begun in *Brown Girl, Brownstones*, what critic Susan Willis calls "an arc of recovery," for Avey has to take a cultural journey back—a journey that Selina began—from the United States through the Caribbean, to an African communal past to regain her sense of wholeness.

In the early 1980s, the Feminist Press reissued Marshall's long out-of-print *Brown Girl, Brownstones* as well as some of her short fiction in *Reena and Other Stories* (1982); *Praisesong for the Widow* received the Before Columbus American Book Award; her most recent novel, *Daughters* (1991), was widely and favorably reviewed. And in 1992, Marshall received the MacArthur Award, an indication that she is finally getting the tribute she deserves, as one of this hemisphere's major contemporary black women writers, as a pioneer in her own right.

Reena

Like most people with unpleasant childhoods, I am on constant guard against the past—the past being for me the people and places associated with the years I served out my girlhood in Brooklyn. The places no longer matter that much since most of them have vanished. The old grammar school, for instance, P.S. 35 ("Dirty 5's" we called it and with justification) has been replaced by a low, coldly functional arrangement of glass and Permastone which bears its name but has none of the feel of a school about it. The small, grudgingly lighted stores along Fulton Street, the soda parlor that was like a church with its stained-glass panels in the door and marble floor have given way to those impersonal emporiums, the supermarkets. Our house even, a brownstone relic whose halls smelled comfortingly of dust and lemon oil, the somnolent street upon which it stood, the tall, muscular trees which shaded it were leveled years ago to make way for a city housing project—a stark, graceless warren for the poor. So that now whenever I revisit that old section of Brooklyn and see these new and ugly forms, I feel nothing. I might as well be in a strange city.

But it is another matter with the people of my past, the faces that in their darkness were myriad reflections of mine. Whenever I encounter them at the funeral or wake, the wedding or christening—those ceremonies by which the past reaffirms its hold—my guard drops and memories banished to the rear of the mind rush forward to rout the present. I almost become the child again—anxious and angry, disgracefully diffident.

Reena was one of the people from that time, and a main contributor to my sense of ineffectualness then. She had not done this deliberately. It was just that whenever she talked about herself (and this was not as often as most people) she seemed to be talking about me also. She ruthlessly analyzed herself, sparing herself nothing. Her honesty was so absolute it was a kind of cruelty.

She had not changed, I was to discover in meeting her again after a separation of twenty years. Nor had I really. For although the years had altered our positions (she was no longer the lord and I the lackey) and I could even afford to forgive her now, she still had the ability to disturb me profoundly by dredging to the surface those aspects of myself that I kept buried. This time, as I listened to her talk over the stretch of one long night, she made vivid without knowing it what is perhaps the most critical fact of my existence—that definition of me, of her and millions like us, formulated by others to serve out their fantasies, a definition we have to combat at an unconscionable cost to the self and even use, at times, in order to survive; the cause of so much shame and rage as well as, oddly enough, a source of pride: simply, what it has meant, what it means, to be a black woman in America.

We met—Reena and myself—at the funeral of her aunt who had been my godmother and whom I had also called aunt, Aunt Vi, and loved, for she and her house had been, respectively, a source of understanding and a place of calm for me as a child. Reena entered the church where the funeral service was being held as though she, not the minister, were coming to officiate, sat down among the immediate family up front, and turned to inspect those behind her. I saw her face then.

It was a good copy of the original. The familiar mold was there, that is, and the configuration of bone beneath the skin was the same despite the slight fleshiness I had never seen there before; her features had even retained their distinctive touches: the positive set to her mouth, the assertive lift to her nose, the same insistent, unsettling eyes which when she was angry became as black as her skin—and this was total, unnerving, and very beautiful. Yet something had happened to her face. It was different despite its sameness. Aging even while it remained enviably young. Time had sketched in, very lightly, the evidence of the twenty years.

As soon as the funeral service was over, I left, hurrying out of the church into the early November night. The wind, already at its winter strength, brought with it the smell of dead leaves and the image of Aunt Vi there in the church, as dead as the leaves—as well as the thought of Reena, whom I would see later at the wake.

Her real name had been Doreen, a standard for girls among West Indians (her mother, like my parents, was from Barbados), but she had changed it to Reena on her twelfth birthday—"As a present to myself"—and had enforced the change on her family by refusing to answer to the old name. "Reena. With two e's!" she would say and imprint those e's on your mind with the indelible black of her eyes and a thin threatening finger that was like a quill.

She and I had not been friends through our own choice. Rather, our mothers, who had known each other since childhood, had forced the relationship. And from the beginning, I had been at a disadvantage. For Reena, as early as the age of twelve, had had a quality that was unique, superior, and therefore dangerous. She seemed defined, even then, all of a piece, the raw edges of her adolescence smoothed over; indeed, she seemed to have escaped adolescence altogether and made one dazzling leap from childhood into the very arena of adult life. At thirteen, for instance, she was reading Zola, Hauptmann, Steinbeck, while I was still in the thrall of the Little Minister and Lorna Doone.[1] When I could only barely conceive of the world beyond Brooklyn, she was talking of the Civil War in Spain, lynchings in the South, Hitler in Poland[2]—and talking with the outrage and passion of a revolutionary. I would try, I remember, to console myself with the thought that she was really an adult masquerading as a child, which meant that I could not possibly be her match.

For her part, Reena put up with me and was, by turns, patronizing and impatient. I merely served as the audience before whom she rehearsed her ideas and the yardstick by which she measured her worldliness and knowledge.

"Do you realize that this stupid country supplied Japan with the scrap iron to make the weapons she's now using against it?" she had shouted at me once.

I had not known that.

Just as she overwhelmed me, she overwhelmed her family, with the result that despite a half dozen brothers and sisters who consumed quantities of bread and jam whenever they visited us, she behaved like an only child and got away with it. Her father, a gentle man with skin the color of dried tobacco and with the nose Reena had inherited jutting out like a crag from his nondescript face, had come from Georgia and was always making jokes about having married a foreigner—Reena's mother being from the West Indies. When not joking, he seemed slightly bewildered by his large family and so in awe of Reena that he avoided her. Reena's mother, a small, dry, formidably black woman, was less a person to me than the abstract principle of force, power, energy. She was alternately strict and indulgent with Reena and, despite the inconsistency, surprisingly effective.

They lived when I knew them in a cold-water railroad flat above a kosher butcher on Belmont Avenue in Brownsville,[3] some distance from us—and this in itself added to Reena's exotic quality. For it was a place where Sunday became Saturday, with all the stores open and pushcarts piled with vegetables and yard goods lined up along the curb, a crowded place where people hawked and spat freely in the streaming gutters and the men looked as if they had just stepped from the pages of the Old Testament with their profuse beards and long, black, satin coats. When Reena was fifteen her family moved to Jamaica in Queens and

---

1. Eponymous heroine of the historical romance by English novelist R. D. Blackmore (1825–1900). "The Little Minister": eponymous hero of the popular sentimental novel by English writer James M. Barrie (1860–1837), who was also the author of Peter Pan. Emile Zola (1840–1902), French novelist, known primarily as an exemplar of literary naturalism. Gerhart Hauptmann (1862–1946), German

dramatist, novelist, and poet. John Steinbeck (1902–1968), American writer, best known for The Grapes of Wrath (1939).
2. Adolf Hitler invaded Poland in 1939, thereby beginning World War II. Civil war raged in Spain from 1936 to 1939.
3. Section of Brooklyn.

since, in those days, Jamaica was considered too far away for visiting, our families lost contact and I did not see Reena again until we were both in college and then only once and not to speak to. . . .

I had walked some distance and by the time I got to the wake, which was being held at Aunt Vi's house, it was well under way. It was a good wake. Aunt Vi would have been pleased. There was plenty to drink, and more than enough to eat, including some Barbadian favorites: coconut bread, pone made with the cassava root, and the little crisp codfish cakes that are so hot with peppers they bring tears to the eyes as you bite into them.

I had missed the beginning, when everyone had probably sat around talking about Aunt Vi and recalling the few events that had distinguished her otherwise undistinguished life. (Someone, I'm sure, had told of the time she had missed the excursion boat to Atlantic City and had her own private picnic—complete with pigeon peas and rice and fricassee chicken—on the pier at 42nd Street.) By the time I arrived, though, it would have been indiscreet to mention her name, for by then the wake had become—and this would also have pleased her—a celebration of life.

I had had two drinks, one right after the other, and was well into my third when Reena, who must have been upstairs, entered the basement kitchen where I was. She saw me before I had quite seen her, and with a cry that alerted the entire room to her presence and charged the air with her special force, she rushed toward me.

"Hey, I'm the one who was supposed to be the writer, not you! Do you know, I still can't believe it," she said, stepping back, her blackness heightened by a white mocking smile. "I read both your books over and over again and I can't really believe it. My Little Paulie!"

I did not mind. For there was respect and even wonder behind the patronizing words and in her eyes. The old imbalance between us had ended and I was suddenly glad to see her.

I told her so and we both began talking at once, but Reena's voice overpowered mine, so that all I could do after a time was listen while she discussed my books, and dutifully answered her questions about my personal life.

"And what about you?" I said, almost brutally, at the first chance I got. "What've you been up to all this time?"

She got up abruptly. "Good Lord, in here's noisy as hell. Come on, let's go upstairs."

We got fresh drinks and went up to Aunt Vi's bedroom, where in the soft light from the lamps, the huge Victorian bed and the pink satin bedspread with roses of the same material strewn over its surface looked as if they had never been used. And, in a way, this was true. Aunt Vi had seldom slept in her bed or, for that matter, lived in her house, because in order to pay for it, she had had to work at a sleeping-in job which gave her only Thursdays and every other Sunday off.

Reena sat on the bed, crushing the roses, and I sat on one of the numerous trunks which crowded the room. They contained every dress, coat, hat, and shoe that Aunt Vi had worn since coming to the United States. I again asked Reena what she had been doing over the years.

"Do you want a blow by blow account?" she said. But despite the flippancy, she was suddenly serious. And when she began it was clear that she had written out the narrative in her mind many times. The words came too easily; the events, the incidents had been ordered in time, and the meaning of her behavior and of the people with whom she had been involved had been painstakingly analyzed. She talked willingly, with desperation almost. And the words by themselves weren't enough. She used her hands to give them form and urgency. I became totally involved with her and all that she said. So much so that as the night wore on I was not certain at times whether it was she or I speaking.

From the time her family moved to Jamaica until she was nineteen or so, Reena's life sounded, from what she told me in the beginning, as ordinary as mine and most of the girls we knew. After high school she had gone on to one of the free city colleges, where she had majored in journalism, worked part time in the school library, and, surprisingly enough, joined a house-plan. (Even I hadn't gone that far.) It was an all-Negro club, since there was a tacit understanding that Negro and white girls did not join each other's houseplans. "Integration, Northern style," she said, shrugging.

It seems that Reena had had a purpose and a plan in joining the group. "I thought," she said with a wry smile, "I could get those girls up off their complacent rumps and out doing something about social issues. . . . I couldn't get them to budge. I remember after the war when a Negro ex-soldier had his eyes gouged out by a bus driver down South I tried getting them to demonstrate on campus. I talked until I was hoarse, but to no avail. They were too busy planning the annual autumn frolic."

Her laugh was bitter but forgiving and it ended in a long, reflective silence. After which she said quietly, "It wasn't that they didn't give a damn. It was just, I suppose, that like most people they didn't want to get involved to the extent that they might have to stand up and be counted. If it ever came to that. Then another thing. They thought they were safe, special. After all, they had grown up in the North, most of them, and so had escaped the southern-style prejudice; their parents, like mine, were struggling to put them through college; they could look forward to being tidy little schoolteachers, social workers, and lab technicians. Oh, they were safe!" The sarcasm scored her voice and then abruptly gave way to pity. "Poor things, they weren't safe, you see, and would never be as long as millions like themselves in Harlem, on Chicago's South Side, down South, all over the place, were unsafe. I tried to tell them this—and they accused me of being oversensitive. They tried not to listen. But I would have held out and, I'm sure, even brought some of them around eventually if this other business with a silly boy hadn't happened at the same time. . . ."

Reena told me then about her first, brief, and apparently innocent affair with a boy she had met at one of the houseplan parties. It had ended, she said, when the boy's parents had met her. "That was it," she said and the flat of her hand cut into the air. "He was forbidden to see me. The reason? He couldn't bring himself to tell me, but I knew. I was too black.

"Naturally, it wasn't the first time something like that had happened. In fact, you might say that was the theme of my childhood. Because I was dark I was always being plastered with Vaseline so I wouldn't look ashy. Whenever I had my picture taken they would pile a whitish powder on my face and make the lights so bright I always came out looking ghostly. My mother stopped speaking to any number of people because they said I would have been pretty if I hadn't been so dark. Like nearly every little black girl, I had my share of dreams of waking up to find myself with long, blond curls, blue eyes, and skin like milk. So I should have been prepared. Besides, that boy's parents were really rejecting themselves in rejecting me.

"Take us"—and her hands, opening in front of my face as she suddenly leaned forward, seemed to offer me the whole of black humanity. "We live surrounded by white images, and white in this world is synonymous with the good, light, beauty, success, so that, despite ourselves sometimes, we run after that whiteness and deny our darkness, which has been made into the symbol of all that is evil and inferior. I wasn't a person to that boy's parents, but a symbol of the darkness they were in flight from, so that just as they—that boy, his parents, those silly girls in the houseplan—were running from me, I started running from them. . . ."

It must have been shortly after this happened when I saw Reena at a debate which was being held at my college. She did not see me, since she was one of the speakers and I was merely part of her audience in the crowded auditorium. The topic had something to do with intellectual freedom in the colleges (McCarthyism[4] was coming into vogue then) and aside from a Jewish boy from City College, Reena was the most effective—sharp, provocative, her position the most radical. The others on the panel seemed intimidated not only by the strength and cogency of her argument but by the sheer impact of her blackness in their white midst.

Her color might have been a weapon she used to dazzle and disarm her opponents. And she had highlighted it with the clothes she was wearing: a white dress patterned with large blocks of primary colors I remember (it looked Mexican) and a pair of intricately wrought silver earrings—long and with many little parts which clashed like muted cymbals over the microphone each time she moved her head. She wore her hair cropped short like a boy's and it was not straightened like mine and the other Negro girls' in the audience, but left in its coarse natural state: a small forest under which her face emerged in its intense and startling handsomeness. I remember she left the auditorium in triumph that day, surrounded by a noisy entourage from her college—all of them white.

"We were very serious," she said now, describing the left-wing group she had belonged to then—and there was a defensiveness in her voice which sought to protect them from all censure. "We believed—because we were young, I suppose, and had nothing as yet to risk—that we could do something about the injustices which everyone around us seemed to take for granted. So we picketed and demonstrated and bombarded Washington with our protests, only to have our names added to the Attorney General's list for all our trouble. We were always standing on street corners handing out leaflets or getting people to sign petitions. We always seemed to pick the coldest days to do that." Her smile held long after the words had died.

4. I.e., the hunt for Communists in every sphere of American life, especially in government, academia, and show business. The hysteria was pro-moted in the early 1950s by Wisconsin senator Joseph R. McCarthy (1908–1957).

"I, we all, had such a sense of purpose then," she said softly, and a sadness lay aslant the smile now, darkening it. "We were forever holding meetings, having endless discussions, arguing, shouting, theorizing. And we had fun. Those parties! There was always somebody with a guitar. We were always singing. . . ." Suddenly, she began singing—and her voice was sure, militant, and faintly self-mocking,

> *"But the banks are made of marble*
> *With a guard at every door*
> *And the vaults are stuffed with silver*
> *That the workers sweated for . . ."*

When she spoke again the words were a sad coda to the song. "Well, as you probably know, things came to an ugly head with McCarthy reigning in Washington, and I was one of the people temporarily suspended from school."

She broke off and we both waited, the ice in our glasses melted and the drinks gone flat.

"At first, I didn't mind," she said finally. "After all, we were right. The fact that they suspended us proved it. Besides, I was in the middle of an affair, a real one this time, and too busy with that to care about anything else." She paused again, frowning.

"He was white," she said quickly and glanced at me as though to surprise either shock or disapproval in my face. "We were very involved. At one point—I think just after we had been suspended and he started working— we even thought of getting married. Living in New York, moving in the crowd we did, we might have been able to manage it. But I couldn't. There were too many complex things going on beneath the surface," she said, her voice strained by the hopelessness she must have felt then, her hands shaping it in the air between us. "Neither one of us could really escape what our color had come to mean in this country. Let me explain. Bob was always, for some odd reason, talking about how much the Negro suffered, and although I would agree with him I would also try to get across that, you know, like all people we also had fun once in a while, loved our children, liked making love—that we were human beings, for God's sake. But he only wanted to hear about the suffering. It was as if this comforted him and eased his own suffering—and he did suffer because of any number of things: his own uncertainty, for one, his difficulties with his family, for another . . .

"Once, I remember, when his father came into New York, Bob insisted that I meet him. I don't know why I agreed to go with him. . . ." She took a deep breath and raised her head very high. "I'll never forget or forgive the look on that old man's face when he opened his hotel-room door and saw me. The horror. I might have been the personification of every evil in the world. His inability to believe that it was his son standing there holding my hand. His shock. I'm sure he never fully recovered. I know I never did. Nor can I forget Bob's laugh in the elevator afterwards, the way he kept repeating: 'Did you see his face when he saw you? Did you? . . .' He had used me, you see. I had been the means, the instrument of his revenge.

"And I wasn't any better. I used him. I took every opportunity to treat him shabbily, trying, you see, through him, to get at that white world which had not only denied me, but had turned my own against me." Her eyes closed. "I went numb all over when I understood what we were doing to, and with, each other. I stayed numb for a long time."

As Reena described the events which followed—the break with Bob, her gradual withdrawal from the left-wing group ("I had had it with them too. I got tired of being 'their Negro,' their pet. Besides, they were just all talk, really. All theories and abstractions. I doubt that, with all their elaborate plans for the Negro and for the workers of the world, any of them had ever been near a factory or up to Harlem")—as she spoke about her reinstatement in school, her voice suggested the numbness she had felt then. It only stirred into life again when she talked of her graduation.

"You should have seen my parents. It was really their day. My mother was so proud she complained about everything: her seat, the heat, the speaker; and my father just sat there long after everybody had left, too awed to move. God, it meant so much to them. It was as if I had made up for the generations his people had picked cotton in Georgia and my mother's family had cut cane in the West Indies. It frightened me."

I asked her after a long wait what she had done after graduating.

"How do you mean, what I did. Looked for a job. Tell me, have you ever looked for work in this man's city?"

"I know." I said, holding up my hand. "Don't tell me."

We both looked at my raised hand which sought to waive the discussion, then at each other and suddenly we laughed, a laugh so loud and violent with pain and outrage it brought tears.

"Girl," Reena said, the tears silver against her blackness. "You could put me blindfolded right now at the Times Building[5] on 42nd Street and I would be able to find my way to every newspaper office in town. But tell me, how come white folks is so *hard*?"

"Just bo'n hard."

We were laughing again and this time I nearly slid off the trunk and Reena fell back among the satin roses.

"I didn't know there were so many ways of saying 'no' without ever once using the word," she said, the laughter lodged in her throat, but her eyes had gone hard. "Sometimes I'd find myself in the elevator, on my way out, and smiling all over myself because I thought I had gotten the job, before it would hit me that they had really said no, not yes. Some of those people in personnel had so perfected their smiles they looked almost genuine. The ones who used to get me, though, were those who tried to make the interview into an intimate chat between friends. They'd put you in a comfortable chair, offer you a cigarette, and order coffee. How I hated that coffee. They didn't know it—or maybe they did—but it was like offering me hemlock. . . .

"You think Christ had it tough?" Her laughter rushed against the air which resisted it. "I was crucified five days a week and half-day on Saturday. I became almost paranoid. I began to think there might be something

5. I.e., the office building of the *New York Times*, in midtown Manhattan.

other than color wrong with me which everybody but me could see, some rare disease that had turned me into a monster.

"My parents suffered. And that bothered me most, because I felt I had failed them. My father didn't say anything but I knew because he avoided me more than usual. He was ashamed, I think, that he hadn't been able, as a man and as my father, to prevent this. My mother—well, you know her. In one breath she would try to comfort me by cursing them: 'But Gor blind them,' "—and Reena's voice captured her mother's aggressive accent—" 'if you had come looking for a job mopping down their floors they would o' hire you, the brutes. But mark my words, their time goin' come, cause God don't love ugly and he ain't stuck on pretty . . .' And in the next breath she would curse me, 'Journalism! Journalism! Whoever heard of colored people taking up journalism. You must feel you's white or something so. The people is right to chuck you out their office. . . .' Poor thing, to make up for saying all that she would wash my white gloves every night and cook cereal for me in the morning as if I were a little girl again. Once she went out and bought me a suit she couldn't afford from Lord and Taylor's. I looked like a Smith girl[6] in blackface in it. . . . So guess where I ended up?"

"As a social investigator for the Welfare Department. Where else?"

We were helpless with laughter again.

"You too?"

"No" I said, "I taught, but that was just as bad."

"No," she said, sobering abruptly. "Nothing's as bad as working for Welfare. Do you know what they really mean by a social investigator? A spy. Someone whose dirty job it is to snoop into the corners of the lives of the poor and make their poverty more vivid by taking from them the last shred of privacy. 'Mrs. Jones, is that a new dress you're wearing?' 'Mrs. Brown, this kerosene heater is not listed in the household items. Did you get an authorization for it?' 'Mrs. Smith, is that a telephone I hear ringing under the sofa?' I was utterly demoralized within a month.

"And another thing. I thought I knew about poverty. I mean, I remember, as a child, having to eat soup made with those white beans the government used to give out free for days running, sometimes, because there was nothing else. I had lived in Brownsville, among all the poor Jews and Poles and Irish there. But what I saw in Harlem, where I had my case load, was different somehow. Perhaps because it seemed so final. There didn't seem to be any way to escape from those dark hallways and dingy furnished rooms. . . . All that defeat." Closing her eyes, she finished the stale whiskey and soda in her glass.

"I remember a client of mine, a girl my age with three children already and no father for them and living in the expensive squalor of a rooming house. Her bewilderment. Her resignation. Her anger. She could have pulled herself out of the mess she was in? People say that, you know, including some Negroes. But this girl didn't have a chance. She had been trapped from the day she was born in some small town down South.

"She became my reference. From then on and even now, whenever I hear people and groups coming up with all kinds of solutions to the quote Negro problem, I ask one question. What are they really doing for that girl, to save her or to save the children? . . . The answer isn't very encouraging."

It was some time before she continued, and then she told me that after Welfare she had gone to work for a private social-work agency, in their publicity department, and had started on her master's in journalism at Columbia. She also left home around this time.

"I had to. My mother started putting the pressure on me to get married. The hints, the remarks—and you know my mother was never the subtle type—her anxiety, which made me anxious about getting married after a while. Besides, it was time for me to be on my own."

In contrast to the unmistakably radical character of her late adolescence (her membership in the left-wing group, the affair with Bob, her suspension from college), Reena's life of this period sounded ordinary, standard—and she admitted it with a slightly self-deprecating, apologetic smile. It was similar to that of any number of unmarried professional Negro women in New York or Los Angeles or Washington: the job teaching or doing social work which brought in a fairly decent salary, the small apartment with kitchenette which they sometimes shared with a roommate; a car, some of them; membership in various political and social action organizations for the militant few like Reena; the vacations in Mexico, Europe, the West Indies, and now Africa; the occasional date. "The interesting men were invariably married," Reena said and then mentioned having had one affair during that time. She had found out he was married and had thought of her only as the perfect mistress. "The bastard," she said, but her smile forgave him.

"Women alone!" she cried, laughing sadly, and her raised opened arms, the empty glass she held in one hand made eloquent their aloneness. "Alone and lonely, and indulging themselves while they wait. The girls of the houseplan have reached their majority only to find that all those years they spent accumulating their degrees and finding the well-paying jobs in the hope that this would raise their stock have, instead, put them at a disadvantage. For the few eligible men around—those who are their intellectual and professional peers, whom they can respect (and there are very few of them)—don't necessarily marry them, but younger women without the degrees and the fat jobs, who are no threat, or they don't marry at all because they are either queer or mother-ridden. Or they marry white women. Now, intellectually I accept this. In fact, some of my best friends are white women . . ." And again our laughter—that loud, searing burst which we used to cauterize our hurt mounted into the unaccepting silence of the room. "After all, our goal is a fully integrated society. And perhaps, as some people believe, the only solution to the race problem is miscegenation.[7] Besides, a man should be able to marry whomever he wishes. Emotionally, though, I am less kind and understanding, and I resent like hell the reasons some black men give for rejecting us for them."

"We're too middle-class-oriented," I said. "Conservative."

"Right. Even though, thank God, that doesn't apply to me."

7. The mixing of races, especially marriage between a white person and a member of another race.

"Too threatening . . . castrating . . ."

"Too independent and impatient with them for not being more ambitious . . . contemptuous . . ."

"Sexually inhibited and unimaginative . . ."

"And the old myth of the excessive sexuality of the black woman goes out the window," Reena cried.

"Not supportive, unwilling to submerge our interests for theirs . . ."

"Lacking in the subtle art of getting and keeping a man . . ."

We had recited the accusations in the form and tone of a litany, and in the silence which followed we shared a thin, hopeless smile.

"They condemn us," Reena said softly but with anger, "without taking history into account. We are still, most of us, the black woman who had to be almost frighteningly strong in order for us all to survive. For, after all, she was the one whom they left (and I don't hold this against them; I understand) with the children to raise, who had to *make* it somehow or the other. And we are still, so many of us, living that history.

"You would think that they would understand this, but few do. So it's up to us. We have got to understand them and save them for ourselves. How? By being, on one hand, persons in our own right and, on the other, fully the woman and the wife. . . . Christ, listen to who's talking! I had my chance. And I tried. Very hard. But it wasn't enough."

The festive sounds of the wake had died to a sober murmur beyond the bedroom. The crowd had gone, leaving only Reena and myself upstairs and the last of Aunt Vi's closest friends in the basement below. They were drinking coffee. I smelled it, felt its warmth and intimacy in the empty house, heard the distant tapping of the cups against the saucers and voices muted by grief. The wake had come full circle: they were again mourning Aunt Vi.

And Reena might have been mourning with them, sitting there amid the satin roses, framed by the massive headboard. Her hands lay as if they had been broken in her lap. Her eyes were like those of someone blind or dead. I got up to go and get some coffee for her.

"You met my husband," she said quickly, stopping me.

"Have I?" I said, sitting down again.

"Yes, before we were married even. At an autograph party for you. He was free-lancing—he's a photographer—and one of the Negro magazines had sent him to cover the party."

As she went on to describe him I remembered him vaguely, not his face, but his rather large body stretching and bending with a dancer's fluidity and grace as he took the pictures. I had heard him talking to a group of people about some issue on race relations very much in the news then and had been struck by his vehemence. For the moment I had found this almost odd, since he was so fair skinned he could have passed for white.

They had met, Reena told me now, at a benefit show for a Harlem day nursery given by one of the progressive groups she belonged to, and had married a month afterward. From all that she said they had had a full and exciting life for a long time. Her words were so vivid that I could almost see them: she with her startling blackness and extraordinary force and he with his near-white skin and a militancy which matched hers; both of them moving among the disaffected in New York, their stand on political and social issues equally uncompromising, the line of their allegiance reaching directly to all those trapped in Harlem. And they had lived the meaning of this allegiance, so that even when they could have afforded a life among the black bourgeoisie of St. Albans or Teaneck,[8] they had chosen to live if not in Harlem so close that there was no difference.

"I—we—were so happy I was frightened at times. Not that anything would change between us, but that someone or something in the world outside us would invade our private place and destroy us out of envy. Perhaps this is what did happen. . . ." She shrugged and even tried to smile but she could not manage it. "Something slipped in while we weren't looking and began its deadly work.

"Maybe it started when Dave took a job with a Negro magazine. I'm not sure. Anyway, in no time, he hated it: the routine, unimaginative pictures he had to take and the magazine itself, which dealt only in unrealities: the high-society world of the black bourgeoisie and the spectacular strides Negroes were making in all fields—you know the type. Yet Dave wouldn't leave. It wasn't the money, but a kind of safety which he had never experienced before which kept him there. He would talk about free-lancing again, about storming the gates of the white magazines downtown, of opening his own studio but he never acted on any one of these things. You see, despite his talent—and he was very talented—he had a diffidence that was fatal.

"When I understood this I literally forced him to open the studio—and perhaps I should have been more subtle and indirect, but that's not my nature. Besides, I was frightened and desperate to help. Nothing happened for a time. Dave's work was too experimental to be commercial. Gradually, though, his photographs started appearing in the prestige camera magazines and money from various awards and exhibits and an occasional assignment started coming in.

"This wasn't enough somehow. Dave also wanted the big, gaudy commercial success that would dazzle and confound that white world downtown and force it to *see* him. And yet, as I said before, he couldn't bring himself to try—and this contradiction began to get to him after awhile.

"It was then, I think, that I began to fail him. I didn't know how to help, you see. I had never felt so inadequate before. And this was very strange and disturbing for someone like me. I was being submerged in his problems— and I began fighting against this.

"I started working again (I had stopped after the second baby). And I was lucky because I got back my old job. And unlucky because Dave saw it as my way of pointing up his deficiencies. I couldn't convince him otherwise: that I had to do it for my own sanity. He would accuse me of wanting to see him fail, of trapping him in all kinds of responsibilities. . . . After a time we both got caught up in this thing, an ugliness came between us, and I began to answer his anger with anger and to trade him insult for insult.

8. Section of Queens, New York, and a town in New Jersey, respectively, with solid middle-class black populations.

"Things fell apart very quickly after that. I couldn't bear the pain of living with him—the insults, our mutual despair, his mocking, the silence. I couldn't subject the children to it any longer. The divorce didn't take long. And thank God, because of the children, we are pleasant when we have to see each other. He's making out very well, I hear."

She said nothing more, but simply bowed her head as though waiting for me to pass judgment on her. I don't know how long we remained like this; but when Reena finally raised her head, the darkness at the window had vanished and dawn was a still, gray smoke against the pane.

"Do you know," she said, and her eyes were clear and a smile had won out over pain, "I enjoy being alone. I don't tell people this because they'll accuse me of either lying or deluding myself. But I do. Perhaps, as my mother tells me, it's only temporary. I don't think so, though. I feel I don't ever want to be involved again. It's not that I've lost interest in men. I go out occasionally, but it's never anything serious. You see, I have all that I want for now."

Her children first of all, she told me, and from her description they sounded intelligent and capable. She was a friend as well as a mother to them, it seemed. They were planning, the four of them, to spend the summer touring Canada. "I will feel that I have done well by them if I give them, if nothing more, a sense of themselves and their worth and importance as black people. Everything I do with them, for them, is to this end. I don't want them ever to be confused about this. They must have their identifications straight from the beginning. No white dolls for them!"

Then her job. She was working now as a researcher for a small progressive news magazine with the promise that once she completed her master's in journalism (she was working on the thesis now) she might get a chance to do some minor reporting. And like most people, she hoped to write someday. "If I can ever stop talking away my substance," she said laughing.

And she was still active in any number of social action groups. In another week or so she would be heading a delegation of mothers down to City Hall "to give the mayor a little hell about conditions in the schools in Harlem." She had started an organization that was carrying on an almost door-to-door campaign in her neighborhood to expose, as she put it, "the blood suckers: all those slumlords and storekeepers with their fixed scales, the finance companies that never tell you the real price of a thing, the petty salesmen that leech off the poor. . . ." In May she was taking her two older girls on a nationwide pilgrimage to Washington to urge for a more rapid implementation of the school desegregation law.

"It's uncanny," she said, and the laugh which accompanied the words was warm, soft with wonder at herself, girlish even, and the air in the room which had refused her laughter before rushed to absorb this now. "Really uncanny. Here I am, practically middle-aged, with three children to raise by myself and with little or no money to do it, and yet I feel, strangely enough, as though life is just beginning—that it's new and fresh with all kinds of possibilities. Maybe it's because I've been through my purgatory and I can't ever be overwhelmed again. I don't know. Anyway, you should see me on evenings after I put the children to bed. I sit alone in the living room (I've repainted it and changed all the furniture since Dave's gone, so that it would at least look different)—I sit there making plans and all of them seem possible. The most important plan right now is Africa. I've already started saving the fare."

I asked her whether she was planning to live there permanently and she said simply, "I want to live and work there. For how long, for a lifetime, I can't say. All I know is that I have to. For myself and for my children. It is important that they see black people who have truly a place and history of their own and who are building for a new and, hopefully, more sensible world. And I must see it, get close to it, because I can never lose the sense of being a displaced person here in America because of my color. Oh, I know I should remain and fight not only for integration (even though, frankly, I question whether I want to be integrated into America as it stands now, with its complacency and materialism, its soullessness) but to help change the country into something better, sounder—if that is still possible. But I have to go to Africa. . . .

"Poor Aunt Vi," she said after a long silence and straightened one of the roses she had crushed. "She never really got to enjoy her bed of roses what with only Thursdays and every other Sunday off. All that hard work. All her life. . . . Our lives have got to make more sense, if only for her."

We got up to leave shortly afterward. Reena was staying on to attend the burial, later in the morning, but I was taking the subway to Manhattan. We parted with the usual promise to get together and exchange telephone numbers. And Reena did phone a week or so later. I don't remember what we talked about though.

Some months later I invited her to a party I was giving before leaving the country. But she did not come.

1962

To Da-Duh, in Memoriam

"... Oh Nana! all of you is not involved in this evil business Death,
Nor all of us in life."
—From "At My Grandmother's Grave," by Lebert Bethune[1]

I did not see her at first I remember. For not only was it dark inside the crowded disembarkation shed in spite of the daylight flooding in from outside, but standing there waiting for her with my mother and sister I was still somewhat blinded from the sheen of tropical sunlight on the water of the bay which we had just crossed in the landing boat, leaving behind us the ship that had brought us from New York lying in the offing. Besides, being only nine years of age at the time and knowing nothing of islands I was busy attending to the alien sights and sounds of Barbados, the unfamiliar smells.

I did not see her, but I was alerted to her approach by my mother's hand which suddenly tightened around mine, and looking up I traced her gaze through the gloom in the shed until I finally made out the small, purposeful, painfully erect figure of the old woman headed our way.

Her face was drowned in the shadow of an ugly rolled-brim brown felt

1. African American historian and poet who wrote for *Ebony* magazine.

hat, but the details of her slight body and of the struggle taking place within it were clear enough—an intense, unrelenting struggle between her back which was beginning to bend ever so slightly under the weight of her eighty-odd years and the rest of her which sought to deny those years and hold that back straight, keep it in line. Moving swiftly toward us (so swiftly it seemed she did not intend stopping when she reached us but would sweep past us out the doorway which opened onto the sea and like Christ walk upon the water!), she was caught between the sunlight at her end of the building and the darkness inside—and for a moment she appeared to contain them both: the light in the long severe old-fashioned white dress she wore which brought the sense of a past that was still alive into our bus-tling present and in the snatch of white at her eye; the darkness in her black high-top shoes and in her face which was visible now that she was closer.

It was as stark and fleshless as a death mask, that face. The maggots might have already done their work, leaving only the framework of bone beneath the ruined skin and deep wells at the temple and jaw. But her eyes were alive, unnervingly so for one so old, with a sharp light that flicked out of the dim clouded depths like a lizard's tongue to snap up all in her view. Those eyes betrayed a child's curiosity about the world, and I wondered vaguely seeing them, and seeing the way the bodice of her ancient dress had col-lapsed in on her flat chest (what had happened to her breasts?), whether she might not be some kind of child at the same time that she was a woman, with fourteen children, my mother included, to prove it. Perhaps she was both, both child and woman, darkness and light, past and present, life and death—all the opposites contained and reconciled in her.

"My Da-duh," my mother said formally and stepped forward. The name sounded like thunder fading softly in the distance.

"Child," Da-duh said, and her tone, her quick scrutiny of my mother, the brief embrace in which they appeared to shy from each other rather than touch, wiped out the fifteen years my mother had been away and re-stored the old relationship. My mother, who was such a formidable figure in my eyes, had suddenly with a word been reduced to my status.

"Yes, God is good," Da-duh said with a nod that was like a tic. "He has spared me to see my child again."

We were led forward then, apologetically because not only did Da-duh prefer boys but she also liked her grandchildren to be "white," that is, fair-skinned; and we had, I was to discover, a number of cousins, the outside children of white estate managers and the like, who qualified. We, though, were as black as she.

My sister being the oldest was presented first. "This one takes after the father," my mother said and waited to be reproved.

Frowning, Da-duh tilted my sister's face toward the light. But her frown soon gave way to a grudging smile, for my sister with her large mild eyes and little broad winged nose, with our father's high-cheeked Barbadian cast to her face, was pretty.

"She's goin' be lucky," Da-duh said and patted her once on the cheek. "Any girl child that takes after the father does be lucky."

She turned then to me. But oddly enough she did not touch me. Instead leaning close, she peered hard at me, and then quickly drew back. I thought I saw her hand start up as though to shield her eyes. It was almost as if she saw not only me, a thin truculent child who it was said took after no one but myself, but something in me which for some reason she found disturbing, even threatening. We looked silently at each other for a long time there in the noisy shed, our gaze locked. She was the first to look away.

"But Adry," she said to my mother and her laugh was cracked, thin, apprehensive. "Where did you get this one here with this fierce look?"

"We don't know where she came out of, my Da-duh," my mother said, laughing also. Even I smiled to myself. After all I had won the encounter. Da-duh had recognized my small strength—and this was all I ever asked of the adults in my life then.

"Come, soul," Da-duh said and took my hand. "You must be one of those New York terrors you hear so much about."

She led us, me at her side and my sister and mother behind, out of the shed into the sunlight that was like a bright driving summer rain and over to a group of people clustered beside a decrepit lorry. They were our relatives, most of them from St. Andrews although Da-duh herself lived in St. Thomas,[2] the women wearing bright print dresses, the colors vivid against their darkness, the men rusty black suits that encased them like straitjackets. Da-duh, holding fast to my hand, became my anchor as they circled round us like a nervous sea, exclaiming, touching us with their calloused hands, embracing us shyly. They laughed in awed bursts: "But look Adry got big-big children!/"And see the nice things they wearing, wrist watch and all!"/"I tell you, Adry has done all right for sheself in New York. . . ."

Da-duh, ashamed at their wonder, embarrassed for them, admonished them the while. "But oh Christ," she said, "why you all got to get on like you never saw people from 'Away' before? You would think New York is the only place in the world to hear wunna. That's why I don't like to go anyplace with you St. Andrews people, you know. You all ain't been colonized."

We were in the back of the lorry finally, packed in among the barrels of ham, flour, cornmeal and rice and the trunks of clothes that my mother had brought as gifts. We made our way slowly through Bridgetown's[3] clogged streets, part of a funereal procession of cars and open-sided buses, bicycles and donkey carts. The dim little limestone shops and offices along the way marched with us, at the same mournful pace, toward the same grave ceremony—as did the people, the women balancing huge baskets on top their heads as if they were no more than hats they wore to shade them from the sun. Looking over the edge of the lorry I watched as their feet slurred the dust. I listened, and their voices, raw and loud and dissonant in the heat, seemed to be grappling with each other high overhead.

Da-duh sat on a trunk in our midst, a monarch amid her court. She still held my hand, but it was different now. I had suddenly become her anchor, for I felt her fear of the lorry with its asthmatic motor (a fear and distrust, I later learned, she held of all machines) beating like a pulse in her rough palm.

2. A parish in the Caribbean island-state of Bar-   3. Capital of Barbados.
bados.

As soon as we left Bridgetown behind though, she relaxed, and while the others around us talked she gazed at the canes standing tall on either side of the winding marl road. "C'dear," she said softly to herself after a time. "The canes this side are pretty enough."

They were too much for me. I thought of them as giant weeds that had overrun the island, leaving scarcely any room for the small tottering houses of sunbleached pine we passed or the people, dark streaks as our lorry hurtled by. I suddenly feared that we were journeying, unaware that we were, toward some dangerous place where the canes, grown as high and thick as a forest, would close in on us and run us through with their stiletto blades. I longed then for the familiar: for the street in Brooklyn where I lived, for my father who had refused to accompany us ("Blowing out good money on foolishness," he had said of the trip), for a game of tag with my friends under the chestnut tree outside our aging brownstone house.

"Yes, but wait till you see St. Thomas canes," Da-duh was saying to me. "They's canes father, bo," she gave a proud arrogant nod. "Tomorrow, God willing, I goin' take you out in the ground and show them to you."

True to her word Da-duh took me with her the following day out into the ground. It was a fairly large plot adjoining her weathered board and shingle house and consisting of a small orchard, a good-sized canepiece and behind the canes, where the land sloped abruptly down, a gully. She had purchased it with Panama money sent her by her eldest son, my uncle Joseph, who had died working on the canal. We entered the ground along a trail no wider than her body and as devious and complex as her reasons for showing me her land. Da-duh strode briskly ahead, her slight form filled out this morning by the layers of sacking petticoats she wore under her working dress to protect her against the damp. A fresh white cloth, elaborately arranged around her head, added to her height, and lent her a vain, almost roguish air.

Her pace slowed once we reached the orchard, and glancing back at me occasionally over her shoulder, she pointed out the various trees. "This here is a breadfruit," she said. "That one yonder is a papaw. Here's a guava. This is a mango. I know you don't have anything like these in New York. Here's a sugar apple." (The fruit looked more like artichokes than apples to me.) "This one bears limes. . . ." She went on for some time, intoning the names of the trees as though they were those of her gods. Finally, turning to me, she said, "I know you don't have anything this nice where you come from." Then, as I hesitated: "I said I know you don't have anything this nice where you come from. . . ."

"No," I said and my world did seem suddenly lacking.

Da-duh nodded and passed on. The orchard ended and we were on the narrow cart road that led through the canepiece, the canes clashing like swords above my cowering head. Again she turned and her thin muscular arms spread wide, her dim gaze embracing the small field of canes, she said—and her voice almost broke under the weight of her pride, "Tell me, have you got anything like these in that place where you were born?"

"No."

"I din' think so. I bet you don't even know that these canes here and the sugar you eat is one and the same thing. That they does throw the canes into some damn machine at the factory and squeeze out all the little life in them to make sugar for you all so in New York to eat. I bet you don't know that."

"I've got two cavities and I'm not allowed to eat a lot of sugar."

But Da-duh didn't hear me. She had turned with an inexplicably angry motion and was making her way rapidly out of the canes and down the slope at the edge of the field which led to the gully below. Following her apprehensively down the incline amid a stand of banana plants whose leaves flapped like elephants ears in the wind, I found myself in the middle of a small tropical wood—a place dense and damp and gloomy and tremulous with the fitful play of light and shadow as the leaves high above moved against the sun that was almost hidden from view. It was a violent place, the tangled foliage fighting each other for a chance at the sunlight, the branches of the trees locked in what seemed an immemorial struggle, one both necessary and inevitable. But despite the violence, it was pleasant, almost peaceful in the gully, and beneath the thick undergrowth the earth smelled like spring.

This time Da-duh didn't even bother to ask her usual question, but simply turned and waited for me to speak.

"No," I said, my head bowed. "We don't have anything like this in New York."

"Ah," she cried, her triumph complete. "I din' think so. Why, I've heard that's a place where you can walk till you near drop and never see a tree."

"We've got a chestnut tree in front of our house," I said.

"Does it bear?" She waited. "I ask you, does it bear?"

"Not anymore," I muttered. "It used to, but not anymore."

She gave the nod that was like a nervous twitch. "You see," she said. "Nothing can bear there." Then, secure behind her scorn, she added, "But tell me, what's this snow like that you hear so much about?"

Looking up, I studied her closely, sensing my chance, and then I told her, describing at length and with as much drama as I could summon not only what snow in the city was like, but what it would be like here, in her perennial summer kingdom.

". . . And you see all these trees you got here," I said. "Well, they'd be bare. No leaves, no fruit, nothing. They'd be covered in snow. You see your canes. They'd be buried under tons of snow. The snow would be higher than your head, higher than your house, and you wouldn't be able to come down into this here gully because it would be snowed under. . . ."

She searched my face for the lie, still scornful but intrigued. "What a thing, huh?" she said finally, whispering it softly to herself.

"And when it snows you couldn't dress like you are now," I said. "Oh no, you'd freeze to death. You'd have to wear a hat and gloves and galoshes and ear muffs so your ears wouldn't freeze and drop off, and a heavy coat. I've got a Shirley Temple coat with fur on the collar. I can dance. You wanna see?"

Before she could answer I began, with a dance called the Truck which was popular back then in the 1930's. My right forefinger waving, I trucked around the nearby trees and around Da-duh's awed and rigid form. After the Truck I did the Suzy-Q, my lean hips swishing, my sneakers sidling zigzag over the ground. "I can sing," I said and did so, starting with "I'm Gonna Sit Right Down and Write Myself a Letter," then without pausing, "Tea For Two," and ending with "I Found a Million Dollar Baby in a Five and Ten Cent Store."

For long moments afterwards Da-duh stared at me as if I were a creature from Mars, an emissary from some world she did not know but which intrigued her and whose power she both felt and feared. Yet something about my performance must have pleased her, because bending down she slowly lifted her long skirt and then, one by one, the layers of petticoats until she came to a drawstring purse dangling at the end of a long strip of cloth tied round her waist. Opening the purse she handed me a penny. "Here," she said half-smiling against her will. "Take this to buy yourself a sweet at the shop up the road. There's nothing to be done with you, soul."

From then on, whenever I wasn't taken to visit relatives, I accompanied Da-duh out into the ground, and alone with her amid the canes or down in the gully I told her about New York. It always began with some slighting remark on her part: "I know they don't have anything this nice where you come from," or "Tell me, I hear those foolish people in New York does do such and such. . . ." But as I answered, recreating my towering world of steel and concrete and machines for her, building the city out of words, I would feel her give way. I came to know the signs of her surrender: the total stillness that would come over her little hard dry form, the probing gaze that like a surgeon's knife sought to cut through my skull to get at the images there, to see if I were lying; above all, her fear, a fear nameless and profound, the same one I had felt beating in the palm of her hand that day in the lorry.

Over the weeks I told her about refrigerators, radios, gas stoves, elevators, trolley cars, wringer washing machines, movies, airplanes, the cyclone at Coney Island, subways, toasters, electric lights: "At night, see, all you have to do is flip this little switch on the wall and all the lights in the house go on. Just like that. Like magic. It's like turning on the sun at night."

"But tell me," she said to me once with a faint mocking smile, "do the white people have all these things too or it's only the people looking like us?"

I laughed. "What d'ya mean," I said. "The white people have even better." Then: "I beat up a white girl in my class last term."

"Beating up white people!" Her tone was incredulous.

"How you mean!" I said, using an expression of hers. "She called me a name."

For some reason Da-duh could not quite get over this and repeated in the same hushed, shocked voice, "Beating up white people now! Oh, the lord, the world's changing up so I can scarce recognize it anymore."

One morning toward the end of our stay, Da-duh led me into a part of the gully that we had never visited before, an area darker and more thickly overgrown than the rest, almost impenetrable. There in a small clearing amid the dense bush, she stopped before an incredibly tall royal palm which rose cleanly out of the ground, and drawing the eye up with it, soared high above the trees around it into the sky. It appeared to be touching the blue dome of sky, to be flaunting its dark crown of fronds right in the blinding white face of the late morning sun.

Da-duh watched me a long time before she spoke, and then she said very quietly, "All right, now, tell me if you've got anything this tall in that place you're from."

I almost wished, seeing her face, that I could have said no. "Yes," I said. "We've got buildings hundreds of times this tall in New York. There's one called the Empire State Building that's the tallest in the world. My class visited it last year and I went all the way to the top. It's got over a hundred floors. I can't describe how tall it is. Wait a minute. What's the name of that hill I went to visit the other day, where they have the police station?"

"You mean Bissex?"

"Yes, Bissex. Well, the Empire State Building is way taller than that."

"You're lying now!" she shouted, trembling with rage. Her hand lifted to strike me.

"No, I'm not," I said. "It really is, if you don't believe me I'll send you a picture postcard of it soon as I get back home so you can see for yourself. But it's way taller than Bissex."

All the fight went out of her at that. The hand poised to strike me fell limp to her side, and as she stared at me, seeing not me but the building that was taller than the highest hill she knew, the small stubborn light in her eyes (it was the same amber as the flame in the kerosene lamp she lit at dusk) began to fail. Finally, with a vague gesture that even in the midst of her defeat still tried to dismiss me and my world, she turned and started back through the gully, walking slowly, her steps groping and uncertain, as if she were suddenly no longer sure of the way, while I followed triumphant yet strangely saddened behind.

The next morning I found her dressed for our morning walk but stretched out on the Berbice chair in the tiny drawing room where she sometimes napped during the afternoon heat, her face turned to the window beside her. She appeared thinner and suddenly indescribably old.

"My Da-duh," I said.

"Yes, nuh," she said. Her voice was listless and the face she slowly turned my way was, now that I think back on it, like a Benin mask, the features drawn and almost distorted by an ancient abstract sorrow.

"Don't you feel well?" I asked.

"Girl, I don't know."

"My Da-duh, I goin' boil you some bush tea," my aunt, Da-duh's youngest child, who lived with her, called from the shed roof kitchen.

"Who tell you I need bush tea?" she cried, her voice assuming for a moment its old authority. "You can't even rest nowadays without some malicious person looking for you to be dead. Come girl," she motioned me to a place beside her on the old-fashioned lounge chair, "give us a tune."

I sang for her until breakfast at eleven, all my brash irreverent Tin Pan Alley songs, and then just before noon we went out into the ground. But it was a short, dispirited walk. Da-duh didn't even notice that the mangoes were beginning to ripen and would have to be picked before the village boys got to them. And when she paused occasionally and looked out across the canes or up at her trees it wasn't as if she were seeing them but something else. Some huge, monolithic shape had imposed itself, it seemed, between her and the land, obstructing her vision. Returning to the house she slept the entire afternoon on the Berbice chair.

She remained like this until we left, languishing away the mornings on the chair at the window gazing out at the land as if it were already doomed; then, at noon, taking the brief stroll with me through the ground during which she seldom spoke, and afterwards returning home to sleep till almost dusk sometimes.

On the day of our departure she put on the austere, ankle length white dress, the black shoes and brown felt hat (her town clothes she called them), but she did not go with us to town. She saw us off on the road outside her house and in the midst of my mother's tearful protracted farewell, she leaned down and whispered in my ear, "Girl, you're not to forget now to send me the picture of that building, you hear."

By the time I mailed her the large colored picture postcard of the Empire State building she was dead. She died during the famous '37 strike[4] which began shortly after we left. On the day of her death England sent planes flying low over the island and in a show of force—so low, according to my aunt's letter, that the downdraft from them shook the ripened mangoes from the trees in Da-duh's orchard. Frightened, everyone in the village fled into the canes. Except Da-duh. She remained in the house at the window so my aunt said, watching as the planes came swooping and screaming like monstrous birds down over the village, over her house, rattling her trees and flattening the young canes in her field. It must have seemed to her lying there that they did not intend pulling out of their dive, but like the hardback beetles which hurled themselves with suicidal force against the walls of the house at night, those menacing silver shapes would hurl themselves in an ecstasy of self-immolation onto the land, destroying it utterly.

When the planes finally left and the villagers returned they found her dead on the Berbice chair at the window.

She died and I lived, but always, to this day even, within the shadow of her death. For a brief period after I was grown I went to live alone, like one doing penance, in a loft above a noisy factory in downtown New York and there painted seas of sugar-cane and huge swirling Van Gogh suns and palm trees striding like brightly-plumed Tutsi warriors across a tropical landscape, while the thunderous tread of the machines downstairs jarred the floor beneath my easel, mocking my efforts.

1967

The Making of a Writer: From the Poets in the Kitchen

Some years ago, when I was teaching a graduate seminar in fiction at Columbia University, a well known male novelist visited my class to speak on his development as a writer. In discussing his formative years, he didn't realize it but he seriously endangered his life by remarking that women

4. Labor riots in the Caribbean that precipitated the struggle for independence for many island-states.

writers are luckier than those of his sex because they usually spend so much time as children around their mothers and their mothers' friends in the kitchen.

What did he say that for? The women students immediately forgot about being in awe of him and began readying their attack for the question and answer period later on. Even I bristled. There again was that awful image of women locked away from the world in the kitchen with only each other to talk to, and their daughters locked in with them.

But my guest wasn't really being sexist or trying to be provocative or even spoiling for a fight. What he meant—when he got around to explaining himself more fully—was that, given the way children are (or were) raised in our society, with little girls kept closer to home and their mothers, the woman writer stands a better chance of being exposed, while growing up, to the kind of talk that goes on among women, more often than not in the kitchen; and that this experience gives her an edge over her male counterpart by instilling in her an appreciation for ordinary speech.

It was clear that my guest lecturer attached great importance to this, which is understandable. Common speech and the plain, workaday words that make it up are, after all, the stock in trade of some of the best fiction writers. They are the principal means by which characters in a novel or story reveal themselves and give voice sometimes to profound feelings and complex ideas about themselves and the world. Perhaps the proper measure of a writer's talent is skill in rendering everyday speech—when it is appropriate to the story—as well as the ability to tap, to exploit, the beauty, poetry and wisdom it often contains.

"If you say what's on your mind in the language that comes to you from your parents and your street and friends you'll probably say something beautiful." Grace Paley [1] tells this, she says, to her students at the beginning of every writing course.

It's all a matter of exposure and a training of the ear for the would-be writer in those early years of apprenticeship. And, according to my guest lecturer, this training, the best of it, often takes place in as unglamorous a setting as the kitchen.

He didn't know it, but he was essentially describing my experience as a little girl. I grew up among poets. Now they didn't look like poets—whatever that breed is supposed to look like. Nothing about them suggested that poetry was their calling. They were just a group of ordinary housewives and mothers, my mother included, who dressed in a way (shapeless housedresses, dowdy felt hats and long, dark, solemn coats) that made it impossible for me to imagine they had ever been young.

Nor did they do what poets were supposed to do—spend their days in an attic room writing verses. They never put pen to paper except to write occasionally to their relatives in Barbados. "I take my pen in hand hoping these few lines will find you in health as they leave me fair for the time being," was the way their letters invariably began. Rather, their day was spent "scrubbing floor," as they described the work they did.

Several mornings a week these unknown bards would put an apron and a

1. American poet and short story writer (b. 1922).

pair of old house shoes in a shopping bag and take the train or streetcar from our section of Brooklyn out to Flatbush.[2] There, those who didn't have steady jobs would wait on certain designated corners for the white housewives in the neighborhood to come along and bargain with them over pay for a day's work cleaning their houses. This was the ritual even in the winter.

Later, armed with the few dollars they had earned, which in their vocabulary became "a few raw-mouth pennies," they made their way back to our neighborhood, where they would sometimes stop off to have a cup of tea or cocoa together before going home to cook dinner for their husbands and children.

The basement kitchen of the brownstone house where my family lived was the usual gathering place. Once inside the warm safety of its walls the women threw off the drab coats and hats, seated themselves at the large center table, drank their cups of tea or cocoa, and talked. While my sister and I sat at a smaller table over in a corner doing our homework, they talked—endlessly, passionately, poetically, and with impressive range. No subject was beyond them. True, they would indulge in the usual gossip: whose husband was running with whom, whose daughter looked slightly "in the way" (pregnant) under her bridal gown as she walked down the aisle. That sort of thing. But they also tackled the great issues of the time. They were always, for example, discussing the state of the economy. It was the mid and late 30's then, and the aftershock of the Depression, with its soup lines and suicides on Wall Street, was still being felt.

Some people, they declared, didn't know how to deal with adversity. They didn't know that you had to "tie up your belly" (hold in the pain, that is) when things got rough and go on with life. They took their image from the bellyband that is tied around the stomach of a newborn baby to keep the navel pressed in.

They talked politics. Roosevelt was their hero. He had come along and rescued the country with relief and jobs, and in gratitude they christened their sons Franklin and Delano and hoped they would live up to the names.

If F.D.R. was their hero, Marcus Garvey[3] was their God. The name of the fiery, Jamaican-born black nationalist of the 20's was constantly invoked around the table. For he had been their leader when they first came to the United States from the West Indies shortly after World War I. They had contributed to his organization, the United Negro Improvement Association (UNIA), out of their meager salaries, bought shares in his ill-fated Black Star Shipping Line, and at the height of the movement they had marched as members of his "nurses' brigade" in their white uniforms up Seventh Avenue in Harlem during the great Garvey Day parades. Garvey: He lived on through the power of their memories.

And their talk was of war and rumors of wars. They raged against World War II when it broke out in Europe, blaming it on the politicians. "It's these politicians. They're the ones always starting up all this lot of war. But

2. Another section of Brooklyn.
3. Leader of the Back to Africa movement (1887–1940).

what they care? It's the poor people got to suffer and mothers with their sons." If it was *their* sons, they swore they would keep them out of the Army by giving them soap to eat each day to make their hearts sound defective. Hitler? He was for them "the devil incarnate."

Then there was home. They reminisced often and at length about home. The old country. Barbados—or Bimshire, as they affectionately called it. The little Caribbean island in the sun they loved but had to leave. "Poor—poor but sweet" was the way they remembered it.

And naturally they discussed their adopted home. America came in for both good and bad marks. They lashed out at it for the racism they encountered. They took to task some of the people they worked for, especially those who gave them only a hard-boiled egg and a few spoonfuls of cottage cheese for lunch. "As if anybody can scrub floor on an egg and some cheese that don't have no taste to it!"

Yet although they caught H in "this man country," as they called America, it was nonetheless a place where "you could at least see your way to make a dollar." That much they acknowledged. They might even one day accumulate enough dollars, with both them and their husbands working, to buy the brownstone houses which, like my family, they were only leasing at that period. This was their consuming ambition: to "buy house" and to see the children through.

There was no way for me to understand it at the time, but the talk that filled the kitchen those afternoons was highly functional. It served as therapy, the cheapest kind available to my mother and her friends. Not only did it help them recover from the long wait on the corner that morning and the bargaining over their labor, it restored them to a sense of themselves and reaffirmed their self-worth. Through language they were able to overcome the humiliations of the work-day.

But more than therapy, that freewheeling, wide-ranging, exuberant talk functioned as an outlet for the tremendous creative energy they possessed. They were women in whom the need for self-expression was strong, and since language was the only vehicle readily available to them they made of it an art form that—in keeping with the African tradition in which art and life are one—was an integral part of their lives.

And their talk was a refuge. They never really ceased being baffled and overwhelmed by America—its vastness, complexity and power. Its strange customs and laws. At a level beyond words they remained fearful and in awe. Their uneasiness and fear were even reflected in their attitude toward the children they had given birth to in this country. They referred to those like myself, the little Brooklyn-born Bajans (Barbadians), as "these New York children" and complained that they couldn't discipline us properly because of the laws here. "You can't beat these children as you would like, you know, because the authorities in this place will dash you in jail for them. After all, these is New York children." Not only were we different, American, we had, as they saw it, escaped their ultimate authority.

Confronted therefore by a world they could not encompass, which even limited their rights as parents, and at the same time finding themselves permanently separated from the world they had known, they took refuge in language. "Language is the only homeland," Czeslaw Milosz, the emigré Polish writer and Nobel Laureate, has said. This is what it became for the women at the kitchen table.

It served another purpose also, I suspect. My mother and her friends were after all the female counterpart of Ralph Ellison's invisible man.[4] Indeed, you might say they suffered a triple invisibility, being black, female and foreigners. They really didn't count in American society except as a source of cheap labor. But given the kind of women they were, they couldn't tolerate the fact of their invisibility, their powerlessness. And they fought back, using the only weapon at their command: the spoken word.

Those late afternoon conversations on a wide range of topics were a way for them to feel they exercised some measure of control over their lives and the events that shaped them. "Soully-gal, talk yuh talk!" they were always exhorting each other. "In this man world you got to take yuh mouth and make a gun!" They were in control, if only verbally and if only for the two hours or so that they remained in our house.

For me, sitting over in the corner, being seen but not heard, which was the rule for children in those days, it wasn't only what the women talked about—the content—but the way they put things—their style. The insight, irony, wit and humor they brought to their stories and discussions and their poet's inventiveness and daring with language—which of course I could only sense but not define back then.

They had taken the standard English taught them in the primary schools of Barbados and transformed it into an idiom, an instrument that more adequately described them—changing around the syntax and imposing their own rhythm and accent so that the sentences were more pleasing to their ears. They added the few African sounds and words that had survived, such as the derisive suck-teeth sound and the word "yam," meaning to eat. And to make it more vivid, more in keeping with their expressive quality, they brought to bear a raft of metaphors, parables, Biblical quotations, sayings and the like:

"The sea ain' got no back door," they would say, meaning that it wasn't like a house where if there was a fire you could run out the back. Meaning that it was not to be trifled with. And meaning perhaps in a larger sense that man should treat all of nature with caution and respect.

"I has read hell by heart and called every generation blessed!" They sometimes went in for hyperbole.

A woman expecting a baby was never said to be pregnant. They never used that word. Rather, she was "in the way" or, better yet, "tumbling big." "Guess who I butt up on in the market the other day tumbling big again!"

And a woman with a reputation of being too free with her sexual favors was known in their book as a "thoroughfare"—the sense of men like a steady stream of cars moving up and down the road of her life. Or she might be dubbed "a free-bee," which was my favorite of the two. I liked the image it conjured up of a woman scandalous perhaps but independent, who flitted from one flower to another in a garden of male beauties, sampling their nectar, taking her pleasure at will, the roles reversed.

---

4. Hero of Ellison's 1952 novel *Invisible Man*.

And nothing, no matter how beautiful, was ever described as simply beautiful. It was always "beautiful-ugly": the beautiful-ugly dress, the beautiful-ugly house, the beautiful-ugly car. Why the word "ugly," I used to wonder, when the thing they were referring to was beautiful, and they knew it. Why the antonym, the contradiction, the linking of opposites? It used to puzzle me greatly as a child.

There is the theory in linguistics which states that the idiom of a people, the way they use language, reflects not only the most fundamental views they hold of themselves and the world but their very conception of reality. Perhaps in using the term "beautiful-ugly" to describe nearly everything, my mother and her friends were expressing what they believed to be a fundamental dualism in life: the idea that a thing is at the same time its opposite, and that these opposites, these contradictions make up the whole. But theirs was not a Manichaean brand of dualism that sees matter, flesh, the body, as inherently evil, because they constantly addressed each other as "soully-gal"—soul: spirit; gal: the body, flesh, the visible self. And it was clear from their tone that they gave one as much weight and importance as the other. They had never heard of the mind/body split.

As for God, they summed up His essential attitude in a phrase. "God," they would say, "don' love ugly and He ain' stuck on pretty."

Using everyday speech, the simple commonplace words—but always with imagination and skill—they gave voice to the most complex ideas. Flannery O'Connor would have approved of how they made ordinary language work, as she put it, "doubletime," stretching, shading, deepening its meaning. Like Joseph Conrad[5] they were always trying to infuse new life in the "old old words worn thin . . . by . . . careless usage." And the goals of their oral art were the same as his: "to make you hear, to make you feel . . . to make you *see*." This was their guiding esthetic.

By the time I was 8 or 9, I graduated from the corner of the kitchen to the neighborhood library, and thus from the spoken to the written word. The Macon Street Branch of the Brooklyn Public Library was an imposing half block long edifice of heavy gray masonry, with glass-paneled doors at the front and two tall metal torches symbolizing the light that comes of learning flanking the wide steps outside.

The inside was just as impressive. More steps—of pale marble with gleaming brass railings at the center and sides—led up to the circulation desk, and a great pendulum clock gazed down from the balcony stacks that faced the entrance. Usually stationed at the top of the steps like the guards outside Buckingham Palace[6] was the custodian, a stern-faced West Indian type who for years, until I was old enough to obtain an adult card, would immediately shoo me with one hand into the Children's Room and with the other threaten me into silence, a finger to his lips. You would have thought he was the chief librarian and not just someone whose job it was to keep the brass polished and the clock wound. I put him in a story called "Barbados" years later and had terrible things happen to him at the end.

5. Polish-born writer of fiction (1857–1924). The quotation is from the preface to *The Nigger of the "Narcissus."* O'Connor (1925–1964), American fiction writer who wrote that the aim of the short story writer is "to make the concrete work double time" (*Mystery and Manners*, 1969).
6. London residence of the British sovereigns; its guards are the famous "Beefeaters."

I sheltered from the storm of adolescence in the Macon Street library, reading voraciously, indiscriminately, everything from Jane Austen to Zane Grey,[7] but with a special passion for the long, full-blown, richly detailed 18th- and 19th-century picaresque tales: "Tom Jones," "Great Expectations," "Vanity Fair."[8]

But although I loved nearly everything I read and would enter fully into the lives of the characters—indeed, would cease being myself and become them—I sensed a lack after a time. Something I couldn't quite define was missing. And then one day, browsing in the poetry section, I came across a book by someone called Paul Laurence Dunbar,[9] and opening it I found the photograph of a wistful, sad-eyed poet who to my surprise was black. I turned to a poem at random. "Little brown-baby wif spa'klin' / eyes / Come to yo' pappy an' set on his knee." Although I had a little difficulty at first with the words in dialect, the poem spoke to me as nothing I had read before of the closeness, the special relationship I had had with my father, who by then had become an ardent believer in Father Divine[1] and gone to live in Father's "kingdom" in Harlem. Reading it helped to ease somewhat the tight knot of sorrow and longing I carried around in my chest that refused to go away. I read another poem. " 'Lias! 'Lias! Bless de Lawd! / Don' you know de day's / erbroad? / Ef you don' get up, you scamp / Dey'll be trouble in dis camp." I laughed. It reminded me of the way my mother sometimes yelled at my sister and me to get out of bed in the mornings.

And another: "Seen my lady home las' night / Jump back, honey, jump back. / Hel' huh han' an' sque'z it tight . . ." About love between a black man and a black woman. I had never seen that written about before and it roused in me all kinds of delicious feelings and hopes.

And I began to search then for books and stories and poems about "The Race" (as it was put back then), about my people. While not abandoning Thackeray, Fielding, Dickens and the others, I started asking the reference librarian, who was white, for books by Negro writers, although I must admit I did so at first with a feeling of shame—the shame I and many others used to experience in those days whenever the word "Negro" or "colored" came up.

No grade school literature teacher of mine had ever mentioned Dunbar or James Weldon Johnson or Langston Hughes. I didn't know that Zora Neale Hurston existed and was busy writing and being published during those years. Nor was I made aware of people like Frederick Douglass and Harriet Tubman[2]—their spirit and example—or the great 19th-century abolitionist and feminist Sojourner Truth. There wasn't even Negro History Week when I attended P.S. 35 on Decatur Street!

What I needed, what all the kids—West Indian and native black American alike—with whom I grew up needed, was an equivalent of the Jewish

---

7. American writer of westerns (1875–1939). Austen (1775–1817), English novelist.
8. Novels by the English authors Henry Fielding (1707–1754), Charles Dickens (1812–1870), and William Thackeray (1811–1863), respectively.
9. American poet (1872–1906).
1. Born George Baker (1880–1965), he became the most popular Harlem religious leader of the 1930s, gaining wealth and attracting many follow-

ers to his cultlike Peace Mission movement.
2. A fugitive slave (1820?–1913) who rescued many other slaves. Johnson (1871–1938), lyricist, writer, and civil rights activist who became secretary of the NAACP. Hughes (1902–1967), author of poetry, fiction, and plays. Hurston (1891–1960), writer and anthropologist. Douglass (1817–1896), orator, author, abolitionist, and supporter of women's rights.

shul,[3] someplace where we could go after school—the schools that were shortchanging us—and read works by those like ourselves and learn about our history.

It was around that time also that I began harboring the dangerous thought of someday trying to write myself. Perhaps a poem about an apple tree, although I had never seen one. Or the story of a girl who could magically transplant herself to wherever she wanted to be in the world—such as Father Divine's kingdom in Harlem. Dunbar—his dark, eloquent face, his large volume of poems—permitted me to dream that I might someday write, and with something of the power with words my mother and her friends possessed.

When people at readings and writers' conferences ask me who my major influences were, they are sometimes a little disappointed when I don't immediately name the usual literary giants. True, I am indebted to those writers, white and black, whom I read during my formative years and still read for instruction and pleasure. But they were preceded in my life by another set of giants whom I always acknowledged before all others: the group of women around the table long ago. They taught me my first lessons in the narrative art. They trained my ear. They set a standard of excellence. This is why the best of my work must be attributed to them; it stands as testimony to the rich legacy of language and culture they so freely passed on to me in the wordshop of the kitchen.

1983

3. School, synagogue (Yiddish).

ADRIENNE KENNEDY
b. 1931

In an autobiographical essay in *Drama Review* in 1977, Adrienne Kennedy describes her playwrighting as a process of the transmutation of images:

> I see my writing as a growth of images. I think all my plays come out of dreams I had two or three years before; I played around with the images for a long period of time to try to get to the most powerful dreams. . . . I think about things for many years and keep loads of notebooks, with images, dreams, ideas I've jotted down.

Kennedy's approach has resulted in plays that combine expressionism and surrealism and remnants of African ritual to create rich, original pieces of theater. In creating her dramatic vision, Kennedy uses various theatrical devices, including masks, nontraditional music, pagan and Christian symbolism, the playing of characters by more than one actor, and the transforming of characters into other characters.

Her unique style, introduced in 1962 with *Funnyhouse of the Negro*, has powerfully influenced conceptions of theater, because it demonstrates the political potential of abstract theatrical language. *New York Times* critic Clive Barnes wrote in a 1969 review that

> while almost every black playwright in the country is fundamentally concerned with realism . . . Miss Kennedy is weaving some kind of dramatic fabric

of poetry. . . . What she writes is a mosaic of feeling, with each tiny stone
stained with the blood of the gray experience.

Kennedy was born Adrienne Lita on September 15, 1931, in Pittsburgh, Pennsylvania, the first child and only daughter of Cornell Wallace Hawkins, executive secretary of the YMCA, and Etra Haugebook Hawkins, a teacher. Kennedy was a gifted
child who learned to read at age three. When she was four, her family moved to an
integrated neighborhood in Cleveland, Ohio. Kennedy compensated for a certain
rigidness in her childhood by developing a dramatic inner life. "I often saw our
family [as] if they were in a play," she recalled, and, indeed, Kennedy's characters
often are composites of people from her childhood, particularly her immediate
family. Her unique autobiography, People Who Led to My Plays (1987), begins
with lists of actual and fictional characters who shaped her early life. However,
Kennedy later adds, "I don't think I felt different from my family at all. I was proud
of my family."

Kennedy graduated from Ohio State University in 1953 with a degree in elementary education. Two weeks later, she married Joseph C. Kennedy. Six months later,
Joseph was sent to Korea. Pregnant, Adrienne returned to her parents' home to await
her husband, during which time she began writing her first plays, including a piece
based on Elmer Rice's Street Scene and another based on Tennessee Williams' Glass
Menagerie. Upon her husband's return from Korea, he decided to continue his education at Columbia's Teachers College, and he and Adrienne along with their son,
Joseph C. Jr., moved to New York. Kennedy studied creative writing at Columbia
University from 1954 to 1956 and at the American Theatre Wing in 1958. In 1961,
the family traveled to Africa, where she began work on Funnyhouse of the Negro.
Due to a difficult pregnancy with her second son, Adam, the family moved to Italy,
where Kennedy finished the play that would launch her career as a playwright.

As drama critic Margaret Wilkerson has noted, in Funnyhouse of a Negro
Kennedy used her experiences as a black woman, her knowledge of the classics,
and her extensive travels in Europe and Africa, from the mammoth statue of Queen
Victoria in front of Buckingham Palace to the murder of Patrice Lumumba in the
Congo to evoke the ambiguities of a people created out of the clash of African and
European cultures. Kennedy submitted the play to Edward Albee's workshop at
Circle-in-the Square in New York, where it was produced with some of the best
actors of the day, Diana Sands, Andre Gregory, Yaphet Kotto. Despite a controversial reception, Albee optioned the play and produced it Off-Broadway in 1964, at
the East End Theatre, where it became the season's cult hit, running for forty-six
performances and winning an Obie Award for Distinguished Play.

Kennedy's next play, The Owl Answers (1965), is her favorite. At the core of this
one act is a black woman's quest for identity in a world dominated by whites.
Kennedy first explores the representing of multiple selves by using composite characters that she transforms back and forth into different parts of themselves. For example, the central character is labeled "SHE who is CLARA PASSMORE who is the
VIRGIN MARY who is the BASTARD who is the OWL."

From 1965 to 1970, Kennedy wrote six more plays: A Beast Story (1966); A Rat's
Mass (1966); A Lesson in a Dead Language (1968); Boats (1969); and Sun: A Poem
for Malcolm X Inspired by His Murder (1970), one of her few dramas dominated by
a male voice. With John Lennon and Victor Spinetti, she wrote The Lennon Play:
In His Own Write (1969), adapted from Lennon's books.

During the late 1960s and the 1970s, Kennedy sustained her writing career
through grants. She received a Guggenheim Fellowship in 1968; Rockefeller Fellowships in 1969, 1973, and 1976; a National Endowment grant in 1973; and the
Creative Artists Public Service Grant in 1974. In that year she and her husband
were divorced. She also began to teach. She has been a fellow at the Yale School of

Drama and a visiting professor at Yale, Princeton, Brown, U.C. Davis, U.C. Berkeley, and most recently Harvard.

In 1976, *A Movie Star Has to Star in Black and White* was produced by Joseph Papp at the New York Shakespeare Festival under the direction of Joseph Chaikin. The play refers back to the fragmented character of Sarah/Clara from *Funnyhouse of a Negro* and *An Owl Answers*, and recalls her 1969 *Cities in Bezique*, in that Clara, the main character, is concerned about the conflict between her role as a wife and mother and her identity as a writer. The play's three overlapping spaces of family scene and movie scene develop the conflict between Clara's inner fantasy life and her outer life.

In the 1980s while teaching, Kennedy continued to write plays, including *Orestes and Electra* (1980), an adaptation commissioned by the Julliard Conservatory of Music, and a children's musical based on Charlie Chaplin's memoirs titled *A Lancashire Lad* (1980), commissioned by the Empire State Youth Theatre Institute. During the latter half of the decade Kennedy also published books: *People Who Led to My Plays* (1987); *Adrienne Kennedy in One Act* (1988); and in 1990, her first fictional work, *Deadly Triplets: A Theatre Mystery and Journal*, which introduces the character of Suzanne Alexander, around whom Kennedy would compose her most recent cycle of plays. In 1992, she published *The Alexander Plays*, which consist of four plays: *She Talks to Beethoven, The Ohio State Murders, The Film Club: A Monologue*, and *The Dramatic Circle*; and in 1993, there was a fifth play concerned with this character: *Letter to My Students on My 61st Birthday by Suzanne Alexander*.

Kennedy's own relationship to her work has shifted, since she first began writing. In her own words: "Obviously, there was always great confusion in my own mind of where I belonged, if anywhere. It's not such a preoccupation now, since I see myself as a writer I don't worry about the rest of it anymore."

A Movie Star Has to Star in Black and White

NOTES: *The movie music throughout is romantic. The ship, the deck, the railings and the dark boat can all be done with lights and silhouettes. All the colors are shades of black and white. These movie stars are romantic and moving, never camp or farcical, and the attitudes of the supporting players to the movie stars is deadly serious. The movie music sometimes plays at intervals when* CLARA's *thought is still.*

CHARACTERS

CLARA
"Leading Roles" are played by actors who look exactly like:
BETTE DAVIS
PAUL HENREID
JEAN PETERS
MARLON BRANDO
MONTGOMERY CLIFT
SHELLEY WINTERS [1]

[They all look exactly like their movie roles.]

---

1. Davis (1908–1989), American actress. Henreid (b. 1907), Australian-born Hollywood actor. Peters (b. 1926), American actress of the 1950s. Brando (b. 1924), American actor. Clift (1920–1966), American actor. Winters (b. 1922), American actress.

Supporting roles by
The MOTHER
The FATHER
The HUSBAND

[*They all look like photographs* CLARA *keeps of them except when they're in the hospital.*]

SCENES:

I. Hospital lobby and *Now Voyager*
II. BROTHER's room and *Viva Zapata*
III. CLARA's old room and *A Place in the Sun*[2]

[*Dark stage. From darkness center appears the* COLUMBIA PICTURES LADY *in a bright light.*]

COLUMBIA PICTURES LADY. Summer, New York, 1955. Summer, Ohio, 1963. The scenes are *Now Voyager, Viva Zapata* and *A Place in the Sun.*

The leading roles are played by Bette Davis, Paul Henreid, Jean Peters, Marlon Brando, Montgomery Clift and Shelley Winters. Supporting roles are played by the mother, the father, the husband. A bit role is played by Clara.

Now Voyager takes place in the hospital lobby.

Viva Zapata takes place in the brother's room.

A Place in the Sun takes place in Clara's old room.

June 1963.

My producer is Joel Steinberg. He looks different from what I once thought, not at all like that picture in *Vogue.* He was in *Vogue* with a group of people who were going to do a musical about Socrates.[3] In the photograph Joel's hair looked dark and his skin smooth. In real life his skin is blotched. Everyone says he drinks a lot.

Lately I think often of killing myself. Eddie Jr. plays outside in the playground. I'm very lonely . . . Met Lee Strasberg: the members of the playwrights unit were invited to watch his scene. Geraldine Page, Rip Torn and Norman Mailer[4] were there. . . . I wonder why I lie so much to my mother about how I feel. . . . My father once said his life has been nothing but a life of hypocrisy and that's why his photograph smiled. While Eddie Jr. plays outside I read Edith Wharton, a book on Egypt and Chinua Achebe.[5] Leroi Jones, Ted Joans and Allen Ginsberg are reading in the Village.[6]

---

2. Titles of films. *Now Voyager* is a 1942 film starring Paul Henreid and Bette Davis, about an overprotected young woman who finds one night of passion. *Viva Zapata* is a 1952 film starring Marlon Brando, Anthony Quinn, and Jean Peters about the Mexican revolutionary Emiliano Zapata. *A Place in the Sun* is a 1951 film starring Montgomery Clift, Elizabeth Taylor, and Shelley Winters, about a poor boy who tries to move up in the world but instead kills his pregnant girlfriend and pays for it with his life.
3. Ancient Greek philosopher, condemned to death by his fellow citizens; an unlikely subject for

a musical.
4. American writer (b. 1923). Page (1924–1987) and Torn (b. 1931) were actors prominent in Off-Broadway theater. Strasberg (1902–1982), founder of the Actors' Studio.
5. Nigerian novelist (b. 1930), best known for *Things Fall Apart* (1958). Wharton (1862–1937), American novelist.
6. I.e., Greenwich Village in New York. Jones, or Amiri Baraka (b. 1934), African American writer. Joans (b. 1928), American poet, musician, painter, and world traveler. Ginsberg (b. 1926), American Beat poet.

Eddie comes every evening right before dark. He wants to know if I'll go back to him for the sake of our son.

[*She fades. At the back of the stage as in a distance a dim light goes on a large doorway in the hospital. Visible is the foot of the white hospital bed and a figure lying upon it. Movie music.* CLARA *stands at the doorway of the room. She is a Negro woman of thirty-three wearing a maternity dress. She does not enter the room but turns away and stands very still. Movie music.*]

CLARA.   [*Reflective; very still facing away from the room.*] My brother is the same . . . my father is coming . . . very depressed.

Before I left New York I got my typewriter from the pawnshop. I'm terribly tired, trying to do a page a day, yet my play is coming together.

Each day I wonder with what or with whom can I co-exist in a true union?

[*She turns and stares into her brother's room. Scene fades out; then bright lights that convey an ocean liner in motion.*]

Scene I

Movie music. On the deck of the ocean liner from Now Voyager *are* BETTE DAVIS *and* PAUL HENREID. *They sit at a table slightly off stage center.* BETTE DAVIS *has on a large white summer hat and* PAUL HENREID *a dark summer suit. The light is romantic and glamorous. Beyond backstage left are deck chairs. It is bright sunlight on the deck.*

BETTE DAVIS.   [*To* PAUL.] June 1955.

When I have the baby I wonder will I turn into a river of blood and die? My mother almost died when I was born. I've always felt sad that I couldn't have been an angel of mercy to my father and mother and saved them from their torment.

I used to hope when I was a little girl that one day I would rise above them, an angel with glowing wings and cover them with peace. But I failed. When I came among them it seems to me I did not bring them peace . . . but made them more disconsolate. The crosses they bore always made me sad.

The one reality I wanted never came true . . . to be their angel of mercy to unite them. I keep remembering the time my mother threatened to kill my father with the shot gun. I keep remembering my father's going away to marry a girl who talked to willow trees.

[*Onto the deck wander the* MOTHER, *the* FATHER, *and the* HUS-BAND. *They are Negroes. The parents are as they were when young in 1929 in Atlanta, Georgia. The* MOTHER *is small, pale and very beautiful. She has on a white summer dress and white shoes. The* FATHER *is small and dark skinned. He has on a Morehouse[7] sweater, knickers and a cap. They both are emotional and nervous. In presence both are romanticized. The* HUSBAND *is twenty-eight and hand-*

---

7. Predominantly black college in Atlanta.

some. He is dressed as in the summer of 1955 wearing a seersucker suit from Kleins [8] *that cost thirteen dollars.*]

BETTE DAVIS.   In the scrapbook that my father left is a picture of my mother in Savannah, Georgia in 1929.

MOTHER.   [*Sitting down in a deck chair, takes a cigarette out of a beaded purse and smokes nervously. She speaks bitterly in a voice with a strong Georgia accent.*] In our Georgia town the white people lived on one side. It had pavement on the streets and sidewalks and mail was delivered. The Negroes lived on the other side and the roads were dirt and had no sidewalk and you had to go to the post office to pick up your mail. In the center of Main Street was a fountain and white people drank on one side and Negroes drank on the other.

When a Negro bought something in a store he couldn't try it on. A Negro couldn't sit down at the soda fountain in the drug store but had to take his drink out. In the movies at Montefore you had to go in the side and up the stairs and sit in the last four rows.

When you arrived on the train from Cincinnati the first thing you saw was the WHITE AND COLORED signs at the depot. White people had one waiting room and we Negroes had another. We sat in only two cars and white people had the rest of the train.

[*She is facing* PAUL HENREID *and* BETTE DAVIS. *The* FATHER *and the* HUSBAND *sit in deck chairs that face the other side of the sea. The* FATHER *also smokes. He sits hunched over with his head down thinking. The* HUSBAND *takes on old test book out of a battered briefcase and starts to study. He looks exhausted and has dark circles under his eyes. His suit is worn.*]

BETTE DAVIS.   My father used to say John Hope Franklin, Du Bois and Benjamin Mays [9] were fine men.

[*Bright sunlight on* FATHER *sitting on other side of deck.* FATHER *gets up and comes toward them . . . to* BETTE DAVIS.]

FATHER.   Cleveland is a place for opportunity, leadership, a progressive city, a place for education, a chance to come out of the back woods of Georgia. We Negro leaders dream of leading our people out of the wilderness.

[*He passes her and goes along the deck whistling. Movie music.* BETTE DAVIS *stands up looking after the* FATHER . . . *then distractedly to* PAUL HENREID.]

BETTE DAVIS.   [*Very passionate.*] I'd give anything in the world if I could just once talk to Jesus.

Sometimes he walks through my room but he doesn't stop long enough for us to talk . . . he has an aureole. [*Then to the* FATHER *who is almost out of sight on the deck whistling.*] Why did you marry the girl who talked to willow trees? [*To* PAUL HENREID.] He left us to marry a girl who talked to willow trees.

[FATHER *is whistling,* MOTHER *is smoking, then the* FATHER *vanishes into a door on deck.* BETTE DAVIS *walks down to railing.* PAUL HENREID *follows her.*]

---

8. Large, cheap department store, formerly in lower Manhattan.
9. President of Morehouse College. Franklin (b. 1915), a preeminent black historian. W. E. B. Du Bois (1868–1963), prominent black educator, writer, and leader.

BETTE DAVIS.   June 1955.

My mother said when she was a girl in the summers she didn't like to go out. She'd sit in the house and help her grandmother iron or shell peas and sometimes she'd sit on the steps.

My father used to come and sit on the steps. He asked her for her first "date." They went for a walk up the road and had an ice cream at Miss Ida's Icecream Parlor and walked back down the road. She was fifteen.

My mother says that my father was one of the most well thought of boys in the town, Negro or white. And he was so friendly. He always had a friendly word for everybody.

He used to tell my mother his dreams how he was going to go up north. There was opportunity for Negroes up north and when he was finished at Morehouse he was going to get a job in someplace like New York.

And she said when she walked down the road with my father people were so friendly.

He organized a colored baseball team in Montefore and he was the Captain. And she used to go and watch him play baseball and everybody called him "Cap."

Seven more months and the baby.

Eddie and I don't talk too much these days.

Very often I try to be in bed by the time he comes home.

Most nights I'm wide awake until at least four. I wake up about eight and then I have a headache.

When I'm wide awake I see Jesus a lot.

My mother is giving us the money for the doctor bill. Eddie told her he will pay it back.

Also got a letter from her; it said I hope things work out for you both. And pray, pray sometimes. Love Mother.

We also got a letter from Eddie's mother. Eddie's brother had told her that Eddie and I were having some problems. In her letter which was enclosed in a card she said when Eddie's sister had visited us she noticed that Eddie and I don't go to church. She said we mustn't forget the Lord, because God takes care of everything . . . God gives us peace and no matter what problems Eddie and I were having if we trusted in Him God would help us. It was the only letter from Eddie's mother that I ever saved.

Even though the card was Hallmark.

July 1955.

Eddie doesn't seem like the same person since he came back from Korea. And now I'm pregnant again. When I lost the baby he was thousands of miles away. All that bleeding. I'll never forgive him. The Red Cross let him send me a telegram to say he was sorry. I can't believe we used to be so in love on the campus and park the car and kiss and kiss. Yet I was a virgin when we married. A virgin who was to bleed and bleed . . . when I was in the hospital all I had was a photograph of Eddie in GI clothes standing in a woods in Korea. [*Pause.*] Eddie and I went to the Thalia on 95th and Broadway. There's a film festival this summer. We

saw *Double Indemnity, The Red Shoes*[1] and *A Place in the Sun.* Next
week *Viva Zapata* is coming. Afterwards we went to Reinzis on Macdou-
gal Street and had Viennese coffee. We forced an enthusiasm we didn't
feel. We took the subway back up to 116th Street and walked to Bencroft
Hall. In the middle of the night I woke up and wrote in my diary.

[*A bright light at hospital doorway.* CLARA *younger, fragile, anxious.
Movie music. She leaves hospital doorway and comes onto the deck
from the door her father entered. She wears maternity dress, white
wedgies,*[2] *her hair is straightened as in the fifties. She has a passive
beauty and is totally preoccupied. She pays no attention to anyone,
only writing in a notebook. Her movie stars speak for her.* CLARA *lets
her movie stars star in her life.* BETTE DAVIS *and* PAUL HENREID *are at
the railing. The* MOTHER *is smoking. The* HUSBAND *gets up and
comes across the deck carrying his battered briefcase. He speaks to*
CLARA *who looks away.* PAUL HENREID *goes on staring at the sea.*]

HUSBAND.   Clara, please tell me everything the doctor said about the delivery and how many days you'll be in the hospital.

[*Instead of* CLARA, BETTE DAVIS *replies.* PAUL HENREID *is oblivious of
him.*]

BETTE DAVIS.   [*Very remote.*] I get very jealous of you Eddie. You're doing
something with your life.

[*He tries to kiss* CLARA. *She moves away and walks along the deck
and writes in notebook.*]

BETTE DAVIS.   [*To* EDDIE.] Eddie, do you think I have floating anxiety?
You said everyone in Korea had floating anxiety. I think I might have it.
[*Pause.*] Do you think I'm catatonic?

EDDIE.   [*Staring at* CLARA.] I'm late to class now. We'll talk when I come
home. [*He leaves.*] When I get paid I'm going to take you to Birdland.
Dizzy's[3] coming back.

[*Movie music.*]

CLARA.   July.

I can't sleep. My head always full of thoughts night and day. I feel so
nervous. Sometimes I hardly hear what people are saying. I'm writing a
lot of my play, I don't want to show it to anyone though. Suppose it's no
good. [*Reads her play.*]

They are dragging his body across the green his white hair hanging
down. They are taking off his shoes and he is stiff. I must get into the
chapel to see him. I must. He is my blood father. God, let me in to his
burial. [*He grabs her down center. She, kneeling.*] I call God and the Owl
answers. [*Softer.*] It haunts my Tower calling, its feathers are blowing
against the cell wall, speckled in the garden on the fig tree, it comes,
feathered, great hollow-eyed with yellow skin and yellow eyes, the flying
bastard. From my Tower I keep calling and the only answer is the Owl,
God. [*Pause. Stands.*] I am only yearning for our kingdom, God.[4]

[*Movie music.*]

---

1. A 1948 film that told a tragic, colorful tale of a
ballet dancer. *Double Indemnity* (1944) was a cynical film about insurance fraud and murder.
2. Shoes with wedge-shaped heels, popular in the
1940s and 1950s.

3. Dizzy Gillespie (1917–1995), prominent jazz
musician. Birdland was a legendary jazz spot in
New York City.
4. This speech is from Kennedy's play *The Owl Answers* (1965); she also quotes it later.

BETTE DAVIS.   [*At railing.*] My father tried to commit suicide once when I was in High School. It was the afternoon he was presented an award by the Mayor of Cleveland at a banquet celebrating the completion of the New Settlement building. It had taken my father seven years to raise money for the New Settlement which was the center of Negro life in our community. He was given credit for being the one without whom it couldn't have been done. It was his biggest achievement.

I went upstairs and found him whistling in his room. I asked him what was wrong. I want to see my dead mama and papa he said, that's all I really live for is to see my mama and papa. I stared at him. As I was about to leave the room he said I've been waiting to jump off the roof of the Settlement for a long time. I just had to wait until it was completed . . . and he went on whistling.

He had tried to jump off the roof but had fallen on a scaffold.

[*Movie music. The deck has grown dark except for the light on* BETTE DAVIS *and* PAUL HENREID *and* CLARA.]

CLARA.   I loved the wedding night scene from *Viva Zapata* and the scene where the peasants met Zapata on the road and forced the soldiers to take the rope from his neck . . . when they shot Zapata at the end I cried.

[*Deck darker. She walks along the deck and into door, leaving* PAUL HENREID *and* BETTE DAVIS *at railing. She arrives at the hospital doorway, then enters her* BROTHER's *room, standing at the foot of his bed. Her* BROTHER *is in a coma.*]

CLARA.   [*To her* BROTHER.] Once I asked you romantically when you came back to the United States on a short leave, how do you like Europe Wally? You were silent. Finally you said, I get into a lot of fights with the Germans. You stared at me. And got up and went into the dining room to the dark sideboard and got a drink.

[*Darkness. Movie music.*]

Scene II

Hospital room and Viva Zapata. *The hospital bed is now totally visible. In it lies* WALLY *in a white gown. The light of the room is twilight on a summer evening.* CLARA's *brother is handsome and in his late twenties. Beyond the bed is steel hospital apparatus.* CLARA *stands by her* BROTHER's *bedside. There is no real separation from the hospital room and* Viva Zapata *and the ship lights as there should have been none in* Now Voyager. *Simultaneously brighter lights come up stage center. Wedding night scene in* Viva Zapata. *Yet it is still the stateroom within the ship. Movie music.* MARLON BRANDO *and* JEAN PETERS *are sitting on the bed. They are both dressed as in* Viva Zapata.

JEAN PETERS.   [*To* BRANDO.] July 11.

I saw my father today. He's come from Georgia to see my brother. He lives in Savannah with his second wife. He seemed smaller and hunched over. When I was young he seemed energetic, speaking before civic groups and rallying people to give money to the Negro Settlement. In the last years he seems introspective, petty and angry. Today he was wearing a white nylon sports shirt that looked slightly too big . . . his dark arms thin. He had on a little straw sport hat cocked slightly to the side.

We stood together in my brother's room. My father touched my brother's bare foot with his hand. My brother is in a coma. [*Silent.*]

Eddie and I were married downstairs in this house. My brother was best man. We went to Colorado, but soon after Eddie was sent to Korea. My mother has always said that she felt if she and my father hadn't been fighting so much maybe I wouldn't have lost the baby. After I lost the baby I stopped writing to Eddie and decided I wanted to get a divorce when he came back from Korea. He hadn't been at Columbia long before I got pregnant again with Eddie Jr.

[MARLON BRANDO *listens. They kiss tenderly. She stands up. She is bleeding. She falls back on her bed.* BRANDO *pulls a sheet out from under her. The sheets are black. Movie music.*]

JEAN PETERS.   The doctor says I have to stay in bed when I'm not at the hospital.

[*From now until the end* MARLON BRANDO *continuously helps* JEAN PETERS *change sheets. He puts the black sheets on the floor around them.*]

CLARA.   [*To her* BROTHER, *at the same time.*] Wally, you just have to get well. I know you will, even though you do not move or speak.

[*Sits down by his bedside watching him. Her* MOTHER *enters. She is wearing a rose colored summer dress and small hat. The* MOTHER *is in her fifties now. She sits down by her son's bedside and holds his hand. Silence in the room. The light of the room is constant twilight. They are in the constant dim twilight while* BRANDO *and* PETERS *star in a dazzling wedding night light. Mexican peasant wedding music, Zapata remains throughout compassionate, heroic, tender. While* CLARA *and her* MOTHER *talk* BRANDO *and* PETERS *sit on the bed, then enact the Zapata teach-me-to-read scene in which* BRANDO *asks* PETERS *to get him a book and teach him to read.*]

MOTHER.   What did I do? What did I do?

CLARA.   What do you mean?

MOTHER.   I don't know what I did to make my children so unhappy.

[JEAN PETERS *gets book for* BRANDO.]

CLARA.   I'm not unhappy mother.

MOTHER.   Yes you are.

CLARA.   I'm not unhappy. I'm very happy. I just want to be a writer. Please don't think I'm unhappy.

MOTHER.   Your family's not together and you don't seem happy. [*They sit and read.*]

CLARA.   I'm very happy mother. Very. I've just won an award and I'm going to have a play produced. I'm very happy.

[*Silence. The* MOTHER *straightens the sheet on her son's bed.*]

MOTHER.   When you grow up in boarding school like I did, the thing you dream of most is to see your children together with their families.

CLARA.   Mother you mustn't think I'm unhappy because I am, I really am, very happy.

MOTHER.   I just pray you'll soon get yourself together and make some deci-

sions about your life. I pray for you every night. Shouldn't you go back to
Eddie especially since you're pregnant?

[*There are shadows of the ship's lights as if* Now Voyager *is still in
motion.*]

CLARA.   Mother, Eddie doesn't understand me.

[*Silence. Twilight dimmer,* MOTHER *holds* WALLY's *hand. Movie light
bright on* JEAN PETERS *and* MARLON BRANDO.]

JEAN PETERS.   My brother Wally's still alive.

CLARA.   [*To her diary.*] Wally was in an accident. A telegram from my
mother. Your brother was in an automobile accident . . . has been unconscious since last night in St. Luke's hospital. Love, Mother.

JEAN PETERS.   Depressed.

CLARA.   Came to Cleveland. Eddie came to La Guardia[5] to bring me
money for my plane ticket and to say he was sorry about Wally who was
best man at our wedding. Eddie looks at me with such sadness. It fills me
with hatred for him and myself.

[BRANDO *is at the window looking down on the peasants. Mexican
wedding music.*]

JEAN PETERS.   Very depressed, and afraid at night since Eddie and I separated. I try to write a page a day on another play. It's going to be called a
Lesson in Dead Language.[6] The main image is a girl in a white organdy
dress covered with menstrual blood.

[CLARA *is writing in her diary. Her* MOTHER *sits holding* WALLY's
hand, BRANDO *stares out the window,* JEAN PETERS *sits on the bed.*
Now Voyager *ship, shadows and light.*]

CLARA.   It is twilight outside and very warm. The window faces a lawn,
very green, with a fountain beyond. Wally does not speak or move. He is
in a coma. [*Twilight dims.*]

It bothers me that Eddie had to give me money for the ticket to come
home. I don't have any money of my own: the option from my play is
gone and I don't know how I will be able to work and take care of Eddie
Jr. Maybe Eddie and I should go back together.

[FATHER *enters the room, stands at the foot of his son's bed. He is in
his fifties now and wears a white nylon sports shirt a little too big, his
dark arms thin, baggy pants and a little straw sports hat cocked to the
side. He has been drinking. The moment he enters the room the
mother takes out a cigarette and starts to nervously smoke. They do
not look at each other. He speaks to* CLARA, *then glances in the direction of the* MOTHER. *He then touches his son's bare feet.* WALLY *is
lying on his back, his hands to his sides.* CLARA *gets up and goes to
the window.* BRANDO *comes back and sits on the bed next to* JEAN
PETERS. *They all remain for a long while silent. Suddenly the*
MOTHER *goes and throws herself into her daughter's arms and cries.*]

MOTHER.   The doctor said he doesn't see how Wally has much of a
chance of surviving: his brain is damaged.

[*She clings to her daughter and cries. Simultaneously.*]

JEAN PETERS.   [*To* BRANDO.] I'm writing on my play. It's about a girl who turns into an owl. Ow. [*Recites from her writings.*] He came to me in the outhouse, in the fig tree. He told me, You are an owl, I am your beginning. I call God and the Owl answers. It haunts my tower, calling.

> [*Silence.* FATHER *slightly drunk goes toward his former wife and his daughter. The* MOTHER *runs out of the room into the lobby.*]

MOTHER.   I did everything to make you happy and still you left me for another woman.

> [CLARA *stares out of the window.* FATHER *follows the* MOTHER *into the lobby and stares at her.* JEAN PETERS *stands up. She is bleeding. She falls back on the bed.* MARLON BRANDO *pulls a sheet out from under her. The sheets are black. Movie music.*]

JEAN PETERS.   The doctor says I have to stay in bed when I'm not at the hospital.

> [*From now until the end* MARLON BRANDO *continuously helps* JEAN PETERS *change sheets. He puts the black sheets on the floor around them.*]

JEAN PETERS.   This reminds me of when Eddie was in Korea and I had the miscarriage. For days there was blood on the sheets. Eddie's letters from Korea were about a green hill. He sent me photographs of himself. The Red Cross, the letter said, says I cannot call you and I cannot come.

For a soldier to come home there has to be a death in the family.

MOTHER.   [*In the hallway she breaks down further.*] I have never wanted to go back to the south to live. I hate it. I suffered nothing but humiliation and why should I have gone back there?

FATHER.   You ought to have gone back with me. It's what I wanted to do.

MOTHER.   I never wanted to go back.

FATHER.   You yellow bastard. You're a yellow bastard. That's why you didn't want to go back.

MOTHER.   You black nigger.

JEAN PETERS.   [*Reciting her play.*] I call God and the Owl answers, it haunts my tower, calling, its feathers are blowing against the cell wall, it comes feathered, great hollow-eyes . . . with yellow skin and yellow eyes, the flying bastard. From my tower I keep calling and the only answer is the Owl.

July 8 I got a telegram from my mother. It said your brother has been in an accident and has been unconscious since last night in St. Luke's hospital. Love, Mother. I came home.

My brother is in a white gown on white sheets.

> [*The* MOTHER *and the* FATHER *walk away from one another. A sudden bright light on the Hospital Lobby and on* WALLY's *room.* CLARA *has come to the doorway and watches her parents.*]

MOTHER.   [*To both her former husband and her daughter.*] I was asleep and the police called and told me Wally didn't feel well and would I please come down to the police station and pick him up. When I arrived at the police station they told me they had just taken him to the hospital because he felt worse and they would drive to the hospital. When I arrived here the doctor told me the truth: Wally's car had crashed into another car at an intersection and Wally had been thrown from the car, his body hitting a mail box and he was close to death.

> [*Darkness.*]

Scene III

JEAN PETERS *and* BRANDO *are still sitting in* Viva Zapata *but now there are photographs above the bed of* CLARA's *parents when they were young, as they were in* Now Voyager. WALLY's *room is dark. Lights of the ship from* Now Voyager.

JEAN PETERS. Wally is not expected to live. [*She tries to stand.*] He does not move. He is in a coma. [*Pause.*] There are so many memories in this house. The rooms besiege me.

My brother has been living here in his old room with my mother. He is separated from his wife and every night has been driving his car crazily around the street where she now lives. On one of these nights was when he had the accident.

[JEAN PETERS *and* BRANDO *stare at each other. A small dark boat from side opposite* WALLY's *room. In it are* SHELLY WINTERS *and* MONTGOMERY CLIFT. CLARA *sits behind* SHELLEY WINTERS *writing in her notebook.* MONTGOMERY CLIFT *is rowing. It is* A Place in the Sun. *Movie music.* BRANDO *and* JEAN PETERS *continue to change sheets.*]

CLARA.   I am bleeding. When I'm not at the hospital I have to stay in bed. I am writing my poems. Eddie's come from New York to see my brother. My brother does not speak or move.

[MONTGOMERY CLIFT *silently rows dark boat across.* CLARA *has on a nightgown and looks as if she has been very sick, and heartbroken by her brother's accident.* MONTGOMERY CLIFT, *as was* HENREID *and* BRANDO, *is mute. If they did speak they would speak lines from their actual movies. As the boat comes across* BRANDO *and* PETERS *are still. Movie music.* EDDIE *comes in room with* JEAN PETERS *and* BRANDO. *He still has his textbook and briefcase.* SHELLEY WINTERS *sits opposite* MONTGOMERY CLIFT *as in* A Place in the Sun. CLARA *is writing in her notebook.*]

EDDIE.   [*To* JEAN PETERS; *simultaneously* CLARA *is writing in her diary.*] Are you sure you want to go on with this?
JEAN PETERS.   This?
EDDIE.   You know what I mean, this obsession of yours?
JEAN PETERS.   Obsession?
EDDIE.   Yes, this obsession to be a writer?
JEAN PETERS.   Of course I'm sure.

[BRANDO *is reading.* CLARA *from the boat.*]

CLARA.   I think the Steinbergs have lost interest in my play. I got a letter from them that said they have to go to Italy and would be in touch when they came back.
EDDIE.   I have enough money for us to live well with my teaching. We could all be so happy.
CLARA.   [*From boat.*] Ever since I was twelve I have secretly dreamed of being a writer. Everyone says it's unrealistic for a Negro to want to write.

Eddie says I've become shy and secretive and I can't accept the passage of time, and that my diaries consume me and that my diaries make me a spectator watching my life like watching a black and white movie.

He thinks sometimes . . . to me my life is one of my black and white movies that I love so . . . with me playing a bit part.

EDDIE.   [*To* JEAN PETERS *looking up at the photographs.*] I wonder about your obsession to write about your parents when they were young. You didn't know them. Your mother's not young, your father's not young and we are not that young couple who came to New York in 1955, yet all you ever say to me is Eddie you don't seem the same since you came back from Korea.

[EDDIE *leaves.* MONTGOMERY CLIFT *rows as* SHELLEY WINTERS *speaks to him. Lights on* BRANDO *and* PETERS *start slowly to dim.*]

SHELLEY WINTERS.   [*To* MONTGOMERY CLIFT.] A Sunday Rain . . . our next door neighbor drove me through the empty Sunday streets to see my brother. He's the same. My father came by the house last night for the first time since he left Cleveland and he and my mother got into a fight and my mother started laughing. She just kept saying see I can laugh ha ha nothing can hurt me anymore. Nothing you can ever do, Wallace, will ever hurt me again, no one can hurt me since my baby is lying out there in that Hospital and nobody knows whether he's going to live or die. And very loudly again she said ha ha and started walking in circles in her white shoes. My father said how goddamn crazy she was and they started pushing each other. I begged them to stop. My father looked about crazily.

I hate this house. But it was my money that helped make a down payment on it and I can come here anytime I want. I can come here and see my daughter and you can't stop me, he said.

CLARA.   [*To diary.*] The last week in March I called up my mother and I told her that Eddie and I were getting a divorce and I wanted to come to Cleveland right away.

She said I'm coming up there.

When, I said. When?

It was four o'clock in the afternoon.

When can you come I said.

I'll take the train tonight. I'll call you from the station.

Should I come and meet you?

No, I'll call you from the station.

She called at 10:35 that morning. She said she would take a taxi. I went down to the courtyard and waited. When she got out of the taxi I will never forget the expression on her face. Her face had a hundred lines on it. I'd never seen her look so sad.

CLARA.   [*Reciting her play.*] They said: I had lost my mind, read so much, buried myself in my books. They said I should stay and teach summer school. But I went. All the way to London. Out there in the black taxi my cold hands were colder than ever. No sooner than I left the taxi and passed down a gray walk through a dark gate and into a garden where there were black ravens on the grass, when I broke down. Oow . . . oww.

SHELLEY WINTERS.   This morning my father came by again. He said Clara I want to talk to you. I want you to know my side. Now, your mother has always thought she was better than me. You know Mr. Harrison raised her like a white girl, and your mother, mark my word, thinks she's better than me. (It was then I could smell the whiskey on his breath . . . he had already taken a drink from the bottle in his suitcase.)

[*She looks anxiously at* MONTGOMERY CLIFT *trying to get him to listen.*]

CLARA.   [*Reading from her notebook.*] He came to me in the outhouse, in the garden, in the fig tree. He told me you are an owl, ow, oww, I am your beginning, ow. You belong here with us owls in the fig tree, not to somebody that cooks for your Goddamn Father, oww, and I ran to the outhouse in the night crying oww. Bastard they say, the people in the town all say Bastard, but I—I belong to God and the owls, ow, and I sat in the fig tree. My Goddamn Father is the Richest White Man in the Town, but I belong to the owls.

[*Putting down her notebook. Lights shift back to* PETERS *and* BRANDO *on the bed.*]

JEAN PETERS.   When my brother was in the army in Germany, he was involved in a crime and was court-martialled. He won't talk about it. I went to visit him in the stockade.

It was in a Quonset hut[7] in New Jersey.

His head was shaven and he didn't have on any shoes. He has a vein that runs down his forehead and large brown eyes. When he was in high school he was in All City track in the two-twenty dash. We all thought he was going to be a great athlete. His dream was the Olympics. After high school he went to several colleges and left them; Morehouse (where my father went), Ohio State (where I went), and Western Reserve.[8] I'm a failure he said. I can't make it in those schools. I'm tired. He suddenly joined the army.

After Wally left the army he worked nights as an orderly in hospitals; he liked the mental wards. For a few years every fall he started to school but dropped out after a few months. He and his wife married right before he was sent to Germany. He met her at Western Reserve and she graduated cum laude while he was a prisoner in the stockade.

[*Movie music. Dark boat with* MONTGOMERY CLIFT *and* SHELLEY WINTERS *reappears from opposite side.* MONTGOMERY CLIFT *rows.* CLARA *is crying.*]

SHELLEY WINTERS and CLARA.   Eddie's come from New York because my brother might die. He did not speak again today and did not move. We don't really know his condition. All we know is that his brain is possibly badly damaged. He doesn't speak or move.

JEAN PETERS.   I am bleeding.

[*Lights suddenly dim on* MARLON BRANDO *and* JEAN PETERS. *Quite suddenly* SHELLEY WINTERS *stands up and falls "into the water." She is in the water, only her head is visible, calling silently.* MONTGOMERY CLIFT *stares at her. She continues to call silently as for help, but* MONTGOMERY CLIFT *only stares at her. Movie music.* CLARA *starts to speak as* SHELLEY WINTERS *continues to cry silently for help.*]

---

7. A type of army barracks; from Quonset Point, a peninsula extending into Narragansett Bay in

Rhode Island, the site of a large U.S. naval station.
8. I.e., Case Western Reserve, a college in Ohio.

CLARA.   The doctor said today that my brother will live; he will be brain damaged and paralyzed.

After he told us, my mother cried in my arms outside the hospital. We were standing on the steps, and she shook so that I thought both of us were going to fall headlong down the steps.

[SHELLEY WINTERS *drowns. Light goes down on* MONTGOMERY CLIFT *as he stares at* SHELLEY WINTERS *drowning. Lights on* CLARA. *Movie music. Darkness. Brief dazzling image of* COLUMBIA PICTURES LADY.]

1976

TONI MORRISON
b. 1931

Toni Morrison has, in the last two decades, published six novels and an essay collection that have transformed our view of American history and literature. In 1993, she was awarded the Nobel Prize for literature, the first time that an African American writer has been so honored, not only for individual achievement but also for her championing of the importance and unique beauty of African American literature.

For Morrison, the history and literature of the United States and of our present world are "incoherent" without an understanding of the African American presence. Her work always engages major contemporary social issues: the interrelatedness of racism, class exploitation and sexism, domination, and imperialism; the spirituality and power of oral folk traditions and values; the mythic scope of the imagination; and the negotiation of slippery boundaries, especially for members of oppressed groups, between personal desire and political urgencies. Her work also articulates perennial human concerns and paradoxes: how are our concepts of the good, the beautiful, and the powerful related; what is goodness and evil; how does our sense of identity derive from community while maintaining individual uniqueness? Morrison has said that

> If anything I do, in the way of writing novels (or whatever I write), isn't about the village or the community or about you, then it is not about anything. I am not interested in indulging myself in some private, closed exercise of my imagination that fulfills only the obligation of my personal dreams—which is to say yes, the work must be political. . . . It seems to me that the best art is political and you ought to make it unquestionably political and irrevocably beautiful at the same time.

As this quotation shows, Morrison insists on a visceral relationship between writer and reader. In an early interview she says that her writing "expects, demands participatory reading, . . . [my] language has some holes and spaces so the reader can come into it." Readers throughout the world have responded to her call, for Morrison not only is a writer praised by literary critics and intellectuals but is also an immensely popular one.

Born Chloe Anthony Wofford to Ramah Willis and George Wofford, in Lorain, Ohio, Morrison has revised the geography we associate with African American literature. Her works take place in midwestern black villages rather than in the traditional settings of the urban North and the rural South. Her first novel, *The Bluest Eye* (1970), is set primarily in Lorain, Ohio; *Sula,* her second novel, in Medallion, Ohio; and *Beloved,* her best known novel, in post–Civil War Ohio. Ohio is central in Morrison's work not only because she was born there or because the state was one of the major stations on the Underground Railroad but also, as Morrison puts it herself, because it represents "an escape from stereotyped black settings . . . being neither plantation nor ghetto."

Morrison's experience of the way immigrants from Europe became "white" and set themselves up in opposition to the black presence in America helped to inform her influential nonfiction collection *Playing in the Dark* (1991), which proposes that America developed a powerful ideology of whiteness because the Europeans in America could unite, whatever their ethnic or class differences, as distinctly different from the blacks. She demonstrates that thesis through her analysis of works by major American writers Herman Melville and Mark Twain, thus contributing to the intellectual debate over what it means to be an American and how we assess American literature.

Morrison's parents were, like so many other African Americans, migrants from the South, and the southern heritage influences her work, especially its major theme of African American displacements—first from Africa, then from the South to North—and what African Americans have created out of their frequent moves. In every one of her novels, a protagonist physically leaves home to learn about her or his interior life and how that life connects to a larger community. Growing up, Morrison experienced a vibrant African American migrant culture; consequently, unlike African American migrant writers such as Richard Wright, she developed an appreciation for her southern black roots. Critic Nellie McKay reports that Morrison's "grandfather played the violin, her parents told thrilling and terrifying ghost stories and her mother sang and played the numbers by decoding dream symbols as they were manifest in a dream book that she kept." Informally educated in her culture, she also read in school the great European writers. She was not exposed to African American literature; she was, however, especially taken with the classic Russian novels, with Flaubert's *Madame Bovary*, and with the works of Jane Austen.

Morrison left Lorain to attend Howard University in Washington, D.C.; at Howard she changed her name to Toni because many people had trouble pronouncing Chloe. While at Howard, Morrison was a member of the Howard Players, where she learned much about voice, pitch, and nuance. She took classes from Alain Locke, one of the major figures of the Harlem Renaissance. Interestingly, Morrison has said that much of the African American literature she encountered while at Howard left her "feeling bereft" for it seemed to be written to someone other than herself or the black people she knew.

After college, Morrison attended Cornell University, where she earned a master's degree in English in 1955. Her thesis, on alienation in the works of William Faulkner and Virginia Woolf, demonstrated that both of these writers were deeply concerned, as Morrison would be, with the interiority of their characters and with innovative approaches to the novel form. Morrison has said that she tries "to incorporate into the traditional genre, the novel, unorthodox novelistic characteristics of Black art," and that she doesn't

> regard Black literature as simply books *by* Black people, or simply as literature written *about* Black people or simply as literature that uses a certain mode of language in which you sort of drop g's. There is something very special and very identifiable about it and it is my struggle to *find* that elusive but identifiable style in the books.

From 1955 to 1957, Morrison taught at Texas Southern University, then returned to Howard to teach English. She married Harold Morrison, a Jamaican architect, and had two sons. They divorced in 1964, and Morrison became a senior editor at Random House, a major publishing company.

Morrison's first novel, *The Bluest Eye* (1970), was published at the height of black cultural nationalism, when most African American literature featured male protagonists and when the women's movement was gaining visibility. Along with Alice Walker's *The Third Life of Grange Copeland, The Bluest Eye* signaled a shift in the shape and emphases of contemporary American literature. Women would begin to occupy a more central role as subjects, the diversity of black communities would be more persistently explored, and relationships among blacks rather than only between blacks and whites would be legitimate topics for African American writers.

After the publication of *The Bluest Eye*, Morrison became a much-sought-after book reviewer. Between 1970 and 1974, she published more than twenty reviews in major outlets, such as the *New York Times*, as well as essays about black history and the women's movement. In so doing, she began to establish her reputation not only as a creative writer but also as an American intellectual articulate about major issues of contemporary life.

Like *The Bluest Eye*, Morrison's second novel *Sula* (1974) foregrounds African American women in the 1920s through the 1940s, this time in relation to friendship—an unusual subject in fiction. Morrison has said that one reason she wrote the novel is that "friendship between women is special, different, and has never been depicted as the major focus of a novel before *Sula*." The novel explores the relationship between Nel Wright and Sula Peace; their relationship to their community, The Bottom; and that community's view of who a woman should be. While Morrison was primarily concerned with what a culture considers good and evil, many feminist critics have seen Sula as the embodiment of "feminist values." In interviews, Morrison has stressed that the qualities of Nel, the traditional nurturing woman, and Sula, the "New World" adventurous woman, are characteristics that African American women have long combined—that they have of necessity had to be both "the ship and the harbor." Praised by some critics for presenting original characters in intense poetic prose, *Sula* upset others, particularly Sarah Blackburn of the *New York Times Book Review*, who felt that Morrison should write about larger subjects than African American women, a point of view that brought letters of protest from writers Alice Walker and Clarence Major. *Sula* was nominated for the 1975 National Book Award in fiction and brought Morrison a wider audience. It also extended her revision of history, for its time span is from World War I through World War II and beyond the Korean War, that is from 1919 to 1965.

It was her third novel, *Song of Solomon* (1977), that brought Morrison national recognition. *Song of Solomon* received the National Book Critics Award and the American Academy and Institute of Arts and Letters Award and was the first book by a black author since Richard Wright's *Native Son* in 1940 to be a Book of the Month Club main selection. In tracing the family history of the Deads, Morrison covered nearly a century of American history, in prose clearly derived from a rich African American oral and musical tradition. While class issues were decidedly a concern in *The Bluest Eye* and *Sula*, the relationship between class and race is central in *Song of Solomon*. Unlike Morrison's first two books, which were spare and which focused on African American women, this novel was praised by reviewers such as Reynolds Price in the *New York Times Book Review* as a "wise and spacious book."

Song of Solomon is based on the African American folktale about captured Africans who flew back to Africa to escape slavery. *Tar Baby*, Morrison's fourth novel, takes its title from another African American folk tale in the Brer Rabbit cycle—as Morrison probed the insights that stories provide to African Americans in a country where they have been systemically oppressed. But *Tar Baby* is different from Morrison's other novels. Not only is it set in the contemporary period (although it inevitably moves backward in time) but also much of the action takes place outside the

United States, and it features white characters as major figures. Immensely popular, *Tar Baby* was on the *New York Times* best-seller list for four months; and it was reviewed both in this country and in Europe. Soon after its publication, Morrison was elected to the American Academy and Institute of Arts and Letters.

Morrison has said that *Beloved* (1987) is the first book in a trilogy she is writing about different kinds of love. This, her fifth novel, explores the nature of mother love and is obsessed with issues of ownership as the basis of American ideology, especially as they are grounded in the institution of slavery and affect even the supposedly personal terrain of motherhood. *Beloved* was generated by a true story that Morrison discovered when she was editing *The Black Book* (1974), a scrapbook of Black history. In a sensational case, Margaret Garner, a runaway slave, killed her daughter rather than allow her to be returned to slavery. Garner was tried not for attempting to kill her child but for the "real" crime, of stealing property—herself and her children—from her master. In *Beloved*, Morrison leaves the historical facts behind, for although Sethe, the runaway slave, does kill her child, Beloved, Sethe is freed and ostracized even from her own black community.

Beloved has generated considerable critical commentary and analysis. Scholars of African American literature have examined its revisioning of the history of American slavery. Feminist critics have written about the mother-daughter relationship at the center of the novel. Marxist critics have probed Morrison's conscious linking of production and reproduction as central to the American slavery system. Formalist critics have delved into its innovative techniques. And students of African myth and culture have begun to explore the relationship between the West African concept of ancestral worship and the mythic core of the novel. A national best-seller and internationally reviewed, *Beloved* won the Pulitzer Prize for fiction in 1988, the Robert F. Kennedy Award, the Melcher Award, the Before Columbus American Book Award, and the Elizabeth Cady Stanton Award from the National Organization for Women. And in 1990, Morrison was awarded the Chianti Ruffino Antico Fattore International Literary Prize.

Morrison's second part of her trilogy, her sixth novel, *Jazz* (1991), is about the 1920s, a period that has often been celebrated in African American history. But Morrison does not cover the jazz clubs and literary circles that have dominated the writing about this period. As with *Beloved*, the novel was sparked by a historical event—a photograph shot by the great African American photographer James Van Zee. Reproduced in Camille Billops's *The Harlem Book of the Dead*, it is the picture of a dead young woman who was literally shot by her sweetheart at a party but who, before she died, refused to identify her assailant. Morrison is not as interested in the love triangle plot as she is in how the story is told. A narrator begins the novel by telling us, "Sth, I know that woman," and then slips in and out of the text, almost like a clicking camera, thinking it has recorded it all, finally beginning to understand that it has not. Like instruments in a jazz suite, the points of view of the major characters play with and against that of the narrator. Praised by some critics such as John Leonard of *The Nation* as "a book that composes itself," it was also criticized by others such as Edna O'Brien in her *New York Times* review as being so much concerned with virtuosity that one does not really care about the characters. Published at the same time as her essay collection, *Jazz* was reviewed with *Playing in the Dark* on the front page of the *New York Times Book Review*, possibly the first time that paper had so situated two books by an African American writer.

Morrison has become a major public intellectual. While a senior editor at Random House, she nurtured African American writers Angela Davis, Gayl Jones, and June Jordan. She taught at the State University of New York at Purchase from 1971 to 1972 and at Yale University from 1976 to 1977, was the Schweitzer Professor of the Humanities at the State University of New York at Albany from 1984 to 1989, was a Regent's Lecturer at the University of California at Berkeley in 1987, and is presently the Robert F. Gooheen Professor of Humanities at Princeton University. Her play *Dreaming Emmett* was first produced in Albany, New York, in 1986. She also edited the volume *Race-ing Justice, EnGendering Power: Essays on Anita Hill, Clarence Thomas and the Construction of Social Reality (1992)*. Currently, she is working on the third part of her trilogy on love, which has the working title of *Paradise*.

Sula

*"Nobody knew my rose of the world
but me. . . . I had too much glory.
They don't want glory like that
in nobody's heart."*
—The Rose Tattoo[1]

Part One

In that place, where they tore the nightshade and blackberry patches from their roots to make room for the Medallion City Golf Course, there was once a neighborhood. It stood in the hills above the valley town of Medallion and spread all the way to the river. It is called the suburbs now, but when black people lived there it was called the Bottom. One road, shaded by beeches, oaks, maples and chestnuts, connected it to the valley. The beeches are gone now, and so are the pear trees where children sat and yelled down through the blossoms to passersby. Generous funds have been allotted to level the stripped and faded buildings that clutter the road from Medallion up to the golf course. They are going to raze the Time and a Half Pool Hall, where feet in long tan shoes once pointed down from chair rungs. A steel ball will knock to dust Irene's Palace of Cosmetology, where women used to lean their heads back on sink trays and doze while Irene lathered Nu Nile into their hair. Men in khaki work clothes will pry loose the slats of Reba's Grill, where the owner cooked in her hat because she couldn't remember the ingredients without it.

There will be nothing left of the Bottom (the footbridge that crossed the river is already gone), but perhaps it is just as well, since it wasn't a town anyway: just a neighborhood where on quiet days people in valley houses could hear singing sometimes, banjos sometimes, and, if a valley man happened to have business up in those hills—collecting rent or insurance payments—he might see a dark woman in a flowered dress doing a bit of cakewalk, a bit of black bottom,[2] a bit of "messing around" to the lively notes of a mouth organ. Her bare feet would raise the saffron dust that floated down on the coveralls and bunion-split shoes of the man breathing music in and out of his harmonica. The black people watching her would laugh and rub their knees, and it would be easy for the valley man to hear the laughter and not notice the adult pain that rested somewhere under the eyelids, somewhere under their head rags and soft felt hats, somewhere in

---

1. Play by American dramatist Tennessee Williams (1911–1983).
2. A popular dance of the 1920s; some saw it as in-

decent. "Cakewalk": a stage dance developed by black entertainers.

the palm of the hand, somewhere behind the frayed lapels, somewhere in the sinew's curve. He'd have to stand in the back of Greater Saint Matthew's and let the tenor's voice dress him in silk, or touch the hands of the spoon carvers (who had not worked in eight years) and let the fingers that danced on wood kiss his skin. Otherwise the pain would escape him even though the laughter was part of the pain.

A shucking, knee-slapping, wet-eyed laughter that could even describe and explain how they came to be where they were.

A joke. A nigger joke. That was the way it got started. Not the town, of course, but that part of town where the Negroes lived, the part they called the Bottom in spite of the fact that it was up in the hills. Just a nigger joke. The kind white folks tell when the mill closes down and they're looking for a little comfort somewhere. The kind colored folks tell on themselves when the rain doesn't come, or comes for weeks, and they're looking for a little comfort somehow.

A good white farmer promised freedom and a piece of bottom land to his slave if he would perform some very difficult chores. When the slave completed the work, he asked the farmer to keep his end of the bargain. Freedom was easy—the farmer had no objection to that. But he didn't want to give up any land. So he told the slave that he was very sorry that he had to give him valley land. He had hoped to give him a piece of the Bottom. The slave blinked and said he thought valley land was bottom land. The master said, "Oh, no! See those hills? That's bottom land, rich and fertile."

"But it's high up in the hills," said the slave.

"High up from us," said the master, "but when God looks down, it's the bottom. That's why we call it so. It's the bottom of heaven—best land there is."

So the slave pressed his master to try to get him some. He preferred it to the valley. And it was done. The nigger got the hilly land, where planting was backbreaking, where the soil slid down and washed away the seeds, and where the wind lingered all through the winter.

Which accounted for the fact that white people lived on the rich valley floor in that little river town in Ohio, and the blacks populated the hills above it, taking small consolation in the fact that every day they could literally look down on the white folks.

Still, it was lovely up in the Bottom. After the town grew and the farm land turned into a village and the village into a town and the streets of Medallion were hot and dusty with progress, those heavy trees that sheltered the shacks up in the Bottom were wonderful to see. And the hunters who went there sometimes wondered in private if maybe the white farmer was right after all. Maybe it was the bottom of heaven.

The black people would have disagreed, but they had no time to think about it. They were mightily preoccupied with earthly things—and each other, wondering even as early as 1920 what Shadrack was all about, what that little girl Sula who grew into a woman in their town was all about, and what they themselves were all about, tucked up there in the Bottom.

1919

Except for World War II, nothing ever interfered with the celebration of National Suicide Day. It had taken place every January third since 1920, although Shadrack,[3] its founder, was for many years the only celebrant. Blasted and permanently astonished by the events of 1917, he had returned to Medallion handsome but ravaged, and even the most fastidious people in the town sometimes caught themselves dreaming of what he must have been like a few years back before he went off to war. A young man of hardly twenty, his head full of nothing and his mouth recalling the taste of lipstick, Shadrack had found himself in December, 1917, running with his comrades across a field in France. It was his first encounter with the enemy and he didn't know whether his company was running toward them or away. For several days they had been marching, keeping close to a stream that was frozen at its edges. At one point they crossed it, and no sooner had he stepped foot on the other side than the day was adangle with shouts and explosions. Shellfire was all around him, and though he knew that this was something called *it*, he could not muster up the proper feeling—the feeling that would accommodate *it*. He expected to be terrified or exhilarated—to feel *something* very strong. In fact, he felt only the bite of a nail in his boot, which pierced the ball of his foot whenever he came down on it. The day was cold enough to make his breath visible, and he wondered for a moment at the purity and whiteness of his own breath among the dirty, gray explosions surrounding him. He ran, bayonet fixed, deep in the great sweep of men flying across this field. Wincing at the pain in his foot, he turned his head a little to the right and saw the face of a soldier near him fly off. Before he could register shock, the rest of the soldier's head disappeared under the inverted soup bowl of his helmet. But stubbornly, taking no direction from the brain, the body of the headless soldier ran on, with energy and grace, ignoring altogether the drip and slide of brain tissue down its back.

When Shadrack opened his eyes he was propped up in a small bed. Before him on a tray was a large tin plate divided into three triangles. In one triangle was rice, in another meat, and in the third stewed tomatoes. A small round depression held a cup of whitish liquid. Shadrack stared at the soft colors that filled these triangles: the lumpy whiteness of rice, the quivering blood tomatoes, the grayish-brown meat. All their repugnance was contained in the neat balance of the triangles—a balance that soothed him, transferred some of its equilibrium to him. Thus reassured that the white, the red and the brown would stay where they were—would not explode or burst forth from their restricted zones—he suddenly felt hungry and looked around for his hands. His glance was cautious at first, for he had to be very careful—anything could be anywhere. Then he noticed two lumps beneath the beige blanket on either side of his hips. With extreme care he lifted one arm and was relieved to find his hand attached to his wrist. He tried the

---

3. The name given to a captive Judean by Nebuchadnezzar, king of the Babylonians (Daniel 1:1–7). Because they refused to worship the golden image, Shadrack and his companions were thrown into the furnace, where they were not burned (Daniel 3:13–27).

other and found it also. Slowly he directed one hand toward the cup and, just as he was about to spread his fingers, they began to grow in higgledy-piggledy fashion like Jack's beanstalk all over the tray and the bed. With a shriek he closed his eyes and thrust his huge growing hands under the covers. Once out of sight they seemed to shrink back to their normal size. But the yell had brought a male nurse.

"Private? We're not going to have any trouble today, are we? Are we, Private?"

Shadrack looked up at a balding man dressed in a green-cotton jacket and trousers. His hair was parted low on the right side so that some twenty or thirty yellow hairs could discreetly cover the nakedness of his head.

"Come on. Pick up that spoon. Pick it up, Private. Nobody is going to feed you forever."

Sweat slid from Shadrack's armpits down his sides. He could not bear to see his hands grow again and he was frightened of the voice in the apple-green suit.

"Pick it up, I said. There's no point to this . . ." The nurse reached under the cover for Shadrack's wrist to pull out the monstrous hand. Shadrack jerked it back and overturned the tray. In panic he raised himself to his knees and tried to fling off and away his terrible fingers, but succeeded only in knocking the nurse into the next bed.

When they bound Shadrack into a straitjacket, he was both relieved and grateful, for his hands were at last hidden and confined to whatever size they had attained.

Laced and silent in his small bed, he tried to tie the loose cords in his mind. He wanted desperately to see his own face and connect it with the word "private"—the word the nurse (and the others who helped bind him) had called him. "Private" he thought was something secret, and he wondered why they looked at him and called him a secret. Still, if his hands behaved as they had done, what might he expect from his face? The fear and longing were too much for him, so he began to think of other things. That is, he let his mind slip into whatever cave mouths of memory it chose.

He saw a window that looked out on a river which he knew was full of fish. Someone was speaking softly just outside the door . . .

Shadrack's earlier violence had coincided with a memorandum from the hospital executive staff in reference to the distribution of patients in high-risk areas. There was clearly a demand for space. The priority or the violence earned Shadrack his release, $217 in cash, a full suit of clothes and copies of very official-looking papers.

When he stepped out of the hospital door the grounds overwhelmed him: the cropped shrubbery, the edged lawns, the undeviating walks. Shadrack looked at the cement stretches: each one leading clearheadedly to some presumably desirable destination. There were no fences, no warnings, no obstacles at all between concrete and green grass, so one could easily ignore the tidy sweep of stone and cut out in another direction—a direction of one's own.

Shadrack stood at the foot of the hospital steps watching the heads of trees tossing ruefully but harmlessly, since their trunks were rooted too deeply in the earth to threaten him. Only the walks made him uneasy. He shifted his weight, wondering how he could get to the gate without stepping on the concrete. While plotting his course—where he would have to leap, where to skirt a clump of bushes—a loud guffaw startled him. Two men were going up the steps. Then he noticed that there were many people about, and that he was just now seeing them, or else they had just materialized. They were thin slips, like paper dolls floating down the walks. Some were seated in chairs with wheels, propelled by other paper figures from behind. All seemed to be smoking, and their arms and legs curved in the breeze. A good high wind would pull them up and away and they would land perhaps among the tops of the trees.

Shadrack took the plunge. Four steps and he was on the grass heading for the gate. He kept his head down to avoid seeing the paper people swerving and bending here and there, and he lost his way. When he looked up, he was standing by a low red building separated from the main building by a covered walkway. From somewhere came a sweetish smell which reminded him of something painful. He looked around for the gate and saw that he had gone directly away from it in his complicated journey over the grass. Just to the left of the low building was a graveled driveway that appeared to lead outside the grounds. He trotted quickly to it and left, at last, a haven of more than a year, only eight days of which he fully recollected.

Once on the road, he headed west. The long stay in the hospital had left him weak—too weak to walk steadily on the gravel shoulders of the road. He shuffled, grew dizzy, stopped for breath, started again, stumbling and sweating but refusing to wipe his temples, still afraid to look at his hands. Passengers in dark, square cars shuttered their eyes at what they took to be a drunken man.

The sun was already directly over his head when he came to a town. A few blocks of shaded streets and he was already at its heart—a pretty, quietly regulated downtown.

Exhausted, his feet clotted with pain, he sat down at the curbside to take off his shoes. He closed his eyes to avoid seeing his hands and fumbled with the laces of the heavy high-topped shoes. The nurse had tied them into a double knot, the way one does for children, and Shadrack, long unaccustomed to the manipulation of intricate things, could not get them loose. Uncoordinated, his fingernails tore away at the knots. He fought a rising hysteria that was not merely anxiety to free his aching feet; his very life depended on the release of the knots. Suddenly without raising his eyelids, he began to cry. Twenty-two years old, weak, hot, frightened, not daring to acknowledge the fact that he didn't even know who or what he was . . . with no past, no language, no tribe, no source, no address book, no comb, no pencil, no clock, no pocket handkerchief, no rug, no bed, no can opener, no faded postcard, no soap, no key, no tobacco pouch, no soiled underwear and nothing nothing nothing to do . . . he was sure of one thing only: the unchecked monstrosity of his hands. He cried soundlessly at the curbside of a small Midwestern town wondering where the window was, and the river, and the soft voices just outside the door . . .

Through his tears he saw the fingers joining the laces, tentatively at first, then rapidly. The four fingers of each hand fused into the fabric, knotted themselves and zigzagged in and out of the tiny eyeholes.

By the time the police drove up, Shadrack was suffering from a blinding headache, which was not abated by the comfort he felt when the policemen pulled his hands away from what he thought was a permanent entanglement with his shoelaces. They took him to jail, booked him for vagrancy and intoxication, and locked him in a cell. Lying on a cot, Shadrack could only stare helplessly at the wall, so paralyzing was the pain in his head. He lay in this agony for a long while and then realized he was staring at the painted-over letters of a command to fuck himself. He studied the phrase as the pain in his head subsided.

Like moonlight stealing under a window shade an idea insinuated itself: his earlier desire to see his own face. He looked for a mirror; there was none. Finally, keeping his hands carefully behind his back he made his way to the toilet bowl and peeped in. The water was unevenly lit by the sun so he could make nothing out. Returning to his cot he took the blanket and covered his head, rendering the water dark enough to see his reflection. There in the toilet water he saw a grave black face. A black so definite, so unequivocal, it astonished him. He had been harboring a skittish apprehension that he was not real—that he didn't exist at all. But when the blackness greeted him with its indisputable presence, he wanted nothing more. In his joy he took the risk of letting one edge of the blanket drop and glanced at his hands. They were still. Courteously still.

Shadrack rose and returned to the cot, where he fell into the first sleep of his new life. A sleep deeper than the hospital drugs; deeper than the pits of plums, steadier than the condor's wing; more tranquil than the curve of eggs.

The sheriff looked through the bars at the young man with the matted hair. He had read through his prisoner's papers and hailed a farmer. When Shadrack awoke, the sheriff handed him back his papers and escorted him to the back of a wagon. Shadrack got in and in less than three hours he was back in Medallion, for he had been only twenty-two miles from his window, his river, and his soft voices just outside the door.

In the back of the wagon, supported by sacks of squash and hills of pumpkins, Shadrack began a struggle that was to last for twelve days, a struggle to order and focus experience. It had to do with making a place for fear as a way of controlling it. He knew the smell of death and was terrified of it, for he could not anticipate it. It was not death or dying that frightened him, but the unexpectedness of both. In sorting it all out, he hit on the notion that if one day a year were devoted to it, everybody could get it out of the way and the rest of the year would be safe and free. In this manner he instituted National Suicide Day.

On the third day of the new year, he walked through the Bottom down Carpenter's Road with a cowbell and a hangman's rope calling the people together. Telling them that this was their only chance to kill themselves or each other.

At first the people in the town were frightened; they knew Shadrack was crazy but that did not mean that he didn't have any sense or, even more important, that he had no power. His eyes were so wild, his hair so long and matted, his voice was so full of authority and thunder that he caused panic on the first, or Charter, National Suicide Day in 1920. The next one, in

1921, was less frightening but still worrisome. The people had seen him a year now in between. He lived in a shack on the riverbank that had once belonged to his grandfather long time dead. On Tuesday and Friday he sold the fish he had caught that morning, the rest of the week he was drunk, loud, obscene, funny and outrageous. But he never touched anybody, never fought, never caressed. Once the people understood the boundaries and nature of his madness, they could fit him, so to speak, into the scheme of things.

Then, on subsequent National Suicide Days, the grown people looked out from behind curtains as he rang his bell; a few stragglers increased their speed, and little children screamed and ran. The tetter heads tried goading him (although he was only four or five years older then they) but not for long, for his curses were stingingly personal.

As time went along, the people took less notice of these January thirds, or rather they thought they did, thought they had no attitudes or feelings one way or another about Shadrack's annual solitary parade. In fact they had simply stopped remarking on the holiday because they had absorbed it into their thoughts, into their language, into their lives.

Someone said to a friend, "You sure was a long time delivering that baby. How long was you in labor?"

And the friend answered, " 'Bout three days. The pains started on Suicide Day and kept up till the following Sunday. Was borned on Sunday. All my boys is Sunday boys."

Some lover said to his bride-to-be, "Let's do it after New Years, 'stead of before. I get paid New Year's Eve."

And his sweetheart answered, "OK, but make sure it ain't on Suicide Day. I ain't 'bout to be listening to no cowbells whilst the weddin's going on."

Somebody's grandmother said her hens always started a laying of double yolks right after Suicide Day.

Then Reverend Deal took it up, saying the same folks who had sense enough to avoid Shadrack's call were the ones who insisted on drinking themselves to death or womanizing themselves to death. "May's well go on with Shad and save the Lamb the trouble of redemption."

Easily, quietly, Suicide Day became a part of the fabric of life up in the Bottom of Medallion, Ohio.

1920

It had to be as far away from the Sundown House as possible. And her grandmother's middle-aged nephew who lived in a Northern town called Medallion was the one chance she had to make sure it would be. The red shutters had haunted both Helene Sabat and her grandmother for sixteen years. Helene was born behind those shutters, daughter of a Creole[4] whore who worked there. The grandmother took Helene away from the soft lights and flowered carpets of the Sundown House and raised her under the dole-

---

4. A person of mixed French and black descent.

some eyes of a multicolored Virgin Mary, counseling her to be constantly on guard for any sign of her mother's wild blood.

So when Wiley Wright came to visit his Great Aunt Cecile in New Orleans, his enchantment with the pretty Helene became a marriage proposal—under the pressure of both women. He was a seaman (or rather a lakeman, for he was a ship's cook on one of the Great Lakes lines), in port only three days out of every sixteen.

He took his bride to his home in Medallion and put her in a lovely house with a brick porch and real lace curtains at the window. His long absences were quite bearable for Helene Wright, especially when, after some nine years of marriage, her daughter was born.

Her daughter was more comfort and purpose than she had ever hoped to find in this life. She rose grandly to the occasion of motherhood—grateful, deep down in her heart, that the child had not inherited the great beauty that was hers: that her skin had dusk in it, that her lashes were substantial but not undignified in their length, that she had taken the broad flat nose of Wiley (although Helene expected to improve it somewhat) and his generous lips.

Under Helene's hand the girl became obedient and polite. Any enthusiasms that little Nel showed were calmed by the mother until she drove her daughter's imagination underground.

Helene Wright was an impressive woman, at least in Medallion she was. Heavy hair in a bun, dark eyes arched in a perpetual query about other people's manners. A woman who won all social battles with presence and a conviction of the legitimacy of her authority. Since there was no Catholic church in Medallion then, she joined the most conservative black church. And held sway. It was Helene who never turned her head in church when latecomers arrived; Helene who established the practice of seasonal altar flowers; Helene who introduced the giving of banquets of welcome to returning Negro veterans. She lost only one battle—the pronunciation of her name. The people in the Bottom refused to say Helene. They called her Helen Wright and left it at that.

All in all her life was a satisfactory one. She loved her house and enjoyed manipulating her daughter and her husband. She would sigh sometimes just before falling asleep, thinking that she had indeed come far enough away from the Sundown House.

So it was with extremely mixed emotions that she read a letter from Mr. Henri Martin describing the illness of her grandmother, and suggesting she come down right away. She didn't want to go, but could not bring herself to ignore the silent plea of the woman who had rescued her.

It was November. November, 1920. Even in Medallion there was a victorious swagger in the legs of white men and a dull-eyed excitement in the eyes of colored veterans.

Helene thought about the trip South with heavy misgiving but decided that she had the best protection: her manner and her bearing, to which she would add a beautiful dress. She bought some deep-brown wool and three-fourths of a yard of matching velvet. Out of this she made herself a heavy but elegant dress with velvet collar and pockets.

Nel watched her mother cutting the pattern from newspapers and moving her eyes rapidly from a magazine model to her own hands. She watched her turn up the kerosene lamp at sunset to sew far into the night.

The day they were ready, Helene cooked a smoked ham, left a note for her lake-bound husband, in case he docked early, and walked head high and arms stiff with luggage ahead of her daughter to the train depot.

It was a longer walk than she remembered, and they saw the train steaming up just as they turned the corner. They ran along the track looking for the coach pointed out to them by the colored porter. Even at that they made a mistake. Helene and her daughter entered a coach peopled by some twenty white men and women. Rather than go back and down the three wooden steps again, Helene decided to spare herself some embarrassment and walk on through to the colored car. She carried two pieces of luggage and a string purse; her daughter carried a covered basket of food.

As they opened the door market COLORED ONLY, they saw a white conductor coming toward them. It was a chilly day but a light skim of sweat glistened on the woman's face as she and the little girl struggled to hold the door open, hang on to their luggage and enter all at once. The conductor let his eyes travel over the pale yellow woman and then struck his little finger into his ear, jiggling it free of wax. "What you think you doin', gal?"

Helene looked up at him.

So soon. So soon. She hadn't even begun the trip back. Back to her grandmother's house in the city where the red shutters glowed, and already she had been called "gal." All the old vulnerabilities, all the old fears of being somehow flawed gathered in her stomach and made her hands tremble. She had heard only that one word; it dangled above her wide-brimmed hat, which had slipped, in her exertion, from its carefully leveled placement and was now tilted in a bit of a jaunt over her eye.

Thinking he wanted her tickets, she quickly dropped both the cowhide suitcase and the straw one in order to search for them in her purse. An eagerness to please and an apology for living met in her voice. "I have them. Right here somewhere, sir . . ."

The conductor looked at the bit of wax his fingernail had retrieved. "What was you doin' back in there? What was you doin' in that coach yonder?"

Helene licked her lips. "Oh . . . I . . ." Her glance moved beyond the white man's face to the passengers seated behind him. Four or five black faces were watching, two belonging to soldiers still in their shit-colored uniforms and peaked caps. She saw their closed faces, their locked eyes, and turned for compassion to the gray eyes of the conductor.

"We made a mistake, sir. You see, there wasn't no sign. We just got in the wrong car, that's all. Sir."

"We don't 'low no mistakes on this train. Now git your butt on in there."

He stood there staring at her until she realized that he wanted her to move aside. Pulling Nel by the arm, she pressed herself and her daughter into the foot space in front of a wooden seat. Then, for no earthly reason, at least no reason that anybody could understand, certainly no reason that Nel understood then or later, she smiled. Like a street pup that wags its tail at the very doorjamb of the butcher shop he has been kicked away from only moments before, Helene smiled. Smiled dazzlingly and coquettishly at the salmon-colored face of the conductor.

Nel looked away from the flash of pretty teeth to the other passengers. The two black soldiers, who had been watching the scene with what appeared to be indifference, now looked stricken. Behind Nel was the bright and blazing light of her mother's smile; before her the midnight eyes of the soldiers. She saw the muscles of their faces tighten, a movement under the skin from blood to marble. No change in the expression of the eyes, but a hard wetness that veiled them as they looked at the stretch of her mother's foolish smile.

As the door slammed on the conductor's exit, Helene walked down the aisle to a seat. She looked about for a second to see whether any of the men would help her put the suitcases in the overhead rack. Not a man moved. Helene sat down, fussily, her back toward the men. Nel sat opposite, facing both her mother and the soldiers, neither of whom she could look at. She felt both pleased and ashamed to sense that these men, unlike her father, who worshiped his graceful, beautiful wife, were bubbling with a hatred for her mother that had not been there in the beginning but had been born with the dazzling smile. In the silence that preceded the train's heave, she looked deeply at the folds of her mother's dress. There in the fall of the heavy brown wool she held her eyes. She could not risk letting them travel upward for fear of seeing that the hooks and eyes in the placket of the dress had come undone and exposed the custard-colored skin underneath. She stared at the hem, wanting to believe in its weight but knowing that custard was all that it hid. If this tall, proud woman, this woman who was very particular about her friends, who slipped into church with unequaled elegance, who could quell a roustabout[5] with a look, if *she* were really custard, then there was a chance that Nel was too.

It was on that train, shuffling toward Cincinnati, that she resolved to be on guard—always. She wanted to make certain that no man ever looked at her that way. That no midnight eyes or marbled flesh would ever accost her and turn her into jelly.

For two days they rode; two days of watching sleet turn to rain, turn to purple sunsets, and one night knotted on the wooden seats (their heads on folded coats), trying not to hear the snoring soldiers. When they changed trains in Birmingham for the last leg of the trip, they discovered what luxury they had been in through Kentucky and Tennessee, where the rest stops had all had colored toilets. After Birmingham there were none. Helene's face was drawn with the need to relieve herself, and so intense was her distress she finally brought herself to speak about her problem to a black woman with four children who had got on in Tuscaloosa.

"Is there somewhere we can go to use the restroom?"

The woman looked up at her and seemed not to understand. "Ma'am?" Her eyes fastened on the thick velvet collar, the fair skin, the high-tone voice.

"The restroom," Helene repeated. Then, in a whisper, "The toilet."

The woman pointed out the window and said, "Yes, ma'am. Yonder."

5. A longshoreman or an unskilled laborer.

Helene looked out of the window halfway expecting to see a comfort station in the distance; instead she saw graygreen trees leaning over tangled grass. "Where?"

"Yonder," the woman said. "Meridian. We be pullin' in direc'lin." Then she smiled sympathetically and asked, "Kin you make it?"

Helene nodded and went back to her seat trying to think of other things—for the surest way to have an accident would be to remember her full bladder.

At Meridian the women got out with their children. While Helene looked about the tiny stationhouse for a door that said COLORED WOMEN, the other woman stalked off to a field of high grass on the far side of the track. Some white men were leaning on the railing in front of the station-house. It was not only their tongues curling around toothpicks that kept Helene from asking information of them. She looked around for the other woman and, seeing just the top of her head rag in the grass, slowly realized where "yonder" was. All of them, the fat woman and her four children, three boys and a girl, Helene and her daughter, squatted there in the four o'clock Meridian sun. They did it again in Ellisville, again in Hattiesburg, and by the time they reached Slidell, not too far from Lake Pontchartrain, Helene could not only fold leaves as well as the fat woman, she never felt a stir as she passed the muddy eyes of the men who stood like wrecked Do-rics[6] under the station roofs of those towns.

The lift in spirit that such an accomplishment produced in her quickly disappeared when the train finally pulled into New Orleans.

Cecile Sabat's house leaned between two others just like it on Elysian Fields.[7] A Frenchified shotgun house, it sported a magnificent garden in the back and a tiny wrought-iron fence in the front. On the door hung a black crepe wreath with purple ribbon. They were too late. Helene reached up to touch the ribbon, hesitated, and knocked. A man in a collar-less shirt opened the door. Helene identified herself and he said he was Henri Martin and that he was there for the settin'-up. They stepped into the house. The Virgin Mary clasped her hands in front of her neck three times in the front room and once in the bedroom where Cecile's body lay. The old woman had died without seeing or blessing her granddaughter.

No one other than Mr. Martin seemed to be in the house, but a sweet odor as of gardenias told them that someone else had been. Blotting her lashes with a white handkerchief, Helene walked through the kitchen to the back bedroom where she had slept for sixteen years. Nel trotted along behind, enchanted with the smell, the candles and the strangeness. When Helene bent to loosen the ribbons of Nel's hat, a woman in a yellow dress came out of the garden and onto the back porch that opened into the bed-room. The two women looked at each other. There was no recognition in the eyes of either. Then Helene said, "This is your . . . grandmother, Nel." Nel looked at her mother and then quickly back at the door they had just come out of.

6. I.e., like columns holding up the roofs.
7. In classical mythology, the home of the blessed after they die; here, a street in New Orleans.

"No. That was your great-grandmother. This is your grandmother. My . . . mother."

Before the child could think, her words were hanging in the gardenia air. "But she looks so young."

The woman in the canary-yellow dress laughed and said she was forty-eight, "an old forty-eight."

Then it was she who carried the gardenia smell. This tiny woman with the softness and glare of a canary. In that somber house that held four Virgin Marys, where death sighed in every corner and candles sputtered, the gardenia smell and canary-yellow dress emphasized the funeral atmosphere surrounding them.

The woman smiled, glanced in the mirror and said, throwing her voice toward Helene, "That your only one?"

"Yes," said Helene.

"Pretty. A lot like you."

"Yes. Well. She's ten now."

"Ten? Vrai?[8] Small for her age, no?"

Helene shrugged and looked at her daughter's questioning eyes. The woman in the yellow dress leaned forward. "Come. Come, chere."

Helene interrupted. "We have to get cleaned up. We been three days on the train with no chance to wash or . . ."

"Comment t'appelle?"

"She doesn't talk Creole."

"Then you ask her."

"She wants to know your name, honey."

With her head pressed into her mother's heavy brown dress, Nel told her and then asked, "What's yours?"

"Mine's Rochelle. Well. I must be going on." She moved closer to the mirror and stood there sweeping hair up from her neck back into its halolike roll, and wetting with spit the ringlets that fell over her ears. "I been here, you know, most of the day. She pass on yesterday. The funeral tomorrow. Henri takin' care." She struck a match, blew it out and darkened her eyebrows with the burnt head. All the while Helene and Nel watched her. The one in a rage at the folded leaves she had endured, the wooden benches she had slept on, all to miss seeing her grandmother and seeing instead that painted canary who never said a word of greeting or affection or . . .

Rochelle continued. "I don't know what happen to de house. Long time paid for. You be thinkin' on it? Oui?" Her newly darkened eyebrows queried Helene.

"Oui."[9] Helene's voice was chilly. "I be thinkin' on it."

"Oh, well. Not for me to say . . ."

Suddenly she swept around and hugged Nel—a quick embrace tighter and harder than one would have imagined her thin soft arms capable of.

" 'Voir![1] 'Voir!" and she was gone.

In the kitchen, being soaped head to toe by her mother, Nel ventured an observation. "She smelled so nice. And her skin was so soft."

8. True (French).   1. Good-bye (French).
9. Yes (French).

Helene rinsed the cloth. "Much handled things are always soft."

"What does 'vwah' mean?"

"I don't know," her mother said. "I don't talk Creole." She gazed at her daughter's wet buttocks. "And neither do you."

When they got back to Medallion and into the quiet house they saw the note exactly where they had left it and the ham dried out in the icebox.

"Lord, I've never been so glad to see this place. But look at the dust. Get the rags, Nel. Oh, never mind. Let's breathe awhile first. Lord, I never thought I'd get back here safe and sound. Whoo. Well, it's over. Good and over. Praise His name. Look at that. I told that old fool not to deliver any milk and there's the can curdled to beat all. What gets into people? I told him not to. Well, I got other things to worry 'bout. Got to get a fire started. I left it ready so I wouldn't have to do nothin' but light it. Lord, it's cold. Don't just sit there, honey. You could be pulling your nose . . ."

Nel sat on the red-velvet sofa listening to her mother but remembering the smell and the tight, tight hug of the woman in yellow who rubbed burned matches over her eyes.

Late that night after the fire was made, the cold supper eaten, the surface dust removed, Nel lay in bed thinking of her trip. She remembered clearly the urine running down and into her stockings until she learned how to squat properly; the disgust on the face of the dead woman and the sound of the funeral drums. It had been an exhilarating trip but a fearful one. She had been frightened of the soldiers' eyes on the train, the black wreath on the door, the custard pudding she believed lurked under her mother's heavy dress, the feel of unknown streets and unknown people. But she had gone on a real trip, and now she was different. She got out of bed and lit the lamp to look in the mirror. There was her face, plain brown eyes, three braids and the nose her mother hated. She looked for a long time and suddenly a shiver ran through her.

"I'm me," she whispered. "Me."

Nel didn't know quite what she meant, but on the other hand she knew exactly what she meant.

"I'm me. I'm not their daughter. I'm not Nel. I'm me. Me."

Each time she said the word *me* there was a gathering in her like power, like joy, like fear. Back in bed with her discovery, she stared out the window at the dark leaves of the horse chestnut.

"Me," she murmured. And then, sinking deeper into the quilts, "I want . . . I want to be . . . wonderful. Oh, Jesus, make me wonderful."

The many experiences of her trip crowded in on her. She slept. It was the last as well as the first time she was ever to leave Medallion.

For days afterward she imagined other trips she would take, alone though, to faraway places. Contemplating them was delicious. Leaving Medallion would be her goal. But that was before she met Sula, the girl she had seen for five years at Garfield Primary but never played with, never knew, because her mother said that Sula's mother was sooty. The trip, perhaps, or her new found me-ness, gave her the strength to cultivate a friend in spite of her mother.

When Sula first visited the Wright house, Helene's curdled scorn turned to butter. Her daughter's friend seemed to have none of the mother's slackness. Nel, who regarded the oppressive neatness of her home with dread, felt comfortable in it with Sula, who loved it and would sit on the redvelvet sofa for ten to twenty minutes at a time—still as dawn. As for Nel, she preferred Sula's woolly house, where a pot of something was always cooking on the stove; where the mother, Hannah, never scolded or gave directions; where all sorts of people dropped in; where newspapers were stacked in the hallway, and dirty dishes left for hours at a time in the sink, and where a one-legged grandmother named Eva handed you goobers from deep inside her pockets or read you a dream.

1921

Sula Peace lived in a house of many rooms that had been built over a period of five years to the specifications of its owner, who kept on adding things: more stairways—there were three sets to the second floor—more rooms, doors and stoops. There were rooms that had three doors, others that opened out on the porch only and were inaccessible from any other part of the house; others that you could get to only by going through somebody's bedroom. The creator and sovereign of this enormous house with the four sickle-pear trees in the front yard and the single elm in the back yard was Eva Peace, who sat in a wagon on the third floor directing the lives of her children, friends, strays, and a constant stream of boarders. Fewer than nine people in the town remembered when Eva had two legs, and her oldest child, Hannah, was not one of them. Unless Eva herself introduced the subject, no one ever spoke of her disability; they pretended to ignore it, unless, in some mood of fancy, she began some fearful story about it— generally to entertain children. How the leg got up by itself one day and walked on off. How she hobbled after it but it ran too fast. Or how she had a corn on her toe and it just grew and grew and grew until her whole foot was a corn and then it traveled on up her leg and wouldn't stop growing until she put a red rag at the top but by that time it was already at her knee.

Somebody said Eva stuck it under a train and made them pay off. Another said she sold it to a hospital for $10,000—at which Mr. Reed opened his eyes and asked, "Nigger gal legs goin' for $10,000 a *piece?*" as though he could understand $10,000 a *pair*—but for *one?*

Whatever the fate of her lost leg, the remaining one was magnificent. It was stockinged and shod at all times and in all weather. Once in a while she got a felt slipper for Christmas or her birthday, but they soon disappeared, for Eva always wore a black laced-up shoe that came well above her ankle. Nor did she wear overlong dresses to disguise the empty place on her left side. Her dresses were mid-calf so that her one glamorous leg was always in view as well as the long fall of space below her left thigh. One of her men friends had fashioned a kind of wheelchair for her: a rocking-chair top fitted into a large child's wagon. In this contraption she wheeled around the room, from bedside to dresser to the balcony that opened out the north side of her room or to the window that looked out on the back yard. The wagon was so low that children who spoke to her standing up were eye level with her, and adults, standing or sitting, had to look down at her. But they didn't know it. They all had the impression that they were looking up at her, up into the open distances of her eyes, up into the soft black of her nostrils and up at the crest of her chin.

Eva had married a man named BoyBoy and had three children: Hannah, the eldest, and Eva, whom she named after herself but called Pearl, and a son named Ralph, whom she called Plum.

After five years of a sad and disgruntled marriage BoyBoy took off. During the time they were together he was very much preoccupied with other women and not home much. He did whatever he could that he liked, and he liked womanizing best, drinking second, and abusing Eva third. When he left in November, Eva had $1.65, five eggs, three beets and no idea of what or how to feel. The children needed her; she needed money, and needed to get on with her life. But the demands of feeding her three children were so acute she had to postpone her anger for two years until she had both the time and the energy for it. She was confused and desperately hungry. There were very few black families in those low hills then. The Suggs, who lived two hundred yards down the road, brought her a warm bowl of peas, as soon as they found out, and a plate of cold bread. She thanked them and asked if they had a little milk for the older ones. They said no, but Mrs. Jackson, they knew, had a cow still giving. Eva took a bucket over and Mrs. Jackson told her to come back and fill it up in the morning, because the evening milking had already been done. In this way, things went on until near December. People were very willing to help, but Eva felt she would soon run her welcome out; winters were hard and her neighbors were not that much better off. She would lie in bed with the baby boy, the two girls wrapped in quilts on the floor, thinking. The oldest child, Hannah, was five and too young to take care of the baby alone, and any housework Eva could find would keep her away from them from five thirty or earlier in the morning until dark—way past eight. The white people in the valley weren't rich enough then to want maids; they were small farmers and tradesmen and wanted hard-labor help if anything. She thought also of returning to some of her people in Virginia, but to come home dragging three young ones would have to be a step one rung before death for Eva. She would have to scrounge around and beg through the winter, until her baby was at least nine months old, then she could plant and maybe hire herself out to valley farms to weed or sow or feed stock until something steadier came along at harvest time. She thought she had probably been a fool to let BoyBoy haul her away from her people, but it had seemed so right at the time. He worked for a white carpenter and toolsmith who insisted on BoyBoy's accompanying him when he went West and set up in a squinchy little town called Medallion. BoyBoy brought his new wife and built them a one-room cabin sixty feet back from the road that wound up out of the valley, on up into the hills and was named for the man he worked for. They lived there a year before they had an outhouse.

Sometime before the middle of December, the baby, Plum, stopped having bowel movements. Eva massaged his stomach and gave him warm water. Something must be wrong with my milk, she thought. Mrs. Suggs gave her castor oil, but even that didn't work. He cried and fought so they couldn't get much down his throat anyway. He seemed in great pain and his shrieks were pitched high in outrage and suffering. At one point, maddened by his own crying, he gagged, choked and looked as though he was strangling to death. Eva rushed to him and kicked over the earthen slop jar, washing a small area of the floor with the child's urine. She managed to soothe him, but when he took up the cry again late that night, she resolved to end his misery once and for all. She wrapped him in blankets, ran her finger around the crevices and sides of the lard can and stumbled to the outhouse with him. Deep in its darkness and freezing stench she squatted down, turned the baby over on her knees, exposed his buttocks and shoved the last bit of food she had in the world (besides three beets) up his ass. Softening the insertion with the dab of lard, she probed with her middle finger to loosen his bowels. Her fingernail snagged what felt like a pebble; she pulled it out and others followed. Plum stopped crying as the black hard stools ricocheted onto the frozen ground. And now that it was over, Eva squatted there wondering why she had come all the way out there to free his stools, and what was she doing down on her haunches with her beloved baby boy warmed by her body in the almost total darkness, her shins and teeth freezing, her nostrils assailed. She shook her head as though to juggle her brains around, then said aloud, "Uh uh. Nooo." Thereupon she returned to the house and her bed. As the grateful Plum slept, the silence allowed her to think.

Two days later she left all of her children with Mrs. Suggs, saying she would be back the next day.

Eighteen months later she swept down from a wagon with two crutches, a new black pocketbook, and one leg. First she reclaimed her children, next she gave the surprised Mrs. Suggs a ten-dollar bill, later she started building a house on Carpenter's Road, sixty feet from BoyBoy's one-room cabin, which she rented out.

When Plum was three years old, BoyBoy came back to town and paid her a visit. When Eva got the word that he was on his way, she made some lemonade. She had no idea what she would do or feel during that encounter. Would she cry, cut his throat, beg him to make love to her? She couldn't imagine. So she just waited to see. She stirred lemonade in a green pitcher and waited.

BoyBoy danced up the steps and knocked on the door.

"Come on in," she hollered.

He opened the door and stood smiling, a picture of prosperity and good will. His shoes were a shiny orange, and he had on a citified straw hat, a light-blue suit, and a cat's-head stickpin in his tie. Eva smiled and told him to sit himself down. He smiled too.

"How you been, girl?"

"Pretty fair. What you know good?" When she heard those words come out of her own mouth she knew that their conversation would start off polite. Although it remained to be seen whether she would still run the ice pick through the cat's-head pin.

"Have some lemonade."

"Don't mind if I do." He swept his hat off with a satisfied gesture. His nails were long and shiny. "Sho is hot, and I been runnin' around all day."

Eva looked out of the screen door and saw a woman in a pea-green dress leaning on the smallest pear tree. Glancing back at him, she was reminded of Plum's face when he managed to get the meat out of a walnut all by himself. Eva smiled again, and poured the lemonade.

Their conversation was easy: she catching him up on all the gossip, he asking about this one and that one, and like everybody else avoiding any reference to her leg. It was like talking to somebody's cousin who just stopped by to say howdy before getting on back to wherever he came from. BoyBoy didn't ask to see the children, and Eva didn't bring them into the conversation.

After a while he rose to go. Talking about his appointments and exuding an odor of new money and idleness, he danced down the steps and strutted toward the peagreen dress. Eva watched. She looked at the back of his neck and the set of his shoulders. Underneath all of that shine she saw defeat in the stalk of his neck and the curious tight way he held his shoulders. But still she was not sure what she felt. Then he leaned forward and whispered into the ear of the woman in the green dress. She was still for a moment and then threw back her head and laughed. A high-pitched big-city laugh that reminded Eva of Chicago. It hit her like a sledge hammer, and it was then that she knew what to feel. A liquid trail of hate flooded her chest.

Knowing that she would hate him long and well filled her with pleasant anticipation, like when you know you are going to fall in love with someone and you wait for the happy signs. Hating BoyBoy, she could get on with it, and have the safety, the thrill, the consistency of that hatred as long as she wanted or needed it to define and strengthen her or protect her from routine vulnerabilities. (Once when Hannah accused her of hating colored people, Eva said she only hated one, Hannah's father BoyBoy, and it was hating him that kept her alive and happy.)

Happy or not, after BoyBoy's visit she began her retreat to her bedroom, leaving the bottom of the house more and more to those who lived there: cousins who were passing through, stray folks, and the many, many newly married couples she let rooms to with housekeeping privileges, and after 1910 she didn't willingly set foot on the stairs but once and that was to light a fire, the smoke of which was in her hair for years.

Among the tenants in that big old house were the children Eva took in. Operating on a private scheme of preference and prejudice, she sent off for children she had seen from the balcony of her bedroom or whose circumstances she had heard about from the gossipy old men who came to play checkers or read the *Courier*, or write her number.[2] In 1921, when her granddaughter Sula was eleven, Eva had three such children. They came with woolen caps and names given to them by their mothers, or grandmothers, or somebody's best friend. Eva snatched the caps off their heads and ignored their names. She looked at the first child closely, his wrists, the shape of his head and the temperament that showed in his eyes and said,

---

2. Eva played the numbers, an illegal lottery that involves betting on certain combinations of digits.

"Well. Look at Dewey. My my mymymy." When later that same year she sent for a child who kept falling down off the porch across the street, she said the same thing. Somebody said, "But, Miss Eva, you calls the other one Dewey."

"So? This here's another one."

When the third one was brought and Eva said "Dewey" again, everybody thought she had simply run out of names or that her faculties had finally softened.

"How is anybody going to tell them apart?" Hannah asked her.

"What you need to tell them apart for? They's all deweys."

When Hannah asked the question it didn't sound very bright, because each dewey was markedly different from the other two. Dewey one was a deeply black boy with a beautiful head and the golden eyes of chronic jaundice. Dewey two was light-skinned with freckles everywhere and a head of tight red hair. Dewey three was half Mexican with chocolate skin and black bangs. Besides, they were one and two years apart in age. It was Eva saying things like, "Send one of them deweys out to get me some Garret, if they don't have Garret, get Buttercup,"[3] or, "Tell them deweys to cut out that noise," or, "Come here, you dewey you," and, "Send me a dewey," that gave Hannah's question its weight.

Slowly each boy came out of whatever cocoon he was in at the time his mother or somebody gave him away, and accepted Eva's view, becoming in fact as well as in name a dewey—joining with the other two to become a trinity with a plural name . . . inseparable, loving nothing and no one but themselves. When the handle from the icebox fell off, all the deweys got whipped, and in dry-eyed silence watched their own feet as they turned their behinds high up into the air for the stroke. When the golden-eyed dewey was ready for school he would not go without the others. He was seven, freckled dewey was five, and Mexican dewey was only four. Eva solved the problem by having them all sent off together. Mr. Buckland Reed said, "But one of them's only four."

"How you know? They all come here the same year," Eva said.

"But that one there was one year old when he came, and that was three years ago."

"You don't know how old he was when he come here and neither do the teacher. Send 'em."

The teacher was startled but not unbelieving, for she had long ago given up trying to fathom the ways of the colored people in town. So when Mrs. Reed said that their names were Dewey King, that they were cousins, and all were six years old, the teacher gave only a tiny sigh and wrote them in the record book for the first grade. She too thought she would have no problem distinguishing among them, because they looked nothing alike, but like everyone else before her, she gradually found that she could not tell one from the other. The deweys would not allow it. They got all mixed up in her head, and finally she could not literally believe her eyes. They spoke with one voice, thought with one mind, and maintained an annoying privacy. Stouthearted, surly, and wholly unpredictable, the deweys re-

3. Brands of snuff.

mained a mystery not only during all of their lives in Medallion but after as well.

The deweys came in 1921, but the year before Eva had given a small room off the kitchen to Tar Baby, a beautiful, slight, quiet man who never spoke above a whisper. Most people said he was half white, but Eva said he was all white. That she knew blood when she saw it, and he didn't have none. When he first came to Medallion, the people called him Pretty John-nie, but Eva looked at his milky skin and cornsilk hair and out of a mixture of fun and meanness called him Tar Baby. He was a mountain boy who stayed to himself, bothering no one, intent solely on drinking himself to death. At first he worked in a poultry market, and after wringing the necks of chickens all day, he came home and drank until he slept. Later he began to miss days at work and frequently did not have his rent money. When he lost his job altogether, he would go out in the morning, scrounge around for money doing odd jobs, bumming or whatever, and come home to drink. Because he was no bother, ate little, required nothing, and was a lover of cheap wine, no one found him a nuisance. Besides, he frequently went to Wednesday-night prayer meetings and sang with the sweetest hill voice imaginable "In the Sweet By-and-By." He sent the deweys out for his liquor and spent most of his time in a heap on the floor or sitting in a chair staring at the wall.

Hannah worried about him a little, but only a very little. For it soon be-came clear that he simply wanted a place to die privately but not quite alone. No one thought of suggesting to him that he pull himself together or see a doctor or anything. Even the women at prayer meeting who cried when he sang "In the Sweet By-and-By" never tried to get him to partici-pate in the church activities. They just listened to him sing, wept and thought very graphically of their own imminent deaths. The people either accepted his own evaluation of his life, or were indifferent to it. There was, however, a measure of contempt in their indifference, for they had little patience with people who took themselves that seriously. Seriously enough to try to die. And it was natural that he, after all, became the first one to join Shadrack—Tar Baby and the deweys—on National Suicide Day.

Under Eva's distant eye, and prey to her idiosyncrasies, her own children grew up stealthily: Pearl married at fourteen and moved to Flint, Michi-gan, from where she posted frail letters to her mother with two dollars folded into the writing paper. Sad little nonsense letters about minor trou-bles, her husband's job and who the children favored. Hannah married a laughing man named Rekus who died when their daughter Sula was about three years old, at which time Hannah moved back into her mother's big house prepared to take care of it and her mother forever.

With the exception of BoyBoy, those Peace women loved all men. It was manlove that Eva bequeathed to her daughters. Probably, people said, be-cause there were no men in the house, no men to run it. But actually that was not true. The Peace women simply loved maleness, for its own sake. Eva, old as she was, and with one leg, had a regular flock of gentleman callers, and although she did not participate in the act of love, there was a good deal of teasing and pecking and laughter. The men wanted to see her lovely calf, that neat shoe, and watch the focusing that sometimes swept down out of the distances in her eyes. They wanted to see the joy in her face as they settled down to play checkers, knowing that even when she beat them, as she almost always did, somehow, in her presence, it was they who had won something. They would read the newspaper aloud to her and make observations on its content, and Eva would listen feeling no obligation to agree and, in fact, would take them to task about their interpretation of events. But she argued with them with such an absence of bile, such a concentration of manlove, that they felt their convictions solidified by her disagreement.

With other people's affairs Eva was equally prejudiced about men. She fussed interminably with the brides of the newly wed couples for not getting their men's supper ready on time; about how to launder shirts, press them, etc. "Yo' man be here direc'lin. Ain't it 'bout time you got busy?"

"Aw, Miss Eva. It'll be ready. We just having spaghetti."

"Again?" Eva's eyebrows fluted up and the newlywed pressed her lips together in shame.

Hannah simply refused to live without the attentions of a man, and after Rekus' death had a steady sequence of lovers, mostly the husbands of her friends and neighbors. Her flirting was sweet, low and guileless. Without ever a pat of the hair, a rush to change clothes or a quick application of paint, with no gesture whatsoever, she rippled with sex. In her same old print wraparound, barefoot in the summer, in the winter her feet in a man's leather slippers with the backs flattened under her heels, she made men aware of her behind, her slim ankles, the dew-smooth skin and the incredible length of neck. Then the smile-eyes, the turn of the head—all so welcoming, light and playful. Her voice trailed, dipped and bowed; she gave a chord to the simplest words. Nobody, but nobody, could say "hey sugar" • like Hannah. When he heard it, the man tipped his hat down a little over his eyes, hoisted his trousers and thought about the hollow place at the base of her neck. And all this without the slightest confusion about work and responsibilities. While Eva tested and argued with her men, leaving them feeling as though they had been in combat with a worthy, if amiable, foe, Hannah rubbed no edges, made no demands, made the man feel as though he were complete and wonderful just as he was—he didn't need fixing— and so he relaxed and swooned in the Hannah-light that shone on him simply because he was. If the man entered and Hannah was carrying a coal scuttle up from the basement, she handled it in such a way that it became a gesture of love. He made no move to help her with it simply because he wanted to see how her thighs looked when she bent to put it down, knowing that she wanted him to see them too.

But since in that crowded house there were no places for private and spontaneous lovemaking, Hannah would take the man down into the cellar in the summer where it was cool back behind the coal bin and the newspapers, or in the winter they would step into the pantry and stand up against the shelves she had filled with canned goods, or lie on the flour sack just under the rows of tiny green peppers. When those places were not available, she would slip into the seldom-used parlor, or even up to her bedroom. She liked the last place least, not because Sula slept in the room with her but because her love mate's tendency was always to fall asleep afterward and Hannah was fastidious about whom she slept with. She would fuck practically anything, but sleeping with someone implied for her a measure of trust and a definite commitment. So she ended up a daylight lover, and it was only once actually that Sula came home from school and found her mother in the bed, curled spoon in the arms of a man.

Seeing her step so easily into the pantry and emerge looking precisely as she did when she entered, only happier, taught Sula that sex was pleasant and frequent, but otherwise unremarkable. Outside the house, where children giggled about underwear, the message was different. So she watched her mother's face and the face of the men when they opened the pantry door and made up her own mind.

Hannah exasperated the women in the town—the "good" women, who said, "One thing I can't stand is a nasty woman"; the whores, who were hard put to find trade among black men anyway and who resented Hannah's generosity; the middling women, who had both husbands and affairs, because Hannah seemed too unlike them, having no passion attached to her relationships and being wholly incapable of jealousy. Hannah's friendships with women were, of course, seldom and short-lived, and the newly married couples whom her mother took in soon learned what a hazard she was. She could break up a marriage before it had even become one—she would make love to the new groom and wash his wife's dishes all in an afternoon. What she wanted, after Rekus died, and what she succeeded in having more often than not, was some touching every day.

The men, surprisingly, never gossiped about her. She was unquestionably a kind and generous woman and that, coupled with her extraordinary beauty and funky elegance of manner, made them defend her and protect her from any vitriol that newcomers or their wives might spill.

Eva's last child, Plum, to whom she hoped to bequeath everything, floated in a constant swaddle of love and affection, until 1917 when he went to war. He returned to the States in 1919 but did not get back to Medallion until 1920. He wrote letters from New York, Washington, D.C., and Chicago full of promises of homecomings, but there was obviously something wrong. Finally some two or three days after Christmas, he arrived with just the shadow of his old dip-down walk. His hair had been neither cut nor combed in months, his clothes were pointless and he had no socks. But he did have a black bag, a paper sack, and a sweet, sweet smile. Everybody welcomed him and gave him a warm room next to Tar Baby's and waited for him to tell them whatever it was he wanted them to know. They waited in vain for his telling but not long for the knowing. His habits were much like Tar Baby's but there were no bottles, and Plum was sometimes cheerful and animated. Hannah watched and Eva waited. Then he began to steal from them, take trips to Cincinnati and sleep for days in his room with the record player going. He got even thinner, since he ate only snatches of things at beginnings or endings of meals. It was Hannah who found the bent spoon black from steady cooking.[4]

So late one night in 1921, Eva got up from her bed and put on her clothes. Hoisting herself up on her crutches, she was amazed to find that

---

4. I.e., from heating and dissolving powdered heroin in water to make a solution for injection.

she could still manage them, although the pain in her armpits was severe. She practiced a few steps around the room, and then opened the door. Slowly, she manipulated herself down the long flights of stairs, two crutches under her left arm, the right hand grasping the banister. The sound of her foot booming in comparison to the delicate pat of the crutch tip. On each landing she stopped for breath. Annoyed at her physical condition, she closed her eyes and removed the crutches from under her arms to relieve the unaccustomed pressure. At the foot of the stairs she redistributed her weight between the crutches and swooped on through the front room, to the dining room, to the kitchen, swinging and swooping like a giant heron, so graceful sailing about in its own habitat but awkward and comical when it folded its wings and tried to walk. With a swing and a swoop she arrived at Plum's door and pushed it open with the tip of one crutch. He was lying in bed barely visible in the light coming from a single bulb. Eva swung over to the bed and propped her crutches at its foot. She sat down and gathered Plum into her arms. He woke, but only slightly.

"Hey, man. Hey. You holdin' me, Mamma?" His voice was drowsy and amused. He chuckled as though he had heard some private joke. Eva held him closer and began to rock. Back and forth she rocked him, her eyes wandering around his room. There in the corner was a half-eaten store-bought cherry pie. Balled-up candy wrappers and empty pop bottles peeped from under the dresser. On the floor by her foot was a glass of strawberry crush and a *Liberty* magazine. Rocking, rocking, listening to Plum's occasional chuckles, Eva let her memory spin, loop and fall. Plum in the tub that time as she leaned over him. He reached up and dripped water into her bosom and laughed. She was angry, but not too, and laughed with him.

"Mamma, you so purty. You so purty, Mamma."

Eva lifted her tongue to the edge of her lip to stop the tears from running into her mouth. Rocking, rocking. Later she laid him down and looked at him a long time. Suddenly she was thirsty and reached for the glass of strawberry crush. She put it to her lips and discovered it was blood-tainted water and threw it to the floor. Plum woke up and said, "Hey, Mamma, whyn't you go on back to bed? I'm all right. Didn't I tell you? I'm all right. Go on, now."

"I'm going, Plum," she said. She shifted her weight and pulled her crutches toward her. Swinging and swooping, she left his room. She dragged herself to the kitchen and made grating noises.

Plum on the rim of a warm light sleep was still chuckling. Mamma. She sure was somethin'. He felt twilight. Now there seemed to be some kind of wet light traveling over his legs and stomach with a deeply attractive smell. It wound itself—this wet light—all about him, splashing and running into his skin. He opened his eyes and saw what he imagined was the great wing of an eagle pouring a wet lightness over him. Some kind of baptism, some kind of blessing, he thought. Everything is going to be all right, it said. Knowing that it was so he closed his eyes and sank back into the bright hole of sleep.

Eva stepped back from the bed and let the crutches rest under her arms. She rolled a bit of newspaper into a tight stick about six inches long, lit it and threw it onto the bed where the kerosene-soaked Plum lay in snug delight. Quickly, as the *whoosh* of flames engulfed him, she shut the door and made her slow and painful journey back to the top of the house.

Just as she got to the third landing she could hear Hannah and some child's voice. She swung along, not even listening to the voices of alarm and the cries of the deweys. By the time she got to her bed someone was bounding up the stairs after her. Hannah opened the door. "Plum! Plum! He's burning, Mamma! We can't even open the door! Mamma!"

Eva looked into Hannah's eyes. "Is? My baby? Burning?" The two women did not speak, for the eyes of each were enough for the other. Then Hannah closed hers and ran toward the voices of neighbors calling for water.

1922

It was too cool for ice cream. A hill wind was blowing dust and empty Camels wrappers about their ankles. It pushed their dresses into the creases of their behinds, then lifted the hems to peek at their cotton underwear. They were on their way to Edna Finch's Mellow House, an ice-cream parlor catering to nice folks—where even children would feel comfortable, you know, even though it was right next to Reba's Grill and just one block down from the Time and a Half Pool Hall. It sat in the curve of Carpenter's Road, which, in four blocks, made up all the sporting life available in the Bottom. Old men and young ones draped themselves in front of the Elmira Theater, Irene's Palace of Cosmetology, the pool hall, the grill and the other sagging business enterprises that lined the street. On sills, on stoops, on crates and broken chairs they sat tasting their teeth and waiting for something to distract them. Every passerby, every motorcar, every alteration in stance caught their attention and was commented on. Particularly they watched women. When a woman approached, the older men tipped their hats; the younger ones opened and closed their thighs. But all of them, whatever their age, watched her retreating view with interest.

Nel and Sula walked through this valley of eyes chilled by the wind and heated by the embarrassment of appraising stares. The old men looked at their stalklike legs, dwelled on the cords in the backs of their knees and remembered old dance steps they had not done in twenty years. In their lust, which age had turned to kindness, they moved their lips as though to stir up the taste of young sweat on tight skin.

Pig meat. The words were in all their minds. And one of them, one of the young ones, said it aloud. Softly but definitively and there was no mistaking the compliment. His name was Ajax, a twenty-one-year-old pool haunt of sinister beauty. Graceful and economical in every movement, he held a place of envy with men of all ages for his magnificently foul mouth. In fact he seldom cursed, and the epithets he chose were dull, even harmless. His reputation was derived from the way he handled the words. When he said "hell" he hit the *h* with his lungs and the impact was greater than the achievement of the most imaginative foul mouth in the town. He could say "shit" with a nastiness impossible to imitate. So, when he said "pig meat" as Nel and Sula passed, they guarded their eyes least someone see their delight.

It was not really Edna Finch's ice cream that made them brave the stretch of those panther eyes. Years later their own eyes would glaze as they cupped their chins in remembrance of the inchworm smiles, the squatting haunches, the track-rail legs straddling broken chairs. The cream-colored trousers marking with a mere seam the place where the mystery curled. Those smooth vanilla crotches invited them; those lemon-yellow gabardines beckoned to them.

They moved toward the ice-cream parlor like tightrope walkers, as thrilled by the possibility of a slip as by the maintenance of tension and balance. The least sideways glance, the merest toe stub, could pitch them into those creamy haunches spread wide with welcome. Somewhere beneath all of that daintiness, chambered in all that neatness, lay the thing that clotted their dreams.

Which was only fitting, for it was in dreams that the two girls had first met. Long before Edna Finch's Mellow House opened, even before they marched through the chocolate halls of Garfield Primary School out onto the playground and stood facing each other through the ropes of the one vacant swing ("Go on." "No. You go."), they had already made each other's acquaintance in the delirium of their noon dreams. They were solitary little girls whose loneliness was so profound it intoxicated them and sent them stumbling into Technicolored visions that always included a presence, a someone, who, quite like the dreamer, shared the delight of the dream. When Nel, an only child, sat on the steps of her back porch surrounded by the high silence of her mother's incredibly orderly house, feeling the neatness pointing at her back, she studied the poplars and fell easily into a picture of herself lying on a flowered bed, tangled in her own hair, waiting for some fiery prince. He approached but never quite arrived. But always, watching the dream along with her, were some smiling sympathetic eyes. Someone as interested as she herself in the flow of her imagined hair, the thickness of the mattress of flowers, the voile[5] sleeves that closed below her elbows in gold-threaded cuffs.

Similarly, Sula, also an only child, but wedged into a household of throbbing disorder constantly awry with things, people, voices and the slamming of doors, spent hours in the attic behind a roll of linoleum galloping through her own mind on a gray-and-white horse tasting sugar and smelling roses in full view of a someone who shared both the taste and the speed.

So when they met, first in those chocolate halls and next through the ropes of the swing, they felt the ease and comfort of old friends. Because each had discovered years before that they were neither white nor male, and that all freedom and triumph was forbidden to them, they had set about creating something else to be. Their meeting was fortunate, for it let them use each other to grow on. Daughters of distant mothers and incomprehensible fathers (Sula's because he was dead; Nel's because he wasn't), they found in each other's eyes the intimacy they were looking for.

Nel Wright and Sula Peace were both twelve in 1922, wishbone thin and easy-assed. Nel was the color of wet sandpaper—just dark enough to

---

5. A sheer, fine fabric.

escape the blows of the pitch-black truebloods and the contempt of old women who worried about such things as bad blood mixtures and knew that the origins of a mule and a mulatto were one and the same.[6] Had she been any lighter-skinned she would have needed either her mother's protection on the way to school or a streak of mean to defend herself. Sula was a heavy brown with large quiet eyes, one of which featured a birthmark that spread from the middle of the lid toward the eyebrow, shaped something like a stemmed rose. It gave her otherwise plain face a broken excitement and blue-blade threat like the keloid scar[7] of the razored man who sometimes played checkers with her grandmother. The birthmark was to grow darker as the years passed, but now it was the same shade as her gold-flecked eyes, which, to the end, were as steady and clean as rain.

Their friendship was as intense as it was sudden. They found relief in each other's personality. Although both were unshaped, formless things, Nel seemed stronger and more consistent than Sula, who could hardly be counted on to sustain any emotion for more than three minutes. Yet there was one time when that was not true, when she held on to a mood for weeks, but even that was in defense of Nel.

Four white boys in their early teens, sons of some newly arrived Irish people, occasionally entertained themselves in the afternoon by harassing black schoolchildren. With shoes that pinched and woolen knickers that made red rings on their calves, they had come to this valley with their parents believing as they did that it was a promised land—green and shimmering with welcome. What they found was a strange accent, a pervasive fear of their religion and firm resistance to their attempts to find work. With one exception the older residents of Medallion scorned them. The one exception was the black community. Although some of the Negroes had been in Medallion before the Civil War (the town didn't even have a name then), if they had any hatred for these newcomers it didn't matter because it didn't show. As a matter of fact, baiting them was the one activity that the white Protestant residents concurred in. In part their place in this world was secured only when they echoed the old residents' attitude toward blacks.

These particular boys caught Nel once, and pushed her from hand to hand until they grew tired of the frightened helpless face. Because of that incident, Nel's route home from school became elaborate. She, and then Sula, managed to duck them for weeks until a chilly day in November when Sula said, "Let's us go on home the shortest way."

Nel blinked, but acquiesced. They walked up the street until they got to the bend of Carpenter's Road where the boys lounged on a disused well. Spotting their prey, the boys sauntered forward as though there was nothing in the world on their minds but the gray sky. Hardly able to control their grins, they stood like a gate blocking the path. When the girls were three feet in front of the boys, Sula reached into her coat pocket and pulled out Eva's paring knife. The boys stopped short, exchanged looks and dropped all pretense of innocence. This was going to be better than they

---

6. Etymologically, *mulatto* (a person of mixed black and white descent) has the same derivation as   *mule* (the sterile offspring of a donkey and a horse).
7. Thick scar.

thought. They were going to try and fight back, and with a knife. Maybe they could get an arm around one of their waists, or tear . . .

Sula squatted down in the dirt road and put everything down on the ground: her lunchpail, her reader, her mittens, her slate. Holding the knife in her right hand, she pulled the slate toward her and pressed her left forefinger down hard on its edge. Her aim was determined but inaccurate. She slashed off only the tip of her finger. The four boys stared open-mouthed at the wound and the scrap of flesh, like a button mushroom, curling in the cherry blood that ran into the corners of the slate.

Sula raised her eyes to them. Her voice was quiet. "If I can do that to myself, what you suppose I'll do to you?"

The shifting dirt was the only way Nel knew that they were moving away; she was looking at Sula's face, which seemed miles and miles away.

But toughness was not their quality—adventuresomeness was—and a mean determination to explore everything that interested them, from one-eyed chickens high-stepping in their penned yards to Mr. Buckland Reed's gold teeth, from the sound of sheets flapping in the wind to the labels on Tar Baby's wine bottles. And they had no priorities. They could be distracted from watching a fight with mean razors by the glorious smell of hot tar being poured by roadmen two hundred yards away.

In the safe harbor of each other's company they could afford to abandon the ways of other people and concentrate on their own perceptions of things. When Mrs. Wright reminded Nel to pull her nose, she would do it enthusiastically but without the least hope in the world.

"While you sittin' there, honey, go 'head and pull your nose."

"It hurts, Mamma."

"Don't you want a nice nose when you grow up?"

After she met Sula, Nel slid the clothespin under the blanket as soon as she got in the bed. And although there was still the hateful hot comb to suffer through each Saturday evening, its consequences—smooth hair—no longer interested her.

Joined in mutual admiration they watched each day as though it were a movie arranged for their amusement. The new theme they were now discovering was men. So they met regularly, without even planning it, to walk down the road to Edna Finch's Mellow House, even though it was too cool for ice cream.

Then summer came. A summer limp with the weight of blossomed things. Heavy sunflowers weeping over fences; iris curling and browning at the edges far away from their purple hearts; ears of corn letting their auburn hair wind down to their stalks. And the boys. The beautiful, beautiful boys who dotted the landscape like jewels, split the air with their shouts in the field, and thickened the river with their shining wet backs. Even their footsteps left a smell of smoke behind.

It was in that summer, the summer of their twelfth year, the summer of the beautiful black boys, that they became skittish, frightened and bold—all at the same time.

In that mercury mood in July, Sula and Nel wandered about the Bottom barefoot looking for mischief. They decided to go down by the river where the boys sometimes swam. Nel waited on the porch of 7 Carpenter's Road while Sula ran into the house to go to the toilet. On the way up the stairs, she passed the kitchen where Hannah sat with two friends, Patsy and Valentine. The two women were fanning themselves and watching Hannah put down some dough, all talking casually about one thing and another, and had gotten around, when Sula passed by, to the problems of child rearing.

"They a pain."

"Yeh. Wish I'd listened to mamma. She told me not to have 'em too soon."

"Any time atall is too soon for me."

"Oh, I don't know. My Rudy minds his daddy. He just wild with me. Be glad when he growed and gone."

Hannah smiled and said, "Shut your mouth. You love the ground he pee on."

"Sure I do. But he still a pain. Can't help loving your own child. No matter what they do."

"Well, Hester grown now and I can't say love is exactly what I feel."

"Sure you do. You love her, like I love Sula. I just don't like her. That's the difference."

"Guess so. Likin' them is another thing."

"Sure. They different people, you know . . ."

She only heard Hannah's words, and the pronouncement sent her flying up the stairs. In bewilderment, she stood at the window fingering the curtain edge, aware of a sting in her eye. Nel's call floated up and into the window, pulling her away from dark thoughts back into the bright, hot daylight.

They ran most of the way.

Heading toward the wide part of the river where trees grouped themselves in families darkening the earth below. They passed some boys swimming and clowning in the water, shrouding their words in laughter.

They ran in the sunlight, creating their own breeze, which pressed their dresses into their damp skin. Reaching a kind of square of four leaf-locked trees which promised cooling, they flung themselves into the four-cornered shade to taste their lip sweat and contemplate the wildness that had come upon them so suddenly. They lay in the grass, their foreheads almost touching, their bodies stretched away from each other at a 180-degree angle. Sula's head rested on her arm, an undone braid coiled around her wrist. Nel leaned on her elbows and worried long blades of grass with her fingers. Underneath their dresses flesh tightened and shivered in the high coolness, their small breasts just now beginning to create some pleasant discomfort when they were lying on their stomachs.

Sula lifted her head and joined Nel in the grass play. In concert, without ever meeting each other's eyes, they stroked the blades up and down, up and down. Nel found a thick twig and, with her thumbnail, pulled away its bark until it was stripped to a smooth, creamy innocence. Sula looked about and found one too. When both twigs were undressed Nel moved easily to the next stage and began tearing up rooted grass to make a bare spot of earth. When a generous clearing was made, Sula traced intricate patterns in it with her twig. At first Nel was content to do the same. But soon she grew impatient and poked her twig rhythmically and intensely into the earth, making a small neat hole that grew deeper and wider with the least manipulation of her twig. Sula copied her, and soon each had a hole the size of a cup. Nel began a more strenuous digging and, rising to her knee, was careful to scoop out the dirt as she made her hole deeper. Together they worked until the two holes were one and the same. When the depression was the size of a small dishpan, Nel's twig broke. With a gesture of disgust she threw the pieces into the hole they had made. Sula threw hers in too. Nel saw a bottle cap and tossed it in as well. Each then looked around for more debris to throw into the hole: paper, bits of glass, butts of cigarettes, until all of the small defiling things they could find were collected there. Carefully they replaced the soil and covered the entire grave with uprooted grass.

Neither one had spoken a word.

They stood up, stretched, then gazed out over the swift dull water as an unspeakable restlessness and agitation held them. At the same instant each girl heard footsteps in the grass. A little boy in too big knickers was coming up from the lower bank of the river. He stopped when he saw them and picked his nose.

"Your mamma tole you to stop eatin' snot, Chicken," Nel hollered at him through cupped hands.

"Shut up," he said, still picking.

"Come up here and say that."

"Leave him 'lone, Nel. Come here, Chicken. Lemme show you something."

"Naw."

"You scared we gone take your bugger away?"

"Leave him 'lone, I said. Come on, Chicken. Look. I'll help you climb a tree."

Chicken looked at the tree Sula was pointing to—a big double beech with low branches and lots of bends for sitting.

He moved slowly toward her.

"Come on, Chicken, I'll help you up."

Still picking his nose, his eyes wide, he came to where they were standing. Sula took him by the hand and coaxed him along. When they reached the base of the beech, she lifted him to the first branch, saying, "Go on. Go on. I got you." She followed the boy, steadying him, when he needed it, with her hand and her reassuring voice. When they were as high as they could go, Sula pointed to the far side of the river.

"See? Bet you never saw that far before, did you?"

"Uh uh."

"Now look down there." They both leaned a little and peered through the leaves at Nel standing below, squinting up at them. From their height she looked small and foreshortened.

Chicken Little laughed.

"Y'all better come on down before you break your neck," Nel hollered.

"I ain't never coming down," the boy hollered back.

"Yeah. We better. Come on, Chicken."

"Naw. Lemme go."

"Yeah, Chicken. Come on, now."

Sula pulled his leg gently.

"Lemme go."

"OK, I'm leavin' you." She started on.

"Wait!" he screamed.

Sula stopped and together they slowly worked their way down.

Chicken was still elated. "I was way up there, wasn't I? Wasn't I? I'm a tell my brovver."

Sula and Nel began to mimic him: "I'm a tell my brovver; I'm a tell my brovver."

Sula picked him up by his hands and swung him outward then around and around. His knickers ballooned and his shrieks of frightened joy startled the birds and the fat grasshoppers. When he slipped from her hands and sailed away out over the water they could still hear his bubbly laughter.

The water darkened and closed quickly over the place where Chicken Little sank. The pressure of his hard and tight little fingers was still in Sula's palms as she stood looking at the closed place in the water. They expected him to come back up, laughing. Both girls stared at the water.

Nel spoke first. "Somebody saw." A figure appeared briefly on the opposite shore.

The only house over there was Shadrack's. Sula glanced at Nel. Terror widened her nostrils. Had he seen?

The water was so peaceful now. There was nothing but the baking sun and something newly missing. Sula cupped her face for an instant, then turned and ran up to the little plank bridge that crossed the river to Shadrack's house. There was no path. It was as though neither Shadrack nor anyone else ever came this way.

Her running was swift and determined, but when she was close to the three little steps that led to his porch, fear crawled into her stomach and only the something newly missing back there in the river made it possible for her to walk up the three steps and knock at the door.

No one answered. She started back, but thought again of the peace of the river. Shadrack would be inside, just behind the door ready to pounce on her. Still she could not go back. Ever so gently she pushed the door with the tips of her fingers and heard only the hinges weep. More. And then she was inside. Alone. The neatness, the order startled her, but more surprising was the restfulness. Everything was so tiny, so common, so unthreatening. Perhaps this was not the house of the Shad. The terrible Shad who walked about with his penis out, who peed in front of ladies and girl-children, the only black who could curse white people and get away with it, who drank in the road from the mouth of the bottle, who shouted and shook in the streets. This cottage? This sweet old cottage? With its made-up bed? With its rag rug and wooden table? Sula stood in the middle of the little room and in her wonder forgot what she had come for until a sound at the door made her jump. He was there in the doorway looking at her. She had not heard his coming and now he was looking at her.

More in embarrassment than terror she averted her glance. When she called up enough courage to look back at him, she saw his hand resting upon the door frame. His fingers, barely touching the wood, were arranged in a graceful arc. Relieved and encouraged (no one with hands like that, no one with fingers that curved around wood so tenderly could kill her), she walked past him out of the door, feeling his gaze turning, turning with her.

At the edge of the porch, gathering the wisps of courage that were fast leaving her, she turned once more to look at him, to ask him . . . had he . . . ?

He was smiling, a great smile, heavy with lust and time to come. He nodded his head as though answering a question, and said, in a pleasant conversational tone, a tone of cooled butter, "Always."

Sula fled down the steps, and shot through the greenness and the baking sun back to Nel and the dark closed place in the water. There she collapsed in tears.

Nel quieted her. "Sh, sh. Don't, don't. You didn't mean it. It ain't your fault. Sh. Sh. Come on, le's go, Sula. Come on, now. Was he there? Did he see? Where's the belt to your dress?"

Sula shook her head while she searched her waist for the belt.

Finally she stood up and allowed Nel to lead her away. "He said, 'Always. Always.' "

"What?"

Sula covered her mouth as they walked down the hill. Always. He had answered a question she had not asked, and its promise licked at her feet.

A bargeman, poling away from the shore, found Chicken late that afternoon stuck in some rocks and weeds, his knickers ballooning about his legs. He would have left him there but noticed that it was a child, not an old black man, as it first appeared, and he prodded the body loose, netted it and hauled it aboard. He shook his head in disgust at the kind of parents who would drown their own children. When, he wondered, will those people ever be anything but animals, fit for nothing but substitutes for mules, only mules didn't kill each other the way niggers did. He dumped Chicken Little into a burlap sack and tossed him next to some egg crates and boxes of wool cloth. Later, sitting down to smoke on an empty lard tin, still bemused by God's curse and the terrible burden his own kind had of elevating Ham's sons,[8] he suddenly became alarmed by the thought that the corpse in this heat would have a terrible odor, which might get into the fabric of his woolen cloth. He dragged the sack away and hooked it over the side, so that the Chicken's body was half in and half out of the water.

Wiping the sweat from his neck, he reported his find to the sheriff at Porter's Landing, who said they didn't have no niggers in their county, but that some lived in those hills 'cross the river, up above Medallion. The bargeman said he couldn't go all the way back there, it was every bit of two miles. The sheriff said whyn't he throw it on back into the water. The bargeman said he never shoulda taken it out in the first place. Finally they

8. Blacks. Ham, whose name means "swarthy" in Hebrew, was a son of Noah and was believed to be the ancestor of both the Egyptians and the Nubians.

got the man who ran the ferry twice a day to agree to take it over in the morning.

That was why Chicken Little was missing for three days and didn't get to the embalmer's until the fourth day, by which time he was unrecognizable to almost everybody who once knew him, and even his mother wasn't deep down sure, except that it just had to be him since nobody could find him. When she saw his clothes lying on the table in the basement of the mortuary, her mouth snapped shut, and when she saw his body her mouth flew wide open again and it was seven hours before she was able to close it and make the first sound.

So the coffin was closed.

The Junior Choir, dressed in white, sang "Nearer My God to Thee" and "Precious Memories," their eyes fastened on the songbooks they did not need, for this was the first time their voices had presided at a real-life event.

Nel and Sula did not touch hands or look at each other during the funeral. There was a space, a separateness, between them. Nel's legs had turned to granite and she expected the sheriff or Reverend Deal's pointing finger at any moment. Although she knew she had "done nothing," she felt convicted and hanged right there in the pew—two rows down from her parents in the children's section.

Sula simply cried. Soundlessly and with no heaving and gasping for breath, she let the tears roll into her mouth and slide down her chin to dot the front of her dress.

As Reverend Deal moved into his sermon, the hands of the women unfolded like pairs of raven's wings and flew high above their hats in the air. They did not hear all of what he said; they heard the one word, or phrase, or inflection that was for them the connection between the event and themselves. For some it was the term "Sweet Jesus." And they saw the Lamb's eye and the truly innocent victim: themselves. They acknowledged the innocent child hiding in the corner of their hearts, holding a sugar-and-butter sandwich. That one. The one who lodged deep in their fat, thin, old, young skin, and was the one the world had hurt. Or they thought of their son newly killed and remembered his legs in short pants and wondered where the bullet went in. Or they remembered how dirty the room looked when their father left home and wondered if that is the way the slim, young Jew[9] felt, he who for them was both son and lover and in whose downy face they could see the sugar-and-butter sandwiches and feel the oldest and most devastating pain there is: not the pain of childhood, but the remembrance of it.

Then they left their pews. For with some emotions one has to stand. They spoke, for they were full and needed to say. They swayed, for the rivulets of grief or of ecstasy must be rocked. And when they thought of all that life and death locked into that little closed coffin they danced and screamed, not to protect God's will but to acknowledge it and confirm once more their conviction that the only way to avoid the Hand of God is to get in it.

In the colored part of the cemetery, they sank Chicken Little in between

9. I.e., Jesus.

his grandfather and an aunt. Butterflies flew in and out of the bunches of field flowers now loosened from the top of the bier and lying in a small heap at the edge of the grave. The heat had gone, but there was still no breeze to lift the hair of the willows.

Nel and Sula stood some distance away from the grave, the space that had sat between them in the pews had dissolved. They held hands and knew that only the coffin would lie in the earth; the bubbly laughter and the press of fingers in the palm would stay aboveground forever. At first, as they stood there, their hands were clenched together. They relaxed slowly until during the walk back home their fingers were laced in as gentle a clasp as that of any two young girlfriends trotting up the road on a summer day wondering what happened to butterflies in the winter.

1923

The second strange thing was Hannah's coming into her mother's room with an empty bowl and a peck of Kentucky Wonders[1] and saying, "Mamma, did you ever love us?" She sang the words like a small child saying a piece at Easter, then knelt to spread a newspaper on the floor and set the basket on it; the bowl she tucked in the space between her legs. Eva, who was just sitting there fanning herself with the cardboard fan from Mr. Hodges' funeral parlor, listened to the silence that followed Hannah's words, then said, "Scat!" to the deweys who were playing chain gang near the window. With the shoelaces of each of them tied to the laces of the others, they stumbled and tumbled out of Eva's room.

"Now," Eva looked up across from her wagon at her daughter. "Give me that again. Flat out to fit my head."

"I mean, did you? You know. When we was little."

Eva's hand moved snail-like down her thigh toward her stump, but stopped short of it to realign a pleat. "No. I don't reckon I did. Not the way you thinkin'."

"Oh, well. I was just wonderin'." Hannah appeared to be through with the subject.

"An evil wonderin' if I ever heard one." Eva was not through.

"I didn't mean nothing by it, Mamma."

"What you mean you didn't *mean* nothing by it? How you gone not mean something by it?"

Hannah pinched the tips off the Kentucky Wonders and snapped their long pods. What with the sound of the cracking and snapping and her swift-fingered movements, she seemed to be playing a complicated instrument. Eva watched her a moment and then said, "You gone can them?"

"No. They for tonight."

"Thought you was gone can some."

"Uncle Paul ain't brought me none yet. A peck ain't enough to can. He say he got two bushels for me."

"Triflin'."

"Oh, he all right."

1. A kind of string bean.

"Sho he all right. Everybody all right. 'Cept Mamma. Mamma the only one ain't all right. Cause she didn't *love* us."

"Awww, Mamma."

"Awww, Mamma? Awww, Mamma? You settin' here with your healthy-ass self and ax me did I love you? Them big old eyes in your head would a been two holes full of maggots if I hadn't."

"I didn't mean that, Mamma. I know you fed us and all. I was talkin' 'bout something else. Like. Like. Playin' with us. Did you ever, you know, play with us?"

"Play? Wasn't nobody playin' in 1895. Just 'cause you got it good now you think it was always this good? 1895 was a killer, girl. Things was bad. Niggers was dying like flies. Stepping tall, ain't you? Uncle Paul gone bring me *two* bushels. Yeh. And they's a melon downstairs, ain't they? And I bake every Saturday, and Shad brings fish on Friday, and they's a pork barrel full of meal, and we float eggs in a crock of vinegar . . ."

"Mamma, what you talkin' 'bout?"

"I'm talkin' 'bout 18 and 95 when I set in that house five days with you and Pearl and Plum and three beets, you snake-eyed ungrateful hussy. What would I look like leapin' 'round that little old room playin' with youngins with three beets to my name?"

"I know 'bout them beets, Mamma. You told us that a million times."

"Yeah? Well? Don't that count? Ain't that love? You want me to tinkle you under the jaw and forget 'bout them sores in your mouth? Pearl was shittin' worms and I was supposed to play rang-around-the-rosie?"

"But Mamma, they had to be some time when you wasn't thinkin' 'bout . . ."

"No time. They wasn't no time. Not none. Soon as I got one day done here come a night. With you all coughin' and me watchin' so TB wouldn't take you off and if you was sleepin' quiet I thought, O Lord, they dead and put my hand over your mouth to feel if the breath was comin' what you talkin' 'bout did I love you girl I stayed alive for you can't you get that through your thick head or what is that between your ears, heifer?"

Hannah had enough beans now. With some tomatoes and hot bread, she thought, that would be enough for everybody, especially since the deweys didn't eat vegetables no how and Eva never made them and Tar Baby was living off air and music these days. She picked up the basket and stood with it and the bowl of beans over her mother. Eva's face was still asking her last question. Hannah looked into her mother's eyes.

"But what about Plum? What'd you kill Plum for, Mamma?"

It was a Wednesday in August and the ice wagon was coming and coming. You could hear bits of the driver's song. Now Mrs. Jackson would be tipping down her porch steps. "Jes a piece. You got a lil ole piece layin' 'round in there you could spare?" And as he had since the time of the pigeons, the iceman would hand her a lump of ice saying, "Watch it now, Mrs. Jackson. That straw'll tickle your pretty neck to death."

Eva listened to the wagon coming and thought about what it must be like in the icehouse. She leaned back a little and closed her eyes trying to see the insides of the icehouse. It was a dark, lovely picture in this heat, until it reminded her of that winter night in the outhouse holding her baby in the dark, her fingers searching for his asshole and the last bit of lard scooped from the sides of the can, held deliberately on the tip of her middle finger, the last bit of lard to keep from hurting him when she slid her finger in and all because she had broken the slop jar and the rags had frozen. The last food staple in the house she had rammed up her baby's behind to keep from hurting him too much when she opened up his bowels to pull the stools out. He had been screaming fit to kill, but when she found his hole at last and stuck her finger up in it, the shock was so great he was suddenly quiet. Even now on the hottest day anyone in Medallion could remember—a day so hot flies slept and cats were splaying their fur like quills, a day so hot pregnant wives leaned up against trees and cried, and women remembering some three-month-old hurt put ground glass in their lovers' food and the men looked at the food and wondered if there was glass in it and ate it anyway because it was too hot to resist eating it—even on this hottest of days in the hot spell, Eva shivered from the biting cold and stench of that outhouse.

Hannah was waiting. Watching her mother's eyelids. When Eva spoke at last it was with two voices. Like two people were talking at the same time, saying the same thing, one a fraction of a second behind the other.

"He give me such a time. Such a time. Look like he didn't even want to be born. But he come on out. Boys is hard to bear. You wouldn't know that but they is. It was such a carryin' on to get him born and to keep him alive. Just to keep his little heart beating and his little old lungs cleared and look like when he came back from that war he wanted to git back in. After all that carryin' on, just gettin' him out and keepin' him alive, he wanted to crawl back in my womb and well . . . I ain't got the room no more even if he could do it. There wasn't space for him in my womb. And he was crawlin' back. Being helpless and thinking baby thoughts and dreaming baby dreams and messing up his pants again and smiling all the time. I had room enough in my heart, but not in my womb, not no more. I birthed him once. I couldn't do it again. He was growed, a big old thing. Godhave-mercy, I couldn't birth him twice. I'd be laying here at night and he be downstairs in that room, but when I closed my eyes I'd see him . . . six feet tall smilin' and crawlin' up the stairs quietlike so I wouldn't hear and opening the door soft so I wouldn't hear and he'd be creepin' to the bed trying to spread my legs trying to get back up in my womb. He was a man, girl, a big old growed-up man. I didn't have that much room. I kept on dreaming it. Dreaming it and I knowed it was true. One night it wouldn't be no dream. It'd be true and I would have done it, would have let him if I'd've had the room but a big man can't be a baby all wrapped up inside his mamma no more; he suffocate. I done everything I could to make him leave me and go on and live and be a man but he wouldn't and I had to keep him out so I just thought of a way he could die like a man not all scrunched up inside my womb, but like a man."

Eva couldn't see Hannah clearly for the tears, but she looked up at her anyway and said, by way of apology or explanation or perhaps just by way of neatness, "But I held him close first. Real close. Sweet Plum. My baby boy."

Long after Hannah turned and walked out of the room, Eva continued to call his name while her fingers lined up the pleats in her dress.

Hannah went off to the kitchen, her old man's slippers plopping down the stairs and over the hardwood floors. She turned the spigot on, letting water break up the tight knots of Kentucky Wonders and float them to the top of the bowl. She swirled them about with her fingers, poured the water off and repeated the process. Each time the green tubes rose to the surface she felt elated and collected whole handfuls at a time to drop in twos and threes back into the water.

Through the window over the sink she could see the deweys still playing chain gang; their ankles bound one to the other, they tumbled, struggled back to their feet and tried to walk single file. Hens strutted by with one suspicious eye on the deweys, another on the brick fireplace where sheets and mason jars[2] were boiled. Only the deweys could play in this heat. Hannah put the Kentucky Wonders over the fire and, struck by a sudden sleepiness, she went off to lie down in the front room. It was even hotter there, for the windows were shut to keep out the sunlight. Hannah straightened the shawl that draped the couch and lay down. She dreamed of a wedding in a red bridal gown until Sula came in and woke her.

But before the second strange thing, there had been the wind, which was the first. The very night before the day Hannah had asked Eva if she had ever loved them, the wind tore over the hills rattling roofs and loosening doors. Everything shook, and although the people were frightened they thought it meant rain and welcomed it. Windows fell out and trees lost arms. People waited up half the night for the first crack of lightning. Some had even uncovered barrels to catch the rain water, which they loved to drink and cook in. They waited in vain, for no lightning no thunder no rain came. The wind just swept through, took what dampness there was out of the air, messed up the yards, and went on. The hills of the Bottom, as always, protected the valley part of town where the white people lived, and the next morning all the people were grateful because there was a dryer heat. So they set about their work early, for it was canning time, and who knew but what the wind would come back this time with a cooling rain. The men who worked in the valley got up at four thirty in the morning and looked at the sky where the sun was already rising like a hot white bitch. They beat the brims of their hats against their legs before putting them on and trudged down the road like old promises nobody wanted kept.

On Thursday, when Hannah brought Eva her fried tomatoes and soft scrambled eggs with the white left out for good luck, she mentioned her dream of the wedding in the red dress. Neither one bothered to look it up for they both knew the number was 522.[3] Eva said she'd play it when Mr. Buckland Reed came by. Later she would remember it as the third strange thing. She had thought it odd even then, but the red in the dream confused her. But she wasn't certain that it was third or not because Sula was acting up, fretting the deweys and meddling the newly married couple. Because she was thirteen, everybody supposed her nature was coming down, but it was hard to put up with her sulking and irritation. The birthmark over her eye was getting darker and looked more and more like a stem and rose. She was dropping things and eating food that belonged to the newly married

2. Used for home canning.
3. I.e., in a dream book, which gives numbers to   specific dreams (the corresponding number can then be played).

couple and started in to worrying everybody that the deweys needed a bath and she was going to give it to them. The deweys, who went wild at the thought of water, were crying and thundering all over the house like colts.

"We ain't got to, do we? Do we got to do what she says? It ain't Saturday." They even woke up Tar Baby, who came out of his room to look at them and then left the house in search of music.

Hannah ignored them and kept on bringing mason jars out of the cellar and washing them. Eva banged on the floor with her stick but nobody came. By noon it was quiet. The deweys had escaped, Sula was either in her room or gone off somewhere. The newly married couple energized by their morning lovemaking, had gone to look for a day's work happily certain that they would find none.

The air all over the Bottom got heavy with peeled fruit and boiling vegetables. Fresh corn, tomatoes, string beans, melon rinds. The women, the children and the old men who had no jobs were putting up for a winter they understood so well. Peaches were stuffed into jars and black cherries (later, when it got cooler, they would put up jellies and preserves). The greedy canned as many as forty-two a day even though some of them, like Mrs. Jackson, who ate ice, had jars from 1920.

Before she trundled her wagon over to the dresser to get her comb, Eva looked out the window and saw Hannah bending to light the yard fire. And that was the fifth (or fourth, if you didn't count Sula's craziness) strange thing. She couldn't find her comb. Nobody moved stuff in Eva's room except to clean and then they put everything right back. But Eva couldn't find it anywhere. One hand pulling her braids loose, the other searching the dresser drawers, she had just begun to get irritated when she felt it in her blouse drawer. Then she trundled back to the window to catch a breeze, if one took a mind to come by, while she combed her hair. She rolled up to the window and it was then she saw Hannah burning. The flames from the yard fire were licking the blue cotton dress, making her dance. Eva knew there was time for nothing in this world other than the time it took to get there and cover her daughter's body with her own. She lifted her heavy frame up on her good leg, and with fists and arms smashed the windowpane. Using her stump as a support on the window sill, her good leg as a lever, she threw herself out of the window. Cut and bleeding she clawed the air trying to aim her body toward the flaming, dancing figure. She missed and came crashing down some twelve feet from Hannah's smoke. Stunned but still conscious, Eva dragged herself toward her firstborn, but Hannah, her senses lost, went flying out of the yard gesturing and bobbing like a sprung jack-in-the-box.

Mr. and Mrs. Suggs, who had set up their canning apparatus in their front yard, saw her running, dancing toward them. They whispered, "Jesus, Jesus," and together hoisted up their tub of water in which tight red tomatoes floated and threw it on the smoke-and-flame-bound woman. The water did put out the flames, but it also made steam, which seared to sealing all that was left of the beautiful Hannah Peace. She lay there on the wooden sidewalk planks, twitching lightly among the smashed tomatoes, her face a mask of agony so intense that for years the people who gathered 'round would shake their heads at the recollection of it.

Somebody covered her legs with a shirt. A woman unwrapped her head rag and placed it on Hannah's shoulder. Somebody else ran to Dick's Fresh Food and Sundries to call the ambulance. The rest stood there as helpless as sunflowers leaning on a fence. The deweys came and stepped in the tomatoes, their eyes raked with wonder. Two cats sidled through the legs of the crowd, sniffing the burned flesh. The vomiting of a young girl finally broke the profound silence and caused the women to talk to each other and to God. In the midst of calling Jesus they heard the hollow clang of the ambulance bell struggling up the hill, but not the "Help me, ya'll" that the dying woman whispered. Then somebody remembered to go and see about Eva. They found her on her stomach by the forsythia bushes calling Hannah's name and dragging her body through the sweet peas and clover that grew under the forsythia by the side of the house. Mother and daughter were placed on stretchers and carried to the ambulance. Eva was wide awake. The blood from her face cuts filled her eyes so she could not see, could only smell the familiar odor of cooked flesh.

Hannah died on the way to the hospital. Or so they said. In any case, she had already begun to bubble and blister so badly that the coffin had to be kept closed at the funeral and the women who washed the body and dressed it for death wept for her burned hair and wrinkled breasts as though they themselves had been her lovers.

When Eva got to the hospital they put her stretcher on the floor, so preoccupied with the hot and bubbling flesh of the other (some of them had never seen so extreme a burn case before) they forgot Eva, who would have bled to death except Old Willy Fields, the orderly, saw blood staining his just-mopped floors and went to find out where it was coming from. Recognizing Eva at once he shouted to a nurse, who came to see if the bloody one-legged black woman was alive or dead. From then on Willy boasted that he had saved Eva's life—an indisputable fact which she herself admitted and for which she cursed him every day for thirty-seven years thereafter and would have cursed him for the rest of her life except by then she was already ninety years old and forgot things.

Lying in the colored ward of the hospital, which was a screened corner of a larger ward, Eva mused over the perfection of the judgment against her. She remembered the wedding dream and recalled that weddings always meant death. And the red gown, well that was the fire, as she should have known. She remembered something else too, and try as she might to deny it, she knew that as she lay on the ground trying to drag herself through the sweet peas and clover to get to Hannah, she had seen Sula standing on the back porch just looking. When Eva, who was never one to hide the faults of her children, mentioned what she thought she'd seen to a few friends, they said it was natural. Sula was probably struck dumb, as anybody would be who saw her own mamma burn up. Eva said yes, but inside she disagreed and remained convinced that Sula had watched Hannah burn not because she was paralyzed, but because she was interested.

1927

Old people were dancing with little children. Young boys with their sisters, and the church women who frowned on any bodily expression of joy

(except when the hand of God commanded it) tapped their feet. Somebody (the groom's father, everybody said) had poured a whole pint jar of
cane liquor into the punch, so even the men who did not sneak out the
back door to have a shot, as well as the women who let nothing stronger
than Black Draught enter their blood, were tipsy. A small boy stood at the
Victrola turning its handle and smiling at the sound of Bert Williams'
"Save a Little Dram for Me."

Even Helene Wright had mellowed with the cane, waving away apologies for drinks spilled on her rug and paying no attention whatever to the
chocolate cake lying on the arm of her red-velvet sofa. The tea roses above
her left breast had slipped from the brooch that fastened them and were
hanging heads down. When her husband called her attention to the children wrapping themselves into her curtains, she merely smiled and said,
"Oh, let them be." She was not only a little drunk, she was weary and had
been for weeks. Her only child's wedding—the culmination of all she
had been, thought or done in this world—had dragged from her energy and
stamina even she did not know she possessed. Her house had to be thoroughly cleaned, chickens had to be plucked, cakes and pies made, and for
weeks she, her friends and her daughter had been sewing. Now it was all
happening and it took only a little cane juice to snap the cords of fatigue
and damn the white curtains that she had pinned on the stretcher only the
morning before. Once this day was over she would have a lifetime to rattle
around in that house and repair the damage.

A real wedding, in a church, with a real reception afterward, was rare
among the people of the Bottom. Expensive for one thing, and most newly-
weds just went to the courthouse if they were not particular, or had the
preacher come in and say a few words if they were. The rest just "took up"
with one another. No invitations were sent. There was no need for that
formality. Folks just came, bringing a gift if they had one, none if they
didn't. Except for those who worked in valley houses, most of them had
never been to a big wedding; they simply assumed it was rather like a funeral except afterward you didn't have to walk all the way out to Beechnut
Cemetery.

This wedding offered a special attraction, for the bridegroom was a
handsome, well-liked man—the tenor of Mount Zion's Men's Quartet,
who had an enviable reputation among the girls and a comfortable one
among men. His name was Jude Greene, and with the pick of some eight
or ten girls who came regularly to services to hear him sing, he had chosen
Nel Wright.

He wasn't really aiming to get married. He was twenty then, and although his job as a waiter at the Hotel Medallion was a blessing to his parents and their seven other children, it wasn't nearly enough to support a
wife. He had brought the subject up first on the day the word got out that
the town was building a new road, tarmac, that would wind through Medallion on down to the river, where a great new bridge was to be built to
connect Medallion to Porter's Landing, the town on the other side. The
war over, a fake prosperity was still around. In a state of euphoria, with a
hunger for more and more, the council of founders cast its eye toward a
future that would certainly include trade from cross-river towns. Towns
that needed more than a house raft to get to the merchants of Medallion.

Work had already begun on the New River Road (the city had always meant to name it something else, something wonderful, but ten years later when the bridge idea was dropped for a tunnel it was still called the New River Road).

Along with a few other young black men, Jude had gone down to the shack where they were hiring. Three old colored men had already been hired, but not for the road work, just to do the picking up, food bringing and other small errands. These old men were close to feeble, not good for much else, and everybody was pleased they were taken on; still it was a shame to see those white men laughing with the grandfathers but shying away from the young black men who could tear that road up. The men like Jude who could do real work. Jude himself longed more than anybody else to be taken. Not just for the good money, more for the work itself. He wanted to swing the pick or kneel down with the string or shovel the gravel. His arms ached for something heavier than trays, for something dirtier than peelings; his feet wanted the heavy work shoes, not the thin-soled black shoes that the hotel required. More than anything he wanted the camaraderie of the road men: the lunch buckets, the hollering, the body movement that in the end produced something real, something he could point to. "I built that road," he could say. How much better sundown would be than the end of a day in the restaurant, where a good day's work was marked by the number of dirty plates and the weight of the garbage bin. "I built that road." People would walk over his sweat for years. Perhaps a sledge hammer would come crashing down on his foot, and when people asked him how come he limped, he could say, "Got that building the New Road."

It was while he was full of such dreams, his body already feeling the rough work clothes, his hands already curved to the pick handle, that he spoke to Nel about getting married. She seemed receptive but hardly anxious. It was after he stood in lines for six days running and saw the gang boss pick out thin-armed white boys from the Virginia hills and the bull-necked Greeks and Italians and heard over and over, "Nothing else today. Come back tomorrow," that he got the message. So it was rage, rage and a determination to take on a man's role anyhow that made him press Nel about settling down. He needed some of his appetites filled, some posture of adulthood recognized, but mostly he wanted someone to care about his hurt, to care very deeply. Deep enough to hold him, deep enough to rock him, deep enough to ask, "How you feel? You all right? Want some coffee?" And if he were to be a man, that someone could no longer be his mother. He chose the girl who had always been kind, who had never seemed hell-bent to marry, who made the whole venture seem like his idea, his conquest.

The more he thought about marriage, the more attractive it became. Whatever his fortune, whatever the cut of his garment, there would always be the hem—the tuck and fold that hid his raveling edges; a someone sweet, industrious and loyal to shore him up. And in return he would shelter her, love her, grow old with her. Without that someone he was a waiter hanging around a kitchen like a woman. With her he was head of a household pinned to an unsatisfactory job out of necessity. The two of them together would make one Jude.

His fears lest his burst dream of road building discourage her were never

realized. Nel's indifference to his hints about marriage disappeared altogether when she discovered his pain. Jude could see himself taking shape
in her eyes. She actually wanted to help, to soothe, and was it true what
Ajax said in the Time and a Half Pool Hall? That "all they want, man, is
they own misery. Ax em to die for you and they yours for life."

Whether he was accurate in general, Ajax was right about Nel. Except
for an occasional leadership role with Sula, she had no aggression. Her
parents had succeeded in rubbing down to a dull glow any sparkle or splut-
ter she had. Only with Sula did that quality have free reign, but their
friendship was so close, they themselves had difficulty distinguishing one's
thoughts from the other's. During all of her girlhood the only respite Nel
had had from her stern and undemonstrative parents was Sula. When Jude
began to hover around, she was flattered—all the girls liked him—and Sula
made the enjoyment of his attentions keener simply because she seemed
always to want Nel to shine. They never quarreled, those two, the way some
girlfriends did over boys, or competed against each other for them. In those
days a compliment to one was a compliment to the other, and cruelty to
one was a challenge to the other.

Nel's response to Jude's shame and anger selected her away from Sula.
And greater than her friendship was this new feeling of being needed by
someone who saw her singly. She didn't even know she had a neck until
Jude remarked on it, or that her smile was anything but the spreading of her
lips until he saw it as a small miracle.

Sula was no less excited about the wedding. She thought it was the perfect thing to do following their graduation from general school. She
wanted to be the bridesmaid. No others. And she encouraged Mrs. Wright
to go all out, even to borrowing Eva's punch bowl. In fact, she handled
most of the details very efficiently, capitalizing on the fact that most people
were anxious to please her since she had lost her mamma only a few years
back and they still remembered the agony in Hannah's face and the blood
on Eva's.

So they danced up in the Bottom on the second Saturday in June,
danced at the wedding where everybody realized for the first time that except for their magnificent teeth, the deweys would never grow. They had
been forty-eight inches tall for years now, and while their size was unusual
it was not unheard of. The realization was based on the fact that they remained boys in mind. Mischievous, cunning, private and completely un-
housebroken, their games and interests had not changed since Hannah
had them all put into the first grade together.

Nel and Jude, who had been the stars all during the wedding, were forgotten finally as the reception melted into a dance, a feed, a gossip session,
a playground and a love nest. For the first time that day they relaxed and
looked at each other, and liked what they saw. They began to dance,
pressed in among the others, and each one turned his thoughts to the night
that was coming on fast. They had taken a housekeeping room with one of
Jude's aunts (over the protest of Mrs. Wright, who had rooms to spare, but
Nel didn't want to make love to her husband in her mother's house) and
were getting restless to go there.

As if reading her thoughts, Jude leaned down and whispered, "Me too."

Nel smiled and rested her cheek on his shoulder. The veil she wore was too heavy to allow her to feel the core of the kiss he pressed on her head. When she raised her eyes to him for one more look of reassurance, she saw through the open door a slim figure in blue, gliding, with just a hint of a strut, down the path toward the road. One hand was pressed to the head to hold down the large hat against the warm June breeze. Even from the rear Nel could tell that it was Sula and that she was smiling; that something deep down in that litheness was amused. It would be ten years before they saw each other again, and their meeting would be thick with birds.

Part Two

1937

Accompanied by a plague of robins, Sula came back to Medallion. The little yam-breasted shuddering birds were everywhere, exciting very small children away from their usual welcome into a vicious stoning. Nobody knew why or from where they had come. What they did know was that you couldn't go anywhere without stepping in their pearly shit, and it was hard to hang up clothes, pull weeds or just sit on the front porch when robins were flying and dying all around you.

Although most of the people remembered the time when the sky was black for two hours with clouds and clouds of pigeons, and although they were accustomed to excesses in nature—too much heat, too much cold, too little rain, rain to flooding—they still dreaded the way a relatively trivial phenomenon could become sovereign in their lives and bend their minds to its will.

In spite of their fear, they reacted to an oppressive oddity, or what they called evil days, with an acceptance that bordered on welcome. Such evil must be avoided, they felt, and precautions must naturally be taken to protect themselves from it. But they let it run its course, fulfill itself, and never invented ways either to alter it, to annihilate it or to prevent its happening again. So also were they with people.

What was taken by outsiders to be slackness, slovenliness or even generosity was in fact a full recognition of the legitimacy of forces other than good ones. They did not believe doctors could heal—for them, none ever had done so. They did not believe death was accidental—life might be, but death was deliberate. They did not believe Nature was ever askew—only inconvenient. Plague and drought were as "natural" as springtime. If milk could curdle, God knows robins could fall. The purpose of evil was to survive it and they determined (without ever knowing they had made up their minds to do it) to survive floods, white people, tuberculosis, famine and ignorance. They knew anger well but not despair, and they didn't stone sinners for the same reason they didn't commit suicide—it was beneath them.

Sula stepped off the Cincinnati Flyer[4] into the robin shit and began the long climb up into the Bottom. She was dressed in a manner that was as

4. A train.

close to a movie star as anyone would ever see. A black crepe dress splashed
with pink and yellow zinnias, foxtails, a black felt hat with the veil of net
lowered over one eye. In her right hand was a black purse with a beaded
clasp and in her left a red leather traveling case, so small, so charming—no
one had seen anything like it ever before, including the mayor's wife and
the music teacher, both of whom had been to Rome.

Walking up the hill toward Carpenter's Road, the heels and sides of her
pumps edged with drying bird shit, she attracted the glances of old men
sitting on stone benches in front of the courthouse, housewives throwing
buckets of water on their sidewalks, and high school students on their way
home for lunch. By the time she reached the Bottom, the news of her return had brought the black people out on their porches or to their windows. There were scattered hellos and nods but mostly stares. A little boy
ran up to her saying, "Carry yo' bag, ma'am?" Before Sula could answer his
mother had called him, "You, John. Get back in here."

At Eva's house there were four dead robins on the walk. Sula stopped
and with her toe pushed them into the bordering grass.

Eva looked at Sula pretty much the same way she had looked at BoyBoy
that time when he returned after he'd left her without a dime or a prospect
of one. She was sitting in her wagon, her back to the window she had
jumped out of (now all boarded up) setting fire to the hair she had combed
out of her head. When Sula opened the door she raised her eyes and said,
"I might have knowed them birds meant something. Where's your coat?"

Sula threw herself on Eva's bed. "The rest of my stuff will be on later."

"I should hope so. Them little old furry tails ain't going to do you no
more good than they did the fox that was wearing them."

"Don't you say hello to nobody when you ain't seen them for ten years?"

"If folks let somebody know where they is and when they coming, then
other folks can get ready for them. If they don't—if they just pop in all sudden like—then they got to take whatever mood they find."

"How you been doing, Big Mamma?"

"Gettin' by. Sweet of you to ask. You was quick enough when you
wanted something. When you needed a little change or . . ."

"Don't talk to me about how much you gave me, Big Mamma, and how
much I owe you or none of that."

"Oh? I ain't supposed to mention it?"

"OK. Mention it." Sula shrugged and turned over on her stomach, her
buttocks toward Eva.

"You ain't been in this house ten seconds and already you starting something."

"Takes two, Big Mamma."

"Well, don't let your mouth start nothing that your ass can't stand. When
you gone to get married? You need to have some babies. It'll settle you."

"I don't want to make somebody else. I want to make myself."

"Selfish. Ain't no woman got no business floatin' around without no
man."

"You did."

"Not by choice."

"Mamma did."

"Not by choice, I said. It ain't right for you to want to stay off by yourself. You need . . . I'm a tell you what you need."

Sula sat up. "I need you to shut your mouth."

"Don't nobody talk to me like that. Don't nobody . . ."

"This body does. Just 'cause you was bad enough to cut off your own leg you think you got a right to kick everybody with the stump."

"Who said I cut off my leg?"

"Well, you stuck it under a train to collect insurance."

"Hold on, you lyin' heifer!"

"I aim to."

"Bible say honor thy father and thy mother that thy days may be long upon the land thy God giveth thee."

"Mamma must have skipped that part. Her days wasn't too long."

"Pus mouth! God's going to strike you!"

"Which God? The one watched you burn Plum?"

"Don't talk to me about no burning. You watched your own mamma. You crazy roach! You the one should have been burnt!"

"But I ain't. Got that? I ain't. Any more fires in this house, I'm lighting them!"

"Hellfire don't need lighting and it's already burning in you . . ."

"Whatever's burning in me is mine!"

"Amen!"

"And I'll split this town in two and everything in it before I'll let you put it out!"

"Pride goeth before a fall."

"What the hell do I care about falling?"

"Amazing Grace."

"You sold your life for twenty-three dollars a month."

"You throwed yours away."

"It's mine to throw."

"One day you gone need it."

"But not you. I ain't never going to need you. And you know what? Maybe one night when you dozing in that wagon flicking flies and swallowing spit, maybe I'll just tip on up here with some kerosene and—who knows—you may make the brightest flame of them all."

So Eva locked her door from then on. But it did no good. In April two men came with a stretcher and she didn't even have time to comb her hair before they strapped her to a piece of canvas.

When Mr. Buckland Reed came by to pick up the number, his mouth sagged at the sight of Eva being carried out and Sula holding some papers against the wall, at the bottom of which, just above the word "guardian," she very carefully wrote Miss Sula Mae Peace.

Nel alone noticed the peculiar quality of the May that followed the leaving of the birds. It had a sheen, a glimmering as of green, rain-soaked Saturday nights (lit by the excitement of newly installed street lights); of lemon-yellow afternoons bright with iced drinks and splashes of daffodils. It showed in the damp faces of her children and the river-smoothness of their voices. Even her own body was not immune to the magic. She would sit on the floor to sew as she had done as a girl, fold her legs up under her or do a little dance that fitted some tune in her head. There were easy sun-washed days and purple dusks in which Tar Baby sang "Abide With Me" at prayer meetings, his lashes darkened by tears, his silhouette limp with regret against the whitewashed walls of Greater Saint Matthew's. Nel listened and was moved to smile. To smile at the sheer loveliness that pressed in from the windows and touched his grief, making it a pleasure to behold.

Although it was she alone who saw this magic, she did not wonder at it. She knew it was all due to Sula's return to the Bottom. It was like getting the use of an eye back, having a cataract removed. Her old friend had come home. Sula. Who made her laugh, who made her see old things with new eyes, in whose presence she felt clever, gentle and a little raunchy. Sula, whose past she had lived through and with whom the present was a constant sharing of perceptions. Talking to Sula had always been a conversation with herself. Was there anyone else before whom she could never be foolish? In whose view inadequacy was mere idiosyncrasy, a character trait rather than a deficiency? Anyone who left behind that aura of fun and complicity? Sula never competed; she simply helped others define themselves. Other people seemed to turn their volume on and up when Sula was in the room. More than any other thing, humor returned. She could listen to the crunch of sugar underfoot that the children had spilled without reaching for the switch; and she forgot the tear in the living-room window shade. Even Nel's love for Jude, which over the years had spun a steady gray web around her heart, became a bright and easy affection, a playfulness that was reflected in their lovemaking.

Sula would come by of an afternoon, walking along with her fluid stride, wearing a plain yellow dress the same way her mother, Hannah, had worn those too-big house dresses—with a distance, an absence of a relationship to clothes which emphasized everything the fabric covered. When she scratched the screen door, as in the old days, and stepped inside, the dishes piled in the sink looked as though they belonged there; the dust on the lamps sparkled; the hair brush lying on the "good" sofa in the living room did not have to be apologetically retrieved, and Nel's grimly intractable children looked like three wild things happily insouciant in the May shine.

"Hey, girl." The rose mark over Sula's eye gave her glance a suggestion of startled pleasure. It was darker than Nel remembered.

"Hey yourself. Come on in here."

"How you doin'?" Sula moved a pile of ironed diapers from a chair and sat down.

"Oh, I ain't strangled nobody yet so I guess I'm all right."

"Well, if you change your mind call me."

"Somebody need killin'?"

"Half this town need it."

"And the other half?"

"A drawn-out disease."

"Oh, come on. Is Medallion that bad?"

"Didn't nobody tell you?"

"You been gone too long, Sula."

"Not too long, but maybe too far."

"What's that supposed to mean?" Nel dipped her fingers into the bowl of water and sprinkled a diaper.

"Oh, I don't know."

"Want some cool tea?"

"Mmmm. Lots of ice, I'm burnin' up."

"Iceman don't come yet, but it's good and cold."

"That's fine."

"Hope I didn't speak too soon. Kids run in and out of here so much." Nel bent to open the icebox.

"You puttin' it on, Nel. Jude must be wore out."

"*Jude* must be wore out? You don't care nothin' 'bout my back, do you?"

"Is that where it's at, in your back?"

"Hah! Jude thinks it's everywhere."

"He's right, it is everywhere. Just be glad he found it, wherever it is. Remember John L.?"

"When Shirley said he got her down by the well and tried to stick it in her hip?" Nel giggled at the remembrance of that teen-time tale. "She should have been grateful. Have you seen her since you been back?"

"Mmm. Like a ox."

"That was one dumb nigger, John L."

"Maybe. Maybe he was just sanitary."

"Sanitary?"

"Well. Think about it. Suppose Shirley was all splayed out in front of you? Wouldn't you go for the hipbone instead?"

Nel lowered her head onto crossed arms while tears of laughter dripped into the warm diapers. Laughter that weakened her knees and pressed her bladder into action. Her rapid soprano and Sula's dark sleepy chuckle made a duet that frightened the cat and made the children run in from the back yard, puzzled at first by the wild free sounds, then delighted to see their mother stumbling merrily toward the bathroom, holding on to her stomach, fairly singing through the laughter: "Aw. Aw. Lord. Sula. Stop." And the other one, the one with the scary black thing over her eye, laughing softly and egging their mother on: "Neatness counts. You know what cleanliness is next to . . ."

"Hush." Nel's plea was clipped off by the slam of the bathroom door.

"What y'all laughing at?"

"Old time-y stuff. Long gone, old time-y stuff."

"Tell us."

"Tell *you?*" The black mark leaped.

"Uh huh. Tell us."

"What tickles us wouldn't tickle you."

"Uh huh, it would."

"Well, we was talking about some people we used to know when we was little."

"Was my mamma little?"

"Of course."

"What happened?"

"Well, some old boy we knew name John L. and a girl name . . ."

Damp-faced, Nel stepped back into the kitchen. She felt new, soft and new. It had been the longest time since she had had a rib-scraping laugh. She had forgotten how deep and down it could be. So different from the miscellaneous giggles and smiles she had learned to be content with these past few years.

"O Lord, Sula. You haven't changed none." She wiped her eyes. "What was all that about, anyway? All that scramblin' we did trying to do it and not do it at the same time?"

"Beats me. Such a simple thing."

"But we sure made a lot out of it, and the boys were dumber than we were."

"Couldn't nobody be dumber than I was."

"Stop lying. All of 'em liked you best."

"Yeah? Where are they?"

"They still here. You the one went off."

"Didn't I, though?"

"Tell me about it. The big city."

"Big is all it is. A big Medallion."

"No. I mean the life. The nightclubs, and parties . . ."

"I was in college, Nellie. No nightclubs on campus."

"Campus? That what they call it? Well. You wasn't in no college for— what—ten years now? And you didn't write to nobody. How come you never wrote?"

"You never did either."

"Where was I going to write to? All I knew was that you was in Nashville. I asked Miss Peace about you once or twice."

"What did *she* say?"

"I couldn't make much sense out of her. You know she been gettin' stranger and stranger after she come out the hospital. How is she anyway?"

"Same, I guess. Not so hot."

"No? Laura, I know, was doing her cooking and things. Is she still?"

"No. I put her out."

"Put her out? What for?"

"She made me nervous."

"But she was doing it for nothing, Sula."

"That's what you think. She was stealing right and left."

"Since when did you get froggy[5] about folks' stealing?"

Sula smiled. "OK. I lied. You wanted a reason."

"Well, give me the real one."

"I don't know the real one. She just didn't belong in that house. Digging around in the cupboards, picking up pots and ice picks . . ."

"You sure have changed. That house was always full of people digging in cupboards and carrying on."

"That's the reason, then."

"Sula. Come on, now."

"You've changed too. I didn't used to have to explain everything to you."

Nel blushed. "Who's feeding the deweys and Tar Baby? You?"

"Sure me. Anyway Tar Baby don't eat and the deweys still crazy."

---

5. Jumpy, nervous.

"I heard one of 'em's mamma came to take him back but didn't know which was hern."

"Don't nobody know."

"And Eva? You doing the work for her too?"

"Well, since you haven't heard it, let me tell you. Eva's real sick. I had her put where she could be watched and taken care of."

"Where would that be?"

"Out by Beechnut."

"You mean that home the white church run? Sula! That ain't no place for Eva. All them women is dirt poor with no people at all. Mrs. Wilkens and them. They got dropsy and can't hold their water—crazy as loons. Eva's odd, but she got sense. I don't think that's right, Sula."

"I'm scared of her, Nellie. That's why . . ."

"Scared? Of Eva?"

"You don't know her. Did you know she burnt Plum?"

"Oh, I heard that years ago. But nobody put no stock in it."

"They should have. It's true. I saw it. And when I got back here she was planning to do it to me too."

"Eva? I can't hardly believe that. She almost died trying to get to your mother."

Sula leaned forward, her elbows on the table. "You ever known me to lie to you?"

"No. But you could be mistaken. Why would Eva . . ."

"All I know is I'm scared. And there's no place else for me to go. We all that's left, Eva and me. I guess I should have stayed gone. I didn't know what else to do. Maybe I should have talked to you about it first. You always had better sense than me. Whenever I was scared before, you knew just what to do."

The closed place in the water spread before them. Nel put the iron on the stove. The situation was clear to her now. Sula, like always, was incapable of making any but the most trivial decisions. When it came to matters of grave importance, she behaved emotionally and irresponsibly and left it to others to straighten out. And when fear struck her, she did unbelievable things. Like that time with her finger. Whatever those hunkies[6] did, it wouldn't have been as bad as what she did to herself. But Sula was so scared she had mutilated herself, to protect herself.

"What should I do, Nellie? Take her back and sleep with my door locked again?"

"No. I guess it's too late anyway. But let's work out a plan for taking care of her. So she won't be messed over."

"Anything you say."

"What about money? She got any?"

Sula shrugged. "The checks come still. It's not much, like it used to be. Should I have them made over to me?"

"Can you? Do it, then. We can arrange for her to have special comforts. That place is a mess, you know. A doctor don't never set foot in there. I ain't figured out yet how they stay alive in there as long as they do."

---

6. Disparaging term for Hungarians, but used often of any whites.

"Why don't I have the checks made over to you, Nellie? You better at this than I am."

"Oh no. People will say I'm scheming. You the one to do it. Was there insurance from Hannah?"

"Yes. Plum too. He had all that army insurance."

"Any of it left?"

"Well I went to college on some. Eva banked the rest. I'll look into it, though."

". . . and explain it all to the bank people."

"Will you go down with me?"

"Sure. It's going to be all right."

"I'm glad I talked to you 'bout this. It's been bothering me."

"Well, tongues will wag, but so long as we know the truth, it don't matter."

Just at that moment the children ran in announcing the entrance of their father. Jude opened the back door and walked into the kitchen. He was still a very good-looking man, and the only difference Sula could see was the thin pencil mustache under his nose, and a part in his hair.

"Hey, Jude. What you know good?"

"White man running it—nothing good."

Sula laughed while Nel, high-tuned to his moods, ignored her husband's smile saying, "Bad day, honey?"

"Same old stuff," he replied and told them a brief tale of some personal insult done him by a customer and his boss—a whiney tale that peaked somewhere between anger and a lapping desire for comfort. He ended it with the observation that a Negro man had a hard row to hoe in this world. He expected his story to dovetail into milkwarm commiseration, but before Nel could excrete it, Sula said she didn't know about that—it looked like a pretty good life to her.

"Say what?" Jude's temper flared just a bit as he looked at this friend of his wife's, this slight woman, not exactly plain, but not fine either, with a copperhead over her eye. As far as he could tell, she looked like a woman roaming the country trying to find some man to burden down with a lot of lip and a lot of mouths.

Sula was smiling. "I mean, I don't know what the fuss is about. I mean, everything in the world loves you. White men love you. They spend so much time worrying about your penis they forget their own. The only thing they want to do is cut off a nigger's privates. And if that ain't love and respect I don't know what is. And white women? They chase you all to every corner of the earth, feel for you under every bed. I knew a white woman wouldn't leave the house after 6 o'clock for fear one of you would snatch her. Now ain't that love? They think rape soon's they see you, and if they don't get the rape they looking for, they scream it anyway just so the search won't be in vain. Colored women worry themselves into bad health just trying to hang on to your cuffs. Even little children—white and black, boys and girls—spend all their childhood eating their hearts out 'cause they think you don't love them. And if that ain't enough, you love yourselves. Nothing in this world loves a black man more than another black man. You hear of solitary white men, but niggers? Can't stay away from one another a whole day. So. It looks to me like you the envy of the world."

Jude and Nel were laughing, he saying, "Well, if that's the only way they got to show it—cut off my balls and throw me in jail—I'd just as soon they left me alone." But thinking that Sula had an odd way of looking at things and that her wide smile took some of the sting from that rattlesnake over her eye. A funny woman, he thought, not that bad-looking. But he could see why she wasn't married; she stirred a man's mind maybe, but not his body.

He left his tie. The one with the scriggly yellow lines running lopsided across the dark-blue field. It hung over the top of the closet door pointing steadily downward while it waited with every confidence for Jude to return.

Could he be gone if his tie is still here? He will remember it and come back and then she would . . . uh. Then she could . . . tell him. Sit down quietly and tell him. "But Jude," she would say, "you *knew* me. All those days and years, Jude, you *knew* me. My ways and my hands and how my stomach folded and how we tried to get Mickey to nurse and how about that time when the landlord said . . . but you said . . . and I cried, Jude. You knew me and had listened to the things I said in the night, and heard me in the bathroom and laughed at my raggedy girdle and I laughed too because I knew you too, Jude. So how could you leave me when you knew me?"

But they had been down on all fours naked, not touching except their lips right down there on the floor where the tie is pointing to, on all fours like (uh huh, go on, say it) like dogs. Nibbling at each other, not even touching, not even looking at each other, just their lips, and when I opened the door they didn't even look for a minute and I thought the reason they are not looking up is because they are not doing that. So it's all right. I am just standing here. They are not doing that. I am just standing here and seeing it, but they are not really doing it. But then they did look up. Or you did. You did, Jude. And if only you had not looked at me the way the soldiers did on the train, the way you look at the children when they come in while you are listening to Gabriel Heatter[7] and break your train of thought—not focusing exactly but giving them an instant, a piece of time, to remember what they are doing, what they are interrupting, and to go on back to wherever they were and let you listen to Gabriel Heatter. And I did not know how to move my feet or fix my eyes or what. I just stood there seeing it and smiling, because maybe there was some explanation, something important that I did not know about that would have made it all right. I waited for Sula to look up at me any minute and say one of those lovely college words like *aesthetic* or *rapport*, which I never understood but which I loved because they sounded so comfortable and firm. And finally you just got up and started putting on your clothes and your privates were hanging down, so soft, and you buckled your pants belt but forgot to button the fly and she was sitting on the bed not even bothering to put on her clothes because actually she didn't need to because somehow she didn't look

___
7. Radio journalist (1890–1972).

naked to me, only you did. Her chin was in her hand and she sat like a visitor from out of town waiting for the hosts to get some quarreling done and over with so the card game could continue and me wanting her to leave so I could tell you privately that you had forgotten to button your fly because I didn't want to say it in front of her, Jude. And even when you began to talk, I couldn't hear because I was worried about you not knowing that your fly was open and scared too because your eyes looked like the soldiers' that time on the train when my mother turned to custard.

Remember how big that bedroom was? Jude? How when we moved here we said, Well, at least we got us a real big bedroom, but it was small then, Jude, and so shambly, and maybe it was that way all along but it would have been better if I had gotten the dust out from under the bed because I was ashamed of it in that small room. And then you walked past me saying, "I'll be back for my things." And you did but you left your tie.

The clock was ticking. Nel looked at it and realized that it was two thirty, only forty-five minutes before the children would be home and she hadn't even felt anything right or sensible and now there was no time or wouldn't be until nighttime when they were asleep and she could get into bed and maybe she could do it then. Think. But who could think in that bed where *they* had been and where they *also* had been and where only she was now?

She looked around for a place to be. A small place. The closet? No. Too dark. The bathroom. It was both small and bright, and she wanted to be in a very small, very bright place. Small enough to contain her grief. Bright enough to throw into relief the dark things that cluttered her. Once inside, she sank to the tile floor next to the toilet. On her knees, her hand on the cold rim of the bathtub, she waited for something to happen . . . inside. There was stirring, a movement of mud and dead leaves. She thought of the women at Chicken Little's funeral. The women who shrieked over the bier and at the lip of the open grave. What she had regarded since as unbecoming behavior seemed fitting to her now; they were screaming at the neck of God, his giant nape, the vast back-of-the-head that he had turned on them in death. But it seemed to her now that it was not a fist-shaking grief they were keening but rather a simple obligation to say something, do something, feel something about the dead. They could not let that heart-smashing event pass unrecorded, unidentified. It was poisonous, unnatural to let the dead go with a mere whimpering, a slight murmur, a rose bouquet of good taste. Good taste was out of place in the company of death, death itself was the essence of bad taste. And there must be much rage and saliva in its presence. The body must move and throw itself about, the eyes must roll, the hands should have no peace, and the throat should release all the yearning, despair and outrage that accompany the stupidity of loss.

"The real hell of Hell is that it is forever." Sula said that. She said doing anything forever and ever was hell. Nel didn't understand it then, but now in the bathroom, trying to feel, she thought, "If I could be sure that I could stay here in this small white room with the dirty tile and water gurgling in the pipes and my head on the cool rim of this bathtub and never have to go out the door, I would be happy. If I could be certain that I never had to get up and flush the toilet, go in the kitchen, watch my children grow up and die, see my food chewed on my plate . . . Sula was wrong. Hell ain't things lasting forever. Hell is change." Not only did men leave and children grow up and die, but even the misery didn't last. One day she wouldn't even have that. This very grief that had twisted her into a curve on the floor and flayed her would be gone. She would lose that too.

"Why, even in hate here I am thinking of what Sula said."

Hunched down in the small bright room Nel waited. Waited for the oldest cry. A scream not for others, not in sympathy for a burnt child, or a dead father, but a deeply personal cry for one's own pain. A loud, strident: "Why me?" She waited. The mud shifted, the leaves stirred, the smell of overripe green things enveloped her and announced the beginnings of her very own howl.

But it did not come.

The odor evaporated; the leaves were still, the mud settled. And finally there was nothing, just a flake of something dry and nasty in her throat. She stood up frightened. There was something just to the right of her, in the air, just out of view. She could not see it, but she knew exactly what it looked like. A gray ball hovering just there. Just there. To the right. Quiet, gray, dirty. A ball of muddy strings, but without weight, fluffy but terrible in its malevolence. She knew she could not look, so she closed her eyes and crept past it out of the bathroom, shutting the door behind her. Sweating with fear, she stepped to the kitchen door and onto the back porch. The lilac bushes preened at the railing, but there were no lilacs yet. Wasn't it time? Surely it was time. She looked over the fence to Mrs. Rayford's yard. Hers were not in bloom either. Was it too late? She fastened on this question with enthusiasm, all the time aware of something she was not thinking. It was the only way she could get her mind off the flake in her throat.

She spent a whole summer with the gray ball, the little ball of fur and string and hair always floating in the light near her but which she did not see because she never looked. But that was the terrible part, the effort it took not to look. But it was there anyhow, just to the right of her head and maybe further down by her shoulder, so when the children went to a monster movie at the Elmira Theater and came home and said, "Mamma, can you sleep with us tonight?" she said all right and got into bed with the two boys, who loved it, but the girl did not. For a long time she could not stop getting in the bed with her children and told herself each time that they might dream a dream about dragons and would need her to comfort them. It was so nice to think about their scary dreams and not about a ball of fur. She even hoped their dreams would rub off on her and give her the wonderful relief of a nightmare so she could stop going around scared to turn her head this way or that lest she see it. That was the scary part—seeing it. It was not coming at her; it never did that, or tried to pounce on her. It just floated there for the seeing, if she wanted to, and O my God for the touching if she wanted to. But she didn't want to see it, ever, for if she saw it, who could tell but what she might actually touch it, or want to, and then what would happen if she actually reached out her hand and touched it? Die probably, but no worse than that. Dying was OK because it was sleep and there wasn't no gray ball in death, was there? Was there? She would have to ask somebody about that, somebody she could confide in and who knew a lot of things, like Sula, for Sula would know or if she didn't she would say something funny that would make it all right. Ooo no, not Sula. Here she was in the midst of it, hating it, scared of it, and again she thought of Sula as though they were still friends and talked things over. That was too much. To lose Jude and not have Sula to talk to about it because it was Sula that he had left her for.

Now her thighs were really empty. And it was then that what those women said about never looking at another man made some sense to her, for the real point, the heart of what they said, was the word *looked*. Not to promise never to make love to another man, not to refuse to marry another man, but to promise and know that she could never afford to look again, to see and accept the way in which their heads cut the air or see moons and tree limbs framed by their necks and shoulders . . . never to look, for now she could not risk looking—and anyway, so what? For now her thighs were truly empty and dead too, and it was Sula who had taken the life from them and Jude who smashed her heart and the both of them who left her with no thighs and no heart just her brain raveling away.

And what am I supposed to do with these old thighs now, just walk up and down these rooms? What good are they, Jesus? They will never give me the peace I need to get from sunup to sundown, what good are they, are you trying to tell me that I am going to have to go all the way through these days all the way, O my god, to that box with four handles with never nobody settling down between my legs even if I sew up those old pillow cases and rinse down the porch and feed my children and beat the rugs and haul the coal up out of the bin even then nobody, O Jesus, I could be a mule or plow the furrows with my hands if need be or hold these rickety walls up with my back if need be if I knew that somewhere in this world in the pocket of some night I could open my legs to some cowboy lean hips but you are trying to tell me no and O my sweet Jesus what kind of cross is that?

1939

When the word got out about Eva being put in Sunnydale, the people in the Bottom shook their heads and said Sula was a roach. Later, when they saw how she took Jude, then ditched him for others, and heard how he bought a bus ticket to Detroit (where he bought but never mailed birthday cards to his sons), they forgot all about Hannah's easy ways (or their own) and said she was a bitch. Everybody remembered the plague of robins that announced her return, and the tale about her watching Hannah burn was stirred up again.

But it was the men who gave her the final label, who fingerprinted her for all time. They were the ones who said she was guilty of the unforgivable thing—the thing for which there was no understanding, no excuse, no compassion. The route from which there was no way back, the dirt that could not ever be washed away. They said that Sula slept with white men. It may not have been true, but it certainly could have been. She was obviously capable of it. In any case, all minds were closed to her when that word was passed around. It made the old women draw their lips together; made small children look away from her in shame; made young men fantasize elaborate torture for her—just to get the saliva back in their mouths when they saw her.

Every one of them imagined the scene, each according to his own predilections—Sula underneath some white man—and it filled them with choking disgust. There was nothing lower she could do, nothing filthier. The fact that their own skin color was proof that it had happened in their own families was no deterrent to their bile. Nor was the willingness of black men to lie in the beds of white women a consideration that might lead them toward tolerance. They insisted that all unions between white men and black women be rape; for a black woman to be willing was literally unthinkable. In that way, they regarded integration with precisely the same venom that white people did.

So they laid broomsticks across their doors at night and sprinkled salt on porch steps.[8] But aside from one or two unsuccessful efforts to collect the dust from her footsteps, they did nothing to harm her. As always the black people looked at evil stony-eyed and let it run.

Sula acknowledged none of their attempts at counter-conjure or their gossip and seemed to need the services of nobody. So they watched her far more closely than they watched any other roach or bitch in the town, and their alertness was gratified. Things began to happen.

First off, Teapot knocked on her door to see if she had any bottles. He was the five-year-old son of an indifferent mother, all of whose interests sat around the door of the Time and a Half Pool Hall. Her name was Betty but she was called Teapot's Mamma because being his mamma was precisely her major failure. When Sula said no, the boy turned around and fell down the steps. He couldn't get up right away and Sula went to help him. His mother, just then tripping home, saw Sula bending over her son's pained face. She flew into a fit of concerned, if drunken, motherhood, and dragged Teapot home. She told everybody that Sula had pushed him, and talked so strongly about it she was forced to abide by the advice of her friends and take him to the county hospital. The two dollars she hated to release turned out to be well spent, for Teapot did have a fracture, although the doctor said poor diet had contributed substantially to the daintiness of his bones. Teapot's Mamma got a lot of attention anyway and immersed herself in a role she had shown no inclination for: motherhood. The very idea of a grown woman hurting her boy kept her teeth on edge. She became the most devoted mother: sober, clean and industrious. No more nickels for Teapot to go to Dick's for a breakfast of Mr. Goodbars and soda pop: no more long hours of him alone or wandering the roads while she was otherwise engaged. Her change was a distinct improvement, although little Teapot did miss those quiet times at Dick's.

Other things happened. Mr. Finley sat on his porch sucking chicken bones, as he had done for thirteen years, looked up, saw Sula, choked on a bone and died on the spot. That incident, and Teapot's Mamma, cleared

8. Traditional methods of warding off witches.

up for everybody the meaning of the birthmark over her eye; it was not a stemmed rose, or a snake, it was Hannah's ashes marking her from the very beginning.

She came to their church suppers without underwear, bought their steaming platters of food and merely picked at it—relishing nothing, exclaiming over no one's ribs or cobbler. They believed that she was laughing at their God.

And the fury she created in the women of the town was incredible—for she would lay their husbands once and then no more. Hannah had been a nuisance, but she was complimenting the women, in a way, by wanting their husbands. Sula was trying them out and discarding them without any excuse the men could swallow. So the women, to justify their own judgment, cherished their men more, soothed the pride and vanity Sula had bruised.

Among the weighty evidence piling up was the fact that Sula did not look her age. She was near thirty and, unlike them, had lost no teeth, suffered no bruises, developed no ring of fat at the waist or pocket at the back of her neck. It was rumored that she had had no childhood diseases, was never known to have chicken pox, croup or even a runny nose. She had played rough as a child—where were the scars? Except for a funny-shaped finger and that evil birthmark, she was free of any normal signs of vulnerability. Some of the men, who as boys had dated her, remembered that on picnics neither gnats nor mosquitoes would settle on her. Patsy, Hannah's one-time friend, agreed and said not only that, but she had witnessed the fact that when Sula drank beer she never belched.

The most damning evidence, however, came from Dessie, who was a big Daughter Elk[9] and knew things. At one of the social meetings she revealed something to her friends.

"Yeh, well I noticed something long time ago. Ain't said nothing 'bout it 'cause I wasn't sure what it meant. Well . . . I did mention it to Ivy but not nobody else. I disremember how long ago. 'Bout a month or two I guess 'cause I hadn't put down my new linoleum yet. Did you see it, Cora? It's that kind we saw in the catalogue."

"Naw."

"Get on with it, Dessie."

"Well, Cora was with me when we looked in the catalogue . . ."

"We all know 'bout your linoleum. What we don't know is . . ."

"OK. Let me tell it, will you? Just before the linoleum come I was out front and seed Shadrack carryin' on as usual . . . up by the well . . . walkin' 'round it salutin' and carryin' on. You know how he does . . . hollerin' commands and . . ."

"Will you get on with it?"

"Who's tellin' this? Me or you?"

"You."

"Well, let me tell it then. Like I say, he was just cuttin' up as usual when Miss Sula Mae walks by on the other side of the road. And quick as that"— she snapped her fingers—"he stopped and cut on over 'cross the road, step-

9. I.e., she held an important office in the Elks, a fraternal organization.

pin' over to her like a tall turkey in short corn. And guess what? He tips his hat."

"Shadrack don't wear no hat."

"I know that but he tipped it anyway. You know what I mean. He acted like he had a hat and reached up for it and tipped it at her. Now you know Shadrack ain't civil to nobody!"

"Sure ain't."

"Even when you buyin' his fish he's cussin'. If you ain't got the right change he cussin' you. If you act like a fish ain't too fresh he snatch it out of your hand like he doin' you the favor."

"Well, everybody know he a reprobate."

"Yeh, so how come he tip his hat to Sula? How come he don't cuss her?"

"Two devils."

"Exactly!"

"What'd she do when he tipped it? Smile and give him a curtsey?"

"No, and that was the other thing. It was the first time I see her look anything but hateful. Like she smellin' you with her eyes and don't like your soap. When he tipped his hat she put her hand on her throat for a minute and *cut* out. Went runnin' on up the road to home. And him still standin' there tippin' away. And—this the point I was comin' to—when I went back in the house a big sty come on my eye. And I ain't never had no sty before. Never!"

"That's 'cause you saw it."

"Exactly."

"Devil all right."

"No two ways about it," Dessie said, and she popped the rubber band off the deck of cards to settle them down for a nice long game of bid whist.

Their conviction of Sula's evil changed them in accountable yet mysterious ways. Once the source of their personal misfortune was identified, they had leave to protect and love one another. They began to cherish their husbands and wives, protect their children, repair their homes and in general band together against the devil in their midst. In their world, aberrations were as much a part of nature as grace. It was not for them to expel or annihilate it. They would no more run Sula out of town than they would kill the robins that brought her back, for in their secret awareness of Him, He was not the God of three faces[1] they sang about. They knew quite well that He had four, and that the fourth explained Sula. They had lived with various forms of evil all their days, and it wasn't that they believed God would take care of them. It was rather that they knew God had a brother and that brother hadn't spared God's son, so why should he spare them?

There was no creature so ungodly as to make them destroy it. They could kill easily if provoked to anger, but not by design, which explained why they could not "mob kill" anyone. To do so was not only unnatural, it was undignified. The presence of evil was something to be first recognized, then dealt with, survived, outwitted, triumphed over.

1. I.e., the Christian Trinity: the Father, the Son, the Holy Spirit.

Their evidence against Sula was contrived, but their conclusions about her were not. Sula was distinctly different. Eva's arrogance and Hannah's self-indulgence merged in her and, with a twist that was all her own imagination, she lived out her days exploring her own thoughts and emotions, giving them full reign, feeling no obligation to please anybody unless their pleasure pleased her. As willing to feel pain as to give pain, to feel pleasure as to give pleasure, hers was an experimental life—ever since her mother's remarks sent her flying up those stairs, ever since her one major feeling of responsibility had been exorcised on the bank of a river with a closed place in the middle. The first experience taught her there was no other that you could count on; the second that there was no self to count on either. She had no center, no speck around which to grow. In the midst of a pleasant conversation with someone she might say, "Why do you chew with your mouth open?" not because the answer interested her but because she wanted to see the person's face change rapidly. She was completely free of ambition, with no affection for money, property or things, no greed, no desire to command attention or compliments—no ego. For that reason she felt no compulsion to verify herself—be consistent with herself.

She had clung to Nel as the closest thing to both an other and a self, only to discover that she and Nel were not one and the same thing. She had no thought at all of causing Nel pain when she bedded down with Jude. They had always shared the affection of other people: compared how a boy kissed, what line he used with one and then the other. Marriage, apparently, had changed all that, but having had no intimate knowledge of marriage, having lived in a house with women who thought all men available, and selected from among them with a care only for their tastes, she was ill prepared for the possessiveness of the one person she felt close to. She knew well enough what other women said and felt, or said they felt. But she and Nel had always seen through them. They both knew that those women were not jealous of other women; that they were only afraid of losing their jobs. Afraid their husbands would discover that no uniqueness lay between their legs.

Nel was the one person who had wanted nothing from her, who had accepted all aspects of her. Now she wanted everything, and all because of *that*. Nel was the first person who had been real to her, whose name she knew, who had seen as she had the slant of life that made it possible to stretch it to its limits. Now Nel was one of *them*. One of the spiders whose only thought was the next rung of the web, who dangled in dark dry places suspended by their own spittle, more terrified of the free fall than the snake's breath below. Their eyes so intent on the wayward stranger who trips into their net, they were blind to the cobalt on their own backs, the moonshine fighting to pierce their corners. If they were touched by the snake's breath, however fatal, they were merely victims and knew how to behave in that role (just as Nel knew how to behave as the wronged wife). But the free fall, oh no, that required—demanded—invention: a thing to do with the wings, a way of holding the legs and most of all a full surrender to the downward flight if they wished to taste their tongues or stay alive. But alive was what they, and now Nel, did not want to be. Too dangerous. Now Nel belonged to the town and all of its ways. She had given herself over to them, and the flick of their tongues would drive her back into her little dry corner where she would cling to her spittle high above the breath of the snake and the fall.

It had surprised her a little and saddened her a good deal when Nel behaved the way the others would have. Nel was one of the reasons she had drifted back to Medallion, that and the boredom she found in Nashville, Detroit, New Orleans, New York, Philadelphia, Macon and San Diego. All those cities held the same people, working the same mouths, sweating the same sweat. The men who took her to one or another of those places had merged into one large personality: the same language of love, the same entertainments of love, the same cooling of love. Whenever she introduced her private thoughts into their rubbings or goings, they hooded their eyes. They taught her nothing but love tricks, shared nothing but worry, gave nothing but money. She had been looking all along for a friend, and it took her a while to discover that a lover was not a comrade and could never be—for a woman. And that no one would ever be that version of herself which she sought to reach out to and touch with an ungloved hand. There was only her own mood and whim, and if that was all there was, she decided to turn the naked hand toward it, discover it and let others become as intimate with their own selves as she was.

In a way, her strangeness, her naïveté, her craving for the other half of her equation was the consequence of an idle imagination. Had she paints, or clay, or knew the discipline of the dance, or strings; had she anything to engage her tremendous curiosity and her gift for metaphor, she might have exchanged the restlessness and preoccupation with whim for an activity that provided her with all she yearned for. And like any artist with no art form, she became dangerous.

She had lied only once in her life—to Nel about the reason for putting Eva out, and she could lie to her only because she cared about her. When she had come back home, social conversation was impossible for her because she could not lie. She could not say to those old acquaintances, "Hey, girl, you looking good," when she saw how the years had dusted their bronze with ash, the eyes that had once opened wide to the moon bent into grimy sickles of concern. The narrower their lives, the wider their hips. Those with husbands had folded themselves into starched coffins, their sides bursting with other people's skinned dreams and bony regrets. Those without men were like sour-tipped needles featuring one constant empty eye. Those with men had had the sweetness sucked from their breath by ovens and steam kettles. Their children were like distant but exposed wounds whose aches were no less intimate because separate from their flesh. They had looked at the world and back at their children, and Sula knew that one clear young eye was all that kept the knife away from the throat's curve.

She was pariah, then, and knew it. Knew that they despised her and believed that they framed their hatred as disgust for the easy way she lay with men. Which was true. She went to bed with men as frequently as she could. It was the only place where she could find what she was looking for: misery and the ability to feel deep sorrow. She had not always been aware that it was sadness that she yearned for. Lovemaking seemed to her, at first, the creation of a special kind of joy. She thought she liked the sootiness of sex and its comedy; she laughed a great deal during the raucous beginnings, and rejected those lovers who regarded sex as healthy or beautiful. Sexual aesthetics bored her. Although she did not regard sex as ugly (ugliness was boring also), she liked to think of it as wicked. But as her experiences multiplied she realized that not only was it not wicked, it was not necessary for her to conjure up the idea of wickedness in order to participate fully. During the lovemaking she found and needed to find the cutting edge. When she left off cooperating with her body and began to assert herself in the act, particles of strength gathered in her like steel shavings drawn to a spacious magnetic center, forming a tight cluster that nothing, it seemed, could break. And there was utmost irony and outrage in lying under someone, in a position of surrender, feeling her own abiding strength and limitless power. But the cluster did break, fall apart, and in her panic to hold it together she leaped from the edge into soundlessness and went down howling, howling in a stinging awareness of the endings of things: an eye of sorrow in the midst of all that hurricane rage of joy. There, in the center of that silence was not eternity but the death of time and a loneliness so profound the word itself had no meaning. For loneliness assumed the absence of other people, and the solitude she found in that desperate terrain had never admitted the possibility of other people. She wept then. Tears for the deaths of the littlest things: the castaway shoes of children; broken stems of marsh grass battered and drowned by the sea; prom photographs of dead women she never knew; wedding rings in pawnshop windows; the tidy bodies of Cornish hens in a nest of rice.

When her partner disengaged himself, she looked up at him in wonder trying to recall his name; and he looked down at her, smiling with tender understanding of the state of tearful gratitude to which he believed he had brought her. She waiting impatiently for him to turn away and settle into a wet skim of satisfaction and light disgust, leaving her to the postcoital privateness in which she met herself, welcomed herself, and joined herself in matchless harmony.

At twenty-nine she knew it would be no other way for her, but she had not counted on the footsteps on the porch, and the beautiful black face that stared at her through the blue-glass window. Ajax.

Looking for all the world as he had seventeen years ago when he had called her pig meat. He was twenty-one then, she twelve. A universe of time between them. Now she was twenty-nine, he thirty-eight, and the lemon-yellow haunches seemed not so far away after all.

She opened the heavy door and saw him standing on the other side of the screen door with two quarts of milk tucked into his arms like marble statues. He smiled and said, "I been lookin' all over for you."

"Why?" she asked.

"To give you these," and he nodded toward one of the quarts of milk.

"I don't like milk," she said.

"But you like bottles don't you?" He held one up. "Ain't that pretty?"

And indeed it was. Hanging from his fingers, framed by a slick blue sky, it looked precious and clean and permanent. She had the distinct impression that he had done something dangerous to get them.

Sula ran her fingernails over the screen thoughtfully for a second and
then, laughing, she opened the screen door.

Ajax came in and headed straight for the kitchen. Sula followed slowly.
By the time she got to the door he had undone the complicated wire cap
and was letting the cold milk run into his mouth.

Sula watched him—or rather the rhythm in his throat—with growing interest. When he had had enough, he poured the rest into the sink, rinsed
the bottle out and presented it to her. She took the bottle with one hand
and his wrist with the other and pulled him into the pantry. There was no
need to go there, for not a soul was in the house, but the gesture came to
Hannah's daughter naturally. There in the pantry, empty now of flour
sacks, void of row upon row of canned goods, free forever of strings of tiny
green peppers, holding the wet milk bottle tight in her arm she stood wide-
legged against the wall and pulled from his track-lean hips all the pleasure
her thighs could hold.

He came regularly then, bearing gifts: clusters of black berries still on
their branches, four meal-fried porgies[2] wrapped in a salmon-colored sheet
of the Pittsburgh *Courier*, a handful of jacks, two boxes of lime Jell-Well, a
hunk of ice-wagon ice, a can of Old Dutch Cleanser with the bonneted
woman chasing dirt with her stick; a page of Tillie the Toiler comics, and
more gleaming white bottles of milk.

Contrary to what anybody would have suspected from just seeing him
lounging around the pool hall, or shooting at Mr. Finley for beating his
own dog, or calling filthy compliments to passing women, Ajax was very
nice to women. His women, of course, knew it, and it provoked them into
murderous battles over him in the streets, brawling thick-thighed women
with knives disturbed many a Friday night with their bloodletting and attracted whooping crowds. On such occasions Ajax stood, along with the
crowd, and viewed the fighters with the same golden-eyed indifference
with which he watched old men playing checkers. Other than his mother,
who sat in her shack with six younger sons working roots,[3] he had never
met an interesting woman in his life.

His kindness to them in general was not due to a ritual of seduction (he
had no need for it) but rather to the habit he acquired in dealing with his
mother, who inspired thoughtfulness and generosity in all her sons.

She was an evil conjure woman, blessed with seven adoring children
whose joy it was to bring her the plants, hair, underclothing, fingernail
parings, white hens, blood, camphor, pictures, kerosene and footstep dust
that she needed, as well as to order Van Van, High John the Conqueror,
Little John to Chew, Devil's Shoe String, Chinese Wash, Mustard Seed
and the Nine Herbs from Cincinnati.[4] She knew about the weather,
omens, the living, the dead, dreams and all illnesses and made a modest
living with her skills. Had she any teeth or ever straightened her back,
she would have been the most gorgeous thing alive, worthy of her sons'
worship for her beauty alone, if not for the absolute freedom she allowed

---

2. A type of fish.   4. Powders and roots to be used in conjuring.
3. Conjuring, performing witchcraft.

them (known in some quarters as neglect) and the weight of her hoary knowledge.

This woman Ajax loved, and after her—airplanes. There was nothing in between. And when he was not sitting enchanted listening to his mother's words, he thought of airplanes, and pilots, and the deep sky that held them both. People thought that those long trips he took to large cities in the state were for some sophisticated good times they could not imagine but only envy; actually he was leaning against the barbed wire of airports, or nosing around hangars just to hear the talk of the men who were fortunate enough to be in the trade. The rest of the time, the time he was not watching his mother's magic or thinking of airplanes, he spent in the idle pursuits of bachelors without work in small towns. He had heard all the stories about Sula, and they aroused his curiosity. Her elusiveness and indifference to established habits of behavior reminded him of his mother, who was as stubborn in her pursuits of the occult as the women of Greater Saint Matthew's were in the search for redeeming grace. So when his curiosity was high enough he picked two bottles of milk off the porch of some white family and went to see her, suspecting that this was perhaps the only other woman he knew whose life was her own, who could deal with life efficiently, and who was not interested in nailing him.

Sula, too, was curious. She knew nothing about him except the word he had called out to her years ago and the feeling he had excited in her then. She had grown quite accustomed to the clichés of other people's lives as well as her own increasing dissatisfaction with Medallion. If she could have thought of a place to go, she probably would have left, but that was before Ajax looked at her through the blue glass and held the milk aloft like a trophy.

But it was not the presents that made her wrap him up in her thighs. They were charming, of course (especially the jar of butterflies he let loose in the bedroom), but her real pleasure was the fact that he talked to her. They had genuine conversations. He did not speak down to her or at her, nor content himself with puerile questions about her life or monologues of his own activities. Thinking she was possibly brilliant, like his mother, he seemed to expect brilliance from her, and she delivered. And in all of it, he listened more than he spoke. His clear comfort at being in her presence, his lazy willingness to tell her all about fixes[5] and the powers of plants, his refusal to baby or protect her, his assumption that she was both tough and wise—all of that coupled with a wide generosity of spirit only occasionally erupting into vengeance sustained Sula's interest and enthusiasm.

His idea of bliss (on earth as opposed to bliss in the sky) was a long bath in piping-hot water—his head on the cool white rim, his eyes closed in reverie.

"Soaking in hot water give you a bad back." Sula stood in the doorway looking at his knees glistening just at the surface of the soap-gray water.

"Soaking in Sula give me a bad back."

"Worth it?"

"Don't know yet. Go 'way."

5. Spells.

"Airplanes?"

"Airplanes."

"Lindbergh know about you?"

"Go 'way."

She went and waited for him in Eva's high bed, her head turned to the boarded-up window. She was smiling, thinking how like Jude's was his craving to do the white man's work, when two deweys came in with their beautiful teeth and said, "We sick."

Sula turned her head slowly and murmured, "Get well."

"We need some medicine."

"Look in the bathroom."

"Ajax in there."

"Then wait."

"We sick now."

Sula leaned over the bed, picked up a shoe and threw it at them.

"Cocksucker!" they screamed, and she leaped out of the bed naked as a yard dog. She caught the redheaded dewey by his shirt and held him by the heels over the banister until he wet his pants. The other dewey was joined by the third, and they delved into their pockets for stones, which they threw at her. Sula, ducking and tottering with laughter, carried the wet dewey to the bedroom and when the other two followed her, deprived of all weapons except their teeth, Sula had dropped the first dewey on the bed and was fishing in her purse. She gave each of them a dollar bill which they snatched and then scooted off down the stairs to Dick's to buy the catarrh remedy they loved to drink.

Ajax came sopping wet into the room and lay down on the bed to let the air dry him. They were both still for a long time until he reached out and touched her arm.

He liked for her to mount him so he could see her towering above him and call soft obscenities up into her face. As she rocked there, swayed there, like a Georgia pine on its knees, high above the slipping, falling smile, high above the golden eyes and the velvet helmet of hair, rocking, swaying, she focused her thoughts to bar the creeping disorder that was flooding her hips. She looked down, down from what seemed an awful height at the head of the man whose lemon-yellow gabardines had been the first sexual excitement she'd known. Letting her thoughts dwell on his face in order to confine, for just a while longer, the drift of her flesh toward the high silence of orgasm.

If I take a chamois and rub real hard on the bone, right on the ledge of your cheek bone, some of the black will disappear. It will flake away into the chamois and underneath there will be gold leaf. I can see it shining through the black. I know it is there . . .

How high she was over his wand-lean body, how slippery was his sliding sliding smile.

And if I take a nail file or even Eva's old paring knife—that will do—and scrape away at the gold, it will fall away and there will be alabaster. The alabaster is what gives your face its planes, its curves. That is why your mouth smiling does not reach your eyes. Alabaster is giving it a gravity that resists a total smile.

The height and the swaying dizzied her, so she bent down and let her breasts graze his chest.

Then I can take a chisel and small tap hammer and tap away at the alabaster. It will crack then like ice under the pick, and through the breaks I will see the loam, fertile, free of pebbles and twigs. For it is the loam that is giving you that smell.

She slipped her hands under his armpits, for it seemed as though she would not be able to dam the spread of weakness she felt under her skin without holding on to something.

I will put my hand deep into your soil, lift it, sift it with my fingers, feel its warm surface and dewy chill below.

She put her head under his chin with no hope in the world of keeping anything at all at bay.

I will water your soil, keep it rich and moist. But how much? How much water to keep the loam moist? And how much loam will I need to keep my water still? And when do the two make mud?

He swallowed her mouth just as her thighs had swallowed his genitals, and the house was very, very quiet.

Sula began to discover what possession was. Not love, perhaps, but possession or at least the desire for it. She was astounded by so new and alien a feeling. First there was the morning of the night before when she actually wondered if Ajax would come by that day. Then there was an afternoon when she stood before the mirror finger-tracing the laugh lines around her mouth and trying to decide whether she was good-looking or not. She ended this deep perusal by tying a green ribbon in her hair. The green silk made a rippling whisper as she slid it into her hair—a whisper that could easily have been Hannah's chuckle, a soft slow nasal hiss she used to emit when something amused her. Like women sitting for two hours under the marcelling irons[6] only to wonder two days later how soon they would need another appointment. The ribbon-tying was followed by other activity, and when Ajax came that evening, bringing her a reed whistle he had carved that morning, not only was the green ribbon still in her hair, but the bathroom was gleaming, the bed was made, and the table was set for two.

He gave her the reed whistle, unlaced his shoes and sat in the rocking chair in the kitchen.

Sula walked toward him and kissed his mouth. He ran his fingers along the nape of her neck.

"I bet you ain't even missed Tar Baby, have you?" he asked.

"Missed? No. Where is he?"

Ajax smiled at her delicious indifference. "Jail."

"Since when?"

"Last Saturday."

"Picked up for drunk?"

"Little bit more than that," he answered and went ahead to tell her about his own involvement in another of Tar Baby's misfortunes.

On Saturday afternoon Tar Baby had stumbled drunk into traffic on the

6. Heated curling irons used for waving hair.

New River Road. A woman driver swerved to avoid him and hit another car. When the police came, they recognized the woman as the mayor's niece and arrested Tar Baby. Later, after the word got out, Ajax and two other men went to the station to see about him. At first they wouldn't let them in. But they relented after Ajax and the other two just stood around for one hour and a half and repeated their request at regular intervals. When they finally got permission to go in and looked in at him in the cell, he was twisted up in a corner badly beaten and dressed in nothing but extremely soiled underwear. Ajax and the other men asked the officer why Tar Baby couldn't have back his clothes. "It ain't right," they said, "to let a grown man lay around in his own shit."

The policeman, obviously in agreement with Eva, who had always maintained that Tar Baby was white, said that if the prisoner didn't like to live in shit, he should come down out of those hills, and live like a decent white man.

More words were exchanged, hot words and dark, and the whole thing ended with the arraignment of the three black men, and an appointment to appear in civil court Thursday next.

Ajax didn't seem too bothered by any of it. More annoyed and inconvenienced than anything else. He had had several messes with the police, mostly in gambling raids, and regarded them as the natural hazards of Negro life.

But Sula, the green ribbon shining in her hair, was flooded with an awareness of the impact of the outside world on Ajax. She stood up and arranged herself on the arm of the rocking chair. Putting her fingers deep into the velvet of his hair, she murmured, "Come on. Lean on me."

Ajax blinked. Then he looked swiftly into her face. In her words, in her voice, was a sound he knew well. For the first time he saw the green ribbon. He looked around and saw the gleaming kitchen and the table set for two and detected the scent of the nest. Every hackle on his body rose, and he knew that very soon she would, like all of her sisters before her, put to him the death-knell question "Where you been?" His eyes dimmed with a mild and momentary regret.

He stood and mounted the stairs with her and entered the spotless bathroom where the dust had been swept from underneath the claw-foot tub. He was trying to remember the date of the air show in Dayton. As he came into the bedroom, he saw Sula lying on fresh white sheets, wrapped in the deadly odor of freshly applied cologne.

He dragged her under him and made love to her with the steadiness and the intensity of a man about to leave for Dayton.

Every now and then she looked around for tangible evidence of his having ever been there. Where were the butterflies? the blueberries? the whistling reed? She could find nothing, for he had left nothing but his stunning absence. An absence so decorative, so ornate, it was difficult for her to understand how she had ever endured, without falling dead or being consumed, his magnificent presence.

The mirror by the door was not a mirror by the door, it was an altar where he stood for only a moment to put on his cap before going out. The red rocking chair was a rocking of his own hips as he sat in the kitchen. Still, there was nothing of his—his own—that she could find. It was as if she were afraid she had hallucinated him and needed proof to the contrary. His absence was everywhere, stinging everything, giving the furnishings primary colors, sharp outlines to the corners of rooms and gold light to the dust collecting on table tops. When he was there he pulled everything toward himself. Not only her eyes and all her senses but also inanimate things seemed to exist because of him, backdrops to his presence. Now that he had gone, these things, so long subdued by his presence, were glamorized in his wake.

Then one day, burrowing in a dresser drawer, she found what she had been looking for: proof that he had been there, his driver's license. It contained just what she needed for verification—his vital statistics: Born 1901, height 5'11", weight 152 lbs., eyes brown, hair black, color black. Oh yes, skin black. Very black. So black that only a steady careful rubbing with steel wool would remove it, and as it was removed there was the glint of gold leaf and under the gold leaf the cold alabaster and deep, deep down under the cold alabaster more black only this time the black of warm loam.

But what was this? Albert Jacks? His name was Albert Jacks? A. Jacks. She had thought it was Ajax. All those years. Even from the time she walked by the pool hall and looked away from him sitting astride a wooden chair, looked away to keep from seeing the wide space of intolerable orderliness between his legs; the openness that held no sign, no sign at all, of the animal that lurked in his trousers; looked away from the insolent nostrils and the smile that kept slipping and falling, falling, falling so she wanted to reach out with her hand to catch it before it fell to the pavement and was sullied by the cigarette butts and bottle caps and spittle at his feet and the feet of other men who sat or stood around outside the pool hall, calling, singing out to her and Nel and grown women too with lyrics like *pig meat* • and *brown sugar* and *jailbait* and *O Lord, what have I done to deserve the wrath*, and *Take me, Jesus, I have seen the promised land*, and *Do, Lord, remember me* in voices mellowed by hopeless passion into gentleness. Even then, when she and Nel were trying hard not to dream of him and not to think of him when they touched the softness in their underwear or undid their braids as soon as they left home to let the hair bump and wave around their ears, or wrapped the cotton binding around their chests so the nipples would not break through their blouses and give him cause to smile his slipping, falling smile, which brought the blood rushing to their skin. And even later, when for the first time in her life she had lain in bed with a man and said his name involuntarily or said it truly meaning *him*, the name she was screaming and saying was not his at all.

Sula stood with a worn slip of paper in her fingers and said aloud to no one, "I didn't even know his name. And if I didn't know his name, then there is nothing I did know and I have known nothing ever at all since the one thing I wanted was to know his name so how could he help but leave me since he was making love to a woman who didn't even know his name.

"When I was a little girl the heads of my paper dolls came off, and it was a long time before I discovered that my own head would not fall off if I bent my neck. I used to walk around holding it very stiff because I thought a strong wind or a heavy push would snap my neck. Nel was the one who told me the truth. But she was wrong. I did not hold my head stiff enough when I met him and so I lost it just like the dolls.

"It's just as well he left. Soon I would have torn the flesh from his face just to see if I was right about the gold and nobody would have understood that kind of curiosity. They would have believed that I wanted to hurt him just like the little boy who fell down the steps and broke his leg and the people think I pushed him just because I looked at it."

Holding the driver's license she crawled into bed and fell into a sleep full of dreams of cobalt blue.

When she awoke, there was a melody in her head she could not identify or recall ever hearing before. "Perhaps I made it up," she thought. Then it came to her—the name of the song and all its lyrics just as she had heard it many times before. She sat on the edge of the bed thinking, "There aren't any more new songs and I have sung all the ones there are. I have sung them all. I have sung all the songs there are." She lay down again on the bed and sang a little wandering tune made up of the words *I have sung all the songs all the songs I have sung all the songs there are* until, touched by her own lullaby, she grew drowsy, and in the hollow of near-sleep she tasted the acridness of gold, left the chill of alabaster and smelled the dark, sweet stench of loam.

1940

"I heard you was sick. Anything I can do for you?"

She had practiced not just the words but the tone, the pitch of her voice. It should be calm, matter-of-fact, but strong in sympathy—for the illness though, not for the patient.

The sound of her voice as she heard it in her head betrayed no curiosity, no pride, just the inflection of any good woman come to see about a sick person who, incidentally, had such visits from nobody else.

For the first time in three years she would be looking at the stemmed rose that hung over the eye of her enemy. Moreover, she would be doing it with the taste of Jude's exit in her mouth, with the resentment and shame that even yet pressed for release in her stomach. She would be facing the black rose that Jude had kissed and looking at the nostrils of the woman who had twisted her love for her own children into something so thick and monstrous she was afraid to show it lest it break loose and smother them with its heavy paw. A cumbersome bear-love that, given any rein, would suck their breath away in its crying need for honey.

Because Jude's leaving was so complete, the full responsibility of the household was Nel's. There were no more fifty dollars in brown envelopes to count on, so she took to cleaning rather than fret away the tiny seaman's pension her parents lived on. And just this past year she got a better job working as a chambermaid in the same hotel Jude had worked in. The tips were only fair, but the hours were good—she was home when the children got out of school.

At thirty her hot brown eyes had turned to agate, and her skin had taken on the sheen of maple struck down, split and sanded at the height of its green. Virtue, bleak and drawn, was her only mooring. It brought her to Number 7 Carpenter's Road and the door with the blue glass; it helped her to resist scratching the screen as in days gone by; it hid from her the true motives for her charity, and, finally, it gave her voice the timbre she wanted it to have: free of delight or a lip-smacking "I told you so" with which the news of Sula's illness had been received up in the Bottom—free of the least hint of retribution.

Now she stood in Eva's old bedroom, looking down at that dark rose, aware of the knife-thin arms sliding back and forth over the quilt and the boarded-up window Eva had jumped out of.

Sula looked up and without a second's pause followed Nel's example of leaving out the greeting when she spoke.

"As a matter of fact, there is. I got a prescription. Nathan usually goes for me but he . . . school don't let out till three. Could you run it over to the drugstore?"

"Where is it?" Nel was glad to have a concrete errand. Conversation would be difficult. (Trust Sula to pick up a relationship exactly where it lay.)

"Look in my bag. No. Over there."

Nel walked to the dresser and opened the purse with the beaded clasp. She saw only a watch and the folded prescription down inside. No wallet, no change purse. She turned to Sula: "Where's your . . ."

But Sula was looking at the boarded-up window. Something in her eye right there in the corner stopped Nel from completing her question. That and the slight flare of the nostrils—a shadow of a snarl. Nel took the piece of paper and picked up her own purse, saying, "OK. I'll be right back."

As soon as the door was shut, Sula breathed through her mouth. While Nel was in the room the pain had increased. Now that this new pain killer, the one she had been holding in reserve, was on the way her misery was manageable. She let a piece of her mind lay on Nel. It was funny, sending Nel off to that drugstore right away like that, after she had not seen her to speak to for years. The drugstore was where Edna Finch's Mellow House used to be years back when they were girls. Where they used to go, the two of them, hand in hand, for the 18-cent ice-cream sundaes, past the Time and a Half Pool Hall, where the sprawling men said "pig meat," and they sat in that cool room with the marble-top tables and ate the first ice-cream sundaes of their lives. Now Nel was going back there alone and Sula was waiting for the medicine the doctor said not to take until the pain got really bad. And she supposed "really bad" was now. Although you could never tell. She wondered for an instant what Nellie wanted; why she had come. Did she want to gloat? Make up? Following this line of thought required more concentration than she could muster. Pain was greedy; it demanded all of her attention. But it was good that this new medicine, the reserve, would be brought to her by her old friend. Nel, she remembered, always thrived on a crisis. The closed place in the water; Hannah's funeral. Nel was the best. When Sula imitated her, or tried to, those long years ago, it always ended up in some action noteworthy not for its coolness but mostly for its being bizarre. The one time she tried to protect Nel, she had cut off her own finger tip and earned not Nel's gratitude but her disgust. From then on she had let her emotions dictate her behavior.

She could hear Nel's footsteps long before she opened the door and put the medicine on the table near the bed.

As Sula poured the liquid into a sticky spoon, Nel began the sickroom conversation.

"You look fine, Sula."

"You lying, Nellie. I look bad." She gulped the medicine.

"No. I haven't seen you for a long time, but you look . . ."

"You don't have to do that, Nellie. It's going to be all right."

"What ails you? Have they said?"

Sula licked the corners of her lips. "You want to talk about that?"

Nel smiled, slightly, at the bluntness she had forgotten. "No. No, I don't, but you sure you should be staying up here alone?"

"Nathan comes by. The deweys sometimes, and Tar Baby . . ."

"That ain't help, Sula. You need to be with somebody grown. Somebody who can . . ."

"I'd rather be here, Nellie."

"You know you don't have to be proud with me."

"Proud?" Sula's laughter broke through the phlegm. "What you talking about? I like my own dirt, Nellie. I'm not proud. You sure have forgotten me."

"Maybe. Maybe not. But you a woman and you alone."

"And you? Ain't you alone?"

"I'm not sick. I work."

"Yes. Of course you do. Work's good for you, Nellie. It don't do nothing for me."

"You never *had* to."

"I never would."

"There's something to say for it, Sula. 'Specially if you don't want people to have to do for you."

"Neither one, Nellie. Neither one."

"You can't have it all, Sula." Nel was getting exasperated with her arrogance, with her lying at death's door still smart-talking.

"Why? I can do it all, why can't I have it all?"

"You *can't* do it all. You a woman and a colored woman at that. You can't act like a man. You can't be walking around all independent-like, doing whatever you like, taking what you want, leaving what you don't."

"You repeating yourself."

"How repeating myself?"

"You say I'm a woman and colored. Ain't that the same as being a man?"

"I don't think so and you wouldn't either if you had children."

"Then I really would act like what you call a man. Every man I ever knew left his children."

"Some were taken."

"Wrong, Nellie. The word is 'left.' "

"You still going to know everything, ain't you?"

"I don't know everything, I just do everything."

"Well, you don't do what I do."

"You think I don't know what your life is like just because I ain't living it? I know what every colored woman in this country is doing."

"What's that?"

"Dying. Just like me. But the difference is they dying like a stump. Me, I'm going down like one of those redwoods. I sure did live in this world."

"Really? What have you got to show for it?"

"Show? To who? Girl, I got my mind. And what goes on in it. Which is to say, I got me."

"Lonely, ain't it?"

"Yes. But my lonely is *mine*. Now your lonely is somebody else's. Made by somebody else and handed to you. Ain't that something? A secondhand lonely."

Nel sat back on the little wooden chair. Anger skipped but she realized that Sula was probably just showing off. No telling what shape she was really in, but there was no point in saying anything other than what was the truth. "I always understood how you could take a man. Now I understand why you can't keep none."

"Is that what I'm supposed to do? Spend my life keeping a man?"

"They worth keeping, Sula."

"They ain't worth more than me. And besides, I never loved no man because he was worth it. Worth didn't have nothing to do with it."

"What did?"

"My mind did. That's all."

"Well I guess that's it. You own the world and the rest of us is renting. You ride the pony and we shovel the shit. I didn't come up here for this kind of talk, Sula . . ."

"No?"

"No. I come to see about you. But now that you opened it up, I may as well close it." Nel's fingers closed around the brass rail of the bed. Now she would ask her. "How come you did it, Sula?"

There was a silence but Nel felt no obligation to fill it.

Sula stirred a little under the covers. She looked bored as she sucked her teeth. "Well, there was this space in front of me, behind me, in my head. Some space. And Jude filled it up. That's all. He just filled up the space."

"You mean you didn't even love him?" The feel of the brass was in Nel's mouth. "It wasn't even loving him?"

Sula looked toward the boarded-up window again. Her eyes fluttered as if she were about to fall off into sleep.

"But . . . ." Nel held her stomach in. "But what about me? What about me? Why didn't you think about me? Didn't I count? I never hurt you. What did you take him for if you didn't love him and why didn't you think about me?" And then, "I was good to you, Sula, why don't that matter?"

Sula turned her head away from the boarded window. Her voice was quiet and the stemmed rose over her eye was very dark. "It matters, Nel, but only to you. Not to anybody else. Being good to somebody is just like being mean to somebody. Risky. You don't get nothing for it."

Nel took her hands from the brass railing. She was annoyed with herself. Finally when she had gotten the nerve to ask the question, the right question, it made no difference. Sula couldn't give her a sensible answer because she didn't know. Would be, in fact, the last to know. Talking to her about right and wrong was like talking to the deweys. She picked at the fringe on Sula's bedspread and said softly, "We were friends."

"Oh, yes. Good friends," Sula said.

"And you didn't love me enough to leave him alone. To let him love me. You had to take him away."

"What you mean take him away? I didn't kill him, I just fucked him. If we were such good friends, how come you couldn't get over it?"

"You laying there in that bed without a dime or a friend to your name having done all the dirt you did in this town and you still expect folks to love you?"

Sula raised herself up on her elbows. Her face glistened with the dew of fever. She opened her mouth as though to say something, then fell back on the pillows and sighed. "Oh, they'll love me all right. It will take time, but they'll love me." The sound of her voice was as soft and distant as the look in her eyes. "After all the old women have lain with the teen-agers; when all the young girls have slept with their old drunken uncles; after all the black men fuck all the white ones; when all the white women kiss all the black ones; when the guards have raped all the jailbirds and after all the whores make love to their grannies; after all the faggots get their mothers' trim; when Lindbergh sleeps with Bessie Smith and Norma Shearer makes it with Stepin Fetchit;[7] after all the dogs have fucked all the cats and every weathervane on every barn flies off the roof to mount the hogs . . . then there'll be a little love left over for me. And I know just what it will feel like."

She closed her eyes then and thought of the wind pressing her dress between her legs as she ran up the bank of the river to four leaf-locked trees and the digging of holes in the earth.

Embarrassed, irritable and a little bit ashamed, Nel rose to go. "Goodbye, Sula. I don't reckon I'll be back."

She opened the door and heard Sula's low whisper. "Hey, girl." Nel paused and turned her head but not enough to see her.

"How you know?" Sula asked.

"Know what?" Nel still wouldn't look at her.

"About who was good. How you know it was you?"

"What you mean?"

"I mean maybe it wasn't you. Maybe it was me."

Nel took two steps out the door and closed it behind her. She walked down the hall and down the four flights of steps. The house billowed around her light then dark, full of presences without sounds. The deweys, Tar Baby, the newly married couples, Mr. Buckland Reed, Patsy, Valentine, and the beautiful Hannah Peace. Where were they? Eva out at the old folks' home, the deweys living anywhere, Tar Baby steeped in wine, and

7. Actor (1902–1985) who played stereotypical Hollywood blacks (lazy, slow, and so forth) in films from the 1920s through the 1950s. Charles Lindbergh (1902–1974), white aviator. Smith (1894?–1937), black blues singer. Shearer (1900–1983), white actress of the 1920s and 1930s.

Sula upstairs in Eva's bed with a boarded-up window and an empty pocket-book on the dresser.

When Nel closed the door, Sula reached for more medicine. Then she turned the pillow over to its cool side and thought about her old friend. "So she will walk on down that road, her back so straight in that old green coat, the strap of her handbag pushed back all the way to the elbow, thinking how much I have cost her and never remember the days when we were two throats and one eye and we had no price."

Pictures drifted through her head as lightly as dandelion spores: the blue eagle that swallowed the E of the Sherman's Mellowe wine that Tar Baby drank; the pink underlid of Hannah's eye as she probed for a fleck of coal dust or a lash. She thought of looking out of the windows of all those trains and buses, looking at the feet and backs of all those people. Nothing was ever different. They were all the same. All of the words and all of the smiles, every tear and every gag just something to do.

"That's the same sun I looked at when I was twelve, the same pear trees. If I live a hundred years my urine will flow the same way, my armpits and breath will smell the same. My hair will grow from the same holes. I didn't mean anything. I never meant anything. I stood there watching her burn and was thrilled. I wanted her to keep on jerking like that, to keep on dancing."

Then she had the dream again. The Clabber Girl Baking Powder lady was smiling and beckoning to her, one hand under her apron. When Sula came near she disintegrated into white dust, which Sula was hurriedly trying to stuff into the pockets of her blue-flannel housecoat. The disintegration was awful to see, but worse was the feel of the powder—its starchy slipperiness as she tried to collect it by handfuls. The more she scooped, the more it billowed. At last it covered her, filled her eyes, her nose, her throat, and she woke gagging and overwhelmed with the smell of smoke.

Pain took hold. First a fluttering as of doves in her stomach, then a kind of burning, followed by a spread of thin wires to other parts of her body. Once the wires of liquid pain were in place, they jelled and began to throb. She tried concentrating on the throbs, identifying them as waves, hammer strokes, razor edges or small explosions. Soon even the variety of the pain bored her and there was nothing to do, for it was joined by fatigue so great she could not make a fist or fight the taste of oil at the back of her tongue.

Several times she tried to cry out, but the fatigue barely let her open her lips, let alone take the deep breath necessary to scream. So she lay there wondering how soon she would gather enough strength to lift her arm and push the rough quilt away from her chin and whether she would turn her cheek to the cooler side of the pillow now or wait till her face was thoroughly soaked and the move would be more refreshing. But she was reluctant to move her face for another reason. If she turned her head, she would not be able to see the boarded-up window Eva jumped out of. And looking at those four wooden planks with the steel rod slanting across them was the only peace she had. The sealed window soothed her with its sturdy termination, its unassailable finality. It was as though for the first time she was completely alone—where she had always wanted to be—free of the possibility of distraction. It would be here, only here, held by this blind window high above the elm tree, that she might draw her legs up to her chest, close her eyes, put her thumb in her mouth and float over and down the tunnels, just missing the dark walls, down, down until she met a rain scent and would know the water was near, and she would curl into its heavy softness and it would envelop her, carry her, and wash her tired flesh always. Always. Who said that? She tried hard to think. Who was it that had promised her a sleep of water always? The effort to recall was too great; it loosened a knot in her chest that turned her thoughts again to the pain.

While in this state of weary anticipation, she noticed that she was not breathing, that her heart had stopped completely. A crease of fear touched her breast, for any second there was sure to be a violent explosion in her brain, a gasping for breath. Then she realized, or rather she sensed, that there was not going to be any pain. She was not breathing because she didn't have to. Her body did not need oxygen. She was dead.

Sula felt her face smiling. "Well, I'll be damned," she thought, "it didn't even hurt. Wait'll I tell Nel."

1941

The death of Sula Peace was the best news folks up in the Bottom had had since the promise of work at the tunnel. Of the few who were not afraid to witness the burial of a witch and who had gone to the cemetery, some had come just to verify her being put away but stayed to sing "Shall We Gather at the River" for politeness' sake, quite unaware of the bleak promise of their song. Others came to see that nothing went awry, that the shallow-minded and small-hearted kept their meanness at bay, and that the entire event be characterized by that abiding gentleness of spirit to which they themselves had arrived by the simple determination not to let anything—anything at all: not failed crops, not rednecks, lost jobs, sick children, rotten potatoes, broken pipes, bug-ridden flour, third-class coal, educated social workers, thieving insurance men, garlic-ridden hunkies, corrupt Catholics, racist Protestants, cowardly Jews, slaveholding Moslems, jack-leg nigger preachers, squeamish Chinamen, cholera, dropsy or the Black Plague, let alone a strange woman—keep them from their God.

In any case, both the raw-spirited and the gentle who came—not to the white funeral parlor but to the colored part of the Beechnut Cemetery—felt that either *because* Sula was dead or just *after* she was dead a brighter day was dawning. There were signs. The rumor that the tunnel spanning the river would use Negro workers became an announcement. Planned, abandoned and replanned for years, this project had finally begun in 1937. For three years there were rumors that blacks would work it, and hope was high in spite of the fact that the River Road leading to the tunnel had encouraged similar hopes in 1927 but had ended up being built entirely by white labor—hillbillies and immigrants taking even the lowest jobs. But the tunnel itself was another matter. The craft work—no, they would not get that. But it was a major job, and the government seemed to favor opening up employment to black workers. It meant black men would not have to sweep Medallion to eat, or leave the town altogether for the steel mills in Akron and along Lake Erie.

The second sign was the construction begun on an old people's home. True, it was more renovation than construction, but the blacks were free, or so it was said, to occupy it. Some said that the very transfer of Eva from the ramshackle house that passed for a colored women's nursing home to the bright new one was a clear sign of the mystery of God's ways, His mighty thumb having been seen at Sula's throat.

So it was with a strong sense of hope that the people in the Bottom watched October close.

Then Medallion turned silver. It seemed sudden, but actually there had been days and days of no snow—just frost—when, late one afternoon, a rain fell and froze. Way down Carpenter's Road, where the concrete sidewalks started, children hurried to the sliding places before shopkeepers and old women sprinkled stove ashes, like ancient onyx, onto the new-minted silver. They hugged trees simply to hold for a moment all that life and largeness stilled in glass, and gazed at the sun pressed against the gray sky like a worn doubloon, wondering all the while if the world were coming to an end. Grass stood blade by blade, shocked into separateness by an ice that held for days.

Late-harvesting things were ruined, of course, and fowl died of both chill and rage. Cider turned to ice and split the jugs, forcing the men to drink their cane liquor too soon. It was better down in the valley, since, as always, the hills protected it, but up in the Bottom black folks suffered heavily in their thin houses and thinner clothes. The ice-cold wind blew what little heat they had through windowpanes and ill-fitting doors. For days on end they were virtually housebound, venturing out only to coal-bins or right next door for the trading of vital foodstuffs. Never to the stores. No deliveries were being made anyway, and when they were, the items were saved for better-paying white customers. Women could not make it down the icy slopes and therefore missed days of wages they sorely needed.

The consequence of all that ice was a wretched Thanksgiving of tiny tough birds, heavy pork cakes, and pithy sweet potatoes. By the time the ice began to melt and the first barge was seen shuddering through the ice skim on the river, everybody under fifteen had croup, or scarlet fever, and those over had chilblains, rheumatism, pleurisy,[8] earaches and a world of other ailments.

Still it was not those illnesses or even the ice that marked the beginning of the trouble, that self-fulfilled prophecy that Shadrack carried on his tongue. As soon as the silvering began, long before the cider cracked the jugs, there was something wrong. A falling away, a dislocation was taking place. Hard on the heels of the general relief that Sula's death brought a restless irritability took hold. Teapot, for example, went into the kitchen and asked his mother for some sugar-butter-bread. She got up to fix it and found that she had no butter, only oleomargarine. Too tired to mix the saffron-colored powder into the hard cake of oleo, she simply smeared the white stuff on the bread and sprinkled the sugar over it. Teapot tasted the difference and refused to eat it. This keenest of insults that a mother

8. Inflammation around the lungs. "Croup" (inflammation of the larynx) and "scarlet fever" (contagious bacterial disease) were once common childhood illnesses. "Chilblains": sores (usually on the hands or feet) caused by prolonged exposure to cold.

can feel, the rejection by a child of her food, bent her into fury and she beat him as she had not done since Sula knocked him down the steps. She was not alone. Other mothers who had defended their children from Sula's malevolence (or who had defended their positions as mothers from Sula's scorn for the role) now had nothing to rub up against. The tension was gone and so was the reason for the effort they had made. Without her mockery, affection for others sank into flaccid disrepair. Daughters who had complained bitterly about the responsibilities of taking care of their aged mothers-in-law had altered when Sula locked Eva away, and they began cleaning those old women's spittoons without a murmur. Now that Sula was dead and done with, they returned to a steeping resentment of the burdens of old people. Wives uncoddled their husbands; there seemed no further need to reinforce their vanity. And even those Negroes who had moved down from Canada to Medallion, who remarked every chance they got that they had never been slaves, felt a loosening of the reactionary compassion for Southern-born blacks Sula had inspired in them. They returned to their original claims of superiority.

The normal meanness that the winter brought was compounded by the small-spiritedness that hunger and scarlet fever produced. Even a definite and witnessed interview of four colored men (and the promise of more in the spring) at the tunnel site could not break the cold vise of that lean and bitter year's end.

Christmas came one morning and haggled everybody's nerves like a dull ax—too shabby to cut clean but too heavy to ignore. The children lay wall-eyed on creaking beds or pallets near the stove, sucking peppermint and oranges in between coughs while their mothers stomped the floors in rage at the cakes that did not rise because the stove fire had been so stingy; at the curled bodies of men who chose to sleep the day away rather than face the silence made by the absence of Lionel trains, drums, crybaby dolls and rocking horses. Teen-agers sneaked into the Elmira Theater in the afternoon and let Tex Ritter[9] free them from the recollection of their fathers' shoes, yawning in impotence under the bed. Some of them had a bottle of wine, which they drank at the feet of the glittering Mr. Ritter, making such a ruckus the manager had to put them out. The white people who came with Christmas bags of rock candy and old clothes were hard put to get a *Yes'm, thank you*, out of those sullen mouths.

Just as the ice lingered in October, so did the phlegm of December—which explained the enormous relief brought on by the first three days of 1941. It was as though the season had exhausted itself, for on January first the temperature shot up to sixty-one degrees and slushed the whiteness overnight. On January second drab patches of grass could be seen in the fields. On January third the sun came out—and so did Shadrack with his rope, his bell and his childish dirge.

He had spent the night before watching a tiny moon. The people, the voices that kept him company, were with him less and less. Now there were long periods when he heard nothing except the wind in the trees and the

9. Known as the "singing cowboy" (1906–1974) of radio, screen, television, and stage.

plop of buckeyes on the earth. In the winter, when the fish were too hard to get to, he did picking-up jobs for small businessmen (nobody would have him in or even near their homes), and thereby continued to have enough money for liquor. Yet the drunk times were becoming deeper but more seldom. It was as though he no longer needed to drink to forget whatever it was he could not remember. Now he could not remember that he had ever forgotten anything. Perhaps that was why for the first time after that cold day in France he was beginning to miss the presence of other people. Shadrack had improved enough to feel lonely. If he was lonely before, he didn't know it because the noise he kept up, the roaring, the busyness, protected him from knowing it. Now the compulsion to activity, to filling up the time when he was not happily fishing on the riverbank, had dwindled. He sometimes fell asleep before he got drunk; sometimes spent whole days looking at the river and the sky; and more and more he relinquished the military habits of cleanliness in his shack. Once a bird flew into his door—one of the robins during the time there was a plague of them. It stayed, looking for an exit, for the better part of an hour. When the bird found the window and flew away, Shadrack was grieved and actually waited and watched for its return. During those days of waiting, he did not make his bed, or sweep, or shake out the little rag-braid rug, and almost forgot to slash with his fish knife the passing day on his calendar. When he did return to housekeeping, it was not with the precision he had always insisted upon. The messier his house got, the lonelier he felt, and it was harder and harder to conjure up sergeants, and orderlies, and invading armies; harder and harder to hear the gunfire and keep the platoon marching in time. More frequently now he looked at and fondled the one piece of evidence that he once had a visitor in his house: a child's purple-and-white belt. The one the little girl left behind when she came to see him. Shadrack remembered the scene clearly. He had stepped into the door and there was a tear-stained face turning, turning toward him; eyes hurt and wondering; mouth parted in an effort to ask a question. She had wanted something—from him. Not fish, not work, but something only he could give. She had a tadpole over her eye (that was how he knew she was a friend—she had the mark of the fish he loved), and one of her braids had come undone. But when he looked at her face he had seen also the skull beneath, and thinking she saw it too—knew it was there and was afraid—he tried to think of something to say to comfort her, something to stop the hurt from spilling out of her eyes. So he had said "always," so she would not have to be afraid of the change—the falling away of skin, the drip and slide of blood, and the exposure of bone underneath. He had said "always" to convince her, assure her, of permanency.

It worked, for when he said it her face lit up and the hurt did leave. She ran then, carrying his knowledge, but her belt fell off and he kept it as a memento. It hung on a nail near his bed—unfrayed, unsullied after all those years, with only the permanent bend in the fabric made by its long life on a nail. It was pleasant living with that sign of a visitor, his only one. And after a while he was able to connect the belt with the face, the tadpole-over-the-eye-face that he sometimes saw up in the Bottom. His visitor, his company, his guest, his social life, his woman, his daughter, his friend—they all hung there on a nail near his bed.

Now he stared at the tiny moon floating high over the ice-choked river. His loneliness had dropped down somewhere around his ankles. Some other feeling possessed him. A feeling that touched his eyes and made him blink. He had seen her again months? weeks? ago. Raking leaves for Mr. Hodges, he had gone into the cellar for two bushel baskets to put them in. In the hallway he passed an open door leading to a small room. She lay on a table there. It was surely the same one. The same little-girl face, same tadpole over the eye. So he had been wrong. Terribly wrong. No "always" at all. Another dying away of someone whose face he knew.

It was then he began to suspect that all those years of rope hauling and bell ringing were never going to do any good. He might as well sit forever on his riverbank and stare out of the window at the moon.

By his day-slashed calendar he knew that tomorrow was the day. And for the first time he did not want to go. He wanted to stay with the purple-and-white belt. Not go. Not go.

Still, when the day broke in an incredible splash of sun, he gathered his things. In the early part of the afternoon, drenched in sunlight and certain that this would be the last time he would invite them to end their lives neatly and sweetly, he walked over the rickety bridge and on into the Bottom. But it was not heartfelt this time, not loving this time, for he no longer cared whether he helped them or not. His rope was improperly tied; his bell had a tinny unimpassioned sound. His visitor was dead and would come no more.

Years later people would quarrel about who had been the first to go. Most folks said it was the deweys, but one or two knew better, knew that Dessie and Ivy had been first. Said that Dessie had opened her door first and stood there shielding her eyes from the sun while watching Shadrack coming down the road. She laughed.

Maybe the sun; maybe the clots of green showing in the hills promising so much; maybe the contrast between Shadrack's doomy, gloomy bell glinting in all that sweet sunshine. Maybe just a brief moment, for once, of not feeling fear, of looking at death in the sunshine and being unafraid. She laughed.

Upstairs, Ivy heard her and looked to see what caused the thick music that rocked her neighbor's breasts. Then Ivy laughed too. Like the scarlet fever that had touched everybody and worn them down to gristle, their laughter infected Carpenter's Road. Soon children were jumping about giggling and men came to the porches to chuckle. By the time Shadrack reached the first house, he was facing a line of delighted faces.

Never before had they laughed. Always they had shut their doors, pulled down the shades and called their children out of the road. It frightened him, this glee, but he stuck to his habit—singing his song, ringing his bell and holding fast to his rope. The deweys with their magnificent teeth ran out from Number 7 and danced a little jig around the befuddled Shadrack, then cut into a wild aping of his walk, his song and his bell-ringing. By now women were holding their stomachs, and the men were slapping their knees. It was Mrs. Jackson, who ate ice, who tripped down off her porch and marched—actually marched—along behind him. The scene was so comic the people walked into the road to make sure they saw it all. In that way the parade started.

Everybody, Dessie, Tar Baby, Patsy, Mr. Buckland Reed, Teapot's Mamma, Valentine, the deweys, Mrs. Jackson, Irene, the proprietor of the Palace of Cosmetology, Reba, the Herrod brothers and flocks of teen-agers got into the mood and, laughing, dancing, calling to one another, formed a pied piper's band[1] behind Shadrack. As the initial group of about twenty people passed more houses, they called to the people standing in doors and leaning out of windows to join them; to help them open further this slit in the veil, this respite from anxiety, from dignity, from gravity, from the weight of that very adult pain that had undergirded them all those years before. Called to them to come out and play in the sunshine—as though the sunshine would last, as though there really was hope. The same hope that kept them picking beans for other farmers; kept them from finally leaving as they talked of doing; kept them knee-deep in other people's dirt; kept them excited about other people's wars; kept them solicitous of white people's children; kept them convinced that some magic "government" was going to lift them up, out and away from that dirt, those beans, those wars.

Some, of course, like Helene Wright, would not go. She watched the ruckus with characteristic scorn. Others, who understood the Spirit's touch which made them dance, who understood whole families bending their backs in a field while singing as from one throat, who understood the ecstasy of river baptisms under suns just like this one, did not understand this curious disorder, this headless display and so refused also to go.

Nevertheless, the sun splashed on a larger and larger crowd that strutted, skipped, marched, and shuffled down the road. When they got down to where the sidewalk started, some of them stopped and decided to turn back, too embarrassed to enter the white part of town whooping like banshees.[2] But except for three or four, the fainthearted were put to shame by the more aggressive and abandoned, and the parade danced down Main Street past Woolworth's and the old poultry house, turned right and moved on down the New River Road.

At the mouth of the tunnel excavation, in a fever pitch of excitement and joy, they saw the timber, the bricks, the steel ribs and the tacky wire gate that glittered under ice struck to diamond in the sun. It dazzled them, at first, and they were suddenly quiet. Their hooded eyes swept over the place where their hope had lain since 1927. There was the promise: leaf-dead. The teeth unrepaired, the coal credit cut off, the chest pains unattended, the school shoes unbought, the rush-stuffed mattresses, the broken toilets, the leaning porches, the slurred remarks and the staggering childish malevolence of their employers. All there in blazing sunlit ice rapidly becoming water.

Like antelopes they leaped over the little gate—a wire barricade that was never intended to bar anything but dogs, rabbits and stray children—and led by the tough, the enraged and the young they picked up the lengths of timber and thin steel ribs and smashed the bricks they would never fire in

---

1. In the tale of the Pied Piper of Hamlin, the elders refused to pay the piper for freeing the town of rats and so he charmed the town's children into following him away forever.
2. Female spirits of Gaelic folklore; their wailing portends the coming of death.

yawning kilns, split the sacks of limestone they had not mixed or even been allowed to haul; tore the wire mesh, tipped over wheelbarrows and rolled forepoles down the bank, where they sailed far out on the icebound river.

Old and young, women and children, lame and hearty, they killed, as best they could, the tunnel they were forbidden to build.

They didn't mean to go in, to actually go down into the lip of the tunnel, but in their need to kill it all, all of it, to wipe from the face of the earth the work of the thin-armed Virginia boys, the bull-necked Greeks and the knife-faced men who waved the leaf-dead promise, they went too deep, too far . . .

A lot of them died there. The earth, now warm, shifted; the first forepole slipped; loose rock fell from the face of the tunnel and caused a shield to give way. They found themselves in a chamber of water, deprived of the sun that had brought them there. With the first crack and whoosh of water, the clamber to get out was so fierce that others who were trying to help were pulled to their deaths. Pressed up against steel ribs and timber blocks young boys strangled when the oxygen left them to join the water. Outside, others watched in terror as ice split and earth shook beneath their feet. Mrs. Jackson, weighing less than 100 pounds, slid down the bank and met with an open mouth the ice she had craved all her life. Tar Baby, Dessie, Ivy, Valentine, the Herrod boys, some of Ajax's younger brothers and the deweys (at least it was supposed; their bodies were never found)—all died there. Mr. Buckland Reed escaped, so did Patsy and her two boys, as well as some fifteen or twenty who had not gotten close enough to fall, or whose timidity would not let them enter an unfinished tunnel.

And all the while Shadrack stood there. Having forgotten his song and his rope, he just stood there high up on the bank ringing, ringing his bell.

1965

Things were so much better in 1965. Or so it seemed. You could go downtown and see colored people working in the dime store behind the counters, even handling money with cash-register keys around their necks. And a colored man taught mathematics at the junior high school. The young people had a look about them that everybody said was new but which reminded Nel of the deweys, whom nobody had ever found. Maybe, she thought, they had gone off and seeded the land and growed up in these young people in the dime store with the cash-register keys around their necks.

They were so different, these young people. So different from the way she remembered them forty years ago.

Jesus, there were some beautiful boys in 1921! Look like the whole world was bursting at the seams with them. Thirteen, fourteen, fifteen years old. Jesus, they were fine. L. P., Paul Freeman and his brother Jake, Mrs. Scott's twins—and Ajax had a whole flock of younger brothers. They hung out of attic windows, rode on car fenders, delivered the coal, moved into Medallion and moved out, visited cousins, plowed, hoisted, lounged on the church steps, careened on the school playground. The sun heated them and the moon slid down their backs. God, the world was *full* of beautiful boys in 1921.

Nothing like these kids. Everything had changed. Even the whores were better then: tough, fat, laughing women with burns on their cheeks and wit married to their meanness: or widows couched in small houses in the woods with eight children to feed and no man. These modern-day whores were pale and dull before those women. These little clothes-crazy things were always embarrassed. Nasty but shamed. They didn't know what shameless was. They should have known those silvery widows in the woods who would get up from the dinner table and walk into the trees with a customer with as much embarrassment as a calving mare.

Lord, how time flies. She hardly recognized anybody in the town any more. Now there was another old people's home. Look like this town just kept on building homes for old people. Every time they built a road they built a old folks' home. You'd think folks was living longer, but the fact of it was, they was just being put out faster.

Nel hadn't seen the insides of this most recent one yet, but it was her turn in Circle Number 5 to visit some of the old women there. The pastor visited them regularly, but the circle thought private visits were nice too. There were just nine colored women out there, the same nine that had been in the other one. But a lot of white ones. White people didn't fret about putting their old ones away. It took a lot for black people to let them go, and even if somebody was old and alone, others did the dropping by, the floor washing, the cooking. Only when they got crazy and unmanageable were they let go. Unless it was somebody like Sula, who put Eva away out of meanness. It was true that Eva was foolish in the head, but not so bad as to need locking up.

Nel was more than a little curious to see her. She had been really active in church only a year or less, and that was because the children were grown now and took up less time and less space in her mind. For over twenty-five years since Jude walked out she had pinned herself into a tiny life. She spent a little time trying to marry again, but nobody wanted to take her on with three children, and she simply couldn't manage the business of keeping boyfriends. During the war she had had a rather long relationship with a sergeant stationed at the camp twenty miles down river from Medallion, but then he got called away and everything was reduced to a few letters— then nothing. Then there was a bartender at the hotel. But now she was fifty-five and hard put to remember what all that had been about.

It didn't take long, after Jude left, for her to see what the future would be. She had looked at her children and knew in her heart that that would be all. That they were all she would ever know of love. But it was a love that, like a pan of syrup kept too long on the stove, had cooked out, leaving only its odor and a hard, sweet sludge, impossible to scrape off. For the mouths of her children quickly forgot the taste of her nipples, and years ago they had begun to look past her face into the nearest stretch of sky.

In the meantime the Bottom had collapsed. Everybody who had made money during the war moved as close as they could to the valley, and the white people were buying down river, cross river, stretching Medallion like two strings on the banks. Nobody colored lived much up in the Bottom any more. White people were building towers for television stations up there and there was a rumor about a golf course or something. Anyway, hill land was more valuable now, and those black people who had moved down right after the war and in the fifties couldn't afford to come back even if they wanted to. Except for the few blacks still huddled by the river bend, and some undemolished houses on Carpenter's Road, only rich white folks were building homes in the hills. Just like that, they had changed their minds and instead of keeping the valley floor to themselves, now they wanted a hilltop house with a river view and a ring of elms. The black people, for all their new look, seemed awfully anxious to get to the valley, or leave town, and abandon the hills to whoever was interested. It was sad, because the Bottom had been a real place. These young ones kept talking about the community, but they left the hills to the poor, the old, the stubborn—and the rich white folks. Maybe it hadn't been a community, but it had been a place. Now there weren't any places left, just separate houses with separate televisions and separate telephones and less and less dropping by.

These were the same thoughts she always had when she walked down into the town. One of the last true pedestrians, Nel walked the shoulder road while cars slipped by. Laughed at by her children, she still walked wherever she wanted to go, allowing herself to accept rides only when the weather required it.

Now she went straight through the town and turned left at its farthest end, along a tree-lined walk that turned into a country road farther on and passed the cemetery, Beechnut Park.

When she got to Sunnydale, the home for the aged, it was already four o'clock and turning chill. She would be glad to sit down with those old birds and rest her feet.

A red-haired lady at the desk gave her a pass card and pointed to a door that opened onto a corridor of smaller doors. It looked like what she imagined a college dormitory to be. The lobby was luxurious—modern—but the rooms she peeped into were sterile green cages. There was too much light everywhere; it needed some shadows. The third door, down the hall, had a little name tag over it that read EVA PEACE. Nel twisted the knob and rapped a little on the door at the same time, then listened a moment before she opened it.

At first she couldn't believe it. She seemed so small, sitting at that table in a black-vinyl chair. All the heaviness had gone and the height. Her once beautiful leg had no stocking and the foot was in a slipper. Nel wanted to cry—not for Eva's milk-dull eyes or her floppy lips, but for the once proud foot accustomed for over a half century to a fine well-laced shoe, now stuffed gracelessly into a pink terrycloth slipper.

"Good evening, Miss Peace. I'm Nel Greene come to pay a call on you. You remember me, don't you?"

Eva was ironing and dreaming of stairwells. She had neither iron nor clothes but did not stop her fastidious lining up of pleats or pressing out of wrinkles even when she acknowledged Nel's greeting.

"Howdy. Sit down."

"Thank you." Nel sat on the edge of the little bed. "You've got a pretty room, a real pretty room, Miss Peace."

"You eat something funny today?"

"Ma'am?"

"Some chop suey? Think back."

"No, ma'am."

"No? Well, you gone be sick later on."

"But I didn't have no chop suey."

"You think I come all the way over here for you to tell me that? I can't make visits too often. You should have some respect for old people."

"But Miss Peace, I'm visiting *you*. This is *your* room." Nel smiled.

"What you say your name was?"

"Nel Greene."

"Wiley Wright's girl?"

"Uh huh. You do remember. That makes me feel good, Miss Peace. You remember me and my father."

"Tell me how you killed that little boy."

"What? What little boy?"

"The one you threw in the water. I got oranges. How did you get him to go in the water?"

"I didn't throw no little boy in the river. That was Sula."

"You. Sula. What's the difference? You was there. You watched, didn't you? Me, I never would've watched."

"You're confused, Miss Peace. I'm Nel. Sula's dead."

"It's awful cold in the water. Fire is warm. How did you get him in?" Eva wet her forefinger and tested the iron's heat.

"Who told you all these lies? Miss Peace? Who told you? Why are you telling lies on me?"

"I got oranges. I don't drink they old orange juice. They puts something in it."

"Why are you trying to make out like I did it?"

Eva stopped ironing and looked at Nel. For the first time her eyes looked sane.

"You think I'm guilty?" Nel was whispering.

Eva whispered back, "Who would know that better than you?"

"I want to know who you been talking to." Nel forced herself to speak normally.

"Plum. Sweet Plum. He tells me things." Eva laughed a light, tinkly giggle—girlish.

"I'll be going now, Miss Peace." Nel stood.

"You ain't answered me yet."

"I don't know what you're talking about."

"Just alike. Both of you. Never was no difference between you. Want some oranges? It's better for you than chop suey. Sula? I got oranges."

Nel walked hurriedly down the hall, Eva calling after her, "Sula?" Nel couldn't see the other women today. That woman had upset her. She handed her pass back to the lady, avoiding her look of surprise.

Outside she fastened her coat against the rising wind. The top button was missing so she covered her throat with her hand. A bright space opened in her head and memory seeped into it.

Standing on the riverbank in a purple-and-white dress, Sula swinging

Chicken Little around and around. His laughter before the hand-slip and the water closing quickly over the place. What had she felt then, watching Sula going around and around and then the little boy swinging out over the water? Sula had cried and cried when she came back from Shadrack's house. But Nel had remained calm.

"*Shouldn't we tell?*"

"*Did he see?*"

"*I don't know. No.*"

"*Let's go. We can't bring him back.*"

What did old Eva mean by *you watched?* How could she help seeing it? She was right there. But Eva didn't say *see*, she said *watched*. "I did not watch it. I just saw it." But it was there anyway, as it had always been, the old feeling and the old question. The good feeling she had had when Chicken's hands slipped. She hadn't wondered about that in years. "Why didn't I feel bad when it happened? How come it felt so good to see him fall?"

All these years she had been secretly proud of her calm, controlled behavior when Sula was uncontrollable, her compassion for Sula's frightened and shamed eyes. Now it seemed that what she had thought was maturity, serenity and compassion was only the tranquillity that follows a joyful stimulation. Just as the water closed peacefully over the turbulence of Chicken Little's body, so had contentment washed over her enjoyment.

She was walking too fast. Not watching where she placed her feet, she got into the weeds by the side of the road. Running almost, she approached Beechnut Park. Just over there was the colored part of the cemetery. She went in. Sula was buried there along with Plum, Hannah and now Pearl. With the same disregard for name changes by marriage that the black people of Medallion always showed, each flat slab had one word carved on it. Together they read like a chant: PEACE 1895–1921, PEACE 1890–1923, PEACE 1910–1940, PEACE 1892–1959.

They were not dead people. They were words. Not even words. Wishes, longings.

All these years she had been harboring good feelings about Eva; sharing, she believed, her loneliness and unloved state as no one else could or did. She, after all, was the only one who really understood why Eva refused to attend Sula's funeral. The others thought they knew; thought the grandmother's reasons were the same as their own—that to pay respect to someone who had caused them so much pain was beneath them. Nel, who did go, believed Eva's refusal was not due to pride or vengeance but to a plain unwillingness to see the swallowing of her own flesh into the dirt, a determination not to let the eyes see what the heart could not hold.

Now, however, after the way Eva had just treated her, accused her, she wondered if the townspeople hadn't been right the first time. Eva *was* mean. Sula had even said so. There was no good reason for her to speak so. Feeble-minded or not. Old. Whatever. Eva knew what she was doing. Always had. She had stayed away from Sula's funeral and accused Nel of drowning Chicken Little for spite. The same spite that galloped all over the Bottom. That made every gesture an offense, every off-center smile a threat, so that even the bubbles of relief that broke in the chest of practically everybody when Sula died did not soften their spite and allow them to go to Mr. Hodges' funeral parlor or send flowers from the church or bake a yellow cake.

She thought about Nathan opening the bedroom door the day she had visited her, and finding the body. He said he knew she was dead right away not because her eyes were open but because her mouth was. It looked to him like a giant yawn that she never got to finish. He had run across the street to Teapot's Mamma, who, when she heard the news, said, "Ho!" like the conductor on the train when it was about to take off except louder, and then did a little dance. None of the women left their quilt patches in disarray to run to the house. Nobody left the clothes halfway through the wringer to run to the house. Even the men just said "uhn," when they heard. The day passed and no one came. The night slipped into another day and the body was still lying in Eva's bed gazing at the ceiling trying to complete a yawn. It was very strange, this stubbornness about Sula. For even when China, the most rambunctious whore in the town, died (whose black son and white son said, when they heard she was dying, "She ain't dead yet?"), even then everybody stopped what they were doing and turned out in numbers to put the fallen sister away.

It was Nel who finally called the hospital, then the mortuary, then the police, who were the ones to come. So the white people took over. They came in a police van and carried the body down the steps past the four pear trees and into the van for all the world as with Hannah. When the police asked questions nobody gave them any information. It took them hours to find out the dead woman's first name. The call was for a Miss Peace at 7 Carpenter's Road. So they left with that: a body, a name and an address. The white people had to wash her, dress her, prepare her and finally lower her. It was all done elegantly, for it was discovered that she had a substantial death policy. Nel went to the funeral parlor, but was so shocked by the closed coffin she stayed only a few minutes.

The following day Nel walked to the burying and found herself the only black person there, steeling her mind to the roses and pulleys. It was only when she turned to leave that she saw the cluster of black folk at the lip of the cemetery. Not coming in, not dressed for mourning, but there waiting. Not until the white folks left—the gravediggers, Mr. and Mrs. Hodges, and their young son who assisted them—did those black people from up in the Bottom enter with hooded hearts and filed eyes to sing "Shall We Gather at the River" over the curved earth that cut them off from the most magnificent hatred they had ever known. Their question clotted the October air, Shall We Gather at the River? The beautiful, the beautiful river? Perhaps Sula answered them even then, for it began to rain, and the women ran in tiny leaps through the grass for fear their straightened hair would beat them home.

Sadly, heavily, Nel left the colored part of the cemetery. Further along the road Shadrack passed her by. A little shaggier, a little older, still energetically mad, he looked at the woman hurrying along the road with the sunset in her face.

He stopped. Trying to remember where he had seen her before. The effort of recollection was too much for him and he moved on. He had to haul some trash out at Sunnydale and it would be good and dark before he got home. He hadn't sold fish in a long time now. The river had killed them all. No more silver-gray flashes, no more flat, wide, unhurried look. No more slowing down of gills. No more tremor on the line.

Shadrack and Nel moved in opposite directions, each thinking separate thoughts about the past. The distance between them increased as they both remembered gone things.

Suddenly Nel stopped. Her eye twitched and burned a little.

"Sula?" she whispered, gazing at the tops of trees. "Sula?"

Leaves stirred; mud shifted; there was the smell of over-ripe green things. A soft ball of fur broke and scattered like dandelion spores in the breeze.

"All that time, all that time, I thought I was missing Jude." And the loss pressed down on her chest and came up into her throat. "We was girls together," she said as though explaining something. "O Lord, Sula," she cried, "girl, girl, girlgirlgirl."

It was a fine cry—loud and long—but it had no bottom and it had no top, just circles and circles of sorrow.

1973

ERNEST J. GAINES
b. 1933

Ernest Gaines's childhood on a Louisiana plantation has been central to his development as a writer. A reservoir of the spoken wisdom and of the stories, historical settings, and dramas of the several generations of Creole, Cajun, and African American country people who still populate southern Louisiana, Gaines's writing draws on his early memories, which themselves are supplemented by frequent trips back to Pointe Coupee Parish.

Born to Manuel and Adrienne Gaines on January 15, 1933, in Oscar, Louisiana, young Ernest worked in the fields from an early age. He was particularly influenced by his aunt Augusteen Jefferson who, though she had no legs, was able to provide for him. She would become the model for the many inspiring older women in his fiction, especially Miss Jane Pittman in his immensely popular *The Autobiography of Miss Jane Pittman* (1971). While Gaines is probably known by most Americans for the television show based on *The Autobiography of Miss Jane Pittman,* he is decidedly a literary craftsman. Beginning with *Catherine Carmier* (1964), his still-neglected first novel, and *Bloodline* (1968), his first collection of short stories, he has dedicated himself to conveying the emotional and physical geographies of the twelve or fifteen plantations that once bound together the two small parishes whose fictional center is Bayonne and whose history he transcribed from "the early forties to the period of civil rights conflict in the sixties."

Gaines moved away from his home, so important to his writing, when he was fifteen and his mother and stepfather decided that there were more opportunities for him in California. In Vallejo, California, he enrolled in junior college. He read widely, especially admiring the works of nineteenth-century Russian novelists such as Turgenev, Gogol, and Tolstoy, whose chronicles of the strains serfdom put on their society were especially resonant for a young man who had just left the segregated South. In fact, Gaines has said that *Catherine Carmier,* while inspired by one of Lightning Hopkins's blues songs, was modeled on Turgenev's *Fathers and Sons.* The relationship between fathers and sons, especially as it relates to a definition of manhood, is a central theme in Gaines's works: in the short stories of *Bloodline*— especially *The Sky Is Gray* and *Three Men*—as well as in his novels *In My Father's House* (1978), *A Gathering of Old Men* (1983), and his most recent, *A Lesson before Dying* (1993).

In interviews, Gaines has explained that contemporary African American novelists Richard Wright and Ralph Ellison and even early-twentieth-century writer Jean Toomer were not influences for him because black writers were simply not on the curriculum of his college. Wright, he points out, would not have been important to him because of his urban focus. Instead, Gaines said, "I learned much about dialogue from Faulkner, especially when we're dealing with southern dialects. I learned rhythms and things from Gertrude Stein." As many critics have noted, Gaines's style is also influenced by that of Ernest Hemingway. Like that modernist Euro-American writer, Gaines has consistently attempted to capture in writing the speech of a particular region in America, in an understated yet vivid prose given to gesture and nuance through the apparently plain sentence.

After a two-year stint in the army, Gaines attended San Francisco State College, graduating in 1957. Then at the height of a literary renaissance triggered by the arrival in the mid-1950s of Beat writers such as Allen Ginsberg, Jack Kerouac, and others migrating from New York City to the West Coast, Gaines found himself living in San Francisco, an ideal place to be a beginning writer. While in college, Gaines had begun publishing his first short stories in a tiny campus publication called *Transfer,* where they were seen by Dorothea Oppenheimer, a literary agent who was instrumental in getting him a Wallace Stegner Fellowship at Stanford and in helping him publish his work. The result was a contract to produce a novel with Dial Press. As Gaines's literary career accelerated, so did his determination to locate his narratives firmly in one region.

"Knowing the place, knowing the people" is a project Gaines conceives of in the broadest possible terms. Understanding locale means being able to tap into a communal store of memories available through folklore and oral storytellers. Gaines has used a variety of strategies to achieve the "transfer" from oral lore to paper. Aware that he is capable, at best, of producing only approximations rather than literal copies of the actual speech each master storyteller uses, Gaines creates a heightened unifying voice "that compensate[s] . . . for not having the audience and the sound and the performance there." Early on, he realized that achieving "voice" meant giving the historical information back to the central characters. This is how Gaines describes this process, which he perfected in his first-person narrative *The Autobiography of Miss Jane Pittman:*

> I went to the Louisiana Room at the LSU library and I went through page after page. . . . Then I said, OK, I've got all this information and now I must go back here, Miss Jane . . . I must in some way—and that's how we come back to the voice thing—give her all this information and let her tell this thing the way she would tell it, as an illiterate black woman a hundred years old talking about these things. . . . I cannot just give her hunks of history and throw them to her, and have her describe, "It was Sunday at seven o'clock and Huey Long was going from New Orleans to such and such a place" . . . because she never would have spoken that way. . . . The historian would have been the one speaking that way.

So powerful was the resulting voice of the 108-year-old narrator that when *The Autobiography,* which became a best-seller, was later produced as a made-for-television movie, its critics protested the inclusion of a white reporter to whom Miss

Pittman narrates her tale. Beginning with childhood on a slave plantation and ending with a promise of desegregation in her native Bayonne, Jane Pittman's "autobiography" is Gaines's longest chronicle of change. Pittman witnesses the violence of the Reconstruction era, the establishment of the Jim Crow laws, and the protests of the early civil rights movement and lives to see legal segregation beginning to crumble.

Gaines's ability to suggest complex moral dilemmas with the barest physical description is his trademark. Not surprisingly, such succinctness has appealed to those who translate literary works into visual media. To date, A Gathering of Old Men and The Sky Is Gray, as well as the Autobiography of Miss Jane Pittman, have been filmed for television.

Gaines lives and writes in San Francisco while teaching as a writer-in-residence part of the year at the University of Southwestern Louisiana in Lafayette.

The Sky Is Gray

1

Go'n be coming in a few minutes. Coming round that bend down there full speed. And I'm go'n get out my handkerchief and wave it down, and we go'n get on it and go.

I keep on looking for it, but Mama don't look that way no more. She's looking down the road where we just come from. It's a long old road, and far's you can see you don't see nothing but gravel. You got dry weeds on both sides, and you got trees on both sides, and fences on both sides, too. And you got cows in the pastures and they standing close together. And when we was coming out here to catch the bus I seen the smoke coming out of the cows's noses.

I look at my mama and I know what she's thinking. I been with Mama so much, just me and her, I know what she's thinking all the time. Right now it's home—Auntie and them. She's thinking if they got enough wood—if she left enough there to keep them warm till we get back. She's thinking if it go'n rain and if any of them go'n have to go out in the rain. She's thinking 'bout the hog—if he go'n get out, and if Ty and Val be able to get him back in. She always worry like that when she leaves the house. She don't worry too much if she leave me there with the smaller ones, 'cause she know I'm go'n look after them and look after Auntie and everything else. I'm the oldest and she say I'm the man.

I look at my mama and I love my mama. She's wearing that black coat and that black hat and she's looking sad. I love my mama and I want put my arm round her and tell her. But I'm not supposed to do that. She say that's weakness and that's crybaby stuff, and she don't want no crybaby round her. She don't want you to be scared, either. 'Cause Ty's scared of ghosts and she's always whipping him. I'm scared of the dark, too, but I make 'tend I ain't. I make 'tend I ain't 'cause I'm the oldest, and I got to set a good sample for the rest. I can't ever be scared and I can't ever cry. And that's why I never said nothing 'bout my teeth. It's been hurting me and hurting me close to a month now, but I never said it. I didn't say it 'cause I didn't want act like a crybaby, and 'cause I know we didn't have enough money to go have it pulled. But, Lord, it been hurting me. And look like it wouldn't start till at night when you was trying to get yourself little sleep. Then soon 's you shut your eyes—ummm-ummm, Lord, look like it go right down to your heartstring.

"Hurting, hanh?" Ty'd say.

I'd shake my head, but I wouldn't open my mouth for nothing. You open your mouth and let that wind in, and it almost kill you.

I'd just lay there and listen to them snore. Ty there, right 'side me, and Auntie and Val over by the fireplace. Val younger than me and Ty, and he sleeps with Auntie. Mama sleeps round the other side with Louis and Walker.

I'd just lay there and listen to them, and listen to that wind out there, and listen to that fire in the fireplace. Sometimes it'd stop long enough to let me get little rest. Sometimes it just hurt, hurt, hurt. Lord, have mercy.

2

Auntie knowed it was hurting me. I didn't tell nobody but Ty, 'cause we buddies and he ain't go'n tell nobody. But some kind of way Auntie found out. When she asked me, I told her no, nothing was wrong. But she knowed it all the time. She told me to mash up a piece of aspirin and wrap it in some cotton and jugg it down in that hole. I did it, but it didn't do no good. It stopped for a little while, and started right back again. Auntie wanted to tell Mama, but I told her, "Uh-uh." 'Cause I knowed we didn't have any money, and it just was go'n make her mad again. So Auntie told Monsieur Bayonne, and Monsieur Bayonne came over to the house and told me to kneel down 'side him on the fireplace. He put his finger in his mouth and made the Sign of the Cross on my jaw. The tip of Monsieur Bayonne's finger is some hard, 'cause he's always playing on that guitar. If we sit outside at night we can always hear Monsieur Bayonne playing on his guitar. Sometimes we leave him out there playing on the guitar.

Monsieur Bayonne made the Sign of the Cross over and over on my jaw, but that didn't do no good. Even when he prayed and told me to pray some, too, that tooth still hurt me.

"How you feeling?" he say.

"Same," I say.

He kept on praying and making the Sign of the Cross and I kept on praying, too.

"Still hurting?" he say.

"Yes, sir."

Monsieur Bayonne mashed harder and harder on my jaw. He mashed so hard he almost pushed me over on Ty. But then he stopped.

"What kind of prayers you praying, boy?" he say.

"Baptist," I say.

"Well, I'll be—no wonder that tooth still killing him. I'm going one way and he pulling the other. Boy, don't you know any Catholic prayers?"

"I know 'Hail Mary,' " I say.

"Then you better start saying it."

"Yes, sir."

He started mashing on my jaw again, and I could hear him praying at the same time. And, sure enough, after while it stopped hurting me.

Me and Ty went outside where Monsieur Bayonne's two hounds was and we started playing with them. "Let's go hunting," Ty say. "All right," I say; and we went on back in the pasture. Soon the hounds got on a trail, and me and Ty followed them all 'cross the pasture and then back in the woods, too. And then they cornered this little old rabbit and killed him, and me and Ty made them get back, and we picked up the rabbit and started on back home. But my tooth had started hurting me again. It was hurting me plenty now, but I wouldn't tell Monsieur Bayonne. That night I didn't sleep a bit, and first thing in the morning Auntie told me to go back and let Monsieur Bayonne pray over me some more. Monsieur Bayonne was in his kitchen making coffee when I got there. Soon 's he seen me he knowed what was wrong.

"All right, kneel down there 'side that stove," he say. "And this time make sure you pray Catholic. I don't know nothing 'bout that Baptist, and I don't want know nothing 'bout him."

3

Last night Mama say, "Tomorrow we going to town."

"It ain't hurting me no more," I say. "I can eat anything on it."

"Tomorrow we going to town," she say.

And after she finished eating, she got up and went to bed. She always go to bed early now. 'Fore Daddy went in the Army, she used to stay up late. All of us sitting out on the gallery or round the fire. But now, look like soon 's she finish eating she go to bed.

This morning when I woke up, her and Auntie was standing 'fore the fireplace. She say: "Enough to get there and get back. Dollar and a half to have it pulled. Twenty-five for me to go, twenty-five for him. Twenty-five for me to come back, twenty-five for him. Fifty cents left. Guess I get little piece of salt meat with that."

"Sure can use it," Auntie say. "White beans and no salt meat ain't white beans."

"I do the best I can," Mama say.

They was quiet after that, and I made 'tend I was still asleep.

"James, hit the floor," Auntie say.

I still made 'tend I was asleep. I didn't want them to know I was listening.

"All right," Auntie say, shaking me by the shoulder. "Come on. Today's the day."

I pushed the cover down to get out, and Ty grabbed it and pulled it back.

"You, too, Ty," Auntie say.

"I ain't getting no teef pulled," Ty say.

"Don't mean it ain't time to get up," Auntie say. "Hit it, Ty."

Ty got up grumbling.

"James, you hurry up and get in your clothes and eat your food," Auntie say. "What time y'all coming back?" she say to Mama.

"That 'leven o'clock bus," Mama say. "Got to get back in that field this evening."

"Get a move on you, James," Auntie say.

I went in the kitchen and washed my face, then I ate my breakfast. I was having bread and syrup. The bread was warm and hard and tasted good. And I tried to make it last a long time.

Ty came back there grumbling and mad at me.

"Got to get up," he say. "I ain't having no teefes pulled. What I got to be getting up for?"

Ty poured some syrup in his pan and got a piece of bread. He didn't wash his hands, neither his face, and I could see that white stuff in his eyes.

"You the one getting your teef pulled," he say. "What I got to get up for. I bet if I was getting a teef pulled, you wouldn't be getting up. Shucks; syrup again. I'm getting tired of this old syrup. Syrup, syrup, syrup. I'm go'n take with the sugar diabetes. I want me some bacon sometime."

"Go out in the field and work and you can have your bacon," Auntie say. She stood in the middle door looking at Ty. "You better be glad you got syrup. Some people ain't got that—hard 's time is."

"Shucks," Ty say. "How can I be strong."

"I don't know too much 'bout your strength," Auntie say; "but I know where you go'n be hot at, you keep that grumbling up. James, get a move on you; your mama waiting."

I ate my last piece of bread and went in the front room. Mama was standing 'fore the fireplace warming her hands. I put on my coat and my cap, and we left the house.

1

I look down there again, but it still ain't coming. I almost say, "It ain't coming yet," but I keep my mouth shut. 'Cause that's something else she don't like. She don't like for you to say something just for nothing. She can see it ain't coming, I can see it ain't coming, so why say it ain't coming. I don't say it, I turn and look at the river that's back of us. It's so cold the smoke's just raising up from the water. I see a bunch of pool-doos not too far out—just on the other side the lilies. I'm wondering if you can eat pool-doos. I ain't too sure, 'cause I ain't never ate none. But I done ate owls and blackbirds, and I done ate redbirds, too. I didn't want kill the redbirds, but she made me kill them. They had two of them back there. One in my trap, one in Ty's trap. Me and Ty was go'n play with them and let them go, but she made me kill them 'cause we needed the food.

"I can't," I say. "I can't."

"Here," she say. "Take it."

"I can't," I say. "I can't. I can't kill him, Mama, please."

"Here," she say. "Take this fork, James."

"Please, Mama, I can't kill him," I say.

I could tell she was go'n hit me. I jerked back, but I didn't jerk back soon enough.

"Take it," she say.

I took it and reached in for him, but he kept on hopping to the back.

"I can't, Mama," I say. The water just kept on running down my face. "I can't," I say.

"Get him out of there," she say.

I reached in for him and he kept on hopping to the back. Then I reached in farther, and he pecked me on the hand.

"I can't, Mama," I say.

She slapped me again.

I reached in again, but he kept on hopping out my way. Then he hopped to one side and I reached there. The fork got him on the leg and I heard his leg pop. I pulled my hand out 'cause I had hurt him.

"Give it here," she say, and jerked the fork out my hand.

She reached in and got the little bird right in the neck. I heard the fork go in his neck, and I heard it go in the ground. She brought him out and helt him right in front of me.

"That's one," she say. She shook him off and gived me the fork. "Get the other one."

"I can't, Mama," I say. "I'll do anything, but don't make me do that."

She went to the corner of the fence and broke the biggest switch over there she could find. I knelt 'side the trap, crying.

"Get him out of there," she say.

"I can't, Mama."

She started hitting me 'cross the back. I went down on the ground, crying.

"Get him," she say.

"Octavia?" Auntie say.

'Cause she had come out of the house and she was standing by the tree looking at us.

"Get him out of there," Mama say.

"Octavia," Auntie say, "explain to him. Explain to him. Just don't beat him. Explain to him."

But she hit me and hit me and hit me.

I'm still young—I ain't no more than eight; but I know now; I know why I had to do it. (They was so little, though. They was so little. I 'member how I picked the feathers off them and cleaned them and helt them over the fire. Then we all ate them. Ain't had but a little bitty piece each, but we all had a little bitty piece, and everybody just looked at me 'cause they was so proud.) Suppose she had to go away? That's why I had to do it. Suppose she had to go away like Daddy went away? Then who was go'n look after us? They had to be somebody left to carry on. I didn't know it then, but I know it now. Auntie and Monsieur Bayonne talked to me and made me see.

5

Time I see it I get out my handkerchief and start waving. It's still 'way down there, but I keep waving anyhow. Then it come up and stop and me and Mama get on. Mama tell me go sit in the back while she pay. I do like she say, and the people look at me. When I pass the little sign that say "White" and "Colored," I start looking for a seat. I just see one of them back there, but I don't take it, 'cause I want my mama to sit down herself. She comes in the back and sit down, and I lean on the seat. They got seats in the front, but I know I can't sit there, 'cause I have to sit back of the sign. Anyhow, I don't want sit there if my mama go'n sit back here.

They got a lady sitting 'side my mama and she looks at me and smiles little bit. I smile back, but I don't open my mouth, 'cause the wind'll get in and make that tooth ache. The lady take out a pack of gum and reach me a slice, but I shake my head. The lady just can't understand why a little boy'll turn down gum and she reach me a slice again. This time I point to my jaw. The lady understands and smiles little bit, and I smile little bit, but I don't open my mouth, though.

They got a girl sitting 'cross from me. She got on a red overcoat and her hair's plaited in one big plait. First, I make 'tend I don't see her over there, but then I start looking at her little bit. She make 'tend she don't see me, either, but I catch her looking that way. She got a cold, and every now and then she h'ist[1] that little handkerchief to her nose. She ought to blow it, but she don't. Must think she's too much a lady or something.

Every time she h'ist that little handkerchief, the lady 'side her say something in her ear. She shakes her head and lays her hands in her lap again. Then I catch her kind of looking where I'm at. I smile at her little bit. But think she'll smile back? Uh-uh. She just turn up her little old nose and turn her head. Well, I show her both of us can turn us head. I turn mine too and look out at the river.

The river is gray. The sky is gray. They have pool-doos on the water. The water is wavy, and the pool-doos go up and down. The bus go round a turn, and you got plenty trees hiding the river. Then the bus go round another turn, and I can see the river again.

I look toward the front where all the white people sitting. Then I look at that little old gal again. I don't look right at her, 'cause I don't want all them people to know I love her. I just look at her little bit, like I'm looking out that window over there. But she knows I'm looking that way, and she kind of look at me, too. The lady sitting 'side her catch her this time, and she leans over and says something in her ear.

"I don't love him nothing," that little old gal says out loud.

Everybody back there hear her mouth, and all of them look at us and laugh.

"I don't love you, either," I say. "So you don't have to turn up your nose, Miss."

"You the one looking," she say.

"I wasn't looking at you," I say. "I was looking out that window, there."

"Out that window, my foot," she say. "I seen you. Everytime I turned round you was looking at me."

"You must of been looking yourself if you seen me all them times," I say.

"Shucks," she say, "I got me all kind of boyfriends."

"I got girlfriends, too," I say.

"Well, I just don't want you getting your hopes up," she say.

I don't say no more to that little old gal 'cause I don't want have to bust her in the mouth. I lean on the seat where Mama sitting, and I don't even look that way no more. When we get to Bayonne, she jugg her little old

1. Hoist.

tongue out at me. I make 'tend I'm go'n hit her, and she duck down 'side her mama. And all the people laugh at us again.

6

Me and Mama get off and start walking in town. Bayonne is a little bitty town. Baton Rouge is a hundred times bigger than Bayonne. I went to Baton Rouge once—me, Ty, Mama, and Daddy. But that was 'way back yonder, 'fore Daddy went in the Army. I wonder when we go'n see him again. I wonder when. Look like he ain't ever coming back home.... Even the pavement all cracked in Bayonne. Got grass shooting right out the side-walk. Got weeds in the ditch, too; just like they got at home.

It's some cold in Bayonne. Look like it's colder than it is home. The wind blows in my face, and I feel that stuff running down my nose. I sniff. Mama says use that handkerchief. I blow my nose and put it back.

We pass a school and I see them white children playing in the yard. Big old red school, and them children just running and playing. Then we pass a café, and I see a bunch of people in there eating. I wish I was in there 'cause I'm cold. Mama tells me keep my eyes in front where they belong.

We pass stores that's got dummies, and we pass another café, and then we pass a shoe shop, and that bald-head man in there fixing on a shoe. I look at him and I butt into that white lady, and Mama jerks me in front and tells me stay there.

We come up to the courthouse, and I see the flag waving there. This flag ain't like the one we got at school. This one here ain't got but a handful of stars. One at school got a big pile of stars—one for every state. We pass it and we turn and there it is—the dentist office. Me and Mama go in, and they got people sitting everywhere you look. They even got a little boy in there younger than me.

Me and Mama sit on that bench, and a white lady come in there and ask me what my name is. Mama tells her and the white lady goes on back. Then I hear somebody hollering in there. Soon's that little boy hear him hollering, he starts hollering, too. His mama pats him and pats him, trying to make him hush up, but he ain't thinking 'bout his mama.

The man that was hollering in there comes out holding his jaw. He is a big old man and he's wearing overalls and a jumper.

"Got it, hanh?" another man asks him.

The man shakes his head—don't want open his mouth.

"Man, I thought they was killing you in there," the other man says. "Hol-lering like a pig under a gate."

The man don't say nothing. He just heads for the door, and the other man follows him.

"John Lee," the white lady says. "John Lee Williams."

The little boy juggs his head down in his mama's lap and holler more now. His mama tells him go with the nurse, but he ain't thinking 'bout his mama. His mama tells him again, but he don't even hear her. His mama picks him up and takes him in there, and even when the white lady shuts the door I can still hear little old John Lee.

"I often wonder why the Lord let a child like that suffer," a lady says to

my mama. The lady's sitting right in front of us on another bench. She's got
on a white dress and a black sweater. She must be a nurse or something
herself, I reckon.

"Not us to question," a man says.

"Sometimes I don't know if we shouldn't," the lady says.

"I know definitely we shouldn't," the man says. The man looks like a
preacher. He's big and fat and he's got on a black suit. He's got a gold
chain, too.

"Why?" the lady says.

"Why anything?" the preacher says.

"Yes," the lady says. "Why anything?"

"Not us to question," the preacher says.

The lady looks at the preacher a little while and looks at Mama again.

"And look like it's the poor who suffers the most," she says. "I don't understand it."

"Best not to even try," the preacher says. "He works in mysterious ways—
wonders to perform."

Right then little John Lee bust out hollering, and everybody turn they
head to listen.

"He's not a good dentist," the lady says. "Dr. Robillard is much better.
But more expensive. That's why most of the colored people come here.
The white people go to Dr. Robillard. Y'all from Bayonne?"

"Down the river," my mama says. And that's all she go'n say, 'cause she
don't talk much. But the lady keeps on looking at her, and so she says,
"Near Morgan."

"I see," the lady says.

7

"That's the trouble with the black people in this country today," somebody else says. This one here's sitting on the same side me and Mama's
sitting, and he is kind of sitting in front of that preacher. He looks like a
teacher or somebody that goes to college. He's got on a suit, and he's got a
book that he's been reading. "We don't question is exactly our problem,"
he says. "We should question and question and question—question everything."

The preacher just looks at him a long time. He done put a toothpick or
something in his mouth, and he just keeps on turning it and turning it. You
can see he don't like that boy with that book.

"Maybe you can explain what you mean," he says.

"I said what I meant," the boy says. "Question everything. Every stripe,
every star, every word spoken. Everything."

"It 'pears to me that this young lady and I was talking 'bout God, young
man," the preacher says.

"Question Him, too," the boy says.

"Wait," the preacher says. "Wait now."

"You heard me right," the boy says. "His existence as well as everything
else. Everything."

The preacher just looks across the room at the boy. You can see he's getting madder and madder. But mad or no mad, the boy ain't thinking 'bout him. He looks at that preacher just 's hard 's the preacher looks at him.

"Is this what they coming to?" the preacher says. "Is this what we educating them for?"

"You're not educating me," the boy says. "I wash dishes at night so that I can go to school in the day. So even the words you spoke need questioning."

The preacher just looks at him and shakes his head.

"When I come in this room and seen you there with your book, I said to myself, 'There's an intelligent man.' How wrong a person can be."

"Show me one reason to believe in the existence of a God," the boy says.

"My heart tells me," the preacher says.

" 'My heart tells me,' " the boy says. " 'My heart tells me.' Sure, 'My heart tells me.' And as long as you listen to what your heart tells you, you will have only what the white man gives you and nothing more. Me, I don't listen to my heart. The purpose of the heart is to pump blood throughout the body, and nothing else."

"Who's your paw, boy?" the preacher says.

"Why?"

"Who is he?"

"He's dead."

"And your mom?"

"She's in Charity Hospital with pneumonia. Half killed herself, working for nothing."

"And 'cause he's dead and she's sick, you mad at the world?"

"I'm not mad at the world. I'm questioning the world. I'm questioning it with cold logic, sir. What do words like Freedom, Liberty, God, White, Colored mean? I want to know. That's why you are sending us to school, to read and to ask questions. And because we ask these questions, you call us mad. No sir, it is not us who are mad."

"You keep saying 'us'?"

" 'Us.' Yes—us. I'm not alone."

The preacher just shakes his head. Then he looks at everybody in the room—everybody. Some of the people look down at the floor, keep from looking at him. I kind of look 'way myself, but soon 's I know he done turn his head, I look that way again.

"I'm sorry for you," he says to the boy.

"Why?" the boy says. "Why not be sorry for yourself? Why are you so much better off than I am? Why aren't you sorry for these other people in here? Why not be sorry for the lady who had to drag her child into the dentist office? Why not be sorry for the lady sitting on that bench over there? Be sorry for them. Not for me. Some way or the other I'm going to make it."

"No, I'm sorry for you," the preacher says.

"Of course, of course," the boy says, nodding his head. "You're sorry for me because I rock that pillar you're leaning on."

"You can't ever rock the pillar I'm leaning on, young man. It's stronger than anything man can ever do."

"You believe in God because a man told you to believe in God," the boy says. "A white man told you to believe in God. And why? To keep you ignorant so he can keep his feet on your neck."

"So now we the ignorant?" the preacher says.

"Yes," the boy says. "Yes." And he opens his book again.

The preacher just looks at him sitting there. The boy done forgot all about him. Everybody else make 'tend they done forgot the squabble, too.

Then I see that preacher getting up real slow. Preacher's a great big old man and he got to brace himself to get up. He comes over where the boy is sitting. He just stands there a little while looking down at him, but the boy don't raise his head.

"Get up, boy," preacher says.

The boy looks up at him, then he shuts his book real slow and stands up. Preacher just hauls back and hit him in the face. The boy falls back 'gainst the wall, but he straightens himself up and looks right back at that preacher.

"You forgot the other cheek," he says.

The preacher hauls back and hit him again on the other side. But this time the boy braces himself and don't fall.

"That hasn't changed a thing," he says.

The preacher just looks at the boy. The preacher's breathing real hard like he just run up a big hill. The boy sits down and opens his book again.

"I feel sorry for you," the preacher says. "I never felt so sorry for a man before."

The boy makes 'tend he don't even hear that preacher. He keeps on reading his book. The preacher goes back and gets his hat off the chair.

"Excuse me," he says to us. "I'll come back some other time. Y'all, please excuse me."

And he looks at the boy and goes out the room. The boy h'ist his hand up to his mouth one time to wipe 'way some blood. All the rest of the time he keeps on reading. And nobody else in there say a word.

8

Little John Lee and his mama come out the dentist office, and the nurse calls somebody else in. Then little bit later they come out, and the nurse calls another name. But fast 's she calls somebody in there, somebody else comes in the place where we sitting, and the room stays full.

The people coming in now, all of them wearing big coats. One of them says something 'bout sleeting, another one says he hope not. Another one says he think it ain't nothing but rain. 'Cause, he says, rain can get awful cold this time of year.

All round the room they talking. Some of them talking to people right by them, some of them talking to people clear 'cross the room, some of them talking to anybody'll listen. It's a little bitty room, no bigger than us kitchen, and I can see everybody in there. The little old room's full of smoke, 'cause you got two old men smoking pipes over by that side door. I think I feel my tooth thumping me some, and I hold my breath and wait. I wait and wait, but it don't thump me no more. Thank God for that.

I feel like going to sleep, and I lean back 'gainst the wall. But I'm scared to go to sleep. Scared 'cause the nurse might call my name and I won't hear her. And Mama might go to sleep, too, and she'll be mad if neither one of us heard the nurse.

I look up at Mama. I love my mama. I love my mama. And when cotton come I'm go'n get her a new coat. And I ain't go'n get a black one, either. I think I'm go'n get her a red one.

"They got some books over there," I say. "Want read one of them?"

Mama looks at the books, but she don't answer me.

"You got yourself a little man there," the lady says.

Mama don't say nothing to the lady, but she must've smiled, 'cause I seen the lady smiling back. The lady looks at me a little while, like she's feeling sorry for me.

"You sure got that preacher out here in a hurry," she says to that boy.

The boy looks up at her and looks in his book again. When I grow up I want be just like him. I want clothes like that and I want keep a book with me, too.

"You really don't believe in God?" the lady says.

"No," he says.

"But why?" the lady says.

"Because the wind is pink," he says.

"What?" the lady says.

The boy don't answer her no more. He just reads in his book.

"Talking 'bout the wind is pink," that old lady says. She's sitting on the same bench with the boy and she's trying to look in his face. The boy makes 'tend the old lady ain't even there. He just keeps on reading. "Wind is pink," she says again. "Eh, Lord, what children go'n be saying next?"

The lady 'cross from us bust out laughing.

"That's a good one," she says. "The wind is pink. Yes sir, that's a good one."

"Don't you believe the wind is pink?" the boys says. He keeps his head down in the book.

"Course I believe it, honey," the lady says. "Course I do." She looks at us and winks her eye. "And what color is grass, honey?"

"Grass? Grass is black."

She bust out laughing again. The boy looks at her.

"Don't you believe grass is black?" he says.

The lady quits her laughing and looks at him. Everybody else looking at him, too. The place quiet, quiet.

"Grass is green, honey," the lady says. "It was green yesterday, it's green today, and it's go'n be green tomorrow."

"How do you know it's green?"

"I know because I know."

"You don't know it's green," the boy says. "You believe it's green because someone told you it was green. If someone had told you it was black you'd believe it was black."

"It's green," the lady says. "I know green when I see green."

"Prove it's green," the boy says.

"Sure, now," the lady says. "Don't tell me it's coming to that."

"It's coming to just that," the boy says. "Words mean nothing. One means no more than the other."

"That's what it all coming to?" that old lady says. That old lady got on a turban and she got on two sweaters. She got a green sweater under a black sweater. I can see the green sweater 'cause some of the buttons on the other sweater's missing.

"Yes ma'am," the boy says. "Words mean nothing. Action is the only thing. Doing. That's the only thing."

"Other words, you want the Lord to come down here and show Hisself to you?" she says.

"Exactly, ma'am," he says.

"You don't mean that, I'm sure?" she says.

"I do, ma'am," he says.

"Done, Jesus," the old lady says, shaking her head.

"I didn't go 'long with that preacher at first," the other lady says; "but now—I don't know. When a person say the grass is black, he's either a lunatic or something's wrong."

"Prove to me that it's green," the boy says.

"It's green because the people say it's green."

"Those same people say we're citizens of these United States," the boy says.

"I think I'm a citizen," the lady says.

"Citizens have certain rights," the boy says. "Name me one right that you have. One right, granted by the Constitution, that you can exercise in Bayonne."

The lady don't answer him. She just looks at him like she don't know what he's talking 'bout. I know I don't.

"Things changing," she says.

"Things are changing because some black men have begun to think with their brains and not their hearts," the boy says.

"You trying to say these people don't believe in God?"

"I'm sure some of them do. Maybe most of them do. But they don't believe that God is going to touch these white people's hearts and change things tomorrow. Things change through action. By no other way."

Everybody sit quiet and look at the boy. Nobody says a thing. Then the lady 'cross the room from me and Mama just shakes her head.

"Let's hope that not all your generation feel the same way you do," she says.

"Think what you please, it doesn't matter," the boy says. "But it will be men who listen to their heads and not their hearts who will see that your children have a better chance than you had."

"Let's hope they ain't all like you, though," the old lady says. "Done forgot the heart absolutely."

"Yes ma'am, I hope they aren't all like me," the boy says. "Unfortunately, I was born too late to believe in your God. Let's hope that the ones who come after will have your faith—if not in your God, then in something else, something definitely that they can lean on. I haven't anything. For me, the wind is pink, the grass is black."

9

The nurse comes in the room where we all sitting and waiting and says the doctor won't take no more patients till one o'clock this evening. My mama jumps up off the bench and goes up to the white lady.

"Nurse, I have to go back in the field this evening," she says.

"The doctor is treating his last patient now," the nurse says. "One o'clock this evening."

"Can I at least speak to the doctor?" my mama asks.

"I'm his nurse," the lady says.

"My little boy's sick," my mama says. "Right now his tooth almost killing him."

The nurse looks at me. She's trying to make up her mind if to let me come in. I look at her real pitiful. The tooth ain't hurting me at all, but Mama say it is, so I make 'tend for her sake.

"This evening," the nurse says, and goes on back in the office.

"Don't feel 'jected, honey," the lady says to Mama. "I been round them a long time—they take you when they want to. If you was white, that's something else; but we the wrong color."

Mama don't say nothing to the lady, and me and her go outside and stand 'gainst the wall. It's cold out there. I can feel that wind going through my coat. Some of the other people come out of the room and go up the street. Me and Mama stand there a little while and we start walking. I don't know where we going. When we come to the other street we just stand there.

"You don't have to make water, do you?" Mama says.

"No, ma'am," I say.

We go on up the street. Walking real slow. I can tell Mama don't know where she's going. When we come to a store we stand there and look at the dummies. I look at a little boy wearing a brown overcoat. He's got on brown shoes, too. I look at my old shoes and look at his'n again. You wait till summer, I say.

Me and Mama walk away. We come up to another store and we stop and look at them dummies, too. Then we go on again. We pass a café where the white people in there eating. Mama tells me keep my eyes in front where they belong, but I can't help from seeing them people eat. My stomach starts to growling 'cause I'm hungry. When I see people eating, I get hungry; when I see a coat, I get cold.

A man whistles at my mama when we go by a filling station. She makes 'tend she don't even see him. I look back and I feel like hitting him in the mouth. If I was bigger, I say; if I was bigger, you'd see.

We keep on going. I'm getting colder and colder, but I don't say nothing. I feel that stuff running down my nose and I sniff.

"That rag," Mama says.

I get it out and wipe my nose. I'm getting cold all over now—my face, my hands, my feet, everything. We pass another little café, but this'n for white people, too, and we can't go in there, either. So we just walk. I'm so cold now I'm 'bout ready to say it. If I knowed where we was going I wouldn't be so cold, but I don't know where we going. We go, we go, we go. We walk clean out of Bayonne. Then we cross the street and we come back. Same thing I seen when I got off the bus this morning. Same old trees, same old walk, same old weeds, same old cracked pave[2]—same old everything.

I sniff again.

"That rag," Mama says.

I wipe my nose real fast and jugg that handkerchief back in my pocket 'fore my hand gets too cold. I raise my head and I can see David's hardware store. When we come up to it, we go in. I don't know why, but I'm glad.

It's warm in there. It's so warm in there you don't ever want to leave. I look for the heater, and I see it over by them barrels. Three white men standing round the heater talking in Creole. One of them comes over to see what my mama want.

"Got any axe handles?" she says.

Me, Mama and the white man start to the back, but Mama stops me when we come up to the heater. She and the white man go on. I hold my hands over the heater and look at them. They go all the way to the back, and I see the white man pointing to the axe handles 'gainst the wall. Mama takes one of them and shakes it like she's trying to figure how much it weighs. Then she rubs her hand over it from one end to the other end. She turns it over and looks at the other side, then she shakes it again, and shakes her head and puts it back. She gets another one and she does it just like she did the first one, then she shakes her head. Then she gets a brown one and do it that, too. But she don't like this one, either. Then she gets another one, but 'fore she shakes it or anything, she looks at me. Look like she's trying to say something to me, but I don't know what it is. All I know is I done got warm now and I'm feeling right smart better. Mama shakes this axe handle just like she did the others, and shakes her head and says something to the white man. The white man just looks at his pile of axe handles, and when Mama pass him to come to the front, the white man just scratch his head and follows her. She tells me come on and we go on out and start walking again.

We walk and walk, and no time at all I'm cold again. Look like I'm colder now 'cause I can still remember how good it was back there. My stomach growls and I suck it in to keep Mama from hearing it. She's walking right 'side me, and it growls so loud you can hear it a mile. But Mama don't say a word.

10

When we come up to the courthouse, I look at the clock. It's got quarter to twelve. Mean we got another hour and a quarter to be out here in the cold. We go and stand 'side a building. Something hits my cap and I look up at the sky. Sleet's falling.

I look at Mama standing there. I want stand close 'side her, but she don't like that. She say that's crybaby stuff. She say you got to stand for yourself, by yourself.

2. I.e., pavement.

"Let's go back to that office," she says.

We cross the street. When we get to the dentist office I try to open the door, but I can't. I twist and twist, but I can't. Mama pushes me to the side and she twist the knob, but she can't open the door, either. She turns 'way from the door. I look at her, but I don't move and I don't say nothing. I done seen her like this before and I'm scared of her.

"You hungry?" she says. She says it like she's mad at me, like I'm the cause of everything.

"No, ma'am," I say.

"You want eat and walk back, or you rather don't eat and ride?"

"I ain't hungry," I say.

I ain't just hungry, but I'm cold, too. I'm so hungry and cold I want to cry. And look like I'm getting colder and colder. My feet done got numb. I try to work my toes, but I don't even feel them. Look like I'm go'n die. Look like I'm go'n stand right here and freeze to death. I think 'bout home. I think 'bout Val and Auntie and Ty and Louis and Walker. It's 'bout twelve o'clock and I know they eating dinner now. I can hear Ty making jokes. He done forgot 'bout getting up early this morning and right now he's probably making jokes. Always trying to make somebody laugh. I wish I was right there listening to him. Give anything in the world if I was home round the fire.

"Come on," Mama says.

We start walking again. My feet so numb I can't hardly feel them. We turn the corner and go on back up the street. The clock on the courthouse starts hitting for twelve.

The sleet's coming down plenty now. They hit the pave and bounce like rice. Oh, Lord; oh, Lord, I pray. Don't let me die, don't let me die, don't let me die, Lord.

11

Now I know where we going. We going back of town where the colored people eat. I don't care if I don't eat. I been hungry before. I can stand it. But I can't stand the cold.

I can see we go'n have a long walk. It's 'bout a mile down there. But I don't mind. I know when I get there I'm go'n warm myself. I think I can hold out. My hands numb in my pockets and my feet numb, too, but if I keep moving I can hold out. Just don't stop no more, that's all.

The sky's gray. The sleet keeps on falling. Falling like rain now—plenty, plenty. You can hear it hitting the pave. You can see it bouncing. Sometimes it bounces two times 'fore it settles.

We keep on going. We don't say nothing. We just keep on going, keep on going.

I wonder what Mama's thinking. I hope she ain't mad at me. When summer come I'm go'n pick plenty cotton and get her a coat. I'm go'n get her a red one.

I hope they'd make it summer all the time. I'd be glad if it was summer all the time—but it ain't. We got to have winter, too. Lord, I hate the winter. I guess everybody hate the winter.

I don't sniff this time. I get out my handkerchief and wipe my nose. My hands's so cold I can hardly hold the handkerchief.

I think we getting close, but we ain't there yet. I wonder where everybody is. Can't see a soul but us. Look like we the only two people moving round today. Must be too cold for the rest of the people to move round in.

I can hear my teeth. I hope they don't knock together too hard and make that bad one hurt. Lord, that's all I need, for that bad one to start off.

I hear a church bell somewhere. But today ain't Sunday. They must be ringing for a funeral or something.

I wonder what they doing at home. They must be eating. Monsieur Bayonne might be there with his guitar. One day Ty played with Monsieur Bayonne's guitar and broke one of the strings. Monsieur Bayonne was some mad with Ty. He say Ty wasn't go'n ever 'mount to nothing. Ty can go just like Monsieur Bayonne when he ain't there. Ty can make everybody laugh when he starts to mocking Monsieur Bayonne.

I used to like to be with Mama and Daddy. We used to be happy. But they took him in the Army. Now, nobody happy no more. . . . I be glad when Daddy comes home.

Monsieur Bayonne say it wasn't fair for them to take Daddy and give Mama nothing and give us nothing. Auntie say, "Shhh, Etienne. Don't let them hear you talk like that." Monsieur Bayonne say, "It's God truth. What they giving his children? They have to walk three and a half miles to school hot or cold. That's anything to give for a paw? She's got to work in the field rain or shine just to make ends meet. That's anything to give for a husband?" Auntie say, "Shhh, Etienne, shhh." "Yes, you right," Monsieur Bayonne say. "Best don't say it in front of them now. But one day they go'n find out. One day." "Yes, I suppose so," Auntie say. "Then what, Rose Mary?" Monsieur Bayonne say. "I don't know, Etienne," Auntie say. "All we can do is us job, and leave everything else in His hand . . ."

We getting closer, now. We getting closer. I can even see the railroad tracks.

We cross the tracks, and now I see the café. Just to get in there, I say. Just to get in there. Already I'm starting to feel little better.

12

We go in. Ahh, it's good. I look for the heater; there 'gainst the wall. One of them little brown ones. I just stand there and hold my hands over it. I can't open my hands too wide 'cause they almost froze.

Mama's standing right 'side me. She done unbuttoned her coat. Smoke rises out of the coat, and the coat smells like a wet dog.

I move to the side so Mama can have more room. She opens out her hands and rubs them together. I rub mine together, too, 'cause this keep them from hurting. If you let them warm too fast, they hurt you sure. But if you let them warm just little bit at a time, and you keep rubbing them, they be all right every time.

They got just two more people in the café. A lady back of the counter, and a man on this side the counter. They been watching us ever since we come in.

Mama gets out the handkerchief and count up the money. Both of us know how much money she's got there. Three dollars. No, she ain't got three dollars, 'cause she had to pay us way up here. She ain't got but two dollars and a half left. Dollar and a half to get my tooth pulled, and fifty cents for us to go back on, and fifty cents worth of salt meat.

She stirs the money round with her finger. Most of the money is change 'cause I can hear it rubbing together. She stirs it and stirs it. Then she looks at the door. It's still sleeting. I can hear it hitting 'gainst the wall like rice.

"I ain't hungry, Mama," I say.

"Got to pay them something for they heat," she says.

She takes a quarter out the handkerchief and ties the handkerchief up again. She looks over her shoulder at the people, but she still don't move. I hope she don't spend the money. I don't want her spending it on me. I'm hungry, I'm almost starving I'm so hungry, but I don't want her spending the money on me.

She flips the quarter over like she's thinking. She's must be thinking 'bout us walking back home. Lord, I sure don't want walk home. If I thought it'd do any good to say something, I'd say it. But Mama makes up her own mind 'bout things.

She turns 'way from the heater right fast, like she better hurry up and spend the quarter 'fore she change her mind. I watch her go toward the counter. The man and the lady look at her, too. She tells the lady something and the lady walks away. The man keeps on looking at her. Her back's turned to the man, and she don't even know he's standing there.

The lady puts some cakes and a glass of milk on the counter. Then she pours up a cup of coffee and sets it 'side the other stuff. Mama pays her for the things and comes on back where I'm standing. She tells me sit down at the table 'gainst the wall.

The milk and the cakes's for me; the coffee's for Mama. I eat slow and I look at her. She's looking outside at the sleet. She's looking real sad. I say to myself, I'm go'n make all this up one day. You see, one day, I'm go'n make all this up. I want say it now; I want tell her how I feel right now; but Mama don't like for us to talk like that.

"I can't eat all this," I say.

They ain't got but just three little old cakes there. I'm so hungry right now, the Lord knows I can eat a hundred times three, but I want my mama to have one.

Mama don't even look my way. She knows I'm hungry, she knows I want it. I let it stay there a little while, then I get it and eat it. I eat just on my front teeth, though, 'cause if cake touch that back tooth I know what'll happen. Thank God it ain't hurt me at all today.

After I finish eating I see the man go to the juke box. He drops a nickel in it, then he just stand there a little while looking at the record. Mama tells me keep my eyes in front where they belong. I turn my head like she say, but then I hear the man coming toward us.

"Dance, pretty?" he says.

Mama gets up to dance with him. But 'fore you know it, she done grabbed the little man in the collar and done heaved him 'side the wall. He hit the wall so hard he stop the juke box from playing.

"Some pimp," the lady back of the counter says. "Some pimp."

The little man jumps up off the floor and starts toward my mama. 'Fore you know it, Mama done sprung open her knife and she's waiting for him.

"Come on," she says. "Come on. I'll gut you from your neighbo[3] to your throat. Come on."

I go up to the little man to hit him, but Mama makes me come and stand 'side her. The little man looks at me and Mama and goes on back to the counter.

"Some pimp," the lady back of the counter says. "Some pimp." She starts laughing and pointing at the little man. "Yes sir, you a pimp, all right. Yes sir-ree."

13

"Fasten that coat, let's go," Mama says.

"You don't have to leave," the lady says.

Mama don't answer the lady, and we right out in the cold again. I'm warm right now—my hands, my ears, my feet—but I know this ain't go'n last too long. It done sleet so much now you got ice everywhere you look.

We cross the railroad tracks, and soon's we do, I get cold. That wind goes through this little old coat like it ain't even there. I got on a shirt and a sweater under the coat, but that wind don't pay them no mind. I look up and I can see we got a long way to go. I wonder if we go'n make it 'fore I get too cold.

We cross over to walk on the sidewalk. They got just one sidewalk back here, and it's over there.

After we go just a little piece, I smell bread cooking. I look, then I see a baker shop. When we get closer, I can smell it more better. I shut my eyes and make 'tend I'm eating. But I keep them shut too long and I butt up 'gainst a telephone post. Mama grabs me and see if I'm hurt. I ain't bleeding or nothing and she turns me loose.

I can feel I'm getting colder and colder, and I look up to see how far we still got to go. Uptown is 'way up yonder. A half mile more, I reckon. I try to think of something. They say think and you won't get cold. I think of that poem, "Annabel Lee."[4] I ain't been to school in so long—this bad weather—I reckon they done passed "Annabel Lee" by now. But passed it or not, I'm sure Miss Walker go'n make me recite it when I get there. That woman don't never forget nothing. I ain't never seen nobody like that in my life.

I'm still getting cold. "Annabel Lee" or no "Annabel Lee," I'm still getting cold. But I can see we getting closer. We getting there gradually.

Soon 's we turn the corner, I see a little old white lady up in front of us. She's the only lady on the street. She's all in black and she's got a long black rag over her head.

"Stop," she says.

Me and Mama stop and look at her. She must be crazy to be out in all

---

3. Knee bone.
4. By American poet and fiction writer Edgar Allen Poe (1809–1849).

this bad weather. Ain't got but a few other people out there, and all of them's men.

"Y'all done ate?" she says.

"Just finish," Mama says.

"Y'all must be cold then?" she says.

"We headed for the dentist," Mama says. "We'll warm up when we get there."

"What dentist?" the old lady says. "Mr. Bassett?"

"Yes, ma'am," Mama says.

"Come on in," the old lady says. "I'll telephone him and tell him y'all coming."

Me and Mama follow the old lady in the store. It's a little bitty store, and it don't have much in there. The old lady takes off her head rag and folds it up.

"Helena?" somebody calls from the back.

"Yes, Alnest?" the old lady says.

"Did you see them?"

"They're here. Standing beside me."

"Good. Now you can stay inside."

The old lady looks at Mama. Mama's waiting to hear what she brought us in here for. I'm waiting for that, too.

"I saw y'all each time you went by," she says. "I came out to catch you, but you were gone."

"We went back of town," Mama says.

"Did you eat?"

"Yes, ma'am."

The old lady looks at Mama a long time, like she's thinking Mama might be just saying that. Mama looks right back at her. The old lady looks at me to see what I have to say. I don't say nothing. I sure ain't going 'gainst my mama.

"There's food in the kitchen," she says to Mama. "I've been keeping it warm."

Mama turns right around and starts for the door.

"Just a minute," the old lady says. Mama stops. "The boy'll have to work for it. It isn't free."

"We don't take no handout," Mama says.

"I'm not handing out anything," the old lady says. "I need my garbage moved to the front. Ernest has a bad cold and can't go out there."

"James'll move it for you," Mama says.

"Not unless you eat," the old lady says. "I'm old, but I have my pride, too, you know."

Mama can see she ain't go'n beat this old lady down, so she just shakes her head.

"All right," the old lady says. "Come into the kitchen."

She leads the way with that rag in her hand. The kitchen is a little bitty little old thing, too. The table and the stove just 'bout fill it up. They got a little room to the side. Somebody in there laying 'cross the bed—'cause I can see one of his feet. Must be the person she was talking to: Ernest or Alnest—something like that.

"Sit down," the old lady says to Mama. "Not you," she says to me. "You have to move the cans."

"Helena?" the man says in the other room.

"Yes, Alnest?" the old lady says.

"Are you going out there again?"

"I must show the boy where the garbage is, Alnest," the old lady says.

"Keep that shawl over your head," the old man says.

"You don't have to remind me, Alnest. Come, boy," the old lady says.

We go out in the yard. Little old back yard ain't no bigger than the store or the kitchen. But it can sleet here just like it can sleet in any big back yard. And 'fore you know it, I'm trembling.

"There," the old lady says, pointing to the cans. I pick up one of the cans and set it right back down. The can's so light, I'm go'n see what's inside of it.

"Here," the old lady says. "Leave that can alone."

I look back at her standing there in the door. She's got that black rag wrapped round her shoulders, and she's pointing one of her little old fingers at me.

"Pick it up and carry it to the front," she says. I go by her with the can, and she's looking at me all the time. I'm sure the can's empty. I'm sure she could've carried it herself—maybe both of them at the same time. "Set it on the sidewalk by the door and come back for the other one," she says.

I go and come back, and Mama looks at me when I pass her. I get the other can and take it to the front. It don't feel a bit heavier than that first one. I tell myself I ain't go'n be nobody's fool, and I'm go'n look inside this can to see just what I been hauling. First, I look up the street, then down the street. Nobody coming. Then I look over my shoulder toward the door. That little old lady done slipped up there quiet 's mouse, watching me again. Look like she knowed what I was go'n do.

"Ehh, Lord," she says. "Children, children. Come in here, boy, and go wash your hands."

I follow her in the kitchen. She points toward the bathroom, and I go in there and wash up. Little bitty old bathroom, but it's clean, clean. I don't use any of her towels; I wipe my hands on my pants legs.

When I come back in the kitchen, the old lady done dished up the food. Rice, gravy, meat—and she even got some lettuce and tomato in a saucer. She even got a glass of milk and a piece of cake there, too. It looks so good, I almost start eating 'fore I say my blessing.

"Helena?" the old man says.

"Yes, Alnest?"

"Are they eating?"

"Yes," she says.

"Good," he says. "Now you'll stay inside."

The old lady goes in there where he is and I can hear them talking. I look at Mama. She's eating slow like she's thinking. I wonder what's the matter now. I reckon she's thinking 'bout home.

The old lady comes back in the kitchen.

"I talked to Dr. Bassett's nurse," she says. "Dr. Bassett will take you as soon as you get there."

"Thank you, ma'am," Mama says.

"Perfectly all right," the old lady says. "Which one is it?"

Mama nods toward me. The old lady looks at me real sad. I look sad, too.

"You're not afraid, are you?" she says.

"No, ma'am," I say.

"That's a good boy," the old lady says. "Nothing to be afraid of. Dr. Bassett will not hurt you."

When me and Mama get through eating, we thank the old lady again.

"Helena, are they leaving?" the old man says.

"Yes, Alnest."

"Tell them I say good-bye."

"They can hear you, Alnest."

"Good-bye both mother and son," the old man says. "And may God be with you."

Me and Mama tell the old man good-bye, and we follow the old lady in the front room. Mama opens the door to go out, but she stops and comes back in the store.

"You sell salt meat?" she says.

"Yes."

"Give me two bits worth."

"That isn't very much salt meat," the old lady says.

"That's all I have," Mama says.

The old lady goes back of the counter and cuts a big piece off the chunk. Then she wraps it up and puts it in a paper bag.

"Two bits," she says.

"That looks like awful lot of meat for a quarter," Mama says.

"Two bits," the old lady says. "I've been selling salt meat behind this counter twenty-five years. I think I know what I'm doing."

"You got a scale there," Mama says.

"What?" the old lady says.

"Weigh it," Mama says.

"What?" the old lady says. "Are you telling me how to run my business?"

"Thanks very much for the food," Mama says.

"Just a minute," the old lady says.

"James," Mama says to me. I move toward the door.

"Just one minute, I said," the old lady says.

Me and Mama stop again and look at her. The old lady takes the meat out of the bag and unwraps it and cuts 'bout half of it off. Then she wraps it up again and juggs it back in the bag and gives the bag to Mama. Mama lays the quarter on the counter.

"Your kindness will never be forgotten," she says. "James," she says to me.

We go out, and the old lady comes to the door to look at us. After we go a little piece I look back, and she's still there watching us.

The sleet's coming down heavy, heavy now, and I turn up my coat collar to keep my neck warm. My mama tells me turn it right back down.

"You not a bum," she says. "You a man."

1963

AUDRE LORDE

1934–1992

Possibly the best-known African American feminist lesbian poet, essayist, and theorist, Audre Lorde was born Audrey Geraldine Lorde in Harlem, New York, to a Grenedian mother, Linda Belmar, and an African American father, Frederic Byron Lorde. In her many writings, Lorde integrated a strong sense of responsibility to the truth with the collective history and experiences of blacks, especially women, in Africa, the Caribbean, and the United States. One result of that fusion was her articulation of the concept of difference as a dialogue, as an energizing charge rather than a threat. The emphasis on difference in Lorde's poetry, and especially in her major essay collection, *Sister Outsider* (1984), was fueled by her belief that she must claim her many identities—"black, lesbian, feminist, mother, lover, poet"—identities that might seem to be in contradiction with one another. Lorde's reevaluation of the meaning of difference was a major theoretical contribution to the study of race, gender, and sexuality.

Lorde's early experiences are a key to her evolution as a poet and thinker. As a child, she had difficulty learning to talk; indeed, she did not speak until she was five, and then in only a limited way. Lorde went to Catholic schools in New York, where she learned early how it felt to be a "sister outsider." In 1951, she enrolled at Hunter College, where she would later be a distinguished professor and where she met poet Diane Di Prima, who would be the editor of her first volume of poems. She did not graduate from Hunter until 1959, because, in order to support herself, she had to work as an x-ray technician and in a factory, among other jobs. She also went for a year, 1954, to the National University of Mexico; there for the first time she began to speak in full sentences. In 1961, she earned an M.A. in library science from Columbia University. She then worked as a librarian in New York City, married, had two children—a daughter and a son—and divorced in 1970.

A crucial experience for Lorde during the 1960s was her time as poet-in-residence at Tougaloo College, in Mississippi. There, during the height of black cultural nationalism, she finished her first volume of poetry, *The First Cities* (1968). This book was innovative for the times because, as black nationalist critic Dudley Randall put it, Lorde "does not wave a black flag, but her blackness is there, implicit in the bone." Her second collection, *Cables to Rage* (1970), explored marital love and betrayal and especially child rearing and included her first explicit reference to her own homosexuality.

During the 1970s, Lorde published most of the poetry for which she is best known—in all, five volumes: *From a Land Where Other People Live* (1973), which was nominated for the National Book Award; *The New York Head Shop and Museum* (1974), considered by critics her most radical volume; *Between Ourselves*, a chapbook of possibly her most quoted poem; *Coal* (1976), her first volume to be released by a major publisher; and *The Black Unicorn* (1978), in which she used African mythology, especially in relation to women. For its provocative and genuine use of African religion, culture, and art, critic Robert Stepto called this volume, "an event in contemporary letters." Feminist poet Adrienne Rich also praised *The Black Unicorn*, for its complexity, its "poems of elemental wildness and healing, nightmare and lucidity."

Central to Lorde's prose, all of which she published in the 1980s, is the claiming of many identities. *The Cancer Journals* (1980) is the first exploration by a black woman of her experience with breast cancer, published some ten years before that disease was acknowledged to be epidemic among American women. A collage of essays and journal entries, A *Burst of Light* (1988) is preoccupied with Lorde's struggle with cancer, as she faced the meaning of her probable death. Between these two volumes, Lorde published her biomythography, *Zami: A New Spelling of My Name* (1984), in which she blurred the literary genres of autobiography, fiction, myth, and poetry—suggesting that literary genres are themselves a construct. *Zami* is also the first account of a black lesbian growing up in homophobic America.

Possibly her most influential book, *Sister Outsider: Essays and Speeches* (1984) charts the development of Lorde's ideas in a distilled, compressed form. Essays such as *Poetry Is Not a Luxury* and *The Transformation of Silence into Language and Action* emphasize an idea central to Lorde's work: that those whom society has marginalized must speak, especially when they are afraid, if they are to empower themselves. *The Uses of the Erotic* explores the power of the erotic as political, an idea central to feminist theory and to the study of sexuality, while essays such as *The Master's Tools Will Never Dismantle the Master's House* and *Age, Race, Class and Sex: Women Redefining Difference* analyze how difference is a "dynamic human force which is enriching rather than threatening to the defined self."

Though Lorde had been known as a poet, and though she continued to write and publish poems in the 1980s, it was her prose that first generated much of the critical response to her work. Ironically, despite her insistence on claiming all her identities, critics often focus on just one part of her person and work. So white feminist-lesbians have tended to respond only to her lesbianism, blacks to her race activism, literary critics to her poetic craft, mother goddess followers to her African goddesses.

In the years just before her death, Audre Lorde returned to the Caribbean, the birthplace of her mother. Knowing that she was near death, she prepared a final volume of poems, which she titled *Undersong: Chosen Poems Old and New* (1992). In her preface she tells us that

> For every poem written, there is the bedrock of experience(s) within which the poem is anchored. A molten hot light shines up through the poem from the core of these experiences. This is the human truth that illuminates the poem surrounding the light that makes it come alive.

In her poetry, prose, and essays, Lorde's integrity illuminates the struggle to generate that "molten hot light," the "undersong" necessary to the just world she envisioned. Following her death in St. Croix in 1992, women throughout the United States, Europe, and the Caribbean held tributes to her; and euologies to her were printed in virtually every major U.S. women's journal, an indication of her importance as a black feminist poet and theorist and a portent of the serious critical attention that is now being given her poetry and essays.

Father Son and Holy Ghost

I have not ever seen my father's grave.
Not that his judgment eyes have been forgotten
Nor his great hands print
On our evening doorknobs
One half turn each night and he would come   5

Misty from the world's business
Massive and silent as the whole day's wish, ready
To re-define each of our shapes—
But that now the evening doorknobs
Wait, and do not recognize us as we pass.   10

Each week a different woman
Regular as his one quick glass each evening—
Pulls up the grass his stillness grows
Calling it weed. Each week
A different woman has my mother's face   15
And he, who time has
Changeless
Must be amazed, who knew and loved but one.

My father died in silence, loving creation
And well-defined response.   20
He lived still judgments on familiar things
And died, knowing a January fifteenth that year me.

Lest I go into dust
I have not ever seen my father's grave.

1960

The Winds of Orisha [1]

I

This land will not always be foreign.
How many of its women ache to bear their stories
robust and screaming like the earth erupting grain
or thrash in padded chains mute as bottles
hands fluttering traces of resistance   5
on the backs of once lovers
half the truth
knocking in the brain like an angry steampipe
how many
long to work or split open   10
so bodies venting into silence
can plan the next move?

Tiresias [2] took 500 years they say to progress into woman
growing smaller and darker and more powerful
until nut-like, she went to sleep in a bottle   15
Tiresias took 500 years to grow into woman
so do not despair of your sons.

1. Gods and goddesses—divine personifications—
of the Yoruba peoples of western Nigeria.
2. In Greek mythology a blind soothsayer who appears in many legends, among them the story of
Oedipus. One account has it that he was turned
into a woman after killing the female of a pair of
mating snakes.

II

Impatient legends speak through my flesh
changing this earths formation
spreading   20
I will become myself
an incantation
dark raucous many-shaped characters
leaping back and forth across bland pages
and Mother Yemanja[3] raises her breasts to begin my labor   25
near water
the beautiful Oshun and I lie down together
in the heat of her body truth my voice comes stronger
Shango will be my brother roaring out of the sea
earth shakes our darkness swelling into each other   30
warning winds will announce us living
as Oya, Oya my sister my daughter
destroys the crust of the tidy beaches
and Eshu's black laughter turns up the neat sleeping sand.

III

The heart of this country's tradition is its wheat men   35
dying for money
dying for water for markets for power
over all people's children
they sit in their chains on their dry earth
before nightfall   40
telling tales as they wait for their time
of completion
hoping the young ones can hear them
earth-shaking fears wreathe their blank weary faces
most of them have spent their lives and their wives   45
in labor
most of them have never seen beaches
but as Oya my sister moves out of the mouths
of their sons and daughters against them
I will swell up from the pages of their daily heralds   50
leaping out of the almanacs
instead of an answer to their search for rain they will read me
the dark cloud
meaning something entire
and different.   55

When the winds of Orisha blow
even the roots of grass
quicken.

                                     1970

---

3. The mother of all the Orisha and also the goddess of oceans; from her breasts are said to flow rivers. The
names in this stanza are those of other Orisha, among them Eshu, the trickster.

Coal

I
Is the total black, being spoken
From the earth's inside.
There are many kinds of open.
How a diamond comes into a knot of flame   5
How a sound comes into a word, coloured
By who pays what for speaking.

Some words are open
Like a diamond on glass windows
Singing out within the crash of passing sun   10
Then there are words like stapled wagers
In a perforated book—buy and sign and tear apart—
And come whatever wills all chances
The stub remains
An ill-pulled tooth with a ragged edge.   15
Some words live in my throat
Breeding like adders. Others know sun
Seeking like gypsies over my tongue
To explode through my lips
Like young sparrows bursting from shell.   20
Some words
Bedevil me.

Love is a word another kind of open—
As a diamond comes into a knot of flame
I am black because I come from the earth's inside   25
Take my word for jewel in your open light.

                                            1976

Now That I Am Forever with Child

How the days went
While you were blooming within me
I remember each up each—
The swelling changed planes of my body—
And how you first fluttered, then jumped   5
And I thought it was my heart.

How the days wound down
And the turning of winter
I recall, with you growing heavy
Against the wind. I thought   10
Now her hands
Are formed, and her hair
Has started to curl
Now her teeth are done
Now she sneezes.   15
Then the seed opened.

I bore you one morning just before spring—
My head rang like a firey piston
My legs were towers between which
A new world was passing.   20

From then
I can only distinguish
One thread within running hairs
You . . . flowing through selves
Toward you.   25

1976

A Litany for Survival

For those of us who live at the shoreline
standing upon the constant edges of decision
crucial and alone
for those of us who cannot indulge
the passing dreams of choice   5
who love in doorways coming and going
in the hours between dawns
looking inward and outward
at once before and after
seeking a now that can breed   10
futures
like bread in our children's mouths
so their dreams will not reflect
the death of ours;

For those of us   15
who were imprinted with fear
like a faint line in the center of our foreheads
learning to be afraid with our mother's milk
for by this weapon
this illusion of some safety to be found   20
the heavy-footed hoped to silence us
For all of us
this instant and this triumph
We were never meant to survive.

And when the sun rises we are afraid   25
it might not remain
when the sun sets we are afraid
it might not rise in the morning
when our stomachs are full we are afraid
of indigestion   30
when our stomachs are empty we are afraid
we may never eat again
when we are loved we are afraid
love will vanish
when we are alone we are afraid   35
love will never return
and when we speak we are afraid

our words will not be heard
nor welcomed
but when we are silent   40
we are still afraid.

So it is better to speak
remembering
we were never meant to survive.

                                                    1978

The Evening News

First rule of the road: attend quiet victims first.

I am kneading my bread Winnie Mandela[1]
while children who sing in the streets of Soweto[2]
are jailed for inciting to riot
the moon in Soweto is mad   5
is bleeding my sister into the earth
is mixing her seed with the vultures'
greeks reap her like olives out of the trees
she is skimmed like salt
from the skin of a hungry desert   10
while the Ganvie fisherwomen with milk-large breasts
hide a fish with the face of a small girl
in the prow of their boats.

Winnie Mandela I am feeling your face
with pain of my crippled fingers   15
our children are escaping their births
in the streets of Soweto and Brooklyn
(what does it mean
our wars
being fought by our children?)   20

Winnie Mandela our names are like olives, salt, sand
the opal, amber, obsidian that hide their shape well.
We have never touched shaven foreheads together
yet how many of our sisters' and daughters' bones
whiten in secret   25
whose names we have not yet spoken
whose names we have never spoken
I have never heard their names spoken.

*Second rule of the road: any wound will stop bleeding if you press
    down hard enough.*

                                                    1979

---

1. Controversial African National Congress activist and leader (b. 1936) and estranged wife of South
African president Nelson Mandela.

2. A group of African townships near Johannesburg, South Africa; in the late 1970s the site of severe rioting and violence.

Poetry Is Not a Luxury

The quality of light by which we scrutinize our lives has direct bearing upon the product which we live, and upon the changes which we hope to bring about through those lives. It is within this light that we form those ideas by which we pursue our magic and make it realized. This is poetry as illumination, for it is through poetry that we give name to those ideas which are—until the poem—nameless and formless, about to be birthed, but already felt. That distillation of experience from which true poetry springs births thought as dream births concept, as feeling births idea, as knowledge births (precedes) understanding.

As we learn to bear the intimacy of scrutiny and to flourish within it, as we learn to use the products of that scrutiny for power within our living, those fears which rule our lives and form our silences begin to lose their control over us.

For each of us as women, there is a dark place within, where hidden and growing our true spirit rises, "beautiful/and tough as chestnut/stanchions against (y)our nightmare of weakness/"[1] and of impotence.

These places of possibility within ourselves are dark because they are ancient and hidden; they have survived and grown strong through that darkness. Within these deep places, each one of us holds an incredible reserve of creativity and power, of unexamined and unrecorded emotion and feeling. The woman's place of power within each of us is neither white nor surface; it is dark, it is ancient, and it is deep.

When we view living in the european mode only as a problem to be solved, we rely solely upon our ideas to make us free, for these were what the white fathers told us were precious.

But as we come more into touch with our own ancient, noneuropean consciousness of living as a situation to be experienced and interacted with, we learn more and more to cherish our feelings, and to respect those hidden sources of our power from where true knowledge and, therefore, lasting action comes.

At this point in time, I believe that women carry within ourselves the possibility for fusion of these two approaches so necessary for survival, and we come closest to this combination in our poetry. I speak here of poetry as a revelatory distillation of experience, not the sterile word play that, too often, the white fathers distorted the word *poetry* to mean—in order to cover a desperate wish for imagination without insight.

For women, then, poetry is not a luxury. It is a vital necessity of our existence. It forms the quality of the light within which we predicate our hopes and dreams toward survival and change, first made into language, then into idea, then into more tangible action. Poetry is the way we help give name to the nameless so it can be thought. The farthest horizons of our hopes and fears are cobbled by our poems, carved from the rock experiences of our daily lives.

As they become known to and accepted by us, our feelings and the honest exploration of them become sanctuaries and spawning grounds for the

---

1. From Lorde's 1973 poem *Black Mother Woman.*

most radical and daring of ideas. They become a safe-house for that difference so necessary to change and the conceptualization of any meaningful
action. Right now, I could name at least ten ideas I would have found intolerable or incomprehensible and frightening, except as they came after
dreams and poems. This is not idle fantasy, but a disciplined attention to
the true meaning of "it feels right to me." We can train ourselves to respect
our feelings and to transpose them into a language so they can be shared.
And where that language does not yet exist, it is our poetry which helps to
fashion it. Poetry is not only dream and vision; it is the skeleton architecture of our lives. It lays the foundations for a future of change, a bridge
across our fears of what has never been before.

Possibility is neither forever nor instant. It is not easy to sustain belief in
its efficacy. We can sometimes work long and hard to establish one beachhead of real resistance to the deaths we are expected to live, only to have
that beachhead assaulted or threatened by those canards we have been so-
cialized to fear, or by the withdrawal of those approvals that we have been
warned to seek for safety. Women see ourselves diminished or softened by
the falsely benign accusations of childishness, of nonuniversality, of
changeability, of sensuality. And who asks the question: Am I altering your
aura, your ideas, your dreams, or am I merely moving you to temporary and
reactive action? And even though the latter is no mean task, it is one that
must be seen within the context of a need for true alteration of the very
foundations of our lives.

The white fathers told us: I think, therefore I am. The Black mother
within each of us—the poet—whispers in our dreams: I feel, therefore I can
be free. Poetry coins the language to express and charter this revolutionary
demand, the implementation of that freedom.

However, experience has taught us that action in the now is also necessary, always. Our children cannot dream unless they live, they cannot live
unless they are nourished, and who else will feed them the real food without which their dreams will be no different from ours? "If you want us to
change the world someday, we at least have to live long enough to grow
up!" shouts the child.

Sometimes we drug ourselves with dreams of new ideas. The head will
save us. The brain alone will set us free. But there are no new ideas still
waiting in the wings to save us as women, as human. There are only old
and forgotten ones, new combinations, extrapolations and recognitions
from within ourselves—along with the renewed courage to try them out.
And we must constantly encourage ourselves and each other to attempt the
heretical actions that our dreams imply, and so many of our old ideas disparage. In the forefront of our move toward change, there is only poetry to
hint at possibility made real. Our poems formulate the implications of ourselves, what we feel within and dare make real (or bring action into accordance with), our fears, our hopes, our most cherished terrors.

For within living structures defined by profit, by linear power, by institutional dehumanization, our feelings were not meant to survive. Kept
around as unavoidable adjuncts or pleasant pastimes, feelings were expected to kneel to thought as women were expected to kneel to men. But
women have survived. As poets. And there are no new pains. We have felt

them all already. We have hidden that fact in the same place where we have hidden our power. They surface in our dreams, and it is our dreams that point the way to freedom. Those dreams are made realizable through our poems that give us the strength and courage to see, to feel, to speak, and to dare.

If what we need to dream, to move our spirits most deeply and directly toward and through promise, is discounted as a luxury, then we give up the core—the fountain—of our power, our womanness; we give up the future of our worlds.

For there are no new ideas. There are only new ways of making them felt—of examining what those ideas feel like being lived on Sunday morning at 7 A.M., after brunch, during wild love, making war, giving birth, mourning our dead—while we suffer the old longings, battle the old warnings and fears of being silent and impotent and alone, while we taste new possibilities and strengths.

1977

COLLEEN McELROY
b. 1935

A poet and short story writer with an intense sense of place, Colleen McElroy was born in St. Louis to Ruth Celeste and Purcia Purcell Rawls. After her parents divorced in 1938, McElroy and her mother moved in with her grandmother, whose full-length boudoir mirror and wind-up Victrola began what McElroy has called "her romance with language." In 1943 her mother married an army sergeant, Jesse Dalton Johnson, and McElroy began the life of an "army brat," moving often. By the time she was twenty-one, she had lived in St. Louis; Wyoming; Munich, Germany, where she attended college; and Kansas City, where she received her B.A. After studying in the speech and hearing program at the University of Pittsburgh, she returned to Kansas City and did graduate work in neurological and language learning patterns, married, had two children, and was divorced. She then migrated to Washington State and became the director of Speech and Hearing Services at Western Washington University. After receiving a Ph.D. in ethnolinguistic patterns of dialect differences and oral traditions from the University of Washington, McElroy became a professor of English at that university. As her poems dramatize, she has traveled extensively, to Europe, South America, Japan, Majorca, Africa, and Southeast Asia.

It was in her thirties that McElroy started writing seriously. She remarried, this time to poet David McElroy, and lived in Bellingham, Washington, the home of many writers. At the same time that she was receiving encouragement to write from poets such as Richard Hugo, Robert Huff, and Denise Levertov, she was also discovering the works of black poets such as Langston Hughes, Joseph S. Cotter, Anne Spencer, Robert Hayden, Gwendolyn Brooks, and Margaret Walker. Both her realization that Keats and Yeats need not be her only role models and her developing passion for the landscape of the Pacific Northwest—the mountains, the ocean, the rain—triggered the writing of her first poems, works that would be collected in a 1973 chapbook, *The Mules Done Long Since Gone*. Another collection, *Winters without Snow*, was published in 1979; McElroy acknowledges that it details the pain of her second divorce. In 1983, McElroy became the first black woman to be promoted to full professor at the University of Washington. Also that year her collection *Queen of the Ebony Isles* was selected for the Wesleyan University Press Poetry Series. *Queen* would receive the American Book Award in 1985.

Since 1985 McElroy has published two short-story collections and two poetic memoirs. In addition, she has demonstrated a talent for drama, writing with Ishmael Reed the choreopoem *The Wild Gardens of the Loup Garou* as well as the play *Follow the Drinking Gourd*, about Harriet Tubman, and many television scripts. One measure of her increasing importance as a poet is the publication of her *What Madness Brought Me Here: Collected Poems, 1968–1988*. Throughout her career, travel and coming face to face with the new remain crucial themes for McElroy. As she herself has said, "Each piece of writing is a new port of call, full of surprises and disappointments, pleasures and intrigue."

Pike Street[1] Bus

Poem, we're going this way,
With that bus,
Its driver fat and full
Of unspent words like you.
Tell them about it, poem.   5

It starts this way,
A slow lumbering thing
Turning the corner.
Then the lead line drops.
The bus is stuck like   10

The driver's face
In the rearview mirror
As he watches sparks dance
In front of Pike Market,[2]
Watches the line throw fire.   15
The broccoli's put away,
Apples gone, fish face sideways
In neat rows under a layer
Of white paper.
There's heavy breathing   20
On the bus.

The driver's face is swollen,
The grey evening settles
In lines around his mouth.
His belly peeks out, dull white   25
Where a missing button
Lets his shirt stand open.
He leaves the bus, catching sight
Of the lead line hanging
Toward the broken pavement.   30
A few faces turn to watch;
Others look sideways.
She stares straight on,
Her black face tired,

1. In Seattle.   2. Large produce, fish, and meat market.

Her arms remembering forty offices,   35
Mop handle imprints still cling
To her palms. Her eyes are old
Before her time.

Say it for her, poem.
Tell her dreams of places   40
Where she's always young,
Smiling and sitting straight
Like the picture that stares out
From her dresser. She's crisp;
Caught by the camera alive,   45
In love, not knowing this night,
This bus.

Ignore the drunk that staggers on,
Lurching toward the coin box.
He hangs at an angle   50
Against Seattle's fading sun.
He leans back, falling
Into his past, using his coins
For balance before diving
For the slot; a handful   55
Of attention on his face
As the change drops.

Plunging toward a seat
Smashing against her feet
And dreams, his mind leaves   60
Him once again. She rubs
Her cleaning woman knees,
Stroking toward the pain on the floor.
Extra fat on her chin bobbing
As she remembers how she last saw   65
Her man; sitting barefoot
Atop a kettledrum, pounding
At an eight-hour day.

                                                       1976

The Griots Who Know Brer Fox[1]

There are old drunks among the tenements,
old men who have been
                    lost
forever from families, shopping centers
starched shirts and   5
                    birthdays.
They are the griots, the storytellers
whose faces are knotted and swollen

---

1. African American folklore character known for his cunning. "Griots": African storytellers who preserve
by performance the history of the group.

into a black patchwork
of open sores and   10
old scabs; disease
transforms the nose
into cabbage   the eyes
are dried egg yolks.
They grind old tobacco between scabby gums   15
like ancient scarabs rolling dung from tombs
in their
                    mother country.
In this country, they are scenic, part of the
view from Route 1, Old Town.   20

Don't miss them; they sit in doorways
of boarded houses in the part of town
nestled between wide roads named for
English kings and tourists.
             These old men sit like moldy stumps   25
             among the broken bricks of narrow
             carriage streets   streets paved
             with the Spirits of '76,
             the Westward Movement and Oz.
These old men never travel the wide roads;   30
they sit in the dusk, dark skinned as Aesop,
remember their youth. They chant stories
to keep themselves awake another day;
             tales of girls bathing in kitchens
             before wood stoves, smells of   35
                    the old South.
             Or Northern tales of babies bitten
             by rats, women who've left them
             or how they were once rich.
They'll spin a new Brer Rabbit story for a nickel;   40
tell you how he slipped past the whistle-slick fox
to become
                    the Abomey[2] king.
But you must listen closely;
it moves fast, their story   45
skipping and jumping childlike;
the moral hidden in an enchanted forest
                    of word games.
             These stories are priceless,
             prized by movie moguls   50
             who dream of Saturday matinees
             and full houses.
You have to look beyond the old men's faces,
beyond the rat that waits to nibble the hand
when they sleep. The face is anonymous,   55
                    you can find it anywhere
but the words are as prized
as the curved tusks of the bull elephant.

                                            1979

2. City in the West African nation of Benin (formerly Dahomey), known for its fine brass figurines.

Tapestries

when I was eight I listened to stories of love
and etiquette while my mother's sisters
sat on Grandma's horsehair sofa
naked under their starched dresses
words flew from their fingers   5
in a dance as old as the moon
but I dreamed of other places
of dark bodies bending
to a language too dreamlike
and concise to decode   10

above them a tapestry desert stretched
into distant corners where I imagined
ancient rituals grotesque and graceful
conjuring up the moon-flecked
seasons of the earth   15
but my mother's sisters wove tales
that collapsed the world
into sarcastic snips of language
their black thighs opened
billows of powdery musk   20
rising from their legs like dust
from some raw and haunting land

I had a choice
two scenes their dark secrets
spread for my viewing   25
the usual desert palm trees camels
a cautious rug merchant one hand
on the tent, face turned towards the horizon
turning back like Thomas Jefferson
towards his black *anima*, like Lot's wife [1]   30
or the thousands of black women
who fled slavery preferring instead
the monastic beds of the River Niger [2]

it is said those waters flowed
red for years   35
shades of ochre fuchsia and russet
as layers of blood sifted
through the silt of the river
the velvet sands on that tapestry
were red and flowed into all corners   40
my aunts sat in a line beneath this scene
refusing to turn back
wagging their heads against the world's sins

1. Lot was a biblical figure, who, warned by two angels, fled from the doomed city of Sodom; his wife looked back to see the destruction and was turned into a pillar of salt (Genesis 19:26).

"*Anima*": soul; in Jungian psychology, the feminine component of the unconscious of a man.
2. In West Africa; it flows from Guinea through Mali, Niger, and Nigeria into the Gulf of Guinea.

I have seen more than my aunts dared to see
how each Sunday they sat bare-assed and defiant   45
their dark female caverns linking thighs
into matching hills of lemon ebony and mocha flesh
how the wooden humps reflected off my grandmother's
whalebone hairpins when she leaned into the light
the crumbling walls of the city of Benin[3]   50
Kamehameha's feathered cape in the Bishop museum[4]

I have seen Buenos Aires
where ladies dine inside their mirrors
Berlin where my blackness
was examined in six languages   55
Bogotá where there are no traffic signals
and even pregnant women are targets
fat clumsy figures playing toreador
with foreign made limousines

in the Middle East fairy chimneys   60
of volcanic tuffs spiral into the sunlight
their colors glowing like stained glass
in the half-light of the desert
shades of ochre russet and ebony
thrust into tidal waves of magma[5]   65
and firestorm of ash
like beads on a rosary linking
village to village

when I was eight my prudish aunts
sat like squat pigeons on the horsehair sofa   70
brazen under their stiff-collared dresses
and I gathered dreams of love
from a tapestry woven in velvet
a blood-colored crescent moon, three palm trees
two burgundy camels, all arched around   75
a shadowy figure entering a tent
the world behind him barren and flat

some days pressed by the low ceiling
of a troubled sky I drift back to that room
the scene spreads before me   80
the delicate red tracery
of some ancient artisan
clinging to threadbare spots
the nomad who is forever coming home
the tent with its doorway of secrets   85
the dark face turned towards the corner

3. Capital of the 15th-century West African empire of Benin; today a city in Nigeria.
4. An anthropological and natural history museum
of Hawaii and Polynesia in Honolulu.

Kamehameha was the name of five rulers of the
Hawaiian Islands from 1795 to 1863.
5. Liquid or molten rock deep in the earth; on
cooling it solidifies to produce igneous rock.

staring at some fixed point
on the amber horizon of that velvet desert
as if to say how vast
and naked the world seems to be   90

                                                  1981

Caledonia [1]

Caledonia, Caledonia
What makes your big head
so hard . . .

The way I hear tell aunt jennie
tapdanced on the hood of her husband's
car because she heard he *might*
have smiled at miz dora emma's daughter
Brand new ford baby pink it was   5
and a convertible right out of days
full of white buck shoes sock hops
and little richard wailing over the local
disc jockey all night party station
Neighbors whooped and laughed seeing her   10
fly straight out the front door swearing
that man would never live another day
seeing mama running down the block
just in time to catch her falling
butt first into the gutter   15
But mama wouldn't laugh because jennie
knew who had not accidentally put too much
red pepper in daddy's beans and rice
that night he came home smelling
of southern comfort and blue grass   20
neither of which mama ever touched
And who bought a one way ticket home
for uncle brother's first wife
stuck up and full of airs
just because she came *from* california   25
in the '40s before it was fashionable

Mama and aunt jennie both hardheaded
and lean on words
inhaling and saying humph and um-um-um
to a chorus of head wagging un-huh's   30
whenever they hear tell I'm having female
problems full of husband troubles
They have been married for as long
as anyone can remember and now so dependent
on their husbands and each other and husbands   35
on them and the other there's no telling
where one begins and ends

1. A famous blues song about a hard-headed woman.

or which sister has religiously whipped
the other into shape
until I've learned that love, like hate   40
is always acted out

                                                                1981

LUCILLE CLIFTON
b. 1936

In his review of *Quilting*, Lucille Clifton's seventh book of poetry, *New York Times* reviewer Bruce Bennet calls her "a passionate, mercurial writer, by turns angry, prophetic, compassionate, shrewd, sensuous, vulnerable and funny." Clifton's prolific career has already spanned more than two decades and includes poetry, autobiography, essays, and children's stories. Drawing on her experience as an African American woman, Clifton creates what one critic has called "precise evocative images that give substance to her rhetorical statements and a frequent duality of vision that lends complexity to her portraits of place and character." A poet read by "ordinary people," as well as by critics, Clifton has stated that

> I use a simple language. I have never believed that for anything to be valid or true or intellectual or "deep" it had to be first complex. . . . I am not interested if anyone knows whether or not I am familiar with big words, I am interested in trying to render big ideas in a simple way. I am interested in being understood not admired.

Clifton's sense that ordinary people need and want poetry may be the result of her own upbringing in Depew, New York, where she was born Thelma Lucille Sayles on June 27, 1936. Her father, Samuel L. Sayles, worked in the steel mills, and her mother, Thelma (Moore) Sayles, in a laundry. Though uneducated, her mother wrote poems, which she read to her four children, and her father often told stories about his ancestors. Much of Clifton's work, specifically her 1976 memoir *Generations*, traces her family ancestry, a line that goes back to her great-great-grandmother Caroline Donald, born in Dahomey, West Africa, in 1822, who (along with her mother, sister, and brother) was kidnapped by slave traders. Clifton's namesake, her great-grandmother Lucille, was the first black woman legally hanged in Virginia (for murdering the white father of her only son).

From 1953 to 1955, Clifton attended Howard University, where she majored in drama and associated with such writers as Amiri Baraka (then LeRoi Jones), A. B. Spellman, and Sterling Brown. In 1955, she transferred to Fredonia State Teachers College (now State University of New York at Fredonia) but did not finish her degree. Instead she decided she wanted to write.

After marrying Fred J. Clifton in 1958, Lucille worked for several years as a claims clerk for the New York State Division of Employment in Buffalo. From 1969 to 1970 she was a literature assistant for the Central Atlantic Regional Educational Laboratory at the U.S. Office of Education in Washington, D.C. Her first book, a collection of poems titled *Good Times*, was published in 1969 and was cited by the *New York Times* as one of the best books of the year. *Good Times* presents realistically drawn family and inner-city community portraits in an economical, musical language; it stresses the resilence and dignity of black families, a theme explored through all of Clifton's work. In 1970, Clifton won the first of two National Endowment for the Arts awards (the second came in 1972); she spent 1971 to 1974 as poet in residence at Coppin State College in Baltimore.

Good Times was followed in 1972 by *Good News about the Earth*, a volume that emphasized the news that "we as [black] people have never hated one another," and that the community has always had heroes—Angela Davis, Bobby Seale, Little Richard—heroes that Clifton groups with biblical figures such as Moses and Jesus. *An Ordinary Woman,* her third volume, was published in 1974 and traces the genealogical line of her great-great grandmother Caroline Donald. The title is intentionally ironic. As Clifton has said, "One of the things I was saying in the title is that the extraordinary woman *is* the ordinary one." Evoking a spiritual sisterhood among Harriet Tubman, Sojourner Truth, her own grandmother, and other "ordinary" women, Clifton insists on the poet's need to "be the pistol / pointed / to be the madwoman / at the rivers edge / warning / be free or die." *Two-Headed Woman* (1980) explores religious and family themes, facing the uncomfortable truth that "there is no such thing / as a bed without affliction."

In 1976, following the deaths of her parents, Clifton wrote *Generations: A Memoir.* In words and photographs, she traces five generations of her family and concludes, "Things don't fall apart. Things hold. Lines connect in thin ways made out of pictures and words just kept." *Good Woman: Poems and a Memoir* (1987) brings together her previous four volumes of poetry as well as *Generations.* In *Next: New Poems,* also published in 1987, Clifton focuses on intense personal experiences, on her own role as "next" in line to inherit and bequeath life's pleasures and pains.

Quilting: Poems 1987–1990 (1991) situates her in the tradition of African American women writers, such as Alice Walker, Toni Morrison, and Gloria Naylor, who have claimed the quilt as a creative legacy bequeathed by African American women of the past to contemporary women. The titles of four of the book's five sections name traditional quilt patterns: Log Cabin, Catalpa Flower, Eight-Pointed Star, and Tree of Life. Like the quilter, who rescues scraps to create a comforting whole, Clifton uses experiences, however ragged-edged they may be, to construct her vision of possibility.

A well-known writer of children's stories, Clifton has published more than sixteen such books to date. Not surprisingly, she credits her own six children with inspiring much of her work: "They keep you aware of life. And you have to stay aware of life, keep growing to write." Most of Clifton's children's works focus on young African Americans as they struggle through their relationships with family and friends. The adventures of Everett Anderson, one of Clifton's best-known characters, fill the pages of six different books.

In all of her work, including her most recent, *Book of Light* (1993), Lucille Clifton immerses herself in the sturdy language, strength, and lineage of "ordinary" black folk, who, despite great deprivations, have created deep spiritual traditions.

[the bodies broken on]

the bodies broken on
the Trail of Tears[1]
and the bodies melted
in Middle Passage[2]
are married to rock and   5

---

1. The forced westward march of the Cherokee Nation in 1838, during which thousands perished from hunger and hardship.

2. The route of the slave trade across the Atlantic from West Africa to the West Indies or America.

ocean by now
and the mountains crumbling on
white men
the waters pulling white men down
sing for red dust and black clay   10
good news about the earth

                                          1972

the lost baby poem

the time i dropped your almost body down
down to meet the waters under the city
and run one with the sewage to the sea
what did i know about waters rushing back
what did i know about drowning   5
or being drowned

you would have been born into winter
in the year of the disconnected gas
and no car   we would have made the thin
walk over genesee hill into the canada wind   10
to watch you slip like ice into strangers' hands
you would have fallen naked as snow into winter
if you were here i could tell you these
and some other things

if i am ever less than a mountain   15
for your definite brothers and sisters
let the rivers pour over my head
let the sea take me for a spiller
of seas   let black men call me stranger
always   for your never named sake   20

later i'll say
i spent my life
loving a great man

later
my life will accuse me   25
of various treasons

not black enough
too black
eyes closed when they should have been open
eyes open when they should have been closed   30

will accuse me for unborn babies
and dead trees

later
when i defend again and again

with this love 35
my life will keep silent
listening to
my body breaking

1972

prayer

lighten up

why is your hand
so heavy
on just poor
me? 5

answer

this is the stuff
i made the heroes
out of
all the saints 10
and prophets and things
had to come by
this

1972

malcolm

nobody mentioned war
but doors were closed
black women shaved their heads
black men rustled in the alleys like leaves
prophets were ambushed as they spoke 5
and from their holes black eagles flew
screaming through the streets

1972

[Kali[1]]

Kali
queen of fatality, she
determines the destiny
of things. nemesis.
the permanent guest 5
within ourselves.

1. Four-armed Hindu mother goddess, consort of
the Hindu god Siva, who combines destructive and
constructive elements. In her manifestation of the
power of time, Kali is often shown black and naked,
wearing a garland of human skulls. As absolute
night, she devours everything. Kali is believed to
protect her devotees against fear and to give them
limitless peace.

woman of warfare,
of the chase, bitch
of blood sacrifice and death.
dread mother. the mystery 10
ever present in us and
outside us. the
terrible hindu woman God
Kali.
who is black. 15

1974

[if mama / could see]

if mama
could see
she would see
lucy sprawling
limbs of lucy 5
decorating the
backs of chairs
lucy hair
holding the mirrors up
that reflect odd 10
aspects of lucy.

if mama
could hear
she would hear
lucysong rolled in the 15
corners like lint
exotic webs of lucysighs
long lucy spiders explaining
to obscure gods.

if mama 20
could talk
she would talk
good girl
good girl
good girl 25
clean up your room.

1974

homage to my hips

these hips are big hips.
they need space to
move around in.
they don't fit into little
petty places. these hips 5
are free hips.

they don't like to be held back.
these hips have never been enslaved,
they go where they want to go
they do what they want to do.   10
these hips are mighty hips.
these hips are magic hips.
i have known them
to put a spell on a man and
spin him like a top!   15

1980

[what spells racoon to me]

what spells raccoon to me
spells more than just his
bandit's eyes
squinting as his furry woman
hunkers down among the fists   5
of berries.
oh coon
which gave my grandfather a name
and fed his wife on more than one
occasion   10
i can no more change my references
than they can theirs.

1987

1. at jonestown [1]

on a day when i would have believed
anything i believed that this white man,
stern as my father, neutral in his coupling
as adam, was possibly who he insisted he was.
now he has brought me to the middle of the   5
jungle of my life. if i have been wrong, again,
father may even this cup in my hand turn against me.

1987

[a woman who loves]

a woman who loves
impossible men
sits a long time indoors

---

1. An agricultural settlement of Americans in Guyana, South America, Jonestown was founded by members of the People's Temple, led by the Reverend Jim Jones. While on a visit to the settlement to investigate charges that some members were being held against their will, Congressman Leo J. Ryan of California, three newsmen, and a defecting member were killed and ten others wounded. In response, Jones ordered his followers to commit suicide, and on November 18, 1978, more than nine hundred people died, most of them from drinking cyanide-laced Kool-Aid.

watching her windows
she has no brother   5
who understands
where she is not going
her sisters offer their
own breasts up, full and
creamy vessels but she   10
cannot drink because
she loves impossible men

a woman who loves
impossible men
listens at night to music   15
she cannot sing
she drinks good sherry
swallowing around the notes
rusted in her throat
but she does not fill   20
she is already full
of love for impossible men

a woman who loves
impossible men
promises each morning   25
that she will take this day in her
hands
disrobe it   lie with it
learn to love it
but she doesn't   she walks by   30
strangers   walks by kin
forgets their birthmarks
their birthdays
remembers only the names
the stains of impossible men   35
                                                              1990

wishes for sons

i wish them cramps.
i wish them a strange town
and the last tampon.
i wish them no 7-11.

i wish them one week early   5
and wearing a white skirt.
i wish them one week late.

later i wish them hot flashes
and clots like you
wouldn't believe.   let the   10
flashes come when they

meet someone special.
let the clots come
when they want to.

let them think they have accepted   15
arrogance in the universe,
then bring them to gynecologists
not unlike themselves.

1990

move

On May 13, 1985 Wilson Goode, Philadelphia's first Black mayor, authorized the bombing of 6221 Osage Avenue after the complaints of
neighbors, also Black, about the Afrocentric back-to-nature group
headquartered there and calling itself Move. All the members of the
group wore dreadlocks and had taken the surname Africa. In the bombing eleven people, including children, were killed and sixty-one homes
in the neighborhood were destroyed.

they had begun to whisper
among themselves   hesitant
to be branded neighbor to the wild
haired women the naked children
reclaiming a continent   5
away

move

he hesitated
then turned his smoky finger
toward africa toward the house   10
he might have lived in might have
owned or saved had he not turned
away

move

the helicopter rose at the command   15
higher at first then hesitating
then turning toward the center
of its own town only a neighborhood
away

move   20

she cried as the child stood
hesitant in the last clear sky
he would ever see the last
before the whirling blades the whirling smoke
and sharp debris carried all clarity   25
away

move

if you live in a mind
that would destroy itself
to comfort itself   30
if you would stand fire
rather than difference
do not hesitate
move
away   35

1993

JUNE JORDAN
b. 1936

June Jordan is one of the most prolific contemporary African American writers. Since *Who Look at Me* (1968), she has published seven other poetry collections, five children's books, three plays, and four books of political essays; in addition, she has edited several anthologies. Currently a columnist for *The Progressive* and a professor of African American and women's studies at the University of California at Berkeley, Jordan has received numerous awards for her work and activism, from a 1970 Prix de Rome in environmental design, the result of a collaboration with Buckminster Fuller, to a 1972 National Book Award nomination for her novel *His Own Where*, to a 1985 New York Foundation for the Arts Fellowship in poetry.

Jordan was born in Harlem on July 9, 1938, to working-class Jamaican parents. Granville Jordan, her father, was a postal clerk, and her mother, Mildred, was a nurse. In her essay *For My American Family* (1993), Jordan describes how her parents escaped a life of poverty in Jamaica by emigrating to the United States and how, though they were always proud to be Americans, America did not always treat them right. Being born the child of black migrant parents and growing up in the black urban ghetto certainly influenced Jordan's writings. In her essays and poems, she details her sometimes turbulent relationship with her father as well as his tenderness for her and his love of literature, from the poetry of the Bible to that of such writers as Shakespeare, Edgar Allen Poe, and Paul Laurence Dunbar. Inspired by that love, Jordan started writing her own poetry at the age of seven and over the years moved through a cycle of influences from the major Romantics to the poetry of African American and women writers to a true "catholicity" of interests, a truly global literary appreciation.

Jordan was also profoundly influenced by the limits of her mother's life, especially her aborted desire to become an artist. In poems such as *Getting Down to Get Over* (1977) and in her essay *Many Rivers to Cross* (1985), Jordan places her mother's life and eventual suicide in the context of the long-neglected history of black women everywhere: "momma / help me / turn the face of history *to your face.*" Certainly throughout her career Jordan herself has sought to redress that neglect, writing on, among others, the women poets of the Harlem Renaissance and Zora Neale Hurston, and critiquing versions of feminism, both American and international, that do not adequately consider children, class, or race.

Characteristic of Jordan's writing is her awareness of "the intimate face of universal struggle," the ways in which the personal and the political cannot be separated. Jordan sees herself as following in the tradition of poets such as Walt Whitman and

Pablo Neruda, who fostered democratic political values and the poetic practices logically derived from such values. The introduction to her first volume of essays, *Civil Wars*, ends with this assertion:

> You begin with your family and the kids on the block, and next you open your eyes to what you call your people and that leads you into land reform into Black English into Angola leads you back to your own bed where you lie by yourself, wondering if you deserve to be peaceful, or trusted or desired or left to the freedom of your own unfaltering heart. And the scale shrinks to the size of a skull; your own interior cage.
>
> And then if you're lucky, and I have been lucky, everything comes back to you.

Jordan's title "Civil Wars" describes not only the race battles of the civil rights era in the United States but also the wars she and others waged within themselves. In 1955, when she was an undergraduate at Barnard College, she married a white Columbia graduate student in anthropology, Michael Meyer, and together they had a son, Christopher David Meyer. In her essay *Letter to Michael*, she describes the difficulties of interracial marriage, especially at a time when it was illegal in forty-three states. During her marriage, Jordan traveled to Baltimore with the Freedom Riders, despite Meyer's worry that she was putting herself and their son in danger. Jordan's decision to join the movement was one reason for the breaking apart of their marriage. For much of her son's childhood, Jordan struggled both to become a self-supporting writer and to support herself and her son on her own.

All descriptions of Jordan's life and work show that she is determined to avoid being pigeonholed in any way, as exemplified by one of her most famous poems, *A Poem about My Rights*, with its defiant refrain: "*I am not wrong: Wrong is not my name* / My name is my own my own my own." Such clear-cut resistance to labeling, to any kind of censorship or limitation, is central to Jordan's second essay collection *On Call*, in which she specifically focuses on worldwide liberation struggles, from that of the Palestinian people to the Nicaraguan revolution and racial segregation in South Africa. In her introduction to this volume, Jordan notes that she regards it as a form of censorship that many of its essays were not accepted for publication in mainstream American venues. Not surprisingly, Jordan's takes on racism and classism are hardly simple; one interesting essay describes her vacation in the Bahamas, where despite her own blackness she is separate and different from the black men who serve her drinks and the black women who make her bed.

Central also to Jordan's writing career is her career in the classroom, which has seen her teaching everywhere from children's writing workshops in Brooklyn, to New York's City College, to such prestigious schools as Sarah Lawrence, Yale, and Berkeley, where Jordan now runs the extremely successful Poetry for the People program, a forum for developing student and community poets. Jordan has for decades been a champion of black English, its beauty and its efficacy. Her first novel, *His Own Where*, was written entirely in black English, twelve years before Alice Walker's celebrated black English novel *The Color Purple* (1982). While Jordan's promotion of black English has not always gone unchallenged, in more than one essay she has skillfully analyzed the relationships between power and language, particularly the quality of resistance embodied in black English.

June Jordan's varied endeavors cannot be isolated from each other. From activism, to teaching, to writing, all are informed by her philosophical assertions that our lives are "an intimate face of universal struggle" and that "by declaring the truth, you create the truth."

In Memoriam: Martin Luther King, Jr.

I

honey people murder mercy U.S.A.
the milkland turn to monsters teach
to kill to violate pull down destroy
the weakly freedom growing fruit
from being born   5

America

tomorrow yesterday rip rape
exacerbate despoil disfigure
crazy running threat the
deadly thrall   10
appall belief dispel
the wildlife burn the breast
the onward tongue
the outward hand
deform the normal rainy   15
riot sunshine shelter wreck
of darkness derogate
delimit blank
explode deprive
assassinate and batten up   20
like bullets fatten up
the raving greed
reactivate a springtime
terrorizing

death by men by more   25
than you or I can

STOP

II

They sleep who know a regulated place
or pulse or tide or changing sky
according to some universal   30
stage direction obvious
like shorewashed shells

we share an afternoon of mourning
in between no next predictable
except for wild reversal hearse rehearsal   35
bleach the blacklong lunging
ritual of fright insanity and more
deplorable abortion
more and
more   40

1968

I Must Become a Menace to My Enemies

Dedicated to the Poet Agostinho Neto, [1]
President of The People's Republic of Angola: 1976

I

I will no longer lightly walk behind
a one of you who fear me:
                Be afraid.
I plan to give you reasons for your jumpy fits
and facial tics   5
I will not walk politely on the pavements anymore
and this is dedicated in particular
to those who hear my footsteps
or the insubstantial rattling of my grocery
cart   10
then turn around
see me
and hurry on
away from this impressive terror I must be:
I plan to blossom bloody on an afternoon   15
surrounded by my comrades singing
terrible revenge in merciless
accelerating
rhythms
But   20
I have watched a blind man studying his face.
I have set the table in the evening and sat down
to eat the news.
Regularly
I have gone to sleep.   25
There is no one to forgive me.
The dead do not give a damn.
I live like a lover
who drops her dime into the phone
just as the subway shakes into the station   30
wasting her message
cancelling the question of her call:

fulminating or forgetful but late
and always after the fact that could save or
condemn me   35

I must become the action of my fate.

II

How many of my brothers and my sisters
will they kill
before I teach myself

---

1. Leader of the liberation movement in Angola, against the colonial power Portugal. He became president of the independent People's Republic of Angola.

retaliation?   40
Shall we pick a number?
South Africa for instance:
do we agree that more than ten thousand
in less than a year but that less than
five thousand slaughtered in more than six   45
months will
WHAT IS THE MATTER WITH ME?

I must become a menace to my enemies.

III

And if I
if I ever let you slide   50
who should be extirpated from my universe
who should be cauterized from earth
completely
(lawandorder jerkoffs of the first the
terrorist degree)   55
then let my body fail my soul
in its bedevilled lecheries

And if I
if I ever let love go
because the hatred and the whisperings   60
become a phantom dictate I o-
bey in lieu of impulse and realities
(the blossoming flamingos of my wild mimosa trees)
then let love freeze me
out.   65

I must become
I must become a menace to my enemies.

                                                                1976

Poem about My Rights

Even tonight and I need to take a walk and clear
my head about this poem about why I can't
go out without changing my clothes my shoes
my body posture my gender identity my age
my status as a woman alone in the evening/   5
alone on the streets / alone not being the point/
the point being that I can't do what I want
to do with my own body because I am the wrong
sex the wrong age the wrong skin and
suppose it was not here in the city but down on the beach/   10
or far into the woods and I wanted to go
there by myself thinking about God/or thinking
about children or thinking about the world/all of it
disclosed by the stars and the silence:

I could not go and I could not think and I could not   15
stay there
alone
as I need to be
alone because I can't do what I want to do with my own
body and   20
who in the hell set things up
like this
and in France they say if the guy penetrates
but does not ejaculate then he did not rape me
and if after stabbing him if after screams if   25
after begging the bastard and if even after smashing
a hammer to his head if even after that if he
and his buddies fuck me after that
then I consented and there was
no rape because finally you understand finally   30
they fucked me over because I was wrong I was
wrong again to be me being me where I was/wrong
to be who I am
which is exactly like South Africa
penetrating into Namibia penetrating into   35
Angola and does that mean I mean how do you know if
Pretoria ejaculates what will the evidence look like the
proof of the monster jackboot ejaculation on Blackland
and if
after Namibia and if after Angola and if after Zimbabwe   40
and if after all of my kinsmen and women resist even to
self-immolation of the villages and if after that
we lose nevertheless what will the big boys say will they
claim my consent:
Do You Follow Me: We are the wrong people of   45
the wrong skin on the wrong continent and what
in the hell is everybody being reasonable about
and according to the *Times* this week
back in 1966 the C.I.A. decided that they had this problem
and the problem was a man named Nkrumah [1] so they   50
killed him and before that it was Patrice Lumumba [2]
and before that it was my father on the campus
of my Ivy League school and my father afraid
to walk into the cafeteria because he said he
was wrong the wrong age the wrong skin the wrong   55
gender identity and he was paying my tuition and
before that
it was my father saying I was wrong saying that
I should have been a boy because he wanted one/a
boy and that I should have been lighter skinned and   60
that I should have had straighter hair and that
I should not be so boy crazy but instead I should
just be one/a boy and before that
it was my mother pleading plastic surgery for

---

1. President of Ghana from 1960 to 1966.
2. Prime minister of the Congo from 1960 until
his assassination in 1961. He was president of the
Congolese National Movement against the colonial power of Belgium and is regarded as a martyr.

my nose and braces for my teeth and telling me   65
to let the books loose to let them loose in other
words
I am very familiar with the problems of the C.I.A.
and the problems of South Africa and the problems
of Exxon Corporation and the problems of white   70
America in general and the problems of the teachers
and the preachers and the F.B.I. and the social
workers and my particular Mom and Dad/I am very
familiar with the problems because the problems
turn out to be   75
me
I am the history of rape
I am the history of the rejection of who I am
I am the history of the terrorized incarceration of
my self   80
I am the history of battery assault and limitless
armies against whatever I want to do with my mind
and my body and my soul and
whether it's about walking out at night
or whether it's about the love that I feel or   85
whether it's about the sanctity of my vagina or
the sanctity of my national boundaries
or the sanctity of my leaders or the sanctity
of each and every desire
that I know from my personal and idiosyncratic   90
and indisputably single and singular heart
I have been raped
be-
cause I have been wrong the wrong sex the wrong age
the wrong skin the wrong nose the wrong hair the   95
wrong need the wrong dream the wrong geographic
the wrong sartorial I
I have been the meaning of rape
I have been the problem everyone seeks to
eliminate by forced   100
penetration with or without the evidence of slime and/
but let this be unmistakable this poem
is not consent I do not consent
to my mother to my father to the teachers to
the F.B.I. to South Africa to Bedford-Stuy[3]   105
to Park Avenue to American Airlines to the hardon
idlers on the corners to the sneaky creeps in
cars
I am not wrong: Wrong is not my name
My name is my own my own my own   110
and I can't tell you who the hell set things up like this
but I can tell you that from now on my resistance
my simple and daily and nightly self-determination
may very well cost you your life

1980

---

3. Abbreviation for the Brooklyn section Bedford Stuyvesant, the largest concentration of blacks in New
York City.

Poem for Guatemala

Dedicated to Rigoberto Manchú [1]

(With thanks to Journey to the Depths, *the testimony of Rigoberto
Manchú, translated into English by Patricia Goedicke, October, 1982)*

No matter how loudly I call you the sound of your name
makes the day soft
Nothing about it sticks to my throat
Guatemala
syllables that lilt into twilight and lust   5
Guatemala
syllables to melt bullets

They call you Indian
They called me West Indian
You learned to speak Spanish when I did   10
We were thirteen
I wore shoes
I ate rice and peas
The beans and the rice in your pot
brought the soldiers   15
to hack off your arms

"Walk like that into the kitchen!
Walk like that into the clearing!
Girl with no arms!"

I had been playing the piano   20

Because of the beans and the rice in your pot
the soldiers arrived with an axe
to claim you guerilla
girl with no arms

An Indian is not supposed to own a pot of food   25
An Indian is too crude
An Indian covers herself with dirt so the cold
times will not hurt her

Cover yourself with no arms!

They buried my mother in New Jersey.   30
Black cars carried her there.
She wore flowers and a long dress.

Soldiers pushed into your mother
and tore out her tongue
and whipped her under a tree   35
and planted a fly in the bleeding
places so that worms

---

1. Nobel Peace Prize awardee for her work on behalf of the indigenous peoples of the Americas.

spread through the flesh
then the dogs
then the buzzards   40
then the soldiers laughing
at the family of the girl
with no arms
guerilla girl
with no arms   45

You go with no arms
among the jungle treacheries
You go with no arms
into the mountains hunting
revenge   50

I watch you
walk like that
into the kitchen
walk like that
into the clearing   55
girl with no arms

I am learning new syllables
of revolution

Guatemala
Guatemala   60
Girl with no arms

                                                    1989

The Female and the Silence of a Man

(c.f. W. B. Yeats' "Leda and the Swan")

And now she knows: The big fist shattering her face.
Above, the sky conceals the sadness of the moon.
And windows light, doors close, against all trace
of her: She falls into the violence of a woman's ruin.

How should she rise against the plunging of his lust?   5
She vomits out her teeth. He tears the slender legs apart.
The hairy torso of his rage destroys the soft last bastion
                              of her trust.
He lacerates her breasts. He claws and squeezes out her heart.

She sinks into a meadow pond of lilies and a swan.   10
She floats above an afternoon of music from the trees.
She vanishes like blood that people walk upon.
She reappears: A mad *bitch* dog that reason cannot sieze;
A fever withering the river and the crops:
A lovely girl protected by her cruel/incandescent energies.   15

                                                    1989

Intifada [1]

In detention
in concentration camps
we trade stories
we take turns sharing the straw mat
or a pencil   5
we watch what crawls in and out
of the sand

As-Salāmm 'Alaykum

The guards do not allow the blue
woolen blanket   10
my family travelled far
to bring
to this crepuscular and gelid cell
where my still breathing infant son
and I   15
defy the purgatory implications
of a state-created hell

Wa 'Alaikum As-Salām

The village trembles from the heavy
tanks that try   20
to terrify the children:
Everyday
my little brother runs behind the rubble
practising the tactics of the stones
against the rock.   25
In January soldiers broke his fingers
one by one. Time has healed
his hands but not the fury that controls
what used to be
his heart.   30

Insha Ā'llāh

Close the villages
Close the clinics
Close the school
Close the house
Close the windows of the house   35
Kill the vegetables languishing under the sun
Kill the milk of the cows left to the swelling of pain
Cut the electricity
Cut the telephones
Confine the people to the people   40

---

1. Shaking off (Arabic, literal trans.); the Palestinian uprising against Israeli occupation of the
West Bank of Jordan and the Gaza Strip, which
began in 1987 and is meant to be ended by the interim accord between Israel and the Palestine Liberation Organization, signed in September 1993.

Do Not Despair of the Mercy of Allah

Fig trees will grow and oranges
erupt from desert
holdings on which plastic   45
bullets (70% zinc, 20% glass, and 10%
plastic) will prove blood
soluble and fertilize the earth
where sheep will graze
and women no longer grieve and beat   50
their breasts
They will beat clean
fine-woven rugs outside a house
smelling of cinnamon
and nutmeg   55

 Ahamdullilah

So says *Iman*
the teacher of peace
the shepherd on the mountain of the lamb
the teacher of peace   60
who will subdue the howling of the lion
so that we may kneel
as we must
five times beginning just after dawn
and ending just before dusk   65
in the *Ibādah*
of prayer

 Allāhu Akbar
 Allāhu Akbar
 Allāhu Akbar   70

GLOSSARY:

As-Salāmm 'Alaykum: peace be unto you
Wa 'Alaikum As-Salām: and peace be unto you
Insha A'llāh: as/if Allah wills it
"Do Not Despair of the Mercy of Allah": verse from *The Qur'ān*
Ahamdullilah: praise be to Allah
Iman: faith
Ibādah: worship in a ritual sense
Allāhu Akbar: Allah is the Greatest

1989

A New Politics of Sexuality [1]

As a young worried mother, I remember turning to Dr. Benjamin Spock's *Common Sense Book of Baby and Child Care* [2] just about as often as I'd pick up the telephone. He was God. I was ignorant but striving to be good: a good Mother. And so it was there, in that best-seller pocketbook of do's and don't's, that I came upon this doozie of a guideline: Do not wear miniskirts or other provocative clothing because that will upset your child, especially if your child happens to be a boy. If you give your offspring "cause" to think of you as a sexual being, he will, at the least, become disturbed; you will derail the equilibrium of his notions about your possible identity and meaning in the world.

It had never occurred to me that anyone, especially my son, might look upon me as an asexual being. I had never supposed that "asexual" was some kind of positive designation I should, so to speak, lust after. I was pretty surprised by Dr. Spock. However, I was also, by habit, a creature of obedience. For a couple of weeks I actually experimented with lusterless colors and dowdy tops and bottoms, self-consciously hoping thereby to prove myself as a lusterless and dowdy and, therefore, excellent female parent.

Years would have to pass before I could recognize the familiar, by then, absurdity of a man setting himself up as the expert on a subject that presupposed women as the primary objects for his patriarchal discourse—on motherhood, no less! Years passed before I came to perceive the perversity of dominant power assumed by men, and the perversity of self-determining power ceded to men by women.

A lot of years went by before I understood the dynamics of what anyone could summarize as the Politics of Sexuality.

I believe the Politics of Sexuality is the most ancient and probably the most profound arena for human conflict. Increasingly, it seems clear to me that deeper and more pervasive than any other oppression, than any other bitterly contested human domain, is the oppression of sexuality, the exploitation of the human domain of sexuality for power.

When I say sexuality, I mean gender: I mean male subjugation of human beings because they are female. When I say sexuality, I mean heterosexual institutionalization of rights and privileges denied to homosexual men and women. When I say sexuality I mean gay or lesbian contempt for bisexual modes of human relationship.

The Politics of Sexuality therefore subsumes all of the different ways in which some of us seek to dictate to others of us what we should do, what we should desire, what we should dream about, and how we should behave ourselves, generally. From China to Iran, from Nigeria to Czechoslovakia, from Chile to California, the politics of sexuality—enforced by traditions of state-sanctioned violence plus religion and the law—reduces to male domi-

1. Adapted from the author's keynote address to the Bisexual, Gay, and Lesbian Student Association at Stanford University on April 29, 1991.
2. First published in 1946, Spock's book (later *Baby and Child Care*) is the best-selling American book on child care and was for years, especially in the 1950s and 1960s, regarded by new parents as the bible of child rearing.

nation of women, heterosexist tyranny, and, among those of us who are in any case deemed despicable or deviant by the powerful, we find intolerance for those who choose a different, a more complicated—for example, an interracial or bisexual—mode of rebellion and freedom.

We must move out from the shadows of our collective subjugation—as people of color/as women/as gay/as lesbian/as bisexual human beings.

I can voice my ideas without hesitation or fear because I am speaking, finally, about myself. I am Black and I am female and I am a mother and I am bisexual and I am a nationalist and I am an antinationalist. And I mean to be fully and freely all that I am!

Conversely, I do not accept that any white or Black or Chinese man—I do not accept that, for instance, Dr. Spock—should presume to tell me, or any other woman, how to mother a child. He has no right. He is not a mother. My child is not his child. And, likewise, I do not accept that anyone—any woman or any man who is not inextricably part of the subject he or she dares to address—should attempt to tell any of us, the objects of her or his presumptuous discourse, what we should do or what we should not do.

Recently, I have come upon gratuitous and appalling pseudoliberal pronouncements on sexuality. Too often, these utterances fall out of the mouths of men and women who first disclaim any sentiment remotely related to homophobia, but who then proceed to issue outrageous opinions like the following:

•That it is blasphemous to compare the oppression of gay, lesbian, or bisexual people to the oppression, say, of black people, or of the Palestinians.

•That the bottom line about gay or lesbian or bisexual identity is that you can conceal it whenever necessary and, so, therefore, why don't you do just that? Why don't you keep your deviant sexuality in the closet and let the rest of us—we who suffer oppression for reasons of our ineradicable and always visible components of our personhood such as race or gender—get on with our more necessary, our more beleaguered struggle to survive?

Well, number one: I believe I have worked as hard as I could, and then harder than that, on behalf of equality and justice—for African-Americans, for the Palestinian people, and for people of color everywhere.

And no, I do not believe it is blasphemous to compare oppressions of sexuality to oppressions of race and ethnicity: Freedom is indivisible or it is nothing at all besides sloganeering and temporary, short-sighted, and short-lived advancement for a few. Freedom is indivisible, and either we are working for freedom or you are working for the sake of your self-interests and I am working for mine.

If you can finally go to the bathroom wherever you find one, if you can finally order a cup of coffee and drink it wherever coffee is available, but you cannot follow your heart—you cannot respect the response of your own honest body in the world—then how much of what kind of freedom does any one of us possess?

Or, conversely, if your heart and your honest body can be controlled by the state, or controlled by community taboo, are you not then, and in that case, no more than a slave ruled by outside force?

What tyranny could exceed a tyranny that dictates to the human heart, and that attempts to dictate the public career of an honest human body?

Freedom is indivisible; the Politics of Sexuality is not some optional "special-interest" concern for serious, progressive folk.

And, on another level, let me assure you: if every single gay or lesbian or bisexual man or woman active on the Left of American politics decided to stay home, there would be *no* Left left.

One of the things I want to propose is that we act on that reality: that we insistently demand reciprocal respect and concern from those who cheerfully depend upon our brains and our energies for their, and our, effective impact on the political landscape.

Last spring, at Berkeley,[3] some students asked me to speak at a rally against racism. And I did. There were four or five hundred people massed on Sproul Plaza, standing together against that evil. And, on the next day, on that same plaza, there was a rally for bisexual and gay and lesbian rights, and students asked me to speak at that rally. And I did. There were fewer than seventy-five people stranded, pitiful, on that public space. And I said then what I say today: That was disgraceful! There should have been just one rally. One rally: freedom is indivisible.

As for the second, nefarious pronouncement on sexuality that now enjoys mass-media currency: the idiot notion of keeping yourself in the closet—that is very much the same thing as the suggestion that black folks and Asian-Americans and Mexican-Americans should assimilate and become as "white" as possible—in our walk/talk/music/food/values—or else. Or else? Or else we should, deservedly, perish.

Sure enough, we have plenty of exposure to white everything so why would we opt to remain our African/Asian/Mexican selves? The answer is that suicide is absolute, and if you think you will survive by hiding who you really are, you are sadly misled: there is no such thing as partial or intermittent suicide. You can only survive if you—who you really are—do survive.

Likewise, we who are not men and we who are not heterosexist—we, sure enough, have plenty of exposure to male-dominated/heterosexist this and that.

But a struggle to survive cannot lead to suicide: suicide is the opposite of survival. And so we must not conceal/assimilate/integrate into the would-be dominant culture and political system that despises us. Our survival requires that we alter our environment so that we can live and so that we can hold each other's hands and so that we can kiss each other on the streets, and in the daylight of our existence, without terror and without violent and sometimes fatal reactions from the busybodies of America.

Finally, I need to speak on bisexuality. I do believe that the analogy is interracial or multiracial identity. I do believe that the analogy for bisexuality is a multicultural, multi-ethnic, multiracial world view. Bisexuality follows from such a perspective and leads to it, as well.

3. I.e., the University of California at Berkeley.

Just as there are many men and women in the United States whose parents have given them more than one racial, more than one ethnic identity and cultural heritage to honor; and just as these men and women must deny no given part of themselves except at the risk of self-deception and the insanities that must issue from that; and just as these men and women embody the principle of equality among races and ethnic communities; and just as these men and women falter and anguish and choose and then falter again and then anguish and then choose yet again how they will honor the irreducible complexity of their God-given human being—even so, there are many men and women, especially young men and women, who seek to embrace the complexity of their total, always-changing social and political circumstance.

They seek to embrace our increasing global complexity on the basis of the heart and on the basis of an honest human body. Not according to ideology. Not according to group pressure. Not according to anybody's concept of "correct."

This is a New Politics of Sexuality. And even as I despair of identity politics—because identity is given and principles of justice/equality/freedom cut across given gender and given racial definitions of being, and because I will call you my brother, I will call you my sister, on the basis of what you *do* for justice, what you *do* for equality, what you *do* for freedom and *not* on the basis of who you are, even so I look with admiration and respect upon the new, bisexual politics of sexuality.

This emerging movement politicizes the so-called middle ground: Bisexuality invalidates either/or formulation, either/or analysis. Bisexuality means I am free and I am as likely to want and to love a woman as I am likely to want and to love a man, and what about that? Isn't that what freedom implies?

If you are free, you are not predictable and you are not controllable. To my mind, that is the keenly positive, politicizing significance of bisexual affirmation:

To insist upon complexity, to insist upon the validity of all of the components of social/sexual complexity, to insist upon the equal validity of all of the components of social/sexual complexity.

This seems to me a unifying, 1990s mandate for revolutionary Americans planning to make it into the twenty-first century on the basis of the heart, on the basis of an honest human body, consecrated to every struggle for justice, every struggle for equality, every struggle for freedom.

1991

CLARENCE MAJOR
b. 1936

In a 1994 interview with critic Larry McCaffery, Clarence Major, a painter and possibly the most celebrated postmodernist African American writer, made this distinction between literature and the other arts:

Literature is unlike the other arts. If we're talking about oral storytelling—the essence of literature—we're talking about pure language. Naturally it's going to be limited to those who can speak and understand it. And it's also always evolving in ways that lines and colors (in painting) and stone (in sculpture) are not. Those materials evolve in their own very different ways and aren't subject to the constant practical communication uses language is subject to. A word's purity can be destroyed in a way that the color yellow, theoretically, cannot.

Major's statement is an important clue to the intensely visual nature of his opus, which consists of seven novels, twelve books of poetry, and many nonfiction works. Though he was born in Atlanta and throughout his childhood visited his grandparents in the rural South, he grew up in Chicago. In that city, he first saw the work of Vincent Van Gogh, among other European painters, and it had such an effect on his inner life that Major decided to become a painter himself. Not surprisingly, this engagement with European art has had a decisive effect on Major's writing; so has his passion for the magical quality of nature in the black southern United States.

Major's has always been a controversial voice. In 1967 he published the frequently anthologized *A Black Criterion* (1967), which called for black poets to resist white standards. He both edited an issue of the *Journal of Black Poetry* and was a member of the primarily white Fiction Collective. With his important anthology *The New Black Poetry* (1970), Major presented a volume of eclectic work by African Americans in a period when "black" was frequently represented in monolithic simplistic terms. And even as he acknowledged both European—Van Gogh, Radiguet, Rimbaud—and African American—Toomer, Wright, Himes—influences on his works, he edited *The Dictionary of Afro-American Slang*.

Truly an original mind, Major produces literary works that insist that fiction creates its own reality—that words are not reality, but rather create a world of their own. Well before the coining of the word *postmodernist*, Major stated one of its major tenets about literature: "You begin with words and you end with words. The content exists in our minds. I don't think that it has to be a reflection of anything. It is a reality that has been created inside of a book. It's put together and exists finally in your mind."

In *Reflex and Bone Structure* (1975), Major deconstructs the genre of the murder mystery, inviting the reader to consider the author of the narrative as the ultimate murderer. His experimentation with the manipulation of signs on the printed page is especially innovative in *Emergency Exits* (1979), a text that includes twenty-six black-and-white reproductions of his own paintings not as illustrations but as part of the narrative. Critic Stuart Klawans has suggested that Cubism serves as "a model, an incitement and a justification" for Major's fifth novel, *My Amputations* (1986).

Insisting that "to some degree doubleness describes the condition of all Americans, whether or not they know it," Major has also written a novel, *Painted Turtle: Woman with Guitar* (1988), and book of poems, *Some Observations of a Stranger at Zuni in the Latter Part of the Century* (1989), that focus on Native Americans and challenge simplistic assessments of their identity. At the same time, his novel *Such Was the Season* (1987) is an exciting, old-fashioned narrative. And he has edited not only the slang dictionary (which was revised in 1994) but also collections of essays and short stories by black American writers.

Major's work has been the subject of many scholarly articles, dissertations, and two special issues of *African American Review* (1979 and 1994). It has been translated into, among other languages, French, German, and Italian. The recipient of numerous awards and fellowships, Major is currently professor of African American literature and creative writing at the University of California at Davis.

Swallow the Lake

Gave me things I
could not use. Then. Now.
Rain night bursting upon & into. I
shine updown into Lake Michigan

like the glow from the cold lights of the Loop. [1]   5
Walks. Deaths. Births.
Streets. Things I could not give back. Nor
use. Or night or day or night or

loneliness. Other ways   feelings I could not
put into words   into themselves into people.   10
Blank monkeys of the hierarchy. More deaths—
stupidity & death turning them on

into the beat of my droopy heart   my middle
passage blues my corroding hate my release
while I come to become neon iron eyes stainless lungs   15
blood zincgripped steel I
come up abstract

not able to take their bricks. Tar. Nor their flesh.
I ran: stung. Loop fumes hung
                              in my smoky lungs.   20

ideas I could not break nor form. Gave me
things I
see break & run down the crawling down the
game.

Illusion illusion, and you   25
would swear before screaming somehow
choked voices in me.

The crawling thing in the blood, the
huge immune loneliness. One becomes immune
to the bricks the feelings. One becomes   30
death.
One becomes each one and every person I
become. I could not
I COULD NOT
I could not whistle and walk in storms   35
along Lake Michigan's shore. Concrete walks.
I could not swallow the lake

                                          1970

1. The shopping and business district in Chicago.

Round Midnight[1]

you know my trouble: story
is they want to make me
liable to punishment
by the-feast-of-Hina-law
for this picture.   5

My spirit is closed,
I'm a delicate engraving
outlined
with semitones, curled
at the edges,   10
nearly worthless,
in mysterious trouble,
in my second story.

I walk the beach
at Scheveningen.[2]   15
Drink myself
blind in The Hague.
Piss in the pretty
bushes at Etten.

I redate all my efforts.   20
Reconsider a cluster
of old houses nearby,
but not the church
behind it. You know
why. It's my spirit!   25

Midnight is round.
So what if I fail
at the total, the whole?
Judith Te Parari
couldn't care less.   30
She swings low
in her sweetness
around midnight as
the diggers dig
the fields stacking mud   35
against gold panels.

When I come to trial
you will hear
in my defense: weavers
and rug-makers, potters,   40
old men leaning on sticks,
people I can trust,
tree-cutters, tree-growers,

1. Famous jazz composition.
2. Bathing resort town in southern Netherlands, part of The Hague, the nation's capital.

folks born
in the month of March.   45

In Harlem or Stuttgart[3]
you can make anything
work: jazz with hard light
against the Rhine; even
a tiny red boat tossed   50
this and that way
along the tired face
of night's season.

You know the story:
I am held captive   55
by winter light
at Nuenen: an ox,
hooked to a cart,
hopeless in
its sincere effort   60
to go on living.

Judith holds the end
of the winter
thread, pushes it
through the needle,   65
into my mouth, sews me
and it together.

My spirit rises: I drink
nectar from her Nefertiti[4]
moon. It's midnight,   70
exactly: I hear the piano
keys. (It's not Rick's
place.)[5] It's sounds
of water at the Gennep
Mill, turning.   75
I am a monk, waiting,
holding a gift:
A token of reprieve
placed in my hands
by my defenders   80
who also wait now
on benches harder
than mine.

1984

3. City in Germany; a center of the arts.
4. Queen of ancient Egypt (c. 1372–1350 B.C.); an
extant bust of her is considered one of the most
beautiful representations of women in antiquity.
5. The nightclub in the famous movie *Casablanca*.

On Watching a Caterpillar Become a Butterfly

It's a slow, slow process
sitting here on the porch

just watching a clumsy male
milkweed caterpillar

slowly turning itself   5
into a graceful butterfly while

hanging from the underside
of a withered leaf dark with life

among a pungent cluster
of other rich leaves   10

from this old branch
leaning over my banister

at a certain point
in its natural growth

probably caterpillar thinks it can   15
decide which way

it wants to go—to fly or die,
by simply taking an oath and dreaming

of having the loveliness
of, say, the male-*crow* butterfly   20

or having the stripes
of the tiger butterfly

or maybe stay in the *chrysalis* stage
of become a *friar* butterfly

caterpillar is a dreamer   25
and a natural schemer

in this changing light where
cuticle-shaped drops of fluid

glow and glow
like red nectar   30

changing itself
as it hangs from the bottom

of this green leaf
wedged tightly

as though bolted   35
with metal springs,

throwing off that light,
a light of silver-purple

outlined in gold—
golden trimmings   40
                                                          1994

Chicago Heat

Hello? Mother? It's me, Floyce. I just got back from the courthouse, me and Russell. You won't believe it. Something terrible has happened. They kept Harley. And it looks like my husband is dead. The police was just here and they took him out of here all covered up on a stretcher. They asked me and Russell all kinds of questions. And we have to go to the police station tomorrow morning because I got to sign some piece of paper. But, Mother, we didn't even *know* Medwin was dead. After the trial we drove home like that with him sitting up in the front seat, kind of all slumped over but still sitting up. And I could've sworn he was just sleeping. And you know, sometimes I have trouble waking him up. He just won't wake up. And I thought this was just another one of them times. 'Cause Medwin was messing up. You know, I told you before that Medwin had been abusing his medication lately, and it wasn't the first time he had passed out and come back hours later. So, that's why we thought he was just passed out again. But he had to have died while we were in the courthouse. Can you imagine that? Sitting out there in that hot car all that time in this Chicago heat just 'cause he didn't want to see Vernon? And August in Chicago, honey, ain't nothing to play with. Wouldn't even come in to Harley's trial. But I guess he didn't have any love to lose on Harley or Russell, for that matter, the way they treated that poor man, beating him up that time and just verbally abusing him all the time. It was like Medwin and Russell had never been friends. And you remember it was Russell who introduced me to Medwin while they were in recovery in the VA hospital. When was that? Already nearly ten years ago. My, how time flies. And you know, Russell brought Medwin home with him, playing on my sympathy, with all this mess about the poor man didn't have no place to live, did we want to see him homeless, out in the street? And *knowing* I had a sympathetic heart. So there was Medwin staying with us. Russell's friend, but a man almost my own age. And, you know, you remember, at first it was all right because it was just Russell and Medwin being friends and sitting around in the front room watching television all day and taking their medication and drinking beer. But when Medwin come just a noticing me and everything, reaching out and touching me when I walked by, no, boy, Russell didn't go for that. Not with *his* mother. Not his friend and his *mother*. He couldn't handle it. But you know, Mother, love is strange, a strange thing. You can't stop it. Once it starts it just gets its own fire and keeps spreading. And there wasn't nothing Russell could do. He's my son and everything and I love him, but he sure did show his ass. I tell you, Mother, that boy gave me a hard time. Did I say *boy?* Shoot! He was a grown man. Grown as he would ever be. Russell was a grown, *grown* man. And is a grown man. And there ain't *no* way you can tell me he didn't know what he was doing, being so evil and all, abusing Medwin, calling him poor white trash. You remember. I told you about it back then. It got so bad I had to put the boy out of the house two or three times. He got to going off his head, talking about how he was going to kill Medwin. I tell you about the time I had to pull that nigger off Medwin? Trying to choke him to death. Right across the bed. And poor Medwin lying there, gasping for his life, all red in the face. Mother, it was something terrible. And you *know* my own health started failing back then. That was the beginning of my downfall, my trouble. I was always healthy before then. You know that. Went to work every day of my life. Never missed a day. But the stress and strain my sons put me through for the last few years has just about killed me, Mother. I myself now have to take medication. Me! I never took medicine in my life before all this mess. The doctor got me on three different kinds of pills. Gave me all kinds of tests. Now they are trying to say I got something called schizophrenia. Well, I know you know more about this sort of stuff than I do. Well, yes, I take the medicine. They say it's supposed to calm me down, keep things from getting on my nerves. But I have to take all kinds of other little pills too. I don't know what most of them are for. But, Mother, I tell you, I'm not going to let these boys kill me. No, no way! They just about finished me off but I'm not going to let them put me in my grave. And Russell himself is so sad about his brother. But you know, Mother, Russell ain't much better off. He just sits around despondent. Won't do nothing but watch television and sleep. Ever since he got out of the Marines, ever since he got back from duty in Germany, that boy ain't been the same. You'd think he saw action or something and got—how do they call it?—got shell-shocked or combat fatigue. And now his younger brother, his baby brother, oh Lord! Harley's in prison just 'cause he got mixed up in the wrong crowd, running around with dope dealers and now they got him for first-degree murder. But I believe Harley, Mother. I believe he wasn't holding the gun. He's just that stupid. Stupid enough to be out there with a bunch of losers, not holding the gun, and end up being the one they nail. You told me yourself you believe these other two boys, Kelley and Pablo, had the gun. And I know you're right. He's got a very gentle, very kind heart. But since the police can't find the gun they can't prove anything. Now, you know they told the police they drove out to the lake and threw the gun in the lake, but Harley told me they didn't do that. They still got the gun hid somewhere. What? Oh, yeah. That's why I called you. Isn't it? Well, it's all just so shocking and new to me I can't get my thoughts straight, Mother. Let's see. What happened in court? What happened with Medwin? Like I said, well, first of all, Medwin didn't want to go into the court building because Vernon, your son Vernon, was there. Vernon, the father of my sons. Good gracious! But Mother, that son of yours is *still* handsome like he was twenty years ago. And, honey, believe me, I kept looking across the courtroom at him. Even with the gray in his hair. I said to myself, Go on, Vernon, with your fine self. But seriously, Mother, I guess it's like they say. You never get over your first love. And you see that's why Medwin didn't want to come into the courthouse. He got this thing about Vernon, what Vernon used to mean to me, Vernon being the father of my boys. And I mean, they were always reminding him that he was just Russell's used-to-be friend and not a stepfather to them. And he better not ever think of himself as their stepfather. And calling him names. It was a shame, Mother. I tell you. Anyway, that's why Medwin didn't go in. He said he'd just sit there in the car and wait for us. But you see, he didn't know, we didn't know, the case would drag on all day, into the afternoon. You know, starting out at nine in the morning, like it did, we thought it would be over before noon. Then it looked like it was going so slow. We went in there, all of us, Russell and me, my mother—you remember my mother Benita, don't you?—bless her heart, she kept so calm. She asked me about you, said, "How come Miss Edmonia ain't here?" and I had to remind her about your heart condition. And who else? Gaye, your daughter, you know, came in with Vernon, and who else? I can't think now—we were all there. But I sure am glad you didn't try to come out there, Mother. Your heart couldn't have stood it. But that place was packed. Even people I didn't know just there out of curiosity, I guess. Who? Oh, yes. The clerk's whole family was there. That's right, Valora. Yes, his name was Gilroy. That's right. You heard it on TV. His sister, Ella they call her, she was there and she was the only one of them they called up to take the stand. And, you know, Mother, I swear I don't even remember much of what she was saying except she kept going on and on about how nice her brother was and how he always tried to help street kids, she said street kids like the boys that killed her brother. Called my son a street kid. And she cried too. Oh, I tell you, she had her performance together, honey. She had that act down to a T. And the judge ate it up. And Harley's criminal friends, Pablo and Kelley, they were there, in custody, but they weren't on trial, just there as witnesses. They're supposed to be having separate trials. And you know, I told you before that I thought Angelo Passano, Harley's lawyer, was really great. He did the best he could, but it was a hard case. That judge—what's his name, some sort of old funny-sounding name?—Judge Yurek Tancik—he was dead-set against Harley from the beginning. The only thing I know now that Angelo did wrong was advising Harley to waive his right to a jury trial. That was a *terrible* mistake. Harley might be free this afternoon, instead of sitting in Cook County Jail, if he had had a jury trial. But I don't blame Angelo. Angelo did what he thought was right. He trusted the judge. And Harley trusted Angelo. He followed Angelo's advice. Told the judge he didn't want a jury. Huh? Oh, the prosecutor's name was Dan Creaver. Same one they had at the pretrial hearing. Remember? Now, you know, I sat there all morning and half the afternoon listening to this Creaver arguing to put my son away and listening to Angelo defending my son's innocence—and I tell you, Mother, that prosecutor did not make any sense, not to me. I mean, I don't see how the judge bought his line. He just didn't present a story that added up to anything like the basis for some conviction. That's what Russell said. And I believe Russell. And Russell has studied law books. He's read up on a lot of things. Russell has a good mind on him but he just won't do nothing with it. Anyway, after hearing Angelo and Creaver we thought surely that judge would say not guilty and let Harley walk out of there. But instead he said, "I find the defendant guilty as charged." And then he turned to the police officer just standing by the exit and in this calm voice like he was bored half to death he said, "Take the prisoner into custody, please." And I almost died. Mother, I tell you, my heart stopped. And it still ain't started beating right again yet. But, anyway, that judge—before you knew it he was calling the next case. But the sentence won't be till a couple of weeks from now. You see, all these Chicago judges want is to get some kind of conviction, set their books clear, honey! They don't care nothing about justice. It's like Russell says, *all* they want is a conviction. Russell says once you get caught in the Chicago criminal justice system charged with something—anything!—your ass is mud. If you're black you can forget it. Your life is just about over. That's what Russell says all the time. And you know he *worked* out there in the courthouse as a guard during that time when he was doing all right, right after service. You remember. Russell knows all the crooked things that goes on out there. Huh? What'd you say, Mother? Oh, yes. Isn't that something? Dying like that. Just up and dying. Dying in the heat. And us driving home with him sitting up like he was still alive.

1994

LEON FORREST
b. 1937

In his novels, poems, operas, and essays, Leon Forrest has consistently combined apparently diverse traditions. From Langston Hughes to Sterling Brown, from Ralph Ellison to Robert Hayden, from Edgar Allan Poe to Herman Melville to William Faulkner, he has drawn on authors of the past to produce his own innovative, original body of work. Not surprisingly, he has been much honored, receiving among other awards the 1978 Sandburg Medallion, the 1984 Carl Sandburg Award, the 1985 Friends of Literature Prize, the 1986 Award for Fiction from the Society of Midland Authors, and the 1993 Book of the Year Award for Fiction from the *Chicago Sun-Times*. Forrest has also been praised by major writers. Toni Morrison edited his first novel and wrote a foreword to the reprint of his second; Ralph Ellison wrote a foreword to the reprint of his first novel; and Michael Harper celebrated him in a poem. In 1985, then Chicago mayor Harold Washington proclaimed April 14 Leon Forrest Day. But despite this profusion of acknowledgment, Forrest may be one of the least known contemporary African American writers.

Born on January 8, 1937, in Chicago and raised in that city, Forrest is the quintessential Chicago writer in that he has reinvented his native town and its surroundings in his "Forest County" novels *There Is a Tree More Ancient Than Eden* (1973), *The Bloodworth Orphans* (1977), *Two Wings to Veil My Face* (1984), and *Divine Days* (1992). His Creole mother's family was Catholic, while his Mississippian father was Protestant, and this divided religious-cultural heritage is a central theme in his work. Though Forrest grew up on the largely segregated South Side of Chicago, he was one of the first black students to attend Hyde Park High School. After taking courses at Roosevelt University and the University of Chicago and serving in the U.S. Army in Germany, Forrest worked first in a bar and a liquor store; then in the late 1960s as a journalist; and from 1969 to 1973 as the associate and managing editor of the Black Muslim paper *Muhammad Speaks,* an experience central to *Divine Days.*

Perhaps the most profound influences on Forrest's work are the traditional oral/ musical forms such as jazz, the sermon, and storytelling. In his essay *A Solo Long-Song, for Lady Day,* Forrest recalls his mother's love of Billie Holiday's music; indeed, a quotation from Holiday's song "Strange Fruit" serves as the epigraph to his first novel. Forrest's inventive prose is clearly influenced by the sounds of bebop musicians such as Charlie Parker, and he has written supremely artistic renditions of African American sermons, certainly a testimony to those he heard at his father's church. Forrest has also remarked on the importance to his work of the storytelling talents of many members of his diverse family, some of whom had heard and passed on stories from their slave ancestors.

Characterized by both historical sweep and mythic profundity, all four of the Forest County novels focus on specific incidents in the life of Nathaniel Turner Witherspoon—e.g., his responses to the death of his mother in *There Is a Tree More Ancient Than Eden* and to the history of his family's slavery in *Two Wings to Veil My Face.* Neither linear nor chronological, the novels use dreams, nightmares, legends, sermons, monologues, and literary allusions to examine the multivoiced, sometimes tragic chronicles of Nathaniel's two families: the Witherspoons and the Bloodworths. Because of Forrest's innovative style and concern with mythical processes, his chronicles refer finally not only to these specific families but also to the general history of blacks in the United States of America.

Leon Forrest has said that African Americans are "constantly remaking everything that was left over from Africa, everything that we got from the Europeans, into something completely new that both the Africans couldn't do and the Europeans couldn't do." As reviewers Frederick Aldama and Cybele Knowles note about *Divine Days,* Forrest's protagonist, and by extension Forrest himself, "unfolds . . . an awesome encyclopedia of the African American consciousness." As Ralph Ellison remarked in his foreword to the 1988 edition of *There Is a Tree More Ancient Than Eden,* "How furiously eloquent is this man Forrest's prose, how zestful his jazz-like invention, his parody, his reference to the classics and commonplaces of literature, folklore, tall-tale and slum-street jive! How admirable the manner in which the great themes of life and literature are revealed in the black-white, white-black American-ness of his characters." That breadth of knowledge combined with a sharp irony is distilled in *The Epistle of Sweetie Reed.*

A well-known and highly respected scholar, Forrest has taught since 1973 at Northwestern University, where he is presently chair of African American Studies and a professor of English.

From There Is a Tree More Ancient Than Eden

The Epistle of Sweetie Reed

Forest County, Illinois
May 7, 1967

The President
Mr. Lyndon Baines Johnson
The White House
Washington, D.C. 20015

Dear President Johnson:

Thank you for your letter congratulating me upon the occasion of my One-Hundredth birthday. Given the grevious history of my people during that epoch of living, it is indeed an honor to still be alive at my age, in this, the United States of America. Indeed, Mr. President, you might say that I was framed by the framers, who tried to keep me out of the picture some three hundred and fifty years ago; however, I am not writing you to play the dozens with our Founding Fathers (some of whom might even truly be *our* American cousins) and some of whom acted-out like motherless children all of their natural days in the White House.

But Mr. President, there is an eagle in my soul, and so I am writing to you personally (and not through a form letter, nor a third party) in order to attempt to set the record straight, yet it won't get straightened out until you and I are straight, and we won't be straight until God straightens us all out in a desegregated graveyard—and He returns to gather up His elect and holds one grand finale-grave eruption-supreme court hearing over this troubled land, concerning the revelations of our genesis . . . When He opens up those graveyards and calls for a show-down of souls—stuffed shirts won't count. When He returns to this troubled land and grave locked-jaws crack, as loose tongues in sinister sleep.

And I also want to give you a few wreathes to place in your memory bank, Mr. President, and at the graves of the unknown soldiers of the Cross: Ladies long since dead in the long-ago past . . .

Now Mr. President, some phased-out folks picture this War on Poverty[1] of yours as the Second Coming, instead of another face on the old second chance. Others see it as yet another trick of yours to get votes. And if *you* were to ask them the time of day, they'd look *you* right dead in the face to see if they could spy a sly quarter moon in back of your eyeballs, at high noon. For them, of course, *you* could never do right for doing wrong, in order to keep the right confused by the left. They don't think you would rightly segregate the chaff from the wheat without your having a deal with Satan to turn that chaff into kindling for Hell's flames in auction for a

---

1. Created during the presidency (1963–68) of Lyndon Johnson (1908–1973), this constellation of government programs aimed to eliminate poverty in the United States.

pitchfork of votes from across the aisle, on Judgement Day . . . So help you God.

. . . And so, Mr. President, when you declared, "And We Shall Overcome"[2] before the Nation (and the Joint Chambers of Congress) many accused you of stealing a line from Dr. King[3] for the sake of tricknology; and when you worked to speed the Voting Rights bill,[4] they were certain that you had what my former husband, a lawyer-jurist, used to call "Ulterior Motives." They even swore that you signed that bill with invisible ink and in ten years that law will be without wisdom teeth, lest fixed bayonets are returned to the South. Some even swear upon a stack of bibles, and with a straight face, that your push for the Public Accommodations bill[5] resulted from secret stock you and Lady Bird have in Neiman and Marcus[6] and that you are trying to open up things so as to close in on all that upper-crust Negro money market in Texas.

Well, I'm not too upset over your accent, Mr. President, I'm more worried about what you accent and don't accent. Why the Public Accommodations bill wouldn't even be ours if you weren't a past master in the art of persuading Mister In-Between and out-reasoning Mr. Go-Between; hurrying up Mister Go-Along to riddle Cousin Gradualism; so that we can all speed up old deliberate Uncle Slow-Down. For as long as you accentuate the Positive, eliminate the Negative—I know you can handle Mr. Go-Slow in Between. (Why rumor even has it you could pull a rabbit out of a tar-baby, without tipping your hand.)

. . . Yes and because winnowing and sifting, angling and scheming, compromising, hog-tying, lying, busting filibusters, re-directing pork barrel, shuffling and switching, stuffing, and excerpting, and revealing and unfolding, as you sealing and zipping up (all the while you appear to stand tall in the feather-bed saddle) is the straight ticket, in the name of a higher goal, and the very needlework of political savvy, in order to sew up a good deal for a more orderly long-suited union . . . Even as these can be the methods—devious—I realize for regress; or on the other hand needed re-dress . . . But when a politician tells all of what he believes to be the truth too much, I know he's bound over to be either a statesman, a preacher, or a simpleton, without the wisdom of a fool, though for sure, let any politician worth his salt have a decent portion of all those aforementioned qualities. And so I say let the President be outraged as Hell about the wrongs, idealistic as the Pope ought to be about spiritual ideals, and slick as an alley cat about how to re-dress; or un-dress bills and tailor-down measures; and not sell the vision out of our eyes so what we see is still, in the main, what we think we can get. Yes and I realize how you have to sometimes dress a politician down in such a way as to not make him feel he's been undressed in the public, privately.

---

2. Anthem of the civil rights movement.
3. Martin Luther King Jr. (1929–1968), African American minister and leader of the civil rights movement. Dedicated to nonviolent resistance, he was awarded the Nobel Peace Prize in 1963 and was assassinated in 1968.
4. Federal legislation passed in 1965 making voter literacy test requirements illegal, thus guaranteeing the vote to African Americans in southern states that had used the literacy test requirement as a means of denying them that right.
5. Bill outlawing the segregation of public accommodations.
6. Exclusive Texas-based department store. "Lady Bird": nickname for President Johnson's wife, Claudia Alta Taylor (b. 1912).

. . . But now given our notorious nation's worship for peddling body and soul (down the Mississippi River for thirty pieces of silver) to make a killing in the marketplace; and then making a killing off that prime slaughter; then splicing, proclaiming and white-washing that second slaying in the stock market, on the air-ways, the killing-ground; the auction bloc in the name of progress, so help us Almighty God, I find it all the more remarkable that an American President would declare a War-on-Poverty . . . lest it be to declare war on the poverty-stricken, because they don't appear humble enough about being poor. For these folks will use anything to put a "proper face" over their misdeeds and sell them to the highest bidder . . . always have.

Why I am told that at Mr. Lincoln's funeral procession a Negro regiment—scurrying down the avenue to be put somewhere back in the line of march, discovered their group locked in a traffic jam, as we would say today, and had to stand at ease where they found themselves. Lucky accident for the liars about our old/new condition—for when the parade began, a few minutes later, the Colored soldiers found themselves placed at the very head of the whole procedure . . . Didn't it go across the land that the new freedmen—the President's grandest achievement—were advanced ahead of all the mourners, as tribute, at the Redeemer's obsequies? Talk about the state of the union. Why the next thing you know, they'll have somebody peddling steamy air in helium balloons to the highest bidder proclaiming it was swooped up from hot air in the sleeping room where Miss Elizabeth Taylor snuggled.

No Mr. President, I, myself, praise you for that part of your effort to eradicate and build—to the highest, but I condemn the make-shift shiftless manifestations of parts of this poverty-stricken program, and some of the rogues in sheep's clothing and the winesap servants in it, that mine eyes have beheld in these vainglorious Urban Progress Centers, in this very Forest County, leastways. Some of their leaders are always defining and re-defining the problem—so that after a while you realize that *they* are the problem, about the same time you commence to remembering what was the question.

Why some of the very folks running these programs—the ones assigned to going around taking names—most truly aren't able to fill out forms properly. Their spelling is as retarded as an unlettered page-boy. Why when my Grandkin, Nathaniel Witherspoon, was in grade school, they had what they called the Dummy Room and some of these self-same people would belong there if I had anything to say about it. I'd also send along Jerry Ford, and that man who comes on television too often, the demented woodpecker, Eric Severeid;[7] he's part of the reason why I stopped watching television, for the most part. Oh we'd have us quite a classroom, alright . . . Maybe you could establish a center for them in the ante-room there in the White House, next to the Rose Garden, so that they can be retrained . . . and watched over for the good of progress. Now not all of them, but a great

---

7. Popular television news anchorman of the 1960s. Gerald Ford (b. 1913), speaker of the house, became vice president under Richard Nixon (1913–1994) after Spiro Agnew (b. 1918) stepped aside when evidence revealed political corruption during his years as governor of Maryland. Ford became the thirty-eighth president when Nixon resigned during the Watergate investigations in 1974.

many of them take too many coffee-breakers, away from the desk. And they got more forms to fill out than those social workers have to fill out to get a pregnant mother an extra bottle of Borden's milk.

It sorely wasn't your intention, but let me hasten to tell you that we are creating yet another flooring for jiving off; they aren't learning anything sound, true, useable, skillful, mathematical, that they can employ at the summit . . . The salaries they are receiving come out to be hush money. They are developing less skill than the numbers runners—who all the time running boot-legging games on our folks down here in the slums . . . Going around taking down numbered dreams, in the Peg-Leg book or writing Clearinghouse.[8] The runners got a flooring in the confusion of awakened dreams but what are these new poverty-folks going to do when you leave office, Mr. President, and the number runs out on their game? Yes, and when things go back to dread, scratch and crunch—which they always do for us—nobody's going to hire them, except maybe the Mafia, or the military. None of these kids and middle-aged adults are getting anything deeper than the worst of Tuskegee[9] trade training (and peanut trees don't grow up in Harlem) to put their kids through school in the year 2000 A.D. which isn't that far off when you think about it. And it's going to backfire on you and them, but mainly us down here in what these nervy and yeasty young Negroes (who started to call themselves "Black People" of late) and the white libs, who try to act like white Negroes in black face, with long hair like the Founding Fathers, all call "The Ghetto." Well, we aren't European Jews, nor are we Indians, even when we attend the Theresa Beauty Parlor, and I don't live on a settled reservation. Indeed if there is one thing you can most often say about a Negro neighborhood—it's that it is an unsettled territory. . . . I like your program Headstart[1] very much, and I would recommend that several of these experts go there first for true-training, in the 3-R's.

But Mr. President, I say this in all seriousness and in due respect: ask yourself, how many of these young and not so young people would you hire to work in the White House on your personal staff and enter the Oval Office—how many would you hire given the training they are receiving—you yourself know the answer to the question you are priming up to ask me, even as you are reading my letter. For if you had a shake-down of these urban progress chaff you might have enough wheat worthy of a loaf of day-old bread; and you can't build a staff of life on crushed crumbs.

Still, the declaration of this War on Poverty is remarkable, just don't trust the generals, nor the captains, and God Almighty help us with these here corporals we are receiving—because all of them are like the soldier boys after the war is over—can't use what they've learned, unless they are going to turn these slums into shooting galleries night and day for gun-slingers, when they return from Viet Nam. (And the Mafia would love that.) Don't trust nobody about nothing who calls himself an expert, and as Edward

8. Perhaps the Publishers Clearinghouse, large-scale seller of magazines and administrator of an annual sweepstakes promising vast sums to the winner.
9. African American college founded by Booker T. Washington (1856–1915) in the late 19th century.

Washington believed that blacks should focus on agricultural and vocational arts and gain economic independence before demanding social equality.
1. War on Poverty program for "disadvantaged" preschoolers.

Kennedy Duke Ellington continues to warn: "Do nothing till you hear from me."

And so I say to you Mr. President go out into the highways and the by-ways, and into the slums and even into the so-called Ghettoes, and see for yourself, and then sneak back into the White House through the backstairs to avoid television peering Thomases. Be sure to see what folks are doing with these white-washed fences for Urban Progress. You were masterful in the Senate in striking up deals. But now you got to get into the highways and the by-ways, down the Stroll and up the Strand, as the street guys say, and out-smart the dealers and the money-lenders and the moneychangers. Out-think the dealers and the hustlers who are peddling your War on Poverty into the poorhouse, like the Black Market during War time. There are outlaws, who are acting as in-laws—who are making a prime killing off the poverty war game, while the true-blue poor remain ragged starvelings, without flush box, chain, or window. Mr. President, as you are well aware, we never did get our forty acres and a mule but after the Civil War Lincoln, through Grant,[2] allowed the secessionist soldiers to keep a mule for a work-horse, no doubt because they knew just how we "former" beasts of burden were now harnessed to freedom.

But if you stay hidden in that Rose Garden—God help our sorry state of affairs; why you might get snake-bit. (Or somebody'll pour some poisonous advice into your ears while you are taking an afternoon's cat-nap in the garden, brooding over the latest polls.) You can't of course be everywhere at once, nor can you be everything to everybody, even though you might want to be in your heart of hearts. But get out of that Oval Office, Mr. Johnson, I'm telling you, you've got a lot to over-come out here in the heartland. Why take the "A" Train, if you really want to get to Harlem, or for that matter Englewood in Chicago.

For if you, Mr. President, had happen to you what recently occurred to me (perhaps because of an especial view of you) then you would roller-coaster to the highways, the underground railroad stations, and the elevated platforms. They tell me you are bound-up in a fitful fever these days, about our troubled land . . . LBJ is too visible; the Presidency seems a distant office; and Lyndon Baines Johnson appears without radiance and a hick-of-horrors to them; they've torn out your eyes with the thorns from bushes of roses that they wouldn't even scatter about your grave. And as the slaves of old used to say Mr. President, *Wings you ain't got on your back you better have in your feet*; you need to catch the first thing smoking and get down here in a big *fat* hurry.

Fact of the business is, some young people have conjured up a Conjure Man[3] named LBJ, he's got the spitting image of your form, all right, but you need to understand what they've placed, or stuffed inside his body. These kids have got a demonic visage of you and our land inside their very jeans, their mind's eye, and their brains are about to explode in one-hundred different directions with what they plainly think is the burden of your long-legged body upon their shoulders. And it's gone all past any idea—

---

2. Ulysses S. Grant (1822–1885), commander in chief of the forces of the North during the Civil War; he was president of the United States from 1869 to 1877.

3. One who can magically call something into being.

now—of them not being able to tell the difference from right and wrong; the left shoe from the right. I also mean to inform you Mr. President—come long or short—somebody's put the Indian sign on you and for a politician, that's worse than a death warrant, signed in blood by the Mafia's Chief Boss . . . Take a Fool's advice . . . For in the beginning was the Word, Mr. President, but when the Maker made it flesh . . . ah that was the rub!

Thank you for sending along that personally autographed picture; I've placed it on my mantel-piece, smack dab between a picture of Martin Luther King on the right, and President Kennedy on your left-hand side. (Also, enclosed please find my personally autographed picture to you; I studied calligraphy at the YWCA a few years back.) But now I confess Mr. Johnson, that you have sorely aged during the time you've been in office. So let this freed-up lady of color send you a set of a few precepts to live by in this letter of response, appreciation and dire warning, from the heartland, or the core-country, in order that you might dare approach my great benchmark of longevity, in the proper manner, with all of your faculties functioning, in time, on time.

1. Avoid all strong drink. (Except hot tea.) I, myself, quit drinking all bottled-up High Spirits, in 1962.

2. Beware of all two-faced coins.

3. After devouring the caviar of all Generals of War be sure to take an enema.

4. Drink one glass of boiling hot water before breakfast each and every morning, just as hot as you can bare it, preferably at the crack of dawn, if you up and about—which you should be, at your age.

5. Stop turning out all of the lights in the White House . . . You might stump your toe in the dark trying to climb up into Mr. Lincoln's bed for inspiration; or you might trip over Sam Houston Johnson's[4] body.

6. Don't harbour any plots against the Negro people, in your heart of hearts.

7. Don't allow any people of the German stock on your personal inner-staff workings.

8. (Never sleep again with another woman, except Lady Bird, your wife, who after all was named by a Negro lady.)

9. Have only indirect telephone conversations with a man known to us all by the name of richard milhouse nixon; but do everything humanely possible to keep him out of the White House—and by whatever means necessary, if you have to stand in the door of the White House to block his way, personally. And if he calls make sure you tape-record anything he says, so that your secret words won't be used against you when he attempts a comeback.

10. Have Mr. J. Edgar Hoover hog-tied and sent to the St. Elizabeth's Hospital[5] under armed guard.

11. Deport Stokely Carmichael.[6]

4. Possibly a combination of two people: Sam Houston (1793–1863), first president of the republic of Texas, also the governor of Tennessee; and Andrew Johnson, a fellow Tennessean, who became president after Lincoln was assassinated.
5. Washington, D.C., area psychiatric hospital,

long known for handling high-profile political patients. Hoover (1895–1972), director of the Federal Bureau of Investigation from 1924 to 1972.
6. African American activist of the 1960s and popularizer of the phrase "Black Power" (b. 1941).

12. Swear to me that you shall never start back to smoking again.

Mr. President, your letter was of course a great honor and it lifted me up out of the very soles of my shoes; but now I'm back down again, with my feet planted on terra firma, where they no doubt do belong; like a bridge over troubled waters. (Bunion-of-onions and all.)

Yet Mr. President, this country is so crazy . . . and our children so willful in their bile-like wickedness and their uncertain profanity, their fatherless, tabboo-breaking, their motherless murder-mouthings . . . puffed out and puffed-up with the dangers of a little learning into a hot-air balloon of self-righteousness. And Mr. President, when it comes to self-righteousness, you and I wrote the book, I realize that, do you?

. . . Why just last week some of those Urban Progress Center representatives called me and invited me over to give a speech at one of the big Universities, where they just recently started to opening up the gates to Colored, in any kind of decent way. It was on the occasion of my One-Hundredth Birthday, and quite late in the day: a Freedom Day Exercise. Earlier that afternoon my Grandkin, Nathaniel Turner Witherspoon, had taken me in hand to a fine downtown restaurant; and we had an excellent plate of lamb. (Nathaniel must be doing better, even paid for our lunch with one of those plastic credit cards, a Master Card, I believe that they call it, or maybe it's a Carte Blanche.)

When we returned home, I received your letter and the photograph by an official post, so I was in a wonderful mood (and from what I can gather from Nathaniel, this is a really rare state of mind these days). Be that as it may, this ceremonial event at the school almost turned into a long-headed riot of a mix-master mess. Why the whole affair gave me a little appreciation for what you, Mr. President, must go through, jailed as you are becoming in that Oval Office, and fearful of crowds, unless you duck out into the Rose Garden, for deliverance from the body politic. Maybe you read something about the catastrophe in the *Washington Post*, or even the *Star*. Or, maybe you saw it on national television—some of the calamity they allowed to go through the airwaves. (My Grandkin, Nathaniel, claims he saw it all replayed on the CBS evening news, with Cronkite,[7] the very evening of that fateful afternoon.) I don't watch television much anymore, if I can help it, because it's bad for my eyes (to say nothing of my brain-power) and I must learn to preserve and protect my sight—before it is too late—lest I lose my insight.

. . . Now Mr. President, my situation is opposite of yours: I was over-glorified, at that Freedom Day celebration, and to a point where Sweetie Reed was no longer there. (Roasted royally you might say without knowing I was burning, I thought I was really radiating in my speech-making). . . . poor old Sweetie. Some of those kids had created an illusion of Sweetie Reed (and used her presence as an excuse for folly) and a call to riot, though born out of tragic even calamitous circumstances, but now mocked into madness by those who only had a thumb-nail sketch portion of the truth, absolutely none of the felt-memory bank of the story, and saw me as but a hang-nail on the scale-ridden hands of time. I'm telling you those kids

---

7. Popular and deeply influential anchor of CBS Evening News during the 1960s and 1970s.

ought to be skinned alive—right along with Mr. Ky—for setting up an old lady like me; for treating me like I was a common bag-lady.

. . . But no, no Mr. President, not an effigy like the ones they sometimes make out of you and then burn up (and I'll get to that too, a little later) as they cry: "LBJ, LBJ / How many kids did you kill today?" (I always have to flinch when I see those mock burnings, because although I love to laugh at pomposity, I have also seen a lynching in my own life-time—and the body was set afire.) Those kids had another Sweetie Reed framed over my living body. Like a shadow, or a scarecrow of Sweetie Reed using her clothing as cover over the body of their own notoriety. For as some of the nicer young people say—"It was wild." And Mr. President, it is going to get wilder. But now I must hasten to confess, in the beginning, I had no idea what was going on except that I did think it odd when I spotted a huge MAY-FLOWER van drawing up to the loading dock when we entered the side of the auditorium; but then I only thought they must be bringing in some furniture that some big-time philanthropist is giving to the University.

Those boys and girls who invited me (in all seriousness, no doubt, at first) turned the Freedom Day celebration into a high-noon drama. Or wanted to—if I hadn't finally woke up from my deep repose of self-righteous glow before the microphone and did an about-face; or if the authorities hadn't arrived, swooping down on us like space-men. I'm telling you Mr. President, I got to feeling after awhile like those Indians must feel nowadays, whose ancestors were duped out of Manhattan Island by Henry Hudson[8] and his gang of rogues, with a mess of trinkets, and glittering, face-changing crystals of colored glass. Angered over their forefathers, and our so-called founding fathers. Here I'd prepared my speech and it was a pretty good one, if I do say so myself. I don't use ghost-writers even though my Grandkin, Nathaniel, always offers to help out, as he hovers over my shoulder.

Now I'm standing behind the wings of the curtain awaiting the University President's arrival, so that we can walk out on the stage, arm-in-arm, as a kind of tribute to the coming together of the generations, the races, and a change in plans from a closed gate to an open-door policy—and besides all of this—it's common courtesy for a gentleman to take the arm of a lady . . . But all of a sudden—before any of this gets started—a delegation of young people . . . Lawd, today my hand trembles even to think of what was to happen, let alone to write you about it, the President of our land; but it is to you especially that I need address the grievance. No, Mr. President I'm not a gossip-spewing woman, like Hedda Hopper;[9] I know all about the proverb, *a tattling woman can't make the bread rise.*

. . . Well, all of a sudden, this delegation of mainly young Negroes descends upon me, like a chariot of energy, coming for to swoop this old body home, and by the arm—but with a plan. Lord what a plan, and now they didn't let me in on the real screwball play below their staged plan—like an invisible trap-door in the flooring of a platform, made for walking over dangerous, new territory.

8. Dutch explorer credited with being the first   9. Powerful Hollywood gossip columnist of the
European to enter the river that later became New   1930s through the 1960s.
York's Hudson, in 1609.

I thought they wanted to add a garland of fine words to stream across the planned bouquet gift of roses, but they had devilment in the rose-bushes prickled with thorns and coated in manure. They lied out loud that their plan was to merely come out on stage sometimes during the early portion of my speech (while I'm giving the tribute part to the University, the Negro Student Union, and the Student body in general for inviting me, etc.), but definitely before I got into the body proper of the speech, "Oh certainly, Mrs. Reed," they said in one big voice, just a-bowing in humility to the weight of my grand years—oh I'm telling you I was quite besides myself, too. Those devils must have been laughing up their sleeves, thinking I was Charlie McCarthy;[1] and that they had my very soul on a string . . . Then they would come from behind the curtains and present me with a bouquet of red roses and a garland streamer, with my name spread across it, with "some added laurel of praise," as one stunning young lady who looked like a combination of Eartha Kitt and Lauren Bacall,[2] put it. I guess I was supposed to look surprised. Yet perhaps all of what was to come to pass served me right for going along with a gimmick for my own self-importance and love for taboo-breaking drama—even though at the time it seemed to be a gentle enough, clever gesture of levity and born out of love, in praise of my longevity, their awe over the rupture between the generations . . . Still and all they spoke right up, and I was proud of this fact there was no back-seat spirit streaking through their dispositions, even though they addressed me in humility.

As I said before all of this gift of roses would occur after the University President introduced me, and shortly before I got into the body and soul of my address . . . I've always been vain and pompous too—something like you, Mr. President—so I went along so they would go along, too, I guess. I know I'm pompous, but then how else could I come to be a One-Hundred-year-old land creature without that bold brass in the pace of a terrapin that courts life on its own terms, and the shell to insult of a turtle? And then too, they were all dressed up so nice, that was what really fooled me. Each introduced herself, or himself, complete with their major subject. One little dark-browned-skinned girl's got her hair dressed ever so nice in an up-sweep—she was the Communication's Major. Then two of the other colored girls . . . One's high brown, with flowing curls, and the other one is a high-yellow girl, she's a Drama Major; they are wearing neat, baby-blue bows in their nicely pressed, shoulder-length hair. (The high-yellow gal's got golden tresses below her shoulders.) Indeed, Mr. President, they almost looked too perfect for words—like those storybook girls of Ebony Fashion Fair in your friend Mr. Johnson's picture-book magazine, where you so seldom see any ebony-skinned maidens modeling anything, in living black and white or color.

Now the boys got nice dark-blue suits and sober, matching ties on. Their hair is close-cut and in fact they look something like those lean and narrow Muslim boys that haunt you down on the corner . . . or run you off the corner to buy their Messenger's paper. I'll take some of that kind of hungry

---

1. Wooden dummy used by comedian Edgar Bergen (1903–1978) in his famed ventriloquist act.
2. Hollywood film star of the 1940s, married to Humphrey Bogart. Kitt, contemporary African American singer, often called a sex kitten; she actively opposed the Vietnam War.

running down in place of what some of those self-same boys used to do when they were fat, sleek and dangerous to a cutting and a shooting. If only they'd relent on the Pork Chops!

But I think to myself: well they can't be Muslim boys, either, because they thought to have a little white girl—spitting image of Jean Harlow, [3] with her curling, rolled, kinked-up to a wave blonde hair—planted smack-dab in the middle of their greeting delegation. They finished getting their bid into me within a twinkling of an eye before the University President's arrival, then vanished. There were all together seven in their numbered flock. Main thing was though, they were so polite, mannerable, well-spoken, and so nicely groomed to a glow. And I remember thinking of all people, of you, at that very moment, Mr. President (because I had just received your letter and photograph shortly before we left home; and you were very much on my mind). I turned to tell Nathaniel this, but then it occurred to me how I had forced him to stay down in the audience, when I met this group. But what I thought was: Why this would be a fitting delegation to meet our President. They might give him another image of his American cousins. They acted so properfied, I thought why they might warm the cockles of Mr. Johnson's heart; he might even want to invite them down to the ranch, for a barbeque. I must confess Mr. President, there was something unique, magical and purely charming about those young people. I think now that perhaps those kids hypnotized me, they were almost bewitching, enchanting . . . Like that time I took little Roy Bobby Brown to the magic-lantern show downtown; or the puppet show that he seemed to love so.

But now what those students did was to let me get knee-deep into my address—and to a point where I had virtually forgotten about their pledge of roses. In the back of my mind, I figured they had called off the ceremony of roses, perhaps they were as nervous over this occasion as I was—for I was nervous down to my cornplasters. . . . That they were screwed up too tightly over what to do and what not to do. Perhaps they were suffering from stage-fright. Or maybe the delivery man had not arrived with the roses, in time, after all, or, as young people will do, some of them had got into an argument about who's who in the pecking order, concerning who was to come out on the stage and make the presentation, and who was to remain in his place, or her place, in the background or in the peanut gallery.

. . . And so Mr. President, I'm wound-up into the bread and wine of my address, like a politician-preacher combine, I don't get the word, nor do I see the gestures out in the multitude of an audience—plain and proper, at first, nor for a long time, because although I'm far-sighted, I appear to be near-sighted. And then again, I'm often just plain blind out of one eye and can't hardly see straight out of the other, for looking; but then when you get One-Hundred years old, Death's eye-shadow always peering over your shoulder, casting her long shade-mascara over your seeing, like hounding hoods of curtain-drooping cataracts. But they were stirring-up something alright and it wasn't Texas Chili, nor were they presenting Oysters Rockefeller; nor grits, side-meat and buttermilk, with lightbread. They had wing-

3. Hollywood film star of the 1930s, called "the blonde bombshell."

clipped peasant, Sweetie Reed, under inspection, under glass, while mean-time, I thought I was high-flying.

For even a President don't have eyes in the back of his head—if he could, he'd take another long look at what history had in store for him in the vine-yard, and take a third view of his sap-headed decisions before he made them with a keener, clearer eye on History's trap-door, long-haul view-point. But mainly, more than anything else, he'd get rid of those advisers, who were with him too long and from the beginning, as a plague upon his house, who can't find the cause for worrying about the termites; fox-trap-ping allies, who were with him too long (so that they blind him with their blind faith in his ambitious, perfect light and they damn near tear his eyes out, as they apologize for his warlike acts) and come to have command-ment over him carrying out of what he thought was the lightning-rod of his decision-making powers. (I know a bit about this Mr. President, for I was married to a man who thought that the very sun rose and set in the power-house light of his beacons of decisions.)

Why Mr. Johnson, those advisers failed the light too, because they carry out the President's decisions—and I mean this second-floor part of power two and three steps down, on the simplest level—too strictly and in the shape of their disguised loyalty to an order beyond his quite simple orders to them.

We elect the President more often then by virtue of the factors of an illusion of his Radiance; his ability to make issues sing into a riddle and then to suggest how we work our way out of our riddled condition by virtue of this new see-through, figuring-out riddle—that sounds so good and looks so right—as the answer for that prime riddle and as a way out of our per-petually riddled human condition . . . And then we precede to roast him, in the fire of experience versus expectations; kill him, one way or another, and then rekindle his ashes . . . his bones . . . his tongues . . . into something that didn't have anything, or very little, to do with the actual presence of the presidency . . . into a fire beyond firelight . . . and a sun beyond radiance . . . into glowing radiance . . . perfect in its nakedness. . . . Then we start to annihilate him, and so it goes . . . and so it goes . . . oh the burden of being buried alive in an unmarked grave . . . via candlelight march. Oh the scab hidden beneath the masquerade.

. . . But meantime back at the ranch, as the saying goes, Mr. President, and *speaking* of can't see for looking, why I'm so busy getting a deep feel for my audience (like I used to do when I got to preaching to raise money for that kitchen Lovelady Breedlove started up over One-Hundred years ago; more about her later); and swaying the feel of my audience into the hollow of my hand, that I missed out on getting the feel of my audience's shifting mood, I guess. I'm so lost in the chambers of my own language, I can't find my way out of the strands I've looped about myself—and now those strands have changed to bars about my body, you might say. Or certainly about my mind, so that I've become a kind of prisoner. Like thirty Who-la-hoops swirling about me head to toe. It's as if a caul over both eyes changes into a sightless mask before the public's eyes; blinds the king-prisoner for the cause of light, as the audience sings out again and again: "How Deep is the Ocean how high is the sky . . ." (*In their hunger to be possessed by a radi-*

*ance forever and ever, while the naked king-prisoner, clothed in visible robes
of royalty stands hidden again before the beastly feast table.)*

Mr. President, my audience now starts to snickering out loud, as I'm well
deep into the very body and soul of my speech, I'm commencing to think
there's a screw loose beneath where I'm standing, in the bridgework of the
platform, for the very floor beneath my feet feels shaky and starts to swaying—like somebody's set loose a tango beat pulsating beneath the motion of
a slow waltz, and besides *that,* I've got a Charleston move swaying in my
temple. For I'm not only wondering what I've said to abuse them so, but
where I'm standing, and something about what I'm standing on. And besides, my corns are beginning to hurt. (I feel like a ship storm-tossed with
direction in a misbegotten sea full of arrows, pointing me in a thousand
different directions and I'm simply trying to steer the ship home through
muddy waters.) And Mr. President, if all of those people are bothered
enough about what I been saying to make faces up in my general direction
(then it's more than General Principles involved, I think to myself) the
ones I can see leastways. Now their gestures have turned to words; plain,
right focussed. At first I thought they were being impolite, impish, and un-
mannerable, but then I started to thinking, maybe—I've been impish and
impolitic . . . Somebody once said that in the enemy's house the very floor
is full of knots. My stomach was sure knotted-up, I know that. Yet in the
beginning this was my audience, I had them eating out of the palm of my
hand . . . And then that's when I hear Lovelady's voice saying to me: "Old
Lady Know-All Died last year." That's when I looked over at the University
President, screwing about in his seat in the front row and I interjected the
words, "Reconstruction isn't necessarily conciliation. I'm not known to
confuse oil and vinegar," but don't nobody seem to understand where I'm
coming from, as the young people continually warn us.

Now if you get to be One-Hundred years old Mr. President, you do have
doubts (from time to time) concerning the quality of actual light you've
cast out from your flesh experience into words. You tend to think your
words are imbued with radiance—but often as not your words can't hold a
candle's light in a darken basement—as you pledge allegiance—like an escaping slave in route with tears in your eyes over those you've left behind in
the white folks' darkness, and you know that your next most trusted light is
the white of their eyes in the next tower, as Lovelady used to talk about.
And now knowing if that next guide is a slavecatcher whose infiltrated the
lines, dressed-up as the contact man, that they (your white friends of freedom) have told you to look for down the road . . .

Then too, Mr. President, I decline to make long-winded utterances
straight from the memory well anymore—but I write long-hand by heart,
and my Grandkin, Nathaniel, types it all down in bold-face print, and tri-
ple-spaced. Indeed, I'm over here as much as anything for him because
he's enrolled in the very University, now, and I'm praying Almighty God
that boy won't drop-out again. He must be thirty years old now, if he's a
civilized day in this uncivilized Forest County.

But in the main, when I dared look up from Nathaniel's typed notes, and
risked losing my place, all I could make out was this sea of blue, red and
white, all of whom have by now, it appeared, elected to stand up, in one

body *Now*, and gesturing and motioning but some are even booing and first I thought maybe they are bored with my speech so far. But surely they are not booing an old lady One-Hundred years young? Over my shoulder? Is there some third party in on all of this two-party-line hook-up between me and my audience, behind my back, or just above my head? If they want me to step down, or to step aside before I'm ready to sit down, then they can forget it. Why even Almighty God has given me a new lease on time and He's yet to say: Sweetie Reed your number's up.

Finally now, Nathaniel himself gets up from his seat there in the front row, and gestures to me—and points to the left of the stage and then sharply to the right and then especially to the rear—like he's trying to say: "Look old lady, either get a seeing-eyed dog, or sit down . . . and quietly shut up . . . I thought you had eyes in the back of your head . . . you better take a second look at what's really going on behind your back," but since he's of a generation before this one, he's only recently started back-talk with gestures and eyes; this one gives you a riot on a mouth organ all of the time.

But now Mr. President, I peer out upon just how many people within the so-called hollow of my hand in this audience are actually getting up— I'm virtually taking names, as if I could, and numbering my flock—and rustling about, maybe some have to go to classes or go to "The John" or "The Euphemism," as Nathaniel and his friends call the toilet . . .

Why even the University President, a former Wall Street executive who was seated in the very front row, had turned purple-red, like a man on the chining exercise bar with puny muscles, whose trying to lift himself up, so he can lift himself out of the way of his tormentors, without hanging.

Mr. President, first thing comes to my fool mind is: Maybe there's a fire somewhere in this very building, in the basement, and it's creeping upwards; Nathaniel's gesturing at me to get down, and he's coming around the stage—for to carry me home?—to help me downwards, but he's moving like a man whose so caught up in what he's looking at that his actual steps are those of slow-motion movement, in the motion pictures. Perhaps he's still angry at me; for I had barred him from coming back-stage with me earlier (when I met with those young people) because sometimes I think he's trying to steal some of the radiance part of this glory of attention I'm receiving as of late—though he has the potential to be something else. But maybe I'm long-gone in my own long-earred corn. He's coming up toward the bank of steps leading to the platform, and his presence comes across my mind as a garland streamer of warming-up-warning words, but in the voice-shape of Hattie Breedlove Wordlaw: "Why Sweetie Reed, stop being as a sacrificial, puffed-up wind-bag in a circus side-show of hot-air—pitched to the North to the delight of the children, for your own name sake, who doesn't know your hot breath is seeded down with bad air . . ." And then I say to myself: Sweetie Reed, don't you understand, someone has bred contentions among the flock—far beyond your poor powers to add or subtract? Extract? Or revise? Sub-Contract? Or compromise? And, anyway, what was your speech about? Or, at least a portion of it?

Mr. President, that was the exact breathing moment when I turned around to see the embankment bouquet behind me . . . a real war of roses, alright? (And I must give them credit for this, those youths did chair up some roses alright—just to show they weren't total liars and I wasn't a total loss, the flowers were spread across something I could not see just then.)

President Johnson, I'm telling you that while I've been up there speech-making at the lectern—and telling my audience what is right and white is not right and black is blue—and unvarnishing the Max Factor[4] face of our Democracy, a whole stage-show, in black and white face has commenced behind my back, like a rear-guard action in a military campaign, but de-voted to shredding up my words into tissue paper tatters for mock rags. I also see before me, yes and with me sent out here on a suicide mission, without my knowledge, or agreement. Or failing this, surely, I've been sent out on a fool's errand. They've formed a mutiny, you might say, these very youngsters I found so charming, yes and magical, earlier. For just beneath my lamentations and meditations over our grievous and ruptured, fabulous and frivolous state of affairs, they're doing a magic show-out act. My speech has been dedicated to mending and healing out of what is left-over from the ruptured and riddled ruins, but what a nightmarish plan of the misbe-gotten has shaped up in the morning glory of dews and damps of my late afternoon—and this Freedom Day Exercise: three students on each ex-treme wing of the stage, appearing apparently out of nowhere? and Lord knows for how long? Six in all—tall Negro males of every color, like a dele-gation from the United Nations—stripped naked to the waist, bare-footed, their heads bowed (as if in silent prayer to some secret long-gone God); their right arms extended with a balled-up, raised fist; and each man bound in chains, about the throat and ankles . . . Like they haven't heard of Mr. Lincoln, Mr. Douglas, *juneteenth*—and the Proclamation wasn't written. And yet, after a stripped-away fashion, they appeared as broken men herded onto the stage of a policeman's line-up, *framed*. And now I fished into my purse and got out my deep-sighted, goldrimmed binocular for a better look. Now my Grandkin, Nathaniel was at my side, helping me on with my spec-tacles, attached to a bright gold chain.

My hearing hasn't been good since I took a blow to the skullbone, in 1906; so no doubt this is why I didn't hear them dragging those chains across the stage, when all of this commotion commenced in silence, like a dance in gestures, beyond words, that is an imitation of a most violent ac-tion. That is right, Mr. President, stripped of their garments to the waist, but one of their number is down to his very loin-cloth, lord his bee-bee'ds, you might say, and all fettered in chains. Then I looked again and to my beholding eyes it was a handsome, dreamy-eyed, young man, whom I had met on the March to Washington, on the train, in 1963. That boy looked the spitting image of Cassius Clay.[5] Lord! But what happened to him, in less than four short years? . . . And when I looked again, he's got so many chains on it appears as if he's dressed up in chains, and naked without them. Yet hard as I can recollect, I could not remember that boy's name rightful, proper; I kept on calling him out of his name, even though we

4. Famous brand of cosmetics.
5. I.e., Muhammad Ali, world heavyweight boxing champion in the 1960s. He became a Black Muslim in 1964 and refused induction into the U.S. Armed Forces in 1967 on religious grounds.

talked a long-time on that train down to Washington . . . but I do remember him saying over and over again something about . . . "For comrades must not ever be confused with confederates."

Some of the others in their troupe, in the rear—forming an audience unto themselves—and holding up placards with the words: *Law and Order;* the letters in bold print and shaped out in script of chain-like links. But that is not all. That is only the commencement of the beginning of the ending, and behind my back. I sure wasn't lying when I said, I couldn't see for looking, even with these gold-rim, especially-made lenses.

For smack-dab in the middle of the stage center were some of those white boys with that long hair, like long ears of corn, and they are doing a pantomime of a slave auction, in the middle of the stage, with that little high-yellow gal smack-dab in their midst. Kneeling like she's being anointed by the accursed; and pleading for pity . . . But now her head is shorn of those golden locks—her wig of gold is draped over the first step of the mock auction bloc. I was fit to be tied. This plainly wasn't in the plan. (Why I had gotten so cocky, at one point in my speech, feeling that those kids were shelling me about the roses, and that they were really stalking horses for Ralph Edwards' troupe, and half way expecting Mr. Edwards himself to take the stage and take me over, proclaiming my One-Hundredth anniversary of living—amongst the spiritually dead land—on This is Your Life, Sweetie Reed.) Not This! This plainly wasn't in my understanding of the plan. All of this has been going on since before I knew when. But now they don't seem to notice—nor care—that even I've turned to them to bear witness now. Just going on right ahead with the planned-out stage of their silent and solemn ceremony, cocky in their peacefulness. I now asked Nathaniel to fish in my purse and extract my vial of smelling salts . . . and yet Mr. President what you have to see through all of these foul and fair and foully feathered deeds reported here too is this: that we sooner work with what we got incubating then overthrow and destroy in alarm . . . Like the egg is to the fowl, we shall fair better sooner having the fowl by hatching the egg, than by smashing it. Now that's separate from the proverb of scolding about throwing out the baby with the bath water . . .

Now some of the Negro kids, I later found out, belong to the Black Panther Party, and some of the audience in this troupe in the rear, were sold for the engagement from what is called, "The Black "P" Stone Ranger Nation,"[6] from Chicago; they fancy themselves, as something out of the badlands of the wild west, and specifically, Mr. President, the Texas Rangers. But in real life, they are punkish rogues who buy, sell, and swindle human suffering, poverty and flesh on the altar-steps of the poverty-stricken. These white kids belong to something called the Spartacus Club devoted to the over-throw of the Republic by any means necessary, or unnecessary, foul or fair. Nathaniel explained to me who they all are as we drove home—but I knew what they were without his telling me; I've had plenty experience

---

6. Chicago gang known for their self-help programs in the black community; poet Gwendolyn Brooks worked with them and has written poems about them. "Black Panther Party": founded in Oakland, California, in 1966, the Black Panthers aimed to bring Black Power to the people by any means necessary.

dealing with Bilbo, Eastland, and your friend, Richard Russell, to get my brains trained on fools, those little scamps on stage were light-work compare to the filibusting bums from down home in the old country.

For Mr. President, I've fought for all of my days, but this minstrel show was integration gone to hell in a wheelbarrow. God's in the plan I keep telling myself, over and over again. But He better hurry up and show His hand if not His face—cause some of these young'ns learning to show-out their natural you know what. . . . For except the Lord keep the city, Mr. President, the watchman waketh, but in vain . . . (Sure hope God and the watchman *ain't* made a compact with gradualism.)

Now one of this Spartacus group wears a black frock coat below his knees. He has a fancy velvet vest on, no shirt and bright rainbow suspenders with double-headed eagles on them, affixed to the suspenders holding up his pants. He is the auctioneer, and he wears a battered, high-top hat on his head (with a ghoulish picture of you, Mr. President, dead center). His golden hair is long with the style of the Founding Fathers, pinched off in a mock, white-whiplash of a pony-tail. And that's also when it comes down to my mind, full circle—Sweetie Reed you been framed . . . again. Framed, *chile*, without you even knowing you were in the picture (much lest the frame) front and center, though in their mind-set you were plainly stripped out of the picture . . . or used as mock-background to set up their picture of things . . . like some people use driftwood in living-room furnishing—even though one day at the beach would leave them with the double pneumonia and the boogie-woogie flu. Merriment turned into malice alright . . . This is your life Sweetie Reed . . . BACKWATER TIME, indeed. Not senile; too stuffed with memory for that, Mr. President. I know what I saw and didn't see in this see-saw side-show that threaten to take over the three ring circus and topple the big top, so help me God.

Why in all respect to you, Mr. Democratic President, I thought I was calling for a split-ticket of unity and here they've fixed the election, stuffed the ballot-box, marked me off as an X, in the place for my name—and I sure ain't no Muslim—and on a fool's straight-jacket, straight-ticket errand. They are maybe a throw-back to the Old Know-Nothing party, or even the do-nothing Whigs, or maybe even the do-nothing 93rd Congress;[7] but they sure made a masquerade out of that natural fool, Sweetie Reed's performance. And here I thought my speech was the main address of the day, something like the elder high-priestess of the tribe—but my real portion was as a blind acolyte selected merely to warm-up the audience for their most souring ceremony . . .

Poor fool Sweetie, I'm not hardly a good-go-between. Those kids might be green-horns, President Johnson, but wasn't slick old screwball Sweetie a gullible stewball? Here I'm always preaching the sermon on: Oh How Have The Mighty Fallen—but mighty Sweetie's been reduced to a midget-matron, like salts flipping backwards through a widow woman's indigestion.

Mr. President, it was an incendiary situation, no two heads about it. Just

---

7. The U.S. Congress in session from 1964 to 1968. "Old Know-Nothing party": secretive American political party of the mid-19th century, which opposed immigration and Catholicism. "Whigs": one of the two dominant political parties in the United States during the first half of the 19th century.

then there appears upon the stage an effigy of *your* head (with blood, no doubt Heinz catch-up, pouring out of the huge elf-like corn-stalk ears) upon a pole rolling around and around-about like the white in the eyes of that fool Mantan Moreland's eyeballs, and carried in by a student dressed in red, white and blue rags, and a stovepipe hat, with chicken feathers attached to his outfit, head to toe, as if someone had tarred and feathered him in the barnyard at the rehearsal for all of this . . . Now the pole with the mock head rises into the air about 30 feet.

Then a fireman's ladder was extended and suddenly (and Lawd God, this following event really staggered me to a shudder of consternation). For just then a little child (at first I must confess Mr. President, that I didn't recognize who he was—scouts honor) enters on tip-toe, with a blow-torch in his trembling right hand, like an uncertain acolyte carrying a candle for a festival of lights, in which he will kick-off the march; I can see right away that the child is no more than a kindergartner, but he's dressed, just like a natural man, in a three-piece, dark-blue suit, and with dark-blue bow tie on, he looks like a miniature replica of little Elijah "Poole" Muhammad, [8] *himself.* And while the stage audience holds that firemen's ladder, this little boy starts to ascend; just then one of their group, lights the torch as the boy's heel touches the seventh step of that rickety ladder, so that they are at eye level. Then he hands it back to the child; as this little boy turns his awful face sharply to the right (and I see him) and I'll believe to the very last day of my life, that he saw me (I needed another whiff of that smelling salt when I saw who the selected child was). And then the little child climbs right on up towards the mock head of the President.

Yes and it was at that very moment—as he turned his head—that I recognized the child, why it was little Roy Bobby Brown. Now he was moving up that ladder like a naughty boy who places lighted candles inside of a Jack O'Lantern's skeleton's skull in the windows of old widows at midnight, in the light of a full and ghastly moon, so that they can think their dead husbands have arrived. Lawd, Mr. President, that child *ain't* nothing but knee-high to a grasshopper, more fit to be rolled up for a Tom Thumb wedding, or a ringbearer, than an agent for the new avengers. Lives right down the street from me. I was floored. My mind was now commencing to know what cauliflower in a pressure cooker must feel like . . . Seems like we were going down in the valley of the shadow without the sweet seasoning sorrow of the cooling off, cleansing shade to temper agony into a steel-blue resolve . . . And come to my mind how many times I had held that little child upon my knee and sang, "What month was Jesus born In? Last Month in the year . . . Born in an ox-cart manger, last month in the year." Or why how often I played games with that little Roy Bobby Brown . . . Knock-Knock jokes and riddles. "What goes through the woods and never touches anything, Roy Bobby?" / "I don't know Great-Mother Sweetie" / "Why your echo," I'd say to him . . . Or I'd tell him: "He who covers himself with cotton should not approach the fire," things like that.

. . . But up goes that little Roy Bobby Brown—on those little skinny legs of his, like the legs of those girls who integrated that school in Little Rock,

---

8. Founder of the Black Muslims (1897–1975).

with such honor—climbing that rickety ladder, made of alabaster timber, with confidence and straight for the paper-mache head of LBJ, just like an experienced traveller (in a no-man's country) up the platform steps, and dead-heading for the best seat on the train soon as the door's open, on the prime car . . . and that was the very moment with the microphone in my hand; I screamed out to him in full flight of anger: "NAW ROY BOBBY BROWN COME BACK HERE SON—DON'T GO CRAZY, JUST BE- CAUSE THEY'VE TOLD YOU, AND *LEARNED* YOU HOW TO PLAY THE FOOL AND ACT AS A JACK-ASS . . . HAVEN'T I WARNED YOU, IF YOU MAKE YOURSELF AN ASS THE WORLD WILL RIDE YOU, BACKWARDS!" But apparently that little cross-eyed angel of the Lord has turned mule-headed and hard-of-hearing at the grand old age of six.

"THIS IS GREAT-MOTHER SWEETIE REED CALLING YOU DOWN, BOY, DON'T BREAK AN OLD LADY'S HEART OF HEARTS . . . BY ACTING UP AND OUT LIKE THE JACK OF DIAMONDS TURNED INSIDE OUT BY A PACK OF JOKERS," I figured a little lev- ity might—also—make him see the light.

But just then Roy Bobby Brown puts the light torch to the paper-mache head of the President of the United States, Mr. Johnson, with the ginger and self-righteousness of a messenger from on high, whose been com- manded to put out the eyes of an evil ogre, by fire. And as he puts the light to the paper-mache head, the troupe drops its collective head, not in shame, but in mock prayer and starts delivering up some mumbling words . . . like murmuring chants of mock-eyed mercy . . . going from grunts to groans to screeching, like a folk before they knew words of a language. God Almighty, this is sternly no laughing matter. For nobody in their right mind would be calling for a national suicide rite, lest they be some of those shell- shocked Viet Nam veterans, begging and wandering the streets of the slums . . . I'm getting mad to furious and heart-sick to weeping as I looked at little Roy Bobby Brown; I'm also getting afraid and even scared, yet for some reason a feeling of guilt starts creeping up the protecting sleeves of my shuddering soul, if for no other reason than the child was under my care and keeping for his first five years on this earth—the so-called crucial years—when his mother worked the grave-yard shift at County Hospital, as a nurse in the Emergency Ward. Lord, they were using my Roy Bobby Brown for a mascot; I'm feeling like those avengers have plucked him from my own nursery garden. Yet something stirs up in my guts and steels up to my mouth to speak: "Sweetie, if you want to keep your milk sweet leave it in the cow." That's Lovelady's voice, pure and simple, I'd know it any- where. Yes, Mr. President, I'm commencing to feel pure guilty too about Roy Bobby Brown, still the most I ever revealed that boy of devilment was to take him to a Punch and Judy puppet-show last year, and then too, as we left, he asked me a lot of questions about the poverty-stricken urchins who were begging for bread or anything else in the streets (in order to buy wine no doubt), as they emerged out of the shadows, into the engulfing sun, near the Stadium, to our awaiting car.

But Mr. President, just now from the left of the stage I see mounted on a huge hog's back, this handsome man, romantic-looking with a black mustache and a snow-white brow, almost swarthy of complexion. He's wearing a Texas Ten Gallon hat, and even as I'm doting upon the lessons learned and especially unlearned by Roy Bobby Brown, I'm thinking this morning, this evening too soon: Roy Bobby Brown, out of the shadows of my shouldering care, even *mothering* care: for I told him of the poverty stricken of that kitchen that Lovelady Breedlove and I kept alive for over One-Hundred years (but now I was too old to keep up the work and nobody else cared anymore to keep things up). And I told him of the story of that man with the long chain clanging and clinging and dragging and banging along through the streets of the back alley, long before I saw the man; then up our three flights of steps . . . Back now Mr. President, over seventy-years ago, in my memory, I was talking about a chain gang, now.

And so the length of our taxi-cab ride home, I told this little fatherless, grandmotherless (papless you, you might say) Roy Bobby Brown about that man, falsely accused of murder, and tried worse than those folks treated to cattle-prods made to give electrical shocks that Bull "Master" Conner used down in bloody Birmingham . . . I told that little child how Lovelady and I fed that man a pan of biscuits and sweet potatoes, because that was all of what he wanted; Roy Bobby Brown couldn't understand why we didn't stop and give those street urchins something.

But the Mayor had sent his personal Caddy for us; and we hurried to the waiting fish-tail. Roy Bobby Brown stroked one of the puppets given to him by the puppeter (a whistling clown) as he asked me other questions. But some how in explaining it all—even to a point of how Lovelady and I broke the man's chains with an axe—I didn't reveal enough material to this precious and questioning little child. Tears ran down his cheeks for the urchins, as I answered yet another question, through example and parable to this man with the long chain on. But it all seemed so long ago, apparently, in his imagination, like trying to relate the story of Job to contemporary woes, in a Bible Class, in this day and age; and knowing that it will all evaporate no sooner than they are outside again, jumping double-dutch, or playing sand lot baseball, stealing bases at every turn. Roy Bobby Brown keeps dragging on with his questions about those folks around the stadium begging for bread, and how can I rightfully answer? He is not quite ready for me to tell them if I gave them bread, or money, they'd be down the street getting some more wine before this very car we are gliding through traffic in—with the siren howling like a wounded animal—can get to the Expressway. I was tired and worn out and so I turned to Nathaniel to pick up the questions, to Face The Nation,[9] and mainly to pick up my answering part and give it new fire, zeal, truth, examples, parables; take it all in the hollow of your hand, Grandkin, I said out loud, to explain and reveal, but mainly to reveal without troubling the child to think past his own understanding. (And that's when it occurred to me Mr. President, that bed-rock don't necessarily mean rock bottom.)

I'm reflecting upon all of this too, Mr. Johnson, and the President of the University has joined us at the lectern (and each of them commences to hold me at my elbows), Nathaniel and the President Dr. Colin d'J Heinz. But now to the right of the stage a troupe member brings out a huge blood-

9. Popular television news program in which guests, mainly politicians, are questioned by journalists.

hound and a stuffed scarecrow with a bunting swept across its body reading: "LBJ, The Rebel." And then right there, for all to see, this bloodhound, on a short-lease of a chain held by a muscular midget, starts
devouring the effigy, that the troupe shaped out of potted-meat, spam,
chicken hearts, and liver, and horse-meat (stolen no doubt from some slum
grocery meat-mart).

I swooned back into Nathaniel's arms, as I watched the bloodhound tear
away at the flesh of these different meats, and at this moment all of the
troupe on stage starts pointing with glee to this side-show event. Nathaniel
swept the smelling salts back and forth beneath my nose. I was holding on
for dear life. I wanted to flag them all down with my white handerchief—
but I thought, well they would misread this too, misunderstand it, anyhow.
Meantime, the President of the University has broken away from Nathaniel
and I; he was rushing toward the general mayhem on stage, his arms waving frantically for all to cease; he was howling in confusion and outrage,
trying to drive all of the troupe offstage . . . The audience was in an up-roar,
they were throwing tomatoes and junk onto the stage; Nathaniel put his
arms about my shoulders for protection's sake.

. . . I'm telling you Mr. President, why dots and dashes splashed before
mine eyes and I wanted to/started to send you a telegram, via Nathaniel:
"What hath God wrought?" But I didn't have the power to pick up the
separate pieces of my imagination, let alone my will (with Nathaniel's aid)
to walk away, and yet a part of me said, no I shall not be driven out, I shall
not be moved! Talk about folks acting as if they had an important rider to
mount upon a sluggish, vulgar steed; now I wandered about the stage freeing my arm from Nathaniel's, let an old lady see what she could do . . . if
they wouldn't listen to the President, then perhaps they'd respect a One-
Hundred year old woman, if they had to face her face to face. But I'm
forced to back off soon enough, because these troupe members have sown
seeds of contentions amongst their own numbers and now they are fighting
with each other. (I heard a fire alarm go off, and I spotted members of the
audience racing off in all directions.) Nathaniel's thrown his body in front
of my own for protection. Meantime the mock head of LBJ is slowly burning, like a slab of bacon under a slow burner.

. . . And I'm now thinking perhaps these new avengers to the constitution
were no more confused than Mr. Jefferson writing out that it was self-
evident that all men were created equal (as long as he didn't have to deal
with the colored ones, he didn't write that in those sacred papers, but he
sure wrote it elsewhere in the dark) even as he slept with a slave lady, and
jamming her people as well as those he created out the crack of his own
loins, as he declared his independence of their solid flesh, and his lily-
white ancestors beyond the pale . . . oh these men, what they won't do in
the dark. Then I looked at the little red Negro on stage there, with features
and face so much like John Connelly, reddish and nappy hair like Malcolm X and the color and glow of Marcus Garvey[1] . . . He was the one who

1. Prominent advocate of black cultural nationalism (1887–1940), who was known for his Back to
Africa movement. Connelly, governor of Texas
(1963–69) and secretary of the treasury (1971–72),
was riding in the car in which President John F.

Kennedy was killed in Dallas in 1963. Malcolm X
(1925–1965), political activist and leader in black
Islamic movement; assassinated in 1965; a major
influence on black thought.

lighted the torch for Roy Bobby Brown . . . What in the world had been on his mind?

I am forever saying if thy left-hand offends, then pluck it off; if my right eye offends pluck it out . . . I believe this from the Bible in a parable way, Mr. President. But this is different and offensive to sight and feel and I got a long-haul view of this short-sighted (short-eyes) Country. So any avengers got to come by me. Yet and still, yet and still beat my heart. I'm still too much of a bell ringer, when I should be sitting down and listening—but they won't listen to me, either. When I invited them by my faint house, using me and my presence only for ceremony—yet I am subject to try to fly out of the upper room at day-break or fall asleep for a half-an-hour amid a solid pattern of good and straightforward recollection from the old memory-bank. Young folks *ain't* got time to be patient, nor time for listening, nor time for dozing, lest they're nodding away on something; especially when they spreading their wings and trying to capture the span of the sun in flight . . . Or maybe some of these are taking that LSD.

But just now Nathaniel's got his handkerchief up to my nose—I've commenced a nose-bleed. I may think I'm clairvoyant about everything but I'm confused right now, as all Hell broke loose. He catches me up just as I go back into his arms again; and smelling salts don't mean a thing, at this level of theater. He puts the chilly house-keys down my back and I shriek, as a startled virgin dunked in cold baptismal waters. Cold-blooded to do this to an old lady, I cry out.

Just then the University security police appeared from out of nowhere and vaulted onto the stage. But to tell the truth and shame Lucifer, Mr. President, at first I thought they might be in on the take (like certain Chicago cops). Or that they might be a part of this whole scene, in what Nathaniel calls Guerrilla Theater[2]—as part of the play . . . This might be Act II, without any intermission, because to also tell the truth, I have never known the police to arrive on time, with such dispatch and short-notice (certainly not when our interests were involved). And if that isn't enough, here comes CBS, with what seems like One-Hundred pieces of equipment and luggage, cameras of all kinds enough to carry on a seven-day expedition, and an in-depth series on the whole war in Viet Nam. Why I'm so shocked that I started to looking for *Walter* to handle this white-paper report, still evolving before my naked eye-balls.

But who had called CBS to be on hand, I wondered?

High upon that ladder I noticed with my glasses wiped off now by Nathaniel, that little Bobby Brown was weeping; and I'm weeping for us all, as I see him weeping. The machie head is burning down now to the neck; little Roy Bobby Brown looks as lost up that ladder as a child in a dream when he sees the tree house turn into an outhouse. Now in comes the fire department and one of those big beefy-faced Irishmen goes up the ladder and leads little Robby down. And I keep thinking that whoever said, "Humor is the mistress of tears," knew more than what he let on about the way a joke lives up the sleeve of pain, but sometimes mocks suffering, wholesale.

---

2. Theater form that promotes rebellion.

I'm feeling like a spectator at my own homage ceremony, and it is very much like standing in the Union Station or the Emergency Ward at the County Hospital; you can't tell for sure from the streaming-through throng, if life has gone from a circus to a freakish side-show pageant. But just now the troupe commences to fight with the police and the CBS cameras are rolling away; Nathaniel pushes a young lady away who comes up to me now to try for an on-the-spot interview, since, I guess, I *was* the one being honored this day . . . But I'm amazed that she knew my name, let alone can speak it aloud enough for me to hear it, amid this bedlam. So I started to praying the 23rd Psalm[3] through all of this to see me through; and to bring peace, since only God can see us through all of this. Because all the smelling salts does is to shock the brain into a keener reality and my keening mind was now beholding too much rawhide reality.

I grabbed the microphone from that television newscaster's hands—that young lady is amazed at my strength, and I start to crying the 23rd Psalm out loud, bellowing it for all I'm worth . . . I'm repeating it over and over again, like those Catholics pray on their rosary beads, over and over again . . . and with that and the cold keys down my back, my nose stops bleeding; now the television cameras turn around and start rolling in my direction; even some of the fighting between the police and the troupe ceases.

Mr. President, I'm telling you prayer has power; I'm not a religious fanatic, but it can work wonders, if not miracles. (You should try it sometimes.) Yes a centenarian, with a microphone in her hand, bellowing out the 23rd Psalm for all she's worth, as if she's yodelling out the National Anthem in Yankee Stadium—does have some slim chance of being heard.

Here I was selected especially for this occasion, and I thought I was being honored in the ceremony. But I'm not talking about "Many are called but few are chosen." And that's when the words of the Good Book come back to haunt me: "God hath chosen the foolish things of the world to confound the wise; and God hath chosen the weak things of this world to confound the things which are mighty . . ." And then the most haunting words and precepts of all from one of the three ladies I want to tell you all about too, Lovelady Breedlove, and her telling me about that former slave who wrote letters on a slate, but sometimes he printed them out with a coal on linen strips torn from a klansman's sheets, and sent them to Northern Colored newspapers, concerning our condition in the South, in a bundle and wrapped about in a band of cotton in a cake-tin. Sheets his mother often washed and didn't know how they were being used by night. (President Johnson, I know that your father fought the Klan in Texas, but I wonder did he know that story.) . . . Now finally this former slave escaped one night by that song "Run, Nigger, Run" which was a warning song at first (long before he was born) but later it became to be a very popular piece sung and played at dances and parties . . .

But now Mr. President, those kids were being lead away by the security police, the city police, the FBI, and the CIA, because they were also wanted for drug charges and the authorities didn't need chains, for these

3. The first verse of this Psalm is "The Lord is my Shepherd; I shall not want."

kids had provided them with their own chains. That one who was the auctioneer is down on both knees, begging not to be lead away, and looking like Al Jolson[4] singing, "Mammy."

But just this afternoon, before the ceremony, at lunch over lamb, in the fine downtown restaurant, didn't I hear streaks on a saxophone from that very song, "Run, Nigger, Run" underneath the piped in music played for our dining pleasure, as the menu said . . . Notes straight from the original melody . . . I'm sure that not one customer in the restaurant knew what they were also listening to and not hearing (I think Nathaniel understood what I was getting at, once I made him listen at what he was hearing) even though I was the only person in that restaurant with a hearing aid. They all were sure that they were a million miles and light years away from a plantation mansion; I started to stand up and reveal it to them, but Nathaniel shooed me down. I wanted them to see the reality they were listening at . . . Like Mrs. Kennedy's blood-stained dress, that she declined to change; or the discolored eyes and upper cheeks of Lincoln's face, not touched up when his body lay in state . . . Yes, let them see this too, too solid deed, streaking through the face of harmonious reality.

I say this with malice towards none, but not with charity for all, President Johnson, sir: this occasion had bled my soul black and blue to red and white and back around again, and so I surrendered to their arms, Nathaniel's and the University President's. Nathaniel, on my right-hand side, led me away and I felt the sway of screws loose within the very flooring all across that stage and down the brief ladder of steps leading me down into what was left of the audience, and they seemed in a state of shock. The President of the University was on my left-hand side, trembling more than Sweetie Reed. Outside we saw that moving van in back which all of the troupe had used and driven up to the loading dock, from which they had swept inside the theater hall like ants forming and forging a new beachhead. The authorities had taken it over . . .

. . . But Lovelady Breedlove's story bears mightily upon all of this, I can assure you of that Mr. President and I believe it touches to the heart of your declared War on Poverty. That's right, her name was Lovelady Breedlove; she was born a slave, in the year 1837; I believe I am correct on that, and I know when she died; I was holding her hand; it was 1907, the very year before you were born, Mr. President. The hour was 3:00 in the afternoon when she gave up her spirit. And she taught me so many things among them: who rules the bee-hive and the importance of the principle of the anthill. She learned me (pardon me for using Negro English, now, or what the youngsters call Black English) she taught me the difference between/ and the links between real refinement, virtue, good manners, and bull S–t. She had her own personal War on Poverty kitchen and long before anybody ever hear of Father Divine's Peace Missions and kitchens to say nothing of the Black Panther Party Members' parents.

Cordially yours,
Sweetie Reed

4. White singer of the 1920s who often performed in blackface (c. 1886–1950).

MICHAEL S. HARPER

b. 1938

In an April 1990 interview with African American editor Charles H. Rowell, Michael Harper was questioned about his repeated assertion that he is "both a black poet and an American poet." Harper responded:

> I myself can't imagine giving up my point of view, my blackness, as a way of seeing the world. But I was born and reared in America, with all its contradictions. . . . . My own perspective on black/America concedes little to those who want to exclude; my investments are too great, in terms of blood.

While lauded for his distinct voice and unusual technique, Harper's creation of a poetry that speaks to both the majority culture and people of color has made him a figure of controversy, particularly among those who advocate a strictly African American aesthetic. But Michael Harper refuses to be pigeonholed and rejects the trendiness of the poetic marketplace. His artistic strength lies in the courage and vigor with which he embraces the American experience while simultaneously exposing the country's history of injustice.

Harper was born in 1938 in Brooklyn, New York, to Walter Warren Harper, a postal supervisor, and Katherine Johnson Harper, a medical stenographer. His parents' jobs provided the family with a comfortable income that enabled them to move in 1951 to a predominantly white neighborhood in west Los Angeles. Although the family had high expectations for their son, Harper's high school placed him in an industrial arts program. Luckily, Harper's father was able to "straighten out" his counselor and enroll him in academic courses, but racial stereotyping followed Harper to college, where he was advised by a zoology professor to give up thoughts of becoming a doctor under the assumption that African Americans could not gain entrance to professional schools.

Despite these dramatic instances of racism, Harper attended Los Angeles State College from 1956 to 1961 and was invited to the Iowa Writer's Workshop in the winter of 1961. As an undergraduate, he was greatly influenced by the rather odd combination of John Keats's letters and Ralph Ellison's *Invisible Man*. At Iowa, Harper became more acutely aware of W. E. B. Du Bois's concept of double-consciousness when he had to live in segregated housing. Further, he was the only African American in his poetry and fiction classes. Harper spent a year in Iowa, then taught for a year at Pasadena City College before returning to receive a master's degree in English from Iowa in 1963.

During the mid to late 1960s, while teaching at various colleges on the West Coast, Harper began to publish his poems in journals, including *Carolina Quarterly, Quarterly Review of Literature, Poetry Northwest, Southern Review, Negro Digest*, and *Poetry*. On the basis of these accomplishments, he received an appointment as associate professor at Brown University in 1970 and was promoted to full professor of English in 1974.

Harper's literary output has been prolific and distinguished. His first book of poetry, *Dear John, Dear Coltrane* (1970), was nominated for the National Book Award. In the next seven years, he published six more collections: *History Is Your Own Heartbeat* (1971); *Photographs: Negatives: History as Apple Tree* (1972); *Song: I Want a Witness* (1972); *Debridgement* (1973); *Nightmare Begins Responsibility* (1975); and *Images of Kin* (1977), which received the Melville-Cane Award and was his second book to be nominated for the National Book Award. In the 1980s and 1990s, Harper has continued to publish poetry, though at a somewhat slower pace. With Robert B. Stepto, he both edited and contributed to the landmark book *Chant of Saints: A Gathering of Afro-American Literature, Art, and Scholarship* (1979). *Healing Song for the Inner Ear* was published in 1984, preceded by *Rhode Island: Eight Poems* in 1980. *Honorable Amendments: Poems* was published in 1995.

Harper's primary emphasis in his work is in exploring the dual conciousness of African Americans and in merging the racist history of the country with the present in a meaningful and constructive way. Throughout Harper's poetry, the redemptive nature of human creativity is celebrated, especially through an emphasis on myth as a structure that remains vital only if it responds to the present. Thus Harper honors African American heroes, not only those of the past such as Paul Laurence Dunbar but also contemporary figures such as Jackie Robinson and Willie Mays. By portraying African American heroes, Harper opens up mythic structures to stories that have not been traditionally told for he believes that closed myths validate the fantasy of a white supremacist America.

Harper's lifelong interest in music has been an enormous presence in his poetry, particularly as it has affected his stylistic choices. His greatest musical influence is John Coltrane, the jazz saxophonist and composer, with whom he had a deep friendship. Referring to Coltrane as "my Orpheus," Harper considers this great musician his "personal signature for competence and rigor" and both celebrates and mourns Coltrane in poems such as *Dear John, Dear Coltrane* and *Here Where Coltrane Is.* Emphasizing the importance of sound in his poetry, Harper asserts: "I'm trying to write a poem for the ear as well as the eye." Consequently, Harper's poetry is rhythmic rather than metric; it is meant to be sung or read aloud. Further, he uses sprung rhythm, blues refrains, enjambment, idioms, cadences, irregular repetition, imbalance, and modulated line lengths to bridge the gap between music and poetry. In an interview with critic Abraham Chapman, Harper describes the importance of modality—poetry based on the performative elements of pitch and tone usually associated with music—not only as a technique but also as a major theme in his work:

> Modality is always about relationships; modality is also about energy, energy irreducible and true only unto itself. What that means is that the Cartesian analogical way of looking at the world will not do for modality . . . the Western orientation of division between denotative/connotative, body/mind, life/spirit, soul/body, mind/heart, that is a way of misunderstanding what modality is; modality is always about unity.

Harper has been critized for an overreliance on such abstract philosophy in his poetry, but his defenders cite his mastery of technique, especially his use of the concrete image, to ground his work and make it accessible. Rather than undercutting the harmony he seeks in his poetry, Harper's improvisational style is philosophically as well as technically rich; his work accepts the diversity that leads to meaningful connections in poetry as well as in the world.

Dear John, Dear Coltrane[1]

a love supreme,[2] a love supreme
a love supreme, a love supreme

Sex fingers toes
in the marketplace
near your father's church   5
in Hamlet, North Carolina[3]—
witness to this love
in this calm fallow
of these minds,
there is no substitute for pain: 10
genitals gone or going,
seed burned out,
you tuck the roots in the earth,
turn back, and move
by river through the swamps,   15
singing: *a love supreme, a love supreme;*
what does it all mean?
Loss, so great each black
woman expects your failure
in mute change, the seed gone.   20
You plod up into the electric city—
your song now crystal and
the blues. You pick up the horn
with some will and blow
into the freezing night: 25
a love supreme, a love supreme—

Dawn comes and you cook
up the thick sin 'tween
impotence and death, fuel
the tenor sax cannibal   30
heart, genitals and sweat
that makes you clean—
a love supreme, a love supreme—

Why you so black?
cause I am   35
why you so funky?
cause I am
why you so black?
cause I am
why you so sweet?   40
cause I am
why you so black?
cause I am
a love supreme, a love supreme:

1. John Coltrane (1926–1967), avant-garde saxophonist and deeply influential jazz composer.
2. A four-part piece (1964) that is one of Coltrane's
most famous recordings.
3. Coltrane's birthplace.

So sick   45
you couldn't play *Naima*, [4]
so flat we ached
for song you'd concealed
with your own blood,
your diseased liver gave   50
out its purity,
the inflated heart
pumps out, the tenor kiss,
tenor love:
a love supreme, a love supreme—   55
a love supreme, a love supreme—

                                                   1970

Deathwatch

Twitching in the cactus
hospital gown, a loon
on hairpin wings,
she tells me how
her episiotomy [1]   5
is perfectly sewn
and doesn't hurt
while she sits in a pile
of blood
which once cleaned   10
the placenta
my third son should be in.
She tells me how early
he is, and how strong,
like his father,   15
and long, like a black-
stemmed Easter rose
in a white hand.

Just under five pounds
you lie there, a collapsed   20
balloon doll, burst in your
fifteenth hour, with the face
of your black father,
his fingers, his toes,
and eight voodoo   25
adrenalin holes in
your pinwheeled hair-lined
chest; you witness
your parents sign the autopsy
and disposal papers   30
shrunken to duplicate
in black ink

---

4. Another of Coltrane's compositions (Naima was
his first wife's name).

1. Surgical enlargement of the vulval opening to
facilitate childbirth.

on white paper
like the country
you were born in,   35
unreal, asleep,
silent, almost alive.

This is a dedication
to our memory
of three sons—   40
two dead, one alive—
a reminder of a letter
to DuBois[2]
from a student
at Cornell—on behalf   45
of his whole history class.
The class is confronted
with a question,
and no one—
not even the professor—   50
is sure of the answer:
"Will you please tell us
whether or not it is true
that negroes
are not able to cry?"   55

America needs a killing.
America needs a killing.
Survivors will be human.

                                                        1970

Here Where Coltrane[1] Is

Soul and race
are private dominions,
memories and modal
songs, a tenor blossoming,
which would paint suffering   5
a clear color but is not in
this Victorian house
without oil in zero degree
weather and a forty-mile-an-hour wind;
it is all a well-knit family: 10
a love supreme.[2]
Oak leaves pile up on walkway
and steps, catholic as apples
in a special mist of clear white
children who love my children.   15
I play "Alabama"

2. W. E. B. Du Bois (1868–1963), prominent African American educator and author.
1. John Coltrane (1926–1967), avant-garde saxophonist and jazz composer.
2. A four-part piece (1964) that is one of Coltrane's
most famous recordings.

on a warped record player
skipping the scratches
on your faces over the fibrous
conical hairs of plastic   20
under the wooden floors.

Dreaming on a train from New York
to Philly, you hand out six
notes which become an anthem
to our memories of you: 25
oak, birch, maple,
apple, cocoa, rubber.
For this reason Martin is dead;
for this reason Malcolm[3] is dead;
for this reason Coltrane is dead;   30
in the eyes of my first son are the browns
of these men and their music.

                                                       1971

Br'er Sterling[1] and the Rocker

Any fool knows a Br'er in a rocker
is a boomerang incarnate; look at the blade
of the rocker, that wondrous crescent
rockin' in harness as poem.

To speak of poetry is the curled line straightened;   5
to speak of doubletalk, the tongue
gone pure, the stoic line a trestle
whistlin', a man a train comin' on:

Listen Br'er Sterling
steel-drivin' man, folk-said, folk-sayin',   10
that chair's a blues-harnessed star
turnin' on its earthy axis;

Miss Daisy, latch on that star's arc,
hold on sweet mama; Br'er Sterling's rocker glows.

for Sterling A. and Daisy T. Brown
16 June 1973

Grandfather

In 1915 my grandfather's
neighbors surrounded his house
near the dayline he ran

3. Malcolm X (1925–1965), African American religious and political leader. Martin Luther King Jr.
(1929–1968), African American clergyman and
civil rights leader.

1. Sterling Brown, to whom, along with his wife,
Daisy, this poem is dedicated, was an African
American poet famous for his writing of dialect po-
etry. "Br'er": brother (dialect).

on the Hudson
in Catskill, NY   5
and thought they'd burn
his family out
in a movie they'd just seen
and be rid of his kind:
the death of a lone black   10
family is *the Birth
of a Nation*, [1]
or so they thought.
His 5'4" waiter gait
quenched the white jacket smile   15
he'd brought back from watered
polish of my father
on the turning seats,
and he asked his neighbors
up on his thatched porch   20
for the first blossom of fire
that would burn him down.

They went away, his nation,
spittooning their torched necks
in the shadows of the riverboat   25
they'd seen, posse decomposing;
and I see him on Sutter
with white bag from your
restaurant, challenged by his first
grandson to a foot-race   30
he will win in white clothes.

I see him as he buys galoshes
for his railed yard near Mineo's
metal shop, where roses jump
as the el circles his house   35
toward Brooklyn, where his rain fell;
and I see cigar smoke in his eyes,
chocolate Madison Square Garden chews
he breaks on his set teeth,
stitched up after cancer,   40
the great white nation immovable
as his weight wilts
and he is on a porch
that won't hold my arms,
or the legs of the race run   45
forwards, or the film
played backwards on his grandson's eyes.

1975

---

1. A 1915 film directed by D. W. Griffith; set in the South during Reconstruction, the film portrays African Americans as violent and dangerous and depicts the "birth" of the Ku Klux Klan (perhaps the "nation" of line 23).

"Goin' to the Territory"[1]

"The prayers of both could not be answered—
that of neither has been answered fully."
—A. Lincoln

Ethical schizophrenia you called it:
come back to haunt the cattle-drive,
Indians coming into blacktown
because it's home; your father's will
lies uncontested, his blood welling up in oil;   5
"Deep Second" hones its marks in Jimmy Rushing;
Charlie Christian's[2] father leads the blind.

Such instruments arrange themselves
at Gettysburg, at Chickamauga;[3]
the whites in Tulsa[4] apologize   10
in the separate library,
all the books you dreamed of,
fairy tales and Satchmo[5] jesting
to the Court of St. James,[6]
infirmary is the saints already home.   15

The hip connected to the thigh
converges in tuberculosis; your mother's
knees spank the planks of rectory,
your father's image sanctified
in documents, in acts won out   20
on hallelujahs of "A" train,
nine Scottsboro Boys[7] spun upward
over thresholds of Duke's[8] dance.

Dance and mask collect their greasepaint,
idioms stand on bandstand, in stove-   25
pipe pants of a riverman, in gambling shoes,
his gold-toothed venom vexing sundown,
the choir at sunrise-service cleansing
a life on a jim crow[9] funeral car.

The first true phrase sings out in barnyard;   30
the hunt in books for quail.

1985

1. Title of Ralph Ellison's 1986 essay collection;
also a reference to Huck Finn's final resolution to
"light out for the Territory."
2. Pioneering jazz guitarist (1917–1942), one of
the first to play the electric guitar as a solo instrument. Rushing (1903–1972), great jazz and blues
singer. His girth was celebrated in the song "Mister
Five by Five"; he was a friend of Ellison's.
3. Sites of major battles of the Civil War.
4. A city in Oklahoma. Oklahoma was known as
"Indian Territory," or simply the "Territory." Ellison was born in Oklahoma shortly after it achieved
statehood.
5. Louis Armstrong (1900–1971), legendary jazz
trumpet player who acquired the name "Satchmo"
when he headlined at the London Palladium in
1932.
6. Foreign ambassadors to Great Britain are received at the Court of St. James, located at the St.
James Palace in London, former royal residence.
7. Nine black youths who were accused in 1931 of
raping two white women on a freight train in Alabama. All were found guilty, and eight were sentenced to death; the Supreme Court twice reversed
the convictions.
8. Edward Kennedy "Duke" Ellington (1899–
1974), jazz composer, pianist, and orchestra leader.
9. A system of laws developed after the Civil War
to segregate blacks from whites in public places
such as transportation, theaters, and parks; they
were not overturned until the mid-1950s.

In Hayden's[1] Collage

Van Gogh[2] would paint the landscape
green—or somber blue;
if you could see the weather
in Amsterdam in June, or August,
you'd cut your lobe too,   5
perhaps simply on heroin,
the best high in the world,
instead of the genius of sunflowers,
blossoming trees. The Japanese
bridge in Hiroshima,   10
precursor to the real impression,
modern life, goes to Windsor, Ontario,
or Jordan, or the Natchez
Trace.[3] From this angle, earless,
a torsioned Django Rhinehart   15
accompanies Josephine.[4] You know
those rainbow children couldn't
get along in this *ole worl'*.

Not over that troubled water;
and when the band would play once   20
too often in Arkansas, or Paris,
you'd cry because the sunset was too
bright to see the true colors,
the first hue, and so nearsighted
you had to touch the spiderman's   25
bouquet; you put your arcane colors
to the spatula and cook
to force the palate in the lion's
den—to find God in all the light
the paintbrush would let in—   30
the proper colors,
the corn, the wheat, the valley,
dike, the shadows, and the heart
of self—minnow of the universe,
your flaccid fishing pole,   35
pieced together, never broken, never end.

                                                          1985

---

1. Robert Hayden (1913–1980), African American
poet.
2. Vincent Van Gogh (1853–1890), Dutch Ex-
pressionist painter.
3. Road frequented by early-19th-century traders,
connecting Nashville, Tennessee, and Natchez,
Mississippi.
4. Josephine Baker (1906–1975), African American jazz singer and dancer. Django Reinhardt
(1910–1953), French jazz guitarist.

The Ghost of Soul-making

"On that day it was decreed who shall live and who shall die."
—Yom Kippur[1] prayer

"Art in its ultimate always celebrates the victory."

The ghost appears in the dark of winter,
sometimes in the light of summer, in the light
of spring, confronts you behind the half-door
in the first shock of morning,
often after-hours, with bad memories to stunt   5
your day, whines in twilight, whines in the umbrella of trees.

He stands outside the locked doors, rain or shine;
he constructs the stuntwork of allegiances
in the form of students, in the form of the half measure
of blankets—he comes to parade rest in the itch of frost   10
on the maple, on the cherry caught in the open field
of artillery; he remembers the battlefields of the democratic
order; he marks each accent through the gates of the orchard
singing in the cadences of books—
you remember books burned, a shattering of crystals,   15
prayers for now, and in the afterlife, Germany of the northern
lights of Kristallnacht,[2] the ashes of synagogues.

The ghost turns to your mother as if he believed
in penance, in wages earned, in truth places these flowers
you have brought with your own hands,   20
irises certainly, and the dalmation rose,
whose fragrance calms every hunger in religious feast or fast.
Into her hands, these blossoms, her fragrant palms.
There is no wedding ring in the life of ghosts,
no sacred asp on the wrist in imperial cool,   25
but there is a bowl on the reception table,
offerings of Swiss black licorice.
On good days the bowl would entice the dream
of husband, children, and grandchildren;
on good days one could build a synagogue in one's own city,   30
call it *city of testimony, conscious city of words.*
In this precinct male and female, the ghost commences, the
      ghost disappears.

What of the lady in the half-door of the enlightenment:
tact, and a few scarves, a small indulgence for a frugal
woman; loyalty learned in the lost records of intricate
      relations: 35
how to remember, how to forget the priceless injuries
on a steno tablet, in the tenured cabinets of the files.

---

1. "The Day of Atonement," one of the high holy days of the Jewish calendar.
2. "Crystal night": on November 9, 1938, Nazi supporters in Germany launched an attack on Jewish businesses and homes, killing hundreds, in-juring thousands, and imprisoning nearly 30,000. It was called *Kristallnacht* because in Berlin the sound of breaking windows was heard throughout the night.

At birth, and before, the ghost taught understanding:
that no history is fully a record, for the food we will eat
is never sour on the tongue, lethal, or not, as a defenseless   40
scapegoat, the tongue turned over, as compost is turned over,
to sainthood which makes the palate sing. These are jewels
in the service of others; this is her song. She reaps
the great reward of praise, where answers do not answer,
when the self, unleashed from the delicate bottle,   45
wafts over the trees at sunrise and forgives the dusk.

—For Ruth Oppenheim

1995

ISHMAEL REED

b. 1938

Ishmael Reed, among the most iconoclastic of contemporary African American writers, was born in Chattanooga, Tennessee, and grew up in Buffalo, New York. Reed, who began writing fiction in second grade, went on to attend the State University of New York at Buffalo. After leaving the university in 1960, in the middle of his junior year, Reed joined Buffalo's *Empire Star Weekly* and for that paper composed stories about the civil rights struggle, police brutality, and other issues of community interest. Through his work on the *Star* he met Malcolm X, and by his conversations with Malcolm, as well as talks with jazz pianist Wade Legge and reading of the *Village Voice*, Reed was inspired to move to New York City.

Once in New York Reed worked as a market researcher, hospital attendant, and clerk at an unemployment office and attended a writing workshop, where he met Tom Dent, the first to call Reed a satirist; Calvin Hernton; Norman Pritchard; Lorenzo Thomas; David Henderson; and several who would later help formulate the Black Arts philosophy, Askia Muhammed Toure and Charles and William Patterson. During this period, the early 1960s, while managing a Newark newspaper and helping guide the underground *East Village Other*, Reed wrote his first novel, *The Free-Lance Pallbearers* (1967), which was inspired by an editorial about politicians who preside over dying cities. Published to mixed reviews, *The Free-Lance Pallbearers* showed the influence of avant-garde music and painting as well as film. Reed, who in 1967 moved to California, quickly became known for his "fresh and arresting diction," in the words of Toni Cade Bambara, and followed with his second novel in 1969, *Yellow Back Radio Broke-Down*, a parody of the American western. Praised enthusiastically by black writers, the novel, which featured a religious African American cowboy, Loop Garoo, was panned by the *New York Times* as "propaganda."

Nineteen seventy-two saw the publication of two books by Reed, *Mumbo Jumbo* and *Conjure*, both of which were nominated for National Book Awards. *Mumbo-Jumbo*, a novel, follows the progress of a metaphysical plague on the United States of the 1920s and earned Reed the title of "anti-Freud." *Conjure*, a poetry collection, consolidated Reed's reputation as a writer who could not be pinned to any one genre. During the 1970s Reed would publish *Chattanooga* (1973), a much-praised poetry collection; *The Last Days of Louisiana Red* (1974), which drew on both Greek myth and popular culture to explore West Coast revolutionary and cultural nationalist politics; and *Flight to Canada* (1976), a novelistic parody of the slave narrative, which both strengthened Reed's reputation as an innovator and aroused controversy, particularly about his portrayal of women characters.

Reed would court further controversy in the 1980s and 1990s, especially with *Reckless Eyeballing* (1986), a lampoon of revisionist feminist theories about Emmett Till, the young black boy lynched for whistling at a white woman in the 1950s South. Not surprisingly, the novel took heat, from sources as divergent as white feminist Susan Brownmiller, black feminist Michele Wallace, and *New York Times* critic Michiko Kakutani. African American novelist Charles Johnson said that *Reckless Eyeballing* was a book he would have been scared to write. Reed's most recent novel, *Japanese by Spring* (1993), is his most commercially successful yet. Replete with historical and contemporary allusions, Reed's work is hard to annotate because the author puts his own idiosyncratic spin on many of the references and revels in juxtaposing dissimilar categories of knowledge. Unglossed, works such as *Neo-HooDoo Manifesto* (1972), Reed's proclamation of his flamboyant, subversive "religion," and *Mumbo Jumbo* present multiple opportunities for amusing and unusual research.

Beside novels and poetry, Ishmael Reed has written essays, plays, operas, and songs. As well he has edited numerous anthologies, including *The Yardbird Reader*, recorded albums of his poetry, and organized with other writers of color to establish the Before Columbus Foundation. Through it all Reed has remained an uncompromising, challenging, and complicated voice.

I am a cowboy in the boat of Ra

'The devil must be forced to reveal any such physical evil
(potions, charms, fetishes, etc.) still outside the body
and these must be burned.' (Rituale Romanum, published
1947, endorsed by the coat-of-arms and introductory
letter from Francis cardinal Spellman)[1]

I am a cowboy in the boat of Ra,[2]
sidewinders in the saloons of fools
bit my forehead   like   O
the untrustworthiness of Egyptologists
who do not know their trips. Who was that   5
dog-faced man?[3] they asked, the day I rode
from town.

School marms with halitosis cannot see
the Nefertiti[4] fake chipped on the run by slick
germans, the hawk behind Sonny Rollins'[5] head or   10
the ritual beard of his axe; a longhorn winding
its bells thru the Field of Reeds.

I am a cowboy in the boat of Ra. I bedded
down with Isis,[6] Lady of the Boogaloo, dove

1. Spellman, an American Roman Catholic, was both archbishop and cardinal of New York City.
2. Ancient Egyptian sun god of Heliopolis; typically represented as a hawk-headed man; father of Osiris, Isis, and Set.
3. Perhaps Anubus, the Egyptian god of the dead, shown typically as a jackal-headed man.
4. Wife of Pharaoh Akenaten (c. 1375–1358 B.C.); a statue of her head was stolen by Germans and chipped in the early 20th century.
5. African American tenor saxophonist.
6. Egyptian nature goddess; sister and wife of Osiris.

down deep in her horny, stuck up her Wells-Far-ago[7]   15
in daring midday getaway. 'Start grabbing the
blue', I said from top of my double crown. [8]

I am a cowboy in the boat of Ra. Ezzard Charles
of the Chisholm Trail. [9] Took up the bass but they
blew off my thumb. Alchemist in ringmanship but a   20
sucker for the right cross.

I am a cowboy in the boat of Ra. Vamoosed from
the temple I bide my time. The price on the wanted
poster was a-going down, outlaw alias copped my stance
and moody greenhorns were making me dance;
        while my mouth's   25
shooting iron got its chambers jammed.

I am a cowboy in the boat of Ra. Boning-up in
the ol West I bide my time. You should see
me pick off these tin cans whippersnappers. I
write the motown long plays for the comeback of   30
Osiris. [1] Make them up when stars stare at sleeping
steer out here near the campfire. Women arrive
on the backs of goats and throw themselves on
my Bowie. [2]

I am a cowboy in the boat of Ra. Lord of the lash,   35
the Loup Garou[3] Kid. Half breed son of Pisces and
Aquarius. I hold the souls of men in my pot. I do
the dirty boogle with scorpions. I make the bulls
keep still and was the first swinger to grape the taste.

I am a cowboy in his boat. Pope Joan[4] of the   40
Ptah Ra. [5] C/mere a minute willya doll?
Be a good girl and
bring me my Buffalo horn of black powder
bring me my headdress of black feathers
bring me my bones of Ju-Ju[6] snake   45
go get my eyelids of red paint.
Hand me my shadow

I'm going into town after Set[7]

I am a cowboy in the boat of Ra

---

7. Wells Fargo was a 19th-century overland stage
company in the American West.
8. Allusion to the combined crowns of the Egyptian cults of Ammon and Ra, which symbolized a
unified Egypt.
9. Most popular of the post-Civil War trails used to
drive cattle from Texas to Kansas, where they were
transported by train into midwestern markets.
1. The Egyptian judge of the dead.
2. Large knife.
3. Werewolf.

4. Apocryphal female pope, said to have ruled
about A.D. 855–58.
5. Ptah: Egyptian deity, chief god of Memphis and
god of craftsmanship. Ra: sun god. The two became Ptah-Ra when the city-states of Memphis and
Heliopolis combined.
6. A fetish or magic charm, amulet or spell used by
tribal peoples of West Africa to counter evil spirits.
7. Egyptian god of the setting sun; he murdered
and dismembered his brother Osiris in order to
steal the throne.

50

look out Set	here I come Set
to get Set	to sunset Set
to unseat Set	to Set down Set

usurper of the Royal couch
imposter Radio of Moses' bush [8]
party pooper O hater of dance
vampire outlaw of the milky way

55

1972

Railroad Bill, a Conjure Man

A HooDoo Suite

Railroad Bill, a conjure man [1]
Could change hisself to a tree
He could change hisself to a
Lake, a ram, he could be
What he wanted to be   5

When a man-hunt came he became
An old slave shouting boss
He went thataway. A toothless
Old slave standing next to a
Hog that laughed as they   10
Galloped away.
Would laugh as they galloped
Away

Railroad Bill was a conjure man
He could change hisself to a bird   15
He could change hisself to a brook
A hill he could be what he wanted
To be

One time old Bill changed hisself
To a dog and led a pack on his   20
Trail. He led the hounds around
And around. And laughed a-wagging
His tail. And laughed
A-wagging his tail

Morris Slater was from Escambia   25
County, he went to town a-toting
A rifle. When he left that
Day he was bounty.
Morris Slater was Railroad Bill
Morris Slater was Railroad Bill   30

8. Yaweh revealed himself to Moses as a burning
bush in Exodus 3:2.
1. Conjurer or witch doctor in the southern
United States and West Indies who can perform
hoodoo—that is, cast spells and practice magic.

Railroad Bill was an electrical
Man he could change hisself into
Watts.[2] He could up his voltage
Whenever he pleased
He could, you bet he could   35
He could, you bet he could

Now look here boy hand over that
Gun, hand over it now not later
I needs my gun said Morris Slater
The man who was Railroad Bill   40
I'll shoot you dead you SOB
let me be whatever I please
The policeman persisted he just
Wouldn't listen and was buried the
Following eve. Was buried the   45
Following eve. Many dignitaries
Lots of speech-making.

Railroad Bill was a hunting man
Never had no trouble fetching game
He hid in the forest for those   50
Few years and lived like a natural
King. Whenever old Bill would
Need a new coat he'd sound out his
Friend the Panther.[3] When Bill got
Tired of living off plants the   55
Farmers would give him some hens.
In swine-killing time the leavings of
Slaughter. They'd give Bill the
Leavings of slaughter. When he
needed love their fine Corinas   60
They'd lend old Bill their daughters

Railroad Bill was a conjure man he
Could change hisself to a song. He
Could change hisself to some blues
Some reds he could be what he wanted   65
To be

E. S. McMillan said he'd get old
Bill or turn in his silver star
Bill told the Sheriff you best
Leave me be said the outlaw from   70
Tombigbee. Leave me be warned
Bill in 1893

Down in Yellowhammer land
By the humming Chattahoochee

2. Perhaps a pun on the number of watts (units of
power) in a lightbulb; also, a reference to the Watts
section of Los Angeles, which is populated largely
by African Americans and in which some of the
worst race riots of the 1960s broke out following the
assassination of Martin Luther King in 1968.
3. Pun on the Black Panthers, a radical political
group of the 1960s that advocated the arming of the
black community against the police.

Where the cajun banjo pickers   75
Strum. In Keego, Volina, and
Astoreth they sing the song of
How come

Bill killed McMillan but wasn't
Willin rather reason than shoot   80
A villain. Rather reason than
Shoot McMillan

"Railroad Bill was the worst old coon [4]
Killed McMillan by the light of the
Moon   85
Was lookin for Railroad Bill
Was lookin for Railroad Bill"

Railroad Bill was a gris-gris [5] man
He could change hisself to a mask
A Ziba, a Zulu   90
A Zambia mask. A Zaramo [6]
Doll as well
One with a necklace on it
A Zaramo doll made of wood

I'm bad, I'm bad said Leonard   95
McGowin. He'll be in hell and dead he
            Said in 1896
Shot old Bill at Tidmore's store
This was near Atmore that Bill was
            Killed in 1896.
He was buying candy for some children
Procuring sweets for the farmers' kids   100

Leonard McGowin and R. C. John as
Cowardly as they come. Sneaked up
On Bill while he wasn't lookin.
Ambushed old Railroad Bill
Ambushed the conjure man. Shot him   105
In the back. Blew his head off.

Well, lawmen came from miles around
All smiles the lawmen came.
They'd finally got rid of
Railroad Bill who could be what   110
He wanted to be

Wasn't so the old folks claimed
From their shacks in the Wawbeek
Wood. That aint our Bill in that
old coffin, that aint our man   115
You killed. Our Bill is in the

---

4. Derogatory term for African Americans, proba-   owner from various dangers.
bly derived from "cooning" (stealing).   6. Presumably references to tribal masks and dolls
5. A voodoo charm or amulet worn to shield the   from various regions of Africa.

Dogwood flower and in the grain
We eat
See that livestock grazing there
That Bull is Railroad Bill   120
The mean one over there near the
Fence, that one is Railroad Bill

Now Hollywood they's doing old
Bill they hired a teacher from
Yale. To treat and script and   125
Strip old Bill, this classics
Professor from Yale.
He'll take old Bill the conjure
Man and give him a-na-ly-sis. He'll
Put old Bill on a leather couch   130
And find out why he did it.
Why he stole the caboose and
Avoided nooses why Bill raised so
Much sand.

He'll say Bill had a complex   135
He'll say it was all due to Bill's
Mother. He'll be playing the
Dozens[7] on Bill, this
Professor from Yale

They'll make old Bill a neurotic   140
Case these tycoons of the silver
Screen. They'll take their cue
From the teacher from Yale they
Gave the pile of green
A bicycle-riding dude from Yale   145
Who set Bill for the screen
Who set Bill for the screen

They'll shoot Bill zoom Bill and
Pan old Bill until he looks plain
Sick. Just like they did old Nat   150
The fox and tried to do Malik
Just like they did Jack Johnson
Just like they did Jack Johnson

But it wont work what these hacks
Will do, these manicured hacks from   155
Malibu cause the people will see
That aint our Bill but a haint of
The silver screen. A disembodied
Wish of a Yalie's dream

Our Bill is where the camellia   160
Grows and by the waterfalls. He's

---

7. General reference to a tradition of oral games, usually obscene (also known as the "dirty dozens"), in which black males insult each other's relatives, especially their mothers (as in "yo' mama"), and in which the object is to test the opponent's emotional strength—the first person to get angry loses.

Sleeping in a hundred trees and in
A hundred skies. That cumulus
That just went by that's Bill's
Old smiling face. He's having a joke   165
On Hollywood
He's on the varmint's case.

Railroad Bill was a wizard. And
His final trick was tame. Wasn't
Nothing to become some celluloid   170
And do in all the frames.
Destroy the original copy
Pour chemicals on the master's
Copy

And how did he manage technology   180
And how did Bill get so modern?
He changed hisself to a production
Assistant and went to work with
The scissors.
While nobody looked he scissored   185
Old Bill he used the scissors.

Railroad Bill was a conjure man
He could change hisself to the end.
He could outwit the chase and throw
Off the scent he didn't care what   190
They sent. He didn't give a damn what
They sent.
Railroad Bill was a conjure man
Railroad Bill was a star he could change
Hisself to the sun, the moon   195
Railroad Bill was free
Railroad Bill was free

                                                    1972

Dualism

in ralph ellison's invisible man[1]

    i am outside of
    history. i wish
    i had some peanuts, it
    looks hungry there in
    its cage   5

    i am inside of
    history. its
    hungrier than i
    thot

                                                    1972

---

1. Ellison's novel was published in 1952.

Chattanooga [1]

1

Some say that Chattanooga is the
Old name for Lookout Mountain
To others it is an uncouth name
Used only by the uncivilised
Our a-historical period sees it   5
As merely a town in Tennessee
To old timers of the Volunteer State
Chattanooga is "The Pittsburgh of
The South"
According to the Cherokee   10
Chattanooga is a rock that
Comes to a point

They're all right
Chattanooga is something you
Can have anyway you want it   15
The summit of what you are
I've paid my fare on that
Mountain Incline #2, Chattanooga
I want my ride up
I want Chattanooga   20

2

Like Nickajack a plucky Blood
I've escaped my battle near
Clover Bottom, braved the
Jolly Roger raising pirates
Had my near miss at Moccasin Bend   25
To reach your summit so
Give into me Chattanooga
I've dodged the Grey Confederate sharpshooters
Escaped my brother's tomahawks with only
Some minor burns   30
Traversed a Chickamauga of my own
Making, so
You belong to me Chattanooga

3

I take your East Ninth Street to my
Heart, pay court on your Market   35
Street of rubboard players and organ
Grinders of Haitian colors rioting

1. Fought between September and November of
1863, the battles known as the Chattanooga Campaign were decisive in allowing Union forces to secure eastern Tennessee and begin the advance into
Georgia, the heart of the Confederacy. Surrounded
by mountains, Chattanooga was held under siege
by Confederate forces after Union armies took the
city on August 16, 1863. But after the Confederate
commander reduced his forces, a Union commander ordered his men to secure the trenches at
the foot of Missionary Ridge. Instead, the soldiers
took the Ridge, breaking the mid and left flanks of
the Confederate forces.

And old Zip Coon Dancers
I want to hear Bessie Smith belt out
I'm wild about that thing in   40
Your Ivory Theatre
Chattanooga
Coca-Cola's homebase
City on my mind

4

My 6th grade teacher asked me to   45
Name the highest mountain in the world
I didn't even hesitate, "Lookout Mountain"
I shouted. They laughed
Eastern nitpickers, putting on the
Ritz[2] laughed at my Chattanooga ways   50
Which means you're always up to it

To get to Chattanooga you must
Have your Tennessee
"She has as many lives as a
cat. As to killing her, even   55
the floods have failed
you may knock the breath out of
her that's all. She will refill her lungs and draw
a longer breath than ever"   60
From a Knoxville editorial—
1870s

5

Chattanooga is a woman to me too
I want to run my hands through her
Hair of New Jersey tea and redroot   65
Aint no harm in that
Be caressed and showered in
Her Ruby Falls
That's only natural
Heal myself in her   70
Minnehaha Springs
58 degrees F. all year
Around. Climb all over her
Ridges and hills
I wear a sign on my chest   75
"Chattanooga or bust"

6

"HOLD CHATTANOOGA AT ALL
HAZARDS"—Grant to Thomas

---

2. Making a display of wealth and luxury, or dressing stylishly by putting on flashy, showy clothing.

When I tasted your big juicy
Black berries ignoring the rattle-   80
Snakes they said came to Cameron
Hill after the rain, I knew I
Had to have you Chattanooga
When I swam in Lincoln Park
Listening to Fats Domino sing   85
I found my thrill on Blueberry
Hill on the loudspeaker
I knew you were mine Chattanooga
Chattanooga whose Howard Negro
Tennyson and Dunbar   90
Whose Miller Bros. Department
Store cheated my Uncle out of
What was coming to him
A pension, he only had 6
Months to go   95
Chattanooooooooooooooooooooga
Chattanooooooooooooooooooooga

"WE WILL HOLD THE TOWN TILL
WE STARVE"—Thomas to Grant

7

To get to Chattanooga you must   100
Go through your Tennessee
I've taken all the scotsboros [3]
One state can dish out
Made Dr. Shockley's [4] "Monkey Trials"
The laughing stock of the Nation   105
Capt. Marvel Dr. Sylvanias shazam
Scientists running from light-
ning, so
Open your borders. Tennessee
Hide your TVA [5]   110
DeSota determined, this
Serpent handler is coming
Through
Are you ready Lookout Mountain?

"Give all of my Generals what he's   115
drinking," Lincoln said, when the
Potomac crowd called Grant a lush

3. Refers to the "Scotsboro boys," nine African American youths accused in 1931 of raping two white girls aboard a freight train in Alabama. Arrested and tried, eight were convicted and sentenced to death (one trial was declared a mistrial). After much public outcry over the unfairness of the trial, the defendants were retried in 1933, and one of the girls recanted, confessing that neither she nor the other girl had been raped. Still, an all-white jury again found the defendants guilty. Following a second appeal, the Supreme Court overturned the convictions, ruling that the racial makeup of the jury had made a fair verdict impossible. But the defendants were tried again, and in 1937 four were acquitted and five sentenced to prison. Not until 1950 was the last "Scotsboro boy" free.
4. American physicist and Nobel prize winner who achieved great notoriety in the late 1960s for arguing that blacks are generally inferior to whites.
5. Tennessee Valley Authority, one of the largest WPA projects undertaken during the Depression; its workforce built many dams and brought electricity to many rural areas.

8

I'm going to strut all over your
Point like Old Sam Grant did
My belly full of good Tennessee   120
Whiskey, puffing on
A .05 cigar
The campaign for Chattanooga
Behind me
Breathing a spell   125
Ponying up for
Appomattox![6]

                                                                    1973

Oakland Blues

Well it's six o'clock in Oakland
and the sun is full of wine
I say, it's six o'clock in Oakland
and the sun is red with wine
We buried you this morning, baby   5
in the shadow of a vine

Well, they told you of the sickness
almost eighteen months ago
Yes, they told you of the sickness
almost eighteen months ago   10
You went down fighting, daddy. Yes
You fought Death toe to toe

O, the egrets fly over Lake Merritt
and the blackbirds roost in trees
O, the egrets fly over Lake Merritt   15
and the blackbirds roost in trees
Without you little papa
what O, what will become of me

O, it's hard to come home, baby
To a house that's still and stark   20
O, it's hard to come home, baby
To a house that's still and stark
All I hear is myself
thinking
and footsteps in the dark   25

                                                                    1988

---

6. Site where General Robert E. Lee surrendered the Confederate Army of Northern Virginia to Ulysses S.
Grant, on April 9, 1865.

Neo-HooDoo Manifesto

Neo-HooDoo is a "Lost American Church" updated. Neo-HooDoo is the music of James Brown without the lyrics and ads for Black Capitalism. Neo-HooDoo is the 8 basic dances of 19-century New Orleans' *Place Congo*—the Calinda the Bamboula the Chacta the Babouille the Conjaille the Juba the Congo and the VooDoo—modernized into the Philly Dog, the Hully Gully, the Funky Chicken, the Popcorn, the Boogaloo and the dance of great American choreographer Buddy Bradley.

Neo-HooDoos would rather "shake that thing" than be stiff and erect. (There were more people performing a Neo-HooDoo sacred dance, the Boogaloo, at Woodstock than chanting Hare Krishna . . . Hare Hare!) All so-called "Store Front Churches" and "Rock Festivals" receive their matrix in the HooDoo rites of Marie Laveau conducted at New Orleans' Lake Pontchartrain, and Bayou St. John in the 1880's. The power of HooDoo challenged the stability of civil authority in New Orleans and was driven underground where to this day it flourishes in the Black ghettos throughout the country. Thats why in Ralph Ellison's modern novel *Invisible Man* New Orleans is described as "The Home of Mystery." "Everybody from New Orleans got that thing," Louis Armstrong said once.

HooDoo is the strange and beautiful "fits" the Black slave Tituba gave the children of Salem. (Notice the arm waving ecstatic females seemingly possessed at the "Pentecostal," "Baptist," and "Rock Festivals," [all fronts for Neo-HooDoo]). The reason that HooDoo isn't given the credit it deserves in influencing American Culture is because the students of that culture both "overground" and "underground" are uptight closet Jeho-vah revisionists. They would assert the American and East Indian and Chinese thing before they would the Black thing. Their spiritual leaders Ezra Pound and T. S. Eliot hated Africa and "Darkies." In Theodore Roszak's book *The Making of a Counter Culture*—there is barely any mention of the Black influence on this culture even though its members dress like Blacks talk like Blacks walk like Blacks, gesture like Blacks wear Afros and indulge in Black music and dance (Neo-HooDoo).

Neo-HooDoo is sexual, sensual and digs the old "heathen" good good loving. An early American HooDoo song says:

Now lady I ain't no mill man
Just the mill man's son
But I can do your grinding
till the mill man comes

Which doesnt mean that women are treated as "sexual toys" in Neo-HooDoo or as one slick Jeho-vah Revisionist recently said, "victims of a raging hormone imbalance." Neo-HooDoo claims many women philosophers and theoreticians which is more than ugh religions Christianity and its offspring Islam can claim. When our theoretician Zora Neale Hurston asked

a *Mambo* (a female priestess in the Haitian VooDoo) a definition of Voo-
Doo the Mambo lifted her skirts and exhibited her Erzulie Seal, her Isis
seal. Neo-HooDoo identifies with Julia Jackson who stripped HooDoo of
its oppressive Catholic layer—Julia Jackson said when asked the origin of
the amulets and talismans in her studio, "I make all my own stuff. It saves
money and it's as good. People who has to buy their stuff ain't using their
heads."

Neo-HooDoo is not a church for egotripping—it takes its "organization"
from Haitian VooDoo of which Milo Rigaud wrote:

*Unlike other established religions, there is no heirarchy of bishops, archbish-
ops, cardinals, or a pope in VooDoo. Each oum'phor is a law unto itself,
following the traditions of VooDoo but modifying and changing the ceremonies and rituals in various ways. Secrets of VooDoo.*

Neo-HooDoo believes that every man is an artist and every artist a priest.
You can bring your own creative ideas to Neo-HooDoo. Charlie "Yardbird
(Thoth)" Parker is an example of the Neo-HooDoo artist as an innovator
and improvisor.

In Neo-HooDoo, Christ the landlord deity ("render unto Caesar") is on
probation. This includes "The Black Christ" and "The Hippie Christ."
Neo-HooDoo tells Christ to get lost. (Judas Iscariot holds an honorary degree from Neo-HooDoo.)

Whereas at the center of Christianity lies the graveyard the organ-drone
and the cross, the center of Neo-HooDoo is the drum the anhk and the
Dance. So Fine, Barefootin, Heard it Through The Grapevine, are all
Neo-HooDoos.

Neo-HooDoo has "seen a lot of things in this old world."

Neo-HooDoo borrows from Ancient Egyptians (ritual accessories of Ancient Egypt are still sold in the House of Candles and Talismans on Stanton Street in New York, the Botanical Gardens in East Harlem, and Min
and Mom on Haight Street in San Francisco, examples of underground
centers found in ghettos throughout America).

Neo-HooDoo borrows from Haiti Africa and South America.
Neo-HooDoo comes in all styles and moods.

Louis Jordon Nellie Lutcher John Lee Hooker Ma Rainey Dinah Wash-
ington the Temptations Ike and Tina Turner Aretha Franklin Muddy Wa-
ters Otis Redding Sly and the Family Stone B.B. King Junior Wells Bessie
Smith Jelly Roll Morton Ray Charles Jimi Hendrix Buddy Miles the 5th
Dimension the Chambers Brothers Etta James and acolytes Creedance
Clearwater Revival the Flaming Embers Procol Harum are all Neo-Hoo-

Doos. Neo-HooDoo never turns down pork. In fact Neo-HooDoo is the Bar-B-Cue of Amerika. The Neo-HooDoo cuisine is Geechee Gree Gree Verta Mae's *Vibration Cooking*. (Ortiz Walton's Neo-HooDoo Jass Band performs at the Native Son Restaurant in Berkeley, California. Joe Overstreet's Neo-HooDoo exhibit will happen at the Berkeley Gallery Sept. 1, 1970 in Berkeley.)

Neo-HooDoo ain't Negritude. Neo-HooDoo never been to France. Neo-HooDoo is "your Mama" as Larry Neal said. Neo-HooDoos Little Richard and Chuck Berry nearly succeeded in converting the Beatles. When the Beatles said they were more popular than Christ they seemed astonished at the resulting outcry. This is because although they could feebly through amplification and technological sham 'mimic' (as if Little Richard and Chuck Berry were Loa [Spirits] practicing ventriloquism on their "Horses") the Beatles failed to realize that they were conjuring the music and ritual (although imitation) of a Forgotten Faith, a traditional enemy of Christianity which Christianity the Cop Religion has had to drive underground each time they meet. Neo-HooDoo now demands a rematch, the referees were bribed and the adversary had resin on his gloves.

The Vatican Forbids Jazz Masses in Italy
Rome, Aug. 6 (UPI)—The Vatican today barred jazz and popular music from masses in Italian churches and forbade young Roman Catholics to change prayers or readings used on Sundays and holy days.
It said such changes in worship were "eccentric and arbitrary."
A Vatican document distributed to all Italian bishops did not refer to similar experimental masses elsewhere in the world, although Pope Paul VI and other high-ranking churchmen are known to dislike the growing tendency to deviate from the accepted form of the mass.
Some Italian churches have permitted jazz masses played by combos while youthful worshipers sang such songs as "We Shall Overcome."
Church leaders two years ago rebuked priests who permitted such experiments. The New York Times, August 7, 1970.

Africa is the home of the loa (Spirits) of Neo-HooDoo although we are building our own American "pantheon." Thousands of "Spirits" (Ka) who would laugh at Jeho-vah's fury concerning "false idols" (translated everybody else's religion) or "fetishes." Moses, Jeho-vah's messenger and zombie swiped the secrets of VooDoo from old Jethro but nevertheless ended up with a curse. (Warning, many White "Black delineators" who practiced HooDoo VooDoo for gain and did not "feed" the Black Spirits of HooDoo ended up tragically. Bix Beiderbecke and Irene Castle (who exploited Black Dance in the 1920s and relished in dressing up as a Nun) are examples of this tragic tendency.

Moses had a near heart attack when he saw his sons dancing nude before the Black Bull God Apis. They were dancing to a "heathen sound" that Moses had "heard before in Egypt" (probably a mixture of Sun Ra and

Jimmy Reed played in the nightclub district of ancient Egypt's "The Domain of Osiris"—named after the god who enjoyed the fancy footwork of the pigmies).

The continuing war between Moses and his "Sons" was recently acted out in Chicago in the guise of an American "trial."

I have called Jeho-vah (most likely Set the Egyptian Sat-on [a pun on the fiend's penalty] Satan) somewhere "a party-pooper and hater of dance." Neo-HooDoos are detectives of the metaphysical about to make a pinch. We have issued warrants for a god arrest. If Jeho-vah reveals his real name he will be released on his own recognizance de-horned and put out to pasture.

A dangerous paranoid pain-in-the-neck a CopGod from the git-go, Jeho-vah was the successful law and order candidate in the mythological relay of the 4th century A.D. Jeho-vah is the God of punishment. The H-Bomb is a typical Jeho-vah "miracle." Jeho-vah is why we are in Vietnam. He told Moses to go out and "subdue" the world.

There has never been in history another such culture as the Western civilization—a culture which has practiced the belief that the physical and social environment of man is subject to rational manipulation and that history is subject to the will and action of man; whereas central to the traditional cultures of the rivals of Western civilization, those of Africa and Asia, is a belief that it is environment that dominates man. The Politics of Hysteria, *Edmund Stillman and William Pfaff.*

"Political leaders" are merely altar boys from Jeho-vah. While the targets of some "revolutionaries" are laundramats and candy stores, Neo-HooDoo targets are TV the museums the symphony halls and churches art music and literature departments in Christianizing (education I think they call it!) universities which propogate the Art of Jeho-vah—much Byzantine Middle Ages Renaissance painting of Jeho-vah's "500 years of civilization" as Nixon put it are Jeho-vah propaganda. Many White revolutionaries can only get together with 3rd world people on the most mundane 'political' level because they are of Jeho-vah's party and don't know it. How much Black music do so called revolutionary underground radio stations play. On the other hand how much Bach?

Neo-HooDoos are Black Red (Black Hawk an American Indian was an early philosopher of the HooDoo Church) and occasionally White (Madamemoiselle Charlotte is a Haitian Loa [Spirit]).

Neo-HooDoo is a litany seeking its text
Neo-HooDoo is a Dance and Music closing in on its words
Neo-HooDoo is a Church finding its lyrics
Cecil Brown Al Young Calvin Hernton

David Henderson Steve Cannon Quincy Troupe
Ted Joans Victor Cruz N.H. Pritchard Ishmael Reed
Lennox Raphael Sarah Fabio Ron Welburn are Neo-
HooDoo's "Manhattan Project" of writing . . .

A Neo-HooDoo celebration will involve the dance music
and poetry of Neo-HooDoo and whatever ideas the
participating artists might add. A Neo-HooDoo seal
is the Face of an Old American Train.
Neo-HooDoo signs are everywhere!
Neo-HooDoo is the Now Locomotive swinging
up the Tracks of the American Soul.

Almost 100 years ago HooDoo was forced to say
Goodbye to America. Now HooDoo is
back as Neo-HooDoo
You can't keep a good church down!

1972

From Mumbo Jumbo

1

A True Sport, the Mayor of New Orleans, spiffy in his patent-leather brown
and white shoes, his plaid suit, the Rudolph Valentino parted-down-the-
middle hair style, sits in his office. Sprawled upon his knees is Zuzu, local
doo-wack-a-doo and voo-do-dee-odo fizgig. A slatternly floozy, her green,
sequined dress quivers.

Work has kept Your Honor late.

The Mayor passes the flask of bootlegged gin to Zuzu. She takes a sip and
continues to spread sprawl and behave skittishly. Loose. She is inhaling
from a Chesterfield cigarette in a shameless brazen fashion.

The telephone rings.

The Mayor removes his hand and picks up the receiver; he recognizes at
once the voice of his poker pardner on the phone.

Harry, you'd better get down here quick. What was once dormant is now a
Creeping Thing.

The Mayor stands up and Zuzu lands on the floor. Her posture reveals a
small flask stuck in her garter as well as some healthily endowed gams.

What's wrong, Harry?

I gots to git down to the infirmary, Zuzu, something awful is happening, the Thing has stirred in its moorings. The Thing that my Grandfather Harry and his generation of Harrys had thought was nothing but a false alarm.

The Mayor, dragging the woman by the fox skins hanging from her neck, leaves city hall and jumps into his Stutz Bearcat parked at the curb. They drive until they reach St. Louis Cathedral where 19th-Century HooDoo Queen Marie Laveau was a frequent worshiper; its location was about 10 blocks from Place Congo. They walk up the steps and the door's Judas Eye swings open.

Joe Sent Me.

What's going on, hon? Is this a speakeasy? Zuzu inquires in her cutesy-poo drawl.

The door opens to a main room of the church which has been converted into an infirmary. About 22 people lie on carts. Doctors are rushing back and forth; they wear surgeon's masks and white coats. Doors open and shut.

1 man approaches the Mayor who is walking from bed to bed examining the sleeping occupants, including the priest of the parish.

What's the situation report, doc? the Mayor asks.

We have 22 of them. The only thing that seems to anesthetize them is sleep.

When did it start?

This morning. We got reports from down here that people were doing "stupid sensual things," were in a state of "uncontrollable frenzy," were wriggling like fish, doing something called the "Eagle Rock" and the "Sassy Bump"; were cutting a mean "Mooche," and "lusting after relevance." We decoded this coon mumbo jumbo. We knew that something was Jes Grewing just like the 1890s flair-up. We thought that the local infestation area was Place Congo so we put our antipathetic substances to work on it, to try to drive it out; but it started to play hide and seek with us, a case occurring in 1 neighborhood and picking up in another. It began to leapfrog all about us.

But can't you put it under 1 of them microscopes? Lock it in? Can't you protective-reaction the dad-blamed thing? Look I got an election coming up—

To blazes with your election, man! Don't you understand, if this Jes Grew becomes pandemic it will mean the end of Civilization As We Know It?

That serious?

Yes. You see, it's not 1 of those germs that break bleed suck gnaw or devour. It's nothing we can bring into focus or categorize; once we call it 1 thing it forms into something else.

No man. This is a *psychic epidemic*, not a lesser germ like typhoid yellow fever or syphilis. We can handle those. This belongs under some ancient Demonic Theory of Disease.

Well, what about the priest?

We tried him but it seized him too. He was shouting and carrying on like any old coon wench with a bass drum.

What about the patients, did you ask any of them about how they knew it?

Yes, 1, Harry. When we thought it was physical we examined his output, and drinking water to determine if we could find some normal germ. We asked him questions, like what he had seen.

What *did* he see?

He said he saw Nkulu Kulu of the Zulu, a locomotive with a red green and black python entwined in its face, Johnny Canoeing up the tracks.

Well Clem, how about his feelings? How did he feel?

He said he felt like the gut heart and lungs of Africa's interior. He said he felt like the Kongo: "Land of the Panther." He said he felt like "deserting his master," as the Kongo is "prone to do." He said he felt he could dance on a dime.

Well, his hearing, Clem. His hearing.

He said he was hearing shank bones, jew's harps, bagpipes, flutes, conch horns, drums, banjos, kazoos.

Go on go on and then what did he say?

He started to speak in tongues. There are no isolated cases in this thing. It knows no class no race no consciousness. It is self-propagating and you can never tell when it will hit.

Well doc, did you get other opinions?

Who do you think some of those other cases are? 6 of them are some of the most distinguished bacteriologists epidemologists and chemists from the University.

There is a commotion outside. The Mayor rushes out to see Zuzu rejoicing. Slapping the attendants who are attempting to placate her. The people
on carts suddenly leap up and do their individual numbers. The Mayor
feels that uncomfortable sensation at the nape and soon he is doing something resembling the symptoms of Jes Grew, and the Doctor who rushes to
his aid starts slipping dipping gliding on out of doors and into the streets.
Shades of windows fly up. Lights flick on in buildings. And before you
know it the whole quarter is in convulsions from Jes Grew's entrance into
the Govi of New Orleans; the charming city, the amalgam of Spanish
French and African culture, is out-of-its-head. By morning there are 10,000
cases of Jes Grew.

• • •

*The foolish Wallflower Order hadn't learned a damned thing. They thought
that by fumigating the Place Congo in the 1890s when people were doing the
Bamboula the Chacta the Babouille the Counjaille the Juba the Congo and
the VooDoo that this would put an end to it. That it was merely a fad. But
they did not understand that the Jes Grew epidemic was unlike physical
plagues. Actually Jes Grew was an anti-plague. Some plagues caused the
body to waste away; Jes Grew enlivened the host. Other plagues were accompanied by bad air (malaria). Jes Grew victims said that the air was as clear as
they had ever seen it and that there was the aroma of roses and perfumes
which had never before enticed their nostrils. Some plagues arise from decomposing animals, but Jes Grew is electric as life and is characterized by ebullience and ecstasy. Terrible plagues were due to the wrath of God; but Jes
Grew is the delight of the gods.*
*So Jes Grew is seeking its words. Its text. For what good is a liturgy without a
text? In the 1890s the text was not available and Jes Grew was out there all
alone. Perhaps the 1920s will also be a false alarm and Jes Grew will evaporate as quickly as it appeared again broken-hearted and double-crossed (++)*

• • •

Once the band starts, everybody starts swaying from one side of the street to
the other, especially those who drop in and follow the ones who have been
to the funeral. These people are known as "the second line" and they may
be anyone passing along the street who wants to hear the music. *The spirit
hits them and they follow*

(My italics)
Louis Armstrong

Mumbo Jumbo

[Mandingo *mā-mā-gyo-mbō*, "magician who makes the troubled spirits of
ancestors go away": *mā-mā*, grandmother+*gyo*, trouble+*mbō*, to leave.]

*The American Heritage Dictionary
of the English Language*

Some *unknown natural phenomenon* occurs
which cannot be explained,
and a new local demigod is named.
—Zora Neale Nurston on the origin of a new loa

The earliest Ragtime song, like Topsy, "jes' grew."

We appropriated about the last one of the "jes' grew" songs.
It was a song which had been sung for years
all through the South. The words were unprintable, but
the tune was irresistible, and belonged to nobody.
                                            —James Weldon Johnson,
                              The Book of American Negro Poetry

                                        2

With the astonishing rapidity of Booker T. Washington's Grapevine Telegraph Jes Grew spreads through America following a strange course. Pine
Bluff and Magnolia Arkansas are hit; Natchez, Meridian and Greenwood
Mississippi report cases. Sporadic outbreaks occur in Nashville and Knoxville Tennessee as well as St. Louis where the bumping and grinding cause
the Gov to call up the Guard. A mighty influence, Jes Grew infects all that
it touches.

                                                                    1972

TONI CADE BAMBARA

1939–1995

Toni Cade Bambara was an activist writer who championed African American
communal traditions, especially the spoken language and storytelling patterns of
black folk. Active in the 1960s Black Arts movement, she edited the anthology *The
Black Woman* (1970), one of the pivotal texts in African American feminist writing.
Her other anthology, *Tales and Stories for Black Folks* (1971), which she called "a
part of our Great Kitchen Tradition," is directly addressed to African American
black youth. Known as one of the finest African American short story writers, she
published two collections, *Gorilla My Love* (1972) and *The Sea Birds Are Still Alive*
(1977), as well as a futuristic revolutionary novel, *The Salt Eaters* (1980). Her second novel, *If Blessings Come* (written in 1987 and still unpublished), deals with the
Atlanta child murders of the 1970s.

Born Toni Cade in New York City on March 25, 1939, she, along with her
brother, Walter, were raised by their mother, Helen Brent Henderson Cade. Cade's
mother refused to distinguish "between how a girl should think and behave and
how a boy should think and behave," expecting her children to actively cultivate
their own judgment and encouraging the development of their inner life. She was
also adamant that black history be accurately taught in any school her children
attended; she would often startle her children's teachers by her frequent appearances in the classroom.

Bambara also acknowledged her unofficial set of second-string "mothers from
the Miss Naomi types . . . women who led a very exciting night life and 'who had
lots of clothes in the closet' and a very shrewd method of dealing with men," to the
"Miss Gladys types . . . who were willing and able to give free advice on everything
from 'how to get your homework done' to which number you should play." Cade
honored her own matrilineal tradition by adding Bambara to her name after she
discovered that her grandmother had adopted it as part of her surname. The sense

of collective mothering so much a part of black communities is central to Bambara's fiction.

Despite frequent childhood moves from borough to borough in New York City, then to Jersey City, New Jersey, as well as to the South, Bambara continued her schooling, frequently holding down several jobs at the same time. After graduating from a joint undergraduate program in theatre arts and English at Queens College in 1959, Bambara went on to graduate study of African fiction at the City College of New York (CCNY), returning there to teach in the SEEK program between 1965 and 1969. In the 1960s, while working at different jobs—as a social worker at the Harlem Welfare Center, as a program director at the Colony House in Brooklyn, as a recreational and occupational therapist in Metropolitan Hospital's psychiatric division, as well as in editing positions at CCNY—she began to publish short fiction in journals such as *Vendome, Massachusetts Review, The Liberator, Prairie Schooner,* and *Redbook.*

But it was not until 1970, after participating in some early women's consciousness groups and after editing *The Black Woman,* that Bambara began to take her literary talents seriously. Before that, as she put it, writing was "rather frivolous . . . something you did because you didn't feel like doing any work." In 1970 too, Bambara had a daughter, Karma. That event was followed by her editing a second anthology, *Tales and Stories for Black Folks* (1971), which combined work by established black writers such as Langston Hughes, Alice Walker, and Ernest Gaines with stories by several of her freshmen composition students at Livingston College, where she had begun teaching in 1969. In the *New York Times Book Review,* Toni Morrison praised this volume for its acknowledgment that children have something to bring to the reading experience and that "*nothing*—not pictures, not binding, not covers can give [children's books] permanent life except language." *Tales and Stories for Black Folks* includes Bambara's much-loved black fairy tales, which sometimes are subversive take-offs of European tales such as "The Little Three Pigs" and which demonstrate the richness of black English and the revolutionary values of the black folk tradition.

Included in this anthology too was Bambara's short story *Raymond's Run,* which features a feisty black adolescent girl, the subject of many of the short stories included in her first collection, the much praised *Gorilla My Love* (1972). Written in rhythmic urban black English, these stories challenged the female victim role in which much of early 1970s feminist literature indulged. *Gorilla My Love* also announced Bambara's most persistent stylistic characteristic, the use of jazz improvisation as the basis of her storytelling. Bambara's second collection, *The Sea Birds Are Still Alive,* shares with her first a focus on the sensibilities of black neighborhoods in big cities and avoids a safe use of linear plots.

Bambara's use of jazz improvisation is even more complex in her first novel, *The Salt Eaters* (1980), a multilayered narrative that explores the high emotional costs of sustained political struggle in the African American community and the extra psychological toll such activism takes on black women. In the novel, a community organizer named Velma Henry attempts suicide after years of battling to save a community center facing chronic funding problems and feuding among the constituencies it serves. Bambara's narrative plunges the reader into the community's attempts to heal Velma, from the chants of the female elders to "traditional folk remedies" and "modern medical techniques."

The novel has been much admired by other African American writers, such as Toni Morrison, who oversaw its publication while working as an editor at Random House, and John Wideman, who compared the narrator's shuttling backward and forward in time and the weaving of conversations, thoughts, and dreams to "concentric circles and the concept of sacred space and sacred time of traditional African religion."

That international tone was evident in Bambara's actions as well as in her writings. In 1973 she traveled to Cuba for the meeting of the Federation of Cuban Women and in 1975 to Vietnam, where she met with the Women's Union. While living in the South in the late 1970s, she helped to found the Southern Collective of African American Writers. She wrote the introduction to the groundbreaking women of color anthology, *This Bridge Called My Back* (1981), edited by Chicana writers and theorists, Gloria Anzaldua and Cherrie Moraga. Bambara also contributed to the West Coast anthology of work by Latina, African American, and gay women, edited by Irene Zahava called *Love Struggle and Change: Stories by Women* (1988).

In the 1980s and early 1990s, Bambara focused on film and video projects. Several of her short stories, *Gorilla My Love, Medley, Witchbird, The Johnson Girls,* and *The Long Night* have been adapted to film. She helped create *The Bombing of Osage Avenue* (1986), a video about the attack on MOVE, the alternative black group bombed by the Philadelphia police. And she was a writer for a series on W. E. B. Du Bois.

Until her death in 1995, Bambara lived in Philadelphia, where she was intensely involved in community media activism. When Bambara died in December 1995, the *New York Times* obituary recalled her unique contribution to American literature and noted the striking way she wove black dialects into her prose, creating a unique, complex language. Writers and readers responded to her death by organizing memorials to her throughout the United States.

Raymond's Run

I don't have much work to do around the house like some girls. My mother does that. And I don't have to earn my pocket money by hustling; George runs errands for the big boys and sells Christmas cards. And anything else that's got to get done, my father does. All I have to do in life is mind my brother Raymond, which is enough.

Sometimes I slip and say my little brother Raymond. But as any fool can see he's much bigger and he's older too. But a lot of people call him my little brother cause he needs looking after cause he's not quite right. And a lot of smart mouths got lots to say about that too, especially when George was minding him. But now, if anybody has anything to say to Raymond, anything to say about his big head, they have to come by me. And I don't play the dozens[1] or believe in standing around with somebody in my face doing a lot of talking. I much rather just knock you down and take my chances even if I am a little girl with skinny arms and a squeaky voice, which is how I got the name Squeaky. And if things get too rough, I run. And as anybody can tell you, I'm the fastest thing on two feet.

There is no track meet that I don't win the first place medal. I used to win the twenty-yard dash when I was a little kid in kindergarten. Nowadays, it's the fifty-yard dash. And tomorrow I'm subject to run the quarter-meter

---

1. Tradition of oral games, often obscene (also known as the "dirty dozens"), in which black males insult each other's relatives, especially their moth- ers (as in "yo' mama"), and in which the object is to test the opponent's emotional strength—the first person to get angry loses.

relay all by myself and come in first, second, and third. The big kids call me Mercury cause I'm the swiftest thing in the neighborhood. Everybody knows that—except two people who know better, my father and me. He can beat me to Amsterdam Avenue with me having a two fire-hydrant headstart and him running with his hands in his pockets and whistling. But that's private information. Cause can you imagine some thirty-five-year-old man stuffing himself into PAL[2] shorts to race little kids? So as far as everyone's concerned, I'm the fastest and that goes for Gretchen, too, who has put out the tale that she is going to win the first-place medal this year. Ridiculous. In the second place, she's got short legs. In the third place, she's got freckles. In the first place, no one can beat me and that's all there is to it.

I'm standing on the corner admiring the weather and about to take a stroll down Broadway so I can practice my breathing exercises, and I've got Raymond walking on the inside close to the buildings, cause he's subject to fits of fantasy and starts thinking he's a circus performer and that the curb is a tightrope strung high in the air. And sometimes after a rain he likes to step down off his tightrope right into the gutter and slosh around getting his shoes and cuffs wet. Then I get hit when I get home. Or sometimes if you don't watch him he'll dash across traffic to the island in the middle of Broadway and give the pigeons a fit. Then I have to go behind him apologizing to all the old people sitting around trying to get some sun and getting all upset with the pigeons fluttering around them, scattering their newspapers and upsetting the waxpaper lunches in their laps. So I keep Raymond on the inside of me, and he plays like he's driving a stage coach which is O.K. by me so long as he doesn't run me over or interrupt my breathing exercises, which I have to do on account of I'm serious about my running, and I don't care who knows it.

Now some people like to act like things come easy to them, won't let on that they practice. Not me. I'll high-prance down 34th Street like a rodeo pony to keep my knees strong even if it does get my mother uptight so that she walks ahead like she's not with me, don't know me, is all by herself on a shopping trip, and I am somebody else's crazy child. Now you take Cynthia Procter for instance. She's just the opposite. If there's a test tomorrow, she'll say something like, "Oh, I guess I'll play handball this afternoon and watch television tonight," just to let you know she ain't thinking about the test. Or like last week when she won the spelling bee for the millionth time, "A good thing you got 'receive,' Squeaky, cause I would have got it wrong. I completely forgot about the spelling bee." And she'll clutch the lace on her blouse like it was a narrow escape. Oh, brother. But of course when I pass her house on my early morning trots around the block, she is practicing the scales on the piano over and over and over and over. Then in music class she always lets herself get bumped around so she falls accidently on purpose onto the piano stool and is so surprised to find herself sitting there that she decides just for fun to try out the ole keys. And what do you know— Chopin's waltzes just spring out of her fingertips and she's the most surprised thing in the world. A regular prodigy. I could kill people like that. I stay up all night studying the words for the spelling bee. And you can see

2. A brand of clothing.

me any time of day practicing running. I never walk if I can trot, and shame on Raymond if he can't keep up. But of course he does, cause if he hangs back someone's liable to walk up to him and get smart, or take his allowance from him, or ask him where he got that great big pumpkin head. People are so stupid sometimes.

So I'm strolling down Broadway breathing out and breathing in on counts of seven, which is my lucky number, and here comes Gretchen and her sidekicks: Mary Louise, who used to be a friend of mine when she first moved to Harlem from Baltimore and got beat up by everybody till I took up for her on account of her mother and my mother used to sing in the same choir when they were young girls, but people ain't grateful, so now she hangs out with the new girl Gretchen and talks about me like a dog; and Rosie, who is as fat as I am skinny and has a big mouth where Raymond is concerned and is too stupid to know that there is not a big deal of difference between herself and Raymond and that she can't afford to throw stones. So they are steady coming up Broadway and I see right away that it's going to be one of those Dodge City scenes cause the street ain't that big and they're close to the buildings just as we are. First I think I'll step into the candy store and look over the new comics and let them pass. But that's chicken and I've got a reputation to consider. So then I think I'll just walk straight on through them or even over them if necessary. But as they get to me, they slow down. I'm ready to fight, cause like I said I don't feature a whole lot of chit-chat, I much prefer to just knock you down right from the jump and save everybody a lotta precious time.

"You signing up for the May Day races?" smiles Mary Louise, only it's not a smile at all. A dumb question like that doesn't deserve an answer. Besides, there's just me and Gretchen standing there really, so no use wasting my breath talking to shadows.

"I don't think you're going to win this time," says Rosie, trying to signify with her hands on her hips all salty, completely forgetting that I have whupped her behind many times for less salt than that.

"I always win 'cause I'm the best," I say straight at Gretchen who is, as far as I'm concerned, the only one talking in this ventriloquist-dummy routine. Gretchen smiles, but it's not a smile, and I'm thinking that girls never really smile at each other because they don't know how and don't want to know how and there's probably no one to teach us how, cause grown-up girls don't know either. Then they all look at Raymond who has just brought his mule team to a standstill. And they're about to see what trouble they can get into through him.

"What grade you in now, Raymond?"

"You got anything to say to my brother, you say it to me, Mary Louise Williams of Raggedy Town, Baltimore."

"What are you, his mother?" sasses Rosie.

"That's right, Fatso. And the next word out of anybody and I'll be *their* mother too." So they just stand there and Gretchen shifts from one leg to the other and so do they. Then Gretchen puts her hands on her hips and is about to say something with her freckle-face self but doesn't. Then she walks around me looking me up and down but keeps walking up Broadway, and her sidekicks follow her. So me and Raymond smile at each other and he says, "Gidyap" to his team and I continue with my breathing exercises, strolling down Broadway toward the ice man on 145th with not a care in the world cause I am Miss Quicksilver herself.

I take my time getting to the park on May Day because the track meet is the last thing on the program. The biggest thing on the program is the May Pole dancing, which I can do without, thank you, even if my mother thinks it's a shame I don't take part and act like a girl for a change. You'd think my mother'd be grateful not to have to make me a white organdy dress with a big satin sash and buy me new white baby-doll shoes that can't be taken out of the box till the big day. You'd think she'd be glad her daughter ain't out there prancing around a May Pole getting the new clothes all dirty and sweaty and trying to act like a fairy or a flower or whatever you're supposed to be when you should be trying to be yourself, whatever that is, which is, as far as I am concerned, a poor Black girl who really can't afford to buy shoes and a new dress you only wear once a lifetime cause it won't fit next year.

I was once a strawberry in a Hansel and Gretel pageant when I was in nursery school and didn't have no better sense than to dance on tiptoe with my arms in a circle over my head doing umbrella steps and being a perfect fool just so my mother and father could come dressed up and clap. You'd think they'd know better than to encourage that kind of nonsense. I am not a strawberry. I do not dance on my toes. I run. That is what I am all about. So I always come late to the May Day program, just in time to get my number pinned on and lay in the grass till they announce the fifty-yard dash.

I put Raymond in the little swings, which is a tight squeeze this year and will be impossible next year. Then I look around for Mr. Pearson, who pins the numbers on. I'm really looking for Gretchen if you want to know the truth, but she's not around. The park is jam-packed. Parents in hats and corsages and breast-pocket handkerchiefs peeking up. Kids in white dresses and light-blue suits. The parkees unfolding chairs and chasing the rowdy kids from Lenox as if they had no right to be there. The big guys with their caps on backwards, leaning against the fence swirling the basketballs on the tips of their fingers, waiting for all these crazy people to clear out the park so they can play. Most of the kids in my class are carrying bass drums and glockenspiels and flutes. You'd think they'd put in a few bongos or something for real like that.

Then here comes Mr. Pearson with his clipboard and his cards and pencils and whistles and safety pins and fifty million other things he's always dropping all over the place with his clumsy self. He sticks out in a crowd because he's on stilts. We used to call him Jack and the Beanstalk to get him mad. But I'm the only one that can outrun him and get away, and I'm too grown for that silliness now.

"Well, Squeaky," he says, checking my name off the list and handing me number seven and two pins. And I'm thinking he's got no right to call me Squeaky, if I can't call him Beanstalk.

"Hazel Elizabeth Deborah Parker," I correct him and tell him to write it down on his board.

"Well, Hazel Elizabeth Deborah Parker, going to give someone else a break this year?" I squint at him real hard to see if he is seriously thinking I should lose the race on purpose just to give someone else a break. "Only six

girls running this time," he continues, shaking his head sadly like it's my
fault all of New York didn't turn out in sneakers. "That new girl should give
you a run for your money." He looks around the park for Gretchen like
a periscope in a submarine movie. "Wouldn't it be a nice gesture if you
were . . . to ahhh . . ."

I give him such a look he couldn't finish putting that idea into words.
Grownups got a lot of nerve sometimes. I pin number seven to myself and
stomp away, I'm so burnt. And I go straight for the track and stretch out on
the grass while the band winds up with "Oh, the Monkey Wrapped His
Tail Around the Flag Pole," which my teacher calls by some other name.
The man on the loudspeaker is calling everyone over to the track and I'm
on my back looking at the sky, trying to pretend I'm in the country, but I
can't, because even grass in the city feels hard as sidewalk, and there's just
no pretending you are anywhere but in a "concrete jungle" as my grandfather says.

The twenty-yard dash takes all of two minutes cause most of the little
kids don't know no better than to run off the track or run the wrong way or
run smack into the fence and fall down and cry. One little kid, though, has
got the good sense to run straight for the white ribbon up ahead so he wins.
Then the second-graders line up for the thirty-yard dash and I don't even
bother to turn my head to watch cause Raphael Perez always wins. He wins
before he even begins by psyching the runners, telling them they're going
to trip on their shoelaces and fall on their faces or lose their shorts or something, which he doesn't really have to do since he is very fast, almost as fast
as I am. After that is the forty-yard dash which I use to run when I was in
first grade. Raymond is hollering from the swings cause he knows I'm about
to do my thing cause the man on the loudspeaker has just announced the
fifty-yard dash, although he might just as well be giving a recipe for angel
food cake cause you can hardly make out what he's saying for the static. I
get up and slip off my sweat pants and then I see Gretchen standing at the
starting line, kicking her legs out like a pro. Then as I get into place I see
that ole Raymond is on line on the other side of the fence, bending down
with his fingers on the ground just like he knew what he was doing. I was
going to yell at him but then I didn't. It burns up your energy to holler.

Every time, just before I take off in a race, I always feel like I'm in a
dream, the kind of dream you have when you're sick with fever and feel all
hot and weightless. I dream I'm flying over a sandy beach in the early
morning sun, kissing the leaves of the trees as I fly by. And there's always
the smell of apples, just like in the country when I was little and used to
think I was a choo-choo train, running through the fields of corn and chugging up the hill to the orchard. And all the time I'm dreaming this, I get
lighter and lighter until I'm flying over the beach again, getting blown
through the sky like a feather that weighs nothing at all. But once I spread
my fingers in the dirt and crouch over the Get on Your Mark, the dream
goes and I am solid again and am telling myself, Squeaky you must win,
you must win, you are the fastest thing in the world, you can even beat your
father up Amsterdam if you really try. And then I feel my weight coming
back just behind my knees then down to my feet then into the earth and
the pistol shot explodes in my blood and I am off and weightless again,

flying past the other runners, my arms pumping up and down and the whole world is quiet except for the crunch as I zoom over the gravel in the track. I glance to my left and there is no one. To the right, a blurred Gretchen, who's got her chin jutting out as if it would win the race all by itself. And on the other side of the fence is Raymond with his arms down to his side and the palms tucked up behind him, running in his very own style, and it's the first time I ever saw that and I almost stop to watch my brother Raymond on his first run. But the white ribbon is bouncing toward me and I tear past it, racing into the distance till my feet with a mind of their own start digging up footfuls of dirt and brake me short. Then all the kids standing on the side pile on me, banging me on the back and slapping my head with their May Day programs, for I have won again and everybody on 151st Street can walk tall for another year.

"In first place . . ." the man on the loudspeaker is clear as a bell now. But then he pauses and the loudspeaker starts to whine. Then static. And I lean down to catch my breath and here comes Gretchen walking back, for she's overshot the finish line too, huffing and puffing with her hands on her hips taking it slow, breathing in steady time like a real pro and I sort of like her a little for the first time. "In first place . . ." and then three or four voices get all mixed up on the loudspeaker and I dig my sneaker into the grass and stare at Gretchen who's staring back, we both wondering just who did win. I can hear old Beanstalk arguing with the man on the loudspeaker and then a few others running their mouths about what the stopwatches say. Then I hear Raymond yanking at the fence to call me and I wave to shush him, but he keeps rattling the fence like a gorilla in a cage like in them gorilla movies, but then like a dancer or something he starts climbing up nice and easy but very fast. And it occurs to me, watching how smoothly he climbs hand over hand and remembering how he looked running with his arms down to his side and with the wind pulling his mouth back and his teeth showing and all, it occurred to me that Raymond would make a very fine runner. Doesn't he always keep up with me on my trots? And he surely knows how to breathe in counts of seven cause he's always doing it at the dinner table, which drives my brother George up the wall. And I'm smiling to beat the band cause if I've lost this race, or if me and Gretchen tied, or even if I've won, I can always retire as a runner and begin a whole new career as a coach with Raymond as my champion. After all, with a little more study I can beat Cynthia and her phony self at the spelling bee. And if I bugged my mother, I could get piano lessons and become a star. And I have a big rep as the baddest thing around. And I've got a roomful of ribbons and medals and awards. But what has Raymond got to call his own?

So I stand there with my new plans, laughing out loud by this time as Raymond jumps down from the fence and runs over with his teeth showing and his arms down to the side, which no one before him has quite mastered as a running style. And by the time he comes over I'm jumping up and down so glad to see him—my brother Raymond, a great runner in the family tradition. But of course everyone thinks I'm jumping up and down because the men on the loudspeaker have finally gotten themselves together and compared notes and are announcing "In first place—Miss Hazel Elizabeth Deborah Parker." (Dig that.) "In second place—Miss Gretchen P.

Lewis." And I look over at Gretchen wondering what the "P" stands for. And I smile. Cause she's good, no doubt about it. Maybe she'd like to help me coach Raymond; she obviously is serious about running, as any fool can see. And she nods to congratulate me and then she smiles. And I smile. We stand there with this big smile of respect between us. It's about as real a smile as girls can do for each other, considering we don't practice real smiling every day, you know, cause maybe we too busy being flowers or fairies or strawberries instead of something honest and worthy of respect . . . you know . . . like being people.

1971

AL YOUNG

b. 1939

Al Young's first novel, *Snakes*, was published in 1970 at the height of the cultural nationalist movement in African American literature. Set in Detroit, the novel revolves around the modest success of a recording single called "Snakes" and the impact that success has on the adolescent band that made the record. M. C., the main character, discovers that it is through music—not through a strictly racial or revolutionary identity—that he can express himself. At the end of the novel, M. C. asserts, "For the first time in my life, I don't feel trapped and I'm going to try and make this feeling last as long as I can."

Despite the artistic excellence of *Snakes*, Young had a hard time finding a publisher because many editors thought his work was "too sweet" for a ghetto novel, an experience that has informed Young's assessment of much published black fiction and poetry:

> You find a one-sidedness that I feel it has been my destiny in part to balance. It is explicitly because most whites still refuse to see black people as people that racism prevails. Blacks turn around and do the same thing to whites, that is, not regard them as human beings, then we turn around and do the same thing to ourselves.

Young combats such stereotyping in literature and in life by creating characters who are both black and well rounded. At the same time, he acknowledges and celebrates the particularities of African American life—the music, the vernacular, the spirituality.

Young was born on May 31, 1939, in Ocean Springs, Mississippi, on the Gulf Coast near Biloxi and New Orleans. His parents were Albert James, a musician and auto worker, and Mary Campbell Young. He lived for a time with his grandparents in the small town of Pachuta, Mississippi, where "the mystery of natural things, the mystery of wilderness affected [him]." After Young's family moved to Detroit in 1945, he traveled back and forth between Michigan and Pachuta. In Detroit he was exposed to industrialism, urban working-class culture, and the rich music scene of Motown, all of which would influence his writing.

Early in life, Young decided to become a writer. He read a great deal and was enthusiastic about authors as different as contemporary American poet Kenneth Patchen, Tang Dynasty poet Li Po, and Irish American novelist James T. Farrell. Fascinated by languages, Young majored in Spanish at the University of Michigan.

In the spring of 1961, Young moved to the San Francisco Bay Area, where he still lives.

Young's six volumes of poetry—*Dancing* (1969), *The Song Turning Back into Itself* (1971), *Geography of the Near Past* (1979), *The Blues Don't Change* (1982), and *Heaven: Collected Poems, 1958–1990* (1990)—reflect the early musical influences in his life and deal with the forces that bind people both to each other and to higher spiritual realities. Young is also well known for his lyrical musical memoirs: *Bodies and Soul* (1981), *Kinds of Blue* (1984), (with Janet Coleman) *Mingus/Mingus* (1989), and *Drowning in the Sea of Love* (1995).

In addition to *Snakes*, Young has written four other novels: *Who Is Angelina* (1975), *Sitting Pretty* (1976), *Ask Me Now* (1980), and *Seduction by Light* (1988). Critics have consistently praised his fiction's warmth and humor, and his work has been compared to Langston Hughes's Jesse B. Semple series and to Jean Toomer's literary explorations of Eastern metaphysics in an African American context. For example, *The Seduction of Light* features the folksy and philosophical voice of Mamie Franklin, a middle-aged black woman who, at the beginning of the novel, lives with her paralyzed husband, Burley Cole. Appearing at first to be the story of their marriage, the novel changes form after Burley dies and comes back as an energetic ghost who wreaks comic havoc on the contemporary L.A. scene. Drawing from Eastern and Western philosophical traditions, *The Seduction of Light* is an ironic *tour de force* in its treatment of the contemporary U.S. West.

Young has worked with many writers of color on the West Coast, one result of which was the editing of *The Yardbird Reader*, with writer Ishmael Reed. While teaching at universities such as Stanford and working on his fiction and poetry, he is one of the few African Americans who have written screenplays for contemporary Hollywood movies: *Nigger* (1972) and *Bustin' Loose* (1979). Versatile above all else, Young celebrates the complex relationships and influences among the many black traditions and nonblack cultural and religious movements such as European modernism and Zen Buddhism.

A Dance for Ma Rainey [1]

I'm going to be just like you, Ma
Rainey this monday morning
clouds puffing up out of my head
like those balloons
that float above the faces of white people   5
in the funnypapers

I'm going to hover in the corners
of the world, Ma
& sing from the bottom of hell
up to the tops of high heaven   10
& send out scratchless waves of yellow
& brown & that basic black honey
misery

I'm going to cry so sweet
& so low   15

1. African American entertainer (1886–1939), often called the "Mother of the Blues."

& so dangerous,
Ma,
that the message is going to reach you
back in 1922
where you shimmer   20
snaggle-toothed
perfumed &
powdered
in your bauble beads
hair pressed & tied back   25
throbbing with that sick pain
I know
& hide so well
that pain that blues
jives the world with   30
aching to be heard
that downness
that bottomlessness
first felt by some stolen delta nigger
swamped under with redblooded american agony;   35
reduced to the sheer shit
of existence
that bred
& battered us all,
Ma,   40
the beautiful people
our beautiful brave black people
who no longer need to jazz
or sing to themselves in murderous vibrations
or play the veins of their strong tender arms   45
with needles
to prove that we're still here

                                                   1969

Conjugal Visits

By noon we'll be deep into it—
    up reading out loud in bed.
Or in between our making love
    I'll paint my toenails red.

Reece say he got to change his name   5
    from Maurice to Malik.
He thinks I need to change mine too.
    Conversion, so to speak.

"I ain't no Muslim yet," I say.
    "Besides, I like my name.   10
Kamisha still sounds good to me.
    I'll let you play that game."

"I'd rather play with you," he say,
   "than trip back to the Sixties."
"The Sixties, eh?" I'm on his case.   15
   "Then I won't do my striptease."

This brother look at me and laugh;
   he know I love him bad
and, worse, he know exactly how much
   loving I ain't had.   20

He grab me by my puffed up waist
   and pull me to him close.
He say, "I want you in my face.
   Or on my face, Miss Toes."

What can I say? I'd lie for Reece,   25
   but I'm not quitting school.
Four mouths to feed, not counting mine.
   Let Urban Studies rule!

I met him in the want ads,
   we fell in love by mail.   30
I say, when people bring this up,
   "Wasn't no one up for sale."

All these Black men crammed up in jail,
   all this I.Q. on ice,
while governments, bank presidents,   35
   the Mafia don't think twice.

They fly in dope and make real sure
   they hands stay nice and clean.
The chump-change Reece made on the street
   —what's that supposed to mean?   40

"For what it cost the State to keep
   you locked down, clothed and fed,
you could be learning Harvard stuff,
   and brilliant skills," I said.

Reece say, "Just kiss me one more time,   45
   then let's get down, make love.
Then let's devour that special meal
   I wish they'd serve more of."

They say the third time out's a charm;
   I kinda think they're right.
My first, he was the Ace of Swords,   50
   which didn't make him no knight.

He gave me Zeus and Brittany;
   my second left me twins.

This third one ain't about no luck;　　　55
we're honeymooners. Friends.

I go see Maurice once a month
　while Moms looks after things.
We be so glad to touch again,
　I dance, he grins, he sings.　　　　　60

When I get back home to my kids,
　schoolwork, The Copy Shop,
ain't no way Reece can mess with me.
They got his ass locked up.

　　　　　　　　　　　　　　　1996

From The Seduction of Light

2A

[BEN FRANKLIN]

It was like I'd sunk straight to the bottom of a dream. You know what that's like, don't you? For one split second you catch yourself hangin between being asleep and awake and then, without anything resemblin a shift, you snap back to the middle of some scene, and it's impossible to tell which one is the real you. Sometime it gets so sweet and cozy and satisfyin out there in the dream world until I dont have any interest in wakin up. And sometime I ask myself: What if the dream kept rollin for a thousand years? You'd never know the difference.

In the part I'd dropped down in the middle of, I was back singin with Chance Franklin's band. The song was "You Go to My Head," and I'd reached my favorite part, the lines that talk about how like a summer with a thousand Julys, you intoxicate my soul with your eyes. Ooo, I love singin that; it use to gimme goosebumps when it came time to project that verse. I would put everything I had into gettin that across. In the dream, Chance could feel the emotion I was puttin out just as if I'd reached around to where he was, in backa me leadin the band, and grabbed him by the wrist.

Whoosh, I got swept up into the words so completely, the music and the lyrics took on a life of their own. The singer, me, Mamie Franklin, disappeared. "You Go to My Head," was suddenly somethin you could taste and smell and feel and see like, well, like the bubbles in a glass of champagne poppin in the air and bein blown by some breeze across the smoky room and out the door of the club. From there I watched myself—that is, the Mamie that'd become the words and the sound—go sailin cross the street. There was a catch to it, tho. I didnt bother floatin across the street in a straight line like you might expect; I just hauled off and rose clean up over all the cars and people on bicycles and motorcycles and trucks and stuff. Just like I was a helicopter made outta nothin, I lifted straight up off the sidewalk and went to reverberatin so strong when I hit the note that goes with the word "eyes" until I thought I would splinter into a zillion pieces.

Mind you, this was all happenin to me the same as I'm tellin you, and when I did come down, oh, I have to laugh. . . . When I did come down it was the tenderest landin imaginable. There was Burley Cole, all decked out in tuxedo, if you can believe it, which you couldnt get him to put on in the other reality even if you were to poke a pistol in his belly. First I saw him as a tiny speck of light down there on the ground, then as I got closer, I could see who he really was. I was tightenin up by then, gettin scared I might not be able to land OK. Burley stretched his arms up toward me, threw em wide open, and suddenly there I was slowin down like I had some kinda parachute attached to me made outta nothin but feathers and silk.

"What taken you so long?" he wanted to know.

"I had to make sure I had it straight," I told Burley, "before we blew all our precious, hard-earned money."

"So do you think you figured it out finally?"

"Sure did."

"OK," he said when we stepped up to the bet-placin window. "I hope you know what you talkin bout, Mamie, cause I plan to shut my eyes and plunk all this money down on a win-place-or-show bet."

"No," I told him, a little sad, just a tad, since that kinda bet woulda reflected how little confidence Burley had in my intuition. "Forget about win-place-or-show. Ben Franklin's gonna win this one hands down, or hooves down, or whatever you say."

Burley laughed again and said, "I can tell by the way your cheeks crinkle up and the way you grin when you say it that you'd practically lay down your life on this hunch."

"You got it, Mr. Burley!"

So that's what we did. We put the whole two grand on Ben Franklin; smacked it down on the counter and just about scared the cashier to death.

"Boy, you guys're either brave or far out, one!" he told us, all big-eyed and shakin his bald head. "That's a 35 to one shot."

"Accordin to the lights out there across the track," I said, "the odds have gone up to 40 to one."

"Well, all I can say is, I guess you know what youre doin."

"We dont know nothin!" Burley said, which was a funny thing to say. No funny ha-ha, but that didnt in no way stop the three of us from laughin.

Then, like magic, the way it happens in dreams, a big crowd popped up to cheer and scream and holler and carry on, the way crowds're suppose to do at racetracks. And the minute the man on the P.A. went, "And they're off!" Burley tried so hard to leap clean outta his skin that he bumped me in the shoulder and almost knocked me down.

It was a seven-horse race and they were runnin the full mile. The track was muddier than I'd ever seen it, but the sun was shinin down so hard you could almost see the dirt and turf dryin up while you looked.

I can't remember all the other horses' names, but the favorite was a French horse named Moulin Rouge, and that old song went to slippin thru my head when I saw it on the program. There were two other horses people were bettin heavy on too—Saturday's Child and Copasetic, Jr. I got a big lump in my throat watching how long it was takin Ben to even get outta the gate. Burley looked at me like he was fixin to dig a hole in the mud and hide in it.

Since I had trouble listenin to the man call the race and watchin the numbers flash on the toteboard at the same time, I told Burley: "You can watch and tell me what's goin on. I'm too wound up to look." Yet, even while I was sayin this, there was a parta me that was as calm as the clouds hangin over the track that afternoon. I knew exactly what was gonna happen, even if I couldna told you *when* it was gonna take place.

Burley grabbed holda my arm and squeezed and squeezed while he hollered in my ear, "Uh-uhhh, Mamie, they comin outta the turn now and, whoa, whoa! I dont believe this shit, I dont believe it!"

"What's happenin, Burley!" I shouted. "Tell me, tell me!"

"No, ma'am," he said, "I want you to open your eyes and see this one for your ownself!"

And when I peeped, then let my eyes pop wide open, I could tell why the crowd was goin nuts. Old Ben was moving up the home stretch so fast it was like some giant invisible hand'd reached down from the sky and was quietly pushin him along past all the others.

"Lookit that!" Burley screamed. "Just lookit! He bout to catch up with Moulin Rouge!"

The words had no sooner left Burley's mouth than Ben Franklin, that 40-to-one shot of ours, leapt right up there neck and neck with the horse from France. Then it was like all the sound clicked off and all the excitement that'd been keepin me from lookin or sayin a word simply cooled down and disappeared. It wasnt even like I was lookin at a horserace any more; it was like I was seein the whole thing from the perspective of one of those flip books. You know, where you be flippin pages with drawins on em and see the picture go to movin.

Ben Franklin, who, accordin to the program, would turn two-years-old that very day, he shot up there so fast it was practically like I had decided to flick the pages across my thumb a little faster than I'd been doin just to see what would happen. When the horses came across the finish line, I let my thumb come to a full stop so I could see for myself what was what. It was Ben Franklin by half a head, but the man on the sound system was sayin: "It's a photo finish, folks! A photo finish! Please save all tickets until the judges have studied the pictures."

Burley was tremblin and stutterin when he talked. "M-M-Mamie," he said, "if this race d-dont t-t-turn out the w-w-way you—"

"Aw, hush!" I told him. "Wont nobody be able to talk to us in a coupla minutes."

Sure enough, the man came back on the loudspeaker, tellin us: "It's official. Ben Franklin's the winner! Moulin Rouge is second and Copasetic, Jr. third. Ladies and gentlemen, this has been one of the most remarkable races I have seen in my 25 years as a track announcer! Ben Franklin the winner, and Joyce Azuela the jockey. They'll be stepping into the Winner's Circle in just a moment. Ben Franklin, ladies and gentlemen, paying 80 dollars on a 2 dollar bet!"

Me and Burley hugged so hard I thought we were gonna come out the other side of one another.

"Mamie, you knew it all along, didnt you, didnt you?"

"Tell me, Burley. How could a horse named Ben Franklin lose? Especially when there's a woman ridin him? Old Ben is my man. Always has been."

"Shoot," Burley said, wipin away tears of joy, "you talk like you musta got it straight from the horse's mouth!"

"Somethin like that," I said in a soft voice. "Yessir, somethin just like that." And then that off-the-wall dream stuff started up. By this I mean there I was, couldnt wait to get my hands on the money. We each had 40 grand comin to us, and I was thinkin how even after the Internal Revenue nailed us right there at the window for their cut we would still have enough left over to do somethin strange and wonderful and wouldnt have to hold back, to do it whole hog! I was thinkin this when I started wakin up, and all I remember about that transition is that the dream went to movin and jumpin around a little on the turbulent side. I mean, the race track, me, Burley, the crowd, the jockeys and the horses, everything—we were shakin quite as if some giant, like the one in Jack and the Beanstalk, was comin back home to roost. It was like his footsteps had turned into stomps that were makin heaven itself jiggle and shake, but I do mean *shake*. The last thing I remember was lookin up at the sky and seein how the clouds had all turned green and it was rainin money.

It was one of those deals where you fight to go on dreamin and not have to click back into the wakin mode, but it was also a fight I knew I wasnt gonna win. Slowly I floated back up to the surface of things, floated to the skin of dreamin, you might say, and got a little shock when I realized where I was.

I was laying next to Burley. That's right. Someplace along the line, I had actually gotten up sleepwalker style and shifted from my bed to his. This'd never happened before. He was as quiet as a blade of grass. I woke up with my hands stretched up in the air so I could catch some of that fallin money, I guess. Isn't it awful the way dreams can jack you around sometime?

But the weirdest thing, tho, was how much control it took for me to keep from throwin myself on topa Burley. There were times—and this was one of em—when I resented Burley's condition, when I felt like havin him all snaked up inside the way we use to could do for hours. I use to love it when his arms'd be wrapped all around me like silk and there I was all snug in my cocoon yet knowin full well the moment was close at hand when pretty soon I'd be wrigglin my way loose and come up out of it the loveliest butterfly you ever wanna see.

While I was tryna stay quiet while I slid outta Burley's bed to make it back across the room to my own, a strange urge overtook me. Suddenly I slipped my hand down to his waist and went to thinkin about how we'd met.

I let my thoughts drift back to the casino. Las Vegas. I'd run my winnins on the nickel machine up to the limit, $7.50. Then I'd hit the quarter slots and then the dollar ones. Burley was standin there next to me, playin the dollar slots too—two at a time, in fact—when I made my first pull and somethin like 200 of them things came tumblin down, he got right up in my face and said: "You wont believe this, but I been lookin for somebody like you all my life. You the one could change my luck."

I mean, it was such a lame come-on I still have trouble believin I went for it. We were both gettin away from our little scenes for the weekend—Burley from that cheese company stuff and me from worryin about Benjie and the lies I'd been tellin him and whatever happened to Mamie Franklin and first-one-thing-and-another there in L.A. As Marvin Gaye would say: "L.A. . . . Now, what I say?"

Say what you will, I decided it wasnt worth it to dwell any longer on that wonderful night; it was too painful. And it clashed too much with the way things stood now. I smoothed my hand over Burley's warm, skinny waist, rememberin how meaty and paunchy he'd been before his health turned bad. Back then when that commercial would come on that asked, "Can you pinch more than an inch?" Burley would grab up a sizable chunka that spare tire of his and turn to me and say, "Pinch an inch? Hell, I can grab a slab?" That's how he was. Burley's the only man I know—not that I've known all that many, mind you—who could be lovin on you so hard you felt like you were about to catch on fire, to burst out in flames like spontaneous combustion, and then in the middle of it he might even crack some joke, mumble somethin like "Yeah, I can grab me a slab!" and the both of us'd be laughin while we shot off like a thousand roman candles in the starry black skies of a thousand Julys, every last one of em the Fourth.

And while I was strokin him, I put as much energy as I could into imaginin the two of us swimmin in pure white light so we would be totally protected from whatever it was that, deep down, I could feel playin around the edges of what I'd just dreamed. In many ways, it felt like a terrible somethin that sooner or later was bound to find someplace to haul off and happen.

It did my heart good to hear Burley let out a little low-pitch chuckle in his sleep—the second one that night—when he turned over again. I knew he was gettin what I was busy thinkin too. The message was sinkin in: All would be well. Now all I had to do was be careful about filterin out what was tiptoin thru the opposite side of my mind: all that tremblin and shakin and turbulence in the racetrack experience I'd just got thru dreamin. I wasnt crazy about that aspect of things, but the more I thought about it the better I felt.

Listen, how many times do you get to be plunked right smack down in the middle of a scene where cash money is fallin out the sky and your longest shot has sailed clean thru like light set free? Dont tell me Old Ben himself didnt have anything to do with this. Goin all the way back to when I was a little girl, he hasnt let me down yet.

The thought of Benjamin Franklin, the real one—the man, not the horse—was enough to clear all the fear outta me. I felt the tension leave my body, even if the lust didnt, while I got up and went back to my own bed and eased back into the sleepytime state. And while sweet sleep was takin its own good time slippin up on me again, I began to pick up little disconnected flashes and bursts that were like pieces in a jigsaw puzzle except made outta vibrations I could see inside myself that had another Benjamin written all over em. I'm talkin now, of course, about Benjie my son. Dont ask how, but I knew he and his girlfriend Tree were curled up under the covers way out there in the freeway distance, lovin one another like lemmings.

But dont get me wrong, I never would use any powers the Lord gave me to violate anybody else's privacy. That stuff can and will bounce back on you, you know. And I do believe in doin unto others the way I expect them to do unto me. Mamie, what you say?

3

[SECONDHAND BUSINESS]

Burley woke up in a pretty good mood for a change. On days like that, I didnt wanna leave him to go to work. When I told him about what'd happened the night before, this mischievous look crept up in his eyes and spread all over the parta his face that wasn't paralyzed.

I said, "What you suppose they coulda been after, tryna break in our garage like that?"

I was wheelin him from the bedroom thru the house, swervin around all the junk stacked up and piled all over the place.

He cocked his head to one side and said, "You know, Mamie, if there was such a thing as a school for fools, I'da had me five or six Ph.D's by now."

Since the kitchen was Burley's favorite mornin spot, I tried to keep it relatively cleared out. I say relatively, and yet there was still too much clutter even in there for the average person to put up with. Miz Wheelock, the housekeeper, was always grumblin about all the shelves fulla old magazines and books and balls of string and busted utensils and jars of nuts and bolts and whatnot.

"Yessir," said Burley, tuggin at the loose skin round his Adam apple— one of his worrisome habits that set my teeth on edge—"I'da done had me at least half a dozen Ph.D's, maybe even a few honorary degrees." He still slurred his words, only it wasnt half as bad as it used to be.

"Burley, I didnt ask you about no Ph.D's and honorary degrees. I asked what you think them devilish burglars mighta been after out there in our garage."

"No tellin," he said, "just no tellin."

He went to yankin at his throat skin again, but I reached over and taken his hands away and said, "How come you cant quit doin that? You know how much it vexes me."

Burley screwed up his face then and said, "What makes you think they had to be after somethin anyway?"

"I was lookin dead at em. Somethin about the way they carried themselves, the way they were actin. It was like . . . well, it was like there was nothin they wanted from the house itself, just the garage. I do believe they knew exactly what they were lookin for, Burley."

"Aw, you and your hunches and notions!"

I heard what Burley was sayin, but I could tell too that there was somethin he wasnt sayin, somethin the new look in his eyes and the tight little wrinkly knot in the middle of his handsome forehead was tryna say instead.

We were at the kitchen table now, right there by the window where Burley liked to sit and read the L.A. Times and look out into the yard. Fog was still rollin like tumbleweed clouds, but I knew the sun would be out by the time I booted Sweepea up thru traffic over to Beverly Hills.

"You might even have a Bachelors or Masters yourself," he said, grinnin at me again.

"Burley, just what in the world are you mumblin about? I'm runnin late as it is, and I do not have time to be hangin around here playin guessin games. The police suppose to be sending a detective around to do some more investigatin."

"Investigatin?" Burley folded his hands in his lap and gazed out the window. He was lookin so serious now, I couldnt tell whether he was studyin the sparrows lined up on the fence out there or the side of the garage. He twisted his neck around and looked at me real hard and said, "I wasnt just playin about that school for fools either. Wouldnt nobody but a coupla fools keep draggin junk into a house like we keep doin."

I was shocked; not by what Burley'd just declared, but by the fact that he'd said it at all. I couldnt agree more. Me, I'd been wantin to clean house and dust my broom years ago. Now, why was he just now gettin around to realizin how stupid we'd been carryin on?

And Burley Cole wasnt just talkin neither, I mean, about junk. Practically every inch of that house, plus the backyard and the garage was crammed with stuff he'd been bringin in there from almost the day he moved in with me. Look like it wasnt nothin he could pass up. Auctions, garage sales, stuff he'd see advertized on supermarket and laundromat bulletin boards or in the classifieds—he made it a point to check em all out, and he didnt hardly ever come away from any expedition empty-handed. I mean, we had televisions, refrigerators, furniture, trunks, suitcases, file cabinets, car batteries, fish tanks, almost every kinda camera and photography equipment you could think of. And we had tape recorders, radios, tools, power mowers, lawn edgers, a small printin press, mattresses, bedsprings, ladders, air conditioners, encyclopedias, electric fans, vacuum cleaners, electric brooms, typewriters, old 78 rpm record albums, boxes of ballpoint pens, crates of old foam rubber turnin yellow, store display racks, sinks, fishin rods, wooden toilet seats, a water cooler, busted water heaters, a coupla outboard motors with no boat to hook em up to. We even had a gang of ski stuff, and the closest I ever got to skiin was the two-three times the Chryslers taken me to Aspen with em. And I wont ever forget that time we all went over to Switzerland where this smooth Frenchman got after me and wouldnt let up. From what Danielle Chrysler'd been tellin me, I'd expected the men over there to be some pretty cold "feesh," as she put it. But the point I'm makin now is that me and Burley had a little some of everything stored around our place. You see, some people get addicted to dope and some to drink, but Burley was addicted to deals. The man was the *original* junkie.

It was dreadful. Burley'd spent the first part of his life tryna get hold to a few dollars so he could buy somethin. The rest of it he spent tumblin and stirrin around in junk. It would get so bad sometime until the city'd be after us to get the yard cleared out; said the neighbors was callin up complainin, and said we were violatin codes and statutes.

"Well," said Burley after he'd sat there awhile. "I want that old trunk moved out from the garage."

"Which one? You forget there's about six or seven of em out there."

"The big one," he said. "That great big green Army trunk, the one that use to belong to Kendall."

Kendall was Burley's only son who'd gotten messed up in Vietnam.

"Where you want it moved to?"

"Someplace safe."

"Someplace safe? It's been out there all this time and nothin's happened to it. How come youre so worried about it all of a sudden?"

"I would just feel better if it wasnt around, that's all."

"Oh yeah? Then tell me, what's in the trunk?"

Burley mighta been sick and slow in his movements and the way he spoke but, lemme tell you, his mind was just as quick as it'd ever been. He just closed his eyes and got real quiet. Now, dont get me wrong. I loved that man and hated seein him in the shape he was in, but like my mother Ruby Franklin use to say—bless her soul—"Every shut eye aint sleep!" Burley rhymes with squirrely, you know, and there were times when I knew good and well that Burley was usin his condition to hide behind and do what he wanted to do just the same as anybody else that's sick.

"What do you think we oughtta do with it?" I gave in and asked.

"Maybe Benjamin could help you move it to his place."

"Now, Burley, you know Benjie moves around too much to be callin any place *his* place. C'mon, cant you tell me what's in that trunk? Who cares about that old beat-up thing anyway?"

"Then maybe you could find a place for it up there at the Big House." Burley loosened up and laughed when he said this. He knew how much I hated him callin the Chrysler's home the Big House. "Yeah," he said. "That's the best idea yet. Why dont you clear it with Mr. Chrysler and have the thing hauled up there for safekeepin."

"That's funny, Burley. As long as the roof's been leakin out there, I never knew we had anything much worth even protectin, much less hide. You mean to tell me after all these years youre still keepin secrets from me?"

"Didnt say nothin about any secrets, Mamie. I was—I was givin some thought to what you said about last night, and that's my conclusion. See, I have a lotta old papers and pictures and souvenirs and things stored away in that trunk I wouldnt want to get lost or anything to happen to em."

"Oh," I said, "Then why didnt you say so? I'll be sure and ask Mr. Chrysler about it first thing."

"First thing, when?"

"The first thing this mornin."

"Good, that makes me feel better."

That was when the tea kettle started whistlin, which made me notice the time on the stove clock. 7:10. Miss Wheelock was runnin a little later than usual.

"What kinda tea you want this mornin, sugar?"

"The peppermint, thank you. Believe I need to lighten up some on that Constant Comment."

"No problem," I told him. "It was the caffeine and the acid the doctor say you needed to cut out."

"Ah but, you know, I still miss my coffee."

"Maybe so, but it means more to me to see you gettin better than to see your health and strength washed away in a silly cup of coffee. That's how I'm givin it up too—to set a good example."

Burley twisted his stiff neck to one side and said, "Betcha anything you still help yourself to some when youre away from around me, when youre up there at the Big House, dont you?"

Thank goodness, I was saved by the bell and didnt have to go makin up some half-lie. Miz Wheelock was here at last and now I could be on my way. On my way to get the door, I said to Burley, "You guys *are* back on good terms, arent you?"

"You mean about the soap battle? Oh, we finally got that worked out, I think. I'm lettin her watch As *the World Turns* on the Motorola in the bedroom while I look at *One Life to Live* on the Big Sony in the livin room and have lunch."

"Well," I said, "maybe that's a decent solution, even tho I'm not all that thrilled about payin her to sit up and look at television."

"Aw, c'mon, Mamie, have a little heart. That's when she eats lunch and picks up the bedroom and cleans the bathroom."

"You really like that old woman, dont you?"

"She's all right in my book, but I'll tell you one thing. I'd like it better if you was here to watch my stories with me. It's more fun having somebody to wisecrack with."

"Well, bless your heart," I said and opened the door to let Miz Wheelock in.

"Mornin, Mamie," she said, lookin all bright-eyes with her glasses steamed up. "Can you help me bring somethin in from the car?"

Quite naturally I was a little put out when the woman didnt offer me no explanation why she was late, but all I said was, "Sure, Miz Wheelock. What is it?"

"Just a little portable television my grandchildren chipped in and got me for my birthday. We packed it back in the box so it oughtta be easy for the two of us to carry."

"But, Miz Wheelock," I said, "we already got seven TV's around here!"

"Oh, I know, Mamie, I know. But all of em but one is black and white. I have to see what the people really look like and what they're wearin and how the rooms and houses is decorated when I catch my stories."

Wasnt nothin else to do but help my help lug that thing out the trunk of that beat-up Cadillac of hers and drag it on up into the house with all the rest of the merchandise. Sometime I think what Burley and me shoulda gone into was the second-hand business.

1989

JOHN EDGAR WIDEMAN
b. 1941

In his preface to *The Homewood Trilogy*, John Edgar Wideman writes about the night of his grandmother's funeral in Pittsburgh in 1974: "It became clear to me . . . that I needn't look any further than the place I was born and the people who'd loved me to find what was significant and lasting in literature. My university training had both thwarted and prepared this understanding." Wideman had already published two well-received novels. After 1974, however, he was to publish the works for which he is best known, works rooted in the terrain of his childhood neighborhood, Homewood. But for Wideman the road back to Homewood was a difficult one: "In America, especially if you're black, there is a temptation to buy a kind of upward mobility. One of the requirements is to forget. Eventually, I felt impoverished by that act."

John Wideman was born on June 14, 1941, in Washington, D.C., the oldest of five children of Edgar and Betty French Wideman. Shortly before his first birthday, the family moved to Homewood, a black neighborhood on the eastern side of Pittsburgh, Pennsylvania. Wideman was to spend the first ten years of his life there, where his great-great-great-grandmother, a fugitive slave, had found freedom in the mid-nineteenth century and where much of his extended family still lived. Wideman's father worked as a waiter, garbage man, and paperhanger. But although the family was poor, his parents, according to Wideman, "followed the traditional striving middle-class pattern." In 1951, the family moved to the predominantly white upper-middle-class neighborhood of Shadyside. There, Wideman attended Peabody High School, where he began to compartmentalize his life by associating with his white friends in the classroom and gym and his African American friends outside of school. Basketball star, senior class president, and valedictorian, Wideman won a Benjamin Franklin Scholarship to the University of Pennsylvania.

In college, Wideman played out what he has called a theatrical performance. As he described it later, in the autobiographical *Brothers and Keepers* (1984), "Just two choices as far as I could tell: either/or. Rich or poor. White or black. Win or lose. . . . To succeed in the man's world you must become like the man and the man sure didn't claim no bunch of nigger relatives in Pittsburgh." Wideman began with a major in psychology but switched to English when he discovered he was to study rats rather than psychoanalytic theory. He earned membership in Phi Beta Kappa, competed in track, and won all-Ivy status as a forward on the basketball team. In his senior year, he traded his dream of becoming an NBA star for that of becoming a writer. In 1963, John Wideman became only the second African American to win a Rhodes Scholarship (Alain Locke had been the first, fifty-five years earlier.) At Oxford University's New College, Wideman studied eighteenth-century literature. He also served as captain and coach of the university's basketball team, leading it to an amateur championship. In 1966, he was awarded a bachelor of philosophy degree and returned to the United States with Judith Ann Goldman, whom he had married in 1965.

From 1966 to 1967, as Kent Fellow at the University of Iowa's Writers' Workshop, Wideman completed his first novel, *A Glance Away* (1967). Choosing to support himself through teaching while he continued to write, Wideman taught at the University of Pennsylvania from 1967 to 1974. His second novel, *Hurry Home*, was published in 1970. Both these early novels deal with African American characters, but the questions Wideman poses in them are not so much racial as existential. *A Glance Away* depicts a day in the lives of Eddie Lawson, an African American and a recovering drug addict, and Robert Thurley, a gay white English professor, as each struggles to understand himself. *Hurry Home* tells the story of Cecil Braithwaite, an African American law school graduate who, at the time the novel opens, is working as a janitor and who decides to travel to Europe and then to Africa in an attempt to somehow merge the two cultures to which he is heir—an attempt at which he ultimately fails. In his use of flashbacks, varying points of view, journals, letters, dreams, and puns, Wideman creates what critic John Leonard called "a rich and complicated novel." Because of the formally complex nature of his work, critics located Wideman in the tradition of Joyce, Eliot, and Faulkner.

Wideman was, at this time, unconnected to the black literary tradition, conceding in a 1968 *Negro Digest* article that he was not familiar with "that school of black writers which seeks to establish the black aesthetic." When two of his undergraduate students at the University of Pennsylvania asked him to teach a course on African American literature in 1968, Wideman at first declined. Then, in a crucial turnabout, he decided to take on the challenge. The course eventually led to the university's first African American studies program and for Wideman personally "awakened in [him] a different sense of self-image and the whole notion of a third world."

That different sense influenced Wideman's third novel, *The Lynchers* (1973), in which race and setting loom large. *The Lynchers* tells the story of a failed conspiracy by a group of black men in a Philadelphia ghetto to lynch one representative white policeman as vengeance for the thousands of black lives lost to lynching. The novel explores themes that would be important in Wideman's later work: relationships between black men and the significance of history, for it begins with a chronicling of lynchings in the United States. For Wideman, the novel's emphasis on pain, degradation, and hopelessness led to an impasse in his writing career. In 1973, wanting "to get away from that Ivy League competitiveness, the pressure to be somebody," he accepted a teaching position at the University of Wyoming at Laramie and moved west with his wife and three children.

In Wyoming, Wideman continued to read nineteenth- and twentieth-century African American writers, to study history and linguistics, and as he put it, "to forge a new language for talking about the places I'd been, the people important to me." That search for a new language, along with a personal event—his younger brother Robby was arrested, tried for murder, and sentenced to life in prison without parole—greatly affected his works of the 1980s and 1990s.

In nearly all of Wideman's subsequent work, he uses both the lyrical language he developed during these years and the technique, dream time, what critic Randall Kenana called Wideman's "own patented stream of consciousness, sliding easily through tense and point of view." *Damballah* (1981), *Hiding Place* (1981), and *Sent for You Yesterday* (1983) established Wideman's reputation as, according to Mel Watkins in the *New York Times Book Review,* "one of America's premier writers of fiction."

As Wideman notes in his preface to *The Homewood Trilogy,* "the tension of multiple traditions, European and Afro-American, the Academy and the Street, animates these texts." In an unusual move, Wideman decided to have each of his Homewood books published originally in paperback to reach more readers, particularly "the people and the world [he] was writing about." All three books revolve around the descendants of Sybela Owens, the great-great-great-grandmother who escaped slavery and settled in Homewood in the late 1850s with the help of her owner's son, who would later become her husband. *Damballah,* the first part of the trilogy, is a collection of twelve interrelated short stories spanning generations; the stories are imagined as "long overdue letters" to Wideman's brother Robby. *Hiding Place,* a novel, traces the life of Tommy, Sybela's great-great-great-grandson, who is wanted for a murder he didn't commit. Featuring the same characters, setting, and language, *Sent for You Yesterday,* the third part of the trilogy, travels back and forth from the 1920s to the 1970s to trace the lives of two Homewood families, the Frenches and the Tates. *Sent for You Yesterday* won the P.E.N./Faulkner Award in 1984.

Wideman's next work, the popular *Brothers and Keepers* (1984), draws inspiration from Homewood but is the author's first venture into nonfiction, as he comes to terms in this autobiographical work with the very different lives he and his younger brother Robby have led. Some reviewers found Wideman's indictment of white society unjustified—especially given his own escape from the ghetto. However, Jonathan Yardley, in the *Washington Post Book World,* observed that in his "effort to understand what happened, to confess and examine his own sense of guilt about his brother's fate (and his own)," Wideman has written "a depiction of the inexorably widening chasm that divides middle-class black Americans from the black underclass." Ironically, in 1986, Wideman's middle child, Jacob, confessed to the murder of his roommate at summer camp, and the eighteen-year-old was sentenced to life in prison.

Reuben, published in 1987, engages the judicial system through its portrayal of a lawyer to the poor and dispossessed black citizenry of Homewood. Though stark in its indictment of the judicial system, *Reuben* did not provoke critics as much as Wideman's next novel, *Philadelphia Fire* (1990), based on the 1985 bombing of the Philadelphia headquarters of MOVE, which was authorized by the city's first African American mayor and led to the deaths of eleven people and the destruction of much of the neighborhood. Against this background, Wideman sets the search by an African American writer named Cudjoe for a small boy reported to have escaped the flames. At the novel's climax, in what critic Rosemary L. Bray called an "act of almost unimaginable boldness," the young boy is transformed into Wideman's own son, Jacob.

Between these two novels, Wideman published his second collection of short stories, *Fever*. Although critics praised *Valaida*, in which a Jewish Holocaust survivor tries to reach out to his African American cleaning woman, and *Little Brother*, about the inability of whites and blacks to live together without mutual hurt, the title story, *Fever*, was considered the prize of the collection. For this story Wideman drew on historical accounts of blacks and whites working side by side during the yellow fever epidemic that hit Philadelphia in 1793.

Wideman's most recent work gathers two previous collections, *Damballah* and *Fever*, together with a new one, *All Stories Are True*. Published in 1992, *The Stories of John Edgar Wideman* arranges the collections in reverse chronological order, with *Damballah* as the anchor.

Wideman was recognized early as an important writer, and his reputation has grown. He has moved from working primarily within a white literary tradition to developing new literary elements based on African American history, literature, and life: a reinvention of black English; the technique, dream time; his engagement with the violence imposed on African Americans; and his contemporary rendition of the inner lives of historical characters, including members of his own family.

John Edgar Wideman currently teaches in the English department of the University of Massachusetts at Amherst.

From Brothers and Keepers

[Robby's Version]

At about the time I was beginning to teach Afro-American literature at the University of Pennsylvania, back home on the streets of Pittsburgh Robby was living through the changes in black culture and consciousness I was reading about and discussing with my students in the quiet of the classroom. Not until we began talking together in prison did I learn about that side of his rebelliousness. *Black Fire* [1] was a book I used in my course. It was full of black rage and black dreams and black love. In the sixties when the

---

1. *Black Fire: An Anthology of Afro-American Writing* (1968), edited by LeRoi Jones (Amiri Baraka) and Larry Neal.

book was published, young black men were walking the streets with, as one of the *Black Fire* writers put it, dynamite growing out of their skulls. I'd never associated Robby with the fires in Homewood and in cities across the land, never envisioned him bobbing in and out of the flames, a constant danger to himself, to everyone around him because "dynamite was growing out of his skull." His plaited naps hadn't looked like fuses to me. I was teaching, I was trying to discover words to explain what was happening to black people. That my brother might have something to say about these matters never occurred to me. The sad joke was, I never even spoke to Robby. Never knew until years later that he was the one who could have told me much of what I needed to hear.

It was a crazy summer. The summer of '68. We fought the cops in the streets. I mean sure nuff punch-out fighting like in them Wild West movies and do. Shit. Everybody in Homewood up on Homewood Avenue duking with the cops. Even the little weeny kids was there, standing back throwing rocks. We fought that whole summer. Cop cars all over the place and they'd come jumping out with night sticks and fists balled up. They wore leather jackets and gloves and sometimes they be wearing them football helmets so you couldn't go upside they heads without hurting your hand. We was rolling. Steady fighting. All you need to be doing was walking down the avenue and here they come. Screeching the brakes. Pull up behind you and three or four cops come busting out the squad car ready to rumble. Me and some the fellas just minding our business walking down Homewood and this squad car pulls up. Hey, you. Hold it. Stop where you are, like he's talking to some silly kids or something. All up in my face. What you doing here, like I ain't got no right to be on Homewood Avenue, and I been walking on Homewood Avenue all my life an ain't no jive police gon get on my case just cause I'm walking down the avenue. Fuck you, pig. Ain't none your goddamn business, pig. Well, you know it's on then. Cop come running at Henry and Henry ducks down on one knee and jacks the motherfucker up. Throw him clean through that big window of Murphy's five-and-dime. You know where I mean. Where Murphy's used to be. Had that cop snatched up in the air and through that window before he knew what hit him. Then it's on for sure. We rolling right there in the middle of Homewood Avenue.

That's the way it was. Seem like we was fighting cops every day. Funny thing was, it was just fighting. Wasn't no shooting or nothing like that. Somebody musta put word out from Downtown. You can whip the niggers' heads but don't be shooting none of em. Yeah. Cause the cops would get out there and fight but they never used no guns. Might bust your skull with a nightstick but they wasn't gon shoot you. So the word must have been out. Cause you know if it was left to the cops they would have blowed us all away. Somebody said don't shoot and we figured that out so it was stone rock 'n' roll and punch-up time.

Sometimes I think the cops dug it too. You know like it was exercise or something. Two or three carloads roll up and it's time to get it on. They was looking for trouble. You could tell. You didn't have to yell pig or nothing. Just be minding your business and here they come piling out the car ready to go ten rounds. I got tired of fighting cops. And getting whipped on. We had some guys go up on the rooves. Brothers was gon waste the mother-fuckers from up there when they go riding down the street but shit, wasn't no sense bringing guns into it long as they wasn't shooting at us. Brothers didn't play in those days. We was organized. Cops jump somebody and in two minutes half of Homewood out there on them cops' ass. We was orga-nized and had our own weapons and shit. Rooftops and them old boarded-up houses was perfect for snipers. Dudes had pistols and rifles and shotguns. You name it. Wouldna believed what the brothers be firing if it come to that but it didn't come to that. Woulda been stone war in the streets. But the shit didn't come down that way. Maybe it woulda been bet-ter if it did. Get it all out in the open. Get the killing done wit. But the shit didn't hit the fan that summer. Least not that way.

Lemme see. I woulda been in eleventh grade. One more year of West-inghouse left after the summer of '68. We was the ones started the strike. Right in the halls of good old Westinghouse High School. Like I said, we had this organization. There was lots of organizations and clubs and stuff like that back then but we had us a mean group. Like, if you was serious business you was wit us. Them other people was into a little bit of this and that, but we was in it all the way. We was gon change things or die trying. We was known as bad. Serious business, you know. If something was com-ing down they always wanted us wit them. See, if we was in it, it was some mean shit. Had to be. Cause we didn't play. What it was called was To-gether. Our group. We was so bad we was having a meeting once and one the brothers bust in. Hey youall. Did youall hear on the radio Martin Lu-ther King[2] got killed? One the older guys running the meeting look up and say, We don't care nothing bout that ass-kissing nigger, we got important business to take care of. See, we just knew we was into something. To-gether was where it was at. Didn't nobody dig what King putting down. We wasn't about begging whitey for nothing and we sure wasn't taking no knots without giving a whole bunch back. After the dude come in hollering and breaking up the meeting we figured we better go on out in the street any-way cause we didn't want no bullshit. You know. Niggers running wild and tearing up behind Martin Luther King getting wasted. We was into plan-ning. Into organization. When the shit went down we was gon be ready. No point in just flying around like chickens with they heads cut off. I mean like it ain't news that whitey is offing niggers. So we go out the meeting to cool things down. No sense nobody getting killed on no humbug.

Soon as we got outside you could see the smoke rising off Homewood Avenue. Wasn't that many people out and Homewood burning already, so we didn't really know what to do. Walked down to Hamilton and checked it out around in there and went up past the A & P. Say to anybody we see, Cool it. Cool it, brother. Our time will come. It ain't today, brother. Cool it. But we ain't really got no plan. Didn't know what to do, so me and Henry torched the Fruit Market and went on home.

Yeah. I was a stone mad militant. Didn't know what I was saying half the time and wasn't sure what I wanted, but I was out there screaming and

---

2. African American clergyman and civil rights leader (1929–1968), advocate of nonviolent resistance.

hollering and waving my arms around and didn't take no shit from nobody. Mommy and them got all upset cause I was in the middle of the school strike. I remember sitting down and arguing with them many a time. All they could talk about was me messing up in school. You know. Get them good grades and keep your mouth shut and mind your own business. Trying to tell me white folks ain't all bad. Asking me where would niggers be if it wasn't for good white folks. They be arguing that mess at me and they wasn't about to hear nothing I had to say. What it all come down to was be a good nigger and the white folks take care of you. Now I really couldn't believe they was saying that. Mommy and Geral[3] got good sense. They ain't nobody's fools. How they talking that mess? Wasn't no point in arguing really, cause I was set in my ways and they sure was set in theirs. It was the white man's world and wasn't no way round it or over it or under it. Got to get down and dance to the tune the man be playing. You know I didn't want to hear nothing like that, so I kept on cutting classes and fucking up and doing my militant thing every chance I got.

I dug being a militant cause I was good. It was something I could do. Rap to people. Whip a righteous message on em. People knew my name. They'd listen. And I'd steady take care of business. This was when Rap Brown and Stokely and Bobby Seale and them on TV. I identified with those cats. Malcolm and Eldridge and George Jackson.[4] I read their books. They was Gods. That's who I thought I was when I got up on the stage and rapped at the people. It seemed like things was changing. Like no way they gon turn niggers round this time.

You could feel it everywhere. In the streets. On the corner. Even in jive Westinghouse High people wasn't going for all that old, tired bullshit they be laying on you all the time. We got together a list of demands. Stuff about the lunchroom and a black history course. Stuff like that and getting rid of the principal. We wasn't playing. I mean he was a mean nasty old dude. Hated niggers. No question about that. He wouldn't listen to nobody. Didn't care what was going on. Everybody hated him. We told them people from the school board his ass had to go first thing or we wasn't coming back to school. It was a strike, see. Started in Westinghouse, but by the end of the week it was all over the city. Langley and Perry and Fifth Avenue and Schenley. Sent messengers to all the schools, and by the end of the week all the brothers and sisters on strike. Shut the schools down all cross the city, so they knew we meant business. Knew they had to listen. The whole Board of Education came to Westinghouse and we told the principal to his face he had to go. The nasty old motherfucker was sitting right there and we told the board, He has to go. The man hates us and we hate him and his ass got to go. Said it right to his face and you ought to seen him turning purple and flopping round in his chair. Yeah. We got on his case. And the thing was they gave us everything we asked for. Yes . . . Yes . . . Yes. Everything we had on the list. Sat there just as nice and lied like dogs. Yes. We agree. Yes.

3. Nickname for Geraldine, Robby's first wife.
4. Leaders in the Black Power movement of the late 1960s. Brown (b. 1943), Southern Nonviolent Coordinating Committee (SNCC) leader. Stokely Carmichael (b. 1941), SNCC leader. Seale (b. 1937), member of the Black Panthers. Malcolm X (1925–1965), powerful political and religious leader, author of The Autobiography of Malcolm X (1965). Eldridge Cleaver (b. 1935), member of the Black Panthers, author of Soul on Ice (1968). Jackson (1941–1971), author of Soledad Brother: The Prison Letters of George Jackson (1970).

You'll have a new principal. I couldn't believe it. Didn't even have to curse them out or nothing. Didn't even raise my voice cause it was yes to this and yes to that before the words out my mouth good.

We's so happy we left that room with the Board and ran over to the auditorium and in two minutes it was full and I'm up there screaming. We did it. We did it. People shouting back Right on and Work out and I gets that whole auditorium dancing in they seats. I could talk now. Yes, I could. And we all happy as could be, cause we thought we done something. We got the black history course and got us a new principal and, shit, wasn't nothing we couldn't do, wasn't nothing could stop us that day. Somebody yelled, Party, and I yelled back, Party, and then I told them, Everybody come on up to Westinghouse Park. We gon stone party. Wasn't no plan or nothing. It all just started in my head. Somebody shouted party and I yelled Party and the next thing I know we got this all-night jam going. We got bands and lights and we partied all night long. Ima tell you the truth now. Got more excited bout the party than anything else. Standing up there on the stage I could hear the music and see the niggers dancing and I'm thinking, Yeah. I'm thinking bout getting high and tipping round, checking out the babes and grooving on the sounds. Got me a little reefer and sipping out somebody's jug of sweet wine and the park's full of bloods[5] and I'm in heaven. That's the way it was too. We partied all night long in Westinghouse Park. Cops like to shit, but wasn't nothing they could do. This was 1968. Wasn't nothing they could do but surround the park and sit out there in they cars while we partied. It was something else. Bands and bongos and niggers singing, *Oh bop she bop* everywhere in the park. Cops sat out in them squad cars and Black Marias, but wasn't nothing they could do. We was smoking and drinking and carrying on all night and they just watched us, just sat in the dark and didn't do a thing. We broke into the park building to get us some lectricity for the bands and shit. And get us some light. Broke in the door and took what we wanted, but them cops ain't moved an inch. It was our night and they knew it. Knew they better leave well enough alone. We owned Westinghouse Park that night. Thought we owned Homewood.

In a way the party was the end. School out pretty soon after that and nobody followed through. We come back to school in the fall and they got cops patrolling the halls and locks on every door. You couldn't go in or out the place without passing by a cop. They had our ass then. Turned the school into a prison. Wasn't no way to get in the auditorium. Wasn't no meetings or hanging out in the halls. They broke up all that shit. That's when having police in the schools really got started. When it got to be a regular everyday thing. They fixed us good. Yes, yes, yes, when we was sitting down with the Board, but when we come back to school in September everything got locks and chains on it.

We was just kids. Didn't really know what we wanted. Like I said. The party was the biggest thing to me. I liked to get up and rap. I was a little Stokely, a little Malcolm in my head but I didn't know shit. When I look back I got to admit it was mostly just fun and games. Looking for a way to get over. Nothing in my head. Nothing I could say I really wanted. Nothing

---

5. Blacks, term of intimacy used by some African Americans.

I wanted to be. So they lied through their teeth. Gave us a party and we
didn't know no better, didn't know we had to follow through, didn't know
how to keep our foot in they ass.

Well, you know the rest. Nothing changed. Business as usual when we
got back in the fall. Hey, hold on. What's this? Locks on the doors. Cops in
the halls. Big cops with big guns. Hey, man, what's going down? But it was
too late. The party was over and they wasn't about to give up nothing no
more. We had a black history class, but wasn't nobody eligible to take it.
Had a new principal, but nobody knew him. Nobody could get to him. And
he didn't know us. Didn't know what we was about except we was trouble.
Troublemakers; and he had something for that. Boot your ass out in a minute. Give your name to the cops and you couldn't get through the door
cause everybody had to have an I.D. Yeah. That was a new one. Locks and
I.D.'s and cops. Wasn't never our school. They made it worse instead of
better. Had our chance, then they made sure we wouldn't have no more
chances.

It was fun while it lasted. Some good times, but they was over in a minute and then things got worser and worser. Sixty-eight was when the dope
came in real heavy too. I mean you could always get dope but in '68 seems
like they flooded Homewood. Easy as buying a quart of milk. Could cop
your works in a drugstore. Dope was everywhere that summer. Cats ain't
never touched the stuff before got into dope and dope got into them. A
bitch, man. It come in like a flood.

Me. I start to using heavy that summer. Just like everybody else I knew.
The shit was out there and it was good and cheap, so why not? What else
we supposed to be doing? It was part of the fun. The good times. The party.

We lost it over the summer, but I still believe we did something hip for a
bunch of kids. The strike was citywide. We shut the schools down. All the
black kids was with us. The smart ones. The dumb ones. It was hip to be on
strike. To show our asses. We had them honkies scared. Got the whole
Board of Education over to Westinghouse High. We lost it, but we had
them going, Bruh. And I was in the middle of it. Mommy and them didn't
understand. They thought I was just in trouble again. The way I always was.
Daddy said one his friends works Downtown told him they had my name
down there. Had my name and the rest of the ringleaders'. He said they
were watching me. They had my name Downtown and I better be cool.
But I wasn't scared. Always in trouble, always doing wrong. But the strike
was different. I was proud of that. Proud of getting it started, proud of being
one the ringleaders. The mad militant. Didn't know exactly what I was
doing, but I was steady doing it.

The week the strike started, think it was Tuesday, could have been Monday but I think it was Tuesday, cause the week before was when some the
students went to the principal's office and said the student council or some
damn committee or something wanted to talk to him about the lunchroom
and he said he'd listen but he was busy till next week, so it could have been
Monday, but I think it was Tuesday cause knowing him he'd put it off long
as he could. Anyway, Mr. Lindsay sitting in the auditorium. Him and vice-
principal Meers and the counselor, Miss Kwalik. They in the second or
third row sitting back and the speakers is up on stage behind the mike but

they ain't using it. Just talking to the air really, cause I slipped in one the side doors and I'm peeping what's going on. And ain't nothing going on. Most the time the principal whispering to Miss Kwalik and Mr. Meers. Lindsay got a tablet propped up on his knee and writes something down every now and then but he ain't really listening to the kids on stage. Probably just taking names cause he don't know nobody's name. Taking names and figuring how he's gon fuck over the ones doing the talking. You. You in the blue shirt, Come over here. Don't none them know your name less you always down in the office cause you in trouble or you one the kiss-ass, nicey-nice niggers they keep for flunkies and spies. So he's taking names or whatever, and every once in a while he says something like, Yes. That's enough now. Who's next? Waving the speakers on and off and the committee, or whatever the fuck they calling theyselves, they ain't got no better sense than to jump when he say jump. Half of them so scared they stuttering and shit. I know they glad when he wave them off the stage cause they done probably forgot what they up there for.

Well, I get sick of this jive real quick. Before I know it I'm up on the stage and I'm tapping the mike and can't get it turned on so I goes to shouting. Talking trash loud as I can. Damn this and damn that and Black Power and I'm somebody. Tell em ain't no masters and slaves no more and we want freedom and we want it now. I'm stone preaching. I'm chirping. Get on the teachers, get on the principal and everybody else I can think of. Called em zookeepers. Said they ran a zoo and wagged my finger at the chief zookeeper and his buddies sitting down there in the auditorium. Told the kids on the stage to go and get the students. You go here. You go there. Like I been giving orders all my life. Cleared the stage in a minute. Them chairs scraped and kids run off and it's just me up there all by my ownself. I runs out of breath. I'm shaking, but I'm not scared. Then it gets real quiet. Mr. Lindsay stands up. He's purple and shaking worse than me. Got his finger stabbing at me now. Shoe's on the other foot now. Up there all by myself now and he's doing the talking.

Are you finished? I hope you're finished cause your ass is grass. Come down from there this instant. You've gone too far this time, Wideman. Get down from there. I want you in my office immediately.

They's all three up now, Mr. Lindsay and Miss Kwalik and Meers, up and staring up at me like I'm stone crazy. Like I just pulled out my dick and peed on the stage or something. Like they don't believe it. And to tell the truth I don't hardly believe it myself. One minute I'm watching them kids making fools of theyselves, next minute I'm badmouthing everything about the school and giving orders and telling Mr. Lindsay to his face he ain't worth shit. Now the whiteys is up and staring at me like I'm a disease, like I'm Bad Breath or Okey Doke the damn fool and I'm looking round and it's just me up there. Don't know if the other kids is gone for the students like I told them or just run away cause they scared.

Ain't many times in life I felt so lonely. I'm thinking bout home. What they gon say when Mr. Lindsay calls and tells them he kicked my ass out for good. Cause I had talked myself in a real deep hole. Like, Burn, baby burn. We was gon run the school our way or burn the motherfucker down. Be our school or wasn't gon be no school. Yeah, I was yelling stuff like that and

I was remembering it all. Cause it was real quiet in there. Could of heard a pin drop in the balcony. Remembering everything I said and then starting to figure how I was gon talk myself out this one. Steady scheming and just about ready to cop a plea. I's sorry boss. Didn't mean it, Boss. I was just kidding. Making a joke. Ha. Ha. I loves this school and loves you Mr. Lindsay. My head's spinning and I'm moving away from the mike but just at that very minute I hears the kids busting into the balcony. It's my people. It's sure nuff them. They bust into the balcony and I ain't by myself no more. I'm hollering again and shaking a power fist and I tells Mr. Lindsay:

You get out. You leave.

I'm king again. He don't say a word. Just splits with his flunkies. The mike starts working and that's when the strike begins.

Your brother was out there in the middle of it. I was good, too. Lot of the time I be thinking bout the party afterward, my heart skipping forward to the party, but I was willing to work. Be out front. Take the weight. Had the whole city watching us, Bruh.

1984

Damballah [1]

Orion [2] let the dead, gray cloth slide down his legs and stepped into the river. He picked his way over slippery stones till he stood calf deep. Dropping to one knee he splashed his groin, then scooped river to his chest, both hands scrubbing with quick, kneading spirals. When he stood again, he stared at the distant gray clouds. A hint of rain in the chill morning air, a faint, clean presence rising from the far side of the hills. The promise of rain coming to him as all things seemed to come these past few months, not through eyes or ears or nose but entering his black skin as if each pore had learned to feel and speak.

He watched the clear water race and ripple and pucker. Where the sun cut through the pine trees and slanted into the water he could see the bottom, see black stones, speckled stones, shining stones whose light came

---

1. In *The Homewood Trilogy* (1985), of which *Damballah* is a part, Wideman quotes from Maya Deren's *Divine Horsemen: The Voodoo Gods of Haiti:*

Damballah Wedo is the ancient, the venerable father; so ancient, so venerable, as of a world before the troubles began; and his children would keep him so; image of the benevolent, paternal innocence, the great father of whom one asks nothing save his blessing. . . . There is almost no precise communication with him, as if his wisdom were of such major cosmic scope and of such grand innocence that it could not perceive the minor anxieties of his human progeny, nor be transmuted to the petty precision of human speech.

Yet it is this very detachment which comforts, and which is evidence, once more, of some original and primal vigor that has somehow remained inaccessible to whatever history, whatever immediacy might diminish it. Damballah's very presence, like the simple, even absent-minded caress of a father's hand, brings peace. . . . Damballah is himself unchanged by life, and so is at once the ancient past and the assurance of the future. . . .

Associated with Damballah as members of the Sky Pantheon, are Badessy, the wind, Sobo and Agarou Tonerre, the thunder. . . . They seem to belong to another period of history. Yet precisely because these divinities are, to a certain extent, vestigial, they give, like Damballah's detachment, a sense of historical extension, of the ancient origin of the race. To invoke them today is to stretch one's hand back to that time and to gather up all history into a solid, contemporary ground beneath one's feet.

One song invoking Damballah requests that he "Gather up the Family."

2. Hunter of Greek myth. Drunk, he raped Merope, to whom he was betrothed. Her father blinded him, but his vision was restored by the sun's rays. Upon his death, Artemis turned him into a constellation.

from within. Above a stump at the far edge of the river, clouds of insects hovered. The water was darker there, slower, appeared to stand in deep pools where tangles of root, bush and weed hung over the bank. Orion thought of the eldest priest chalking a design on the floor of the sacred *obi*.[3] Drawing the watery door no living hands could push open, the crossroads where the spirits passed between worlds. His skin was becoming like that in-between place the priest scratched in the dust. When he walked the cane rows and dirt paths of the plantation he could feel the air of this strange land wearing out his skin, rubbing it thinner and thinner until one day his skin would not be thick enough to separate what was inside from everything outside. Some days his skin whispered he was dying. But he was not afraid. The voices and faces of his fathers bursting through would not drown him. They would sweep him away, carry him home again.

In his village across the sea were men who hunted and fished with their voices. Men who could talk the fish up from their shadowy dwellings and into the woven baskets slung over the fishermen's shoulders. Orion knew the fish in this cold river had forgotten him, that they were darting in and out of his legs. If the whites had not stolen him, he would have learned the fishing magic. The proper words, the proper tones to please the fish. But here in this blood-soaked land everything was different. Though he felt their slick bodies and saw the sudden dimples in the water where they were feeding, he understood that he would never speak the language of these fish. No more than he would ever speak again the words of the white people who had decided to kill him.

The boy was there again hiding behind the trees. He could be the one. This boy born so far from home. This boy who knew nothing but what the whites told him. This boy could learn the story and tell it again. Time was short but he could be the one.

"That Ryan, he a crazy nigger. One them wild African niggers act like he fresh off the boat. Kind you stay away from less you lookin for trouble." Aunt Lissy had stopped popping string beans and frowned into the boy's face. The pause in the steady drumming of beans into the iron pot, the way she scrunched up her face to look mean like one of the Master's pit bulls told him she had finished speaking on the subject and wished to hear no more about it from him. When the long green pods began to shuttle through her fingers again, it sounded like she was cracking her knuckles, and he expected something black to drop into the huge pot.

"Fixin to rain good. Heard them frogs last night just a singing at the clouds. Frog and all his brothers calling down the thunder. Don't rain soon them fields dry up and blow away." The boy thought of the men trudging each morning to the fields. Some were brown, some yellow, some had red in their skins and some white as the Master. Ryan black, but Aunt Lissy blacker. Fat, shiny blue-black like a crow's wing.

---

3. Or obeah, a form of witchcraft or magic practiced in Africa and also in parts of the South and in the West Indies.

"Sure nuff crazy." Old woman always talking. Talking and telling silly stories. The boy wanted to hear something besides an old woman's mouth. He had heard about frogs and bears and rabbits too many times. He was almost grown now, almost ready to leave in the mornings with the men. What would they talk about? Would Orion's voice be like the hollers the boy heard early in the mornings when the men still sleepy and the sky still dark and you couldn't really see nobody but knew they were there when them cries and hollers came rising through the mist.

Pine needles crackled with each step he took, and the boy knew old Ryan knew somebody spying on him. Old nigger guess who it was, too. But if Ryan knew, Ryan didn't care. Just waded out in that water like he the only man in the world. Like maybe wasn't no world. Just him and that quiet place in the middle of the river. Must be fishing out there, some funny old African kind of fishing. Nobody never saw him touch victuals Master set out and he had to be eating something, even if he was half crazy, so the nigger must be fishing for his breakfast. Standing there like a stick in the water till the fish forgot him and he could snatch one from the water with his beaky fingers.

A skinny-legged, black waterbird in the purring river. The boy stopped chewing his stick of cane, let the sweet juice blend with his spit, a warm syrup then whose taste he prolonged by not swallowing, but letting it coat his tongue and the insides of his mouth, waiting patiently like the figure in the water waited, as the sweet taste seeped away. All the cane juice had trickled down his throat before he saw Orion move. After the stillness, the illusion that the man was a tree rooted in the rocks at the riverbed, when motion came, it was too swift to follow. Not so much a matter of seeing Orion move as it was feeling the man's eyes inside him, hooking him before he could crouch lower in the weeds. Orion's eyes on him and through him boring a hole in his chest and thrusting into that space one word *Damballah*. Then the hooded eyes were gone.

On a spoon you see the shape of a face is an egg. Or two eggs because you can change the shape from long oval to moons pinched together at the middle seam or any shape egg if you tilt and push the spoon closer or farther away. Nothing to think about. You go with Mistress to the chest in the root cellar. She guides you with a candle and you make a pouch of soft cloth and carefully lay in each spoon and careful it don't jangle as up and out of the darkness following her rustling dresses and petticoats up the earthen steps each one topped by a plank which squirms as you mount it. You are following the taper she holds and the strange smell she trails and leaves in rooms. Then shut up in a room all day with nothing to think about. With rags and pieces of silver. Slowly you rub away the tarnished spots; it is like finding something which surprises you though you knew all the time it was there. Spoons lying on the strip of indigo: perfect, gleaming fish you have coaxed from the black water.

Damballah was the word. Said it to Aunt Lissy and she went upside his head, harder than she had ever slapped him. Felt like crumpling right there in the dust of the yard it hurt so bad but he bit his lip and didn't cry out, held his ground and said the word again and again silently to himself, pretending nothing but a bug on his burning cheek and twitched and sent it flying. Damballah. Be strong as he needed to be. Nothing touch him if he don't want. Before long they'd cut him from the herd of pickaninnies. No more chasing flies from the table, no more silver spoons to get shiny, no fat, old woman telling him what to do. He'd go to the fields each morning with the men. Holler like they did before the sun rose to burn off the mist. Work like they did from can to caint. From first crack of light to dusk when the puddles of shadow deepened and spread so you couldn't see your hands or feet or the sharp tools hacking at the cane.

He was already taller than the others, a stork among the chicks scurrying behind Aunt Lissy. Soon he'd rise with the conch horn and do a man's share so he had let the fire rage on half his face and thought of the nothing always there to think of. In the spoon, his face long and thin as a finger. He looked for the print of Lissy's black hand on his cheek, but the image would not stay still. Dancing like his face reflected in the river. Damballah. "Don't you ever, you hear me, ever let me hear that heathen talk no more. You hear me, boy? You talk Merican, boy." Lissy's voice like chicken cackle. And his head a barn packed with animal noise and animal smell. His own head but he had to sneak round in it. Too many others crowded in there with him. His head so crowded and noisy lots of time don't hear his own voice with all them braying and cackling.

Orion squatted the way the boy had seen the other old men collapse on their haunches and go still as a stump. Their bony knees poking up and their backsides resting on their ankles. Looked like they could sit that way all day, legs folded under them like wings. Orion drew a cross in the dust. Damballah. When Orion passed his hands over the cross the air seemed to shimmer like it does above a flame or like it does when the sun so hot you can see waves of heat rising off the fields. Orion talked to the emptiness he shaped with his long black fingers. His eyes were closed. Orion wasn't speaking but sounds came from inside him the boy had never heard before, strange words, clicks, whistles and grunts. A singsong moan that rose and fell and floated like the old man's busy hands above the cross. Damballah like a drum beat in the chant. Damballah a place the boy could enter, a familiar sound he began to anticipate, a sound outside of him which slowly forced its way inside, a sound measuring his heartbeat then one with the pumping surge of his blood.

The boy heard part of what Lissy saying to Primus in the cooking shed: "Ryan he yell that heathen word right in the middle of Jim talking bout Sweet Jesus the Son of God. Jump up like he snake bit and scream that word so everybody hushed, even the white folks what came to hear Jim preach. Simple Ryan standing there at the back of the chapel like a knot poked out on somebody's forehead. Lookin like a nigger caught wid his hand in the chicken coop. Screeching like some crazy hoot owl while Preacher Jim praying the word of the Lord. They gon kill that simple nigger one day."

Dear Sir:

The nigger Orion which I purchased of you in good faith sight unseen on your promise that he was of sound constitution "a full grown and able-bodied house servant who can read, write, do sums and cipher" to recite the exact words of your letter dated April 17, 1852, has proved to be a burden, a deficit to the economy of my plantation rather than the asset I fully believed I was receiving when I agreed to pay the price you asked. Of the vaunted intelligence so rare in his kind, I have seen nothing. Not an English word has passed through his mouth since he arrived. Of his docility and tractability I have seen only the willingness with which he bares his leatherish back to receive the stripes constant misconduct earn him. He is a creature whose brutish habits would shame me were he quartered in my kennels. I find it odd that I should write at such length about any nigger, but seldom have I been so struck by the disparity between promise and performance. As I have accrued nothing but expense and inconvenience as a result of his presence, I think it only just that you return the full amount I paid for this flawed *piece of the Indies.*

You know me as an honest and fair man and my regard for those same qualities in you prompts me to write this letter. I am not a harsh master, I concern myself with the spiritual as well as the temporal needs of my slaves. My nigger Jim is renowned in this county as a preacher. Many say I am foolish, that the words of scripture are wasted on these savage blacks. I fear you have sent me a living argument to support the critics of my Christianizing project. Among other absences of truly human qualities I have observed in this Orion is the utter lack of a soul.

She said it time for Orion to die. Broke half the overseer's bones knocking him off his horse this morning and everybody thought Ryan done run away sure but Mistress come upon the crazy nigger at suppertime on the big house porch naked as the day he born and he just sat there staring into her eyes till Mistress screamed and run away. Aunt Lissy said Ryan ain't studying no women, ain't gone near to woman since he been here and she say his ain't the first black butt Mistress done seen all them nearly grown boys walkin round summer in the onliest shirt Master give em barely come down to they knees and niggers man nor woman don't get drawers the first. Mistress and Master both seen plenty. Wasn't what she saw scared her less she see the ghost leaving out Ryan's body.

The ghost wouldn't steam out the top of Orion's head. The boy remembered the sweaty men come in from the fields at dusk when the nights start to cool early, remembered them with the drinking gourds in they hands scooping up water from the wooden barrel he filled, how they throw they heads back and the water trickles from the sides of they mouth and down they chin and they let it roll on down they chests, and the smoky steam curling off they shoulders. Orion's spirit would not rise up like that but wiggle out his skin and swim off up the river.

The boy knew many kinds of ghosts and learned the ways you get round their tricks. Some spirits almost good company and he filled the nothing with jingles and whistles and took roundabout paths and sang to them when he walked up on a crossroads and yoo-hooed at doors. No way you fool the haunts if a spell conjured strong on you, no way to miss a beating if it your day to get beat, but the ghosts had everything in they hands, even the white folks in they hands. You know they there, you know they floating up in the air watching and counting and remembering them strokes Ole Master laying cross your back.

They dragged Orion across the yard. He didn't buck or kick but it seemed as if the four men carrying him were struggling with a giant stone rather than a black bag of bones. His ashy nigger weight swung between the two pairs of white men like a lazy hammock but the faces of the men all red and twisted. They huffed and puffed and sweated through they clothes carrying Ryan's bones to the barn. The dry spell had layered the yard with a coat of dust. Little squalls of yellow spurted from under the men's boots. Trudging steps heavy as if each man carried seven Orions on his shoulders. Four grown men struggling with one string of black flesh. The boy had never seen so many white folks dealing with one nigger. Aunt Lissy had said it time to die and the boy wondered what Ryan's ghost would think dropping onto the dust surrounded by the scowling faces of the Master and his overseers.

One scream that night. Like a bull when they cut off his maleness. Couldn't tell who it was. A bull screaming once that night and torches burning in the barn and Master and the men coming out and no Ryan.

Mistress crying behind a locked door and Master messing with Patty down the quarters.

In the morning light the barn swelling and rising and teetering in the yellow dust, moving the way you could catch the ghost of something in a spoon and play with it, bending it, twisting it. That goldish ash on everybody's bare shins. Nobody talking. No cries nor hollers from the fields. The boy watched till his eyes hurt, waiting for a moment when he could slip unseen into the shivering barn. On his hands and knees hiding under a wagon, then edging sideways through the loose boards and wedge of space where the weathered door hung crooked on its hinge.

The interior of the barn lay in shadows. Once beyond the sliver of light coming in at the cracked door the boy stood still till his eyes adjusted to the darkness. First he could pick out the stacks of hay, the rough partitions dividing the animals. The smells, the choking heat there like always, but rising above these familiar sensations the buzz of flies, unnaturally loud, as if the barn breathing and each breath shook the wooden walls. Then the boy's eyes followed the sound to an open space at the center of the far wall. A black shape there. Orion there, floating in his own blood. The boy ran at the blanket of flies. When he stomped, some of the flies buzzed up from the carcass. Others too drunk on the shimmering blood ignored him except to join the ones hovering above the body in a sudden droning peal of annoyance. He could keep the flies stirring but they always returned from the recesses of the high ceiling, the dark corners of the building, to gather in a cloud above the body. The boy looked for something to throw. Heard his breath, heavy and threatening like the sound of the flies. He sank to the dirt floor, sitting cross-legged where he had stood. He moved only once, ten slow paces away from Orion and back again, near enough to be sure, to see again how the head had been cleaved from the rest of the body, to see how the ax and tongs, branding iron and other tools were scattered around the corpse, to see how one man's hat and another's shirt, a letter that must have come from someone's pocket lay about in a helter-skelter way as if the men had suddenly bolted before they had finished with Orion.

Forgive him, Father. I tried to the end of my patience to restore his lost soul. I made a mighty effort to bring him to the Ark of Salvation but he had walked in darkness too long. He mocked Your Grace. He denied Your Word. Have mercy on him and forgive his heathen ways as you forgive the soulless beasts of the fields and birds of the air.

She say Master still down slave row. She say everybody fraid to go down and get him. Everybody fraid to open the barn door. Overseer half dead and the Mistress still crying in her locked room and that barn starting to stink already with crazy Ryan and nobody gon get him.

And the boy knew his legs were moving and he knew they would carry him where they needed to go and he knew the legs belonged to him but he could not feel them, he had been sitting too long thinking on nothing for too long and he felt the sweat running on his body but his mind off somewhere cool and quiet and hard and he knew the space between his body and mind could not be crossed by anything, knew you mize well try to stick the head back on Ryan as try to cross that space. So he took what he needed out of the barn, unfolding, getting his gangly crane's legs together under him and shouldered open the creaking double doors and walked through the flame in the center where he had to go.

Damballah said it be a long way a ghost be going and Jordan chilly and wide and a new ghost take his time getting his wings together. Long way to go so you can sit and listen till the ghost ready to go on home. The boy wiped his wet hands on his knees and drew the cross and said the word and settled down and listened to Orion tell the stories again. Orion talked and he listened and couldn't stop listening till he saw Orion's eyes rise up through the back of the severed skull and lips rise up through the skull and the wings of the ghost measure out the rhythm of one last word.

Late afternoon and the river slept dark at its edges like it did in the mornings. The boy threw the head as far as he could and he knew the fish would hear it and swim to it and welcome it. He knew they had been waiting. He knew the ripples would touch him when he entered.

1985

SAMUEL R. DELANY

b. 1942

Samuel R. (Chip) Delany Jr., one of very few African American science fiction writers, is one of the most important authors in the genre. During a career that began in 1962, he has published over twenty novels and over eight works of nonfiction and has repeatedly won the Hugo and Nebula awards, the most coveted prizes in science fiction. Because science fiction is often characterized as marginal, Delany has had to defend the field in order to be seen as a serious writer. Not surprisingly, both through the richness of his own science fiction and through his four collections of essays about the genre, he has done so passionately, maintaining at times that "the science fictional enterprise is richer than the enterprise of mundane fiction." Critics have listened, comparing him to Kierkegaard, Kafka, and Joyce and hailing his contribution not just to science fiction but to contemporary American literature as a whole.

The son of Margaret and Samuel R. Delany Sr., Samuel R. Delany Jr. was born and raised in Harlem. His father, a prosperous funeral director, sent him to the progressive and white Dalton School. Delany's struggle with undiagnosed dyslexia, and possibly his shifting back and forth between the world of Harlem and the world of Dalton, resulted in his leading a tumultuous and difficult childhood. After Dalton, Delany went to the Bronx High School of Science, where he concentrated on math and physics. At the same time, he played the guitar, wrote a violin concerto, and studied acting and ballet. Between 1954 and 1961, he wrote several apprentice novels.

At the age of nineteen, in 1961, Delany married the poet Marilyn Hacker, who encouraged him to submit a manuscript to Ace Books, where she worked. This first book, *The Jewels of Aptor* (1962), explores themes of quest, of the capabilities of technology, and of the status of the artist, themes to which Delany would often come back. Between 1962 and 1965, Delany published five novels. After a nervous breakdown in 1965, he slowed his pace and from 1966 to 1969 produced *Babel-17* (1966); *The Einstein Intersection* (1967), for which he won the Nebula award; and *Nova* (1969), the culmination of his traditional science fiction phase. For the next seven years Delany lived in the Heavenly Breakfast commune in New York City. During this time, he played in a rock band and published what has been called a pornographic novel, *The Tides of Lust* (1973).

In 1975 Delany published the novel that established him as a major American writer: *Dhalgren*. In an important 1977 essay on Delany, critic Peter Alterman notes that, within Delany's novels and especially within *Dhalgren*, "time, logic and point of view are cut loose from traditional literary positions, and function relativistically." Kid, *Dhalgren*'s narrator, is dyslexic and epileptic, and the narrative itself is somewhat disorienting. Nonetheless, in *Dhalgren*, as in Delany's later novels, time, logic, and point of view are rigidly controlled by the rules of a relativistic universe. Delany's vision, as Alterman points out, is both grounded in the concrete, sensual, "realistic" world and celebratory of the mythic, metaphoric elements of language. Such concern with language is central to all Delany's writing: the early, more traditional science fiction; the nonfiction; and the "postmodernist" novels of the 1970s and 1980s. Definitely it makes itself felt in *Atlantis: Model 1924* (1995), which by its abundance of wordplay and literary allusion weaves a dense but dancing network of humor, myth, and madness.

Delany's science fiction is notable too for its black and mixed-blood characters, unusual in science fiction, and for its exploration of sexuality—the final frontier for the genre. *Triton* (1976) features more than forty different sexes. *The Tides of Lust,* Delany's "pornographic" novel, ponders the politics of sexual desire. A bisexual himself, Delany focused on issues of sexuality in his memoir *The Motion of Light in Water* (1988).

In 1975, after his divorce from Hacker and partly as result of his correspondence with literary critic Leslie Fiedler, Delany became the Butler Professor of English at the State University of New York; in 1977 he was named senior fellow at the Center for Twentieth Century Studies at the University of Wisconsin, Milwaukee. He is presently professor of contemporary literature at the University of Massachusetts, Amherst.

From Atlantis: Model 1924

d

> The One remains, the many change and pass;
> Heaven's light forever shines, Earth's shadows fly;
> Life, like a dome of many-coloured glass,
> Stains the white radiance of Eternity.
> —PERCY BYSSHE SHELLEY,[1] *Adonaïs*

> . . . plough through thrashing glister toward
> fata morgana's lucent melting shore,
> weave toward New World littorals that are
> mirage and myth and actual shore.
> —ROBERT HAYDEN,[2] "Middle Passage"

Sam turned on the bench, to see, standing behind him, the man he'd bumped when he'd been staring through the planks.

"Yes," Sam said. "That's right. I am."

"I know it's none of my business," the man said. "But I'd bet a lot of people meet you and think you're white."

Well, a lot of people up here did. "Some of them."

"The reason I suspected, I suppose, is that I have a colored friend—a writer. A marvelous writer. He writes stories, but they're much more like poems. You read them, and you can just *see* the sunlight on the fields and hear the sound of the Negro girls' laughter. His name is Jean—"

"—Toomer?"[3] Sam supplied.

"Now don't tell me you're related to him . . . ?" The man laughed. "Though you look somewhat like him. You know, Jean just ran off with the wife of my very good friend, Waldo—so I don't think I'm really *supposed* to like him right through here—it's the kind of thing you don't write your mother about. But I do—like him, that is. He's handsome, brilliant, talented. How could one help it? Maybe that's why I took a chance and spoke to you—because you do look something like him. New York is the biggest of cities, but the smallest of worlds. Everybody always turns out to know everyone else—"

1. English Romantic poet (1792–1822); his elegy *Adonais* was written in memory of fellow poet John Keats, who died of tuberculosis in 1821.
2. African American poet (1913–1980); *Middle Passage* (1945) depicts the famous mutiny on the slave ship *Amistad.*
3. African American poet and fiction writer (1894–1967); his experimental novel *Cane* (1923) was one of the major works of the Harlem Renaissance.

"No," Sam said. "No. I'm not his relative. But he's a friend of my . . ." How did you explain about your brother's strange girlfriend—who was the one who *knew* everybody. "A friend of my brother's. Well, a friend of a girl my brother knows." Though Clarice had said he looked like Toomer, she hadn't mentioned the absconsion. "She was the one who told me about him." He couldn't imagine Clarice approving of such carryings on.

"Oh, well, there—you see. You know, that man you were watching, in the boat—do you mind if I sit down?"

"No. Sure . . . !"

The young man stepped around the bench's end, flopped to the seat, and flung both arms along the back: "Lord, he was hung! Like a stallion! Pissed like a racehorse, too!" He looked over, grinning behind his glasses. "To see it from up here at all, someone's got to throw a stream as thick as a fire hose. It was something, 'ey?"

Sam was surprised—and found himself grinning at the ridiculousness of it. People didn't strip down to stand up and make water before all New York—but if someone did, even less did you talk about it. That both had happened within the hour seemed to overthrow the anxiety of the last minutes, and struck him as exorbitantly comic.

"But did you see what he did?" Sam asked. "Did you see?"

"I saw as much as you, I bet—maybe more, the way you ran off." The fellow hit him playfully on the shoulder with the back of his hand.

"I mean, he must have jumped in . . . for a swim. Or maybe—"

"No," the man said. "I don't think he'd have done that." He seemed suddenly pensive. "It's much too cold. The water's still on the nippy side, this early in spring."

"But he *must* have," Sam said. He'd stopped laughing. "I saw the boat, later on—over there." He pointed toward Brooklyn. "There was no one in it. I know it was the same boat. Because of the hat, and . . . because of his hat."

"No one in it?" The man seemed surprised.

"It was floating empty. He must have fallen overboard—or jumped in. Then he couldn't get back up. The boat was just drifting, turning in circles. Really—there was no one in it at all!"

The man narrowed his eyes, then looked pensively out at the sky while a train's open-air trundle filled the space beneath them. Through the green v's of the beams supporting the rail, over the walkway's edge, Sam could see the car tops moving toward the city. Finally the man said: "No, I don't think that's what happened. He was probably one of the Italian fishermen living over there. I live over there, too—not too far from them. A clutch of Genovesi."[4] He too waved toward Brooklyn. "God, those guineas are magnificent animals! Swim like porpoises—at least the boys do. You can watch them, frisking about in the water just down from where I live. Fell in? *Naw* . . . !" He burlesqued the word, speaking it in an exaggerated tone of someone who didn't use it naturally. "It's a bold swimmer who jumps into the midst of his own pee. You think he went under in his own maelstrom, while your white aeroplane of Help soared overhead? Oh, no. The East

---

4. Natives of Genoa, a seaport in northern Italy.

River's not really a river, you know. It's a saltwater estuary—complete with tides. So even that whole herd of pissers from the Naval Shipyard, splattering off the concrete's edge every day, doesn't significantly change the taste. Jump? I'll tell you what's more likely. After he spilled his manly quarts, he lay down in the bottom and let his boat float, with the sunlight filling it up around him as if it were a tub and the light was a froth of suds. And when, finally, he drifts into the dago docks, he'll jump up, grab hold of it, and shake that long-skinned guinea pizzle for the little Genoese lassies out this afternoon to squeal over, go running to their mothers, and snigger at. No, suicidal or otherwise, his kind doesn't go in for drowning."

Sam started to repeat that the boat had been empty. But—well, *was* there a chance he'd missed the form stretched on the bottom? Sam said: "You live in Brooklyn?" because that was all he could think to say. (No. He remembered the oar. The boat had been empty, he was sure of it—almost.)

The man inclined his head: "Sebastian Melmouth, at your service. One-ten Columbia Heights, Apartment c33." The man took his glasses off, held them up to the sky, examining them for dust, then put them back on.

Sam said: "I think he fell over. Maybe he was drunk or crazy or . . . drunk. Maybe that's why he took his clothes off—?"

"—to piss in the river?" The man cocked his head, quizzical. "It's possible. Those guineas drink more than I do. A couple of quarts of dago red'll certainly make your spigot spout." He looked over at Sam, suddenly sober-faced. "My name isn't really Sebastian Melmouth. Do you know who Sebastian Melmouth was?"

Sam shook his head.

"That was the name Wilde used, after he got out of Reading and was staying incognito in France. Oscar Wilde [5]—you know, *The Ballad of Reading Gaol*—'each man kills the thing he loves'?"

"*The Importance of Being Earnest*," Sam answered.

"The importance of being earnest to be *sure!*" The man nodded deeply.

"They did that down on the school campus—the play—where I grew up."

"School?" The man raised an eyebrow.

"The college—it's a Negro college, in North Carolina. My father works there. My mama's Dean of Women. The students put it on, three years ago, I guess. We all went to see it."

The man threw back his head and barked a single syllable of laughter. "I'm sorry—but the idea of *The Importance of Being Earnest* in blackface— well, not blackface. But as a minstrel—" The man's laughter fractured his own sentence. ". . . Really!" He bent forward, rocked back, recovering. "That's just awful of me. But maybe—" he turned, sincere questioning among his features nudging through the laugh's detritus—"they only used the lighter-skinned students for the—?"

"No," Sam said, suppressing the indignation from his voice. "No, they had students of *all* colors, playing whichever part they did best. They just had to be able to speak the lines."

---

5. Irish poet, playwright, novelist, and critic (1854–1900); imprisoned from 1895 to 1897 because of his homosexuality.

"Really?" the man asked, incredulously.

Sam put his hands on his thighs, ready to stand and excuse himself. There seemed no need at all to continue this.

"You know," the man said, sitting back again, again looking at the sky. "I would have *loved* to have seen that production! Actually, it sounds quite exciting. More than exciting—it might even have been important. In fact, I wouldn't be surprised if it's the sort of thing that *all* white people should be made to see—Shakespeare and Wilde and Ibsen, with Negro actors of all colors, taking whichever parts. It would probably do us some good!"

Surprised once more, Sam took his hands from his thighs. His sister Jules, who had played Gwendolen Fairfax (and was as light as his mother), had said much the same thing after it was over—though the part of Cecily Cardew had been taken by pudgy little black-brown Milly Potts ("Memory, my dear Cecily, is the diary we all carry about with us . . ."), who'd jazzed up the lines unmercifully, strutting and flaunting every phrase as much as it could bear and then some, rolling her eyes, shooting her hands in the air, and making the whole audience, including Papa, rock in their seats, clutch their stomachs and howl (the women's cackles cutting over and continuing after the men's bellowings)—to the point where the other actors couldn't say their own lines, trying to hold their laughter. Later, a more serious Papa had said that though it was *supposed* to be funny, it *wasn't* supposed to be funny in the way Milly had made it so. But now it was hard to think of the play any other way.

The man said: "I don't live in Apartment C 33, actually. You know what that was? That was the cell number Wilde had at Reading. 'The brave man does it with a sword, the coward with a—' "

"What?" Sam asked.

"Kills the thing he loves," the man intoned. "I was going to put C 33 on my door, once. But then I thought better. It's a nice room, though. It's right in front of Roebling's old room."

"Roebling . . . ?"

"Washington Roebling. He's the man who made this bridge." The man raised his head, to take in caging cables. "Who hung these lines here? *He* took over the job from his father, John Augustus Roebling.[6] The Bridge killed his father, John, you know. He'd already completed the plans and was at the waterfront, surveying to start the work—when a runaway cart sliced open his foot. It became infected until, three weeks later, tetanus did him in—with spasms that near broke his bones, with crying out for water. So the son, Washington, took it up. The problem, you see, was to dig the foundations out for those great stone towers." The man gestured left, then right. "How to excavate them, there in the water, the both of them, with those gigantic dredging machines. They had to dig out, beneath the river, two areas a hundred-seventy-two feet by a hundred-two—for each about a third the size of a football field! You know how they did it? They built two immense, upside-down iron and wooden boxes. The bottoms—or, better, the roofs—were made of five layers of foot-square pine timbers, bolted to-

---

6. John Augustus (1806–1869) and Washington Roebling (1837–1926), designer and chief engineer, respectively, of the Brooklyn Bridge.

gether. They caulked them within an inch of their lives, covered them over
with sheet tin, then covered over the whole with wood again. Then they
dropped those upside-down caissons into the drink, with the air still in
them. They let the workers down through shafts that were pressurized to
keep the air in and the water out. Working on the bottom, the poor bo-
hunks and square-heads they had in there dredged out muck and mud till
they hit bedrock—seventy-eight feet six inches below the high-tide line on
the Manhattan side and forty-four feet six inches below on the Brooklyn
side. The workers had a nine-foot high space to dig in, all propped up with
six-by-six beams. The pressure was immense—and they used what they
called clamshell buckets to haul out the dredgings. Right at the very beginning, young Roebling was down in the caissons inspecting—came up too
fast and got the bends. He was a cripple for the rest of his life. So he stayed
in the room at the back of where I live now, surveying the work through the
window with a telescope and directing it through his wife—the bridge—
who went down to the docks every day to bring his orders and take back her
report: spying through his glass at the stanchions he'd raised—twin gno-
mons swinging their shadows around the face of the sound, insistently
marking out his days, till new navigators remap those voyages to and
beyond love's peripheries, till another alphabet, another hunt can reconfig-
ure the word. There're twenty corpses down under those towers. When
it was all done, they poured concrete through the air shafts into the
work space, filled it up, sealed it down to the bedrock. Twenty corpses, at
least—"

"They buried the men in the caissons?" Sam asked, surprised.

"I'm speaking figuratively. Some twenty workers died in the bridge's
construction—and do you know, no one is really sure of their names? I like
to think of those towers as their tombstones. This one falling from the top of
some steam-powered boom derrick, that one hit in the head by a swinging
beam. I see them, buried, all twenty, in those hypogea at the river bottom,
while the stanchions' shadows sweep away the years between their deaths
and the sea's mergence with the sun, while the noon signal sirens all the
dead swimmers through the everyday . . ." For a moment he was pensive.
(Uncomfortable Sam thought again of the . . . Italian fisherman?) "Everybody always talks about John Augustus—a kraut, you see," the man went
on. "There's nothing dumber than a dumb kraut, but there's nothing
smarter than a smart one—we all know that. The war taught it to us if it
taught us anything. John built bridges all over kingdom come: over the
Allegheney, over the Monongahela, over Niagara Falls, the Ohio—each
runs under a Roebling bridge. You'd think, sometimes, he was out to build
a single bridge across the whole of the country. And the plans for this one
were, yes, his. But I want to write the life of Washington. (Don't think it's
an accident John named his son after our good first president!)" Again, he
nodded deeply. "Roebling—Washington A. Roebling—*was* this bridge; this
bridge was Washington Roebling. He was born into it, through his father:
every rivet and cable you see around us sings of him. Write such a life? It
shouldn't be too hard. To get the feel of it, all I have to do is to go into the
back room, look out the window, and imagine . . . *this*, cable by cable,
rising over the river."

When the man was quiet, Sam said with some enthusiasm: "The plaque says the bridge was opened to traffic in 1883. That's the year they started the first commercial electricity in New York City and Hartford, Connecticut!" because, along with and among his magic and tricks, Sam had lots of such informations—like the sixty stories of the Woolworth Building—and this was a man who might appreciate it.

"*Really—?*" the young man asked, conveying more surprise than was reasonable.

"That's right."

"In May it was—since you're being so particular—the very month we're in: on the twenty-fourth, that's when they started to roll and stroll across. Though your plaque doesn't say *that!* Nor does it say how, on the first day, when they opened the walkway here to the curious hordes, going down those steps there a woman tripped and screamed—and the crowds, thinking the whole structure was collapsing, stampeded. Twelve people were trampled to death. It's a strange bridge, a dangerous bridge in its way; things happen here. I mean things in your mind—" a wicked smile behind his glasses gave way to a warm one—"that you wouldn't ordinarily think of." The man held out his hand. "My name's Harold. Harold Hart.[7] People call me Hart. A few folks—especially in the family—call me Harry. But I'm becoming Hart more and more these days."

Sam seized the hand to shake—in his own hand with their nails like helmets curving the tops of the enlarged first joints, their forward rims like visors. "Sam." He shook vigorously—let go, and put his hands down beside him. "My name is Sam." No, the man was not particularly looking at them. "My birthday's just coming up—" he felt suddenly expansive—"and it happens during the transit of Mercury."

"Does it now? And the last year of construction on this bridge, here—in 1882—took place under the last transit of Venus! A fascinating man," the man said, leaving Sam for a moment confused. "When you live in the same room as someone, realize when you go to the bathroom, or leave by the front door, or simply stop to gaze out the window, you're doubtless doing exactly what he did, walking the same distances, seeing what he saw, feeling what he felt, it gives you an access to the bodily reality of a fellow you could never get at any other way—unless, of course, you went out in a boat on the river yourself, and, underneath, stood up, pulled down your pants, and let fly into the flood!" Playfully the man hit at Sam's shoulder once more, then turned to the water, sniggering.

At contact, realizing what the man was referring to, Sam felt the anxiety from the bridge's Brooklyn end flood back. Perhaps, he thought, he *should* excuse himself and go.

But the man said, snigger now a smile and face gone thoughtful: "Sam—now *that's* the name of a poet. There's the biography I should *really* write."

A tug pulled out from under the traffic way's edge—as the dinghy had floated out when Sam had been nearer Brooklyn.

"Pardon?"

---

7. Presumably Harold Hart Crane (1899–1932), American Modernist poet who in 1930 published a poem called *The Bridge*, which used the Brooklyn Bridge as its unifying figure.

ATLANTIS: MODEL 1924 2349

"A marvelous, wonderful, immensely exciting poet—named Sam. Another kraut. Roebling—John Augustus—was born in Prussia—Mühlhausen!" He pronounced it with a crisp, German accent, like some vaudeville comic (Mr. Horstein?) taking off Kaiser Wilhelm.[8] "But Sam was born in Vienna. His parents brought him here when he was seven or eight. No grammar, no spelling, and scarcely any form, but a quality to his work that's unspeakably eerie—and the most convincing gusto. Still, by the time he was your age, Sam was as American as advertising or apple pie. He died about seven years ago—I never met him. But—do you know Woodstock?"

"Pardon?" Sam repeated.

"Amazing little town, in upstate New York—full of anarchists and artists and—" he leaned closer to whisper, the snigger back—"free lovers!" He sat back again. "It's full of all the things that make life really fine in this fatuous age. It's a place to learn the measurement of art and to what extent it's an imposition—a fulcrum of shifted energy! It's a town where, on Christmas Eve morning, leaves blow in a wailing, sunny wind, all about outside the house, over the snow patches. It's a good place to roast turkeys and dance till dawn. A good place to climb mountains, or to curl up with a volume of the *Bough*[9]—though you can get bored there, sweeping, drawing pictures, masturbating the cat . . . Well, that's where I spent this past winter. That's where I discovered Sam—somewhere between making heaps of apple sauce and cooking the turkey in front of an open fire in a cast-iron pig! I've been growing this mustache since about then. How do you think it looks?"

"It looks fine." It looked rather thin for all that time—certainly thinner than Hubert's. "You found Sam's books?"

"Alas, poor Sam never *had* a book. But I found his notebooks and his manuscripts—a friend of mine had them. He let me borrow them so I could copy some of them out."

"He lived in Woodstock?"

"Sam? No, he lived right here in the city—within walking distance of the bridge." This time he gestured toward Manhattan. "Oh, Sam was very much a city poet. He lived just on the Lower East Side, there. Went to P.S. One-sixty at Suffolk and Rivington Street. Worked in the sweatshops—stole what time he could to go to the Metropolitan Museum, take piano lessons. He played piano just beautifully—that's what my friend said. And drew his pictures; and wrote his poems. He wrote a poem once, right here, while he was walking across the bridge with his oldest brother, Daniel—there were eight boys in the family, I believe." Again the man spread his arms along the bench back; one hand went behind Sam's shoulder. "Late in November—just a month before Christmas—they were walking across, from Brooklyn, talking, like you and me, when Sam pulled out his notebook and started writing." He closed his eyes, lifted his chin: " 'Is this the river "East", I heard? / Where the ferry's, tugs, and sailboats stirred / And the reaching wharves from the inner land / Outstretched like the harmless re-

8. William II (1859–1941), emperor of Germany, king of Prussia, and aggressive Central Powers leader during World War I.

9. I.e., *The Golden Bough*, a twelve-volume study of myth and religion, written by James Frazer (1854–1941).

ceiving hand . . . . / But look! at the depths of the dripling tide / That dripples, re-ripples like locusts astride / As the boat turns upon the silvery
spread / It leaves strange—a shadow—dead . . .' "

Through the cables, the dark, flat, and—yes—dead green spread behind
the tug. Ripples crawled to the wake's rim, like silver beetles, to quiver and
glitter at, though unable to cross, the widening borders.

"The river's very beautiful," Sam said, because beauty was the aspect of
nature and poetry it seemed safest to speak of.

"Oh, not for Sam the poet. If anything, for him it was terrifying. He was
to die, looking out at it, from a window of the Manhattan Hospital for the
Destitute, up on Ward's Island. They keep the dying there—and the insane.
It's only an island away from Brother's, where the *General Slocum* beached
after it burned up a thousand krauts and drenched them till they drowned,
back in 'aught-four—makes you wonder what we needed a war for. It was
the dust and the airless walls of his brother Adolf's leather shop where he
worked that first seated in the floor of Sam's breath that terrible, spiritual,
stinking illness—have you ever visited anyone dying of TB?[1] They do stink,
you know? Here in the city, you learn to recognize the stench—if you hang
out in the slums. Nobody ever talks about that, but—*Lord!*—they smell.
The lungs bleed and die and rot in their chests; and their breath and their
bodies erupt with the putrefaction of it—in a way it's a purification too, I
suppose. But before he was nineteen, Sam had already learned the rustle of
nurses around his bed, like the husks of summer locusts. All the nuns—and
he'd been reading Poe, the ghoul-haunted woodlands, that sort of stuff—
once made our rogue tanton bolt St. Anthony's at Woodhaven, in terror for
his life. That's where they first packed him off to die. For a while after that
he stayed in New Jersey—Paterson—with Morris, another brother. But a
few months later, he was back in another hospital—Sea View this time, on
Staten Island." Without closing his eyes, again the man recited: " 'And the
silvery tinge that sparkles aloud / Like brilliant white demons, which a tide
has towed / From the rays of the morning sun / Which it doth ceaselessly
shine upon.' But that was written some years before, when he was well—
walking across the bridge here with Daniel. Still: 'loud, brilliant white demons . . .'? He had a very excitable poetic apprehension—like any true poet
would want to or—really—must have. Don't you think?"

By now Sam was feeling somewhat sulky there'd been no praise of his
own eccentric bit of electrical information. He was not about to condone
all this biography. "It doesn't sound all *that* good of a poem."

"Well, in a way, it's not. But it's what poetry—real poetry—is made of:
'. . . The dripling tide that dripples, re-ripples . . .' Really, for any word-
lover, that's quite wonderful! Words must create and tear down whole visions, cities, worlds!" (Sam was not sure if he was saying Sam—the other
Sam—did this or didn't.) "And then, Sam was only a child when he died—
twenty-three. I'm twenty-four now. A year older than Sammy. But I suppose
he was too young, or too uneducated—too unformed to make *real* poems.
But then, Keats, Rimbaud[2]—all that material: you can feel its sheer verbal

---

1. Tuberculosis.
2. Arthur Rimbaud (1854–1891), French Symbolist poet who wrote all his works between the ages of fifteen and twenty. John Keats (1795–1821), English Romantic poet.

excitement, can't you?" He chuckled, as if to himself. "Twenty-four? In a moment I'll sneeze—and be *older* than Keats!"

Sam looked at the face now looking past his; at first he'd put it at Hubert's age. But there was a dissoluteness to it—the skin was not as clear as it might be, the eyes were not as bright as they should be; and, of course, just the way he spoke—that made the man seem older than twenty-four. Sam asked: "Don't poems have to make sense, besides just sounding nice?" A teacher down in Raleigh had once explained to them why Edgar Poe was not really a good poet, even after they'd all applauded her recitation of "The Bells." Apparently Poe had not been a very good man—and people who were not good men, while they could write fun poems, simply *couldn't* write great ones.

"Oh, do they, now? But there're many interesting ways to seem not to be making sense while you're actually making very good sense indeed—using myths, symbols, poetic associations and rhetorical gestures. I never wrote my mother about Sam—just as I never wrote her about Jean's scooting off with Margy. I haven't written her about Emil yet, either—but I'll have to do that, soon. I wonder if I'll write her about you? Grace proffers the truth in a regular Sunday Delivery, and I send her back lies—of omission mostly. (Can you imagine, telling her about some wild afternoon I had at Sand Street, skulking down behind the piled-up planks and plates beside the Yard?) So I just assume they can be corrected later. I dare say it's all quite incoherent to you. But it's leading up to something—a bigger truth. I just have to get my gumption up to it. At any rate—" he chuckled—"Sam was not only a poet. He drew pictures. He played the piano beautifully, as I said—at least that's what my friend who'd known him told me. You see, it was a poetic sensibility in embryo, struggling to express itself in all the arts. Do you play an instrument?"

"The cornet." Playing the cornet, Sam had always figured, was like knowing about electricity in Hartford and the number of stories in the Woolworth Building. Or maybe a couple of magic tricks.

"Well, then, you see?" the man said. "You and little Sammy Greenberg are very much alike!"

"He was a jewboy!" Sam exclaimed—because till then, for all he'd been trying to withhold, he'd really begun to identify with his strange namesake who had once walked across the bridge and had seen, as had he, the water dripple, re-ripple . . .

"Yes, he was, my young, high-yellow, towering little whippersnapper!" The man laughed.

Once more Sam started, because, though he knew the term—high-yellow—, nobody had ever actually called him that before. (He'd been called "nigger" by both coloreds *and* whites and knew what to do when it happened. But this was a new insult, though it was given so jokingly, he wondered if it was worth taking offense.) Sam put his hands on his thighs again, then put them back on the bench, to arch his fingertips against the wood, catching his nails in weathered grain. Was *this* man, Sam wondered a moment, Jewish? Wasn't there something Semitic in his features? Sam asked: "Do you write poems, too?"

"Me?" The young man brought one hand back, the slender fingers splayed wide against the sweater he wore under his corduroy jacket. "Do I write poems? *Me?*" He took a breath. "I'm in advertising, actually. Ah, but I *should* be writing poems. I *will* be writing poems. Have I ever written poems?" He scowled, shook his head. "*Perhaps* I've written poems. Once I found a beautiful American word: 'findrinny.' But no American writer ever wrote it down save Melville. And since it never made it from *Moby-Dick* into any dictionary (I've looked in half a dozen), I've finally settled on 'spindrift.' Go look *it* up! It's equally lovely in the lilt and lay of what it means. Believe me, if I wrote a real poem, everyone would be talking about it—writing about it. When I write a poem—find its lymph and sinew, fix a poem that speaks with a tongue more mine than any you'll ever actually hear me talking with—you'll know it! Boni and Liveright did *Cane* last year, *Beyond the Pleasure Principle*[3] this year; I just wonder when they'll get to me. I can promise you—Crane," he said suddenly, sat forward, and scowled. "Isn't that endlessly ironic?" He shook his head. "Crane—that's whom they're all mad about now. Someone showed me the manuscript. And, dammit, some of them are actually good! They're planning to get endorsements from Benét[4] and Nunnally Johnson—he lives in Brooklyn, too."

"A poet? Named Crane?" Sam asked.

The man nodded, glancing over. "Nathalia Crane. She lives in Flatbush, out where it builds up again and Brooklyn starts to look at least like a town; and she's in love with the janitor's boy—some snub-nosed freckle-cheeked mick named Jones."

"In the heart of Brooklyn?" Sam said.

"If Brooklyn can be said to have a heart. I wonder why, no matter how hard I try to get away, I always end up working with sweets—Dad makes chocolates, you see. Well, I've lived off them long enough. Personally, I think Brooklyn, once you leave the Heights, is a heartless place. For heart, you go downtown into the Village. Really, the irony's just beyond me. She's supposed to be ten—or was, a couple of years ago. They go on about her like she was Hilda Conkling or Helen Adam.[5] And they actually gave me the thing for review! I mean, I told them—under no *circumstances* would I! Could you think of anything more absurd—*me* reviewing *that?* If I liked it, people would think I was joking. If I hated it, they'd think I was simply being malicious. *They* thought it would be fun. No—I said; I certainly wouldn't be trapped into *that* one. Poetry's more serious than—" Again he broke off and turned, to regard Sam with a fixity that, as the silence grew, grew uncomfortable with it. "I mean, any poem worth its majority must pell-mell through its stages of love, meditation, evocation, and beauty. It's got to hie through tragedy, war, recapitulation, ecstasy, and final declaration. But sometimes I think *she's* got more of the Great War in her poems than I do. I wonder if that makes the geeky girl a better poet? No, I'm not going to be able to take these engineering specifications, instruction manu-

---

3. A study in psychoanalysis by Sigmund Freud (1856–1939), first published in German in 1920. Boni and Liveright was an innovative publishing company of the early 20th century.
4. William Benét (1886–1950), American poet, novelist, and editor, who was on the staff of the New York *Evening Post Literary Review* in the early 1920s.
5. Child prodigies, both poets, of the early 1920s.

als, and giant architectural catalogs much longer—Lord, they're real door-
stoppers! Soon, I'm going to leave that job—the only question is, at my behest or theirs?"

"You're quitting your—?"

"*Nobody* can write poems and have a job at the same time. It's impossible!"

"You don't think so?" He wondered if he should mention that Clarice
worked as a secretary to the principal in the school where Hubert taught—
and seemed to turn out her share.

"Do you think I should quit my job because they—not the people I work
for, but the people I sometimes write for—asked me to review that silly little
girl's silly little book? Of poems?" He crossed his arms severely, hunched
his shoulders as if it had suddenly grown chill. "And, of course, they're not
silly. Really. They're quite good—a handful of them. But they're not as
good as poems I wrote when I was that age. (But doesn't every poet feel like
that?) And they're certainly not as good as the poems I could write now!"
He rocked a few times on the bench, then declared: "Now who do you
think it was who wrote,

> "Here's Crane with a seagull and Lola the Drudge,
> With one pound of visions and one of Pa's fudge.

"Do you think there's that much fudge—and does anybody ever really notice? Fidge, perhaps? Well, Lowell[6] did in Poe . . ." He rocked a few more
times, then began, softly, intensely, voiced, yes, but quiet as a whisper:

> "And midway on that structure I would stand
> One moment, not as diver, but with arms
> That open to project a disk's resilience
> Winding the sun and planets in its face.
> Water should not stem that disk, nor weigh
> What holds its speed in vantage of all things
> That tarnish, creep, or wane; and in like laughter,
> Mobile yet posited beyond even that time
> The Pyramids shall falter, slough into sand,—
> And smooth and fierce above the claim of wings,
> And figured in that radiant field that rings
> The Universe:—I'd have us hold one consonance
> Kinetic to its poised and deathless dance."

He broke off, turning aside, then added: "No, wait a minute. What about
this." Now the voice was louder:

> "To be, Great Bridge, in vision bound of thee,
> So widely belted, straight and banner-wound,
> Multi-colored, river-harboured and upbourne

6. James Russell Lowell (1819–1891), American poet. His *Fable for Critics* (1848) includes the lines
"There comes Poe with his raven, like Barnaby Rudge, / Three-fifths of him genius and two-fifths sheer
fudge."

Through the bright drench and fabric of our veins,—
With white escarpments swinging into light,
Sustained in tears the cities are endowed
And justified, conclamant with the fields
Revolving through their harvests in sweet torment.

"And steady as the gaze incorporate
Of flesh affords, we turn, surmounting all
In keenest transience to that sear arch-head,—
Expansive center, purest moment and electron
That guards like eyes that must always look down
Through blinding cables to the ecstasy
That crashes manifoldly on us when we hear
The looms, the wheels, the whistles in concord
Teathered and antiphonal to a dawn
Whose feet are shuttles, silvery with speed
To tread upon and weave our answering world,
Recreate and resonantly risen in this dome."

Again the man sat back, relaxed his arms. "All right—tell me: is that the greatest—" he growled *greatest* in mock exaggeration—"poem you've ever heard? Or is it?"

Sam looked up, where arch ran into arch, along great cables. "What's it *about?*" he asked, looking back. "The bridge?"

"It's called . . . 'Finale'!" The man seemed, now, absolutely delighted, eyes bright behind his lenses.

"I get the parts about . . . the bridge, I think. But what's the dome?"

"Ah, that's Sam's 'starry splendor dome'—from a poem he wrote, called 'Words.' 'One sad scrutiny from my warm inner self / That age hath—but the pleasure of its own / And that which rises from my inner tomb / Is but the haste of the starry splendor dome / O though, the deep hath fear of thee. . . .' It goes on like that—and ends: '. . . Another morning must I wake to see— / That lovely pain, O that conquering script / cannot banish me.' Conquering script—I like that idea: that the pen is mightier; that writing conquers." His eyes had gone up to tangle in the harp of slant and vertical cables, rising toward the beige-stone doubled groin. "Yes, I think I'll use it, make that one mine—too."

"Can you do that?" Sam asked. "If you write your own poems, can you just take words and phrases from someone else's?"

The man looked down. "Did you ever see a poem by a man named Eliot[7]—read it in *The Dial* a couple of Novembers back. No, you probably didn't. But his poem is nothing *but* words and phrases borrowed from other writers: Shakespeare, Webster, Wagner[8]—all sorts of people."

"Taking other people's poems," Sam said, "that doesn't sound right to me."

"Then I'll link Sam's words to words of mine, engulf them, digest and transform them, *make* them words of my own. Really, it's all right. You said

7. T. S. Eliot (1888–1965), Modernist poet. The work alluded to is *The Waste Land* (1922).
8. Richard Wagner (1813–1883), German composer, especially of large-scale operas. John Webster (1580–1625), English dramatist.

you grew up on a college campus?" Leaning forward, his face became a bit wolfish. "The word is . . . 'allusion'!"

"I grew up there," Sam said. "But I didn't go to school there."

"I see. But look what I've managed to call up! Go on—take a look there, now." The man nodded toward Manhattan. "What's that city, do you think?"

Sam turned, about to say . . . But the city had changed, astonishingly, while they'd been sitting. The sunlight, in lowering, had smelted its copper among the towers, to splash the windows of the southernmost skyscrapers, there the Pulitzer, in the distance the Fuller, there the Woolworth Building itself.

"Risen from the sea, just off the Pillars of Hercules—that's Atlantis,[9] boy—a truly wonder-filled city, far more so than any you've ever visited yet, or certainly ever lived in." Behind Sam the man lowered his voice: "I'm a kind of magician who makes things appear and disappear. But not just doves and handkerchiefs and coins. I'm one of O'Shaunessey's movers and shakers, an archæologist of evening. I call up from the impassive earth the whole of the world around you, Sam—stalking the wild nauga and bringing it all down to words, paired phalluses, bridge between man and man. I create and crumble worlds, cities, visions! No, friend! It is Atlantis that I sing. And poets have been singing it since Homer, son; still, it's amazing what, at any moment, might be flung up by the sea. So: *ecce* Atlantic Irrefragable, corymbulous of towers, each tower a gnomon[1] on the gold afternoon, flinging around it its metric shadow! And you should see it by moonlight—! They speak a wonder-filled language there, Sam: not like any tongue you've ever heard. My pop—C.A.—thinks poetry should be a pleasure taken up in the evening—but not so in Atlantis! No! There, Raphèl maì amècche zabì almi makes as lucid sense as mene, mene tekel upharsin[2] or Mon sa me el kirimoor—nor is it anywhere near as dire as Daniel. But we *need* Asia's, Africa's fables! In Atlantis, when I stand on the corner and howl my verses, no one looks at me and asks, 'Whadja say?' Because mine's the tongue they speak there. In Atlantis I'll get back my filched *Ulysses*[3] with the *proper* apology. I tell you, all twenty of those dead workers are up and dancing there with savage sea-girls, living high and healthy in garden-city splendor, their drinking late into the dawn putting out Liberty's light each morning. And the niggers and the jewboys, the wops and the krauts say hey, hi, and howdy—and quote Shakespeare and Adelaide Crapsey[4] all evening to each other. And even if I were to pull a Steve Brodie[5] this moment from the brink of the trolley lane there—watchman, what of the track?—, as long

9. In Greek myth, Atlantis was a large island in the western sea; Plato described it as a utopia that was destroyed by earthquake. "The Pillars of Hercules": two great rocks on either side of the Strait of Gibraltar, supposedly placed by Hercules during one of his Twelve Labors.
1. Object whose shadow indicates the time of day, as the pointer on a sundial. "*Ecce*": behold (Latin). "Irrefragable": impossible to break. "Corymbulous": made up of several separate stalks all rising to the same height; usually used to describe a flower such as Queen Anne's Lace.
2. Numbered, weighed divisions (Aramaic, literal

trans.); from Daniel, 6:25–28: ". . . God hath numbered thy kingdom, and finished it. . . . Thou art weighed in the balances, and art found wanting. . . . Thy kingdom is divided."
3. Stream-of-consciousness novel by Irish writer James Joyce (1882–1941), published in 1922 but banned for obscenity in the United States until 1933.
4. Adelaide Crapsey (1878–1914), minor American poet best known for developing a five-line form called a "cinquain."
5. I.e., jump off the bridge.

as that city's up, the river would float me, singing on my back, straight into its docks at a Sutton gone royal, no longer a dead end, and I'd walk its avenues in every sort of splendor. You say you saw the empty boat of our dark friend a-dribble over his gunwale? Well, if it was empty, it's because he's found safe harbor there. And he's happy, happy—oh, he's happy, Sam, as only a naked stallion (may St. Titus protect your foreskin in these heathen lands) prancing in the city can be!"

Sam said: "Wow . . . !" though his "Wow" was at the gilded stones, the burnished panes, the towers before him, rather than at the words that wove from behind through the woof of towers ahead. He glanced back at the man, then turned to the city again, where, in a building he couldn't name, copper light fell from one window—"Oh . . . !" Sam breathed—to the window below. "Wow . . ."

"Atlantis," the man repeated. "And the only way to get there is the bridge: the arched nave of this loom, the temple of this stranded warp, the pick of some epiphenomenal gull among them as it shuttles tower to tower, bobbin, spool, and spindle. The bridge—that's what brings us exhausted devils, in the still and tired evening, to Atlantis."

"That's . . . I mean—"

"Atlantis? There, you can see it, when the sun's like this—the city whose kings ordered this bridge be built. Better, the city grows, weaves, wavers from the bridge, boy—not the bridge from the city. For the bridge is a woob—orbly and woob are Sammy's words: a woob's something halfway between a womb and a web. Roebling's bridge, Stella's bridge, my bridge! Trust me—it wasn't gray, girder-grinding, grim and grumpy New York that wove out from this mill. Any dull, seamy era can throw up an Atlantis— Atlantis, I say: city of mirrors, City of Dreadful Night, there a-glittering in the sun! Vor cosma saga. Look at those towers—those molte alti torri, those executors of Mars, like those 'round Montereggione. Vor shalmer raga. Look at them, listen: O Jerusalem and Nineveh—among them you can hear Nimrod's[6] horn bleating and Ephialtes' chain a-rattle. Whose was the last funeral you tagged behind, when the bee drowsed with the bear? What primaveral prince, priest, pauper, Egyptian mummy was it, borne off to night, fire, and forever? What mother's son—or daughter—was it, boxed now and buried? Per crucem ad lucem. Everything living arcs to an end. Nabat. Kalit. The hour to suffer. It's a dangerous city, Sam. Et in Arcadia ego.[7] Anything can be stolen from you any moment. But all you get bringing up the rear of funerals in November is shattered by the sea—for death's as marvelous a mystery as either birth or madness. Go strolling in our city parks, Caina, Ptolomea, Judecca. (The only one I don't have to worry about getting frozen into, I guess, is Antenora—if only thanks to the change of season). Li jorz iert clers e sanz grant vent. Go on, ask: 'Maestro, di, che terra è questa?'[8] No, not penitence, but song. I'm still not ready for repentance. See, I'm looking for Atlantis, too, Sam—sometimes I think the worst

---

6. Grandson of Noah and a noted hunter (Genesis 10:8–10). "Molte alti torri": very high towers (Italian). "Executors of Mars": i.e., towers tall as the twin giants of Greek mythology, Otus and Ephialtes, who captured and chained up the god of war. Jerusalem is a city in Israel, the holy land of the Jews, Christians, and Muslims. Nineveh was the ancient capital of Assyria (now Iraq).
7. And I too in Arcadia (Latin). Arcadia was a region of ancient Greece known for its pastoral tranquility.
8. Master, what land is this? (Italian).

that can happen is that I'll be stuck with the opportunists in the vestibule—maybe even allowed to loll among the pages of the virtuous *Pagan*. But then I'm afraid you're more likely to find me running in circles on burning sand, under a slow fall of fire—that's if I don't just snap and end up in the trees, where harpies peck the bleeding bark. Mine and Amfortas's wounds both could use us some of Achilles' rust—if not a little general ataraxy.[9] In Atlantis you spend *every* night carousing with Charlie Chaplin[1]—and celebrate each dawn with randy icemen at your knees. In Atlantis, you can strut between Jim Harris and the emperor every day, Mike Drayton squiring Goldilocks behind. In Atlantis, all poets wake up in the morning *real* advertising successes—and cheese unbinds, like figs. Step right up, sit down with your own Sammy, drink a glass of malmsey,[2] and share a long clay stem. When this Orlando is to his dark tower come[3]—when I split my ivory horn in two, bleeding from lip and ear (you think my pop will be my Ganelon and finally pluck me from my santa gesta?[4])—will they hear me eight miles or thirty leagues away, the note borne by an angel? You're sensitive, boy—sensitive to beauty. I can tell from your 'Wow!'—it's a sensitive 'Wow!' So—*Wow!*—I know you know what I'm talking of. As well, you're a handsome boy—like Jean. Only *handsomer* than Jean; I'd say it if anyone asked me. But there—I *have* said it; and it's still true! That's the job of poets, you know—to speak the terrifying, simple truths, that, for most people, are so difficult they stick in the throat from embarrassment. I mean, what's poetry for, anyway? To write a reply on the back of a paper somebody slips you at the baths with their address on it whom you don't feel like fucking? To celebrate some black theft of goose, cigar, and perfume—rather than toss it out the window at Thompson's?"

Sam had been used to people down home saying, "The Bishop has some *fine* looking boys!" He'd even had two or three girls at the school get moony and giggly about him, fascinated with the silliest thing he'd say. But the notion of himself as *really* handsome . . . ? He pushed his fingertips over the green bench planks, beneath his thighs.

"Actually," the man said behind him (again Sam looked at the city), "I'm probably as good a poet as I am because I'm quite brave. I'm not some Jonathan Yankee nor yet, really, a Pierrot. But I've trod far shadowier grounds than those Wordsworth[5] preluded his excursion to cover—precisely because they are *not* in the mind of man. Sure. I mean, here a logical fellow must ask: okay, what finally keeps me from it? We have the river's flow—instead of certainty. I could be any old priestess of Hesperus[6]—wrecked on whatever. Am I really going to sing three times? It's a pretty easy argument that, whether in Egypt or at the Dardanelles, with any two

9. A state of calmness, free from emotional distress. "Harpies": half bird, half woman creatures of Greek mythology.
1. Preeminent comedic star of early silent films (1889–1977).
2. Sweet Madeira wine.
3. From Shakespeare's *King Lear* 3.4.170–73: "Child Rowland to the dark tower came" is a line of nonsense verse quoted by Edgar pretending to be insane. Orlando is the Italian name for "Roland" (see n. 4, below).

4. Godly achievements (Italian). Ganelon was a French warrior in the *Song of Roland*, who arranges for his stepson Roland's defeat and death in battle.
5. William Wordsworth (1770–1850), English Romantic poet. "Pierrot": a stock character of French pantomime, usually depicted as a clown dressed in white and black.
6. The morning star. Also a reference to Henry Wadsworth Longfellow's poem *The Wreck of the Hesperus*.

towns divided by water, one can always play Abydos to the other's Sestos: for every Hero somewhere there's a Leander, and every Hero has her Hellespont.[7] There's always hope as long as he remembers how to swim. I mean what are you going to do with Eve, La Gioconda, and Delilah[8]— replace the latter two with Magdalene or Mary? Do I covet the extinction of light in dark waters? Three Marys will rise up and calm the roar: sure— Mary Garden, Merry Andrews, and Mary Baker Eddy.[9]

"But we have the bridge.

"Oh, surely, it starts with your having a satori[1] in the dentist chair, and the next you know you're at work on your hieros gamos and giggling over what Dol Common said to Sir Epicure.[2] There are some folks to whom the thunder speaks; but there are others who need poets to rend and read into it their own trap-clap. (I hope you're not sure, either, who that their own refers to.) It ends, however, here, with me talking to you—I certainly didn't think I would be, half an hour ago. Not when I first saw you. The ones who terrify me are always the short, muscular blonds—and the tall, dark, handsome ones. Like you. 'Tall, dark, and handsome'? That's trite for terror. But it's true. I live with a short, muscular blond. We have a nice, six-dollar a week room. Only, I confess, it's the eight dollar room I lust after. That's Roebling's room. My blond's a sailor. His old man's the building owner. Now he's got the view—but he tells me I can come in and use it whenever I want. They're nice, that way. You can't imagine what it took, getting up nerve to speak to him—but I said, his name's Emil—to talk with him; and really talking with someone is different from simply speaking. I mean, you and I are speaking. But are we talking yet? Perhaps we ought to find out if we can. Still, suddenly, Emil and I—my handsome sailor, my golden wanderer, off after his own fleece—we were talking—telling each other how we felt. About one another. About the world. We talked till the sun came up; then he kissed my eyes with a speech entirely beyond words, and I've been able to do nothing but babble my happiness since. We decided it really would be terrible if we ever left each other. So he asked me to move in with him. All life is a bridge, I told him. Even the whole world. He's like an older brother—it's like living with a brother. And once again I'm hearing things before dawn. I'm three years younger than he—and two inches taller! But sometimes, it's true, I feel like I'm the elder. His father can't imagine that anything could be going on that shouldn't be—if anything is going on at all." Sam heard him shrug . . . "It's a hoot. The last person to pick him up and suckle at his schlong was Lauritz Melchior. Now, because they both speak Danish, we get to lurk backstage at the Met,[3] about as regular as The Brooklyn Eagle. But it's very pure. Very severe, between us— Emil and me. But he is a sailor—and he goes on voyages. He's away, now— in South America. But in Atlantis, I live forever, in my room with my Vic-

7. Or the Dardanelles, a strait separating Europe and Asia Minor. Hero and Leander were lovers who lived on either side of the water; every night Leander would swim from his town, Abydos, to Hero's town, Sestos, guided by the light of Hero's torch. He drowned one night when the torch blew out; Hero killed herself when she found his body. 8. Samson's mistress who betrays him to his enemies (Judges 16:5). "La Giaconda": the cheerful woman (Italian); the title of Leonardo da Vinci's Mona Lisa. 9. Founder of the Christian Science Church (1821–1910). Garden (1877–1967), soprano opera star of the early 20th century. 1. A state of sudden enlightenment. 2. A swindler and the greedy fool she dupes in Ben Jonson's satire The Alchemist (1610). 3. I.e., the Metropolitan Opera House.

trola and my love. It makes my dark room light and light." Suddenly the man leaned forward again. (Sam could hear him, not see him, closer at his back.) "Tell me, Sam: Have you ever tried to kiss the sun? I mean, deep kiss it—French kiss it as they've just begun to say. Maul it with your lips and tongue? Flung your arms around it, pulled it down on top of you, till it seared your chest and toasted the white wafer cheek of love, poached the orbs in your skull, even while you thrust your mouth out and into its fires till the magma at its core blackened the wet muscle of all articulation? Well, Atlantis is the town in which everybody, man and woman, can kiss the sun and still have the moon smile down on them—not this stock, market culture of the stock market. And believe me, sometimes when the sun's away, you'll find yourself needs reaching for the moon. All I do is sweat with imagined jealousies while he's gone—Emil, I mean. But someday, he's going to come home, just while I'm in the throes of it, down on the daybed, with you or some guinea fisherman's randy brat—does it matter which? And . . ." The man sat back. Sam couldn't see him for the city— though he heard his fingers snap: "That'll be it! But that's not for today. That's for another time. Do you want to come back to the place with me— have a drink? We could be alone. I'm a good man to get soused with, if you like to get soused—and what self-respecting Negro doesn't? Come on, relax. Spend a little time—come with me, boy-oh-boy, and we'll get boozy and comfortable."

Was it the mention of the fisherman? Was it the mention of the moon? Suddenly Sam stood and turned around. "Look," he said. "I'm going to get a policeman."

The man frowned, put his head to the side.

"I'm going to get a *policeman*. This isn't right—" He thought: How do you explain to this fellow that the boat was really empty, that a man had *really* drowned?

"But you don't have to do—"

"I'm sorry! But I have tell *somebody!* Look, we just can't—"

The man was looking at Sam's hands—which, in his excitement, had come loose to wave all over the day.

"I know all about it—the force of the club in the hand of the working man. Really," the man added, with a worried look, "policemen are *so* dull. Laughter's what you want here. Celebration of the city. Beauty. Higher thoughts. Get yourself lost in that lattice of flame. Humor's the artist's only weapon against the proletariat—and, in this city, my friend, the police are as proletarian as they come. Hey, I'm not going to make you do anything you don't—I mean I only *asked* . . . only offered you a sociable drink—"

"I'm going to get a policeman," Sam repeated. "Now." He added: "Maybe we'll be back—!" He started away. "In a few minutes."

From behind him the man called out, almost petulantly: "*That's* not the way to Atlantis!"

Sam glanced back.

"And you're a damned fool if you think I'm going to wait around for *you*." The man stood now, one hand on the bench back, like someone poised to run. His final salvo: "Don't think you'll ever get to it calling the law on people like *me!*"

Sam started again. Really, the fellow was a fool! What in the world had made him sit there listening, letting the man drench him in his lurid monologue? Sam broke into a lope, into a run—turned and, practically dancing backwards, looked once more:

The man was hurrying off, into Brooklyn, into Flatbush, or wherever he'd said he lived, moving away almost as fast as Sam was moving toward the city. Sam turned ahead, in time to take the stairs down the Manhattan stanchion—two at a step. Three minutes later, he almost missed the narrow entrance down to Rose. He had to swing around the rail, come back, and, at the entrance, plunge in silence by gray stone.

He found a policeman coming along the black metal railing by City Hall Park, where tall buildings' shadows had already darkened the lower stories to gray—save when Sam passed an east-west street, gilded with sudden sun. He hurried up to the officer. "Excuse me, sir. Please." On the other side of the park's grass, light glinted on the edge of the sprawling trolley terminal's tin roof—where some of the green paint had come away . . . ? "But I think someone's drowned—in the river, sir. I was up walking across, into Brooklyn, and—"

"You saw someone do a Brodie off the bridge?" Below the midnight visor, webbed in forty-plus years' wrinkles, river-green eyes were perfectly serious.

"Someone jump, you mean? No. He was in a boat. I could see it, down in the water. And later on, I saw the boat again—and it was empty. A green rowboat—I think."

The policeman said: "Oh. You saw him go over?"

Sam watched the man's dull squint and his ordinary thumb laid up against the belly of his shirt between his jacket flaps, like something inevitable. He thought about putting his own hands in his pockets, but kept them hanging by force. "Well, no—not really. I mean, I didn't actually *see* it. But later—I saw the same boat. The oar was floating behind it. And there was nobody in it."

"Oh," the policeman said again. The ordinary thumb rose, and the officer scratched ash-blown blond, cap edge a-joggling on the walnuts of his knuckles. "And how long ago was this?"

"Just a few minutes," Sam said, trying to figure how long he'd been talking with the man on the bridge. "Maybe twenty, twenty-five minutes." Probably it was over thirty. Could it have been an hour? "But, well, you know. It takes some time to get all the way back over, to this side, from Brooklyn."

"It was on the Brooklyn side?"

"It was closer to the Brooklyn side than ours."

"Then why didn't you try to get some help over there?" The officer dropped his hand to put a fist on his bullet-belt.

"I didn't see anybody over there. And I was coming back this way, anyway—I mean, I don't think there's anything anybody could have done. Not now. Even then. But I still thought I ought to tell somebody. An officer. That it happened—that it probably happened . . . I mean."

"Oh," the policeman said a third time. "I see."

Sam looked around, looked at the policeman, who seemed to be waiting for him to leave, and finally said a hurried, "I just wanted to tell you—Thank you, sir," and ducked around him, embarrassment reddening his cheeks, rouging his neck.

At the corner, Sam glanced back, hoping the officer would be marking it down on his pad—at least the time or the place or something—in case, later, it came up. (Above, incomplete construction marked the day with girders and derrick, flown against the clouds in sight of the sound; for a moment Sam recalled the white workers who, with saw and torch, would hang there, humming, through the week.) *Would* that white man remember? But the officer was walking on, crossing silver tracks in a fan of sunlight, one untroubled hand flipping his billyclub down, around, and up—now one way, now the other.

Starting purposefully uptown, Sam mulled, block after block, toward the twilight city, now on the disappearance of the fisherman, now on the ravings of the stranger on the bridge, now on the three girls coming down the steps when he'd arrived at the underpass, whose delicate descent had innocently initiated it all, now on the policeman who'd brought the afternoon to its inconclusive close. A knot had tied low in his throat—an anxious thing that wouldn't be swallowed, that kept him walking, kept him thinking, kept him rehearsing and revising bits of the day in their dialogue—till, stalking some greater understanding still eluding him, he got as far as Fifty-second Street.

Nestled in the grip of gilded tritons and swept round by cast nereids'[4] metal drapes, up on the pediment of a bank, with its brazen disk, from arrow-tipped hands, down-cast, short one right and long one left (a wonderful water clock, he thought suddenly and absurdly, in which the water had all run out), Sam realized it was just after . . . twenty-five-to-five!

Along all four legs of the intersection, he looked with electric attention for a subway stop's green globes. He'd been due at Elsie and Corey's almost forty minutes ago!

1995

4. Sea nymphs.

SHERLEY ANNE WILLIAMS
b. 1944

Short story writer, dramatist, critic, poet, and novelist Sherley Anne Williams combines in her work a keen sense of the tradition of black oral and Western literary forms with the concerns of class that are often camouflaged by race in contemporary American literature. Williams feels an affinity with "protest fiction" and claims kin with Alice Walker, Sterling Brown, Langston Hughes, James Baldwin, Zora Neale Hurston, Ernest Gaines, Amiri Baraka, and Toni Morrison, writers who render black life as significant in and of itself and not simply as an adjunct to the white experience or as an irritation in the history of the United States.

Williams was born, the third of four daughters, on August 25, in Bakersfield,

California, to Fesse Winson and Lelia Marie (Silers) Williams. Her parents were laborers, and as a child Williams worked alongside them in the fruit and cotton fields. Her father died of tuberculosis when she was eight, and her mother when she was sixteen. Ruise, Sherley's older sister, then became her guardian. Encouraged by a high school science teacher, Williams studied at Fresno State. After earning a B.A. in history in 1966, she began to write short stories. In 1967, the *Massachusetts Review* published *Tell Martha Not to Moan*.

Williams studied and taught as she wrote. Between 1966 and 1967, she did graduate work at Howard University; from 1970 to 1972, she worked as a community educator in Washington, D.C. In 1972 she taught in the black studies department at Brown University and earned her master's degree. That same year, the manuscript she had worked on during her time at Howard and Brown was published as *Give Birth to Brightness: A Thematic Study in Neo-Black Literature*. In *Give Birth*, Williams contrasts Amiri Baraka's *Dutchman* and *The Slave* with James Baldwin's *Blues for Mister Charlie* and Ernest Gaines's *Of Love and Dust*, arguing that while Baraka draws his characters from a Western tradition, Baldwin and Gaines find theirs in the life of the collective black community.

While researching the history and literature of African Americans and teaching at California State University at Fresno and then at the University of California at San Diego, Williams continued to write. Her first volume of poetry, *The Peacock Poems* (1975), which was nominated for the National Book Award, both draws on her childhood in Bakersfield and gives glimpses of her son, John Malcolm. Her second collection, *Some One Sweet Angel Chile* (1982), employs the point of view of women from different historical eras: nineteenth-century Hannah in *Letters from a New England Negro*, twentieth-century blues singer Bessie Smith in *Regular Reefer*, and her own past self in *The Iconography of Childhood*.

In 1986 Williams published her novel *Dessa Rose*, which she had revised and expanded from a short story titled *Meditations on History* (1980). Like Williams's poetry, the novel reflects her deep knowledge of African American history as well as the musicality of its oral tradition. Williams based her story on two historical events: an 1829 slave uprising in Kentucky led by a pregnant black woman, which is discussed in Angela Davis's essay *Reflections on the Black Woman's Role in the Community of Slaves*, and the giving of sanctuary to runaway slaves in North Carolina by a white woman living on an isolated farm in 1830, which Williams first read about in Davis's essay and then more deeply in Herbert Aptheker's *American Slave Revolts*. Although inspired by historical sources, *Dessa Rose* is not determined by them, for Williams has these two women, who challenge the stereotypes of African American slave women and antebellum southern white women, meet. *Dessa Rose* is also Williams's outraged response to William Styron's *Confessions of Nat Turner* (1967), which, Williams points out, in its limitations is an indication of how "African Americans remain at the mercy of literature and writing." In structuring her novel as if it were being told, so that we hear the difference between Dessa Rose's memory of her experience, her telling of it to a white man, and that man's interpretation of her story, Williams highlights an important aspect of the slave narrative tradition—that is, that these narratives were often told to whites who did not necessarily understand or sympathize with the slave's story but who, because they could write, became the transmitters of the slave experience. Called "artistically brilliant, emotionally affecting and totally unforgettable" in its uncompromising portrayal of American slavery by *New York Times* reviewer David Bradley, *Dessa Rose* was both a critical and a popular success, going into its third printing only a few months after publication.

Williams combines the life of the creative writer with that of the scholar, continuing her own impressive literary efforts while teaching African American literature at the University of California at San Diego.

The Peacock Poems: 1

the trimming of the feathers

I wish I could still stay
down by the fire at the end of the row
and jes watch the baby but Daddy
say I'm a big girl now

not big enough to have my own sack   5
jes only to help pile the cotton
in the middle of the row fo Mamma to put
in her'n. I gots to keep my jacket button;

it's cold. Mamma say I move
mo faster I wouldn't be feelin it so much.   10
I can't do what her and Daddy do move
slow and fast togetha and get a bunch

of cotton and keep warm and watch
the baby, Le'rn. Maybe I get old
as Jesmarie even Ruise I can do a   15
hundred pounds a day hold

the baby—but she won't need no holdin
by then. Mamma sing Daddy hum.
He pickin the row side Ruise
and Jesmarie and they pickin side-a us. We come   20

early fo it's even light and Mamma
face be so dark under them white
head rags and by the end of the day
they be dirty wid sweat. It be gettin on to night

then. Us all be tired. I be thinkin bout   25
the beans Mamma cook. Jack
come wid the bus. Daddy take
the baby and Mamma drag the sack.

1975

I Want Aretha [1] to Set This to Music

I Want Aretha to Set
  This to Music:
                I surprise girlhood
                in your face; I know
                my own, have been a   5
                prisoner of my own
                dark skin and fleshy
                lips, walked that same high
                butty strut despite

1. Aretha Franklin (b. 1942), African American singer known as the "queen of Soul."

all this; rejected   10
the mask my mother
wore so stolidly
through womanhood and
wear it now myself.

I see the mask, sense   15
the girl and the woman
you became, wonder
if mask and woman
are one, if pain is
the sum of all your   20
knowing, victim the
only game you learned.

Old and in pain and
bearing up bearing up
and hurt and age These   25
are the signs of our
womanhood but I'll
make book Bessie[2] did
more than just endure.

•

hear it?   30
hear it?

Oh I'm lonesome now
  but I won't be lonesome long
Say I'm lonely now
  but I don't need to be lonesome long 35
You know it take a man wid some style and passion
  to make a single woman sing these lonely songs

   one-sided bed Blues

Never had a man talk to me
  to say the things he say   40
Never had a man talk like this, honey,
  say the things you say.
Man talk so strong
  till I can't tell Night from Day.

His voice be low words come slow 45
  and he be movin all the while
His voice be low words come slow
  and he be movin, Lawd! all the while.
I'm his radio and he sho
  know how to tune my dial.   50

2. Bessie Smith (1898?–1937), African American singer known as the "empress of the Blues." "Make book": bet.

My bed one-sided from me
    sleepin alone all the time
My bed *wop*-sided from me
    sleepin alone so much of the time
And the fact that it empty   55
    show how this man is messin wid my mind.

•

    what's out there knockin
    Is what the world
    don't get enough of

•

1982

Tell Martha Not to Moan

My mamma is a big woman, tall and stout, and men like her cause she soft and fluffy-looking. When she round them it all smiles and dimples and her mouth be looking like it couldn't never be fixed to say nothing but darling and honey.

They see her now, they sho see something different. I should not even come today. Since I had Larry things ain't been too good between us. But— that's my mamma and I know she gon be there when I need her. And sometime when I come, it okay. But this ain't gon be one a them times. Her eyes looking all ove me and I know it coming. She snort cause she want to say god damn but she don't cuss. "When it due, Martha?"

First I start to say, what. But I know it ain't no use. You can't fool old folks bout something like that, so I tell her.

"Last part of November."

"Who the daddy?"

"Time."

"That man what play piano at the Legion?"

"Yeah."

"What he gon do bout it?"

"Mamma, it ain't too much he can do, now is it? The baby on its way."

She don't say nothing for a long time. She sit looking at her hands. They all wet from where she been washing dishes and they all wrinkled like yo hand be when they been in water too long. She get up and get a dish cloth and dry em, then sit down at the table. "Where he at now?"

"Gone."

"Gone? Gone where?" I don't say nothing and she start cussing then. I get kinda scared cause mamma got to be real mad foe she cuss and I don't know who she cussing—me or Time. Then she start talking to me. "Martha, you just a fool. I told you that man wan't no good first time I seed him. A musician the worst kind of men you can get mixed up with. Look at you. You ain't even eighteen years old yet, Larry just barely two, and here you is pregnant again." She go on like that for a while and I don't say nothing. Couldn't no way. By the time I get my mouth fixed to say something, she done raced on so far ahead that what I got to say don't have nothing to do with what she saying right then. Finally she stop and ask, "What you gon do now? You want to come back here?" She ain't never liked me living with Orine and when I say no, she ask, "Why not? It be easier for you."

I shake my head again. "If I here, Time won't know where to find me, and Time coming; he be back. He gon to make a place for us, you a see."

"Hump, you just played the fool again, Martha."

"No Mamma, that not it at all; Time want me."

"Is that what he say when he left?"

"No, but . . ."

Well, like the first night we met, he come over to me like he knowed me for a long time and like I been his for awmost that long. Yeah, I think that how it was. Cause I didn' even see him when we come in the Legion that first night.

Me and Orine, we just got our checks that day. We went downtown and Orine bought her some new dresses. But the dress she want to wear that night don't look right so we go racing back to town and change it. Then we had to hurry home and get dressed. It Friday night and the Legion crowded. You got to get there early on the weekend if you want a seat. And Orine don't want just any seat; she want one right up front. "Who gon see you way back there? Nobody. You don't dance, how you gon meet people? You don't meet people, what you doing out?" So we sit up front. Whole lots a people there that night. You can't even see the bandstand cross the dance floor. We sharing the table with some more people and Orine keep jabbing me, telling me to sit cool. And I try cause Orine say it a good thing to be cool.

The set end and people start leaving the dance floor. That when I see Time. He just getting up from the piano. I like him right off cause I like men what look like him. He kind of tall and slim. First time I ever seed a man wear his hair so long and nappy[1]—he tell me once it an African Bush—but he look good anyway and he know it. He look round all cool. He step down from the bandstand and start walking toward me. He come over to the table and just look. "You," he say, "you my Black queen." And he bow down most to the floor.

Ah shit! I mad cause I think he just trying to run a game. "What you trying to prove, fool?" I ask him.

"Ah man," he say and it like I cut him. That the way he say it. "Ah man. I call this woman my Black queen—tell her she can rule my life and she call me a fool."

"And sides what, nigga," I tell him then, "I ain't black." And I ain't, I don't care what Time say. I just a dark woman.

"What's the matter, you shamed of being Black? Ain't nobody told you Black is pretty?" He talk all loud and people start gathering round. Somebody say, "Yeah, you tell her bout it, soul." I embarrassed and I look over at Orine. But she just grinning, not saying nothing. I guess she waiting to see what I gon do so I stand up.

"Well if I is black, I is a fine black." And I walk over to the bar. I walk just like I don't know they watching my ass, and I hold my head up. Time follow me right on over to the bar and put his arm round my shoulder.

"You want a drink?" I start to say no cause I scared. Man not supposed to make you feel like he make me feel. Not just like doing it—but, oh, like it right for him to be there with me, touching me. So I say yes. "What's your name?" he ask then.

I smile and say, "They call me the player." Orine told a man that once in Berkeley and he didn't know what to say. Orine a smart woman.

"Well they call me Time and I know yo mamma done told you Time ain't nothing to play with." His smile cooler than mine. We don't say nothing for a long while. He just stand there with his arm round my shoulder looking at us in the mirror behind the bar. Finally he say, "Yeah, you gon be my Black queen." And he look down at me and laugh. I don't know what to do, don't know what to say neither, so I just smile.

"You gon tell me your name or not?"

"Martha."

He laugh. "That a good name for you."

"My mamma name me that so I be good. She name all us kids from the Bible,"[2] I tell him laughing.

"And is you good?"

I nod yes and no all at the same time and kind of mumble cause I don't know what to say. Mamma really did name all us kids from the Bible. She always saying, "My mamma name me Veronica[3] after the woman in the Bible and I a better woman for it. That why I name all my kids from the Bible. They got something to look up to." But mamma don't think I'm good, specially since I got Larry. Maybe Time ain't gon think I good neither. So I don't answer, just smile and move on back to the table. I hear him singing soft-like, "Oh Mary don't you weep, tell yo sister Martha not to moan." And I kind of glad cause most people don't even think bout that when I tell em my name. That make me know he really smart.

We went out for breakfast after the Legion close. Him and me and Orine and German, the drummer. Only places open is on the other side of town and at first Time don't want to go. But we finally swade him.

Time got funny eyes, you can't hardly see into em. You look and you look and you can't tell nothing from em. It make me feel funny when he look at me. I finally get used to it, but that night he just sit there looking and don't say nothing for a long time after we order.

"So you don't like Black?" he finally say.

"Do you?" I ask. I think I just ask him questions, then I don't have to talk so much. But I don't want him to talk bout that right then, so I smile and say, "Let's talk bout you."

"I am not what I am." He smiling and I smile back, but I feel funny cause I think I supposed to know what he mean.

"What kind of game you trying to run?" Orine ask. Then she laugh. "Just cause we from the country don't mean we ain't hip to niggas trying to be big-time. Ain't that right, Martha?"

2. In the New Testament, Martha is the sister of Mary of Bethany; symbol of active religious service.
3. She gave Jesus a cloth with which to wipe his face on the way to the Crucifixion; legend held that his image was impressed on it.

I don't know what to say, but I know Time don't like that. I think he was going to cuss Orine out, but German put his arm round Orine and he laugh. "He just mean he ain't what he want to be. Don't pay no mind to that cat. He always trying to blow some shit." And he start talking that talk, rapping to Orine.

I look at Time. "That what you mean?"

He all lounged back in the seat, his legs stretched way out under the table. He pour salt in a napkin and mix it up with his finger. "Yeah, that's what I mean. That's all about me. Black is pretty, Martha." He touch my face with one finger. "You let white people make you believe you ugly. I bet you don't even dream."

"I do too."

"What do you dream?"

"Huh?" I don't know what he talking bout. I kind of smile and look at him out the corner of my eye. "I dreams bout a man like you. Why, just last night, I dream—"

He start laughing. "That's all right. That's all right."

The food come then and we all start eating. Time act like he forgot all bout dreams. I never figure out how he think I can just sit there and tell him the dreams I have at night, just like that. It don't seem like what I dream bout at night mean as much as what I think bout during the day.

We leaving when Time trip over this white man's feet. That man's feet all out in the aisle but Time don't never be watching where he going no way. "Excuse me," he say kind of mean.

"Say, watch it buddy." That white man talk most as nasty as Time. He kind of old and maybe he drunk or an Okie.

"Man, I said excuse me. You the one got your feet in the aisle."

"You," that man say, starting to get up, "you better watch yourself boy."

And what he want to say that for? Time step back and say real quiet, "No, motherfucker. You the one. You better watch yourself and your daughter too. See how many babies she gon have by boys like me." That man get all red in the face, but the woman in the booth with him finally start pulling at him, telling him to sit down, shut up. Cause Time set to kill that man.

I touch Time's arm first, then put my arm round his waist. "Ain't no use getting messed behind somebody like that."

Time and that man just looking at each other, not wanting to back down. People was gon start wondering what going on in a few minutes. I tell him, "Got something for you, baby," and he look down at me and grin. Orine pick it up. We go out that place singing, "Good loving, good, good loving, make you feel so clean."

"You like to hear me play?" he ask when we in the car.

"This the first time they ever have anybody here that sound that good."

"Yeah," Orine say. "How come you all staying round a little jive-ass town like Ashley?"

"We going to New York pretty soon," Time say kind of snappy.

"Well, shit, baby, you—"

"When you going to New York?" I ask real quick. When Orine in a bad mood, can't nobody say nothing right.

"Couple of months." He lean back and put his arm round me. "They doing so many things with music back there. Up in the City, they doing one maybe two things. In L.A. they doing another one, two things. But, man, in New York, they doing everything. Person couldn't never get stuck in one groove there. So many things going on, you got to be hip, real hip to keep up. You always growing there. Shit, if you 'live and playing, you can't help but grow. Say, man," he reach and tap German on the shoulder, "let's leave right now."

We all crack up. Then I say, "I sorry but I can't go, got to take care of my baby."

He laugh, "Sugar, you got yo baby right here."

"Well, I must got two babies then."

We pull in front of the partment house then but don't no one move. Finally Time reach over and touch my hair. "You gon be my Black queen?"

I look straight ahead at the night. "Yeah," I say. "Yeah."

We go in and I check first on Larry cause sometimes that girl don't watch him good. When I come in some nights, he be all out the cover and shivering but too sleepy to get back under em. Time come in when I'm pulling the cover up on Orine two kids.

"Which one yours," he ask.

I go over to Larry bed. "This my baby," I tell him.

"What's his name?"

"Larry."

"Oh, I suppose you name him after his daddy?"

I don't like the way he say that, like I was wrong to name him after his daddy. "Who else I gon name him after?" He don't say nothing and I leave him standing there. I mad now and I go in the bedroom and start pulling off my clothes. I think, That nigga can stand up in the living room all night, for all I care; let Orine talk to German and him, too. But Time come in the bedroom and put his arms round me. He touch my hair and my face and my tittie, and it scare me. I try to pull away but he hold me too close. "Martha," he say, "Black Martha." Then he just stand there holding me, not saying nothing, with his hand covering one side on my face. I stand there trembling but he don't notice. I know a woman not supposed to feel the way I feel bout Time, not right away. But I do.

He tell me things nobody ever say to me before. And I want to tell him that I ain't never liked no man much as I like him. But sometime you tell a man that and he go cause he think you liking him a whole lot gon hang him up.

"You and me," he say after we in bed, "we can make it together real good." He laugh. "I used to think all I needed was that music, but it take a woman to make that music sing, I think. So now stead of the music and me, it be the music and me and you."

"You left out Larry," I tell him. I don't think he want to hear that. But Larry my baby.

"How come you couldn't be free," he say real low. Then, "How you going when I go if you got a baby?"

"When you going?"

He turn his back to me. "Oh, I don't know. You know what the song say,

'When a woman take the blues, She tuck her head and cry. But when a man catch the blues, he grab his shoes and slide.' Next time I get the blues," he laugh a little, "next time the man get too much for me, I leave here and go someplace else. He always chasing me. The god damn white man." He turn over and reach for me. "You feel good. He chasing me and I chasing dreams. You think I'm crazy, huh? But I'm not. I just got so many, many things going on inside me I don't know which one to let out first. They all want out so bad. When I play—I got to be better, Martha. You gon help me?"

"Yes, Time, I help you."

"You see," and he reach over and turn on the light and look down at me, "I'm not what I am. I up tight on the inside but I can't get it to show on the outside. I don't know how to make it come out. You ever hear Coltrane[4] blow? That man is together. He showing on the outside what he got on the inside. When I can do that, then I be somewhere. But I can't go by myself. I need a woman. A Black woman. Them other women steal your soul and don't leave nothing. But a Black woman—" He laugh and pull me close. He want me and that all I care bout.

Mamma come over that next morning and come right on in the bedroom, just like she always do. I kind of shamed for her to see me like that, with a man and all, but she don't say nothing cept scuse me, then turn away. "I come to get Larry."

"He in the other bedroom," I say, starting to get up.

"That's okay; I get him." And she go out and close the door.

I start to get out the bed anyway. Time reach for his cigarettes and light one. "Your mamma don't believe in knocking, do she?"

I start to tell him not to talk so loud cause Mamma a hear him, but that might make him mad. "Well, it ain't usually nobody in here with me for her to walk in on." I standing by the bed buttoning my house coat and Time reach out and pull my arm, smiling. "I know you ain't no tramp, Martha. Come on, get back in bed."

I pull my arm way and start out the door. "I got to get Larry's clothes together," I tell him. I do got to get them clothes together cause when Mamma come for Larry like that on Sadday morning, she want to keep him for the rest of the weekend. But—I don't know. It just don't seem right for me to be in the bed with a man and my mamma in the next room.

I think Orine and German still in the other bedroom. But I don't know; Orine don't too much like for her mens to stay all night. She say it make a bad impression on her kids. I glad the door close anyway. If Mamma gon start talking that "why don't you come home" talk the way she usually do, it best for Orine not to hear it.

Orine's two kids still sleep but Mamma got Larry on his bed tickling him and playing with him. He like that. "Boy, you sho happy for it to be so early in the morning," I tell him.

Mamma stop tickling him and he lay there breathing hard for a minute. "Big Mamma," he say laughing and pointing at her. I just laugh at him and go get his clothes.

4. John Coltrane (1926–1967), African American jazz musician.

"You gon marry this one?" Every man I been with since I had Larry, she ask that about.

"You think marrying gon save my soul, Mamma?" I sorry right away cause Mamma don't like me to make fun of God. But I swear I gets tired of all that. What I want to marry for anyway? Get somebody like Daddy always coming and going and every time he go leave a baby behind. Or get a man what stay round and beat me all the time and have my kids thinking they big shit just cause they got a daddy what stay with them, like them saddity kids at school. Shit, married or single they still doing the same thing when they goes to bed.

Mamma don't say nothing else bout it. She ask where he work. I tell her and then take Larry in the bathroom and wash him up.

"The older you get, the more foolish you get, Martha. Them musicians ain't got nothing for a woman. Lots sweet talk and babies, that's all. Welfare don't even want to give you nothing for the one you got now, how you gon—" I sorry but I just stop listening. Mamma run her mouth like a clatterbone on a goose ass sometime. I just go on and give her the baby and get the rest of his things ready.

"So your mamma don't like musicians, huh?" Time say when I get back in the bedroom. "Square-ass people. Everything they don't know about, they hate. Lord deliver me from a square-ass town with square-ass people." He turn over.

"You wasn't calling me square last night."

"I'm not calling you square now, Martha."

I get back in the bed then and he put his arm round me. "But they say what they want to say. Long as they don't mess with me things be okay. But that's impossible. Somebody always got to have their little say about your life. They want to tell you where to go, how to play, what to play, where to play it—shit, even who to fuck and how to fuck em. But when I get to New York—"

"Time, let's don't talk now."

He laugh then. "Martha, you so Black." I don't know what I should say so I don't say nothing, just get closer and we don't talk.

That how it is lots a time with me and him. It seem like all I got is lots little pitchers in my mind and can't tell nobody what they look like. Once I try to tell him bout that, bout the pitchers, and he just laugh. "Least your head ain't empty. Maybe now you got some pictures, you get some thoughts." That make me mad and I start cussing, but he laugh and kiss me and hold me. And that time, when we doing it, it all—all angry and like he want to hurt me. And I think bout that song he sing that first night bout having the blues. But that the only time he mean like that.

Time and German brung the piano a couple days after that. The piano small and all shiny black wood. Time cussed German when German knocked it against the front door getting it in the house. Time went to put it in the bedroom but I want him to be thinking bout me, not some damn piano when he in there. I tell him he put it in the living room or it don't come in the house. Orine don't want it in the house period, say it too damn noisy—that's what she tell me. She don't say nothing to Time. I think she halfway scared of him. He pretty good bout playing it though. He don't never play it when the babies is sleep or at least he don't play loud as he can. But all he thinking bout when he playing is that piano. You talk to him, he don't answer; you touch him, he don't look up. One time I say to him, "Pay me some tention," but he don't even hear. I hit his hand, not hard, just playing. He look at me but he don't stop playing. "Get out of here, Martha." First I start to tell him he can't tell me what to do in my own self's house, but he just looking at me. Looking at me and playing and not saying nothing. I leave.

His friends come over most evenings when he home, not playing. It like Time is the leader. Whatever he say go. They always telling him how good he is. "Out of sight, man, the way you play." "You ought to get out of this little town so somebody can hear you play." Most times, he just smile and don't say nothing, or he just say thanks. But I wonder if he really believe em. I tell him, sometime, that he sound better than lots a them men on records. He give me his little cool smile. But I feel he glad I tell him that.

When his friends come over, we sit round laughing and talking and drinking. Orine like that cause she be playing up to em all and they be telling her what a fine ass she got. They don't tell me nothing like that cause Time be sitting right there, but long as Time telling me, I don't care. It like when we go to the Legion, after Time and German started being with us. We all the time get in free and then get to sit at one a the big front tables. And Orine like that cause it make her think she big-time. But she still her same old picky self; all the time telling me to "sit cool, Martha," and "be cool, girl." Acting like cool the most important thing in the world. I finally just tell her, "Time like me just the way I am, cool or not." And it true; Time always saying that I be myself and I be fine.

Time and his friends, they talk mostly bout music, music and New York City and white people. Sometime I get so sick a listening to em. Always talking bout how they gon put something over on the white man, gon take something way from him, gon do this, gon do that. Ah shit! I tell em. But they don't pay me no mind.

German say, one night, "Man, this white man come asking if I want to play at his house for—"

"What you tell him, man, 'Put money in my purse'?" Time ask. They all crack up. Me and Orine sit there quiet. Orine all swole up cause Time and them running some kind of game and she don't know what going down.

"Hey, man, yo all member that time up in Frisco when we got fired from that gig and wan't none of our old ladies working?" That Brown, he play bass with em.

"Man," Time say, "all I remember is that I stayed high most of the time. But how'd I stay high if ain't nobody had no bread? Somebody was putting something in somebody's purse." He lean back laughing a little. "Verna's mamma must have been sending her some money till she got a job. Yeah, yeah man, that was it. You remember the first time her mamma sent that money and she gave it all to me to hold?"

"And what she wanna do that for? You went out and gambled half a it away and bought pot with most of the rest." German not laughing much as Time and Brown.

"Man, I was scared to tell her, cause you remember how easy it was for her to get her jaws tight. But she was cool, didn't say nothing. I told her I was going to get food with the rest of the money and asked her what she wanted, and—"

"And she say cigarettes," Brown break in laughing, "and this cat, man, this cat tell her, 'Woman, we ain't wasting this bread on no nonessentials!' " He doubled over laughing. They all laughing. But I don't think it that funny. Any woman can give a man money.

"I thought the babe was gon kill me, her jaws was so tight. But even with her jaws tight, Verna was still cool. She just say, 'Baby, you done fucked up fifty dollars on nonessentials; let me try thirty cents.' "

That really funny to em. They all cracking up but me. Time sit there smiling just a little and shaking his head. Then, he reach out and squeeze my knee and smile at me. And I know it like I say; any woman can give a man money.

German been twitching round in his chair and finally he say, "Yeah, man, this fay dude want me to play at his house for fifty cent." That German always got to hear hisself talk. "I tell him take his fifty cent and shove it up his ass—oh scuse me. I forgot that baby was here—but I told him what to do with it. When I play for honkies, I tell him, I don't play for less than two hundred dollars and he so foolish he gon pay it." They all laugh, but I know German lying. Anybody offer him ten cent let lone fifty, he gon play.

"It ain't the money, man," Time say. "They just don't know what the fuck going on." I tell him Larry sitting right there. I know he ain't gon pay me no mind, but I feel if German can respect my baby, Time can too. "Man they go out to some little school, learn a few chords, and they think they know it all. Then, if you working for a white man, he fire you and hire him. No, man, I can't tie shit from no white man."

"That where you wrong," I tell him. "Somebody you don't like, you supposed to take em for everything they got. Take em and tell em to kiss yo butt."

"That another one of your pictures, I guess," Time say. And they all laugh cause he told em bout that, too, one time when he was mad with me.

"No, no," I say. "Listen, one day I walking downtown and this white man offer me a ride. I say okay and get in the car. He start talking and hinting round and finally he come on out and say it. I give you twenty dollars, he say. I say okay. We in Chinatown by then and at the next stop light he get out his wallet and give me a twenty-dollar bill. 'That what I like bout you colored women,' he say easing all back in his seat just like he already done got some and waiting to get some more. 'Yeah,' he say, 'you all so easy to get.' I put that money in my purse, open the door and tell him, 'Motherfucker, you ain't got shit here,' and slam the door."

"Watch your mouth," Time say, "Larry sitting here." We all crack up.

"What he do then?" Orine ask.

"What could he do? We in Chinatown and all them colored folks walking round. You know they ain't gon let no white man do nothing to me."

Time tell me after we go to bed that night that he kill me if he ever see me with a white man.

I laugh and kiss him. "What I want with a white man when I got you?" We both laugh and get in the bed. I lay stretched out waiting for him to reach for me. It funny, I think, how colored men don't never want no colored women messing with no white mens but the first chance he get, that colored man gon be right there in that white woman's bed. Yeah, colored men sho give colored womens a hard way to go. But I know if Time got to give a hard way to go, it ain't gon be for scaggy fay babe, and I kinda smile to myself.

"Martha—"

"Yeah, Time," I say turning to him.

"How old you—eighteen? What you want to do in life? What you want to be?"

What he mean? "I want to be with you," I tell him.

"No, I mean really. What you want?" Why he want to know, I wonder. Everytime he start talking serious-like, I think he must be hearing his sliding song.

"I don't want to have to ask nobody for nothing. I want to be able to take care of my own self." I won't be no weight on you, Time, I want to tell him. I won't be no trouble to you.

"Then what are you doing on the Welfare?"

"What else I gon do? Go out and scrub somebody else's toilets like my mamma did so Larry can run wild like I did? No. I stay on Welfare awhile, thank you."

"You see what the white man have done to us, is doing to us?"

"White man my ass," I tell him. "That was my no good daddy. If he'd gone out and worked, we woulda been better off."

"How he gon work if the man won't let him?"

"You just let the man turn you out. Yeah, that man got yo mind."

"What you mean?" he ask real quiet. But I don't pay no tention to him. "You always talking bout music and New York City, New York City and the white man. Why don't you forget all that shit and get a job like other men? I hate that damn piano."

He grab my shoulder real tight. "What you mean, 'got my mind?' What you mean?" And he start shaking me. But I crying and thinking bout he gon leave.

"You laugh cause I say all I got in my mind is pitchers but least they better some old music. That all you ever think about, Time."

"What you mean? What you mean?"

Finally I scream. "You ain't gon no damn New York City and it ain't the white man what gon keep you. You just using him for a scuse cause you scared. Maybe you can't play." That the only time he ever hit me. And I cry cause I know he gon leave for sho. He hold me and say don't cry, say he sorry, but I can't stop. Orine bamming on the door and Time yelling at her to leave us lone and the babies crying and finally he start to pull away. I say, "Time . . ." He still for a long time, then he say, "Okay, Okay, Martha."

No, it not like he don't want me no more, he—

"Martha. Martha. You ain't been listening to a word I say."

"Mamma." I say it soft cause I don't want to hurt her. "Please leave me lone. You and Orine—and Time too, sometime—yo all treat me like I don't know nothing. But just cause it don't seem like to you that I know what I'm doing, that don't mean nothing. You can't see into my life."

"I see enough to know you just get into one mess after another." She shake her head and her voice come kinda slow. "Martha, I named you after that woman in the Bible cause I want you to be like her. Be good in the same way she is. Martha, that woman ain't never stopped believing. She humble and patient and the Lord make a place for her." She lean her hands on the table. Been in them dishes again, hands all wrinkled and shiny wet. "But that was the Bible. You ain't got the time to be patient, to be waiting for Time or no one else to make no place for you. That man ain't no good. I told you—"

Words coming faster and faster. She got the cow by the tail and gon on down shit creek. It don't matter though. She talk and I sit here thinking bout Time. "You feel good . . . You gon be my Black queen? . . . We can make it together . . . You feel good . . ." He be back.

1967

ALICE WALKER
b. 1944

Alice Walker is the best known southern African American writer of the second half of this century, perhaps because of the controversy generated by her Pulitzer Prize–winning *The Color Purple* (1982), the first novel by an African American woman to win this award. She has, however, published many other works—to date, four other novels, five volumes of poetry, three essay collections, two children's books, and two short story collections. But *The Color Purple* is a point of demarcation in Walker's oeuvre in that it is both the completion of the cycle of novels she announced in the early 1970s and the beginning of new emphases for her as a writer.

Fourteen years before *The Color Purple*, with the publication of *Once: Poems* (1968), written when she was barely twenty-three, Walker declared herself an African American woman writer committed to exploring the lives of black women. In a 1973 interview with critic Mary Helen Washington, Walker described the three types of black women characters she felt were missing from much of the literature of the United States. The first were those who were exploited both physically and emotionally, whose lives were narrow and confining, and who were driven sometimes to madness, such as Margaret and Mem Copeland in Walker's first novel, *The Third Life of Grange Copeland* (1970). The second were those who were victims not so much of physical violence as of psychic violence, women who are alienated from their own culture. The third type of black woman character, represented most effectively by Celie and Shug in *The Color Purple*, are those African American women who, despite the oppressions they suffer, achieve some wholeness and create spaces for other oppressed communities.

Walker was certainly aware of the ways in which southern black women had always been artists, even when that word was not applied to them. Born in 1944 to sharecroppers Minnie Lou Grant and Willie Lee Walker, she grew up in the small town of Eatonville, Georgia. Her mother, who worked as a domestic and made everything Alice and her seven siblings used, was known for the incredible gardens she grew, gardens her literary daughter commemorated in the classic essay *In Search of Our Mothers' Gardens: The Legacy of Southern Black Women* (1974). From her mother's artistry, Walker learned that African American women's experience and art are based on spirituality, especially as it relates to nature. Though not admitted to libraries or schools, and definitely lacking any rooms of their own, they expressed themselves in the media allowed to them: cooking, gardening, storytelling, quilting.

When Walker was eight, one of her brothers "accidentally" shot her with a gun he'd received for Christmas, resulting in the loss of one eye. Not only did this experience make Walker feel like an outcast, but also it caused her to begin to notice relationships and to start recording her observations and feelings in a notebook. Her early experience of being different may be in some sense responsible for her tendency to pursue "forbidden" subjects in her writing, the most recent example being her protest of female genital circumcision, which she redefines as mutilation, in her fifth novel, *Possessing the Secret of Joy* (1992).

Walker left Eatonville in 1961 to go to college, first at Spelman, a black women's college in Atlanta, then two years later at Sarah Lawrence, in the suburbs of New York City. Both educational experiences had a lasting effect on her writing. Her years at Spelman coincided with the rise of the civil rights movement, the subject of many of her short stories, essays, and her second novel *Meridian* (1976). While at Sarah Lawrence, she became pregnant, at a time when abortion was illegal. Deciding to commit suicide because of the shame her family would feel and because of the powerlessness she felt, especially in relation to her own body, Walker instead began writing, and soon published her first book, *Once*.

The works Walker published during the 1970s had a decisive effect on the literary world. Her focus on southern African American women's voices helped to galvanize an explosion of African American women's creative and critical expressions. In *The Third Life of Grange Copeland*, she explored familial cruelty, especially as it is triggered by societal forces such as racism, unemployment, sexism, and the like. She challenged the 1960s African American cultural nationalist position, which idealized "black manhood" and seldom acknowledged the oppression of women. In her second poetry collection, *Revolutionary Petunias* (1972) and in *In Love & Trouble: Stories of Black Women* (1973), Walker continued to articulate African American women's resistance against injustice. She traced the radical actions of southern black peasant women, such as the supposedly backward Sammy Lou, of the poem *Revolutionary Petunias*, and Mrs. Johnson, the guardian of southern black culture in the story *Everyday Use*.

From 1965 to 1968 Walker was actively involved in the civil rights movement, including voter registration drives in Georgia and campaigns for welfare rights and children's programs in Mississippi. She also lived for a time on the Lower East Side of New York City, where she worked for the welfare department, an experience that inspired her story *Advancing Luna*. In 1967 she married Melvyn Leventhal, a white civil rights lawyer. At a time when interracial marriage was illegal in Mississippi, Walker and Leventhal lived in that state and there had a daughter, Rebecca. Together they worked to desegregate the Mississippi schools. They divorced in 1977, at which time Walker moved first to New York City and then to northern California, where she still lives.

During the 1970s Walker published several important essays, among them *Saving the Life That Is Your Own: The Importance of Models in the Artist's Life* (1976) and *One Child of One's Own* (1979). Her most important contribution to literary history may well be her rescue of the classic works of her southern maternal ancestor Zora Neale Hurston, especially the novel *Their Eyes Were Watching God* (1937). In the essay *Looking for Zora* (1975), contained in her edition of Hurston's then forgotten works, *I Love Myself When I Am Laughing* . . . (1979), and in poems in *Good Night Willie Lee* (1979), Walker described her search for Hurston, which included the placing of a headstone on Hurston's unmarked grave, without doubt an important symbolic moment in the reconstruction of a black female literary tradition.

Walker's works of the 1980s and 1990s continue her emphatic exploration of the lives of black women. She began her first published collection of essays, *In Search of Our Mothers' Gardens: Womanist Prose* (1983), by coining a new word, *womanism*. In so doing, Walker replaced the European-sounding *feminist* with a word derived from a black folk expression ("womanish") and thereby refuted any narrow definition of *feminist*. The title of her second collection of stories, *You Can't Keep a Good Woman Down* (1981), demonstrates Walker's belief in the remarkableness of African American women, despite the twin afflictions of sexism and racism. Blatantly topical, the stories in this collection, such as *The Abortion* and *Advancing Luna*, are a bridge between her novels of the 1970s and *The Color Purple*.

Since the publication of Richard Wright's *Native Son* in 1941, few works written by an African American have generated as much controversy as *The Color Purple*, which won not only the Pulitzer Prize but also the National Book Award and American Book Award. Some critics saw Walker's exposé of incest and wife beating as well as her articulation of lesbianism as evidence of her having sold out to white feminists, while others praised the novel for its originality and courage and for its clear-sighted analysis of the sexual politics of black life. Still others took issue with the African section, calling it too monolithic, a comment made also about her most recent novel, *Possessing the Secret of Joy*. Contributing further to the controversy was Steven Spielberg's film adaptation of the novel, which was released in 1985. Not only did many feel the film prettified the difficult issues of Walker's narrative, but some criticized its supposedly negative portrayal of black men, even more loudly than they had the novel's depiction of these characters. Walker chronicled the personal difficulties and joys she experienced as a result of the book and film in her most recent book, *The Same River Twice* (1996).

Walker's recent works have continued the global direction first taken by *The Color Purple*. *The Temple of My Familiar* (1989) is set in Central America, Europe, and Africa as well as in the United States, and *Possessing the Secret of Joy* (1992) in the United States, Europe, and Africa. Walker too has demonstrated increasing concern with the relationship between human beings and nature. In *Horses Make the Landscape Look More Beautiful* (1984) and *Living by the Word* (1988), she illuminates the connections between the social violations of sexism and racism and violations against nature. Also in the 1980s Walker founded Wild Trees Press, which has published many books, including the first short story collection of California Cooper, another contemporary African American woman writer. A further confirmation of her stature with her public and with her publishers is the issuing in 1991 of Walker's collected poems, one of the few such volumes by an African American woman: *Her Blue Body Everything We Know: Earthling Poems: 1965–1990* (1991). A prolific writer and a courageous thinker, Walker is without question one of the major African American feminist/womanist writers of this century.

Women

They were women then
My mama's generation
Husky of voice—Stout of
Step
With fists as well as   5
Hands
How they battered down
Doors
And ironed

Starched white   10
Shirts
How they led
Armies
Headragged Generals
Across mined   15
Fields
Booby-trapped
Ditches
To discover books
Desks   20
A place for us
How they knew what we
Must know
Without knowing a page
Of it   25
Themselves.

                              1970

Outcast

for Julius Lester

Be nobody's darling;
Be an outcast.
Take the contradictions
Of your life
And wrap around   5
You like a shawl,
To parry stones
To keep you warm.

Watch the people succumb
To madness   10
With ample cheer;
Let them look askance at you
And you askance reply.

Be an outcast;
Be pleased to walk alone   15
(Uncool)
Or line the crowded
River beds
With other impetuous
Fools.   20

Make a merry gathering
On the bank
Where thousands perished
For brave hurt words
They said.   25

Be nobody's darling;
Be an outcast.
Qualified to live
Among your dead.

1973

On Stripping Bark from Myself

(for Jane, who said trees die from it)

because women are expected to keep silent about
their close escapes I will not keep silent
and if I am destroyed (naked tree!) someone will please
mark the spot
where I fall and know I could not live   5
silent in my own lies
hearing their "how *nice* she is!"
whose adoration of the retouched image
I so despise.

No. I am finished with living   10
for what my mother believes
for what my brother and father defend
for what my lover elevates
for what my sister, blushing, denies or rushes
to embrace.   15

I find my own
small person
a standing self
against the world
an equality of wills   20
I finally understand.

Besides:

My struggle was always against
an inner darkness: I carry within myself
the only known keys   25
to my death—to unlock life, or close it shut
forever. A woman who loves wood grains, the color yellow
and the sun, I am happy to fight
all outside murderers
as I see I must.   30

1979

"Good Night, Willie Lee, I'll See You in the Morning"

Looking down into my father's
dead face
for the last time
my mother said without
tears, without smiles   5
without regrets
but with *civility*
"Good night, Willie Lee, I'll see you
in the morning."
And it was then I knew that the healing   10
of all our wounds
is forgiveness
that permits a promise
of our return
at the end.   15

1979

In Search of Our Mothers' Gardens

> I described her own nature and temperament. Told how they needed a
> larger life for their expression. . . . I pointed out that in lieu of proper
> channels, her emotions had overflowed into paths that dissipated them.
> I talked, beautifully I thought, about an art that would be born, an art
> that would open the way for women the likes of her. I asked her to
> hope, and build up an inner life against the coming of that day. . . . I
> sang, with a strange quiver in my voice, a promise song.
> —JEAN TOOMER,[1] "AVEY," CANE
>
> The poet speaking to a prostitute who falls asleep while he's talking—

When the poet Jean Toomer walked through the South in the early
twenties, he discovered a curious thing: black women whose spirituality
was so intense, so deep, so *unconscious*, that they were themselves unaware
of the richness they held. They stumbled blindly through their lives: creatures so abused and mutilated in body, so dimmed and confused by pain,
that they considered themselves unworthy even of hope. In the selfless abstractions their bodies became to the men who used them, they became
more than "sexual objects," more even than mere women: they became
"Saints." Instead of being perceived as whole persons, their bodies became
shrines: what was thought to be their minds became temples suitable for
worship. These crazy Saints stared out at the world, wildly, like lunatics—or
quietly, like suicides; and the "God" that was in their gaze was as mute as a
great stone.

Who were these Saints? These crazy, loony, pitiful women?

Some of them, without a doubt, were our mothers and grandmothers.

In the still heat of the post-Reconstruction South,[2] this is how they

---

1. A writer of the Harlem Renaissance (1894–
1967). *Cane* is a mixture of narrative prose and
lyric poetry.
2. I.e., the South after home rule (and thus white

supremacy) was restored following the Confederacy's social and political "reconstruction" (1865–
77).

seemed to Jean Toomer: exquisite butterflies trapped in an evil honey, toiling away their lives in an era, a century, that did not acknowledge them, except as "the *mule* of the world."[3] They dreamed dreams that no one knew—not even themselves, in any coherent fashion—and saw visions no one could understand. They wandered or sat about the countryside crooning lullabies to ghosts, and drawing the mother of Christ in charcoal on courthouse walls.

They forced their minds to desert their bodies and their striving spirits sought to rise, like frail whirlwinds from the hard red clay. And when those frail whirlwinds fell, in scattered particles, upon the ground, no one mourned. Instead, men lit candles to celebrate the emptiness that remained, as people do who enter a beautiful but vacant space to resurrect a God.

Our mothers and grandmothers, some of them: moving to music not yet written. And they waited.

They waited for a day when the unknown thing that was in them would be made known; but guessed, somehow in their darkness, that on the day of their revelation they would be long dead. Therefore to Toomer they walked, and even ran, in slow motion. For they were going nowhere immediate, and the future was not yet within their grasp. And men took our mothers and grandmothers, "but got no pleasure from it." So complex was their passion and their calm.

To Toomer, they lay vacant and fallow as autumn fields, with harvest time never in sight: and he saw them enter loveless marriages, without joy; and become prostitutes, without resistance; and become mothers of children, without fulfillment.

For these grandmothers and mothers of ours were not Saints, but Artists; driven to a numb and bleeding madness by the springs of creativity in them for which there was no release. They were Creators, who lived lives of spiritual waste, because they were so rich in spirituality—which is the basis of Art—that the strain of enduring their unused and unwanted talent drove them insane. Throwing away this spirituality was their pathetic attempt to lighten the soul to a weight their work-worn, sexually abused bodies could bear.

What did it mean for a black woman to be an artist in our grandmothers' time? In our great-grandmothers' day? It is a question with an answer cruel enough to stop the blood.

Did you have a genius of a great-great-grandmother who died under some ignorant and depraved white overseer's lash? Or was she required to bake biscuits for a lazy backwater tramp, when she cried out in her soul to paint watercolors of sunsets, or the rain falling on the green and peaceful pasturelands? Or was her body broken and forced to bear children (who were more often than not sold away from her)—eight, ten, fifteen, twenty children—when her one joy was the thought of modeling heroic figures of rebellion, in stone or clay?

How was the creativity of the black woman kept alive, year after year and century after century, when for most of the years black people have been in

---

3. Allusion to a statement in Zora Neale Hurston's (1891–1960) *Their Eyes Were Watching God* (1937): "De nigger woman is de mule uh de world."

America, it was a punishable crime for a black person to read or write? And
the freedom to paint, to sculpt, to expand the mind with action did not
exist. Consider, if you can bear to imagine it, what might have been the
result if singing, too, had been forbidden by law. Listen to the voices of
Bessie Smith, Billie Holiday, Nina Simone, Roberta Flack, and Aretha
Franklin,[4] among others, and imagine those voices muzzled for life. Then
you may begin to comprehend the lives of our "crazy," "Sainted" mothers
and grandmothers. The agony of the lives of women who might have been
Poets, Novelists, Essayists, and Short-Story Writers (over a period of centuries), who died with their real gifts stifled within them.

And, if this were the end of the story, we would have cause to cry out in
my paraphrase of Okot p'Bitek's[5] great poem:

> O, my clanswomen
> Let us all cry together!
> Come,
> Let us mourn the death of our mother,
> The death of a Queen
> The ash that was produced
> By a great fire!
> O, this homestead is utterly dead
> Close the gates
> With *lacari* thorns,
> For our mother
> The creator of the Stool is lost!
> And all the young women
> Have perished in the wilderness!

But this is not the end of the story, for all the young women—our mothers and grandmothers, *ourselves*—have not perished in the wilderness. And
if we ask ourselves why, and search for and find the answer, we will know
beyond all efforts to erase it from our minds, just exactly who, and of what,
we black American women are.

One example, perhaps the most pathetic, most misunderstood one, can
provide a backdrop for our mothers' work: Phillis Wheatley,[6] a slave in the
1700s.

Virginia Woolf,[7] in her book *A Room of One's Own,* wrote that in order
for a woman to write fiction she must have two things, certainly: a room of
her own (with key and lock) and enough money to support herself.

What then are we to make of Phillis Wheatley, a slave, who owned not
even herself? This sickly, frail black girl who required a servant of her own
at times—her health was so precarious—and who, had she been white,
would have been easily considered the intellectual superior of all the
women and most of the men in the society of her day.

Virginia Woolf wrote further, speaking of course not of our Phillis, that
"any woman born with a great gift in the sixteenth century [insert "eigh-

---

4. Black American female singers from the 1920s
to the present.
5. African poet (b. 1931). Walker has changed the
original masculine nouns in *Song of Lawino* (1966)
to feminine equivalents.

6. Highly educated black slave (1753–1784) who
wrote formal, neoclassical poems.
7. British novelist and essayist (1882–1941). *A
Room of One's Own* was published in 1929.

teenth century," insert "black woman," insert "born or made a slave"]
would certainly have gone crazed, shot herself, or ended her days in some
lonely cottage outside the village, half witch, half wizard [insert "Saint"],
feared and mocked at. For it needs little skill and psychology to be sure that
a highly gifted girl who had tried to use her gift for poetry would have been
so thwarted and hindered by contrary instincts [add "chains, guns, the lash,
the ownership of one's body by someone else, submission to an alien religion"], that she must have lost her health and sanity to a certainty."

The key words, as they relate to Phillis, are "contrary instincts." For
when we read the poetry of Phillis Wheatley—as when we read the novels
of Nella Larsen[8] or the oddly false-sounding autobiography of that freest of
all black women writers, Zora Hurston—evidence of "contrary instincts" is
everywhere. Her loyalties were completely divided, as was, without question, her mind.

But how could this be otherwise? Captured at seven, a slave of wealthy,
doting whites who instilled in her the "savagery" of the Africa they "rescued" her from . . . one wonders if she was even able to remember her
homeland as she had known it, or as it really was.

Yet, because she did try to use her gift for poetry in a world that made
her a slave, she was "so thwarted and hindered by . . . contrary instincts,
that she . . . lost her health. . . ." In the last years of her brief life, burdened not only with the need to express her gift but also with a penniless, friendless "freedom" and several small children for whom she was
forced to do strenuous work to feed, she lost her health, certainly. Suffering from malnutrition and neglect and who knows what mental agonies,
Phillis Wheatley died.

So torn by "contrary instincts" was black, kidnapped, enslaved Phillis
that her description of "the Goddess"—as she poetically called the Liberty
she did not have—is ironically, cruelly humorous. And, in fact, has held
Phillis up to ridicule for more than a century. It is usually read prior to
hanging Phillis's memory as that of a fool. She wrote:

> The Goddess comes, she moves divinely fair,
> Olive and laurel binds her *golden* hair.
> Wherever shines this native of the skies,
> Unnumber'd charms and recent graces rise. [My italics][9]

It is obvious that Phillis, the slave, combed the "Goddess's" hair every
morning; prior, perhaps, to bringing in the milk, or fixing her mistress's
lunch. She took her imagery from the one thing she saw elevated above all
others.

With the benefit of hindsight we ask, "How could she?"

But at last, Phillis, we understand. No more snickering when your stiff,
struggling, ambivalent lines are forced on us. We know now that you were
not an idiot or a traitor; only a sickly little black girl, snatched from your
home and country and made a slave; a woman who still struggled to sing
the song that was your gift, although in a land of barbarians who praised

---

8. Black woman novelist (1893–1964) of the Har-   9. From Wheatley's *To His Excellency, General*
lem Renaissance.   *Washington* (1775).

you for your bewildered tongue. It is not so much what you sang, as that you kept alive, in so many of our ancestors, *the notion of song.*

Black women are called, in the folklore that so aptly identifies one's status in society, "the *mule* of the world," because we have been handed the burdens that everyone else—*everyone* else—refused to carry. We have also been called "Matriarchs," "Superwomen," and "Mean and Evil Bitches." Not to mention "Castraters" and "Sapphire's[1] Mama." When we have pleaded for understanding, our character has been distorted; when we have asked for simple caring, we have been handed empty inspirational appellations, then stuck in the farthest corner. When we have asked for love, we have been given children. In short, even our plainer gifts, our labors of fidelity and love, have been knocked down our throats. To be an artist and a black woman, even today, lowers our status in many respects, rather than raises it: and yet, artists we will be.

Therefore we must fearlessly pull out of ourselves and look at and identify with our lives the living creativity some of our great-grandmothers were not allowed to know. I stress *some* of them because it is well known that the majority of our great-grandmothers knew, even without "knowing" it, the reality of their spirituality, even if they didn't recognize it beyond what happened in the singing at church—and they never had any intention of giving it up.

How they did it—those millions of black women who were not Phillis Wheatley, or Lucy Terry or Frances Harper or Zora Hurston or Nella Larsen or Bessie Smith; or Elizabeth Catlett, or Katherine Dunham,[2] either—brings me to the title of this essay, "In Search of Our Mothers' Gardens," which is a personal account that is yet shared, in its theme and its meaning, by all of us. I found, while thinking about the far-reaching world of the creative black woman, that often the truest answer to a question that really matters can be found very close.

In the late 1920s my mother ran away from home to marry my father. Marriage, if not running away, was expected of seventeen-year-old girls. By the time she was twenty, she had two children and was pregnant with a third. Five children later, I was born. And this is how I came to know my mother: she seemed a large, soft, loving-eyed woman who was rarely impatient in our home. Her quick, violent temper was on view only a few times a year, when she battled with the white landlord who had the misfortune to suggest to her that her children did not need to go to school.

She made all the clothes we wore, even my brothers' overalls. She made all the towels and sheets we used. She spent the summers canning vegetables and fruits. She spent the winter evenings making quilts enough to cover all our beds.

During the "working" day, she labored beside—not behind—my father in the fields. Her day began before sunup, and did not end until late at

1. Wife of "the Kingfish" in *Amos and Andy*, a popular early radio and television show.
2. Black American dancer and choreographer (b. 1910). Terry (1730–1821), black poet. Harper (1825–1911), black poet and activist. Catlett (b. 1915?), black educator and sculptor.

night. There was never a moment for her to sit down, undisturbed, to unravel her own private thoughts; never a time free from interruption—by
work or the noisy inquiries of her many children. And yet, it is to my
mother—and all our mothers who were not famous—that I went in search
of the secret of what has fed that muzzled and often mutilated, but vibrant,
creative spirit that the black woman has inherited, and that pops out in wild
and unlikely places to this day.

But when, you will ask, did my overworked mother have time to know or
care about feeding the creative spirit?

The answer is so simple that many of us have spent years discovering it.
We have constantly looked high, when we should have looked high—and
low.

For example: in the Smithsonian Institution in Washington, D.C., there
hangs a quilt unlike any other in the world. In fanciful, inspired, and yet
simple and identifiable figures, it portrays the story of the Crucifixion. It is
considered rare, beyond price. Though it follows no known pattern of
quilt-making, and though it is made of bits and pieces of worthless rags, it is
obviously the work of a person of powerful imagination and deep spiritual
feeling. Below this quilt I saw a note that says it was made by "an anonymous Black woman in Alabama, a hundred years ago."

If we could locate this "anonymous" black woman from Alabama, she
would turn out to be one of our grandmothers—an artist who left her mark
in the only materials she could afford, and in the only medium her position
in society allowed her to use.

As Virginia Woolf wrote further, in A Room of One's Own:

> Yet genius of a sort must have existed among women as it must have
> existed among the working class. [Change this to "slaves" and "the
> wives and daughters of sharecroppers."] Now and again an Emily
> Brontë or a Robert Burns [change this to "a Zora Hurston or a Richard
> Wright"[3]] blazes out and proves its presence. But certainly it never got
> itself on to paper. When, however, one reads of a witch being ducked,
> of a woman possessed by devils [or "Sainthood"], of a wise woman sell-
> ing herbs [our root workers], or even a very remarkable man who had a
> mother, then I think we are on the track of a lost novelist, a suppressed
> poet, of some mute and inglorious Jane Austen. . . . Indeed, I would
> venture to guess that Anon, who wrote so many poems without signing
> them, was often a woman. . . .

And so our mothers and grandmothers have, more often than not anonymously, handed on the creative spark, the seed of the flower they themselves never hoped to see: or like a sealed letter they could not plainly
read.

And so it is, certainly, with my own mother. Unlike "Ma" Rainey's[4]
songs, which retained their creator's name even while blasting forth from
Bessie Smith's mouth, no song or poem will bear my mother's name. Yet so

---

3. Black American novelist (1908–1960). Brontë   4. Gertrude Pridgett Rainey (1886–1939), black
(1819–1848), English novelist and poet. Burns   blues singer and songwriter.
(1759–1796), Scottish poet.

many of the stories that I write, that we all write, are my mother's stories. Only recently did I fully realize this: that through years of listening to my mother's stories of her life, I have absorbed not only the stories themselves, but something of the manner in which she spoke, something of the urgency that involves the knowledge that her stories—like her life—must be recorded. It is probably for this reason that so much of what I have written is about characters whose counterparts in real life are so much older than I am.

But the telling of these stories, which came from my mother's lips as naturally as breathing, was not the only way my mother showed herself as an artist. For stories, too, were subject to being distracted, to dying without conclusion. Dinners must be started, and cotton must be gathered before the big rains. The artist that was and is my mother showed itself to me only after many years. This is what I finally noticed:

Like Mem, a character in *The Third Life of Grange Copeland*,[5] my mother adorned with flowers whatever shabby house we were forced to live in. And not just your typical straggly country stand of zinnias, either. She planted ambitious gardens—and still does—with over fifty different varieties of plants that bloom profusely from early March until late November. Before she left home for the fields, she watered her flowers, chopped up the grass, and laid out new beds. When she returned from the fields she might divide clumps of bulbs, dig a cold pit, uproot and replant roses, or prune branches from her taller bushes or trees—until night came and it was too dark to see.

Whatever she planted grew as if by magic, and her fame as a grower of flowers spread over three counties. Because of her creativity with her flowers, even my memories of poverty are seen through a screen of blooms—sunflowers, petunias, roses, dahlias, forsythia, spirea, delphiniums, verbena . . . and on and on.

And I remember people coming to my mother's yard to be given cuttings from her flowers; I hear again the praise showered on her because whatever rocky soil she landed on, she turned into a garden. A garden so brilliant with colors, so original in its design, so magnificent with life and creativity, that to this day people drive by our house in Georgia—perfect strangers and imperfect strangers—and ask to stand or walk among my mother's art.

I notice that it is only when my mother is working in her flowers that she is radiant, almost to the point of being invisible—except as Creator: hand and eye. She is involved in work her soul must have. Ordering the universe in the image of her personal conception of Beauty.

Her face, as she prepares the Art that is her gift, is a legacy of respect she leaves to me, for all that illuminates and cherishes life. She has handed down respect for the possibilities—and the will to grasp them.

For her, so hindered and intruded upon in so many ways, being an artist has still been a daily part of her life. This ability to hold on, even in very simple ways, is work black women have done for a very long time.

This poem is not enough, but it is something, for the woman who literally covered the holes in our walls with sunflowers:

---

5. Walker's first novel.

They were women then
My mama's generation
Husky of voice—Stout of
Step
With fists as well as
Hands
How they battered down
Doors
And ironed
Starched white
Shirts
How they led
Armies
Headragged Generals
Across mined
Fields
Booby-trapped
Kitchens
To discover books
Desks
A place for us
How they knew what we
Must know
Without knowing a page
Of it
Themselves.

Guided by my heritage of a love of beauty and a respect for strength—in search of my mother's garden, I found my own.

And perhaps in Africa over two hundred years ago, there was just such a mother; perhaps she painted vivid and daring decorations in oranges and yellows and greens on the walls of her hut; perhaps she sang—in a voice like Roberta Flack's—*sweetly* over the compounds of her village; perhaps she wove the most stunning mats or told the most ingenious stories of all the village storytellers. Perhaps she was herself a poet—though only her daughter's name is signed to the poems that we know.

Perhaps Phillis Wheatley's mother was also an artist.

Perhaps in more than Phillis Wheatley's biological life is her mother's signature made clear.

1974

Everyday Use

for your grandmama

I will wait for her in the yard that Maggie and I made so clean and wavy yesterday afternoon. A yard like this is more comfortable than most people know. It is not just a yard. It is like an extended living room. When the hard clay is swept clean as a floor and the fine sand around the edges lined with tiny, irregular grooves, anyone can come and sit and look up into the elm tree and wait for the breezes that never come inside the house.

Maggie will be nervous until after her sister goes: she will stand hopelessly in corners, homely and ashamed of the burn scars down her arms and legs, eying her sister with a mixture of envy and awe. She thinks her sister has held life always in the palm of one hand, that "no" is a word the world never learned to say to her.

You've no doubt seen those TV shows where the child who has "made it" is confronted, as a surprise, by her own mother and father, tottering in weakly from backstage. (A pleasant surprise, of course: What would they do if parent and child came on the show only to curse out and insult each other?) On TV mother and child embrace and smile into each other's faces. Sometimes the mother and father weep, the child wraps them in her arms and leans across the table to tell how she would not have made it without their help. I have seen these programs.

Sometimes I dream a dream in which Dee and I are suddenly brought together on a TV program of this sort. Out of a dark and soft-seated limousine I am ushered into a bright room filled with many people. There I meet a smiling, gray, sporty man like Johnny Carson who shakes my hand and tells me what a fine girl I have. Then we are on the stage and Dee is embracing me with tears in her eyes. She pins on my dress a large orchid, even though she has told me once that she thinks orchids are tacky flowers.

In real life I am a large, big-boned woman with rough, man-working hands. In the winter I wear flannel nightgowns to bed and overalls during the day. I can kill and clean a hog as mercilessly as a man. My fat keeps me hot in zero weather. I can work outside all day, breaking ice to get water for washing; I can eat pork liver cooked over the open fire minutes after it comes steaming from the hog. One winter I knocked a bull calf straight in the brain between the eyes with a sledge hammer and had the meat hung up to chill before nightfall. But of course all this does not show on television. I am the way my daughter would want me to be: a hundred pounds lighter, my skin like an uncooked barley pancake. My hair glistens in the hot bright lights. Johnny Carson has much to do to keep up with my quick and witty tongue.

But that is a mistake. I know even before I wake up. Who ever knew a Johnson with a quick tongue? Who can even imagine me looking a strange white man in the eye? It seems to me I have talked to them always with one foot raised in flight, with my head turned in whichever way is farthest from them. Dee, though. She would always look anyone in the eye. Hesitation was no part of her nature.

"How do I look, Mama?" Maggie says, showing just enough of her thin body enveloped in pink skirt and red blouse for me to know she's there, almost hidden by the door.

"Come out into the yard," I say.

Have you ever seen a lame animal, perhaps a dog run over by some careless person rich enough to own a car, sidle up to someone who is ignorant enough to be kind to him? That is the way my Maggie walks. She has been like this, chin on chest, eyes on ground, feet in shuffle, ever since the fire that burned the other house to the ground.

Dee is lighter than Maggie, with nicer hair and a fuller figure. She's a woman now, though sometimes I forget. How long ago was it that the other house burned? Ten, twelve years? Sometimes I can still hear the flames and feel Maggie's arms sticking to me, her hair smoking and her dress falling off her in little black papery flakes. Her eyes seemed stretched open, blazed open by the flames reflected in them. And Dee. I see her standing off under the sweet gum tree she used to dig gum out of; a look of concentration on her face as she watched the last dingy gray board of the house fall in toward the red-hot brick chimney. Why don't you do a dance around the ashes? I'd wanted to ask her. She had hated the house that much.

I used to think she hated Maggie, too. But that was before we raised the money, the church and me, to send her to Augusta to school. She used to read to us without pity; forcing words, lies, other folks' habits, whole lives upon us two, sitting trapped and ignorant underneath her voice. She washed us in a river of make-believe, burned us with a lot of knowledge we didn't necessarily need to know. Pressed us to her with the serious way she read, to shove us away at just the moment, like dimwits, we seemed about to understand.

Dee wanted nice things. A yellow organdy dress to wear to her graduation from high school; black pumps to match a green suit she'd made from an old suit somebody gave me. She was determined to stare down any disaster in her efforts. Her eyelids would not flicker for minutes at a time. Often I fought off the temptation to shake her. At sixteen she had a style of her own: and knew what style was.

I never had an education myself. After second grade the school was closed down. Don't ask me why: in 1927 colored asked fewer questions than they do now. Sometimes Maggie reads to me. She stumbles along good-naturedly but can't see well. She knows she is not bright. Like good looks and money, quickness passed her by. She will marry John Thomas (who has mossy teeth in an earnest face) and then I'll be free to sit here and I guess just sing church songs to myself. Although I never was a good singer. Never could carry a tune. I was always better at a man's job. I used to love to milk till I was hooked in the side in '49. Cows are soothing and slow and don't bother you, unless you try to milk them the wrong way.

I have deliberately turned my back on the house. It is three rooms, just like the one that burned, except the roof is tin; they don't make shingle roofs any more. There are no real windows, just some holes cut in the sides, like the portholes in a ship, but not round and not square, with rawhide holding the shutters up on the outside. This house is in a pasture, too, like the other one. No doubt when Dee sees it she will want to tear it down. She wrote me once that no matter where we "choose" to live, she will manage to come see us. But she will never bring her friends. Maggie and I thought about this and Maggie asked me, "Mama, when did Dee ever *have* any friends?"

She had a few. Furtive boys in pink shirts hanging about on washday after school. Nervous girls who never laughed. Impressed with her they worshiped the well-turned phrase, the cute shape, the scalding humor that erupted like bubbles in lye. She read to them.

When she was courting Jimmy T she didn't have much time to pay to us, but turned all her faultfinding power on him. He *flew* to marry a cheap city girl from a family of ignorant flashy people. She hardly had time to recompose herself.

When she comes I will meet—but there they are!

Maggie attempts to make a dash for the house, in her shuffling way, but I stay her with my hand. "Come back here," I say. And she stops and tries to dig a well in the sand with her toe.

It is hard to see them clearly through the strong sun. But even the first glimpse of leg out of the car tells me it is Dee. Her feet were always neat-looking, as if God himself had shaped them with a certain style. From the other side of the car comes a short, stocky man. Hair is all over his head a foot long and hanging from his chin like a kinky mule tail. I hear Maggie suck in her breath. "Uhnnnh," is what it sounds like. Like when you see the wriggling end of a snake just in front of your foot on the road. "Uhnnnh."

Dee next. A dress down to the ground, in this hot weather. A dress so loud it hurts my eyes. There are yellows and oranges enough to throw back the light of the sun. I feel my whole face warming from the heat waves it throws out. Earrings gold, too, and hanging down to her shoulders. Bracelets dangling and making noises when she moves her arm up to shake the folds of the dress out of her armpits. The dress is loose and flows, and as she walks closer, I like it. I hear Maggie go "Uhnnnh" again. It is her sister's hair. It stands straight up like the wool on a sheep. It is black as night and around the edges are two long pigtails that rope about like small lizards disappearing behind her ears.

"Wa-su-zo-Tean-o!" she says, coming on in that gliding way the dress makes her move. The short stocky fellow with the hair to his navel is all grinning and he follows up with "Asalamalakim, my mother and sister!" He moves to hug Maggie but she falls back, right up against the back of my chair. I feel her trembling there and when I look up I see the perspiration falling off her chin.

"Don't get up," says Dee. Since I am stout it takes something of a push. You can see me trying to move a second or two before I make it. She turns, showing white heels through her sandals, and goes back to the car. Out she peeks next with a Polaroid. She stoops down quickly and lines up picture after picture of me sitting there in front of the house with Maggie cowering behind me. She never takes a shot without making sure the house is included. When a cow comes nibbling around the edge of the yard she snaps it and me and Maggie *and* the house. Then she puts the Polaroid in the back seat of the car, and comes up and kisses me on the forehead.

Meanwhile Asalamalakim is going through motions with Maggie's hand. Maggie's hand is as limp as a fish, and probably as cold, despite the sweat, and she keeps trying to pull it back. It looks like Asalamalakim wants to shake hands but wants to do it fancy. Or maybe he don't know how people shake hands. Anyhow, he soon gives up on Maggie.

"Well," I say. "Dee."

"No, Mama," she says. "Not 'Dee,' Wangero Leewanika Kemanjo!"

"What happened to 'Dee'?" I wanted to know.

"She's dead," Wangero said. "I couldn't bear it any longer, being named after the people who oppress me."

"You know as well as me you was named after your aunt Dicie," I said. Dicie is my sister. She named Dee. We called her "Big Dee" after Dee was born.

"But who was *she* named after?" asked Wangero.

"I guess after Grandma Dee," I said.

"And who was she named after?" asked Wangero.

"Her mother," I said, and saw Wangero was getting tired. "That's about as far back as I can trace it," I said. Though, in fact, I probably could have carried it back beyond the Civil War through the branches.

"Well," said Asalamalakim, "there you are."

"Uhnnnh," I heard Maggie say.

"There I was not," I said, "before 'Dicie' cropped up in our family, so why should I try to trace it that far back?"

He just stood there grinning, looking down on me like somebody inspecting a Model A car. Every once in a while he and Wangero sent eye signals over my head.

"How do you pronounce this name?" I asked.

"You don't have to call me by it if you don't want to," said Wangero.

"Why shouldn't I?" I asked. "If that's what you want us to call you, we'll call you."

"I know it might sound awkward at first," said Wangero.

"I'll get used to it," I said. "Ream it out again."

Well, soon we got the name out of the way. Asalamalakim had a name twice as long and three times as hard. After I tripped over it two or three times he told me to just call him Hakim-a-barber. I wanted to ask him was he a barber, but I didn't really think he was, so I didn't ask.

"You must belong to those beef-cattle peoples down the road," I said. They said "Asalamalakim" when they met you, too, but they didn't shake hands. Always too busy: feeding the cattle, fixing the fences, putting up salt-lick shelters, throwing down hay. When the white folks poisoned some of the herd the men stayed up all night with rifles in their hands. I walked a mile and a half just to see the sight.

Hakim-a-barber said, "I accept some of their doctrines, but farming and raising cattle is not my style." (They didn't tell me, and I didn't ask, whether Wangero (Dee) had really gone and married him.)

We sat down to eat and right away he said he didn't eat collards and pork was unclean. Wangero, though, went on through the chitlins and corn bread, the greens and everything else. She talked a blue streak over the sweet potatoes. Everything delighted her. Even the fact that we still used the benches her daddy made for the table when we couldn't afford to buy chairs.

"Oh, Mama!" she cried. Then turned to Hakim-a-barber. "I never knew how lovely these benches are. You can feel the rump prints," she said, running her hands underneath her and along the bench. Then she gave a sigh and her hand closed over Grandma Dee's butter dish. "That's it!" she said. "I knew there was something I wanted to ask you if I could have." She

jumped up from the table and went over in the corner where the churn
stood, the milk in it clabber by now. She looked at the churn and looked
at it.

"This churn top is what I need," she said. "Didn't Uncle Buddy whittle
it out of a tree you all used to have?"

"Yes," I said.

"Uh huh," she said happily. "And I want the dasher, too."

"Uncle Buddy whittle that, too?" asked the barber.

Dee (Wangero) looked up at me.

"Aunt Dee's first husband whittled the dash," said Maggie so low you
almost couldn't hear her. "His name was Henry, but they called him
Stash."

"Maggie's brain is like an elephant's," Wangero said, laughing. "I can
use the churn top as a centerpiece for the alcove table," she said, sliding a
plate over the churn, "and I'll think of something artistic to do with the
dasher."

When she finished wrapping the dasher the handle stuck out. I took it
for a moment in my hands. You didn't even have to look close to see where
hands pushing the dasher up and down to make butter had left a kind of
sink in the wood. In fact, there were a lot of small sinks; you could see
where thumbs and fingers had sunk into the wood. It was beautiful light
yellow wood, from a tree that grew in the yard where Big Dee and Stash
had lived.

After dinner Dee (Wangero) went to the trunk at the foot of my bed and
started rifling through it. Maggie hung back in the kitchen over the dishpan. Out came Wangero with two quilts. They had been pieced by
Grandma Dee and then Big Dee and me had hung them on the quilt
frames on the front porch and quilted them. One was in the Lone Star
pattern. The other was Walk Around the Mountain. In both of them were
scraps of dresses Grandma Dee had worn fifty and more years ago. Bits and
pieces of Grandpa Jarrell's Paisley shirts. And one teeny faded blue piece,
about the size of a penny matchbox, that was from Great Grandpa Ezra's
uniform that he wore in the Civil War.

"Mama," Wangero said sweet as a bird. "Can I have these old quilts?"

I heard something fall in the kitchen, and a minute later the kitchen
door slammed.

"Why don't you take one or two of the others?" I asked. "These old
things was just done by me and Big Dee from some tops your grandma
pieced before she died."

"No," said Wangero. "I don't want those. They are stitched around the
borders by machine."

"That'll make them last better," I said.

"That's not the point," said Wangero. "These are all pieces of dresses
Grandma used to wear. She did all this stitching by hand. Imagine!" She
held the quilts securely in her arms, stroking them.

"Some of the pieces, like those lavender ones, come from old clothes her
mother handed down to her," I said, moving up to touch the quilts. Dee
(Wangero) moved back just enough so that I couldn't reach the quilts.
They already belonged to her.

"Imagine!" she breathed again, clutching them closely to her bosom.

"The truth is," I said, "I promised to give them quilts to Maggie, for when she marries John Thomas."

She gasped like a bee had stung her.

"Maggie can't appreciate these quilts!" she said. "She'd probably be backward enough to put them to everyday use."

"I reckon she would," I said. "God knows I been saving 'em for long enough with nobody using 'em. I hope she will!" I didn't want to bring up how I had offered Dee (Wangero) a quilt when she went away to college. Then she had told me they were old-fashioned, out of style.

"But they're *priceless!*" she was saying now, furiously; for she has a temper. "Maggie would put them on the bed and in five years they'd be in rags. Less than that!"

"She can always make some more," I said. "Maggie knows how to quilt."

Dee (Wangero) looked at me with hatred. "You just will not understand. The point is these quilts, *these* quilts!"

"Well," I said, stumped. "What would *you* do with them?"

"Hang them," she said. As if that was the only thing you *could* do with quilts.

Maggie by now was standing in the door. I could almost hear the sound her feet made as they scraped over each other.

"She can have them, Mama," she said, like somebody used to never winning anything, or having anything reserved for her. "I can 'member Grandma Dee without the quilts."

I looked at her hard. She had filled her bottom lip with checkerberry snuff and it gave her face a kind of dopey, hangdog look. It was Grandma Dee and Big Dee who taught her how to quilt herself. She stood there with her scarred hands hidden in the folds of her skirt. She looked at her sister with something like fear but she wasn't mad at her. This was Maggie's portion. This was the way she knew God to work.

When I looked at her like that something hit me in the top of my head and ran down to the soles of my feet. Just like when I'm in church and the spirit of God touches me and I get happy and shout. I did something I never had done before: hugged Maggie to me, then dragged her on into the room, snatched the quilts out of Miss Wangero's hands and dumped them into Maggie's lap. Maggie just sat there on my bed with her mouth open.

"Take one or two of the others," I said to Dee.

But she turned without a word and went out to Hakim-a-barber.

"You just don't understand," she said, as Maggie and I came out to the car.

"What don't I understand?" I wanted to know.

"Your heritage," she said. And then she turned to Maggie, kissed her, and said, "You ought to try to make something of yourself, too, Maggie. It's really a new day for us. But from the way you and Mama still live you'd never know it."

She put on some sunglasses that hid everything above the tip of her nose and her chin.

Maggie smiled; maybe at the sunglasses. But a real smile, not scared. After we watched the car dust settle I asked Maggie to bring me a dip of snuff. And then the two of us sat there just enjoying, until it was time to go in the house and go to bed.

1973

Advancing Luna—and Ida B. Wells [1]

I met Luna the summer of 1965 in Atlanta where we both attended a political conference and rally. It was designed to give us the courage, as temporary civil rights workers, to penetrate the small hamlets farther south. I had taken a bus from Sarah Lawrence [2] in New York and gone back to Georgia, my home state, to try my hand at registering voters. It had become obvious from the high spirits and sense of almost divine purpose exhibited by black people that a revolution was going on, and I did not intend to miss it. Especially not this summery, student-studded version of it. And I thought it would be fun to spend some time on my own in the South.

Luna was sitting on the back of a pickup truck, waiting for someone to take her from Faith Baptist, where the rally was held, to whatever gracious black Negro home awaited her. I remember because someone who assumed I would also be traveling by pickup introduced us. I remember her face when I said, "No, no more back of pickup trucks for me. I know Atlanta well enough, I'll walk." She assumed of course (I guess) that I did not wish to ride beside her because she was white, and I was not curious enough about what she might have thought to explain it to her. And yet I was struck by her passivity, her *patience* as she sat on the truck alone and ignored, because someone had told her to wait there quietly until it was time to go.

This look of passively waiting for something changed very little over the years I knew her. It was only four or five years in all that I did. It seems longer, perhaps because we met at such an optimistic time in our lives. John Kennedy and Malcolm X had already been assassinated, but King had not been and Bobby Kennedy had not been. Then too, the lethal, bizarre elimination by death of this militant or that, exiles, flights to Cuba, shootouts between former Movement friends sundered forever by lies planted by the FBI, the gunning down of Mrs. Martin Luther King, Sr., as she played the Lord's Prayer on the piano in her church (was her name Alberta?), were still in the happily unfathomable future.

We believed we could change America because we were young and bright and held ourselves *responsible* for changing it. We did not believe we would fail. That is what lent fervor (revivalist fervor, in fact; we would *revive* America!) to our songs, and lent sweetness to our friendships (in the beginning almost all interracial), and gave a wonderful fillip to our sex (which, too, in the beginning, was almost always interracial).

What first struck me about Luna when we later lived together was that she did not own a bra. This was curious to me, I suppose, because she also

1. African American journalist and activist (1862–1931). Her *Red Report* (1895), which proved that the lynching of black men in the South was not related to the rape of white women, helped to initiate the antilynching campaigns of the 1890s.
2. College in Bronxville, New York, a suburb of New York City.

did not need one. Her chest was practically flat, her breasts like those of a child. Her face was round, and she suffered from acne. She carried with her always a tube of that "skin-colored" (if one's skin is pink or eggshell) medication designed to dry up pimples. At the oddest times—waiting for a light to change, listening to voter registration instructions, talking about her father's new girlfriend, she would apply the stuff, holding in her other hand a small brass mirror the size of her thumb, which she also carried for just this purpose.

We were assigned to work together in a small, rigidly segregated South Georgia town that the city fathers, incongruously and years ago, had named Freehold. Luna was slightly asthmatic and when overheated or nervous she breathed through her mouth. She wore her shoulder-length black hair with bangs to her eyebrows and the rest brushed behind her ears. Her eyes were brown and rather small. She was attractive, but just barely and with effort. Had she been the slightest bit overweight, for instance, she would have gone completely unnoticed, and would have faded into the background where, even in a revolution, fat people seem destined to go. I have a photograph of her sitting on the steps of a house in South Georgia. She is wearing tiny pearl earrings, a dark sleeveless shirt with Peter Pan collar, Bermuda shorts, and a pair of those East Indian sandals that seem to adhere to nothing but a big toe.

The summer of '65 was as hot as any other in that part of the South. There was an abundance of flies and mosquitoes. Everyone complained about the heat and the flies and the hard work, but Luna complained less than the rest of us. She walked ten miles a day with me up and down those straight Georgia highways, stopping at every house that looked black (one could always tell in 1965) and asking whether anyone needed help with learning how to vote. The simple mechanics: writing one's name, or making one's "X" in the proper column. And then, though we were required to walk, everywhere, we were empowered to offer prospective registrants a car in which they might safely ride down to the county courthouse. And later to the polling places. Luna, almost overcome by the heat, breathing through her mouth like a dog, her hair plastered with sweat to her head, kept looking straight ahead, and walking as if the walking itself was her reward.

I don't know if we accomplished much that summer. In retrospect, it seems not only minor, but irrelevant. A bunch of us, black and white, lived together. The black people who took us in were unfailingly hospitable and kind. I took them for granted in a way that now amazes me. I realize that at each and every house we visited I *assumed* hospitality, I *assumed* kindness. Luna was often startled by my "boldness." If we walked up to a secluded farmhouse and half a dozen dogs ran up barking around our heels and a large black man with a shotgun could be seen whistling to himself under a tree, she would become nervous. I, on the other hand, felt free to yell at this stranger's dogs, slap a couple of them on the nose, and call over to him about his hunting.

That month with Luna of approaching new black people every day taught me something about myself I had always suspected: I thought black people superior people. Not simply superior to white people, because even without thinking about it much, I assumed almost everyone was superior to them; but to everyone. Only white people, after all, would blow up a Sunday-school class and grin for television over their "victory," *i.e.*, the death of four small black girls. Any atrocity, at any time, was expected from them. On the other hand, it never occurred to me that black people *could* treat Luna and me with anything but warmth and concern. Even their curiosity about the sudden influx into their midst of rather ignorant white and black Northerners was restrained and courteous. I was treated as a relative, Luna as a much welcomed guest.

Luna and I were taken in by a middle-aged couple and their young school-age daughter. The mother worked outside the house in a local canning factory, the father worked in the paper plant in nearby Augusta. Never did they speak of the danger they were in of losing their jobs over keeping us, and never did their small daughter show any fear that her house might be attacked by racists because we were there. Again, I did not expect this family to complain, no matter what happened to them because of us. Having understood the danger, they had assumed the risk. I did not think them particularly brave, merely typical.

I think Luna liked the smallness—only four rooms—of the house. It was in this house that she ridiculed her mother's lack of taste. Her yellow-and-mauve house in Cleveland, the eleven rooms, the heated garage, the new car every year, her father's inability to remain faithful to her mother, their divorce, the fight over the property, even more bitter than over the children. Her mother kept the house and the children. Her father kept the car and his new girlfriend, whom he wanted Luna to meet and "approve." I could hardly imagine anyone disliking her mother so much. Everything Luna hated in her she summed up in three words: *"yellow and mauve."*

I have a second photograph of Luna and a group of us being bullied by a Georgia state trooper. This member of Georgia's finest had followed us out into the deserted countryside to lecture us on how misplaced—in the South—was our energy, when "the Lord knew" the North (where he thought all of us lived, expressing disbelief that most of us were Georgians) was just as bad. (He had a point that I recognized even then, but it did not seem the point where we were.) Luna is looking up at him, her mouth slightly open as always, a somewhat dazed look on her face. I cannot detect fear on any of our faces, though we were all afraid. After all, 1965 was only a year after 1964 when three civil rights workers had been taken deep into a Mississippi forest by local officials and sadistically tortured and murdered. Luna almost always carried a flat black shoulder bag. She is standing with it against her side, her thumb in the strap.

At night we slept in the same bed. We talked about our schools, lovers, girlfriends we didn't understand or missed. She dreamed, she said, of going to Goa. I dreamed of going to Africa. My dream came true earlier than hers: an offer of a grant from an unsuspected source reached me one day as I was writing poems under a tree. I left Freehold, Georgia, in the middle of summer, without regrets, and flew from New York to London, to Cairo, to Kenya, and, finally, to Uganda, where I settled among black people with the same assumptions of welcome and kindness I had taken for granted in Georgia. I was taken on rides down the Nile as a matter of course, and accepted all invitations to dinner, where the best local dishes were superbly prepared in my honor. I became, in fact, a lost relative of the people, whose ancestors had foolishly strayed, long ago, to America.

I wrote to Luna at once.

But I did not see her again for almost a year. I had graduated from college, moved into a borrowed apartment in Brooklyn Heights, and was being evicted after a month. Luna, living then in a tenement on East 9th Street, invited me to share her two-bedroom apartment. If I had seen the apartment before the day I moved in I might never have agreed to do so. Her building was between Avenues B and C and did not have a front door. Junkies, winos, and others often wandered in during the night (and occasionally during the day) to sleep underneath the stairs or to relieve themselves at the back of the first-floor hall.

Luna's apartment was on the third floor. Everything in it was painted white. The contrast between her three rooms and kitchen (with its red bathtub) and the grungy stairway was stunning. Her furniture consisted of two large brass beds inherited from a previous tenant and stripped of paint by Luna, and a long, high-backed church pew which she had managed somehow to bring up from the South. There was a simplicity about the small apartment that I liked. I also liked the notion of extreme contrast, and I do to this day. Outside our front window was the decaying neighborhood, as ugly and ill-lit as a battleground. (And allegedly as hostile, though somehow we were never threatened with bodily harm by the Hispanics who were our neighbors, and who seemed, more than anything, *bewildered* by the darkness and filth of their surroundings.) Inside was the church pew, as straight and spare as Abe Lincoln lying down, the white walls as spotless as a monastery's, and a small, unutterably pure patch of blue sky through the window of the back bedroom. (Luna did not believe in curtains, or couldn't afford them, and so we always undressed and bathed with the lights off and the rooms lit with candles, causing rather nun-shaped shadows to be cast on the walls by the long-sleeved high-necked nightgowns we both wore to bed.)

Over a period of weeks, our relationship, always marked by mutual respect, evolved into a warm and comfortable friendship which provided a stability and comfort we both needed at that time. I had taken a job at the Welfare Department during the day, and set up my typewriter permanently in the tiny living room for work after I got home. Luna worked in a kindergarten, and in the evenings taught herself Portuguese.

It was while we lived on East 9th Street that she told me she had been raped during her summer in the South. It is hard for me, even now, to relate my feeling of horror and incredulity. This was some time before Eldridge Cleaver wrote of being a rapist / revolutionary; of "practicing" on black women before moving on to white. It was also, unless I'm mistaken, before LeRoi Jones (as he was then known; now of course Imamu Baraka,[3]

---

3. African American poet, playwright, and essayist (b. 1934); one of the major figures of the Black Arts movement of the 1960s. Cleaver (b. 1935), ex-Black Panther leader and author of *Soul on Ice* (1968).

which has an even more presumptuous meaning than "the King") wrote his advice to young black male insurrectionaries (women were not told what to do with *their* rebelliousness): "Rape the white girls. Rape their fathers." It was clear that he meant this literally and also as: to rape a white girl *is* to rape her father. It was the misogynous cruelty of this latter meaning that was habitually lost on black men (on men in general, actually), but nearly always perceived and rejected by women of whatever color.

"Details?" I asked.

She shrugged. Gave his name. A name recently in the news, though in very small print.

He was not a Movement star or anyone you would know. We had met once, briefly. I had not liked him because he was coarse and spoke of black women as "our" women. (In the early Movement, it was pleasant to think of black men wanting to own us as a group; later it became clear that owning us meant exactly *that* to them.) He was physically unattractive, I had thought, with something of the hoodlum about him: a swaggering, unnecessarily mobile walk, small eyes, rough skin, a mouthful of wandering or absent teeth. He was, ironically, among the first persons to shout the slogan everyone later attributed solely to Stokeley Carmichael—Black Power! Stokeley was chosen as the originator of this idea by the media, because he was physically beautiful and photogenic and articulate. Even the name—Freddie Pye—was diminutive, I thought, in an age of giants.

"What did you do?"

"Nothing that required making a noise."

"Why didn't you scream?" I felt I would have screamed my head off.

"You know why."

I did. I had seen a photograph of Emmett Till's[4] body just after it was pulled from the river. I had seen photographs of white folks standing in a circle roasting something that had talked to them in their own language before they tore out its tongue. I knew why, all right.

"What was he trying to prove?"

"I don't know. Do you?"

"Maybe you filled him with unendurable lust," I said.

"I don't think so," she said.

Suddenly I was embarrassed. Then angry. Very, very angry. *How dare she tell me this!* I thought.

Who knows what the black woman thinks of rape? Who has asked her? Who *cares*? Who has even properly acknowledged that *she* and not the white woman in this story is the most likely victim of rape? Whenever interracial rape is mentioned, a black woman's first thought is to protect the lives of her brothers, her father, her sons, her lover. A history of lynching has bred this reflex in her. I feel it as strongly as anyone. While writing a fictional account of such a rape in a novel, I read Ida B. Wells's autobiography three times, as a means of praying to her spirit to forgive me.

---

4. Thirteen-year-old African American who was killed in Mississippi in 1955, supposedly because he whistled at a white woman. His death became symbolic of the racial injustices of the South. His killers were acquitted.

My prayer, as I turned the pages, went like this: *"Please forgive me. I am a writer."* (This self-revealing statement alone often seems to me sufficient reason to require perpetual forgiveness; since the writer is guilty not only of always wanting to know—like Eve—but also of trying—again like Eve—to find out.) *"I cannot write contrary to what life reveals to me. I wish to malign no one. But I must struggle to understand at least my own tangled emotions about interracial rape. I know, Ida B. Wells, you spent your whole life protecting, and trying to protect, black men accused of raping white women, who were lynched by white mobs, or threatened with it. You know, better than I ever will, what it means for a whole people to live under the terror of lynching. Under the slander that their men, where white women are concerned, are creatures of uncontrollable sexual lust. You made it so clear that the black men accused of rape in the past were innocent victims of white criminals that I grew up believing black men literally did not rape white women. At all. Ever. Now it would appear that some of them, the very twisted, the terribly ill, do. What would you have me write about them?"*

Her answer was: *"Write nothing. Nothing at all. It will be used against black men and therefore against all of us. Eldridge Cleaver and LeRoi Jones don't know who they're dealing with. But you remember. You are dealing with people who brought their children to witness the murder of black human beings, falsely accused of rape. People who handed out, as trophies, black fingers and toes. Deny! Deny! Deny!"*

And yet, I have pursued it: *"Some black men themselves do not seem to know what the meaning of raping someone is. Some have admitted rape in order to denounce it, but others have accepted rape as a part of rebellion, of 'paying whitey back.' They have gloried in it."*

"They know nothing of America," she says. *"And neither, apparently, do you. No matter what you think you know, no matter what you feel about it, say nothing. And to your dying breath!"*

Which, to my mind, is virtually useless advice to give to a writer.

Freddie Pye was the kind of man I would not have looked at then, not even once. (Throughout that year I was more or less into exotica: white ethnics who knew languages were a peculiar weakness; a half-white hippie singer; also a large Chinese mathematician who was a marvelous dancer and who taught me to waltz.) There was no question of belief.

But, in retrospect, there was a momentary *suspension* of belief, a kind of *hope* that perhaps it had not really happened; that Luna had made up the rape, "as white women have been wont to do." I soon realized this was unlikely. I was the only person she had told.

She looked at me as if to say: "I'm glad *that* part of my life is over." We continued our usual routine. We saw every interminable, foreign, depressing, and poorly illuminated film ever made. We learned to eat brown rice and yogurt and to tolerate kasha and odd-tasting teas. My half-black hippie singer friend (now a well-known reggae singer who says he is from "de I-lands" and not Sheepshead Bay) was "into" tea and kasha and Chinese vegetables.

And yet the rape, the knowledge of the rape, out in the open, admitted,

pondered over, was now between us. (And I began to think that perhaps—
whether Luna had been raped or not—it had always been so; that her power
over my life was exactly the power *her word on rape* had over the lives of
black men, over *all* black men, whether they were guilty or not, and therefore over my whole people.)

Before she told me about the rape, I think we had assumed a lifelong
friendship. The kind of friendship one dreams of having with a person one
has known in adversity; under heat and mosquitoes and immaturity and
the threat of death. We would each travel, we would write to each other
from the three edges of the world.

We would continue to have an "international list" of lovers whose amo-
rous talents or lack of talents we would continue (giggling into our dotage)
to compare. Our friendship would survive everything, be truer than everything, endure even our respective marriages, children, husbands—assuming we *did*, out of desperation and boredom someday, marry, which did not
seem a probability, exactly, but more in the area of an amusing idea.

But now there was a cooling off of our affection for each other. Luna was
becoming mildly interested in drugs, because everyone we knew was. I was
envious of the open-endedness of her life. The financial backing to it.
When she left her job at the kindergarten because she was tired of working,
her errant father immediately materialized. He took her to dine on scampi
at an expensive restaurant, scolded her for living on East 9th Street, and
looked at me as if to say: "Living in a slum of this magnitude must surely
have been your idea." As a cullud, of course.

For me there was the welfare department every day, attempting to get
the necessary food and shelter to people who would always live amid the
dirty streets I knew I must soon leave. I was, after all, a Sarah Lawrence girl
"with talent." It would be absurd to rot away in a building that had no front
door.

I slept late one Sunday morning with a painter I had met at the Welfare
Department. A man who looked for all the world like Gene Autry,[5] the
singing cowboy, but who painted wonderful surrealist pictures of birds and
ghouls and fruit with *teeth*. The night before, three of us—me, the painter,
and "an old Navy buddy" who looked like his twin and who had just arrived
in town—had got high on wine and grass.

That morning the Navy buddy snored outside the bedrooms like a puppy
waiting for its master. Luna got up early, made an immense racket getting
breakfast, scowled at me as I emerged from my room, and left the apartment, slamming the door so hard she damaged the lock. (Luna had made it
a rule to date black men almost exclusively. My insistence on dating, as she
termed it, "anyone" was incomprehensible to her, since in a politically
diseased society to "sleep with the enemy" was to become "infected" with
the enemy's "political germs." There is more than a grain of truth in this, of
course, but I was having too much fun to stare at it for long. Still, coming
from Luna it was amusing, since she never took into account the risk her
own black lovers ran by sleeping with "the white woman," and she had

---

5. Singing cowboy film star of the 1930s through the 1950s.

apparently been convinced that a summer of relatively innocuous political work in the South had cured her of any racial, economic, or sexual political disease.)

Luna never told me what irked her so that Sunday morning, yet I remember it as the end of our relationship. It was not, as I at first feared, that she thought my bringing the two men to the apartment was inconsiderate. The way we lived allowed us to *be* inconsiderate from time to time. Our friends were varied, vital, and often strange. Her friends especially were deeper than they should have been into drugs.

The distance between us continued to grow. She talked more of going to Goa.[6] My guilt over my dissolute if pleasurable existence coupled with my mounting hatred of welfare work, propelled me in two directions: south and to West Africa. When the time came to choose, I discovered that *my* summer in the South had infected me with the need to return, to try to understand, and write about, the people I'd merely lived with before.

We never discussed the rape again. We never discussed, really, Freddie Pye or Luna's remaining feelings about what had happened. One night, the last month we lived together, I noticed a man's blue denim jacket thrown across the church pew. The next morning, out of Luna's bedroom walked Freddie Pye. He barely spoke to me—possibly because as a black woman I was expected to be hostile toward his presence in a white woman's bedroom. I was too surprised to exhibit hostility, however, which was only a part of what I felt, after all. He left.

Luna and I did not discuss this. It is odd, I think now, that we didn't. It was as if he was never there, as if he and Luna had not shared the bedroom that night. A month later, Luna went alone to Goa, in her solitary way. She lived on an island and slept, she wrote, on the beach. She mentioned she'd found a lover there who protected her from the local beachcombers and pests.

Several years later, she came to visit me in the South and brought a lovely piece of pottery which my daughter much later dropped and broke, but which I glued back together in such a way that the flaw improves the beauty and fragility of the design.

Afterwords, Afterwards Second Thoughts

That is the "story." It has an "unresolved" ending. That is because Freddie Pye and Luna are still alive, as am I. However, one evening while talking to a friend, I heard myself say that I had, in fact, written *two* endings. One, which follows, I considered appropriate for such a story published in a country truly committed to justice, and the one above, which is the best I can afford to offer a society in which lynching is still reserved, at least subconsciously, as a means of racial control.

I said that if we in fact lived in a society committed to the establishment of justice for everyone ("justice" in this case encompassing equal housing, education, access to work, adequate dental care, et cetera), thereby placing Luna and Freddie Pye in their correct relationship to each other, *i.e.*, that

6. Coastal region of southwestern India, formerly a Portuguese colony.

of brother and sister, *compañeros*, then the two of them would be required to struggle together over what his rape of her had meant.

Since my friend is a black man whom I love and who loves me, we spent a considerable amount of time discussing what this particular rape meant to us. Morally wrong, we said, and not to be excused. Shameful; politically corrupt. Yet, as we thought of what might have happened to an indiscriminate number of innocent young black men in Freehold, Georgia, had Luna screamed, it became clear that more than a little of Ida B. Wells's fear of probing the rape issue was running through us, too. The implications of this fear would not let me rest, so that months and years went by with most of the story written but with me incapable, or at least unwilling, to finish or to publish it.

In thinking about it over a period of years, there occurred a number of small changes, refinements, puzzles, in angle. Would these shed a wider light on the continuing subject? I do not know. In any case, I returned to my notes, hereto appended for the use of the reader.

LUNA: IDA B. WELLS—DISCARDED NOTES

Additional characteristics of Luna: At a time when many in and out of the Movement considered "nigger" and "black" synonymous, and indulged in a sincere attempt to fake Southern "hip" speech, Luna resisted. She was the kind of WASP who could not easily imitate another's ethnic style, nor could she even exaggerate her own. She was what she was. A very straight, clear-eyed, coolly observant young woman with no talent for existing outside her own skin.

IMAGINARY KNOWLEDGE

Luna explained the visit from Freddie Pye in this way:

"He called that evening, said he was in town, and did I know the Movement was coming north? I replied that I did know that."

When could he see her? he wanted to know.

"Never," she replied.

He had burst into tears, or something that sounded like tears, over the phone. He was stranded at wherever the evening's fund-raising event had been held. Not in the place itself, but outside, in the street. The "stars" had left, everyone had left. He was alone. He knew no one else in the city. Had found her number in the phone book. And had no money, no place to stay.

Could he, he asked, crash? He was tired, hungry, broke—and even in the South had had no job, other than the Movement, for months. Et cetera.

When he arrived, she had placed our only steak knife in the waistband of her jeans.

He had asked for a drink of water. She gave him orange juice, some cheese, and a couple of slices of bread. She had told him he might sleep on the church pew and he had lain down with his head on his rolled-up denim jacket. She had retired to her room, locked the door, and tried to sleep. She was amazed to discover herself worrying that the church pew was both too narrow and too hard.

At first he muttered, groaned, and cursed in his sleep. Then he fell off the narrow church pew. He kept rolling off. At two in the morning she unlocked her door, showed him her knife, and invited him to share her bed.

Nothing whatever happened except they talked. At first, only he talked. Not about the rape, but about his life.

"He was a small person physically, remember?" Luna asked me. (She was right. Over the years he had grown big and, yes, burly, in my imagination, and I'm sure in hers.) "That night he seemed tiny. A child. He was still fully dressed, except for the jacket and he, literally, hugged his side of the bed. I hugged mine. The whole bed, in fact, was between us. We were merely hanging to its edges."

At the fund-raiser—on Fifth Avenue and 71st Street, as it turned out—his leaders had introduced him as the unskilled, barely literate, former Southern fieldworker that he was. They had pushed him at the rich people gathered there as an example of what "the system" did to "the little people" in the South. They asked him to tell about the thirty-seven times he had been jailed. The thirty-five times he had been beaten. The one time he had lost consciousness in the "hot" box. They told him not to worry about his grammar. "Which, as you may recall," said Luna, "was horrible." Even so, he had tried to censor his "ain'ts" and his "us'es." He had been painfully aware that he was on exhibit, like Frederick Douglass had been for the Abolitionists. But unlike Douglass he had no oratorical gift, no passionate language, no silver tongue. He knew the rich people and his own leaders perceived he was nothing: a broken man, unschooled, unskilled at anything. . . .

Yet he had spoken, trembling before so large a crowd of rich, white Northerners—who clearly thought their section of the country would never have the South's racial problems—begging, with the painful stories of his wretched life, for their money.

At the end, all of them—the black leaders, too—had gone. They left him watching the taillights of their cars, recalling the faces of the friends come to pick them up: the women dressed in African print that shone, with elaborately arranged hair, their jewelry sparkling, their perfume exotic. They were so beautiful, yet so strange. He could not imagine that one of them could comprehend his life. He did not ask for a ride, because of that, but also because he had no place to go. Then he had remembered Luna.

Soon Luna would be required to talk. She would mention her confusion over whether, in a black community surrounded by whites with a history of lynching blacks, she had a right to scream as Freddie Pye was raping her. For her, this was the crux of the matter.

And so they would continue talking through the night.

This is another ending, created from whole cloth. If I believed Luna's story about the rape, and I did (had she told anyone else I might have dismissed it), then this reconstruction of what might have happened is as probable an accounting as any is liable to be. Two people have now become "characters."

I have forced them to talk until they reached the stumbling block of the rape, *which they must remove themselves,* before proceeding to a place from which it will be possible to insist on a society in which Luna's word alone on rape can never be used to intimidate an entire people, and in which an innocent black man's protestation of innocence of rape is unprejudicially heard. Until such a society is created, relationships of affection between black men and white women will always be poisoned—from within as from without—by historical fear and the threat of violence, and solidarity among black and white women is only rarely likely to exist.

Postscript: Havana, Cuba, November 1976

I am in Havana with a group of other black American artists. We have spent the morning apart from our Cuban hosts bringing each other up to date on the kind of work (there are no apolitical artists among us) we are doing in the United States. I have read "Luna."

High above the beautiful city of Havana I sit in the Havana Libre pavilion with the muralist/photographer in our group. He is in his mid-thirties, a handsome, brown, erect individual whom I have known casually for a number of years. During the sixties he designed and painted street murals for both SNCC[7] and the Black Panthers, and in an earlier discussion with Cuban artists he showed impatience with their explanation of why we had seen no murals covering some of the city's rather dingy walls: Cuba, they had said, unlike Mexico, has no mural tradition. "But the point of a revolution," insisted Our Muralist, "is to make new traditions!" And he had pressed his argument with such passion for the *usefulness*, for revolutionary communication, of his craft, that the Cubans were both exasperated and impressed. They drove us around the city for a tour of their huge billboards, all advancing socialist thought and the heroism of men like Lenin, Camilo, and Che Guevara, and said, "These, *these* are our 'murals'!"

While we ate lunch, I asked Our Muralist what he'd thought of "Luna." Especially the appended section.

"Not much," was his reply. "Your view of human weakness is too biblical," he said. "You are unable to conceive of the man without conscience. The man who cares nothing about the state of his soul because he's long since sold it. In short," he said, "you do not understand that some people are simply evil, a disease on the lives of other people, and that to remove the disease altogether is preferable to trying to interpret, contain, or forgive it. Your 'Freddie Pye,'" and he laughed, "was probably raping white women on the instructions of his government."

Oh ho, I thought. Because, of course, for a second, during which I stalled my verbal reply, this comment made both very little and very much sense.

"I *am* sometimes naive and sentimental," I offered. I am sometimes both, though frequently by design. Admission in this way is tactical, a stimulant to conversation.

"And shocked at what I've said," he said, and laughed again. "Even though," he continued, "you know by now that blacks could be hired to blow up other blacks, and could be hired *by someone* to shoot down Brother Malcolm, and hired *by someone* to provide a diagram of Fred

7. Southern Nonviolent Coordinating Committee. One of the major civil rights activist organizations of the 1960s; it launched the voter registration drives in the South in the early 1960s.

Hampton's [8] bedroom so the pigs could shoot him easily while he slept, you find it hard to believe a black man could be hired *by someone* to rape white women. But think a minute, and you will see why it is the perfect disruptive act. Enough blacks raping or accused of raping enough white women and any political movement that cuts across racial lines is doomed.

"Larger forces are at work than your story would indicate," he continued. "You're still thinking of lust and rage, moving slowly into aggression and purely racial hatred. But you should be considering money—which the rapist would get, probably from your very own tax dollars, in fact—and a maintaining of the status quo; which those hiring the rapist would achieve. I know all this," he said, "because when I was broke and hungry and selling my blood to buy the food and the paint that allowed me to work, I was offered such 'other work.' "

"But you did not take it."

He frowned. "There you go again. How do you know I didn't take it? It paid, and I was starving."

"You didn't take it," I repeated.

"No," he said. "A black and white 'team' made the offer. I had enough energy left to threaten to throw them out of the room."

"But even if Freddie Pye *had been* hired *by someone* to rape Luna, that still would not explain his second visit."

"Probably nothing will explain that," said Our Muralist. "But assuming Freddie Pye *was* paid to disrupt—by raping a white woman—the black struggle in the South, he may have wised up enough later to comprehend the significance of Luna's decision not to scream."

"So you are saying he *did have* a conscience?" I asked.

"Maybe," he said, but his look clearly implied I would never understand anything about evil, power, or corrupted human beings in the modern world.

But of course he is wrong.

1981

From The Color Purple

[*The Color Purple* traces about thirty years in the life of Celie, a southern black woman born at the turn of the twentieth century. In her teens, she is raped by her stepfather, who sells the two children she bears him. Her sister, Nettie, runs away because of the treatment they receive from their stepfather and, unbeknownst to Celie, is adopted by a black missionary couple who takes her to Africa. Celie is married off to Albert, a relatively comfortable landowner whom she calls "Mister," an indication of his control over her. Albert expects Celie, as a wife, to work in his fields and to accept his beatings, a common belief in the world among husbands at that time.

At first, the only relief Celie has in her marriage is her relationship with Sophia, the wife of Albert's son, Harpo, and the letters she writes to Nettie. Sophia refuses to be abused by her husband but is beaten and jailed because she won't be the maid for the children of the white mayor's wife. Then Shug Avery, a blues singer and the

---

8. Black Panther thought to have been murdered by the Chicago police.

woman whom Albert loves, becomes ill and is taken care of by Celie. Strengthened by her friendship and sexual love with Shug, Celie leaves her marriage. Her husband, Mister, becomes more nurturing as a result of the women's struggle to become their whole selves. At the close of the novel, Celie is united with her sisters as well as with her children.

The novel consists of three sets of letters: Celie's letters to God, about the incest and abuse she cannot speak or write of to anyone else; Nettie's letters to Celie, which are included within Celie's letters to God after she's met Shug; and Celie's letters to Nettie, emphasizing the theme of sisterhood at the core of this novel's concerns. The excerpt that follows is letter 73, in which Shug articulates the central spiritual concern of the novel, which is the image of the color purple to embody the unity and enjoyment that is her view of God, a view that sees no separation between the body and the spirit and expresses the spirit of the oneness of the universe.]

[God Love All Them Feelings]

Dear Nettie,

I don't write to God no more, I write to you.

What happen to God? ast Shug.

Who that? I say.

She look at me serious.

Big a devil as you is, I say, you not worried bout no God, surely.

She say, Wait a minute. Hold on just a minute here. Just because I don't harass it like some peoples us know don't mean I ain't got religion.

What God do for me? I ast.

She say, Celie! Like she shock. He gave you life, good health, and a good woman that love you to death.

Yeah, I say, and he give me a lynched daddy, a crazy mama, a lowdown dog of a step pa and a sister I probably won't ever see again. Anyhow, I say, the God I been praying and writing to is a man. And act just like all the other mens I know. Trifling, forgitful and lowdown.

She say, Miss Celie. You better hush. God might hear you.

Let 'im hear me, I say. If he ever listened to poor colored women the world would be a different place, I can tell you.

She talk and she talk, trying to budge me way from blasphemy. But I blaspheme much as I want to.

All my life I never care what people thought bout nothing I did, I say. But deep in my heart I care about God. What he going to think. And come to find out, he don't think. Just sit up there glorying in being deef, I reckon. But it ain't easy, trying to do without God. Even if you know he ain't there, trying to do without him is a strain.

I is a sinner, say Shug. Cause I was born. I don't deny it. But once you find out what's out there waiting for us, what else can you be?

Sinners have more good times, I say.

You know why? she ast.

Cause you ain't all the time worrying bout God, I say.

Naw, that ain't it, she say. Us worry bout God a lot. But once us feel loved by God, us do the best us can to please him with what us like.

You telling me God love you, and you ain't never done nothing for him? I mean, not go to church, sing in the choir, feed the preacher and all like that?

But if God love me, Celie, I don't have to do all that. Unless I want to. There's a lot of other things I can do that I speck God likes.

Like what? I ast.

Oh, she say. I can lay back and just admire stuff. Be happy. Have a good time.

Well, this sound like blasphemy sure nuff.

She say, Celie, tell the truth, have you ever found God in church? I never did. I just found a bunch of folks hoping for him to show. Any God I ever felt in church I brought in with me. And I think all the other folks did too. They come to church to *share* God, not find God.

Some folks didn't have him to share, I said. They the ones didn't speak to me while I was there struggling with my big belly and Mr. _____ children.

Right, she say.

Then she say: Tell me what your God look like, Celie.

Aw naw, I say. I'm too shame. Nobody ever ast me this before, so I'm sort of took by surprise. Besides, when I think about it, it don't seem quite right. But it all I got. I decide to stick up for him, just to see what Shug say.

Okay, I say. He big and old and tall and graybearded and white. He wear white robes and go barefooted.

Blue eyes? she ast.

Sort of bluish-gray. Cool. Big though. White lashes, I say.

She laugh.

Why you laugh? I ast. I don't think it so funny. What you expect him to look like, Mr. _____?

That wouldn't be no improvement, she say. Then she tell me this old white man is the same God she used to see when she prayed. If you wait to find God in church, Celie, she say, that's who is bound to show up, cause that's where he live.

How come? I ast.

Cause that's the one that's in the white folks' white bible.

Shug! I say. God wrote the bible, white folks had nothing to do with it.

How come he look just like them, then? she say. Only bigger? And a heap more hair. How come the bible just like everything else they make, all about them doing one thing and another, and all the colored folks doing is gitting cursed?

I never thought bout that.

Nettie say somewhere in the bible it say Jesus' hair was like lamb's wool, I say.

Well, say Shug, if he came to any of these churches we talking bout he'd have to have it conked[1] before anybody paid him any attention. The last thing niggers want to think about they God is that his hair kinky.

That's the truth, I say.

Ain't no way to read the bible and not think God white, she say. Then

---

1. Straightened and waved.

she sigh. When I found out I thought God was white, and a man, I lost interest. You mad cause he don't seem to listen to your prayers. Humph! Do the mayor listen to anything colored say? Ask Sofia, she say.

But I don't have to ast Sofia. I know white people never listen to colored, period. If they do, they only listen long enough to be able to tell you what to do.

Here's the thing, say Shug. The thing I believe. God is inside you and inside everybody else. You come into the world with God. But only them that search for it inside find it. And sometimes it just manifest itself even if you not looking, or don't know what you looking for. Trouble do it for most folks, I think. Sorrow, lord. Feeling like shit.

It? I ast.

Yeah. It. God ain't a he or a she, but a It.

But what do it look like? I ast.

Don't look like nothing, she say. It ain't a picture show. It ain't something you can look at apart from anything else, including yourself. I believe God is everything, say Shug. Everything that is or ever was or ever will be. And when you can feel that, and be happy to feel that, you've found It.

Shug a beautiful something, let me tell you. She frown a little, look out cross the yard, lean back in her chair, look like a big rose.

She say, My first step from the old white man was trees. Then air. Then birds. Then other people. But one day when I was sitting quiet and feeling like a motherless child, which I was, it come to me: that feeling of being part of everything, not separate at all. I knew that if I cut a tree, my arm would bleed. And I laughed and I cried and I run all round the house. I knew just what it was. In fact, when it happen, you can't miss it. It sort of like you know what, she say, grinning and rubbing high up on my thigh.

Shug! I say.

Oh, she say. God love all them feelings. That's some of the best stuff God did. And when you know God loves 'em you enjoys 'em a lot more. You can just relax, go with everything that's going, and praise God by liking what you like.

God don't think it dirty? I ast.

Naw, she say. God made it. Listen, God love everything you love—and a mess of stuff you don't. But more than anything else, God love admiration.

You saying God vain? I ast.

Naw, she say. Not vain, just wanting to share a good thing. I think it pisses God off if you walk by the color purple in a field somewhere and don't notice it.

What it do when it pissed off? I ast.

Oh, it make something else. People think pleasing God is all God care about. But any fool living in the world can see it always trying to please us back.

Yeah? I say.

Yeah, she say. It always making little surprises and springing them on us when us least expect.

You mean it want to be loved, just like the bible say.

Yes, Celie, she say. Everything want to be loved. Us sing and dance, make faces and give flower bouquets, trying to be loved. You ever notice that trees do everything to git attention we do, except walk?

Well, us talk and talk bout God, but I'm still adrift. Trying to chase that old white man out of my head. I been so busy thinking bout him I never truly notice nothing God make. Not a blade of corn (how it do that?) not the color purple (where it come from?). Not the little wildflowers. Nothing.

Now that my eyes opening, I feels like a fool. Next to any little scrub of a bush in my yard, Mr. _____'s evil sort of shrink. But not altogether. Still, it is like Shug say, You have to git man off your eyeball, before you can see anything a'tall.

Man corrupt everything, say Shug. He on your box of grits, in your head, and all over the radio. He try to make you think he everywhere. Soon as you think he everywhere, you think he God. But he ain't. Whenever you trying to pray, and man plop himself on the other end of it, tell him to git lost, say Shug. Conjure up flowers, wind, water, a big rock.

But this hard work, let me tell you. He been there so long, he don't want to budge. He threaten lightening, floods and earthquakes. Us fight. I hardly pray at all. Every time I conjure up a rock, I throw it.

Amen
1982

AUGUST WILSON

b. 1945

August Wilson is one of only seven American dramatists ever to win two Pulitzer Prizes (one for *Fences*, and one for *A Piano Lesson*) as well as the first African American to have two plays *(Fences* and *Joe Turner's Come and Gone)* running simultaneously on Broadway. Director-producer Lloyd Richards hails Wilson as the "culmination of political, social and aesthetic objectives presaged by the Harlem Renaissance in the twenties and the Black Arts Movement of the sixties."

Wilson became a playwright to "tell a history that has never been told. His major works are all part of a cycle of ten plays, each of which explores a central issue facing African Americans in a different decade of the twentieth century. In the 1991 preface to *Three Plays*, Wilson reports that his exploration of African American historical experience began in 1965 with "a typewritten yellow-labeled record titled 'Nobody in Town Can Bake a Sweet Jellyroll Like Mine' by someone named Bessie Smith. . . . It was the beginning of my consciousness that I was a representative of a culture and the carrier of some very valuable antecedents." Wilson evoked that memory in his first big hit, *Ma Rainey's Black Bottom*, set in the 1920s. His cycle has continued with *Joe Turner's Come and Gone*, set in the second decade of the century; *Fences*, set in the 1950s; *The Piano Lesson*, set in the 1930s; *Two Trains Running*, set in the 1960s; and *Seven Guitars*, set in the 1940s.

August Wilson was born in 1945 in Pittsburgh, Pennsylvania, the fourth of six children and the eldest son of German American Frederick August Kittel and African American Daisy Wilson. He grew up in a poor, racially mixed section of Pittsburgh called "the Hill." Actively raised by his African American stepfather, David Belford, Wilson remembers his biological father only as "a sporadic presence."

When his stepfather relocated the family to a predominantly white suburb in the late 1950s, August experienced racial prejudice: the throwing of bricks at his house, classmates who would not sit with him, notes saying "Nigger go home." At fifteen, after an African American history teacher falsely accused him of plagiarism, he quit school: "Basically the years from fifteen to twenty I spent in the library educating myself." As well as his own reading, Wilson was also deeply affected by the oral tradition passed on from one generation of black men to the next:

> About 21 living in Pittsburgh, it was very difficult . . . and I wasn't quite sure I was going to be 22. And I looked up and saw this old man walking down the street and I said I didn't know how he lived to be 65. . . . I followed him and went into this place called Pat's place, which was a cigar store. And there these guys would stand around every day and I would stand around in the background and listen to them. . . . Little did I know that many years later . . . I would make use of them in my plays.

In the late 1960s, Wilson became involved in the Black Power movement and began writing poetry and short stories, publishing early works in small black journals. In 1969, he married Brenda Burton, a Muslim, with whom he had a daughter, Sakin Ansair. The marriage ended in 1972. In 1978, he moved to St. Paul, where he wrote his first plays, *Jitney* and *Fullerton Street*. In 1981, he married Judy Oliver, a social worker.

With the support of Lloyd Richards, dean of the Yale School of Drama and the artistic director of the Yale Repertory Theatre, Wilson's play *Ma Rainey's Black Bottom* opened on Broadway at the Cort Theatre in 1984 and was a commercial and critical success, running for 275 performances and winning the New York Drama Critics Circle Award as well as several Tony nominations. Critics such as the *New York Times*'s Frank Rich hailed Wilson as "a major find for the American theater" and praised him for writing "with compassion, raucous humor and penetrating wisdom."

The production history of Wilson's next play, *Fences*, overlaps that of *Ma Rainey's Black Bottom*, establishing what has become a typical work pattern for Wilson. He usually has several pieces in progress at the same time. After four years of polishing *Fences*, and productions at several venues, Wilson opened the play at the 46th Street Theater in New York on March 26, 1987. Starring James Earl Jones as Troy Maxson, the play was a tremendous critical success, winning the New York Drama Critics Circle Award, four Tony awards (including Best Play), and the Pulitzer Prize for drama. As Richards describes it, the play places a father-son conflict in a specific context, showing it as "a rite of passage which is often misconstrued as a struggle between father and son for dominance when, in fact, there are no rights shared by sons with fathers in traditional African American households." Wilson's use of myth too elicited praise from critics, with the *Village Voice*'s Michael Feingold proclaiming Wilson "a mythmaker who sees his basically naturalistic panorama plays as sages in an allegorical history of black America."

Wilson's next play, *Joe Turner's Come and Gone* was lauded by Frank Rich as "a spiritual allegory" that "will give a lasting voice to a generation of uprooted black Americans." Set in a boarding house in Pittsburgh in 1911, *Joe Turner's Come and Gone* explores the lives of characters in danger of being cut off from their African and southern roots by their migration to the North. In his customary fashion, while *Joe Turner* wended its way to Broadway, Wilson wrote his next play, *The Piano Lesson*, which premiered at the Yale Repertory Theater in 1987, opened on Broadway in 1990, and won the Pulitzer Prize.

The Piano Lesson is set in 1937 in Pittsburgh and revolves around the conflict between a brother and a sister, Boy Willie and Berniece, and their relationship to a piano, which comes to symbolize the "choice between revering symbols of African ancestry and converting them to functional use." Some critics noted the scarcity of complicated female characters. Others praised the "music of the dialogue" and how "phrase by phrase and speech by speech, Wilson is as sheerly listenable as Handel."

Wilson's next play in his cycle, *Two Trains Running*, opened at the Walter Kerr Theater on Broadway in April 1992. The play is again set in Pittsburgh, this time in a luncheonette in the late 1960s. Although the characters are not directly involved in the turbulent events of the period, one critic noted that the play "embodies the entire black political dialectic from that time to this—isolation vs. assimilation, hostility toward vs. cooperation with whites, clinging to bitter memory vs. moving on into a better world." Others such as Cheryl McCourtie of the *Crisis* noted how the play resonated with her own life experience: "Sitting in on *Two Trains Running* about the workers and 'regulars' in a Pittsburgh restaurant in 1969 is like eavesdropping on a group of family members."

No one playwright can be expected to counteract the long history of underrepresentation and misrepresentation of African Americans in American theater. Nevertheless, Wilson's plays represent a powerful vision, and his work has greatly enlarged the dramatic landscape. By developing his gift for poetic dialogue and by using that gift to relate material from his own past, he has found a way of incorporating politics and history, as well as aspects of a distinctive African American culture, into plays that appeal to a mass audience. His most recent play, *Seven Guitars*, opened on Broadway in 1995 to rave reviews.

Fences

When the sins of our fathers visit us
We do not have to play host.
We can banish them with forgiveness
As God, in His Largeness and Laws.
—AUGUST WILSON

CHARACTERS

TROY MAXSON
JIM BONO, TROY's *friend*
ROSE, TROY's *wife*
LYONS, TROY's *oldest son by previous marriage*
GABRIEL, TROY's *brother*
CORY, TROY *and* ROSE's *son*
RAYNELL, TROY's *daughter*

Setting

The setting is the yard which fronts the only entrance to the MAXSON *household, an ancient two-story brick house set back off a small alley in a big-city neighborhood. The entrance to the house is gained by two or three steps leading to a wooden porch badly in need of paint.*

A relatively recent addition to the house and running its full width, the porch lacks congruence. It is a sturdy porch with a flat roof. One or two chairs of dubious value sit at one end where the kitchen window opens onto the porch. An old-fashioned icebox stands silent guard at the opposite end.

The yard is a small dirt yard, partially fenced, except for the last scene, with a wooden sawhorse, a pile of lumber, and other fence-building equipment set off to the side. Opposite is a tree from which hangs a ball made of rags. A baseball bat leans against the tree. Two oil drums serve as garbage receptacles and sit near the house at right to complete the setting.

The Play

Near the turn of the century, the destitute of Europe sprang on the city with tenacious claws and an honest and solid dream. The city devoured them. They swelled its belly until it burst into a thousand furnaces and sewing machines, a thousand butcher shops and bakers' ovens, a thousand churches and hospitals and funeral parlors and money-lenders. The city grew. It nourished itself and offered each man a partnership limited only by his talent, his guile, and his willingness and capacity for hard work. For the immigrants of Europe, a dream dared and won true.

The descendants of African slaves were offered no such welcome or participation. They came from places called the Carolinas and the Virginias, Georgia, Alabama, Mississippi, and Tennessee. They came strong, eager, searching. The city rejected them and they fled and settled along the riverbanks and under bridges in shallow, ramshackle houses made of sticks and tar-paper. They collected rags and wood. They sold the use of their muscles and their bodies. They cleaned houses and washed clothes, they shined shoes, and in quiet desperation and vengeful pride, they stole, and lived in pursuit of their own dream. That they could breathe free, finally, and stand to meet life with the force of dignity and whatever eloquence the heart could call upon.

By 1957, the hard-won victories of the European immigrants had solidified the industrial might of America. War had been confronted and won with new energies that used loyalty and patriotism as its fuel. Life was rich, full, and flourishing. The Milwaukee Braves won the World Series, and the hot winds of change that would make the sixties a turbulent, racing, dangerous, and provocative decade had not yet begun to blow full.

Act One

SCENE ONE

It is 1957. TROY *and* BONO *enter the yard, engaged in conversation.* TROY *is fifty-three years old, a large man with thick, heavy hands; it is this largeness that he strives to fill out and make an accommodation with. Together with his blackness, his largeness informs his sensibilities and the choices he has made in his life.*

Of the two men, BONO *is obviously the follower. His commitment to their friendship of thirty-odd years is rooted in his admiration of* TROY's *honesty, capacity for hard work, and his strength, which* BONO *seeks to emulate.*

It is Friday night, payday, and the one night of the week the two men engage in a ritual of talk and drink. TROY *is usually the most talkative and*

*at times he can be crude and almost vulgar, though he is capable of rising
to profound heights of expression. The men carry lunch buckets and wear
or carry burlap aprons and are dressed in clothes suitable to their jobs as
garbage collectors.*

BONO.   Troy, you ought to stop that lying!

TROY.   I ain't lying! The nigger had a watermelon this big.
  [*He indicates with his hands.*]
  Talking about . . . "What watermelon, Mr. Rand?" I liked to fell out!
  "What watermelon, Mr. Rand?" . . . And it sitting there big as life.

BONO.   What did Mr. Rand say?

TROY.   Ain't said nothing. Figure if the nigger too dumb to know he carrying a watermelon, he wasn't gonna get much sense out of him. Trying to
  hide that great big old watermelon under his coat. Afraid to let the white
  man see him carry it home.

BONO.   I'm like you . . . I ain't got no time for them kind of people.

TROY.   Now what he look like getting mad cause he see the man from the
  union talking to Mr. Rand?

BONO.   He come to me talking about . . . "Maxson gonna get us fired." I
  told him to get away from me with that. He walked away from me calling
  you a troublemaker. What Mr. Rand say?

TROY.   Ain't said nothing. He told me to go down the Commissioner's office next Friday. They called me down there to see them.

BONO.   Well, as long as you got your complaint filed, they can't fire you.
  That's what one of them white fellows tell me.

TROY.   I ain't worried about them firing me. They gonna fire me cause I
  asked a question? That's all I did. I went to Mr. Rand and asked him,
  "Why?" Why you got the white mens driving and the colored lifting?"
  Told him, "what's the matter, don't I count? You think only white fellows got sense enough to drive a truck. That ain't no paper job! Hell,
  anybody can drive a truck. How come you got all whites driving and the
  colored lifting? He told me "take it to the union." Well, hell, that's what
  I done! Now they wanna come up with this pack of lies.

BONO.   I told Brownie if the man come and ask him any questions . . . just
  tell the truth! It ain't nothing but something they done trumped up on
  you cause you filed a complaint on them.

TROY.   Brownie don't understand nothing. All I want them to do is change
  the job description. Give everybody a chance to drive the truck. Brownie
  can't see that. He ain't got that much sense.

BONO.   How you figure he be making out with that gal be up at Taylors' all
  the time . . . that Alberta gal?

TROY.   Same as you and me. Getting just as much as we is. Which is to say
  nothing.

BONO.   It is, huh? I figure you doing a little better than me . . . and I ain't
  saying what I'm doing.

TROY.   Aw, nigger, look here . . . I know you. If you had got anywhere near
  that gal, twenty minutes later you be looking to tell somebody. And the
  first one you gonna tell . . . that you gonna want to brag to . . . is gonna
  be me.

BONO.   I ain't saying that. I see where you be eyeing her.

TROY.   I eye all the women. I don't miss nothing. Don't never let nobody tell you Troy Maxson don't eye the women.

BONO.   You been doing more than eyeing her. You done bought her a drink or two.

TROY.   Hell yeah, I bought her a drink! What that mean? I bought you one, too. What that mean cause I buy her a drink? I'm just being polite.

BONO.   It's alright to buy her one drink. That's what you call being polite. But when you wanna be buying two or three . . . that's what you call eyeing her.

TROY.   Look here, as long as you known me . . . you ever known me to chase after women?

BONO.   Hell yeah! Long as I done known you. You forgetting I knew you when.

TROY.   Naw, I'm talking about since I been married to Rose?

BONO.   Oh, not since you been married to Rose. Now, that's the truth, there. I can say that.

TROY.   Alright then! Case closed.

BONO.   I see you be walking up around Alberta's house. You supposed to be at Taylors' and you be walking up around there.

TROY.   What you watching where I'm walking for? I ain't watching after you.

BONO.   I seen you walking around there more than once.

TROY.   Hell, you liable to see me walking anywhere! That don't mean nothing cause you see me walking around there.

BONO.   Where she come from anyway? She just kinda showed up one day.

TROY.   Tallahassee. You can look at her and tell she one of them Florida gals. They got some big healthy women down there. Grow them right up out the ground. Got a little bit of Indian in her. Most of them niggers down in Florida got some Indian in them.

BONO.   I don't know about that Indian part. But she damn sure big and healthy. Woman wear some big stockings. Got them great big old legs and hips as wide as the Mississippi River.

TROY.   Legs don't mean nothing. You don't do nothing but push them out of the way. But them hips cushion the ride!

BONO.   Troy, you ain't got no sense.

TROY.   It's the truth! Like you riding on Goodyears!

[ROSE *enters from the house. She is ten years younger than* TROY, *her devotion to him stems from her recognition of the possibilities of her life without him: a succession of abusive men and their babies, a life of partying and running the streets, the Church, or aloneness with its attendant pain and frustration. She recognizes* TROY's *spirit as a fine and illuminating one and she either ignores or forgives his faults, only some of which she recognizes. Though she doesn't drink, her presence is an integral part of the Friday night rituals. She alternates between the porch and the kitchen, where supper preparations are under way.*]

ROSE.   What you all out here getting into?

TROY.   What you worried about what we getting into for? This is men talk, woman.

ROSE.   What I care what you all talking about? Bono, you gonna stay for supper?

BONO.   No, I thank you, Rose. But Lucille say she cooking up a pot of pigfeet.

TROY.   Pigfeet! Hell, I'm going home with you! Might even stay the night if you got some pigfeet. You got something in there to top them pigfeet, Rose?

ROSE.   I'm cooking up some chicken. I got some chicken and collard greens.

TROY.   Well, go on back in the house and let me and Bono finish what we was talking about. This is men talk. I got some talk for you later. You know what kind of talk I mean. You go on and powder it up.

ROSE.   Troy Maxson, don't you start that now!

TROY.   [Puts his arm around her.] Aw, woman . . . come here. Look here, Bono . . . when I met this woman . . . I got out that place, say, "Hitch up my pony, saddle up my mare . . . there's a woman out there for me somewhere. I looked here. Looked there. Saw Rose and latched on to her." I latched on to her and told her—I'm gonna tell you the truth—I told her, "Baby, I don't wanna marry, I just wanna be your man." Rose told me . . . tell him what you told me, Rose.

ROSE.   I told him if he wasn't the marrying kind, then move out the way so the marrying kind could find me.

TROY.   That's what she told me. "Nigger, you in my way. You blocking the view! Move out the way so I can find me a husband." I thought it over two or three days. Come back—

ROSE.   Ain't no two or three days nothing. You was back the same night.

TROY.   Come back, told her . . . "Okay, baby . . . but I'm gonna buy me a banty[1] rooster and put him out there in the backyard . . . and when he see a stranger come, he'll flap his wings and crow . . ." Look here, Bono, I could watch the front door by myself . . . it was that back door I was worried about.

ROSE.   Troy, you ought not talk like that. Troy ain't doing nothing but telling a lie.

TROY.   Only thing is . . . when we first got married . . . forget the rooster . . . we ain't had no yard!

BONO.   I hear you tell it. Me and Lucille was staying down there on Logan Street. Had two rooms with the outhouse in the back. I ain't mind the outhouse none. But when that goddamn wind blow through there in the winter . . . that's what I'm talking about! To this day I wonder why in the hell I ever stayed down there for six long years. But see, I didn't know I could do no better. I thought only white folks had inside toilets and things.

ROSE.   There's a lot of people don't know they can do no better than they doing now. That's just something you got to learn. A lot of folks still shop at Bella's.

---

1. Or bantam, an aggressive and spirited small domestic fowl.

TROY. Ain't nothing wrong with shopping at Bella's. She got fresh food.

ROSE. I ain't said nothing about if she got fresh food. I'm talking about what she charge. She charge ten cents more than the A&P.

TROY. The A&P ain't never done nothing for me. I spends my money where I'm treated right. I go down to Bella, say, "I need a loaf of bread, I'll pay you Friday." She give it to me. What sense that make when I got money to go and spend it somewhere else and ignore the person who done right by me? That ain't in the Bible.

ROSE. We ain't talking about what's in the Bible. What sense it make to shop there when she overcharge?

TROY. You shop where you want to. I'll do my shopping where the people been good to me.

ROSE. Well, I don't think it's right for her to overcharge. That's all I was saying.

BONO. Look here . . . I got to get on. Lucille going be raising all kind of hell.

TROY. Where you going, nigger? We ain't finished this pint. Come here, finish this pint.

BONO. Well, hell, I am . . . if you ever turn the bottle loose.

TROY. [*Hands him the bottle.*] The only thing I say about the A&P is I'm glad Cory got that job down there. Help him take care of his school clothes and things. Gabe done moved out and things getting tight around here. He got that job. . . . He can start to look out for himself.

ROSE. Cory done went and got recruited by a college football team.

TROY. I told that boy about that football stuff. The white man ain't gonna let him get nowhere with that football. I told him when he first come to me with it. Now you come telling me he done went and got more tied up in it. He ought to go and get recruited in how to fix cars or something where he can make a living.

ROSE. He ain't talking about making no living playing football. It's just something the boys in school do. They gonna send a recruiter by to talk to you. He'll tell you he ain't talking about making no living playing football. It's a honor to be recruited.

TROY. It ain't gonna get him nowhere. Bono'll tell you that.

BONO. If he be like you in the sports . . . he's gonna be alright. Ain't but two men ever played baseball as good as you. That's Babe Ruth and Josh Gibson.[2] Them's the only two men ever hit more home runs than you.

TROY. What it ever get me? Ain't got a pot to piss in or a window to throw it out of.

ROSE. Times have changed since you was playing baseball, Troy. That was before the war. Times have changed a lot since then.

TROY. How in hell they done changed?

ROSE. They got lots of colored boys playing ball now. Baseball and football.

---

2. Negro National Baseball League catcher (1911–1947), elected to the Baseball Hall of Fame. George Herman "Babe" Ruth (1895–1948), pitcher for the Boston Red Sox and outfielder for the New York Yankees; he hit 714 home runs, played in ten World Series, set fifty-four Major League records, and was elected to the Baseball Hall of Fame.

BONO. You right about that, Rose. Times have changed, Troy. You just come along too early.

TROY. There ought not never have been no time called too early! Now you take that fellow . . . what's that fellow they had playing right field for the Yankees back then? You know who I'm talking about, Bono. Used to play right field for the Yankees.

ROSE. Selkirk?[3]

TROY. Selkirk! That's it! Man batting .269, understand? .269. What kind of sense that make? I was hitting .432 with thirty-seven home runs! Man batting .269 and playing right field for the Yankees! I saw Josh Gibson's daughter yesterday. She walking around with raggedy shoes on her feet. Now I bet you Selkirk's daughter ain't walking around with raggedy shoes on her feet! I bet you that!

ROSE. They got a lot of colored baseball players now. Jackie Robinson[4] was the first. Folks had to wait for Jackie Robinson.

TROY. I done seen a hundred niggers play baseball better than Jackie Robinson. Hell, I know some teams Jackie Robinson couldn't even make! What you talking about Jackie Robinson. Jackie Robinson wasn't nobody. I'm talking about if you could play ball then they ought to have let you play. Don't care what color you were. Come telling me I come along too early. If you could play . . . then they ought to have let you play.

[TROY *takes a long drink from the bottle.*]

ROSE. You gonna drink yourself to death. You don't need to be drinking like that.

TROY. Death ain't nothing. I done seen him. Done wrassled with him. You can't tell me nothing about death. Death ain't nothing but a fastball on the outside corner. And you know what I'll do to that! Lookee here, Bono . . . am I lying? You get one of them fastballs, about waist high, over the outside corner of the plate where you can get the meat of the bat on it . . . and good god! You can kiss it goodbye. Now, am I lying?

BONO. Naw, you telling the truth there. I seen you do it.

TROY. If I'm lying . . . that 450 feet worth of lying!

[*Pause.*]

That's all death is to me. A fastball on the outside corner.

ROSE. I don't know why you want to get on talking about death.

TROY. Ain't nothing wrong with talking about death. That's part of life. Everybody gonna die. You gonna die, I'm gonna die. Bono's gonna die. Hell, we all gonna die.

ROSE. But you ain't got to talk about it. I don't like to talk about it.

TROY. You the one brought it up. Me and Bono was talking about baseball . . . you tell me I'm gonna drink myself to death. Ain't that right, Bono? You know I don't drink this but one night out of the week. That's Friday night. I'm gonna drink just enough to where I can handle it. Then I cuts it loose. I leave it alone. So don't you worry about me drinking myself to death. 'Cause I ain't worried about Death. I done seen him. I done wrestled with him.

3. George A. "Twinkletoes" Selkirk (1908–1987), American baseball player.
4. First African American player in the Major Leagues (1919–1972), played second base for the Brooklyn Dodgers and was elected to the Baseball Hall of Fame.

Look here, Bono . . . I looked up one day and Death was marching straight at me. Like Soldiers on Parade! The Army of Death was marching straight at me. The middle of July, 1941. It got real cold just like it be winter. It seem like Death himself reached out and touched me on the shoulder. He touch me just like I touch you. I got cold as ice and Death standing there grinning at me.

ROSE.   Troy, why don't you hush that talk.

TROY.   I say . . . What you want, Mr. Death? You be wanting me? You done brought your army to be getting me? I looked him dead in the eye. I wasn't fearing nothing. I was ready to tangle. Just like I'm ready to tangle now. The Bible say be ever vigilant. That's why I don't get but so drunk. I got to keep watch.

ROSE.   Troy was right down there in Mercy Hospital. You remember he had pneumonia? Laying there with a fever talking plumb out of his head.

TROY.   Death standing there staring at me . . . carrying that sickle in his hand. Finally he say, "You want bound over for another year?" See, just like that . . . "You want bound over for another year?" I told him, "Bound over hell! Let's settle this now!"
It seem like he kinda fell back when I said that, and all the cold went out of me. I reached down and grabbed that sickle and threw it just as far as I could throw it . . . and me and him commenced to wrestling.
We wrestled for three days and three nights. I can't say where I found the strength from. Every time it seemed like he was gonna get the best of me, I'd reach way down deep inside myself and find the strength to do him one better.

ROSE.   Every time Troy tell that story he find different ways to tell it. Different things to make up about it.

TROY.   I ain't making up nothing. I'm telling you the facts of what happened. I wrestled with Death for three days and three nights and I'm standing here to tell you about it.
      [Pause.]
Alright. At the end of the third night we done weakened each other to where we can't hardly move. Death stood up, throwed on his robe . . . had him a white robe with a hood on it. He throwed on that robe and went off to look for his sickle. Say, "I'll be back." Just like that. "I'll be back." I told him, say, "Yeah, but . . . you gonna have to find me!" I wasn't no fool. I wasn't going looking for him. Death ain't nothing to play with. And I know he's gonna get me. I know I got to join his army . . . his camp followers. But as long as I keep my strength and see him coming . . . as long as I keep up my vigilance . . . he's gonna have to fight to get me. I ain't going easy.

BONO.   Well, look here, since you got to keep up your vigilance . . . let me have the bottle.

TROY.   Aw hell, I shouldn't have told you that part. I should have left out that part.

ROSE.   Troy be talking that stuff and half the time don't even know what he be talking about.

TROY.   Bono know me better than that.

BONO.   That's right. I know you. I know you got some Uncle Remus[5] in your blood. You got more stories than the devil got sinners.

TROY.   Aw hell, I done seen him too! Done talked with the devil.

ROSE.   Troy, don't nobody wanna be hearing all that stuff.

[LYONS *enters the yard from the street. Thirty-four years old,* TROY'S *son by a previous marriage, he sports a neatly trimmed goatee, sport coat, white shirt, tieless and buttoned at the collar. Though he fancies himself a musician, he is more caught up in the rituals and "idea" of being a musician than in the actual practice of the music. He has come to borrow money from* TROY, *and while he knows he will be successful, he is uncertain as to what extent his lifestyle will be held up to scrutiny and ridicule.*]

LYONS.   Hey, Pop.

TROY.   What you come "Hey, Popping" me for?

LYONS.   How you doing, Rose?

[*He kisses her.*]

Mr. Bono. How you doing?

BONO.   Hey, Lyons . . . how you been?

TROY.   He must have been doing alright. I ain't seen him around here last week.

ROSE.   Troy, leave your boy alone. He come by to see you and you wanna start all that nonsense.

TROY.   I ain't bothering Lyons.

[*Offers him the bottle.*]

Here . . . get you a drink. We got an understanding. I know why he come by to see me and he know I know.

LYONS.   Come on, Pop . . . I just stopped by to say hi . . . see how you was doing.

TROY.   You ain't stopped by yesterday.

ROSE.   You gonna stay for supper, Lyons? I got some chicken cooking in the oven.

LYONS.   No, Rose . . . thanks. I was just in the neighborhood and thought I'd stop by for a minute.

TROY.   You was in the neighborhood alright, nigger. You telling the truth there. You was in the neighborhood cause it's my payday.

LYONS.   Well, hell, since you mentioned it . . . let me have ten dollars.

TROY.   I'll be damned! I'll die and go to hell and play blackjack with the devil before I give you ten dollars.

BONO.   That's what I wanna know about . . . that devil you done seen.

LYONS.   What . . . Pop done seen the devil? You too much, Pops.

TROY.   Yeah, I done seen him. Talked to him too!

ROSE.   You ain't seen no devil. I done told you that man ain't had nothing to do with the devil. Anything you can't understand, you want to call it the devil.

5. Slave and folk philosopher whose stories and proverbs were recorded by Joel Chandler Harris (1848–1908).

TROY.   Look here, Bono . . . I went down to see Hertzberger about some furniture. Got three rooms for two-ninety-eight. That what it say on the radio. "Three rooms . . . two-ninety-eight." Even made up a little song about it. Go down there . . . man tell me I can't get no credit. I'm working every day and can't get no credit. What to do? I got an empty house with some raggedy furniture in it. Cory ain't got no bed. He's sleeping on a pile of rags on the floor. Working every day and can't get no credit. Come back here—Rose'll tell you—madder than hell. Sit down . . . try to figure what I'm gonna do. Come a knock on the door. Ain't been living here but three days. Who know I'm here? Open the door . . . devil standing there bigger than life. White fellow . . . got on good clothes and everything. Standing there with a clipboard in his hand. I ain't had to say nothing. First words come out of his mouth was . . . "I understand you need some furniture and can't get no credit." I liked to fell over. He say "I'll give you all the credit you want, but you got to pay the interest on it." I told him, "Give me three rooms worth and charge whatever you want." Next day a truck pulled up here and two men unloaded them three rooms. Man what drove the truck give me a book. Say send ten dollars, first of every month to the address in the book and everything will be alright. Say if I miss a payment the devil was coming back and it'll be hell to pay. That was fifteen years ago. To this day . . . the first of the month I send my ten dollars, Rose'll tell you.

ROSE.   Troy lying.

TROY.   I ain't never seen that man since. Now you tell me who else that could have been but the devil? I ain't sold my soul or nothing like that, you understand. Naw, I wouldn't have truck with the devil about nothing like that. I got my furniture and pays my ten dollars the first of the month just like clockwork.

BONO.   How long you say you been paying this ten dollars a month?

TROY.   Fifteen years!

BONO.   Hell, ain't you finished paying for it yet? How much the man done charged you.

TROY.   Aw hell, I done paid for it. I done paid for it ten times over! The fact is I'm scared to stop paying it.

ROSE.   Troy lying. We got that furniture from Mr. Glickman. He ain't paying no ten dollars a month to nobody.

TROY.   Aw hell, woman. Bono know I ain't that big a fool.

LYONS.   I was just getting ready to say . . . I know where there's a bridge for sale.

TROY.   Look here, I'll tell you this . . . it don't matter to me if he was the devil. It don't matter if the devil give credit. Somebody has got to give it.

ROSE.   It ought to matter. You going around talking about having truck with the devil . . . God's the one you gonna have to answer to. He's the one gonna be at the Judgment.

LYONS.   Yeah, well, look here, Pop . . . let me have that ten dollars. I'll give it back to you. Bonnie got a job working at the hospital.

TROY.   What I tell you, Bono? The only time I see this nigger is when he wants something. That's the only time I see him.

LYONS.   Come on, Pop, Mr. Bono don't want to hear all that. Let me have the ten dollars. I told you Bonnie working.

TROY.   What that mean to me? "Bonnie working." I don't care if she working. Go ask her for the ten dollars if she working. Talking about "Bonnie working." Why ain't you working?

LYONS.   Aw, Pop, you know I can't find no decent job. Where am I gonna get a job at? You know I can't get no job.

TROY.   I told you I know some people down there. I can get you on the rubbish if you want to work. I told you that the last time you came by here asking me for something.

LYONS.   Naw, Pop . . . thanks. That ain't for me. I don't wanna be carrying nobody's rubbish. I don't wanna be punching nobody's time clock.

TROY.   What's the matter, you too good to carry people's rubbish? Where you think that ten dollars you talking about come from? I'm just supposed to haul people's rubbish and give my money to you cause you too lazy to work. You too lazy to work and wanna know why you ain't got what I got.

ROSE.   What hospital Bonnie working at? Mercy?

LYONS.   She's down at Passavant working in the laundry.

TROY.   I ain't got nothing as it is. I give you that ten dollars and I got to eat beans the rest of the week. Naw . . . you ain't getting no ten dollars here.

LYONS.   You ain't got to be eating no beans. I don't know why you wanna say that.

TROY.   I ain't got no extra money. Gabe done moved over to Miss Pearl's paying her the rent and things done got tight around here. I can't afford to be giving you every payday.

LYONS.   I ain't asked you to give me nothing. I asked you to loan me ten dollars. I know you got ten dollars.

TROY.   Yeah, I got it. You know why I got it? Cause I don't throw my money away out there in the streets. You living the fast life . . . wanna be a musician . . . running around in them clubs and things . . . then, you learn to take care of yourself. You ain't gonna find me going and asking nobody for nothing. I done spent too many years without.

LYONS.   You and me is two different people, Pop.

TROY.   I done learned my mistake and learned to do what's right by it. You still trying to get something for nothing. Life don't owe you nothing. You owe it to yourself. Ask Bono. He'll tell you I'm right.

LYONS.   You got your way of dealing with the world . . . I got mine. The only thing that matters to me is the music.

TROY.   Yeah, I can see that! It don't matter how you gonna eat . . . where your next dollar is coming from. You telling the truth there.

LYONS.   I know I got to eat. But I got to live too. I need something that gonna help me to get out of the bed in the morning. Make me feel like I belong in the world. I don't bother nobody. I just stay with my music cause that's the only way I can find to live in the world. Otherwise there ain't no telling what I might do. Now I don't come criticizing you and how you live. I just come by to ask you for ten dollars. I don't wanna hear all that about how I live.

TROY.   Boy, your mama did a hell of a job raising you.

LYONS.   You can't change me, Pop. I'm thirty-four years old. If you wanted
to change me, you should have been there when I was growing up. I
come by to see you . . . ask for ten dollars and you want to talk about how
I was raised. You don't know nothing about how I was raised.

ROSE.   Let the boy have ten dollars, Troy.

TROY.   [To LYONS.] What the hell you looking at me for? I ain't got no ten
dollars. You know what I do with my money.
    [To ROSE.]
Give him ten dollars if you want him to have it.

ROSE.   I will. Just as soon as you turn it loose.

TROY.   [Handing ROSE the money.] There it is. Seventy-six dollars and
forty-two cents. You see this, Bono? Now, I ain't gonna get but six of that
back.

ROSE.   You ought to stop telling that lie. Here, Lyons.
    [She hands him the money.]

LYONS.   Thanks, Rose. Look . . . I got to run . . . I'll see you later.

TROY.   Wait a minute. You gonna say, "thanks, Rose" and ain't gonna
look to see where she got that ten dollars from? See how they do me,
Bono?

LYONS.   I know she got it from you, Pop. Thanks. I'll give it back to
you.

TROY.   There he go telling another lie. Time I see that ten dollars . . . he'll
be owing me thirty more.

LYONS.   See you, Mr. Bono.

BONO.   Take care, Lyons!

LYONS.   Thanks, Pop. I'll see you again.
    [LYONS exits the yard.]

TROY.   I don't know why he don't go and get him a decent job and take
care of that woman he got.

BONO.   He'll be alright, Troy. The boy is still young.

TROY.   The boy is thirty-four years old.

ROSE.   Let's not get off into all that.

BONO.   Look here . . . I got to be going. I got to be getting on. Lucille
gonna be waiting.

TROY.   [Puts his arm around ROSE.] See this woman, Bono? I love this
woman. I love this woman so much it hurts. I love her so much . . . I
done run out of ways of loving her. So I got to go back to basics. Don't
you come by my house Monday morning talking about time to go to
work . . . 'cause I'm still gonna be stroking!

ROSE.   Troy! Stop it now!

BONO.   I ain't paying him no mind, Rose. That ain't nothing but gin-talk.
Go on, Troy. I'll see you Monday.

TROY.   Don't you come by my house, nigger! I done told you what I'm
gonna be doing.
    [The lights go down to black.]

SCENE TWO

The lights come up on ROSE *hanging up clothes. She hums and sings softly to herself. It is the following morning.*

ROSE. [*Sings.*] Jesus, be a fence all around me every day
          Jesus, I want you to protect me as I travel on my way.
          Jesus, be a fence all around me every day.
          [TROY *enters from the house.*]
ROSE. [*Continued.*] Jesus, I want you to protect me
                    As I travel on my way.
          [*To* TROY.]
    'Morning. You ready for breakfast? I can fix it soon as I finish hanging up
    these clothes?
TROY.   I got the coffee on. That'll be alright. I'll just drink some of that this
    morning.
ROSE.   That 651 hit yesterday. That's the second time this month. Miss
    Pearl hit for a dollar . . . seem like those that need the least always get
    lucky. Poor folks can't get nothing.
TROY.   Them numbers don't know nobody. I don't know why you fool
    with them. You and Lyons both.
ROSE.   It's something to do.
TROY.   You ain't doing nothing but throwing your money away.
ROSE.   Troy, you know I don't play foolishly. I just play a nickel here and a
    nickel there.
TROY.   That's two nickels you done thrown away.
ROSE.   Now I hit sometimes . . . that makes up for it. It always comes in
    handy when I do hit. I don't hear you complaining then.
TROY.   I ain't complaining now. I just say it's foolish. Trying to guess out of
    six hundred ways which way the number gonna come. If I had all the
    money niggers, these Negroes, throw away on numbers for one week—
    just one week—I'd be a rich man.
ROSE.   Well, you wishing and calling it foolish ain't gonna stop folks from
    playing numbers. That's one thing for sure. Besides . . . some good things
    come from playing numbers. Look where Pope done bought him that
    restaurant off of numbers.
TROY.   I can't stand niggers like that. Man ain't had two dimes to rub to-
    gether. He walking around with his shoes all run over bumming money
    for cigarettes. Alright. Got lucky there and hit the numbers . . .
ROSE.   Troy, I know all about it.
TROY.   Had good sense, I'll say that for him. He ain't throwed his money
    away. I seen niggers hit the numbers and go through two thousand dol-
    lars in four days. Man brought him that restaurant down there . . . fixed it
    up real nice . . . and then didn't want nobody to come in it! A Negro go
    in there and can't get no kind of service. I seen a white fellow come in
    there and order a bowl of stew. Pope picked all the meat out the pot for
    him. Man ain't had nothing but a bowl of meat! Negro come behind
    him and ain't got nothing but the potatoes and carrots. Talking about

what numbers do for people, you picked a wrong example. Ain't done nothing but make a worser fool out of him than he was before.

ROSE. Troy, you ought to stop worrying about what happened at work yesterday.

TROY. I ain't worried. Just told me to be down there at the Commissioner's office on Friday. Everybody think they gonna fire me. I ain't worried about them firing me. You ain't got to worry about that.

[*Pause.*]

Where's Cory? Cory in the house? [*Calls.*] Cory?

ROSE. He gone out.

TROY. Out, huh? He gone out 'cause he know I want him to help me with this fence. I know how he is. That boy scared of work.

[GABRIEL *enters. He comes halfway down the alley and, hearing* TROY's *voice, stops.*]

TROY. [*Continues.*] He ain't done a lick of work in his life.

ROSE. He had to go to football practice. Coach wanted them to get in a little extra practice before the season start.

TROY. I got his practice . . . running out of here before he get his chores done.

ROSE. Troy, what is wrong with you this morning? Don't nothing set right with you. Go on back in there and go to bed . . . get up on the other side.

TROY. Why something got to be wrong with me? I ain't said nothing wrong with me.

ROSE. You got something to say about everything. First it's the numbers . . . then it's the way the man runs his restaurant . . . then you done got on Cory. What's it gonna be next? Take a look up there and see if the weather suits you . . . or is it gonna be how you gonna put up the fence with the clothes hanging in the yard.

TROY. You hit the nail on the head then.

ROSE. I know you like I know the back of my hand. Go on in there and get you some coffee . . . see if that straighten you up. 'Cause you ain't right this morning.

[TROY *starts into the house and sees* GABRIEL. GABRIEL *starts singing.* TROY's *brother, he is seven years younger than* TROY. *Injured in World War II, he has a metal plate in his head. He carries an old trumpet tied around his waist and believes with every fiber of his being that he is the Archangel Gabriel.*[6] *He carries a chipped basket with an assortment of discarded fruits and vegetables he has picked up in the strip district and which he attempts to sell.*]

GABRIEL. [*Singing.*]

Yes, ma'am, I got plums
You ask me how I sell them
Oh ten cents apiece
Three for a quarter
Come and buy now

---

6. The divine messenger of God, seen in Christian tradition as the trumpeter of the Last Judgment.

'Cause I'm here today
And tomorrow I'll be gone
　　　[GABRIEL *enters.*]
　Hey, Rose!
ROSE.　How you doing, Gabe?
GABRIEL.　There's Troy . . . Hey, Troy!
TROY.　Hey, Gabe.
　　　[*Exit into kitchen.*]
ROSE.　[*To* GABRIEL.] What you got there?
GABRIEL.　You know what I got, Rose. I got fruits and vegetables.
ROSE.　[*Looking in basket.*] Where's all these plums you talking about?
GABRIEL.　I ain't got no plums today, Rose. I was just singing that. Have
　some tomorrow. Put me in a big order for plums. Have enough plums
　tomorrow for St. Peter and everybody.
　　　[TROY *re-enters from kitchen, crosses to steps.*]
　　　[*To* ROSE.]
　Troy's mad at me.
TROY.　I ain't mad at you. What I got to be mad at you about? You ain't
　done nothing to me.
GABRIEL.　I just moved over to Miss Pearl's to keep out from in your way. I
　ain't mean no harm by it.
TROY.　Who said anything about that? I ain't said anything about that.
GABRIEL.　You ain't mad at me, is you?
TROY.　Naw . . . I ain't mad at you, Gabe. If I was mad at you I'd tell you
　about it.
GABRIEL.　Got me two rooms. In the basement. Got my own door too.
　Wanna see my key?
　　　[*He holds up a key.*]
　That's my own key! Ain't nobody else got a key like that. That's my key!
　My two rooms!
TROY.　Well, that's good, Gabe. You got your own key . . . that's good.
ROSE.　You hungry, Gabe? I was just fixing to cook Troy his breakfast.
GABRIEL.　I'll take some biscuits. You got some biscuits? Did you know
　when I was in heaven . . . every morning me and St. Peter would sit
　down by the gate and eat some big fat biscuits? Oh, yeah! We had us a
　good time. We'd sit there and eat us them biscuits and then St. Peter
　would go off to sleep and tell me to wake him up when it's time to open
　the gates for the judgment.
ROSE.　Well, come on . . . I'll make up a batch of biscuits.
　　　[ROSE *exits into the house.*]
GABRIEL.　Troy . . . St. Peter got your name in the book. I seen it. It
　say . . . Troy Maxon. I say . . . I know him! He got the same name like
　what I got. That's my brother!
TROY.　How many times you gonna tell me that, Gabe?
GABRIEL.　Ain't got my name in the book. Don't have to have my name. I
　done died and went to heaven. He got your name though. One morning
　St. Peter was looking at his book . . . marking it up for the judgment
　. . . and he let me see your name. Got it in there under M. Got Rose's
　name . . . I ain't seen it like I seen yours . . . but I know it's in there. He

got a great big book. Got everybody's name what was ever been born. That's what he told me. But I seen your name. Seen it with my own eyes.

TROY.   Go on in the house there. Rose going to fix you something to eat.

GABRIEL.   Oh, I ain't hungry. I done had breakfast with Aunt Jemimah. She come by and cooked me up a whole mess of flapjacks. Remember how we used to eat them flapjacks?

TROY.   Go on in the house and get you something to eat now.

GABRIEL.   I got to go sell my plums. I done sold some tomatoes. Got me two quarters. Wanna see?

[He shows TROY his quarters.]

I'm gonna save them and buy me a new horn so St. Peter can hear me when it's time to open the gates.

[GABRIEL stops suddenly. Listens.]

Hear that? That's the hellhounds. I got to chase them out of here. Go on get out of here! Get out!

[GABRIEL exits singing.]

Better get ready for the judgment
Better get ready for the judgment
My Lord is coming down

[ROSE enters from the house.]

TROY.   He gone off somewhere.

GABRIEL.   [Offstage.]

Better get ready for the judgment
Better get ready for the judgment morning
Better get ready for the judgment
My God is coming down

ROSE.   He ain't eating right. Miss Pearl say she can't get him to eat nothing.

TROY.   What you want me to do about it, Rose? I done did everything I can for the man. I can't make him get well. Man got half his head blown away . . . what you expect?

ROSE.   Seem like something ought to be done to help him.

TROY.   Man don't bother nobody. He just mixed up from that metal plate he got in his head. Ain't no sense for him to go back into the hospital.

ROSE.   Least he be eating right. They can help him take care of himself.

TROY.   Don't nobody wanna be locked up, Rose. What you wanna lock him up for? Man go over there and fight the war . . . messin' around with them Japs, get half his head blown off . . . and they give him a lousy three thousand dollars. And I had to swoop down on that.

ROSE.   Is you fixing to go into that again?

TROY.   That's the only way I got a roof over my head . . . cause of that metal plate.

ROSE.   Ain't no sense you blaming yourself for nothing. Gabe wasn't in no condition to manage that money. You done what was right by him. Can't nobody say you ain't done what was right by him. Look how long you took care of him . . . till he wanted to have his own place and moved over there with Miss Pearl.

TROY.   That ain't what I'm saying, woman! I'm just stating the facts. If my brother didn't have that metal plate in his head . . . I wouldn't have a pot to piss in or a window to throw it out of. And I'm fifty-three years old. Now see if you can understand that!

[TROY *gets up from the porch and starts to exit the yard.*]

ROSE. Where you going off to? You been running out of here every Saturday for weeks. I thought you was gonna work on this fence?

TROY. I'm gonna walk down to Taylors'. Listen to the ball game. I'll be back in a bit. I'll work on it when I get back.

[*He exits the yard. The lights go to black.*]

SCENE THREE

The lights come up on the yard. It is four hours later. ROSE *is taking down the clothes from the line.* CORY *enters carrying his football equipment.*

ROSE. Your daddy like to had a fit with you running out of here this morning without doing your chores.

CORY. I told you I had to go to practice.

ROSE. He say you were supposed to help him with this fence.

CORY. He been saying that the last four or five Saturdays, and then he don't never do nothing, but go down to Taylors'. Did you tell him about the recruiter?

ROSE. Yeah, I told him.

CORY. What he say?

ROSE. He ain't said nothing too much. You get in there and get started on your chores before he gets back. Go on and scrub down them steps before he gets back here hollering and carrying on.

CORY. I'm hungry. What you got to eat, Mama?

ROSE. Go on and get started on your chores. I got some meat loaf in there. Go on and make you a sandwich . . . and don't leave no mess in there.

[CORY *exits into the house.* ROSE *continues to take down the clothes.* TROY *enters the yard and sneaks up and grabs her from behind.*]

Troy! Go on, now. You liked to scared me to death. What was the score of the game? Lucille had me on the phone and I couldn't keep up with it.

TROY. What I care about the game? Come here, woman.

[*He tries to kiss her.*]

ROSE. I thought you went down Taylors' to listen to the game. Go on, Troy! You supposed to be putting up this fence.

TROY. [*Attempting to kiss her again.*] I'll put it up when I finish with what is at hand.

ROSE. Go on, Troy. I ain't studying you.

TROY. [*Chasing after her.*] I'm studying you . . . fixing to do my homework!

ROSE. Troy, you better leave me alone.

TROY. Where's Cory? That boy brought his butt home yet?

ROSE. He's in the house doing his chores.

TROY. [*Calling.*] Cory! Get your butt out here, boy!

[ROSE *exits into the house with the laundry.* TROY *goes over to the pile of wood, picks up a board, and starts sawing.* CORY *enters from the house.*]

TROY.   You just now coming in here from leaving this morning?

CORY.   Yeah, I had to go to football practice.

TROY.   Yeah, what?

CORY.   Yessir.

TROY.   I ain't but two seconds off you noway. The garbage sitting in there overflowing . . . you ain't done none of your chores . . . and you come in here talking about "Yeah."

CORY.   I was just getting ready to do my chores now, Pop . . .

TROY.   Your first chore is to help me with this fence on Saturday. Everything else come after that. Now get that saw and cut them boards.

[CORY *takes the saw and begins cutting the boards.* TROY *continues working. There is a long pause.*]

CORY.   Hey, Pop . . . why don't you buy a TV?

TROY.   What I want with a TV? What I want one of them for?

CORY.   Everybody got one. Earl, Ba Bra . . . Jesse!

TROY.   I ain't asked you who had one. I say what I want with one?

CORY.   So you can watch it. They got lots of things on TV. Baseball games and everything. We could watch the World Series.

TROY.   Yeah . . . and how much this TV cost?

CORY.   I don't know. They got them on sale for around two hundred dollars.

TROY.   Two hundred dollars, huh?

CORY.   That ain't that much, Pop.

TROY.   Naw, it's just two hundred dollars. See that roof you got over your head at night? Let me tell you something about that roof. It's been over ten years since that roof was last tarred. See now . . . the snow come this winter and sit up there on that roof like it is . . . and it's gonna seep inside. It's just gonna be a little bit . . . ain't gonna hardly notice it. Then the next thing you know, it's gonna be leaking all over the house. Then the wood rot from all that water and you gonna need a whole new roof. Now, how much you think it cost to get that roof tarred?

CORY.   I don't know.

TROY.   Two hundred and sixty-four dollars . . . cash money. While you thinking about a TV, I got to be thinking about the roof . . . and whatever else go wrong around here. Now if you had two hundred dollars, what would you do . . . fix the roof or buy a TV?

CORY.   I'd buy a TV. Then when the roof started to leak . . . when it needed fixing . . . I'd fix it.

TROY.   Where you gonna get the money from? You done spent it for a TV. You gonna sit up and watch the water run all over your brand new TV.

CORY.   Aw, Pop. You got money. I know you do.

TROY.   Where I got it at, huh?

CORY.   You got it in the bank.

TROY.   You wanna see my bankbook? You wanna see that seventy-three dollars and twenty-two cents I got sitting up in there.

CORY.   You ain't got to pay for it all at one time. You can put a down payment on it and carry it on home with you.

TROY.   Not me. I ain't gonna owe nobody nothing if I can help it. Miss a payment and they come and snatch it right out your house. Then what you got? Now, soon as I get two hundred dollars clear, then I'll buy a TV. Right now, as soon as I get two hundred and sixty-four dollars, I'm gonna have this roof tarred.

CORY.   Aw . . . Pop!

TROY.   You go on and get you two hundred dollars and buy one if ya want it. I got better things to do with my money.

CORY.   I can't get no two hundred dollars. I ain't never seen two hundred dollars.

TROY.   I'll tell you what . . . you get you a hundred dollars and I'll put the other hundred with it.

CORY.   Alright, I'm gonna show you.

TROY.   You gonna show me how you can cut them boards right now.

[CORY *begins to cut the boards. There is a long pause.*]

CORY.   The Pirates won today. That makes five in a row.

TROY.   I ain't thinking about the Pirates. Got an all-white team. Got that boy . . . that Puerto Rican boy . . . Clemente.[7] Don't even half-play him. That boy could be something if they give him a chance. Play him one day and sit him on the bench the next.

CORY.   He gets a lot of chances to play.

TROY.   I'm talking about playing regular. Playing every day so you can get your timing. That's what I'm talking about.

CORY.   They got some white guys on the team that don't play every day. You can't play everybody at the same time.

TROY.   If they got a white fellow sitting on the bench . . . you can bet your last dollar he can't play! The colored guy got to be twice as good before he get on the team. That's why I don't want you to get all tied up in them sports. Man on the team and what it get him? They got colored on the team and don't use them. Same as not having them. All them teams the same.

CORY.   The Braves got Hank Aaron and Wes Covington.[8] Hank Aaron hit two home runs today. That makes forty-three.

TROY.   Hank Aaron ain't nobody. That's what you supposed to do. That's how you supposed to play the game. Ain't nothing to it. It's just a matter of timing . . . getting the right follow-through. Hell, I can hit forty-three home runs right now!

CORY.   Not off no major-league pitching, you couldn't.

TROY.   We had better pitching in the Negro leagues. I hit seven home runs off of Satchel Paige.[9] You can't get no better than that!

CORY.   Sandy Koufax.[1] He's leading the league in strikeouts.

TROY.   I ain't thinking of no Sandy Koufax.

CORY.   You got Warren Spahn and Lew Burdette.[2] I bet you couldn't hit no home runs off of Warren Spahn.

TROY.   I'm through with it now. You go on and cut them boards.

[*Pause.*]

---

7. Roberto Clemente Walker (1934–1972), eighteen-year right fielder for the Pittsburgh Pirates; died in a plane crash while ferrying aid to Nicaraguan earthquake victims.
8. Players for the Atlanta Braves. Aaron (b. 1934) hit 755 home runs.

9. Baseball player (1906–1982), first African American pitcher in the American League (1948).
1. American baseball player (b. 1935), star pitcher for the Dodgers (1955–1966).
2. Spahn (b. 1921) and Burdette (b. 1926), American baseball players.

Your mama tell me you done got recruited by a college football team? Is
that right?

CORY.   Yeah. Coach Zellman say the recruiter gonna be coming by to talk
to you. Get you to sign the permission papers.

TROY.   I thought you supposed to be working down there at the A&P. Ain't
you suppose to be working down there after school?

CORY.   Mr. Stawicki say he gonna hold my job for me until after the football season. Say starting next week I can work weekends.

TROY.   I thought we had an understanding about this football stuff? You
suppose to keep up with your chores and hold that job down at the A&P.
Ain't been around here all day on a Saturday. Ain't none of your chores
done . . . and now you telling me you done quit your job.

CORY.   I'm gonna be working weekends.

TROY.   You damn right you are! And ain't no need for nobody coming
around here to talk to me about signing nothing.

CORY.   Hey, Pop . . . you can't do that. He's coming all the way from North
Carolina.

TROY.   I don't care where he coming from. The white man ain't gonna let
you get nowhere with that football noway. You go on and get your book-
learning so you can work yourself up in that A&P or learn how to fix cars
or build houses or something, get you a trade. That way you have something can't nobody take away from you. You go on and learn how to put
your hands to some good use. Besides hauling people's garbage.

CORY.   I get good grades, Pop. That's why the recruiter wants to talk with
you. You got to keep up your grades to get recruited. This way I'll be
going to college. I'll get a chance . . .

TROY.   First you gonna get your butt down there to the A&P and get your
job back.

CORY.   Mr. Stawicki done already hired somebody else 'cause I told him I
was playing football.

TROY.   You a bigger fool than I thought . . . to let somebody take away your
job so you can play some football. Where you gonna get your money to
take out your girlfriend and whatnot? What kind of foolishness is that to
let somebody take away your job?

CORY.   I'm still gonna be working weekends.

TROY.   Naw . . . naw. You getting your butt out of here and finding you
another job.

CORY.   Come on, Pop! I got to practice. I can't work after school and play
football too. The team needs me. That's what Coach Zellman say . . .

TROY.   I don't care what nobody else say. I'm the boss . . . you understand?
I'm the boss around here. I do the only saying what counts.

CORY.   Come on, Pop!

TROY.   I asked you . . . did you understand?

CORY.   Yeah . . .

TROY.   What?!

CORY.   Yessir.

TROY.   You go on down there to that A&P and see if you can get your job
back. If you can't do both . . . then you quit the football team. You've got
to take the crookeds with the straights.

CORY.   Yessir.
    [*Pause.*]
    Can I ask you a question?
TROY.   What the hell you wanna ask me? Mr. Stawicki the one you got the
    questions for.
CORY.   How come you ain't never liked me?
TROY.   Liked you? Who the hell say I got to like you? What law is there say
    I got to like you? Wanna stand up in my face and ask a damn fool-ass
    question like that. Talking about liking somebody. Come here, boy,
    when I talk to you.
        [CORY *comes over to where* TROY *is working. He stands slouched over
        and* TROY *shoves him on his shoulder.*]
    Straighten up, goddammit! I asked you a question . . . what law is there
    say I got to like you?
CORY.   None.
TROY.   Well, alright then! Don't you eat every day?
    [*Pause.*]
    Answer me when I talk to you! Don't you eat every day?
CORY.   Yeah.
TROY.   Nigger, as long as you in my house, you put that sir on the end of it
    when you talk to me!
CORY.   Yes . . . sir.
TROY.   You eat every day.
CORY.   Yessir!
TROY.   Got a roof over your head.
CORY.   Yessir!
TROY.   Got clothes on your back.
CORY.   Yessir.
TROY.   Why you think that is?
CORY.   Cause of you.
TROY.   Aw, hell I know it's 'cause of me . . . but why do you think that is?
CORY.   [*Hesitant.*] Cause you like me.
TROY.   Like you? I go out of here every morning . . . bust my butt . . .
    putting up with them crackers[3] every day . . . cause I like you? You about
    the biggest fool I ever saw.
    [*Pause.*]
    It's my job. It's my responsibility! You understand that? A man got to take
    care of his family. You live in my house . . . sleep you behind on my
    bedclothes . . . fill you belly up with my food . . . cause you my son. You
    my flesh and blood. Not 'cause I like you! Cause it's my duty to take care
    of you. I owe a responsibility to you! Let's get this straight right here . . .
    before it go along any further . . . I ain't got to like you. Mr. Rand don't
    give me my money come payday cause he likes me. He gives me cause
    he owe me. I done give you everything I had to give you. I gave you your
    life! Me and your mama worked that out between us. And liking your
    black ass wasn't part of the bargain. Don't you try and go through life

---

3. Disparaging term for poor white people, especially of the rural southeastern United States.

worrying about if somebody like you or not. You best be making sure they doing right by you. You understand what I'm saying, boy?

CORY. Yessir.

TROY. Then get the hell out of my face, and get on down to that A&P.

[ROSE *has been standing behind the screen door for much of the scene. She enters as* CORY *exits.*]

ROSE. Why don't you let the boy go ahead and play football, Troy? Ain't no harm in that. He's just trying to be like you with the sports.

TROY. I don't want him to be like me! I want him to move as far away from my life as he can get. You the only decent thing that ever happened to me. I wish him that. But I don't wish him a thing else from my life. I decided seventeen years ago that boy wasn't getting involved in no sports. Not after what they did to me in the sports.

ROSE. Troy, why don't you admit you was too old to play in the major leagues? For once . . . why don't you admit that?

TROY. What do you mean too old? Don't come telling me I was too old. I just wasn't the right color. Hell, I'm fifty-three years old and can do better than Selkirk's .269 right now!

ROSE. How's was you gonna play ball when you were over forty? Sometimes I can't get no sense out of you.

TROY. I got good sense, woman. I got sense enough not to let my boy get hurt over playing no sports. You been mothering that boy too much. Worried about if people like him.

ROSE. Everything that boy do . . . he do for you. He wants you to say "Good job, son." That's all.

TROY. Rose, I ain't got time for that. He's alive. He's healthy. He's got to make his own way. I made mine. Ain't nobody gonna hold his hand when he get out there in that world.

ROSE. Times have changed from when you was young, Troy. People change. The world's changing around you and you can't even see it.

TROY. [*Slow, methodical*] Woman . . . I do the best I can do. I come in here every Friday. I carry a sack of potatoes and a bucket of lard. You all line up at the door with your hands out. I give you the lint from my pockets. I give you my sweat and my blood. I ain't got no tears. I done spent them. We go upstairs in that room at night . . . and I fall down on you and try to blast a hole into forever. I get up Monday morning . . . find my lunch on the table. I go out. Make my way. Find my strength to carry me through to the next Friday.

[*Pause.*]

That's all I got, Rose. That's all I got to give. I can't give nothing else.

[TROY *exits into the house. The lights go down to black.*]

SCENE FOUR

It is Friday. Two weeks later. CORY *starts out of the house with his football equipment. The phone rings.*

CORY. [*Calling.*] I got it!

[*He answers the phone and stands in the screen door talking.*]

Hello? Hey, Jesse. Naw . . . I was just getting ready to leave now.

ROSE. [*Calling.*] Cory!

CORY. I told you, man, them spikes is all tore up. You can use them if you want, but they ain't no good. Earl got some spikes.

ROSE. [*Calling.*] Cory!

CORY. [*Calling to* ROSE.] Mam? I'm talking to Jesse.

[*Into phone.*]

When she say that? [*Pause.*] Aw, you lying, man. I'm gonna tell her you said that.

ROSE. [*Calling.*] Cory, don't you go nowhere!

CORY. I got to go to the game, Ma!

[*Into the phone.*]

Yeah, hey, look, I'll talk to you later. Yeah, I'll meet you over Earl's house. Later. Bye, Ma.

[CORY *exits the house and starts out the yard.*]

ROSE. Cory, where you going off to? You got that stuff all pulled out and thrown all over your room.

CORY. [*In the yard.*] I was looking for my spikes. Jesse wanted to borrow my spikes.

ROSE. Get up there and get that cleaned up before your daddy get back in here.

CORY. I got to go to the game! I'll clean it up *when I get back.*

[CORY *exits.*]

ROSE. That's all he need to do is see that room all messed up.

[ROSE *exits into the house.* TROY *and* BONO *enter the yard.* TROY *is dressed in clothes other than his work clothes.*]

BONO. He told him the same thing he told you. Take it to the union.

TROY. Brownie ain't got that much sense. Man wasn't thinking about nothing. He wait until I confront them on it . . . then he wanna come crying seniority.

[*Calls.*]

Hey, Rose!

BONO. I wish I could have seen Mr. Rand's face when he told you.

TROY. He couldn't get it out of his mouth! Liked to bit his tongue! When they called me down there to the Commissioner's office . . . he thought they was gonna fire me. Like everybody else.

BONO. I didn't think they was gonna fire you. I thought they was gonna put you on the warning paper.

TROY. Hey, Rose!

[*To* BONO.]

Yeah, Mr. Rand like to bit his tongue.

[TROY *breaks the seal on the bottle, takes a drink, and hands it to* BONO.]

BONO. I see you run right down to Taylors' and told that Alberta gal.

TROY. [*Calling.*] Hey Rose! [*To* BONO.] I told everybody. Hey, Rose! I went down there to cash my check.

ROSE. [*Entering from the house.*] Hush all that hollering, man! I know you out here. What they say down there at the Commissioner's office?

TROY.   You supposed to come when I call you, woman. Bono'll tell you that.

    [*To* BONO.]

Don't Lucille come when you call her?

ROSE.   Man, hush your mouth. I ain't no dog . . . talk about "come when you call me."

TROY.   [*Puts his arm around* ROSE.] You hear this, Bono? I had me an old dog used to get uppity like that. You say, "C'mere, Blue!" . . . and he just lay there and look at you. End up getting a stick and chasing him away trying to make him come.

ROSE.   I ain't studying you and your dog. I remember you used to sing that old song.

TROY.   [*He sings.*] Hear it ring! Hear it ring! I had a dog his name was Blue.

ROSE.   Don't nobody wanna hear you sing that old song.

TROY.   [*Sings.*] You know Blue was mighty true.

ROSE.   Used to have Cory running around here singing that song.

BONO.   Hell, I remember that song myself.

TROY.   [*Sings.*] You know Blue was a good old dog.

    Blue treed a possum in a hollow log.

  That was my daddy's song. My daddy made up that song.

ROSE.   I don't care who made it up. Don't nobody wanna hear you sing it.

TROY.   [*Makes a song like calling a dog.*] Come here, woman.

ROSE.   You come in here carrying on, I reckon they ain't fired you. What they say down there at the Commissioner's office?

TROY.   Look here, Rose . . . Mr. Rand called me into his office today when I got back from talking to them people down there . . . it come from up top . . . he called me in and told me they was making me a driver.

ROSE.   Troy, you kidding!

TROY.   No I ain't. Ask Bono.

ROSE.   Well, that's great, Troy. Now you don't have to hassle them people no more.

    [LYONS *enters from the street.*]

TROY.   Aw hell, I wasn't looking to see you today. I thought you was in jail. Got it all over the front page of the *Courier* about them raiding Sefus' place . . . where you be hanging out with all them thugs.

LYONS.   Hey, Pop . . . that ain't got nothing to do with me. I don't go down there gambling. I go down there to sit in with the band. I ain't got nothing to do with the gambling part. They got some good music down there.

TROY.   They got some rogues . . . is what they got.

LYONS.   How you been, Mr. Bono? Hi, Rose.

BONO.   I see where you playing down at the Crawford Grill tonight.

ROSE.   How come you ain't brought Bonnie like I told you. You should have brought Bonnie with you, she ain't been over in a month of Sundays.

LYONS.   I was just in the neighborhood . . . thought I'd stop by.

TROY.   Here he come . . .

BONO.   Your daddy got a promotion on the rubbish. He's gonna be the first colored driver. Ain't got to do nothing but sit up there and read the paper like them white fellows.

LYONS.   Hey, Pop . . . if you knew how to read you'd be alright.

BONO.   Naw . . . naw . . . you mean if the nigger knew how to *drive* he'd be all right. Been fighting with them people about driving and ain't even got a license. Mr. Rand know you ain't got no driver's license?

TROY.   Driving ain't nothing. All you do is point the truck where you want it to go. Driving ain't nothing.

BONO.   Do Mr. Rand know you ain't got no driver's license? That's what I'm talking about. I ain't asked if driving was easy. I asked if Mr. Rand know you ain't got no driver's license.

TROY.   He ain't got to know. The man ain't got to know my business. Time he find out, I have two or three driver's licenses.

LYONS.   [*Going into his pocket.*] Say, look here, Pop . . .

TROY.   I knew it was coming. Didn't I tell you, Bono? I know what kind of "Look here, Pop" that was. The nigger fixing to ask me for some money. It's Friday night. It's my payday. All them rogues down there on the avenue . . . the ones that ain't in jail . . . and Lyons is hopping in his shoes to get down there with them.

LYONS.   See, Pop . . . if you give somebody else a chance to talk sometime, you'd see that I was fixing to pay you back your ten dollars like I told you. Here . . . I told you I'd pay you when Bonnie got paid.

TROY.   Naw . . . you go ahead and keep that ten dollars. Put it in the bank. The next time you feel like you wanna come by here and ask me for something . . . you go on down there and get that.

LYONS.   Here's your ten dollars, Pop. I told you I don't want you to give me nothing. I just wanted to borrow ten dollars.

TROY.   Naw . . . you go on and keep that for the next time you want to ask me.

LYONS.   Come on, Pop . . . here go your ten dollars.

ROSE.   Why don't you go on and let the boy pay you back, Troy?

LYONS.   Here you go, Rose. If you don't take it I'm gonna have to hear about it for the next six months.

[*He hands her the money.*]

ROSE.   You can hand yours over here too, Troy.

TROY.   You see this, Bono. You see how they do me.

BONO.   Yeah, Lucille do me the same way.

[GABRIEL *is heard singing offstage. He enters.*]

GABRIEL.   Better get ready for the Judgment! Better get ready for . . . Hey! . . . Hey! . . . There's Troy's boy!

LYONS.   How you doing, Uncle Gabe?

GABRIEL.   Lyons . . . The King of the Jungle! Rose . . . hey, Rose. Got a flower for you.

[*He takes a rose from his pocket.*]

Picked it myself. That's the same rose like you is!

ROSE.   That's right nice of you, Gabe.

LYONS.   What you been doing, Uncle Gabe?

GABRIEL.   Oh, I been chasing hellhounds and waiting on the time to tell St. Peter[4] to open the gates.

LYONS.   You been chasing hellhounds, huh? Well . . . you doing the right thing, Uncle Gabe. Somebody got to chase them.

GABRIEL.   Oh, yeah . . . I know it. The devil's strong. The devil ain't no pushover. Hellhounds snipping at everybody's heels. But I got my trumpet waiting on the judgment time.

LYONS.   Waiting on the Battle of Armageddon, huh?

GABRIEL.   Ain't gonna be too much of a battle when God get to waving that Judgment sword. But the people's gonna have a hell of a time trying to get into heaven if them gates ain't open.

LYONS.   [*Putting his arm around* GABRIEL.] You hear this, Pop. Uncle Gabe, you alright!

GABRIEL.   [*Laughing with* LYONS.] Lyons! King of the Jungle.

ROSE.   You gonna stay for supper, Gabe. Want me to fix you a plate?

GABRIEL.   I'll take a sandwich, Rose. Don't want no plate. Just wanna eat with my hands. I'll take a sandwich.

ROSE.   How about you, Lyons? You staying? Got some short ribs cooking.

LYONS.   Naw, I won't eat nothing till after we finished playing.
     [*Pause.*]
You ought to come down and listen to me play, Pop.

TROY.   I don't like that Chinese music. All that noise.

ROSE.   Go on in the house and wash up, Gabe . . . I'll fix you a sandwich.

GABRIEL.   [*To* LYONS, *as he exits.*] Troy's mad at me.

LYONS.   What you mad at Uncle Gabe for, Pop?

ROSE.   He thinks Troy's mad at him cause he moved over to Miss Pearl's.

TROY.   I ain't mad at the man. He can live where he want to live at.

LYONS.   What he move over there for? Miss Pearl don't like nobody.

ROSE.   She don't mind him none. She treats him real nice. She just don't allow all that singing.

TROY.   She don't mind that rent he be paying . . . that's what she don't mind.

ROSE.   Troy, I ain't going through that with you no more. He's over there cause he want to have his own place. He can come and go as he please.

TROY.   Hell, he could come and go as he please here. I wasn't stopping him. I ain't put no rules on him.

ROSE.   It ain't the same thing, Troy. And you know it.
     [GABRIEL *comes to the door.*]
Now, that's the last I wanna hear about that. I don't wanna hear nothing else about Gabe and Miss Pearl. And next week . . .

GABRIEL.   I'm ready for my sandwich, Rose.

ROSE.   And next week . . . when that recruiter come from that school . . . I want you to sign that paper and go on and let Cory play football. Then that'll be the last I have to hear about that.

TROY.   [*To* ROSE *as she exits into the house.*] I ain't thinking about Cory nothing.

---

4. Apostle (d. ca. A.D. 67), traditionally regarded as guarding the gates to Heaven.

LYONS.   What . . . Cory got recruited? What school he going to?

TROY.   That boy walking around here smelling his piss . . . thinking he's grown. Thinking he's gonna do what he want, irrespective of what I say. Look here, Bono . . . I left the Commissioner's office and went down to the A&P . . . that boy ain't working down there. He lying to me. Telling me he got his job back . . . telling me he working weekends . . . telling me he working after school . . . Mr. Stawicki tell me he ain't working down there at all!

LYONS.   Cory just growing up. He's just busting at the seams trying to fill out your shoes.

TROY.   I don't care what he's doing. When he get to the point where he wanna disobey me . . . then it's time for him to move on. Bono'll tell you that. I bet he ain't never disobeyed his daddy without paying the consequences.

BONO.   I ain't never had a chance. My daddy came on through . . . but I ain't never knew him to see him . . . or what he had on his mind or where he went. Just moving on through. Searching out the New Land. That's what the old folks used to call it. See a fellow moving around from place to place . . . woman to woman . . . called it searching out the New Land. I can't say if he ever found it. I come along, didn't want no kids. Didn't know if I was gonna be in one place long enough to fix on them right as their daddy. I figured I was going searching too. As it turned out I been hooked up with Lucille near about as long as your daddy been with Rose. Going on sixteen years.

TROY.   Sometimes I wish I hadn't known my daddy. He ain't cared nothing about no kids. A kid to him wasn't nothing. All he wanted was for you to learn how to walk so he could start you to working. When it come time for eating . . . he ate first. If there was anything left over, that's what you got. Man would sit down and eat two chickens and give you the wing.

LYONS.   You ought to stop that, Pop. Everybody feed their kids. No matter how hard times is . . . everybody care about their kids. Make sure they have something to eat.

TROY.   The only thing my daddy cared about was getting them bales of cotton in to Mr. Lubin. That's the only thing that mattered to him. Sometimes I used to wonder why he was living. Wonder why the devil hadn't come and got him. "Get them bales of cotton in to Mr. Lubin" and find out he owe him money . . .

LYONS.   He should have just went on and left when he saw he couldn't get nowhere. That's what I would have done.

TROY.   How he gonna leave with eleven kids? And where he gonna go? He ain't knew how to do nothing but farm. No, he was trapped and I think he knew it. But I'll say this for him . . . he felt a responsibility toward us. Maybe he ain't treated us the way I felt he should have . . . but without that responsibility he could have walked off and left us . . . made his own way.

BONO.   A lot of them did. Back in those days what you talking about . . . they walk out their front door and just take on down one road or another and keep on walking.

LYONS. There you go! That's what I'm talking about.

BONO. Just keep on walking till you come to something else. Ain't you never heard of nobody having the walking blues? Well, that's what you call it when you just take off like that.

TROY. My daddy ain't had them walking blues! What you talking about? He stayed right there with his family. But he was just as evil as he could be. My mama couldn't stand him. Couldn't stand that evilness. She run off when I was about eight. She sneaked off one night after he had gone to sleep. Told me she was coming back for me. I ain't never seen her no more. All his women run off and left him. He wasn't good for nobody.

When my turn come to head out, I was fourteen and got to sniffing around Joe Canewell's daughter. Had us an old mule we called Greyboy. My daddy sent me out to do some plowing and I tied up Greyboy and went to fooling around with Joe Canewell's daughter. We done found us a nice little spot, got real cozy with each other. She about thirteen and we done figured we was grown anyway . . . so we down there enjoying ourselves . . . ain't thinking about nothing. We didn't know Greyboy had got loose and wandered back to the house and my daddy was looking for me. We down there by the creek enjoying ourselves when my daddy come up on us. Surprised us. He had them leather straps off the mule and commenced to whupping me like there was no tomorrow. I jumped up, mad and embarrassed. I was scared of my daddy. When he commenced to whupping on me . . . quite naturally I run to get out of the way.

[Pause.]

Now I thought he was mad cause I ain't done my work. But I see where he was chasing me off so he could have the gal for himself. When I see what the matter of it was, I lost all fear of my daddy. Right there is where I become a man . . . at fourteen years of age.

[Pause.]

Now it was my turn to run him off. I picked up them same reins that he had used on me. I picked up them reins and commenced to whupping on him. The gal jumped up and run off . . . and when my daddy turned to face me, I could see why the devil had never come to get him . . . cause he was the devil himself. I don't know what happened. When I woke up, I was laying right there by the creek, and Blue . . . this old dog we had . . . was licking my face. I thought I was blind. I couldn't see nothing. Both my eyes were swollen shut. I layed there and cried. I didn't know what I was gonna do. The only thing I knew was the time had come for me to leave my daddy's house. And right there the world suddenly got big. And it was a long time before I could cut it down to where I could handle it.

Part of that cutting down was when I got to the place where I could feel him kicking in my blood and knew that the only thing that separated us was the matter of a few years.

[GABRIEL *enters from the house with a sandwich.*]

LYONS. What you got there, Uncle Gabe?

GABRIEL. Got me a ham sandwich. Rose gave me a ham sandwich.

TROY. I don't know what happened to him. I done lost touch with everybody except Gabriel. But I hope he's dead. I hope he found some peace.

LYONS.   That's a heavy story, Pop. I didn't know you left home when you was fourteen.

TROY.   And didn't know nothing. The only part of the world I knew was the forty-two acres of Mr. Lubin's land. That's all I knew about life.

LYONS.   Fourteen's kinda young to be out on your own. [*Phone rings.*] I don't even think I was ready to be out on my own at fourteen. I don't know what I would have done.

TROY.   I got up from the creek and walked on down to Mobile. I was through with farming. Figured I could do better in the city. So I walked the two hundred miles to Mobile.

LYONS.   Wait a minute . . . you ain't walked no two hundred miles, Pop. Ain't nobody gonna walk no two hundred miles. You talking about some walking there.

BONO.   That's the only way you got anywhere back in them days.

LYONS.   Shhh. Damn if I wouldn't have hitched a ride with somebody!

TROY.   Who you gonna hitch it with? They ain't had no cars and things like they got now. We talking about 1918.

ROSE.   [*Entering.*] What you all out here getting into?

TROY.   [*To* ROSE.] I'm telling Lyons how good he got it. He don't know nothing about this I'm talking.

ROSE.   Lyons, that was Bonnie on the phone. She say you supposed to pick her up.

LYONS.   Yeah, okay, Rose.

TROY.   I walked on down to Mobile and hitched up with some of them fellows that was heading this way. Got up here and found out . . . not only couldn't you get a job . . . you couldn't find no place to live. I thought I was in freedom. Shhh. Colored folks living down there on the riverbanks in whatever kind of shelter they could find for themselves. Right down there under the Brady Street Bridge. Living in shacks made of sticks and tarpaper. Messed around there and went from bad to worse. Started stealing. First it was food. Then I figured, hell, if I steal money I can buy me some food. Buy me some shoes too! One thing led to another. Met your mama. I was young and anxious to be a man. Met your mama and had you. What I do that for? Now I got to worry about feeding you and her. Got to steal three times as much. Went out one day looking for somebody to rob . . . that's what I was, a robber. I'll tell you the truth. I'm ashamed of it today. But it's the truth. Went to rob this fellow . . . pulled out my knife . . . and he pulled out a gun. Shot me in the chest. It felt just like somebody had taken a hot branding iron and laid it on me. When he shot me I jumped at him with my knife. They told me I killed him and they put me in the penitentiary and locked me up for fifteen years. That's where I met Bono. That's where I learned how to play baseball. Got out that place and your mama had taken you and went on to make life without me. Fifteen years was a long time for her to wait. But that fifteen years cured me of that robbing stuff. Rose'll tell you. She asked me when I met her if I had gotten all that foolishness out of my system. And I told her, "Baby, it's you and baseball all what count with me." You hear me, Bono? I meant it too. She say, "Which one comes first?" I told her, "Baby, ain't no doubt it's baseball . . . but you stick and get old with me and we'll both outlive this baseball." Am I right, Rose? And it's true.

ROSE.   Man, hush your mouth. You ain't said no such thing. Talking about, "Baby, you know you'll always be number one with me." That's what you was talking.

TROY.   You hear that, Bono. That's why I love her.

BONO.   Rose'll keep you straight. You get off the track, she'll straighten you up.

ROSE.   Lyons, you better get on up and get Bonnie. She waiting on you.

LYONS.   [Gets up to go.] Hey, Pop, why don't you come on down to the Grill and hear me play?

TROY.   I ain't going down there. I'm too old to be sitting around in them clubs.

BONO.   You got to be good to play down at the Grill.

LYONS.   Come on, Pop . . .

TROY.   I got to get up in the morning.

LYONS.   You ain't got to stay long.

TROY.   Naw, I'm gonna get my supper and go on to bed.

LYONS.   Well, I got to go. I'll see you again.

TROY.   Don't you come around my house on my payday.

ROSE.   Pick up the phone and let somebody know you coming. And bring Bonnie with you. You know I'm always glad to see her.

LYONS.   Yeah, I'll do that, Rose. You take care now. See you, Pop. See you, Mr. Bono. See you, Uncle Gabe.

GABRIEL.   Lyons! King of the Jungle!

[LYONS exits.]

TROY.   Is supper ready, woman? Me and you got some business to take care of. I'm gonna tear it up too.

ROSE.   Troy, I done told you now!

TROY.   [Puts his arm around BONO.] Aw hell, woman . . . this is Bono. Bono like family. I done known this nigger since . . . how long I done know you?

BONO.   It's been a long time.

TROY.   I done known this nigger since Skippy was a pup. Me and him done been through some times.

BONO.   You sure right about that.

TROY.   Hell, I done know him longer than I known you. And we still standing shoulder to shoulder. Hey, look here, Bono . . . a man can't ask for no more than that.

[Drinks to him.]

I love you, nigger.

BONO.   Hell, I love you too . . . but I got to get home see my woman. You got yours in hand. I got to go get mine.

[BONO starts to exit as CORY enters the yard, dressed in his football uniform. He gives TROY a hard, uncompromising look.]

CORY.   What you do that for, Pop?

[He throws his helmet down in the direction of TROY.]

ROSE. What's the matter? Cory . . . what's the matter?

CORY. Papa done went up to the school and told Coach Zellman I can't play football no more. Wouldn't even let me play the game. Told him to tell the recruiter not to come.

ROSE. Troy . . .

TROY. What you Troying me for. Yeah, I did it. And the boy know why I did it.

CORY. Why you wanna do that to me? That was the one chance I had.

ROSE. Ain't nothing wrong with Cory playing football, Troy.

TROY. The boy lied to me. I told the nigger if he wanna play football . . . to keep up his chores and hold down that job at the A&P. That was the conditions. Stopped down there to see Mr. Stawicki . . .

CORY. I can't work after school during the football season, Pop! I tried to tell you that Mr. Stawicki's holding my job for me. You don't never want to listen to nobody. And then you wanna go and do this to me!

TROY. I ain't done nothing to you. You done it to yourself.

CORY. Just cause you didn't have a chance! You just scared I'm gonna be better than you, that's all.

TROY. Come here.

ROSE. Troy . . .

[CORY *reluctantly crosses over to* TROY.]

TROY. Alright! See. You done made a mistake.

CORY. I didn't even do nothing!

TROY. I'm gonna tell you what your mistake was. See . . . you swung at the ball and didn't hit it. That's strike one. See, you in the batter's box now. You swung and you missed. That's strike one. Don't you strike out!

[*Lights fade to black.*]

Act Two

SCENE ONE

The following morning. CORY *is at the tree hitting the ball with the bat. He tries to mimic* TROY, *but his swing is awkward, less sure.* ROSE *enters from the house.*

ROSE. Cory, I want you to help me with this cupboard.

CORY. I ain't quitting the team. I don't care what Poppa say.

ROSE. I'll talk to him when he gets back. He had to go see about your Uncle Gabe. The police done arrested him. Say he was disturbing the peace. He'll be back directly. Come on in here and help me clean out the top of this cupboard.

[CORY *exits into the house.* ROSE *sees* TROY *and* BONO *coming down the alley.*]

Troy . . . what they say down there?

TROY. Ain't said nothing. I give them fifty dollars and they let him go. I'll talk to you about it. Where's Cory?

ROSE. He's in there helping me clean out these cupboards.

TROY. Tell him to get his butt out here.

[TROY *and* BONO *go over to the pile of wood.* BONO *picks up the saw and begins sawing.*]

TROY.   [*To* BONO.] All they want is the money. That makes six or seven times I done went down there and got him. See me coming they stick out their *hands.*

BONO.   Yeah. I know what you mean. That's all they care about . . . that money. They don't care about what's right.

[*Pause.*]

Nigger, why you got to go and get some hard wood? You ain't doing nothing but building a little old fence. Get you some soft pine wood. That's all you need.

TROY.   I know what I'm doing. This is outside wood. You put pine wood inside the house. Pine wood is inside wood. This here is outside wood. Now you tell me where the fence is gonna be?

BONO.   You don't need this wood. You can put it up with pine wood and it'll stand as long as you gonna be here looking at it.

TROY.   How you know how long I'm gonna be here, nigger? Hell, I might just live forever. Live longer than old man Horsely.

BONO.   That's what Magee used to say.

TROY.   Magee's a damn fool. Now you tell me who you ever heard of gonna pull their own teeth with a pair of rusty pliers.

BONO.   The old folks . . . my granddaddy used to pull his teeth with pliers. They ain't had no dentists for the colored folks back then.

TROY.   Get clean pliers! You understand? Clean pliers! Sterilize them! Besides we ain't living back then. All Magee had to do was walk over to Doc Goldblums.

BONO.   I see where you and that Tallahassee gal . . . that Alberta . . . I see where you all done got tight.

TROY.   What you mean "got tight"?

BONO.   I see where you be laughing and joking with her all the time.

TROY.   I laughs and jokes with all of them, Bono. You know me.

BONO.   That ain't the kind of laughing and joking I'm talking about.

[CORY *enters from the house.*]

CORY.   How you doing, Mr. Bono?

TROY.   Cory? Get that saw from Bono and cut some wood. He talking about the wood's too hard to cut. Stand back there, Jim, and let that young boy show you how it's done.

BONO.   He's sure welcome to it.

[CORY *takes the saw and begins to cut the wood.*]

Whew-e-e! Look at that. Big old strong boy. Look like Joe Louis.[5] Hell, must be getting old the way I'm watching that boy whip through that wood.

CORY.   I don't see why Mama want a fence around the yard noways.

TROY.   Damn if I know either. What the hell she keeping out with it? She ain't got nothing nobody want.

BONO.   Some people build fences to keep people out . . . and other people build fences to keep people in. Rose wants to hold on to you all. She loves you.

---

5. African American boxer (1914–1981) who held the heavyweight title from 1937 to 1949.

TROY.   Hell, nigger, I don't need nobody to tell me my wife loves me. Cory . . . go on in the house and see if you can find that other saw.

CORY.   Where's it at?

TROY.   I said find it! Look for it till you find it!

[CORY *exits into the house.*]

What's that supposed to mean? Wanna keep us in?

BONO.   Troy . . . I done known you seem like damn near my whole life. You and Rose both. I done know both of you all for a long time. I remember when you met Rose. When you was hitting them baseball out the park. A lot of them old gals was after you then. You had the pick of the litter. When you picked Rose, I was happy for you. That was the first time I knew you had any sense. I said . . . My man Troy knows what he's doing . . . I'm gonna follow this nigger . . . he might take me somewhere. I been following you too. I done learned a whole heap of things about life watching you. I done learned how to tell where the shit lies. How to tell it from the alfalfa. You done learned me a lot of things. You showed me how to not make the same mistakes . . . to take life as it comes along and keep putting one foot in front of the other.

[*Pause.*]

Rose a good woman, Troy.

TROY.   Hell, nigger, I know she a good woman. I been married to her for eighteen years. What you got on your mind, Bono?

BONO.   I just say she a good woman. Just like I say anything. I ain't got to have nothing on my mind.

TROY.   You just gonna say she a good woman and leave it hanging out there like that? Why you telling me she a good woman?

BONO.   She loves you, Troy. Rose loves you.

TROY.   You saying I don't measure up. That's what you trying to say. I don't measure up cause I'm seeing this other gal. I know what you trying to say.

BONO.   I know what Rose means to you, Troy. I'm just trying to say I don't want to see you mess up.

TROY.   Yeah, I appreciate that, Bono. If you was messing around on Lucille I'd be telling you the same thing.

BONO.   Well, that's all I got to say. I just say that because I love you both.

TROY.   Hell, you know me . . . I wasn't out there looking for nothing. You can't find a better woman than Rose. I know that. But seems like this woman just stuck onto me where I can't shake her loose. I done wrestled with it, tried to throw her off me . . . but she just stuck on tighter. Now she's stuck on for good.

BONO.   You's in control . . . that's what you tell me all the time. You responsible for what you do.

TROY.   I ain't ducking the responsibility of it. As long as it sets right in my heart . . . then I'm okay. Cause that's all I listen to. It'll tell me right from wrong every time. And I ain't talking about doing Rose no bad turn. I love Rose. She done carried me a long ways and I love and respect her for that.

BONO.   I know you do. That's why I don't want to see you hurt her. But what you gonna do when she find out? What you got then? If you try and juggle both of them . . . sooner or later you gonna drop one of them. That's common sense.

TROY.   Yeah, I hear what you saying, Bono. I been trying to figure a way to work it out.

BONO.   Work it out right, Troy. I don't want to be getting all up between you and Rose's business . . . but work it so it come out right.

TROY.   Aw hell, I get all up between you and Lucille's business. When you gonna get that woman that refrigerator she been wanting? Don't tell me you ain't got no money now. I know who your banker is. Mellon don't need that money bad as Lucille want that refrigerator. I'll tell you that.

BONO.   Tell you what I'll do . . . when you finish building this fence for Rose . . . I'll buy Lucille that refrigerator.

TROY.   You done stuck your foot in your mouth now!

[TROY *grabs up a board and begins to saw.* BONO *starts to walk out the yard.*]

Hey, nigger . . . where you going?

BONO.   I'm going home. I know you don't expect me to help you now. I'm protecting my money. I wanna see you put that fence up by yourself. That's what I want to see. You'll be here another six months without me.

TROY.   Nigger, you ain't right.

BONO.   When it comes to my money . . . I'm right as fireworks on the Fourth of July.

TROY.   Alright, we gonna see now. You better get out your bankbook.

[BONO *exits, and* TROY *continues to work.* ROSE *enters from the house.*]

ROSE.   What they say down there? What's happening with Gabe?

TROY.   I went down there and got him out. Cost me fifty dollars. Say he was disturbing the peace. Judge set up a hearing for him in three weeks. Say to show cause why he shouldn't be re-committed.

ROSE.   What was he doing that cause them to arrest him?

TROY.   Some kids was teasing him and he run them off home. Say he was howling and carrying on. Some folks seen him and called the police. That's all it was.

ROSE.   Well, what's you say? What'd you tell the judge?

TROY.   Told him I'd look after him. It didn't make no sense to recommit the man. He stuck out his big greasy palm and told me to give him fifty dollars and take him on home.

ROSE.   Where's he at now? Where'd he go off to?

TROY.   He's gone on about his business. He don't need nobody to hold his hand.

ROSE.   Well, I don't know. Seem like that would be the best place for him if they did put him into the hospital. I know what you're gonna say. But that's what I think would be best.

TROY.   The man done had his life ruined fighting for what? And they wanna take and lock him up. Let him be free. He don't bother nobody.

ROSE.   Well, everybody got their own way of looking at it I guess. Come on and get your lunch. I got a bowl of lima beans and some cornbread in the oven. Come on get something to eat. Ain't no sense you fretting over Gabe.

[ROSE *turns to go into the house.*]

TROY. Rose . . . got something to tell you.

ROSE. Well, come on . . . wait till I get this food on the table.

TROY. Rose!

[*She stops and turns around.*]
I don't know how to say this.
[*Pause.*]
I can't explain it none. It just sort of grows on you till it gets out of hand. It starts out like a little bush . . . and the next thing you know it's a whole forest.

ROSE. Troy . . . what is you talking about?

TROY. I'm talking, woman, let me talk. I'm trying to find a way to tell you . . . I'm gonna be a daddy. I'm gonna be somebody's daddy.

ROSE. Troy . . . you're not telling me this? You're gonna be . . . what?

TROY. Rose . . . now . . . see . . .

ROSE. You telling me you gonna be somebody's daddy? You telling your *wife* this?

[GABRIEL *enters from the street. He carries a rose in his hand.*]

GABRIEL. Hey, Troy! Hey, Rose!

ROSE. I have to wait eighteen years to hear something like this.

GABRIEL. Hey, Rose . . . I got a flower for you.
[*He hands it to her.*]
That's a rose. Same rose like you is.

ROSE. Thanks, Gabe.

GABRIEL. Troy, you ain't mad at me is you? Them bad mens come and put me away. You ain't mad at me is you?

TROY. Naw, Gabe, I ain't mad at you.

ROSE. Eighteen years and you wanna come with this.

GABRIEL. [*Takes a quarter out of his pocket.*] See what I got? Got a brand new quarter.

TROY. Rose . . . it's just . . .

ROSE. Ain't nothing you can say, Troy. Ain't no way of explaining that.

GABRIEL. Fellow that give me this quarter had a whole mess of them. I'm gonna keep this quarter till it stop shining.

ROSE. Gabe, go on in the house there. I got some watermelon in the frigidaire. Go on and get you a piece.

GABRIEL. Say, Rose . . . you know I was chasing hellhounds and them bad mens come and get me and take me away. Troy helped me. He come down there and told them they better let me go before he beat them up. Yeah, he did!

ROSE. You go on and get you a piece of watermelon, Gabe. Them bad mens is gone now.

GABRIEL. Okay, Rose . . . gonna get me some watermelon. The kind with the stripes on it.

[GABRIEL *exits into the house.*]

ROSE. Why, Troy? Why? After all these years to come dragging this in to me now. It don't make no sense at your age. I could have expected this ten or fifteen years ago, but not now.

TROY. Age ain't got nothing to do with it, Rose.

ROSE. I done tried to be everything a wife should be. Everything a wife could be. Been married eighteen years and I got to live to see the day you tell me you been seeing another woman and done fathered a child by her. And you know I ain't never wanted no half nothing in my family. My whole family is half. Everybody got different fathers and mothers . . . my two sisters and my brother. Can't hardly tell who's who. Can't never sit down and talk about Papa and Mama. It's your papa and your mama and my papa and my mama . . .

TROY. Rose . . . stop it now.

ROSE. I ain't never wanted that for none of my children. And now you wanna drag your behind in here and tell me something like this.

TROY. You ought to know. It's time for you to know.

ROSE. Well, I don't want to know, goddamn it!

TROY. I can't just make it go away. It's done now. I can't wish the circumstance of the thing away.

ROSE. And you don't want to either. Maybe you want to wish me and my boy away. Maybe that's what you want? Well, you can't wish us away. I've got eighteen years of my life invested in you. You ought to have stayed upstairs in my bed where you belong.

TROY. Rose . . . now listen to me . . . we can get a handle on this thing. We can talk this out . . . come to an understanding.

ROSE. All of a sudden it's "we." Where was "we" at when you was down there rolling around with some godforsaken woman? "We" should have come to an understanding before you started making a damn fool of yourself. You're a day late and a dollar short when it comes to an understanding with me.

TROY. It's just . . . She gives me a different idea . . . a different understanding about myself. I can step out of this house and get away from the pressures and problems . . . be a different man. I ain't got to wonder how I'm gonna pay the bills or get the roof fixed. I can just be a part of myself that I ain't never been.

ROSE. What I want to know . . . is do you plan to continue seeing her. That's all you can say to me.

TROY. I can sit up in her house and laugh. Do you understand what I'm saying. I can laugh out loud . . . and it feels good. It reaches all the way down to the bottom of my shoes.

[Pause.]

Rose, I can't give that up.

ROSE. Maybe you ought to go on and stay down there with her . . . if she a better woman than me.

TROY. It ain't about nobody being a better woman or nothing. Rose, you ain't the blame. A man couldn't ask for no woman to be a better wife than you've been. I'm responsible for it. I done locked myself into a pattern trying to take care of you all that I forgot about myself.

ROSE. What the hell was I there for? That was my job, not somebody else's.

TROY. Rose, I done tried all my life to live decent . . . to live a clean . . . hard . . . useful life. I tried to be a good husband to you. In every way I knew how. Maybe I come into the world backwards, I don't know. But

. . . you born with two strikes on you before you come to the plate. You got to guard it closely . . . always looking for the curve-ball on the inside corner. You can't afford to let none get past you. You can't afford a call strike. If you going down . . . you going down swinging. Everything lined up against you. What you gonna do. I fooled them, Rose. I bunted. When I found you and Cory and a halfway decent job . . . I was safe. Couldn't nothing touch me. I wasn't gonna strike out no more. I wasn't going back to the penitentiary. I wasn't gonna lay in the streets with a bottle of wine. I was safe. I had me a family. A job. I wasn't gonna get that last strike. I was on first looking for one of them boys to knock me in. To get me home.

ROSE.   You should have stayed in my bed, Troy.

TROY.   Then when I saw that gal . . . she firmed up my backbone. And I got to thinking that if I tried . . . I just might be able to steal second. Do you understand after eighteen years I wanted to steal second.

ROSE.   You should have held me tight. You should have grabbed me and held on.

TROY.   I stood on first base for eighteen years and I thought . . . well, god-damn it . . . go on for it!

ROSE.   We're not talking about baseball! We're talking about you going off to lay in bed with another woman . . . and then bring it home to me. That's what we're talking about. We ain't talking about no baseball.

TROY.   Rose, you're not listening to me. I'm trying the best I can to explain it to you. It's not easy for me to admit that I been standing in the same place for eighteen years.

ROSE.   I been standing with you! I been right here with you, Troy. I got a life too. I gave eighteen years of my life to stand in the same spot with you. Don't you think I ever wanted other things? Don't you think I had dreams and hopes? What about my life? What about me. Don't you think it ever crossed my mind to want to know other men? That I wanted to lay up somewhere and forget about my responsibilities? That I wanted someone to make me laugh so I could feel good? You not the only one who's got wants and needs. But I held on to you, Troy. I took all my feelings, my wants and needs, my dreams . . . and I buried them inside you. I planted a seed and watched and prayed over it. I planted myself inside you and waited to bloom. And it didn't take me no eighteen years to find out the soil was hard and rocky and it wasn't never gonna bloom.

But I held on to you, Troy. I held you tighter. You was my husband. I owed you everything I had. Every part of me I could find to give you. And upstairs in that room . . . with the darkness falling in on me . . . I gave everything I had to try and erase the doubt that you wasn't the finest man in the world. And wherever you was going . . . I wanted to be there with you. Cause you was my husband. Cause that's the only way I was gonna survive as your wife. You always talking about what you give . . . and what you don't have to give. But you take too. You take . . . and don't even know nobody's giving!

[ROSE *turns to exit into the house;* TROY *grabs her arm.*]

TROY.   You say I take and don't give!

ROSE.   Troy! You're hurting me!

TROY.   You say I take and don't give.

ROSE.   Troy . . . you're hurting my arm! Let go!

TROY.   I done give you everything I got. Don't you tell that lie on me.

ROSE.   Troy!

TROY.   Don't you tell that lie on me!

[CORY *enters from the house.*]

CORY.   Mama!

ROSE.   Troy. You're hurting me.

TROY.   Don't you tell me about no taking and giving.

[CORY *comes up behind* TROY *and grabs him.* TROY, *surprised, is thrown off balance just as* CORY *throws a glancing blow that catches him on the chest and knocks him down.* TROY *is stunned, as is* CORY.]

ROSE.   Troy. Troy. No!

[TROY *gets to his feet and starts at* CORY.]

Troy . . . no. Please! Troy!

[ROSE *pulls on* TROY *to hold him back.* TROY *stops himself.*]

TROY.   [*To* CORY.] Alright. That's strike two. You stay away from around me, boy. Don't you strike out. You living with a full count.[6] Don't you strike out.

[TROY *exits out the yard as the lights go down.*]

SCENE TWO

It is six months later, early afternoon. TROY *enters from the house and starts to exit the yard.* ROSE *enters from the house.*

ROSE.   Troy, I want to talk to you.

TROY.   All of a sudden, after all this time, you want to talk to me, huh? You ain't wanted to talk to me for months. You ain't wanted to talk to me last night. You ain't wanted no part of me then. What you wanna talk to me about now?

ROSE.   Tomorrow's Friday.

TROY.   I know what day tomorrow is. You think I don't know tomorrow's Friday? My whole life I ain't done nothing but look to see Friday coming and you got to tell me it's Friday.

ROSE.   I want to know if you're coming home.

TROY.   I always come home, Rose. You know that. There ain't never been a night I ain't come home.

ROSE.   That ain't what I mean . . . and you know it. I want to know if you're coming straight home after work.

TROY.   I figure I'd cash my check . . . hang out at Taylors' with the boys . . . maybe play a game of checkers . . .

ROSE.   Troy, I can't live like this. I won't live like this. You livin' on borrowed time with me. It's been going on six months now you ain't been coming home.

TROY.   I be here every night. Every night of the year. That's 365 days.

ROSE.   I want you to come home tomorrow after work.

6. In baseball, a count of three balls and two strikes.

TROY.   Rose . . . I don't mess up my pay. You know that now. I take my pay and I give it to you. I don't have no money but what you give me back. I just want to have a little time to myself . . . a little time to enjoy life.

ROSE.   What about me? When's my time to enjoy life?

TROY.   I don't know what to tell you, Rose. I'm doing the best I can.

ROSE.   You ain't been home from work but time enough to change your clothes and run out . . . and you wanna call that the best you can do?

TROY.   I'm going over to the hospital to see Alberta. She went into the hospital this afternoon. Look like she might have the baby early. I won't be gone long.

ROSE.   Well, you ought to know. They went over to Miss Pearl's and got Gabe today. She said you told them to go ahead and lock him up.

TROY.   I ain't said no such thing. Whoever told you that is telling a lie. Pearl ain't doing nothing but telling a big fat lie.

ROSE.   She ain't had to tell me. I read it on the papers.

TROY.   I ain't told them nothing of the kind.

ROSE.   I saw it right there on the papers.

TROY.   What it say, huh?

ROSE.   It said you told them to take him.

TROY.   Then they screwed that up, just the way they screw up everything. I ain't worried about what they got on the paper.

ROSE.   Say the government send part of his check to the hospital and the other part to you.

TROY.   I ain't got nothing to do with that if that's the way it works. I ain't made up the rules about how it work.

ROSE.   You did Gabe just like you did Cory. You wouldn't sign the paper for Cory . . . but you signed for Gabe. You signed that paper.

[*The telephone is heard ringing inside the house.*]

TROY.   I told you I ain't signed nothing, woman! The only thing I signed was the release form. Hell, I can't read, I don't know what they had on that paper! I ain't signed nothing about sending Gabe away.

ROSE.   I said send him to the hospital . . . you said let him be free . . . now you done went down there and signed him to the hospital for half his money. You went back on yourself, Troy. You gonna have to answer for that.

TROY.   See now . . . you been over there talking to Miss Pearl. She done got mad cause she ain't getting Gabe's rent money. That's all it is. She's liable to say anything.

ROSE.   Troy, I seen where you signed the paper.

TROY.   You ain't seen nothing I signed. What she doing got papers on my brother anyway? Miss Pearl telling a big fat lie. And I'm gonna tell her about it too! You ain't seen nothing I signed. Say . . . you ain't seen nothing I signed.

[ROSE *exits into the house to answer the telephone. Presently she returns.*]

ROSE.   Troy . . . that was the hospital. Alberta had the baby.

TROY.   What she have? What is it?

ROSE.   It's a girl.

TROY.   I better get on down to the hospital to see her.

ROSE. Troy . . .

TROY. Rose . . . I got to go see her now. That's only right . . . what's the matter . . . the baby's alright, ain't it?

ROSE. Alberta died having the baby.

TROY. Died . . . you say she's dead? Alberta's dead?

ROSE. They said they done all they could. They couldn't do nothing for her.

TROY. The baby? How's the baby?

ROSE. They say it's healthy. I wonder who's gonna bury her.

TROY. She had family, Rose. She wasn't living in the world by herself.

ROSE. I know she wasn't living in the world by herself.

TROY. Next thing you gonna want to know if she had any insurance.

ROSE. Troy, you ain't got to talk like that.

TROY. That's the first thing that jumped out your mouth. "Who's gonna bury her?" Like I'm fixing to take on that task for myself.

ROSE. I am your wife. Don't push me away.

TROY. I ain't pushing nobody away. Just give me some space. That's all. Just give me some room to breathe.

[ROSE *exits into the house.* TROY *walks about the yard.*]

TROY. [*With a quiet rage that threatens to consume him.*] Alright . . . Mr. Death. See now . . . I'm gonna tell you what I'm gonna do. I'm gonna take and build me a fence around this yard. See? I'm gonna build me a fence around what belongs to me. And then I want you to stay on the other side. See? You stay over there until you're ready for me. Then you come on. Bring your army. Bring your sickle. Bring your wrestling clothes. I ain't gonna fall down on my vigilance this time. You ain't gonna sneak up on me no more. When you ready for me . . . when the top of your list say Troy Maxson . . . that's when you come around here. You come up and knock on the front door. Ain't nobody else got nothing to do with this. This is between you and me. Man to man. You stay on the other side of that fence until you ready for me. Then you come up and knock on the front door. Anytime you want. I'll be ready for you.

[*The lights go down to black.*]

SCENE THREE

The lights come up on the porch. It is late evening three days later. ROSE *sits listening to the ball game waiting for* TROY. *The final out of the game is made and* ROSE *switches off the radio.* TROY *enters the yard carrying an infant wrapped in blankets. He stands back from the house and calls.*

[ROSE *enters and stands on the porch. There is a long, awkward silence, the weight of which grows heavier with each passing second.*]

TROY. Rose . . . I'm standing here with my daughter in my arms. She ain't but a wee bittie little old thing. She don't know nothing about grownups' business. She innocent . . . and she ain't got no mama.

ROSE. What you telling me for, Troy?

[*She turns and exits into the house.*]

TROY. Well . . . I guess we'll just sit out here on the porch.

[*He sits down on the porch. There is an awkward indelicateness about the way he handles the* BABY. *His largeness engulfs and seems to swallow it. He speaks loud enough for* ROSE *to hear.*]
A man's got to do what's right for him. I ain't sorry for nothing I done. It felt right in my heart.
[*To the* BABY.]
What you smiling at? Your daddy's a big man. Got these great big old hands. But sometimes he's scared. And right now your daddy's scared cause we sitting out here and ain't got no home. Oh, I been homeless before. I ain't had no little baby with me. But I been homeless. You just be out on the road by your lonesome and you see one of them trains coming and you just kinda go like this . . .
[*He sings a lullaby.*]
Please, Mr. Engineer let a man ride the line
Please, Mr. Engineer let a man ride the line
I ain't got no ticket please let me ride the blinds
[ROSE *enters from the house.* TROY *hearing her steps behind him, stands and faces her.*]
She's my daughter, Rose. My own flesh and blood. I can't deny her no more than I can deny them boys.
[*Pause.*]
You and them boys is my family. You and them and this child is all I got in the world. So I guess what I'm saying is . . . I'd appreciate it if you'd help me take care of her.
ROSE.   Okay, Troy . . . you're right. I'll take care of your baby for you . . . cause . . . like you say . . . she's innocent . . . and you can't visit the sins of the father upon the child. A motherless child has got a hard time.
[*She takes the* BABY *from him.*]
From right now . . . this child got a mother. But you a womanless man.
[ROSE *turns and exits into the house with the* BABY. *Lights go down to black.*]

SCENE FOUR

It is two months later. LYONS *enters from the street. He knocks on the door and calls.*

LYONS.   Hey, Rose! [*Pause.*] Rose!
ROSE.   [*From inside the house.*] Stop that yelling. You gonna wake up Raynell. I just got her to sleep.
LYONS.   I just stopped by to pay Papa this twenty dollars I owe him. Where's Papa at?
ROSE.   He should be here in a minute. I'm getting ready to go down to the church. Sit down and wait on him.
LYONS.   I got to go pick up Bonnie over her mother's house.
ROSE.   Well, sit it down there on the table. He'll get it.
LYONS.   [*Enters the house and sets the money on the table.*] Tell Papa I said thanks. I'll see you again.
ROSE.   Alright, Lyons. We'll see you.

[LYONS *starts to exit as* CORY *enters.*]

CORY. Hey, Lyons.

LYONS. What's happening, Cory. Say man, I'm sorry I missed your graduation. You know I had a gig and couldn't get away. Otherwise, I would
have been there, man. So what you doing?

CORY. I'm trying to find a job.

LYONS. Yeah I know how that go, man. It's rough out here. Jobs are
scarce.

CORY. Yeah, I know.

LYONS. Look here, I got to run. Talk to Papa . . . he know some people.
He'll be able to help get you a job. Talk to him . . . see what he say.

CORY. Yeah . . . alright, Lyons.

LYONS. You take care. I'll talk to you soon. We'll find some time to talk.

[LYONS *exits the yard.* CORY *wanders over to the tree, picks up the bat
and assumes a batting stance. He studies an imaginary pitcher and
swings. Dissatisfied with the result, he tries again.* TROY *enters. They
eye each other for a beat.* CORY *puts the bat down and exits the yard.*
TROY *starts into the house as* ROSE *exits with* RAYNELL. *She is carrying
a cake.*]

TROY. I'm coming in and everybody's going out.

ROSE. I'm taking this cake down to the church for the bakesale. Lyons was
by to see you. He stopped by to pay you your twenty dollars. It's laying in
there on the table.

TROY. [*Going into his pocket.*] Well . . . here go this money.

ROSE. Put it in there on the table, Troy. I'll get it.

TROY. What time you coming back?

ROSE. Ain't no use in you studying me. It don't matter what time I come
back.

TROY. I just asked you a question, woman. What's the matter . . . can't I
ask you a question?

ROSE. Troy, I don't want to go into it. Your dinner's in there on the stove.
All you got to do is heat it up. And don't you be eating the rest of them
cakes in there. I'm coming back for them. We having a bakesale at the
church tomorrow.

[ROSE *exits the yard.* TROY *sits down on the steps, takes a pint bottle
from his pocket, opens it and drinks. He begins to sing.*]

TROY.
Hear it ring! Hear it ring!
Had an old dog his name was Blue
You know Blue was mighty true
You know Blue as a good old dog
Blue trees a possum in a hollow log
You know from that he was a good old dog
[BONO *enters the yard.*]

BONO. Hey, Troy.

TROY. Hey, what's happening, Bono?

BONO. I just thought I'd stop by to see you.

TROY. What you stop by and see me for? You ain't stopped by in a month
of Sundays. Hell, I must owe you money or something.

BONO.   Since you got your promotion I can't keep up with you. Used to see you everyday. Now I don't even know what route you working.

TROY.   They keep switching me around. Got me out in Greentree now . . . hauling white folks' garbage.

BONO.   Greentree, huh? You lucky, at least you ain't got to be lifting them barrels. Damn if they ain't getting heavier. I'm gonna put in my two years and call it quits.

TROY.   I'm thinking about retiring myself.

BONO.   You got it easy. You can *drive* for another five years.

TROY.   It ain't the same, Bono. It ain't like working the back of the truck. Ain't got nobody to talk to . . . feel like you working by yourself. Naw, I'm thinking about retiring. How's Lucille?

BONO.   She alright. Her arthritis get to acting up on her sometime. Saw Rose on my way in. She going down to the church, huh?

TROY.   Yeah, she took up going down there. All them preachers looking for somebody to fatten their pockets.

   [*Pause.*]

Got some gin here.

BONO.   Naw, thanks. I just stopped by to say hello.

TROY.   Hell, nigger . . . you can take a drink. I ain't never known you to say no to a drink. You ain't got to work tomorrow.

BONO.   I just stopped by. I'm fixing to go over to Skinner's. We got us a domino game going over his house every Friday.

TROY.   Nigger, you can't play no dominoes. I used to whup you four games out of five.

BONO.   Well, that learned me. I'm getting better.

TROY.   Yeah? Well, that's alright.

BONO.   Look here . . . I got to be getting on. Stop by sometime, huh?

TROY.   Yeah, I'll do that, Bono. Lucille told Rose you bought her a new refrigerator.

BONO.   Yeah, Rose told Lucille you had finally built your fence . . . so I figured we'd call it even.

TROY.   I knew you would.

BONO.   Yeah . . . okay. I'll be talking to you.

TROY.   Yeah, take care, Bono. Good to see you. I'm gonna stop over.

BONO.   Yeah. Okay, Troy.

   [BONO *exits.* TROY *drinks from the bottle.*]

TROY.

   Old Blue died and I dig his grave
   Let him down with a golden chain
   Every night when I hear old Blue bark
   I know Blue treed a possum in Noah's Ark.
   Hear it ring! Hear it ring!

       [CORY *enters the yard. They eye each other for a beat.* TROY *is sitting in the middle of the steps.* CORY *walks over.*]

CORY.   I got to get by.

TROY.   Say what? What's you say?

CORY.   You in my way. I got to get by.

TROY.   You got to get by where? This is my house. Bought and paid for. In

full. Took me fifteen years. And if you wanna go in my house and I'm
sitting on the steps . . . you say excuse me. Like your mama taught you.

CORY.   Come on, Pop . . . I got to get by.

[CORY *starts to maneuver his way past* TROY. TROY *grabs his leg and
shoves him back.*]

TROY.   You just gonna walk over top of me?

CORY.   I live here too!

TROY.   [*Advancing toward him.*] You just gonna walk over top of me in my
own house?

CORY.   I ain't scared of you.

TROY.   I ain't asked if you was scared of me. I asked you if you was fixing to
walk over top of me in my own house? That's the question. You ain't
gonna say excuse me? You just gonna walk over top of me?

CORY.   If you wanna put it like that.

TROY.   How else am I gonna put it?

CORY.   I was walking by you to go into the house cause you sitting on the
steps drunk, singing to yourself. You can put it like that.

TROY.   Without saying excuse me???

[CORY *doesn't respond.*]

I asked you a question. Without saying excuse me???

CORY.   I ain't got to say excuse me to you. You don't count around here no
more.

TROY.   Oh, I see . . . I don't count around here no more. You ain't got to
say excuse me to your daddy. All of a sudden you done got so grown that
your daddy don't count around here no more . . . Around here in his own
house and yard that he done paid for with the sweat of his brow. You
done got so grown to where you gonna take over. You gonna take over
my house. Is that right? You gonna wear my pants. You gonna go in there
and stretch out on my bed. You ain't got to say excuse me cause I don't
count around here no more. Is that right?

CORY.   That's right. You always talking this dumb stuff. Now, why don't
you just get out my way.

TROY.   I guess you got someplace to sleep and something to put in your
belly. You got that, huh? You got that? That's what you need. You got
that, huh?

CORY.   You don't know what I got. You ain't got to worry about what I got.

TROY.   You right! You one hundred percent right! I done spent the last
seventeen years worrying about what you got. Now it's your turn, see? I'll
tell you what to do. You grown . . . we done established that. You a man.
Now, let's see you act like one. Turn your behind around and walk out
this yard. And when you get out there in the alley . . . you can forget
about this house. See? Cause this is my house. You go on and be a man
and get your own house. You can forget about this. 'Cause this is mine.
You go on and get yours cause I'm through with doing for you.

CORY.   You talking about what you did for me . . . what'd you ever give
me?

TROY.   Them feet and bones! That pumping heart, nigger! I give you more
than anybody else is ever gonna give you.

CORY.   You ain't never gave me nothing! You ain't never done nothing but hold me back. Afraid I was gonna be better than you. All you ever did was try and make me scared of you. I used to tremble every time you called my name. Every time I heard your footsteps in the house. Wondering all the time . . . what's Papa gonna say if I do this? . . . What's he gonna say if I do that? . . . What's Papa gonna say if I turn on the radio? And Mama, too . . . she tries . . . but she's scared of you.

TROY.   You leave your mama out of this. She ain't got nothing to do with this.

CORY.   I don't know how she stand you . . . after what you did to her.

TROY.   I told you to leave your mama out of this!

    [*He advances toward* CORY.]

CORY.   What you gonna do . . . give me a whupping? You can't whup me no more. You're too old. You just an old man.

TROY.   [*Shoves him on his shoulder.*] Nigger! That's what you are. You just another nigger on the street to me!

CORY.   You crazy! You know that?

TROY.   Go on now! You got the devil in you. Get on away from me!

CORY.   You just a crazy old man . . . talking about I got the devil in me.

TROY.   Yeah, I'm crazy! If you don't get on the other side of that yard . . . I'm gonna show you how crazy I am! Go on . . . get the hell out of my yard.

CORY.   It ain't your yard. You took Uncle Gabe's money he got from the army to buy this house and then you put him out.

TROY.   [TROY *advances on* CORY.] Get your black ass out of my yard!

    [TROY'*s advance backs* CORY *up against the tree.* CORY *grabs up the bat.*]

CORY.   I ain't going nowhere! Come on . . . put me out! I ain't scared of you.

TROY.   That's my bat!

CORY.   Come on!

TROY.   Put my bat down!

CORY.   Come on, put me out.

    [CORY *swings at* TROY, *who backs across the yard.*]

  What's the matter? You so bad . . . put me out!

    [TROY *advances toward* CORY.]

CORY.   [*Backing up.*] Come on! Come on!

TROY.   You're gonna have to use it! You wanna draw that bat back on me . . . you're gonna have to use it.

CORY.   Come on! . . . Come on!

    [CORY *swings the bat at* TROY *a second time. He misses.* TROY *continues to advance toward him.*]

TROY.   You're gonna have to kill me! You wanna draw that bat back on me. You're gonna have to kill me.

    [CORY, *backed up against the tree, can go no farther.* TROY *taunts him. He sticks out his head and offers him a target.*]

  Come on! Come on!

    [CORY *is unable to swing the bat.* TROY *grabs it.*]

TROY.   Then I'll show you.

    [CORY *and* TROY *struggle over the bat. The struggle is fierce and fully*

engaged. TROY *ultimately is the stronger, and takes the bat from* CORY
and stands over him ready to swing. He stops himself.]
  Go on and get away from around my house.
    [CORY, *stung by his defeat, picks himself up, walks slowly out of the
    yard and up the alley.*]
CORY.   Tell Mama I'll be back for my things.
TROY.   They'll be on the other side of that fence.
    [CORY *exits.*]
TROY.   I can't taste nothing. Helluljah! I can't taste nothing no more.
    [TROY *assumes a batting posture and begins to taunt Death, the fastball in
    the outside corner.*] Come on! It's between you and me now! Come on!
    Anytime you want! Come on! I be ready for you . . . but I ain't gonna be
    easy.
    [*The lights go down on the scene.*]

SCENE FIVE

The time is 1965. The lights come up in the yard. It is the morning of TROY's
*funeral. A funeral plaque with a light hangs beside the door. There is a small
garden plot off to the side. There is noise and activity in the house as* ROSE,
GABRIEL *and* BONO *have gathered. The door opens and* RAYNELL, *seven years
old, enters dressed in a flannel nightgown. She crosses to the garden and
pokes around with a stick.* ROSE *calls from the house.*

ROSE.   Raynell!
RAYNELL.   Mam?
ROSE.   What you doing out there?
RAYNELL.   Nothing.
    [ROSE *comes to the door.*]
ROSE.   Girl, get in here and get dressed. What you doing?
RAYNELL.   Seeing if my garden growed.
ROSE.   I told you it ain't gonna grow overnight. You got to wait.
RAYNELL.   It don't look like it never gonna grow. Dag!
ROSE.   I told you a watched pot never boils. Get in here and get dressed.
RAYNELL.   This ain't even no pot, Mama.
ROSE.   You just have to give it a chance. It'll grow. Now you come on and
  do what I told you. We got to be getting ready. This ain't no morning to
  be playing around. You hear me?
RAYNELL.   Yes, mam.
    [ROSE *exits into the house.* RAYNELL *continues to poke at her garden
    with a stick.* CORY *enters. He is dressed in a Marine corporal's uni-
    form, and carries a duffel bag. His posture is that of a military man,
    and his speech has a clipped sternness.*]
CORY.   [*To* RAYNELL.] Hi.
    [*Pause.*]
  I bet your name is Raynell.
RAYNELL.   Uh huh.
CORY.   Is your mama home?
    [RAYNELL *runs up on the porch and calls through the screendoor.*]

RAYNELL.   Mama . . . there's some man out here. Mama?

[ROSE *comes to the door.*]

ROSE.   Cory? Lord have mercy! Look here, you all!

[ROSE *and* CORY *embrace in a tearful reunion as* BONO *and* LYONS *enter from the house dressed in funeral clothes.*]

BONO.   Aw, looka here . . .

ROSE.   Done got all grown up!

CORY.   Don't cry, Mama. What you crying about?

ROSE.   I'm just so glad you made it.

CORY.   Hey Lyons. How you doing, Mr. Bono.

[LYONS *goes to embrace* CORY.]

LYONS.   Look at you, man. Look at you. Don't he look good, Rose. Got them Corporal stripes.

ROSE.   What took you so long.

CORY.   You know how the Marines are, Mama. They got to get all their paperwork straight before they let you do anything.

ROSE.   Well, I'm sure glad you made it. They let Lyons come. Your Uncle Gabe's still in the hospital. They don't know if they gonna let him out or not. I just talked to them a little while ago.

LYONS.   A Corporal in the United States Marines.

BONO.   Your daddy knew you had it in you. He used to tell me all the time.

LYONS.   Don't he look good, Mr. Bono?

BONO.   Yeah, he remind me of Troy when I first met him.

[*Pause.*]

Say, Rose, Lucille's down at the church with the choir. I'm gonna go down and get the pallbearers lined up. I'll be back to get you all.

ROSE.   Thanks, Jim.

CORY.   See you, Mr. Bono.

LYONS.   [*With his arm around* RAYNELL.] Cory . . . look at Raynell. Ain't she precious? She gonna break a whole lot of hearts.

ROSE.   Raynell, come and say hello to your brother. This is your brother, Cory. You remember Cory.

RAYNELL.   No, Mam.

CORY.   She don't remember me, Mama.

ROSE.   Well, we talk about you. She heard us talk about you.

[*To* RAYNELL.] This is your brother, Cory. Come on and say hello.

RAYNELL.   Hi.

CORY.   Hi. So you're Raynell. Mama told me a lot about you.

ROSE.   You all come on into the house and let me fix you some breakfast. Keep up your strength.

CORY.   I ain't hungry, Mama.

LYONS.   You can fix me something, Rose. I'll be in there in a minute.

ROSE.   Cory, you sure you don't want nothing. I know they ain't feeding you right.

CORY.   No, Mama . . . thanks. I don't feel like eating. I'll get something later.

ROSE.   Raynell . . . get on upstairs and get that dress on like I told you.

[ROSE *and* RAYNELL *exit into the house.*]

LYONS.   So . . . I hear you thinking about getting married.

CORY.   Yeah, I done found the right one, Lyons. It's about time.

LYONS.   Me and Bonnie been split up about four years now. About the time Papa retired. I guess she just got tired of all them changes I was putting her through.

   [*Pause.*]

   I always knew you was gonna make something out yourself. Your head was always in the right direction. So . . . you gonna stay in . . . make it a career . . . put in your twenty years?

CORY.   I don't know. I got six already, I think that's enough.

LYONS.   Stick with Uncle Sam and retire early. Ain't nothing out here. I guess Rose told you what happened with me. They got me down the workhouse. I thought I was being slick cashing other people's checks.

CORY.   How much time you doing?

LYONS.   They give me three years. I got that beat now. I ain't got but nine more months. It ain't so bad. You learn to deal with it like anything else. You got to take the crookeds with the straights. That's what Papa used to say. He used to say that when he struck out. I seen him strike out three times in a row . . . and the next time up he hit the ball over the grandstand. Right out there in Homestead Field. He wasn't satisfied hitting in the seats . . . he want to hit it over everything! After the game he had two hundred people standing around waiting to shake his hand. You got to take the crookeds with the straights. Yeah, Papa was something else.

CORY.   You still playing?

LYONS.   Cory . . . you know I'm gonna do that. There's some fellows down there we got us a band . . . we gonna try and stay together when we get out . . . but yeah, I'm still playing. It still helps me to get out of bed in the morning. As long as it do that I'm gonna be right there playing and trying to make some sense out of it.

ROSE.   [*Calling.*] Lyons, I got these eggs in the pan.

LYONS.   Let me go on and get these eggs, man. Get ready to go bury Papa.

   [*Pause.*]

   How you doing? You doing alright?

   [CORY *nods.* LYONS *touches him on the shoulder and they share a moment of silent grief.* LYONS *exits into the house.* CORY *wanders about the yard.* RAYNELL *enters.*]

RAYNELL.   Hi.

CORY.   Hi.

RAYNELL.   Did you used to sleep in my room?

CORY.   Yeah . . . that used to be my room.

RAYNELL.   That's what Papa call it. "Cory's room." It got your football in the closet.

   [ROSE *comes to the door.*]

ROSE.   Raynell, get in there and get them good shoes on.

RAYNELL.   Mama, can't I wear these. Them other one hurt my feet.

ROSE.   Well, they just gonna have to hurt your feet for a while. You ain't said they hurt your feet when you went down to the store and got them.

RAYNELL.   They didn't hurt then. My feet done got bigger.

ROSE.   Don't you give me no backtalk now. You get in there and get them shoes on.

[RAYNELL *exits into the house.*]

Ain't too much changed. He still got that piece of rag tied to that tree. He was out here swinging that bat. I was just ready to go back in the house. He swung that bat and then he just fell over. Seem like he swung it and stood there with this grin on his face . . . and then he just fell over. They carried him on down to the hospital, but I knew there wasn't no need . . . why don't you come on in the house?

CORY.   Mama . . . I got something to tell you. I don't know how to tell you this . . . but I've got to tell you . . . I'm not going to Papa's funeral.

ROSE.   Boy, hush your mouth. That's your daddy you talking about. I don't want hear that kind of talk this morning. I done raised you to come to this? You standing there all healthy and grown talking about you ain't going to your daddy's funeral?

CORY.   Mama . . . listen . . .

ROSE.   I don't want to hear it, Cory. You just get that thought out of your head.

CORY.   I can't drag Papa with me everywhere I go. I've got to say no to him. One time in my life I've got to say no.

ROSE.   Don't nobody have to listen to nothing like that. I know you and your daddy ain't seen eye to eye, but I ain't got to listen to that kind of talk this morning. Whatever was between you and your daddy . . . the time has come to put it aside. Just take it and set it over there on the shelf and forget about it. Disrespecting your daddy ain't gonna make you a man, Cory. You got to find a way to come to that on your own. Not going to your daddy's funeral ain't gonna make you a man.

CORY.   The whole time I was growing up . . . living in his house . . . Papa was like a shadow that followed you everywhere. It weighed on you and sunk into your flesh. It would wrap around you and lay there until you couldn't tell which one was you anymore. That shadow digging in your flesh. Trying to crawl in. Trying to live through you. Everywhere I looked, Troy Maxson was staring back at me . . . hiding under the bed . . . in the closet. I'm just saying I've got to find a way to get rid of that shadow, Mama.

ROSE.   You just like him. You got him in you good.

CORY.   Don't tell me that, Mama.

ROSE.   You Troy Maxson all over again.

CORY.   I don't want to be Troy Maxson. I want to be me.

ROSE.   You can't be nobody but who you are, Cory. That shadow wasn't nothing but you growing into yourself. You either got to grow into it or cut it down to fit you. But that's all you got to make life with. That's all you got to measure yourself against that world out there. Your daddy wanted you to be everything he wasn't . . . and at the same time he tried to make you into everything he was. I don't know if he was right or wrong . . . but I do know he meant to do more good than he meant to do harm. He wasn't always right. Sometimes when he touched he bruised. And sometimes when he took me in his arms he cut.

When I first met your daddy I thought . . . Here is a man I can lay down with and make a baby. That's the first thing I thought when I seen him. I was thirty years old and had done seen my share of men. But when he walked up to me and said, "I can dance a waltz that'll make you dizzy," I thought, Rose Lee, here is a man that you can open yourself up to and be filled to bursting. Here is a man that can fill all them empty spaces you been tipping around the edges of. One of them empty spaces was being somebody's mother.

I married your daddy and settled down to cooking his supper and keeping clean sheets on the bed. When your daddy walked through the house he was so big he filled it up. That was my first mistake. Not to make him leave some room for me. For my part in the matter. But at that time I wanted that. I wanted a house that I could sing in. And that's what your daddy gave me. I didn't know to keep up his strength I had to give up little pieces of mine. I did that. I took on his life as mine and mixed up the pieces so that you couldn't hardly tell which was which anymore. It was my choice. It was my life and I didn't have to live it like that. But that's what life offered me in the way of being a woman and I took it. I grabbed hold of it with both hands.

By the time Raynell came into the house, me and your daddy had done lost touch with one another. I didn't want to make my blessing off of nobody's misfortune . . . but I took on to Raynell like she was all them babies I had wanted and never had.

[*The phone rings.*]

Like I'd been blessed to relive a part of my life. And if the Lord see fit to keep up my strength . . . I'm gonna do her just like your daddy did you . . . I'm gonna give her the best of what's in me.

RAYNELL. [*Entering, still with her old shoes.*] Mama . . . Reverend Tollivier on the phone.

[ROSE *exits into the house.*]

RAYNELL. Hi.

CORY. Hi.

RAYNELL. You in the Army or the Marines?

CORY. Marines.

RAYNELL. Papa said it was the Army. Did you know Blue?

CORY. Blue? Who's Blue?

RAYNELL. Papa's dog what he sing about all the time.

CORY. [*Singing.*] Hear it ring! Hear it ring!
I had a dog his name was Blue
You know Blue was mighty true
You know Blue was a good old dog
Blue treed a possum in a hollow log
You know from that he was a good old dog.
Hear it ring! Hear it ring!

[RAYNELL *joins in singing.*]

CORY and RAYNELL. Blue treed a possum out on a limb
Blue looked at me and I looked at him
Grabbed that possum and put him in a sack
Blue stayed there till I came back

Old Blue's feets was big and round
Never allowed a possum to touch the ground.

Old Blue died and I dug his grave
I dug his grave with a silver spade
Let him down with a golden chain
And every night I call his name
Go on Blue, you good dog you
Go on Blue, you good dog you

RAYNELL. Blue laid down and died like a man
Blue laid down and died . . .

BOTH. Blue laid down and died like a man
Now he's treeing possums in the Promised Land
I'm gonna tell you this to let you know
Blue's gone where the good dogs go
When I hear old Blue bark
When I hear old Blue bark
Blue treed a possum in Noah's Ark
Blue treed a possum in Noah's Ark.

[ROSE *comes to the screen door.*]

ROSE. Cory, we gonna be ready to go in a minute.

CORY. [*To* RAYNELL.] You go on in the house and change them shoes like Mama told you so we can go to Papa's funeral.

RAYNELL. Okay, I'll be back.

[RAYNELL *exits into the house.* CORY *gets up and crosses over to the tree.* ROSE *stands in the screen door watching him.* GABRIEL *enters from the alley.*]

GABRIEL. [*Calling.*] Hey, Rose!

ROSE. Gabe?

GABRIEL. I'm here, Rose. Hey Rose, I'm here!

[ROSE *enters from the house.*]

ROSE. Lord . . . Look here, Lyons!

LYONS. See, I told you, Rose . . . I told you they'd let him come.

CORY. How you doing, Uncle Gabe?

LYONS. How you doing, Uncle Gabe?

GABRIEL. Hey, Rose. It's time. It's time to tell St. Peter to open the gates. Troy, you ready? You ready, Troy. I'm gonna tell St. Peter to open the gates. You get ready now.

[GABRIEL, *with great fanfare, braces himself to blow. The trumpet is without a mouthpiece. He puts the end of it into his mouth and blows with great force, like a man who has been waiting some twenty-odd years for this single moment. No sound comes out of the trumpet. He braces himself and blows again with the same result. A third time he blows. There is a weight of impossible description that falls away and leaves him bare and exposed to a frightful realization. It is a trauma that a sane and normal mind would be unable to withstand. He begins to dance. A slow, strange dance, eerie and lifegiving. A dance of atavistic signature and ritual.* LYONS *attempts to embrace him.* GABRIEL *pushes* LYONS *away. He begins to howl in what is an attempt*]

at song, or perhaps a song turning back into itself in an attempt at
speech. He finishes his dance and the gates of heaven stand open as
wide as God's closet.]
That's the way that go!
[*BLACKOUT.*]

1987

MICHELLE CLIFF

b. 1946

In Michelle Cliff's work—the stories, poems, and essays that she has been publishing since the late 1970s—race, sexuality, and the tensions experienced both in the United States and in Britain by its Caribbean immigrants come together with particular force.

Born on November 2, 1946, in Kingston, Jamaica, Cliff emigrated to the United States when she was three years old. Until she was ten, she lived in New York City with her mother and sister, then returned to Jamaica, where, fair-skinned enough to pass for white herself, she was shocked by the island's attention to color, especially prominent in the private girls' school that she attended. In the mid-1960s she left to continue her education in London, receiving an A.B. from Wagner College in 1969, and in 1974 an M.Phil. in comparative literature from the Warburg Institute, with a thesis on the historical study of the Renaissance.

Despite the academic start to her career, Cliff sees her essay *Notes on Speechlessness*, published in the lesbian-feminist magazine *Conditions* II in 1977, as her first real piece of writing. In *Notes on Speechlessness* Cliff identifies with Victor, the Wild Boy of Aveyron, who, "after his rescue from the forest and wildness by a well-meaning doctor of Enlightenment Europe, became 'civilized' but never came to speech." Certainly this is a surprising identification, especially for a woman who had worked as a journalist, researcher, editor, teacher, and historian, all jobs requiring excellent written or verbal skills. Ultimately, it points to one of Cliff's main concerns, that is with "speech," by which she means not outward oral expression but instead the complex surfacing of material hidden from both the self and others.

A second major concern of Cliff's is her return to Jamaica, whose dispersed images she must reclaim, almost as if she were part of the diaspora brought about by slavery. Having lived in both the United States and the Caribbean, and in England, the country responsible for Jamaica's colonial past, Cliff turns constantly from one cultural identification to another, trying to sort them out, an activity that is central to her first novel, *Abeng* (1984), and to *No Telephone to Heaven* (1987). These same concerns surface in the short story *Columba*, from her 1990 collection *Bodies of Water*, in which the narrator, a twelve-year-old girl just returned to Jamaica from New York, experiences the sensory power of the tropical world at the same time that she apprehends its colonial scars and its domestic mysteries.

Michelle Cliff has received both a Macdowell fellowship and a fellowship from the National Endowment for the Arts. She has taught at the New School, Hampshire College, the University of Massachusetts at Amherst, Vista College, and Trinity College. Her most recent novel, *Free Enterprise*, was published in 1993.

Within the Veil

Color ain't no faucet
You can't turn it off and on
I say, color ain't no faucet
You can't turn it off and on
Tell the world who you are   5
Or you might as well be gone.

Now, the whiteman makes the rules
But we got to learn to turn them down
Yes, baby, the whiteman makes the rules
But we got to learn to turn them down   10
Can't abide this shit no longer
We got to swing the thing around.

You can pass[1] in many ways, mama
This is one thing that I know
I say, you can pass in many ways, mama   15
This is one thing that I know
Unless you quit your passing, honey
You only gonna come to woe.

Oh, we can call them ofay[2]
By that we mean the foe   20
Yes, sisters, we can call them ofay
By that we mean the foe
But that's only half the battle
You lie if you tell me you don't know.

Now Zora[3] was a genius   25
But there were some did call her fool
I say, Zora was a genius
But there were some did call her fool
Now, you consider mules and men[4]
And how many times she broke the whiteman's rule.   30

Some of us come from islands
And some of us born in the U.S.A.
Some of us come from islands
And some of us born in the U.S.A.
There are those of us who marry   35
And others who will always be gay.

No two people are the same
It's what gives life a thrilling twist
No two people are the same, children

1. I.e., pass for white.
2. Derogatory term for a white person (*foe* in Pig Latin).
3. Zora Neale Hurston (1903–1960), African American writer and anthropologist, best known for her novel *Their Eyes Were Watching God*.

4. Reference to Hurston's book *Mules and Men* (1935), a class of African American ethnography, in which Hurston documented the oral folklore traditions of southern blacks as well as some of their musical and religious practices.

That's what gives life a thrilling twist   40
How dare anyone object
Tell me I had better not exist.

Some of us use the hot comb[5]
And some of us have natural hair
Yes, sisters, some of us use the hot comb   45
And some of us have natural hair
You should ponder Madame C. J. Walker[6]
Before you suck your teeth and stare.

Sister Lorraine[7] talked revolution
Talked of "the beauty of things Black"   50
Yes, Lorraine talked revolution, baby
Talked of "the beauty of things Black"
And then she was killed by cancer
Just like a well-aimed shot in her strong brown back.

Your best friend's a bulldagger[8]   55
That is very plain to see
I say, your best friend's a bulldagger
That is very plain to see
Now that you been told it
Can you tell them you love me?   60

We got to love each other
That is what is known as the bottom line
I say, we got to love each other
That is what they call the bottom line
Can't say to each other   65
To hell with you, this piece of the world is mine.

Some of us part Indian
And some of us part white
Yes, sisters, some of us part Indian
And some of us part white   70
But we still will call you sisters
Even if you judge our skin too light.

Gold chains are love-symbols
You tell me where they are found
Yes, gold chains are love-symbols   75
You tell me where gold is found
There are deep mines in South Africa
Where our brothers sweat their lives underground.

5. Presumably refers to conking, or using heated lye to straighten hair.
6. Highly successful businesswoman (1867–1919), developer of cosmetic and hair preparations for African American women.
7. Lorraine Hansberry (1930–1965), African American playwright, best known for *A Raisin in the Sun* (1959).
8. Female homosexual who takes the masculine role in a lesbian relationship; a variation of *bull dyke*.

God loves the babies in Soweto[9]
And the babies in Harlem too   80
I say, God loves the babies in Soweto
And the babies in Harlem too
But his love alone can't save them
We got to figure what we can do.

If we say Third World Revolution   85
The white folks say World War III
If we say Third World Revolution, baby
The white folks say World War III
Seems they imagine Armageddon
Is prettier than if we be free.   90

I got brothers and sisters in prison
All across the U.S.A.
Yes, I got brothers and sisters in prison
All across the U.S.A.
Some folks broke the rules   95
Others just been put away.

Elijah Pate was gunned down
Shot five times by the Boston cops
Yes, Brother Elijah was gunned down
Shot five times by the Boston cops   100
And the d.a. won't bring charges
Says Elijah gunned his car and wouldn't stop.

They want us in their factories
And they want us in their homes
I say, they want us in their factories   105
and they want us in their homes
They'll take some for their armed forces
And some more for their astrodomes.

They see our brothers as monsters
Or as harmless smart-assed little boys   110
they judge our brothers to be monsters
Want to keep them harmless little boys
Let just one speak his piece
And watch the guns replace the toys.

Don't overstep your boundaries   115
Act like you have a little sense
No, don't overstep your boundaries, girl
Act like you have a little sense
Was the lesson my mama taught me
To live surrounded by a whiteman's fence.   120

It's all about survival
And about how to get by

9. Black townships southwest of Johannesburg, South Africa; the site of much poverty and unrest.

Yes, it's all about survival
And about how to get by
But we got to do it better   125
Else we might as well lay down and die.

1985

Columba

When I was twelve my parents left me in the hands of a hypochondriacal
aunt and her Cuban lover, a ham radio operator. Her lover, that is, until
she claimed their bed as her own. She was properly a family friend, who
met my grandmother when they danced the Black Bottom[1] at the Glass
Bucket. Jamaica in the twenties was wild.

This woman, whose name was Charlotte, was large and pink and given
to wearing pink satin nighties—flimsy relics, pale from age. Almost all was
pink in that room, so it seemed; so it seems now, at this distance. The lace
trim around the necks of the nighties was not pink; it was yellowed and
frazzled, practically absent. Thin wisps of thread which had once formed
flowers, birds, a spider's web. Years of washing in hard water with brown
soap had made the nighties loose, droop, so that Charlotte's huge breasts
slid outside, suddenly, sideways, pink falling on pink like ladylike camouflage, but for her livid nipples. No one could love those breasts, I think.

Her hair stuck flat against her head, bobbed and straightened, girlish
bangs as if painted on her forehead. Once she had resembled Louise
Brooks.[2] No longer. New moons arced each black eye.

Charlotte was also given to drinking vast amounts of water from the crystal carafes standing on her low bedside table, next to her *Information Please
Almanac*—she had a fetish for detail but no taste for reading—linen hankies
scented with bay rum, and a bowl of soursweet tamarind[3] balls. As she
drank, so did she piss, ringing changes on the walls of chamber pots lined
under the bed, all through the day and night. Her room, her pink expanse,
smelled of urine and bay rum and the wet sugar which bound the tamarind
balls. Ancestral scents.

I was to call her Aunt Charlotte and to mind her, for she was officially *in
loco parentis.*[4]

The Cuban, Juan Antonio Corona y Mestee, slept on a safari cot next to
his ham radio, rum bottle, stacks of *Punch, Country Life,*[5] and something
called *Gent.* His room was a screened-in porch at the side of the verandah.
Sitting there with him in the evening, listening to the calls of the radio, I
could almost imagine myself away from that place, in the bush awaiting
capture, or rescue, until the sharp PING! of Charlotte's water cut across
even my imaginings and the scratch of faraway voices.

One night a young man vaulted the rail of a cruise ship off Tobago[6] and

---

1. A popular dance; also, slang name for the area
where the poorer black population of any town or
city resides.
2. Early film star (1896–1985), popular during the
1920s; her best-known film, the classic *Pandora's
Box*, was made in Germany.
3. Fruit of the tropical evergreen tree; its acid pulp
is used in making drinks and candies.
4. Taking the place of normal parental authority

(Latin).
5. British magazine displaying life among upper-
class Britons, especially those living on country estates. "*Punch*": British magazine satirizing life
among upper-class Britons.
6. West Indian island off the northeast coast of
Venezuela, now part of the independent republic
of Trinidad and Tobago.

we picked up the distress call. A sustained SPLASH! followed Charlotte's PING! and the young man slipped under the waves.

I have never been able to forget him, and capture him in a snap of that room, as though he floated through it, me. I wonder still, why that particular instant? That warm evening, the Southern Cross[7] in clear view? The choice of a sea-change?

His mother told the captain they had been playing bridge with another couple when her son excused himself. We heard all this on the radio, as the captain reported in full. Henry Fonda sprang to my movie-saturated mind, in *The Lady Eve*,[8] with Barbara Stanwyck. But that was blackjack, not bridge, and a screwball comedy besides.

Perhaps the young man had tired of the coupling. Perhaps he needed a secret sharer.[9]

The Cuban was a tall handsome man with blue-black hair and a costume of unvarying khaki. He seemed content to stay with Charlotte, use the whores in Raetown[1] from time to time, listen to his radio, sip his rum, leaf through his magazines. Sitting on the side of the safari cot in his khaki, engaged in his pastimes, he seemed like a displaced white hunter (except he wasn't white, a fact no amount of relaxers or wide-brimmed hats could mask) or a mercenary recuperating from battle fatigue, awaiting further orders.

Perhaps he did not stir for practical reasons. This was 1960; he could not return to Cuba in all his hyphenated splendor, and had no marketable skills for the British Crown Colony in which he found himself. I got along with him, knowing we were both there on sufferance, unrelated dependants. Me, because Charlotte owed my grandmother something, he, for whatever reason he or she might have.

One of Juan Antonio's duties was to drop me at school. Each morning he pressed a half-crown into my hand, always telling me to treat my friends. I appreciated his largesse, knowing the money came from his allowance. It was a generous act and he asked no repayment but one small thing: I was to tell anyone who asked that he was my father. As I remember, no one ever did. Later, he suggested that I say "Goodbye, Papá"—with the accent on the last syllable—when I left the car each morning. I hesitated, curious. He said, "Never mind," and the subject was not brought up again.

I broke the chain of generosity and kept his money for myself, not willing to share it with girls who took every chance to ridicule my American accent and call me "salt."[2]

I used the money to escape them, escape school. Sitting in the movies, watching them over and over until it was time to catch the bus back.

Charlotte was a woman of property. Her small house was a cliché of colonialism, graced with calendars advertising the coronation of ER II, the

---

7. Southern Hemisphere constellation with four bright stars situated as if at the ends of a Latin cross.
8. A 1941 film about the outwitting of a female cardsharper and her father by a millionaire simpleton.
9. Perhaps an allusion to Joseph Conrad's story

The Secret Sharer, in which the young captain of a ship hides a fugitive who begins to seem like a mysterious twin of himself.
1. A district in Kingston, Jamaica.
2. Perhaps a reference to the narrator's skin color.

marriage of Princess Margaret Rose, the visit of Alice, Princess Royal.[3] Bamboo and wicker furniture was sparsely scattered across dark mahogany floors—settee there, end table here—giving the place the air of a hotel lobby, the sort of hotel carved from the shell of a great house, before Hilton and Sheraton made landfall. Tortoiseshell lampshades. Ashtrays made from coconut husks. Starched linen runners sporting the embroideries of craftswomen.

The house sat on top of a hill in Kingston, surrounded by an unkempt estate—so unkempt as to be arrogant, for this was the wealthiest part of the city, and the largest single tract of land. So large that a dead quiet enveloped the place in the evening, and we were cut off, sound and light absorbed by the space and the dark and the trees, abandoned and wild, entangled by vines and choked by underbrush, escaped, each reaching to survive.

At the foot of the hill was a cement gully which bordered the property— an empty moat but for the detritus of trespassers. Stray dogs roamed amid Red Stripe beer bottles, crushed cigarette packets, bully-beef tins.

Trespassers, real and imagined, were Charlotte's passion. In the evening, after dinner, bed-jacket draped across her shoulders against the soft trade winds, which she said were laden with typhoid, she roused herself to the verandah and took aim. She fired and fired and fired. Then she excused herself. "That will hold them for another night." She was at once terrified of invasion and confident she could stay it. Her gunplay was ritual against it.

There was, of course, someone responsible for cleaning the house, feeding the animals, filling the carafes and emptying the chamber pots, cooking the meals and doing the laundry. These tasks fell to Columba, a fourteen-year-old from St. Ann, where Charlotte had bartered him from his mother; a case of condensed milk, two dozen tins of sardines, five pounds of flour, several bottles of cooking oil, permission to squat on Charlotte's cane-piece—fair exchange. His mother set up housekeeping with his brothers and sisters, and Columba was transported in the back of Charlotte's black Austin[4] to Kingston. A more magnanimous, at least practical, landowner would have had a staff of two, even three, but Charlotte swore against being taken advantage of, as she termed it, so all was done by Columba, learning to expand his skills under her teaching, instructions shouted from the bed.

He had been named not for our discoverer, but for the saint buried on Iona, discoverer of the monster in the loch. A Father Pierre, come to St. Ann from French Guiana,[5] had taught Columba's mother, Winsome, to write her name, read a ballot, and know God. He said he had been assistant to the confessor on Devil's Island,[6] and when the place was finally shut down in 1951 he was cast adrift, floating around the islands seeking a berth. His word was good enough for the people gathered in his seaside chapel

3. Members of the British royal family, especially Queen Elizabeth II ("ER II"), the reigning monarch.
4. British automobile.
5. Country in northeast South America. Iona is an

Inner Hebrides Island, off the coast of Scotland. In 563 St. Columba founded a monastery there and spread Christianity to Scotland.
6. Island off French Guiana, until 1951 the site of a penal colony used mostly for political prisoners.

of open sides and thatched roof, used during the week to shelter a woman smashing limestone for the road, sorting trilobite[7] from rock. On Sunday morning people sang, faces misted by spray, air heavy with the scent of sea grapes, the fat purple bunches bowing, swinging, brushing the glass sand, bruised. Bruises releasing more scent, entering the throats of a congregation fighting the smash of the sea. On Sunday morning Father Pierre talked to them of God, dredging his memory for every tale he had been told.

This was good enough for these people. They probably couldn't tell a confessor from a convict—which is what Father Pierre was—working off his crime against nature by boiling the life out of yam and taro[8] and salted beef for the wardens, his keepers.

Even after the *Gleaner* had broadcast the real story, the congregation stood fast: he was white; he knew God—they reasoned. Poor devils.

Father Pierre held Columba's hand at the boy's baptism. He was ten years old then and had been called "Junior" all his life. Why honor an un-named sire? Father Pierre spoke to Winsome. "Children," the priest intoned, "the children become their names." He spoke in an English as broken as hers.

What Father Pierre failed to reckon with was the unfamiliar nature of the boy's new name; Columba was "Collie" to some, "Like one damn dawg," his mother said. "Chuh, man. Hignorant smaddy cyaan[9] accept not'ing new." Collie soon turned Lassie and he was shamed.

To Charlotte he became "Colin," because she insisted on Anglicization. It was for his own good, she added for emphasis, and so he would recognize her kindness. His name-as-is was foolish and feminine and had been given him by a *pedophile*, for heaven's sake.

Charlotte's shouts reached Columba in the kitchen. He was attempting to put together a gooseberry fool[1] for the mistress's elevenses. The word *pedophile* smacked the stucco of the corridor between them, each syllable distinct, perversion bouncing furiously off the walls. I had heard—who hadn't?—but the word was beyond me. I was taking Latin, not Greek.

I softly asked Juan Antonio and he, in equally hushed tones, said, "Mariposa[2] . . . butterfly."

Charlotte wasn't through. "Fancy naming a boy after a bird. A black boy after a white bird. And still people attend that man. . . . Well, they will get what they deserve," she promised. "You are lucky I saved you from that." She spoke with such conviction.

I was forbidden to speak with Columba except on matters of household business, encouraged by Charlotte to complain when the pleat of my school tunic was not sharp enough. I felt only awkward that a boy two years older than myself was responsible for my laundry, for feeding me, for making my bed. I was, after all, an American now, only here temporarily. I did not keep the commandment.

I sought him out in secret. When Juan Antonio went downtown and

---

7. A fossil animal.
8. A tropical plant with edible tubers.
9. Somebody can't (Jamaican patois).

1. Dessert made of fruit, custard, and cream.
2. Butterfly (Spanish, literal trans.); here, male homosexual.

while Charlotte dozed, the coast was clear. We sat behind the house under an ancient guava,[3] concealed by a screen of bougainvillea. There we talked. Compared lives. Exchanged histories. We kept each other company, and our need for company made our conversations almost natural. The alternative was a dreadful loneliness; silence, but for the noises of the two adults. Strangers.

His questions about America were endless. What was New York like? Had I been to Hollywood? He wanted to know every detail about Duke Ellington, Marilyn Monroe, Stagger Lee, Jackie Wilson, Ava Gardner, Billy the Kid, Dinah Washington, Tony Curtis, Spartacus, John Wayne. Everyone, every name he knew from the cinema, where he slipped on his evening off; every voice, ballad, beat, he heard over Rediffusion,[4] tuned low in the kitchen.

Did I know any of these people? Could you see them on the street? Then, startling me: what was life like for a black man in America? An ordinary black man, not a star?

I had no idea—not really. I had been raised in a community in New Jersey until this interruption, surrounded by people who had made their own world and "did not business" with that sort of thing. Bourgeois separatists. I told Columba I did not know and we went back to the stars and legends.

A Tuesday during rainy season: Charlotte, swathed in a plaid lap-robe lifted from the *Queen Mary*, is being driven by Juan Antonio to an ice factory she owns in Old Harbour. There is a problem with the overseer; Charlotte is summoned. You would think she was being transported a thousand miles up the Amazon into headhunter territory, so elaborate are the preparations.

She and Juan Antonio drop me at school. There is no half-crown this morning. I get sixpence and wave them off. I wait for the Austin to turn the corner at St. Cecilia's Way, then I cut to Lady Musgrave Road to catch the bus back.

When I return, I change and meet Columba out back. He has promised to show me something. The rain drips from the deep green of the escaped bush which surrounds us. We set out on a path invisible but to him, our bare feet sliding on slick fallen leaves. A stand of mahoe[5] is in front of us. We pass through the trees and come into a clearing.

In the clearing is a surprise: a wreck of a car, thirties Rover.[6] Gut-sprung, tired and forlorn, it slumps in the high grass. Lizards scramble through the vines which wrap around rusted chrome and across black hood and boot. We walk closer. I look into the wreck.

The leather seats are split and a white fluff erupts here and there. A blue gyroscope[7] set into the dash slowly rotates. A pennant of the Kingston Yacht Club dangles miserably from the rearview.

This is not all. The car is alive. Throughout, roaming the seats, perched on the running board, spackling the crystal face of the clock, are doves.

---

3. Small tropical tree with sweet fruit.
4. The broadcasting or rebroadcasting of a radio or television program (British).

5. Tropical hibiscus tree.
6. British automobile.
7. Probably part of the car's steering system.

White. Speckled. Rock. Mourning. Wreck turned dovecote is filled with
their sweet coos.

"Where did you find them?"

Columba is pleased, proud too, I think. "Nuh find dem nestin' all over
de place? I mek dem a home, give dem name. Dat one dere nuh Stagger
Lee?" He points to a mottled pigeon hanging from a visor. "Him is rascal fe
true."

Ava Gardner's feet click across the roof where Spartacus is hot in her
pursuit.

Columba and I sit among the birds for hours.

I thank him for showing them to me, promising on my honor not to tell.

That evening I am seated across from Charlotte and next to Juan Antonio in the dining room. The ceiling fan stirs the air, which is heavy with
the day's moisture.

Columba has prepared terrapin [8] and is serving us one by one. His head
is bowed so our eyes cannot meet, as they never do in such domestic moments. We—he and I—split our lives in this house as best we can. No one
watching this scene would imagine our meeting that afternoon, the wild
birds, talk of flight.

The turtle is sweet. A turtling man traded it for ice that morning in Old
Harbour. The curved shell sits on a counter in the kitchen. Golden. Delicate. Representing our island. Representing the world.

I did not tell them about the doves.

They found out easily, stupidly.

Charlotte's car had developed a knock in the engine. She noticed it on
the journey to the ice factory, and questioned me about it each evening
after that. Had I heard it on the way to school that morning? How could she
visit her other properties without proper transport? Something must be
done.

Juan Antonio suggested he take the Austin to the Texaco station at
Matilda's Corner. Charlotte would have none of it. She asked little from
Juan Antonio, the least he could do was maintain her automobile. What
did she suggest? he asked. How could he get parts to repair the Austin;
should he fashion them from bamboo?

She announced her solution: Juan Antonio was to take a machete and
chop his way through to the Rover. The car had served her well, she said,
surely it could be of use now. He resisted, reminding her that the Rover was
thirty years old, probably rusted beyond recognition, and not of any conceivable use. It did not matter.

The next morning Juan Antonio set off to chop his way through the
bush, dripping along the path, monkey wrench in his left hand, machete in
his right. Columba was in the kitchen, head down, wrapped in the heat of
burning coals as he fired irons to draw across khaki and satin.

The car, of course, was useless as a donor, but Juan Antonio's mission
was not a total loss. He was relieved to tell Charlotte about the doves. Why,
there must be a hundred. All kinds.

8. Turtle.

Charlotte was beside herself. Her property was the soul of bounty. Her trees bore heavily. Her chickens laid through hurricanes. Edible creatures abounded!

Neither recognized that these birds were not for killing. They did not recognize the pennant of the Kingston Yacht Club as the colors of this precious colony within a colony.

Columba was given his orders. Wring the necks of the birds. Pluck them and dress them and wrap them tightly for freezing. Leave out three for that evening's supper.

He did as he was told.

Recklessly I walked into the bush. No notice was taken.

I found him sitting in the front seat of the dovecote. A wooden box was beside him, half-filled with dead birds. The live ones did not scatter, did not flee. They sat and paced and cooed, as Columba performed his dreadful task.

"Sorry, man, you hear?" he said softly as he wrung the neck of the next one. He was weeping heavily. Heaving his shoulders with the effort of execution and grief.

I sat beside him in silence, my arm around his waist. This was not done.

1990

WANDA COLEMAN

b. 1946

Writer of drama, poetry, and short stories, and recipient of National Endowment for the Arts and Guggenheim fellowships, Wanda Coleman has for two decades been known in the classrooms, community centers, and rock clubs of Los Angeles as "an electrifying performer/reader" of her stark commentaries about those who have been excluded from the American Dream.

Coleman was born on November 13, 1946, in Los Angeles to George and Lewana (Scott) Evans. Her father was in advertising; her mother was a seamstress. After attending college for two years in Los Angeles, Coleman was writer in residence at Studio Watts from 1968 to 1969. From the beginning of her career in the late 1960s, Coleman was never an academic poet. She worked as a production assistant, a proofreader, a magazine editor, a waitress, and a recruiter for Peace Corps/ VISTA. She was a staff writer for the NBC daytime drama *Days of Our Lives* from 1975 to 1976 and won the 1976 Emmy Award for best writing in a daytime drama. From 1979 to 1981 Coleman worked as a medical transcriber and insurance billing clerk.

Since the 1970s Coleman's poems and stories have appeared in many periodicals, among them *Bachy, Partisan Review, Black American Literature Forum, Callaloo*, and *Michigan Quarterly Review*. Her first collection, *Art in the Court of the Blue Fag*, was published as a chapbook in 1977 and was followed in 1979 by *Mad Dog, Black Lady. Imagoes*, a collection of poetry and stories, appeared in 1983, to be followed by *Heavy Daughter Blues* (1987), *War of Eyes and Other Stories* (1988), and *African Sleeping Sickness* (1990). Her latest work is *Hard Dance* (1993).

Early in her career, Coleman stated, "I have one desire—to write. And through writing control, destroy, and create social institutions. I want to wield the power that belongs to the pen." *Los Angeles Times* reviewer Holly Prado has noted that Coleman's "heated and economical language and head-on sensibility take her work beyond brutality to fierce dignity." Many of Coleman's poems focus on women trying to survive the dual burdens of racism and sexism. Coming as it does from the street rather than from the academy, Coleman's work challenges the critical methods traditionally brought to bear on literature. Not surprisingly, the full impact of her uncompromising poetry remains to be felt.

Emmett Till [1]

1

river jordan [2] run red

rainfall panes the bottom acreage—rain
black earth blacker still

blackness seeps in seeps down
the mortal gravity of hate-inspired poverty   5
Jim Crow nidus [3]

the alabama the apalachicola the arkansas the aroostook
the altamaha [4]

killing of 14-year-old
stirs nation. there will be a public wake   10

works its way underground
scarred landscape veined by rage
sanctified waters flow
go forth

the bighorn the brazos   15

along roan valley walls blue rapids
wear away rock
flesh current quickly courses thru
the front page news amber fields purple mountains
muddies   20

the chattahoochee the cheyenne the chippewa the cimarron
the colorado the columbia the connecticut the cumberland

---

1. A fourteen-year-old black youth from Chicago who when visiting his grandparents in Mississippi in 1955 was tortured and killed for allegedly flirting with a white woman. His two white murderers were acquitted by an all-white jury, even though one of them admitted his guilt.
2. Important in both Judaism and Christianity. After the exodus from bondage in Egypt, the Israelites crossed the Jordan to the Promised Land; John the Baptist baptized Jesus in the Jordan.
3. A breeding place (usually of insects). "Jim Crow": laws adopted by southern states after Reconstruction to enforce racial segregation in schools, public transportation, theaters, hotels, and restaurants.
4. Rivers of the United States, listed throughout the poem (in alphabetical order, for the most part).

waftage

spirit uplifted eyes head heart
imitation of breath chest aheave   25
that grotesque swim up the styx[5]
level as rainwater culls into its floodplain

the des moines

blood river born

2

ebony robe aflow   30
swathed hair of the black madonna
bereft of babe

the flint

that hazel eye sees
the woman   35
she fine mighty fine
she set the sun arising in his thighs

the hudson the humboldt the illinois

and he let go a whistle
a smooth long all-american hallelujah whistle   40
appreciation. a boy

the james the klamath

but she be a white woman. but he be
a black boy

the maumee the minnesota the mississippi the missouri   45
the mohican

raping her with that hazel eye

the ohio

make some peckerwood pass water mad
make a whole tributary of intolerance   50

the pearl the pecos the pee dee the penobscot
the north platte the south platte the potomac

vital fluid streaming forth in holy torrents

---

5. The mythical river, encircling the Greek underworld of Hades, over which Charon the boatman ferries
the souls of the dead.

think about it. go mad go blind
go back to africa go civil rights go go   55

the red the white the green

run wine

3

silt shallows the slow sojourn seaward

they awakened him from sleep
that early fall morning   60
they made him dress
they hurried Emmett down to the water's edge

the roanoke

after the deed
they weighted him down   65
tossed him in
for his violation

the sacramento the salt the san juan the savannah
the smoke

from the deep dank murk of consciousness a birth   70
oh say do you see the men off
the bank dredging in that
strange jetsam

the tennessee the trinity

a lesson   75
he had to be taught—crucified (all a nigger
got on his mind) for rape by eye that
wafer-round hazel offender plucked out
they crown him

the wabash   80

cuz she was white woman virtue and he
be a black boy lust

the yazoo the yellowstone

oh say Emmett Till can you see Emmett Till
crossed over into campground   85

spill tears
nimbus threatening downpour
sweetwater culls into its soulplain

come forth to carry the dead child home

4

at my mouth forking   90

autumn 1955, lord!
kidnapped from his family visit
            lord!
      money road shanty
            lord!   95
         his face smashed in
            lord! lord!
his body beaten beyond cognition

      river mother carries him
            laid in state   100
         sovereign at last

   that all may witness true majesty
            cast eyes upon

               murder

      the youth's body too light   105
was weighted down in barbed wire & steel

dumped into the river agape a ripple a wave
         (once it was human)

   aweigh. awade in water. bloated
            baptized   110

      and on that third day awaft
from the mulky arm of the tallahatchie
   stretched cross cotton-rich flats
            of delta

         on that third day   115
            he rose

and was carried forth to that promised land

                                                   1990

Today I Am a Homicide in the North of the City

on this bus to oblivion i bleed in the seat
numb silent rider
bent to poverty/my blackness covers me like the
american flag over the coffin of some hero killed in action
unlike him i have remained unrecognized, unrewarded   5
eyes cloaked in the shroud of hopelessness
search advancing avenues for a noisy haven

billboards press against my face
reminders of what i can't afford to buy
laughing fantasies speed past in molded steel luxury   10
i get off at a dark corner
and in my too tight slacks
move into the slow graceful mood of shadow

i know my killer is out there

1990

be quiet. go away

VOICES

i hear voices. i hear them often. i've heard them
since childhood. soft persistences
shapeless. they come unexpected. hover on my sleep
pierce and distract my study   5
speaking in rainbow they discuss me as if i'm
the ghost. say wrong things about me. tell me
i'm different i don't belong
i hear them. the voices. the noise of lies & analyses
threatening to follow me into life   10

1991

At the Record Hop

bobby-soxers exchange clandestine feels
in dark hallways of junior high gym
young black bodies humped hard to
hully gully shimmy peanut butter

puberty   5

embarrassment
menstrual red stains white pleated skirt
catching on to 2-tone socks
when nylons are in
losing worn elastic in cotton panties   10
threatening to drop
a cherry bomb
into the eyes of hungry young men

the only girl not asked to dance

allegiance is pledged earnest honk honk   15
of low rider bird horn and street racers rule turf
with hot rubber and zip guns
me/the intellectual square looks on in maimed silence
wish

lonely bus ride home   20
up front staring straight ahead

in the back of the bus
giggles. eager hands. lips learn to french

wonder why boys don't like me

                                                        1991

American Sonnet (10)

after Lowell

our mothers wrung hell and hardtack from row
          and boll. fenced others'
gardens with bones of lovers. embarking
          from Africa in chains
reluctant pilgrims stolen by Jehovah's[1] light   5
          planted here the bitter
seed of blight and here eternal torches mark
          the shame of Moloch's[2] mansions
built in slavery's name. our hungered eyes
          do see/refuse the dark   10
illuminate the blood-soaked steps of each
          historic gain. a yearning
yearning to avenge the raping of the womb
          from which we spring

                                                        1993

Bedtime Story

bed calls. i sit in the dark in the living room
trying to ignore them

in the morning, especially Sunday mornings
it will not let me up. you must sleep
longer, it says   5

facing south
the bed makes me lay heavenward on my back
while i prefer a westerly fetal position
facing the wall

the bed sucks me sideways into it when i   10
sit down on it to put on my shoes. this
persistence on its part forces me to dress in
the bathroom where things are less subversive

1. God of the Old Testament.   worship included human sacrifice, ordeals by fire,
2. Malevolent deity in the Old Testament whose   and self-mutilation.

the bed lumps up in anger springs popping out to
scratch my dusky thighs 15

my little office sits in the alcove adjacent to
the bed. it makes strange little sighs
which distract me from my work
sadistically i pull back the covers
put my typewriter on the sheet and turn it on 20

the bed complains that i'm difficult duty
its slats are collapsing. it bitches when i
blanket it with books and papers. it tells me
it's made for blood and bone

lately spiders ants and roaches 25
have invaded it searching for food

1993

Mastectomy

the fall of
velvet plum points and umber aureolae

remember living

forget cool evening air kisses the rush of
liberation freed from the brassiere 5

forget the cupping of his hands the pleasure
his eyes looking down/anticipating

forget his mouth. his tongue at the nipples
his intense hungry nursing

forget sensations which begin either 10
on the right or the left. go thru the body
linger between thighs

forget the space once grasped during his ecstasy

sweet sweet mama you taste so

1993

OCTAVIA BUTLER

b. 1947

Since the late 1970s, Octavia Butler has been writing an extended cycle of science
fiction novels that have been popular among African American women as well as
the mainstream. Her Patternist series, which includes *Patternmaster* (1976), *Mind*

of My Mind (1977), *Survivor* (1978), *Wild Seed* (1980), and *Clay's Ark* (1984), immerses the reader in a fully rendered universe whose central figure is a four-thousand-year-old immortal named Doro. Able to move at will, from body to body and across time periods, Doro sustains himself by appropriating the bodies of others, regardless of gender or race, although he prefers to inhabit black males. A powerful Nubian patriarch who maintains his supremacy by using his exceptional psychic powers and physical strength, Doro has fathered enough descendants to build a dynasty known as "the Pattern." In this series, Butler has also created Mary, one of Doro's daughters, an exceptionally gifted telepath, as well as Emma, who adopts Mary and is a strong, elegant female figure, in many ways a prototypical feminist science fiction character.

Born in Pasadena, California, in 1947, and raised by her mother and grandmother (her father died shortly after her birth), Butler, an introspective only child in a strict Baptist household, was drawn early to magazines such as *Amazing, Fantasy and Science Fiction*, and *Galaxy* and soon began reading all the science fiction classics. She was particularly impressed by Ursula Le Guin's *Dispossessed* and the first of Frank Herbert's Dune series. California, with its highly fluid, ethnically mixed population, has long been a congenial birthplace for science fiction about imaginative mixes of societies, time periods, and races, producing some of the genre's finest writers, including A. E. Van Vogt, Philip K. Dick, and Harlan Ellison, who discovered Butler through the "Open Door" program of the Writer's Guild. After a short time writing "terrible stories about thirty-year-old men who drank and smoked too much," Butler began composing early versions of what would become the Patternist series.

Butler's best-known book, *Kindred* (1988), was originally intended to be a Patternist novel, but was too realistic to fit into its futurist frame. In *Kindred*, Dana, a twenty-six-year-old black woman, is transported from the 1970s Los Angeles suburb where she lives with her white husband, to a Maryland plantation in the antebellum South; there she finds herself the property of a family whose eldest son, Rufus, has summoned her to save him. Throughout this fantasy, Butler describes how the imprint of slavery is carried not only in the minds but also on the bodies of all African Americans, as symbolized in the novel by Dana's loss of an arm during her ordeal.

Although Butler writes short fiction only infrequently, *Bloodchild*, anthologized here, is one of her most powerful, well-crafted efforts. As do her novels, Butler's story challenges our contemporary ideas about gender and race in a futuristic way that few African American writers have attempted. Her most recent book is *Parable of the Sower* (1993).

Bloodchild

My last night of childhood began with a visit home. T'Gatoi's sisters had given us two sterile eggs. T'Gatoi gave one to my mother, brother, and sisters. She insisted that I eat the other one alone. It didn't matter. There was still enough to leave everyone feeling good. Almost everyone. My mother wouldn't take any. She sat, watching everyone drifting and dreaming without her. Most of the time she watched me.

I lay against T'Gatoi's long, velvet underside, sipping from my egg now and then, wondering why my mother denied herself such a harmless pleasure. Less of her hair would be gray if she indulged now and then. The eggs prolonged life, prolonged vigor. My father, who had never refused one in his life, had lived more than twice as long as he should have. And toward the end of his life, when he should have been slowing down, he had married my mother and fathered four children.

But my mother seemed content to age before she had to. I saw her turn away as several of T'Gatoi's limbs secured me closer. T'Gatoi liked our body heat, and took advantage of it whenever she could. When I was little and at home more, my mother used to try to tell me how to behave with T'Gatoi—how to be respectful and always obedient because T'Gatoi was the Tlic government official in charge of the Preserve, and thus the most important of her kind to deal directly with Terrans. It was an honor, my mother said, that such a person had chosen to come into the family. My mother was at her most formal and severe when she was lying.

I had no idea why she was lying, or even what she was lying about. It *was* an honor to have T'Gatoi in the family, but it was hardly a novelty. T'Gatoi and my mother had been friends all my mother's life, and T'Gatoi was not interested in being honored in the house she considered her second home. She simply came in, climbed onto one of her special couches and called me over to keep her warm. It was impossible to be formal with her while lying against her and hearing her complain as usual that I was too skinny.

"You're better," she said this time, probing me with six or seven of her limbs. "You're gaining weight finally. Thinness is dangerous." The probing changed subtly, became a series of caresses.

"He's still too thin," my mother said sharply.

T'Gatoi lifted her head and perhaps a meter of her body off the couch as though she were sitting up. She looked at my mother and my mother, her face lined and old-looking, turned away.

"Lien, I would like you to have what's left of Gan's egg."

"The eggs are for the children," my mother said.

"They are for the family. Please take it."

Unwillingly obedient, my mother took it from me and put it to her mouth. There were only a few drops left in the now-shrunken, elastic shell, but she squeezed them out, swallowed them, and after a few moments some of the lines of tension began to smooth from her face.

"It's good," she whispered. "Sometimes I forget how good it is."

"You should take more," T'Gatoi said. "Why are you in such a hurry to be old?"

My mother said nothing.

"I like being able to come here," T'Gatoi said. "This place is a refuge because of you, yet you won't take care of yourself."

T'Gatoi was hounded on the outside. Her people wanted more of us made available. Only she and her political faction stood between us and the hordes who did not understand why there was a Preserve—why any Terran could not be courted, paid, drafted, in some way made available to them. Or they did understand, but in their desperation, they did not care. She parceled us out to the desperate and sold us to the rich and powerful for their political support. Thus, we were necessities, status symbols, and an independent people. She oversaw the joining of families, putting an end to the final remnants of the earlier system of breaking up Terran families to suit impatient Tlic. I had lived outside with her. I had seen the desperate eagerness in the way some people looked at me. It was a little frightening to know that only she stood between us and that desperation that could so easily swallow us. My mother would look at her sometimes and say to me, "Take care of her." And I would remember that she too had been outside, had seen.

Now T'Gatoi used four of her limbs to push me away from her onto the floor. "Go on, Gan," she said. "Sit down there with your sisters and enjoy not being sober. You had most of the egg. Lien, come warm me."

My mother hesitated for no reason that I could see. One of my earliest memories is of my mother stretched alongside T'Gatoi talking about things I could not understand, picking me up from the floor and laughing as she sat me on one of T'Gatoi's segments. She ate her share of eggs then. I wondered when she had stopped and why.

She lay down now against T'Gatoi, and the whole left row of T'Gatoi's limbs closed around her, holding her loosely, but securely. I had always found it comfortable to lie that way but except for my older sister, no one else in the family liked it. They said it made them feel caged.

T'Gatoi meant to cage my mother. Once she had, she moved her tail slightly, then spoke. "Not enough egg, Lien. You should have taken it when it was passed to you. You need it badly now."

T'Gatoi's tail moved once more, its whip motion so swift I wouldn't have seen it if I hadn't been watching for it. Her sting drew only a single drop of blood from my mother's bare leg.

My mother cried out—probably in surprise. Being stung doesn't hurt. Then she sighed and I could see her body relax. She moved languidly into a more comfortable position within the cage of T'Gatoi's limbs. "Why did you do that?" she asked, sounding half asleep.

"I could not watch you sitting and suffering any longer."

My mother managed to move her shoulders in a small shrug. "Tomorrow," she said.

"Yes. Tomorrow you will resume your suffering—if you must. But for now, just for now, lie here and warm me and let me ease your way a little."

"He's still mine, you know," my mother said suddenly. "Nothing can buy him from me." Sober, she would not have permitted herself to refer to such things.

"Nothing," T'Gatoi agreed, humoring her.

"Did you think I would sell him for eggs? For long life? My son?"

"Not for anything," T'Gatoi said stroking my mother's shoulders, toying with her long, graying hair.

I would like to have touched my mother, shared that moment with her. She would take my hand if I touched her now. Freed by the egg and the sting, she would smile and perhaps say things long held in. But tomorrow, she would remember all this as a humiliation. I did not want to be part of a remembered humiliation. Best just to be still and know she loved me under all the duty and pride and pain.

"Xuan Hoa, take off her shoes," T'Gatoi said. "In a little while I'll sting her again and she can sleep."

My older sister obeyed, swaying drunkenly as she stood up. When she had finished, she sat down beside me and took my hand. We had always been a unit, she and I.

My mother put the back of her head against T'Gatoi's underside and tried from that impossible angle to look up into the broad, round face. "You're going to sting me again?"

"Yes, Lien."

"I'll sleep until tomorrow noon."

"Good. You need it. When did you sleep last?"

My mother made a wordless sound of annoyance. "I should have stepped on you when you were small enough," she muttered.

It was an old joke between them. They had grown up together, sort of, though T'Gatoi had not, in my mother's lifetime, been small enough for any Terran to step on. She was nearly three times my mother's present age, yet would still be young when my mother died of age. But T'Gatoi and my mother had met as T'Gatoi was coming into a period of rapid development—a kind of Tlic adolescence. My mother was only a child, but for a while they developed at the same rate and had no better friends than each other.

T'Gatoi had even introduced my mother to the man who became my father. My parents, pleased with each other in spite of their very different ages, married as T'Gatoi was going into her family's business—politics. She and my mother saw each other less. But sometime before my older sister was born, my mother promised T'Gatoi one of her children. She would have to give one of us to someone, and she preferred T'Gatoi to some stranger.

Years passed. T'Gatoi traveled and increased her influence. The Preserve was hers by the time she came back to my mother to collect what she probably saw as her just reward for her hard work. My older sister took an instant liking to her and wanted to be chosen, but my mother was just coming to term with me and T'Gatoi liked the idea of choosing an infant and watching and taking part in all the phases of development. I'm told I was first caged within T'Gatoi's many limbs only three minutes after my birth. A few days later, I was given my first taste of egg. I tell Terrans that when they ask whether I was ever afraid of her. And I tell it to Tlic when T'Gatoi suggests a young Terran child for them and they, anxious and ignorant, demand an adolescent. Even my brother who had somehow grown up to fear and distrust the Tlic could probably have gone smoothly into one of their families if he had been adopted early enough. Sometimes, I think for his sake he should have been. I looked at him, stretched out on the floor across the room, his eyes open, but glazed as he dreamed his egg dream. No matter what he felt toward the Tlic, he always demanded his share of egg.

"Lien, can you stand up?" T'Gatoi asked suddenly.

"Stand?" my mother said. "I thought I was going to sleep."

"Later. Something sounds wrong outside." The cage was abruptly gone.

"What?"

"Up, Lien!"

My mother recognized her tone and got up just in time to avoid being dumped on the floor. T'Gatoi whipped her three meters of body off her couch, toward the door, and out at full speed. She had bones—ribs, a long spine, a skull, four sets of limbbones per segment. But when she moved that way, twisting, hurling herself into controlled falls, landing running, she seemed not only boneless, but aquatic—something swimming through the air as though it were water. I loved watching her move.

I left my sister and started to follow her out the door, though I wasn't very steady on my own feet. It would have been better to sit and dream, better yet to find a girl and share a waking dream with her. Back when the Tlic saw us as not much more than convenient big warm-blooded animals, they would pen several of us together, male and female, and feed us only eggs. That way they could be sure of getting another generation of us no matter how we tried to hold out. We were lucky that didn't go on long. A few generations of it and we would have *been* little more than convenient big animals.

"Hold the door open, Gan," T'Gatoi said. "And tell the family to stay back."

"What is it?" I asked.

"N'Tlic."[1]

I shrank back against the door. "Here? Alone?"

"He was trying to reach a call box, I suppose." She carried the man past me, unconscious, folded like a coat over some of her limbs. He looked young—my brother's age perhaps—and he was thinner than he should have been. What T'Gatoi would have called dangerously thin.

"Gan, go to the call box," she said. She put the man on the floor and began stripping off his clothing.

I did not move.

After a moment, she looked up at me, her sudden stillness a sign of deep impatience.

"Send Qui," I told her. "I'll stay here. Maybe I can help."

She let her limbs begin to move again, lifting the man and pulling his shirt over his head. "You don't want to see this," she said. "It will be hard. I can't help this man the way his Tlic could."

"I know. But send Qui. He won't want to be of any help here. I'm at least willing to try."

She looked at my brother—older, bigger, stronger, certainly more able to help her here. He was sitting up now, braced against the wall, staring at the man on the floor with undisguised fear and revulsion. Even she could see that he would be useless.

"Qui, go!" she said.

He didn't argue. He stood up, swayed briefly, then steadied, frightened sober.

"This man's name is Bram Lomas," she told him, reading from the man's arm band. I fingered my own arm band in sympathy. "He needs T'Khotgif Teh. Do you hear?"

"Bram Lomas, T'Khotgif Teh," my brother said. "I'm going." He edged around Lomas and ran out the door.

Lomas began to regain consciousness. He only moaned at first and clutched spasmodically at a pair of T'Gatoi's limbs. My younger sister, finally awake from her egg dream, came close to look at him, until my mother pulled her back.

T'Gatoi removed the man's shoes, then his pants, all the while leaving

1. Presumably, without a Tlic guardian or protector.

him two of her limbs to grip. Except for the final few, all her limbs were equally dexterous. "I want no argument from you this time, Gan," she said.

I straightened. "What shall I do?"

"Go out and slaughter an animal that is at least half your size."

"Slaughter? But I've never—"

She knocked me across the room. Her tail was an efficient weapon whether she exposed the sting or not.

I got up, feeling stupid for having ignored her warning, and went into the kitchen. Maybe I could kill something with a knife or an ax. My mother raised a few Terran animals for the table and several thousand local ones for their fur. T'Gatoi would probably prefer something local. An achti, perhaps. Some of those were the right size, though they had about three times as many teeth as I did and a real love of using them. My mother, Hoa, and Qui could kill them with knives. I had never killed one at all, had never slaughtered any animal. I had spent most of my time with T'Gatoi while my brother and sisters were learning the family business. T'Gatoi had been right. I should have been the one to go to the call box. At least I could do that.

I went to the corner cabinet where my mother kept her larger house and garden tools. At the back of the cabinet there was a pipe that carried off waste water from the kitchen—except that it didn't any more. My father had rerouted the waste water before I was born. Now the pipe could be turned so that one half slid around the other and a rifle could be stored inside. This wasn't our only gun, but it was our most easily accessible one. I would have to use it to shoot one of the biggest of the achti. Then T'Gatoi would probably confiscate it. Firearms were illegal in the Preserve. There had been incidents right after the Preserve was established—Terrans shooting Tlic, shooting N'Tlic. This was before the joining of families began, before everyone had a personal stake in keeping the peace. No one had shot a Tlic in my lifetime or my mother's, but the law still stood—for our protection, we were told. There were stories of whole Terran families wiped out in reprisal back during the assassinations.

I went out to the cages and shot the biggest achti I could find. It was a handsome breeding male and my mother would not be pleased to see me bring it in. But it was the right size, and I was in a hurry.

I put the achti's long, warm body over my shoulder—glad that some of the weight I'd gained was muscle—and took it to the kitchen. There, I put the gun back in its hiding place. If T'Gatoi noticed the achti's wounds and demanded the gun, I would give it to her. Otherwise, let it stay where my father wanted it.

I turned to take the achti to her, then hesitated. For several seconds, I stood in front of the closed door wondering why I was suddenly afraid. I knew what was going to happen. I hadn't seen it before but T'Gatoi had shown me diagrams, and drawings. She had made sure I knew the truth as soon as I was old enough to understand it.

Yet I did not want to go into that room. I wasted a little time choosing a knife from the carved, wooden box in which my mother kept them. T'Gatoi might want one, I told myself, for the tough, heavily furred hide of the achti.

"Gan!" T'Gatoi called, her voice harsh with urgency.

I swallowed. I had not imagined a simple moving of the feet could be so difficult. I realized I was trembling and that shamed me. Shame impelled me through the door.

I put the achti down near T'Gatoi and saw that Lomas was unconscious again. She, Lomas, and I were alone in the room, my mother and sisters probably sent out so they would not have to watch. I envied them.

But my mother came back into the room as T'Gatoi seized the achti. Ignoring the knife I offered her, she extended claws from several of her limbs and slit the achti from throat to anus. She looked at me, her yellow eyes intent. "Hold this man's shoulders, Gan."

I stared at Lomas in panic, realizing that I did not want to touch him, let alone hold him. This would not be like shooting an animal. Not as quick, not as merciful, and, I hoped, not as final, but there was nothing I wanted less than to be part of it.

My mother came forward. "Gan, you hold his right side," she said. "I'll hold his left." And if he came to, he would throw her off without realizing he had done it. She was a tiny woman. She often wondered aloud how she had produced, as she said, such "huge" children.

"Never mind," I told her, taking the man's shoulders. "I'll do it."

She hovered nearby.

"Don't worry," I said. "I won't shame you. You don't have to stay and watch."

She looked at me uncertainly, then touched my face in a rare caress. Finally, she went back to her bedroom.

T'Gatoi lowered her head in relief. "Thank you, Gan," she said with courtesy more Terran than Tlic. "That one . . . she is always finding new ways for me to make her suffer."

Lomas began to groan and make choked sounds. I had hoped he would stay unconscious. T'Gatoi put her face near his so that he focused on her.

"I've stung you as much as I dare for now," she told him. "When this is over, I'll sting you to sleep and you won't hurt any more."

"Please," the man begged. "Wait . . ."

"There's no more time, Bram. I'll sting you as soon as it's over. When T'Khotgif arrives she'll give you eggs to help you heal. It will be over soon."

"T'Khotgif!" the man shouted, straining against my hands.

"Soon, Bram." T'Gatoi glanced at me, then placed a claw against his abdomen slightly to the right of the middle, just below the last rib. There was movement on the right side—tiny, seemingly random pulsations moving his brown flesh, creating a concavity here, a convexity there, over and over until I could see the rhythm of it and knew where the next pulse would be.

Lomas's entire body stiffened under T'Gatoi's claw, though she merely rested it against him as she wound the rear section of her body around his legs. He might break my grip, but he would not break hers. He wept helplessly as she used his pants to tie his hands, then pushed his hands above his head so that I could kneel on the cloth between them and pin them in place. She rolled up his shirt and gave it to him to bite down on.

And she opened him.

His body convulsed with the first cut. He almost tore himself away from me. The sounds he made . . . I had never heard such sounds come from anything human. T'Gatoi seemed to pay no attention as she lengthened and deepened the cut, now and then pausing to lick away blood. His blood vessels contracted, reacting to the chemistry of her saliva, and the bleeding slowed.

I felt as though I were helping her torture him, helping her consume him. I knew I would vomit soon, didn't know why I hadn't already. I couldn't possibly last until she was finished.

She found the first grub. It was fat and deep red with his blood—both inside and out. It had already eaten its own egg case, but apparently had not yet begun to eat its host. At this stage, it would eat any flesh except its mother's. Let alone, it would have gone on excreting the poisons that had both sickened and alerted Lomas. Eventually it would have begun to eat. By the time it ate its way out of Lomas's flesh, Lomas would be dead or dying—and unable to take revenge on the thing that was killing him. There was always a grace period between the time the host sickened and the time the grubs began to eat him.

T'Gatoi picked up the writhing grub carefully, and looked at it, somehow ignoring the terrible groans of the man.

Abruptly, the man lost consciousness.

"Good," T'Gatoi looked down at him. "I wish you Terrans could do that at will." She felt nothing. And the thing she held . . .

It was limbless and boneless at this stage, perhaps fifteen centimeters long and two thick, blind and slimy with blood. It was like a large worm. T'Gatoi put it into the belly of the achti, and it began at once to burrow. It would stay there and eat as long as there was anything to eat.

Probing through Lomas's flesh, she found two more, one of them smaller and more vigorous. "A male!" she said happily. He would be dead before I would. He would be through his metamorphosis and screwing everything that would hold still before his sisters even had limbs. He was the only one to make a serious effort to bite T'Gatoi as she placed him in the achti.

Paler worms oozed to visibility in Lomas's flesh. I closed my eyes. It was worse than finding something dead, rotting, and filled with tiny animal grubs. And it was far worse than any drawing or diagram.

"Ah, there are more," T'Gatoi said, plucking out two long, thick grubs. You may have to kill another animal, Gan. Everything lives inside you Terrans."

I had been told all my life that this was a good and necessary thing Tlic and Terran did together—a kind of birth. I had believed it until now. I knew birth was painful and bloody, no matter what. But this was something else, something worse. And I wasn't ready to see it. Maybe I never would be. Yet I couldn't *not* see it. Closing my eyes didn't help.

T'Gatoi found a grub still eating its egg case. The remains of the case were still wired into a blood vessel by their own little tube or hook or whatever. That was the way the grubs were anchored and the way they fed. They took only blood until they were ready to emerge. Then they ate their stretched, elastic egg cases. Then they ate their hosts.

T'Gatoi bit away the egg case, licked away the blood. Did she like the taste? Did childhood habits die hard—or not die at all?

The whole procedure was wrong, alien. I wouldn't have thought anything about her could seem alien to me.

"One more, I think," she said. "Perhaps two. A good family. In a host animal these days, we would be happy to find one or two alive." She glanced at me. "Go outside, Gan, and empty your stomach. Go now while the man is unconscious."

I staggered out, barely made it. Beneath the tree just beyond the front door, I vomited until there was nothing left to bring up. Finally, I stood shaking, tears streaming down my face. I did not know why I was crying, but I could not stop. I went farther from the house to avoid being seen. Every time I closed my eyes I saw red worms crawling over redder human flesh.

There was a car coming toward the house. Since Terrans were forbidden motorized vehicles except for certain farm equipment, I knew this must be Lomas's Tlic with Qui and perhaps a Terran doctor. I wiped my face on my shirt, struggled for control.

"Gan," Qui called as the car stopped. "What happened?" He crawled out of the low, round, Tlic-convenient car door. Another Terran crawled out the other side and went into the house without speaking to me. The doctor. With his help and a few eggs, Lomas might make it.

"T'Khotgif Teh?" I said.

The Tlic driver surged out of her car, reared up half her length before me. She was paler and smaller than T'Gatoi—probably born from the body of an animal. Tlic from Terran bodies were always larger as well as more numerous.

"Six young," I told her. "Maybe seven, all alive. At least one male."

"Lomas?" she said harshly. I liked her for the question and the concern in her voice when she asked it. The last coherent thing he had said was her name.

"He's alive," I said.

She surged away to the house without another word.

"She's been sick," my brother said, watching her go. "When I called, I could hear people telling her she wasn't well enough to go out even for this."

I said nothing. I had extended courtesy to the Tlic. Now I didn't want to talk to anyone. I hoped he would go in—out of curiosity, if nothing else.

"Finally found out more than you wanted to know, eh?"

I looked at him.

"Don't give me one of *her* looks," he said. "You're not her. You're just her property."

One of her looks. Had I picked up even an ability to imitate her expressions?

"What'd you do, puke?" He sniffed the air. "So now you know what you're in for."

I walked away from him. He and I had been close when we were kids. He would let me follow him around when I was home and sometimes T'Gatoi would let me bring him along when she took me into the city. But something had happened when he reached adolescence. I never knew what. He began keeping out of T'Gatoi's way. Then he began running away—until he realized there was no "away." Not in the Preserve. Certainly not outside. After that he concentrated on getting his share of every egg that came into the house, and on looking out for me in a way that made me all but hate him—a way that clearly said, as long as it was all right, he was safe from the Tlic.

"How was it, really?" he demanded, following me.

"I killed an achti. The young ate it."

"You didn't run out of the house and puke because they ate an achti."

"I had . . . never seen a person cut open before." That was true and enough for him to know. I couldn't talk about the other. Not with him.

"Oh," he said. He glanced at me as though he wanted to say more, but he kept quiet.

We walked, not really headed anywhere. Toward the back, toward the cages, toward the fields.

"Did he say anything?" Qui asked. "Lomas, I mean."

Who else would he mean? "He said 'T'Khotgif.' "

Qui shuddered. "If she had done that to me, she'd be the last person I'd call for."

"You'd call for her. Her sting would ease your pain without killing the grubs in you."

"You think I'd care if they died?"

No. Of course he wouldn't. Would I?

"Shit!" He drew a deep breath. "I've seen what they do. You think this thing with Lomas was bad? It was nothing."

I didn't argue. He didn't know what he was talking about.

"I saw them eat a man," he said.

I turned to face him. "You're lying!"

"*I saw them eat a man.*" He paused. "It was when I was little. I had been to the Hartmund house and I was on my way home. Halfway here, I saw a man and a Tlic and the man was N'Tlic. The ground was hilly. I was able to hide from them and watch. The Tlic wouldn't open the man because she had nothing to feed the grubs. The man couldn't go any farther and there were no houses around. He was in so much pain he told her to kill him. He begged her to kill him. Finally, she did. She cut his throat. One swipe of one claw. I saw the grubs eat their way out, then burrow in again, still eating."

His words made me see Lomas's flesh again, parasitized, crawling. "Why didn't you tell me that?" I whispered.

He looked startled, as though he'd forgotten I was listening. "I don't know."

"You started to run away not long after that, didn't you?"

"Yeah. Stupid. Running inside the Preserve. Running in a cage."

I shook my head, said what I should have said to him long ago. "She wouldn't take you, Qui. You don't have to worry."

"She would . . . if anything happened to you."

"No. She'd take Xuan Hoa. Hoa . . . wants it." She wouldn't if she had stayed to watch Lomas.

"They don't take women," he said with contempt.

"They do sometimes." I glanced at him. "Actually, they prefer women. You should be around them when they talk among themselves. They say women have more body fat to protect the grubs. But they usually take men to leave the women free to bear their own young."

"To provide the next generation of host animals," he said, switching from contempt to bitterness.

"It's more than that!" I countered. Was it?

"If it were going to happen to me, I'd want to believe it was more, too."

"It *is* more!" I felt like a kid. Stupid argument.

"Did you think so while T'Gatoi was picking worms out of that guy's guts?"

"It's not supposed to happen that way."

"Sure it is. You weren't supposed to see it, that's all. And him. Tlic was supposed to do it. She could sting him unconscious and the operation wouldn't have been as painful. But she'd still open him, pick out the grubs, and if she missed even one, it would poison him and eat him from the inside out."

There was actually a time when my mother told me to show respect for Qui because he was my older brother. I walked away hating him. In his way, he was gloating. He was safe and I wasn't. I could have hit him, but I didn't think I would be able to stand it when he refused to hit back, when he looked at me with contempt and pity.

He wouldn't let me get away. Longer-legged, he swung ahead of me and made me feel as though I were following him.

"I'm sorry," he said.

I strode on, sick and furious.

"Look, it probably won't be that bad with you. T'Gatoi likes you. She'll be careful."

I turned back toward the house, almost running from him.

"Has she done it to you yet?" he asked, keeping up easily. "I mean, you're about the right age for implantation. Has she—"

I hit him. I didn't know I was going to do it, but I think I meant to kill him. If he hadn't been bigger and stronger, I think I would have.

He tried to hold me off, but in the end, had to defend himself. He only hit me a couple of times. That was plenty. I don't remember going down, but when I came to, he was gone. It was worth the pain to be rid of him.

I got up and walked slowly toward the house. The back was dark. No one was in the kitchen. My mother and sisters were sleeping in their bedrooms—or pretending to.

Once I was in the kitchen, I could hear voices—Tlic and Terran from the next room. I couldn't make out what they were saying—didn't want to make it out.

I sat down at my mother's table, waiting for quiet. The table was smooth and worn, heavy and well-crafted. My father had made it for her just before he died. I remembered hanging around underfoot when he built it. He didn't mind. Now I sat leaning on it, missing him. I could have talked to him. He had done it three times in his long life. Three clutches of eggs, three times being opened and sewed up. How had he done it? How did anyone do it?

I got up, took the rifle from its hiding place, and sat down again with it. It needed cleaning, oiling.

All I did was load it.

"Gan?"

She made a lot of little clicking sounds when she walked on bare floor, each limb clicking in succession as it touched down. Waves of little clicks.

She came to the table, raised the front half of her body above it, and surged onto it. Sometimes she moved so smoothly she seemed to flow like water itself. She coiled herself into a small hill in the middle of the table and looked at me.

"That was bad," she said softly. "You should not have seen it. It need not be that way."

"I know."

"T'Khotgif—Ch'Khotgif now—she will die of her disease. She will not live to raise her children. But her sister will provide for them, and for Bram Lomas." Sterile sister. One fertile female in every lot. One to keep the family going. That sister owed Lomas more than she could ever repay.

"He'll live then?"

"Yes."

"I wonder if he would do it again."

"No one would ask him to do that again."

I looked into the yellow eyes, wondering how much I saw and understood there, and how much I only imagined. "No one ever asks us," I said. "You never asked me."

She moved her head slightly. "What's the matter with your face?"

"Nothing. Nothing important." Human eyes probably wouldn't have noticed the swelling in the darkness. The only light was from one of the moons, shining through a window across the room.

"Did you use the rifle to shoot the achti?"

"Yes."

"And do you mean to use it to shoot me?"

I stared at her, outlined in moonlight—coiled, graceful body. "What does Terran blood taste like to you?"

She said nothing.

"What are you?" I whispered. "What are we to you?"

She lay still, rested her head on her topmost coil. "You know me as no other does," she said softly. "You must decide."

"That's what happened to my face," I told her.

"What?"

"Qui goaded me into deciding to do something. It didn't turn out very well." I moved the gun slightly, brought the barrel up diagonally under my own chin. "At least it was a decision I made."

"As this will be."

"Ask me, Gatoi."

"For my children's lives?"

She would say something like that. She knew how to manipulate people, Terran and Tlic. But not this time.

"I don't want to be a host animal," I said. "Not even yours."

It took her a long time to answer. "We use almost no host animals these days," she said. "You know that."

"You use us."

"We do. We wait long years for you and teach you and join our families to yours." She moved restlessly. "You know you aren't animals to us."

I stared at her, saying nothing.

"The animals we once used began killing most of our eggs after implantation long before your ancestors arrived," she said softly. "You know these things, Gan. Because your people arrived, we are relearning what it means to be a healthy, thriving people. And your ancestors, fleeing from their homeworld, from their own kind who would have killed or enslaved them—they survived because of us. We saw them as people and gave them the Preserve when they still tried to kill us as worms."

At the word "Worms" I jumped. I couldn't help it, and she couldn't help noticing it.

"I see," she said quietly. "Would you really rather die than bear my young, Gan?"

I didn't answer.

"Shall I go to Xuan Hoa?"

"Yes!" Hoa wanted it. Let her have it. She hadn't had to watch Lomas. She'd be proud. . . . Not terrified.

T'Gatoi flowed off the table onto the floor, startling me almost too much.

"I'll sleep in Hoa's room tonight," she said. "And sometime tonight or in the morning, I'll tell her."

This was going too fast. My sister. Hoa had had almost as much to do with raising me as my mother. I was still close to her—not like Qui. She could want T'Gatoi and still love me.

"Wait! Gatoi!"

She looked back, then raised nearly half her length off the floor and turned it to face me. "These are adult things, Gan. This is my life, my family!"

"But she's . . . my sister."

"I have done what you demanded. I have asked you!"

"But—"

"It will be easier for Hoa. She has always expected to carry other lives inside her."

Human lives. Human young who would someday drink at her breasts, not at her veins.

I shook my head. "Don't do it to her, Gatoi." I was not Qui. It seemed I could become him, though, with no effort at all. I could make Xuan Hoa my shield. Would it be easier to know that red worms were growing in her flesh instead of mine?

"Don't do it to Hoa," I repeated.

She stared at me, utterly still.

I looked away, then back at her. "Do it to me."

I lowered the gun from my throat and she leaned forward to take it.

"No," I told her.

"It's the law," she said.

"Leave it for the family. One of them might use it to save my life some-day."

She grasped the rifle barrel, but I wouldn't let go. I was pulled into a standing position over her.

"Leave it here!" I repeated. "If we're not your animals, if these are adult things, accept the risk. There is risk, Gatoi, in dealing with a partner."

It was clearly hard for her to let go of the rifle. A shudder went through her and she made a hissing sound of distress. It occurred to me that she was afraid. She was old enough to have seen what guns could do to people. Now her young and this gun would be together in the same house. She did not know about our other guns. In this dispute, they did not matter.

"I will implant the first egg tonight," she said as I put the gun away. "Do you hear, Gan?"

Why else had I been given a whole egg to eat while the rest of the family was left to share one? Why else had my mother kept looking at me as though I were going away from her, going where she could not follow? Did T'Gatoi imagine I hadn't known?

"I hear."

"Now!" I let her push me out of the kitchen, then walked ahead of her toward my bedroom. The sudden urgency in her voice sounded real. "You would have done it to Hoa tonight!" I accused.

"I must do it to someone tonight."

I stopped in spite of her urgency and stood in her way. "Don't you care who?"

She flowed around me and into my bedroom. I found her waiting on the couch we shared. There was nothing in Hoa's room that she could have used. She would have done it to Hoa on the floor. The thought of her doing it to Hoa at all disturbed me in a different way now, and I was suddenly angry.

Yet I undressed and lay down beside her. I knew what to do, what to expect. I had been told all my life. I felt the familiar sting, narcotic, mildly pleasant. Then the blind probing of her ovipositor.[2] The puncture was painless, easy. So easy going in. She undulated slowly against me, her muscles forcing the egg from her body into mine. I held on to a pair of her limbs until I remembered Lomas holding her that way. Then I let go, moved inadvertently, and hurt her. She gave a low cry of pain and I expected to be caged at once within her limbs. When I wasn't, I held on to her again, feeling oddly ashamed.

"I'm sorry," I whispered.

She rubbed my shoulders with four of her limbs.

"Do you care?" I asked. "Do you care that it's me?"

She did not answer for some time. Finally, "You were the one making choices tonight, Gan. I made mine long ago."

"Would you have gone to Hoa?"

"Yes. How could I put my children into the care of one who hates them?"

---

2. A pointed tubular organ with which a female insect deposits her eggs.

"It wasn't . . . hate."

"I know what it was."

"I was afraid."

Silence.

"I still am." I could admit it to her here, now.

"But you came to me . . . to save Hoa."

"Yes." I leaned my forehead against her. She was cool velvet, deceptively soft. "And to keep you for myself," I said. It was so. I didn't understand it, but it was so.

She made a soft hum of contentment. "I couldn't believe I had made such a mistake with you," she said. "I chose you. I believed you had grown to choose me."

"I had, but . . ."

"Lomas."

"Yes."

"I have never known a Terran to see a birth and take it well. Qui has seen one, hasn't he?"

"Yes."

"Terrans should be protected from seeing."

I didn't like the sound of that—and I doubted that it was possible. "Not protected," I said. "Shown. Shown when we're young kids, and shown more than once. Gatoi, no Terran ever sees a birth that goes right. All we see is N'Tlic—pain and terror and maybe death."

She looked down at me. "It is a private thing. It has always been a private thing."

Her tone kept me from insisting—that and the knowledge that if she changed her mind, I might be the first public example. But I had planted the thought in her mind. Chances were it would grow, and eventually she would experiment.

"You won't see it again," she said. "I don't want you thinking any more about shooting me."

The small amount of fluid that came into me with her egg relaxed me as completely as a sterile egg would have, so that I could remember the rifle in my hands and my feelings of fear and revulsion, anger and despair. I could remember the feelings without reviving them. I could talk about them.

"I wouldn't have shot you," I said. "Not you." She had been taken from my father's flesh when he was my age.

"You could have," she insisted.

"Not you." She stood between us and her own people, protecting, interweaving.

"Would you have destroyed yourself?"

I moved carefully, uncomfortably. "I could have done that. I nearly did. That's Qui's 'away.' I wonder if he knows."

"What?"

I did not answer.

"You will live now."

"Yes." *Take care of her,* my mother used to say. Yes.

"I'm healthy and young," she said. "I won't leave you as Lomas was left—alone, N'Tlic. I'll take care of you."

1984

YUSEF KOMUNYAKAA

b. 1947

Winner of the 1993 Pulitzer Prize for Poetry for *Neon Vernacular,* Yusef Komunyakaa draws much of his material from his boyhood hometown of Bogalusa, Louisiana, near New Orleans. He has published six collections of poetry, including *Dien
Cai Dau* (1988), a volume about his experience as a soldier and war correspondent
in Vietnam. He has also edited, with Sascha Feinstein, *The Jazz Poetry Anthology*
(1991). Most critics agree with poet Alvin Aubert, who remarks on the "quality of
the language of Komunyakaa's poetry, a freshness marked by a delightful figurative-
ness and a wit that never cloys." A graduate of the University of California, Irvine,
Komunyakaa's M.F.A. thesis was titled "Premonitions of the Bread Line."
Komunyakaa is presently a professor of English at Indiana University.

February in Sydney[1]

Dexter Gordon's[2] tenor sax
plays "April in Paris"
inside my head all the way back
on the bus from Double Bay.
Round Midnight,[3] the '50's,   5
cool cobblestone streets
resound footsteps of Bebop[4]
musicians with whiskey-laced voices
from a boundless dream in French.
Bud, Prez, Webster & The Hawk,[5]   10
their names run together
like mellifluous riffs.
Painful gods jive talk through
bloodstained reeds & shiny brass
where music is an anesthetic.   15
Unreadable faces from the human void
float like torn pages across the bus
windows. An old anger drips into my throat,
& I try thinking something good,
letting the precious bad   20
settle to the salty bottom.
Another scene keeps repeating itself:
I emerge from the dark theatre,
passing a woman who grabs her red purse
& hugs it to her like a heart attack.   25
Tremolo. Dexter comes back to rest
behind my eyelids. A loneliness
lingers like a silver needle
under my black skin,

1. City in southeastern Australia.
2. American jazz musician.
3. French film (1986), directed by Bertrand Taver-
nier; story of the friendship between a young Parisian jazz devotee and an aging jazz musician.

4. Jazz characterized by complex melodies and
harmonies and shifting accents; often played very
fast.
5. American jazz musicians: Bud Powell, Lester
Young, Ben Webster, and Coleman Hawkins.

as I try to feel how it is   30
to scream for help through a horn.

1989

Facing It

My black face fades,
hiding inside the black granite.
I said I wouldn't,
dammit: No tears.
I'm stone. I'm flesh.   5
My clouded reflection eyes me
like a bird of prey, the profile of night
slanted against morning. I turn
this way—the stone lets me go.
I turn that way—I'm inside   10
the Vietnam Veterans Memorial[1]
again, depending on the light
to make a difference.
I go down the 58,022 names,
half-expecting to find   15
my own in letters like smoke.
I touch the name Andrew Johnson;
I see the booby trap's white flash.
Names shimmer on a woman's blouse
but when she walks away   20
the names stay on the wall.
Brushstrokes flash, a red bird's
wings cutting across my stare.
The sky. A plane in the sky.
A white vet's image floats   25
closer to me, then his pale eyes
look through mine. I'm a window.
He's lost his right arm
inside the stone. In the black mirror
a woman's trying to erase names: 30
No, she's brushing a boy's hair.

1988

Sunday Afternoons

They'd latch the screendoors
& pull venetian blinds,
Telling us not to leave the yard.
But we always got lost
Among mayhaw & crabapple.   5

1. In Washington, D.C.

Juice spilled from our mouths,
& soon we were drunk & brave
As birds diving through saw vines.
Each nest held three or four
Speckled eggs, blue as rage.   10

Where did we learn to be unkind,
There in the power of holding each egg
While watching dogs in June
Dust & heat, or when we followed
The hawk's slow, deliberate arc?   15

In the yard, we heard cries
Fused with gospel on the radio,
Loud as shattered glass
In a Saturday-night argument
About trust & money.   20

We were born between Oh Yeah
& Goddammit. I knew life
Began where I stood in the dark,
Looking out into the light,
& that sometimes I could see   25

Everything through nothing.
The backyard trees breathed
Like a man running from himself
As my brothers backed away
From the screendoor. I knew   30

If I held my right hand above my eyes
Like a gambler's visor, I could see
How their bedroom door halved
The dresser mirror like a moon
Held prisoner in the house.   35

1992

Banking Potatoes

Daddy would drop purple-veined vines
Along rows of dark loam
& I'd march behind him
Like a peg-legged soldier,
Pushing down the stick   5
With a V cut into its tip.

Three weeks before the first frost
I'd follow his horse-drawn plow
That opened up the soil & left
Sweet potatoes sticky with sap,   10
Like flesh-colored stones along a riverbed
Or diminished souls beside a mass grave.

They lay all day under the sun's
Invisible weight, & by twilight
We'd bury them under pine needles   15
& then shovel in two feet of dirt.
Nighthawks scalloped the sweaty air,
Their wings spread wide

As plowshares. But soon the wind
Knocked on doors & windows   20
Like a frightened stranger,
& by mid-winter we had tunneled
Back into the tomb of straw,
Unable to divide love from hunger.

1992

Birds on a Powerline

Mama Mary's counting them
Again. Eleven black. A single
Red one like a drop of blood

Against the sky. She's convinced
They've been there two weeks.   5
I bring her another cup of coffee

& a Fig Newton. I sit here reading
Frances Harper[1] at the enamel table
Where I ate teacakes as a boy,

My head clear of voices brought back.   10
The green smell of the low land returns,
Stealing the taste of nitrate.

The deep-winter eyes of the birds
Shine in summer light like agate,
As if they could love the heart   15

Out of any wild thing. I stop,
With my finger on a word, listening.
They're on the powerline, a luminous

Message trailing a phantom
Goodyear blimp. I hear her say   20
Jesus, I promised you. Now

He's home safe, I'm ready.
My travelling shoes on. My teeth
In. I got on clean underwear.

1993

---

1. African American writer and activist (1825–1911), particularly involved in the abolitionist movement.

NATHANIEL MACKEY

b. 1947

Nathaniel Mackey's writings are intensely involved with music, especially jazz. In a 1995 interview in *Callaloo*, Mackey commented on why music is so important to his writing: "Music includes so much: it's social, it's religious, it's metaphysical, it's aesthetic, it's expressive, it's creative, it's destructive. It just covers so much." In his four chapbooks, two volumes of poetry, three works of fiction, and essay collection, Mackey consistently combines the innovations of postbop jazz pioneers with the experiments of the major avant-garde American poets.

Mackey was born in 1947 in Miami to Sadie Jane Wilcox and Alexander Obadiah Mackey. When Mackey was four, his parents separated, and he moved with his mother to California. In his teens, he began listening to bebop, then to free jazz. Simultaneously, he discovered the poetry of William Carlos Williams and Amiri Baraka and as a student at Princeton read Donald Allen's *The New American Poetry*, which included the black Mountain "Projectivist" poets Charles Olson, Robert Creeley, and Robert Duncan. The Black Arts movement also influenced his thinking at the time; his senior thesis was titled "The Conversion of LeRoi Jones."

After graduating from college, Mackey taught mathematics for a year, then earned a Ph.D. in English and American literature at Stanford. Since 1978, when he published his first chapbook, *Four for Trane*, Mackey has been characterized as a postmodern poet. Critic Mark Scruggins describes Mackey's work as a "dense web of intertextual reference," which contains allusions to other texts, to musical compositions, and to Mackey's own writing. Some of the many cultural influences one might encounter in Mackey's poems are jazz; Haitian *vodoun* and Cuban *santeria*; the Koran and Islamic music and writers; the philosophy of Dogon; and the works of the Guayanese novelist Wilson Harris, the African American writer Amiri Baraka, the modernist poet Ezra Pound, and the avant-garde poet Robert Duncan.

That quality of multiplicity, that eager embracing of variety, is also central to Mackey's fiction. To date he has published *Bedouin Hornbook* (1986) and *Djbout Baghostus' Run* (1993), installments of *From a Broken Bottle Traces of Perfume Still Emanate*. Each section of this series is composed as a letter from "N.," a jazz musician and member of the band called the Mystic Horn Society, to the mysterious Angel of Dust. Influenced by the dreamlike work of Wilson Harris as well as by jazz ensembles such as the Art Ensemble of Chicago, each of these letters circles around one of the band's rehearsals or performances.

A teacher and scholar, Mackey has taught at the University of Wisconsin at Madison and the University of Southern California. Since 1979 he has taught in the American studies and literature programs at the University of California at Santa Cruz, where he is now a full professor. In addition to writing poetry and fiction and publishing *Hambone*, a major little magazine for innovative poetry and art, Mackey hosts a radio program featuring African American and third world music and has composed a series of essays about music and literature called *Discrepant Engagement: Dissonance, Cross-Culturality and Experimental Writing* (1993).

Falso Brilhante [1]

for Elis Regina [2]

I wake up chasing my breath, my
dead lungs undone by alcohol and cocaine,
   a rope of dust at my throat . . .
   Raw thread of a dirge woven into the
     wind, all night I wonder   5
               what
but unruliness ranges the heart . . .

                 A blunt featherless
     bird hovering close to my chest as
I wake up, what but ennui that I'd even   10
wonder, what but a whim, the clouded rum
       I drink   drains me of light
     I dream I hang from, dangling,
                 draped
   as in rags, white fractured sky from which   15
                  I fall . . .
   White sky made blue by the blackness
beyond it, withered light, wind says *Better*
                not
  to have been born.   20
         Breath caught in
a cloud, I cross myself, *So be it,*
               my self-embrace
    a rickety crib I serenade
             myself   25
             inside . . .
And I'm singing all the songs that made me a
   star, my arms like wings as though
   they were not quite my own anymore . . .

                Leaned   30
on by a ghost, I launch a prayer to Iansã, Ogum [3]
   at my back, my torn voice haloed
    by an orbiting chorus as it bleeds,
hand on my heart as if I were taking an
           oath,   35
             a faint, fading
    spark, the seeds of this parting planted
  who knows how far back . . .

     A see-thru lid on the coffin I rest in.
  See-thru exit, see-thru sign of the times . . .   40
     Weepers fill the streets of São Paulo, [4]
   I wake up gasping,   chasing my breath,
             another

---

1. False brilliance (Portuguese).
2. Popular Brazilian singer who died in the early
1980s from respiratory problems after drinking
rum.
3. Or Ogoun, the Yoruba god of hunters and
blacksmiths. Iansã, the Yoruba goddess of the river
Niger, is often associated with St. Barbara and was
the patron saint of Elis Regina.
4. A city in Brazil.

snuffed-out star.   Prophetic wingtip skimming
the water . . .   45
    A crystalline cut color makes
                    in time . . .
    In every crack the same suffocating sweat,
                                   this
world with its arrows . . .   50
        Its rosary of worms, its
    neon angels, its megatons . . .

                            One eye with
God, the other eye with Satan, I watch the
    empty-eyed, pipe-smoking saints . . .   55

The keepers of bread do with the world as they
                        will,
    whose cards collapse . . .
                  The way the
wind has of having its way   60
                with a falling
                    leaf

                                  1985

Song of the Andoumboulou:[1] 8

—maitresse erzulie[2]—

One hand on her hip, one hand
    arranging her hair,
                blue heaven's
    bride. Her beaded hat she hangs
    from a nail on the danceroom   5
                  wall . . .

    As though an angel sought
    me out in my sleep or I sat up
    sleepless, eyes like rocks,
                  night   10
like so many such nights I've known.
    Not yet asleep I'm no longer
        awake,   lie awaiting what
    stalks the unanswered air,
                  still   15
    awaiting what blunts the running
                  flood
or what carries, all Our Mistress's
                whispers,
                    thrust   20
    of a crosscut saw . . .

1. Funeral prayer of the Dogon, a West African group.
2. Mistress erzulie (French creole). Erzulie is the Haitian vodoun (goddess) of love; flirtatious and sensuous, she is often called "mistress."

Who sits at her feet fills his
head with wings, oils his
                    mouth
        with rum, readies her way
    with perfume . . .
                From whatever glimpse
    of her I get I take heart, I hear them
                            say,
        By whatever bit of her I touch
    I take
        hold

1994

26.IX.81

Dear Angel of Dust,

Thank you for your letter. It arrived yesterday. I'm glad to hear you're doing well and that the various demands on your time that you mention have eased up. I'd begun to wonder why I hadn't heard from you for so long. Things here have been busy as well. We've had a number of gigs recently and we've all been doing a fair amount of writing—which means we've also been putting in more rehearsal time. No, we haven't (to answer your question) found a drummer yet. We've been too busy to really apply ourselves to the search. Furthermore, the drum-dreams we had a few weeks back, I've begun to feel, did more to confuse than to clarify matters. Whether it's a drummer named Penny or a drummer named Djeannine we should be looking for we've been unable to reach an agreement on.

I have, however, given some thought to the second letter you wrote me in July, the one regarding my after-the-fact lecture/libretto. The questions you posed have stayed with me—most of all the big one you dropped on me, "Why opera?" I must admit I'm not a fan of opera. Nor do I especially know anything about it. But since anything, it seems, can be an opera nowadays, I could easily answer by asking, "Why not?" The roots of either "why," I suspect, have to do with certain suppositions regarding social and artistic arrival and/or elevation—antithetically to do with a Eurocentric ladder whose "axiomaticness" makes one ask with no real hope of ascertaining why. The roots of either "why" and of my reasons why, in other words, concern opera's aura more than anything else.

It goes back to a movie I saw as a kid in the early fifties, my first exposure to "opera," *Carmen Jones*.[1] Dorothy Dandridge and Harry Belafonte starred in it. Max Roach and Pearl Bailey[2] were in it as well and on one of his recordings of "What Is This Thing Called Love?" Bird[3] throws in a

1. Famous musical film of the 1950s with African American characters based on French composer Georges Bizet's opera *Carmen*.
2. African American singer and actor (1918–1990). Dandridge (1922–1963), first African American woman to become a major film star in the United States. Belafonte (b. 1927), one of the first African American men to become a major film star in the United States. Roach (b. 1925), jazz drummer.
3. Charlie "Bird" Parker (1920–1955), one of the greatest bebop musicians.

quote from the score. My older brother took me to see it and what I remember most is that it struck us as funny, that whenever someone burst into song we broke out laughing. At one point we laughed so loud and so long an usher came over to quiet us down. We laughed loudest at the end of the movie. When Belafonte choked Carmen to death and then started singing my brother and I thought we'd die.

What made us laugh was the incongruity—the unreality and the inappropriateness of singing, the gap between song and circumstance. That gap, that incongruity, obeyed a principle of non-equivalence, an upfront absence of adequation I've since made a case for regarding as apt. Such a case calls non-equivalence post-equivalence. That is, the post-equivalent slide of a pointedly unsecured address makes for an apt, operatic inappropriateness—an accusative, therefore apt incongruity. Call it fiddling while Rome burns. This is largely, though not entirely, what I'm up to.

It was exactly this I was thinking about the other night when an uncanny coincidence occurred. The notion of operatic incongruity, of an elevated, broken vessel the sound of whose shattering antithetically rings true, was much on my mind as I got up to turn the television on. I pushed in the knob and what came on was the tail-end of a Memorex commercial: Ella Fitzgerald[4] hitting an extremely high note while in the foreground a wine glass shattered. I could hardly believe it. I immediately thought of two things: 1) Rahsaan's[5] piece "Rip, Rig and Panic," whose opening section ends with the sound of breaking glass, and 2) Aunt Nancy's phrase "an eye made of opera glass."

The coincidence turned out to be catalytic. The sense of a straining see-thru mode which telescopes its own demise immediately had me under its spell. Turning away from the TV set, I sat down and began a new after-the-fact lecture/libretto, the first paragraph of which came so effortlessly it seemed to be writing itself:

> Jarred Bottle's I made of opera glass dropped out. Orb and vessel both (i.e., glass eye, reading glass and wine glass rolled into one), it dropped out, fell to the floor and shattered, having turned lower-case and taken the place of Aunt Nancy's u. An apostrophe had already pried the n and the t apart, opening the door thru which Ain't Nancy had come in and which remained ajar, a concrete epigraph endorsed in namesake fashion by a Platonic/Pythagorean pun. Jarred Bottle had begun his lecture by reading a quote: "Some clever fellow, making a play with words, called the soul a jar, because it can easily be jarred by persuasive words into believing this or that."

I quickly found myself at a loss as to where to go from there. Not only did words no longer come effortlessly but now they didn't come at all. I found myself put off by and caught up in qualms about the patness of the "shattered I," its apparent endorsement of currently fashionable notions of a nonexistent self, a dead subject and such. My own effortless recourse to

---

4. Jazz singer (1918–1993). A reference to a television commercial in which Fitzgerald's voice recorded on a Memorex cassette tape was clear enough to break a wineglass.

5. Rahsaan Roland Kirk (1936–1977), saxophonist, clarinetist, and flutist, famous for playing three horns at once.

some such implication turned me off. That the self gets all the more talked about by way of its widely insisted-upon disappearance turns out to be an irony I'm evidently not able to get beyond.

Thus the paragraph turned out to be no more than a heuristic wedge, an impromptu foot-in-the-door whose playing back of imprints availed itself of a suspect effortlessness which could now be and had to be parted with, put aside. It was a possible music I now turned my attention to. Abandoning paper and pen, I turned off the TV, took out my alto and began working on a solo which would hopefully both allude to and bridge Bird's *Carmen Jones* quote and Rahsaan's "Rip, Rig and Panic." (Rahsaan, by the way, alludes to Bird's quote in the course of his solo on "Wham Bam Thank You Ma'am" on Mingus's[6] album *Oh Yeah.*) The solo would be a part of my antithetical opera.

The working out of it went pretty well. I came up with a number of combinations and transitions, the more complex and oblique of which built upon a sensation of spindly support, a Platonic rapport between panicky stritch and impromptu aria somewhat like impishness and trauma holding hands. My playing grew possessed of a geometric high, a Pythagorean dismay (almost outrage at points) before incommensurables—but only in order not to console "Pythagorean" expectations, only in order to acknowledge or arouse a sense of aliquant excess, an elegant post-equivalent drift. I took out staff paper and as I went along wrote out the passages I felt I might not otherwise remember.

There were some wrinkles which at first refused to be ironed out. I tinkered, fine-tuned and tested for quite a while, working out most of them though a few went on getting the best of me. I arrived at a point where putting it all aside for a while seemed to be the best thing to do, so I set the horn in the stand on the floor and got up and turned the TV back on. There was a Peter Lorre[7] movie on the Late Show and I sat back down to watch it, my mind still mainly on the impasse I'd reached in my impromptu post-equivalent solo.

Not long after sitting back down I fell asleep. I must've slept for quite some time. By the time I woke up, that is, there was a test pattern on the TV screen. What woke me up was the sound of an alto playing a familiar tune, a tune whose name was on the tip of my tongue though as I slept I couldn't for the life of me recall what it was. The effort to do so woke me up.

I awoke, rubbed the sleep from my eyes and looked around, noticing the test pattern on the TV screen and the fact that the sound I'd heard was no dream but was coming from my alto sitting on the floor. I rubbed my eyes again and shook my head as if to clear it of cobwebs, taken aback by the sight of the horn apparently playing itself. I looked on in disbelief as keys were pressed and let go, the horn fingered by invisible hands. The tune, I realized after a while, was "The Inflated Tear," Rahsaan's lament recalling a nurse's mistake which had left him blind.

I sat glued to my chair, the horn's captive. There was a lush but alarmed quality to its tone, a namesake fluidity which not only bordered on but

---

6. Charles Mingus (1922–1979), jazz bassist and composer.

7. Film star of the 1930s and 1940s, who often played villains (1904–1964).

clearly crossed over into effortlessness. Indeed, the horn was possessed of a virtuosity which amounted to the ultimate in effortlessness: automatism. I sat entranced by its utter fluency, the utter finesse with which it held forth on the emotional flood to which it owed itself. Automatic alto spoke of a blind Atlantean[8] reservoir of feeling, an inordinate rush and/or capacity from which it ever so lightly held back, all the more insistent, all the more extrapolatively brought into being by its doing so. Automatic alto (effortless alto) spoke eloquently as well as at length of operatic inflation and of its related, residual theme of aliquant excess, the very theme which had been so much on my mind.

Every now and then, however, automatic alto tripped itself up, critiqued its own effortlessness by deliberately having a beginner's difficulty with fourth-line D. By resorting to a beginner's unsuccessful effort to avoid the "break" in using the octave key automatic alto not only brought the issue of human agency to the fore but brought me more actively into the picture. I found I couldn't, that is, help trying to correct automatic alto's lapses into awkwardness. With each problematic D I lent it a bit of body English, gesturing as though I were holding it and playing it, correctly coordinating my left thumb's roll with the appropriate changes in lip and tongue pressure. In doing so I contracted a host of automatic stigmata. I could actually feel the weight of the horn pull the strap against the back of my neck, feel the reed against my lower lip, feel the octave key underneath my thumb and so forth. It was as though automatic alto were playing me, as if I were its axe, its instrument. Even so, its voice broke like that of a boy entering puberty. I could do nothing, body English notwithstanding, to assist it.

But the more automatic alto faltered the more deeply it had me under its spell. I was its axe, its instrument, no "as if" about it. With each "break" it indicated its own suspect effortlessness, but in doing so it implicated a fallible human hand, a broken vessel—namely, in this instance, me. The more it faltered the more I lent it support. But the more support I lent it—the more I gestured, the more body English I resorted to—the more inept its non-avoidance of the "break" became. With each lapse into awkwardness it brought me abreast of my own ineffectuality, seemed intent on teaching me humility—which, in a sense, it very effectively did. Automatic alto (awkward alto) clearly had a mind of its own.

What awkward alto seemed intent on saying was that I was the problem, not the solution, that aliquant excess provided not a see-thru advance but a before-the-fact Atlantean collapse. This, of course, I'd long suspected and, in that sense, already knew, but the way in which awkward alto went on to both base itself upon and embroider a blend of precipitous forethought and residual truth not only renewed but ever so expertly strengthened its hold on me. Residual truth turned into precipitous afterthought. I couldn't help noting that even though I was its axe awkward alto (aliquant[9] alto) had apparently gotten me under its skin. I was a ghost, a grain of salt in the machine. Mine was the salt- or sand-anointed voice, the unavoided "break."

---

8. Symbol of high civilization as used in Plato and W. É. B. Du Bois.

9. Designating a part of a number that divides the number evenly and leaves no remainder.

After the last of these non-avoidances "The Inflated Tear" gave way to "L'oiseau rebelle,"[1] a quote of Rahsaan's quote of Bird's quote of *Carmen Jones*'s quote of *Carmen*. Aliquant alto might as well have meant aliquant elevation, aliquant/operatic aura come home to roost. It belabored the fact that what it quoted was already a quote of a quote of a quote, as though in so doing it thumbed a long since remaindered book. This accounted for the "break," the inept employment of the octave key, the lack of the appropriate tongue and lip coordination. Aliquant alto, it invited one to say, was "all thumb."

Having made its joke and having tossed out its quote of a quote of a quote of a quote, aliquant alto again took up "The Inflated Tear," playing it now without the slightest lapse into awkwardness. The finesse and facility with which it now played almost blew me away. I sat entranced as it ran the gamut from a velvety calm reminiscent of Johnny Hodges to a nervous, on-the-edge intensity worthy of Jimmy Lyons,[2] a nervous, pistol-pointed-at-one's-head sense of emergency.

Automatic alto had now come full circle, clearly come to be the host of a circuitous muse. In attempting to sidestep or critique its own technical finesse, it was now willing to admit, it had simply replaced what it took to be artificial wholeness, artificial health, with artificial breakage, artificial debris. This was a dilemma one couldn't help addressing, it went on to announce, in a period haunted by (hemmed in by) artifice, operatic reflex. Was there no way to be genuinely broken it rhetorically asked by way of a distraught, strangled, bittersweet cry, a Braxtonian[3] mix confronting form with flight. Was there no way to be genuinely whole it rhetorically asked by way of a smooth, unhurried blaze of ballad warmth, ballad hearth, ballad health.

I was now even more deeply entranced as automatic alto came full circle by playing the tune straight. Its unhurried blaze of ballad warmth brought Benny Carter[4] to mind, causing me to see that "The Inflated Tear" was the watery, post-equivalent bridge I'd been after, the sunken, lush, dreamless Atlantean drift I'd been looking for.

Automatic alto's Carteresque ballad warmth gradually gave way to a benedictory aubade which made one think of Carlos Ward[5] (more specifically, the edge he puts on "Desireless" on Don Cherry's[6] *Relativity Suite*). It was on this note of salt-inflected fluidity—with its related sense of endless flotation and a requisite regard for longstanding limbo—that automatic alto brought its recital to a close.

Everything was now silent except for the hum of the TV set. I sat riveted to my seat, mulling over the implications of the upstart serenade the horn had treated me to. Automatic alto (upstart alto) had overcome the impasse I'd arrived at in my impromptu post-equivalent solo, ironed out the wrin-

---

1. Rebellious bird (French); the title of an aria from *Carmen* and a song from *Carmen Jones*. Also a reference to Parker's nickname.
2. Alto saxophonist, who played in Cecil Taylor's demanding jazz orchestra. Hodges (1906–1970), alto saxophonist in Duke Ellington's orchestra.
3. From Anthony Braxton (b. 1945); avant-garde

African American composer.
4. Great arranger, composer, and multitalented brass jazz musician (b. 1907).
5. Panamanian alto saxophonist.
6. Jazz and avant-garde composer and trumpet player (1936–1996).

kles I'd been unable to correct. Exactly how it'd done so I now sat trying to figure out.

It took me a while but I eventually figured it out—the result of which please give a listen to on the cassette you'll find enclosed: "Robotic Aria for Prepared and Unprepared Alto." As you'll hear, I've availed myself not only of automatic alto's technical solutions but of its theme of built-in obstruction as well. The aria consists of two parts, "prepared" and "unprepared." For the former I taped a sawed-off popsicle stick under the octave key. The latter begins, as you can hear, with the sound of me peeling off the tape and the popsicle stick falling to the floor.

I find the aria notable, even if I do say so myself, for the head-on hedging mixed with head-on address it carries off, its dredging up of a watery precipitate (post-equivalent bridge and post-equivalent debris rolled into one).

As always, I look forward to your response.

Yours,

N.

1986

CHARLES JOHNSON

b. 1948

Winner of the 1990 National Book Award for the novel *Middle Passage*, only the second African American man to receive this honor, Charles Johnson is concerned that the complexity of African American truths has yet to be told. In his critical study *Being and Race* (1988), he argues that African American authors have been too narrow in their description of New World black life, that instead of presenting its multiplicities and its underlying philosopical concerns, they have repeated the limited observations of sociologists and historians. As a result, Johnson has contended, many African American writers have participated in their own stereotyping. Johnson's writing is dedicated to breaking those stereotypes and exploring the philosophical traditions that African Americans have both used and transformed. He has created revisionary fables of traditional African American narratives and related them to a variety of philosophical constructs: Western philosophies such as phemonology, Eastern philosophies such as Buddhism, and African cosmologies that have not been given their full due as philosophies.

Johnson was born in Evanston, Illinois, in 1948. His father came from a poor, large family and had only a second-grade education, but his mother finished high school and maintained a devotion to books throughout her life. She introduced Johnson to literature and to art, which fueled his desire to become a visual artist. Johnson was also inspired by his father, a practical resourceful person, and his uncle, who built many houses in Evanston. Because of the strengths of his family, Johnson understood, despite national rhetoric about blacks as underprivileged, that his own folk had contributed to the development of the United States.

When his father objected to a career in art because he was worried about how Johnson would make a living, Charles majored in journalism, but enrolled in a mail-order cartooning course and after two years began publishing drawings in various publications. Upon entering Southern Illinois University in 1967, Johnson went directly to the college newspaper with his political sketches. By the time he graduated, Johnson had published a book of cartoons, called *Black Humor* (1970).

At twenty-two, just after his marriage, an idea for a novel occurred to him. For the next few years, while a graduate student in philosophy at Southern Illinois University, Johnson wrote seven novels, none of which he published. It was his exploration of Western philosophy and his relationship with author John Gardner that helped him to draw the connection between the African American historical experience and various philosophical traditions. *Faith and the Good Thing* (1974), his first published novel, was written under Gardner's tutelage and reflects Johnson's concern with philosophical traditions as a source of imaginative writing.

While working on his Ph.D., Johnson found himself slowly molding a novel in which he would break new artistic ground, a novel that would have been impossible without the scholarship on African American history and literature that was inspired by the movements of the 1960s. Later Johnson would say about the origins of *The Oxherding Tale* (1974) that

> it became increasingly clear to me as I read criticism, that one of the most indigenous native forms of literature that we have in this country is the slave narrative. And I wanted to take the slave narrative and do something philosophical with it.

Johnson's personal discovery of the ten Zen Buddhist oxherding pictures by the twelfth-century Chinese artist Kaakuan Shien was important. These drawings explore the Chinese symbol for the self and the polarity between the self and the world. They suggested to Johnson links between that clearly articulated Eastern philosophical system and the slave histories of African Americans.

Oxherding Tale is one of the first African American novels to explore American slavery from the point of view of the different epistemologies embodied in his characters' conceptions of knowledge and reality. As the result of a practical joke between master and slave, Andrew Hawkins, the narrator, is "accidentally" conceived. His mother is the mistress of the plantation and his father is a house slave doomed to be an oxherder after Andrew's conception and birth. Johnson's narrative reminds us that U.S. slaveowners read the philosophers of their day. Thus when Andrew turns five and his father decides to educate him, he engages as his teachers Ezekiel, an anarchist-transcendalist-mystic, as well as the European philosopher Karl Marx, who is visiting America. Johnson also explores gender politics by having Andrew become sexually enslaved to Flou Hatfield, a widow who owns a cotton plantation; from her he learns variations of sexual pleasure, another way of knowing. The tension between Horace Bannon, the Soulcatcher in the novel, who uses his intuition to detect the feelings and consciousness of the escaped slaves he sets out to capture, and the philosophically aware Andrew is the basis of a unique African American philosophical mystery. *Oxherding Tale* was not an easy book to sell, for it did not fit the publishing trends in African American literature of the day. It went to more than twenty publishers before it was accepted by Indiana University Press.

While Johnson wrote *Oxherding Tale*, he taught writing at the University of Washington in Seattle. He had become a Buddhist and an active martial arts devotee. The title story of *The Sorcerer's Apprentice* (1986) contains a main character from the Allmuseri tribe of Africa, the origin of Mingo in *The Education of Mingo* as well as a central element in *Middle Passage* (1990).

Middle Passage tells the story of an educated, recently emancipated slave from Indiana who ends up in New Orleans and who, as a result of his attempt to escape from the clutches of a black schoolmarm, ends up as a stowaway on the ironically named illegal slave ship *The Republic*. Without question, Rutherford is a rogue, a trickster, a long-standing character type in African American literature. His experiences as a "black" with the forty members of the Allmuseri who are captured and destined to become slaves, but who rebel on the ship, changes his view of himself and possible modes of existence. The novel probes the underlying concepts of philosophy in the West, especially those that resulted in the peculiar institution of slavery. At the same time, it confronts the philosophically advanced but perhaps overly refined cosmology of the Allmuseri. *Middle Passage* was a best-seller and won the 1990 National Book Award. Although most reviewers praised it, some found its comic tone inappropriate for the seriousness of its subject.

Charles Johnson is a startling and innovative writer who blends African American, Eastern, and Western philosophies in his work, even as he explores specific African American literatures, especially those of the nineteenth century. He currently teaches at the University of Washington in Seattle.

The Education of Mingo

Once, when Moses Green took his one-horse rig into town on auction day, he returned to his farm with a bondsman[1] named Mingo. He came early in a homespun suit, stayed through the sale of fifteen slaves, and paid for Mingo in Mexican coin. A monkeylike old man, never married, with tangled hair, ginger-colored whiskers like broomstraw, and a narrow knot of a face, Moses, without children, without kinfolk, who seldom washed because he lived alone on sixty acres in southern Illinois, felt the need for a field hand and helpmate—a friend, to speak the truth plainly.

Riding home over sumps[2] and mudholes into backcountry imprecise yet startlingly vivid in spots as though he were hurtling headlong into a rigid New Testament parable, Moses chewed tobacco on that side of his mouth that still had good teeth and kept his eyes on the road and ears of the Appaloosa[3] in front of his rig; he chattered mechanically to the boy, who wore tow-linen trousers a size too small, a straw hat, no shirt, and shoes repaired with wire. Moses judged him to be twenty. He was the youngest son of the reigning king of the Allmuseri,[4] a tribe of wizards, according to the auctioneer, but they lied anyways, or so thought Moses, like abolitionists and Red Indians; in fact, for Moses Green's money nearly everybody in the New World from Anabaptists to Whigs[5] was an outrageous liar and twisted the truth (as Moses saw it) until nothing was clear anymore. He was a dark boy. A wild, marshy-looking boy. His breastbone was broad as a barrel; he had thick hands that fell away from his wrists like weights and, on his sharp cheeks, a crescent motif. "Mingo," Moses said in a voice like gravel scrunching under a shoe, "you like rabbit? That's what I fixed for tonight. Fresh rabbit, sweet taters, and cornbread. Got hominy[6] made from Indian corn on the fire, too. Good eatings, eh?" Then he remembered that Mingo spoke no English, and he gave the boy a friendly thump on his thigh. " 'S all right. I'm going to school you myself. Teach you everything I know, son, which ain't so joe-fired much—just common sense—but it's better'n not knowing nothing, ain't it?" Moses laughed till he shook; he liked to laugh and let his hair down whenever he could. Mingo, seeing his strangely un-

---

1. Slave.
2. Marshy pits or swamps.
3. North American horse with white or solid-colored coat covered with small spots.
4. African tribe.

5. A dominant political party in early 19th-century America. "Anabaptists": 16th-century European Christian sect that held that only true believers should be baptized.
6. Hulled corn kernels cooked into a pudding.

filed teeth, laughed, too, but his sounded like barking. It made Moses jump a foot. He swung 'round his head and squinted. "Reckon I'd better teach you how to laugh, too. That half grunt, half whinny you just made'll give a body heart failure, son." He screwed up his lips. "You sure got a lot to learn."

Now Moses Green was not a man for doing things halfway. Education, as he dimly understood it, was as serious as a heart attack. You had to have a model, a good Christian gentleman like Moses himself, to wash a Moor[7] white in a single generation. As he taught Mingo farming and table etiquette, ciphering with knotted string, and how to cook ashcakes,[8] Moses constantly revised himself. He tried not to cuss, although any mention of Martin Van Buren or Free-Soilers[9] made his stomach chew itself; or sop cornbread in his coffee; or pick his nose at public market. Moses, policing all his gestures, standing the boy behind his eyes, even took to drinking gin from a paper sack so Mingo couldn't see it. He felt, late at night when he looked down at Mingo snoring loudly on his corn-shuck mattress, now like a father, now like an artist fingering something fine and noble from a rude chump of foreign clay. It was like aiming a shotgun at the whole world through the African, blasting away all that Moses, according to his lights, tagged evil, and cultivating the good; like standing, you might say, on the sixth day, feet planted wide, trousers hitched, and remaking the world so it looked more familiar. But sometimes it scared him. He had to make sense of things for Mingo's sake. Suppose there was lightning dithering in dark clouds overhead? Did that mean rain? Or the Devil whaling his wife? Or— you couldn't waffle on a thing like that. "Rain," said Moses, solemn, scratching his neck. "For sure, it's a storm. Electri-city, Mingo." He made it a point to despoil meanings with care, choosing the ones that made the most common sense.

Slowly, Mingo got the hang of farm life, as Moses saw it—patience, grit, hard work, and prayerful silence, which wasn't easy, Moses knew, because *every*thing about him and the African was as different as night and day, even what idealistic philosophers of his time called structures of intentional consciousness[1] (not that Moses Green called it that, being a man for whom nothing was more absolute than an ax handle, or the weight of a plow in his hands, but he knew sure enough they didn't see things quite the same way). Mingo's education, to put it plainly, involved the evaporation of one coherent, consistent, complete universe and the embracing of another one alien, contradictory, strange.

Slowly, Mingo conquered knife and spoon, then language. He picked up the old man's family name. Gradually, he learned—soaking them up like a sponge—Moses's gestures and idiosyncratic body language. (Maybe too well, for Moses Green had a milk leg[2] that needed lancing and hobbled, favoring his right knee; so did Mingo, though he was strong as an ox.

---

7. Africans were often referred to by whites as "Moors."
8. Cornmeal cakes baked in hot ashes.
9. Members of a U.S. political party formed in 1847–48 to oppose the extension of slavery into territories gained from Mexico; it ran Martin Van Buren (1782–1862) for president, but he was de-

feated by Zachary Taylor. Van Buren had already served as president from 1837 to 1841.
1. A reference to rationalism in Enlightenment philosophy, which Johnson often parodies.
2. A leg painfully swollen by inflammation of and clotting in the veins.

His *t*'s had a reedy twang like the quiver of a ukulele string; so did Mingo's.) That African, Moses saw inside a year, was exactly the product of his own way of seeing, as much one of his products and judgments as his choice of tobacco; was, in a sense that both pleased and bum-squabbled the crusty old man, himself: a homunculus,[3] or a distorted shadow, or—as Moses put it to his lady friend Harriet Bridgewater—his own spitting image.

"How you talk, Moses Green!" Harriet sat in a Sleepy Hollow chair on the Sunday afternoons Moses, in his one-button sack coat and Mackinaw hat,[4] visited her after church services. She had two chins, wore a blue dress with a flounce of gauze and an apron of buff satin, above which her bosom slogged back and forth as she chattered and knitted. There were cracks in old Harriet Bridgewater's once well-stocked mind (she had been a teacher, had traveled to places Moses knew he'd never see), into which she fell during conversations, and from which she crawled with memories and facts that, Moses suspected, Harriet had spun from thin air. She was the sort of woman who, if you told her of a beautiful sunset you'd just seen, would, like as not, laugh—a squashing sound in her nose—and say, "Why, Moses, that's not beautiful at all!" And then she'd sing a sunset more beautiful— like the good Lord coming in a cloud—in some faraway place like Crete or Brazil, which you'd probably never see. That sort of woman: haughty, worldly, so clever at times he couldn't stand it. Why Moses Green visited her . . .

Even he didn't rightly know why. She wasn't exactly pretty, what with her gull's nose, great heaps of red-gold hair, and frizzy down on her arms, but she had a certain silvery beauty intangible, elusive, inside. It was comforting after Reverend Raleigh Liverspoon's orbicular[5] sermons to sit a spell with Harriet in her religiously quiet, plank-roofed common room. He put one hand in his pocket and scratched. She knew things, that shrewd Harriet Bridgewater, like the meaning of Liverspoon's gnomic[6] sermon on property, which Moses couldn't untangle to save his life until Harriet spelled out how being and having were sorta the same thing: "You kick a man's mule, for example, and isn't it just like ramming a boot heel in that man's belly? Or suppose," she said, wagging a knitting needle at him, "you don't fix those chancy steps of yours and somebody breaks his head—his relatives have a right to sue you into the poorhouse, Moses Green." This was said in a speech he understood, but usually she spoke properly in a light, musical voice, such that her language, as Moses listened, was like song. Her dog, Ruben—a dog so small he couldn't mount the bitches during rutting season and, crazed, jumped Harriet's chickens instead—ran like a fleck of light around her chair. Then there was Harriet's three-decked stove, its sheet-iron stovepipe turned at a right angle, and her large wooden cupboard—all this, in comparison to his own rude, whitewashed cabin, and Harriet's endless chatter, now that her husband, Henry, was dead (when eating fish, he had breathed when he should have swallowed, then swallowed when he should have breathed), gave Moses, as he sat in his Go-to-meeting clothes nibbling egg bread (his palm under his chin to catch

3. Miniature adult.
4. A hat made of heavy wool, often plaid.
5. Circular.

6. Full of aphorisms, or short statements of principles or truths.

crumbs), a lazy feeling of warmth, well-being, and wonder. Was he sweet on Harriet Bridgewater? His mind weathervaned—yes, no; yes, no—when he thought about it. She was awesome to him. But he didn't exactly like her opinions about his education of young Mingo. Example: "There's only *so* much he can learn, being a salt-water African and all, don't-chooknow?"

"So?"

"You know he'll never completely adjust."

"So?" he said.

"You know everything here's strange to him."

"So?" he said again.

"And it'll *always* be a little strange—like seeing the world through a fun house mirror?"

Moses knocked dottle[7] from his churchwarden pipe, banging the bowl on the hard wooden arm of his chair until Harriet, annoyed, gave him a tight look. "You oughta see him, though. I mean, he's right smart—r'ally. It's like I just shot out another arm and that's Mingo. Can do anything I do, like today—he's gonna he'p Isaiah Jenson fix some windows and watcher-mercallems"—he scratched his head—"fences, over at his place." Chuckling, Moses struck a friction match on his boot heel. "Only thing Mingo won't do is kill chicken hawks; he feeds 'em like they was his best friends, even calls 'em Sir." Lightly, the old man laughed again. He put his left ankle on his right knee and cradled it. "But otherwise, Mingo says just what I says. Feels what I feels."

"Well!" Harriet said with violence. Her nose wrinkled—she rather hated his raw-smelling pipe tobacco—and testily laid down a general principle. "Slaves are tools with life in them, Moses, and tools are lifeless slaves."

The old man asked, "Says who?"

"Says Aristotle." She said this arrogantly, the way some people quote Scripture. "He owned thirteen slaves (they were then called *banausos*), sage Plato,[8] fifteen, and neither felt the need to elevate their bondsmen. The institution is old, Moses, old, and you're asking for a peck of trouble if you keep playing God and get too close to that wild African. If he turns turtle on you, what then?" Quotations followed from David Hume,[9] who, Harriet said, once called a preposterous liar one New World friend who informed him of a bondsman who could play any piece on the piano after hearing it only once.

"P'raps," hemmed Moses, rocking his head. "I reckon you're right."

"I know I'm right, Moses Green." She smiled.

"Harriet—"

The old woman answered, "Yes?"

"You gets me confused sometimes. Abaht my feelings. Half the time I can't rightly hear what you say, 'cause I'm all taken in by the way you say it." He struggled, shaking saliva from the stem of his pipe. "Harriet, your Henry, d'ya miss him much? I mean, abaht now you should be getting married again, don't you think? You get along okay by yourself, but I been thinking I . . . Sometimes you make me feel—"

---

7. Unburned or partially burned tobacco.
8. In ancient Greece, during the time of Plato and Aristotle, slavery was common. "Banausos": artisan (Greek); the word also has to do with things utilitarian or with moneymaking.
9. Scottish philosopher and historian (1711–1776); as a radical skeptic, he denied the possibility of certain knowledge.

"Yes?" She brightened. "Go on."

He didn't explain how he felt.

Moses, later on the narrow, root-covered road leading to Isaiah Jenson's cabin, thought Harriet Bridgewater wrong about Mingo and, strange to say, felt closer to the black African than to Harriet. So close, in fact, that when he pulled his rig up to Isaiah's house, he considered giving Mingo his farm when he died, God willing, as well as his knowledge, beliefs, and prejudices. Then again, maybe that was overdoing things. The boy was all Moses wanted him to be, his own emanation, but still, he thought, himself. Different enough from Moses so that he could step back and admire him.

Swinging his feet off the buckboard,[1] he called, "Isaiah!" and, hearing no reply, hobbled, bent forward at his hips, toward the front door— "H'lo?"—which was halfway open. Why could he see no one? "Jehoshaphat!" blurted Moses. From his lower stomach a loamy feeling crawled up to his throat. "Y'all heah? Hey!" The door opened with a burst at his fingertips. Snatching off his hat, ducking his head, he stepped inside. It was dark as a poor man's pocket in there. Air within had the smell of boiled potatoes and cornbread. He saw the boy seated big as life at Isaiah's table, struggling with a big lead-colored spoon and a bowl of hominy. "You two finished al-raid-y, eh?" Moses laughed, throwing his jaw forward, full of pride, as Mingo fought mightily, his head hung over his bowl, to get food to his mouth. "Whar's that fool Isaiah?" The African pointed over his shoulder, and Moses's eyes, squinting in the weak light, followed his wagging finger to a stream of sticky black fluid like the gelatinous trail of a snail flowing from where Isaiah Jenson, cold as stone, lay crumpled next to his stove, the image of Mingo imprisoned on the retina of his eyes. Frail moonlight funneled through cracks in the roof. The whole cabin was unreal. Simply unreal. The old man's knees knocked together. His stomach jerked. Buried deep in Isaiah's forehead was a meat cleaver that exactly split his face and disconnected his features.

"Oh, my Lord!" croaked Moses. He did a little dance, half juba,[2] half jig, on his good leg toward Isaiah, whooped, "Mingo, what'd you *do?*" Then, knowing full well what he'd done, he boxed the boy behind his ears, and shook all six feet of him until Moses's teeth, not Mingo's, rattled. The old man sat down at the table; his knees felt rubbery, and he groaned: "Lord, *Lord, Lord!*" He blew out breath, blenched, his lips skinned back over his tobacco-browned teeth, and looked square at the African. "Isaiah's daid! You understand that?"

Mingo understood that; he said so.

"And you're responsible!" He stood up, but sat down again, coughing, then pulled out his handkerchief and spit into it. "Daid! You know what daid means?" Again, he hawked and spit. "Responsible—you know what *that* means?"

He did not; he said, "Nossuh, don't know as I know that one, suh. Not Mingo, boss. Nossuh!"

Moses sprang up suddenly like a steel spring going off and slapped the boy till his palm stung. Briefly, the old man went bananas, pounding the

---

1. Four-wheeled carriage with a floor made of long boards.

2. Southern plantation dance that includes clapping the hands and slapping the knees and thighs.

boy's chest with his fists. He sat down again. Jumping up so quick made his head spin and legs wobble. Mingo protested his innocence, and it did not dawn on Moses why he seemed so indifferent until he thought back to what he'd told him about chicken hawks. Months ago, maybe five, he'd taught Mingo to kill chicken hawks and be courteous to strangers, but it got all turned around in the African's mind (how was he to know New World customs?), so he was courteous to chicken hawks (Moses groaned, full of gloom) and killed strangers. "You idjet!" hooted Moses. His jaw clamped shut. He wept hoarsely for a few minutes like a steer with the strangles.[3] "Isaiah Jenson and me was friends, and—" He checked himself; what'd he said was a lie. They weren't friends at all. In fact, he thought Isaiah Jenson was a pigheaded fool and only tolerated the little yimp in a neighborly way. Into his eye a fly bounded. Moses shook his head wildly. He'd even sworn to Harriet, weeks earlier, that Jenson was so troublesome, always borrowing tools and keeping them, he hoped he'd go to Ballyhack[4] on a red-hot rail. In his throat a knot tightened. One of his eyelids jittered up, still itchy from the fly; he forced it down with his finger, then gave a slow look at the African. "Great Peter," he mumbled. "You couldn'ta known that."

"Go home now?" Mingo stretched out the stiffness in his spine. "Powerful tired, boss."

Not because he wanted to go home did Moses leave, but because he was afraid of Isaiah's body and needed time to think things through. Dry the air, dry the evening down the road that led them home. As if to himself, the old man grumped, "I gave you thought and tongue, and look at what you done with it—they gonna catch and kill you, boy, just as sure as I'm sitting heah."

"Mingo?" The African shook his long head, sly; he touched his chest with one finger. "Me? Nossuh."

"Why the hell you keep saying that?" Moses threw his jaw forward so violently muscles in his neck stood out. "You kilt a man, and they gonna burn you crisper than an ear of corn. Ay, God, Mingo," moaned the old man, "you gotta act responsible, son!" At the thought of what they'd do to Mingo, Moses scrooched the stalk of his head into his stiff collar. He drilled his gaze at the smooth-faced African, careful not to look him in the eye, and barked, "What're you thinking now?"

"What Mingo know, Massa Green know. Bees like what Mingo sees or don't see is only what Massa Green taught him to see or don't see. Like Mingo lives through Massa Green, right?"

Moses waited, suspicious, smelling a trap. "Yeah, all that's true."

"Massa Green, he owns Mingo, right?"

"Right," snorted Moses. He rubbed the knob of his red, porous nose. "Paid good money—"

"So when Mingo works, it bees Massa Green workin', right? Bees Massa Green workin', thinkin', doin' through Mingo—ain't that so?"

Nobody's fool, Moses Green could latch onto a notion with no trouble at all; he turned violently off the road leading to his cabin, and plowed on toward Harriet's, pouring sweat, remembering two night visions he'd had,

---

3. Infectious disease of horses and cattle, marked by inflammation of mucous membranes. 4. Hell (slang).

recurrent, where he and Mingo were wired together like say two ventriloquist's dummies, one black, one white, and there was somebody—who he
didn't know, yanking their arm and leg strings simultaneously—how he
couldn't figure, but he and Mingo said the same thing together until his
liver-spotted hands, the knuckles tight and shriveled like old carrot skin,
flew up to his face and, shrieking, he started hauling hips across a cold
black countryside. But so did Mingo, *his* hands on *his* face, pumping his
knees right alongside Moses, shrieking, their voice inflections identical;
and then the hazy dream doorwayed luxuriously into another where he was
greaved[5] on one half of a thrip—a coin halfway between a nickel and a
dime—and on the reverse side was Mingo. Shaking, Moses pulled his rig
into Harriet Bridgewater's yard. His bowels, burning, felt like boiling tar.
She was standing on her porch in a checkered Indian shawl, staring at
them, her book still open, when Moses scrambled, tripping, skinning his
knees, up her steps. He shouted, "Harriet, this boy done kilt Isaiah Jenson
in cold blood." She lost color and wilted back into her doorway. Her hair
was swinging in her eyes. Hands flying, he stammered in a flurry of anxiety,
"But it wasn't altogether Mingo's fault—he didn't know what he was doin'."

"Isaiah? You mean Izay-yah? He didn't kill Izay-yah?"

"Yeah, aw no! Not really—" His mind stuttered to a stop.

"Whose fault is it then?" Harriet gawked at the African picking his nose
in the wagon (Moses had, it's true, not policed himself as well as he'd
wanted). A shiver quaked slowly up her left side. She sloughed off her confusion, and flashed, "I can tell you whose fault it is, Moses. Yours! Didn't I
say not to bring that wild African here? Huh? Huh? Huh? You both should
be—put to sleep."

"Aw, woman! Hesh up!" Moses threw down his hat and stomped it out of
shape. "You just all upsetted." Truth to tell, he was not the portrait of composure himself. There were rims of dirt in his nails. His trouser legs had
blood splattered on them. Moses stamped his feet to shake road powder off
his boots. "You got any spirits in the house? I need your he'p to untangle
this thing, but I ain't hardly touched a drop since I bought Mingo, and my
throat's pretty dr—"

"You'll just have to get it yourself—on the top shelf of the cupboard."
She touched her face, fingers spread, with a dazed gesture. There was suddenly in her features the intensity found in the look of people who have a
year, a month, a minute only to live. "I think I'd better sit down." Lowering
herself onto her rocker, she cradled on her lap a volume by one M. Shelley,
a recent tale of monstrosity and existential horror,[6] then she demurely settled her breasts. "It's just like you, Moses Green, to bring all your bewilder-
ments to me."

The old man's face splashed into a huge, foamy smile. He kissed her
gently on both eyes, and Harriet, in return, rubbed her cheek like a cat
against his gristly jaw. Moses felt lighter than a feather. "Got to have somebody, don't I?"

In the common room, Moses rifled through the cupboard, came up with

---

5. Engraved.
6. I.e., *Frankenstein* (1818), by the English writer Mary Shelley (1797–1851).

a bottle of luke-warm bourbon and, hands trembling, poured himself three fingers' worth in a glass. Then, because he figured he deserved it, he refilled his glass and, draining it slowly, sloshing it around in his mouth, considered his options. He could turn Mingo over to the law and let it go at that, but damned if he couldn't shake loose the idea that killing the boy somehow wouldn't put things to rights; it would be like they were killing Moses himself, destroying a part of his soul. Besides, whatever the African'd done, it was what he'd learned through Moses, who was not the most reliable lens for looking at things. You couldn't rightly call a man responsible if, in some utterly alien place, he was without power, without privilege, without property—was, in fact, property—if he had no position, had nothing, or virtually next to nothing, and nothing was his product or judgment. "Be damned!" Moses spit. It was a bitter thing to siphon your being from someone else. He knew that now. It was like, on another level, what Liverspoon had once tried to deny about God and man: *If* God was (and now Moses wasn't all that sure), and *if* He made the world, then a man didn't have to answer for anything. Rape or murder, it all referred back to who-or-whatever was responsible for that world's make-up. Chest fallen, he tossed away his glass, lifted the bottle to his lips, then nervously lit his pipe. Maybe . . . maybe they could run, if it came to that, and start all over again in Missouri, where he'd teach Mingo the difference between chicken hawks and strangers. But, sure as day, he'd do it again. He couldn't change. What was *was*. They'd be running forever, across all space, all time—so he imagined—like fugitives with no fingers, no toes, like two thieves or yokefellows, each with some God-awful secret that could annihilate the other. Naw! Moses thought. His blood beat up. The deep, powerful stroke of his heart made him wince. His tobacco maybe. Too strong. He sent more whiskey crashing down his throat. Naw! You couldn't have nothing and just go as you pleased. How strange that owner and owned magically dissolved into each other like two crossing shafts of light (or, if he'd known this, which he did not, particles, subatomic, interconnected in a complex skein of relatedness). Shoot him maybe, reabsorb Mingo, was that more merciful? Naw! He was fast; fast. Then manumit[7] the African? Noble gesture, that. But how in blazes could he disengage himself when Mingo shored up, sustained, *let be* Moses's world with all its sores and blemishes every time he opened his oily black eyes? Thanks to the trouble he took cementing Mingo to his own mind, he could not, by thunder, do without him now. Giving him his freedom, handing it to him like a rasher of bacon, would shackle Mingo to him even more. There seemed, just then, no solution.

Undecided, but mercifully drunk now, his pipebowl too hot to hold any longer, Moses, who could not speak his mind to Harriet Bridgewater unless he'd tied one on, called out: "I come to a decision. Not about Mingo, but you'n' me." It was then seven o'clock. He shambled, feet shuffling, toward the door. "Y'know, I was gonna ask you to marry me this morning"—he laughed; whiskey made his scalp tingle—"but I figured living alone was better when I thought how married folks—and sometimes wimmin with dogs—got to favoring each other . . . like they was wax candles flowing

7. Release from slavery.

tergether. Hee-hee." He stepped gingerly, holding the bottle high, his ears brick red, face streaky from wind-dried sweat, back onto the quiet porch. He heard a moan. It was distinctly a moan. "Harriet? Harriet, I ain't put it too well, but I'm asking you now." On the porch her rocker slid back, forth, squeaking on the floorboards. Moses's bottle fell—*bip!*—down the stairs, bounced out into the yard, rolled, and bumped into Harriet Bridgewater. Naw, he thought. Aw, naw. By the wagon, by a chopping block near a pile of split faggots, by the ruin of an old handpump caked with rust, she lay on her side, the back fastenings of her dress burst open, her mouth a perfect O. The sight so wounded him he wept like a child. It was then seven-fifteen.

October 7 of the year of grace 1855.

Midnight found Moses Green still staring down at her. He felt sick and crippled and dead inside. Every shadowed object thinging in the yard beyond, wrenched up from its roots, hazed like shapes in a hallucination, was a sermon on vanity; every time he moved his eyes he stared into a grim homily on the deadly upas[8] of race and relatedness. Now he had no place to stand. Now he was undone. "Mingo . . . come ovah heah." He was very quiet.

"Suh?" The lanky African jumped down from the wagon, faintly innocent, faintly diabolical. Removed from the setting of Moses's farm, the boy looked strangely elemental; his skin had the texture of plant life, the stones of his eyes an odd, glossy quality like those of a spider, which cannot be read. "Talky old hen daid now, boss."

The old man's face shattered. "I was gonna marry that woman!"

"Naw." Mingo frowned. From out of his frown a huge grin flowered. "You say—I'm quoting you now, suh—a man needs a quiet, patient, uncomplaining woman, right?"

Moses croaked, "When did I say that?"

"Yesstiday." Mingo yawned. He looked sleepy. "Go home now, boss?"

"Not just yet." Moses Green, making an effort to pull himself to his full height, failed. "You lie face down—heah me?—with your hands ovah your head till I come back." With Mingo hugging the front steps, Moses took the stairs back inside, found the flintlock[9] Harriet kept in her cupboard on account of slaves who swore to die in the skin of freemen, primed it, and stepped back, so slowly, to the yard. Outside, the air seemed thinner. Bending forward, perspiring at his upper lip, Moses tucked the cold barrel into the back of Mingo's neck, cushioning it in a small socket of flesh above the African's broad shoulders. With his thumb he pulled the hammer back. Springs in the flintlock whined. Deep inside his throat, as if he were speaking through his stomach, he talked to the dark poll of the boy's back-slanting head.

"You ain't never gonna understand why I gotta do this. You a saddle across my neck, always will be, even though it ain't rightly all your fault. Mingo, you more me than I am myself. Me planed away to the bone! Ya understand?" He coughed and went on miserably: "All the wrong, all the good you do, now or tomorrow—it's me indirectly doing it, but without the lies and excuses, without the feeling what's its foundation, with all the po-

<hr/>

8. Harmful or poisonous influence or institution.   9. A type of gun.

lite make-up and apologies removed. It's an empty gesture, like the swing of a shadow's arm. You can't never see things exactly the way I do. I'm guilty. It was me set the gears in motion. Me . . ." Away in the octopoid darkness a wild bird—a nighthawk maybe—screeched. It shot noisily away with blurred wings askirring when the sound of hoofs and wagons rumbled closer. Eyes narrowed to slits, Moses said—a dry whisper—"Get up, you damned fool." He let his round shoulders slump. Mingo let his broad shoulders slump. "Take the horses," Moses said; he pulled himself up to his rig, then sat, his knees together beside the boy. Mingo's knees drew together. Moses's voice changed. It began to rasp and wheeze; so did Mingo's. "Missouri," said the old man, not to Mingo but to the dusty floor of the buckboard, "if I don't misremember, is off thataway somewheres in the west."

1986

NTOZAKE SHANGE
b. 1948

In a 1976 interview in *Time* magazine, Ntozake Shange recalled the circumstances that prompted the writing of A *Nite with Beau Willie*, one of the most powerful poems in the work for which she is best known, *for colored girls who have considered suicide/when the rainbow is enuf*:

> It was hot. I was broke. I didn't have enough money for a subway token. I was miserable. The man in the next room was beating up his old lady. It went on for hours and hours. She was screaming. He was laughing. Every time he hit her I would think, yeah, man, well that has already happened to me. So I sat down and wrote "Beau Willie." All my anger came out.

Shange's young adult experiences while living in a Harlem boardinghouse were a far cry from her "rich and somewhat protected" childhood. She was born Paulette Williams on October 18, 1948, in Trenton, New Jersey, the daughter of Eloise Williams, a psychiatric social worker and educator, and Paul T. Williams, a surgeon, for whom she was named. When she was eight, her family moved to St. Louis, Missouri. Shange remembers the difficulties she encountered when she was bused to a formerly segregated German-American school: "I was not prepared for it. . . . I was being harrassed and chased around by these white kids. My parents were busy being proud."

The family moved back to Trenton when she was thirteen, and the adolescent Shange began a period of intense reading, devouring the works of Dostoevsky, Melville, Carson McCullers, Edna St. Vincent Millay, Simone de Beauvoir, and Jean Genet, among others. In addition, Shange's artistic development was nourished by her parents' friendships with prominent performers such as Josephine Baker, Dizzy Gillespie, Chuck Berry, Charlie Parker, and Miles Davis. W. E. B. Du Bois was also a visitor in her family's home. Shange enrolled at Barnard College, in New York City, in 1966. Despite emotional upheaval, marked by a series of suicide attempts and a difficult separation from her law-student husband, she graduated with honors in 1970. In 1971, while studying for a master's degree in African American studies at UCLA, she took an African name. Ntozake translates as "she who comes with her own things," and Shange as "who walks like a lion."

From 1972 to 1975, Shange taught humanities, women's studies, and African American studies at various colleges in California. At the same time, she was reciting poetry and dancing with West Coast performance groups, including her own company, For Colored Girls Who Have Considered Suicide. She moved to New York in 1975 during the Public Theater's production of her choreopoem—poems that are performed much like the movements of a dramatic dance sequence—*for colored girls who have considered suicide/when the rainbow is enuf*. The play went on to become the second by an African American woman to reach Broadway (Hansberry's *Raisin in the Sun* opened on Broadway in 1958). In addition to tremendous popular success, the play won Obie and Outer Critics Circle awards and was nominated for the Emmy, Grammy, and Tony awards.

for colored girls is a mesh of poetry, music, dancing, and light. Seven women, dressed in the colors of the rainbow plus brown, the color of the earth and the body, perform twenty poems, without any set or props. In her introduction to the piece, Shange writes that *for colored girls* is about "our struggle to become all that is forbidden, all that is forfeited by our gender, all that we have forgotten." Tracing the women's emotions from youth to maturity, the piece focuses on the lack of communication between men and women and on the misunderstanding of women, exploring particularly the theme of unrequited love. Although many of the poems center on the physical, psychological, and emotional pain experienced by its characters, the piece also asserts the possibility of surviving and developing self-esteem with the support of other women. Many critics praised *for colored girls* as witty and unpredictable; others faulted it for undeveloped characterizations and especially for a lack of sympathetic male figures. Not surprisingly, it sparked much debate in African American intellectual circles.

After *for colored girls*, Shange went on to publish a novella, *Sassafrass* (1977); two novels, *Sassafrass, Cypress, and Indigo* (1982) and *Betsey Brown* (1985); and several volumes of poetry, including *Nappy Edges* (1978) and *Ridin' the Moon in Texas: Word Paintings* (1987), in which her resistance to conventional grammar and spelling reflect a rejection of the hierarchies inherent in standard English, as well as a connection with the African American oral tradition. Two of her plays were produced by Joseph Papp's New York Shakespeare Festival, *Spell #7* and *A Photograph: Lovers-in-Motion*, and in 1980 she won a second Obie, for her adaptation of Brecht's *Mother Courage*, which featured a black family during the American Civil War. Her essay collection *See No Evil: Prefaces, Essays and Accounts, 1976–1983*, appeared in 1984.

Throughout her innovative, productive career, Ntozake Shange's work has been a celebration of language. As she told a *New Yorker* interviewer in 1976, "I listen to words, and when people can't say what they mean they are in trouble."

From for colored girls who have considered suicide/when the rainbow is enuf

* * *

lady in green
somebody almost walked off wid alla my stuff
not my poems or a dance i gave up in the street
but somebody almost walked off wid alla my stuff
like a kleptomaniac workin hard & forgettin while stealin
this is mine/ this aint yr stuff/   5
now why dont you put me back & let me hang out in my own self
somebody almost walked off wid alla my stuff

& didnt care enuf to send a note home saying
i waz late for my solo conversation
or two sizes too small for my own tacky skirts 10
what can anybody do wit somethin of no value on
a open market/ did you getta dime for my things/
hey man/ where are you goin wid alla my stuff/
this is a woman's trip & i need my stuff/
to ohh & ahh abt/ daddy/ i gotta mainline number 15
from my own shit/ now wontchu put me back/ & let
me play this duet/ wit this silver ring in my nose/
honest to god/ somebody almost run off wit alla my stuff/
& i didnt bring anythin but the kick & sway of it
the perfect ass for my man & none of it is theirs 20
this is mine/ ntozake "her own things" [1]/ that's my name/
now give me my stuff/ i see ya hidin my laugh/ & how i
sit wif my legs open sometimes/ to give my crotch
some sunlight/ & there goes my love my toes my chewed
up finger nails/ niggah/ wif the curls in yr hair/ 25
mr. louisiana hot link/ i want my stuff back/
my rhythms & my voice/ open my mouth/ & let me talk ya
outta/ throwin my shit in the sewar/ this is some delicate
leg & whimsical kiss/ i gotta have to give to my choice/
without you runnin off wit alla my shit/ 30
now you cant have me less i give me away/ & i waz
doin all that/ til ya run off on a good thing/
who is this you left me wit/ some simple bitch
widda bad attitude/ i wants my things/
i want my arm wit the hot iron scar/ & my leg wit the 35
flea bite/ i want my calloused feet & quik language back
in my mouth/ fried plantains/ pineapple pear juice/
sun-ra & joseph & jules [2]/ i want my own things/ how i lived them/
& give me my memories/ how i waz when i waz there/
you cant have them or do nothin wit them/ 40
stealin my shit from me/ dont make it yrs/ makes it stolen/
somebody almost run off wit alla my stuff/ & i waz standin
there/ lookin at myself/ the whole time
& it waznt a spirit took my stuff/ waz a man whose
ego walked round like Rodan's [3] shadow/ waz a man faster 45
n my innocence/ waz a lover/ i made too much
room for/ almost run off wit alla my stuff/
& i didn't know i'd give it up so quik/ & the one running wit it/
dont know he got it/ & i'm shoutin this is mine/ & he dont
know he got it/ my stuff is the anonymous ripped off treasure 50
of the year/ did you know somebody almost got away with me/
me in a plastic bag under their arm/ me
danglin on a string of personal carelessness/ i'm spattered wit
mud & city rain/ & no i didnt get a chance to take a douche/
hey man/ this is not your perogative/ i gotta have me in my 55

1. The word *ntozake* means "she who comes with
her own things."
2. Perhaps a reference to Shange's friends Joseph
Jarmin, member of the Chicago Art Ensemble, and
Jules Allen, photographer. Sun Ra (1914?–1993),
African American jazz musician and composer.
3. Perhaps a reference to Rodan, a winged God-
zilla-like monster of a 1950s Japanese science fiction film.

pocket/ to get round like a good woman shd/ & make the poem
in the pot or the chicken in the dance/ what i got to do/
i gotta have my stuff to do it to/
why dont ya find yr own things/ & leave this package
of me for my destiny/ what ya got to get from me/   60
i'll give it to ya/ yeh/ i'll give it to ya/
round 5:00 in the winter/ when the sky is blue-red/
& Dew City is gettin pressed/ if it's really my stuff/
ya gotta give it to me/ if ya really want it/ i'm
the only one/ can handle it   65

    lady in blue
that niggah will be back tomorrow, sayin 'i'm sorry'

    lady in yellow
get this, last week my ol man came in sayin, 'i don't know
how she got yr number baby, i'm sorry'

    *   *   *

                                  1977

Nappy Edges*

*the roots of your hair/ what
turns back when we sweat, run,
make love, dance, get afraid, get
happy: the tell-tale sign of living/
nappy edges (a cross country sojourn)   5

    st. louis/ such a colored town/ a whiskey
black space of history & neighborhood/ forever ours/
    to lawrenceville [1]/ where the only road open
to me/ waz cleared by colonial slaves/ whose children never
moved/ never seems like/ mended the torments of the Depression   10
the stains of demented spittle/ dropped from lips of crystal women/
still makin independence flags/
    from st. louis/ on a halloween's eve to the veiled prophet/
usurpin the mystery of mardi gras/ made it mine tho the queen
waz always fair/ that parade/ of pagan floats & tambourines/   15
commemoratin me/ unlike the lonely walks wit liberal trick or
treaters/ back to my front door/ bag half empty/
    my face enuf to scare anyone i passed/ a colored kid/
whatta gas

        1) here   20
           a tree
           wonderin the horizon
           dipped in blues &
           untended bones
           usedta hugs drawls   25
           rhythm & decency

1. An Illinois town, south of St. Louis.

          here a tree
          waitin to be hanged

     sumner[2] high school/ squat & pale on the corner/ like
our vision/ waz to be vague/ our memory   30
of the war/ that made us free to be forgotten
becomin paler/ a linear movement from south carolina
to missouri/ freedmen/ landin in jackie wilson's[3] yelp/ daughters of
the manumitted swimmin in tina turner's[4] grinds/ this is chuck
berry's town/ disavowin misega-nation[5]/ in any situation/ & they let   35
us be/ electric blues & bo diddley's[6] cant/ rockin pneumonia &
boogie-woogie flu/ the slop & short-fried heads/ runnin always to
the river

          / from chambersbourg[7]/ lil italy/ i passed everyday
at the sweet shoppe/ & waz afraid/ the cops raided truants/   40
regularly/ after dark i wd not be seen/ wit any other colored/
sane/ lovin my life/
          in the 'bourg/ seriously expectin to be gnarled/
hey niggah/ over here/
          & behind the truck lay five hands claspin chains/   45
round the trees/ 4 more sucklin steel/
                              hey niggah/ over here
this is the borderline/
a territorial dispute/
                              hey/ niggah/   50
over here/
          cars loaded wit families/ fellas from the factory/ one or two
practical nurses/ black/ become our trenches/ some dig into cement
wit elbows/ under engines/ do not be seen/ in yr hometown/ after
sunset we suck up our shadows/   55

          2) i will sit here
          my shoulders brace an enormous oak
          dreams waddle in my lap
          round to miz bertha's where lil richard[8]
          gets his process   60
          run backwards to the rosebushes/ a drunk man/ lyin
          down the block to the nuns in pink habits
          prayin in a pink chapel
          my dreams run to meet aunt marie
          my dreams draw blood from ol sores   65
              these stains & scars are mine
              this is my space
              i am not movin

                                                        1978

2. A town in southeastern Illinois.
3. African American singer and boxer (1934–1984).
4. African American soul and pop singer (b. 1939). "Manumitted": freed from slavery.
5. A play on the word *miscegenation*, which means sexual relations between a man and a woman of different races. Berry (b. 1926), African American rock music guitarist, songwriter, and singer.
6. African American blues singer and musician (b. 1928).
7. Illinois town.
8. African American singer, songwriter (b. 1932), known for his sleek, wavy ("processed") hairdo.

Bocas:[1] A Daughter's Geography

i have a daughter/ mozambique
i have a son/ angola[2]
our twins
salvador & johannesburg[3]/ cannot speak
the same language   5
but we fight the same old men/ in the new world

we are so hungry for the morning
we're trying to feed our children the sun
but a long time ago/ we boarded ships/ locked in
depths of seas our spirits/ kisst the earth   10
on the atlantic side of nicaragua costa rica
our lips traced the edges of cuba puerto rico
charleston & savannah/ in haiti[4]
we embraced &
made children of the new world   15
but old men spit on us/ shackled our limbs
but for a minute
our cries are the panama canal/ the yucatan[5]
we poured thru more sea/ more ships/ to manila[6]
ah ha we're back again   20
everybody in manila awready speaks spanish

the old men sent for the archbishop of canterbury[7]
"can whole continents be excommunicated?"
"what wd happen to the children?"
"wd their allegiance slip over the edge?"   25
"dont worry bout lumumba/ don't even think bout
ho chi minh[8]/ the dead cant procreate"
so say the old men

but i have a daughter/ la habana
i have a son/ guyana[9]   30
our twins
santiago & brixton[1]/ cannot speak
the same language
yet we fight the same old men

the ones who think helicopters rhyme with hunger   35
who think patrol boats can confiscate a people
the ones whose dreams are full of none of our
children
they see mae west & harlow[2] in whittled white cafes
near managua/ listening to primitive rhythms in   40
jungles near pétionville[3]
with bejeweled benign natives
ice skating in abidjan[4]
unaware of the rest of us in chicago
all the dark urchins   45
rounding out the globe/ primitively whispering
the earth is not flat old men

there is no edge
no end to the new world
cuz i have a daughter/ trinidad   50
i have a son/ san juan[5]
our twins
capetown & palestine[6]/ cannot speak the same
language/ but we fight the same old men
the same men who thought the earth waz flat   55
go on over the edge/ go on over the edge old men
you'll see us in luanda.[7] or the rest of us
in chicago
rounding out the morning/
we are feeding our children the sun   60

1983

2. Mae West (1892?–1980) and Jean Harlow (1911–1937), American film stars known for their sultry personas and spicy wit. Managua is the capital of Nicaragua.
3. City in Haiti.
4. Former capital of the Ivory Coast, a country in west Africa.
5. The capital of Puerto Rico. Trinidad is one of the islands of the Caribbean nation of Trinidad and Tobago.
6. Historically, a region comprising parts of modern Israel, Egypt, and Jordan; also, the nation of the Palestinian people. Capetown is the capital of South Africa.
7. The capital of Angola; in the 16th to the 19th centuries, it was the center of slave trade to Brazil.

JAMAICA KINCAID

b. 1949

Born Elaine Potter Richardson on May 25, 1949, in St. John's, Antigua, in the British West Indies, Jamaica Kincaid remembers life on that former British Colony as a series of ongoing tensions between appearance and reality: "I was always being told I should be something, and then my whole upbringing was something I was not: English." The evocation of that sense of dislocation and an intense exploration of the mother-daughter relationship are the major elements of Kincaid's much-celebrated works. She has published *At the Bottom of the River* (1983), a densely poetic prose work; *Annie John* (1985), short stories that became a novel; *A Small Place* (1988), a critique of colonialism in Antigua; *Lucy* (1990), a sparse, beautifully precise novel that evokes what critic and writer Thulani Davis calls "the psychological space between leaving and arriving," and *An Autobiography of My Mother* (1996), praised by critics for its hypnotic yet disturbing language.

Kincaid has portrayed life for an immigrant from the West Indies to the United States in styles—the metaphoric quality of *Annie John*, the minimalism of *Lucy*—that reflect modernist influences. Certainly her work does feel indebted to the modernist writings of Virginia Woolf and James Joyce. In an interview with Selvyn Cudjoe, she recalls reading stories by French *nouveau roman* writer Alain Robbe-Grillet for the first time:

> I cannot describe them except that they broke every rule. When I read them, the top of my head came off and I thought, "This is really living!" And I knew that whatever I did, I would not be interested in realism.

Although her work has been praised by critics for its feminist investigation of the mother-daughter relationship in a third world and immigrant context, Kincaid herself views her writing as much more of an individual phenomenon:

> I don't really want to be placed in that category. I don't mind if people put me in it, but I don't claim to be in it. But that's just me as an individual. I mean, I always see myself as alone. I can't bear to be in a group of any kind, or in the school of anything.

A precocious child, Jamaica Kincaid, then Elaine Richardson, won scholarships to colonial schools in Antigua, including the much-hated Princess Margaret School, where she has said her education was so "Empire" that she "thought all the great writing had been done before 1900." At sixteen she came to New York as an au pair, eventually intending to become a nurse—an experience that is the basis for her second novel, *Lucy*. Instead, Kincaid studied photography and wrote for various magazines, including an early breakthrough interview with Gloria Steinem for the magazine *Ingenue*. Changing her name from Elaine Potterson to Jamaica Kincaid, she graduated to the *New Yorker*, which published sections of *At the Bottom of the River* and *Annie John*.

At the Bottom of the River is a collection of short stories, dreams, and reflections, which won the Morton Dauwen Zabel Award from the American Academy and Institute of Arts and Letters. While critics such as novelist Anne Tyler noted "its almost insultingly obscure quality," they also praised its poetic exploration of two themes: "the wonderful terrible strength of a loving mother" and "the mysteriousness of ordinary life." Those two themes are also central to Kincaid's first novel, *Annie John*.

Annie John is the work of Kincaid's that is most often assumed to be autobiographical. The story chronicles, in richly detailed prose, the childhood of a young girl in Antigua who gradually becomes estranged from her mother. When asked in a 1985 interview about its correspondence to her own childhood, Kincaid answered, "The feelings in it are autobiographical, yes. I didn't want to say it was autobiographical because I felt that would be somehow admitting something about myself, but it is, and so that's that."

Perhaps her most analytical work, her third published book *A Small Place* is an essay addressed to a tourist from North America or Europe, traveling in Antigua, that in stark sentences describes the destructive effects of colonialism. Some reviewers were upset by its rage, while others, especially in Europe, praised its powerful critique of imperialism.

In 1990, Kincaid published *Lucy*, in many ways complementary to her first novel. Lucy is a young Antiguan woman who comes to New York to work as an au pair for a young white couple with four children and feels estranged from the mother she left, even as she cannot connect with her life in New York. Kincaid's *An Autobiography of My Mother* also focuses on the theme of motherhood. Xuela Claudette Richardson, the daughter of a Carib mother and a half-Scottish, half-African father, delivers a book-length monologue that powerfully evokes the loss of the mother she never knew.

Still a young writer, Jamaica Kincaid has already been recognized as a talented, unique stylist. She lives with her husband, Allen Shawn, and their two children in Bennington, Vermont.

From Annie John

Chapter Two

THE CIRCLING HAND

During my holidays from school, I was allowed to stay in bed until long after my father had gone to work. He left our house every weekday at the stroke of seven by the Anglican[1] church bell. I would lie in bed awake, and I could hear all the sounds my parents made as they prepared for the day ahead. As my mother made my father his breakfast, my father would shave, using his shaving brush that had an ivory handle and a razor that matched; then he would step outside to the little shed he had built for us as a bathroom, to quickly bathe in water that he had instructed my mother to leave outside overnight in the dew. That way, the water would be very cold, and he believed that cold water strengthened his back. If I had been a boy, I would have gotten the same treatment, but since I was a girl, and on top of that went to school only with other girls, my mother would always add some hot water to my bathwater to take off the chill. On Sunday afternoons, while I was in Sunday school, my father took a hot bath; the tub was half filled with plain water, and then my mother would add a large caldron-ful of water in which she had just boiled some bark and leaves from a bay-leaf tree. The bark and leaves were there for no reason other than that he liked the smell. He would then spend hours lying in this bath, studying his pool coupons or drawing examples of pieces of furniture he planned to make. When I came home from Sunday school, we would sit down to our Sunday dinner.

My mother and I often took a bath together. Sometimes it was just a plain bath, which didn't take very long. Other times, it was a special bath in which the barks and flowers of many different trees, together with all sorts of oils, were boiled in the same large caldron. We would then sit in this bath in a darkened room with a strange-smelling candle burning away. As we sat in this bath, my mother would bathe different parts of my body; then she would do the same to herself. We took these baths after my mother had consulted with her obeah[2] woman, and with her mother and a trusted friend, and all three of them had confirmed that from the look of things

---

1. Of the episcopal Church of England.
2. Religious ritual practiced in Africa and in parts of the American South and the West Indies.

around our house—the way a small scratch on my instep had turned into a small sore, then a large sore, and how long it had taken to heal; the way a dog she knew, and a friendly dog at that, suddenly turned and bit her; how a porcelain bowl she had carried from one eternity and hoped to carry into the next suddenly slipped out of her capable hands and broke into pieces the size of grains of sand; how words she spoke in jest to a friend had been completely misunderstood—one of the many women my father had loved, had never married, but with whom he had had children was trying to harm my mother and me by setting bad spirits on us.

When I got up, I placed my bedclothes and my nightie in the sun to air out, brushed my teeth, and washed and dressed myself. My mother would then give me my breakfast, but since, during my holidays, I was not going to school, I wasn't forced to eat an enormous breakfast of porridge, eggs, an orange or half a grapefruit, bread and butter, and cheese. I could get away with just some bread and butter and cheese and porridge and cocoa. I spent the day following my mother around and observing the way she did everything. When we went to the grocer's, she would point out to me the reason she bought each thing. I was shown a loaf of bread or a pound of butter from at least ten different angles. When we went to market, if that day she wanted to buy some crabs she would inquire from the person selling them if they came from near Parham, and if the person said yes my mother did not buy the crabs. In Parham was the leper colony, and my mother was convinced that the crabs ate nothing but the food from the lepers' own plates. If we were then to eat the crabs, it wouldn't be long before we were lepers ourselves and living unhappily in the leper colony.

How important I felt to be with my mother. For many people, their wares and provisions laid out in front of them, would brighten up when they saw her coming and would try hard to get her attention. They would dive underneath their stalls and bring out goods even better than what they had on display. They were disappointed when she held something up in the air, looked at it, turning it this way and that, and then, screwing up her face, said, "I don't think so," and turned and walked away—off to another stall to see if someone who only last week had sold her some delicious christophine[3] had something that was just as good. They would call out after her turned back that next week they expected to have eddoes or dasheen[4] or whatever, and my mother would say, "We'll see," in a very disbelieving tone of voice. If then we went to Mr. Kenneth, it would be only for a few minutes, for he knew exactly what my mother wanted and always had it ready for her. Mr. Kenneth had known me since I was a small child, and he would always remind me of little things I had done then as he fed me a piece of raw liver he had set aside for me. It was one of the few things I liked to eat, and, to boot, it pleased my mother to see me eat something that was so good for me, and she would tell me in great detail the effect the raw liver would have on my red blood corpuscles.

We walked home in the hot midmorning sun mostly without event. When I was much smaller, quite a few times while I was walking with my

3. Chayote, a pear-shaped vegetable native to the   4. Tropical plants whose roots are edible.
Americas.

mother she would suddenly grab me and wrap me up in her skirt and drag me along with her as if in a great hurry. I would hear an angry voice saying angry things, and then, after we had passed the angry voice, my mother would release me. Neither my mother nor my father ever came straight out and told me anything, but I had put two and two together and I knew that it was one of the women that my father had loved and with whom he had had a child or children, and who never forgave him for marrying my mother and having me. It was one of those women who were always trying to harm my mother and me, and they must have loved my father very much, for not once did any of them ever try to hurt him, and whenever he passed them on the street it was as if he and these women had never met.

When we got home, my mother started to prepare our lunch (pumpkin soup with droppers, banana fritters with salt fish stewed in antroba and tomatoes, fungie with salt fish stewed in antroba and tomatoes, or pepper pot,[5] all depending on what my mother had found at market that day). As my mother went about from pot to pot, stirring one, adding something to the other, I was ever in her wake. As she dipped into a pot of boiling something or other to taste for correct seasoning, she would give me a taste of it also, asking me what I thought. Not that she really wanted to know what I thought, for she had told me many times that my taste buds were not quite developed yet, but it was just to include me in everything. While she made our lunch, she would also keep an eye on her washing. If it was a Tuesday and the colored clothes had been starched, as she placed them on the line I would follow, carrying a basket of clothespins for her. While the starched colored clothes were being dried on the line, the white clothes were being whitened on the stone heap. It was a beautiful stone heap that my father had made for her: an enormous circle of stones, about six inches high, in the middle of our yard. On it the soapy white clothes were spread out; as the sun dried them, bleaching out all stains, they had to be made wet again by dousing them with buckets of water. On my holidays, I did this for my mother. As I watered the clothes, she would come up behind me, instructing me to get the clothes thoroughly wet, showing me a shirt that I should turn over so that the sleeves were exposed.

Over our lunch, my mother and father talked to each other about the houses my father had to build; how disgusted he had become with one of his apprentices, or with Mr. Oatie; what they thought of my schooling so far; what they thought of the noises Mr. Jarvis and his friends made for so many days when they locked themselves up inside Mr. Jarvis's house and drank rum and ate fish they had caught themselves and danced to the music of an accordion that they took turns playing. On and on they talked. As they talked, my head would move from side to side, looking at them. When my eyes rested on my father, I didn't think very much of the way he looked. But when my eyes rested on my mother, I found her beautiful. Her head looked as if it should be on a sixpence. What a beautiful long neck, and long plaited hair, which she pinned up around the crown of her head because when her hair hung down it made her too hot. Her nose was the shape of a flower on the brink of opening. Her mouth, moving up and

5. A West Indian stew.

down as she ate and talked at the same time, was such a beautiful mouth I
could have looked at it forever if I had to and not mind. Her lips were wide
and almost thin, and when she said certain words I could see small parts of
big white teeth—so big, and pearly, like some nice buttons on one of my
dresses. I didn't much care about what she said when she was in this mood
with my father. She made him laugh so. She could hardly say a word before
he would burst out laughing. We ate our food, I cleared the table, we said
goodbye to my father as he went back to work, I helped my mother with the
dishes, and then we settled into the afternoon.

   When my mother, at sixteen, after quarreling with her father, left his
house on Dominica and came to Antigua,[6] she packed all her things in an
enormous wooden trunk that she had bought in Roseau for almost six shillings. She painted the trunk yellow and green outside, and she lined the
inside with wallpaper that had a cream background with pink roses printed
all over it. Two days after she left her father's house, she boarded a boat and
sailed for Antigua. It was a small boat, and the trip would have taken a day
and a half ordinarily, but a hurricane blew up and the boat was lost at sea
for almost five days. By the time it got to Antigua, the boat was practically in
splinters, and though two or three of the passengers were lost overboard,
along with some of the cargo, my mother and her trunk were safe. Now,
twenty-four years later, this trunk was kept under my bed, and in it were
things that had belonged to me, starting from just before I was born. There
was the chemise, made of white cotton, with scallop edging around the
sleeves, neck, and hem, and white flowers embroidered on the front—the
first garment I wore after being born. My mother had made that herself,
and once, when we were passing by, I was even shown the tree under
which she sat as she made this garment. There were some of my diapers,
with their handkerchief hemstitch that she had also done herself; there was
a pair of white wool booties with matching jacket and hat; there was a blanket in white wool and a blanket in white flannel cotton; there was a plain
white linen hat with lace trimming; there was my christening outfit; there
were two of my baby bottles: one in the shape of a normal baby bottle, and
the other shaped like a boat, with a nipple on either end; there was a ther-
mos in which my mother had kept a tea that was supposed to have a soothing effect on me; there was the dress I wore on my first birthday: a yellow
cotton with green smocking on the front; there was the dress I wore on my
second birthday: pink cotton with green smocking on the front; there was
also a photograph of me on my second birthday wearing my pink dress and
my first pair of earrings, a chain around my neck, and a pair of bracelets, all
specially made of gold from British Guiana; there was the first pair of shoes
I grew out of after I knew how to walk; there was the dress I wore when I
first went to school, and the first notebook in which I wrote; there were the
sheets for my crib and the sheets for my first bed; there was my first straw
hat, my first straw basket—decorated with flowers—my grandmother had
sent me from Dominica; there were my report cards, my certificates of
merit from school, and my certificates of merit from Sunday school.

6. Both Antigua and Dominica are islands in the British West Indies.

From time to time, my mother would fix on a certain place in our house and give it a good cleaning. If I was at home when she happened to do this, I was at her side, as usual. When she did this with the trunk, it was a tremendous pleasure, for after she had removed all the things from the trunk, and aired them out, and changed the camphor balls,[7] and then refolded the things and put them back in their places in the trunk, as she held each thing in her hand she would tell me a story about myself. Sometimes I knew the story first hand, for I could remember the incident quite well; sometimes what she told me had happened when I was too young to know anything; and sometimes it happened before I was even born. Whichever way, I knew exactly what she would say, for I had heard it so many times before, but I never got tired of it. For instance, the flowers on the chemise, the first garment I wore after being born, were not put on correctly, and that is because when my mother was embroidering them I kicked so much that her hand was unsteady. My mother said that usually when I kicked around in her stomach and she told me to stop I would, but on that day I paid no attention at all. When she told me this story, she would smile at me and say, "You see, even then you were hard to manage." It pleased me to think that, before she could see my face, my mother spoke to me in the same way she did now. On and on my mother would go. No small part of my life was so unimportant that she hadn't made a note of it, and now she would tell it to me over and over again. I would sit next to her and she would show me the very dress I wore on the day I bit another child my age with whom I was playing. "Your biting phase," she called it. Or the day she warned me not to play around the coal pot, because I liked to sing to myself and dance around the fire. Two seconds later, I fell into the hot coals, burning my elbows. My mother cried when she saw that it wasn't serious, and now, as she told me about it, she would kiss the little black patches of scars on my elbows.

As she told me the stories, I sometimes sat at her side, leaning against her, or I would crouch on my knees behind her back and lean over her shoulder. As I did this, I would occasionally sniff at her neck, or behind her ears, or at her hair. She smelled sometimes of lemons, sometimes of sage, sometimes of roses, sometimes of bay leaf. At times I would no longer hear what it was she was saying; I just liked to look at her mouth as it opened and closed over words, or as she laughed. How terrible it must be for all the people who had no one to love them so and no one whom they loved so, I thought. My father, for instance. When he was a little boy, his parents, after kissing him goodbye and leaving him with his grandmother, boarded a boat and sailed to South America. He never saw them again, though they wrote to him and sent him presents—packages of clothes on his birthday and at Christmas. He then grew to love his grandmother, and she loved him, for she took care of him and worked hard at keeping him well fed and clothed. From the beginning, they slept in the same bed, and as he became a young man they continued to do so. When he was no longer in school and had started working, every night, after he and his grandmother had eaten their dinner, my father would go off to visit his friends. He would

---

7. Used to keep insects out of storage places.

then return home at around midnight and fall asleep next to his grand-mother. In the morning, his grandmother would awake at half past five or so, a half hour before my father, and prepare his bath and breakfast and make everything proper and ready for him, so that at seven o'clock sharp he stepped out the door off to work. One morning, though, he overslept, because his grandmother didn't wake him up. When he awoke, she was still lying next to him. When he tried to wake her, he couldn't. She had died lying next to him sometime during the night. Even though he was overcome with grief, he built her coffin and made sure she had a nice funeral. He never slept in that bed again, and shortly afterward he moved out of that house. He was eighteen years old then.

When my father first told me this story, I threw myself at him at the end of it, and we both started to cry—he just a little, I quite a lot. It was a Sunday afternoon; he and my mother and I had gone for a walk in the botanical gardens. My mother had wandered off to look at some strange kind of thistle, and we could see her as she bent over the bushes to get a closer look and reach out to touch the leaves of the plant. When she returned to us and saw that we had both been crying, she started to get quite worked up, but my father quickly told her what had happened and she laughed at us and called us her little fools. But then she took me in her arms and kissed me, and she said that I needn't worry about such a thing as her sailing off or dying and leaving me all alone in the world. But if ever after that I saw my father sitting alone with a faraway look on his face, I was filled with pity for him. He had been alone in the world all that time, what with his mother sailing off on a boat with his father and his never seeing her again, and then his grandmother dying while lying next to him in the middle of the night. It was more than anyone should have to bear. I loved him so and wished that I had a mother to give him, for, no matter how much my own mother loved him, it could never be the same.

When my mother got through with the trunk, and I had heard again and again just what I had been like and who had said what to me at what point in my life, I was given my tea—a cup of cocoa and a buttered bun. My father by then would return home from work, and he was given his tea. As my mother went around preparing our supper, picking up clothes from the stone heap, or taking clothes off the clothesline, I would sit in a corner of our yard and watch her. She never stood still. Her powerful legs carried her from one part of the yard to the other, and in and out of the house. Sometimes she might call out to me to go and get some thyme or basil or some other herb for her, for she grew all her herbs in little pots that she kept in a corner of our little garden. Sometimes when I gave her the herbs, she might stoop down and kiss me on my lips and then on my neck. It was in such a paradise that I lived.

The summer of the year I turned twelve, I could see that I had grown taller; most of my clothes no longer fit. When I could get a dress over my head, the waist then came up to just below my chest. My legs had become more spindlelike, the hair on my head even more unruly than usual, small tufts of hair had appeared under my arms, and when I perspired the smell was strange, as if I had turned into a strange animal. I didn't say anything about it, and my mother and father didn't seem to notice, for they didn't say anything, either. Up to then, my mother and I had many dresses made out of the same cloth, though hers had a different, more grownup style, a boat neck or a sweetheart neckline, and a pleated or gored skirt, while my dresses had high necks with collars, a deep hemline, and, of course, a sash that tied in the back. One day, my mother and I had gone to get some material for new dresses to celebrate her birthday (the usual gift from my father), when I came upon a piece of cloth—a yellow background, with figures of men, dressed in a long-ago fashion, seated at pianos that they were playing, and all around them musical notes flying off into the air. I immediately said how much I loved this piece of cloth and how nice I thought it would look on us both, but my mother replied, "Oh, no. You are getting too old for that. It's time you had your own clothes. You just cannot go around the rest of your life looking like a little me." To say that I felt the earth swept away from under me would not be going too far. It wasn't just what she said, it was the way she said it. No accompanying little laugh. No bending over and kissing my little wet forehead (for suddenly I turned hot, then cold, and all my pores must have opened up, for fluids just flowed out of me). In the end, I got my dress with the men playing their pianos, and my mother got a dress with red and yellow overgrown hibiscus, but I was never able to wear my own dress or see my mother in hers without feeling bitterness and hatred, directed not so much toward my mother as toward, I suppose, life in general.

As if that were not enough, my mother informed me that I was on the verge of becoming a young lady, so there were quite a few things I would have to do differently. She didn't say exactly just what it was that made me on the verge of becoming a young lady, and I was so glad of that, because I didn't want to know. Behind a closed door, I stood naked in front of a mirror and looked at myself from head to toe. I was so long and bony that I more than filled up the mirror, and my small ribs pressed out against my skin. I tried to push my unruly hair down against my head so that it would lie flat, but as soon as I let it go it bounced up again. I could see the small tufts of hair under my arms. And then I got a good look at my nose. It had suddenly spread across my face, almost blotting out my cheeks, taking up my whole face, so that if I didn't know I was me standing there I would have wondered about that strange girl—and to think that only so recently my nose had been a small thing, the size of a rosebud. But what could I do? I thought of begging my mother to ask my father if he could build for me a set of clamps into which I could screw myself at night before I went to sleep and which would surely cut back on my growing. I was about to ask her this when I remembered that a few days earlier I had asked in my most pleasing, winning way for a look through the trunk. A person I did not recognize answered in a voice I did not recognize, "Absolutely not! You and I don't have time for that anymore." Again, did the ground wash out from under me? Again, the answer would have to be yes, and I wouldn't be going too far.

Because of this young-lady business, instead of days spent in perfect harmony with my mother, I trailing in her footsteps, she showering down on me her kisses and affection and attention, I was now sent off to learn one thing and another. I was sent to someone who knew all about manners and how to meet and greet important people in the world. This woman soon asked me not to come again, since I could not resist making farting-like noises each time I had to practice a curtsy, it made the other girls laugh so. I was sent for piano lessons. The piano teacher, a shriveled-up old spinster from Lancashire, England, soon asked me not to come back, since I seemed unable to resist eating from the bowl of plums she had placed on the piano purely for decoration. In the first case, I told my mother a lie—I told her that the manners teacher had found that my manners needed no improvement, so I needn't come anymore. This made her very pleased. In the second case, there was no getting around it—she had to find out. When the piano teacher told her of my misdeed, she turned and walked away from me, and I wasn't sure that if she had been asked who I was she wouldn't have said, "I don't know," right then and there. What a new thing this was for me: my mother's back turned on me in disgust. It was true that I didn't spend all my days at my mother's side before this, that I spent most of my days at school, but before this young-lady business I could sit and think of my mother, see her doing one thing or another, and always her face bore a smile for me. Now I often saw her with the corners of her mouth turned down in disapproval of me. And why was my mother carrying my new state so far? She took to pointing out that one day I would have my own house and I might want it to be a different house from the one she kept. Once, when showing me a way to store linen, she patted the folded sheets in place and said, "Of course, in your own house you might choose another way." That the day might actually come when we would live apart I had never believed. My throat hurt from the tears I held bottled up tight inside. Sometimes we would both forget the new order of things and would slip into our old ways. But that didn't last very long.

In the middle of all these new things, I had forgotten that I was to enter a new school that September. I had then a set of things to do, preparing for school. I had to go to the seamstress to be measured for new uniforms, since my body now made a mockery of the old measurements. I had to get shoes, a new school hat, and lots of new books. In my new school, I needed a different exercise book for each subject, and in addition to the usual—English, arithmetic, and so on—I now had to take Latin and French, and attend classes in a brand-new science building. I began to look forward to my new school. I hoped that everyone there would be new, that there would be no one I had ever met before. That way, I could put on a new set of airs; I could say I was something that I was not, and no one would ever know the difference.

On the Sunday before the Monday I started at my new school, my mother became cross over the way I had made my bed. In the center of my bedspread, my mother had embroidered a bowl overflowing with flowers and two lovebirds on either side of the bowl. I had placed the bedspread on my bed in a lopsided way so that the embroidery was not in the center of my bed, the way it should have been. My mother made a fuss about it, and I could see that she was right and I regretted very much not doing that one little thing that would have pleased her. I had lately become careless, she said, and I could only silently agree with her.

I came home from church, and my mother still seemed to hold the bedspread against me, so I kept out of her way. At half past two in the after-noon, I went off to Sunday school. At Sunday school, I was given a certifi-cate for best student in my study-of-the-Bible group. It was a surprise that I would receive the certificate on that day, though we had known about the results of a test weeks before. I rushed home with my certificate in hand, feeling that with this prize I would reconquer my mother—a chance for her to smile on me again.

When I got to our house, I rushed into the yard and called out to her, but no answer came. I then walked into the house. At first, I didn't hear any-thing. Then I heard sounds coming from the direction of my parents' room. My mother must be in there, I thought. When I got to the door, I could see that my mother and father were lying in their bed. It didn't inter-est me what they were doing—only that my mother's hand was on the small of my father's back and that it was making a circular motion. But her hand! It was white and bony, as if it had long been dead and had been left out in the elements. It seemed not to be her hand, and yet it could only be her hand, so well did I know it. It went around and around in the same circular motion, and I looked at it as if I would never see anything else in my life again. If I were to forget everything else in the world, I could not forget her hand as it looked then. I could also make out that the sounds I had heard were her kissing my father's ears and his mouth and his face. I looked at them for I don't know how long.

When I next saw my mother, I was standing at the dinner table that I had just set, having made a tremendous commotion with knives and forks as I got them out of their drawer, letting my parents know that I was home. I had set the table and was now half standing near my chair, half draped over the table, staring at nothing in particular and trying to ignore my mother's presence. Though I couldn't remember our eyes having met, I was quite sure that she had seen me in the bedroom, and I didn't know what I would say if she mentioned it. Instead, she said in a voice that was sort of cross and sort of something else, "Are you going to just stand there doing nothing all day?" The something else was new; I had never heard it in her voice before. I couldn't say exactly what it was, but I know that it caused me to reply, "And what if I do?" and at the same time to stare at her directly in the eyes. It must have been a shock to her, the way I spoke. I had never talked back to her before. She looked at me, and then, instead of saying some squelching thing that would put me back in my place, she dropped her eyes and walked away. From the back, she looked small and funny. She carried her hands limp at her sides. I was sure I could never let those hands touch me again; I was sure I could never let her kiss me again. All that was finished.

I was amazed that I could eat my food, for all of it reminded me of things that had taken place between my mother and me. A long time ago, when I wouldn't eat my beef, complaining that it involved too much chewing, my mother would first chew up pieces of meat in her own mouth and then feed it to me. When I had hated carrots so much that even the sight of them would send me into a fit of tears, my mother would try to find all sorts of ways to make them palatable for me. All that was finished now. I didn't think that I would ever think of any of it again with fondness. I looked at my parents. My father was just the same, eating his food in the same old way, his two rows of false teeth clop-clopping like a horse being driven off to market. He was regaling us with another one of his stories about when he was a young man and played cricket on one island or the other. What he said now must have been funny, for my mother couldn't stop laughing. He didn't seem to notice that I was not entertained.

My father and I then went for our customary Sunday-afternoon walk. My mother did not come with us. I don't know what she stayed home to do. On our walk, my father tried to hold my hand, but I pulled myself away from him, doing it in such a way that he would think I felt too big for that now.

That Monday, I went to my new school. I was placed in a class with girls I had never seen before. Some of them had heard about me, though, for I was the youngest among them and was said to be very bright. I liked a girl named Albertine, and I liked a girl named Gweneth. At the end of the day, Gwen and I were in love, and so we walked home arm in arm together.

When I got home, my mother greeted me with the customary kiss and inquiries. I told her about my day, going out of my way to provide pleasing details, leaving out, of course, any mention at all of Gwen and my overpowering feelings for her.

1985

DAVID BRADLEY

b. 1950

In an interview with critics Susan Blake and James Millner published in the journal *Callaloo*, David Bradley spoke of the pleasure that he received from writing:

> When you sit down at your typewriter, you're having a good time. I can make you spend hours finding out about somebody that you would not invite to your dining room table. I can make people love winos, and hookers, and you wouldn't have them in your house. I think that's real politics.

Through the art of novel writing, Bradley opens worlds that are mysteries to many Americans, simultaneously informing and entertaining.

Born in 1950 to the Reverend D. H. Bradley and Harriet M. Jackson Bradley, he was reared in rural Pennsylvania, where he attended local schools, graduated from high school in 1968, and was named a Benjamin Franklin Scholar, National Achievement Scholar, and Presidential Scholar. He graduated summa cum laude from the University of Pennsylvania in 1972.

Bradley's first novel, *South Street* (1975), evolved from the reminiscences of friends he made during his undergraduate years. Alienated from the urban, political students he met in college, he found that the working-class people of the South Street neighborhood of Philadelphia provided the small town, caring environment he needed. Drawing on the traditional African American meaning of community, Bradley's first novel focuses on the three main meeting places in his fictionalized South Street: Lightin' Ed's Bar and Grill, the Elysium Hotel, and the nondenominational World of Life Church. Despite its innovative qualities, such as frequent shifts in perspective, Bradley's first novel earned little critical attention.

But *The Chanysville Incident* (1981), Bradley's second novel, received great critical acclaim, winning the 1982 Pen/Faulkner Prize and being chosen as a Book of
the Month Club alternative selection. Bradley had worked for more than ten years
to tell this story, which he first heard during his mother's historical research for a
hometown bicentennial. Harriet was able to prove the truth of a local tale of thirteen runaway slaves who chose death over recapture; hearing this story sparked
David to write an unpublished short narrative based on it while still in college.
Bradley's graduate work at King's College in London led to his first academic study
of this incident and then to his consistently praised second novel.

An assistant professor of English at Temple University in Philadelphia, Bradley
continues to write fiction and frequently publishes reviews in the *New York Times
Book Review* and the *Washington Post Book World*.

From The Chaneysville Incident

[Old Jack]

[John Washington, a young black historian who lives in Philadelphia, returns home
to rural western Pennsylvania because his surrogate father, Old Jack Crawley, is ill.
After Jack dies, John visits his parents' home, where he becomes intrigued by his
late father's (whose name was Moses) collection of old papers. John's research into
the papers helps him understand his father's suicide and how it relates to the legend
of the town: thirteen fugitive slaves, en route to freedom on the Underground Railroad, asked to be killed when they realized that they were to be recaptured.

Much of the novel is told in flashbacks as John's return home triggers memories
of the stories Old Jack told him. Immersed in his father's historical collection and
captivated by his memories, John learns as a historian how imagination is as important as facts, how empathy with those long dead is as important as registering exactly
what took place. Consequently, he is able to reconstruct the thinking of his father as
well as of the thirteen slaves. As he learns more about the papers, John relates his
findings to his white psychiatrist girlfriend. That telling helps him understand more
about the true function of history.]

He had left me standing in the open doorway while he went to light the
lamp, and waited there while I looked around, letting me take my time.
After a few minutes he came toward me and placed his hand on my shoulder. "You pack a pretty good wallop for a youngster," he said.

It took me a while to figure out that he was talking about my hitting him,
but once I had I felt a flush of a curiously mixed emotion: embarrassment
at the praise, fear at the thought of reprisal, pride at my sudden capacity for
violence. "I'm sorry," I said. "I hope I didn't hurt you."

"Hurt," he roared. "Hell, you damn near kilt me. But you ain't got no
need to be sorry. If you hadda kilt me it woulda served me right—I didn't
have no business comin' up there like that, stickin' ma face up in yours. It
was the wrong way to go about things. I always was like that, get the idea
'bout what oughta be done, an' then haul off an' do it jest backwards. Your
daddy now, he always thought things out, knowed what he wanted to do *an'*
what was the right way to go about it. He—" He stopped, looked at me.
"Damn, I guess I'm doin' it again. I hadn't oughta be speakin' a your daddy
now."

"I don't mind," I said.

He must have heard indifference, or something, in my voice. "You don't care if he's gone, do you?"

I didn't say anything.

"It ain't nothin' to be ashamed of," he said. "Can't nobody make you feel somethin' you don't feel, an' there ain't no point in tryin' to pretend you feel it. Hell, I bet you didn't even like him."

I didn't say anything.

"Me," he said, "I guess you could say I loved him. He saved my life moren one time. But I'll tell you the truth—way Moses went about things, he was like to save your butt by kickin' you in it to get you movin' in the right direction. You mighta loved him for it later on, but right off you wasn't likely to be too damn grateful."

He had been hypnotizing me. He must have been, for somehow I found that I had left the door and was standing in the middle of the cabin, near an odd slate-topped table, and the door was shut behind me. I looked around for some other way out; there wasn't any. I started to edge back towards the door.

"Don't jest stand there, boy," he snapped. "Siddown."

I had to decide then whether to break for the door or not. There was no question about what I *wanted* to do, but my mother had told me to obey the commands of adults without question; besides, I was curious. So I moved forward towards a handmade hickory chair that butted up against the table. I pulled it out and got up on it, to sit with my legs dangling.

Meanwhile Old Jack had been busy, stirring up the stove, setting a kettle over an open hole. "You drink, boy?"

"Sure," I said. "Everybody drinks."

"Damn, son," he said. "I don't mean buttermilk an' root beer, I mean do you drink whiskey?"

"Oh, no," I said.

He peered at me. "Why the hell don't you?"

"Why, because it's bad."

"What's so bad about it?"

"Well . . . it's bad for you, that's all. It makes you do bad things. And it makes you sick. And . . ." I trailed off; I couldn't remember any more of the reasons they had always given for avoiding Demon Rum.

He shook his head. "You been talkin' to them Christians too much," he said. "Hell, boy, you could say all those things about women. Bet you them old biddies didn't tell you that, did they?"

"No," I admitted.

"You don't mess around with women, do you?"

"No," I almost shouted, even though I didn't know what he meant, precisely.

"That's good," he said. "Women's got their uses, but you're too young to 'preciate 'em. You stay clear of 'em for a good while yet. And stay clear a girls. I know, kissin' girls is fun, but you get to like the taste, an' you keep on likin' it you don't notice when they stop bein' girls an' start bein' women, an' women do more harm to a man than whiskey ever did. But I bet you don't even like the taste of whiskey."

"I . . . don't know," I said. "I never tasted whiskey."

"What?" He was shocked. "You ain't never tasted whiskey? You mean to tell me your daddy never even give you a taste?"

"He didn't drink whiskey," I snapped.

"Lord," Old Jack said. He left the stove and came over to the table. "Boy," he said, "how old are you?"

"Nine," I said. "Almost ten."

"Then it's time you learned the truth about a few things. An' the first thing you better learn is that your daddy drank enough whiskey in his time to float a battleship, an' he *made* enough to float the whole damn Navy. And the second thing you better learn is that you're damn lucky he did, because otherwise you wouldn't be eatin' tomorrow, 'less it was by some white man's handout." He glared at me for a minute, and then turned and stomped back to the stove, stood with his back to me. "He cooked the meanest moonshine a man could ever hope to taste. And he tasted. And I tasted it with him. Folks said a lot of things about that, but when he done somethin' for 'em, you didn't never see 'em turnin' the kindness away." He whirled then and looked at me hard. "You go over to that Sunday school an' let them holy-butted biddies tell you how bad whiskey is, but let me tell you somethin': they never give back a penny a what he put into the collection plate. I don't know why the hell he done it, but he did. He'd sneak in there durin' the week an' leave money for Sunday. They'd find it. They'd know where it come from. But they'd keep it. An' then whatever dumb-butted preacher they had over there would stand up on Sunday an' talk about how bad whiskey was, an' take his damn five dollars an' go home. Livin' on whiskey money. An' I'll tell you somethin' else they ain't told you: that Jesus Christ they pray to was a moonshiner Hisself; He turned water straight into wine. An', like Mose useta say, he didn't pay no damn tax on it neither." He came away from the stove then, and set a steaming cup in front of me. "That there's a toddy," he said. "Some folks makes 'em fancy. I make 'em the way Mose taught me, with hot water and honey. An' whiskey. Right now, yours ain't got no whiskey in it. I'll put some in if you want it. But you gotta make up your own mind." He stood there, patient and unmoving, while I made up my mind.

"He really drank whiskey?" I said finally.

"Indeed he did."

"I'll take some."

He nodded, went back to the stove, and returned with another cup and a bottle. "This ain't your daddy's whiskey," he said. "I ain't got much a that left, an' it packs a kick. This here's good enough for now." He reached out and dribbled some whiskey into my cup. Cheap bourbon, but the smell of the steam that rose to my nose was wonderful. "Stir it with your finger," he said, "an' take care you don't burn yourself."

I did as he said, burned myself anyway, but didn't say anything. Then I cautiously raised the cup to my lips and tasted. It was mostly water, but I could taste the whiskey, and in a minute I could feel the warmth growing in my stomach.

"It's good," I said.

"Course it's good," Old Jack said. "Hell, why you think them Christians don't want nobody to drink it?"

We sat there for a while, drinking the toddies. I found myself getting sleepy, but I struggled to keep my eyes open. Presently he got up and mixed another toddy for each of us. By the time I was halfway through it, the room was starting to swim, and the heat from the stove was becoming thick.

"He liked you," Old Jack said suddenly.

"What?" I said.

"Your daddy. He liked you. He was proud a you. An' he was worried about you. That was jest about the last thing he said to me; probly the last thing he said to anybody." He took a sip from his cup. "He come over here with a jug; guess that's the last jug a Moses Washington Black Lightning left. He come in here an' we talked for a while. He was talkin' about you. Said you was too much your mama's child. Said he was worried you was gonna end up bein' a preacher or a sissy or somethin', on account a the way that woman carried on around you, fussin' with your clothes an' fixin' you food an' things that a man oughta be able to do for hisself. Said he wasn't worried about your brother, there wasn't enough woman in him for it to be dangerous. But you was different. He said there was a lot a woman in you. He didn't mean nothin' bad by that—jest meant that you was the kind that trusted people. Kind that believed there was always gonna be somebody to help you get through things. It ain't jest women that thinks that way— there's a lotta panty-waisted fellas runnin' around these days, get into trou- ble an' all they know to do is to pray to Jesus or the government—but women's the only ones that can afford it, on accounta they know that there's gonna be a man around somewheres to haul their wagon outa the mud, and that when the whistle blows they get first crack at the lifeboats. I ain't actually sayin' it's wrong for a man to believe that, but it's damn dan- gerous. On accounta he can't afford it. A man can't carry hisself, folks laugh at him. The women won't have nothin' to do with him. 'Cause what they want is a man that can haul their wagon outa the mud.

"Anyways, that was what your daddy was afraid was gonna happen: you'd spend so much time with women that the woman would come out in you and you'd end up rubbin' your hands an' cryin' 'stead a doin' what needed to be done. He was afraid your mama would do for you so much you wasn't never gonna be able to do for yourself, wasn't gonna end up fit for nothin' 'cept gettin' turned over to another woman an' goin' to work for a white man, an' end up the kinda fool that can't go to sleep lessen he knows 'xactly where he's gonna get his pussy an' his next pay. An' he said that was all right for some, but not for you, on accounta you was special. That's what he said. Special. Said you had a lot a woman in you, but you had one hell of a lot a man in you to go with it. He told me some a the things you done, things he was real proud of. You know what they was?"

"No," I said, wondering how Moses Washington had seen me doing any- thing, since I had learned early on that the best way to get along with him was to stay pretty much out of sight.

"He told me 'bout them books you read. Told me how you go down there to the library an' steal the ones they say you ain't old enough to read, an' how if you get one an' you start it, then you by God finish it, even if you don't know what the hell it's all about, an' how you read 'em over an' over until you think you do. He liked that. Told me how when your brother give you a lickin' you wouldn't say nothin' to nobody, you'd jest wait till didn't nobody think you was mad anymore, an' then you'd clobber that boy good. He liked that; he surely did. Course he did say he had to whup you for doin' your clobberin' with that there ax handle, but he didn't mind you gettin' the idea. Not at all. He liked all that. Course he jest about had to, on accounta that was jest the way he was." He smiled at me. "You know what he said he liked best about you?"

"No," I said.

"He said he liked the way you hated him."

I didn't say anything.

"He didn't mind; most folks hated him. I hated him some myself. He was a real hateable man. He wanted things his way all the time, an' if he didn't get what he wanted, he took it. He wasn't kind to people 'less it suited him; all he cared about was what got him where he wanted to go. He didn't give a good God damn about anybody in the world. Oh, he cared, but you knowed that if it come down to a question a him or you, it woulda been you, an' he mighta been sorry, but that was all. Matter a fact, the only time I ever seen him do anything to make me think he cared much about anybody was when he come over here an' ast me to take care a you if anything was to happen to him, to make sure you learned how to be a man. What he said was, says, 'Jack, if anything happens to me, you take that boy an' teach him to hunt, an' teach him to fish, an' drink whiskey an' cuss. Teach him to track.' That's what he said. An' then the damn fool went out huntin' groundhog."

He paused, and I looked at him and saw the lamplight reflected in his eyes—they were glistening. "Hell," he said finally, "you gotta be mighty hungry to eat a groundhog. Meat's greasy an' stringy an' tough all at the same time. Seems to me if a man was gonna get kilt out huntin', the least thing he could do was to be huntin' somethin' worth huntin'. I recall a time when Moses Washington woulda rather drunk warm water than be huntin' a groundhog. Matter a fact, I don't recall him ever huntin' no groundhog before. An' I don't guess he's gonna be doin' it again. The damn fool." He rose then, and went to the stove and mixed himself another toddy. The smell of it reached me, and I knew he was making it stronger this time. He drank it down in a few gulps without coming back to the table, without even turning around, and then he mixed another, just as strong.

"You don't mind me talkin' 'bout your daddy the way I do?" he said.

"No," I said.

"Well," he said, "that's good. An' I don't guess it changes nothin' to speak of him. Everybody else is. They *been* speakin' of him. Most folks, they gotta be dead an' gone 'fore there's a chance anybody'll talk about 'em. Not Mose. They was probly talkin' about Moses Washington 'fore he was ever born. Wasn't nobody that knowed nothin' about him, though. I knowed some. Josh knowed a bit, but he wasn't the kind a man that set too much store by where a man come from, or where he went when he was outa sight. An' he's dead anyways. But not knowin' facts don't stop folks talkin'; hell, it just sets 'em goin'. Most folks'd a hell of a lot rather listen to rumors than go around the corner to see what's what. And Mose helped 'em right along. He let 'em talk, an' if they was to ast him a question—an' there wasn't many that had the nerve—he'd just smile an' let 'em think what they wanted. Pretty soon you couldn't go anywheres in the County without everybody knowed his name, an' who run with him, an' three or four stories about what we done. Wasn't half of it true. Fact is, you found out somethin' about Moses Washington, you knowed for sure either he wanted you to find it out jest 'xactly the way you done it, or it was a lie. An' most times, it was both." He stopped then, sipped at the toddy, and looked at me hard. It frightened me, and I stirred uneasily and looked over my shoulder towards the door.

"You goin' somewheres?" he said.

"Well . . ." I said.

"You scared a the boogeyman?"

It must have been the lateness of the hour, making me cranky, or perhaps it was the whiskey. "Don't you make fun of me," I said.

His eyes grew wide for a moment, and then he nodded his head. "I'm sorry, son," he said. "I forgot you was Mose's boy. You want some more?" He gestured with the bottle.

"No," I said.

"Hell, son, I said I was sorry. Now, when a man apologizes, you either take his hand or you let him be, but you don't sit around takin' little bites out a him all day long; that's what women does. Now, you want some more or not?"

"I'll take a little."

He nodded, took my cup, and mixed the toddy. His hand was a little unsteady; he put in more whiskey than he should have. But I didn't notice it. All I knew was that the taste was strong and sweet and good, and that the warmth of it moved through me like joy. I sipped with abandon, and put the cup down. He watched me, then came, bringing his own cup, and sat down across from me.

"You wanna know how I met your daddy?" he said.

I looked at him, or tried to; my eyes wouldn't focus right, and all I could see was a dark face swimming in the darkness somewhere beyond the lamp's glow.

"Do you?" he said. "You want a story?"

"Yes," I said. "Yes, please."

"Then fetch me the candle," he said. "It's there, by the door."

He nodded to show me the direction, and I clambered down from the chair and felt my way through the darkness. I found the candle, a brand-new one, on a small shelf next to a flat, round coffee can.

"Bring the matches too," he said. "There, in the can. Can't have light without strikin' fire."

I took the candle and the can and brought them back to the table, moving slowly, unsure of my footing. He took them from me, opened the can, extracted a match. I stood beside him while he struck it, feeling the acid fumes tickle my nose. He lit the candle and extinguished the match, then he held the candle sideways, over the table. I watched, fascinated, as the melted wax formed a pool on the slate. When he judged it big enough he set the candle in the pool, held it while the wax hardened. We waited then, while the flame steadied, the light from the candle added to that from the lamp making the room seem almost too bright. He leaned over then and blew out the lamp, and the light faded.

"Put the matches back," he said. "Always put things back where you found 'em so you'll know where they are when you need 'em again."

There was no answer. The clouds of condensation blossomed in front of my face. I waited, listening. I could hear the sound of my own breathing, the pounding of blood in my ears. I wanted to push the door open and just go in, but you do not do that to a man, not even to save his life. And so I waited, and waited, and raised my hand to knock again. Then I heard the sound coming from behind the weather-ravished door: a long, racking cough. I shoved the door open and stepped inside. "Jack?" I said, as the door swung to behind me.

He coughed again. His breath came in harsh asthmatic whistles, and after each exhalation I could hear the squeaky sucking sounds of mucus shifting in his chest. Pneumonia. But I didn't mind; at least he was breathing. I moved towards where he lay and looked down, although I knew I could not see him. I could smell him, though. He stank of urine and feces and unhealthy perspiration. "Jack," I said stupidly, "you all right?"

He chuckled, the same deep, throaty chuckle he had always had, and my heart lifted. But then the chuckle ended in a cough, not a rumbling cough, but a high, deep, tight one. I shuddered at the sound of it, for I knew what it was like to lie in a bed feeling the vise closing down on your chest, knew that he would be feeling no relief, just a harsh burning every time he tried to clear his lungs. I waited silently until he stopped coughing, feeling the pain as if it were in my own chest, wishing that my feeling it would somehow make it less for him, knowing it would not.

He stopped coughing. I could hear his mouth working as he got up some spit and swallowed it to soothe his throat. "Hey," he said finally, "if it ain't the Perfessor. What brings you up this way?" His voice was a croak, but I could hear the bitterness in it; it had been a long time.

I didn't say anything.

"It does me good to see you, Johnny," he said, finally.

"It does me good to see you," I said. I reached out through the darkness, but I stopped myself before I touched him; he would not want that, not now, when it would feel like the touch of a nurse. He would rather die than have that.

1981

GLORIA NAYLOR

b. 1950

When Gloria Naylor read Toni Morrison's *The Bluest Eye* as a twenty-seven-year-old sophomore at Brooklyn College in 1978, she felt that she had been given "the authority . . . to enter this forbidden terrain" of prose. Assured by Morrison's work that "not only is your story worth telling but it can be told in words so painstakingly eloquent that it becomes a song," Naylor wrote her first novel, *The Women of Brewster Place* (1982). Immensely successful, that work was followed by three others: *Linden Hills* (1985), *Mama Day* (1988), and *Bailey's Cafe* (1992). Naylor has said that these four novels constitute a quartet intended to appeal to readers black and white. One of the first African American women writers who has studied both her African ancestors and the European tradition, Naylor consciously draws on Western sources even as her writings reflect the complexity of the African American female experience.

Gloria Naylor was born on January 25, 1950, in New York City because her mother, Alberta (McAlpin) Naylor, had made her husband, Roosevelt Naylor, promise that none of their children would be born in Mississippi. A dedicated reader in a state that did not allow blacks to enter libraries, Naylor's mother passed onto her eldest daughter a respect for education and the written word. Although Naylor's potential was recognized early on, she joined the Jehovah's Witnesses after graduating from high school and from 1968 to 1975 served as a missionary in New York, North Carolina, and Florida. After becoming disenchanted with the Witnesses, she moved to New York, where she briefly studied nursing and then enrolled in Brooklyn College. Her B.A. in English was followed by a master's degree from Yale, a partial fulfillment of which was the writing of her second novel, *Linden Hills*.

With the publication of *The Women of Brewster Place* in 1982, Naylor was quickly recognized as an important new voice in American fiction at a time when other African American women writers, Toni Morrison and Alice Walker among them, were receiving much attention. Praised for the richness of its prose and the intense humaneness of its vision, *Brewster Place* won the 1983 American Book Award. Some faulted it, however, along with Walker's *The Color Purple* (1982), for what was seen as a conscious effort to portray males negatively and to repeatedly cast women as the victims of male violence, both physical and emotional. Such criticism extended even to Naylor's portrayal of Lorraine and Theresa, the lesbians of *The Two*. Notwithstanding these caveats, the novel continues to be seen as a paean to the diversity of the African American experience, and it was made into a television movie by Oprah Winfrey.

Naylor's second novel, *Linden Hills*, moves from the ghetto to a middle-class black suburb. Set in the 1980s, the novel traces the journey of Willie Mason, a young African American poet, as he travels with a fellow poet through the exclusive black neighborhood looking for odd jobs and meeting the inhabitants. Like LeRoi Jones's *The Systems of Dante's Hell* (1965), *Linden Hills* is, among other things, an ambitious rewriting of the *Inferno*. In its sharing a general geography with *Brewster Place*, as well as some characters, *Linden Hills* signaled the almost Faulkernian importance of place to Naylor. *Mama Day*, Naylor's third novel, moves away from the inner city and the suburb to Willow Springs, an island off the southeastern coast of the United States that has been owned by Mama Day's family since before the Civil War. Just as *Linden Hills* reminds us that the black middle class is at least a hundred years old, *Mama Day* reiterates the existence of a three-hundred-year-old African American folk tradition. The last of Naylor's quartet is *Bailey's Cafe*, which is written in the form of a jazz suite. Set in a 1948 Brooklyn neighborhood, the novel explores the disruption of lives by sexual abuse and violence.

Gloria Naylor has taught at George Washington University, Princeton, the University of Pennsylvania, New York University, Boston University, Brandeis, and Cornell. She has received both a National Endowment for the Arts fellowship and a Guggenheim fellowship. Without doubt she is a powerful presence in contemporary African American literature.

From The Women of Brewster Place

The Two

At first they seemed like such nice girls. No one could remember exactly when they had moved into Brewster. It was earlier in the year before Ben was killed—of course, it had to be before Ben's death. But no one remembered if it was in the winter or spring of that year that the two had come. People often came and went on Brewster Place like a restless night's dream, moving in and out in the dark to avoid eviction notices or neighborhood bulletins about the dilapidated condition of their furnishings. So it wasn't until the two were clocked leaving in the mornings and returning in the evenings at regular intervals that it was quietly absorbed that they now claimed Brewster as home. And Brewster waited, cautiously prepared to claim them, because you never knew about young women, and obviously single at that. But when no wild music or drunken friends careened out of the corner building on weekends, and especially, when no slightly eager husbands were encouraged to linger around that first-floor apartment and run errands for them, a suspended sigh of relief floated around the two when they dumped their garbage, did their shopping, and headed for the morning bus.

The women of Brewster had readily accepted the lighter, skinny one. There wasn't much threat in her timid mincing walk and the slightly protruding teeth she seemed so eager to show everyone in her bell-like good mornings and evenings. Breaths were held a little longer in the direction of the short dark one—too pretty, and too much behind. And she insisted on wearing those thin Qiana [1] dresses that the summer breeze molded against the maddening rhythm of the twenty pounds of rounded flesh that she swung steadily down the street. Through slitted eyes, the women watched their men watching her pass, knowing the bastards were praying for a wind. But since she seemed oblivious to whether these supplications went answered, their sighs settled around her shoulders too. Nice girls.

And so no one even cared to remember exactly when they had moved into Brewster Place, until the rumor started. It had first spread through the block like a sour odor that's only faintly perceptible and easily ignored until it starts growing in strength from the dozen mouths it had been lying in, among clammy gums and scum-coated teeth. And then it was everywhere—lining the mouths and whitening the lips of everyone as they wrinkled up their noses at its pervading smell, unable to pinpoint the source or time of its initial arrival. Sophie could—she had been there.

It wasn't that the rumor had actually begun with Sophie. A rumor needs no true parent. It only needs a willing carrier, and it found one in Sophie. She had been there—on one of those August evenings when the sun's absence is a mockery because the heat leaves the air so heavy it presses the naked skin down on your body, to the point that a sheet becomes unbearable and sleep impossible. So most of Brewster was outside that night when the two had come in together, probably from one of those air-conditioned

1. Nylon.

movies downtown, and had greeted the ones who were loitering around their building. And they had started up the steps when the skinny one tripped over a child's ball and the darker one had grabbed her by the arm and around the waist to break her fall. "Careful, don't wanna lose you now." And the two of them had laughed into each other's eyes and went into the building.

The smell had begun there. It outlined the image of the stumbling woman and the one who had broken her fall. Sophie and a few other women sniffed at the spot and then, perplexed, silently looked at each other. Where had they seen that before? They had often laughed and touched each other—held each other in joy or its dark twin—but where had they seen *that* before? It came to them as the scent drifted down the steps and entered their nostrils on the way to their inner mouths. They had seen that—done that—with their men. That shared moment of invisible communion reserved for two and hidden from the rest of the world behind laughter or tears or a touch. In the days before babies, miscarriages, and other broken dreams, after stolen caresses in barn stalls and cotton houses, after intimate walks from church and secret kisses with boys who were now long forgotten or permanently fixed in their lives—that was where. They could almost feel the odor moving about in their mouths, and they slowly knitted themselves together and let it out into the air like a yellow mist that began to cling to the bricks on Brewster.

So it got around that the two in 312 were *that* way. And they had seemed like such nice girls. Their regular exits and entrances to the block were viewed with a jaundiced eye. The quiet that rested around their door on the weekends hinted of all sorts of secret rituals, and their friendly indifference to the men on the street was an insult to the women as a brazen flaunting of unnatural ways.

Since Sophie's apartment windows faced theirs from across the air shaft, she became the official watchman for the block, and her opinions were deferred to whenever the two came up in conversation. Sophie took her position seriously and was constantly alert for any telltale signs that might creep out around their drawn shades, across from which she kept a religious vigil. An entire week of drawn shades was evidence enough to send her flying around with reports that as soon as it got dark they pulled their shades down and put on the lights. Heads nodded in knowing unison—a definite sign. If doubt was voiced with a "But I pull my shades down at night too," a whispered "Yeah, but you're not *that* way" was argument enough to win them over.

Sophie watched the lighter one dumping their garbage, and she went outside and opened the lid. Her eyes darted over the crushed tin cans, vegetable peelings, and empty chocolate chip cookie boxes. What do they do with all them chocolate chip cookies? It was surely a sign, but it would take some time to figure that one out. She saw Ben go into their apartment, and she waited and blocked his path as he came out, carrying his toolbox.

"What ya see?" She grabbed his arm and whispered wetly in his face.

Ben stared at her squinted eyes and drooping lips and shook his head slowly. "Uh, uh, uh, it was terrible."

"Yeah?" She moved in a little closer.

"Worst busted faucet I seen in my whole life." He shook her hand off his arm and left her standing in the middle of the block.

"You old sop bucket," she muttered, as she went back up on her stoop. A broken faucet, huh? Why did they need to use so much water?

Sophie had plenty to report that day. Ben had said it was terrible in there. No, she didn't know exactly what he had seen, but you can imagine—and they did. Confronted with the difference that had been thrust into their predictable world, they reached into their imaginations and, using an ancient pattern, weaved themselves a reason for its existence. Out of necessity they stitched all of their secret fears and lingering childhood nightmares into this existence, because even though it was deceptive enough to try and look as they looked, talk as they talked, and do as they did, it had to have some hidden stain to invalidate it—it was impossible for them both to be right. So they leaned back, supported by the sheer weight of their numbers and comforted by the woven barrier that kept them protected from the yellow mist that enshrouded the two as they came and went on Brewster Place.

Lorraine was the first to notice the change in the people on Brewster Place. She was a shy but naturally friendly woman who got up early, and had read the morning paper and done fifty sit-ups before it was time to leave for work. She came out of her apartment eager to start her day by greeting any of her neighbors who were outside. But she noticed that some of the people who had spoken to her before made a point of having something else to do with their eyes when she passed, although she could almost feel them staring at her back as she moved on. The ones who still spoke only did so after an uncomfortable pause, in which they seemed to be peering through her before they begrudged her a good morning or evening. She wondered if it was all in her mind and she thought about mentioning it to Theresa, but she didn't want to be accused of being too sensitive again. And how would Tee even notice anything like that anyway? She had a lousy attitude and hardly ever spoke to people. She stayed in that bed until the last moment and rushed out of the house fogged-up and grumpy, and she was used to being stared at—by men at least—because of her body.

Lorraine thought about these things as she came up the block from work, carrying a large paper bag. The group of women on her stoop parted silently and let her pass.

"Good evening," she said, as she climbed the steps.

Sophie was standing on the top step and tried to peek into the bag. "You been shopping, huh? What ya buy?" It was almost an accusation.

"Groceries." Lorraine shielded the top of the bag from view and squeezed past her with a confused frown. She saw Sophie throw a knowing glance to the others at the bottom of the stoop. What was wrong with this old woman? Was she crazy or something?

Lorraine went into her apartment. Theresa was sitting by the window, reading a copy of *Mademoiselle*. She glanced up from her magazine. "Did you get my chocolate chip cookies?"

"Why good evening to you, too, Tee. And how was my day? Just wonderful." She sat the bag down on the couch. "The little Baxter boy brought in a puppy for show-and-tell, and the damn thing pissed all over the floor and then proceeded to chew the heel off my shoe, but, yes, I managed to hobble to the store and bring you your chocolate chip cookies."

Oh, Jesus, Theresa thought, she's got a bug up her ass tonight.

"Well, you should speak to Mrs. Baxter. She ought to train her kid better than that." She didn't wait for Lorraine to stop laughing before she tried to stretch her good mood. "Here, I'll put those things away. Want me to make dinner so you can rest? I only worked half a day, and the most tragic thing that went down was a broken fingernail and that got caught in my typewriter."

Lorraine followed Theresa into the kitchen. "No, I'm not really tired, and fair's fair, you cooked last night. I didn't mean to tick off like that; it's just that . . . well, Tee, have you noticed that people aren't as nice as they used to be?"

Theresa stiffened. Oh, God, here she goes again. "What people, Lorraine? Nice in what way?"

"Well, the people in this building and on the street. No one hardly speaks anymore. I mean, I'll come in and say good evening—and just silence. It wasn't like that when we first moved in. I don't know, it just makes you wonder; that's all. What are they thinking?"

"I personally don't give a shit what they're thinking. And their good evenings don't put any bread on my table."

"Yeah, but you didn't see the way that woman looked at me out there. They must feel something or know something. They probably—"

"They, they, they!" Theresa exploded. "You know, I'm not starting up with this again, Lorraine. Who in the hell are they? And where in the hell are we? Living in some dump of a building in this God-forsaken part of town around a bunch of ignorant niggers with the cotton still under their fingernails because of you and your theys. They knew something in Linden Hills, so I gave up an apartment for you that I'd been in for the last four years. And then they knew in Park Heights, and you made me so miserable there we had to leave. Now these mysterious theys are on Brewster Place. Well, look out that window, kid. There's a big wall down that block, and this is the end of the line for me. I'm not moving anymore, so if that's what you're working yourself up to—save it!"

When Theresa became angry she was like a lump of smoldering coal, and her fierce bursts of temper always unsettled Lorraine.

"You see, that's why I didn't want to mention it." Lorraine began to pull at her fingers nervously. "You're always flying up and jumping to conclusions—no one said anything about moving. And I didn't know your life has been so miserable since you met me. I'm sorry about that," she finished tearfully.

Theresa looked at Lorraine, standing in the kitchen door like a wilted leaf, and she wanted to throw something at her. Why didn't she ever fight back? The very softness that had first attracted her to Lorraine was now a frequent cause for irritation. Smoked honey. That's what Lorraine had reminded her of, sitting in her office clutching that application. Dry autumn days in Georgia woods, thick bloated smoke under a beehive, and the first glimpse of amber honey just faintly darkened about the edges by the burning twigs. She had flowed just that heavily into Theresa's mind and had stuck there with a persistent sweetness.

But Theresa hadn't known then that this softness filled Lorraine up to the very middle and that she would bend at the slightest pressure, would be constantly seeking to surround herself with the comfort of everyone's good-will, and would shrivel up at the least touch of disapproval. It was becoming a drain to be continually called upon for this nurturing and support that she just didn't understand. She had supplied it at first out of love for Lorraine, hoping that she would harden eventually, even as honey does when exposed to the cold. Theresa was growing tired of being clung to—of being the one who was leaned on. She didn't want a child—she wanted someone who could stand toe to toe with her and be willing to slug it out at times. If they practiced that way with each other, then they could turn back to back and beat the hell out of the world for trying to invade their territory. But she had found no such sparring partner in Lorraine, and the strain of fighting alone was beginning to show on her.

"Well, if it was that miserable, I would have been gone a long time ago," she said, watching her words refresh Lorraine like a gentle shower.

"I guess you think I'm some sort of a sick paranoid, but I can't afford to have people calling my job or writing letters to my principal. You know I've already lost a position like that in Detroit. And teaching is my whole life, Tee."

"I know," she sighed, not really knowing at all. There was no danger of that ever happening on Brewster Place. Lorraine taught too far from this neighborhood for anyone here to recognize her in that school. No, it wasn't her job she feared losing this time, but their approval. She wanted to stand out there and chat and trade makeup secrets and cake recipes. She wanted to be secretary of their block association and be asked to mind their kids while they ran to the store. And none of that was going to happen if they couldn't even bring themselves to accept her good evenings.

Theresa silently finished unpacking the groceries. "Why did you buy cottage cheese? Who eats that stuff?"

"Well, I thought we should go on a diet."

"If we go on a diet, then you'll disappear. You've got nothing to lose but your hair."

"Oh, I don't know. I thought that we might want to try and reduce our hips or something." Lorraine shrugged playfully.

"No, thank you. We are very happy with our hips the way they are," Theresa said, as she shoved the cottage cheese to the back of the refrigerator. "And even when I lose weight, it never comes off there. My chest and arms just get smaller, and I start looking like a bottle of salad dressing."

The two women laughed, and Theresa sat down to watch Lorraine fix dinner. "You know, this behind has always been my downfall. When I was coming up in Georgia with my grandmother, the boys used to promise me penny candy if I would let them pat my behind. And I used to love those jawbreakers—you know, the kind that lasted all day and kept changing colors in your mouth. So I was glad to oblige them, because in one afternoon I could collect a whole week's worth of jawbreakers."

"Really. That's funny to you? Having some boy feeling all over you."

Theresa sucked her teeth. "We were only kids, Lorraine. You know, you remind me of my grandmother. That was one straight-laced old lady. She had a fit when my brother told her what I was doing. She called me into the smokehouse and told me in this real scary whisper that I could get pregnant from letting little boys pat my butt and that I'd end up like my cousin Willa. But Willa and I had been thick as fleas, and she had already given me a step-by-step summary of how she'd gotten into her predicament. But I sneaked around to her house that night just to double-check her story, since that old lady had seemed so earnest. 'Willa, are you sure?' I whispered through her bedroom window. 'I'm tellin' ya, Tee,' she said. 'Just keep both feet on the ground and you home free.' Much later I learned that advice wasn't too biologically sound, but it worked in Georgia because those country boys didn't have much imagination."

Theresa's laughter bounced off of Lorraine's silent, rigid back and died in her throat. She angrily tore open a pack of the chocolate chip cookies. "Yeah," she said, staring at Lorraine's back and biting down hard into the cookie, "it wasn't until I came up north to college that I found out there's a whole lot of things that a dude with a little imagination can do to you even with both feet on the ground. You see, Willa forgot to tell me not to bend over or squat or—"

"Must you!" Lorraine turned around from the stove with her teeth clenched tightly together.

"Must I what, Lorraine? Must I talk about things that are as much a part of life as eating or breathing or growing old? Why are you always so uptight about sex or men?"

"I'm not uptight about anything. I just think it's disgusting when you go on and on about—"

"There's nothing disgusting about it, Lorraine. You've never been with a man, but I've been with quite a few—some better than others. There were a couple who I still hope to this day will die a slow, painful death, but then there were some who were good to me—in and out of bed."

"If they were so great, then why are you with me?" Lorraine's lips were trembling.

"Because—" Theresa looked steadily into her eyes and then down at the cookie she was twirling on the table. "Because," she continued slowly, "you can take a chocolate chip cookie and put holes in it and attach it to your ears and call it an earring, or hang it around your neck on a silver chain and pretend it's a necklace—but it's still a cookie. See—you can toss it in the air and call it a Frisbee or even a flying saucer, if the mood hits you, and it's still just a cookie. Send it spinning on a table—like this—until it's a wonderful blur of amber and brown light that you can imagine to be a topaz or rusted gold or old crystal, but the law of gravity has got to come into play, sometime, and it's got to come to rest—sometime. Then all the spinning and pretending and hoopla is over with. And you know what you got?"

"A chocolate chip cookie," Lorraine said.

"Uh-uh." Theresa put the cookie in her mouth and winked. "A lesbian."

She got up from the table. "Call me when dinner's ready, I'm going back to read." She stopped at the kitchen door. "Now, why are you putting gravy on that chicken, Lorraine? You know it's fattening."

The Brewster Place Block Association was meeting in Kiswana's apartment. People were squeezed on the sofa and coffee table and sitting on the floor. Kiswana had hung a red banner across the wall, "Today Brewster— Tomorrow America!" but few understood what that meant and even fewer cared. They were there because this girl had said that something could be done about the holes in their walls and the lack of heat that kept their children with congested lungs in the winter. Kiswana had given up trying to be heard above the voices that were competing with each other in volume and length of complaints against the landlord. This was the first time in their lives that they felt someone was taking them seriously, so all of the would-be-if-they-could-be lawyers, politicians, and Broadway actors were taking advantage of this rare opportunity to display their talents. It didn't matter if they often repeated what had been said or if their monologues held no relevance to the issues; each one fought for the space to outshine the other.

"Ben ain't got no reason to be here. He works for the landlord."

A few scattered yeahs came from around the room.

"I lives in this here block just like y'all," Ben said slowly. "And when you ain't got no heat, I ain't either. It's not my fault 'cause the man won't deliver no oil."

"But you stay so zooted[2] all the time, you never cold no way."

"Ya know, a lot of things ain't the landlord's fault. The landlord don't throw garbage in the air shaft or break the glass in them doors."

"Yeah, and what about all them kids that be runnin' up and down the halls."

"Don't be talking 'bout my kids!" Cora Lee jumped up. "Lot of y'all got kids, too, and they no saints."

"Why you so touchy—who mentioned you?"

"But if the shoe fits, steal it from Thom McAn's."

"Wait, please." Kiswana held up her hands. "This is getting us nowhere. What we should be discussing today is staging a rent strike and taking the landlord to court."

"What we should be discussin'," Sophie leaned over and said to Mattie and Etta, "is that bad element that done moved in this block amongst decent people."

"Well, I done called the police at least a dozen times about C. C. Baker and them boys hanging in that alley, smoking them reefers, and robbing folks," Mattie said.

"I ain't talkin' 'bout them kids—I'm talkin' 'bout those two livin' 'cross from me in 312."

"What about 'em?"

"Oh, you know, Mattie," Etta said, staring straight at Sophie. "Those two girls who mind their business and never have a harsh word to say 'bout nobody—them the two you mean, right, Sophie?"

2. Drunk.

"What they doin'—livin' there like that—is wrong, and you know it." She turned to appeal to Mattie. "Now, you a Christian woman. The Good Book say that them things is an abomination against the Lord. We shouldn't be havin' that here on Brewster and the association should do something about it."

"My Bible also says in First Peter not to be a busybody in other people's matters, Sophie. And the way I see it, if they ain't botherin' with what goes on in my place, why should I bother 'bout what goes on in theirs?"

"They sinning against the Lord!" Sophie's eyes were bright and wet.

"Then let the Lord take care of it," Etta snapped. "Who appointed you?"

"That don't surprise me comin' from *you*. No, not one bit!" Sophie glared at Etta and got up to move around the room to more receptive ears.

Etta started to go after her, but Mattie held her arm. "Let that woman be. We're not here to cause no row over some of her stupidness."

"The old prune pit," Etta spit out. "She oughta be glad them two girls are that way. That's one less bed she gotta worry 'bout pullin' Jess out of this year. I didn't see her thumpin' no Bible when she beat up that woman from Mobile she caught him with last spring."

"Etta, I'd never mention it in front of Sophie 'cause I hate the way she loves to drag other people's business in the street, but I can't help feelin' that what they're doing ain't quite right. How do you get that way? Is it from birth?"

"I couldn't tell you, Mattie. But I seen a lot of it in my time and the places I've been. They say they just love each other—who knows?"

Mattie was thinking deeply. "Well, I've loved women, too. There was Miss Eva and Ciel, and even as ornery as you can get, I've loved you practically all my life."

"Yeah, but it's different with them."

"Different how?"

"Well . . ." Etta was beginning to feel uncomfortable. "They love each other like you'd love a man or a man would love you—I guess."

"But I've loved some women deeper than I ever loved any man," Mattie was pondering. "And there been some women who loved me more and did more for me than any man ever did."

"Yeah." Etta thought for a moment. "I can second that, but it's still different, Mattie. I can't exactly put my finger on it, but . . ."

"Maybe it's not so different," Mattie said, almost to herself. "Maybe that's why some women get so riled up about it, 'cause they know deep down it's not so different after all." She looked at Etta. "It kinda gives you a funny feeling when you think about it that way, though."

"Yeah, it does," Etta said, unable to meet Mattie's eyes.

Lorraine was climbing the dark narrow stairway up to Kiswana's apartment. She had tried to get Theresa to come, but she had wanted no part of it. "A tenants' meeting for what? The damn street needs to be condemned." She knew Tee blamed her for having to live in a place like Brewster, but she could at least try to make the best of things and get involved with the community. That was the problem with so many black people—they just sat back and complained while the whole world tumbled down around their heads. And grabbing an attitude and thinking you were

better than these people just because a lot of them were poor and uneducated wouldn't help, either. It just made you seem standoffish, and Lorraine wanted to be liked by the people around her. She couldn't live the
way Tee did, with her head stuck in a book all the time. Tee didn't seem to
need anyone. Lorraine often wondered if she even needed her.

But if you kept to yourself all the time, people started to wonder, and
then they talked. She couldn't afford to have people talking about her, Tee
should understand that—she knew from the way they had met. Understand. It was funny because that was the first thing she had felt about her
when she handed Tee her application. She had said to herself, I feel that I
can talk to this woman, I can tell her why I lost my job in Detroit, and she
will understand. And she had understood, but then slowly all that had
stopped. Now Lorraine was made to feel awkward and stupid about her
fears and thoughts. Maybe Tee was right and she was too sensitive, but
there was a big difference between being personnel director for the Board
of Education and a first-grade teacher. Tee didn't threaten their files and
payroll accounts but, somehow, she, Lorraine, threatened their children.
Her heart tightened when she thought about that. The worst thing she had
ever wanted to do to a child was to slap the spit out of the little Baxter boy
for pouring glue in her hair, and even that had only been for a fleeting
moment. Didn't Tee understand that if she lost this job, she wouldn't be so
lucky the next time? No, she didn't understand that or anything else about
her. She never wanted to bother with anyone except those weirdos at that
club she went to, and Lorraine hated them. They were coarse and bitter,
and made fun of people who weren't like them. Well, she wasn't like them
either. Why should she feel different from the people she lived around?
Black people were all in the same boat—she'd come to realize this even
more since they had moved to Brewster—and if they didn't row together,
they would sink together.

Lorraine finally reached the top floor; the door to Kiswana's apartment
was open but she knocked before she went in. Kiswana was trying to break
up an argument between a short light-skinned man and some woman who
had picked up a potted plant and was threatening to hit him in the mouth.
Most of the other tenants were so busy rooting for one or the other that
hardly anyone noticed Lorraine when she entered. She went over and
stood by Ben.

"I see there's been a slight difference of opinion here," she smiled.

"Just nigger mess, miss. Roscoe there claim that Betina ain't got no right
being secretary 'cause she owe three months' rent, and she say he owe more
than that and it's none of his never mind. Don't know how we got into all
this. Ain't what we was talkin' 'bout, no way. Was talkin' 'bout havin' a
block party to raise money for a housing lawyer."

Kiswana had rescued her Boston Fern from the woman and the two people were being pulled to opposite sides of the room. Betina pushed her way
out of the door, leaving behind very loud advice about where they could
put their secretary's job along with the block association, if they could find
the space in that small an opening in their bodies.

Kiswana sat back down, flushed and out of breath. "Now we need someone else to take the minutes."

"Do they come with the rest of the watch?" Laughter and another series of monologues about Betina's bad-natured exit followed for the next five minutes.

Lorraine saw that Kiswana looked as if she wanted to cry. The one-step-forward-two-steps-backwards progression of the meeting was beginning to show on her face. Lorraine swallowed her shyness and raised her hand. "I'll take the minutes for you."

"Oh, thank you." Kiswana hurriedly gathered the scattered and crumpled papers and handed them to her. "Now we can get back down to business."

The room was now aware of Lorraine's presence, and there were soft murmurs from the corners, accompanied by furtive glances while a few like Sophie stared at her openly. She attempted to smile into the eyes of the people watching her, but they would look away the moment she glanced in their direction. After a couple of vain attempts her smile died, and she buried it uneasily in the papers in her hand. Lorraine tried to cover her trembling fingers by pretending to decipher Betina's smudged and misspelled notes.

"All right," Kiswana said, "now who had promised to get a stereo hooked up for the party?"

"Ain't we supposed to vote on who we wants for secretary?" Sophie's voice rose heavily in the room, and its weight smothered the other noise. All of the faces turned silently toward hers with either mild surprise or coveted satisfaction over what they knew was coming. "I mean, can anybody just waltz in here and get shoved down our throats and we don't have a say about it?"

"Look, I can just go," Lorraine said. "I just wanted to help, I—"

"No, wait." Kiswana was confused. "What vote? Nobody else wanted to do it. Did you want to take the notes?"

"She can't do it," Etta cut in, "unless we was sitting here reciting the ABC's, and we better not do that too fast. So let's just get on with the meeting."

Scattered approval came from sections of the room.

"Listen here!" Sophie jumped up to regain lost ground. "Why should a decent woman get insulted and y'll take sides with the likes of them?" Her finger shot out like a pistol, which she swung between Etta and Lorraine.

Etta rose from her seat. "Who do you think you're talkin' to, you old hen's ass? I'm as decent as you are, and I'll come over there and lam you in the mouth to prove it!"

Etta tried to step across the coffee table, but Mattie caught her by the back of the dress; Etta turned, tried to shake her off, and tripped over the people in front of her. Sophie picked up a statue and backed up into the wall with it slung over her shoulder like a baseball bat. Kiswana put her head in her hands and groaned. Etta had taken off her high-heeled shoe and was waving the spiked end at Sophie over the shoulders of the people who were holding her back.

"That's right! That's right!" Sophie screamed. "Pick on me! Sure, I'm the one who goes around doin' them filthy, unnatural things right under your noses. Every one of you knows it; everybody done talked about it, not just me!" Her head moved around the room like a trapped animal's. "And any woman—any woman who defends that kind of thing just better be watched. That's all I gotta say—where there's smoke, there's fire, Etta Johnson!"

Etta stopped struggling against the arms that were holding her, and her chest was heaving in rapid spasms as she threw Sophie a look of wilting hate, but she remained silent. And no other woman in the room dared to speak as they moved an extra breath away from each other. Sophie turned toward Lorraine, who had twisted the meeting's notes into a mass of shredded paper. Lorraine kept her back straight, but her hands and mouth were moving with a will of their own. She stood like a fading spirit before the ebony statue that Sophie pointed at her like a crucifix.

"Movin' into our block causin' a disturbance with your nasty ways. You ain't wanted here!"

"What have any of you ever seen me do except leave my house and go to work like the rest of you? Is it disgusting for me to speak to each one of you that I meet in the street, even when you don't answer me back? Is that my crime?" Lorraine's voice sank like a silver dagger into their consciences, and there was an uneasy stirring in the room.

"Don't stand there like you a Miss Innocent," Sophie whispered hoarsely. "I'll tell ya what I seen!"

Her eyes leered around the room as they waited with a courtroom hush for her next words.

"I wasn't gonna mention something so filthy, but you forcin' me." She ran her tongue over her parched lips and narrowed her eyes at Lorraine. "You forgot to close your shades last night, and I saw the two of you!"

The silence in the room tightened into a half-gasp.

"There you was, standin' in the bathroom door, drippin' wet and as naked and shameless as you please . . ."

It had become so quiet it was now painful.

"Calling to the other one to put down her book and get you a clean towel. Standin' in that bathroom door with your naked behind. I saw it—I did!"

Their chests were beginning to burn from a lack of air as they waited for Lorraine's answer, but before the girl could open her mouth, Ben's voice snaked from behind her like a lazy breeze.

"Guess *you* get out the tub with your clothes on, Sophie. Must make it mighty easy on Jess's eyes."

The laughter that burst out of their lungs was such a relief that eyes were watery. The room laid its head back and howled in gratitude to Ben for allowing it to breathe again. Sophie's rantings could not be heard above the wheezing, coughing, and backslapping that now went on.

Lorraine left the apartment and grasped the stairway railing, trying to keep the bile from rising into her throat. Ben followed her outside and gently touched her shoulder.

"Miss, you all right?"

She pressed her lips tightly together and nodded her head. The lightness of his touch brought tears to her eyes, and she squeezed them shut.

"You sure? You look 'bout ready to keel over."

Lorraine shook her head jerkily and sank her nails deeply into her palm as she brought her hand to her mouth. I mustn't speak, she thought. If I open my mouth, I'll scream. Oh, God, I'll scream or I'll throw up, right here, in front of this nice old man. The thought of the churned up bits of her breakfast and lunch pouring out of her mouth and splattering on Ben's trouser legs suddenly struck her as funny, and she fought an overwhelming desire to laugh. She trembled violently as the creeping laughter tried to deceive her into parting her lips.

Ben's face clouded over as he watched the frail body that was so bravely struggling for control. "Come on now, I'll take you home." And he tried to lead her down the steps.

She shook her head in a panic. She couldn't let Tee see her like this. If she says anything smart to me now, I'll kill her, Lorraine thought. I'll pick up a butcher knife and plunge it into her face, and then I'll kill myself and let them find us there. The thought of all those people in Kiswana's apartment standing over their bleeding bodies was strangely comforting, and she began to breathe more easily.

"Come on now," Ben urged quietly, and edged her toward the steps.

"I can't go home." She barely whispered.

"It's all right, you ain't gotta—come on."

And she let him guide her down the stairs and out into the late September evening. He took her to the building that was nearest to the wall on Brewster Place and then down the outside steps to a door with a broken dirty screen. Ben unlocked the door and led her into his damp underground rooms.

He turned on the single light bulb that was hanging from the ceiling by a thick black cord and pulled out a chair for her at the kitchen table, which was propped up against the wall. Lorraine sat down, grateful to be able to take the weight off of her shaky knees. She didn't acknowledge his apologies as he took the half-empty wine bottle and cracked cup from the table. He brushed off the crumbs while two fat brown roaches raced away from the wet cloth.

"I'm makin' tea," he said, without asking her if she wanted any. He placed a blackened pot of water on the hot plate at the edge of the counter, then found two cups in the cabinet that still had their handles intact. Ben put the strong black tea he had brewed in front of her and brought her a spoon and a crumpled pound bag of sugar. Lorraine took three heaping teaspoons of sugar and stirred the tea, holding her face over the steam. Ben waited for her face to register the effects of the hot sweet liquid.

"I liked you from first off," he said shyly, and seeing her smile, he continued. "You remind me lots of my little girl." Ben reached into his hip pocket and took out a frayed billfold and handed her a tiny snapshot.

Lorraine tilted the picture toward the light. The face stamped on the celluloid paper bore absolutely no resemblance to her at all. His daughter's face was oval and dark, and she had a large flat nose and a tiny rounded mouth. She handed the picture back to Ben and tried to cover her confusion.

"I know what you thinkin'," Ben said, looking at the face in his hands. "But she had a limp—my little girl. Was a breech baby, and the midwife broke her foot when she was birthed and it never came back right. Always kinda cripped along—but a sweet child." He frowned deeply into the picture and paused, then looked up at Lorraine. "When I seen you—the way you'd walk up the street all timid-like and tryin' to be nice to these-here folks and the look on your face when some of 'em was just downright rude—you kinda broke up in here." He motioned toward his chest. "And you just sorta limped along inside. That's when I thought of my baby."

Lorraine gripped the teacup with both hands, but the tears still squeezed through the compressed muscles in her eyes. They slowly rolled down her face but she wouldn't release the cup to wipe them away.

"My father," she said, staring into the brown liquid, "kicked me out of the house when I was seventeen years old. He found a letter one of my girlfriends had written me, and when I wouldn't lie about what it meant, he told me to get out and leave behind everything that he had ever bought me. He said he wanted to burn them." She looked up to see the expression on Ben's face, but it kept swimming under the tears in her eyes. "So I walked out of his home with only the clothes on my back. I moved in with one of my cousins, and I worked at night in a bakery to put myself through college. I would send him a birthday card each year, and he always returned them unopened. After a while I stopped putting my return address on the envelopes so he couldn't send them back. I guess he burned those too." She sniffed the mucus up into her nose. "I still send those cards like that— without a return address. That way I can believe that, maybe, one year before he dies, he'll open them."

Ben got up and gave her a piece of toilet paper to blow her nose in.

"Where's your daughter now, Mr. Ben?"

"For me?" Ben sighed deeply. "Just like you—livin' in a world with no address."

They finished their tea in silence and Lorraine got up to go.

"There's no way to thank you, so I won't try."

"I'd be right hurt if you did." Ben patted her arm. "Now come back anytime you got a mind to. I got nothing, but you welcome to all of that. Now how many folks is that generous?"

Lorraine smiled, leaned over, and kissed him on the cheek. Ben's face lit up the walls of the dingy basement. He closed the door behind her, and at first her "Good night, Mr. Ben" tinkled like crystal bells in his mind. Crystal bells that grew larger and louder, until their sound was distorted in his ears and he almost believed that she had said "Good night, Daddy Ben"— no—"Mornin' Daddy Ben, mornin' Daddy Ben, mornin' . . ." Ben's saliva began to taste like sweating tin, and he ran a trembling hand over his stubbled face and rushed to the corner where he had shoved the wine bottle. The bells had begun almost to deafen him and he shook his head to relieve the drumming pain inside of his ears. He knew what was coming next, and he didn't dare waste time by pouring the wine into a cup. He lifted the bottle up to his mouth and sucked at it greedily, but it was too late. *Swing low, sweet chariot*. The song had started—the whistling had begun.

It started low, from the end of his gut, and shrilled its way up into his ears and shattered the bells, sending glass shards flying into a heart that should have been so scarred from old piercings that there was no flesh left to bleed.

But the glass splinters found some minute, untouched place—as they always did—and tore the heart and let the whistling in. And now Ben would have to drink faster and longer, because the melody would now ride on his body's blood like a cancer and poison everywhere it touched. *Swing low, sweet chariot.* It mustn't get to his brain. He had a few more seconds before it got to his brain and killed him. He had to be drunk before the poison crept up his neck muscles, past his mouth, on the way to his brain. If he was drunk, then he could let it out—sing it out into the air before it touched his brain, caused him to remember. *Swing low, sweet chariot.* He couldn't die there under the ground like some animal. Oh, God, please make him drunk. And he promised—he'd never go that long without a drink again. It was just the meeting and then that girl that had kept him from it this long, but he swore it would never happen again—just please, God, make him drunk.

The alcohol began to warm Ben's body, and he felt his head begin to get numb and heavy. He almost sobbed out his thanks for this redeeming answer to his prayers, because the whistling had just reached his throat and he was able to open his mouth and slobber the words out into the room. The saliva was dripping from the corners of his mouth because he had to take huge gulps of wine between breaths, but he sang on—drooling and humming—because to sing was salvation, to sing was to empty the tune from his blood, to sing was to unremember Elvira, and his daughter's "Mornin', Daddy Ben" as she dragged her twisted foot up his front porch with that song hitting her in the back.
Swing low
"Mornin', Ben. Mornin', Elvira."
Sweet chariot
The red pick-up truck stopped in front of Ben's yard.
Comin' for to carry me home
His daughter got out of the passenger side and began to limp toward the house.
Swing low
Elvira grinned into the creviced face of the white man sitting in the truck with tobacco stains in the corner of his mouth. "Mornin', Mr. Clyde. Right nice day, ain't it, sir?"
Sweet chariot
Ben watched his daughter come through the gate with her eyes on the ground, and she slowly climbed up on the porch. She took each step at a time, and her shoes grated against the rough boards. She finally turned her beaten eyes into his face, and what was left of his soul to crush was taken care of by the bell-like voice that greeted them. "Mornin', Daddy Ben. Mornin', Mama."
"Mornin', baby," Ben mumbled with his jaws tight.
Swing low
"How's things up at the house?" Elvira asked. "My little girl do a good job for you yesterday?"
Sweet chariot
"Right fine, Elvira. Got that place clean as a skinned rat. How's y'all's crops comin'?"

"Just fine, Mr. Clyde, sir. Just fine. We sure appreciate that extra land you done rented us. We bringin' in more than enough to break even. Yes, sir, just fine."

The man laughed, showing the huge gaps between his tobacco-rotted teeth. "Glad to do it. Y'all some of my best tenants. I likes keepin' my people happy. If you needs somethin', let me know."

"Sure will, Mr. Clyde, sir."

"Aw right, see y'all next week. Be by the regular time to pick up the gal."

"She be ready, sir."

The man started up the motor on the truck, and the tune that he whistled as he drove off remained in the air long after the dust had returned to the ground. Elvira grinned and waved until the red of the truck had disappeared over the horizon. Then she simultaneously dropped her arm and smile and turned toward her daughter. "Don't just stand there gawkin'. Get in the house—your breakfast been ready."

"Yes, Mama."

When the screen door had slammed shut, Elvira snapped her head around to Ben. "Nigger, what is wrong with you? Ain't you heard Mr. Clyde talkin' to you, and you standin' there like a hunk of stone. You better get some sense in you head 'fore I knock some in you!"

Ben stood with his hands in his pockets, staring at the tracks in the dirt where the truck had been. He kept balling his fists up in his overalls until his nails dug into his palms.

"It ain't right, Elvira. It just ain't right and you know it."

"What ain't right?" The woman stuck her face into his and he backed up a few steps. "That that gal work and earn her keep like the rest of us? She can't go to the fields, but she can clean house, and she'll do it! I see it's better you keep your mouth shut 'cause when it's open, ain't nothin' but stupidness comin' out." She turned her head and brushed him off as she would a fly, then headed toward the door of the house.

"She came to us, Elvira." There was a leaden sadness in Ben's voice. "She came to us a long time ago."

The thin woman spun around with her face twisted into an airless knot. "She came to us with a bunch of lies 'bout Mr. Clyde 'cause she's too damn lazy to work. Why would a decent widow man want to mess with a little black nothin' like her? No, anything to get out of work—just like you."

"Why she gotta spend the night then?" Ben turned his head slowly toward her. "Why he always make her spend the night up there alone with him?"

"Why should he make an extra trip just to bring her tail home when he pass this way every Saturday mornin' on the way to town? If she wasn't lame, she could walk it herself after she finish work. But the man nice enough to drop her home, and you want to bad-mouth him along with that lyin' hussy."

"After she came to us, you remember I borrowed Tommy Boy's wagon and went to get her that Friday night. I told ya what Mr. Clyde told me. 'She ain't finished yet, Ben.' Just like that—'She ain't finished yet.' And then standin' there whistlin' while I went out the back gate." Ben's nails dug deeper into his palms.

"So!" Elvira's voice was shrill. "So it's a big house. It ain't like this shit you got us livin' in. It take her longer to do things than most folks. You know that, so why stand there carryin' on like it mean more than that?"

"She ain't finished yet, Ben." Ben shook his head slowly. "If I was half a man I woulda—"

Elvira came across the porch and sneered into his face. "If you was half a man, you coulda given me more babies and we woulda had some help workin' this land instead of a half-grown woman we gotta carry the load for. And if you was even quarter a man, we wouldn't be a bunch of miserable sharecroppers on someone else's land—but we is, Ben. And I'll be damned if I see the little bit we got taken away 'cause you believe that gal's lowdown lies! So when Mr. Clyde come by here, you speak—hear me? And you act as grateful as your pitiful ass should be for the favors he done us."

Ben felt a slight dampness in his hands because his fingernails had broken through the skin of his palms and the blood was seeping around his cuticles. He looked at Elvira's dark braided head and wondered why he didn't take his hands out of his pockets and stop the bleeding by pressing them around it. Just lock his elbows on her shoulders and place one hand on each side of her temples and then in toward each other until the blood stopped. His big calloused hands on the bones of her skull pressing in and in, like you would with a piece of dark cloth to cover the wounds on your body and clot the blood. Or he could simply go into the house and take his shotgun and press his palms around the trigger and handle, emptying the bullets into her sagging breasts just long enough—just pressing hard enough—to stop his palms from bleeding.

But the gram of truth in her words was heavy enough to weigh his hands down in his pockets and keep his feet nailed to the wooden planks in the porch, and the wounds healed over by themselves. Ben discovered that if he sat up drinking all night Friday, he could stand on the porch Saturday morning and smile at the man who whistled as he dropped his lame daughter home. And he could look into her beaten eyes and believe that she had lied.

The girl disappeared one day, leaving behind a note saying that she loved them very much, but she knew that she had been a burden and she understood why they had made her keep working at Mr. Clyde's house. But she felt that if she had to earn her keep that way, she might as well go to Memphis where the money was better.

Elvira ran and bragged to the neighbors that their daughter was now working in a rich house in Memphis. And she was making out awful well because she always sent plenty of money home. Ben would stare at the envelopes with no return address, and he found that if he drank enough every time a letter came, he could silence the bell-like voice that came chiming out of the open envelope—"Mornin' Daddy Ben, mornin' Daddy Ben, mornin' . . ." And then if he drank enough every day he could bear the touch of Elvira's body in the bed beside him at night and not have his sleep stolen by the image of her lying there with her head caved in or her chest ripped apart by shotgun shells.

But even after they lost the sharecropping contract and Elvira left him for a man who farmed near the levee and Ben went north and took a job on

Brewster, he still drank—long after he could remember why. He just knew that whenever he saw a mailman, the crystal bells would start, and then that strange whistling that could shatter them, sending them on that deadly journey toward his heart.

He never dreamed it would happen on a Sunday. The mailman didn't run on Sundays, so he had felt safe. He hadn't counted on that girl sounding so much like the bells when she left his place tonight. But it was okay, he had gotten drunk in time, and he would never take such a big chance again. No, Lord, you pulled me through this time, and I ain't pressin' your mercy no more. Ben stumbled around his shadowy damp rooms, singing now at the top of his voice. The low, trembling melody of "Swing Low, Sweet Chariot" passed through his greasy windows and up into the late summer air.

Lorraine had walked home slowly, thinking about the old man and the daughter who limped. When she came to her stoop, she brushed past her neighbors with her head up and didn't bother to speak.

Theresa got off the uptown bus and turned the corner into Brewster Place. She was always irritable on Friday evenings because they had to do payroll inventories at the office. Her neck ached from bending over endless lists of computer printouts. What did that damn Board of Education think—someone in accounting was going to sneak one of their relatives on the payroll? The biggies had been doing that for years, but they lay awake at night, thinking of ways to keep the little guys from cashing in on it too. There was something else that had been turning uncomfortably in her mind for the last few weeks, and just today it had lain still long enough for her to pinpoint it—Lorraine was changing. It wasn't exactly anything that she had said or done, but Theresa sensed a firmness in her spirit that hadn't been there before. She was speaking up more—yes, that was it—whether the subject was the evening news or bus schedules or the proper way to hem a dress. Lorraine wasn't deferring to her anymore. And she wasn't apologizing for seeing things differently from Theresa.

Why did that bother her? Didn't she want Lorraine to start standing up for herself? To stop all that sniveling and hand-wringing every time Theresa raised her voice? Weren't things the way she had wanted them to be for the last five years? What nagged at Theresa more than the change was the fact that she was worrying about it. She had actually thought about picking a fight just to see how far she could push her—push her into what? Oh, God, I must be sick, she thought. No, it was that old man—that's what it was. Why was Lorraine spending so much time with that drunk? They didn't have a damn thing in common. What could he be telling her, doing for her, that was causing this? She had tried—she truly had—to get Lorraine to show some backbone. And now some ignorant country winehead was doing in a few weeks what she couldn't do for the last five years.

Theresa was mulling this over when a little girl sped past her on skates, hit a crack in the sidewalk, and fell. She went to walk around the child, who looked up with tears in her eyes and stated simply, "Miss, I hurt myself." She said it with such a tone of wonder and disappointment that Theresa smiled. Kids lived in such an insulated world, where the smallest disturbance was met with cries of protest. Oh, sweetheart, she thought, just live on and you'll wish many a day that the biggest problem in your life would be a scraped knee. But she was still just a little girl, and right now she wanted an audience for her struggle with this uninvited disaster.

Theresa bent down beside her and clucked her teeth loudly. "Oh, you did? Let's see." She helped her off the ground and made an exaggerated fuss over the scraped knee.

"It's bleeding!" The child's voice rose in horror.

Theresa looked at the tiny specks of blood that were beading up on the grimy knee. "Why, it sure is." She tried to match the note of seriousness in the child's tone. "But I think we have a little time before you have to worry about a transfusion." She opened her pocketbook and took out a clean tissue. "Let's see if we can fix it up. Now, I want you to spit on this for me and I'll wipe your knee."

The girl spit on the tissue. "Is it gonna hurt?"

"No, it won't hurt. You know what my grandma used to call spit? God's iodine. Said it was the best thing for patching anything up—except maybe a broken leg."

She steadied the girl's leg and gently dabbed at the dirty knee. "See, it's all coming off. I guess you're gonna live." She smiled.

The child looked at her knee with a solemn face. "I think it needs a Band-Aid."

Theresa laughed. "Well, you're out of luck with me. But you go on home and see if your mama has one for you—if you can remember which knee it was by then."

"What are you doing to her?" The voice pierced the air between the child and Theresa. She looked up and saw a woman rushing toward them. The woman grabbed the child to her side. "What's going on here?" Her voice was just half an octave too high.

Theresa stood up and held out the dirty and bloody tissue. "She scraped her knee." The words fell like dead weights. "What in the hell did you think I was doing?" She refused to let the woman avoid her eyes, enjoying every minute of her cringing embarrassment.

"Mama, I need a Band-Aid, you got a Band-Aid?" The child tugged on her arm.

"Yes, yes, honey, right away." The woman was glad to have an excuse to look down. "Thank you very much," she said, as she hurried the child away. "She's always so clumsy. I've told her a million times to be careful on those skates, but you know . . ."

"Yeah, right," Theresa said, watching them go. "I know." She balled the tissue in her hand and quickly walked into the building. She slammed the apartment door open and heard Lorraine running water in the bathroom.

"Is that you, Tee?"

"Yeah," she called out, and then thought, No, it's not me. It's not me at all. Theresa paced between the kitchen and living room and then realized that she still had the tissue. She threw it into the kitchen garbage and turned on the faucet to its fullest pressure and started washing her hands. She kept lathering and rinsing them, but they still felt unclean. Son-of-a-bitch, she thought, son-of-a-fucking-bitch! She roughly dried her hands

with some paper towels and fought the impulse to wash them again by starting dinner early. She kept her hands moving quickly, chopping more onions, celery, and green peppers than she really needed. She vigorously
seasoned the ground beef, jabbing the wooden spoon repeatedly into the
red meat.

When she stopped to catch her breath and glanced toward the kitchen
window, a pair of squinty black eyes were peering at her from the corner of
a shade across the air shaft. "What the hell . . . ?" She threw down her
spoon and ran over to the window.

"You wanna see what I'm doing?" The shade was pulled up with such
force it went spinning on its rollers at the top of the window. The eyes disappeared from the corner of the shade across the air shaft.

"Here!" Theresa slammed the window up into its casing. "I'll even raise
this so you can hear better. I'm making meat loaf, you old bat! Meat loaf!"
She stuck her head out of the window. "The same way other people make
it! Here, I'll show you!"

She ran back to the table and took up a handful of chopped onions and
threw them at Sophie's window. "See, that's the onions. And here, here's
the chopped peppers!" The diced vegetables hit against the windowpane.
"Oh, yeah, I use eggs!" Two eggs flew out of the window and splattered
against Sophie's panes.

Lorraine came out of the bathroom, toweling her hair. "What's all the
shouting for? Who are you talking to?" She saw Theresa running back and
forth across the kitchen, throwing their dinner out of the window. "Have
you lost your mind?"

Theresa picked up a jar of olives. "Now, here's something *freaky* for
you—olives! I put olives in my meat loaf! So run up and down the street and
tell that!" The jar of olives crashed against the opposite building, barely
missing Sophie's window.

"Tee, stop it!"

Theresa put her head back out the window. "Now olives are definitely
weird, but you gotta take that one up with my grandmother because it's her
recipe! Wait! I forgot the meat—can't have you think I would try to make
meat loaf without meat." She ran back to the table and grabbed up the
bowl.

"Theresa!" Lorraine rushed into the kitchen.

"No, can't have you thinking that!" Theresa yelled as she swung back
her arm to throw the bowl through Sophie's window. "You might feel I'm a
pervert or something—someone you can't trust your damn children
around!"

Lorraine caught her arm just as she went to hurl the bowl out of the
window. She grabbed the bowl and shoved Theresa against the wall.

"Look," Lorraine said, pressing against the struggling woman, "I know
you're pissed off, but ground sirloin is almost three dollars a pound!"

The look of sincere horror on Lorraine's face as she cradled the bowl of
meat in her arm made Theresa giggle, and then slowly she started laughing
and Lorraine nodded her head and laughed with her. Theresa laid her
head back against the wall, and her plump throat vibrated from the full
sounds passing through it. Lorraine let her go and put the bowl on the
table. Theresa's sides were starting to ache from laughing, and she sat down

in one of the kitchen chairs. Lorraine pushed the bowl a little further down the table from her, and this set them off again. Theresa laughed and rocked in the chair until tears were rolling down her cheeks. Then she crossed that fine line between laughter and tears and started to sob. Lorraine went over to her, cradled her head in her chest, and stroked her shoulders. She had no idea what had brought on all of this, but it didn't matter. It felt good to be the one who could now comfort.

The shade across the air shaft moved a fraction of an inch, and Sophie pressed one eye against her smeared and dripping windowpane. She looked at the two women holding each other and shook her head. "Um, um, um."

The next day Lorraine was on her way back from the supermarket, and she ran into Kiswana, who was coming out of their building, carrying an armful of books.

"Hi," she greeted Lorraine, "you sure have a full load there."

"Well, we ran out of vegetables last night." Lorraine smiled. "So I picked up a little extra today."

"You know, we haven't seen you at the meetings lately. Things are really picking up. There's going to be a block party next weekend, and we can use all the help we can get."

Lorraine stopped smiling. "Did you really think I'd come back after what happened?"

The blood rushed to Kiswana's face and she stared uncomfortably at the top of her books. "You know, I'm really sorry about that. I should have said something—after all, it was my house—but things just sort of got out of hand so quickly, I'm sorry, I . . ."

"Hey, look, I'm not blaming you or even that woman who made such a fuss. She's just a very sick lady, that's all. Her life must be very unhappy if she has to run around and try to hurt people who haven't done anything to her. But I just didn't want any more trouble, so I felt I ought to stay away."

"But the association is for all of us," Kiswana insisted, "and everyone doesn't feel the way she did. What you do is your own business, not that you're doing anything, anyway. I mean, well, two women or two guys can't live together without people talking. She could be your cousin or sister or something."

"We're not related," Lorraine said quietly.

"Well, good friends then," Kiswana stammered. "Why can't good friends just live together and people mind their own business. And even if you're not friends, even . . . well, whatever." She went on miserably, "It was my house and I'm sorry, I . . ."

Lorraine was kind enough to change the subject for her. "I see you have an armful yourself. You're heading toward the library?"

"No." Kiswana gave her a grateful smile. "I'm taking a few classes on the weekends. My old lady is always on my back about going back to school, so I enrolled at the community college." She was almost apologetic. "But I'm only studying black history and the science of revolution, and I let her know that. But it's enough to keep her quiet."

"I think that's great. You know, I took quite a few courses in black history when I went to school in Detroit."

"Yeah, which ones?"

While they were talking, C. C. Baker and his friends loped up the block. These young men always moved in a pack, or never without two or three. They needed the others continually near to verify their existence. When they stood with their black skin, ninth-grade diplomas, and fifty-word vocabularies in front of the mirror that the world had erected and saw nothing, those other pairs of tight jeans, suede sneakers, and tinted sunglasses imaged nearby proved that they were alive. And if there was life, there could be dreams of that miracle that would one day propel them into the heaven populated by their gods—Shaft and Superfly.[3] While they grew old awaiting that transformation they moved through the streets, insuring that they could at least be heard, if not seen, by blasting their portable cassette players and talking loudly. They continually surnamed each other Man and clutched at their crotches, readying the equipment they deemed necessary to be summoned at any moment into Superfly heaven.

The boys recognized Kiswana because her boyfriend, Abshu, was director of the community center, and Lorraine had been pointed out to them by parents or some other adult who had helped to spread the yellow mist. They spotted the two women talking to each other, and on a cue from C. C., they all slowed as they passed the stoop. C. C. Baker was greatly disturbed by the thought of a Lorraine. He knew of only one way to deal with women other than his mother. Before he had learned exactly how women gave birth, he knew how to please or punish or extract favors from them by the execution of what lay curled behind his fly. It was his lifeline to that part of his being that sheltered his self-respect. And the thought of any woman who lay beyond the length of its power was a threat.

"Hey, Swana, better watch it talkin' to that dyke—she might try to grab a tit!" C. C. called out.

"Yeah, Butch, why don't ya join the WACS[4] and really have a field day."

Lorraine's arms tightened around her packages, and she tried to push past Kiswana and go into the building. "I'll see you later."

"No, wait." Kiswana blocked her path. "Don't let them talk to you like that. They're nothing but a bunch of punks." She called out to the leader, "C. C., why don't you just take your little dusty behind and get out of here. No one was talking to you."

The muscular tan boy spit out his cigarette and squared his shoulders. "I ain't got to do nothin'! And I'm gonna tell Abshu you need a good spankin' for taking up with a lesbo." He looked around at his reflections and preened himself in their approval. "Why don't ya come over here and I'll show ya what a real man can do." He cupped his crotch.

Kiswana's face reddened with anger. "From what I heard about you, C. C., I wouldn't even feel it."

His friends broke up with laughter, and when he turned around to them, all he could see mirrored was respect for the girl who had beat him at the dozens.[5] Lorraine smiled at the absolutely lost look on his face. He curled his lips back into a snarl and tried to regain lost ground by attacking what instinct told him was the weaker of the two.

3. Larger-than-life heroes of 1970s black action films.
4. Women's Army Corps.

5. Informal but serious game of mutual insult, the playing of which offers the possibility of proving one's verbal superiority over an opponent.

"Ya laughing at me, huh, freak? I oughta come over there and stick my fist in your cunt-eatin' mouth!"

"You'll have to come through me first, so just try it." Kiswana put her books on the stoop.

"Aw, Man, come on. Don't waste your time." His friends pulled at his arm. "She ain't nothing but a woman."

"I oughta go over there and slap that bitch in her face and teach her a lesson."

"Hey, Man, lay light, lay light," one whispered in his ear. "That's Abshu's woman, and that big dude don't mind kickin' ass."

C. C. did an excellent job of allowing himself to be reluctantly pulled away from Kiswana, but she wasn't fooled and had already turned to pick up her books. He made several jerky motions with his fist and forefinger at Lorraine.

"I'm gonna remember this, Butch!"

Theresa had watched the entire scene out of the window and had been ready to run out and help Kiswana if the boy had come up on the stoop. That was just like Lorraine to stand there and let someone else take up for her. Well, maybe she'd finally learned her lesson about these ignorant nothings on Brewster Place. They weren't ever going to be accepted by these people, and there was no point in trying.

Theresa left the window and sat on the couch, pretending to be solving a crossword puzzle when Lorraine came in.

"You look a little pale. Were the prices that bad at the store today?"

"No, this heat just drains me. It's hard to believe that we're in the beginning of October." She headed straight for the kitchen.

"Yeah," Theresa said, watching her back intently. "Indian Summer and all that."

"Mmm." Lorraine dumped the bags on the table. "I'm too tired to put these away now. There's nothing perishable in there. I think I'll take some aspirin and lay down."

"Do that," Theresa said, and followed her into the bedroom. "Then you'll be rested for later. Saddle called—he and Byron are throwing a birthday party at the club, and they want us to come over."

Lorraine was looking through the top dresser drawer for her aspirin. "I'm not going over there tonight. I hate those parties."

"You never hated them before." Theresa crossed her arms in the door and stared at Lorraine. "What's so different now?"

"I've always hated them." Lorraine closed the drawer and started searching in the other one. "I just went because you wanted to. They make me sick with all their prancing and phoniness. They're nothing but a couple of fags."

"And we're just a couple of dykes." She spit the words into the air.

Lorraine started as if she'd been slapped. "That's a filthy thing to say, Tee. You can call yourself that if you want to, but I'm not like that. Do you hear me? I'm not!" She slammed the drawer shut.

So she can turn on me but she wouldn't say a word to that scum in the streets, Theresa thought. She narrowed her eyes slowly at Lorraine. "Well, since my friends aren't good enough for the Duchess from Detroit," she said aloud, "I guess you'll go spend another evening with your boyfriend.

But I can tell you right now I saw him pass the window just before you came up the block, and he's already stewed to the gills and just singing away. What do you two do down there in that basement—harmonize? It must get kinda boring for you, he only knows one song."

"Well, at least he's not a sarcastic bitch like some people."

Theresa looked at Lorraine as if she were a stranger.

"And I'll tell you what we do down there. We talk, Theresa—we really, really talk."

"So you and I don't talk?" Theresa's astonishment was turning into hurt. "After five years, you're going to stand there and say that you can talk to some dried-up wino better than you can to me?"

"You and I don't talk, Tee. You talk—Lorraine listens. You lecture—Lorraine takes notes about how to dress and act and have fun. If I don't see things your way, then you shout—Lorraine cries. You seem to get a kick out of making me feel like a clumsy fool."

"That's unfair, Lorraine, and you know it. I can't count the times I've told you to stop running behind people, sniveling to be their friends while they just hurt you. I've always wanted you to show some guts and be independent."

"That's just it, Tee! You wanted me to be independent of other people and look to you for the way I should feel about myself, cut myself off from the world, and join you in some crazy idea about being different. When I'm with Ben, I don't feel any different from anybody else in the world."

"Then he's doing you an injustice," Theresa snapped, "because we are different. And the sooner you learn that, the better off you'll be."

"See, there you go again. Tee the teacher and Lorraine the student, who just can't get the lesson right. Lorraine, who just wants to be a human being—a lousy human being who's somebody's daughter or somebody's friend or even somebody's enemy. But they make me feel like a freak out there, and you try to make me feel like one in here. The only place I've found some peace, Tee, is in that damp ugly basement, where I'm not different."

"Lorraine." Theresa shook her head slowly. "You're a lesbian—do you understand that word?—a butch, a dyke, a lesbo, all those things that kid was shouting. Yes, I heard him! And you can run in all the basements in the world, and it won't change that, so why don't you accept it?"

"I have accepted it!" Lorraine shouted. "I've accepted it all my life, and it's nothing I'm ashamed of. I lost a father because I refused to be ashamed of it—but it doesn't make me any *different* from anyone else in the world."

"It makes you damned different!"

"No!" She jerked open the bottom drawer of her dresser and took out a handful of her underwear. "Do you see this? There are two things that have been a constant in my life since I was sixteen years old—beige bras and oatmeal. The day before I first fell in love with a woman, I got up, had oatmeal for breakfast, put on a beige bra, and went to school. The day after I fell in love with that woman, I got up, had oatmeal for breakfast, and put on a beige bra. I was no different the day before or after that happened, Tee."

"And what did you do when you went to school that next day, Lorraine?

Did you stand around the gym locker and swap stories with the other girls about this new love in your life, huh? While they were bragging about their boyfriends and the fifty dozen ways they had lost their virginity, did you jump in and say, 'Oh, but you should have seen the one I gave it up to last night?' Huh? Did you? Did you?"

Theresa was standing in front of her and shouting. She saw Lorraine's face crumple, but she still kept pushing her.

"You with your beige bras and oatmeal!" She grabbed the clothes from Lorraine's hand and shook them at her. "Why didn't you stand in that locker room and pass around a picture of this great love in your life? Why didn't you take her to the senior prom? Huh? Why? Answer me!"

"Because they wouldn't have understood," Lorraine whispered, and her shoulders hunched over.

"That's right! There go your precious 'theys' again. They wouldn't understand—not in Detroit, not on Brewster Place, not anywhere! And as long as they own the whole damn world, it's them and us, Sister—them and us. And that spells different!"

Lorraine sat down on the bed with her head in her hands, and heavy spasms shook her shoulders and slender back. Theresa stood over her and clenched her hands to keep herself from reaching out and comforting her. Let her cry. She had to smarten up. She couldn't spend the rest of her life in basements, talking to winos and building cardboard worlds that were just going to come crashing down around her ears.

Theresa left the bedroom and sat in the chair by the living room window. She watched the autumn sky darken and evening crystallize over the tops of the buildings while she sat there with the smugness of those who could amply justify their methods by the proof of their victorious ends. But even after seven cigarettes, she couldn't expel the sour taste in her mouth. She heard Lorraine move around in the bedroom and then go into the shower. She finally joined her in the living room, freshly clothed. She had been almost successful in covering the puffiness around her eyes with makeup.

"I'm ready to go to the party. Shouldn't you start getting dressed?"

Theresa looked at the black pumps and the green dress with black print. Something about the way it hung off of Lorraine's body made her feel guilty.

"I've changed my mind. I don't feel up to it tonight." She turned her head back toward the evening sky, as if the answer to their tangled lives lay in its dark face.

"Then I'm going without you." The tone of Lorraine's voice pulled her face unwillingly from the window.

"You won't last ten minutes there alone, so why don't you just sit down and stop it."

"I have to go, Tee." The urgency in her words startled Theresa, and she made a poor attempt of hiding it.

"If I can't walk out of this house without you tonight, there'll be nothing left in me to love you. And I'm trying, Theresa; I'm trying so hard to hold on to that."

Theresa would live to be a very old woman and would replay those words in her mind a thousand times and then invent a thousand different things she could have said or done to keep the tall yellow woman in the green and black dress from walking out of that door for the last time in her life. But tonight she was a young woman and still in search of answers, and she made the fatal mistake that many young women do of believing that what never existed was just cleverly hidden beyond her reach. So Theresa said nothing to Lorraine that night, because she had already sadly turned her face back to the evening sky in a mute appeal for guidance.

Lorraine left the smoky and noisy club and decided to walk home to stretch the time. She had been ready to leave from the moment she had arrived, especially after she saw the disappointment on everyone's face when she came in without Theresa. Theresa was the one who loved to dance and joke and banter with them and could keep a party going. Lorraine sat in a corner, holding one drink all night and looking so intimidated by the people who approached her that she killed even the most persistent attempts at conversation. She sensed a mood of quiet hysteria and self-mockery in that club, and she fled from it, refusing to see any possible connection with her own existence.

She had stuck it out for an hour, but that wasn't long enough. Tee would still be up, probably waiting at that window, so certain that she would be returning soon. She thought about taking a bus downtown to a movie, but she really didn't want to be alone. If she only had some friends in this city. It was then that she thought about Ben. She could come up the street in back of Brewster Place and cut through the alley to his apartment. Even if Tee was still in that window, she couldn't see that far down the block. She would just tap lightly on his door, and if he wasn't too drunk to hear her, then he wouldn't be too far gone to listen tonight. And she had such a need to talk to someone, it ached within her.

Lorraine smelled the claw-edged sweetness of the marijuana in the shadowy alley before she had gone more than fifty feet in. She stopped and peered through the leaden darkness toward the end and saw no one. She took a few more cautious steps and stopped to look again. There was still no one. She knew she would never reach Brewster like this; each time she stopped her senseless fears would multiply, until it would be impossible to get through them to the other side. There was no one there, and she would just have to walk through quickly to prove this to her pounding heart.

When she heard the first pair of soft thuds behind her, she willed herself not to stop and look back because there was no one there. Another thud and she started walking a little faster to reassure herself of this. The fourth thud started her to running, and then a dark body that had been pressed against the shadowy building swung into her path so suddenly she couldn't stop in time, and she bumped into it and bounced back a few inches.

"Can't you say excuse me, dyke?" C. C. Baker snarled into her face.

Lorraine saw a pair of suede sneakers flying down behind the face in front of hers and they hit the cement with a dead thump. Her bladder began to loosen, and bile worked its way up into the tightening throat as she realized what she must have heard before. They had been hiding up on the wall, watching her come up that back street, and they had waited. The face pushed itself so close to hers that she could look into the flared nostrils and smell the decomposing food caught in its teeth.

"Ain't you got no manners? Stepping on my foot and not saying you sorry?"

She slowly backed away from the advancing face, her throat working convulsively. She turned to run in the direction of the formless thuds behind her. She hadn't really seen them so they weren't there. The four bodies that now linked themselves across the alley hit her conscious mind like a fist, and she cried out, startled. A hand shot itself around her mouth, and her neck was jerked back while a hoarse voice whispered in her ear.

"You ain't got nothing to say now, huh? Thought you was real funny laughing at me in the streets today? Let's see if you gonna laugh now, dyke!" C. C. forced her down on her knees while the other five boys began to close in silently.

She had stepped into the thin strip of earth that they claimed as their own. Bound by the last building on Brewster and a brick wall, they reigned in that unlit alley like dwarfed warrior-kings. Born with the appendages of power, circumcised by a guillotine, and baptized with the steam from a million nonreflective mirrors, these young men wouldn't be called upon to thrust a bayonet into an Asian farmer, target a torpedo, scatter their iron seed from a B-52 into the wound of the earth, point a finger to move a nation, or stick a pole into the moon—and they knew it. They only had that three-hundred-foot alley to serve them as stateroom, armored tank, and executioner's chamber. So Lorraine found herself, on her knees, surrounded by the most dangerous species in existence—human males with an erection to validate in a world that was only six feet wide.

"I'm gonna show you somethin' I bet you never seen before." C. C. took the back of her head, pressed it into the crotch of his jeans, and jerkily rubbed it back and forth while his friends laughed. "Yeah, now don't that feel good? See, that's what you need. Bet after we get through with you, you ain't never gonna wanna kiss no more pussy."

He slammed his kneecap into her spine and her body arched up, causing his nails to cut into the side of her mouth to stifle her cry. He pushed her arched body down onto the cement. Two of the boys pinned her arms, two wrenched open her legs, while C. C. knelt between them and pushed up her dress and tore at the top of her pantyhose. Lorraine's body was twisting in convulsions of fear that they mistook for resistance, and C. C. brought his fist down into her stomach.

"Better lay the fuck still, cunt, or I'll rip open your guts."

The impact of his fist forced air into her constricted throat, and she worked her sore mouth, trying to form the one word that had been clawing inside of her—"Please." It squeezed through her paralyzed vocal cords and fell lifelessly at their feet. Lorraine clamped her eyes shut and, using all of the strength left within her, willed it to rise again.

"Please."

The sixth boy took a dirty paper bag lying on the ground and stuffed it into her mouth. She felt a weight drop on her spread body. Then she opened her eyes and they screamed and screamed into the face above hers—the face that was pushing this tearing pain inside of her body. The screams tried to break through her corneas out into the air, but the tough rubbery flesh sent them vibrating back into her brain, first shaking lifeless the cells that nurtured her memory. Then the cells went that contained her powers of taste and smell. The last that were screamed to death were those that supplied her with the ability to love—or hate.

Lorraine was no longer conscious of the pain in her spine or stomach. She couldn't feel the skin that was rubbing off of her arms from being pressed against the rough cement. What was left of her mind was centered around the pounding motion that was ripping her insides apart. She couldn't tell when they changed places and the second weight, then the third and fourth, dropped on her—it was all one continuous hacksawing of torment that kept her eyes screaming the only word she was fated to utter again and again for the rest of her life. Please.

Her thighs and stomach had become so slimy from her blood and their semen that the last two boys didn't want to touch her, so they turned her over, propped her head and shoulders against the wall, and took her from behind. When they had finished and stopped holding her up, her body fell over like an unstringed puppet. She didn't feel her split rectum or the patches in her skull where her hair had been torn off by grating against the bricks. Lorraine lay in that alley only screaming at the moving pain inside of her that refused to come to rest.

"Hey, C. C., what if she remembers that it was us?"

"Man, how she gonna prove it? Your dick ain't got no fingerprints." They laughed and stepped over her and ran out of the alley.

Lorraine lay pushed up against the wall on the cold ground with her eyes staring straight up into the sky. When the sun began to warm the air and the horizon brightened, she still lay there, her mouth crammed with paper bag, her dress pushed up under her breasts, her bloody pantyhose hanging from her thighs. She would have stayed there forever and have simply died from starvation or exposure if nothing around her had moved. There was no wind that morning, so the tin cans, soda bottles, and loose papers were still. There wasn't even a stray cat or dog rummaging in the garbage cans for scraps. There was nothing moving that early October morning—except Ben.

Ben had come out of the basement and was sitting in his usual place on an old garbage can he had pushed up against the wall. And he was singing and swaying while taking small sips from the pint bottle he kept in his back pocket. Lorraine looked up the alley and saw the movement by the wall. Side to side. Side to side. Almost in perfect unison with the sawing pain that kept moving inside of her. She crept up on her knees, making small grunting sounds like a wounded animal. As she crawled along the alley, her hand brushed a loose brick, and she clawed her fingers around it and dragged it along the ground toward the movement on Brewster Place. Side to side. Side to side.

Mattie left her bed, went to the bathroom, and then put on her tea kettle. She always got up early, for no reason other than habit. The timing mechanism that had been embedded in her on the farm wasn't aware that she now lived in a city. While her coffee water was heating up, she filled a pitcher to water her plants. When she leaned over the plants at the side of the apartment, she saw the body crawling up the alley. She raised the window and leaned out just to be sure the morning light wasn't playing tricks with her eyes. "Merciful Jesus!" She threw a coat over her nightgown, slipped on a pair of shoes, and tried to make her arthritic legs hurry down the steps.

Lorraine was getting closer to the movement. She raised herself up on her bruised and stiffened knees, and the paper bag fell out of her mouth. She supported herself by sliding against the wall, limping up the alley toward the movement while clawing her brick and mouthing her silent word. Side to side. Side to side. Lorraine finally reached the motion on top of the garbage can. Ben slowly started to focus her through his burgundy fog, and just as he opened his lips to voice the words that had formed in his brain—"My God, child, what happened to you?"—the brick smashed down into his mouth. His teeth crumbled into his throat and his body swung back against the wall. Lorraine brought the brick down again to stop the moving head, and blood shot out of his ears, splattering against the can and bottom of the wall. Mattie's screams went ricocheting in Lorraine's head, and she joined them with her own as she brought the brick down again, splitting his forehead and crushing his temple, rendering his brains just a bit more useless than hers were now.

Arms grabbed her around the waist, and the brick was knocked from her hand. The movement was everywhere. Lorraine screamed and clawed at the motions that were running and shouting from every direction in the universe. A tall yellow woman in a bloody green and black dress, scraping at the air, crying, "Please. Please."

1982

TERRY McMILLAN
b. 1951

Terry McMillan's phenomenal success has been achieved by talent, hard work, and classic American publicity and promotion. Not only have McMillan's novels come to the center of the U.S. publishing and bookselling industry, but McMillan herself has become something of a celebrity, in many ways the apotheosis of the renaissance in writing by African American women.

Born in Port Huron, Michigan, in 1951, to working-class parents, McMillan went on to earn a bachelor's degree in journalism at the University of California, Berkeley, in 1978, and a graduate degree from the film school of Columbia University. McMillan, who had published her first short story while at Berkeley, published her first novel, *Mama*, in 1987 and quickly undertook the promotion of the book herself, contacting bookstores, colleges and universities, and other sales outlets. Not surprisingly, her efforts were well rewarded. *Mama*, the moving story of a mother of five children who must negotiate the difficulties of family life at the same time that she creates a life for herself, was reviewed positively; McMillan gave many well-attended readings; and in less than two months, the book had been reprinted three times. *Disappearing Act* (1989) continued McMillan's success. In her second novel she narrates the love affair between a black man and a black woman. Unusual in being told from the point of view of both protagonists, *Disappearing Act,* like *Mama,* maintains a quick pace and offers healthy doses of humor. In 1990 McMillan edited and published *Breaking Ice: An Anthology of Contemporary African American Fiction,* partly to redress what she saw as the consistent exclusion of such writing from other collections of the time.

To date McMillan's biggest success has been *Waiting to Exhale* (1992), her frank and occasionally hilarious treatment of four black women and their relationships with men: lovers, husbands, sons. An enormous best-seller, one that novelist Charles Johnson called "a tough love letter to black males everywhere," *Waiting to Exhale* became a successful movie in 1995, and McMillan moved even farther on her way to literary celebrityhood.

In 1996 McMillan published *How Stella Got Her Groove Back.* Truly a force to be reckoned with, Terry McMillan and her honest, entertaining, and intelligent chronicles of the complex lives of middle-class black women have widened the readership for novels by and about African American women and have upped the ante for those writing after her. As in *Quilting on the Rebound,* the story anthologized here, McMillan's focus in no way ignores life's difficulties but it also in no way neglects the possibility of a rebound, of "getting one's groove back."

Quilting on the Rebound

Five years ago, I did something I swore I'd never do—went out with someone I worked with. We worked for a large insurance company in L.A. Richard was a senior examiner and I was a chief underwriter. The first year, we kept it a secret, and not because we were afraid of jeopardizing our jobs. Richard was twenty-six and I was thirty-four. By the second year, everybody knew it anyway and nobody seemed to care. We'd been going out for three years when I realized that this relationship was going nowhere. I probably could've dated him for the rest of my life and he'd have been satisfied. Richard had had a long reputation for being a Don Juan of sorts, until he met me. I cooled his heels. His name was also rather ironic, because he looked like a black Richard Gere. The fact that I was older than he was made him feel powerful in a sense, and he believed that he could do for me what men my own age apparently couldn't. But that wasn't true. He was a challenge. I wanted to see if I could make his head and heart turn 360 degrees, and I did. I blew his young mind in bed, but he also charmed me into loving him until I didn't care how old he was.

Richard thought I was exotic because I have slanted eyes, high cheekbones, and full lips. Even though my mother is Japanese and my dad is black, I inherited most of his traits. My complexion is dark, my hair is nappy, and I'm five-six. I explained to Richard that I was proud of both of my heritages, but he has insisted on thinking of me as being mostly Japanese. Why, I don't know. I grew up in a black neighborhood in L.A., went to Dorsey High School—which was predominantly black, Asian, and Hispanic—and most of my friends are black. I've never even considered going out with anyone other than black men.

My mother, I'm glad to say, is not the stereotypical passive Japanese wife either. She's been the head nurse in Kaiser's cardiovascular unit for over twenty years, and my dad has his own landscaping business, even though he should've retired years ago. My mother liked Richard and his age didn't bother her, but she believed that if a man loved you he should marry you. Simple as that. On the other hand, my dad didn't care who I married just as long as it was soon. I'll be the first to admit that I was a spoiled-rotten brat because my mother had had three miscarriages before she finally had me and I was used to getting everything I wanted. Richard was no exception. "Give him the ultimatum," my mother had said, if he didn't propose by my thirty-eighth birthday.

But I didn't have to. I got pregnant.

We were having dinner at an Italian restaurant when I told him. "You want to get married, don't you?" he'd said.

"Do you?" I asked.

He was picking through his salad and then he jabbed his fork into a tomato. "Why not, we were headed in that direction anyway, weren't we?" He did not eat his tomato but laid his fork down on the side of the plate.

I swallowed a spoonful of my clam chowder, then asked, "Were we?"

"You know the answer to that. But hell, now's as good a time as any. We're both making good money, and sometimes all a man needs is a little incentive." He didn't look at me when he said this, and his voice was strained. "Look," he said, "I've had a pretty shitty day, haggling with one of the adjusters, so forgive me if I don't appear to be boiling over with excitement. I am happy about this. Believe me, I am," he said, and picked up a single piece of lettuce with a different fork and put it into his mouth.

My parents were thrilled when I told them, but my mother was nevertheless suspicious. "Funny how this baby pop up, isn't it?" she'd said.

"What do you mean?"

"You know exactly what I mean. I hope baby doesn't backfire."

I ignored what she'd just said. "Will you help me make my dress?" I asked.

"Yes," she said. "But we must hurry."

My parents—who are far from well off—went all out for this wedding. My mother didn't want anyone to know I was pregnant, and to be honest, I didn't either. The age difference was enough to handle as it was. Close to three hundred people had been invited, and my parents had spent an astronomical amount of money to rent a country club in Marina Del Rey. "At your age," my dad had said, "I hope you'll only be doing this once." Richard's parents insisted on taking care of the caterer and the liquor, and my parents didn't object. I paid for the cake.

About a month before the Big Day, I was meeting Richard at the jeweler because he'd picked out my ring and wanted to make sure I liked it. He was so excited, he sounded like a little boy. It was beautiful, but I told him he didn't have to spend four thousand dollars on my wedding ring. "You're worth it," he'd said and kissed me on the cheek. When we got to the parking lot, he opened my door and stood there staring at me. "Four more weeks," he said, "and you'll be my wife." He didn't smile when he said it, but closed the door and walked around to the driver's side and got in. He'd driven four whole blocks without saying a word and his knuckles were almost white because of how tight he was holding the steering wheel.

"Is something wrong, Richard?" I asked him.

"What would make you think that?" he said. Then he laid on the horn because someone in front of us hadn't moved and the light had just barely turned green.

"Richard, we don't have to go through with this, you know."

"I know we don't *have* to, but it's the right thing to do, and I'm going to do it. So don't worry, we'll be happy."

But I *was* worried.

I'd been doing some shopping at the Beverly Center when I started getting these stomach cramps while I was going up the escalator, so I decided to sit down. I walked over to one of the little outside cafés and I felt something lock inside my stomach, so I pulled out a chair. Moments later my skirt felt like it was wet. I got up and looked at the chair and saw a small red puddle. I sat back down and started crying. I didn't know what to do. Then a punkish-looking girl came over and asked if I was okay. "I'm pregnant, and I've just bled all over this chair," I said.

"Can I do something for you? Do you want me to call an ambulance?" She was popping chewing gum and I wanted to snatch it out of her mouth.

By this time at least four other women had gathered around me. The punkish-looking girl told them about my condition. One of the women said, "Look, let's get her to the rest room. She's probably having a miscarriage."

Two of the women helped me up and all four of them formed a circle around me, then slowly led me to the ladies' room. I told them that I wasn't in any pain, but they were still worried. I closed the stall door, pulled down two toilet seat covers, and sat down. I felt as if I had to go, so I pushed. Something plopped out of me and it made a splash. I was afraid to get up but I got up and looked at this large dark mass that looked like liver. I put my hand over my mouth because I knew that was my baby.

"Are you okay in there?"

I went to open my mouth, but the joint in my jawbone clicked and my mouth wouldn't move.

"Are you okay in there, miss?"

I wanted to answer, but I couldn't.

"Miss." I heard her banging on the door.

I felt my mouth loosen. "It's gone," I said. "It's gone."

"Honey, open the door," someone said, but I couldn't move. Then I heard myself say, "I think I need a sanitary pad." I was staring into the toilet bowl when I felt a hand hit my leg. "Here, are you sure you're okay in there?"

"Yes," I said. Then I flushed the toilet with my foot and watched my future disappear. I put the pad on and reached inside my shopping bag, pulled out a Raiders sweatshirt I'd bought for Richard, and tied it around my waist. When I came out, all of the women were waiting for me. "Would you like us to call your husband? Where are you parked? Do you feel light-headed, dizzy?"

"No, I'm fine, really, and thank you so much for your concern. I appreciate it, but I feel okay."

I drove home in a daze and when I opened the door to my condo, I was glad I lived alone. I sat on the couch from one o'clock to four o'clock without moving. When I finally got up, it felt as if I'd only been there for five minutes.

I didn't tell Richard. I didn't tell anybody. I bled for three days before I went to see my doctor. He scolded me because I'd gotten some kind of an infection and had to be prescribed antibiotics, then he sent me to the outpatient clinic, where I had to have a D & C.

Two weeks later, I had a surprise shower and got enough gifts to fill the housewares department at Bullock's. One of my old girlfriends, Gloria, came all the way from Phoenix, and I hadn't seen her in three years. I hardly recognized her, she was as big as a house. "You don't know how lucky you are, girl," she'd said to me. "I wish I could be here for the wedding but Tarik is having his sixteenth birthday party and I am not leaving a bunch of teenagers alone in my house. Besides, I'd probably have a heart attack watching you or anybody else walk down an aisle in white. Come to think of it, I can't even remember the last time I went to a wedding."

"Me either," I said.

"I know you're gonna try to get pregnant in a hurry, right?" she asked, holding out her wrist with the watch on it.

I tried to smile. "I'm going to work on it," I said.

"Well, who knows?" Gloria said, laughing. "Maybe one day you'll be coming to my wedding. We may both be in wheelchairs, but you never know."

"I'll be there," I said.

All Richard said when he saw the gifts was, "What are we going to do with all this stuff? Where are we going to put it?"

"It depends on where we're going to live," I said, which we hadn't even talked about. My condo was big enough and so was his apartment.

"It doesn't matter to me, but I think we should wait a while before buying a house. A house is a big investment, you know. Thirty years." He gave me a quick look.

"Are you getting cold feet?" I blurted out.

"No, I'm not getting cold feet. It's just that in two weeks we're going to be man and wife, and it takes a little getting used to the idea, that's all."

"Are you having doubts about the idea of it?"

"No."

"Are you sure?"

"I'm sure," he said.

I didn't stop bleeding, so I took some vacation time to relax and finish my dress. I worked on it day and night and was doing all the beadwork by hand. My mother was spending all her free time at my place trying to make sure everything was happening on schedule. A week before the Big Day I was trying on my gown for the hundredth time when the phone rang. I thought it might be Richard, since he hadn't called me in almost forty-eight hours, and when I finally called him and left a message, he still hadn't returned my call. My father said this was normal.

"Hello," I said.

"I think you should talk to Richard." It was his mother.

"About what?" I asked.

"He's not feeling very well," was all she said.

"What's wrong with him?"

"I don't know for sure. I think it's his stomach."

"Is he sick?"

"I don't know. Call him."

"I did call him but he hasn't returned my call."

"Keep trying," she said.

So I called him at work, but his secretary said he wasn't there. I called him at home and he wasn't there either, so I left another message and for the next three hours I was a wreck, waiting to hear from him. I knew something was wrong.

I gave myself a facial, a manicure, and a pedicure and watched Oprah Winfrey while I waited by the phone. It didn't ring. My mother was downstairs hemming one of the bridesmaid's dresses. I went down to get myself a glass of wine. "How you feeling, Marilyn Monroe?" she asked.

"What do you mean, how am I feeling? I'm feeling fine."

"All I meant was you awful lucky with no morning sickness or anything, but I must say, hormones changing because you getting awfully irritating."

"I'm sorry, Ma."

"It's okay. I had jitters too."

I went back upstairs and closed my bedroom door, then went into my bathroom. I put the wineglass on the side of the bathtub and decided to take a bubble bath in spite of the bleeding. I must have poured half a bottle of Secreti in. The water was too hot but I got in anyway. Call, dammit, call. Just then the phone rang and scared me half to death. I was hyperventilating and couldn't say much except, "Hold on a minute," while I caught my breath.

"Marilyn?" Richard was saying. "Marilyn?" But before I had a chance to answer he blurted out what must have been on his mind all along. "Please don't be mad at me, but I can't do this. I'm not ready. I wanted to do the right thing, but I'm only twenty-nine years old. I've got my whole life ahead of me. I'm not ready to be a father yet. I'm not ready to be anybody's husband either, and I'm scared. Everything is happening too fast. I know you think I'm being a coward, and you're probably right. But I've been having nightmares, Marilyn. Do you hear me, nightmares about being imprisoned. I haven't been able to sleep through the night. I doze off and wake up dripping wet. And my stomach. It's in knots. Believe me, Marilyn, it's not that I don't love you because I do. It's not that I don't care about the baby, because I do. I just can't do this right now. I can't make this kind of commitment right now. I'm sorry. Marilyn? Marilyn, are you still there?"

I dropped the portable phone in the bathtub and got out.

My mother heard me screaming and came tearing into the room. "What happened?"

I was dripping wet and ripping the pearls off my dress but somehow I managed to tell her.

"He come to his senses," she said. "This happen a lot. He just got cold feet, but give him day or two. He not mean it."

Three days went by and he didn't call. My mother stayed with me and did everything she could to console me, but by that time I'd already flushed the ring down the toilet.

"I hope you don't lose baby behind this," she said.

"I've already lost the baby," I said.

"What?"

"A month ago."

Her mouth was wide open. She found the sofa with her hand and sat down. "Marilyn," she said and let out an exasperated sigh.

"I couldn't tell anybody."

"Why not tell somebody? Why not me, your mother?"

"Because I was too scared."

"Scared of what?"

"That Richard might change his mind."

"Man love you, dead baby not change his mind."

"I was going to tell him after we got married."

"I not raise you to be dishonest."

"I know."

"No man in world worth lying about something like this. How could you?"

"I don't know."

"I told you it backfire, didn't I?"

For weeks I couldn't eat or sleep. At first, all I did was think about what was wrong with me. I was too old. For him. No. He didn't care about my age. It was the gap in my teeth, or my slight overbite, from all those years I used to suck my thumb. But he never mentioned anything about it and I was really the only one who seemed to notice. I was flat-chested. I had cellulite. My ass was square instead of round. I wasn't exciting as I used to be in bed. No. I was still good in bed, that much I did know. I couldn't cook. I was a terrible housekeeper. That was it. If you couldn't cook and keep a clean house, what kind of wife would you make?

I had to make myself stop thinking about my infinite flaws, so I started quilting again. I was astonished at how radiant the colors were that I was choosing, how unconventional and wild the patterns were. Without even realizing it, I was fusing Japanese and African motifs and was quite excited by the results. My mother was worried about me, even though I had actually stopped bleeding for two whole weeks. Under the circumstances, she thought that my obsession with quilting was not normal, so she forced me to go to the doctor. He gave me some kind of an antidepressant, which I refused to take. I told him I was not depressed, I was simply hurt. Besides, a pill wasn't any antidote or consolation for heartache.

I began to patronize just about every fabric store in downtown Los Angeles, and while I listened to the humming of my machine, and concentrated on designs that I couldn't believe I was creating, it occurred to me that I wasn't suffering from heartache at all. I actually felt this incredible sense of relief. As if I didn't have to anticipate anything else happening that was outside of my control. And when I did grieve, it was always because I had lost a child, not a future husband.

I also heard my mother all day long on my phone, lying about some tragedy that had happened and apologizing for any inconvenience it may have caused. And I watched her, bent over at the dining room table, writing hundreds of thank-you notes to the people she was returning gifts to. She even signed my name. My father wanted to kill Richard. "He was too young, and he wasn't good enough for you anyway," he said. "This is really a blessing in disguise."

I took a leave of absence from my job because there was no way in hell I could face those people, and the thought of looking at Richard infuriated me. I was not angry at him for not marrying me, I was angry at him for not being honest, for the way he handled it all. He even had the nerve to come over without calling. I had opened the door but wouldn't let him inside. He was nothing but a little pipsqueak. A handsome, five-foot-seven-inch pipsqueak.

"Marilyn, look, we need to talk."

"About what?"

"Us. The baby."

"There is no baby."

"What do you mean, there's no baby?"

"It died."

"You mean you got rid of it?"

"No, I lost it."

"I'm sorry, Marilyn," he said and put his head down. How touching, I thought. "This is all my fault."

"It's not your fault, Richard."

"Look. Can I come in?"

"For what?"

"I want to talk. I need to talk to you."

"About what?"

"About us."

"Us?"

"Yes, us. I don't want it to be over between us. I just need more time, that's all."

"Time for what?"

"To make sure this is what I want to do."

"Take all the time you need," I said and slammed the door in his face. He rang the buzzer again, but I just told him to get lost and leave me alone.

I went upstairs and sat at my sewing machine. I turned the light on, then picked up a piece of purple and terra-cotta cloth. I slid it under the pressure foot and dropped it. I pressed down on the pedal and watched the needle zigzag. The stitches were too loose so I tightened the tension. Richard is going to be the last in a series of mistakes I've made when it comes to picking a man. I've picked the wrong one too many times, like a bad habit that's too hard to break. I haven't had the best of luck when it comes to keeping them either, and to be honest, Richard was the one who lasted the longest.

When I got to the end of the fabric, I pulled the top and bobbin threads together and cut them on the thread cutter. Then I bent down and picked up two different pieces. They were black and purple. I always want what I can't have or what I'm not supposed to have. So what did I do? Created a pattern of choosing men that I knew would be a challenge. Richard's was his age. But the others—all of them from Alex to William—were all afraid of something, namely, committing to one woman. All I wanted to do was seduce them hard enough—emotionally, mentally, and physically—so they wouldn't even be aware that they were committing to anything. I just wanted them to crave me, and no one else but me. I wanted to be their healthiest addiction. But it was a lot harder to do than I thought. What I found out was that men are a hard nut to crack.

But some of them weren't. When I was in my late twenties, early thirties—before I got serious and realized I wanted a long-term relationship—I'd had at least twenty different men fall in love with me, but of course these were the ones I didn't want. They were the ones who after a few dates or one rousing night in bed, ordained themselves my "man" or were too quick to want to marry me, and even some considered me their "property." When it was clear that I was dealing with a different species of man, a hungry element, before I got in too deep, I'd tell them almost immediately that I hope they wouldn't mind my being bisexual or my being unfaithful because I was in no hurry to settle down with one man, or that I had a tendency of always falling for my man's friends. Could they tolerate that? I even went so far as to tell them that I hoped having herpes wouldn't cause a problem, that I wasn't really all that trustworthy because I was a habitual liar, and that if they wanted the whole truth they should find themselves another woman. I told them that I didn't even think I was good enough for them, and they should do themselves a favor, find a woman who's truly worthy of having such a terrific man.

I had it down to a science, but by the time I met Richard, I was tired of lying and conniving. I was sick of the games. I was whipped, really, and allowed myself to relax and be vulnerable because I knew I was getting old.

When Gloria called to see how my honeymoon went, I told her the truth about everything. She couldn't believe it. "Well, I thought I'd heard 'em all, but this one takes the cake. How you holding up?"

"I'm hanging in there."

"This is what makes you want to castrate a man."

"Not really, Gloria."

"I know. But you know what I mean. Some of them have a lot of nerve, I swear they do. But really, Marilyn, how are you feeling for real, baby?"

"I'm getting my period every other week, but I'm quilting again, which is a good sign."

"First of all, take your behind back to that doctor and find out why you're still bleeding like this. And, honey, making quilts is no consolation for a broken heart. It sounds like you could use some R and R. Why don't you come visit me for a few days?"

I looked around my room, which had piles and piles of cloth and half-sewn quilts, from where I'd changed my mind. Hundreds of different-colored threads were all over the carpet, and the satin stitch I was trying out wasn't giving me the effect I thought it would. I could use a break, I thought. I could. "You know what?" I said. "I think I will."

"Good, and bring me one of those tacky quilts. I don't have anything to snuggle up with in the winter, and contrary to popular belief, it does get cold here come December."

I liked Phoenix and Tempe, but I fell in love with Scottsdale. Not only was it beautiful but I couldn't believe how inexpensive it was to live in the entire area, which was all referred to as the Valley. I have to thank Gloria for being such a lifesaver. She took me to her beauty salon and gave me a whole new look. She chopped off my hair, and one of the guys in her shop showed me how to put on my makeup in a way that would further enhance what assets he insisted I had.

We drove to Tucson, to Canyon Ranch for what started out as a simple Spa Renewal Day. But we ended up spending three glorious days and had the works. I had an herbal wrap, where they wrapped my entire body in hot thin linen that had been steamed. Then they rolled me up in flannel blankets and put a cold washcloth on my forehead. I sweated in the dark for a half hour. Gloria didn't do this because she said she was claustrophobic and didn't want to be wrapped up in anything where she couldn't move. I had a deep-muscle and shiatsu massage on two different days. We steamed. We Jacuzzied. We both had a mud facial, and then this thing called aromatherapy—where they put distilled essences from flowers and herbs on your face and you look like a different person when they finish. On the last day, we got this Persian Body Polish where they actually buffed our skin with crushed pearl creams, sprayed us with some kind of herbal spray, then used an electric brush to make us tingle. We had our hands and feet moisturized and put in heated gloves and booties, and by the time we left, we couldn't believe we were the same women.

In Phoenix, Gloria took me to yet another resort where we listened to live music. We went to see a stupid movie and I actually laughed. Then we went on a two-day shopping spree and I charged whatever I felt like. I even bought her son a pair of eighty-dollar sneakers, and I'd only seen him twice in my life.

I felt like I'd gotten my spirit back, so when I got home, I told my parents I'd had it with the smog, the traffic, the gangs, and L.A. in general. My mother said, "You cannot run from heartache," but I told her I wasn't running from anything. I put my condo on the market, and in less than a month it sold for four times what I paid for it. I moved in with my mother and father, asked for a job transfer for health reasons, and when it came through, three months later, I moved to Scottsdale.

The town house I bought feels like a house. It's twice the size of the one I had and cost less than half of what I originally spent. My complex is pretty standard for Scottsdale. It has two pools and four tennis courts. It also has vaulted ceilings, wall-to-wall carpet, two fireplaces, and a garden bathtub with a Jacuzzi in it. The kitchen has an island in the center and I've got a 180-degree view of Phoenix and mountains. It also has three bedrooms. One I sleep in, one I use for sewing, and the other is for guests.

I made close to forty thousand dollars after I sold my condo, so I sent four to my parents because the money they'd put down for the wedding was nonrefundable. They really couldn't afford that kind of loss. The rest I put in an IRA and CDs until I could figure out something better to do with it.

I hated my new job. I had to accept a lower-level position and less money, which didn't bother me all that much at first. The office, however, was much smaller and full of rednecks who couldn't stand the thought of a black woman working over them. I was combing the classifieds, looking for a comparable job, but the job market in Phoenix is nothing close to what it is in L.A.

But thank God Gloria's got a big mouth. She'd been boasting to all of her clients about my quilts, had even hung the one I'd given her on the wall at the shop, and the next thing I know I'm getting so many orders I couldn't keep up with them. That's when she asked me why didn't I consider opening my own shop? That never would've occurred to me, but what did I have to lose?

She introduced me to Bernadine, a friend of hers who was an accountant. Bernadine in turn introduced me to a good lawyer, and he helped me draw up all the papers. Over the next four months, she helped me devise what turned out to be a strong marketing and advertising plan. I rented an 800-square-foot space in the same shopping center where Gloria's shop is, and opened Quiltworks, Etc.

It wasn't long before I realized I needed to get some help, so I hired two seamstresses. They took a lot of the strain off of me, and I was able to take some jewelry-making classes and even started selling small pieces in the shop. Gloria gave me this tacky T-shirt for my thirty-ninth birthday, which gave me the idea to experiment with making them. Because I go overboard in everything I do, I went out and spent a fortune on every color of metallic and acrylic fabric paint they made. I bought one hundred 100-percent cotton heavy-duty men's T-shirts and discovered other uses for sponges, plastic, spray bottles, rolling pins, lace, and even old envelopes. I was having a great time because I'd never felt this kind of excitement and gratification doing anything until now.

I'd been living here a year when I found out that Richard had married another woman who worked in our office. I wanted to hate him, but I didn't. I wanted to be angry, but I wasn't. I didn't feel anything toward him, but I sent him a quilt and a wedding card to congratulate him, just because.

To be honest, I've been so busy with my shop, I haven't even thought about men. I don't even miss having sex unless I really just *think* about it. My libido must be evaporating, because when I *do* think about it, I just make quilts or jewelry or paint T-shirts and the feeling goes away. Some of my best ideas come at these moments.

Basically, I'm doing everything I can to make Marilyn feel good. And at thirty-nine years old my body needs tightening, so I joined a health club and started working out three to four times a week. Once in a while, I babysit for Bernadine, and it breaks my heart when I think about the fact that I don't have a child of my own. Sometimes, Gloria and I go out to hear some music. I frequent most of the major art galleries, go to just about every football and basketball game at Arizona State, and see at *least* one movie a week.

I am rarely bored. Which is why I've decided that at this point in my life,

I really don't care if I ever get married. I've learned that I don't need a man in order to survive, that a man is nothing but an intrusion, and they require too much energy. I don't think they're worth it. Besides, they have too much power, and from what I've seen, they always seem to abuse it. The one thing I *do* have is power over my own life. I like it this way, and I'm not about to give it up for something that may not last.

The one thing I do want is to have a baby. Someone I could love who would love me back with no strings attached. But at thirty-nine, I know my days are numbered. I'd be willing to do it alone, if that's the only way I can have one. But right now, my life is almost full. It's fun, it's secure, and it's safe. About the only thing I'm concerned about these days is whether or not it's time to branch out into leather.

1991

RITA DOVE
b. 1952

Rita Dove is the first African American to be named poet laureate of the United States, an office in which she served from 1993 to 1995, as well as the first African American since Gwendolyn Brooks to be awarded the Pulitzer Prize for poetry. Often seen by critics as speaking for a younger generation of poets, Dove rejected what she perceived to be the narrowness of the 1960s Black Arts movement in favor of a more inclusive sensibility. In a 1991 interview published in *Callaloo*, she asserted her intention to present characters who are seen as individuals, "as persons who have their very individual lives, and whose histories make them react to the world in different ways." Although her work often responds to social injustice, she has declared that

> As an artist, I shun political considerations and racial or gender partiality; for example I would find it a breach of my integrity as a writer to create a character for didactic or propaganda purposes, like concocting a strong black heroine, an idealized so-called role model, just to promote a positive image.

Dove was born in 1952 in Akron, Ohio, to parents who greatly valued education. Her father, Ray A. Dove, was the only sibling among ten children to go to college. Despite being at the top of his class when he received his master's degree, Ray Dove had to work as an elevator operator at Goodyear for a number of years before becoming the first black chemist in the tire and rubber industry. While shielding their children from such discrimination, Ray and Elvira (Hurd) Dove retained their faith in education. Their daughter, Rita, began writing plays and stories at an early age and became interested in writing as a career when a high-school teacher took her to a local writers conference.

The first major recognition of Dove's talent came in 1970 with her invitation to the White House as a Presidential Scholar, an award given to the top one hundred high school seniors each year. A National Achievement Scholar, she enrolled in Miami University in Oxford, Ohio. Following her graduation in 1973, Dove received a Fulbright scholarship to study at Tubingen University in West Germany, a locale that would influence her work. Later she did graduate work at the University of Iowa's Writers Workshop. As early as 1974, her poetry began to appear in major periodicals. In addition to four chapbooks, Dove has published five volumes of poems, a book of short stories, and a novel. *Thomas and Beulah* (1986), Dove's third collection of poetry, was awarded the Pulitzer Prize in poetry, solidifying her reputation and furthering critical interest in her work.

Dove's earliest published volumes were the chapbooks *Ten Poems* (1977) and *The Only Dark Spot in the Sky* (1980), both of which contain poems later reprinted in *The Yellow House on the Corner* (1980). Although some critics saw *The Yellow House* as overly autobiographical, others noted its tight control and discipline. While the volume is concerned with the movement from girlhood to womanhood, Dove avoids a mundane treatment of this topic by her unusual use of biblical imagery, as she imagines the laying on of hands to be a healing through sexuality. Further, in *The Yellow House*, monumental events of history merge with everyday events so that the reader feels the continuity between the private moment and the public happening. Dove's second major volume, *Museum* (1983), mixes autobiographical poems with those that cross cultures. Such poems as *My Father's Telescope* and *Why I Turned Vegetarian* provide family snapshots, while others, especially the travel poems, contrast the personal and the historical. Dove's gathering together of European women as well as women from other parts of the world separates her from the many African American poets whose interests are primarily those of their own communities.

In *Thomas and Beulah*, Dove returned to her own history to present, in narrative verse, the saga of her family. Based loosely on the lives of her maternal grandparents, Thomas and Beulah Hord who lived in Akron, Ohio, *Thomas and Beulah* gracefully compresses personal and social history into two sections: "Mandolin," which contains twenty-three poems and is told from Thomas's perspective, and "Canary in Bloom," which consists of twenty-one poems and is told from Beulah's perspective. Helpful to the reader in interpreting the poems is a chronology, giving a dated guide to the family's myths. In explaining her use of this guide, Dove notes that

> In a certain way it's also a parody on history because private dates are put on equal footing with dates of publicly important happenings. But significant events in the private sphere are rarely written up in history books, although they make up the life-sustaining fabric of humanity.

Further undercutting a monolithic construct of history are Thomas's and Beulah's differing versions of the same events. Nonetheless, the lasting impression of *Thomas and Beulah* is that both parents manage to maintain their goodness despite the struggles they undergo, and that both are able to pass on to their children the value of dignity and the power of the imagination. *Thomas and Beulah* received great praise, with many critics noting Dove's economy of style and the way in which she artfully wedded biography and lyric.

That economy of style is further exhibited in her chapbook *The Other Side of the House* (1988) and in *Grace Notes* (1989). In *Mother Love* (1995), her most recent book of poems, Dove takes her explorations of relationships into the realm of Greek myth. In a series of sonnets, she examines the mother-daughter love between Demeter and Persephone.

In addition to her poetry, Dove has also published *Fifth Sunday* (1985), a collection of eight short stories as well as a novel, *Through the Ivory Gate* (1992). As in her poetry, Dove communicates the story through a remarkable use of concrete detail, especially of color and shape. More important, the novel, like many of Dove's poems, concerns itself with the uncovering of history, as represented by the protagonist Virginia King and her lifelong association with masks, dolls, and puppets.

A prolific writer, Dove has also taught creative writing for more than a decade at various universities, including Arizona State and Tuskegee, and has traveled extensively in Europe, northern Africa, and Israel. In addition to her Pulitzer and laureate elections, she has received a Guggenheim, a Lavan Younger Poets award, and a Walt Whitman award. Currently she is Commonwealth Professor of English at the University of Virginia and lives near Charlottesville with her husband, Fred Viebahn, and their daughter.

David Walker [1] (1785–1830)

Free to travel, he still couldn't be shown how lucky
he was: *They strip and beat and drag us about
like rattlesnakes.* Home on Brattle Street, he took in the sign
on the door of the slop shop. All day at the counter—
white caps, ale-stained pea coats. Compass: needles,   5
eloquent as tuning forks, shivered, pointing north.
Evenings, the ceiling fan sputtered like a second pulse.
Oh Heaven! I am full!! I can hardly move my pen!!!

On the faith of an eye-wink, pamphlets were stuffed
into trouser pockets. Pamphlets transported   10
in the coat linings of itinerant seamen, jackets
ringwormed with salt traded drunkenly to pursers
in the Carolinas, pamphlets ripped out, read aloud:
Men of colour, who are also of sense.
Outrage. Incredulity. Uproar in state legislatures.   15

*We are the most wretched, degraded and abject set
of beings that ever lived since the world began.*
The jewelled canaries in the lecture halls tittered,
pressed his dark hand between their gloves.
Every half-step was no step at all.   20
Every morning, the man on the corner strung a fresh
bunch of boots from his shoulders. "I'm happy!" he said.
"I never want to live any better or happier than
when I can get a-plenty of boots and shoes to clean!"

A second edition. A third.   25
The abolitionist press is *perfectly appalled.*
*Humanity, kindness and the fear of the Lord
does not consist in protecting devils.* A month—
his person (is that all?) found face-down
in the doorway at Brattle Street,   30
his frame slighter than friends remembered.

                                                                          1980

---

1. A Boston dealer in old clothes and a militant abolitionist. His *Appeal in Four Articles* (1829) urged blacks the world over to revolt against their oppressors; when he died mysteriously in June 1830, it was rumored that he had been poisoned.

Parsley[1]

1. The Cane[2] Fields

There is a parrot imitating spring
in the palace, its feathers parsley green.
Out of the swamp the cane appears

to haunt us, and we cut it down. El General
searches for a word; he is all the world   5
there is. Like a parrot imitating spring,

we lie down screaming as rain punches through
and we come up green. We cannot speak an R—
out of the swamp, the cane appears

and then the mountain we call in whispers *Katalina*.[3]   10
The children gnaw their teeth to arrowheads.
There is a parrot imitating spring.

El General has found his word: *perejil*.
Who says it, lives. He laughs, teeth shining
out of the swamp. The cane appears   15

in our dreams, lashed by wind and streaming.
And we lie down. For every drop of blood
there is a parrot imitating spring.
Out of the swamp the cane appears.

2. The Palace

The word the general's chosen is parsley.   20
It is fall, when thoughts turn
to love and death; the general thinks
of his mother, how she died in the fall
and he planted her walking cane at the grave
and it flowered, each spring stolidly forming   25
four-star blossoms. The general

pulls on his boots, he stomps to
her room in the palace, the one without
curtains, the one with a parrot
in a brass ring. As he paces he wonders   30
Who can I kill today. And for a moment
the little knot of screams
is still. The parrot, who has traveled

all the way from Australia in an ivory
cage, is, coy as a widow, practising   35

---

1. On October 2, 1957, Rafael Trujillo (1891–
1961), dictator of the Dominican Republic, ordered 20,000 blacks killed because they could not
pronounce the letter "r" in *perejil*, the Spanish
word for parsley [Dove's note].
2. I.e., sugar cane.
3. Katarina (because "We cannot speak an R").

spring. Ever since the morning
his mother collapsed in the kitchen
while baking skull-shaped candies
for the Day of the Dead,[4] the general
has hated sweets. He orders pastries   40
brought up for the bird; they arrive

dusted with sugar on a bed of lace.
The knot in his throat starts to twitch;
he sees his boots the first day in battle
splashed with mud and urine   45
as a soldier falls at his feet amazed—
how stupid he looked!—at the sound
of artillery. *I never thought it would sing*
the soldier said, and died. Now

the general sees the fields of sugar   50
cane, lashed by rain and streaming.
He sees his mother's smile, the teeth
gnawed to arrowheads. He hears
the Haitians sing without R's
as they swing the great machetes: 55
Katalina, they sing, *Katalina*,

mi madle, mi amol en muelte.[5] God knows
his mother was no stupid woman; she
could roll an R like a queen. Even
a parrot can roll an R! In the bare room   60
the bright feathers arch in a parody
of greenery, as the last pale crumbs
disappear under the blackened tongue. Someone

calls out his name in a voice
so like his mother's, a startled tear   65
splashes the tip of his right boot.
My mother, my love in death.
The general remembers the tiny green sprigs
men of his village wore in their capes
to honor the birth of a son. He will   70
order many, this time, to be killed

for a single, beautiful word.

                                                        1983

---

4. All Soul's Day, November 2. An Aztec festival
for the spirits of the dead that coincides with the
Catholic calendar. In Latin America and the
Caribbean, friends and relatives of the dead move
in procession to cemeteries, bearing candles, flowers, and food, all of which may be shaped to resemble symbols of death, such as skulls or coffins.
5. I.e., *mi madre, mi amor en muerte:* "my mother,
my love in death" (Spanish).

Receiving the Stigmata [1]

There is a way to enter a field
empty-handed, your shoulder
behind you and air tightening.

The kite comes by itself,
a spirit on a fluttering string.   5

Back when people died for
the smallest reasons, there was
always a field to walk into.
Simple men fell to their knees
below the radiant crucifix   10
and held out their palms

in relief. Go into the field
and it will reward. Grace

is a string growing straight
from the hand. Is   15
the hatchet's shadow on the
rippling green.

                                        1983

FROM THOMAS AND BEULAH [1]

The Event

Ever since they'd left the Tennessee ridge
with nothing to boast of
but good looks and a mandolin,

the two Negroes leaning
on the rail of a riverboat   5
were inseparable: Lem plucked

to Thomas' silver falsetto.
But the night was hot and they were drunk.
They spat where the wheel

1. Wounds or marks on a person that resemble the five wounds received by Jesus Christ at the Crucifixion.
1. The story in this sequence of poems begins with Thomas making his way north to Akron, Ohio. He loses his best friend, who, on a drunken dare from Thomas, drowns, leaving behind his mandolin. Thomas carries the instrument with him and eventually hangs it on his parlor wall. He and Beulah (Hebrew for "married one" or "possessed"; in the Bible it refers to the Promised Land) marry and have four daughters. Thomas works at the Goodyear Zeppelin factory (a zeppelin is a cylindrical airship kept aloft by gas). The Depression puts him out of work, so he cleans offices for a living until Goodyear rehires him at the start of World War II. Beulah works in a dress shop and later makes hats. Thomas dies at sixty-three from a heart attack; Beulah dies six years later.

churned mud and moonlight,   10
they called to the tarantulas
down among the bananas

to come out and dance.
You're so fine and mighty; let's see
what you can do, said Thomas, pointing   15

to a tree-capped island.
Lem stripped, spoke easy: *Them's chestnuts,*
I believe. Dove

quick as a gasp. Thomas, dry
on deck, saw the green crown shake   20
as the island slipped

under, dissolved
in the thickening stream.
At his feet

a stinking circle of rags,   25
the half-shell mandolin.
Where the wheel turned the water

gently shirred.[2]

                                                          1986

Motherhood

She dreams the baby's so small she keeps
misplacing it—it rolls from the hutch
and the mouse carries it home, it disappears
with his shirt in the wash.
Then she drops it and it explodes   5
like a watermelon, eyes spitting.

Finally they get to the countryside;
Thomas has it in a sling.
He's strewing rice along the road
while the trees chitter with tiny birds.   10
In the meadow to their right three men
are playing rough with a white wolf. She calls

warning but the wolf breaks free
and she runs, the rattle
rolls into the gully, then she's   15
there and tossing the baby behind her,
listening for its cry as she straddles
the wolf and circles its throat, counting
until her thumbs push through to the earth.

2. Drew together.

White fur seeps red. She is hardly breathing.   20
The small wild eyes
go opaque with confusion and shame, like a child's.

                                                                 1986

Daystar

She wanted a little room for thinking:
but she saw diapers steaming on the line,
a doll slumped behind the door.

So she lugged a chair behind the garage
to sit out the children's naps.   5

Sometimes there were things to watch—
the pinched armor of a vanished cricket,
a floating maple leaf. Other days
she stared until she was assured
when she closed her eyes   10
she'd see only her own vivid blood.

She had an hour, at best, before Liza appeared
pouting from the top of the stairs.
And just *what* was mother doing
out back with the field mice? Why,   15

building a palace. Later
that night when Thomas rolled over and
lurched into her, she would open her eyes
and think of the place that was hers
for an hour—where   20
she was nothing,
pure nothing, in the middle of the day.

                                                                 1986

The Oriental Ballerina

twirls on the tips of a carnation
while the radio scratches out a morning hymn.
Daylight has not ventured as far

as the windows—the walls are still dark,
shadowed with the ghosts   5
of oversized gardenias. The ballerina

pirouettes to the wheeze of the old
rugged cross, she lifts
her shoulders past the edge

of the jewelbox lid. Two pink slippers   10
touch the ragged petals, no one
should have feet that small! In China

they do everything upside down:
this ballerina has not risen but drilled
a tunnel straight to America   15

where the bedrooms of the poor
are papered in vulgar flowers
on a background the color of grease, of

teabags, of cracked imitation walnut veneer.
On the other side of the world   20
they are shedding robes sprigged with

roses, roses drifting with a hiss
to the floor by the bed
as, here, the sun finally strikes the windows

suddenly opaque,   25
noncommital as shields. In this room
is a bed where the sun has gone

walking. Where a straw nods over
the lip of its glass and a hand
reaches for a tissue, crumpling it to a flower.   30

The ballerina had been drilling all night!
She flaunts her skirts like sails,
whirling in a disk so bright,

so rapidly she is standing still.
The sun walks the bed to the pillow   35
and pauses for breath (in the Orient,

breath floats like mist
in the fields), hesitating
at a knotted handkerchief that has slid

on its string and has lodged beneath   40
the right ear which discerns
the most fragile music

where there is none. The ballerina dances
at the end of a tunnel of light,
she spins on her impossible toes—   45

the rest is shadow.
The head on the pillow sees nothing
else, though it feels the sun warming

its cheeks. *There is no China;*
no cross, just the papery kiss   50
of a kleenex above the stink of camphor,

the walls exploding with shabby tutus. . . .

1986

Pastoral

Like an otter, but warm,
she latched onto the shadowy tip
and I watched, diminished
by those amazing gulps. Finished
she let her head loll, eyes   5
unfocused and large: milk-drunk.

I liked afterwards best, lying
outside on a quilt, her new skin
spread out like meringue. I felt then
what a young man must feel   10
with his first love asleep on his breast:
desire, and the freedom to imagine it.

1989

From Mother Love [1]

Persephone Abducted

She cried out for Mama, who did not
hear. She left with a wild eye thrown back,
she left with curses, rage
that withered her features to a hag's.
No one can tell a mother how to act: 5
there are no laws when laws are broken, no names
to call upon. Some say there's nourishment for pain,

and call it Philosophy.
That's for the birds, vulture and hawk,
the large ones who praise   10
the miracle of flight because
they use it so diligently.
She left us singing in the field, oblivious
to all but the ache of our own bent backs.

1995

---

1. This volume of Dove's poetry, from which the
next six poems are taken, examines the dilemmas of
the mother-daughter relationship within the context of the Demeter-Persephone story. In Greek
mythology, Persephone, the daughter of Zeus and
Demeter, was abducted by Pluto, who held her
captive in Hades and allowed her to return each
spring and summer.

Statistic: The Witness

No matter where I turn, she is there
screaming. No matter how
I run, pause to catch a breath—
until I am the one screaming
as the drone of an engine overtakes   5
the afternoon.

I know I should stop looking, do
as my mother says—turn my head
to the wall and tell Jesus—but
I keep remembering things,   10
clearer and smaller: his watch,
his wrist, the two ashen ovals
etched on her upturned sandals.

Now I must walk this faithless earth
which cannot readjust an abyss   15
into flowering meadow.
I will walk until I reach
green oblivion . . . then
I will lie down in its kindness,
in the bottomless lull of her arms.   20

1995

Mother Love

Who can forget the attitude of mothering?
          Toss me a baby and without bothering
to blink I'll catch her, sling him on a hip.
          Any woman knows the remedy for grief
is being needed: duty bugles and we'll   5
          climb out of exhaustion every time,
bare the nipple or tuck in the sheet,
          heat milk and hum at bedside until
they can dress themselves and rise, primed
          for Love or Glory—those one-way mirrors   10
girls peer into as their fledgling heroes slip
          through, storming the smoky battlefield.

So when this kind woman approached at the urging
          of her bouquet of daughters,
(one for each of the world's corners,   15
          one for each of the winds to scatter!)
and offered up her only male child for nursing
          (a smattering of flesh, noisy and ordinary),
I put aside the lavish trousseau of the mourner
          for the daintier comfort of pity: 20
I decided to save him. Each night
          I laid him on the smoldering embers,

sealing his juices in slowly so he might
                be cured to perfection. Oh, I know it
looked damning: at the hearth a muttering crone   25
                bent over a baby sizzling on a spit
as neat as a Virginia ham. Poor human—
                to scream like that, to make me remember.

                                                        1995

Demeter Mourning

Nothing can console me. You may bring silk
to make skin sigh, dispense yellow roses
in the manner of ripened dignitaries.
You can tell me repeatedly
I am unbearable (and I know this):   5
still, nothing turns the gold to corn,
nothing is sweet to the tooth crushing in.

I'll not ask for the impossible;
one learns to walk by walking.
In time I'll forget this empty brimming,   10
I may laugh again at
a bird, perhaps, chucking the nest—
but it will not be happiness,
for I have known that.

                                                        1995

History

Everything's a metaphor, some wise
guy said, and his woman nodded, wisely.
Why was this such a discovery
to him? Why did history
happen only on the outside?   5
She'd watched an embryo track an arc
across her swollen belly from the inside
and knew she'd best
think *knee*, not *tumor* or *burrowing mole*, lest
it emerge a monster. Each craving marks   10
the soul: splashed white upon a temple the dish
of ice cream, coveted, broken in a wink,
or the pickle duplicated just behind the ear. *Every wish
will find its symbol*, the woman thinks.

                                                        1995

Demeter's Prayer to Hades

This alone is what I wish for you: knowledge.
To understand each desire has an edge,
to know we are responsible for the lives
we change. No faith comes without cost,
no one believes without dying.   5
Now for the first time
I see clearly the trail you planted,
what ground opened to waste,
though you dreamed a wealth
of flowers.   10

There are no curses—only mirrors
held up to the souls of gods and mortals.
And so I give up this fate, too.
Believe in yourself,
go ahead—see where it gets you.   15

1995

WALTER MOSLEY

b. 1952

While he has only been publishing for slightly over half a decade, Walter Mosley
has swiftly entered into the company of contemporary American novelists whose
work is expected to last. Even more striking then the speed of his literary arrival,
though, is his chosen vehicle: a series of mystery novels set in postwar Los Angeles
featuring a reluctant black investigator, Easy Rawlins. In American literary history
only three other crime writers—Edgar Allen Poe, inventor of the detective story;
Dashiell Hammett, creator of detectives Sam Spade and the Continental Op; and
Raymond Chandler, whose classic hard-boiled private eye novels featuring Philip
Marlowe are frequently cited as precursors to Mosley's work—have received similar
critical scrutiny as "serious" (as opposed to pure genre) figures. There does exist a
somewhat submerged genre of black crime writing, stretching from Rudolph
Fisher's Harlem-based voodoo novel *The Conjure Man Dies* (1932) to Chester
Himes's Coffin Ed and Gravedigger Jones police procedurals in the 1960s, but
Mosley's books are the first to capture mainstream attention, including appearances
on bestseller lists, film adaptations, and even the enthusiastic endorsement of a sitting president, Bill Clinton. In a real sense he has single-handedly integrated a formerly white literary genre, in the process lending it a new level of moral complexity
and a hard-headed racial realism.

Walter Mosley was born in the South Central section of Los Angeles in 1952 and
was educated in public schools there. His mother, Ella Mosley, is a Bronx-born
Jewish schoolteacher and administrator; his father, Leroy Mosley, was a school custodian who died of cancer in 1993. In his private life Mosley's bi-racial parentage is
not an apparent issue, although miscegenation and mixed parentage do figure
prominently in more than one of his mysteries. Mosley has acknowledged his literary debt to his father, a gifted storyteller who bequeathed to him both the language
and the tales drawn from his own growing up in south Texas and Louisiana. There

are obvious parallels between Leroy Mosley and Easy Rawlins: both grew up in Houston's black Fifth Ward, both were combat veterans of World War II, and both were (or are) mesmerizing narrators. Three of Walter Mosley's novels are dedicated to his father.

Mosley lived a somewhat knockabout existence after graduation from Johnson State College in Vermont in 1977, working as a potter, a caterer, and a computer programmer. He began writing in earnest in the middle 1980s, first poetry, and then fiction at the City College of New York. His first completed novel, *Gone Fishin'*, which is narrated by Easy Rawlins, did not find a publisher. But when he placed Easy in a classic hard-boiled mystery in *Devil in a Blue Dress* (1990), critical and commercial success was quick in coming—as were succeeding volumes—*A Red Death* (1991), *White Butterfly* (1992), *Black Betty* (1994), and *A Little Yellow Dog* (1996). In 1995 he published *R.L.'s Dream*, his first book outside the mystery genre, a blues novel centered around the legendary Robert Johnson. Not surprisingly, Mosley has emerged as an important public figure in the black literary community. His 1996 decision to publish *Gone Fishin'* with a small black-owned press and forego any advance was a widely remarked upon gesture of solidarity with the community of African American writers and publishers.

The Easy Rawlins novels are unique in American crime fiction in a number of respects. For one thing, they unfold in real historical time: *Devil in a Blue Dress* being set in the postwar Los Angeles of 1948, *A Little Yellow Dog* taking place just before the assassination of John F. Kennedy in 1963. The critic R. W. B. Lewis has noted that the novels are less a series than a *saga*, one that recalls William Faulkner's Yoknapatawpha novels in the density with which it peoples and animates its home around South Central L.A. They are also unique in the candor with which they confront racism in American life; when Mosley's black characters collide with white Los Angeles police officers echoes of the 1992 Rodney King beating are impossible to ignore. In no sense, though, are these "protest" novels; the teeming and vibrant community that Mosley creates is full of autonomous and unpredictable characters, not typecast victims.

Their real uniqueness, though—and most lasting literary value—resides in the figure of Easy Rawlins, a man of quicksilver sensibility who must wrestle with his own demons as well as the villains, white and black, whom he encounters in his perambulations around Los Angeles. Mosley has said that his conception of Easy owes much to the novels of Albert Camus, and there is something distinctly existential in the way this black man must work out his private conceptions of morality by acting in an often absurd, white-controlled world where justice can be—and usually is—denied to him. Not a detective per se, but rather an operative in the "favor business" in the black community, Easy carves out a domain for himself with a home, a string of rental properties, and an unconventional family of two adopted children, all of it concealed from the scrutiny of white officialdom. In this habit of underground existence, of hiding in plain sight, Easy Rawlins recalls the narrator of Ralph Ellison's *Invisible Man*. Like Ellison's narrator, Easy inhabits a dangerous, predatory world, one in which he must constantly face up to the capacity for violence in himself and others, a capacity that presents itself most vividly in the person of one Raymond "Mouse" Alexander, his gleefully murderous friend and sidekick whose shoot-first approach to existence plays wonderfully against Easy's brooding, ruminative temperament.

What follows are the first three chapters of *Devil in a Blue Dress*, in which Easy Rawlins strides onto the literary stage for the first time in economic prose that conveys both submerged menace and genuine hope. It is hard not to read these pages as a shot across Raymond Chandler's bow—here is *my* hard-boiled detective, *my* Los Angeles.

From Devil in a Blue Dress

1

I was surprised to see a white man walk into Joppy's bar. It's not just that he was white but he wore an off-white linen suit and shirt with a Panama straw hat and bone shoes over flashing white silk socks. His skin was smooth and pale with just a few freckles. One lick of strawberry-blond hair escaped the band of his hat. He stopped in the doorway, filling it with his large frame, and surveyed the room with pale eyes; not a color I'd ever seen in a man's eyes. When he looked at me I felt a thrill of fear, but that went away quickly because I was used to white people by 1948.

I had spent five years with white men, and women, from Africa to Italy, through Paris, and into the Fatherland[1] itself. I ate with them and slept with them, and I killed enough blue-eyed young men to know that they were just as afraid to die as I was.

The white man smiled at me, then he walked to the bar where Joppy was running a filthy rag over the marble top. They shook hands and exchanged greetings like old friends.

The second thing that surprised me was that he made Joppy nervous. Joppy was a tough ex-heavyweight who was comfortable brawling in the ring or in the street, but he ducked his head and smiled at that white man just like a salesman whose luck had gone bad.

I put a dollar down on the bar and made to leave, but before I was off the stool Joppy turned my way and waved me toward them.

"Com'on over here, Easy. This here's somebody I want ya t'meet."

I could feel those pale eyes on me.

"This here's a ole friend'a mines, Easy. Mr. Albright."

"You can call me DeWitt, Easy," the white man said. His grip was strong but slithery, like a snake coiling around my hand.

"Hello," I said.

"Yeah, Easy," Joppy went on, bowing and grinning. "Mr. Albright and me go way back. You know he prob'ly my oldest friend from L.A. Yeah, we go ways back."

"That's right," Albright smiled. "It must've been 1935 when I met Jop. What is it now? Must be thirteen years. That was back before the war, before every farmer, and his brother's wife, wanted to come to L.A."

Joppy guffawed at the joke; I smiled politely. I was wondering what kind of business Joppy had with that man and, along with that, I wondered what kind of business that man could have with me.

"Where you from, Easy?" Mr. Albright asked.

"Houston."

"Houston, now that's a nice town. I go down there sometimes, on business." He smiled for a moment. He had all the time in the world. "What kind of work you do up here?"

1. Germany.

Up close his eyes were the color of robins' eggs; matte and dull.

"He worked at Champion Aircraft up to two days ago," Joppy said when I didn't answer. "They laid him off."

Mr. Albright twisted his pink lips, showing his distaste. "That's too bad. You know these big companies don't give a damn about you. The budget doesn't balance just right and they let ten family men go. You have a family, Easy?" He had a light drawl like a well-to-do southern gentleman.

"No, just me, that's all," I said.

"But they don't know that. For all they know you could have ten kids and one on the way but they let you go just the same."

"That's right!" Joppy shouted. His voice sounded like a regiment of men marching through a gravel pit. "Them people own them big companies don't never even come in to work, they just get on the telephone to find out how they money is. And you know they better get a good answer or some heads gonna roll."

Mr. Albright laughed and slapped Joppy on the arm. "Why don't you get us some drinks, Joppy? I'll have scotch. What's your pleasure, Easy?"

"Usual?" Joppy asked me.

"Sure."

When Joppy moved away from us Mr. Albright turned to look around the room. He did that every few minutes, turning slightly, checking to see if anything had changed. There wasn't much to see though. Joppy's was a small bar on the second floor of a butchers' warehouse. His only usual customers were the Negro butchers and it was early enough in the afternoon that they were still hard at work.

The odor of rotted meat filled every corner of the building; there were few people, other than butchers, who could stomach sitting in Joppy's bar.

Joppy brought Mr. Albright's scotch and a bourbon on the rocks for me. He put them both down and said, "Mr. Albright lookin' for a man to do a lil job, Easy. I told him you outta work an' got a mortgage t'pay too."

"That's hard." Mr. Albright shook his head again. "Men in big business don't even notice or care when a working man wants to try to make something out of himself."

"And you know Easy always tryin' t'be better. He just got his high school papers from night school and he been threatenin' on some college." Joppy wiped the marble bar as he spoke. "And he's a war hero, Mr. Albright. Easy went in with Patton. Volunteered! You know he seen him some blood."

"That a fact?" Albright said. He wasn't impressed. "Why don't we go have a chair, Easy? Over there by the window."

Joppy's windows were so dingy that you couldn't see out onto 103rd Street. But if you sat at a small cherry table next to them, at least you had the benefit of the dull glow of daylight.

"You got a mortgage to meet, eh, Easy? The only thing that's worse than a big company is the bank. They want their money on the first and if you miss the payment, they will have the marshal knocking down your door on the second."

"What's my business got to do with you, Mr. Albright? I don't wanna be rude, but I just met you five minutes ago and now you want to know all my business."

"Well, I thought that Joppy said you needed to get work or you were going to lose your house."

"What's that got to do with you?"

"I just might need a bright pair of eyes and ears to do a little job for me, Easy."

"And what kind of work is it that you do?" I asked. I should have gotten up and walked out of there, but he was right about my mortgage. He was right about the banks too.

"I used to be a lawyer when I lived in Georgia. But now I'm just another fella who does favors for friends, and for friends of friends."

"What kind of favors?"

"I don't know, Easy." He shrugged his great white shoulders. "Whatever somebody might need. Let's say that you need to get a message to someone but it's not, um, convenient for you to do it in person; well, then you call me and I take the job. You see I always do the job I'm asked to do, everybody knows that, so I always have lots of work. And sometimes I need a little helper to get the job done. That's where you come in."

"And how's that?" I asked. While he talked it dawned on me that Albright was a lot like a friend I had back in Texas—Raymond Alexander was his name but we called him Mouse. Just thinking about Mouse set my teeth on edge.

"I need to find somebody and I might need a little help looking."

"And who is it you want to—"

"Easy," he interrupted. "I can see that you're a smart man with a lot of very good questions. And I'd like to talk more about it, but not here." From his shirt pocket he produced a white card and a white enameled fountain pen. He scrawled on the card and then handed it to me.

"Talk to Joppy about me and then, if you want to try it out, come to my office any time after seven tonight."

He downed the shot, smiled at me again, and stood up, straightening his cuffs. He tilted the Panama hat on his head and saluted Joppy, who grinned and waved from behind the bar. Then Mr. DeWitt Albright strolled out of Joppy's place like a regular customer going home after his afternoon snort.

The card had his name printed on it in flourished letters. Below that was the address he'd scribbled. It was a downtown address; a long drive from Watts.[2]

I noted that Mr. DeWitt Albright didn't pay for the drinks he ordered. Joppy didn't seem in a hurry to ask for his money though.

2

[JOPPY]

"Where'd you meet this dude?" I asked Joppy.

"I met him when I was still in the ring. Like he said, before the war."

---

2. Section of South Central Los Angeles, mainly African American in population.

Joppy was still at the bar, leaning over his big stomach and buffing the marble. His uncle, a bar owner himself, had died in Houston ten years earlier, just when Joppy decided to give up the ring. Joppy went all the way back home to get that marble bar. The butchers had already agreed to let him open his business upstairs and all he could think of was getting that marble top. Joppy was a superstitious man. He thought that the only way he could be successful was with a piece of his uncle, already a proven success, on the job with him. Every extra moment Joppy had was spent cleaning and buffing his bar top. He didn't allow roughhousing near the bar and if you ever dropped a pitcher or something heavy he'd be there in a second, looking for chips.

Joppy was a heavy-framed man, almost fifty years old. His hands were like black catcher's mitts and I never saw him in shirt-sleeves that didn't strain at the seams from bulging muscle. His face was scarred from all the punishment he had taken in the ring; the flesh around his big lips was jagged and there was a knot over his right eye that always looked red and raw.

In his years as a boxer Joppy had had moderate success. He was ranked number seven in 1932 but his big draw was the violence he brought to the ring. Joppy would come out swinging wildly, taking everything any boxer could dish out. In his prime no one could knock Joppy down and, later on, he always went the distance.

"He got something to do with the fights?" I asked.

"Wherever they's a little money to be made Mr. Albright got his nose to the ground," Joppy said. "An' he don't care too much if that money got a little smudge or sumpin' on it neither."

"So you got me tied up with a gangster?"

"Ain't no gangster, Ease. Mr. Albright just a man with a finger in a whole lotta pies, thas all. He's a businessman and you know when you in business sellin' shirts and a man come up to you with a box he say done falled off a truck, well . . . you just give that man a couple'a dollars and look t'other way." He waved his catcher's mitt at me. "Thas business."

Joppy was cleaning one area on his counter until it was spotless, except for the dirt that caked in the cracks. The dark cracks twisting through the light marble looked like a web of blood vessels in a newborn baby's head.

"So he's just a businessman?" I asked.

Joppy stopped wiping for a moment and looked me in the eye. "Don't get me wrong, Ease. DeWitt is a tough man, and he runs in bad company. But you still might could get that mortgage payment an' you might even learn sumpin' from 'im."

I sat there looking around the small room. Joppy had six tables and seven high stools at his bar. A busy night never saw all his chairs full but I was jealous of his success. He had his own business; he owned something. He told me one night that he could sell that bar even though he only rented the room. I thought he was lying but later on I found out that people will buy a business that already has customers; they wouldn't mind paying the rent if there was money coming in.

The windows were dirty and the floor was rutted but it was Joppy's place and when the white butcher-boss came up to collect the rent he always said, "Thank you, Mr. Shag." Because he was happy to get his money.

"So what he want with me?" I asked.

"He just want you t'look for somebody, leastwise that what he said."

"Who?"

"Some girl, I dunno." Joppy shrugged. "I ain't ax him his business if it don't gotta do wit' me. But he just payin' you to *look*, ain't nobody says you gotta find nuthin'."

"And what's he gonna pay?"

"Enough fo' that mortgage. That's why I called you in on this, Easy, I know'd you need some fast money. I don't give a damn 'bout that man, or whoever it is he lookin' fo' neither."

The thought of paying my mortgage reminded me of my front yard and the shade of my fruit trees in the summer heat. I felt that I was just as good as any white man, but if I didn't even own my front door then people would look at me like just another poor beggar, with his hand outstretched.

"Take his money, man. You got to hold on to that little bit'a property," Joppy said as if he knew what I was thinking. "You know all them pretty girls you be runnin' wit' ain't gonna buy you no house."

"I don't like it, Joppy."

"You don't like that money? Shit! I'll hold it for ya."

"Not the money . . . It's just . . . You know that Mr. Albright reminds me of Mouse."

"Who?"

"You remember, he was a little man lived down in Houston. He married EttaMae Harris."

Joppy turned his jagged lips into a frown. "Naw, he must'a come after my time."

"Yeah, well, Mouse is a lot like Mr. Albright. He's smooth and a natty dresser and he's smilin' all the time. But he always got his business in the front'a his mind, and if you get in the way you might come to no good." I always tried to speak proper English in my life, the kind of English they taught in school, but I found over the years that I could only truly express myself in the natural, "uneducated" dialect of my upbringing.

" 'Might come to no good' is a bitch, Easy, but sleepin' in the street ain't got no 'might' to it."

"Yeah, man. I'm just feelin' kinda careful."

"Careful don't hurt, Easy. Careful keep your hands up, careful makes ya strong."

"So he's just a businessman, huh?" I asked again.

"Thas right!"

"And just exactly what kind of business is it he does? I mean, is he a shirt salesman or what?"

"They gotta sayin' for his line'a work, Ease."

"What's that?"

"Whatever the market can bear." He smiled, looking like a hungry bear himself. "Whatever the market can bear."

"I'll think about it."

"Don't worry, Ease, I'll take care'a ya. You just call ole Joppy now and then and I'll tell ya if it sounds like it's gettin' bad. You just keep in touch with me an' you be just fine."

"Thanks for thinkin'a me, Jop," I said, but I wondered if I'd still be thankful later on.

3

[DAPHNE MONET]

I drove back to my house thinking about money and how much I needed to have some.

I loved going home. Maybe it was that I was raised on a sharecropper's farm or that I never owned anything until I bought that house, but I loved my little home. There was an apple tree and an avocado in the front yard, surrounded by thick St. Augustine grass. At the side of the house I had a pomegranate tree that bore more than thirty fruit every season and a banana tree that never produced a thing. There were dahlias and wild roses in beds around the fence and African violets that I kept in a big jar on the front porch.

The house itself was small. Just a living room, a bedroom, and a kitchen. The bathroom didn't even have a shower and the back yard was no larger than a child's rubber pool. But that house meant more to me than any woman I ever knew. I loved her and I was jealous of her and if the bank sent the county marshal to take her from me I might have come at him with a rifle rather than to give her up.

Working for Joppy's friend was the only way I saw to keep my house. But there was something wrong, I could feel it in my fingertips. DeWitt Albright made me uneasy; Joppy's tough words, though they were true, made me uneasy. I kept telling myself to go to bed and forget it.

"Easy," I said, "get a good night's sleep and go out looking for a job tomorrow."

"But this is June twenty-five," a voice said. "Where is the sixty-four dollars coming from on July one?"

"I'll get it," I answered.

"How?"

We went on like that but it was useless from the start. I knew I was going to take Albright's money and do whatever he wanted me to, providing it was legal, because that little house of mine needed me and I wasn't about to let her down.

And there was another thing.

DeWitt Albright made me a little nervous. He was a big man, and powerful by the look of him. You could tell by the way he held his shoulders that he was full of violence. But I was a big man too. And, like most young men, I never liked to admit that I could be dissuaded by fear.

Whether he knew it or not, DeWitt Albright had me caught by my own pride. The more I was afraid of him, I was that much more certain to take the job he offered.

The address Albright had given me was a small, buff-colored building on Alvarado. The buildings around it were taller but not as old or as distinguished. I walked through the black wrought-iron gates into the hall of the Spanish-styled entrance. There was nobody around, not even a directory, just a wall of cream-colored doors with no names on them.

"Excuse me."

The voice made me jump.

"What?" My voice strained and cracked as I turned to see the small man.

"Who are you looking for?"

He was a little white man wearing a suit that was also a uniform.

"I'm looking for, um . . . ah . . . ," I stuttered. I forgot the name. I had to squint so that the room wouldn't start spinning.

It was a habit I developed in Texas when I was a boy. Sometimes, when a white man of authority would catch me off guard, I'd empty my head of everything so I was unable to say anything. "The less you know, the less trouble you find," they used to say. I hated myself for it but I also hated white people, and colored people too, for making me that way.

"Can I help you?" the white man asked. He had curly red hair and a pointed nose. When I still couldn't answer he said, "We only take deliveries between nine and six."

"No, no," I said, trying to remember.

"Yes we do! Now you better leave."

"No, I mean I . . ."

The little man started backing toward a small podium that stood against the wall. I figured that he had a nightstick back there.

"Albright!" I yelled.

"What?" he yelled back.

"Albright! I'm here to see Albright!"

"Albright who?" There was suspicion in his eye, and his hand was behind the podium.

"Mr. Albright. Mr. DeWitt Albright."

"Mr. Albright?"

"Yes, that's him."

"Are you delivering something?" he asked, holding out his scrawny hand.

"No. I have an appointment. I mean, I'm supposed to meet him." I hated that little man.

"You're supposed to meet him? You can't even remember his name."

I took a deep breath and said, very softly, "I am supposed to meet Mr. DeWitt Albright tonight, any time after seven."

"You're supposed to meet him at seven? It's eight-thirty now. He's probably gone."

"He told me *any time* after seven."

He held out his hand to me again. "Did he give you a note saying you're to come in here after hours?"

I shook my head at him. I would have liked to rip the skin from his face like I'd done once to another white boy.

"Well, how am I to know that you aren't just a thief? You can't even remember his name and you want me to take you somewhere in there. Why you could have a partner waiting for me to let you in . . ."

I was disgusted. "Forget it man," I said. "You just tell him, when you see him, that Mr. Rawlins was here. You tell him that the next time he better give me a note because you cain't be lettin' no street niggahs comin' in yo' place wit' no notes!"

I was ready to leave. That little white man had convinced me that I was in the wrong place. I was ready to go back home. I could find my money another way.

"Hold on," he said. "You wait right there and I'll be back in a minute." He sidled through one of the cream-colored doors, shutting it as he went. I heard the lock snap into place a moment later.

After a few minutes he opened the door a crack and waved at me to follow him. He looked from side to side as he let me through the door; looking for my accomplices I suppose.

The doorway led to an open courtyard that was paved with dark red brick and landscaped with three large palm trees that reached out beyond the roof of the three-story building. The inner doorways on the upper two floors were enclosed by trellises that had vines of white and yellow sweetheart roses cascading down. The sky was still light at that time of year but I could see a crescent moon peeking over the inner roof.

The little man opened another door at the other side of the courtyard. It led down an ugly metal staircase into the bowels of the building. We went through a dusty boiler room to an empty corridor that was painted drab green and draped with gray cobwebs.

At the end of the hall there was a door of the same color that was chipped and dusty.

"That's what you want," the little man said.

I said thank you and he walked away from me. I never saw him again. I often think of how so many people have walked into my life for just a few minutes and kicked up some dust, then they're gone away. My father was like that; my mother wasn't much better.

I knocked on the ugly door. I expected to see Albright, but instead the door opened into a small room that held two strange-looking men.

The man who held the door was tall and slight with curly brown hair, dark skin like an India Indian, and brown eyes so light they were almost golden. His friend, who stood against a door at the far wall, was short and looked a little like he was Chinese around the eyes, but when I looked at him again I wasn't so sure of his race.

The dark man smiled and put out his hand. I thought he wanted to shake but then he started slapping my side.

"Hey, man! What's wrong with you?" I said, pushing him away. The maybe-Chinese man slipped a hand in his pocket.

"Mr. Rawlins," the dark man said in an accent I didn't know. He was still smiling. "Put your hands up a little from your sides, please. I'm just checking." The smile widened into a grin.

"You could just keep your hands to yourself, man. I don't let nobody feel on me like that."

The little man pulled something, I couldn't tell what, halfway out of his pocket. Then he took a step toward us. The grinner tried to put his hand against my chest but I grabbed him by the wrist.

The dark man's eyes glittered, he smiled at me for a moment, and then said to his partner, "Don't worry, Manny. He's okay."

"You sure, Shariff?"

"Yeah. He's alright, just a little shaky." Shariff's teeth glinted between his dusky lips. I still had his wrist.

Shariff said, "Let him know, Manny."

Manny put his hand back in his pocket and then took it out again to knock on the door behind.

DeWitt Albright opened the door after a minute.

"Easy," he smiled.

"He doesn't want us to touch him," Shariff said as I let him go.

"Leave it," Albright answered. "I just wanted to make sure he was solo."

"You're the boss." Shariff sounded very sure of himself; even a little arrogant.

"You and Manny can go now," Albright smiled. "Easy and I have some business to talk over."

Mr. Albright went behind a big blond desk and put his bone shoes up next to a half-full bottle of Wild Turkey. There was a paper calendar hanging on the wall behind him with a picture of a basket of blackberries as a design. There was nothing else on the wall. The floor was bare too: plain yellow linoleum with flecks of color scattered through it.

"Have a seat, Mr. Rawlins," Mr. Albright said, gesturing to the chair in front of his desk. He was bare-headed and his coat was nowhere in sight. There was a white-leather shoulder holster under his left arm. The muzzle of the pistol almost reached his belt.

"Nice friends you got," I said as I studied his piece.

"They're like you, Easy. Whenever I need a little manpower I give them a call. There's a whole army of men who'll do specialized work for the right price."

"The little guy Chinese?"

Albright shrugged. "No one knows. He was raised in an orphanage, in Jersey City. Drink?"

"Sure."

"One of the benefits of working for yourself. Always have a bottle on the table. Everybody else, even the presidents of these big companies, got the booze in the bottom drawer, but I keep it right out in plain sight. You want to drink it? That's fine with me. You don't like it? Door's right there behind you." While he talked he poured two shots into glasses that he had taken from a desk drawer.

The gun interested me. The butt and the barrel were black; the only part of DeWitt's attire that wasn't white.

As I leaned over to take the glass from his hand he asked, "So, you want the job, Easy?"

"Well, that depends on what kind of job you had in mind?"

"I'm looking for somebody, for a friend," he said. He pulled a photograph from his shirt pocket and put it down on the desk. It was a picture of the head and shoulders of a pretty young white woman. The picture had been black and white originally but it was touched up for color like the

photos of jazz singers that they put out in front of nightclubs. She had light
hair coming down over her bare shoulders and high cheekbones and eyes
that might have been blue if the artist got it right. After staring at her for a
full minute I decided that she'd be worth looking for if you could get her to
smile at you that way.

"Daphne Monet," Mr. Albright said. "Not bad to look at but she's hell to
find."

"I still don't see what it's got to do with me," I said. "I ain't never laid eyes
on her."

"That's a shame, Easy." He was smiling at me. "But I think you might be
able to help me anyway."

"I can't see how. Woman like this don't hardly know my number. What
you should do is call the police."

"I never call a soul who isn't a friend, or at least a friend of a friend. I
don't know any cops, and neither do my friends."

"Well then get a—"

"You see, Easy," he cut me off, "Daphne has a predilection for the company of Negroes. She likes jazz and pigs' feet and dark meat, if you know
what I mean."

I knew but I didn't like to hear it. "So you think she might be down
around Watts?"

"Not a doubt in my mind. But, you see, I can't go in those places looking
for her because I'm not the right persuasion. Joppy knows me well enough
to tell me what he knows but I've already asked him and all he could do was
to give me your name."

"So what do you want with her?"

"I have a friend who wants to apologize, Easy. He has a short temper and
that's why she left."

"And he wants her back?"

Mr. Albright smiled.

"I don't know if I can help you, Mr. Albright. Like Joppy said, I lost a job
a couple of days ago and I have to get another one before the note comes
due."

"Hundred dollars for a week's work, Mr. Rawlins, and I pay in advance.
You find her tomorrow and you keep what's in your pocket."

"I don't know, Mr. Albright. I mean, how do I know what I'm getting
mixed up in? What are you—"

He raised a powerful finger to his lips, then he said, "Easy, walk out your
door in the morning and you're mixed up in something. The only thing
you can really worry about is if you get mixed up to the top or not."

"I don't want to get mixed up with the law is what I mean."

"That's why I want you to work for me. I don't like the police myself.
Shit! The police enforce the law and you know what the law is, don't
you?"

I had my own ideas on the subject but I kept them to myself.

"The law," he continued, "is made by the rich people so that the poor
people can't get ahead. You don't want to get mixed up with the law and
neither do I."

He lifted the shot glass and inspected it as if he were checking for fleas, then he put the glass on the desk and placed his hands, palms down, around it.

"I'm just asking you to find a girl," he said. "And to tell me where she is. That's all. You just find out where she is and whisper it in my ear. That's all. You find her and I'll give you a bonus mortgage payment and my friend will find you a job, maybe he can even get you back into Champion."

"Who is it wants to find the girl?"

"No names, Easy, it's better that way."

"It's just that I'd hate to find her and then have some cop come up to me with some shit like I was the last one seen around her—before she disappeared."

The white man laughed and shook his head as if I had told a good joke.

"Things happen every day, Easy," he said. "Things happen every day. You're an educated man, aren't you?"

"Why, yes."

"So you read the paper. You read it today?"

"Yes."

"Three murders! Three! Last night alone. Things happen every day. People with everything to live for, maybe they even got a little money in the bank. They probably had it all planned out what they'd be doing this weekend, but that didn't stop them from dying. Those plans didn't save them when the time came. People got everything to live for and they get a little careless. They forget that the only thing you have to be sure of is that nothing bad comes to you."

The way he smiled when he sat back in his chair reminded me of Mouse again. I thought of how Mouse was always smiling, especially when misfortune happened to someone else.

"You just find the girl and tell me, that's all. I'm not going to hurt her and neither is my friend. You don't have a thing to worry about."

He took a white secretary-type wallet from a desk drawer and produced a stack of bills. He counted out ten of them, licking his square thumb for every other one, and placed them in a neat stack next to the whiskey.

"One hundred dollars," he said.

I couldn't see why it shouldn't be my one hundred dollars.

When I was a poor man, and landless, all I worried about was a place for the night and food to eat; you really didn't need much for that. A friend would always stand me a meal, and there were plenty of women who would have let me sleep with them. But when I got that mortgage I found that I needed more than just friendship. Mr. Albright wasn't a friend but he had what I needed.

He was a fine host too. His liquor was good and he was pleasant enough. He told me a few stories, the kind of tales that we called "lies" back home in Texas.

One story he told was about when he was a lawyer in Georgia.

"I was defending a shit-kicker who was charged with burning down a banker's house," DeWitt told me as he stared out toward the wall behind my head. "Banker had foreclosed on the boy the minute the note was due. You know he didn't even give him any chance to make extra arrangements. And that boy was just as guilty as that banker was."

"You get him off?" I asked.

DeWitt smiled at me. "Yeah. That prosecutor had a good case on Leon, that's the shit-kicker. Yeah, the honorable Randolph Corey had solid proof that my client did the arson. But I went down to Randy's house and I sat at his table and pulled out this here pistol. All I did was talk about the weather we'd been having, and while I did that I cleaned my gun."

"Getting your client off meant that much to you?"

"Shit. Leon was trash. But Randy had been riding pretty high for a couple'a years and I had it in mind that it was time for him to lose a case." Albright straightened his shoulders. "You have to have a sense of balance when it comes to the law, Easy. Everything has to come out just right."

After a few drinks I started talking about the war. Plain old man-talk, about half of it true and the rest just for laughs. More than an hour went by before he asked me, "You ever kill a man with your hands, Easy?"

"What?"

"You ever kill a man, hand-to-hand?"

"Why?"

"No reason really. It's just that I know you've seen some action."

"Some."

"You ever kill somebody up close? I mean so close that you could see it when his eyes went out of focus and he let go? When you kill a man it's the shit and piss that's worst. You boys did that in the war and I bet it was bad. I bet you couldn't dream about your mother anymore, or anything nice. But you lived with it because you knew that it was the war that forced you to do it."

His pale blue eyes reminded me of the wide-eyed corpses of German soldiers that I once saw stacked up on a road to Berlin.

"But the only thing that you have to remember, Easy," he said as he picked up the money to hand me across the table, "is that some of us can kill with no more trouble than drinking a glass of bourbon." He downed the shot and smiled.

Then he said, "Joppy tells me that you used to frequent an illegal club down on Eighty-ninth and Central. Somebody saw Daphne at that very same bar not long ago. I don't know what they call it but they have the big names in there on weekends and the man who runs it is called John. You could start tonight."

The way his dead eyes shined on me I knew our party was over. I couldn't think of anything to say so I nodded, put his money in my pocket, and moved to leave.

I turned back at the door to salute him goodbye but DeWitt Albright had filled his glass and shifted his gaze to the far wall. He was staring into some-place far from that dirty basement.

1990

ESSEX HEMPHILL

1957–1995

In his poetry and prose collection *Ceremonies* (1992), Essex Hemphill wrote of the double alienation that occurs when a man tries to assert his identity as both a homosexual and an African American. His short essay *Loyalty* rejects the notion that he has sinned against "nature and the race" and renounces the silence that has been imposed on black gays with the following declaration:

> I speak for thousands, perhaps hundreds of thousands of men who live and die in the shadows of secrets, unable to speak of the love that helps them endure and contribute to the race. Their ordinary kisses, stolen or shared behind facades of heroic achievement, their kisses of sweet spit and loyalty are scrubbed away by the propaganda makers of the race, the "Talented Tenth" who would just as soon have us believe Black people can fly, rather than reveal that Black men have been longing to kiss one another, and have done so, for centuries.

By aggressively insisting on the truth, Hemphill forced awareness of a presence that a homophobic society would rather ignore. Although he was known primarily as a poet, his compelling prose as well as his poetry gained him increasing recognition and popularity in the early 1990s.

Born on April 16, 1957, in Chicago, Hemphill was reared in a southeast Washington, D.C., neighborhood, which he described as "a ghetto that had not yet suffered the fatal wounds and injuries caused by drugs and Black-on-Black crime." After graduating from high school in 1975, Hemphill pursued his interests in English and journalism at the University of Maryland. Later, he studied English at the University of the District of Columbia.

Hemphill's *Earth Life*, a chapbook, was published in 1985, with *Conditions*, his second collection, following in 1986. He edited and contributed to *Brother to Brother: New Writings by Black Gay Men* (1991), an anthology initiated by the late Joseph Fairchild Beam; *Brother to Brother* won the American Library Association's 1993 Gay and Lesbian Book Award. During the early 1990s, Hemphill participated in several gay black film projects, including *Looking for Langston, Out of the Shadows,* and *Tongues Untied. Ceremonies,* a collection of poetry and prose, was his first large collection and included both new work and pieces that had been seen in anthologies such as *In the Life, Men & Intimacy,* and *Gay and Lesbian Poetry in Our Time.*

Fueling Hemphill's work was his scorn for "watered-down versions of Black life in America." Instead, Hemphill confronted his reader with "the ass-splitting truth," thereby hoping to reestablish, uncloseted, his connection to the larger community. Although his style in both poetry and prose can be blunt, verging on the violent, Hemphill's intent was not to sever ties with the straight world, but rather to come home to a world where the mothers of gay men understand this lesson: "Do not feel shame for how I live / I chose this tribe / of warriors and outlaws." His powerful language and images construct an alternative to the sad, doomed stereotype of gay life. In Hemphill's new, erotic world, men transform old institutions to fit their needs, as in *American Wedding,* where "Everytime we kiss / we confirm the new world coming."

In recognition of his achievements, Hemphill became an artist in residence at the Getty Museum in Los Angeles in 1993. That same year, he won the Gregory Kolovakos award for AIDS writing.

Essex Hemphill died on November 4, 1995. To recognize his accomplishments, members of the Gay Men of African Descent (GMAD) and Black Nations/Queer Nations declared December 10, 1995, as the National Day of Remembrance. Memorials were held throughout the United States acknowledging Hemphill as a pioneer in the literary arts as they related to gay and lesbian peoples throughout the world.

From Conditions

XXI

You judge a woman
by the length of her skirt,
by the way she walks,
talks, looks, and acts;
by the color of her skin you judge   5
and will call her "bitch!"
"Black bitch!"
if she doesn't answer your:
"Hey baby, whatcha gonna say
to a man."   10

You judge a woman
by the job she holds,
by the number of children she's had,
by the number of digits on her check;
by the many men she may have lain with   15
and wonder what jive murphy[1]
you'll run on her this time.

You tell a woman
every poetic love line
you can think of,   20
then like the desperate needle
of a strung out junkie
you plunge into her veins,
travel wild through her blood,
confuse her mind, make her hate   25
and be cold to the men to come,
destroying the thread of calm
she held.

You judge a woman
by what she can do for you alone   30
but there's no need
for slaves to have slaves.

1. Pick-up lines (slang), specifically used to talk someone into a sexual encounter.

You judge a woman
by impressions you think you've made.
Ask and she gives,   35
take without asking,
beat on her and she'll obey,
throw her name up and down the streets
like some loose whistle—
knowing her neighbors will talk.   40
Her friends will chew her name.
Her family's blood will run loose
like a broken creek.
And when you're gone,
a woman is left   45
healing her wounds alone.
But we so called men,
we so called brothers
wonder why it's so hard
to love *our* women   50
when we're about loving them
the way america
loves us.

XXII

If there were seven blind men
one of them unable to hear
would be father.
He would be the one
promising to deliver   5
what never arrives.
He is the bridge
which on one side
I stand feeling doomed
to never forgive him   10
for the violence in our past,
while on the other side
he vigorously waves to me
to cross over,
but he doesn't know   15
the bridge has fallen through.

If there were seven blind men
the deaf one would be father.
The mute, his son.

XXIV

In america
I place my ring
on your cock
where it belongs.
No horsemen   5
bearing terror,

no soldiers of doom
will swoop in
and sweep us apart.
They're too busy   10
looting the land
to watch us.
They don't know
we need each other
critically.   15
They expect us to call in sick,
watch television all night,
die by our own hands.
They don't know
we are becoming powerful.   20
Everytime we kiss
we confirm the new world coming.

What the rose whispers
before blooming
I vow to you.   25
I give you my heart,
a safe house.
I give you promises other than
milk, honey, liberty.
I assume you will always   30
be a free man with a dream.
In america,
place your ring
on my cock
where it belongs.   35
Long may we live
to free this dream.

1986

1492–1773

1492 Pedro Alonzo Nino, traditionally considered the first of many New World explorers of African descent, sails with Christopher Columbus

1526 First African slaves brought to what is now the United States by the Spanish

1619 Twenty Africans brought to Jamestown, Virginia, on Dutch ship and sold as indentured servants

1623 Birth of William Tucker, in Jamestown—first black child born in the English North American colonies

1641 Massachusetts becomes the first colony to legally recognize slavery

1645 First American slave ships sail, from Boston; triangular trade route brings African slaves to West Indies in exchange for sugar, tobacco, and wine, which are then sold for manufactured goods in Massachusetts

1646 John Wham and his wife are freed, becoming first recorded free blacks in New England

1652 Rhode Island passes first North American law against slavery

1662 Virginia is the first colony to declare that mother's status determines whether a child is born free or into slavery

1663 Major conspiracy by black and white indentured servants in Virginia is betrayed by servant

1688 Pennsylvania Quakers sign first official written protest against slavery in North America

1712 New York City slave revolt is quelled by militia • Pennsylvania becomes first colony to outlaw slave trade

1734 "Great Awakening" religious revival begins; Methodist and Baptist churches attract blacks by offering "Christianity for all"

1739 South Carolina slaves launch Stono Rebellion, killing 30 whites

1740 In response to the Stono Rebellion, South Carolina outlaws teaching slaves to write

1746 Lucy Terry writes *Bars Fight,* the first poem extant written by an African American (not published until 1895)

1756–63 African Americans fight in French and Indian War

1757 Phillis Wheatley purchased in Boston

1758 First black Baptist church in colonies is erected on plantation in Virginia

1760 Jupiter Hammon, *An Evening Thought: Salvation by Christ with Penitential Cries*, printed as a broadside, the first poetry published by an African American

1773 Phillis Wheatley, *Poems on Various Subjects, Religious and Moral,* published in London, first book published by an African American and second book published by an American woman • Slaves in Massachusetts petition legislature for freedom for first time

Boldface titles indicate works in or excerpted in the anthology.

1774 Continental Congress prohibits importation of slaves after December 1, 1774

1775–83 American Revolutionary War; battles fought by African Americans include Bunker Hill, Lexington, and Concord

1775 First antislavery society organized by Philadelphia Quakers • Royal governor of Virginia offers freedom to any slave joining British army; 800 respond to form "Ethiopian Regiment" • Second Continental Congress resolves against importation of slaves

1776 Declaration of Independence adopted without antislavery statement proposed by Thomas Jefferson

1777 Vermont is one of the first states to abolish slavery in state constitution • New York is the first state to extend vote to black males, but limits voting in 1815 and 1821 with permit, property, and residency requirements

1780 Pennsylvania becomes the first state to allow interracial marriage • Free blacks in Massachusetts protest "taxation without representation" and petition for exemption from taxes

1783 Massachusetts Supreme Court grants black taxpayers suffrage

1786 Free blacks join in Shay's Rebellion, protesting the lack of concern over harsh conditions of farmers by Massachusetts government

1787 Constitution ratified, classifying one slave as three-fifths of one person for congressional apportionment, postponing prohibition of slave importation until 1808, and demanding return of fugitive slaves to masters • Congress passes Northwest Ordinance, banning slavery in Northwest Territories and all land north of Ohio River • Absalom Jones and Richard Allen organize Philadelphia Free African Society • Rhode Island free blacks establish African Union Society to promote repatriation to Africa, a position opposed by Philadelphia Free African Society

1789 Olaudah Equiano, *The Interesting Narrative of the Life of Olaudah Equiano, or Gustavus Vassa, the African*

1790 Pennsylvania abolitionists submit first antislavery petitions to U.S. Congress

1793 U.S. Congress passes first Fugitive Slave Law • Invention of cotton gin increases demand for slaves in South

1794 U.S. Congress prohibits slave trade with foreign countries • French National Convention abolishes slavery in French territories (ban will be repealed by Napoleon in 1802) • Richard Allen founds first African Methodist Episcopal church (AME), in Philadelphia

1796 Lucy Terry Prince becomes first woman to argue before Supreme Court, successfully defending against a white man trying to steal her family's land • Joshua Johnson, first black portrait painter to gain recognition in the United States, opens studio in Baltimore

1798 Georgia is last state to abolish slave trade

1800 U.S. citizens are prohibited from exporting slaves • Pennsylvania free blacks petition U.S. Congress to outlaw slavery • Gabriel Prosser and Jack Bowler organize 1,000 fellow slaves to seize Richmond, but plan is quelled by militia and leaders are executed along with many others

1802 Haitians force French government to end slavery in Haiti; François-Dominique Toussaint-Louverture is made governor

1803 Louisiana Purchase doubles size of the United States

1804 York, a slave, serves as guide for Lewis and Clark expedition to Pacific • Ohio sets precedent with passage of first "Black Laws" restricting rights and movements of free blacks in North

1807 United States outlaws importation of new slaves after January 1, 1808, but law is widely ignored • Britain abolishes slave trade

1811 Slave revolt in Louisiana led by Charles Deslandres ends with over 100 slaves killed or executed by U.S. troops

1812 Slaves and free blacks fight in War of 1812

1815 Quaker Levi Coffin establishes Underground Railroad to help slaves escape to Canada

1816–18 First Seminole War involving runaway slaves and Native Americans fighting U.S. federal government in Florida

1816 American Colonization Society formed in Washington, D.C., to promote African repatriation of freed slaves to ease U.S. race problems; the society is supported by leading white congressmen

1817 Over 3,000 free blacks in Philadelphia meet to oppose American Colonization Society

1818 President given power to use armed vessels in Africa to halt illegal slave trade • U.S. Congress allots $100,000 to transport illegally imported slaves back to Africa

1820 Missouri Compromise reached, allowing Maine into Union as free state, Missouri as slave state in 1821, and outlawing slavery in all new Northern Plains states • American Colonization Society sends expedition to begin establishment of Liberia, a black republic in West Africa; first repatriation ship, *Mayflower of Liberia*, leaves from New York City with 86 blacks

1821 African Grove Theatre, first all-black U.S. acting troupe, begins performances in New York City

1822 Denmark Vesey organizes slave revolt to take over Charleston, South Carolina, but is betrayed by a servant • Liberia formally founded by African American colonizers

1823 Alexander L. Twilight graduates from Middlebury College, Vermont, becoming first African American college graduate

1826 First U.S. colony for free blacks, Nashoba, established near Memphis, Tennessee

1829 David Walker, *David Walker's Appeal* • George Moses Horton, *The Hope of Liberty* • Three-day race riot breaks out in Cincinnati; more than 1,000 blacks flee to Canada after whites attack them and burn their homes

1830 First National Negro Convention convenes in Philadelphia

1831 Maria W. Stewart, *Religion and the Pure Principles of Morality, the*

Sure Foundation on Which We Must Build • Nat Turner leads slave uprising in Southampton County, Virginia; at least 57 whites are killed; 3,000 soldiers and Virginia militiamen react by killing blacks indiscriminately; Turner is captured and hanged

1832 Maria W. Stewart, first American woman to engage in public political debates, begins speaking tour in Boston

1833 Oberlin College is founded as first coeducational U.S. college and is integrated from its inception

1834 Henry Blair, inventor of corn planter, is first recorded African American to receive patent • Antiabolitionist riots in Philadelphia and New York • British Parliament abolishes slavery in British Empire

1835–42 Second Seminole War

1836 U.S. House of Representatives passes first "gag rule," preventing any antislavery petition or bill from being introduced, read, or discussed

1837 Victor Séjours's *The Mulatto* published

1838 Frederick Douglass escapes from slavery • Joshua Giddings of Ohio is first abolitionist elected to U.S. Congress

1839 Cinque leads successful slave revolt on Spanish ship *Amistad* • U.S. State Department rejects passport application by Philadelphia black man on basis that African Americans are not citizens

1840 Pope Gregory XVI states opposition to slave trade and slavery

1841 Quintuple Treaty signed by England, France, Russia, Austria, and Prussia, allowing mutual search of vessels on high seas to halt slave trade • Frederick Douglass makes his first antislavery speech, in Nantucket, Massachusetts

1843 Henry Highland Garnet delivers *An Address to the Slaves of the United States* at National Negro Convention, Buffalo, New York • Vermont and Massachusetts defy 1793 Fugitive Slave Act

1845 Frederick Douglass, *Narrative of the Life of Frederick Douglass, an American Slave, Written by Himself*

1847 William Wells Brown, *Narrative of William W. Brown* • Liberia declares independence and becomes first African republic

1848 Frederick Douglass speaks at first Women's Rights Convention in Seneca Falls, New York • Ohio reverses "Black Laws"

1849 Harriet Tubman escapes from slavery and begins work with Underground Railroad • Massachusetts Supreme Court upholds "separate but equal" ruling in first U.S. integration suit

1850 Clay Compromise strengthens 1793 Fugitive Slave Act, outlaws slave trade in Washington, D.C., admits California as free state, and admits Utah and New Mexico as either slave or free • Lucy Session becomes first recorded African American woman college graduate, receiving her degree from Oberlin College, in Ohio

1851 Sojourner Truth delivers *Ar'n't I a Woman?* at Women's Rights Conference in Akron, Ohio

1852 Harriet Beecher Stowe, *Uncle Tom's Cabin*

1853 Brown, *Clotel* • J. M. Whitfield, *America and Other Poems*

1854–64, 1885–89 Charlotte Forten Grimké writes **journals**

1854 Frances E. W. Harper, *Poems on Miscellaneous Subjects* • Kansas-Nebraska Act repeals Missouri Compromise of 1820 • Republican Party founded to oppose extension of slavery

1855 Douglass, *My Bondage and My Freedom* • "Bleeding Kansas" fighting begins as antislavery and proslavery settlers hold separate state conventions • John Mercer Langston is elected clerk of Brownhelm Township, Ohio, becoming first African American elected to political office

1857 Supreme Court declares African Americans are not citizens in *Dred Scott* decision

1859 Harriet Adams Wilson, *Our Nig,* first novel published in America by an African American • John Brown leads abolitionist raid in Harpers Ferry, West Virginia • Last U.S. slave ship lands in Alabama

1860 South Carolina is first state to secede from Union

1861–65 American Civil War

1861 Harriet Jacobs, *Incidents in the Life of a Slave Girl* • Harper's *The Two Offers* is first short story published by an African American woman

1862 Congress bans slavery in District of Columbia and U.S. territories •

President Lincoln issues Emancipation Proclamation, effective January 1, 1863, freeing slaves in rebel states • U.S. recognizes Liberia as free nation

1863 Slavery abolished in all Dutch colonies

1864 Fugitive Slave Laws repealed

1865 General Sherman orders up to 40 acres given to each black family, but President Johnson later reverses policy • Slavery outlawed by 13th Amendment • Freedmen's Bureau established • "Black Codes" issued in former Confederate states, severely limiting rights of freed women and men • President Lincoln assassinated • Ku Klux Klan founded in Tennessee

1866 Congress passes first Civil Rights Act declaring freed blacks U.S. citizens and nullifying black codes • Edward G. Walker and Charles L. Mitchel are first blacks elected to state legislature

1867 Congress passes First Reconstruction Act, granting suffrage to black males in rebel states, among other rights

1868 Congress passes 14th Amendment, granting blacks equal citizenship and civil rights

1869 National Women's Suffrage Association formed • Wyoming Territory grants women first suffrage in the United States

1870 Congress passes 15th Amendment, guaranteeing suffrage to all male U.S. citizens • Congress passes Enforcement Acts to control Ku Klux Klan and to federally guarantee civil and political rights • Rev. Hiram R. Revels of Mississippi is first black U.S. senator • Joseph H. Rainey is seated as first black U.S. representative; 5 other black men are also elected to U.S. House of Representatives • Richard T. Greener is first African American graduate of Harvard College

1871 Congress passes second Ku Klux Klan Act to enforce 14th Amendment

1874 Women's Christian Temperance Union founded in Ohio

1875 Congress passes Civil Rights Act of 1875, giving equal treatment in public places and access to jury duty

1877 Federal troops withdraw from South, officially ending Reconstruction

1881 Booker T. Washington founds Tuskegee Institute

1883 Supreme Court overturns Civil Rights Act of 1875

1884 Moses Fleetwood Walker plays baseball for Toledo Blue Stockings as one of first black major leaguers

1890 Oklahoma admitted as first state with women's suffrage • Mississippi limits black suffrage through "understanding" test, setting precedent for other southern states

1892 Anna Julia Cooper, *A Voice from the South* • Harper, *Iola Leroy*

1893 Paul Laurence Dunbar, *Oak and Ivy*

1894 *The Woman's Era*, later to become the official organ of the National Association of Colored Women, begins publication

1895 Booker T. Washington delivers *Atlanta Exposition Speech* • Alice Moore Dunbar Nelson, *Violets and Other Tales* • Ida B. Wells-Barnett, *A Red Record* • Dunbar, *Majors and Minors*

1896 Supreme Court approves segregation with "separate but equal" ruling in *Plessy v. Ferguson* • National League of Colored Women and National Federation of Afro-American Women merge to form National Association of Colored Women with Mary Church Terrell as president

1898 Spanish-American War

1899 Charles W. Chesnutt, *The Conjure Woman, The Wife of His Youth and Other Stories of the Color Line*

1900 Washington, *Up From Slavery* • Pauline E. Hopkins, *Contending Forces*

1902 James D. Corrothers, *The Black Cat Club*

1903 W. E. B. Du Bois, *The Souls of Black Folk*

1904 William Stanley Braithwaite, *Lyrics of Life and Love* • AME *Church Review* calls for a "New Negro Renaissance"

1905 Sutton E. Griggs, *The Hindered Hand; or, The Reign of the Repressionist* • Niagara Movement, dedicated to "aggressive action" for equal rights, is founded by W. E. B. Du Bois and others

1906 Madame C. J. Walker opens hair-care business, eventually becoming one of the first female American millionaires

1907 Alain Locke is first African American Rhodes Scholar

1908 Braithwaite, *The House of Falling Leaves with Other Poems* • Jack Johnson becomes first African American heavyweight champion of the world

1909 National Association for the Advancement of Colored People (NAACP) founded by Du Bois

1910–30 Great Migration of over 1 million southern blacks to northern cities

1912 James Weldon Johnson, *The Autobiography of an Ex-Colored Man* • Claude McKay, *Songs of Jamaica* and *Constab Ballads*

1913 Fenton Johnson, *A Little Dreaming*

1914–18 World War I

1916 Angelina Weld Grimke's *Rachel* is performed in Washington, D.C., the first full-length play written, performed, and produced by African Americans in the twentieth century • Marcus Garvey comes to the United States from Jamaica and begins "Back to Africa" movement with establishment of Universal Negro Improvement Association • Margaret Sanger opens first birth control clinic in the United States

1917 United States enters World War I

1918 Georgia Douglas Johnson, *The Heart of a Woman* • Marcus Garvey establishes the newspaper *Negro World*

1919 Du Bois organizes first Pan-African Congress in Paris • 83 lynchings recorded during "Red Summer of Hate" • American Communist Party organized

1920 Du Bois, *Darkwater* • Ratification of 19th Amendment, granting suffrage to women

1922–33 Harlem Renaissance

1922 Johnson, *The Book of American Negro Poetry* • McKay, *Harlem Shadows* • Dyer Anti-Lynching bill passes U.S. House of Representatives but fails in Senate

1923–25 Marcus Garvey, *The Philosophy and Opinions of Marcus Garvey*

1923 Jean Toomer, *Cane* • Oklahoma declares martial law to curb KKK

1925–27 Annual literary contests sponsored by *Crisis* and *Opportunity* magazines

1925 Alain Locke, *The New Negro* • Countee Cullen, *Color* • 40,000 KKK members parade in Washington, D.C. • Josephine Baker becomes sensation in Paris through *La Revue Negre*

1926 Eric Walrond, *Tropic Death* • Langston Hughes, *The Weary Blues*

1927 Charles S. Johnson's anthology *Ebony and Topaz* • Cullen's anthology of black poetry *Caroling the Dusk* • *The Jazz Singer* is first "talkie" motion picture, with white actor Al Jolson as black-faced minstrel singer

1928 McKay, *Home to Harlem* • Marita Bonner, *The Purple Flower* • Nella Larsen, *Quicksand* and *Passing*

1929 Jessie Fauset, *Plum Bun* • Wallace Thurman, *The Blacker the Berry* • Stock Market Crash ushers in Great Depression

1930–1951

1930 W. D. Fard founds Nation of Islam

1931 Arna Bontemps, *God Sends Sunday* • "Scotsboro boys" unjustly convicted of raping two white women in Alabama, prompting nationwide protest

1932 Sterling A. Brown, *Southern Road* • Thurman, *Infants of the Spring*

1933 President Roosevelt pushes "New Deal" through Congress

1934 Nancy Cunard, *Negro, An Anthology*

1935 Zora Neale Hurston, *Mules and Men* • National Council of Negro Women founded

1936 Bontemps, *Black Thunder* • Jesse Owens wins four gold medals at "Nazi Olympics" in Berlin

1937 Hurston, *Their Eyes Were Watching God* • Joe Louis becomes world boxing heavyweight champion

1938 Richard Wright, *Uncle Tom's Children* • Crystal Bird Fauset elected to Pennsylvania House of Representatives, becoming first African American woman state legislator

1939–45 World War II

1939 Contralto Marian Anderson sings at Lincoln Memorial for 75,000 after her concert at Constitution Hall was prevented by Daughters of American Revolution

1940 Wright, *Native Son* • Hughes, *The Big Sea* • Robert Hayden, *Heart-Shape in the Dust*

1941 United States enters war after Japanese attack on Pearl Harbor • A. Philip Randolph of the Brotherhood of Sleeping Car Porters organizes march on Washington to protest segregation in the military and employment discrimination; President Roosevelt issues executive order forbidding racial and religious discrimination in government training programs and defense industries; Randolph calls off march

1942 Hurston, *Dust Tracks on a Road* • Margaret Walker, *For My People*

1943 First successful "sit-in" demonstration staged by Congress of Racial Equality (CORE) • Over 40 killed in race riots in Detroit and Harlem

1944 Melvin B. Tolson, *Rendezvous with America*

1945 Wright, *Black Boy* • Gwendolyn Brooks, *A Street in Bronzeville*

1946 Ann Petry, *The Street*

1947 Tolson named Poet Laureate of Liberia

1948 Dorothy West, *The Living Is Easy* • President Truman approves desegregation of the military and creates Fair Employment Board

1950–53 Korean War

1950 Brooks wins Pulitzer Prize for *Annie Allen* (1949) • Gwendolyn Brooks is first African American to win Pulitzer Prize in any category • Ralph J. Bunche is first African American to receive Nobel Peace Prize

1951 Hughes, *Montage of a Dream Deferred*

1952 Ralph Ellison, *Invisible Man*

1953 Tolson, *Libretto for the Republic of Liberia* • Brooks, *Maud Martha* • James Baldwin, *Go Tell It on the Mountain* • Wright, *The Outsider*

1954 In *Brown v. Board of Education*, Supreme Court declares segregated schools unconstitutional, overturning *Plessy v. Ferguson* (1896)

1955 Baldwin, *Notes of a Native Son* • Rosa Parks arrested for refusing to give seat on bus to white man, setting off bus boycott led by Dr. Martin Luther King Jr. • 14-year-old Emmett Till lynched in Mississippi • Supreme Court orders speedy integration of schools • Interstate Commerce Commission orders integration of buses, trains, and waiting rooms for interstate travel

1956 101 southern congressmen sign "Southern Manifesto" against school desegregation

1957 Congress approves Civil Rights Act of 1957 • Federal troops sent to Alabama to enforce school desegregation • Ghana is first African nation to gain independence from colonial rule

1959 Lorraine Hansberry's *A Raisin in the Sun* is first Broadway play by an African American woman • Paule Marshall, *Brown Girl, Brownstones*

1960 Sit-in staged by 4 black students at Woolworth's lunch counter in North Carolina • Student Non-violent Coordinating Committee (SNCC) founded • Congress passes Civil Rights Act of 1960

1961 Hughes, *The Best of Simple* • Hoyt Fuller revives *Negro Digest* • LeRoi Jones (Amiri Baraka), *Preface*

to a Twenty Volume Suicide Note • Baraka, *Dutchman* • 13 "freedom riders" sponsored by CORE take bus trip across South to force integration of terminals

1962 First Production of Adrienne Kennedy's Obie Award–winning play *Funnyhouse of a Negro* • Hayden, *Ballad of Remembrance* • Baldwin, *Another Country* • Riots break out after Supreme Court orders University of Mississippi to accept James H. Meredith as first black student; 12,000 federal troops are employed to restore order and ensure Meredith's admission

1963 Martin Luther King writes *Letter from Birmingham Jail* • National support for civil rights roused after police attack Alabama demonstration led by King • Civil rights "March on Washington" attracts over 200,000 demonstrators; King delivers *I Have a Dream* speech • President Kennedy assassinated

1964 Tolson, *Harlem Gallery* • Ellison, *Shadow and Act* • Baraka's *Dutchman* wins Obie Award • Malcolm X founds Organization of Afro-American Unity, officially splitting with Elijah Muhammad and the Black Muslims • 3 civil rights workers murdered in Mississippi by white segregationists, setting off Mississippi "Freedom Summer" • King wins Nobel Peace Prize • 24th Amendment ratified, outlawing poll tax used to limit black suffrage • Congress passes Civil Rights Act of 1964 and Economic Opportunity Act • Sidney Poitier wins Academy Award for *Lilies of the Field* • Cassius Clay wins world heavyweight boxing championship, subsequently converts to Islam and changes name to Muhammad Ali

1965–73 Vietnam War

1965 Malcolm X, *The Autobiography of Malcolm X* • A. B. Spellman, *The Beautiful Days* • King leads march from Selma to Montgomery, Alabama • Malcolm X assassinated in New York City • Watts riot is most serious single racial disturbance in U.S. history • Black Arts Movement started by Amiri Baraka in Harlem

1966 Black Panther Party founded • National Organization for Women founded • Senator Edward W. Brooke (R-MA) becomes first elected black senator since Reconstruction • "Black Power" concept is adopted by CORE and SNCC

1967 Haki R. Madhubuti, *Think Black* • Jay Wright, *Death as History* • Ishmael Reed, *The Free-Lance Pallbearers* • King announces opposition to Vietnam War • Worst race riot in U.S. history in Detroit kills 43; major riots in Newark and Chicago • Thurgood Marshall becomes first black U.S. Supreme Court justice • Supreme Court overturns law against interracial marriage

1968 Etheridge Knight, *Poems from Prison* • Nikki Giovanni, *Black Feeling* • Eldridge Cleaver, *Soul on Ice* • Quincy Troupe's anthology *Watts Poets: A Book of New Poetry and Essays* • Carolyn Rodgers, *Paper Soul* • Earnest Gaines, *Bloodline* • Audre Lorde, *The First Cities* • June Jordan, *Who Look at Me* • Alice Walker, *Once: Poems* • King assassinated in Memphis • Senator Robert F. Kennedy assassinated in Los Angeles • Shirley Chisholm becomes first black woman elected to U.S. Congress

1969 Sonia Sanchez, *homecoming* • Jayne Cortez, *Pisstained Stairs and the Monkey Man's Wares* • Lucille Clifton, *Good Times* • Al Young, *Dancing: Poems* • Major antiwar demonstrations in Washington

1970 Charles Gordon wins Pulitzer Prize for *No Place to Be Somebody* (1969) • Mari Evans, *I Am a Black Woman* • Maya Angelou, *I Know Why the Caged Bird Sings* • Toni Morrison, *The Bluest Eye* • Michael S. Harper, *Dear John, Dear Coltrane* • Toni Cade Bambara edits *The Black Woman*

1971 Addison Gayle, *The Black Aesthetic* • Angelou, *Just Give Me A Cool Drink of Water 'fore I Diiie* • Gaines, *Autobiography of Miss Jane Pittman* • Supreme Court approves busing as method of desegregation • Supreme Court rules closing of Mississippi swimming pools to avoid desegregation is constitutional

1972 Reed, *Mumbo Jumbo* • Congress passes Equal Rights Amendment, which goes to states for ratification • Chisholm is first black woman to run for U.S. president

1973 Knight, *Belly Song and Other Poems* • Morrison, *Sula* • Supreme Court prohibits state restrictions on abortions in *Roe v. Wade*

1974 Charles Johnson, *Oxherding Tale* • Albert Murray, *Train Whistle Guitar*

1975 Ntozake Shange's *for colored girls who have considered suicide/when the rainbow is enuf* is second play by an African American woman to reach Broadway • Sherley Anne Williams, *Peacock Poems* • Gayl Jones, *Corregidora*

1976 Alex Haley awarded special Pulitzer Prize for *Roots* • Kennedy, *A Movie Star Has to Star in Black and White* • Octavia Butler, *Patternmaster*

1977 Wanda Coleman, *Art in the Court of the Blue Fag* • Rita Dove, *Ten Poems* • TV miniseries based on Alex Haley's *Roots* attracts more viewers than any television program in history

1978 James Alan McPherson wins Pulitzer Prize for his 1977 *Elbow Room* • Shange, *Nappy Edges* • Supreme Court disallows quotas for college admissions but gives limited approval to affirmative action programs

1979 Walker edits *I Love Myself When I Am Laughing: A Zora Neale Hurston Reader* • Butler, *Kindred*

1980 Bambara, *The Salt Eaters* • Liberian president William Tolbert ousted by Staff Sargeant Samuel K. Doe, ending over 130 years of Americo-Liberian rule over indigenous Africans

1981 David Bradley, *The Chaneysville Incident*

1982 Charles Fuller wins Pulitzer Prize for his 1981 *A Soldier's Play* • Marshall, *Reena and Other Stories* • Lorde, *Zami: a new spelling of my name* • Gloria Naylor, *The Women of Brewster Place* • Equal Rights Amendment fails after 10 years, 3 states short of ratification

1983 Alice Walker wins Pulitzer Prize for her 1982 *The Color Purple*

1984 John Wideman, *Brothers and Keepers* • August Wilson's *Ma Rainey's Black Bottom* opens on Broadway • Rev. Jesse Jackson is first

serious black contender for the U.S. presidency, winning 17 percent of popular vote in democratic primary • Vanessa Williams crowned first black Miss America

1985 Wideman, *The Homewood Trilogy* • Michelle Cliff, *The Land of Look Behind* • Jamaica Kincaid, *Annie John*

1986 Williams, *Dessa Rose* • Essex Hemphill, *Conditions* • Martin Luther King's birthday officially celebrated as federal holiday • Wole Soyinka of Nigeria is first person of African descent to win Nobel Prize for Literature

1987 Wilson wins Pulitzer Prize for Broadway play *Fences* (1986) • Dove wins Pulitzer Prize for *Thomas and Beulah* (1986)

1988 Morrison wins Pulitzer Prize for *Beloved* (1987) • Young, *Seduction by Light* • Naylor, *Mama Day*

1989 500,000 march in Washington for prochoice rally • L. Douglas Wilder of Virginia is first elected black governor • General Colin Powell becomes first black Chief of Staff for U.S. Armed Forces • Supreme Court approves state limits on abortion

1990 Wilson wins Pulitzer Prize for *The Piano Lesson* • Johnson's *Middle Passage* wins National Book Award • Cliff, *Bodies of Water* • Kincaid, *Lucy* • Walter Mosley, *Devil in a Blue Dress*

1991 Clarence Thomas confirmed Supreme Court justice, despite Anita Hill's sexual harassment testimony

1992 Jordan, *Technical Difficulties* • Dove, *Through the Ivory Gate* • Terry

McMillan, *Waiting to Exhale* • Police acquitted of beating Rodney King, setting off riots in Los Angeles • Carol Moseley Braun of Illinois becomes first African American woman elected to the U.S. Senate • Supreme Court rules against state bans of "hate speech" • Derek Walcott is first West Indian to win Nobel Prize for Literature

1993 Yusef Komunyakaa wins Pulitzer Prize for *Neon Vernacular* • Cornel West, *Race Matters* • Sarah and A. Elizabeth Delany, *Having Our Say: The Delany Sisters' First 100 Years* • Toni Morrison is first African American to win Nobel Prize for Literature • Maya Angelou reads *On the Pulse of Morning* at Clinton inauguration, becoming the first black poet to participate in a U.S. presidential inauguration • Supreme Court disallows congressional districts drawn to increase black representation

1994 Henry Louis Gates Jr., *Colored People* • Nathan McCall, *Makes Me Wanna Holler: A Young Black Man in America* • Brent Staples, *Parallel Time: Growing Up in Black and White* • Rita Dove named U.S. Poet Laureate • O.J. Simpson accused of murdering ex-wife and her friend; ensuing trial grips nation

1995 Dorothy West, *The Wedding* • Jamaica Kincaid, *The Autobiography of My Mother* • Rita Dove, *Mother Love* • O.J. Simpson acquitted of murder charges • Million Man March in Washington organized by Nation of Islam minister Louis Farrakhan • Colin Powell is first African American seriously considered as a presidential candidate of a major party

1996 Walter Mosley, *A Little Yellow Dog* • Terry McMillan, *How Stella Got Her Groove Back* • August Wilson, *Seven Guitars*, on Broadway

Selected Bibliographies

THE VERNACULAR TRADITION

Studies of the African American vernacular have been many and varied; most refer to this area either as "folklore" or as "popular culture." (This anthology prefers "vernacular" because it is relatively free of the baggage associated with other terms and because certain vernacular forms, such as jazz, should not be categorized as "folk" expression.) Some of the most outstanding general studies of the field are Alan Dundes, ed., *Mother Wit from the Laughing Barrel: Readings in the Interpretation of Afro-American Folklore* (1977); Lawrence Levine's *Black Culture and Black Consciousness* (1977); Roger Abrahams and John Szwed, eds., *After Africa* (1983); and Sterling Stuckey's *Slave Culture: Nationalist Theory and the Foundations of Black America* (1987). For a general introduction to the meaning of vernacular materials, see also Melville Herskovitz's *The Myth of the Negro Past* (1941); Albert Murray's *The Omni-Americans* (1970); Robert F. Thompson's *Flash of the Spirit: African and Afro-American Art and Philosophy* (1983); and Ralph Ellison's *Collected Essays* (1995). Useful reference books for tracking down data concerning the vernacular include John Szwed and Roger Abrahams, eds., *Afro-American Folk Culture: An Annotated Bibliography* (1978); William R. Ferris Jr., ed., *Encyclopedia of Southern Culture* (1989); and Jack Salzman, Cornel West, and David L. Smith, eds., *Encyclopedia of African American History and Culture* (1995).

For information concerning spirituals and gospel music, James Weldon Johnson and J. Rosamond Johnson's *Book of American Negro Spirituals* (1925–26) is indispensable. Also very important are W. E. B. Du Bois's *Souls of Black Folk* (1903), particularly the chapter "The Sorrow Songs"; Howard W. Odum and Guy B. Johnson's *Negro and His Songs* (1925); Bernard Katz, ed., *Social Implications of Early Negro Music in the United States* (1969); Tony Heilbut's *Gospel Sound* (1971); John Lovell's *Forge and the Flame* (1972); James Cone's *Spirituals and the Blues* (1972); and Eileen Southern's *Music of Black Americans* (3rd ed., 1997). Michael W. Harris's *Rise of Gospel Blues: The Music of Thomas Andrew Dorsey* (1992) is an extremely useful study of this music and one of its major composers.

Studies of blues music might start with relevant chapters in Sterling A. Brown, Arthur P. Davis, Ulysses Lee, eds., *The Negro Caravan* (1941);

Langston Hughes and Arna Bontemps, eds., *Book of American Negro Folklore* (1958); Amiri Baraka (LeRoi Jones)'s *Blues People* (1963); Charles Keil's *Urban Blues* (1966); Jeff Todd Titon's *Early Downhome Blues* (1977); and Robert Palmer's *Deep Blues* (1981) are excellent studies of the history of the blues. W. C. Handy's autobiography, *Father of the Blues* (1976), is a very important document. Albert Murray's *Stomping the Blues* (1976) offers the most significant analysis of the music's meaning. See also the study by Houston A. Baker Jr., *Blues, Ideology, and Afro-American Literature* (1980).

Secular rhymes and songs (beyond the blues) have been studied with care by Howard W. Odum and Guy B. Johnson in their *Negro Workaday Songs* (1926). Also available are Harold Courlander's *Negro Folk Music USA* (1963); Roger Abrahams's *Deep Down in the Jungle* (1970); Dana Epstein's *Sinful Tunes and Spirituals* (1977); and Abrahams's *Singing the Master* (1992). Consult also Sterling A. Brown, "Negro Folk Expression: Spirituals, Seculars, Ballads and Work Songs," *Phylon* (1953).

For an overview of jazz, consult Barry Ulanov's *History of Jazz in America* (1952); Marshall W. Stearns's *Story of Jazz* (1956); and Gunther Schuller's *Early Jazz* (1968) and *The Swing Era* (1989). The most reliable books on the meaning of the music are Amiri Baraka (LeRoi Jones)'s *Blues People* (1963); Ralph Ellison's *Shadow and Act* (1964); Albert Murray's *Stomping the Blues* (1976); and Martin Williams's *Jazz Tradition* (1983). Consult also these autobiographies: Willie "the Lion" Smith's *Music on My Mind* (1964), Duke Ellington's *Music Is My Mistress* (1973), and Dizzy Gillespie's *To Be or Not to Bop* (1979).

For studies of black sermons and prayers, consult James Weldon Johnson's *God's Trombones* (1927), Zora Neale Hurston's *Sanctified Church* (1983), and Gerald L. Davis's *I Got the Word in Me and I Can Sing It, You Know* (1985). See also Charles V. Hamilton's *Black Preacher in America* (1972).

The language of black tale-telling traditions has been studied by Geneva Smitherman in her *Talking and Testifyin'* (1977) and *Black Talk* (1994). Tales themselves have been collected in Joel Chandler Harris's *Uncle Remus: His Songs and Sayings* (1880); William Wells Brown's *Southern Home* (1882); Richard Dorson's *American Negro*

Folktales (1967); Roger Abrahams's *Afro-American Folktales* (1985); and E. C. L. Adams's *Tales of the Congaree* (1987). Zora Neale Hurston's *Mules and Men* (1935) is particularly useful because it presents tales in their social/ritual contexts. Hurston's book brings the material to life and comments, indirectly, on its meanings for its creators. For a collection of contemporary tales, see Daryl Dance's *Shuckin' and Jivin'* (1978).

The best study of rap music is Tricia Rose's *Black Noise* (1993). For background, see Nelson George's *The Death of Rhythm and Blues* (1991). For specific data about rap groups, David Toop's *Rap Attack 2* (1992) is a key source.

THE LITERATURE OF SLAVERY AND FREEDOM
1746–1865

William Wells Brown

The most informative edition of Brown's *Narrative* was done by Larry Gara in 1969. The definitive biography is William Edward Farrison's *William Wells Brown: Author and Reformer* (1969). Substantive treatments of Brown as an autobiographer and/or novelist appear in Vernon Loggins's *The Negro Author* (1931), J. Saunders Redding's *To Make a Poet Black* (1939), Jean Fagan Yellin's *The Intricate Knot* (1972), Robert B. Stepto's *From Behind the Veil* (1979), William L. Andrews's *To Tell a Free Story* (1986), Bernard W. Bell's *The Afro-American Novel and Its Tradition* (1987), Blyden Jackson's *A History of Afro-American Literature. Vol. 1. The Long Beginning* (1989), and Ann duCille's *The Coupling Convention* (1993).

Frederick Douglass

The definitive edition of the writings of Frederick Douglass is currently being published by Yale University Press under the general editorship of John W. Blassingame. Handy editions of Douglass's *Narrative* have been fashioned by Houston A. Baker Jr. (1982), David W. Blight (1993), and William L. Andrews and William S. McFeely (1996). Andrews has also edited Douglass's second autobiography, *My Bondage and My Freedom* (1987) and the *Oxford Frederick Douglass Reader* (1996). Douglass's novella, *The Heroic Slave*, is available in *Three Classic African-American Novels* (1990), also edited by Andrews. The 1892 version of the *Life and Times of Frederick Douglass* appears in a modern reprint introduced by Rayford W. Logan (1962). *Frederick Douglass: Autobiographies* (1994), with notes by Henry Louis Gates Jr., puts the *Narrative*, *My Bondage and My Freedom*, and the 1892 version of the *Life and Times* in a single volume. William S. McFeely's *Frederick Douglass* (1991) is the best complete biography, although Dickson J. Preston's *Young Frederick Douglass* is excellent on Douglass's years in slavery and Benjamin Quarles's *Frederick Douglass* (1948) is always informative. Waldo E. Martin Jr.'s *The Mind of Frederick Douglass* (1984) offers a comprehensive intellectual portrait. Valuable critical studies can be found in Vernon Loggins's *The Negro Author* (1931), Stephen Butterfield's *Black Autobiography in America* (1974), Houston A. Baker Jr.'s *The Journey Back* (1980) and *Blues, Ideology, and Afro-American Literature* (1984), William L. Andrews's *To Tell a Free Story* (1986) and *Critical Essays on Frederick Douglass* (1991), Eric Sundquist's edited *Frederick Douglass: New Literary and Historical Essays* (1990), and Sundquist's *To Wake the Nations* (1993).

Olaudah Equiano

Paul Edwards, the foremost authority on Equiano, has produced a useful, two-volume facsimile edition of the *Narrative* (1969). A valuable, copiously annotated modernized edition of the *Narrative*, edited by Vincent Caretta, was published in 1995. The most thorough analysis of Equiano and the *Narrative* in the context of eighteenth-century black writing is Angelo Costanzo's *Surprizing Narrative: Olaudah Equiano and the Beginnings of Black Autobiography* (1987). Critical evaluations and commentary on the *Narrative* appear in Vernon Loggins's *The Negro Author* (1931), Stephen Butterfield's *Black Autobiography in America* (1974), and Houston A. Baker Jr.'s *The Journey Back* (1980).

Ada [Sarah L. Forten]

Sarah Forten's poems and essays have never been collected, nor has much information about her life been assembled. In *We Are Your Sisters: Black Women in the Nineteenth Century* (1984), Dorothy Sterling provides useful biographical information and a sampling from Forten's letters.

Henry Highland Garnet

Garnet's writing has suffered editorial neglect in the twentieth century. There is no collection of his speeches and essays. Modern studies of Garnet are headed by Earl Ofari's *Let Your Motto Be Resistance* (1972) and Joel Schor's *Henry Highland Garnet: A Voice of Black Radicalism in the Nineteenth Century* (1977). Sterling Stuckey's *Slave Culture* (1987) also contains an important analysis of Garnet's significance.

Frances E. W. Harper

The most comprehensive collections of Frances Harper's poems, essays, and short fiction are Frances Smith Foster's *A Brighter Coming Day: A Frances E. W. Harper Reader* (1990) and Mary Emma Graham's *The Complete Poems of Frances E. W. Harper* (1988). The best current editions of Harper's best known novel, *Iola Leroy; or, Shadows Uplifted*, are edited by Hazel V. Carby (1987), and Foster (1988). Three recently rediscovered serial novels by Harper, edited by Foster, were published in 1994. The first full-length biography of Harper has been written by Melba Boyd (1994). The best nineteenth-century source on Harper's life is William Still's The Underground Railroad (1871; rpt. 1970). Influential critical examinations of Harper's work may be found in Carby's Reconstructing Womanhood (1987), Mary Helen Washington's Invented Lives (1988), and Foster's Written by Herself: Literary Production of Early African American Women Writers (1993).

George Moses Horton

Horton's poems have been widely anthologized, but there is no standard edition. The most complete biography is Richard Walser's The Black Poet: The Story of George Moses Horton, a North Carolina Slave (1966). As a preface to his second collection of poems, the Poetical Works, Horton wrote a brief autobiography that covers his life up to the early 1830s. Useful critical studies include J. Saunders Redding's To Make a Poet Black (1939), Blyden Jackson and Louis D. Rubin Jr.'s Black Poetry in America (1974), Merle A. Richmond's Bid the Vassal Soar (1974), and Joan R. Sherman's Invisible Poets (1989).

Harriet Ann Jacobs

The best introduction to and most reliable edition of Incidents in the Life of a Slave Girl are to be found in Jean Fagan Yellin's annotated edition of Incidents (1987), which also contains a generous sampling of Jacobs's correspondence. Yellin is also at work on the first biography of Jacobs. Among the better studies of Incidents are discussions in William L. Andrews's To Tell a Free Story (1986), Hazel V. Carby's Reconstructing Womanhood (1987), Valerie Smith's Self-Discovery and Authority in Afro-American Narrative (1987), Joanne M. Braxton's Black Women Writing Autobiography (1989), Dana D. Nelson's The Word in Black and White (1992), and Carla L. Peterson's Doers of the Word: African-American Women Speakers and Writers in the North (1830–1880) (1995).

Victor Séjour

Although there is no biography of Séjour, sketches of his life and work by Thomas Bonner in Afro-American Writers before the Harlem Renaissance (1986), edited by Trudier Harris, and by Philip Barnard in the Oxford Companion to African American Literature (to be published in 1997), edited by William L. Andrews, Frances Smith Foster, and Trudier Harris, are useful. See also Charles Edwards O'Neill's "Nineteenth-Century Black Artists and Authors," in Louisiana's Black Heritage (1979), edited by Robert R. MacDonald et al., and J. John Perret's "Victor Séjour, Black French Playwright from Louisiana," French Review 57 (1983).

Maria W. Stewart

The most complete biographical and critical treatment of Stewart is included in Maria W. Stewart, America's First Black Woman Political Writer (1987), Marilyn Richardson's edition of Stewart's essays and speeches. Excerpts from Stewart's writing, along with biographical information, appear in Dorothy Sterling's We Are Your Sisters (1984). Paula Giddings discusses Stewart's historical importance in When and Where I Enter (1984). Carla L. Peterson comments on Stewart's religious writing and sermons in "Doers of the Word": African-American Women Speakers and Writers in the North (1830–1880).

Lucy Terry

What little is known about Lucy Terry is in George Sheldon's A History of Deerfield, Massachusetts (1895), vol. 1, and Lorenzo J. Green's The Negro in Colonial New England (1942). Frances Smith Foster offers an analysis of Bars Fight in Written by Herself: Literary Production of Early African American Women Writers (1993).

Sojourner Truth

Two editions of the Narrative of Sojourner Truth are reliable: that of Margaret Washington (1993), which reprints the 1850 edition of the Narrative accompanied by a historical introduction and notes, and that of Jeffrey Stewart (1991), which reprints the 1878 edition of the Narrative along with the History of Her Labors and Correspondence Drawn from Her "Book of Life." Modern biographies include Carlton Mabee's (with Susan Mabee Newhouse) Sojourner Truth (1993) and Nell Irvin Painter's Sojourner Truth, a Life, a Symbol (1996). Helpful studies of Truth in historical and cultural context are Dorothy Sterling's We Are Your Sisters: Black Women in the Nineteenth Century (1984) and Jean Fagan Yellin's Women and Sisters: The Antislavery Feminists in American Culture (1989).

David Walker

Herbert Aptheker's One Continual Cry (1965) and Charles M. Wiltse's David Walker's Appeal (1965) are two useful editions of the Appeal that remain valuable today. Vernon Loggins in The Negro Author (1931) comments on Walker, as does Lerone Bennett's Pioneers in Protest (1968). In Long Black Song (1972), Houston A. Baker Jr. develops a comparative analysis of the style and substance of Walker's writing and that of Douglass.

Phillis Wheatley

Three fine editions of Wheatley's poems and prose are available: William H. Robinson's Phillis Wheatley and Her Writings (1984), John C. Shields's The Collected Works of Phillis Wheatley (1988), and Julian Mason's The Poems of Phillis Wheatley (1989). Robinson's Phillis Wheatley: A Bio-Bibliography is the place to start for reliable biographical or bibliographical facts about Wheatley. Robinson is also the editor of Critical Essays on Phillis Wheatley (1981), which surveys the development of her literary critical reputation from the eighteenth century to the present. The following books contain influential studies of Wheatley: Vernon Loggins's *The Negro Author* (1931), J. Saunders Redding's *To Make a Poet Black* (1939), Merle A. Richmond's *Bid the Vassal Soar* (1974), Houston A. Baker Jr.'s *The Journey Back* (1980), Henry Louis Gates Jr.'s *Figures in Black* (1987), and Frances Smith Foster's *Written by Herself: Literary Production of Early African American Women Writers* (1993).

James M. Whitfield

Although Whitfield's poetry has been often anthologized, it has never been collected and edited in a scholarly manner. No book-length biography of the poet exists. Brief critical discussions appear in Vernon Loggins's *The Negro Author* (1931) and Blyden Jackson's *A History of Afro-American Literature. Vol. 1. The Long Beginning* (1989). The most thorough biographical and analytic treatment of

Whitfield and his work is in Joan R. Sherman's *Invisible Poets* (1989).

Harriet E. Wilson

The 1983 facsimile edition of *Our Nig*, with an introduction and notes by Henry Louis Gates Jr., is the best single way to begin the study of Wilson and her novel. Gates also has a useful essay on *Our Nig* in his *Figures in Black* (1987). Shorter discussions of the novel appear in James Kinney's *Amalgamation!* (1985), Bernard W. Bell's *The Afro-American Novel and Its Tradition* (1987), Hazel V. Carby's *Reconstructing Womanhood* (1987), and Ann duCille's *The Coupling Convention* (1993). A recent essay by Barbara A. White, " 'Our Nig' and the She-Devil: New Information about Harriet Wilson and the 'Bellmont Family,' " *American Literature* 65 (1993), combines original historical research with thoughtful analytic criticism.

THE LITERATURE OF THE RECONSTRUCTION TO THE NEW NEGRO RENAISSANCE: 1865–1919

William Stanley Braithwaite

Lyrics of Life and Love and *The House of Falling Leaves, with Other Poems* were reissued by Mnemosyne in 1969. *The William Stanley Braithwaite Reader* (1972) makes available additional selections of his work. The best overall treatment of Braithwaite's contributions can be found in Kenny Williams's "Invisible Partnership and Unlikely Relationship: William Stanley Braithwaite and Harriet Moore," *Callaloo* 10 (1987).

Charles W. Chesnutt

Chesnutt's novels and short stories are all in print in a variety of inexpensive editions.

The two most valuable book-length studies of Chesnutt are Frances Richardson Keller's *An American Crusade: The Life of Charles Waddell Chesnutt* (1978) and William L. Andrews's *The Literary Career of Charles W. Chesnutt* (1980), which gives a comprehensive critical assessment. Helen M. Chesnutt's *Charles Waddell Chesnutt: Pioneer of the Color Line* (1952) provides an intimate view of her father's life and writing. Richard Brodhead's *The Journals of Charles W. Chesnutt* (1993) is carefully edited. Useful critical discussions of Chesnutt's fiction appear in Robert Bone's *Down Home: Origins of the Afro-American Short Story* (1975), Arlene A. Elder's *The "Hindered Hand"* (1978), Sylvia Lyons Render's *Charles W. Chesnutt* (1980), Bernard W. Bell's *The Afro-American Novel and Its Tradition* (1987), Dickson D. Bruce Jr.'s *Black American Writing from the Nadir* (1989), Richard Brodhead's *Cultures of Letters* (1993), and Eric J. Sundquist's *To Wake the Nations* (1993).

Anna Julia Cooper

A Voice from the South (1892, rpt. 1988) has been edited and introduced by Mary Helen Washington. Louise Daniel Hutchinson's *Anna J. Cooper, A Voice from the South* and Leona Gabel's *From*

Slavery to the Sorbonne and Beyond are full-length studies of Cooper's life and writings. Other important scholarship on Cooper may be found in *Black Women in Nineteenth-Century American Life* (1976), edited by Bert J. Loewenberg and Ruth Bogin; *The Afro-American Woman* (1978), edited by Sharon Harley and Rosalyn Terborg-Penn; and *When and Where I Enter* (1984), by Paula Giddings.

James D. Corrothers

Corrothers's two book-length publications are *The Black Cat Club* (1902) and *In Spite of the Handicap* (1916). For an example of early critical commentary on his work, see James Weldon Johnson, ed., *The Book of American Negro Poetry* (1931). Notable examples of more recent scholarship include Dickson D. Bruce Jr.'s "James Corrothers Reads a Book: Or, the Lives of Sandy Jenkins," *African-American Review* 26 (1992); Kevin Gaines's "Assimilationist Minstrelsy as Racial Uplift Ideology: James D. Corrothers's Literary Quest for Black Leadership," *American Quarterly* 45 (1993); and James Robert Payne's "Griggs and Corrothers: Historical Reality and Black Fiction," *Explorations in Ethnic Studies* 6 (1983).

W. E. B. Du Bois

The *Complete Published Works of W. E. B. Du Bois* (1973–86), edited by Herbert Aptheker, Du Bois's literary executor, numbers thirty-six volumes. In addition, Aptheker has edited the three-volume *Correspondence of W. E. B. Du Bois* (1973–78). *W. E. B. Du Bois: Writings* (1986), edited by Nathan Irvin Huggins, contains *The Suppression of the African Slave-Trade, The Souls of Black Folk, Dusk of Dawn,* and a sizable selection of representative essays and articles by Du Bois. Selections from Du Bois's work appear in *The Seventh Son: The Thought and Writings of W. E. B. Du Bois* (1971), edited by Julius Lester; W. E. B. Du Bois: A Reader (1995), edited by David Levering Lewis; and the Oxford W. E. B. Du Bois Reader (1996), edited by Eric J. Sundquist. Aptheker's Annotated Bibliography of the Published Writings of W. E. B. Du Bois (1973) provides a detailed listing of almost two thousand items.

Earlier biographies—Francis Broderick's W. E. B. Du Bois: Negro Leader in a Time of Crisis (1959) and Elliott M. Rudwick's W. E. B. Du Bois: A Study in Minority Group Leadership (1960)—pay little attention to Du Bois's literary career. The first to give full attention to this dimension of Du Bois's life was Arnold Rampersad's The Art and Imagination of W. E. B. Du Bois (1976). Jack B. Moore's W. E. B. Du Bois (1981) also reviews Du Bois's life through the lens of his writing. David Levering Lewis's W. E. B. Du Bois: Biography of a Race 1868–1919 (1993), the first of a projected two-volume biography, was much praised. Shamoon Zamir's Dark Voices: W. E. B. Du Bois and American Thought, 1888–1903 (1995) discusses Du Bois's ideas.

Among the noteworthy critical books that devote significant space to Du Bois's writing are J. Saunders Redding's To Make a Poet Black (1939), Nathan Irvin Huggins's Harlem Renaissance (1971), Houston A. Baker Jr.'s Long Black Song (1972), Robert B. Stepto's From Behind the Veil: A Study of Afro-American Narrative (1979), Albert E. Stone's Autobiographical Occasions and Original Acts (1982), Wilson J. Moses's Black Messiahs and Uncle Toms (1982), Sterling Stuckey's Slave Culture (1987), Richard Kostelanetz's Politics in the African-American Novel (1991), Michel Fabre's From Harlem to Paris (1991), David L. Dudley's My Father's Shadow: Intergenerational Conflict in African American Men's Autobiography (1991), and Eric J. Sundquist's To Wake the Nations (1993). A useful sampling of important critical studies of Du Bois is William L. Andrews, ed., Critical Essays on W. E. B. Du Bois (1985). Keith Byerman's Seizing the Word: History, Art, and Self in the Work of W. E. B. Du Bois (1994) offers a thorough assessment of Du Bois as a man of letters.

Paul Laurence Dunbar
The most complete edition of Dunbar's poetry is The Collected Poetry of Paul Laurence Dunbar (1993), edited by Joanne M. Braxton. Dunbar's fiction exists in various reprint editions. A handy sampling of his work in a variety of genres appears in The Paul Laurence Dunbar Reader (1975), edited by Jay Martin and Gossie H. Hudson. Reliable biographical treatments are Benjamin Brawley's Paul Laurence Dunbar: Poet of His People (1936), Addison Gayle's Oak and Ivy: A Biography of Paul Laurence Dunbar (1971), and Peter Revell's Paul Laurence Dunbar (1979). Balanced critical assessments of Dunbar appear in J. Saunders Redding's To Make a Poet Black (1939) and Dickson D. Bruce Jr.'s Black American Writing from the Nadir (1989). A Singer in the Dawn: Reinterpretations of Paul

Laurence Dunbar (1975), edited by Jay Martin, offers a thoughtful collection of revisionist analyses of Dunbar's work. Houston A. Baker Jr.'s Singers at Daybreak (1974) and Blues, Ideology, and Afro-American Literature (1984) discuss Dunbar insightfully. Dunbar's contribution to African American fiction is reviewed in Hugh M. Gloster's Negro Voices in American Fiction (1948), Robert Bone's The Negro Novel in America (1965) and Down Home: Origins of the Afro-American Short Story (1975), Arlene A. Elder's The "Hindered Hand": Cultural Implications of Early African-American Fiction (1978), and Bernard W. Bell's The Afro-American Novel and Its Tradition (1987).

Alice Moore Dunbar Nelson
Gloria T. Hull has edited in three volumes The Works of Alice Dunbar-Nelson (1988) and provides insightful analyses of her work in Color, Sex, and Poetry (1987). Also helpful is Dickson D. Bruce Jr.'s Black American Writing from the Nadir (1989). Selections from Dunbar Nelson's diaries have been brilliantly edited by Hull in Give Us Each Day: The Diary of Alice Dunbar-Nelson (1984).

Sutton E. Griggs
Griggs's most important work consists of his five novels: Imperium in Imperio (1899), Overshadowed (1901), Unfettered (1902), The Hindered Hand; or, The Reign of the Repressionist (1905), and Pointing the Way (1908). Among his nonfiction, Wisdom's Call (1911) and The Story of My Struggles (1914) are noteworthy. Helpful critical evaluations of Griggs's work are Robert E. Fleming's "Sutton E. Griggs: Militant Black Novelist," Phylon 34 (1973) and Arlene A. Elder's The "Hindered Hand" (1978).

Charlotte Forten Grimké
Grimké's complete journals have been finely introduced and edited by Brenda Stevenson in The Journals of Charlotte Forten Grimké (1988). An abridged version of the journals (1953), edited by Ray Allen Billington, provides helpful notes and is the basis for Polly Longsworth's fictionalized I, Charlotte Forten, Black and Free (1970). Anna Julia Cooper's Life and Writings of the Grimké Family (1951) has the advantage of having been written by a scholar who was also a lifetime friend. Joan R. Sherman's Invisible Poets: Afro-Americans of the Nineteenth Century (1974) and Joan M. Braxton's Black Women Writing Autobiography (1989) provide cogent discussions of Grimké's writings.

Pauline E. Hopkins
Hopkins's major fiction consists of Contending Forces: A Romance of Negro Life North and South (1900, 1988) and her three novels originally serialized in Colored American Magazine: Hagar's Daughter: A Story of Southern Caste Prejudice (as Sarah A. Allen, 1901–02), Winona: A Tale of Negro Life in the South and Southwest (1902), and Of One Blood; Or, the Hidden Self (1902–03); they are

now available in *The Magazine Novels of Pauline Hopkins* (1988).

For critical commentary on Hopkins's work, see the introductions to *Contending Forces* and *The Magazine Novels* by Richard Yarborough and Hazel V. Carby, respectively. See also Hazel V. Carby's *Reconstructing Womanhood: The Emergence of the Afro-American Woman Novelist* (1987); Ann Allen Shockley's "Pauline Elizabeth Hopkins: A Biographical Excursion into Obscurity," *Phylon* 33 (1972); Claudia Tate's "Pauline Hopkins: Our Literary Foremother," in *Conjuring: Black Women, Fiction, and Literary Tradition* (1985), edited by Marjorie Pryse and Hortense J. Spillers; and *The Unruly Voice: Rediscovering Pauline Elizabeth Hopkins* (1996), edited by John Cullen Greusser.

Fenton Johnson

Johnson's most important publications include *A Little Dreaming* (1913), *Visions of the Dusk* (1915), *Songs of the Soil* (1916), and *Tales of Darkest America* (1920). For critical commentary, see J. Saunders Redding's *To Make a Poet Black* (1939), Eugene Redmond's *Drumvoices: The Mission of Afro-American Poetry* (1976), and Jean Wagner's *Black Poets of the United States from Paul Laurence Dunbar to Langston Hughes* (1973), translated by Kenneth Douglas.

James Weldon Johnson

There is no collected edition of Johnson's writing. His major work of fiction, *The Autobiography of an Ex-Colored Man*, exists in a number of convenient paperback editions. Notable volumes of his poetry are *Fifty Years and Other Poems* (1917, rpt. 1975), *God's Trombones: Seven Negro Sermons in Verse* (1927, rpt. 1976), and *Saint Peter Relates an Incident* (1935, rpt. 1993). Two volumes of *The Selected Writings of James Weldon Johnson* (1995), comprising editorials and social, political, and literary essays, have been edited by Sondra Kathryn Wilson.

Eugene D. Levy's *James Weldon Johnson: Black Leader* (1973) and Robert E. Fleming's *James Weldon Johnson* (1987) offer compact biographical portraits. Critical considerations of Johnson's work can be found in Benjamin Griffith Brawley's *The Negro in Literature and Art in the United States* (1929); Stephen H. Bronz's *Roots of Negro Racial Consciousness in the 1920s* (1964); Jean Wagner's *Black Poets of the United States* (1973), translated by Kenneth Douglas; Robert B. Stepto's *From Behind the Veil: A Study of Afro-American Narrative* (1979); Bernard Bell's *The Afro-American Novel and Its Tradition* (1987); Dickson D. Bruce Jr.'s *Black American Writing from the Nadir: The Evolution of a Literary Tradition, 1877–1915* (1989); Richard Kostelanetz's *Politics in the African-*

American Novel (1991); and Eric J. Sundquist's *The Hammers of Creation: Folk Culture in Modern African-American Fiction* (1992). For a guide to secondary work on Johnson, see *James Weldon Johnson and Arna Wendell Bontemps* (1978), edited by Robert E. Fleming.

Booker T. Washington

The standard edition of Washington's writings is the fourteen-volume *Booker T. Washington Papers* (1972–89), edited by Louis R. Harlan et al. A Norton Critical Edition of *Up From Slavery*, with salient historical and analytical essays, was published in 1996, edited by William L. Andrews. Harlan's *Booker T. Washington: The Making of a Black Leader, 1856–1901* (1972) and *Booker T. Washington: The Wizard of Tuskegee, 1901–1915* (1983) comprise the definitive biography.

Among studies of Washington as a social leader, the following are important: August Meier's *Negro Thought in America, 1880–1915* (1963), Rayford W. Logan's *The Betrayal of the Negro from Rutherford B. Hayes to Woodrow Wilson* (1965), William Toll's *The Resurgence of Race: Black Social Theory from Reconstruction to the Pan-African Conferences* (1979), and James D. Anderson's *The Education of Blacks in the South, 1860–1935* (1988). Rhetorical and cultural analyses of *Up From Slavery* appear in Hugh Hawkins's *Booker T. Washington and His Critics* (1974), Sidonie Smith's *Where I'm Bound: Patterns of Slavery and Freedom in Black American Autobiography* (1974), Robert B. Stepto's *From Behind the Veil: A Study of Afro-American Narrative* (1979), Houston A. Baker Jr.'s *Modernism and the Harlem Renaissance* (1987), James Cox's *Recovering Literature's Lost Ground: Essays in American Autobiography* (1989), and David Dudley's *My Father's Shadow: Intergenerational Conflict in African American Men's Autobiography* (1991).

Ida B. Wells-Barnett

Three of Wells-Barnett's works—*Southern Horrors, A Red Record,* and *Mob Rule in New Orleans*—have been collected in *On Lynchings* (1969). Additional selections may be found in Ann Allen Shockley's *Afro-American Women Writers, 1796–1933* (1988) and *Selected Works of Ida B. Wells-Barnett*. The principal sources of biographical information on Wells-Barnett are her memoirs, collected and edited by her daughter Alfreda Duster as *Crusade for Justice: The Autobiography of Ida B. Wells-Barnett* (1970); *Ida B. Wells-Barnett* (1990), by Mildred Thompson; and *The Memphis Diary of Ida B. Wells* (1995), edited by Miriam Decosta-Willis. Other useful sources include Paula Gidding's *When and Where I Enter* (1984), Gerda Lerner's *Black Women in White America* (1972), and Dorothy Sterling's *Black Foremothers* (1979).

HARLEM RENAISSANCE: 1919–1940

Gwendolyn B. Bennett

Bennett's art regularly appeared on the covers of *Opportunity* and *Messenger*; her column "The Ebony Flute" appeared regularly in *Opportunity*; and other writing (poetry, short stories, essays, reviews) was published in such journals and anthologies as *American Mercury*, *Crisis*, *Fire!!*, *Palms*, *Caroling Dusk* (1927) edited by Countee Cullen, and *Ebony and Topaz* (1927) edited by Charles S. Johnson. Bennett's papers are located at the Schomburg Center for Research in Black Culture, the New York Public Library. For an introduction to her life and work, see Gloria Hull's essay in *Negro American Literature Forum* 9 (1975).

Marita Bonner

Bonner's short stories and essays were published from 1924 to 1941 in *Opportunity*, *Crisis*, *Black Life*, and *Ebony and Topaz* (1927) edited by Charles S. Johnson. Her plays are *The Pot Maker* (1927), *The Purple Flower* (1928), and *Exit, an Illusion* (1929). See *Frye Street and Environs: The Collected Works of Marita Bonner* (1987), edited by Joyce Flynn and Joyce Occomy Stricklin, for her short stories, many of which were previously unpublished. For an introduction to her life and work, see Doris E. Abramson's essay in SAGE 2 (1985) and Lorraine Elena Roses and Ruth Elizabeth Randolph's article in *Black American Literature Forum* 21 (1987).

Arna Bontemps

Bontemps was a prolific writer in a variety of genres: the novels *God Sends Sunday* (1931), *Black Thunder* (1936), and *Drums at Dusk* (1939); the short story collections *They Seek a City* (1945), with Jack Conroy, and *The Old South: "A Summer Tragedy" and Other Stories of the Thirties* (1973); the volume of poetry *Personals* (1963); and numerous children's books, including *Popo and Fifina* (1932), with Langston Hughes. He also edited a number of important works, including *The Poetry of the Negro, 1746–1949* (1949) and *The Book of Negro Folklore* (1958), both with Langston Hughes; *American Negro Poetry* (1963), *Great Slave Narratives* (1969), and *The Harlem Renaissance Remembered* (1972). See also *The Arna Bontemps–Langston Hughes Letters* (1980), edited by Charles Nichols. For bibliographical, biographical, and critical studies, see Arthur P. Davis's *From the Dark Tower* (1974), Robert Bone's *Down Home* (1975), Robert Fleming's *James Weldon Johnson and Arna Wendell Bontemps: A Research Guide* (1978), Nicolas Canady's article in *Callaloo* 4 (1981), Mary Kemp Davis's article in *Black American Literature Forum* 23 (1989), and Kirkland Jones's *Renaissance Man from Louisiana* (1992).

Sterling A. Brown

Brown's poetry can be found in *The Collected Poems of Sterling Brown* (1980), edited by Michael Harper, as well as *Southern Road* (1932); *The Last Ride of Wild Bill and Eleven Narrative Poems* (1975); and, along with essays and reviews, such periodicals as *Opportunity*, *New Republic*, *Nation*, *Journal of Negro Education*, *Phylon*, and *Crisis*. His important critical studies include *Outline for the Study of Poetry of American Negroes* (1931), *The Negro in American Fiction* (1937), and *Negro Poetry and Drama* (1937). He coedited *The Negro Caravan*, an important Harlem Renaissance anthology, in 1941.

Important critical studies and commentaries include Houston Baker's *Long Black Song* (1972); *Sterling A. Brown: A UMUM Tribute* (1976), edited by the Black History Museum Collective; Stephen Henderson's essay in *Black American Literature Forum* 14 (1980); essays in *Callaloo* 5 (1982); Joanne V. Gabbin's *Sterling A. Brown: Building the Black Aesthetic Tradition* (1985); Henry Louis Gates Jr.'s *Figures in Black* (1987); and essays in *Black American Literature Forum* 23 (1989).

Countee Cullen

Cullen's books of poetry include *Color* (1925), *The Ballad of the Brown Girl* (1927), *Copper Sun* (1927), *The Black Christ and Other Poems* (1929), *One Way to Heaven* (1932), *The Medea and Some Poems* (1935). His works have been collected in *On These I Stand: An Anthology of the Best Poems of Countee Cullen* (1947) and *My Soul's High Song: The Collected Writings of Countee Cullen, Voice of the Harlem Renaissance* (1991), edited by Gerald Early. He published two books of short stories, *The Lost Zoo* (1940) and *My Lives and How I Lost Them* (1942), the play *St. Louis Woman* (1946), cowritten with Arna Bontemps, and various essays in *Crisis*, *Opportunity*, and other important periodicals. In 1927, he edited *Caroling Dusk*, an important anthology of the Harlem Renaissance.

Blanche E. Ferguson's biography, *Countee Cullen and the Negro Renaissance* (1966), is useful, but should be supplemented by Margaret Perry's *A Bio-Bibliography of Countee P. Cullen, 1903–1946* (1971) and Alan R. Shucard's *Countee Cullen* (1984). Important critical studies and commentaries include J. Saunders Redding's *To Make a Poet Black* (1939), Stephen H. Bronz's *Roots of Negro Racial Consciousness* (1964), Barbara Christian's *Spirit Bloom in Harlem* (1970), Nathan I. Huggins's *Harlem Renaissance* (1971), Darwin T. Turner's *In a Minor Chord* (1971), Jean Wagner's *Black Poets of the United States* (1973), Houston Baker's *A Many-Colored Coat of Dreams* (1974), Arthur P. Davis's *From the Dark Tower* (1974), Blyden Jackson's *The Waiting Years* (1976), and Bernard W. Bell's *The Afro-American Novel and Its Traditions* (1987).

Jessie Redmon Fauset

Fauset's novels include *There Is Confusion* (1924), *Plum Bun: A Novel without a Moral* (1929), *The Chinaberry Tree* (1931), and *Comedy, American*

Style (1933). She published many poems, short stories, articles, essays, biographical sketches, and reviews in W. E. B. Du Bois's *Crisis* between 1910 and 1933 and, with Du Bois, published a children's magazine, *The Brownies' Book*. For brief introduction to Fauset's life and work, see *Modern American Women Writers* (1991), edited by Elaine Showalter. Important biographical and critical analyses include Robert Bone's *The Negro Novel in America* (1965); Abby Arthur Johnson's article in *Phylon 39* (1978); Joseph J. Feeney's article in *CLA Journal* 22 (1979); Barbara Christian's *Black Women Novelists* (1980); Carolyn Sylvander's *Jessie Redmon Fauset, Black American Writer* (1981); Mary Dearborn's *Pocahontas's Daughters* (1985); Deborah McDowell's article in *Conjuring: Black Women, Fiction, and Literary Tradition* (1985), edited by Marjorie Pryse and Hortense Spillers; Elizabeth Ammons's *Conflicting Stories: American Women Writers at the Turn into the Twentieth Century* (1992); and Ann duCille's *The Coupling Convention: Sex, Text, and Tradition in Black Women's Fiction* (1993).

Rudolph Fisher

Fisher's novels include *The Walls of Jericho* (1928) and *The Conjure Man Dies* (1932). His short stories can be found in *The City of Refuge: The Collected Stories of Rudolph Fisher* (1987), edited by John McCluskey Jr., and *The Short Fiction of Rudolph Fisher* (1987), edited by Margaret Perry.

Important critical studies include Benjamin Brawley's *The Negro Genius* (1937), Sterling A. Brown's *The Negro in American Fiction* (1937), Hugh M. Gloster's *Negro Voices in American Fiction* (1948), Arthur P. Davis's *From the Dark Tower* (1974), Robert Bone's *Down Home* (1975), and Leonard J. Deutsch's essay in *Obsidian* 6 (1980).

Marcus Garvey

Important collections of Garvey's works include *The Philosophy and Opinions of Marcus Garvey* (1923–25), edited by Amy Jacques-Garvey; *The Poetical Works of Marcus Garvey* (1983), edited by Tony Martin; *Message to the People: The Course of African Philosophy* (1986), edited by Tony Martin; and *The Marcus Garvey and the Universal Negro Improvement Association Papers* (1983–87), edited by Robert Hill.

For brief introductions to Garvey's life and work, see *Black Literature Criticism* (1992), edited by James Draper, and J. A. Rogers's, *World's Great Men of Color* (1947), vol. 2. For biographical and historical information, see Rupert Lewis's *Marcus Garvey: Anti-Colonial Champion* (1988), Tony Martin's *Race First: The Ideological and Organizational Struggles of Marcus Garvey and the Universal Negro Improvement Association* (1986), and Amy Jacques-Garvey's *Garvey and Garveyism* (1978). Useful critical assessments and commentaries include Charles Willis Simmons's essay in *The Negro History Bulletin* 25 (1961); Adolph Ed-

wards's *Marcus Garvey, 1887–1940* (1967); *Marcus Garvey and the Vision of Africa* (1973), edited by John Henrik Clarke; Henry J. Young's *Major Black Religious Leaders: 1755–1940* (1977); Lawrence Levine's *Black Leaders of the Twentieth Century* (1982); Tony Martin's *Literary Garveyism* (1983); John Runcie's essay in *Afro-Americans in New York Life and History* 10 (1986); and *Marcus Garvey: A Centenary, 1887–1987* (1988), edited by Erich Huntley. See also Lenwood G. Davis's *Marcus Garvey: An Annotated Bibliography* (1980).

Angelina Weld Grimké

Grimké's poetry appeared in *Opportunity* and in such important Harlem Renaissance anthologies as *The New Negro* (1925), edited by Alain Locke; *Caroling Dusk* (1927), edited by Countee Cullen; and *Ebony and Topaz* (1927), edited by Charles S. Johnson. Her short story *The Closing Door* appeared in Margaret Sanger's *Birth Control Review* in 1919, and her play *Rachel* was first performed in 1916 and published in 1921. The recently released *Selected Works of Angelina Weld Grimké* (1991), edited by Carolivia Herron, collects much of her published and unpublished writings. Her unpublished poems, along with her letters, diaries, scrapbooks, and manuscripts, are with the Grimké family papers at Howard University's Moorland-Spingarn Research Center. For critical analyses of Grimké's work, see Jeanne-Marie A. Miller's article in *CLA Journal* 21 (1978), Doris E. Abramson's article in *SAGE* 2 (1985), Gloria T. Hull's *Color, Sex, and Poetry* (1987) and her article in *Conditions: Five* 2 (1979), Patricia Young's article in *Women and Language* 15 (1992), and David A. Hirsch's essay in *African American Review* 26 (1992).

Langston Hughes

The most important of Hughes's many books of poetry include *The Weary Blues* (1926), *Fine Clothes to the Jew* (1927), *Montage of a Dream Deferred* (1951), and *Ask Your Mama: Twelve Moods for Jazz* (1961). His poetry has been collected in *Selected Poems* (1959) and *The Collected Poems of Langston Hughes* (1994), edited by Arnold Rampersad and David Roessel. Other important books include *Not without Laughter* (1930), *The Ways of White Folks* (1934), and his two autobiographies, *The Big Sea* (1940) and *I Wonder as I Wander* (1956). Anthologies of his writings include *The Langston Hughes Reader* (1958); *The Best of Simple* (1961); *Five Plays by Langston Hughes* (1963), edited by Webster Smalley; and *Good Morning, Revolution: Uncollected Social Protest Writings by Langston Hughes* (1973), edited by Faith Berry. Hughes also wrote many plays, children's books, edited or coedited several important anthologies, including *The Poetry of the Negro, 1746–1949* (1949), *The Book of Negro Folklore* (1958), *New Negro Poets USA* (1964), and *The Best Short Stories by Negro Writers* (1967), and translated books of poetry by Lorca and Guillén, among others. Interested readers should also see *The Arna Bontemps–Langston Hughes Letters* (1980), edited by Charles Nichols.

Arnold Rampersad's biography *The Life of Langston Hughes—Vol. 1, 1902–1941: I, Too, Sing America* (1986), and *Vol. 2, 1941–1967: I Dream a World* (1988)—is essential. Also important is Faith Berry's *Langston Hughes, Before and Beyond Harlem* (1983). For a brief introduction to Hughes's life and work, see *American Writers* (1991), edited by Lea Baechler and A. Walton Litz. Important critical studies of Hughes's works include James A. Emanuel's *Langston Hughes* (1967), Nathan I. Huggins's *Harlem Renaissance* (1971), Jean Wagner's *Black Poets of the United States* (1973), Richard Barksdale's *Langston Hughes: The Poet and His Critics* (1977), Onwuchekwa Jemie's *Langston Hughes: An Introduction to the Poetry* (1977), Edward J. Mullen's *Langston Hughes in the Hispanic World and Haiti* (1977), Steven C. Tracy's *Langston Hughes & the Blues* (1988), and R. Baxter Miller's *The Art and Imagination of Langston Hughes* (1989). For collections of critical essays, see *Langston Hughes, Black Genius: A Critical Evaluation* (1971), edited by Therman O'Daniel; *Black American Literature Forum* 15 (1981); *Critical Essays on Langston Hughes* (1986), edited by Edward J. Mullen; *Langston Hughes* (1989), edited by Harold Bloom; *Langston Hughes: Critical Perspectives Past and Present* (1993), edited by Henry Louis Gates Jr. and K. A. Appiah; *Langston Hughes: The Man, His Art, and His Continuing Influence* (1995), edited by C. James Trotman; and articles in the journal *The Langston Hughes Review*. Important bibliographies include Donald C. Dickinson's *A Bio-Bibliography of Langston Hughes, 1902–1967* (1967), R. Baxter Miller's *Langston Hughes and Gwendolyn Brooks: A Reference Guide* (1978), Thomas A. Mikolyzk's *Langston Hughes: A Bio-Bibliography* (1990), and Sharryn Etheridge's essay in *The Langston Hughes Review* 11 (1992).

Zora Neale Hurston

Hurston's novels include *Jonah's Gourd Vine* (1934), *Their Eyes Were Watching God* (1937), *Moses, Man of the Mountain* (1939), and *Seraph on the Sewanee* (1948). *Mules and Men* (1935) and *Tell My Horse* (1938) combine anthropological material, short stories, and folklore. Her plays include *Color Struck* (1926) and *Mule Bone* (performed 1930, published 1991), which was coauthored by Langston Hughes. Her autobiography *Dust Tracks on a Road* was published in 1942. Important collections of prose include *I Love Myself When I Am Laughing . . . & Then Again When I Am Looking Mean & Impressive* (1979), edited by Alice Walker; *The Sanctified Church* (1981), edited by Toni Cade Bambara; and *Spunk: The Short Stories of Zora Neale Hurston* (1985).

For brief introductions to Hurston's life and work, see *Modern American Women Writers* (1991), edited by Elaine Showalter, and Alice Walker's *In Search of Our Mothers' Gardens* (1983). Robert Hemenway's biography, *Zora Neale Hurston* (1977), is essential. Important critical studies include Darwin T. Turner's *In a Minor Chord* (1971), Robert Bone's *Down Home* (1975), Robert Stepto's *From Behind a Veil* (1979), Barbara Christian's *Black Women Novelists* (1980), Lillie P. Howard's *Zora Neale Hurston* (1980), Mary Helen Washington's *Invented Lives* (1987), Susan Willis's *Specifying* (1987), Karla Holloway's *The Character of the Word* (1987), Barbara Johnson's *A World of Difference* (1987), Henry Louis Gates Jr.'s *The Signifying Monkey* (1988), Michele Wallace's article in *VLS* 64 (1988), and Michael Awkward's *Inspiriting Influences* (1989). Important collections of critical essays on Hurston include *Zora Neale Hurston: Critical Perspectives Past and Present* (1993), edited by Henry Louis Gates Jr. and K. A. Appiah, and *Zora Neale Hurston* (1986), edited by Harold Bloom. *New Essays on Their Eyes Were Watching God* (1990), edited by Michael Awkward, and *Zora Neale Hurston's Their Eyes Were Watching God* (1987), edited by Harold Bloom, are valuable collections of critical essays on Hurston's most important novel. For bibliographical information, see Adele Newson's *Zora Neale Hurston* (1987) and Craig Werner's *Black American Women Novelists: An Annotated Bibliography* (1989).

Georgia Douglas Johnson

Johnson's poetry appeared in such anthologies as *The New Negro* (1925), edited by Alain Locke; *Caroling Dusk* (1927), edited by Countee Cullen; and *Ebony and Topaz* (1927), edited by Charles S. Johnson, and was collected in four books: *The Heart of a Woman and Other Poems* (1918), *Bronze* (1922), *An Autumn Love Cycle* (1928), and *Share My World: A Book of Poems* (1962). For critical and biographical studies, see Cedric Dover's article in *Crisis* 59 (1952), Doris E. Abramson's article in *SAGE* 2 (1985), Jeffrey C. Stewart's article in *Washington Studies* 12 (1986), Gloria Hull's *Color, Sex, and Poetry* (1987), and Jeanne-Marie A. Miller's essay in *CLA Journal* 33 (1990).

Helene Johnson

Johnson's poetry appeared in such journals as *Fire!!, Messenger, Opportunity, Palms,* and *Vanity Fair* and such anthologies as *Caroling Dusk* (1927), edited by Countee Cullen, and *Ebony and Topaz* (1927), edited by Charles S. Johnson. For an introduction to her works, see Gloria T. Hull's article in *Sturdy Black Bridges* (1979), edited by Roseann Bell et al.

Nella Larsen

Larsen's novels include *Quicksand* (1928) and *Passing* (1929). Her essays, reviews, and a short story appeared in such publications as *Opportunity, Forum,* and *The Brownies' Book* and have recently been published in *An Intimation of Things Distant: The Collected Fiction of Nella Larsen* (1992), edited by Charles Larson.

For an introduction to her life and work, see *American Women Writers* (1980), edited by Lina

Mainiero and Langdon Lynne Faust. For important critical and biographical studies, see Hortense Thornton's essay in *CLA Journal* 16 (1973); Addison Gayle Jr.'s *The Way of the New World* (1975); Claudia Tate's article in *Black American Literature Forum* 14 (1980); Cheryl Wall's article in *Black American Literature Forum* 20 (1986); Hazel Carby's *Reconstructing Womanhood: The Emergence of the Afro-American Woman Novelist* (1987); Henry Louis Gates Jr.'s *Figures in Black* (1987); Deborah McDowell's essay in *Black Feminist Criticism and Critical Theory* (1988), edited by Joe Weixlmann and Houston Baker; Elizabeth Ammons's *Conflicting Stories: American Women Writers at the Turn into the Twentieth Century* (1992); Charles R. Larson's *Invisible Darkness: Jean Toomer and Nella Larsen* (1993); Ann duCille's *The Coupling Convention: Sex, Text, and Tradition in Black Women's Fiction* (1993); and Thadious Davis's *Nella Larsen, Novelist of the Harlem Renaissance: A Woman's Life Unveiled* (1994).

Alain Locke

Locke's books include *A Decade of Negro Self-Expression* (1928), *The Negro in America* (1933), *The Negro and His Music* (1936), and *Negro Art: Past and Present* (1936). He edited *Four Negro Poets* (1927), *Plays of Negro Life* (1927), *The Negro in Art* (1940), and *When People Meet: A Study in Race and Culture Contacts* (1942); he is best known, however, for editing the groundbreaking anthology *The New Negro* (1925). For collections of his essays and addresses, see *The Critical Temper of Alain Locke* (1983), edited by Jeffrey Stewart, and *Race Contacts and Interracial Relations* (1992), edited by Jeffrey Stewart. Useful critical studies include *Alain Locke: Reflections on a Modern Renaissance Man* (1982), edited by Russell J. Linneman; Johnny Washington's *Alain Locke and Philosophy: A Quest for Cultural Pluralism* (1986); *The Philosophy of Alain Locke: Harlem Renaissance and Beyond* (1989), edited by Leonard Harris; Everett H. Akam's essay in *American Literary History* 3 (1991); Tommy Lott's essay in *Contemporary Philosophical Perspectives on Pluralism and Multiculturalism* (1994), edited by Lawrence Foster; and George Hutchinson's *The Harlem Renaissance in Black and White* (1995). See also John Edgar Tidwell and John Wright's bibliography in *Callaloo* 4 (1981).

Claude McKay

McKay's books of poetry include *Songs of Jamaica* (1912), *Constab Ballads* (1912), *Spring in New Hampshire and Other Poems* (1920), and *Harlem Shadows* (1922). His writings have been collected in *Selected Poems of Claude McKay* (1953); *The Dialect Poetry of Claude McKay* (1972), edited by Wayne Cooper; and *The Passion of Claude McKay: Selected Poetry and Prose, 1912–1948* (1973), also edited by Cooper. McKay also wrote the novels *Home to Harlem* (1928), *Banjo: A Story without a Plot* (1929), and *Banana Bottom* (1933); the short

story collections *Gingertown* (1932), *Trial by Lynching* (1977), and *My Green Hills of Jamaica* (1979); the autobiography *A Long Way from Home* (1937); and two books of essays, *Harlem: Negro Metropolis* (1940) and *The Negroes in America* (1979).

Useful biographies include Tyrone Tillery's *Claude McKay: A Black Poet's Struggle for Identity* (1991), Wayne F. Cooper's *Claude McKay—Rebel Sojourner in the Harlem Renaissance: A Biography* (1987), and James R. Giles's *Claude McKay* (1976). For important critical analyses and commentaries, see J. Saunders Redding's *To Make a Poet Black* (1939), Stephen H. Bronz's *Roots of Negro Racial Consciousness* (1964), Harold Cruse's *The Crisis of the Negro Intellectual* (1967), Addison Gayle Jr.'s *Claude McKay: The Black Poet at War* (1972), George E. Kent's *Blackness and the Adventure of Western Culture* (1972), Jean Wagner's *Black Poets of the United States* (1973), Robert Bone's *Down Home* (1975), Marian B. McLeod's essay in *CLA Journal* 23 (1980), Robert M. Greenberg's essay in *CLA Journal* 24 (1981), P. S. Chauhan's essay in *CLA Journal* 34 (1990), A. L. McLeod's edited *Claude McKay: Centennial Studies* (1992), and George Hutchinson's *The Harlem Renaissance in Black and White* (1995).

Arthur A. Schomburg

Schomburg's writings have been collected in *The Arthur A. Schomburg Papers* (1991). Elinor Des Verney Sinnette's *Arthur Alphonso Schomburg, Black Bibliophile and Collector* (1989) is a valuable biography.

George Samuel Schuyler

Schuyler's works include *Black No More* (1931), a novel of satire and science fiction, and *Slaves Today* (1931), a muckraking novel; an autobiography, *Black and Conservative: The Autobiography of George S. Schuyler* (1966); two other books, *Racial Intermarriage in the United States* (1929) and *The Communist Conspiracy against the Negro* (1947); and many essays appearing in such journals as *Nation*, *Phylon*, and *American Mercury*. His short fiction has been collected in *Black Empire* (1991), edited by Robert A. Hill and R. Kent Rasmussen, and *Ethiopian Stories* (1995), edited by Robert Hill. For critical studies of Schuyler's works, see Arthur P. Davis's *From the Dark Tower* (1974), Ann Rayson and John Reilly's articles in *Black American Literature Forum* 12 (1978), Michael Peplow's *George S. Schuyler* (1980), Henry Louis Gates Jr.'s essay in the *New York Times Book Review* (Sept. 20, 1992), and George Hutchinson's *The Harlem Renaissance in Black and White* (1995).

Anne Spencer

Spencer's poetry appeared in such important journals as *Opportunity*, *Palms*, and *Crisis* as well as the central anthologies of the Harlem Renaissance, but her unpublished poetry and essays have not yet been collected. The largest collection of her papers is located at the Anne Spencer House Historic Landmark at Lynchburg, Virginia; several letters are at the Beinecke Rare Book and Manuscript Library at Yale University. A good introduction to Spencer's life and work is J. Lee Greene's *Time's Unfading Garden: Anne Spencer's Life and Poetry* (1977).

Wallace Thurman

Thurman is the author of three novels: *The Blacker the Berry* (1929); *Infants of the Spring* (1932); and *The Interne* (1932), with Abraham L. Furman. He collaborated with William Jourdan Rapp on the drama *Harlem* (1929) and was the author of two screenplays: *Tomorrow's Children* (1934) and *High School Girl* (1935). He wrote the nonfictional *Negro Life in New York's Harlem* in 1928. For biographical and critical studies, see Sterling Brown's *The Negro in American Fiction* (1937), Hugh Gloster's *Negro Voices in American Fiction* (1948), Robert Bone's *The Negro Novel in America* (1965), Nathan I. Huggins's *The Harlem Renaissance* (1971), and Eleonore van Notten's *Wallace Thurman's Harlem Renaissance* (1994).

Jean Toomer

Toomer's best-known work is *Cane* (1923), but he also wrote a collection of aphorisms, *Essentials* (1931, rpt. 1991), and two other books. While many of his writings have been collected in *The Wayward and the Seeking: A Collection of Writings by Jean Toomer* (1980), edited by Darwin Turner, and *The Collected Poems of Jean Toomer* (1988), edited by Robert Jones and Margery Toomer Latimer, some short stories, poems, essays, and a play remain uncollected.

Nellie Y. McKay's *Jean Toomer, Artist: A Study of His Literary Life and Work, 1894–1936* (1984),

Cynthia Earl Kerman and Richard Eldridge's *The Lives of Jean Toomer: A Hunger for Wholeness* (1987), and Rudolph P. Byrd's *Jean Toomer's Years with Gurdjieff: Portrait of an Artist, 1923–1936* (1990) are important biographies. Important critical studies and commentaries include Robert Bone's *The Negro Novel in America* (1965); Darwin T. Turner's *In a Minor Chord* (1971); Houston Baker's *Singers of Daybreak* (1975); Bryan Joseph Benson and Mabel Mayle Dillard's *Jean Toomer* (1980); Donald B. Gibson's *The Politics of Literary Expression* (1981); Robert Jones's essay in *Black American Literature Forum* 21 (1987); Henry Louis Gates Jr.'s *Figures in Black* (1987); George Hutchinson's articles in *American Literature* 63 (1991) and *Texas Studies in Literature and Language* 35 (1993); and Charles R. Larson's *Invisible Darkness: Jean Toomer and Nella Larsen* (1993). For collections of critical essays, see *CLA Journal* 17 (1974) and *Jean Toomer: A Critical Evaluation* (1988), edited by Therman B. O'Daniel. For useful bibliographies, see McKay's *Jean Toomer, Artist*, and C. Lynn Munro's essay in *Black American Literature Forum* 21 (1987).

Eric Walrond

Walrond published a collection of short stories, *Tropic Death* (1926), as well as essays and short stories in such periodicals as *New Republic, Opportunity, Messenger*, and *Current History*. For a short time he edited the UNIA's weekly newspaper, *Negro World*. For critical studies of Walrond's life and work, see Hugh Gloster's *Negro Voices in American Fiction* (1948), Robert Bone's *Down Home* (1975), and David Levering Lewis's *When Harlem Was in Vogue* (1981).

REALISM, NATURALISM, MODERNISM: 1940–1960

James Baldwin

Baldwin's novels are *Go Tell It on the Mountain* (1953), *Giovanni's Room* (1956), *Another Country* (1962), *Tell Me How Long the Train's Been Gone* (1968), *If Beale Street Could Talk* (1974), and *Just above My Head* (1979). Baldwin published a short story collection, *Going to Meet the Man* (1965). His essays and other nonfiction are collected in *The Price of the Ticket* (1985). He wrote two plays: *Blues for Mr. Charlie* (1964) and *The Amen Corner* (1968).

James Campbell's *Talking at the Gates: A Life of James Baldwin* (1991) is a recent biography. Critical treatments of Baldwin include Fern Maria Eckman's *The Furious Passage of James Baldwin* (1966), Horace A. Porter's *Stealing the Fire: The Art and Protest of James Baldwin* (1989), and Quincy Troupe's *James Baldwin: The Legacy* (1989). Collections of critical essays are Harold Bloom, ed., *James Baldwin* (1986); Fred L. Stanley and Nancy V. Burt, eds., *Critical Essays on James Baldwin* (1988); and Jakob Kollhofer, ed., *James Baldwin: His Place in American Literary History and His Reception in Europe* (1991).

Gwendolyn Brooks

Volumes of poetry by Brooks include *A Street in Bronzeville* (1945), *Annie Allen* (1949), *Bronzeville Boys and Girls* (1956), *The Bean Eaters* (1960), *Selected Poems* (1963), *In the Mecca* (1968), *Family Pictures* (1970), *Riot* (1970), *Aloneness* (1971), *Beckonings* (1975), *Primer for Blacks* (1981), and *To Disembark* (1981). Brooks's prose works include *Maud Martha* (1953, 1974); the autobiographical *Report from Part One* (1972); "Keziah," *TriQuarterly* 75 (1989); and "45 Years in Culture and Creative Writing; Many Talented New Voices Have Emerged to Comment on Our Complex Turbulent Times," *Ebony* 46 (1990). *The World of Gwendolyn Brooks* (1971) and *Blacks* (1987, 1991) are collections of her poetry and prose. Brooks edited *A Broadside Treasury* (1971), *Jump Bad: A New Chicago Anthology* (1971), and *A Capsule Course in Black Poetry Writing* (1975) as well as the short-lived journal *The Black Position* in 1971.

General critical and biographical information on Brooks can be found in R. Baxter Miller's *Langston Hughes and Gwendolyn Brooks: A Reference*

Guide (1978); Harry B. Shaw's Gwendolyn Brooks (1980); Brian Lanker and Maya Angelou's "I Dream a World," National Geographic 176 (1989); and Martha Satch's "Honest Reporting: An Interview with Gwendolyn Brooks," Southwest Review 74 (1989).

Recent critical considerations of Brooks's work include Mary Helen Washington's "Taming All That Anger Down: Rage and Silence in Gwendolyn Brooks' Maud Martha," Massachusetts Review 24 (1983); Hortense J. Spillers's "'An Order of Constancy': Notes on Brooks and the Feminine," The Centennial Review 29 (1985); Charles Whitaker's "Gwendolyn Brooks—A Poet for All Ages," Ebony 42 (1987); John C. Gruesser's "Afro-American Travel Literature and Africanist Discourse," Black American Literature Forum 24 (1990); Ann Folwell Stanford's "Dialectics of Desire: War and the Resistive Voice in Gwendolyn Brooks's 'Negro Hero' and 'Gay Chaps at the Bar,'" African American Review 26 (1992); Henry Taylor's "Gwendolyn Brooks: An Essential Sanity," The Kenyon Review 13 (1991); Ann Folwell Stanford's "'Like narrow banners for some gathering war': Readers, Aesthetics, and Gwendolyn Brooks's 'The Sundays of Satin-Legs Smith,'" College Literature 17 (1990); Gertrude Reif Hughes's "Making It Really New: Hilda Doolittle, Gwendolyn Brooks, and the Feminist Potential of Modern Poetry," American Quarterly 42 (1990); Malin Lavon Walther's "Re-Wrighting Native Son: Gwendolyn Brooks's Domestic Aesthetic in Maud Martha," Tulsa Studies in Women's Literature 13 (1994); and Brooke Kenton Horvath's "The Satisfactions of What's Difficult in Gwendolyn Brooks's Poetry," American Literature 62 (1990).

Book-length considerations of Brooks's work include Maria K. Mootry and Gary Smith's A Life Distilled: Gwendolyn Brooks, Her Poetry and Fiction (1987), D. H. Melhem's Gwendolyn Brooks: Poetry and the Heroic Voice (1987), George E. Kent's A Life of Gwendolyn Brooks (1990), and Susan Marie Schweik's A Gulf So Deeply Cut: American Women Poets and the Second World War (1991).

Ralph Ellison

Ellison's works include the novel Invisible Man (1952) and two collections of essays, Shadow and Act (1964) and Going to the Territory (1986).

Book-length treatments of Ellison's work include Robert G. O'Meally's The Craft of Ralph Ellison (1980), Robert N. List's Dedalus in Harlem: The Joyce-Ellison Connection (1982), Alan Nadel's Invisible Criticism: Ralph Ellison and the American Canon (1988), Kerry McSweeney's Invisible Man: Race and Identity (1988), and Jerry Gafio Watts's The Black Intellectual: Ralph Ellison, Politics, and Afro-American Intellectual Life (1994). Some collections of essays are John Hersey, ed., Ralph Ellison: A Collection of Critical Essays (1974); Harold Bloom, ed., Ralph Ellison: Modern Critical Views (1986); John M. Reilly, ed., Twentieth Century In-

terpretations of Invisible Man (1970); and Robert G. O'Meally, ed., New Essays on Invisible Man (1988).

Lorraine Hansberry

A Raisin in the Sun (1959) and The Sign in Sidney Brustein's Window (1965) are available in a paperback edited by Robert Nemiroff. Also edited by Nemiroff is Lorraine Hansberry: The Collected Last Plays (1983), which contains Les Blancs, The Drinking Gourd, and What Use Are Flowers? Hansberry wrote the text for a photohistory, The Movement: Documentary of a Struggle for Equality (1964); notable among her essays is "The Negro Writer and His Roots," Black Scholar 12 (1981).

To Be Young, Gifted and Black: An Informal Autobiography of Lorraine Hansberry (1969), edited by Nemiroff, contains biographical material; Nemiroff produced a play with this title. Elizabeth C. Phillips, The Works of Lorraine Hansberry, appeared in 1973. Critical discussions include Harold Cruse's The Crisis of the Negro Intellectual (1967) and Lloyd W. Brown's "Lorraine Hansberry as Ironist," Journal of Black Studies 4 (1974). Important essays by James Baldwin, Nikki Giovanni, Alex Haley, Adrienne Rich, and Margaret B. Wilkerson appear in Lorraine Hansberry: Art of Thunder, Vision of Light, a special issue of Freedomways 4 (1979), edited by Jean Carey Bond. More recent essays, by Steven R. Carter, are "Commitment amid Complexity: Lorraine Hansberry's Life-in-Action," MELUS 7 (1980), and "Images of Men in Lorraine Hansberry's Writing," Black American Literature Forum 19 (1985). Dean Peerman's "A Raisin in the Sun: The Uncut Version," The Christian Century 25 (1989), discusses material cut from the original production of the play. See also Anne Cheney's Lorraine Hansberry (1984) and Margaret Wilkerson's "A Raisin in the Sun: Anniversary of an American Classic," Theatre Journal 38 (1986).

Robert Hayden

The standard collection of Hayden's poetry is Collected Poems (1985), edited by Frederick Glaysher. A large collection of Hayden's poems that reprinted works from earlier volumes, A Ballad of Remembrance (1962), was revised and published in 1966 as Selected Poems. Individual volumes of poetry include Heart-Shape in the Dust: Poems (1940), The Lion and the Archer: Poems (1948), Figure of Time (1955), Words in the Mourning Time: Poems (1970), The Night-Blooming Cereus (1972), Angle of Ascent: New and Selected Poems (1975), and American Journal (1978, 1982). His prose is collected in Collected Prose: Poets on Poetry (1984). Among the numerous anthologies Hayden edited are Kaleidoscope: Poems by American Negro Poets (1967); Afro-American Literature: An Introduction (1971), edited with David J. Burrows and Frederick Lapides; American Models: A Collection of Modern Stories (1973), edited with James E. Miller Jr. and Robert O'Neal; Person, Place and Point of View: Factual Prose for Interpretation and Extension

(1974); and *The Human Condition: Literature Written in the English Language* (1974). Hayden published two surveys of American poetry in the 1970s: "A Portfolio of Recent American Poems," *World Order* 5 (1971), and "Recent American Poetry—Portfolio II," *World Order* 9 (1975). He also wrote the introduction to the *Counterpoise Series* (1948) and the preface to the 1968 edition of Alain Locke's *The New Negro*.

Biographical information on Hayden can be found in Fred M. Fetrow's *Robert Hayden* (1984). Recent critical consideration of Hayden's work includes Xavier Nicholas's "Robert Hayden: Some Introductory Notes," *Michigan Quarterly Review* 31 (1992); Ann M. Gallagher's "Hayden's 'Those Winter Sundays,'" *The Explicator* 51 (1993); Alan Shapiro's "In Praise of the Impure: Narrative Consciousness in Poetry," *TriQuarterly* 81 (1991); Fred M. Fetrow's "Minority Reporting and Psychic Distancing in the Poetry of Robert Hayden," *CLA Journal* 33 (1989); Michael Collins's "On the Track of the Universal: 'Middle Passage' and America," *Parnassus: Poetry in Review* 17 (1992); and Xavier Nicholas "Robert Hayden and Michael Harper: A Literary Friendship," *Callaloo* 17 (1994). Book-length treatments of Hayden's work include John Hatcher's *From the Auroral Darkness: The Life and Poetry of Robert Hayden* (1984) and Pontheolla T. Williams's *Robert Hayden: A Critical Analysis of His Poetry* (1987).

Chester B. Himes

Himes wrote fifteen novels, among them *If He Hollers Let Him Go* (1945), *Lonely Crusade* (1947), *Third Generation* (1954), *The Primitive* (1955), *Cast the First Stone* (1955), *For Love of Imabelle* (1957), *Pinktoes* (1961), and *Cotton Comes to Harlem* (1965). His autobiographies, *The Quality of Hurt* and *My Life of Absurdity*, were published in 1972 and 1976, respectively.

Critical discussions include Stephen F. Milliken's *Chester Himes: A Critical Appraisal* (1976) and Edward Margolies's "The Thrillers of Chester Himes," *Studies in Black Literature* 1 (1970). Very informative is a chapter on Himes in Michel Fabre's *From Harlem to Paris: Black American Writers in Paris* (1991).

Bob Kaufman

Kaufman's work includes the broadside *Abomunisto Manifesto* (1959) and the books *Solitudes Crowded with Loneliness* (1965), *Golden Sardine* (1967), and *The Ancient Rain: Poems 1956–1978* (1981). Critical studies include Kathryne V. Lindberg's "Bob Kaufman, Sir Real, and His Rather Surreal Self-Presentation," *Talisman* 11 (1993); Barbara Christian's "Whatever Happened to Bob Kaufman?," in *Beats: Essays in Criticism* (1981), edited by Lee Bartlett; and Kush's "The Duende of Bob Kaufman," *Third Rail* 8 (1987).

Ann Petry

Petry's novels are *The Street* (1946), *Country Place* (1947), and *The Narrows* (1953). She's also pub-

lished *Miss Muriel and Other Stories* (1971) as well as four children's books: *The Drugstore Cat* (1949), *Harriet Tubman: Conductor of the Underground Railway* (1955), *Tituba of Salem Village* (1988), and *Legends of the Saints* (1964).

Critical discussion of Petry includes George R. Adams's "Riot as Ritual: Ann Petry's *In Darkness and Confusion*," *Negro Literature Forum* 6 (1968); Vernon E. Lattin's "Ann Petry and the American Dream," *Black American Literature Forum* 12 (1978); Margaret McDowell's "*The Narrows*: A Fuller View of Ann Petry," *Black American Literature Forum* 14 (1980); Thelma Shinn's "Women in the Novels of Ann Petry," *Critique* 16 (1984); Gladys J. Washington's "A World Made Cunningly: A Closer Look at Ann Petry's Fiction," *CLA Journal* 30 (1986); Sybil Weir's "*The Narrows*: A Black New England Novel," *Studies in American Fiction* 15 (1987); and Richard Yarborough's "The Quest for the American Dream in Three Afro-American Novels: *If He Hollers Let Him Go*, *The Street*, and *Invisible Man*," *MELUS* 8 (1981).

Melvin B. Tolson

Tolson's poetry includes *Libretto for the Republic of Liberia* (1953), *Harlem Gallery: Book I, The Curator* (1965), and *A Gallery of Harlem Portraits* (1979). His other major works are *Rendezvous with America* (1944), and *Caviar and Cabbage: Selected Columns by Melvin B. Tolson from the Washington Tribune* (1982).

Biographical information on Tolson can be found in Joy Flasch's *Melvin B. Tolson* (1972). Recent critical considerations of Tolson's work include Michael Bérubé's "Masks, Margins, and African American Modernism: Melvin Tolson's *Harlem Gallery*," *PMLA* 105 (1990); Melvin B. Tolson Jr.'s "The Poetry of Melvin B. Tolson," *World Literature Today* 64 (1990); Craig Werner's "Blues for T. S. Eliot and Langston Hughes: The Afro-Modernist Aesthetic of *Harlem Gallery*," *Black American Literature Forum* 24 (1990); and Aldon L. Nielsen's "Melvin B. Tolson and the De-Territorialization of Modernism," *African American Summer Review* 26 (1992). Book-length treatments of Tolson's work include Mariann Russell's *Melvin B. Tolson's Harlem Gallery: A Literary Analysis* (1980), Robert M. Farnsworth's *Melvin B. Tolson, 1898–1966: Plain Talk and Poetic Prophecy*, (1984), and Bérubé's *Marginal Forces/Cultural Centers: Tolson, Pynchon, and the Politics of the Canon* (1992).

Margaret Walker

Walker's poetry is collected in *This Is My Century: New and Collected Poems* (1988). Her individual volumes are *For My People* (1942), *Prophets for a New Day* (1970), and *October Journey* (1973). She has also published the novel *Jubilee* (1966) as well as *How I Wrote "Jubilee"* (1972), *A Poetic Equation: Conversations between Nikki Giovanni and Margaret Walker* (1974), *For Farish Street Green* (1988), and a work on fellow author and friend

Wright: *Richard Wright, Daemonic Genius: A Portrait of the Man, a Critical Look at His Work* (1988). Her articles include "New Poets," in *Black Expressions* (1969), edited by Addison Gayle Jr.; "Willing to Pay the Price," in *Many Shades of Black* (1969), edited by Stanley Wormley and Louis H. Fenderson; "Richard Wright," in *Richard Wright: Impressions and Perspectives* (1973), edited by David Ray and Robert Farnsworth; and "On Being Female, Black and Free," in *The Writer on Her Work* (1980), edited by Janet Sternburg.

Critical essays and biographical material for Walker include Eugenia Collier's "Fields and Watered Blood: Myth and Ritual in the Poetry of Margaret Walker," in *Black Women Writers (1950–1980): A Critical Evaluation* (1984), edited by Mari Evans; Gloria Hull's "Black Women Poets from Wheatley to Walker," *Negro American Literature Forum* 9 (1975); John Griffin Jones's "Margaret Walker Alexander," in his *Mississippi Writers Talking*, vol. II (1983); and Charles Rowell's "Poetry, History and Humanism: An Interview with Margaret Walker," *Black World* 25 (1975).

Dorothy West
West's novels are *The Living Is Easy* (1948) and *The Wedding* (1995). Among her short stories are *The Typewriter* (1926); *An Unimportant Man* (1928); *The Richer, the Poorer*, reprinted in *The Best Short Stories by Negro Writers* (1967), edited by Langston Hughes; and *Jack in the Pot*, reprinted in *Harlem: Voices from the Soul of Black America* (1970), edited by John Henrik Clarke.

Biographical sources for West include her interviews for *The Black Women Oral History Project* (1991), edited by Ruth Edmonds Hill; *As I Remember It: A Portrait of Dorothy West* (1991), a film produced by Mekuria Productions in association with WGBH; and West's *Papers, 1914–1985*, at the Schlesinger Library. Critical work on West began with the reissue of *The Living Is Easy* in 1982 and includes Dorothy A. Clark's "Rediscovering Dorothy West," *American Visions* 8 (1993); Lawrence R. Rodgers's "Dorothy West's *The Living Is Easy* and the Ideal of Southern Folk Community," *African American Review* 26 (1992); and Mary Helen Washington's "I Sign My Mother's Name: Maternal Power in Dorothy West's Novel *The Living Is*

Easy," in her *Invented Lives: Narratives of Black Women (1860–1960)* (1987).

Richard Wright
Wright's fiction includes *Uncle Tom's Children* (1938), *Native Son* (1940), *The Outsider* (1953), *The Long Dream* (1958), *Eight Men* (1961), and *Lawd Today* (1963). *Black Boy*, his autobiography, was published in 1945; and a second installment, titled *American Hunger*, was published posthumously in 1977. Wright's account of his experience in the Communist Party is included in *The God That Failed* by Richard Crossman (1959). The two-volume Library of America edition, prepared by Arnold Rampersad, presents Wright's major works in unrevised and unabbreviated form, based on Wright's original typescripts and proofs.

Biographies of Wright include Michel Fabre's *The Unfinished Quest of Richard Wright* (1973), translated from the French by Isabel Barzun; Constance Webb's *Richard Wright: A Biography* (1968); and Margaret Walker's *Richard Wright: Daemonic Genius* (1988). Critical essays on Wright include James Baldwin's "Everybody's Protest Novel" and "Many Thousands Gone" in his *Notes of a Native Son* (1955); Irving Howe's "Black Boys and Native Sons" in *A World More Attractive* (1963); Ralph Ellison's response to Howe in "The World and the Jug" in *Shadow and Act* (1964). See also Ellison's "Richard Wright's Blues" in *Shadow and Act* and "Remembering Richard Wright" in *Going to the Territory* (1986). More recent criticism of Wright includes Robert Stepto's "I Thought I Knew These People: Richard Wright and the Afro-American Literary Tradition," in *Chant of Saints* (1979); Sherley Anne Williams's "Papa Dick and Sister-Woman: Reflections on Women in the Fiction of Richard Wright" in *American Novelists Revisited: Essays in Feminist Criticism* (1982), edited by Fritz Fleischmann; Houston Baker's *Blues, Ideology, and Afro-American Literature: A Vernacular Theory* (1984); Joyce Ann Joyce's *Richard Wright: Art of Tragedy* (1986); Kenneth Kinnamon, ed., *New Essays on Native Son* (1990); Yoshinobu Hakutani, ed., *Critical Essays on Richard Wright* (1982); and Harold Bloom, ed., *Richard Wright: Modern Critical Views* (1987).

THE BLACK ARTS MOVEMENT: 1960–1970

Amiri Baraka
Baraka's *Selected Poetry* and his *Selected Plays and Prose* appeared in 1979. His other volumes include *Preface to a Twenty Volume Suicide Note* (1962), *The Dead Lecturer* (1965), *Black Art* (1966), *Black Magic: Poetry 1961–1967* (1969), *Spirit Reach* (1972), *Afrikan Revolution* (1973), *Hard Facts* (1976), and *Reggae or Not!* (1982). Baraka has also written several important and well-received plays, among them *Dutchman* (1964), *The Baptism* and

The Toilet (1967), and *Four Black Revolutionary Plays* (1969). His prose writings include *Home: Social Essays* (1966); *Raise Race Rays Raze* (1972); *Daggers and Javelins: Essays 1974–1979* (1984); *The Autobiography of LeRoi Jones/Amiri Baraka* (1984); and *The Music: Reflections on Jazz and Blues* (1987). Critical studies include Werner Sollors's *Amiri Baraka/LeRoi Jones: The Quest for a 'Populist Modernism'* (1978), Lloyd Brown's *Amiri Baraka* (1980), and William J. Harris's *Poetry and*

Poetics of Amiri Baraka: The Jazz Aesthetic (1985). Imamu Amiri Baraka (1979), edited by Kimberly W. Benston, is a collection of critical essays.

Ed Bullins
Among Bullins's many writings are Electronic Nigger (1969), The Gentleman Caller (1969), Goin'a Buffalo (1969), In the Wine Time (1969), Death List (1970), The Devil Catchers (1970), It Bees Dat Way (1970), Night of the Beast: A Screenplay (1970), In New England Winter (1971), Next Time (1972), The Reluctant Rapist (1973), The Taking of Miss Janie (1975), I Am Lucy Terry (1976), The Mystery of Phyllis Wheatley (1976), Storyville (1977), C'mon Back to Heavenly House (1978), and Steve and Velma (1980).

Eldridge Cleaver
Cleaver's Soul on Ice was published in 1968. Some of his speeches are collected in Black Panther Leaders Speak: Huey P. Newton, Bobby Seale, Eldridge Cleaver and Company Speak Out through the Black Panther Party's Official Newspaper (1976), edited by G. Louis Heath. Cleaver published Soul on Fire in 1978.

Jayne Cortez
Cortez's publications include Pisstained Stairs and the Monkey Man's Wares (1969), Festivals and Funerals (1971), Scarifications (1973), Mouth on Paper (1977), Firespitter (1982), Merveilleux Coup de Foudre: Poetry of Jayne Cortez and Ted Joans (1982), and Coagulations: New and Selected Poems (1984). Among her recordings are Celebrations and Solitudes: The Poetry of Jayne Cortez (1975), Unsubmissive Blues (1980), There It Is (1983), and Maintain Control (1986). Her films include Poetry in Motion (1982) and War on War (1982), and among her video productions are Jayne Cortez in Concert 1 (1982) and Life and Influences of Jayne Cortez (1987), produced in Sao Paolo by Museu da Literatura in 1987.

Cortez's poems have been included in numerous anthologies, among them We Speak as Liberators: Young Black Poets (1970), edited by Orde Coombs; A Rock against the Wind: Black Love Poems (1973), edited by Lindsay Patterson; Black Sister: Poetry by Black American Women, 1746–1980 (1981), edited by Erlene Stetson; and Confirmations: An Anthology of African American Women (1983), edited by Amina Baraka and Amiri Baraka.

Mari Evans
Evans's collections of poetry are I Am a Black Woman (1970), Nightstar, 1973–1978 (1981), and A Dark and Splendid Mass (1992). Black Women Writers, 1950–1980: A Critical Evaluation is a work of literary criticism she published in 1984. Among her children's books are Singing Black (1976) and Jim Flying High (1979). See also Evans's essay "Ethos and Creativity: The Impulse as Malleable," in David Hoppe, ed., Where We Live: Essays about Indiana (1989).

Hoyt Fuller
Among Fuller's many publications are "An Aperitive in the Plaza," Negro Digest (June 1961); "Notes from an African in Exile: A Personal Odyssey," Journal of Black Poetry 1 (1970–71); "Identity, Reality, and Responsibility: Elusive Poles of the World of Black Literature," Journal of Negro History (1972); "The Question of Aesthetics," Black World (1974); "Plundered World," Nowmo 1 (1975); "Africa: Homeland to My Heart," Black World (1975); and "Racism in Literary Anthologies," The Black Scholar (1987).

Addison Gayle Jr.
Gayle's works include The Black Situation (1970), The Black Aesthetic (1971), Oak and Ivy: A Biography of Paul Laurence Dunbar (1971), Claude McKay: The Black Poet at War (1972), The Way of the New World: The Black Novel in America (1975), Wayward Child: A Personal Odyssey (1977), and Richard Wright: Ordeal of a Native Son (1980). In addition, he edited the collections Black Expression: Essays by and about Black Americans in the Creative Arts (1969) and Bondage, Freedom, and Beyond: The Prose of Black Americans (1971).

Nikki Giovanni
Among Giovanni's most noted collections of poetry are Black Feeling, Black Talk (1967), Ego Tripping and Other Poems for Young People (1974), My House: Poems (1972), and Cotton Candy on a Rainy Day (1978). Her autobiographical work is Gemini: An Extended Autobiographical Statement on My First Twenty-Five Years of Being a Black Poet (1974). Other work includes the collections Re: Creation (1970); Dialogue (1973), with James Baldwin; A Poetic Equation: Conversations between Nikki Giovanni and Margaret Walker (1974); Conversations with Nikki Giovanni (1992), edited by Virginia Fowler; and Racism 101 (1994).

Maulena Karenga
Karenga is the author of numerous scholarly articles and books. Among his publications are Introduction to Black Studies (1982), Kwanzaa: A Celebration of Family, Community and Culture, and Selections from the Husia: Sacred Wisdom of Ancient Egypt. In addition, he coedited The Million Man March/Day of Absence: A Commemorative Anthology (1996).

James Alan McPherson
McPherson's writings include Hue and Cry (1969), Railroad (1976), and Elbow Room (1977). See also his December 1970 Atlantic article, written with Ralph Ellison, "Indivisible Man."

Haki Madhubuti
Madhubuti's early poetry collections include Black Pride Poems (1968), Think Black (1969), and Don't Cry Scream (1969). He has also edited various anthologies of poems and essays, including Dynamite Voices 1: Black Poets of the 1960s (1971), To Gwen with Love: An Anthology Dedicated to Gwendolyn Brooks (1971), and Confusion by Any Other Name:

Essays *Exploring the Negative Impact of "The Black Man's Guide to Understanding Women"* (1990). Other works include *Killing Memory, Seeking Ancestors* (1987) and *Black Men, Obsolete, Single, Dangerous* (1988). His latest work is *Claiming Earth: Race Rage, Rape, Redemption: Blacks Seeking a Culture of Enlightened Empowerment* (1994).

Martin Luther King Jr.
King's works include *Stride toward Freedom: The Montgomery Story* (1959), *Strength to Love* (1963), *Why We Can't Wait* (1964), *Where Do We Go from Here?* (1967), and *Trumpet of Conscience* (1968). See also James M. Washington's *A Testament of Hope: The Essential Writings of Martin Luther King* (1986) and James Cone's *Martin and Malcolm and America: A Dream or a Nightmare* (1991). Also valuable is Keith D. Miller's *Voice of Deliverance: The Language of Martin Luther King, Jr., and Its Sources* (1992).

Etheridge Knight
Knight's collections include *Poems from Prison* (1968), *A Poem for Brother/man* (1972), *Belly Song and Other Poems* (1973), *Born of a Women: New and Selected Poems* (1980), and *The Essential Etheridge Knight* (1986). Along with other inmates of Indiana State Prison, Knight wrote and edited *Black Voices from Prison* (1970). For critical discussions of Knight and his work, see Stephen Henderson's *Understanding the New Black Poetry: Black Speech and Black Music as Poetic References* (1973); Patricia L. Hill's " 'The Violent Space': An Interpretation of the Function of the New Black Aesthetic as Seen in Etheridge Knight's Poetry," *Black American Literature Forum* 14 (1980), and also Hill's " 'Blues for a Mississippi Black Boy': Etheridge Knight's Craft in the Black Oral Tradition," *Mississippi Quarterly* 36 (1982–83); and Sanford Pinsker's "A Conversation with Etheridge Knight," *Black American Literature Forum* 18 (1984).

Malcolm X
The Autobiography of Malcolm X was coauthored with Alex Haley and published posthumously in 1965. Malcolm X's speeches and statements have been published in several collections, including *Malcolm X Speaks* (1965), *The Speeches of Malcolm X at Harvard* (1968), *By Any Means Necessary: Speeches, Interviews and a Letter* (1970), and *Malcolm X: The Last Speeches* (1989). For general background, see Clifton E. Marsh's *From Black Muslims to Muslims: The Transition from Separatism to Islam, 1930–1980* (1984). See also George Breitman's *The Last Year of Malcolm X* (1968), Peter Goldman's *The Death and Life of Malcolm X* (1973), James Cone's *Martin and Malcolm and America: A Dream or a Nightmare* (1991), Bruce Perry's *Malcolm* (1991), Clayborne Carson's *Malcolm X: The FBI File* (1991), and Michael Eric Dyson's *Making Malcolm: The Myth and Meaning of Malcolm X* (1995). Also of interest is the collec-

tion, edited by Joe Wood, *Malcolm X: In Our Own Image* (1992).

Larry Neal
Neal's books include *Black Boogaloo: Notes on Black Liberation* (1969) and *Hoodoo Hollerin' Bebop Ghosts* (1971). With Amiri Baraka and A. B. Spellman, he wrote *Trippin': A Need for Change* (1969). Neal's plays are *The Glorious Monster in the Bell of the Horn* (1976) and *In an Upstate Motel* (1981). With Baraka he edited *Black Fire: An Anthology of Afro-American Writing* (1968).
Neal's critical essays were published in many journals. Among them are "The Negro in the Theater," *Drama Critique* (1964); "Cultural Front," *Liberator* (1965); "Black Writer's Views on Literary Lions and Values," *Negro Digest* (1968); and "The Black Arts Movement," *Drama Review* (1968).

Carolyn M. Rodgers
Rodgers has published several collections of poetry, including *Paper Soul* (1968), *Songs of a Black Bird* (1969), *2 Love Raps* (1969), *how I got ivah: New and Selected Poems* (1975), and *The Heart as Ever Green* (1978). In addition, her work has been included in numerous anthologies, including *Black Sister: Poetry by Black American Women, 1746–1980* (1981), edited by Erlene Stetson.

Sonia Sanchez
Among Sonia Sanchez's poetry collections are *home coming* (1969), *We a Baddddd People* (1970), *It's a New Day: Poems for Young Brothas and Sistuhs* (1971), *Love Poems* (1973), *Blues Book for Blue Black Magical Women* (1974), *Selected Poems, 1974* (1975), *homegirls & handgrenades* (1984), *I've Been a Woman: New and Selected Poems* (1985), *Generations: poetry, 1969–1985* (1986), *Under a Soprano Sky* (1987), and *Wounded in the House of a Friend* (1995).
Sanchez has edited a collection of stories under the title *We Be Word Sorcerers: 25 Stories by Black Americans* (1973). "Crisis and Culture: The Poet as a Creator of Social Values" (1983) is a critical essay by Sanchez. Sanchez's collections of children's stories are *The Adventures of Fathead, Smallhead, and Squarehead* (1973) and *A Sound Investment: Short Stories for Young Readers* (1980). See the discussion of Sanchez's poetry in D. H. Melham's *Heroism in the New Black Poetry: The Will and the Spirit* (1990).

A. B. Spellman
Spellman's poetry collection, *The Beautiful Days*, was published in 1965. As well as publishing essays and reviews in numerous magazines and journals, he has also written *Four Lives in the Bebop Business* (1966).

Quincy Troupe
Troupe's poetry collections include *Embryo Poems, 1967–1971* (1972); *Snake-Back Solos: Selected Poems, 1969–1977* (1978), and *Skulls along the River* (1984). In addition, Troupe has edited two anthologies: *Watts Poets: A Book of New Poetry and*

Essays (1968) and *Talk: An Anthology of Third World Writings* (1975, with Rainer Schulte). With David Wolper he wrote *The Inside Story of TV's "Roots"* (1978). With Miles Davis he wrote *Miles, the Autobiography* (1989). In 1989 he edited *James Baldwin: The Legacy.*

John Alfred Williams
Williams's publications include *Angry Ones* (1960); *Night Song* (1961); *Sissie* (1963); *The Man Who Cried I Am* (1967); *Sons of Darkness, Sons of Light, A Novel of Some Probability* (1969); *Captain*

Blackman (1972); *Mothersill and the Foxes* (1975); *The Junior Bachelor Society* (1976); *!Click Song* (1982); *Berhama Account* (1985); and *Jacob's Ladder* (1987). In addition, he has edited *Angry Black* (1962), *Beyond the Angry Black* (1966), and *Bridges: Literature across Cultures* (1994, with Gilbert H. Muller). See also his *The King God Didn't Save: Reflections on the Life and Death of Martin Luther King, Jr.* (1971); *Flashbacks: A Twenty-Year Diary of Article Writing* (1973); and *If I Stop, I'll Die: The Comedy and Tragedy of Richard Pryor* (1990, with Dennis A. Williams).

LITERATURE SINCE 1970

Maya Angelou
Angelou's autobiographical works include *I Know Why the Caged Bird Sings* (1970), *Gather Together in My Name* (1974), *Oh Pray My Wings Are Gonna Fit Me Well* (1975), *Singin' and Swingin' and Getting Merry Like Christmas* (1976), *The Heart of a Woman* (1981), *All God's Children Need Traveling Shoes* (1986), and *Wouldn't Take Nothing for My Journey Now* (1993). Her poetry is collected in *The Complete Collected Poems of Maya Angelou* (1994). She has published a children's book, *My Painted House, My Friendly Chicken, and Me* (1994), and has edited *I Dream a World: Portraits of Black Women Who Changed America* (1989), with photographs and interviews by Brian Lanker.

A book-length critical work on Angelou's autobiographies is Dolly Aimee McPherson's *Order Out of Chaos: The Autobiographical Works of Maya Angelou* (1990). General critical and biographical information can be found in Jeffrey M. Elliot's *Conversations with Maya Angelou* (1989).

Toni Cade Bambara
Bambara published two collections of short stories, *Gorilla, My Love: Short Stories* (1972) and *The Sea Birds Are Still Alive: Collected Stories* (1977), and a novel, *The Salt Eaters* (1980). She edited two anthologies: *The Black Woman: An Anthology* (1970) and *Tales and Stories for Black Folks* (1971). Other published works are "Black Theater," in *Black Expressions: Essays by and about Black Americans in the Creative Arts* (1969), edited by Addison Gayle Jr.; "Toni Cade Bambara," in *The Writer and Her Work* (1980), edited by Janet Sternberg; "Programming with 'School Daze,' " in *Five for Five: The Films of Spike Lee* (1991), edited by Spike Lee; "Deep Sight & Rescue Missions," in *Lure and Loathing: Race, Identity, Assimilation* (1993), edited by Gerald Early; and "Julie Dash and the Black Independent Film Movement, Black Cinema," in *Black Cinema* (1993), edited by Mantia Diawara.

A bibliography on Bambara's work up to 1984 is Martha Vertreace's "Toni Cade Bambara: The Dance of Character and Community," in *American Women Writing Fiction: Memory, Identity, Family Space* (1989), edited by Mickey Pearlman.

Post-1984 essays and books about Bambara include Susan Willis's *Specifying: Black Women Writing the American Experience* (1987); Elliot Butler-Evans's *Race, Gender and Desire: Narrative Strategies in the Fiction of Toni Cade Bambara, Toni Morrison and Alice Walker* (1989); Wendy K. Komar's "Dialectics of Connectedness: Supernatural Elements in Novels by Bambara, Cisneros, Grahn and Erdich," *Haunting the House of Fiction* (1991); Nancy Porter's "Women's Interracial Friendships and Visions in *Meridian, The Salt Eaters, Civil Wars,* and *Dessa Rose,*" in her *Traditions and the Talents of Women* (1991).

David Bradley
Bradley's major works are the novels *South Street* (1975) and *The Chaneysville Incident* (1981). His published essays include "The Happiness of the Long Distance Runner," *Village Voice* (Aug. 1975); "Eye Witness News," *Tracks* (1978); "City of the Big Sleep," *Signature* (Aug. 1979); and "Looking behind *Cane,*" *The Southern Review* (1985). Critical and biographical information on Bradley can be found in Susan L. Blake and James A. Millner's "The Business of Writing: An Interview with David Bradley," *Callaloo* (1984).

Octavia Butler
Butler's works include *Patternmaster* (1976), *Mind of My Mind* (1977), *Survivor* (1978), *Kindred* (1979), *Wild Seed* (1980), *Clay's Ark* (1984), *Adulthood Rites: Xenogenesis* (1988), *Imago* (1989), and *Parable of the Sower* (1993). A critical essay is Thelma J. Shinn's "The Wise Witches: Black Women Mentors in the Fiction of Octavia E. Butler," in *Conjuring: Black Women, Fiction and Literary Tradition* (1985), edited by Hortense Spillers and Marjorie Pryse. General critical and biographical information on Butler can be found in Joe Weixlmann's "An Octavia E. Butler Bibliography," *Black American Literature Forum* (1984) and Larry McCaffery's *Across the Wounded Galaxies: Interviews with Contemporary American Science Fiction Writers* (1990).

Michelle Cliff
Cliff's works include *Claiming an Identity They Taught Me to Despise* (1980), *Abeng* (1984), *The*

Land of Look Behind: Prose and Poetry (1985), *No Telephone to Heaven* (1987), *Bodies of Water* (1990), and *Free Enterprise* (1993). Her critical essays include "A Journey into Speech," in *Multi-Cultural Literacy* (1988), "Clare Savage as a Crossroads Character," in *Caribbean Woman Writers: Essays from the First International Conference* (1990), and "Women Warriors: Black Writers Load the Canon," *Village Voice Literary Supplement* (May 1990). Cliff edited *The Winner Names the Age: A Collection of Writings by Lillian Eugenia Smith* (1978).

A recent critical consideration of Cliff's work is Francoise Lionnet's "Of Mangoes and Maroons: Language, History, and the Multicultural Subject of Michelle Cliff's *Abeng*" in *De/Colonizing the Subject: The Politics of Gender in Women's Autobiography* (1992), edited by Julia Watson. General critical and biographical information can be found in Judith Raiskin's "The Art of History: An Interview with Michelle Cliff," *The Kenyon Review* (1993); Meryl Schwartz's "An Interview with Michelle Cliff," *Contemporary Literature* (1993); and Opal Palmer Adisa's "Journey into Speech: A World between Two Worlds," *African American Review* (1994).

Lucille Clifton

Clifton's collections of poetry include *Good Times* (1969), *Good News about the Earth* (1972), *An Ordinary Woman* (1974), *Two-Headed Woman* (1980), *Good Woman: Poems and a Memoir, 1969–1980* (1987), *Next* (1987), *Ten Oxherding Pictures* (1988), *Quilting* (1991), and *The Book of Light* (1993). She has published a memoir, *Generations* (1976). Clifton's many children's books include *Some of the Days of Everett Anderson* (1970), *The Black BC's* (1970), *Everett Anderson's Christmas Coming* (1972), *The Boy Who Didn't Believe in Spring* (1973), *All Us Come Cross the Water* (1973), *Everett Anderson's Friend* (1976), *Amifika* (1977), *The Lucky Stone* (1979), *My Friend Jacob* (1980), *Sonora Beautiful* (1981), *Everett Anderson's Goodbye* (1983), and *Everett Anderson's Year* (1992).

Critical treatments of Clifton's work can be found in Alicia Ostriker's "Kin and Kin: The Poetry of Lucille Clifton," *American Poetry Review* 22 (1993).

Wanda Coleman

Collections of Coleman's short stories and poetry include *Art in the Court of the Blue Fag* (1977), *Mad Dog, Black Lady* (1979), *Imagoes* (1987), *Heavy Daughter Blues* (1987), *A War of Eyes and Other Stories* (1988), *African Sleeping Sickness* (1990), *Hand Dance* (1993), and *American Sonnets* (1994). Coleman's nonfiction includes "Surviving the Riot Watch," *The Nation* (May 17, 1993). She also wrote (with Jeff Spurrier) the text for *Twenty-four Hours in the Life of Los Angeles* (1984), edited by Kalus Fabricius and Red Saunders (1984) and edited (with Joana Leedom-Ackerman) *Women for*

All Seasons: Prose and Poetry about the Transitions in Women's Lives (1988).

Biographical and critical work on Coleman includes Ton Magistrale's "Doing Battle With the Wolf: A Critical Introduction to Wanda Coleman's Poetry," *Black American Literature Forum* (1989) and his interview (with Patricia Ferreira) of Coleman, "Sweet Mama Wanda Tells Fortunes," *Black American Literature Forum* (1990).

Samuel R. Delany

Delaney's novels are *The Jewels of Aptor* (1962); *Captives of the Flame* (1963, rev. as *Out of the Dead City*, 1968); *The Towers of Toron* (1964, rev. 1968); *The Ballad of Beta-2* (1965); *City of a Thousand Suns* (1965, rev. 1969); *Babel-17* (1966); *Empire Star* (1966); *The Einstein Intersection* (1967, corr. ed. 1968); *Nova* (1968); *The Fall of the Towers* (1970), which was published as three earlier novels, *Captives of the Flame, The Towers of Toron, City of a Thousand Suns; The Tides of Lust* (1973); *Dhalgren* (1975); *Triton* (1976); *Empire* (with Howard V. Chaykin, 1978); *Distant Stars* (1981); *Neveryona, or The Tale of Signs and Cities* (1983); *Stars in My Pocket Like Grains of Sand* (1984); *Flight from Neveryon* (1985); *The Bridge of Lost Desire* (1987); *They Fly at Ciron* (1993); *The Mad Man* (1994); *Hogg* (1994); and *Atlantis: Three Tales* (1995). He has also published a novella, *Time Considered as a Helix of Semi-Precious Stones*, in *World's Best Science Fiction* (1969). Delany's collections of short stories are *Driftglass: Ten Tales of Speculative Fiction* (1971) and *The Complete Nebula Award-Winning Fiction* (1986). Nonfiction by Delany is *The Jewel-Hinged Jaw: Notes on the Language of Science Fiction* (1977); *The American Shore* (1978); *Heavenly Breakfast* (1979); *Starboard Wine: More Notes on the Language of Science Fiction* (1984); *The Motion of Light in Water: Sex and Science Fiction Writing in the East Village, 1957–1965* (1988); *Straits of Messina: Essays* (1988); *Wagner/Artaud: A Play of Nineteenth- and Twentieth-Century Critical Fictions* (1988); *Silent Interviews on Language, Race, Sex, Science Fiction and Some Comics* (1994); and *Longer Views: Essays* (1996).

Critical book-length works on Delany are Robert Elliot Fox's *Conscientious Sorcerers: The Black Postmodernist Fiction of LeRoi Jones/Amiri Baraka, Ishmael Reed, and Samuel R. Delaney* (1987), and Jane Branhan Weedman's *Samuel R. Delany* (1982). A biography is Seth McEvoy's *Samuel R. Delany* (1984). The most recent bibliography is Michael W. Peplow and Robert S. Bravard's *Samuel R. Delany: A Selective Primary and Secondary Bibliography, 1979–1983*, in *Black American Literature Forum* 18 (1984), a special issue devoted to Delany's writings.

Rita Dove

Dove's poetry can be found in *Ten Poems* (1977), *The Only Dark Spot in the Sky* (1980), *The Yellow House on the Corner* (1980), *Museum* (1983),

Thomas and Beulah (1986), *Grace Notes* (1989), *Selected Poems* (1993), and *Mother Love* (1995). Her prose work includes a collection of stories, *Fifth Sunday* (1985), as well as the novel *Through the Ivory Gate* (1992). Her other works include *Mandolin* (1982), *The Other Side of the House* (1988), and *The Darker Face of the Earth: A Verse Play in Fourteen Scenes* (1994).

General critical and biographical information on Dove can be found in Mohammed B. Taleb-Khyar's "An Interview with Maryse Conde and Rita Dove," *Callaloo* (1991). Dove's work is treated in Robert McDowell's "The Assembling Vision of Rita Dove," in *Conversant Essays: Contemporary Poets on Poetry* (1990), edited by James McCorkle, and Helen Vendler's *The Given and the Made: Strategies of Poetic Redefinition* (1995).

Leon Forrest

Forrest's novels are *There Is a Tree More Ancient Than Eden* (1973; rpt. with a new section, 1988), *The Bloodworth Orphans* (1977), *Two Wings to Veil My Face* (1984), and *Divine Days* (1992). As well as two poems—"Ezekiel, Notes Towards a Suicide: Poem," *Negro Digest* 15 (1966), and "Richard Hunt's Ladder," *Black American Literature Forum* 18 (1986)—Forrest has published several major essays: "In the Light of the Likeness—Transformed," *Contemporary Authors, Autobiography Series* (1988); "Luminosity at the Lower Frequencies: An Essay on Ralph Ellison's *Invisible Man*," *Carlton Miscellany* 18 (1980); and "A Solo Long-Song for Lady Day," *Callaloo* 16 (1993). His published plays are *Theatre of the Soul: A Three-Act Play* (1967) and *Recreation: A One-Act Verse Play* (1978). He has published a short story, "Oh Say Can You See," *Story/Quarterly* 15–16 (1982). Biographical, critical, and bibliographical material can be found in *Callaloo* 16 (1993), a special issue devoted to Forrest's work.

Ernest Gaines

Gaines's novels include *Catherine Carmier* (1964), *Of Love and Dust* (1967), *The Autobiography of Miss Jane Pittman* (1971), *In My Father's House* (1978), *A Gathering of Old Men* (1983), and *A Lesson Before Dying* (1993). His short story collection is *Bloodline* (1968). He also published two short works, "Home: A Photo Essay" and "Miss Jane and I," both in *Callaloo* (May 1978).

The most recent bibliography of Gaines's work is Frank Shelton's "Ernest J. Gaines," in *Fifty Southern Writers after 1900: A Biographical Sourcebook* (1987). Book-length studies on Gaines include Valerie Babb's *Ernest Gaines* (1991), Anne K. Simpson's *A Gathering of Gaines: The Man and the Writer* (1991), David C. Estes's *Critical Reflections on the Fiction of Ernest J. Gaines* (1994), Herman Beavers's *Wrestling Angels into Song: The Fictions of Ernest J. Gaines and James Alan McPherson* (1995). Biographical and critical information can also be obtained from Marcia Gaudet and Carl Wooton's *Porch Talk with Ernest Gaines: Conversa-*

tions on the Writer's Craft (1990) and John Lowe's *Conversations with Ernest Gaines* (1995).

Michael S. Harper

Harper's poetry collections include *History Is Your Own Heartbeat* (1971), *Dear John, Dear Coltrane* (1972), *Photographs: Negatives: History as Apple Tree* (1972), *Song: I Want a Witness* (1972), *Debridgement* (1973), *Nightmare Begins Responsibility* (1975), *Images of Kin: New and Selected Poems* (1977), *Rhode Island: Eight Poems* (1981), and *Healing Song for the Inner Ear* (1984). He authored, with Larry Kart and Al Young, "Jazz and Letters: A Colloquy," *Triquarterly* (1986). Harper has also served as editor of *The Collected Poems of Sterling A. Brown* (1980) and as coeditor with Robert B. Stepto of *Chant of Saints: A Gathering of Afro-American Literature, Art and Scholarship* (1979), with John Wright for "A Ralph Ellison Festival," *Carlton Miscellany* (1980), and with Anthony Walton for *Every Shut Eye Ain't Asleep: An Anthology of Poetry by Americans Since 1945* (1994). Critical treatments of Harper's work include John F. Callahan's "'Close Roads': The Friendship Songs of Michael Harper" and Niccolo N. Donzella's "The Rage of Michael Harper," both published in *Callaloo* (1990). General critical and biographical information can be found in David Lloyd's "Interview with Michael S. Harper," *Triquarterly* (1986).

Essex Hemphill

Collections of Hemphill's poetry include *Earth Life* (1985), *Conditions* (1986), and, including prose as well, *Ceremonies* (1992). With Joseph Fairchild Beam, he edited *Brother to Brother: New Writings by Black Gay Men* (1991). His work is included in *In the Life: A Black Gay Anthology* (1985), edited by Martin Humphries; *New Men, New Minds: Breaking Male Tradition* (1987), edited by Franklin Abbott; and *Gay and Lesbian Poetry in Our Time* (1988), edited by Joan Larkin and Carl Morse.

Charles Johnson

Johnson's novels are *Faith and the Good Thing* (1974), *Oxherding Tale* (1982), and *Middle Passage* (1990). His short fiction is collected in *The Sorcerer's Apprentice* (1986). Other works include *Black Humor* (1970), *Half-Past Nation Time* (1972), *Being and Race: Black Writing Since 1970* (1988), and *In Search of a Voice: Charles Johnson and Ron Chernow* (1991). Critical considerations of Johnson's works include Elizabeth Schultz's "The Heirs of Ralph Ellison," *CLA Journal* (Dec. 1978). Critical and biographical information can be found in "Reflections on Fiction, Philosophy and Film: An Interview with Charles Johnson," *Callaloo* (Oct. 1978).

June Jordan

Jordan's collections of poetry include *Who Look at Me* (1969), *New Days: Poems of Exile and Return* (1974), *Things That I Do in the Dark: Selected Po-*

etry (1977), *Passion: New Poems* (1980), *Living Room: New Poems* (1985), *Lyrical Campaigns: Selected Poems* (1989), *Naming Our Destiny: New and Selected Poems* (1989), and *Haruko/Love Poems* (1993). Collections of essays are *Civil Wars* (1981), *On Call: Political Essays* (1985), and *Technical Difficulties: African American Notes on the State of the Union* (1992). Her children's books are *His Own Where* (1971), *Dry Victories* (1972), *Fannie Lou Hamer* (1972), *New Life: New Room* (1975), and *Kimako's Story* (1981). She has also edited *Soulscript: Afro-American Poetry* (1970); with Terri Bush, *The Voices of the Children* (1970); and *Some Changes* (1971). Jordan has also written the plays *In the Spirit of Sojourner Truth* (1979) and *The Issue* (1985), and the libretto and lyrics for the opera *I Was Looking at the Ceiling and Then I Saw the Sky: Earthquake/Romance* (1995), music composed by John Adams.

Critical and biographical information on Jordan can be found in *Diverse Voices: Essays on Twentieth-Century Women Writers in English* (1991), edited by Harriet Devine Jump. A critical essay on her work is Peter Erickson's "The Love Poetry of June Jordan," *Callaloo* 9 (1986).

Adrienne Kennedy

Kennedy's work includes *Cities in Bezique* (1969), *Funnyhouse of a Negro* (1969), *People Who Led to My Plays* (1987), *Adrienne Kennedy: In One Act* (1988), *Deadly Triplets: A Theatre Mystery and Journal* (1990), *She Talks to Beethoven* (1991), and *The Alexander Plays* (1992). She also co-authored, with John Lennon and Victor Spinetti, *The Lennon Play: In His Own Write* (1969). Kennedy has also written, with Margaret B. Wilkerson, "Adrienne Kennedy: Reflections," *City Arts Monthly* (Feb. 1982). Her work has been given critical attention in Paul Carter Harrison's *The Drama of Nommo* (1972), Linda Kintz's *The Subject's Tragedy: Political Poetics, Feminist Theory and Drama* (1992), and Paul K. Bryant-Jackson and Lois More Overbeck's edited *Intersecting Boundaries: The Theatre of Adrienne Kennedy* (1992).

Jamaica Kincaid

Kincaid has published three novels, *Annie John* (1985), *Lucy* (1990), and *Autobiography of My Mother* (1996). Her collection of short stories is titled *At the Bottom of the River* (1983). She has also published a book-length essay, *A Small Place* (1988). Studies of Kincaid's work are Moira Ferguson's *Jamaica Kincaid: Where the Land Meets the Body* (1994) and Diane Simmons's *Jamaica Kincaid* (1994). Some biographical and critical information can be obtained from Selwyn R. Cudjoe's interview with Jamaica Kincaid in *Callaloo*, 12 (1989).

Yusef Komunyakaa

Komunyakaa's books of poetry are *Lost in the Bonewheel Factory* (1979), *Copaceti* (1984), *I Apologize for the Eyes in My Head* (1986), *Dien Cai Dau* (1988), *Magic City* (1992), and *Neon Vernacular* (1993). Komunyakaa coedited, with Sascha Feinstein, *The Jazz Poetry Anthology* (1991). An interview with Komunyakaa is "Jazz and Poetry," *Georgia Review* 6 (1992).

Audre Lorde

Lorde's books of poetry are *The First Cities* (1968), *Cables to Rage* (1970), *From a Land Where Other People Live* (1973), *New York Head Shop and Museum* (1974), *Between Ourselves* (1976), *Coal* (1976), *The Black Unicorn* (1978), *Chosen Poems: Old and New* (1982), *Our Dead behind Us* (1986), *Undersong: Chosen Poems Old and New* (1992), and *The Marvellous Arithemetic of Difference* (1994), which includes poems published only posthumously. Her nonfiction and theoretical works are *The Cancer Journals* (1980); her automythobiography, *Zami: A New Spelling of My Name* (1982); *Sister Outsider* (1984); *I Am Your Sister: Black Women Organizing across Sexualities* (1985); and *A Burst of Light* (1988). Important critical essays on Lorde are Mary DeShazer's chapter on Lorde, in her *Imagining the Muse* (1987); Gloria T. Hull's "Living on the Line: Audre Lorde and *Our Dead behind Us*," in *Changing Our Own Words* (1990), edited by Cheryl A. Wall; and Chinasole's "*Zami: A New Spelling of My Name*: Audre Lorde and Matrilineal Diaspora: 'Moving History beyond Nightmare Into Structures for the Future . . . ,'" (1990) in *Wild Women in the Whirlwind* (1990), edited by J. Braxton and A. McLaughlin.

Colleen McElroy

McElroy's poetry is collected in *What Madness Brought Me Here: Collected Poems, 1968–1988*. Her short-story collections are *Jesus and Fat Tuesday* (1987) and *Driving under the Cardboard Pines* (1990). Other publications are *Speech and Language Development of the Preschool Child: A Survey* (1972); with Ishmael Reed, *The Wild Gardens of the Loup Garou*, a choreopoem (1982); and *Follow the Drinking Gourd* (1987).

Terry McMillan

McMillan's novels are *Mama* (1987), *Disappearing Acts* (1989), *Waiting to Exhale* (1992), and *How Stella Got Her Groove Back* (1996). She has also edited *Breaking Ice: An Anthology of Contemporary African American Fiction* (1990).

Nathaniel Mackey

Mackey has published four chapbooks of poetry: *Four for Trane* (1978), *Septet for the End of Time* (1983), *Outlandish* (1992), and *Song of the Andoumboulou: 18–20* (1994). His two books of poetry are *Eroding Witness* (1985) and *School of Udhra* (1993). *Strick: Song of the Andoumboulou 16–25* is a compact disc recording of poems read with musical accompaniment (1995). Mackey is also the author of an ongoing prose composition, *From a Broken Bottle Traces of Perfume Still Emanate*, of which two volumes have been published: *Bedouin Hornbook* (1986) and *Djbot Baghostus's Run* (1993). He has written a book of critical essays,

Discrepant Engagement: Dissonance, Cross-Cultur-ality and Experimental Writing (1993), and is the editor of the literary magazine *Hambone* and coedi-tor, with Art Lange, of the anthology *Moment's No-tice: Jazz in Poetry and Prose* (1993). Biographical and critical material on Mackey can be found in a special edition of *Talisman: A Journal of Contem-porary Poetry and Poetics* 9 (1992).

Clarence Major

Major's books of poetry are the chapbooks *The Fires That Burn in Heaven* (1954), *Love Poems of a Black Man* (1965), and *Human Juices* (1966), and his published collections *Swallow the Lake* (1970), *Private Line* (1971), *Symptoms and Madness* (1972), *The Cotton Club: New Poems* (1972), *The Syncopated Cakewalk* (1974), *The Other Side of the Wall* (1982), *Inside Diameter: The France Poems* (1985), *Surfaces and Masks* (1988), *Some Observa-tions of a Stranger at Zuni in the Latter Part of the Century* (1989), and *Parking Lots* (1992). His nov-els are *All-Night Visitors* (1969), *No* (1973), *Reflex and Bone Structure* (1975), *Emergency Exit* (1979), *My Amputations* (1987), *Such Was the Season* (1987), and *Painted Turtle: Woman with Guitar* (1988). He has also published a collection of short stories, *Fun and Games* (1990), and a collection of essays, *The Dark and Feeling: Black American Writ-ers and Their Work* (1974), and has edited *Man Is Like a Child: An Anthology of Creative Writing by Students* (1968), *Dictionary of Afro-American Slang* (1970), revised as *Juba to Jive: A Dictionary of Afri-can American Slang* (1994), *Calling the Wind: Twentieth Century African American Short Stories* (1993), and *The Garden Thrives: Twentieth-Century African-American Poetry* (1996).

Two special issues of *African American Review* 13 (1979) and 28 (1994) have been published on Major's work. The primary bibliography on Major is Joe Weixlmann and Clarence Major, "Toward a Primary Bibliography of Clarence Major," in *Black American Literature Forum* 13 (1979).

Paule Marshall

Marshall's published novels are *Brown Girl, Brown-stones* (1959), *The Chosen Place, the Timeless Peo-ple* (1969), *Praisesong for the Widow* (1983), and *Daughters* (1991). She has published a collection of novellas. *Soul Clap Hands and Sing* (1961), and a collection of novellas and short stories, *Reena and Other Stories* (1983). Uncollected essays are "The Negro Woman in American Literature," *Freedom-ways* 6 (1966); "Shaping the World of My Art," *New Letters* 40 (Oct. 1972); and "From the Poets of the Kitchen," *New York Times Book Review*, Jan. 9, 1983.

Two book-length studies of Marshall's work are Joyce Pettis's *Toward Wholeness in Paule Mar-shall's Fiction* (1995) and Stelamaris Coser's *Bridg-ing the Americas: The Literature of Paule Marshall, Toni Morrison and Gayl Jones* (1995). Important essays in books are Barbara T. Christian's "Sculp-ture and Space: The Interdependency of Character

and Culture in the Novels of Paule Marshall," in her *Black Women Novelists* (1980); Hortense Spill-ers's "The Chosen Place, the Timeless People: Some Figurations in the New World," in *Conjuring: Black Women: Fiction and Literary Tradition*, (1985), edited by Marjorie Pryse and Hortense Spillers; and Susan Willis's "Describing Arcs of Re-covery: Paule Marshall's Relationship to Afro-American Culture," in her *Specifying: Black Women Writing the American Experience* (1987). A special *Callaloo* issue, 18 (1983), is devoted to her writings.

Toni Morrison

Morrison's novels include *The Bluest Eye* (1970), *Sula* (1973), *Song of Solomon* (1977), *Tar Baby* (1980), *Beloved* (1987), and *Jazz* (1992). A collec-tion of essays is *Playing in the Dark* (1992). Essays not collected include "What the Black Woman Thinks about Women's Lib," *New York Times Magazine* (Aug. 22, 1971); "Cooking Out," *New York Times Book Review* (June 10, 1971); "Behind the Making of the *Black Book*," *Black World* (Feb. 1974); "Rediscovering Black History," *New York Times Magazine* (Aug. 11, 1974); "City Limits, Vil-lage Values: Concepts of the Neighborhood in Black Fiction," in *Black Literature and the Urban Experience* (1981), edited by Michale C. Jaye and Ann Chalmers Watts; "Memory, Creation and Writing," *Thought* (Dec. 1984); "Rootedness: The Ancestor as Foundation," in *Black Women Writers (1950–1980)* (1984), edited by Mari Evans; "Un-speakable Things Unspoken: The Afro-American Presence in American Literature," *Michigan Quar-terly Review* (1989); and *Toni Morrison: The Nobel Lecture in Literature* (1993). Morrison has also ed-ited *Race-ing Justice, Engendering Power: Essays on Anita Hill, Clarence Thomas, and the Construction of Social Reality* (1992).

The most recent bibliography of Morrison's work is David Middleton's *Toni Morrison: An An-notated Bibliography* (1987). Since 1987, the book-length studies on Morrison's work include Terry Otten's *The Crime of Innocence in the Fiction of Toni Morrison* (1989), Henry Louis Gates Jr. and Anthony Appiah's *Toni Morrison: Critical Perspec-tives, Past and Present* (1991), Doreatha D. Mbalia's *Toni Morrison's Developing Class Con-sciousness* (1991), Barbara Hill Rigney's *The Voices of Toni Morrison* (1991), Trudier Harris's *Fiction and Folklore: The Novels of Toni Morrison* (1991), Patrick Bjork's *The Novels of Toni Morrison: The Search for Self and Place within the Community* (1992), Denise Heinze's *The Dilemma of "Double-Consciousness": Toni Morrison's Novels* (1993), Karen Carmean's *Toni Morrison's World of Fiction* (1993), Wendy Martin and Jacky Martin's *A World of Difference: An Intercultural Study of Toni Morri-son's Novels* (1994), and Valerie Smith's *New Es-says on Song of Solomon* (1995). Morrison's work is also treated in Marilyn Sanders Mobley's *Folk Roots and Mythic Wings in Sarah Orne Jewett and Toni Morrison: The Cultural Function of Narrative*

(1991), and Stelamaris Coser's *Bridging the Americas: The Literature of Paule Marshall, Toni Morrison and Gayl Jones* (1995). Some biographical information on Morrison can be obtained from Danielle Taylor-Guthrie's *Conversations with Toni Morrison* (1994).

Walter Mosley

Mosley's novels are *Devil in a Blue Dress* (1990), *A Red Death* (1991), *White Butterfly* (1992), *Black Betty* (1994), *R.L.'s Dream* (1995), *A Little Yellow Dog* (1996), and *Gone Fishin'* (forthcoming).

Albert Murray

Murray's novels are *South to a Very Old Place* (1971), *Train Whistle Guitar* (1974), *The Spyglass Tree* (1991), and *The Seven League Boots* (1996). He has also written *The Omni-Americans: Black Experience and American Culture* (1970) and *Stomping the Blues* (1976). In addition, he has published essay-and-lecture collections *The Hero and the Blues* (1973) and *The Blue Devils of Nada* (1996). *Good Morning, Blues* (1985) is the autobiography of Count Basie as told to Murray. Two interesting articles on Murray are James Alan McPherson's "The View from the Chinaberry Tree," *Atlantic* (Dec. 1974) and John Wideman's "Stomping the Blues: Ritual in Black Music and Speech," *American Poetry Review* (1978).

Gloria Naylor

Naylor's novels are *The Women of Brewster Place* (1982), *Linden Hills* (1985), *Mama Day* (1988), and *Bailey's Cafe* (1992). Her short fiction includes "A Life on Beekman Place," *Essence* (Mar. 1980) and "When Mama Comes to Call," *Essence* (Aug. 1982). She has also written the critical essays "Until Death Do Us Part . . . ," *Essence* (May 1985); "The Myth of the Matriarch," *Life* (1988); and "Love and Sex in the Afro-American Novel," *Yale Review* (1988). She also edited *Children of the Night: The Best Short Stories by Black Writers, 1967 to the Present* (1991). Her conversation with Toni Morrison, which was published in *Southern Review* (1985), illuminates both writers. A variety of critical points of view are featured in Henry Louis Gates Jr. and Anthony Appiah, eds., *Gloria Naylor: Critical Perspectives, Past and Present* (1993).

Ishmael Reed

Reed's novels include *The Free-Lance Pallbearers* (1967), *Yellow Back Radio Broke-Down* (1969), *Mumbo Jumbo* (1972), *The Last Days of Louisiana Red* (1974), *Flight to Canada* (1976), *The Terrible Twos* (1982), *Reckless Eyeballing* (1986), *The Terrible Threes* (1989), and *Japanese by Spring* (1993). His poems are collected in *New and Collected Poems* (1988). Among his book-length prose works are the essay collections *Shrovetide in Old New Orleans: Essays* (1978), *God Made Alaska for the Indians: Selected Essays* (1982), *Writing Is Fighting: Thirty-Seven Years of Boxing on Paper* (1988), and *Airing Dirty Laundry* (1993). Reed has edited numerous works, among them *19 Necromancers from Now* (1970), *Califia: The California Poetry* (1979), *The Before Columbus Foundation Fiction Anthology* (1992), and *The Before Columbus Foundation Poetry Anthology* (1992). Reed has also written several journal articles, including "Larry Neal: A Remembrance," *Callaloo* (1985), and "Henry Dumas: The Poet of Resurrection," *Black American Literature Forum* (1988). He also wrote the introduction to Richard Negler's *Oakland Rhapsody: The Secret Soul of a Downtown: Photographs by Richard Negler* (1995).

A bibliography of Reed's work up to 1982 is Elizabeth A. Settle's *Ishmael Reed: A Primary and Secondary Bibliography* (1982). Recent book-length critical treatments are Robert Elliot Fox's *Conscientious Sorcerers: The Black Postmodernist Fiction of LeRoi Jones (Amiri Baraka), Ishmael Reed, and Samuel Delany* (1987), Reginald Martin's *Ishmael Reed and the New Black Aesthetic Critics* (1988), and Jay Boyer's *Ishmael Reed* (1993). Helpful and interesting journal articles are Robert Fox, "Blacking the Zero: Towards a Semiotics of Neo-Hoodoo," *Black American Literary Forum* 18 (1984); Michael Boccia, "Form of the Mystery: Ishmael Reed's *Mumbo Jumbo*," *Journal of Popular Literature* 3 (1987); Theodore Mason, "Performance, History, and Myth: The Problem of Ishmael Reed's *Mumbo Jumbo*," *Modern Fiction Studies* 34 (1988); and Reginald Martin, "Ishmael Reed's Syncretic Use of Language: Bathos as Popular Discourse," *Modern Language Studies* 20 (1990).

Ntozake Shange

Shange's plays include *for colored girls who have considered suicide/when the rainbow is enuf* (1975), *Spell #7: A Theatre Piece in Two Acts* (1981), *A Photograph: Lovers in Motion: Poemplay* (1981), *Three Pieces* (1982), *The Love Space Demans* (1991), and *I Heard Eric Dolphy in His Eyes* (1992). Her poetry volumes include *Matrilineal Poems* (1983), *From Okra to Greens: A Different Kinda Love Story* (1984), *Nappy Edges* (1978), *A Daughter's Geography* (1983), *Ridin' the Moon in Texas: Word Paintings* (1987), and *I Live in Music: Poem* (1995). Shange's prose works include *Melissa & Smith* (1978), *Sassafrass: A Novella* (1976), *Sassafrass, Cypress and Indigo: A Novel* (1983), *Betsy Brown: A Novel* (1985), and *Liliane* (1994). Other works include *Natural Disasters and Other Festive Occasions* (1977), *Between Itaporica y Itapua* (1978), *Some Men* (1981), and *See No Evil: Prefaces, Essays and Accounts, 1976–1983* (1984). She also wrote the foreword to Robert Mapplethorpe's *Black Book* (1986).

Book-length treatments of Shange's works include Neal Lester's *Ntozake Shange: A Critical Study of the Plays* (1995), Tejumola Olaniyan's *Scars of Conquest/Masks of Resistance: The Invention of Cultural Identities in African, African-American and Caribbean Drama* (1995), and Neal Lester's *Ntozake Shange: A Critical Study of the Plays* (1995). Shange's work has also received critical treatment in Carol Christ's *Diving Deep and*

Surfacing: Women Writers on Spiritual Quests (1980); Mary Helen Washington's *Black Eyed Susans: Stories by and about Black Women* (1980); Carolyn Mitchell's "A Laying On of Hands: Transcending the City in Ntozake Shange's *for colored girls*," in *Women Writers and the City: Essays in Feminist Literary Criticism* (1984), edited by Susan Merrill Squier; Barbara T. Christian's *Black Feminist Criticism* (1985); and Melissa Walker's *Down from the Mountaintop: Black Women's Novels in the Wake of the Civil Rights Movement, 1966–1989* (1991).

Alice Walker

Walker's novels are *The Third Life of Grange Copeland* (1970), *Meridian* (1976), *The Color Purple* (1982), *The Temple of My Familiar* (1989), and *Possessing the Secret of Joy* (1992). Her two volumes of short fiction are *In Love & Trouble* (1973) and *You Can't Keep a Good Woman Down* (1979), collected in *The Complete Stories* (1994). Her children's stories are *Langston Hughes: American Poet* (1974), *To Hell with Dying* (1988), and *Finding the Green Stone* (1991). Walker's poems are collected in *Her Blue Body Everything We Know: Earthling Poems, 1965–1990* (1991), and her collections of essays, including autobiographical material, are *In Search of Our Mothers' Gardens* (1983) and *Living by the Word* (1988). Walker has also edited *I Love Myself When I Am Laughing: A Zora Neale Hurston Reader* (1979). Her work includes *Warrior Marks: Female Genital Mutilation and the Sexual Blinding of Women* (1993), with Pratibha Parmar, and *The Same River Twice* (1996).

Bibliographies are Louis and Darnell Pratt's *Alice Malsenior Walker: An Annotated Bibliography, 1968–1986* (1988), and Erma D. Banks and Keither Byerman's *Alice Walker: An Annotated Bibliography* (1989). Significant book-length critical studies published since these bibliographies include Elliot Butler-Evans's *Race, Gender and Desire: Narrative Strategies in the Fiction of Toni Cade Bambara, Toni Morrison and Alice Walker* (1989); Molly Hite's *The Other Side of the Story: Structures and Strategies of Contemporary Feminist Narrative* (1989); Donna Haisty Winchell's *Alice Walker* (1992); Henry Louis Gates Jr. and Anthony Appiah's *Alice Walker: Critical Perspectives Past and Present*; Lillie P. Howard's *Alice Walker and Zora Neale Hurston: The Common Bond* (1993); and Barbara T. Christian's *"Everyday Use" by Alice Walker: A Casebook* (1994).

John Edgar Wideman

Wideman has published seven novels: *A Glance Away* (1967), *Hurry Home* (1970), *The Lynchers* (1973), *Hiding Place* (1981), *Sent for You Yesterday* (1983), *Reuben* (1987), and *Philadelphia Fire* (1990). His short stories are collected in *The Short Stories of John Edgar Wideman* (1992). Another collection of short stories, *All Stories Are True*, was published in 1993. Other works include *The Home-*

wood Trilogy (1985), a collection of three earlier novels; the autobiographical *Brothers and Keepers* (1984); *Fatheralong: A Meditation on Fathers and Sons, Race and Society* (1994); and "Playing Dennis Rodman," *The New Yorker*, Apr. 29 and May 6, 1996. Among Wideman's critical essays are "Charles W. Chesnutt: *The Marrow of Tradition*," *American Scholar* (1972–73); "Frame and Dialect: The Evolution of the Black Voice in Fiction," *American Poetry Review* 5 (1976); "Defining the Black Voice in Fiction," *Black American Literature Forum* (Fall 1977); "Of Love and Dust: A Reconsideration," *Callaloo* (May 1978); and "Stomping the Blues' Ritual in Black Music and Speech," *American Poetry Review* (July–August 1978). Other writings include "The Divisible Man," *Life* 7 (1988); "Michael Jordan Leaps the Great Divide," *Esquire* (Nov. 1990); and "Dead Black Men and Other Fallout from the American Dream," *Esquire* (Sept. 1992).

James Coleman's *Blackness and Modernism: The Literary Career of John Edgar Wideman* is a major critical treatment of John Edgar Wideman.

Sherley Anne Williams

Williams's poetry is collected in *The Peacock Poems* (1975; under Shirley Williams) and *Some One Sweet Angel Chile* (1982). Her fiction includes the short stories "Tell Martha Not to Moan," anthologized here, and "The Lawd Don't Like Ugly," in *Between Mothers and Daughters: Stories across Generations* (1985), edited by Susan Koppelman; the novel *Dessa Rose* (1986); and the children's book *Working Cotton* (1992). Her critical works include *Give Birth to Brightness: A Thematic Study in Neo-Black Literature* (1972); "The Blues Roots of Contemporary Afro-American Poetry," *Massachusetts Review* (1977); "Anonymous in America," *Boundary* (1978); "Meditations on History," in *Midnight Birds, Black-Eyed Susans* (1980), edited by Mary Helen Washington; and "Some Implications of Womanist Theory," in *Reading Black, Reading Feminist* (1990), edited by Henry Louis Gates Jr. Her play *Letters from a New England Negro* was published in *Callaloo* 5 (1979).

Recent critical considerations include Deborah McDowell's "Negotiating between Tennessees: Witnessing Slavery Father Freedom: *Dessa Rose*," in *Slavery and the Literary Imagination* (1989), edited by D. McDowell and A. Rampersad; Barbara T. Christian's "Somebody Forgot to Tell Somebody Something": African American Women's Historical Novels," in *Wild Women in the Whirlwind* (1990), edited by J. Braxton and A. McLaughlin (1990); Mae Henderson's *Speaking in Tongues*," in *Reading Black, Reading Feminist* (1990), edited by Gates; and Melissa Walker's *Down from the Mountaintop: Black Women's Novels in the Wake of the Civil Rights Movement, 1966–1989* (1991).

August Wilson

Wilson's plays include *Ma Rainey's Black Bottom* (1985), *The Janitor* (in short pieces from *New*

Dramatists, 1985), *Fences* (1986), *Joe Turner's Come and Gone* (1988), *The Piano Lesson* (1988, 1990), *Testimonies: Four Monologues* (1991), *Three Plays* (1991), and *Two Trains Running* (1992), and *Seven Guitars* (1995). His poetry has appeared in several periodicals as well as in *The Poetry of Black Americans: Anthology of the Twentieth Century* (1973), edited by Arnold Adoff. Wilson's work has been treated in *August Wilson: A Casebook* (1994), edited by Marilyn Elkins; *May All Your Fences Have Gates: Essays on the Drama of August Wilson* (1994), edited by Alan Nadel; Kim Pereira's *August Wilson and the African American Odyssey* (1995); and Sandra Shannon's *The Dramatic Vision of August Wilson* (1995).

Al Young

Al Young's poetry is collected in *Heaven: Collected Poems, 1958–1990*. His novels include *Snakes* (1970), *Who Is Angelina?* (1975), *Sitting Pretty* (1976), and *Seduction by Light* (1988). He has also authored four musical memoirs: *Bodies & Soul* and *Kinds of Blue* (1984), with Janet Coleman; *Mingus/ Mingus* (1989), with Janet Coleman; and *Drowning in the Sea of Love* (1995). Young also co-authored with Larry Kart and Michael S. Harper "Jazz and Letters: A Colloquoy," *Triquarterly* (1987).

Biographical information can be found in Nathaniel Mackey's "Interview with Al Young," *MELUS* (1978); John O'Brien's *Interviews with Black Writers* (1979); and William J. Harris's "Interview with Al Young," *Greenfield Review* (1982). A critical discussion of Young's work can be found in "The Dimensions of Freedom," *The Afro-American Novel Since 1960* (1982), edited by Peter Bruck and Wolfgang Karrer.

Harlem River Writers, 1991; "Conversation Overheard," © Quincy Troupe, from MS. 1969; "Impressions of Chicago: for Howlin' Wolf" from WEATHER REPORTS, published by Harlem River Writers, 1991. Reprinted by permission of the author.

Alice Walker: "Women" from REVOLUTIONARY PETUNIAS AND OTHER POEMS, copyright © 1970 by Alice Walker, reprinted by permission of Harcourt Brace & Company. "Be Nobody's Darling" from REVOLUTIONARY PETUNIAS AND OTHER POEMS, copyright © 1972 by Alice Walker, reprinted by permission of Harcourt Brace & Company. "In Search of Our Mothers' Gardens" from IN SEARCH OF OUR MOTHERS' GARDENS: WOMANIST PROSE, copyright © 1974 by Alice Walker, reprinted by permission of Harcourt Brace & Company. "Everyday Use" from IN LOVE & TROUBLE: STORIES OF BLACK WOMEN, copyright © 1973 by Alice Walker, reprinted by permission of Harcourt Brace & Company. "Advancing Luna and Ida B. Wells" from YOU CAN'T KEEP A GOOD WOMAN DOWN, copyright © 1977 by Alice Walker, reprinted by permission of Harcourt Brace & Company. Excerpts from THE COLOR PURPLE, copyright © 1982 by Alice Walker, reprinted by permission of Harcourt Brace & Company. Reprinted by permission of David Higham Associates.

Margaret Walker: From THIS IS MY CENTURY: NEW AND COLLECTED POEMS by Margaret Walker Alexander. Copyright © 1989. Reprinted by permission of University of Georgia Press.

Eric Walrond: From TROPIC DEATH by Eric Walrond. Copyright 1926 by Boni & Liveright, Inc., renewed 1954 by Eric Walrond. Reprinted by permission of Liveright Publishing Corporation.

Dorothy West: Reprinted, by permission, from Dorothy West, THE LIVING IS EASY, (New York: The Feminist Press at City University of New York, 1982), pp. 3-36. © 1948, 1975, 1982 Dorothy West. All rights reserved.

Phillis Wheatley: From THE POEMS OF PHILLIS WHEATLEY, revised and enlarged edition, edited with an Introduction by Julian D. Mason, Jr. Copyright © 1989 by the University of North Carolina Press. Used by permission of the publisher.

John Wideman: From BROTHERS AND KEEPERS by John Wideman. Copyright © 1984 by John Wideman. Reprinted by permission of Henry Holt & Company. Reprinted by permission of The Wylie Agency. From DAMBALLAH by John Wideman. Copyright © 1988 by John Edgar Wideman. Reprinted by permission of Vintage Books, a division of Random House, Inc. Reprinted by permission of The Wylie Agency.

John Alfred Williams: Excerpt from THE MAN WHO CRIED I AM, © 1967, 1988. Used by permission of the Author.

Sherley Anne Williams: "Peacock Poem #1" from PEACOCK POEMS © 1974 by Sherley Anne Williams and Wesleyan University Press. Reprinted by permission of University Press of New England. "I Want Aretha to Set This to Music" and "Tell Martha Not to Moan" are reprinted by permission of Sherley Anne Williams.

August Wilson: From FENCES by August Wilson. Copyright © 1986 by August Wilson. Used by permission of Dutton Signet, a division of Penguin Books USA Inc.

Richard Wright: "Blueprint for Negro Writing" from NEW CHALLENGE. Copyright © 1937 by Richard Wright. Reprinted by permission of John Hawkins & Associates, Inc. "The Ethics of Jim Crow" from UNCLE TOM'S CHILDREN by Richard Wright. Copyright 1937 by Richard Wright. Copyright renewed 1965 by Ellen Wright. Reprinted by permission of HarperCollins Publishers, Inc. "Long Black Song" pages 103-129 from UNCLE TOM'S CHILDREN by Richard Wright. Copyright 1936, 1937, 1938 by Richard Wright. Copyright © renewed 1964, 1965, 1966 by Ellen Wright. Reprinted by permission of HarperCollins Publishers, Inc. "The Man Who Lived Underground" from EIGHT MEN by Richard Wright. Copyright © 1944 by L. B. Fischer Publishing Corp., copyright © 1961 by Richard Wright. Reprinted by permission of HarperCollins Publishers, Inc. Reprinted by permission of John Hawkins & Associates, Inc. Chapters 13 and 16 from BLACK BOY by Richard Wright. Copyright 1937, 1942, 1944, 1945 by Richard Wright. Copyright renewed 1973 by Ellen Wright. Reprinted by permission of HarperCollins Publishers, Inc.

Malcolm X: From THE AUTOBIOGRAPHY OF MALCOLM X with Alex Haley. Copyright © 1964 by Alex Haley and Malcolm X. Copyright © 1965 by Alex Haley and Betty Shabazz. Reprinted by permission of Random House, Inc. "The Ballot or the Bullet" from MALCOLM X SPEAKS. Copyright © 1965, 1989 by Betty Shabazz and Pathfinder Press. Text reprinted with the permission of Pathfinder Press.

Al Young: Reprinted by permission of the author.

Index

Prophets for a New Day, 1575
Prove It on Me Blues, 27
Public Enemy, 65
Put on yo' red silk stockings, 1262

Quadroon mermaids, Afro angels, black saints, 1509
Queen Latifah, 68
Quicksand, 1066
Quiet Has a Hidden Sound, 923
Quilting on the Rebound, 2572

Raga of the drum, the drum the drum the drum the drum, the heartbeat, 1723
Railroad Bill, 49
Railroad Bill, a Conjure Man, 2288
Rain, 1258
Raisin in the Sun, A, 1728
Raymond's Run, 2307
Razaf, Andy, 57
Receiving the Stigmata, 2587
Red Record, A, 596
Red Silk Stockings, 1262
Reed, Ishmael, 2285
Reena, 2052
Religion and the Pure Principles of Morality, the Sure Foundation on Which We Must Build, 202
Remember Not, 1317
Remember not the promises we made, 1317
Revolutionary Theatre, The, 1899
Revolution Will Not Be Televised, The, 61
Rich, flashy, puffy-faced, 1222
Riot, 1596
Rites for Cousin Vit, The, 1586
river jordan run red, 2473
Rodgers, Carolyn M., 2007
Round Midnight, 2244
Runagate Runagate, 1506
Run, Nigger, Run, 40
Runs falls rises stumbles on from darkness into darkness, 1506

Sadie and Maud, 1580
St. Isaac's Church, Petrograd, 987
St. Louis Blues, 24
Salute to the Passing, 1468
Sam Smiley, 1225
Sanchez, Sonia, 1902
Sank through easeful, 1499
Satchmo, 1358
Saturday's Child, 1306
Scarlet Woman, The, 928
Schomburg, Arthur A., 937
Schuyler, George Samuel, 1170
Scott-Heron, Gil, 61
Seduction of Light, The, 2317
Seems lak to me de stars don't shine so bright, 768
Seems like I heard, 36
Seen my lady home las' night, 888
See, See Rider, 27
See, See Rider, see what you've done done!, 27
See! There he stands; not brave, but with an air, 773
Séjour, Victor, 286
Self-Reliance, 406
Sence You Went Away, 768
Sent for You Yesterday, 34

Setting in the house with everything on my mind, 30
Shange, Ntozake, 2518
She cried out for Mama, who did not, 2591
She dreams the baby's so small she keeps, 2588
She leaned her head upon her hand, 415
She wanted a little room for thinking, 2589
Shine and the Titanic, 51
Shroud of Color, The, 1307
Sic Vita, 922
Signifying Monkey, The, 42
Singing Hallelujia, 925
Sinking of the Titanic, 51
Sky Is Gray, The, 2182
Slave Mother, The, 414
Slim Greer, 1218
Snapping of the Bow, The, 762
Soledad, 1511
Solo Song: For Doc, A, 1986
Some are teethed on a silver spoon, 1306
somebody almost walked off wid alla my stuff, 2519
Some say that Chattanooga is the, 2293
Some things are very dear to me, 1228
Song for a Dark Girl, 1262
song in the front yard, a, 1580
Song of the Andoumboulou: 8, 2501
Song of the Smoke, The, 612
Song of the Whirlwind, 926
Songs for the People, 421
Sonnet—2, 1228
Sonnet to a Negro in Harlem, 1317
Sonny's Blues, 1694
Soon I Will Be Done, 11
Soon I will be done with the troubles of the world, 11
SOS, 1883
Soul and race, 2279
Soul on Ice, 1947
Souls of Black Folk, The, 613
Southern Mansion, 1244
Southern Road, 1213
Spellman, A. B., 1955
Spencer, Anne, 946
Sporting Beasley, 1224
Stackolee, 50
Stand by Me, 21
Statistic: The Witness, 2592
Status Symbol, 1807
Steal Away to Jesus, 13
Stewart, Maria W., 201
Still I Rise, 2039
Stranger in the Village, 1670
Street, The, 1484
Strong Men, 1215
Sula, 2098
Summer Tragedy, A, 1244
Summer Words of a Sistuh Addict 1905
Sunday Afternoons, 2496
Sundays of Satin-Legs Smith, The, 1582
Sunnyland, 36
Swallow the Lake, 2243
Sweat, 999
Sweet beats of jazz impaled on slivers of wind, 1718
Swing dat hammer—hunh, 1213
Swing Low, Sweet Chariot, 13
Sylvester's Dying Bed, 1264
Sympathy, 900